Tall, blond and incredibly handsome, Paul remained hard to ignore.

"I have a proposition for you," he said.

Her gaze narrowed on Paul. "What do you mean a proposition?"

"I could stay with you at night until we catch him."

Elise's heart fluttered and her hands grew cold and clammy. She hadn't lived in the same house with a man since she'd left North Dakota. Heck, she hadn't trusted herself with another man since.

The last time she'd been with Paul, he'd played with her children in the evacuation shelter. She'd been drawn to the sexy federal agent more than she wanted to admit. But that didn't matter. She couldn't get involved with anyone, not now or ever.

ELLE JAMES

OPERATION XOXO

HARLEQUIN®

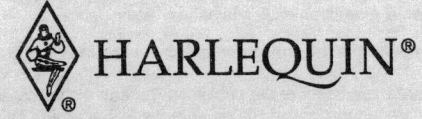

TORONTO • NEW YORK • LONDON
AMSTERDAM • PARIS • SYDNEY • HAMBURG
STOCKHOLM • ATHENS • TOKYO • MILAN • MADRID
PRAGUE • WARSAW • BUDAPEST • AUCKLAND

This book is dedicated to Texas.
I loved all 20 lovely years I lived there. It's rugged, it's beautiful and it's full of wonderful cowboys and heroes just right for Intrigue. God Bless Texas!

ISBN-13: 978-0-373-69439-6

OPERATION XOXO

This edition published by arrangement with Harlequin Books S.A.

www.eHarlequin.com

Printed in U.S.A.

ABOUT THE AUTHOR

Golden Heart winner for Best Paranormal Romance in 2004, Elle James started writing when her sister issued a Y2K challenge to write a romance novel. She has managed a full-time job, raised three wonderful children and she and her husband even tried their hands at ranching exotic birds (ostriches, emus and rheas) in the Texas Hill Country. Ask her and she'll tell you what it's like to go toe-to-toe with an angry 350-pound bird! After leaving her successful career in Information Technology Management, Elle is now pursuing her writing full-time. She loves building exciting stories about heroes, heroines, romance and passion. Elle loves to hear from fans. You can contact her at ellejames@earthlink.net or visit her Web site at www.ellejames.com.

Books by Elle James

HARLEQUIN INTRIGUE

906—BENEATH THE TEXAS MOON
938—DAKOTA MELTDOWN
961—LAKOTA BABY
987—COWBOY SANCTUARY
1014—BLOWN AWAY
1033—ALASKAN FANTASY
1052—TEXAS-SIZED SECRETS
1080—UNDER SUSPICION, WITH CHILD
1100—NICK OF TIME
1127—BABY BLING
1156—AN UNEXPECTED CLUE
1172—OPERATION XOXO

CAST OF CHARACTERS

Paul Fletcher—The FBI special agent never met a woman he wanted to protect more than the brave and vulnerable ex-wife of a serial killer.

Elise Johnson—She moved to Texas and changed her name to give herself and her sons a chance to start over without the stigma of being the wife and children of the Dakota Strangler.

Luke & Brandon Johnson—Elise Johnson's sons are also the sons of a serial killer.

Stan Klaus—The Dakota Strangler supposedly died in a fire and flood two years ago. His body was never found.

Melissa Bradley—The FBI special agent was also involved in the Dakota Strangler case.

Gerri Finch—This cheerleader's mom is out to get Elise fired for interfering with her daughter's cheer competition.

Colton West—The police officer assigned to high-school campus duty has access to Elise, and he knew Lauren and Mary. But is he a killer?

George Slater—Luke's mystery friend lives on the other side of the hedge. Some say he's crazy. Crazy like a killer?

Trevor Cain—This FBI special agent wanted the job Paul Fletcher got. Now he has to report to the man who stole his promotion.

Caesar Valdez—An angry teenage bully, he's bent on stirring up trouble in Elise's high-school classroom.

Alex Mendoza—Elise's star student and class brainiac sticks up for Elise when the class bully gets rough.

Kendall Laughlin—A teenager in a family of cops, she wants to be an FBI agent when she grows up.

Chapter One

"Caesar Valdez, please return to your seat." Elise Johnson struggled to look calm and keep her voice even. She pushed a hand through her damp hair and sighed. Why was the air conditioner on the fritz again? How could she teach in such stifling heat?

Caesar glared at her and slumped into his assigned seat, grumbling, "I don't know why we have to study history, anyway. It's lame. Only losers care about history."

Elise couldn't blame the students for being fractious. The temperature in the room had to be nearing the mideighties. Outside the South Texas summer had stretched well into the one hundreds and it was October, for heaven's sake!

A transplant from North Dakota, Elise suffered in anything above seventy degrees Fahrenheit. She sighed. If she could just make it another few minutes, the day would be done and they could all go home. "Can anyone tell Caesar why we study world history?"

Ashley Finch flicked her straight strawberry-blond hair over her shoulder and looked down her perfect nose at Elise. "Because teachers like to torture teenagers?"

The students laughed.

Elise nodded, already used to the young people posturing in front of their peers. A cheerleader, Ashley liked to be the center of attention and had no trouble speaking up in class; it got her in trouble often. She never knew when to shut up. After several conferences with Ashley's mother, Elise understood where the girl got her mouth and attitude.

"Thank you, Ashley." She stared around at the sea of bored faces, each watching the clock on the wall, waiting for the bell to ring and school to end for the day. "Anyone else know of another reason why we might want to study history?"

Alex Mendoza glanced from left to right and inched his hand upward.

As one, the entire class moaned.

Alex was the brainiac of the class. He'd already blown the class curve, earning him the disdain of his less fortunate and less studious classmates.

Elise liked him because he was voracious in his desire to learn and his ability to retain what he'd digested. "Yes, Alex?"

"We study history so that we don't repeat the mistakes of our past. If we don't learn from the past, we are destined to do it all over again." His words started out slow, tentative, and sped up as if he were afraid the class would pummel him with spit wads for being so verbose. "Who wants another Hitler or Hussein?"

Before the class could bombard him with a barrage of answers to his question, the bell rang.

Students grabbed their books and backpacks and scrambled for the door.

Elise straightened her desk and gathered the quiz papers from a previous class. She liked to be home when the boys got off the bus. As a teacher, she had the latitude to be with her young sons when they got out of school. As a single parent, she liked to maintain a certain amount of stability in their lives. They'd been through so much.

Alex Mendoza and Kendall Laughlin were the last to leave, as usual. The two were best friends and partners on the school newspaper. They went everywhere together—joined at the hip, as Elise's mother would have said before she passed away last year.

Kendall stopped in front of Elise's desk. "Ms. Johnson, remember if you need me to babysit, all you have to do is let me know. I'm available practically anytime, and you're just down the street, so I could ride my bike."

Elise chewed her bottom lip. She hadn't been out with adults since she'd come to Breuer, Texas, the small traditionally German town on the outskirts of San Antonio. "Thanks, Kendall, I'll keep you in mind."

For when she actually met some adults she could hang out with after teaching school all day.

"Alex, don't let Caesar's comments get you down. You two will go far because you aren't afraid or too lazy to learn."

Alex shrugged. "I wasn't worried. While I'm at Stanford earning my doctorate, Caesar will still be bagging groceries."

"Come on, Alex," Kendall said. "My mom's waiting to take us to the library so we can dig up more scoop on Jack the Ripper."

A chill slithered its way down Elise's spine. "Why are you doing a report on Jack the Ripper?"

"We had to pick someone famous in history, and who wants to do the same ol' same ol'?" Kendall grinned.

Alex rolled his eyes. "It was her idea. I wanted Albert Einstein."

Kendall's eyes glowed with enthusiasm. "There's something about an unsolved mystery that appeals to me." She jerked her head toward the door. "Are we going or not? My mom's probably waiting in the parking lot."

Alex smiled and scooted out the door after Kendall.

After the kids had cleared the room Elise hurried down the hallway, her footsteps clicking along the tiled floors. She had to stop at the office where she'd drop off parent permission forms for their field trip to Enchanted Rock at the end of next week.

Elise tried to shake the uneasy feeling creeping across her skin. All Alex and Kendall's talk of Jack the Ripper brought up memories best forgotten.

Students and teachers milled in and out of the office. Elise had to squeeze through to get to the front desk.

"Hi, Elise." Becky McNabb, the school secretary, looked up from her computer terminal at her desk. "How was class?"

"Challenging," she answered, her tone flat, her lips twisting into a wry grin.

"I don't know how you teachers do it." She glanced back at the computer. "I'd have to shoot myself."

"They have their moments." Both good and bad. Elise handed Becky the stack of crumpled papers. "Could you file these?"

"Sure." She stuck a paper clip on them and laid them on the stack in her in-box. "Hey, don't forget to check your cubby before you leave. You got mail today."

Behind the counter a plain white envelope leaned to the side of her box. She retrieved it and stuffed it in her purse for later.

The small town was just what she and her boys had needed. Not much traffic and plenty of room to grow. Most of all, it was a long way from North Dakota. A long way from the past she'd tried her damnedest to erase. She'd changed her name and her sons' to ensure no one could trace them or know their real identities. The only people who knew where they'd gone were her sister, Brenna, and Brenna's FBI husband, Nick Tarver—the only people she trusted with her children's lives.

For the past four months, she and her sons had lived in the small Texas town with no one aware of what had happened in North Dakota.

A long funeral procession wended its way down Main Street, bringing traffic to a complete standstill. Elise glanced at the clock on the dash. She had a good fifteen minutes before Luke and Brandon got off the bus and she was only five minutes from home once the procession made it past. After shifting her metallic gray sedan into Park, she reached into her purse for the envelope, slipped her fingernail beneath the flap and ripped it open. The sharp edge of the flap sliced into her skin and she jerked her hand back.

Damn. She hated paper cuts. She dabbed at the dot of blood oozing from her finger and opened the envelope. Inside she found a single white sheet of paper.

Careful not to bleed on the writing, she unfolded the paper and flattened it. The message was short and it didn't take Elise long to read the three simple lines.

Dear Alice,
For better or worse, until death do us part.
Let death begin.

Cold consumed her, penetrating straight to her bones.

No. This was a mistake. No one knew her here. No one.

She grabbed the envelope. On the outside written in crisp clean computer print was *Elise Johnson.* There was no postage, no return address.

Her hands shook so hard, the paper and envelope fluttered from her grip and fell to the seat beside her.

Brenna. I have to call Brenna. She hesitated for a few seconds. Should she? Married now, Brenna was eight months pregnant with her first child. Should Elise call her and upset her?

The words on the note stared up at her, pushing her past any kind of reason. She had to talk to her sister. Brenna would know what to do.

Elise fumbled in her purse for her cell phone and hit the speed-dial button that would connect her with her sister living in Minneapolis.

After four rings, Elise's teeth were chattering and she almost threw the phone out the window. "Where is she?"

"Al—Elise?" Brenna was still trying to get used to the different name, but her voice sounded so calm over the line.

"Brenna." Elise Johnson's fingers trembled as she held the phone to her ear with one hand and snatched up the letter in the other.

"What's wrong?" Her younger sister had a way of reading her voice, even from over a thousand miles away.

"Brenna. I'm scared."

"Are the boys okay?" Brenna's voice, clear and crisp, snapped over the line.

"The boys are f-fine." Elise sucked in a deep breath and fought back the sob rising in her throat. Fear clenched a hand around her gut and squeezed. "I got a letter today."

"From whom?"

As the procession of cars crawled by one by one with their headlights on like so many zombies, Elise whispered, "I don't know."

"What did it say?"

For several seconds, Elise stared down at the boxy print, her hand shaking so hard, she couldn't read the words. But then, she didn't have to. She could recite them word for word without seeing the paper.

"Elise!" At Brenna's shout, Elise pulled herself together.

She took a deep breath. "The letter said, 'Dear Alice, For better or for worse, until death do us part. Let death begin.'"

"What the hell does that mean?" A street cop turned detective, Brenna didn't tone down her words. "And who the hell knows you're Alice?"

"I don't know. But I'm so scared I can't think." A car honked behind her. Elise jumped and glanced around, realizing the funeral procession had passed and traffic had resumed, except where she held up a dozen cars. "I'm in traffic and I have to go. I'll call you when I get home." She wished her sister was in Texas where she could go straight to her.

"Do that. And, Elise, don't worry. We'll figure this out."

God, she hoped so. This all had to be a big mistake—a really big mistake. The letter was much like the ones Brenna had received in North Dakota when she'd been on the trail of a serial killer.

That serial killer had turned out to be none other than Elise's husband. He'd very nearly killed Brenna. Hysterical laughter bubbled up in her throat. What woman ever suspected her husband of being a serial killer? Especially a deacon in the church, a man most of the community looked up to and trusted.

They'd told her Stan had died in the fire he'd set in his attempt to kill Brenna. Elise still had nightmares about that time. She'd almost lost her only sister.

Elise had always wondered if Stan really died in that fire.

Memories flowed in like the floodwaters of the Red River that had swept away the burning house with Stan inside two years ago. No body had been recovered, but then he'd been burned and carried away, so what had they expected to find?

Her husband the serial killer was dead.

Elise shifted the car into gear and pulled forward, suddenly overwhelmed with the need to hug her children. She wished she had someone big and strong to hug her.

How could anyone know where she was? How could he have found out her secret? Was it really Stan?

Damn it. Stan Klaus *had* to be dead.

Elise couldn't live through all that again.

Then again…maybe that was the plan.

PAUL FLETCHER STEPPED OUT into the bright afternoon sun. The heat radiating off the pavement warmed his air-conditioner-chilled arms. The contrast between the conference room inside and the South Texas heat had to be at least thirty degrees. He might never acclimate if he didn't get out of the office more often.

He marveled at the number of trucks in the parking lot. Hardly anyone in the urban areas of the East Coast owned pickups. Paul had succumbed to the lure of the four-wheel-drive vehicle within a week of arriving and bought a pewter-gray 4x4 truck, glad he'd passed on shiny black like the SUV parked in the space next to his. It looked good, but in the Texas sunshine, black absorbed more heat, making it blistering hot in the long summers.

Before he stepped off the curb onto the sticky black asphalt, Melissa Bradley's bright red truck pulled up next to him. Her automatic window slid down. "Get in."

"Why? I was on my way to the house for a cold beer."

"Change of plans."

Paul climbed into the passenger seat, the dream of relaxing by the apartment-complex pool with a beer fading as Melissa pulled onto Interstate 10, headed toward El Paso. "Where are we going?"

"Breuer." Dressed in jeans and Dingo boots, Melissa had made the transition from the East Coast like she'd been born and raised in Texas. She'd even picked up a little of the local dialect.

"Why Breuer?"

"Remember Alice Klaus?" She glanced at him before returning her attention to the San Antonio afternoon traffic. Slowing, she allowed cars from the access ramp to ease onto the busy interstate, headed to the suburbs after a day at work.

"Alice from the Dakota Strangler case in North Dakota?" An image of a pretty lady with pale blond hair and two cute little boys swam into his head. "The wife of the serial killer Alice?"

"That's the one."

"What does she have to do with Breuer?"

"Her sister, Brenna, called a few minutes ago. Apparently, Alice Klaus, now Elise Johnson, settled in Breuer and hired on as a high school history teacher."

A smile lifted the corners of Paul's lips. He remembered her, all right. Pretty blonde, killer husband. "She changed her name." He nodded. "A good thing."

"Yeah. Only someone's found her."

Paul tensed and sucked in his breath. "Found her or killed her?" He'd barely known the woman more than a few days, but he remembered feeling regret. If the circumstances had been different, she was someone he wouldn't mind getting to know better.

Melissa shot a glance at Paul. "Found. She's alive."

Paul let the air out of his lungs and leaned back in his seat for the twenty-minute drive to the hill country outside San Antonio.

WHEN THEY PULLED ONTO Main Street in Breuer, Paul scanned the small town with a critical eye. White limestone buildings intermingled with old, German-style gingerbread houses.

People smiled and waved to each other from the sidewalks and children played in their front yards. Paul would bet most residents didn't even lock their doors at night.

A veritable nightmare if a killer ran loose in their midst.

"Here's Highland Street." Melissa turned left onto the street lined with gnarled live oaks whose branches shaded the curbs, giving the impression of a leafy arched bower instead of a city street.

Melisa parked in front of a yellow cottage with a three-foot-tall, white picket fence surrounding the yard, front and back. "How cute. Reminds me of my grandmother's house in Wisconsin."

Paul climbed from the passenger side of the truck and pushed through the rickety gate. Before he got halfway to the house, two little boys burst through the front door and raced out into the yard.

"Luke, Brandon! Come back inside right now!" A beautiful woman with long blond hair flung the screen door open and raced out onto the porch, a worried frown creasing her forehead. When she spied Paul, she stopped, her eyes widening. She pressed a hand to her mouth as tears bubbled up and spilled over.

Somewhere in her past life, she had to have been the high school beauty queen. She was so perfect in every way except the tears now pouring down her cheeks.

For a man who avoided crying females like the plague, Paul couldn't resist moving forward and taking her into his arms. "Shh." He smoothed her hair and spoke to her in a soothing tone. "Everything's going to be okay."

"He's supposed to be dead." She pushed away to stare up into Paul's eyes, her jaw clenched, angry light refracting off the tears in her eyes. "He's supposed to be dead."

Chapter Two

She clutched his shirt like she was grasping for purchase on the face of a drop-off. She felt like she had fallen over the edge of a cliff, straight into her past.

Just seeing Paul and Melissa made the memories of the nightmare all too vivid. These two talented FBI agents had been in Riverton and assisted in the investigation that ultimately identified the Dakota Strangler as Stan Klaus, Elise's husband. During the evacuation of the flooded town of Riverton, Paul had been the one to help get her, the boys and her aging mother out of the evacuation center when the press converged on her.

The solid wall of Paul's chest and the security of his arms triggered all the emotions she'd repressed. All the fear, desperation and disbelief rushed in and threatened to swamp her.

She'd held it together for the boys, but now that help had arrived, sobs rose in her throat and she pressed her mouth to his chest to keep from crying out and scaring the children. She needed to stay strong for the boys and so far she wasn't doing a good job of it. Her shoulders shook with the force of her sobs and she huddled in Paul's arms, wanting to stay hidden from the world.

"Hey, boys," Melissa said behind her. "Why don't you show me that swing set I see in your backyard. Think I can swing on it?"

From the corner of her eye she saw Brandon run around Paul's side and stare up at the man, his eyes narrowed into tight slits. "Did you make my mother cry?"

"No, I didn't." Thankfully, Paul shielded Elise from her son's view.

"Did you hurt her?" the boy demanded, his voice rising.

"No, sir."

Elise gulped back more tears and tried to collect herself enough to face her oldest son.

Brandon crossed his arms over his little chest. "Let my mother go."

"It's okay, Brandon. Paul's a nice guy," Elise said into Paul's damp shirt, her sobs drying and turning into hiccups.

"Let her go." Brandon stuck his hands between them and attempted to split them apart.

Paul glanced to Melissa for help.

"Let her go!" Brandon's rage turned to tears when all the pushing he did resulted in nothing. He balled his fists and beat against the backs of Paul's legs.

Elise pushed away from the warmth of Paul's arms and squatted next to Brandon, gathering him close. Luke edged in on the hug, his little face creased in a frown to match his brother's.

Melissa lifted him into her arms. "Come here, little man."

Elise's lack of control over her emotions made her sons uneasy. Both boys needed reassurance as much as she did, if not more. She was the adult. Adults must be strong. Then why the hell did she feel like she was falling apart? "It's okay, Brandon. Paul's not hurting me." She scrubbed at the tears on her cheeks and pushed her hair back from her forehead. "I'm okay. I was crying because I was so happy to see Paul and Melissa. Do you remember them?"

In the circle of his mother's arms, Brandon glared from Paul to Melissa, his gaze returning to Paul as if he expected Paul to make another move on his mother.

Elise had never told Brandon why his father had died in a fire or that he was a bad man. She had told him that he was now the man of the house and it was up to him to help her. He'd taken his responsibilities seriously over the past two years, sometimes forgetting it was okay to be an eight-year-old boy.

Kendall Laughlin pulled up beside the picket fence on her bicycle and braked to a halt. "Hi, Ms. Johnson. Hi, Luke. Yo, Brandon."

Luke squirmed in Melissa's arms. "Kenny!" Melissa set the child on his feet and he was off like a shot and through the gate. "I have a bike now. You wanna see?" He grabbed her hand and pulled her toward the gate.

Kendall laughed and smiled down at the six-year-old. "Let me get off mine first." She shot a curious look at Elise. "Is everything okay?"

Elise stood, her hand lingering on Brandon's shoulder. "Yes, Kendall, everything's okay." *My world is catching up to me and my killer husband might be alive, but everything's just fine and dandy.* She attempted a smile that turned into a grimace. "Kendall, could you do me a big favor?"

"Sure." She climbed off her bike and rolled it into the yard.

"Could you watch the boys for a few minutes while I talk to…my old friends, Paul and Melissa?" *And please don't ask too many questions.* Her students couldn't know about her past. Her principal couldn't know or her peaceful life would be shattered. Who wanted the wife of a serial killer teaching children in their school? Elise had never hurt another human in her life. But her husband had killed five people that she knew of.

"I'd love to. Luke and I are old friends already. Aren't we, buddy?" She ruffled the boy's hair.

Luke jumped up and down. "Come see my new bike."

Brandon stuck by Elise's side, his hand creeping into hers. "I don't want to play."

"Go with Kendall. I promise, everything's okay." She stared down into her son's eyes. "As the man of the house, you need to help me keep an eye on your brother."

His face scrunched into a fierce pout and he glared again at Paul. "Kendall can watch him."

"She doesn't know all his hiding places." She let go of his hand. "You do. So it's up to you to keep your brother safe and in the yard. Neither one of you is to leave the yard, understand?"

Brandon nodded.

She patted his shoulder instead of bending down to hug him close. He wouldn't appreciate being treated like a child in front of the other adults. "I need a few minutes to talk to Mr. Fletcher and Ms. Bradley, alone."

"Come on, Brandon," Luke called out. "You can show Kenny your new bike, too." With Kendall's hand clutched in his, Elise's youngest son tugged the teen across the yard, grabbed his brother's hand and headed for the back.

Brandon pulled loose of Luke's grip and gave his mother one last look as if to say, *Are you sure?*

Elise nodded, a reassuring smile plastered to her face. "Go on, honey. We'll be in the house."

Dragging his feet, Brandon followed Luke and Kendall around the side of the house to the shed where the bicycles were stored.

Paul's gaze followed the boys. When they were out of sight, he turned to Elise. "Want to show me the note?"

The mention of the note set her heart racing again. If she could she'd have burned it and scattered the ashes to the winds, as if by doing so, her troubles would blow away. "It's in the house."

She led the way into the living room, taking no pleasure in all the warm and colorful furnishings that were so different from the Spartan look Stan had preferred. The note had turned her happy and sunny home sinister, a place where evil lurked, waiting to pounce. She crossed to the kitchen and glanced out the window.

Brandon and Luke had their bicycles out of the shed. Kendall smiled and laughed with the boys, admiring their new wheels.

Elise pulled the letter out of her purse and held it out for Paul to see. "I don't know what to make of it, but I'll tell you…it has me scared."

Paul pulled a rubber glove from his hip pocket and stretched it over his large, capable hand before he took the note from her. He turned it over, inspecting the outside of the envelope. "Where did you find it?"

"It was in my mailbox cubby at school today." Elise spun away and paced across the ceramic kitchen tiles. This was her home, a place where she could make new friends and her boys could grow up unencumbered by their father's crimes. Fear turned to anger and she marched back across the tile to face the two agents. "Tell me, guys. What really happened to Stan? Did he, or did he not die in that fire?"

Elise's blue eyes blazed, the anger a welcome change from the defeated and frightened young woman of a moment ago. Paul remembered the shock and disbelief in her face after she'd learned what her husband had done two years ago.

She'd suffered through the stares and whispers of the people she'd sat beside in church for years. They'd shunned her as if she'd been the one to kill those innocent women. They couldn't understand how her husband could have committed all those crimes with her unaware. Didn't she live in the same house?

Paul had heard the whispers, the catty remarks and the name-calling. When the reporters descended on her, he'd been there to get her out and relocate her to a private room where she, the boys and her mother remained out of the spotlight. All the while, she'd put up a strong front for Brandon and Luke, shielding them from the ugliness as best she could. They had been too young to understand and hopefully too young to remember.

He stared down at the letter, like so many others he'd seen on the case in Riverton, North Dakota. Had Stan Klaus lived through the fire and flood? They'd never found his body. "We'll have the letter examined by our lab."

Melissa pulled out an evidence bag from her back pocket and opened it.

Paul dropped the letter inside. "What did it say?"

Elise inhaled through her mouth, her lip quivering ever so slightly. "'Dear Alice, for better or for worse, until death do us part. Let death begin.'" She said it in a flat, emotionless tone. When she finished, her body trembled from head to toe.

"Alice? He specifically said 'Dear Alice'?" Melissa asked.

Elise nodded. She'd put that name behind her, even went so far as to consider her old self as someone who'd died along with Stan. Alice Klaus had been young, naive and stupid. Elise Johnson was savvy, aware and would never harbor a killer in her home. Ever.

"Have you or the boys told anyone your former names?"

"No. The two years we spent in Minneapolis gave us time

to adjust to the new names. When we moved here, we started our new lives. No one knows who we are."

Melissa snorted. "Someone does."

"Question is who?" Paul held the evidence bag up. "Who would write a note like that and for what purpose?"

"Could be just a scare tactic." Melissa shrugged. "Who have you made mad since you moved here?"

Scratching through her recent memories, Elise could think of only a couple people she'd angered. "One of my students' parents, or maybe a student?"

Paul glanced up, his blond brows rising on his tanned forehead. "A student?"

"I have a bully and a talker. I sent the talker to detention for two days straight. Her mother read me the riot act, claiming I was denying her daughter an education, although she gets the same work at the detention center as in the classroom. In fact, she gets more. The only thing she doesn't get is cheer practice and she's benched for the next game."

"Do you think that student could be using your past against you?" Paul asked.

"Ashley?" Elise shook her head. "She's more interested in her next boyfriend than exacting revenge on a teacher."

Melissa's mouth thinned. "You'd be surprised what kids can do."

Elise pressed her fingers to her temples where a dull ache grew into a steady pounding. "I'd be more afraid of her mother than Ashley. Gerri Finch is a nightmare in heels. Your basic overachieving stage mother."

Melissa stared across the evidence to Paul. "Wouldn't hurt to question her."

"Does that mean you're taking the case? Or should I have turned this in to the police?"

"Technically, we don't have a case," Melissa said. "No one's been hurt."

"Yet. That's the whole idea. I don't want anyone else hurt by my husband or whoever sent this. I don't want to be responsible for any more murders."

Paul lifted one of Elise's hands. "Elise, your husband murdered those women, not you."

She pulled her hand from Paul's grasp, wanting the comfort, but feeling unworthy of it. "I should have seen through those late-night service calls." She threw her arms in the air. "At the very least, I should have suspected *something*. Good God, I lived with the man." The manipulative, verbally abusive, domineering son of a—

"You weren't the only one who trusted him. He had an entire community snowed." Melissa moved up beside Paul. "In most cases involving serial killers, the people closest to them never saw it coming."

Elise rolled her eyes, a shaky laugh erupting from her throat. "Oh, that makes me feel so much better about the women my husband killed."

"I know it's not much. But it took us a while to figure him out, as well." Melissa gave her a crooked smile. "Hell, we were almost too late to save your sis—"

"Mel, let me handle this," Paul said.

Melissa's face turned pink and she backed away. "Yeah, maybe you should."

Elise felt sorry for Melissa having to walk on eggshells around her. Elise didn't need people feeling sorry for her any more than she wanted their blame for the deaths. After two years, she'd managed to start over and put the horror behind her, only for it to resurface and slap her squarely in the face. Would she ever be free of Stan Klaus?

"Elise." Paul was talking to her. "For now, we're going to do some checking without opening a case. The local police would be handling this one if we were to turn it in, which we might do soon if we need their help."

"I'd rather the locals didn't know any more than they have to. We have to live here. I can't keep uprooting my children and moving every time someone recognizes me."

"Or threatens you and your children?"

Her blood ran cold. She drew in a deep breath and let it out. "If my husband is still alive, he'll come after his sons. I won't let him have them. I swear I'll kill the monster first."

PAUL AND MELISSA RODE BACK to San Antonio in silence. Paul immersed in his memories of North Dakota and the first contact he'd had with Alice Klaus. He remembered thinking how unfair life was to dump this horrific burden on such a nice woman and her kids. He'd gone to the evacuation shelter and played with Brandon and Luke to help her out and give her a break while her hometown flooded and her life fell apart.

She'd been strong then, but now he recognized her behavior as that of a person in shock and denial. The Texas sunshine had done her good, tanning her pale northern skin. She was too young to be widowed and too pretty to live alone. Elise Johnson needed a man around to run interference for her and provide some kind of protection. Either that or a gun.

The sound of little boys shouting in the backyard had grounded Paul in Elise's reality. A gun in the house wasn't a good idea, either. Not with curious boys on the loose.

Stan had set fire to the house he supposedly died in. When Paul, Melissa, Nick and Brenna left the house, the river had already flooded the road and the house was a raging inferno. By the time they were able to return, the house had been swept away in the floodwaters. Stan's vehicle had been found along the banks of the Red River, five miles south of Riverton. Empty.

Had Stan Klaus survived? If so, why had he showed up now? Why not sooner?

Paul turned to Melissa. "Until we get something solid to go on, I want this case kept between you and me."

"You're the boss." Melissa gave him a mock salute. "It really is hard calling you boss."

"You didn't have to take this assignment, you know. And if you recall, I tried to talk you out of it."

"And miss my one and only opportunity to transfer to Texas?" She gunned the accelerator of her cherry-red F150 four-wheel-drive pickup. "I'd take a job with the devil himself just to leave the snow behind."

AT 7:00 P.M., PAUL ENTERED the Bureau building in San Antonio and headed for his office, Melissa close on his heels.

As they passed Special Agent Trevor Cain's desk, the agent looked up from his conversation on the telephone. His eyes widened and he smiled up at them. "*Muy bien. Adios,*" he said into the receiver and hung up. "Hey, Bradley, Fletch. Where've you been?" Cain rose from his desk and followed them down the hall.

"Cain." Paul acknowledged the man with a nod before he entered his office.

"You're pulling a late night," Melissa commented, standing in the doorway. "Still working those applicant background investigations?"

"Yeah." Trevor moved as if to enter, but Mel wasn't in a hurry to make way. She crossed her arms and leaned against the doorjamb, effectively blocking his entrance.

Thank goodness Mel had decided to transfer to San Antonio

with Paul. She understood him, could read him like only a close friend could. Paul smothered a grin.

"Your ability to speak Spanish is a plus around here," Mel commented.

Paul fought impatience. He was ready for the conversation to end and for Cain to disappear so that he could discuss Elise with Mel.

Cain shrugged, his attention focused on Paul. "It comes in handy."

"Making any headway?" Paul asked.

"Some. There's just so many, it doesn't feel like it. I'd rather sink my teeth into something more interesting."

"We all do our jobs." Paul refused to be drawn into another discussion about what FBI agents *should* be doing. He knew Trevor wanted a case more substantial than applicant background checks, but everyone had to do them. Trevor just needed to do his share.

Cain snorted. "We can't all get the national headliners like you two, huh?" His tone held more of a bite than just another agent joking with his comrades.

"No, we can't." Paul glanced at Melissa. "Could you close my door? I have some calls to make."

"Will do." Melissa closed the door, luring Trevor away.

Paul owed her for that one. Trevor might be a good agent, but he was too impatient for the next big case. What he seemed to forget was that when they got a big case, it meant people were being either kidnapped or murdered. While Trevor was looking for a thrill, others were just trying to survive or keep someone else from being hurt.

Trevor had a lot to learn about being a good agent. In his new supervisory role, Paul hoped he'd have the patience to teach the man.

For now, he wanted to fish and see if Elise's note had more guts behind it than just paper and ink.

His first call was to the Kendall County Sheriff's Department. Now how did he phrase his question in a manner that wouldn't raise too much suspicion?

"Kendall County Sheriff's Department."

Paul identified himself, stating his position with the FBI in the San Antonio field office.

"What can I help you with, Agent Fletcher?" the woman asked.

"Have there been any missing persons reported in the past forty-eight hours, particularly women?"

After a long pause, the woman spoke. "No, sir. Do you want me to notify you if something should come up in that respect?"

"Yes, please." He gave her his number, hung up and repeated his query at the sheriff's office for the next county over and got the same response. So far, so good. Maybe there wasn't anything to the note after all.

His gut told him differently and his gut was rarely wrong.

A light knock sounded at the door and Melissa stuck her head in. "Mind if I join you?"

"Trevor head home?" he countered.

"No, he's at his desk, slogging through more background checks." She chuckled. "He's not at all happy about it, either."

"He'll get over it." Paul tipped his head to the side. "Come in."

Melissa entered, sinking into the seat across from Paul's desk. "What are you going to do about the note?"

"I made a few calls to outlying counties. I haven't called the Bexar County Sheriff or San Antonio Police Department yet. They're next on my list."

"What exactly are you asking them?"

"I'm inquiring about missing persons reported in the past forty-eight hours." He glanced at Melissa. "You got any other ideas?"

"I'll run the envelope and letter over to Forensics to see if we can lift any prints."

"Thanks."

"What do you think? Is it a real threat or a prank?"

Paul tapped a pencil to his desk blotter. "I don't know. But I have a bad feeling about it. Elise and her kids are on their own. Vulnerable."

"Why don't you assign an agent to them?"

"A note isn't enough to go on. By rights, it should be a local case, not even in FBI jurisdiction."

"Unless Stan Klaus really is alive and up to his old tricks again."

The phone on Paul's desk rang. "Let's hope not."

Paul lifted the receiver. "This is Fletcher."

"Agent Fletcher, this is Rita at the Kendall County Sheriff's Office. We just had a woman reported missing. Last seen at ten o'clock last night. Normally a missing-persons report isn't filed until twenty-four hours after the person has supposedly gone missing, but you wanted to know."

Chapter Three

Elise spent two hours lying in bed that night willing herself to sleep with very little luck. Shortly after midnight, due to sheer exhaustion, she dozed off.

The dream started with her as a teenager during the first flood when her family had evacuated Riverton. Her father, mother and sister were all there, alive and well. The dream transitioned into the flood of two years ago, when the Riverton Police Department and the FBI were hot on the case of a serial killer.

They didn't know who it was, but she did. She was lying in bed next to her husband in her house in North Dakota. Her husband was the killer, but he didn't know she knew. Terrified, she lay there, afraid to look at him lest he see in her eyes that she knew. When she worked up the courage and looked at Stan, he was gone.

Afraid for her boys, she leaped out of bed and ran down the longest hallway of her life. She didn't remember the hall being that long, but the more she ran, the longer it became. When she finally reached the boys' room and peered in, their beds were empty and floodwaters had seeped through the walls.

She searched through the house, the water rising from her

ankles to her knees, dragging at her nightgown, pulling her down. With water up to her waist, she couldn't find the front door to the house. Where were the boys? They weren't good swimmers. Had Stan taken them? Would he murder his own sons like he'd murdered those women?

When she finally found the front door, she grabbed the handle beneath the surface of the water and pulled, but the door wouldn't open. The water kept it from moving and had risen to just below her chin.

"Help!" she cried. "Help me!" No one heard her, no one came. When the water covered her face, the door opened and she poured out into the cold, dark street. The flood had only been in her house. The streets were dry and everyone was gone.

She was completely alone.

Elise knew in her heart it was all a dream, but when the fear and emptiness threatened to choke off her air, she forced herself awake. She was the only one who could stop the nightmare from sucking her into a black abyss of despair. She was the only one who could make the evil go away.

At two o'clock, she woke, her body shaking. The covers had slid to the floor and the air conditioner had done an excellent job of keeping the house cool. Too cool.

A subtle creaking sound reached her from the living room. Was someone in the house or was she going to start imagining that every noise was Stan trying to break into her home?

She slid her feet over the edge of the bed and stepped onto the floor, glad it was dry and not flooding like the house in her dream. Padding quietly down the hallway, she confirmed both boys were still in the house. As if they sensed their mother's restlessness, they'd tossed off the covers from their matching twin beds. She tucked them in, kissed their foreheads and trudged back to her room.

By four o'clock, Elise gave up her pretense at sleeping, afraid she'd go right back to the same nightmare. Instead, she paced, working through every possible scenario. If the note wasn't from Stan, who would be sick enough to send it to her? Since it hadn't gone through the postal system, someone who had access to the school had to have left it there. How many people could she have angered in the past few months? Angry enough to send her threatening notes? One of her students? A parent? The garbage man? Her next-door neighbor? Who? Her head ached and she still hadn't come up with one viable suspect.

INSTEAD OF LETTING THE BOYS ride the bus that morning, she dropped them off at school. If Stan were alive, he'd want his boys. How could she keep them safe? She couldn't stay home and lock the doors forever, could she?

Before the boys got out of the car, she warned them that she was the only person allowed to pick them up and they were not to talk to strangers. Ever.

Brandon nodded, his face somber.

Luke bounced out of the car, shouting, "Okay, Mom."

On her drive to work, she almost wrecked when she saw a man who vaguely resembled Stan. She circled the street, looking for him, but he'd disappeared. By the time she arrived at the school, she swore she'd seen at least a dozen Stan Klaus look-alikes.

This is crazy! How could she live like this, scared of every man with brown hair and brown eyes?

Afraid someone would stop her in the hallway and ask her what was wrong, she ducked into her classroom and hid behind her computer, hoping no one would talk to her before class started. What could she say? *I'm not sleeping well because my demented, serial-killer husband is not dead like I thought.*

Ten minutes before the bell rang for second period and Elise's first class, Gerri Finch flounced into the room, a sullen Ashley in tow. "Ms. Johnson, what do you mean by giving my Ashley three tardies in your class?"

At barely eight in the morning, after a sleepless night of worry, Elise was in no mood to put up with Gerri. "Did you ask Ashley?"

"Don't get flippant with me. I pay your salary out of the god-awful amount of taxes I pay each year. Don't think I can't pull the plug on your little vendetta against my little girl."

Elise would bet Gerri Finch hadn't worked a day in her life and if she had, she hadn't paid a dime of taxes. As the general manager of one of the larger auto dealerships in San Antonio, her husband raked in a six-figure salary plus bonuses, enabling him to keep his wife and daughter in the manner to which they'd become accustomed.

"Oh, Mom." Ashley tugged against her mother's clawlike grip. "Just leave it."

"I will not. She's been out to get you since the first day of school and I won't have it." Gerri's voice rose with each word she said until she was yelling.

"Ms. Finch, my class starts in five minutes. Unless you plan to stay and keep quiet, I suggest you take your complaint to the principal's office." To Ashley, she said, "You've been late to class five times. The rule says three tardies and you're in Saturday school. I gave you two freebies." Elise raised her brows at the girl. "Didn't I, Ashley?"

Ashley shrugged instead of answering.

Gerri stepped between Ashley and Elise. "If she goes to Saturday school, she'll miss the cheer competition. She's captain of the cheerleading squad, for chrissake."

"Then maybe she should set the example for her peers and

get to class on time." Elise stood and herded the mother and daughter toward the door where students waited to get in. "I'm following the rules, Ms. Finch. Now, if you'll excuse me, the bell is about—"

As Elise opened the classroom door, the earsplitting school bell blared in the hallway.

Teenagers filed in looking no more rested than she felt, but probably possessing a lot more energy.

Elise braced herself for the day ahead, wondering if she'd get a moment to call Paul and Melissa for an update.

Gerri glared at her over the heads of the teens. "I'll take this matter to the principal. Just you wait. We're not through yet."

Oh, goody. One more thing to worry about. As if she didn't have enough on her mind with a death threat. She stared after Gerri Finch. Could the pushy mother be the one who'd sent her the letter? She certainly had access to the school. She volunteered on occasion and knew every teacher by name.

Elise made a mental note to talk to Paul about Gerri. In the meantime, she had a full day of teaching to get through before she could meet up with the FBI agents later that afternoon.

The day passed much like the others in her teaching job. With the added stress of the note, she fought to be patient with the teens. Every minor thing was a major problem to them. Drama, always drama. The "me" mentality wouldn't let them see past their own little worlds to the bigger, harsher world outside Breuer, Texas.

On good days, Elise put herself in their shoes and tried to empathize, but today...not a chance. What to wear to the football game on Friday was the last thing she considered important.

How to survive a serial killer ranked just a bit higher on her list.

If the constant chatter wasn't bad enough, Caesar Valdez

was up to his usual tricks, as well, in her last class of the day. Her challenging class, as the seasoned teachers called it. The young man couldn't sit still to save his life. After Elise had told him to return to his seat for the fourth time, she snapped.

"Caesar, I can't teach when you're interrupting the class constantly. Go to the principal's office. You can spend the rest of the week in the Student Alternative Center."

Caesar stood, puffed out his chest and said, "No."

Elise blinked, surprised by his blatant refusal to do as he was told. "What do you mean by no?"

He shrugged, his lip curling into a sneer. "No."

The bell chose that moment to ring, indicating the end of the longest day of Elise's life.

While most of the students grabbed their books and raced for the door, Caesar stood his ground.

"That's fine, Caesar. I'll inform the principal of your behavior. She can deal with it."

"Why don't *you* deal with it?" He stepped forward until he was only two feet away from her.

Her personal space threatened, Elise refused to back down. "Just because you're bigger than me, doesn't mean you can push me around, Caesar. Back off."

"You heard her, Caesar. Back off." Kendall dropped her backpack on her desk and stepped up beside Elise.

"That's right. We're tired of you pushing people around." Alex moved to stand on Elise's other side.

Caesar's brows rose at the united front. After a quick glance around at the room still full of his peers, Caesar's glare returned. "You three don't scare me. You can't do anything to me."

"Maybe they can't, but I can." Paul Fletcher stepped through the doorway and stood a good six inches taller than Caesar. His muscular chest was developed and solid. Not to mention, Paul was a trained federal agent and he looked like it, from the way he stood to the cold look he directed toward Caesar.

Elise let the breath out that she'd been holding. Glad for the interference, she knew she'd ultimately pay for not dealing with the problem herself. Now that Paul had stepped in, Caesar would find another time to test her and possibly Kendall and Alex. Not good.

Caesar stared at Paul as if weighing his options and then he shrugged. "I got better things to do." He pushed past Paul and left the room.

"You okay?" Paul looked at her with a concerned frown.

With a half-dozen students still gawking, she squared her shoulders and nodded. "Yes. I'm fine. Just another day in the classroom." She shot a glance at the teens still standing around, her eyebrows rising. "Don't you have homes to go to?"

They ducked their heads and scurried out the door, except for Alex and Kendall.

"I can't believe what Caesar tried to pull. Someone needs to take him down." Kendall threw back her shoulders as if she'd like to be the one to do it—all five foot two of girl with attitude. "We've got enough going on around here without him playing the class jerk."

Elise grabbed Kendall's arm. "You be careful around him. He's got a lot more bulk to him than you, and apparently he's not afraid to throw it around."

"He doesn't scare us," Alex said, standing as tall as his five-foot-four-inch frame would go. "I'm a black belt in tae kwon do."

"Yeah, but he has eighty pounds on you," Elise reminded him.

The teen's eyes narrowed. "Doesn't matter how big you are. What matters is how you use what you have."

"Yeah," Kendall added. "I took self-defense, too." When Alex shot her a surprised look, she blushed. "My dad insisted." Kendall's brows rose. "It could happen to anybody. Look at that woman who disappeared last night. She was taken from her home right here in Breuer."

The blood in Elise's head rushed to her stomach and she swayed. "A woman disappeared?" She frowned at Kendall. "How did you know?"

"My dad works for the sheriff's department." Kendall laughed. "I guess the cop thing runs in the family."

Elise's gaze connected with Paul's. "Did you know about this?"

Paul nodded, wishing he'd taken Melissa's advice last night and called Elise as soon as he'd heard. "I got word about it last night."

Elise's face went from white to red. Instead of blasting him, she turned calmly toward the teens. "Kendall, Alex, did you need me for anything?"

"No, ma'am," Kendall responded.

Kendall and Alex left Paul and Elise alone in the classroom with the door half-closed.

Paul braced himself.

As soon as the kids were out of earshot, Elise launched her attack. "Why didn't you call me?"

"We don't know whether or not the woman's disappearance had anything to do with the note." Paul knew his answer wouldn't be good enough for her. She wanted to be in on every little detail, to stay on top of the threat to herself and her children.

"Still, I want to know what's going on." She paced across the classroom and back, only to stop directly in front of him. "I can't believe you didn't tell me. How could you? You know what it means to me. You know I'm scared."

"Exactly. If I'd told you about the woman, you wouldn't have slept a wink."

"You think I slept last night?" She dropped her voice to just above a whisper. "I had nightmares about him all night. This morning, I swear I saw Stan in every face on the street. Is he or is he not dead?"

Paul sighed. "We don't know with absolute certainty."

"That's not good enough, damn it." Her eyes glazed with moisture and she stepped closer. "You don't know what it's like to look over your shoulder every second of the day. Or the hell you go through when you let your children out of your sight to go to school. To school, for heaven's sake." Her voice cracked and tears spilled over the edges of her eyelids and down her face. "Why didn't you make sure he was dead then? If he is alive, what have I done to this town? What have I brought with me by moving here?"

"You haven't brought anything. We don't know if it's your husband or someone playing a prank on you. You have to give us time." He clasped her arms and stared down into her tear-streaked face.

"Time?" She looked up at him through hazy blue eyes. "Does that missing woman have time?"

A noise at the door drew Paul's attention, saving him from answering truthfully.

Kendall stood there, her eyes wide, her hand hovering, as if to knock. "I—I'm sorry. I didn't mean to interrupt." Her glance darted to Elise and then to the desk where her backpack lay. "I forgot something."

"Get it," Elise said through her teeth, turning her back to the girl.

Kendall dove for the backpack and almost made it out the door when Elise swung back.

"Kendall, wait." She scrubbed her hand over her cheeks and frowned at the teen. "How much of our conversation did you overhear?"

The girl eased around. "Not much." She didn't look Elise in the eye when she responded. "I have to go." She spun toward the door.

"Kendall." Paul stepped in front of her. "How much did you hear?"

"Nothing I'll repeat. I swear." Kendall looked around Paul to Elise. "Alex and I like you, Ms. Johnson. You're our favorite teacher. We'd never do or say anything that would hurt you."

Elise stared at her for a long moment. "It's very important that whatever you think you might have heard doesn't go outside this room."

The girl nodded, her eyes wide, scared. "I promise, it won't."

"Go home, Kendall." Elise gave her a crooked smile, but the smile faded and she added, "And lock your doors."

When the young lady had gone, Elise glanced up at Paul, a worried frown drawing her brows together. "If word gets out about my problem, I'll be kicked out of this school so fast, I won't know what hit my backside."

"I don't think the kid will rat on you." Paul stared into her tearstained face. "Are you ready to leave?"

"Yes." She glanced around the room one last time as if checking for stray students. "My boys will be home soon."

But she didn't move yet. "Maybe I should turn in my resignation now and save the school the worry."

"Don't borrow trouble, Elise. You're a good teacher. You have a right to a life."

"Yeah, so do the rest of the people of Breuer." She looked up into his eyes, her face pale and pinched. "So did the woman who disappeared."

What could he say to that? Paul fought the urge to pull Elise into his arms and shield her from all the ugliness the world had to offer.

After Elise slung her handbag over her shoulder, Paul hurried her out of the classroom and off campus.

"We'll take my truck." He waved toward a big, dark gray pickup parked in the visitors' parking area.

"No, I'll need my car." When she tried to step around him and go to her car, he snagged her arm.

"That's what I came here to talk to you about." He held the passenger door open. "Before the boys get home, I have something to tell you and I don't want you driving while I tell you."

"You mean there's more?" She closed her eyes, her face going dangerously pale.

"Yeah. Get in." He all but lifted her into the seat and closed the door. When he'd climbed in beside her and had the door safely shut, he turned in his seat. "They found Lauren Pendley this afternoon. She was the missing woman."

"Oh, God." Elise pressed her fist to her lips, her blue eyes wide and shining with unshed tears. "Where?"

Paul wished he didn't have to tell her. This woman had gone through so much already. He hesitated.

Elise laid her fist in her lap and her chin rose. "Just tell me."

"They found her in the Guadalupe River bound with Ethernet cable."

"Oh, God, oh, God." Elise wrapped her arms around herself and rocked back and forth in her seat.

The woman had been strangled, tied with Ethernet cable and dumped, just like the women in the Dakota Strangler case.

"One other disturbing item to note… She went by Lauren, but her first name was Alice."

Chapter Four

Elise's eyes burned, tears held in check by the cold wash of fear snaking through her body, stiffening her limbs. "It's him."

"We don't know that, but Mel and I will be working with the local sheriff's department and city police to find the man responsible."

"It's him." Her voice sounded hollow, even to her own ears. "He didn't die in the fire."

"That wasn't his usual M.O." Paul shifted into Drive and pulled out of school parking lot, careful not to hit loitering teens waiting for parents to get off work. "Stan didn't care about first names. He chose smart women."

True. Her grip on the armrest loosened slightly. She no longer believed in coincidence, not since the Dakota Strangler. She wouldn't let herself. "But it's too much of a coincidence. It has to be him." And if it was him, even the kids at school could be in danger, especially the girls. Elise scrambled for the button to lower the window so that she could shout out a warning to the female students still loitering on school grounds. Her hands shook and the tears filling her eyes made it impossible to see. "How do I open the window?"

Paul brought the truck to a halt. He reached across her lap and laid a hand over her shaking one. "Alice, it'll be all right."

She jerked her face toward his, heat rising up her neck and into her cheeks. "Don't call me that! Alice Klaus is dead as far as I'm concerned. She was stupid and deserved to die along with all the other women her husband killed."

Paul grabbed her hand and kept her from lowering her window. "No. Alice didn't die. You're alive and kicking and living in Texas."

"No, she's not." Her faith in herself had died a little more with each one of the women Stan murdered. How could this man think she was the same woman?

"Alice—Elise." He turned her to face him. "You're beautiful and smart enough to realize you aren't to blame for what happened. Stan, and only Stan, was responsible."

"How can you say that? I lived with the man. I should have stopped him. Now that maniac is out there. These kids could be in danger. I have to let them know."

"You can't, Elise. You'll have an entire town up in arms and like you said, you'll lose your job."

Anger burned in her chest and she wanted to take it out on Paul, but she knew it wasn't his fault. He'd been nothing but kind to her and her children when her world had shattered. Even back then, she remembered thinking how nice it would have been to be married to a man like Paul—a man who cared enough to protect them from harm.

The steam fizzled out of her and she slumped in her seat, pulling her hand free of his. Paul was a nice man. Stan was nice, too, when Elise married him. But people changed. She'd changed.

She stared out at the lingering teens. She wanted to warn them. Warn everyone that she was the plague. That a killer had followed her all the way to Texas. "It's not right for me to keep this secret. So many could be at risk."

"We can't be certain that Stan did it. We don't know if you or anyone around you is the real target. This could all be a fluke."

"I don't think so." She shook her head and stared out at the stunted live oak trees, gnarled and twisted by weather. "But you're right. I can't leave. I used all my savings to move us to Texas. I don't have any money left to keep running."

"You can't keep running." Paul spoke in low, steady tones, his voice caressing her with a calm she couldn't manage on her own.

She breathed in and out, willing her heart rate to slow. But then it cranked up again. "We don't know where he'll strike next."

"If he strikes," Paul said.

Elise stared out at the clear blue sky, mocking her dark thoughts. How could it be so bright and sunny when a killer stalked the streets? "We can't let him hurt anyone else." She sat up straighter, squaring her shoulders. Now wasn't the time to go soft. She had to be strong. A glance at the clock made her blood race. "I won't let him take my boys. Can you go a little faster, Agent Fletcher? Their bus will be there in less than five minutes."

"Yes, ma'am." A hint of a smile flashed on Paul's face before he pulled out onto the street, focused on beating the traffic.

For the first couple of minutes, she remained silent, her thoughts churning over her options. She didn't have the money to gather her belongings and move to another city. Her house wasn't wired with a security system and she'd used the last of her meager savings to replace the air conditioner, a must in the blazing heat of a South Texas Indian summer. "Do you think the bank would loan me enough money to install a security system?"

"You don't know until you ask."

With a sigh, she forced herself to lean back in her seat. "How long does it take to install one?"

"Depends on the contractor."

Elise snorted softly. "Maybe a gun would be the better investment. More immediate."

"There's usually a waiting period to purchase a gun." He shot a glance at her. "Do you even know how to use one?"

"No." Her lips twisted. "Actually, they scare me."

"And you don't want to risk your boys getting their hands on a loaded gun, and loaded is the only way a gun is of use to you."

Hopelessness washed over her and she shook her head. "So what you're telling me is that I'm basically defenseless in my own home."

"Not quite. I have a proposition for you."

Her gaze narrowed on Paul. "What do you mean, a proposition?"

He didn't look at her, but kept his attention on navigating the turn into her driveway. "I could stay with you at night until we catch him."

Elise's heart fluttered and her hands grew cold and clammy. She hadn't lived in the same house with a man since North Dakota. Heck, she hadn't trusted herself with another man since.

The last time she'd been with Paul, he'd played with her children in the evacuation shelter. She'd been drawn to the sexy federal agent more than she wanted to admit, but chalked it up to vulnerability. Tall, blond and incredibly handsome, Paul remained hard to ignore. But that didn't matter. She couldn't get involved with anyone, not now or ever. "No. That's not possible."

Her voice quivered and her hands shook as she fumbled for her seat belt, the interior of the truck suddenly too closed in, the air thick with tension. The scent of Paul's aftershave drifted beneath her defenses, making her think thoughts she hadn't dared to in a very long time.

Before she could climb down, he was out and holding the door for her. He helped her down and held her arms in his hands. "Please reconsider, Elise."

The big, yellow bus turned onto Highland Street, its brakes screeching as it came to a halt halfway down the block. The doors opened and a backpack flew off the bus, landing on the pavement. Luke leaped to the ground, laughing.

Brandon clambered down after him, his gaze shooting immediately to where Elise stood in Paul's arms. His eyes narrowed and he grabbed Luke's hand, hurrying him home.

"You should go." Elise could see the storm brewing in Brandon's eyes.

"Okay, but I'll be back later." He stared down into her eyes. "To stay."

"I'll think about it."

Paul climbed into his truck, feeling like he was running away when every instinct told him to stay. He, too, had seen the look on Brandon's young face. The little guy had been through enough, losing more than a father. Elise wanted to handle her children her own way. He'd give her the space.

For now.

At least until he could get back to the office and have a powwow with Mel. He hadn't planned on staying with Elise, but he didn't see any other way to protect her during the dark hours when most people slept.

He slid his cell phone open and speed-dialed the Kendall County Sheriff's department. "This is Special Agent Fletcher. I'd like to speak to Sheriff Engel."

He pulled into a church parking lot and waited while the operator made the transfer.

"This is the sheriff. What can I do for you, Agent Fletcher?"

"I'd like to meet with you concerning the woman found murdered."

"This case isn't in your jurisdiction, unless you've got something to share from the FBI?"

"I understand." He'd known he'd have to dance around Elise's connection, but he had to open the lines of communication with the men actually working the case. "We can discuss it in further detail when we meet."

"How's nine o'clock in the morning? The Denny's in Breuer. I'm partial to their chicken-fried steak. Just don't tell my wife I eat it for breakfast. She's trying to get me on some danged low-fat diet."

"Your secret's safe with me." Paul's stomach rumbled at the mention of food. He hadn't eaten since he'd grabbed a biscuit at the McDonald's on his way to work that morning. "I'll be there at nine. Thanks." He clicked the end button and hit the speed-dial button for Agent Melissa Bradley.

"Hey, Fletcher," Melissa answered on the first ring. "How did Alice take the news?"

"Elise. She insists we call her Elise. I just left her house." His grip tightened on the phone. "She's pretty shaken. Wants to buy a gun."

"I would be, too." Mel snorted. "Does she even know how to use one?"

"Not a clue."

"Almost as scary a thought as a serial killer returned from the dead."

"I'm not buying that it's Stan. That house was in flames. If the fire didn't get him, the smoke would have."

"Yeah, but we didn't find the body." Mel's voice dropped to barely above a whisper. "We can't rule it out."

"If he's alive, he had to have been in a hospital for burns or smoke inhalation."

"I'll check with all the hospitals in the Riverton area around that time frame."

"Good. And also check the hospitals farther down along the Red River. If Klaus did live, he could have ended up miles down river."

"Hey, boss, here's a chance for you to get to know Cain's abilities. Want me to get him to help make the calls?"

Paul hesitated. On the one hand, Cain had been itching for a case with more meat. Then again, he still didn't know how much he could trust Cain to keep his mouth shut. Paul had only been on the job for two months, not long enough to get a good feel for the other man's capabilities or loyalties. Not to mention, Cain hadn't been overly pleased with an outsider moving into his territory. "I don't know what to think about Cain yet."

"What? He hasn't warmed up to the ol' Fletcher charm yet?"

"No, the district coordinator warned me that some of the men had been up for the job I got. I wonder if he was one of them."

"Sour grapes?"

"Could be. I don't want him involved until I get a better feel for his work. Especially with Ali—Ms. Johnson's need for confidentiality."

"Gotcha. Mum's the word around Cain." Mel paused. "You want me to take lead on this one, boss?"

"No, I'll take lead."

"Not trying to overstep your authority to decide, but I just want to remind you that you're the boss now. You're *supposed* to delegate duties."

"Point taken." He grinned. "I'm still taking the lead."

Melissa chuckled. "You got it. Do we need to assign protection to her?"

A twinge of guilt pinched his nerves, but he quickly shrugged it aside. "I've got that covered."

"Going to use the local police force?"

Here goes. Explanation time. "No, I'm going to stay with her." He braced himself for the onslaught of questions.

A long pause stretched from the other end of the line.

Paul heaved a sigh. "Go ahead, I know you're holding back."

"You sure you can handle that?" Mel asked. "Last time you were around her, you were pretty taken with her, serial killer husband and all."

Damn, nothing escaped Mel's notice. That's what made her such a good agent. "I'm taken with all the ladies, you know that."

"No, boss, this was different. You were really taken with her, not your usual love-'em-and-leave-'em style."

Paul's fingers tightened on the steering wheel. Mel hit too close to home with her observation. He had felt something back then. He'd chalked it up to pity for the beautiful bride of the Dakota Strangler. Still, he wanted to be the one to see to Elise's safety. "I was only doing what anyone would have done to help her through the trauma."

Mel chuckled. "Yeah, right. Whatever you say, boss. And she's agreed to this plan?"

Paul's lips firmed into a straight line. "Not yet. But she will. I'm on my way to the Bexar County coroner's office."

"I'll meet you there as soon as I get those calls started."

"Good deal." He slid the phone shut, tossed it into the cup holder and pressed his foot to the accelerator, shooting his truck out onto the narrow streets of Breuer. The coroner's office in San Antonio only stayed open until five. He'd just make it if he hurried.

As he merged into the interstate traffic, his cell phone vibrated, rattling against the hard plastic cup holder. He risked a glance down at the caller ID.

Cain.

Great. What did he want?

Paul slid the phone open. “Fletcher.”

“Did you hear about the body they found in Breuer?” Cain asked.

“Yes.” Paul held his hand steady, not in any mood to talk with Cain, but unwilling to show his hand. “Are you finished with that stack of background checks?”

“I’ve made some headway. I just wondered if you wanted me to look into the Breuer case.”

“Not yet. It’s a local issue at this point. Until the local officials invite us in, it’s in their ballpark. We have no jurisdiction.”

“Right. But we could offer our services. Up to them to refuse.”

Paul squashed his irritation. The man really was hungry for something interesting. “Not yet. Tell you what, why don’t you get with Alvarez on the government fraud case. I’ll call and let him know you’ll be assisting.”

“I’d rather help out with the Breuer case.”

“Not on your radar, Cain.” So his voice was a little too sharp. Cain was starting to get on his nerves.

“Yes, sir,” Cain answered, his own response prickly.

“We’ll talk in the morning when I get to the office.” Paul could swear he heard muttered curses, but he couldn’t be sure as a tractor-trailer rig chose that moment to roar past him on the interstate.

“Roger.” Cain clicked off.

He’d been giving Cain the benefit of the doubt since he’d arrived in the San Antonio office. But if his attitude toward his new boss didn't improve soon, Cain would have to be dealt with. Either they'd get their differences out in the open and start over, or Paul would recommend a transfer for Agent Cain.

In the meantime, he had a case to work, even though he wasn't supposed to be working it.

HE PULLED INTO the coroner's office five minutes to five. The front door was still open and he slipped inside, quickly making his way to the examination room where he met Gordon Smithson, the county medical examiner.

"Dr. Smithson, I'm Agent Fletcher." He nodded toward the woman lying on the table. He jammed his hands into his back pockets to keep from touching anything and tried to ignore the scent of decaying bodies and formaldehyde permeating the room. "Is this Alice Lauren Pendley?"

"Agent Fletcher. Glad you made it. I was just finishing up my examination of the body."

The door opened behind him. Mel entered and closed the distance between them. "Sorry I'm late," she said, then turned a smile toward the coroner. "Special Agent Bradley."

Smithson returned her smile, showing more animation than when Paul had introduced himself. Mel had that effect on most men. She was engaging without trying. Someone others automatically wanted to confide in.

"Do we have a cause of death?" she asked, her gaze shifting from Dr. Smithson to the body stretched out on the examination table.

Smithson's attention reverted to the victim. "Asphyxiation. Most probably someone came at her from behind and hooked an arm around her neck. She put up a fight. See the way her fingernails are broken off? She was found naked with

Ethernet cable securing her hands behind her back and tied around her ankles. But she was dead before he bound her."

"Isn't that overkill?" Mel said.

Paul cringed at her poor choice of words, but the killer had made his point. He was either Stan Klaus or a copycat. Newspapers around the country had printed stories detailing the Dakota Strangler's methods. A book on serial killers had an entire chapter dedicated to him. Anyone with a sick mind could copy his methods.

What they shouldn't have been able to do was find his wife.

Unless one of the children had unintentionally let the secret leak out. Brandon was old enough to remember his real name. Luke had been four when his father disappeared: he probably didn't even remember the man.

Paul made a mental note to ask Brandon. Not that he expected the boy to open up to him. For some reason, Brandon viewed Paul as a threat to his mother.

Paul had little experience with children, but how hard could it be to get the boy to warm up to him? He'd just turn up the old Fletcher charm, as Mel called it. After he stopped by his apartment and packed an overnight kit.

He wasn't taking no for an answer from Elise. She needed protection. Whether the killer was Stan or a copycat, he definitely had something in mind for Elise Johnson.

Chapter Five

Elise threw herself into the normal routine of homework with the boys, grading papers and then fixing dinner for her small family. The work should have helped her to calm down after Paul's revelation and pending return.

But she couldn't help what her mind kept conjuring. A woman floating in the Guadalupe, her blond hair streaming out beside her, her hands and feet tied in Ethernet cable. Every time the image surfaced, a cool chill she couldn't attribute to the new air-conditioning shook Elise's body.

When she finally dropped into her chair at the dinner table to eat the boys' favorite, mac and cheese, her shoulders were stiff and her appetite nonexistent. She forced a smile, determined to act like normal. "How was your day, Luke?"

Luke gave her a cheesy grin and spoke around the food in his mouth. "I got four stars today for helping clean the classroom."

"Very good, Luke. I'm sure Mrs. Dobratka was impressed with your thoughtfulness."

He nodded, stuffing another heaping forkful of orangey macaroni into his mouth, half of it falling back to his plate.

"Smaller bites, big guy." Elise turned to Brandon. He'd been quiet since he'd gotten off the bus, following her around the small house, if not physically, then with his penetrating gaze. Sometimes she thought he could see more into situations than an eight-year-old should.

"How about you, Brandon? How was your day? Did Ms. Tingle give you a spelling test today?" She placed a small bite in her mouth and pretended enjoyment.

Her oldest son set his fork beside his plate and gave her a narrow stare. "Why was that man here again?"

Glad for the little bit of food in her mouth, Elise chewed slowly before answering. "Paul is an old friend. He didn't know we lived here until yesterday. I guess he just wanted to come visit."

Brandon lifted his fork and stabbed at the food on his plate. "I don't like him."

"Why?"

"He made you cry." The boy's brows drew together in a fierce frown.

It was times like these when he looked most like his father. Elise prayed that he wouldn't take after the man. "I told you, I cried because I was happy to see him." This was only a partial lie. She had cried because she was scared out of her mind, but she'd been very glad to see Paul when he'd shown up yesterday. Maybe a little too glad. He'd been her pillar of strength when she really needed him. He was a man any girl could easily fall in love with. Any girl but her. She couldn't trust her instincts.

"Isn't he the man from where we used to live?"

Brandon's words broke into Elise's thoughts and she set her fork down, fighting back a jolt of nervous tension. Since they'd left North Dakota, she hadn't talked with the boys about any of what had happened. She'd only told them that their father had died and that they were going to start a new life with new names.

Brandon hadn't asked questions at the time. If Elise wasn't mistaken, her oldest son seemed relieved that he didn't have to suffer his father's abuse. The man had leaned toward obsessive-compulsive behavior in the way he'd demanded perfection from his boys. They hadn't been allowed to run and play in their own home. Once free of his father, Brandon had taken a long time to loosen up and remember that he was a kid.

Looking at the young man across from her, Elise recognized the same little boy who'd sat straight in his chair while his father blasted him for dropping his fork on the floor.

Elise had tried to interfere with the harsh lectures once and had her face slapped so hard she'd hit the wall behind her. Every time she stepped in the middle, their punishment became harsher and Brandon became more resentful.

How much did Brandon remember? And how much talk had he overheard when they'd been in the evacuation shelter? Did he know his father was a killer?

"Yes. We knew Paul from where we used to live." She hoped his questions would end there. "Want some more?" Elise jumped to her feet and grabbed the pan from the stove.

"Did he know our father?" Brandon asked. "Was he his friend?"

Elise's hand shook and she set the pan back on the stove before she dropped it. "No, Brandon. He didn't know your father and he wasn't his friend."

Brandon sat staring at his food for a long moment. "I don't like him."

"He only wants to make sure we're okay and take care of us."

Her son straightened in his chair. "I'm the man of the house. I'll take care of us. I promised, remember?"

Elise dropped to a crouch next to his chair and pulled him

into her arms. "Yes, sweetheart. You are the man of the house. It's just that sometimes we need a little more help around here."

"No, we don't." Brandon pushed her away, his lips set in a stubborn line.

As much as she wanted to agree with Brandon, the more Elise thought about it, the more she felt she needed Paul around. If Stan really was alive, he'd be coming after her and the boys any minute. She might as well prepare the boys for Paul's "visit" before he showed up with his suitcase. "Brandon, you're the man of the house. However, Mr. Fletcher offered to stay with us for a few days. I hope you'll be nice to him and treat him as a guest."

"We don't need him around here." Brandon pushed his chair away from the table. "We don't need anyone. I'll take care of you." He stood straight, his fists clenched beside him.

Tears threatened to well in Elise's eyes, but she refused to let Brandon see them and willed them away, though her eyes burned with the effort. "I know you will, honey. But Paul—Mr. Fletcher…" What? What could she say to convince Brandon that it was all right for Paul to stay several nights at their house? Then a thought surfaced. "He's going to help us build a fence in the backyard."

"We already have a fence," Brandon argued.

"A different fence, one that doesn't have big gaps in it."

"So we can get a dog?" Luke jumped out of his chair and ran around the kitchen table whooping. "We're going to get a dog!"

Brandon glared at his brother. "A dog?" His glare transferred to his mother. "They make a mess."

God, that was his father talking. Stan hadn't let the boys have a dog, claiming they were filthy. He had to have everything in perfect order.

Elise let a smile spill across her face. A little bit of revenge filling her veins. She didn't know why she hadn't thought about it until now. Maybe she'd taken a little too long to loosen up after being released from Stan's controlling ways. "Yes, Brandon. But not a dog. A puppy."

"A puppy!" Luke ran to his mother and threw his arms around her neck. "I'm gonna tell George. We're getting a puppy." He raced for the back door. Before Elise could stop him, he was outside, the screen slamming back in place.

"Luke!" His words sank in and she turned to Brandon. "Who's George?"

Brandon shrugged. "I don't know."

Elise hurried to the back door and watched as Luke ran to the back corner of the yard where the picket fence was overgrown with bushes and bramble.

The little guy yelled, "George! Guess what?"

Who was George? Elise strained to see through the overgrown hedges to the house on the other side, but could only make out the roofline. For that matter, she didn't know any of her neighbors. She'd been too busy moving in and getting the boys settled in school and setting up her own classroom that she hadn't taken the time to stroll down the block. Elise made a mental note to get to know her neighbors. For all she knew, Stan could be one of them. Another chill shook her from head to toe.

Luke yelled again and again. When no one seemed to respond, he ran back to the house. "Can I tell Kenny? Can I, Mom?"

A stab of fear lanced through her. Kendall lived a block away over the top of a slight rise in Highland Street, just enough of a rise you couldn't see her house from theirs. Luke and Brandon had been there once when Kendall had taken them there to see her Sheltie. They knew where it was. Would they try to go there on their own? Elise squatted next to her youngest son. "You're not to go to her house without me. Do you understand?"

Luke's eyes widened, his gaze going from his mother to where her hands pinched his arms. "I promise."

Elise's gaze followed his to where her hands clenched around his thin upper arms. She immediately let go, her fingers burning. Memories of Stan manhandling her blasting through her mind. "I'm sorry. I just don't want you or Brandon leaving the house without me."

"Even to play in the yard?" Brandon asked, stepping up to his brother.

"Yes." She couldn't look into her oldest son's eyes. She didn't want him to see the fear in hers. "Just for a few days, anyway."

"Is it because of him?" Brandon persisted. "The man from North Dakota?"

Elise's heart skipped several beats before she realized Brandon was talking about Paul, not his father. "No. Not at all. Agent Fletcher is just coming to help build the fence in the backyard." Speaking of which, she'd have to come up with funds to buy the materials. Maybe she could open an account with the local hardware store until she could afford to pay it off. "Right now, why don't we go out in the backyard and see what needs to be cleaned up to get started."

Anything to get Brandon's mind off Paul until the man showed up at his door. She'd deal with his attitude then. At least Luke was on board. It didn't take much to get Luke excited. Especially with the promise of a puppy.

"Can we get our puppy today?" Luke asked, bounding down the back steps into the overgrown grass.

"Not today. We need a fence that will hold him before we can bring one home." The more she thought about it, the more she liked the idea of having a dog. A lone woman with two small children to protect could always use a dog. She'd make sure it grew into a big dog, one that protected her boys. Paul could help her find just the right breed.

As she wandered around the yard, picking up sticks and toys, she kept a close eye on the boys. The skin on the back of her neck prickled as though someone was watching her. Twice she spun around, sure someone would be there.

No one was.

At this rate, she'd be a nervous wreck before Paul returned at sundown.

AFTER LEAVING THE CORONER and Mel, Paul swung by the office. Only a few agents remained at their desks, and Paul breathed a sigh when he walked by Cain's empty desk. At least he didn't have to confront the man and his attitude. He wanted to place a few calls and then get back to Breuer before nightfall.

Paul stepped into his office and jerked to a halt.

Agent Cain leaped from Paul's chair, ruddy red color filling his cheeks. "Sorry. Always wondered what it was like from the other side of this desk."

Paul tamped down the anger that flared inside. "Just don't make it a habit."

"I won't." He hurried around the desk then danced around Paul, giving him enough room to take his seat.

The seat was warm. How long had Cain been sitting there? Paul's gaze panned the files and paperwork neatly stacked on his desk. Had anything moved? Had Cain been snooping through his work? He'd lock his door next time he left the office. A new file lay square in the middle of his desk.

Agent Cain sat in the cracked leather seat across from Paul and leaned back, pressing his fingertips together in a steeple. "I hope you don't mind, but after I met Alvarez on the fraud case I did some research on similar murders as the one in Breuer."

"It's not in our jurisdiction." Paul fished for a pen from his desk drawer and then stared across at the man.

"I know, but it should be."

Paul's fingers tightened around his pen. "Stay out of it, Cain. It's not your case to work." He didn't trust the man yet. Especially with a case as sensitive as Elise's.

"But there are a number of serial murder cases it could be related to. Cases where the killer was never found."

The man didn't give up, and Paul was past being patient with him. With anger sizzling just beneath the surface of his control, Paul leaned forward. "Agent Cain, what part of 'it's not your case' did you fail to understand?"

"But I think we might have a serial killer in Breuer. Don't you care?"

Paul stood up so fast his chair rolled back and hit the wall. "You are not to go near Breuer. You are not to contact anyone concerning the murder. And you are not to bring up this subject again with me or anyone else. Is that understood?"

Cain shot to his feet, his face stained a mottled red, his nostrils flaring. "But—"

Rounding his desk, Paul came to a halt in front of Cain, nose to nose. "Do you have a problem following orders, Agent Cain?"

"No, sir." Right answer, wrong inflection.

But Paul accepted it. "Next time I have to remind you of your orders, I'll write you up."

Cain straightened, his lips drawn into a thin line, his eyes burning hatred. "Yes, sir."

"Dismissed."

Special Agent Cain spun on his heels and marched out the door, slamming it behind him with enough force to shake

Paul's framed college diploma from the wall. It fell to the floor with a crash, the glass front shattering into a million shards.

Damn. If Cain didn't suspect Paul's involvement in the murder case before, he sure as hell would by now. So be it. He'd been warned.

Paul made a call to Elise's sister's home in Minneapolis.

His friend and former partner, Nick Tarver, answered. "Hello."

"Hey, Nick. How's the weather up there?"

"Getting darned cold." He laughed. "I hear you're having a warm fall. I could use a little of that about now."

An excellent FBI Special Agent, Nick had always been there when Paul needed help. And he needed it now. "I need a favor."

"Shoot."

"Can you check and see if anyone has accessed Alice Klaus's files? You know, if anyone in the system knows what she changed her name to?"

"What's happening?"

"Found a body this morning in Breuer."

"Alice?"

"No, but whoever killed her wanted it to look like Stan Klaus. And the victim's first name was Alice."

"Damn. Brenna won't be happy about that. She'll want to hop the first plane south."

"No. Don't let her. Not in her condition." At eight months pregnant, she'd be more of a hindrance than a help to him. "Mel and I are handling it from here. If you could dig around and see if her files have been tampered with, that would help."

"You got it. If you need more help, I'll come. All you have to do is say so."

"I know." Paul allowed a tight smile to stretch across his lips. Nick was one of his true friends. A man he could count on when he needed a hand. But this was his command. He had to handle things on his own. "Thanks."

He hung up, grabbed the spare shaving kit he kept in his desk drawer for the times he worked through the night and headed out the door.

A bad feeling crept across his skin, raising gooseflesh across his forearm. His footsteps quickened, urging him faster. Once he reached the parking lot, he broke into a run.

Chapter Six

The sun had dipped below the horizon, the last lingering hints of daylight glowing a dull gray, casting the world in deep shadows. Not quite dark, but hard to see nonetheless. Paul parked in Elise's driveway and climbed down from his truck. Rustling and voices sounded from the back corner of Elise's house, making the hairs on his arms prickle.

Though it could be a cat mewing for his supper, Paul didn't want to take the chance that it might be something else. He vaulted over the picket fence, landing softly in the grass. Slipping into the shadows beside the house, he hurried in the direction of the sound. A small dark form hovered near the very back of the lot, leaning into the bushes.

A giggle sounded like that of a child.

"Luke?" Paul called out.

A gasp was followed by the rustle of leaves on the bushes between the back of Elise's property and the house behind it.

The little boy raced for the back door, his small feet making little sound in the grass. The rustling on the other side of the bushes faded and disappeared in the opposite direction.

Luke had his hand on the door handle when Paul caught him by the collar of his pajamas.

"Let me go!" Luke's arms flailed, his feet hammering against Paul's shins.

Paul chuckled. "It's okay, it's just me. Paul Fletcher."

Luke continued his frenzied effort to free himself. "Let me go or Mom will be mad."

The back porch light blinked on and the door swung open. "Luke!" Elise stood in a silk robe, her hair twisted up in a towel, her eyes brilliant blue saucers in her pale face. "Paul!" The older child stood behind her, his eyes round and anxious.

"Did you lose this?" He smiled, hoping to wipe some of the fear off her pretty face.

She opened the screen and folded her son into her arms. "Luke, baby, don't ever scare me like that again!"

Brandon stared up at Paul over his mother's shoulder, his gaze narrow, unfriendly.

Paul had his work cut out for him. The boy didn't trust him. It was his job to figure out why and turn him around. The child's life could depend on it.

"Mom, I had to tell George about the puppy." Luke struggled against his mother's hold.

Elise loosened her arms enough to look into his face without letting go. "I told you you couldn't go out in the yard without me anymore."

"But George is my friend," Luke wailed.

"I don't even know George." Her eyes narrowed and her forehead creased into fine lines Paul wanted to smooth away. "Until I meet him and talk to his mother, you aren't to talk to him again. Do you understand?"

Luke's face pinched into a frown and he pushed away from his mother's arms. "Mom! George is my friend!"

Paul stood on the back steps, feeling the boy's pain, but understanding the danger involved. "Your mother is right. We need to meet George and his parents before you play with him." How could he keep the little guy from playing in his own yard without telling him that a really nasty bad guy might steal him away? The boy would have night terrors for the rest of his life.

As if just remembering who Paul was, Luke glanced up at him, his frown turning upside down into a face-splitting grin. "Are you really going to build a fence for our puppy?" His hand slipped into Paul's and he pulled him through the door into the kitchen.

Broadsided by Luke's question, Paul allowed himself to be led to the kitchen table.

Brandon backed away, not having uttered a single word so far.

"What's this about a fence?" Paul asked.

Elise's mouth twisted. "Sorry, I'll explain in a minute." She leaned down to her son. "Go wash the dirt off your feet and get to bed. It's way past your bedtime."

"But…"

"No buts. Go." She stood with her arms crossed over her chest, her face set in stern lines. The entire effect muted by her soft pink robe and makeup-free face. If Paul wasn't mistaken, her lips twitched at the corners.

Luke's body drooped so much even the faces of the cartoon cars on his pajamas appeared dejected. "I want our puppy now."

"We can't get one until we get the fence up and that isn't going to be tonight. Go on." Elise swatted at the little boy's bottom, urging him toward the hallway leading to the bedrooms.

Brandon stood at a distance, his body stiff and unmoving.

"You, too, Brandon. You have school tomorrow and need to get some sleep."

Brandon shook his head. "*I'm* the man of the house. I

shouldn't have a bedtime." He glared at Paul as if daring him to disagree.

So that was it. Brandon was feeling threatened by a new man in the house. That explained the immediate animosity toward him. How to fix it? Paul hadn't a clue, not having dealt with children before.

"Part of being the man of the house is knowing when to do as you're told." Elise didn't talk down to him as though he was a baby. She spoke to him like any other adult, presenting the facts without discouraging the boy. "Paul—Agent Fletcher and I need to talk about…the fence."

When Brandon still didn't move, Elise tipped her head slightly. "I'll be just fine and I'm not going anywhere. Now go to bed, please."

Brandon sighed and turned toward his bedroom. As he passed through his door, his glance shot toward Paul, his eyes narrowing. Then he disappeared.

"And close the door," Elise called out.

The door closed with a soft snick.

Elise sighed and pulled the towel off her head. Long strands of damp hair dropped to her shoulders. "I'm sorry. I meant to be more prepared for when you got here." She buried her fingers in the lengths and shook them, the scent of strawberries filling the air around him. "When I couldn't find Luke, I swear I almost had a heart attack."

With Elise standing so close in little more than a silk, calf-length robe, the teasing scent of her shampoo wrapping around his senses, Paul fought to concentrate on her words. "You don't have to 'be prepared' for me. I'm here to make sure you and the boys are all right."

"I know, but still…" Her hand waved vaguely and she stared around at the clutter of toys littering the otherwise neat living room. Tears filled her eyes and she sniffed, a pathetic whimper like a dog who'd been abused.

The hint of tears glazing her cornflower-blue eyes was his undoing. "A little mess never hurt anyone." Paul gave up the fight and grabbed her hand, pulling her into his arms.

She stood stiff at first, then her fingers clutched at his shirt and she leaned into him. "I'm so scared, I don't know what to do."

"That's why I'm here. We'll figure this thing out and you can get back to your normal life."

"I don't think my life will ever be normal." She sniffed and leaned back, tears staining her cheeks. "How can it be when you're the wife of a serial killer?"

Paul didn't have an answer for her, not when all he wanted to do was kiss the tears from her cheeks. Now wasn't the time to take advantage of Elise. She was vulnerable, scared and likely to cling to anyone. But those eyes, the full, trembling lips…

Before he could think through another thought, Paul's head tipped forward.

Elise's eyes widened briefly, then she stretched upward on her toes, her eyelids sinking to half-mast, her lips rising to meet his.

He might have pulled back at the last minute if she hadn't met him halfway. Like kinetic energy unleashed, he couldn't stop himself once he'd committed to kissing Elise Johnson. The scent of strawberries wafted around him, lured him into a deeper embrace, his hands resting on her lower back, pulling her against him. If she didn't know she'd aroused him before, she'd surely guess it now.

Instead of backing away, Elise's hands climbed up to his shoulders, lacing into the hair at his nape.

His lips slanted over hers, his tongue pushing past her teeth to taste the sweet depths of her mouth. Mint toothpaste tingled against his tongue, dragging him deeper. His hand slid up her back, the silk of her robe like a promise of the smoothness of the skin beneath, her damp hair evoking images of her naked in the shower. He wanted more. He wanted to swing her up into his arms and carry her to her bed where he'd make sweet love to her, pushing aside all her worries if only for a moment.

All too soon, the fantasy ended.

Elise gasped against his mouth, planted her hands against his chest and pushed him away.

He let go, shocked at his own loss of control.

Elise staggered backward, her knuckles skimming across swollen lips. The front of her robe hung open, giving Paul a peek of one fully rounded, naked breast.

He groaned, battling the urge to pursue her and take more of what he'd just tasted. Clenching his hands into fists to keep from reaching out to her, he nodded. "I'm sorry. I shouldn't have done that." He kept his voice low so as not to disturb the boys.

Her eyes, round and blue, stared at him for a long moment, like a deer caught in the path of a predator. Then she turned away, gathering the lapels of her robe close around her. "No, I'm sorry. It wouldn't have happened if I'd been stronger. I'm such a wimp." She laughed softly with no hint of mirth reflected in the sound.

His arms rose to pull her back against him, but dropped to his sides before he could follow through. "You're not a wimp. You're a worried mother. And rightly so."

"Rightly so?" She spun to face him. "Tell me something new. Did you find out who's doing this? Is it Stan?"

The hopeful look on her face made him want to tell her they'd nailed the bad guy. "We don't know much more than before."

"Stan killed five women before you caught up with him in North Dakota. Please tell me he won't kill five more before they find him this time."

"We can only do the best we can. We haven't got much to go on. It's not even in the FBI jurisdiction yet. Look, I'll check on this George kid and his parents for you. And I'm meeting with the sheriff tomorrow to offer our assistance in the case."

"He has to let you help. You're the only ones who understand what Stan is capable of."

"Elise, we don't know that it's Stan. The killer could be a copycat."

"But he wrote the note to *me!*" she beseeched in a hushed whisper. "How do you explain that?"

He couldn't. "Honestly, that's what has me worried."

She snorted. "You and me both. Only a few people were supposed to know of my whereabouts and name change. How does someone get that information?"

"I have your brother-in-law working on that." It wasn't much, but between Mel's hospital search and Nick's check on her file, those were the only leads they had to go on. Tomorrow he'd meet with the sheriff and get on the inside of the case. "Look, Elise, it's getting late. You might as well turn in and get some rest."

Her answering chuckle ended in a choked sob. For a moment, she stared at the ground, her fingers clenching and unclenching. Then she straightened and looked him square in the eye. "I'm tired of being scared."

"I know."

How could he know? She'd been the one targeted with the note. Someone had walked right into the school and stuck it in her cubby. She couldn't have the police checking at the school or her cover would be blown.

Paul stared across at her, his brows dipping low. "You're not planning on doing something crazy, are you?"

Her gaze slipped to the side and down. She hadn't asked before, because she didn't know how without alerting her coworkers to her dilemma. But somehow, tomorrow, she'd ask the secretary at the office if she'd seen who delivered that note. She'd make up some excuse about a secret admirer or something to throw her off. "No." At least that wasn't a lie.

"Good, because I can't be with you all the time. I need to know you're not going to go off anywhere and investigate on your own."

"I'm going to school and home." While at school she might find out something from the staff.

"If you want me to, I can come into the school and ask around about the note."

Her gaze shot back to him. Had he read her mind? "No!" Heat rose up her neck and spread across her cheekbones. She pressed her palms to her face. "I don't want the principal or the other teachers to suspect anything. I want a chance to live here in peace. No one can know about my past."

Paul sighed. "Sure makes it hard to follow up on that note."

"I know. But that's the way it has to be." She'd find out what she could tomorrow on her own, without alerting the entire school to the possibility of a serial killer in their midst.

"You might as well hit the sack." Paul rolled his shoulders. "Mind if I look around before calling it a night?"

"Please do. I've checked that all the windows and doors are secure, but it wouldn't hurt to double-check."

"Exactly. Plus, I want to look for other vulnerable areas."

A chill snaked down the back of her robe, reminding Elise she was practically naked in front of a virtual stranger. Though somehow, she didn't consider Paul much of a stranger even though they'd only been in each other's company no more times than she could count on one hand. Her lips tingled, still aching a little from the kiss they'd shared. When she glanced down, she realized her nipples were poking out against the thin silk of her robe, the turgid peaks glaringly obvious.

She wasn't immune to Paul's presence. Nor was she unfazed by his kiss, but she didn't need to advertise the fact. Her cheeks burning again, she crossed her arms over the evidence and ducked her head, refusing to meet his gaze. "I'll go to bed now."

"I take it I can have the couch?"

"Oh, right, yes." Why was she stuttering like an adolescent? He was there to protect her. "I'll get you a blanket." She hurried toward the cabinet in the hallway.

As her hand reached upward to open the upper cabinet door, a large, tanned hand caught hers. "Here, let me get it. You know you don't have to wait on me."

His heat radiated warmth through the silk clinging to her skin. Although he wasn't touching her, she could sense the hard planes of his body only a breath away. All she had to do was lean back to absorb his strength.

His hand slid down her raised arm, his fingers brushing against the curve of her breast. "You feel it, don't you?"

Elise's breath caught in her throat, her body aching for his, heat pooling low in her belly, begging for release. She couldn't deny her attraction to him. Couldn't deny the lust threatening to overwhelm her and make her do things she knew she shouldn't. But she wanted to so badly. Her body poised to turn into his arm when a door opened behind them.

Paul backed away, his hands coming away with a blanket and a pillow from the top shelf.

Elise ducked beneath his arm and confronted her oldest son.

"Mom?" Although he spoke to his mother, Brandon stared up at Paul. "Something made a noise outside my window. I'm scared."

Fear spiked in Elise's veins, freezing out any thoughts of making love with the sexy FBI agent. What had she been thinking, anyway? She had the world's worst instincts where men were concerned. Her choices couldn't be trusted. If a serial killer could disguise himself as a fine, upstanding citizen, a deacon of the church, why couldn't he disguise himself as an police officer, a school janitor or an FBI agent?

Chapter Seven

Paul spent the night on the couch, getting up every hour to go outside and check the perimeter. The noise Brandon had heard had been the branch of a mountain laurel pushed into the glass by a steadily increasing northerly breeze. Indian summer had come to an end in Breuer, the temperature plummeting thirty degrees overnight.

Before five o'clock, Paul headed out. The gray light of dawn edged the darkness out of the sky as he headed south-east into San Antonio. Rather than wake the woman he'd almost made love to last night, he'd left a note on the table telling her he'd be back that evening and for her not to go anywhere without letting him know first. He'd scribbled his cell-phone number at the bottom of the note.

First stop, his apartment on the northwest side of town for a quick shower, shave and clean clothing. The office would be practically empty at six-thirty. Most agents didn't arrive until closer to seven-thirty or eight if they weren't out working a case. He liked the early hours all to himself without interruptions. Paperwork was hard enough to wade through on a good day.

As he walked out the front door of his apartment, he noticed the light on his answering machine blinking. He turned back to discover he had two missed calls.

He punched the play button. The first message was a call from a telemarketer wanting his mortgage business. Irritation made him hit the skip button harder than necessary. The second call started with dead air.

Paul sighed, his hand halfway to the skip button when a disembodied voice rumbled from the machine. "Stay away from the teacher if you know what's good for you."

His heart skipped a beat, then kicked back into high gear, adrenaline shooting through his veins. He replayed the message again and again. The voice was so garbled, he couldn't recognize it. Unplugging the phone from the wall, he headed for the office, hitting the speed dial for Brian Thomas, the district's techno guru. Between the recording and the phone records maybe they'd get a new lead on the killer before he took another life.

He managed to get into the office, meet with Brian, complete some pressing paperwork and leave without being interrupted more than ten times before eight-thirty. Mel had headed for Breuer first thing that morning to question the victim's family. Cain had his head down for once, working the mound of background checks.

Paul avoided the man, not in the mood for another pissing contest on Cain's assignment. He had a date to keep with the sheriff of Kendall County and he had just enough time to get there, if he hurried.

BEFORE ELISE HAD THE CHANCE to set her purse in her desk drawer at school, Gerri Finch marched into her room towing an already frazzled Principal Ford behind her.

"Ms. Johnson, I've spoken to the principal concerning your behavior toward my daughter and she agrees you're picking on her."

"No, Mrs. Finch, I did not agree." Principal Ford gave Elise a tight smile. "I agreed to listen to both sides of the story and that's all."

"Ashley has the right to free speech just like anyone else in the United States of America. It says so in the Declaration."

"The Constitution, Mrs. Finch. Everyone has the right to free speech, but we have classroom rules to maintain order so that all students can learn. And these rules are what the students and the parents all agree to at the beginning of the school year."

"I don't remember agreeing to any rules." Gerri Finch tapped her alligator-skin stilettos against the shiny linoleum tiles, making an angry staccato sound that beat in rhythm with the headache pounding against Elise's temples.

Principal Ford sighed. "When you signed the signature sheet at the back of the student handbook, you agreed to the rules contained within."

"Well, if I'd known it had such stupid rules in it, I wouldn't have signed it."

"Nevertheless, you did and you and your child are bound by the rules."

Elise fought back the smile of gratitude. At least one person was on her side this morning.

"We'll see about that. Any way it goes, Ms. Johnson is picking on my daughter."

The principal turned to Elise.

"Ashley likes to talk in class to the point she disrupts others from getting their work done," Elise explained.

"She can't help it she's smarter than the others." Gerri's chest swelled forward. "She gets it from both sides."

"Ashley has also been late to class five times."

The principal's brows rose as she turned back to Mrs. Finch. "Three tardies is enough to send her to Saturday school. Five is two more chances than she deserved."

"But Saturday is the cheer competition. Ashley's the captain. She has to be there."

"She should have thought of that before she arrived late for class for the fifth time." The principal held the door open for Gerri. "Now, if you'll come this way, we can continue this discussion in my office and let Ms. Johnson get on with teaching her class."

Gerri Finch glared at Elise. "This isn't over yet. I know your game. I'll make you regret targeting my daughter with your petty vindictiveness. You'll be gone before you collect your next paycheck." The woman's voice dripped with venom, but she allowed the principal to hook an arm through her elbow and drag her away.

Elise let out the breath she'd been holding, sagging into her chair behind her desk. Wasn't it enough she had someone sticking death threats in her cubby? Did she have to put up with overindulgent moms, as well?

Her eyes narrowed on the retreating form of Gerri Finch. What did she mean by "I know your game"? Would she know about Elise's background? She shook her head. If she did, she'd have shouted it from the rooftops of the school by now and had Elise canned so fast she wouldn't have time to mutter the word *but*.

She shook off the thought and got down to the business of shaping young minds with lessons from the past. If only the past wasn't prone to repeat performances.

PAUL ARRIVED AT DENNY'S at exactly nine. His gaze panned the tables and booths for the heavyset sheriff, spying him in the far left corner.

The sheriff waved a hand toward the opposite booth seat. "I've already ordered," he said, lifting his cup of coffee toward the waitress and nodding at Paul.

Taking her cue, the young brunette hurried to the pot of coffee warming at the counter and collected a clean cup. She returned to their table and smiled at Paul. "You're new around here." She set the mug in front of him and poured steaming, fragrant coffee into it. "Need to see a menu?"

He hadn't realized just how hungry he was until she'd asked. "No, thanks. I'll have two eggs over-medium and wheat toast."

She nodded without taking down a word he spoke. "That's what I like, a man who knows what he wants."

The sheriff's chuckle followed her retreating form. "Mandy's a pretty little thing. Watch out, though. She's tough. Comes from hardy stock. Her parents own a small angora goat ranch in the hill country near Sisterdale."

Paul's gaze followed the pretty Mandy, but his thoughts kept to a certain blonde he'd wanted more than anything to keep kissing last night. "Thanks for the recommendation. But I'm not interested." He leaned back against the slick vinyl seat and sipped his coffee. "What can you tell me about Alice Lauren Pendley?"

The sheriff's mouth pulled into a tight line. "Lauren was a good kid. Grew up here in Breuer, member of the 4-H club, graduated from University of Texas at San Antonio two years ago." He shook his head, his gaze directed toward the window. "Her parents were so proud. Neither one had ever been to college. Hardworking folks, always looking out for others. It's a damned shame. And Lauren was engaged to be married next spring."

Paul listened, waiting for the sheriff to get to the pertinent details of the murder investigation.

"Her mother called us the night before last when she didn't come home from work."

"Where did she work?"

"At the drugstore. She wanted to go to pharmacy school next fall. Had her acceptance and everything."

"Did anyone see her leave?"

"The manager walked her to her car every night. Only, he was off that night. She left by herself. No one saw her get into her car."

"Is there a security camera for the parking lot?"

"Already checked it. The manager insisted the cameras were aimed at the guest parking up front and the employee parking in the rear of the building. Again, not that night. We don't know if someone with killing on his mind shifted the camera to point at the treetops, but that's all that was on the recording from eight o'clock that night until we confiscated the video at eight the next morning."

Paul leaned forward. "How do you know the shift happened at eight?"

"We watched from the time Lauren got to work until she was scheduled to leave. We could see the camera shift around eight o'clock."

"Fingerprints on the camera?"

The sheriff shook his head. "Not a one. But we found a brick close by and a dent in the camera casing. We did the math. It wasn't the wind."

"Could you trace the brick?"

"It was from the stack in Mrs. Veatch's backyard behind

the drugstore." The sheriff looked up as Mandy delivered their plates.

Steam rose from the sheriff's fried bacon and sausage, sending waves of tempting aromas toward Paul. His own eggs and toast didn't seem quite as appealing as the plate of heart attack the sheriff planned to consume. "Did you review the indoor videos for customers entering and leaving around eight that night?"

"We've gone over and over the video. Neither the officers nor the store employees recognized most of the customers."

"This is a small town. Wouldn't you know a majority of the people here?" Paul took up his fork, suddenly ravenous, his stomach aching for nourishment.

"We're small, but we get a lot of transients from the interstate who come in for over-the-counter medications." The sheriff shrugged. "Short of questioning all the hotel clerks and RV park attendants about whether or not they've seen the people in that clip before, I don't have much to go on."

Paul set his cup on the table. "What about the crime scene? Did the state crime lab process it?"

"Yeah, they had a team come in and comb over the area. Because of the lack of rain, the river's way down. Heck, it's more like a creek. The girl didn't float far from where he dumped her in the water."

"Any footprints?"

"No. The guy was careful. He obviously knew to cover his tracks. The Ethernet was standard cable used by just about everyone in the industry. No tracks, no witnesses. He did it by the books, leaving no traces."

How did he catch a killer who didn't want to be caught? A man trying to make a point with Elise. He had to be in on the ground-level with the sheriff's office, investigating alongside Breuer's finest to ensure not a stone remained unturned. Something their less experienced eyes might miss, he might pick up on. "Do you want the FBI's help on this one?"

The sheriff stared across the table at Paul. "I don't want the FBI taking over our case, if that's what you're askin'."

Paul nodded. "Fair enough. But we might have more resources available that could help speed up the investigation."

"Look, I don't mind a little help. We're always shorthanded, what with cattle getting out of fences and domestic disputes we answer to, but I don't want some yahoo muckin' around and messin' up my investigation, got that?"

"Yes, sir." Paul liked the old coot, despite his belligerence. "How about if me and my partner, Special Agent Bradley, work alongside you until we find the guy who did this?"

"Is Agent Bradley like you?"

"A little, only she fancies herself a Texan even though she grew up in Boston."

The sheriff's stern face settled into a grin. "Can't be all bad if she wants to be a Texan. Not everyone can be one, though. It's something you gotta live, breathe and defend." He nodded at Paul. "Not everyone opens up to people with funny accents."

"Like me, right?" Paul returned the sheriff's grin. "I'll work on that."

"My advice to you is to get a hat." The sheriff nodded at his on the seat beside him. Paul was saved from a response when the sheriff's cell phone chirped and he reached for it. "Excuse me."

Paul ate several bites of the greasy eggs, his stomach churning over the lack of evidence he could sink his teeth into.

The sheriff listened to the caller, the smile on his face

fading, dipping into a fierce frown. He set his napkin beside his plate. "You tell Mrs. Holzhauer I'll be there in five minutes. Don't let anyone inside the girl's apartment until the state crime lab can get there and process the scene."

Paul couldn't feign indifference to the call. Every hackle he had stood at full attention.

When the sheriff disconnected, he stood, leaving the majority of his food untouched. "We've had another woman reported missing at the Hilltop Apartments. Ready to go to work?"

Paul rose, tossing enough cash on the table to cover the meal for both of them and a sizable tip for Mandy. "Let's go. I'll follow you."

A FEW MINUTES BEFORE the last class of Elise's day, Kendall McKenzie rushed in, followed by Alex Mendoza. "Ms. Johnson." She stopped short and let out a relieved sigh. "Oh, good, you're still here."

Elise smiled at the girl. "Of course I'm here. We have class at this time." She laughed. "Why would you think otherwise?"

Alex nudged Kendall in the side hard enough to take the wind out of her next words. "No reason."

It wasn't like Alex to lie about something. "No really, why wouldn't I be in my classroom?"

"Because my mother is going to have you fired." Ashley Finch flounced into the room and slung her backpack on the floor beside her desk.

Elise fought not to roll her eyes.

Students filed in and took their seats just as the tardy bell buzzed in the hallway.

Elise had a job to do, whether she felt like it or not. And she definitely didn't feel like forcing history into the closed minds of hormonal teenagers when a killer ran free in the same town. But what else would she do? Run home and hide under the bed until the danger passed?

She refused to cower. If her sister could bring criminals to justice while being personally targeted, Elise should at least be able to teach a few high school kids without running screaming.

She'd pulled out her history book and opened it to the current chapter when Caesar strolled through the door, bumped Alex out of his seat and plopped down in it.

"Hey!" Alex picked himself up off the floor and glared at Caesar. "That's my seat."

Caesar glanced down at the desk and back at Alex. "Doesn't have your name on it."

Elise inhaled, let it out and crossed her arms over her chest. "Out."

Caesar's dark brows rose into the long, unruly hair hanging down in his eyes. "Who, me?"

"Now." Elise's eyes narrowed into slits.

"And what are you going to do if I don't leave?" His mouth twisted into an irritating smirk. "Your boyfriend isn't here today."

Elise didn't bother arguing with the young man. She spun on her heel and marched to the intercom attached to the wall. Before she could punch the button, Caesar was on his feet and across the room.

His big hand clamped down over the keypad, blocking her from making the call to the office. "What are you going to do now?" he challenged.

She made a move to step around him and head for the door.

He blocked her exit, the wall of his body effectively trapping her inside the classroom.

"Very well." She glanced toward the students who watched with varying expressions on their faces. Some had wide-eyed looks, shock and fear rooting them to their seats. Her glance returned to Caesar. "Someone go get the principal…and security." She refused to show fear. Bullies like Caesar thrived on fear.

"Do it and you won't live to graduate," Caesar warned.

The classroom remained silent. No one moved toward the door.

Elise rolled her eyes. "Good grief, Caesar, what do you really think this little power game you're playing is going to buy you?"

"A little satisfaction." He flicked his finger at the vee in her blouse. "If you want a real man to keep you warm at night, you need to get rid of that boyfriend of yours. Besides, a pretty teacher like you shouldn't be sleeping around. Word gets out to the school board and you might not have a job anymore."

Her frown deepened. "What do you know about…" She clamped her teeth down on her bottom lip. Had he been spying on her? Hanging around her house? She'd assumed Caesar was relatively harmless for the most part. As the class bully, he pushed people around, but she hadn't heard of him breaking any laws or seriously harming anyone. Would he, now that she'd made him mad?

Movement caught Elise's attention. Alex and Kendall had eased toward the door and stood poised for flight. With his back to them, Caesar couldn't see them slide out and race down the hall toward the administrative offices.

"Hey—" Ashley began.

"Caesar, what's this really about?" Elise asked, desperate to keep Caesar's attention.

"I don't like being pushed around."

Elise snorted. "But you don't mind pushing others around. That makes a lot of sense."

"What do you know? You're a white girl in a white man's world. You don't know nothin'."

"You don't know anything," Elise corrected automatically.

"What are you, my English teacher now?"

Elise sighed. "No, but if you don't tell me what's really wrong, you'll only end up in trouble every time."

"I don't care. Why should I?" He stepped closer to her. "School's just stupid."

The hairs on her arms raised and she fought to keep from moving backward. She had to take a stand, even if she got hurt in the process. Bullies like Caesar pushed and pushed until they hit a brick wall. She meant to be his brick wall.

"Well, you're not scaring me, Caesar. You need to leave the class and let me get on with teaching the people who want to make something of their lives."

He jerked his head toward the others. "You think history is going to get them out of this town?"

"Maybe not directly, but it might help them to make better decisions, like when to pick a fight and when not to."

Footsteps echoed from the hallway. Officer West, the Breuer police officer assigned to the high school, Principal Ford and a couple of the bigger coaches hurried toward Elise's classroom.

Caesar glanced over his shoulder and snorted. "You got lucky, teach." He faced her, his eyes narrowing. "This time. You won't always." Then he vaulted across a desk, opened a window to the outside and jumped through.

The police officer burst through the door. Elise pointed at the open window. Caesar had dropped to the ground and taken off running.

The officer followed Caesar out the window, his belt catching on the metal window frame, slowing him down.

Students erupted into chatter. Principal Ford dismissed all but one of the coaches while Elise collapsed into her chair.

The rush of adrenaline that had kept her toe-to-toe with Caesar receded, leaving her drained.

"Ms. Johnson? Elise?" The principal leaned over her. "Why don't you and I take a break. Coach Ueker will sit with your class."

Great. Three times in the past two days her abilities as a teacher responsible for a classroom of teenagers had been in question. Was Principal Ford about to fire her? If so, what would she do for a job? How would she pay the mortgage?

"Principal Ford, Ms. Johnson didn't do anything to make Caesar mad." Bless Alex. The kid might be half the size of Caesar, but he had a heart.

"It's okay, Alex. I'll explain what happened to Principal Ford. Everyone open your books to page…" She stared at her desk and the book lying open where she'd intended to begin the class lecture. "Page 242. I want you to start reading there and answer the questions in the back of the chapter. I'll be back shortly." She hoped.

Elise stood, her legs shaking beneath her, and followed the principal to her office.

Chapter Eight

Paul accompanied the sheriff to the apartment.

The Hilltop Apartments manager, Mrs. Holzhauer, stood at the open door to Mary Alice Fenton's second-floor apartment, clutching a folded paper in her hand. "I didn't touch anything, just like you said. Well, except when I went inside to ask why Miss Fenton left her door open. The place was a mess, but Miss Fenton wasn't home. If the door hadn't been standing wide open, I wouldn't have thought anything of it." The older woman sucked in a breath and let it out. "I called her work number and they said she didn't report to work this morning. They left a message on her voice mail, but she didn't call back."

"You did all the right things, Mrs. Holzhauer." Sheriff Engel patted the woman's shoulder.

She wrung her hands; her narrow frame clad in a gray polyester pantsuit looked as gray as the overcast sky. "I saw the local news. I know they found a woman murdered just yesterday, but they hadn't released her name. I just wondered…"

Paul hung back and let the sheriff take the lead.

"It wasn't Mary Alice, Mrs. Holzhauer." Sheriff Engel took a notebook out of his pocket. "Do you have Miss Fenton's cell-phone number?"

"It's not on her application." Mrs. Holzhauer stared at the paper in her hand. "I know she had one because I saw her talking on one when she drove out of here yesterday morning to go to work."

The sheriff leaned over Mrs. Holzhauer's shoulder to look at the paper she held. "What about an emergency contact?"

Mrs. Holzhauer shoved the paper toward him. "I pulled her application from the file. The number listed is her mother's." The older woman shook her head. "It's a horrible thing to report to a mother."

The sheriff shook his head as he scanned the application. "Now, Mrs. Holzhauer, we don't know that anything untoward has happened to Mary Alice. Don't go borrowin' trouble."

"I know, I know, but still…" She wrung her hands, her gaze following the sheriff through the door of the empty apartment. "You think the same guy that got the other lady might have Mary Alice?"

Paul stepped forward. "Mrs. Holzhauer, we don't know, but we'll do the best we can to find out. For now, we need to look around. Will you be all right by yourself in your office?"

Mrs. Holzhauer nodded, backing away, taking Paul's hint. "I called my sister-in-law. She said she'd come keep me company the rest of the day if necessary. If you need anything, just ask." She hurried down the metal steps, glancing all around before she exited the building to walk across the parking lot.

Paul shook his head. Lousy way to live when a woman had to be afraid of walking from one building to another in broad daylight. He followed Sheriff Engel into the apartment, careful not to disturb anything that could be classified as evidence. The police officer who'd been the first on scene waited in the parking lot for the state crime lab team.

Technically, the woman hadn't been reported missing by her family and she hadn't been missing long enough to qualify for a missing-persons report. But with the discovery of a murdered woman only a day prior to Mary Alice's disappearance, the sheriff had to take action.

The small apartment had a collection of mismatched furniture, likely thrift-shop specials or hand-me-downs from family members. A pair of jeans hung from the corner of a door, stretched out as if to dry. A plate with a piece of leftover pizza was on the table, the pizza only half-eaten as if Mary Alice had planned to finish it.

The sheriff's gaze panned the room. "No signs of forced entry, no signs of struggle. You see anything different?"

Paul shook his head, staring at the pizza. "She might have been eating the pizza when someone came to the door."

"With no signs of forced entry, I'd venture to guess she opened the door. The chain is still intact so she didn't feel threatened by whoever stood on the other side."

"Someone she knew, maybe."

"Or someone she'd trust."

"What about her purse?" Paul nodded toward the black leather bag on the counter, a set of car keys lying next to it.

The sheriff used his pen to push the purse open and peered inside. "The wallet's inside."

"Cell phone?"

"No." The sheriff pulled out his own phone and hit the speed dial. "I'll get her cell-phone number from her employer. I hate to think we might have a serial killer on our hands. But with one woman dead already, I'm willing to bet Mary Alice's disappearance is related."

While the sheriff placed his call to the state police, Paul worked his way around the room and into the bedroom, careful not to touch anything. The covers on the bed lay in disarray but not like a struggle had taken place. More like someone who didn't make the bed after sleeping in it. In the bathroom, cosmetics and perfume littered the counter but no sign of a cell phone.

The sheriff's voice carried to him from the other room.

When he emerged, the sheriff was hitting the off button on his cell phone.

"Not a robbery or they would have taken the purse and the car." Paul circled the living room, pausing to stare at a picture sitting on the end table beside a faded blue couch. Both people in the photo were smiling. The young man possibly in his late twenties, the young woman vaguely familiar with long blond hair and blue eyes. Paul's heart plunged to his stomach, making the food he'd eaten earlier churn. "This must be Mary Alice."

The sheriff moved to join Paul by the couch. "I've seen her around town. Always had a smile."

"Know the guy in this picture?"

The sheriff bent forward and stared hard at the man in the picture. "He looks like the police officer assigned to the high school."

"What?" Paul straightened, his heart leaping against his chest, pounding so hard he couldn't hear himself think.

The sheriff frowned at him. "Is there something wrong with that? I've met him once or twice at football games at the high school stadium. Last name's West." The sheriff scratched his chin. "Colton West, if I'm not mistaken. Kinda new. Only been on the city police force for two or three months."

The urge to get to the high school and find Officer Colton West hit Paul hard, but he kept his cool in front of the sheriff. He wanted to get to Elise as quickly as possible. Whoever had left Elise the note in her box had access to the school. A campus police officer had access to every place on campus, including the front office. "Let's start there. Maybe he can help us pinpoint the last time she'd been seen."

"Yeah. As soon as the state police crime scene investigators arrive, I'm on it."

"I have to make some calls to check in with the office. Want to meet up at the high school in, say, an hour?"

"I'll meet you there." The sheriff returned his attention to the notebook in his hand, scribbling words on the page.

Paul left the apartment complex and pushed the posted speed limits on his way to the high school on the other side of Breuer.

At a stoplight, he dialed Brian.

"Hey, Fletcher."

"Anything on that phone call?"

"Got an electronic copy of your phone records just a few minutes ago. The fastest I've ever gotten anything from the phone company. Gotta love technology."

Paul wanted to tell Brian to get to the point. The light changed and he concentrated on making a left turn onto Main Street.

"Anyway, I scanned for the time you gave me and sure enough there was a phone call from a cell phone. Only, the cell phone is one of those disposable types you can't trace."

"Great." Another dead end and his killer was using all the tricks.

"I'm trying to trace the phone back to the dealer. Maybe we can get an ID on the person who bought it."

"Thanks, Brian." Paul hung up and resisted the urge to throw his cell phone out the window. They were running out of time on this case. Another woman could be fighting for her life as they chased dead-end clues.

The afternoon had passed and school would be getting out soon. As he pulled into the parking lot, the boy he'd caught giving Elise hell sprinted past him. A man dressed in the solid black uniform of the Breuer Police Department pounded the pavement after the kid. The kid had a good hundred yards on the officer. Unless he was in better shape than a seventeen-year-old, he didn't stand a chance of capturing the punk.

Unfortunately, the cop chasing the kid was the one Paul wanted to talk to.

The best way to speed this up was to slow the kid down.

Paul whipped his vehicle around and raced after the punk, pulling in front of him. He spun his steering wheel hard to the left, spinning the car broadside on the road leading out of the high school campus. Paul leaped out and gave chase.

The young man changed directions and ran for the five-foot-tall, chain-link fence bordering the road. With the ease of youth, he grabbed the wire and vaulted over the top, dropping to the ground on the other side and disappearing between the tightly packed houses of a neighborhood.

By the time Paul could get over the fence, the kid would be long gone.

The cop skidded to a halt in front of Paul. "Give me one good reason why I shouldn't haul your butt to jail for driving like that on a school campus." He sucked in enough air to fill his lungs, his dark-eyed gaze angry.

Raising his hands, Paul smiled. "Hey, I was only trying to slow him down."

"We know where he lives. I'll catch up with him later."

Paul pulled out his FBI credentials. "FBI Special Agent Paul Fletcher."

The cop's hands slid off his hips and he relaxed a little. "Okay, that's a reason. I'm not so sure it's a good enough one to justify reckless driving on campus, but I'll give you the benefit of the doubt. What brings you here?"

Paul studied him. He didn't appear to be nervous about an FBI agent showing up. If he'd had anything to do with his girlfriend's disappearance, he wasn't giving any signs via body language.

"You know Mary Alice Fenton?" Paul asked.

The cop stiffened, his eyes narrowing. "Yeah, why?"

"When was the last time you saw her?"

"Last night around eleven o'clock." His eyes widened. "Is Mary okay? What's this all about?"

Paul hadn't planned to question the boyfriend until the sheriff arrived, but he was here and the opportunity had presented itself. "Her apartment door was open this morning. The manager got concerned and called her office. She didn't show up for work today. Did she say anything to you about that?"

Officer West shoved a hand through his hair. "Jesus. No. No, she didn't say anything about missing work." He looked around. "I should go check on her."

"I just came from Miss Fenton's apartment. The Kendall County sheriff is there now, waiting for state crime scene investigators. Do you know if Miss Fenton has a cell phone?"

"Yeah, she does." Officer West pulled his own cell phone out of his pocket and punched one of the numbers, his expression hopeful.

Paul waited, quietly.

After a long minute, the younger man hit the off button, his body sagging. "Her voice mail picked up."

If the cell phone had been in the apartment, the sheriff would have found it by now. But why would she leave her apartment with her cell phone and not her purse or keys?

"I really should go over to her place."

Paul shook his head. "They wouldn't let you in and she's

not there." His gut told him the police officer had nothing to do with his girlfriend's disappearance, but he wasn't ruling anything out yet.

Officer West held out his hands. "What am I supposed to do? I can't do nothing."

"You can start by getting on the phone to all your mutual friends. See if anyone has seen her." Paul pulled a card out of his wallet and handed it to the officer. "If you hear anything at all, give me a call or call the sheriff."

"I will." Officer West tucked the card into his pocket and stared at the fence the young punk had jumped.

Paul would bet he wasn't seeing the kid or the fence.

The school bell rang. Paul glanced at his watch. Elise was getting off work now. He could meet her at her classroom and escort her home. First thing, he'd better move his car out of the middle of the road before the stampede of teenagers exited campus.

When he passed through the main entrance, Elise was leaving the office, a tissue clutched in her hand and her eyes red-rimmed. When she spotted him, she hurried toward him.

Paul opened his arms and she fell into them.

"Wooo, Ms. Johnson." A passing student snickered, the smirk on his face freezing when Paul glared at him.

Elise pushed Paul to arm's length and then stepped away. "I'm sorry. It's just been a really bad day."

"Want to tell me about it?"

She gave him a half smile. "Later. I need to get home to my boys."

"I'll take you."

"No, I need my car. I like to have my own transportation. You can't be playing chauffeur for me. You have a job."

"You need protection."

"Yeah, that and a bucket of money." She touched his arm. "Please. I need to do things on my own. I'll be careful."

Paul didn't like letting her out of his sight, but she was right. He had work to do and so did she. As long as he provided protection at night, she ought to be okay. The two women who'd disappeared had done so after dark, as far as he could ascertain. "Okay. I'll meet you at your place this evening. Don't open your door for anyone and keep a close eye on the boys."

"I won't and I will." She grinned. "Later?" She turned to go back to her classroom, stopped and came back to the office. "Will you do me a big favor?"

When she looked up at him with those big blue eyes, he would have walked off a cliff for her. "Anything."

"This may sound stupid, but I forgot to check my mailbox in the office." Elise remembered how the Dakota Strangler left messages every time he killed another woman. Maybe subconsciously she'd avoided her mailbox because she didn't want to find another note. Another note meant another death.

"You want me to check it?" Paul's voice penetrated her musings.

Elise shook off the morbid worries and straightened her shoulders. "No, no. I'll do it, but will you wait until I do...just in case?"

"I'll be right here."

Elise walked back into the administrative office, her footsteps dragging. If another note showed up in her box from whoever was tormenting her, she didn't know what she'd do.

Without looking at her box, she turned to the secretary. "Becky, did you see who put the note in my box the day before yesterday, by chance?"

The slightly plump and perky secretary tipped her head to the side. "No, I don't recall seeing who left it. I think it might have been there before I came in that morning. Why?"

"No reason."

"Wasn't there a name on it?" Becky asked.

"No."

The secretary's eyes widened and a smile blossomed on her face. "A secret admirer?" She clapped her hands together. "How sweet."

Elise almost burst out laughing, but she was afraid her laughter would turn to tears all too easily. "Uh, no. Not a secret admirer."

Becky's smile slipped. "Oh."

To avoid further questions, Elise braced herself and turned toward her box. An envelope lay tilted to the left.

Her hand shook as she reached for it. On the front written in blue ink were the words *Ms. Johnson's insurance forms.*

All the air left Elise's lungs in a rush and she dragged in more, a nervous giggle rising to the top of her throat. All that worry for nothing. Elise took another steadying breath and turned a smile toward Becky. "See you tomorrow."

"Those insurance forms are due back in the office by Friday," Becky called out.

Outside, Paul's gaze questioned her without a word being spoken.

She smiled. "Just insurance papers." Tucking the envelope inside her purse, she headed for the door, glad Paul had met her at school. Her day hadn't been the best, but with a hunky agent spending the night at her house, things were looking up.

Paul inspected her car inside and out before he opened her door for her. Elise didn't question him, but a chill slithered down her back. What if someone had tampered with it while it sat in the school parking lot overnight? She really should have brought it home yesterday. Elise shrugged. Anyone could just as easily tamper with it outside her home.

She'd had the car for two years, but getting inside it now gave her no comfort.

"I'll see you home, then I need to head to the office for a couple hours to check in."

"You don't have to babysit me, you know," Elise insisted, feeling more and more like a burden. "I hate to be such a problem."

He touched a finger to her lips, startling her into silence.

"Ms. Johnson, you are not the problem." He winked and stepped away, closing her door firmly between them.

She sat for a moment, her tongue sliding across her lips, the salty taste of his finger giving her entirely different tingles than the scary ones of earlier.

Get a grip, girl. You're not on the market. A cold slap of reality hit her. She didn't need to get involved now or ever. All her concentration should be on raising her sons and keeping them safe.

With the little pep talk firmly in mind, she shifted into Drive and blended into the line of cars filled with teens and their parents eager to get away from the school and back home.

Once off campus she headed for Highland Street, cutting through the back roads. Paul followed.

A red light caught him. Without a good place to pull off the road, Elise continued toward home, turning left at the next intersection. She still couldn't see Paul and slowed. No one was behind her so she slowed even more until she was almost at a standstill.

As she peered into her rearview mirror a dark object sailed into her peripheral vision and something smashed into the front windshield. Elise screamed and flung one of her hands up to protect her face. Glass shattered, tiny shards projecting through the air. Elise slammed her foot to the brake and squeezed her eyes shut.

Too late. Little slivers of glass prickled behind her eyelids. Afraid to open her eyes and unable to move, she sat frozen in her seat, her heart hammering in her chest.

Chapter Nine

At least five times in the two minutes he sat at the red light, Paul debated running it. Each time he talked himself down. What could happen to Elise in two minutes?

The light changed. Just as Paul pressed his foot to the accelerator, a young woman driving a burgundy sports car and talking on a cell phone ran the red light.

"Damn!" Paul slammed his foot on the brakes to keep from hitting the oblivious idiot. As soon as she passed, Paul checked for oncoming traffic. Nothing. He hit the accelerator and sped forward, determined to catch up with Elise before she got home.

At the next corner, he barely slowed, taking the turn a little faster than was safe for the normal driver. His tires squealed and he slowed. That's when he saw Elise's metallic-gray, four-door sedan with the blue and gold Minnesota Vikings bumper sticker parked in the middle of the road.

Paul slammed his foot to the brakes and skidded to a halt behind her. He engaged his emergency blinker and jumped from his truck.

As he rounded the side of the vehicle, shards of glass on the ground caught the sunlight and twinkled up at him. Elise sat inside, her body rigid, her hands covering her face.

Paul's heart jumped into his throat and he jerked at the door handle. "Elise!" The door was locked.

"Elise, unlock the door." With desperation trumping reason, Paul yanked on the door, knowing it wouldn't open until she unlocked it.

Her eyes still shut, Elise dropped her left hand to the armrest and fumbled to locate the power switch for the door lock.

At the faint click, Paul jerked the door handle and flung open the door. "Elise?"

Both hands were covering her eyes again. "I have glass in my eyes. I'm afraid to do anything in case it cuts me."

"Just be still. I have a bottle of water in my truck. I'll be right back."

"I'm not going anywhere."

Reluctant to leave her, Paul ran back to his truck and rummaged in the backseat for the bottle of water he kept handy for after a workout. By the time he got back to her, Elise had turned sideways in her seat and set her feet on the pavement.

"Here, let me help you." He hooked an arm around her waist and helped her straighten without bumping her head. He steered her to the curb. "How bad does it hurt?"

"Just prickles like big grains of sand in my eyes. But I'm afraid to blink or open my eyes until I have something to get the glass out."

When she'd straightened, Paul slid his hand from around her waist up beneath the hair at the back of her neck. "Lean back and I'll flush your eyes with the water."

She tipped her head back, a small chuckle escaping her. "You're going to smear my mascara."

That she could laugh at a time like this was more than Paul could take and not kiss her. He pressed his lips to her temple.

"I promise not to laugh." Holding the bottle poised over her left eye, he said, "Tilt your head a bit to the left so we don't wash it out of one eye into the other."

Oblivious to the cars creeping around them in the street, Paul poured water over her eyelid. "Open slowly."

Elise's left eyelid fluttered open. "That's good." She eased her eyelid closed and opened again. "Better. Now the other."

Paul repeated the routine on the other side until he emptied the bottle. "Feel like we got it all?"

"I think so. When I get home, I'll get under the shower."

"No, I'm taking you to an optometrist. You don't mess with your eyesight."

"I'll be fine. I need to get home to my sons. I promise I'll make an appointment tomorrow." Elise pushed her damp hair out of her face and crossed the pavement to examine her car. The front windshield was shattered. She wouldn't be driving the car until she replaced the windshield. "What did I hit?"

Paul surveyed the car and the surrounding area. He knelt beside her back left tire and lifted a large red brick and held it up, anger burning in his chest. "Did you see who threw it?"

Elise's face blanched. "I was looking in the rearview mirror. All I saw was a shadow of the brick when it hit."

Paul made a mental note of the street name and numbers to report to the sheriff and the wrecker service. If he knew who'd thrown the brick, he'd skip the sheriff altogether and perform a little vigilante justice himself. First he had to get Elise home safe. "Come on. We'll pick up the boys on the way to the optometrist."

Elise shook her head, her lips twisting into a wry grin. "You really should run screaming from me. I'm beginning to think my life is jinxed." Although she smiled, her voice cracked and she sniffed.

His heart constricting inside his chest, Paul reached out and held her arms, staring down into watery blue eyes with black smudges beneath them where her mascara had run. He couldn't recall anyone more beautiful. "You're okay." Then he bent to brush her lips with his.

Her eyes widened and her fingers rose to touch where his lips had been. "Please don't do that again."

"I'm sorry. There's something about you that I can't seem to resist." When he bent to kiss her again, she pressed her hands against his chest, stopping him.

"Remember? I'm the wife of a serial killer."

"No, as you reminded me, you're Elise Johnson." He'd already stepped way over the line of FBI agent and protected citizen, so he held off. As much as he wanted to kiss her again, it had to be her choice.

The hands on his chest bunched in the fabric of his shirt and pulled him down until his lips met hers. "I know I'm going to regret this, but…" She pressed her lips to his, her tongue sweeping past his teeth to tangle with his.

A bright yellow school bus eased around their parked cars.

As though just remembering where she was, Elise straightened, her eyes going wide. "I must be out of my mind."

"Because you kissed me?"

"I didn't kiss you, you kissed me."

"No, sweet Elise, you kissed me."

She pressed her fingers to her lips and stared at the bus, thinking of all the reasons she shouldn't be kissing Paul and not caring about even one of them at that moment. A sea of faces peered through the glass windows of the school bus at her and the wrecked car. Among the faces, a familiar one stood out.

Brandon.

Sometimes being a mom was tough. Especially when you

wanted to be yourself. "We have to get going." She stepped out of Paul's arms and reached inside her car for her purse and the stack of papers that needed grading. "Think the car will be all right if we leave it here?"

"I'll get a wrecker to pick it up. There's plenty of room for other cars to go around in the meantime." Paul held open the passenger-seat door to his truck.

Once she'd buckled herself into the leather seat, Elise scrubbed at the black under her eyes, while Paul rounded the hood of the pickup and slipped in beside her. "Do you think whoever wrote the note also threw the brick?"

Paul frowned. "No."

Elise waited for more, but it wasn't forthcoming. "No?"

"Whoever is behind the murder victim and the missing girl wouldn't be so sloppy as to throw a brick and risk being seen." Paul shifted into gear and pulled around the stranded car, picking up speed to catch the bus.

Paul placed a call to Sheriff Engel while Elise called her insurance company, each reporting the damage.

When they reached Highland Street, the bus had just pulled away from the bus stop. Brandon walked toward the house, his shoulders slumped. Luke dragged his backpack behind him by one of the loose straps.

Elise shook her head. "I can't keep that child in backpacks." Though she was talking about Luke, her heart went out to her oldest son. As soon as Luke turned and saw the truck, he let out a whoop. "It's Paul! It's Paul!"

Brandon didn't look back, but continued toward the house.

Paul rolled the window down and called out to Luke. "Climb in the backseat."

"Yay! I get to ride in the monster truck!" Luke climbed up on the running board and jerked the door open. He slung his backpack onto the floorboard and clambered up into the truck. "Can we go to the rodeo? Can we?"

"Luke, honey. The rodeo has already come and gone. We'll have to wait until next fall when it comes back."

"Are you going to start on the fence? Can we get our puppy?"

Paul laughed out loud. "Do you ever breathe?"

"Sure. All the time." He huffed in and out and patted his chest. "See?"

Brandon reached the house before the truck pulled into the drive. He dug in a side pocket of his backpack, unearthing a key. Without glancing their way, he inserted the key in the door and pushed it open.

Paul shifted into Park, his gaze on the boy.

What would it take for Brandon to warm up to Paul? The boy had lost one parent already. He might be thinking of Paul as someone who might take his mother away from him. How could he convince the child that would never happen?

Luke burst out of the truck and dropped to the ground. He rounded the house and ran into the backyard.

Paul glanced across at Elise. "Want me to talk to Brandon?"

"No. I will." She sighed. "Give me a minute, will you?"

Elise gathered her purse and the papers and headed into the house.

Once inside, she dropped the papers on the counter and hurried down the hall to Brandon's room. Only, he wasn't there. He'd stopped in front of Elise's room and stood just inside the doorway, staring at the wall, his eyes round, his face pale.

"Brandon?" Elise closed the distance between them and dropped to her knees beside her son. "Baby, what's wrong?"

He didn't look at her, just kept staring straight ahead. "I didn't do it, Mommy."

Elise's heart flipped in her chest and she turned her head so slowly she felt she was in a time warp.

On the clean white wall over the headboard of her bed were words scrawled in bold black letters.

Roses are red

Her eyes were blue

She was a blonde

And looked just like you.

Lying below the note, neatly stretched across the snowy-white pillowcase, was a lock of long blond hair.

"Elise?" Paul called out from the living room.

Elise straightened and turned Brandon away from her room. "It's okay, Brandon. I know you didn't do it."

"But who? Who would have done it?" he whispered. Then his gaze locked on Paul and his body stiffened.

Before Elise realized what was happening, Brandon flew at Paul, scratching and kicking, screaming at the top of his voice. "You did it! It's all your fault! You never should have come!"

Paul gripped the boy by the shoulders, but found no relief from his swinging feet.

"Brandon!" Elise tried to get to her son.

Paul's voice stopped her. "Elise, let me handle this."

"Brandon," he called out over the child's screams. "Brandon!"

The little boy kept on kicking and screaming, tears running down his cheeks. "It's all your fault."

Just when Elise couldn't take it anymore, Paul lifted Brandon and wrapped him in a hug tight enough the boy couldn't move his arms or legs. He grunted his frustration, the tears coursing. "If you hadn't come, this wouldn't have happened."

"No, Brandon." Elise moved up behind him and laid a hand on his back. "Someone is trying to scare us."

"It's him!"

"No, Paul is here to protect us. Aunt Brenna sent him. He helped us up in North Dakota. He'll help us now."

"No, he's the one doing this."

"No, sweetheart, he's not. Agent Fletcher is one of the good guys."

Brandon looked into Paul's eyes, his own blue eyes filled with distrust. "You took Daddy away, didn't you?"

"Brandon, your dad died in a fire."

"No, he didn't!" Brandon shot an accusing glance at Elise.

The force of the look almost made her stagger. She couldn't deny Brandon's claim. With the notes and the woman who'd disappeared, she truly believed her husband was back and that he wanted revenge.

The anger and hurt dissolved as he stared at her. "Mom, is it true? Did our dad kill all those women?"

Elise's heart broke into a million pieces. She'd never wanted her sons to know the extent of their father's horrible legacy.

"Brandon, some people get sick in ways that aren't like a cold or flu. They get sick here." Paul loosened his grip enough to touch his finger to his temple.

Brandon switched his attention to Paul, the frown still furrowing his young brow. "Like crazy people?"

"Yes." Elise pounced on that. "Your father couldn't help it. His brain was sick."

Brandon pushed against Paul's arms. "You can put me down. I won't hurt you."

If Elise weren't so upset, she would have smiled at the little boy telling the hulking agent he wouldn't hurt him.

Brandon stood there, all straight and serious, like a little old man, not a boy of eight. "Am I going to get sick like my father?"

Elise dropped to her knees and pulled her son into her arms. "No, Brandon. You are not going to get sick like your father."

He pushed her to arm's length. "What about Luke? Is he going to get sick like our father?"

Tears welled in Elise's eyes. "No, baby, you both are going to be just fine. You'll grow up into wonderful, loving men and have children and families who love you."

Brandon stood for a long moment, staring into his mother's eyes, seeking reassurance. Finally, he nodded. "I'd better go check on Luke."

"That's a good idea." Elise stood, scrubbing the tears from her eyes. "Please have him come inside, will you?"

As Brandon turned toward the back door, Paul laid a hand on his shoulder. "You have a mighty good kick."

Brandon hung his head and scuffed his shoe against the carpet. "I'm sorry, Mr. Fletcher. I shouldn't have done that."

"It's okay. At least I know you can defend your mother like a pro."

Brandon looked up at Paul, his eyes burning fiercely bright. "I won't let anyone hurt her."

"And nor will I. I promise." Paul held out his hand, man-to-man.

With all the dignity of a statesman, Brandon shook Paul's hand. Then he ran for the back door, yelling, "Luke! Luke, you get in here right now!"

Elise faced her bedroom again and pushed the door open. "It's another note."

"Yeah." Paul nodded.

Elise shivered, her thoughts going back to the spring in North Dakota as one woman after another disappeared only to be found dead days later. "If he follows the same pattern as last time, he's going to kill again," she whispered.

When Paul didn't answer, she looked up into his eyes. "How can we keep him from taking another woman?"

For a moment, Paul refused to meet her gaze. When he did, his blue eyes were the flat color of slate. “We can’t.”

Elise’s heart flipped over, all the blood leaving her head in a rush. She leaned a hand against the wall to steady herself. “Dear God. He already has another.”

Paul nodded. “Last night.”

Chapter Ten

"Ms. Johnson, mind if we come in?" Two students Paul had seen in Elise's class appeared at the back door of her house, one on either side of Luke, each holding one of his hands.

"Mom, watch this!" Luke reared back and swung forward, kicking his feet high in the air. He flipped over and landed on his feet, still holding on to the teens' hands.

Paul muttered a curse beneath his breath for the untimely interruption. He'd wanted to reassure Elise in some way before she faced the others.

"Wow, Luke, that's amazing." Elise's voice was strained, not her normal soft, melodious sound, and her face had lost most of its color. "Kendall, Alex, what brings you here?"

The young man held up a notebook. "You wouldn't believe all the information Kenny and I have come up with on Jack the Ripper. We are *so* going to make an A on our research paper."

Paul opened the screen door, cringing inwardly at the subject Alex mentioned. Jack the Ripper? Why do a research paper on a killer that was never caught? He glanced at Elise.

Her mouth turned up on the corners, though her lips looked a bit too tight for the smile to be natural.

As he held the door for the kid, Luke shot through and headed straight for his room. "Alex, come see the Spider-Man Aunt Brenna sent me," he yelled over his shoulder.

"I will, in a minute." Alex grinned, following Kendall through the door. "I had a collection of Spider-Man and Hulk action figures when I was a kid. I know, it's hard to picture now." He tipped his head to the side. "Come to think of it, I might still have them buried in my closet. I should dig them out. Luke might like them."

Kendall turned toward the door. "Brandon, aren't you coming in?"

A sullen Brandon tromped up the steps and entered.

Paul released the door and stood back.

"Brandon, go wash your hands for dinner, please," Elise said.

When the boy complied without argument, Paul knew he probably was still traumatized by the writing on the wall in Elise's bedroom. He gave her door a wide breadth as he passed, his gaze flickering to the wall inside.

Kendall's pale brows inched up her forehead. "You don't mind, do you? Us coming over and all?"

Elise waved her hand absently, her gaze dull. "No, not at all. But do your parents know where you are?"

"Yeah, I told Mom I was going to get some help on my history homework." Kendall beamed. "Not that I need help on that. I totally get it."

"Uh, good, good." Elise's gaze flickered to Paul.

Paul stepped toward Elise and almost put his arm around her when he had second thoughts in front of the teens. "Maybe now isn't a good time. Ms. Johnson is having an unusually bad day and needs some time to wind down."

Kendall touched Elise's arm. "Is that why your makeup is all smeared? I didn't want to say anything."

Elise scrubbed at her eyes and gave a shaky laugh. "That bad, is it?"

"No, not really, just a little black around the corners. But your eyes are a little red-rimmed, too." Kendall's lips compressed into a line. "Does your bad day have to do with what happened in class?"

Alex stepped closer. "Caesar was out of line. He shouldn't have threatened you."

Paul sent a piercing look at Elise. "What happened in class?"

She shrugged, her lips twisting. "One of my students has anger management issues."

Alex harrumphed. "Understatement of the year, if you ask me."

Every protective instinct in Paul rose with the hairs on the back of his neck. "Was he the kid being chased across campus by the campus cop?"

"You saw that?" Alex's eyes widened.

"Yeah." Paul's gaze remained on Elise. "I spoke with the police officer, too."

Kendall nodded. "That would be our Caesar. Jumped out the window of the classroom when Officer West came in. Did he catch him?"

"Unfortunately, no." Paul faced Elise. "Could he be the one who threw the brick?"

Elise shrugged. "I told you, I don't know. I didn't see who threw it. Like I said, I was looking in the rearview mirror."

Looking for him. Paul could have kicked himself for not tailing her more closely.

"Brick?" Kendall latched on to the word, her gaze on Elise's pale face. "Someone threw a brick? Did it hit you?"

"No, it didn't hit me. It did hit the windshield of my car," she said, her voice low. She shot a glance toward the hallway where the boys had disappeared.

"I'm glad you're okay, anyway." Kendall wrapped her arms around Elise and hugged her. "That jerk should be kicked out of school."

"Alex, are you gonna come see my Spider-Man?" Luke called out from his bedroom.

Alex grinned. "Guess I better check it out."

Elise gave him a wan smile. "Thanks."

Alex sauntered down the hall peering into the open bedroom doors. "Where are you, Luke?"

"In here!" Luke shouted.

Before Alex arrived at Luke's door farther down the hallway, he came to a sudden halt in front of Elise's bedroom door.

"Wait, Alex!" Elise lunged toward the teen.

Paul realized their mistake at about the same time as Elise and they collided at the entrance to the hallway.

Alex stood transfixed, staring into the bedroom. "Wow, Ms. Johnson. Someone did a number on your wall."

"It's nothing." Elise reached for the door handle, but before she could close the door, Kendall ducked around her and entered.

"Holy crap!" the blond-haired teen said, her jaw dropping. "Who did this?"

Elise stared at Paul, her eyes pooling with more tears. "I don't know."

"Oh my God!" Kendall's hand covered her mouth. "Does this have to do with the woman they found dead? She was a blonde, wasn't she?" Kendall faced Elise, her eyes wide. "Was this why you were all creeped out when I stopped by the other day?"

Paul pulled Elise into the crook of his arm, unconcerned about what the teens might think of their relationship.

Her body shook as though she were chilled. "Yes."

"Oh, Ms. Johnson." Kendall reached for her hands and held them. "This is terrible. Did you go to the police?"

"She went to the FBI," Paul answered for Elise.

Alex's eyes rounded. "You're an FBI agent?"

Paul nodded.

"Wow." Alex's teeth shone in a huge grin. "That's so cool."

"Alex! Ms. Johnson could be in trouble. She's blond and everything, like the note on the wall."

Alex looked at her sideways. "Kenny, so are you, in case you didn't notice. And so are half the girls at school."

Kendall's face blanched. "That's right." She stood for a moment, staring at the wall, then she reached into her back pocket, pulled out her cell phone and held it up and clicked a button.

"What are you doing?" Elise grabbed her arm and pulled it down.

"Getting a picture." Kendall turned the phone over and viewed the picture she'd just taken. "We could be involved in an honest-to-God murder case. This is evidence."

Elise snatched the camera from Kendall's hand. "You can't show this to anyone."

"Why? It's part of solving the case. The police need to see it."

"I have my reasons." Elise clicked the buttons on the phone, trying to delete the picture. "How do you delete it? You have to delete it!"

"It's okay, Ms. Johnson." Kendall reached around and touched her finger to two buttons. The display asked her to cancel or delete. Kendall pressed the key for delete and the picture of Elise's wall disappeared. "I'm sorry. I wouldn't have taken the picture if I'd known it would upset you so much."

"No, I'm sorry." Elise shoved the phone back into Kendall's hands. "I shouldn't have overreacted."

"Is there anything we can do? Do you want me to keep the boys while you talk with the police?" Kendall asked. "I've had the Red Cross CPR and babysitting courses."

"No, no. We'll manage." Elise placed a hand on Kendall's arm and one on Alex's. "Please, don't say anything to anyone about this. Please."

"We won't, Ms. Johnson," Alex answered automatically.

Kendall bit on her bottom lip, but didn't say anything.

Alex jabbed her in the ribs. "Right, Kenny?"

The teen frowned and rubbed her ribs. "Right, right. We won't tell anyone. But I think you need to take it to the police."

Elise's hand fluttered up to Paul's chest. "I have the FBI working on it. They know what to do."

Paul grabbed her hand and held it trapped against his shirt, wishing he'd thought to close the door before Alex and Kendall saw the writing. The more people knew about it, the more likely it would get around. Elise's new life looked to be blowing wide open.

Alex grabbed Kendall's arm and pulled her toward the door. "Come on, Kendall. Ms. Johnson has enough to worry about. Let's go home."

"Thanks, Alex," Elise said. "I'll see you two tomorrow."

"Seven-thirty, right?" Kendall asked.

Elise's brow furrowed. "Seven-thirty?"

"Didn't you need help setting up for a movie?"

Elise softly snorted, her smile unconvincing. "Yes, yes I did."

"We'll be there," Alex said.

"Good. I might need help with the audio-visual equipment. We're supposed to watch a DVD for class tomorrow and I haven't a clue how to work the machine."

Alex's face lit up. "Cool!" Then he toned down his enthusiasm, his face getting serious. "Be careful, Ms. Johnson."

Elise leaned against Paul and tears glistened in the corners of her eyes. "Thanks, Alex, Kendall. Go straight home, will you?"

Kendall's shoulders pushed back and her jaw set firmly. "Don't worry, Ms. Johnson." She dragged Alex out the front door and the room faded into silence.

"I guess I should be packing my bags." Elise pulled away from Paul and stood looking around her living room, her eyes swimming with unshed tears.

Paul reached for her, but she stepped away. "You can't give up now."

"I feel as though there is a line forming to throw more bricks my way."

"I'd say the brick was the act of a juvenile—an angry juvenile."

"You think it was Caesar?" Elise nodded. "Yeah, you're probably right. He likes to scare people. It's the only way he knows how to get attention." Her gaze went to the bathroom where the door opened and Brandon came out, his hands wet and dripping. Her eyes shone with love for her son. She'd do anything for her boys.

Her oldest son glanced their way. After a long moment, he ducked into the bedroom he shared with Luke.

Elise's shoulders sagged. "What am I going to do?"

"What you always do. Stand tall and make sure your boys are okay." If he could, Paul would wrap her in his arms and shield her from all that was bad in the world, shoulder her burdens so she didn't have to. But she'd pushed him away, determined to manage her fear alone, and he had a job to do. Standing around here wasn't getting it done. "Are you going to be all right until nightfall? I have to go to the office and check on a few things. I'll be back before eleven tonight."

"I'll keep the door locked."

"Good. And don't open it for anyone but me."

"Don't worry," she said in a tone low enough Brandon wouldn't overhear. "I'm scared enough now to follow orders."

"And I know this won't make you feel any better, but leave the note on the wall. I want someone from our forensics team to take a look at it."

Elise shook her head. "No."

"Okay, how about I get Mel to catalog the evidence, take pictures and run it through evidence with the location undisclosed. Deal?"

Elise chewed on her lower lip, the action making him want to taste that lip himself. "Okay. But just Mel."

"I'll have her here as soon as possible." He turned for the door.

"Paul?" Her voice pulled him back to stand in front of her.

"Yes?"

She stared up at him through dew-kissed blue eyes. "Thanks." She leaned up on her toes and pressed a sweet kiss to his lips.

Paul fought the urge to crush her in his arms and deepen the kiss. Instead, he ended the kiss and stepped away. "You don't have to thank me. It's my job."

Elise's tears trickled out of the corners of her eyes, then she turned and fled for the boys' bedroom.

As Paul closed the front door behind him, Luke's voice called out, muffled by the heavy wood door, "Hey, where'd Alex go? I wanted to show him my Spider-Man."

A smile crossed Paul's face. A boy like Luke would be fine no matter what. Brandon knew too much for his own good. That child acted more like an old man.

Anger surged in Paul's gut. The boy's childhood had been stolen from him by his abusive father and now by this new threat.

And Elise…how much torture could one woman stand? The fear she must be feeling had to be overwhelming.

Paul climbed into his truck and headed for the sheriff's office. He had to tell Sheriff Engel about the notes. Holding back information was almost as bad as committing the crime.

ELISE WANDERED AROUND THE HOUSE, checking each window lock, door lock and dead bolt. Her cozy little house felt more like a cage than a home. She needed a fortress, not a house of sticks.

The cell phone rang and she hurried to answer, thinking it might be Paul with another round of cautions. She didn't care; she felt more secure in his presence, even when it was only his voice. The caller ID displayed "out of area." Paul's cell phone probably was unlisted in caller ID, given his line of business.

"Did you forget something?" she asked, her voice slightly breathless, the feel of Paul's lips still tingling on hers.

"No, I remember every detail." The voice wasn't Paul's. It was mechanical and disguised. "Did you like my artwork?"

Cold chills shook Elise so hard her teeth rattled. "Who is this?"

"You know who."

"No, I don't."

"After eight years of marital bliss you'd forget me so soon?"

"My husband is dead."

"Are you sure I'm dead? Did you bury me yourself? Did you see my body?"

"No," she whispered, her hand shaking so hard she almost dropped the telephone.

"Does the fed make you scream in bed like I did?"

"Shut up! My husband is dead."

"Does he make you cry out his name?"

"None of your business!"

"Get rid of the new boyfriend, Alice. He'll never be enough man for you. He didn't catch me. He's not the hero everyone makes him out to be."

"What do you know about being a man? Do you think real men are supposed to hurt women?" She forced a laugh she didn't feel. "Any man who hurts women is a coward. You must be afraid of other men, if you have to hurt women to get off."

She must have struck a chord in him because the phone remained silent for several long moments.

"Do you hear me?" Elise turned away from her boys' bedroom door and walked into the kitchen, placing distance between her children and her. They didn't need to know. They shouldn't have to know. "You're a coward."

"Don't make me mad, Alice."

"Why? Can't you take it like a man?" Why didn't she just shut up? Why was she egging on a killer? Why was she so angry? Because her anger masked her fear, stiffened her spine and made her want to take action.

Elise Johnson was tired of being afraid. Tired of running. Tired of men controlling her life. "Leave me the hell alone."

"Sorry, baby. I can't." The mechanical voice breathed into the phone, the static crackling in Elise's ear. "Say goodbye to pretty Mary Alice."

A woman screamed in the background.

"No! Wait!" Elise gulped past the horror clogging her throat.

"Change your mind? Want me to visit you instead?"

"No! Don't hurt that woman. Please."

"Why? Are you willing to take her place?"

Elise thought of her boys. If she gave herself to this maniac, they'd be orphaned. "Don't hurt her. It's me you want, not her."

"True, but I want you to suffer like you made me suffer."

"What do you want from me? Why are you doing this?"

"Like the rhyme said…" He laughed. "They remind me of everything I lost because of you…Alice."

Chapter Eleven

Paul strode through the office, heels hitting hard on the tiled floor. "Mel? You here?"

Mel's head popped up over the top of her cubicle. "I'm here, though I'd rather be out of this stuffy office. Whatcha got?"

"In my office, ASAP." He paced behind his desk until Mel closed the door.

She stood with her shoulders back, her hands crossed at the small of her back in a perfect parade rest. "What happened, boss?"

"Whoever left Elise that note broke into her home and wrote another across the wall in her bedroom."

"Shoot." Mel let out a long breath. "The woman could use some better locks."

"I need you out there to collect any evidence you can find. And get a locksmith. I want all the doors on her house rekeyed."

"I should get hold of Joe in forensics."

"No, I promised her we wouldn't get any more people involved than we have already. She's expecting you and the sooner you're out there the better I'll feel."

"Gotcha." Mel dug a small steno pad out of the back pocket of her jeans. "I spent my day out in Breuer as well, interviewing the first victim's friends and family. Seems Lauren Alice Pendley worked in the high school cafeteria as a lunch lady. She quit just a month ago to go to work at the pharmacy."

"Elise's high school?"

Mel nodded. "One and the same."

"I think I need to spend more time on campus."

"On campus in general, or with Elise in particular?" Mel's smile came and went with the searing glare Paul aimed her way. "Anything else, boss?"

"Yeah, keep an eye open for a Hispanic teen about six feet tall. Caesar Valdez. He threatened Elise in school today and I think he was also responsible for throwing a brick at her car windshield."

"Think our Alice Klaus has enough people gunning for her?" Mel shook her head. "And here I thought you were just out enjoying the cool hill-country weather."

Paul ran a hand through his hair, his shoulders tense, the muscles screaming for the release of a good workout. And maybe a workout would help him clear his mind and body of the feeling of Elise's lips on his, her body pressed to him. He really needed to clear his mind of her. If he hurried through the paperwork, he might get in a run before dark. "She's scared, Mel. Go easy on her."

"You don't have to tell me, Paul. I can just imagine. Seems like the world is gangin' up on her."

"Tread lightly around the kids, too. The oldest boy knows about his father."

Mel sucked air past her clamped teeth. "That's a darn shame. Gotta be a blow to the kid to know that much."

"Yeah." Paul frowned at Mel. "When did you start talking like a Texan?"

Mel shrugged. "It grows on you."

He glared at her. "Quit it, it doesn't sound right on someone from the East Coast."

"You might not like Texas, but I plan on staying here as long as the Bureau lets me. I want to become a Texan and the sooner I sound like one the better." She hooked her thumbs in the belt loops of her jeans and rocked back on her cowboy-boot heels.

Paul shook his head. "Go on. I don't like Elise being without protection too long."

"You kinda like her, don't you?"

Paul jerked his thumb toward the door. "Get the hell out of here, will ya?" As soon as Mel closed the door behind her, Paul stared down at his desk.

A neat stack of papers sat in the middle with a note on top from Agent Cain. *Assignment complete. Next?*

He rose to check Trevor's desk. The man wasn't there, the desk was clean and the pencils neatly standing in a coffee mug. What did he expect, that every agent in the office should work overtime every night like him?

"He's been gone most of the day." Alvarez walked up behind Paul.

"Working the fraud case?" Paul held out his hand to Agent Alvarez.

Alvarez shook his hand and nodded toward Cain's empty desk. "That's what I thought, but I called one of the witnesses he was supposed to talk to today and he hadn't seen him. So I called some of the others Cain was supposed to have checked with and they all said the same thing. Did you give him an alternate mission?"

"No." He'd have to talk with Cain first thing in the morning. Paul sighed. He really needed to spend more time with the man and either mentor or transfer him. Cain obviously had an issue with his new boss and assignments.

The cell phone clipped to his belt buzzed. "Fletcher."

"We found Mary Alice." Sheriff Engel's voice came across the line old and tired.

Paul scrubbed a hand over his face, his chest constricting, making it hard for him to breathe. "Where?"

"Same river, different bridge. And the body's fresh." The sheriff called out orders, his voice muffled by his hand over the receiver. "He's getting sloppy."

"How's that?"

"It's not dark yet and we have a witness who may have seen the vehicle drive away."

"Yeah? Did they get a make and model?"

"Not a make and model, but he said a dark SUV, either black or navy blue, entered the highway from the access road beside the river bridge around five-thirty this afternoon."

"Did they get a license plate?"

"No." The sheriff paused. "Does the FBI have anything they want to share about this case? What about the idea that you suggested about this being a copycat of the Dakota Strangler? Anything new in that department?"

"As a matter of fact, I was just about to call you. I need a favor."

After the sheriff agreed to keep Elise's identity secret, Paul filled him in on the notes and the writing on the wall.

"Agent Fletcher, you know I'll have to see it," Sheriff Engel said.

"I know. I have Agent Bradley on her way out to collect the evidence. I'll have her let you in."

"If it helps, I'll swing by my house, change into plain clothes and then head over to Ms. Johnson's."

"Thanks, Sheriff." Paul agreed to meet with him the following day to compare notes and clues. In the meantime, he had duties as the head of the regional office to complete before he returned to Breuer.

He hung up and called his buddy Agent Nick Tarver.

"I was about to call you." Nick didn't bother with pleasantries. It wasn't his style.

Paul grinned. "Good to hear from you, too."

"I didn't find anything. No John Does, Smiths or Joneses checked into any hospitals downstream of the flooding with burn wounds or smoke inhalation during the six weeks following the flood two years ago."

"What about the hospitals within a 200-mile radius?"

"Checked them. No one fitting his description. No unidentified patients, no one in a coma with burns or smoke inhalation there, either."

"No body, no patient lying in a hospital. Nothing." Paul voiced his thoughts aloud.

"You got it."

"This guy has to be a copycat."

"Agreed. Brenna checked out the local library for all the books written that mention the Dakota Strangler. Each of them details how the victim was strangled and tied up with Ethernet cable."

"Yeah, but the Dakota Strangler strangled his victims *with* the cable, then tied them with the murder weapon."

"This guy didn't?"

"The first victim was strangled, the coroner thinks with an arm around her throat. No signs of the cable around her throat. Then she was bound at the hands and feet and tossed into the Guadalupe River."

Nick heaved a sigh. "Not quite the same."

"Which could mean something or nothing. It's been two years. If Stan Klaus is still alive, he might have changed his method. Then again, if it's a copycat, how did he find out Elise

Johnson is really Alice Klaus?" Paul paused to breathe. "Hell, I didn't even know who she was and where she'd relocated until you and Brenna called."

"Any chance the kids inadvertently let it slip?"

Paul hesitated. Brandon knew his father had killed. "Maybe. But to whom? They go to elementary school. So far the victims have all had some connection to the high school in some way."

"How big is Breuer?"

"Just under ten thousand people."

"A small town where everyone knows everyone else's business?"

"Not quite. Most of the people who live here in the hill country commute to San Antonio. It's like a really large suburb of the city."

"Still, word could have gotten around."

Paul didn't like the idea of questioning Brandon, but he had to follow all the leads. "I'll see what I can find out."

He ended the call and had just set his cell phone down when it rang again. The name on the caller ID made him pick up. "What's wrong, Elise?"

"I got a call from him."

The tone of Elise's voice told Paul all he needed to know about who "him" was.

Paul gripped the phone hard. "Tell me."

ELISE BUSIED HERSELF with getting the boys through homework and their nightly routine. She didn't want to slow down long enough to think about what the killer had said, nor did she want to relive the scream she'd heard in the background. She'd probably hear that scream echoing in her nightmares for the rest of her life.

Promptly at eight-thirty, she had Luke and Brandon bathed and tucked into their beds, forcing herself to take the time to read a story to them, when all she wanted was to run screaming through the house. Normalcy was what they needed in their lives. Normalcy was what she prayed for every day, though her prayers had gone unanswered.

Agent Melissa Bradley had called thirty minutes earlier to say she'd be there around eight forty-five with the sheriff.

The entire time Elise read to her boys, her thoughts strayed to that phone call and anger surged through her veins. Surged and ebbed away and surged again.

She knew she had to tell the police about the notes and the phone call, but still Elise couldn't help dreading the exposure of her and her children to the scrutiny of the police and ultimately the press.

Elise leaned over Brandon and kissed his forehead. Nowadays he only let her kiss him when he was sleeping. Kissing was for babies, and Brandon was the man of the house. She'd told him so and he'd taken his responsibilities seriously.

Elise stared down at him as he lay snuggled in his twin-size bed, the exact match of his brother's beside him. Her heart swelled with the pain and love she felt for her sons.

Brandon knew. All this time she'd avoided talking with Brandon about what had happened back in North Dakota. She hoped he'd forget, that his young mind would let it go. Maybe he wouldn't remember the news reporters pushing microphones into his mother's face, asking her if she'd known that her husband had been killing women.

He'd probably seen the reports on television displaying the picture of his father, calling him the Dakota Strangler. What must that have done to him? And for Brandon to hold that inside all this time must have been hard.

A lump choked her throat and she struggled to swallow past it.

She'd thought moving this far south, where no one knew her and her sons, would safeguard them from the torment of the press. Never in a million years had she imagined that her husband might still be alive and want revenge.

Elise scrubbed at the tears now streaming down her cheeks.

Would this nightmare ever end?

She trudged into the living room and stared around at the scattered toys, shoes and books, with no desire to clean. The familiar cracking sound the house made occasionally made her jump. A cat squalled outside the side window, sending shivers up and down Elise's arms. Despite her desire for independence, she found herself clock-watching, waiting for Paul's return. In the meantime, she couldn't sit around twitching at every noise.

Elise switched on the television to mask the noises of the encroaching night. No sooner had she tuned in to a favorite sitcom and settled into her lounge chair, than she got a shock during the first commercial break.

A San Antonio anchorman looked into the camera, but Elise felt as if he were talking directly to her. "Another young woman was found murdered in the Guadalupe River this afternoon. Stay tuned to the news at ten for more on this breaking story."

Elise's heart fisted in her gut, churning the mac and cheese she'd eaten for dinner into bile. The sick bastard had killed Mary Alice. She bent over and moaned. No. This couldn't be happening.

A soft knock sounded from the front door, jerking her out of her anguish and back into stark terror.

Her heart hammering in her chest, Elise leaped to her feet and ran for the door. Her hand paused on the knob. She didn't have a peephole to identify the person on the other side. "Who is it?" she said, inwardly cursing how much her voice shook.

"Elise, it's me, Melissa Bradley."

Elise crossed to the window and parted the vinyl blinds.

Agent Bradley stood in her faded blue jeans, crisp white blouse, a navy blue wool blazer and mock-ostrich-skin cowboy boots. Behind her stood an older man in sweatpants and a sweatshirt with Kendall Country Sheriff written in bold black letters over his right breast.

Darkness crept in on the quiet street, edging out the last rays of sun. Wind buffeted the gnarled live oak in the front yard. For all her neighbors knew, two normal people had shown up to pay Elise Johnson a visit. Not that it mattered. Elise couldn't keep her identity a secret much longer. Not when the lives of more women were at stake.

She sighed and unlocked the dead bolt, relieved and apprehensive at the same time. "Please, come in."

Melissa entered with a camera around her neck, carrying what looked like a toolbox. She turned to the man behind her. "Elise Johnson, this is Kendall County Sheriff Thomas Engel."

The sheriff held out a meaty hand and nodded. "Ms. Johnson. I understand you've had some trouble. I'm here to help."

Elise shook hands with the sheriff, dreading the questioning to come, yet knowing it had to be addressed. "If you'll follow me. Please try to keep it down. The boys are sleeping."

"We'll make this as painless as possible. Unfortunately, some of this stuff can be messy." Agent Bradley nodded. "Lead the way."

When Elise opened the door to her bedroom a cold wave of dread swept her all over again. The lettering hadn't changed since Brandon found it earlier that day, yet it hung over her bed, taunting her with an oppressive threat.

Melissa set the toolbox on the floor then started snapping pictures. "Has anything been disturbed since you found it?"

"No." She hadn't even gone into her room since Alex and Kendall had been there.

"Good." Melissa covered the room's every angle and closed in on the writing on the wall.

Elise tried to imagine what the room looked like from her viewpoint. A full-sized bed in the middle of the room. Only one pillow and fluffy yellow bedding and a child's action figure lying on the nightstand. Lonely, female, single parent without a sex life.

On her limited budget, Elise had gone for soft and feminine decor. The exact opposite of what Stan had insisted she buy for their bedroom. She hadn't wanted to be reminded of her former husband in any way whatsoever, preferring to completely erase him from her existence. So much for erasing him. "Sheriff, the news said another woman was found this afternoon."

"Good news travels fast." The lines around his eyes deepened. "Bad news even faster."

"Was she a blonde, Sheriff Engel?" Elise asked, her voice barely above a whisper, as her gaze traveled over the writing on the wall and her mind rolled over the words the killer had spoken on the phone only a few short hours ago.

The sheriff stared at the message on the wall and nodded, his lips set in a grim line. "Yes, ma'am."

"And the woman from the other day?" Elise knew the answer before she asked.

"Blondes on both counts." The sheriff flipped open a notepad and jotted something down. "Seems we might have us a serial killer with a penchant for blondes on our hands."

Blondes by the name of Alice.

Elise stood outside her bedroom, not sure she'd ever be able to sleep there again. "Whoever killed those two women was in this house."

Melissa dropped to her haunches beside the toolbox and flipped the metal latches open. "I have a locksmith on his way. Should be here any minute. The boss wants to make sure you're rekeyed and secure before you go to bed tonight. Or we could move you and the boys to a safe house."

A small amount of relief loosened some of the tension in her shoulders. "No, thanks. New locks will be sufficient." At least she could rest somewhat assured the killer wouldn't have a key to the new locks.

Elise paced the hallway, stopping to peek in on the boys who slept oblivious to the visitors. Thank goodness. How would she explain to Brandon that everything was all right when their world was falling apart around them?

When she returned, Melissa was brushing black powder on surfaces throughout the room. "I'm sorry, this is a mess, but I'm hoping we'll find a fingerprint or two."

"I don't mind. I'd like to know how he got in," Elise stated.

"We would, too." Melissa dusted black powder on the wall near the writing. "Did you check all your windows and doors before you left this morning?"

"Ever since I got the first note, I've been very careful to lock everything."

"Are you certain the kids didn't unlock a window or leave a door unlocked?"

"I double-checked everything before we left for school."

Melissa shook her head. "Then he's either good at lock-picking or he's got a master key similar to what a locksmith would carry."

"Are you telling me new locks won't keep him out?" Elise

laughed, although no amount of humor reflected in the sound. "That's reassuring."

"I'd get the new locks, just in case he's gotten hold of one of your keys from somewhere."

"Where?"

"Do you leave your keys with a garage attendant when you get your oil changed?" the sheriff asked.

"No, I only leave my car key."

Sheriff Engel made a note on his pad. "Do you keep a spare house key anywhere?"

"Only at school in my desk drawer and I keep that locked when I'm not there."

"Have you checked that lock lately to be sure someone hasn't tampered with it?"

"No, it never occurred to me."

"I wouldn't put it past this guy." Melissa shrugged. "I wouldn't put anything past this guy. You might consider buying a big dog or a gun."

"I'm seriously considering a gun." Then she told Mel and the sheriff about her phone conversation with the killer.

Chapter Twelve

Paul parked along the side of the street a block over from Elise's house. He wanted to get a quick run in before he called it a night and camped out on her couch.

He climbed out of his truck, wearing a pair of gray sweatpants and a plain gray T-shirt. The wind whipped across his biceps, raising goose bumps along his exposed skin. He debated the sweatshirt on the backseat, but decided against it. Forty-five degrees didn't bother him as long as he kept moving. After the months of record heat, a little cold air would be refreshing. And he needed to move to get rid of the cobwebs crowding his thoughts so that he could think more clearly and get some perspective on this case.

He took off at a steady jog. Darkness claimed the day, settling like a shroud over the small town. He'd told Melissa he'd work out before he arrived at Elise's house and that Elise should expect him around ten o'clock. Instead of jogging the track close to his apartment in San Antonio, he'd decided to take his workout to Breuer and make some use of it, scouting the neighborhood around the Johnsons' house.

Melissa had informed him that she'd completed collecting evidence and the sheriff had asked all the questions he could possibly ask Elise. The locksmith had come and gone, leaving brand-new locks on all the doors and giving his nod over the ones on the windows. All that and the boys hadn't woken up once.

Paul smiled, not surprised that Luke hadn't woken up, knowing how busy the little guy was when he was awake. The kid could sleep through a tornado, as much energy as he burned during the day. Brandon, on the other hand, was an entirely different case. Paul would have thought any little sound would wake the older of the two boys. Given the amount of emotional trauma he'd experienced finding the note on the wall and owning up to knowledge of his father's career as a killer, the kid probably had nightmares.

Only a block over from Elise's little cottage, Paul found himself headed her way first. As soon as he turned west, the wind thrust against him, penetrating the single layer of his T-shirt and chilling his skin. He picked up the pace, passing the front of her house, pushing hard to encourage his body to warm quickly.

From the outside, all was peaceful, but inside a frightened woman was probably pacing the floor, wondering where the killer would strike next.

He lengthened his stride, passing half a dozen little houses. At the next street, he turned left and made another left on the street running parallel to Highland.

He wanted to see the house behind hers. With all the brush and overgrown hedges, he'd only glimpsed the rooftop. If the house was anything like the hedges, it would probably be run-down and in need of work.

The opposite was the case. The house behind Elise's was a single-story dwelling spread out over the lot. The yard and garden in front were well-maintained and neatly kempt. Whoever took care of the front yard obviously didn't have a hand in the care of the backyard. Two rockers sat on the front porch, rocking gently in the wind.

Paul slowed to a stop beneath the heavy limbs of a bare native pecan tree and stared into the shadowy backyard.

Luke had stood at his back fence calling through the hedges to someone on this side. But who? Paul made a note to introduce himself to this neighbor.

As he studied the house, he didn't get any idea about its occupants from the neat appearance. If anything, he'd guess a little old lady lived there who liked to sit on the porch and rock during the warmer weather. But then who was the guy Luke referred to as George? A little boy?

Paul saw no signs of a little boy. No toys or swing set in the yard, no bicycle propped against the house. He moved toward the backyard, careful to be quiet and not disturb the occupants. He didn't need to scare an old woman into a heart attack thinking she had a Peeping Tom. As he peered into the darkness of the backyard, ancient live oaks and native pecan trees cast impenetrable, inky shadows.

Paul squinted, his eyes struggling to adjust to the limited light of the dark yard beyond. Hunkering low and keeping away from the few beams of light cast across the grass by the street light out front, he moved toward the side of the house, blending with the bushes lining the boundary.

Movement caught the corner of his eye. It wasn't in the backyard of this house, but in Elise's.

Adrenaline spiked in Paul's veins, shooting through his muscles, warming them from the inside out. He ran for the back row of overgrown bushes and hedges. The more he pushed and shoved, the more he realized he wasn't getting through them and had to go around.

Angry at having wasted even a minute trying to push through,

Paul sprinted back around the line of bushes to close on Elise's house. The shadow had disappeared by the time he got there.

A vehicle engine revved in the distance. Paul raced out to the pavement in time to see brake lights flash before they disappeared around a dark corner. The driver hadn't bothered to turn on the car's exterior lights, no headlights or taillights. What fool would drive around in the dark without their lights on? Someone bent on stirring up trouble. Someone who didn't want to get caught.

Paul ran full out, arriving at the corner in time to see… nothing.

The vehicle had completely vanished.

Breathing hard from the sprint and the anger surging through his body, Paul gave up on his run and hurried back to his truck. If nothing else, having the truck in Elise's driveway should ward off unwanted visits.

Paul pulled up in the driveway and shut off the engine. No sooner had he climbed down from the cab than the blinds flickered in the window.

Before he rounded the truck, the front door opened. Elise stood in the hazy glow of the front porch light, her hair whipped by the wind and shining a golden blur around her head. Her tired smile made his heart flip over and then ram against his chest.

Paul hurried toward her, wanting to pull her into his arms and hold her there until all the bad things stopped. Elise started to take a step, stopped and stared down at something on the front stoop.

Her eyes widened and she froze.

Halfway to her, Paul wondered what she stared at. His heartbeat kicked up a notch and he rushed forward. "Elise?"

She looked up at him, her eyes filling with tears. "Who is doing this to me?"

On the ground at her feet was a fashion doll with golden blond hair like Elise's, wearing a blue skirt and white blouse like she'd worn earlier that day. What sent cold chills down Paul's spine was the Ethernet cable tied around the doll's neck.

He opened his arms and she fell into them, sobbing against his chest. Leaving the doll on the stoop, Paul lifted Elise into his arms and carried her across the threshold into the house, kicking the door shut behind him. He set her on her feet and turned to twist the shiny new dead-bolt lock, one arm still around her waist, holding her against him.

Elise pressed her face into his T-shirt, her fingers bunching the material in her grip. "Why?" she sobbed quietly.

"I don't know. But it doesn't matter. You are not going to be next on any killer's list."

"I can't die." She laid her cheek against his chest, sniffing loudly. "What would Brandon and Luke do? They only have one parent."

The warmth of her tears soaking his shirt made him want to shield her from the terror of the day. "You're not going anywhere. You're going to see Brandon and Luke grow up. You'll have the pleasure of suffering when they go through puberty. You'll sprout a few gray hairs teaching them to drive." Paul stroked the back of her hair, wishing he could be there when she got those gray hairs. He bet she'd be just as beautiful as she was today.

She chuckled. "Oh, please, you're not helping."

He tipped her head up and stared down into her eyes. "You're a good mother, Elise, and I promise I'll do everything in my power to make sure you have the opportunity to raise those boys yourself."

Her blue eyes filled with a fresh wave of tears. "I can't even sleep in my own bedroom. That monster was in there, writing on my wall."

"Then sleep out here." He nodded toward the couch. "You can have the couch. I'll sleep in the lounge chair. Either way, I'm not going anywhere."

She sucked in a long, shaky breath and let it out, resting her forehead against his chest. "I promised myself I wouldn't let another man control my life."

"Is that what you think this is? Me controlling your life?"

"No." She smiled up at him, her eyes awash in unshed tears. "You aren't controlling my life. The killer is. He's making me afraid to step outside my door. Afraid to go to work. Afraid to answer my own telephone."

"We'll get him."

"When? After another woman dies?" Her voice caught in her throat and she glanced toward the hallway where her boys slept. "Or after I die?"

Paul pushed a long strand of golden-blond hair behind her ear and bent to press a kiss to her temple. "You're not going to die."

She turned her face to his, their lips only a breath away. "Why do you care? You don't even know me."

With his mouth hovering over hers, he stared into her eyes. "I've known you since I first met you and the boys in North Dakota."

"You were only around for a week, tops."

"It was enough." Since then, she'd haunted his dreams. The beauty had no idea how her sad eyes had penetrated his reserve where women were concerned. Her bravery in the face of the media circus, the accusations, the police hounding her for answers. She'd kept a stiff upper lip, protecting her boys like a mama bear, always composed under the glare of the cameras. She was the kind of woman he'd only dreamed about, the kind a man married and lived with happily ever after. The kind he'd shied away from, certain he had nothing to offer.

But the timing had been way off.

Seemed like Paul's timing continued to be off. Yet he couldn't ignore the way she felt, her body pressed against his, her breath warm against his lips.

"I want to..." Her voice trailed off, her eyelids drifting to half-mast. "But I shouldn't."

"No, we shouldn't." He stared into eyes so blue they rivaled the summer sky, his heart pounding against his ribs, the erratic beats having nothing to do with his earlier run. He couldn't control himself. He pulled her against him and kissed her.

At first stiff, Elise pressed her hands to his chest. Then she melted into his arms, her soft moan warming the inside of his mouth, touching him in places he didn't think accessible.

His tongue slipped across the seam of her lips. When they parted, he dove in past the slick smoothness of minty-fresh teeth to the warm, soft wetness of her tongue.

Her hands crept up his chest to wrap around his neck, dragging him closer.

He complied, his fingers gripping her hips, pulling her closer. The hard ridge of his erection pressed through the soft material of his sweats, nudging against her belly. Holding her hard against him, one hand crept up beneath her T-shirt, his thumb connecting with the soft swell of her naked breast.

Elise leaned into his touch, her lungs filling, pushing her breasts closer.

His thumb found the beaded nipple, flicked over the tip until Elise gasped into his mouth.

The featherlight touch of her hands slipped down his back. She grasped the hem of his T-shirt and tugged it upward.

Paul released his hold on her breast and lifted his arms.

Elise tugged the shirt higher.

Impatient to get his hands back on her beautiful body,

Paul grabbed the shirt and yanked it over his head, tossing it to the floor.

Elise's eyes widened, her mouth opening on a soft gasp.

For a moment, Paul thought she'd change her mind. He held back, unwilling to push her into anything she might regret. The choice was clearly hers. If she wanted to call a halt at this point... He sucked in a deep breath and let it out slowly. *So be it.*

Her tongue swept across kiss-swollen lips and she reached out, her fingers weaving into the hairs on his chest. "I want this," she whispered almost too softly to hear.

But Paul heard and his body rejoiced. Still, he had to take it slowly, carefully.

It took every ounce of his own self-control to keep from ripping her clothes off and making passionate, noisy love to her there on the living room floor.

Her gaze roamed over his chest, her fingers tracing a path to his hard brown nipples. A quick glance over her shoulder must have reassured her that the boys still slept. The door to their bedroom remained firmly closed. "This is so wrong."

He captured her hand beneath his, pressing it against the pounding of his heart. "Then don't." It cost him to make the offer.

"But I want to." She tugged her hand from his and reached for the hem of her own shirt, dragging it up her torso.

Every inch the shirt moved exposed pale, silky skin and the curve of her waist. Then a breast appeared and the other. When she raised her arms above her head, Paul could hold back no longer.

With her hands high, the shirt still tangled around her forearms, Paul reached out and cupped both breasts in his palms, a groan rising in his throat. "You're beautiful, Elise."

She tugged the shirt from her arms and let it drop to the floor. "I'm scared."

He kissed the tip of her nose, massaging the rounded flesh weighing lightly in his hands. "Of the killer?" He kissed her, his mouth slanting over hers, his tongue flicking across her lips. "Or me?"

"The killer, yes." Her head dropped back, her hair cascading around her, reaching past her bottom. "But most of all afraid of myself."

"I won't hurt you," Paul promised. Despite the passion of the moment, threatening to carry him away, he knew how important it was to reassure Elise. "I will never force you to do anything you don't want to."

"That's just it. I want this so much, I can't think." Her hands ran across his chest in a frenzy, then dipped lower, following the narrowing line of hair to the waistband of his sweats.

Oh, sweet heaven. Paul captured her hand before she went lower. "Don't go there unless you're certain. I can only take so much."

"Paul, I'm not as fragile as you might think." Her shoulders pushed back, forcing her bare breasts deeper into his hands. She looked up into his eyes, her own darker than the usual sunny-sky blue, smoldering a smoky gray. "I want this." Her hand skimmed over the hard ridge, making his sweats jut out in a tent. "You obviously want it, so shut up and let me before one of the boys decides to wake up."

Paul grinned and grabbed her around the waist, swinging her around the room, before gently setting her on her feet. "You're an amazing woman."

Elise was feeling pretty amazing, and scared, and filled with an overpowering desire to make love to this man. Now. Before she came to her senses and chickened out. Once he set her back on her feet, she gulped in a fortifying breath and reached for the button on her jeans.

"Let me." His fingers closed over hers and together they flicked it loose, sliding the zipper down to expose the pink lace of her panties.

Elise thanked the laundry gods for the loads of laundry she had yet to wade through. If not for getting behind, she wouldn't have been forced to wear the lacy panties her sister had given her last Christmas instead of the sensible briefs she usually wore.

The jeans came off and she stood in nothing but those stupid pink panties, the cool air raising gooseflesh on her skin.

Paul hooked his thumbs in the elastic waistband of his sweats.

Elise reached out, her fingers colliding with his, sending electric current all the way up her arms.

He halted the downward progress of his sweats, the elastic catching on that part of him straining for release. "Change your mind?"

Elise could tell it took a lot of effort for him to ask that question by the tightness around his lips. She shook her head and shoved his hands out of the way. "No. Let me."

She tugged on the front of the sweatpants, pushing them far enough down his hips that he sprang free.

Her breath caught in her throat. The man was hard, erect and magnificent. Elise hadn't been with any other man but her late husband. But in comparison just between the two of them, Paul's muscular body, trim waist and everything else was so much more…manly, and larger than life…than Stan had ever been.

She curled her hands around his buttocks, sliding the sweats and his briefs over the curve of his muscles and down the backs of his legs. Dropping to her knees, she skimmed over the crisp hairs of his thighs and downward to his taut, well-defined calves.

Paul cupped the back of her head, his fingers digging into her hair. "I never knew sweats could be so sexy."

"Me, either." She smiled up at him from her position at his feet. Her fingers circled his ankles, pushing the pants down as he stepped free.

As she rose slowly to her feet, she cupped him in her palm, loving the smooth feel of velvety skin over steely hardness. The juncture between her thighs ached to have him inside her, filling her, making her whole.

"Wait." He leaned over and pulled his wallet from the back pocket of his sweats, slipping a foil packet from its interior.

Elise smiled. "I'm glad you remembered." She had been well on her way to forgetting everything in the moment. That scared her. Was she doing the right thing? Would she be giving Paul the wrong message? Would he expect more from her than she was able to give? More than the sex she so craved? The feel of his body against her, making her remember she was alive and a woman with needs he could satisfy, if only temporarily.

Paul tipped her chin upward and pressed a kiss to her temple. "You're thinking too much." He held her face between his palms, his thumbs stroking her chin, her lips. "Just say no and I'll walk away, no questions asked. I won't be angry."

She stared into his eyes and knew he spoke the truth and knew deep down she was tired of being alone. Tired of being scared and way past due for sex. She inhaled and let the breath out slowly and raised her leg, sliding it along the outside of Paul's calf. Her hands slipped over the muscular bulges of his shoulders and upward to wrap around his neck. She laced her fingers behind his head and pulled his mouth down to hers. "Although I appreciate the out you're offering, I think you're talking too much. Shut up and kiss me."

She wrapped her leg around his, rubbing the damp space between her legs over the rough hairs on his thigh. Fire ignited, flaming throughout her body.

Paul's hands slid down her naked backside. He cupped her bottom and lifted her, draping her legs around his waist, his member pressing against her opening. Then he strode across the room, ripped a throw blanket off the back of the couch, tossed it to the carpeted floor and lowered her onto her back.

Elise's feet dropped to the floor and she opened her legs as he slid into her, filling her as she'd wanted since he'd entered her home tonight.

He moved in and out of her, gently easing his way deeper and deeper, the speed of his penetration increasing until they rocked back and forth in unison. Tension knotted deep inside her, a sweet, good kind of tension she had never experienced, even with her husband. The knot of pressure built to a ragged edge and then exploded throughout her system, sending shards of pulsing sensations rocketing through her body.

Elise's fingers dug into Paul's shoulders and she rode the wave of feeling until she collapsed against the blanket, gasping for breath. She'd never felt quite this replete. Ever.

As she lay curled in Paul's arms, fear crept back in. Fear for her boys' lives, fear for her own and most of all, perhaps the most frightening of all, fear that she was falling in love. How could she let that happen?

A panic attack big enough to launch a rocket hit her full force. Her chest tightened, her muscles bunched and she sucked in a deep breath, ready to bolt.

Paul sighed, pulled her close and kissed her on the tip of her nose. "You're going to run, aren't you?" He stared down into her eyes.

She couldn't move, couldn't breathe, couldn't answer his question.

He nodded in answer to his own question and a slow, sad smile crossed his face. "Just know this—I'll let you go now, but I don't give up easily." Paul rolled to his feet and grabbed his sweatpants, shoving his legs into them.

Elise grabbed her jeans and shirt and ran for the bathroom. She couldn't go back into the living room and face Paul. Not when she didn't know what she wanted from him, from herself, from anything. She couldn't sleep in her bedroom under the writing on the wall aimed to scare her. It had done its job and scared the fool out of her.

Elise washed her face and combed her fingers through her hair then stepped back out into the living room, dreading facing Paul, completely at a loss for an explanation for her actions.

Paul lay on the couch, his back to her, wrapped in the throw blanket. He didn't budge or acknowledge her presence. And was that him snoring? Elise suspected he was faking to put her at ease.

A smile curled the corners of her mouth. Grabbing a blanket from the hall closet, Elise slipped into the lounge chair and lay back. Her body still hummed from making love with Paul and danged if she didn't want to do it again. But she couldn't. Not now.

Not when she suspected she was falling in love with him.

Chapter Thirteen

Alex dumped his backpack on the floor beside the roller cart with the television on it. "Ms. Johnson, where's the disc you wanted to play for the class?"

"I left it in the machine yesterday afternoon. I couldn't figure out how to make the video display on the screen. Think you can work some magic on it?"

Elise had arrived on time but everything conspired against her getting the audio-visual equipment going for her first class. Thank goodness her first class was actually the second hour of the day and not the first. Alex and Kendall served as her assistants during their study hall.

Elise knew teachers weren't supposed to show favoritism to students; however, Alex and Kendall were always willing to help and loved learning. How could she not favor them? And they helped keep her mind off the writing on her wall and what she'd done with Paul on the floor of her living room last night.

Her cheeks burned as her mind conjured the image of Paul lying beside her, naked and beautiful in all his macho maleness. What kind of thoughts were those to have at school?

"These cables are backward. The input is in the output slot." Alex switched the cables and turned on the television.

Black-and-white static filled the screen and speaker.

Kendall busied herself erasing the previous day's assignment from the big white dry-erase board. "Alex, you're such an audio-visual geek. I'm going to have to work on you to make you date-worthy."

"Girls." Alex snorted. "Who needs 'em?"

"Hey!" Kendall planted her fists on her narrow hips. "I resent that."

"You know. You're not like a girl." Alex turned away, a smirk twisting his lips.

"It's worse that I thought." Kendall shook her head at Elise. "He doesn't even know what a girl is."

Elise smiled for what felt like the first time in a long time.

"What did the police have to say about the note on your wall, Ms. Johnson?" Kendall asked, her voice stiff and unnaturally cheerful as if she was trying too hard to make the question more casual than it was.

"Kendall." Alex shot a warning glance at the girl. "You promised you wouldn't be nosy."

"I can't help asking questions. It's my nature." She smiled at Elise. "After all, someday I want to work for the FBI like Agent Fletcher."

Elise cast a glance at the door. It was closed and hopefully no one out in the hallway could hear what was being said. "The sheriff and the FBI took pictures and dusted for fingerprints. I guess it's up to them to figure out who did it."

Kendall heaved a sigh. "Wish I could have been there when they collected the evidence."

"What, so you could ask dumb questions? Just kick her out when she gets to botherin' you too much, Ms. Johnson." Alex plugged a cable into the back of the television and the power cord into the wall. "That ought to do it."

"I've been thinking, Ms. Johnson." Kendall tipped her head to the side, a frown pressing her blond brows closer together. "Do you think the killer will come after you next? My mom won't even let me ride my bicycle down the street right now."

Elise squeezed her eyes shut to keep the ready tears from spilling. Was she doing the right thing by staying in Breuer? Was her very presence there placing all the other blond women in danger? "I don't know, Kendall."

"Why would he write that note on your wall?"

"Kendall, shut up." Alex straightened from the back of the television and glared at his friend.

Kendall held her hands up in surrender. "What? I'm just asking."

"Maybe Ms. Johnson doesn't want to answer all your crazy questions."

"But I could be at risk, too, for all we know." She lifted the end of her blond ponytail, her brows raised.

"Yeah and your name isn't Alice."

"Neither is Ms. Johnson's." Kendall turned her gaze back to Elise. "Your first name is Elise, isn't it? Why did the note call you Alice? I mean, it sounds kinda like Alice but it's different."

"Enough, Kendall!" Alex stalked toward her.

Kendall ducked behind Elise's desk. "Leave me alone, you geek. I mean it. One step closer and I'll let you have it."

Alex took that one step and a couple more.

"You're impossible." Kendall tossed the eraser at Alex's head and missed. The eraser bounced off the front of the video player, triggering the unit to switch on.

Instead of the documentary on ancient Egypt and the pyramids, a news clip came on.

Kendall's attention shifted to the television screen. "Is that the local news channel?"

Alex returned to the set and fiddled with the buttons, changing the channels. On any other channel he either got a blue screen or static. He hit the eject button and reloaded the disc.

Once again the screen filled with a news clip. People were standing out in the rain, wearing heavy coats, and the news reporter held a microphone up to a woman clutching the hands of two small boys.

Elise's heart stumbled in her chest, her vision going blurry around the edges. She knew that woman. Knew those boys.

"Turn it off," she said, barely able to force air past her vocal cords.

Alex and Kendall moved closer to the television.

Kendall pointed at the oldest boy. "Hey, isn't that Brandon?" When she turned back to Elise, her face blanched. "Ms. Johnson, are you okay?"

Alex turned the sound up on the television, oblivious to Kendall and Elise.

"Mrs. Klaus, did you know your husband was a serial killer?"

"No." Elise's lips formed the words the woman on the screen said, the sound from the television echoing in her head as though it came from a cave.

Another reporter shoved a microphone in her face and demanded, "How could you live in the same house with a killer and not know it?"

"Please, leave us alone. I didn't have anything to do with it. I knew nothing."

The segment cut to a well-coiffed reporter. "Here in Riverton, North Dakota, with the banks of the Red River overflowing in what's been the worst flooding since 1997, authorities are searching for the body of the Dakota Strangler, thought to have perished in a farmhouse fire. In the background, the FBI and state police are transporting the killer's wife to the police station for questioning. She claims to know nothing of her husband's connection to the deaths of five Riverton women."

The video cut to another reporter outside a school gymnasium, rain dripping off the edges of his black umbrella. "It's rumored that the Dakota Strangler's wife, Alice Klaus, and her two sons are taking refuge in this evacuation shelter. Meanwhile the body of the Dakota Strangler has yet to be recovered.

"Experts say he may never be found, his body may even be carried as far as the Gulf of Mexico. Remnants of the house in which he'd last been seen have been found rammed against a railroad bridge crossing the Red River. No signs of the strangler himself. Authorities say the debris is too unstable to pick through at this time. With the snow melting and the continued rain, the river isn't expected to crest for another twenty-four hours."

Elise collapsed in the chair behind her desk and laid her face on the cool wooden surface. "Please, turn it off. Please." Tears spilled out of the corners of her eyes, dripping onto the calendar desk pad, smearing the ink of a note she'd jotted in a hurry.

Kendall ran for the television and hit the power button. "Ms. Johnson." Her hand touched Elise's shoulder, but Elise could barely feel it. Her entire body had gone numb. Nightmares of reporters hounding her and the boys, the terror of outrunning the flooding in the streets, losing everything in her home and life, the accusations by the police and the press all jumbled in her mind.

"Ms. Johnson?" Alex called to her.

Elise couldn't lift her head. She moved her lips but couldn't force words to come out. I'm all right, she wanted to say, but couldn't.

She wasn't all right. Nothing was all right. Her secret was out and soon all of Breuer would blame her for the deaths of women she didn't even know. Wasn't she to blame? She'd come to this town hoping to escape the death that found its way here.

"Alex, go get the principal," Kendall ordered somewhere on the other side of the haze that crowded her.

No. Elise cried out, but no sound came out. She couldn't tell the principal. With parents like Gerri Finch ready to file lawsuits, she wouldn't want that kind of scandal at her school.

"It's okay, Ms. Johnson. I have the disc in my pocket. Alex and I won't tell anyone if you don't want us to."

Tainted relief flooded in on a wave of blackness and the world went dark.

PAUL STRODE INTO THE OFFICE by eight-thirty that morning. That's where Mel cornered him.

"Tell me you have something," Paul said without the usual greeting.

"Wish I could. All I know is this guy has to be a copycat. From what we knew about Stan Klaus, he killed women who were smart because he didn't want his wife, our Elise, to get ideas about going back to school or getting smarter than him."

"We still can't rule him out." Paul pushed his hand through his hair and paced the room. "I don't like being away from her any more than we have to. My gut tells me that he'll eventually make a grab for her."

Melissa crossed her arms over her chest. "Then why are you here?"

"I have a job to do. I can't run a department from Breuer."

"Don't worry about the department right now. These guys have assignments. They're big agents who can operate independently. You said so yourself."

"Everyone except maybe Agent Cain."

"What's up with him?"

"He's been playing a disappearing act with Alvarez. I plan to get to the bottom of it tomorrow morning first thing."

"Just what you need when you have so much more on your mind." Melissa's brows rose. "Want me to check it out?"

Paul nodded. "If I'm not in first thing in the morning, tail him. See what he's up to."

"Will do." Melissa jerked her head toward the door. "But right now, you need to get back to Breuer. Elise will be biting her nails until you get there. After seeing the writing on the wall, I don't blame her."

"I know. She says she doesn't like me hanging around, but I think she feels safer when I'm there. She's more afraid people will start asking questions and find out about her past."

"It's a tough past to live with. But maybe if she would let her secret out, others around her would be on the lookout for her and keep her all the safer."

"It's hard convincing her." Paul paced the length of the office again, needing the release of exercise or hitting something, someone.

"Okay, tough guy. If you think you're needed here, why aren't you sitting at your desk pushing paper like a good supervisor should?" Melissa's words acted as a finger poked in a wound, gouging a hole in the thin veneer of reason he kept on his tightly strung control.

Sitting behind his desk would make him want to crawl right out of his skin, and damned if Melissa didn't know that. He couldn't leave Elise exposed to whoever was killing women in Breuer. "I'm going back to the school. I have a feeling there's something we're missing."

"How so?"

"The first note appeared in her box at school."

"Did you find out how it got there?"

"No. Elise didn't want me nosing around the school alerting the staff to her situation. But I want to know how that note got in her box." Paul glanced at the paperwork piling up on his desk, a twinge of guilt eating at his gut, but not enough to stop him.

"Leave the drudgery." Melissa waved at the documents and reports. "It'll still be there once we've apprehended the Breuer Killer."

"You sound confident we'll get him soon."

"I know you and you've got that look in your eye."

"What look?"

"That look you get when you're on the trail of someone and won't let it go until you find him."

Paul shrugged. "I don't know what you're talking about." He stepped out of his office, Melissa following close on his heels. "So tomorrow while I'm out of the office you're going to keep up with Cain."

"Yes, sir." Mel followed him. "You know, I've never known a person Paul Fletcher couldn't get along with."

Paul strode past Cain's empty desk, noting the papers stacked in neat piles and the pens standing in an FBI coffee mug. The guy liked things orderly. If he handled his cases like he did his office, he'd be thorough. So why was he skipping out on his assigned duties? Paul made a mental note to review Cain's past cases to get to know his style more and have a talk with him in the morning. He wanted his people to work as a team.

"I have another assignment for you this afternoon. I told Elise and the boys that you would be at their house when the boys get off the school bus. She insists on being at the school for parent-teacher night."

Mel's brows rose. "What do I know about babysitting boys?"

"About as much as I do."

"Why don't *you* pick them up?"

"I'm going to the school to keep an eye on Elise."

Mel grinned. "You get the girl. I get the kids. One of the perks of being the boss, right? Just don't take all night, will you? I might have had plans."

"It's business," Paul insisted. Although what they'd done last night had nothing to do with business. His jeans tightened at the memory. "And you? Plans? When was the last time you had a date?"

Mel bristled. "I've had dates."

"Yeah? When?"

"Well, I could have had a date if I wasn't working." Mel's lips twisted into a wry grin. "Okay, so I haven't had a date in a while. What's it to you?"

Paul shook his head. "Just be there, will you?"

"Yes, boss." She pulled her gun from inside her jacket, checked the clip and slammed it back into the handle. "I guess I can pick up pizza on the way. Kids like pizza, don't they?"

"I don't know anyone who doesn't like pizza. Leave the stinky fish off." Paul smiled at Mel as he hit the door leading out of the office. "Thanks, Mel. I'll let you know if we're going to be really late."

"Don't worry about us. I can come up with something to do with the boys."

"Just don't let them play with your weapon. And keep a close eye on Luke. He's got a habit of sneaking out the back door."

She grinned. "Check."

"I'm headed over to the coroner's to check on our latest victim."

Melissa shook her head. "Shame about Mary Alice. She was only twenty-six. I did a background check on her boyfriend. He came up clean."

Paul snorted. "So did Stan Klaus."

"HOW ARE YOU FEELING NOW?" The school nurse pressed a cool compress to Elise's forehead as she lay on the couch in the nurse's office.

Principal Ford poked her head in the door. "How is she?"

Elise pushed to a sitting position, removing the compress from her forehead. "I'm fine. Really. I should get back to my class before they destroy my room."

Principal Ford waved a hand. "I got Coach Hensley to stand in. He'll have them bench-pressing their desks to keep them busy." Her smile went a long way toward making Elise feel more at ease. The older woman nodded at the nurse. "Could we have a few minutes?"

The nurse glanced at Elise. "I'll get you a bottle of water from the lounge."

"Thanks." Elise gave the woman a wan smile, her gaze following her out the door. She wished she could escape as easily. It seemed as though the time for confession was upon her.

Principal Ford took the seat across from her and leaned forward, her hands clasped, elbows resting on her knees. "What happened?"

Elise hated lying. "I got light-headed and must have passed out."

"Elise, I know something is going on. For the past few days you've been pale, tense and jumpy. If there's anything you'd like to tell me, maybe I can help."

If only she could. "I'm not getting much sleep." That wasn't a lie.

"Does it have to do with the man that keeps showing up around here?"

Elise's eyes widened. "What man?"

Principal Ford frowned. "The one who got Caesar to back

down in your class the other day. You know, tall, blond and gorgeous. He showed us his badge in the office. FBI." She paused, giving Elise all the opportunity she needed to spill her guts.

But she just couldn't, could she? She sat silently biting her lower lip.

"Is he really your boyfriend or is he here on official business?"

Elise smiled for the first time in what felt like days, her cheeks warming at the images of what they'd done on her couch last night. Paul had obviously told the office staff he was her boyfriend to avoid generating suspicion. "He's really my b-boyfriend."

"Are the incidents with Caesar getting to you?"

"No, although that was pretty scary."

"Rumor has it he threw a brick at your car. Is that true?"

Elise shrugged. "I didn't see who threw it."

"If we find out he did it, we can press charges." The lines in Principal Ford's forehead deepened. "I don't like it when my teachers are threatened or hurt by students. I won't tolerate it. His parents have been notified that upon his return from suspension, he will be placed in the alternative center until his attitude improves."

"For his sake, I hope he returns. He needs an education. All teens need an education."

"I wish they could see that as clearly." The principal sighed. "I'm sorry. I shouldn't have lumped all the hard cases in your final class of the day. Between Caesar Valdez and Ashley Finch, you've had more than you share of trouble."

"I can handle them."

"Yeah, but you shouldn't have to handle Ashley's mother. The woman is a force to be reckoned with. If she even hints at anything resembling a threat, a reprisal or a lawsuit, you bring it straight to me."

Elise gave her boss a mock salute. "Yes, ma'am."

Principal Ford sat back in her chair, pressing her fingertips together in a steeple. "You know, Elise, I've liked you from the start. That's why I hired you. You're fresh, you're personable and you're really interested in making a difference with the students. I'd like to think you could confide in me and let me help you with any issues you might be having here at school or even outside of school. I only want to help."

Ready tears welled in Elise's eyes. For a moment she teetered on the verge of telling the other woman everything, right down to the note in her mailbox, but reason took hold and she straightened. "Thanks, Principal Ford. I'll keep that in mind. I'm sorry for the spectacle I must have made in my classroom. I won't let it happen again."

Principal Ford rose and crossed to Elise, extending her hand to help her up from the couch. "You can't help it when you aren't feeling well. If you'd like to take the rest of the day to recuperate, please do. I can get a substitute in."

"No. I think I'll be fine. I must have skipped breakfast this morning. A little food in my stomach and I'll be fine for the rest of the day. Besides, this evening we have parent-teacher conferences scheduled. I can't miss those. Most of my students are doing well and their parents need to hear that from me."

"They'll understand if you're not feeling well. I can stand in for you."

"No, really, I feel like such a bother already."

"No bother. I just don't want to lose one of my shining new stars. It's hard to find high school teachers who can inspire their students and who actually care whether or not they learn."

"Thanks for your confidence in me." Elise leaned across

and hugged the other woman. Maybe someday she'd share her secret with her. Just not now.

Principal Ford hugged her back, then pulled away, brushing a hand over her blazer. "Remember, my door is open if you need anything. Anything at all."

I need more than you could imagine just to survive this ordeal. "I'll remember." Elise left the room and went in search of her two pupils with a disc she needed back in her possession ASAP.

Chapter Fourteen

Paul left the coroner's office within fifteen minutes of arriving with the same story as his previous visit. The victim had been choked from behind by an arm, not by Ethernet cable.

He had a couple places he wanted to check out today before heading to the high school to hang out with Elise during her parent-teacher conferences.

Clouds hovered over San Antonio and north into the hill country. Dark clouds laden with moisture from a system moving in from the northwest. A cool breeze promised an end to the Indian summer. Fall had officially arrived in central Texas. Tiny drops of rain hit his windshield as Paul left the city behind and followed the interstate northwest toward El Paso. The closer he came to the exit for Breuer, the harder the rain fell until he slowed his truck to compensate for the limited visibility and to keep from hydroplaning on the oily asphalt. Cars moved at a snail's pace through the small town, clumping at stoplights and inching forward when the light flashed a blurry green.

First stop on Paul's list were the houses surrounding Elise's. Someone might have seen a man enter her house during the day while she'd been gone to work. Surely in the old neighborhood where Elise lived, some elderly lady with a herd of cats kept a vigilant eye out her window.

Paul parked in Elise's driveway and dropped down into a puddle of water. The rain pounded against his shoulders and face. He pulled an umbrella from behind his seat and popped it open. With the rain coming in sideways, he had to tip it to keep from being soaked all over, but he couldn't help the drenching on his legs. Thank goodness he wore boots. Water ran along the sides of the curbs a foot deep, racing down the street to a drain.

The first house he came to was a modest, white wood-framed house with a screened-in porch whose screens had seen better days. A rosebush climbed up the side of one screen, thorns poking holes in the metal mesh.

He pulled the screen door open and stepped onto the semi-dry porch, shaking off the rain from his umbrella. When the screen slammed behind him a cacophony of yapping erupted from inside the little house.

He pressed the doorbell and waited. The dogs inside let up a frenzy of noise. One pushed his nose through the thin slats of aluminum blinds, its white hairy face and black button eyes shaking with eagerness to see the visitor.

Paul rang the doorbell again. Either the dogs made too much noise for the bell to be heard or they were the only ones at home. He lifted his umbrella, ready to step off the porch when the door opened and a white-haired old lady peeked out.

"Yes?"

"Pardon me, ma'am. I'm Special Agent Paul Fletcher with the FBI. I'm hoping you can help me." He flipped his credentials out.

The woman's eyes narrowed and her head tipped back so that she could look at his documentation through her bifocals. She opened the door a little wider. "What is it you need?"

"Your neighbor, Ms. Johnson, had a break-in yesterday during the day while she was teaching at the high school. Did you happen to see any vehicles parked along the street or notice anyone enter or leave her house?"

The old woman's hand shook as she pressed it to her chest. "Oh, my. That's terrible." She glanced around as if the culprit might be lurking, waiting to break into her own home.

"Yes, ma'am." Paul wished the woman would hurry and answer his question, but knew it took time. "Did you happen to see anything?"

She shook her head. "No, no. Nothing out of the ordinary." She frowned, her head tipping to the right. "I did see one of those bug extermination trucks drive by and park several doors down around noon."

In this part of Texas, an exterminator truck was common with the amount of scorpions, fire ants and sugar ants in the area. "Could you point out which house it stopped in front of?"

"The rock house three doors down, I think." She nodded. "Yes, that's the one." She smiled up at him. "That's the only vehicle I saw parked on our street during the day."

"Do you look out often?"

"Son, I sit by the window all day. I like to see what's going on since I don't get out much lately and my children only visit once or twice a year."

Paul smiled. The woman was probably lonely, watching the world pass her by out her front window.

"Do you remember the logo on the truck? Any distinguishing marks, the name?"

She shook her head. "Noooo..." Then her eyes brightened. "But it was one of those trucks with the big bug on top. Does that help?"

"No other vehicles?"

"No, that's it."

"Thank you, Mrs...?"

"Thompson. It's Mrs. Thompson." She stuck her hand through the door.

Paul took her shriveled, frail fingers and shook her hand gently. "Thank you, Mrs. Thompson. You've been a big help."

He left the covered porch, hurrying out into the rain to the house on the other side of Elise's, hoping to get a corroborating story.

After knocking on the doors of the houses on either side and in front of Elise's house with no luck, he cut through the backyard to the one behind her where he'd seen movement the night before.

There wasn't a doorbell so Paul opened the screen door and tapped his knuckles against the wood-paneled front door and stepped back, letting the screen door close.

At first he suspected no one was home. But then a round, dark face peered around a curtain at him from the window closest to the door. The curtain jerked closed when the viewer realized she was being viewed.

Still the door didn't open.

Impatient to be on his way, but certain someone in this house had information that could help him, he knocked louder. "This is the FBI. Please open the door."

Footsteps pattered against wooden floors inside headed away from the front door. Whoever was inside was running away from him.

Adrenaline kicked in and Paul leaped from the porch and down into the soggy yard. He rounded the side of the house so fast, he slipped and almost fell.

A door at the rear of the house slammed shut.

Paul sped up, racing after a small figure, bundled in an

old coat with the hood pulled up, making a break for the side of the house.

"Stop!" Paul yelled.

The figure glanced over her shoulder, dark eyes wide, mouth open in surprise.

Paul was almost onto the escapee when she came to a halt, shoulders sagging and breaths coming in ragged gasps. *"Por favor!"*

Paul grabbed an arm and spun the person around to discover a Hispanic woman, her eyes rounded, fearful. "Who are you?"

She shook her head. *"No hablo Inglés."*

Just what he didn't need, to scare some illegal alien into a heart attack. He thanked his Spanish teachers from high school and college for the little bit he could speak. He switched to his broken Spanish. *"Cómo te llamas?"*

"Maria."

"Do you live there?" He pointed to the house she'd come out of.

She stared at the house and back to him, her brow furrowed.

Frustration hit hard. What were the words in Spanish? *"Vive en esa casa?"*

Her face brightened but she shook her head. "No. *Me limpio la casa.*" She moved her hand in a circular motion. "Clean *la casa.*"

Ah, Maria was the cleaning lady. Paul nodded. "*Necesito respuestas.* I need answers." He pointed to Elise's house.

Rain dripped off her face as she tipped her head back to look up into Paul's face.

He held the umbrella over her head and smiled down at her reassuringly, though he kept a firm grip on her arm. "I won't hurt you or turn you in to the authorities. I just need to know if you've seen anyone hanging around that house. *Has visto a nadie alrededor de la casa?*" He hoped he'd said that right. His luck, he was asking which way to the farm.

She shook her head. *"No, sólo a la mujer con dos niños."*

"Were you here yesterday during the day? *Aquí fueron ayer?*"

"Sí." She nodded. *"Me limpio la casa de la Señora Slater."*

An image of little Luke talking through the bushes to his friend came to Paul's mind. Was this where George lived? *"George no vive aquí?"*

The woman nodded and she looked around as if to see if anyone else was watching her. *"Señor George es retrasado."*

Paul didn't recognize the word. He shook his head. *"No entiendo."*

She looked around as if trying to come up with a way to tell him. Finally she shrugged and circled her finger beside her temple. *"George es muy loco."*

Crazy? *"George es poco?"* Paul held his hand out at about Luke's height.

The woman in front of him shook her head and raised her hand to the same height as Paul.

Luke had been talking through the fence with a crazy man? What had he told him? Could he have let it slip what their last names used to be? Would the little boy have remembered?

"Dónde está George?" he asked.

The lady shrugged, her body drenched from the rain. She glanced longingly over her shoulder at a beat-up, rusty car parked in the gravel driveway. "I go. *Tengo que ir.*"

"Where is George?" Paul insisted.

"En la escuela." She pulled free of the hand he still had on her arm and ran for the car.

At the school. George was at the school.

Before Maria had her car cranked, Paul had circled around

to Elise's house and jumped into his truck. Which school? Which school was George at?

Shifting into Reverse, he spun the truck out of the driveway and shot into the street. Then he pressed the accelerator to the floor, spitting water up behind him as he blasted down Highland Street toward the high school.

Managing the turns with one hand, he slid his cell phone open with the other and dialed Agent Bradley. "Mel, check all the bug extermination companies in Breuer and the San Antonio area for a truck scheduled for Highland Street in Breuer."

Mel didn't respond right away and then cleared her throat. "Okaayy, I'll bite. Has Elise got bug problems?"

"One of her neighbors saw an exterminator truck parked on the street yesterday. One with the bug on top of it."

"That ought to narrow it down some. I'm on it. Where are you headed now?"

"To the high school. One of Elise's neighbors works at the high school. I'm going to check him out."

"Think he was the one to leave the note in her box?"

Paul's jaw tightened. If this guy was loco as Maria indicated, there was no telling what he was capable of. "I don't know, but I plan on finding out."

Cars left the parking lot in a steady stream as campus cleared of students. An equally steady stream of cars entered and filled the parking lot as parents trudged through the puddles of water, hunkered beneath newspapers or umbrellas to get indoors.

Paul climbed out, forgoing the umbrella since he was already soaked through to the skin. He just wanted to get to Elise.

Tables had been set up in the entrance where parents stood in line for course schedules with class numbers for each of their children. Paul bypassed the masses and hurried toward Elise's classroom.

A dark-haired woman in a navy-blue skirt suit stepped into his path. "Agent Fletcher, is it?" She stuck her hand out, forcing him to stop and shake it. "I'm Anita Ford, the principal here at Breuer High School."

"Nice to meet you." He shook her hand, his gaze shooting past her to the hallway where Elise's classroom was located.

"Are you here on official business, or personal?" Her brows rose on her forehead, her mouth stretched in a thin line.

What was this all about? Paul shifted his full attention to Principal Ford. If he told her it was official, he'd be obliged to give her some of the details, which he wasn't prepared to impart to the woman. "Personal."

"As the principal of this school, I'm responsible for the students as well as the teachers. If this is official business, I have a right to know what it's all about."

"It's personal."

"Ms. Johnson is new to us here at Breuer, yet I like to think I treat all my teachers the same, new or tenured. If she's in any kind of trouble, I'd like to know what I can do to help."

Paul studied the woman. She seemed sincere, yet it wasn't his place to tell her anything about Elise's past. If Elise wanted her to know, she'd have told her. "Thank you, Principal Ford. As Elise's…fiancé…" Hopefully, knowing Paul was Elise's fiancé ought to keep her from questioning his continued presence at the high school. "I'm relieved to know someone is looking out for her welfare."

"Fiancé?" Her lips curved into a smile. "Is this something new?"

Paul forced a smile, hoping it looked natural and not strained. "Well as soon as I pop the question and she says yes. You won't say anything to her, will you? I'd planned on surprising her this Friday."

Principal Ford was all grins. "You have my word. She should be in her classroom."

While he had the principal's attention, he might as well ask. "Principal Ford, do you have a man working here by the name of George Slater?"

The lady's smile softened. "Why, yes. George is a janitor here at the high school." She paused. "Why do you ask?"

"Is he working now? I know he lives close to Elise and I haven't had the opportunity to meet him."

"I'm sure he's around somewhere. He usually does the cleaning at the end of the school day after the students leave." She turned toward the office. "I can have him paged."

"That won't be necessary. I can meet him another time." Paul smiled. "I'm more interested in seeing Elise first."

"If you're certain." She motioned toward the office. "Won't take a minute to put an announcement over the intercom system."

The offer was not Paul's idea of subtle. "No, that's okay. Maybe next time." Paul sprinted down the hallway toward Elise's room, more anxious than ever to see that she was truly all right, almost certain she would be, surrounded by parents and other teachers and students.

It gnawed at him that George was an employee of the school. In a perfect position to have access to Elise's mailbox. If the boys had somehow alerted him to their former name and circumstances, he might be the one threatening her and killing the women.

First he'd check on Elise, then he'd find George. His gut twisted at the thought of young Luke standing at the back fence talking to the crazy man. How close to death had the boys been in their own backyard?

His cell phone rang and he answered. "Fletcher."

"Hey, Paul. I called the bug exterminator company you

mentioned before I picked up the boys. I got hold of their dispatch office in Breuer and found out something interesting."

"What's that?"

"One of the bug trucks was stolen yesterday morning before their office opened."

"Has it been located?" He couldn't imagine a truck as distinctive as one with a giant bug on it could go missing for long.

"As a matter of fact, yes. It was located a mile away in an empty lot. The police think it was kids taking it for a joyride."

"I'll bet it was our killer. Did the police have the truck dusted for prints?"

"Yup. Only the regular drivers' prints showed."

Whoever had stolen it knew the ropes. Leaving no trace evidence. Paul headed toward the cafeteria. Could a high school janitor be the culprit behind such an elaborate operation? Or was Paul wasting his time and the real killer was out there preparing to strike again? He feared Elise would be his next target. Maybe Elise was right and it was Stan Klaus. Who else would have sufficient motivation to kill others to torment her? Who else would have motivation to ultimately kill her?

"Oh, and, Paul, while I was still at the office, Cain showed up for all of five minutes. I couldn't follow him because I had to pick up the boys. He looked like he was in a hurry. He left at the same time as I did. Pealed out of the parking lot in his SUV without so much as a word to me."

Paul's jaw tightened. Between protecting a woman from a crazed killer and dealing with a troubled employee, he had his share of frustrations. "I'll deal with him when I get in to the office tomorrow."

ELISE SAT BEHIND HER DESK with her grade sheets neatly printed, waiting for parents to show up and ask about their child's progress. For all outward appearances, she hoped she appeared calm and relaxed. While inside her stomach churned, her palms sweated and she still felt a little light-headed.

Every time a person appeared in the doorway, Elise teetered at the edge of terror. What if Stan entered carrying an Ethernet cable, ready to take her out like he had the other women he'd killed?

Her more hopeful side watched the door, hoping Paul would step through and allay her fears. She fought the urge to call home and check on the boys. Agent Bradley had been there to see them off the bus. She'd called as soon as they arrived and again when they were safely tucked inside the house with the doors locked.

Elise would rather have skipped the parent-teacher conference night, but she feared for her job. Especially after passing out in the classroom and then lying to the principal about why.

She hadn't seen Alex and Kendall since the earlier incident. They hadn't shown up for class, either. She'd called their homes and left a message, but they hadn't checked in. Now, not only did she have to worry about her own children, she was worried about her students. The burden of her situation weighed heavily on her.

Just when she thought things couldn't get worse, Geri Finch walked in, her three-inch stilettos clicking sharply against the tiles. Ashley followed her mother, her head down, her cheeks pale.

"I've had about all I can take of this school, Ms. Johnson." Geri plopped her Gucci bag on Elise's desk and planted her hands on her hips. "My daughter will be at the cheer competition on Saturday, do you understand? If she's not, I'll hold you responsible and do my best to have you fired."

All the frustration, fear and anger that had built up over the past couple of days rocketed up inside Elise. She stood, heat rising up her neck into her face and all the way to her scalp. "Mrs. Finch." Elise sucked in a deep breath in hope of calming her rising fury. "Ashley is responsible for whether or not she performs on Saturday. She needs to understand that there are consequences for her actions. And you, as her parent, should know that and provide the guidance she so desperately needs and obviously isn't getting."

"Mom, leave it alone." Ashley grabbed her mother's arm and tried to pull her away from Elise's desk. "So I'll miss one competition. The world won't end."

"Shut up, Ashley. You'll be there if I have to file a lawsuit against this school and particularly against this teacher."

Ashley's face reddened and she shot a helpless glance at Elise. "But I don't want you to sue the school. I like it here. I have friends."

Mrs. Finch's cheeks flushed an unbecoming beet-red. "I said shut up! If you had kept your mouth shut in the first place and gotten to class on time, you wouldn't be in this situation. Let go of me!" Geri Finch jerked her arm loose and raised her hand as if to strike her daughter.

Ashley flinched and backed away, color draining from her face.

Elise gasped. "Mrs. Finch!"

"Don't." Paul's deep voice penetrated the woman's rage and halted her hand in midair.

Relief washed over Elise and she rushed across the room and into his open arms.

Geri's hand remained frozen, hovering over her daughter's head, her breath coming in ragged gasps. "You have to be at the competition."

"Why, Mom?" Ashley's color came back, tears filling her eyes. "*You're* the one who wanted me to cheer. *You're* the one who made me go to all those gymnastics lessons. Did you ever ask me what I wanted? I hate gymnastics. I hate cheering!"

Geri stared at her raised hand and back at her daughter. Her hand dropped to her side, her shoulders sagging. "I wanted you to have all the things I didn't."

"But I don't want them, Mom. I just want to go to school, graduate and get the hell out of the house. Away from my crazy mother who won't quit embarrassing me in front of the entire school!"

Geri's own eyes glazed as she stared across at her daughter as if for the first time. "But you're my baby. I love you."

"Just let me live *my* life, *my* way." Ashley's face softened. "Come on, Mom. Let's get out of here."

"One question before you leave." Paul stood between them and the doorway. "Did either one of you throw a brick at Ms. Johnson's car yesterday around four o'clock?"

Ashley and Geri Finch both blinked.

"I was getting a facial at that time," Geri answered.

"I have cheer practice every day after school," Ashley said. "Someone threw a brick at your car?" The young woman turned to Elise, her forehead creased in a frown. "I might have been mad at you, but not that mad."

"It wasn't them." A tall Hispanic man with a heavy accent pushed Caesar Valdez through the door, his hand clenched around the boy's collar. "Tell them."

Caesar, his chin tucked into his chest, scuffed his toe on the tile. "I threw the brick, Ms. Johnson. I'm sorry."

Elise couldn't stop the gasp, but when Paul tensed beside her, she put out a hand to hold him back. She nodded at Ashley and her mother. "I'll see you in class tomorrow, Ashley?"

Ashley's gaze shot from Caesar to Elise and back. She looked like she wanted to stay for the show.

"You two have a lot to talk about at home." Elise followed them to the door, ushering them out. "Goodbye, Ashley, Mrs. Finch." She closed the door and turned to Caesar, her heart pounding against her chest. "Surely you knew that throwing a brick at my car could hurt me, maybe even kill me."

"I wanted to hurt you." He threw back his head and glared at her. "I'm tired of school. It's a waste of time. If I wasn't stuck in class, I could get out and get a job now."

"A job paying no more than minimum wage for the rest of your life. You can do better than that. You can do better than me." The man beside Caesar stuck out his hand. "Raul Valdez. Caesar's father."

The man's large paw engulfed Elise's small hand, the rough calluses from hard physical labor scraping against her softer skin.

"What Caesar isn't saying is that he's having trouble with all of his classes and he wants to give up," his father said. "He wants to quit school so he's acting up in all his classes hoping they'll kick him out."

Elise stepped forward. "Caesar, you can't give up."

"When will I ever use stupid history? How will it help me get a job?"

"There are teachers all over this school who want to help you. All you have to do is be willing to try. We have after-school tutoring for every subject. I have early-morning help in my class. Some of my students tutor."

"I spend enough time in this hellhole. Why would I want to spend more?"

"Because you're an intelligent young man and you can do anything you set your mind to," Elise said.

"I'm not. I barely get by in this class and I'm failing in others."

Elise laid a hand on his arm. "I'll help you."

"Why do you want to help me?" He stared at the hand on his arm. "I threw a freakin' brick at your car."

"Yes, you did." Elise's lips pressed into a line. "And you'll pay to have it replaced. But to keep me from filing a report to the police, you'll come to my class early every morning and study with me. Bring whatever subject you're having difficulties with and I'll help."

Caesar stared into Elise's eyes, his own brown ones brooding and suspicious. "Why?"

"Because, though you might think all teachers are here to torture you, we do care about our students' futures." Elise smiled and removed her hand from his arm. "And once upon a time, I didn't think I could do anything with my life," she said softly. "But I was wrong."

All the years of marriage to Stan Klaus. How he controlled her life, how he insisted on her being a stay-at-home mom. Not so much for the sake of her boys, but because he didn't want her to be smarter than him. He didn't want her to go out into the world and be more important than he was.

"I want you to be successful, Caesar. I want you to know you can do better than pushing people around who are smaller than you. But you need to know that I won't tolerate you threatening me or any other student ever again."

"I understand if you want to press charges. He deserves it." Caesar's father glared at his son. "I also want you to understand that I raised him better, and he will make it up to you if you give him a chance. I'll see to that."

Elise raised her hands palms up. "It's completely up to Caesar. Will you show up every day and work hard without complaint?"

Caesar sucked in a deep breath and let it out, thinking about her offer for a long minute. Finally he shrugged. "Okay."

His father nudged him hard with his elbow. "Say, 'Yes, ma'am.'"

Caesar's mouth twisted and he rubbed his ribs. "Yes, ma'am."

"I'll see you in the morning, then." Elise grinned. "And, Caesar, bring your books."

The Valdezes left her room and Elise stared after them.

Paul gripped her shoulders and leaned her against him. "Tough day?"

"You have no idea." She turned and buried her face in his chest, her arms wrapping around his waist. "I didn't think it could get more stressful. But it continues to do so."

"I understand you were under the weather earlier?" He tipped her chin up and studied her face.

Elise could stand there forever, melting into his gaze, warming her body with the heat from his. "I had a gift left in my DVD player." Before she could fill him in on what had happened earlier that day, a parent arrived at her door.

Elise forced a smile, gave the parent an update on her student and thanked her for coming.

Paul stood in a far corner, staring at a map on the wall, probably trying to be inconspicuous.

It wasn't working. Paul's broad shoulders and tough-guy stance made him hard to ignore. Elise's gaze slipped to him more than she intended.

As soon as the mother left the room, Paul was beside her. "What gift?"

"A video of the news reports filmed two years ago after the Dakota Strangler went missing."

Paul's fingers gripped her arms. "Where is the DVD?"

"I don't have it. Alex and Kendall hid it before the principal could see it. I haven't seen them since. And frankly, I'm worried."

"Can you leave now?"

"I'm supposed to stay until seven o'clock, but I guess I could ask the principal to fill in for me." She glanced at the clock. "Could you give me a few minutes to put my papers in order?"

"Yes, I have something I want to check on. Promise you won't step outside this room until I get back?"

Elise smiled. If it had been Stan, he'd have demanded that she do exactly as he instructed. With Paul, he made it sound like she had a choice. "Yes, I promise to stay right here until you get back. Where are you going?"

"Do you know George the janitor?"

Elise remembered seeing the janitors in the hallway, but she didn't stick around after school long enough to get to know them. "No, not really, why?"

"Did you know that one of the janitors lives behind you?"

Her eyes widened. "Really?"

"I think it's the same George that Luke has been talking to through the fence."

"Is that a bad thing?" Elise asked.

"I don't know, but I wanted to check him out while I was here."

"I think the janitors are here at this time. They usually come in after school gets out. I think the male janitor takes the cafeteria and the woman works the front offices." She shrugged. "I try not to stay late very often. If I do, the boys are with me."

Paul nodded. "I'll be back in a minute." He wanted to talk to both janitors.

"I'll be here."

Paul left the room. A few more parents wandered in. Elise gave them grade reports and talked about their students, while her mind wandered to what Paul was up to.

Could the janitor be the one terrorizing her and the women of Breuer? A janitor? Had Luke told him what their last names used to be? Elise didn't think he would have remembered.

After what seemed a long time of watching her door, meeting with parents and generally gnashing her teeth, Elise straightened her desk, grabbed her purse and keys and headed for her classroom door. She'd stop by the principal's office and let Principal Ford know she was leaving early.

As she stepped into the hallway, a loud boom shook the entire school. Elise dropped to the floor and covered her head as a blast of smoke and dust blew through the hallway.

Chapter Fifteen

Paul slammed back against the concrete walls of the building, the air knocked from his lungs. When the explosion rocked the school, he'd been on his way to the cafeteria where a teacher had said she'd last seen George Slater headed.

Adrenaline got his heart going and he sucked in a long, deep breath, restoring oxygen to his brain. Then he was on his feet and running through the darkened hallways. His path snarled with screaming women and crying children. Unable to move through them, he located an exit and helped the frightened parents outside. Cloud-cloaked skies made night fall before its time. The rain continued to pour down in torrents, soaking his view and blinding him to the darkness. Had Elise made it out? Were there others trapped in the building?

Bright flames licked through the roof of the building in the direction of the cafeteria. Paul ducked back inside; he had to get to Elise.

"Help me, please!" A woman grabbed his arm, coughed and pulled him toward the smoke. "My son was in the cafeteria getting a soda from the machine. I think he's still in there."

"What's his name?"

"Michael."

"Paul? Paul? Is that you?" Elise materialized out of the smoke, her wool scarf pulled up over her nose and eyes, a flashlight shaking in her hands. "Oh, thank God!"

"Elise, get this woman outside. I'm going back in."

"I'm going with you."

"No, it will be faster if I go without you. Please take this woman outside."

"My son is in there. I have to find him." The woman headed toward the cafeteria, tears streaming from her eyes.

Elise grabbed her arm and held tight. "You have to let Paul find him. He's trained in this kind of thing." She handed him the flashlight she'd been holding and unwound the scarf from her neck. "Take these and hurry!"

Paul wrapped the scarf around his nose and mouth, hunkered low and ran down the hallway toward the cafeteria.

He shone his light in the open doorways searching for victims too scared or disoriented to find their way out. When he made it to the cafeteria, the smoke was getting so thick his eyes burned and the scarf was doing little to keep the smoke from his lungs. He coughed and yelled through the fabric, "Michael!"

Was that a groan? Paul closed his eyes to the smoke and listened.

Another groan.

Paul ducked low and peered beneath the layer of rising smoke, shining his flashlight across the floor. He spotted what looked like two lumps of rags near the vending machines. One moved.

"Michael!"

"Over here," a scratchy voice called out, followed by coughing.

Paul crawled on his hands and knees toward the sound, tucking the scarf securely around his face. "Gotta get out of here."

"No, duh." More coughing led Paul to the downed boy. "Are you hurt?"

"My ankle hurts." A coughing fit racked his body. When he tried to stand, he yelped and dropped to the floor. "I can't walk."

"Grab around my neck and hold on." Paul hooked his arm around the boy's back and lifted.

"Wait. There's someone else over there."

Paul glanced over his shoulder at the limp form on the floor. "I can only move one of you at a time."

"It's…" Michael coughed. "The janitor."

The very person Paul had been looking for. "First let's get you out, then I'll come back for him."

Running low to the ground, Paul hauled Michael out of the cafeteria and down the hall toward the exit, the boy hopping on his good foot. One of the parents met them close to the exit and took over. Paul, his lungs burning, blinking back the smoky tears in his eyes, jogged back into the wreckage. He found his way to the cafeteria, the smoke nearly overcoming him. He slid to his knees and crawled the rest of the way to the man lying on the floor near the vending machines.

He was a full-size adult, weighing as much if not more than Paul. Fighting the effects of the smoke, Paul grabbed the man underneath his arms and dragged him back the way he'd come, one slow, agonizing tile at a time.

By the time he'd reached the hallway leading toward the exit, other hands took over. Firemen in yellow jackets and oxygen masks lifted the man off the floor and carried him the rest of the way out of the building. Another fireman hooked an arm beneath Paul's and hefted him to his feet, leading, half carrying him out into the rain where they laid him on the soggy ground.

Blessedly cool water pelted his face, washing away a layer of soot and smoke, clearing the raw stinging sensation from his eyes. Paul dragged clean fresh air into his lungs and coughed. "Elise." He stared around at the crowd of emergency responders tending to the fire and the injured.

Where was Elise? When he tried to stand, his legs shook and he staggered, landing on his knees.

"Here." An EMT shoved an oxygen mask over his face. "Breathe."

Paul didn't want to breathe, he wanted to find Elise. What if the explosion had been intentional? What if the killer had set it off to confuse everyone?

He sucked in a deep breath and handed the mask back to the technician. "Where's the guy I pulled out of there?"

"They're loading him into the ambulance over there." The EMT pointed at a group of medical technicians shoving a gurney in through the back door of a waiting ambulance.

While watching out for Elise, Paul lurched to his feet and caught the door before it closed. "Is he alive?"

"Yeah, you know this guy?" one of the techs asked. "You a relative or something?"

"No. I'm just concerned. I got him out of the cafeteria."

"Oh, well, thanks. You probably saved his life. The principal was concerned about him, said he would need family around when he came to."

"Why?" Paul asked.

"She said that he's mentally retarded and he'll be scared. I was hoping you were family."

Paul backed away and the door to the ambulance closed. The lights flickered on and the siren flared.

George was mentally retarded?

Which took him off the list of suspects, although he could have been tricked into dropping a letter into Elise's mailbox, if he could read well enough to know which was hers.

Back to square one. Paul forced himself to think through the facts. The M.O. wasn't exactly the same on the killings. The method was close, but not exact. Even if it were the Dakota Strangler, how would he have found Elise? Did he stalk Elise's sister, Brenna, and glean information from her phone records?

Brenna was too good a cop to let it slip where her sister was. If not from Brenna, how did someone learn the whereabouts of a person in the witness protection program?

An insider?

Paul's heart stuttered in his chest. Who had sufficient motivation to kill women other than the original Dakota Strangler? Someone angry at Elise? He shook his head. She'd done nothing. Her husband was the killer, not her. If it was an insider, could it be someone involved in the original case? The FBI agents on the case had been Paul, Melissa and Nick. Brenna had been working for the state on the crimes. He'd trust every one of the team with his life and Elise's.

Then who? Someone who wanted the Dakota Strangler to be alive again. But why? Who was he really after?

Paul filtered through the crowd of emergency workers and victims, frantically searching for the woman he was as near as he'd ever come to falling in love with. Where was Elise?

THE FIREMEN HAD FORCED all onlookers back to clear the way for them to perform their search and rescue routine. Unlike so many others, Elise had been fortunate enough to escape her classroom with her purse and keys.

She strained to see over the shoulders of the parents searching for their children and past the firemen running hoses to the fire. The cool rain helped to keep it from spreading quickly, but it also chilled her to the bone. Still she stood in the rain and waited for Paul to emerge from the smoky building.

She felt her cell phone buzz in her purse against her leg. She scrambled through her purse to reach it. When she did and read the text message on the screen, her blood ran colder than the air outside.

Where's Paul? Luke is missing. It was from Melissa Bradley.

Elise ran to the nearest fireman. "Did Paul Fletcher come out of there yet?"

"Lady, I couldn't tell you if the Pope stepped out right now. Please stay back while the emergency personnel work."

Desperate to find Paul, Elise placed a hand on the fireman's arm. "But I have to find him. It's an emergency."

"No kidding about the emergency. You and half a dozen other people are looking for loved ones. If you don't stay back, we can't do our jobs and find them."

"But—" She backed away, her heart racing in her chest. She couldn't wait for Paul. She had to do something. Luke could be in trouble. If Stan really was alive, he could have snatched the boy and run with him.

A sob welled up in her throat. She was torn, afraid to leave before making sure the man she was seriously in danger of losing her heart to made it out of the burning building alive. Paul was a grown man. There were emergency personnel crawling all over the place; they'd make sure he got out okay.

In the meantime, her son was missing. A defenseless little boy against a crazed killer didn't stand a chance. Agent Bradley had her hands tied watching over Brandon. She couldn't go after Luke when Elise's other son was in danger, as well.

Elise made the decision. She yanked a piece of paper from a pad in her purse and scribbled a note on it, telling Paul where she'd gone and why. She handed the note to the first policeman she came to. "Please make sure FBI Agent Paul Fletcher gets this note."

"Lady, I don't know who he is." He tried to hand it back to her. "Give it to him yourself."

"I can't. He's tall and blond and he went back into that building to save a woman's son. When he comes out, give him this." She shoved the note into the man's hand, refusing to let him give it back. "It's a matter of life and death."

With one last glance toward the building, Elise ran toward her little gray car that had been delivered with a new windshield early that afternoon. Thank goodness she had rescued her purse from her classroom. She dialed Paul's number. The connection went directly to his voice mail. Damn! With no other recourse, she left a message and climbed into her car.

Rain dripped off the end of her nose and down inside her jacket. The cold penetrated her clothing, sinking all the way to her heart. If someone had taken Luke, she wouldn't begin to know where to look. Tears filled her eyes, making it impossible to drive. She blinked them back, fiercely determined to be strong for her sons, strong for Paul and most of all strong for herself. She couldn't fail Luke.

Elise inched her way out of the parking lot, careful to avoid emergency vehicles and gawkers. "Move, please!" She slammed her palm against her steering wheel, fear for her son making her want to slam her foot down on the accelerator and fly home. The longer Luke was missing, the farther away the killer could get with him.

As soon as the roadway cleared ahead of her, Elise dropped her foot to the floor, urging her little car beyond the posted speed limits, only slowing for stop signs to avoid wrecking and further delaying her arrival at her house. Several times she hydroplaned on the slick roads, her heart in her throat as she slid close to mailboxes only to right herself and press forward.

Melissa's red pickup stood in the driveway outside Elise's

house. Skidding in next to it, she slammed on her brakes, shoved the shift into Park and leaped out.

Agent Bradley met her at the door. "Where's Paul?" She stared closer at Elise. "What happened?"

"There was an explosion at the school. I left. He was still helping people out of the building." Elise pushed past Melissa. "Where's Brandon?"

"I'm here." Brandon stood in the middle of the living room, his backpack on, fully clothed in jeans, jacket and shoes.

"How long has Luke been gone?" Elise asked.

"Around fifteen minutes, twenty tops. I tried to call you as soon as I discovered he was missing," Mel said.

Elise dropped to her haunches next to her oldest son. "Are you all right?"

"I'm fine. We have to find Luke. It's raining outside." Brandon waved a hand toward the door, his brow furrowed into a frown that was too heavy for a boy his age. "Luke gets scared when there's thunder."

"I know, I know, honey. We'll find him." She hugged Brandon and turned back to Melissa, straightening. "How did he get out of the house?"

"I went to answer my phone and the next thing I knew, he'd gone out the back door."

"He went to find George. He wanted to show him a picture of the puppy he wants to get." Brandon's eyes filled. "It's all my fault. If I hadn't shown him the picture, he'd still be here."

"It's not your fault, Brandon. You can't keep an eye on Luke all the time. He's fast and determined to do what he wants to do." Elise recognized the same guilt in Brandon as she felt herself. She should have been here—she should have guarded her sons.

"But I'm supposed to be the man of the house." The tears

spilled out of the corners of his eyes. "I didn't save him. Now he's going to die."

Elise's heart burned in her chest. "Listen to me, Brandon. Luke is not going to die. And this is not your fault. Luke shouldn't have left the house. He knows better." If anyone was at fault it was her. She shouldn't have left her children, knowing a killer was loose, threatening her and her family.

"I'm sorry, Elise. I turned my back for a moment. I never thought he'd leave the house."

Elise wanted to yell at Melissa, wanted to scream and cry, but she couldn't. All of this was her fault. She should have moved farther away, maybe Mexico or South America. Someplace where no one could find out about her past and no one could trace her or her children. Was there such a place? She shook her head. "The important thing right now is to find Luke."

"Right. Now that you're here, I can get out and start canvassing the neighborhood. The sooner we find him the better. Problem is that I can't wait for Paul to get back to protect you two."

"We'll be fine, just go!"

"Lock the doors. Don't let anyone inside."

"But I can't just stand here and do nothing. I have to look for Luke, too. You can't expect me to stay locked in my house while my son is in danger."

"You have two sons, Elise. You need to take care of this one." She shot a pointed look at Brandon, who scrubbed at his eyes, trying to act brave when he was probably falling apart inside.

Elise ached for her oldest son. He shouldn't have been through so much in his short life. She was lucky he wasn't more screwed up than he was. "Okay. We'll wait until Paul gets here. But then we have to find him."

Melissa ran for the door, shrugging into her leather jacket, her cowboy boots tapping against the entrance tiles. "I'll have my cell phone. Call if you hear or see anything."

The screen door slammed behind Melissa.

Elise stood at the door for a moment, staring out into the cool, wet night, her heart squeezing in her chest. She strained to hear over the water dripping off the eaves. Elise listened hard, hoping to hear her young son's voice calling out to her from the shadows.

A small hand tugged the back of her wet jacket. "Mom, we have to go out and look for Luke."

She turned to stare down into her son's face. "Oh, darling, we have to wait here in case he comes home. What if he found his way home and no one was here to let him in?"

"He would already be home if he could get here. Luke needs us." Brandon pulled her hand, urging her toward the door. "I know his hiding places. I can find him."

"It's dark and wet out there, baby. I can't risk losing you, too." And she couldn't risk exposing Brandon to the killer.

"But Luke is part of our family. We won't be a family without him."

Elise dropped to her knees and hugged her son. "I know, honey, I know."

The cell phone in her pocket rang, the vibration startling her. She jumped to her feet and fumbled in her jacket to locate the device. It could be Melissa, she could have found Luke.

An out-of-area message displayed on the caller ID screen. Cold fingers of dread clutched her chest and squeezed. She pressed the talk button and held the phone to her ear, her hand shaking. "Hello?"

"Mama, I'm scared." Luke's plaintive cry echoed in her ear. He sniffed and called out in a little above a whisper, "I want to come home."

"Luke?" Elise clutched the phone, wishing she could reach through and hold on to her son. "Luke?" She could hear him crying in the distance, but she could do nothing to comfort him.

"He's fine as long as you do exactly as you're told." That familiar mechanical voice sounded in her ear.

"Who is this? Where have you taken my son?"

"Shut up and listen or the kid dies."

Elise took a breath and forced a calm she didn't feel. The killer had her son. If she stood any chance of seeing him again, she had to do as he said. "What do you want?"

"I want you." The three words echoed in her head as though bouncing off the walls of a long tunnel. Silence followed when all she could hear was the blood pounding in her eardrums.

"Don't hurt Luke. I'll do whatever you say." Cold determination settled over her. She avoided looking down at Brandon, knowing he understood more than any eight-year-old should and would get the gist of her conversation.

"Good girl. Drive out to the Guadalupe River Bridge on Highway 474 north of town. Luke and I will be waiting for you there. If you tell anyone, if anyone follows you, I'll kill him. Do you understand? I'll kill your son."

The nightmare had returned. Her husband's legacy had followed her to Texas and turned on her sons. She couldn't run from it, she couldn't hide. She had to stand and fight to win her freedom from the terror, to save her sons from their father's horrifying past. She'd been a doormat to Stan Klaus, someone he could walk all over and abuse mentally, if not physically. She wouldn't let anyone do that to her again. And she wouldn't let anyone threaten her sons and get away with it.

Her shoulders thrown back, her head held high, she knew what she had to do. "I understand. I'll be there. Alone."

Chapter Sixteen

Paul couldn't find her. He'd searched the thinning crowd several times, but he couldn't find Elise. He turned to the parking lot and searched through the cars to find her little gray sedan with the Minnesota Vikings bumper sticker. It had been there earlier when he'd arrived at the school. The automobile service had gone the extra mile, had the car's windshield fixed and delivered the car to her school today, as good as new.

Of all the times for an automobile service to be efficient. Why couldn't they have taken more time? Then Elise would have been stranded at the high school and she would have had to rely on him to get her where she needed to go. The only place she could be was back home. Something must be wrong with the boys. The other more disturbing thought he brushed aside, refusing to entertain. The killer had not taken Elise. He couldn't have.

Paul dug in his jacket pocket to find his cell phone. He cursed at the broken screen. He must have fallen on it. He tried the speed-dial number for Elise, but couldn't even get a dial tone.

Mounting dread pressed against his chest. The explosion in the high school hadn't been an accident. The firemen might not know that yet, but Paul did. It had been a diversion. A chance for someone to lure Elise away from the grounds, maybe even kidnap her.

Without a cell phone, Paul had only one choice; he had to get to Elise's house. Worst-case scenario, he'd find Melissa and a telephone. Best case, Elise had gotten tired of waiting for him and gone home. He'd find her there tucking Luke and Brandon into bed, kissing them good-night, just like every other night. Just like normal.

This day had been anything but normal so far; why should that change now? Paul inched his truck around the emergency vehicles and out into the street where he slammed the gas pedal to the floorboard.

The two miles to Elise's little house on Highland passed painfully slowly and filled him with terrifying possibilities. What if Elise had been taken by the killer? What if Melissa and the boys were hurt? What if Paul was too late?

Even without a firm suspect, Paul still couldn't believe the Dakota Strangler had survived the fire and flood. His gut told him to look elsewhere. But who would want to hurt Elise and why? The witness had reported a black SUV leaving the bridge access road. An image of a black SUV popped into his mind as clearly as if he'd seen it. And he had, but where?

Then he remembered. One had been parked next to his truck in the parking lot of the Bureau building the day this all began.

Paul shook his head. No, it was just a coincidence. There were hundreds of black SUVs all over San Antonio.

Could someone in the Bureau have gotten hold of the information of Elise's whereabouts? Someone who knew how the witness protection program worked?

He skidded around the corner a block away from Highland

Street and almost ran into Melissa on foot, waving at him from the sidewalk.

Jamming his foot on the brake, he slid to a halt, popping the automatic door locks open.

Melissa slid in, rain dripping off her jacket onto the seat, breathing hard, her face screwed into a scared frown. "Luke is gone."

"What?" The bottom fell out of Paul's stomach. Luke was a bright, active little boy with an imagination and charm that had endeared him to Paul. He'd be proud to have such a little boy as his son. "How did that happen?"

Agent Bradley shrugged, shaking her wet head. "I don't know. One minute he was there, the next he was gone."

"Does Elise know?" How would she react? God, she needed someone to be with her. Paul needed to be with her.

"I called her as soon as I realized he was gone. She came within fifteen minutes."

A cold tingling sensation began at the back of Paul's neck and snaked its way down his spine. "Where is Elise now?"

"I left Elise and Brandon at the house while I searched the neighborhood. I called the police, but they're tied up at the school fire. Jeez, Paul, why haven't you answered your phone?" She took a deep breath, her brown hair hanging in lank, wet ropes along the sides of her face. "I lost the kid, Paul. I can't believe I lost the kid. It was just like you said, he slipped out the back door when I wasn't looking."

Paul took the corner onto Highland Street too fast for the rain-slicked road. The rear tires fishtailed on the slippery surface and straightened.

Light shone on Elise's porch, but that didn't make Paul feel any better. Not until he saw Elise, Brandon and Luke all standing in their living room, safe, well and happy would he feel better.

Mel's red truck stood in the driveway. Alone.

"Oh, God, her car's gone. I shouldn't have left her." Mel jumped from Paul's truck before it came to a complete halt and ran for the house. Paul wasn't far behind and caught her as she reached the door. It was unlocked and easily swung open when given a gentle push.

Lights blazed from all the rooms in the house, but it stood eerily silent. A few toy cars littered the floor, lying neglected and forgotten.

Paul ran from room to room, knowing before he completed his search that he wouldn't find them. He'd let Elise and her boys down. He hadn't been there to stop a crazed killer from taking them from their home.

"What now?" Melissa stood by the door, her face glum, her lips pressed into a tight line.

"Ms. Johnson!" A voice drifted through the open door. "Ms. Johnson?" The sound of light metal clashing against concrete was followed by Elise's students, Kendall and Alex, bursting through the door.

"Where's Ms. Johnson?" Kendall blurted, then sucked in a deep breath. Her hair clung to her cheeks in wet strands and water ran in rivulets down her jacket onto the tile entrance.

"She's missing," Paul answered, his tone as flat as his heart.

"Oh, no! We were afraid someone might hurt her." Kendall pulled at Alex's coat. "Give them the disc."

Alex frowned and jerked away from Kendall's hands. "Let me unzip my jacket, will ya?" He ripped the zipper down and a DVD fell to the floor.

"What's this?" Paul grabbed the disc.

"It's the disc that was in Ms. Johnson's audio-visual equipment this morning. It had film clips from news reports of the Dakota Strangler on it."

"Why do you have it?" Paul carried it to the DVD player above the television and fed it into the machine.

Kendall's cheeks reddened. "When Ms. Johnson passed out in her room, we got scared. We promised we wouldn't let anyone else see the disc so we took it."

"Then the bright one here—" Alex jerked his thumb toward Kendall "—decided we should see if we could come up with some clues as to who put it there."

"We just *know* it had something to do with the writing on the wall in Ms. Johnson's house, so we spent the day asking around—"

Alex rolled his eyes. "Ditching class, you mean."

"I wanted to find out if anyone saw someone coming in or out of Ms. Johnson's room. I couldn't go to class, knowing someone wanted to scare her like that. Heck, I was scared, too."

"And did you?" Melissa asked. "Find anyone who saw something?"

Kendall's face brightened. "Yeah, we sure did." She grinned at Alex. "Thanks to Alex, who can speak fluent Spanish."

Alex shrugged, his cheeks turning a ruddy red. "I'm not Latino for nothin'."

"There's a cafeteria worker who doesn't speak English very well," Kendall said. "Anyway, she confessed to letting a man in the cafeteria door early this morning and also two days ago."

Paul grabbed Alex by the arms, past his level of endurance. Past the need for patience. "Did she give a description of the man?"

"Not much of one. Brown hair, brown eyes, so high." Alex raised his hand to somewhere between Melissa's and Paul's height. "Could be anyone."

Kendall nudged Alex. "Oh, but when Alex asked her why she let him in when it was against the rules, she got all shaky.

We had to promise we wouldn't tell anyone before she'd tell us why." Kendall frowned. "I guess we're gonna have to break that promise."

Alex picked up where Kendall stopped. "She said the man threatened her. He said he'd fixed her background check and could unfix it if she didn't help him."

Kendall looked to Alex. "We weren't sure what that meant, but anything could be important in a case, right? Even the smallest detail?" She gave Paul a weak smile.

Paul's glance clashed with Melissa's. "What does Cain drive?"

Melissa frowned. "He bought a black SUV about the same time as you bought your truck."

His chest tightened. "A witness saw a black SUV leaving the scene of the second murder. It all makes sense now." Paul's eyes squeezed shut. "This isn't about Elise at all. It's about me. Why didn't I see it?"

"Who would have thought someone on our own team would be behind this? We're supposed to be the good guys." Melissa snorted. "I knew there was a reason I didn't like that guy."

Paul pulled his thoughts together. "Have Brian run the GPS tracker on Cain's cell phone."

Thank goodness each of their department cell phones was equipped with the ability to track them via the global positioning system. He didn't know where Elise had gone or how long it would take to find her. But he did know Cain wouldn't hesitate to kill again. Why hadn't he heeded the warning signs? Why hadn't he put a tail on Cain when he first suspected something fishy?

Melissa placed a hand over his forearm, the other holding her cell phone to her ear. "You can't blame yourself."

Paul's back teeth ground together. He sure as hell could. "Tell Brian to hurry."

When Elise reached the bridge spanning the Guadalupe River, she slowed, scanning the bridge for Luke and his captor.

"Where is he, Mom? Where's Luke?" Brandon's breath warmed her shoulder.

"Get down!" She hadn't wanted to leave Brandon alone in case the killer had set up yet another trap to capture her other son. She hadn't wanted to alert Melissa or the police and give the killer a reason to force his hand and kill Luke. Instead, she'd made Brandon promise to stay low and if anything bad happened, he should run as fast as he could. She'd given him her cell phone and made him promise not to use it until he absolutely had to.

Brandon ducked down below the seat. "I'm scared."

"Me, too, baby. Me, too." The rain had slackened but still came down in a heavy drizzle, keeping the highway slick with water flowing into the ditches.

On the opposite side of the bridge, she found a dirt road that led down to the river twenty feet below. Already, weather reports on the radio had indicated the river had risen well above its normal levels. Usually no more than a meandering stream, the Guadalupe River was known to rise up over the bridge twenty or more feet above the riverbed. Elise, being new to the area, had yet to witness what the locals called the forces of nature in action. She hoped she wasn't about to capture her first glimpse.

Elise wasn't sure her car could make it down and back up the muddy road. Unwilling to risk Brandon's safety any more than she had, she parked her car at the top and turned in her seat. "Brandon."

"Yes, mama?" His head popped up over the back of the seat, his eyes wide and shiny in the lights from the dashboard.

"I'm going to get Luke." She touched the cell phone in his

hand. "If I don't come back in ten minutes, you dial the number two on the phone and hold it down until it rings. It's the speed dial for Agent Fletcher. Tell him you're at the Guadalupe River Bridge on Highway 474."

"Why don't you call him now?"

"The man who has Luke said I shouldn't call anyone or he'd hurt Luke."

"Then why do you want me to call?"

"In case Luke and I don't come back, you need to get help for yourself."

"I want to go with you."

"You can't. As the man of the house, you need to do what I tell you."

His lip trembled. "I don't want to be the man of the house. I want to go with you."

"Please, Brandon. Please do as I say. Wait ten minutes and call Paul. He'll help." She reached for the door handle, peering through the windshield into the dark. Tires had spun up the mud on the tracks leading down to the river, but she couldn't see what awaited her there. She turned back to her oldest son. "Brandon, if anyone but me comes back up here, you get out of the car and run as fast as you can away from here before you call Paul. Do you understand?"

He nodded, a tear trickling down his cheek.

"I love you, Brandon. And I promise that I'll do my best to come back. With your brother." She leaned across the seat and hugged him, pressing a kiss to his forehead. "I love you so much."

Elise dug a flashlight out from beneath her seat and got out of the car. She slipped and caught herself on the door, fumbling to keep the light in her hand. After righting herself, she set off down the muddy track to the river and her youngest son. Rain blurred her vision, mixing with the tears welling in her eyes. Blinking only seemed to make it worse.

She couldn't go soft now. Luke needed her. Brandon needed her and Luke to return. Her oldest son would never forgive himself if something happened to either one of them. Failure was *not* an option. She slipped in the mud, water filling her shoes and soaking her stockings. As usual, hindsight was twenty-twenty and she should have changed into tennis shoes before she left the house. In the flat pumps she'd worn to school that day, she got little traction in the miniature river flowing down the hill in the rutted tire tracks.

Elise fell on her butt in the mud, rose and continued her descent into the darkness, shaking the slick, cold slop from her hands and holding the flashlight as steady as possible. She shone the light back and forth, hoping to catch a glimpse of Luke.

When she reached the bottom of the road near the banks of the river, her heart beat an erratic pace and she began to think maybe the killer had set a trap for her or her son. Frantic now, she whirled, her light barely penetrating the rain that had picked up since she'd left her house. A black SUV stood beside the river, the interior dark and menacing. Elise shone her light into the interior, but nothing moved. Luke was nowhere to be seen.

The river flowed heavy, swollen from the rain to ten feet deeper than usual. The dull roar of water rushing past masked most noises.

A faint cry carried over the top of the truck, over the noise of the river. Elise spun toward the bridge. Had the cry come from there? Elise shone the flashlight beam toward the underpinnings of the bridge. At first she could see nothing but dark shadows and rain. Then the shadows moved and a man holiding a small figure emerged.

"Luke!" Elise ran toward them, her light bouncing across the gravel and brush, flashing on and off the man and boy. "Luke!" she called out, tears streaming from her eyes, washed away by the drenching rain.

"That's far enough," the man yelled.

Elise halted, holding her flashlight on the man and boy.

He had something pointed at Luke's head.

Her stomach tumbled over and over as she realized what it was. Oh, God, he had a gun pointed at her son's head and it wasn't Stan. It wasn't even a man she recognized. Yes, he had brown hair and dark eyes like her former husband, but it wasn't Stan. Elise wasn't sure if she should be relieved or not. He'd already killed two women and he held her son at gunpoint. But knowing it wasn't Stan had a strange impact on her. Almost relief, if she could have allowed herself the luxury of relief in such dire circumstances.

"Mama!" Luke reached out his arms.

Elise stumbled and fell to her knees. "Please, don't hurt him." Her chest tightened, her breath catching in her throat on a silent sob. "Please. You want me, not him."

"You got that right."

"Let him go. I'll go with you. I won't even put up a fight."

"Very convenient. The other ladies didn't put up a fight, either. They thought they were with someone safe." When Luke wiggled to get out of his arms, he shook the boy. "Be still!"

"Let him go!" Elise staggered to her feet and ran forward.

Luke kicked out, landing a foot in the man's privates.

He threw Luke to the side and doubled over, his hand coming up to aim the gun at Elise. "Don't come any closer."

Luke lay on the concrete beneath the bridge, his body limp, unmoving.

"What have you done to my son, you monster?" she growled through gritted teeth, anger overcoming her fear.

He grunted and halfway straightened, the barrel of the gun level with her chest. "Not nearly what I plan to do to you."

"Why? Why are you doing this to me? I don't even know you."

"Yeah, but somehow you and your family have managed to kill my career. I feel like I should return the favor."

PAUL DIDN'T WAIT FOR ALVAREZ to get back with him on the GPS location of Cain's cell phone. "Get in the truck, Mel."

"Where are we going? We don't know where Cain took her until we hear back from Alvarez." Despite her arguments, she left Elise's house on Paul's heels and climbed into the truck beside him.

"He killed the other two women out by the river."

"Yeah, in two different locations. Each up different highways. If you take the wrong route, you could double our time getting back to the right one."

"I can't wait while he's got her." Paul's throat tightened. "He'll kill her."

"All because of a promotion he didn't get?" Mel shook her head. "Unbelievable."

"I should have had him transferred as soon as I came in. None of this would have happened if I'd dealt with the problem instead of ignoring it." Paul slammed his palm against the steering wheel. "It's all my fault!"

Mel gripped the handle above the door when the truck swerved. "You didn't know he'd go psycho. You couldn't have guessed he'd do what he's doing."

"I should have." He should have seen the signs much earlier. "Two women died, Mel! Because of me!"

"Paul, you're not a mind reader. You can't go around believing the worst in everyone. Cain was supposed to be on our side—one of the good guys."

"I should have seen it. Then at least two innocent women wouldn't have become victims. Maybe even three." His throat closed off on the last word. He couldn't let Elise be the third victim. Whatever it took, he had to get there in time to stop Cain.

"If you believed the worst in people, you'd never have fallen in love with Elise."

"Who said I'm in love with Elise?" Although he tossed the words at Mel, he couldn't deny it. What he felt was stronger than any emotion he'd ever experienced with any other woman. If she died, he'd never get the chance to follow through, explore the possibilities of a happily ever after.

Mel snorted, rolling her eyes his way. "You are in love with her, so don't try to scam me. A woman can tell."

His stomach knotted. How had he let this happen? How had he fallen in love with her when he'd only known her a few days? And how hopeless was loving Elise? "She doesn't want another man in her life. Stan really did a number on her."

"Yeah, but if I'm not mistaken, she's falling in love with you, too." Mel stared across the interior of the truck at him, her eyes shining in the light from the dashboard. "Given time, you two can work past the killer-ex thing."

Paul whipped out of the driveway onto the road. "None of it matters if Cain kills her."

"Then let's find her." Mel stared out the window. "You know she might have tried to call you on your cell phone. Have you checked your messages remotely?"

"Call my cell phone number." He gave her the instructions to access his messages, tapping his fingers on the steering wheel as he waited in the middle of the road.

"Here. Your messages are coming up. You have two." Mel shoved the phone against his ear.

"Paul! Luke is missing." Elise's panicked voice filled his ear. "I can't wait for you, I have to find him. I'm sorry I'm breaking my promise to stay put, but I have to go home."

Paul's jaw tightened at the fear in Elise's voice. He quickly skipped to the next message.

"Agent Fletcher, sir. This is Brandon Johnson." The boy sniffed into the phone. "Please come help my mom. We're at the Guadalupe River bridge on Highway 474. Please hurry."

Paul dropped the phone into Mel's lap and swung the truck in the direction of Highway 474 leading north out of Breuer.

"Who was it?" Mel asked.

"Brandon Johnson." A scared little boy who might not live to see the next day. And if he did, he might not have a mother or little brother to go home to.

"You know where they are, don't you?" Mel held on to the handle above her door, her expression grim.

"Yes." He told her what he'd heard. "Ten minutes. It takes ten minutes to get there."

"Make it five." Melissa grabbed the handle above the door and held on.

Paul held the steering wheel so tightly his knuckles turned white. They had to get there in time. Elise needed him and he wouldn't let her down. Not again.

Chapter Seventeen

"Please, take me. Don't hurt my son," Elise begged from her knees in the mud. She'd say anything, *do* anything to keep her son safe. As she pushed against the ground to rise to her feet, her hand closed around a stone the size of a baseball. She curled her fingers around it and hid it behind her back, hoping her aim was as good as it had been when she played softball in high school. She'd have to be good. The rock and her brain were her only weapons in the face of certain death.

"What you don't understand, *Alice,* is that I'm in charge here. You don't get a say in what happens."

"My name is Elise." Anger washed over Elise's fear, pushing it aside to make room for more rage. "Who are you, anyway?"

"Your boyfriend doesn't talk about me? He never mentioned Trevor Cain?" He snorted. "Figures."

"What boyfriend? I've never heard of you, and I don't have a boyfriend."

"The man you slept with last night. Don't play dumb with me. I know what's going on." He kicked at the boy lying on the ground. "You and these brats are all he cares about."

"Did Paul have you sent to prison or something?"

The man laughed. "Hardly. I'm one of the good guys. I put

the bad guys behind bars. Besides, he's not smart enough to figure out who's responsible for the deaths of those women. And I'm not going to give him the opportunity to figure it out. Helps when you don't leave any witnesses."

Elise's body went cold and she gulped hard to keep from screaming. She'd suspected as much. This man wouldn't be telling her as much as he was if he planned on letting her go. That went for Luke as well, which made it all the more imperative that she keep a level head and figure a way out of this on her own. "Paul's smarter than you are. At least he doesn't have to go around killing innocent women to prove he's a man."

The man's mouth tightened until his jaw twitched. "Fletcher hasn't got anything on me, except pure dumb luck. He couldn't even figure out this case before two women died. Make that three." He nodded at the gun in his hand. "Now, not only will he lose his golden-boy prestige, he'll lose the woman he's gotten stupid over. Seems like a fair trade to me. My career for his girlfriend. I'll bet you even helped him solve the Dakota Strangler case. What, were you and him doing it on the side while your husband killed those women?"

Anger flared inside her over his callous words. Like Paul had said, *Stan* was responsible for the murders in North Dakota, not her. And just like Stan, this man was responsible for the deaths of Lauren and Mary. She couldn't let her emotions take over. She had to use her head. How ironic, when her husband hadn't wanted her to be smart, to think for herself. Now she *had* to…or die.

She sucked in a deep, calming breath. "I don't know what you're talking about. None of this is making any sense." She inched closer, her worry for Luke outweighing her concern over the gun pointed at her chest. In order for the rock in her hand to be of any use, she had to get close enough to hit her mark. "What is your career, anyway? Murdering women?" Keep him talking, maybe she'd figure out some way to disarm him and get Luke away. Far away.

"No, murdering women was only my way of showing the world Mr. Perfect Agent Fletcher isn't so great after all. While he was out playing with you, women were dying and he could do nothing to stop it."

"Paul will stop you." If she didn't stop him first.

"Sorry, but he won't. And he won't in time to save you or your son. Now won't that just kill him?" His laughter echoed off the concrete and steel of the underside of the bridge. "And the beauty of it all is that once you're gone, he'll lose his job and I'll be promoted in his place. With no one the wiser. The country will think the Dakota Strangler is still alive and killing."

Her heartbeat faltered. She knew Cain was a murderer, but hearing him promise to kill her and her son made it all the more frightening. What he might not fully appreciate was that she wasn't going to die yet, nor was Luke, and she refused to go down without a helluva fight.

While he'd been talking, bragging about his prowess as a crafty murderer, Elise had worked her way closer until she stood within range to do some damage with her rock, *if* her aim struck true. *Please, please, please remember everything Coach Wright taught you about throwing a ball in high school.*

One shot was all she'd get.

"It's time." Cain turned his gun on Luke. "Should I start with him or you?"

Her arm tensed. As she drew it from behind her back, a flurry of motion burst into her peripheral vision. Before she could react, a small, dark shadow slammed into the man's arm, knocking the gun loose. It flew across the sloping concrete, skittering to a stop three feet short of the rising river water.

Oh, God, it was Brandon. Elise held her breath as her son scurried across the concrete to stand in front of Luke, his face fierce and scared at the same time.

"You little brat!" Cain dove for the gun.

"Duck, Brandon!" Elise cocked her arm, prayed for a miracle and let loose. Throwing into a stationary catcher's glove was a lot easier than at a moving target. But her rock hit Cain in the head, stopping him short of his gun. He stumbled and fell, rolling over and over until he tumbled into the water. The current picked him up and carried him downstream, past the bridge and out of sight of the flashlight Elise held.

Brandon ran for the gun and kicked it into the dark, muddy water roaring past.

"Run, Brandon!" Elise scooped Luke up in her arms. His little body wiggled against hers, filling her with relief. "Hold still, little guy. We'll get you home."

Uncertain whether Cain had been revived by the cold river water, Elise knew she had to get to her car as quickly as possible.

Brandon stumbled behind her, slipping in the muddy ruts left by Cain's truck.

Weighed down by Luke, Elise slowed and turned, extending the hand holding the flashlight for him. "Grab the flashlight and hold on."

Brandon latched on to the light and pulled himself up next to her. Then he let go and charged forward. "Come on!"

Getting to the top of the hill seemed to take forever. Elise slipped at least another five times, crashing to the ground on her elbows. She rolled to the side to keep from crushing Luke.

Brandon had disappeared, hopefully making it to the car and the cell phone to call for help.

Luke wiggled to get free. "Let go, Mom. I can walk."

Unable to push herself back to her feet without letting go, Elise released him.

Once free, Luke stood in the mud, slipped and scrambled to his feet, running after Brandon.

With rain dripping down in her eyes, mud coating her arms and legs, Elise struggled to get up.

Before she could take a step, the ground shook behind her and a large hand grabbed her ankle.

Barely balanced to begin with, Elise crashed to the drenched earth, the wind knocked from her lungs. But she held on to the flashlight, its heavy batteries making it the only weapon she had left to save herself and her boys. "Run, Luke! Run, Brandon! Hide!"

Fingers grabbed the back of her calf and Trevor Cain crawled up her body, one hand at a time.

Trapped on her stomach, Elise rolled from side to side, unable to flip onto her back. She swung the flashlight out to the side.

His grunt told her she'd made contact, but not enough to get him off her back.

Again, she swung the heavy flashlight.

He let go of one of her legs long enough to grab the flashlight and yank it from her grip, tossing it into the bushes, the light shining off in another direction.

Now it was her against him. Darkness swallowed them, rain pelting her face and running into her eyes. She kicked, she rolled, but he was heavy and the mud made it too slippery for her to gain purchase. Elise needed a miracle about now to save her and her boys.

Cain climbed onto her back, straddling her hips with his.

He yanked a handful of her hair, pulling back hard until she thought her neck would snap.

"I should have killed you first." He slammed her face into the mud.

If the ground hadn't been so soft and moist, the force of his brutal slam would surely have broken her nose. As it was, her mouth and nostrils filled with mud, choking off her air.

He lifted her head again for another slam.

Elise spit and blew the mud from her nose, gasping for breath. Was this the way it would end? She prayed Luke and Brandon were far, far away and hiding low in the bushes. She prayed it would all end very quickly and painlessly.

"Say goodbye to your boys. They're next." His hand tightened on her hair and his body tensed for the next slam.

Then Cain jerked off her back and fell across her legs, sliding down the muddy slope.

Stunned, Elise kicked free of Cain's legs and rolled to the side, scuttling to her feet to bump into a broad, solid chest.

"Paul!" She fell into his arms, her body sliding against his, coating him in a layer of mud.

Paul clutched her to him, regardless of the mud. Feeling her soft body against him helped to slow his heartbeat and steady his breathing. He'd never been more scared in his life than when he'd seen Cain brutalizing her. Now, he didn't want to let go of her. Ever again.

"Stay with Elise. I want to take care of this." Melissa pushed around Paul's side, gun drawn, and stalked down the hill toward the man who'd terrorized Breuer for the past week.

"Don't kill him, Melissa," Paul called out. Much as he wanted to see the man die for all he'd done, Paul knew he had to live by the laws he'd sworn to uphold. "The families of the victims will want justice."

"I'll show him justice." In the limited glow from the fallen flashlight, Melissa stopped in front of Cain. "Come on, coward. Your murdering days are done."

"What's wrong, Fletcher," Cain called out from flat on his back in the mud. "Not man enough to take me on? Have to send a *woman* to do your job? Took you long enough to figure it out. So much for being a hero."

"Cuff him and read him his rights, Mel." Paul's arm tightened around Elise and he pushed a muddy strand of hair from her face. "Are you okay?"

Elise nodded and snuggled into his chest.

Paul couldn't tell if it was tears or more rain that soaked his shirt.

She looked up at him, her face filthy but the most beautiful face he'd ever seen. "Luke and Brandon?"

"Safe in my truck, although I think they're pretty scared." He returned his attention to Cain. "You should join them." Although he said the words, he didn't loosen his grip on her.

Melissa bent toward Cain, handcuffs outstretched. "Take a swing, try something. I'd love to get one in for the women you terrorized and murdered."

"Don't, Mel," Paul said. "He's not worth it. He's nothing but a coward. He didn't get the job I did, not because of me, but because he couldn't handle it."

"Don't ignore me, Fletcher. You'll never be the agent I am. You're just not that good. You didn't deserve that promotion. I did!" The man on the muddy ground surged to his feet with a roar and shoved at Mel hard.

Caught off guard, she slipped and fell in the mud, cursing her own stupidity.

But before Cain could reach Paul, Melissa flung out her leg, catching the killer in the shins, bringing him to his knees.

Then she was on his back, slamming his body into the ground, her arm around his throat, pulling hard until he gasped for air.

"Like the way that feels?" she said, her voice low and angry. "Like being helpless and scared? You ought to try it sometime. I'm sure the guys in the prison you're going to will love practicing on you. They eat agents for lunch."

"Mel." Paul set Elise to the side and went to Cain. "He's not worth it."

For a moment she hesitated, her eyes blazing. Then she loosened her hold on Cain's throat and stood, bringing one of his arms up hard between his shoulder blades, keeping the man immobile, his cheek in the mud.

Paul retrieved a plastic slip tie out of his pocket and cinched the man's hands together behind him, then yanked him to his feet. "It's over, Cain. The killing, your career…it's over."

Sirens penetrated the roar of the river and the drenching rain. Flashing lights pierced the darkness as several police cars skidded to a stop on the road above them.

Paul's gaze scanned the dimly lit path leading up to Elise's car. She'd disappeared. Probably headed for her boys. Which was just as well. He had a lot to explain to the police and his boss at the Bureau before he could check on her, Luke and Brandon.

Though the murders had been solved and Elise and her boys were alive, Paul couldn't help his confusion. Now that Trevor had confessed to the killings, would Elise still want to stay in Breuer?

Paul hoped she'd stay. The last time he'd been with her in North Dakota, the timing hadn't been right. He couldn't count this encounter as good timing, either. But if he'd learned one thing out of all of this mess, he couldn't wait for perfect timing. He had to reach out for what he wanted and hope that she wanted it, too.

"Let's go, Cain. I'm ready for this night to be over." He hauled the killer up the mud-slick road to the highway above, delivering him into the hands of Sheriff Engel.

An ambulance stood to the side, the back door open, Elise climbing in to join Brandon and Luke. More than anything Paul wanted to go with them to make sure the boys and their mother were all right. Luke had sported a nasty bruise on his forehead when Paul had run across him and Brandon standing on the highway, crying and scared for their mother.

A fresh wave of anger washed over him. He thought he'd lost Elise. Seeing her facedown in the mud with Cain beating the crap out of her had nearly driven him over the edge. He'd kicked the man so hard, he wouldn't be surprised if he'd cracked a few of Cain's ribs.

The ambulance drove away as Paul answered questions for the sheriff. He'd catch up with them at the hospital. They'd need a ride home.

When the sheriff took off in the squad car with Trevor Cain, Paul headed for his truck.

Melissa ducked into the driver's side of Elise's car. "Keys are here. I'll take her car back by her house to pick up my truck. You're going to the hospital, right?" Melissa grinned at Paul.

"Yeah. Thanks." Now that he was free for the moment, he wondered if Elise would care to see him anymore. Had their one night of passion been a fluke? Adrenaline sex for tough times? Would she want anything to do with him after all that had happened?

Paul wouldn't be surprised if she wanted to forget all about North Dakota and Breuer. Heck, she'd probably want to pack up and leave as soon as she could. Start over once again.

His jaw tightened as he pulled out on the highway. Somehow, he had to convince her that she didn't have to leave. That she could start over right here in Breuer. Maybe give their relationship more than a fighting chance. One thing was certain—he needed help.

ELISE SAT BESIDE BRANDON in the waiting room of the emergency room at Santa Rosa Children's Hospital in San Antonio. Luke had a cold compress on his forehead and was sleeping stretched across Elise's lap. The doctor told her to wake him several times during the night in case of concussion, but that he should be all right.

Agent Melissa Bradley had called to tell her that someone would be there in a few minutes to take her home. She wouldn't have to come in to the police station to answer questions until tomorrow and Trevor Cain was securely locked up in jail.

As she sat with one arm around Brandon and the other cradling Luke, she wondered if it was time to move on.

As if on cue, her cell phone rang. Hoping it would be Paul, she answered, her voice breathless. "Hello."

"Alice!" Her sister's voice shouted in her ear. "I just heard. Oh my God, I can't believe all this happened to you. I'm taking a leave of absence and getting on a plane in the morning. I would have been out tonight, but they've got some wind advisories keeping all planes from entering or leaving Minneapolis tonight."

"It's okay, Brenna. I'm fine, the boys are fine. It's all over."

"When I got the call from Fletcher, I couldn't believe it. I should have been there with you."

"Really, I'm okay." Elise smiled, for what seemed the first time in a week. "You don't need to come down here. You have to think of yourself and your baby. Flying at eight months pregnant probably isn't a good idea. I'm sure you'd make the flight attendants nervous. Besides, they caught the guy."

"That's what I heard. I can't believe it was another agent." Her sister sighed. "Are you sure you're okay? I'd feel better seeing you in person."

Elise thought of the bruise on her cheek and Luke's forehead and shook her head. The outward wounds would heal quickly. Getting Brandon and Luke over the trauma of the kidnapping might take a little longer. But they'd muddle through together. "No. We'll be okay."

"If you're sure…"

"I'm sure."

"I tried to call you earlier but my cell-phone reception stunk. I wanted to tell you that I'd spent the day on the phone with a number of agencies and hospitals located along the Red River south of Riverton."

Elise's heart rate kicked up a notch. Although they'd captured the Breuer killer, they still didn't have a definitive answer about her husband. For all she knew, he could still be out there, waiting for his chance to make her life hell. "Did they find anything?"

"Hospitals came up blank. But I found a small town along the river who'd recovered a John Doe skeleton just recently. They'd done a dental X-ray but couldn't find a match locally. I had the North Dakota crime lab run a comparison against Stan's dental records and guess what?"

Elise's eyes filled with tears and her hand shook. "It matched?" she whispered, afraid voicing her heartfelt hopes would jinx her yet again.

"It matched, sweetie. Stan Klaus is well and truly dead. You don't have to run anymore."

With her eyes blurred by tears, Elise didn't see the group of people walking in the door. Brandon jumped up from his seat beside her, shouting, "Kenny! Alex!"

Elise brushed the moisture from her eyes and cheeks and

looked up at the group walking toward her in the emergency room lobby. Principal Ford, Kendall and Alex.

"What's going on?" Brenna asked in Elise's ear.

"I have to go. I'll call you back later." Brenna kept talking, but Elise hit the off button and stood, hugging Luke's sleeping body next to her. Had word gotten out? Had she been exposed for the serial killer's wife? Was her entire world about to crash around her?

Principal Ford stepped forward. "Ms. Johnson…Elise." She held out her arms and engulfed Elise in a giant hug, taking in Luke and her in the effort. Kendall and Alex crowded in, all trying to hug her, everyone talking at once.

The one face she didn't see was Paul's. She'd thought when Melissa said someone would be there to pick her up that it would be Paul. Throughout the outpouring of well-wishes, hugs and love, Elise tried to hide her disappointment.

Kendall nudged Principal Ford. "Are you going to tell her?"

The principal smiled and winked at Kendall and Alex. "No, I think you two should."

Kendall cleared her throat. "Ms. Johnson, we just wanted to let you know how much of a difference you've made in our lives."

Elise wanted to laugh, but tears choked her throat from making any noises. Those tears flowed down her cheeks now.

"Yeah, and we know about what happened to you up in North Dakota," Alex said.

Lead dropped to the pit of Elise's gut, followed by overwhelming sadness. She'd have to leave. To uproot the boys once again and leave.

Kendall pulled Brandon under one arm, hugging him. "We know about the Dakota Strangler and what you, Brandon and Luke have had to live through since then."

Yeah, her days in Breuer were definitely numbered. She

stared at Kendall, Alex and Principal Ford. She'd miss them. Had it been too much to hope she could find a home for herself and her boys? Were they destined to move from town to town the rest of their lives? "Does everyone know?"

"Yeah, pretty much." Kendall nodded. "The news got hold of it and aired it when they captured Agent Cain."

"When Agent Fletcher put the call out to me and Kendall, we knew we had to do something to convince you."

"Agent Fletcher?" Through the darkness of her depressing thoughts, a light of hope burned like a reviving ember buried deep in the ashes.

"Yes, Agent Fletcher." His deep voice rumbled from the lobby entrance, and the students and principal parted, letting him come through to the front.

Paul stood with a cowboy hat in his hands, his shirt muddy from when she'd clung to him out by the river and his face streaked with grime. But he was the most beautiful man she'd ever seen. She stood, holding Luke in her arms, afraid to move, afraid to say anything to douse the tiny flickers of optimism daring to build inside.

"As soon as I heard the radio make a big announcement about the capture of the copycat Dakota Strangler, I knew you'd be thinking about leaving." Paul's brows rose, challenging her to deny it.

She couldn't. Even now, everyone in Breuer would know she'd been married to a killer. Leaving would be her only choice.

"Mom, I don't want to leave," Brandon said, looking up to Kendall and Alex. "I have friends here."

"I know, honey. I know." She hugged Luke tighter and he stirred, his eyes opening.

Her youngest son blinked once, then again, focusing on the tall man in front of him. Then he held out his arms to Paul.

Paul lifted him and laid him on his shoulder. "How are you, big guy?" The small boy and the big man with the sandy-blond hair and blue eyes almost the color of hers looked right together.

For a fleeting moment, Elise wished Paul were a permanent part of her family. The father the boys deserved, the man she could possibly learn to love. "I can't stay. You of all people know why."

"You can't go. We need more teachers like you," Principal Ford insisted. "I suspected you had a history and that something wasn't quite right, but I also saw how much you wanted the job, how much you cared whether or not the students did well."

"Yeah, besides, we love you, Ms. Johnson." Kendall hugged Brandon. "And we love Brandon and Luke."

"Yeah," Alex said. "You can't leave us. What would the school do without you?"

Paul smiled over Luke's head. "You see? It's unanimous. Everyone wants you to stay in Breuer."

Suddenly shy and with nothing to hold in front of her, Elise felt exposed, raw, emotional. More tears pushed their way into her eyes and spilled down her cheeks. "Everyone?"

"Everyone." Paul reached out and brushed his thumb across her cheek. "Including me."

"Why? I don't know if we can be anything more than friends."

Paul's smile faded, his blue eyes serious. "Then I'll settle for that."

"You'd be my friend?" Elise's heart swelled at that. "Stan had never wanted to be my friend."

"I keep telling you, I'm not Stan." Paul laughed. "When are you going to start believing me?"

"He's really dead," she whispered.

Paul tucked a strand of hair behind her ear. "Yes, he is."

"Brenna told you?"

"News on the grapevine travels fast."

Elise couldn't stop the sob rising up her throat. "I'm free."

Paul pulled her into his arms and held her, Luke crushed between them. Brandon broke away from Kendall and pushed his way in between Elise and Paul so they stood hugging, just like a family. "So what's it going to be? Are you going to stay and give these folks a chance to know and love you?"

Elise nodded, for the first time in two years daring to hope. "On one condition."

"And that is?" Paul kissed the tip of her nose.

"I get to know you, as well." She leaned up on her toes and pressed her lips to his.

"Good, because I still have a fence to build and a puppy to get settled. I promised the boys." Then he kissed her long and hard and a cheer went up from the crowd. When he came up for air, he smiled and held her close. "Then it's settled. You're coming home."

She nestled into his chest, her arms around him and her boys. The promise of a bright future ahead, with the chance to get to know this tall, handsome man filled her with a happiness she never dreamed would come her way. "I'm coming home."

* * * * *

Celebrate 60 years of pure reading pleasure
with Harlequin®!
Just in time for the holidays,
Silhouette Special Edition® is proud to present
New York Times *bestselling author*
Kathleen Eagle's
ONE COWBOY, ONE CHRISTMAS.

Rodeo rider Zach Beaudry was a travelin' man—until he broke down in middle-of-nowhere South Dakota during a deep freeze. That's when an angel came to his rescue....

"Don't die on me. Come on, Zel. You know how much I love you, girl. You're all I've got. Don't do this to me here. Not *now*."

But Zelda had quit on him, and Zach Beaudry had no one to blame but himself. He'd taken his sweet time hitting the road, and then miscalculated a shortcut. For all he knew he was a hundred miles from gas. But even if they were sitting next to a pump, the ten dollars he had in his pocket wouldn't get him out of South Dakota, which was not where he wanted to be right now. Not even his beloved pickup truck, Zelda, could get him much of anywhere on fumes. He was sitting out in the cold in the middle of nowhere. And getting colder.

He shifted the pickup into Neutral and pulled hard on the steering wheel, using the downhill slope to get her off the blacktop and into the roadside grass, where she shuddered to a standstill. He stroked the padded dash. "You'll be safe here."

But Zach would not. It was getting dark, and it was already too damn cold for his cowboy ass. Zach's battered body was a barometer, and he was feeling South Dakota, big-time. He'd have given his right arm to be climbing into a hotel hot tub instead of a brutal blast of north wind. The right was his free arm anyway. Damn thing had lost altitude, touched some part of the bull and caused him a scoreless ride last time out.

It wasn't scoring him a ride this night, either. A carload of teenagers whizzed by, topping off the insult by laying on the horn as they passed him. It was at least twenty minutes before another vehicle came along. He stepped out and waved both arms this time, damn near getting himself killed. Whatever happened to *do unto others?* In places like this, decent people didn't leave each other stranded in the cold.

His face was feeling stiff, and he figured he'd better start walking before his toes went numb. He struck out for a distant yard light, the only sign of human habitation in sight. He couldn't tell how distant, but he knew he'd be hurting by the time he got there, and he was counting on some kindly old man to be answering the door. No shame among the lame.

It wasn't like Zach was fresh off the operating table—it had been a few months since his last round of repairs—but he hadn't given himself enough time. He'd lopped a couple of weeks off the near end of the doc's estimated recovery time, rigged up a brace, done some heavy-duty taping and climbed onto another bull. Hung in there for five seconds—four seconds past feeling the pop in his hip and three seconds short of the buzzer.

He could still feel the pain shooting down his leg with every step. Only, this time he had to pick the damn thing up, swing it forward and drop it down again on his own.

Pride be damned, he just hoped *somebody* would be answering the door at the end of the road. The light in the front window was a good sign.

The four steps to the covered porch might as well have been four hundred, and he was looking to climb them with a lead weight chained to his left leg. His eyes were just as screwed up as his hip. Big black spots danced around with tiny red flashers, and he couldn't tell what was real and what wasn't. He stumbled over some shrubbery, steadied himself on the porch railing and peered between vertical slats.

There in the front window stood a spruce tree with a silver star affixed to the top. Zach was pretty sure the red sparks were all in his head, but the white lights twinkling by the hundreds throughout the huge tree, those were real. He wasn't too sure about the woman hanging the shiny balls. Most of her hair was caught up on her head and fastened in a curly clump, but the light captured by the escaped bits crowned her with a golden halo. Her face was a soft shadow, her body a willowy silhouette beneath a long white gown. If this was where the mind ran off to when cold started shutting down the rest of the body, then Zach's final worldly thought was, *This ain't such a bad way to go.*

If she would just turn to the window, he could die looking into the eyes of a Christmas angel.

* * * * *

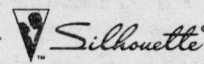

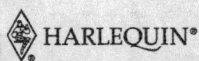

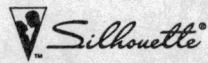

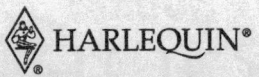

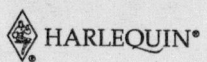

THE AUTHORITY SINCE 1868

THE WORLD ALMANAC® & BOOK OF FACTS 1978

David Livingston

NEA

Published Annually by
NEWSPAPER ENTERPRISE ASSOCIATION, INC.
New York

THE WORLD ALMANAC® & BOOK OF FACTS

The editors acknowledge with thanks the many letters of helpful comment and criticism from users of THE WORLD ALMANAC, and invite further suggestions and observations. Because of the volume of mail directed to the editorial offices, it is not possible personally to reply to each letter writer. However, every communication is read by the editors and all comments and suggestions receive careful attention.

THE WORLD ALMANAC is published annually in November.

Inquiries regarding contents and purchase orders should be sent to: The World Almanac, 230 Park Avenue, New York, NY 10017.

THE WORLD ALMANAC does not decide wagers.

The first edition of THE WORLD ALMANAC, a 120-page volume with 12 pages of advertising, was published by the New York World in 1868, 110 years ago. Annual publication was suspended in 1876. Joseph Pulitzer, publisher of the New York World, revived THE WORLD ALMANAC in 188 with the goal of making it a "compendium of universal knowledge." It has been published annually since then. In 1931, it was acquired by the Scripps-Howard Newspapers; until 1951, it bore the imprint of the New York World-Telegram and thereafter, until 1967, that of the New York World-Telegram and Sun. It is now published in paper and clothbound editions by Newspaper Enterprise Association, Inc., a Scripps-Howard company.

THE WORLD ALMANAC & BOOK OF FACTS 1978

Library of Congress Catalog Card Number 4-3781
International Standard Serial Number (ISSN) 0084-1382
Newspaper Enterprise Association, Inc. ISBN 0-911818-08-1
Doubleday and Co., Inc. ISBN 0-385-13560-2
Microfilm Edition since 1868: Bell and Howell Co.
Printed in the United States of America

NEWSPAPER ENTERPRISE ASSOCIATION, INC.
230 Park Avenue, New York, NY 10017

GENERAL INDEX

— D —

— G —

—H—

—J—

— M —

—U—

—V—

Late News, Addenda, Changes

Colleges and Universities (pp. 154-177)

Bennett College, Millbrook, N.Y., closed down, Aug. 9, 1977 (p. 169).

Briarcliff College, Pleasantville, N.Y., became the Briarcliff campus of Pace University in 1977 (p. 155).

Bronx (N.Y.) Community College, president is Roscoe C. Brown Jr. (p. 170).

Univ. of Colorado, Boulder, president is Roland C. Rautenstraus (p. 156).

Hostos Community College, Bronx, N.Y., acting president is Anthony Santiago (p. 172).

Kent (O.) State Univ., president is Brage Golding (p. 160).

Manhattan Community College, New York, N.Y., president is Joshua Smith (p. 173).

New York, (N.Y.) City Univ. of: Queens College, acting president is Nathaniel H. Siegel (p. 162).

New York, State Univ. of, chancellor is Clifton R. Wharton Jr. (p. 162).

New York City Community College, acting president is Peter Caffrey (p. 174).

Notre Dame College, St. Louis, Mo., closed, May 1977.

St. Joseph's College, Brentwood, N.Y., address should be Brooklyn, NY 11205 (p. 165).

Univ. of Wisconsin, system president is Edwin Young (p. 168), Madison chancellor is Irving Shain (p. 169).

U.S. Population (187-243)

Changing Population Patterns: The Bureau of the Census reported in August that the U.S. population (including armed forces overseas) was 216,817,000 as of July 1, 1977 (p. 187).

West Virginia: Boone County population, Apr. 1, 1970, was 25,118, not 2,118 (p. 242).

State Governments (pp. 249-252)

Arizona: governor is Wesley Bolin, D. (p. 249).

Judiciary (pp. 253-255)

New York: Eastern: Eugene H. Nickerson and Charles P. Sifton were sworn in as District Court judges, Oct. 26, 1977 (p. 255).

Congress (pp. 288-296)

Washington: Jack Cunningham (R) was elected, May 17, in the 7th district to replace Brock Adams (D), who became transportation secretary. Cunningham defeated Marvin Durning (D), 43,441 votes to 37,-229 (p. 296).

Associations and Societies (pp. 333-346)

Big Brothers of America merged, June 1977, w Big Sisters International to form **Big Brothers/ Sisters of America;** national address: 220 Subur Station Building, Philadelphia, PA 19103 (p. 334).

The National Institute of Social Sciences' new tional address is: 150 Amsterdam Ave., N.Y., 10023 (p. 344).

Religious Information (pp. 347-358)

Eastern Orthodox Churches: Greek Ortho Archdio.: should be 535 churches, not 530 (p. 347).

Greek Orthodox Church: should be Archdioc not Church (p. 349).

Orthodox Church in America: new primate Metropolitan Archbishop Theodosius (elected Oct. 1977) (p. 350).

1977 Awards, Prizes (pp. 404-416)

Nobel Peace Prize: Mairead Corrigan and Be Williams, leaders of a Northern Ireland peace mo ment, were belatedly granted the Nobel Peace Pr for 1976, and awarded $140,000 to share betw them. Amnesty International, a voluntary gr monitoring human rights around the world, won 1977 prize of $145,000 (p. 405).

Nobel Prize in Literature: Spanish surrealist p Vicente Aleixandre; cash prize, $145,000 (p. 405).

Nobel Prize in Physiology or Medicine: Dr. Rosa S. Yalow, U.S., for her development of radioim noassay, $72,500; Dr. Roger C.L. Guillemin and Andrew V. Schally, both U.S., shared $72,500 for search into hormone production in the brain (p. 40

Nobel Memorial Prize in Economic Science: Be Ohlin, Sweden, and James E. Meade, Britain, sha $145,000, for their theory of international trade 405).

Nobel Prize in Physics: Dr. Philip W. Anderson a Dr. John H. Van Vleck, both U.S., and Sir Nevill Mott, Britain, shared $145,000 for work in solid-st physics (p. 404).

Nobel Prize in Chemistry: Dr. Ilya Prigogine, B gium, for his theory of dissipative structures (p. 40

Emmy Awards, by Academy of Television Arts Sciences (a selection from among 316 winners in categories): comedy series: Mary Tyler Moore Sh variety special: Barry Manilow Special; vari

(Continued on Page

110th ANNIVERSARY EDITION

The World Almanac

and Book of Facts for 1978

The Top 10 News Stories of 1977

Georgian **Bert Lance**, President Carter's close friend and Director of the U.S. Office of Management and Budget, resigned in face of a barrage of criticism for massive personal bank overdrafts and unusual loans incurred while he was president of two banks. In spite of his spirited self-defense before a Senate committee, Lance was unable to overcome public doubt about the ethics and legality of his financial dealings.

With the U.S. now importing 40% of its oil, President Carter called for the country to make "the moral equivalent of war" on energy waste as he presented to Congress a comprehensive, if moderate, **energy program** which emphasized conservation over increased production. The program was the major piece of legislation before Congress during the year.

Ending 13 years of negotiations under 3 U.S. administrations, the U.S. and Panama signed a **new canal treaty** which would turn the canal over to full Panamanian control at the end of 1999. In spite of support of the treaty by senior officials of present and past administrations, Senate ratification of the treaty seemed doubtful.

"No member of the United Nations can claim that mistreatment of its citizens is solely its own business." With these words and a variety of actions, Carter pushed forward his international campaign for **human rights**, to the discomfiture of the USSR, Eastern Europe, and several U.S. allies.

Details of **Korean gifts to U.S. congressmen** began to emerge from House Ethics Committee hearings led by former Watergate prosecutor Leon Jaworski. Several million dollars in cash, possibly from U.S. aid funds, were given by South Korean government agents to more than 150 U.S. Senators and Representatives in an attempt to buy favorable votes and statements.

Over 300 New York City policemen, working full-time on the city's largest man-hunt, were unable to prevent the psychopathic killer, **Son of Sam**, from claiming two more victims before a parking ticket led the police to the apartment of David Berkowitz. Berkowitz was accused of killing 5 young women and a young man and wounding 7 other people during a year-long murder-spree.

Likud, Israel's conservative coalition led by Menahem Begin, ended 30 years of Labor rule, as the party of David Ben Gurion and Golda Meir, beset by scandal and faltering leadership, went down to defeat in **Israel's national elections**. The new government moved quickly to take a hard-line stand in relations with the Arab nations.

Young Kunta Kinte and his daughter Kizzy, ancestors of ***Roots*** author Alex Haley, captured the imagination of America, as the largest TV audiences in history viewed the dramatization of Haley's book. Over 36 million American families saw at least one episode of the 8-part series, and thousands began to trace their own ancestral roots.

North America experienced the worst **weather extremes** in the 20th century as the North, East, and South suffered through a record cold winter and the Far West underwent a drought that brought severe water rationing to much of northern California.

Death by firing squad finally came to **Gary Gilmore** in the first execution in the U.S. in 10 years. While capital punishment foes fought against Gilmore's death sentence for murder, Gilmore himself loudly proclaimed his desire to die.

Carter's Promises

At the beginning of the Carter Administration, the White House staff prepared a list of all of Carter's campaign promises, over 600. The following is a list of some of those promises on which definite action has been taken. The Republican National Committee and the White House were both consulted in compiling this data.

Economy

To provide federal funds for public employment of those whom private business cannot and will not hire.

Kept. The Administration submitted legislation to increase public service employment by 415,000. Legislation enacted in previous Congress provided 310,000 public service jobs. P.L. 95-28.

To support the full Employment Act of 1976. (Humphrey-Hawkins Bill)

Broken. There has been no sign of support for the Humphrey-Hawkins bill.

To support counter-cyclical assistance to deal with fiscal and employment needs of cities particularly hard hit by the recession.

Kept. $1.25 billion is included in the Public Service Jobs Bill, P.L. 95-28. Carter's economic stimulus package included counter-cyclical aid and extended the program for an additional year with an authorization of $2.25 billion.

(continued)

To provide strong work incentives, public jobs creation, and job training for those on welfare able to work.	**Kept.** Included in welfare reform proposals of 8/6/7

Taxes

Not to increase taxes for working people and lower and middle-income groups.	**Partly broken.** Carter's energy tax proposals w tied to rebates which would return most of the re nues to taxpayers. Carter's Social Security proposals would tax employers and the best-paid t much greater extent, but lower- and middle-inco workers would still pay more tax. Carter inco proposals provide for tax cuts for lower- and midd tax income groups.
To prefer a more progressive plan to increase gradually the maximum amount of earnings subject to the Social Security tax (rather than increasing the Social Security contribution rate).	**Kept.** In his Social Security message, Carter asked for a $14 billion transfusion from general re nue funds to the Social Security Trust Fund. would require employers to pay Social Security ta on all employees' wages from 1981 on. The additio cost to employers from 1979 through 1982 would $30 billion. Carter has also proposed increasing wage base on which workers pay tax by $2,400 1985.

Energy

To establish most energy programs in one Cabinet-level Department.	**Kept.** Energy Department established August, 1977
To prevent a further increase in reliance on imported oil.	**Debatable.** The Library of Congress' Congressio Research Service (CRS) said that Carter's estim that his energy plan would reduce oil imports under 7 million barrels per day by 1985 was in err The CRS estimated imports at 11.8 million barr per day. The General Accounting Office estima 1985 import levels of 10.3 million barrels per day, proximately the amount imported at present.

Environment

To oppose the lowering of the standards of the Water Pollution Control Act of 1972.	**Kept.** Included in Environment Message.
To support passage of rigid strip mining laws.	**Kept.** Carter signed such a law in August, 1977.

Agriculture

To support agricultural prices equal to at least the cost of production.	**Kept.** The new agriculture bill (signed 9/29/77) t farm price supports to production costs.

Health

To initiate immediate fundamental management reform in the way in which medicaid/medicare programs pay hospitals; to adopt the concept of prospective reimbursements under which reasonable rates will be forecast and fixed in advance.	**Kept.** On 3/8/77, HEW Secretary Joseph A. Calif Jr. announced the creation of a Health Care Fina ing Administration. The new agency will be respo ble for oversight and policy control over Medic and Medicaid; and be involved in detecting and c trolling fraud, abuse, and overpayments.
To increase federal expenditures to expand educational rights of the handicapped.	**Kept.** Carter asked for, and on 6/17/77 signed, Education of the Handicapped Amendments of 19 that extended through fiscal 1982 eight progra that provide centers, materials and personnel training the handicapped.

Justice

To establish independent judicial selection commissions to recommend persons as federal judges and prosecutors and to select from those recommended.	**In process.** Carter on 2/15/77 issued an execut order setting up advisory panels to recommend no nees for the 11 Federal Circuit Courts. He made individual senators the request that they voluntai set up merit selection panels for district judges a prosecutors. The White House says that if th voluntary panels are not set up or don't work, Car will act to carry through on his promise.
To issue a blanket pardon for those who violated Selective Service laws during the Vietnam War.	**Kept.** Carter granted a pardon to all Vietnam dr evaders who had not been involved in a violent act.

Government Organization

To reduce the number of federal agencies (about 1,900) to no more than 200.	**In process.** After taking office, Carter discove that of the so-called 1,900 federal agencies, 1, were advisory committees. The White House plans eliminate 480 committees by abolishing 261 and c solidating the others into 78 committees. The Wh House estimates saving $15 million.
To schedule public interrogation sessions to allow the full bodies of the Congress to question cabinet members.	**Broken.** Nothing further has been heard of this p liamentary procedure.
To make mandatory financial disclosure for the	**Kept.** Financial information on cabinet members a

president, vice president and anyone appointed to major policy-making positions in the administration.

top White House staff was made public, but the controversy over OMB Director Lance's financial situation raised questions about this process.

Foreign Policy

To support efforts of the UN and other bodies to attract world attention to the denial of freedom.

Kept. Carter has repeatedly stressed the importance of human rights in every nation.

To reduce present defense expenditures by about $5-7 billion annually.

Kept. In his budget revisions for FY 1978 submitted February 1977, Carter asked for $2.7 billion less in budget authority for defense, $3.5 billion less in defense outlays than in Ford's last budget.

To favor negotiations to reduce the present SALT ceilings on offensive weapons before both sides start a new arms race and before new missile systems are committed for production.

Kept. Carter's initial attempts at reaching an agreement on offensive weapons ended in failure. Since that point there have been hints of some progress in the negotiations.

The New Panama Canal Treaty

The new Panama Canal agreement consists of 2 treaties which were signed in Washington on Sept. 7, 1977. Both treaties must still be ratified by the legislatures of the U.S. and Panama. Ratification in the U.S. requires a two-thirds majority (67 votes) of the Senate. If the treaties are ratified, notices of ratification will be exchanged in formal ceremonies in Panama. The treaties will enter into force 6 months after that exchange.

The first treaty, the *Panama Canal Treaty* itself, is concerned with the timetable for the transfer to Panama of control of the canal. The second treaty, *Treaty Concerning the Permanent Neutrality of the Panama Canal*, only defines the obligations of Panama to maintain the neutrality of the canal.

The first treaty, which will expire at the end of 1999, clearly states that the U.S. has the "primary responsibility" for defending the canal. The second treaty, which is permanent, declares simply that the U.S. and Panama "agree to maintain the regime of neutrality" of the canal.

The Timetable

When the *Panama Canal Treaty* enters into force, the Canal Zone and the Canal Zone Government will cease to exist. About 65% of present Zone territory will immediately come under full Panamanian control. In the remaining 35%, the U.S. will have the right to use certain designated military bases, canal operating areas, and U.S. citizen employee housing areas, and will continue to have full operating control of the canal.

Except at U.S. military bases and a few official buildings, only the Panamanian flag will be flown in the area of the former Zone.

The present Panama Canal Company will cease to exist and its canal operating functions will be taken over by a Panama Canal Commission. The Commission will not be permitted to engage in the kind of general commercial activity which the former Company carried on. That is, the supermarkets, movie houses, restaurants, gasoline stations, etc., which the Company operated for the benefit of Zone residents will become part of the Panamanian free enterprise economy.

The 9-man Commission board of directors will consist of 5 Americans and 4 Panamanians. Until Jan. 1, 1990, the Administrator will be an American and his deputy a Panamanian. After that date the national roles will be reversed.

Payments to Panama

The U.S. will pay Panama $10 million a year for services — police, fire protection, etc. — to be provided by Panama in the areas used by the U.S. Another $10 million will be paid to Panama annually from canal operating revenues. A further $10 million per year will be paid to Panama out of any canal revenues that exceed expenditures. If revenues are not sufficient to meet that payment, it can be delayed. Finally, the U.S. will pay Panama 30 cents for each cargo-ton passing through the canal; this sum could amount to over $35 million per year.

At noon, Panama time, December 31, 1999, Panama will assume full control of canal operations and of the canal area.

Panama Canal Facts

1. The 1903 Panama Canal Treaty was not signed by a Panamanian. Phillippe Bunau-Varilla, a French engineer and adventurer, originally with the bankrupt French Panama Canal Company, helped arrange the revolution which gained Panama's independence from Colombia. He then inveigled a weak Panamanian leadership into making him Panama's minister to the U.S. with full power to negotiate a canal treaty. In 24 hours he wrote a treaty which gave every advantage to the U.S., for he wanted the U.S. to sign the treaty before a delegation of Panamanians arrived in Washington. He signed the treaty for Panama. Immediately afterward, he retired to France to write his memoirs, in which he stated that, through his canal machinations, "I had safeguarded the work of French genius; I had avenged its honor; I had served France."

2. The treaty granted to the U.S. "all rights, power and authority within the zone which the U.S. would possess if it were the sovereign of the territory." The titular sovereignty of Panama over the Canal Zone was recognized by Wm. H. Taft, then secretary of war, in a letter to President Theodore Roosevelt in 1904. A 1936 treaty between the U.S. and Panama referred to the Zone as "territory of Panama under the jurisdiction" of the U.S.

3. The Canal Zone occupies about 2% of Panama's area. A proportionate area taken from the center of the U.S. would include all of Missouri and 5 adjacent counties of Kansas.

4. An estimated 225 million cubic yards of earth were excavated to build the canal, enough to bury Miami under 6 feet of dirt. The total cost of the canal was approximately $375 million.

5. Over 20,000 lives were sacrificed to the French effort to build the canal. The dead were overwhelmingly laborers from neighboring Caribbean islands. At the peak of the U.S. effort, over 40,000 men from 97 countries were at work on the canal; Americans were never more than 20% of this work force. Deaths during American construction, 1904-1914, amounted to about 7,000.

6. The U.S. originally paid Panama $10 million for

its rights in the Canal Zone. Panama, in addition, received $250,000 a year from 1914 to 1936; $430,000 per year from 1936 to 1955; and $1.93 million per year beginning in 1955. Since then the annual payment has risen to $2.3 million.

7. Only 7% of U.S. interstate trade and 8% of U.S. international trade passes through the canal, but this small proportion makes up 70% of the canal's traffic.

8. Aircraft carriers, the largest cargo ships and tankers, and some passenger liners are too large to pass through the canal.

9. Some 35,000 Americans are estimated to live in the Zone. Of these, about 10% are employed by the Panama Canal Company, which employs a total 13,000 people. Another 30% of Americans in the Zo are members of the armed forces. The Zone funne about $260 million each year into the Panamani economy through Company purchases and wages Panamanian workers. U.S. investments in Panan outside the Zone are estimated at $250 million.

10. The property, plant, and equipment of the U. in the Canal Zone are presently estimated to worth about $6.5 billion. Capital expenditures on t canal are now running about $25 million per yea while operating costs and general expenses are abo $83 million. Total toll income from the canal ru about $135 million a year.

(Continued from Page 34)

series: Van Dyke and Co.; limited series: Roots; drama series: Upstairs, Downstairs; drama or comedy special: Eleanor and Franklin, The White House Years and Sybil (tie); actor in single performance: Louis Gossett Jr., Roots, Edward Asner, Roots; actress in single performance: Beulah Bondi, Waltons; Rita Moreno, Muppet Show; Olivia Cole, Roots; actor in series: Christopher Plummer, Money Changers, James Garner, Rockford Files; actress in series: Patty Duke Astin, Captains and the Kings; Lindsay Wagner, Bionic Woman; supporting actor in series: Gary Burghoff, M-A-S-H, Gary Frank, Family, Tim Conway, Carol Burnett Show; supporting actress in series: Mary Kay Place, Mary Hartman, Mary Hartman, Kristy McNichol, Family; supporting actor in special: Burgess Meredith, Tail Gunner Joe; supporting actress in special: Diana Hyland, Boy in the Plastic Bubble (p. 413).

ABC Theater Award, by ABC Entertainment, for television play, $10,000: George Rubino for **The Last Tenant** (p. 413).

Albert Gallatin Medal by New York Univ., for contributions to society: Avery Fisher (p. 414).

Louisa Gross Horwitz Prize, by Columbia Univ., for biology research, $25,000: Michael Heidelberger, Elvin A. Kabat, Henry G. Kunkel (p. 414).

Lamont Poetry Selection, by Academy of American Poets, for second book: Gerald Stern, for **Lucky Life** (p. 411).

Loeb Memorial Award, by Univ. of California, L.A., for business reporting: Leonard Silk, N.Y. Times (p. 412).

Samuel Eliot Morison Award, by American Heritage Publishing Co., for history: Joseph P. Lash, for **Roosevelt and Churchill, 1939-1941** (p. 411).

National Press Club Award, for consumer journalism, $1,000: Herb Denenberg, Philadelphia Bulletin (p. 412).

Bradford Washburn Award, by Boston Museum of Science, for popular science writing: Arthur C. Clarke (p. 411).

World Facts (pp. 431-453)

Important Islands: Samoa Is., Western Samoa is now called Samoa (p. 438).

Nations of the World (pp. 511-595)

China: The Tangshan earthquake occurred in 1976, not 1977 (p. 523).

Kampuchea: Pol Pot is Prime Minister and secretary of the central committee of the communist party (p. 550).

Thailand: A military coup Oct. 21, 1977, deposed the civilian government. Adm. Sa-ngad Chaloryu headed the new council of military officers (p. 580).

Yemen Arab Republic: Pres. Ibrahim al-Hamidi and his brother, Col. Abdullah Mohammed al-Hamidi were assassinated, Oct. 10, 1977. Lieut. Col. Ahmed Hussein al-Ghashmi assumed leadership of the ruling command council (p. 592).

Ambassadors (pp. 599-600)

New U.S. ambassadors are:
William B. Schwartz to Bahamas.
Mari-Luci Jaramillo to Honduras.
Maurice D. Bean to Burma (nominated).
Arthur J. Goldberg, Ambassador-at-Large.

New envoys to the U.S., as of August, 1977, are:
Afghanistan: Abdul Wahed Karim, Amb.
Algeria: Abdelaziz Maoui, Amb.
Argentina: Raul H. Castro, Amb.
Canada: Peter M. Towe, Amb.
Colombia: Virgilio Barco, Amb.
Ethiopia: Getachew Tadesse, Charge.
Guinea: Mamadi Toure, Charge.
Kenya: Mbogna was elevated to ambassadorial rank.
Morocco: Ali Bengelloun, Amb.
Nigeria: Olujimi Jolaoso, appointed Amb.
United Kingdom: Peter Jay, Amb.
Zambia: Putteho M. Ngonda, Amb.

States of the Union (pp. 681-710)

Alaska: state song is "Alaska's Flag" (p. 681).

Canal Zone and Panama Canal: The 1903 Panan Canal treaty technically did not grant the U.S. pe petual sovereignty over the Canal Zone. It on granted the U.S. such rights, powers and authority it would exercise "if it were sovereign" (p. 710).

Memorable Dates (pp. 713-745)

1920: Sacco and Vanzetti were executed Aug. 2 1927, not Aug. 22 (p. 730).

Disasters (pp. 746-753)

Earthquakes: 1976, July 28, China, Tangsha should be 750,000 deaths, not 655,235; 1976, Feb. Guatemala: should be 22,836 deaths, not 22,778 (747).

Floods, Tidal Waves: At least 68 persons we killed and 31 missing when a flood swept throug Johnstown, Penn., and surrounding areas, July 19-2 1977. Property damage was reported at $200 milli (p. 747).

Historic Assassinations: Unidentified assassi killed Yemen Arabic Republic President Ibrahim a Hamidi and his brother, Col. Abdullah Mohamme al-Hamidi, Oct. 10, 1977 (p. 752).

Sports (pp. 818-913)

New York Marathon: Bill Rodgers took his secor consecutive first place in the 1977 New York Mar thon, running the 26 miles 385 yards in 2 hours 1

(Continued on Page 3

Governors of States and Possessions

Reflecting Nov. 8, 1977 election

State	Capital	Governor	Party	Term years	Term expires	Annual salary
Alabama	Montgomery	George C. Wallace	Dem.	4	Jan. 1979	$28,955
Alaska	Juneau	Jay Hammond	Rep.	4	Dec. 1978	50,000
Arizona	Phoenix	Wesley Bolin	Dem.	4	Jan. 1979	40,000
Arkansas	Little Rock	David Pryor	Dem.	2	Jan. 1979	35,000
California	Sacramento	Edmund G. Brown Jr.	Dem.	4	Jan. 1979	49,100
Colorado	Denver	Richard D. Lamm	Dem.	4	Jan. 1979	40,000
Connecticut	Hartford	Ella T. Grasso	Dem.	4	Jan. 1979	42,000
Delaware	Dover	Pierre S. du Pont	Rep.	4	Jan. 1981	35,000
Florida	Tallahassee	Reubin Askew	Dem.	4	Jan. 1979	50,000
Georgia	Atlanta	George Busbee	Dem.	4	Jan. 1979	50,000
Hawaii	Honolulu	George R. Ariyoshi	Dem.	4	Dec. 1978	50,000
Idaho	Boise	John V. Evans	Dem.	4	Jan. 1979	33,000
Illinois	Springfield	James R. Thompson	Rep.	4	Jan. 1981	50,000
Indiana	Indianapolis	Otis R. Bowen	Rep.	4	Jan. 1981	36,000
Iowa	Des Moines	Robert D. Ray	Rep.	4	Jan. 1979	40,000
Kansas	Topeka	Robert F. Bennett	Rep.	4	Jan. 1979	35,000
Kentucky	Frankfort	Julian Carroll	Dem.	4	Dec. 1979	35,000
Louisiana	Baton Rouge	Edwin W. Edwards	Dem.	4	May 1980	50,000
Maine	Augusta	James Longley	Ind.	4	Jan. 1979	35,000
Maryland	Annapolis	Blair Lee 3d	Dem.	4	Jan. 1979	25,000
Massachusetts	Boston	Michael S. Dukakis	Dem.	4	Jan. 1979	40,000
Michigan	Lansing	William G. Milliken	Rep.	4	Jan. 1979	58,000
Minnesota	St. Paul	Rudy Perpich	Dem.	4	Jan. 1979	58,000
Mississippi	Jackson	Charles C. Finch	Dem.	4	Jan. 1980	43,000
Missouri	Jefferson City	Joseph P. Teasdale	Dem.	4	Jan. 1981	37,500
Montana	Helena	Thomas L. Judge	Dem.	4	Jan. 1981	30,000
Nebraska	Lincoln	J. James Exon	Dem.	4	Jan. 1979	40,000
Nevada	Carson City	Mike O'Callaghan	Dem.	4	Jan. 1979	40,000
New Hampshire	Concord	Meldrim Thomson Jr.	Rep.	2	Jan. 1979	34,070
New Jersey	Trenton	Brendan T. Byrne	Dem.	4	Jan. 1982	65,000
New Mexico	Sante Fe	Jerry Apodaca	Dem.	4	Jan. 1979	26,000
New York	Albany	Hugh L. Carey	Dem.	4	Jan. 1979	85,000
North Carolina	Raleigh	James B. Hunt Jr.	Dem.	4	Jan. 1981	45,000
North Dakota	Bismarck	Arthur A. Link	Dem.	4	Jan. 1981	27,500
Ohio	Columbus	James A. Rhodes	Rep.	4	Jan. 1979	50,000
Oklahoma	Oklahoma City	David Boren	Dem.	4	Jan. 1979	42,500
Oregon	Salem	Robert Straub	Dem.	4	Jan. 1979	42,350
Pennsylvania	Harrisburg	Milton J. Shapp	Dem.	4	Jan. 1979	60,000
Rhode Island	Providence	J. Joseph Garrahy	Dem.	2	Jan. 1979	42,500
South Carolina	Columbia	James B. Edwards	Rep.	4	Jan. 1979	39,000
South Dakota	Pierre	Richard F. Kneip	Dem.	4	Jan. 1979	25,000
Tennessee	Nashville	Ray Blanton	Dem.	4	Jan. 1979	50,000
Texas	Austin	Dolph Briscoe	Dem.	4	Jan. 1979	66,800
Utah	Salt Lake City	Scott M. Matheson	Dem.	4	Jan. 1981	40,000
Vermont	Montpelier	Richard A. Snelling	Rep.	2	Jan. 1979	36,100
Virginia	Richmond	John Dalton	Rep.	4	Jan. 1982	50,000
Washington	Olympia	Dixy Lee Ray	Dem.	4	Jan. 1981	34,300
West Virginia	Charleston	John D. Rockefeller 4th	Dem.	4	Jan. 1981	50,000
Wisconsin	Madison	Patrick J. Lucey	Dem.	4	Jan. 1979	44,292
Wyoming	Cheyenne	Ed Herschler	Dem.	4	Jan. 1979	37,500
Possessions						
Guam	Agana	Ricardo J. Bordallo	Rep.	4	Jan. 1981	35,000
Puerto Rico	San Juan	Carlos Romero Barcelo	N.P.	4	Jan. 1981	36,200
Virgin Isls.	Charlotte Amalie	Cyril E. King	ICM	4	Jan. 1979	35,505

The Races for Governor[1]

In 1977, there were 37 Democratic and 12 Republican governors. As result of the November 8 election, the roster became 36 Democrats to 13 Republicans. There is one independent governor, in Maine.

State	Democrats	Vote	Republicans	Vote
New Jersey	**Brendan T. Byrne**	1,168,468	Raymond H. Bateman	870,043
Virginia	Henry Howell	542,529	**John Dalton**	703,827

*Incumbent. **Bold face type** denotes the winner. (1) Preliminary unofficial returns.

(Continued from Page 38)

minutes 28.2 seconds; top woman finisher Miki Gorman came in 190th place overall at 2:43:10. Starters totalled 4,823 (p. 836).

Cy Young Award: Sparky Lyle, New York Yankees, won the 1977 American League Cy Young Award; Steve Carlton, Philadelphia Phillies, won the 1977 National League Cy Young Award (p. 898).

Mayors and City Managers of Larger North American Cities

Reflecting Nov. 8, 1977 elections

*Asterisk before name denotes city manager. All others are mayors. For mayors, dates are those of expiration of term, for city managers; they are dates of appointment.

D, Democrat; R, Republican; N-P, Non-Partisan

City	Name	Term
Abilene, Tex.	*Fred Sandlin	1974, May
Abington, Pa.	*William J. Jobling	1977, Feb.
Akron, Oh.	John S. Ballard, R	1979, Dec.
Alameda, Cal.	*John Goss	1973, Dec.
Albany, Ga.	*S. A. Roos	1961, Aug.
Albany, N.Y.	Erastus Corning 2d, D	1979, Dec.
Albuquerque, N.M.	Mel Aragon, D	1981, Dec.
Alexandria, La.	Carroll E. Lanier, D	1981, Dec.
Alexandria, Va.	Frank Mann, N-P	1979, July
Alhambra, Cal.	*Donald L. Russell	1976, July
Allen Park, Mich.	Frank J. Lada, N-P	1979, Nov.
Allentown, Pa.	Frank Fischl Jr., R	1982, Jan.
Alton, Ill.	Paul A. Lenz, N-P	1981, Apr.
Altoona, Pa.	William C. Stouffer, R	1979, Dec.
Amarillo, Tex.	Jerry Hodge, N-P	1979, Apr.
Ames, Ia.	*Terry Sprenkel	1976, Apr.
Anaheim, Cal.	*William O. Talley	1976, July
Anchorage, Alas.	George Sullivan, N-P	1978, Oct.
Anderson, Ind.	Robert Rock, D	1979, Dec.
Anderson, S.C.	Darwin H. Wright, D	1978, June
Ann Arbor, Mich.	Albert Wheller, D	1979, Apr.
Appleton, Wis.	James P. Sutherland, N-P	1980, Apr.
Arcadia, Cal.	*Lyman H. Cozad	1966, July
Arlington, Mass.	*Donald R. Marquis	1966, Nov.
Arlington, Tex.	S.J. Stovall, N-P	1979, Apr.
Arlington, Va.	*W.V. Ford	1976, Feb.
Arlington Hts., Ill.	*L.A. Hanson	1959, June
Arvada, Col.	*Craig Kocian	1977, Feb.
Asheville, N.C.	Otis Michael, R	1979, Nov.
Athens, Ga.	Upshaw Bentley, D	1979, Nov.
Atlanta, Ga.	Maynard Jackson, N-P	1981, Dec.
Atlantic City, N.J.	Joseph Lazarow, R	1980, May
Auburn, N.Y.	Paul W. Lattimore, D	1979, Dec.
Augusta, Ga.	Lewis A. Newman, N-P	1978, Nov.
Aurora, Col.	*W. Robert Semple	1972, Feb.
Aurora, Ill.	Jack Hill, N-P	1981, Apr.
Austin, Tex.	Carole K. McClellan, N-P	1979, May
Bakersfield, Cal.	*Harold E. Bergen	1966, July
Baldwin Park, Cal.	*James Sexton	1976, Mar.
Baltimore, Md.	William Schaefer, D	1979, Dec.
Bangor, Me.	*John W. Flynn	1977, Feb.
Baton Rouge, La.	W.W. Dumas, D	1980, Dec.
Battle Creek, Mich.	*Gordon Jaeger	1976, Mar.
Bay City, Mich.	*Carlton Laird	1975, July
Baytown, Tex.	*Fritz Lanham	1972, May
Beaumont, Tex.	*Howard McDaniel (act.)	1975, June
Belleville, Ill.	Charles E. Nichols, N-P	1981, Apr.
Belleville, N.J.	Michael Marotti, D	1979, May
Bellevue, Wash.	*Richard C. Cushing	1977, Oct.
Bellflower, Cal.	*Jean S. Koch	1977, July
Beloit, Wis.	*H. Herbert Holt	1971, Mar.
Berkeley, Cal.	*Elijah B. Rogers	1976, July
Bessemer, Ala.	Ed Porter, D	1978, Sept.
Bethlehem, Pa.	Paul M. Marcincin, D	1982, Jan.
Billings, Mont.	William Fox, N-P	1981, May
Biloxi, Miss.	Jerry O'Keefe, D	1981, July
Binghamton, N.Y.	Alfred J. Libous, D	1981, Dec.
Birmingham, Ala.	David Vann, D	1979, Nov.
Bismarck, N.D.	Robert Heskin, N-P	1978, Apr.
Bloomfield, N.J.	John W. Kinder, R	1980, Dec.
Bloomington, Ill.	*William Vail	1977, Oct.
Bloomington, Ind.	Francis X. McCloskey, D	1979, Dec.
Bloomington, Minn.	*John Pidgeon	1967, Dec.
Boise, Ida.	Dick Eardley, N-P	1981, Dec.
Bossier City, La.	Marvin E. Anding, D	1981, Jan.
Boston, Mass.	Kevin White, D	1979, Dec.
Boulder, Col.	*Robert Westdyke	1976, Aug.
Bowie, Md.	*G.C. Moore	1976, Apr.
Bowling Green, Ky.	*Charles W. Coates	1977, Feb.
Bridgeport, Conn.	John Mandanici, D	1979, Nov.
Bristol, Conn.	Michael Werner, R	1979, Nov.
Brockton, Mass.	David L. Crosby, D	1979, Dec.
Brookfield, Wis.	William Mitchell Jr., N-P	1978, Apr.
Brookline, Mass.	Board of Selectmen	
Brooklyn Center, Minn.	*Gerald G. Splinter	1977, Oct.
Brownsville, Tex.	Ruben Edelstein, N-P	1979, Nov.
Bryan, Tex.	*J. Louis Odle	1974, May
Buffalo, N.Y.	James D. Griffen, D	1981, Dec.
Burbank, Cal.	D. Verner Gibson, R	1979, Apr.
Burlington, Vt.	Gordon H. Paquette, D	1979, Apr.
Calumet City, Ill.	Robert C. Stefaniak, D	1981, Apr.
Cambridge, Mass.	*James L. Sullivan	1974, Apr.
Camden, N.J.	Angelo Errichetti, D	1981, July
Canton, Oh.	Stanley A. Cmich, R	1979, Dec.
Cape Girardeau, Mo.	Howard Tooke, R	1979, Apr.
Carson, Cal.	*E. Frederick Bien	1968, June
Casper, Wyo.	*Kenneth Erickson	1969, Oct.
Cedar Rapids, Ia.	Donald J. Canney, N-P	1979, Dec.
Champaign, Ill.	*V. Eugene Miller	1974, Sept.
Charleston, S.C.	Joseph P. Riley Jr., D	1979, Dec.
Charleston, W. Va.	*John G. Hutchinson, D	1979, May
Charlotte, N.C.	*David A. Burkhalter	1971, May
Charlottesville, Va.	*Cole Hendrix	1971, Jan.
Chattanooga, Tenn.	Charles A. Rose, N-P	1979, May
Chesapeake, Va.	Marian P. Whitehurst, D	1980, June
Chester, Pa.	John Nacrelli, R	1980, Jan.
Cheyenne, Wyo.	Donald Erickson, N-P	1980, Dec.
Chicago, Ill.	Michael A. Bilandic, D	1979, Apr.
Chicago Hts., Ill.	Charles Panici, R	1979, Apr.
Chicopee, Mass.	John Moylan, N-P	1980, Jan.
Chula Vista, Cal.	Will T. Hyde	1981, Apr.
Cicero, Ill.	Christy Berkos	1980, Apr.
Cincinnati, Oh.	Gerald Springer, N-P	1979, Nov.
Clarksville, Tenn.	Charles W. Crow, D	1979, Jan.
Clearwater, Fla.	Gabriel Cazares, N-P	1979, Mar.
Cleveland, Oh.	Dennis J. Kucinich, D	1979, Nov.
Cleveland Hgts., Oh.	*Robert A. Edwards	1975, June
Clifton, N.J.	*William Holster	1957, Jan.
Col. Spgs., Col.	*George H. Fellows	1966, July
Columbia, Mo.	*Terry Novak	1974, Feb.
Columbia, S.C.	*Graydon V. Olive Jr.	1970, Mar.
Columbus, Ga.	Jack P. Mickle, D	1978, Dec.
Columbus, Oh.	Tom Moody, R	1979, Dec.
Commerce, Cal.	Robert Eula, N-P	1980, Mar.
Compton, Cal.	*Allen Parker	1975, Dec.
Concord, Cal.	Richard La Pointe, R	1978, Mar.
Concord, N.H.	*John E. Henchey	1968, Jan.
Coon Rapids, Minn.	*John K. Cottingham	1969, July
Coral Gables, Fla.	*J. Martin Gainer	1975, Jan.
Corpus Christi, Tex.	*R. Marvin Townsend	1968, Jan.
Corvallis, Ore.	*C. Dean Smith	1968, Jan.
Costa Mesa, Cal.	Norma Hertzog, D	1978, Mar
Council Bluffs, Ia.	*M. Don Harmon	1968, Feb
Covington, Ky.	George Wermeling, D	1979, Nov
Cranston, R.I.	James L. Taft Jr., R	1978, Dec
Crystal, Minn.	*John Irving	1964, Jan.
Culver City, Cal.	*Dale Jones	1969, Jun
Cuyahoga Falls, Oh.	Robert Quirk, D	1981, Dec
Dallas, Tex.	Robert S. Folsom, N-P	1979, May
Daly City, Cal.	*David R. Rowe	1969, Aug.
Danbury, Conn.	Donald Boughton, R	1979, Dec.
Danville, Ill.	David S. Palmer, D	1979, Apr.
Danville, Va.	*James W. Lord	1971, Nov
Dayton, Oh.	*James Alloway	1974, Feb.
Daytona Bch., Fla.	*Russell C. Smith	1971, Apr.
Dearborn, Mich.	John O'Reilly, N-P	1982, Jan.
Decatur, Ala.	Bill Dukes, D	1980, Oct.
Decatur, Ill.	*Leslie T. Allen	1972, Sept
Denton, Tex.	Elinor O. Hughes, N-P	1979, Apr.
Denver, Col.	William H. McNichols, D	1979, July
Des Moines, Ia.	Richard E. Olson, R	1980, Jan.
Des Plaines, Ill.	H. H. Volberding Sr., N-P	1981, Apr.
Detroit, Mich.	Coleman A. Young, N-P	1981, Dec
Dotham, Ala.	*Christian P. Morris	1974, Mar.
Downers Grove, Ill.	*James R. Griesemer	1972, Sept
Dubuque, Ia.	*Gilbert D. Chavenelle	1960, July
Duluth, Minn.	Robert Beaudin, D	1979, Dec.
Durham, N.C.	*I. Harding Hughes Jr.	1963, Feb

City	Name	Term
E. Chicago, Ind.	Robert A. Pastrick, D.	1979, Dec.
E. Cleveland, Oh.	*Edwin M. Robinson	1976, Sept.
E. Detroit, Mich.	Allyn Carl Weinert, N-P	1979, Nov.
E. Hartford, Conn.	Richard H. Blackstone, D.	1979, Nov.
E. Lansing, Mich.	*vacant	
E. Orange, N.J.	Thomas H. Cooke, Jr., D.	1981, Dec.
E. Providence, R.I.	*Paul A. Flynn	1972, Oct.
E. St. Louis, Ill.	William Mason, D.	1979, May
Eau Claire, Wis.	*Ray E. Wachs	1970, June
Edina, Minn.	James Van Valkenburg, R.	1981, Jan.
Edison, N.J.	Anthony Yelencsics, N-P	1981, Dec.
El Cajon, Cal.	Robert L. Cornett, N-P	1980, Mar.
Elgin, Ill.	Richard L. Verbic, R.	1979, May
Elizabeth, N.J.	Thomas G. Dunn, D.	1980, Dec.
Elkhart, Ind.	Peter Sarantos, R.	1979, Dec.
Elmhurst, Ill.	*Robert T. Palmer	1953, June
Elmira, N.Y.	*Joseph E. Sartori	1972, June
El Monte, Cal.	*Kenneth Botts	1969, Aug.
El Paso, Tex.	Ray Salazar, D.	1979, Apr.
Elyria, Oh.	Marguerite Bowman, R.	1979, Dec.
Enfield, Conn.	*Robert F. Ledger Jr.	1977, Mar.
Enid, Okla.	Paul Russell, N-P	1979, May
Erie, Pa.	Louis J. Tullio, D.	1981, Dec.
Escondido, Cal.	*Kenneth Lounsbery	1976, Aug.
Euclid, Oh.	Anthony Sustarsic, N-P.	1979, Dec.
Eugene, Ore.	*Charles T. Henry	1975, July
Evanston, Ill.	*Edward A. Martin	1971, Jan.
Evansville, Ind.	Russell Lloyd, R.	1979, Dec.
Everett, Mass.	George R. McCarthy, D.	1979, Dec.
Everett, Wash.	Bill Moore, N-P	1982, Jan.
Fairborn, Oh.	*William Burns	1977, Feb.
Fairfield, Cal.	*B. Gale Wilson	1956, Mar.
Fairfield, Conn.	John J. Sullivan, D.	1979, Nov.
Fair Lawn, N.J.	*Frank Peruggi	1977, July
Fall River, Mass.	Carlton Viveiros, N-P	1980, Jan.
Fayetteville, Ark.	*Donald Grimes	1972, Apr.
Fayetteville, N.C.	Beth Finch, D.	1979, Dec.
Fitchburg, Mass.	David Gilmartin, N-P	1980, Jan.
Flagstaff, Ariz.	Robert Moody, N-P	1978, Apr.
Flint, Mich.	*Peter Kleinpell	1976, Jan.
Florissant, Mo.	James J. Eagan, D.	1979, Apr.
Fond du Lac, Wis.	*Myron J. Medin Jr.	1967, Nov.
Ft. Collins, Col.	*John Arnold	1977, Oct.
Ft. Lauderdale, Fla.	*Richard E. Anderson	1975, July
Ft. Lee, N.J.	*Charles Melchior	1975, Jan.
Ft. Smith, Ark.	Jack Freeze, N-P	1979, Dec.
Ft. Wayne, Ind.	Robert Armstrong, R.	1979, Dec.
Ft. Worth, Tex.	*Rodger Line	1971, Apr.
Fremont, Cal.	*Don Driggs	1967, Jan.
Fresno, Cal.	*Ralph W. Hanley	1973, Sept.
Fullerton, Cal.	*Leslie R. White	1976, July
Gadsden, Ala.	Steve Means, D	1978, Oct.
Gainesville, Fla.	*B. Harold Farmer	1968, Nov.
Galesburg, Ill.	*Thomas B. Herring	1960, Nov.
Galveston, Tex.	John Unbehagen, N-P	1979, May
Gardena, Cal.	*Craig McDowell	1973, Dec.
Garden Grove, Cal.	*Richard R. Powers	1972, Apr.
Garfield Hts., Oh.	Raymond Stachewicz, D.	1979, Dec.
Garland, Tex.	Charles Clack, N-P	1978, Apr.
Gary Ind.	Richard G. Hatcher, D.	1979, Dec.
Gastonia, N.C.	*Gary Hicks	1973, Dec.
Glendale, Ariz.	*S. F. Van De Putte	1960, Aug.
Glendale, Cal.	*J. Keithley	1972, Sept.
Grand Forks, N.D.	Cyril P. O'Neill, D.	1980, Apr.
Gr. Island, Neb.	*Earl Ahlschwede	1977, Mar.
Gr. Prairie, Tex.	Weldon Parkhill, N-P	1978, Apr.
Gr. Rapids, Mich.	*Joseph G. Zainea	1976, Oct.
Granite City, Ill.	Paul Schuler, D.	1978, Apr.
Great Falls, Mont.	*Richard D. Thomas	1973, May
Green Bay, Wis.	Michael Monfils, N-P	1979, Apr.
Greensboro, N.C.	Jim Melvin, N-P	1979, Dec.
Greensville, S.C.	*John J. Dullea	1971, Oct.
Greenwich, Conn.	Ruth L. Sims, D.	1979, Dec.
Groton, Conn.	Donald Sweet, R.	1979, May
Gulfport, Miss.	Jack Barnett, D	1981, July
Hackensack, N.J.	*Joseph J. Squillace	1964, Oct.
Hagerstown, Md.	Varner L. Paddack, R.	1981, Apr.
Hamden, Conn.	Charles Haleach, R.	1979, Nov.
Hamilton, Oh.	Frank Witt	1979, Dec.
Hammond, Ind.	Edward J. Raskowsky, D.	1979, Dec.
Hampton, Va.	*C. E. Johnson	1958, May
Harlingen, Tex.	*W. T. Snyder Jr.	1974, Dec.
Harrisburg, Pa.	Paul Doutrich, R.	1982, Jan.

City	Name	Term
Hartford, Conn.	*James B. Daken	1976, Oct.
Harvey, Ill.	James A. Haines, R	1979, Apr.
Hattiesburg, Miss.	A.L. Gerrard Jr., D.	1981, July
Haverhill, Mass.	George K. Katsaros, N-P	1979, Dec.
Hawthorne, Cal.	*R. Kenneth Jue	1977, Jan.
Hayward, Cal.	Ilene Weinreb, N-P	1978, Apr.
Hempstead, N.Y.	Dalton R. Miller, R.	1981, Apr.
Hialeah, Fla.	Dale Bennett, D.	1979, Dec.
High Point, N.C.	*Cyrus L. Brooks	1976, Aug.
Highland Pk., Ill.	Robert Buhai, N-P.	1979, Apr.
Hoboken, N.J.	Steve Cappiello, D	1981, July
Holyoke, Mass.	Earnest Proulx, D.	1980, Jan.
Hollywood, Fla.	*James Chandler	1976, Nov.
Honolulu, Ha.	Frank F. Fasi, D	1981, Jan.
Hot Springs, Ark.	Tom Ellsworth, N-P	1978, Dec.
Houston, Tex.	Fred Hofheinz, D.	1978, Jan.
Huntington, W. Va.	*Barry R. Evans	1973, Mar.
Huntington Beach, Cal.	*David D. Rowlands	1972, Feb.
Huntsville, Ala.	Joe W. Davis, N-P	1980, Oct.
Hutchinson, Kan.	John Corey, N-P	1978, Apr.
Independence, Mo.	*Lyle Alberg	1968, Sept.
Indianapolis, Ind.	William Hudnut, R	1979, Dec.
Inglewood, Cal.	*Douglas W. Ayres	1968, Apr.
Inkster, Mich.	Terrel LeCesne, N-P	1979, Nov.
Iowa City, Ia.	*Neal Berlin	1975, Mar.
Irving, Tex.	Marvin Randle, N-P	1979, Apr.
Irvington, N.J.	Robert Miller, R.	1978, July
Jackson, Mich.	*S.W. McAllister Jr.	1974, Mar.
Jackson, Miss.	Dale Danks, D.	1981, July
Jackson, Tenn.	Bob Conger, D	1979, July
Jacksonville, Fla.	Hans Tanzler Jr., D	1979, July
Jamestown, N.Y.	Steve Carlson, D.	1979, Dec.
Janesville, Wis.	*Philip L. Deaton	1976, Mar.
Jefferson City, Mo.	Robert Hyder, D.	1979, Apr.
Jersey City, N.J.	Thomas F.X. Smith, D.	1981, July
Johnson City, Tenn.	*William Ricker	1971, Oct.
Johnstown, Pa.	Charles Tomljanovic, D.	1982, Jan.
Joliet, Ill.	*Robert H. Oldland	1977, Aug.
Joplin, Mo.	*James P. Berzina	1977, Mar.
Kalamazoo, Mich.	Francis Hamilton, N-P	1979, Nov.
Kansas City, Kan.	John Reardon, D.	1979, Apr.
Kansas City, Mo.	*Robert A. Kipp	1974, Jan.
Kenosha, Wis.	Paul Saftig, N-P	1980, Apr.
Kettering, Oh.	*John W. Laney	1976, Mar.
Key West, Fla.	*Robert J. Stack	1974, June
Killeen, Tex.	Major E. Blair, N-P	1978, Apr.
Knoxville, Tenn.	Randell L. Tyree, D	1979, Dec.
Kokomo, Ind.	Arthur LaDow, R	1980, Jan.
LaCrosse, Wis.	Patrick Zielke, N-P	1979, Apr.
Lafayette, Ind.	James Riehle, D.	1979, Dec.
Lafayette, La.	Kenneth Bowen, D	1980, June
La Habra, Cal.	*Lee Risner	1970, Nov.
La Mesa, Cal.	*Gayle T. Martin	1975, June
La Mirada, Cal.	*Claude J. Klug	1971, Aug.
Lake Charles, La.	William E. Boyer, D	1981, July
Lakeland, Fla.	*Robert V. Youkey	1960, Jan.
Lakewood, Cal.	*Howard L. Chambers	1976, June
Lakewood, Col.	*Ray Wells	1974, Sept.
Lakewood, Oh.	Robert M. Lawther, R.	1979, Dec.
Lancaster, Pa.	Richard Scott, R.	1982, Jan.
Lansing, Mich.	Gerald Graves, N-P	1981, Dec.
Laredo, Tex.	J.C. Martin Jr., N-P	1978, May
Las Cruces, N.M.	*Kenneth E. Ohler	1977, Aug.
Las Vegas, Nev.	*William E. Adams	1976, Mar.
Lawrence, Kan.	*Buford M. Watson Jr.	1970, Jan.
Lawrence, Mass.	Lawrence LeFebre, N-P	1979, Dec.
Lawton, Okla.	*Robert Metzinger	1977, Jan.
Lexington, Ky.	James Amato, D	1982, Jan.
Lima, Oh.	Harry Moyer, R.	1981, Nov.
Lincoln, Neb.	Helen Boosalis, D	1979, May
Linden, N.J.	John Gregorio, D.	1978, Dec.
Little Rock, Ark.	*Carleton E. McMullin	1973, Nov.
Livermore, Cal.	*William H. Parness	1957, Oct.
Livonia, Mich.	Edward H. McNamara, N-P	1980, Jan.
Lombard, Ill.	Mardyth E. Pollard, N-P	1981, May
Long Beach, Cal.	*John Dever	1977, Jan.
Long Beach, N.Y.	*Laurence P. Farbstein	1976, June
Longview, Tex.	*Harry G. Mosley	1952, July

City	Name	Term
Los Angeles, Cal.	Thomas Bradley, D	1981, June
Louisville, Ky.	William Stansbury, D.	1979, Nov.
Lowell, Mass.	*William Taupier	1975, Oct.
L. Merion, Pa.	*Thomas B. Fulweiler	1968, Jan.
Lubbock, Tex.	*Larry Cunningham	1976, Aug.
Lynchburg, Va.	*David B. Norman	1970, Nov.
Lynn, Mass.	Antonio J. Marino, N-P	1980, Jan.
Lynwood, Cal.	*Edward J. Valliere	1976, Nov.
Macon, Ga.	Buckner Melton, D	1979, Nov.
Madison, Wis.	Paul Soglin, N-P	1979, Apr.
Madison Heights, Mich.	George Suarez, N-P	1979, Apr.
Malden, Mass.	James Conway, D.	1980, Jan.
Manchester, Conn.	*Robert B. Weiss	1966, Jan.
Manchester, N.H.	Charles Stanton, D.	1979, Dec.
Manitowoc, Wis.	Anthony V. Dufek, N-P.	1979, Apr.
Mansfield, Oh.	Richard A. Porter, R.	1979, Dec.
Marion, Ind.	Anthony Maidenberg, D.	1979, Dec.
McKeesport, Pa.	Thomas Fullard, R	1980, Jan.
Medford, Mass.	*James Nicholson	1970, Oct.
Melbourne, Fla.	*Ernest E. Watkins	1963, Oct.
Memphis, Tenn.	Wyeth Chandler, N-P	1979, Dec.
Mentor, Oh.	*Arthur V. Dickard	1969, Sept.
Meridian, Miss.	*Joel W. Forrester	1959, July
Mesa, Ariz.	Wayne Pomeroy, N-P.	1978, June
Mesquite, Tex.	B. J. Smith, N-P	1979, Apr.
Miami, Fla.	*Joseph Grassie	1976, July
Miami Beach, Fla.	*Frank Spence	1972, Nov.
Middletown, Oh.	*Dale F. Helsel	1970, Oct.
Midland, Tex.	Ernest Angelo Jr., N-P	1978, Apr.
Midwest City, Okla.	Marion C. Reed, N-P.	1978, Apr.
Milford, Conn.	Henry A. Povinelli, R	1979, Nov.
Milwaukee, Wis.	Henry W. Maier, D.	1980, Apr.
Minneapolis, Minn.	Albert Hofstede, N-P	1980, Jan.
Minnetonka, Minn.	*Carsten D. Leikvold	1973, Dec.
Minot, N.D.	*vacant	
Mobile, Ala.	Lambert C. Mims, N-P	1978, Sept.
Modesto, Cal.	*Garth Lipsky	1974, Jan.
Moline, Ill.	Lawrence Lorenson, D.	1981, Apr.
Monroe, La.	W. L. Howard, D.	1980, June
Monclair, N.J.	Grant M. Gille, N-P.	1980, May
Montebello, Cal.	*Roy Pederson	1969, Jan.
Monterey Park, Cal.	George Ige, D	1978, Mar.
Montgomery, Ala	Jim Robinson, D.	1979, Nov.
Mt. Prospect, Ill.	*Robert J. Eppley	1971, Aug.
Mt. Vernon, N.Y.	Thomas E. Sharpe, D.	1979, Dec.
Mountain View, Cal.	*Bruce Liedstrand	1976, Aug.
Muncie, Ind	Robert Cunningham, D	1979, Dec.
Mundelein, Ill.	Colin McRae, N-P	1981, Apr.
Muskegon, Mich.	*Paul F. Frederick	1970, June
Muskogee, Okla.	W. Robert Collins, D.	1978, Apr.
Napa, Cal.	*William Bopf	1976, Dec.
Nashua, N.H.	Morris Arel, N-P	1980, Jan.
Nashville, Tenn.	Richard Fulton, D.	1979, Aug.
National City, Cal.	Kile Morgan, D	1978, Mar.
New Bedford, Mass.	John Markey, N-P	1980, Jan.
New Britain, Conn.	William J. McNamara, D.	1979, Nov.
New Brunswick, N.J.	Richard J. Mulligan	1978, Dec.
New Castle, Pa.	Francis J. Rogan, D	1979, Dec.
New Haven, Conn.	Frank Logue, D	1979, Dec.
New Kensington, Pa.	Verle N. Bevan, D	1981, Dec.
New Orleans, La.	Moon Landrieu, D	1978, Apr.
New Rochelle, N.Y.	*C. Samuel Kissinger	1975, Apr.
New York, N.Y.	Edward Koch, D.	1981, Dec.
Newark, N.J.	Kenneth Gibson, D.	1978, July
Newport, R.I.	H. J. Donnelly 3d, N-P.	1979, Nov.
Newport Beach, Cal.	*Robert L. Wynn	1971, Aug.
Newport News, Va.	*Frank Smiley	1976, Oct.
Newton, Mass.	Theodore Mann, R	1981, Dec.
Niagara Falls, N.Y.	*Donald J. O'Hara	1976, May
Niles, Ill.	Nicholas B. Blase, D	1981, Apr.
Norfolk, Va.	*Julian Hirst	1975, Apr.
Norman, Okla.	*James D. Crosby	1976, Oct.
No. Charleston, S.C.	John Bourne, R	1978, June
North Chicago, Ill.	Leo F. Kukla, D	1981, Apr.
No. Little Rock, Ark.	Eddie Powell, D.	1980, Dec.
Norwalk, Cal.	*William H. Kraus	1972, May
Norwalk, Conn.	William A. Collins, D.	1979, Nov.
Norwich, Conn.	*Charles Whitty	1973, June
Novato, Cal.	*Phillip J. Brown	1974, May
Oak Lawn, Ill.	*Richard E. O'Neill	1976, Sept.
Oak Park, Ill.	*Jack Gruber, act.	1976, June
Oak Park, Mich	*James B. Thompson	1970, Aug.

City	Name	Term
Oak Ridge, Tenn.	A. K. Bissell, N-P.	1979, Ju
Oakland, Cal.	*Cecil S. Riley	1972, S
Oceanside, Cal.	*Daniel E. Stone	1975, D
Odessa, Tex.	*Ronald J. Neighbors	1968, N
Ogden, Ut.	*L.D. Hunter	1977, S
Oklahoma City, Okla.	Patience Latting, N-P	1979, A
Omaha, Neb.	Al Veys, D	1981, Ju
Ontario, Cal	Paul Treadway, N-P.	1978, M
Orange, Cal.	Robert Hoyt, N-P	1978, M
Orange, N.J.	Carmine Capone, N-P	1980, Ju
Orlando, Fla.	Carl Langford, N-P.	1980, Oc
Oshkosh, Wis.	*W. O. Frueh	1976, Au
Overland Park, Kan.	Ben Sykes, D	1981, Ap
Owensboro, Ky.	Jack C. Fisher, D.	1980, Ja
Oxnard, Cal.	*Paul E. Wolven	1953, Fe
Pacifica, Cal.	*Donald Weidner	1974, Oc
Palm Springs, Cal.	*Don Blubaugh	1973, Au
Palo Alto, Cal.	*George Sipel	1972, Fe
Parkersburg, W. Va.	Alvin K. Smith, D	1981, De
Parma, Oh	John Petruska, D	1979, De
Pasadena, Cal.	*Donald F. McIntyre	1973, Ju
Pasadena, Tex.	John Ray Harrison, D.	1981, Ma
Passaic, N.J.	Robert Hare, N-P	1981, Ju
Paterson, N.J.	Lawrence Kramer, R.	1978, Ju
Pawtucket, R.I.	Dennis Lynch, D.	1980, Ja
Pekin, Ill.	William L. Waldmeier, D.	1979, Ap
Pensacola, Fla.	*Frank A. Faison	1971, Ap
Peoria, Ill.	Richard E. Carver, R.	1981, Ma
Perth Amboy, N.J.	George J. Otlowski, D	1980, Ju
Petersburg, Va.	Hermanze Fauntleroy Jr., D.	1978, Ju
Philadelphia, Pa.	Frank L. Rizzo	1980, Ja
Phoenix, Ariz.	*Marvin Andrews	1976, Oc
Pico Rivera, Cal	*John Donlevy	1977, Ma
Pine Bluff, Ark.	Charles Moore, D.	1980, Ja
Pittsburgh, Pa.	Richard S. Caliguiri, D.	1981, De
Pittsfield, Mass.	Paul Brindle, N-P	1979, De
Plainfield, N.J.	Paul O'Keefe, R	1982, Ja
Pocatello, Ida.	*Charles W. Moss	1970, Se
Pomona, Cal.	*Jerrold R. Gonce	1973, Oc
Pompano Bch., Fla.	*John Schoeberlein	1975, Oc
Pontiac, Mich.	*vacant	
Port Arthur, Tex.	Bernis Sadler, N-P	1979, Ap
Port Huron, Mich.	*Gerald R. Bouchard	1965, Ju
Portage, Mich.	*Donald Ziemke	1974, Au
Portland, Me.	*A. J. Wilson Jr.	1976, Ma
Portland, Ore.	Neil Goldschmidt, N-P	1979, De
Portsmouth, Oh.	*Barry Feldman	1977, Ja
Portsmouth, Va.	*Robert T. Williams	1975, Ap
Poughkeepsie, N.Y.	John Kennedy, D.	1979, De
Prichard, Ala.	A.J. Cooper Jr.	1980, Oc
Providence, R.I.	Vincent Cianci Jr., R.	1979, Ja
Provo, Ut.	Jim Ferguson, N-P.	1982, Ja
Pueblo, Col.	*Fred E. Weisbroad	1967, Fe
Quincy, Ill.	C. David Nuessen, R.	1981, Ap
Quincy, Mass.	Arthur H. Tobin	1980, Ja
Racine, Wis.	Stephen Olson, N-P.	1981, Ap
Raleigh, N.C.	Isabell Cannon, N-P.	1979, De
Rapid City, S.D.	Arthur La Croix, R.	1979, Ma
Reading, Pa.	Joseph Kuzminski, D	1980, Ja
Redlands, Cal.	Charles G. DeMirjyn, D.	1978, Ap
Redondo Beach, Cal.	David K. Hayward, D.	1981, Ap
Redwood City, Cal.	Marguerite Leipzig, N-P	1980, Ap
Reno, Nev.	*Robin Bogich	1977, Au
Revere, Mass.	William Reinstein, D.	1980, Ja
Richardson, Tex.	Raymond Noah, N-P.	1979, Ap
Richfield, Minn.	*Wayne Burggraaff	1968, De
Richmond, Cal.	*Kenneth Smith	1967, Se
Richmond, Ind.	Clifford Dickman, R.	1979, De
Richmond, Va.	*William J. Leidinger	1972, Ju
Riverside, Cal.	*William F. Cornett	1976, Ja
Roanoke, Va.	*Byron E. Haner	1973, Ja
Rochester, Minn.	Alex Smekta, N-P	1979, Ap
Rochester, N.Y.	*Elisha Freedman	1974, Ja
Rock Hill, S.C.	*Max Holland	1965, Ma
Rock Island, Ill.	*Raymond P. Botch	1961, Fe
Rockford, Ill.	Robert McGaw, D.	1981, Ma
Rockville, Md.	*Larry N. Blick	1972, No
Rome, N.Y.	William A. Valentine, R.	1979, De
Rosemead, Cal.	*Frank Tripepi	1974, Oc
Roseville, Mich.	*B. J. Nardelli	1976, Ap
Roseville, Minn.	*James Andre	1974, Ma
Rosewell, N.M.	Jerry Smith, D	1978, Ma
Royal Oak, Mich.	*William Baldridge	1975, Se

City	Name	Term
Sacramento, Cal.	Phillip Isenberg, D.	1979, Nov.
Saginaw, Mich.	*E. H Potthoff Jr.	1961, July
St. Clair Shores, Mich.	*Donald J. Harm	1962, Jan.
St. Cloud, Minn.	Alcuin Loehr N-P.	1980, Apr.
St. Joseph, Mo.	W. J. Bennett, D.	1978, Apr.
St. Louis, Mo.	James F. Conway, D.	1981, Apr.
St. Louis Pk., Minn.	*Chris Cherches	1968, Oct.
St. Paul, Minn.	George Latimer, D.	1978, June
St. Petersburg, Fla.	Corinne Freeman, N-P.	1979, Apr.
Salem, Mass.	Jean Levesque, D.	1980, Jan.
Salem, Ore.	*Robert S. Moore	1968, Aug.
Salina, Kan.	*Norris D. Olson.	1964, May
Salinas, Cal.	*Robert Christofferson	1972, Dec.
Salt Lake City, Ut.	Ted Wilson, D	1980, Jan.
San Angelo, Tex.	Tom Parrett, N-P.	1978, May
San Antonio, Tex.	Lila Cockrell, N-P.	1979, Apr.
San Bernardino, Cal.	*Marshall Julian	1971, Nov.
San Buenaventura, Cal.	*Edward McCombs.	1970, Feb.
San Diego, Cal.	*Hugh McKinley.	1975, Apr.
San Francisco, Cal.	George Moscone, D.	1980, Jan.
San Jose, Cal.	*Ted Tedesco	1973, Feb.
San Leandro, Cal.	Jack Maltester, D	1978, Apr.
San Mateo, Cal.	*Richard Delong	1976, Sept.
San Rafael, Cal.	*William, J. Bielser	1973, Jan.
Sandusky, Oh.	*Frank Link	1972, Jan.
Santa Ana, Cal.	*Bruce C. Spragg	1972, Sept.
Santa Barbara, Cal.	*Richard Thomas.	1977, Jan.
Santa Cruz, Cal.	*David C. Koester	1962, Oct.
Santa Fe, N.M.	Sam Pick, N-P	1978, Mar.
Santa Maria, Cal.	*Robert Grogan	1963, Jan.
Santa Monica, Cal.	*James D. Williams.	1973, Oct.
Santa Rosa, Cal.	*Kenneth R. Blackman	1970, July
Sarasota, Fla.	*Kenneth Thompson.	1950, Feb.
Savannah, Ga.	*Arthur A. Mendonsa	1971, Sept.
Schenectady, N.Y.	*Wayne V. Chapman	1977, May
Scottsdale, Ariz.	William Jenkins, N-P.	1980, Apr.
Scranton, Pa.	Eugene Hickey, D.	1981, Dec.
Seattle, Wash.	Charles Royer, N-P.	1981, Dec.
Shaker Heights, Oh.	Walter C. Kelley, D.	1979, Dec.
Sheboygan, Wis.	Richard Suscha, R.	1981, Apr.
Shreveport, La.	L. Calhoun Allen Jr., D	1978, Nov.
Simi Valley, Cal.	*Richard Malcolm	1974, May
Sioux City, Ia.	*Gary F. Pokorny	1974, Jan.
Sioux Falls, S.D.	Rick Knobe, R.	1979, May
Skokie, Ill.	Albert J. Smith, R	1981, Apr.
Somerville, Mass.	Thomas F. August.	1980, Jan.
South Bend, Ind.	Peter J. Nemeth, D.	1979, Dec.
So. Gate, Cal.	*Carl Zeise.	1966, Oct.
So. S. F., Cal.	*vacant	
Southfield, Mich.	*Peter Cristiano	1968, July
Southgate, Mich.	*William Valusek.	1972, Feb.
Spartanburg, S.C.	*W. H. Carstarphen	1975, Mar.
Spokane, Wash.	*Glen A. Yake	1977, Aug.
Springfield, Ill.	William C. Telford, N-P	1979, Apr.
Springfield, Mass.	Theodore Dimauro.	1980, Jan.
Springfield, Mo.	*Don. G. Busch.	1971, Oct.
Springfield, Oh.	*Richard T. Bennett	1977, Mar.
Stamford, Conn.	Louis A. Clapes, R	1979, Nov.
Sterling Hts. Mich.	*Leonard Hendricks,	1975, Jan.
Stillwater, Okla.	Jon Patton, N-P	1979, May
Stockton, Cal.	*Gerald Davenport.	1977, Jan.
Stratford, Conn.	*H. B. Ewert	1976, Aug.
Sunnyvale, Cal.	*Lee Ayres.	1977, Mar.
Syracuse, N.Y.	Lee Alexander, D	1981, Dec.
Tacoma, Wash.	*Erling O. Mork	1975, June
Tallahassee, Fla.	*Daniel A. Kleman	1974, Aug.
Tampa, Fla.	William Poe, N-P.	1979, Sept.
Taunton, Mass.	Joseph Amaral, N-P.	1979, Dec.
Taylor, Mich.	Donald L. Zub, N-P	1981, Nov.
Teaneck, N.J.	*Werner H. Schmid.	1959, Mar.
Tempe, Ariz.	William LoPiano, R.	1978, June
Temple, Tex.	William Courtney.	1978, Apr.
Terre Haute, Ind.	William Brighton, D	1979, Dec.
Thousand Oaks, Cal.	*Glenn Kendall	1966
Titusville, Fla.	Robert Telfer Jr., N-P.	1978, Mar.
Toledo, Oh.	*Walter Kane	1977, Mar.
Topeka, Kan.	William McCormick, N-P.	1979, Apr.
Torrance, Cal.	*Edward J. Ferraro	1964, Mar.
Trenton, N.J.	Arthur Holland, N-P.	1978, July
Troy, Mich.	Richard Doyle, N-P	1980, Apr.
Troy, N.Y.	*J. Duncan Barrett	1977, Aug.
Tucson, Ariz.	Lewis Murphy, R.	1979, Dec.
Tulsa, Okla.	Robert La Fortune, R	1978, May
Tuscaloosa, Ala.	Ernest Collins, N-P	1981, Oct.
Tyler, Tex.	Robert M. Nall, N-P.	1978, Apr.

City	Name	Term
Univ City, Mo.	*Victor Ellman	1975, Dec.
Upland, Cal.	George M. Gibson, N-P	1980, Mar.
Upper Arlington, Oh.	*H. W. Hyme.	1968, May
Urbana, Ill.	Jeffrey Markland, R.	1981, May
Utica, N.Y.	Stephen Pawlinga, D	1979, Dec.
Vallejo, Cal.	*Gerald R. Davis.	1975, Mar.
Vancouver, Wash.	*Alan Harvey	1969, May
Ventura, Cal.	*Edward E. McCombs	1970, Mar.
Victoria, Tex.	C.C. Carsner Jr., D.	1979, May
Vineland, N.J.	Patrick R. Fiorilli, N-P.	1980, July
Virginia Beach, Va.	Clarence A. Holland, N-P.	1978, June
Waco, Tex.	*David F. Smith Jr.	1971, Sept.
Walnut Creek, Cal.	James Hazard, R.	1978, Mar.
Waltham, Mass.	Arthur J. Clarke	1980, Jan.
Warren, Mich.	Ted Bates, N-P	1979, Nov.
Warwick, R.I.	Joseph Walsh, D.	1979, Jan.
Wash, D.C.	Walter Washington, D.	1979, Jan.
Waterbury, Conn.	Edward Bergin, D.	1979, Dec.
Waterloo, Ia.	Leo Rooff, N-P	1980, Jan.
Waukegan, Ill.	Mel Morris, D.	1981, Apr.
Waukesha, Wis.	Paul Vrakas, N-P	1978, Apr.
Wauwatosa, Wis.	James A. Benz, N-P.	1980, Apr.
West Allis, Wis.	Jack Barlich, N-P	1980, Apr.
W. Covina, Cal.	*Herman Fast	1976, Aug.
W. Hartford, Conn.	*Richard H. Custer.	1962, Sept.
W. Haven, Conn.	Robert A. Johnson, D.	1979, Dec.
W. New York, N.J.	Anthony DeFino, D.	1979, May
W. Orange, N.J.	William F. Cuozzi, D.	1978, June
W. Palm Beach, Fla.	*Richard Simmons.	1969, Sept.
Westland, Mich.	Thomas F. Taylor, N-P.	1981, Dec.
Westminster, Cal.	*Robert J. Huntley	1967, July
Weymouth, Mass.	Board of Selectmen	
Wheaton, Ill.	Ralph Barger, R.	1979, Apr.
Wheeling, W. Va.	John Fahey, N-P.	1979, June
White Plains, N.Y.	Alfred Del Vecchio, R.	1980, Jan.
Wichita, Kan.	*E. H. Denton.	1976, July
Wichita Falls, Tex.	J. C. Boyd Jr., N-P	1978, Apr.
Wilkes-Barre, Pa.	Walter Lisman, D	1979, Dec.
Williamsport, Pa.	Daniel Kirby, D.	1980, Jan.
Wilmington, Del	William T. McLaughlin, D	1981, Jan.
Wilmington, N.C.	Ben Halderman, N-P.	1979, Dec.
Winston-Salem, N.C.	*Orville W. Powell	1972, Nov.
Woonsocket, R.I.	Gerard Bouley, D	1979, Nov.
Worcestor, Mass.	*Francis J. McGrath.	1951, May
Wyandotte, Mich.	*William L. Cook, N-P.	1979, Apr.
Wyoming, Mich.	*vacant	
Yakima, Wash.	*George Eastman.	1977, Feb.
Yonkers, N.Y.	*Vincent Castaldo.	1976, Feb.
York, Pa.	Elizabeth Marshall, D.	1982, Jan.
Youngstown, Oh.	J. Philip Richley, D	1979, Dec.
Zanesville, Oh.	*Frank Patrizio.	1974, Sept.

Canadian Cities

City	Name	Term
Calgary, Alta.	Rod Sykes	1977, Oct.
Dartmouth, N.S.	D.P. Brownlow	1978, Oct.
Edmonton, Alta.	T. J. Cavanagh.	1977, Oct.
Guelph, Ont.	N. Jary	1978, Dec.
Halifax, N.S.	Edmund L. Morris.	1977, Oct.
Hamilton, Ont.	Jack MacDonald	1978, Dec.
Hull, Que.	Gilles Rocheleau.	1979, Nov.
Kingston, Ont.	Ken Keyes	1978, Dec.
Kitchener, Ont.	Morley Rosenberg	1978, Dec.
Lachine, Que.	Guy Descary	1977, Nov.
La Salle, Que.	Gerald Raymond.	1979, Nov.
Laval, Que.	Lucien Paliement	1977, Nov.
London, Ont.	Mrs. Jane Bigelow.	1978, Dec.
Moncton, N.B.	G.D. Wheeler	1980, June
Montreal, Que.	Jean Drapeau	1978, Nov.
Oshawa, Ont.	J. H. Potticary.	1978, Dec.
Ottawa, Ont.	Lorry Greenberg	1978, Dec.
Peterborough, Ont.	Cameron Wasson	1978, Dec.
Quebec, Que.	J. Gilles Lamontagne	1977, Nov.
Regina, Sask.	Henry H.P. Baker	1979, Oct.
St. John, N.B.	S. Davis	1980, June
Saskatoon, Sask.	C. Wright	1979, Oct.
Sault Ste. Marie, Ont.	Nicholas Trbovich	1978, Dec.
Sherbrooke, Que.	Jacques O'Bready	1977, Nov.
Sudbury, Ont.	J. Gordon	1978, Dec.
Toronto, Ont.	David Crombie	1978, Dec.
Vancouver, B.C.	Jack Volrich	1978, Nov.
Victoria, B.C.	M. Young	1978, Nov.
Waterloo, Ont.	H. A. Epp.	1978, Dec.
Windsor, Ont.	Bert Weeks	1978, Dec.
Winnipeg, Man.	Stephen Juba	1977, Oct.

Laws Passed During 95th Congress, First Session, 1977

The 95th Congress convened its First Session Jan. 4, 1977, amid heavy pressure from congressmen and public opinion to tighten ethical standards and improve congressional performance.

In the House, committee quorum rules and floor procedures were changed (Jan. 4) to expedite legislation. In the Senate, the number of standing committees was cut sharply, and senators were limited to 11 memberships each on committees and sub-committees (Feb. 4).

The House approved an ethics code (Mar. 2), which required extensive financial disclosures, limited outside earnings to 15% of a representative's salary ($8,625) per year, banned unofficial office accounts, and forbade travel abroad at government expense by "lame duck" congressmen. Official office allowances were raised to $7,000 from $2,000.

The new Senate ethics code (Apr. 1) contained essentially the same provisions, but also provided for periodic audits of members' financial disclosures. It also forbade a senator from serving as a member of the board of a private company unless he had been on the board for at least 2 years prior to election.

Proponents of the income limit cited the new congressional pay raise from $44,625 to $57,500 (effective Feb. 20) as sufficient to cover a congressman's needs. Congress later turned down, for itself and other federal officials, a scheduled cost of living increase which would have added $3,500 to congressmen's pay.

Bills passed and signed and other major actions during the First Session included:

Rhodesian Chrome. Banned the import of Rhodesian chrome, bringing the U.S. into compliance with a 1966 UN resolution (signed Mar. 18). An earlier ban had been rescinded in 1971.

Common Site Picketing. House defeated (217-205) a bill granting construction workers the right to picket an entire building site even if they were striking against only one sub-contractor (Mar. 23). A similar bill, passed in 1974, was vetoed by Pres. Ford.

Congressional Pay. Required recorded votes in both houses on congressional pay raise recommendations (signed Apr. 4). The previous procedure made a raise automatic upon the president's recommendation unless one house rejected it within 30 days.

Government Reorganization. Authorized the president to reorganize the government (signed Apr. 6). The President would be able to abolish bureaucracies (except cabinet-level departments and independent agencies) or reorganize them unless the proposed change was disapproved by Congress within 60 days of its formal proposal. Similar powers were granted presidents from 1949 to 1973, but had been allowed to lapse under Pres. Nixon.

Drought, Unemployment

Drought Relief. Authorized $100 million for emergency drought relief in Western and Plains states (signed Apr. 7). Another $225 million was authorized to subsidize water supply projects (signed May 23).

Unemployment Benefits. Extended supplemental unemployment benefits through Jan. 31, 1978, to those who had exhausted regular benefits (signed Apr. 12).

Supplemental Funds. Appropriated $28.9 billion in supplemental funds for fiscal 1977, the largest supplemental funding bill since World War II (signed May 4).

Public Works. Authorized $4 billion through fiscal 1978 to fund public works projects. States with unemployment of 6.5% or more would receive 35% of the funds, while 65% would be allocated to all states on the basis of the actual number of unemployed (signed May 13).

Economic Stimulus. Appropriated $20.1 billion in fiscal 1977 to fund public works, additional public service jobs in state and local governments, youth training and job programs, and other anti-recessio and unemployment measures (signed May 13).

Tax Cuts. Set standard deductions for the 1977 ta year at $2,200 for single and $3,200 for married pe sons; extended the tax credit of $35 through 1978; e tended the earned income credit and corporate ta reductions through 1978; and granted businesses $2,000 tax credit for each additional employee hire over a "normal" 2% increase in employees up to maximum of $100,000 (signed May 23).

Boycott of Israel. Banned participation by U. companies in the Arab boycott of trade with Isra and with companies doing business with Isra (signed June 22).

Weapons Procurement. Authorized $36.1 billio for weapons procurement, research, and develo ment, for civil defense in fiscal 1978 (signed June 30

Strip Mining. Required strip miners to resto stripped land to its approximate original contou and established a tax on coal to reclaim land prev ously damaged by coal mining (signed Aug. 3).

SBA Funds. Authorized $2.96 billion in Small Bus ness Administration funds for fiscal 1978 and 197 Also allowed the SBA to make economic injury loa in areas of exceptional natural conditions, econom dislocation, or natural disaster even if there is no of cial "disaster area" declaration (signed Aug. 4).

Foreign Aid

Foreign Military Aid. Authorized $3.2 billion foreign military aid in fiscal 1978, nearly two-thir of it for the Middle East. Barred aid to Argenti (signed Aug. 4).

Foreign Economic Aid. Authorized $1.6 billion foreign economic aid for fiscal 1978, including $5 million in food and nutrition projects and $252 m lion in support of international organizations (sign Aug. 4).

Youth Jobs. Authorized several new programs, i cluding a Young Adult Conservation Corps, to he place young people in jobs (signed Aug. 5).

Water Projects, Energy Research, Neutron Bom Appropriated $10.4 billion for public works, inclu ing 9 of 18 water projects Carter had tried to halt; f the Energy Research and Development Agency (billion); and for the development of the neutr bomb (signed Aug. 8).

Clean Air. Delayed new auto emission standar for 2 years, retaining the 1977 standards until t 1980 model year, and set restrictions on new pol tion sources (signed Aug. 8).

Agriculture Funds. Appropriated $12.7 billion f various agriculture department programs in fis 1978, including $5.6 billion for the food stamp pr gram (signed Aug. 12).

Fiscal 1978 Budget Levels. Set upper limit $458.25 billion on outlays against estimated revenu of $397 billion for a deficit of $61.25 billion (clear Sept. 15). Figures based on an estimated 4.8% grow in real GNP and 6.5% unemployment. Outlay limit stricts only Congress.

Farm Support. Keyed farm support target prices production costs and thus raised farm suppo (signed Sept. 29).

Veterans' Benefits. Denied benefits to veter whose discharges have been upgraded to "gener unless such veterans go through another review pr ess to determine if their military conduct had be consistent with historical standards for honora discharges (signed Oct. 8).

Housing. Authorized $14.7 billion housing p gram, including additional rent subsidies and panded community development progran especially in older cities of the Northeast and Mid West (signed Oct. 12).

Minimum Wage. Raised minimum wage from $2 to $2.65 in 1978, to $2.90 in 1979, to $3.10 in 1980, a to $3.35 in 1981 (signed Nov. 1).

Major Decisions of the U.S. Supreme Court, 1976-77

Among notable actions in 1976-77, the Supreme Court:

Let stand, by a 4-4 vote, a U.S. Court of Appeals decision that a company in Berea, Ky. had violated the Civil Rights Act of 1964 when it discharged an employee who refused, on religious grounds, to work on Saturday (Nov. 2, 1976).

Upheld closed primary elections by refusing to review a decision by a Federal court in Connecticut that permitted the exclusion from primary elections of voters not affiliated with either major political party (Dec. 6, 1976).

Ruled 6-3 that exclusion of pregnancy from an employer's program of disability benefits is not necessarily a violation of the Civil Rights Act of 1964 (Dec. 7, 1976).

Ruled unanimously that divorced women can, under the current Social Security law, be excluded from a Social Security "wife's insurance benefit" program for mothers caring for dependent children (Dec. 13, 1976).

By a vote of 6-3, vacated a ruling by a federal appeals court upholding a desegregation plan for Indianapolis public schools, under which black children from the city were to be bused to schools in suburban districts. The court directed the lower court to decide whether there had been discriminatory "intent" (Jan. 25).

Decided, 6-3, that police may ask a suspect to appear at a station house and, if the appearance is voluntary, may question the suspect about the case without the usual Miranda warning (Jan. 25).

Ruled unanimously that the federal government has the authority to limit the quantity of pollutants that factories may dump in the nation's waterways (Feb. 23).

Widowers' Rights

Decided, 5-4, that the provision of the Social Security Act that made it more difficult for widowers than for widows to collect survivors benefits, was unconstitutional sex discrimination (Mar. 2).

By a vote of 7-1, decided that a New York State reapportionment plan may use racial quotas in some instances to insure that certain legislative districts have non-white majorities (Mar. 1).

Ruled that material concerning juvenile defendants that is revealed in open court may be published in the media. The decision reversed a ruling by the Oklahoma Supreme Court (Mar. 7).

Upheld, unanimously, a 5% tax levied by Mississippi on interstate businesses operating within the state. The Court maintained that the operator made use of state services and was liable to taxes necessary to support these services (Mar. 7).

Decided 5-4 that spanking of schoolchildren by teachers or other school officials does not violate constitutional restrictions against cruel and unusual punishment (Apr. 19).

Ruled 6-3 that state prisoners who want to challenge the fairness of their trials must be provided with adequate legal help in doing so, though states need not provide a lawyer (Apr. 28).

Ruled 7-2 that testimony given by a grand jury witness suspected of wrongdoing could be used against him in a later prosecution even though he had not been warned that he was a potential defendant (May 3).

Ruled unanimously that state and local governments can enter into "agency shop" agreements with labor unions under which a union is the exclusive agent for employees and all employees must contribute to the union (May 23).

Ruled 5-4 that individuals are subject to federal controls on sending obscenity through the mail even though the state where they are acting has more permissive standards (May 23).

Decided 7-2 that seniority systems that perpetuate the effects of racial discrimination that occurred before 1965, are not necessarily illegal, as long as there is no intent to discriminate (May 31).

Ruled 8-0 that states may refuse to pay unemployment benefits to a worker who is laid off because of a strike against his employer, whether or not the worker is participating in the strike himself (May 31).

In a 6-3 vote, ruled that customs inspectors may open mail entering the U.S. if there is "reasonable cause to suspect" that the envelopes contain narcotics or other contraband (June 6).

Ruled 5-4 that the kind of advertising and promotion given sexually-oriented motion pictures can properly affect a jury's judgement of whether the films themselves are obscene (June 6).

Death Penalty Restriction

Ruled 5-4 that states may not make the death penalty mandatory and automatic for persons convicted of murdering police officers (June 6).

Ruled 7-2 that it is unconstitutional for states to insist that nonprescription contraceptives be sold only in drug stores or by physicians, or to prohibit advertising of contraceptives; states may not forbid persons under age 16 to get nonprescription contraceptives (June 9).

Ruled 7-2 that an employer need not arrange Saturdays off for employees who celebrate their Sabbath on Saturday if to do so the employer would incur such costs as overtime pay for replacements (June 16).

Held 6-3 that the Constitution's double-jeopardy clause forbids a trial for an offense if the defendant has already been convicted of another, less serious, charge growing out of the same incident (June 16).

Ruled 7-2 that eyewitness identification is admissible even when the initial identification was obtained by police in questionable fashion (June 16).

Upheld by a 6-3 vote a death sentence imposed under Florida's new death penalty law for murders committed before the law was in effect; a different death penalty law then in effect was later ruled unconstitutional (June 17).

Held 5-4 that states may deny welfare benefits to children of fathers who are dismissed for misconduct, go on strike, or quit work (June 20).

Ruled 6-3 that states are not required by the Constitution or federal law to spend Medicaid funds for elective abortions (June 20).

Lawyers Can Advertise

Declared unconstitutional, by a 5-4 vote, an Arizona state bar rule that prohibited attorneys from advertising their fees for routine legal services (June 27).

Ruled unanimously that federal courts in desegregation cases may order school districts to provide remedial education to help repair the effects of illegal segregation (June 27).

Held 8-1 that employment requirements for height and weight discriminate illegally against women when employers fail to demonstrate that the tests have some relation to ability to handle the job (June 27).

Overturned a Georgia law providing the death penalty for rapists when the victim was an adult (June 29).

Let stand two lower court rulings which allowed local school officials in New Jersey and Washington State to dismiss teachers because they were admitted homosexuals (Oct. 3).

Let stand a decision allowing the Chicago police force to implement a program in which 40% of promotions were reserved for blacks and Hispanics (Oct. 3).

Let stand a lower court ruling that New Jersey could pay welfare benefits to families of striking workers (Oct. 3).

Refused to overturn a pollution plan mandated by the Environmental Protection Agency that would, in stages, sharply restrict automobile traffic in Manhattan (Oct. 17).

Using the Consumer Price Index

To measure the impact of inflation, the indispensable tool is the Consumer Price Index (CPI) published monthly by the Bureau of Labor Statistics. The index has been specifically designed to apply to a worker family's pattern of purchases. Unless your own budget is markedly different from this norm, you should be able to employ the CPI to interpret your own affairs. The index is reported each month by most of the news media, often specifically for your own city, and what follows tells, step by step, how to employ the figures to analyze your own financial affairs.

The CPI emerges each month as a single number. In June 1977 it stood at 181.8, meaning that all the goods and services it measured cost 81.8% more that month than they did in the base year 1967. It can be considered this way: the 1967 value was 100.0%; by June 1977 another 81.8% had been added to living costs. The total comes to 181.8, the term "index" having the same sense as percent, merely omitting the percent sign.

The change in the price level for consumer good and services can be calculated by comparing the CP readings in one period against another. The June 1977 CPI of 181.8 may be compared to the June reading for 1976 of 170.1. Dividing 181.8 by 170.1, the excess over 1 is the percentage increase over the 12 month period: in this case, 6.88%. A similar year-to year comparison may be made each month — indeed these percentage changes often figure in the news releases when the month's CPI is announced.

We determined above that the CPI increased b 6.88% between June 1976 and June 1977. Did your in come do the same? To make the comparison yo might dig out your paycheck stubs for the sam months and follow the arithmetic below.

The comparison can be made in terms of your bas

Average Consumer Price Indexes

Source: Bureau of Labor Statistics, U. S. Labor Department

The Consumer Price Index measures the average change in prices of goods and services purchased by urban wage-earner an clerical-worker families and single workers living alone. Data for 56 large, medium size, and small cities are combined for the all-cit average.

(1967 — 100) Year and month	All items	Food	Housing: Total	Housing: Rent	Housing: Gas and electricity	Housing: Fuel and utilities	Housing: Household furnishings & operation	Apparel and upkeep	Transportation	Medical care	Personal care	Reading and recreation	Other goods and services
1970	116.3	114.9	118.9	110.1	107.3	107.6	113.4	116.1	112.7	120.6	113.2	113.4	116
1971	121.3	118.4	124.3	115.2	114.7	115.1	118.1	119.8	118.6	128.4	116.8	119.3	120
1972	125.3	123.5	129.2	119.2	120.5	120.1	121.0	122.3	119.9	132.5	119.8	122.8	125
1973	133.1	141.4	135.0	124.2	126.4	126.9	124.9	126.8	123.8	137.7	125.2	125.9	129
1974	147.7	161.7	150.6	130.6	145.8	150.2	140.5	136.2	137.7	150.5	137.3	133.8	137
1975	161.2	175.4	166.8	137.3	169.6	167.8	158.1	142.3	150.6	168.6	150.7	144.4	147
1976	170.5	180.8	177.2	144.7	189.0	182.7	168.5	147.6	165.5	184.7	160.5	151.2	153
1977, Jan.	175.3	183.4	183.1	149.5	204.2	194.8	172.6	150.0	172.1	194.1	166.2	154.9	156
Feb.	177.1	187.7	184.3	150.2	205.4	196.4	173.6	150.8	173.3	195.8	166.7	155.5	156
Mar.	178.2	188.6	185.5	150.8	208.5	198.5	174.6	151.7	174.8	197.6	167.3	155.8	157
Apr.	179.6	190.9	186.7	151.6	209.8	199.4	175.4	152.3	176.8	199.1	168.4	156.0	157
May	180.6	191.7	187.6	152.2	210.9	200.2	175.9	153.4	178.2	200.5	169.5	156.8	158
June	181.8	193.6	189.0	152.9	213.0	201.8	177.1	153.9	179.2	201.8	170.6	157.6	158
July	182.6	194.6	190.5	153.6	216.0	203.5	177.4	153.4	179.3	203.5	171.3	157.7	159

Indexes of Retail Prices of Foods

Details of "Food" column in table above.

Year and month	All food	Food away from home	Food prepared at home: Food at home	Cereals, bakery	Beef, veal	Pork	Other meats	Poultry	Fish	Dairy products	Fruits, vegetables	Other foods	Nonalcoholic beverages
1971	118.4	126.1	116.4	113.9	124.9	105.0	115.6	109.0	130.2	115.3	119.1	115.9	121
1972	123.5	131.1	121.6	114.7	136.6	121.6	124.0	110.4	141.9	117.1	125.0	116.7	121
1973	141.4	141.4	141.4	127.7	161.1	161.7	154.4	154.8	162.8	127.9	142.5	130.3	130
1974	161.7	159.4	162.4	166.1	168.5	161.0	159.2	146.9	187.7	151.9	165.8	162.8	155
1975	175.4	174.3	175.8	184.8	170.0	196.9	168.5	162.4	203.3	156.6	171.0	184.8	178
1976	180.8	196.1	179.5	180.6	164.5	199.5	178.4	155.7	227.3	169.3	175.3	189.9	214
1977 Jan.	183.4	192.2	181.2	179.9	162.1	180.1	172.6	144.5	258.0	171.3	177.6	206.1	257
Feb.	187.7	193.6	186.2	180.0	161.5	185.1	173.6	162.9	241.1	171.1	194.7	213.0	273
Mar.	188.6	195.2	186.9	181.3	160.7	184.1	174.5	158.3	241.5	171.2	196.8	213.2	286
Apr.	190.9	197.5	189.3	182.6	161.2	181.7	173.7	157.7	244.0	171.4	203.0	219.1	31
May	191.7	199.3	189.8	182.5	162.8	182.0	175.1	157.6	248.8	173.1	195.1	224.6	334
June	193.6	200.6	191.9	182.8	164.8	187.0	178.0	157.6	250.8	174.3	196.8	228.0	348
July	194.6	201.7	192.8	183.3	164.2	192.0	179.0	161.2	254.3	174.1	194.1	231.4	34

ıy — your basic rate of earnings — or in terms of hat you actually take home after standard deducons. Both gross and takehome comparisons are ely to be of interest to you, but take care to comre equals. Overtime pay should be omitted. When aling with takehome pay, look out for changes in ductions which are unrelated to inflation, such as ded exemptions, credit union deductions, payroll nds, and the like.

Measuring Your Paycheck

A. To compare the year-to-year earnings in percent rm, divide your June 1977 earnings by your June 76 earnings and express the result as a percent. If u earned the wage of the average U.S. worker, for ample, your paycheck showed $175.81 per week in ne 1976 as compared with 189.64 in June of 1977, increase of 7.87%. Since prices rose by 6.88% durg the same 12-month period, the average worker ade a slight gain in real income that year.

B. Another way of dealing with the same figures kes a dollar form. For this calculation, assume your age in June 1976 was 175.81 per week. Prices ineased by 6.88%, according to the CPI. To match that ice, your wage should have gone to 187.91 ($175.81 nes 1.0688) by June of 1977. If your earnings did not up by that amount, you lost money to inflation, hile the average worker gained.

Single readings on a weekly or monthly basis could misleading; the inflation rate changes rapidly, rnings are affected by special situations unrelated inflation. Repeated readings over a period of months provide a broader look. For this purpose you may consider an entire year as the appropriate period for measuring the total impact of inflation on your earnings.

The CPI provides us with an index of 161.2 for the year 1975 as a whole and 170.5 for 1976. Dividing 170.5 by 161.2, we get 1.05769; the excess over 1 shows price increases of 5.77% over the year. If you compare your earnings for the same years by the methods we have described, your shortfall due to or gain over inflation can be ascertained in percent or dollar form. You can readily determine your annual earnings on your income tax return or from your W-2 statements.

The figures cited above measure an individual's progress as compared with the rate of inflation, as if matching the rate were the sole target. Nothing is said about your personal capacity for advancement. Figuring your loss to inflation is only the first step of the reckoning, a way to true up your income figures so you can check your real progress and advancement.

Savings

Less visible to the average individual than the loss on earnings is the attrition inflation brings to his savings. Narrowly considered, savings are the funds salted away in some savings institution. Although such funds earn interest, it is clear that during double-digit inflation of 10% to 12%, interest rates of 5% to 8% cause a real loss in the value of the savings.

The apparent loss in the value of savings — the

Consumer Price Indexes by Cities

(1967=100)

City	Annual Average All Items 1975	All Items 1976	Food 1975	Food 1976
U.S. city average	161.2	170.5	175.4	180.8
Atlanta, Ga.	161.7	169.2	181.8	185.8
Baltimore, Md.	165.2	173.9	178.2	184.3
Boston, Mass.	162.1	174.5	175.2	183.1
Buffalo, N.Y.	161.8	170.6	173.6	178.6
Chicago, Ill.	157.6	165.1	175.1	180.1
Cincinnati, Oh.	160.3	170.1	177.4	184.0
Cleveland, Oh.	160.9	169.0	175.8	185.9
Dallas, Tex.	158.2	167.7	172.5	176.9
Detroit, Mich.	160.3	168.8	171.6	175.6
Honolulu, Ha.	154.4	162.8	176.7	183.0
Houston, Tex.	164.9	177.3	181.2	187.6
Kansas City, Mo.	157.9	166.5	177.8	180.8
s Angeles, Cal.	157.6	168.0	170.1	173.5
lwaukee, Wis.	157.0	167.1	171.9	180.0
nneapolis, Minn.	160.9	170.9	178.9	186.6
w York, N.Y.	166.6	176.3	179.6	185.4
iladelphia, Pa.	164.2	172.4	179.6	186.2
ttsburgh, Pa.	160.0	168.3	177.4	181.1
rtland, Ore.	156.5	167.0	168.4	177.3
Louis, Mo.	156.1	165.1	174.3	180.5
n Diego, Cal.	160.8	170.7	173.9	179.2
n Francisco, Cal.	159.1	168.0	171.2	173.9
ranton, Pa.	164.7	170.9	172.9	178.4
attle, Wash.	155.8	164.5	169.6	175.0
ashington, D.C.	161.6	171.2	180.7	186.5

Latest Month, 1977[1]

City	All Items (Month)	Food (July)
S. city average	182.6 (7)	194.6
lanta, Ga.	179.1 (6)	197.3
ltimore, Md.	185.8 (6)	199.2
ston, Mass.	185.0 (7)	194.4
ffalo, N.Y.	181.3 (5)	190.9
icago, Ill.	176.4 (7)	192.9
ncinnati, Oh.	182.3 (6)	199.1
eveland, Oh.	179.9 (5)	192.5
llas, Tex.	179.4 (5)	193.1
etroit, Mich.	182.5 (7)	189.3
nolulu, Ha.	170.5 (6)	194.2
uston, Tex.	191.6 (7)	201.0
nsas City, Mo.	179.0 (6)	196.7
Los Angeles, Cal.	180.4(7)	187.6
Milwaukee, Wis.	178.0(5)	193.0
Minneapolis, Minn.	184.5(7)	200.2
New York, N.Y.	186.4(7)	197.8
Philadelphia, Pa.	184.8(7)	200.5
Pittsburgh, Pa.	180.6(7)	196.0
Portland, Ore.	181.5(7)	191.8
St. Louis, Mo.	177.4(6)	195.6
San Diego, Cal.	180.6(5)	190.4
San Francisco, Cal.	180.7(6)	[2]190.0
Scranton, Pa.	179.0(5)	187.8
Seattle, Wash.	176.2(5)	190.2
Washington, D.C.	182.2(5)	201.1

All items indexes are computed monthly in 5 areas and on a rotating cycle in other areas: (7) =July, (6)=June, =May. (2) In May.

amount of goods and services the funds will ultimately buy — should be considered in terms of a broadened view of savings. In addition to funds placed at interest, savings would include the paid-u value of a home or insurance policy and the value savings bonds.

Purchasing Power of the Dollar

Source: Bureau of Labor Statistics, U.S. Labor Department

1967=$1.00

Beginning 1961, wholesale prices include data for Alaska and Hawaii; and, beginning 1964, consumer prices include them. O tained by dividing the average price index for 1967 base period (100.0) by the price index for given period and expressing the result dollars and cents.

Year	Monthly average as measured by— Wholesale prices	Consumer prices	Year	Monthly average as measured by— Wholesale prices	Con sum price
1940	$2.469	$2.381	1966	$1.002	$1.02
1950	1.222	1.387	1967	1.000	1.00
1955	1.139	1.247	1968	.976	.96
1957	1.072	1.186	1969	.939	.91
1958	1.057	1.155	1970	.906	.86
1959	1.055	1.145	1971	.878	.82
1960	1.054	1.127	1972	.840	.79
1961	1.058	1.116	1973	.744	.75
1962	1.055	1.104	1974	.625	.67
1963	1.058	1.091	1975	.572	.62
1964	1.056	1.076	1976	.546	.58
1965	1.035	1.058	1977, July	.513	.54

Average Weekly Earnings of Production Workers[1]

Source: Bureau of Labor Statistics, U.S. Labor Department

Year and month	Private nonagricultural workers						Manufacturing workers					
	Gross average weekly earnings		Spendable average weekly earnings[2]				Gross average weekly earnings		Spendable average weekly earnings[2]			
			Worker with no dependents		Worker with 3 dependents				Worker with no dependents		Worker with 3 dependents	
	Current dollars	1967 dollars	Current dollars	1967 dollars	Current dollars	1967 dollars	Current dollars	1967 dollars	Current dollars	1967 dollars	Current dollars	1967 dolla
1971	127.28	104.93	103.78	85.56	112.41	92.67	142.44	117.43	114.97	94.78	124.24	102.4
1972	136.16	108.67	111.65	89.11	121.09	96.64	154.69	123.46	125.32	100.02	135.56	108.1
1973	145.43	109.26	117.54	88.31	127.41	95.73	165.65	124.46	132.00	99.17	142.90	107.3
1974	154.45	104.57	124.14	84.05	134.37	90.97	176.00	119.16	139.80	94.52	150.94	102.1
1975	163.89	101.67	132.74	82.34	145.93	90.53	189.51	117.56	150.71	93.49	165.33	102.5
1976	176.29	103.40	145.90	84.40	156.50	91.79	207.60	121.76	166.55	97.68	180.03	105.5
1977 Jan.	179.48	102.38	146.20	83.40	158.90	90.64	212.94	121.47	170.54	97.28	184.04	104.9
Feb.	182.73	103.18	148.55	83.88	161.34	91.10	216.66	122.34	173.33	97.87	186.84	105.5
Mar.	183.96	103.23	149.44	83.86	162.27	91.06	220.30	123.63	176.05	98.79	189.58	106.3
April	185.40	103.23	150.48	83.79	163.35	90.95	220.80	122.94	176.42	98.23	189.95	105.7
May	187.36	103.74	151.89	84.10	164.82	91.26	224.07	124.07	178.86	99.04	192.41	106.5
June (p)	189.64	104.31	157.17	86.45	173.21	95.28	228.48	125.68	184.52	101.50	202.61	111.4
July (p)	190.90	104.55	158.07	86.57	174.20	95.40	225.76	123.64	182.62	100.01	200.57	109.8

(1) Data relate to production workers in mining and manufacturing; to construction workers in contract construction; and to nonsu pervisory workers in transportation and public utilities; wholesale and retail trade; finance, insurance, and real estate; and services. (Spendable average weekly earnings are based on gross average weekly earnings less the estimated amount of the worker's Federa social security, and income taxes. (p)—preliminary.

Annual Percent Change in Productivity and Related Data, 1966-76

Source: Bureau of Labor Statistics, U.S. Labor Department

Item	1966	1967	1968	1969	1970	1971	1972	1973	1974	1975	197
Private business sector:											
Output per hour of all persons	3.2	2.3	3.3	0.3	0.7	3.2	2.9	1.9	2.7	1.8	4.
Real compensation per hour	4.0	2.7	3.3	1.5	1.1	2.2	2.3	1.8	−1.4	0.5	3.
Unit labor cost	3.7	3.3	4.1	6.6	6.4	3.2	2.7	6.2	12.4	7.7	4.
Unit nonlabor payments	2.2	2.1	3.6	1.0	1.3	6.9	5.4	5.0	4.3	16.1	5.
Implicit price deflator	3.2	2.9	3.9	4.7	4.7	4.4	3.6	5.8	9.8	10.3	4.
Nonfarm business sector:											
Output per hour of all persons	2.5	1.9	3.2	−0.2	0.2	2.9	3.0	1.7	2.8	1.6	4.
Real compensation per hour	3.1	2.9	3.0	1.0	0.7	2.2	2.4	1.4	−1.4	0.5	2.
Unit labor cost	3.4	3.8	3.9	6.6	6.5	3.5	2.7	6.0	12.6	7.9	4.
Unit nonlabor payments	2.0	2.3	4.0	0.4	1.7	6.8	4.0	0.3	5.9	17.8	6.
Implicit price deflator	2.9	3.3	4.0	4.5	4.9	4.5	3.1	4.1	10.5	10.9	5.
Manufacturing:											
Output per hour of all persons	1.6	0.3	3.6	1.2	−0.4	5.6	5.2	2.9	−5.5	3.1	6.
Real compensation per hour	1.7	2.2	2.7	1.1	0.8	2.2	2.2	1.0	1.1	1.9	2.
Unit labor cost	3.1	4.8	3.3	5.2	7.2	1.0	0.4	4.3	16.1	7.8	1.
Unit nonlabor payments	−0.8	−2.4	3.9	−4.4	−3.2	9.0	2.5	−1.0	0.7	20.7	10.
Implicit price deflator	1.8	2.5	3.5	2.3	4.2	3.1	1.0	2.8	11.5	11.0	4.

Federal Individual Income Tax

Source: Internal Revenue Service, U.S. Treasury Department.

Who Must File

Every individual under 65 years of age who resided the United States and had a gross income of $2,950 more during the year must file a federal income x return. Anyone 65 or older on the last day of the x year is not required to file a return unless he had oss income of $3,700 or more during the year. A arried couple both 65 or older, need not file unless eir gross income exceeds $6,200.

A taxpayer with gross income of less than $2,950 r less than $3,700 if 65 or older) should file a return claim the refund of any taxes withheld, even if he listed as a dependent by another taxpayer.

Forms to Use

A taxpayer may, at his election, use form 1040 or rm 1040A. However, those taxpayers who choose itemize deductions must use the longer form 1040.

Deductions

A taxpayer may either itemize deductions or oose the standard deduction. For single taxpayers standard deduction is $2,200. For married tax- yers filing a joint return it is $3,200. For married payers filing separate returns the deduction is 600 each.

Dates for Filing Returns

or individuals using the calendar year, Apr. 15 is l date (unless it falls on a Saturday, Sunday, or a al holiday) for filing income tax returns and for ment of any tax due, and the first quarterly in- lment of the estimated tax. Other installments of mated tax to be paid June 15, Sept. 15, and Jan.

pr. 15 is final date for filing declaration of esti- ed tax. Amended declarations may be filed June Sept. 15, and Jan. 15.

stead of paying the 4th installment a final income rn may be filed Jan. 31. Farmers may file a final rn Mar. 1 to satisfy estimated tax requirements.

Joint Return

husband and wife may make a return jointly, n if one has no income personally. Their tax will twice the tax imposed if the income were cut in and taxed at the married filing separate rate.

ne provision stipulates that if one spouse dies, the vivor may compute his tax using joint return rates the first two taxable years following, provided he he also was entitled to file a joint return the year e death, and furnishes over half the cost of main- ing in his household a home for a dependent child tepchild. If the taxpayer remarries before the of the taxable year these privileges are lost but s permitted to file a joint return with his new use. An individual legally separated or divorced is considered married.

Estimated Tax

total tax exceeds withheld tax by at least $100, arations of estimated tax are required from (1) e individuals, heads of a household or surviving ses, or a married person entitled to file a joint rn whose spouse does not receive wages, who ex- s a gross income over $20,000; (2) married indi- als with over $10,000 where both spouses receive es; (3) married individuals with over $5,000 not led to file a joint return; and (4) individuals e gross income can reasonably be expected to in- clude more than $500 from sources other than wages subject to withholdings.

Exemptions

Personal exemption is $750.

Every individual has an exemption of $750, to be deducted from gross income. A husband and a wife are each entitled to a $750 exemption. A taxpayer 65 or over on the last day of the year gets another exemption of $750. A person blind on the last day of the year gets another exemption of $750.

Exemption for dependents, over one-half of whose total support comes from the taxpayer and for whom the other dependency tests have been met, is $750. This applies to a child, stepchild, or adopted child as well as certain other relatives with less than $750 gross income; also to a child, stepchild, or adopted child of the taxpayer who is under 19 at the end of the year or was a full-time student during 5 months of the year even if he makes $750 or more. A dependent can be a non-relative if a member of the taxpayer's household and living there all year. There is a special $35 tax credit per dependent for 1976 or 2% of the first $9,000 of taxable income, whichever is greater.

In 1977, taxpayers can use $35 for age and $35 for blindness in computing general tax credit. However, most taxpayers will not have to compute this credit because it is incorporated into the new tax tables.

Taxpayer gets the exemption for his child who is a student regardless of the student's age or earnings, provided the taxpayer provides over half of the student's total support. If the student gets a scholarship, this is not counted as support.

Child and Disabled Dependent Care

To qualify, a taxpayer must be employed and provide over one-half the cost of maintaining a household for a dependent child under 15, a disabled dependent of any age, or a disabled spouse.

Taxpayers may be allowed a credit of an amount equal to 20% of employment related expenses.

For further information consult your local IRS office or the instructional material attached to your return form.

Life Insurance

Life insurance paid to survivors is not taxed as income. Interest on life insurance left with the insurance company and paid to survivors at intervals is taxable when available. Surviving spouse has an exclusion of the prorata amount of principal payable at death plus up to $1,000 per year of interest earned when life insurance proceeds are payable in installments.

Regular payments under the Railroad Retirement Act, and those received as social security, are exempt.

Dividends

The first $100 in dividends can be excluded from income. If husband and wife both receive $100 on their joint return they can exclude $200.

The exclusion does not apply to dividends from tax-exempt corporations, mutual savings banks, building and loan associations, and several others.

Dividends paid in stock or in stock rights are generally exempt from tax, except when paid in place of preferred stock dividends of the current or preceding year, or when the stockholder has an option to take stock or property or when the stock distribution is disproportionate.

Deductible Medical Expenses

Expenses for medical care, not compensated for by insurance or other payment for taxpayer, spouse, and dependents, in excess of 3% of adjusted gross income are deductible. There is not limit to the maximum amount of medical expense that can be deducted.

Medical care includes diagnosis, treatment and prevention of disease or for the purpose of affecting any structure or function of the body, and amounts paid for insurance to reimburse for hospitalization, surgical fees and other medical expenses.

Only medicine and drugs in excess of 1% of adjusted gross income may be included in medical expenses.

One-half the cost of medical care insurance premiums up to $150 can be deducted without regard to the 3% limitation. The other half plus any excess over $150 is included with other medical expenses subject to the 3% limit.

Medical expenses for a decedent paid by his estate within one year after his death may be treated as expenses of the decedent taxpayer.

Medical and hospital benefits provided by the employer may be exempt from individual income tax.

Disability income payments are excludable only if the payee is totally and permanently disabled and under age 65 at the end of the tax year. Up to $5,200 can be excluded but must be reduced by income above certain limits.

Deductions for Contributions

Deductions up to 50% of taxpayers' adjusted gross income may be taken for contribution to most publicly supported charitable organizations, including churches or associations of churches, tax-exempt educational institutions, tax-exempt hospitals, and medical research organizations associated with a hospital. The deduction is generally limited to 20% for such organizations as private nonoperating foundations, and certain organizations that do not qualify for the 50% limitation.

Taxpayers also are permitted to carry over for five years certain contributions, generally to publicly supported organizations, which exceed the 50% allowable deduction the year the contribution was made.

Also permissible is the deduction as a charitable contribution of unreimbursed amounts up to $50 a school month spent to maintain an elementary or high school student, other than a dependent or relative, in taxpayer's home. There must be a written agreement between you and a qualified organization.

Deductions for Interest Paid

Interest paid by the taxpayer is deductible.

If personal property is bought under a contract providing for payment by installments, and in which carrying charges are stated but interest is not ascertainable, then subject to limitation payments are held to include interest equal to 6% on average unpaid balance.

However, the amount charged to a customer's revolving charge account is solely for the privilege of deferring payment and is interest.

Prizes and Awards

All prizes and awards must be reported in gross income, except when received without action by recipient. To be exempt, awards must be recei primarily in recognition of religious, charita scientific, educational, artistic, literary, or c achievement. (Nobel and Pulitzer prizes exempt.)

Deductions for Employees

An employee may take the standard deduction a deduct as well the following if in connection with employment: transportation, except commuti automobile expense, including gas, oil, and depre tion; however, meals and lodging are deductible traveling expense only if the employee is away fr home overnight.

An outside salesman—a salesman who works f time outside the office, using the latter only for i dentals—may deduct both the standard deduct and all his business expenses.

An employee who is reimbursed and is required account to his employer for his business expen will not be required to report either the reimbu ment or the expenses on his tax return. Any all ance to the employee in excess of his expenses m be included in gross income. If he claims a deduct for an excess of expenses over reimbursement will have to report the reimbursement and cla actual expenses.

An employee who is not required to account to employer must report on his return the total amou of reimbursements and expenses for travel, tra portation, entertainment, etc., that he incurs unde reimbursement arrangement with his employer.

The expense of moving to a new place of empl ment may be deducted under certain circumstan regardless of whether the taxpayer is a new or c tinuing employee, or whether he pays his o expenses or is reimbursed by his employer. Re bursement must be reported as income.

Tax Credit for the Elderly

Subject to certain rules or exclusions, taxpayers or older may claim a credit which varies accordin filing status. Taxpayers should read IRS instructi carefully for full details.

The credit is limited to 15% of $2,500 for single t payers; 15% of $2,500 for married taxpayers filin joint return when only one taxpayer is 65 or old 15% of $3,750 for married taxpayers both 65 or ol filing a joint return; and 15% of $1,875 for a marr taxpayer filing a separate return.

Net Capital Losses

An individual taxpayer may deduct capital los up to $2,000 against his ordinary income. Howeve takes $2 of net long-term capital loss to get $1 of set against other income. He may carry the rest o to subsequent years at the same rate, no legal limit the number of years.

Income Averaging

Individuals with large fluctuations in their ann income may be able to take advantage of averag provisions available to taxpayers whose income fo particular year exceeds 120% of their average come for the prior 4 years, if the excess is more th $3,000.

Returns with Itemized Deductions for 1975

Size of adjusted gross income		Total deductions: No. of returns	Total deductions: Amount (thousands)	Standard deduction: No. of returns	Standard deduction: Amount (thousands)	Itemized deductions: No. of returns	Itemized deductions: %²	Itemized deductions: Amount (thousanc
Total, all returns		82,176,778	$222,800,634	56,120,953	$100,922,250	26,055,825	31.7	$121,878,
$1.00 to	$1,000	4,743,930	7,612,777	4,724,263	7,569,492	19,667	0.4	43,
1,000 to	2,000	5,395,830	8,633,911	5,344,610	8,533,027	51,220	0.9	100,
2,000 to	3,000	5,006,686	8,250,763	4,912,353	7,981,039	94,333	1.9	269,
3,000 to	4,000	4,570,066	7,800,418	4,351,415	4,178,888	218,651	4.8	621,
4,000 to	5,000	4,543,152	7,881,427	4,214,721	6,990,495	328,431	7.2	890,
5,000 to	6,000	4,725,853	8,494,005	4,236,976	7,098,029	488,877	10.3	1,395,
6,000 to	7,000	4,161,744	7,735,519	3,557,476	5,998,433	604,268	14.5	1,737,
7,000 to	8,000	3,840,802	7,517,536	3,123,800	5,344,622	717,002	18.7	2,173,

ize of djusted ross income	Total deductions: No. of returns	Total deductions: Amount (thousands)	Standard deduction: No. of returns	Standard deduction: Amount (thousands)	Itemized deductions: No. of returns	Itemized deductions: %[2]	Itemized deductions: Amount (thousands)
8,000 to 9,000	3,727,395	7,616,941	2,830,464	4,884,389	896,931	24.1	2,732,552
9,000 to 10,000	3,468,929	7,616,253	2,423,112	4,221,839	1,045,817	30.1	3,394,414
10,000 to 11,000	3,283,312	7,418,949	2,174,456	3,880,955	1,108,856	33.8	3,537,994
11,000 to 12,000	3,118,000	7,517,767	1,927,173	3,593,275	1,190,827	38.2	3,924,492
12,000 to 13,000	2,948,366	7,561,332	1,712,251	3,403,347	1,236,115	41.9	4,157,985
13,000 to 14,000	2,926,496	8,147,501	1,600,133	3,434,074	1,326,363	45.3	4,713,427
14,000 to 15,000	2,682,731	8,002,639	1,389,498	3,198,624	1,293,233	48.2	4,804,015
15,000 to 20,000	10,355,874	35,478,832	4,526,601	11,617,366	5,729,273	55.3	23,861,466
20,000 to 25,000	5,601,031	22,751,249	1,524,668	3,902,488	4,076,363	72.8	18,848,761
25,000 to 30,000	2,737,048	13,428,662	472,136	1,207,664	2,264,912	82.8	12,220,998
30,000 to 50,000	2,742,948	17,782,764	297,798	761,711	2,445,150	89.2	17,021,053
50,000 to 100,000	781,056	9,080,486	43,307	110,250	737,749	94.5	8,970,236
100,000 to 200,000	152,466	3,578,551	4,186	10,616	148,280	97.3	3,567,935
200,000 to 500,000	29,561	1,687,443	570	1,429	28,991	98.1	1,686,014
500,000 to 1,000,000	3,411	564,347	33	81	3,378	99.0	564,266
000,000 or more	1,149	640,562	11	27	1,138	99.0	640,535

ize of ljusted oss income otal, all returns	Medical and dental: No. of returns 19,482,182	Medical and dental: Amount (thousands) $11,413,472	Taxes paid: No. of returns 25,914,234	Taxes paid: Amount (thousands) $44,109,545	Contributions: No. of returns 24,635,851	Contributions: Amount (thousands) $15,426,157
$1 to $1,000	12,762	13,842	15,606	9,943	9,378	1,257
1,000 to 2,000	23,891	20,128	49,746	24,546	26,971	5,629
2,000 to 3,000	61,798	118,363	91,638	62,629	65,281	13,670
3,000 to 4,000	181,395	218,701	207,631	160,602	179,271	63,960
4,000 to 5,000	285,270	296,646	303,481	234,722	279,417	109,836
5,000 to 6,000	419,406	403,172	478,928	339,294	432,204	168,384
6,000 to 7,000	501,645	433,902	596,182	470,889	531,209	182,248
7,000 to 8,000	622,618	569,762	708,803	539,835	658,633	252,483
8,000 to 9,000	745,923	561,264	891,543	754,293	809,655	304,866
9,000 to 10,000	847,979	706,505	1,037,703	905,451	961,994	367,030
10,000 to 11,000	884,327	559,307	1,102,489	1,032,219	1,018,725	386,841
11,000 to 12,000	951,189	574,044	1,188,131	1,180,535	1,106,605	439,431
12,000 to 13,000	938,223	513,001	1,228,543	1,305,887	1,155,447	453,156
13,000 to 14,000	998,554	518,317	1,322,808	1,484,889	1,250,328	508,535
14,000 to 15,000	975,639	543,070	1,285,807	1,539,981	1,206,887	534,927
15,000 to 20,000	4,148,646	2,100,912	5,712,796	8,260,975	5,483,422	2,570,254
20,000 to 25,000	2,936,910	1,287,968	4,070,804	7,299,319	3,965,708	2,116,808
25,000 to 30,000	1,642,557	679,111	2,260,696	5,008,254	2,208,548	1,509,535
30,000 to 50,000	1,732,298	864,796	2,442,614	7,256,500	2,386,379	2,219,147
50,000 to 100,000	468,382	321,973	736,701	3,877,866	721,854	1,448,416
100,000 to 200,000	84,127	82,873	148,096	1,449,307	145,171	757,732
200,000 to 500,000	16,144	22,049	28,976	599,470	28,330	485,455
500,000 to 1,000,000	1,897	3,255	3,375	164,370	3,312	201,109
000,000 or more	602	511	1,137	147,769	1,122	325,448

e of usted ss income al, all returns	Miscellaneous[3]: No. of returns 21,930,790	Miscellaneous[3]: Amount (thousands) $12,307,099	Taxable returns: No. of returns 61,752,767	Taxable returns: Taxable income (thousands) $590,917,794	Taxable returns: Total tax (thousands) $124,757,875	Taxable returns: Total tax as % of taxable income 21.1
$1 to $1,000	9,344	2,850	—[1]	—[1]	—[1]	—[1]
1,000 to 2,000	15,507	12,249	52,005	30,940	3,021	9.8
2,000 to 3,000	53,995	16,080	1,319,860	631,858	49,748	7.9
3,000 to 4,000	146,744	46,477	2,730,168	2,972,765	352,702	11.9
4,000 to 5,000	224,379	72,269	3,165,316	5,885,392	794,373	13.5
5,000 to 6,000	369,473	139,348	3,557,236	9,372,954	1,347,977	14.4
6,000 to 7,000	440,766	155,538	3,537,168	11,769,992	1,694,459	14.4
7,000 to 8,000	566,987	224,906	3,548,416	14,198,478	2,130,613	15.0
8,000 to 9,000	722,644	272,317	3,522,697	16,851,197	2,654,497	15.8
9,000 to 10,000	866,699	351,288	3,340,902	18,302,244	2,938,603	16.1
10,000 to 11,000	921,018	426,799	3,205,174	20,182,473	3,337,514	16.5
11,000 to 12,000	1,015,577	419,489	3,063,220	21,504,103	3,587,694	16.7
12,000 to 13,000	1,067,356	473,045	2,909,206	22,593,899	3,836,260	17.0
13,000 to 14,000	1,151,920	519,180	2,887,336	24,367,243	4,167,797	17.1
14,000 to 15,000	1,138,144	530,324	2,655,696	24,371,237	4,248,374	17.4
15,000 to 20,000	5,028,736	2,602,111	10,263,539	116,865,067	21,196,422	18.1
20,000 to 25,000	3,526,823	1,721,998	5,573,476	86,742,403	17,033,865	19.6
25,000 to 30,000	1,914,949	1,153,798	2,727,690	53,657,532	11,379,270	21.2
30,000 to 50,000	2,012,491	1,533,813	2,729,930	74,597,805	18,192,156	24.4
50,000 to 100,000	586,537	926,301	776,468	40,146,648	13,383,693	33.3
00,000 to 200,000	121,830	384,557	151,818	15,917,429	6,876,261	43.2
00,000 to 500,000	24,922	192,213	29,386	6,485,754	3,379,633	52.1
00,000 to 1,000,000	2,962	67,010	3,369	1,704,475	1,011,273	59.3
00,000 or more	1,027	63,139	1,136	1,765,906	1,148,856	65.1

stimate not shown because sample base is too small. (2) Percent of returns, in each income category, which are itemized. (3) All deductions except those for interest paid.

Individual Income Tax Returns for 1975

Source: Internal Revenue Service U.S. Treasury Department

Size of adjusted gross income	All returns				Taxable returns		
	Returns		Adjusted gross income less deficit		Returns		Adjusted gross incom less defici
	Number	Percent of total	Amount ($000)	Average (dollars)	Number	Percent of total	Amount ($000)
Total	**82,176,778**	**100.0**	**948,093,716**	**11,537**	**61,752,767**	**100.0**	**899,722,8**
No adjusted gross income	629,942	0.8	−5,670,297	−9,001	1,495	(1)	−187,2
$1 under $1,000	4,743,930	5.8	2,717,411	573	(1)	(1)	(
$1,000 under $2,000	5,395,830	6.6	8,056,692	1,493	52,005	0.1	80,2
$2,000 under $3,000	5,006,686	6.1	12,459,543	2,489	1,319,860	2.1	3,634,5
$3,000 under $4,000	4,570,066	5.6	15,974,216	3,495	2,730,168	4.4	9,586,7
$4,000 under $5,000	4,543,152	5.5	20,489,822	4,510	3,165,316	5.1	14,311,8
$5,000 under $6,000	4,725,853	5.8	25,908,449	5,482	3,557,236	5.8	19,533,2
$6,000 under $7,000	4,161,744	5.1	27,001,139	6,488	3,537,168	5.7	22,978,2
$7,000 under $8,000	3,840,802	4.7	28,789,923	7,496	3,548,416	5.7	26,603,2
$8,000 under $9,000	3,727,395	4.5	31,696,096	8,504	3,522,697	5.7	29,958,7
$9,000 under $10,000	3,468,929	4.2	32,955,087	9,500	3,340,902	5.4	31,743,5
$10,000 under $11,000	3,282,312	4.0	34,467,151	10,501	3,205,174	5.2	33,661,7
$11,000 under $12,000	3,118,000	3.8	35,862,420	11,502	3,063,220	5.0	35,235,5
$12,000 under $13,000	2,948,366	3.6	36,857,431	12,501	2,909,206	4.7	36,369,8
$13,000 under $14,000	2,926,496	3.6	39,503,969	13,499	2,887,336	4.7	38,974,7
$14,000 under $15,000	2,682,731	3.3	38,880,370	14,493	2,655,696	4.3	38,490,1
$15,000 under $20,000	10,355,874	12.6	179,008,508	17,286	10,263,539	16.6	177,444,7
$20,000 under $25,000	5,601,031	6.8	124,361,878	22,203	5,573,476	9.0	123,754,3
$25,000 under $30,000	2,737,048	3.3	74,430,257	27,194	2,727,690	4.4	74,175,0
$30,000 under $50,000	2,742,948	3.3	99,974,292	36,448	2,729,930	4.4	99,483,7
$50,000 under $100,000	781,056	1.0	51,523,925	65,967	776,468	1.3	51,226,0
$100,000 under $200,000	152,466	0.2	19,925,531	130,688	151,818	0.2	19,840,5
$200,000 under $500,000	29,561	(1)	8,242,889	278,843	29,386	(1)	8,193,4
$500,000 under $1,000,000	3,411	(1)	2,270,172	665,544	3,369	(1)	2,242,7
$1,000,000 or more	1,149	(1)	2,406,842	2,094,728	1,136	(1)	2,386,9

Size of adjusted gross income	Taxable returns—continued					
	Taxable income	Income tax after credits		Total income tax		
	Amount ($000)	Number of returns	Amount ($000)	Amount ($000)	Percent of adjusted gross income	Average (dollars)
Total	**590,917,794**	**61,746,457**	**124,623,677**	**124,757,875**	**13.9**	**2,020**
No adjusted gross income	—	—	—	12,461	—	8,335
$1 under $1,000	—	—	—	—	—	—
$1,000 under $2,000	30,940	51,997	2,870	3,021	3.8	58
$2,000 under $3,000	631,858	1,319,803	49,575	49,748	1.4	38
$3,000 under $4,000	2,972,765	2,730,132	352,480	352,702	3.7	129
$4,000 under $5,000	5,885,392	3,165,301	794,264	794,373	5.6	251
$5,000 under $6,000	9,372,954	3,556,400	1,347,365	1,347,977	6.9	379
$6,000 under $7,000	11,769,992	3,536,942	1,694,267	1,694,459	7.4	479
$7,000 under $8,000	14,198,478	3,548,397	2,130,509	2,130,613	8.0	600
$8,000 under $9,000	16,851,197	3,522,665	2,654,356	2,654,497	8.9	754
$9,000 under $10,000	18,302,244	3,340,896	2,938,463	2,938,603	9.3	880
$10,000 under $11,000	20,182,473	3,205,154	3,337,408	3,337,514	9.9	1,041
$11,000 under $12,000	21,504,103	3,063,155	3,587,487	3,587,694	10.2	1,171
$12,000 under $13,000	22,593,899	2,909,154	3,836,205	3,836,260	10.5	1,319
$13,000 under $14,000	24,367,243	2,887,313	4,167,675	4,167,797	10.7	1,443
$14,000 under $15,000	24,371,237	2,655,668	4,248,100	4,248,374	11.0	1,600
$15,000 under $20,000	116,865,067	10,262,773	21,195,026	21,196,422	11.9	2,065
$20,000 under $25,000	86,742,403	5,573,055	17,031,943	17,033,865	13.8	2,056
$25,000 under $30,000	53,657,532	2,726,957	11,378,244	11,379,270	15.3	4,172
$30,000 under $50,000	74,597,805	2,729,355	18,185,723	18,192,156	18.3	6,664
$50,000 under $100,000	40,146,648	776,078	13,366,825	13,383,693	26.1	17,237
$100,000 under $200,000	15,917,429	151,519	6,853,450	6,876,261	34.7	45,293
$200,000 under $500,000	6,485,754	29,274	3,351,519	3,379,633	41.2	115,008
$500,000 under $1,000,000	1,704,475	3,342	997,850	1,011,273	45.1	300,170
$1,000,000 or more	1,765,906	1,119	1,122,071	1,148,856	48.1	1,011,317

(1) Less than 0.05 per cent.

Social Security Programs

Source: Social Security Administration, U.S. Dept. of Health, Education and Welfare

Medicare; Old-Age, Survivors and Disability Insurance; Supplemental Security Income

Under a March 1977 reorganization of the Department of Health, Education, and Welfare, the federal-ate assistance program of aid to families with de-endent children became the responsibility of the So-al Security Administration. The reorganization aced the Medicare program under the newly eated Health Care Financing Administration, hich also now administers Medicaid, the federal-ate medical assistance program. The Social Se-rity Administration continues to provide services, ch as those relating to contributions and premiums d maintenance of beneficiary records, for the edicare program.

The cost-of-living increase in 1977 in the social se-rity benefit called for a redetermination of the aximum on taxable earnings under the social se-rity program, as well as the amount of earnings a neficiary may have without any loss of benefits. ese amounts will be superseded by later legisla-n.

The third cost-of-living increase in social security nefits — amounting to 5.9% — went into effect in ne 1977 and was reflected in monthly checks re-ved in July by all persons on the rolls in May ex-pt those affected by the special minimum benefit ovision. Since Federal SSI payments administered the Social Security Administration are also af-ted by the automatic provisions, they rose at the ne rate, effective for July. The next automatic t-of-living increase will be based on the rise in the asumer price index from the first quarter of 1977 there is no legislated increase) to the first quarter 1978; if the index rises 3% or more, the benefit el will be raised as of June 1978 by the same per-tage.

he 1977 benefit increase made necessary two er automatic adjustments, effective for 1978: (1) maximum taxable and creditable earnings base s raised from $16,500 to $17,700, and (2) the annual mpt earnings amount for social security benefici-es was increased from $3,000 to $3,240 (or $270 in onth).

Medicare, following the required annual review ospital costs under the program, increases were de in the hospital insurance deductible amount at the patient must pay for hospital services be-reimbursement can begin) and in the cost-shar-for days above the number specified in the law.

he Commissioner of Social Security is James B. dwell. There are 632 district offices with 682 nch offices, and 30 teleservice centers where the lic may obtain information about benefit rights.

Medicare

nder Medicare, protection against the costs of pital care is provided for social security and rail-d retirement beneficiaries aged 65 and over inning July 1966) and, effective July 1973, for sons entitled for 24 months to receive a social se-ty disability benefit, certain persons with chronic ey disease and their dependents, and, on a volun-basis with payment of a special premium, sons aged 65 and over not otherwise eligible for ital benefits; all those eligible for hospital bene-may enroll for medical benefits and pay a thly premium and so may persons aged 65 and who are not eligible for hospital benefits.

ersons eligible for both hospital and medical rance or for medical insurance only may choose ave their covered services provided through a lth Maintenance Organization (a prepaid group th or other capitation plan that meets prescribed dards).

ospital insurance. — In the 11th year of operation 1976-June 1977) about $58.7 billion was with-wn from the hospital insurance trust fund for ital and related benefits. About 25,316,000 persons were enrolled under the program as of July 1976 —2,392,000 of them disabled beneficiaries under age 65.

The hospital insurance program pays the cost of covered services for hospital and posthospital care as follows:

- Up to 90 days of hospital care during a benefit period (spell of illness) starting the first day that care as a bed-patient is received in a hospital or skilled-nursing facility and ending when the individual has not been a bed-patient for 60 consecutive days. For the first 60 days, the hospital insurance pays for all but the first $144 of expenses; for the 61st day to 90th day, the program pays all but $36 a day for covered services. In addition, each person has a 60-day lifetime reserve that can be used after the 90 days of hospital care in a benefit period are exhausted, and all but $72 a day of expenses during the reserve days are paid. Once used, the reserve days are not replaced. (Payment for care in a mental hospital is limited to 190 days.)
- Up to 100 days' care in a skilled-nursing facility (skilled-nursing home) in each benefit period. Hospital insurance pays for all covered services for the first 20 days and all but $18 daily for the next 80 days. At least 3 days' hospital stay must precede these services, and the skilled-nursing facility must be entered within 14 days after leaving the hospital. (The 1972 law permits more than 14 days in certain circumstances.)
- Up to 100 visits by nurses or other health workers (not doctors) from a home health agency in the 365 days after release from a hospital or extended-care facility.

Money to pay these benefits comes from special the self-employed. The 1977 rate was 0.9% on earnings up to $16,500 (the maximum taxable for that year). It is 1.1% on earnings up to $17,700 for 1978, unless changed by pending legislation.

Medical insurance. Aged persons can receive benefits under this supplementary program only if they sign up for them and agree to a monthly premium ($7.70 to July 1978). The Federal Government pays the rest of the cost. In December of each year the Secretary of Health, Education, and Welfare announces the amount of the premium payable starting in July of the following year. The premiums are to be increased only when there is a general benefit increase in the year and it will rise no more than the percent by which the cash benefits have been increased since the last premium increase.

About 140 million bills were reimbursed under the medical insurance program from Jan. 1976 to July 1977 for a total of $7.5 billion. As of July 1976, 24,614,400 persons were enrolled — 2,168,500 of them disabled persons under age 65.

The medical insurance program pays 80% of the reasonable charges (after the first $60 in each calendar year) for the following services:

- Physicians' and surgeons' services, whether in the doctor's office, a clinic, or hospital or at home (but physician's charges for X-ray or clinical laboratory services for hospital bed-patients are paid in full and without meeting the deductible).
- Other medical and health services, such as diagnostic tests, surgical dressings and splints, and rental or purchase of medical equipment. Services of a physical therapist in independent practice, furnished in his office or the patient's home. A hospital or extended-care facility may provide covered outpatient physical therapy services under the medical insurance program to its patients who have exhausted their hospital insurance coverage.
- Physical therapy services furnished under the supervision of a practicing hospital, clinic, skilled nursing facility, or agency.
- Certain services by podiatrists.
- All outpatient services of a participating hospital (including diagnostic tests).

- Outpatient speech pathology services, under the same requirements as physical therapy.
- Services of licensed chiropractors who meet uniform standards, but only for treatment by means of manual manipulation of the spine and treatment of subluxation of the spine demonstrated by X-ray.
- Supplies related to colostomies are considered prosthetic devices and payable under the program.
- Home health services even without a hospital stay (up to 100 visits a year) are paid up to 100%.

To get medical insurance protection, persons approaching age 65 may enroll in the 7-month period that includes 3 months before the 65th birthday, the month of the birthday, and 3 months after the birthday, but if they wish coverage to begin in the month they reach 65 they must enroll in the 3 months **before** their birthday. Persons not enrolling within their first enrollment period may enroll later, during the first 3 months of each year but their premium is 10% higher for each 12-month period elapsed since they first could have enrolled.

The monthly premium is deducted from the cash benefit for persons receiving social security, railroad retirement, or civil service retirement benefits. Income from the medical premiums and the Federal matching payments are put in a Supplementary Medical Insurance Trust Fund, from which benefits and administrative expenses are paid.

Medicare card. Persons qualifying for hospital insurance under social security receive a health insurance card similar to cards now used by Blue Cross and other health agencies. The card indicates whether the individual has taken out medical insurance protection. It is to be shown to the hospital, skilled nursing facility, home health agency, doctor, or whoever provides the covered services.

Payments are made only in the 50 States, Puerto Rico, the Virgin Islands, Guam, and American Samoa, except that hospital services may be provided in border areas immediately outside the U.S. if comparable services are not accessible in the U.S. for a beneficiary who becomes ill or is injured in the U.S.

Old-Age, Survivors, and Disability Insurance

Retired and disabled workers and their families and the survivors of deceased workers received $6.13 billion in social security cash benefits for Aug. 1977; the average benefit being received by a retired worker was about $241; for retired workers just coming on the rolls, the average benefit award was about $255. For a disabled worker, the average Aug. check was $263 and new disabled-worker beneficiaries were awarded $293, on the average.

Old-age, survivors, and disability insurance covers almost all jobs in which people work for wages or salaries, as well as most work of self-employed persons, whether in a city job, or in business, or on a farm.

Old-age, survivors, and disability insurance is paid for by a tax on earnings (for 1977 up to $16,500 and for 1978 up to $17,700; the taxable earnings base is now subject to adjustment when cost-of-living benefit increases have been made). The employed worker and his employer share the tax equally (cash tips count as covered wages if they amount to $20 or more from one place of employment. The worker reports them to his employer, who includes them in his social security tax reports, but only the worker pays contributions on the amount of the tips).

The employer deducts the tax each payday and sends it, with an equal amount as his own share, to the District Director of Internal Revenue. The collected taxes are deposited in the Federal Old-Age and Survivors Insurance Trust Fund and the Federal Disability Insurance Trust Fund; they can be used only to pay benefits, the costs of rehabilitation services, and administrative expenses.

Amount of Work Required

To qualify for benefits for himself and his family, the worker must have been in covered employment long enough to become insured. Just how long pends on his date of birth (or if he dies or beco disabled, the date of his death or disability).

A person is fully covered if he has one quarte coverage for every year after 1950 (or year reaches age 21) up to but not including the yea which he reaches age 62 or dies.

Certain provisions in the law permit spec monthly payments under the social security progr to persons aged 72 and over who are not eligible regular social security benefits since they had li or no opportunity to earn social security work cre during their working lifetime.

To get disability benefits, the worker must have credit for 5 out of 10 years before he becor disabled. Persons disabled before age 31 can qua with a briefer period of coverage.

Work Years Required

The following table shows the number of w years required to be fully insured for old-age survivors benefits, according to the year wor reaches retirement age or dies.

Work credit for retirement benefits

If you reach 62 in	Years you need	If you reach 62 in	Ye yc ne
1974	6*	1979	7
1975	6	1981	7
1976	6¼	1983	8
1977	6½	1987	9
1978	6¾	1991 or later	1

*For 1974 a woman needs only 5¾ years.

Deceased's work credit for survivor's benefits

Born after 1929, die at	Born before 1930, die before age 62	Yea neec
28 or younger		1
30		2
32		2
34		3
36		3
38		4
40		4
42		5
44	1973	5
45	1974	5
46	1975	6
48	1977	6
50	1979	7
52	1981	7
54	1983	8
56	1985	8
58	1987	9
60	1989	9
62 or older	1991 or later	1

Self-Employed

A self-employed person who has earnings of $ or more in a year must report his earnings for inco tax and social security tax purposes. If he is nc farmer he reports only net returns from his busin He need not add income from real estate, savir dividends, loans, pensions or insurance policie these are not part of his business.

A self-employed person who has net earnings $400 or more in a year gets 4 quarters of coverage that year. If his earnings are less than $400 in a y they do not count toward social security credits. nonfarm self-employed person must make estima payments of his social security taxes, on a quarte basis, for taxable years after 1966, if combined e mated income tax and social security tax amoun at least $40.

The self-employed now have the option, compa ble to that for farm workers, of reporting th earnings as ⅔ of their gross income from self- ployment but not more than $1,600 a year. option can be used only if actual net earnings fr self-employment income is less than $1,600 and than ⅔ of gross income and may be used only 5 tim

When a person has both taxable wages and earnings from self-employment, only as much of the self-employment income as will bring total earnings up to the current taxable maximum is subject to tax for social security purposes. A self-employed person pays the tax at a lower rate than the combined rate for an employee and his employer — about 1 1/2 times what the employee alone pays.

Farm Owners and Workers

Self-employed farmers whose gross annual earnings from farming are under $2,400 may report 2/3 of their gross earnings instead of net earnings for social security purposes. Cash or crop shares received from a tenant or share farmer count if the owner participated materially in production or management. The self-employed farmer pays contributions at the same rate as other self-employed, but he may make his tax returns annually.

Farm workers. Earnings from farm work count toward benefits (1) if the employer pays $150 or more in cash during the year; (2) if the employee works on 20 or more days for cash pay figured on a time basis. Under these rules a person gets credit for one calendar quarter for each $100 in cash pay in a year but no more than four quarters in any one year.

Foreign farm workers admitted to the United States on a temporary basis are not covered.

Household Workers

Anyone working as maid, cook, laundress, nursemaid, baby-sitter, chauffeur, gardener and at other household tasks in the house of another, is covered by social security if he or she earns $50 or more in cash in three months from any one employer. Room and board do not count, but carfare counts if paid in cash. The job does not have to be regular or fulltime. The employee should get a card at the social security office and show it to the employer.

The employer deducts the amount of the social security tax from the worker's pay, adds an identical amount as his own tax and sends the total amount to the Federal Government, with the number of the employee's social security card.

What Aged Workers Get

When a person has enough work in covered employment and reaches retirement age (65 for full benefit, 62 for reduced benefit), he may retire and get monthly old-age benefits. If he continues to work and has earnings of more than $3,240, $1 in benefits will be withheld for every $2 above $3,240. The amount that can be earned in a month without loss of any benefits is $270. The annual exempt amount and the monthly test are raised automatically or according to the rise in general earnings levels. The eligible worker who is 72 receives the full amount of benefit, regardless of earnings.

A worker's benefit will be raised by 1% for each year after 1970 for which the worker between 65 and 72 did not receive benefits because of earnings from work. No increases are to be paid to the worker's dependents or survivors under this provision.

A special minimum benefit is payable to persons who worked 20 or more years under social security as an alternative to the regular minimum ($114.30 in June 1977) if a higher amount results. The highest minimum under this provision would be $180 a month for a person ($270 for a couple) with 30 or more years of coverage.

When a person receives old-age benefits, payments can also be made to certain of his dependents, including a wife 62 or over, dependent children under 18 or who became totally disabled before age 22 or who are full-time students not yet aged 22, a wife (regardless of age) if caring for an eligible child, and a dependent husband 62 or over.

The special benefit for persons aged 72 or over who do not meet the regular coverage requirements is $78.40 a month ($117.60 for a couple if both members are eligible). Like the monthly benefits, these payments are now subject to cost-of-living increases. The special payment is not made to persons on the public assistance or supplemental security income rolls.

Social Security benefits are not subject to income taxes.

A woman worker is eligible for a full old-age benefit at age 65, but she may retire at 62 and get 80% of her full benefit for the rest of her life; the nearer she is to 65 when she begins collecting her benefit, the larger it will be. (Benefits for men retiring before 65 are reduced at the same rate as benefits for women retiring before 65.)

A child can get benefits based on his mother's earnings on the same conditions as those entitling a child to benefits based on his father's earnings record.

Benefits for Worker's Spouse

The wife of a man who is getting social security retirement or disability payments may become entitled to wife's insurance benefits in a reduced amount when she reaches 62, or she may wait until she reaches 65 and get the entire amount of the wife's benefit, which is one-half of the husband's benefit. Benefits are also payable to the divorced wife of an insured worker if she was married to him for at least 20 years and he was contributing to or was ordered by a court to contribute to her support.

If a woman worker entitled to an old-age benefit has a dependent husband aged 65 or over, he may draw a benefit similar to a wife's benefit at 65 (or a reduced benefit at age 62).

Benefits for Children of Retired or Disabled Workers

If a worker has children under 18 when he retires for age or disability they will get a benefit that is half his benefit, and so will his wife, even if she is under 62. Total benefits paid on a worker's earnings record are subject to a maximum and if the total paid to a family exceeds that maximum, the individual dependents' benefits are adjusted downward. (Total benefits paid to the family of a worker who retired in 1975 at age 65 with average monthly earnings of $1,175 can be no higher than $1,031.)

When his children reach 18, their benefits will stop, except that a child permanently and totally disabled before 22 may get a benefit as long as his disability meets the definition in the law. In addition, child's benefits are payable until the child reaches his 22nd birthday if he is attending school as a full-time student. Benefits may now be paid to a grandchild or step-grandchild of a worker or of his spouse, in special circumstances.

What Disabled Workers Get

If a worker becomes so severely disabled that he is unable to work, he may be eligible to receive a monthly disability benefit that is the same amount he would receive as an old-age benefit if he were 65 at the start of his disability. When he reaches 65, his disability benefit becomes an old-age benefit.

Benefits like those provided for dependents of retired-worker beneficiaries may be paid to dependents of disabled beneficiaries.

Survivor Benefits

If a worker should die while insured, one or more types of benefits would be payable to survivors.

1. A cash payment to cover burial expenses that amounts to 3 times the basic benefit but not more than $255, paid at the death of every insured worker.

2. A benefit for each child until the child reaches 18 (or up to age 22, if he is attending school). The monthly benefit of each child of a worker who has died is three-quarters of the amount the worker would have received if he had lived and drawn retirement benefits. A child with a permanent disability that began before age 22 may receive his benefit after that age.

3. A mother's benefit for the widow, if children under 18 are left in her care. Her benefit is 75% of the basic benefit and she draws it until the youngest child reaches 18. Payments stop then even if the

child's benefit continues because he is attending school. They will start again when she is 62 (or 60), unless she marries. If she marries and the marriage is ended, she regains benefit rights. If she has a disabled child beneficiary aged 18 or over in her care, her benefits also continue.

Disabled widows and widowers qualify for benefits at age 50 at reduced rates that depend on age at entitlement. The widow or widower must have become totally disabled before or within 7 years after the spouse's death.

4. If there are no children entitled to receive benefits, the widow will receive a benefit that is 100% of the husband's basic amount, if it is first payable when she is 65. She may choose to get her benefit when she is 60; her benefit is then reduced by 19/40 of 1% for each month it is paid before she is 65. However, for widows aged 62 and over whose husbands claimed their benefits before 65, the benefit is the reduced amount he would be getting if he were alive but not less than 82 1/2% of his basic benefit. Dependent widowers aged 60 or over are entitled to survivor benefits on same basis as widows.

5. Dependent parents may be eligible for benefits, if they have been receiving at least half their support from the worker before his death, have reached age 62, and (except in certain circumstances) have not remarried since the worker's death. Each parent gets 75% of the basic benefit except that if only one parent survives the benefit is 82 1/2%.

The survivors of a woman worker receive benefits on the same basis as those of men workers. (Beginning March 1975, widowed father's benefits are payable on same basis as widowed mother's benefits).

Maximum Benefits Payable

The illustrative table below shows a column heading for average earnings of $10,000, but the benefit amounts shown in the column are not in general payable yet, since it will be some time before workers can have an average that high (years when the maximum creditable amount of earnings was lower than $14,100 — the 1975 maximum — must currently be included when the average is figured). Benefit amounts larger than those shown in the table will eventually be payable to persons who raise their average yearly earnings for social security purposes by earning, for a sufficient period, the highest creditable amount in years with the higher maximums specified in the law — $16,500 in 1977 and $17,700 in 1978 (higher amounts in the future whenever the base is raised under the automatic adjustment procedure).

Examples of Monthly OASDI Cash Payments
Average yearly earnings after 1950

Benefits can be paid to:	$923 or less	$3,000	$4,000	$5,000	$6,000	$8,000	$10,000
Worker:							
Retired at 65	114.30	236.40	278.10	322.50	364.50	453.10	502.00
Under 65 and disabled	114.30	236.40	278.10	322.50	364.50	453.10	502.00
Retired at 62	91.50	189.20	222.50	258.00	291.60	362.50	401.60
Spouse:							
at 65	57.20	118.20	139.10	161.30	182.30	226.60	251.00
at 62, with no child	42.90	88.70	104.40	121.00	136.80	170.00	188.30
Under 65 and one dependent child	57.20	125.00	197.20	272.60	304.20	339.80	376.60
Surviving spouse:							
At 65 (if worker never received reduced retirement benefits)	114.30	236.40	278.10	322.50	364.50	453.10	502.00
at 60 (if sole survivor)	81.80	169.10	198.90	230.60	260.70	324.00	359.00
at 50 and disabled (if sole survivor)	57.30	118.30	139.20	161.30	182.40	226.60	251.10
Widowed parent caring for one child	171.50	354.60	417.20	483.80	546.80	679.80	753.00
Maximum family payment	171.50	361.40	475.30	595.10	668.60	792.90	878.50

*Generally, average earnings are figured over the period from 1951 until the worker reaches retirement age, becomes disabled, or dies. Up to 5 years of low earnings or no earnings can be excluded. The maximum earnings creditable for social security are $3,600 for 1951-1954; $4,200 for 1955-1958; $4,800 for 1959-65; $6,600 for 1966-67; $7,800 for 1968-71; $9,000 for 1972; $10,800 for 1973; $13,200 for 1974; $14,100 for 1975; $15,300 for 1976; $16,500 for 1977; and $17,700 for 1978. As the text under the heading "Maximum Benefits Payable" explains, amounts shown in the last column will generally not be payable until later. When a person is entitled to more than one benefit, the amount actually payable is limited to the larger of the benefits.

Contribution Rate for Employees, Employers, and Self-Employed

	Percent of Covered Earnings					
	Employees and employers each			Self-employed		
Years	OASDI Benefits	Hospital Insurance	Total	OASDI Benefits	Hospital Insurance	Total
1974-77	4.95	0.90	5.85	7.0	0.90	7.90
1978-80	4.95	1.10	6.05	7.0	1.10	8.10
1981-85	4.95	1.35	6.30	7.0	1.35	8.35
1986-97	4.95	1.50	6.45	7.0	.50	8.50
1998-2010*	4.95	(1.50)	(6.45)	7.0	(1.50)	(8.50)
2011 and thereafter	5.95	(1.50)	(7.45)	7.0	(1.50)	(8.50)

*Costs of hospital insurance estimated only through 1997.

Supplemental Security Income

On Jan. 1, 1974, the supplemental security income program established by the 1972 Social Security Act amendments replaced the former Federal grants to States for aid to the needy aged, blind, and disabled in the 50 States and the District of Columbia. The program provides both for Federal payments based on uniform national standards and eligibility requirements and for State supplementary payments varying from State to State. The Social Security Administration administers the Federal payments financed from general funds of the Treasury — and the State supplements as well, if the State elects to have its supplementary program federally administered. The States may supplement the Federal payment for all recipients and must supplement it for persons otherwise adversely affected by the transition from the former public assistance programs. In Aug. 1977, the number of persons receiving Federal payments and federally administered State payments was 4,237,000, and the amount of these payments was $529,882,000. The average amount of combined federal payments and federally administered state payments was $125 for that month.

As a result of the 5.9 percent cost-of-living increase in social security benefits in June, 1977, the Federal SSI payment levels were raised in July, 1977, from

$167.80 per month for an individual and $251.80 for a couple to $177.80 and $266.70 respectively.

Public Assistance

In May 1977, 11.1 million persons received cash payments of $839.6 million under the Federal-State program of aid to families with dependent children that averaged $234.03 per family and $75.56 per recipient. Under the child-support enforcement provisions of the Social Security Act, $34.3 million was collected and applied against assistance expenditures. In 42 States, 877,523 persons were receiving general assistance, financed entirely by State and local governments, that averaged $119.40. Emergency assistance was provided in 21 States for 41,348 families at an average payment of $165.70.

Social Security Trust Funds

Old-Age, Survivors, and Disability Insurance Trust Funds, 1937-1977

(thousands)

Fiscal year:	Receipts: Net contrib. inc., transfers, and reimb. from gen'l rev.	Receipts: Net interest received	Expenditures: Cash benefit payments and rehab. services	Expenditures: Transfers to R.R. ret. acct. Acct.	Expenditures: Administrative expenses	Total assets at end of period
1937	$ 265,000	$ 2,262	$ 27	$. . . .	$ 26,840	$ 267,235
1940	550,000	42,489	15,805	. . . .	12,288	1,744,698
1945	1,309,919	123,854	239,834	. . . .	26,950	6,613,381
1950	2,109,912	256,778	727,266	. . . .	56,841	12,892,612
1955	5,087,154	438,029	4,333,147	-9,551	103,202	21,141,001
1960	10,829,664	564,040	10,798,013	573,606	234,291	22,995,939
1965	17,032,456	648,372	16,618,084	459,253	379,145	22,187,184
1970	34,554,182	1,572,375	29,062,772	589,257	623,055	37,719,951
1975	63,872,883	2,803,838	62,547,281	1,010,299	1,100,693	48,138,321
1976	67,867,099	2,815,197	71,462,416	1,238,669	1,200,326	44,919,209
1976 (July-Sept.)[1]	18,264,999	93,726	19,459,572	. . . .	304,448	43,513,811
1977 (Oct. 1976-June 1977)	57,922,104	2,547,921	60,652,293	1,207,523	1,071,521	41,025,829
Cumulative to June 1977	**672,018,519**	**31,463,054**	**637,539,125**	**11,826,744**	**13,061,919**	**43,513,811**

(1) Transitional quarter. Beginning Oct. 1976, federal fiscal year begins Oct. 1.

Hospital Insurance Trust Fund, 1966-77

(thousands)

Fiscal year:	Receipts: Net contribution income[1]	Receipts: Transfers from general revenues[2]	Receipts: Transfers from railroad retirement account[3]	Receipts: Net interest[4]	Expenditures: Net hospital and related service benefits[5]	Expenditures: Administrative expenses[6]	Total assets
1966	$908,797	. . . .	. . . .	$5,970	. . . .	$63,564	$851,204
1967	2,688,684	$337,850	$16,200	45,903	$2,507,773	88,848	1,343,221
1970	4,784,789	628,262	61,307	139,423	4,804,242	148,660	2,677,401
1972	5,225,891	551,351	63,782	190,105	6,109,139	166,370	2,858,725
1973	7,663,119	429,415	61,222	197,844	6,648,819	192,839	4,368,666
1974	10,606,551	498,780	96,163	408,273	7,785,596	258,066	7,934,772
1975	11,296,773	529,353	126,749	614,989	10,355,390	256,134	9,870,039
1976	12,039,194	658,430	130,904	715,744	12,270,382	308,215	10,835,714
1976 (July-Sept.)[7]	3,367,940	135,863	. . . .	11,951	3,315,251	88,408	10,947,810
1977 (Oct. 1976-June 1977)	10,077,873	944,000	. . . .	759,994	11,064,558	237,735	11,427,384
July 1966-June 1977	**81,494,865**	**6,641,752**	**716,971**	**3,430,377**	**78,715,510**	**2,141,082**	**11,427,384**

(1)Represents amounts appropriated (estimated tax collections with suitable subsequent adjustments), after deductions for refund of estimated amount of employee-tax overpayment. (2)Represents Federal Government transfers from general funds appropriations to meet costs of benefits for persons not insured for cash benefits under OASDHI or railroad-retirement and for costs of benefits arising from military wage credits. (3)Represents receipts under the financial interchange with railroad retirement account with respect to contributions for hospital insurance coverage of railroad workers. (4)Represents interest and profit on investments after transfers of interest on administrative expenses reimbursed to the OASI trust fund and on amounts transferred from railroad accounts. (5)-Represents (1) payment vouchers on letters of credit issued to fiscal intermediaries under sec. 1816 and (2) direct payments to providers of services under sec. 1815 of the Social Security Act. (6)Subject to subsequent adjustment among all 4 social security trust funds, for allocated cost of each operation. (7)Transitional quarter. Beginning Oct. 1976, federal fiscal year begins Oct. 1.

Supplementary Medical Insurance Trust Fund, 1966-77

(thousands)

Fiscal year:	Receipts: Premium income[1]	Receipts: Transfers from general revenues[2]	Receipts: Net interest[3]	Expenditures: Net medical service benefits[4]	Expenditures: Administrative expenses[5]	Total assets
1967	$646,682	$623,000	$14,052	$664,261	$133,682	$485,791
1970	36,000	928,151	11,536	1,979,287	216,993	57,181
1973	1,462,607	1,430,451	45,049	2,391,232	245,861	745,722
1974	1,703,189	2,028,926	75,924	2,869,132	409,146	1,275,483
1975	1,886,962	2,329,590	105,539	3,765,397	404,458	1,424,413
1976	1,951,221	2,939,338	103,645	4,671,847	528,214	1,218,555
1976 (July-Sept.)[6]	538,648	878,000	4,420	1,269,038	132,077	1,238,508
1977 (Oct. 1976-June 1977)	1,616,976	3,854,870	131,248	4,320,114	351,040	2,170,451
July 1966-June 1977	**14,901,741**	**19,241,188**	**581,817**	**29,259,358**	**3,294,940**	**2,170,451**

(1)Represents voluntary premium payments from and in behalf of insured persons. (2)Represents Federal Government transfers from general funds appropriations to match aggregate premiums paid. (3)Represents interest and profit on investments after transfer of interest on administrative expenses reimbursed to the OASI trust fund (see footnote 5). (4)Represents payment vouchers on letters of credit issued to carriers under section 1842 of the Social Security Act. (5)Subject to subsequent adjustment among all 4 social security trust funds for allocated cost of each operation. (6)Transitional quarter. Beginning Oct. 1976, federal fiscal year begins Oct. 1.

Employment and Training Services and Unemployment Insurance

Source: Employment and Training Administration, U.S. Labor Department

Employment Service

The Federal-State Employment Service consists of the U.S. Employment Service and affiliated state employment services with their network of about 2,500 local offices. During calendar year 1976, these offices made a total of 5.3 million placements, of which 4.9 million were in nonagricultural and 400,000 agricultural industries. Overall, 3.4 million different individuals were placed in employment.

The employment service works to refer employable applicants to job openings that use their highest skills and helps the unemployed obtain services or training to make them employable. It also provides special attention to help meet the needs of older workers, youth, minorities, the poor, handicapped workers, migrants, seasonal farmworkers, and workers who lose their jobs because of foreign trade competition. Special efforts are being made to improve services in rural areas.

The employment service helps employers find needed workers and offers many employer services. To give employers a wider choice of workers and applicants access to more job openings, it has developed job banks, which provide computerized daily lists of all available jobs in a city or area. Statewide networks of job banks now serve about 85% of the nation's population.

Special Veterans Service

Veterans receive special services and absolute preference in placements at all employment service offices. During calendar year 1976, these offices placed over 600,000 veterans in jobs, two-thirds of them veterans of the Vietnam era. The requirement that federal contractors list job openings with the employment service continues to be of particular benefit to veterans.

Community Manpower System

The Comprehensive Employment and Training Act of 1973 sets up a community manpower system to give people training and job-related services and place them in jobs. Under this system, which replaces certain federal manpower programs, all states and cities, counties, and combinations of local units with populations of 100,000 or more receive federal grants to plan and run comprehensive manpower programs in their localities. The job-related services provided vary from one area to another, according to local decisions on the needs of the area's workers and the demands of its labor market. Among them are work experience, classroom and on-the-job training, education, job referral, and needed services such as child care and medical aid.

Besides operating comprehensive programs, local governments plan and provide public service jobs for unemployed workers. CETA supports a permanent program of transitional public employment for areas with high unemployment rates plus an emergency program for all parts of the country. In May 1977, the Economic Stimulus Appropriations Act provided funding for 415,000 new public service jobs, bringing the national total to 725,000 jobs.

National Activities

The federal role in the system is to provide support and technical assistance to local programs, insure proper use of federal money, and serve groups with special job disadvantages.

In addition to continuing programs for Indians and migrant and seasonal farmworkers, there are new and expanded efforts for youth and veterans. Programs authorized by the Youth Employment and Demonstration Projects Act of 1977 include the Young Adult Conservation Corps, which hires unemployed young people to work on public lands; Youth Incentive Entitlement Pilot Projects, providing part-time jobs and training to youth attending school; and Youth Community Conservation and Improvement Projects, which give unemployed youth paid work in community betterment. The act also provides for Youth Employment and Training Programs to improve young people's job prospects. In addition, continuing programs are increasing opportunities for young people. Job Corps, which was training disadvantaged youth at 60 residential centers in mid-1977, plans to double the number of centers it operates so that it can serve 100,000 youth per year by October 1978, and the Summer Program for Economically Disadvantaged Youth supported over a million part-time jobs in 1977.

Help Through Industry Retraining and Employment (HIRE) is a new national program to place veterans and other unemployed workers in on-the-job training in private industry, with CETA money paying employer training costs. Another action to assist veterans is the effort to place them in 35% of the public service jobs funded in 1977.

In addition to carrying out activities under CETA, the Employment and Training Administration acts as the federal partner in the employment service system and the unemployment insurance program and administers national programs authorized by other laws.

Unemployment Insurance

Unlike old-age and survivors insurance, entirely a federal program, the unemployment insurance program is a Federal-State system which provides insured wage earners with partial replacement of wages lost during involuntary unemployment. The program protects most workers in industry. By calendar year 1978, an estimated 86.2 million jobs in commerce, industry, agriculture, and government, including the armed forces, will be covered under the Federal-State system. In addition, an estimated 500,000 railroad workers will be insured against unemployment by the Railroad Retirement Board.

Each state, as well as the District of Columbia and Puerto Rico, has its own law and operates its own program. The amount and duration of the weekly benefits are determined by state laws, based on prior wages and length of employment. States are required to extend the duration of benefits when unemployment rises to and remains above specified state or national levels; costs of extended benefits are shared by the state and federal governments.

Under the Federal Unemployment Tax Act, as amended in 1976, the tax rate is 3.4% on the first $6,000 paid to each employee of employers with one or more employees in 20 weeks of the year or a quarterly payroll of $1,500. A credit of up to 2.7% is allowed for taxes paid under state unemployment insurance laws that meet certain criteria, leaving the federal share at 0.7% of taxable wages, from which the federal government pays its share of the cost of extended benefits and makes grants to the states to cover the administrative costs of the unemployment insurance and employment service programs. Grants from this source for employment service administrative costs are limited to that proportion of total employment service costs that is attributable to the covered work force.

Social Security Requirement

The Social Security Act requires, as a condition of such grants, prompt payment of due benefits. The Federal Unemployment Tax Act provides safeguards for workers' right to benefits if they refuse jobs that fail to meet certain labor standards. Through the Unemployment Insurance Service of the Employment and Training Administration, the Secretary of Labor determines whether states qualify for grants and for tax offset credit for employers.

Benefits are financed solely by employer contributions, except in Alaska, Alabama, and New Jersey, where employees also contribute. Benefits are paid through the public employment offices, at which unemployed workers must register for work and to which they must report regularly for referral to a ossible job during the time when they are drawing weekly benefit payments. During the 1976 calendar ear, $9.0 billion in benefits was paid under state nemployment insurance programs to 8,600,000 eneficiaries, representing compensation for 155,560,200 weeks of unemployment. They received an average weekly payment of $75.16 for total unemployment for an average of 14.9 weeks.

Federal Worker Benefits

Title 5, chapter 85 of the U.S. Code provided unemployment insurance protection during calendar year 976 to about 2,900,200 federal civilian employees and about 2,144,300 members of the armed forces. Benefits for unemployed federal workers and ex-servicemen are financed through direct federal appropriations but are paid by the state agencies as agents of the federal government.

During calendar year 1976, a total of $305,385,263 was paid to 144,500 unemployed federal civilian workers for a total of 2,597,100 weeks of unemployment. The average weekly payment was $77.05 and was paid for an average of 17.3 weeks. A total of $593,002,700 was paid to 281,600 unemployed ex-servicemen for 5,100,900 weeks of unemployment. The average weekly benefit was $79.39 and was paid for the average of 18.0 weeks.

Employment Security

Source: Employment and Training Administration, U.S. Labor Department

Selected unemployment insurance data by state.
Calendar year 1976, state programs only

State	Insured claimants[1] (1,000)	Beneficiaries[2] (1,000)	Exhaustions[3] (1,000)	Initial claims[4] (1,000)	Benefits paid[5] (1,000)	Avg. weekly benefit for total unemp'ment	Funds available for benefits Dec. 31, 1976 (millions)	Employers subject to state law Dec. 31, 1976 (1,000)
labama	166	151	46	301	$111,417	$66.50	$ 11	58
laska	49	44	7	74	53,797	81.82	95	9
rizona	72	66	30	165	67,704	72.63	35	51
rkansas	109	80	25	218	55,439	63.29	8	43
alifornia	1,487	1,101	391	2,514	1,123,454	71.11	641	451
olorado	91	70	34	162	61,274	84.58	36	56
onnecticut	216	202	71	415	238,013	79.18	21	70
elaware	31	27	11	58	36,519	83.89	2	13
istrict of Columbia	38	32	16	49	54,487	99.17	2	17
lorida	283	234	132	527	218,883	64.04	24	166
eorgia	256	203	88	426	135,882	68.52	223	88
awaii	48	40	19	63	57,822	85.23	−12	18
daho	37	34	10	78	22,779	70.13	54	20
linois	465	455	206	914	692,298	91.64	−505	196
ndiana	201	133	61	428	110,281	63.57	212	84
owa	89	79	29	148	92,672	87.23	47	62
ansas	68	60	20	103	51,410	70.49	143	48
entucky	146	120	39	269	96,971	67.42	126	58
ouisiana	139	104	37	210	100,247	69.14	165	64
aine	62	70	22	198	43,637	63.02	7	22
aryland	142	126	25	296	129,741	73.21	−20	70
assachusetts	326	270	121	545	329,808	76.76	94	113
ichigan	522	460	185	1,220	487,646	87.82	180	149
innesota	169	148	65	239	162,641	80.82	−19	77
ississippi	78	55	15	135	33,736	50.81	98	36
issouri	226	176	68	507	150,222	73.07	89	86
ontana	38	27	10	67	23,428	66.19	1	20
ebraska	37	36	16	75	29,913	68.12	39	33
evada	35	40	19	110	38,933	73.28	11	15
ew Hampshire	50	39	4	76	22,032	65.19	34	20
ew Jersey	496	414	199	766	525,897	77.72	15	149
ew Mexico	29	25	9	70	23,517	59.66	32	24
ew York	939	691	316	1,949	993,700	73.53	205	385
orth Carolina	351	304	71	704	173,802	63.92	265	95
orth Dakota	19	16	4	40	14,942	70.38	20	16
hio	408	332	104	853	376,242	84.60	190	178
klahoma	81	66	33	145	55,271	60.82	14	51
regon	132	112	34	314	102,129	69.06	36	54
ennsylvania	755	650	177	1,612	822,995	87.37	18	193
uerto Rico	146	141	99	272	93,517	43.29	4	42
hode Island	87	61	25	163	58,928	72.38	−54	23
outh Carolina	168	118	36	309	81,309	64.43	81	46
outh Dakota	14	13	4	27	9,100	66.14	16	16
ennessee	252	163	55	330	117,036	61.47	174	67
exas	270	191	77	447	128,718	55.35	205	215
tah	44	40	13	73	34,325	74.24	24	25
ermont	66	21	7	51	21,747	68.97	(7)	12
irginia	147	105	35	249	88,724	68.99	91	80
ashington	177	169	70	524	183,182	76.28	−88	79
est Virginia	86	75	15	139	47,632	58.76	72	29
isconsin	239	164	64	421	181,189	85.32	165	86
yoming	12	8	2	15	7,562	71.89	35	12
Total	**10,594**	**8,560**	**3,270**	**20,065**	**8,974,546**	**75.16**	**3,362**	**4,092**

(1) Claimants whose base-period earnings or whose employment — covered by the unemployment insurance program — was ufficient to make them eligible for unemployment insurance benefits as provided by state law. (2) Based on number of first payments.) Based on final payments. Some claimants shown, therefore, actually experienced their final week of compensable unemployment ward the end of the previous calendar year but received their final payments in the current calendar year. Similarly, some claimants no served their last week of compensable unemployment toward the end of the current calendar year did not receive their final ayment in this calendar year and hence are not shown. A final week of compensable unemployment in a benefit year results in the haustion of benefit rights for the benefit year. Claimants who exhaust their benefit rights in one benefit year may be entitled to further enefits in the following benefit year. (4) Excludes intrastate transitional claims to reflect more nearly instances of new unemployment. cludes claims filed by interstate claimants in the Virgin Islands. (5) Adjusted for voided benefit checks and transfers under interstate mbined wage plan. (6) Sum of balance in state clearing accounts, benefit payment accounts, and unemployment trust fund accounts aintained in the U.S. Treasury. (7) Less than $500,000.

Canadian Income Tax Rates

Source: 1976 Income Tax Return

1976 Rates of Federal Income Tax

Taxable income	Tax	Taxable income	Tax
$ 654 or less	6%	$11,763	$ 2,470 + 27% on next $ 2,614
654	$ 39 + 18% on next $ 653	14,377	3,176 + 31% on next 3,921
1,307	157 + 19% on next 1,307	18,298	4,392 + 35% on next 13,070
2,614	405 + 20% on next 1,307	31,368	8,966 + 39% on next 19,605
3,921	667 + 21% on next 2,614	50,973	16,612 + 43% on next 27,447
6,535	1,216 + 23% on next 2,614	78,420	28,414 + 47% on remainder
9,149	1,817 + 25% on next 2,614		

1976 Rates of Provincial Income Tax

Newfoundland	41%	Manitoba	42.5%
Prince Edward Island	36%	Saskatchewan	40%
Nova Scotia	38.5%	Alberta	26%
New Brunswick	41.5%	British Columbia	31.5%
Ontario	30.5%		

Canada: Taxable Returns by Income, 1974

Source: Taxation Statistics

Total Income in dollars	Number	Per-cent	Total income (millions)	Per-cent	Taxed income (millions)	Federal tax[1] (millions)	Per-cent
0-1,500	25,793	.29	$ 22.8	.03	$ 7.4	$ .0	.0
1,500-2,000	47,371	.82	89.2	.12	10.2	.5	.0
2,000-3,000	427,755	5.61	1,080.5	1.33	233.4	1.3	.0
3,000-4,000	619,814	12.55	2,185.9	3.77	778.2	32.4	.3
4,000-5,000	761,852	21.08	3,437.0	7.60	1,518.5	126.0	1.1
5,000-10,000	3,580,241	61.17	26,308.3	36.95	15,269.7	2,113.9	19.9
10,000-15,000	2,155,194	85.31	26,221.3	66.20	17,585.1	3,089.6	29.1
15,000-20,000	779,873	94.04	13,271.8	81.01	9,440.4	1,888.9	17.8
20,000-25,000	257,830	96.93	5,685.9	87.35	4,163.5	908.1	8.5
25,000-50,000	224,527	99.44	7,303.0	95.50	5,615.8	1,384.2	13.0
50,000-100,000	41,931	99.91	2,745.3	98.56	2,280.5	682.9	6.4
100,000-200,000	6,745	99.99	874.6	99.54	747.1	259.7	2.4
200,000-& over	1,306	100.00	414.2	100.00	351.1	128.6	1.2
Total	**8,930,232**	**100.00**	**89,639.7**	**100.00**	**58,000.9**	**10,616.0**	**100.0**

(1) Federal taxes include income taxes, social development tax, and old age security tax.

Federal Taxes in Selected Canadian Cities, 1974

Source: Taxation Statistics

City	Rank[1]	No. of returns[2]	Average income	Avg. tax
Barrie	51	18,351	$9,844	$1,231
Belleville	58	19,660	9,652	1,155
Brantford	47	32,696	9,876	1,262
Brockville	63	12,148	9,601	1,201
Calgary	25	206,215	10,364	1,364
Cambridge	92	34,358	8,830	1,038
Charlottetown	99	10,699	8,393	906
Chatham	26	20,984	10,348	1,331
Chicoutimi	34	24,822	10,161	869
Cornwall	96	19,467	8,747	995
Dartmouth	57	31,240	9,666	1,146
Dawson Creek	85	6,512	9,113	1,073
Drummondville	88	17,199	8,963	728
Edmonton	33	244,569	10,218	1,327
Fredericton	61	21,502	9,254	1,075
Guelph	42	29,840	9,997	1,258
Halifax	62	65,876	9,606	1,164
Hamilton	15	219,455	10,578	1,407
Hull	21	51,433	10,455	1,019
Kamloops	23	25,233	10,407	1,353
Kingston	48	41,809	9,873	1,246
Kitchener-Waterloo	54	84,910	9,760	1,233
Lethbridge	52	20,326	9,824	1,186
Levis	30	18,117	10,295	933
London	35	118,305	10,151	1,309
Longueuil	48	43,290	9,873	859
Mississauga	4	98,750	11,298	1,631
Moncton	95	28,762	8,808	965
Montreal	8	798,436	10,872	1,073
New Westminister	29	21,095	$10,302	$1,360
Niagara Falls	65	30,864	9,532	1,117
North Bay	36	20,426	10,149	1,257
Oakville	2	30,920	12,212	1,834
Oshawa	22	48,510	10,435	1,391
Ottawa	6	225,569	11,099	1,528
Pembroke	98	8,113	8,673	943
Peterborough	50	30,734	9,848	1,195
Prince George	7	26,640	11,004	1,512
Quebec	13	147,666	10,616	1,03
Regina	46	64,688	9,890	1,213
St. Catharines	20	60,886	10,460	1,338
Saint John, N.B.	89	37,326	8,889	1,00
St. John's, Nfld.	84	44,397	9,157	1,11
Sarnia	5	34,907	11,204	1,537
Saskatoon	60	57,706	9,624	1,13
Saulte Ste. Marie	17	33,482	10,517	1,366
Sherbrooke	44	32,374	9,989	89
Sudbury	37	60,900	10,139	1,26
Sydney-Glace Bay	100	40,025	8,331	85
Thunder Bay	37	50,928	10,139	1,30
Timmins	68	17,577	9,491	1,14
Toronto	19	1,158,990	10,481	1,44
Trois-Rivieres	40	21,362	10,111	92
Vancouver	12	505,354	10,629	1,43
Victoria	41	102,288	10,077	1,23
Welland	77	19,410	9,310	1,12
Windsor	11	105,908	10,766	1,38
Winnipeg	73	262,891	9,463	1,12

(1) Rank refers to position in order of average income. (2) Taxable returns only.

State Individual Income Taxes: Rates, Exemptions

Source: Tax Foundation, Inc. Data as of July 1, 1977
Footnotes at end of table.

State	Taxable income	Percentage rates	Taxable income	Percentage rates	Personal exemp. Single	Personal exemp. Married family head	Credit per depend.
Alabama[1]	First $1,000	1.5	$2,001-$5,000	4.5	$1,500	$3,000	$300
	1,001- 2,000	3	Over 5,000	5			
Alaska	Rates range from 3% on first $4,000 to 14.5% over $400,000				Federal exemptions		
Arizona[1 2]	First 1,000	2	3,001- 4,000	5	1,000	2,000	600
	1,001- 2,000	3	4,001- 5,000	6			
	2,001- 3,000	4	5,001- 6,000	7	Over 6,000	8	
Arkansas[3]	First 2,999	1	9,000-14,999	4.5	17.50	35	6
	3,000- 5,999	2.5	15,000-24,999	6	(tax credit)		
	6,000- 8.999	3.5	25,000 and over	7			
California[1 2]	First 2,000	1	8,001- 9,500	6	(tax credit) 25	50	8
	2,001- 3,500	2	9,501-11,000	7			
	3,501- 5,000	3	11,001-12,500	8	Heads of households have slightly lower tax rates.		
	5,001- 6,500	4	12,501-14,000	9			
	6,501- 8,000	5	14,001-15,500	10	Over 15,500	11	
Colorado[1 4]	First 1,000	3	6,001- 7,000	6	750	1,500	750
	1,001- 2,000	3.5	7,001- 8,000	6.5			
	2,001- 3,000	4	8,001- 9,000	7			
	3,001- 4,000	4.5	9,001-10,000	7.5	Surtax on intangible income over $5,000, 2%. A credit equal to 1/2 of 1% of net taxable income is allowed for income under $9,000.		
	4,001- 5,000	5	Over 10,000	8			
	5,001- 6,000	5.5					
Connecticut	Capital gains tax; range from 1% on $20,000 through 9% on $100,000 and over						
Delaware[3]	First 1,000	1.6	6,001- 8,000	7.7	Federal exemptions		
	1,001- 2,000	2.2	8,001-20,000	8.8			
	2,001- 3,000	3.3	20,001-25,000	9.3			
	3,001- 4,000	4.4	25,001-30,000	9.9		50,001- 75,000	15.4
	4,001- 5,000	5.5	30,001-40,000	12.1		75,001-100,000	16.5
	5,001- 6,000	6.6	40,001-50,000	13.2		Over 100,000	19.8
Dist. of Col.[1 4]	First 1,000	2	5,001-10,000	7	Federal exemptions		
	1,001-2,000	3	10,001-13,000	8			
	2,001-3,000	4	13,001-17,000	9			
	3,001-4,000	5	17,001-25,000	10			
	4,001-5,000	6	Over 25,000	11			
Georgia[3 5]	First 750	1	5,251- 7,000	5	1,500	3,000	700
	751- 2,250	2	Over 7,000	6			
	2,251- 3,750	3					
	3,751- 5,250	4					
	For married persons filing separately, rates range from 1% on the first $500 to 6% on $5,000 or more. For married couples filing jointly and heads of households, rates range from 1% on the first $1,000 to 6% on $10,000 or more.						
Hawaii[1]	First 500	2.25	5,001-10,000	8.5	750	1,500	750
	501- 1,000	3.25	10,001-14,000	9.5			
	1,001- 1,500	4.5	14,001-20,000	10			
	1,501- 2,000	5	20,001-30,000	10.5	Special tax rates for heads of households.		
	2,001- 3,000	6.5	Over 30,000	11			
	3,001- 5,000	7.5					
Idaho[2 3 4]	First 1,000	2	3,001- 4,000	5.5	Federal exemptions		
	1,001- 2,000	4	4,001- 5,000	6.5	Plus tax credit of $15 for each exemption.		
	2,001- 3,000	4.5	Over 5,000	7.5			
Illinois	Total net income		2.5		1,000	2,000	1,000
Indiana[4]	Adjusted gross	2			1,000	*2,000	500
	*Lesser of $1,000 or adjusted gross income of each spouse, but not less than $500.						
Iowa[3]	First 1,000	0.5	3,001- 4,000	3.5	(tax credit) 15	30	10
	1,001- 2,000	1.25	4,001- 7,000	5	Net incomes $4,000 or less are not taxable.		
	2,001- 3,000	2.75	7,001- 9,000	6	On up to 13% over $75,000		
Kansas[1 4]	First 2,000	2	5,001- 7,000	5	750	1,500	750
	2,001- 3,000	3.5	7,001-10,000	6.5	20,001-25,000	8.5	
	3,001- 5,000	4	10,001-20,000	7.5	Over 25,000	9.5	
Kentucky[1]	First 3,000	2	4,001- 5,000	4	(tax credit) 20	40	20
	3,001- 4,000	3	5,001- 8,000	5	Over 8,000	6	

State	Taxable income	Percentage rates	Taxable income	Percentage rates	Personal exemp. Single	Personal exemp. Married family head	Credit per depend.
Louisiana[1,2]	First 10,000	2	Over 50,000	6	2,500	5,000	400
	10,001-50,000	4					
Credits are allowed new income which is taxed at 2%; additional $1,000 exemp. for blindness allowed for dependents.							
Maine[1]	First 2,000	1	8,001-10,000	7	1,000	2,000	1,000
	2,001- 4,000	2	10,001-15,000	8			
	4,001- 6,000	4	15,001-25,000	9			
	6,001- 8,000	6	Over 25,000	10	on up to 8% over 50,000		
Maryland[1,4]	First 1,000	2	2,001- 3,000	4	800	1,600	800
	1,001- 2,000	3	Over 3,000	5			
An additional exemption of $800 is allowed for each dependent 65 or over.							
Massachusetts	Earned and business income:	5*			2,000	2,600-4,600	600
	Interest, divs., capital gains on intangibles:	10*					
The exemptions shown are those allowed against business income, including salaries and wages. A specific exemption of $2,000 is allowed for each taxpayer. In addition, a dependency exemption of $600 is allowed for a dependent spouse who has income from all sources of less than $2,000. In the case of a joint return, the exemption is the smaller of (1) $4,600 or (2) $2,600 plus the income of the spouse having the smaller income.							
*Plus 7.5% surtax.							
Michigan[4]	All taxable income	4.6			1,500	3,000	1,500
Minnesota[1,4]	First 500	1.6	5,001- 7,000	10.2	21	42	2
	501- 1,000	2.2	7,001- 9,000	11.5			
	1,001- 2,000	3.5	9,001-12,500	12.8			
	2,001- 3,000	5.8	12,501-20,000	14			
	3,001- 4,000	7.3	Over 20,000	15	An additional tax credit of $21 is allowed for each taxpayer 65 years old.		
	4,001- 5,000	8.8					
Mississippi[3]	First 5,000	3	Over 5,000	4	4,500	6,500	750
Missouri[1]	First 1,000	1.5	5,001- 6,000	4	1,200	2,400	400
	1,001- 2,000	2	6,001- 7,000	4.5			
	2,001- 3,000	2.5	7,001- 8,000	5			
	3,001- 4,000	3	8,001- 9,000	5.5	An additional $800 exemption is allowed unmarried head of household.		
	4,001- 5,000	3.5	Over 9,000	6			
Montana[3]	First 1,000	2	8,001-10,000	7	650	1,300	650
	1,001-2,000	3	10,001-14,000	8			
	2,001-4,000	4	14,001-20,000	9	Additional surtax of 10% on tax liability.		
	4,001-6,000	5	20,001-35,000	10			
	6,001-8,000	6	Over 35,000	11			
Nebraska[3,4]					Federal exemptions		
The tax is imposed as a % of the taxpayer's Fed. income tax liability (not including surtax) before credits, with limited adjustments. For the year 1977 the rate was set at 18% by State Board of Equalization and Assessment.							
New Hampshire.	Interest and dividends (except interest on savings accounts).	5	4% commuter tax		600	600-1,200	
Each spouse with taxable income is allowed a $600 exemption.							
New Jersey[3]	First 20,000	2			1,000	1,000	1,000
	Over 20,000	2.5			Additional credit of $35 allowed for the elderly and disabled.		
Commuter tax from 1.6% on net income under $1,000 to 19.8% on income over $100,000.							
New Mexico[2,3]	First 500	0.9	6,001-7,000	3.0	Federal exemptions		
	501-1,000	1.1	7,001-8,000	3.3			
	1,001-1,500	1.3	8,001-10,000	3.6			
	1,501-2,000	1.5	10,001-12,000	4.3	The income classes reported are for individuals. For joint returns and heads of households, a separate rate schedule is provided. A credit is allowed for state and local taxes for gross income of less than $8,000.		
	2,001-3,000	1.6	12,001-20,000	6.1			
	3,001-4,000	1.9	20,001-50,000	8.0			
	4,001-5,000	2.3	50,001-100,000	8.5			
	5,001-6,000	2.4	Over 100,000	9.0			
New York[1]	First 1,000	2	13,001-15,000	9	650	1,300	650
	1,001- 3,000	3	15,001-17,000	10	Tax credits of $10.00 for single persons, $12.50 for married persons filing separately and $25 for married persons filing jointly and heads of households are allowed.		
	3,001- 5,000	4	17,001-19,000	11			
	5,001- 7,000	5	19,001-21,000	12			
	7,001- 9,000	6	21,001-23,000	13			
	9,001-11,000	7	23,001-25,000	14			
	11,001-13,000	8	Over 25,000	15			
Income from unincorporated business is taxed at 5.5%. The following credit is allowed: $110 tax or less, full amount; $110 to $550 difference between $137.50 and 25% of amount of tax; $550 or more, no credit. A 2.5% surtax is imposed.							

State	Taxable income	Percentage rates	Taxable income	Percentage rates	Personal exemp. Single	Personal exemp. Married family head	Credit per depend.
North Carolina[3]	First 2,000	3	6,001-10,000	6	1,000	2,000*	600
	2,001-4,000	4	Over 10,000	7			
	4,001-6,000	5					

*An additional exemption of $1,000 is allowed the spouse having the lower income; joint returns are not permitted.

North Dakota[3]	First 1,000	1	6,001-8,000	7.5	750	1,500	750
	1,001-3,000	2	Over 8,000	10			
	3,001-5,000	3					
	5,001-6,000	5					

A credit of 25% of income tax liability is allowed up to a maximum of $100.

Ohio[4]	First 5,000	0.5	15,001-20,000	2.5	650	1,300	650
	5,001-10,000	1	20,001-40,000	3			
	10,001-15,000	2	Over 40,000	3.5			

Maximum personal exemption is $3,000 per return. Taxpayers age 65 or older are allowed a $25 credit, or if they have received a lump sum distribution from a pension, retirement or profit sharing plan during the tax year, they are allowed a credit equal to $25 times the taxpayer's expected remaining life. Credit may not exceed tax otherwise due. Credit is also allowed for an amount paid during the school year for elementary and secondary education or instruction or training of dependents who do not have a high school diploma.

Oklahoma[1]	First 1,000	0.5	5,001-6,250	4	750	1,500	750
	1,001-2,500	1	6,251-7,500	5			
	2,501-3,750	2	Over 7,500	6			
	3,751-5,000	3					

For joint returns the rates shown apply to income classes twice as large. Rates of heads of households range from 1/2% on the first $1,500 to 6% on taxable income over $11,250. Non-residents are taxed at a flat rate of 6% of Oklahoma taxable income.

Oregon[3]	First $500	4	3,001-4,000	8	750	1,500	750
	501-1,000	5	4,001-5,000	9			
	1,001-2,000	6	Over 5,000	10			
	2,001-3,000	7					

A credit is provided in an amount and equal to 25% of the federal retirement income tax credit to the extent that such a credit is based on Oregon taxable income.

Pennsylvania	All taxable income	2					
Rhode Island	17% of federal income tax liability				Federal Exemptions.		
South Carolina[1]	First 2,000	2	6,001- 8,000	5	800	1,600	800
	2,001-4,000	3	8,001-10,000	6			
	4,001-6,000	4	Over 10,000	7			
Tennessee	Interest and dividends	6					

Dividends from corporations, 75% of whose property is taxable in Tenn., are taxed at 4%.

Utah	First 750	2.25	2,251-3,000	5.25	Federal exemptions		
	751-1,500	3.25	3,001-3,750	6.25	Over 4,500	7.75	
	1,501-2,250	4.25	3,751-4,500	7.25			
Vermont					Federal exemptions.		

The tax is imposed at a rate of 25% of the fed. income tax liability of the taxpayer for the taxable year after certain credits (retirement income, investment, foreign tax, child and dependent care, and tax-free covenant bonds) but before any surtax on fed. liability, reduced by a % equal to the % of the taxpayer's adjusted gross income for the taxable year which is not Vermont income. A 9% surcharge is imposed for 1974, and thereafter.

Virginia[3]	First 3,000	2	5,001-12,000	5	600	1,200	600
	3,001-5,000	3	Over 12,000	5.75			
West Virginia[1]	First 2,000	2.1	26,001-32,000	6.5	600	1,200	600
	2,001-4,000	2.3	32,001-38,000	6.8			
	4,001-6,000	2.8	38,001-44,000	7.2			
	6,001-8,000	3.2	44,001-50,000	7.5			
	8,001-10,000	3.5	50,001-60,000	7.9			
	10,001-12,000	4	60,001-70,000	8.2			
	12,001-14,000	4.6	70,001-80,000	8.6			
	14,001-16,000	4.9	80,001-90,000	8.8			
	16,001-18,000	5.3	90,001-100,000	9.1			
	18,001-20,000	5.4	100,001-150,000	9.3			
	20,001-22,000	6	150,001-200,000	9.5			
	22,001-26,000	6.1	Over 200,000	9.6			

For joint returns and a return of a surviving spouse, a separate rate schedule is provided.

Wisconsin[4]	First 1,000	3.1	8,001-9,000	8.2	(Tax Credit) 20	40	20
	1,001-2,000	3.4	9,001-10,000	8.8			
	2,001-3,000	3.6	10,001-11,000	9.3			
	3,001-4,000	4.8	11,001-12,000	9.9			

(continued)

State	Taxable income	Percentage rates	Taxable income	Percentage rates	Personal exemp. Single	Married family head	Credit depend
Wisconsin (cont.)	4,001-5,000	5.4	12,001-13,000	10.5			
	5,001-6,000	5.9	13,001-14,000	11.1			
	6,001-7,000	6.5	Over 14,000	11.4			
	7,001-8,000	7.6					

(1) A standard deduction and optional tax table are provided. In Louisiana, only optional tax table is provided.
(2) Community property state in which, in general, one-half of the community income is taxable to each spouse.
(3) A standard deduction is allowed.
(4) A limited tax credit is allowed for sales taxes in Colorado, Idaho, Massachusetts, Nebraska, and Vermont; for property taxes on homesteads of the elderly in Arizona, Colorado, Indiana, Kansas, Michigan, Minnesota, Missouri, New Jersey, Oklahoma, and Vermont; for property taxes and city income taxes in Michigan; and for personal property taxes in Maryland and Wisconsin; for property taxes in D.C. if household income is less than $7,000.
(5) Tax credits are allowed: $15 for single person or married person filing separately if AGI is $3,000 or less. (For each dollar by which the federal AGI exeeeds $3,000 the credit is reduced by $1 until no credit is allowed if federal AGI is $3,015 or more.) $30 for heads of households or married persons filing jointly with $6,000 or less AGI. (For each dollar by which federal AGI exceeds $6,000, credit is reduced by $1 until no credit is all owed if federal AGI is $6,030 or more.)

State Retail Sales Taxes: Types and Rates

Source: Advisory Commission on Intergovernmental Relations

State	Tangible personal property	Admissions	Selected service: Rest. meals	Transient lodging	Public utilities	Rates on other services and nonretail business
Alabama[2]	4%[3]	4%	4%	4%	. . .	Gross rcpts of amus't operators, 4% agric., mining and mfg. mach., 1.5%.
Arizona[2]	4	4	4	3	4	Timbering, 1.5%; storage, apt., office rental, 3%.
Arkansas[2]	3	3	3	3	3	Printing, photographic services; rcpts from coin-operated dev.; repair services incl. auto and elect., 3%.
California[2]	4.75[5]	. . .	4.75	. . .	[14]	Renting, leasing, producing, fabricating processing, printing, 4.75%.
Colorado[2]	3	. . .	3	3[10]	3	
Connecticut	7	. . .	7[7]	7[10]	7[13]	Storing for use or consumption of personal property items, 7%.
D. of C.	5[3]	5	6	6	5	Duplicating, mailing, addressing and public stenographic services, 5%; sales of food for off-premise consumption, nonprescription medicines, 2%
Florida	4	4	4	4	. . .	Rental income of amus't. mach., 4%.
Georgia	3	3	3	3	3	Levies on amus't dev., 3%.
Hawaii[1]	4	4	4	4	. . .	Sugar processors, pineapple farmers and selected businesses, 0,5%; insur. solicitors, 2%; contractors, sales rep., professions, radio stations, 4%
Idaho[6]	3	3	3	3	. . .	Closed circuit TV boxing, wrestling, 5%.
Illinois[2]	4	. . .	4	. . .	. . .	Property sold in connection with a sale of service, 4%; remodeling, repairing and reconditioning of tangible personal property, 4%
Indiana	4	. . .	4	4	4	
Iowa	3	3	3	3	3	Laundry, dry cleaning, automobile and cold storage, photography, printing, repairs, barber and beauty parlor services, advt., dry cleaning equip. rentals and gross rcpts from amus't dev., 3%
Kansas[2]	3	3	3	3	3	Gross rcpts. from operation of coin-operated devices; commer. amus't, 3%.
Kentucky[2]	5	5	5	5	5	Storage, sewer services, photog. and photo fin., 5%; ticket sales to boxing or wrestling on closed circuit TV 5% of gross rcpts; tax also applies to pay'ts for right to broadcast matches
Louisiana[2]	3	3	3	3	. . .	Food and prescpt'n. drugs, exempt.
Maine	5	. . .	5	5	5	Proceeds from closed circuit TV, 5%.
Maryland[2]	4[3]	[11]	4[7]	4	4	Farm equip., 2%; mfg. equip., including that used in generation of electricity or in R.&S. sold to mfrs., 2%; watercraft, 3%
Mass.	5	. . .	[7]	5.7[9]	. . .	
Michigan	4	. . .	4	4	4	
Minnesota[2]	4[3]	4	4	4	4	Food, medicines and clothing are exempt; coin-operated vending mach., 3% of gross sales

State	Tangible personal property	Admissions	Selected service: Rest. meals	Selected service: Transient lodging	Selected service: Public utilities	Rates on other services and nonretail business
Mississippi[1]	5[3]		5	5	5	Wholesaling, 0.125% (0.5% on sales of meat for human consumption; 5% on beer, alc. bevs., soft drinks and motor fuel); extracting or mining of minerals, specified miscellaneous bus. incl. bowling, pool halls, warehouses, laundry and dry cleaning, pest control services, specified repair services, 5%; cotton ginning, 15c per bale; sales of materials to railroads for use in track structures, 3%; tractors, indust. fuel and mfg. mach. sales over $500, 1%.
Missouri[2]	3	3	3	3	3	
Nebraska[2]	2.5	2.5	2.5	2.5	2.5	
Nevada[2]	3[10]	...	3	...	...	
New Jersey[1 2]	5	5[11]	5	5[9]	...	
New Mexico[1 2]	4[3]	4	4	4	4	
New York[2]	4	4[11]	4[7]	4[9]	4	Safe deposit rentals, 4%.
North Carolina[2]	3[3]	...	3	3	...	Farm and industrial machinery, 1% ($80 max.); airplanes, boats and locomotives, 2% ($120 max.); sales of horses and mules, 1%.
North Dakota	4[3]	4	4	4	4	Severance of sand or gravel from the soil, 4%.
Ohio[2]	4	...	4	4	...	
Oklahoma[2]	2[3]	2	2	2	2	Advert. (exclusive of newspapers, periodicals, billboards), printing, auto storage, gross proceeds from amusement dev., 2%.
Pennsylvania[2]	6	...	6[7]	6	6	Cleaning, polishing, lubr. and insp. motor vehicles, rental income of coin-operated amuse. dev., 6%.
Rhode Island	6	...	6	6	6	
South Carolina	4	...	4	4	4	
South Dakota[1 2]	4[3]	4	4	3	3	Farm mach. and agric. irrigation equip., 2%; gross rcpts. from professions (other than medical), 4%.
Tennessee[2]	4.5	...	4.5	4.5	4.5	Vending machines, 1.5% (except tobacco products, 2.5%); industrial, farm equipment and machinery, 1%.
Texas[2]	4[3]	...	4	...	4	
Utah[2]	4	4	4	4	4	
Vermont	3	3	[12]	[12]	3	
Virginia[2]	3[3]	...	3	3	...	
Washington[1 2]	4.6	4.6	4.6	4.6	...	Rentals, auto, parking, other specified services, amusements, recreations, 4.5% (unless subject to county or city adm. taxes, when they remain taxable under the state business, occupation levy, 1%).
West Virginia[1]	3[3]	3	3	3	...	All services except public util. and personal and professional sevices, 3%.
Wisconsin[2]	4	4[11]	4	4	4	
Wyoming[2]	3	3	3	3	3	

(1) All but a few states levy sales taxes of the single-stage retail type. Ha. and Miss. levy multiple-stage sales taxes. The N.M. and S.D. taxes have broad bases with respect to taxable services but they are not multiple-stage taxes. Wash. and W.Va. levy gross receipts taxes on all business, distinct from their sales taxes. Alaska also levies a gross receipts tax on businesses. The rates applicable to retailers, with exceptions, under these gross receipts taxes are as follows: Alaska 0.5% on gross receipts of $20,000-$100,000 and 0.25% on gross receipts in excess of $100,000; Wash., 0.44%, plus a 6% surtax; and W.Va., 0.55%. N.J. imposes a tax of 0.05% on retail stores with income in excess of $150,000, and an unincorporated business tax at the rate of 0.25% of 1% if gross receipts exceed $5,000.

(2) In addition to the State tax, sales taxes are also levied by certain cities and/or counties.

(3) Motor vehicles are taxed at the general sales tax rates with the following exceptions: Ala., 1.5%; Miss., 3%; and N.C., 2% ($120 maximum). Motor vehicles are exempt from the general sales and use taxes but are taxed under motor vehicle tax laws in Md., 4%; Minn., 4%; N.M., 2%; N.D. 4%; Okla., 2%; S.D. and W.Va., 3%; Tex., 4%; Va., 2%; and the D.C., 4%.

(4) Ariz. and Miss. also tax the transportation of oil and gas by pipeline. Ga., Mo., Okla., and Utah do not tax transportation of property. Miss. taxes taxicab transportation at the rate of 2%. Okla. does not tax fares of 15c or less on local transportation. Utah does not tax street railway fares.

(5) "Lease" excludes the use of tangible personal property for a period of less than one day for a charge of less than $10 when the privilege of using the property is restricted to use on the premises or at a business location of the grantor.

(6) A limited credit (or refund) in the form of a flat dollar amount per personal exemption is allowed against the personal income tax to compensate for (1) sales taxes paid on food in Col., D.C., and Neb.; and (2) all sales taxes paid in Ida., Mass. and Vt. Low-income taxpayers (adjusted gross income not over $6,000) are allowed a credit against D.C. tax liability ranging from $2 to $6 per personal exemption, depending on taxpayer's income bracket. A refund is allowed if credit exceeds tax liability.

(7) Restaurant meals below a specified price are exempt: Conn. and Md. less than $1; N.Y. less than $1 (when alcoholic beverages are sold, meals are taxable regardless of price); and Pa., 50c or less. In Mass., restaurant meals ($1 or more) which are taxed at 8% under the meals excise tax are exempt.

(8) Conn., exempts clothing for children under 10 years of age. Pa. and Wisc. exempt clothing with certain exceptions.

(9) In Col. and Conn., the first 30 consecutive days of rental or occupancy of rooms is taxable. Over 30 days is exempt. In

Mass., transient lodging (in excess of $2 a day) is subject to a 5.7% (5% plus 14% surtax) room occupancy excise tax. In N.J. and N.Y., rooms which rent for $2 a day or less are exempt.

(10) Includes a statewide mandatory 1% county sales tax collected by the state and paid to the counties for support of local school districts.

(11) Md. taxes at 0.5% gross receipts derived from charges for rentals of sporting or recreational equipment, and admissions, cover charges for tables, services or merchandise at any roof garden or cabaret. In N.J., admissions to a place of amusement are taxable if the charge is in excess of 75c. N.Y. taxes admissions when the charge is over 10c; exempt are participating sports (such as bowling and swimming), motion picture theaters, race tracks, boxing, wrestling, and live dramatic or musical performances. In Wis., sales of admissions to motion picture theaters costing 75c or less are exempt.

(12) Meals and rooms are exempt from sales tax, but are subject to a special excise tax of 5%.

(13) Gas, water, electricity, telephone and telegraph services provided to consumers through mains, lines or pipes are exempt. Gas and electric energy used for domestic heating are exempt. Interstate telephone calls are exempt, as are calls from coin-operated telephones.

(14) Beginning Jan. 1, 1975, a surcharge for efficiency is imposed at the rate of 1/10th mill ($0.0001) per kwh.

State Estate Tax Rates and Exemptions

Source: Compiled by Tax Foundation from Commerce Clearing House data

As of Sept. 1, 1977. *See index for state inheritance tax rates and exemptions.*

State (a)	Rates (on net estate after exemptions) (b)	Maximum rate applies above	Exemption
Alabama	Maximum federal credit (c, d)	$10,040,000	$60,000
Alaska	Maximum federal credit (c, d)	10,040,000	60,000
Arizona	0.8% on first $50,000 to 16% (e)	10,000,000	100,000 (f, g)
Arkansas	Maximum federal credit (c, d)	10,040,000	60,000 (g)
Florida	Maximum federal credit (c, d)	10,040,000	60,000
Georgia	Maximum federal credit (c, d)	10,040,000	60,000
Massachusetts	5% on first $50,000 to 16%	4,000,000	30,000 (h)
Mississippi	1% on first $60,000 to 16%	10,000,000	60,000 (f, g)
New Mexico	Maximum federal credit (c, d)	10,040,000	60,000
New York	2% on first $50,000 to 21% (e,i)	10,100,000	(f, g, j)
North Dakota	4% on first $10,000 to 18% (e)	80,000	60,000 (g)
Ohio	2% on first $40,000 to 7% (e)	500,000	5,000 (g, k)
Oklahoma	1% on first $10,000 to 10% (e)	10,000,000	60,000 (g,l,m
South Carolina	4% on first $40,000 to 6%	100,000	60,000 (g)
Utah	Maximum federal credit (c, d)	10,400,000	60,000 (g)
Vermont	Maximum federal credit (e, n)	10,040,000	60,000 (g)

(a) Excludes states shown in table on page 67 which levy an estate tax, in addition to their inheritance taxes, to assure full absorption of the federal credit.

(b) The rates generally are in addition to graduated absolute amounts.

(c) Maximum federal credit allowed under the 1954 code for state estate taxes paid is expressed as a percentage of the taxable estate (after $60,000 exemption) in excess of $40,000, plus a graduated absolute amount.

(d) A tax on nonresident estates is imposed on the proportionate share of the net estate which the property located in the state bears to the entire estate wherever situated.

(e) An additional estate tax is imposed to assure full absorption of the federal credit.

(f) Insurance receives special treatment.

(g) Transfers to religious, charitable, educational, and municipal corporations are fully exempt. Limited in Mississippi to those located in U.S. or its possessions.

(h) Applies to net estates above $60,000.

(i) On net estate before exemption.

(j) The specific exemptions ($20,000 of the net estate transferred to spouse and $5,000 to lineal ancestors and descendants and certain other named relatives) are allowed in an amount equal to 2% of the first $50,000 and 3% of the next $100,000.

(k) Property is exempt to the extent transferred to surviving spouse not exceeding $30,000; for a child under 18, $7,000, and for each child 18 or over, $3,000.

(l) An estate valued at $100 or less is exempt.

(m) Exemption is a total aggregate of $60,000 for father, mother, child, and other named relatives.

(n) The tax is 30% of the federal estate tax liability. Taxes on estates of decedents dying after 12/31/76, but before 1/1/79, are reduced by the percentage that $120 000 is of the amount of the federal taxable estate; after 12/31/78, $240,000. The reduction shall not be more than 100%.

City Income Tax in U.S. Cities over 50,000

Compiled by Tax Foundation from Commerce Clearing House data and other sources.

City	Rates % 1977	Rates % Orig.	Year began
Cities with 500,000 or more inhabitants			
Baltimore, Md.	(50% of state tax)	1.0	1966
Cleveland, Oh.	1.0	0.5	1967
Columbus, Oh.	1.5	0.5	1947
Detroit, Mich.	2.0	1.0	1965
Kansas City, Mo.	1.0	0.5	1964
New York, N.Y.	0.9-4.3	0.4-2.0	1966
Philadelphia, Pa.	4.3125	1.5	1939
Pittsburgh, Pa.	1.0	1.0	1954
St. Louis, Mo.	1.0	.25	1948
Cities with 100,000 to 499,999 inhabitants			
Akron, Oh.	1.5	1.0	1962
Allentown, Pa.	1.0	1.0	1958
Birmingham, Ala.	1.0	1.0	1970
Canton, Oh.	1.5	0.6	1954
Cincinnati, Oh.	2.0	1.0	1954
Dayton, Oh.	1.75	0.5	1949
Erie, Pa.	1.0	1.0	1948
Flint, Mich.	1.0	1.0	1965
Grand Rapids, Mich.	1.0	1.0	1967
Lansing, Mich.	1.0	1.0	1968
Lexington, Ky.	2.0	1.0	1952
Louisville, Ky.	2.0	1.0	1948
Parma, Oh.	1.0	0.5	1967

City	Rates % 1977	Rates % Orig.	Yea bega
Scranton, Pa.	2.0	1.0	1948
Toledo, Oh.	1.5	1.0	1946
Youngstown, Oh.	1.5	0.3	1948
Cities with 50,000 to 99,999 inhabitants			
Altoona, Pa.	1.0	1.0	194
Bethlehem, Pa.	1.0	1.0	195
Chester, Pa.	1.0	1.0	195
Covington, Ky.	2.5	1.0	195
Euclid, Oh.	1.0	0.5	196
Gadsden, Ala.	2.0	1.0	195
Hamilton, Oh.	1.5	0.8	196
Harrisburg, Pa.	1.0	1.0	196
Lakewood, Oh.	1.0	1.0	196
Lancaster, Pa.	0.5	0.5	195
Lima, Oh.	1.0	.75	195
Lorain, Oh.	1.0	0.5	196
Pontiac, Mich.	1.0	1.0	196
Reading, Pa.	1.0	1.0	196
Saginaw, Mich.	1.0	1.0	196
Springfield, Oh.	2.0	1.0	194
Warren, Oh.	1.0	0.5	195
Wilkes-Barre, Pa.	1.0	1.0	196
Wilmington, Del.	1.25	0.5	197
York, Pa.	1.0	1.0	196

State Inheritance Tax Rates and Exemptions

Source: Compiled by Tax Foundation from Commerce Clearing House data.
As of Sept. 1, 1977

State (a)	Rates (b) (per cent)			Max. rate applies above ($1,000)	Exemptions (c) ($1,000)			
	Spouse, child, or parent	Brother or sister	Other than relative		Spouse	Child or parent	Brother or sister	Other than relative
California	3-14	6-20	10-24	400	60 (d)	5 (e)	2	0.3
Colorado (f)	2-8	3-10	10-19	500	30	10 (e)	2	0.5 (g)
Connecticut (i)	2-8	4-10	8-14	1,000	50	10	3	0.5
Delaware	1-6	5-10	10-16	200	70	3	1	None
District of Columbia	1-8	5-23	5-23	1,000	5	5	1	1
Hawaii	1.5-7.5	3.5-9	3.5-9	250	20	5	0.5	0.5
Idaho	2-15	4-20	8-30	500	30 (d)	15 (e)	10	10
Illinois	2-14	2-14	10-30	500	20	20	10	0.1
Indiana	1-10	7-15	10-20	1,500 (h)	60	2 (e)	0.5	0.1
Iowa	1-8	5-10	10-15	150	80	10 (e)	None	None
Kansas	0.5-5	3-12.5	10-15	500	75	15	5	0.2 (g)
Kentucky	2-10	4-16	6-16	500 (j)	20	5 (e)	1	0.5
Louisiana	2-3	5-7	5-10	25	5 (d)	5	1	0.5
Maine	5-10	8-14	14-18	250	50	25	1	1
Maryland (k)	1	10	10	(l)	.15 (g)	.15 (g)	0.15 (g)	0.15 (g)
Massachusetts (m)	1.8-11.8	5.5-19.3	8-19.3	1,000	30 (n)	15 (n)	5 (n)	5 (n)
Michigan	2-8 (o)	2-8 (o)	10-15 (o)	750	30 (e)	5	5	None
Minnesota	1.5-10	6-25	8-30	1,000	60	6 (e)	1.5	0.5
Missouri	1-6	3-18	5-30	400	20 (p)	5 (e)	0.5	0.1 (g)
Montana	2-8	4-16	8-32	100	40	7 (e)	1.0	None
Nebraska	1	1	6-18	60	10	10	10	0.5
New Hampshire	(q)	15	15	(l)	(q)	(q)	None	None
New Jersey	1-16	11-16	15-16	3,200	5	5	0.5 (g)	0.5 (g)
North Carolina	1-12	4-16	8-17	3,000	10	2 (e)	None	None
Oregon	3-12	3-12 (r)	3-12 (r)	500	(r, s)	(r, s)	3	0.5
Pennsylvania	6	15	15	(l)	None (t)	None (t)	None	None
Rhode Island	2-9	3-10	8-15	1,000 (u)	10	10	5	1
South Dakota (a)	(v)	4-16	6-24	100	60 (v)	3 (e)	0.5	0.1
Tennessee	5.5-9.5	6.5-20	6.5-20	500	60	60	1	1
Texas	1-6	3-10	5-20	1,000	25 (d)	25	10	0.5
Virginia	1-5	2-10	5-15	1,000	5	5	2	1
Washington	1-10	3-20	10-25	500	5 (d)	5	1	None
West Virginia	3-13	4-18	10-30	1,000	30	10	10	None
Wisconsin	1.25-12.5	5-25	10-30(w)	500	50	4	1	0.5
Wyoming	2	2	6	(l)	60	10	10	None

(a) In addition to an inheritance tax, all states listed also levy an estate tax, generally to assure full absorption of the federal credit. Exception is S. D.

(b) Rates generally apply to excess above graduated absolute amounts.

(c) Generally, transfers to governments or to solely charitable, educational, scientific, religious, literary, public, and other similar organizations in the U.S. are wholly exempt. Some states grant additional exemptions either for insurance, homestead, joint deposits, support allowance, disinherited minor children, orphaned, incompetent or blind children, and for previously or later taxed transfers. In many states, exemptions are deducted from the first bracket only. Adopted children generally receive the same consideration as natural children.

(d) Community property state in which, in general, either all community property to the surviving spouse is exempt, or only one-half of the community property is taxable on the death of either spouse.

(e) Exemption for child (in thousands): $15 in Iowa; and $30 in S. D. Exemption for minor child is (in thousands): $12 in Cal.; $15 in Col.; $30 in Idaho; $5 in Ind.; $10 in Ky.; $30 in Minn.; $15 in Mon.; $5 in N.C. In Mo. the exemption for an insane, blind or otherwise incapacitated lineal descendant is (thousands) $15. In Mich. a widow receives $5,000 for every minor child to whom no property is transferred in addition to the normal exemption for a spouse.

(f) Col. imposes an additional tax of 10% upon the amount of tax computed at above rates.

(g) No exemption if share exceeds amount stated.

(h) Maximum rate for brother or sister and other than relative is $1 million

(i) On estates an additional inheritance tax equal to 30% of the basic tax is imposed.

(j) Estates over $3 million are not subject to the inheritance tax but are subject to an estate tax equal to the amount of the federal credit.

(k) Where property of a decedent subject to administration in Md. is $5,000 or less, no inheritance taxes are due.

(l) Rate applies to entire share.

(m) Mass. imposes a 14% surtax in addition to the inheritance tax on all property or interests. This tax is suspended with respect to estates of decedents dying on or after 1/1/76.

(n) No exemption if share exceeds amount stated except that the tax shall not reduce the share below the amount of the exemption. In addition there are certain exemptions for the spouse's home.

(o) There is no tax on the share of any beneficiary if the value of the share is less than $100. In addition to the above rates each county collects an additional 0.5% of the tax collected.

(p) In addition, an exemption of one-half of the decedent's estate, or one-third if decedent is survived by lineal descendants.

(q) Spouses, minor children, and minor adopted children in the decedent's line of succession are entirely exempt. Parents have no exemption and are taxable at the flat rate of 15%.

(r) An additional tax of 3-25% is levied on all beneficiaries other than grandparents, parents, spouse, children, stepchildren, or lineal descendants. These categories of beneficiaries are exempt from the additional taxes.

(s) A credit of $300,000 is allowed against the tax base for spouse, minor child, or child incapable of self-support.

(t) However, the $2,000 family exemption is specifically allowed as a deduction.

(u) Estates of $250,000 or more are taxed at rates from 1.4-14.92% in addition to the rates above.

(v) The rates range from 4.5-6% for a spouse and from 3-12% for a child or parents. Effective 7/1/78, exemption for spouse is $80,000.

(w) Maximum rate applies above $50,000.

Federal Estate and Gift Tax

Source: Tax Foundation, Inc.

As a result of sweeping changes introduced by the Tax Reform Act of 1976, the federal government now taxes estates, and gifts on an entirely different basis than previously applied. The major changes include the unification of estate and gift rates, the substitution of a unified credit for the previous estate and gift tax exemptions, and a new tax on generation-skipping.

Estate Tax

Instead of the specific exemptions which were subtracted from the total estate (previously $60,000) or the lifetime gift total (previously $30,000), the new law provides for a unified credit against combined estate and gift taxes. For estates of decedents who die in 1977, the unified credit is $30,000; in 1978, $34,000; in 1979, $38,000; in 1980, $42,500; in 1981 and thereafter $47,000. The 1977 credit is in general equivalent to an exemption of $120,660; by 1981, to $175,625.

Estate taxes are computed by applying the unified rate schedule, shown below, to the total estate (minus allowable deductions) plus taxable gifts made after 1976. Gift taxes paid are subtracted from tax due, and credit also may be taken for state death taxes. The amount of the state tax credit is determined by the schedule shown in the table below or the actual state taxes paid, whichever is less. No state tax credit is available to an adjusted taxable estate (i.e., taxable estate minus $60,000) smaller than $40,000.

Deductions may be taken from the gross estate for funeral expenses, administration expenses, debts, charitable contributions, and, within limitations, bequests to the surviving spouse. A special deduction is allowed for estates passing to orphans, up to $5,000 per child multiplied by the number of years by which 21 exceeds the child's age. For instance, two orphaned children aged 7 and 9 would be entitled to a deduction of $130,000.

The marital deduction for small and medium-sized estates is increased to the larger of 50 percent of the adjusted gross estate or $250,000. A fractional interest rule eliminates the previous requirement for a consideration-furnished test. In general, each spouse's interest will be one-half, where property is jointly held with rights of survivorship and joint tenancy is created by a transfer subject to gift tax provisions.

The new law provides for real property passed on to family members for use in a closely held business, such as farming, to be valued on basis of such use, rather than fair market value on basis of highest and best use. In no case may this special valuation reduce the gross estate by more than $500,000.

Generation-skipping transfers which occur after April 30, 1976, in general are now subject to taxes substantially equivalent to those which would have been imposed had the property been transferred outright to each successive generation. However, an exclusion is provided for transfers to grandchildren up to $250,000 for each child of the decedent who serves as a conduit for the transfer (not for each grandchild).

A return must be filed for the estate of every U.S. citizen or resident whose gross estate exceeds $120,000 ($60,000 if the decedent died before 1977; $36,000 for the estate of a nonresident not a citizen). The return is due nine months after death unless an extension is granted.

Gift Tax

Any citizen or resident alien whose gifts to any one person exceed $3,000 within a calendar year will be liable for payment of a gift tax, at rates determined under the unified estate and gift tax schedule. Gift tax returns are filed on a quarterly basis and ordinarily are due a month and a half following any quarter in which a taxable gift was made (i.e., May 15, August 15, November 15, and February 15). After 1976, however, quarterly filing is not required until cumulative taxable gifts during the year exceed $25,000.

Gifts made by husband and wife to a third party may be considered as having been made one-half by each, provided both spouses consent to such division. For gifts between spouses, there is an unlimited deduction for the first $100,000 of lifetime gifts.

Unified Rate Schedule for Estate and Gift Tax

If the amount with respect to which the tentative tax to be computed is:				The tentative tax is:		
Not over $10,000				18 percent of such amount.		
Over	$10,000	but not over	$20,000	$1,800, plus 20%	of the excess over	$10,000.
Over	$20,000	but not over	$40,000	$3,800, plus 22%	of the excess over	$20,000.
Over	$40,000	but not over	$60,000	$8,200, plus 24%	of the excess over	$40,000.
Over	$60,000	but not over	$80,000	$13,000, plus 26%	of the excess over	$60,000.
Over	$80,000	but not over	$100,000	$18,200, plus 28%	of the excess over	$80,000.
Over	$100,000	but not over	$150,000	$23,800, plus 30%	of the excess over	$100,000.
Over	$150,000	but not over	$250,000	$38,800, plus 32%	of the excess over	$150,000.
Over	$250,000	but not over	$500,000	$70,800, plus 34%	of the excess over	$250,000.
Over	$500,000	but not over	$750,000	$155,800, plus 37%	of the excess over	$500,000.
Over	$750,000	but not over	$1,000,000	$248,300, plus 39%	of the excess over	$750,000.
Over	$1,000,000	but not over	$1,250,000	$345,800, plus 41%	of the excess over	$1,000,000.
Over	$1,250,000	but not over	$1,500,000	$448,300, plus 43%	of the excess over	$1,250,000.
Over	$1,500,000	but not over	$2,000,000	$555,800 plus 45%	of the excess over	$1,500,000
Over	$2,000,000	but not over	$2,500,000	$780,800, plus 49%	of the excess over	$2,000,000.
Over	$2,500,000	but not over	$3,000,000	$1,025,800, plus 53%	of the excess over	$2,500,000.
Over	$3,000,000	but not over	$3,500,000	$1,290,800, plus 57%	of the excess over	$3,000,000.
Over	$3,500,000	but not over	$4,000,000	$1,575,800, plus 61%	of the excess over	$3,500,000.
Over	$4,000,000	but not over	$4,500,000	$1,880,800. plus 65%	of the excess over	$4,000,000.
Over	$4,500,000	but not over	$5,000,000	$2,205,800, plus 69%	of the excess over	$4,500,000.
Over $5,000,000				$2,550,800, plus 70%	of the excess over	$5,000,000.

State Death Tax Credit for Estate Tax

Adjusted taxable estate from	to	Credit= +	%	Of excess over	Adjusted taxable estate from	to	Credit= +	%	Of excess over
$ 0	$ 40,000	$ 0	0	$ 0	2,540,000	3,040,000	146,800	8.8	2,540,000
40,000	90,000	0	.8	40,000	3,040,000	3,540,000	190,800	9.6	3,040,000
90,000	140,000	400	1.6	90,000	3,540,000	4,040,000	238,800	10.4	3,540,000
140,000	240,000	1,200	2.4	140,000	4,040,000	5,040,000	290,800	11.2	4,040,000
240,000	440,000	3,600	3.2	240,000	5,040,000	6,040,000	402,800	12	5,040,000
440,000	640,000	10,000	4	440,000	6,040,000	7,040,000	522,800	12.8	6,040,000
640,000	840,000	18,000	4.8	640,000	7,040,000	8,040,000	650,800	13.6	7,040,000
840,000	1,040,000	27,600	5.6	840,000	8,040,000	9,040,000	786,800	14.4	8,040,000
1,040,000	1,540,000	38,800	6.4	1,040,000	9,040,000	10,040,000	930,800	15.2	9,040,000
1,540,000	2,040,000	70,800	7.2	1,540,000	10,040,000		1,082,800	16	10,040,000
2,040,000	2,540,000	106,800	8	2,040,000					

(1) The adjusted taxable estate equals the taxable estate minus $60,000.

Savings by Individuals in the U. S.

Source: Federal Reserve System
Seasonally adjusted annual rates (billions of dollars).

	1970	1972	1973	1974	1975	1976	1977[1]
Increase in financial assets	78.5	128.1	142.8	140.5	161.7	191.4	221.4
Currency and demand deposits	8.9	14.8	12.9	5.6	7.1	8.2	31.2
Savings accounts	43.6	71.0	67.8	57.2	84.9	108.8	91.8
Securities	-3.6	1.7	20.6	33.2	16.7	2.7	12.0
U.S. Savings Bonds	0.3	3.3	2.7	3.0	4.0	4.7	5.0
Other U.S. Treasury sec.	-13.3	-0.1	12.8	6.8	8.2	-8.0	0.3
U.S. Govt. agency securities	4.6	-3.5	2.0	3.9	-1.2	2.2	-0.6
State & local obligations	-0.9	2.3	5.3	8.9	5.0	4.2	10.6
Corporation & foreign bonds	9.5	4.4	1.3	4.7	8.2	4.0	0.9
Commercial paper	-3.2	-0.2	3.4	8.1	-3.5	-0.5	0.3
Investment company shares	2.8	-0.5	-1.2	-0.7	-0.1	-1.0	-3.3
Other corporate stock	-3.5	-4.0	-5.7	-1.5	-3.9	-2.9	-1.0
Private life insurance reserves	5.1	6.5	7.2	6.4	5.3	6.7	7.6
Private insured pension reserves	3.3	4.3	5.5	6.2	9.7	15.6	15.5
Private noninsured pension reserves	7.1	6.9	8.5	10.9	12.8	12.8	14.6
Government ins. & pension reserves	8.9	11.6	11.8	12.6	15.0	18.5	27.3
Miscellaneous financial assets	5.3	11.3	8.6	8.5	10.2	18.1	21.4
Gross investment in tangible assets	142.8	195.3	218.5	201.8	214.8	257.4	297.1
Nonfarm homes	25.2	40.6	45.0	42.9	42.9	57.6	72.5
Noncorporate business construction & equipment	32.3	41.6	45.2	40.9	38.3	41.3	45.1
Consumer durables	84.9	111.2	123.7	122.0	132.9	158.9	179.1
Inventories	0.4	1.9	4.6	-4.0	0.6	-0.4	0.5
Capital consumption allowances	103.6	118.1	131.1	148.9	172.1	184.8	204.6
Nonfarm homes	12.8	14.7	17.1	19.8	22.2	24.8	26.9
Noncorporate business plant and equipment	23.2	25.7	29.3	34.1	39.7	43.4	47.3
Consumer durables	67.5	77.6	84.8	95.0	110.3	116.6	130.4
Net investment in tangible assets	39.2	77.3	87.3	52.9	42.7	72.6	92.5
Nonfarm homes	12.4	25.9	27.9	23.1	20.8	32.8	45.5
Noncorporate business construction and equipment	9.0	15.9	15.8	6.8	-1.4	-2.1	-2.2
Consumer durables	17.4	33.6	39.0	27.0	22.7	42.3	48.7
Inventories	0.4	1.9	4.6	-4.0	0.6	-0.4	0.5
Increase in debt	34.2	92.8	98.2	65.8	64.8	114.4	153.0
Mortgage debt on nonfarm homes	14.7	41.6	46.9	35.4	38.0	61.2	82.1
Noncorporate business mortgage debt	8.2	16.8	16.0	12.7	7.5	10.8	16.9
Consumer credit	5.9	18.9	22.0	10.2	9.4	23.6	38.0
Security credit	-1.8	4.5	-4.3	-1.8	0.8	4.7	3.6
Policy loans	2.3	1.0	2.2	2.7	1.6	1.4	2.0
Other debt	4.8	10.1	15.3	6.5	7.5	12.7	10.4
Individual saving	83.6	112.6	132.0	127.6	139.6	149.6	160.9
Less-Govt. ins. & pen. reserves	8.9	11.6	11.8	12.6	15.0	18.5	27.3
Net inv. in cons. dur.	17.4	33.6	39.0	27.0	22.7	42.3	48.7
Capital gains dividends from invest. cos.	0.9	1.4	0.9	0.5	0.2	0.5	1.4
Net savings by farm crops	-0.1	0.1	0.4	-0.1	0.2	0.2	0.1
Equals pers. saving, F/F basis	56.5	65.8	80.0	87.7	101.5	88.2	83.5
Personal saving, NIA basis	50.6	49.4	70.3	71.7	80.2	65.9	71.6
Difference	5.9	16.5	9.6	16.1	21.3	22.3	11.9

(1) 2d quarter, 1977.

Major Federal Tax Expenditures (Loopholes)

Source: Office of Management and Budget
(Estimates for fiscal year 1976)

Income tax provisions resulting in tax expenditures are defined as exceptions to the "normal structure" of individual and corporate income tax. They reduce tax liabilities for particular groups of taxpayers. The normal structure is nowhere defined in the tax code. Existing rates are accepted as "normal"; when the rate structure is changed, for whatever reason, the new rate structure becomes the new norm.

The following features of the tax system are defined as part of the normal tax structure and therefore **do not result in tax expenditures:** progressive rate schedules for individual income tax; personal exemptions and the minimum standard deduction; separate schedules for single and married persons, married persons filing separately, and heads of households, deduction of business expenses; exclusion of unrealized capital gains and losses; exclusion of gifts and bequests received; exclusion of the value of government services received in kind (e.g., food stamps); foreign tax credits; treatment of individuals and corporations as separate tax paying entities.

Item	Amount (millions) Individual	Corporate
State and local tax deduction	$7,255	—
Investment credit	1,810	$7,685
Capital gains, lower tax on	7,770	865
Home mortgage interest deduction	4,870	—
Employer pension contribution exclusion	7,290	—
Charitable contributions deduction	4,870	540
Home property tax deduction	4,030	—
Interest on state and local bonds exclusion	1,645	3,100
Corporate profits, lower tax on first $50,000	—	4,170
Employer medical care and insurance payments exclusion	4,490	—
Social security retirement benefits exclusion	2,725	—
Percentage depletion allowance	285	1,010

Item	Amount (millions) Individual	Corporate
Medical expense deduction	2,315	—
Unemployment insurance benefits exclusion	3,335	—
Interest on life insurance savings exclusion	1,655	—
Excess of percentage standard deduction over low income allowance	1,140	—
Consumer credit interest deduction	2,105	—
Deferral for domestic international sales corporations	—	1,220
Additional exemption for over 65	1,145	—
Armed Forces personnel benefits exclusion	1,020	—
Self-employed pension contributions exclusion	1,060	—
Expensing of research and development	25	1,325

How and Where to Get Help on Consumer Complaints

by Kenneth C. Johnston

Efforts to establish a federal consumer protection agency, stymied earlier by opposition in the Ford administration, got a boost Apr. 6, 1977, when Pres. Carter told Congress he endorsed creation of such a unit, though one with limited powers.

The proposed Agency for Consumer Advocacy would be "tiny" but would give the consumer a voice in government to counter lobbyists for producers, Carter said. Rather than issuing rules, it would "improve the way rules, regulations, and decisions are made and carried out," he said. The agency would be empowered to help consumer groups represent themselves before courts and government units. Congressional action on the proposals was awaited.

Meanwhile, there were many places to which a customer, dissatisfied with faulty merchandise or shoddy repair work, could turn for help:

- Many big businesses now provide phone numbers (some toll-free) or addresses where complainants can receive courteous consideration and have some hope of action (see below).
- There are also many existing government agencies, federal, state, and local, which provide a wide range of aids to consumers (see latter part of this article).

What Corporations Provide

Here's what some big companies suggest you do if you can't get satisfaction from your local dealer:

A & P: See store manager or phone book under Great Atlantic & Pacific Tea Co. for Customer Relations Dept. (in 23 cities); finally, write Executive Office, A & P Food Stores. 2 Paragon Dr., Montvale, NJ 07645.

Admiral Corporation: Write Frank Williamson, Consumer Relations, Admiral Corp., 200 Murray Hill Parkway, East Rutherford, NJ 07073.

American Motors: Contact zone office (see owner's manual); then write AMC Sales Corp., Owner Relations Dept., 14250 Plymouth Rd., Detroit, MI 48232.

Atlantic Richfield: See phone book or dealer for Atlantic Richfield district office or write to ARCO, Consumer Relations, P.O. Box 2679 T.A., Los Angeles, CA 90051. On credit cards, use free "800" phone no. shown on bill.

Avis: Write Customer Service Dept., Avis Rent A Car System, 900 Old Country Road, Garden City, NY 11530.

Chrysler: Phone or write Chrysler Corp., Customer Service (ask dealer or see phone book); or write to: Consumer Affairs, Chrysler Corp., P.M. Box 856, Detroit, MI 48288; include your own phone no.

Du Pont: See dealer or phone book under Du Pont de Nemours, Product Information (in 8 major cities), or write Du Pont Co., Wilmington, DE 19898.

Exxon: Write to John B. Boatwright, Marketing Dept., Exxon Co., USA, Box 2180, Houston, TX 77001, on product, service, or credit card complaints.

Firestone: See dealer or phone book, under Firestone Tire & Rubber Co., for district office, contact Customer Service representative there (in some 35 cities); or phone 800 321-9638 (free call), or write Director of Consumer Affairs, Firestone, 1200 Firestone Pkwy., Akron, OH 44317.

Ford: Phone or write Ford Parts & Service Div., district office (see phone book or ask local Ford dealer); or phone 800 648-4848 (free call) for all vehicles made by Ford (from Nevada, phone 800-992-5777).

General Electric: On small appliances, write Consumer Counseling Manager, GE, 1285 Boston Ave., Bridgeport, Conn. 06602; large, Product Service Manager, GE, Appliance Park, Louisville, KY 40225.

General Foods: Write to General Foods Corp., 250 North St., White Plains, NY 10625.

General Motors: Phone or write Divisional Owner Relations Office (listed in owner's manual), or GM Customer Relations, Central Office, 3044 Grand Boulevard, Detroit, MI 48202.

Goodyear: See dealer or phone book for Goodyear Tire & Rubber Co. customer service representative at district office, or write Director of Consumer Affairs, Goodyear Tire & Rubber Co., 1144 E. Market St., Akron, OH 44316.

Gulf Oil: See phone book or dealer for nearest Gulf Oil district office or write Gulf Oil Corp., Consumer Affairs, P.O. Box 1563, Houston, TX 77001.

Hertz: Phone 212 598-4921 or write Consumer Relations, RCA Corp., 30 Rockefeller Plaza, New York, NY 10020.

Kodak: See phone book under Eastman Kodak Co. for Kodak Consumer Center (in some 35 cities) for free minor adjustments and advice; write Eastman Kodak Co., 343 State St., Rochester, NY 14650, attention—Dept. 841.

Kresge's: See section supervisor; then, store manager; finally, get from manager address of S.S. Kresge Co. regional office, write to Customer Relations there.

Mobil Oil: See dealer or contact local district sales office or regional marketing offices in Los Angeles; Scarsdale, N.Y.; Valley Forge, Pa., or Woodfield, Ill. For credit card troubles, contact Mobil Oil Credit Corp., 210 W. 10th St., Kansas City, Mo. 64105.

Panasonic: Write nearest regional office listed on card accompanying product or write Panasonic Consumer Affairs Div., 1 Panasonic Way, Secaucus, NJ 07094.

J. C. Penney: See store manager; if unsatisfied, write Dolores M. Jones, Customer Relations Dept., J. C. Penney Co., 1301 Avenue of the Americas, New York, NY 10019.

Procter & Gamble: Write Consumer Services, P.O. Box 599, Cincinnati, OH 45201. If possible, include your phone number, times you can be reached and name and serial number from the product package.

RCA: On any RCA product, phone 212 598-4921 or write Consumer Relations, RCA Corp., 30 Rockefeller Plaza, New York, NY 10020.

Sears, Roebuck: Ask for Customer Service at the store; then, the store manager; finally, write Sears, Roebuck & Co., Customer Relations, Sears Tower, Chicago, IL 60684.

Texaco: See retailer or phone book for nearest Texaco, Inc., division office; otherwise, write Texaco, Assistant General Manager (Resale), Marketing Dept. —U.S., 2000 Westchester Ave., White Plains, NY 10650.

Union Carbide: The product or the guarantee has address to write to: or write Union Carbide Corp., Consumer Information, 270 Park Ave., New York, NY 10017.

United Van Lines: Call toll-free 800-325-3870, ask for Bette Malone. (On interstate moves, call destination agent first.).

Volkswagen (also Audis and Porsches): Try Customer Assistance Dept. at regional office (see owner's manual); or write Customer Assistance, Volkswagen of America. Englewood Cliffs, NJ 07632.

Whirlpool: Round-the-clock, toll-free service through 800 253-1301.

Woolworth's: See store manager; if not satisfied, write F.W. Woolworth Co., 233 Broadway, New York, NY 10007; Attention Consumer Relations Dept.

Other Industry Aids

Within industry groups there are industry and trade associations which may be helpful. One which claims an excellent record in handling a large number of complaints is MACAP, the **Major Appliance Consumer Action Panel,** 20 North Wacker Drive, Chicago, IL 60606. You may write or make a free, collect phone call to 312 236-3165, if you don't get satisfaction from a manufacturer of home laundry equipment, range, refrigerator, freezer, room air conditioner, water heater, dehumidifier, dishwasher, disposer, gas incinerator, or humidifier. Give full details.

A similar organization is CRICAP, the **Carpet and Rug Industry Consumer Action Panel**, Box 1568, Dalton, GA 30720. Write them, if the dealer and maker won't cooperate, giving full details and your phone number. They will recommend appropriate action to the company involved; they claim good results, especially among firms that are members of the Carpet & Rug Institute.

Among industry complaint centers sponsored by the U.S. Chamber of Commerce are:

American Apparel Manufacturers Assn., 1611 N. Kent St., Arlington, VA 22209.

American Footwear Manufacturers Assn., 342 Madison Ave., NY 10017.

Direct Mail Advertising Assn., 230 Park Ave., New York, NY 10017.

Direct Selling Assn., 1730 M St. NW., Washington, DC 20036. (On door-to-door sales.)

Master Photo Dealers and Finishers Assn., 603 Lansing Ave., Jackson, MI 49202.

Mobile Homes Manufacturing Assn., 14650 Lee Rd., Chantilly, VA 22021.

National Assn. of Furniture Manufacturers, 8401 Connecticut Ave., Suite 911, Washington, DC 20015.

National Employment Assn., 2000 K St. N.W., Washington, DC 20006. (For employment agencies.)

National Automobile Dealers Assn., 2000 K St. Connecticut Ave., Suite 911, Washington, DC 20015.

National Consumer Finance Assn., 1000 16th St. N.W., Washington, DC 20036.

National Employment Assn., 2000 K St. N.W., Washington, DC 20006. (On employment agencies.)

National Institute of Drycleaning, 909 Burlington Ave., Silver Spring, MD 20910.

The Council of Better Business Bureaus has a central office; complaints about nationwide products, especially, may be sent to it: Council of Better Business Bureaus, Trade Practices Dept., 1150 17th St. N.W., Washington, DC 20036. The council will seek solutions for complaints.

Government Agencies

There are numerous government agencies which can be helpful:

Cities: Some have Offices of Consumer Complaints or Depts. of Consumer Affairs (see phone book). In N.Y. City, for example, the department will investigate the complaint, then may try to work out a settlement; it may sue on behalf of a consumer, issue violation notices, hold hearings and fine a company or revoke or suspend a company's license to operate in the city.

Many **towns** and **counties** also have consumer protection agencies.

States likewise offer aid to the unhappy consumer. Usually, it is a part of the Attorney General's office. Write or phone the Attorney General, Attention Consumer Protection Office, in your state.

Nationally, one may write to the Bureau of Consumer Protection, Federal Trade Commission, Washington, DC 20580, or the nearest FTC regional office.

The Consumer Product Safety Commission, a federal agency, offers a toll-free number, 800 638-2666, where you can find out if a particular product has been declared unsafe or complain about one you believe is hazardous. If enough complaints are received, the commission will investigate and can order the product banned. Address: Washington, DC 20207.

For a complaint against an airline (fares, baggage, service, delays), write Office of the Consumer Advocate, Civil Aeronautics Board, Washington, DC 20428.

In **Canada**, one may write the Director, Trade Practices Branch, Dept. of Consumer and Corporate Affairs, 219 Laurier Ave. West, Ottawa, Ont.

Don't Forget

As a complaining consumer you will find it helpful to provide whatever agency you appeal to with copies of receipts and guarantees (not the actual receipts). Be as specific as possible about the dealer's name and address, purchase date, price, name, and serial number (if any) of the product, places you may already have sought relief, with dates. Don't forget your name, address, and phone number (some companies or agencies may want to serve you as rapidly as possible and may need further information).

The consumer may even return the favor in some cases and help the manufacturer: as a Procter & Gamble spokesman points out, some manufacturers will want the consumer to hold on to the offending product so that the maker can analyze it, find out what went wrong, and try to prevent its happening again.

Consumers' Association of Canada

The Consumers' Association of Canada, CAC, is a voluntary, non-profit organization, founded in 1947. The National Office is located at 801-251 Laurier Avenue West, Ottawa, Ontario, K1P 5Z7. Editorial and Testing Departments, at 200 First Avenue, Ottawa, Ontario K1S 2G6. CAC's aims are:

(a) to unite the strength of consumers,
(b) to study consumer problems and make recommendations for their solutions,
(c) to enunciate the views and concerns of consumers,
(d) to establish a two-way channel of communication between governments, trade and industry, regulatory bodies, and the consumer,
(e) to provide information on consumer legislation, research and test consumer goods and services, encourage conservation and to inform and monitor the metric conversion.

CAC publishes bi-monthly, bilingual magazines, CANADIAN CONSUMER and LE CONSOMMATEUR CANADIEN; circulation 140,000. Across Canada there are 10 provincial and 2 territorial branches and 93 English and 14 French local associations and consumer committees.

CAC has attained notable achievements in implementing better packaging and labelling, improved safety standards and selling practices and updating food and drug regulations.

Consumer Installment Credit

Source: Federal Reserve System (estimated amounts outstanding, millions of dollars)

		By holder				By type				
End of year or month	Total	Commercial banks	Finance companies	Credit unions	Retailers and others	Automobile	Mobile homes	Home improvement	Revolving	All other
1973	146,434	71,871	35,404	19,609	19,550	50,065	11,698	6,950	9,092	68,629
1974	157,454	75,846	36,087	21,895	23,626	52,871	14,618	8,522	11,078	70,364
1975	164,955	78,667	35,994	25,666	24,628	55,879	14,423	9,405	12,311	72,937
1976	185,489	89,511	38,639	30,546	26,793	66,116	14,572	10,990	14,392	79,418
1977, June	196,157	95,307	40,712	33,750	26,387	72,459	14,551	11,742	14,664	82,742

Interest Laws and Consumer Finance Loan Rates

Source: Revised by Christian T. Jones, Editor Consumer Finance Law Bulletin, Chicago.

Most states have laws regulating interest rates. These laws fix a legal or conventional rate which applies when there is no contract for interest. They also fix a general maximum contract rate, but in many states there are so many exceptions that the general contract maximum actually applies only to exceptional cases.

Legal rate of interest. The legal or conventional rate of interest applies to money obligations when no interest rate is contracted for and also to judgments. The rate is usually 6% a year; 5% or 7% in some states.

General maximum contract rates. General interest laws in most states set the maximum rate between 8% and 12% per year. The general maximum is fixed by the state constitution rather than by statute at 10% per year in Arkansas, California, Tennessee, and Texas. Loans to corporations are frequently exempted or subject to a higher maximum. In recent years, it has also been common to provide special rates for home mortgage loans. Courts generally hold that installment sale charges are not interest, but installment sale charges are limited by laws in many states.

Specific enabling acts. In many states special statutes permit industrial loan companies and banks to charge interest and fees without regard to installment payments which yield 1.5% a month or more. Laws regulating charge accounts and credit cards generally limit charges to 1.5% per month. Credit unions may generally charge 1% a month. Pawnbrokers' rates vary widely. Building and loan associations, and loans insured by the Federal Housing Administration, are also specially regulated.

Consumer finance loan statutes. Most consumer finance loan statutes are based on early models drafted by the Russell Sage Foundation (1916-42) to provide small loans to wage earners under license and other protective regulations. Since 1969, however, the model has frequently been the Uniform Consumer Credit Code which applies to credit sales and loans for consumer purposes up to $25,000. In general, licensed lenders may charge 2.5% or 3% a month for $300 or less and reduced rates for additional amounts up to $2,000 or more. A number of states permit add-on rates of 17% to 20% ($17 to $20 per $100) a year of the original principal for $300 and lower rates for additional amounts. An add-on of 17% ($17 per $100) per year yields about 2.5% per month when the loan is paid in equal monthly installments. In the table below unless otherwise stated, monthly and annual rates are based on reducing principal balances, annual add-on rates are based on the original principal for the full term, and two or more rates apply to different portions of balance or original principal.

States with consumer finance loan laws and the rates of charge as of Oct. 1, 1977.
Maximum rate monthly unless otherwise stated.

Ala. . . . . Annual add-on: 15% to $500, 10% to $1,000, 8% to $2,000. Over $2,000, 8% add-on on entire balance. Higher rates for loans up to $300.
Alas. . . . 3% to $400, 2% to $800, 1% to $1,500. 5% to $50.
Ariz. . . . . 3% to $300, 2% to $600, 1.5% to $1,500, 1% to $2,500.
Cal. . . . . 2.5% to $225, 2% to $625, 1.5% to $1,650, 1% to $10,000 (1.5% min.).
Colo. . . . 36% per annum to $300, 21% to $1,000, 15% to $25,000 (18% min.).
Conn. . . Annual Add-on: 17% to $300, 11% to $5,000, 11% over $1,800 to $5,000 for certain secured loans.
Del. . . . . Annual Discount: 9% for 1st 36 mos., 6% for remaining months; plus 2% fee.
Fla. . . . . 30% per annum to $500, 24% to $1,000, 16% to $2,500.
Ga. . . . . 8% per annum discount for 18 months, add-on to 36½ months; 8% fee to $600, 4% on excess plus $2 per month; max. $3,000.
Ha. . . . . 3.5% to $100, 2.5% to $300.
Ida. . . . . 36% per annum to $480, 21% to $1,600, 15% to $40,000 (18% min.).
Ill. . . . . . 2.5% to $300, 2% to $600, 1.5% to $1,500.
Ind. . . . . 36% per annum to $390, 21% to $1,300, 15% to $32,500 (18% min.).
Ia. . . . . . 3% to $250, 2% to $400, 1.5% to $1,000.
Kan. . . . 36% per year to $300, 21% to $1,000, 14.45% to $25,000. (18% min.).
Ky. . . . . 3% to $500, 2% to $1,200, 1.5% to $1,500.
La. . . . . 36% per annum to $800, 27% to $2,000, 21% to $3,500, 15% to $25,000 (18% min.).
Me. . . . . 30% per annum to $480, 21% to $1,600, 15% to $40,000 (18% min.).
Md. . . . . 2.75% to $300, 2% to $500, 1.25% to $1,200, 1.75 to $3,500, 1.5% to $6,000.
Mass. . . 18% per year plus $15 fee.
Mich. . . . 2.5% to $400, 1.25% to $1,500.
Minn. . . . 2.75% to $300, 1.5% to $600, 1.25% to $1,200 plus fee of $1 per $100.
Miss. . . . 36% per annum to $600, 33% to $1,800, 24% to $4,500, 12% over $4,500.
Mo. . . . . 2.218% to $500, 10% per annum on any remainder.
Mont. . . . Annual add-on; 20% to $300, 16% to $500, 12% to $1,000, 10% to $7,500. Special rate to $90.
Neb. . . . 30% per annum to $300, 24% to $500, 18% to $1,000, 12% to $3,000.
Nev. . . . 36% per annum to $300, 21% to $1,000, 15% to $10,000 (1.5% min.)
N.H. . . . 2% to $600, 1.5% to $1,500; 1.5% on entire amount over $1,500 to $5,000.
N.J. . . . . 24% per annum to $500, 22% to $1,500, 18% to $2,500.
N.M. . . . 3% to $150, 2.5% to $300, 1% to $2,500 (1.5% min.).
N.Y. . . . . 2.5% to $100, 2% to $300, 1.5% to $900, 1.25% to $2,500.
N.C. . . . . 3% to $300, 1.5% to $1,500.
N.D. . . . . 2.5% to $250, 2% to $500, 1.75% to $750, 1.5% to $1,000; 1.5% on entire amount over $1,000 to $3,500.
Ohio . . . Annual add-on: 16% to $750, 11% to $1,500, 9% to $3,000; or equivalent simple interest rate.
Okla. . . . 30% per annum to $300, 21% to $1,000, 15% to $25,000. (18% min.). Special rates to $100.
Ore. . . . . 3% to $300, 1.75% to $1,000, 1.25% to $5,000. Over $5,000, 1.5%.
Pa. . . . . 9.5% per annum discount to 36 months, 6% for remaining time plus 2% fee; $5,000 max.
P.R. . . . . Annual Add-on: 20% to $300, 7% to $600.
R.I. . . . . 3% to $300, 2.5% for loans between $300 and $800; 2% for larger loans to $2,500.
S.C. . . . . 36% per annum to $300, 21% to $1,000, 15% to $25,000 (18% min.). Special rate to $150.
S.D. . . . . 2.5% to $300, 2% to $1,000, 1.5% to $1,500, 1% to $2,500; 1.5% on entire amount to $5,000. $2 minimum.
Tenn. . . . 7.5% per annum discount plus fees; no size limit.
Texas. . Annual add-on: 18% to $300, 8% to $2,500. Special rates to $100.
Utah . . . 36% per annum to $480, 21% to $1,600, 15% to $40,000 (18% min.).
Vt. . . . . . Annual add-on of 14% to $1,500.
Va. . . . . 2.5% to $500, 1.5% to $1,500; annual add-on of 17% to $500, 13% to $1,000, 11% to $1,500.
Wash. . . 2.5% to $500, 1.75% to $1,000, 1% to $2,500.
W.Va. . . 36% per year to $200, 24% to $600, 18% to $1,200.
Wis. . . . Annual Discount: 9.5% on first $1,000, 8% to $3,000 up to 36 months; 18% per annum for larger loans.
Wyo. . . . 36% per annum to $300, 21% to $1,000, 15% to $25,000 (18% min.).

U.S. Budget Receipts and Outlays—1975-1977

Source: Treasury Department; Office of Management and Budget.
(1975 and 1976 fiscal years ended June 30; 1977 fiscal year ended Sept. 30)
(thousands of dollars)

Classification	Fiscal 1975	Fiscal 1976	Transitional Quarter 1976	Fiscal 1977[1]
Net Receipts				
Individual income taxes	122,385,980	131,602,555	38,800,969	158,300,000
Corporation income taxes	40,621,179	41,408,703	8,460,466	54,600,000
Social insurance taxes and contributions:				
Federal old-age and survivors insurance	55,207,343	58,702,690	15,885,848	(NA)
Federal disability insurance	7,250,217	7,686,092	2,130,051	(NA)
Federal hospital insurance	11,257,522	11,995,098	3,458,803	(NA)
Railroad retirement taxes	1,489,333	1,525,144	328,310	(NA)
Total employment taxes and contributions	**75,204,416**	**79,909,024**	**21,803,012**	**(NA)**
Other insurance and retirement:				
Unemployment	6,770,706	8,053,658	2,697,903	(NA)
Federal supplementary medical insurance	1,900,887	1,937,296	538,648	(NA)
Federal employees retirement	2,512,548	2,760,167	706,247	(NA)
Civil service retirement and disability	52,434	54,231	13,323	(NA)
Total social insurance taxes and contributions	**86,440,989**	**92,714,377**	**25,759,134**	**108,800,000**
Excise taxes	16,550,686	16,962,582	4,472,698	17,800,000
Estate and gift taxes	4,611,125	5,216,229	1,454,592	7,300,000
Customs duties	3,675,532	4,074,176	1,212,173	5,000,000
Deposits of earnings-Federal Reserve Banks	5,776,550	5,450,824	1,500,459	(NA)
Petroleum import license fees	442,615	1,890,326	-49,812	(NA)
All other miscellaneous receipts	532,810	685,305	162,088	6,600,000
Net Budget Receipts	**281,037,466**	**300,005,077**	**81,772,766**	**358,300,000**
Net Outlays				
Legislative Branch	726,199	779,052	224,882	1,100,000
The Judiciary	283,754	325,021	85,188	400,000
Executive Office of the President:				
The White House Office	15,294	15,791	4,136	(NA)
Office of Management and Budget	21,736	23,591	5,373	(NA)
Office of Telecommunications Policy	7,754	9,009	2,136	(NA)
Total Executive Office	**92,939**	**79,224**	**16,206**	**100,000**
Funds appropriated to the President:				
Appalachian regional development	311,374	319,283	73,539	(NA)
Disaster relief	205,858	291,137	71,321	(NA)
Foreign assistance-security	1,394,870	1,101,398	468,084	(NA)
Foreign assistance-development-multilateral	684,699	1,045,829	429,712	(NA)
Foreign assistance-development-bilateral	870,462	623,516	179,348	(NA)
Total funds appropriated to the President	**3,986,277**	**3,524,692**	**1,221,437**	**3,000,000**
Agriculture Department:				
Food stamp program	4,598,956	5,774,500	1,366,642	(NA)
Child Nutrition Program	1,452,267	1,801,566	346,012	(NA)
Total Agriculture Department	**9,727,716**	**12,796,311**	**3,849,622**	**16,700,000**
Commerce Department	1,582,752	2,020,005	533,952	3,000,000
Defense Department:				
Military personnel	24,967,611	25,063,518	6,358,317	(NA)
Retired military personnel	6,241,772	7,295,679	1,947,333	(NA)
Operation and maintenance	26,329,633	27,901,590	7,260,781	(NA)
Procurement	16,041,841	15,963,849	3,766,420	(NA)
Research and development	8,866,499	8,923,023	2,205,681	(NA)
Military construction	1,461,767	2,018,627	376,211	(NA)
Family housing	1,124,297	1,191,772	295,954	(NA)
Civil defense	86,404	79,835	17,621	(NA)
Corps of Engineers and other civil	2,050,662	2,124,252	582,545	(NA)
Total Defense Department	**87,017,373**	**90,160,407**	**22,508,760**	**98,300,000**
Health, Education and Welfare Department:				
National Institutes of Health	1,889,343	2,349,289	471,704	(NA)
Old-age and survivors benefits	54,838,818	62,164,263	17,109,799	(NA)
Public assistance (including health care and social services)	14,009,701	16,675,438	4,399,141	(NA)
Education Division	6,514,748	6,903,749	1,751,003	(NA)
Total HEW	**112,409,704**	**128,784,967**	**34,340,745**	**147,800,000**
Housing and Urban Development Department	7,488,207	7,079,133	1,397,090	6,500,000
Interior Department	2,171,404	2,293,480	787,617	3,400,000
Justice Department:				
Federal Bureau of Investigation	438,501	468,764	130,177	(NA)
Total Justice Department	**2,066,769**	**2,241,574**	**550,633**	**2,400,000**
Labor Department:				
Unemployment Trust Fund	13,211,123	17,920,413	3,543,844	(NA)
Total Labor Department	**17,648,632**	**25,742,379**	**5,905,346**	**22,900,000**
State Department	828,694	1,061,820	316,144	1,200,000
Transportation Department	9,246,454	11,936,056	3,002,507	12,400,000
Treasury Department:				
Internal Revenue Service	1,959,041	2,924,389	600,805	(NA)
Interest on the public debt	32,665,008	37,063,211	8,101,561	(NA)
General revenue sharing	6,137,917	6,242,926	1,587,642	(NA)
Total Treasury Department	**41,173,936**	**44,335,468**	**9,699,089**	**49,800,000**
Energy Research and Development Agency	3,198,973	3,759,025	1,051,211	5,000,000
Environmental Protection Agency	2,530,466	3,117,746	1,108,362	4,800,000

Classification	Fiscal 1975	Fiscal 1976	Transitional Quarter 1976	Fiscal 1977[1]
Net Outlays (cont'd)				
General Services Administration	—621,448	—92,142	3,202	200,000
National Aeronautics and Space Administration	3,329,924	3,669,502	953,026	3,900,000
Veterans Administration	16,571,969	18,414,835	3,957,459	18,100,000
Independent agencies:				
Action	178,166	177,011	47,840	(NA)
Arms Control and Disarmament Agency	9,726	10,704	2,642	(NA)
Board for International Broadcasting	49,858	59,340	21,265	(NA)
Civil Aeronautics Board	80,884	90,939	22,193	(NA)
Civil Service Commission	7,036,236	8,320,440	2,352,986	(NA)
Commission on Civil Rights	6,920	7,863	1,873	(NA)
Community Services Administration	546,314	448,733	123,700	(NA)
Consumer Product Safety Commission	34,212	38,351	10,189	(NA)
Corporation for Public Broadcasting	62,000	70,000	26,000	(NA)
District of Columbia	429,312	464,738	173,110	(NA)
Emergency Loan Guarantee Board	—7,144	—5,570	—3,872	(NA)
Equal Employment Opportunity Commission	56,120	56,143	16,204	(NA)
Federal Communications Commission	47,938	52,486	12,756	(NA)
Federal Deposit Insurance Corporation	—407,682	—478,330	133,280	(NA)
Federal Energy Administration	120,672	140,603	—26,593	(NA)
Federal Home Loan Bank Board	924,200	—78,853	—178,167	(NA)
Federal Maritime Commission	7,229	7,784	1,892	(NA)
Federal Mediation and Conciliation Service	15,497	17,908	4,335	(NA)
Federal Power Commission	34,407	35,704	8,639	(NA)
Federal Trade Commission	38,703	43,729	11,117	(NA)
Historical and Memorial Commissions	11,581	12,788	5,839	(NA)
Intergovernmental Agencies	177,663	174,099	52,689	(NA)
International Trade Commission	8,296	9,715	2,472	(NA)
Interstate Commerce Commission	43,962	47,440	12,582	(NA)
Legal Services Corporation	—	84,634	51,769	(NA)
National Credit Union Administration	—13,537	—19,896	3,532	(NA)
National Foundation on the Arts and Humanities	128,082	151,860	43,895	(NA)
National Labor Relations Board	60,889	67,466	15,717	(NA)
National Science Foundation	662,161	731,905	206,475	(NA)
Nuclear Regulatory Commission	52,792	179,956	45,819	(NA)
Postal Service	1,877,112	1,719,650	937,742	(NA)
Railroad Retirement Board	3,083,036	3,482,102	936,792	(NA)
Securities and Exchange Commission	44,395	50,618	11,568	(NA)
Selective Service System	48,544	37,493	3,993	(NA)
Small Business Administration	617,893	436,164	78,144	(NA)
Smithsonian Institution	102,852	112,772	30,423	(NA)
Temporary Study Commissions	12,239	13,602	3,153	(NA)
Tennessee Valley Authority	767,225	930,318	232,130	(NA)
U.S. Information Agency	239,806	257,034	73,035	(NA)
U.S. Railway Association	22,700	329,020	3,150	(NA)
Water Resources Council	9,415	10,943	2,026	(NA)
Other independent agencies	37,339	52,031	12,710	(NA)
Total independent agencies	**17,258,013**	**18,285,947**	**5,527,046**	**20,700,000**
Undistributed offsetting receipts	—14,007,119	—14,704,375	—2,566,530	—15,200,000
Net Budget Outlays	**324,641,586**	**365,610,129**	**94,472,996**	**406,400,000**
Less net receipts	281,037,466	300,005,077	81,772,766	358,300,000
Deficit	**—43,604,120**	**—65,605,052**	**—12,700,230**	**—48,100,000**

(1) Estimate. (NA) Not available.

U.S. Net Receipts and Outlays

Source: Treasury Department; annual statements for year ending June 30[3]

(thousands of dollars)

Yearly average	Receipts	Expenditures	Yearly average	Receipts	Expenditures	Yearly average	Receipts	Expenditures
1789-1800[1]	5,717	5,776	1871-1875	336,830	287,460	1911-1915	710,227	720,252
1801-1810[2]	13,056	9,086	1876-1880	288,124	255,598	1916-1920[6]	3,483,652	8,065,333
1811-1820[2]	21,032	23,943	1881-1885	366,961	257,691	1921-1925	4,306,673	3,578,989
1821-1830[2]	21,928	16,162	1886-1890	375,448	279,134	1926-1930	4,069,138	3,182,807
1831-1840[2]	30,461	24,495	1891-1895	352,891	363,599	1931-1935[4]	2,770,973	5,214,874
1841-1850[2]	28,545	34,097	1896-1900	434,877	457,451	1936-1040[4]	4,960,614	10,192,367
1851-1860	60,237	60,163	1901-1905	559,481	535,559	1941-1945[4]	25,951,137	66,037,928
1861-1865	160,907	683,785	1906-1910	628,507	639,178	1946-1950[5] [7]	39,047,243	42,334,534
1866-1870	447,301	377,642						

Fiscal year	Receipts	Expenditures	Fiscal year	Receipts	Expenditures	Fiscal year	Receipts	Expenditures
1955	60,389,744	64,569,973	1964	89,458,664	97,684,375	1972[8]	215,262,639	238,285,907
1959	67,915,349	80,342,335	1965	93,071,797	96,506,904	1973	232,191,842	246,603,359
1960	77,763,460	76,539,413	1968[9]	153,675,705	172,803,186	1974	264,847,484	268,342,952
1961	77,659,425	81,515,167	1970	193,843,791	194,968,258	1975	281,037,466	324,641,586
1962	81,409,092	87,786,767	1971	188,332,129	210,652,667	1976	300,005,077	365,610,129
1963	86,357,020	92,589,764				1976 Transitional quarter[3]	81,772,766	94,472;996
						1977 Estimate[3]	358,300,000	406,400,000

(1) Average for period March 4, 1789, to Dec. 31, 1800. (2) Years ended Dec. 31, 1801 to 1842; average for 1841-1850 is for the period Jan. 1, 1841, to June 30, 1850. (3) Effective fiscal year 1977, fiscal year is reckoned Oct. 1-Sept. 30; transition quarter covers July 1, 1976-Sept. 30, 1976. (4) Expenditures for years 1932 through 1946 have been revised to include Government corps. (wholly owned) etc. (net). (5) Effective January 3, 1949, amounts refunded by the Government, principally for the overpayment of taxes, are being reported as deductions from total receipts rather than as expenditures. Also, effective July 1, 1948, payments to the Treasury, principally by wholly owned Government corporations for retirement of capital stock and for disposition of earnings, are excluded in reporting both budget receipts and expenditures. Neither of these changes affects the size of the budget surplus or deficit. Beginning 1931 figures in each case have been adjusted accordingly for comparative purposes. (6) Figures for 1918 through 1946 are revised to exclude statutory debt retirement (sinking fund, etc.). (7) Excludes $3 billion transferred to Foreign Economics Corporation Trust Fund, and includes $3 billion representing expenditures made from the FEC Trust Fund. (8) Effective fiscal year 1972 loan repayments and loan disbursements will be netted against expenditures and known as outlays. (9) From 1968, figures include trust funds (e.g. Social Security).

Summary of U.S. Receipts by Source and Outlays by Function

Source: U.S. Treasury Department, Office of Management and Budget
(in thousands)

Net Receipts	Fiscal 1976	7/1-9/30 1976[1]	Fiscal 1977[2]
vidual income taxes	$131,602,555	$38,800,969	$158,300,000
poration income taxes	41,408,703	8,460,466	54,600,000
ial insurance taxes and contributions	92,714,377	25,759,134	108,800,000
mployment taxes and contributions	79,909,024	21,803,012	(NA)
nemployment insurance	8,053,658	2,697,903	(NA)
ontributions for other insurance and retirement	4,751,695	1,258,218	(NA)
ise taxes	16,962,582	4,472,698	17,800,000
ate and gift taxes	5,216,229	1,454,592	7,300,000
stoms	4,074,176	1,212,173	5,000,000
cellaneous	8,026,454	1,612,734	6,600,000
otal	**300,005,077**	**81,772,766**	**358,300,000**
Outlays			
ional defense	90,215,930	22,388,851	96,900,000
rnational affairs	4,461,848	1,449,751	6,500,000
neral science, space, and technology	4,196,683	1,128,573	4,600,000
ural resources, environment, and energy	11,674,436	3,591,726	15,500,000
iculture	1,994,004	760,073	4,800,000
nmerce and transportation	17,238,524	4,684,861	15,400,000
nmunity and regional development	5,022,863	1,505,295	7,500,000
ication, training, employment and social services	17,678,274	4,683,016	20,700,000
alth	33,600,713	8,992,124	39,000,000
ome security	126,895,958	32,838,104	137,500,000
erans benefits and services	18,444,339	3,974,959	18,100,000
v enforcement and justice	3,325,494	859,667	3,700,000
neral government	2,951,242	854,162	3,800,000
venue sharing and general purpose scal assistance	7,114,160	2,024,055	9,500,000
rest	35,500,036	7,304,310	38,000,000
distributed offsetting receipts	-14,704,375	-2,566,530	-15,200,000
Total	**365,610,129**	**94,472,996**	**406,400,000**

1) Transitional quarter; up to 1976, fiscal year ended June 30; beginning with 1977, fiscal year ends Sept. 30 of the year indicated.
Estimate. (NA) Not available.

U. S. Customs and Internal Revenue Receipts

Source: Treasury Department

Gross. Not reduced by appropriations to Federal old-age and survivors insurance trust fund or refunds or receipts.

cal ar	Customs	Internal Revenue	Fiscal year	Customs	Internal Revenue	Fiscal year	Customs	Internal Revenue
30	$587,000,903	$3,039,295,014	1955	$606,396,634	$66,288,691,586	1972	$3,284,922,000	$209,900,000,000
35	343,353,034	3,277,690,028	1960	1,123,037,579	91,774,802,823	1973	3,175,268,000	237,800,000,000
40	348,590,635	5,303,133,988	1965	1,477,548,820	114,428,991,753	1974	3,334,127,000	269,000,000,000
45	354,775,542	43,902,001,929	1970	2,429,799,000	195,700,000,000	1975	3,665,929,000	293,800,000,000
50	422,650,329	39,448,607,109	1971	2,589,973,339	191,600,000,000			

U.S. Direct Investments Abroad, Countries and Industries

Source: Bureau of Economic Analysis, U.S. Commerce Department
(millions of dollars)

	Direct investment position		Net capital outflows		Reinvested earnings		Balance of payments income		Earnings	
	1975	1976	1975	1976	1975	1976	1975	1976	1975	1976
Bulk all areas	124,212	137,244	6,264	4,596	8,048	7,714	8,567	11,127	16,434	18,843
veloped countries	90,923	101,150	2,898	3,354	4,900	6,176	4,609	5,217	9,445	11,298
anada	31,038	33,927	419	102	2,173	2,459	1,239	1,376	3,364	3,782
Petroleum	6,220	7,153	−57	−53	548	722	303	279	871	1,011
Manufacturing	14,691	15,984	130	80	1,106	1,208	522	628	1,641	1,847
Other	10,127	10,790	346	75	519	529	414	469	852	924
urope	49,533	55,906	2,338	2,914	2,345	3,110	2,643	2,996	4,981	6,058
Petroleum	11,393	13,445	1,293	1,838	142	33	381	499	470	425
Manufacturing	26,013	28,702	769	579	1,261	2,029	1,330	1,553	2,623	3,626
Other	12,128	13,759	276	497	942	1,048	932	944	1,888	2,007
ther	10,352	11,317	141	338	382	607	727	845	1,100	1,458
Petroleum	2,745	3,064	−25	156	126	164	142	184	252	344
Manufacturing	4,723	5,013	22	18	173	261	242	275	432	557
Other	2,884	3,240	144	164	83	182	343	386	416	557
veloping countries	26,222	29,050	3,702	1,665	3,083	1,204	3,619	5,763	6,623	7,112
atin America	22,101	23,536	1,215	145	1,621	1,302	1,600	2,098	3,163	3,354
Petroleum	3,324	2,940	−214	−574	173	227	254	222	431	453
Manufacturing	8,562	9,242	246	176	801	495	359	486	1,150	997
Other	10,215	11,354	1,183	543	647	580	987	1,390	1,582	1,904
ther	4,121	5,514	2,487	1,520	1,462	−98	2,019	3,665	3,460	3,758
Petroleum	−805	−58	2,202	1,384	1,068	−595	1,575	3,115	2,647	2,723
Manufacturing	1,897	2,120	133	75	109	133	94	117	206	255
Other	3,029	3,452	152	61	285	364	350	433	607	780
rnational and unallocated	7,067	7,044	335	423	66	333	338	147	367	435

Gross National Product, National Income, and Personal Income

Source: Office of Economic Analysis, U.S. Commerce Department
Includes Alaska and Hawaii beginning in 1960 (millions of dollars)

	1950	1960	1970	1974	1975	19
Gross national product	**284,769**	**503,734**	**977,080**	**1,412,889**	**1,528,822**	**1,706,**
Less: Capital consumption allowances	18,342	43,408	87,254	137,651	162,531	179,
Equals: Net national product	**266,427**	**460,326**	**889,826**	**1,275,238**	**1,366,291**	**1,527,**
Less: Indirect business tax and nontax liability	23,334	45,200	93,461	128,582	138,701	150,
Business transfer payments	778	1,878	3,989	5,886	7,008	8,
Statistical discrepancy	1,488	—1,031	—6,392	5,763	5,862	5,
Plus: Subsidies minus current surplus of government enterprises	247	243	1,694	952	2,264	
Equals: National income	**241,074**	**414,522**	**800,462**	**1,135,959**	**1,216,984**	**1,364,**
Less: Corporate profits and inventory valuation adjustment	37,669	49,904	69,240	83,553	99,264	128,
Contributions for social insurance	6,870	20,672	57,708	103,805	110,120	123,
Wage accruals less disbursement	24	0	0	—530	0	
Plus: Government transfer payment to persons	14,294	26,609	75,119	134,940	169,825	184,
Personal income interest	7,198	15,083	30,998	103,014	115,598	130,
Dividends	8,838	13,437	24,680	30,963	32,399	35,
Business transfer payments	778	1,878	3,989	5,886	7,008	8,
Equals: Personal income	**227,619**	**400,953**	**808,290**	**1,154,936**	**1,253,367**	**1,382,**

National Income by Type of Income

(millions of dollars)

	1960	1965	1970	1974	1975	19
Compensation of employees	**294,226**	**393,844**	**603,869**	**875,771**	**930,341**	**1,036,**
Wage and salaries	270,844	358,885	541,976	764,054	805,705	891,
Private	222,108	289,621	426,875	604,076	630,278	704,
Government	48,736	69,264	115,101	159,978	175,427	187,
Supplements to wages, salary	23,382	34,959	61,893	111,717	124,636	144,
Employer contrib. for social insurance	11,380	16,217	29,717	56,113	59,761	68,
Other labor income	12,002	18,742	32,176	55,604	64,875	75,
Proprietors' income	**46,209**	**57,253**	**66,919**	**86,247**	**85,995**	**88,**
Business and professional	34,244	42,416	50,017	60,863	62,826	69,
Inventory valuation adj.	—19	—380	—706	—3,630	—1,194	—1,
Farm	11,965	14,837	16,902	25,384	23,169	18,
Rental income of persons	**15,822**	**18,952**	**23,938**	**33,672**	**36,831**	**39,**
Corp. prof., with inv. adjust.	**49,904**	**76,070**	**69,240**	**83,553**	**99,264**	**128,**
Corp. profits before tax	49,712	77,787	74,041	126,921	123,516	156,
Corp. profits tax liability	23,032	31,326	34,789	52,375	50,154	64,
Corp. profits after tax	26,680	46,461	39,252	74,546	73,362	92,
Dividends	13,437	19,808	24,680	30,963	32,399	35,
Undistributed profits	13,243	26,653	14,572	43,583	40,963	56,
Inventory valuation adj.	192	—1,717	—4,801	—40,422	—12,029	—14.
Net interest	**8,361**	**18,217**	**36,496**	**68,998**	**79,063**	**88,**
National income	**414,522**	**564,336**	**800,462**	**1,135,959**	**1,216,984**	**1,364,**

Public Debt of the U. S.

Source: U.S. Treasury Department

Fiscal year	Gross debt	Per cap.	Fiscal year	Gross debt	Per cap.	Fiscal year	Gross debt	Per ca
						1971	$398,129,744,455	$1,923.
1870	$2,436,453,269	$61.06	1930	$16,185,309,831	$131.51	1972	427,260,460,940	2,046
1880	2,090,908,872	41.60	1940	42,967,531,038	367.48	1973	458,141,605,312	2,177
1890	1,132,396,584	17.80	1950	257,357,352,351	1,696.67	1974	475,059,815,732	2,241
1900	1,263,416,913	16.60	1960	286,330,760,848	1,584.70	1975	533,188,263,000	2,495
1910	1,146,939,969	12.41	1965	317,273,898,984	1,630.46	1976	620,432,257,000	2,893
1920	24,299,321,467	228.23	1970	370,918,706,950	1,811.12	1977	675,557,000,000	3,117

Appropriations by the Federal Government

Source: U.S. Treasury Department (fiscal year)

Year	Appropriations	Year	Appropriations	Year	Appropriations	Year	Appropriatior
1890	$395,430,284.26	1940	$13,349,202,681.73	1953	$94,916,821,231.67	1965	$107,555,087,622
1895	492,477,759.97	1944	118,411,173,965.24	1954	74,744,844,304.88	1967	140,861,235,376
1900	698,912,982.83	1945	73,067,712,071.39	1955	54,761,172,461.58	1968	195,908,743,535
1905	781,288,215.95	1946	76,597,999,662.67	1956	63,857,731,203.86	1969	203,049,351,090
1910	1,044,433,622.64	1947	40,823,734,061.18	1957	70,717,305,080.55	1970	222,200,021,901
1915	1,122,471,919.12	1948	42,098,608,820.42	1958	77,145,934,082.25	1971	247,623,820,964
1920	6,454,596,649.56	1949	47,357,993,957.59	1959	82,055,863,758.58	1972	247,638,104,722
1925	3,748,651,750.35	1950	52,867,672,466.21	1960	80,169,728,902.87	1973	275,554,945,383
1930	4,665,236,678.04	1951	67,966,083,088.46	1961	89,229,575,129.94	1974	311,728,034,120
1935	7,527,559,327.66	1952	127,788,153,262.97	1962	91,447,827,731.00	1975	374,124,469,875
				1963	102,149,886,566.52	1976	403,740,395,600

(1) This appropriation for 1968 incorporates for the first time the changes in the President's Budget for 1969, in consonance with th recommendations of the President's Commission on Budget Concepts which were adopted and implemented during fiscal year 196

National Income by Industry

Source: Bureau of Economic Analysis, U.S. Commerce Department

(millions of dollars)

	1960	1965	1970	1973	1974	1975	1976
Agricul., forestry, fisheries	**16,852**	**21,017**	**25,582**	**47,003**	**42,199**	**42,662**	**40,785**
Farms	15,857	19,630	23,639	43,835	38,692	39,134	36,656
Agri. services, forestry, fisheries	995	1,417	1,943	3,168	3,507	3,528	4,129
Mining	**5,732**	**6,116**	**7,682**	**10,149**	**15,539**	**17,979**	**19,384**
Metal mining	817	908	1,177	1,489	1,596	1,637	1,755
Coal mining	1,253	1,332	2,157	2,869	5,208	6,352	6,567
Crude petroleum, natural gas	2,734	2,754	3,048	3,908	6,661	7,762	8,765
Nonmetallic min. & quar.	928	1,122	1,300	1,883	2,074	2,228	2,297
Contract construction	**20,810**	**29,116**	**42,791**	**59,749**	**62,233**	**61,732**	**67,684**
Manufacturing	**125,822**	**172,572**	**217,505**	**283,540**	**297,833**	**311,530**	**364,994**
Nondurable goods	**52,208**	**66,482**	**88,902**	**107,094**	**119,285**	**127,123**	**146,902**
Food, kindred products	12,225	14,495	19,530	20,958	23,672	29,511	32,623
Tobacco manufactures	1,017	1,111	1,738	1,775	1,687	2,296	2,587
Textile mill products	4,488	5,837	7,419	8,704	9,915	8,770	10,419
Apparel, other fabric prod.	4,953	6,556	8,634	10,287	10,426	10,771	12,389
Paper, allied products	4,707	5,929	7,970	10,881	11,898	11,944	14,293
Printing, pub., allied industry	6,655	8,746	11,929	14,872	15,212	16,553	18,900
Chemicals, allied products	9,159	12,648	16,342	19,936	21,268	23,843	27,080
Petroleum refining, related ind.	4,586	5,381	7,342	8,509	13,977	12,424	15,531
Rubber, misc. plastic products	2,809	3,949	5,776	8,806	8,811	8,649	10,370
Leather, leather products	1,609	1,830	2,222	2,368	2,419	2,362	2,710
Durable goods	**73,614**	**106,090**	**128,603**	**176,446**	**178,548**	**184,407**	**218,092**
Lumber, wood, except furn.	3,255	4,212	5,135	10,560	10,596	8,989	11,593
Furniture and fixtures	2,092	2,870	3,657	4,690	4,792	4,565	5,333
Stone, clay, glass products	4,640	5,713	6,894	9,750	9,690	9,872	11,799
Primary metal industries	11,103	14,735	15,961	21,148	26,631	24,523	26,584
Fabricated metal products	8,113	11,518	14,635	22,397	22,815	24,324	27,554
Machinery, except electrical	11,861	18,357	24,296	32,107	33,455	36,857	41,754
Electrical equip. and supplies	10,469	14,850	20,327	25,874	25,762	26,409	31,091
Transport equip. exc. autos	8,270	11,361	14,347	13,806	14,064	15,430	17,218
Motor vehicles equipment	8,532	15,432	13,801	23,089	17,712	19,278	28,956
Instruments	2,954	4,170	5,843	8,000	8,176	8,889	10,322
Misc. manufacturing	2,325	2,872	3,707	5,025	4,855	5,271	5,888
ransportation	**18,177**	**23,150**	**29,824**	**41,056**	**44,248**	**44,497**	**50,621**
Railroad	6,718	7,047	7,358	9,712	10,139	9,882	11,074
Local suburban highway passenger	1,639	1,897	2,285	2,503	2,763	2,935	3,093
Motor freight trans., warehousing	5,840	8,317	11,632	17,544	18,692	18,447	21,054
Water transportation	1,654	1,990	2,502	2,799	3,305	3,362	3,682
Air transportation	1,400	2,697	4,374	6,412	6,914	7,034	8,586
Pipeline transportation	355	401	518	594	641	876	927
Transportation service	571	801	1,155	1,492	1,794	1,961	2,205
ommunication	**8,237**	**11,241**	**16,787**	**22,648**	**24,516**	**27,142**	**30,934**
Telephone and telegraph	7,304	9,991	15,074	20,374	22,167	24,365	27,654
Radio broadcasting, television	933	1,250	1,713	2,274	2,349	2,777	3,280
ectric, gas, sanitary services	**8,934**	**11,447**	**14,718**	**18,759**	**18,442**	**24,411**	**25,915**
holesale and retail trade	**64,396**	**84,302**	**121,274**	**161,583**	**174,973**	**195,407**	**220,739**
Wholesale trade	23,126	30,341	44,430	65,737	76,639	82,403	91,144
Retail trade	41,270	53,961	76,844	95,846	98,334	113,004	129,595
nance, ins. and real estate	**45,940**	**61,857**	**89,948**	**116,657**	**128,409**	**143,112**	**160,827**
Banking	7,276	8,989	16,437	18,368	19,621	21,132	23,508
Credit agencies, holding, other investment co.	—435	—505	—1,873	—6,223	—6,831	—6,570	—7,038
Security, commodity brokers	1,243	1,903	2,675	3,198	3,017	4,219	4,626
Insurance carriers	4,641	5,186	8,544	12,767	12,100	12,659	15,389
Insurance agents, brokers, service	1,948	2,671	3,871	5,665	5,852	6,769	7,450
Real estate	31,267	43,613	60,294	83,027	93,216	103,129	114,776
rvices	**44,371**	**64,076**	**102,876**	**136,842**	**150,224**	**168,223**	**188,152**
Hotels, other lodging places	2,111	2,788	4,236	5,835	6,193	6,990	7,638
Personal services	4,608	5,993	7,433	7,730	8,052	8,319	8,805
Misc. business services	5,093	8,413	13,984	20,324	22,030	23,758	27,026
Automobile repair, serv., garages	1,762	2,450	3,628	5,119	5,389	5,935	6,635
Misc. repair services	1,105	1,501	2,117	2,829	3,276	3,453	3,851
Motion pictures	894	1,205	1,565	1,700	1,745	1,643	1,846
Amusement, recreation services	1,661	2,221	3,244	4,312	4,622	5,326	5,970
Medical, other health services	10,724	16,256	29,942	40,875	46,250	54,224	62,439
Legal services	2,636	4,069	6,443	9,672	10,669	11,894	13,030
Education services	2,402	4,191	7,231	7,794	8,651	10,030	11,112
Nonprofit membership org.	3,815	5,306	8,376	13,054	14,212	15,992	17,260
Misc. professional services	3,761	5,719	9,847	12,196	13,548	14,856	16,129
Private households	3,799	3,964	4,830	5,402	5,587	5,803	6,411
vernment, government enterprises	**52,891**	**75,233**	**126,850**	**165,785**	**180,415**	**199,475**	**214,860**
Federal	21,868	33,458	53,414	62,407	66,708	72,014	76,434
General Government	25,524	28,450	45,164	51,923	54,903	58,999	62,386
Government enterprises	3,658	5,008	8,250	10,484	11,805	13,015	14,048
State & local	25,615	41,775	73,436	103,378	113,707	127,461	138,426
General Government	27,367	39,345	69,553	97,139	106,458	119,226	129,237
Government enterprises	1,752	2,430	3,883	6,239	7,249	8,235	9,189
mestic income	**412,162**	**560,157**	**795,837**	**1,063,771**	**1,139,031**	**1,236,170**	**1,384,895**
est of the world	**2,360**	**4,179**	**4,625**	**9,058**	**13,052**	**10,543**	**14,359**
ll industries, total	**414,522**	**564,336**	**800,462**	**1,072,829**	**1,152,083**	**1,246,713**	**1,399,254**

State Finances

Revenues, Expenditures, Debts, Taxes, U.S. Aid, Military Contracts

For fiscal 1976 (year ending June 30, 1976, except: Alabama, Sept. 30; New York, Mar. 31; Texas, Aug. 31).

Sources: Census Bureau. U.S. Treasury and Defense Depts. *Military prime contracts. Taxes are state income and sales (or gross receipts) taxes, and vehicle, etc., fees.

State	Receipts (thousands)	Outlays (thousands)	Total debt (thousands)	Per cap. debt	Per cap. taxes	Per cap. U.S. aid	*Mltry cntrcts (thousands
Alabama	$2,826,853	$2,844,643	$979,022	$267.13	$339.22	$274.58	$418,249
Alaska	1,188,279	1,032,889	827,846	2,167.14	1,567.55	903.68	144,754
Arizona	1,864,083	1,838,885	91,821	40.45	448.33	237.32	614,288
Arkansas	1,492,345	1,482,793	129,659	61.48	343.79	289.69	77,176
California	22,124,617	20,533,635	6,465,717	300.45	500.05	273.63	8,949,118
Colorado	2,167,903	1,996,742	126,214	48.86	373.38	47.52	311,334
Connecticut	2,678,703	2,651,232	3,068,950	984.58	405.46	233.80	1,913,08
Delaware	661,580	702,412	737,502	1,267.19	616.12	277.38	36,565
Florida	5,178,835	5,157,603	1,739,834	206.61	348.59	182.50	972,00
Georgia	3,357,513	3,324,401	1,289,771	259.51	337.22	288.28	476,917
Hawaii	1,330,484	1,381,535	1,304,493	1,470.68	720.63	357.11	363,358
Idaho	711,110	708,116	39,443	47.46	395.67	322.20	16,528
Illinois	9,148,441	9,477,017	3,356,892	298.95	425.94	250.71	474,328
Indiana	3,493,933	3,522,701	599,654	113.10	361.29	187.42	785,230
Iowa	2,314,349	2,346,284	125,870	43.86	417.95	229.48	229,98
Kansas	1,644,976	1,596,955	408,101	176.67	369.67	228.37	307,38
Kentucky	2,746,691	2,641,107	1,996,558	582.43	409.49	299.08	188,28
Louisiana	3,497,916	3,412,868	1,457,976	379.58	431.03	299.44	302,71
Maine	1,051,158	1,036,176	535,347	500.32	495.86	354.68	283,75
Maryland	3,590,346	3,861,429	2,517,334	607.46	472.93	273.07	981,62
Massachusetts	5,727,697	5,531,537	4,960,606	853.95	469.55	312.20	1,956,14
Michigan	8,803,753	8,711,398	1,882,527	206.78	414.04	285.51	965,16
Minnesota	4,090,202	3,840,302	1,019,908	257.23	559.62	277.10	690,53
Mississippi	1,836,834	1,825,708	774,505	329.02	371.36	333.63	934,61
Missouri	2,894,819	2,850,813	336,697	70.47	302.18	217.99	2,294,70
Montana	737,101	687,758	85,055	112.95	368.85	385.64	22,83
Nebraska	1,006,610	983,070	64,051	41.24	315.14	255.93	43,66
Nevada	689,035	589,920	53,163	87.15	481.84	327.48	19,02
New Hampshire	589.303	631,766	303,795	369.58	223.57	252.58	147,44
New Jersey	5,739,354	5,853,457	4,013,414	547.08	312.49	254.34	975,32
New Mexico	1,244,706	1,071,351	186,768	159.90	492.36	372.11	124,94
New York	21,022,373	21,027,229	20,451,198	1,130.90	540.81	353.71	3,304,12
North Carolina	3,874,953	4,165,676	709,221	129.68	376.66	233.80	346,96
North Dakota	649,692	575,856	70,081	108.99	446.93	322.54	154,56
Ohio	8,086,425	7,737,614	3,029,677	283.41	309.70	198.18	921,0
Oklahoma	2,032,489	1,968,534	947,997	342.73	361.61	253.90	254,87
Oregon	2,322,644	2,161,043	2,001,580	859.42	354.57	347.78	51,73
Pennsylvania	10,596,881	11,133,842	5,888,110	496.38	432.22	263.74	1,252,40
Rhode Island	1,007,025	980,430	508,691	548.75	419.35	335.97	94,44
South Carolina	2,162,617	2,265,776	1,045,189	366.99	366.04	247.02	156,7
South Dakota	496,264	492,032	91,767	133.77	280.09	358.78	14,1
Tennessee	2,643,189	2,807,698	950,969	225.67	302.14	258.46	341,75
Texas	7,942,919	7,386,147	2,081,822	166.72	337.49	212.68	2,095,43
Utah	1,118,467	1,072,396	152,292	124.02	386.46	297.61	145,20
Vermont	537,515	530,955	421,172	884.82	431.29	375.01	129,23
Virginia	3,648,728	3,551,768	710,951	141.29	362.15	238.43	1,607,65
Washington	3,976,086	3,638,718	1,227,331	339.79	511.64	276.15	1,289,25
West Virginia	1,771,748	1,726,426	1,174,605	645.03	455.13	382.31	85,33
Wisconsin	4,400,184	4,190,261	1,362,143	295.54	525.29	252.70	250,9
Wyoming	493,505	454,245	75,335	193.17	495.13	445.60	20,91
Total or average	**$185,213,233**	**$181,966,149**	**$84,378,624**	**$394.37**	**$417.17**	**$294.77**	**$38,949,2**

U.S. Money in Circulation, by Denominations

Source: Fiscal Service, Bureau of Government Financial Operations, U.S. Treasury Department Outside Treasury and Federal Reserve Banks. (millions of dollars)

End of year	Total in circulation	Coin and small denomination							Large denomination currency						
		Total	Coin	$1	$2	$5	$10	$20	Total	$50	$100	$500	$1,000	$5,000	$10,00
1950	27,741	19,305	1,554	1,113	64	2,049	5,998	8,529	8,438	2,422	5,043	368	588	4	12
1960	32,869	23,521	2,427	1,533	88	2,246	6,691	10,536	9,348	2,815	5,954	249	316	3	10
1970	57,093	39,639	6,281	2,310	136	3,161	9,170	18,581	17,454	4,896	12,084	215	252	3	4
1975	86,547	54,866	8,959	2,809	135	3,841	10,777	28,344	31,681	8,157	23,139	175	204	2	4
1976	93,716	57,644	9,483	2,858	637	3,905	10,775	29,986	36,072	9,026	26,668	172	200	2	4

Bureau of the Mint

Source: Bureau of the Mint, U.S. Treasury Department

The first United States Mint was established in Philadelphia, Pa., then the nation's capital, by the Act of April 2, 1792, which provided for gold, silver, and copper coinage. Originally, supervision of the Mint was a function of the secretary of state, but it became (1799) an independent agency reporting directly to the president. When the Coinage Act of 1873 was passed, all mint and assay office activities were placed under a newly organized Bureau of the Mint in the Department of the Treasury.

The Bureau of the Mint manufactures all U.S. coins and distributes them through the Federal Reserve banks and branches. The Mint also maintains physical custody of the Treasury's monetary stocks of gold and silver, and refines and processes silver bullion. Functions performed by the Mint on a reimbursable basis include: the manufacture and sale of medals of a national character, the production and sale of numismatic coins and coin sets, and, as scheduling permits, the manufacture of foreign coins.

Amendments to the Coinage Act of 1965 (Public Law 91-607, Dec 31, 1970) authorized the production of dollar coins and provided that the dollar and half dollar coins for general circulation be of the same nonsilver clad composition as the quarter dollars and dimes. The cladding is an alloy of 75 percent copper and 25 percent nickel, bonded to a core of pure copper. The coins were first minted in calendar year 1971. The legislation authorized the secretary of the treasury to mint and issue not more than 150 million one dollar pieces containing 40-percent silver for sale to the public at premium prices. The dollar coins which bore the likeness of President Eisenhower and a reverse design emblematic of the Apollo 11 moon landing were minted and issued from 1971 until early in 1975.

Public Law 93-127, Oct. 18, 1973, authorized the minting for issue after July 4, 1975, of dollar, half dollar, and quarter dollar coins with reverse designs emblematic of the Bicentennial and the obverse dates 1776-1976, for general issue; and the production of 45 million numismatic 40-percent silver coins of the same designs and denominations to be sold to the public at premium prices.

The composition of the five cent coin continues to be 75 percent copper, 25 percent nickel, while the one cent coins are 95 percent copper and 5 percent zinc.

Calendar year 1976 coinage production follows:

Domestic Coinage Executed During Calendar Year 1976

Denomination	Philadelphia	Denver	San Francisco	Total value	Total pieces
Dollars - non-silver					
Bicentennial	$ 34,329,000.00	$ 24,555,564.00	-0-	$ 58,884,564.00	58,884,564
Total dollars	**$ 34,329,000.00**	**$ 24,555,564.00**	**-0-**	**$ 58,884,564.00**	**58,884,564**
Subsidiary					
Half-dollars - Bicentennial	$ 35,620,000.00	$ 36,059,624.00	-0-	$ 71,679,624.00	143,359,248
Quarters - Bicentennial	92,766,004.00[1]	120,567,709.75	-0-	213,333,713.75	853,334,855
Dimes	56,876,000.00	69,522,277.40	-0-	126,398,277.40	1,263,982,774
Total subsidiary	**$185,262,004.00**	**$226,149,611.15**	**-0-**	**$411,411,615.15**	**2,260,676,877**
Minor					
Five-cent pieces	$ 18,356,200.00	$ 28,198,207.35	-0-	$ 46,554,407.35	931,088,147
One-cent pieces	46,742,924.26[2]	42,215,924.55	-0-	88,958,848.81	-8,895,884,881
Total minor	**$ 65,099,124.26**	**$ 70,414,131.90**	**-0-**	**$135,513,256.16**	**9,826,973,028**
Total domestic coinage	**$284,690,128.26**	**$321,119,307.05**	**-0-**	**$605,809,435.31**	**12,146,534,469**

Manufactured at San Francisco Assay Office

1976 proof coin sets - 4,149,730
40% silver Bicentennial proof coin sets - 1,045,412
40% silver Bicentennial uncirculated sets - 1,398,200

(1) $94,004.00 manufactured at West Point Depository.
(2) $15,407,124.26 manufactured at West Point Depository.

Coinage executed for foreign governments

Country	No. of pieces
Haiti	24,000
Liberia	6,000
Peru	313,224,000
Philippines	249,118,000
Total	**562,372,000**

Large Denominations of U.S. Currency Discontinued

The largest denomination of United States currency now being issued is the $100 bill. Issuance of currency in denominations of $500, $1,000, $5,000 and $10,000 has been discontinued because their use has declined sharply over the past two decades.

As large denomination bills reach the Federal Reserve Bank they are removed from circulation.

Because some of the discontinued currency is expected to be in the hands of holders for many years, the description of the various denominations below is continued:

Portraits on U.S. Currency

Amt.	Portrait	Embellishment on back	Amt.	Portrait	Embellishment on back
$ 1	Washington	Great Seal of U.S.	$ 100	Franklin	Independence Hall
2	Jefferson	Signers of Declaration	500*	McKinley	Ornate denominational marking
5	Lincoln	Lincoln Memorial	1,000*	Cleveland	Ornate denominational marking
10	Hamilton	U.S. Treasury	5,000*	Madison	Ornate denominational marking
20	Jackson	White House	10,000*	Chase	Ornate denominational marking
50	Grant	U.S. Capitol	100,000*	Wilson	Ornate denominational marking

*For use only in transactions between Federal Reserve System and Treasury Department.

Portraits on U.S. Treasury Bills, Bonds, Notes and Savings Bonds

Denomination	Savings bonds	Treas. bills	Treas. bonds	Treas. notes
25	Washington			
50	Jefferson		Jefferson	
75	Kennedy			
100	Cleveland		Jackson	
200	F.D. Roosevelt			
500	Wilson		Washington	
1,000	Lincoln	H.McCulloch	Lincoln	Lincoln
5,000		J.G. Carlisle	Monroe	Monroe
10,000	T. Roosevelt	J. Sherman	Cleveland	Cleveland
50,000		C. Glass		
100,000		A. Gallatin	Grant	Grant
1,000,000		O. Wolcott	T. Roosevelt	T. Roosevelt
100,000,000				Madison
500,000,000				McKinley

U.S. Currency and Coin — June 30, 1977

Source: U.S. Treasury Department

Amounts in Circulation and Outstanding

	Amounts in circulation	Add amounts held by: United States Treasury	Add amounts held by: Federal Reserve Banks	Amounts outstanding
Currency[1]				
Federal Reserve Notes	$86,314,616,869	$11,008,195	$4,923,754,857	$91,249,379,921
United States Notes	318,260,217	4,278,799		322,539,016
Currency No Longer Issued	281,038,266	189,422	25,996	281,253,684
Total	**86,913,915,352**	**15,476,416**	**4,923,780,853**	**91,853,172,621**
Coin[2]				
Dollars[3]	$988,303,283	$48,862,073	$46,200,542	[3] $1,083,365,898
Fractional Coin	8,750,232,051	375,946,336	267,613,613	9,393,792,000
Total	**9,738,535,334**	**424,808,409**	**313,814,155**	**10,477,157,898**
Total currency and coin	**96,652,450,686**	**440,284,825**	**5,237,595,008**	**102,330,330,519**

Currency in Circulation by Denominations

Denomination	Total currency in circulation	Federal Reserve Notes[4]	United States Notes	Currency no longer issued
1 Dollar	$2,823,841,772	$2,667,913,461	$144,003	$155,784,308
2 Dollars	645,930,678	510,836,118	135,081,164	13,396
5 Dollars	3,835,933,586	3,678,340,660	116,053,750	41,539,176
10 Dollars	10,674,563,670	10,648,134,460	10,555	26,418,655
20 Dollars	30,930,206,234	30,909,690,670	3,870	20,511,694
50 Dollars	9,330,960,575	9,318,697,000	25	12,263,550
100 Dollars	28,298,193,850	28,207,351,500	66,964,850	23,877,500
500 Dollars	170,644,500	170,437,000	2,000	205,500
1,000 Dollars	198,095,000	197,866,000		229,000
5,000 Dollars	1,865,000	1,800,000		65,000
10,000 Dollars	3,680,000	3,550,000		130,000
Fractional parts	487			487
Total currency	**86,913,915,352**	**86,314,616,869**	**318,260,217**	**281,038,266**

Comparative Totals of Money in Circulation — Selected Dates

Date	Amounts (in millions)	Per capita[5]	Date	Amounts (in millions)	Per capita[5]	Date	Amounts (in millions)	Per capita[5]
June 30, 1977	$96,652.5[6]	$445.81	June 30, 1955	$30,229.3	$182.90	June 30, 1930	$4,522.0	$36.74
June 30, 1976	88,877.7	413.18[7]	June 30, 1950	27,156.3	179.03	June 30, 1925	4,815.2	41.56
June 30, 1970	54,351.0	265.39	June 30, 1945	26,746.4	191.14	June 30, 1920	5,467.6	51.36
June 30, 1965	39,719.8	204.14	June 30, 1940	7,847.5	59.40	June 30, 1915	3,319.6	33.01
June 30, 1960	32,064.6	177.47	June 30, 1935	5,567.1	43.75	June 30, 1910	3,148.7	34.07

(1) Excludes gold certificates, 1934 Series — $1,277,800, at 6/30/74 which are issued only to Federal Reserve banks and do not appear in circulation. (2) Excludes coin sold to collectors at premium prices. (3) Includes $481,781,898 in standard silver dollars (4) Issued on and after July 1, 1929. (5) Based on Bureau of the Census estimates of population. (6) Highest amount to date. (7) Revised.

The requirement for a gold reserve against U.S. notes' was repealed by Public Law 90-269 approved Mar. 18, 1968. Silver certificates issued on and after July 1, 1929 became redeemable from the general fund on June 24, 1968. The amount of security after those dates has been reduced accordingly.

Seigniorage on Coin and Silver Bullion

Seigniorage is the profit from coining money; it is the difference between the monetary value of coins and their cost, including the manufacturing expense.

Source: Fiscal Service, U.S. Treasury Department
(Jan. 1, 1935 to June 30, 1976)

	Total	Potential[1]
Fiscal Year Jan. 1, 1935-June 30, 1965, cumulative	$2,525,927,763.84	$ 6,560,393.72[2]
1968	383,141,339.00[3]	759,844,047.56
1969	250,170,276.34	700,000,000.00
1970	274,217,884.01	
1971	399,652,811.18	
1972	580,586,683.00	
1973	399,799,682.00	
1974	320,706,638.49	
1975	660,898,070.69	
1976	769,722,066.00	
Cumulative Jan. 1, 1935-June 30, 1976	8,050,361,580.69	

(1) Not cumulative, as coinage metals held by the Treasurer of the United States changes, the potential seigniorage changes. Potential seigniorage also changes depending on the denomination of the coins manufactured.
(2) Represents potential seigniorage as of June 30, 1965.
(3) Revised to include seigniorage on clad coins.

Federal Deposit Insurance Corporation (FDIC)

The primary purpose of the Federal Deposit Insurance Corporation (FDIC) is to insure the deposits of all banks entitled to insurance benefits under the Federal Deposit Insurance Act. The major functions of the FDIC are to pay off depositors of insured banks closed without adequate provision having been made to pay depositors' claims, to act as receiver for all national banks placed in receivership and for state banks placed in receivership when appointed receiver by state authorities, and to prevent the continuance or development of unsafe and unsound banking practices. The FDIC's entire income consists of assessments on insured banks and income from investments; it receives no appropriations from Congress. It may borrow from the U.S. Treasury not to exceed $3 billion outstanding at any one time, but has made no such borrowings since it was organized in 1933. The FDIC surplus (Deposit Insurance Fund) as of Dec. 31, 1976, was 7.26 billion.

World Gold Production

Source: Bureau of Mines, U.S. Interior Department (in ounces)

Year	Estimated world prod.	Africa: South Africa	Africa: Ghana	Africa: Zaire	North and South America: United States	North and South America: Canada	North and South America: Mexico	North and South America: Nicaragua	North and South America: Colombia	Other: Australia	Other: India	Other: Japan	Other: Philippines	Other: All other
1970	47,522,342	32,164,107	707,900	180,590	1,743,322	2,408,574	198,241	115,173	201,519	619,922	104,200	255,189	602,715	8,220,890
1971	46,494,837	31,388,631	697,517	171,685	1,495,108	2,243,000	150,915	121,134	188,847	672,106	118,569	255,255	637,048	8,355,022
1972	44,843,374	29,245,273	724,051	140,724	1,449,943	2,078,567	146,061	112,340	188,137	754,866	105,776	243,027	606,730	9,047,879
1973	43,296,755	27,494,603	722,531	133,642	1,175,750	1,954,340	132,557	85,051	215,876	554,278	105,390	188,274	572,250	9,962,213
1974	39,941,080	24,388,203	566,617	130,603	1,126,886	1,698,392	134,454	82,639	265,195	522,127	101,114	139,727	536,338	10,248,785
1975	38,574,162	22,937,820	523,889	103,217	1,052,252	1,674,000	132,236	70,281	299,366	514,186	91,437	143,489	501,776	10,530,213
1976p	NA	22,935,988	532,473	NA	1,048,037	1,685,998	162,811	75,855	NA	497,700	100,374	NA	501,197	NA

(p) preliminary. (NA) not available.

Gold Reserves of Central Banks and Governments

Source: Federal Reserve Board

Millions of dollars; valued at $35 per ounce through 1971, at $38 for 1972, and $42.22 thereafter.

Dec.	Total World (est.)[1]	Int'l Monetary Fund	United States	Canada	Rest of world (est.)	Belgium	France	West Germany	Italy	Netherlands	Switzerland	United Kingdom
1960	40,540	2,439	17,804	885	20,295	1,170	1,641	2,971	2,203	1,451	2,185	2,800
1965	43,230	1,869	13,806	1,151	27,285	1,558	4,706	4,410	2,404	1,756	3,042	2,265
1970	41,275	4,339	11,072	791	25,865	1,470	3,532	3,980	2,887	1,787	2,732	1,349
1971	41,175	4,732	10,206	792	26,235	1,544	3,523	4,077	2,884	1,909	2,909	775
1972	44,890	5,830	10,487	834	28,575	1,638	3,826	4,459	3,130	2,059	3,158	800
1973	49,850	6,478	11,652	927	30,793	1,781	4,261	4,966	3,483	2,294	3,513	886
1974	49,800	6,478	11,652	927	30,733	1,781	4,262	4,966	3,483	2,294	3,513	888
1975	49,740	6,478	11,599	927	30,738	1,781	4,262	4,966	3,483	2,294	3,513	888

(1) Excludes USSR, other Eastern European countries, and People's Republic of China.

Reserves not listed above, Dec. 1975. Algeria 231, Argentina 169, Australia 312, Austria 882, Republic of China (Taiwan) 97, Denmark 76, Egypt 103, Greece 153, India 293, Iran 158, Iraq 173, Japan 891, Kuwait 169, Lebanon 389, Libya 103, Mexico 154, Pakistan 67, Portugal 1,170, Saudi Arabia 129, South Africa 749, Spain 602, Sweden 244, Thailand 99, Turkey 151, Uruguay 135, Venezuela 472, Bank for International Settlements (net) 246.

U.S. and World Silver Production

Source: Bureau of Mines, U.S. Interior Department

Largest production of silver in the United States in 1915—74,961,075 fine ounces.

Year (Cal.)	United States Fine ozs.	United States Value	World Fine ozs.	Year (Cal.)	United States Fine ozs.	United States Value	World Fine ozs.
1930	50,748,127	$19,538,000	248,708,426	1960	36,000,000	$33,305,858	241,300,000
1935	45,924,454	33,008,000	220,704,231	1965	39,806,033	51,469,201	257,415,000
1940	69,585,734	49,483,000	275,387,000	1970	45,006,000	79,697,000	310,891,000
1945	29,063,255	20,667,200	162,000,000	1974	33,762,000	159,018,000	294,935,000
1950	43,308,739	38,291,545	203,300,000	1975	34,938,000	154,424,000	294,268,000
1955	36,469,610	33,006,839	224,000,000	1976p	34,328,000	149,328,00	NA

(p) preliminary (NA) not available.

Bank Rates on Short-term Business Loans

Source: Federal Reserve System

Percent per annum. Estimates based on reports from banks in 35 centers. Short-term loans mature within one year.

	All size loans: Avg. 35 cities	N.Y. C.	7 Other N.E.	8 No. Cent.	7 S.E.	8 S.W.	4 West	Size of loan in $1,000: 1-9	10-99	100 to 499	500 to 999	1,000 and over
1967 Aug. 1-15	5.95	5.66	6.29	5.92	5.92	6.01	6.02	6.58	6.46	6.16	5.89	5.72
Nov. 1-15	5.96	5.71	6.29	5.91	5.94	6.03	6.03	6.60	6.48	6.17	5.90	5.73
1970 Aug. 1-15	8.50	8.24	8.89	8.47	8.49	8.53	8.54	9.15	9.07	8.75	8.46	8.25
Nov. 1-15	8.07	7.74	8.47	8.05	8.15	8.08	8.16	8.89	8.79	8.34	8.09	7.74
1971 Aug.	6.51	6.25	6.77	6.46	6.77	6.64	6.54	7.68	7.27	6.88	6.58	6.27
Nov.	6.18	5.86	6.40	6.13	6.47	6.43	6.21	7.51	7.05	6.51	6.26	5.93
1973 Aug.	9.24	9.08	9.49	9.24	9.25	9.16	9.25	8.95	9.25	9.50	9.31	9.14
Nov.	10.08	9.90	10.51	10.02	9.96	10.08	10.04	9.80	10.14	10.43	10.18	9.95
1974 Feb.	9.91	9.68	10.28	9.98	9.80	9.93	9.78	9.86	10.09	10.28	10.06	9.75
May	11.15	11.08	11.65	11.09	10.88	10.82	11.19	10.50	11.06	11.41	11.32	11.06
1975 Feb.	9.94	9.61	10.31	9.87	10.24	10.01	9.99	10.94	10.73	10.25	9.93	9.73
May	8.16	7.88	8.37	8.00	8.70	8.34	8.33	9.57	9.10	8.52	8.18	7.90
1976 Aug.	7.80	7.48	8.18	7.70	7.95	7.75	8.15	8.85	9.41	8.65	9.33	9.26
Nov.	7.28	6.88	7.62	7.28	7.51	7.33	7.52	8.56	9.22	8.45	9.13	8.69

NOTE:—The Quarterly Survey of Interest Rates Charged by Banks on Business Loans has been revised beginning with the survey period of February 1971. The revision incorporates a number of technical changes in coverage, sampling, and interest rate calculations. These include elimination of accounts receivable loans from the survey, shortening the sample period for respondent banks in most districts, and calculation of effective annual interest rates on discounted loans using a revised formula based on annual rather than quarterly compounding of interest. As a result of the above changes, new weights derived from this survey have been used to calculate the weighted average rates.

U. S. Commercial Banks with Deposits over $1 Billion

A compilation of the 300 largest commercial banks in the U.S. is made twice a year by the American Banker, daily banking newspaper, 525 W. 42 St., New York, NY 10036. Of these the first 101 banks had deposits of more than $1 billion on June 30, 1977. They are listed below. (Copyright 1977, by American Banker)

Rank	Bank	Deposits
1	Bank of America NT&SA, San Francisco	$60,963,239,000
2	Citibank NA, New York	53,562,659,000
3	Chase Manhattan Bank NA, New York	38,735,165,547
4	Manufacturers Hanover Trust Co., N.Y.	25,952,350,000
5	Morgan Guaranty Trust Co., New York	21,848,328,000
6	Chemical Bank, New York	21,596,944,000
7	Bankers Trust Co., New York	16,400,807,000
8	Continental Illinois NB&T Co., Chicago	16,133,091,000
9	First National Bank, Chicago	15,517,547,000
10	Security Pacific Nat'l Bk, Los Angeles	13,975,979,446
11	Wells Fargo Bank NA, San Francisco	11,372,476,000
12	Marine Midland Bank, Buffalo, N.Y.	9,505,319,000
13	Crocker National Bank, San Francisco	9,385,125,000
14	United California Bank, Los Angeles	8,234,470,000
15	Irving Trust Co., New York	7,689,020,127
16	First National Bank, Boston	6,735,120,000
17	Mellon Bank NA, Pittsburgh	6,730,610,001
18	National Bank of Detroit	6,265,109,000
19	Bank of New York	4,723,925,081
20	First Pennsylvania Bank NA, Philadelphia	4,269,463,000
21	Seattle-First National Bank, Wash.	4,264,889,000
22	Republic National Bank, Dallas	3,993,579,000
23	First National Bank, Dallas	3,866,568,000
24	Harris Trust & Savings Bank, Chicago	3,841,267,000
25	Union Bank, Los Angeles	3,657,229,571
26	Valley National Bank, Phoenix, Ariz.	3,027,979,066
27	Philadelphia National Bank	3,016,121,000
28	First City National Bank, Houston, Tex.	3,013,663,000
29	Cleveland Trust Co.	2,971,219,000
30	North Carolina National Bank, Charlotte	2,917,002,000
31	Northern Trust Co., Chicago	2,874,217,000
32	Detroit Bank & Trust Co.	2,848,714,000
33	Wachovia B&T NA, Winston-Salem, N.C.	2,815,024,400
34	Girard Bank, Philadelphia	2,689,887,000
35	Manufacturers National Bank, Detroit	2,672,811,000
36	Citizens & Southern NB, Atlanta, Ga.	2,611,995,000
37	First National Bank of Oregon, Portland	2,607,193,000
38	Texas Commerce Bank NA, Houston	2,600,667,000
39	European-American B&T Co., New York	2,600,328,000
40	United States NB of Oregon, Portland	2,592,081,000
41	National Bk of No. America, New York	2,581,453,000
42	Rainier National Bank, Seattle, Wash.	2,568,041,604
43	Bank of California NA, San Francisco	2,486,939,000
44	Pittsburgh National Bank	2,398,075,240
45	Fidelity Bank, Philadelphia	2,183,697,000
46	Maryland National Bank, Baltimore	2,143,709,942
47	California First Bank, San Francisco	2,091,927,255
48	Bank of Tokyo Trust Co., New York	2,056,456,546
49	First National Bank of Arizona, Phoenix	2,001,543,000
50	First Wisconsin National Bank, Milwaukee	1,959,268,000
51	National City Bank, Cleveland	1,790,023,000
52	Republic National Bank of New York	$1,745,723,753
53	Equibank NA, Pittsburgh	1,711,378,000
54	Virginia National Bank, Norfolk	1,676,820,000
55	Riggs National Bank, Washington, D.C.	1,605,378,141
56	First Union NB of North Car., Charlotte	1,589,595,000
57	American Fletcher NB&T Co., Indianapolis	1,560,621,099
58	Hartford National B&T Co., Conn.	1,551,229,469
59	First National Bank, Atlanta, Ga.	1,516,535,000
60	Industrial NB of Rhode Island, Providence	1,514,734,000
61	Northwestern NB, Minneapolis, Minn.	1,495,296,000
62	Connecticut Bank & Trust Co., Hartford	1,451,549,136
63	Southeast First National Bank, Miami	1,408,185,000
64	Michigan National Bank, Lansing	1,383,113,000
65	Lloyds Bank, California, Los Angeles	1,382,524,000
66	American National B&T Co., Chicago	1,374,183,584
67	Mercantile Trust Co. NA, St. Louis, Mo.	1,353,992,000
68	Trust Co. Bank, Atlanta, Ga.	1,344,272,000
69	Central National Bank, Cleveland	1,335,030,000
70	Shawmut Bank of Boston NA	1,301,232,789
71	Manuf. & Traders Trust Co., Buffalo, N.Y.	1,299,349,549
72	Provident National Bank, Philadelphia	1,292,929,000
73	First National Bank, St. Louis, Mo.	1,289,560,000
74	First National Bank, Minneapolis, Minn.	1,285,690,000
75	Indiana National Bank, Indianapolis	1,279,156,326
76	State Street Bank & Trust Co., Boston	1,218,617,000
77	New England Merchants NB, Boston	1,211,241,448
78	Banco Popular de Puerto Rico, San Juan	1,204,093,070
79	Equitable Trust Co., Baltimore, Md.	1,190,983,000
80	American Security Bank NA, Wash., D.C.	1,189,291,750
81	Bank of Hawaii, Honolulu	1,177,819,147
82	Mercantile National Bank, Dallas	1,146,421,380
83	First National Bank, Baltimore, Md.	1,139,700,000
84	First National State Bank of N.J., Newark	1,132,155,000
85	First National Bank, St. Paul, Minn.	1,126,293,000
86	Whitney National Bank, New Orleans, La.	1,124,703,341
87	American Bank & Trust Co., Reading, Pa.	1,112,420,000
88	Northwestern Bk., North Wilkesboro, N.C.	1,109,088,494
89	Continental Bank, Norristown, Pa.	1,085,838,903
90	Michigan National Bank of Detroit	1,085,610,000
91	United Jersey Bank, Hackensack, N.J.	1,082,638,000
92	Idaho First National Bank, Boise	1,081,650,550
93	First & Merchants NB, Richmond, Va.	1,071,239,671
94	Bank of the Southwest NA, Houston, Tex.	1,065,318,000
95	National Central Bank, Lancaster, Pa.	1,046,120,738
96	Ohio National Bank, Columbus	1,044,852,319
97	Arizona Bank, Phoenix	1,037,260,409
98	First American NB, Nashville, Tenn.	1,021,792,441
99	First-Citizens B&T Co., Raleigh, N.C.	1,016,634,188
100	Society National Bank, Cleveland	1,008,097,000
101	First Tennessee Bank NA, Memphis	1,002,319,000

Largest Bank in Each of 47 Foreign Countries

Source: 500 Largest Banks in the Free World, compiled by the American Banker, New York. (Copyright 1977) Based on deposits Jan. 1, 1977, or nearest fiscal year-end. For Canada, see Index.

(thousands)

Country, bank	Deposits in U.S. $
Argentina, Banco de la Nacion	1,095,926
Australia, Commonwealth Bkng. Corp.	12,893,224
Austria, Creditanstalt-Bankverein	7,514,712
Belgium, Societe Generale de Banque	15,324,016
Brazil, Banco do Brasil	23,748,997
Denmark, Copenhagen Handelsbank	3,454,008
Egypt, National Bank of Egypt	5,308,674
Finland, Kansallis-Osake Pankki	2,922,984
France, Credit Agricole Mutuel	40,812,177
Germany, Deutsche Bank	41,512,713
Greece, National Bank of Greece	5,818,717
Hong Kong, Hongkong & Shanghai	10,271,765
India, State Bank of India	5,224,701
Indonesia, Bank Bumi Daya	1,853,716
Iran, Bank Melli Iran	7,017,404
Iraq, Rafidain Bank	3,138,455
Ireland, Allied Irish Banks Ltd.	2,825,494
Israel, Bank Leumi le-Israel	8,344,625
Italy, Banca Nazionale del Lavoro	21,039,307
Japan, Dai-Ichi Kangyo Bank Ltd.	29,016,843
Jordan, Arab Bank, Ltd.	2,092,597
Korea, Bank of Seoul & Trust Co.	1,572,133
Kuwait, National Bank of	1,717,511
Libya, National Commercial Bank	892,844
Luxembourg, Cie, Luxembourgeoise	5,191,941
Malaysia, Malayan Banking Berhad	844,357
Mexico, Banco Nacional de Mexico	2,092,592
Netherlands, Algemene Bank Nederland	20,387,835
New Zealand, Bank of	1,699,509
Nigeria, Standard Bank Nigeria Ltd.	1,767,199
Norway, Norske Creditbank	1,961,149
Pakistan, Habib Bank Ltd.	1,440,982
Peru, Banco de la Nacion	2,405,138
Philippines, Philippine National Bank	900,138
Portugal, Banco Pinto & Sotto Mayor	1,517,528
Saudi Arabia, National Commercial Bank	2,707,716
Singapore, Oversea-Chinese Banking Corp.	1,143,758
South Africa, Standard Bank of	2,601,010
Spain, Banco Espanol de Credito	9,483,971
Sweden, Post-Och Kreditbanken	9,867,924
Switzerland, Swiss Bank Corp.	19,347,532
Taiwan, Bank of	3,243,564
Thailand, Bangkok Bank Ltd.	1,877,406
Turkey, Turkiye Is Bankasi	2,752,285
United Arab Emirates, Nat'l Bank of Abu Dhabi	1,808,960
United Kingdom, Barclays Bank Ltd.	29,366,659
Venezuela, Banco Nacional de Descuento	1,166,875

Corporations and Stocks

Stock Exchanges Trade Record 7.04 Billion Shares in U.S. Firms

The Securities and Exchange Commission reported in 1977 that a record 7.04 billion shares of stock were traded on the New York, American, and other U.S. stock exchanges in 1976.

The N.Y. Stock Exchange listed 2,169 issues of 1,575 companies for a total of 25.7 billion shares, valued on July 31, 1977, at $816 billion. Average daily trading was 21,014,779 through Aug. 31, 1977, compared to 13,365,138 in 1974.

The American Stock Exchange listed 1,191 issues of 1,138 companies, totaling 3.2 billion shares, valued Aug. 31, 1977, at $36.4 billion. Average daily volume through Aug. 31 was 2.7 million shares.

A 1975 count indicated that 25.3 million persons owned shares in American corporations. More recent counts are not available.

50 U.S. Companies with Largest Annual Sales or Revenues

Reprinted by special permission from the Fortune Directory, as listed for 1976; copyright 1977, Time Inc.

Company	Revenues (thousands)	Net profit (thousands)	Company	Revenues (thousands)	Net profit (thousands)
Exxon Corp.	$48,630,817	$2,640,964	Occidental Petroleum	$5,525,451	$183,721
General Motors Corp.	47,181,000	2,902,800	International Harvester	5,488,123	174,088
Ford Motor Co.	28,839,600	983,100	Eastman Kodak	5,438,170	650,618
Texaco Inc.	26,451,851	869,731	Sun Co.	5,387,064	356,182
Mobil	26,062,570	942,523	Union Oil of Cal.	5,350,693	268,815
Standard Oil Co. of Cal.	19,434,133	880,127	RCA Corp.	5,328,500	177,400
Gulf Oil Corp.	16,451,000	816,000	Esmark Inc.	5,300,566	82,550
Int'l. Business Machines	16,304,333	2,398,093	Bethlehem Steel Corp.	5,248,000	168,000
General Electric Co.	15,697,300	930,600	Rockwell International	5,220,100	123,400
Chrysler Corp.	15,537,788	422,631	United Technologies	5,166,264	157,403
Int'l. Tel. & Tel. Corp.	11,764,106	494,467	Caterpillar Tractor Co.	5,042,300	383,200
Standard Oil Co. (Ind.)	11,532,048	892,968	Kraft Corp.	4,976,643	135,650
Shell Oil Co.	9,229,950	705,838	Beatrice Foods Co.	4,690,569	153,107
U.S. Steel Corp.	8,604,200	410,300	LTV Corp.	4,496,893	30,700
Atlantic Richfield Co.	8,462,524	575,178	Xerox Corp.	4,403,897	358,906
E. I. Du Pont de Nemours	8,361,000	459,300	R. J. Reynolds Industries	4,291,149	353,893
Continental Oil Co.	7,957,620	459,994	Monsanto Co.	4,270,200	366,300
Western Electric Co.	6,930,942	217,383	Ashland Oil Inc.	4,086,845	135,983
Procter & Gamble Co.	6,512,728	401,098	General Foods Corp.	3,978,294	150,428
Tenneco	6,389,236	383,500	Cities Service Co.	3,964,600	217,000
Union Carbide Corp.	6,345,700	441,200	Firestone Tire & Rubber	3,939,107	96,003
Westinghouse Electric	6,145,152	223,217	Boeing	3,918,535	102,895
Goodyear Tire & Rubber	5,791,494	121,967	Amerada Hess	3,914,595	152,637
Phillips Petroleum	5,697,516	411,656	Greyhound	3,727,306	77,081
Dow Chemical	5,652,070	612,767	W.R. Grace	3,615,153	131,882

30 Largest Industrial Companies Outside the U.S.

Reprinted by special permission from the Fortune Directory, as listed for 1976; copyright 1977, Time Inc.

Company	Sales (thousands)	Net profit (or loss) (thousands)	Company	Sales (thousands)	Net profit (or loss) (thousands)
Royal Dutch Shell, N-B	$36,087,130	$2,347,766	Siemens, G	$8,060,411	$221,969
National Iranian Oil, Ir.	19,671,064	17,175,182	Thyssen, G	7,947,640	105,499
British Petroleum, B	19,103,330	324,615	Toyota Motor, J	7,695,997	345,433
Unilever, B-N	15,762,219	517,614	Nestle, S	7,627,869	348,922
Philips Gloilampnfab, N	11,521,549	212,940	ELF Aquitaine, F	7,536,225	340,108
ENI, It.	9,983,105	(37,026)	Imperial Chem Inds, B	7,465,412	442,328
Cie Francaise Petroles, F	9,927,775	34,731	Peugeot-Citroen, F	7,346,998	287,426
Renault, F	9,352,884	N.A.	Petrobas (Brazil Oil), Br.	7,252,110	934,579
Hoechst, G	9,332,979	188,010	Hitachi, J	6,680,423	200,377
BASF (Badische Anilin), G	9,202,592	241,176	BAT (Br-Am Tobacco), B	6,668,743	323,541
Petroleos Venezuela, V	9,083,587	876,153	Nissan Motor, J	6,583,517	273,005
Daimler-Benz, G	8,938,321	164,182	Mitsubishi Heavy Inds, J	6,137,230	47,711
Volkswagenwerk, G	8,513,304	399,164	St-Gobain-Pont-Mssn, F	5,979,469	98,775
Bayer, G	8,297,808	181,364	Montedison, It	5,826,432	(195,019)
Nippon Steel, J	8,089,530	38,572	Matsushita El Ind, J	5,736,562	220,641

Nation of hqs: B, Britain; Br, Brazil; F, France; G, West Germany; Ir, Iran; It, Italy; J, Japan; N, Netherlands; S, Switzerland; V, Venezuela.

50 Stocks Most Widely Held by Investment Cos., Insurance Cos., Trust Funds

As listed in 1977 by the N.Y. Stock Exchange
(In order of number of institutions, etc., which held shares, 1977)

Intl. Bus. Machs.	Citicorp	S.S. Kresge	Warner-Lambert	Avon Products
Exxon Corp.	Merck & Co.	Burroughs Corp.	Texas Utilities	Tenneco Inc.
Amer. Tel. & Tel.	Mobil Corp.	Gulf Oil	Philip Morris	Alcan Aluminum
Eastman Kodak	Dow Chemical	Amer. Home Prods.	Johnson & Johnson	Eli Lilly & Co.
General Motors	Minn. Mng. Mfg.	E.I. Du Pont	Pfizer Inc.	Weyerhaeuser Co.
General Electric	Standard Oil, Ind.	Caterpillr Tractr	Int'l. Paper	McDonald's Corp.
Xerox Corp.	Ford Motor	Procter & Gamble	Halliburton Co.	Int'l. Tel. & Tel.
Texaco Inc.	Union Carbide	Continental Oil	Coca-Cola Co.	Schering-Plough
Sears, Roebuck	Phillips Petroleum	Standard Oil, Cal.	Goodyear Tire	J.C. Penney
Atlantic Richfld.	General Tel. & El.	Schlumberger, Ltd.	Monsanto Co.	Commonwealth Ed.

N.Y. Stock Exchange Transactions and Seat Prices

Source: New York Stock Exchange

Year	Yearly volumes: Stock shares	Yearly volumes: Bonds Par values	Seat price: High	Seat price: Low
1900	138,981,000	$579,293,000	$47,500	$37,500
1905	260,569,000	1,026,254,000	85,000	72,000
1910	163,705,000	634,863,000	94,000	65,000
1915	172,497,000	961,700,000	74,000	38,000
1920	227,636,000	3,868,422,000	115,000	85,000
1925	459,717,623	3,427,042,210	150,000	99,000
1929	1,124,800,410	2,996,398,000	625,000	550,000
1930	810,632,546	2,720,301,800	480,000	205,000
1935	381,635,752	$3,339,458,000	$140,000	$65,000
1940	207,599,749	1,669,438,000	60,000	33,000
1945	377,563,575	2,261,985,110	95,000	49,000
1950	524,799,621	1,112,425,170	54,000	46,000
1960	766,693,818	1,346,419,750	162,000	135,000
1970	2,937,359,448	4,494,864,600	320,000	130,000
1975	4,693,427,000	5,178,300,000	138,000	55,000
1976	*5,360,116,000	5,262,107,000	104,000	40,000

*Record high for trading in stocks and bonds.

American Stock Exchange Transactions and Seat Prices

Source: American Stock Exchange

Year	Yearly volumes: Stock shares	Yearly volumes: Bonds Par values	Seat price: High	Seat price: Low
1929	476,140,375	$513,551,000	$254,000	$150,000
1930	222,270,065	863,541,000	225,000	70,000
1940	42,928,337	303,902,000	7,250	6,900
1945	143,309,392	167,333,000	32,000	12,000
1950	107,792,340	47,549,000	11,000	6,500
1960	286,039,982	$32,670,000	$60,000	$51,000
1965	534,221,999	146,927,000	80,000	55,000
1970	843,116,260	641,270,000	180,000	70,000
1975	457,610,360	259,128,000	72,000	34,000
1976	648,297,321	301,054,000	68,000	40,000

U.S. Business Indexes

Source: Federal Reserve System (1967=100, except as noted)
Data are seasonally adjusted unless otherwise noted.

Period	Industrial production: Total	Market Products: Total	Final: Total	Final: Consumer goods	Final: Equipment	Intermediate	Materials	Industry: Manufacturing	Capacity utilization in mfg.	Construction contracts	Nonagricultural employment—Total[1]	Manufacturing[2]: Employment	Manufacturing[2]: Payrolls	Total retail sales[3]	Prices[4]: Consumer	Prices[4]: Wholesale commodity
1963..	76.5	76.4	75.5	81.3	67.5	79.9	76.7	75.8	83.5	86.1	86.1	87.7	76.0	79	91.8	94.5
1965..	89.8	88.2	87.6	92.6	80.7	90.6	92.4	89.7	89.5	93.2	92.3	93.9	88.1	90	94.5	96.6
1970..	107.8	106.9	105.3	109.0	100.1	112.9	109.2	106.4	79.2	123.1	107.7	98.0	114.1	119	116.3	110.4
1971..	109.6	108.5	106.3	114.7	94.7	116.7	111.3	108.2	78.0	145.4	108.1	94.1	116.7	130	121.3	113.9
1972..	119.7	118.0	115.7	124.4	103.8	126.5	122.3	118.9	83.1	166.1	111.9	97.5	131.5	142	125.3	119.1
1973..	129.8	127.1	124.4	131.5	114.5	137.2	133.9	129.8	87.5	183.3	116.8	103.2	149.2	160	133.1	134.7
1974..	129.3	127.3	125.1	128.9	120.0	135.3	132.4	129.4	84.2	173.9	119.1	102.1	157.1	171	147.7	160.1
1975..	117.8	119.3	118.2	124.0	110.2	123.1	115.5	116.3	73.6	162.3	116.9	91.3	151.0	186	161.2	174.9
1976..	129.8	129.3	127.3	136.8	114.3	136.8	130.5	129.4	80.1	190.2	120.6	95.2	170.7	207	171.2	183.0
1977[5]..	139.0	138.9	136.9	145.3	125.6	146.6	139.1	138.8	83.4	...	125.0	99.2	...	224	182.6	194.8

(1) Employees only: excludes personnel in the Armed Forces. (2) Production workers only. Revised back to 1973. (3) F.R. index based on Census Bureau figures. (4) Prices are not seasonally adjusted. Latest figure is final. (5) July 1977.

Wholesale Price Indexes

Source: Bureau of Labor Statistics, U. S. Labor Department

The Wholesale Primary Market Price Index is designed to show the rate and direction of the composite of price movements, and to measure price changes not influenced by quality, quantity, terms of sale, etc. Wholesale refers to sales in quantities, not to prices received or paid by wholesalers.

Commodity group (1967 = 100)	1977 June	1977 Jan.	1976 Avg.	1975 Avg.
All commodities	194.4	188.0	183.0	174.9
Farm products, processing foods, and feeds	191.5	184.8	183.1	184.2
Farm products	192.7	193.5	191.0	186.7
Processed foods and feeds	190.1	179.3	178.0	182.6
All commodities except farm products	193.9	187.0	181.7	173.4
Industrial commodities	194.6	188.4	182.4	171.5
Textile products and apparel	154.4	150.3	148.2	137.9
Hides, skins, leathers, and related products	179.7	174.5	167.8	148.5
Fuels and related products and power	304.0	278.7	265.6	245.1
Chemicals and allied products	193.9	188.9	187.2	181.3
Rubber and plastic products	167.4	164.5	159.2	150.2
Lumber and wood products	228.7	222.7	205.6	176.9
Pulp, paper, and allied products	187.3	182.9	179.4	170.4
Metals and metal products	207.8	201.8	195.9	185.6
Machinery and equipment	180.8	177.0	171.0	161.4
Furniture and household durables	151.3	148.6	145.6	139.7
Nonmetallic mineral products	200.4	192.3	186.3	174.0
Transportation equipment (Dec. 1968 = 100)	159.4	157.1	151.1	141.5
Miscellaneous products	163.5	160.2	153.7	147.7

Assets and Liabilities of Insured Commercial Banks

Source: Federal Deposit Insurance Corp.
As of December 31, 1976 (thousands of dollars)

State	Loans and securities	Total assets	Total deposits	Total liabilities	Equity capital
Ala. . .	10,221,520	11,872,788	10,169,563	10,959,921	912,867
Alas. . .	1,276,743	1,593,077	1,374,073	1,472,792	120,285
Ariz. . .	6,353,246	7,538,655	6,733,694	7,161,575	377,080
Ark. . .	6,414,165	7,586,435	6,612,326	7,029,633	556,802
Cal. . .	83,560,739	108,705,404	88,902,503	102,424,091	6,281,313
Col. . .	7,911,382	9,675,139	8,317,471	8,981,753	693,386
Conn. .	7,016,994	8,990,751	7,613,682	8,350,627	640,124
Del. . .	2,457,010	2,770,463	2,268,666	2,584,445	186,018
D.C. . .	3,843,013	4,551,476	3,885,286	4,159,086	392,390
Fla. . . .	25,359,222	30,500,016	26,752,065	28,085,178	2,414,838
Ga. . . .	12,638,960	15,964,523	12,891,389	14,672,747	1,291,776
Ha. . . .	2,726,293	3,244,624	2,893,434	3,048,228	196,396
Ida. . . .	2,798,612	3,302,747	2,950,020	3,098,699	204,048
Ill.	67,031,547	78,647,460	61,685,161	73,016,779	5,630,681
Ind. . . .	19,743,753	23,084,814	19,579,739	21,461,042	1,623,772
Ia.	12,746,725	14,606,004	13,035,214	13,521,784	1,084,220
Kan. . .	9,580,461	11,126,867	9,747,739	10,230,701	896,166
Ky. . . .	10,551,882	12,290,516	10,613,845	11,339,372	951,144
La. . . .	12,799,312	15,369,442	13,106,310	14,247,363	1,122,079
Me. . . .	2,151,041	2,451,315	2,156,771	2,270,098	181,217
Md. . . .	9,397,078	11,204,340	9,472,695	10,374,677	829,663
Mass. .	14,384,249	18,789,098	14,777,612	17,378,193	1,410,905
Mich. .	31,207,514	36,914,335	31,755,790	34,295,956	2,618,379
Minn. .	16,872,757	19,619,451	16,210,337	18,287,124	1,332,327
Miss. .	6,086,647	7,259,947	6,403,979	6,714,028	545,919
Mo. . . .	19,218,090	23,132,310	19,012,207	21,418,946	1,713,364
Mon. . .	3,112,402	3,569,264	3,203,247	3,322,872	246,392
Neb. . .	6,491,425	7,701,682	6,718,439	7,106,206	595,476
Nev. . .	2,002,835	2,372,489	2,143,151	2,206,271	166,218
N.H. . .	1,828,269	2,110,409	1,881,128	1,939,703	170,706
N.J. . .	22,786,963	26,807,588	23,463,784	24,915,126	1,892,462
N.M. . .	3,106,147	3,698,846	3,319,732	3,449,267	249,579
N.Y. . .	118,753,173	170,495,528	127,302,682	157,219,429	13,276,099
N.C. . .	12,971,689	15,867,202	13,086,229	14,780,389	1,086,813
N.D. . .	2,794,436	3,135,917	2,824,394	2,898,230	237,687
Oh. . . .	33,527,233	40,070,154	33,295,721	36,773,993	3,296,161
Okla. .	10,989,420	13,290,285	11,535,853	12,323,691	966,594
Ore. . .	6,465,563	8,300,191	6,775,979	7,808,772	491,419
Pa. . . .	49,981,384	58,817,221	46,869,129	54,678,168	4,139,053
R.I. . . .	3,579,816	4,228,764	3,441,223	3,954,100	274,664
S.C. . .	4,263,486	5,107,695	4,427,318	4,693,804	413,891
S.D. . .	3,124,677	3,558,907	3,229,056	3,308,339	250,568
Tenn. .	13,511,567	16,421,590	14,249,009	15,272,607	1,148,983
Tex. . .	50,968,702	63,381,265	52,999,363	58,883,992	4,497,273
Ut. . . .	3,568,450	4,293,731	3,801,934	4,024,427	269,304
Vt. . . .	1,485,246	1,637,867	1,486,037	1,530,207	107,660
Va. . . .	14,470,672	16,994,111	14,854,842	15,733,902	1,260,209
Wash.	10,326,490	12,993,499	10,613,291	12,226,894	766,605
W.Va. .	6,399,426	7,252,811	6,195,486	6,657,972	594,839
Wis. . .	16,411,831	19,022,003	16,485,504	17,711,687	1,310,316
Wy. . .	1,779,703	2,099,297	1,877,756	1,945,192	154,105
*Others	5,527,695	7,308,892	5,922,264	7,118,341	190,551
U.S.	**809,049,960**	**1,004,020,313**	**825,001,858**	**931,950,078**	**72,070,235**

*Includes American Samoa, Guam, Puerto Rico, and Virgin Islands.

Bank Suspensions

Source: Federal Deposit Insurance Corp. Deposits in thousands of dollars. The figures represent banks which, during the periods shown, closed temporarily or permanently on account of financial difficulties; does not include banks whose deposit liabilities were assumed by other banks.

Year	Susp.	Deposits	Year	Susp.	Deposits	Year	Susp.	Deposits	Year	Susp.	Deposits
1929 . . .	659	230,643	1936 . . .	42	11,241	1959 . . .	3	2,593	1967 . . .	4	10,878
1930 . .	1,352	853,363	1937 . . .	50	14,960	1960 . . .	1	6,930	1969 . . .	4	9,011
1931 . .	2,294	1,690,669	1938 . . .	50	10,296	1961 . . .	5	8,936	1970 . . .	4	34,040
1932 . .	1,456	715,626	1939 . . .	32	32,738	1963 . . .	2	23,444	1971 . . .	5	74,605
1933*.	4,004	3,598,975	1940 . . .	19	5,657	1964 . . .	7	23,438	1972 . . .	1	20,482
1934 . . .	9	1,968	1955(a) .	4	6,503	1965 . . .	3	42,889	1973 . . .	3	25,811
1935 . . .	24	9,091	1958 . . .	3	4,156	1966 . . .	1	774	1975 . . .	1	18,248
									1976 . . .	3	18,859

*Figures for 1933 comprise 628 banks with deposits of $360,413,000 suspended before or after the banking holiday (the holiday began March 6 and closed March 15) or placed in receivership during the holiday; 2,124 banks with deposits of $2,520,391,000 which were not licensed following the banking holiday and were placed in liquidation or receivership; and 1,252 banks with deposits of $718,171,000 which had not been licensed by June 20, 1933. (a) No suspensions in years 1945-1954, 1962, 1968, 1974.

Federal Reserve System

The Federal Reserve System, central banking system of the United States, was established Dec. 23, 1913, by an Act of Congress to give the country an elastic currency, to provide facilities for discounting commercial paper, and to improve supervision of banking. Today it is generally recognized that the primary function of the System is to foster a flow of credit and money that will facilitate orderly economic growth, a stable dollar, and a long-run balance in international payments.

The Federal Reserve System consists of the (1) Board of Governors of the Federal Reserve System; (2) Federal Open Market Committee; (3) 12 Fed. Reserve Banks and 25 branches; (4) member banks; (5) Fed. Advisory Council, and (6) the Consumer Advisory Council.

The 7 members of the Board of Governors in Washington are appointed by the President with the advice and consent of the Senate; Dr. Arthur F. Burns is chairman. One of the Board's principal functions is in the area of monetary policy. The Board has authority to approve changes in discount rates, to change member bank reserve requirements within specified limits, to set margin requirements for certain kinds of stock transactions, and to set maximum interest rates payable on member banks' savings and time deposits. Another important duty of the Board relates to supervision of Federal Reserve Banks, state chartered member banks, and bank holding companies. Expenses of the Board of Governors are paid out of assessments upon the Reserve Banks. The Federal Reserve has also been given responsibility by the Congress for rule writing and enforcement of a number of consumer credit protection laws.

The Federal Open Market Committee is composed of the 7 members of the Board of Governors and 5 Federal Reserve Bank presidents elected annually. The Committee establishes System open market policy for the purchases and sales of securities and for operations in foreign currencies.

Rather than having one central bank in the political capital, as in central banking systems of most countries, the Federal Reserve System is divided into 12 districts, each with a Federal Reserve Bank—in Boston, New York, Philadelphia, Cleveland, Richmond, Atlanta, Chicago, St. Louis, Minneapolis, Kansas City, Dallas, and San Francisco. Reserve Banks are operated for public service. By statute, their stock is held entirely by member banks, which include all national banks and such state banks and trust companies as have been admitted to membership. Ownership of Reserve Bank stock is in the nature of an obligation incident to membership in the System and does not carry with it the attributes of control and financial interest ordinarily attached to stock ownership in corporations that are operated for profit. The amount of stock that member banks own is specified by law and dividends are limited to 6% per annum. In case of the liquidation of any Reserve Bank, its surplus would be paid entirely to the United States. Each Reserve Bank has 9 directors, 6 of whom are chosen by member banks and 3 by the Board of Governors, including the chairman of the Reserve Bank board.

U.S. Balance of International Payments

Source: Bureau of Economic Analysis, U.S. Commerce Department

(millions of dollars)

	1955	1960	1965	1970	1973	1974	1975	1976
Exports of goods and services	**19,948**	**27,595**	**39,548**	**62,483**	**101,697**	**138,303**	**147,600**	**163,271**
Merchandise, adjusted	14,424	19,650	26,461	42,469	71,410	98,306	107,088	114,700
Transfers under U.S. military agency sales contracts	200	335	830	1,501	2,342	2,952	3,919	5,213
Receipts of income on U.S. investments abroad	2,817	3,350	5,899	8,575	13,540	19,763	17,330	21,369
Other services	2,507	4,261	6,359	9,938	14,405	17,281	19,263	21,990
Imports of goods and services	**−17,795**	**−23,555**	**−32,443**	**−59,571**	**−98,177**	**−136,143**	**−131,436**	**−159,571**
Merchandise, adjusted	−11,527	−14,758	−21,510	−39,866	−70,499	−103,673	−98,043	−123,917
Direct defense expenditures	−2,901	−3,087	−2,952	−4,855	−4,629	−5,035	−4,795	−4,847
Payments of income on foreign investments in the U.S.	−520	−1,063	−1,730	−5,082	−8,744	−11,019	−11,376	−11,561
Other services	−2,847	−4,646	−6,252	−9,771	−14,306	−16,416	−17,221	−19,247
Unilateral transfers, net	−2,498	−2,308	−2,854	−3,294	−3,887	−7,188	−4,612	−5,023
Official reserve assets, net	182	2,145	1,222	2,477	209	−1,434	−607	−2,530
Government assets, other than official reserve assets, net	−310	−1,100	−1,605	−1,589	−2,645	365	−3,463	−4,213
Private assets, net	−1,255	−3,878	−3,793	−7,052	−12,230	−25,960	−27,478	−36,216
Foreign official assets in the U.S., net }		1,473	132	6,907	6,299	10,981	6,960	17,945
Other foreign assets in the U.S., net }	1,357	647	249	−984	11,454	22,631	7,376	16,575
Allocations of special drawing rights	—	—	—	867	—	—	—	—
Statistical discrepancy	371	−1,019	−457	−244	−2,720	−1,555	5,660	9,763
Memoranda:								
Balance on merchandise trade	2,897	4,892	4,951	2,603	911	−5,367	9,045	−9,217
Balance on goods and services	2,153	4,040	7,105	2,912	3,520	2,160	16,164	3,699
Balance on goods, services, and remittances	1,556	3,404	6,059	1,354	1,572	447	14,444	1,822
Balance on current account	−345	1,732	4,251	−382	−367	−5,028	11,552	−1,324

Note: — details may not add to totals because of rounding.

All Banks in U. S.—Number, Deposits

Source: Federal Reserve System

Comprises all national banks in the United States and all state commercial banks, trust companies, mutual and stock savings banks, private and industrial banks, and special types of institutions that are treated as banks by the federal bank supervisory agencies.

Year	Number of banks						Total deposits (millions of dollars)					
		F.R.S. members			Nonmembers			F.R.S. members			Nonmembers	
(As of June 30)	Total all banks	Total	Nat'l	State	Mutual savings	Other	Total all banks	Total	Nat'l	State	Mutual savings	Other
1925	**26,479**	9,538	8,066	1,472	621	18,320	**51,641**	32,457	19,912	12,546	7,089	12,095
1930	**23,855**	8,315	7,247	1,068	604	14,936	**59,828**	38,069	23,235	14,834	9,117	12,642
1935	**16,047**	6,410	5,425	985	569	9,068	**51,149**	34,938	22,477	12,461	9,830	6,381
1940	**14,955**	6,398	5,164	1,234	551	8,008	**70,770**	51,729	33,014	18,715	10,631	8,410
1945	**14,542**	6,840	5,015	1,825	539	7,163	**151,033**	118,378	76,534	41,844	14,413	18,242
1950	**14,674**	6,885	4,971	1,914	527	7,262	**163,770**	122,707	82,430	40,277	19,927	21,137
1955	**14,309**	6,611	4,744	1,867	525	7,173	**208,850**	154,670	98,636	56,034	27,310	26,870
1960	**14,006**	6,217	4,542	1,675	513	7,276	**249,163**	179,519	116,178	63,341	35,316	34,328
1965	**14,295**	6,235	4,803	1,432	504	7,556	**362,611**	259,743	171,528	88,215	50,980	51,889
1970	**14,167**	5,803	4,637	1,166	496	7,868	**502,658**	346,229	254,261	91,967	69,285	87,145
1974, Dec. 31	**14,944**	5,780	4,706	1,074	479	8,685	**847,663**	575,838	431,039	144,799	99,371	172,454
1975, Dec. 31	**15,108**	5,787	4,741	1,046	475	8,846	**897,101**	590,999	447,590	143,409	110,569	195,533
1976, Dec. 31	**15,145**	5,758	4,735	1,023	473	8,914	**961,980**	618,859	469,378	149,481	123,654	219,467

Bank Clearings in Major U.S. Cities

Source: Dun & Bradstreet, Inc.

Year (Cal.)	New York $1,000	Chicago $1,000	Phila. $1,000	Los Ang. $1,000	Boston $1,000	San Fran. $1,000	Detroit $1,000	Dallas $1,000
1935	181,551,008	13,194,988	16,909,000	5,852,244	10,645,822	6,478,835	4,523,167	1,969,290
1940	160,878,038	16,684,672	21,455,000	7,543,880	11,943,665	6,773,877	6,312,233	2,986,774
1945	334,432,654	27,279,588	34,710,000	17,144,078	19,589,725	15,743,086	16,472,971	6,634,514
1950	399,308,634	40,674,983	51,102,000	26,504,731	25,348,336	21,982,689	22,855,273	14,451,332
1955	530,883,498	52,818,527	59,962,000	42,818,633	32,472,726	31,492,157	36,364,754	21,678,567
1960	738,604,276	66,651,600	56,716,000	53,635,826	40,759,040	39,787,147	39,101,854	27,811,939
1965	1,280,402,568	82,507,560	69,116,728	111,587,481	60,318,717	87,095,481	56,068,833	42,414,327
1970	3,752,515,518	110,219,418	94,003,896	174,153,125	125,033,163	122,929,389	136,965,556	51,886,403
1974	13,163,126,958	148,493,173	129,756,288	254,091,476	117,527,838	188,674,386	212,028,019	74,039,017
1975	13,189,673,325	153,368,143	129,025,577	274,825,654	100,151,380	200,376,308	195,847,574	76,064,440
1976	15,472,872,646	174,385,134	137,997,731	321,080,091	109,226,791	213,044,616	190,376,840	85,679,209

Year (Cal.)	Kan. City $1,000	Houston $1,000	Pittsburgh $1,000	Cleveland $1,000	St. Louis $1,000	Minneap. $1,000	Baltimore $1,000	Atlanta $1,000
1935	4,348,113	1,420,404	5,245,718	3,417,055	3,940,654	3,044,735	2,910,637	2,204,500
1940	4,997,593	2,568,518	7,074,775	5,734,407	4,822,016	3,787,088	4,201,985	3,430,900
1945	10,856,497	5,982,318	12,978,668	11,529,428	9,723,815	8,196,279	8,315,468	8,263,900
1950	16,707,120	11,922,307	16,782,419	17,683,829	14,896,444	14,113,814	12,154,904	12,910,100
1955	20,057,800	19,199,929	21,142,527	26,426,614	18,481,105	18,496,868	17,071,914	18,597,100
1960	24,967,583	21,887,889	23,913,706	32,364,009	21,138,861	25,129,318	20,423,684	22,993,200
1965	33,936,377	33,938,170	29,070,474	44,600,090	28,399,392	34,029,120	25,893,740	34,371,000
1970	53,509,523	39,855,427	42,418,973	52,690,067	33,611,932	43,112,445	29,964,761	53,784,237
1974	51,771,171	80,517,773	87,752,769	69,231,013	37,993,730	61,765,880	34,858,768	80,579,538
1975	52,681,392	88,375,890	93,419,382	66,424,707	35,009,486	62,917,478	37,954,018	78,791,721
1976	60,322,939	99,029,673	93,612,263	69,300,835	40,142,197	68,866,898	42,266,842	88,733,176

Per Capita Personal Income, by States and Regions

Source: Bureau of Economic Analysis, U.S. Commerce Department (dollars)

State and region	1970	1973	1974	1975	1976
nited States	3,966	5,049	5,486	5,902	6,441
ew England	4,300	5,227	5,668	6,098	6,590
Connecticut	4,917	5,929	6,487	6,973	7,373
Maine	3,302	4,158	4,536	4,786	5,385
Massachusetts	4,340	5,262	5,667	6,114	6,585
New Hampshire	3,737	4,633	4,986	5,315	5,973
Rhode Island	3,959	4,873	5,355	5,841	6,498
Vermont	3,468	4,296	4,602	4,960	5,480
ideast	4,471	5,479	5,968	6,433	6,975
Delaware	4,524	5,846	6,284	6,748	7,290
Dist. of Columbia	5,079	6,420	7,043	7,742	8,648
Maryland	4,309	5,453	5,973	6,474	7,036
New Jersey	4,701	5,718	6,242	6,722	7,269
New York	4,712	5,657	6,120	6,564	7,100
Pennsylvania	3,971	4,989	5,485	5,943	6,466
reat Lakes	4,135	5,311	5,731	6,121	6,793
Illinois	4,507	5,750	6,268	6,789	7,432
Indiana	3,772	4,959	5,295	5,653	6,257
Michigan	4,180	5,509	5,846	6,173	6,994
Ohio	4,020	5,063	5,481	5,810	6,432
Wisconsin	3,812	4,831	5,281	5,669	6,293
lains	3,751	5,115	5,364	5,785	6,130
Iowa	3,751	5,344	5,561	6,077	6,439
Kansas	3,853	5,276	5,615	6,023	6,495
Minnesota	3,859	5,112	5,469	5,807	6,153
Missouri	3,781	4,794	5,065	5,510	6,005
Nebraska	3,789	5,251	5,379	6,087	6,240
North Dakota	3,086	5,768	5,698	5,737	5,400
South Dakota	3,123	4,957	4,860	4,924	4,796
Southeast	3,257	4,346	4,740	5,055	5,544
Alabama	2,948	3,905	4,284	4,643	5,105
Arkansas	2,878	3,952	4,379	4,620	5,073
Florida	3,738	5,107	5,406	5,638	6,108
Georgia	3,354	4,441	4,798	5,086	5,571
Kentucky	3,112	4,048	4,565	4,871	5,423
Louisiana	3,090	3,961	4,456	4,904	5,386
Mississippi	2,626	3,579	3,837	4,052	4,575
North Carolina	3,252	4,300	4,649	4,952	5,409
South Carolina	2,990	3,972	4,390	4,618	5,126
Tennessee	3,119	4,206	4,567	4,895	5,432
Virginia	3,712	4,902	5,377	5,785	6,276
West Virginia	3,061	3,989	4,480	4,918	5,394
Southwest	3,546	4,567	5,019	5,487	6,040
Arizona	3,665	4,833	5,152	5,355	5,817
New Mexico	3,077	3,927	4,299	4,775	5,213
Oklahoma	3,387	4,336	4,823	5,250	5,657
Texas	3,606	4,632	5,106	5,631	6,243
Rocky Mountain	3,590	4,785	5,222	5,576	6,072
Colorado	3,855	5,137	5,549	5,985	6,503
Idaho	3,290	4,489	5,140	5,159	5,726
Montana	3,500	4,781	5,079	5,422	5,600
Utah	3,227	4,186	4,539	4,923	5,482
Wyoming	3,815	4,945	5,644	6,131	6,723
Far West	4,374	5,403	5,976	6,481	7,048
California	4,493	5,497	6,089	6,593	7,164
Nevada	4,563	5,742	6,161	6,647	7,337
Oregon	3,719	4,848	5,398	5,769	6,331
Washington	4,053	5,146	5,646	6,247	6,772
Alaska	4,644	6,005	7,037	9,448	10,178
Hawaii	4,623	5,570	6,010	6,658	6,969

Per capita personal income for each state is derived by division of total personal income for the calendar year by resident population as estimated by the Bureau of the Census) as of July 1. Personal income consists of wage and salary disbursements, other labor come, proprietors' income, less personal contributions for social insurance plus a residence adjustment, plus property income (divi- ends, interest, and rent), plus transfer payments, such as unemployment benefits and relief, welfare, and social insurance payments.

Average Percent Increase in Earnings

Source: Bureau of Labor Statistics, U.S. Labor Department

July 1975 to July 1976	All industries				Manufacturing			
rea	Office clerical	Industrial nurses	Skilled maintenance	Unskilled plant	Office clerical	Industrial nurses	Skilled maintenance	Unskilled plant
nited States	7.4	8.1	8.6	9.0	7.8	8.2	8.6	8.8
Northeast	7.2	7.8	8.5	8.7	7.9	8.2	8.5	8.4
South	7.2	8.2	8.9	9.0	7.3	7.9	9.1	9.4
North Central	7.8	8.3	8.4	8.8	7.9	8.4	8.4	8.9
West	7.6	7.9	8.7	10.0	7.7	8.3	8.9	8.6

Indexes of Manufacturing, Industrial Countries

Source: Bureau of Labor Statistics, U.S. Labor Department (1967=100)

ountry	1960	1965	1970	1972	1973	1974	1975	1976
Output per hour								
nited States	78.8	98.2	104.5	116.0	119.4	112.8	116.3	124.2
1 foreign countries	68.3	89.9	123.8	139.0	149.6	155.2	154.4	NA
anada	75.5	94.4	115.2	127.4	132.2	132.3	134.4	137.6
apan	52.6	79.1	146.5	163.9	184.3	187.5	181.7	205.2
elgium	69.9	87.5	129.5	153.2	166.7	178.8	188.6	NA
enmark	66.6	86.7	129.3	150.7	159.8	166.9	177.3	196.3
rance	68.7	88.5	121.2	137.0	144.1	149.8	148.9	166.1
/. Germany	66.4	90.4	116.6	130.3	138.9	147.6	153.3	165.8
aly	65.1	91.6	117.8	132.9	147.8	155.9	150.2	161.5
etherlands	67.5	87.8	134.4	154.8	170.6	182.1	178.0	NA
weden	63.1	88.5	124.5	137.9	147.4	152.1	152.8	153.2
witzerland	80.4	90.5	125.5	137.9	147.7	150.7	144.8	156.8
nited Kingdom	76.8	92.4	109.1	121.1	128.2	127.9	124.3	129.3
vg. 9 European countries	69.0	90.7	119.3	134.6	143.4	149.6	149.4	NA
riginal EC	67.8	90.8	120.1	135.5	145.1	152.7	154.4	NA
Unit labor costs in U.S. dollars								
nited States	97.7	92.6	116.5	118.1	123.2	143.1	154.3	156.9
foreign countries	82.6	97.5	111.8	142.5	171.7	194.4	234.1	NA
anada	106.3	91.3	111.5	121.9	126.6	145.4	160.3	180.0
pan	82.5	102.5	113.3	160.1	194.3	233.4	272.0	262.3
elgium	74.9	94.3	101.4	128.6	153.6	175.1	216.7	NA
enmark	74.7	91.8	104.4	117.3	147.6	168.4	201.6	192.2
ance	81.7	98.3	98.9	119.9	147.1	155.0	207.4	188.5
. Germany	78.1	95.7	124.6	162.5	207.8	232.1	262.4	249.3
ly	76.5	97.1	119.2	152.2	172.5	183.1	246.2	213.2
etherlands	65.4	91.8	108.4	138.8	173.5	200.1	251.5	NA
weden	80.5	93.3	105.1	132.8	148.5	165.9	216.3	247.4
vitzerland	71.1	95.6	99.8	129.5	165.2	194.9	250.2	242.4
nited Kingdom	85.7	98.7	106.0	126.2	134.1	157.2	199.0	180.7
g. 9 European countries	79.3	96.5	112.6	141.9	172.6	191.8	234.5	NA
iginal EC	77.8	96.2	115.6	147.1	183.0	201.0	242.9	NA

A) Not available

U. S. Labor Force, Employment and Unemployment

Source: Bureau of the Census, U. S. Commerce Department; Bureau of Labor Statistics, U. S. Labor Department
(Unemployment by sex, age, race and other characteristics)
(numbers in thousands)

	1974	1975	1976	1977 Jan.	Feb.	Mar.	Apr.	May	Jun
U.S. pop. (incl. armed forces overseas)	211,894[1]	213,631[1]	215,118[1]	215,998	216,123	216,237	216,376	216,504	216,64
Labor force[2]									
Labor force, persons 16 years of age and over	93,240	94,793	—	—	—	—	—	—	—
Civilian labor force	91,011	92,613	94,773	94,704	95,340	95,771	95,826	96,193	99,13
Employed, total	85,935	84,783	87,485	86,856	87,231	88,215	89,258	90,042	91,68
Agriculture	3,492	3,380	3,297	2,672	2,709	2,804	3,140	3,478	3,82
Nonagricultural industries	82,443	81,403	84,188	84,184	84,522	85,411	86,118	86,564	87,86
Unemployed, total	5,076	7,830	7,288	7,848	8,109	7,556	6,568	6,151	7,45
Long term, 15 weeks and over	937	2,483	2,339	2,260	2,409	2,448	2,357	2,078	1,83
Seasonally adjusted[3]									
Civilian labor force	—	—	—	95,516	96,145	96,539	96,760	97,158	97,64
Employed, total	—	—	—	88,558	88,962	89,475	90,023	90,408	90,67
Agriculture	—	—	—	3,090	3,090	3,116	3,260	3,386	3,33
Nonagricultural industries	—	—	—	85,468	85,872	86,359	86,763	87,022	87,34
Unemployed, total	—	—	—	6,958	7,183	7,064	6,737	6,750	6,96
Long term, 15 weeks and over	—	—	—	2,283	2,182	1,923	1,816	1,836	1,73
Rates (unemployed in each group as percent of total in group):									
All civilian workers	5.6	8.5	7.7	7.3	7.5	7.3	7.0	6.9	7.
Males, 20 years and over	3.8	6.7	5.9	5.6	5.8	5.4	5.0	5.3	5.
Females, 20 years and over	5.5	8.0	7.4	6.9	7.2	7.2	7.0	6.6	7.
Both sexes, 16-19 years	16.0	19.9	19.0	18.7	18.5	18.8	17.8	17.9	18.
White	5.0	7.8	7.0	6.7	6.7	6.6	6.3	6.2	6.
Black and other	9.9	13.9	13.1	12.5	13.1	12.7	12.3	12.9	13.
Household heads	3.3	5.8	5.1	4.8	4.9	4.6	4.4	4.5	4.
Married men	2.7	5.1	4.2	3.8	4.1	3.7	3.6	3.6	3.
Occupation of last job									
White-collar workers	3.3	4.7	4.6	4.5	4.6	4.7	4.4	4.3	4.
Blue-collar workers	6.7	11.7	9.4	8.4	8.7	8.3	7.8	7.9	7.
Industry of last job (nonagricultural)									
Private wage & salary workers	5.7	9.2	7.9	7.4	7.6	7.4	7.0	7.1	6.
Construction	10.6	18.1	15.6	14.9	15.2	14.2	12.0	13.0	12.
Manufacturing	5.7	10.9	7.9	6.9	7.1	6.6	6.7	6.2	6.
Durable goods	5.4	11.3	7.7	6.5	7.0	6.1	6.0	5.7	5.

(1) As of July 1. (2) Effective January 1972, data reflect adjustment to the 1970 Census of Population. For example th civilian labor force and employment totals were increased by a little more than 300,000; unemployment levels and rate were essentially unchanged. A subsequent census adjustment, primarily affecting whites and black and other groups, wa introduced into the survey for March 1973. As a result, the white labor force and employment levels were lowered by abou 150,000, while black levels were raised by 210,000. Consequently, the overall labor force and employment showed a ne increase of about 60,000. Unemployment levels and rates were not affected significantly. Comparisons with data prior t these two dates should take these adjustments into account. (3) Monthly data only. Revisions in the U.S. pop. (includin armed forces): 1975—213,540; 1974—211,901.

Employed Persons by Major Occupational Groups and Sex

Source: Bureau of Labor Statistics, U.S. Labor Department

Annual averages 1976

Occupational group	Thousands of persons: Both sexes	Males	Females	Percent distribution: Both sexes	Males	Females
Total employed	87,485	52,391	35,095	100.0	100.0	100.0
White-collar workers	43,700	21,551	22,148	49.9	41.1	63.1
Professional and technical	13,329	7,725	5,603	15.2	14.7	16.0
Managers and administrators, except farm	9,315	7,373	1,942	10.6	14.1	5.5
Sales workers	5,497	3,140	2,357	6.3	6.0	6.7
Clinical workers	15,558	3,314	12,245	17.8	6.3	34.9
Blue-collar workers	28,958	23,852	5,106	33.1	45.5	14.5
Craft and kindred workers	11,278	10,733	545	12.9	20.5	1.6
Operatives, except transport	10,085	6,135	3,949	11.5	11.7	11.3
Transport equipment operatives	3,271	3,062	209	3.7	5.8	.6
Nonfarm laborers	4,325	3,922	403	4.9	7.5	1.1
Service workers	12,005	4,622	7,384	13.7	8.8	21.0
Private household workers	1,125	30	1,095	1.3	.1	3.1
Other service workers	10,880	4,592	6,289	12.4	8.8	17.9
Farm workers	2,822	2,365	458	3.2	4.5	1.3
Farmers and farm managers	1,514	1,423	90	1.7	2.7	.3
Farm laborers and supervisors	1,309	942	367	1.5	1.8	1.0

Employment and Unemployment in the U.S.

Civilian labor force, persons 16 years of age and over (in thousands)

Year	Civilian labor force	Employed	Unem-ployed	Year	Civilian labor force	Employed	Unem-ployed
1940	52,705	45,070	7,635	1970	82,715	78,627	4,088
1950	62,208	58,920	3,288	1972	86,542	81,702	4,840
1960	69,628	65,778	3,852	1973	88,714	84,409	4,304
1965	74,455	71,088	3,366	1974	91,011	85,936	5,076
1967	77,347	74,372	2,975	1975	92,613	84,783	7,830
1969	80,734	77,902	2,832	1976	94,773	87,485	7,288

Civilian Employment of the Federal Government

Source: Workforce Analysis and Statistics Division, U.S. Civil Service Commission; data as of June 30, 1977

Agency	All areas	United States: Total	United States: Full-time	United States: Part-time & intermittent	Outside United States: Total	Outside United States: Territories	Outside United States: Foreign countries
Total, all agencies[1]	**2,893,335**	**2,765,331**	**2,534,924**	**230,407**	**128,004**	**33,426**	**94,578**
Percent distribution	**100**	**96**	**88**	**8**	**4**	**1**	**3**
Legislative branch	**40,715**	**40,630**	**39,552**	**1,078**	**85**	**11**	**74**
Congress	19,117	19,117	19,117	...	...	...	...
Senate	7,114	7,114	7,114	...	...	...	...
House of Representatives	11,989	11,989	11,989	...	...	...	...
Comm. on Security and Coop. in Europe	14	14	14	...	...	...	...
Architect of the Capitol	2,289	2,289	2,004	285	...	...	...
General Accounting Office	5,608	5,533	5,346	187	75	11	64
Government Printing Office	7,986	7,986	7,676	310	...	...	...
Library of Congress	5,062	5,052	4,804	248	10	...	10
Tax Court	194	194	190	4	...	...	...
Judicial branch	**12,471**	**12,337**	**11,680**	**657**	**134**	**134**	...
United States Courts	12,139	12,005	11,377	628	134	134	...
Supreme Court	332	332	303	29	...	...	...
Executive branch	**2,840,149**	**2,712,364**	**2,483,692**	**228,672**	**127,785**	**33,281**	**94,504**
Executive Office of the President	1,828	1,828	1,718	110	...	...	...
White House Office	478	478	464	14	...	...	...
Office of the Vice President	25	25	23	2	...	...	...
Office of Management and Budget	769	769	743	26	...	...	...
Council of Economic Advisors	41	41	39	2	...	...	...
Council on Environmental Quality	64	64	64	...	...	...	...
Council on Internt'l Economic Policy	22	22	21	1	...	...	...
Council on Wage and Price Stability	47	47	43	4	...	...	...
Domestic Council	35	35	34	1	...	...	...
Executive Mansion and Grounds	80	80	80	...	...	...	...
Office of Drug Abuse Policy	14	14	12	2	...	...	...
Office of Special Representatives Trade Negotiations	59	59	53	6	...	...	...
Office of Telecommunications Policy	72	72	59	13	...	...	...
Office of Science and Technology Policy	48	48	22	26	...	...	...
National Security Council	74	74	61	13	...	...	...
Executive departments	**1,749,392**	**1,647,260**	**1,572,206**	**75,054**	**102,132**	**14,180**	**87,952**
State[2]	30,578	10,873	10,251	622	19,705	...	19,705
Treasury	127,321	126,431	120,669	5,762	890	555	335
Defense	1,008,690	931,917	919,137	12,780	76,773	10,500	66,273
Department of the Army	368,415	332,667	327,597	5,070	35,748	3,671	32,077
Department of the Navy	315,141	293,015	289,140	3,875	22,126	4,863	17,263
Department of the Air Force	252,385	236,830	233,553	3,277	15,555	1,770	13,785
Defense Logistics Agency	49,338	48,815	48,648	167	523	55	468
Other defense activities	23,411	20,590	20,199	391	2,821	141	2,680
Justice	53,259	52,392	51,214	1,178	867	365	502
Interior	87,437	87,054	78,296	8,758	383	308	75
Agriculture	131,756	130,327	101,775	28,552	1,429	749	680
Commerce	39,661	39,393	33,056	6,337	268	80	188
Labor	17,096	17,016	16,166	850	80	63	17
Health, Education, and Welfare	159,469	158,700	149,932	8,768	769	724	45
Housing and Urban Development	17,948	17,783	17,379	404	165	165	...
Transportation	76,177	75,374	74,331	1,043	803	671	132
Independent agencies	**1,088,929**	**1,063,276**	**909,768**	**153,508**	**25,653**	**19,101**	**6,552**
ACTION	2,089	1,557	1,446	111	532	18	514
Board of Governors, Fed. Res. System	1,521	1,521	1,485	36	...	...	...
Canal Zone Government	3,207	...	...	...	3,207	3,207	...
Civil Service Commission	8,700	8,679	7,042	1,637	21	21	...
Community Service Admin.	1,085	1,085	1,077	8	...	...	...
Energy Research and Dev. Admin.	9,772	9,762	9,444	318	10	1	9
Environmental Protection Agency	12,290	12,280	11,001	1,279	10	10	...
Federal Communications Comm.	2,137	2,130	2,130	...	7	7	...
Federal Energy Admin.	3,675	3,675	3,655	20	...	...	...
Federal Power Commission	1,387	1,387	1,379	8	...	...	...
Federal Trade Commission	1,756	1,756	1,683	73	...	...	...
General Services Admin.	37,786	37,697	36,180	1,517	89	84	5
Information Agency	8,571	3,243	3,210	33	5,328	...	5,328
Interstate Commerce Commission	2,144	2,144	2,118	26	...	...	...
National Aeronautics and Space Admin.	25,613	25,587	25,383	204	26	1	25
National Labor Relations Board	2,830	2,809	2,790	19	21	21	...
Nuclear Regulatory Commission	2,959	2,959	2,813	146	...	...	...
Panama Canal Company	10,761	81	81	...	10,680	10,680	...
Securities & Exchange Commission	1,922	1,922	1,890	32	...	...	...
Selective Service System	80	80	79	1	...	...	...
Small Business Admin.	5,013	4,901	4,778	123	112	112	...
Tennessee Valley Authority	35,736	35,732	35,373	359	4	...	4
U. S. Postal Service	658,390	655,595	527,709	127,886	2,795	2,795	...
Veterans Admin.	224,178	221,847	203,597	18,250	2,331	2,049	282
All Other Agencies	25,327	24,847	23,425	1,422	480	95	385

(1) Excludes employees of Central Intelligence Agency, National Security Agency (not reported to the Civil Service Commission) and uncompensated employees. June 1977 total includes 41,622 employees exempted from personnel ceilings in the Youth Programs and Worker Trainee Opportunities Program. (2) Includes 6,229 employees in Agency for International Development (2,784 in the Washington, D.C. metropolitan area); employees in foreign countries include 573 paid from local currency trust funds established by foreign governments.

Foreign Direct Investment in the U.S.

Source: Bureau of Economic Analysis, U.S. Commerce Department

*Consists of interest, dividends, and branch profits received by foreign owners from direct investments in the U
NOTE: All the data series relating to foreign direct investment in the U.S. have been revised substantially and are r
comparable to previously published data.

(Millions of dollars)	Book value	Net Cap. inflows	Earnings: Total	Earnings: Pay-ments*	Earnings: Reinv'd.
1975	27,662	1,414	2,181	1,046	1,189
1976 Total (prelim.)	30,182	2,176	2,299	1,360	1,585
By country:					
Canada	5,859	247	373	215	267

(Millions of dollars)	Book value	Net Cap. inflows	Earnings: Total	Earnings: Pay-ments*	Earnings: Reinv
United Kingdom	5,699	351	429	351	27
Netherlands	6,184	369	689	220	46
Switzerland	2,284	93	66	170	5
Other	10,156	1,116	742	404	51

Canadian Labor Force

Source: Statistics Canada; Apr., 1976, seasonally adjusted (thousands of workers)

	Can.	Nfld.	P.E.I.	N.S.	N.B.	Que.	Ont.	Man.	Sask.	Alta.	B
Labor force	10,308	183	48	326	261	2,716	3,931	449	403	856	1,1
Employed	9,572	158	44	295	232	2,479	3,689	428	387	822	1,0
Unemployed	736	25	5	31	29	236	242	21	16	33	
Percent unemployed	7.1	13.6	9.8	9.6	11.1	8.7	6.2	4.7	4.0	3.9	

Canadian Labor Force Characteristics

Source: Statistics Canada (thousands of workers)

		Employed						
		All workers[1]			Paid workers			
Year	Labor force	Total	Agri-culture	Non-agri-culture	Total	Non-agri-culture	Unem-ployed	Unem-ployed %
1950	5,163	4,976	1,018	3,958	3,522	3,411	186	3.6
1955	5,610	5,364	819	4,546	4,133	4,027	245	4.4
1960	6,411	5,965	683	5,282	4,843	4,732	446	7.0
1965	7,141	6,862	594	6,268	5,760	5,655	280	3.9
1970	8,374	7,879	511	7,368	6,839	6,740	495	5.9
1973	9,279	8,759	467	8,292	7,757	7,661	520	5.6
1974	9,662	9,137	473	8,664	8,105	8,006	525	5.4
1975	10,060	9,363	486	8,877	8,448	8,310	697	6.9
1976	10,308	9,572	474	9,098	8,631	8,488	736	7.1

(1) Including self-employed.

Average Weekly Canadian Wages and Salaries, by Province

Source: Canadian Statistical Review, Apr. 1977 (Canadian dollars)

Year & month	Canada	Nfld.	P.E.I.	N.S.	N.B.	Que.	Ont.	Man.	Sask.	Alta.	B.C
1970	126.82	117.70	83.82	104.21	104.01	122.38	131.52	115.88	114.87	128.15	137.
1974	178.09	168.48	126.92	149.98	154.58	172.89	181.43	162.71	160.99	178.72	200.
1975	203.34	196.50	149.84	172.40	182.40	199.22	204.86	186.01	188.31	207.39	229.
1976 Jan.	217.03	211.36	166.98	183.86	194.95	211.25	218.58	195.33	202.04	225.60	246.
Apr.	224.40	217.40	167.56	189.79	199.68	219.09	225.51	203.02	210.10	231.63	255.
July	230.11	223.85	173.15	198.24	202.22	223.31	230.74	214.26	216.24	239.93	263.
Oct.	235.03	227.63	176.02	198.34	208.24	228.74	235.82	215.82	222.73	244.89	266.

Canadian Provincial Unemployment Rates, 1973-1976

Source: Statistics Canada

Year	Can.	Nfld.	P.E.I.	N.S.	N.B.	Que.	Ont.	Man.	Sask.	Alta.	B.C.
1973	5.6	12.8	...	6.8	9.2	7.4	4.0	3.9	3.6	4.0	6.5
1974	5.4	16.7	...	6.7	9.2	7.3	4.1	3.1	2.8	2.7	6.0
1975	6.9	12.2	...	7.8	9.9	8.1	6.3	4.5	2.9	4.1	8.5
1976	7.1	13.6	9.8	9.6	11.1	8.7	6.2	4.7	4.0	3.9	8.6

Canadian Unemployment Insurance Commission

Source: Canadian Statistical Review, Apr., 1977
(Canadian dollars)

	Claims data			Benefits paid					
Year and month	Benefi-ciaries[1 2] (000)	Claims received (000)	Weeks paid (000)	Total paid[3] (thousands of dollars)	Regular	Sickness	Maternity	Retirement	Fishi
1975	...	2,857	37,326	3,144,020	2,907,715	110,989	102,161	5,834	23,6
1976	701	2,675	36,189	3,342,246	3,019,686	129,802	139,624	18,048	28,8
Jan.	878	277	3,746	341,825	314,180	9,761	9,713	1,842	5,3
1977 Jan.	878	267	3,948	395,158	356,223	13,820	13,679	1,070	9,4

(1) Refer to the number of persons receiving $1.00 or more in unemployment insurance benefits during a specific we
each month. (2) Annual figures are average of 12 months. (3) Includes adjustments for cancellation of warrants and c
lection of overpayments.

Total Value of Canadian Construction Work

Source: Statistics Canada (thousands of Canadian dollars)

Province	1975 New	1975 Repair	1975 Total	1976 New	1976 Repair	1976 Total
Canada	23,895,420	4,238,025	28,133,445	26,809,741	4,639,118	31,448,859
Newfoundland	548,946	77,214	626,160	652,065	88,544	740,609
Prince Edward Island	82,318	17,406	99,724	72,179	17,786	89,965
Nova Scotia	630,253	129,653	759,906	758,158	137,505	895,663
New Brunswick	742,275	112,079	854,354	736,939	122,839	859,778
Quebec	5,967,072	951,644	6,918,716	6,444,634	1,032,660	7,477,294
Ontario	7,480,855	1,523,023	9,003,878	8,156,744	1,639,748	9,796,492
Manitoba	858,988	186,068	1,045,056	974,096	195,053	1,169,149
Saskatchewan	884,105	195,420	1,079,525	1,100,604	218,299	1,318,903
Alberta	3,331,420	502,710	3,834,130	4,262,401	564,749	4,827,150
British Columbia	3,369,188	542,808	3,911,996	3,651,921	621,935	4,273,856

Includes residential, commercial, institutional, marine, road, highway and aerodrome, waterworks and sewage systems, and all other construction.

Canadian Pulpwood, Wood Pulp, and Newsprint

Source: Canadian Statistical Review, Apr. 1977 (thousands of tons)

Year and month	Pulpwood production (thousand units[1])	Wood pulp production[2] Total	Mechanical	Chemical	Wood pulp exports[3]	News-print production	Newsprint shipments Total	Domestic	Exports[4]
1972	18,805	18,593.3	7,520.8	11,033.9	6,071.2	8,660.8	8,739.4	779.7	7,959.8
1974	2,640	21,168	7,870	12,001	7,057	9,548	9,597	886	8,711
1975	16,444	—	—	—	5,496	7,679	7,727	864	6,863
1976	15,093	—	—	—	6,722	8,906	8,703	885	7,818

(1) 100 cu. ft. of solid wood; pulpwood produced for domestic use and excluding exports, but including receipts of purchased roundwood. (2) Total pulp production covers "screenings" which are already included in exports. "Screenings" are excluded throughout from mechanical and chemical pulp. (3) Customs exports. (4) Mill shipments destined for export.

Telephones in North American Cities

Source: American Telephone and Telegraph Co., and Trans-Canada Telephone Systems (Jan. 1, 1976)

City	Number
Akron	337,183
Albany, N.Y.	164,772
Albuquerque	261,410
Alexandria, Va.	224,808
Allentown, Pa.	138,004
Amarillo	121,458
Anaheim, Cal.	205,242
Anchorage	103,759
Ann Arbor, Mich.	118,669
Atlanta, Ga.	831,341
Augusta, Ga.	129,867
Austin, Tex.	277,289
Bakersfield, Cal.	152,243
Baltimore	1,222,448
Baton Rouge	246,563
Birmingham	409,664
Boise	104,759
Boston	517,687
Bridgeport	172,833
Buffalo	432,611
Calgary, Alta.	352,967
Cambridge, Mass.	112,812
Canton	125,755
Cedar Rapids	117,700
Champaign	100,539
Charleston, S.C.	185,679
Charleston, W. Va.	159,273
Charlotte	314,900
Chattanooga	226,653
Chicago	2,486,886
Cincinnati	705,465
Clearwater	179,229
Cleveland	903,365
Colorado Springs	191,982
Columbia, S.C.	245,438
Columbus, Ga.	126,988
Columbus, Oh.	470,791
Corpus Christi	133,221
Covington	112,492
Dallas	759,066
Davenport	109,300
Dayton	388,620
Denver	1,067,054
Des Moines	260,300
Detroit	1,459,001
Durham, N.C.	103,332
East Orange, N.J.	131,186
Edmonton, Alta.	329,239
El Paso	240,133

City	Number
Erie	133,160
Eugene-Springfield, Ore.	127,960
Evansville	119,257
Fayetteville	121,692
Flint	207,810
Ft. Lauderdale	348,006
Fort Wayne	159,987
Fort Worth	317,606
Fremont City	114,013
Fresno	231,143
Gary	129,618
Grand Rapids	276,436
Greensboro	175,591
Greenville, S.C.	159,419
Guadalajara, Mex.	171,143
Halifax, N.S.	135,219
Hamilton, Ont.	199,119
Harrisburg	198,462
Hartford	309,532
Hayward, Cal.	133,313
Hollywood, Fla.	198,890
Honolulu	333,412
Houston	1,234,854
Huntington Beach	116,702
Huntsville, Ala.	133,505
Indianapolis	633,216
Jackson, Miss.	187,417
Jacksonville	400,225
Jersey City	175,171
Kalamazoo	140,749
Kansas City, Kan.	163,069
Kansas City, Mo.	339,405
Kitchener, Ont.	109,654
Knoxville	196,005
Lancaster, Pa.	102,530
Lansing	207,372
Las Vegas	304,078
Lexington	146,683
Lincoln	150,500
Little Rock	203,050
Livonia, Mich.	166,402
London, Ont.	165,435
Los Angeles (Area)	5,481,756
Louisville	519,017
Lubbock, Tex.	143,746
Macon, Ga.	107,786
Madison, Wis.	182,722

City	Number
Memphis	551,735
Mexico City	1,404,266
Miami	952,919
Milwaukee	798,112
Minn.-St. Paul	1,513,600
Mobile	206,178
Modesto, Cal.	101,842
Monterey, Mex.	167,247
Montgomery	138,347
Montreal, Que.	1,198,894
Mt. Vernon, N.Y.	121,248
Nashville	369,328
New Haven	257,022
New Orleans	661,188
New York	5,965,684
Newark	314,658
Newport Beach	110,069
Newport News	195,681
Norfolk (Area)	417,136
Oak Lawn, Ill.	108,606
Oklahoma City	550,954
Omaha	411,800
Orange, Cal.	100,676
Orlando	226,766
Ottawa, Ont.	417,377
Overland Pk., Kan.	112,868
Palo Alto	146,195
Passaic	134,797
Paterson	120,642
Pensacola	135,927
Peoria	181,515
Philadelphia	1,647,178
Phoenix	829,706
Pittsburgh	786,122
Pomona	166,329
Pompano Beach	152,430
Pontiac	111,082
Portland, Ore.	460,407
Providence	263,780
Quebec City	252,835
Raleigh	174,326
Reading, Pa.	152,708
Regina, Sask.	105,655
Reno	118,554
Richmond, Va.	360,601
Riverside, Cal.	142,038
Roanoke, Va.	120,098
Rochester, N.Y.	364,491
Rockford, Ill.	173,147

City	Number
Royal Oak, Mich.	191,660
Sacramento	463,497
Saginaw, Mich.	120,383
St. Louis	566,831
St. Petersburg	278,108
Salt Lake City	431,759
San Antonio	386,289
San Diego (area)	957,976
San Francisco	778,547
San Jose	535,951
San Mateo	119,951
Santa Ana	377,966
Santa Barbara	125,417
Savannah	132,213
Schenectady	127,535
Seattle	590,083
Shreveport	191,725
Skokie, Ill.	135,587
South Bend	131,721
Southfield, Mich.	109,659
Spokane	198,457
Springfield, Ill.	140,176
Springfield, Mass.	148,260
Springfield, Mo.	114,150
Stamford, Conn.	107,375
Stockton, Cal.	128,047
Sunnyvale, Cal.	101,466
Syracuse	257,587
Tacoma	219,737
Tampa	364,918
Toledo	300,074
Topeka	112,983
Toronto, Ont.	1,956,879
Tucson	283,114
Tulsa	368,747
Union City, N.J.	119,627
Vancouver, B.C.	417,372
Victoria, B.C.	130,049
Warren, Mich.	287,674
Washington, D.C.	992,330
West Palm Beach	257,099
Wichita	210,264
Wilmington, Del.	193,725
Windsor, Ont.	118,820
Winnipeg, Man.	372,822
Winston-Salem	155,392
Winter Park	115,558
Worcester	137,195
Youngstown	184,804

Nuclear Power Reactors in U.S.

Source: U.S. Energy Research and Development Administration (June 30, 1977)

State	Site	Plant name	Capacity (kilowatts)	Utility	Commercial operation
Alabama	Decatur	Browns Ferry Unit 1	1,065,000	Tennessee Valley Authority	1974
	Decatur	Browns Ferry Unit 2	1,065,000	Tennessee Valley Authority	1975
	Decatur	Browns Ferry Unit 3	1,065,000	Tennessee Valley Authority	1977
	Dothan	Joseph M. Farley Unit 1	829,000	Alabama Power Co.	1977
	Dothan	Joseph M. Farley Unit 2	829,000	Alabama Power Co.	1979
Arkansas	Russellville	Arkansas Unit 1	850,000	Ark. Power & Light Co.	1974
	Russellville	Arkansas Unit 2	912,000	Ark. Power & Light Co.	1978
California	Eureka	Humboldt Bay Unit 3	63,000	Pacific Gas & Electric Co.	1963
	San Clemente	San Onofre Unit 1	430,000	So. Calif. Ed. & San Diego Gas & El. Co.	1968
	Diablo Canyon	Diablo Canyon Unit 1	1,084,000	Pacific Gas & Electric Co.	1977
	Diablo Canyon	Diablo Canyon Unit 2	1,106,000	Pacific Gas & Electric Co.	1978
	Clay Station	Rancho Seco Station	918,000	Sacramento Munic. Utility District	1975
Colorado	Platteville	Ft. St. Vrain Station	330,000	Public Service Co. of Colorado	1977
Connecticut	Haddam Neck	Haddam Neck	575,000	Conn. Yankee Atomic Power Co.	1968
	Waterford	Millstone Unit 1	652,000	Northeast Nuclear Energy Co.	1971
	Waterford	Millstone Unit 2	828,000	Northeast Nuclear Energy Co.	1975
Florida	Florida City	Turkey Point Unit 3	693,000	Fla. Power & Light Co.	1972
	Florida City	Turkey Point Unit 4	693,000	Fla. Power & Light Co.	1973
	Red Level	Crystal River Unit 3	825,000	Florida Power Corp.	1977
	Ft. Pierce	St. Lucie Unit 1	810,000	Fla. Power & Light Co.	1976
Georgia	Baxley	Edwin I. Hatch Unit 1	786,000	Georgia Power Co.	1975
Illinois	Morris	Dresden Unit 1	200,000	Commonwealth Edison Co.	1960
	Morris	Dresden Unit 2	794,000	Commonwealth Edison Co.	1970
	Morris	Dresden Unit 3	794,000	Commonwealth Edison Co.	1971
	Zion	Zion Unit 1	1,040,000	Commonwealth Edison Co.	1973
	Zion	Zion Unit 2	1,040,000	Commonwealth Edison Co.	1974
	Cordova	Quad-Cities Unit 1	789,000	Comm. Ed. Co.-Ia.-Ill. Gas & Elec. Co.	1972
	Cordova	Quad-Cities Unit 2	789,000	Comm. Ed. Co.-Ia.-Ill. Gas & Elec. Co.	1972
	Seneca	LaSalle County Unit 1	1,078,000	Commonwealth Edison Co.	1979
Iowa	Palo	Duane Arnold Unit 1	538,000	Iowa Electric Light and Power Co.	1975
Maine	Wiscasset	Maine Yankee	790,000	Me. Yankee Atomic Power Co.	1972
Maryland	Lusby	Calvert Cliffs Unit 1	845,000	Baltimore Gas & Electric Co.	1975
	Lusby	Calvert Cliffs Unit 2	845,000	Baltimore Gas & Electric Co.	1977
Massachusetts	Rowe	Yankee Station	175,000	Yankee Atomic Electric Co.	1961
	Plymouth	Pilgrim Unit 1	655,000	Boston Edison Co.	1972
Michigan	Big Rock Point	Big Rock Point	72,000	Consumers Power Co.	1965
	South Haven	Palisades Station	668,000	Consumers Power Co.	1971
	Bridgman	Donald C. Cook Unit 1	1,054,000	Ind. & Michigan Electric Co.	1975
	Bridgman	Donald C. Cook Unit 2	1,060,000	Ind. & Michigan Electric Co.	1978
Minnesota	Monticello	Monticello	545,000	Northern States Power Co.	1971
	Red Wing	Prairie Island Unit 1	530,000	Northern States Power Co.	1973
	Red Wing	Prairie Island Unit 2	530,000	Northern States Power Co.	1974
Nebraska	Fort Calhoun	Ft. Calhoun Unit 1	457,000	Omaha Public Power District	1973
	Brownville	Cooper Station	778,000	Neb. Pub. Power Dist.-Ia. Power & Light Co.	1974
New Jersey	Toms River	Oyster Creek Unit 1	650,000	Jersey Central Power & Light Co.	1969
	Salem	Salem Unit 1	1,090,000	Public Service Electric & Gas, N.J.	1977
	Salem	Salem Unit 2	1,115,000	Public Service Electric & Gas, N.J.	1979
New York	Indian Point	Indian Point Unit 1	265,000	Consolidated Edison Co.	1962
	Indian Point	Indian Point Unit 2	873,000	Consolidated Edison Co.	1973
	Indian Point	Indian Point Unit 3	873,000	Power Authority of State of N.Y.	1976
	Scriba	Nine Mile Point Unit 1	610,000	Niagara Mohawk Power Co.	1969
	Ontario	R.E. Ginna Unit 1	490,000	Rochester Gas & Electric Co.	1970
	Brookhaven	Shoreham Station	819,000	Long Island Lighting Co.	1979
	Scriba	James A. FitzPatrick	821,000	Power Authority of State of N.Y.	1975
North Carolina	Southport	Brunswick Steam Unit 1	821,000	Carolina Power & Light Co.	1977
	Southport	Brunswick Steam Unit 2	821,000	Carolina Power & Light Co.	1975
	Cowans Ford Dam	Wm. B. McGuire Unit 1	1,180,000	Duke Power Co.	1979
Ohio	Oak Harbor	Davis-Besse Unit 1	906,000	Toledo Edison-Cleveland El. Illum. Co.	1977
	Moscow	Wm. H. Zimmer Unit 1	810,000	Cincinnati Gas & Electric Co.	1979
Oregon	Prescott	Trojan Unit 1	1,130,000	Portland Gen. Electric Co.	1975
Pennsylvania	Peach Bottom	Peach Bottom Unit 2	1,065,000	Philadelphia Electric Co.	1974
	Peach Bottom	Peach Bottom Unit 3	1,065,000	Philadelphia Electric Co.	1974
	Shippingport	Shippingport Station	90,000	U.S. Energy Research & Devel. Admin.	1957
	Shippingport	Beaver Valley Unit 1	852,000	Duquesne Light Co.-Ohio Edison Co.	1977
	Middletown	Three Mile Island Unit 1	819,000	Metropolitan Edison Co.	1974
	Middletown	Three Mile Island Unit 2	906,000	Jersey Central Power & Light Co.	1978
South Carolina	Hartsville	H. B. Robinson Unit 2	712,000	Carolina Power & Light Co.	1971
	Seneca	Oconee Unit 1	887,000	Duke Power Co.	1973
	Seneca	Oconee Unit 2	887,000	Duke Power Co.	1974
	Seneca	Oconee Unit 3	887,000	Duke Power Co.	1974
Tennessee	Daisy	Sequoyah Unit 1	1,148,000	Tennessee Valley Authority	1978
	Daisy	Sequoyah Unit 2	1,148,000	Tennessee Valley Authority	1979
	Spring City	Watts Bar Unit 1	1,177,000	Tennessee Valley Authority	1979
Vermont	Vernon	Vermont Yankee Station	514,000	Vt. Yankee Nuclear Power Corp.	1972
Virginia	Gravel Neck	Surry Unit 1	822,000	Va. Electric & Power Co.	1972
	Gravel Neck	Surry Unit 2	822,000	Va. Electric & Power Co.	1973
	Mineral	North Anna Unit 1	907,000	Va. Electric & Power Co.	1977
	Mineral	North Anna Unit 2	907,000	Va. Electric & Power Co.	1977
Washington	Richland	N-Reactor/WPPSS Steam	850,000	U.S. Energy Research & Devel. Admin.	1966
Wisconsin	La Crosse	Genoa Station	50,000	Dairyland Power Cooperative	1969
	Two Creeks	Point Beach Unit 1	497,000	Wis. Mich. Power Co.	1970
	Two Creeks	Point Beach Unit 2	497,000	Wis. Mich. Power Co.	1973
	Carlton	Kewaunee Unit 1	535,000	Wis. Public Service Corp.	1974

Nuclear plant capacity (kilowatts): operable 47,606,000; being built 95,308,500; planned 87,914,000; Total 230,828,500.

World Nuclear Power

Source: Federal Energy Administration

Country	Operational reactors	Capacity[1]	Generation[2] April 1977
Canada	7	3,930,000	2.08
France	11	3,970,000	1.53
Germany, West	10	6,410,000	3.46
Great Britain	31	7,950,000	3.22
India	3	620,000	0.14
Italy	3	630,000	0.39
Japan	13	7,430,000	1.62
Spain	3	1,120,000	0.44
Sweden	6	3,880,000	1.73
Switzerland	3	1,060,000	0.76
United States	63	46,090,000	20.40
Total	**153**	**83,090,000**	**35.76**

(1) Kilowatts (2) Billion kilowatt-hours

World Production of Crude Petroleum[1]

Source: Bureau of Mines, U.S. Interior Department
(thousands of 42-gallon barrels)

Country	1976	1975	Percent of change
North America:			
Canada	488,680	520,666	−6.1
Mexico[1]	327,285	294,254	+11.2
United States[2]	2,971,686	3,052,048	−2.6
Cuba (e)	775	775	0.0
Total	**3,788,426**	**3,867,743**	**−2.1**
South America:			
Argentina	145,561	144,364	+0.8
Barbados	110	123	−10.6
Bolivia	[2]14,856	14,732	+0.8
Brazil	61,026	62,766	−2.8
Chile	8,372	8,946	−6.4
Colombia	53,376	57,259	−6.8
Ecuador	68,463	58,753	+16.5
Peru	27,936	26,384	+5.9
Trinidad	81,984	78,613	+4.3
Venezuela	839,737	856,364	−1.9
Total	**1,301,421**	**1,308,304**	**−0.5**
Western Europe:			
Austria	13,466	14,205	−5.2
Denmark	1,098	1,327	+17.3
France	7,710	7,460	+3.4
Germany, West	39,902	41,470	−3.8
Italy	7,553	6,743	+12.0
Netherlands	10,538	9,676	+8.9
Norway	101,900	68,900	+47.9
Spain	11,552	14,822	−22.1
United Kingdom	[2]89,006	8,000	+1012.6
Yugoslavia	28,739	27,347	+5.1
Total	**311,464**	**199,950**	**+55.8**
Middle East:			
Bahrain	21,228	20,805	+2.0
Iran	2,168,237	1,952,650	+11.0
Iraq	834,810	825,521	+1.1
Israel	(e)366	27,345	−98.7
Kuwait	700,000	670,918	+4.3
Neutral Zone	171,669	181,431	−5.4
Oman	133,795	124,600	+7.4
Qatar	178,120	159,482	+11.7
Saudi Arabia	3,053,887	2,491,834	+22.6
Syria	(e) 70,094	65,930	+6.3
Turkey	25,254	22,167	+13.9
United Arab Emirates	692,106	618,310	+11.9
Total	**8,049,566**	**7,160,993**	**+12.4**
Africa:			
Algeria	[2]383,816	350,753	+9.4
Angola	33,217	57,943	−42.7
Congo	14,274	13,460	+6.0
Egypt	120,180	84,348	+42.5
Gabon	82,042	81,948	+0.1
Libya	704,011	551,150	+27.7
Morocco	35	171	−79.5
Nigeria	756,064	651,890	+16.0
Tunisia	28,600	34,567	−17.3
Zaire	9,075	25	+36,200.0
Total	**2,131,314**	**1,826,255**	**+16.7**
Asian area:			
Australia	152,522	149,873	+1.8
Brunei	75,030	65,932	+13.8
Burma	8,183	6,700	+22.1
India	64,632	61,611	+4.9
Indonesia	550,319	477,055	+15.4
Japan	4,241	4,378	−3.1
Malaysia	60,547	35,774	+69.2
New Zealand[2]	(e) 1,420	1,423	−0.2
Pakistan	2,562	2,190	+17.0
Taiwan	1,555	1,351	+15.1
Thailand	57	(e) 42	+35.7
Total	**921,068**	**806,329**	**+14.2**
East Europe and China:			
Albania	(e) 15,012	15,012	0.0
Bulgaria	(e) 730	913	−20.0
Czechoslovakia	(e) 949	1,017	−6.7
Germany, East	(e) 2,500	2,500	0.0
Hungary	16,343	15,306	+6.8
China	645,897	571,590	+13.0
Poland	3,376	4,103	−17.7
Romania	(e) 108,814	108,739	−0.1
USSR[2]	3,822,000	3,608,850	+5.9
Total	**4,615,621**	**4,328,030**	**+6.6**
Total World	**21,118,880**	**19,497,604**	**+8.3**

(e) Estimate. (1) Includes condensate and absorptive liquid production. (2) Includes lease condensate.

U.S. Crude Petroleum Production by Chief States

Source: Bureau of Mines, U.S. Interior Department (thousands of 42-gallon barrels)

Year	Ark.	Cal.	Ill.	Kan.	La.	Miss.	N.M.	N.D.	Okla.	Tex.	Wyo.
1950	31,108	327,607	62,028	107,586	208,965	38,236	47,367	....	164,599	829,874	61,631
1960	30,117	305,352	77,341	113,453	400,832	51,673	107,380	21,992	192,913	927,479	133,910
1965	25,930	316,428	63,708	104,733	594,853	56,183	119,166	26,350	203,441	1,000,749	138,314
1970	18,035	372,191	43,747	84,853	906,907	65,119	128,184	21,998	223,574	1,249,697	160,345
1972	18,519	347,022	34,874	73,744	891,827	61,100	110,525	20,624	207,633	1,301,685	140,011
1973	18,016	336,075	30,669	66,227	831,524	56,102	100,986	20,235	191,204	1,294,671	141,914
1974	16,527	323,003	27,553	61,691	737,324	50,779	98,695	19,697	177,785	1,262,126	139,997
1975	16,133	322,199	26,067	59,106	650,840	46,614	95,063	20,452	163,123	1,221,929	135,943
1976	18,097	326,021	26,272	58,714	606,501	46,072	92,130	21,725	161,426	1,189,523	134,149

World Oil Supply and Demand Projections

Source: Central Intelligence Agency

(million barrels per day)

	1976	1977	1978	1979	1980	1985
Demand (non-Communist)	**48.4**	**49.8-50.5**	**51.2-52.2**	**52.5-54.1**	**54.9-56.7**	**68.3-72.6**
United States	16.7	17.8-18.3	18.2-19.0	18.4-19.7	19.3-20.7	22.2-25.6
West Europe	13.6	13.9-14.3	13.8-14.2	13.7-14.4	13.7-14.7	15.8-18.2
Japan	5.2	5.3-5.4	5.5-5.8	5.9-6.2	6.2-6.6	8.1-8.8
Canada	2.0	2.0-2.1	2.1-2.2	2.2-2.3	2.2-2.4	2.9-3.5
Other developed[1]	1.2	1.2	1.3	1.3	1.4	1.9
Non-OPEC LDCs[2]	6.7	7.1	7.5	7.8	8.5	12.0
OPEC[3] countries	2.1	2.3	2.5	2.8	3.0	4.0
Other demand[4]	0.9	0	0	0	0	0
Non-OPEC supply[5]	**17.5**	**18.5**	**20.1**	**21.2**	**22.0**	**20.4-22.4**
United States	9.7	9.6	10.2	10.2	10.0	10.0-11.0
West Europe	0.9	1.8	2.5	3.1	3.7	4.0-5.0
Japan	0	0	0	0	0	0.1
Canada	1.6	1.6	1.5	1.5	1.5	1.3-1.5
Other developed[1]	0.5	0.5	0.5	0.5	0.5	0.4
Non-OPEC LDCs	3.7	4.1	4.6	5.3	6.1	8.0-9.0
Net Communist trade[6]						
USSR-East Europe	0.9	0.7	0.5	0.2	−0.3	−3.5 −4.5
China	0.2	0.2	0.3	0.4	0.5	0
Required OPEC production[7]	**30.9**	**31.3-32.0**	**31.1-32.1**	**31.3-32.9**	**32.9-34.7**	**46.7-51.2**

(1) Australia, Israel, New Zealand, South Africa. (2) LDCs: less developed countries. (3) OPEC: Organization of Petroleum Exporting Countries. (4) Including stock changes and statistical discrepancy. (5) Including natural gas liquids. (6) Difference of Communist countries' exports and imports; minus sign indicates net Communist imports. (7) OPEC production capacity will reach 27.5-29.4 million barrels per day by 1985, exclusive of Saudi Arabia; Saudi projections are uncertain.

U.S. Natural Gas Reserves

Source: American Gas Association

Estimates of proved reserves, which can be recovered under existing economic and operating conditions.

	Natural gas (millions of cu. ft.)				Natural gas liquids (1,000 42-gallon barrels)		
Year	Discoveries, revisions and extensions	Change in underground storage[1]	Production[4]	Proved reserves at end of year	Discoveries, revisions and extensions	Production[4]	Proved reserves at end of year
1946	17,632,864	(2)	4,915,774	159,703,813	(2)	129,262	3,163,219
1947	10,921,187	(2)	5,599,235	165,025,765	251,538	160,782	3,253,975
1948	13,823,090	51,202	5,975,001	172,925,056	470,557	183,749	3,540,783
1949	12,605,615	82,146	6,211,124	179,401,693	386,776	198,547	3,729,012
1950	11,985,361	52,935	6,855,244	184,584,745	766,062	227,411	4,267,663
1951	15,965,808	132,030	7,923,673	192,758,910	723,991	267,052	4,724,602
1952	14,267,606	197,766	8,592,716	198,631,566	556,838	284,789	4,996,651
1953	20,341,933	513,629[3]	9,188,365	210,298,763	743,969	302,698	5,437,922
1954	9,547,074	90,408	9,375,314	210,560,931	107,350	300,815	5,244,457
1955	21,897,616	87,164	10,063,167	222,482,544	514,508	320,400	5,438,565
1956	24,716,115	133,241	10,848,685	236,483,215	809,820	346,053	5,902,332
1957	20,008,051	178,761	11,439,890	245,230,137	137,392	352,364	5,687,360
1958	18,896,724	57,582	11,422,651	252,761,792	858,206	341,548	6,204,018
1959	20,621,249	160,453	12,373,063	261,170,431	703,444	385,154	6,522,308
1960	13,893,978	281,273	13,019,356	262,326,326	725,130	431,379	6,816,059
1961	17,166,421	159,544	13,378,649	266,273,642	694,686	461,649	7,049,096
1962	19,483,958	159,231	13,637,973	272,278,858	732,549	470,128	7,311,517
1963	18,164,667	253,733	14,546,025	276,151,233	878,120	515,659	7,673,978
1964	20,252,139	195,110	15,347,028	281,251,454	608,744	536,090	7,746,632
1965	21,319,279	150,483	16,252,293	286,468,923	832,312	555,410	8,023,534
1966	20,220,432	134,523	17,491,073	289,332,805	894,116	588,684	8,328,966
1967	21,804,333	151,403	18,380,838	292,907,703	929,758	644,493	8,614,231
1968	13,697,008	118,568	19,373,427	287,349,852	685,659	701,782	8,598,108
1969	8,375,004	107,169	20,723,190	275,108,835	281,028	735,962	8,143,174
1970	37,196,359	402,018	21,960,804	290,746,408	307,579	747,812	7,702,941
1971	9,825,421	310,301	22,076,512	278,805,618	347,720	746,434	7,304,227
1972	9,634,563	156,563	22,511,898	266,084,846	238,273	755,941	6,786,559
1973	6,825,049	(354,282)	22,605,406	249,950,207	408,979	740,831	6,454,707
1974	8,679,184	(178,424)	21,318,470	237,132,497	619,841	724,099	6,350,449
1975	10,483,688	302,561	19,718,570	228,200,176	618,504	701,123	6,267,830
1976	7,555,468	(187,550)	19,542,020	216,026,074	834,766	700,629	6,401,967

(1) Parentheses indicate decline. (2) Not estimated. (3) All native gas in storage reservoirs formerly classified as proved reserves is included in this figure. (4) Preliminary net production.

U.S. Crude Oil Reserves

Source: American Petroleum Institute

Estimates of proved reserves, which can be recovered under present economic relationships and known technology. Improved technology or higher world prices would increase estimates of reserves. Cumulative production for all years through Dec. 31, 1976 was 111,850,236 thousand barrels.

(thousands of 42-gallon barrels)

Year	Discoveries, revisions, extensions	Production	Proved reserves at end of year	Change from previous year[1]
1946	2,658,062	1,726,348	20,873,560	931,714
1947	2,464,570	1,850,445	21,487,685	614,125
1948	3,795,207	2,002,448	23,280,444	1,792,759
1949	3,187,845	1,818,800	24,649,489	1,369,045
1950	2,562,685	1,943,776	25,268,398	618,909
1951	4,413,954	2,214,321	27,468,031	2,199,633
1952	2,749,288	2,256,765	27,960,554	492,523
1953	3,296,130	2,311,856	28,944,828	984,274
1954	2,873,037	2,257,119	29,560,746	615,918
1955	2,870,724	2,419,300	30,012,170	451,424
1956	2,974,336	2,551,857	30,434,649	422,479
1957	2,424,800	2,559,044	30,300,405	(134,244)
1958	2,608,242	2,372,730	30,535,917	235,512
1959	3,666,745	2,483,315	31,719,347	1,183,430
1960	2,365,328	2,471,464	31,613,211	(106,136)
1961	2,657,567	2,512,273	31,758,505	145,294
1962	2,180,896	2,550,178	31,389,223	(369,282)
1963	2,174,110	2,593,343	30,969,990	(419,233)
1964	2,664,767	2,644,247	30,990,510	20,520
1965	3,048,079	2,686,198	31,352,391	361,881
1966	2,963,978	2,864,242	31,452,127	99,736
1967	2,962,122	3,037,579	31,376,670	(75,457)
1968	2,454,635	3,124,188	30,707,117	(669,553)
1969	2,120,036	3,195,291	29,631,862	(1,075,255)
1970	12,688,918	3,319,445	39,001,335	9,369,473
1971	2,317,732	3,256,110	38,062,957	(938,378)
1972	1,557,848	3,281,397	36,339,408	(1,723,549)
1973	2,145,831	3,185,400	35,299,839	(1,039,569)
1974	1,993,573	3,043,456	34,249,956	(1,049,883)
1975	1,318,463	2,886,292	32,682,127	(1,567,829)
1976	1,085,291	2,825,252	30,942,166	(1,739,961)

(1) Parentheses indicate decline.

U. S. Petroleum and Natural Gas Production

Source: Bureau of Mines, U.S. Interior Department

Year	Crude oil		Natural gas liquids		Total oil & N.G.L.	Natural gas	
	Production 1,000 bbls.	Value $1,000	Production 1,000 bbls.	Value $1,000	1,000 bbls.	Marketed mil. cu. ft.	Value $1,000
1945	1,713,655	2,094,250	112,004	187,564	1,828,539	3,944,021	191,006
1950	1,973,574	4,963,380	181,961	419,605	2,155,693	6,282,060	408,521
1955	2,484,428	6,870,380	281,371	619,006	2,766,325	9,405,351	978,357
1960	2,574,933	7,420,181	340,157	808,385	2,915,365	12,771,038	1,789,970
1965	2,848,514	8,158,298	441,556	911,603	3,290,083	16,042,753	2,494,542
1970	3,517,450	11,173,726	605,916	1,275,112	4,123,366	21,920,642	3,745,680
1971	3,453,914	11,692,998	617,815	1,386,054	4,071,729	22,493,012	4,085,482
1972	3,455,368	11,706,510	638,216	1,452,233	4,093,584	22,531,698	4,180,462
1973	3,360,903	13,057,905	634,423	1,857,073	3,995,326	22,647,549	4,894,072
1974	3,202,585	21,580,549	616,098	3,087,927	3,818,683	21,600,522	6,573,402
1975	3,056,779	23,116,059	595,958	2,772,588	3,652,737	20,108,661	8,945,062
1976	2,976,180	24,229,540	587,045	3,284,089	3,563,225	19,952,438	11,571,776

U. S. Total Fuel Supply and Demand

Source: Bureau of Mines, U.S. Interior Department

(thousands of 42-gallon barrels)

Year	Gasoline[1]		Kerosene[2]		Distillate fuel oil		Residual fuel oil	
	Production	Total demand	Production	Total demand	Production	Total demand	Production	Total demand
1950[3]	1,024,181	1,019,011	118,512	119,922	398,912	75,435	425,217	570,021
1960	1,522,497	1,525,126	136,842	133,188	667,050	695,165	332,147	577,934
1965	1,733,258	1,756,419	201,788	219,932	765,430	779,644	268,567	601,893
1970	2,135,838	2,165,598	313,544	358,146	897,097	928,109	257,510	824,073
1971	2,231,157	2,246,025	306,847	365,308	912,097	974,077	274,684	851,262
1972	2,352,310	2,384,734	313,554	379,984	963,625	1,067,321	292,519	937,707
1973	2,434,943	2,487,580	327,818	384,063	1,030,178	1,127,548	354,597	1,029,165
1974	2,371,004	2,436,681	290,780	346,706	974,025	1,076,771	390,491	968,185
1975	2,420,962	2,479,857	308,034	347,399	968,650	1,040,838	450,957	903,914
1976[4]	2,549,627	2,601,112	323,114	351,371	1,070,209	1,146,066	503,953	1,023,798

Demand usually exceeds the production; the difference is made up by dipping into stocks or by imports. (1) Includes special naphtha production. (2) Includes kerosene type jet fuel. (3) 1950 figures are on a 48-state basis. (4) Preliminary.

U.S. Motor Fuel Supply and Demand

Source: Bureau of Mines, U.S. Interior Department

(thousands of 42-gallon barrels)

Year	Supply[1]		Demand	
	Production	Daily average	Domestic	Export
1945	793,431	2,174	696,333	88,059
1950	1,024,481	2,806	994,290	24,721
1955	1,373,950	3,764	1,329,788	34,521
1960[2]	1,522,497	4,171	1,511,670	13,456
1965	1,733,258	4,749	1,750,028	6,391
1970	2,135,838	5,852	2,162,642	2,956
1971	2,231,157	6,113	2,242,921	3,104
1972	2,352,310	6,445	2,382,569	2,165
1973	2,434,943	6,671	2,484,262	3,318
1974	2,371,004	6,496	2,434,368	2,313
1975	2,420,962	6,633	2,477,786	2,071
1976[3]	2,549,627	6,985	2,597,302	3,810

(1) Includes special naphtha. (2) Beginning with 1960 Alaska and Hawaii are included. (3) Preliminary.

Fuel Economy in 1978 Autos; Comparative Miles per Gallon

New 1978 model cars continued the fuel economy improvements of the last few years, according to tests by the U. S. Environmental Protection Agency.

Cars were tested on a dynamometer, simulating varied driving conditions for both city (at an average of 20 miles per hour) and highway (49 mph). The tests showed that substantial reductions in exhaust emissions accompanied the improved economy, the EPA reported.

Make & model	Cu. in. displcmt.	Cylinders	City mpg	Hwy mpg
AMC Gremlin	121	4	22	34
AMC Gremlin	232	6	20	28
AMC Gremlin	258	6	16	25
AMC Pacer	232	6	19	26
AMC Matador	360	8	12	17
Audi Fox	97	4	23	37
Audi 5000	131	5	15	22
Buick Opel	111	4	24	34
Buick Skylark	231	6	16	26
Buick Skyhawk	231	6	16	28
Buick Century, Regl	196	6	19	33
Buick Century, Regl	305	8	18	26
Buick Electra	350	8	15	22
Cadillac Seville	350	8	14	20
Cadillac Eldorado	425	8	10	15
Chevrolet Chevette	98	4	30	40
Chevrolet Monza	151	4	24	34
Chevrolet Nova	250	6	19	26
Chevrolet Nova	350	8	15	21
Chevrolet Camaro	250	6	18	27
Chevrolet Monte Carlo	231	6	16	28
Chevrolet Monte Carlo	305	8	17	25
Chevrolet Malibu	200	6	21	29
Chevrolet Malibu	305	8	17	25
Chevrolet	250	6	17	24
Chevrolet	350	8	15	21
Chevrolet Corvette	350	8	15	21
Chrysler Cordoba	318	8	14	21
Chrysler Cordoba	400	8	13	20
Chrysler LeBaron	225	6	17	25
Chrysler LeBaron	360	8	14	22
Datsun 2-Seater 280Z	168	6	18	27
Datsun B-210	85	4	36	48
Datsun 510	119	4	25	35
Dodge Colt	98	4	34	45
Dodge Aspen	225	6	20	28
Dodge Aspen	360	8	15	22
Dodge Challenger	98	4	29	40
Dodge Charger	318	8	14	21
Dodge Charger	400	8	13	20
Dodge Diplomat	225	6	17	25
Dodge Diplomat	360	8	14	22
Dodge Monaco	225	6	17	24
Dodge Monaco	360	8	14	22
Dodge Monaco	440	8	10	14
Fiat X 1/9	79	4	20	31
Fiat 124 Sport	107	4	19	28
Fiat 128	79	4	20	31
Ford Fiesta	98	4	34	46
Ford Pinto	140	4	25	35
Ford Pinto	171	6	18	22
Ford Mustang II	140	4	23	33
Ford Mustang II	171	6	20	26
Ford Mustang II	302	8	16	23
Ford Fairmont	140	4	23	33
Ford Fairmont	302	8	16	23
Ford Granada	250	6	18	26
Ford Granada	302	8	16	25
Ford LTD II	302	8	15	22
Ford LTD II	400	8	13	18
Ford	302	8	15	22
Ford	460	8	12	17
Lincoln Contntl Mk V	400	8	13	19
Mazda GLC	78	4	35	44
Mazda RX-3 (Rotary)	70	2	19	28
Mercury Bobcat	140	4	25	35
Mercury Bobcat	171	6	18	22
Mercury Zephyr	140	4	23	33
Mercury Zephyr	302	8	16	23
Mercury Monarch	250	6	18	26
Mercury Monarch	302	8	16	25
Merc. Cougar XR-7	302	8	15	22
Merc. Cougar XR-7	400	8	13	19
Oldsmobile Omega	231	6	16	28
Oldsmobile Omega	305	8	15	21
Oldsmobile Cutlass	231	6	16	28
Oldsmobile Cutlass	260	8	20	29
Oldsmobile Cutlass	305	8	18	26
Oldsmobile Delta 88	231	6	17	25
Oldsmobile Delta 88	403	8	14	20
Oldsmobile Delta 88 Dsl.	350	8	21	30
Oldsmobile 98	350	8	15	22
Oldsmobile 98	403	8	14	20
Oldsmobile Starfire	151	4	24	34
Oldsmobile Toronado	403	8	13	19
Peugeot Diesel	141	4	28	34
Plym. Arrow	98	4	29	39
Plym. Sapporo	98	4	29	40
Plym. Volare	225	6	20	28
Plym. Volare	360	8	15	22
Plymouth Fury	225	6	17	24
Plymouth Fury	318	8	14	21
Plymouth Fury	360	8	14	22
Plymouth Fury	440	8	10	14
Pontiac Sunbird	151	4	24	34
Pontiac Firebird	231	6	16	25
Pontiac Firebird	400	8	12	16
Pontiac Phoenix	151	4	21	27
Pontiac Phoenix	305	8	15	21
Pontiac Grand Prix	231	6	16	28
Pontiac Grand Prix	301	8	18	25
Pontiac LeMans	231	6	16	28
Pontiac LeMans	301	8	18	25
Pontiac	231	6	17	25
Pontiac	400	8	14	19
Renault LeCar	79	4	26	41
Subaru	97	4	31	46
Toyota Corolla	71	4	34	46
Toyota Corolla	97	4	28	38
Toyota Corona	134	4	20	29
Toyota Celica	134	4	20	34
Triumph TR-8	215	8	16	26
Volkswgn Diesl Rabt	90	4	40	53
Volswgn Dasher	97	4	23	37
Volswgn Rabt, Scirocco	89	4	25	38
Volswgn Beetle	97	4	21	30

Carpooling Could Save You $1,390 a Year

Carpooling, the Federal Highway Administration has figured out, can save you anywhere from $281 a year, by sharing your subcompact with one person on a 10-mi. home-to-work trip, to $1,390, by sharing your standard sized car on a 25-mi. trip.

The FHA has a handy chart for all sized cars, various mileages, and different numbers of car-sharers, one to 5.

It tells you, the car-owner, how much to charge your fellow carpoolers in each case. The FHA figured what your yearly costs are, adding in gas and oil, maintenance and repair, parking, insurance, and depreciation.

If you travel with one person, you charge that person half of the FHA-determined cost; if you share your car with 4 persons, each owes a fifth of the cost.

For a drive of 10 mi. each way, between home and work, your yearly cost of driving, according to the FHA, is $646 in a subcompact, $749 in a compact, $948 in a standard.

For 15 mi., it's $815, $964, $1,255; for 20 mi., $982, $1,177, $1,561; for 25 mi., $1,149, $1,392, $1,868.

How to Figure Charges

In a 2-person pool, these costs are cut in half. You charge your passenger half the above figure.

In a 5-person pool (4 passengers), divide the costs 5 ways. Your savings can run, in a 5-person pool, from $425, 4/5ths of the subcompact cost for 10 mi., to $1,390, 4/5ths of the standard car cost for 25 mi. Each of your fellow poolers saves the same amount.

In its chart, the FHA included Pintos, Datsuns, Vegas, VWs, and Colts in subcompacts; Novas, Darts, Mavericks, and Pacers in compacts, and Matadors, Cutlasses, LTDs and Caprices in standards.

If your pooler thinks you are overcharging, tell him or her to write to Federal Highway Administration, Washington, DC 20590, for the carpooling cost table, or show your pooler this article.

Production of Electricity in the U.S. by Source

Source: Federal Power Commission

Amounts include both privately-owned and publicly-owned utilities

Calendar Year	Net production million kwh	Percentage produced by source: Coal	Oil	Gas	Nuclear	Hydro	Other[1]	Fuel Consumption: Coal 1,000 sht. tns.	Oil 1,000 bbls.	Gas million cu. ft.
1974	1,867,103	44.5	16.0	17.2	6.1	16.1	0.1	392,423	536,245	3,443,293
1975	1,917,638	44.5	15.1	15.6	9.0	15.6	0.2	406,029	506,128	3,157,585
1976	2,037,415	46.4	15.7	14.4	9.4	13.9	0.2	448,426	555,819	3,078,317
1977[2]	357,422	46.7	20.3	11.1	11.7	10.0	0.2	80,104	126,635	405,805

(1) Includes electricity produced from geothermal, wood, and waste. (2) Two months.

Measuring Energy

Source: House of Representatives Subcommittee on Energy

The following tables of equivalents contain those figures commonly used to compare different types of energy sources and their various measurements.

Btu - a British thermal unit — the amount of heat required to raise one pound of water one degree Fahrenheit. Equivalent to 1,055 joules or about 252 gram calories. A **therm** is usually 100,000 Btu but is sometimes used to refer to other units.

Calorie - the amount of heat required to raise one gram of water one degree Centigrade; abbreviated cal.; equivalent to about .003968 Btu. More common is the kilogram calorie, also called a **kilocalorie** and abbreviated Cal. or Kcal; equivalent to about 3.97 Btu. (One Kcal is equivalent to one food calorie.)

Btu Values of Energy Sources

(These are conventional or average values, not precise equivalents.)

Coal (per 2,000 lb. ton):

Anthracite	= 25.4 x 10^6 Btu
Bituminous	= 26.2 x 10^6
Sub-bituminous	= 19.0 x 10^6
Lignite	= 13.4 x 10^6

Average heating value of coal used to generate electricity in 1969 was 27.7 x 10^6 Btu.

Natural gas (per cubic foot):

Dry	= 1,031 Btu
Wet	= 1,103
Liquid (avg.)	= 4,100

Electricity — 1 kwn = 3,413 Btu

Petroleum (per barrel):

Crude oil	= 5.60 x 10^6 Btu
Residual fuel oil	= 6.29 x 10^6
Distillate fuel oil	= 5.83 x 10^6
Gasoline (including av gas)	= 5.25 x 10^6
Jet fuel (kerosene)	= 5.67 x 10^6
Jet fuel (naphtha)	= 5.36 x 10^6
Kerosene	= 5.67 x 10^6

Nuclear — gram of fissioned U-235 = 74x10^6 Btu

The Btu and cajorie, being small amounts of energy, are usually expressed as follows when large numbers are involved.

1 x 10^3 Btu	= 1,000
1 x 10^6	= 1,000,000
1 x 10^9	= 1,000,000,000
1 x 10^{12}	= 1 trillion
1 x 10^{15}	= 1 quadrillion
1 x 10^{18}	= 1 quintillion or 1 Q unit
One Q unit	= 38.46 billion tons of coal
	= 172.4 billion tons of oil
	= 968.9 trillion cubic ft. of natural gas

Other Conversion Factors

Electricity — 1 kwh = 0.88 lbs. of coal
= 0.076 gallon of oil
= 10.4 cu. ft. of natural gas

Natural gas — 1 tcf (trillion cubic feet) = 39.3x10^6 tons of coal
= 184x10^6 barrels of oil

Coal — 1 mtce (million tons of coal equivalent) = 4.48 x 10^6 barrels of oil
= 67 tons of oil
= 25.19 x 10^{12} cu. ft. of natural gas

Oil — 1 million tons (6.65x10^6 barrels)
= 4x10^9 kwh of electricity (when used to generate power)
= 12x10^9 kwh uncoverted
= 1.5x10^6 tons of coal
= 41.2x10^9 cu. ft. of natural gas

Approximate Conversion Factors for Oils

To convert	Barrels to metric tons	Metric tons to barrels	Barrels/days to tons/year	Tons/year to barrels/day
	Multiply by —			
Crude oil [1] . .	.136	7.33	49.8	.0201
Gasoline . . .	.118	8.45	43.2	.0232
Kerosene . . .	.128	7.80	46.8	.0214
Diesel fuel . .	.133	7.50	48.7	.0205
Fuel oil	.149	6.70	54.5	.0184

[1] Based on world average gravity (excluding natural gas liquids).

Coal and Coke Production in the U.S.

Source: Bureau of Mines. U.S. Interior Department

ear	Penn. anthracite — Production 1,000 net tons	Penn. anthracite — Value $1,000	Bituminous — Production 1,000 net tons	Bituminous — Value $1,000
945	54,934	323,944	577,617	1,768,204
950	44,077	392,398	516,311	2,500,374
955	26,205	206,097	464,633	2,092,383
960	18,817	147,116	415,512	1,950,421
962	16,894	134,094	422,149	1,891,555
963	18,267	153,503	458,928	2,013,390
964	17,184	148,648	486,998	2,165,582
965	14,866	122,021	512,088	2,276,022
966	12,941	100,663	533,881	2,421,293

Year	Penn. anthracite — Production 1,000 net tons	Penn. anthracite — Value $1,000	Bituminous — Production 1,000 net tons	Bituminous — Value $1,000
1967	12,256	96,160	552,026	2,555,377
1968	11,461	97,245	545,245	2,546,340
1969	10,473	100,769	560,505	2,795,509
1970	9,729	105,341	602,932	3,772,662
1971	8,727	103,469	552,192	3,901,496
1972	7,106	85,251	595,386	4,561,983
1973	6,830	90,260	591,738	5,049,612
1974	6,617	144,695	603,406	9,502,347
1975	6,203	198,481	648,438	12,472,486
1976 est. . . .	6,200	211,000	665,000	13,000,000

Coke production (1,000 net tons—value in $1,000)—(1968) 63,653, $1,157,359; (1969) 64,757, $1,355,260; (1970) 66,525, ,849,160; (1971) 57,436, $1,745,693; (1972) 60,507, $2,012,486; (1973) 64,325, $2,442,151; (1974) 61,581, $4,510,150; (1975) ,207, $4,835,654.

Coke exports (short tons)—(1968) 791,909; (1969) 1,629,000; (1970) 2,478,338; (1971) 1,508,639; (1972) 1,231,633; (1973) 394,980; (1974) 1,277,681; (1975) 1,272,905; (1976) 1,314,725. **imports** —(1968) 94,085; (1969) 173,052; (1970) 152,879; (1971) 3,914; (1972) 185,023; (1973) 1,077,737; (1974) 3,540,326; (1975) 1,818,981; (1976) 1,311,472.

Anthracite exports (net tons)—(1966) 766,025; (1967) 594,797; (1968) 518,159; (1969) 627,492; (1970) 789,499; (1971) 671,024; 972) 743,451; (1973) 716,546; (1974) 735,173; (1975) 639,601; (1976) 615,167.

World's Largest Hydroelectric Generating Plants

Source: Bureau of Reclamation, U.S. Interior Department
UC—Under construction. Year—Initial operation.

Name	Present megawatts	Ultimate megawatts	Year
Itaipu, Brazil/Paraguay	—	12,600	UC
Grand Coulee, U.S.	2,161	9,780	1941
Paulo Afonso, Brazil	1,299	6,774	1955
Guri, Venezuela	524	6,500	1967
Tucurui, Brazil	—	6,480	UC
Sayanskaya, USSR	—	6,400	UC
Krasnoyarsk, USSR	6,096	6,096	1968
La Grande, Canada	—	5,416	UC
Churchill Falls, Canada	5,225	5,225	1971
Bratsk, USSR	4,100	4,600	1964
Sukhovo, USSR	—	4,500	UC
Ust-Ipimsk, USSR	720	4,320	1974
Irha Solteira, Brazil	3,200	4,100	1973
Cabora Bassa, Mozambique	2,000	4,000	1975
Inga, Zaire	350	3,700	UC
Rogunsky, USSR	—	3,600	UC
Inga, Zaire	350	2,820	UC
John Day, U.S.	2,160	2,700	1968
Nurek, USSR	—	2,700	UC
Sao Simao, Brazil	—	2,680	UC
Volgograd-22nd Congress, USSR	2,560	2,560	1958
Chicoasen, Mexico	—	2,400	UC
Volga-V.I. Lenin, USSR	2,300	2,300	1955
W.A.C. Bennett, Canada	1,816	2,270	1969
Foz Do Areia, Brazil	—	2,250	UC
High Aswan (Sadd-el-Aali), Egypt	2,100	2,100	1967
Iron Gate, Romania/Yugoslavia	2,100	2,100	1970
Bath County(1), U.S.	—	2,100	UC
Itumbiara, Brazil	—	2,100	UC
Chief Joseph, U.S.	1,024	2,069	1956

Name	Present megawatts	Ultimate megawatts	Year
Salto Santiago, Brazil	—	2,000	UC
Robert Moses-Niagara, U.S.	1,950	1,950	1961
Salto Grando, Argentina	—	1,890	UC
Dinorwic(1), Great Britain	—	1,880	UC
Ludington(1), U.S.	1,872	1,872	1973
St. Lawrence Power Dam, U.S./Canada	1,824	1,824	1958
The Dalles, U.S.	1,807	1,807	1957
Karakaya, Turkey	—	1,800	UC
Mica, Canada	—	1,740	UC
Beauharnois, Canada	1,021	1,670	1950
Kemano, Canada	813	1,670	1954
Blue Ridge(1), U.S.	—	1,600	UC
Patia, Colombia	—	1,540	UC
Racoon Mountain(1), U.S.	1,530	1,530	1975
Kariba, Rhodesia	600	1,500	1959
Tumut-3, Australia	750	1,500	1972
Marimbondo, Brazil	1,440	1,440	1975
Jupia, Brazil	1,411	1,411	1966
McNary, U.S.	980	1,406	1953
Cheboksary, USSR	1,404	1,404	1972
Agua Vermelha, Brazil	—	1,380	UC
Saratov, USSR	1,360	1,360	1967
Daniel Johnson, Canada	650	1,353	1970
Hoover, U.S.	1,345	1,345	1936
Wanapum, U.S.	831	1,330	1964
Inguri, USSR	—	1,300	UC
Zeya, USSR	300	1,290	1975
Takase, Japan	—	1,280	UC
Priest Rapids, U.S.	789	1,262	1959

(1) Pumped storage installation.

Non-Federal Hydroelectric Plants in U.S.

Capacities of 150,000 Kilowatts or More as of Jan. 1, 1977
Source: Bureau of Power, Federal Power Commission
Auxiliary and pumped storage units are not included in hydroelectric capacities.

Plant	State	Owner	Kilowatts
Robert Moses, (Niagara)	New York	Power Authority State of New York	1,953,900
Rocky Reach	Washington	Chelan County District No. 1	1,213,100
Robert Moses, (Massena)	New York	Power Authority State of New York	912,000
Wanapum	Washington	Grant County District No. 2	831,250
Priest Rapids	Washington	Grant County District No. 2	788,500
Wells	Washington	Douglas County PUD No. 1	774,300
Boundary	Washington	Seattle Department of Lighting	551,000
Conowingo	Maryland	Philadelphia Electric Company	474,480
Hells Canyon	Oregon	Idaho Power Company	391,50
Brownlee	Idaho	Idaho Power Company	360,400
Ross	Washington	Seattle Department of Lighting Company	360,000
Edward Hyatt	California	California Department of Water Resources	351,000
Cowans Ford	North Carolina	Duke Power Company	350,000
Upper Smith Mt.	Virginia	Appalachian Power Company	300,20
Mossyrock	Washington	City of Tacoma	300,00
New Colgate	California	Yuba County Water Agency	284,400
Noxon Rapids	Montana	The Washington Water Power Company	282,880
Round Butte	Oregon	Portland General Electric Company	247,05
Safe Harbor	Pennsylvania	Safe Harbor Water Power Corporation	226,500
Walter Bouldin(1)	Alabama	Alabama Power Company	225,00
Rock Island	Washington	Chelan County District No. 1	212,10
Swift No. 1	Washington	Pacific Power and Light Company	204,00
Cabinet Gorge	Idaho	The Washington Water Power Company	200,00
Saluda	South Carolina	South Carolina Electric and Gas Company	197,50
Oxbow	Oregon	Idaho Power Company	190,00
White Rock	California	Sacramento Municipal Utility District	190,00
Caribou No. 1 & 2	California	Pacific Gas and Electric Company	184,80
Gaston	North Carolina	Virginia Electric and Power Company	177,92
Lay Dem	Alabama	Alabama Power Company	177,00
Osage	Missouri	Union Electric Company of Missouri	172,000
Kerr	Montana	The Montana Power Company	168,000
Lewis Smith	Alabama	Alabama Power Company	157,500
Keowee	South Carolina	Duke Power Company	157,500
James B. Black	California	Pacific Gas and Electric Company	154,800
Martin Dam	Alabama	Alabama Power Company	154,200

(1) Units out of service Feb. 1975 in dam failure.

World Electricity Production

Source: UN Monthly Bulletin of Statistics, July 1977 (1976 production in million kilowatt-hours)

Country	Production	Country	Production	Country	Production	Country	Production
United States	2,117,628	France	191,196	East Germany	89,148	Czechoslovakia	62,62
USSR	1,110,960	Italy	160,560	Sweden	84,312	Netherlands	58,05
Japan(3)	475,800	China(1)(e)	112,000	Norway	82,188	Romania(3)	53,72
West Germany	333,648	Poland	104,100	South Africa	80,712	Belgium	47,35
Canada	293,412	Spain	90,600	Brazil(3)	78,072	Mexico	46,23
United Kingdom	276,972	India(2)	89,208	Australia	76,500	Yugoslavia	43,57

(e) Estimate. (1) 1974. (2) Excluding generation by industrial establishments. (3) 1975.

MANUFACTURES AND MINERALS

General Statistics for Major Industry Groups

Source: Bureau of the Census

The estimates for 1975 in the following table are based upon reports from a representative sample of about 70,000 manufacturing establishments.

Industry	All employees		Production workers			Value added by mf'r
	Number (1,000)	Payroll (millions)	Number (1,000)	Man-hours (millions)	Wages (millions)	(millions)
Food and kindred products	1,527.3	$ 15,891.2	1,056.8	2,071.4	$ 9,861.2	$48,142.0
Tobacco manufactures	66.2	654.6	56.3	104.2	513.0	3,722.0
Textile mill products	838.4	6,418.2	727.7	1,386.8	4,931.6	12,109.9
Apparel and other textile products	1,212.5	7,688.7	1,056.7	1,885.0	5,762.2	13,381.2
Lumber and wood products	591.7	5,268.6	509.0	951.1	4,079.1	
Furniture and fixtures	397.8	3,322.6	326.6	611.0	2,349.3	6,310.6
Paper and allied products	589.5	6,984.5	454.4	902.5	4,873.4	17,926.8
Printing and publishing	1,072.8	11,675.3	629.8	1,144.6	6,252.8	24,503.6
Chemicals and allied products	848.1	11,303.8	511.2	1,003.4	5,870.5	45,116.0
Petroleum and coal products	141.1	2,143.8	98.0	197.6	1,355.8	10,090.2
Rubber and plastics products	587.4	5,944.9	453.0	877.8	4,002.1	13,674.2
Leather and leather products	240.0	1,652.4	209.3	377.9	1,251.5	3,187.2
Stone, clay, and glass products	591.6	6,402.6	464.0	905.9	4,601.1	15,337.6
Primary metal industries	1,090.6	15,015.0	856.3	1,638.5	11,047.1	30,554.4
Fabricated metal products	1,419.9	16,359.0	1,072.7	2,091.2	11,048.4	34,095.8
Machinery, except electrical	1,979.2	24,702.0	1,349.8	2,661.1	14,853.8	51,471.0
Electric, electronic equipment	1,520.9	17,392.0	1,017.8	1,946.5	9,627.8	34,804.4
Transportation equipment	1,604.4	22,770.3	1,137.9	2,217.3	14,418.8	45,155.2
Instruments and related products	502.0	5,854.2	310.4	590.8	2,835.4	14,116.2
Miscellaneous manufacturing industries	394.9	3,499.7	303.2	566.8	2,173.5	7,695.9
Administrative and auxiliary[1]	1,128.4	19,014.8	—	—	—	—
All industries total	**18,344.7**	**209,958.2**	**12,601.0**	**24,131.5**	**121,708.5**	**441,850.0**

(1) In addition to the employment and payroll for operating manufacturing establishments, manufacturing concerns reorted separately for central administrative offices or auxiliary units (e.g., research laboratories, storage warehouses, ower plants, garages, repair shops, etc.) which serve the manufacturing establishments of a company rather than the ublic.

Manufacturing Production Worker Statistics

Source: Bureau of Labor Statistics, U.S. Labor Department (p — preliminary)

Year	All employees	Production workers	Payroll index 1967=100	Avg. weekly earnings	Avg. hourly earnings	Avg. hrs. per wk.
955	16,882,000	13,288,000	61.1	$75.70	$ 1.86	40.7
960	16,796,000	12,586,000	68.9	89.72	2.26	39.7
965	18,062,000	13,434,000	88.1	107.53	2.61	41.2
970	19,349,000	14,020,000	114.1	133.73	3.36	39.8
972	19,090,000	13,957,000	131.5	159.69	3.81	40.6
973	20,068,000	14,760,000	149.2	166.06	4.08	40.7
974	20,046,000	14,613,000	157.1	176.40	4.41	40.0
975	18,347,000	13,070,000	151.0	189.51	4.81	39.4
976	18,956,000	13,625,000	172.4	207.60	5.19	40.0
977, Jan.	19,001,000	13,606,000	176.4	212.94	5.46	39.0
Feb.	19,005,000	13,600,000	179.6	216.66	5.43	39.9
Mar.	19,183,000	13,763,000	184.5	220.30	5.48	40.2
Apr.	19,327,000	13,893,000	187.0	220.80	5.52	40.0
May	19,470,000	14,021,000	191.5	224.07	5.56	40.3
June (p)	19,758,000	14,259,000	198.3	228.48	5.60	40.8
July (p)	19,606,000	14,089,000	193.6	225.76	5.63	40.1

Hourly Earnings in Manufacturing Industries

Source: Bureau of Labor Statistics, U.S. Labor Department (p-preliminary)

Year and month (annual average)	Manufacturing		Durable goods		Nondurable goods	
	Gross	Excluding overtime	Gross	Excluding overtime	Gross	Excluding overtime
50	$1.440	$1.39	$1.52	$1.46	$1.35	$1.31
55	1.86	1.79	1.99	1.91	1.67	1.62
60	2.26	2.20	2.43	2.36	2.05	1.99
65	2.61	2.51	2.79	2.67	2.36	2.27
70	3.36	3.24	3.55	3.43	3.08	2.97
72	3.81	3.66	4.06	3.89	3.47	3.33
73	4.08	3.89	4.34	4.13	3.68	3.53
74	4.41	4.24	4.69	4.50	3.99	3.84
75	4.81	4.66	5.14	4.98	4.35	4.20
76	5.19	5.00	5.55	5.34	4.68	4.51
7, Jan.	5.46	5.25	5.81	5.59	4.95	4.77
Feb.	5.43	5.24	5.79	5.57	4.93	4.75
Mar.	5.48	5.27	5.84	5.61	4.95	4.77
Apr.	5.52	5.31	5.88	5.65	4.99	4.81
May	5.56	5.34	5.95	5.70	4.99	4.81
June (p)	5.60	5.37	6.00	5.74	5.03	4.83
July (p)	5.63	5.41	6.00	5.75	5.09	4.90

General Manufacturing Statistics for States

Source: Bureau of the Census, U.S. Commerce Department

1975 Divisions, Regions, and States	All employees Number (1,000)	All employees Payroll (millions)	Production workers Number (1,000)	Production workers Man-hrs. (millions)	Production workers Wages (millions)	Value added by mfr. (millions)	Value of shipments (millions)	Capital expend. (millions)
New England Division	1,318	$14,440	878	1,683	$7,758	$27,482	$52,667	$1,818
Maine	96	834	79	150	602	1,758	3,847	315
New Hampshire	86	809	64	122	558	1,606	3,081	97
Vermont	40	410	28	53	225	782	1,682	77
Massachusetts	588	6,500	382	731	3,389	12,554	24,009	622
Rhode Island	109	1,017	83	155	625	2,020	3,987	123
Connecticut	399	4,870	242	472	2,359	8,762	16,061	584
Middle Atlantic Division	3,609	42,952	2,305	4,399	22,331	82,456	176,997	5,290
New York	1,490	18,033	910	1,735	8,606	35,031	69,854	2,127
New Jersey	777	9,615	471	911	4,606	17,878	40,823	1,207
Pennsylvania	1,342	15,304	924	1,753	9,119	29,547	66,320	1,956
East North Central Division	4,674	59,815	3,199	6,167	36,223	118,715	282,521	9,114
Ohio	1,278	16,043	872	1,685	9,882	32,436	73,720	2,202
Indiana	653	7,984	470	891	5,154	16,290	38,236	1,504
Illinois	1,251	15,573	819	1,580	8,813	32,133	75,066	2,229
Michigan	973	14,125	670	1,307	8,535	24,845	64,178	2,298
Wisconsin	519	6,090	368	704	3,839	13,011	31,321	881
West North Central Division	1,246	13,981	839	1,594	8,169	31,352	85,122	2,345
Minnesota	322	3,798	198	375	1,957	7,458	18,751	502
Iowa	226	2,726	160	307	1,752	7,018	19,127	692
Missouri	407	4,503	273	511	2,562	9,387	23,439	608
North Dakota	14	120	9	17	74	324	1,128	23
South Dakota	22	189	16	29	129	424	1,497	37
Nebraska	87	892	63	123	580	2,391	8,408	162
Kansas	168	1,753	120	232	1,115	4,350	12,772	321
South Atlantic Division	2,681	24,352	1,996	3,771	15,612	55,589	129,481	5,317
Delaware	63	934	31	58	324	1,247	3,960	18
Maryland	243	2,892	162	307	1,616	5,583	13,120	45
District of Columbia	20	279	9	15	116	503	888	1
Virginia	398	3,837	301	572	2,480	8,355	17,750	67
West Virginia	118	1,353	87	165	892	3,070	6,790	36
North Carolina	716	5,873	568	1,061	3,887	13,643	31,573	1,22
South Carolina	341	2,841	271	514	1,932	5,942	13,749	80
Georgia	454	4,106	346	660	2,574	9,785	25,276	75
Florida	328	3,237	221	419	1,791	7,461	16,375	83
East South Central Division	1,225	11,334	948	1,794	7,652	27,002	64,726	2,64
Kentucky	265	2,713	200	375	1,789	7,395	17,618	48
Tennessee	453	4,144	339	647	2,667	9,298	21,809	83
Alabama	313	2,906	252	474	2,071	6,623	15,781	1,06
Mississippi	194	1,571	157	298	1,125	3,686	9,518	26
West South Central Division	1,294	13,787	912	1,795	8,223	38,878	105,516	5,62
Arkansas	175	1,424	141	265	1,011	3,701	9,299	32
Louisiana	183	2,079	136	276	1,374	7,346	22,048	1,15
Oklahoma	152	1,590	99	189	856	3,451	8,904	30
Texas	784	8,694	536	1,065	4,982	24,380	65,265	3,83
Mountain Division	411	4,599	278	527	2,648	10,351	26,024	1,22
Montana	21	228	16	30	168	532	2,203	7
Idaho	47	498	36	68	338	1,295	3,045	14
Wyoming	7	78	5	9	49	267	846	2
Colorado	138	1,668	88	171	902	3,391	8,357	36
New Mexico	27	239	20	38	147	484	1,303	16
Arizona	96	1,102	60	113	568	2,711	5,532	29
Utah	64	659	45	84	398	1,361	4,100	12
Nevada	11	127	8	14	78	310	638	2
Pacific Division	2,013	25,030	1,328	2,537	13,740	53,362	120,144	4,03
Washington	242	3,188	163	300	1,810	7,279	17,038	8
Oregon	181	2,042	138	253	1,426	4,426	10,295	45
California	1,558	19,450	1,004	1,943	10,287	40,536	90,195	2,5
Alaska	8	113	6	12	84	449	828	12
Hawaii	24	237	17	29	133	672	1,788	[illegible]
Total	**18,471**	**210,290**	**12,683**	**24,267**	**122,356**	**445,187**	**1,043,198**	**37,4**

Employees in Non-Agricultural Establishments

Source: Bureau of Labor Statistics, U.S. Labor Department (p-preliminary)
(thousands)

Annual Average by Industry Division

Year	Total	Mining	Contr./construction	Manufacturing	Trans. and public utilities	Whole., retail trade	Finance, insur., real estate	Service, miscellaneous	Gove[rn]me[nt]
1955	50,675	792	2,802	16,882	4,141	10,535	2,335	6,274	6,9
1960	54,234	712	2,885	16,796	4,004	11,391	2,669	7,423	8,3
1965	60,815	632	3,186	18,062	4,036	12,716	3,023	9,087	10,0
1970	70,920	623	3,536	19,369	4,504	15,040	3,687	11,621	12,5
1973	76,896	644	4,015	20,068	4,644	16,674	4,091	13,021	13,7
1974	78,413	694	3,957	20,046	4,696	17,017	4,208	13,617	14,1
1975	77,051	745	3,512	18,347	4,498	17,000	4,223	14,006	14,7
1976	79,443	783	3,594	18,956	4,509	17,694	4,316	14,644	14,9
1977 July (p)	82,159	835	4,144	19,606	4,615	18,297	4,565	15,473	14,6

Profits of Manufacturing Corporations by Industry Groups

Source: Federal Trade Commission

Industry Group (Amounts estimated in millions of dollars)	Before Income Taxes 1976	Pct. of sales 1976	Pct. of sales 1975	Profits After Taxes 1976	Pct. of sales 1976	Pct. of sales 1975
ɪrable goods	**50,658**	**8.6**	**6.8**	**30,770**	**5.2**	**4.1**
Transportation equipment	11,357	8.1	4.3	6,786	4.8	2.5
Motor vehicles and equipment[1]	8,470	9.2	4.0	5,099	5.6	2.3
Electrical and electronic equipment	7,262	8.0	5.8	4,073	4.5	3.2
Machinery, except electrical	12,600	11.7	10.2	7,889	7.3	6.4
Fabricated metal products	5,568	8.3	7.4	3,196	4.8	4.2
Primary iron and steel	2,893	5.7	7.5	2,085	4.1	5.0
Primary nonferrous metal	1,291	5.3	4.1	913	3.8	3.1
Stone, clay, and glass products	2,356	8.1	5.8	1,447	5.0	3.7
Instruments and related products	3,646	13.5	12.3	2,144	7.9	7.7
Other durable goods	3,687	6.9	5.1	2,237	4.2	2.8
ndurable goods	**54,263**	**8.8**	**8.2**	**33,748**	**5.5**	**5.1**
Food and kindred products	9,743	5.7	5.5	5,826	3.4	3.2
Tobacco manufactures	1,833	15.3	16.5	1,011	8.5	9.2
Textile mill products	1,525	4.5	3.1	809	2.4	1.5
Paper and allied products	3,643	9.3	9.1	2,270	5.8	5.6
Printing and publishing	3,961	9.4	8.5	2,147	5.1	4.6
Chemicals and allied products	12,431	12.2	12.3	7,610	7.5	7.6
Petroleum and coal products	16,903	12.0	10.9	11,725	8.3	7.6
Rubber and miscellaneous plastic products	1,876	6.6	5.4	1,079	3.8	3.1
Other nondurable products	2,350	5.2	4.4	1,272	2.8	2.4
Manufacturing Corps.	**104,921**	**8.7**	**7.5**	**64,519**	**5.4**	**4.6**

ɔluded in major industry above.

Occupational Earnings in Selected Metropolitan Areas

Source: Bureau of Labor Statistics, U.S. Labor Department

Average earnings[1] for selected occupations studied in 6 bread industry divisions: manufacturing, transportation, com- .nication, and other public utilities; wholesale trade; retail trade; finance, insurance, and real estate; and selected serv- s, March-May 1977)

Occupations	Birmingham, Ala.	Detroit, Mich.	Norfolk-Virginia Beach-Portsmouth, Va.-N.C.	St. Louis, Mo.-Ill.	San Jose, Calif.	Toledo, Ohio-Mich.	Worcester, Mass.
			Average weekly earnings, straight-time				
ice workers							
ɔounting clerks[2]	$194.50	$233.50	$172.00	$207.00	$188.50	$208.50	$193.50
nputer operators[2]	204.50	303.00	—	252.00	264.00	230.00	218.00
nputer programmers, usiness[2]	301.00	377.50	—	300.00	377.50	277.00	328.00
nputer systems analysts, usiness[2]	366.50	438.00	344.00	390.50	445.00	371.50	363.00
fters[2]	302.00	416.50	—	315.00	299.00	313.50	272.00
clerks[2]	149.00	197.00	—	160.50	—	—	—
punch operators[2]	149.50	198.00	138.00	184.50	200.00	198.50	164.50
ssengers	131.00	148.50	—	133.00	163.00	135.50	123.50
istered industrial nurses	227.00	311.00	—	258.00	278.00	260.50	236.00
retaries	183.50	257.50	172.50	194.00	217.50	211.50	189.00
nographers, general	164.50	191.00	154.50	170.00	189.00	192.00	164.00
ists[2]	145.50	197.00	162.50	172.00	197.50	162.00	158.00
			Average hourly earnings, straight-time				
ntenance, custodial, and aterial movement workers							
penters	$6.44	$8.34	$ —	$7.11	$7.68	$7.12	$5.93
tricians	6.89	8.60	6.92	7.64	8.19	7.77	6.49
ionary engineers	7.03	8.24	—	7.28	7.59	7.12	6.17
les helpers	5.56	6.69	4.38	6.11	6.10	6.33	4.21
hinists	6.85	8.12	5.92	7.54	7.97	7.35	6.69
hanics (motor vehicles)	5.90	8.10	5.83	7.12	8.45	7.82	6.58
ters	5.95	8.33	—	7.20	7.83	7.21	—
rds and watchmen	2.74	4.89	3.36	3.21	3.90	3.37	3.56
tors, porters and cleaners	2.74	4.95	3.03	3.80	4.62	4.61	3.70
erial handling laborers	3.66	6.41	3.75	5.71	5.41	6.10	5.05
ping packers	4.12	6.08	—	5.19	4.51	5.85	4.42
ping clerks	4.99	7.07	4.26	5.51	—	5.93	4.56
kdrivers, local	4.63	7.14	4.36	7.09	7.74	7.20	6.06

) Weekly earnings relate to regular straight-time salaries that are paid for standard workweeks. Hourly earnings exclude premium for overtime, weekends, holidays, or late shifts. (2) More than one skill level surveyed. Earnings are for the highest level surveyed.

Annual Rates of Profit on Stockholders' Equity

Source: Federal Trade Commission

(Each rate is the arithmetic mean of 4 quarterly rates, each on an annual basis.)

By industry after taxes: by percent	1950	1960	1965	1969[1]	1970	1974[2]	1975	19
All manufacturing corporations, except newspapers	15.4	9.2	13.0	11.5	9.3	14.9	11.6	13
Durable goods industries	16.8	8.6	13.8	11.4	8.3	12.6	10.3	13
Metals and metal fabricating industries	16.9	8.6	14.2	11.2	*	*	*	
Transportation equipment	21.5	11.7	18.5	12.0	6.3	8.0	7.5	16
Motor vehicles and equipment	25.2	13.5	19.5	12.6	6.1	6.9	6.2	17
Aircraft and parts	*	7.4	15.1	10.6	6.8	10.6	11.0	12
Electrical machinery, equipment and supplies	20.8	9.5	13.5	11.1	9.1	11.1	9.0	12
Machinery, except electrical	14.0	7.6	14.1	12.2	9.9	13.2	13.7	15
Metalworking machinery and equipment	*	5.3	14.4	11.6	8.3	*	*	
Other fabricated metal products	15.9	5.6	13.2	11.3	8.6	16.6	13.2	15
Primary metal industries	14.5	7.2	10.6	9.5	7.0	16.4	8.6	8
Blast furnaces, steel works and foundries	14.3	7.2	9.8	7.6	4.3	16.8	10.9	9
Nonferrous metals	15.0	7.1	11.9	12.2	10.7	15.8	5.0	7
Other durable goods industries	16.3	8.6	12.2	12.4	*	*	*	
Lumber and wood products, except furniture	17.4	3.6	10.0	13.2	5.9	*	*	
Furniture and fixtures	15.1	6.5	13.3	12.6	7.9	*	*	
Stone, clay and glass products	17.6	9.9	10.2	9.2	6.9	10.6	8.3	11
Instruments and related products	16.7	11.6	17.5	15.6	14.2	16.1	13.5	14
Miscellaneous manufacturing and ordnance	12.2	9.2	10.7	11.6	10.0	*	*	
Nondurable goods industries	14.0	9.8	12.2	11.5	10.3	17.2	12.9	14
Chemicals: petroleum, rubber, and plastics	15.4	10.8	13.0	12.0	*	*	*	
Chemicals and allied products	17.8	12.2	15.2	12.8	11.5	18.2	15.2	15
Basic chemicals and related products	*	11.1	14.3	10.5	8.5	17.4	13.3	14
Drugs	*	16.8	20.3	18.4	17.6	18.8	17.8	18
Petroleum refining and related industries	13.8	10.1	11.8	11.7	11.0	21.0	12.5	14
Petroleum refining	*	10.1	11.8	11.7	11.0	*	*	
Rubber and miscellaneous plastics products	16.7	9.1	11.7	10.4	7.1	14.4	8.0	10
Other nondurable goods industries	12.8	8.5	11.1	10.8	*	*	*	
Food and kindred products	12.3	8.7	10.7	10.9	10.8	14.0	14.4	14
Dairy products	*	*	10.6	10.1	10.2	*	*	
Bakery products	*	*	9.3	8.6	8.8	*	*	
Alcoholic beverages	*	7.1	9.3	10.3	10.5	*	*	
Tobacco manufacturers	11.5	13.4	13.5	14.4	15.7	15.6	15.9	1
Textile mill products	12.6	5.8	10.8	7.9	5.1	8.2	4.2	[illegible]
Apparel and other fabricated textile products	10.1	7.7	12.6	9.3	11.9	*	*	
Paper and allied products	16.1	8.5	9.4	10.1	7.0	17.8	12.6	1
Printing and publishing, except newspapers	11.5	10.6	14.1	12.6	11.2	13.2	12.8	1
Leather and leather products	10.9	6.3	11.6	9.3	9.4	*	*	

*—Not available. (1) Includes newspapers for the first time. (2) Profits for 1974 include equity in earnings (net of taxes) of noncons- dated subsidiaries. In prior years this component was included in adjustment to earned surplus.

Personal Consumption Expenditures for the U.S.

Source: Bureau of Economic Analysis, U.S. Commerce Department

(millions of dollars)

Product	1950	1955	1960	1965	1970	1974	1975	197
Food and tobacco	58,120	72,236	87,510	107,183	141,181	203,660	224,164	241,
Clothing, accessories and jewelry	23,709	27,982	33,032	43,318	62,834	76,336	82,048	89,
Personal care	2,438	3,461	5,324	7,578	10,420	13,461	14,309	15,
Housing	21,286	33,738	46,305	63,509	90,926	136,512	150,784	167,
Household operation	29,461	37,322	46,906	61,789	87,360	130,616	142,816	160,
Medical care	8,788	12,755	19,116	28,082	47,401	76,898	90,303	106,
Personal business	6,858	10,049	14,974	21,879	35,314	45,476	51,824	55,
Transportation	24,672	35,574	43,134	58,154	77,776	115,090	125,142	150,
Recreation	11,147	14,078	18,295	26,298	40,653	60,892	66,171	72,
Private educ. and research	1,618	2,339	3,718	5,927	10,363	13,758	15,434	16,
Religious and welfare activities	2,282	3,257	4,748	5,972	8,601	11,622	12,460	13,
Foreign travel and other—net	630	1,590	2,179	3,150	4,815	5,282	4,954	4,
Total personal consumption expenditures	**191,009**	**254,381**	**325,241**	**432,839**	**617,644**	**889,603**	**980,409**	**1,093,**

Work Stoppages (Strikes) in the U.S.

Source: Bureau of Labor Statistics, U.S. Labor Department

	Number stoppages	Workers involved	Man days idle
Average 1935-1939	2,862	1,130,000	16,900,000
War Period Dec. 8, 1941-Aug. 14, 1945	14,371	6,744,000	36,300,000
Year			
1947-49	3,573	2,380,000	39,700,000
1950	4,843	2,410,000	38,800,000
1955	4,320	2,650,000	28,200,000
1960	3,333	1,320,000	19,100,000
1965	3,963	1,550,000	23,300,000
1969	5,700	2,481,000	42,869,000
1970	5,716	3,305,000	66,414,000

Year	Number stoppages	Workers involved	Man days i
1971	5,138	3,280,000	47,589,
1972	5,010	1,714,000	27,066,
1973	5,353	2,251,000	27,948,
1974	6,074	2,778,000	47,991,
1975	5,031	1,746,000	31,237,
1976	5,648	2,421,000	37,800,
1977 (p) Jan.	351	109,000	1,160,
Feb.	314	158,000	1,356,
Mar.	391	222,000	2,094,
Apr.	615	202,000	3,045,
May	551	254,000	4,131,
June	664	205,000	3,292,

Retail Store Sales

Source: Bureau of the Census, U.S. Commerce Department (millions of dollars)

Kind of business	1975	1976
All retail stores	**584,423**	**651,884**
Durable goods stores	**180,725**	**214,169**
Automotive group	102,105	125,625
Motor vehicle, other automotive dealers	93,046	115,631
Tire, battery, accessory dealers	9,059	9,994
Furniture and appliance group	26,123	28,963
Furniture, home furnishings stores	15,283	17,053
Household appliance, radio TV stores	8,420	9,200
Lumber, building, hardware group	23,974	28,168
Lumber, building materials dealers	18,202	21,946
Hardware stores	5,772	6,222

Kind of business	1975	1976
Nondurable goods stores	**403,698**	**437,715**
Apparel group	26,749	28,612
Men's and boys' wear stores	6,085	6,325
Women's apparel, accessory stores	10,396	11,123
Shoe stores	4,123	4,373
Food group	131,723	140,984
Grocery stores	122,666	131,133
General merchandise group with stores	95,402	104,168
Department stores, excl. mail order	60,719	68,011
Mail order (catalog sales)	5,995	6,584
Variety stores	9,120	8,529
Eating and drinking places	47,514	52,290
Gasoline service stations	43,895	47,731
Drug and proprietary stores	18,098	19,704
Liquor stores	10,974	11,411

Total Retail Stores Sales (millions of dollars) — (1955) 183,851; (1956) 189,729; (1957) 200,002; (1958) 200,353; (1959) 215,-13; (1960) 219,529; (1961) 218,992; (1962) 235,563; (1963) 246,666; (1964) 261,870; (1965) 284,128; (1966) 303,956; (1967) 313,-09; (1968) 341,876; (1969) 357,885; (1970) 375,527; (1971) 408,850; (1972) 448,379; (1973) 503,317; (1974) 537,782; (1975) 584,-23.

Cotton, Wool, Silk, and Man-Made Fibers Production

Source: Economic Research Service, U.S. Agriculture Department

Cotton and wool from reports of the Agriculture Department; silk, rayon, and non-celluosic man-made fibers from Textile Organon, a publication of the Textile Economics Bureau, Inc.

Year	Cotton[1] U.S. (million bales)	Cotton[1] World (million bales)	Wool[2] U.S. (million pounds)	Wool[2] World (million pounds)	Silk World (mil. lbs.)	Man-made fibers[3] Rayon & acetate U.S. (million pounds)	Man-made fibers[3] Rayon & acetate World (million pounds)	Man-made fibers[3] Non-cellulosic[4] U.S.[4] (million pounds)	Man-made fibers[3] Non-cellulosic[4] World (million pounds)
940	12.6	31.2	434.0	4,180	130	471.2	2,485.3	4.6	4.6
950	10.0	30.6	249.3	4,000	42	1,259.4	3,552.8	145.9	177.4
960	14.2	46.2	298.9	5,615	68	1,028.5	5,749.1	854.2	1,779.1
965	15.0	55.0	224.8	5,836	72	1,527.0	7,359.4	2,062.4	4,928.9
967	7.4	49.7	211.4	6,040	75	1,388.1	7,297.4	2,662.1	6,013.0[6]
968	10.9	54.7	197.9	6,295	82	1,594.3	7,779.0	3,632.1	7,906.0
969	10.0	53.2	182.8	6,261	86	1,576.2	7,835.0	4,029.3	9,211.0
970	10.2	53.6	176.8	6,163	90	1,373.2	7,564.0	4,053.5	10,363.0
971	10.5	59.8	172.2	6,033	90	1,390.9	7,590.0	4,761.0	12,352.0
972	13.7	62.9	168.6	5,631	93	1,394.3	7,838.0	5,927.0	14,043.0
973	13.0	63.2	153.2	5,508	97	1,357.0	8,071.0	6,997.4	16,820.0
974	11.5	64.3	138.7	5,728	99	1,198.8	7,803.0	6,906.5	16,486.0
975	8.3	54.3	123.4	5,732	106	749.0	6,536.0	6,432.2	16,233.0
976	10.6	57.5	113.9	5,580	108	848.1	6,980.0	7,293.7	18,760.0

(1) Year beginning Aug. 1. (2) Grease basis. (3) Includes filament yarn and staple and tow fiber. (4) Includes textile glass fiber. 5) 480-pound net weight bales, U.S. beginning 1960 and world beginning 1965. (6) 1966 to date, excludes Olefin.

World Production of Natural Rubber

Source: Domestic and International Business Administration, U.S. Commerce Department

(metric tons)

Year	Far East	Tropical America	Africa	Total	Year	Far East	Tropical America	Africa	Total
970	2,857,500	32,000	213,000	3,102,500	1940	1,379,000	26,000	16,000	1,421,000
972	2,873,200	34,800	212,000	3,120,000	1945	173,000	49,000	54,000	276,000
973	3,241,700	33,400	229,900	3,505,000	1950	1,771,500	27,000	55,000	1,853,500
974	3,178,900	29,600	231,500	3,440,000	1955	1,798,000	27,500	98,500	1,924,000
975	3,058,600	31,300	210,100	3,300,000	1960	1,825,100	29,900	148,000	2,002,000
976	3,295,000	37,300	197,700	3,530,000	1965	2,156,950	36,300	159,250	2,352,500

Full-time and Part-time Status of Civilian Labor Force

Source: Bureau of Labor Statistics, U.S. Labor Department

(Numbers in thousands seasonally adjusted)

mployment status...	1976 July	1976 Aug.	1976 Sept.	1976 Oct.	1976 Nov.	1976 Dec.	1977 Jan.	1977 Feb.	1977 Mar.	1977 April	1977 May	1977 June
otal, 16 years and over:												
ull time												
Civilian labor force	81,006	81,177	80,977	81,297	81,786	82,048	81,730	81,946	82,074	82,222	82,738	83,306
Employed	75,128	75,092	74,879	75,135	75,601	75,923	76,223	76,295	76,606	76,886	77,349	77,905
Unemployed	5,878	6,085	6,098	6,162	6,185	6,125	5,507	5,651	5,468	5,343	5,389	5,401
Unemployment rate	7.3	7.5	7.5	7.6	7.6	7.5	6.7	6.9	6.7	6.5	6.5	6.5
art time												
Civilian labor force	14,181	14,351	14,340	14,059	14,046	13,912	13,980	14,265	14,426	14,587	14,435	14,192
Employed	12,681	12,922	12,963	12,610	12,577	12,546	12,549	12,736	12,820	13,146	13,006	12,668
Unemployed	1,500	1,429	1,377	1,449	1,469	1,366	1,431	1,529	1,606	1,441	1,429	1,524
Unemployment rate	10.6	10.0	9.6	10.3	10.5	9.8	10.2	10.7	11.1	9.9	9.9	10.7

Labor Union Membership

Source: U.S. Labor Department
AFL-CIO unions with a membership of 25,000 or over (Aug., 1977)

Union	Members
Actors and Artists of America, Associated	85,000
Air Line Pilots Association	44,000
Aluminum Workers International Union	27,000
Bakery and Confectionery Workers International Union of America	108,000
Barbers, Hairdressers and Cosmetologists' International Union of America, the Journeymen	33,000
Boilermakers, Iron Ship Builders, Blacksmiths, Forgers and Helpers, International Brotherhood of	130,000
Boot and Shoe Workers' Union	29,000
Bricklayers, Masons, and Plasterers International Union of America	118,000
Carpenters and Joiners of America, United Brotherhood of	650,000
Cement, Lime and Gypsum Workers International Union, United	28,000
Chemical Workers Union, International	50,000
Clothing and Textile Workers Union, Amalgamated	295,000
Communications Workers of America	485,000
Dolls, Toys, Playthings, Novelties and Allied Products of the United States and Canada, AFL-CIO, International Union of	33,000
Electrical, Radio and Machine Workers, International Union of	238,000
Electrical Workers, International Brotherhood of	815,000
Engineers, International Union of Operating	300,000
Fire Fighters, International Association of	150,000
Firemen and Oilers, International Brotherhood of	36,000
Furniture Workers of America, United	26,000
Garment Workers of America, United	32,000
Garment Workers Union, International Ladies'	340,000
Glass and Ceramic Workers of North America, United	26,000
Glass Bottle Blowers' Association of the United States and Canada	75,000
Glass Workers Union, American Flint	32,000
Government Employees, American Federation of	255,000
Grain Millers, American Federation of	36,000
Graphic Arts International Union	81,000
Hotel and Restaurant Employees' and Bartenders' International Union	397,000
Industrial Workers of America, International Union, Allied	85,000
Iron Workers, International Association of Bridge and Structural	160,000
Laborers' International Union of North America	475,000
Leather Goods, Plastics and Novelty Workers Union, International	30,000
Letter Carriers, National Association of	151,000
Longshoremen's Association, International	63,000
Machinists and Aerospace Workers, International Association of	630,000
Maintenance of Way Employees, Brotherhood of	73,000
Maritime Union of America, National	30,000
Meat Cutters and Butcher Workmen of North America, Amalgamated	427,000
Molders and Allied Workers Union, International	50,000
Musicians, American Federation of	183,000
Newspaper Guild, The	26,000
Office and Professional Employees International Union	78,000
Oil, Chemical and Atomic Workers International Union	145,000
Painters & Allied Trades of the United States and Canada, International Brotherhood of	160,000
Paper Workers International Union, United	265,000
Plasterers' & Cement Masons' International Association of the United States and Canada, Operative	50,000
Plumbing and Pipe Fitting Industry of the United States & Canada, United Association of Journeymen & Apprentices of the	228,000
Postal Workers Union, American	247,000
Printing and Graphics Communications Union, International	98,000
Railway, Airline and Steamship Clerks, Freight Handlers, Express & Station Employes, Brotherhood of	104,000
Railway Carmen of the United States & Canada, Brotherhood	51,000
Retail Clerks International Association	620,0
Retail, Wholesale and Department Store Union	131,0
Roofers, Damp & Waterproof Workers Association, United Slate, Tile & Composition	27,0
Rubber, Cork, Linoleum & Plastic Workers of America, United	156,0
Seafarers International Union of North America	95,0
Service Employees International Union, AFL-CIO	507,0
Sheet Metal Workers International Association	120,0
Stage Employes & Moving Picture Machine Operators of the United States & Canada, International Alliance of Theatrical	50,0
State, County & Municipal Employees, American Federation of	679,0
Steelworkers of America, United	960,0
Teachers, American Federation of	415,0
Textile Workers of America, United	31,0
Tobacco Workers International Union	25,0
Transit Union, Amalgamated	92,0
Transport Workers Union of America	95,0
Transportation Union, United	122,0
Typographical Union, International	59,0
Upholsterers' International Union of North America	45,0
Utility Workers Union of America	52,0
Woodworkers of America, International	53,0

Independent Unions

(Jan., 1976)

Automobile, Aerospace and Agricultural Implement Workers of America, Intl. Union, United	1,393,5
Distributive Workers of America	50,0
Education Assn., National	1,165,6
Electrical, Radio, and Machine Workers of America, United	165,0
Federal Employees, Nat'l. Federation of	85,0
Government Employees, Nat'l. Assn. of	100,0
Letter Carriers Assn., Nat'l. Rural	46,3
Locomotive Engineers, Brotherhood of	37,6
Longshoremen's and Warehousemen's Union Int'l.	58,0
Mine Workers of America, United	213,1
Nurses' Assn., American	156,6
Police, Fraternal Order of Police	125,0
Postal and Federal Employees, Nat'l. Alliance of	45,0
Postal Supervisors, Nat'l. Assn. of	32,9
Teamsters, Chauffeurs, Warehousemen and Helpers of America, Int'l. Brotherhood of	1,854,6
Telecommunications International Union	50,0
Treasury Employees Union, Nat'l.	33,0
University Professors, American Assn. of	85,6

Canadian Unions

Independent Unions (1976)

Government Employees' Union, Quebec	30,1
Teachers' Corporation, Quebec	85,0
Teachers' Federation, Ontario Secondary School	34,4

CNTU Unions (1975)

Public Service Employees Inc., Federation of	29,6
Social Affairs Federation	61,1

CLC Unions (1976)

Automobile, Aerospace and Agricultural Implement Workers of America, International Union, United	130,0
Civil Service Assn. of Alberta, The	26,3
Civil Service Assn. of Ontario, The	63,3
Government Employees' Union, British Columbia	27,6
Paperworkers Union, Canadian	56,0
Public Employees, Canadian Union of	228,6
Public Service Alliance of Canada	159,4
Railway, Transport and General Workers, Canadian Brotherhood of	40,6

U.S. Mineral Production

Source: Bureau of Mines, U.S. Interior Department

Production as measured by mine shipments, sales, or marketable production (including consumption by producers)

Mineral fuels	Unit	1975 Quantity	1975 Value (thousands)	1976[p] Quantity	1976[p] Value (thousands)
sphalt and related bitumens (native):					
Bituminous limestone & sandstone & gilsonite	short tons	1,901,715	$19,838	e1,889,000	e$19,850
arbon dioxide, natural (e)	thousand cubic feet	1,070,024	279	1,060,000	285
oal: Bituminous and lignite[1]	thousand short tons	648,438	12,472,486	665,000	12,500,000
Pennsylvania anthracite	thousand short tons	6,203	198,481	6,200	211,000
elium: Crude	million cubic feet	334	4,008	585	7,020
Grade A	million cubic feet	745	19,915	754	18,928
latural gas	million cubic feet	20,108,661	8,945,062	19,952,438	11,571,776
latural gas liquids: Gasoline products	thousand 42-gal. bbls.	151,872	878,698	149,679	985,442
LP gases	thousand 42-gal. bbls.	444,086	1,893,890	437,366	2,298,647
eat	thousand short tons	746	12,294	970	17,131
etroleum (crude)	thousand 42-gal. bbls.	3,056,779	23,116,059	2,976,180	24,229,540
Total mineral fuels		**XX**	**47,561,000**	**XX**	**51,859,619**
Non metals (except fuels)					
brasive stones[2]	short tons	2,953	1,060	2,339	1,337
sbestos	short tons	98,654	14,220	114,842	23,693
arite	thousand short tons	1,318	21,100	1,234	28,689
oron minerals	thousand short tons	1,172	158,772	1,246	184,852
romine	thousand pounds	407,163	113,126	439,538	107,653
alcium-magnesium chloride	short tons	594,400	29,047	648,979	32,889
ement: Portland	thousand short tons	65,214	2,015,626	609,069	2,247,336
Masonry	thousand short tons	2,868	111,800	3,454	144,010
Natural and slag	thousand short tons	W	W	53,014	510,923
lays	thousand short tons	49,047	424,556	631,380	54,982
iatomite	short tons	573,000	45,812	2,957	W
eldspar	short tons	684,898	11,893	681,380	55,000
luorspar	short tons	139,913	10,888	188,270	17,927
arnet (abrasive)	short tons	17,204	1,690	25,661	2,740
em stones (e)		NA	13,900	NA	7,900
ypsum	thousand short tons	9,751	44,654	11,980	59,888
ime	thousand short tons	19,133	523,805	19,974	574,253
lagnesium compounds from sea water and brine (except for metals)	short tons, MgO equivalent	W	W	W	W
lica: Scrap	thousand short tons	135	5,219	127	5,686
Sheet	pounds	5,000	3	5,000	3
erlite	short tons	512,000	7,282	553,000	9,400
hosphate rock	thousand short tons	48,816	1,122,184	49,241	949,365
otassium salts	thousand short tons, K_2O equivalent	2,501	223,098	24,000	202,370
umice	thousand short tons	3,892	11,203	4,134	10,500
yrites	thousand long tons	625	4,776	750	8,213
alt	thousand short tons	41,030	368,063	44,191	426,792
and and gravel	thousand short tons	789,436	1,416,346	770,000	1,524,600
odium carbonate (natural)	thousand short tons	4,328	182,620	5,216	259,253
odium sulfate (natural)	thousand short tons	667	27,667	663	32,655
tone[3]	thousand short tons	902,900	2,123,049	890,000	2,130,000
ulfur: Frasch process mines	thousand long tons	6,077	304,843	5,860	299,999
alc, soapstone, and pyrophyllite	short tons	927,548	8,309	1,134,000	11,500
ripoli	short tons	80,562	565	126,323	807
ermiculite	thousand short tons	330	13,761	304	14,032
Value of items that cannot be disclosed: Aplite, brucite, emery, graphite, iodine, kyanite, lithium minerals, magnesite, greensand marl, olivine, staurolite, wollastonite, and values of nonmetal items indicated by symbol W:			157,180	XX	171,974
Total nonmetals		**XX**	**9,518,000**	**XX**	**10,111,221**
Metals					
ntimony ore concentrate, antimony content	short tons	886	2,131	283	600
auxite	thousands long tons, dried equivalent	1,772	25,083	1,958	26,645
eryllium concentrate	short tons, gross weight	W	W	W	W
opper (recoverable content of ores, etc.)	short tons	1,413,366	1,814,763	1,605,586	2,234,975
old (recoverable content of ores, etc.)	troy ounces	1,052,252	169,928	1,048,037	131,340
on ore (excluding iron sinter)	thousand long tons, gr. wgt.	75,695	1,620,599	77,076	1,870,993
ead (recoverable content of ores, etc.)	short tons	621,464	267,230	609,546	281,610
langanese ore (35% or more Mn)	short tons, gross weight	—	—	—	—
langaniferous ore (5 to 35% Mn)	short tons, gross weight	159,225	1,413	256,633	2,260
lercury	76-pound flasks	7,366	1,165	23,133	2,806
lolybdenum (content of concentrate)	thousand pounds	105,170	259,328	114,527	33,494
lickel (content of ore and concentrate)	short tons	16,987	W	16,469	W
are-earth metal concentrates	short tons	W	W	W	W
ilver (recoverable content of ores, etc.)	thousand troy ozs.	3434,938	154,424	34,328	149,328
itanium concentrate, ilmenite	short tons, gross weight	702,252	26,946	617,896	27,578
ungsten ore and concentrate	thousand pounds	5,490	29,090	5,869	37,266
ranium (Recoverable content U_3O_8)	thousand pounds	22,877	281,388	13,572	404,830
anadium (recoverable in ore and concentrate)	short tons	4,743	49,329	7,376	81,279
inc (recoverable content of ores, etc.)	short tons	469,355	366,097	484,513	358,541
alue of items that cannot be disclosed: symbol W		XX	127,459	XX	13,316
Total metals		**XX**	**5,196,000**	**XX**	**5,522,056**
Grand total mineral production		**XX**	**62,275,000**	**XX**	**67,492,896**

e) Estimate. (NA) Not available. (W) Withheld to avoid disclosing individual company confidential data: included with "Value of items hat cannot be disclosed." (XX) Not applicable. (p) Preliminary.
1) Includes a small quantity of anthracite mined in states other than Pennsylvania.
2) Grindstones, pulpstones, grinding pebbles, sharpening stones, and tube mill liners.
3) Excludes abrasive stone, bituminous limestone, bituminous sandstone, and soapstone, all included elsewhere.

U.S. Mineral Production—Leading States

Source: Bureau of Mines, U.S. Interior Department

State 1975	Value (thousands)	Percent of U.S. total	Principal minerals, in order of value
Texas	$15,529,931	24.94	Petroleum, natural gas, natural gas liquids, cement.
Louisiana	8,513,275	13.67	Petroleum, natural gas, natural gas liquids, sulfur.
West Virginia	3,390,212	5.44	Coal, natural gas, petroleum, natural gas liquids.
California	3,152,937	5.06	Petroleum, cement, natural gas, sand and gravel.
Pennsylvania	2,907,838	4.67	Coal, cement, stone, lime.
Kentucky	2,738,859	4.40	Coal, petroleum, stone, natural gas.
Oklahoma	2,267,095	3.64	Petroleum, natural gas, natural gas liquids, coal.
New Mexico	2,091,541	3.36	Petroleum, natural gas, potassium salts, copper.
Florida	1,775,500	2.85	Phosphate rock, petroleum, stone, cement.
Wyoming	1,644,438	2.64	Petroleum, sodium compounds, coal, natural gas.

Value of U.S. Mineral Production

Source: Bureau of Mines, U.S. Interior Department
(millions of dollars)
Production as measured by mine shipments sales or marketable production.

Year[1]	Fuels	Nonmetallic	Metals	Total[2]	Year[1]	Fuels	Nonmetallic	Metals	Total[2]
1930	2,500	973	501	3,980	1970	20,152	5,712	3,928	29,792
1940	2,662	784	752	4,198	1971	21,247	6,058	3,406	30,711
1950	8,689	1,882	1,351	11,862	1972	22,061	6,482	3,642	32,185
1960	12,142	3,868	2,022	18,032	1973	25,012	7,413	4,362	36,787
1965	14,047	4,933	2,544	21,524	1974	40,937	8,642	5,552	55,131
1968	16,820	5,449	2,698	24,966	1975	47,561	9,518	5,196	62,275
1969	17,965	5,624	3,333	26,921	1976p	52,140	10,025	5,587	67,752

(1) Excludes Alaska and Hawaii, 1930-53. (2) Data may not add to total because of rounding figures. (P) Preliminary.

U.S. Copper, Lead, and Zinc Production

Source: Bureau of Mines, U.S. Interior Department

Year	Copper Mil. lbs.	Copper $1,000	Lead[1] Short tons	Lead[1] $1,000	Zinc Short tons	Zinc Mil. dol.
1950	1,823	379,122	418,809	113,078	591,454	167
1960	2,286	733,708	228,899	53,562	334,101	87
1965	2,703	957,028	301,147	93,959	611,153	178
1970	3,439	1,984,484	571,767	178,609	534,136	164
1972	3,330	1,704,796	618,915	186,046	478,318	170
1973	3,436	2,044,346	603,024	196,465	478,850	198
1974	3,194	2,468,964	668,870	298,742	499,872	359
1975	2,827	1,814,763	621,464	267,230	469,355	366
1976	3,211	2,234,975	609,546	281,610	484,513	359

(1) Production from domestic ores.

U.S. Pig Iron and Steel Output

Source: American Iron and Steel Institute (net tons)

Year	Total pig iron	Pig iron and ferro-alloys	Raw steel	Year	Total pig iron	Pig iron and ferro-alloys	Raw steel
1940	46,071,666	47,398,529	66,982,686	1970	91,435,000	93,851,000	131,514,000
1945	53,223,169	54,919,029	79,701,648	1972	88,942,000	91,338,000	133,241,000
1950	64,586,907	66,400,311	96,836,075	1973	100,837,000	103,089,000	150,799,000
1955	76,857,417	79,263,865	117,036,085	1974	95,909,000	98,332,000	145,720,000
1960	66,480,648	68,566,384	99,281,601	1975	101,208,000	103,345,000	116,642,000
1965	88,184,901	90,918,040	131,461,601	1976	NA	NA	128,000,000

Steel figures include only that portion of the capacity and production of steel for castings used by foundries which were operated by companie producing steel ingots.

Raw Steel Production

(thousands of net tons)

State	1975	1976	State	1975	1976
New York	3,401	4,799	Indiana	19,807	22,17
Pennsylvania	25,761	26,696	Illinois	9,552	11,03
R.I., Conn., N.J., Del., Md.	5,094	5,870	Michigan	9,093	10,38
Va., W. Va., Ga., Fla., N.C., S.C.	4,795	5,403	Minn., Mo., Okla., Texas	5,399	5,07
Kentucky	2,081	2,206	Ariz., Colo., Utah, Wash., Ore., Hawaii	4,380	4,43
Ala., Tenn., Miss., Ark.	4,308	4,109	California	3,351	3,39
Ohio	19,620	22,419	**Total**	**116,642**	**128,00**

U.S. Primary Aluminum Production

Source: The Aluminum Association

Year	Short tons	Year	Short tons	Year	Short tons	Year	Short ton
1883-1902	13,981	1930	114,518	1965	2,754,478	1973	4,529,11
1903-1912	108,412	1940	206,280	1969	3,793,062	1974	4,903,42
1913-1923	282,722	1950	718,622	1970	3,976,148	1975	3,879,00
1924-1925	145,340	1960	2,014,498	1972	4,122,392	1976	4,200,00

Major Aluminum Markets

1976 Market	Millions of lbs.	Percent	1976 Market	Millions of lbs.	Perce
Building & construction	2,957	23.2	Containers & packaging	2,570	20.2
Transportation	2,454	19.2	Exports	842	6.6
Consumer durables	1,035	8.1	Other	657	5.2
Electrical	1,328	10.4			
Machinery & equipment	904	7.1	**Total industry**	**12,747**	**100.0**

TRADE AND TRANSPORTATION

Notable Steamships and Motorships

Source: Lloyd's Register of Shipping as of Aug. 23, 1977

Gross tonnage is a measurement of enclosed space (1 gross ton = 100 cu. ft.). Deadweight tonnage is the weight (long tons) of cargo, fuel, etc., which a vessel is designed to carry safely.

Oil Tankers

Name-registry	Dwght. ton.	Lgth. Ft.	Bdth. Ft.
Bellamya, Fr.	553,662	1359	206
Batillus, Fr.	550,000	1312	206
Nissei Maru, Jap.	484,337	1243	203
Globtik London, Br.	483,939	1243	203
Globtik Tokyo, Br.	483,664	1243	203
Homeric, Liber.	446,500	1241	223
Berge Empress, Nor.	423,700	1252	223
Esso Deutschland, W. Ger.	421,678	1240	226
Al Rekkah, Kuw.	414,366	1200	229
Berge Emperor, Nor.	414,000	1285	223
Jinko Maru	413,549	1200	229
Chevron So. America, Liber.	413,159	1200	229
Aiko Maru, Jap.	413,012	1200	229
Chevron No. America, Liber.	412,612	1200	229
Porthos, Liber.	412,000	1174	209
Golar Patricia, Liber.	409,500	1236	226
Coraggio, It.	409,500	1240	226
Hilda Knudson, Nor.	409,500	1240	226
David Packard, Liber.	406,592	1200	229
Esso Tokyo, Liber.	406,258	1187	229
Esso Japan, Liber.	402,000	1148	229
Shat-Al Araq, Iraq	392,623	1213	209
Bonn, W. Ger.	392,607	1214	209
Wahran, Alger.	392,372	1221	210
Andros Petros, Liber.	388,916	1241	223
Berlin, Liber.	386,612	1213	210
Brazilian Hope, Liber.	386,600	1213	210
Bremen, Liber.	386,600	1213	210
Jarmada, Nor.	380,000	1225	210
Esso Le Havre, Liber.	380,000	1225	210
Esso Madrid, Liber.	380,000	1225	210
Titus, Nor.	380,000	1225	209
Malmros Mariner, Swed.	372,280	1193	208
Hemland, Swed.	372,201	1193	208
Nisseki Maru, Jap.	366,813	1138	179
La Santa Maria, Sp.	362,946	1189	175
Al Andalus, Kuw.	362,946	1188	175
Kimizuru Maru, Jap.	172,181	948	157
Oder Maru, Jap.	171,500	984	157
Sir John Hunter, Br.	171,400	965	145
Cedros, Liber.	170,418	995	142
Cetra Centaurus, Fr.	170,414	981	143
Cetra Vela, Fr.	169,317	967	155
Champagne, Fr.	169,300	967	155
Garden Green, Liber.	169,147	967	155
English Bridge, Br.	169,080	965	145
Sir Alexander Glen, Br.	169,080	965	144

Bulk, Ore, Bulk Oil & Ore Oil Carriers

Name-registry	Dwght. ton.	Lgth. Ft.	Bdth. Ft.
Svealand, Swed.	282,450	1109	179
Docecanyon, Liber.	271,235	1113	180
Licorne Pacifique, Fr.	271,000	1111	176
Jose Bonifacio, Braz.	270,358	1106	179
Tarfala, Swed.	265,000	1099	170
Mary R. Koch, Liber.	265,000	1099	170
Torne, Swed.	265,000	1099	170
Usa Maru, Jap.	264,523	1105	179
Nordic Conqueror, Br.	264,485	1101	176
Lauderdale, Br.	260,424	1101	176
Licorne Atlantique, Fr.	258,268	1101	176
Seiko Maru, Jap.	248,300	1069	170
La Loma, Br.	245,288	1069	170
Hoegh Hood, Nor.	244,677	1069	170
Hoegh Hill, Nor.	241,447	1069	170
Konkar Dinos, Gr.	231,045	1075	160
Berge Vanga, Liber.	227,561	1030	164
Berge Adria, Nor.	227,561	1030	164
Andros Antares, Liber.	227,480	1061	158
San Giusto, It.	227,408	1091	149
World Recovery, Liber.	227,406	1075	161
Ambrosiana, It.	227,400	1091	149
Berge Brioni, Nor.	227,187	1030	165
Konkar Theodoros, Liber.	225,000	1091	164
Andros Atlas, Gr.	224,074	1061	158
Andros Aries, Gr.	223,808	1061	158
Sysla, Nor.	223,500	1096	149
Alva Bay, Br.	222,331	1091	149
Alva Sea, Br.	221,457	1090	149
Tartar, Nor.	215,621	1075	164
Jarl Malmros, Swed.	215,500	1075	164
Tantalus, Br.	214,592	1075	164
Atsuta Maru, Jap.	214,017	1075	164
Tsurumi Maru, Jap.	213,842	1075	164
Sensho Maru, Jap.	191,018	983	154
Adria Maru, Jap.	183,572	1023	156
Arafura Maru, Jap.	180,626	1023	156
arina, Liber.	175,927	984	157
Romantic, Liber.	174,107	995	151
Rhetoric, Liber.	173,668	995	151

World's Largest Passenger Ships

Name-registry	Gross ton.	Lgth. Ft.	Bdth. Ft.
Queen Elizabeth 2, Br.	66,852	963	105
France, Fr.	66,348	1035	110
Raffaello, It.	45,933	904	101
Michelangelo, It.	45,911	904	101
Canberra, Br.	44,807	818	102
Oriana, Br.	41,910	804	97
United States, U.S.	38,216	990	101
Rotterdam, Neth. Antil.	37,783	748	94
Windsor Castle, Br.	36,277	783	92
Leonardo Da Vinci, It.	33,340	767	92
Eugenio C., It.	30,567	713	96
S.A. Vaal, S. Afr.	30,213	760	90

Container, Liquefied Gas, Misc. Ships

LNG Aquarius, U.S.	87,000	936	143
Golar Freeze, Liber.	85,158	943	142
Gimi, Liber.	84,855	963	136
Hilli, Liber.	84,855	961	136
Mostefa Ben Boulaid, Alger	82,243	914	134
Ben Franklin, Fr.	80,071	894	134
Gastor, Pan.	79,040	902	138
LNG Challenger, Br.	76,496	857	131
Norman Lady, Br.	76,416	818	131
Ben M'hiri Larbi, Alger.	74,000	924	136
El Paso Paul Kayser, Liber.	66,808	920	136
El Paso Consolidated, Liber.	66,808	920	141
El Paso Sonatrach, Liber.	66,807	920	136
Palace Tokyo, Jap.	64,378	807	131
Cardigan Bay, Br.	58,899	950	106
Kowloon Bay, Br.	58,889	950	106
Liverpool Bay, Br.	58,889	950	106
Tokyo Bay, Br.	58,889	950	106
Osaka Bay, Br.	58,889	950	106
Nedlloyd Delft, Neth.	58,716	941	106
Nedlloyd Dejima, Neth.	58,716	941	106
City of Edinburgh, Br.	58,440	950	106
Benavon, Br.	58,440	950	106
Benalder, Br.	58,440	950	106
Hamburg Express, W. Ger.	58,088	943	105
Tokio Express, W. Ger.	58,082	943	105
Bremen Express, W. Ger.	57,535	941	106
Hongkong Express, W. Ger.	57,525	941	106
Kasuga Maru, Jap.	57,500	948	105
Korrigan, Fr.	57,249	946	105
Esso Fuji, Pan.	55,896	807	131
Geomitra, Br.	53,128	846	114
Genota, Br.	53,128	846	113
Toyama, Nor.	52,196	902	106
Elbe Maru, Jap.	51,623	882	105
Kitano Maru, Jap.	51,159	856	105
Kurama Maru, Jap.	51,139	856	105
Kamakura Maru, Jap.	51,139	856	105
Rhine Maru, Jap.	51,085	856	105
Nihon, Swed.	50,805	902	105
Selandia, Den.	49,890	900	106
Jutlandia, Den.	49,890	900	106
Gouldia	48,662	844	114
Gari, Br.	48,662	842	114
Gastrana, Br.	48,662	842	114
Gadila, Br.	48,662	842	114
Gadinia, Br.	48,662	842	114
Hoegh Swallow, Nor.	48,500	752	105
Yusho Maru, Jap.	47,783	744	114

Name-registry	Gross ton.	Lgth. Ft.	Bdth. Ft.
Sun River, Jap.	45,647	734	106
Polar Alaska, Liber.	44,088	798	111
Arctic Tokyo, Liber.	44,088	798	111
Act 7, Br.	43,992	815	106
Australian Venture, Austral.	43,878	824	106
Nyhammer, Nor.	43,000	757	105
Gas Gemini, Liber.	42,252	748	120
Remuera Bay, Br.	42,007	824	105
Kanayama Maru, Jap.	41,939	734	113
Sea-Land Exchange, U.S.	41,555	946	105
Sea-Land Commerce, U.S.	41,127	946	105
Sea-Land Trade, U.S.	41,127	946	105
Sea-Land Market, U.S.	41,127	946	105
Sea-Land Resource, U.S.	41,127	946	105
Sea-Land Finance, U.S.	41,127	946	105
Sea-Land Galloway, U.S.	41,127	946	105
Sea-Land Mclean, U.S.	41,127	946	105
Bridgestone Maru No. 5, Jap.	40,934	690	106
Pioneer Louise, Liber.	40,300	698	120
World Vigour, Liber.	39,500	734	106
World Concord, Liber.	39,500	734	106
World Creation, Liber.	39,411	734	106
Verrazano Bridge, Jap.	39,153	867	105
Seven Seas Bridge, Jap.	39,152	867	105
Tokuho Maru, Jap.	39,117	705	105
Izumisan Maru, Jap.	38,872	705	105
New York Maru, Jap.	38,825	862	105
Kiso Maru, Jap.	38,540	857	105
Svendborg Maersk, Den.	38,540	856	105
Kurobe Maru, Jap.	37,845	854	105
Ogden General, Liber.	37,809	746	113
New Jersey Maru, Jap.	37,799	863	105

Nuclear Powered Merchant Ships

Name-registry	Gross ton.	Lgth. Ft.	Bdth. Ft.
Arktika, USSR	18,172	492	98
Otto Hahn, W. Ger.	16,871	564	76
Savannah, U.S.	15,585	595	78
Lenin, USSR	14,067	439	90
Mutsu, Jap.	8,214	428	62

U.S. Exports and Imports of Leading Commodities

Source: Bureau of International Commerce, U.S. Commerce Department (millions of dollars)

Commodity	Exports 1974	Exports 1975	Exports 1976	Imports 1974	Imports 1975	Imports 1976
Total	**$98,506**	**$107,652**	**$114,997**	**$100,972**	**$96,140**	**$120,677**
Food and live animals	**13,983**	**15,487**	**15,710**	**9,379**	**8,509**	**10,267**
Meat	381	528	798	1,344	1,141	1,447
Dairy products and eggs	67	134	128	...	...	...
Cheese	...	...	...	236	165	207
Fish	196	268	332	1,499	1,356	1,855
Grains and preparations	10,331	11,643	10,911	171	180	150
Wheat and wheat flour	4,589	5,292	4,041	...	...	...
Rice	852	858	629	...	...	...
Corn	3,772	4,448	5,223	...	...	...
Fruit and nuts	757	871	976	627	637	760
Vegetables	391	406	559	387	355	426
Sugar	...	...	...	2,256	1,870	1,154
Coffee, green	...	...	...	1,504	1,561	2,632
Beverages and tobaccos	**1,247**	**1,310**	**1,523**	**1,321**	**1,419**	**1,624**
Alcoholic beverages	...	...	...	1,028	1,033	1,174
Tobacco, unmanufactured	832	853	921	255	343	392
Crude materials, inedible other than fuels	**10,934**	**9,784**	**10,891**	**5,915**	**5,564**	**7,014**
Synthetic rubber	290	261	329	...	...	...
Ores and metal scrap	1,475	1,355	1,285	1,838	1,977	2,251
Coal	2,436	3,259	2,910	...	...	...
Petroleum and products	792	907	998	24,210	24,814	31,794
Animal and vegetable oils and fats	**1,423**	**944**	**978**	**544**	**554**	**464**
Chemicals	**8,822**	**8,705**	**9,958**	**3,991**	**3,696**	**4,772**
Medicinal and pharmaceutical	800	866	996	214	235	269
Machinery and transport equipment	**38,189**	**45,710**	**49,510**	**24,713**	**23,465**	**29,824**
Automotive engines	673	763	943	1,013	1,040	1,384
Agricultural machinery	545	706	707	440	474	496
Tractors and parts	483	752	928	412	430	456
Metalworking machinery	639	920	953	305	361	362
Textile and leather machinery	528	486	457	609	518	636
Other nonelectrical machinery	1,930	2,245	2,337	1,384	1,156	1,29
Electrical apparatus	7,019	7,587	9,278	5,417	4,911	7,424
Transport equipment	**13,871**	**16,495**	**17,399**	**12,630**	**11,495**	**14,37**
New motor vehicles	3,681	5,135	5,385	7,544	7,130	8,928
Aircraft and parts	5,766	6,171	6,116	510	519	43
Other manufactured goods	**16,516**	**16,590**	**17,777**	**27,507**	**23,929**	**30,17**
Rubber manufactures	544	544	491	...	...	...
Paper and manufactures	1,522	1,448	1,624	1,831	1,673	2,10
Diamonds excluding industrial	305	237	306	775	730	1,01
Metals and manufactures	1,665	1,891	2,089	11,383	8,944	9,898
Iron and steel-mill products	2,491	2,382	1,833	5,013	4,037	3,80
Nonferrous base metals	1,300	1,090	1,089	3,042	2,063	2,94
Textiles other than clothing	1,795	1,625	1,970	1,629	1,219	1,63
Clothing	372	382	488	1,323	2,562	3,634
Other transactions	**2,587**	**3,162**	**2,749**	**2,252**	**2,529**	**2,53**

U.S. Merchandise Exports and Imports, by Continent

Source: International Trade Analysis Division, U.S. Commerce Department (millions of dollars)

Year	Exports: Western Hemis.	Exports: Europe	Exports: Asia & Oceania	Exports: Africa	General imports: Western Hemis.	General imports: Europe	General imports: Asia & Oceania	General imports: Africa
1965	9,932	9,397	7,129	1,071	9,257	6,292	4,999	867
1970	15,611	14,817	11,294	1,502	16,928	11,395	10,515	1,090
1972	19,694	16,180	12,407	1,500	21,930	15,744	16,279	1,578
1973	25,003	23,157	20,395	2,081	27,229	19,687	19,614	2,552
1974	35,745	30,878	28,129	3,204	40,702	24,636	29,073	6,547
1975	38,873	32,732	31,281	4,266	37,796	21,466	28,591	8,277
1976	41,082	35,903	33,231	4,396	43,356	23,640	41,130	12,547

U.S. Foreign Trade with Leading Countries

Source: Bureau of International Commerce, U.S. Commerce Department
(millions of dollars)

Exports from the U.S. to the following areas and countries and imports into the U.S. from those areas and countries:	Exports			Imports		
	1974	1975	1976	1974	1975	1976
Total	**$98,506**	**$107,652**	**$114,997**	**$100,972**	**$96,140**	**$120,677**
Western Hemisphere	**35,745**	**38,873**	**41,082**	**40,702**	**37,796**	**43,356**
Canada	19,932	21,759	24,109	22,282	21,747	26,238
19 American Republics	14,504	15,670	15,492	13,678	11,840	13,227
Central American Common Market	1,033	968	1,153	788	825	1,209
Latin American Free Trade Ass'n.	12,571	...	...	12,199	...	...
Dominican Republic	410	453	432	471	634	520
Panama	364	317	358	108	194	142
Bahamas	253	208	199	958	880	670
Jamaica	337	381	285	233	308	312
Netherlands Antilles	193	228	248	2,018	1,558	1,170
Trinidad and Tobago	192	256	309	1,273	1,170	1,500
Europe	**30,071**	**32,726**	**35,903**	**24,636**	**21,466**	**23,640**
OECD Countries (Excludes depend and Yugo.)	28,268	29,569	32,052	23,470	20,471	22,393
Western Europe	28,639	29,939	32,401	23,745	20,735	22,784
European Economic Community	22,069	22,862	25,406	19,205	16,610	17,848
Belgium and Luxembourg	2,285	2,427	2,991	1,681	1,190	1,119
France	2,942	3,031	3,449	2,305	2,137	2,509
Germany, Federal Republic of	4,986	5,194	5,730	6,428	5,382	5,591
Italy	2,752	2,867	3,068	2,593	2,397	2,530
Netherlands	3,979	4,183	4,645	1,453	1,083	1,080
United Kingdom	4,574	4,525	4,799	4,021	3,784	4,254
Denmark	360	445	444	477	461	561
Ireland	193	190	280	247	176	205
European Free Trade Association	2,984	...	...	3,068	...	...
Austria	148	181	197	457	238	237
Finland	201	261	243	212	148	189
Iceland	38	32	35	75	85	120
Norway	498	510	500	307	403	646
Portugal	407	427	400	241	156	128
Sweden	908	925	1,036	876	877	918
Switzerland	1,150	1,153	1,173	900	867	1,025
Greece	488	450	591	158	111	146
Spain	1,899	2,161	2,021	899	831	914
Turkey	463	608	451	141	145	222
Yugoslavia	310	328	298	268	260	385
Eastern Europe	1,432	2,787	3,502	891	731	856
Asia	**26,239**	**28,942**	**30,541**	**27,570**	**27,083**	**39,459**
Near East	**5,557**	**8,977**	**10,047**	**4,735**	**5,432**	**9,103**
Egypt	455	683	810	70	28	92
Iraq	285	310	382	1	19	110
Iran	1,734	3,242	2,776	2,132	1,400	1,480
Israel	1,206	1,551	1,409	282	313	423
Jordan	105	195	234	...	1	1
Kuwait	209	366	472	13	111	38
Lebanon	287	402	49	30	33	5
Saudi Arabia	835	1,502	2,774	1,671	2,625	5,213
Japan	10,679	9,565	10,144	12,455	11,268	15,504
East and South Asia	9,196	10,095	10,214	10,264	10,224	14,648
China, Republic of (Taiwan)	1,427	1,660	1,635	2,108	1,938	2,989
Hong Kong	882	808	1,115	1,637	1,575	2,413
India	760	1,290	1,135	561	548	708
Indonesia	531	810	1,036	1,688	2,221	3,004
Korea, Republic of	1,546	1,761	2,015	1,460	1,416	2,404
Malaysia	377	395	536	773	766	940
Singapore	988	994	965	553	532	695
Pakistan	398	372	394	61	49	70
Philippines	747	832	819	1,091	754	883
Thailand	369	357	347	184	217	276
Vietnam	675	213	1	8	6	1
Oceania	**2,697**	**2,339**	**2,690**	**1,503**	**1,508**	**1,671**
Australia	2,157	1,816	2,185	1,042	1,147	1,211
New Zealand and Western Samoa	454	414	415	348	246	330
Africa	**3,204**	**4,267**	**4,396**	**6,547**	**8,277**	**12,547**
North Africa excluding Egypt	826	1,339	1,342	1,224	2,498	4,644
Algeria	315	632	487	1,091	1,359	2,209
Ethiopia	33	70	78	64	49	94
Libya	139	232	277	1	1,046	2,243
Morocco	184	200	297	20	10	17
Tunisia	87	90	82	21	26	56
Western and equatorial Africa	827	1,170	1,418	4,287	4,457	6,090
Angola	62	53	35	378	426	264
Ghana	77	100	133	126	150	155
Ivory Coast	49	78	64	95	160	248
Liberia	70	90	85	96	97	99
Nigeria	286	536	770	3,286	3,282	4,938
Central and southern Africa	1,552	1,763	1,641	1,034	1,323	1,811
Kenya	49	49	43	39	36	60
South Africa	1,160	1,302	1,348	609	841	925
Zaire	145	188	99	68	67	189

Important Waterways and Canals

The St. Lawrence & Great Lakes Waterway, the largest inland navigation system on the continent, extends from the Atlantic Ocean to Duluth at the western end of Lake Superior, a distance of 2,342 miles. With the deepening of channels and locks to 27 ft., ocean carriers are able to penetrate to ports in the Canadian interior and the American midwest.

The major canals are those of the St. Lawrence-Great Lakes waterway — the 3 new canals of the St. Lawrence Seaway, with their 7 locks, providing navigation for vessels of 26-foot draught from Montreal to Lake Ontario; the Welland Ship Canal by-passing the Niagara River between Lake Ontario and Lake Erie with its 8 locks, and the Sault Ste. Marie Canal and lock between Lake Huron and Lake Superior. These 16 locks overcome a drop of 580 ft. from the head of the lakes to Montreal. From Montreal to Lake Ontario the former bottleneck of narrow, shallow canals and of slow passage through 22 locks has been overcome, giving faster and safer movement for larger vessels. The new locks and linking channels now accommodate all but the largest ocean-going vessels and the upper St. Lawrence and Great Lakes are open to 80% of the world's saltwater fleet.

Subsidiary Canadian canals or branches include the St. Peters Canal between Bras d'Or Lakes and the Atlantic Ocean in Nova Scotia; the St. Ours and Chambly Canals on the Richelieu River, Quebec; the Ste. Anne and Carillon Canals on the Ottawa River; the Rideau Canal between the Ottawa River and Lake Ontario, the Trent and Murray Canals between Lake Ontario and Georgian Bay in Ontario and the St. Andrew's Canal on the Red River. The commercial value of these canals is not great but they are maintained to control water levels and permit the passage of small vessels and pleasure craft. The Canso Canal, completed 1957, permits shipping to pass through the causeway connecting Cape Breton Island with the Nova Scotia mainland.

The 1976 Navigation season began on April 3 and ended when the last commercial vessel cleared the St. Lawrence Seaway system at St. Lambert Lock near Montreal on December 24. This marked the latest closing in the 18-year history of the waterway.

Cargo tonnage on the Montreal - Lake Ontario Section of the Seaway reached 54.4 million tons during 1976 — the second best tonnage year. Bulk cargo, totaling 49.9 million tons, was principally responsible for the overall increase. General cargo in 1976 rose 25% and accounted for 4.5 million tons.

St. Lawrence Seaway provides a navigational channel with a minimum water depth of 27 ft. to link the Great Lakes to the Atlantic Ocean. A vessel entering the Great Lakes from the Atlantic ascends 20 ft. above sea level in the 1,000-mile-long reach up the Gulf of St. Lawrence and St. Lawrence River to Montreal, Quebec. At Montreal, the vessel enters the first of 7 new locks, 5 of which are in Canadian waters and 2 within United States waters, which raise or lower shipping a total of 226 ft. in the 182-mile stretch of the St. Lawrence River between Montreal and Lake Ontario. Crossing Lake Ontario, the vessel enters Canada's 28-mile-long Welland Canal, with 8 locks to compensate for the difference in elevation of 326 ft. between Lake Ontario and Lake Erie.

The signing of the Merchant Marine Bill of 1970 removed the major obstacles to the future development of the St. Lawrence Seaway. The bill eliminated interest payments on the Seaway's debt, gave official "fourth seacoast" identity to the Great Lakes-St. Lawrence Waterway, and enabled lake shipbuilders to qualify for federal shipbuilding subsidies.

Addresses: St. Lawrence Seaway Development Corporation (U.S.), P.O. Box 520, Massena, N.Y., David W. Oberlin, Administrator, and St. Lawrence Seaway Authority (Canada), Ottawa, Ont., Mr. Paul D. Normandeau, president.

The Welland Canal overcomes the 326-ft. drop of Niagara Falls and the rapids of the Niagara River. It has 8 locks, each 859 ft. long, 80 ft. wide and 30 ft. deep. Regulations permit ships of 730-ft. length and 75-ft. beam to transit.

The Welland Section cargo tonnage totaled 64.3 million in comparison with 61.5 million tons for 1975. The principal commodities carried in the Welland Section in order of tonnage were: iron ore, wheat, coal, corn, manufactured iron and steel, and barley.

Sault Ste. Marie Canal reported 90,992,366 short tons of freight passed through during the season of 1976 compared with 88,829,075 for 1975.

Panama Canal

The Panama Canal is a lock and lake canal, crossing the Isthmus of Panama from the Caribbean Sea in a southeasterly direction to the Bay of Panama of the Pacific Ocean. It is 50 mi. long from deep water to deep water, at least 500 ft. wide at the bottom of excavated channels, 110 ft. wide in lock chambers, which have a usable length of 1,000 ft. Depth varies, but is not less than 40 ft. Time in transit is about 8 hours.

Gatun Dam blocks the Chagres River near its Atlantic mouth, creating Gatun Lake, 23 3/4 mi. long, 85 ft. above sea level, about 45 ft. deep. Ships ascend to the lake by locks and then pass through Gaillard (formerly Culebra) Cut, 8 mi. long.

Cargo tonnage on the Panama Canal in fiscal 1976 amounted to 117.4 million compared with 140.6 million tons in 1975. Transit of oceangoing ships in fiscal 1976 totaled 12,280 compared with 13,786 in fiscal 1975. Toll collections in fiscal 1976 were $135.0 million, $143.3 million in 1975.

Improvements have included the widening of the 8-mile long channel through Gaillard Cut from 300 to 500 ft., costing $60 million; illumination of Gaillard Cut and installation of new towing locomotives at the locks costing $8 million.

Thatcher Ferry Bridge, opened 1962, spans Panama Canal 201 ft. above the water level near Balboa. It is a steel-arch bridge, about one mi. long, with 3 spans and 4 lanes. It cost $20 million authorized by the U.S. Congress in 1956.

Other Foreign Canals

One of the busiest canals in Europe is the Gota, in Sweden, 115 mi. long. Others: Kiel Canal, Germany, connecting the Baltic with the North Sea, 61 mi.; Elbe, Germany, 41 mi.; Amsterdam, Netherlands, 16 mi. Also the Manchester Ship Canal, England, 35.5 mi.

U. S. Foreign Trade, by Economic Classes

Source: International Trade Analysis Div., U.S. Commerce Department (millions of dollars)

	Value of domestic exports					Value of imports				
Year	Crude mater'ls	Crude foods	Manu'd foods	Semi manuf's	Finish. manuf's	Crude mater'ls	Crude foods	Manu'd foods	Semi-manuf's	Finish. manuf's
1965.	2,887	2,587	1,590	4,114	16,008	3,709	2,008	1,877	4,964	8,871
1970.	4,492	2,748	1,921	6,866	26,563	4,126	2,579	3,519	7,263	22,464
1974.	11,150	10,246	4,196	14,913	56,638	19,995	3,720	6,810	22,067	48,380
1975.	10,883	11,804	4,221	12,815	66,434	23,568	3,642	5,972	17,323	46,435
1976.	11,850	11,420	4,764	13,969	71,365	32,080	5,225	6,277	20,495	57,716

Total agricultural exports were valued as follows (millions of dollars): 1965—1,942; 1968—2,177; 1969—2,057; 1970—2,524; 1971—2,884; 1972—3,325; 1973—5,290; 1974—6,981; 1975—5,747; 1976—6,765 Agricultural imports for consumption (millions of dollars): 1965—864; 1968—834; 1969—909; 1970—797; 1971—685; 1972—801; 1973—1,080; 1974—1,348; 1975—1,280; 1976—1,620.

Shortest Navigable Distances Between Ports

Source: Distances Between Ports, 1965. Defense Mapping Agency Hydrographic Center

Distances shown are in nautical miles (1,852 meters or about 6,076.115 feet).

To get statute miles, multiply by 1.15 (one statute mile equals 5280 feet).

TO / FROM	New York	Montreal	Colon[1]
Algiers, Algeria	3,617	3,600	4,745
Amsterdam, Netherlands	3,438	3,162	4,825
Baltimore, Md.	417	1,769	1,901
Barcelona, Spain	3,714	3,697	4,842
Boston, Mass.	386	1,308	2,157
Buenos Aires, Argentina	5,817	6,455	5,472
Cape Town, S. Africa[2]	6,786	7,118	6,494
Cherbourg, France	3,154	2,878	4,541
Cobh, Ireland	2,901	2,603	4,308
Copenhagen, Denmark	3,846	3,570	5,233
Dakar, Senegal	3,335	3,566	3,694
Galveston, Tex.	1,882	3,165	1,492
Gibraltar[3]	3,204	3,187	4,332
Glasgow, Scotland	3,086	2,691	4,508
Halifax, N.S.	600	895	2,295
Hamburg, W. Germany	3,674	3,398	5,061
Hamilton, Bermuda	697	1,572	1,659
Havana, Cuba	1,186	2,473	998
Helsinki, Finland	4,309	4,033	5,696
Istanbul, Turkey	5,001	4,984	6,129
Kingston, Jamaica	1,474	2,690	551
Lagos, Nigeria	4,883	5,130	5,049
Lisbon, Portugal	2,972	2,943	4,152
Marseille, France	3,891	3,874	5,019
Montreal, Quebec	1,460		3,126
Naples, Italy	4,181	4,164	5,309
Nassau, Bahamas	962	2,274	1,166
New Orleans, La.	1,708	2,991	1,389
New York, N.Y.		1,460	1,974
Norfolk, Va.	294	1,700	1,779
Oslo, Norway	3,827	3,165	5,053
Piraeus, Greece	4,688	4,671	5,816
Port Said, Egypt	5,123	5,106	6,251
Rio de Janeiro, Brazil	4,770	5,354	4,367
St. John's, Nfld.	1,093	1,043	2,695
San Juan, Puerto Rico	1,399	2,445	993
Southampton, England	3,189	2,913	4,576

TO / FROM	San. Fran.	Vancouver	Panama[1]
Acapulco, Mexico	1,833	2,613	1,426
Anchorage, Alas.	1,872	1,444	5,093
Bombay, India	9,794	9,578	12,962
Calcutta, India	8,991	8,728	12,154
Colon, Panama[1]	3,298	4,076	44
Jakarta, Indonesia	7,641	7,360	10,637
Haiphong, Vietnam	6,496	6,231	9,673
Hong Kong	6,044	5,777	9,195
Honolulu, Hawaii	2,091	2,423	4,685
Los Angeles, Cal.	371	1,161	2,913
Manila, Philippines	6,221	5,976	9,347
Melbourne, Australia	6,970	7,343	7,928
Pusan, S. Korea	4,914	4,623	8,074
Saigon, Vietnam	6,878	6,664	10,017
San Francisco, Cal.		812	3,245
Seattle, Wash.	807	126	4,020
Shanghai, China	5,396	5,110	8,566
Singapore	7,353	7,078	10,505
Suva, Fiji	4,749	5,183	6,325
Valparaiso, Chile	5,140	5,915	2,616
Vancouver, B.C.	812		4,032
Vladivostok, USSR	4,563	4,378	7,741
Yokohama, Japan	4,536	4,262	7,682

TO / FROM	Port Said	Cape Town[2]	Singapore
Bombay, India	3,049	4,616	2,441
Calcutta, India	4,695	5,638	1,649
Dar es Salaam, Tanzania	3,238	2,365	4,042
Jakarta, Indonesia	5,293	5,276	525
Hong Kong	6,462	7,006	1,454
Kuwait	3,360	5,176	3,833
Manila, Philippines	6,348	6,777	1,330
Melbourne, Australia	7,842	5,963	3,844
Saigon, Vietnam	5,667	6,263	649
Singapore	5,018	5,614	
Yokohama, Japan	7,907	8,503	2,889

(1) Colon on the Atlantic is 44 nautical miles from Panama (port) on the Pacific. (2) Cape Town is 35 nautical miles northwest of the Cape of Good Hope. (3) Gibraltar (port) is 24 nautical miles east of the Strait of Gibraltar.

Mississippi River System and Gulf Intracoastal Waterway

Source: Corps of Engineers, Department of the Army.

Note—The Mississippi River System comprises main channels and all tributaries of the Mississippi, Illinois, Missouri, and Ohio rivers. The Gulf Intracoastal Waterway, 1,137 miles long, extends from Apalachee Bay, Florida, to the Mexican border.

Freight moved

Port	1971 Tonnage	1974 Tonnage	1975 Tonnage
Minneapolis	825,429	2,528,968	3,177,355
St. Paul	4,210,106	5,143,251	4,925,554
Metropolitan St. Louis*		21,662,116	23,082,359
Memphis	7,024,509	11,096,770	11,648,641
Helena	1,740,938	3,238,699	2,783,445
Greenville	1,250,608	2,427,011	2,783,043
Lake Providence		375,257	320,055
Vicksburg	1,258,508	2,854,131	2,525,399
Natchez	582,942	1,162,865	759,479
Baton Rouge	30,272,282	59,126,282	60,225,734
New Orleans	79,130,710	144,189,409	140,409,268

*Port limits expanded in 1972

Reach	1971 Tonnage	1974 Tonnage	1975 Tonnage
Mississippi R. System	271,319,518	442,844,560	453,412,723
Minneapolis to the Gulf	157,807,291	302,589,614	311,239,484
Minneapolis to St. Louis	30,943,237	62,013,644	63,238,667
St. Louis to Cairo	35,726,911	69,995,050	71,623,162
Cairo to Baton Rouge	49,370,417	111,381,795	108,926,777
Baton Rouge to New Orleans	69,913,376	185,988,142	201,600,768
New Orleans to the Gulf	99,554,315	193,370,192	203,134,329
Gulf Intracoastal Waterway	67,320,002	103,076,142	96,950,849

Ton-Mileage of Freight Carried on Inland Waterways

Source: Corps of Engineers, Department of the Army

System	1971	1974	1975
Atlantic coast waterways	28,619,707,000	35,391,955,000	31,849,833,000
Gulf coast waterways	30,473,095,000	33,510,277,000	30,777,423,000
Pacific coast waterways	8,525,013,000	10,253,815,000	9,698,501,000
Mississippi River system, including Ohio River and tributaries	142,385,476,000	168,274,841,000	170,712,931,000
Great Lakes System, U.S. Commerce	105,027,016,000	107,450,897,000	99,171,007,000
Total	**315,030,307,000**	**354,881,785,000**	**342,209,695,000**

Commerce at Principal North American Ports

Source: Corps of Engineers, Department of the Army; Statistics Canada

U.S. data 1975; Canadian data 1976 (short tons)
Excluding Great Lakes shipping

Major Ports

Port of New York, N.Y. & N.J.	177,814,618
New Orleans, La.	140,409,268
Houston, Tex.	83,674,039
Baton Rouge, La.	60,225,734
Baltimore Hbr. and channels, Md.	52,661,448
Philadelphia Hbr., Pa.	52,029,803
Norfolk Hbr., Va.	49,742,717
Tampa Hbr., Fla.	39,857,660
Corpus Christi, Tex.	35,487,454
Mobile Hbr., Ala.	32,452,912
Los Angeles Hbr., Cal.	30,746,362
Beaumont, Tex.	30,582,512
Portland Hbr., Me.	27,565,807
Paulsboro, N.J. and vicinity	27,132,019
Port Arthur, Tex.	26,597,557
Long Beach, Cal.	26,587,134
Boston, Mass.	24,719,452
Marcus Hook, Pa. and vicinity	24,395,291
Texas City, Tex.	23,863,770
Port of metropolitan St. Louis	23,082,359
Pascagoula Hbr., Miss.	19,950,992
Portland, Ore.	19,600,466
Lake Charles, La.	17,462,574
Port of Newport News, Va.	17,258,771
Seattle Hbr., Wash.	15,008,395
Richmond Hbr., Cal.	14,358,284
Huntington, W. Va.	13,625,926
Jacksonville Hbr., Fla.	13,495,764
Memphis, Tenn.	11,648,641
New Haven Hbr., Conn.	11,432,920
New Castle, Del. and vicinity	11,224,013
Port Everglades Hbr., Fla.	10,552,161
Clairton-Elizabeth, Pa.	10,291,182
Cincinnati, Oh.	9,437,973
Port of Albany, N.Y.	9,260,233
Pittsburgh, Pa.	8,771,080
Penn Manor, Pa. and vicinity	8,639,482
Charleston Hbr., S.C.	8,379,831
Louisville, Ky.	8,290,993
Providence River and Hbr., R.I.	8,266,295
Freeport Hbr., Tex.	8,194,136
Tacoma Hbr., Wash.	7,897,699
Camden-Gloucester, N.J.	7,803,177
Savannah Hbr., Ga.	7,593,297

Other U.S. Ports

Longview, Wash.	7,380,419
Port of Wilmington, N.C.	7,372,232
El Segundo, Cal.	7,043,051
Coos, Bay, Ore.	6,376,127
Harbor Island, Tex.	6,348,824
Oakland Hbr., Cal.	6,186,033
Galveston, Tex.	5,971,160
Aliquippa-Rochester, Pa.	5,640,986
St. Paul, Minn.	4,925,554
Anacortes Hbr., Wash.	4,851,539
Fall River, Hbr., Mass.	4,834,393
Everett Hbr., Wash.	4,366,723
Port Jefferson Hbr., N.Y.	4,346,392
Matagorda Ship Channel, Port Lavaca, Tex.	4,342,515
Mount Vernon, Ind.	3,684,005
Miami Hbr., Fla.	3,585,001
New London Hbr., Conn.	3,480,918
Vancouver, Wash.	3,466,913
Astoria, Ore.	3,233,588
Wilmington Hbr., Del.	3,226,559
Minneapolis, Minn.	3,177,355
Victoria, Tex.	3,030,897
Portsmouth Hbr., N.H.	2,943,343
Canaveral Hbr., Fla.	2,937,221
Nashville, Tenn.	2,894,514
Bridgeport Hbr., Conn.	2,860,171
Brownsville, Tex.	2,829,009
Helena, Ark.	2,783,445
Greenville, Miss.	2,783,043
Port Angeles Hbr., Wash.	2,726,513
Grays Hbr. and Chehalis River, Wash.	2,587,183
Vicksburg, Miss.	2,525,399
San Francisco Hbr., Cal.	2,497,188
San Diego Hbr., Cal.	2,351,306
Hempstead Hbr., N.Y.	2,298,906
Pensacola Hbr., Fla.	2,262,084
Charlotte Hbr., Fla.	2,259,601
Salem Hbr., Mass.	1,936,086
Bellingham Bay and Hbr., Wash.	1,883,484
Stockton, Cal.	1,856,470
Ventura Hbr., Cal.	1,685,404
Kansas City, Mo.	1,651,918
Panama City Hbr., Fla.	1,616,293
Chattanooga, Tenn.	1,590,922
Morehead City Hbr., N.C.	1,522,208
Port of Richmond, Va.	1,519,899
Brunswick Hbr., Ga.	1,430,354
Washington Hbr., D.C.	1,405,513
Searsport Hbr., Me.	1,365,860
Georgetown Hbr., S.C.	1,359,697
Humboldt Hbr. and Bay, Cal.	1,357,544
Trenton Hbr., N.J.	1,242,500
Port of Hopewell, Va.	1,233,679
San Luis Obispo Hbr., Cal.	1,159,907
Hammersley Inlet (Shelton Hbr.), Wash.	1,115,658
Port Townsend Hbr., Wash.	1,106,892
Guntersville, Ala.	1,047,552
Palm Beach Hbr., Fla.	1,022,628
Gulfport Hbr., Miss.	922,379
Orange, Tex.	912,014
Norwalk Hbr., Conn.	847,490
Stamford Hbr., Conn.	846,148
Natchez, Miss.	759,479
Moss Landing Hbr., Cal.	747,518
Sabine Pass Hbr., Tex.	513,062
Rondout Hbr., N.Y.	511,037
Tarrytown Hbr., N.Y.	492,129
Port Gamble Hbr., Wash.	482,499
Chester, Pa.	471,184
Port St. Joe Hbr., Fla.	463,062
Olympia Hbr., Wash.	459,047
Weedon Island, Fla.	448,467
Burlington Hbr., Vt.	429,932
Redwood City Hbr., Cal.	429,211
Plattsburgh, N.Y.	427,309
Carpinteria, Cal.	392,160
Oregon Slough (North Portland Hbr.), Ore.	362,504
New Bedford, Fairhaven Hbr., Mass.	361,026
Fernandina Hbr., Fla.	354,344
St. Petersburg Hbr., Fla.	331,994
Knoxville, Tenn.	310,956
Port Chester Hbr., N.Y.	289,248
Port Isabel, Tex.	255,938
Huntington Hbr., N.Y.	242,122
Crescent City Hbr., Cal.	228,792
Beverly Hbr., Mass.	222,470
Ellwood, Cal.	211,127
Gloucester Hbr., Mass.	188,173
Alexandria, Va.	143,886
Peekskill Hbr., N.Y.	134,578
Willapa River and Hbr., Naselle River, Wash.	99,112
Port of St. Helens, Ore.	68,560
Gaviota, Santa Barbara County, Cal.	43,254

Alaska, Hawaii, Puerto Rico, Canada

Sept-Isles, Que.	26,305,716
Vancouver, B.C.	24,929,971
Thunder Bay, Ont.	20,027,820
Montreal, Que.	18,632,938
Port Cartier, Que.	17,627,889
Hamilton, Ont.	14,270,367
Quebec, Que. (includes St. Romuald)	12,496,009
Halifax, N.S.	11,742,732
Saint John, N.B. (1975)	10,850,676
Roberts Bank, B.C.	10,591,348
San Juan Hbr., P.R.	10,522,051
Sarnia, Ont.	9,090,425
Honolulu, Hbr., Oahu, Ha.	7,935,183
Port Hawkesbury, N.S.	7,718,427
Barbers Point, Oahu, Ha.	5,185,659
Anchorage, Alas.	2,936,159
Ketchikan Hbr., Alas.	1,562,507
Skagway Hbr., Alas.	1,416,177
Kahului Hbr., Maui, Ha.	1,109,485
Hilo Hbr., Hawaii, Ha.	1,053,879
Wrangell Hbr., Alas.	956,170
Whittier Hbr., Alas.	667,112
Ponce Hbr., P.R.	566,400
Nawiliwili Hbr., Kauai, Ha.	532,978
Sitka Hbr., Alas.	387,510
Kaunakakai Hbr., Molokai, Ha.	371,340
St. Thomas Hbr., V.I.	350,834
Iliuliuk Hbr., Alas.	300,953
Mayaguez Hbr., P.R.	292,635
Kawaihae Hbr., Hawaii, Ha.	279,687
Pearl Hbr., Oahu, Ha.	276,319
Kaumalapau Hbr., Lanai, Ha.	261,095
Guam	181,537
Guanica Hbr., P.R.	179,687
Juneau Hbr., Alas.	149,160

Commerce at Great Lakes Ports

Source: Corps of Engineers, Department of the Army

Calendar Year 1975 (short tons)

Port of Chicago, Ill.	42,589,058
Duluth - Superior Hbr., Minn. & Wis.	33,607,024
Port of Detroit, Mich.	26,487,866
Toledo Hbr., Oh.	23,628,827
Conneaut Hbr., Oh.	19,192,311
Cleveland Hbr., Oh.	18,145,180
Indiana Hbr., Ind.	17,126,086
Taconite Hbr., Minn.	11,900,507
Calcite, Mich.	11,645,917
Escanaba, Mich.	10,876,331
Silver Bay, Minn.	10,353,673
Gary Hbr., Ind.	9,812,754
Ashtabula Hbr., Oh.	8,738,094
Stoneport, Mich.	8,533,242
Lorain Hbr., Oh.	7,650,341
Port of Buffalo, NY	7,614,212
Sandusky Hbr., Oh.	4,532,500
Presque Isle Hbr., Mich.	3,846,960
Port Dolomite, Mich.	3,608,490
Milwaukee Hbr., Wis.	3,508,683
Port Inland, Mich.	3,248,529
Fairport Hbr., Oh.	3,020,122
Alpena Hbr., Mich.	2,855,580
St. Clair, Mich.	2,686,497
Green Bay Hbr., Wis.	2,608,177
Drummond Island, Mich.	2,341,074
Ludington Hbr., Mich.	2,123,507
Huron Hbr., Oh.	2,115,680
Buffington Hbr., Ind.	1,947,958
Muskegon Hbr., Mich.	1,945,311
Marblehead, Oh.	1,461,055
Marquette Hbr., Mich.	1,233,323
Erie Hbr., Pa.	1,218,153
Good Haven Hbr. & Good River, Mich.	1,138,133
Kewaunee Hbr., Wis.	1,084,288
Port Washington Hbr., Wis.	876,913
Oswego Hbr., NY	847,987
Manitowoc Hbr., Wis.	653,503
Frankfort Hbr., Mich.	644,659
Marysville, Mich.	559,728
Petoskey Penn Dixie Hbr., Mich.	468,960
Port Gypsum, Mich.	382,132
Traverse City Hbr., Mich.	364,777
Waukegan Hbr., Ill.	341,781
Holland Hbr., Mich.	338,089
Ashland Hbr., Wis.	333,555
Sheboygan Hbr., Wis.	302,887
St. Joseph Hbr., Mich.	244,963
Ogdensburg Hbr., NY	235,448
Oak Creek, Wis.	226,340
Rochester (Charlotte) Hbr., NY	225,861
Manistee Hbr., Mich.	220,002
Alabaster, Mich.	217,120
Port Huron, Mich.	213,613
Gladstone Hbr., Mich.	194,084
Wells, Mich.	123,720
Menominee Hbr., Mich. & Wis.	118,116
St. Ignace, Mich.	112,845
Mackinaw City, Mich.	98,441
Sault Ste. Marie, Mich.	86,224
Detour, Mich.	78,904
Racine Hbr., Wis.	77,337
Cheboygan Hbr., Mich.	69,432
Lime Island, Mich.	56,391
Two Rivers Hbr., Wis.	6,378
Manistique Hbr., Mich.	144
Michigan City Hbr., Ind.	89

Total Exports and Exports Financed by Foreign Aid

Source: Bureau of International Commerce, U.S. Commerce Department

(millions of dollars)	1965	1970	1972	1973	1974	1975	1976
Exports, total	27,530	43,224	49,778	71,314	98,506	107,652	114,997
Agricultural commodities	6,306	7,349	9,505	17,855	22,257	22,097	23,274
Nonagricultural commodities	20,445	35,310	39,714	52,943	75,650	85,094	91,533
Manufactured goods (domestic)	17,439	29,343	33,742	44,702	63,527	71,005	77,245
Military grant—aid	779	565	560	516	599	461	190
Export financed under P.L. 480	1,323	1,021	1,064	750	760	1,181	NA
Sales for foreign currency	899	276	70	4	—	—	—
Donations, including disaster relief	253	255	376	209	272	257	NA
Barter for strategic goods	19	—	—	—	—	—	—
Long-term dollar credit sales	152	490	618	537	488	924	NA

Value of Principal Agricultural Exports

(millions of dollars)	Avg. 1961-1965	Avg. 1966-1970	1965	1970	1974	1975	1976
Bread grains & preparations	1,268	1,197	1,214	1,144	4,678	5,292	4,041
Coarse grains, except rice	841	1,082	1,162	1,099	4,727	5,492	6,241
Rice	178	311	244	314	853	858	629
Fodders and feeds	179	386	278	496	1,287	987	1,358
Vegetable oils, oilseeds, etc.	774	1,182	1,029	1,642	4,865	NA	NA
Cotton, unmanufactured	639	408	495	377	1,353	991	1,049

Value of U.S. Merchandise Exports and Imports

Source: International Trade Analysis Division, U.S. Commerce Department

(millions of dollars)

Year	U.S. exports					U.S. imports		
	Total	Domestic and foreign: Military aid	Domestic and foreign: Excl. military aid	Domestic merchandise	Foreign merchandise	General	For consumption	Gross merchandise balance[1]
1950	10,279	[2]282	9,997	10,146	133	8,954	8,844	1,043
1955	15,554	1,256	14,298	15,426	128	11,566	11,519	2,732
1960	20,608	949	19,659	20,408	201	15,073	15,069	4,586
1965	27,521	779	26,742	27,178	343	21,427	21,345	5,315
1970	43,224	565	42,659	42,590	634	39,952	39,756	2,707
1973	71,314	516	70,798	70,223	1,091	69,121	68,656	1,347
1974	98,506	599	97,907	97,143	1,363	100,972	99,391	−3,065
1975	107,592	462	107,130	106,102	1,489	96,116	95,704	11,014
1976	114,997	190	114,807	113,323	1,674	120,677	120,014	—5,870

(1) Balance represents exports excluding military grant-aid valued f.a.s. less imports which are valued generally at the market value in the foreign country. Export values include both commercially-financed shipments and shipments under government-financed programs. (2) Includes data from April when shipments under the program began.

Merchant Fleets of the World

Source: Maritime Administration, U.S. Dept. of Commerce

Oceangoing steam and motor ships of 1,000 gross tons and over as of June 30, 1976; excludes ships operating exclusively on the Great Lakes and inland waterways and special types such as channel ships, icebreakers, cable ships, etc., and merchant ships owned by any military force.

Tonnage is in thousands. Gross tonnage is a volume measurement; each cargo gross ton represents 100 cubic ft. of enclosed space. Deadweight tonnage is the carrying capacity of a ship in long tons (2,240 lbs.).

Country of registry	Total no.	Gross tons	Dwt. tons	Bulk carriers		Freighters		Tankers	
				No.	Dwt.	No.	Dwt.	No.	Dwt.
Total - All Countries	23,134	343,996	578,749	4,397	155,129	11,622	95,875	5,349	318,705
United States [1]	843	12,407	17,989	18	529	497	6,957	263	10,086
Privately owned	577	10,291	15,455	18	529	304	4,978	249	9,898
Government owned	266	2,116	2,534	-	-	193	1,979	14	188
British Commonwealth									
United Kingdom	1,552	32,853	54,812	341	14,609	616	5,890	442	32,763
Australia	87	1,114	1,646	34	849	37	343	16	454
Bangladesh	16	83	122	-	-	14	118	2	4
British colonies	98	1,821	3,088	30	988	32	201	27	1,883
Canada	68	378	523	11	176	22	82	25	253
Cyprus	565	3,179	4,667	48	613	455	3,155	45	831
Ghana	19	127	166	-	-	18	163	-	-
India	321	4,620	7,386	80	3,316	199	2,273	30	1,719
Malaysia	31	395	575	8	344	17	136	4	91
New Zealand	30	131	180	9	31	16	68	2	51
Nigeria	20	135	191	1	16	19	175	-	-
Pakistan	53	471	630	2	31	43	514	1	27
Singapore	429	5,150	8,671	48	1,754	267	2,028	82	4,740
Algeria	31	348	567	3	36	18	87	10	444
Argentina	158	1,342	1,869	15	298	67	605	50	821
Belgium	78	1,332	2,136	23	1,066	29	385	18	633
Brazil	266	2,896	4,648	36	1,325	161	1,268	55	1,994
Bulgaria	115	880	1,323	29	384	57	365	20	532
Chile	46	411	623	7	156	30	295	6	160
China (Taiwan)	155	1,466	2,251	32	819	92	718	13	614
*China (People's Rep.)	388	3,032	4,436	48	858	254	2,323	49	1,104
Colombia	35	204	269	1	2	33	237	1	30
*Cuba	67	448	615	4	35	44	466	7	76
Czechoslovakia	13	144	214	5	160	8	54	-	-
Denmark	351	4,922	8,053	43	1,169	221	1,725	65	5,061
Ecuador	19	164	247	-	-	6	53	11	181
Egypt	62	321	449	-	-	41	188	12	215
Finland	189	1,886	2,986	18	323	101	587	52	2,031
France	449	10,962	19,016	57	2,436	195	1,989	155	14,371
Gabon	5	106	183	1	15	3	28	1	140
Germany (West)	616	8,331	13,485	78	3,977	414	3,576	84	5,640
*Germany (East)	152	1,275	1,744	18	369	106	771	12	514
Greece	1,816	23,088	38,736	500	13,819	887	8,498	334	15,991
Indonesia	174	661	848	11	65	113	558	20	131
Iran	46	640	1,052	-	-	37	470	9	582
Iraq	21	543	1,002	-	-	8	85	13	917
Ireland	17	164	247	9	229	5	11	3	7
Israel	52	467	605	9	277	35	252	-	-
Italy	636	10,621	17,256	152	6,663	175	1,312	241	9,005
Ivory Coast	16	122	164	-	-	14	153	-	-
Japan	2,079	38,609	65,557	560	22,383	859	7,069	541	35,670
Korea (South)	169	1,337	2,236	26	388	107	673	32	1,160
Kuwait	43	1,053	1,803	1	9	33	491	8	1,294
Lebanon	49	165	215	4	10	40	187	-	-
Liberia	2,609	74,170	141,172	961	38,486	551	5,741	1,031	96,533
Libya	11	378	702	-	-	3	9	8	693
Maldives	39	113	148	1	6	34	133	-	-
Mexico	48	464	692	3	61	17	143	27	484
Morocco	26	106	157	2	50	12	54	3	17
Netherlands	453	5,350	8,355	35	919	305	2,411	83	4,901
Norway	991	27,861	49,302	316	17,011	293	2,480	332	29,628
Panama	1,585	14,195	22,969	242	5,042	1,031	7,192	230	10,363
Peru	42	370	556	9	217	27	257	5	77
Philippines	156	854	1,268	6	119	94	601	30	489
Poland	296	2,915	4,378	77	1,740	184	1,539	14	1,005
Portugal	102	1,079	1,609	6	125	61	472	23	931
*Romania	98	812	1,224	18	397	67	370	7	433
Saudi Arabia	30	315	539	-	-	17	89	6	434
Somalia	245	1,817	2,658	30	601	194	1,720	15	306
South Africa	53	440	558	4	88	38	316	3	61
Spain	458	5,199	8,850	63	1,946	221	1,063	115	5,645
Sweden	319	7,322	12,409	85	4,564	126	1,145	80	6,459
Switzerland	26	245	364	5	172	17	182	2	7
Thailand	28	149	244	1	2	17	90	10	152
Turkey	108	884	1,231	10	268	60	473	23	518
Uruguay	17	156	240	-	-	8	47	7	180
*U.S.S.R. [2]	2,420	14,576	18,678	150	1,768	1,440	9,199	470	6,095
Venezuela	44	433	612	3	16	24	172	16	415
Vietnam	21	80	118	1	3	17	72	3	43
Yugoslavia	227	1,865	2,713	37	888	158	1,369	17	382
Zaire	11	106	152	-	-	9	127	-	-

*Source material limited. (1) Excludes 34 non-merchant type ships which are currently in the National Defense Reserve Fleet. (2) Includes U.S. government-owned ships transferred to USSR under lend-lease agreements, 38 of which are still under that registry and 2 under North Korean registry.

Notable Ocean Passages by Ships

Time	From	To	Distance Naut. mi.	Date	Ship
Sailing Vessels					
16d	Liverpool	New York	3,150	Nov. 1846	Yorkshire
76d 6h	San Francisco	Boston	...	1853	Northern Light
12d 6h	Boston Light	Light Rock	...	1854	James Baines
89d	New York	San Francisco	15,091	1854	Flying Cloud
89d 20h	New York	San Francisco	13,700	1860	Andrew Jackson
63d 18h 15m	Liverpool	Melbourne	...	1868-69	Thermopylae
13d 1h 25m	New York	Liverpool	3,150	...	Red Jacket
36d	50 S. Lat.	Golden Gate	...	...	Starr King
12d 12h	Equator	San Francisco	...	...	Golden Fleece
12d 4h 1m	Sandy Hook	England	3,013	1905	Atlantic
23d	England	Sandy Hook	3,013	1928	Atlantic
22d 6h 7m	Bishop's Rock	Boston Light	...	1936	Yankee
Atlantic Crossings by Power Vessels					
29d 4h	Savannah	Liverpool	...	May 22, 1819	Savannah (Amer.) (a)
15d	Bristol	New York	...	Apr. 1838	Great Western (Br.)
14d 8h	Liverpool	New York	3,150	July 1840	Britannia (Br.) (b)
9d 13h	Liverpool	New York	3,054	Aug. 1852	Baltic (Amer.)
8d 1h 45m	Queenstown	New York	2,780	1856	Persia
8d 2h 48m	Queenstown	New York	2,780	1866	Scotia
7d 4h 1m	Queenstown	New York	...	1867	City of Paris (Br.)
7d 22h 3m	Queenstown	New York	2,780	1869	City of Brussels (Br.)
7d 20h 9m	Queenstown	New York	2,780	1873	Baltic (Br.)
7d 15h 48m	Queenstown	New York	2,780	1875	City of Berlin (Br.)
7d 11h 37m	Queenstown	New York	2,780	1876	Germanic (Br.)
7d 10h 53m	Queenstown	New York	2,780	1877	Britannic (Br.)
7d 8h 0m	New York	Queenstown	...	1879	Arizona (Br.)
6d 7h 23m	Queenstown	New York	2,780	1880	Arizona (Br.)
6d 18h 37m	New York	Queenstown	2,780	1882	Alaska (Br.)
6d 21h 40m	Queenstown	New York	2,780	1883	Alaska (Br.)
6d 10h 40m	New York	Queenstown	2,780	1884	Oregon (Br.)
6d 4h 34m	Queenstown	New York	2,780	1887	Umbria (Br.)
5d 1h 55m	Queenstown	New York	2,780	1888	Etruria (Br.)
5d 22h 50m	New York	Queenstown	2,780	1889	City of Paris (Br.)
5d 16h 31m	Queenstown	New York	2,780	1891	Teutonic (Br.)
5d 14h 24m	Queenstown	New York	2,780	1892	City of Paris (Br.)
5d 9h 6m	Queenstown	New York	2,780	1893	Campania (Br.)
5d 7h 23m	Queenstown	New York	2,780	1894	Lucania (Br.)
5d 15h 20m	Southampton	New York	3,189	1898	Kaiser Wilhelm Der Grosse (Ger.)
5d 7h 38m	Sandy Hook	Plymouth	3,082	Sept. 1900	Deutschland (Ger.)
4d 11h 42m	Queenstown	New York	2,780	1909	Lusitania (Br.)
4d 10h 41m	Queenstown	New York	2,780	1910	Mauretania (Br.)
5d 6h 21m	New York	Cherbourg	3,227	Oct. 1924	Leviathan (Amer.)
4d 17h 42m	Cherbourg	Ambrose Lt.	3,164	July 1929	Bremen (Ger.)*
4d 14h 30m	New York	Plymouth	3,082	July 1929	Bremen (Ger.)
4d 19h 57m	Ambrose Lt.	Cherbourg	3,196	June 1933	Europa (Ger.)
4d 16h 48m	Cherbourg	New York	3,149	July 1933	Europa (Ger.)
4d 13h 58m	Gibraltar	Ambrose Lt.	3,181	Aug. 1933	Rex (Ital.)
4d 14h 27m	Cherbourg	Ambrose Lt.	3,092	Nov. 1934	Bremen (Ger.)
4d 12h 24m	Cherbourg	Ambrose Lt.	3,158	May-June, 1936	Queen Mary (Br.)*
3d 23h 02m	Bishop's Rock	Ambrose Lt.	2,906	July-Aug., 1937	Normandie (Fr.)
3d 22h 07m	New York	Southampton	2,936	Aug. 1937	Normandie (Fr.)
3d 20h 42m	Ambrose Lt.	Bishop's Rock	3,120	Aug. 10-14, 1938	Queen Mary (Br.)
3d 21h 48m	Bishop's Rock	Ambrose Lt.	3,120	Aug. 3-8, 1948	Queen Mary (Br.)
3d 10h 40m	Ambrose Lt.	Bishop's Rock	2,942	July 3-7, 1952	United States (U.S.)* (e)
3d 12h 12m	Bishop's Rock	Ambrose Lt.	2,902	July 11-14, 1952	United States (U.S.) (e)
3d 11h 24m	Bishop's Rock	Ambrose Lt.	2,912	Aug. 20, 1973	Sea-Land Exchange (U.S.) (j)
Other Ocean Passages					
3d 00h 36m	San Pedro	Honolulu	2,226	June 1928	U.S.S. Lexington
86d	Halifax	Vancouver	7,295	July-Sept. 1944	St. Roch (Can.) (c)
3d 2h 30m	San Francisco	Oahu, Hawaii	2,091	July 16-19, 1945	U.S.S. Indianapolis (d)
4d 8h 51m	Gibraltar	Newport News	3,360	Nov. 26, 1945	U.S.S. Lake Champlain
7d 18h 36m	Japan	San Francisco	5,000	July-Aug. 4, 1950	U.S.S. Boxer
7d 13h	Yokosuka	Alameda	5,000	June 1-9, 1951	U.S.S. Philippine Sea
8d 11h	Nantucket	Portland, Eng.	3,161	Feb. 25-Mar. 4, '58	U.S.S. Skate (f)
7d 5h	Lizard Head	Nantucket, Mass.	...	Mar. 23-29, 1958	U.S.S. Skate (f)
15d	Pearl Harbor	Iceland (via N. Pole)	...	July 23-Aug. 7, '58	U.S.S. Nautilus (g)
84d	New London	Rehoboth, Del.	41,500	Feb. 16-May 10, '60	U.S.S. Triton (h)
6d	Baffin Bay	NW Passage, Pac	850	Aug. 15-20, 1960	U.S.S. Seadragon (i)
12d 16h 22m	New York	Cape Town	6,786	Oct. 30-Nov. 11, '62	African Comet*
5d 6h	Kobe	Race Rock, B.C.	4,126	Aug. 24, 1973	Sea-Land Trade (U.S.)

*Maiden voyage. (a) The Savannah, a fully rigged sailing vessel with steam auxiliary (over 300 tons, 98.5 ft. long, beam 25.8 ft., depth 12.9 ft.) was launched in the East River in 1818. It was the first ship to use steam in crossing any ocean. It was supplied with engines and detachable iron paddle wheels. On its famous voyage it used steam 105 hours. (b) First Cunard liner. (c) First ship to complete NW Passage in one season. (d) Carried Hiroshima atomic bomb in World War II. (e) Set world speed record; average speed eastbound on maiden voyage 35.59 knots (about 41 m.p.h.): westbound, 34.51 knots. (f) First atomic submarine to cross Atlantic both ways submerged. (g) World's first atomic submarine also first to make undersea voyage under polar ice cap, 1,830 mi. from Point Barrow, Alaska, to Atlantic Ocean, Aug. 1-4, 1958, reaching North Pole Aug. 3. Second undersea transit of the North Pole made by submarine USS Skate Aug. 11, 1958, during trip from New London, Conn., and return. (h) World's largest submarine. Nuclear-powered Triton was submerged during nearly all its voyage around the globe. It duplicated the route of Ferdinand Magellan's circuit (1519-1522) 30,708 mi., starting from St. Paul Rocks off the NE coast of Brazil, Feb. 24-Apr. 25, 1960, then sailed to Cadiz, Spain, before returning home. (i) First underwater transit of Northwest Passage. (j) Fastest freighter crossing of Atlantic.

Fastest Scheduled Train Runs in U.S. and Canada

Source: Donald M. Steffee; figures are based on 1977 timetables

Electric Traction-Passenger-(81 mph and over)

Railroad	Train	From	To	Dis.	Time	Speed
Amtrak	Metroliners(7)	Baltimore	Wilmington	68.4	44	93.3
Amtrak	Metroliners(4)	Wilmington	Baltimore	68.4	44	93.3
Amtrak	Metroliners(6)	Wilmington	Baltimore	68.4	45	91.2
Amtrak	Metroliners(5)	Baltimore	Wilmington	68.4	45	91.2
Amtrak	Metroliner	No. Philadelphia	Metro Park	61.9	41	90.6
Amtrak	Metroliners(2)	Wilmington	Baltimore	68.4	46	89.2
Amtrak	Metroliner	Newark	Trenton	48.1	34	84.9
Amtrak	Metroliner	Metro Park	Trenton	33.9	24	84.7
Amtrak	Metroliner	Metro Park	Philadelphia	66.3	47	84.6
Amtrak	Metroliner	Baltimore	Philadelphia	94.0	67	84.2
Amtrak	Metroliners(3)	Newark	Philadelphia	80.5	58	83.3
Amtrak	Metroliners(3)	Metro Park	Philadelphia	66.3	48	82.9
Amtrak	Metroliners(2)	Trenton	Newark	48.1	35	82.4
Amtrak	Metroliners(5)	Philadelphia	Newark	80.5	59	81.9
Amtrak	Metroliner	Newark	Philadelphia	80.5	59	81.9
Amtrak	Metroliner	Philadelphia	Baltimore	94.0	69	81.7
Amtrak	Metroliner	Trenton	Metro Park	33.9	25	81.3
Amtrak	Metroliner	Philadelphia	Metro Park	66.3	49	81.2
Amtrak	Metroliner	New York	Trenton	58.1	43	81.1
Diesel Traction—Passenger—(75 mph and over)						
Canadian National	Turbotrain	Kingston	Guildwood	145.1	102	85.4
Canadian National	Turbotrains(2)	Kingston	Dorval	165.8	120	82.9
Canadian National	Turbotrains(2)	Dorval	Kingston	165.8	121	82.2
Canadian National	Turbotrain	Guildwood	Kingston	145.1	106	82.1
Amtrak	Southwest Limited	Garden City	Lamar	99.9	73	82.1
Canadian National	Turbotrain	Kingston	Guildwood	145.1	107	81.4
Amtrak	Southwest Limited	Dodge City	Hutchinson	120.1	90	80.1
Canadian National	Turbotrain	Guildwood	Kingston	145.1	111	78.4
Amtrak	Lone Star	Marceline	Carrollton	39.1	30	78.2
Amtrak	Southwest Limited	Lamar	Garden City	99.9	77	77.8
Canadian National	Rapidos(2)	Dorval	Kingston	165.8	128	77.7
Canadian National	Rapidos(2)	Guildwood	Kingston	145.1	113	77.0
Amtrak	San Francisco Zephyr	Denver	Fort Morgan	78.0	62	75.5
Amtrak	San Francisco Zephyr	Akron	McCook	143.0	114	75.3
Diesel Traction—Freight—(62 mph and over)						
Sante Fe	No. 991	Seligman	Kingman	88.1	80	66.1
Union Pacific	BASV	North Platte	Cheyenne	225.4	205	66.0
Union Pacific	Super Van	North Platte	Cheyenne	225.4	215	62.9
Sante Fe	Five trains	Winslow	Gallup	125.8	120	62.9
Sante Fe	Two trains	Winslow	Gallup	125.8	120	62.9
Sante Fe	No. 199	Kingman	Seligman	88.1	85	62.2

Fastest Scheduled Passenger Train Runs in Japan and European Countries

Country	Train	From	To	Dis.	Time	Speed
Japan	Hikari Train	Nagoya	Shizouka	108.2	59	110.0
Great Britain	High Speed Trains (4)	Swindon	Reading	41.3	24	103.2
France	Etendard	St. Pierre des Corps	Poitiers	62.7	37	101.5
West Germany	Nymphenburg	Dortmund	Bielefeld	61.0	41	89.3
Russia	Aurora	Moscow	Bologoe	205.5	147	83.9
Italy	Three Trains	Rome	Naples	130.3	95	82.3
	Two trains	Naples	Rome	130.3	95	82.3
Sweden	No. 121	Hallsberg	Skovde	70.8	56	75.9
	No. 130	Skovde	Hallsberg	70.8	56	75.9

Japanese Hikari Trains Average over 100 mph Including Intermediate Stops

On the standard-gauged Shinkanson Line, 107 daily Hikari express trains make the 320.1 mile run between Tokyo and Osaka, including stops at Nagoya and Kyoto, in 3 hr. 10 min. at an average overall speed of 101.1 mph. With the extension of the line to Hakata in March, 1975, the runs of many Hikari trains were extended to provide service over the new line. Fastest time for the 663.9 mile run between Tokyo and Hakata is 6 hr. 56 min. — at 95.8 mph including six stops.

British High Speed Trains Average 90 to over 100 mph on Short Runs

The new HST trains placed in service on the Western Region of British Rail have revolutionized service between London and Bristol and to South Wales. The schedules call for some remarkably high speeds for short distances. Among these is London-Reading, 35.9 miles in 22 minutes — at 97.8 mph and Swindon to Didcot, 24.2 miles in 15 minutes at 96.8 mph. This last is the world's fastest for a distance of less than 25 miles between station stops.

Paris to Bordeaux at 93.9 mph

As result of upgrading the entire Paris-Bordeaux mainline (359.8 miles) to 125 mph standards, French National Railways has cut the nonstop time between these cities to 3 hr. 50 min. This is Europe's fastest intercity service.

New Canadian Speed Records Set in 1976

During a series of tests of the new LRC (light, rapid, comfortable train conducted on March 10th on Canadian Pacific's Adirondack subdivision, an average of 124.5 mph was made over a one mile stretch of track wherein a top speed of 129 mph was attained.

The above record was broken on April 22 as a nine-car Canadian National Turbotrain accelerated from 95 to 140.6 mph over a smooth 20-mile stretch of welded rail east of Prescott, Ont. (miles 104 to 84). This run was staged "to attract attention to Canadian National's new passenger service in the Quebec-Ontario Corridor."

Some Fast Railway Runs in the U. S. and Canada

Date	Railroad	Run	Miles	H.	M.	S.	MPH
May, 1876	Pennsylvania-Chicago & Northwestern-Union Pacific-Central Pacific	Jersey City-Oakland	3310.8	83	45		39.5
July, 1885	New York, West Shore & Buffalo	East Buffalo-Weehawken	422.6	9	23		45.0
Aug., 1886	New York Central & Hudson River	Syracuse-Buffalo	148.7	2	24		61.9
Aug., 1894	Atlantic Coast Line Route	Jacksonville-Washington	780.9	15	49		49.4
Sept., 1895	New York Central & Hudson River	New York-Buffalo	436.32	6	51	56	66.54
Oct., 1895	Lake Shore & Michigan Southern	Chicago-Buffalo	510.1	8	1	7	63.61
May, 1905	Atlantic City	Camden-Atlantic City	55.5		42	33	78.3
July, 1905	Atchison, Topeka & Santa Fe	Los Angeles-Chicago	2244.5	44	54		50.0
April, 1911	Lake Shore & Michigan Southern	Toledo-Elkhart	133.0	1	46		75.28
Nov., 1925	Canadian National	Montreal-Vancouver	2937.5	67	0	0	43.8
May, 1934	Chicago, Burlington & Quincy	Denver-Chicago	1015.31	13	5	44	77.6
July, 1934	Chicago, Milwaukee, St. Paul & Pac.	Chicago-Milwaukee	85.0	1	7	35	75.46
Oct., 1934	Union Pacific	Cheyenne-Omaha	506.7	6	11	0	81.95
Oct., 1934	Union Pacific, Chicago & North-western, New York Central	Los Angeles-New York	3257.6	56	55		57.2
Jan., 1935	Pennsylvania	Philadelphia-Washington	134.2	1	50		73.2
April, 1935	New York, New Haven & Hartford	Providence-Boston	43.8		32	35	80.6
Oct., 1936	Chicago, Burlington & Quincy	Chicago-Denver	1017.23	12	12	27	83.3
May, 1937	Atchison, Topeka & Santa Fe	Los Angeles-Chicago	2228.6	36	49		60.5
July, 1966	New York Central	Bryan, Ohio (MP 350-345)	5.0		1	39¾	181.0*
May, 1967	Pennsylvania	County Tower-Milheim Tower	21.2		11†		115.66†
Jan., 1968	Atchison, Topeka & Santa Fe	Corwith-Hobart Yards (Super C Frgt.)	2202.1	34	35	40	63.6

*The official speed measured by ground instruments was 183.85 mph on passing mile post 347 + 13 over an accurately measured 300 feet of track. This is the highest speed on rails ever recorded in the United States. The run was made by a single Budd Rail Diesel car fitted with two turbo-jet J-47 aircraft engines mounted on forward end. †Time and speed calculated from standing start at County Tower to passing Milheim Tower (end of test track) at 80-mph, after which the train was gradually braked down on regular track to a stop in Trenton passenger station. Between mileposts 46 and 51, speed was 150 mph or over, a momentary peak of 156 mph, was reached in the vicinity of milepost 47.

Intercity Truck Tonnage

Source: American Trucking Associations

Based on operations of 2,004 Class I & II intercity motor carriers (tons)

Region	1975	1976
New England	16,628,667	17,234,411
Middle Atlantic	115,786,850	128,536,124
Central	150,422,484	177,619,380
Southern	104,011,046	119,747,209
Northwestern	46,819,034	51,382,877
Midwestern	42,232,027	47,837,829
Southwestern	57,206,216	63,852,707
Rocky Mountain	22,603,641	23,552,503
Pacific	50,379,232	55,341,872
United States	606,089,197	685,104,912

Commodity Class	1975	1976
General Freight	195,291,903	225,008,938
Household Goods	1,937,959	2,094,972
Heavy Machinery	8,390,415	9,606,658
Liquid Petroleum	161,319,957	176,632,408
Refrig. Solids & Liquids	19,364,552	21,072,433
Agricultural Commodities	12,336,644	12,846,552
Motor Vehicles	20,860,159	25,618,412
Building Materials	22,189,642	26,688,857
All Other Classes	164,397,966	185,535,682
All Commodities	606,089,197	685,104,912

Car, Truck, and Bus Drivers in the U.S.

Source: Federal Highway Administration, estimated total licenses in force during 1976.

State	No. of drivers	State	No. of drivers	State	No. of drivers	State	No. of drivers
Alabama	1,986,000	Indiana	3,483,000	Nebraska	1,084,000	South Carolina	1,676,000
Alaska	242,000	Iowa	1,926,000	Nevada	441,000	South Dakota	425,000
Arizona	1,369,000	Kansas	1,703,000	New Hampshire	543,000	Tennessee	2,490,000
Arkansas	1,356,000	Kentucky	2,021,000	New Jersey	4,432,000	Texas	7,737,000
California	13,961,000	Louisiana	2,215,000	New Mexico	770,000	Utah	737,000
Colorado	1,738,000	Maine	634,000	New York	8,934,000	Vermont	317,000
Connecticut	1,940,000	Maryland	2,526,000	North Carolina	3,433,000	Virginia	3,092,000
Delaware	378,000	Massachusetts	3,590,000	North Dakota	384,000	Washington	2,233,000
Florida	6,051,000	Michigan	6,238,000	Ohio	7,917,000	West Virginia	1,324,000
Georgia	3,132,000	Minnesota	2,431,000	Oklahoma	1,730,000	Wisconsin	2,779,000
Hawaii	545,000	Mississippi	1,538,000	Oregon	1,569,000	Wyoming	304,000
Idaho	528,000	Missouri	3,036,000	Pennsylvania	7,068,000	Dist. of Col.	340,000
Illinois	6,481,000	Montana	534,000	Rhode Island	533,000	**Total**	**133,874,000**

Minimum Legal Age for Purchase of Alcoholic Beverages

In the U.S. and Canada

	Years		Years		Years		Years
Alabama	19	Indiana	21	New Brunswick	19	Quebec	18
Alaska	19	Iowa	18	Newfoundland	19	Rhode Island	18
Alberta	18	Kansas (a)	21	New Hampshire	18	Saskatchewan	19
Arizona	19	Kentucky	21	New Jersey	18	South Carolina (d)	21
Arkansas	21	Louisiana	18	New Mexico	21	South Dakota (a)	21
British Columbia	19	Maine	20	New York	18	Tennessee	18
California	21	Manitoba	18	North Carolina (b)	21	Texas	18
Colorado (c)	21	Maryland (b)	21	North Dakota	21	Utah	21
Connecticut	18	Massachusetts	18	Northwest Territories	19	Vermont	18
Delaware	20	Michigan	18	Nova Scotia	19	Virginia (f)	21
Dist. of Col. (b)	21	Minnesota	19	Ohio (a)	21	Washington	21
Florida	18	Mississippi (e)	21	Oklahoma (a)	21	West Virginia	18
Georgia	18	Missouri	21	Oregon	21	Wisconsin	18
Hawaii	18	Montana	18	Ontario	18	Wyoming	19
Idaho	19	Nebraska	19	Pennsylvania	21	Yukon Territory	19
Illinois (c)	21	Nevada	21	Prince Edward Island	18		

(a) 3.2 Beer 18. (b) Light wine, beer 18. (c) Wine, beer 19. (d) Wine, beer 18. (e) Beer not over 4% by wgt. and wine 18. (f) Beer 18.

Trucking: Employees, Payroll, Registration

Source: American Trucking Assns.; U.S. Transportation Department

1975	Employees	Annual payroll ($)	Truck registration 1974	Truck registration 1975
Alabama	162,500	1,576,900,000	527,174	563,022
Alaska	15,200	264,343,200	61,392	76,535
Arizona	114,800	1,214,239,600	374,561	376,749
Arkansas	134,200	1,144,323,400	383,167	402,127
California	1,187,700	14,485,189,200	2,379,693	2,514,473
Colorado	146,200	1,551,766,800	445,022	462,332
Connecticut	127,000	1,455,039,000	139,577	132,530
Delaware	29,800	342,610,600	55,108	57,707
Dist. of Col.	10,900	155,216,000	9,728	12,807
Florida	273,000	2,737,644,000	839,462	815,497
Georgia	216,000	2,130,840,000	671,949	662,263
Hawaii	21,200	225,313,600	59,325	61,484
Idaho	49,400	463,421,400	212,873	225,538
Illinois	340,600	4,084,475,200	853,199	926,850
Indiana	320,100	3,522,060,300	693,366	717,453
Iowa	164,800	1,624,928,000	494,619	524,215
Kansas	148,700	1,426,925,200	511,683	542,671
Kentucky	153,700	1,518,248,600	514,117	544,547
Louisiana	167,300	1,679,022,800	491,232	497,566
Maine	55,000	481,745,000	133,253	138,376
Maryland	123,000	1,352,631,000	322,597	326,415
Mass.	167,500	1,790,575,000	283,136	296,858
Michigan	317,000	4,051,260,000	808,897	860,530
Minnesota	190,800	1,986,228,000	553,001	540,753
Mississippi	105,600	891,897,600	355,156	364,867
Missouri	240,800	2,526,714,400	659,561	665,186
Montana	50,800	474,218,000	212,318	221,840
Nebraska	91,600	848,216,000	324,133	339,931
Nevada	42,300	463,100,400	109,052	109,022
New Hamp.	28,300	265,144,400	78,545	72,784
New Jersey	212,100	2,506,597,800	352,412	350,419
New Mexico	56,200	553,570,000	216,881	257,249
New York	408,500	5,048,651,500	728,472	763,203
N. Carolina	311,600	2,806,892,800	718,957	756,335
N. Dakota	37,200	334,874,400	197,846	211,960
Ohio	333,500	3,620,476,000	813,243	833,574
Oklahoma	167,900	1,634,506,500	616,360	650,242
Oregon	120,400	1,289,484,000	274,373	282,151
Penna.	452,200	4,992,288,000	893,047	1,013,848
R. Island	35,600	344,038,400	63,597	59,419
S. Carolina	144,000	1,280,880,000	313,976	348,708
S. Dakota	37,900	317,715,700	165,799	174,177
Tennessee	142,700	1,344,947,500	549,627	600,371
Texas	681,100	6,875,704,500	1,928,529	2,051,738
Utah	59,900	593,668,900	211,161	247,781
Vermont	18,600	173,017,200	50,953	49,544
Virginia	180,800	1,825,356,800	484,835	510,018
Washington	194,200	2,233,300,000	580,029	617,338
W. Va.	87,900	1,050,580,800	222,000	220,959
Wisconsin	156,500	1,646,849,500	411,884	428,838
Wyoming	25,200	261,828,000	111,606	126,908
U.S. Total	9,059,800	97,469,465,000	23,462,479	24,607,708
1974 Totals	**9,065,300**	**88,295,403,600**		

Total Road and Street Mileage in U. S.

Source: Federal Highway Administration, U.S. Transportation Department (1975)

State	Rural	Urban	Surfaced	Total
Ala.	68,370	18,104	82,143	86,474
Alas.	8,344	1,597	6,161	9,941
Ariz.	44,248	7,354	25,637	51,602
Ark.	67,613	10,223	65,123	77,836
Cal.	123,191	47,909	126,327	171,100
Colo.	77,113	8,432	56,198	85,545
Conn.	5,501	13,445	18,852	18,946
Del.	4,382	812	5,180	5,194
Fla.	74,297	27,241	66,389	101,538
Ga.	85,022	16,444	70,753	101,466
Ha.	2,696	1,054	3,603	3,750
Ida.	54,108	3,381	31,541	57,489
Ill.	102,122	29,409	125,559	131,531
Ind.	74,910	16,322	87,870	91,232
Ia.	99,011	13,343	106,601	112,354
Kan.	123,138	11,553	102,646	134,691
Ky.	64,061	6,070	63,606	70,131
La.	42,867	11,830	51,557	54,697
Me.	19,009	2,571	20,283	21,580
Md.	21,678	4,271	25,919	25,949
Mass.	14,245	18,584	32,829	32,829
Mich.	98,808	19,982	102,500	118,790
Minn.	110,575	17,808	117,810	128,383
Miss.	60,055	7,433	65,913	67,488
Mo.	99,028	17,979	110,525	117,007
Mon.	75,625	2,552	46,539	78,177
Neb.	90,051	7,057	79,789	97,108
Nev.	47,773	1,969	16,198	49,742
N.H.	10,302	4,955	12,721	15,257
N.J.	13,751	19,285	31,609	33,036
N.M.	65,257	5,364	22,275	70,621
N.Y.	65,010	43,625	104,986	108,635
N.C.	75,480	15,330	82,136	90,810
N.D.	102,683	3,289	71,293	105,972
Oh.	86,363	24,257	109,139	110,620
Okla.	93,264	16,135	84,874	109,399
Ore.	98,193	6,284	66,855	104,477
Pa.	90,381	24,806	101,017	115,187
R.I.	971	4,557	5,288	5,528
S.C.	53,731	7,214	43,285	60,945
S.D.	79,236	3,057	62,898	82,293
Tenn.	68,964	12,308	79,629	81,272
Tex.	198,552	57,335	194,292	255,887
Ut.	44,091	4,763	23,491	48,854
Vt.	12,848	1,038	12,946	13,886
Va.	53,055	9,712	61,621	62,767
Wash.	73,872	10,443	68,420	84,315
W. Va.	33,318	3,666	27,731	36,984
Wis.	90,259	14,912	99,685	105,171
Wyo.	31,174	1,384	19,360	32,558
D.C.	—	1,102	1,102	1,102
Total	**3,198,596**	**639,550**	**3,100,704**	**3,838,146**

Automobile Factory Sales

Source: Motor Vehicle Manufacturers Association, Detroit, Mich.—wholesale values

Year	Passenger Cars		Motor Trucks, Buses		Total	
	Number	Value	Number	Value	Number	Value
1900	4,192	$4,899,443	...	...	4,190	$4,899,443
1905	24,250	38,670,000	350	$1,330,000	24,600	240,000,000
1910	181,000	215,340,000	6,000	9,660,000	187,000	225,000,000
1915	895,930	575,978,000	74,000	125,800,000	969,930	701,778,000
1920	1,905,560	1,809,170,963	321,789	423,249,410	2,227,349	2,232,420,373
1925	3,735,171	2,458,370,026	530,659	458,400,277	4,265,830	2,916,770,303
1930	2,787,456	1,644,083,152	575,364	390,752,061	3,362,820	2,034,853,213
1935	3,273,874	1,707,836,325	697,367	380,997,330	3,971,241	2,088,833,655
1940	3,717,385	2,370,654,083	754,901	567,820,414	4,472,286	2,938,474,497
1945	69,532	57,254,655	655,683	1,181,955,532	725,215	1,239,210,187
1950	6,665,863	8,468,137,000	1,337,193	1,707,748,000	8,003,056	10,175,885,000
1955	7,920,186	12,452,871,000	1,249,106	2,020,973,000	9,169,292	14,473,844,000
1960	6,674,796	12,164,234,000	1,194,475	2,350,680,000	7,869,271	14,514,914,000
1965	9,305,561	18,380,036,000	1,751,805	3,733,664,000	11,057,366	22,113,700,000
1970	6,546,817	14,630,217,000	1,692,440	4,819,752,000	8,239,257	19,449,969,000
1974	7,331,256	21,653,000,000	2,727,313	10,163,203,000	10,058,569	31,816,239,000
1975	6,712,852	23,400,000,000*	2,272,160	9,900,000,000*	8,985,012	33,300,000,000*
1976	8,497,603	NA	2,979,049	NA	11,476,652	NA

After July 1, 1964 all tactical vehicles are excluded. Federal excise taxes are excluded in all years. *Preliminary.

Highway Mileage Between Selected Canadian and U.S. Cities

	CALGARY	EDMONTON	HALIFAX	LONDON	MONCTON	MONTREAL	OTTAWA	QUEBEC	REGINA	ST. JOHN	SAULT STE. MARIE	THUNDER BAY	TORONTO	VANCOUVER	WINNIPEG
BANGOR, ME.	2592	2595	450	762	287	310	436	241	2115	188	936	1331	651	3250	1760
BOSTON, MASS.	2620	2639	683	675	520	333	458	390	2142	421	958	1403	564	3168	1812
BUFFALO, N.Y.	2106	2125	1141	142	978	383	350	533	1628	879	532	977	102	2878	1377
BUTTE, MONT.	378	561	2950	1859	2787	2309	2033	2470	629	2739	1533	1303	1972	764	875
CALGARY, ALTA.		183	3073	2246	2910	2282	2202	2432	478	2862	1601	1271	2142	659	832
DETROIT, MICH.	1915	1934	1336	122	1204	576	475	738	1437	1156	246	691	235	2505	1149
DULUTH, MINN.	1240	1243	1842	777	1679	1051	925	1199	763	1631	425	195	865	1898	408
EDMONTON, ALTA.	183		3076	2249	2913	2285	2205	2435	497	2865	1632	1274	2145	842	835
FARGO, N.D.	989	1172	2092	1048	1929	1502	1175	1764	511	1881	675	445	1161	1654	233
HALIFAX, N.S.	3073	3076		1243	163	791	917	657	2596	262	1417	1812	1132	3731	2241
LONDON, ONT.	2246	2249	1243		1080	452	359	602	1769	1032	403	985	111	2904	1414
MONCTON, N.B.	2910	2913	163	1080		628	754	494	2433	99	1254	1649	969	3568	2078
MONTREAL, QUE.	2282	2285	791	452	628		126	150	1805	580	626	1021	341	2940	1450
OTTAWA, ONT.	2202	2205	917	359	754	126		274	1725	706	500	941	248	2860	1370
QUEBEC, QUE.	2432	2435	657	602	494	150	274		1955	446	774	1171	491	3090	1600
REGINA, SASK.	478	497	2596	1769	2433	1805	1725	1955		2385	1146	794	1665	1136	355
ST. JOHN, N.B.	2862	2865	262	1032	99	580	706	446	2385		1206	1601	921	3520	2030
SAULT STE. MARIE	1601	1632	1417	403	1254	626	500	774	1146	1206		445	440	2201	797
SEATTLE, WASH.	762	945	3494	2489	3331	2693	2577	2934	1092	3283	2077	1883	2600	146	1444
THUNDER BAY, ONT.	1271	1274	1812	985	1649	1021	941	1171	794	1601	445		881	1929	439
TORONTO, ONT.	2142	2145	1132	111	969	341	248	491	1665	921	440	881		2800	1310
VANCOUVER, B.C.	659	842	3731	2904	3568	2940	2860	3090	1136	3520	2201	1929	2800		1490
WINNIPEG, MAN.	832	835	2241	1414	2078	1450	1370	1600	355	2030	797	439	1310	1490	

Passenger Car Production, U.S. Plants

Source: Motor Vehicle Manufacturers Association of the U.S., Inc.

	1975	1976	1977 7 mos.
American Motors Corp.			
Gremlin	51,471	39,419	15,266
Hornet	69,557	63,722	34,838
Pacer	140,996	74,030	26,533
Matador	61,772	36,747	13,355
Total American	**323,796**	**213,918**	**89,992**
Chrysler Corp.			
Voyager (Valiant)	215,761	50,664	7,250
Volare	33,416	435,625	203,715
Fury	122,703	114,265	73,000
Gran Fury	71,670	57,466	30,822
Total Plymouth	**443,550**	**658,020**	**314,787**
Chrysler	102,940	127,466	91,615
Imperial (Le Baron)	1,930	—	50,678
Total Chry.-Plym.	**548,420**	**785,486**	**457,080**
Sportsman (Dart)	203,473	77,906	26,538
Aspen	25,129	342,509	162,824
Coronet (Monaco)	72,417	77,656	48,075
Dodge (Diplomat)	53,463	49,845	65,292
Total Dodge	**354,482**	**547,916**	**302,729**
Total Chrylser Corp.	**902,902**	**1,333,402**	**759,809**
Ford Motor Co.			
Ford	191,405	248,550	165,493
Torino (Ltd II)	153,510	198,307	166,449
Elite	90,738	105,989	—
Club Wagon	34,639	34,982	27,664
Granada	336,864	415,390	243,527
Maverick	105,418	92,378	48,792
Pinto	163,510	108,140	60,799
Mustang	187,554	183,369	93,375
Thunderbird (Elite)	37,776	106,949	219,785
Total Ford	**1,301,414**	**1,494,054**	**1,025,884**
Mercury	79,507	91,509	106,956
Montego	52,751	33,238	—
Cougar (Montego)	57,215	105,811	147,507
Monarch	108,103	133,734	79,766
Comet	46,822	31,510	12,237
Bobcat	60,706	39,063	22,763
Total Mercury	**405,104**	**434,865**	**369,229**
Lincoln	55,499	64,584	67,929
Mark IV, Mark V	46,021	60,296	48,650
Versailles	—	—	14,431
Total Lincoln	**101,520**	**124,880**	**131,010**
Total Ford Motor	**1,808,038**	**2,053,799**	**1,526,123**
General Motors Corp.			
Chevrolet	318,400	370,934	358,004
Corvette	45,948	47,431	27,628
Monte Carlo	266,578	364,233	237,365
Chevelle	246,759	319,812	173,823
Camaro	156,400	201,653	141,166
Nova	296,413	391,309	227,935
Vega	193,245	136,284	40,361
Monza Notchback	82,954	21,064	6,225
Chevette	80,394	154,381	79,454
Total Chevrolet	**1,687,091**	**2,012,412**	**1,294,187**
Pontiac	104,073	151,695	134,785
Grand Prix	112,896	271,276	180,508
Le Mans	88,364	89,713	39,554
Firebird	94,198	125,018	103,394
Ventura	60,405	86,750	49,919
Astre	55,805	43,103	20,019
Sunbird	7,728	17,076	7,012
Total Pontiac	**523,469**	**784,631**	**535,191**
Oldsmobile	226,845	304,071	242,484
Toronado	22,535	24,781	21,124
Cutlass	363,814	560,055	402,127
Omega	37,261	67,127	35,955
Starfire	3,887	8,391	—
Total Oldsmobile	**654,342**	**964,425**	**701,690**
Buick	227,732	309,099	240,039
Riviera	16,759	22,940	13,374
Century	212,948	345,201	187,410
Apollo/Skylark	74,443	128,599	62,256
Skyhawk	3,938	11,830	—
Total Buick	**535,820**	**817,669**	**503,079**
Cadillac	193,444	233,575	162,504
Eldorado	48,134	39,995	32,507
Seville	36,826	39,275	29,086
Total Cadillac	**278,404**	**312,845**	**224,097**
Total Gen. Mts.	**3,679,126**	**4,891,982**	**3,258,244**
Checker Motors	**3,181**	**4,792**	**2,777**
Total Passenger Cars	**6,717,043**	**8,497,893**	**5,636,945**

Automotive Exports from U.S.

Source: Bureau of Economic Analysis, U.S. Commerce Department (in millions)

	Total value Vehicles	Total value Automotive*
1940	$147	$259
1950	406	746
1955	747	1,276
1960	634	1,266
1965	$739	$1,929
1969	1,554	3,888
1970	1,397	3,652
1972	2,008	5,119
1973	$2,678	$6,343
1974	3,684	8,162
1975	4,979	10,077
1976	5,259	11,238

*Includes new and used passenger cars and trucks, trailers, parts for assembly, and garage equipment.

Highway Mileage Between Selected Cities

Cities In The East*	ALBANY, N.Y.	ATLANTA, GA.	BALTIMORE, MD.	BANGOR, ME.	BIRMINGHAM, ALA.	BOSTON, MASS.	BUFFALO, N.Y.	CHARLESTON, W. VA.	CHICAGO, ILL.	CINCINNATI, OHIO	CLEVELAND, OHIO	DETROIT, MICH.	INDIANAPOLIS, IND.	JACKSON, MISS.	JACKSONVILLE, FLA.
ALBANY		988	321	366	1091	170	283	712	807	707	466	536	766	1379	1117
ATLANTA	988		671	1315	155	1070	876	519	707	467	692	726	539	400	315
BALTIMORE	321	671		632	800	400	366	391	690	497	348	510	565	998	794
BANGOR	366	1315	632		1407	233	652	1018	1174	1094	827	892	1136	1635	1426
BIRMINGHAM	1091	155	800	1407		1210	932	589	661	499	742	743	492	243	427
BOSTON	170	1070	400	233	1210		458	781	974	861	640	707	931	1446	1201
BUFFALO	283	876	366	652	932	458		439	520	428	186	249	486	1115	1080
CHARLESTON	712	519	391	1018	589	781	439		483	202	268	357	301	786	671
CHICAGO	807	707	690	1174	661	974	520	483		294	345	269	188	747	1017
CINCINNATI	707	467	497	1094	499	861	428	202	294		244	251	104	678	783
CLEVELAND	466	692	348	827	742	640	186	268	345	244		168	300	924	971
DETROIT	536	726	510	892	743	707	249	357	269	251	168		277	931	1039
INDIANAPOLIS	766	539	565	1136	492	931	486	301	188	104	300	277		631	852
JACKSON	1379	400	998	1635	243	1446	1115	786	747	678	924	931	631		597
JACKSONVILLE	1117	315	794	1426	427	1201	1080	671	1017	783	971	1039	852	597	
LOUISVILLE	827	428	602	1198	362	964	537	266	304	108	351	363	114	573	766
MEMPHIS	1217	366	951	1594	247	1340	924	615	548	487	737	726	444	210	672
MIAMI	1468	665	1143	1773	765	1539	1431	1043	1377	1133	1322	1387	1197	920	345
NASHVILLE	1090	251	732	736	201	1126	717	409	452	289	532	544	293	375	577
NEW ORLEANS	1476	517	1153	1747	359	1556	1248	936	929	820	1060	1077	839	182	568
NEW YORK	147	863	192	450	988	211	367	566	828	635	486	626	716	1232	979
NORFOLK	560	592	249	881	753	543	561	397	874	600	531	699	698	996	661
PHILADELPHIA	233	771	99	541	897	303	360	481	758	571	425	578	639	1153	889
PITTSBURGH	457	737	230	819	763	576	220	233	459	278	127	287	355	972	893
PORTLAND, ME.	275	1185	513	128	1325	106	574	895	1089	967	752	817	1037	1552	1293
RICHMOND	472	545	144	773	697	543	473	309	786	512	443	611	620	944	646
ST. LOUIS	1016	553	804	1379	503	1188	723	538	291	338	540	513	239	505	881
TAMPA	1331	464	986	1620	552	1383	1263	884	1187	948	1166	1201	1005	678	194
TRENTON	223	783	128	520	915	289	358	513	780	590	435	594	660	1163	921
WASHINGTON	367	640	39	673	767	440	372	355	687	497	362	516	567	1000	754

	LOUISVILLE, KY.	MEMPHIS, TENN.	MIAMI, FLA.	NASHVILLE, TENN.	NEW ORLEANS, LA.	NEW YORK, N.Y.	NORFOLK, VA.	PHILADELPHIA, PA.	PITTSBURGH, PA.	PORTLAND, ME.	RICHMOND, VA.	ST. LOUIS, MO.	TAMPA, FLA.	TRENTON, N.J.	WASHINGTON, D.C.
ALBANY	827	1217	1468	1090	1476	147	560	233	457	275	472	1016	1331	223	367
ATLANTA	428	366	665	251	517	863	592	771	737	1185	545	553	464	783	640
BALTIMORE	602	951	1143	732	1153	192	249	99	230	513	144	804	986	128	39
BANGOR	1198	1594	1773	736	1747	450	881	541	819	128	773	1379	1620	520	673
BIRMINGHAM	362	247	765	201	359	988	753	897	763	1325	697	503	552	915	767
BOSTON	964	1340	1539	1126	1556	211	543	303	576	106	543	1188	1383	289	440
BUFFALO	537	924	1431	717	1248	367	561	360	220	574	473	723	1263	358	372
CHARLESTON	266	615	1043	409	936	566	397	481	233	895	309	538	884	513	355
CHICAGO	304	548	1377	452	929	828	874	758	459	1089	786	291	1187	780	687
CINCINNATI	108	487	1133	289	820	635	600	571	278	967	512	338	948	590	497
CLEVELAND	351	737	1322	532	1060	486	531	425	127	752	443	540	1166	435	362
DETROIT	363	726	1387	544	1077	626	699	578	287	817	611	513	1201	594	516
INDIANAPOLIS	114	444	1197	293	839	716	698	639	355	1037	620	239	1005	660	567
JACKSON	573	210	920	375	182	1232	996	1153	972	1552	944	505	678	1163	1000
JACKSONVILLE	766	672	345	577	568	979	661	889	893	1293	646	881	194	921	754
LOUISVILLE		365	1078	180	719	759	693	682	398	1070	575	267	865	705	605
MEMPHIS	365		1017	220	399	1142	958	1057	786	1446	845	294	782	1064	917
MIAMI	1078	1017		916	878	1327	1013	1230	1237	1649	994	1222	248	1276	1105
NASHVILLE	180	220	916		536	929	713	838	568	1232	625	295	908	853	697
NEW ORLEANS	719	399	878	536		1353	1101	1239	1113	1655	1057	699	644	1270	1150
NEW YORK	759	1142	1327	929	1353		441	91	363	317	330	961	1176	70	226
NORFOLK	693	958	1013	713	1101	441		348	400	649	88	930	859	359	195
PHILADELPHIA	682	1057	1230	838	1239	91	348		294	409	240	881	1083	32	136
PITTSBURGH	398	786	1237	568	1113	363	400	294		682	312	599	1045	205	229
PORTLAND, ME.	1070	1446	1649	1232	1655	317	649	409	682		649	1294	1488	395	549
RICHMOND	575	845	994	625	1057	330	88	240	312	649		842	842	277	107
ST. LOUIS	267	294	1222	295	699	961	930	881	599	1294	842		1030	897	804
TAMPA	865	782	248	908	644	1176	859	1083	1045	1488	842	1030		1109	947
TRENTON	705	1064	1276	853	1270	70	359	32	205	395	277	897	1109		169
WASHINGTON	605	917	1105	697	1150	226	195	136	229	549	107	804	947	169	

*Directions for Use of Mileage Charts

To measure mileage between the east and west charts there are 5 key cities: Chicago, Jackson (Miss.), Memphis, New Orleans and St. Louis.

Plot your course between the city listed nearest your home town and whichever of the 5 key cities you desire to pass through to the city of your destination. Add the mileage shown and this will give you the approximate total mileage.

For example: The mileage between Cheyenne and Philadelphia through St. Louis: Philadelphia to St. Louis - 881 miles, St. Louis to Cheyenne - 910; the total is 1,791 miles.

Highway Mileage Between Selected Cities

Cities In The West	ALBUQUERQUE, N.M.	BOISE, IDA.	CHEYENNE, WY.	CHICAGO, ILL.	DALLAS, TEX.	DENVER, COL.	DES MOINES, IA.	FARGO, N.D.	HELENA, MON.	HOUSTON, TEX.	JACKSON, MISS.	KANSAS CITY, MO.	LITTLE ROCK, ARK.	LOS ANGELES, CAL.	MEMPHIS, TENN.
ALBUQUERQUE		980	545	1285	650	432	1032	1310	1111	844	1062	791	901	805	1032
BOISE	980		766	1726	1637	867	1397	1228	494	1825	2063	1446	1833	887	1913
CHEYENNE	545	766		967	880	101	632	823	700	1143	1282	657	1053	1182	1127
CHICAGO	1285	1726	967		936	1018	330	657	1478	1092	747	505	652	2106	548
DALLAS	650	1637	880	936		784	704	1110	1571	245	411	498	330	1410	468
DENVER	432	867	101	1018	784		674	901	792	1028	1219	613	962	1162	1058
DES MOINES	1032	1397	632	330	704	674		491	1162	948	828	207	581	1788	608
FARGO, N.D.	1310	1228	823	657	1110	901	491		822	1364	1271	636	1054	1935	1061
HELENA	1111	494	700	1478	1571	792	1162	822		1813	1922	1261	1666	1234	1720
HOUSTON	844	1825	1143	1092	245	1028	948	1364	1813		433	744	439	1554	572
JACKSON	1062	2063	1282	747	411	1219	828	1271	1922	433		613	257	1864	210
KANSAS CITY	791	1446	657	505	498	613	207	636	1261	744	613		409	1620	467
LITTLE ROCK	901	1833	1053	652	330	962	581	1045	1666	439	257	409		1698	139
LOS ANGELES	805	887	1182	2106	1410	1162	1788	1935	1234	1554	1864	1620	1698		1823
MEMPHIS	1032	1913	1127	548	468	1058	627	1061	1720	572	210	467	139	1823	
MILWAUKEE	1390	1763	1019	87	1063	1039	358	573	1392	1163	826	564	727	2145	632
MINNEAPOLIS	1223	1446	821	418	964	845	254	239	1056	1211	1062	461	833	1996	852
NEW ORLEANS	1145	2140	1376	929	500	1284	1028	1479	2070	358	182	846	434	1916	399
OKLAHOMA CITY	545	1489	702	826	212	616	566	900	1392	458	587	357	350	1353	482
OMAHA	892	1267	491	465	672	537	139	436	1056	917	882	208	623	1698	671
PHOENIX	449	1020	924	1753	1021	826	1449	1726	1147	1158	1456	1238	1337	389	1470
PORTLAND, ORE.	1461	435	1211	2131	2057	1285	1819	1590	657	2282	2506	1901	2284	994	2367
RENO	1036	427	995	1970	1695	1040	1638	1639	905	1888	2104	1665	2030	476	2083
ST. LOUIS	1057	1701	910	291	651	863	349	812	1498	801	505	254	357	1862	294
SALT LAKE CITY	612	363	457	1443	1262	512	1089	1215	500	1453	1685	1118	1444	730	1570
SAN FRANCISCO	1132	654	1209	2183	1773	1267	1851	1873	1134	1955	2203	1893	2032	403	2162
SEATTLE	1511	529	1279	2031	2136	1377	1766	1505	611	2354	2601	1904	2273	1177	2362
SIOUX FALLS	1082	1295	654	525	844	655	282	230	960	1110	1013	390	799	1817	858
TUCSON	454	1191	999	1739	951	845	1462	1746	1270	1070	1362	1255	1278	512	1417
WICHITA	620	1663	590	711	386	512	403	731	1241	629	733	202	472	1384	549

	MILWAUKEE, WIS.	MINNEAPOLIS, MINN.	NEW ORLEANS, LA.	OKLAHOMA CITY, OKLA.	OMAHA, NEB.	PHOENIX, ARIZ.	PORTLAND, ORE.	RENO, NEV.	ST. LOUIS MO.	SALT LAKE CITY, UTAH	SAN FRANCISCO, CAL.	SEATTLE, WASH.	SIOUX FALLS, S.D.	TUCSON, ARIZ.	WICHITA, KAN.
ALBUQUERQUE	1390	1223	1145	545	892	449	1461	1036	1057	612	1132	1511	1082	454	620
BOISE	1763	1446	2140	1489	1267	1020	435	427	1701	363	654	525	1295	1191	1663
CHEYENNE	1019	821	1376	702	491	924	1211	995	910	457	1209	1279	654	999	590
CHICAGO	87	418	929	826	465	1753	2131	1970	291	1443	2183	2031	525	1739	711
DALLAS	1063	964	500	212	672	1021	2057	1695	651	1262	1773	2136	844	951	386
DENVER	1039	845	1284	616	537	826	1285	1040	863	512	1267	1377	655	845	512
DES MOINES	358	254	1028	566	139	1449	1819	1638	349	1089	1851	1766	282	1462	403
FARGO, N.D.	573	239	1479	900	436	1726	1590	1639	812	1215	1873	1505	230	1746	731
HELENA	1392	1056	2070	1392	1056	1147	657	905	1498	500	1134	611	960	1270	1241
HOUSTON	1163	1211	358	458	917	1158	2282	1888	801	1453	1955	2354	1110	1070	629
JACKSON	826	1062	182	587	882	1456	2506	2104	505	1685	2203	2601	1013	1362	733
KANSAS CITY	564	461	846	357	208	1238	1901	1665	254	1118	1893	1904	390	1255	202
LITTLE ROCK	727	833	434	350	623	1337	2284	2030	357	1444	2032	2273	799	1278	472
LOS ANGELES	2145	1996	1916	1353	1698	389	994	476	1862	730	403	1177	1817	512	1384
MEMPHIS	632	852	399	482	671	1470	2367	2083	294	1570	2162	2362	858	1417	549
MILWAUKEE		334	1034	905	501	1833	2069	2003	371	1502	2203	2045	507	1819	792
MINNEAPOLIS	334		1251	818	364	1671	1721	1797	553	1246	2001	1673	221	1677	650
NEW ORLEANS	1034	1251		684	1065	1527	2591	2199	699	1773	2278	2645	1265	1436	840
OKLAHOMA CITY	905	818	648		477	989	1926	1529	523	1112	1692	1975	644	941	168
OMAHA	1501	364	1065	477		1325	1700	1500	453	955	1720	1657	187	1341	309
PHOENIX	1833	1671	1527	989	1325		1273	762	1492	688	794	1510	1481	123	1040
PORTLAND, ORE.	2069	1721	2591	1926	1700	1273		566	2113	807	669	173	1580	1396	1854
RENO	2003	1797	2199	1529	1500	762	566		1906	531	227	760	1472	912	1542
ST. LOUIS	371	553	699	523	453	1492	2113	1879		1381	2133	2102	632	1457	460
SALT LAKE CITY	1502	1246	1773	1112	953	688	807	531	1381		755	869	941	820	1020
SAN FRANCISCO	2203	2001	2278	1692	1720	794	669	227	2133	755		858	1696	921	1730
SEATTLE	2045	1673	2645	1975	1657	1510	173	760	2102	869	858		1526	1666	1842
SIOUX FALLS	507	221	1265	644	187	1481	1580	1472	632	941	1696	1526		1536	493
TUCSON	1819	1677	1436	941	1341	123	1396	912	1457	820	921	1666	1536		1074
WICHITA	792	650	840	168	309	1040	1854	1542	460	1020	1730	1842	493	1074	

Motor Vehicle Registrations, Taxes, Motor Fuel, Drivers' Ages

Source: Federal Highway Adm.

State, 1976	Driver's age Jan. 1, 1976 (1) Regular	(2) Juvenile	Registered autos, buses & trucks[3] number	State gas tax per gal. cents	Motor fuel gross tax collections[3] $1,000	Motor fuel consumption[3] Highway 1,000 gallons	Non-highway 1,000 gallons	Total 1,000 gallons
Alabama	16		2,590,000	7	156,355	2,185,259	45,201	2,230,460
Alaska	16		255,000	8	16,695	201,220	41,319	242,539
Arizona	16		1,491,000	8	108,725	1,352,465	48,041	1,400,506
Arkansas	16		1,327,000	8.5	116,484	1,384,906	29,810	1,414,716
California	16/18	14	14,102,000	7	785,142	11,435,212	231,599	11,666,811
Colorado	21	16	1,994,000	7	102,329	1,525,248	51,343	1,576,591
Connecticut	16/18		2,009,000	10	153,441	1,449,749	23,707	1,473,456
Delaware	16/18		360,000	9	29,128	326,329	6,992	333,321
Florida	16/18		5,603,000	8	369,855	4,645,835	130,993	4,776,828
Georgia	16		3,263,000	7.5	238,847	3,209,447	49,844	3,259,291
Hawaii	15		483,000	8.5	25,911	301,645	10,954	312,599
Idaho	16	14	681,000	8.5	47,116	523,979	42,416	566,395
Illinois	16/18		6,542,000	7.5	400,755	5,553,695	254,046	5,807,741
Indiana	16/18		3,382,000	8	248,350	3,146,853	79,660	3,226,513
Iowa	16/18	14	2,157,000	7	127,018	1,798,619	189,934	1,988,553
Kansas	16	14	1,848,000	7	110,925	1,459,920	121,430	1,581,350
Kentucky	16		2,350,000	9	186,379	1,960,442	31,993	1,992,435
Louisiana	17	15	2,277,000	8	168,321	2,096,678	50,997	2,147,675
Maine	15/17	15	680,000	9	53,184	599,530	11,460	610,990
Maryland	16/18		2,508,000	9	183,467	2,018,115	26,475	2,044,590
Massachusetts	18	16½	3,192,000	8.5	211,082	2,507,502	28,356	2,535,858
Michigan	16/18	14	5,723,000	9	411,193	4,875,996	186,122	5,062,118
Minnesota	16/18	15	2,576,000	9	189,486	2,149,099	170,762	2,319,861
Mississippi	15		1,424,000	9	125,668	1,367,150	28,622	1,395,772
Missouri	16		2,924,000	7	197,923	2,895,297	143,758	3,039,055
Montana	15/16		620,000	7.75	41,303	519,015	37,712	556,727
Nebraska	16	14	1,218,000	8.5	81,368	970,857	81,797	1,052,654
Nevada	16	14	476,000	6	29,082	484,293	16,073	500,366
New Hampshire	16/18	16	504,000	9	38,642	428,356	6,375	434,731
New Jersey	17	16	4,312,000	8	291,364	3,630,704	61,869	3,692,573
New Mexico	15/16		863,000	7	60,515	862,165	15,292	877,457
New York	17/18	16	7,758,000	8	508,266	5,954,385	152,243	6,106,628
North Carolina	16/18		3,837,000	9	283,064	3,168,741	78,982	3,247,723
North Dakota	16	14	569,000	7	27,061	402,092	97,658	499,750
Ohio	16/18	14	7,469,000	7	384,113	5,606,667	155,400	5,762,067
Oklahoma	16		2,181,000	6.5	119,130	1,866,078	50,509	1,916,587
Oregon	16	14	1,678,000	7	88,973	1,439,224	51,080	1,490,304
Pennsylvania	17/18	16	7,979,000	9	486,865	5,323,256	118,462	5,441,718
Rhode Island	16/18		576,000	10	41,928	402,957	11,887	414,844
South Carolina	16	15	1,877,000	8	137,768	1,713,531	35,160	1,748,691
South Dakota	16	14	549,000	8	36,114	451,933	70,076	522,009
Tennessee	16	14	2,858,000	7	186,190	2,620,913	42,807	2,663,720
Texas	16/18	15	8,674,000	5	429,213	8,572,251	166,907	8,739,158
Utah	16		881,000	7	48,891	717,713	25,443	743,156
Vermont	18	16	294,000	9	22,896	268,988	5,871	274,859
Virginia	16/18		3,398,000	9	262,644	2,878,890	52,058	2,930,948
Washington	16/18		2,666,000	9	177,532	1,955,631	60,903	2,016,534
West Virginia	16/18		1,003,000	8.5	80,386	947,835	10,009	957,844
Wisconsin	16/18	14	2,683,000	7	165,912	2,381,742	114,443	2,496,185
Wyoming	16	14	358,000	7	29,756	373,778	36,464	410,242
District Of Columbia	18	16	265,000	10	25,274	261,554	4,262	265,816
Total United States			**137,287,000**		**8,848,026**	**115,173,739**	**3,595,576**	**118,769,315**

(1) Unrestricted operation of private passenger car. When 2 ages are shown, license is issued at lower age upon completion of approved driver education course. (2) Juvenile license issued for use between home and school in Cal., Iowa, Kan., Me., Mich., Neb., Nev., N.H., N.D., Oreg.; restricted to daylight or curfew hours in Idaho, Ill., La., Mass., Minn., N.Y., Pa., S.C., S.D., Tenn., Wis.; hardship cases in Ohio and Texas; for agricultural pursuits in N.J. (3) Estimated.

Auto Registrations, Taxes, Motor Fuel, Drivers' Ages in Canada

Source: Statistics Canada

Province	Driver's age (1975) Minimum	Minor	Registered[1] road motor vehicles (1975[4])	Province gas tax per gal. (1975[4])	Motor fuel[2] gross tax collect's (C$1,000) (1975)	Fuel consumption on roads and highways 1975[3] Gasoline 1,000 gallons	Diesel 1,000 gallons	Liquified petroleum 1,000 gallons
Newfoundland	17	—	170,612	27	34,280	118,846	18,220	86
P.E.I.	16	*	55,459	21	8,219	36,821	2,072	2
Nova Scotia	16	*	345,198	21	56,039	239,305	16,548	147
New Brunswick	18	16	288,658	20	46,216	208,504	21,114	26
Quebec	17	16	2,702,272	19	419,771	1,798,628	280,508	817
Ontario	16	—	4,079,108	19	577,987	2,617,374	283,591	1,052
Manitoba	16	*	535,808	18	58,206	290,407	32,924	954
Saskatchewan	16	—	613,269	15	45,329	296,322	39,395	593
Alberta	16	14	1,073,020	10	82,429	646,398	84,353	2,626
British Columbia	19	16	1,554,081	17	170,910	729,614	84,043	913
Yukon and N.W.T.	—	—	25,158	14	6,011	19,385	15,557	—
Total			**11,442,643**		**1,505,397**	**7,001,606**	**888,327**	**7,218**

(1) Registrations include: passenger automobiles (including taxis and for-hire cars) 8,870,307; trucks and truck tractors 2,111,945; buses 45,859; motorcycles 331,347; registered mopeds 29,527, and other road vehicles (ambulances, fire trucks, etc.) 53.658. (2) Includes some taxes on other fuels (i.e. not highway). (3) Net sales of gasoline diesel fuel, and liquified petroleum gas at road-use tax rates. (4) Fiscal year Apr. 1, 1975 to Mar. 31, 1976. *No minor permit issued.

Memorable Manned Space Flights

Sources: National Aeronautics and Space Administration and The World Almanac.

Crew, date	Mission name	Orbits[1]	Duration	Remarks
Yuri A. Gagarin (4/12/61)	Vostok 1	1	1h 48m	First manned orbital flight.
Alan Z. Shepard Jr. (5/5/61)	Mercury-Redstone 3	(2)	15m 22s	First American in space.
Virgil I. Grissom (7/21/61)	Mercury-Redstone 4	(2)	15m 37s	Spacecraft sank, Grissom rescued.
Gherman S. Titov (8/6-7/61)	Vostok 2	16	25h 18m	First space flight of more than 24 hrs.
John H. Glenn Jr. (2/20/62)	Mercury-Atlas 6	3	4h 55m 23s	First American in orbit.
M. Scott Carpenter (5/24/62)	Mercury-Atlas 7	3	4h 56m 05s	Manual retrofire error caused 250 mi. landing overshoot.
Andrian G. Nikolayev (8/11-15/62)	Vostok 3	64	94h 22m	Vostok 3 and 4 made first group flight.
Pavel R. Popovich (8/12-15/62)	Vostok 4	48	70h 57m	On first orbit it came within 3 miles of Vostok 3.
Walter M. Schirra, Jr. (10/3/62)	Mercury-Atlas 8	6	9h 13m 11s	Closest splashdown to target to date (4.5 mi.).
L. Gordon Cooper (5/15-16/63)	Mercury-Atlas 9	22	34h 19m 49s	First U.S. evaluation of effects on man of one day in space.
Valery F. Bykovsky (6/14-6/19/63)	Vostok 5	81	119h 06m	Vostok 5 and 6 made 2d group flight.
Valentina V. Tereshkova (6/16-19/63)	Vostok 6	48	70h 50m	First woman in space.
Vladimir M. Komarov, Konstantin P. Feoktistov, Boris B. Yegorov (10/12/64)	Voskhod 1	16	24h 17m	First 3-man orbital flight; first without space suits.
Pavel I. Belyayev, Aleksei A. Leonov (3/18/65)	Voskhod 2	17	26h 02m	Leonov made first "space walk" (10 min.).
Virgil I. Grissom, John W. Young (3/23/65)	Gemini-Titan 3	3	4h 53m 00s	First manned spacecraft to change its orbital path.
James A. McDivitt, Edward H. White 2d, (6/3-7/65)	Gemini-Titan 4	62	97h 56m 11s	White was first American to "walk in space" (20 min.).
L. Gordon Cooper Jr., Charles Conrad Jr. (8/21-29/65)	Gemini-Titan 5	120	190h 55m 14s	First use of fuel cells for electric power; evaluated guidance and navigation system.
Frank Borman, James A. Lovell Jr. (12/4-18/65)	Gemini-Titan 7	206	330h 35m 31s	Longest duration Gemini flight.
Walter M. Schirra Jr., Thomas P. Stafford (12/15-16/65)	Gemini-Titan 6-A	16	25h 51m 24s	Completed world's first space rendezvous with Gemini 7.
Neil A. Armstrong, David R. Scott (3/16-17/66)	Gemini-Titan 8	6.5	10h 41m 26s	First docking of one space vehicle with another; mission aborted, control malfunction.
John W. Young, Michael Collins (7/18-21/66)	Gemini-Titan 10	43	70h 46m 39s	First use of Agena target vehicle's propulsion systems; rendezvoused with Gemini 8.
Charles Conrad Jr., Richard F. Gordon Jr. (9/12-15/66)	Gemini-Titan 11	44	71h 17m 08s	Docked, made 2 revolutions of earth tethered; set Gemini altitude record (739.2 mi.).
James A. Lovell Jr., Edwin E. Aldrin Jr. (11/11-15/66)	Gemini-Titan 12	59	94h 34m 31s	Final Gemini mission; record 5½ hrs. of extravehicular activity.
Vladimir M. Komarov (4/23/67)	Soyuz 1	17	26h 40m	Crashed after re-entry killing Komarov.
Walter M. Schirra Jr., Donn F. Eisele, R. Walter Cunningham (10/11-22/68)	Apollo-Saturn 7	163	260h 09m 03s	First manned flight of Apollo spacecraft command-service module only.
Georgi T. Beregovoi (10/26-30/68)	Soyuz 3	64	94h 51m	Made rendezvous with unmanned Soyuz 2.
Frank Borman, James A. Lovell Jr., William A. Anders (12/21-27/68)	Apollo-Saturn 8	10[3]	147h 00m 42s	First flight to moon (command-service module only); views of lunar surface televised to earth.
Vladimir A. Shatalov (1/14-17/69)	Soyuz 4	45	71h 14m	Docked with Soyuz 5.
Boris V. Volyanov, Aleksei S. Yeliseyev, Yevgeny V. Khrunov (1/15-18/69)	Soyuz 5	46	72h 46m	Docked with Soyuz 4; Yeliseyev and Khrunov transferred to Soyuz 4.

(continued)

Crew, date	Mission name	Orbits[1]	Duration	Remarks
James A. McDivitt, David R. Scott, Russell L. Schweickart (3/3-13/69)	Apollo-Saturn 9	151	241h 00m 54s	First manned flight of lunar module.
Thomas P. Stafford, Eugene A. Cernan, John W. Young (5/18-26/69)	Apollo-Saturn 10	31[4]	192h 03m 23s	First lunar module orbit of moon.
Neil A. Armstrong, Edwin E. Aldrin Jr., Michael Collins (7/16-24/69)	Apollo-Saturn 11	30[3]	195h 18m 35s	First lunar landing made by Armstrong and Aldrin; collected 48.5 lbs. of soil, rock samples; lunar stay time 21 h, 36 m, 21 s.
Georgi S. Shonin, Valery N. Kubasov (10/11-16/69)	Soyuz 6	79	118h 42m	First welding of metals in space.
Anatoly V. Filipchenko, Vladislav N. Volkov, Viktor V. Gorbatko (10/12-17/69)	Soyuz 7	79	118h 41m	Space lab construction tests made; Soyuz 6, 7 and 8 — first time 3 spacecraft 7 crew orbited earth at once.
Vladimir A. Shatalov, Aleksei S. Yeliseyev (10/13-18/69)	Soyuz 8	79	118h 41m	Orbiting space laboratory construction tests were made.
Charles Conrad Jr., Richard F. Gordon, Alan L. Bean (11/14-24/69)	Apollo-Saturn 12	45[3]	244h 36m 25s	Conrad and Bean made 2d moon landing; collected 74.7 lbs. of samples, lunar stay time 31 h, 31 m.
James A. Lovell Jr., Fred W. Haise Jr., John L. Swigart Jr. (4/11-17/70)	Apollo-Saturn 13	. .	142h 54m 41s	Aborted after service module oxygen tank ruptured; crew returned safely using lunar module oxygen and power.
Alan B. Shepard Jr., Stuart A. Roosa, Edgar D. Mitchell (1/31-2/9/71)	Apollo-Saturn 14	34[3]	216h 01m 57s	Shepard and Mitchell made 3d moon landing, collected 96 lbs. of lunar samples; lunar stay 33 h, 31 m.
Vladimir A. Shatalov, Aleksei S. Yeliseyev, Nikolai Rukavishnikov (4/22-24/71)	Soyuz 10	32	47h 46m	Docked with prototype Salyut orbiting space station for 5½ hrs, then mission was aborted.
Georgi T. Dobrovolsky, Vladislav N. Volkov, Viktor I. Patsayev (6/6-30/71)	Soyuz 11	360	569h 40m	Docked with Salyut space station; and orbited in Salyut for 23 days; crew died during re-entry from loss of pressurization.
David R. Scott, Alfred M. Worden, James B. Irwin (7/26-8/7/71)	Apollo-Saturn 15	74[3]	295h 11m 53s	Scott and Irwin made 4th moon landing; first lunar rover use; first deep space walk; 170 lbs. of samples; 66 h, 55 m, stay.
Charles M. Duke Jr., Thomas K. Mattingly, John W. Young (4/16-27/72)	Apollo-Saturn 16	64[3]	265h 51m 05s	Young and Duke made 5th moon landing; collected 213 lbs. of lunar samples; lunar stay time 71 h, 2 m.
Eugene A. Cernan, Ronald E. Evans, Harrison H. Schmitt (12/7-19/72)	Apollo-Saturn 17	75[3]	301h 51m 59s	Cernan and Schmitt made 6th manned lunar landing; collected 243 lbs. of samples; record lunar stay of 75 h.
Charles Conrad Jr., Joseph P. Kerwin, Paul J. Weitz (5/25-6/22/73)	Skylab 2	. .	672h 49m 49s	First American manned orbiting space station; made long-flights tests, crew repaired damage caused during boost.
Alan L. Bean, Jack R. Lousma, Owen K. Garriott (7/28-9/25/73)	Skylab 3	. .	1,427h 09m 04s	Crew systems and operational tests, exceeded pre-mission plans for scientific activities; space walk total 13 h, 44 m.
Gerald P. Carr, Edward G. Gibson, William Pogue (11/16/73-2/8/74)	Skylab 4	. .	2,017h 16m 30s	Final Skylab mission; record space walk of 7 h, 1 m., record space walks total for a mission 22 h, 21 m.
Alexi Leonov, Valeri Kubason (7/15-7/21/75)	Soyuz 19	96	143h 31m	
Vance Brand, Thomas P. Stafford, Donald K. Slayton (7/15-7/24/75)	Apollo 18	136	217h 30m	U.S.-USSR joint flight. Crews linked-up in space, conducted experiments, shared meals, and held a joint news conference.

(1) The Americans measure orbital flights in revolutions while the Soviets use "orbits." (2) suborbital. (3) Moon orbits in command module. (4) Moon orbits.

Fire aboard spacecraft Apollo I on the ground at Cape Kennedy, Fla. killed Virgil I. Grissom, Edward H. White and Roger B. Chaffee on Jan. 27, 1967. They were the only U.S. astronauts killed in space tests.

Notable Ocean and Intercontinental Flights

(Certified by the Federation Aeronautique Internationale as of Jan., 1977)

Pilot, plane	From	To	Miles	Time	Date
		Dirigible Balloons			
British R-34 (1)	East Fortune, Scot	Mineola, N.Y.		108 hrs.	July 2-6, 1919
	Mineola, N.Y.	Pulham, Eng.		75 hrs.	July 9-13, 1919
Amundsen-Ellsworth-Nobile expedition	Spitsbergen	Teller, Alas.		80 hrs.	May 11-14, 1926
Graf Zeppelin	Friedrichshafen	Lakehurst, N.J.	6,630	4d 15h 46m	Oct. 11-15, 1928
Hindenburg Zeppelin	Germany	Lakehurst, N.J.		51h 17m	June 30-July 2, 1936
	Lakehurst, N.J.	Frankfort, Ger.	.....	42h 53m	Aug. 9-11, 1936
USN ZPG-2 Blimp	S. Weymouth, Mass.	Africa			
	Africa	Key West, Fla.	7,000	275h	Mar. 4-16, 1957
		Airplanes			
USN NC-4	Rockaway, N.Y.	Lisbon, Port	.....	....	May 8-27, 1919
John Alcock-A. W. Brown (2)	St. John's, Nfld.	Clifden, Ireland	1,960	16h 12m	June 14-15, 1919
Richard E. Byrd(3)	Spitsbergen	North Pole	1,545	15h 30m	May 9, 1926
Charles Lindbergh (4)	Mineola, N.Y.	Paris	3,610	33h 29m 30s	May 20-21, 1927
C. Levin-	Roosevelt Field				
C. Chamberlin (5)	Mineola, N.Y.	Isleben, Germany	3,911	42h 31m	June 4-6, 1927
Baron G. von Huenefeld, crew (6)	Dublin	Greenly Isl., Lab	.....	37 hrs.	Apr. 12-13, 1928
Sir Hubert Wilkins (9)	Point Barrow, Alaska	Spitsbergen	.....	.....	Apr. 16, 1928
Sir Chas. Kingsford-Smith, crew (7)	Oakland, Cal	Brisbane, Aust		.....	May 31-June 8, 1928
Amelia Earhart Putnam, W. Stultz, L. Gordon	Trepassy, Nfld	Burry Port, Wales	.....	20h 40m	June 17-18, 1928
Richard E. Byrd (8)	Bay of Wales	South Pole	.....	....	Nov. 28-29, 1929
D. Coste-M. Bellonte	Paris	Valley Stream, N.Y.	4,100	37h 18m 30s	Sept. 1-2, 1930
Wiley Post-Harold Gatty	Harbor Grace, Nfld	England	2,200	16h 17m	June 23-24, 1931
Clyde Pangborn-Hugh Herndon Jr. (10)	Tokyo	Wenatchee, Wash	4,458	41h 34m	Oct. 3-5, 1931
Amelia Earhart Putnam (11)	Harbor Grace, Nfld	Ireland	2,026	14h 56m	May 20-21, 1932
James A. Mollison (12)	Portmarnock, Ire.	Pennfield, N.B.	.....	....	Aug. 18, 1932
China Clipper (Pan	San Francisco	Manila, P.I.	.....	....	Nov. 22-28, 1935
Am. Airways) (13)	Manila, P.I.	San Francisco	.....	....	Dec. 1-6, 1935
Gromoff, Yumasheff, Danilin (USSR)	Moscow, USSR	San Jacinto, Cal	6,262	62h 02m	July 12-14, 1937
Douglas C. Corrigan	New York	Dublin, Ire.	.....	28h 13m	July 17-18, 1938
B-29 (C.J. Miller)	Honolulu	Washington, D.C.	4,640	17h 21m	Sept. 1, 1945
C-54 (Maj. G.E. Cain)	Tokyo	Washington, D.C.		31h 24m	Sept. 3, 1945
Col. David C. Schilling, USAF (14)	England	Limestone, Me	3,300	10h 01m	Sept. 22, 1950
Chas. F. Blair Jr.	New York	London	3,500	7h 48m	Jan. 31, 1951
Chas. F. Blair Jr. (15)	Bardufoss, Norway	Fairbanks, Alas.	3,300	10h 29m	May 29, 1951
Chas. F. Blair Jr.	Fairbanks, Alaska	New York	3,450	9h 31m	May 30, 1950
Canberra Bomber	England	Australia	.....	20h 20m	Mar. 16, 1952
Two U. S. S-55 Helicopters (16)	Westover AFB, Mass.	Prestwick, Scotland	3,410	42h 30m	July 15-31, 1952
Canberra Bomber (17)	Aldergrove, N.Ire.	Gander, Nfld	2,073	4h 34m	Aug. 26, 1952
	Gander, Nfld	Aldergrove, N.Ire.	2,073	3h 25m	Aug. 26, 1952
British Comet	London-Tokyo	Tokyo-London	20,400	74h 52m	Apr. 3-7, 1953
British Comet	London	Rio de Janeiro	6,000	12h 30m	Sept. 13-14, 1953
Max Conrad (solo)	New York	Paris	.....	22h 23m	Nov. 7, 1954
	Gander, Nfld	Aldergrove, N.Ire.	2,073	3h 25m	Aug. 26, 1952
Canberra Bomber	London (round trip)	New York	6,920	14h 21m 45.4s	Aug. 23, 1955
Capt. William F. Judd	New York	Paris	.....	24h 11m	Jan. 29-30, 1956
Three USAF F-100Cs	London	Los Angeles	6,710	14h 5m	May 13, 1957
Spirit of St. Louis II (USAF F-100F jet)	McGuire AFB, N.J.	Le Bourget, Paris	.....	6h 38m	May 21, 1957
USAF KC-135	Tokyo	Lajes AFB, Azores	10,230	18h 48m	Apr. 7-8, 1958
Max Conrad (solo)	New York	Palermo, Sicily	4,440	32h 55m	June 22-23, 1958
Capt. Marion Boling	Manila, P.I.	Pendleton, Ore	6,979	45h 42m	July 31-Aug. 1, 1958
USAF KC-135	Yokota AB, Japan	Washington, D.C.	7,100	12h 28m	Sept. 12, 1958
Max Conrad (solo)	Chicago	Rome	5,000	34h 3m	Mar. 5-6, 1959
Max Conrad (solo)	Casablanca, Mor.	Los Angeles	7,700	58h 36m	June 2-4, 1959
USSR TU-114 (18)	Moscow	New York	5,092	11h 6m	June 28, 1959
Boeing 707 airliner	San Francisco	Sydney, Australia	7,630	16h 10m	July 2, 1959
Boeing 707-320	New York	Moscow	c.5,090	8h 54m	July 23, 1959
Max Conrad (solo)	Casablanca, Mor	El Paso, Tex	6,911	56h 26m	Nov. 22-26, 1959
Col. J.B. Swindal	Washington, D.C.	Moscow	5,004	8h 39m 02.2s	May 19, 1963
Mrs. Jerrie Mock (19)	Columbus, Oh.	Columbus, Oh.	23,206	29d 11h 59m	Mar. 19-Apr. 18, 1964
Joan Merriam (20)	Oakland, Cal	Oakland, Cal	27,750	56d	Mar. 17-May 12, 1964
Elgen Long (solo) (21)	San Francisco	San Francisco	38,896	28d 00h 43m	Nov. 5-Dec. 3, 1971

Notable first flights: (1) Atlantic aerial round trip. (2) Non-stop transatlantic flight. (3) Polar flight. (4) Solo transatlantic flight in the Ryan monoplane the "Spirit of St. Louis." (5) Transatlantic passenger flight. (6) East-West transatlantic crossing. (7) U.S. to Australia flight. (8) South Pole flight. (9) Trans-Arctic flight. (10) Non-stop Pacific flight. (11) Woman's transoceanic solo flight. (12) Westbound transatlantic solo flight. (13) Pacific airmail and U.S. to Philippines crossing. (14) Non-stop jet transatlantic flight. (15) Solo across North Pole. (16) Transatlantic helicopter flight. (17) Transatlantic round trip on same day. (18) Non-stop between Moscow and New York. (19) First woman pilot to circle globe; First woman to fly both North Atlantic and Pacific. (20) Followed route Amelia Earhart partly completed in 1937. (21) Speed record around the world over both the earth's poles.

International Aeronautical Records

Source: The National Aeronautic Association, 806 15th St. NW, Washington, DC 20005, representative in the United States of the Federation Aeronautique Internationale, certifying agency for world aviation and space records. The International Aeronautical Federation was formed in 1905 by representatives from Belgium, France, Germany, Great Britain, Spain, Italy, Switzerland, and the United States, with headquarters in Paris. Regulations for the control of official records were signed Oct. 14, 1905. World records are defined as maximum performance, regardless of class or type of aircraft used. Records to Dec., 1976.

World Air Records—Maximum Performance in Any Class

Speed over a straight course — 3,529.56 kph. (2,193.16 mi.) — Capt. Elden W. Joersz, USAF, Lockheed SR-71; Beale AFB Cal., July 28,1976.

Speed over a closed circuit — 3,367,221 kph. (2,092,294 mph) — Maj. Adolphus H. Bledsoe Jr., USAF, Lockheed SR-71 Beale AFB, Cal., July 27, 1976.

Distance in a straight line — 20,168.78 kms (12,532.28 mi.) — Maj. Clyde P. Evely, USAF, Boeing B52-P; Kadena Okinawa, to Madrid, Spain, Jan. 12, 1962.

Distance over a closed circuit — 18,245.5 kms (11,336.92 mi.) — Capt. William Stevenson, USAF, Boeing B52-H; Seymour Johnson, N.C., June 6-7, 1962.

Altitude — 95.935.99 meters (314,750 feet) — Maj. Robert M. White, USAF, North American X-15-1; Edwards AFB, Cal. July 17, 1962.

Altitude in horizontal flight — 25,929,031 meters (85,068,997 ft.) — Capt. Robert C. Helt, USAF, Lockheed SR-71; Beale AFB, Cal., July 28, 1976.

Manned Space Craft

Duration — 84 days 1 hr. 15 min. 30.8 sec. — Gerald P. Carr, Edward G. Gibson, William R. Pogue, U.S.; Skylab 3; Nov. 16, 1973-Feb. 8, 1974.

Altitude — 377,668.9 kms (234,672.5 mi.) — Frank Borman, James A. Lovell Jr., William Anders, Apollo 8; Dec. 21-27, 1968.

Greatest mass lifted — 127,980 kgs. (282,197 lbs) — Frank Borman, James S. Lovell Jr., William Anders, Apollo 8; Dec. 21-27, 1968.

Distance — 55,560,000 kms. (34,523,000 mi.) — Gerald P. Carr, Edward G. Gibson, William R. Pogue, U.S.; Skylab 3; Nov. 16, 1973-Feb. 8, 1974.

World "Class" Records

All other records, international in scope, are termed World "Class" records and are divided into classes: airships, free balloons, airplanes, seaplanes, amphibians, gliders, and rotorplanes. Airplanes (Class C) are sub-divided into four groups: Group 1 — piston engine aircraft, Group II — turboprop aircraft, Group III — jet aircraft, Group IV — rocket powered aircraft. A partial listing of world records follows:

Airplanes (Class C, Group I — piston engine)

Distance, closed circuit — 14,441.26 kms (8,974 mi.) — James R. Bede, U.S.; BD-2, Columbus, Oh. to Kansas City course, Nov. 7-9, 1969.

Distance in a straight line. Airline (international) — 18,081,990 kms. (11,235.6 miles) — Cmdr. Thomas D. Davies, USN; Cmdr. Eugene P. Rankin, USN; Cmdr. Walter S. Reid, USN, and Lt. Cmdr. Ray A. Tabeling, USN; Lockheed P2V-1; from Pearce Field, Perth, Australia, to Port Columbus, Oh., Sept. 29-Oct. 1, 1946.

Maximum speed over 3-kilometer measured course (international) — 776,449 kph. (482.462 mph) — Darryl Grecnamyer Grumman F8F Bearcat; Edwards AFB, Cal., Aug. 16, 1969.

Speed for 100 kilometers (62.137 miles) without payload (international) — 755.668 kph. (469.549 mph.) — Jacqueline Cochran, U.S.; North American P-51; Coachella Valley, Cal., Dec. 10, 1947.

Speed for 1,000 kilometers (621.369 miles) without payload — 693.78 kph. (431.09 mph.) — Jacqueline Cochran, U.S. North American P-51; Santa Rosasummit, Cal. — Flagstaff, Ariz. course, May 24, 1948.

Speed for 5,000 kilometers (3,106.849 miles) without payload — 544.59 kph. (338.39 mph.) — Capt. James Bauer, USAF Boeing B-29; Dayton, Oh., June 28, 1946.

Speed around the world — 327.73 kph (203.64 mph) — D.N. Dalton, Australia; Beechcraft Duke; Brisbane, Aust., July 20-25, 1975. Time: 5 days, 2 hours, 19 min., 57 sec.

Light Airplanes—(Class C-1.d)

Distance in a straight line — 12,341.26 kms. (7,668.48 miles) — Max Conrad, U.S.; Piper Comanche; Casablanca, Morocco to Los Angeles, June 2-4, 1959.

Speed for 100 kilometers — (62,137 miles) in a closed circuit — 519.480 kph. (322.780 mph.) — Miss R. M. Sharpe, Great Britain; Vickers Supermarine Spitfire 5-B; Wolverhampton, June 17, 1950.

Helicopters (Class E-1)

Distance in a straight line — 3,561.55 kms. (2,213.04 miles) — Robert G. Ferry, U.S.; Hughes YOH-6A helicopter; Culver City, Cal., to Daytona Beach, Fla., Apr. 6-7, 1966.

Speed over 3-km. course — 348.971 kph. (216.839 mph.) — Byron Graham, U.S.; Sikorsky S-67 helicopter; Windsor Locks Conn., Dec. 14, 1970.

Gliders (Class D—single-place)

Distance, straight line — 1,460.8 kms. (907.7 miles) — Hans Werner Grosse, West Germany; ASK12 sailplane; Luebeck to Biarritz, Apr. 25, 1972.

Altitude above sea level — 14,102 meters (46,267 feet) — Paul F. Bikle, U.S.; Sailplane Schweizer SCG 123E; Mojave Lancaster, Cal., Feb. 25, 1961.

Airplanes (Class C, Group II—Turboprop)

Distance in a straight line — 14,052.95 kms. (8,732.09 miles) — Lt. Col. Edgar L. Allison Jr., USAF, Lockheed HC-130 Hercules aircraft; Taiwan to Scott AFB, Ill.; Feb. 20, 1972.

Speed over a 15-25 km. course —Cmdr. D.H. Lilienthal, USN, Lockheed P3C Orion aircraft; 806.10 kph. (501.44 mph) Jan. 27, 1971.

Altitude — 15,549 meters (51,014 ft.) — Donald R. Wilson, U.S.; LTV L450F aircraft; Greenville, Tex., Mar. 27, 1972.

Speed for 1,000 kilometers (621.369 miles) without payload — 871.38 kph. (541.449 mph.) — Ivan Soukhomline, USSR TU-114 swept wing monoplane, Sternberg, USSR; Mar. 24, 1960.

Speed for 5,000 kilometers (3,106.849 miles) without payload — 877.212 kph. (545.072 mph.) — Ivan Soukhomline, USSR TU-114 swept wing monoplane, Sternberg, USSR; Apr. 9, 1960.

Airplanes (Class C-1, Group III—Jet-powered)

Distance in a straight line — 20,168.78 kms. (12,532.28 mi.) — Maj. Clyde P. Evely, USAF, Boeing B52-H, Kadena, Okinawa, to Madrid, Spain, Jan. 10-11, 1962.

Distance in a closed circuit — 18,245.05 kms. (11,336.92 miles) — Capt. William Stevenson, USAF, Boeing B52H, Seymour-Johnson, N.C., June 6-7, 1962.

Altitude — 36,240 meters (118,898 ft.) — Alexander Fedotov, USSR; E-266 Airplane; Podmoskovnoye, USSR, July 25, 1973.

Speed over a 3-kilometer course — 1,452.777 kph. (902.769 mph) — Lt. Hunt Hardisty, USN; McDonnell F4H Phantom, White Sands, N.M., Aug. 29, 1961.

Speed for 100 kilometers in a closed circuit — 2,605 kph. (1,618.7 mph.) — Alexander Fedotov, USSR; E-266 airplane, Apr. 8, 1973.

Speed for 500 kilometers in a closed circuit — 2,981.5 kph, (1,852.61 mph.) — Mikhall Komarov, USSR; E-266 airplane, Oct. 5, 1967.

Speed for 1,000 kilometers in a closed circuit — 3,367.221 kph (2,192.294 mph) — Maj. Adolphus H. Bledsoe Jr., USAF Lockheed SR-71; Beale, AFB, Cal., July 27, 1976.

Speed for 2,000 kilometers in closed circuit — 1,708.817 kph. (1,061.808 mph.) — Maj. H. J. Deutschendorf Jr., USA, Convair B-58 Hustler Bomber; Edwards AFB, Cal., Jan. 12, 1961.

Free Balloons (Tenth category, 4001 cu. meters or more)

Altitude — 34,668 meters (113,739.9 feet) — Cmdr. Malcolm D. Ross, USNR; Lee Lewis Memorial Winzen Research Balloon; Gulf of Mexico, May 4, 1961.

FAI Course Records

Los Angeles to New York — 1,954.79 kph (1,214.65 mph) — Capt. Robert G. Sowers, USAF; Convair B58 Hustler; 4 GEj795B engines; elapsed time: 2 hrs. 58.71 sec., Mar. 5, 1962.

New York to Los Angeles — 1,741 kph (1,081.80 mph)—Capt. Robert G. Sowers, USAF; Convair B58 Hustler; elapsed time: 2 hrs. 15 min. 50.08 sec., Mar. 5, 1962.

New York to Paris — 1,753.068 kph (1,089.36 mph) — Maj. W. R. Payne, U.S.; Convair B58 Hustler; elapsed time: 3 hrs. 19 min. 44 sec., May 26, 1961.

London to New York — 945.423 kph (587.457 mph) — Maj. Burl B. Davenport, USAF; Boeing KC-135; London International Airport to Idlewild International Airport, New York, June 27, 1958; elapsed time: 5 hrs. 53 min. 12.77 sec.

Baltimore to Moscow, USSR — 906.64 kph (563.36 mph)—Col. James B. Swindal, USAF; Boeing VC-137 (707); elapsed time: 8 hrs. 33 min. 45.4 sec., May 19, 1963.

Belfast to Gander, Newfoundland — 774.25 kph (481.099 mph) — Wing Commander R. P. Beamont, Great Britain; Canberra bomber, Aug. 31, 1951; elapsed time: 4 hrs. 18 min. 24.4 sec.

New York to London — 2,908.026 kph (1,810.964 mph)—Maj. James V. Sullivan, USAF; Lockheed SR-71; elapsed time 1 hr. 54 min. 56.4 sec., Sept. 1, 1974.

London to Los Angeles — 2,310.353 kph (1,435.587 mph)—Capt. Harold B. Adams, USAF; Lockheed SR-71; elapsed time: 3 hrs. 47 min. 39 sec., Sept. 13, 1974.

Aviation Hall of Fame

The Aviation Hall of Fame at Dayton, Oh., is dedicated to honoring aviation's outstanding pioneers.

Allen, William P.
Arnold, Henry "Hap"
Balchen, Bernt
Baldwin, Thomas S.
Beachly, Lincoln
Beech, Walter H.
Bell, Alexander Graham
Bell, Lawrence D.
Boeing, William E.
Byrd, Richard E.
Chamberlin, Clarence D.
Chanute, Octave
Chennault, Claire L.
Cunningham, Alfred A.
Curtiss, Glenn H.
deSeversky, Alexander P
Doolittle, James H.
Douglas, Donald W.
Eaker, Ira C.
Earhart, (Putnam), Amelia
Ellyson, Theodore G.
Ely, Eugene B.
Fleet, Reuben H.
Foulois, Benjamin D.
Glenn Jr., John
Goddard, George W.
Goddard, Robert H.
Gross, Robert E.
Grumman, Leroy R.
Guggenheim, Harry F.
Hegenberger, Albert F.
Hughes, Howard
Johnson, Clarence L.
Kenney, George C.
Kindelberger, James H.
Knabenshue, A. Roy
Lahm, Frank P.
Langley, Samuel P.
LeMay, Curtis
Lindbergh, Charles A.
Link, Edwin A.
Loening, Grover Cleveland
Luke Jr., Frank
MacReady, John A.
Martin, Glenn A.
McDonnell, James S.
Mitchell, William "Billy"
Montgomery, John J.
Moss, Sanford A.
Northrop, John K.
Odlum, Jacqueline Cochran
Patterson, William A.
Post, Wiley H.
Read, Albert C.
Reeve, Robert C.
Rickenbacker, Edward V.
Rodgers, Calbraith P.
Rogers, "Will"
Ryan, T. Claude
Selfridge, Thomas E.
Shepard Jr., Alan B.
Sikorsky, Igor I.
Smith, C. R.
Spaatz, Carl A.
Sperry Sr., Elmer A.
Taylor, Charles E.
Towers, John H.
Trippe, Juan T.
Turner, Roscoe
Twining, Nathan F.
Wade, Leigh
Walden, Henry W.
Wright, Orville
Wright, Wilbur
Yeager, Charles E.

U.S. Scheduled Airline Traffic

Source: Air Transport Association of America (thousands)

	1974	1975	1976
Passenger traffic			
Revenue passengers enplaned	207,458	205,062	223,313
Revenue passenger miles	162,918,594	162,810,160	172,987,543
Available seat miles	297,006,062	303,006,243	322,820,561
Cargo traffic (ton miles)	6,121,752	5,892,606	6,210,421
Freight	4,890,026	4,766,119	5,074,175
Express	80,845	29,190	22,003
U.S. Mail	1,150,881	1,097,297	1,114,243
Overall traffic and service			
Nonscheduled traffic—total ton miles	1,474,997	1,348,205	1,588,119
Total revenue ton miles—all services	23,900,208	23,533,743	25,708,984
Total available ton miles—all services	48,941,526	49,288,695	51,708,666

Notable Trips Around the World

(Certified by Federation Aeronautique Internationale as of Jan., 1977)

Fast circuits of the earth have been a subject of wide interest since Jules Verne, French novelist, described an imaginary trip by Phileas Fogg in Around the World in 80 Days, assertedly occurring Oct. 2 to Dec. 20, 1872.

Craft, Pilot	Terminal	Miles	Time	Date
Nellie Bly	New York, N.Y.		72d 06h 11m	1889
George Francis Train	New York, N.Y.		67d 12h 03m	1890
Charles Fitzmorris	Chicago		60d 13h 29m	1901
J. W. Willis Sayre	Seattle		54d 09h 42m	1903
Henry Frederick			54d 07h 02m	1903
Col. Burnlay-Campbell			40d 19h 30m	1907
Andre Jaeger-Schmidt			39d 19h 42m 38s	1911
John Henry Mears			35d 21h 36m	1913
Two U.S. Army airplanes	Seattle (57 hops, 21 countries)	26,103	35d 01h 11m	1924
Edward S. Evans and Linton Wells (New York World) (1)	New York	18,400	28d 14h 36m 05s	June 16-July 14, 1926
John H. Mears and Capt. C. B. D. Collyer	New York		23d 15h 21m 03s	June 29-July 22, 1928
Graf Zeppelin	Friedrichshafen, Ger. via Tokyo, Los Angeles, Lakehurst, N.J.	21,700	20d 04h	Aug. 14-Sept. 4, 1929
Wiley Post and Harold Gatty (Monoplane Winnie Mae)	Roosevelt Field, via Arctic Circle	15,474	8d 15h 51m	June 23-July 1, 1931
Wiley Post (Monoplane Winnie Mae) (2)	Floyd Bennett Field, via Arctic Circle	15,596	115h 36m 30s	July 15-22, 1933
H. R. Ekins (Scripps-Howard Newspapers in race) (Zeppelin Hindenburg to Germany, airplanes from Frankfurt)	Lakehurst, N.J., via Frankfurt, Germany	25,654	18d 11h 14m 33s	Sept. 30-Oct. 19, 1936
Howard Hughes and 4 assistants	New York, Paris, Moscow, Siberia, Fairbanks	14,824	3d 19h 08m 10s	July 10-13, 1938
Mrs. Clara Adams (Pan American Clipper)	Port Washington, N.Y., return Newark, N.J.		16d 19h 04m	June 28-July 15, 1939
Globester, U.S. Air Transport Command	Washington, D.C.	23,279	149h 44m	Sept. 28-Oct. 4, 1945
Capt. William P. Odom (A-26 Reynolds Bombshell)	New York, via Paris, Cairo, Tokyo, Alaska	20,000	78h 55m 12s	Apr. 12-16, 1947
America, Pan American 4-engine Lockheed Constellation (3)	New York, eastward	22,219	101h 32m	June 17-30, 1947
Col. Edward P. F. Eagan	New York	20,559	147h 15m	Dec. 13, 1948
USAF B-50 Lucky Lady II (Capt. James Gallagher) (4)	Fort Worth, Texas	23,452	94h 01m	Feb. 26-Mar. 2, 1949
Jean-Marie Audibert	Paris		4d 19h 38m	Dec. 11-15, 1952
Pamela Martin	Midway Airport, Chicago		90h 59m	Dec. 5-8, 1953
Three USAF B-52 Stratofortresses (5)	Merced, Cal., via Nfld., Morocco, Saudi Arabia, India, Ceylon, P.I., Guam	24,325	45h 19m	Jan. 15-18, 1957
Joseph Cavoli	Cleveland, Oh.		89h 13m 37s	Jan. 31-Feb. 4, 1958
Peter Gluckmann (solo)	San Francisco	22,800	29d	Aug. 22-Sept. 20, 1959
Milton Reynolds	San Francisco		51h 45m 22s	Jan. 12-14, 1960
Sue Snyder	Chicago	21,219	62h 59m	June 22-24, 1960
Max Conrad (solo)	Miami, Fla.	25,946	8d 18h 35m 57s	Feb. 28-Mar. 8, 1961
Sam Miller & Louis Fodor	New York		46h 28m	Aug. 3-4, 1963
Henry G. Beaird	Wichita, Kan.	22,992	65h 38m 49s	May 23-26, 1966
Robert & Joan Wallick (6)	Manila, Philippines	23,129	5d 6h 17m 10s	June 2-7, 1966
Arthur Godfrey, Richard Merrill Fred Austin, Karl Keller	New York	23,333	86h 9m 01s	June 4-7, 1966
Trevor K. Brougham	Darwin, Australia	24,800	5d 05h 57m	Aug. 5-10, 1972

(1) Mileage by train and auto, 4,110; by plane, 6,300; by steamship, 8,000. (2) First to fly solo around northern circumference of the world, also first to fly twice around the world. (3) Inception of regular commercial global air service. (4) First non-stop round-the-world flight, refueled 4 times in flight. (5) First non-stop global flight by jet planes; refueled in flight by KC-97 aerial tankers; average speed approx. 525 mph. (6) Official world record for light planes.

The Busiest Airports, 1976

(Total take-offs and landings)

United States

Source: U.S. Transportation Department

O'Hare (Chicago)	718,174	(1)
Santa Ana, Cal.	627,199	
Van Nuys, Cal.	618,689	
Long Beach, Cal.	551,815	
Atlanta, Ga.	490,002	(2)
Los Angeles, Cal.	482,587	(3)
San Jose, Cal.	469,982	
Torrence, Cal.	439,134	
Phoenix, Ariz.	425,375	
Denver, Col.	418,753	
Opa Locka, Fla. (Miami)	404,042	
Oakland, Cal.	398,948	

Canada

Source: Transport Canada

Edmonton Municipal, Alta.	279,867	
St. Hubert, Que.	265,396	
Pitt Meadows, B. C.	248,037	
Toronto International, Ont.	244,849	(1
Hamilton City, Ont.	243,825	
Vancouver International, B.C.	216,622	(3
Buttonville, Ont.	211,530	
St. Andrews, Man.	208,085	
Springbank, Alta.	203,467	
Langley, B. C.	200,352	
Montreal International, Que.	160,178	(2

Numbers in parentheses indicate top 3 in air carrier operations only.

Air Line Distances Between Selected Cities of the World

Source: Defense Mapping Agency Aerospace Center (statute miles)
Point-to-point measurements are usually from City Hall

	Bangkok	Berlin	Cairo	Cape-town	Caracas	Chicago	Hong Kong	Hono-lulu	Lima	London
Bangkok	....	5,352	4,523	6,300	10,555	8,570	1,077	6,609	1,244	5,944
Berlin	5,352	....	1,797	5,961	5,238	4,414	5,443	7,320	6,896	583
Cairo	4,523	1,797	....	4,480	6,342	6,141	5,066	8,848	7,726	2,185
Capetown	6,300	5,961	4,480	....	6,366	8,491	7,376	11,535	6,072	5,989
Caracas	10,555	5,238	6,342	6,366	....	2,495	10,165	6,021	1,707	4,655
Chicago	8,570	4,414	6,141	8,491	2,495	....	7,797	4,256	3,775	3,958
Hong Kong	1,077	5,443	5,066	7,376	10,165	7,797	....	5,556	11,418	5,990
Honolulu	6,609	7,320	8,848	11,535	6,021	4,256	5,556	....	5,947	7,240
London	5,944	583	2,185	5,989	4,655	3,958	5,990	7,240	6,316	....
Madrid	6,337	1,165	2,087	5,308	4,346	4,189	6,558	7,872	5,907	785
Melbourne	4,568	9,918	8,675	6,425	9,717	9,673	4,595	5,505	8,059	10,500
Mexico City	9,793	6,056	7,700	8,519	2,234	1,690	8,788	3,789	2,639	5,558
Montreal	8,338	3,740	5,427	7,922	2,438	745	7,736	4,918	3,970	3,254
Moscow	4,389	1,006	1,803	6,279	6,177	4,987	4,437	7,047	7,862	1,564
New Delhi	1,813	3,598	2,758	5,769	8,833	7,486	2,339	7,412	10,432	4,181
New York	8,669	3,979	5,619	7,803	2,120	714	8,060	4,969	3,639	3,469
Paris	5,877	548	1,998	5,786	4,732	4,143	5,990	7,449	6,370	214
Peking	2,046	4,584	4,698	8,044	8,950	6,604	1,217	5,077	10,349	5,074
Rio de Janeiro	9,994	6,209	6,143	3,781	2,804	5,282	11,009	8,288	2,342	5,750
Rome	5,494	737	1,326	5,231	5,195	4,824	5,774	8,040	6,750	895
San Francisco	7,931	5,672	7,466	10,248	3,902	1,859	6,905	2,398	4,518	5,367
Singapore	883	6,164	5,137	6,008	11,402	9,372	1,605	6,726	11,689	6,747
Stockholm	5,089	528	2,096	6,423	5,471	4,331	5,063	6,875	7,166	942
Tokyo	2,865	5,557	5,958	9,154	8,808	6,314	1,791	3,859	9,631	5,959
Warsaw	5,033	322	1,619	5,935	5,559	4,679	5,147	7,366	7,215	905
Washington, D.C.	8,807	4,181	5,822	7,895	2,047	596	8,155	4,838	3,509	3,674

	Madrid	Mel-bourne	Mexico City	Mon-treal	Mos-cow	Nai-robi	New Delhi	New York	Paris	Peking
Bangkok	6,337	4,568	9,793	8,338	4,389	4,483	1,813	8,669	5,877	2,046
Berlin	1,165	9,918	6,056	3,740	1,006	3,949	3,598	3,979	548	4,584
Cairo	2,087	8,675	7,700	5,427	1,803	2,186	2,758	5,619	1,998	4,698
Capetown	5,308	6,425	8,519	7,922	6,279	2,542	5,769	7,803	5,786	8,044
Caracas	4,346	9,717	2,234	2,438	6,177	7,178	8,833	2,120	4,732	8,950
Chicago	4,189	9,673	1,690	745	4,987	8,011	7,486	714	4,143	6,604
Hong Kong	6,558	4,595	8,788	7,736	4,437	5,449	2,339	8,060	5,990	1,217
Honolulu	7,872	5,505	3,789	4,918	7,047	10,741	7,412	4,969	7,449	5,077
London	785	10,500	5,558	3,254	1,564	4,231	4,181	3,469	214	5,074
Madrid	....	10,758	5,643	3,448	2,147	3,841	4,530	3,593	655	5,745
Melbourne	10,758	....	8,426	10,395	8,950	7,153	6,329	10,359	10,430	5,643
Mexico City	5,643	8,426	....	2,317	6,676	9,219	9,120	2,090	5,725	7,753
Montreal	3,448	10,395	2,317	....	4,401	7,267	7,012	331	3,432	6,519
Moscow	2,147	8,950	6,676	4,401	....	3,930	2,698	4,683	1,554	3,607
New Delhi	4,530	6,329	9,120	7,012	2,698	3,374	....	7,318	4,102	2,353
New York	3,593	10,359	2,090	331	4,683	7,364	7,318	....	3,636	6,844
Paris	655	10,430	5,725	3,432	1,554	4,022	4,102	3,636	....	5,120
Peking	5,745	5,643	7,753	6,519	3,607	5,727	2,353	6,844	5,120	....
Rio de Janeiro	5,045	8,226	4,764	5,078	7,170	5,560	8,753	4,801	5,684	10,768
Rome	851	9,929	6,377	4,104	1,483	3,339	3,684	4,293	690	5,063
San Francisco	5,803	7,856	1,887	2,543	5,885	9,597	7,691	2,572	5,577	5,918
Singapore	7,080	3,759	10,327	9,203	5,228	4,638	2,571	9,534	6,673	2,771
Stockholm	1,653	9,630	6,012	3,714	716	4,281	3,414	3,986	1,003	4,133
Tokyo	6,706	5,062	7,035	6,471	4,660	6,999	3,638	6,757	6,053	1,307
Warsaw	1,427	9,598	6,337	4,022	721	3,801	3,277	4,270	852	4,325
Washington, D.C.	3,792	10,180	1,885	489	4,876	7,551	7,500	205	3,840	6,942

	Rio de Janiero	Rome	San Fran-cisco	Singa-pore	Stock-holm	Teheran	Tokyo	Vienna	Warsaw	Wash., D.C.
Bangkok	9,994	5,494	7,931	883	5,089	3,391	2,865	5,252	5,033	8,807
Berlin	6,209	737	5,672	6,164	528	2,185	5,557	326	322	4,181
Cairo	6,143	1,326	7,466	5,137	2,096	1,234	5,958	1,481	1,619	5,822
Capetown	3,781	5,231	10,248	6,008	6,423	5,241	9,154	5,656	5,935	7,895
Caracas	2,804	5,195	3,902	11,402	5,471	7,320	8,808	5,372	5,559	2,047
Chicago	5,282	4,824	1,859	9,372	4,331	6,502	6,314	4,698	4,679	596
Hong Kong	11,009	5,774	6,905	1,605	5,063	3,843	1,791	5,431	5,147	8,155
Honolulu	8,288	8,040	2,398	6,726	6,875	8,070	3,859	7,632	7,366	4,838
London	5,750	895	5,367	6,747	942	2,743	5,959	771	905	3,674
Madrid	5,045	851	5,803	7,080	1,653	2,978	6,706	1,128	1,427	3,792
Melbourne	8,226	9,929	7,856	3,759	9,630	7,826	5,062	9,790	9,598	10,180
Mexico City	4,764	6,377	1,887	10,327	6,012	8,184	7,035	6,320	6,337	1,885
Montreal	5,078	4,104	2,543	9,203	3,714	5,880	6,471	4,009	4,022	489
Moscow	7,170	1,483	5,885	5,228	716	1,532	4,660	1,043	721	4,876
New Delhi	8,753	3,684	7,691	2,571	3,414	1,583	3,638	3,465	3,277	7,500
New York	4,801	4,293	2,572	9,534	3,986	6,141	6,757	4,234	4,270	205
Paris	5,684	690	5,577	6,673	1,003	2,625	6,053	645	852	3,840
Peking	10,768	5,063	5,918	2,771	4,133	3,490	1,307	4,648	4,325	6,942
Rio de Janeiro	....	5,707	6,613	9,785	6,683	7,374	11,532	6,127	6,455	4,779
Rome	5,707	....	6,259	6,229	1,245	2,127	6,142	477	820	4,497
San Francisco	6,613	6,259	....	8,448	5,399	7,362	5,150	5,994	5,854	2,441
Singapore	9,785	6,229	8,448	....	5,936	4,103	3,300	6,035	5,843	9,662
Stockholm	6,683	1,245	5,399	5,936	....	2,173	5,053	780	494	4,183
Tokyo	11,532	6,142	5,150	3,300	5,053	4,775	....	5,689	5,347	6,791
Warsaw	6,455	820	5,854	5,843	494	1,879	5,689	347	....	4,472
Washington, D.C.	4,779	4,497	2,441	9,662	4,183	6,341	6,791	4,438	4,472	....

World and Regional Food Production, 1971 to 1976

Source: UN Food and Agriculture Organization

Region	1971	1972	1973	1974	1975	1976[1]	Charge 1975 to 1976	Annual rate of change 1961-70	1970-76
			1961-65 = 100				%		
Developing market economies[2]. . . .	126	125	129	132	140	146	+ 4	3.0	2.7
Latin America.	128	129	132	138	142	151	+ 7	3.5	2.8
Far East.	126	122	133	131	143	145	+ 2	2.7	2.8
Near East.	127	137	130	141	151	158	+ 5	3.2	4.0
Africa.	121	119	115	123	126	131	+ 4	2.6	1.5
Asian centrally planned economies.	126	125	130	134	138	140	+ 2	2.9	2.4
Total, developing countries.	**126**	**125**	**130**	**133**	**140**	**144**	**+ 3**	**2.9**	**2.6**
Developed market economies[2]. . . .	123	122	125	128	132	134	+ 2	2.4	2.4
Western Europe.	120	119	123	129	127	125	− 1	2.3	1.5
North America.	124	122	124	126	135	140	+ 3	2.3	3.1
Oceania.	127	126	139	131	141	148	+ 5	3.4	3.1
Eastern Europe and the USSR. . . .	126	124	146	139	131	143	+10	3.1	2.1
Total, developed countries.	**124**	**122**	**131**	**131**	**132**	**137**	**+ 4**	**2.6**	**2.3**
World.	**125**	**123**	**130**	**132**	**135**	**140**	**+ 3**	**2.8**	**2.4**

Note: Food production covers crops and livestock only. In addition to other non-food products, the index numbers now also exclude coffee, tea, linseed, and hempseed, and are therefore not completely comparable with those published earlier.

(1) Preliminary. (2) Including countries in other regions not specified.

Food Production Per Capita in Developing Regions, 1971-76

Source: UN Food and Agriculture Organization

Region	1971	1972	1973	1974	1975	1976[1]	Change 1975 to 1976	Annual rate of change 1961-70	1970-76
			1961-65 = 100				%	%	%
Developing market economies[2]. . . .	102	99	100	100	103	104	+1	0.4	+0.1
Latin America.	103	101	101	103	102	107	+4	0.7	+0.1
Far East.	103	97	104	99	106	105	−1	0.2	+0.2
Near East.	103	108	100	105	109	109	—	0.5	+0.9
Africa.	99	95	89	93	93	94	+1	—	−1.2
Asian centrally planned economies.	110	107	110	111	112	112	—	1.1	+0.6
Total developing countries.	**105**	**102**	**103**	**103**	**106**	**107**	+	**0.6**	**+0.3**

(1) Preliminary. (2) Including countries in other regions not specified.

Dietary Energy Supplies Per Capita in Developing Regions

Source: UN Food and Agriculture Organization

Region	Average 1969-71	Average 1970-1971	1972	1973	1974	Requirements		Nutritional
			Percentage of requirements					Kilocalories per caput per day
Latin America.	106	107	106	106	106	107	107	2,380
Far East.	94	93	94	95	93	90	93	2,210
Near East.	98	99	98	98	99	99	102	2,460
Africa.	92	91	92	92	90	90	90	2,330

World Cereal Production

Source: UN Food and Agricultural Organization

	1973	1974	1975	1976[1]	Change 1976 over 1975
		(million tons)			(per cent)
Wheat	377	360	355	411	+15.8
Rice (milled)	216	214	230	228	− 0.9
Coarse grains	677	653	661	717	+ 8.5
Total	**1,270**	**1,227**	**1,246**	**1,356**	**+ 8.8**

(1) Preliminary.

World Cereal Production by Regions

Source: UN Food and Agriculture Organization

	Rice (paddy[1])			Wheat			Coarse grains		
	1975	1976 prelim.	1977 fore-cast	1975	1976 prelim.	1977 fore-cast	1975	1976 prelim.	1977 fore-cast
					million tons				
Far East	**314.6**	**309.7**		**74.2**	**81.5**	**79**	**128.1**	**128.4**	**128**
Bangladesh	19.1	18.5		0.1	0.2		0.1	0.1	
Burma	9.2	9.4		—	—		0.1	0.1	
China[2]	116.3	116.6		41.0	43.0		81.1	83.1	
India	74.2	70.5		24.1	28.3		29.8	28.6	
Indonesia	22.6	23.0	25.3	—	—		2.6	2.5	
Japan	17.1	15.3		0.2	0.2		0.3	0.3	
Pakistan	3.9	3.9		7.7	8.6		1.5	1.4	
Philippines	6.2	6.4		—	—		2.7	2.7	
Thailand	15.3	15.1		—	—		3.2	2.9	
Others	30.7	31.0		1.1	1.2		6.7	6.7	
Near East	**4.6**	**5.1**		**28.6**	**31.6**	**31**	**19.9**	**21.0**	**21**
Egypt	2.4	2.5	2.6	2.0	2.0		3.7	3.6	
Iran	1.4	1.7		5.5	6.0		1.5	1.6	
Turkey	0.2	0.3		14.8	16.5		7.1	7.7	
Others	0.6	0.6		6.3	7.1		7.6	8.1	
Africa	**5.3**	**5.4**		**7.4**	**8.4**	**7**	**43.8**	**44.7**	**47**
Madagascar	1.9	1.8		—	—		0.1	0.1	
Morocco	—	—		1.6	2.1		2.1	3.4	
Nigeria	0.4	0.4		—	—		7.8	8.0	
South Africa	—	—		1.8	2.1		9.7	7.7	
Others	3.0	3.2		4.0	4.2		24.1	25.5	
Latin America	**13.6**	**15.3**		**15.0**	**19.5**	**17**	**50.8**	**52.4**	**58**
Argentina	0.4	0.3	0.3	8.6	11.2		14.2	13.0	
Brazil	7.5	9.6	8.7	1.8	3.2		16.9	18.5	
Mexico	0.5	0.4		2.8	3.4		11.8	12.9	
Others	5.2	5.0		1.8	1.7		7.9	8.0	
North America	**5.8**	**5.3**	**4.5**	**75.2**	**81.9**	**71**	**204.9**	**214.3**	**210**
Canada	—	—	—	17.1	23.5		20.0	21.2	
U.S.	5.8	5.3	4.5	58.1	58.4		184.9	193.1	
Western Europe	**1.7**	**1.6**	**1.6**	**53.0**	**56.9**	**58**	**92.0**	**82.8**	**93**
EC	1.0	1.0	1.1	38.1	39.5		59.0	51.3	
Spain	0.4	0.4		4.3	4.2		9.5	7.6	
Sweden	—	—		1.5	1.8		3.8	3.7	
Yugoslavia	—	—		4.4	6.0		10.6	10.2	
Others	0.3	0.2		4.7	5.4		9.1	10.0	
Eastern Europe	**0.2**	**0.2**	**0.2**	**24.1**	**28.3**	**29**	**49.1**	**50.1**	**52**
Hungary	0.1	0.1		4.0	5.1		8.2	6.6	
Poland	—	—		5.2	5.7		14.4	15.1	
Romania	0.1	0.1		4.9	6.7		10.3	13.0	
Others	—	—		10.0	10.8		16.2	15.4	
USSR	**2.0**	**2.1**		**66.1**	**96.9**	**95**	**66.5**	**115.3**	**103**
Oceania	**0.4**	**0.4**	**0.5**	**12.2**	**12.4**	**11**	**6.0**	**5.9**	**6**
Australia	0.4	0.4	0.5	12.0	12.0		5.4	5.3	
World	**348.2**	**345.2**		**355.8**	**417.4**	**398**	**661.1**	**714.9**	**7187**

Forecast for 1977 as of May 20, 1977 (1) The conventional extraction rate to convert paddy to milled rice is 66.7%. (2) Including Taiwan.

Estimated World Carryover Stocks of Cereals

Source: UN Food and Agriculture Organization (in millions of tons)

	Crop year ending in					
Commodity	**1972**	**1973**	**1974**	**1975**	**1976**	**1977[1]**
Wheat	69	47	43	49	59	84
Rice stocks	21	13	14	13	17	16
Coarse grain stocks	75	60	50	47	46	59
Total cereals	**165**	**120**	**107**	**109**	**122**	**159**
Proportion of total consumption	**19%**	**14%**	**13%**	**12%**	**14%**	**17%**

Excluding China and USSR. FAO estimates a minimum ratio of 17-18% to assure world food security.
(1) Preliminary.

World Trade in Wheat and Coarse Grains

Source: UN Food and Agriculture Organization

	Wheat			Coarse grains		
	1975/76	1976/77 preliminary	1977/78[2] projected	1975/76	1976/77 preliminary	1977/78[2] projected
	(million tons)					
Far East	-	-	-	2.7	2.3	2.5
Thailand	-	-		2.5	2.2	
Near East	0.1	0.3	0.5	0.2	0.3	0.5
Africa	0.1	0.2	-	3.7	2.2	3.0
South Africa Rep.	-	0.2		3.4	2.1	
Latin America	3.3	5.6	4.5	6.8	8.0	8.5
Argentina	3.2	5.5		5.4	6.5	
North America	43.6	36.0	37.0-39.0	51.2	51.0	40.0-43.0
Canada	12.1	12.0		4.9	4.8	
United States	31.5	24.0		46.3	46.2	
Western Europe	9.0	5.3	6.5-7.5	3.2	1.4	2.5
EEC[1]	7.9	4.2		2.5	0.6	
Eastern Europe	1.2	1.3	1.5	2.0	1.3	2.0
U.S.S.R.	0.7	2.5	2.0	-	2.0	2.0
Oceania	7.9	7.8	8.0	3.3	3.0	3.0
Australia	7.9	7.7		3.2	2.9	
World	**65.9**	**59.0**	**60.0-63.0**	**73.1**	**71.5**	**64.0-67.0**
Imports						
Far East	23.3	20.3	20.0-22.0	17.8	18.6	19.0-20.0
China	2.3	3.5		0.2	-	
India	6.8	3.5		0.5	-	
Japan	5.9	5.6		13.5	14.8	
Near East	7.7	8.0	9.0	2.5	2.7	3.0
Egypt	3.6	4.0		0.5	0.5	
Africa	5.0	4.5	6.0	1.0	1.1	1.0
Latin America	9.0	8.5	9.0	4.7	3.5	4.0
Brazil	3.7	3.0		-	-	
Mexico	-	-		2.3	1.2	
North America	-	-	-	0.9	1.1	1 0
Western Europe	8.1	6.5	6.5	25.3	32.0	26.0-28.0
EEC[1]	6.4	5.0		17.8	24.0	
Eastern Europe	4.0	6.0	5.0	6.0	7.5	6.0
USSR	10.2	5.0	4.0-5.0	14.7	5.0	4.0
Oceania	0.2	0.2	0.5	-	-	-
World	**67.5**	**59.0**	**60.0-63.0**	**72.9**	**71.5**	**64.0-67.0**

(1) Excluding trade between EC member countries. (2) Oceania and unspecified.

European Community: Food Aid in Cereals for 1976-77

Source: EC Commission

Recipient countries	EC Total aid	Community actions	National actions
	(thousand tons)		
Latin America	**15.0**	**11.0**	**4.0**
Bolivia	2.5	2.5	—
Haiti	3.0	—	3.0
Honduras	1.0	1.0	—
Peru	8.5	7.5	1.0
Africa	**263.93**	**127.63**	**136.3**
Angola	11.5	10.0	1.5
Benin	2.5	2.5	—
Botswana	0.5	0.5	—
Burundi	4.5	1.0	3.5
Cape Verde	9.5	8.5	1.0
Cent. Af. Emp.	1.0	1.0	—
Congo P.R.	3.0	—	3.0
Ethiopia	11.5	2.5	9.0
Ghana	3.5	3.5	—
Guinea	6.5	3.5	3.0
Guinea Bissau	4.5	3.0	1.5
Lesotho	0.13	0.13	—
Liberia	3.0	3.0	—
Mauritius	6.5	3.5	3.0
Mozambique	32.3	15.0	17.3
Rwanda	5.0	2.5	2.5
Sao Tome & Principe	1.5	1.5	—
Senegal	11.0	8.0	3.0
Somalia	34.0	25.0	9.0
Sudan	3.5	3.5	—
Tanzania	15.0	5.0	10.0
Tunisia	26.5	3.5	23.0
Zaire	15.0	15.0	—
Zambia	6.0	6.0	—
Unspecified[1]	4.0	—	4.0
Not yet allocated	42.0	—	42.0
Near East	**221.5**	**160.0**	**61.5**
Egypt	150.0	100.0	50.0
Jordan	21.0	18.0[3]	3.0
Lebanon	32.5	25.0	7.5
Syria	5.0	5.0	—
Yemen A.R.	6.0	6.0	—
Yemen P.D.R.	7.0	6.0	1.[illegible]
Far East	**347.5**	**202.5**	**145.0**
Bangladesh	142.0	100.0	42.0
Indonesia	31.5	10.0	21.5
Laos	—	—	—
Pakistan	49.0	25.0	24.0
Philippines	10.5	7.5	3.0
Sri Lanka	69.5	30.0	39.5
Vietnam	30.0	30.0	—
Unspecified[2]	15.0	—	15.0
Other countries	**5.5**	**1.0**	**4.5**
Malta	5.5	1.0	4.5
Reserve	**183.97**	**78.37**	**105.[illegible]**
Total	**1,287.0**	**720.5**	**566.[illegible]**

(1) To be distributed between Ethiopia and Mozambique. (2) To be distributed between Laos and Vietnam. (3) For Palestinian refugees.

Grain, Hay, Potato, Cotton, Tobacco Production

Source: Statistical Reporting Service: U.S. Agriculture Department

1976 State	Barley 1,000 bushels	Corn, grain 1,000 bushels	Cotton' lint 1,000 bales	All hay 1,000 tons	Oats 1,000 bushels	Potatoes 1,000 cwt.	Rye 1,000 bushels	Tobacco 1,000 pounds	All wheat 1,000 bushels
Alabama	—	49,352	350	1,105	1,080	2,799	—	1,152	3,375
Alaska	—	—	—	—	—	—	—	—	—
Arizona	7,600	1,680	810	1,570	—	1,836	—	—	32,325
Arkansas	—	2,520	780	1,241	5,320	—	—	—	27,690
California	56,560	31,900	2,530	7,554	5,635	24,188	—	—	59,720
Colorado	13,475	62,400	—	2,814	2,350	11,025	161	—	47,990
Connecticut	—	—	—	174	—	494	—	7,323	—
Delaware	880	18,275	—	48	—	1,160	207	—	1,085
Florida	—	30,240	7.6	427	600	6,293	—	30,013	660
Georgia	450	133,920	200	1,070	5,100	85,175	2,420	123,760	3,565
Hawaii	—	—	—	—	—	—	—	—	—
Idaho	43,200	2,465	—	4,201	3,192	—	—	—	68,320
Illinois	520	1,250,830	—	3,375	23,780	513	315	—	72,150
Indiana	378	693,000	—	2,150	10,560	1,570	230	17,390	57,600
Iowa	—	1,147,500	—	6,768	87,025	537	140	—	2,975
Kansas	2,584	170,050	—	4,535	10,080	—	255	—	339,000
Kentucky	1,110	138,720	0.7	2,988	350	—	60	490,039	10,230
Louisiana	—	5,916	555	710	480	195	—	—	1,115
Maine	—	—	—	433	1,924	27,440	—	145	—
Maryland	4,230	57,330	—	589	1,350	306	297	28,750	5,244
Massachusetts	—	—	—	238	—	704	—	1,932	—
Michigan	882	141,450	—	3,010	19,635	9,622	676	—	37,620
Minnesota	34,830	330,400	—	5,765	92,700	13,055	2,048	—	130,482
Mississippi	—	8,084	1,145	1,130	966	190	—	—	5,220
Missouri	320	173,850	165	4,998	6,800	—	210	5,980	54,450
Montana	52,065	825	—	4,059	10,810	1,806	—	—	167,295
Nebraska	1,368	514,600	—	6,163	26,880	1,654	1,020	—	94,400
Nevada	864	—	1.7	939	144	5,320	—	—	1,027
New Hampshire	—	—	—	182	—	104	—	—	—
New Jersey	980	8,600	—	298	408	1,976	240	—	2,310
New Mexico	1,020	9,240	80	924	—	576	—	—	6,089
New York	492	37,884	—	5,352	16,380	13,032	360	—	5,940
North Carolina	2,340	150,440	70	477	3,600	2,425	380	900,505	6,960
North Dakota	81,320	7,200	—	3,996	44,840	16,940	2,831	—	287,830
Ohio	564	395,920	—	3,593	27,500	3,079	196	24,510	66,000
Oklahoma	3,570	8,645	178	3,427	5,940	—	684	—	151,200
Oregon	7,360	990	—	2,410	4,160	28,913	225	—	60,301
Pennsylvania	6,321	103,500	—	4,325	18,250	7,140	364	23,125	9,450
Rhode Island	—	—	—	18	—	1,029	—	—	—
South Carolina	805	46,690	145	460	2,870	—	510	153,375	3,625
South Dakota	5,950	37,200	—	2,840	42,600	286	1,485	—	39,520
Tennessee	532	56,485	225	1,845	1,440	447	54	135,228	12,395
Texas	2,028	180,000	3,250	5,370	14,430	3,453	378	—	103,400
Utah	6,930	1,350	—	1,820	684	1,248	—	—	6,519
Vermont	—	—	—	913	—	205	—	—	—
Virginia	4,738	46,740	0.5	1,279	1,890	3,506	322	153,868	7,680
Washington	21,060	4,620	—	2,474	2,565	55,800	176	—	144,050
West Virginia	378	5,368	—	839	656	274	—	3,150	448
Wisconsin	1,280	148,240	—	8,126	55,040	15,370	252	18,315	3,238
Wyoming	8,280	1,653	—	1,854	2,438	1,701	171	—	6,875
Total U.S.	**377,264**	**6,216,032**	**10,493.5**	**120,876**	**562,452**	**353,386**	**16,667**	**2,118,560**	**2,147,408**

(1) Equiv. 480 lbs.

Grain Receipts at U.S. Grain Centers

Source: Chicago Board of Trade (thousands bushels)

1976	Wheat	Corn	Oats	Rye	Barley	Soybeans	Total
Chicago	21,079	116,933	584	189	85	22,487	161,357
Duluth	131,548	12,430	7,384	799	46,014	—	198,175
Enid	77,706	—	—	—	—	—	77,706
Hutchinson	66,843	33	—	—	—	—	66,876
Kansas City	97,780	51,378	559	2	—	9,873	159,592
Milwaukee	225	20,104	59	—	19,373	174	39,935
Minneapolis	117,230	89,292	32,467	4,094	42,442	29,270	314,795
Omaha	20,165	41,511	2,191	53	—	3,946	67,866
Peoria	200	21,004	8	72	—	48	21,332
Sioux City	2,371	6,248	5,147	—	8	16,216	29,990
St. Joseph	3,870	9,086	3,813	—	—	3,914	20,683
St. Louis	35,104	23,467	477	—	—	21,866	80,914
Toledo	20,004	108,838	5,564	—	2	44,135	176,543
Wichita	51,822	2,901	—	—	285	6,201	61,209
Total	**644,698**	**497,521**	**57,454**	**5,209**	**108,203**	**142,332**	**1,455,417**

Production of Chief U. S. Crops

Source: Statistical Reporting Service, U.S. Agriculture Department

Year	Corn grain 1,000 bushels	Oats 1,000 bushels	Barley 1,000 bushels	Sorghums for grain 1,000 bushels	All wheat 1,000 bushels	Rye 1,000 bushels	Flax-seed 1,000 bushels	Cotton lint 1,000 bales	Cotton seed 1,000 tons
1965...	4,102,867	929,554	393,055	672,698	1,315,603	33,307	35,402	14,938	6,087
1970...	4,151,938	917,159	416,139	683,571	1,351,558	36,840	29,548	10,192	4,068
1972...	5,573,320	691,973	423,461	809,264	1,544,936	29,183	13,909	13,704	5,393
1973...	5,646,806	666,867	421,527	930,012	1,705,167	26,263	16,091	12,974	5,016
1974...	4,663,631	613,777	304,112	629,222	1,796,187	19,293	13,541	11,540	4,510
1975...	5,797,048	657,640	383,920	760,069	2,134,833	17,875	15,019	8,302	3,030
1976...	6,216,032	562,452	377,264	723,679	2,147,408	7,356	7,356	10,557	4,035

Year	Tobacco 1,000 lbs.	All hay 1,000 tons	Beans dry edible 1,000 cwt.	Peas dry field 1,000 cwt.	Peanuts 1,000 lbs.	Soy-beans 1,000 bushel	Pota-toes 1,000 cwt.	Sweet pota-toes 1,000 cwt.
1965........	1,854,568	125,610	16,457	3,031	2,389,596	845,608	291,109	15,469
1970........	1,906,453	126,971	17,399	3,315	2,979,465	1,127,100	325,752	13,409
1972........	1,749,085	128,614	18,118	2,103	3,274,761	1,270,630	295,955	12,453
1973........	1,742,105	134,751	16,389	1,665	3,473,837	1,547,165	299,410	12,534
1974........	1,989,728	127,143	20,343	3,228	3,667,604	1,214,802	342,060	13,921
1975........	2,181,775	132,729	17,422	2,731	3,857,122	1,546,120	319,834	13,567
1976........	2,118,560	120,876	17,216	2,150	3,735,435	1,264,890	353,386	13,703

Year	Five seed crops* 1,000 lbs.	Sugar and seed 1,000 tons	Sugar beets 1,000 tons	Pecans 1,000 tons	Al-monds 1,000 tons	Wal-nuts 1,000 tons	Fil-berts 1,000 tons	Oranges and tan-gerines 1,000 boxes	Grape-fruit 1,000 boxes
1965..............	302,592	23,663	20,918	125.6	72.9	80.3	7.7	139,650	46,695
1970..............	254,429	23,996	26,427	77.6	124.0	111.8	9.3	194,790	60,560
1972..............	165,876*	28,332	28,410	91.6	125.0	116.8	10.2	229,790	65,640
1973..............	172,957	25,827	24,499	137.9	134.0	175.0	12.3	221,050	65,100
1974..............	177,400	24,812	22,123	68.6	189.0	156.5	6.7	221,050	65,500
1975..............	160,697	28,523	29,704	123.4	160.0	199.3	12.1	243,240	61,580
1976..............	137,946	28,790	29,427	49.9	230.0	185.7	7.1	247,790	70,090

*Five seed crops include alfalfa, red clover, sweet clover, lespedeza, and timothy. Beginning 1972 sweet clover was discontinued.

Production of Principal Field Crops in Canada

Source: Statistics Canada

1976	Wheats 1,000 bushels	Oats 1,000 bushels	Barley 1,000 bushels	Ryes 1,000 bushels	Flaxseed 1,000 bushels
Canada[1]..........................	**864,326**	**321,676**	**473,245**	**22,089**	**11,700**
Prince Edward Island................	469	3,158	1,475	—	—
Nova Scotia..........................	170	901	343	—	—
New Brunswick......................	180	2,193	354	—	—
Quebec................................	2,529	24,304	2,268	49	—
Ontario................................	24,978	16,520	14,805	1,260	—
Manitoba..............................	103,000	61,000	65,000	2,900	6,300
Saskatchewan........................	548,000	103,000	135,000	9,300	3,800
Alberta................................	182,000	106,000	245,000	8,400	1,600
British Columbia....................	3,000	4,600	9,000	180	—

	Mixed grains 1,000 bushels	Corn grains 1,000 bushels	Soybeans 1,000 bushels	Rapeseed 1,000 bushels	Potatoes 1,000 c.w.t.
Canada[1]..........................	**83,158**	**144,669**	**9,250**	**41,000**	**58,229**
Prince Edward Island................	5,365	—	—	—	13,853
Nova Scotia..........................	560	—	—	—	616
New Brunswick......................	258	—	—	—	11,838
Quebec................................	5,425	10,719	—	—	8,622
Ontario................................	38,400	133,000	9,250	—	11,700
Manitoba..............................	8,100	950	—	4,500	4,500
Saskatchewan........................	7,300	—	—	19,400	550
Alberta................................	17,500	—	—	16,500	3,800
British Columbia....................	250	—	—	600	2,750

	Mustard seed 1,000 pounds	Sunflower seed 1,000 pounds	Tame hay 1,000 tons	Fodder corn 1,000 tons	Sugar beets 1,000 tons
Canada[1]..........................	**115,400**	**53,000**	**25,322**	**13,665**	**1,277**
Prince Edward Island................	—	—	244	140	—
Nova Scotia..........................	—	—	319	215	—
New Brunswick......................	—	—	298	135	—
Quebec................................	—	—	5,211	2,850	117
Ontario................................	—	—	6,750	9,675	—
Manitoba..............................	14,400	53,000	2,400	300	386
Saskatchewan........................	67,000	—	3,000	—	—
Alberta................................	34,000	—	5,400	—	774
British Columbia....................	—	—	1,700	350	—

(1) Excluding Newfoundland. Estimates as indicated on or about November 15, 1976.

Harvested Acreage of Principal U.S. Crops

Source: Statistical Reporting Service: U.S. Agriculture Department (thousands of acres)

State	1974	1975	1976	State	1974	1975	1976
Alabama	3,345	3,524	3,652	Nebraska	17,548	17,669	18,101
Arizona	1,211	1,208	1,329	Nevada	492	503	516
Arkansas	7,531	7,907	8,024	New Hampshire	108	110	115
California	6,284	6,418	6,511	New Jersey	417	423	473
Colorado	5,762	5,611	5,576	New Mexico	966	1,239	978
Connecticut	152	154	151	New York	4,057	4,078	4,140
Delaware	495	502	501	North Carolina	4,757	4,779	4,735
Florida	1,340	1,383	1,492	North Dakota	19,436	19,589	20,611
Georgia	4,896	4,882	4,929	Ohio	10,661	10,731	10,869
Hawaii	101	112	105	Oklahoma	10,162	10,371	10,070
Idaho	4,277	4,291	4,405	Oregon	2,664	2,643	2,769
Illinois	22,270	22,906	23,133	Pennsylvania	4,465	4,475	4,474
Indiana	12,192	12,259	12,595	Rhode Island	17	17	17
Iowa	24,057	24,259	24,379	South Carolina	2,781	2,741	2,708
Kansas	21,467	21,661	21,520	South Dakota	15,669	15,261	12,886
Kentucky	4,635	4,699	4,781	Tennessee	4,462	4,610	4,762
Louisiana	3,951	3,760	4,165	Texas	19,581	23,043	21,495
Maine	438	422	414	Utah	1,147	1,155	1,116
Maryland	1,502	1,530	1,554	Vermont	574	580	577
Massachusetts	153	153	154	Virginia	2,834	2,854	2,842
Michigan	6,188	6,291	6,350	Washington	4,772	4,826	4,941
Minnesota	20,256	20,368	21,252	West Virginia	755	759	741
Mississippi	5,438	5,533	6,061	Wisconsin	9,148	9,164	9,213
Missouri	12,872	13,240	13,466	Wyoming	1,713	1,808	1,824
Montana	8,949	9,094	9,248	**Total U. S.**	**318,948**	**325,595**	**326,720**

Crop acreages included are corn, sorghum, oats, barley, wheat, rice, rye, soybeans, flaxseed, peanuts, sunflower seed (1975, 1976), popcorn, cotton, all hay, dry edible beans, dry edible peas, potatoes, sweet potatoes, tobacco, sugarcane and sugar beets.

Livestock on Farms in the U.S.

Source: Statistical Reporting Service: U.S. Agriculture Department (thousands)

Year (On Jan. 1)	All cattle	Milk cows	All sheep	Hogs	Horses* and mules
1890	60,014	15,000	44,518	48,130	18,054
1900	59,739	16,544	48,105	51,055	21,004
1910	58,993	19,450	50,239	48,072	24,211
1920	70,400	21,455	40,743	60,159	25,742
1925	63,373	22,575	38,543	55,770	22,569
1930	61,003	23,032	51,565	55,705	19,124
1935	68,846	26,082	51,808	39,066	16,683
1940	68,039	24,940	52,107	61,165	14,478
1945	85,573	27,770	46,520	59,373	11,950
1950	77,963	23,853	29,826	58,937	7,781
1955	96,592	23,462	31,582	50,474	4,309
1960	96,236	19,527	33,170	59,026	3,089

Year (On Jan. 1)	All cattle	Milk cows	All sheep	Hogs
1965	109,000	[2]15,380	25,127	57,030
1967	108,783	13,725	23,953	[3]57,125
1968	109,371	13,115	22,223	[3]58,818
1969	110,015	12,550	21,350	[3]60,829
1970	112,369	12,091	20,423	[3]57,046
1971	114,578	11,909	19,686	[3]67,433
1972	117,862	11,778	18,710	[3]62,507
1973	121,534	11,624	17,724	[3]59,180
1974	127,540	11,286	16,394	61,106
1975[1]	131,826	11,211	14,512	55,062
1976	127,976	11,087	13,376	49,602
1977	122,896	11,031	12,710	[3]55,085

*Discontinued in 1960. (1) Total estimated value on farms as of Jan. 1, 1975, was as follows (avg. value per head in parentheses): cattle and calves $20,963,981 ($159.00); sheep and lambs $442,271 ($30.40); hogs $2,481,644 ($45.10); chickens $652,-799 ($1.71); turkeys $29,223,000 ($9.84) (2) New series, milk cows and heifers that have calved beginning 1965. (3) Dec. 1, preceding year.

Egg Production in the U.S.

Source: Statistical Reporting Service: U.S. Agriculture Department (millions of eggs)

State	1974	1975	1976	State	1974	1975	1976	State	1974	1975	1976	State	1974	1975	1976
Ala.	2,945	2,951	2,919	Ind.	2,639	2,609	2,774	Neb.	723	782	737	S.C.	1,301	1,384	1,282
Alas.	6.4	5.0	6.0	Ia.	2,069	2,006	1,949	Nev.	5	4	5	S.D.	770	701	622
Ariz.	149	159	143	Kan.	601	599	564	N.H.	275	283	260	Tenn.	1,026	949	922
Ark.	3,601	3,594	—	Ky.	527	518	541	N.J.	736	620	548	Tex.	2,292	2,360	2,357
Cal.	8,485	8,467	8,953	La.	664	658	671	N.M.	197	234	270	Ut.	311	321	283
Col.	385	473	505	Me.	1,656	1,650	1,790	N.Y.	2,030	1,984	1,903	Vt.	131	105	—
Conn.	864	817	913	Md.	335	331	314	N.C.	3,037	2,802	2,756	Va.	760	765	799
Del.	134	115	127	Mass.	509	537	442	N.D.	151	132	120	Wash.	1,089	1,084	1,060
Fla.	2,852	2,779	2,846	Mich.	1,375	1,303	1,293	Oh.	2,057	1,999	1,913	W.Va.	248	256	230
Ga.	5,827	5,284	5,591	Minn.	2,385	2,209	2,289	Okla.	428	430	458	Wis.	1,183	1,194	1,159
Ha.	207	209	218	Miss.	1,908	1,707	1,719	Ore.	543	519	532	Wy.	30	30	26
Ida.	186	184	192	Mo.	1,149	1,241	1,195	Pa.	3,490	3,299	3,153	**Total**			
Ill.	1,543	1,483	1,392	Mon.	202	196	178	R.I.	65.4	70	65	**U.S.**	**66,083**	**64,391**	**64,821**

Gross income from farm eggs 1973, $2,912,454,000; 1974, $2,935,998,000; 1975, $2,813,412,000. Prices received by farmers per dozen eggs 1973, 52.5c; 1974, 53.3c; 1975, 52.3c. Gross income from farm chickens 1973, $174,098,000; 1974, $122,904,000; 1975, $108,705,000. Commercial broilers produced 1973, 3,008,667,000 ($2,690,362,000); 1974, 2,992,334,000 ($2,435,861,000); 1975, 2,932,711,000 ($2,899,183,000). Gross income from eggs and chickens 1973, $5,776,914,000; 1974, $5,500,000,000; 1975, $5,800,000,000.

U.S. Meat and Lard Production and Consumption

Source: Economic Research Service: U.S. Agriculture Department (million lbs.)

Year	Beef		Veal		Lamb and mutton		Pork (exclud. lard)		All meats		Lard	
	Production	Consumption	Production	Consumption	Production	Consumption	Production	Consumption	Production	Consumption	Production	Consumption
1940	7,175	7,257	981	981	876	873	10,044	9,701	19,076	18,812	2,288	1,901
1950	9,534	9,529	1,230	1,206	597	596	10,714	10,390	22,075	21,721	2,631	1,891
1960	14,753	15,147	1,109	1,093	768	852	11,607	11,566	28,237	28,658	2,562	1,358
1965	18,727	19,060	1,020	992	651	716	11,141	11,235	31,539	32,003	2,045	1,225
1970	21,685	22,926	588	581	551	657	13,436	13,391	36,260	37,555	1,913	939
1974	23,138	24,489	486	493	465	483	13,805	13,962	37,894	39,427	1,366	680
1975	23,975	25,397	873	876	410	431	11,504	11,576	36,762	38,280	1,012	632
1976	25,972	27,458	857	865	372	398	12,443	12,402	39,644	41,123	1,025	565

Grain Storage Capacity at Principal Grain Centers in U.S. and Canada

Source: Chicago Board of Trade
(bushels)

United States	Capacity
Atlantic Coast	35,500,000
Great Lakes	
Toledo	32,200,000
Buffalo	16,700,000
Chicago	59,900,000
Milwaukee	5,600,000
Duluth	67,000,000
River Points	
Minneapolis	115,700,000
Peoria	6,600,000
St. Louis	25,500,000
Sioux City	11,600,000
Omaha-Council Bluffs	35,300,000
Atchinson	24,500,000
St. Joseph	20,600,000
Kansas City	72,400,000
Southwest	
Fort Worth	57,600,000
Texas High Plains	89,500,000
Enid	66,100,000
Gulf Points	
South Mississippi	48,500,000
North Texas Gulf	28,200,000
South Texas Gulf	14,000,000
Plains	
Wichita	59,600,000
Topeka	61,600,000
Salina	26,300,000
Hutchinson	42,000,000
Hastings-Grand Island	22,000,000
Lincoln	39,600,000
Des Moines	9,700,000
Pacific N.W.	
Puget Sound	12,500,000
Portland	33,100,000
California Ports	14,300,000

Canada	Capacity
Bae Comeau, Que.	13,778,000
Calgary, Alta.	2,500,000
Churchill, Man.	5,000,000
Collingwood, Ont.	2,000,000
Edmonton, Alta.	2,350,000
Goderich, Ont.	4,600,000
Halifax, N.S.	5,125,500
Kingston, Ont.	2,350,000
Lethbridge, Alta.	1,250,000
Midland, Ont.	11,550,000
Montreal, Que.	19,600,000
Moose Jaw, Sask.	5,500,000
North Vancouver, B.C.	5,472,000
Owen Sound, Ont.	4,000,000
Port Cartier, Que.	10,462,000
Port Colbourne, Ont.	5,250,000
Port McNicoll, Ont.	6,500,000
Prescott, Ont.	5,500,000
Prince Rupert, B.C.	2,250,000
Quebec, Que.	8,000,000
Saint John, N.B.	400,000
Sarnia, Ont.	5,400,000
Saskatoon, Sask.	5,500,000
Sorel, Que.	5,230,000
Three Rivers, Que.	5,880,000
Thunder Bay, B.C.	85,768,100
Toronto, Ont.	4,000,000
Vancouver, B.C.	18,056,000
Victoria, B.C.	1,040,000
West St. John, N.B.	2,576,800

Atlantic Coast — Albany, N.Y., Philadelphia, Pa., Baltimore, Md., Norfolk, Va., North Charleston, S.C. Gulf Points: S. Miss. — New Orleans, Baton Rouge, AMA, Belle Chasse, La., Mobile, Ala., Pascagoula, Miss.; N. Texas Gulf — Houston, Galveston, Beaumont, Port Arthur, Texas; S. Texas Gulf — Corpus Christi, Brownsville, Texas. Pacific N.W. — Seattle, Tacoma, Wash., Portland, Ore., Columbia River. Calif. Ports — San Francisco, Stockton, Sacramento, Los Angeles. Texas High Plains — Amarillo, Lubbock, Hereford, Plainview, Texas.

Grain Receipts at Western Canadian Grain Centers

Source: Canadian Grain Commission (thousands of bushels)

Crop year 1974-75 Province	Wheat	Oats	Barley	Rye	Flaxseed	Rapeseed	Total
Western Canada	**422,431**	**40,280**	**209,224**	**10,435**	**10,797**	**41,217**	**734,385**
Manitoba	49,693	12,535	32,368	1,911	5,028	6,300	107,834
Saskatchewan	280,184	13,486	80,482	3,984	3,880	19,637	401,653
Alberta and British Columbia	92,554	14,258	96,374	4,540	1,890	15,281	224,898

Egg Production in Canada

Source: Statistics Canada
(thousand dozens)

Province	1974	1975	1976
Newfoundland	7,857	6,740	6,749
Prince Edward Island	2,363	2,373	2,568
Nova Scotia	19,297	17,756	16,134
New Brunswick	8,770	8,852	8,532
Quebec	64,613	67,419	75,035
Ontario	189,323	175,966	165,506
Manitoba	50,498	49,757	48,871
Saskatchewan	21,019	20,722	18,635
Alberta	40,769	42,039	39,964
British Columbia	54,942	53,301	55,096
Total	**459,451**	**444,925**	**437,090**

Realized gross farm income from eggs (1973) $255,302,000; (1974) $283,871,000; (1975) $274,467,000; (1976) $297,292,000. Average price of eggs sold for consumption taking the month of February (1973) $.45; (1974) $.63; (1975) $.56; (1976) $.63. Realized gross farm income from chickens (1973) $324,992,000; (1974) $344,839,000; (1975) $317,688,000; (1976) $354,773,-000. Fowl produced (1973) 23,965,000, $13,567,000; (1974) 23,764,000, $9,412,000; (1975) 22,909,000, $6,605,000; (1976) 21,279,000, $6,192,000. Realized gross farm income from eggs, chicken and fowl (1973) $580,294,000; (1974) $628,710,000; (1975) $592,155,000; (1976) $652,065,000.

Canadian Production of Sawn Lumber

Source: Canadian Statistical Review (May, 1977)
(million feet, board measure)

Year	Canada[1]	N.S.	N.B.	Que.	Ont.	Sask.	Alta.	B.C.
1972	13,887.5	179.2	313.6	2,146.9	1,082.9	135.6	580.0	9,446.9
1974	13,499	188	342	2,210	1,260	139	618	8,755
1975	11,283	162	256	1,930	948	127	391	7,469
1976	15,432	159	321	2,364	1,175	156	511	10,745

(1) Excludes Newfoundland, P.E.I., Manitoba, the Yukon, and the Northwest Territories which, together, account for less than 1% of the total.

U.S. Farms by State — Number, Acreage, and Value

Source: Bureau of the Census

State 1970	Farms	2,000 acres or more	10-49 acres	Average acreage	$ Value per acre	Total acreage
Alabama	72,491	629	21,439	188.3	$199.60	13,654,215
Alaska	322	35	32	4,831.9	12.73	1,604,211
Arizona	5,890	897	1,229	6,486.0	69.72	38,202,667
Arkansas	60,433	625	10,935	259.7	260.03	15,694,527
California	77,875	2,926	28,915	458.7	474.65	35,722,348
Colorado	27,950	4,166	3,048	1,312.9	94.58	36,697,132
Connecticut	4,490	6	1,245	120.5	921.19	541,372
Delaware	3,710	14	872	181.6	498.96	673,895
Florida	35,586	1,062	12,413	394.3	354.58	14,031,998
Georgia	67,431	693	13,737	234.4	234.00	15,805,892
Hawaii	3,896	70	1,281	528.2	296.82	2,058,087
Idaho	25,475	1,218	4,382	565.9	176.55	14,416,521
Illinois	123,565	145	13,487	242.0	489.52	29,913,190
Indiana	101,479	65	19,522	173.1	406.05	17,572,865
Iowa	140,354	84	9,586	239.1	391.73	33,569,629
Kansas	86,057	3,341	5,231	573.9	158.78	49,390,369
Kentucky	125,069	114	26,761	127.6	253.05	15,968,243
Louisiana	42,269	536	13,610	231.5	321.33	9,788,662
Maine	7,971	25	948	220.7	160.79	1,759,700
Maryland	17,181	41	3,733	163.1	639.63	2,803,442
Massachusetts	5,703	7	1,622	122.8	564.63	700,578
Michigan	77,946	43	14,334	152.7	326.31	11,900,689
Minnesota	110,747	305	6,459	260.4	225.76	28,845,240
Mississippi	72,577	894	17,060	221.0	233.53	16,039,665
Missouri	137,067	396	16,823	236.5	224.22	32,420,284
Montana	24,951	7,596	1,485	2,521.6	59.57	62,918,247
Nebraska	72,257	3,509	3,113	677.4	154.38	48,949,376
Nevada	2,112	333	305	5,070.2	53.35	10,708,346
New Hampshire	2,902	6	443	211.1	238.78	612,750
New Jersey	8,493	13	2,471	121.9	1,092.31	1,035,678
New Mexico	11,641	2,660	1,704	4,019.6	41.87	46,792,302
New York	51,909	50	6,589	195.5	273.13	10,148,359
North Carolina	119,386	205	42,911	106.6	333.31	12,733,751
North Dakota	46,381	3,157	721	929.6	93.82	43,117,831
Ohio	111,332	53	19,729	153.6	398.51	17,111,459
Oklahoma	83,037	2,024	7,655	433.6	172.58	36,007,719
Oregon	29,063	1,739	9,000	619.9	150.22	18,017,850
Pennsylvania	62,824	38	10,428	141.6	372.88	8,900,767
Rhode Island	700	...	235	98.1	733.75	68,720
South Carolina	39,559	286	12,129	176.7	261.23	6,991,718
South Dakota	45,726	4,148	1,402	996.9	83.69	45,584,164
Tennessee	121,406	212	35,117	124.0	267.50	15,056,907
Texas	213,550	9,941	27,315	667.6	148.49	142,566,826
Utah	13,045	849	3,159	867.2	91.90	11,312,951
Vermont	6,874	17	465	278.6	223.73	1,915,520
Virginia	64,572	206	15,169	164.9	286.13	10,649,862
Washington	34,033	1,693	10,817	515.9	223.83	17,559,187
West Virginia	23,142	67	3,808	187.5	135.69	4,340,554
Wisconsin	98,973	81	8,118	182.9	231.98	18,109,273
Wyoming	8,838	2,689	473	4,014.0	40.73	35,476,374
Total	**2,730,242**	**59,909**	**473,465**	**390.5**	**—**	**1,066,218,650**

Net Income per Farm by States

Source: Economic Research Service, U.S. Agriculture Department

State	1968	1969	1970	1971	1972	1973	1974	1975
Alabama	$ 2,447	$ 2,853	$ 2,723	$ 2,873	$ 4,144	$ 6,159	$ 3,039	$ 4,642
Alaska	3,619	2,797	4,681	3,452	4,203	4,813	5,219	11,020
Arizona	17,190	22,722	19,350	24,029	21,068	42,615	61,178	37,594
Arkansas	3,635	3,892	4,357	4,110	5,066	11,078	7,910	10,152
California	16,849	17,683	15,778	17,351	23,148	36,395	39,966	34,634
Colorado	6,035	5,576	6,119	7,709	10,072	17,596	19,055	15,630
Connecticut	8,165	9,381	9,517	9,291	9,699	12,280	8,408	9,880
Delaware	6,907	10,890	7,902	8,954	11,752	26,583	21,405	23,564
Florida	10,071	12,285	10,751	14,219	19,005	23,056	19,316	26,412
Georgia	3,682	4,374	4,225	4,545	6,046	9,558	7,049	8,056
Hawaii	12,035	9,802	10,848	14,526	17,389	16,401	89,553	28,128
Idaho	4,308	6,105	6,273	6,643	9,569	14,765	21,045	14,203
Illinois	5,780	6,121	6,159	4,819	6,528	11,746	15,189	9,116
Indiana	3,680	4,895	3,846	4,440	4,112	10,245	9,503	7,354
Iowa	5,605	7,898	8,016	5,741	8,119	16,908	17,041	10,294
Kansas	3,033	3,992	5,384	6,042	10,488	15,032	14,921	7,483
Kentucky	2,572	2,931	2,995	2,441	3,453	4,220	3,856	3,940
Louisiana	4,173	4,018	4,107	4,452	5,531	10,483	9,446	6,021
Maine	3,631	6,249	6,188	4,956	6,673	20,595	17,621	10,356
Maryland	4,314	5,955	5,381	4,886	6,752	10,016	8,247	9,423
Massachusetts	6,001	6,626	6,407	6,376	6,683	8,357	5,621	6,587
Michigan	2,751	3,368	3,012	3,291	3,745	7,408	6,324	5,885
Minnesota	4,628	5,729	6,578	5,902	7,816	15,647	16,465	9,775
Mississippi	3,220	3,614	3,095	3,918	4,384	7,086	4,460	2,966
Missouri	2,350	3,066	2,711	2,585	3,769	5,492	4,222	4,206
Montana	5,690	6,952	7,962	7,071	13,993	18,556	17,785	12,165
Nebraska	5,061	6,221	7,232	5,659	8,977	13,329	17,034	13,744
Nevada	2,040	8,608	11,262	11,398	17,570	25,414	15,872	9,991
New Hampshire	4,603	5,271	4,917	5,444	7,104	9,537	6,394	7,087
New Jersey	7,402	7,657	7,078	6,276	6,111	10,183	10,558	6,959
New Mexico	5,333	6,526	9,398	9,488	9,276	16,808	7,767	16,065
New York	5,608	6,267	5,892	5,604	5,613	6,663	4,317	4,199
North Carolina	2,748	3,612	3,761	3,656	4,918	7,897	7,483	8,027
North Dakota	4,387	5,805	6,780	6,164	13,817	29,008	32,233	17,055
Ohio	3,057	3,329	3,166	2,681	3,653	5,735	5,895	6,598
Oklahoma	1,489	2,176	3,219	2,090	3,624	6,992	3,032	3,855
Oregon	3,656	4,484	4,070	3,785	6,005	10,633	12,656	8,358
Pennsylvania	3,381	3,973	4,041	3,836	4,478	5,208	4,151	4,556
Rhode Island	5,678	6,740	8,815	8,373	8,100	5,694	4,647	12,963
South Carolina	2,285	2,685	2,891	2,613	3,865	5,442	5,719	4,485
South Dakota	6,056	6,789	7,166	6,385	11,163	17,343	19,776	12,432
Tennessee	1,559	1,713	1,715	1,506	2,054	3,327	1,118	1,788
Texas	2,399	3,269	3,745	3,108	3,233	8,632	4,490	5,252
Utah	3,560	3,602	4,212	4,705	6,552	10,513	5,504	5,569
Vermont	5,518	6,372	6,502	6,966	8,737	9,575	7,092	6,867
Virginia	1,781	2,090	2,254	1,936	2,714	4,570	3,692	4,029
Washington	6,545	6,958	5,555	5,633	10,643	18,704	17,170	18,320
West Virginia	529	641	699	488	962	1,383	626	897
Wisconsin	4,684	5,167	5,199	5,187	6,729	8,697	6,853	7,456
Wyoming	4,506	4,836	4,284	5,318	11,690	15,083	5,198	4,428
Total U.S.	**3,972**	**4,733**	**4,788**	**4,550**	**6,204**	**10,529**	**9,826**	**8,079**

Farm Income—Cash Receipts from Marketings

Source: Economic Research Service: U.S. Agriculture Department

($1,000)

1976 State	Crops	Live-stock	Gov't pay'ts	Total
Alabama	624,722	993,226	13,115	1,631,063
Alaska	5,216	4,126	151	9,493
Arizona	699,005	541,115	4,936	1,245,056
Arkansas	1,237,025	1,059,002	9,097	2,305,124
California	6,148,682	2,953,178	12,983	9,114,843
Colorado	530,591	1,446,017	22,780	1,999,388
Connecticut	93,678	137,281	443	231,402
Delaware	98,757	182,805	290	281,852
Florida	1,840,106	692,680	5,440	2,538,226
Georgia	1,103,337	1,165,684	9,783	2,278,804
Hawaii	260,847	62,410	391	323,648
Idaho	793,330	455,090	9,277	1,257,697
Illinois	4,243,954	1,866,939	9,700	6,120,593
Indiana	1,995,998	1,334,757	6,016	3,336,771
Iowa	2,967,826	4,041,870	26,767	7,036,463
Kansas	1,614,397	1,917,163	50,824	3,582,384
Kentucky	896,536	729,592	6,591	1,632,719
Louisiana	868,417	405,489	7,453	1,281,359
Maine	174,987	268,081	2,083	445,151
Maryland	255,071	428,292	1,514	684,877
Massachusetts	100,560	114,163	599	215,322
Michigan	884,776	815,799	7,300	1,707,875
Minnesota	1,720,943	2,181,606	59,085	3,961,634
Mississippi	989,588	682,220	28,557	1,700,365
Missouri	1,053,027	1,577,728	30,874	2,661,629
Montana	543,594	453,381	10,497	1,007,472
Nebraska	1,690,740	2,176,886	36,614	3,904,240
Nevada	42,288	107,484	1,323	151,095
New Hampshire	21,610	57,688	689	79,987
New Jersey	224,717	109,603	833	335,153
New Mexico	193,923	518,402	15,502	727,827
New York	474,757	1,223,614	5,979	1,704,350
North Carolina	1,748,541	1,073,071	7,784	2,829,396
North Dakota	1,171,511	484,362	22,744	1,678,617
Ohio	1,617,874	1,163,911	7,297	2,789,082
Oklahoma	663,084	1,248,848	27,679	1,939,611
Oregon	666,702	355,774	5,277	1,027,753
Pennsylvania	500,069	1,300,409	5,774	1,806,252
Rhode Island	15,082	12,956	87	28,125
South Carolina	553,932	285,482	5,285	844,699
South Dakota	372,451	1,417,116	88,068	1,877,635
Tennessee	635,168	675,368	11,392	1,321,928
Texas	3,109,198	3,189,219	111,735	6,410,152
Utah	97,121	262,186	5,611	364,918
Vermont	18,492	244,825	1,187	264,504
Virginia	482,101	554,976	7,225	1,044,302
Washington	1,231,157	523,110	5,007	1,759,274
West Virginia	37,190	103,442	2,591	143,223
Wisconsin	541,755	2,486,884	14,282	3,042,921
Wyoming	82,781	303,320	7,113	393,214
Total U.S.	**47,937,214**	**46,388,630**	**733,624**	**95,059,468**

Average Prices Received by U.S. Farmers

Source: Statistical Reporting Service; U.S. Agriculture Department

The figures represent dollars per 100 lbs. for hogs, beef cattle, veal calves, sheep, lamb, and milk (wholesale), dollars per head for milk cows; cents per lb. for milk fat (in cream), chickens, broilers, turkeys, and wool; cents for eggs per dozen.

Weighted calendar year prices for livestock and livestock products other than wool. 1943 through 1963, wool prices are weighted on marketing year basis. The marketing year has been changed (1964) from a calendar year to a Dec.-Nov. basis for hogs, chickens, broilers and eggs.

Year	Hogs	Cattle (beef)	Calves (veal)	Sheep	Lambs	Cows (milk)	Milk (wholesale)	Milk fat (in cream)	Chickens (excl. broilers)	Broilers	Turkeys	Eggs	Wool
1930	8.84	7.71	9.68	4.74	7.76	74.20	2.21	34.5	...	...	20.2	23.7	19.5
1940	5.39	7.56	8.83	3.95	8.10	61.00	1.82	28.0	13.0	17.3	15.2	18.0	28.4
1950	18.00	23.30	26.30	11.60	25.10	198.00	3.89	62.0	22.0	27.4	32.9	36.3	62.1
1960	15.30	20.40	22.90	5.61	17.90	223.00	4.21	60.5	12.2	16.9	25.4	36.1	42.0
1965	19.60	19.90	22.00	6.34	22.80	212.00	4.23	61.1	8.9	15.0	22.2	33.7	47.1
1970	22.70	27.10	34.50	7.51	26.40	332.00	5.71	70.0	9.1	13.6	22.6	39.1	35.5
1972	25.10	33.50	44.70	7.28	29.10	397.00	6.07	67.5	8.9	14.1	22.2	30.9	35.0
1973	38.40	42.80	56.60	12.70	35.10	496.00	7.14	67.2	15.1	24.0	38.2	52.5	82.7
1974	34.20	35.60	35.20	11.30	37.00	500.00	8.33	63.5	9.7	21.5	28.0	53.3	59.1
1975	46.10	32.30	27.20	11.20	42.10	412.00	8.75	71.0	9.9	26.3	34.8	52.5	44.7
1976	43.30	33.70	34.10	13.20	46.90	477.00	9.66	83.4	13.0	23.6	31.7	58.4	65.7

The figures represent cents per lb. for cotton, apples, and peanuts; dollars per bushel for oats, wheat, corn, barley, and soybeans; dollars per 100 lbs. for rice, sorghum, and potatoes; dollars per ton for cottonseed and baled hay.

Weighted crop year prices. Crop years are as follows: apples, June-May; wheat, oats, barley, hay and potatoes, July-June; cotton, rice, peanuts and cottonseed, August-July; soybeans, September-August; and corn and sorghum grain, October-September.

Crop Year	Corn	Wheat	Upland Cotton[1]	Oats	Barley	Rice	Soy-beans	Sor-ghum	Peanuts	Cotton-seed	Hay	Potatoes	Apples
1930	.663	:550	9.46	31.1	.420	1.74	1.34	1.02	3.46	22.00	11.00	1.47	...
1940	.674	.601	9.83	29.8	.393	1.80	.892	.873	3.33	21.70	9.78	.850	...
1950	2.00	1.52	39.90	78.8	1.19	5.09	2.47	1.88	10.9	86.60	21.10	1.50	...
1960	1.74	.997	30.08	59.8	.838	4.55	2.13	1.49	10.0	42.50	21.70	2.00	4.79
1965	1.35	1.16	29.26	62.2	1.02	4.93	2.54	1.76	11.4	46.70	23.20	2.53	4.32
1970	1.33	1.33	22.81	62.3	.973	5.17	2.85	2.04	12.8	56.50	26.10	1.21	4.54
1972	1.57	1.76	27.20	72.5	1.21	6.73	4.37	2.45	14.5	49.50	31.30	3.01	6.43
1973	2.55	3.95	44.40	118.0	2.13	13.80	5.68	3.82	16.2	100.10	41.60	4.89	8.80
1974	3.03	4.09	42.70	153.0	2.80	11.20	6.64	4.96	17.9	135.50	50.90	4.01	8.40
1975	2.54	3.55	51.10	146.0	2.43	8.34	4.92	4.23	19.6	97.00	52.00	4.48	6.40
1976	2.32	2.85	64.70	155.0	2.29	6.63	7.32	3.70	20.0	103.00	60.40	3.36	8.80

(1) Beginning 1964, 480 lb. net weight bales.

Index Numbers of Prices Received by Farmers

Source: Statistical Reporting Service; U.S. Agriculture Department (index 1910-14=100 per cent)

Year	All farm products	All crops	Livestock[1]	Food grains	Feed grains and Hay	Feed grains	Cotton	Tobacco	Oil-bearing crops	Fruit	Commercial vegetables[2]	Potatoes sweetpot[3]	Meat animals	Dairy products	Poultry and eggs	Wool
1910	104	105	102	109	96	97	118	84	120	100	...	83	101	100	104	117
1920	211	235	190	249	202	209	262	233	208	188	...	294	171	202	222	214
1930	125	115	134	93	106	109	104	140	111	149	128	162	133	142	128	119
1940	100	90	109	84	85	86	83	134	103	81	122	89	108	120	98	160
1950	258	233	280	224	193	198	282	402	276	194	211	166	340	249	186	341
1960	239	222	253	203	152	151	254	500	214	244	230	203	296	259	160	235
1965	245	230	260	163	174	—	245	513	265	240	262	293	315	260	144	—
1970	274	225	325	162	179	—	183	604	265	217	292	218	405	350	147	—
1974	481	504	454	529	423	—	433	821	625	319	403	543	553	510	214	—
1975	463	452	474	426	400	—	348	899	529	313	458	400	567	537	235	—
1976	465	444	485	354	379	—	504	907	550	300	456	377	569	591	233	—

(1) Livestock and livestock products. (2) For fresh market and processing beginning 1952. (3) Including dry edible beans.

Average Farm Wages

(dollars per hour)

	1974	1975	1976
Method of pay:			
All hired farm workers	2.25	2.43	2.66
Paid by piece-rate	2.58	2.96	3.14
Paid by other than piece-rate	2.21	2.38	2.61
Paid by hour only[1]	2.23	2.39	2.60
Paid cash wages only[2]	2.43	2.60	2.81
Paid by hour cash wages only[3]	2.32	·2.45	2.65
Type of work performed:			
Field and livestock workers	2.08	2.26	2.47

	1974	1975	1976
Packinghouse workers	2.41	2.52	2.80
Machine operators	2.25	2.50	2.72
Maintenance and bookkeeping	2.85	3.15	3.45
Supervisors	3.77	4.00	4.39
Other agricultural workers	2.40	2.76	2.82
Indexes[4]			
(1910-14=100)	1,466	1,612	1,764
(1967=100)	173	190	208

(1) May include perquisites such as room and board, includes only those paid by the hour. (2) Does not include perquisites, includes all methods of pay. (3) Does not include perquisites, includes only those paid by the hour. (4) Indexes are based on all hired farm workers and are adjusted for seasonal variation.

Government Payments by Programs, by States

Source: Economic Research Service: U.S. Agriculture Department ($1,000)

1975 State	Conservation[1]	Sugar Act	Feed Grain Program	Wheat Program	Cotton	Cropland Adjustment	Great Plains Conservation	Misc. Program[2]	Total
Alabama	5,189	—	528	22	4,450	1,817	—	314	12,320
Alaska	77	—	—	—	—	—	—	7	84
Arizona	2,040	584	17	—	2,243	122	—	747	5,753
Arkansas	3,872	—	188	139	11,183	207	—	439	16,028
California	4,660	8,568	144	313	108	92	—	1,946	15,831
Colorado	3,029	2,655	2,279	7,238	—	683	1,402	708	17,994
Connecticut	297	—	—	—	—	59	—	17	373
Delaware	185	—	1	5	—	26	—	5	222
Florida	3,798	7,506	336	—	294	893	—	48	12,875
Georgia	5,473	—	678	60	1,703	2,473	—	384	10,771
Hawaii	243	8,377	—	—	—	—	—	—	8,620
Idaho	2,415	3,612	358	1,519	—	33	—	723	8,660
Illinois	7,662	—	28,951	1,529	14	618	—	159	38,933
Indiana	5,457	—	9,811	684	—	711	—	120	16,783
Iowa	7,233	—	44,286	460	—	668	—	474	53,121
Kansas	6,875	857	15,603	13,090	—	769	1,040	160	38,394
Kentucky	5,338	—	695	36	89	1,055	—	65	7,278
Louisiana	3,046	8,599	180	64	6,410	53	—	311	18,663
Maine	2,068	—	—	—	—	37	—	87	2,192
Maryland	1,074	—	11	5	—	62	—	52	1,204
Massachusetts	488	—	—	—	—	36	—	69	593
Michigan	4,488	3,254	2,717	533	—	1,926	—	358	13,276
Minnesota	6,395	4,536	18,968	1,798	—	1,553	—	627	33,877
Mississippi	3,898	—	503	80	14,910	467	—	249	20,107
Missouri	7,697	—	23,536	2,626	4,198	1,737	—	166	39,960
Montana	4,548	1,408	413	1,338	—	151	602	890	9,350
Nebraska	5,197	775	55,010	8,017	—	1,426	961	285	71,671
Nevada	670	—	—	18	—	—	—	133	821
New Hampshire	578	—	—	—	—	1	—	55	634
New Jersey	536	—	(3)	—	—	112	—	23	668
New Mexico	2,149	16	2,576	1,201	1,554	2,665	591	594	11,346
New York	4,909	—	29	14	—	677	—	292	5,921
North Carolina	5,528	—	847	85	1,058	1,030	—	331	8,879
North Dakota	4,273	3,222	5,200	9,430	—	943	748	1,067	24,883
Ohio	4,342	1,047	1,644	222	(7)	1,014	—	560	8,822
Oklahoma	4,864	—	1,823	6,515	3,577	718	1,008	272	18,777
Oregon	3,104	546	53	297	—	37	—	607	4,644
Pennsylvania	4,030	—	150	42	—	791	—	297	5,310
Rhode Island	61	—	—	—	—	—	—	6	67
South Carolina	2,712	—	234	36	1,891	1,680	—	192	6,745
South Dakota	3,579	—	18,961	6,866	—	1,093	850	1,466	32,815
Tennessee	4,047	—	1,727	221	9,601	942	—	63	16,601
Texas	14,184	1,742	32,595	11,273	74,956	5,124	3,670	3,018	146,562
Utah	1,434	379	84	648	—	38	—	716	3,299
Vermont	1,174	—	6	—	—	11	—	66	1,257
Virginia	5,001	—	35	113	6	406	—	263	5,824
Washington	3,451	2,640	6	70	—	23	—	733	6,923
West Virginia	1,733	—	7	3	—	28	—	163	1,934
Wisconsin	4,026	—	7,504	47	—	2,146	—	360	14,083
Wyoming	2,084	778	75	319	—	35	473	1,569	5,333
Total U.S.	**181,211**	**61,101**	**278,766**	**76,976**	**138,238**	**37,188**	**11,345**	**22,256**	**807,081**

(1) Includes amounts paid under other similar programs not listed separately. (2) Includes Wool, Milk Indemnity Program, Bee Keepers Indemnity Program, Water Bank Program, Public Access and other miscellaneous programs.

Cooperative Farm Credit System

Loans outstanding to farmers and farmers' co-ops from banks and associations supervised by the Farm Credit Admin.

Calendar year	Farm mortgage loans Federal land banks	Farm production loans Production credit ass'ns	Loans to cooperatives by banks for cooperatives	FICB loans and discounts other than interagency	Total
1950	$946,469,000	$455,472,000	$344,979,000	$70,020,000	$1,816,940,000
1955	1,497,165,000	653,478,000	370,683,000	70,785,000	2,592,111,000
1960	2,563,772,000	1,490,138,000	648,859,000	91,951,000	4,794,720,000
1965	4,280,675,000	2,598,460,000	1,055,163,000	146,091,000	8,080,389,000
1970	7,187,140,000	5,334,495,000	2,029,864,000	222,099,000	14,773,598,000
1974	13,863,752,000	9,560,649,000	3,575,483,000	403,402,000	27,403,286,000
1975	16,563,886,000	10,825,963,000	3,978,861,000	372,860,000	31,741,570,000
1976	19,126,749,000	12,297,052,000	5,061,669,000	385,185,000	36,870,655,000

Farm Employment—Annual Averages

Source: Statistical Reporting Service: U.S. Agriculture Department (Index 1910-14=100 per cent)

Year	Total		Family		Hired	
	Aver. no. (1,000)	Index %	Aver. no. (1,000)	Index %	Aver. no. (1,000)	Index %
1920	13,432	99	10,041	99	3,391	100
1930	12,497	92	9,307	92	3,190	94
1940	10,979	82	8,300	81	2,679	79
1950	9,926	75	7,597	73	2,329	69
1960	7,057	52	5,172	52	1,885	55
1970	4,523	34	3,348	33	1,175	35
1975	4,342	32	3,025	30	1,317	35
1976	4,376	32	2,999	80	1,377	37

Farm-Real Estate Debt Outstanding by Lender Groups

Source: Economic Research Service, U.S. Agriculture Department

	Total farm-real estate debt[1]	Federal land banks[1]	Amounts held by principal lender groups: Farmers Home Administration[2]	Life insurance companies[3]	All commercial banks	Other[4]
	$1,000	$1,000	$1,000	$1,000	$1,000	$1,000
1951	6,112,286	991,439	256,724	1,352,635	985,954	2,525,534
1952	6,662,327	1,026,906	290,529	1,541,874	1,017,360	2,785,658
1953	7,240,937	1,095,257	330,087	1,716,022	1,069,398	3,030,173
1954	7,930,931	1,187,046	352,199	1,892,773	1,091,949	3,215,964
1955	8,245,278	1,279,787	378,108	2,051,784	1,161,308	3,374,291
1956	9,012,016	1,480,204	412,670	2,271,784	1,275,429	3,571,929
1957	9,821,525	1,722,381	462,942	2,476,543	1,298,113	3,861,546
1958	10,382,475	1,897,187	540,762	2,578,958	1,315,530	4,050,038
1959	11,091,390	2,065,372	608,101	2,661,229	1,407,548	4,349,140
1960	12,082,409	2,335,124	676,224	2,819,542	1,523,051	4,728,468
1961	12,820,304	2,539,044	722,870	2,974,609	1,591,762	4,992,019
1962	13,899,105	2,803,103	948,346	3,161,757	1,640,790	5,345,109
1963	15,167,821	3,024,013	1,057,923	3,391,183	1,870,216	5,824,486
1964	16,803,505	3,281,797	1,171,373	3,780,537	2,136,571	6,433,227
1965	18,894,240	3,686,755	1,284,913	4,287,671	2,416,634	7,218,267
1966	21,186,886	4,240,227	1,497,313	4,801,677	2,607,404	8,040,265
1967	23,077,186	4,914,522	1,663,067	5,213,587	2,770,010	8,516,000
1968	25,142,401	5,563,204	1,844,046	5,539,600	3,060,551	9,135,000
1969	27,397,370	6,081,229	2,054,382	5,763,500	3,333,259	10,165,000
1970	29,182,766	6,671,222	2,279,620	5,733,900	3,545,024	10,953,000
1971	30,346,083	7,145,363	2,440,043	5,610,300	3,772,377	11,378,000
1972	32,207,666	6,879,753	2,618,131	5,564,300	4,218,482	11,927,000
1973	35,757,754	9,050,067	2,835,202	5,643,300	4,792,185	13,437,000
1974	41,252,870	10,901,352	3,013,440	5,964,800	5,458,278	15,915,000
1975	46,288,419	13,402,441	3,214,657	6,297,400	5,966,282	17,407,639
1976	51,068,946	15,949,720	3,368,747	6,726,000	6,296,286	18,728,193
1977[5]	56,056,182	18,454,578	3,655,146	7,270,084	6,781,410	19,894,964

(1) Includes data for joint stock land banks and Federal Farm Mortgage Corporations. (2) Includes loans made directly by FmHA for farm ownership, soil and water loans to individuals, recreation loans to individuals, Indian tribe land acquisition, grazing associations, and irrigation drainage and soil conservation associations. Also includes loans for rural housing on farm tracts and labor housing. (3) Taken from Life Insurance Institute Tally sheet. (4) Estimated by ERS, USDA 1965-73 revised June, 1974. (5) Preliminary.

Canadian Farm Cash Receipts

Source: Canadian Statistical Review (May, 1977)
(millions of Canadian dollars)

Cash receipts from farming operations excluding supplementary payments. Excludes Newfoundland.

Crops

Year and quarter		Total cash receipts	Total crops	Wheat[1]	Oats[1]	Barley[1]	C.W.B. advance payments[3]	Other grains[2]	Sugar beets	Potatoes	Fruits	Vegetables	Tobacco	Other crops[3]
1973		6,828.42	2,672.70	1,201.26	43.59	330.27	6.47	539.99	88.28	159.97	137.42	172.39	142.81	231.38
1974		8,836.54	4,150.46	2,033.30	54.17	554.30	11.43	728.30	43.80	213.94	195.49	191.64	207.68	207.55
1975		9,877.03	4,688.60	2,538.02	88.45	620.78	-13.90	564.26	39.90	164.79	126.84	183.46	198.18	247.31
1976		9,737.70	4,466.37	2,066.17	84.29	512.48	58.43	563.60	36.26	220.42	125.91	219.03	210.16	219.01
1977	1	2,608.26	1,428.17	331.55	26.24	149.77	-4.42	162.87	0.67	55.62	12.42	28.48	103.97	32.16

Livestock and Products

Year & quarter		Total	Cattle	Hogs	Sheep	Dairy products	Poultry	Eggs	Other	Total forest and maple products	Dairy supplementary payments	Deficiency payments[4]
1973		2,969.58	1,479.51	825.49	10.67	849.46	437.94	243.79	74.73	42.63	181.02	60.49
1974		4,328.01	1,620.58	787.72	12.87	1,087.74	472.15	269.09	77.85	40.96	131.02	36.04
1975		4,813.88	1,817.96	886.45	13.81	1,348.39	412.52	258.34	76.67	42.34	259.76	22.58
1976		4,888.82	1,922.54	820.04	13.88	1,301.08	469.11	282.73	79.34	27.38	258.85	23.19
1977	1	1,123.41	467.02	199.62	2.10	264.32	96.12	70.36	23.83	8.01	41.97	1.68

(1) Represents participation payments made by the Canadian Wheat Board direct to producers on crops delivered in previous years. (2) Includes rye, flaxseed, rapeseed, soybeans, and corn. (3) Includes clover and grass seed, hay, clover, greenhouse products, mustard seed, sunflower seed, hops, dry beans and dry peas and miscellaneous products. (4) Made under the authority of the Agricultural Stabilization Act.

Canadian Farm Cash Receipts by Province

Source: Statistics Canada
(C$1,000)

Province	1972	1973	1974	1975	1976
Prince Edward Island	44,840	73,304	84,693	83,427	104,869
Nova Scotia	73,572	96,499	103,537	116,236	124,029
New Brunswick	64,955	95,822	103,233	100,043	113,967
Quebec	776,355	980,080	1,149,617	1,342,037	1,359,766
Ontario	1,622,681	1,992,585	2,486,908	2,649,785	2,769,932
Manitoba	487,812	619,429	825,371	935,004	897,160
Saskatchewan	1,202,828	1,467,146	2,039,831	2,468,789	2,286,186
Alberta	917,353	1,201,211	1,686,475	1,876,103	1,847,633
British Columbia	246,750	335,230	389,199	426,765	471,484
Total	**5,437,146**	**6,861,306**	**8,868,864**	**9,998,189**	**9,975,026**

U.S. Farm Marketing, Supply, Related Service Cooperatives

Source: Farmer Cooperative Service, U.S. Agriculture Department

Marketing season 1973-74[1]; a marketing season includes the period during which the farm products of a specified year are moved into the channels of trade. Marketing seasons overlap.

State	Cooperatives No.	Memberships	Net business[2] ($1,000)	State	Cooperatives No.	Memberships	Net business[2] ($1,000)
Alabama	71	80,000	331,428	Nebraska	340	262,095	1,259,415
Alaska	2	350	3,648	Nevada	5	935	6,954
Arizona	17	85,135	194,605	New Hampshire	7	3,765	52,740
Arkansas	108	108,350	825,669	New Jersey	36	16,965	211,463
California[2]	293	91,925	2,996,793	New Mexico	22	7,315	65,806
Colorado	85	50,095	437,085	New York	285	139,370	1,508,506
Connecticut	11	5,375	113,113	North Carolina	31	146,250	421,389
Delaware	8	13,355	42,559	North Dakota	671	262,450	1,333,438
Florida	93	54,280	737,830	Ohio	202	216,545	1,176,477
Georgia	89	169,865	567,305	Oklahoma	154	140,665	689,284
Hawaii[2]	19	2,385	22,153	Oregon	72	57,070	570,753
Idaho	68	47,675	323,212	Pennsylvania	105	77,830	804,221
Illinois	307	316,900	2,136,149	Rhode Island	1	920	11,497
Indiana	111	409,890	925,920	South Carolina	22	40,915	130,572
Iowa	462	371,790	2,820,230	South Dakota	321	175,275	614,030
Kansas	268	201,445	1,615,583	Tennessee	105	151,505	364,241
Kentucky	82	204,835	379,340	Texas	453	141,825	1,943,689
Louisiana	100	17,430	274,518	Utah	43	27,535	239,008
Maine	10	9,975	94,341	Vermont	10	6,980	150,082
Maryland	39	44,380	345,946	Virginia	117	179,735	529,080
Massachusetts	18	10,275	152,248	Washington	149	102,930	917,124
Michigan	146	124,805	914,926	West Virginia	63	48,930	88,506
Minnesota	1,073	589,185	2,626,788	Wisconsin	511	420,955	1,838,411
Mississippi	138	126,030	666,756	Wyoming	31	11,285	42,855
Missouri	156	248,045	906,220				
Montana	225	81,440	241,378	**Total U.S.**	**7,755**	**6,105,530**	**35,775,549**

(1) Preliminary. (2) The volume of an Hawaiian sugar co-op based in California is included in the dollar volume of California.

Food Stamps—Costs and Benefits

Source: Food and Nutrition Service, U.S. Agriculture Department

Fiscal year	Average persons participating per month	Value per year: Total purchase	Value per year: Bonus	Avg. bonus per participant per month: Current $	Avg. bonus per participant per month: 1967 $
1962	142,817	$ 35,202,266	$ 13,152,695	7.67	8.47
1965	424,652	85,471,989	32,505,096	6.38	6.75
1970	4,340,030	1,089,960,761	549,663,811	10.55	9.07
1971	9,367,908	2,713,273,217	1,522,749,091	13.55	11.17
1973	12,165,682	3,883,952,103	2,131,404,604	14.60	11.67
1974	12,861,526	4,727,450,579	2,718,296,427	17.61	11.87
1975	17,064,196	7,265,641,706	4,385,501,248	21.41	13.62
1976p	18,526,728	8,691,149,536	5,319,886,500	23.93	–
1977p	16,939,206	8,187,748,731	4,965,166,236	24.43	–

(p) preliminary. The Food Stamp Program enables low-income families to buy more food of greater variety to improve their diets. If a household meets eligibility requirements it receives a food stamp "bonus" based on its net income and the number of people in the household. Major reform measures will go into effect this year to: lower net income eligibility standards to the official poverty level ($5850 for a family of four in 1977); eliminate the food stamp purchase requirement; and streamline administration. County and city welfare departments administer the program locally.

Federal Food Program Costs

Source: Food and Nutrition Service, U.S. Agriculture Department (millions of dollars)

Calendar year	Food stamps: Total value	Food stamps: Bonus[1]	Food distribution[2]: Needy families	Food distribution[2]: Supp. food	Food distribution[2]: Schools	Food distribution[2]: Institutions	Child nutrition: School lunch	Child nutrition: School bkfst.	Child nutrition: Special food	Child nutrition: Special milk	Total costs
1971	3,105	1,699	318	13	296	26	647	22	34	92	**3,147**
1974	5,868	3,498	114	16	393	21	1,164	70	101	89	**5,466**
1975	8,325	5,073	12	18	364	15	1,385	99	122	133	**7,221**
1976p	8,588	5,241	10	16	510	15	1,559	127	236	150	**7,864**
1977 1st qtr. p	2,144	1,311	3	4	205	5	540	46	29	48	**2,191**
2nd qtr. p	2,027	1,219	3	4	100	4	408	38	42	38	**1,856**

(1) Includes Food Certificate Program (2) Cost of food delivered to state distribution centers.

Harvested Acreage of Principal Canadian Crops

Source: Statistics Canada (thousands of acres)

Province	1973	1974	1975	1976	Province	1973	1974	1975	1976
Prince Edward Island	328	333	357	356	Manitoba	12,619	12,129	12,208	13,151
Nova Scotia	191	192	205	209	Saskatchewan	42,768	41,860	40,917	43,626
New Brunswick	288	291	296	295	Alberta	22,937	22,167	22,445	23,810
Quebec	3,910	3,941	3,990	4,005	British Columbia	976	1,031	1,041	1,082
Ontario	7,970	8,058	8,130	8,208	**Total**	**92,211**	**90,199**	**89,800**	**94,990**

Crops included are winter wheat, spring wheat, oats, barley, fall rye, spring rye, flaxseed, mixed grains, corn for grain, buckwheat, peas, dry beans, soybeans, rapeseed, potatoes, mustard seed, sunflower seed, tame hay, fodder corn, field roots, and sugar beets.

Agricultural Products — U. S. and World Production and Exports

Source: Foreign Agricultural Service, U.S. Agriculture Department

976

Commodity[1]	Unit	Production U.S.	Production World	Production % U.S.	Exports U.S.	Exports World	Exports % U.S.
Vheat, Grain only	Mil Mt	58	350	16.6	31.7[2,3]	72.6[2,3]	43.7
)ats	Mil Mt	8	47	17.0	0.2[2]	1.6[2]	12.5
orn	Mil Mt	158	322	49.1	43.2[2]	61.2[2]	70.6
arley	Mil Mt	8	144	5.5	0.5[2]	13.3[2]	3.8
oybeans	Mil Mt	34.4	58.9	58.4	15.1	19.2	78.6
ice	Mil Mt	6	352	1.7	2.0[4]	8.0[4]	25.0
ard[5]	1000 Mt	473	N/A	[9]	82	N/A	[9]
allow & grease[5]	1000 Mt	2574	N/A	[9]	1057	N/A	[9]
obacco, unmftd.[5]	1000 Mt	945	5404	17.5	262	1224	21.4
dible veg. oils[6]	Mil Mt	8.1	33.2	24.4	3818[7,10]	11574[8,10]	33.0
otton	1000 Bales	8302	54317	15.3	3311	18810	17.6

1) Crop 1975-76 as follows: wheat, oats, and barley beginning July 1; corn, October 1; soybeans, September 1; rice and cotton, ugust 1. Excludes Alaska, Hawaii and Puerto Rico except for exports. (2) Fiscal year 1975-76. (3) Includes wheat flour in grain quivalent. (4) Milled rice. (5) Calendar year 1976. (6) Includes palm oils. (7) Includes oil equivalent of exported oilseeds. (8) Exports rom producing countries. (9) Percentage not available. (10) 1000 metric tons. (11) Sales of 480 lbs., net wgt. N/A=not available

Civilian Consumption of Major Food Commodities per Person

Source: Economic Research Service: U.S. Agriculture Department

Commodity[1]	Avg. (pounds) 1957-59	1974	1975
leats (carcass wt.)	156.6	188.0	181.1
Beef	82.1	116.8	120.1
Veal	7.1	2.3	4.2
Lamb and mutton	4.4	2.3	2.0
Pork (excl. lard)	63.0	66.6	54.8
ish (edible wt.)	10.5	12.2	12.2
oultry products			
Eggs (farm basis, number)	356	288	279
Chicken (ready to cook)	27.5	41.1	40.9
Turkey (ready to cook)	6.0	8.9	8.6
airy products			
Cheese	7.9	14.6	14.5
Cond. and evap. milk	14.8	5.6	5.2
Fluid milk and cream	337	246	248
Ice Cream (prod. wt.)	18.4	17.5	18.6
ats and oils-Total fat content	45.3	53.2	53.3
Butter (actual wt.)	8.2	4.6	4.8
Margarine (act. wt.)	8.9	11.3	11.2
Lard	9.3	3.2	3.0
Shortening	11.4	17.0	17.3
Other edible fats and oils	10.8	20.3	20.3
ruits			
Fresh	95.5	83.4	85.8
Citrus	34.0	27.6	29.8
Apples	21.0	15.9	17.8
Other (excl. melons)	40.5	40.2	38.2
Processed:			
Canned fruit	22.4	19.7	19.2
Canned juice	13.5	14.7	14.8
Frozen (incl juices)	8.6	11.2	12.6
Dried	3.3	2.5	3.1
Vegetables			
Fresh[2]	104.1	101.1	101.5
Canned (excl. potatoes)	43.3	53.3	52.5
Frozen (excl. potatoes)	6.6	10.2	10.3
Potatoes, fresh equiv.	106.9	114.2	122.5
Sweet potatoes, fresh	8.3	5.2	5.5
Grains			
Cornmeal and flour	7.4	7.6	7.7
Corn syrup	9.4	25.0	28.5
Corn sugar	3.6	5.3	5.5
Wheat flour[3]	120	106	107
Wheat cereals	2.8	2.9	2.9
Rice, milled	5.4	7.6	7.7
Other			
Coffee (green beans)	15.7	12.9	12.4
Tea	.58	0.8	0.8
Cocoa beans	3.5	3.7	3.3
Peanuts (shelled)	4.6	6.4	6.6
Melons	25.1	19.0	19.3
Sugar (refined)	96.1	96.6	90.2

1) Quantity in pounds except for eggs. Data on calendar year basis except for dried fruits, which are on pack-year basis, fresh citrus uits and peanuts on a crop-year basis, and rice on August 1 year. Fresh citrus year begins in previous October and rice year begins in revious August. (2) Commercial production for sale as fresh produce. (3) Includes white, whole wheat, and semolina flour.

Recommended Daily Dietary Allowances

Source: Food and Nutrition Board, National Research Council

The allowances are amounts of nutrients recommended as adequate for maintenance of good nutrition in healthy per- ons in the U.S. Diets should be based on a variety of common foods in order to provide other nutrients for which human equirements have been less well defined.

	Years From-up to	Weight (kg)	Weight (lbs.)	Hgt. (in.)	Calories	Protein (grams)	Calcium (mg.)	Iron (mg.)	Vit A (I.U.)	Thiamin (mg.)	Riboflavin (mg.)	Niacin (mg.)	Ascorbic acid (mg.)
nfants	0.0-0.5	6	14	24	kg × 117	kg × 2.2	360	10	1,400	0.3	0.4	5	35
	0.5-1.0	9	20	28	kg × 108	kg × 2.0	540	15	2,000	0.5	0.6	8	35
hildren	1-3	13	28	34	1,300	23	800	15	2,000	0.7	0.8	9	40
	4-6	20	44	44	1,800	30	800	10	2,500	0.9	1.1	12	40
	7-10	30	66	54	2,400	36	800	10	3,500	1.2	1.2	16	40
lales	11-14	44	97	63	2,800	44	1,200	18	5,000	1.4	1.5	18	45
	15-18	61	134	69	3,000	54	1,200	18	5,000	1.5	1.8	20	45
	19-22	67	147	69	3,000	54	800	10	5,000	1.5	1.8	20	45
	23-50	70	154	69	2,700	56	800	10	5,000	1.4	1.6	18	45
	51+	70	154	69	2,400	56	800	10	5,000	1.2	1.5	16	45
emales	11-14	44	97	62	2,400	44	1,200	18	4,000	1.2	1.3	16	45
	15-18	54	119	65	2,100	48	1,200	18	4,000	1.1	1.4	14	45
	19-22	58	128	65	2,100	46	800	18	4,000	1.1	1.4	14	45
	23-50	58	128	65	2,000	46	800	18	4,000	1.0	1.2	13	45
	51+	58	128	65	1,800	46	800	10	4,000	1.0	1.1	12	45
Pregnant	...	...	...	...	+300	+30	1,200	+18	5,000	+0.3	+0.3	+2	60
Lactating	...	...	...	...	+500	+20	1,200	18	6,000	+0.3	+0.5	+4	80

Nutritive Value of Food (Calories, Proteins, etc.)

Source: Home and Garden Bulletin No. 72 (revised April 1977), U.S. Agriculture Department

Available for $1.05 from Supt. of Documents, U. S. Government Printing Office, Washington, DC 20402

Food	Measure	Food energy (calories)	Protein (grams)	Fat (grams)	Saturated fats (grams)	Carbohydrate (grams)	Calcium (milligrams)	Iron (milligrams)	Vitamin A (I.U.)	Thiamin (milligrams)	Riboflavin (milligrams)	Niacin (milligrams)	Ascorbic acid (milligrams)
Dairy products													
Cheese, cheddar	1 oz.	115	7	9	6.1	T	204	.2	300	.01	.11	T	0
Cheese, cottage, small curd	1 cup	220	26	9	6.0	6	126	.3	340	.04	.34	.3	T
Cheese, cream	1 oz.	100	2	10	6.2	1	23	.3	400	T	.06	T	0
Cheese, Swiss	1 oz.	105	8	8	5.0	1	272	T	240	.01	.10	T	0
Cheese, pasteurized process spread, American	1 oz.	82	5	6	3.8	2	159	.1	220	.01	.12	T	0
Half-and-Half	1 tbsp.	20	T	2	1.1	1	16	T	20	.01	.02	T	T
Cream, sour	1 tbsp.	25	T	3	1.6	1	14	T	90	T	.02	T	T
Milk, whole	1 cup	150	8	8	5.1	11	291	.1	310	.09	.40	.2	2
Milk, nonfat (skim)	1 cup	85	8	T	.3	12	302	.1	500	.09	.37	.2	2
Buttermilk	1 cup	100	8	2	1.3	12	285	.1	80	.08	.38	.1	2
Milkshake, chocolate	10.6 oz.	355	9	8	5.0	63	396	.9	260	.14	.67	.4	0
Ice Cream, hardened	1 cup	270	5	14	8.9	32	176	.1	540	.05	.33	.1	1
Sherbet	1 cup	270	2	4	2.4	59	103	.3	190	.03	.09	.1	4
Yogurt, fruit-flavored	8 oz.	230	10	3	1.8	42	343	.2	120	.08	.40	.2	1
Eggs													
Fried in butter	1	85	5	6	2.4	1	26	.9	290	.03	.13	T	0
Hard-cooked	1	80	6	6	1.7	1	28	1.0	260	.04	.14	T	0
Scrambled in butter	1	95	6	7	2.8	1	47	.9	310	.04	.16	T	0
Fats & oils													
Butter	1 tbsp.	100	T	12	7.2	T	3	T	430	T	T	T	0
Margarine	1 tbsp.	100	T	12	2.1	T	3	T	470	T	T	T	0
Salad dressing, blue cheese	1 tbsp.	75	1	8	1.6	1	12	T	30	T	.02	T	T
Salad dressing, French	1 tbsp.	65	T	6	1.1	3	2	.1	—	—	—	—	—
Salad dressing, Italian	1 tbsp.	85	T	9	1.6	1	2	T	T	T	T	T	—
Mayonnaise	1 tbsp.	100	T	11	2.0	T	3	.1	40	T	.01	T	—
Meat, poultry, fish													
Bluefish, baked with butter or margarine	3 oz.	135	22	4	—	0	25	0.6	40	.09	.08	1.6	—
Clams, raw, meat only	3 oz.	65	11	1	—	2	59	5.2	90	.08	.15	1.1	8
Crabmeat, white or king, canned	1 cup	135	24	3	.6	1	61	1.1	—	.11	.11	2.6	—
Fish sticks, breaded, cooked, frozen	1 oz.	50	5	3	—	2	3	.1	0	.01	.02	.5	—
Salmon, pink, canned	3 oz.	120	17	5	.9	0	167	.7	60	.03	.16	6.8	—
Sardines, Atlantic, canned in oil	3 oz.	175	20	9	3.0	0	372	2.5	190	.02	.17	4.6	—
Shrimp, French fried	3 oz.	190	17	9	2.3	9	61	1.7	—	.03	.07	2.3	—
Tuna, canned in oil	3 oz.	170	24	7	1.7	0	7	1.6	70	.04	.10	10.1	—
Bacon, broiled or fried, crisp	2 slices	85	4	8	2.5	T	2	.5	0	.08	.05	.8	—
Ground beef, broiled, 10% fat	3 oz.	185	23	10	4.0	0	10	3.0	20	.08	.20	5.1	—
Roast beef, relatively lean	3 oz.	165	25	7	2.8	0	11	3.2	10	.06	.19	4.5	—
Beef steak, lean and fat	3 oz.	330	20	27	11.3	0	9	2.5	50	.05	.15	4.0	—
Beef & vegetable stew	1 cup	220	16	11	4.9	15	29	2.9	2,400	.15	.17	4.7	17
Lamb, chop, lean and fat	3.1 oz.	360	18	32	14.8	0	8	1.0	—	.11	.19	4.1	—
Ham, light cure, lean and fat	3 oz.	245	18	19	6.8	0	8	2.2	0	.40	.15	3.1	—
Pork, chop, lean and fat	2.7 oz.	305	19	25	8.9	0	9	2.7	0	.75	.22	4.5	—
Bologna	1 slice	85	3	8	3.0	T	2	.5	—	.05	.06	.7	—
Frankfurter, cooked	1	170	7	15	5.6	1	3	.8	—	.08	.11	1.4	—
Sausage, pork link, cooked	1 link	60	2	6	2.1	T	1	.3	0	.10	.04	.5	—
Veal, cutlet, braised or broiled	3 oz.	185	23	9	4.0	0	9	2.7	—	.06	.21	4.6	—
Chicken, drumstick, fried, bones removed	1.3 oz.	90	12	4	1.1	T	6	.9	50	.03	.15	2.7	—
Chicken, half broiler, broiled, bones removed	6.2 oz.	240	42	7	2.2	0	16	3.0	160	.09	.34	15.5	—
Chicken a la king	1 cup	470	27	34	12.7	12	127	2.5	1,130	.10	.42	5.4	12
Chicken potpie, baked, 1/3 of 9 in. diam. pie	1 piece	545	23	31	11.3	42	70	3.0	3,090	.34	.31	5.5	5
Fruits & products													
Apple, raw, 2-3/4 in. diam.	1	80	T	1	—	20	10	.4	120	.04	.03	.1	6
Applejuice	1 cup	120	T	T	—	30	15	1.5	—	.02	.05	.2	2
Applesauce, canned, sweetened	1 cup	230	1	T	—	61	10	1.3	100	.05	.03	.1	3
Banana, raw	1	100	1	T	—	26	10	.8	230	.06	.07	.8	12
Cherries, sweet, raw	10	45	1	T	—	12	15	.3	70	.03	.04	.3	7
Fruit cocktail, canned, in heavy syrup	1 cup	195	1	T	—	50	23	1.0	360	.05	.03	1.0	5
Grapefruit, raw, medium, white	1/2	45	1	T	—	12	19	.5	10	.05	.02	.2	44
Grapes, Thompson seedless	10	35	T	T	—	9	6	.2	50	.03	.02	.2	2
Lemonade, frozen, diluted	1 cup	105	T	T	—	28	2	.1	10	.01	.02	.2	17
Cantaloupe, 5-in. diam.	1/2	80	2	T	—	20	38	1.1	9,240	.11	.08	1.6	90
Orange, 2-5/8 in. diam.	1	65	1	T	—	16	54	.5	260	.13	.05	.5	66
Orange juice, frozen, diluted	1 cup	120	2	T	—	29	25	.2	540	.23	.03	.9	120
Peach, raw, 2-1/2 in. diam.	1	40	1	T	—	10	9	.5	1,330	.02	.05	1.0	7
Peaches, canned in syrup	1 cup	200	1	T	—	51	10	.8	1,100	.03	.05	1.5	8
Pear, raw, Bartlett, 2-1/2 in. diam.	1	100	1	1	—	25	13	.5	30	.03	.07	.2	7
Pineapple, heavy syrup pack, crushed, chunks	1 cup	190	1	T	—	49	28	.8	130	.20	.05	.5	18
Raisins, seedless	1 cup	420	4	T	—	112	90	5.1	30	.16	.12	.7	1
Strawberries, whole	1 cup	55	1	1	—	13	31	1.5	90	.04	.10	.9	88
Watermelon, 4 by 8 in. wedge	1 wedge	110	2	1	—	27	30	2.1	2,510	.13	.13	.9	30
Grain products													
Bagel, egg	1	165	6	2	.5	28	9	1.2	30	.14	.10	1.2	0
Biscuit, 2 in. diam., from home recipe	1	105	2	5	1.2	13	34	.4	T	.08	.08	.7	T
Bread, raisin	1 slice	65	2	1	.2	13	18	.6	T	.09	.06	.6	T
Bread, white, enriched, soft-crumb	1 slice	70	2	1	.2	13	21	.6	T	.10	.06	.8	T
Bread, whole wheat, soft-crumb	1 slice	65	3	1	.1	14	24	.8	T	.09	.03	.8	T
Oatmeal or rolled oats	1 cup	130	5	2	.4	23	22	1.4	0	.19	.05	.2	0
Bran flakes (40% bran), added sugar, salt, iron, vitamins	1 cup	105	4	1	—	28	19	12.4	1,650	.41	.49	4.1	12
Corn flakes, added sugar, salt, iron, vitamins	1 cup	95	2	T	—	21	*	0.6	1,180	.29	.35	2.9	9
Rice, puffed, added iron, thiamin, niacin	1 cup	60	1	T	—	13	3	.3	0	.07	.01	.7	0

Food	Measure	Food energy (calories)	Protein (grams)	Fat (grams)	Saturated fats (grams)	Carbohydrate (grams)	Calcium (milligrams)	Iron (milligrams)	Vitamin A (I.U.)	Thiamin (milligrams)	Riboflavin (milligrams)	Niacin (milligrams)	Ascorbic acid (milligrams)
Wheat, shredded, plain, 1 biscuit or 1/2 cup	1 serving	90	2	1	—	20	11	.9	0	.06	.03	1.1	0
Cake, angel food, 1/12 of cake	1	135	3	T	—	32	50	.2	0	.03	.08	.3	0
Coffeecake, 1/6 of cake	1	230	5	7	2.0	38	44	1.2	120	.14	.15	1.3	T
Cupcake, 2-1/2 in. diam., with chocolate icing	1	130	2	5	2.0	21	47	.4	60	.05	.06	.4	T
Cake, devil's food with chocolate icing, 1/16 of 2 layer cake	1	235	3	8	3.1	40	41	1.0	100	.07	.10	.6	T
Boston cream pie with custard filling, 1/12 of cake	1	210	3	6	1.9	34	46	.7	140	.09	.11	.8	T
Fruitcake, dark, 1/30 of loaf	1	55	1	2	.5	9	11	.4	20	.02	.02	.2	T
Cake, pound, 1/17 of loaf	1	160	2	10	2.5	16	6	.5	80	.05	.06	.4	0
Brownies, with nuts, from commercial recipe	1	85	1	4	.9	13	9	.4	20	.03	.02	.2	T
Cookies, chocolate chip, from home recipe	4	205	2	12	3.5	24	14	.8	40	.06	.06	.5	T
Vanilla wafers	10	185	2	6	—	30	16	.6	50	.10	.09	.8	0
Crackers, graham	2	55	1	1	.3	10	6	.5	0	.02	.08	.5	0
Crackers, saltines	4	50	1	1	.3	8	2	.5	0	.05	.05	.4	0
Danish pastry, round piece	1	275	5	15	4.7	30	33	1.2	200	.18	.19	1.7	T
Doughnut, cake type	1	100	1	5	1.2	13	10	.4	20	.05	.05	.4	T
Macaroni and cheese, from home recipe	1 cup	430	17	22	8.9	40	362	1.8	860	.20	.40	1.8	T
Muffin, corn	1	125	3	4	1.2	19	42	.7	120	.10	.10	.7	T
Noodles, enriched, cooked	1 cup	200	7	2	—	37	16	1.4	110	.22	.13	1.9	0
Pancake, plain, from home recipe	1	60	2	2	.5	9	27	.4	30	.06	.07	.5	T
Pie, apple, 1/7 of pie	1	345	3	15	3.9	51	11	.9	40	.15	.11	1.3	2
Pie, banana cream, 1/7 of pie	1	285	6	12	3.8	40	86	1.0	330	.11	.22	1.0	1
Pie, cherry, 1/7 of pie	1	350	4	15	4.0	52	19	.9	590	.16	.12	1.4	T
Pie, lemon meringue, 1/7 of pie	1	305	4	12	3.7	45	17	1.0	200	.09	.12	.7	4
Pie, pecan, 1/7 of pie	1	495	6	27	4.0	61	55	3.7	190	.26	.14	1.0	T
Pie, pumpkin, 1/7 of pie	1	275	5	15	5.4	32	66	1.0	3,210	.11	.18	1.0	T
Pizza, cheese, 1/8 of 12 in. diam. pie	1	145	6	4	1.7	22	86	1.1	230	.16	.18	1.6	4
Popcorn, popped, plain	1 cup	25	1	T	T	5	1	.2	—	—	.01	.1	0
Pretzels, stick	10	10	T	T	—	2	1	T	0	.01	.01	.1	0
Rice, white, enriched, instant, cooked	1 cup	180	4	T	T	40	5	1.3	0	.21	**	1.7	0
Rolls, enriched, brown & serve	1	85	2	2	.4	14	20	.5	T	.10	.06	.9	T
Rolls, frankfurter & hamburger	1	120	3	2	.5	21	30	.8	T	.16	.10	1.3	T
Spaghetti with meat balls & tomato sauce, from home recipe	1 cup	330	19	12	3.3	39	124	3.7	1,590	.25	.30	4.0	22
Legumes, nuts, seeds													
Beans, Great Northern, cooked	1 cup	210	14	1	—	38	90	4.9	0	.25	.13	1.3	0
Peanuts, roasted in oil, salted	1 cup	840	37	72	13.7	27	107	3.0	—	.46	.19	24.8	0
Peanut butter	1 tbsp.	95	4	8	1.5	3	9	.3	—	.02	.02	2.4	0
Sugars & sweets													
Candy, caramels	1 oz.	115	1	3	1.6	22	42	.4	T	.01	.05	.1	T
Candy, milk chocolate	1 oz.	145	2	9	5.5	16	65	.3	80	.02	.10	.1	T
Fudge, chocolate	1 oz.	115	1	3	1.3	21	22	.3	T	.01	.03	.1	T
Candy, hard	1 oz.	110	0	T	—	28	6	.5	0	0	0	0	0
Honey	1 tbsp.	65	T	0	0	17	1	.1	0	T	.01	.1	T
Jams & Preserves	1 tbsp.	55	T	T	—	14	4	.2	T	T	.01	T	T
Vegetables													
Asparagus, canned, spears	4 spears	15	2	T	—	3	15	1.5	640	.05	.08	.6	12
Beans, lima, thick-seeded	1 cup	170	10	T	—	32	34	2.9	390	.12	.09	1.7	29
Beans, green, from frozen, cuts	1 cup	35	2	T	—	8	54	.9	780	.09	.12	.5	7
Beets, canned, diced or sliced	1 cup	65	2	T	—	15	32	1.2	30	.02	.05	.2	5
Broccoli, cooked	1 stalk	45	6	1	—	8	158	1.4	4,500	.16	.36	1.4	162
Cabbage, raw, coarsely shredded or sliced	1 cup	15	1	T	—	4	34	.3	90	.04	.04	.02	33
Carrots, raw, 7-1/2 by 1-1/8 in.	1	30	1	T	—	7	27	.5	7,930	.04	.04	.4	6
Cauliflower, raw	1 cup	31	3	T	—	6	29	1.3	70	.13	.12	.8	90
Celery, raw	1 stalk	5	T	T	—	2	16	.1	110	.01	.01	.1	4
Corn, sweet, cooked	1 ear	70	2	1	—	16	2	.5	310	.09	.08	1.1	7
Corn, cream style	1 cup	210	5	2	—	51	8	1.5	840	.08	.13	2.6	13
Cucumber, with peel	6-8 slices	5	T	T	—	1	7	.3	70	.01	.01	.1	3
Lettuce, Iceberg, chopped	1 cup	5	T	T	—	2	11	.3	180	.03	.03	.2	3
Mushrooms, raw	1 cup	20	2	T	—	3	4	.6	T	.07	.32	2.9	2
Peas, frozen, cooked	1 cup	110	8	T	—	19	30	3.0	960	.43	.14	2.7	21
Potatoes, baked, peeled	1	145	4	T	—	33	14	1.1	T	.15	.07	2.7	31
Potatoes, mashed, milk added	1 cup	135	4	2	.7	27	50	.8	40	.17	.11	2.1	21
Potato chips	10	115	1	8	2.1	10	8	.4	T	.04	.01	1.0	3
Potato salad	1 cup	250	7	7	2.0	41	80	1.5	350	.20	.18	2.8	28
Sauerkraut, canned	1 cup	40	2	T	—	9	85	1.2	120	.07	.09	.5	33
Spinach, chopped, from frozen	1 cup	45	6	1	—	8	232	4.3	16,200	.14	.31	.8	39
Squash, summer, cooked	1 cup	30	2	T	—	7	53	.8	820	.11	.17	1.7	21
Sweet potatoes, baked in skin, peeled	1	160	2	1	—	37	46	1.0	9,230	.10	.08	.8	25
Tomatoes, raw	1	25	1	T	—	6	16	.6	1,110	.07	.05	.9	28
Tomato catsup	1 tbsp.	15	T	T	—	4	3	.1	210	.01	.01	.2	2
Tomato juice	1 cup	45	2	T	—	10	17	2.2	1,940	.12	.07	1.9	39
Miscellaneous													
Beer	12 fl. oz.	150	1	0	0	14	18	T	—	.01	.11	2.2	—
Gin, rum, vodka, whisky, 86 proof	1¹/₂ fl. oz.	105	—	—	0	T	—	—	—	—	—	—	—
Wine, table	3¹/₂ fl. oz.	85	T	0	0	4	9	.4	—	T	.01	.1	—
Cola-type beverage	12 fl. oz.	145	0	0	0	37	—	—	0	0	0	0	0
Ginger ale	12 fl. oz.	115	0	0	0	29	—	—	0	0	0	0	0
Gelatin dessert	1 cup	140	4	0	0	34	—	—	—	—	—	—	—
Mustard, prepared	1 tsp.	5	T	T	—	T	4	.1	—	—	—	—	—
Olives, pickled, green	4 medium	15	T	2	.2	T	8	.2	40	—	—	—	—
Pickles, dill, whole	1	5	T	T	—	1	17	.7	70	T	.01	T	4
Popsicle, 3 fl. oz.	1	70	0	0	0	18	0	T	0	0	0	0	0
Soup, cream of chicken, prepared with milk	1 cup	180	7	10	4.2	15	172	.5	610	.05	.27	.7	2
Soup, cream of mushroom, prepared with milk	1 cup	215	7	14	5.4	16	191	.5	250	.05	.34	.7	1
Soup, tomato, prepared with water	1 cup	90	2	3	.5	16	15	.7	1,000	.05	.05	1.2	12

T — Indicates trace * — Varies by brand

Giant Trees of the U.S.

Source: The American Forestry Association

There are approximately 1,180 different species of trees native to the continental U.S., including a few imports that have become naturalized to the extent of reproducing themselves in the wild state.

The oldest living trees in the world are reputed to be the bristlecone pines, the majority of which are found growing on the arid crags of California's White Mts. Some of them are estimated to be more than 4,600 years old. The largest known bristlecone pine is the "Patriarch," believed to be 1,500 years old. The oldest known redwoods are about 3,500 years old.

Recognition as the National Champion of each species is determined by total mass of each tree, based on this formula: the circumference in inches as measured at a point 4 1/2 feet above the ground plus the total height of the tree, plus 1/4 of the average crown spread in feet. In case of a tie the Champion is determined on the basis of circumference. It is not possible, due to lack of space, to list all the 865 trees registered with the American Forestry Assn.

(Figure in parentheses is last year tree was reported)

Species	Height (Ft.)	Location
Acacia, Koa (1969)	140	Kau, Ha.
Ailanthus, Tree-of-Heaven (1972)	60	Long Island, N.Y.
Alder, European (1974)	68	Princeton, Ill.
Apple, Southern Crab (1976)	46	Williamsburg, Va.
Ash, Blue (1972)	86	Danville, Ky.
Aspen, Bigtooth (1963)	95	Walker, N.Y.
Bald Cypress, Common (1954)	122	nr. Sharon, Tenn.
Basswood, American (1971)	115	Grand Traverse City, Mich.
Bayberry, Pacific (1972)	38	Siuslaw Natl. Forest, Ore.
Beech, American (1976)	161	Three Oaks, Mich.
Birch, River (1974)	95	Cumberland For., Va.
Blackbead, Catclaw (1976)	88	Sarasota, Fla.
Blackhaw, Rusty (1961)	25	nr. Washington, Ark.
Bladdernut, American (1972)	36	nr. Utica, Mich.
Boxelder (1976)	95	Milan, Mich.
Buckeye, Painted (1972)	144	Union County, Ga.
Buckthorn, Cascara (1976)	37	Seaside, Ore.
Buckwheat tree (1967)	30	nr. Crooked Creek, Fla.
Buffaloberry, Silver (1975)	22	Malheur Co., Ore.
Bumelia, Gum (1977)	80	Robertson Co., Tex.
Butternut (1973)	102	Portland, Ore.
Buttonbush, Common (1976)	29	Oakland Co., Mich.
Button-Mangrove (1974)	52	Palm Beach, Fla.
Cajeput (1975)	66	Sarasota, Fla.
Camphor-tree (1977)	72	Hardee Co., Fla.
Casuarina, Horsetail (1968)	89	Olowalo, Maui, Ha.
Catalpa, Northern (1972)	94	Lansing, Mich.
Cedar, Port-Orford (1972)	219	Siskiyou Natl. Forest, Ore.
Cercocarpus, Birchleaf (1972)	34	Central Point, Ore.
Cherry, Black (1972)	114	Lawrence, Mich.
Chestnut, American (1977)	66	Sherwood, Ore.
Chinaberry (1967)	75	Kaohe, S. Kona, Ha.
Chinkapin, Golden (1954)	127	nr. Annapolis, Cal.
Chokecherry, Common (1972)	66	Ada, Mich.
Coconut (1968)	94	Hilo, Ha.
Coffeetree, Kentucky (1976)	110	Van Buren Co., Mich.
Cottonwood, Black (1969)	147	Unionvalle, Ore.
Cypress, Monterey (1975)	97	Brookings, Ore.
Dahoon (1975)	72	Osceola For., Fla.
Desert Willow (1976)	56	Gila Co., Ariz.
Devil's-walkingstick (1976)	51	San Felasco Hammock, Fla.
Devilwood (1972)	37	Mayo, Fla.
Dogwood, Pacific (1975)	50	nr. Clatskanie, Ore.
Douglas Fir (1975)	302	Coos Bay, Ore.
Doveplum (1965)	45	Miami, Fla.
Elder, Blackbead (1972)	42	nr. Prescott, Ore.
Elm, American (1974)	92	White Creek, N.Y.
False-Mastic (1975)	70	Lignumvitae Key, Fla.
Fig, Florida Strangler (1973)	80	Old Cutler Hammock, Fla.
Fir, Noble (1972)	278	Gifford Pinchot Natl. Forest, Wash.
Franklinia (1973)	38	McLean, Va.
Grapefruit (1972)	38	Ellenton, Fla.
Gumbo-limbo (1973)	50	Homestead, Fla.
Hackberry, Common (1972)	118	Wayland, Mich.
Hawthorn (1967)	50	Glenview, Ill.
Hemlock, Western (1972)	163	Olympic Natl. Pk., Wash.
Hercules-club (1961)	38	Little Rock, Ark.
Hickory, Pignut (1972)	125	nr. Brunswick, Ga.
Holly, Tawnyberry (1973)	55	Homestead, Fla.
Honeylocust, Thornless (1976)	130	Washtenaw Co., Mich.
Hophornbeam, Eastern (1976)	73	Traverse Co., Mich.
Hoptree, Common (1972)	31	Ada, Mich.
Hornbeam, American (1975)	65	Milton, N.Y.
Joshua-tree (1967)	32	San Bernardino Natl. Forest, Cal.
Juniper, Western (1954)	87	Stanislaus Natl. Forest Cal.
Larch, Western (1972)	177	nr. Kootenai Natl. Forest, Mont.
Laurelcherry, Carolina (1972)	44	Dellwood, Fla.
Lebbek (1968)	65	Lahina, Maui, Ha.
Loblolly-Bay (1972)	84	Hugh's Island, Fla.
Locust, Black (1974)	96	Dansville, N.Y.
Lysiloma, Bahama (1973)	79	Homestead, Fla.
Madrone, Pacific (1955)	80	Humboldt Co., Cal.
Magnolia, Cucumber tree (1974)	92	Bel Air, Md.
Mangrove, Red (1975)	75	Everglades Natl. Pk., Fla.
Maple, Red (1972)	125	nr. Armada, Mich.
Mesquite, Velvet (1972)	55	Coronado Natl. Forest, Ariz.
Mountain-Ash, Showy (1972)	58	nr. Gould City, Mich.
Mountain-Laurel (1972)	20	Chattahoochee Natl. Forest, Ga.
Mulberry, White (1976)	82	Battle Creek, Mich.
Oak, California white (1967)	120	nr. Gridley, Cal.
Oleander, Common (1963)	22	Phoenix, Ariz.
Osage-Orange (1972)	51	Charlotte Co., Va.
Palmetto, Cabbage (1972)	90	Highlands Hammock State Pk., Fla.
Paloverde, Blue (1976)	53	Riverside Co., Cal.
Paulownia, Royal (1969)	105	Philadelphia Co., Pa.
Pawpaw, Blue (1972)	41	nr. Smith Mills, Ky.
Pear (1976)	57	Clawson, Mich.
(1972)	74	Leslie Co., Ky.
Pecan (1973)	124	Mer Rouge, La.
Peppertree (1972)	47	San Juan Capistrano, Cal.
Pinckneya (1972)	21	nr. Mt. Pleasant, Fla.
Pine, Ponderosa (1974)	223	Plumas, Cal.
Plum, American (1972)	35	Oakland Co., Mich.
Poison Sumac (1972)	20	Robin's Island, N.Y.
Pondcypress (1972)	135	nr. Newton, Ga.
Poplar, Balsam (1976)	128	Champion, Mich.
Possumhaw (1976)	30	Congaree Swamp, S.C.
Redbay (1972)	58	Randolph Co., Ga.
Redwood, Coast (1972)	362	Humboldt Redwoods State Park, Cal.
Royalpalm, Florida (1973)	80	Homestead, Fla.
Sassafras (1972)	100	Owensboro, Ky.
Seagrape (1972)	57	Miami, Fla.
Sequoia, Giant (1961)	272	Sequoia Natl. Pk., Cal.
Serviceberry, Downy (1975)	50	New Philadelphia, Oh.
Silk-oak (1972)	78	nr. La Belle, Fla.
Silktree (1971)	41	Gilmer, Tex.
Silverbell, Two-wing (1971)	55	Tallahassee, Fla.
Smoketree, American (1974)	47	Lewiston, Ida.
Soapberry, Western (1972)	67	Newton County, Tex.
Sourwood (1972)	118	nr. Robbinsville, N.C.
Sparkleberry Tree (1972)	29	Keltys, Tex.
Spruce, Sitka (1973)	216	Seaside, Ore.
Sugarberry (1976)	78	Society Hill, S.C.
Sumac, Shining (1974)	55	Grenada Co., Miss.
Sweetleaf, Common (1972)	55	Tallahassee, Fla.
Sycamore, Cal. (1945)	116	nr. Santa Barbara, Cal.
Tamarack (1972)	95	Jay, Me.
Tamarisk, Five-Stamen (1972)	37	Albuquerque, N.M.

(Continued)

(continued)

Tanoak (1969)	100	Kneeland, Cal.
Tesota (1972)	31.6	nr. Quartzsite, Ariz.
Torreya, Cal. (1945)	141	nr. Mendocino, Cal.
Trifoliate-Orange (1968)	26	Harrisburg, Pa.
Tupelo, Black (1969)	117	Harrison Co., Tex.
(1971)	139	nr. Houston, Tex.
Wahoo, Eastern (1974)	20	Warrensburg, Mo.
Walnut, Cal. (1973)	116	Santa Rosa, Cal.
Willow, Crack (1972)	112	nr. Utica, Mich.
Winterberry, Common (1971)	40	Wildwood, Fla.
Witch-Hazel, Common (1976)	43	Muskegon, Mich.
Yaupon (1972)	45	nr. Devers, Tex.
Yellow-Poplar (1972)	124	Bedford, Va.
Yellowwood (1967)	58	Morrisville, Pa.
Yew, Pacific (1959)	60	nr. Mineral, Wash.
Yucca, Aloe (1976)	15	Lakeland, Fla.

The 1975-1976 Wildfire Season

Source: Forest Service, U.S. Agriculture Department
Federal, State and Private Protected Areas

In 1975 two of the Nation's major forest fires were on the Angeles National Forest, California. They spread out of control for 8 days, damaging some 69,000 acres of watershed and damaging or destroying over 40 structures.

Over 96 percent of all fires were controlled at 10 acres or less in size on the 201 million acres of Forest Service protected lands. Less than one percent were large fires burning over 300 acres. Forest fires burned .66 acres for each 1,000 acres protected.

All fires decreased 20 percent over previous years. However, 10,804 fires burned only 133,198 acres. Aggressive prevention measures followed by hard-hitting attack forces reduced the potential for major conflagrations on national forests.

On all federal, state and private forest and nonforested watershed lands during 1976, a total of 241,699 fires were reported, an increase of 106,827 above the 134,872 reported during 1975. Acreage burned on all lands totalled 5,109,926, an increase of 3,318,599 above the 1,791,327 burned during 1975.

Through carelessness or incendiarism, man is blamed for the largest portion of wildfires. During 1976 some 161,108 or 93% of the 172,835 reported as having burned on protected land were man-caused. Lightning-started fires amounted to 11,727 or 7% of the protected area fires. Causes of the 68,864 which occurred on unprotected lands are not known.

More than 739,228,000 acres of state and private forest and nonforested watershed lands are protected under the Federal-State cooperative Forest Fire Control Program. Since the area qualifying for protection under the program is 838,420,000 acres, the goal of the program is to bring protection to the more than 99,192,000 acres not now receiving protection. All states participate in the cooperative forest fire protection effort. The record on state and private protected lands for 1976 follows:

Group	Number of fires	Acres burned
Rocky Mountain	8,676	347,765
Pacific	12,586	200,587
North Central	23,697	298,508
Southern	89,750	1,123,062
Eastern	22,326	148,787
Total	**157,035**	**2,118,709**

The record on state and private unprotected lands is:

Rocky Mountain	264	8,035
Pacific	No data	No data
North Central	5,468	51,628
Southern	43,132	2,398,125
Eastern	20,000	15,000
Total	**68,804**	**2,492,428**

Total Fires and Acres Burned — National Forest Protection

Calendar year	Lightning	Man caused	Total	Acres burned
1970	7,804	7,172	14,976	519,978
1971	5,876	6,363	12,239	171,867
1972	8,406	5,748	14,154	116,703
1973	6,376	6,048	12,424	168,692
1974	6,601	6,937	13,538	208,721
1975	4,891	5,913	10,804	133,198
Average 1970-75	7,013	6,454	13,467	237,192

National Forest Areas

Source: Forest Service, U.S. Agriculture Department.
Data as of Sept. 30, 1976

States	Acres	States	Acres	States	Acres	States	Acres
Alabama	640,054	Kansas	107,906	N. Hampshire	683,944	Tennessee	620,080
Alaska	20,710,329	Kentucky	655,440	N. Mexico	9,244,681	Texas	781,353
Arizona	11,271,164	Louisiana	595,591	New York	13,232	Utah	8,045,666
Arkansas	2,464,784	Maine	51,483	N. Carolina	1,146,136	Vermont	261,591
California	20,265,390	Michigan	2,701,561	N. Dakota	1,105,585	Virgin Islands	147
Colorado	14,385,255	Minnesota	2,785,107	Ohio	166,557	Virginia	1,602,804
Connecticut	10	Mississippi	1,138,322	Oklahoma	291,000	Washington	9,071,917
Florida	1,082,252	Missouri	1,453,821	Oregon	15,582,993	W. Virginia	960,802
Georgia	856,200	Montana	16,744,501	Pennsylvania	506,490	Wisconsin	1,492,685
Idaho	20,370,772	Nebraska	351,509	Puerto Rico	27,846	Wyoming	9,251,264
Illinois	255,984	Nevada	5,112,685	S. Carolina	607,240	**Total acreage**	**187,639,754**
Indiana	180,401			S. Dakota	1,995,220		

National Forest System

Administered by the Forest Service, U.S. Agriculture Department, the National Forest System is made up of 155 national forests, 19 national grasslands, 17 land utilization projects, and other minor acreages which total 187,639,754 acres in 44 states, Puerto Rico, and the Virgin Islands. All lands within the National Forest System are managed under two guiding principles: multiple use — the management of lands to make each area yield the combination of uses best suited to public needs; and sustained yield — maintenance of a continuous supply of all forest resources through wise use, management, and protection.

National forest lands which supply water for agriculture, industry, recreation, and domestic use, for example, also are managed to prevent erosion and help control floods, yet there also may be camping, skiing, and timber harvesting on the same land.

The scenic beauty and recreation opportunities available on national forests yearly draw millions of Americans to these lands to hunt, fish, camp, picnic, boat, recreational play, swim, hike, ski, and to make pack trips into the wilderness. Use reached 192,915,800 visitor days during calendar year 1974.

Giant Trees of Canada

Source: Native Trees of Canada by R. C. Hosie; Canadian Forestry Service, Dept. of Fisheries & Forestry

There are nearly 140 species of trees native to Canada on which information is easily available. A "native" tree is defined as a single-stemmed perennial woody plant growing to a height of more than 10 feet, and which is indigenous to Canada. Most of the "giant" trees in Canada are to be found in the forest regions. These regions reflect differences caused by terrain, soil, and climate. The 9 forest regions are: The Grassland, Boreal, Great Lakes-St. Lawrence, Columbia, Deciduous, Coast, Subalpine, Acadian, and Montane.

Species	Height (ft.)	Forest region
Alpine Fir	65-100	Subalpine; N.W. Boreal
Amabilis Fir	80-125	Coast & coastal parts of Subalpine
Balsam Poplar	60-80	Boreal, Great Lakes-St. Lawrence & Acadian
Black Cottonwood	80-125	Throughout B.C. and western Alberta
Black Maple	80-90	Ontario to Montreal Is.
Douglas Fir	150-200	Coast
Eastern Cottonwood	75-100	Gt. Lakes-St. Lawrence
Eastern White Pine	100-175	Through east Canada
Engelmann Spruce	100-120	Southern Subalpine
Grand Fir	100-125	S. Coast & Columbia
Mockernut Hickory	75-90	Deciduous
Silver Maple	80-90	S.E. parts of G. Lakes-St. Lawrence

It is difficult to obtain precise records of single trees of outstanding heights. Given below are several common species of trees native to Canada showing the usual or normal height of the species. But many exceptions have been noted. For example, the Douglas Fir, whose average range in height is given at 150 to 200 ft. with diameters of up to 9 ft., occasionally may attain heights above 300 ft. and diameters of 15 ft. or more. The Sitka Spruce is also known to have reached heights of at least 280 ft., and the Western White Pine is recorded as having attained 200 ft.

Species	Height (ft.)	Forest region
Sitka Spruce	125-175	Coast
Sugar Maple	80-90	Gt. Lakes-St. Lawrence
Sycamore	Up to 150	Deciduous
Western Hemlock	120-160	Coast & Columbia
Western Larch	100-180	Southern part of Columbia & Montane, B.C.
Western Red Cedar	150-200	Coast & Columbia
Western White Pine	90-110	S. Coast & Columbia
White Birch	Med.-80	Throughout Canada
White Elm	60-80	G. Lakes-St. Lawrence & Acadian
White Oak	Med.-100	Southern Ontario
White Spruce	80-120	Boreal
Yellow Cypress	60-80	Coast & in coastal parts of Subalpine

The 1974 Forest Fire Season in Canada

Source: Environment Canada-Canadian Forestry Service

Most of the fire activity in Canada in 1974 was concentrated within a narrow band along the Ontario-Manitoba border. Both provinces experienced generally cool, wet weather conditions throughout the early part of the fire season followed by a period of unusually hazardous fire conditions extending from mid-June through the early part of August. By the time nature took a hand and fairly frequent rainfalls helped to bring the fire situation under control, close to 400,000 acres of forest land had been burned over in Manitoba, while the losses in Ontario had climbed to an astounding 1,254,625 acres, the highest since 1923.

At the peak of the emergency, in Ontario, periods of restricted forest travel were instituted and on July 6th some 1,700 people had to be evacuated from the Vermilion Bay area.

A total of 7,871 forest fires were reported on all provincial and federal lands in 1974, which is only slightly more than that reported in 1973. It is fortunate, however, that little or no direct relationship exists between number of fires and total area burned. Indeed, despite the higher fire occurrence, acreage burned has dropped by almost one million acres from the corresponding figure for the previous year.

Success of the fire control effort is borne out by the fact that 88% of all fires reported did not exceed 10 acres in size. Furthermore, only 306 fires, or 3.8% of all fires started, could not be contained at 100 acres or less.

Lightning was by far the greatest bugbear for fire control people in 1974 with 94% of the total area burned being attributed to this cause. However, human negligence and incendiarism continued to be responsible for the greatest proportion of forest fires. Man started 5,705 fires, or 72% of the national total. Although woods workers, land clearing and railroads are important sources of man-caused fires, recreationists — campers, hunters, fishermen — are still the major offenders.

The total area afforded some form of organized protection in 1974 was approximately 1,689,000 square miles.

Forest Fires on Provincial and Federal Protected Lands, 1974

	No. of fires	Acres burned
Provincial lands		
Newfoundland	(1)	(1)
Nova Scotia	579	4,473
Prince Edward Island	52	377
New Brunswick	465	2,571
Quebec	910	7,500
Ontario	1,625	1,294,629
Manitoba	491	398,224
Saskatchewan	197	64,348
Alberta	598	45,450
British Columbia	2,560	51,805
Federal lands		
Yukon	93	3,830
Northwest Territories	183	91,716
National parks	94	953
Other federal lands	24	511
Total all lands	**7,871**	**1,966,387**

Total Fires and Acres Burned, by Causes

Year	Man-caused		Lightning	
	No. of fires	Acres burned	No. of fires	Acres burned
1969	5,003	809,063	1,658	1,522,641
1970	6,014	400,447	3,299	2,217,690
1971	6,287	699,978	2,918	3,448,933
1972	5,739	716,932	2,524	1,211,000
1973	5,524	141,525	2,081	2,785,185
Average '69-'73	5,713	553,589	2,496	2,237,090
1974[1]	5,705	121,653	2,166	1,844,734

(1) Figures for Newfoundland are not available.

ENVIRONMENT

Estimated Total Pollution Control Expenditures

Source: Council on Environmental Quality (billions of 1975 dollars)
Does not include land reclamation, or research, conservation, and enhancement programs.

Pollutant/ source	1975 O&M[1]	1975 Capital costs[2]	1975 Total annual costs[3]	1984 O&M[1]	1984 Capital costs[2]	1984 Total annual costs[3]	Cumulative—1975-84 O&M[1]	Cumulative—1975-84 Capital costs[2]	Cumulative—1975-84 Total costs[3]
Air pollution									
Public	0.1	0.1	0.2	0.6	0.2	0.8	4.2	1.8	6.0
Private									
Mobile	3.4	1.5	4.9	1.3	4.4	5.7	20.9	31.7	52.6
Industrial	2.1	2.4	4.5	4.9	5.6	10.5	34.8	39.5	74.3
Utilities	1.0	1.0	2.0	3.5	3.5	7.0	21.0	21.0	42.0
Total	**6.6**	**5.0**	**11.6**	**10.3**	**13.7**	**24.0**	**80.9**	**94.0**	**174.9**
Water pollution									
Public									
Federal	0.2	(4)	0.2	0.2	0.1	0.3	2.1	0.4	2.5
State and local	2.3	7.6	9.9	6.2	15.1	21.3	41.7	113.7	155.4
Private									
Industrial	1.9	1.7	3.6	7.4	5.7	13.1	40.6	33.0	73.6
Utilities	0.6	0.4	1.0	1.4	0.8	2.2	10.5	6.3	16.8
Total	**5.0**	**9.7**	**14.7**	**15.2**	**21.7**	**36.9**	**94.9**	**153.4**	**248.3**
Radiation									
Nuclear powerplants	(4)	(4)	(4)	(4)	(4)	(4)	0.1	(4)	0.2
Solid waste									
Public	1.5	0.3	1.8	2.1	0.6	2.7	18.2	4.2	22.4
Private	2.9	0.7	3.6	3.9	1.1	5.0	28.4	8.8	37.2
Total	**4.4**	**1.0**	**5.4**	**6.0**	**1.7**	**7.7**	**46.6**	**13.0**	**59.6**
Noise	NA	NA	NA	0.3	0.3	0.6	1.8	1.6	3.4
Grand total	**16.0**	**15.7**	**31.7**	**31.8**	**37.4**	**69.2**	**244.2**	**262.0**	**486.2**

(1) Operating and maintenance costs. (2) Interest and depreciation. (3) O&M plus capital costs. (4) Less than 0.05. (NA) Not available.

Investment for Pollution Control by U.S. Industries

Source: Bureau of Economic Analysis, U.S. Commerce Department
(millions of dollars)

	1976 Pollution statement Air	Water	Solid waste	Total	Percent of investment[2]	1977[1] Pollution abatement Air	Water	Solid waste	Total	Percent of investment[2]
All industries[3]	**3,593**	**2,743**	**426**	**6,762**	**5.58**	**3,832**	**3,159**	**521**	**7,512**	**5.57**
Manufacturing	**2,105**	**1,993**	**284**	**4,382**	**8.27**	**2,177**	**2,276**	**283**	**4,736**	**7.95**
Durable goods	952	537	72	1,560	6.61	998	765	84	1,847	6.98
Primary metals	661	250	12	923	15.69	680	376	16	1,072	17.30
Blast furnaces, steel works	272	173	1	446	15.10	316	281	1	597	19.10
Nonferrous metals	323	71	11	405	18.93	287	80	14	380	17.15
Electrical machinery	44	86	19	148	5.61	47	57	16	120	4.10
Machinery, except electrical	40	30	10	80	1.59	50	71	15	135	2.42
Transportation equipment	53	51	21	125	3.39	65	110	23	198	4.15
Motor vehicles	32	39	19	90	3.62	49	80	20	149	4.37
Aircraft	20	11	2	32	3.26	15	14	2	31	2.83
Stone, clay, and glass	74	25	5	103	6.15	79	32	6	118	6.74
Other durables	81	95	5	181	3.86	76	120	9	205	3.91
Nondurable goods	1,153	1,456	212	2,821	9.60	1,180	1,511	199	2,889	8.73
Food including beverage	90	75	10	175	4.48	95	102	7	204	4.91
Textiles	11	24	2	37	4.40	11	24	1	36	3.85
Paper	182	304	25	511	14.71	212	329	26	567	14.08
Chemicals	287	433	45	765	11.38	298	403	48	749	10.20
Petroleum	554	594	126	1,275	10.86	527	626	109	1,262	9.48
Rubber	20	14	3	37	3.39	21	13	4	38	2.73
Other nondurables	9	11	2	23	1.43	17	14	4	34	1.75
Nonmanufacturing	**1,488**	**750**	**142**	**2,381**	**3.49**	**1,655**	**883**	**238**	**2,775**	**3.68**
Mining	47	29	10	86	2.17	40	41	49	130	2.95
Railroad	8	17	2	27	1.15	1	19	1	21	0.81
Air transportation	12	2	2	16	1.21	11	2	1	14	0.84
Other transportation	11	26	1	38	1.06	17	23	1	40	1.56
Public utilities	1,332	600	100	2,032	9.06	1,503	717	159	2,378	9.29
Electric	1,312	579	99	1,990	10.51	1,488	702	158	2,348	10.87
Gas and other	20	21	1	42	1.20	15	15	1	31	0.76
Communication, commercial and other[4]	79	76	27	182	0.53	84	82	27	193	0.50

(1) Planned. (2) Pollution control as a percent of total plant and equipment investment. (3) Excludes agricultural business; real estate operators; medical, legal, educational, and cultural services; and nonprofit organizations. (4) Includes trade, service, construction, finance, and insurance.

U.S. Forest Land by State and Region

Source: Forest Service, U.S. Agriculture Department

State or region	Land area (1,000) acres	Area forested	Percent forested
Connecticut	3,116	2,186	70
Maine	19,797	17,748	90
Massachusetts	5,013	3,520	70
New Hampshire	5,781	5,131	89
Rhode Island	671	433	65
Vermont	5,935	4,391	74
New England	**40,314**	**33,410**	**83**
Delaware	1,268	391	31
Maryland	6,369	2,960	47
New Jersey	4,820	2,463	51
New York	30,636	17,377	57
Pennsylvania	28,816	17,832	62
West Virginia	15,413	12,172	79
Mid Atlantic	**87,324**	**53,196**	**61**
Michigan	36,492	19,273	53
Minnesota	50,745	18,984	37
North Dakota	44,339	421	1
South Dakota (east)	41,727	334	1
Wisconsin	34,858	14,945	43
Lake States	**208,162**	**53,959**	**26**
Illinois	35,761	3,789	11
Indiana	23,161	3,908	17
Iowa	35,867	2,455	7
Kansas	52,515	1,344	3
Kentucky	25,504	11,968	47
Missouri	44,189	14,919	34
Nebraska	48,974	1,045	2
Ohio	26,251	6,498	25
Central	**292,225**	**45,928**	**16**
Alabama	32,678	21,770	67
Arkansas	33,324	18,277	55
Florida	35,179	17,932	51
Georgia	37,295	25,545	69
Louisiana	28,867	15,380	53
Mississippi	30,290	16,913	56
North Carolina	31,367	20,613	66
Oklahoma	44,149	9,340	21
South Carolina	19,366	12,493	65
Tennessee	26,474	13,136	50
Texas	168,300	24,091	14
Virginia	25,496	16,389	64
South	**512,791**	**211,884**	**41**
Alaska	365,481	119,051	33
California	100,091	42,408	42
Hawaii	4,106	1,974	48
Oregon	61,574	30,404	49
Washington	42,665	23,098	54
Pacific Coast	**573,917**	**216,935**	**38**
Arizona	72,688	18,583	26
Colorado	66,485	22,534	34
Idaho	52,933	21,591	41
Montana	93,248	22,777	24
Nevada	70,264	7,660	11
New Mexico	77,766	18,313	24
South Dakota (west)	6,878	1,399	20
Utah	52,697	15,288	29
Wyoming	62,342	10,085	16
Rocky Mountain	**555,315**	**138,234**	**25**
Total U.S.	**2,270,050**	**(1)753,549**	**33**

(1) Of this total, 499,697,000 acres are of commercial quality (136 million acres are government-owned); 17,246,000 acres are productive but reserved; 2,281,000 acres are deferred for possible reserve status; and 233,891,000 acres are unproductive or awaiting survey.

Gestation, Longevity, and Incubation of Animals

Longevity figures were supplied by Ronald T. Reuther, of the Zoological Society of Philadelphia. They refer to animals in captivity; the potential life span of animals is rarely attained in nature. Maximum longevity figures are from the Biology Data Book, 1972. Figures on gestation and incubation are averages based on estimates by leading authorities.

Animal	Gestation (days)	Average longevity (years)	Maximum longevity (yrs., mos.)
Ass	365	12	35-10
Baboon	187	20	35-7
Bear: Black	219	18	36-10
Grizzly	225	25	—
Polar	240	20	34-8
Beaver	122	5	20-6
Buffalo (American)	278	15	—
Bactrian camel	406	12	29-5
Cat (domestic)	63	12	28
Chimpanzee	231	20	44-6
Chipmunk	31	6	8
Cow	284	15	30
Deer (white-tailed)	201	8	17-6
Dog (domestic)	61	12	20
Elephant (African)	—	35	60
Elephant (Asian)	645	40	70
Elk	250	15	26-6
Fox (red)	52	7	14
Giraffe	425	10	33-7
Goat (domestic)	151	8	18
Gorilla	257	20	39-4
Guinea pig	68	4	7-6
Hippopotamus	238	25	—
Horse	330	20	46
Kangaroo	42	7	—
Leopard	98	12	19-4
Lion	100	15	25-1
Monkey (rhesus)	164	15	—
Moose	240	12	—
Mouse (meadow)	21	3	—
Mouse (dom. white)	19	3	3-6
Opossum (American)	14-17	1	—
Pig (domestic)	112	10	27
Puma	90	12	19
Rabbit (domestic)	37	5	13
Rhinocerous (black)	450	15	—
Rhinocerous (white)	—	20	—
Sea lion (California)	350	12	28
Sheep (domestic)	154	12	20
Squirrel (gray)	44	10	—
Tiger	105	16	26-3
Wolf (maned)	63	5	—
Zebra (Grant's)	365	15	—

Incubation time (days)

Chicken	21
Duck	30
Goose	30
Pigeon	18
Turkey	26

A Collection of Animal Collectives

The English language boasts an abundance of names to describe groups of things, particularly pairs or aggregations of animals. Some of these words have fallen into comparative disuse, but many of them are still in service, helping to enrich the vocabularies of those who like their language to be precise, who tire of hearing a group referred to as "a bunch of," or who enjoy the sound of words that aren't overworked.

band of gorillas
bed of clams, oysters
bevy of quail, swans
brace of ducks
brood of chicks
cast of hawks
cete of badgers
charm of goldfinches
chattering of choughs
cloud of gnats
clowder of cats
clutch of chicks
clutter of cats
colony of ants
congregation of plovers
covey of quail, partridge
cry of hounds
down of hares
drift of swine
drove of cattle, sheep
exaltation of larks
flight of birds
flock of sheep, geese
gaggle of geese
gam of whales
gang of elks
grist of bees
herd of elephants
hive of bees
horde of gnats
husk of hares
kindle or **kendle** of kittens
knot of toads
leap of leopards
leash of greyhounds, foxes
litter of pigs

mob of kangaroos
murder of crows
muster of peacocks
mute of hounds
nest of vipers
nest, nide of pheasants
pack of hounds, wolves
pair of horses
pod of whales, seals
pride of lions
school of fish
sedge or **siege** of cranes
shoal of fish, pilchards
skein of geese
skulk of foxes
sleuth of bears
sounder of boars, swine
span of mules
spring of teals
swarm of bees
team of ducks, horses
tribe or **trip** of goats
troop of kangaroos, monkeys
volery of birds
watch of nightingales
wing of plovers
yoke of oxen

Speeds of Animals

Source: *Natural History* magazine, March 1974.

Animal	Mph	Animal	Mph	Animal	Mph
Cheetah	70	Mongolian wild ass	40	Human	27.89
Pronghorn antelope	61	Greyhound	39.35	Elephant	25
Wildebeest	50	Whippet	35.50	Black mamba snake	20
Lion	50	Rabbit (domestic)	35	Six-lined race runner	18
Thomson's gazelle	50	Mule deer	35	Wild turkey	15
Quarter horse	47.5	Jackal	35	Squirrel	12
Elk	45	Reindeer	32	Pig (domestic)	11
Cape hunting dog	45	Giraffe	32	Chicken	9
Coyote	43	White-tailed deer	30	Spider (Tegenaria atrica)	1.17
Gray fox	42	Wart hog	30	Giant tortoise	0.17
Hyena	40	Grizzly bear	30	Three-toed sloth	0.15
Zebra	40	Cat (domestic)	30	Garden snail	0.03

Most of these measurements are for maximum speeds over approximate quarter-mile distances. Exceptions are the lion and elephant, whose speeds were clocked in the act of charging; the whippet, which was timed over a 200-yard course; the cheetah over a 100-yard distance; man for a 15-yard segment of a 100-yard run (of 13.6 seconds); and the black mamba, six-lined race runner, spider, giant tortoise, three-toed sloth, and garden snail, which were measured over various small distances.

Young of Animals Have Special Names

The young of many animals, birds and fish have come to be called by special names. A young eel, for example, is an elver. Many young animals, of course, are often referred to simply as infants, babies, younglets, or younglings.

bunny: rabbit.
calf: cattle, elephant, antelope, rhino, hippo, whale, etc.
cheeper: grouse, partridge, quail.
chick, chicken: fowl.
cockerel: rooster.
codling, sprag: codfish.
colt: horse (male).
cub: lion, bear, shark, fox, etc.
cygnet: swan.
duckling: duck.
eaglet: eagle.
elver: eel.
eyas: hawk, others.
fawn: deer.
filly: horse (female).
fingerling: fish generally.
flapper: wild fowl.
fledgling: birds generally.
foal: horse, zebra, others.
fry: fish generally.
gosling: goose.
heifer: cow.
joey: kangaroo, others.
kid: goat.
kit: fox, beaver, rabbit, cat.
kitten, kitty, catling: cats, other fur-bearers.
lamb, lambkin, cosset, hog: sheep.
leveret: hare.
nestling: birds generally.
owlet: owl.
parr, smolt, grilse: salmon.
piglet, shoat, farrow, suckling: pig.
polliwog, tadpole: frog.
poult: turkey.
pullet: hen.
pup: dog, seal, sea lion, fox.
puss, pussy: cat.
spike, blinker, tinker: mackerel.
squab: pigeon.
squeaker: pigeon, others.
whelp: dog, tiger, beasts of prey.
yearling: cattle, sheep, horse, etc.

Some Endangered Species in North America

Source: U.S. Fish and Wildlife Service, U.S. Interior Department

Common name	Scientific name	Range
Mammals		
Wood bison	Bison bison athabascae	Canada (Alberta)
Black-footed ferret	Mustela nigripes	U.S., Canada
Northern kit fox	Vulpus velox hebes	Canada
West Indian (Florida) manatee	Trichechus manatus	Caribbean (once U.S.)
Sonoran pronghorn	Antilocapra americana sonoriensis	U.S., Mexico
Hawaiian monk seal	Monachus schauinslandi	U.S. (Hawaii)
Eastern timber wolf	Canis lupus lycaon	U.S. (Minn., Mich.)
Northern Rocky Mountain wolf	Canis lupus irremotus	U.S. (Wy., Mont.)
Red wolf	Canis rufus	U.S. (Tex., La.)
Eastern cougar	Felis concolor cougar	U.S., Canada
Birds		
Southern bald eagle	Haliaeetus leucocephalus leucocephalus	U.S. (south of 40° parallel)
Masked bobwhite (quail)	Colinus virginianus ridgwayi	U.S., Mexico
California condor	Gymnogyps californianus	U.S. (Cal.)
Whooping crane	Grus americana	U.S., Canada
Eskimo curlew	Numenius borealis	Canada to Argentina
American peregrine falcon	Falco peregrinus anatum	Canada to Mexico
Arctic peregrine falcon	Falco peregrinus tundrius	Canada to Mexico
Aleutian Canada goose	Branta canadensis leucopareia	U.S., Japan
Brown pelican	Pelecanus occidentalis	U.S. to South America
Attwater's greater prairie chicken	Tympanuchus cupido attwateri	U.S. (Tex.)
Bachman's warbler	Vermivora bachmanii	U.S., Cuba

Kirtland's warbler	Dendroica kirtlandii	U.S., Bahamas
Ivory-billed woodpecker	Campephilus principalis	U.S., Cuba
Reptiles		
American alligator	Alligator mississippiensis	U.S. (Southeast)
American crocodile	Crocodylus acutus	U.S. (Fla.)

Some Other Endangered Species in the World

Source: U.S. Fish and Wildlife Service, U.S. Interior Department

Common name	Scientific name	Range
Mammals		
Asian wild ass	Equus hemionus	Iran to Mongolia
Dugong	Dugong dugon	East Africa to Okinawa
Slender-horned (Rhin) gazelle	Gazella leptoceros	North Africa
Mountain gorilla	Gorilla gorilla	Central and West Africa
Orangutan	Pongo pygmaeus	Indonesia, Malaysia, Brunei
Great Indian rhinoceros	Rhinoceros unicornus	India, Nepal
Javan rhinoceros	Rhinoceros sondaicus	Indonesia, Burma, Thailand
Sumatran rhinoceros	Didermocerus sumatrensis	Bangladesh to Vietnam to Indonesia
Northern white rhinoceros	Ceratotherium simum cottoni	Sudan, Zaire, Uganda, Central African Empire
Blue whale	Balaenoptera musculus	Oceanic
Humpback whale	Megaptera novaeangliae	Oceanic
Sperm whale	Physeter catodon	Oceanic
Birds		
Great Indian bustard	Choriotis nigriceps	India, Pakistan
Japanese crane	Grus japonensis	Japan, China, Korea, USSR
Chinese egret	Egretta eulophotes	China, Korea
Japanese crested ibis	Nipponia nippon	Japan, China, Korea, USSR

Major U.S. Public Zoological Parks

Source: Ronald T. Reuther, President, Zoological Society of Philadelphia. Figures are for 1976; budget, metro population and attendance are in millions. (e) estimate

Zoo	Budget	Metro. pop.	Atten-dance	Acres	Species	Major attractions
San Diego	$10.7	1.6	3.2	128	1,017	Bus tours, primates, walk-through bird cages.
National (Washington, D.C.)	6.2	3.1	3.5e	168	600	Giant pandas, flight cage, lions & tigers.
Brookfield (Chicago)	5.7	7.8	2.0	200	597	Porpoise show, tropical world, baboon island.
Bronx (N.Y.C.)	5.0+	17.3	2.0	252	640	World of Darkness, World of Birds, sky ride.
St. Louis	4.0	2.3	2.0e	83	724	Cat country, aquatic house.
Los Angeles	3.7+	8.9	1.5	113	570	Zoogeographic design, hoofed animals, birds.
Detroit	3.3	4.5	1.3	122	349	Penguinarium, great ape house.
Philadelphia	3.2	5.3	1.1	42	532	Reptiles, African plains, great apes, monorail.
Milwaukee	3.1	1.4	1.6	184	846	Zoogeographic design, bird house, aquarium.
San Francisco	2.0+	4.8	.9	98	309	Great apes, monkey island, bears.
San Antonio	1.5	.9	.8	50	692	Hoofed animals, great apes.
Lincoln Park (Chicago)	1.3+	7.8	4.0e	35	582	Small mammal house, great ape house, sea lions.
Pittsburgh	1.3	2.1	.6	65	374	Underground zoo, aquazoo, children's zoo.
Baltimore	1.3	2.1	.4	142	324	Pachyderm building, children's zoo.
Buffalo	1.3	1.4	.5	235	327	Children's zoo, giraffe house.
Oklahoma City	1.2	.8	.5	225	510	Hoofed animals, carnivores, birds of prey.
Memphis	1.2	.8	.6	36	317	Great ape house, aquarium.
Cleveland	1.2	2.4	.5	125	301	Children's farm, pachyderm building, hoofed animals.
Columbus	1.2		.4	90	623	Reptiles, great apes.
Toledo	1.2	.8	.9	43	458	Birds, reptiles, primates, museum.
Houston	1.1+	2.4	1.7e	43	529	Small mammals, reptiles, great apes, bird house.
Denver	1.1	1.3	.9	80	402	Walk-through bird house, primates, hoofed animals, cats.
Dallas	1.0	2.7	.6	50	750	Birds and reptiles, hoofed animals, primates, pachyderms.
Phoenix	1.0	1.4	.7	125	320	Safari train, Arizona wildlife, children's zoo.
Cincinnati	1.0	1.5	.8	62	602	Walk-through cat exhibit, great apes, aquarium.

Environmental Quality Index

Source: National Wildlife Federation.
Adapted from the Feb.-Mar., 1977 issue of *National Wildlife* magazine.

In 1969, the National Wildlife Federation began to record an index of environmental quality which measures progress or decline in 7 environmental areas. The index represents the rough judgment of environmental protection experts and advocates influenced by very high standards of environmental quality. While their judgment is, in part, subjective and open to dispute, it does provide a relative indication of success and failure in achieving one set of goals.

Wildlife: Natural habitat for wildlife continued to shrink in 1976, as a result of human activities such as drainage projects (particularly in the Mississippi Delta) and subdivision of Western lands for mining and logging, and of drying of some wetlands through drought. But some new gains promise benefits for the future: new federal timber managing guidelines; the new 200-mile offshore limits; more federal funds for land and water acquisition; better habitat impact survey techniques for federal programs; and a Supreme Court ruling that the federal government has the power to manage wildlife on federal lands.

Air: Air quality has on the whole continued to improve, especially in urban areas. Urban sulfur dioxide levels were 30% below 1970 concentrations; particulate matter in the air is decreasing at a 5% annual rate. Some 90% of the nation's 20,000 major stationary pollution sources are either complying with emission limits or on compliance schedules. New federal pollution standards were issued for copper, lead, and zinc smelters. And technological advances have brought full economic pollution control within the capability of auto manufacturers, On the other hand, industrial and political opposition to further advances has increased, and strengthening amendments to the 1970 Clean Air Act were defeated. Air has deteriorated in rural areas. And the ever-increasing number of synthetic toxic chemicals pose health problems that are only now being appreciated.

Minerals: The U.S. is using more minerals than ever before, but it is producing less and importing more. Energy consumption, though lower than in 1973, is on the rise again. Domestic oil production dropped to the lowest level in over ten years, and imports filled 41% of all petroleum needs. The U.S. is still without a national energy policy. Conservation and recycling efforts could be expanded greatly, and more research should be funded into alternatives such as solar energy and nuclear fusion. More than half of the nation's supply of 20 important minerals now comes from abroad. Recycling, seabed exploitation, and materials development could alleviate this dependency.

Soil: Three million acres of farmland are still being lost each year to urbanization or flooding by ponds and reservoirs. On producing farmland, 4 billion tons of topsoil are lost yearly to wind and water erosion, from which only half the nation's cropland is adequately protected. There is growing concern over the effects of herbicides, insecticides, and fertilizers. The President's Council on Environmental Quality took a giant step in advising federal agencies to include farmland in environmental impact statements.

Forests: New timber growth on private lands continues to gain steadily, though the national forests, with half the softwood stock, have shown net losses. Much timberland is still being lost to other uses, and wasteful practices are still tolerated, especially on small private plots. The new National Forest Management Act lays down guidelines on clearcutting and long-range planning.

Living space: Among positive steps were the enactment of a plan by California to control development along its 1,100-mile coast; the designation of a million additional acres as wilderness land; and a big increase in federal funds for buying recreation land. But over a million acres of rural land is lost to development yearly.

Water: Nonpoint water pollution, from runoff, air pollution fallout, strip mining, and construction has hardly been touched by anti-pollution programs, which have had some success against municipal and industrial polluters. More than half of federally authorized pollution-cleanup funds have remained unspent locally. Toxic chemicals, like PCBs, which may cause cancer, remain a major health threat. A new toxic substances law, and EPA action to control 65 toxic industrial wastes, may bring future gains.

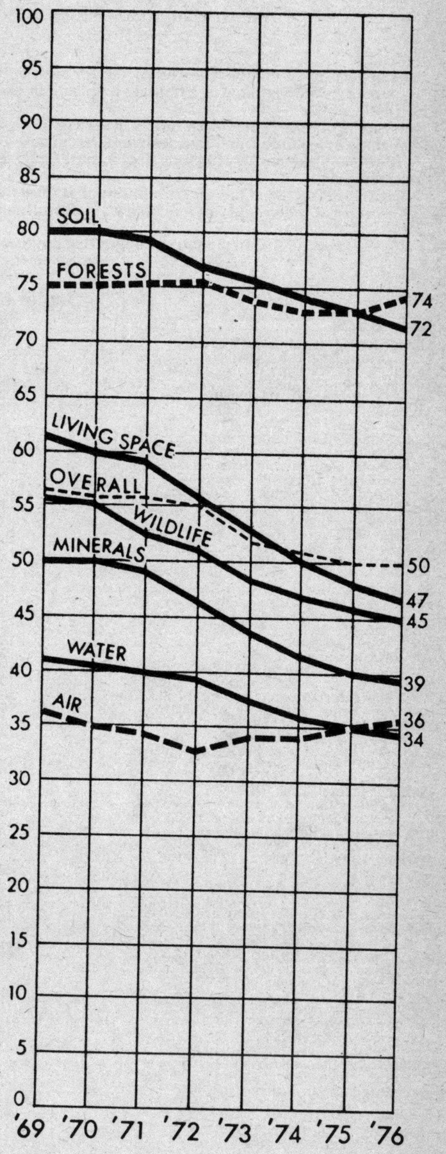

EDUCATION

American Colleges and Universities

Student and Faculty Figures for Spring Term, 1977

Source: World Almanac questionnaires and U.S. Office of Education.

(For Canadian Colleges and Universities, see Index.)

All coeducational unless followed by (M) for men only, or (W) for women only. Even though marked (M) or (W) some are coeducational at graduate level and in evening and summer divisions. Asterisk (*) denotes land-grant college.

Governing official is president unless otherwise designated. Year is that of founding. The word college is part of the name listed unless another designation is given.

Affiliation: C-county; D-religious denomination; Di-district; F-federal; Mu-municipal; P-private; S-state; T-territorial govt.

Each institution listed has an enrollment of at least 200 students of college grade. Number of teachers is the total number of individuals on teaching staff. Enrollment and faculty in italics includes all branches and campuses.

(A) Designates colleges that have not provided up-to-date information.

(See Index for typical tuition fees)

Senior Colleges

Name, address	Year	Governing official and affiliation		Students	Teachers
Abilene Christian, Abilene, TX 79601	1906	John C. Stevens	P	*4,555*	*200*
Adams State, Alamosa, CO 81102	1925	John A. Marvel	S	2,700	144
Adelphi Univ., Garden City, NY 11530	1896	Timothy Costello	P	10,500	360
Adrian, Adrian, MI 49221	1859	John H. Dawson	P	969	92
Agnes Scott, Decatur, GA 30030	1889	Marvin Perry Jr.	P	597	79
Akron, Univ. of, Akron, OH 44325	1870	Dominic J. Guzzetta	S	*22,802*	*894*
Alabama A&M Univ., Normal, AL 35762	1875	Richard D. Morrison	S	4,564	247
Alabama State Univ., Montgomery, AL 36104	1874	Levi Watkins	S	4,150	219
Alabama, Univ. of, University, AL 35486	1831	David Mathews	S	15,460	1,177
at Birmingham, Birmingham, AL 35294	1966	S. R. Hill Jr.	S	12,539	1,271
at Huntsville, Huntsville, AL 35807	1969	Benjamin B. Graves	S	3,421	200
Alaska, Univ. of*, Fairbanks, AK 99701	1917	Robert W. Hiatt	S	*18,254*	*422*
Albany Coll. of Pharmacy, Albany, NY 12208	1881	Dean Walter Singer	P	600	35
Albany State, Albany, GA 31705	1903	Charles Hays	S	2,220	127
Albertus Magnus (W), New Haven, CT 06511	1925	Sr. Francis Heffernan	D	512	61
Albion, Albion, MI 49224	1835	Bernard Tagg Lomas	P	1,668	109
Albright, Reading, PA 19604	1856	Arthur Schultz	D	1,402	96
Albuquerque, Univ. of, Albuquerque, NM 87140	1920	Laurence Smith	D	2,993	190
Alcorn State Univ., Lorman, MS 39096	1871	Walter Washington	S	2,653	124
Alderson-Broaddus, Philippi, WV 26416	1871	Richard E. Shearer	P,D	868	72
Alfred Univ., Alfred, NY 14802	1836	M. Richard Rose	P	2,100	180
Allegheny, Meadville, PA 16335	1815	Lawrence L. Pelletier	P	1,850	127
Alma, Alma, MI 48801	1886	Robert D. Swanson	D	1,150	70
Alvernia, Reading, PA 19607	1958	Sister Mary Victorine	P,D	767	46
Alverno (W), Milwaukee, WI 53215	1936	Sister Joel Read	D	857	104
American Cons. of Music, Chicago, IL 60603	1886	Leo Heim	P	383	171
American International, Springfield, MA 01109	1885	Harry J. Courniotes	P	2,213	98
American Univ., Washington DC 20016	1893	Joseph J. Sisco	D	13,881	763
Amherst, Amherst, MA 01002	1821	John William Ward	P	1,485	157
Anderson, Anderson, IN 46011	1917	Robert H. Reardon	P,D	1,919	151
Andrews Univ., Berrien Springs, MI 49104	1874	Joseph Smoot	D	2,061	255
Angelo State Univ., San Angelo, TX 76901	1928	Lloyd Vincent	S	4,660	190
Annhurst, Woodstock CT 06260	1941	Paul Buchanan	P	329	53
Antioch, Yellow Spgs., OH 45387	1852	Vacant	P	1,300	75
Appalachian Bible Inst., Bradley, WV 25818	1950	Lester E. Pipkin	P	265	15
Appalachian State Univ., Boone, NC 28608	1899	Herbert W. Wey, Chan.	S	9,121	470
Aquinas, Grand Rapids, MI 49506	1922	Norbert J. Hruby	P	1,800	119
Arizona, State Univ., Tempe, AZ 85281	1885	John W. Schwada	S	34,366	1,257
Arizona, Univ. of*, Tucson, AZ 85721	1885	John Paul Schaefer	S	30,146	1,828
Arkansas, Batesville, AR 72501	1872	Dan C. West	D,P	515	43
Arkansas Polytechnic, Russellville, AR 72801	1909	Kenneth Kersh	S	2,400	130
Arkansas State Univ., State Univ., AR 72467	1909	Ross Pritchard	S	*7,920*	*373*
Arkansas, State Coll. of, Conway, AR 72032	1907	Jefferson Farris	S	5,280	212
Arkansas, Univ. of*, Fayetteville, AR 72701	1871	Charles Bishop	S	*29,610*	*1,565*
at Little Rock, Little Rock, AR 72204	1927	G. Robert Ross, Chan.	S	10,000	450
at Pine Bluff, Pine Bluff, AR 71601	1873	Herman Smith Jr.	S	3,135	162
Armstrong, Berkeley, CA 94704	1918	John E. Armstrong	P	623	70
Armstrong State, Savannah, GA 31406	1935	Henry L. Ashmore	S	3,719	165
Art Center Coll. of Design, Pasadena, CA 91103	1930	Donald R. Kubly	P	1,310	171
Art Inst. of Chicago, Chicago, IL 60603	1869	Donald Irving, Dir.	P	1,560	133
Asbury, Wilmore, KY 40390	1890	Dennis F. Kinlaw	P	1,257	94
Ashland, Ashland, OH 44805	1878	Glenn L. Clayton	P	2,013	133
Assumption, Worcester, MA 01609	1904	Pasquale DiPasquale	D	1,763	122
Athens State, Athens AL 35611	1822	Sidney Sandridge	S	1,175	48
Atlanta College of Art, Atlanta, GA 30309	1928	William Voos	P	575	50
Atlantic Christian, Wilson, NC 27893	1902	Milton Adams, Act.	D	1,688	96
Atlantic Union, So. Lancaster, MA 01561	1882	R. Dale McCune	P	730	86
Auburn Univ.*, Auburn, AL 36830	1856	Harry Philpott	S	*21,380*	*1,240*
Augsburg, Minneapolis, MN 55454	1869	Oscar A. Anderson	D,P	1 587	118
Augusta, Augusta, GA 30904	1925	George A. Christenberry	S	3,233	147
Augustana, Rock Island, IL 61201	1860	J. Thomas Tredway	D	2,128	113
Augustana, Sioux Falls, SD 57102	1860	Charles L. Balcer	P	2,263	149
Aurora, Aurora, IL 60507	1893	Lloyd Richardson	P	840	87
Austin, Sherman, TX 75090	1849	John D. Moseley	D,P	1,216	93
Austin Peay State Univ., Clarksville, TN 37040	1927	Robert O. Riggs	S	4,600	225
Averett, Danville, VA 24541	1859	Conwell A. Anderson	P,D	1,086	50
Avila, Kansas City, MO 64145	1916	Sister Olive Dallavis	D,P	1,864	185

Name, address	Year	Governing official and affiliation		Students	Teachers
Azusa Pacific, Azusa, CA 91702	1899	Paul Sago	D	1,445	96
Babson, Babson Park, MA 02157	1919	Ralph Sorenson	P	2,449	130
Baker Univ., Baldwin City, KS 66006	1858	Jerald C. Walker	P	955	78
Baldwin-Wallace, Berea, OH 44017	1845	A.B. Bonds Jr.	D	2,392	160
Ball State Univ., Muncie, IN 47306	1918	John J. Pruis	S	17,547	881
Baltimore, Univ. of, Baltimore, MD 21201	1925	H. Mebane Turner	S	5,316	254
Baptist Bible College of Pa., Clarks Summit, PA 18411	1932	Ernest Pickering	D,P	869	40
Baptist Coll. at Charleston, Charleston, SC 29411	1960	John Hamrick	D	2,290	95
Barat (W), Lake Forest, IL 60045	1858	Judith Cagney	P	839	72
Barber-Scotia, Concord, NC 28025	1867	Mable McLean	P	526	38
Bard, Annandale, NY 12504	1934	Leon Botstein	P	648	77
Barnard (W), New York, NY 10027	1889	Jacquelyn Mattfeld	P	1,950	150
Barrington, Barrington, RI 02806	1900	Harold Fickett Jr.	P	597	60
Barry, Miami Shores, FL 33161	1940	Sister M. Trinita Flood	P,D	1,592	125
Bates, Lewiston, ME 04240	1864	Thomas H. Reynolds	P	1,322	105
Baylor Univ., Waco, TX 76703	1845	Abner V. McCall	D	*8,947*	*430*
Beaver, Glenside, PA 19038	1853	Edward D. Gates	P	1,890	96
Belhaven, Jackson, MS 39202	1883	Howard J. Cleland	D	859	51
Bellarmine, Louisville, KY 40205	1950	Eugene Petrick	D	1,705	93
Bellevue, Bellevue, NE 68005	1965	Richard Winchell	P	1,543	49
Belmont, Nashville, TN 37203	1951	Herbert C. Gabhart	D	1,160	79
Belmont Abbey, Belmont, NC 28012	1876	Rev. John Bradley	D	767	52
Beloit, Beloit, WI 53511	1846	Martha Peterson	P	1,194	91
Bemidji State, Bemidji, MN 56601	1919	Robert Decker	S	4,384	225
Benedict, Columbia, SC 29204	1870	Henry Ponder	P	1,982	113
Benedictine, Atchison KS 66002	1971	Rev. Gerard Senecal	D,P	*979*	*85*
Benjamin Franklin Univ., Washington, DC 20036	1925	Mrs. Clephane Kennedy	P	1,000	34
Bennett (W), Greensboro, NC 27420	1873	Isaac H. Miller	D	618	59
Bennington, Bennington, VT 05201	1935	Joseph Iseman, Act.	D	597	82
Bentley, Waltham, MA 02154	1917	Gregory Adamian	P	4,871	224
Berea, Berea, KY 40404	1855	W.D. Weatherford	P	1,500	145
Berry, Mount Berry, GA 30149	1902	John R. Bertrand	P	1,671	77
Bethany, Lindsborg, KS 67456	1881	Arvin Hahn	D	784	61
Bethany, Bethany, WV 26032	1840	William Tucker	P,D	1,029	82
Bethany Bible, Santa Cruz, CA 95066	1919	C. Morse Ward	D,P	576	30
Bethany Nazarene, Bethany, OK 73008	1899	John Knight	P,D	1,272	75
Bethel, Mishawaka, IN 46544	1947	Albert Beutler	P	448	31
Bethel, North Newton, KS 67117	1887	Harold Schultz	D	638	44
Bethel, McKenzie, TN 38201	1842	William L. Odom	P,D	304	34
Bethel, St. Paul, MN 55112	1871	Carl Lundquist	D	1,680	115
Bethune-Cookman, Daytona Beach, FL 32015	1904	O. P. Bronson	D	1,464	85
Biola, La Mirada, CA 90639	1908	J. Richard Chase	P	2,282	130
Birmingham Southern, Birmingham, AL 35204	1856	Neal R. Berte	Mu	1,006	70
Biscayne, Miami, FL 33054	1962	Rev. John McDonnell	D	14,974	83
Bishop, Dallas, TX 75241	1881	Milton K. Curry Jr.	P	1,733	91
Black Hills State, Spearfish, SD 57783	1883	M. Fitzgerald, Act.	S	2,366	115
Blackburn, Carlinville, IL 62626	1837	John Alberti	D	643	55
Bloomfield, Bloomfield, NJ 07003	1868	Merle F. Allshouse	P	1,800	90
Bloomsburg State, Bloomsburg, PA 17815	1839	James McCormick	S	6,149	290
Blue Mountain (W), Blue Mountain, MS 38610	1873	E. Harold Fisher	D	325	35
Bluefield State, Bluefield, WV 24701	1895	J. Wade Gilley	S	*1,523*	*103*
Bluffton, Bluffton, OH 45817	1899	Benjamin Sprunger	P	690	58
Bob Jones Univ., Greenville, SC 29614	1927	Bob Jones, Chan.	D	4,924	323
Boca Raton, Boca Raton, FL 33431	1963	Thomas Carlin	P	510	34
Boise State, Boise, ID 83725	1932	John Barnes	S	9,757	463
Boston, Chestnut Hill, MA 02167	1863	Rev. J. Donald Monan	D	12,000	700
Boston State, Boston, MA 02115	1852	Kermit C. Merrissey	S	5,805	295
Boston Conserv. of Music, Boston, MA 02215	1867	George Brambilla	P	479	99
Boston Univ., Boston, MA 02215	1869	John Silber	P	22,671	1,880
Bowdoin, Brunswick, ME 04011	1794	Roger Howell Jr.	P	1,331	110
Bowie State*, Bowie, MD 20715	1865	Samuel L. Myers	S	1,817	157
Bowling Green State Univ., Bowling Green, OH 43403	1910	Hollis A. Moore Jr.	S	*17,042*	*716*
Bradley Univ., Peoria, IL 61625	1897	Martin G. Abegg	P	5,000	259
Brandeis Univ., Waltham, MA 02154	1948	Marver Bernstein	P	2,777	389
Brenau, Gainesville, GA 30501	1878	James T. Rogers	P	596	45
Brescia, Owensboro, KY 42301	1950	Sister Geo. Ann Cecil	P	930	87
Briar Cliff, Sioux City, IA 51104	1930	Kasper Marking	D,P	764	61
Briarcliff, Briarcliff Manor, NY 10510	1903	Josiah Bunting	P	400	58
Bridgeport Engineering Inst., Bridgeport, CT 06606	1924	William J. Owens	P	381	56
Bridgeport, Univ. of, Bridgeport, CT 06602	1927	Leland Miles	P	7,150	507
Bridgewater, Bridgewater, VA 22812	1880	Wayne F. Geisert	D	778	65
Bridgewater State, Bridgewater, MA 02324	1840	Adrian Rondileau	S	7,550	280
Brigham Young Univ., Provo, UT 84602	1875	Dallin U. Oaks	P,D	*26,470*	*1,259*
Brooklyn Law School, Brooklyn, NY 11201	1901	Raymond Lisle, Dean	P	1,036	55
Brown Univ., Providence, RI 02912	1764	Howard R. Swearer	P	5,055	432
Bryan, Dayton, TN 37321	1930	Theodore Mercer	P	549	37
Bryant, Smithfield RI 02917	1863	William O'Hara	P	5,000	131
Bryn Mawr (W), Bryn Mawr, PA 19010	1885	Harris L. Wofford Jr.	P	1,601	188
Bucknell Univ., Lewisburg, PA 17837	1846	George O'Brien	P	3,200	261
Buena Vista, Storm Lake, IA 50588	1891	Keith G. Briscoe	D	*879*	*47*
Butler Univ., Indianapolis, IN 46208	1850	Paul Stewart, Act.	P	4,117	360
Caldwell, Caldwell, NJ 07006	1939	Sr. M. Anne John O'Laughlin	D,P	850	73
California Baptist, Riverside, CA 92504	1950	James R. Staples	D	822	51
Cal. Coll. of Arts and Crafts, Oakland, CA 94618	1907	Harry Xavier Ford	P	1,150	110
Cal. College of Podiatric Med., San Francisco, CA 94120	1900	H. D. Bailey	P	*440*	*62*
Cal. Inst. of the Arts, Valencia, CA 91355	1968	Robert Fitzpatrick	P	629	66
Cal. Inst. of Tech., Pasadena, CA 91125	1920	Robert Christy, Act.	P	1,541	738
Cal. Lutheran, Thousand Oaks, CA 91360	1959	Mark Mathews	P	2,487	263
Cal. Maritime Academy, Vallejo, CA 94590	1929	R. Adm. Joseph Rizza	S	468	28
Cal. State Polytechnic, San Luis Obispo, CA 93407	1901	Robert Kennedy	S	15,158	800
Cal. State, Bakersfield, CA 93309	1970	Jacob Frankel	S	3,035	194
Cal. State, California, PA 15419	1852	George Roadman	S	4,968	333
Cal. State, Dominguez Hills, CA 90747	1960	Donald Gerth	S	6,000	310
Cal. State, Rohnert Park, CA 94928	1960	P. Diamandopoulos	S	6,024	424

Name, address	Year	Governing official and affiliation		Students	Teachers
Cal. State, San Bernardino, CA 92407	1965	John Pfau	S	4,002	232
Cal. State, Turlock, CA 95380	1957	Walter Olson	S	3,307	212
Cal. State Polytechnic Univ., Pomona, CA 91768	1938	Robert C. Kramer	S	13,471	757
Cal. State Univ., Northridge, CA 91330	1958	James W. Cleary	S	26,000	1,500
Cal. State Univ., Chico, CA 95929	1887	Stanford Cazier	S	*13,383*	*933*
Cal. State Univ., Fresno, CA 93740	1911	Norman Baxter	S	14,951	944
Cal. State Univ., Fullerton, CA 92634	1959	L. Donald Shields	S	21,572	1,181
Cal. State Univ., Hayward, CA 94542	1957	Ellis McCune	S	12,800	750
Cal. State Univ., Long Beach, CA 90840	1949	Stephen Horn	S	31,157	1,601
Cal. State Univ., Los Angeles, CA 90032	1947	J. A. Greenlee	S	25,600	1,460
Cal. State Univ., Sacramento, CA 95819	1947	James Bond	S	20,415	1,115
Cal. State Univ., San Francisco, CA 94132	1899	Paul F. Romberg	S	23,409	1,500
Cal., Univ. of*, Berkeley, CA 94720	1868	David S. Saxon	S	*128,478*	*7,000*
Berkeley Campus, Berkeley, CA 94720	1873	Albert H. Bowker, Chan.	S	30,001	2,429
Davis Campus, Davis, CA 95616	1905	James Meyer, Chan.	S	17,197	1,260
Irvine Campus, Irvine, CA 92717	1965	D. G. Aldrich, Chan.	S	9,682	718
Los Angeles Campus, Los Angeles, CA 90024	1919	Charles Young, Chan.	S	32,131	2,265
Riverside Campus, Riverside, CA 92502	1907	Ivan Hinderaker, Chan.	S	5,058	766
San Diego Campus, La Jolla, CA 92093	1912	William D. McElroy, Chan.	S	8,875	946
San Francisco Campus, San Francisco, CA 94122	1873	F. A. Sooy, Chan.	S	3,295	1,414
Santa Barbara Campus, Santa Barbara, CA 93106	1898	Vernon Cheadle, Chan.	S	14,584	947
Santa Cruz Campus, Santa Cruz, CA 95064	1965	R. L. Sinsheimer, Chan.	S	6,134	337
Calumet, E. Chicago, IN 46312	1951	Rev. James McCabe	D,P	1,658	98
Calvary Bible, Kansas City, MO 64111	1932	Leslie Madison	P	295	25
Calvin, Grand Rapids, MI 49506	1876	Anthony Dickema	P	3,915	200
Cameron, Lawton, OK 73505	1908	Don Owen	S	5,538	234
Campbell, Buies Creek, NC 27506	1887	Norman A. Wiggins	D	*2,500*	*155*
Campbellsville, Campbellsville, KY 42718	1906	William R. Davenport	P,D	686	50
Canisius, Buffalo, NY 14208	1870	Rev. James Demske	P	4,287	263
Capital Univ., Columbus, OH 43209	1850	Thomas H. Langevin	D	2,619	163
Capitol Inst. of Tech., Kensington, MD 20795	1927	Harold Johnson, Act.	P	*300*	*22*
Cardinal Stritch, Milwaukee, WI 53217	1937	Sister M. Kliebhan	D	1,206	102
Carleton, Northfield, MN 55057	1866	Robert Edwards	P	1,674	168
Carlow (W), Pittsburgh, PA 15213	1929	Sister Jane Scully	D,P	901	96
Carnegie-Mellon Univ., Pittsburgh, PA 15213	1900	Richard M. Cyert	P	4,996	426
Carroll, Helena, MT 59601	1909	Francis Kevins	D,P	1,433	115
Carroll, Waukesha, WI 53186	1846	Robert V. Cramer	D	1,225	103
Carson-Newman, Jefferson City, TN 37760	1851	John A. Fincher	P,D	1,540	110
Carthage, Kenosha, WI 53140	1847	Erno Dahl	D	1,604	103
Case Western Reserve Univ., Cleveland OH 44106	1826	L. A. Toepfer	P	8,178	1,250
Castleton State, Castleton, VT 05735	1787	Donald Wilson	S	2,069	87
Catawba, Salisbury, NC 28144	1851	M. L. Shotzberger	P,D	935	84
Cathedral (M), Douglaston, NY 11362	1914	Rev. Thomas Gradilone	D	208	40
Catholic Univ. of America, Washington, DC 20064	1887	Clarence C. Walton	D	7,399	592
Cath. Univ. of Puerto Rico, Ponce, PR 00731	1948	F. J. Carreras	D,P	*10,026*	*426*
Cedar Crest (W), Allentown, PA 18104	1867	Pauline Tompkins	D	745	82
Cedarville, Cedarville, OH 45314	1887	James Jeremiah	D,P	1,217	53
Centenary (W), Hackettstown, NJ 07840	1867	Charles Dick	P	511	44
Central Bible, Springfield, MO 65802	1922	Rev. Philip Crouch	D,P	1,147	51
Central, Pella, IA 50219	1853	Kenneth J. Weller	P	*1,352*	*92*
Central Connecticut State, New Britain, CT 06050	1849	F. Don James	S	12,757	655
Central Methodist, Fayette, MO 65248	1854	Thomas Field	D	581	69
Central Mich. Univ., Mt. Pleasant, MI 48859	1892	Harold Abel	S	16,004	750
Central Missouri St. Univ., Warrensburg, MO 64093	1871	Warren C. Lovinger	S	10,145	419
Central State Univ., Edmond, OK 73034	1890	Bill Lillard	S	11,382	432
Central State Univ., Wilberforce, OH 45384	1887	Lionel H. Newsom	S	2,280	113
Central Washington State, Ellensburg, WA 98926	1890	James E. Brooks	S	7,666	330
Central Wesleyan, Central, SC 29630	1906	Claude Rickman	D	347	29
Centre Coll. of Ky, Danville, KY 40422	1819	Thos. Spragens	P	799	77
Chadron State, Chadron, NE 69337	1911	Edwin Nelson	S	1,907	95
Chaminade Col. of Honolulu, Honolulu, HI 96816	1955	Rev. Charles Lees	D	1,600	181
Chapman, Orange, CA 92666	1861	D. Chamberlin, Act.	D	*3,551*	*180*
Charleston, Coll. of, Charleston, SC 29401	1770	Theodore Stern	S	4,562	215
Chatham (W), Pittsburgh, PA 15232	1869	Edward D. Eddy	P	614	78
Chestnut Hill (W), Philadelphia, PA 19118	1924	Sister Mary Xavier	D	857	83
Cheyney State, Cheyney, PA 19319	1837	Wade Wilson	S	2,801	220
Chicago Academy of Fine Arts, Chicago, IL 60601	1902	Richard Hamper	P	257	30
Chicago Coll. (Osteopathic), Chicago, IL 60615	1900	Thaddeus Kawalek	P	381	185
Chicago State Univ., Chicago, IL 60628	1869	Benjamin Alexander	S	6,880	268
Chicago Technical, Chicago, IL 60616	1904	Leslie Morey	P	451	16
Chicago, Univ. of, Chicago, IL 60637	1892	John Wilson	P	8,888	1,045
Christian Brothers, Memphis, TN 38104	1871	Bro. Bernard LoCoco	D	940	71
Cincinnati, Univ. of, Cincinnati, OH 45221	1870	Warren G. Bennis	S,Mu	*38,841*	*3,161*
Citadel, The (Military) (M), Charleston, SC 29409	1842	Lt. Gen. George Seignious	S	3,276	150
Claflin, Orangeburg, SC 29115	1869	Hubert V. Manning	D	895	56
Claremont Men's, Claremont, CA 91711	1946	Jack Lee Stark	P	800	90
Clarion State, Clarion, PA 16214	1867	Clayton Sommers	S	*4,861*	*279*
Clark, Atlanta, GA 30314	1869	Chas. Knight, Act.	P	1,759	127
Clark Univ., Worcester, MA 01610	1887	Mortimer Appley	P	2,777	205
Clarke (W), Dubuque, IA 52001	1843	Robert Giroux	D,P	656	63
Clarkson Coll. of Tech. Potsdam, NY 13676	1896	Robert A. Plane	P	3,147	213
Cleary, Ypsilanti, MI 48197	1883	James Perry	P	1,200	42
Clemson Univ.*, Clemson, SC 29631	1889	Robert C. Edwards	S	11,383	695
Cleveland Inst. of Art, Cleveland, OH 44106	1882	Joseph McCullough	P	782	82
Cleveland Inst. of Music, Cleveland, OH 44106	1920	Grant Johannesen	P	233	83
Cleveland State Univ., Cleveland, OH 44115	1964	Walter Waetjen	S	16,467	700
Coe, Cedar Rapids, IA 52402	1851	Leo Nussbaum	P	1,074	100
Colby, Waterville, ME 04901	1813	Robert E. L. Strider II	P	1,593	135
Colby-Sawyer, New London NH 03257	1837	Louis Vaccaro	P	720	70
Colgate Univ., Hamilton, NY 13346	1819	Thomas Bartlett	D	2,485	214
Colorado, Colo. Spgs., CO 80903	1874	Lloyd E. Worner	P	1,830	148
Colorado Sch. of Mines, Golden, CO 80401	1874	Guy McBride Jr.	S	2,204	133
Colorado State Univ.*, Fort Collins, CO 80523	1879	A. R. Chamberlain	S	17,426	952
Colorado, Univ. of (A), Boulder, CO 80302	1876	Frederick P. Thieme	S	*30,428*	*2,729*
Colorado Springs, Colorado Springs, CO 80907	1965	Lawrence Silverman	S	3,765	130
Colorado Women's (W), Denver, CO 80220	1888	Marjorie Chambers	P	568	45
Columbia (W), Columbia, SC 29203	1854	R. Wright Spears	P,D	850	64
Columbia, Columbia, MO 65201	1851	W. Merle Hill	P	2,218	74

Name, address	Year	Governing official and affiliation		Students	Teachers
Columbia Bible, Columbia, SC 29203	1923	J. Robertson McQuilkin	P	834	38
Columbia Union, Takoma Park, MD 20012	1904	Colin Standish	D	947	70
Columbia Univ., New York, NY 10027	1754	William McGill	P	18,000	6,000
Teachers College, New York, NY 10027	1887	L. A. Cremin	P	5,922	403
Columbus, Columbus, GA 31907	1958	Thomas Y. Whitley	S	5,277	256
Columbus Coll. of Art & Design, Columbus, OH 43215	1870	Joseph Canzani, Dean	P	593	54
Concord, Athens, WV 24712	1872	Meredith Freeman	S	1,675	90
Concordia, Bronxville, NY 10708	1881	Robert Schnabel	D	625	58
Concordia, Moorhead, MN 56560	1891	Paul Dover	D	2,402	200
Concordia, St. Paul, MN 55104	1893	Gerhardt Ryatt	D	668	54
Concordia Teachers, River Forest, IL 60305	1864	Paul A. Zimmerman	D	1,206	103
Concordia Teachers, Seward, NE 68434	1894	Vance Hinrichs, Act.	D	1,125	111
Connecticut, New London, CT 06320	1911	Oakes Ames	P	1,908	196
Connecticut Univ. of, Storrs, CT 06268	1939	Glenn Fergusen	S	22,450	1,375
Converse (W), Spartanburg, SC 29301	1889	Robert T. Coleman Jr.	P	840	70
Cooper Union, New York, NY 10003	1859	John White	P	937	138
Coppin State, Baltimore, MD 21216	1900	Calvin Burnett	S	3,000	175
Cornell, Mt. Vernon, IA 52314	1853	Philip Secor	P	900	79
Cornell Univ.*, Ithaca, NY 14853	1865	Frank Rhodes	S	18,421	1,507
Creighton Univ., Omaha, NE 68178	1878	Rev. Joseph Labaj	D, P	4,797	812
Culver-Stockton, Canton, MO 63435	1853	Harold Doster	P	553	46
Cumberland, Williamsburg, KY 40769	1889	J.M. Boswell	D,P	1,850	100
Curry, Milton, MA 02186	1879	John S. Hafer	P	912	53
Daemen, Amherst, NY 14226	1948	R.S. Marshall	D	1,300	100
Dakota State, Madison, SD 57042	1881	Robert DeZonia	S	922	55
Dakota Wesleyan Univ., Mitchell, SD 57301	1885	Donald E. Messer	D	555	59
Dallas Baptist, Dallas, TX 75211	1965	W. E. Thorn	D,P	1,226	64
Dallas, Univ. of, Irving, TX 75061	1956	Damian Fandal, Act.	P	1,685	129
Dana, Blair, NE 68008	1884	Earl Mezoff	P	549	46
Dartmouth, Hanover, NH 03755	1769	John George Kemeny	P	3,960	363
David Lipscomb, Nashville, TN 37203	1891	Athens C. Pullias	P	2,154	112
Davidson, Davidson, NC 28036	1837	Samuel R. Spencer Jr.	P,D	1,356	95
Davis & Elkins, Elkins, WV 26241	1904	Gordon Hermanson	P,D	938	82
Dayton, Univ. of, Dayton, OH 45469	1850	Rev. R. A. Rosech	D,P	8,807	527
Defiance, Defiance, OH 43512	1850	M. Ludwig	P,D	800	63
Delaware State*, Dover, DE 19901	1891	Luna I. Mishoe	S	2,046	124
Delaware, Univ. of*, Newark, DE 19711	1833	E. A. Trabant	S	18,446	885
Del. Valley Coll. of S&A, Dolyestown, PA 18901	1896	Joshua Feldstein	P	1,467	80
Delta State Univ., Cleveland, MS 38733	1924	Kent Wyatt	S	3,175	190
Denison Univ., Granville, OH 43023	1831	Robert C. Good	P	2,180	157
Denver, Univ. of, Denver, CO 80210	1864	Maurice B. Mitchell	P	7,835	457
DePaul Univ., Chicago, IL 60604	1898	Rev. J. R. Cortelyou	P	11,052	554
DePauw Univ., Greencastle, IN 46135	1837	Richard Rosser	P,D	2,384	145
Detroit Bible, Detroit, MI 48235	1945	Wendell Johnston	P,D	510	36
Detroit Coll. of Business, Dearborn, MI 48126	1962	Robert Sneden	D	2,540	195
Detroit Coll. of Law, Detroit, MI 48201	1891	G. Cameron Buchanan	P	984	49
Detroit Inst. of Tech., Detroit, MI 48201	1877	H. Thompson	P	1,400	145
Detroit, Univ. of, Detroit, MI 48221	1877	Rev. M. Carron	P	7,633	543
DeVry Inst. of Tech., Dallas, TX 75235	1969	Douglas Kerr	P	752	42
DeVry Inst. of Tech, Chicago, IL 60618	1931	Samuel Edmonds	P	2,907	100
DeVry Inst. of Tech, Phoenix, AZ 85016	1967	F. Roger Hess	P	2,220	89
Dickinson (A), Carlisle, PA 17013	1773	Howard L. Rubendal	P	1,711	120
Dickinson School of Law, Carlisle, PA 17013	1834	Dale F. Shughart	P	445	32
Dickinson State, Dickinson, ND 58601	1918	R. C. Gillund	S	1,100	70
Dillard Univ., New Orleans, LA 70122	1869	Samuel Cook	D,P	1,141	89
District of Columbia, Univ. of, Washington, DC 20009	1851	Wendell Russell	Mu	1,310	132
Doane, Crete, NE 68333	1872	Philip C. Heckman	P	625	43
Dr. Martin Luther, New Ulm, MN 56073	1884	Rev. Conrad Frey	D	739	70
Dominican Coll. of Blauvelt, Blauvelt, NY 10913	1952	Sister Natalie Casey	D	1,135	78
Dominican Coll. of San Rafael, San Rafael, CA 94901	1890	Sister M. Samuel Conlan	D,P	722	112
Dordt, Sioux Center, IA 51250	1955	B. J. Haan	D	990	50
Dowling, Oakdale, NY 11769	1959	V. P. Meskill	P	2,224	219
Drake Univ., Des Moines, IA 50311	1881	Wilbur C. Miller	P	6,458	277
Drew Univ., Madison, NJ 07940	1866	Paul Hardin	P	2,112	173
Drexel Univ., Philadelphia, PA 19104	1891	William W. Hagerty	P	10,183	310
Drury, Springfield, MO 65802	1873	William Everheart	P	2,214	156
Dubuque, Univ. of, Dubuque, IA 52001	1852	Walter F. Peterson	P,D	788	59
Duke Univ., Durham, NC 27706	1838	Terry Sanford	P,D	9,970	1,253
Duquesne Univ., Pittsburgh, PA 15219	1878	Rev. J. McAnulty	P	7,457	462
Dyke, Cleveland, OH 44114	1848	John Corfias	P	1,396	60
D'Youville, Buffalo, NY 14201	1908	Sister Mary C. Barton	P,D	1,400	90
Earlham, Richmond, IN 47374	1847	Franklin Wallin	D,P	1,082	118
East Carolina Univ, Greenville, NC 27834	1907	L. W. Jenkins, Chan.	S	13,399	714
East Central Univ., Ada, OK 74820	1909	Stanley Wagner	S	3,441	140
East Stroudsburg State, E. Stroudsburg, PA 18301	1893	Darrell Holmes	S	3,940	195
East Tennessee State Univ., Johnson City, TN 37601	1911	Delos Culp	S	10,288	426
East Texas Baptist, Marshall, TX 75670	1912	Jerry Dawson	D	727	45
East Texas State Univ., Commerce, TX 75428	1889	F. H. McDowell	S	9,827	425
Eastern, St. Davids, PA 19087	1952	Daniel E. Weiss	D,P	658	63
Eastern Conn. State, Willimantic, CT 06226	1889	Charles Richard Webb	S	2,342	210
Eastern Illinois Univ., Charleston, IL 61920	1895	Daniel Marvin	S	9,923	505
Eastern Kentucky Univ., Richmond, KY 40475	1906	Julius Powell	S	13,510	569
Eastern Mennonite, Harrisonburg, VA 22801	1917	Myron S. Augsburger	P,D	1,007	68
Eastern Michigan Univ., Ypsilanti, MI 48197	1849	James Brickley	S	18,931	752
Eastern Montana, Billings, MT 59101	1927	J. Van de Wetering, Act.	S	3,303	147
Eastern Nazarene, Wollaston, MA 02170	1918	Donald Irwin	D	817	60
Eastern New Mexico Univ., Portales, NM 88130	1934	Warren Armstrong	S	3,901	190
Eastern Oregon State, LaGrande, OR 97850	1929	Rodney A. Briggs	S	1,471	105
Eastern Washington State, Cheney, WA 99004	1890	H. G. Frederickson	S	7,000	350
Eckerd, St. Petersburg, FL 33733	1958	Billy D. Wireman	D	863	60
Edgecliff, Cincinnati, OH 45206	1935	Sr. M. Molitor	D	971	94
Edgewood, Madison, WI 53711	1927	Sister Cecilia Carey	P,D	624	60
Edinboro State, Edinboro, PA 16444	1857	Chester T. McNerney	S	6,755	434
Eisenhower, Seneca Falls, NY 13148	1965	Joseph Coffee Jr.	P	550	61

Name, address	Year	Governing official and affiliation		Students	Teachers
Elizabeth City State Univ., Eliz. City, NC 27909	1891	Marion Thorpe, Chan.	S	1,629	114
Elizabethtown, Elizabethtown, PA 17022	1899	Morely J. Mays	P	1,633	143
Elmhurst, Elmhurst, IL 60126	1871	Ivan Frick	P,D	2,653	178
Elmira, Elmira, NY 14901	1855	Leonard Grant	P	3,139	246
Elon, Elon College, NC 27244	1889	J. F. Young	P	2,175	94
Embry Riddle Aero. Univ., Daytona Beach, FL 32014	1926	Jack R. Hunt	P	2,250	156
Emerson, Boston, MA 02116	1880	Gus Turbeville	P	1,434	84
Emmanuel (W), Boston, MA 02115	1919	Sister Mary McCarthy	D,P	1,390	107
Emory & Henry, Emory, VA 24327	1836	Thomas F. Chilcote	D	794	58
Emory Univ., Atlanta, GA 30322	1836	S. S. Atwood	D,P	7,334	950
Emporia Kansas State, Emporia, KS 66801	1857	John Visser	S	6,007	334
Erskine, Due West, DC 29639	1839	M. S. Bell	D	771	52
Eureka, Eureka, IL 61530	1855	Daniel Gilbert	D	450	28
Evangel, Springville, MO 65802	1955	Robert Spence	P	1,133	72
Evansville, Univ. of, Evansville, IN 47702	1854	Wallace B. Graves	D	4,904	277
Evergreen State, Olympia, WA 98505	1967	Daniel Evans	S	2,566	169
Fairfield Univ., Fairfield, CT 06430	1942	Rev. Thomas Fitzgerald	P	4,752	320
Fairleigh Dickinson Univ., Rutherford, NJ 07070	1942	Jerome Pollack	P	19,021	1,538
Fairmont State, Fairmont, WV 26554	1867	Eston K. Feaster	S	5,072	180
Faith Baptist Bible, Ankeny, IA 50021	1921	David Nettleton	P	600	32
Fayetteville St. Univ., Fayetteville, NC 28301	1877	Charles Lyons Jr.	S	3,540	145
Felician, Lodi, NJ 07644	1942	Sr. Mary Lawniczak	P,D	822	66
Ferris State, Big Rapids, MI 49507	1884	Robert Ewigleben	S	9,934	535
Ferrum, Ferrum, VA 24088	1913	Joseph T. Hart	D,P	1,344	70
Findlay, Findlay, OH 45840	1882	Glen R. Rasmussen	P,D	931	74
Fisk Univ., Nashville, TN 37203	1867	Walter Leonard	P	1,281	79
Fitchburg State, Fitchburg, MA 01420	1894	Vincent J. Mars	S	6,626	284
Flagler, St. Augustine, FL 32084	1968	William L. Proctor	P	680	30
Florida Atlantic Univ., Boca Raton, FL 33431	1961	G. L. Creech	S	7,000	350
Florida A.&M. Univ.*, Tallahassee, FL 32307	1887	Benjamin Luther Perry Jr.	S	5,725	384
Florida Inst. of Tech., Melbourne, FL 32901	1958	Jerome P. Keuper	P	4,287	312
Florida Memorial, Miami, FL 33054	1879	P. V. Moore, Act.	D,P	492	34
Florida Southern, Lakeland, FL 33802	1885	Robert Davis	D	1,581	80
Florida State Univ., Tallahassee, FL 32306	1857	Bernard Sliger	S	21,604	1,100
Florida Tech. Univ., Orlando, FL 32816	1963	Charles N. Millican	S	9,504	365
Florida Univ. of*, Gainesville, FL 32611	1853	Robert Marston	S	27,838	2,868
Fontbonne, St. Louis, MO 63105	1917	Sister Jane Hassett	P,D	901	79
Fordham Univ., Bronx, NY 10458	1841	Rev. James C. Finley	P	15,027	407
Ft. Hays State, Hays, KS 67601	1902	G. Tomanek	S	4,303	269
Ft. Lauderdale, Ft. Lauderdale, FL 33301	1940	Lyle E. Anderson	P	750	35
Fort Lewis, Durango, CO 81301	1911	Rexer Berndt	S	2,800	160
Fort Valley State*, Fort Valley, GA 31030	1895	Cleveland W. Pettigrew	S	1,800	151
Fort Wayne Bible, Fort Wayne, IN 46807	1904	Timothy Warner	D,P	607	45
Fort Wright, Spokane, WA 99204	1907	Sr. Katherine Gray	D,P	460	57
Framingham State, Framingham, MA 01701	1839	D. Justin McCarthy	S	4,400	175
Francis Marion, Florence, SC 29501	1970	Walter D. Smith	S	2,720	117
Franklin, Franklin, IN 46131	1834	Edwin A. Penn	P,D	685	64
Franklin Univ., Columbus, OH 43215	1902	Joseph Frasch	P	3,875	130
Franklin and Marshall, Lancaster, PA 17604	1787	Keith Spalding	P	1,974	126
Franklin Pierce, Rindge, NH 03461	1962	Walter Peterson	P	1,102	53
Freed-Hardeman, Henderson, TN 38340	1908	E. Claude Gardner	D	1,453	90
Free Will Baptist Bible, Nashville, TN 37205	1942	L. C. Johnson	D,P	550	25
Friends Univ., Wichita, KS 67213	1898	Harold C. Cope	D,P	858	65
Frostburg State, Frostburg, MD 21532	1898	Nelson Guild	S	3,186	203
Furman Univ., Greenville, SC 29613	1826	John Johns	P	2,721	185
Gallaudet, Washington, DC 20002	1864	Edward C. Merrill Jr.	P	943	126
Gannon, Erie, PA 16501	1944	Rev. Msgr. W. J. Nash	D	3,644	212
Gardner-Webb, Boiling Springs, NC 28017	1905	C. Williams	D,P	1,308	79
General Motors Inst., Flint, MI 48502	1919	W. Cottingham	P	2,175	150
Geneva, Beaver Falls, PA 15010	1848	Edwin C. Clarke	D	1,362	94
George Fox, Newberg, OR 97132	1891	David Le Shana	D,P	630	45
George Mason Univ., Fairfax, VA 22030	1956	Robert Krug, Act.	S	8,771	315
Geo. Peabody Coll. for Teachers, Nashville, TN 37203	1875	John Dunworth	P	2,000	150
Geo. Washington Univ., Washington, DC 20052	1821	Lloyd H. Elliott	P	20,839	2,661
George Williams, Downers Grove, IL 60515	1890	Richard E. Hamlin	P	1,895	75
Georgetown, Georgetown, KY 40324	1829	Robert L. Mills	D	1,020	64
Georgetown Univ. (A), Washington DC 20057	1789	Rev. Timothy Healy	D	10,359	1,013
Georgia, Milledgeville, GA 31061	1889	J. Whitney Bunting	S	3,510	173
Georgia Inst. Of Tech.*, Atlanta, GA 30332	1885	Joseph M. Pettit	S	10,741	755
Georgia Southern, Statesboro, GA 30458	1906	Pope A. Duncan	S	6,114	303
Georgia Southwestern, Americus, GA 31709	1908	William B. King	S	2,409	129
Georgia State Univ., Atlanta, GA 30303	1913	Noah N. Langdale Jr.	S	28,921	1,079
Georgia, Univ. of*, Athens, GA 30602	1785	Fred C. Davison	S	21,442	1,694
Georgian Court, Lakewood, NJ 08701	1908	Sister Maria Cordis	P,D	950	84
Gettysburg, Gettysburg, PA 17325	1832	Chas. Glassick	P	1,900	137
Glassboro State, Glassboro, NJ 08028	1923	Mark Chamberlain	S	10,331	403
Glenville State, Glenville, WV 26351	1872	Wm. Simmons	S	1,406	74
Goddard, Plainfield, VT 05667	1938	John Hall, Act.	P	1,800	75
Golden Gate Univ., San Francisco, CA 94105	1901	Otto Butz	P	9,155	847
Gonzaga Univ., Spokane, WA 99258	1887	Bernard Coughlin	D	3,200	175
Gordon, Wenham, MA 01984	1889	Richard Gross	P	1,088	57
Goshen, Goshen, IN 46526	1894	J. Lawrence Burkholder	D,P	1,214	99
Goucher (W), Towson, MD 21204	1885	Rhoda Dorsey	P	899	109
Governors State Univ., Park Forest South, IL 60466	1969	L. Malamuth II	S	3,600	152
Grace Coll. of the Bible, Omaha, NE 68108	1943	Robert Benton	P	500	34
Graceland, Lamoni, IA 50140	1895	Franklin Hough, Act.	P,D	1,234	88
Grambling State Univ., Grambling, LA 71245	1901	Ralph W. E. Jones	S	3,749	208
Grand Canyon, Phoenix, AZ 85061	1949	William R. Hintze	D,P	1,137	63
Grand Valley State, Allendale, MI 49401	1960	Arend Lubbers	S	7,540	284
Grand View, Des Moines, IA 50316	1896	Karl F. Langrock	D,P	1,063	66
Great Falls, Coll. of, Great Falls, MT 59405	1932	Msgr. A. M. Brown	P,D	1,223	89
Green Mountain, Poultney, VT 05764	1834	Raymond Withey	P	475	43
Greenville, Greenville, IL 62246	1892	O. R. Herron	D,P	856	66
Grinnell, Grinnell, IA 50112	1846	A. Richard Turner	P	1,158	102
Grove City, Grove City, PA 16127	1876	Charles S. MacKenzie	P	2,177	116

Name, address	Year	Governing official and affiliation		Students	Teachers
Guilford, Greensboro, NC 27410	1837	Grimsley T. Hobbs	D	1,649	100
Gulf-Coast Bible, Houston, TX 77008	1953	John Conley	D,P	363	21
Gustavus Adolphus, St. Peter, MN 56082	1862	Edward Lindell	D,P	2,130	132
Gwynedd-Mercy, Gwynedd Valley, PA 19437	1948	Sister Isabelle Keiss	D,P	1,092	113
Hahnemann Medical, Philadelphia, PA 19102	1848	Wharton R. Shober	P	710	214
Hamilton (M), Clinton, NY 13323	1812	J. M. Carovano	P	976	89
Hamline Univ., St. Paul, MN 55104	1854	Jerry E. Hudson	P	1,816	148
Hampden-Sydney (M), Hampden-Sydney, VA 23943	1776	Josiah Bunting III	D,P	736	56
Hampton Institute, Hampton, VA 23668	1868	Carl M. Hill, Act.	P	2,618	248
Hanover, Hanover, IN 47243	1827	John E. Horner	D	932	72
Hardin-Simmons Univ., Abilene, TX 79601	1891	Elwin L. Skiles	D	1,641	117
Harding, Searcy, AR 72143	1924	Clinton L. Ganus Jr.	D	2,987	157
Harris Teachers, St. Louis, MO 63103	1857	Richard Stumpe	MU	1,300	65
Hartford, Univ. of, W. Hartford, CT 06117	1877	A. M. Woodruff	P	8,984	553
Hartwick, Oneonta, NY 13820	1928	Earl Deubler Jr., Act.	P	*1,550*	*120*
Harvard Univ.**(1), Cambridge, MA 20138	1636	Derek Curtis Bok	P	*20,498*	*3,860*(2)
Harvey Mudd, Claremont, CA 91711	1955	D. Kenneth Baker	P	481	52
Hastings, Hastings, NE 68901	1882	Clyde B. Matters	P,D	712	53
Haverford (M), Haverford, PA 19401	1833	John R. Coleman	P	800	101
Hawaii, Univ. of, Honolulu, HI 96822	1907	Fujio Matsuda	S	*47,214*	*2,302*
Heald Engineering, San Francisco, CA 94109	1863	James Dietz	P	1,000	70
Heidelberg, Tiffin, OH 44883	1850	Leslie H. Fishel Jr.	P,D	1,018	107
Henderson State Univ., Arkadelphia, AR 71923	1890	Martin Garrison	S	*3,333*	*175*
Hendrix, Conway, AR 72032	1884	Roy Shilling, Jr.	D	1,058	54
High Point, High Point, NC 27262	1924	Wendell M. Patton	D	1,132	60
Hillsdale, Hillsdale, MI 49242	1844	George C. Roche III	P	1,029	70
Hiram, Hiram, OH 44234	1850	Elmer Jagow	P,D	1,156	110
Hobart & William Smith, Geneva, NY 14456	1822	Allan A. Kuusisto	P	1,757	122
Hofstra Univ., Hempstead, NY 11550	1935	James Shuart	P	9,420	604
Hollins (W), Hollins Coll., VA 24020	1842	Carroll Brewster	P	990	91
Holy Cross, Coll. of the, Worcester, MA 01610	1843	Rev. John Brooks	D	2,565	195
Holy Family, Philadelphia, PA 19114	1954	Sister Mary Lillian	D,P	1,102	84
Holy Names, Oakland, CA 94619	1868	Sister M. Irene Woodward	P	641	96
Hood, Frederick, MD 21701	1893	Martha Church	P,D	1,506	117
Hope, Holland, MI 49423	1866	Gordon Van Wylen	P	2,290	160
Houghton, Houghton, NY 14744	1883	D. R. Chamberlain	P,D	*1,220*	*84*
Houston Baptist Univ., Houston, TX 77074	1960	William Hinton	D	1,632	106
Houston, Univ. of, Houston, TX 77004	1927	Philip G. Hoffman	S	*38,500*	*1,750*
Downtown College, Houston, TX 77002	1974	J. Don Boney, Chan.	S	4,517	179
Howard Payne, Brownwood, TX 76801	1889	Roger L. Brooks	P	*1,422*	*90*
Howard Univ., Washington, DC 20059	1867	James E. Cheek	P	*9,815*	*1,908*
Humboldt State Univ., Arcata, CA 95521	1913	Alistair McCrone	S	7,442	425
Huntingdon, Montgomery, AL 36106	1854	Allen Jackson	D,P	651	52
Huntington, Huntington, IN 46750	1897	E. DeWitt Baker	P,D	565	55
Huron, Huron, SD 57350	1883	Richard Hill	D	373	28
Husson, Bangor, ME 04401	1898	Franklin Peters	P	903	93
Huston-Tillotson, Austin, TX 78702	1876	John T. King	D	707	49
Idaho, Coll. of, Caldwell, ID 83605	1891	William Cassell	P	843	57
Idaho State Univ., Pocatello, ID 83209	1901	Myron Coulter	S	9,843	499
Idaho, Univ. of*, Moscow, ID 83843	1889	Richard D. Gibb	S	8,168	493
Illinois, Jacksonville, IL 62650	1829	Donald Mundinger	P,D	755	69
Illinois Benedictine, Lisle, IL 60532	1887	Richard Becker	P,D	1,405	87
Illinois Coll. of Optometry, Chicago, IL 60616	1872	Alfred Rosenbloom	P	574	65
Illinois Coll. of Pod. Med., Chicago, IL 60610	1912	P.R. Brachman	P	596	90
Illinois Inst. of Technology, Chicago, IL 60616	1892	Thomas L. Martin Jr.	P	*6,806*	*757*
Illinois State Univ., Normal, IL 61761	1857	Gene Budig	S	17,986	949
Illinois, Univ. of*, Urbana, IL 61801	1867	John E. Corbally	S	*64,531*	*7,558*
Chicago Circle*, Chicago, IL 60680	1965	Donald Riddle, Chan.	S	20,252	975
Medical Center*, Chicago, IL 60680	1896	Joseph Begando, Chan.	S	4,538	3,801
Urbana-Champaign*, Urbana, IL 61801	1867	Jack W. Peltason, Chan.	S	33,552	2,261
Illinois Wesleyan Univ., Bloomington, IL 61701	1850	Robert Eckley	P,D	1,682	124
Immaculata, Immaculata, PA 19345	1920	Sister Mary Antione	P,D	1,038	137
Immaculate Heart, Los Angeles, CA 90027	1916	Sister Helen Kelley	P,D	675	79
Incarnate Word, San Antonio, TX 78209	1881	Sr. Margaret Slattery	D,P	1,450	84
Indiana Central Univ., Indianapolis, IN 46227	1902	Gene Sease	P,D	3,316	138
Indiana Inst. of Tech., Ft. Wayne, IN 46803	1931	Thomas Scully	P	323	37
Indiana State Univ., Terre Haute, IN 47809	1865	Richard Landini	S	*15,593*	*700*
Indiana Univ., Bloomington, IN 47401	1820	John W. Ryan	S	*77,948*	*3,223*
Indiana Univ. of Pa. Indiana, PA 15701	1875	Robert C. Wilburn	S	*11,420*	*610*
Insurance, Coll. of., New York, NY 10038	1962	A. Leslie Leonard	P	1,809	140
Inter Amer. Univ. of P.R. San Juan, PR 00936	1921	Sol Luis Descartes	P	*26,379*	*1,100*
Iona, New Rochelle, NY 10801	1940	John Driscoll	P,D	4,926	256
Iowa State Univ.*, Ames, IA 50011	1858	W. Robert Parks	S	21,831	1,518
Iowa, Univ. of., Iowa City, IA 52242	1847	Willard L. Boyd	S	21,271	1,193
Iowa Wesleyan, Mt. Pleasant, IA 52641	1842	Louis Haselmayer	P,D	678	70
Ithaca, Ithaca, NY 14850	1892	James J. Whalen	P	4,681	368
Jackson State Univ., Jackson, MS 39217	1877	John A. Peoples Jr.	S	7,928	882
Jacksonville State Univ., Jacksonville, AL 36265	1883	Ernest Stone	S	7,000	342
Jacksonville Univ., Jacksonville, FL 32211	1934	Robert H. Spiro	P	2,014	135
James Madison Univ., Harrisonburg, VA 22801	1908	Ronald Carrier	S	7,659	380
Jamestown, Jamestown, ND 58401	1883	J. N. Anderson	P,D	543	52
Jarvis Christian, Hawkins, TX 75765	1912	E. W. Rand	P	517	48
Jersey City State, Jersey City, NJ 07305	1926	William Maxwell	S	8,200	400
John Brown Univ., Siloam Springs, AR 72761	1919	John E. Brown Jr.	P	617	51
John Carroll Univ., Cleveland, OH 44118	1886	Rev. Henry Birkenhauer	P,D	3,711	251
John F. Kennedy Univ., Orinda, CA 94563	1964	Robert Fisher	P	650	85
John Marshall Law School, Chicago, IL 60604	1899	Louis Bird	P	1,500	80
John Wesley, Owosso, MI 48867	1909	H. C. Roost	P	520	45
Johns Hopkins Univ., Baltimore, MD 21218	1876	Steven Muller	P	*10,000*	*700*
Johnson C. Smith Univ., Charlotte, NC 28216	1867	Wilbert Greenfield	P,D	1,635	75

(1) Includes Radcliffe College (2) Includes teaching fellows.
**Oldest college in the United States.

Name, address	Year	Governing official and affiliation		St. dents	Teach-ers
Johnson State, Johnston, VT 05656	1866	E. Elmendorf	S	1,253	100
Johnson & Wales, Providence, RI 02903	1914	Morris J. Gaebe	P	8,341	450
Jones, Jacksonville, FL 32211	1918	Delores C. Jones	P	432	16
at Orlando, Orlando, FL 32803	1953	Jack Jones	P	1,565	48
Judson, Marion, AL 36756	1838	N. McCrummen	D	431	38
Juilliard School, The, New York, NY 10023	1905	Peter Mennin	P	1,000	200
Juniata, Huntingdon, PA 16652	1876	Frederick M. Binder	P	1,140	80
Kalamazoo, Kalamazoo, MI 49007	1833	George N. Rainsford	D	1,501	83
Kan. City Art Inst., Kansas City, MO 64111	1885	John W. Lottes	P	701	58
Kan. City Coll. of Osteop. Med., Kansas City, MO 64124	1916	Rudolph Bremen	P	578	117
Kansas Newman, Wichita, KS 67213	1933	Rev. Roman S. Galiardi	D,P	598	58
Kansas State, Pittsburg, KS 66762	1903	James Appleberry	S	5,284	334
Kansas State Univ.*, Manhattan, KS 66506	1863	Duane Acker	S	18,220	975
Kansas, Univ. of., Lawrence, KS 66045	1865	Archie R. Dykes, Chan.	S	24,372	1,286
Kansas Wesleyan, Salina, KS 67401	1886	Daniel Bratton	D	427	37
Kean Coll. of New Jersey, Union, NJ 07083	1855	Nathan Weiss	S	12,450	359
Kearney State, Kearney, NE 68847	1905	Brendan McDonald	S	5,814	238
Keene State, Keene, NH 03431	1909	Leo Redfern	S	2,998	147
Kent State Univ., Kent, OH 44240	1910	Glenn A. Olds	S	28,024	1,111
Kentucky State Univ.*, Frankfort, KY 40601	1886	W. A. Butts	S	2,389	220
Kentucky, Univ. of*., Lexington, KY 40506	1865	Otis A. Singletary	S	40,083	1,545
Kentucky Wesleyan (A), Owensboro, KY 42301	1858	William James	P	931	71
Kenyon, Gambier, OH 43022	1824	Philip Jordan Jr.	P	1,384	124
Keuka (W), Keuka Park, NY 14478	1890	William Boyle Jr.	P	600	51
King, Bristol, TN 37620	1867	Powell A. Fraser	D	301	40
King's, Briarcliff Manor, NY 10510	1938	Robert A. Cook	P	792	64
King's, Wilkes-Barre, PA 18711	1946	Rev. Charles Sherrer	D	2,088	106
Kirksville Coll. of Osteop. Med., Kirksville, MO 63501	1892	H. C. Moore	P	491	85
Knox, Galesburg, IL 61401	1837	E. Inman Fox	P	1,100	87
Knoxville, Knoxville, TN 37921	1875	Rutherford Adkins	D,P	851	57
Kutztown State, Kutztown, PA 19530	1866	Lawrence M. Stratton	S	5,322	279
Ladycliff (W), Highland Falls, NY 10928	1933	Rev. Francis J. Breidenbach	P,D	472	54
Lafayette, Easton, PA 18042	1826	K. R. Bergethon	P,D	2,147	167
LaGrange, LaGrange, GA 30240	1831	Waights Henry Jr.	D	800	50
Lake Erie (W), Painesville, OH 44077	1856	Paul Newland, Act.	P	498	80
Lake Forest, Lake Forest, IL 60045	1857	Eugene Hotchkiss	P,D	1,072	83
Lakeland, Sheboygan, WI 53081	1864	Ralph Mirse	D	576	42
Lake Superior State, Sault Ste. Marie, MI 49783	1946	Kenneth Shouldice	S	2,457	135
Lamar Univ., Beaumont, TX 77710	1923	John E. Gray	S	12,723	414
Lander, Greenwood, SC 29646	1872	Larry Jackson	S	1,578	93
Lane, Jackson, TN 38301	1882	Herman Stone Jr.	D,P	551	48
Langston Univ.*, Langston, OK 73050	1897	Thos. English	S	1,201	63
LaRoche, Pittsburgh, PA 15237	1963	Mary Coultas	D,P	1,009	90
La Salle, Philadelphia, PA 19141	1863	Bro. Patrick Ellis	D,P	5,600	375
La Verne, La Verne, CA 91750	1891	Armen Sarafian	P	2,737	253
Lawrence Inst. Of Tech., Southfield, MI 48075	1932	W. H. Buell	P	4,584	200
Lawrence Univ., Appleton, WI 54911	1847	Thomas S. Smith	P	1,300	125
Lebanon Valley, Annville, PA 17003	1866	Frederick Sample	D	1,100	110
Lee, Cleveland, TN 37311	1918	Charles Conn	D,P	1,197	55
Lehigh Univ., Bethlehem, PA 18015	1865	W. Deming Lewis	P	6,261	605
Le Moyne, Syracuse, NY 13214	1946	W. O'Halloran	P,D	1,767	140
Le Moyne-Owen, Memphis, TN 38126	1870	Walter Walker	P	1,040	61
Lenoir-Rhyne, Hickory, NC 28601	1891	Albert Anderson	D,P	1,139	96
Lesley (W), Cambridge, MA 02138	1909	Don A. Orton	P	1,311	109
Lewis Univ., Lockport, IL 60441	1930	Bro. Vincent Neil, Act.	P,D	4,222	210
Lewis & Clark, Portland, OR 97219	1867	John R. Howard	P	2,976	203
Limestone, Gaffney, SC 29340	1845	Jack Jones Early	P	835	63
Lincoln Christian, Lincoln, IL 62656	1944	Robert Phillips	P,D	820	63
Lincoln Memorial Univ., Harrogate, TN 37752	1897	Frank W. Welch	P	917	68
Lincoln Univ., Jefferson City, MO 65101	1866	James Frank	S	2,400	165
Lincoln Univ., Lincoln Univ., PA 19352	1854	Herman Branson	S	1,103	103
Lincoln Univ., San Francisco, CA 94118	1919	T. Kong Lee, Chan.	P	867	50
Lindenwood, St. Charles, MO 63301	1827	William Spencer	P	1,596	113
Linfield, McMinnville, OR 97128	1849	Charles Walker	P	1,000	81
Livingston Univ., Livingston, AL 35470	1835	Asa Green	S	1,430	71
Livingstone, Salisbury, NC 28144	1879	F. George Shipman	D	909	56
Lock Haven State, Lock Haven, PA 17745	1870	Francis Hamblin	S	2,157	180
Loma Linda Univ., Loma Linda, CA 92354	1905	V. Norskov Olsen	D	4,832	1,469
Lone Mountain, San Francisco, CA 94118	1898	Sister Gertrude Patch	P	900	60
Long Island Univ., Brooklyn, NY 11201	1926	Edward Clark	P	7,000	250
C. W. Post, Greenvale, NY 11548	1954	Edward Cook	P	10,803	331
Longwood, Farmville, VA 23901	1839	Henry I. Willett, Jr.	S	2,150	150
Loras, Dubuque, IA 52001	1839	Msgr. Francis P. Friedl	D	1,501	97
Los Angeles Baptist, Newhall, CA 91321	1927	John Dunkin	D	317	16
Louisiana, Pineville, LA 71360	1906	Robert Lynn	P	1,170	56
Louisiana St. Univ.*, Baton Rouge LA 70803	1860	Martin Woodin	S	46,315	4,239
Baton Rouge Campus, Baton Rouge LA 70803	1860	Paul Murrill, Chan.	S	24,596	1,223
Medical Center, New Orleans LA 70112	1931	Allen Copping, Chan.	S	2,079	1,960
New Orleans Campus, New Orleans, LA 70122	1956	Homer L. Hitt, Chan.	S	14,047	443
Shreveport Campus, Shreveport, LA 71105	1967	Donald Shipp, Chan.	S	3,095	127
Louisiana Tech. Univ., Ruston, LA 71272	1894	F. J. Taylor	S	9,017	336
Louisville, Univ. of, Louisville, KY 40208	1798	James G. Miller	S	16,300	1,278
Lowell, Univ. of, Lowell, MA 01854	1894	John B. Duff	S	11,000	400
Loyola, Baltimore, MD 21210	1852	Rev. J. A. Sellinger	D,P	4,529	239
Loyola Univ., Chicago, IL 60611	1870	Rev. R. C. Baumhart	D	14,917	1,140
Loyola Univ., New Orleans, LA 70118	1912	Rev. James Carter	D	4,500	256
Loyola Marymount Univ., Los Angeles, CA 90045	1911	Rev. D. P. Merrifield	D	5,303	335
Lubbock Christian, Lubbock, TX 79407	1957	H.M. Pruitt	P	1,051	97
Luther, Decorah, IA 52101	1861	Elwin D. Farwell	P	1,849	146
Lycoming, Williamsport, PA 17701	1812	F. Blumer	D	1,337	83
Lynchburg, Lynchburg, VA 24504	1903	Carey Brewer	P	2,158	127
Lyndon State, Lyndonville, VT 05851	1911	Edward Stevens	S	1,073	81
Macalester, St. Paul, MN 55105	1874	John B. Davis Jr.	P,D	1,637	136
MacMurray, Jacksonville, IL 62650	1846	John Wittich	P,D	730	67

Name, address	Year	Governing official and affiliation		Students	Teachers
Madonna, Livonia, MI 48150	1947	Sr. Mary VandeVeyver	P,D	2,208	111
Maine Maritime Academy, Castine, ME 04421	1941	E. A. Rodgers, Supt	S	640	45
Maine System, Univ. of*, Bangor, ME 04401	1865	P. McCarthy, Chan	S	*26,750*	*1,136*
at Augusta, Augusta, ME 04330	1965	K. Allen, Act	S	2,966	232
at Farmington, Farmington, ME 04938	1864	Einar Olsen	S	1,898	95
at Ft. Kent, Ft. Kent, ME 04743	1878	Richard J. Spath	S	598	28
at Machias, Machias, ME 04654	1909	Arthur Buswell	S	743	56
at Ornoo*, Orono, ME 04473	1865	Howard Neville	S	*10,688*	*656*
at Portland-Gorham, Portland, ME 40438	1878	N. E. Miller	S	*7,602*	*544*
at Presque Isle, Presque Isle, ME 04769	1903	P. McCarthy, Chan	S	1,269	69
Malone, Canton, OH 44709	1892	Lon D. Randall	D	896	69
Manchester, N. Manchester, IN 46962	1889	Alfred B. Helman	D	1,171	91
Manhattan, Riverdale, NY 10471	1853	Brother J.S. Sullivan	P	4,310	325
Manhattan Sch. of Music, New York, NY 10027	1917	John O. Crosby	P	750	185
Manhattanville, Purchase, NY 10577	1841	Barbara K. Debs	P	2,296	151
Mankato State Univ., Mankato, MN 56001	1867	Douglas Moore	S	12,827	565
Mansfield State, Mansfield, PA 16933	1857	Lawrence Park	S	2,900	260
Marian, Indianapolis, IN 46222	1851	Louis C. Gatto	D,P	808	84
Marian Coll. of Fond du Lac, Fon du Lac, WI 54935	1936	James Hanlon	P,D	517	55
Marietta, Marietta, OH 45750	1835	Sherrill Cleland	P	1,647	115
Marion, Marion, IN 46952	1920	Robert Luckey	D	860	70
Marist, Poughkeepsie, NY 12601	1946	Linus Richard Foy	P	1,881	118
Marlboro, Marlboro, VT 05344	1946	Thomas B. Ragle	P	205	35
Marquette Univ., Milwaukee, WI 53233	1881	Rev. J. P. Raynor	P	12,422	750
Mars Hill, Mars Hill, NC 28754	1856	Fred Blake Bentley	D	1,756	120
Marshall Univ., Huntington, WV 25701	1837	Robert B. Hayes	S	11,160	490
Mary Baldwin, Staunton, VA 24401	1842	Virginia Lester	D,P	671	60
Mary Hardin Baylor, Belton, TX 76513	1845	Bobby E. Parker	D,P	1,117	165
Mary Washington, Fredericksburg, VA 22401	1908	Prince B. Woodard	S	2,292	138
Marycrest, Davenport, IA 52804	1939	Ron Van Ryswyk	P	1.084	98
Marygrove, Detroit, MI 48221	1910	Raymond Fleck	D	1,700	164
Maryland Inst. of Art, Baltimore, MD 21217	1826	T. E. Klitzke, Act	P	1,923	110
Maryland, Univ. of*, College Park, MD 20742	1859	Wilson Elkins	S	35,890	3,454
Eastern Shore, Princess Anne, MD 21853	1882	William P. Hytche, Chan	S	1,014	88
Marylhurst, Marylhurst, OR 97036	1893	Sr. V. A. Baxter	D	*1,828*	74
Marymount, Salina, KS 67401	1922	Sr. Mary Buser	D,P	832	70
Marymount (W)., Tarrytown, NY 10591	1907	Robert Christin	P	922	115
Marymount Coll. of Va., Arlington, VA 22207	1950	Sr. M. Majella Berg	D	734	89
Marymount Manhattan, New York, NY 10021	1936	Colette Mahoney	P	1,851	150
Maryville, Maryville, TN 37801	1819	Wayne Anderson	D,P	580	50
Maryville, St. Louis, MO 63141	1872	C. Pritchard, Act	P,D	1,072	92
Marywood, Scranton, PA 18509	1915	Sister M. Coleman Nee	P	2,956	211
Massachusetts Coll. Of Art, Boston, MA 02215	1873	John Nolan	S	1,736	120
Mass. Coll. of Pharmacy, Boston, MA 02115	1823	Raymond A. Gosselin	P	1,300	120
Mass. Institute of Tech.*, Cambridge, MA 02139	1861	Jerome Wiesner	P	7,972	972
Mass. Maritime Academy, Buzzards Bay, MA 02532	1891	Lee Harrington	S	850	44
Massachusetts, Univ. of*, Boston, MA 02108	1863	Robert C. Wood	S	*29,045*	*1,892*
Boston Campus, Boston, MA 02125	1964	Carlo L. Golino, Chan	S	6,600	500
Mayville State, Mayville, ND 58257	1889	James Schobel	S	824	55
McKendree, Lebanon, IL 62254	1828	Julian Murphy	D	740	54
McMurry, Abilene, TX 79605	1923	Tom K. Kim	D,P	1,218	73
McNeese State Univ., Lake Charles, LA 70609	1939	Thomas S. Leary	S	5,806	344
McPherson, McPherson, KS 67460	1887	Paul Hoffman	P,D	513	44
Medaille, Buffalo, NY 14214	1875	Robert Hesse	P	966	60
Medical Coll. of Ga., Augusta, GA 30902	1828	William Moretz	S	2,224	440
Medical Coll. of Pa., Philadelphia, PA 19129	1850	Robert J. Slater	P	836	423
Medical Univ. of S.C., Charleston, SC 29401	1824	William McCord	S	2,020	630
Meharry Medical, Nashville, TN 37208	1876	Lloyd C. Elam	P	790	240
Memphis Academy of Arts, Memphis, TN 38112	1936	Jameson Jones	P	220	18
Memphis State Univ., Memphis, TN 38152	1912	Billy Jones	S	21,451	771
Menlo, Menlo Park, CA 94025	1927	Richard O'Brien	P	890	80
Mercer Univ., Macon, GA 31207	1833	Rufus C. Harris	P,D	*3,622*	*150*
Mercy, Dobbs Ferry, NY 10522	1950	Donald Grunewald	P	5,675	340
Mercy Coll. of Detroit, Detroit, MI 48219	1941	Sister Agnes Mary Mansour	D	1,936	120
Mercyhurst, Erie, PA 16501	1926	Marion Shane	P	1,426	104
Meredith (W), Raleigh, NC 27611	1891	John Edgar Weems	D,P	1,544	114
Merrimack, No. Andover, MA 01845	1947	Rev. John A. Coughlan	D	1,875	118
Mesa, Grand Junction, CO 81501	1925	John Tomlinson	S	2,716	163
Messiah, Grantham, PA 17027	1909	D. Ray Hostetter	P	*966*	*86*
Methodist, Fayetteville, NC 28301	1956	Richard Pearce	P	803	50
Metropolitan State, Denver, CO 80204	1965	James D. Palmer	S	12,921	602
Miami Univ., Oxford, OH 45056	1809	Phillip R. Shriver	S	*17,534*	*827*
Miami, Univ. of, Coral Gables, FL 33124	1926	Henry K. Stanford	P	*16,877*	*1,290*
Michigan State Univ., East Lansing, MI 48824	1855	Clifton R. Wharton Jr.	S	43,459	2,687
Michigan Tech Univ., Houghton, MI 49931	1885	Raymond L. Smith	S	6,387	342
Michigan, Univ. of, Ann Arbor, MI 48104	1817	Robben W. Fleming	S	*44,372*	*5,362*
Mid-America Nazarene, Olathe, KS 66061	1968	R. Curtis Smith	D	1,033	60
Middle Tenn. State Univ., Murfreesboro, TN 37132	1911	M. G. Scarlett	S	10,400	457
Middlebury, Middlebury, VT 05753	1800	Olin Robinson	P	1.917	155
Midland Lutheran, Fremont, NE 68025	1883	L. Dale Lund	D,P	852	78
Midwestern State Univ., Wichita Falls, TX 76308	1922	John Barker	S	4,600	157
Miles, Birmingham, AL 35208	1905	W. Clyde Williams	D	*1,245*	*89*
Millersville State, Millersville, PA 17551	1854	William Duncan	S	6,292	329
Milligan, Milligan Coll., TN 37682	1866	Jess W. Johnson	P	695	60
Millikin Univ., Decatur, IL 62522	1901	J. Roger Miller	P,D	1,520	122
Mills (W), Oakland, CA 94613	1852	Barbara White	P	957	109
Millsaps, Jackson, MS 39210	1890	Edward Collins	D	955	77
Milton, Milton, WI 53563	1867	Joseph Kipper	P	500	46
Milwaukee Sch. of Eng., Milwaukee, WI 53201	1903	Karl O. Werwath	P	1,311	73
Mpls. Coll. of Art & Design, Minneapolis, MN 55404	1886	J. Hausman	P	960	78
Minnesota, Univ. of*, Minneapolis, MN 55455	1851	C.P. Magrath	S	*82,401*	*5,601*
Duluth Campus*, Duluth, MN 55812	1947	Robt. Heller (Prov.)	S	6,561	466
Morris Campus*, Morris, MN 56267	1960	John Imholte (Prov.)	S	1,740	104
Minot State, Minot, ND 58701	1913	Gordon Olson	S	2,026	136
Misericordia, Dallas, PA 18612	1924	Sister Ann Gallagher	D	933	100

Name, address	Year	Governing official and affiliation		Students	Teachers
Mississippi, Clinton, MS 39058	1826	Lewis Nobles	D,P	3,088	150
Mississippi Industrial, Holly Springs, MS 38635	1905	E.E. Rankin	D,P	400	24
Miss. Univ. for Women (W), Columbus, MS 39701	1884	Charles P. Hogarth	S	3,010	170
Mississippi State Univ.*, Miss. State, MS 39762	1878	James McComas	S	*11,829*	*626*
Mississippi, Univ. of, University, MS 38677	1848	P.L. Fortune Jr., Chan.	S	*8,989*	*546*
Mississippi Valley State Univ., Itta Bena, MS 38941	1950	E.A. Boykins	S	3,228	140
Missouri Baptist, St. Louis, MO 63141	1968	R. Sutherland	D,P	525	32
Missouri Inst. of Tech., Kansas City, MO 64108	1931	C.R. LeValley	P	624	29
Missouri Southern State, Joplin, MO 64801	1966	Leon Billingsly	S	3,659	160
Missouri, Univ. of*, Columbia, MO 65201	1839	C. Brice Ratchford	S	*51,100*	*2,722*
at Columbia*, Columbia, MO 65201	1839	H. W. Schooling, Chan.	S	23,500	3,515
at Kansas City*, Kansas City, MO 64110	1933	Wesley Dale, Act. Chan.	S	*11,257*	*551*
at Rolla*, Rolla, MO 65401	1870	R. Bisplinghoff, Chan.	S	4,350	670
at St. Louis*, St. Louis, MO 63121	1963	A. Grobman, Chan.	S	11,863	535
Missouri Valley, Marshall, MO 65340	1889	Donald Zimeke	P	513	43
Missouri Western State, St. Joseph, MO 64507	1915	Marvin Looney	S	3,488	175
Mobile, Mobile, AL 36613	1961	William K. Weaver Jr.	P	919	60
Molloy, Rockville Ctre, NY 11570	1955	Sister Janet Fitzgerald	D	1,284	154
Monmouth, Monmouth, IL 61462	1853	DeBow Freed	P,D	700	65
Monmouth, W. Long Branch, NJ 07764	1933	Richard Stonesifer	P	3,936	200
Montana Coll. of Mineral Science & Tech., Butte, MT 59701	1893	Fred W. DeMoney	S	1,008	65
Montana State Univ., Bozeman, MT 59715	1893	Carl McIntosh	S	9,400	500
Montana, Univ. of, Missoula, MT 59812	1893	Richard Bowers	S	8,381	498
Montclair State, Upper Montclair, NJ 07043	1908	David W.D. Dickson	S	15,018	484
Monterey Inst. of Foreign Studies, Monterey, CA 93940	1955	Stuart McIntyre	P	424	60
Montevallo, Univ. of (A), Montevallo, AL 35115	1896	Kermit Johnson	S	3,600	160
Moody Bible Institute, Chicago, IL 60610	1883	George Sweeting	P,D	*3,159*	*112*
Moore Coll. of Art (W), Philadelphia, PA 19103	1844	H.J. Burgart	P	700	72
Moorehead State, Moorehead, MN 56560	1887	Roland Dille	S	4,821	340
Moravian, Bethlehem, PA 18018	1807	Herman E. Collier Jr.	D,P	1,524	137
Morehead State Univ., Morehead, KY 40351	1923	Morris Norfleet	S	7,318	340
Morehead (M), Atlanta, GA 30314	1867	Hugh Gloster	P	1,405	105
Morgan State, Baltimore, MD 21239	1867	A. Billingsley	S	6,361	286
Morningside, Sioux City, IA 51106	1893	Thomas S. Thompson	D,P	1,559	87
Morris Brown, Atlanta, GA 30314	1881	Robert Threatt	P,D	1,503	95
Morris Harvey, Charleston, WV 25304	1888	Robert L. Bliss	P	2,197	133
Mt. Holyoke (W), S. Hadley, MA 01075	1837	David Bicknell Truman	P	*1,850*	*200*
Mt. Marty, Yankston, SD 57078	1936	Bruce Weier	D,P	700	65
Mt. Mary (W), Milwaukee, WI 53222	1913	Sister Mary Nora Barber	P,D	*1,125*	*154*
Mt. Mercy, Cedar Rapids, IA 52402	1928	Sister Mary Hennessey	P,D	900	82
Mt. St. Joseph (W), Mt. St. Joseph, OH 45051	1920	Robert Wolverton	P,D	894	104
Mt. St. Mary (W), Hooksett, NH 03106	1934	Sister Amy Hoey	P,D	205	42
Mt. St. Mary, Newburgh, NY 12550	1959	Sr. Ann Sakac	P,D	973	82
Mt. St. Mary's Los Angeles, CA 90049	1925	Sr. Magdalen Coughlin	D,P	*1,066*	*125*
Mt. St. Mary's, Emmitsburg, MD 21727	1808	Robt. Wickenheiser	D,P	1,318	65
Mt. St. Vincent, Coll. of, Riverdale, NY 10471	1847	Sister Doris Smith	P	1,106	84
Mt. Senario, Ladysmith, WI 54848	1962	Robert Lovett	P	410	35
Mt. Union, Alliance, OH 44601	1846	Ronald Weber	P,D	1,149	97
Mt. Vernon, Washington, DC 20007	1875	Peter Pelham	P	450	50
Mt. Vernon Nazarene, Mount Vernon, OH 43050	1964	L. Guy Nees	D	879	58
Muhlenberg, Allentown, PA 18104	1848	John H. Morey	P,D	1,825	118
Multnomah Sch. of the Bible, Portland, OR 97220	1936	Willard M. Aldrich	P	746	43
Mundelein, Chicago, IL 60660	1930	Sr. Susan Rink	D	1,425	160
Murray State Univ., Murray, KY 42071	1922	C. Curris	S	7,355	355
Muskingum, New Concord, OH 43762	1837	John A. Brown Jr.	P	993	88
National Coll. of Business, Rapid City, SD 57709	1941	John Hauer	P,D	*3,400*	*222*
National Coll. of Chiropractic, Lombard, IL 60148	1906	Joseph Janse	P	811	55
National Coll. of Education, Evanston, IL 60201	1886	Calvin Gross	P	*3,610*	*144*
Nazareth Coll, Nazareth, MI 49074	1924	John S. Lore	P,D	435	66
Nazareth Coll. of Rochester, Rochester, NY 14610	1924	Alice Foley	P	2,590	142
Nebraska, Univ. of*, Lincoln, NE 68583	1869	R. Roskens, Act.	S	*38,815*	*2,461*
at Omaha, Omaha, NE 68101	1908	Ronald Roskens	S	14,294	581
Nebraska Wesleyan Univ., Lincoln, NE 68504	1887	John White Jr.	P	1,152	95
Nevada Univ. of*, Reno, NV 89557	1864	Max Milam	S	8,073	625
at Las Vegas, Las Vegas, NV 89154	1951	Donald Baepler	S	8,698	278
New England, Henniker, NH 03242	1946	J.K.Cummiskey	P	1,482	131
New England Cons. of Music, Boston, MA 02115	1867	J.S. Ballinger	P	785	130
New Hampshire, Manchester, NH 03104	1932	Edward Shaprio	P	3,295	133
New Hampshire, Univ. of*, Durham, NH 03824	1866	Eugene Mills	S	*11,220*	*659*
New Haven, Univ. of*, New Haven, CT 06516	1920	Phillip Kaplan	P	6,607	131
New Jersey Inst. of Tech., Newark, NJ 07102	1881	Paul H. Newell Jr.	S	5,665	245
New Mexico Highlands Univ., Las Vegas, NM 87701	1893	John Aragon	S	2,100	130
N. Mexico Inst. of Min. & Tech., Socorro, NM 87801	1889	Kenneth Ford	S	929	75
New Mexico State Univ.*, Las Cruces, NM 88003	1888	Gerald W. Thomas	S	*13,539*	*460*
New Mexico, Univ. of*, Albuquerque, NM 87131	1889	William Davis	S	*23,685*	*1,171*
New Rochelle, Coll. of (W), New Rochelle, NY 10801	1904	Sister Dorothy Ann Kelly	P	*2,979*	*230*
New School for Soc. Research, New York, NY 10011	1919	John R. Everett	P	25,000	1,050
New York City, Univ. of, New York, NY 10021	1847	Robert J. Kibbee, Chan.	Mu	*269,929*	*15,116*
Bernard M. Baruch, New York, NY 10010	1919	Joel Segall	Mu	17,271	980
Brooklyn, Brooklyn, NY 11210	1930	John W. Kneller	Mu	22,320	1,450
City, New York, NY 10031	1847	Robert E. Marshak	Mu	15,708	1,200
Medgar Evers, Brooklyn, NY 11225	1969	Richard D. Trent	Mu	3,500	180
Hunter, New York, NY 10021	1870	Jacqueline G. Wexler	Mu	19,015	1,313
John Jay Coll. of Criminal Just., New York, NY 10019	1965	Gerald Lynch	Mu	7,000	277
Herbert H. Lehman, Bronx, NY 10468	1931	Leonard Lief	Mu	10,796	793
Queens, Flushing, NY 11367	1937	Joseph Murphy	Mu	28,735	1,612
Staten Island, Staten Island, NY 10301	1965	Edmond Volpe	Mu	*12,322*	*421*
York, Jamaica, NY 11432	1966	Milton G. Bassin	Mu	6,771	419
N.Y. Inst. of Technology, Old Westbury, NY 11568	1955	Alexander Schure	P	*17,589*	*600*
New York Law School, New York, NY 10013	1891	E. Shapiro	P	1,232	100
New York Medical (A), New York, NY 10029	1860	Lawrence Slobody	P	613	1,200
New York, State Univ. of, Albany, NY 12210	1948	J. F. Kelly, Act. Chan.	S	*342,855*	*14,451*
State Univ., Albany, NY 12222	1844	Emmet B. Fields	S	14,673	760
" " Buffalo, NY 14214	1846	Robert Ketter	S	21,955	979
" " Binghamton, NY 13901	1946	Clifford D. Clark	S	9,523	451

Name, address	Year	Governing official and affiliation		Students	Teachers
" " Stony Brook, NY 11790	1957	John Toll	S	15,350	643
State Univ. Colleges, Brockport, NY 14420	1867	Albert W. Brown	S	10,730	536
" " " Buffalo, NY 14222	1867	Elbert K. Fretwell	S	11,850	581
" " " Cortland, NY 13045	1868	Richard Jones	S	5,529	324
" " " Fredonia, NY 14063	1866	Dallas Beal	S	5,203	278
" " " Geneseo, NY 14454	1871	Robert Mac Vittie	S	5,845	301
" " " New Paltz, NY 12561	1885	Stanley K. Coffman	S	8,262	371
" " " Oneonta, NY 13820	1887	Cliffored Craven	S	6,230	356
" " " Oswego, NY 13126	1867	V. L. Radley, Act.	S	8,672	457
" " " Old Westbury, NY 11568	1965	John Maguire	S	2,104	85
" " " Plattsburgh, NY 12901	1889	Joseph C. Burke	S	5,970	313
" " " Potsdam, NY 13676	1867	Thomas Barrington	S	4,934	278
" " " Purchase, NY, 10577	1965	Abbott Kaplan	S	2,686	116
" " " Utica, NY 13502	1966	William Kunsela	S	2,852	46
" " Empire State, Saratoga Spgs., NY 12866	1971	James Hall	S	3,136	98
Buffalo Health Sciences Ctr., Buffalo, NY 14214	1846	F. C. Pannill, V.P.	S	3,055	346
College of Ceramics, Alfred, NY 14802	1900	W. G. Lawrence, Dean	S	601	39
Env'm't'l. Sci. & Forestry, Syracuse, NY 13210	1911	Edward Palmer	S	2,349	105
Downstate Medical Center, Brooklyn, NY 11203	1858	Calvin H. Plimpton	S	1,458	472
Health Sciences Center, Stony Brook, NY 11790	1970	James H. Oaks, V.P.	S	1,221	229
Maritime (M), Bronx, NY 10465	1874	Sheldon Kinney	S	1,045	66
Upstate Medical Center, Syracuse, NY 13210	1834	Richard P. Schmidt	S	916	495
New York Univ., New York, NY 10003	1831	John Sawhill	P	*40,199*	*5,160*
Newberry, Newberry, SC 29108	1856	Glenn Whitesides	D,P	843	69
Niagara Univ., Niagara Univ., NY 14109	1856	V. Rev. G. Mahoney	D	4,460	246
Nicholls State Univ., Thibodaux, LA 70301	1948	Vernon Galliano	S	6,410	262
Nichols, Dudley, MA 01570	1815	Darcy C. Coyle	P	584	37
Norfolk State, Norfolk, VA 23540	1935	Lyman Brooks	S	6,260	405
North Adams State, North Adams, MA 01247	1894	James Amsler	S	2,671	130
North Alabama, Univ., Florence, AL 35630	1872	Robt. Guillot	S	5,000	200
North Carolina Central U., Durham, NC 27707	1910	A. Whiting, Chan.	S	4,765	350
North Carolina, Univ. of, Chapel Hill, NC 27514	1972	William Friday	S	*104,786*	*6,325*
A&T State Univ., Greensboro, NC 27411	1891	Lewis Dowdy, Chan.	S	5,515	316
at Asheville, Asheville, NC 28804	1927	William Highsmith	S	1,618	85
at Chapel Hill, Chapel Hill, NC 27514	1776	N. F. Taylor	S	20,293	1,730
at Charlotte, Charlotte, NC 28223	1946	D. W. Colvard, Chan.	S	7,815	387
at Greensboro, Greensboro, NC 27412	1891	J. S. Ferguson, Chan.	S	9,733	592
at Wilmington, Wilmington, NC 28401	1947	Wm. H. Wagoner, Chan.	S	3,373	199
N.C. School of the Arts, Winston-Salem, NC 27104	1965	R. Suderburg, Chan.	S	600	145
N.C. State Univ. at Raleigh, NC 27607	1887	Joab Thomas	S	*17,500*	*1,200*
North Carolina Wesleyan, Rocky Mount, NC 27801	1956	S. Bruce Petteway	D,P	551	33
North Central Bible, Minneapolis, MN 55404	1930	E. M. Clark	D	580	36
North Central, Naperville, IL 60540	1861	Gael D. Swing	P	1,021	65
North Dakota State Univ., Fargo, ND 58102	1890	L.D. Loftsgard	S	*6,600*	*475*
North Dakota, Univ. of*, Grand Forks, ND 58202	1883	Thomas Clifford	P	8,858	640
North Florida, Univ. of, Jacksonville, FL 32216	1969	Thos. Carpenter	S	4,600	155
North Georgia, Dahlonega, GA 30533	1873	John H. Owen	S	1,753	110
North Park, Chicago, IL 60625	1891	Lloyd Ahlem	D	1,313	109
North Texas State Univ., Denton, TX 76203	1890	C. C. Nolen	S	*17,016*	*639*
Northeast Louisiana Univ., Monroe, LA 71209	1931	Dwight Vines	S	9,143	391
Northeast Missouri St., Univ., Kirksville, MD 63501	1867	Charles T. McClain	S	5,009	355
Northeastern Illinois Univ., Chicago, IL 60625	1867	Ronald Williams	S	10,040	421
Northeastern Okla. State, Tahlequah, OK 74464	1909	Robert Collier	S	5,469	226
Northeastern Univ., Boston, MA 02115	1898	Kenneth Ryder	P	*37,440*	*2,189*
Northern Arizona Univ., Flagstaff, AZ 86011	1899	J. Lawrence Walkup	S	11,502	572
Northern Colorado, Univ. of, Greeley, CO 80639	1890	Richard R. Bond	S	10,965	734
Northern Ill. Univ., DeKalb, IL 60625	1895	Richard Nelson	S	21,269	1,017
Northern Iowa, Univ. of, Cedar Falls, IA 50613	1876	John Kamerick	S	12,054	595
Northern Ky. Univ., Highland Hts., KY 41076	1968	A.D. Albright	S	7,000	320
Northern Michigan Univ., Marquette, MI 49855	1899	John X. Jamrich	S	8,533	345
Northern Montana, Havre, MT 59501	1929	Joseph R. Crowley	S	1,020	62
Northern State, Aberdeen, SD 57401	1901	Lester Clarke, Act.	S	2,530	113
Northland, Ashland, WI 54806	1892	Malcolm McLean	D	709	51
Northrop Univ., Inglewood, CA 90306	1942	B. J. Shell	P	1,778	91
Northwest, Kirkland, WA 98033	1934	D. V. Hurst	D	573	30
Northwest Christian, Eugene, OR 97401	1895	Barton A. Dowdy	D	431	21
Northwest Missouri State, Univ., Maryville, MO 64468	1905	Robert P. Foster	S	4,333	248
Northwest Nazarene, Nampa, ID 83651	1913	Kenneth Pearsall	D,P	1,142	81
Northwestern, Orange City, IA 51041	1882	H. Rowenhorst	D	760	46
Northwestern State Univ., Nathicohes, LA 71457	1884	Arnold R. Kilpatrick	S	*6,685*	*313*
Northwestern Okla. St. Univ., Alva, OK 73717	1897	Joe Struckle	S	1,868	90
Northwestern Univ., Evanston, IL 60201	1851	Robert Henry Strotz	P	*15,225*	*1,681*
Norwich, Univ., Northfield, VT 05663	1849	Loring Hart	P	*1,700*	*105*
Northwood Inst., Midland, MI 48640	1959	T. J. Brown, V.P.	P	2,000	75
Notre Dame, Coll of, Belmont CA 94002	1868	Sr. Catharine Cunningham	P	1,058	107
Notre Dame, Manchester, NH 03104	1950	Sr. Jeannette Vezeau	P,D	537	56
Notre Dame (W), Cleveland, OH 44121	1922	Sister Mary Marthe	D,P	618	61
Notre Dame of Maryland, Baltimore, MD 21210	1973	Sister Kathleen Feeley	D	803	75
Notre Dame, Univ. of, Notre Dame, IN 46556	1842	Rev. T.M. Hesburgh	D,P	8,556	780
Nova Univ., Ft. Lauderdale, FL 33314	1964	Abraham Fischler	P	6,305	305
Nyack, Nyack, NY 10960	1882	Thomas Bailey	D,P	682	55
Oakland City, Oakland City, IN 47660	1885	J.W. Murray	D,P	450	29
Oakland Univ., Rochester, MI 48063	1957	Donald D. O'Dowd	S	10,457	488
Oakwood, Huntsville, AL 35806	1896	C. B. Rock	P	1,068	91
Oberlin, Oberlin, OH 44074	1833	E. Danenberg	P	2,700	226
Occidental, Los Angeles, CA 90041	1887	Richard C. Gilman	P	1,650	120
Oglethorpe Univ, Atlanta, GA 30319	1835	Manning Pattilo Jr.	D	804	47
Ohio Dominican, Columbus, OH 43219	1911	Sister M. Suzanne Uhrhane	D	969	70
Ohio Coll. of Podiatric Med., Cleveland, OH 44106	1916	Abe Rubin	P	469	72
Ohio Inst. of Technology, Columbus, OH 43209	1952	Richard A. Czerniak	P	2,978	102
Ohio Northern Univ., Ada, OH 45810	1871	R. B. Loeschner	D,P	2,533	163
Ohio State Univ.*, Columbus, OH 43210	1870	Harold L. Enarson	S	*54,579*	*3,363*
Ohio Univ., Athens, OH 45701	1804	Charles J. Ping	S	*18,045*	*700*

Name, address	Year	Governing official and affiliation		Students	Teachers
Ohio Wesleyan Univ., Delaware, OH 43015	1842	Thomas Wenzlau	D,P	2,240	160
Oklahoma Baptist Univ., Shawnee, OK 74801	1910	W. E. Neptune, Act.	D,P	1,723	125
Oklahoma Christian, Oklahoma City, OK 73111	1950	J. Johnson	P,D	1,322	56
Oklahoma City Univ., Oklahoma City, OK 73106	1904	Dolphus Whitten Jr.	D,P	2,735	178
Okla. Coll. of Liberal Arts, Chickasha, OK 73018	1908	Roy Troutt	S	1,267	74
Oklahoma Panhandle St. Univ., Goodwell, OK 73939	1909	Thomas L. Palmer	S	1,115	74
Oklahoma State Univ.*, Stillwater, OK 74074	1890	Lawrence Roger	S	*24,754*	*1,277*
Oklahoma Univ. of, Norman, OK 73019	1890	Paul F. Sharp	S	*25,329*	*1,343*
Old Dominion Univ., Norfolk, VA 23508	1930	A. B. Rollins Jr.	S	13,254	545
Olivet, Olivet, MI 49076	1844	Ray B. Loeschner	P	750	50
Olivet Nazarene, Kankakee, IL 60901	1907	Leslie Parrott	P,D	1,880	111
Oral Roberts Univ., Tulsa, OK. 74171	1963	Oral Roberts	P	3,500	229
Orangeburg-Calhoun Tech, Orangeburg, SC 29115	1968	M. Rudy Groomes	S	1,400	51
Oregon College of Educ., Monmouth, OR 97361	1856	G. Leinwand	S	3,555	208
Oregon Inst. of Tech., Klamath Falls, OR 97601	1947	Kenneth Light	S	2,345	170
Oregon State Univ.*, Corvallis, OR 97331	1868	R. MacVicar	S	16,236	2,972
Oregon, Univ. of, Eugene, OR 97403	1876	William Boyd	S	17,384	1,062
Ottawa Univ., Ottawa, KS 66067	1865	Peter H. Armacost	P,D	*1,550*	75
Otterbein, Westerville, OH 43081	1847	Thomas Jefferson Kerr	D,P	1,447	79
Ouachita Baptist Univ., Arkadelphia, AR 71923	1886	Daniel R. Grant	D,S	1,563	104
Our Lady of Angels, Aston, PA 19014	1965	Sr. Marie Cunningham	D	589	55
Our Lady of Elms, Col. of (W), Chicopee, MA 01013	1928	Edward D'Alessio	D,P	410	60
Our Lady of the Lake, Univ., San Antonio, TX 78285	1911	Gerald Burns	D	1,813	142
Ozarks, Coll. of the, Clarksville, AR 72830	1834	Robert Qualls	D,P	556	39
Ozarks, School of the, Pt. Lookout, MO 65726	1906	M. Graham Clark	P	1,150	81
Pace Univ., New York, NY 10038	1906	Edward J. Mortola	P	*14,575*	*789*
Pacific, Fresno, CA 93702	1944	Edmund Janzen	P	437	27
Pacific Christian, Fullerton, CA 92631	1928	Medford Jones	D,P	749	47
Pacific Lutheran Univ., Tacoma, WA 98447	1890	William Rieke	P,D	3,428	279
Pacific States Univ., Los Angeles, CA 90006	1928	Steven Kase	P	*40*	*52*
Pacific Union, Angwin, CA 94508	1882	J. W. Cassel, Jr.	D	2,140	150
Pacific Univ. Forest Grove, OR 97116	1849	James Miller	P,D	1,086	76
Pacific, Univ. of the, Stockton, CA 95211	1851	Stanley McCaffrey	P	*5,600*	*375*
Paine, Augusta, GA 30901	1882	J. S. Scott Jr.	P	776	67
Palm Beach Atlantic, W. Palm Beach, FL 33401	1968	Warner Fusselle	P	458	53
Pan American Univ., Edinburg, TX 78539	1927	Ralph Schilling	S	*7,183*	*321*
Park, Parkville, MO 64152	1875	Harold Condit	P	*2,511*	*66*
Parsons School of Design, New York, NY 10011	1896	John R. Everett	P	3,000	250
Paul Quinn, Waco, TX 76704	1872	R. D. Manning, Act	D	547	35
Peabody Cons. of Music, Baltimore, MD 21202	1857	Richard F. Goldman	P	505	90
Pembroke St. Univ., Pembroke, NC 28372	1887	English E. Jones	S	1,874	112
Penn Col. of Optometry, Philadelphia, PA 19141	1919	Norman F. Wallis	P	545	90
Penn. State Univ.*, University Park, PA 16802	1855	John W. Oswald	S	*67,138*	*3,052*
Pennsylvania, Univ. of, Philadelphia, PA 19104	1740	Martin Meyerson	P	20,538	4,306
Pepperdine Univ., Malibu, CA 90265	1937	William S. Banowsky	D,P	*9,400*	*695*
Peru State (A), Peru, NE 68421	1867	Douglas Pearson	S	685	46
Pfeiffer, Misenheimer, NC 28109	1885	Douglas Reid Sasser	D	1,036	68
Phila. College of Art, Philadelphia, PA 19102	1876	Thomas Schutte	P	1,600	180
Phila. Coll. of Bible, Philadelphia, PA 19103	1913	D. B. MacCorkle	P,D	1,534	69
Phila. Coll. of Osteopathic Med., Philadelphia, PA 19131	1898	Thomas Rowland Jr	P	*318*	*208*
Phila. Coll. of Pharm. & Science, Philadelphia, PA 19104	1821	John Bergen	P	1,113	89
Phila. Coll. of Textiles & Science, Philadelphia, PA 19144	1884	D. B. Partridge, Act	P	2,202	83
Philander Smith, Little Rock, AR 72203	1868	Walter Hazzard	D	701	52
Phillips Univ., Enid, OK 73701	1907	Samuel Curl	P	1,379	88
Piedmont, Demerest, GA 30535	1897	James E. Walker	P	400	24
Piedmont Bible, Winston-Salem, NC 27101	1946	Donald Drake	D	453	26
Pikeville, Pikeville, KY 41501	1889	Jackson Hall	D,P	650	50
Pittsburgh, Univ. of, Pittsburgh, PA 15260	1787	Wesley W. Posvar	S	*24,182*	*2,204*
Pitzer, Claremont, CA 91711	1963	Robert Atwell	P	760	70
Plymouth State, Plymouth, NH 03264	1871	Harold E. Hyde	S	3,014	124
Point Park, Pittsburgh, PA 15222	1960	John Hopkins	P	1,809	113
Polytechnic Institute (A), Brooklyn, NY 11201	1854	George Bugliarello	P	*4,500*	*230*
Pomona, Claremont, CA 91711	1887	David Alexander	P	1,300	130
Portland State Univ., Portland, OR 97207	1946	Joseph Blumel	S	14,016	732
Portland, Univ. of, Portland, OR 97203	1901	Rev. P. E. Waldschmidt	P	2,301	147
Pratt Institute, Brooklyn, NY 11205	1887	Richardson Pratt Jr.	P	4,400	350
Presbyterian, Clinton, SC 29325	1880	Marc C. Weersing	D	850	62
Princeton Univ., Princeton, NJ 08540	1746	William G. Bowen	P	*5,920*	*785*
Principia, Elsah, IL 62028	1898	David K. Andrews	P	864	77
Providence, Providence RI 02918	1917	Rev. T. R. Peterson	P	5,123	207
Puerto Rico, Univ. of*, San Juan, PR 00936	1903	A. Carrion	S	*50,225*	*2,644*
Puget Sound, Univ. of, Tacoma, WA 98416	1888	Philip M. Phibbs	P	*5,375*	*264*
Purdue Univ.*, W. Lafayette, IN 47907	1869	Arthur G. Hansen	S	*40,997*	*2,376*
Queens (W), Charlotte, NC 28274	1857	Alfred Canon	D,P	631	70
Quincy, Quincy, IL 62301	1859	Rev. G. Brinkman	D	1,550	88
Quinnipiac, Hamden, CT 06518	1929	Leonard Kent	P	3,471	286
Radcliffe (W), Cambridge, MA 02138	1879	Matina Souretia Horner	P	(a)	(a)
Radford, Radford, VA 24142	1910	Donald N. Dedmon	S	5,112	279
Ramapo, Coll. of N.J., Mahwah, NJ 07430	1969	George T. Potter	S	3,963	200
Randolph-Macon, Ashland, VA 23005	1830	Luther W. White III	P,D	799	70
Randolph-Macon Woman's (W), Lynchburg, VA 24503	1891	William F. Quillian Jr.	D,P	807	85
Redlands, Univ. of, Redlands, CA 92373	1907	Eugene Dawson	P	2,598	205
Reed, Portland, OR 97202	1911	Paul Bragdon	D	1,213	116
Regis, Denver, CO 80221	1877	Rev. David M. Clarke	D,P	1,087	69
Regis (W), Weston, MA 02193	1927	Sister Therese Higgins	P	853	85
Rensselaer Poly. Inst., Troy, NY 12181	1824	George M. Low	P	5,349	321
Rhode Island, Providence, RI 02908	1854	Charles B. Willard	S	*8,714*	*364*

(a) See Harvard University

Name, address	Year	Governing official and affiliation		Students	Teachers
R.I. School of Design, Providence, RI 02903	1877	Ms. Lee Hall	P	1,458	188
Rhode Island, Univ. of, Kingston, RI 02881	1888	Frank Newman	S	*16,527*	*846*
Rice Univ., Houston, TX 77001	1891	Norman Hackerman	P	3,648	429
Richmond, Univ. of, Richmond, VA 23173	1830	E. Bruce Heilman	P	4,052	311
Ricker, Houlton, ME 04730	1848	W. Abbott	P	709	55
Rider, Lawrenceville, NJ 08648	1865	Frank N. Elliott	P	5,680	300
Rio Grande, Rio Grande, OH 45674	1876	Paul Hayes	S	1,035	52
Ripon, Ripon, WI 54971	1951	Bernard S. Adams	P	923	70
Rivier, Nashua, NH 03060	1933	Sister Doris Benoit	P	1,455	93
Roanoke, Salem, VA 24153	1842	Norman Fintel	P	1,198	73
Robert Morris, Coraopolis, PA 15108	1921	Charles Sewall	P	*3,699*	*124*
Roberts Wesleyan, Rochester, NY 14624	1866	Paul L. Adams	D	672	80
Rochester Inst. of Tech., Rochester, NY 14623	1829	Paul A. Miller	P	12,192	1,017
Rochester, Univ. of, Rochester, NY 14627	1850	Robert Sproull	P	*8,094*	*1,228*
Rockford, Rockford, IL 61101	1847	John A. Howard	P	1,118	100
Rockhurst, Kansas City, MO 64110	1910	Rev. M.E. Van Ackeren	P,D	3,225	206
Rocky Mountain, Billings, MT 59102	1848	B. Alton	D,P	1,100	50
Roger Williams, Bristol, RI 02809	1948	Ralph Gauvey	P	2,661	69
Rollins, Winter Park, FL 32789	1885	Jack Critchfield	P	*4,546*	*362*
Roosevelt Univ., Chicago, IL 60605	1945	Rolf A. Weil	P	7,047	259
Rosary, River Forest, IL 60305	1901	Sister Candida Lund	P	772	140
Rosary Hill, Buffalo, NY 14226	1948	Robert S. Marshall	P	1,200	115
Rose-Hulman Inst. of Tech., Terre Haute, IN 47803	1874	S. F. Hulbert	P	1,100	87
Rosemont, Rosemont, PA 19010	1921	Sister Ann Marie Durst	D	610	84
Russell Sage (A), Troy, NY 12180	1916	William Kahl	P	*3,671*	*259*
Rust, Holly Spgs., MS 38635	1866	W.A. McMillan	D,P	785	46
Rutgers Univ.*, New Brunswick, NJ 08903	1766	Edward J. Bloustein	S	*46,491*	*1,580*
Sacred Heart, Coll. of the (A), Santurce, PR 00914	1935	Pedro Gonzalez Ramos	D	2,779	147
Sacred Heart Univ., Bridgeport, CT 06606	1963	Robert Kidera	P	2,481	139
Saginaw Valley State, Univ. Center, MI 48710	1964	Jack Ryder	S	3,046	183
St. Ambrose, Davenport, IA 52803	1882	William Bakrow	D,P	1,454	112
St. Andrews Presbyterian, Laurinburg, NC 28352	1962	A.P. Perkinson Jr.	D	568	55
St. Anselm's, Manchester, NH 03102	1889	Rev. B.P. Donnelly	D	1,830	138
St. Augustine's, Raleigh, NC 27611	1867	Prezell R. Robinson	D	1,579	78
St. Benedict, Coll. of (W), St. Joseph, MN 56374	1927	Beverly Miller	D	1,560	107
St. Bernard, St. Bernard, AL 35138	1891	Robert Kaffer	D	450	52
St. Bonaventure Univ., St. Bonaventure, NY 14778	1856	V. Rev. M. Doyle	P	2,605	185
St. Catherine, Coll. of (W), St. Paul, MN 55105	1905	Sister Alberta Huber	P,D	1,985	130
St. Cloud State Univ., St. Cloud, MN 56301	1869	Charles J. Graham	S	11,038	575
St. Edward's Univ., Austin, TX 78704	1885	Bro. Stephen Walsh	P	1,800	121
St. Elizabeth, Coll. of (W), Convent Station, NJ 07961	1899	Sister Eliz. Ann Maloney	D,P	714	79
St. Francis, Fort Wayne, IN 46808	1890	Sister M. Jo Ellen Scheetz	D	1,329	75
St. Francis, Biddeford, ME 04005	1953	Jack S. Ketchum	P	350	21
St. Francis, Brooklyn, NY 11201	1884	Bro. Donald Sullivan	P	3,755	192
St. Francis, Loretto, PA 15940	1847	Rev. Sean Sullivan	D,P	1,419	85
St. Francis, Coll. of, Joliet, IL 60435	1930	John Orr	P,D	2,827	174
St. John Fisher, Rochester, NY 14618	1948	Rev. C.J. Lavery	P,D	1,842	111
St. John's, Annapolis, MD 21404	1695	Richard D. Weigle	P	*666*	*92*
St. John's Univ. (M), Collegeville, MN 56321	1857	V. Rev. Michael Blecker	D,P	1,837	140
St. John's Univ., Jamaica, NY 11439	1870	V. Rev. Joseph T. Cahill	P,D	*15,838*	*730*
St. Joseph, West Hartford, CT 06117	1932	Sr. Mary O'Connor	D,P	1,038	96
St. Joseph's, Rensselaer, IN 47978	1889	Rev. Charles Banet	D	1,052	75
St. Joseph's, Brentwood, NY 11717	1916	Sr. G.A. O'Connor	D,P	*1,014*	*120*
St. Joseph's, North Windham, ME 04062	1912	Bernard Currier	D	568	47
St. Joseph's, Philadelphia, PA 19131	1851	Rev. Donald MacLean	D	5,482	125
St. Lawrence Univ., Canton, NY 13617	1856	Frank Peter Piskor	P	2,200	150
St. Leo, St. Leo, FL 33574	1963	Thomas Southard	P,D	940	67
St. Louis Coll. of Pharmacy, St. Louis, MO 63110	1864	Charles C. Rabe	P	692	35
St. Louis Univ., St. Louis, MO 63103	1818	Rev. D. O'Connell	P	*10,167*	*1,767*
Park, Cahokia, IL 62206	1927	Leon Z. Seltzer (Dean)	D	717	53
St. Martin's, Olympia, WA 98503	1895	Fr. John C. Scott	D	*857*	*86*
St. Mary, Coll. of, Omaha, NE 68124	1924	Sister Mary A. Costello	P	533	75
St. Mary (W), Leavenworth, KS 66048	1923	Sr. Mary J. McGilley	D	825	65
St. Mary-of the Woods (W), St. Mary-of-the-Woods, IN 47876	1840	Sister Jeanne Knoerle	D,P	620	75
St. Mary's (W), Notre Dame, IN 46556	1844	John Duggan	D,P	1,784	156
St. Mary's, Winona, MN 55987	1912	Peter Clifford	D,P	1,185	99
St. Mary's Coll. of Cal., Moraga, CA 94575	1863	Bro. Mel Anderson	D,P	1,473	94
St. Mary's Coll. of Maryland, St. Mary's City, MD 20686	1839	J. Renwick Jackson Jr.	S	1,115	90
St. Mary's Dominican (W), New Orleans, LA 70118	1910	Sr. Mary Eugene Cazayoux	D,P	917	75
St. Mary's Univ., San Antonio, TX 78284	1852	Rev. James Young	D,P	3,376	155
St. Michael's, Winooski, VT 05404	1903	Edward L. Henry	P	1,685	94
St. Norbert, DePere, WI 54115	1898	Neil Webb	D	1,519	96
St. Olaf, Northfield, MN 55057	1874	Sidney A. Rand	D,P	2,888	242
St. Paul Bible, Bible College, MN 55375	1916	Francis W. Grubbs	D,P	562	38
St. Paul's, Lawrenceville, VA 23868	1888	James Alvin Russell Jr.	D	661	38
St. Peter's, Jersey City, NJ 07306	1872	V. Rev. V.R. Yanitelli	D	*4,700*	*337*
St. Rose, Coll. of, Albany, NY 12203	1920	Thomas Manion	P	2,083	167
St. Scholastica, Coll. of, Duluth, MN 55811	1912	Bruce Stender	D,P	1,274	105
St. Teresa, Coll. of (W), Winona, MN 55987	1907	Sister Joyce Rowland	P	1,171	130
St. Thomas Aquinas, Sparkill, NY 10976	1952	D. McNelis	P	*970*	*65*
St. Thomas, Coll. of, St. Paul, MN 55105	1885	Msgr. Terrence Murphy	D,P	3,650	202
St. Thomas, Univ. of, Houston, TX 77006	1947	Rev. Patrick Braden	D	1,746	186
St. Vincent (M), Latrobe, PA 15650	1846	Rev. Cecil Diethrich	P	960	89
St. Xavier, Chicago, IL 60655	1847	Sr. M. Chekouras	D	1,450	141
Salem (W), Winston-Salem, NC 27108	1772	M. Cuningim	P,D	625	70
Salem, Salem, WV 26426	1888	Dallas Bailey Jr.	P	*1,250*	*60*
Salem State, Salem, MA 01970	1854	Vincent Mara	S	7,910	294
Salisbury State, Salisbury, MD 21801	1925	Norman Crawford Jr.	S	4,107	155
Salve Regina, Newport, RI 02840	1934	Sister Lucille McKillop	D	1,605	120
Sam Houston State Univ., Huntsville, TX 77340	1879	E. T. Bowers	S	10,593	386
Samford Univ., Birmingham, AL 35209	1841	Leslie S. Wright	D,P	3,846	191
San Diego, Univ. Of, San Diego, CA 92110	1949	Author E. Hughes	P	3,100	150

Name, address	Year	Governing official and affiliation		Students	Teachers
San Diego State, San Diego, CA 92182	1897	Brage Golding	S	*31,000*	*2,025*
San Francisco Art Inst., San Francisco, CA 94133	1871	A. Herstand	P	907	65
San Francisco, Univ. of, San Francisco, CA 94117	1855	Rev. J. LoSchiavo	P	5,818	351
Sangamon State Univ., Springfield, IL 62708	1969	Robert Spencer	S	3,792	185
San Jose State Univ., San Jose, CA 95192	1857	John H. Bunzel	S	27,271	1,570
Santa Clara, Univ. of, Santa Clara, CA 95053	1851	William Rewak	D	6,829	371
Sante Fe, Coll. of, Sante Fe, NM 87501	1947	Bro. Cyprian Luke Roney	D,P	1,273	80
Sarah Lawrence, Bronxville, NY 10708	1926	Charles DeCarlo	P	863	149
Savannah State, Savannah, GA 31404	1890	Prince Jackson Jr.	S	2,600	140
Scranton, Univ. of, Scranton, PA 18510	1888	Rev. William Byron	D	4,298	227
Scripps (W), Claremont, CA 91711	1926	John Chandler	P	590	65
Seattle Pacific Univ., Seattle, WA 98119	1891	David L. McKenna	D,P	*2,296*	*159*
Seattle Univ., Seattle, WA 98122	1891	Rev. William Sullivan	P,D	3,500	234
Selma Univ. (A), Selma, AL 36701	1878	M.C. Cleveland Jr.	D	361	23
Seton Hall Univ., S. Orange, NJ 07079	1856	John Cole, Act	D	*9,800*	*356*
Seton Hill (W), Greensburg, PA 15601	1883	Miss E. Farrell	D	867	80
Shaw Coll. at Detroit, Detroit, MI 48202	1936	Romallus Murphy	P	1,242	85
Shaw Univ., Raleigh, NC 27611	1865	Richard Fields, Act.	D	1,318	90
Shenandoah Coll. of Music, Winchester, VA 22601	1875	Robert P. Parker	D	742	91
Shepherd, Shepherdstown, WV 25443	1871	James Butcher	S	2,399	115
Shippensburg State, Shippensburg, PA 17257	1871	Gilmore B. Seavers	S	6,041	276
Shorter, Rome GA 30161	1873	Randall H. Minor	D,P	875	58
Siena, Loundonville, NY 12211	1937	Rev. Hugh F. Hines	P, D	2,063	107
Siena Heights, Adrian, MI 49221	1919	Hugh L. Thompson	D,P	1,054	75
Simmons (W), Boston, MA 02115	1899	William J. Holmes Jr	P	*2,615*	*175*
Simpson, Indianola, IA 50125	1860	Richard Lancaster	P	835	77
Simpson, San Francisco, CA 94134	1921	Mark W. Lee	D	*700*	*50*
Sioux Falls, Sioux Falls, SD 57101	1883	Owen Halleen	D,P	685	46
Skidmore, Saratoga Spgs, NY 12866	1922	Joseph C. Palamountian Jr.	P	*2,350*	*165*
Slippery Rock State, Slippery Rock, PA 16057	1889	James Roberts, Act.	S	5,754	327
Smith (W), Northampton, MA 01060	1875	Thomas C. Mendenhall	P	2,518	240
South Univ. of the, Sewanee, TN 37375	1857	James J. Bennett	D,P	1,112	108
South Alabama, Univ. of, Mobile, AL 36688	1963	Frederick Whiddon	S	6,508	465
South Carolina St.*, Orangeburg, SC 29117	1896	M. M. Nance Jr.	S	3,823	224
South Carolina, Univ. of*, Columbia, SC 29208	1801	William Patterson	S	*22,285*	*1,453*
S.D. Sch. of Mines & Tech., Rapid City, SD 57701	1885	Richard Schleusener	S	1,682	109
South Dakota State Univ.*, Brookings, SD 57006	1881	Sherwood Berg	S	6,373	510
South Dakota, Univ. of, Vermillion, SD 57069	1862	Richard E. Bowen	S	*5,601*	*475*
South Florida, Univ of, Tampa, FL 33620	1956	Wm. Smith Jr., Act.	S	*22,243*	*1,080*
South Texas Coll. of Law, Houston, TX 77002	1923	G. R. Walker	P	1,013	47
Southeast Missouri St. Univ., Cape Girardeau, MO 63701	1873	Robert Leestampter	S	8,368	390
Southeastern, Washington, DC 20024	1879	B. Kibarian	P	831	120
Southeastern Bible, Lakeland, FL 33801	1935	Cyril Homer	D	957	25
Southeastern Louisiana Univ., Hammond, LA 70402	1925	Clea E. Parker	S	*6,972*	*278*
Southeastern Mass. Univ., N. Dartmouth, MA 02747	1895	Donald E. Walker	S	7,272	284
Southeastern Okla. St. Univ., Durant, OK 74701	1909	Leon Hibbs	S	4,486	169
Southern California, Costa Mesa, CA 92626	1920	Wayne Kraiss	D	606	46
Southern Cal., Univ. of, Los Angeles, CA 90007	1880	John R. Hubbard	P	28,402	9,973
S. Cal. College of Optometry, Fullerton, CA 92631	1904	Richard Hopping	P	300	79
Southern Coll. of Optometry, Memphis, TN 38104	1932	Spurgeon B. Eure	P	623	54
Southern Colorado, Univ. of, Pueblo, CO 81001	1961	Harry P. Bowes	S	*5,770*	*327*
Southern Conn. State, New Haven, CT 06515	1893	Manson Van B. Jennings	S	11,901	584
Southern Illinois Univ., Edwardsville, IL 62026	1965	Kenneth Shaw	S	*12,509*	*588*
Southern Illinois Univ., Carbondale, IL 62901	1869	Warren Brandt	S	*27,000*	*1,849*
Southern Methodist Univ., Dallas, TX 75275	1911	J. Zumberge	D	9,105	630
Southern Missionary, Collegedale, TN 37315	1892	Frank Knittel	D	*1,682*	*120*
Southern Miss. Univ of, Hattiesburg, MS 39401	1910	Aubrey Lucas	S	*11,511*	*580*
Southern Oregon State, Ashland, OR 97520	1926	James K. Sours	S	4,500	251
Southern State, Magnolia, AR 71753	1909	Harold T. Brinson	S	*2,325*	*200*
Southern Tech. Inst., Marietta, GA 30060	1948	Joseph Pettit	S	1,938	90
Southern Univ., Baton Rouge, LA 70813	1880	Jesse Stone Jr.	S	*9,022*	*476*
Southern Utah State, Cedar City, UT 84720	1897	R. C. Braithwaite	S	1,912	120
Southwest Baptist, Bolivar, MO 65613	1878	James L. Sells	P,D	1,328	89
Southwest St. Univ., Marshall, MN 56258	1963	C. Tisinger, Act.	S	1,672	126
Southwest Mo. St. Univ., Springfield, MO 65802	1905	Duane Meyer	S	*12,661*	*701*
Southwest Texas St. Univ., San Marcos, TX 78666	1899	Lee Smith	S	13,561	455
Southwestern, Winfield, KS 67150	1885	Donald Ruthenberg	D,P	693	48
Southwestern La., Univ. of, Lafayette, LA 70504	1898	Ray Authement	S	12,895	581
Southwestern at Memphis, Memphis, TN 38112	1848	James Daughdrill Jr	D	985	112
Southwestern Okla. St. Univ., Weatherford, OK 73096	1901	Leonard Campbell	S	4,784	216
Southwestern Union, Keene, TX 76059	1893	Donald McAdams	D	747	46
Southwestern Univ., Georgetown, TX 78626	1840	Durwood Fleming	D	856	61
Spalding, Lousville, KY 40203	1920	Sister Eileen Egan	D	1,132	93
Spelman (W), Atlanta, GA 30314	1881	Albert E. Manley	P	1,155	100
Spring Arbor, Spring Arbor, MI 49283	1873	E. A. Voller	D	890	75
Spring Garden, Philadelphia, PA 19118	1850	Robert H. Thompson	P	850	60
Spring Hill, Mobile, AL 36608	1830	Rev. Paul S. Tipton	P	790	62
Springfield, Springfield, MA 01109	1885	Wilbert Locklin	P	2,600	150
Stanford Univ., Stanford, CA 94305	1885	Richard W. Lyman	P	11,710	1,755
Stephen F. Austin State Univ., Nacogdoches, TX 75962	1923	Wm. Johnson	S	11,029	415
Stephens (W), Columbia, MO 65201	1833	Arland Christ-Janer	P	1,800	148
Sterling, Sterling, KS 67579	1887	C. Schoenherr	P	527	44
Stetson Univ., De Land, FL 32720	1883	Geo. Borders	D,P	*2,806*	*146*
Steubenville, Coll. of, Steubenville, OH 43952	1946	Rev. M. Scanlon	D,P	837	39
Stevens Inst. of Tech., Hoboken, NJ 07030	1870	Kenneth C. Rogers	P	2,050	130
Stillman, Tuscaloosa, AL 35401	1876	Harold N. Stinson	D,P	812	41
Stockton State, Pomona, NJ 08240	1969	Richard Bjork	S	4,079	170
Stonehill, N. Easton, MA 02356	1948	Rev. Ernest Bartell	D	2,200	160
Strayer, Washington, DC 20005	1904	Murray Donoho	P	1,550	65
Suffolk Univ, Boston, MA 02114	1906	Thomas Fulham	P	6,419	271
Sul Ross State Univ., Alpine, TX 79830	1917	C. R. Richadson	S	2,425	81
Susquehanna Univ., Selinsgrove, PA 17870	1858	Gustave W. Weber	P	1,700	115
Swarthmore, Swarthmore, PA 19081	1864	Theodore Friend	P	1,223	163
Sweet Briar, Sweet Briar, VA 24595	1901	Harold B. Whiteman Jr.	P	664	88
Syracuse Univ., Syracuse, NY 13210	1870	M A. Eggers, Chan.	P	18,877	1,059

Name, address	Year	Governing official and affiliation		Students	Teachers
Tabor, Hillsboro, KS 67063	1908	Roy Just	P,D	489	51
Talladega, Talladgea, AL 35160	1867	Joseph Gayles	P	625	45
Tampa, Tampa, FL 33609	1890	Jack H. Jones	P	1,274	70
Tampa, Univ. of, Tampa, FL 33606	1931	Fred Learey, Act.	P	2,366	129
Tarkio, Tarkio, MO 64491	1883	Eldon E. Breazier	P,D	387	35
Taylor Univ., Upland, IN 46989	1846	Robert Baptista	P	1,400	86
Temple Univ., Philadelphia, PA 19122	1884	Marvin Wachman	S	35,600	2,426
Tennessee State Univ.*, Nashville, TN 37203	1912	F. Humphries	S	5,326	226
Tennessee System, Univ. of*, Knoxville, TN 37916	1968	Edward Boling	S	49,123	3,217
at Nashville*, Nashville, TN 37203	1947	Charles Smith, Act. Chan.	S	5,616	131
at Chattanooga*, Chattanooga, TN 37403	1886	James Drinnon Jr., Chan.	S	6,162	336
at Knoxville*, Knoxville, TN 37916	1794	Jack Reese, Chan.	S	29,711	1,741
at Martin*, Martin, TN 38237	1900	Larry T. McGhee, Chan.	S	5,082	257
Ctr. for Health Sci.*, Memphis, TN 38103	1911	T. Farmer, Chan.	S	2,552	752
Tennessee Tech. Univ., Cookeville, TN 38501	1915	Arliss Roaden	S	7,120	339
Tennessee Temple, Chattanooga, TN 37404	1946	Lee Roberson, Chan.	P,D	3,781	142
Tennessee Wesleyan, Athens, TN 37303	1857	George Naff Jr.	D	445	32
Texas, Tyler, TX 75701	1894	Allen C. Hancock	P	592	37
Texas A & I Univ., Kingsville, TX 78363	1925	Gerald Robins	S	6,369	209
Texas A & M Univ.*, College Station, TX 77843	1876	Jack K. Williams	S	28,000	2,000
Prairie View A. & M. Univ., Prairie View, TX 77445	1876	Alvin Thomas	S	5,007	716
Tarleton State Univ., Stephenville, TX 76402	1899	William O. Trogdon	S	2,983	150
Texas Christian Univ., Fort Worth, TX 76129	1873	J. M. Moudy, Chan.	P,D	6,028	466
Texas Eastern Univ., Tyler, TX 75701	1971	James Stewart Jr.	S	1,653	68
Texas Lutheran, Segiun, TX 78155	1891	Chas. Oestreich	Mu	1,194	73
Texas Southern Univ., Houston, TX 77004	1947	Granville Sawyer	S	9,147	453
Texas System, Univ. of, Austin, TX 78701	1883	Charles A. LeMaistre, Chan.	S	92,346	5,639
at Arlington, Arlington, TX 76019	1895	Wendell Nedderman	S	16,745	690
at Austin, Austin, TX 78712	1883	L. Rogers	S	41,387	2,228
at Dallas, Dallas, TX 75080	1969	Bryce Jordan	S	4,416	267
at El Paso, El Paso, TX 79968	1913	Arleigh Templeton	S	14,795	468
Health Science Center, Dallas, TX 75235	1943	Charles Sprague	S	1,240	335
at Houston, Houston, TX 77025	1905	Truman Blocker Jr.	S	1,905	448
at San Antonio, San Antonio, TX 78284	1959	Frank Harrison	S	1,551	448
Medical Branch, Galveston, TX 77550	1881	William Levin	S	1,338	378
at Permian Basin, Odessa, TX 79762	1969	V. R. Cardozier	S	1,471	93
at San Antonio, San Antonio, TX 78285	1969	Peter Flawn	S	7,498	284
Texas Tech. Univ., Lubbock, TX 79409	1923	Cecil Mackey	S	22,176	1,386
Texas Wesleyan, Fort Worth, TX 76105	1891	William Pearce	D	1,876	72
Texas Woman's Univ. (W), Denton, TX 76204	1901	Mary B. Huey	S	8,728	528
Thiel, Greenville, PA 16125	1866	Louis Almen	D	1,050	61
Thomas, Waterville, ME 04901	1894	John L. Thomas Jr.	P	660	30
Thomas Jefferson Univ., Philadelphia, PA 19107	1824	Geo. Norwood Jr., Act.	P	1,700	1,400
Thomas More, Ft. Mitchell, KY 41017	1921	Richard A. DeGraff	D,P	1,003	96
Tiffin Univ., Tiffin, OH 44883	1918	Richard Pfeiffer	P	611	30
Tift (W), Forsyth, GA 31029	1847	Robert W. Jackson	P	457	35
Toledo, Univ. of, Toledo, OH 43606	1872	Glen R. Driscoll	S	17,500	680
Tougaloo, Tougaloo, MS 39174	1869	George A. Owens	P	710	57
Towson State Univ., Baltimore, MD 21204	1866	James L. Fisher	S	14,400	462
Transylvania Univ., Lexington, KY 40508	1780	William Kelly	P	722	59
Trenton State, Trenton, NJ 08625	1855	C. B. Brower	S	8,800	546
Trevecca Nazarene, Nashville, TN 37210	1901	Mark Moore	D,P	1,008	53
Trinity, Hartford, CT 06106	1823	Theodore Lockwood	P	1,783	135
Trinity, Deerfield, IL 60015	1897	Harry Evans	P	854	53
Trinity, Burlington, VT 05401	1925	Catherine McNamee	D	475	56
Trinity, Washington, DC 20017	1897	Sr. Roseanne Fleming	D	900	109
Trinity Univ., San Antonio, TX 78284	1869	M. B. Thomas, Act.	P	3,566	228
Tri-State Univ., Angola, IN 46703	1884	Carl Elliott	P	1,510	84
Troy State Univ. System, Troy, AL 36081	1887	Ralph W. Adams	S	10,530	584
Tufts Univ., Medford, MA 02155	1852	Jean Mayer	P	6,483	904
Tulane Univ., New Orleans, LA 70118	1834	Sheldon Hackney	P	9,100	700
Tulsa, Univ. of, Tulsa, OK 74104	1894	J. Paschal Twyman	P,D	6,540	362
Tusculum, Greenville, TN 37743	1794	Thomas Voss	P	434	28
Tuskegee Institute, Tuskegee Inst., AL 36088	1881	Luther H. Foster	P	3.590	316
Union, Barbourville, KY 40906	1879	Mahlon A. Miller	D,P	1,151	71
Union, Lincoln, NE 68506	1891	Myrl O. Manley	D	975	81
Union, Schenectady, NY 12308	1795	Thomas Bonner	P	3,045	150
Union Univ., Jackson, TN 38301	1825	Robert E. Craig	D,P	947	70
U.S. Air Force Academy, Col. Springs, CO 80840	1955	Lt. Gen. J. Allen, Supt.	F	4,000	550
U.S. Coast Guard Acad., New London, CT 06320	1876	R. Adm. W. Jenkins, Supt.	F	1,134	122
U.S. International Univ., San Diego, CA 92131	1952	William Rust	P	3,000	203
U.S. Merch. Marine Acad., Kings Point, NY 11024	1943	Rear Adm. A. Engel, Supt.	F	1,036	88
U.S. Military Academy, West Point, NY 10996	1802	A. J. Goodpaster, Supt.	F	4,400	600
U.S. Naval Academy, Annapolis, MD 21402	1845	Kinnaird McKee, Supt.	F	4,300	540
Unity, Unity, ME 04988	1966	Allan Karstetter	P	394	24
Upper Iowa Univ., Fayette, IA 52142	1857	Aldrich Paul	P	509	41
Upsala, E. Orange, NJ 07019	1893	W. Weller Jr., Chan.	P	1,701	129
Urbana, Urbana, OH 43078	1850	Roland Patzer	P,D	465	34
Ursinus, Collegeville, PA 19426	1869	Richard Richter	P	1,776	108
Ursuline, Cleveland, OH 44124	1871	Sister M. Kenan Dulzer	D,P	815	87
Utah State Univ.*, Logan, UT 84322	1888	Glen L. Taggart	S	9,113	462
Utah, Univ. of, Salt Lake City, UT 84112	1850	David P. Gardner	S	21,661	1,050
Valdosta State, Valdosta, GA 31601	1913	S. Walter Martin	S	5,012	237
Valley City State, Valley City, ND 58072	1890	Ted DeVries	S	890	52
Valparaiso Univ., Valparaiso, IN 46383	1859	Albert Huegli	P	3,537	343
Vanderbilt Univ., Nashville, TN 37240	1873	Alexander Heard, Chan.	P	6,833	1,687
Vassar, Poughkeepsie, NY 12601	1861	Virginia Smith	P	2,250	221
Vermont, Univ. of*, Burlington, VT 05401	1791	Lattie Coor	S	10,271	682
Villa Maria (W), Erie, PA 16415	1925	Sr. M. Lawrence Antoun	P	508	72
Villanova Univ., Villanova, PA 19085	1842	Rev. John M. Driscoll	D,P	9,619	572
Virgin Island, Coll. of the, St. Thomas, VI 00801	1962	L. C. Wanlass	T	2,122	150
Virginia Commonwealth Univ., Richmond, VA 23284	1838	H. I. Willett, Act.	S	18,099	1,777
Virginia Intermont, Bristol, VA 24201	1884	Floyd Turner	D,P	657	43
Virginia Military Inst. (M), Lexington, VA 24450	1839	Lt. Gen. R. Irby	S	1,349	132

Name, address	Year	Governing official and affiliation		Students	Teachers
Virginia Poly. Inst. & State Univ.*, Blacksburg, VA 24061	1871	William Lavery	S	21,277	1,070
Virginia State*, Petersburg, VA 23803	1882	Thomas Law	S	4,980	253
Virginia Union Univ., Richmond, VA 23220	1865	Allix B. James	P,D	1,424	139
Virginia, Univ. of, Charlottesville, VA 22903	1819	F. Hereford Jr.	S	15,529	1,660
Virginia Wesleyan, Norfolk, VA 23502	1961	Lambuth M. Clarke	P,D	657	33
Viterbo, La Crosse, WI 54601	1931	Rev. J. Thomas Finucan	P,D	900	112
Voorhees, Denmark, SC 29042	1897	Harry Graham	D,P	1,050	61
Wabash (M), Crawfordsville, IN 47933	1832	Thaddeus Seymour	P	851	70
Wagner, Staten Island NY 10301	1883	John Satterfield	P	*2,600*	*237*
Wake Forest Univ., Winston-Salem, NC 27109	1834	James R. Scales	D	*4,516*	*781*
Walla Walla, College Place, WA 99324	1892	N.C. Sorensen	D	*1,947*	*130*
Walsh, Canton, OH 44720	1960	Bro. Robert Francoeur	D,P	625	61
Walsh Coll. of Accounting, Troy, MI 48084	1922	Jeffrey Barry	P	1,172	72
Warner Pacific, Portland, OR 97215	1937	E. J. Gilliam	D,P	649	38
Warren Wilson, Swannanoa, NC 28778	1894	Reuben H. Holden	P,D	505	59
Wartburg, Waverly, IA 50677	1852	W. Jellema	P,D	1,197	79
Washburn Univ. of Topeka, Topeka, KS 66621	1865	John W. Henderson	Mu	5,488	317
Washington, Chestertown, MD 21620	1782	Joseph McLain	P	731	68
Washington and Jefferson, Washington, PA 15301	1781	Howard J. Burnett	P	1,239	99
Washington and Lee Univ., Lexington, VA 24450	1749	Robert Huntley	P	1,706	147
Washington State Univ., Pullman, WA 99164	1890	Glenn Terrell	S	16,693	1,013
Washington Tech. Inst., Washington, DC 20008	1966	C. L. Dennard	S	*4,142*	*194*
Washington Univ., St. Louis, MO 63130	1853	W. H. Danforth, Chan.	P	*11,265*	*2,141*
Washington, Univ. of*, Seattle, WA 98195	1861	John R. Hogness	S	36,000	3,891
Way Coll. of Emporia, The, Emporia, KS 66801	1882	V. P. Wierwille	D	476	64
Wayland Baptist, Plainview, TX 79072	1908	Roy C. McClung	D	1,126	55
Wayne State, Wayne, NE 68787	1910	Lyle Seymour	S	2,280	86
Wayne State Univ., Detroit, MI 48202	1868	George Gullen Jr.	S	*34,818*	*1,600*
Waynesburg, Waynesburg, PA 15370	1849	Joseph Marsh	D,P	802	61
Weber State, Ogden, UT 84408	1889	Joseph Bishop	S	9,668	485
Webster, St. Louis, MO 63119	1915	Leigh Gerdine	P	4,393	244
Wellesley (W), Wellesley, MA 02181	1875	Barbara W. Newell	P	2,093	261
Wells (W), Aurora, NY 13026	1868	Frances Farenthold	P	513	69
Wesleyan (W), Macon, GA 31201	1836	W. Earl Strickland	D	570	53
Wesleyan Univ., Middletown, CT 06457	1831	Colin G. Campbell	P	2,500	250
West Chester State, West Chester, PA 19380	1871	Charles Mayo	S	9,152	519
West Coast Univ., Los Angeles, CA 90020	1909	Victor Elconin	P	*1,240*	*200*
West Florida, Univ. of, Pensacola, FL 32504	1967	James Robinson	S	*4,978*	*294*
West Georgia, Carrollton, GA 30117	1933	Maurice Townsend	S	5,366	269
West Liberty State, West Liberty, WV 26074	1837	James L. Chapman	S	2,686	148
West Texas State Univ, Canyon, TX 79016	1909	Lloyd Watkins	S	6,558	348
W. Va. Inst. of Tech., Montgomery, WV 25136	1895	Leonard C. Nelson	S	3,034	175
West Virginia State, Institute, WV 25112	1891	Harold M. McNeill	S	3,519	186
West Virginia Univ.*, Morgantown, WV 26505	1867	Gene Budig	S	*20,964*	*1,175*
W. Virginia Wesleyan, Buckhannon, WV 26201	1890	R. E. Sleeth	D	1,805	132
Western Baptist Bible, Salem, OR 97302	1946	W. T. Younger	D,P	438	38
Western Carolina Univ., Cullonhee, NC 28723	1889	H. F. Robinson, Chan.	S	6,380	307
Western Conn. State, Danbury, CT 06810	1903	Robert Bersi	S	4,981	251
Western Illinois Univ., Macomb, IL 61455	1899	L. Malpass	S	14,744	773
Western Kentucky Univ., Bowling Green, KY 42101	1906	Dero Downing	S	13,386	626
Western Maryland, Westminster, MD 21157	1867	Ralph C. John	P	2,147	146
Western Mich. Univ., Kalamazoo, MI 49008	1903	John T. Bernhard	S	21,033	888
Western Montana, Dillon, MT 59725	1893	George Bandy	S	823	43
Western New England, Springfield, MA 01119	1919	Richard Gottier	P	*4989*	*266*
Western New Mexico Univ, Silver City, NM 88061	1893	John Snedeker	S	1,916	60
Western State Col. of Colo., Gunnison, CO 81230	1901	John Mellon	S	3,350	130
Western Washington St., Bellingham, WA 98225	1899	Paul Olscamp	S	8,697	439
Westfield State, Westfield, MA 01085	1839	Robert L. Randolph	S	3,900	155
Westmar, Le Mars, IA 51031	1890	Ben F. Wade	D	642	50
Westminster, Fulton, MO 65251	1851	J. H. Saunders	P	700	60
Westminster, New Wilmington, PA 16142	1852	Earland I. Carlson	P	1,850	113
Westminster, Salt Lake City, UT 84105	1875	Helmut Hofmann	P	1,671	75
Westminster Choir, Princeton, NJ 08540	1926	Ray E. Robinson	P	460	57
Westmont, Santa Barbara, CA 93108	1940	David Winter	P	*954*	*86*
Wheaton, Wheaton, IL 60187	1860	Hudson T. Armerding	P	2,135	180
Wheaton (W), Norton, MA 02766	1834	William C. H. Prentice	P	1,112	117
Wheeling, Wheeling, WV 26003	1954	Rev Charles Currie	D	1,041	77
Wheelock, Boston, MA 02215	1889	Gordon L. Marshall	P	907	95
White Plains, Coll. of, White Plains, NY 10603	1923	Edward Mortola	P	800	55
Whitman, Walla Walla, WA 99362	1859	Robert Skotheim	P	1,112	88
Whittier, Whittier, CA 90608	1901	W. R. Newsom	P	*1,785*	*126*
Whitworth, Spokane, WA 99251	1890	Edward B. Lindaman	P	1,868	152
Wichita State Univ., Wichita, KS 67208	1895	Clark Ahlberg	S	14,842	852
Widener, Chester, PA 19013	1821	Clarence R. Moll	P	3,341	236
Wilberforce Univ., Wilberforce, OH 45384	1856	Charles Taylor	D,P	1,107	62
Wiley, Marshall, TX 75670	1873	Robert Hayes Sr.	D	544	41
Wilkes, Wilkes-Barre, PA 18703	1933	Robert Capin	P	2,767	158
Willamette Univ., Salem, OR 97301	1842	Robert Lisensky	P	1,753	148
William Carey, Hattiesburg, MS 39401	1906	J. Ralph Noonkester	D	*2,042*	*90*
William Jewell, Liberty, MO 64068	1849	Thomas Field	P,D	1,619	133
Wm. and Mary, Coll. of, Williamsburg, VA 23185	1693	Thomas A. Graves Jr.	S	6,011	464
Wm. Mitchell Coll. of Law, St. Paul, MN 55105	1900	Ronald Hachey	P	1,050	100
Wm. Paterson, Wayne, NJ 07470	1855	William McKeefery	S	12,999	443
William Penn, Oskaloosa, IA 52577	1873	Duane Moon	P	650	40
William Woods (W), Fulton, MO 65251	1870	Randall B. Cutlip	P	1,086	100
Williams, Williamstown, MA 01267	1793	John W. Chandler	P	1,863	160
Wilmington, Wilmington, OH 45177	1870	Robert E. Lucas	D	1,022	102
Wilmington, New Castle, DE 19720	1967	Donald E. Ross	P	710	32
Wilson (W), Chambersburg, PA 17201	1869	Margaret Waggoner	P,D	285	50
Winona State Univ., Winona, MN 55987	1858	Robt. DuFresne	S	4,750	202
Winston-Salem St. Univ., Winston-Salem, NC 27102	1892	Kenneth Williams, Chan.	S	1,987	140
Winthrop, Rock Hill, SC 29733	1886	Charles Vail	S	4,000	277
Wisconsin, Univ. of*, Madison, WI 53706	1971	John Weaver	S	*143,440*	*6,615*
Eau Claire, Eau Claire, WI 54701	1916	Leonard Haas, Chan.	S	9,974	501
Green Bay, Green Bay, WI 54302	1969	Edward W. Weidner, Chan.	S	3,641	160
La Crosse, La Crosse, WI. 54601	1909	Kenneth Lindner, Chan.	S	7,756	333

Name, address	Year	Governing official and affiliation		Students	Teachers
Madison, Madison, WI 53706	1849	Edwin Young, Chan.	S	37,857	2,275
Milwaukee, Milwaukee, WI 53201	1885	Werner Baum, Chan.	S	24,686	846
Oshkosh, Oshkosh, WI 54901	1871	Robert Birnbaum, Chan.	S	10,225	547
Parkside, Kenosha, WI 53140	1969	Alan Guskin, Chan.	S	4,984	167
Platteville, Platteville, WI 53818	1866	Warren Carrier, Chan.	S	4,447	247
River Falls, River Falls, WI 54022	1874	George Field, Chan.	S	4,873	238
Stevens Point, Stevens Point, WI 54481	1894	Lee S. Dreyfus, Chan.	S	8,522	435
Stout, Menomonie, WI 54751	1893	Robert Swanson, Chan.	S	6,066	293
Superior, Superior, WI 54880	1896	Karl W. Meyer, Chan.	S	2,450	155
Whitewater, Whitewater, WI 53190	1868	James Connor, Chan.	S	9,388	418
Wittenberg Univ., Springfield, OH 45501	1845	W. A. Kinnison	P,D	4,355	156
Wofford, Spartanburg, SC 29301	1854	J. M. Lesesne Jr.	P,D	1,000	100
Woodbury, Los Angeles, CA 90017	1884	Bethel Johnson	P	1,600	75
Wooster, Coll. of, Wooster, OH 44691	1866	Henry Copeland	P	1,896	141
Worcester Polytechnic Inst., Worcester, MA 01609	1865	George W. Hazzard	P	2,887	233
Worcester State, Worcester, MA 01602	1874	Joseph Orze	S	5,524	185
Wright State Univ., Dayton, OH 45431	1964	R. J. Kegerreis	S	*13,669*	*596*
Wyoming, Univ. of*, Laramie, WY 82071	1886	William Carlson	S	8,718	839
Xavier Univ. of La., New Orleans, LA 70125	1925	Norman C. Francis	D	1,700	158
Xavier Univ., Cincinnati, OH 45207	1831	Rev. Robert Mulligan	P	6,225	285
Yale Univ., New Haven, CT 06520	1701	Kingman Brewster Jr.	P	9,600	1,450
Yankton, Yankton, SD 57078	1881	Alfred M. Gibbens	D	318	45
Yeshiva Univ., New York, NY 10033	1886	Norman Lamm	P	*6,508*	*2,500*
York College of Pa., York, PA 17405	1941	R. V. Iosue	P	3,150	153
Youngstown State Univ., Youngstown, OH 44503	1908	John J. Coffelt	S	13,917	760

Community and Junior Colleges

Enrollment and faculty figures in italics includes all branches and campuses

Abraham Baldwin Agric., Tifton, GA 31794	1908	Stanley Anderson	S	2,431	111
Adirondacks Community, Glens Falls, NY 12801	1960	Charles R. Eisenhart	S	1,693	66
Aeronautics, Academy of, Flushing, NY 11371	1932	Walter M. Hartung	P	1,325	53
Aims Comm., Greeley, CO 80631	1968	Richard Laughlin	C	4,000	200
Alabama Christian, Montgomery, AL 36069	1942	E.R. Brannan	D,P	*1,352*	*105*
Alameda, Coll. of, Alameda, CA 94501	1970	Jeanette Poore	C,S	7,337	241
Albany Junior, Albany, GA 31707	1966	B.R. Tilley	S	2,148	100
Albany, Junior Coll. of, Albany, NY 12208	1957	William Kahl	P	1,045	42
Albemarle, Coll. of the, Elizabeth City, NC 27909	1960	J.P. Chesson Jr.	S	1,100	58
Alexander City State Jr., Alexander City, AL 35010	1965	W. Byron Causey	S	1,291	92
Allen Co. Comm. Jr., Iola, KS 66749	1923	Bill R. Spencer	C	747	52
Alice Lloyd, Pippa Passes, KY 41844	1923	Jerry Davis	P	241	25
Allan Hancock Comm., Santa Maria, CA 93454	1920	Walter E. Conrad	Di.	8,941	528
Allegany Community, Cumberland, MD 21502	1961	W. Ardell Haines	C,S	1,813	124
Allegheny Co., Comm. Coll. of, Pittsburgh, PA 15222	1965	John B. Hirt	C	*38,480*	*1,510*
Alpena Community, Alpena, MI 49707	1952	Herbert N. Stoutenberg	C	1,850	110
Alvin Comm., Alvin, TX 77511	1948	A.R. Allbright	S	2,603	79
Amarillo, Amarillo, TX 79178	1929	Charles Lutz Jr.	Mu	4,069	197
American International, Springfield, MA 01109	1885	Harry Courniotes	P	2,231	154
American River, Sacramento, CA 95841	1955	Kenneth Boettcher	Di	*17,364*	*497*
Anderson, Anderson, SC 29621	1911	J. Cordell Maddox	D	1,231	63
Andrew, Cuthbert, GA 31740	1854	Walter Murphy	D	352	25
Angelina, Lufkin, TX 75901	1968	Jack W. Hudgins	S	1,475	88
Anne Arundel Comm., Arnold, MD 21012	1961	Justus D. Sundermann	C,S	5,668	265
Anoke-Ramsey Comm., Coon Rapids, MN 55433	1965	Neil Christenson	S	2,747	72
Anson Tech. Inst., Ansonville, NC 28007	1962	H. B. Monroe	S	6,277	61
Antelope Valley, Lancaster, CA 93534	1929	Clinton Stine	S	4,665	200
Aquinas Junior, Milton, MA 02186	1956	Sr. Mary Morgan	D	378	23
Aquinas Junior, Nashville, TN 37205	1961	Sister Henry Suso Fletcher	D	408	36
Arapahoe Community, Littleton, CO 80120	1966	Joseph K. Bailey	S	5,100	300
Arizona Western, Yuma, AZ 85364	1963	Marvin Knudson	S	*3,900*	*421*
Asheville Buncombe Tech. Inst., Asheville, NC 28801	1959	Harvey Haynes	S	1,686	135
Ashland Community, Ashland, KY 41101	1957	Robert Goodpaster	S	1,253	62
Atlantic Comm., Mays Landing, NJ 08330	1964	L. R. Winchell Jr.	C,S	2,307	123
Austin Comm., Austin, MN 55912	1940	Arlan Burmeister	S	900	50
Bacone, Muskogee, OK 74401	1880	Charles D. Holleyman	P,D	600	35
Bakersfield, Bakersfield, CA 93305	1913	John J. Collins	S	*13,083*	*452*
Baltimore, Com. Col. of, Baltimore, MD 21215	1947	Harry Bard	Mu	*11,700*	*350*
Barstow Community, Barstow, CA 92311	1960	Wm. R. Graham	Mu	2,019	82
Barton County Comm., Great Bend, KS 67530	1965	Jimmie Downing	C	1,902	109
Bay de Noe Comm., Escanaba, MI 49829	1962	Edwin E. Wuehle	C	1,121	85
Bay Path Junior, Longmeadow, MA 01106	1897	Randle Elliott	P	607	34
Beal, Business, Bangor, ME 04401	1891	David Tibbetts	P	*380*	*30*
Beaufort Co. Tech. Inst., Washington, NC 27889	1967	James P. Blanton	S	1,542	100
Beaver Co. Com. Col. of, Monaca, PA 15061	1966	Richard Adams	S	2,000	63
Becker Junior, Worcester, MA 01609	1784	Lloyd H. Van Buskirk	P	*1,300*	*60*
Beckley, Beckley, WV 25801	1933	John Saunders	P,D	1,230	63
Bee County, Beeville, TX 78102	1965	Grady C. Hogue	S	2,219	125
Belleville Area, Belleville, IL 62221	1946	William Keel	S	10,000	664
Bellevue Community, Bellevue, WA 98007	1966	Merle Landerholm	S	7,580	347
Belmont Technical, St. Clairsville, OH 43950	1970	Paul Tien	S	1,200	70
Bennett, Millbrook, NY 12545	1891	J. William Nystrom	P	249	35
Bergen Community, Paramus, NJ 07652	1965	Sidney Silverman	C,S	9,743	513
Berkeley School, The (W), Little Falls, NJ 07424	1931	Larry Luing	P	*1,936*	*87*
Berkshire Community, Pittsfield, MA 01201	1960	Vacant	S	3,200	160
Big Bend Community, Moses Lake, WA 98837	1962	Robert J. Wallenstein	S	2,600	117
Biscayne Southern, Charlotte, NC 28232	1972	Charles Palmer	P	*425*	*32*
Bismarck Junior (A), Bismarck, ND 58501	1939	Ralph Werner	Mu	1,900	85
Black Hawk, Moline, IL 61265	1946	Alban E. Reid	S,C	*9,257*	*698*
Blackhawk Technical Inst., Janesville, WI 53545	1968	O. L. Johnson (Dir.)	Di	*1,693*	*97*

Name, address	Year	Governing official and affiliation		Students	Teachers
Blinn, Brenham, TX 77833	1883	James H. Atkinson	C	2,100	70
Bliss, Columbus, OH 43214	1899	Gerald J. Wickham	P	530	28
Bluefield, Bluefield, VA 24605	1922	Charles L. Tyer	D	634	33
Blue Mountain Comm., Pendleton, OR 97801	1962	Ronald L. Daniels	C,S	1,820	91
Blue Ridge Comm., Weyers Cave, VA 24486	1967	James A. Armstrong	S	1,967	66
Brandywine, Wilmington, DE 19803	1966	C.R. Moll	D	*1,375*	*45*
Brazosport, Lake Jackson, TX 77566	1968	J. R. Jackson	S	3,270	73
Brevard, Brevard, NC 28712	1853	J.C. Martinson Jr.	D,P	550	41
Brevard Comm. (A), Coca, FL 32922	1960	Maxwell King	S	*7,600*	*300*
Brewton Parker, Mt. Vernon, GA 30445	1904	J. Theodore Phillips	D	1,052	48
Bristol Community, Fall River, MA 02722	1965	Jack Hudnall	S	*5,000*	*200*
Bronx Community, Bronx, NY 10453	1957	M. Rosenstock, Act.	Mu	10,000	593
Brookdale Comm., Lincroft, NJ 07738	1967	Donald H. Smith	C	8,314	354
Broome Community, Binghamton, NY 13902	1946	Peter Blomerley	S	4,634	154
Broward Community, Ft. Lauderdale, FL 33301	1960	Hugh Adams	S	*16,000*	*275*
Brunswick Junior, Brunswick, GA 31520	1961	John W. Teel	S	1,068	54
Bucks County Comm., Newtown, PA 18940	1965	Charles Rollins	C,S	7,609	347
Butler County Comm., Butler, PA 16001	1966	Thomas Ten Hoeve Jr.	C	2,012	126
Butler County Comm. Jr., El Dorado, KS 67042	1927	Edwin J. Walbourn	C	1,509	85
Butte Community, Oroville, CA 95965	1967	Albert Schlueter	S	7,716	350
Cabrillo Comm. Coll., Aptos, CA 95003	1959	J.C. Petersen	S	9,400	328
Caldwell Comm. Coll. & Tech. Inst., Lenoir, NC 28645	1964	H. Edwin Beam	C,S	*1,300*	*120*
Camden County, Blackwood, NJ 08012	1967	Otto R. Mauke	C	*6,660*	*342*
Canada, Redwood City, CA 94061	1968	J.W. Wenrich	C	8,300	350
Canyons, Coll. of the, Valencia, CA 91355	1968	Robert Rockwell	C	3,439	109
Cape Cod Comm., W. Barnstable, MA 02668	1960	James F. Hall	S	4,685	220
Cape Fear Tech. Inst., Wilmington, NC 28401	1964	M. J. McLeod	S	3,902	400
Carl Albert Junior, Poteau, OK 74953	1934	Joe E. White	S	1,375	40
Carl Sandburg, Galesburg, IL 61401	1966	Eltis Henson	S	2,400	191
Carteret Tech. Inst., Morehead City, NC 28557	1964	Donald Bryant	S	*913*	*64*
Casper, Casper, WY 82601	1945	Tilghman Aley	S	3,584	188
Catawba Valley Tech Inst., Hickory, NC 28601	1958	Robert E. Paap	S	2,228	120
Catonsville Comm., Baltimore, MD 21228	1957	Robert Barringer	C,S	*8,881*	*413*
Cayuga Co. Comm., Auburn, NY 13021	1953	John Anthony	S	2,735	83
Cazenovia (W), Cazenovia, NY 13035	1824	Stephen Schneeweiss	P	350	38
Cecil Community, North East, MD 21901	1968	William O'Connor	C,S	1,472	96
Central Arizona, Coolidge, AZ 85228	1969	Don Pence	C	4,200	50
Central Carolina Tech. Inst., Sanford, NC 27330	1962	James F. Hockaday	S	1,870	72
Central, McPherson, KS 67460	1884	Bruce L. Kline	P	212	23
Central Florida Comm., Ocala, FL 32670	1957	Henry E. Goodlett	S	2,357	185
Central Oregon Comm., Bend, OR 97701	1949	Frederick Boyle	S	2,500	80
Central Piedmont Comm., Charlotte, NC 28204	1963	Richard H. Hagemeyer	S	18,947	692
Central Nebr. Tech. Comm., Grand Island, NE 68801	1966	Chester Gausman	C	*16,072*	*132*
Central Texas, Killeen, TX, 76541	1967	L. M. Morton Jr.	S.	*5,000*	*125*
Central Virginia Comm., Lynchburg, VA 24502	1966	Donald Puyear	S	3,003	121
Central Wyoming, Riverton, WY 82501	1966	William Day	C	640	100
Central YMCA Comm., Chicago, IL 60606	1960	Donald A. Canar	P	3,885	370
Centralia, Centralia, WA 98531	1925	Nels W. Hanson	S	4,182	200
Cerritos Community, Norwalk, CA 90650	1955	Wilford Michael	S	22,063	720
Cerro Coso Comm., Ridgecrest, CA 93555	1973	Richard Meyers	S	4,527	68
Chabot, Hayward, CA 94545	1961	Reed L. Buffington	Di	*19,348*	*900*
Chaffey, Alta Loma, CA 91701	1883	K.C. Hinrichsen	S	11,644	461
Champlain, Burlington, VT 05402	1878	C. Bader Brouilette	P	1,174	63
Charles Co. Comm., La Plata, MD 20646	1958	J. N. Carsey	S	2,146	115
Charles S. Mott Comm., Flint, MI 48503	1923	Charles Pappas	C	9,710	430
Chattanooga St. Tech. Comm., Chattanooga, TN 37406	1973	Charles W. Branch	S	5,000	76
Chemeketa Comm., Salem, OR 97309	1969	G.R. Edelbrock, Act.	Di	*31,382*	*900*
Chicago, City Colleges of, Chicago, IL 60601	1911	Oscar Shabat, Chan.	Mu	*106,774*	*1,400*
Kennedy-King, Chicago, IL 60621	1935	Ewen Akin	S	9,668	229
Loop, Chicago, IL 60601	1962	David H. Heller	S	14,605	205
Malcolm X. Chicago, IL 60612	1911	Samuel Huffman	S	5,830	156
Olive-Harvey, Chicago, IL 60628	1957	Eugene T. Speller	S	5,050	184
Daley, Chicago, IL 60652	1960	Virginia R. Keehan	S	5,479	140
Wilbur Wright, Chicago, IL 60634	1934	Ernest Clements	S	7,384	227
Chipola Junior, Marianna, FL 32446	1947	Raymond M. Deming	S	999	47
Chowan, Murfreesboro, NC 27855	1848	Bruce E. Whitaker	P,D	1,060	69
Cisco Junior, Cisco, TX 76437	1940	Norman Wallace Jr.	S	2,598	110
Citrus, Azusa, CA 91702	1915	Robert Haugh	S	10,049	174
Clackamas Comm., Oregon City, OR 97045	1966	John Hakanson	S	9,000	745
Claremore Junior, Claremore, OK 74017	1971	Richard Mosier	S	2,100	87
Clarendon, Clarendon, TX 79226	1898	Kenneth D. Vaughan	S	525	33
Clark, Vancouver, WA 98663	1933	I. S. Hakanson	S	5,755	225
Clark Co. Comm., N. Las Vegas, NV 89030	1971	Chas. Donnelly	S	5,800	60
Clark Tech., Springfield, OH 45501	1962	Richard Brinkman	S	2,010	110
Clarke, Newton, MS 39345	1908	W. L. Compere	D	252	18
Clatsop Community, Astoria, OR 97103	1962	Philip Bainer	S	6,545	148
Clayton Junior, Morrow, GA 30260	1965	Harry S. Downs	S	3,095	128
Cleveland Co. Tech. Inst., Shelby, NC 28150	1965	James Petty	S	1,810	130
Cleveland State Comm., Cleveland, TN 37311	1967	D. F. Adkisson	S	3,600	94
Clinton Community, Clinton, IA 52732	1946	Dean F. Travis	S	*804*	*57*
Clinton Community, Plattsburgh, NY 12901	1966	Albert B. Light	S	1,303	31
Cloud County Comm., Concordia, KS 66901	1965	James P. Ihrig	C	1,275	90
Coahoma Junior, Clarksdale, MS 38614	1949	James Earl Miller	S	1,302	66
Coastal Carolina Comm., Jacksonville, NC 28540	1964	James Henderson Jr.	S	2,500	256
Cochise Comm., Douglas, AZ 85607	1962	John R. Edwards Jr.	C	*4,173*	*284*
Coffeyville Comm. Jr., Coffeyville, KS 67337	1923	Russell Graham	S	744	49
Colby Comm., Colby, KS 67701	1964	James Tangeman	S	1,996	81
Colorado Mountain, Glenwood Spgs., CO 81601	1967	Elbie L. Gann	C	*5,238*	*244*
Colorado Northwestern Comm., Rangely, CO 81648	1962	James H. Bos	Di	3,680	121
Columbia Greene Comm., Hudson, NY 12534	1966	Edward J. Owen	S	1,142	34
Columbia Junior, Columbia, CA 95310	1968	Harvey Rhodes	S	3,000	150
Columbia State Comm., Columbia, TN 38401	1966	Harold S. Pryor	S	2,156	91
Columbus Tech. Inst., Columbus, OH 43215	1963	Clarence Schauer	S	4,966	264
Compton Comm., Compton, CA 90221	1927	Abel B. Sykes Jr.	S	6,832	268
Concordia, Portland, OR 97211	1905	E.P. Weber	D	200	2
Concordia, Milwaukee, WI 53208	1881	Wilbert Rosin	D	476	4
Concordia Lutheran, Austin, TX 78705	1926	Ray F. Martens	P	302	2

Name, address	Year	Governing official and affiliation		Students	Teachers
Connors State, Warner, OK 74469	1908	Melvin Self	S	1,800	64
Cooke County, Gainesville, TX 76240	1924	Alton Laird	S	1,718	116
Copiah-Lincoln Junior, Wesson, MS 39191	1928	Billy Thames	C	*1,365*	*98*
Corning Community, Corning, NY 14830	1956	Donald H. Hangen	S	2,784	103
Cottey (W), Nevada, MO 64772	1884	Evelyn Milam	P	355	34
Cowley County Comm., Arkansas City, KS 67005	1922	Owen Nelson	C	1,221	60
Crafton Hills, Yucaipa, CA 92399	1972	Wm. Moore	S	3,416	167
Craven Comm., New Bern, NC 28560	1965	Thurman E. Brock	S	1,293	65
Crowder, Neosho, MO 64850	1964	Dell Reed	S	1,000	53
Cuesta, San Luis Obispo, CA 93406	1963	Frank Martinez	C	5,445	238
Cumberland County, Vineland, NJ 08360	1963	Philip Phelan	C	1,750	65
Curry, Milton, MA 02186	1879	John S. Hafer	P	1,027	54
Cuyahoga Community, Cleveland, OH 44115	1962	Nolen Ellison, Chan.	C	*28,102*	*1,253*
Cypress, Cypress, CA 90630	1966	Omar Scheidt	C	11,363	452
Dabney S. Lancaster Comm., Clifton Forge, VA 24422	1967	John F. Backels	S	900	55
Dallas Co. Comm. Col. System, Dallas, TX 75202	1965	Bill J. Priest	C	*32,790*	*2,412*
Dalton Jr., Dalton, GA 30720	1967	Derrell Roberts	S	1,600	75
Danville Junior, Danville, IL 61832	1946	William Langas	S	3,441	172
Davenport Coll. of Business, Grand Rapids, MI 49502	1866	Robert W. Sneden	P	1,311	46
Davidson County Comm, Lexington, NC 27292	1959	Grady Love	S	2,597	198
Davis Jr. Coll. of Business, Toledo, OH 43604	1858	Ruth L. Davis	P	1,197	41
Dawson Comm., Glendive, MT 59330	1940	James Hoffman	C	730	43
Daytona Beach Comm., Daytona Beach, FL 32015	1958	Charles Polk	S	4,835	415
Dean Junior, Franklin, MA 02038	1865	Richard Crockford	P	1,486	64
De Anza, Cupertino, CA 95014	1967	A. Robert DeHart	C	21,000	755
DeKalb Community, Clarkston, GA 30021	1964	W.W. Scott, Act.	C	*15,574*	*468*
Delgado Junior, New Orleans, LA 70119	1921	Marvin E. Thames	S	10,445	540
Del Mar, Corpus Christi, TX 78404	1935	Jean Richardson	S	7,937	235
Delaware County Comm., Media, PA 19063	1967	Douglas Libby Jr.	C	4,800	250
Delaware Tech. Comm., Dover, DE 19901	1966	P.K. Weatherly	S	*3,500*	*600*
Delta, University Ctr., MI 48710	1957	Donald Carlyon	C	8,150	385
Denver, Comm. Coll. of, Denver, CO 80203	1968	G.O. Smith, Act.	S	*15,739*	*766*
Des Moines Area Comm., Ankeny, IA 50021	1966	Paul Lowery	S	*12,887*	*224*
Desert, Coll. of the, Palm Desert, CA 92260	1958	F.D. Stout	S	*11,352*	*303*
Diablo Valley, Pleasant Hill, CA 94523	1949	William P. Niland	Di	17,040	552
District One Tech. Inst., Eau Claire, WI 54701	1912	Norbert Wurtzel, Dir.	S	*2,147*	*120*
Dixie, St. George, UT 84770	1911	Wm. Kerr	S	1,343	75
Dodge City Community, Dodge City, KS 67801	1935	Charles M. Barnes	C	1,200	73
Donnelly, Kansas City, KS 66102	1949	Rev. Raymond Davern	D	844	42
Dundalk Community, Baltimore, MD 21222	1969	John E. Ravekes	C	2,200	65
Du Page, Coll. of, Glen Ellyn, IL 60137	1965	Rodney Berg	S	16,000	264
Durham Tech. Inst., Durham, NC 27703	1965	John Crumpton Jr.	S,C	2,000	130
Dutchess Community, Poughkeepsie, NY 12601	1957	John J. Connolly	S	5,700	131
Dyersburg State Comm., Dyersburg, TN 38024	1969	Edward Eller	S	1,191	70
East Central Junior, Decatur, MS 39327	1928	Charles V. Wright	S	1,000	55
East Central Junior, Union, MO 63084	1968	Donald D. Shook	Di	1,400	82
East Los Angeles, Los Angeles, CA 90022	1945	A. Rodriguez	Di	*18,000*	*700*
East Mississippi Jr., Scooba, MS 39358	1927	C. Cheatham	S	*1,311*	*49*
Eastern Arizona, Thatcher, AZ 85552	1888	W. M. McGrath	S,C	*3,826*	*239*
Eastern Iowa Comm., Davenport, IA 52806	1966	Gerald Clemmensen (Supt.)	S,Di	*2,773*	*163*
Eastern Maine Voc. Tech., Bangor, ME 04401	1965	Francis Sprague, Dir.	S	2,280	100
Eastern Oklahoma State, Wilburton, OK 74578	1907	James Miller	S	*1,785*	*89*
Eastern Utah, Coll. Of, Price, UT 84501	1937	Dean McDonald	S	1,885	75
Eastern Wyoming, Torrington, WY 82240	1948	Charles Rogers	Di	1,500	120
Eastfield, Mesquite, TX 75149	1970	Byron McClenney	C	11,800	402
Edgecombe Tech. Inst., Tarboro, NC 27886	1968	Charles McIntyre	C,S	*1,000*	*60*
Edison Community, Ft. Myers, FL 33901	1962	David G. Robinson	S	*3,400*	*121*
Edmonds Community, Lynnwood, WA 98036	1965	James Warren	S	4,600	185
El Camino, Torrance, CA 90506	1947	Stuart E. Marsee	Di	28,454	620
El Centro, Dallas, TX 75202	1966	Ruby H. Herd	C	7,733	193
El Paso Comm., Colorado Springs, CO 80904	1967	D.W. McInnis	S	5,684	326
El Paso Community, El Paso, TX 79904	1971	Ray Salazan	C	*9,800*	*347*
El Reno Jr., El Reno, OK 73036	1938	Bill S. Cole	S	801	57
Elgin Community, Elgin, IL 60120	1949	Mark L. Hopkins	S	5,500	340
Elizabeth Seton, Yonkers, NY 10701	1960	Sr. Mary Ellen Brosnan	P	989	81
Elizabethtown Comm., Elizabethtown, KY 42701	1964	James Owen, Dir.	S	1,440	65
Ellsworth Comm., Iowa Falls, IA 50126	1890	G.P. Warford (Dean)	S	724	*54*
Emmanuel, Franklin Spgs., GA 30639	1919	C.Y. Melton	P,D	415	26
Endicott Junior (W), Beverly, MA 01915	1939	Eleanor Tupper	P	841	64
Erie Community, Buffalo, NY 14221	1946	Robert H. Stauffer	S	9,508	276
Essex Community, Baltimore, MD 21237	1957	Vernon Wanty	C	9,467	413
Essex County, Newark, NJ 07102	1968	J. Harry Smith	C	6,749	257
Everett Comm., Everett, WA 98201	1941	Norman Clark	S	6,528	273
Fashion Inst. of Tech., New York, NY 10001	1944	Marvin J. Feldman	S	7,625	152
Faulkner State Jr., Bay Minette, AL 36507	1963	L. Sibert	S	2,347	78
Fayetteville Tech. Inst., Fayetteville, NC 28303	1961	Howard Boudreau	S	3,955	218
Feather River, Quincy, CA 95971	1968	Dale P. Wren	S	*1,837*	*53*
Fergus Falls Comm., Fergus Falls, MN 56537	1960	W. A. Waage	S	614	39
Finger Lakes, Comm. Coll. of, Canandaigua, NY 14424	1965	Charles Meder	S	2,342	57
Fisher Junior, Boston, MA 02116	1903	Scott Fisher	P	*2,115*	*97*
Flathead Valley Comm., Kalispell, MT 59901	1967	R. C. Mattson, Act.	S,C	1,407	100
Florida, Temple Terrace, FL 33617	1946	James R. Cope	P	474	34
Florida Jr., Jacksonville, FL 32202	1966	Benjamin R. Wygal	S	*75,158*	*1,580*
Florida Key Comm., Key West, FL 33040	1965	John S. Smith	S	1,267	55
Florissant Valley Comm. (A), St. Louis, MO 63135	1962	Raymond J. Stith	Di	6,869	350
Floyd Junior, Roma, GA 30161	1970	David McCorkle	S	1,646	103
Foothill, Los Altos Hills, CA 94022	1958	James Fitzgerald	Di	*14,415*	*606*
Forest Park Comm. (A), St. Louis, MO 63110	1962	Ralph H. Lee	Di	5,828	367
Forsyth Tech. Inst., Winston-Salem, NC 27103	1960	Harley Affeldt	S	*2,174*	*127*
Ft. Steilacoom Comm., Tacoma, WA 98498	1967	Marion O. Oppelt	S	10,050	424
Fox Valley Tech. Inst., Appleton, WI 54911	1967	William Sirek, Dir.	D	*6,750*	*675*
Franklin Inst., Boston, MA 01778	1908	Michael Mazzola, Dir.	P	952	63
Fresno City, Fresno, CA 93741	1910	Clyde McCully	S	16,470	561
Fullerton, Fullerton, CA 92634	1913	John Casey	S	20,710	671
Fulton-Montgomery Comm., Johnstown, NY 12095	1963	Hadley S. DePuy	S	1,642	53

Name, address	Year	Governing official and affiliation		Students	Teachers
Gadsden State Junior, E. Gadsden, AL 35903	1963	A. D. Naylor	S	7,109	145
Gainesville Junior, Gainesville, GA 30501	1964	Hugh Mills Jr.	S	1,550	60
Galveston, Galveston, TX 77550	1967	Melvin M. Plexco	S	*2,203*	*80*
Garden City Comm. Jr., Garden City, KS 67846	1919	Raymond Wamsley	C,S	1,464	64
Gaston, Dallas, NC 28034	1963	Joseph L. Mills	S	3,000	91
Gateway Tech. Inst., Kenosha, WI 53140	1911	Keith Stoehr, Dir.	Di	*12,188*	*225*
Gavilan, Gilroy, CA 95020	1919	Rudy Melone	S	2,500	145
Genesee Community, Batavia, NY 14020	1966	Stuart Steiner	S	2,420	85
George C. Wallace St. Comm., Dothan, AL 36301	1965	Phillip J. Hamm	S	2,239	96
Germanna Comm., Locust Grove, VA 22508	1970	Arnold E. Wirtala	S	1,050	45
Glen Oaks Comm., Centreville, MI 49032	1965	Justus Sundermann	S	900	66
Glendale Comm., Glendale, CA 91208	1927	John Grande	S	7,752	360
Gloucester County, Sewell, NJ 08080	1966	William Apetz	C	2,500	114
Gogebic Community, Ironwood, MI 49938	1932	R. Ernest Dear	S	1,200	50
Golden West, Huntgtn. Bch., CA 92647	1965	R. Dudley Boyce	S	23,063	555
Goldey Beacom, Wilmington, DE 19808	1886	William Ott	P	1,450	125
Gordon Junior, Barnesville, GA 30204	1852	Jerry M. Williamson	S	1,104	53
Grahm Junior, Boston, MA 02215	1950	Arthur Griffin	P	831	72
Grand Rapids Junior, Grand Rapids, MI 49502	1914	Richard Calkins	Mu	7,301	230
Grand View, Des Moines, IA 50316	1896	K. F. Langrock	P	858	40
Grays Harbor, Aberdeen, WA 98520	1930	Joseph Malik	S	3,399	160
Grayson County Junior, Denison, TX 75020	1964	Truman Wester	S,C	4,900	183
Greater Hartford Comm., Hartford, CT 06105	1967	Arthur C. Banks Jr.	S	2,600	130
Green River Comm., Auburn, WA 98002	1964	Melvin Lindbloom	S	6,990	215
Greenfield Comm., Greenfield, MA 01301	1962	Lewis Turner	S	2,000	100
Greenville Tech., Greenville, SC 29606	1962	Thomas Barton Jr.	S	10,000	132
Grossmont, El Cajon, CA 92020	1961	Erv. F. Metzgar	S	16,181	630
Guilford Tech. Inst., Jamestown, NC 27282	1958	Woodrow Sugg	C	*3,300*	*240*
Gulf Coast Comm., Panama City, FL 32401	1957	Lawrence Tyree	S	3,000	200
Hagerstown Junior, Hagerstown, MD 21740	1946	Atlee Kepler	C	1,972	100
Halifax Co. Tech. Inst., Weldon, NC 27890	1967	Phillip W. Taylor	S,C	*840*	*90*
Harcum Junior, Bryn Mawr, PA 19010	1915	Michael A. Duzy	P	750	61
Harrisburg Area Comm., Harrisburg, PA 17110	1964	S. James Manilla	Di	4,400	157
Hartford Community, Bel Air, MD 21014	1957	A.C. O'Connell	S	2,630	83
Hartford Col. for Wm. (W), Hartford, CT 06105	1939	Joan Davis	P	231	35
Hartford State Tech., Hartford, CT 06106	1946	L. Barrell	S	1,419	84
Hartnell, Salinas, CA 93901	1920	Gibb R. Madsen	S	7,309	279
Haskell Indian Junior, Lawrence, KS 66044	1884	Wallace Galluzzi	F	1,086	81
Hawkeye Inst. of Tech., Waterloo, IA 50704	1966	John Hawse	S	21,642	442
Haywood Tech. Inst., Clyde, NC 28721	1965	J. H. Nanney	S	1,600	160
Hazard Community, Hazard, KY 41701	1968	J. Marvin Jolly, Dir.	S	292	24
Henderson Community, Henderson, KY 42420	1960	Marshall Arnold, Dir.	S	803	50
Henderson County, Athens, TX 75751	1946	T. M. Harvey	C	*1,786*	*95*
Henry Ford Comm., Dearborn, MI 48128	1938	Stuart M. Bundy	Mu	14,856	609
Herkimer Co. Comm., Herkimer, NY 13350	1966	Robert McLaughlin	S	1,666	57
Hesston, Hesston, KS 67062	1909	Laban Peachey	D	650	75
Hibbing Comm., Hibbing, MN 55746	1916	Jennis Bapst	S	575	47
Highland Comm., Freeport, IL 61032	1961	Howard Sims	S	1,814	101
Highland Comm., Highland, KS 66035	1858	Jack D. Nutt	S	996	33
Highline Comm., Midway, WA 98031	1961	Shirley Gordon	S	7,095	356
Hilbert, Hamburg, NY 14075	1957	Sr. E. Paczesny	P	690	44
Hill Junior, Hillsboro, TX 76645	1962	Oran Bailey	S	*700*	*51*
Hillsborough Comm., Tampa, FL 33622	1968	F. Scaglione	C	*11,045*	*261*
Hinds Junior, Raymond, MS 39154	1917	Robert Mayo	C,S	*8,516*	*337*
Hiwassee, Madisonville, TN 37354	1849	Horace N. Barker	D	650	33
Hocking Technical, Nelsonville, OH 45764	1968	John J. Light	S	2,020	130
Holding Tech. Inst., Raleigh, NC 27603	1963	R. LeMay Jr.	S	1,362	83
Holmes Junior, Goodman, MS 39079	1925	Frank Branch	S	1,338	68
Holy Cross Junior, Notre Dame, IN 46556	1966	Bro. John Driscoll	D	272	23
Holyoke Community, Holyoke, MA 01040	1946	David Bartley	S	4,996	285
Honolulu Comm., Honolulu, HI 96817	1920	C. Yoshioka	S	*6,544*	*492*
Hopkinsville Comm, Hopkinsville, KY 42240	1965	Thomas Riley	S	1,345	65
Horry-Georgetown Tech., Conway, SC 29526	1965	W.F. Anderson	S	*3,300*	*65*
Hostos Community, Bronx, NY 10451	1968	Candido De Leon	C	2,871	202
Housatonic Comm., Bridgeport, CT 06608	1966	V. Darnowski	S	2,724	107
Houston Comm. Coll., Houston, TX 77007	1971	J.B. Whiteley	S	*26,000*	*1,375*
Howard Community, Columbia, MD 21044	1970	Alfred Smith Jr.	C	1,450	69
Howard, Big Spring, TX 79720	1945	Charles Hays	S,C	1,600	78
Hudson Valley Comm., Troy, NY 12180	1953	J. Fitzgibbons	S	7,012	250
Humphreys, Stockton, CA 95207	1896	John Humphreys	P	299	21
Hutchinson Comm. Jr., Hutchinson, KS 67501	1928	A.H. Elland	S	2,416	174
Illinois Central, E. Peoria, IL 61635	1967	Leon Perley	S	23,000	700
Illinois Eastern Comm., Olney, IL 62450	1968	James Spencer, Chan.	C	*5,262*	*88*
Illinois Valley Comm., Oglesby, IL 61348	1924	Alfred Wisgoski	S	3,100	143
Imperial Valley, Imperial, CA 92251	1922	Terrell Spencer	S	4,565	213
Independence Comm. Jr., Independence, KS 67301	1925	Neil Edds	C	937	73
Indian Hills Comm., Ottumwa, IA 52501	1966	Lyle A. Hellyer	C	1,095	93
Indian Hills Comm., Centerville, IA 52544	1930	Lyle Hellyer	S	1,228	96
Indian River Comm., Ft. Pierce, FL 33450	1959	Herman Heise	S	4,300	87
Indian Valley, Novato, CA 94947	1971	Ernest H. Berg	C	3,064	145
Indiana Vocational Tech., Indianapolis, IN 46206	1963	Glenn W. Sample	S	*12,042*	*919*
Inver Hills Comm., Inver Grove Hts., MN 55075	1970	Curtis Johnson	S	3,000	160
Iowa Central Comm., Ft. Dodge, IA 50501	1966	Edwin Barbour	S	*2,520*	*141*
Iowa Lakes Comm., Estherville, IA 51334	1967	Richard Blacker, Supt.	S,C	*1,372*	*86*
Isothermal Comm., Spindale, NC 28160	1966	Fred J. Eason	S	*1,046*	45
Itasca Comm., Grand Rapids, MN 55744	1922	Bruce M. Bauer	S	513	37
Itawamba Junior, Fulton, MS 38843	1948	W. O. Benjamin	S	*2,172*	*106*
Jackson Comm., Jackson, MI 49201	1928	Harold Sheffer	S	9,041	325
Jackson State Comm., Jackson, TN 38301	1965	W. L. Nelms	S	2,001	100
Jamestown Community, Jamestown, NY 14701	1950	C. W. Ingler, Act.	S	3,346	109
Jeff Davis State Jr., Brewton, AL 36426	1965	W. P. Patterson	S	900	45
Jefferson Community, Louisville, KY 40201	1968	Ronald Horvath, Dir.	S	*6,086*	*300*
Jefferson Comm., Hillsboro, MO 63050	1963	B. R. Henry	Di	5,200	206
Jefferson Community, Watertown, NY 13601	1961	James McVean	C	1,520	47

Name, address	Year	Governing official and affiliation		Students	Teachers
Jefferson State Jr., Birmingham, AL 35215	1965	George Layton	S	8,118	200
John A. Logan, Carterville, IL 62918	1967	Robert Tarvin	S	4,183	75
John C. Calhoun St. Comm., Decatur, AL 35601	1965	J.R. Chasteen	S	5,000	220
John Tyler Comm., Chester, VA 23831	1967	James Walpole	S	909	83
Johnson County Comm., Overland Park, KS 66210	1968	John E. Cleek	C	5,013	229
Joliet Junior, Joliet, IL 60436	1901	H.D. McAninch	S	9,000	565
Jones County Junior, Ellisville, MS 39437	1911	Terrell Tisdale	S	3,156	141
Kalamazoo Valley Comm., Kalamazoo, MI 49009	1966	Dale B. Lake	C	6,314	199
Kankakee Comm., Kankakee, IL 60901	1966	L.H. Horton Jr.	S	3,526	99
Kan. City Kan. Comm. Jr., Kansas City, KS 66112	1923	A. L. Davies	C,S	6,123	240
Kapiolani Comm., Honolulu, HI 96814	1965	J. S. Tsunoda, Prov.	S	4,500	95
Kaskaskia, Centralia, IL 62801	1965	Paul Blowers	S	1,600	54
Katharine Gibbs School, New York, NY 10017	1917	Miss Edith Foster	P	1,000	25
Kauai Community, Lihue, HI 96766	1965	Edward White, Provost	S	1,256	75
Kellogg Community, Battle Creek, MI 49016	1956	Richard F. Whitmore	S	6,635	232
Kendall, Evanston,IL 60204	1934	Andrew Cothran	D	400	25
Kennesaw Junior, Marietta, GA 30061	1963	Horace W.Sturgis	S	3,211	94
Kettering Coll. of Med. Arts, Kettering, OH 45429	1967	Winton Beaven, Dean	D	412	40
Keystone Junior, La Plume, PA 18440	1868	John B. Hibbard	P	850	52
Kilgore, Kilgore, TX 75662	1935	Randolph C. Watson	S	3,696	130
Kingsborough Comm., Brooklyn, NY 11235	1963	Leon M. Goldstein	C	8,772	357
Kirtland Comm., Roscommon, MI 48653	1966	Robert A. Stenger	S	1,100	75
Kirkwood Comm., Cedar Rapids, IA 52406	1966	Selby Ballantyne (Supt.)	S	4,128	266
Kishwaukee, Malta, IL 60150	1968	W. Lamar Fly	S	3,028	203
Labette Comm. Jr., Parsons, KS 67357	1923	James J. Altendorf	C,S	736	52
Lackawanna Jr., Scranton, PA 18503	1894	S. J. Budash	P	1,798	201
LaGuardia Comm., Long Island City, NY 11101	1968	Joseph Shenker	Mu	6,120	315
Lake City Comm., Lake City, FL 32055	1947	Herbert E. Phillips	S	2,996	139
Lake County, Coll. of, Grayslake, IL 60030	1968	Richard Erzen	S	8,401	405
Lake Land, Hattoon, IL 61938	1966	Robert D. Webb	Di	3,980	347
Lakeland, Mentor, OH 44060	1966	Wayne Rodehorst	C	6,342	280
Lake Michigan, Benton Harbor, MI 49022	1946	James Lehman	S	3,104	207
Lake Region Jr., Devils Lake, ND 58301	1941	Merril Berg	S	1,132	57
Lake Sumter Comm., Leesburg, FL 32748	1962	Paul P. Williams	Di	2,135	115
Lakeshore Tech Inst., Cleveland, WI 53015	1912	Frederick Nierode	Mu	3,958	115
Lakewood Comm., White Bear L., MN 55110	1967	N. Christenson, Act	S	2,474	93
Lamar Community, Lamar, CO 81052	1937	Carl Westbrook	S	501	43
Lane Community, Eugene, OR 97405	1965	Eldon G. Schafer	C	13,685	361
Lansing Community, Lansing, MI 48914	1957	Philip Gannon	S	15,901	816
Laramie County Comm., Cheyenne, WY 82001	1968	Harlan L. Heglar	S,C	3,205	205
Laredo Junior, Laredo, TX 78040	1946	D. Arechiga	Mu	3,206	135
Lasell Junior (W), Newton, MA 02166	1851	Arthur Griffin	P	631	76
Lassen Comm., Susanville, CA 96130	1925	Robert Theiler	Di	3,100	215
Latter-Day Saints Bus., Salt Lake City, UT 84111	1886	R. F. Kirkham	P	800	25
Lee, Baytown, TX 77520	1934	Jim Sturgeon	Di	5,009	169
Lees-McRae, Banner Elk, NC 28604	1900	H. C. Evans Jr.	D	750	45
Lehigh County Comm., Schnecksville, PA 18078	1966	John G. Berrier	C	2,452	102
Leicester Jr., Leicester, MA 01524	1784	L. Van Burkirk	P	209	26
Lenoir Comm., Kinston, NC 28501	1960	Jesse L. McDaniel	S	1,972	111
Lewis and Clark Comm., Godfrey, IL 62035	1971	Wilbur R. L. Trimpe	S	4,153	184
Lexington Technical Inst., Lexington, KY 40506	1965	William Price	S	1,600	85
Lima Technical, Lima, OH 45804	1971	James S. Biddle	S	1,050	47
Lincoln Land Comm., Springfield, IL 62708	1967	Robert L. Poorman	S,C	5,972	255
Lincoln, Lincoln, IL 62656	1865	Dale Brummet	D	487	48
Lincoln Trail, Robinson, IL 62454	1969	Joseph Piland	S	2,000	103
Linn Benton Comm., Albany, OR 97321	1967	Raymond J. Needham	S	6,333	552
Long Beach City, Long Beach, CA 90808	1927	Frank Pearce	Mu	31,065	1,187
Longview Community, Lee's Summit, MO 64063	1969	William D. Hatley	Di	5,138	229
Lorain County Comm., Elyria, OH 44035	1964	Omar Olson	C,S	5,298	239
Los Angeles City, Los Angeles, CA 90029	1929	J. L. Heinselman, Act	C,S	19,727	650
Los Angeles Harbor, Wilmington, CA 90744	1949	Eugene A. Pimentel	S	12,258	425
Los Angeles Pierce, Woodland Hills, CA 91364	1947	Edward Liston	S	23,500	750
Los Angeles Southwest, Los Angeles, CA 90047	1967	Franklin Turner	S	6,250	225
L.A. Trade Technical, Los Angeles, CA 90015	1949	Fred Brinkman	Mu	18,528	945
Los Angeles Valley, Van Nuys, CA 91401	1949	Alice Thurston	S	21,523	640
Louisburg, Louisburg, NC 27549	1787	J. Allen Norris Jr.	D	576	39
Louisiana State Univ.					
at Alexandria, Alexandria, LA 71301	1960	R. Cleveland	S	1,550	100
at Eunice, Eunice, LA 70535	1967	Anthony Mumphrey, Chan.	S	904	50
Lower Columbia, Longview, WA 98632	1934	David Story	S	2,685	84
Lurleen B. Wallace St. Jr., Andalusia, AL 36420	1969	W. H. McWhorter	S	1,072	50
Luzerne County Comm., Nanticoke, PA 18634	1966	Byron Rinehimer	C	1,800	120
Macomb County Comm., Warren, MI 48093	1963	R. F. Roelofs	S	24,000	865
MacCormac Junior, Chicago, IL 60604	1904	Gordon Borchardt	P	400	21
Macon Junior, Macon, GA 31206	1968	William Wright	S	2,506	82
Madison Area Technical, Madison, WI 53703	1912	Norman P. Mitby, Dir.	Di	7,383	220
Madison Business, Madison, WI 53703	1856	Stuart E. Sears	D	296	17
Maine, Univ of					
at Augusta, ME 04330	1965	K. W. Allen, Act	S	3,160	232
Mainland, Coll. of the, Texas City, TX 77590	1967	Fred Taylor	Di	2,080	239
Malcolm X, Chicago, IL 60612	1911	Samuel Huffman	Mu	6,830	215
Manatee Junior, Bradenton, FL 33507	1957	W. Wetzler	S	4,161	198
Manchester Comm., Manchester, CT 06040	1963	Ronald Denison	S	5,000	110
Manhattan Comm., New York, NY 10019	1963	Edgar Draper	Mu	10,909	457
Manor Jr., Jenkintown, PA 19046	1947	Sr. Mirian Claire	P	300	37
Maple Woods Comm., Kansas City, MO 64156	1969	John M. Gazda	Mu	1,972	39
Maria, Albany, NY 12208	1958	Sr. L. Fitzgerald	D	488	48
Maricopa Tech. Comm., Phoenix, AZ 85004	1968	N. Bruemmer, Dean	C	5,196	366
Marin, Coll. of, Kentfield, CA 94904	1926	I. P. Diamond	S	7,390	225
Marion Institute, Marion, AL 36756	1842	Maj. Gen. Barfield	P	370	35
Marshalltown Comm., Marshalltown, IA 50158	1927	Paul Kegel	S	1,034	65
Martin, Pulaski, TN 38478	1870	Bill Starnes	D	300	24
Martin Tech. Inst., Williamston NC 27892	1968	Joseph B. Carter	S,C	1,250	65
Mass. Bay Comm., Watertown, MA 02181	1961	John McKenzie	S	4,096	248
Massasoit Comm., Brockton, MA 02402	1966	John Musselman	S	5,900	300

Name, address	Year	Governing official and affiliation		Students	Teachers
Mater Dei, Ogdensburg, NY 13669	1960	Sr. Patricia Burke	D	313	55
Mattatuck Comm., Waterbury CT 06708	1967	Charles B. Kinney	S	*3,088*	*120*
Maui Community, Kahului, HI 96732	1965	Sanae Moikeha, Provost	S	1,615	82
McCook, McCook, NE 69001	1926	Elmer Kuntz	C	646	46
McDowell Tech. Inst., Marion, NC 28752	1964	John Price	S	514	36
McHenry County, Crystal Lake, IL 60014	1967	James Davis	Di	4,100	130
McLennan Comm., Waco, TX 76708	1965	Wilbur Ball	S	3,535	176
Medgar Evers, Brooklyn, NY 11225	1968	Richard D. Trent	Mu	3,500	180
Meramec Community, St. Louis, MO 63122	1962	Glynn E. Clark	Di	7,070	378
Merced Merced, CA 95340	1962	Lowell Barker	S	*7,706*	*300*
Mercer County Comm., Trenton, NJ 08690	1966	John P. Hanley	D	*7,274*	*158*
Mercy, Dobbs Ferry, NY 10522	1950	Donald Grunewald	P	4,300	275
Meridian Jr., Meridian, MS 39301	1937	William F. Scaggs	Mu	2,857	221
Merritt, Oakland, CA 94619	1964	Donald Godbold	Di	10,500	350
Mesa (A), Gd. Junction, CO 81501	1925	Theodore E. Albers	S	3,573	125
Mesabi Comm., Virginia, MN 55792	1918	Gilbert Staupe	S	850	37
Metropolitan Comm., Minneapolis, MN 55403	1967	Rafael Cortada	S	4,000	160
Metropolitan Comm., Kansas City, MO 64111	1916	Ervin Harlacher, Chan.	S	*15,329*	*277*
Miami-Dade Comm., Miami, FL 33176	1960	Peter Masiko Jr.	S	*40,296*	*886*
Miami-Jacobs Jr. Coll. of Bus., Dayton, OH 45401	1860	Charles P. Harbottle	P	1,003	59
Michael J. Owens Tech., Perrysburg, OH 43551	1967	Jacob H. See	S	2,991	63
Michigan Christian Jr., Rochester, MI 48063	1959	Don E. Gardner	D,P	347	19
Midland, Midland, TX 79701	1972	Al G. Langford	S	1,600	101
Mid Michigan Comm., Harrison, MI 48625	1965	Eugene W. Gillaspy	S	2,000	83
Mid-Plains Comm., No. Platte, NE 69101	1967	Kenneth L. Aten	C	1,748	64
Mid-State Tech. Inst., Wis. Rapids, WI 54494	1967	Earl F. Jaeger	Di,S	*6,000*	250
Middle Georgia, Cochran, GA 31014	1884	Louis C. Alderman Jr.	S	1,695	109
Middlesex Comm., Middletown, CT 06457	1966	Philip Wheaton	S	2,166	45
Middlesex County, Edison, NJ 08817	1966	Robert Harris	C	14,600	257
Midlands Tech., Columbia, SC 29250	1974	Robert Grigsby Jr.	S,C	*8,500*	*250*
Miles Comm., Miles City, MT 59301	1939	Vernon R. Kailey	Di	850	49
Milwaukee Area Tech., Milwaukee, WI 53203	1911	William Ramsey	Di	*77,600*	*2,336*
Mineral Area, Flat River, MO 63601	1922	Richard Caster	Di	917	53
Mira Costa, Oceanside, CA 92054	1934	John MacDonald	S	5,400	190
Mississippi Delta Jr., Moorhead, MS 38761	1926	J.T. Hall	S,C	1,441	9
Mississippi Gulf Coast Jr., Perkinston, MS 39573	1925	J.J. Hayden Jr.	S	*8,672*	25
Mitchell, New London, CT 06320	1938	Robert C. Weller	P	732	4
Mitchell Comm., Statesville, NC 28677	1852	Charles Poindexter	S	1,581	6
Moberly Area Junior, Moberly, MO 65270	1927	Andrew Komar Jr.	S	765	6
Modesto Junior, Modesto, CA 95350	1921	Kenneth Griffin	S	*17,058*	*56*
Mohawk Valley Comm., Utica, NY 13501	1946	G.H. Robertson	S	6,449	14
Mohegan Comm., Norwich, CT 06360	1970	Robert N. Rue	S	1,841	9
Monroe Community, Rochester, NY 14623	1961	Moses Kock	S	9,739	29
Monroe County Comm., Monroe, MI 48161	1964	Ronald Campbell	C,S	2,100	5
Montcalm Comm., Sidney, MI 48885	1965	C.J. Bedore	C	1,050	2
Monterey Peninsula, Monterey, CA 93940	1947	George J. Faul	S	*8,000*	*42*
Montgomery Comm., Rockville, MD 20850	1946	William Strasser	C	*13,984*	*69*
Montgomery Co. Comm., Blue Bell, PA 19422	1964	Leroy Brendlinger	C	5,813	31
Montreat-Anderson, Montreat, NC 28757	1916	Silas M. Vaughn	P	449	2
Moorpark, Moorpark, CA 93021	1967	W. Ray Hearon	C	9,397	45
Morame Valley Comm., Palos Hills, IL 60465	1968	James Koeller	S	10,516	37
Morgan Comm., Ft. Morgan, CO 807'1	1970	Robert W. Johnson	S	1,000	1
Morris, County Coll. of, Dover, NJ 07801	1965	Sherman H. Masten	C	8,717	35
Morristown, Morristown, TN 37814	1881	Raymond White	D	233	1
Morse Sch. of Bus. Inc., Hartford, CT 06103	1860	Michael Taub	P	350	3
Motlow State Comm., Tullahoma, TN 37388	1969	Harry D. Wagner	S	1,140	4
Mt. Aloysius Junior, Cresson, PA 16630	1939	J.P. Gallagher	P	489	3
Mt. Hood Comm., Gresham, OR 97030	1965	R.S. Nicholson	Di	*10,000*	*60*
Mt. Ida Junior, Newton Centre, MA 02159	1899	B.E. Carlson	P	710	4
Mt. Olive, Mt. Olive, NC 28365	1951	Williams B. Raper	D,P	377	3
Mt. San Antonio, Walnut, CA 91789	1946	Eldon Pearce	Di	23,815	75
Mt. San Jacinto, San Jacinto, CA 92383	1963	Milo P. Johnson	S	2,500	4
Mt. St. Clare, Clinton, IA 52732	1928	Sr. Eileen Smith	D	230	3
Mt. Wachusett Comm., Gardner, MA 01440	1963	Arthur F. Haley	S	*2,969*	*17*
Mountain View, Dallas, TX 75211	1970	David Sims	S	*6,500*	*25*
Murray State, Tishomingo, OK 73460	1908	Clyde Kindell	S	1,357	4
Muskegon Business, Muskegon, MI 49442	1885	Robert Jewell	P	750	5
Muskegon Comm., Muskegon, MI 49442	1926	J.G. Thompson	C	4,762	20
Napa, Napa, CA 94558	1962	George Clark	C	8,000	38
Nash Tech. Inst., Rocky Mount, NC 27801	1968	Jack D. Ballard	S	813	3
Nassau Community, Garden City, NY 11530	1959	George Chambers	C	17,456	44
Navarro, Corsicana, TX 75110	1946	Kenneth Walker	S	2,018	11
Nebraska Western, Scottsbluff, NE 69361	1928	Alex Easton	Mu	761	5
Neosho County Comm. Jr., Chanute, KS 66720	1936	J.C. Sanders	C	622	4
New Hampshire Tech. Inst., Concord, NH 03301	1965	D. Larrabee Sr.	S	2,200	1
New Hampshire Voc. Tech., Manchester, NH 03102	1945	R.E. Mandeville, Dir.	S	700	
New Mexico Junior, Hobbs, NM 88240	1965	Jodie Smith	S	1,154	
New Mexico Military Inst. (M), Roswell, NM 88201	1891	Robert Kemble	S	940	
New River Community, Dublin, VA 24084	1966	H.R. Edwards	S	2,325	1
N.Y. City Community, Brooklyn, NY 11201	1946	Herbert M. Sussman	Mu	18,367	1,4
New York, State Univ. of					
Agric. & Tech. Inst., Alfred, NY 14802	1908	David H. Huntington	S	4,256	2
" " " Canton, NY 13617	1906	Earl MacArthur	S	2,581	1
" " " Cobleskill, NY 12043	1911	Walton A. Brown	S	2,608	1
" " " Delhi, NY 13753	1913	Francis Hennessy	S	2,714	1
" " " Farmingdale, NY 11735	1912	Mauro Zulli, Act.	S	13,269	3
" " " Morrisville, NY 13408	1908	Royson N. Whipple	S	2,903	1
Niagara County Comm., Sanborn, NY 14132	1962	Jack C. Watson	S	4,050	1
Normandale Comm., Bloomington, MN 55431	1968	Dale Lorenz	S	4,500	1
North Central Michigan, Petoskey, MI 49770	1958	A.D. Shankland	S,C	1,569	
North Central Tech. Inst., Wausau, WI 54401	1912	L.B. Hoyt, Dir.	C	*2,502*	4
North County Comm., Saranac Lake, NY 12983	1967	P.J. Cayan	S	1,135	
N. Dak. St. Sch. of Science, Wahpeton, ND 58075	1903	Clair I. Blikre	S	3,176	
North Florida Junior, Madison, FL 32340	1958	Stephen McMahon	S	1,034	
North Greenville, Tigerville, SC 29688	1892	George Silver	D,P	632	
North Harris County, Houston, TX 77037	1972	W.W. Thorne	S	1,500	
North Hennepin Comm., Brooklyn Pk., MN 55445	1966	John F. Helling	S	3,372	1
North Idaho, Coeur d'Alene, ID 83814	1933	Barry Schuler	Di	2.337	1

Name, address	Year	Governing official and affiliation		Students	Teachers
North Iowa Area Comm., Mason City, IA 50401	1918	David Randall Pierce	S	2,014	90
North Shore Community, Beverly, MA 01915	1965	George Traicoff	S	6,392	358
Northampton Co. Area Comm., Bethlehem, PA 18017	1966	Richard Richardson Jr.	C	3,900	209
Northeast Alabama State Jr., Rainsville, AL 35986	1965	E.R. Knox	S	2,978	148
Northeast Miss. Junior, Booneville, MS 38829	1948	Harold T. White	S	1,556	95
Northeast Neb. Tech. Comm., Norfolk, NE 68701	1973	Robert P. Cox	S	1,166	91
Northeast Wisc. Tech. Inst., Green Bay, WI 54303	1916	K.W. Hanbenschild, Dir.	Di	*3,050*	*650*
Northeastern Junior, Sterling, CO 80751	1941	Ervin S. French	C	1,977	110
Northeastern Okla. A&M, Miami, OK 74354	1919	D.D. Creech	S	2,561	129
Northern Essex Comm., Haverhill, MA 01830	1960	J.R. Dimitry	S	5,857	347
Northern Oklahoma, Tonkawa, OK 74653	1901	Edwin Vineyard	S	2,023	67
Northern Virginia Comm., Annandale, VA 22003	1965	Richard Ernst	S	*26,557*	*1,477*
Northland Comm., Thief R. Falls, MN 56701	1965	Alex Easton	S	650	27
Northwest Community, Powell, WY 82435	1946	Sinclair Orendorff	S	1,409	88
Northwest Miss. Junior, Senotobia, MS 38668	1927	Henry B. Koon	S	*2,743*	*130*
Northwestern Conn. Comm., Winsted, CT 06098	1965	Regina Duffy	S	1,901	58
Northwestern Michigan, Traverse City, MI 49684	1951	William J. Yankee	S	*2,605*	*97*
Norwalk Community, Norwalk, CT 06854	1961	E.I.L. Baker	S	2,887	92
Norwalk State Tech., Norwalk, CT 06854	1961	P.A. Marino	S	2,000	65
Oakland Comm., Bloomfield Hills, MI 48013	1965	Joseph Hill	C	*18,000*	245
Oakton Comm., Morton Grove, IL 60053	1969	William Koehnline	S	11,694	751
Ocean County, Toms River, NJ 08753	1964	Andrews S. Moreland	C	4,634	230
Odessa, Odessa, TX 79760	1946	Philip Speegle	S	3,650	125
Ohlone, Fremont, CA 94538	1966	W.B. Richter	Di	7,860	350
Okaloosa-Walton Jr., Niceville, FL 32578	1963	J.E. McCracken	S	2,866	155
Oklahoma Sch. of Business, Acctg., Law & Finance, Tulsa, OK 74103	1919	H. Everett Pope Jr.	P	489	28
Olney Central, Olney, IL 62450	1963	Paul Thompson	S	1,576	63
Olympic, Bremerton, WA 98310	1946	Henry Milander	S	7,500	350
Onondaga Comm., Syracuse, NY 13215	1961	Roger J. Manges	S	6,211	189
Orange Coast, Costa Mesa, CA 92626	1948	Robert Moore	C	*25,529*	*898*
Orange County Comm., Middletown, NY 10940	1950	Robert T. Novak	S	5,163	136
Oscar Rose Junior, Midwest City, OK 73110	1970	Joe Leone	S	8,091	144
Otero Junior, La Junta, CO 81050	1941	William L. McDivitt	S	921	47
Ottumwa Heights, Ottumwa, IA 52501	1925	Jerry Solloway	P	310	27
Paducah Comm., Paducah, KY 42001	1932	Donald J. Clemens, Dir.	S	1,320	76
Palm Beach Junior, Lake Worth, FL 33461	1933	Harold C. Manor	S	10,868	244
Palomar Comm., San Marcos, CA 92069	1946	Frederick R. Huber	S	15,515	600
Palo Verde, Blythe, CA 92225	1947	George W. Pennell	S	750	20
Panola Junior, Carthage, TX 75633	1947	Arthur Johnson	S	850	39
Paris Junior, Paris, TX 75460	1924	Louis B. Williams	Di	2,430	107
Parkersburg Comm., Parkersburg, WV 26101	1971	Jerry Jones	S	3,672	88
Parkland, Champaign, IL 61820	1966	William M. Staerkel	Di,S	6,967	318
Pasadena City, Pasadena, CA 91106	1924	E. H. Floyd	S	20,700	712
Pasco-Hernando Comm., Dade City, FL 33525	1972	Milton O. Jones	S	1,700	174
Passaic Co. Comm., Paterson, NJ 07505	1968	Gustavo Mellander	C	1,236	94
Patrick Henry State Jr., Monroeville, AL 36460	1965	Cecil Murphy	S	1,013	57
Paul D. Camp Comm., Franklin, VA 23851	1968	Perry Adams	S	1,253	54
Paul Smith's Coll. of Arts & Sci., Paul Smiths, NY 12970	1937	T.N. Stainback	P	1,246	81
Peace (W), Raleigh, NC 27604	1857	S. David Frazier	D	531	34
Pearl River Junior, Poplarville, MS 39470	1921	M.R. White	S	2,500	106
Peirce Junior, Philadelphia, PA 19102	1865	Thomas M. Peirce III	P	1,407	71
Peninsula, Port Angeles, WA 98362	1961	Paul G. Cornaby	S	2,463	120
Penn Valley Comm., Kansas City, MO 64112	1915	Thomas M. Law	S	6,219	237
Pensacola Jr., Pensacola, FL 32504	1948	T. Felton Harrison	S	*14,635*	*470*
Peralta Comm., Oakland, CA 94610	1964	Thos. Fryer Jr.	Di	*34,559*	*1,108*
Philadelphia, Comm., Coll. of, Philadelphia, PA 19107	1964	Allen T. Bonnell	Mu	11,000	617
Phillips County Comm., Helena, AR 72342	1965	John Easley	S	4,724	100
Phoenix, Phoenix, AZ 85013	1920	William Berry	C	15,000	650
Piedmont Tech., Greenwood, SC 29646	1966	Lex Walters	S	*3,300*	*300*
Piedmont Tech. Inst., Roxboro, NC 27573	1970	Edward W. Cox	S	*877*	*59*
Piedmont Virginia Comm., Charlottesville, VA 22901	1972	James Walpole	S	2,028	107
Pima Comm., Tucson, AZ 85709	1970	Irwin Spector	S	*19,996*	*998*
Pine Manor Junior (W), Chestnut Hill, MA 02167	1911	Rosemary Ashby	P	377	47
Pitt Tech. Inst., Greenville, NC 27834	1961	W.E. Fulford Jr.	S,C	1,626	90
Polk Comm., Winter Haven, FL 33880	1964	Frederick T. Lenfestey	S	5,428	185
Porterville, Porterville, CA 93257	1927	O.H. Shires	S	*3,686*	*143*
Portland Comm., Portland, OR 97219	1961	Amo De Bernardis	C	*29,832*	*2,200*
Post Junior, Waterbury, CT 06708	1890	Harold Harlow	P	1,320	63
Potomac State, Keyser, WV 26726	1901	A.G. Slonaker, Dean	S	1,005	57
Prairie State, Chicago Hts., IL 60411	1957	Richard Creal	Di	5,800	301
Pratt Community, Pratt, KS 67124	1938	Norman Myers	C	1,638	74
Prince George's Comm., Largo, MD 20870	1958	Robert Bickford	C	11,830	569
Puerto Rico Jr., Rio Piedras, PR 00928	1949	Federico J. Modesto	P	*5,691*	*218*
Queensborough Comm., Bayside, NY 11364	1958	Kurt R. Schmeller	C	*13,000*	*367*
Quincy Jr., Quincy, MA 02169	1958	Edward Pierce	Mu	*4,201*	*150*
Quinebaug Valley Comm., Danielson, CT 06239	1971	Robert E. Miller	S	614	38
Quinsigamond Comm., Worcester, MA 01606	1963	Paul Preus	S	5,107	309
Randolph Tech. Inst., Asheboro, NC 27203	1962	M.H. Branson	S	8,159	130
Ranger Junior, Ranger, TX 76470	1926	Jack Elsom	S	*850*	*50*
Reading Area Comm., Reading, PA 19603	1971	Lewis Ogle	S	887	74
Redwoods, Coll. of the, Eureka, CA 95501	1964	Donald Weichert	S	8,767	500
Reedley, Reedley, CA 93654	1926	R.A. Cattant	S	3,401	157
Reinhardt, Waleska, CA 30183	1893	Allen O. Jernigan	D	797	44
Rend Lake, Ina, IL 62846	1967	W.T. Martin Jr.	S	2,475	146
Rhode Island Jr., Warwick, RI 02886	1964	William F. Flanagan	S	*8,500*	*474*
Richard J. Daley, Chicago, IL 60652	1960	Virginia Keehan	C	7,766	185
Richland, Dallas, TX 75243	1972	E. Biggerstaff Jr.	C	11,200	428
Richland Comm., Decatur, IL 62523	1971	Murray Deutsch	Di	3,422	88
Richmond Tech. Inst., Hamlet, NC 28345	1964	Joseph Nanney	S	1,122	78
Ricks, Rexburg, ID 83440	1888	Henry B. Eyring	D	5,740	234
Rio Hondo, Comm., Whittier, CA 90608	1960	L.A. Grandy	C,S	13,656	555
Riverside City, Riverside, CA 92506	1916	Foster Davidoff	S	14,064	469
Robeson Tech. Inst., Lumberton, NC 28358	1965	R. Craig Allen	S	1,225	54

Name, address	Year	Governing official and affiliation		Stu-dents	Teach- er
Rochester Comm., Rochester, MN 55901	1915	Charles Hill	S	2,950	14
Rockland Comm., Suffern, NY 10901	1957	Seymour Eskow	S	7,994	15
Rock Valley, Rockford, IL 61101	1964	Karl Jacobs	S	7,485	12
Rockingham Comm., Wentworth, NC 27375	1963	Gerald B. James	S	1,600	6
Rogue Comm., Grants Pass, OR 97526	1971	Henry O. Pete	C,S	1,490	5
Sacramento City, Sacramento, CA 95822	1916	Sam Kipp	S	49,024	56
Saddleback, Mission Viejo, CA 92675	1967	R.A. Lombardi	S	13,773	68
St. Clair County Comm., Pt. Huron, MI 48060	1923	Richard L. Norris	C	3,316	17
St. John's, Winfield KS 67156	1893	Rev. M.J. Stelmachowicz	D	285	3
St. John's River Junior, Palatka, FL 32077	1958	Robert L. McLendon	S	1,388	4
St. Louis Community, St. Louis, MO 63110	1962	Richard Greenfield	C	*30,000*	*1,50*
at Florissant Valley, St. Louis, MO 63135	1962	Raymond Smith	Di	9,337	47
at Forest Park, St. Louis, MO 63139	1963	Ralph H. Lee	Di	9,613	50
at Meramec, St. Louis, MO 63122	1962	Glynn Clark	Di	9,039	43
St. Mary's Jr., Minneapolis, MN 55454	1964	Sr. Anne Joachim Moore	D,P	821	10
St. Mary's (W), Raleigh, NC 27611	1842	John T. Rice	D	510	4
St. Petersburg Junior, St. Petersburg, FL 33733	1927	Michael Bennett	S	*13,018*	29
Salem Community, Penns Grove, NJ 08069	1972	Herbert C. Donaghay	C	923	5
Sampson Tech Inst., Clinton, NC 28328	1965	Bruce Howell	S	745	8
San Antonio, San Antonio, TX 78284	1925	Jerome Weynand	S	21,402	1,19
San Bernardino Valley, San Bernardino, CA 92403	1926	Arthur Jensen	S	15,585	49
San Diego City, San Diego, CA 92101	1914	Allen Repashy	S	5,250	14
San Diego, Mesa, San Diego, CA 92111	1963	Ellis Benson	C	9,214	34
San Francisco, City Coll. of, San Francisco, CA 94112	1935	K.S. Washington	C,Mu	24,498	98
San Jacinto, Pasadena, TX 77505	1961	Thomas M. Spencer	S	11,448	48
San Joaquin Delta Comm., Stockton, CA 95207	1935	Dale Parnell	S,Di	20,710	54
San Jose City, San Jose, CA 95128	1921	Theodore Murguia	C	14,713	75
San Luis Obispo Co. Comm., San Luis Obispo, CA 93406	1965	Merlin Eisenbise	C	5,504	20
San Mateo, Coll. of, San Mateo, CA 94402	1922	David H. Mertes	C	17,000	60
Sandhills Comm., Southern Pines, NC 28387	1963	Raymond A. Stone	S	1,592	8
Santa Ana, Santa Ana, CA 92706	1915	John E. Johnson	S	23,288	78
Santa Barbara City, Santa Barbara, CA 93109	1908	Glenn Gooder	Di,S	8,613	24
Santa Fe Community, Gainesville, FL 32602	1965	Alan Robertson	S	6,056	32
Santa Moinca, Santa Monica, CA 90405	1929	Richard Moore	Mu	*20,144*	73
Santa Rosa Junior, Santa Rosa, CA 95401	1918	Roy Mikalson	C	15,861	56
Sauk Valley, Dixon, IL 61021	1965	George Cole	S	3,261	15
Schenectady Co. Comm., Schenectady, NY 12305	1967	Robert Larsson	S	3,042	4
Schoolcraft, Livonia, MI 48151	1964	C. Nelson Grote	S	6,816	91
Schreiner, Kerrville, TX 78028	1923	Sam Junkin	D,P	477	3
Scottsdale Comm., Scottsdale, AZ 85251	1970	Ray Cattan, Exec. Dean	C	5,100	20
S.D. Bishop State Jr., Mobile, AL 36603	1965	Sanford Bishop	S	1,650	7
Seattle Central Comm., Seattle, WA 98122	1966	Robert Terry	S	8,129	33
Selma Univ., Selma, AL 36701	1878	M.C. Cleveland Jr.	D,P	652	3
Seminole Comm., Sanford, FL 32771	1965	E.S. Weldon	S	5,809	30
Sequoias, Coll. of the, Visalia, CA 93277	1925	Ivan Crookshanks	Di	6,592	33
Seward County Comm., Liberal, KS 67901	1967	Wade Kirk	C,S	1,059	4
Shasta, Redding, CA 96001	1950	Dale Miller	C	12,800	48
Shelby State Comm., Memphis TN 38104	1972	Jess Parrish	S	*4,326*	23
Sheldon Jackson, Sitka, AK 99835	1878	H. H. Holloway	D	297	2
Sheridan, Sheridan, WY 82801	1948	Gordon Ward	S	720	5
Shoreline Comm., Seattle, WA 98133	1964	Richard S. White	S	8,000	32
Sierra, Rocklin, CA 95677	1914	G. C. Angove	C	8,328	35
Sinclair Comm., Dayton, OH 45402	1887	David Ponitz	C	12,634	55
Siakiyous, Coll. of the Weed, CA 96094	1957	Eugene Schumacher	Di	3,500	16
Skagit Valley, Mt. Vernon, WA 98273	1926	Norwood Cole	S	*15,662*	*37*
Skyline, San Bruno, CA 94066	1969	J. C. Petersen	C	7,842	28
Snead State Jr., Boaz, AL 35957	1935	Virgil McCain Jr.	S	1,635	13
Snow, Ephraim, UT 84627	1888	J. M. Higbee	S	1,103	4
Solano Comm., Suisun City, CA 94585	1945	William Wilson	S	9,285	33
Somerset Comm., Somerset, KY 42501	1965	Roscoe Kelley	S	800	4
Somerset County, Somerville, NJ 08876	1968	Joseph Fink	C,S	3,700	15
South Florida Jr., Avon Park, FL 33825	1965	William Stallard	S	1,400	3
South Georgia, Douglas, GA 31533	1906	Denton Coker	S	1,263	7
South Oklahoma City, Oklahoma City, OK 73159	1972	Dale L. Gibson	S	5,458	14
South Plains, Levelland, TX 79336	1957	Marvin L. Baker	Di	*2,538*	*17*
Southeast Comm., Fairbury, NE 68352	1941	Daniel Gerber, Dir.	C,S	*852*	3
Southeastern Comm., Burlington, IA 52655	1966	C. W. Callison, Supt.	S	*1,782*	*13*
Southeastern Comm., Keokuk, IA 52632	1953	C. W. Callison	C	414	3
Southeastern Comm., Whiteville, NC 28472	1965	W. R. McCarter	S	1,666	10
Southeastern Illinois, Harrisburg, IL 62946	1960	Harry Abell	S	1,850	6
Southern Baptist, Walnut Ridge, AR 72476	1941	D. J. Nicholas	P	694	4
Southern Idaho, Coll. of, Twin Falls, ID 83301	1965	James L. Taylor	S	3,190	8
Southern Ohio, Cincinnati, OH 45202	1927	H. W. Nagel	P	*1,600*	6
Southern Seminary Jr., Buena Vista, VA 24416	1867	J. T. Kanipe Jr.	P	293	2
Southern Union State Jr., Wadley AL 36276	1922	Ray Jones	S	1,710	5
Southwest Mississippi Jr., Summit, MS 39666	1929	Horace Holmes	S	1,105	5
Southwest Texas Junior, Uvalde, TX 78801	1946	Wayne Matthews	S	2,129	14
Southwest Virginia Comm., Richlands, VA 24641	1968	Charles King	S	2,003	11
Southwestern, Chula Vista, CA 92010	1961	C. S. DeVore	S	11,761	40
Southwestern, Okla. City, OK 73127	1946	Hugh Morgan	D	1,500	7
Southwestern Comm., Creston, IA 50801	1966	John A. Smith	S	550	4
Southwestern Michigan, Dowagiac, MI 49047	1966	R. M. Owens	C	2,000	10
Southwestern Oregon Comm., Coos Bay, OR 97420	1961	Jack E. Brookins	S	3,429	20
Spartanburg Methodist, Spartanburg, SC 29301	1911	James S. Barrett	D	1,008	6
Spartanburg Tech., Spartanburg, SC 29303	1963	Joe D. Gault	S	3,097	21
Spokane Comm., Spokane, WA 99202	1963	Lloyd Stannard	S	*3,600*	*34*
Spokane Falls Comm., Spokane, WA 99204	1970	Gerald Saling	S	3,904	13
Spoon River, Canton, IL 61520	1959	Hearl C. Bishop	S	*1,476*	4
Springfield Tech. Comm., Springfield, MA 01105	1967	Robert Geitz	S	5,794	20
Springfield Coll. in Illinois, Springfield, IL 62702	1929	Sr. Mary Ann Luth	D	541	4
State Fair Comm., Sedalia, MO 65301	1966	Fred E. Davis	Di	1,545	9
State Tech Inst., Memphis, TN 38134	1967	Charles Whitehead	S	4,527	26
Staten Island Comm., Staten Island, NY 10301	1955	William M. Birenbaum	Mu	12,325	54
Sue Bennett, London, KY 40741	1897	Earl F. Hays	D	287	2
Suffolk County Comm., Selden, NY 11784	1959	Albert M. Ammerman	S	17,928	36
Sullivan County Comm., Loch Sheldrake, NY 12759	1962	Richard F. Grego	S	1,794	6
Sumter Area Tech, Sumter, SC 29150	1962	James M. Morris Jr.	S	2,187	12

Name, address	Year	Governing official and affiliation		Students	Teachers
Suomi, Hancock, MI 49930	1896	Ralph J. Jalkanen	P,D	371	30
Surry Community, Dobson, NC 27017	1964	Swanson Richards	S	1,358	73
Tacoma Comm., Tacoma, WA 98465	1965	L. P. Stevens	S	*5,753*	*250*
Taft, Taft, CA 93268	1922	Wendell Reeder	Di	1,056	46
Tallahassee Comm., Tallahassee, FL 32304	1965	Fred W. Turner	S	2,900	114
Tarrant County Junior, Ft. Worth, TX 76102	1965	Joe B. Rushing	S,C	*19,103*	*386*
Tech. Inst. of Alamance, Burlington, NC 27215	1958	William Taylor	S	9,783	2,207
Temple Junior, Temple, TX 76501	1926	Marvin Felder	S	1,914	101
Texarkana, Texarkana, TX 75501	1927	Carl M. Nelson	S	2,946	128
Texas Southmost, Brownsville, TX 78520	1926	A. L. Oliveira	Mu	4,600	125
Thomas Nelson Comm., Hampton, VA 23670	1968	Gerald O. Cannon	S	4,662	194
Thornton Comm., So. Holland, IL 60473	1927	Nathan A. Ivey	Di	11,077	331
Three Rivers Comm., Poplar Bluff, MO 63901	1966	J.L. Bottenfield	S	1,411	51
Tidewater Comm., Portsmouth, VA 23703	1968	George Pass	S	*11,250*	*216*
Tomkins-Courtland Comm., Groton, NY 13053	1967	Hushang Bahar	S	2,742	57
Treasure Valley Comm., Ontario, OR 97914	1962	Emery Skinner	Di	1,441	52
Tri-County Tech. Inst., Murphy, NC 28906	1964	Vincent W. Crisp	S	540	32
Tri-County Tech. Pendleton, SC 29670	1962	Don Garrison	S	*2,304*	*362*
Trident Tech, Charleston, SC 29411	1964	Richard Waldroup Jr.	S	*7,356*	*241*
Trinidad State Junior, Trinidad, CO 81082	1925	Thomas Sullivan	S	1,400	143
Triton, River Grove, IL 60171	1964	Brent Knight	Mu	23,675	1,183
Truett McConnell, Cleveland, GA 30528	1946	Ronald Weitman	D	730	48
Tulsa Junior (A), Tulsa, OK 74119	1968	Alfred M. Phillips	S	5,002	225
Tunxis Community, Farmington, CT 06032	1970	Benjamin G. Davis	S	2,557	134
Tyler Junior, Tyler, TX 75701	1926	Harry E. Jenkins	S	5,908	303
Ulster County Comm., Stone Ridge, NY 12484	1961	Robert T. Brown	S	2,685	83
Umpqua Comm., Roseburg, OR 97470	1964	I.S. Hakanson	Di	3,600	145
Union, Cranford, NJ 07016	1933	Saul Orkin	C	5,000	250
Union County Tech. Inst., Scotch Plains, NJ 07076	1960	Harvey Charles	C	4,188	300
Utica Junior, Utica, MS 39175	1903	J.Louis Stokes	S	1,412	69
Valencia Comm. (A), Orlando, FL 32802	1967	James F. Gollattscheck	S	5,432	222
Ventura, Ventura, CA 93003	1927	Richard A. Glenn	S	13,739	481
Vermillion Comm., Ely, MN 55731	1922	C.Donald Miller	S	421	20
Vermont, Comm. Coll. of, Montpelier, VT 05602	1970	Peter Smith	S	2,000	455
Vermont Technical, Randolph Center, VT 05061	1957	Ned Herrin Jr.	S	600	46
Victor Valley, Victorville, CA 92392	1961	B.W. Wadsworth	Di	3,200	156
Victoria, Victoria, TX 77901	1925	Roland E. Bing	C	2,258	85
Villa Julie, Stevenson, MD 21153	1952	Sister Mary Stephen	P	593	65
Vincennes Univ., Vincennes, IN 47591	1801	Isaac K. Beckes	S	*4,518*	*250*
Virginia Highlands Comm., Abingdon, VA 24210	1969	Emma Schulken	S	1,333	66
Virginia Western Comm., Roanoke, VA 24015	1966	Harold H. Hopper	S	*4,002*	*166*
Wabash Valley, Mt. Carmel, IL 62863	1960	John Gwaltney	S	2,800	94
Wake Tech. Inst., Raleigh, NC 27603	1963	Robert LeMay Jr.	S	1,422	98
Waldorf, Forest City, IA 50436	1903	Paul Mork	D	492	33
Walker, Jasper, AL 35501	1938	David J. Rowland	P	674	40
Walla Walla Comm, Walla Walla, WA 99362	1967	Eldon Dietrich	S	3,602	95
Walters State Comm., Morristown, TN 37814	1970	Jack E. Campbell	S	2,200	150
Washington State Comm., Spokane, WA 92207	1963	Max M. Synder	S	*18,978*	*326*
Washtenaw Comm., Ann Arbor, MI 48106	1965	Gunder Myran	C	6,800	359
Waterbury State Tech, Waterbury, CT 06708	1964	Kenneth Fogg	S	1,234	76
Waubonsee Comm.,Sugar Grove, IL 60554	1966	F.D. Etheredge	C	5,334	245
Waukesha Co. Tech. Inst., Pewaukee, WI 53072	1923	R. Anderson	S,Di	*30,000*	*812*
Wayne Community, Goldsboro, NC 27530	1957	Clyde Erwin Jr.	S	2,000	120
Wayne County Comm., Detroit, MI 48201	1967	Reginald Wilson	S	*16,177*	*735*
Weatherford Jr., Weatherford, TX 76086	1869	E.W. Mince	C	*1,453*	*74*
Wenatchee Valley, Wenatchee, WA 98801	1939	William Steward	S	3,689	168
Wentworth Institue, Boston, MA 02115	1904	Edward I. Kirkpatrick	P	1,900	191
Wesley, Dover, DE 19901	1873	R.J.Cooke	D	1,053	56
West Hills, Coalinga, CA 93210	1932	Robert A. Annand	S	2,000	150
West Los Angeles, Culver City, CA 90230	1968	H. Zeitlin	Di	7,483	244
West Shore Comm., Scottville, MI 49454	1967	John Eaton	S	2,745	86
West Valley, Saratoga, CA 95070	1963	James P. Hardy	S	*23,000*	*750*
West Virginia North, Comm., Wheeling, WV 26003	1972	Daniel B. Crowder	S	*5,103*	*153*
Westark Comm., Ft. Smith, AR 72901	1528	James Kraby	S	3,339	129
Westbrook (W), Portland, ME 04103	1831	James F. Dickinson	P	796	70
Westchester Comm., Valhalla, NY 10595	1946	Joseph N. Hankin	S	7,856	176
Western Iowa Tech., Sioux City, IA 51102	1966	Robert Kiser	S	1,324	82
Western Okla. State, Altus, OK 73521	1926	W. C. Burris	S	1,612	43
Western Piedmount Comm., Morganton, NC 28655	1964	Gordon Blank	S	1,560	55
Western Texas, Snyder, TX 79549	1969	Robert Clinton	C,S	*1,182*	*80*
Western Wisc. Tech. Inst., LaCrosse, WI 54601	1912	Charles Richardson, Dir.	C,Mu	3,584	175
Wharton County Junior, Wharton, TX 77488	1946	Theodore Nicksick Jr.	S	2,011	96
Wilkes Community, Wilkesboro, NC 28697	1964	Howard Thompson	S	2,225	101
William Rainey Harper, Palatine, IL 60067	1965	Robert E. Lahti	S	19,575	933
Williamsport Area Comm., Williamsport, PA 17701	1965	William Fedderson	S,C	*3,065*	*210*
Willmar Comm., Willmar, MN 56201	1962	John Torgelson	S	765	47
Wingate, Wingate, NC 28174	1896	Thomas Corts	D	1,323	72
Wisconsin Center, Univ. of					
at Barron, Rice Lake, WI 54868	1966	John Meggers, Dean	S	466	28
at Manitowoc, Manitowoc, WI 54220	1933	C.Natunewicz, Dean	S	309	12
at Marathon, Wausau, WI 54401	1947	W.R. Peters, Dean	S	840	35
at Marshfield/Wood, Marshfield, WI 54449	1964	Norbert Koopman, Dean	S	500	22
at Richland, Richland Ctr., WI 53581	1967	Marjorie Wallace, Dean	S	326	9
at Rock County, Janesville, WI 53545	1966	T.Walterman, Dean	S	622	27
at Sheboygan, Sheboygan, WI 53081	1933	K.M. Bailey, Dean	S	631	24
at Washington, West Bend, WI 53095	1968	R.O. Thompson, Dean	S	590	22
Worcester Junior, Worcester, MA 01608	1905	Ross Dixon	P	1,250	75
Worthington Comm., Worthington, MN 56187	1936	Leon Flancher	S	762	47
Yakima Valley (A), Yakima, WA 98902	1929	William Russell	S	4,505	140
Yavapai, Prescott, AZ 86301	1966	Joseph Russo	C,S	*4,751*	*195*
York, York, NE 68467	1890	Dale Larsen	D,P	345	23
York Technical, Rock Hill, SC 29730	1964	Baxter Hood	S,C	2,500	65
Young Harris, Young Harris, GA 30582	1886	Ray Farley	D,P	534	28
Yuba Comm., Marysville, CA 95901	1927	Daniel G. Walker	C,S	7,047	223

Canadian Colleges and Universities

Source: Statistics Canada

All coeducational unless followed by (M) for men only. Governing official is president unless otherwise desig nated. Year is that of founding. The word college is part of the name listed unless another designation is given Each institution listed has an enrollment of at least 200 students of college grade. Number of teachers is th total number of individuals on teaching staff. Enrollment and faculty in italics include all branches and cam puses.

Name	Location	Year	Governing official	Students[1]	Teacher
Acadia Univ.	Wolfville, N.S.	1838	J.M.R. Beveridge	2,589	17
Alberta, Univ. of	Edmonton, Calgary, Alta.	1906	Harry E. Gunning	19,156	1,48
Bishop's Univ.	Lennoxville, Que.	1843	Christopher Nicholl	721	7
Brandon Univ.	Brandon, Man.	1899	H. J. Perkins	959	10
British Columbia, Univ. of	Vancouver, B.C.	1908	Douglas T. Kenny	19,296	1,78
Brock Univ.	St. Catharines, Ont.	1964	A. J. Earp	2,291	21
Calgary, Univ. of	Calgary, Alta.	1945	W. A. Cochrane	9,569	85
Carleton, Univ.	Ottawa, Ont.	1942	Michael Oliver	8,444	60
Concordia Univ.	Montreal, Que.	1974	John O'Brien, Rector	9,407	60
Dalhousie Univ.	Halifax, N.S.	1818	Henry D. Hicks	7,042	69
Guelph, Univ. of	Guelph, Ont.	1964	Donald F. Forster	9,381	70
King's Coll., Univ. of	Halifax, N.S.	1789	J. Graham Morgan	—	1
Lakehead Univ.	Thunder Bay, Ont.	1965	A. D. Booth	2,388	23
Laurentian Univ.	Sudbury, Ont.	1960	Edward J. Monahan	*2,693*	26
Laval Universite	Quebec, Que.	1852	Jean-Guy Paquet	*13,074*	1,26
Lethbridge, Univ. of	Lethbridge, Alta.	1967	W. E. Beckel	1,154	13
Manitoba, Univ. of	Winnipeg, Man.	1877	Ralph Campbell	14,025	1,21
McGill Univ.	Montreal, Que.	1821	Robert E. Bell, Prin.	16,106	1,25
McMaster Univ.	Hamilton, Ont.	1887	A.N. Bourns	9,546	77
Mem. Univ. of Newfoundland	St. John's, Nfld.	1925	M. O.Morgan	5,987	74
Moncton, Univ. of	Moncton, N.B.	1963	M. Jean Cadieux, Rector	3,080	26
Montreal, Universite de	Montreal, Que.	1920	M. Paul Lacoste, Rector	12,231	1,26
Mount Allison Univ.	Sackville, N.B.	1840	W. S. H. Crawford	1,405	12
Mount St. Vincent Univ.	Halifax, N.S.	1925	Sr. Mary Albertus	1,179	8
New Brunswick, Univ. of	Fredericton, N.B.	1785	John M. Anderson	5,204	51
Notre Dame Univ.	Nelson, B.C.	1963	Roland F. Grant	353	4
Nova Scotia Coll. of Arts & Design	Halifax, N.S.	1887	Garry Neill Kennedy	401	3
Nova Scotia Technical	Halifax, N.S.	1907	Clair Callghan	468	6
Ontario Inst. for Studies in Education	Toronto, Ont.	1965	Clifford C. Pitt	—	13
Ottawa, Univ. of	Ottawa, Ont.	1848	Rev. Roger Guindon	*10,584*	90
Prince Edward Island, Univ. of	Charlottetown, P.E.I.	1834	Ronald J. Baker	1,343	11
Quebec, Universite de	Montreal, Que.	1969	M. Robert Despres	*10,080*	1,08
Queen's Univ.	Kingston, Ont.	1841	R. L. Watts	9,792	86
Regina, Univ. of	Regina, Sask.	1974	Lloyd I. Barber	*3,638*	38
Royal Military Coll. of Can. (M)	Kingston, Ont.	1876	J. R. Dacey	653	11
Ryerson Polytechnical	Toronto, Ont.	1948	Walter G. Pitman	8,672	62
St. Francis Xavier Univ.	Antigonish, N.S.	1853	Rev. M. MacDonell	2,133	15
St. Mary's Univ.	Halifax, N.S.	1802	D. Owen Carrigan	2,331	16
St. Paul Univ.	Ottawa, Ont.	1866	Rev. Marcel Patry	330	3
Saskatchewan, Univ. of	Saskatoon, Sask.	1907	R. W. Begg	*9,566*	88
Sherbrooke, Univ. of	Sherbrooke, Que.	1954	Yves Martin	*5,071*	57
Simon Fraser Univ.	Burnaby, B.C.	1965	Pauline Jewett	5,305	37
Toronto, Univ. of	Toronto, Ont.	1827	John Robert Evans	*32,011*	2,22
Trent Univ.	Peterborough, Ont.	1963	T. E. W. Nind	2,004	17
Victoria, Univ. of	Victoria, B.C.	1963	Howard E. Petch	5,215	43
Waterloo, Univ. of	Waterloo, Ont.	1959	B. C. Matthews	13,425	74
Western Ontario, Univ. of	London, Ont.	1878	D. Carlton Williams	*17,201*	1,26
Wilfrid Laurier Univ.	Waterloo, Ont.	1973	F. C. Peters	2,658	17
Windsor, Univ. of	Windsor, Ont.	1857	John Francis Leddy	6,001	49
Winnipeg, Univ. of	Winnipeg, Man.	1871	Henry E. Duckworth	2,516	18
York Univ.	Downsview, Ont.	1959	H. Ian Macdonald	11,561	1,05

(1) Total full-time enrollment including undergraduates and graduates for the academic year 1974-75.

Typical Tuition Fees at Canadian Colleges and Universities

Source: Statistics Canada

Undergraduate tuition fees at universities and colleges with enrollment of 5,000 full day-time students or more. Fee i for 1976-77 academic year.

Institution	Tuition
Alberta, University of	$500-750
British Columbia, University of	428-644
Calgary, University of	250-500 (1)
Carleton University, Ottawa	580-640
Concordia University	450-540
Dalhousie University	720-835
Guelph, University of	288-393 (1)
Laval Universite	225-300 (3)
Manitoba, University of	450-725
Montreal, University de	270-370 (2)
Memorial University of Newfoundland	250 (1)
McGill University	570-719
McMaster University	580-645
New Brunswick, University of	$74
Ottawa, University of	565-73
Queen's University of Kingston	600-72
Quebec, Universite de	250 (2
Ryerson Polytechnical Institute	42
Saskatchewan, University of	520-75
Simon Fraser University	214 (3
Toronto, University of	655-91
Victoria, University of	42
Waterloo, University of	625-78
Western Ontario, University of	580-77
Windsor, University of	580-64
York University	653-66

(1) Per semester. (2) Per session. (3) Per trimester.

Typical Tuition Fees at U.S. Colleges and Universities

Source: World Almanac Questionnaire

The College Entrance Examination Board has estimated that the average cost in a private college in the fall of 1977 was $4,905, a 4% increase over the previous year. The cost at a public college averaged $3,005.

Fees for tuition charged per year by colleges and universities for courses, use of libraries, laboratories and other facilities, are a major part of student expenses. Tuition varies considerably, depending on the type of institution, its control and location. The lowest tuition fees are those of state-controlled or other public-controlled institutions for residents of their state, city, etc. Students from other states or areas have to pay more. In the following list, such state or other public institutions are shown with two figures. The lower one is the tuition fee for residents, the higher one the tuition fee for students from other states or areas.

(Tuition does not include room, board, or other expenses.)

School	Tuition
Adams State	$283-886
Adelphi Univ.	2,940
Akron, Univ. of	840-1,800
Alabama State	480-796
Alabama, Univ. of	645-1,275
Albertus Magnus	2,750
Albion	3,427
Albright	3,050
Albuquerque, Univ. of	1,620
Allegheny	3,350
Alma	4,456
Amherst	4,300
Anderson	2,400
Appalachian State Univ.	282-1,930
Arizona, Univ. of	450-1,640
Arkansas, Univ. of	380-760
Auburn	549-1,074
Austin Peay State Univ.	441-1,337
Avila	1,859
Baldwin-Wallace	3,060
Ball State	720-1,440
Baylor	1,500
Bethany	3,420
Bethune-Cookman	1,822
Black Hills State	651
Bloomfield	2,350
Blue Mountain	1,225
Bob Jones	1,207
Boca Raton, College of	2,496
Boston	3,890
Bowdoin	4,180
Bowie State	750-1,450
Bowling Green State	876-2,076
Brandeis Univ.	4,315
Bridgeport, Univ. of	3,360
Brown	4,300
Bryan	3,290
Bryn Mawr	4,725
Bucknell Univ.	4,015
Cabrini	2,195
Cal. Lutheran	2,700
Canisius	2,530
Carleton	5,277
Carnegie-Mellon	3,400
Case Western Reserve Univ.	3,770
Central Conn. State	711-1,701
Central Missouri State	345-945
Central New England	1,800
Centre College of Ky.	3,125
Chatham	3,450
Cheyney State	990-1,810
Chicago, Univ. of	4,050
Clemson Univ.	830-1,780
Cleveland State Univ.	795-1,590
Dakota State	682-1,306
Dallas, Univ. of	1,130
Dana	2,270
Dayton, Univ. of	2,350
Delaware, Univ. of	945-2,075
Denver, Univ. of	3,375
Doane Univ.	2,430
Drake Univ.	2,930
Drexel Univ.	2,974
Duke Univ.	3,530
Duquesne Univ.	2,830
Evansville, Univ. of	2,300
Florida State Univ.	705-1,740
Fordham Univ.	2,830
Furman Univ.	2,592
Gonzaga Univ.	2,590
Hampton Institute	2,170
Holy Cross	3,675
Idaho, Univ. of	434-1,634
Indiana Univ.	722-1,640
Indiana State Univ.	744-1,457
Iona	2,380
Jacksonville Univ.	2,180
John Carroll Univ.	2,400
Johns Hopkins Univ.	3,750
Kansas, Univ. of	690-1,690
Kansas State Univ.	680-1,670
Kentucky, Univ. of	530-1,260
Lewis and Clark	3,391
Louisville, Univ. of	340-990
Marquette Univ.	2,900
Memphis State Univ.	448-936
Minnesota, Univ. of	1,038-2,062
Mississippi, Univ. of	703-1,478
Montana, Univ. of	585-1,368
Montana State Univ.	510-1,482
Muskingum	2,970
New Hampshire, Univ. of	1,000-2,990
New Mexico, Univ. of	520-1,515
Notre Dame, Univ. of	3,230
Oberlin	3,675
Ohio Univ.	930-2,205
Oklahoma State Univ.	600-1,500
Old Dominion Univ.	620-1,150
Oral Roberts Univ.	1,600
Pennsylvania State Univ.	2,379-4,956
Pittsburgh, Univ. of	1,234-2,444
Portland, Univ. of	2,400
Princeton Univ.	4,400
Purdue Univ.	750-1,700
Radcliffe	4,450
Rhode Island, Univ. of	954-2,099
Richmond, Univ. of	2,820
Rutgers Univ.	951-1,711
St. Bonaventure Univ.	2,750
St. Louis Univ.	2,800
St. Olaf	3,050
St. Paul Bible	1,140
Selma Univ.	1,083
Southern Methodist Univ.	3,138
Southern Miss., Univ. of	660-750
Temple Univ.	1,400-2,500
Tennessee, Univ. of	480-1,380
Tulane Univ.	3,240
Utah, Univ. of	545-1,420
Vanderbilt Univ.	3,400
Vassar	3,875
Vermont, Univ. of	1,348-3,378
Virginia State	762-1,222
Wake Forest Univ.	2,700
Walla Walla	3,100
Washburn Univ. of Topeka	850-1,330
Wellesley	3,850
Wyoming, Univ. of	434-1,400
Yale Univ.	4,750

Federal Funds for Education, 1977

Source: Office of Education, U. S. Health, Education and Welfare Department

Includes grants, loans, and directly administered services. Estimated. (thousands of dollars)

Type of support, level, and program	
Elementary-secondary education	**$4,680,049**
School asst.—federally affected areas	438,463
Educationally deprived/Economic Opportunity Programs	2,773,268
Supporting services	318,219
Teacher Corps	36,138
Vocational education	333,133
Dependents' schools abroad	269,004
Public lands revenue for schools	81,050
Assistance in special areas	107,775
Veterans' education	79,500
Emergency school asst.	203,934
Other	39,565
Higher education	**8,088,497**
Basic research	1,273,000
Research facilities	180,000
Training grants, fellowships and traineeships	813,666
Facilities and equipment	250,973
Other institutional support	395,732
Other student assistance	5,175,126
Vocational-tech. and continuing ed.	**3,837,523**
Vocational-technical education	2,911,000
Veterans' education	783,400
General continuing education	123,588
Training State and local personnel	19,535
Grants, total	**16,606,069**
Loans, total	**454,705**
Student loan program, Nat. Def. Ed. Act	398,075
College facilities loans	56,630
Total grants and loans	**17,060,774**
Other federal funds, total	**6,267,975**
Applied research and development	2,001,000
School lunch and milk programs	2,000,000
Training of federal personnel	1,194,318
U.S. Academies	314,030
Professional training, military	842,911
Civilian education and training in non-federal facilities	37,377
Library services	**243,491**
Grants to public libraries	26,600
National library services	216,891
International education	**106,496**
Educational exchange program	35,620
AID projects	63,972
ACTION (including Peace Corps)	4,976
Other international educ. and training	1,928

(continued)

(Continued)

Other	**722,670**	Other education and training	134,815
Agricultural extension service	219,678	Value of surplus property transferred:	
Educational television facilities	77,170	acquisition cost of personal property	254,990
Education in federal correctional inst.	12,191	Fair value of real property	23,826

Fall Enrollment and Teachers in Full-time Day Schools

Public Elementary and Secondary Day Schools, Fall 1976

Source: Office of Education, U. S. Health, Education, and Welfare Department

	Pupils enrolled[1]		Teachers[2]	H. S. graduates[1]	
	Elementary	Secondary		Male	Female
United States	**30,072,000**	**14,321,000**	**2,208,000**	**1,389,353**	**1,433,670**
Alabama	511,000	239,000	36,760	22,518	24,115
Alaska	65,000	24,000	4,590	2,140	2,080
Arizona	346,000	142,000	23,030	12,892	12,773
Arkansas	314,000	139,000	21,300	13,405	13,431
California	2,948,000	1,429,000	205,460	133,653	139,758
Colorado	379,000	185,000	26,810	17,438	17,525
Connecticut	444,000	204,000	35,750	21,105	21,687
Delaware	81,000	43,000	6,350	3,990	4,245
District of Columbia	93,000	36,000	6,660	2,168	3,199
Florida	1,043,000	493,000	73,000	42,809	43,672
Georgia	741,000	342,000	47,490	28,697	31,106
Hawaii	117,000	56,000	7,880	5,627	5,656
Idaho	134,000	65,000	9,030	6,337	6,294
Illinois	1,514,000	732,000	113,840	69,811	71,505
Indiana	839,000	373,000	52,700	36,824	37,178
Iowa	403,000	205,000	33,170	21,435	21,570
Kansas	289,000	155,000	25,730	15,777	16,681
Kentucky	468,000	216,000	32,030	20,803	21,565
Louisiana	584,000	255,000	41,150	22,582	25,109
Maine	170,000	79,000	12,330	7,288	7,542
Maryland	595,000	275,000	42,470	26,541	28,867
Massachusetts	800,000	385,000	64,240	39,500	39,500
Michigan	1,400,000	651,000	90,050	66,253	69,256
Minnesota	562,000	308,000	44,880	32,918	33,617
Mississippi	350,000	156,000	23,930	12,949	14,294
Missouri	634,000	320,000	49,390	31,098	31,277
Montana	113,000	56,000	9,070	6,145	6,148
Nebraska	205,000	106,000	17,750	11,119	11,130
Nevada	94,000	44,000	5,760	3,735	3,497
New Hampshire	118,000	55,000	8,790	5,318	5,732
New Jersey	982,000	461,000	80,590	47,213	48,787
New Mexico	180,000	91,000	12,910	9,066	9,372
New York	2,248,000	1,121,000	189,550	104,577	106,690
North Carolina	805,000	367,000	52,500	34,103	35,991
North Dakota	81,000	48,000	7,610	5,264	5,426
Ohio	1,508,000	760,000	106,110	77,888	80,291
Oklahoma	404,000	186,000	29,830	19,066	18,743
Oregon	318,000	157,000	23,860	15,354	15,314
Pennsylvania	1,460,000	764,000	116,510	81,666	81,458
Rhode Island	118,000	55,000	9,220	5,302	5,740
South Carolina	434,000	187,000	28,760	18,725	19,587
South Dakota	99,000	52,000	8,100	5,907	5,818
Tennessee	620,000	250,000	39,940	23,591	25,772
Texas	1,961,000	830,000	143,710	79,500	79,987
Utah	209,000	97,000	11,930	9,874	9,794
Vermont	71,000	31,000	6,440	3,207	3,248
Virginia	749,000	347,000	58,460	31,015	34,555
Washington	521,000	256,000	33,770	25,150	25,840
West Virginia	280,000	120,000	19,630	12,263	12,368
Wisconsin	613,000	341,000	51,960	34,865	36,114
Wyoming	57,000	32,000	5,220	2,882	2,766
Outlying areas	**515,000**	**249,000**	**29,246**	**(3)**	**(3)**
American Samoa	8,000	2,000	343	217	231
Canal Zone	8,000	3,000	407	366	363
Guam	21,000	7,000	1,232	578	539
Puerto Rico	459,000	232,000	25,853	11,952	15,119
Virgin Islands	19,000	5,000	1,411	(3)	(3)

(1) Estimated. (2) Full and part-time classroom teachers. (3) Data not available.

National Spelling Bee Champions

The National Spelling Bee, conducted by Scripps-Howard Newspapers and other newspapers since 1939, was instituted by the Louisville (Ky.) Courier-Journal in 1925. Children under 16 years of age sponsored by participating newspapers are eligible to compete for the cash prizes and prize trips.

In the 1977 spelldown, the runner-up misspelled sesquipedelian (which means having many syllables), giving it an "e" in place of the first "i." The winner spelled it correctly and also the final word, cambist, an exchange dealer.

Recent winners are:

1976 — 1. Tim Kneale, 13, Nedrow, N.Y. (Syracuse Herald-Journal-American). 2. Rachel Wachtel, 13, Shreve, Oh. (Akron Beacon Journal). 3. William M. Mulhern, 13, Beattie, Kan. (Topeka Daily Capital).

1977 — 1. John Paola, 14, Pittsburgh (Pittsburgh Press). 2. Joan O'Leary, 13, Yonkers, N.Y. (N.Y. Daily News). 3. Joseph Fumic, 13, Cleveland (Cleveland Press).

Public School Attendance, Teachers, Expenditures

Source: National Center for Education Statistics, U.S. Health, Education and Welfare Department

(salaries cover supervisors, principals, and teachers)

School year	Pop. 5 to 17 yrs.	Pupils: Enrolled	Pupils: Av. daily attend.	Teachers'[1]: Male	Teachers'[1]: Female	Teachers'[1]: Total	Teachers'[1]: Salary[2]	Total expend.
1900	21,404,322	15,503,110	**10,632,772**	126,588	296,474	**423,062**	$325	**$214,964,618**
1910	24,239,948	17,813,852	**12,827,307**	110,481	412,729	**523,210**	485	**426,250,434**
1920	27,728,788	21,578,316	**16,150,035**	95,654	583,648	**679,302**	871	**1,036,151,209**
1930	31,571,322	25,678,015	**21,264,886**	141,771	712,492	**854,263**	1,420	**2,316,790,384**
1940	29,805,259	25,433,542	**22,042,151**	194,725	680,752	**875,477**	1,441	**2,344,048,927**
1950	30,788,000	25,111,427	**22,283,845**	194,968	718,703	**913,671**	3,010	**5,837,643,000**
1960	43,881,000	36,086,771	**32,477,440**	392,700	962,300	**1,355,000**	5,174	**15,613,255,000**
1968 (Fall)	52,288,000	44,961,662	**41,157,000**	617,805	1,324,980	**1,942,785**	8,200	**35,511,170,000**
1970 (Fall)	52,435,000	45,909,088	**42,495,346**	649,250	1,411,865	**2,061,115**	9,570	**44,423,865,000**
1971 (Fall)	52,133,000	46,081,000	**42,544,000**	668,000	1,395,000	**2,063,000**	10,100	**48,513,986,000**
1972 (Fall)	51,637,000	45,744,000	**42,408,000**	702,000	1,400,000	**2,102,000**	10,608	**51,905,025,000**
1974	51,485,000	46,441,189	**41,438,054**	722,868	1,432,580	**2,155,448**	11,185	**56,970,355,000**
1975 (Fall) P	50,364,000	44,838,490	**41,373,473**	748,000	1,455,000	**2,203,000**	13,967	**67,102,569,000**

(1) Prior to 1954 includes other nonsupervisory instructional staff (librarians and guidance and psychological personnel). (2) Average annual salary per member of instructional staff. (P) preliminary.

Cost per Pupil by State

Source: Office of Education, U. S. Health, Education and Welfare Department

Estimated expenditures per pupil in average daily attendance in public elementary and secondary day schools, 1975-76.

State	Expenditure per pupil: Total	Current	Capital outlay	Interest on school debt
United States	**$1,581**	**$1,388**	**$145**	**$48**
labama	1,199	1,090	102	7
laska	2,705	2,096	500	109
rizona	1,742	1,415	283	44
rkansas	1,045	881	135	29
alifornia	1,440	1,320	75	45
olorado	1,769	1,422	290	57
onnecticut	1,741	1,659	33	49
elaware	1,803	1,606	128	69
istrict of Columbia	2,202	1,954	248	. .
lorida	1,765	1,381	353	31
eorgia	1,235	1,114	75	46
awaii	1,704	1,545	153	6
daho	1,491	1,112	323	56
linois	1,650	1,452	155	43
ndiana	1,471	1,160	274	37
wa	1,684	1,455	200	29
ansas	1,589	1,475	91	23
entucky	1,093	986	67	40
ouisiana	1,208	1,082	94	32
laine	1,302	1,197	79	26
laryland	1,828	1,516	266	46
lassachusetts	(1)	(1)	(1)	(1)
lichigan	1,560	1,366	147	47
linnesota	1,831	1,516	248	67
lississippi	1,062	997	56	9
lissouri	1,335	1,186	118	31
lontana	1,643	1,554	67	22
ebraska	1,345	1,302	27	16
evada	1,450	1,261	118	71
New Hampshire	$1,343	$1,175	$134	$34
New Jersey	2,076	1,892	125	59
New Mexico	1,572	1,261	292	19
New York	2,360	2,179	99	82
North Carolina	1,242	1,099	131	12
North Dakota	1,373	1,207	142	24
Ohio	1,413	1,264	119	30
Oklahoma	1,258	1,130	114	14
Oregon	1,722	1,501	188	33
Pennsylvania	1,901	1,660	148	93
Rhode Island	1,721	1,481	102	138
South Carolina	1,177	1,030	119	28
South Dakota	1,270	1,094	161	15
Tennessee	1,183	969	171	43
Texas	1,300	1,094	148	58
Utah	1,384	1,084	270	30
Vermont	1,581	1,398	141	42
Virginia	1,408	1,197	184	27
Washington	1,572	1,443	96	33
West Virginia	1,311	1,071	217	23
Wisconsin	1,797	1,618	133	46
Wyoming	1,688	1,489	162	37
Outlying areas:				
American Samoa	(1)	(1)	(1)	. .
Canal Zone	2,040	1,958	82	. .
Guam	1,258	1,258	. .	. .
Puerto Rico	593	571	22	. .
Virgin Islands	1,441	1,441	. .	. .

(1) Data not available.

Canadian Fall Enrollment, Teachers, Expenditures in Day Schools

Full-time Public Elementary and Secondary Day Schools — 1975-1976

Source: Statistics Canada

	Enrollment(p): Elementary Kdgn-Gr. 8	Enrollment(p): Secondary Gr. 9 and up	Enrollment(p): Total	Teachers(p): Elementary Kdgn.-Gr. 8(e)	Teachers(p): Secondary Gr.9 and up(e)	Teachers(p): Total(p)	School board expenditure per pupil(e): Total	Operating	Capital
anada	**3,745,475**	**1,625,756**	**5,371,231**	**171,142**	**91,387**	**262,529**	**$1,347**	**$1,201**	**$146**
ld.	124,667	33,101	157,768	5,427	2,000	7,427	967	792	175
E.I.	20,236	7,614	27,850	968	476	1,444	1,024	913	111
S.	146,951	55,655	202,606	2,331	3,450	10,781	1,056	966	90
B.	115,142	49,857	164,990	5,069	2,800	7,869	906	906	N/A
ue.	972,581	396,184	1,374,765	46,700(e)	24,000(e)	70,700(e)	1,484	1,334	150
nt.	1,359,476	635,162	1,994,638	59,110(e)	34,900(e)	94,010(e)	1,355	1,197	158
an.	160,346	67,781	228,127	7,270	4,201	11,471	1,287	1,155	132
ask.	154,899	66,074	220,973	7,223	3,531	10,754	1,149	1,059	90
a.	299,818	139,536	439,354	14,060	7,120	21,180	1,393	1,231	162
C.	371,137	171,543	542,680	17,212	8,759	25,971	1,386	1,231	155
k.	3,744	1,231	4,975	207	64	271	2,143	1,853	290
W.T.	10,478	2,018	12,496	565	86	651	1,922	1,816	106

(e) estimate (p) preliminary

Public Libraries in Selected North American Cities

Source: World Almanac Questionnaire

Figure in parenthesis denotes number of branches; asterisk (*) indicates county library jurisdiction; (A) designates library has not provided up-to-date information.

City	No. of volumes	Circulation	Cost of operation
Akron, Oh.* (17)	850,054	2,070,623	$ 3,141,974
Albany, N.Y. (5)	264,741	505,721	1,044,853
Albuquerque, N.M. (8)	325,000	1,350,000	1,680,000
Atlanta, Ga. (26)	939,864	2,376,028	3,300,000
Augusta, Ga.* (5)	335,491	731,130	849,906
Baltimore, Md. (32)	2,293,214	2,528,926	8,309,734
Baton Rouge, La.* (9)	326,405	858,120	1,028,716
Birmingham, Ala. (17) A	977,855	2,141,668	1,976,026
Boston, Mass. (26)	4,070,851	2,515,794	9,238,359
Bridgeport, Conn. (4)	484,672	493,795	1,087,180
Buffalo, N.Y.* (60)	3,010,577	5,792,911	8,800,000
Calgary, Alta. (12)	619,033	2,577,639	3,705,439
Charleston, W.Va.* (5) A	412,812	857,005	826,979
Charlotte, N.C.* (16)	638,367	1,503,647	1,953,530
Chattanooga, Tenn.*(2)	268,200	581,469	1,332,639
Chicago, Ill. (88)	5,997,370	[illegible],792,922	31,894,420
Cincinnati, Oh.* (36)	3,122,523	5,566,728	7,384,140
Cleveland, Oh. (35)	3,123,191	2,847,009	12,090,000
Columbus, Oh.* (22)	1,133,436	2,948,044	3,555,019
Corpus Christi, Tex. (3) A	319,540	677,280	665,708
Dallas, Tex. (12)	1,757,958	3,664,786	6,543,065
Dayton, Oh.* (19)	1,266,126	4,357,941	3,393,813
Denver, Col. (21)	1,617,623	2,964,847	6,963,189
Des Moines, Ia. (5)	402,000	1,203,300	1,314,000
Detroit, Mich. (26) A	2,325,146	2,644,164	10,865,834
El Paso, Tex. (6)	398,975	927,060	1,244,915
Erie, Pa.* (7)A	390,000	1,000,000	1,350,000
Evansville, Ind.* (7)	476,306	1,035,962	1,137,714
Halifax, N.S.* (2)	218,852	692,189	849,799
Hamilton, Ont. (10) A	723,113	1,923,660	3,394,735
Hartford, Conn. (9)	462,036	459,060	1,339,875
Honolulu, Ha.* (18)	750,067	2,426,657	2,214,207
Houston, Tex. (25)	1,803,979	5,168,726	6,840,734
Jacksonville, Fla. (10) A	965,811	1,944,402	1,982,707
Kansas City, Kan. (2)	302,656	379,066	710,185
Kansas City, Mo. (12) A	1,159,653	1,206,562	2,560,000
Kitchener, Ont. (2) A	334,677	853,851	1,271,712
Knoxville, Tenn.* (19)	517,266	1,514,472	1,608,081
Little Rock, Ark.* (5)	419,754	709,601	715,790
Los Angeles, Cal.* (116)	4,074,905	11,344,100	20,252,476
Louisville, Ky. (23) A	1,441,291	1,588,436	2,963,149
Memphis, Tenn.* (20)	1,366,464	2,755,561	4,098,838
Miami, Fla.* (19)	1,051,438	2,645,929	8,987,700
Milwaukee, Wis. (12)	2,422,998	3,044,870	6,276,159
Minneapolis, Minn. (15)	1,417,099	2,590,325	5,470,517
Montreal, Que. (28)	1,197,563	2,033,149	$ 2,738,320
Nashville, Tenn.* (14)	484,128	1,424,312	2,860,785
New Orleans, La. (11)	731,264	1,428,133	2,605,504
New York City	5,511,927	None	17,524,000
N.Y.C. branches (81)	3,357,490	9,972,831	24,082,000
Brooklyn* (57)	3,720,839	7,321,514	14,730,760
Queens* (55) A	3,073,715	6,481,352	16,256,039
Norfolk, Va. (10)	574,917	1,276,347	2,000,863
Okla. City, Okla.* (12) A	600,000	1,540,842	2,031,074
Omaha, Neb. (9)	512,134	1,609,428	1,937,442
Orlando, Fla. (12) A	483,077	177,551	3,222,309
Ottawa, Ont. (7)	575,667	1,992,062	4,300,000
Philadelphia, Pa. (49)	2,950,779	5,605,062	16,634,606
Phoenix, Ariz. (9) A	998,012	2,997,859	3,809,260
Pittsburgh, Pa. (21)	2,049,828	3,301,311	7,152,323
Portland, Me. (4)	253,269	404,400	729,375
Portland, Ore.* (16)	1,092,711	2,691,193	3,890,000
Providence, R. I. (9)	613,146	697,297	1,669,176
Regina, Sask. (4)	282,051	1,086,625	2,300,000
Richmond, Va. (5)	547,818	1,073,021	1,347,545
Roanoke, Va. (5)	308,536	424,706	622,220
Rochester, N.Y. (12)	829,650	1,632,359	3,751,700
Sacramento, Cal. (28)	988,846	4,069,475	6,208,511
St. Louis, Mo. (22)	1,366,828	2,572,250	4,079,849
St. Paul, Minn. (10)	742,911	1,952,492	2,548,711
St. Petersburg, Fla. (3)	368,239	1,228,209	973,986
Salt Lake City, Ut. (4)	906,771	851,811	1,433,997
San Antonio, Tex. (8) A	869,388	2,317,104	2,212,445
San Diego, Cal. (26)	1,421,927	4,274,105	4,624,773
San Francisco, Cal. (27) A	1,581,115	2,945,258	6,458,570
San Jose, Cal. (15)	908,582	3,060,000	3,234,300
Saskatoon, Sask. (2) A	295,218	980,740	1,485,195
Seattle, Wash. (15) A	1,500,000	4,000,000	6,000,000
Syracuse, N.Y.* (8)	494,447	1,003,359	2,297,066
Tallahassee, Fla.* (2) A	180,000	499,990	511,565
Tampa, Fla. (14)	548,000	2,100,000	3,300,000
Toledo, Oh.* (17)	1,126,576	2,863,989	4,081,989
Toronto, Ont. (25)	1,026,016	4,111,046	10,013,540
Tucson, Ariz. (7)	600,000	2,414,260	3,352,844
Tulsa, Okla.* (20)	700,000	1,552,587	2,470,000
Vancouver, B.C. (15)	787,642	4,159,905	6,106,595
Washington, D.C. (26)	1,930,341	1,784,743	8,831,787
Wichita, Kan. (9)	354,328	1,116,043	1,464,276
Winnipeg, Man. (7) A	457,651	1,395,175	1,735,910
Winston-Salem, N.C.* (8)	300,000	1,100,000	1,350,000

Major U. S. Academic Libraries

Source: World Almanac Questionnaire

(A) designates library has not provided up-to-date information.

Institution	No. of volumes	Microfilm units	Enrollment	Staff Prof.	Staff Total	Annual expenditure
Harvard Univ.	9,383,255	1,273,351	16,201	219	874	$15,346,73
Yale Univ. (A)	6,518,848	893,165	9,427	185	602	10,773,00
Univ. of Illinois, Urbana-Champaign	5,368,666	1,323,640	32,969	174	417	2,059,97
Univ. of Michigan, Ann Arbor	4,790,805	1,178,964	35,990	158	593	8,157,96
Univ. of California, Berkeley (A)	4,649,533	896,411	28,499	165	543	8,420,44
Columbia Univ.	4,623,344	1,386,267	15,978	142	539	8,371,74
Cornell Univ.	4,370,000	1,486,120	21,747	120	415	7,000,00
Indiana Univ.	4,220,978	955,974	54,137	168	659	8,234,92
Stanford Univ.	4,175,976	1,231,888	12,350	138	479	9,724,37
Univ. of Texas, Austin	3,878,535	1,359,212	43,998	119	464	7,766,38
Univ. of Chicago	3,866,972	568,761	8,888	67	519	5,500,00
Univ. of California, Los Angeles	3,632,831	1,397,718	30,410	145	441	9,734,26
Ohio State Univ.	3,142,500	1,019,047	58,956	92	294	5,394,76
Univ. of Wisconsin, Madison	3,132,863	1,246,940	36,450	112	446	6,848,49
Univ. of Minnesota (A)	3,046,816	794,035	45,723	118	388	6,150,06
Princeton Univ. (A)	2,812,253	924,526	5,675	100	350	5,934,00
Duke Univ.	2,764,348	226,611	8,789	83	232	4,166,50
Univ. of Pennsylvania	2,713,905	1,027,044	14,739	92	317	4,870,21
Northwestern Univ.	2,536,611	617,150	12,769	98	330	5,213,23
Michigan State Univ.	2,250,000	980,000	43,000	73	298	4,200,00
Univ. of North Carolina, Chapel Hill	2,192,224	1,097,671	20,536	79	246	5,014,47
Univ. of Pittsburgh	2,075,909	840,282	26,471	128	329	4,485,39
Univ. of Iowa	1,965,214	901,502	22,393	72	237	4,000,61
Rutgers Univ.	1,927,021	1,079,289	37,440	99	314	6,097,56
Univ. of Missouri, Columbia	1,836,458	1,659,253	22,000	47	166	2,682,1
Univ. of Florida	1,807,242	861,381	24,413	77	252	3,350,05
Johns Hopkins Univ. (A)	1,717,534	872,250	8,267	65	164	6,976,48
Univ. of Colorado, Boulder	1,656,245	1,457,998	20,000	43	187	3,284,85
Syracuse Univ.	1,585,163	1,588,888	16,241	50	258	2,945,84

105 Years of Public Schools

Source: National Center for Education Statistics, U.S. Health, Education and Welfare Department

Pupils and teachers (thousands)	1869-70	1899-1900	1909-10	1919-20	1929-30	1939-40	1949-50	1959-60	1969-70	1973-74
Total U.S. population	39,818	75,995	90,492	104,512	121,770	130,880	148,665	179,323	203,212	209,843
Population 5-17 years of age	12,055	21,573	24,009	27,556	31,417	30,150	30,168	43,881	52,490	51,485
Percent aged 5-17 years	30.3	28.4	26.5	26.4	25.8	23.0	20.3	24.5	25.8	24.5
Enrollment (thousands)										
Elementary and secondary	6,872	15,503	17,814	21,578	25,678	25,434	25,111	36,087	45,619	45,409
Percent pop. 5-17 enrolled	57.0	71.9	74.2	78.3	81.7	84.4	83.2	82.2	86.9	88.2
Percent in high schools	1.2	3.3	5.1	10.2	17.1	26.0	22.7	23.5	28.5	31.0
High school graduates	....	62	111	231	592	1,143	1,063	1,627	2,589	2,762
Average school term (in days)	132.2	144.3	157.5	161.9	172.7	175.0	177.9	178.0	178.9	178.7
Total instructional staff	....	....	....	678	880	912	962	1,464	2,253	2,425
Teachers, librarians: Men	78	127	110	93	140	195	195	402	691	766
Women	123	296	413	565	703	681	719	985	1,440	1,521
Percent men	38.7	29.9	21.1	14.1	16.6	22.2	21.3	29.0	33.4	33.5
Receipts & expenditures (millions)										
Total receipts	....	$219	$433	$970	$2,088	$2,260	$5,437	$14,746	$40,267	$58,231
Total expenditures	$63	214	426	1,036	2,316	2,344	5,837	15,613[1]	40,683	56,970
Current, elem. and secondary	....	179	356	861	1,843	1,941	4,687	12,329	34,218	50,025
Capital outlay	....	35	69	153	370	257	1,014	2,661	4,659	4,979
Interest on school debt	....	....	....	18	92	130	100	489	1,171	1,514
Other	....	....	....	3	9	13	35	132	636	453
Salaries and pupil cost				(Data in unadjusted dollars)						
Average annual teacher salary[2]	$189	$325	$485	$2,130	$3,869	$3,894	$5,928	$8,213	$10,917	$11,185
Expenditure per capital total pop.	1.59	2.83	4.71	24.24	51.85	48.40	77.34	138.21	247.23	271.49
Current expenditure per pupil ADA[3]	....	16.67	27.85	130.41	236.25	238.05	411.29	595.50	1,007.65	1,207.21

(1) Because of a modification of the scope, "current expenditures for elementary and secondary schools" data for 1959-60 and later years are not entirely comparable with data for prior years. (2) Includes supervisors, principals, teachers and other non-supervisory instructional staff. (3) "ADA" means average daily attendance in elementary and secondary day schools.

Income Disparities: Male and Female, Black and White

Source: U. S. Bureau of the Census

Total money income (Includes full and part-time workers, 25 and over, Mar. 1976)		Years of schooling					
	Total	7 or less	8	9-11	12	13-15	18 or more
White males with income (1,000)	49,632	4,833	4,802	6,817	16,365	7,072	9,743
Percent	100.0	100.0	100.0	100.0	100.0	100.0	100.0
Loss to $2,999	8.5	26.5	16.3	9.8	4.8	5.2	3.7
$3,000 to $5,999	14.6	34.0	28.0	18.7	10.4	9.3	6.4
$6,000 to $7,999	9.5	13.3	14.6	13.2	9.4	7.0	4.4
$8,000 to $9,999	10:1	8.4	11.3	13.1	11.7	8.7	6.7
$10,000 to $14,999	26.2	13.2	20.0	27.9	32.9	30.0	20.9
$15,000 and over	30.9	4.5	10.0	17.2	30.9	39.8	57.9
Mean income	$12,726	$6,096	$7,890	$9,881	$12,648	$14,287	$19,389
Black males with income (1,000)	4,916	1,446	430	950	1,302	470	317
Percent	100.0	100.0	100.0	100.0	100.0	100.0	100.0
Loss to $2,999	20.9	39.3	26.0	18.6	10.3	6.6	3.7
$3,000 to $5,999	24.1	31.2	29.0	26.7	19.7	15.1	8.4
$6,000 to $7,999	12.7	10.9	13.4	17.3	12.3	10.4	11.3
$8,000 to $9,999	11.4	8.0	8.8	9.8	16.7	13.2	10.3
$10,000 to $14,999	21.0	8.0	16.5	21.6	28.7	37.5	28.8
$15,000 and over	9.9	2.6	6.1	5.8	12.4	17.4	37.3
Mean income	$7,665	$4,978	$6,457	$7,170	$9,014	$10,429	$13,399
Mean income, Full-time males	$15,446	$9,225	$10,853	$11,960	$14,251	$16,369	$21,301
White females with income (1,000)	40,454	3,834	4,093	6,128	15,795	5,257	5,348
Percent	100.0	100.0	100.0	100.0	100.0	100.0	100.0
Loss to $2,999	39.2	64.6	57.1	44.8	35.0	30.0	22.8
$3,000 to $5,999	27.4	27.5	30.2	34.0	28.6	25.8	15.8
$6,000 to $7,999	12.0	5.0	7.4	11.9	14.7	13.5	10.8
$8,000 to $9,999	8.4	1.7	2.5	5.1	10.3	11.7	12.6
$10,000 to $14,999	9.8	1.1	2.4	3.6	9.4	15.1	24.9
$15,000 and over	3.3	0.2	0.5	0.8	2.2	4.0	13.0
Mean income	$5,097	$2,836	$3,348	$3,952	$5,121	$5,971	$8,435
Black females with income (1,000)	5,393	1,215	511	1,230	1,574	470	392
Percent	100.0	100.0	100.0	100.0	100.0	100.0	100.0
Loss to $2,999	43.5	78.3	56.0	44.6	26.5	21.7	8.9
$3,000 to $5,999	27.7	19.0	36.2	36.8	30.9	23.1	8.7
$6,000 to $7,999	11.1	1.6	6.3	12.0	17.9	14.1	13.0
$8,000 to $9,999	8.1	0.4	1.4	2.5	14.2	19.0	22.0
$10,000 to $14,999	7.8	0.6	0.4	3.4	9.6	17.9	35.1
$15,000 and over	1.6	—	—	0.6	0.9	4.0	12.3
Mean income	$4,577	$2,292	$3,018	$3,909	$5,474	$6,787	$9,543
Mean income, Full-time females	$8,633	$5,316	$6,042	$6,728	$8,074	$9,344	$11,884

(Percentages may not add to 100.0 due to rounding;—represents zero or rounds to zero.)

Explanation: The tables above demonstrate that while income tends to rise with educational attainment, it rises far less for women and blacks than for white men. For every year of schooling, the black man tends to gain less than his white counterpart. (Black women appear to improve their incomes in comparison with white women, but this is probably because more black women tend to work full-time.)

Educational Attainment by Age, Race, and Sex

Source: U.S. Bureau of the Census (Number of persons in thousands)

1975 Age, race and sex	Total Pop.	Elementary 5 years	Elementary 6 & 7 years	Elementary 8 years	High School 1 year	High School 2 years	High School 3 years	High School 4 years	College 1 year	College 2 years	College 3 years	College 4 years	College 5 or more
White													
Total, 14 years and over	**140,967**	**1,383**	**7,689**	**15,240**	**9,119**	**10,382**	**8,144**	**49,371**	**7,647**	**8,122**	**3,416**	**10,405**	**6,485**
14 and 15 years	7,142	23	1,779	3,452	1,746	90	10	10	—	—	—	—	—
16 and 17 years	7,051	5	83	406	1,698	2,991	1,682	156	4	12	—	—	—
18 and 19 years	6,826	9	59	101	226	495	1,448	3,526	847	63	7	3	—
20 and 21 years	6,635	13	75	126	206	278	302	2,997	965	1,062	500	75	2
22 to 24 years	9,248	18	100	168	266	316	291	3,875	878	958	601	1,480	267
25 years and over	104,065	1,315	5,592	10,987	4,977	6,211	4,411	38,807	4,953	6,028	2,309	8,847	6,216
Male, 14 years and over	**67,655**	**698**	**3,866**	**7,359**	**4,308**	**4,714**	**3,925**	**21,183**	**3,748**	**4,195**	**1,804**	**5,623**	**4,388**
14 and 15 years	3,642	18	988	1,737	825	45	6	3	—	—	—	—	—
16 and 17 years	3,571	3	56	246	900	1,514	792	44	—	5	—	—	—
18 and 19 years	3,354	6	22	59	114	254	816	1,622	406	24	4	—	—
20 and 21 years	3,268	10	30	63	104	114	158	1,451	534	530	231	21	—
22 to 24 years	4,561	6	52	70	118	142	136	1,770	463	495	371	763	166
25 years and over	49,259	655	2,718	5,183	2,248	2,646	2,018	16,293	2,344	3,140	1,198	4,839	4,222
25 to 29 years	7,147	18	111	197	185	217	206	2,635	622	669	324	1,109	768
30 to 34 years	5,956	13	139	223	213	253	237	2,220	366	473	176	758	818
35 to 44 years	9,745	91	357	554	411	512	395	3,687	473	657	255	1,052	1,095
45 to 54 years	10,194	125	476	994	491	645	503	3,642	428	626	206	978	764
55 to 64 years	8,324	147	602	1,330	489	566	429	2,716	261	425	120	481	443
65 to 74 years	5,264	138	642	1,170	352	342	193	1,042	143	227	76	324	242
75 years and over	2,629	122	392	715	107	111	55	350	52	62	41	137	92
Female, 14 years and over	**73,312**	**684**	**3,822**	**7,881**	**4,810**	**5,667**	**4,219**	**28,188**	**3,899**	**3,928**	**1,613**	**4,781**	**2,096**
14 and 15 years	3,500	5	791	1,714	921	45	4	7	—	—	—	—	—
16 and 17 years	3,480	2	27	160	798	1,477	890	112	4	7	—	—	—
18 and 19 years	3,472	3	37	42	112	242	632	1,903	441	39	3	3	—
20 and 21 years	3,367	3	45	63	101	165	144	1,546	431	532	269	53	2
22 to 24 years	4,687	12	48	99	148	174	155	2,105	415	462	230	717	101
25 years and over	54,806	660	2,873	5,804	2,730	3,565	2,393	22,514	2,608	2,888	1,111	4,008	1,994
25 to 29 years	7,238	25	134	155	218	346	280	3,346	523	522	227	1,009	392
30 to 34 years	6,032	37	135	206	251	347	257	2,826	411	345	157	638	362
35 to 44 years	10,073	45	294	475	487	688	483	4,938	547	542	227	766	410
45 to 54 years	10,851	87	449	909	530	752	533	5,209	472	538	199	615	347
55 to 64 years	9,299	133	586	1,385	555	691	469	3,599	323	419	143	449	251
65 to 74 years	6,897	157	757	1,467	447	513	251	1,771	214	330	106	359	164
75 years and over	4,416	176	518	1,206	242	229	120	825	118	193	53	172	67
Negro & other races													
Total, 14 years and over	**18,980**	**522**	**1,743**	**1,838**	**1,578**	**1,874**	**1,536**	**5,095**	**792**	**761**	**337**	**875**	**483**
14 and 15 years	1,292	18	422	527	273	26	5	2	—	—	—	—	—
16 and 17 years	1,249	3	34	149	345	454	233	26	—	2	—	—	—
18 and 19 years	1,130	4	16	34	81	159	286	455	79	9	3	—	—
20 and 21 years	1,053	—	15	37	28	75	115	465	138	99	52	16	—
22 to 24 years	1,424	10	44	53	73	91	107	600	120	97	63	129	31
25 years and over	12,832	488	1,212	1,039	779	1,069	791	3,546	456	555	218	729	452
Male, 14 years and over	**8,693**	**271**	**816**	**832**	**718**	**836**	**663**	**2,137**	**367**	**360**	**165**	**395**	**289**
14 and 15 years	646	15	217	271	118	7	5	2	—	—	—	—	—
16 and 17 years	621	3	23	86	182	218	99	6	—	—	—	—	—
18 and 19 years	524	—	15	19	39	79	149	184	32	3	—	—	—
20 and 21 years	483	—	6	17	13	48	64	195	70	37	21	3	—
22 to 24 years	642	6	28	9	36	32	53	274	51	40	44	47	16
25 years and over	5,777	247	528	429	330	451	293	1,476	214	280	100	345	273
25 to 29 years	900	6	28	33	37	76	40	357	61	87	24	90	57
30 to 34 years	772	8	19	19	29	71	40	296	41	42	30	84	74
35 to 44 years	1,247	20	99	73	85	120	88	363	44	73	20	95	83
45 to 54 years	1,171	61	132	118	87	97	76	260	47	36	14	47	39
55 to 64 years	857	71	122	105	51	69	44	125	15	28	7	16	9
65 to 74 years	561	43	98	58	37	18	5	52	3	6	5	12	8
75 years and over	268	39	30	24	3	1	—	23	1	7	—	1	4
Female, 14 years and over	**10,287**	**251**	**927**	**1,007**	**860**	**1,038**	**873**	**2,958**	**425**	**400**	**172**	**480**	**194**
14 and 15 years	646	3	206	256	155	18	—	—	—	—	—	—	—
16 and 17 years	628	—	11	63	162	236	134	20	—	2	—	—	—
18 and 19 years	606	4	1	15	42	80	137	271	47	5	3	—	—
20 and 21 years	570	—	10	19	15	26	51	271	68	61	31	13	—
22 to 24 years	782	4	16	44	36	60	53	326	69	57	19	82	15
25 years and over	7,055	241	684	609	450	618	497	2,070	242	275	119	384	179
25 to 29 years	1,107	11	34	22	46	88	90	468	64	71	40	115	47
30 to 34 years	939	3	33	35	45	102	70	397	55	48	26	99	23
35 to 44 years	1,542	29	102	121	102	161	141	543	58	61	30	87	56
45 to 54 years	1,369	51	139	142	114	151	112	368	48	54	18	47	25
55 to 64 years	1,006	61	144	137	90	80	48	183	15	23	4	22	22
65 to 74 years	702	60	156	114	39	26	29	71	—	13	1	11	4
75 years and over	390	26	76	38	14	10	8	40	2	6	—	5	2

Education Pays — Black or White

Source: U.S. Bureau of the Census

(— represents zero or rounds to zero)

Race, age, income, occupation (March 1975)	Total (1,000)	Percent Distribution, Years of Schooling 0-8	9-11	12	13-15	16	16+	Median Years
White employed males, age 25-44	**19,976**	**1,609**	**2,170**	**7,480**	**3,528**	**2,711**	**2,478**	**12.8**
Under $3,000	793	141	98	231	139	104	79	12.7
$3,000-$5,999	1,654	349	217	530	251	151	156	12.5
$6,000-$9,999	4,342	538	721	1,733	635	421	295	12.5
$10,000-$14,999	7,011	419	727	3,034	1,360	809	661	12.8
$15,000 & over	6,176	162	407	1,952	1,143	1,226	1,287	14.5
White-collar workers	**9,713**	**117**	**360**	**2,407**	**2,087**	**2,355**	**2,388**	**15.8**
Under $6,000	824	23	45	191	188	173	203	15.4
$6,000 & over	8,890	93	315	2,216	1,899	2,182	2,184	15.9
Blue-collar workers	**8,443**	**1,219**	**1,565**	**4,247**	**1,125**	**242**	**45**	**12.3**
Under $6,000	1,059	302	206	364	136	44	7	12.1
$6,000 & over	7,384	918	1,358	3,883	989	198	38	12.4
Service workers	**1,211**	**135**	**160**	**562**	**250**	**73**	**31**	**12.6**
Under $6,000	287	68	33	113	39	14	19	12.4
$6,000 & over	924	67	127	448	210	59	13	12.6
Farm workers	**609**	**137**	**85**	**265**	**67**	**41**	**14**	**12.3**
Under $6,000	278	98	30	94	27	23	7	12.1
$6,000 & over	332	40	56	170	40	17	8	12.4
Black employed males, age 25-44	**1,827**	**255**	**407**	**696**	**259**	**145**	**65**	**12.4**
Under $3,000	150	43	29	50	17	8	2	12.1
$3,000-$5,999	336	83	103	97	33	17	3	11.5
$6,000-$9,999	579	96	146	220	65	45	8	12.2
$10,000-$14,999	570	28	109	252	102	54	24	12.6
$15,000 & over	193	5	19	77	42	21	28	12.9
White-collar workers	**432**	—	**26**	**123**	**102**	**117**	**63**	**15.0**
Under $6,000	66	—	9	22	15	15	5	13.4
$6,000 & over	366	—	17	101	86	101	58	15.2
Blue-collar workers	**1,079**	**194**	**309**	**445**	**107**	**23**	**2**	**12.1**
Under $6,000	286	83	90	82	24	7	—	11.0
$6,000 & over	792	112	219	363	83	16	2	12.2
Service workers	**269**	**29**	**63**	**121**	**50**	**5**	—	**12.3**
Under $6,000	91	16	26	36	10	3	—	12.1
$6,000 & over	177	14	37	85	41	2	—	12.5
Farm workers	**47**	**33**	**8**	**6**	—	—	—	**7.9**
Under $6,000	40	28	6	6	—	—	—	7.9
$6,000 & over	7	6	2	—	—	—	—	8.0
White employed males, age 45-64	**14,976**	**2,926**	**2,462**	**5,344**	**1,813**	**1,325**	**1,106**	**12.4**
Under $3,000	585	244	112	170	33	13	12	10.3
$3,000-$5,999	1,109	441	208	311	68	38	44	10.6
$6,000-$9,999	3,015	920	578	1,069	222	138	90	12.0
$10,000-$14,999	4,757	881	981	1,909	573	244	168	12.3
$15,000 & over	5,510	441	583	1,884	918	892	793	12.9
White-collar workers	**6,840**	**366**	**608**	**2,300**	**1,302**	**1,199**	**1,065**	**13.3**
Under $6,000	441	81	68	151	49	41	49	12.5
$6,000 & over	6,399	287	539	2,149	1,252	1,157	1,015	13.5
Blue-collar workers	**6,346**	**1,918**	**1,491**	**2,423**	**394**	**98**	**21**	**11.5**
Under $6,000	690	320	154	181	28	6	2	9.5
$6,000 & over	5,655	1,598	1,337	2,241	366	92	19	11.8
Service workers	**1,005**	**314**	**229**	**365**	**77**	**8**	**13**	**11.5**
Under $6,000	200	89	40	61	10	—	1	9.9
$6,000 & over	804	223	189	305	68	7	12	11.8
Farm workers	**785**	**328**	**134**	**255**	**40**	**20**	**8**	**10.4**
Under $6,000	362	195	59	88	13	4	3	8.8
$6,000 & over	424	134	75	167	27	17	4	12.0
Black employed males, age 45-64	**1,185**	**563**	**258**	**224**	**87**	**31**	**23**	**9.3**
Under $3,000	137	109	14	8	5	—	1	5.9
$3,000-$5,999	252	163	45	30	9	4	1	8.0
$6,000-$9,999	381	182	106	65	20	8	—	9.3
$10,000-$14,999	287	86	71	90	24	9	5	11.4
$15,000 & over	128	27	22	30	29	10	15	12.7
White-collar workers	**188**	**26**	**16**	**64**	**41**	**20**	**20**	**12.8**
Under $6,000	36	15	5	6	6	2	2	10.8
$6,000 & over	151	11	11	58	36	19	18	12.9
Blue-collar workers	**721**	**394**	**173**	**110**	**36**	**5**	**3**	**8.6**
Under $6,000	239	185	33	16	6	—	—	6.9
$6,000 & over	482	208	140	94	31	5	2	9.7
Service workers	**229**	**100**	**66**	**48**	**10**	**5**	—	**9.6**
Under $6,000	71	36	17	13	3	2	—	8.9
$6,000 & over	157	64	48	35	6	3	—	9.9
Farm workers	**47**	**43**	**3**	**1**	—	—	—	**4.0**
Under $6,000	41	37	3	1	—	—	—	3.9
$6,000 & over	5	5	—	—	—	—	—	4.2

The Principal Languages of the World

Source: Sidney S. Culbert, Assoc. Professor of Psychology, University of Washington

Total number of speakers of languages spoken by at least one million persons (Midyear 1977)

Language	Millions
Afrikaans (S. Africa)	6
Albanian	3
Amharic (Ethiopia)	9
Arabic	134
Armenian	4
Assamese[1] (India)	13
Aymara (Bolivia; Peru)	1
Azerbaijani (USSR; Iran)	8
Bahasa (See Malay-Indonesian)	
Balinese	3
Baluchi (Pakistan; Iran)	3
Batak (Indonesia)	2
Bemba (S. Central Africa)	2
Bengali[1] (Bangladesh; India)	131
Berber[2] (N. Africa)	
Bhili (India)	4
Bihari (India)	23
Bikol (Philippines)	2
Bisaya (see Cebuano, Panay-Hiligaynon, and Samar-Leyte)	
Bugi (Indonesia)	2
Bulgarian	9
Burmese	24
Byelorussian (mainly USSR)	9
Cambodian (Cambodia; Asia)	7
Canarese (see Kannada)	
Cantonese (China)	48
Catalan (Spain; France; Andorra)	6
Cebuano (Philippines)	9
Chinese[3]	
Chuang[7] (China)	
Chuvash (USSR)	2
Czech	11
Danish	5
Dayak (Borneo)	1
Dutch (see Netherlandish)	
Edo (W. Africa)	1
Efik	2
English	369
Esperanto	1
Estonian	1
Ewe (W. Africa)	3
Fang-Bulu (W. Africa)	1
Finnish	5
Flemish (see Netherlandish)	
French	95
Fula (W. Africa)	8
Galician (Spain)	3
Galla (see Oromo)	
Ganda (or Luganda) (E. Africa)	3
Georgian (USSR)	3
German	120
Gilaki (Iran)	2
Gondi (India)	2
Greek	10
Guarani (mainly Paraguay)	3
Gujarati[1] (India)	31
Hakka (China)	21
Hausa (W. and Central Africa)	19
Hebrew	3
Hindi[1,4]	218
Hindustani[4]	
Hungarian (or Magyar)	13
Ibibio (see Efik)	
Ibo (or Igbo) (W. Africa)	11
Ijaw (W. Africa)	1
Ilocano (Philippines)	4
Iloko (see Ilocano)	
Indonesian (see Malay-Indonesian)	
Italian	61
Japanese	113
Javanese	45
Kamba (E. Africa)	1
Kanarese (see Kannada)	
Kannada[1] (India)	29
Kanuri (W. and Cent. Africa)	3
Kashmiri[1]	3
Kazakh (USSR)	6
Khalkha (Mongolia)	2
Kikongo (see Kongo)	
Kikuyu (or Gekoyo) (Kenya)	3
Kimbundu (see Mbundu-Kim.)	
Kirghiz (USSR)	2
Kituba (Congo River)	3
Kongo (Congo River)	2
Konkani (India)	2
Korean	55
Kumauni (India)	1
Kurdish (S.W. of Caspian Sea)	7
Kurukh (or Oraon) (India)	1
Lao[5] (Laos, Asia)	3
Latvian (or Lettish)	2
Lingala (see Ngala)	
Lithuanian	3
Luba-Lulua (Zaire)	3
Luganda (see Ganda)	
Luhya (or Luhia) (Kenya)	1
Luo (Kenya)	2
Luri (Iran)	2
Macedonian (Yugoslavia)	2
Madurese (Indonesia)	8
Makua (S.E. Africa)	3
Malagasy (Madagascar)	8
Malay-Indonesian	101
Malayalam[1] (India)	27
Malinke-Bambara-Dyula (Africa)	6
Mandarin (China)	670
Marathi[1] (India)	53
Mazandarani (Iran)	2
Mbundu (Umbundu group) (S. Angola)	3
Mbundu (Kimbundu group) (Angola)	2
Mende (Sierra Leone)	1
Meo (see Miao)	
Miao (and Meo) (S.E. Asia)	3
Min (China)	39
Moldavian (inc. w/Romanian)	
Mongolian (see Khalkha)	
Mordvin (USSR)	1
More (see Mossi)	
Mossi (W. Africa)	3
Ndongo (see Mbundu-Kimbundu)	
Nepali (Nepal; India)	10
Netherlandish (Dutch and Flem.)	20
Ngala (or Lingala) (Africa)	2
Norwegian	5
Nyamwezi-Sukuma (S.E. Africa)	2
Nyanja (S.E. Africa)	3
Oraon (see Kurukh)	
Oriya[1] (India)	24
Oromo (Ethiopia)	7
Panay-Hiligaynon (Philippines)	4
Panjabi (see Punjabi)	
Pashto (see Pushtu)	
Pedi (see Sotho, Northern)	
Persian	26
Polish	36
Portuguese	133
Provencal (Southern France)	5
Punjabi[1] (India; Pakistan)	58
Pushtu (mainly Afghanistan)	16
Quechua (S. America)	7
Rajasthani (India)	22
Romanian	22
Ruanda (S. Central Africa)	7
Rundi (S. Central Africa)	4
Russian (Great Russian only)	246
Samar-Leyte (Philippines)	1
Sango (Central Africa)	2
Santali (India)	4
Sepedi (see Sotho, Northern)	
Serbo-Croatian (Yugoslavia)	19
Shan (Burma)	2
Shona (S.E. Africa)	4
Siamese (see Thai)	
Sindhi[1] (India; Pakistan)	10
Sinhalese (Sri Lanka)	11
Slovak	5
Slovene (Yugoslavia)	2
Somali (E. Africa)	5
Sotho, Northern (S. Africa)	2
Sotho, Southern (S. Africa)	3
Spanish	225
Sundanese (Indonesia)	15
Swahili (E. Africa)	23
Swedish	10
Tagalog (Philippines)	22
Tajiki (USSR)	3
Tamil[1] (India; Sri Lanka)	55
Tatar (or Kazan-Turkic) (USSR)	7
Telugu[1] India	55
Thai[5]	32
Thonga (S.E. Africa)	1
Tibetan	6
Tigrinya (Ethiopia)	4
Tiv (E. Central Nigeria)	1
Tswana (S. Africa)	2
Tulu (India)	1
Turkish	41
Turkoman (USSR)	2
Twi-Fante (or Akan) (W. Africa)	5
Uighur-(Sinkiang, China)	5
Ukrainian (mainly USSR)	42
Umbundu (see Mbundu-Umbundu)	
Urdu[1] (Pakistan; India)	60
Uzbek (USSR)	10
Vietnamese	38
Visayan (see Cebuano, Panay-Hiligaynon, and Samar-Leyte)	
White Russian (see Byelorussian)	
Wolof (W. Africa)	3
Wu (China)	43
Xhosa (S. Africa)	5
Yi (China)	4
Yiddish[6]	3
Yoruba (W. Africa)	13
Zhuang[7] (China)	9
Zulu (S. Africa)	5

(1) One of the 15 languages of the Constitution of India. (2) Here considered a group of dialects. (3) See Mandarin, Cantonese, Wu, Min, and Hakka. The "national language" (Guoyu) is a standardized form of Mandarin as spoken in the area of Peking. (4) Hindi and Urdu are essentially the same language, Hindustani. As the official language of India it is written in the Devanagari script and called Hindi. As the official language of Pakistan it is written in a modified Arabic script and called Urdu. (5) Thai includes Central, Southwestern, Northern, and Northeastern Thai. The distinction between Northeastern Thai and Lao is political rather than linguistic. (6) Yiddish is usually considered a variant of German, though it has its own standard grammar, dictionaries, a highly developed literature, and is written in Hebrew characters. (7) A group of Thai-like dialects.

UNITED STATES POPULATION

Changing Population Patterns

By Manuel D. Plotkin
Director, U.S. Bureau of the Census

The United States began 1977 with an estimated ›pulation of 216.0 million, an increase of 1.6 million, r 0.7 percent, over the January 1, 1976 figure. The ensus Bureau estimates that the net gain resulted om about 3.2 million births, 1.9 million deaths, and et immigration of about 300,000.

In 1976, blacks made up 11 percent of the popula- on and totaled 24.2 million. There were also 11.1 illion persons of Spanish origin, comprising five ercent of the population. Persons of Spanish origin icluded 6.6 million of Mexican origin; 1.8 million of uerto Rican origin; 0.8 million of Central or South merican origin; 0.7 million of Cuban origin; and 1.3 illion of other Spanish origin.

The U.S. population has been growing at a slower ite for several years, and the past trends in the num- er of births are gradually changing the country's age ructure. Since 1970, the number of children under ge 14 has declined by 5.5 million. During the same eriod, however, the population 65 and over has rown by three million, or 14.8 percent. Over 10 per- ent of the population is now 65 or older. The median ge of the population, therefore, has risen from 27.9 ears in 1970 to 29.0 in 1976.

Fertility Rate Down Again

The total fertility rate in 1976 was 1.76 — which eans that an estimated 1,760 children would be orn to each 1,000 women during their lifetimes if ey were to experience the 1976 birth rates over eir entire reproductive lives. (In 1975, the total fer- ility rate was 1.80). The present rate is well below e natural replacement level of 2.1 children per oman. Because of the large number of women of ildbearing age, however, it would still be many ears before the U.S. could attain zero population owth even if present low fertility rates were to con- nue indefinitely.

The shifting age structure is also apparent in the 2 percent drop in elementary school enrollment in e past six years. Nursery school enrollment, which ad increased by 60 percent between 1970 and 1975, opped by 13 percent between 1975 and 1976. Kind- garten enrollment continued to climb slightly hile the number of high school students rose by even percent from 1970 to 1976.

Between 1970 and 1976, college enrollment grew a dramatic 34 percent. The largest increases in ollege enrollment occurred among persons older an traditional college students (18 to 21 years). En- ollment rose 80 percent during this time for persons 5 to 29 years old and by 96 percent for those 30 to 34 ears old. This compares with a rise of about 32 per- ent for students in their early twenties and 13 ercent for persons 18 and 19. The number of college udents 35 and over rose by 52 percent between 1972 nd 1976. Thus, in 1976 one-fourth of all college stu- ents were 25 years old or more.

Marriage Down, Divorce Up

Other social changes are, in turn, having their effect on the number of children born. The number of divorces rose to 1,077,000 in 1976, whereas, the number of marriages fell to 2,133,000. The divorce rate per 1,000 population doubled from 2.5 in 1966 to 5.0 in 1976, but the marriage rate has been declining since it peaked at 11.0 in 1972. By 1976 there were 9.9 marriages per 1,000 population.

The Census Bureau estimates that if recent trends continue, one in every three married persons between 25 and 35 years of age in 1975 may end their first marriage in divorce.

More young people are also postponing marriage — or deciding not to marry at all. The percentage of single men between 20 and 24 years old increased from 53 percent in 1960 to 62 percent in 1976. Forty-three percent of all women in this age group (the age when men and women have traditionally married), were still single in 1976, compared to 28 percent in 1960.

As more women have postponed marriage and childbearing, or have become separated and/or divorced, the college enrollment of women 25 to 35 years old has more than doubled — from 409,000 in 1970 to 971,000 in 1976.

The number of unmarried persons of the opposite sex sharing the same living quarters has also doubled since 1970, the Bureau reports. In addition, the number of households in which persons live alone or with nonrelatives has increased by 41 percent since 1970, while the number of families maintained by a woman with no husband present increased by one-third.

Moving From Old Cities

In the past six years, Americans have not only been changing how they live but where they live. The population of metropolitan areas only increased by four percent between 1970 and 1976, while nonmetropolitan areas increased by eight percent. None of the eight metropolitan areas of three million people or more has grown by as much as four percent, although several smaller metropolitan areas (especially in the South), have grown faster than the nonmetropolitan areas next to them.

The black population in the suburbs has increased faster than the white population with average annual rates of increase since 1970 amounting to 5.2 percent for blacks and 1.4 percent for whites.

Central cities lost 4.6 million persons and gained only 2.7 million through internal migration between 1975 and 1976. Suburban parts of metropolitan areas gained 4.8 million between 1975 and 1976 and lost 3.2 million. Those who left nonmetropolitan areas tended to move to metropolitan suburbs rather than to central cities (1.3 million versus 0.8 million).

West and South Grow

Among the States, the largest numerical population gains between 1970 and 1976 occurred in Florida

(1.6 million increase); California (1.5 million); and Texas (1.3 million). The largest rates of increase during this period were in Arizona (28 percent); Alaska (26 percent); Nevada (25 percent); and Florida (24 percent).

Approximately four percent of the Nation's population, or 8.3 million persons, lived on farms in 1976, as the decline in farm population continued. In just six years, there has been a net loss of almost 1.5 million people living on farms, with 40 percent of the loss occurring in the past year alone.

The farm population is also becoming older, with the sharpest decline in population occurring among children. The total of those under age 14 dropped by one-third, compared to a nine percent decline among those 14 and older.

Population of the U.S., 1960-1970

Region, Division, and State	1970 Census	1960 Census	Pct. + or -	1970 Urban	1970 Rural	1970 Pct. Urban	Rank 1970	Rank 1960
United States	**203,235,298**	**179,323,175**	**13.3**	**149,324,930**	**53,886,996**	**73.5**	...	..
Regions:								
Northeast	48,999,999	44,677,819	9.7	39,449,818	9,590,885	80.4	...	..
North Central	56,577,067	51,619,139	9.6	40,480,760	16,090,903	71.6	...	..
South	62,798,347	54,973,113	14.2	40,539,961	22,255,406	64.6	...	..
West	34,809,359	28,053,104	24.1	28,854,391	5,949,802	82.9	...	..
New England	**11,847,186**	**10,509,367**	**12.7**	**9,043,517**	**2,798,146**	**76.4**	...	..
Maine	993,663	969,265	2.5	504,157	487,891	50.8	38	[illegible]
New Hampshire	737,681	606,921	21.5	416,040	321,641	56.4	42	[illegible]
Vermont	444,732	389,881	14.1	142,889	301,441	32.2	49	[illegible]
Massachusetts	5,689,170	5,148,578	10.5	4,810,449	878,721	84.6	10	[illegible]
Rhode Island	949,723	859,488	10.5	824,930	121,795	87.1	39	[illegible]
Connecticut	3,032,217	2,535,234	19.6	2,345,052	686,657	77.4	24	[illegible]
Middle Atlantic	**37,152,813**	**34,168,452**	**8.7**	**30,406,301**	**6,792,739**	**81.7**	...	..
New York	18,241,266	16,782,304	8.4	15,602,486	2,634,481	85.6	2	[illegible]
New Jersey	7,168,164	6,066,782	18.2	6,373,405	794,759	88.9	8	[illegible]
Pennsylvania	11,793,909	11,319,366	4.2	8,430,410	3,363,499	71.5	3	[illegible]
East North Central	**40,252,678**	**36,225,024**	**11.1**	**30,091,847**	**10,160,629**	**74.8**	...	..
Ohio	10,652,017	9,706,397	9.7	8,025,775	2,625,242	75.3	6	[illegible]
Indiana	5,193,669	4,662,498	11.4	3,372,060	1,821,609	64.9	11	[illegible]
Illinois	11,113,976	10,081,158	10.2	9,229,821	1,884,155	83.0	5	[illegible]
Michigan	8,875,083	7,823,194	13.4	6,553,773	2,321,310	73.8	7	[illegible]
Wisconsin	4,417,933	3,951,777	11.8	2,910,418	1,507,313	65.9	16	[illegible]
West North Central	**16,324,389**	**15,394,115**	**6.0**	**10,388,913**	**5,930,274**	**63.7**	...	..
Minnesota	3,805,069	3,413,864	11.5	2,527,308	1,277,663	66.4	19	[illegible]
Iowa	2,825,041	2,757,537	2.4	1,616,405	1,207,971	57.2	25	[illegible]
Missouri	4,677,399	4,319,813	8.3	3,277,662	1,398,839	70.1	13	[illegible]
North Dakota	617,761	632,446	-2.3	273,442	344,319	44.3	46	[illegible]
South Dakota	666,257	680,514	-2.1	296,628	368,879	44.6	45	[illegible]
Nebraska	1,483,791	1,411,330	5.1	912,598	570,895	61.5	35	[illegible]
Kansas	2,249,071	2,178,611	3.2	1,484,870	761,708	66.1	28	[illegible]
South Atlantic	**30,671,337**	**25,971,732**	**18.1**	**19,523,920**	**11,147,417**	**63.7**	...	..
Delaware	548,104	446,292	22.8	395,569	152,535	72.2	47	[illegible]
Maryland	3,922,399	3,100,689	26.5	3,003,935	918,464	76.6	18	[illegible]
District of Columbia	756,510	763,956	-1.0	756,510	...	100.0	41	[illegible]
Virginia	4,648,494	3,966,949	17.2	2,934,841	1,713,653	63.1	14	[illegible]
West Virginia	1,744,237	1,860,421	-6.2	679,491	1,064,746	39.0	34	[illegible]
North Carolina	5,082,059	4,556,155	11.5	2,285,168	2,796,891	45.0	12	[illegible]
South Carolina	2,590,516	2,382,594	8.7	1,232,195	1,358,321	47.6	26	[illegible]
Georgia	4,589,575	3,943,116	16.4	2,768,074	1,821,501	60.3	15	[illegible]
Florida	6,789,443	4,951,560	37.1	5,468,137	1,321,306	80.5	9	[illegible]
East South Central	**12,804,552**	**12,050,126**	**6.3**	**6,987,943**	**5,815,527**	**54.6**	...	..
Kentucky	3,219,311	3,038,156	6.0	1,684,053	1,534,653	52.3	23	[illegible]
Tennessee	3,924,164	3,567,089	10.0	2,305,307	1,618,380	58.7	17	[illegible]
Alabama	3,444,165	3,266,740	5.4	2,011,941	1,432,224	58.4	21	[illegible]
Mississippi	2,216,912	2,178,141	1.8	986,642	1,230,270	44.5	29	[illegible]
West South Central	**19,322,458**	**16,951,255**	**14.0**	**14,028,098**	**5,292,462**	**72.6**	...	..
Arkansas	1,923,295	1,786,272	7.7	960,865	962,430	50.0	32	[illegible]
Louisiana	3,643,180	3,257,022	11.9	2,406,150	1,235,156	66.1	20	[illegible]
Oklahoma	2,559,253	2,328,284	9.9	1,740,137	819,092	68.0	27	[illegible]
Texas	11,196,730	9,579,677	16.9	8,920,946	2,275,784	79.7	4	[illegible]
Mountain	**8,283,585**	**6,855,060**	**20.8**	**6,054,979**	**2,226,583**	**73.1**	...	..
Montana	694,409	674,767	2.9	370,676	323,733	53.4	44	[illegible]
Idaho	713,008	667,191	6.9	385,434	327,133	54.1	43	[illegible]
Wyoming	332,416	330,066	0.7	201,111	131,305	60.5	50	[illegible]
Colorado	2,207,259	1,753,947	25.8	1,733,311	473,948	78.5	30	[illegible]
New Mexico	1,016,000	951,023	6.8	708,775	307,225	69.8	37	[illegible]
Arizona	1,772,482	1,302,161	36.1	1,408,864	362,036	79.6	33	[illegible]
Utah	1,059,273	890,627	18.9	851,472	207,801	80.4	36	[illegible]
Nevada	488,738	285,278	71.3	395,336	93,402	80.9	48	[illegible]
Pacific	**26,525,774**	**21,198,044**	**25.1**	**22,799,412**	**3,723,219**	**86.0**	...	..
Washington	3,409,169	2,853,214	19.5	2,476,468	932,701	72.6	22	[illegible]
Oregon	2,091,385	1,768,687	18.2	1,402,704	688,681	67.1	31	[illegible]
California	19,953,134	15,717,204	27.0	18,136,045	1,817,089	90.9	1	[illegible]
Alaska	302,173	226,167	33.6	145,512	154,870	48.4	51	[illegible]
Hawaii	769,913	632,772	21.7	638,683	129,878	83.1	40	[illegible]

Urban and rural figures do not equal total 1970 population because of errors discovered by Census Bureau after tabulation.

U.S. Area and Population: 1790 to 1970

Source: U.S. Bureau of the Census

Area figures represent area on indicated date including in some cases considerable areas not then organized or settled. and not covered by the census. Area figures have been adjusted to bring them into agreement with remeasurements made in 1940. *Changes in land and water area between 1960 and 1970 due to construction of dams and reservoirs. Also total area of Texas reduced approximately one square mile in the Chamizal agreement between U.S. and Mexico.

Census Date	Area (square miles) Gross	Land	Water	Population Number	Per sq. mile of land	Increase over preceding census Number	%
790 (Aug. 2)	888,811	864,746	24,065	3,929,214	4.5		
800 (Aug. 4)	888,811	864,746	24,065	5,308,483	6.1	(X)	(X)
810 (Aug. 6)	1,716,003	1,681,828	34,175	7,239,881	4.3	1,379,269	35.1
820 (Aug. 7)	1,788,006	1,749,462	38,544	9,638,453	5.5	1,931,398	36.4
830 (June 1)	1,788,006	1,749,462	38,544	12,866,020	7.4	2,398,572	33.1
840 (June 1)	1,788,006	1,749,462	38,544	17,069,453	9.8	3,227,567	33.5
850 (June 1)	2,992,747	2,940,042	52,705	23,191,876	7.9	4,203,433	32.7
860 (June 1)	3,022,387	2,969,640	52,747	31,443,321	10.6	6,122,423	35.9
870 (June 1)	3,022,387	2,969,640	52,747	39,818,449[1]	13.4	8,251,445	35.6
880 (June 1)	3,022,387	2,969,640	52,747	50,155,783	16.9	8,375,128	26.6
890 (June 1)	3,022,387	2,969,640	52,747	62,947,714	21.2	10,337,334	26.0
900 (June 1)	3,022,387	2,969,834	52,553	75,994,575	25.6	12,791,931	25.5
910 (Apr. 15)	3,022,387	2,969,565	52,822	91,972,266	31.0	13,046,861	20.7
920 (Jan. 1)	3,022,387	2,969,451	52,936	105,710,620	35.6	15,977,691	21.0
930 (Apr. 1)	3,022,387	2,977,128	45,259	122,775,046	41.2	13,738,354	14.9
940 (Apr. 1)	3,022,387	2,977,128	45,259	131,669,275	44.2	17,064,426	16.1
950 (Apr. 1)[2]	3,615,211	3,552,206	63,005	151,325,798	42.6	8,894,229	7.2
960 (Apr. 1)[2]	3,615,123	3,540,911	74,212	179,323,175	50.5	19,161,229	14.5
970* (Apr. 1)[2]	3,615,122	3,536,855	78,267	203,211,926	57.5	27,997,377	18.5
						23,888,751	13.3

(X) Not applicable. (1) Revised to include adjustments for underenumeration in Southern States; unrevised number is 8,558,371. (2) Includes Alaska and Hawaii.

Population, Urban and Rural, by Race: 1960 and 1970

Source: U. S. Bureau of the Census

n urbanized area comprises at least one city of 50,000 inhabitants (central city) plus contiguous, closely settled areas (urban fringe). (thousands)

Year and Area	1960 Total	White	Negro and other	1970 Total	White	Negro and other
Population, total	**179,323**	**158,832**	**20,491**	**203,212**	**177,749**	**25,463**
rban	125,269	110,428	14,840	149,325	128,773	20,552
Inside urbanized areas	95,848	83,770	12,070	118,447	100,952	17,495
Central cities	57,975	47,627	10,348	63,922	49,547	14,375
Urban fringe	37,873	36,143	1,731	54,525	51,405	3,120
Outside urbanized areas	29,420	26,658	2,762	30,878	27,822	3,057
ıral	54,054	48,403	5,651	53,887	48,976	4,911

Congressional Apportionment

	1970	1960		1970	1960		1970	1960		1970	1960		1970	1960
a....	7	8	Ida....	2	2	Minn...	8	8	N. D....	1	2	Vt.....	1	1
as....	1	1	Ill.....	24	24	Miss...	5	5	Oh.....	23	24	Va.....	10	10
iz...	4	3	Ind.....	11	11	Mo.....	10	10	Okla...	6	6	Wash...	7	7
k....	4	4	Ia.....	6	7	Mon....	2	2	Ore....	4	4	W. Va..	4	5
al....	43	38	Kan....	5	5	Neb....	3	3	Pa.....	25	27	Wis....	9	10
ol....	5	4	Ky.....	7	7	Nev....	1	1	R. I....	2	2	Wy.....	1	1
onn...	6	6	La.....	8	8	N. H....	2	2	S. C....	6	6			
el....	1	1	Me.....	2	2	N. J....	15	15	S. D....	2	2	**Totals.**	**435**	**435**
a.....	15	12	Md.....	8	8	N. M...	2	2	Tenn...	8	9			
a.....	10	10	Mass...	12	12	N. Y....	39	41	Tex....	24	23			
a.....	2	•2	Mich...	19	19	N. C....	11	11	Ut.....	2	2			

The chief reason why the Constitution provided for a census of the population every 10 years was to give a basis for apportionment of representatives among the states. This apportionment has largely determined the number of electoral votes allotted to each state.

The number of representatives of each state in Congress determined by the state's population, except that each state is entitled to one representative regardless of population. A Congressional apportionment has been made after each decennial census except that of 1920.

Under provisions of a law that became effective Nov. 15, 1941, apportionment of representatives is made by the method of equal proportions. In the application of this method, the apportionment is made so that the average population per representative has the least possible variation between one state and any other. The first House of Representatives, in 1790, had 65 members, or one representative for each 30,000 of the estimated population, as provided by the Constitution. As the population grew, the number of representatives was increased but the total membership has been fixed at 435 since 1912.

U.S. Population by Official

(Members of the Armed Forces overseas or

State	1790	1800	1810	1820	1830¹	1840¹	1850	1860	1870	1880
Ala.	.....	1,250	9,046	127,901	309,527	590,756	771,623	964,201	996,992	1,262,505
Ariz.	.....	....	....	....	....	....	....	....	9,658	40,440
Ark.	.....	....	1,062	14,273	30,388	97,574	209,897	435,450	484,471	802,525
Cal.	.....	....	....	....	....	....	92,597	379,994	560,247	864,694
Col.	.....	....	....	....	....	....	....	34,277	39,864	194,327
Conn.	237,946	251,002	261,942	275,248	297,675	309,978	370,792	460,147	537,454	622,700
Del.	59,096	64,273	72,674	72,749	76,748	78,085	91,532	112,216	125,015	146,608
D.C.	.....	14,093	24,023	33,039	39,834	43,712	51,687	75,080	131,700	177,624
Fla.	.....	....	....	....	34,730	54,477	87,445	140,424	187,748	269,493
Ga.	82,548	162,686	252,433	340,989	516,823	691,392	906,185	1,057,286	1,184,109	1,542,180
Ida.	.....	....	....	....	....	....	....	....	14,999	32,610
Ill.	.....	....	12,282	55,211	157,445	476,183	851,470	1,711,951	2,539,891	3,077,871
Ind.	.....	5,641	24,520	147,178	343,031	685,866	988,416	1,350,428	1,680,637	1,978,301
Ia.	.....	....	....	....	....	43,112	192,214	674,913	1,194,020	1,624,615
Kan.	.....	....	....	....	....	....	....	107,206	364,399	996,096
Ky.	73,677	220,995	406,511	564,317	687,917	779,828	982,405	1,155,684	1,321,011	1,648,690
La.	.....	....	76,556	153,407	215,739	352,411	517,762	708,002	726,915	939,946
Me.	96,540	151,719	228,705	298,335	399,455	501,793	583,169	628,279	626,915	648,936
Md.	319,728	341,548	380,546	407,350	447,040	470,019	583,034	687,049	780,894	934,943
Mass.	378,787	422,845	472,040	523,287	610,408	737,699	994,514	1,231,066	1,457,351	1,783,085
Mich.	.....	....	4,762	8,896	31,639	212,267	397,654	749,113	1,184,059	1,636,937
Minn.	.....	....	....	....	....	....	6,077	172,023	439,706	780,773
Miss.	.....	8,850	40,352	75,448	136,621	375,651	606,526	791,305	827,922	1,131,597
Mo.	.....	....	19,783	66,586	140,455	383,702	682,044	1,182,012	1,721,295	2,168,380
Mon.	.....	....	....	....	....	....	....	....	20,595	39,159
Neb.	.....	....	....	....	....	....	....	28,841	122,993	452,402
Nev.	.....	....	....	....	....	....	....	6,857	42,491	62,266
N. H.	141,885	183,858	214,460	244,161	269,328	284,574	317,976	326,073	318,300	346,991
N. J.	184,139	211,149	245,562	277,575	320,823	373,306	489,555	672,035	906,096	1,131,116
N. M.	.....	....	....	....	....	....	61,547	93,516	91,874	119,565
N. Y.	340,120	589,051	959,049	1,372,812	1,918,608	2,428,921	3,097,394	3,880,735	4,382,759	5,082,871
N. C.	393,751	478,103	555,500	638,829	737,987	753,419	869,039	992,622	1,071,361	1,399,750
N. D.	.....	....	....	....	....	....	....	....	*2,405	36,909
Oh.	.....	45,365	230,760	581,434	937,903	1,519,467	1,980,329	2,339,511	2,665,260	3,198,062
Okla.	.....	....	....	....	....	....	....	....	....	....
Ore.	.....	....	....	....	....	....	13,294	52,465	90,923	174,768
Pa.	434,373	602,365	810,091	1,049,458	1,348,233	1,724,033	2,311,786	2,906,215	3,521,951	4,282,891
R. I.	68,825	69,122	76,931	83,059	97,199	108,830	147,545	174,620	217,353	276,531
S. C.	249,073	345,591	415,115	502,741	581,185	594,398	668,507	703,708	705,606	995,577
S. D.	.....	....	....	....	....	....	....	*4,837	*11,776	98,268
Tenn.	35,691	105,602	261,727	422,823	681,904	829,210	1,002,717	1,109,801	1,258,520	1,542,359
Tex.	.....	....	....	....	....	....	212,592	604,215	818,579	1,591,749
Ut.	.....	....	....	....	....	....	11,380	40,273	86,786	143,963
Vt.	85,425	154,465	217,895	235,981	280,652	291,948	314,120	315,098	330,551	332,286
Va.	821,287	880,200	974,600	1,065,366	1,211,405	1,239,797	1,421,661	1,596,318	1,225,163	1,512,565
Wash.	.....	....	....	....	....	....	1,201	11,594	23,955	75,116
W. Va.	.....	....	....	....	....	....	....	....	442,014	618,457
Wis.	.....	....	....	....	....	30,945	305,391	775,881	1,054,670	1,315,497
Wyo.	.....	....	....	....	....	....	....	....	9,118	20,789
U.S.	**3,929,214**	**5,308,483**	**7,239,881**	**9,638,453**	**12,866,020**	**17,069,453**	**23,191,876**	**31,443,321**	**38,558,371**	**50,155,78**

*1860 figure is for Dakota Territory; 1870 figures are for parts of Dakota Territory. (1) U.S. total includes persons (5,318 in 1830 an 6,100 in 1840) on public ships in the service of the United States not credited to any region, division, or state.

Density of Population by States

(Per square mile, land area only)

State	1920	1960	1970	State	1920	1960	1970	State	1920	1960	197
Ala.	45.8	64.2	67.9	Ky.	60.1	76.2	81.2	N. D.	9.2	9.1	8
Alas.*	0.1	0.4	0.5	La.	39.6	72.2	81.0	Oh.	141.4	236.6	260
Ariz.	2.9	11.5	15.6	Me.	25.7	31.3	32.1	Okla.	29.2	33.8	37
Ark.	33.4	34.2	37.0	Md.	145.8	313.5	396.6	Ore.	8.2	18.4	21
Cal.	22.0	100.4	127.6	Mass.	479.2	657.3	727.0	Pa.	194.5	251.4	262
Col.	9.1	16.9	21.3	Mich.	63.8	137.6	156.2	R. I.	566.4	819.3	905
Conn.	286.4	520.6	623.7	Minn.	29.5	43.0	48.0	S. C.	55.2	78.7	85
Del.	113.5	225.2	276.5	Miss.	38.6	46.0	46.9	S. D.	8.3	9.0	8
D. C.	7,292.9	12,523.9	12,401.8	Mo.	49.5	62.6	67.8	Tenn.	56.1	86.2	94
Fla.	17.7	91.5	125.5	Mon.	3.8	4.6	4.8	Tex.	17.8	36.4	42
Ga.	49.3	67.8	79.0	Neb.	16.9	18.4	19.4	Ut.	5.5	10.8	12
Ha.*	39.9	98.5	119.8	Nev.	.7	2.6	4.4	Vt.	38.6	42.0	47
Ida.	5.2	8.1	8.6	N. H.	49.1	67.2	81.7	Va.	57.4	99.5	116
Ill.	115.7	180.4	199.4	N. J.	420.0	805.5	953.1	Wash.	20.3	42.8	51
Ind.	81.3	128.8	143.9	N. M.	2.9	7.8	8.4	W. Va.	60.9	77.2	72
Ia.	43.2	49.2	50.5	N. Y.	217.9	350.6	381.3	Wis.	47.6	72.6	81
Kan.	21.6	26.6	27.5	N. C.	52.5	93.2	104.1	Wyo.	2.0	3.4	3
								U.S.	***29.9**	**50.6**	**57**

*For purposes of comparison, Alaska and Hawaii included in above tabulation for 1920, even though not states then.

Census from 1790 to 1970

other U.S. nationals overseas are not included.)

State	1890	1900	1910	1920	1930	1940	1950	1960	1970
Ala.	1,513,401	1,828,697	2,138,093	2,348,174	2,646,248	2,832,961	3,061,743	3,266,740	3,444,164
Alas.	....	....	....	....	....	....	....	226,167	302,173
Ariz.	88,243	122,931	204,354	334,162	435,573	499,261	749,587	1,302,161	1,772,482
Ark.	1,128,211	1,311,564	1,574,449	1,752,204	1,854,482	1,949,387	1,909,511	1,786,272	1,923,295
Cal.	1,213,398	1,485,053	2,377,549	3,426,861	5,677,251	6,907,387	10,586,223	15,717,204	19,953,134
Col.	413,249	539,700	799,024	939,629	1,035,791	1,123,296	1,325,089	1,753,947	2,207,259
Conn.	746,258	908,420	1,114,756	1,380,631	1,606,903	1,709,242	2,007,280	2,535,234	3,032,217
Del.	168,493	184,735	202,322	223,003	238,380	266,505	318,085	446,292	548,104
D.C.	230,392	278,718	331,069	437,571	486,869	663,091	802,178	763,956	756,510
Fla.	391,422	528,542	752,619	968,470	1,468,211	1,897,414	2,771,305	4,951,560	6,789,443
Ga.	1,837,353	2,216,331	2,609,121	2,895,832	2,908,506	3,123,723	3,444,578	3,943,116	4,589,575
Ha.	....	....	....	....	....	....	....	632,772	769,913
Ida.	88,548	161,772	325,594	431,866	445,032	524,873	588,637	667,191	713,008
Ill.	3,826,352	4,821,550	5,638,591	6,485,280	7,630,654	7,897,241	8,712,176	10,081,158	11,113,976
Ind.	2,192,404	2,516,462	2,700,876	2,930,390	3,238,503	3,427,796	3,934,224	4,662,498	5,193,669
Ia.	1,912,297	2,231,853	2,224,771	2,404,021	2,470,939	2,538,268	2,621,073	2,757,537	2,825,041
Kan.	1,428,108	1,470,495	1,690,949	1,769,257	1,880,999	1,801,028	1,905,299	2,178,611	2,249,071
Ky.	1,858,635	2,147,174	2,289,905	2,416,630	2,614,589	2,845,627	2,944,806	3,038,156	3,219,311
La.	1,118,588	1,381,625	1,656,388	1,798,509	2,101,593	2,363,880	2,683,516	3,257,022	3,643,180
Me.	661,086	694,466	742,371	768,014	797,423	847,226	913,774	969,265	993,663
Md.	1,042,390	1,188,044	1,295,346	1,449,661	1,631,526	1,821,244	2,343,001	3,100,689	3,922,399
Mass.	2,238,947	2,805,346	3,366,416	3,852,356	4,249,614	4,316,721	4,690,514	5,148,578	5,689,170
Mich.	2,093,890	2,420,982	2,810,173	3,668,412	4,842,325	5,256,106	6,371,766	7,823,194	8,875,083
Minn.	1,310,283	1,751,394	2,075,708	2,387,125	2,563,953	2,792,300	2,982,483	3,413,864	3,805,069
Miss.	1,289,600	1,551,270	1,797,114	1,790,618	2,009,821	2,183,796	2,178,914	2,178,141	2,216,912
Mo.	2,679,185	3,106,665	3,293,335	3,404,055	3,629,367	3,784,664	3,954,653	4,319,813	4,677,399
Mon.	142,924	243,329	376,053	548,889	537,606	559,456	591,024	674,767	694,409
Neb.	1,062,656	1,066,300	1,192,214	1,296,372	1,377,963	1,315,834	1,325,510	1,411,330	1,483,791
Nev.	47,355	42,335	81,875	77,407	91,058	110,247	160,083	285,278	488,738
N.H.	376,530	411,588	430,572	443,083	465,293	491,524	533,242	606,921	737,681
N.J.	1,444,933	1,883,669	2,537,167	3,155,900	4,041,334	4,160,165	4,835,329	6,066,782	7,168,164
N.M.	160,282	195,310	327,301	360,350	423,317	531,818	681,187	951,023	1,016,000
N.Y.	6,003,174	7,268,894	9,113,614	10,385,227	12,588,066	13,479,142	14,830,192	16,782,304	18,241,266
N.C.	1,617,949	1,893,810	2,206,287	2,559,123	3,170,276	3,571,623	4,061,929	4,556,155	5,082,059
N.D.	190,983	319,146	577,056	646,872	680.845	641,935	619,636	632,446	617,761
Oh.	3,672,329	4,157,545	4,767,121	5,759,394	6,646,697	6,907,612	7,946,627	9,706,397	10,652,017
Okla.	258,657	790,391	1,657,155	2,028,283	2,396,040	2,336,434	2,233,351	2,328,284	2,559,253
Ore.	317,704	413,536	672,765	783,389	953,786	1,089,684	1,521,341	1,768,687	2,091,385
Pa.	5,258,113	6,302,115	7,665,111	8,720,017	9,631,350	9,900,180	10,498,012	11,319,366	11,793,909
R.I.	345,506	428,556	542,610	604,397	687,497	713,346	791,896	859,488	949,723
S.C.	1,151,149	1,340,316	1,515,400	1,683,724	1,738,765	1,899,804	2,117,027	2,382,594	2,509,516
S.D.	348,600	401,570	583,888	636,547	692,849	642,961	652,740	680,514	666,257
Tenn.	1,767,518	2,020,616	2,184,789	2,337,885	2,616,556	2,915,841	3,291,718	3,567,089	3,924,164
Tex.	2,235,527	3,048,710	3,896,542	4,663,228	5,824,715	6,414,824	7,711,194	9,579,677	11,196,730
Ut.	210,779	276,749	373,351	449,396	507,847	550,310	688,862	890,627	1,059,273
Vt.	332,422	343,641	355,956	352,428	359,611	359,231	377,747	389,881	444,732
Va.	1,655,980	1,854,184	2,061,612	2,309,187	2,421,851	2,677,773	3,318,680	3,966,949	4,648,494
Wash.	357,232	518,103	1,141,990	1,356,621	1,563,396	1,736,191	2,378,962	2,853,214	3,409,169
W. Va.	762,794	958,800	1,221,119	1,463,701	1,729,205	1,901,974	2,005,553	1,860,421	1,744,237
Wis.	1,693,330	2,069,042	2,333,860	2,632,067	2,939,006	3,137,587	3,434,575	3,951,777	4,417,933
Wyo.	62,555	92,531	145,965	194,402	225,565	250,742	290,529	330,066	332,416
U.S.	**62,947,714**	**75,994,575**	**91,972,266**	**105,710,620**	**122,775,046**	**131,669,275**	**150,697,361**	**179,323,175**	**203,235,298**

U.S. Center of Population, 1790-1970

Center of population is that point which may be considered as center of population gravity of the U.S. or that point upon which the U.S. would balance if it were a rigid plane without weight and the population distributed thereon with each individual being assumed to have equal weight and to exert an influence on a central point proportional to his distance from that point.

Year	N. Lat. °	'	"	W. Long. °	'	"	Approximate location
1790	39	16	30	76	11	12	23 miles east of Baltimore, Md.
1800	39	16	6	76	56	30	18 miles west of Baltimore, Md.
1810	39	11	30	77	37	12	40 miles northwest by west of Washington, D.C. (in Va.)
1820	39	5	42	78	33	0	16 miles east of Moorefield, W. Va.[1]
1830	38	57	54	79	16	54	19 miles west-southwest of Moorefield, W. Va.
1840	39	2	0	80	18	0	16 miles south of Clarksburg, W. Va.[1]
1850	38	59	0	81	19	0	23 miles southeast of Parkersburg, W. Va.[1]
1860	39	0	24	82	48	48	20 miles south by east of Chillicothe, Oh.
1870	39	12	0	83	35	42	48 miles east by north of Cincinnati, Oh.
1880	39	4	8	84	39	40	8 miles west by south of Cincinnati, Oh. (in Ky.)
1890	39	11	56	85	32	53	20 miles east of Columbus, Ind.
1900	39	9	36	85	48	54	6 miles southeast of Columbus, Ind.
1910	39	10	12	86	32	20	In the city of Bloomington, Ind.
1920	39	10	21	86	43	15	8 miles south-southeast of Spencer, Owen County, Ind.
1930	39	3	45	87	8	6	3 miles northeast of Linton, Greene County, Ind.
1940	38	56	54	87	22	35	2 miles southeast by east of Carlisle, Haddon township, Sullivan County, Ind.
1950 (Inc. Alaska & Hawaii)	38	48	15	88	22	8	3 miles northeast of Louisville, Clay County, Ill.
1960	38	35	58	89	12	35	6 1/2 miles northwest of Centralia, Ill.
1970	38	27	47	89	42	22	5 miles east southeast of Mascoutah, St. Clair County, Ill.

(1) West Virginia was set off from Virginia Dec. 31, 1862, and admitted as a state June 20, 1863.

Rankings of U.S. Standard Metropolitan Statistical Areas

Source: U.S. Bureau of the Census

Metropolitan areas are ranked by 1974 provisional population size based on new SMSA definitions and compared with a ranking of areas as defined in the 1970 census. Included are 259 of the 272 Standard Metropolitan Statistical Areas (SMSAs) as defined through December 1975 by the Office of Management and Budget, excluding 4 areas in Puerto Rico not covered in the report.

Asterisk (*) indicates 13 New England County Metropolitan Areas comprised of 26 New England SMSAs.

SMSA	1974 (P) Rank	1974 (P) Pop.	1970 Rank	1970 Pop.
New York, N.Y.-N.J.	1	9,634,400	1	9,973,716
Chicago, Ill.	2	6,971,200	3	6,977,611
Los Angeles-Long Beach, Cal.	3	6,926,100	2	7,041,980
Philadelphia, Pa.-N.J.	4	4,809,900	4	4,824,110
Detroit, Mich.	5	4,434,300	5	4,435,051
Boston-Lowell-Brockton-Lawrence-Haverhill, Mass.-N.H.*	6	3,918,400	6	3,848,593
San Francisco-Oakland, Cal.	7	3,135,900	7	3,108,782
Washington, D.C.-Md.-Va.	8	3,015,300	8	2,910,111
Nassau-Suffolk, N.Y.[1]	9	2,620,700	9	2,555,868
Dallas-Ft. Worth, Tex.[3]	10	2,498,500	12	2,378,353
St. Louis, Mo.-Ill.	11	2,371,400	10	2,410,492
Pittsburgh, Pa.	12	2,333,600	11	2,401,362
Houston, Tex.	13	2,222,700	16	1,999,316
Baltimore, Md.	14	2,140,400	13	2,071,016
Newark, N.J.	15	2,019,200	15	2,057,468
Minneapolis-St. Paul, Minn.-Wis.	16	2,010,800	17	1,965,391
Cleveland, Oh.	17	1,984,100	14	2,063,729
Atlanta, Ga.	18	1,776,000	18	1,595,517
Anaheim-Santa Ana-Garden Grove, Cal.	19	1,660,900	20	1,421,233
San Diego, Cal.	20	1,518,000	23	1,357,854
Miami, Fla.	21	1,415,900	26	1,267,792
Milwaukee, Wis.	22	1,415,400	21	1,403,884
Seattle-Everett, Wash.	23	1,396,400	19	1,424,605
Denver-Boulder, Col.	24	1,391,100	27	1,239,477
Cincinnati, Oh.-Ky.-Ind.	25	1,375,800	22	1,385,103
Tampa-St. Petersburg, Fla.	26	1,332,900	30	1,088,549
Buffalo, N.Y.	27	1,330,700	24	1,349,211
Kansas City, Mo.-Kan.	28	1,301,600	25	1,273,926
Riverside-San Bernardino-Ontario, Cal.	29	1,213,900	28	1,141,307
San Jose, Cal.	30	1,181,600	31	1,065,313
Phoenix, Ariz.	31	1,172,200	36	969,425
Indianapolis, Ind.	32	1,143,700	29	1,111,352
New Orleans, La.	33	1,090,200	32	1,046,470
Portland, Ore.-Wash.	34	1,079,700	34	1,007,130
Columbus, Oh.	35	1,067,000	33	1,017,847
Hartford-New Britain-Bristol, Conn.*	36	1,058,700	35	1,035,195
San Antonio, Tex.	37	979,900	38	888,179
Rochester, N.Y.	38	966,400	37	961,516
Louisville, Ky.-Ind.	39	892,500	39	867,330
Sacramento, Cal.	40	882,600	42	803,793
Providence-Warwick-Pawtucket, R.I.*	41	854,400	45	855,495
Memphis, Tenn.-Ark.-Miss.	42	853,100	41	834,103
Dayton, Oh.	43	844,800	40	852,531
Fort Lauderdale-Hollywood, Fla.	44	806,800	61	620,100
Albany-Schenectady-Troy, N.Y.	45	799,400	44	777,977
Bridgeport-Stamford-Norwalk-Danbury, Conn.*	46	791,000	43	792,814
Birmingham, Ala.	47	785,000	46	767,230
Toledo, Oh.-Mich.	48	781,000	47	762,658
Oklahoma City, Okla.	49	766,200	53	699,092
Norfolk-Virginia Beach-Portsmouth, Va.-N.C.	50	766,000	49	732,600
Salt Lake City-Ogden Ut.[3]	51	765,500	51	705,458
New Haven-West Haven-Waterbury-Meriden, Conn.*	52	759,700	48	744,948
Greensboro-Winston-Salem-High Point, N.C.	53	759,500	50	724,129
Nashville-Davidson, Tenn.	54	744,600	52	699,271
Honolulu, Ha.	55	691,200	58	630,528
Jacksonville, Fla.	56	674,900	60	621,827
Akron, Oh.	57	671,300	54	679,239
Worcester-Fitchburg-Leominster, Mass.*	58	648,400	55	637,037
Syracuse, N.Y.	59	645,800	56	636,596
Gary-Hammond-East Chicago, Ind.	60	643,900	57	633,367
Northeast Pennsylvania[3]	61	633,100	59	621,882
Allentown-Bethlehem-Easton, Pa.-N.J.	62	616,600	63	594,382
New Brunswick-Perth Amboy-Sayreville, N.J.[1]	63	590,200	64	583,813
Springfield-Chicopee-Holyoke, Mass.*	64	589,700	65	583,031
Charlotte-Gastonia, N.C.	65	589,300	66	557,785
Jersey City, N.J.	66	583,000	62	607,839
Orlando, Fla.	67	578,600	77	453,270
Tulsa, Okla.	68	576,100	67	549,154
Omaha, Nebr.-Ia.	69	575,100	68	542,646
Richmond, Va.	70	569,500	69	542,242
Grand Rapids, Mich.	71	558,700	70	539,225
Youngstown-Warren, Oh.	72	542,900	71	537,124
Greenville-Spartanburg, S. C.	73	522,200	74	473,454
Flint, Mich.	74	522,200	72	508,664
Wilmington, Del.-N.J.-Md.	75	513,300	73	499,493
Long Branch-Asbury Park, N.J.[1]	76	485,700	75	461,849
New Bedford/Fall River, Mass.*	77	463,700	78	444,301
Raleigh/Durham, N.C.[3]	78	462,300	80	419,394
Paterson/Clifton-Passaic, N.J.	79	456,200	76	460,782
West Palm Beach-Boca Raton, Fla.	80	433,600	96	348,993
Lansing-East Lansing, Mich.	81	440,600	79	424,271
Fresno, Cal.	82	439,400	81	413,329
Tucson, Ariz.	83	433,500	95	351,667
Oxnard-Simi Valley-Ventura, Cal.	84	430,200	87	378,497
Knoxville, Tenn.	85	427,700	84	409,409
Harrisburg, Pa.	86	425,500	83	410,505
El Paso, Tex.	87	410,000	94	359,291
Baton Rouge, La.	88	407,200	89	375,628
Canton, Oh.	89	404,500	85	393,789
Tacoma, Wash.	90	397,600	82	412,344
Mobile, Ala.	91	396,400	88	476,690
Johnson City-Kingsport-Bristol, Tenn.-Va.[1]	92	391,700	90	373,591
Chattanooga, Tenn.-Ga.	93	390,300	91	370,857
Austin, Tex.	94	388,600	107	323,158
Wichita, Kan.	95	379,000	86	389,352
Albuquerque, N.M.	96	378,900	102	333,266
Fort Wayne, Ind.	97	373,200	93	361,984
Davenport-Rock Island-Moline, Ia.-Ill.	98	364,400	92	362,638
Charleston-North Charleston, S. C.	99	362,000	100	336,125
Columbia, S.C.	100	360,800	108	322,880
Little Rock-North Little Rock, Ark.	101	356,100	106	323,296
Peoria, Ill.	102	352,000	98	341,979
Newport News-Hampton, Va.	103	346,800	103	333,140
York, Pa.	104	345,900	105	329,540
Beaumont-Port Arthur-Orange, Tex.	105	344,600	97	347,568
Shreveport, La.	106	343,400	101	333,826
Utica-Rome, N.Y.	107	337,900	99	340,670
Lancaster, Pa.	108	337,900	109	320,079
Bakersfield, Cal.	109	337,600	104	330,234
Des Moines, Ia.	110	328,400	110	313,562
Las Vegas, Nev.	111	319,600	124	273,288
Trenton, N.J.	112	319,100	111	304,116
Reading, Pa.	113	304,500	113	296,382
Spokane, Wash.	114	303,800	116	287,487
Madison, Wis.	115	303,000	115	290,272
Binghamton, N. Y.-Pa.	116	300,400	112	302,672
Stockton, Cal.	117	299,200	114	291,073
Corpus Christi, Tex.	118	295,100	119	284,832
Colorado Springs, Col.	119	293,200	138	239,288

SMSA	1974 (P) Rank	1974 (P) Pop.	1970 Rank	1970 Pop.
luntington-Ashland, W. Va.-Ky.-Oh.	120	290,400	117	286,935
:vansville, Ind.-Ky.	121	288,600	118	284,959
exington-Fayette, Ky.	122	286,300	126	266,701
luntsville, Ala.	123	285,200	120	282,450
ppleton-Oshkosh, Wis.	124	281,800	122	276,948
;anta Barbara-Santa Maria-Lompoc, Cal.	125	281,800	128	264,324
;outh Bend, Ind.	126	280,400	121	280,031
ackson, Miss.	127	278,600	131	258,906
ugusta, Ga.-S. C.	128	273,900	123	275,787
:rie, Pa.	129	273,700	129	263,654
Rockford, Ill.	130	270,300	125	272,063
'allejo-Fairfield-Napa, Cal.	131	267,700	135	251,129
ohnstown, Pa.	132	266,000	130	262,822
orain-Elyria, Oh.	133	265,800	134	156,843
'ensacola, Fla.	134	263,600	137	243,075
akeland-Winter Haven, Fla.[1]	135	263,200	143	228,515
)uluth-Superior, Minn.-Wis.	136	262,200	127	265,350
<alamazoo-Portage, Mich.	137	261,600	132	257,723
;alinas-Seaside-Monterey, Cal.	138	260,600	136	247,450
:harlestown, W. Va.	139	253,700	133	257,140
nn Arbor, Mich.	140	250,100	140	234,103
/lontgomery, Ala.	141	248,400	146	225,911
;anta Rosa, Cal.	142	242,600	154	204,885
łamilton-Middletown, Oh.	143	242,300	145	226,207
lew London-Norwich, Conn.*	144	239,700	141	230,654
/lanchester-Nashua, N.H.*	145	238,500	147	223,941
:ugene-Springfield, Ore.	146	236,600	150	215,401
/lacon, Ga.	147	235,500	144	226,782
'oughkeepsie, N.Y.[1]	148	233,300	148	222,295
/lelbourne-Titusville-Cocoa, Fla.[1]	149	229,400	142	230,006
'ortland, Me.*	150	227,300	157	225,386
;aginaw, Mich.	151	226,900	149	219,743
'ayetteville, N.C.	152	223,100	151	212,042
;olumbus, Ga.-Ala.	153	218,000	139	238,584
IcAllen-Pharr-Edinburg, Tex.	154	217,600	161	181,535
Roanoke, Va.	155	212,200	155	203,153
Aodesto, Cal.	156	211,100	156	194,506
.ima, Oh.	157	210,800	152	210,074
<illeen-Temple, Tex.[1]	158	202,200	180	159,794
;alem, Ore.	159	201,800	159	186,658
)aytona Beach, Fla.[1]	160	199,600	171	169,487
;avannah, Ga.	161	199,100	153	207,987
.ubbock, Tex.	162	194,500	164	179,295
tlantic City, N.J.	163	190,000	167	175,043
;pringfield, Oh.	164	187,500	158	187,606
;pringfield, Mo.	165	187,400	172	168,053
Vheeling, W. Va.-Oh.	166	182,900	160	181,954
.incoln, Neb.	167	182,200	173	167,972
3attle Creek, Mich.	168	181,900	163	180,129
'opeka, Kan.[1]	169	179,500	162	180,619
;alveston-Texas City, Tex.	170	179,100	170	169,812
;pringfield, Ill.	171	177,500	168	171,020
/luskegon-Norton Shores-Muskegon Heights, Mich.	172	176,700	165	175,410
'erre Haute, Ind.	173	173,700	166	175,143
Racine, Wis.	174	173,500	169	170,838
3iloxi-Gulfport, Miss.	175	173,200	179	160,070
'ort Smith, Ark.-Okla.	176	172,700	178	160,421
3rownsville-Harlingen-San Benito, Tex.	177	168,300	189	140,368
;teubenville-Weirton, Oh.-W. Va.	178	166,800	174	165,627
;reen Bay, Wis.	179	166,600	181	158,244
sheville, N.C.	180	166,300	177	161,059
;edar Rapids, Ia.	181	164,600	176	163,213
'rovo-Orem, Ut.	182	163,000	191	137,776
;hampaign-Urbana-Ranroul, Ill.	183	163,000	175	163,281
arasota, Fla.[1]	184	158,900	209	120,413
Vaco, Tex.	185	154,400	184	147,553
ort Myers, Fla.[1]	186	154,100	228	105,216
akima, Wash.[1]	187	151,200	186	145,212
ittsfield, Mass.*	188	150,500	182	149,402
marillo, Tex.	189	150,200	187	144,396
arkersburg-Marietta, W. Va.-Oh.[2]	190	150,000	183	148,132
.ake Charles, La.	191	149,300	185	145,415
Anchorage, Alas.	192	148,800	202	126,385
St. Cloud, Minn.[1]	193	148,300	193	134,585
Santa Cruz, Cal.[1]	194	147,200	204	123,790
Jackson, Mich.	195	145,000	188	143,274
Fayetteville-Springdale, Ark.[1]	196	144,900	201	127,846
Reno, Nev.	197	142,700	207	121,068
Lynchburg, Va.	198	141,500	194	133,258
Clarksville-Hopkinsville, Tenn.-Ky.[1]	199	140,000	211	118,945
Anderson, Ind.	200	139,400	190	138,522
Alexandria, La.[2]	201	136,100	196	131,749
Altoona, Pa.	202	135,600	192	135,356
Tallahassee, Fla.	203	132,700	225	109,355
Waterloo-Cedar Falls, Ia.	204	132,300	195	132,916
Boise City, Ida.	205	131,500	222	112,230
Vineland-Millville-Bridgeton, N.J.	206	131,400	206	121,374
Mansfield, Oh.	207	131,200	197	129,997
Muncie, Ind.	208	130,600	198	129,219
Abilene, Tex.	209	128,400	205	122,164
Wichita Falls, Tex.	210	127,300	200	128,642
Wilmington, N.C.	211	126,900	227	107,219
Fargo-Moorhead, N.D.-Minn.	212	125,600	210	120,261
Decatur, Ill.	213	125,200	203	125,010
Petersburg-Colonial Heights-Hopewell, Va.	214	124,300	199	128,809
Pueblo, Col.	215	124,300	212	118,238
Longview, Tex.	216	124,200	208	120,770
Gainesville, Fla.	217	124,000	229	104,764
Eau Claire, Wis.	218	123,700	219	114,936
Monroe, La.	219	122,600	218	115,387
Tuscaloosa, Ala.	220	122,500	217	116,029
Lafayette, La.	221	122,200	223	111,643
Kenosha, Wis.	222	122,100	213	117,917
Florence, Ala.[1]	223	120,900	214	117,743
Bay City, Mich.	224	119,400	215	117,339
Sioux City, Ia.-Neb.	225	118,500	216	116,189
Williamsport, Pa.[1]	226	116,400	221	113,296
Fort Collins, Col.	227	114,900	244	89,900
Bloomington-Normal, Ill.	228	114,400	230	104,389
Texarkana, Tex.-Ark.	229	114,200	220	113,488
Lafayette-West Lafayette, Ind.	230	112,200	224	109,378
Greeley, Col.	231	106,600	245	89,297
Anniston, Ala.[1]	232	105,900	231	103,092
Tyler, Tex.	233	105,700	235	97,096
Lawton, Okla.	234	105,400	226	108,144
Pascagoula-Moss Point, Miss.	235	104,200	246	87,975
Albany, Ga.	236	100,700	236	96,683
St. Joseph, Mo.	237	99,400	233	98,828
Burlington, N.C.[1]	238	99,400	237	96,362
Elmira, N.Y.[1]	239	99,300	232	101,537
Sioux Falls, S. D.	240	98,400	238	95,209
Richland-Kennewick, Wash.[1]	241	97,100	240	93,356
Kankakee, Ill.[1]	242	95,900	234	97,250
Lewiston-Auburn, Me.*	243	94,700	242	91,279
Gadsden, Ala.	244	94,700	239	94,144
Billings, Mon.	245	94,500	247	87,367
Odessa, Tex.	246	93,900	241	92,660
Dubuque, Ia.	247	91,600	243	90,609
Bloomington, Ind.	248	89,100	249	85,221
Rochester, Minn.	249	88,600	250	84,104
Columbia, Mo.	250	86,400	253	80,935
Great Falls, Mon.	251	84,400	252	81,804
Pine Bluff, Ark.	252	84,000	248	85,329
La Crosse, Wis.	253	83,300	254	80,468
Owensboro, Ky.	254	81,000	255	79,486
Laredo, Tex.	255	78,100	256	72,859
Sherman-Denison, Tex.	256	77,500	251	83,225
San Angelo, Tex.	257	74,600	257	71,047
Bryan-College Station, Tex.	258	67,900	259	47,978
Midland, Tex.	259	66,000	258	65,433

(1) New SMSA established since 1970 census.
(2) New SMSA established in Nov. 1971, and area definition changed in Apr. 1973.
(3) Merger of 2 existing SMSAs since 1970 census; rank and population given for 1970 definition refer to the larger of the 2 merged SMSAs.

How the Cities Grew

Source: U. S. Bureau of the Census
(cities over 100,000 ranked by 1975 population estimates)

Rank	City	1975	1970	1960	1950	1900	1850	1790
1	New York, N.Y.	7,481,613	7,895,563	7,781,984	7,891,957	3,437,202	[1]696,115	[1]49,401
	Bronx	1,355,482	1,471,701	1,424,815	1,451,277	200,507	8,032	1,781
	Brooklyn	2,408,234	2,602,012	2,627,319	2,738,175	1,166,582	138,882	4,495
	Manhattan	1,429,033	1,539,233	1,698,281	1,960,101	1,850,093	515,547	33,131
	Queens	1,963,705	1,987,174	1,809,578	1,550,849	152,999	18,593	6,159
	Staten Island	325,159	295,443	221,991	191,555	67,021	15,061	3,835
2	Chicago, Ill.	3,099,391	3,369,357	3,550,404	3,620,962	1,698,575	29,963	...
3	Los Angeles, Cal.	2,727,399	2,811,801	2,479,015	1,970,358	102,479	1,610	...
4	Philadelphia, Pa.	1,815,808	1,949,996	2,002,512	2,071,605	1,293,697	121,376	28,522
5	Detroit, Mich.	1,335,085	1,514,063	1,670,144	1,849,568	285,704	21,019	...
6	Houston, Tex.	1,326,809	1,253,479	938,219	596,163	44,633	2,396	...
7	Baltimore, Md.	851,698	905,787	939,024	949,708	508,957	169,054	13,603
8	Dallas, Tex.	812,797	844,303	679,684	434,462	42,638	...	...
9	San Diego, Cal.	773,996	697,027	573,224	334,387	17,700	...	...
10	San Antonio, Tex.	773,248	708,582	587,718	408,442	53,321	3,488	...
11	Indianapolis, Ind.	725,077	740,000	476,258	427,173	169,164	8,091	...
12	Washington, D. C.	711,518	756,668	763,956	802,178	278,718	40,001	...
13	Honolulu, Ha.	705,381	630,528	294,194	248,034	39,306	...	...
14	Milwaukee, Wis.	665,796	717,372	741,324	637,392	285,315	20,061	...
15	Phoenix, Ariz.	664,721	589,016	439,170	106,818	5,544	...	...
16	San Francisco, Cal.	664,520	715,674	740,316	775,357	342,782	[2]34,776	...
17	Memphis, Tenn.	661,319	657,007	497,524	396,000	102,320	8,841	...
18	Cleveland, Oh.	638,793	750,879	876,050	914,808	381,768	17,034	...
19	Boston, Mass.	636,725	641,071	697,197	801,444	560,892	136,881	18,320
20	Jacksonville, Fla.	562,283	528,865	201,030	204,517	28,429	1,045	...
21	New Orleans, La.	559,770	593,471	627,525	570,445	287,104	116,375	...
22	San Jose, Cal.	555,707	461,212	204,196	95,280	21,500	...	...
23	Columbus, Oh.	535,610	540,025	471,316	375,901	125,560	17,832	...
24	St. Louis, Mo.	524,964	622,236	750,026	856,796	575,238	77,860	...
25	Seattle, Wash.	487,091	530,831	557,087	467,591	80,671	...	...
26	Denver, Col.	484,531	514,678	493,887	415,786	133,859	...	...
27	Kansas City, Mo.	476,529	507,330	475,539	456,622	163,752	...	...
28	Pittsburgh, Pa.	458,651	520,089	604,332	676,806	321,616	46,601	...
29	Nashville-Davidson, Tenn.[3]	446,941	447,877	170,874	174,307	80,865	10,165	...
30	Atlanta, Ga.	436,057	495,039	487,455	331,314	89,872	2,572	...
31	Cincinnati, Oh.	412,564	453,514	502,550	503,998	325,902	115,435	...
32	Buffalo, N.Y.	407,160	462,768	532,759	580,132	352,387	42,261	...
33	El Paso, Tex.	385,691	322,261	276,687	130,435	15,906	...	...
34	Minneapolis, Minn.	378,112	434,400	482,872	521,718	202,718	...	...
35	Omaha, Neb.	371,455	358,452	301,598	251,117	102,555	...	...
36	Toledo, Oh.	367,650	383,062	318,003	303,616	131,822	3,829	...
37	Oklahoma City, Okla.	365,916	368,164	324,253	243,504	10,037	...	...
38	Miami, Fla.	365,082	334,859	291,688	249,276	1,681	...	...
39	Fort Worth, Tex.	358,364	393,455	356,263	278,778	26,688	...	...
40	Portland, Ore.	356,732	382,352	372,676	373,628	90,426	...	...
41	Newark, N.J.	339,568	381,930	405,220	438,776	246,070	38,894	...
42	Louisville, Ky.	335,954	361,706	390,639	369,129	204,731	43,194	200
43	Long Beach, Cal.	335,602	361,427	344,168	250,767	2,252	...	...
44	Tulsa, Okla.	331,726	330,350	261,685	182,740	1,390	...	...
45	Oakland, Cal.	330,651	361,561	367,548	384,575	66,960	...	...
46	Austin, Tex.	301,147	255,869	186,545	132,459	22,258	629	...
47	Tucson, Ariz.	296,457	267,418	212,892	45,454	7,531	...	...
48	Baton Rouge, La.	294,394	271,922	152,419	125,629	11,269	3,905	...
49	Norfolk, Va.	286,694	307,951	304,869	213,513	46,624	14,326	2,95
50	Charlotte, N.C.	281,417	274,640	201,564	134,042	18,091	1,065	...
51	Tampa, Fla.	280,340	277,714	274,970	124,681	15,839	...	...
52	St. Paul, Minn.	279,535	309,866	313,411	311,349	163,065	1,112	...
53	Albuquerque, N. M.	279,401	243,751	201,189	96,815	6,238	...	...
54	Birmingham, Ala.	276,273	305,893	340,887	326,037	38,415	...	...
55	Rochester, N.Y.	267,173	295,011	318,611	332,488	162,608	36,403	...
56	Wichita, Kan.	264,901	276,554	254,698	168,279	24,671	...	...
57	Sacramento, Cal.	260,822	257,105	191,667	137,572	29,282	6,820	...
58	Akron, Oh.	251,747	275,425	290,351	274,605	42,728	3,266	...
59	Jersey City, N.J.	243,756	260,350	276,101	299,017	206,433	6,856	...
60	St. Petersburg, Fla.	234,389	216,159	181,298	96,738	1,575	...	...
61	Richmond, Va.	232,652	249,431	219,958	230,310	85,050	27,570	3,76
62	Corpus Christi, Tex.	214,838	204,525	167,690	108,287	4,703	...	...
63	Virginia Beach, Va.	213,954	172,106	8,091	5,390	...	...	...
64	Dayton, Oh.	205,986	244,564	262,332	243,872	85,333	10,977	...
65	Mobile, Ala.	196,441	190,026	194,856	129,009	38,469	20,515	...
66	Des Moines, La.	194,168	201,404	208,982	177,965	62,139	...	...
67	Anaheim, Cal.	193,616	166,408	104,184	14,566	1,456	...	...
68	Yonkers, N.Y.	192,509	204,297	190,634	152,798	47,931	...	...
69	Grand Rapids, Mich.	187,946	197,649	177,313	176,515	87,565	2,686	...
70	Lexington-Fayette, Ky.[5]	186,048	174,323	62,810	55,534	26,369	8,159	83
71	Shreveport, La.	185,711	182,064	164,372	127,206	16,013	1,728	...
72	Fort Wayne, Ind.	185,299	184,989	161,776	133,607	45,115	4,282	...
73	Knoxville, Tenn.	183,383	174,587	111,827	124,769	32,637	2,076	...
74	Syracuse, N.Y.	182,543	197,297	216,038	220,583	103,374	22,271	...
75	Colorado Springs, Col.	179,584	140,512	70,194	45,472	21,038	...	...
76	Santa Ana, Cal.	177,304	155,710	100,350	45,533	4,933	...	...
77	Fresno, Cal.	176,528	167,427	133,929	91,699	12,470	...	...
78	Flint, Mich.	174,218	193,317	196,940	163,143	13,103	...	...
79	Spokane, Wash.	173,698	170,516	181,608	161,721	36,848	...	...

Rank	City	1975	1970	1960	1950	1900	1850	1790
80	Warren, Mich.	172,755	179,260	89,246	727	350	...	...
81	Worcester, Mass.	171,566	176,572	186,587	203,486	118,421	17,049	2,095
82	Springfield, Mass.	170,790	163,905	174,463	162,399	62,059	11,766	1,574
83	Salt Lake City, Ut.	169,917	175,885	189,454	182,121	53,531	...	...
84	Madison, Wis.	168,196	171,809	126,706	96,056	19,164	1,525	...
85	Kansas City, Kan.	168,153	178,889	121,901	129,553	51,418	...	...
86	Providence, R. I.	167,724	179,116	207,493	248,674	175,597	41,513	6,380
87	Gary, Ind	167,546	188,398	178,320	133,911	...	...	...
88	Jackson, Miss.	166,512	162,380	144,422	98,271	7,816	1,881	...
89	Lubbock, Tex.	163,525	149,101	128,691	71,747	...	...	...
90	Lincoln, Neb.	163,112	152,639	128,521	98,884	40,159	...	...
91	Chattanooga, Tenn.	161,978	166,947	130,009	131,041	30,154	...	...
92	Anchorage, Alas.	161,018	126,385	44,237	11,254	...	...	...
93	Columbus, Ga.	160,103	167,377	116,779	79,611	17,614	5,942	...
94	Greensboro, N.C.	155,848	147,948	119,574	74,389	10,035	...	...
95	Montgomery, Ala.	153,343	140,102	134,393	106,525	30,346	8,728	...
96	Fort Lauderdale, Fla.	152,959	139,590	83,648	36,328	...	...	...
97	Tacoma, Wash.	151,267	154,407	147,979	143,673	37,714	...	...
98	Riverside, Cal.	150,612	140,089	84,332	46,764	7,973	...	...
99	Huntington Beach, Cal.	149,706	115,960	11,492	5,237	...	...	...
100	Las Vegas, Nev.	146,030	125,787	64,405	24,624	...	...	...
101	Rockford, Ill.	145,459	147,370	126,706	92,927	31,051	...	...
102	Bridgeport, Conn.	142,960	156,542	156,748	158,809	70,996	6,080	...
103	Little Rock, Ark.	141,143	132,483	107,813	102,213	38,307	2,167	...
104	Winston-Salem, N.C.(4)	141,018	133,683	111,135	87,811	13,650	...	...
105	Torrance, Cal.	139,776	134,968	100,991	22,241	...	...	...
106	Newport News, Va.	138,760	138,177	113,662	42,358	19,635	...	...
107	Amarillo, Tex.	138,743	127,010	137,969	74,246	1,442	...	...
108	Hartford, Conn.	138,152	158,017	162,178	177,397	72,850	13,555	2,683
109	Huntsville, Ala.	136,419	139,282	72,365	16,437	8,068	2,863	...
110	Paterson, N.J.	136,098	144,824	143,663	139,336	105,171	11,334	...
111	Raleigh, N.C.	134,231	122,830	93,931	65,679	13,643	4,518	...
112	Evansville, Ind.	133,566	138,764	141,543	128,635	59,007	3,235	...
113	Glendale, Cal.	132,360	132,664	119,442	95,702	...	...	...
114	Youngstown, Oh.	132,203	140,909	166,689	168,330	44,885	...	...
115	Springfield, Mo.	131,557	120,096	95,865	66,731	23,267	415	...
116	Erie, Pa.	127,895	129,265	138,440	130,803	52,733	5,858	...
117	New Haven, Conn.	126,845	137,707	152,048	164,443	108,027	20,345	4,487
118	Lansing, Mich.	126,805	131,403	107,807	92,129	16,485	...	...
119	Peoria, Ill.	125,983	126,963	103,162	111,856	56,100	5,095	...
120	Hampton, Va.	125,013	120,779	89,258	5,966	2,764	...	...
121	Macon, Ga.	121,157	122,423	69,764	70,252	23,272	5,720	...
122	Lakewood, Col.	120,350	92,743	...	...	...	...	...
123	Topeka, Kan.	119,203	125,011	119,484	76,791	33,608	...	...
124	Hollywood, Fla.	119,002	106,873	35,237	14,351	...	...	...
125	Garden Grove, Cal.	118,454	121,155	84,238	...	...	...	...
126	Aurora, Col.	118,060	76,477	48,548	11,421	202	...	...
127	Fremont, Cal.	117,862	100,869	43,790	...	...	...	...
128	Hialeah, Fla.	117,682	102,452	66,972	19,676	...	...	...
129	Stockton, Cal.	117,600	109,963	86,321	70,853	17,506	...	...
130	South Bend, Ind.	117,478	127,328	132,445	115,911	35,999	1,652	...
131	Livonia, Mich.	114,881	110,109	66,702	17,534	...	...	...
132	Beaumont, Tex.	113,696	117,548	119,175	94,014	9,427	...	...
133	Orlando, Fla.	113,179	100,081	88,135	52,367	2,481	...	...
134	Columbia, S. C.	111,616	113,542	97,433	86,914	21,103	6,060	...
135	Independence, Mo.	111,481	111,630	62,328	36,963	6,974	...	...
136	Garland, Tex.	111,322	81,437	38,501	10,571	819	...	...
137	Arlington, Tex.	110,543	90,229	44,775	7,692	1,079	...	...
138	Berkeley, Cal.	110,465	114,091	111,268	113,805	13,214	...	...
139	Savannah, Ga.	110,348	118,349	149,245	119,638	54,244	15,312	...
140	Albany, N.Y.	110,311	115,781	129,726	134,995	94,151	50,763	3,498
141	Cedar Rapids, Ia.	108,998	110,642	92,035	72,296	25,656	...	...
142	Portsmouth, Va.	108,674	110,963	114,773	80,039	17,427	8,626	...
143	Pasadena, Cal.	108,220	112,951	116,407	104,577	3,117	...	...
144	Waterbury, Conn.	107,065	108,033	107,130	104,477	45,859	...	...
145	Allentown, Pa.	106,624	109,871	108,347	106,756	35,416	3,779	...
146	Pueblo, Col.	105,312	99,978	91,181	63,685	28,157	...	...
147	Alexandria, Va.	105,220	110,927	91,023	61,787	14,528	8,734	2,748
148	Stamford, Conn.	105,151	108,798	92,713	74,293	15,997	...	...
149	Hammond, Ind.	104,892	107,983	111,698	87,594	12,376	...	...
150	Chesapeake, Va.	104,459	89,580	73,637	110,371	...	...	...
151	Elizabeth, N.J.	104,405	112,654	107,698	112,817	52,130	5,583	...
152	Irving, Tex.	103,703	98,961	45,985	2,621	...	...	...
153	Ann Arbor, Mich.	103,542	100,035	67,340	48,251	14,509	...	...
154	Sunnyvale, Cal.	102,462	95,976	52,898	9,829	...	...	...
155	Cambridge, Mass.	102,420	100,361	107,761	120,740	91,886	15,215	2,115
156	San Bernardino, Cal.	102,076	109,203	91,992	63,058	6,150	...	...
157	Canton, Oh.	101,852	110,053	113,631	118,912	30,667	2,603	...
158	Trenton, N.J.	101,365	104,786	114,167	128,009	73,307	6,461	...
159	Durham, N.C.	101,224	95,438	78,302	71,311	6,679	...	...
160	Roanoke, Va.	100,585	105,637	97,110	91,921	21,495	8,477	...

) Population shown for years prior to 1900 is for New York and its boroughs as constituted under the act of consolidation in 1898. (2) opulation shown is for 1862 as given in State census for that year; 1850 returns for San Francisco were destroyed by fire. (3) Figure r 1970 is for the Metropolitan Government of Nashville and Davidson County (consolidated 1963); figures for previous years are for ashville city. (4) Winston city and Salem town consolidated as Winston-Salem city between 1910 and 1920. Figure for 1900 represents combined population of Winston and Salem. (5) Lexington city and Fayette county governments consolidated in 1974. Figure r 1970 is for combined populations; figures for previous years are for Lexington city. N./A.—not available.

Foreign Born and 2d Generation in U.S.; Countries of Origin

Source: U.S. Bureau of the Census (1970 census)

The table below shows, state by state, the country of origin of U.S. residents who were either foreign born or had at lea one foreign-born parent. "Mixed" means one native and one foreign-born parent.

In the table, Germany includes both East and West Germany; West Asia includes European Turkey; and China includ both the mainland and Taiwan.

	Ala.	Alas.	Ariz.	Ark.	Cal.	Col.	Conn.	Del.	D. C.	Fla.
Mixed parents	47,742	24,842	219,830	29,269	3,234,089	219,579	708,193	48,710	39,340	695,69
Foreign born	15,988	7,763	76,570	8,287	1,757,990	60,311	261,614	15,648	33,562	540,28
U.K.	8,944	3,081	19,866	3,797	373,495	26,377	71,532	7,949	5,638	114,87
Ireland	1,912	804	5,670	1,056	109,888	7,804	60,366	4,244	3,553	36,38
Norway	643	2,501	4,745	408	69,278	4,787	5,513	510	504	12,28
Sweden	678	1,565	6,903	1,100	103,913	13,193	23,427	676	773	26,94
Denmark	555	632	3,180	559	61,757	5,508	5,471	231	426	9,94
Netherlands	526	215	2,947	537	63,772	3,609	3,586	485	408	10,80
Switzerland	408	201	1,629	989	44,483	2,419	4,291	309	533	6,90
France	1,799	630	2,972	1,010	63,449	3,695	8,388	686	1,881	14,83
Germany	12,074	3,526	25,653	9,806	360,656	43,172	60,290	5,991	5,642	123,42
Poland	2,097	765	7,930	1,331	115,833	7,882	103,820	7,263	2,787	50,59
Czech	989	536	3,483	1,170	44,964	5,074	19,871	865	804	16,22
Austria	1,556	603	5,370	1,027	77,382	9,242	24,595	1,819	1,612	35,89
Hungary	819	169	3,144	310	58,097	3,035	21,641	952	847	23,05
Yugo	421	361	2,592	198	53,868	6,079	3,447	331	474	5,72
USSR	1,854	679	8,812	912	221,198	28,023	48,150	3,523	5,597	81,83
Lithuania	415	169	1,591	355	22,063	1,146	20,469	487	953	8,93
Greece	2,092	208	2,009	500	43,645	3,111	10,933	1,117	1,716	11,63
Italy	5,771	866	12,498	2,284	340,675	21,411	227,782	12,112	4,657	84,88
Other Europe	1,358	1,208	6,952	854	189,979	7,252	32,304	1,648	2,368	47,36
Western Asia	1,753	103	2,501	672	64,565	2,272	8,655	457	1,614	13,75
China	554	282	3,162	661	136,860	1,697	2,195	523	2,099	3,11
Japan	1,392	1,203	2,310	625	144,335	6,005	1,492	516	602	4,84
Other Asia	1,797	1,808	3,488	945	222,709	4,418	6,008	1,690	4,084	10,96
Canada	5,232	6,499	26,136	3,016	439,862	21,580	126,305	4,047	3,914	114,61
Mexico	975	766	113,816	862	1,112,008	24,759	1,220	246	611	11,04
Cuba	680	56	505	86	47,699	945	5,772	483	902	252,52
Other Amer	2,146	576	3,586	572	176,586	3,519	18,844	1,239	11,514	44,41

	Ga.	Ha.	Ida.	Ill.	Ind.	Ia.	Kan.	Ky.	La.	Me.
Mixed parents	78,528	180,577	60,972	1,572,843	268,060	257,342	147,206	56,080	100,221	149,74
Foreign born	32,988	75,595	12,572	628,898	83,198	40,217	27,842	16,553	39,542	43,01
U.K.	14,517	5,114	10,406	115,891	30,039	22,008	15,986	7,619	9,252	12,07
Ireland	3,461	1,056	1,653	101,856	9,931	9,441	4,853	3,156	3,240	6,52
Norway	933	664	3,534	34,922	2,934	20,418	1,920	457	1,331	1,23
Sweden	1,641	841	5,333	98,254	8,274	21,108	9,622	817	1,284	2,74
Denmark	759	532	3,627	22,021	2,269	20,024	3,200	473	729	1,05
Netherlands	971	355	1,568	27,189	6,760	19,213	1,692	555	1,005	44
Switzerland	517	275	1,736	11,827	3,710	3,476	3,256	1,650	608	22
France	2,684	811	865	19,266	5,372	2,911	2,775	1,848	5,420	1,05
Germany	20,951	5,112	9,894	312,070	64,883	101,974	43,252	21,438	14,237	4,48
Poland	4,574	775	684	299,316	34,590	3,323	4,046	2,147	2,771	2,53
Czech	1,456	385	1,118	88,259	13,681	10,995	4,978	857	977	74
Austria	2,646	746	1,091	65,026	10,441	3,347	5,581	1,626	1,751	82
Hungary	1,286	342	357	35,822	14,108	1,007	938	1,103	1,267	24
Yugo	824	198	421	59,280	14,410	2,202	3,815	451	1,412	13
USSR	5,831	828	3,136	110,321	9,933	4,563	17,664	2,531	3,073	2,87
Lithuania	798	207	151	58,285	4,265	1,226	507	545	358	1,17
Greece	2,984	371	657	48,669	7,852	2,085	965	861	1,560	1,28
Italy	5,220	1,656	1,595	228,984	17,935	7,683	4,552	4,499	29,031	6,08
Other Europe	3,668	8,318	3,966	67,143	15,478	6,160	3,810	2,092	4,149	2,98
Western Asia	2,457	344	177	18,270	4,098	1,670	1,738	1,523	2,758	1,07
China	1,278	20,939	456	11,833	1,976	1,073	786	539	1,117	28
Japan	1,775	105,223	1,322	12,948	1,888	787	2,435	1,056	1,308	22
Other Asia	4,068	79,410	571	28,637	4,948	2,448	3,066	2,324	3,109	92
Canada	10,021	5,865	10,452	80,611	21,920	13,297	10,425	4,823	6,090	136,80
Mexico	1,562	1,159	5,669	117,268	18,325	4,546	13,728	692	4,865	27
Cuba	3,816	235	73	19,649	1,690	382	796	556	6,711	22
Other Amer	3,880	1,371	371	31,276	4,208	1,538	2,011	1,998	18,235	80

	Md.	Mass.	Mich.	Minn.	Miss.	Mo.	Mon.	Neb.	Nev.	N.H.
Mixed parents	329,813	1,397,064	1,259,961	609,218	22,862	245,948	101,688	175,556	50,274	133,50
Foreign born	124,345	494,660	424,309	98,056	8,125	65,744	19,634	28,796	18,179	37,04
U.K.	40,291	152,741	148,612	25,672	3,910	23,080	11,293	11,083	6,969	14,04
Ireland	18,267	218,798	28,667	11,900	816	15,470	5,274	4,846	1,991	8,43
Norway	3,385	8,969	12,899	114,221	347	2,257	14,595	3,183	1,163	1,21
Sweden	4,546	38,753	33,639	114,512	445	6,274	6,177	17,099	1,670	2,77
Denmark	2,461	5,163	11,951	22,762	294	2,879	4,302	13,202	1,485	59
Netherlands	3,312	5,656	72,763	13,166	237	2,425	2,731	1,754	796	61
Switzerland	2,437	3,845	5,442	4,282	160	5,204	1,225	2,054	1,103	42
France	6,519	12,342	12,149	3,766	733	5,297	1,160	1,296	1,959	1,26
Germany	59,680	54,846	184,192	137,442	4,960	77,748	15,593	62,726	7,023	6,30
Poland	39,334	117,992	214,085	26,931	730	15,469	1,781	8,333	1,578	6,88
Czech	11,111	6,434	32,176	17,905	377	7,504	2,171	19,551	796	42
Austria	13,516	16,898	40,730	17,266	576	11,755	3,464	3,612	1,483	1,29
Hungary	7,817	5,583	39,202	3,741	266	5,861	828	1,060	751	48
Yugo	3,148	1,776	30,375	12,266	574	6,517	3,020	1,599	957	22
USSR	46,332	104,223	65,606	18,666	534	19,127	11,365	14,160	2,247	2,98
Lithuania	9,090	32,617	16,908	2,445	152	2,168	242	1,428	282	1,92
Greece	12,508	39,669	19,519	2,833	471	4,209	541	859	1,205	5,04

(Continued)

Continued from previous page)

	Md.	Mass.	Mich.	Minn.	Miss.	Mo.	Mon.	Neb.	Nev.	N.H.
aly	49,619	294,318	117,064	12,910	3,957	30,114	3,415	6,414	7,927	6,465
ther Europe	15,069	117,653	94,603	41,228	954	9,085	4,157	3,823	3,645	3,952
estern Asia	8,124	27,159	31,579	2,411	1,249	3,279	377	771	633	1,281
nina	5,975	11,324	5,725	1,998	1,078	2,337	245	543	811	541
apan	3,784	3,390	4,952	2,206	394	2,618	675	1,106	1,084	370
ther Asia	13,832	10,897	12,925	4,749	945	5,301	746	1,428	2,148	662
anada	25,300	466,942	353,154	57,604	2,496	15,532	21,106	8,247	7,587	96,834
exico	2,714	2,136	31,067	4,575	783	8,353	1,485	5,552	5,760	209
uba	4,931	6,915	3,231	765	241	1,131	45	608	1,306	195
ther Amer.	19,309	27,299	13,339	3,390	1,427	3,857	426	1,017	1,147	728

	N.J.	N.M.	N.Y.	N.C.	N.D.	Oh.	Okla.	Ore.	Pa.	R.I.
lixed parents	1,521,045	66,170	3,885,445	65,661	127,689	994,850	72,713	229,357	1,687,145	237,233
oreign born	634,818	22,510	2,109,776	28,620	18,437	316,496	20,160	66,149	445,895	74,374
.K.	172,308	6,000	334,424	12,826	3,537	108,027	9,812	28,525	198,190	34,178
eland	122,600	1,718	386,403	2,506	1,248	37,941	2,386	7,175	118,174	21,041
lorway	17,474	872	47,605	773	38,722	4,382	901	18,085	5,251	1,093
weden	19,366	1,681	52,058	1,401	8,434	12,539	1,962	17,830	20,370	6,669
enmark	11,000	721	20,911	728	3,442	4,492	1,396	8,792	4,935	574
letherlands	28,440	655	32,043	1,444	1,120	6,539	1,101	4,776	5,691	749
witzerland	13,219	557	23,773	678	426	12,337	1,200	6,816	8,039	522
rance	22,152	1,219	56,861	1,820	402	13,640	1,669	3,263	18,484	3,261
ermany	219,178	7,438	516,216	16,614	21,004	188,386	21,475	40,242	202,611	768
oland	217,509	1,422	557,478	3,037	1,952	116,262	2,670	4,855	243,752	13,389
zech	51,599	763	90,641	1,132	2,473	93,187	3,411	4,144	118,855	763
ustria	83,165	1,483	237,836	1,664	2,254	62,829	1,893	5,294	145,815	2,896
lungary	70,424	687	115,474	1,190	1,590	82,944	793	2,298	62,014	589
ugo	16,202	899	41,756	449	194	73,843	400	3,220	54,424	278
SSR	143,234	1,725	569,813	2,928	33,177	54,520	5,463	15,709	157,348	11,198
ithuania	22,658	371	42,863	545	117	13,979	559	778	43,183	1,459
reece	25,703	747	90,886	3,883	168	22,210	667	3,480	23,198	2,242
aly	515,889	3,916	1,330,057	4,658	485	166,629	3,531	9,644	444,841	73,255
ther Europe	69,176	1,725	197,966	2,764	4,076	48,002	2,584	13,752	52,748	33,222
Vestern Asia	23,415	865	87,036	2,536	770	18,246	2,488	2,348	20,191	4,211
hina	7,748	506	66,407	1,178	150	4,987	758	4,423	6,010	1,069
apan	6,064	1,029	17,304	2,988	391	5,169	1,810	3,983	4,480	783
ther Asia	16,085	1,137	51,785	3,583	555	14,066	2,539	5,345	15,248	2,278
anada	58,720	5,663	286,047	10,334	15,630	63,258	7,811	53,002	47,827	66,003
lexico	3,301	37,822	12,249	1,770	276	13,349	6,071	7,739	4,707	407
uba	71,233	418	98,479	1,330	46	3,593	352	689	5,195	516
ther Amer.	54,867	1,484	415,906	3,012	378	11,679	2,114	2,887	20,183	2,788

	S.C.	S.D.	Tenn.	Tex.	Ut.	Vt.	Va.	Wash.	W.Va.	Wis.
lixed parents	35,436	98,147	49,368	889,246	102,036	62,680	179,518	481,586	57,358	617,479
oreign born	14,364	10,899	19,024	309,772	29,573	18,482	72,281	156,020	16,662	130,669
.K.	7,779	4,562	8,682	49,185	28,531	7,008	32,737	60,522	8,259	28,446
eland	1,336	1,980	2,087	12,143	1,416	3,071	10,162	13,266	1,742	9,433
orway	392	18,898	600	5,442	4,113	651	3,077	60,427	191	52,681
weden	686	7,790	1,081	10,873	7,477	1,142	4,144	45,251	601	27,352
enmark	325	6,584	630	4,801	10,464	476	2,195	14,422	170	18,959
etherlands	516	5,126	698	4,722	7,617	518	2,690	13,297	223	15,315
witzerland	576	950	802	4,314	3,392	529	1,640	7,675	762	14,316
rance	1,069	399	1,333	8,992	1,014	759	6,210	6,145	881	4,457
ermany	9,193	26,792	11,675	104,726	14,179	4,195	32,596	71,353	6,960	234,767
oland	1,701	1,052	2,789	16,328	904	2,797	9,423	9,821	6,360	71,534
zech	704	3,507	776	29,536	668	393	4,675	6,137	2,996	26,465
ustria	935	1,305	1,354	13,397	1,436	614	6,827	10,332	2,572	27,343
ungary	479	503	995	4,852	394	602	3,814	4,269	2,931	12,448
ugo	391	280	376	2,992	1,337	84	1,775	7,580	2,549	19,873
SSR	1,661	14,041	3,649	16,149	1,151	1,171	11,129	23,466	1,996	24,246
thuania	228	140	388	2,069	112	211	2,040	1,436	602	5,796
reece	2,188	284	1,563	6,168	3,372	504	5,712	4,061	1,894	4,746
aly	2,653	616	6,054	26,886	4,688	4,982	18,026	21,422	17,906	30,513
ther Europe	1,658	2,659	1,678	15,713	2,396	1,707	8,005	24,907	2,564	22,142
estern Asia	1,382	523	1,579	9,219	672	652	6,248	3,411	2,522	3,388
hina	408	270	1,032	7,606	983	165	2,936	8,107	135	2,141
apan	892	273	1,352	8,388	2,834	66	4,691	15,777	433	1,871
ther Asia	2,106	403	2,726	12,465	1,533	449	14,060	18,701	1,704	4,928
anada	4,805	6,617	6,213	35,900	11,194	46,176	24,048	136,546	2,492	36,888
exico	668	472	1,036	711,058	7,710	111	3,167	17,892	513	9,160
uba	860	58	894	7,749	116	7	4,479	570	110	787
ther Amer.	1,405	303	1,593	21,300	1,593	356	10,538	5,173	772	3,834

Wyoming

lixed parents	31,014	Germany	5,721	Other Europe	1,194
oreign born	6,989	Poland	1,033	Western Asia	177
.K.	5,367	Czech	824	China	177
eland	1,066	Austria	1,300	Japan	341
orway	1,257	Hungary	250	Other Asia	385
weden	2,156	Yugo.	1,263	Canada	3,069
enmark	1,505	USSR	2,913	Mexico	2,638
etherlands	332	Lithuania	82	Cuba	...
witzerland	563	Greece	728	Other Amer.	277
ance	504	Italy	1,750		

Poverty by Family Status, Sex, and Race

Source: U.S. Bureau of the Census
(In 1975, according to poverty level defined in table below. Thousands)

	1975		1974r		1973		1972	
	No.	%*	No.	%*	No.	%*	No.	%*
Total poor	**25,877**	**12.3**	**23,370**	**11.2**	**22,973**	**11.1**	**24,460**	**11.9**
In families	**20,789**	**10.9**	**18,817**	**9.9**	**18,299**	**9.7**	**19,577**	**10.3**
Head	5,450	9.7	4,922	8.8	4,828	8.8	5,075	9.3
Related children	10,882	16.8	9,967	15.1	9,453	14.2	10,082	14.9
Other relatives	4,457	6.4	3,928	5.7	4,018	5.9	4,420	6.6
Unrelated individuals	5,088	25.1	4,553	24.1	4,674	25.6	4,883	29.0
In male-head families	**11,943**	**7.1**	**10,355**	**6.2**	**10,121**	**6.0**	**11,463**	**6.8**
Head	3,020	6.2	2,598	5.4	2,635	5.5	2,917	6.1
Related children	5,284	9.8	4,605	8.3	4,282	7.6	4,988	8.6
Other relatives	3,638	5.7	3,151	5.0	3,204	5.1	3,558	5.7
Unrelated male individuals	1,667	19.9	1,547	19.5	1,495	19.8	1,410	21.1
In female-head families	**8,846**	**37.5**	**8,462**	**36.5**	**8,178**	**37.5**	**8,114**	**38.2**
Head	2,430	32.5	2,324	32.1	2,193	32.2	2,158	32.7
Related children	5,597	52.7	5,361	51.5	5,171	52.1	5,094	53.1
Other relatives	819	15.0	777	14.1	814	16.0	862	17.0
Unrelated female individuals	3,422	28.9	3,007	27.3	3,179	29.7	3,473	34.3
Total white poor	**17,770**	**9.7**	**15,736**	**8.6**	**15,142**	**8.4**	**16,203**	**9.0**
In families	**13,799**	**8.3**	**12,181**	**7.3**	**11,412**	**6.9**	**12,268**	**7.4**
Head	3,838	7.7	3,352	6.8	3,219	6.6	3,441	7.1
Female	1,394	25.9	1,289	24.8	1,190	24.5	1,135	24.3
Related children	6,748	12.5	6,079	11.0	5,462	9.7	5,784	10.1
Other relatives	3,213	5.2	2,750	4.5	2,731	4.5	3,043	5.1
Unrelated individuals	3,972	22.7	3,555	21.8	3,730	23.7	3,935	27.1
Total black poor	**7,545**	**31.3**	**7,182**	**30.3**	**7,388**	**31.4**	**7,710**	**33.3**
In families	**6,533**	**30.1**	**6,255**	**29.3**	**6,560**	**30.8**	**6,841**	**32.4**
Head	1,513	27.1	1,479	26.9	1,527	28.1	1,529	29.0
Female	1,004	50.1	1,010	52.2	974	52.7	972	53.3
Related children	3,884	41.4	3,713	39.6	3,822	40.6	4,025	42.7
Other relatives	1,136	16.9	1,063	16.4	1,211	18.7	1,287	20.0
Unrelated individuals	1,011	42.1	927	39.3	828	37.9	870	42.9

r-revised. *Percent of total population in that general category who fell below poverty level. For example, of all black female heads of households in 1974, 52.2 per cent were poor.

Estimated Poverty Level, 1976, by Family Size and Sex of Head

		Non-Farm			Farm		
Number of family members	**Total**	**Total**	**Male**	**Female**	**Total**	**Male**	**Female**
1 member	$2,870	$2,880	$3,020	$2,790	$2,440	$2,530	$2,350
Under 65 yrs.	2,950	2,960	3,070	2,840	2,530	2,610	2,410
65 yrs. and over	2,720	2,730	2,760	2,720	2,320	2,340	2,310
2 members	3,690	3,710	3,720	3,660	3,130	3,130	3,000
Head under 65 yrs.	3,810	3,830	3,850	3,730	3,260	3,260	3,100
Head 65 yrs. and over	3,420	3,440	3,450	3,420	2,930	2,930	2,930
3 members	4,520	4,540	4,570	4,420	3,850	3,860	3,680
4 members	5,780	5,820	5,820	5,790	4,970	4,970	4,880
5 members	6,840	6,870	6,880	6,810	5,870	5,870	5,920
6 members	7,690	7,740	7,740	7,690	6,580	6,590	6,460
7 members or more	9,450	9,540	9,580	9,330	8,080	8,080	8,090

Poverty Level, 1975

		Non-Farm			Farm		
Numbers of family members	**Total**	**Total**	**Male**	**Female**	**Total**	**Male**	**Female**
1 member	$2,717	$2,724	$2,851	$2,635	$2,305	$2,396	$2,224
Under 65 yrs.	2,791	2,797	2,902	2,685	2,396	2,466	2,282
65 years and over	2,572	2,581	2,608	2,574	2,196	2,216	2,187
2 members	3,485	3,506	3,515	3,460	2,955	2,963	2,834
Head under 65 yrs.	3,599	3,617	3,636	3,530	3,079	3,086	2,933
Head 65 yrs. and over	3,232	3,257	3,260	3,237	2,772	2,772	2,770
3 members	4,269	4,293	4,317	4,175	3,643	3,652	3,480
4 members	5,469	5,500	5,502	5,473	4,695	4,697	4,616
5 members	6,463	6,499	6,504	6,434	5,552	5,552	5,595
6 members	7,272	7,316	7,322	7,270	6,224	6,230	6,105
7 members or more	8,939	9,022	9,056	8,818	7,639	7,639	7,647

Income Distribution by Population Fifths

Source: U.S. Bureau of the Census

	Top income of each fifth				Average	Percent distribution of total income					
Families, 1975	**Lowest**	**Second**	**Third**	**Fourth**	**Top 5%**	**Lowest fifth**	**Second fifth**	**Third fifth**	**Fourth fifth**	**Highest fifth**	**Top 5%**
Total	$6,914	$11,465	$16,000	$22,037	$34,144	5.4	11.8	17.6	24.1	41.1	15.5
White	7,430	12,000	16,450	22,614	35,000	5.7	12.1	17.6	23.9	40.7	15.4
Black and other	4,100	7,364	11,358	17,017	26,600	4.7	10.1	16.7	25.1	43.3	15.4
Black	3,966	6,850	10,696	16,000	24,850	4.9	10.2	16.8	25.3	42.9	14.7

Aid to Families with Dependent Children

Source: Social and Rehabilitation Service, U.S. Health, Education and Welfare Department

State	No. of Families	Number of recipients: Total[1]	Number of recipients: Children	Payments to recipients: Total amount	Payments to recipients: Average per family	Payments to recipients: Average per recipient	% change from January 1977: No. of recip.	% change from January 1977: Amount
Alabama	54,043	166,798	122,772	6,124,017	113.32	36.72	0.1	24.1
Alaska	3,944	10,526	7,721	1,159,819	294.07	110.19	-1.8	8.0
Arizona	18,962	58,177	43,309	2,690,624	141.90	46.25	-14.3	-2.5
Arkansas	30,822	95,314	70,926	4,154,844	134.80	43.59	-12.3	-3.4
California	477,201	1,448,332	986,270	142,144,507	297.87	98.14	0.2	15.1
Colorado	31,427	91,684	64,339	6,419,468	204.27	70.02	-7.1	-5.8
Connecticut	43,189	134,633	95,818	11,659,114	269.96	86.60	0.2	4.0
Delaware	10,622	31,702	22,701	2,186,033	205.80	68.96	0.4	9.1
Dist. of Columbia	30,596	94,488	67,394	7,448,038	243.43	78.83	-9.2	-2.2
Florida	81,244	243,429	180,058	11,335,983	139.53	46.57	-0.3	16.0
Georgia	87,577	252,188	187,811	8,477,460	96.80	33.62	-17.1	-13.4
Guam	1,129	4,274	3,261	215,600	190.97	50.44	27.9	30.2
Hawaii	17,034	55,364	37,742	6,158,315	361.53	111.23	2.4	10.4
Idaho	6,854	19,894	13,860	1,714,345	250.12	86.17	0.8	2.8
Illinois	227,480	777,957	558,324	61,414,454	269.98	78.94	-3.9	-4.4
Indiana	56,185	168,758	122,646	9,455,134	168.29	56.03	-5.1	-4.9
Iowa	31,454	95,933	64,972	7,799,855	247.98	81.31	0.6	-5.4
Kansas	27,457	75,859	55,301	6,262,982	228.10	82.56	0.7	13.0
Kentucky	68,114	210,175	145,132	11,622,001	170.63	55.30	5.7	4.1
Louisiana	66,186	221,697	166,006	7,919,027	119.65	35.72	-4.7	-4.4
Maine	19,775	60,059	41,899	3,707,975	187.51	61.74	-10.3	0.5
Maryland	74,720	214,903	150,864	12,889,264	172.50	59.98	-2.0	-0.7
Massachusetts	119,988	371,686	255,912	35,986,561	299.92	96.82	3.1	4.9
Michigan	204,065	653,012	453,039	59,773,639	292.91	91.54	-4.1	-0.7
Minnesota	46,080	132,214	91,419	12,532,238	271.97	94.79	1.2	5.6
Mississippi	52,730	175,294	134,160	2,526,862	47.92	14.41	-6.0	-5.7
Missouri	89,550	271,661	193,418	12,132,151	135.48	44.66	-0.8	-1.9
Montana	6,472	18,056	12,908	1,121,787	173.33	62.13	-4.2	5.4
Nebraska	11,340	34,057	24,318	2,304,537	203.22	67.67	-7.5	-5.4
Nevada	4,419	12,552	8,990	686,477	155.35	54.69	-19.6	-20.8
New Hampshire	8,518	25,313	17,536	1,909,004	224.11	75.42	-6.5	-3.6
New Jersey	137,683	448,132	318,104	36,287,956	263.56	80.98	-1.2	-4.6
New Mexico	17,541	55,773	40,009	2,458,751	140.17	44.08	-6.9	-5.4
New York	378,543	1,244,524	859,939	138,297,937	365.34	111.13	1.1	1.9
North Carolina	70,855	200,813	147,861	10,918,172	154.09	54.37	4.5	3.4
North Dakota	4,764	13,807	9,868	1,235,358	259.31	89.47	1.3	10.7
Ohio (e)	186,508	568,864	388,506	36,165,647	193.91	63.58	-3.0	-5.5
Oklahoma	28,654	89,681	66,980	5,811,431	202.81	64.80	0.5	10.4
Oregon	42,952	123,994	81,817	11,040,888	257.05	89.04	7.0	15.7
Pennsylvania	204,099	654,430	445,241	58,381,401	286.04	89.21	2.1	5.8
Puerto Rico	43,877[2]	193,693[2]	140,524[2]	2,009,185[2]	45.79	10.37	-8.8	-1.0
Rhode Island	17,126	53,064	36,873	4,531,463	264.60	85.40	2.9	7.3
South Carolina	46,284	139,109	101,435	3,919,609	84.69	28.18	0.2	-0.7
South Dakota	8,096	24,180	17,800	1,649,193	203.70	68.20	-3.6	-2.7
Tennessee	68,900	202,991	148,035	7,141,209	103.65	35.18	-4.3	-2.0
Texas	98,893	320,059	238,339	10,278,262	103.93	32.11	-10.5	-10.6
Utah	12,095	36,113	26,407	2,987,484	247.00	82.73	-3.3	-2.0
Vermont	6,963	22,790	14,927	1,762,199	253.08	77.32	-8.1	-8.9
Virgin Islands	1,151[2]	3,766[2]	3,063[2]	147,651[2]	128.28	39.21	-1.7	2.4
Virginia	59,074	173,322	124,227	11,233,620	190.16	64.81	-3.4	-2.6
Washington	49,875	146,580	95,240	13,071,181	262.08	89.17	-2.6	2.5
West Virginia	21,370	65,183	45,054	3,703,896	173.32	56.82	-12.1	-8.2
Wisconsin	68,053	202,087	140,228	19,355,274	284.41	95.78	8.0	3.8
Wyoming	2,386	6,519	4,738	466,704	195.60	71.59	0.6	13.9
Total	•3,584,919	11,215,463	7,896,041	$844,786,586	$235.65	$75.32	-2.0	2.7

(e) Estimated. (1) Includes as recipients the children and one or both parents or one caretaker relative other than a parent in families in which the requirements of such adults were considered in determining the amount of assistance. (2) Incomplete. Data for foster care not reported by Puerto Rico and the Virgin Islands.

Recipients and Payments, 1950-1976

Category		1950, Dec.	1955, Dec.	1960, Dec.	1965, Dec.	1970, Dec.	1975, Dec. (b)	1976, Dec.
Old-age:	Recipients	2,786,000	2,538,000	2,305,000	2,087,000	2,082,000	2,333,685	2,175,442
	Total amt.	$119,955,000	$127,003,000	$135,759,000	$131,674,000	$161,642,000	$217,002,000	$209,553,000
	Avg. amt.	$43.05	$50.05	$58.90	$63.10	$77.65	$92.99	$96.33
	(a) Avg. real $	52.60	62.41	66.38	66.75	66.78	57.65	56.50
AFDC:	Recipients	2,233,000	2,192,000	3,073,000	4,396,000	9,659,000	11,389,000	11,215,463
	Total amt.	$46,529,000	$51,472,000	$87,051,000	$144,355,000	$485,877,000	$824,648,000	$844,786,586
	Avg. amt.	$20.85	$23.50	$28.35	$32.85	$50.30	$72.40	$75.32
	(a) Avg. real $	25.47	29.30	31.95	34.76	43.26	44.89	44.18
Blind	Recipients	97,500	104,000	107,000	85,100	81,000	75,315	77,223
	Total amt.	$4,481,000	$5,803,000	$7,215,000	$6,922,000	$8,446,000	$11,220,000	$11,991,000
	Avg. amt.	$46.00	$55.55	$67.45	$81.35	$104.35	$148.97	$155.28
	(a) Avg. real $	56.21	69.27	76.02	86.07	89.74	92.36	91.07
Disabled	Recipients	68,800	241,000	369,000	557,000	935,000	1,950,625	2,033,487
	Total amt.	$3,033,000	$11,750,000	$20,711,00C	$37,035,000	$91,325,000	$279,073,000	$299,723,000
	Avg. amt.	$44.10	$48.75	$56.15	$66.50	$97.65	$143.07	$147.39
	(a) Avg. real $	53.89	60.79	63.28	70.36	83.98	88.70	86.45

(a) Dollar amounts adjusted to represent actual purchasing power in terms of average value of dollar during 1967. (b) Administration of the public assistance programs of Old-age Assistance, Aid to the Blind, and Aid to the Disabled was transferred to the Social Security Administration by Public Law 92-603 effective 1/1/74.

Jewish Population by Countries and Cities

Source: Jewish Statistical Bureau, Dr. H. S. Linfield, Exec. Secy. (latest estimates)

North America	6,145,500
Central and South America	756,685
Europe	4,142,750
Asia	3,001,210
Australia and New Zealand	77,000
Africa	185,200
World Total	**14,308,345**

Europe

Albania	300
Austria	12,000
Belgium	41,000
Bulgaria	7,000
Czechoslovakia	14,000
Denmark	6,500
Finland	1,300
France	550,000
Germany	32,000
Gibraltar	600
Great Britain	450,000
Greece	6,500
Hungary	80,000
Irish Free State	4,000
Italy	35,000
Luxembourg	1,000
Malta	50
Netherlands	30,000
Norway	900
Poland	8,000
Portugal	600
Romania	80,000
Soviet Union	2,700,000
Spain	9,000
Sweden	15,000
Switzerland	21,000
Turkey	30,000
Yugoslavia	7,000

North America

Canada	308,000
United States	5,800,000
Mexico	37,500

Central and South America

Argentina	475,000
Barbados	85
Bolivia	2,000
Brazil	155,000
Chile	30,000
Colombia	12,000
Costa Rica	1,500
Cuba	1,500
Curacao	700
Dominican Rep.	200
Surinam	650
Ecuador	1,000
El Salvador	300
Guatemala	1,900
Haiti	150
Honduras	200
Jamaica	500
Nicaragua	200
Panama	2,000
Paraguay	1,200
Peru	5,300
Trinidad	300
Uruguay	50,000
Venezuela	15,000

Asia

Afghanistan	200
Burma	200
Cyprus	30
China	30
Hong Kong	200
India	12,000
Indonesia	100
Iran	80,000
Iraq	500
Israel	3,400,000[1]
Japan	500
Lebanon	2,000
Pakistan	250
Philippines	200
Singapore	500
Syria	4,000
Yemen	500

Africa

Algeria	1,000
Congo	250
Egypt	500
Ethiopia	20,000
Kenya	200
Libya	50
Morocco	30,000
Rhodesia	4,800
Tunisia	8,000
Rep. of South Africa	120,000
Zambia	400

Australia and New Zealand

Australia	72,000
New Zealand	5,000

(1.) Includes about 500,000 Christians and Mohammedans.

Estimated Jewish Population in Foreign Cities

Amsterdam	20,000
Antwerp	13,000
Ascalon[1]	46,700
Ashdod[1]	48,200
Athens	2,800
Basle	2,500
Beersheba[1]	93,400
Belgrade	1,500
Berlin	6,000
Bet Shean[1]	12,000
Birmingham	6,000
B'nai B'rak	81,000
Bordeaux	6,400
Brussels	24,500
Bucharest	40,000
Budapest	65,000
Buenos Aires	350,000
Casablanca	30,000
Copenhagen	6,000
Czernowitz	70,000
Elat[1]	4,000
Glasgow	13,000
Haifa[1]	210,000
Istanbul	22,000
Jerusalem[1]	284,500
Johannesburg	63,000
Kharkov	80,000
Kiev	170,000
Kovno	8,000
Leeds	18,000
Leningrad	165,000
Liverpool	6,500
Lod (Lydda)[1]	30,200
London (Gr.)	280,000
Lvov	40,000
Lyons	20,000
Marseilles	65,000
Manchester and Salford	35,000
Melbourne	34,000
Milan	10,000
Minsk	47,000
Montreal	114,000
Moscow	285,000
Nazareth[1]	35,400
Nazareth Illet[1]	18,000
Nice	20,000
Odessa	120,000
Ottawa	7,000
Paris	300,000
Petach Tikvah	107,000
Ramath Gan[1]	121,000
Rehovoth	46,400
Riga	40,000
Rio de Janeiro	50,000
Rome	15,000
Safed	14,400
Santiago	25,000
Sao Paulo	65,000
Stockholm	8,000
Strasbourg	12,000
Sydney	28,000
Teheran	50,000
Tel Aviv-Jaffa[1]	394,000
Tiberias[1]	35,300
Toronto	110,000
Toulouse	18,000
Vancouver	11,500
Vienna	9,000
Warsaw	5,000
Winnipeg	20,000
Zurich	6,150

(1.) Includes some Christians, Moslems.

Estimated Jewish Population Centers in U.S.

Albany	13,500
Alexandria, Arlington and Fairfax cos., Va.	15,000
Atlanta	18,000
Atlantic City	10,000
Baltimore	94,000
Bergen Co., N.J.	100,000
Boston	180,000
Bridgeport	14,500
Buffalo	23,500
Camden	26,000
Chicago	253,000
Cincinnati	30,000
Cleveland	80,000
Columbus	13,000
Dallas	20,000
Denver	26,000
Detroit	80,000
Elizabeth*	50,000
Hartford	23,000
Hollywood, Fla.	25,000
Houston	22,000
Jersey City	10,000
Kansas City	22,000
Long Beach, Cal.	16,000
Los Angeles*	463,000
Lynn	19,000
Miami*	225,000
Milwaukee	23,900
Minneapolis	22,085
Montg'y Co., Md.	50,000
New B'nswick*	18,000
New Haven	20,000
New Orleans	10,500
New York City	1,228,000
Manhattan	171,000
Bronx	143,000
Brooklyn	514,000
Queens	379,000
Richmond	21,000
N.Y. City environs:	
Nassau and Suffolk cos.	605,000
Westchester Co.	165,000
Newark:	
Essex Co., N.J.	95,000
Oakland:	
Alameda and Contra Costa cos., Cal.*	21,000
Orange Co., Cal.	37,500
Passaic	9,200
Paterson*	28,000
Philadelphia*	350,000
Phoenix*	14,000
Pittsburgh	52,000
Prince George Co., Md.	15,000
Providence*	22,000
Richmond, Va.	10,000
Rochester	21,500
Rockland Co., N.Y.	25,000
St. Louis	60,000
St. Paul	10,000
San Diego	15,000
San Francisco*	75,000
Seattle	13,000
Springfield, Mass.	11,000
Stanford	10,800
Syracuse	11,000
Trenton, N.J.	9,900
Washington, D.C.	112,500
Worcester*	10,000

*Indicates greater area.

Black Population by States

Source: Bureau of the Census (1970)

Ala.	903,467
Alas.	8,911
Ariz.	53,344
Ark.	352,445
Cal.	1,400,143
Col.	66,411
Conn.	181,177
Del.	78,276
D.C.	537,712
Fla.	1,401,651
Ga.	1,187,149
Ha.	7,573
Ida.	2,130
Ill.	1,425,674
Ind.	357,464
Ia.	32,596
Kan.	106,977
Ky.	230,793
La.	1,086,832
Me.	2,800
Md.	699,479
Mass.	175,817
Mich.	991,066
Minn.	34,868
Miss.	815,770
Mo.	480,172
Mon.	1,995
Neb.	39,911
Nev.	27,762
N. H.	2,505
N. J.	770,292
N. M.	19,555
N. Y.	2,168,949
N. C.	1,126,478
N. D.	2,494
Oh.	970,477
Okla.	171,892
Ore.	26,308
Pa.	1,016,514
R. I.	25,338
S. C.	789,041
S. D.	1,627
Tenn.	621,261
Tex.	1,399,005
Ut.	6,617
Vt.	761
Va.	861,368
Wash.	71,308
W. Va.	67,342
Wis.	128,224
Wy.	2,568
Total	**22,580,289**

U.S. Places of 5,000 or More Population—with ZIP Codes

Source: U.S. Bureau of the Census; U.S. Postal Service

The listings below show the official urban population of the United States. "Urban population" is defined as all persons living in (a) places of 5,000 inhabitants or more, incorporated as cities, villages, boroughs (except Alaska), and towns (except in New England, New York, New Jersey, Pennsylvania and Wisconsin), but excluding those persons living in the rural portions of extended cities; (b) unincorporated places of 5,000 inhabitants or more; and (c) other territory, incorporated or unincorporated, included in urbanized areas.

The non-urban portion of an extended city contains one or more areas, each at least 5 square miles in extent and with a population density of less than 100 persons per square mile. The area or areas constitute at least 25 percent of the legal city's land area of a total of 25 square miles or more.

In New England, New York, New Jersey, Pennsylvania, and Wisconsin, minor civil divisions called "towns" often include rural areas and one or more urban areas. Only the urban areas of these "towns" are included here, except in the case of New England where entire town populations, which may include some rural population, are shown in italics. Boroughs in Alaska may contain one or more urban areas which are included here.

(u) means place is unincorporated.

Where special censuses were taken after April 1, 1970, the year appears after the name of the place.

The ZIP Code of each place appears before the name of that place, if it is obtainable.

CAUTION—Where an asterisk (*) appears before the ZIP Code, ask your local postmaster for the correct ZIP Code for a specific address within the place listed.

ZIP code	Place	1970	1960
	Alabama		
35950	Albertville	9,963	8,250
35010	Alexander City	12,358	13,140
36420	Andalusia	10,092	10,263
36201	Anniston	31,533	33,657
.....	Anniston Northwest(u)	6,609	......
35611	Athens	14,360	9,330
36502	Atmore	8,293	8,173
35954	Attalla	7,510	8,257
36830	Auburn	22,767	16,261
36507	Bay Minette	6,727	5,197
35020	Bessemer	33,428	33,052
*35203	Birmingham	300,910	340,887
35226	Bluff Park(u)	12,431	......
35957	Boaz	5,635	4,654
36426	Brewton	6,747	6,309
35215	Center Point(u)	15,675	......
36611	Chickasaw	8,447	10,002
35045	Clanton	5,868	5,683
35055	Cullman	12,601	10,883
36322	Daleville	5,182	693
35601	Decatur	38,044	29,217
36732	Demopolis	7,651	7,377
36301	Dothan	36,733	31,440
36330	Enterprise	15,591	11,410
36027	Eufaula	9,102	8,357
35064	Fairfield 1975	12,976	15,816
36532	Fairhope	5,720	4,858
35630	Florence	34,031	31,649
35214	Forestdale(u)	6,091	......
36201	Fort McClellan(u)	5,334	......
35967	Fort Payne	8,435	7,029
36360	Fort Rucker(u)	14,242	......
35068	Fultondale	5,163	2,001
*35901	Gadsden	53,928	58,088
35071	Gardendale	6,537	4,712
36037	Greenville	8,033	6,894
35976	Guntersville	6,491	6,592
35640	Hartselle	7,355	5,000
35209	Homewood	21,137	20,289
35020	Hueytown 1976	12,127	5,997
*35804	Huntsville	139,282	72,365
35210	Irondale 1975	5,200	3,501
36545	Jackson	5,957	4,959
36265	Jacksonville	7,715	5,678
35501	Jasper	10,798	10,799
36863	Lanett	6,908	7,674
35094	Leeds	6,991	6,162
35228	Midfield	6,340	3,556
*36601	Mobile	190,026	194,856
*36104	Montgomery	133,386	134,393
35223	Mountain Brook	19,509	12,680
35660	Muscle Shoals	6,907	4,084
35476	Northport	9,435	5,245
36801	Opelika	19,027	15,678
36467	Opp	6,493	5,535
36360	Ozark	13,555	9,534
35125	Pell City	5,602	4,165
36867	Phenix City	25,281	27,630
36272	Piedmont	5,063	4,794
35127	Pleasant Grove	5,090	3,097
36067	Prattville	13,116	6,616
36610	Prichard	41,578	47,371
36274	Roanoke	5,251	5,288
35653	Russellville	7,814	6,628
36571	Saraland	7,840	4,595
35768	Scottsboro 1976	12,917	6,449
36701	Selma	27,379	28,385
35660	Sheffield	13,115	13,491
35150	Sylacauga	12,255	12,857
35160	Talladega	17,662	17,742
35217	Tarrant City	6,835	7,810
36081	Troy	11,482	10,234
35401	Tuscaloosa	65,773	63,370
35674	Tuscumbia	8,828	8,994
36083	Tuskegee	11,028	7,240
35216	Vestavia Hills 1975	14,199	4,029
36201	West End—Cobb(u)	5,515	5,485
	Alaska		
*99502	Anchorage	48,081	44,237
99702	Eielson(u)	6,149	......
99506	Elmendorf(u)	6,018	......
99701	Fairbanks	14,771	13,311
99505	Fort Richardson(u)	10,751	......
99703	Fort Wainwright(u)	9,097	......
99801	Juneau	6,050	6,797
99901	Ketchikan	6,994	6,483
99503	Spenard(u)	18,089	9,074
	Arizona		
85321	Ajo(u)	5,881	7,049
85323	Avondale 1975	6,526	6,151
85603	Bisbee	8,328	9,914
85222	Casa Grande 1975	13,598	8,311
85224	Chandler 1975	20,034	9,531
85533	Clifton	5,087	4,191
85228	Coolidge 1975	6,711	4,990
85607	Douglas 1975	12,422	11,925
85231	Eloy 1975	6,493	4,899
86001	Flagstaff 1975	31,370	18,214
85613	Fort Huachuca(u)	6,659	......
*85301	Glendale 1975	67,298	15,893
85501	Globe 1975	6,396	6,217
86025	Holbrook 1975	5,093	3,438
86401	Kingman 1975	7,397	4,525
85301	Luke(u)	5,047	......
*85201	Mesa 1975	100,763	33,772
85621	Nogales	8,946	7,286
86040	Page(u) 1975	5,892	2,960
85253	Paradise Valley 1975	9,121	......
85345	Peoria 1975	7,758	2,593
*85026	Phoenix 1975	669,005	439,170
86301	Prescott 1975	16,888	12,861
85546	Safford 1975	5,947	4,648
*85251	Scottsdale 1975	78,065	10,026
85635	Sierra Vista 1975	20,121	3,121
85713	South Tucson 1975	6,218	7,004
85351	Sun City(u)	13,670	......
*85282	Tempe 1975	93,882	24,897
*85726	Tucson 1975	*298,683	212,892
85364	West Yuma(u)	5,552	2,781
86047	Winslow 1975	7,663	8,862
85364	Yuma 1975	30,081	23,974
	Arkansas		
71923	Arkadelphia 1975	10,227	8,069
72501	Batesville 1974	7,085	6,207
72015	Benton 1975	16,724	10,399
72712	Bentonville 1975	6,707	3,649
72315	Blytheville	24,752	20,797
72021	Brinkley	5,275	4,636
71701	Camden	15,147	15,823
72032	Conway 1973	16,772	9,791
71635	Crossett 1975	6,295	5,370
71639	Dumas 1974	5,290	3,540
71730	El Dorado	25,283	25,292
72701	Fayetteville 1976	34,036	20,274
72335	Forrest City	12,521	10,544
72901	Fort Smith 1973	65,393	52,991
72601	Harrison 1975	8,867	6,580

ZIP code	Place	1970	1960
72342	Helena 1971	10,201	11,500
71801	Hope	8,830	8,399
71901	Hot Springs	35,631	28,337
72076	Jacksonville 1975	24,391	14,488
72401	Jonesboro 1974	28,962	21,418
*72201	Little Rock 1974	139,703	107,813
71753	Magnolia 1973	11,527	10,651
72104	Malvern 1974	9,848	9,566
72360	Marianna	6,196	5,134
71655	Monticello 1972	7,034	4,412
72110	Morrilton	6,814	5,997
72653	Mountain Home 1976	6,415	2,105
72112	Newport 1976	7,854	7,007
*72114	North Little Rock 1976	62,040	58,032
72370	Osceola 1975	8,371	6,189
72450	Paragould	10,639	9,947
72455	Pocahantas 1974	5,448	3,665
71601	Pine Bluff	57,389	44,037
72756	Rogers 1976	14,982	5,700
72801	Russellville 1975	13,909	8,921
72143	Searcy 1973	10,867	7,272
72116	Sherwood 1976	6,744	1,222
72761	Siloam Springs 1975	6,433	3,953
72204	Southwest Little Rock (u)	13,231	....
72764	Springdale 1974	19,962	10,076
72160	Stuttgart	10,477	9,661
75501	Texarkana 1976	21,192	19,788
72472	Trumann 1974	6,402	4,511
72956	Van Buren 1975	9,452	6,787
71671	Warren	6,433	6,752
72390	West Helena 1973	10,838	8,385
72301	West Memphis 1973	28,236	19,374
72396	Wynne 1974	7,292	4,922

California

ZIP code	Place	1970	1960
94501	Alameda	70,968	63,855
94507	Alamo-Danville (u)	14,059	....
94706	Albany	14,674	14,804
*91802	Alhambra	62,125	54,807
90249	Alondra Park (u)	12,193	....
91001	Altadena (u)	42,415	40,568
95116	Alum Rock (u)	18,355	18,942
*92803	Anaheim	166,408	104,184
96007	Anderson	5,492	4,492
94509	Antioch	28,060	17,305
92307	Apple Valley (u)	6,702	....
95003	Aptos (u)	8,704	....
91006	Arcadia	45,138	41,005
95521	Arcata	8,985	5,235
95825	Arden-Arcade (u)	82,492	73,352
93420	Arroyo Grande	7,454	3,291
90701	Artesia	14,757	9,993
93203	Arvin 1975	6,014	....
94577	Ashland (u)	14,810	....
93422	Atascadero (u)	10,290	5,983
94025	Atherton	8,085	7,717
95301	Atwater	11,640	7,318
95603	Auburn	6,570	5,586
92505	August School Area (u)	6,735	....
91746	Avocado Heights (u)	9,810	....
91702	Azusa	25,217	20,497
*93302	Bakersfield	69,515	56,848
91706	Baldwin Park	47,285	33,951
92220	Banning	12,034	10,250
92311	Barstow 1975	16,812	11,644
95903	Beale East (u)	7,029	....
92223	Beaumont	5,484	4,288
90201	Bell	21,836	19,450
90706	Bellflower	51,454	45,909
90201	Bell Gardens	29,308	....
94002	Belmont	23,538	15,996
94510	Benicia	7,349	6,070
*94704	Berkeley	116,716	111,268
*90213	Beverly Hills	33,416	30,817
92314	Big Bear (u)	5,268	1,562
92316	Bloomington (u)	11,957	....
92225	Blythe	7,047	6,023
92227	Brawley 1974	13,940	12,703
92621	Brea	18,447	8,487
95605	Broderick-Bryte (u)	12,782	....
*90620	Buena Park	63,646	46,401
*91505	Burbank	88,871	90,155
94010	Burlingame	27,320	24,036
92231	Calexico 1974	12,829	7,992
93725	Calwa	5,191	....
93010	Camarillo	19,219	....
93010	Camarillo Heights (u)	5,892	1,704
95124	Cambrian Park (u)	5,316	....
95008	Campbell	24,770	11,863
95010	Capitola	5,080	2,021
92007	Cardiff-by-the-Sea (u)	5,724	3,149
92008	Carlsbad	14,944	9,253
95608	Carmichael (u)	37,625	20,455
93013	Carpinteria	6,982	....
90744	Carson	71,150	....
94546	Castro Valley (u)	44,760	37,120
95307	Ceres	6,029	4,406
90701	Cerritos	15,856	3,508
94541	Cherryland (u)	9,969	....
95926	Chico	19,580	14,757
95926	Chico North (u)	6,656	....
93555	China Lake (u)	11,105	....
91710	Chino 1975	27,490	10,305
*92010	Chula Vista	67,901	42,034
95610	Citrus Heights (u)	21,760	....
91711	Claremont	23,464	12,633
93612	Clovis	13,856	5,546
92236	Coachella	8,353	4,854
93210	Coalinga	6,161	5,965
92324	Colton 1975	18,686	18,666
90022	Commerce	10,536	9,555
*90220	Compton	78,547	71,812
*94520	Concord	85,164	36,000
93212	Corcoran	5,249	4,976
91720	Corona	27,519	13,336
92118	Coronado	20,020	18,039
94925	Corte Madera	8,464	5,962
*92626	Costa Mesa	72,660	37,550
*91722	Covina	30,395	20,124
91730	Cucamonga (u)	5,796	....
90201	Cudahy	16,998	....
90230	Culver City	34,451	32,163
95014	Cupertino	18,216	3,664
90630	Cypress	31,569	1,753
*94017	Daly City	66,922	44,791
95616	Davis	23,488	8,910
90250	Del Aire (u)	11,930	....
93215	Delano	14,559	11,913
91765	Diamond Bar (u)	10,576	....
93618	Dinuba	7,917	6,103
90810	Dominguez (u)	5,980	....
*90241	Downey	88,445	82,505
91010	Duarte	14,981	13,962
94566	Dublin (u)	13,641	....
90220	East Compton (u)	5,853	....
90638	East La Mirada (u)	12,339	....
90022	East Los Angeles (u)	105,033	104,270
94303	East Palo Alto (u)	18,099	....
93523	Edwards (u)	10,331	....
*92020	El Cajon	52,273	37,618
92243	El Centro 1973	21,134	16,811
94530	El Cerrito	25,190	25,437
93017	El Encanto Heights (u)	6,225	....
*91734	El Monte	69,892	13,163
93446	El Paso de Robles	7,168	6,677
93030	El Rio (u)	6,173	6,966
90245	El Segundo	15,620	14,219
92630	El Toro (u)	8,654	....
92709	El Toro Station (u)	6,970	....
92024	Encinitas (u)	5,375	2,786
96001	Enterprise (u)	11,486	4,946
*92025	Escondido	36,792	16,377
95501	Eureka	24,337	28,137
94930	Fairfax	7,661	5,813
94533	Fairfield	44,146	14,968
95628	Fair Oaks (u)	11,256	....
92028	Fallbrook (u)	6,945	4,814
93015	Fillmore	6,285	4,808
90001	Florence-Graham (u)	42,895	38,164
95828	Florin (u)	9,646	....
95630	Folsom	5,810	3,925
92335	Fontana 1975	23,629	14,659
94404	Foster City (u)	9,522	....
92708	Fountain Valley	31,886	2,068
95019	Freedom (u)	5,563	4,206
*94536	Fremont	100,869	43,790
*93706	Fresno	165,972	133,929
*92631	Fullerton	85,987	56,180
*90247	Gardena	41,021	35,943
95205	Garden Acres (u)	7,870	....
*92640	Garden Grove	120,967	84,238
92392	George (u)	7,404	....
95020	Gilroy	12,665	7,348
92509	Glen Avon (u)	5,759	3,416
*91209	Glendale	132,664	119,442
91740	Glendora	31,380	20,752
92324	Grand Terrace (u)	5,901	....
95945	Grass Valley	5,149	4,876
92041	Grossmont-Mt. Helix (u)	8,723	....
93433	Grover City	5,939	5,210
91745	Hacienda Heights (u)	35,969	....
93230	Hanford	15,179	10,133
90716	Hawaiian Gardens	9,052	....
90250	Hawthorne	53,304	33,035
*94544	Hayward	93,058	72,700
95448	Healdsburg	5,438	4,816
92343	Hemet	12,252	5,416
92343	Hemet East (u)	8,598	1,936
90254	Hermosa Beach	17,412	16,115
92346	Highland (u)	12,669	....
94010	Hillsborough	8,753	7,554
95023	Hollister	7,663	6,071
91720	Home Gardens (u)	5,116	1,541
*92647	Huntington Beach	115,960	11,492
90255	Huntington Park 1976	37,851	29,920
92032	Imperial Beach	20,244	17,773
92201	Indio	14,459	9,745

ZIP code	Place	1970	1960
*90306	Inglewood	89,985	63,390
93017	Isla Vista (u)	13,441	....
94707	Kensington (u)	5,823	....
91011	La Canada-Flintridge (u)	20,652	18,338
91214	La Crescenta-Montrose(u)	19,620	....
90045	Ladera Heights(u)	6,535	....
94549	Lafayette	20,484	7,114
*92651	Laguna Beach	14,550	9,288
92653	Laguna Hills(u)	13,676	....
90631	La Habra	41,350	25,136
92040	Lakeside(u)	11,991	....
*90714	Lakewood	83,025	67,126
92041	La Mesa	39,178	30,441
90638	La Mirada	30,808	22,444
93241	Lamont(u)	7,007	6,177
93534	Lancaster(u)	32,728	26,012
90624	La Palma	9,687	622
*91747	La Puente	31,092	24,723
94939	Larkspur	10,487	5,710
91750	La Verne	12,965	6,516
90260	Lawndale	24,825	21,740
92045	Lemon Grove(u)	19,690	19,348
93245	Lemoore Station(u)	9,210	....
90304	Lennox(u)	16,121	31,224
95207	Lincoln Village(u)	6,112	....
95901	Linda(u)	7,731	6,129
93247	Lindsay	5,206	5,397
95062	Live Oak(u) (Santa Cruz)	6,443	3,518
94550	Livermore	37,703	16,058
95240	Lodi 1975	32,065	22,229
92354	Loma Linda 1975	7,651	....
90717	Lomita	19,784	....
93436	Lompoc	25,284	14,415
*90801	Long Beach	358,879	344,168
90720	Los Alamitos	11,346	4,312
94022	Los Altos	24,726	19,696
94022	Los Altos Hills	6,865	3,412
*90052	Los Angeles	2,809,813	2,479,015
93635	Los Banos	9,188	5,272
95030	Los Gatos	23,735	9,036
90262	Lynwood	43,354	31,614
93637	Madera	16,044	14,430
90266	Manhattan Beach	35,352	33,934
95336	Manteca 1975	17,488	8,242
93933	Marina(u)	8,343	3,310
94553	Martinez	16,506	9,604
95901	Marysville	9,353	9,553
95655	Mather(u)	7,027	....
90270	Maywood	16,996	14,588
93023	Meiners Oaks-Mira Monte(u)	7,025	....
94025	Menlo Park	26,826	26,957
95340	Merced	22,670	20,068
94030	Millbrae	20,792	15,873
94941	Mill Valley	12,942	10,411
95035	Milpitas	27,149	6,572
91752	Mira Loma(u)	8,482	3,982
92675	Mission Viejo(u)	11,933	....
*95350	Modesto	61,712	36,585
91016	Monrovia	30,562	27,079
91763	Montclair 1975	21,072	13,546
90640	Montebello	42,807	32,097
93940	Monterey	26,302	22,618
91754	Monterey Park	49,166	37,821
94556	Moraga(u)	14,205	....
95037	Morgan Hill	6,485	3,151
93442	Morro Bay	7,109	....
*94042	Mountain View	54,304	30,889
92405	Muscoy(u)	7,091	....
94558	Napa	35,978	22,170
92050	National City	43,184	32,771
94560	Newark	27,153	9,884
91321	Newhall(u)	9,651	4,705
*92660	Newport Beach	49,422	26,564
91760	Norco	14,511	....
94025	North Fair Oaks(u)	9,740	....
95660	North Highlands(u)	31,854	21,271
92135	North Island(u)	6,892	....
90650	Norwalk	91,827	88,739
94947	Novato	31,006	17,881
95361	Oakdale	6,594	4,980
*94615	Oakland	361,561	367,548
92054	Oceanside	40,494	24,971
93308	Oildale(u)	20,879	....
93023	Ojai	5,591	4,495
95961	Olivehurst(u)	8,100	4,835
*91761	Ontario 1975	63,186	46,617
95060	Opal Cliffs(u)	5,425	3,825
*92667	Orange	77,365	26,444
95662	Orangevale(u)	16,493	....
93454	Orcutt(u)	8,500	1,414
94563	Orinda Village(u)	6,790	5,568
95965	Oroville	7,536	6,115
92010	Otay-Castle Park(u)	15,445	....
93030	Oxnard	71,225	40,265
94044	Pacifica	36,020	20,995
93950	Pacific Grove	13,505	12,121
93550	Palmdale	8,511	....
92260	Palm Desert(u)	6,171	1,295
92262	Palm Springs	20,936	13,468
*94302	Palo Alto	55,835	52,287
90274	Palos Verdes Estates	13,631	9,564
90274	Palos Verdes Peninsula(u)	38,918	....
95969	Paradise(u)	14,539	8,268
90723	Paramount	34,734	27,249
95823	Parkway-Sacramento So.(u)	28,574	....
*91109	Pasadena	112,951	116,407
92055	Pendleton North(u)	11,803	....
92055	Pendleton South(u)	13,692	....
94952	Petaluma	24,870	14,035
90660	Pico Rivera	54,170	49,150
94611	Piedmont	10,917	11,117
94564	Pinole	13,266	6,064
94565	Pittsburg	20,651	19,062
92670	Placentia	21,948	5,861
95667	Placerville	5,416	4,439
94523	Pleasant Hill	24,610	23,844
94566	Pleasanton	18,328	4,203
*91766	Pomona	87,384	67,157
93257	Porterville	12,602	7,991
93257	Porterville West(u)	6,200	....
93041	Port Hueneme	14,295	11,067
92064	Poway(u)	9,422	1,921
95670	Rancho Cordova(u)	30,451	7,429
95014	Rancho Rinconada(u)	5,149	....
96080	Red Bluff	7,676	7,202
96001	Redding	16,659	12,773
92373	Redlands 1975	36,566	26,829
*90277	Redondo Beach	57,451	46,986
*94064	Redwood City	55,686	46,290
93654	Reedley	8,131	5,850
92376	Rialto 1975	31,069	18,567
*94802	Richmond	79,043	71,854
93555	Ridgecrest	7,629	....
95673	Rio Linda(u)	7,524	2,189
*92502	Riverside	140,089	84,332
94572	Rodeo(u)	5,356	....
94928	Rohnert Park	6,133	....
90274	Rolling Hills Estates	6,735	3,941
95401	Roseland(u)	5,105	4,510
91770	Rosemead	40,972	15,476
95678	Roseville	18,221	13,421
90720	Rossmoor(u)	12,922	....
91745	Rowland Heights(u)	16,881	....
92509	Rubidoux(u)	13,969	....
*95813	Sacramento	257,105	191,667
93901	Salinas	58,896	28,957
94960	San Anselmo	13,031	11,584
*92403	San Bernardino 1975	102,303	91,922
94066	San Bruno	36,254	29,063
......	San Buenaventura *(See Ventura)*		
94070	San Carlos	26,053	21,370
92672	San Clemente	17,063	8,527
*92109	San Diego	697,027	573,224
91773	San Dimas	15,692	....
*91340	San Fernando	16,571	16,093
*94101	San Francisco	715,674	740,316
91776	San Gabriel	29,336	22,561
93657	Sanger	10,088	8,072
*95101	San Jose	445,779	204,196
*94577	San Leandro	68,698	65,962
94580	San Lorenzo(u)	24,633	23,773
93401	San Luis Obispo	28,036	20,437
91108	San Marino	14,177	13,658
*94402	San Mateo	78,991	69,870
94806	San Pablo	21,461	19,687
*94901	San Rafael	38,977	20,460
*92711	Santa Ana	155,762	100,350
*93102	Santa Barbara	70,215	58,768
*95050	Santa Clara	87,717	58,880
95060	Santa Cruz	32,076	25,596
90670	Santa Fe Springs	14,750	16,342
93454	Santa Maria	32,749	20,027
93454	Santa Maria South(u)	7,129	....
*90406	Santa Monica	88,289	83,249
93060	Santa Paula	18,001	13,279
*95402	Santa Rosa	50,006	31,027
92071	Santee(u)	21,107	....
95070	Saratoga	27,110	14,861
94965	Sausalito	6,158	5,331
90740	Seal Beach	24,441	6,994
93955	Seaside	35,935	19,353
93662	Selma	7,459	6,934
93263	Shafter	5,327	4,576
91024	Sierra Madre	12,140	9,732
90806	Signal Hill	5,588	4,627
*93065	Simi Valley	59,832	....
92075	Solana Beach(u)	5,023	....
95073	Soquel(u)	5,795	....
91733	South El Monte	13,443	4,850
90280	South Gate	56,909	53,831
95705	South Lake Tahoe	12,921	....
95350	South Modesto(u)	7,889	5,465
91030	South Pasadena	22,979	19,706
94080	South San Francisco	46,646	39,418
91770	South San Gabriel(u)	5,051	....
91744	South San Jose Hills(u)	12,386	....
90605	South Whittier(u)	46,641	....
95991	South Yuba(u)	5,352	3,200

ZIP code	Place	1970	1960
*92077	Spring Valley(u)	29,742	....
94305	Stanford(u)	8,691	....
90680	Stanton	18,186	11,163
*95204	Stockton 1975	117,986	86,321
92381	Sun City(u)	5,519	....
92388	Sunnymead(u)	6,708	3,404
*94086	Sunnyvale	95,408	52,898
96130	Susanville	6,608	5,598
91780	Temple City	31,034	....
*91360	Thousand Oaks	35,873	....
94920	Tiburon	6,209	....
*90510	Torrance	134,968	100,991
95396	Tracy 1975	16,055	11,289
93274	Tulare	16,235	13,824
95380	Turlock	13,992	9,116
92680	Tustin	21,180	2,006
92705	Tustin-Foothills(u)	26,598	....
92277	Twentynine Palms(u)	5,667	....
92278	Twentynine Palms Base(u)	5,647	....
95482	Ukiah	10,095	9,900
94587	Union City	14,724	6,618
91786	Upland 1975	37,253	15,918
95688	Vacaville	21,690	10,898
91744	Valinda(u)	18,837	....
94590	Vallejo	71,710	60,877
93437	Vandenburg(u)	13,193	....
*93001	Ventura	57,964	29,114
92392	Victorville 1975	12,344	....
90043	View Park-Windsor Hills(u)	12,268	....
93277	Visalia	27,268	15,791
92083	Vista	24,688	....
91789	Walnut	5,992	934
*94596	Walnut Creek	39,844	9,903
94596	Walnut Creek West(u)	8,330	....
90255	Walnut Park(u)	8,925	....
93280	Wasco	8,269	6,841
95076	Watsonville	14,569	13,293
90044	West Athens(u)	13,311	....
90502	West Carson(u)	15,918	....
90247	West Compton(u)	5,605	....
*91793	West Covina	68,034	50,645
90069	West Hollywood(u)	34,622	28,870
92683	Westminster	59,874	25,750
95351	West Modesto(u)	6,135	1,897
90047	Westmont(u)	29,310	....
94565	West Pittsburg(u)	5,969	5,188
91746	West Puente Valley(u)	20,733	....
95691	West Sacramento(u)	12,002	....
*90606	West Whittier-Los Nietos(u)	20,845	....
*90605	Whittier	72,863	33,663
90222	Willowbrook(u)	32,328	....
95695	Woodland	20,677	13,524
92686	Yorba Linda	11,856	....
96097	Yreka City	5,394	4,759
95991	Yuba City	13,986	11,507
92399	Yucaipa(u)	19,284	....

Colorado

ZIP code	Place	1970	1960
81101	Alamosa	6,985	6,205
80401	Applewood(u)	8,214	....
*80001	Arvada	49,083	19,242
80010	Aurora	74,974	48,548
*80302	Boulder	66,870	37,718
80601	Brighton	8,309	7,055
80020	Broomfield	7,261	....
81212	Canon City	9,206	8,973
*80901	Colorado Springs	135,060	70,194
80022	Commerce City	17,407	8,970
81321	Cortez	6,032	6,764
*80202	Denver	514,678	493,887
80022	Derby(u)	10,206	10,124
81301	Durango	10,333	10,530
80110	Englewood	33,695	33,398
80913	Fort Carson(u)	19,399	....
80521	Fort Collins	43,337	25,027
80701	Fort Morgan	7,594	7,379
80401	Golden	9,817	7,118
81501	Grand Junction	20,170	18,694
80631	Greeley	38,902	26,314
81050	La Junta	7,938	8,026
80215	Lakewood	92,743	....
81052	Lamar	7,797	7,369
80120	Littleton	26,466	13,670
80120	Littleton Southeast(u)	22,899	....
80501	Longmont	23,209	11,489
80537	Loveland	16,220	9,734
81401	Montrose	6,496	5,044
80233	North Glenn	27,937	....
81501	Orchard Mesa(u)	5,824	4,956
*81003	Pueblo	97,453	91,181
80911	Security-Widefield(u)	15,297	9,017
80221	Sherrelwood(u)	18,868	....
80751	Sterling	10,636	10,751
80906	Stratton Meadows(u)	6,223	....
80229	Thornton	13,326	11,353
81082	Trinidad	9,901	10,691
80229	Welby(u)	6,875	....
80030	Westminster	19,432	13,850
80221	Westminster East(u)	7,576	....
80033	Wheat Ridge	29,778	....

Connecticut

See Note on Page 201

ZIP code	Place	1970	1960
06401	Ansonia	21,160	19,819
06001	*Avon*	8,352	5,273
06037	*Berlin*	14,149	11,250
06801	*Bethel*	10,945	8,200
06002	*Bloomfield*	18,301	13,613
06405	*Branford*	20,444	16,610
*06602	Bridgeport	156,542	156,748
06010	Bristol	55,487	45,499
06804	*Brookfield*	9,688	3,405
06019	*Canton*	6,868	4,783
06410	*Cheshire*	19,051	13,383
06413	*Clinton*	10,267	4,166
06413	Clinton Center(u)	5,957	2,693
06415	*Colchester*	6,603	4,648
06340	Conning Towers-Nautilus Park(u)	9,791	3,457
06238	*Coventry*	8,140	6,356
06416	*Cromwell*	7,400	6,780
06810	Danbury	50,781	22,928
06820	Darien	20,411	18,437
06418	Derby	12,599	12,132
06424	*East Hampton*	7,078	5,403
06108	*East Hartford*	57,583	43,977
06512	*East Haven*	25,120	21,388
06333	*East Lyme*	11,399	6,782
06016	*East Windsor*	8,513	7,500
06029	*Ellington*	7,707	5,580
06082	*Enfield*	46,189	31,464
06430	*Fairfield*	56,487	46,183
06032	*Farmington*	14,390	10,813
06033	*Glastonbury*	20,651	14,497
06035	*Granby*	6,150	4,968
06830	*Greenwich*	59,755	53,793
06351	*Griswold*	7,763	6,472
06340	Groton	38,244	29,937
06340	Groton Borough	8,933	10,111
06437	*Guilford*	12,033	7,913
06514	*Hamden*	49,357	41,056
*06101	Hartford	158,017	162,178
06239	*Killingly*	13,573	11,298
06339	*Ledyard*	14,837	5,395
06759	*Litchfield*	7,399	6,264
06443	*Madison*	9,768	4,567
06040	*Manchester*	47,994	42,102
06250	*Mansfield*	19,994	14,638
06450	Meriden	55,959	51,850
06762	*Middlebury*	5,542	4,785
06457	Middletown	36,924	33,250
06460	Milford	50,858	41,662
06468	*Monroe*	12,047	6,402
06353	*Montville*	15,662	7,759
06770	Naugatuck	23,034	19,511
*06050	New Britain	83,441	82,201
06840	*New Canaan*	17,455	13,466
06810	*New Fairfield*	6,991	3,355
*06510	New Haven	137,707	152,048
06111	*Newington*	26,037	17,664
06320	New London	31,630	34,182
06776	*New Milford*	14,601	8,318
06470	*Newtown*	16,942	11,373
06471	*North Branford*	10,778	6,771
06473	*North Haven*	22,194	15,935
06856	Norwalk	79,113	67,775
06360	Norwich	41,739	38,506
06475	*Old Saybrook*	8,468	5,274
06477	*Orange*	13,524	8,547
02891	Pawcatuck(u)	5,255	4,389
06374	*Plainfield*	11,957	8,884
06062	*Plainville*	16,733	13,149
06782	*Plymouth*	10,321	8,981
06480	*Portland*	8,812	7,496
06712	*Prospect*	6,543	4,367
06260	Putnam	6,918	6,952
......	*Putnam*	8,598	8,412
06875	*Redding*	5,590	3,359
06877	Ridgefield Center(u)	5,878	2,954
......	*Ridgefield*	18,188	8,165
06067	*Rocky Hill*	11,103	7,404
06483	*Seymour*	12,776	10,100
06484	Shelton	27,165	18,190
06070	*Simsbury*	17,475	10,138
06071	*Somers*	6,893	3,702
06488	*Southbury*	7,852	5,186
06489	*Southington*	30,946	22,797
06074	*South Windsor*	15,553	9,460
06075	*Stafford*	8,680	7,476
*06904	Stamford	108,798	92,713
06378	*Stonington*	15,940	13,969
06268	Storrs(u)	10,691	6,054
06497	*Stratford*	49,775	45,012
06078	*Suffield*	8,634	6,779
06787	*Thomaston*	6,233	5,850
06277	*Thompson*	7,580	6,217

ZIP code	Place	1970	1960
06084	Tolland	7,857	2,950
06790	Torrington	31,952	30,045
06611	Trumbull	31,394	20,379
06060	Vernon	27,237	16,961
06492	Wallingford	35,714	29,920
*06701	Waterbury	108,033	107,130
06385	Waterford	17,227	15,391
06795	Watertown	18,610	14,837
06107	West Hartford	68,031	62,382
06516	West Haven	52,851	43,002
06880	Weston	7,417	4,039
06880	Westport	27,414	20,955
06109	Wethersfield	26,662	20,561
06226	Willimantic	14,402	13,881
06897	Wilton	13,572	8,026
06094	Winchester	11,106	10,496
06280	Windham	19,626	16,973
06095	Windsor	22,502	19,467
06096	Windsor Locks	15,080	11,411
06098	Winsted	8,954	8,136
06716	Wolcott	12,495	8,889
06525	Woodbridge	7,673	5,182
06798	Woodbury	5,869	3,910

Delaware

ZIP code	Place	1970	1960
19711	Brookside Park(u)	7,856	......
19703	Claymont(u)	6,584	......
19901	Dover	17,488	7,250
19901	Dover Base(u)	8,106	......
19805	Elsmere	8,415	7,319
19963	Milford	5,314	5,795
19711	Newark	21,298	11,404
19973	Seaford	5,537	4,430
*19899	Wilmington	80,386	95,827
19720	Wilmington Manor—Chelsea—Leedom	10,134	......

District of Columbia

ZIP code	Place	1970	1960
*20013	Washington	756,510	763,956
	Northeast	184,439	197,536
	Northwest	347,337	374,165
	Southeast	194,365	173,988
	Southwest	30,369	18,267

Florida

ZIP code	Place	1970	1960
33821	Arcadia	5,658	5,889
33823	Auburndale	5,386	5,595
33825	Avon Park	6,712	6,073
32807	Azalea Park(u)	7,367	......
33830	Bartow	12,891	12,849
33505	Bayshore Gardens(u)	9,255	2,297
33430	Belle Glade	15,949	11,273
33432	Boca Raton	28,506	6,961
33435	Boynton Beach	18,115	10,467
*33506	Bradenton	21,040	19,380
33511	Brandon(u)	12,749	1,665
33314	Broadview Park-Rock Hill(u)	6,049	......
33311	Browardale(u)	17,444	......
33142	Browns Village(u)	23,442	......
33054	Bunche Park(u)	5,773	......
33904	Cape Coral(u)	10,193	......
33055	Carol City(u)	27,361	21,749
33023	Carver Ranch Estates(u)	5,515	......
32707	Casselberry	9,438	2,463
33505	Cedar Hammock-Bradenton South(u)	10,820	......
32324	Chattahoochee	7,944	9,699
*33515	Clearwater	52,074	34,653
32922	Cocoa	16,110	12,294
32931	Cocoa Beach	9,952	3,475
32922	Cocoa West(u)	5,779	3,975
33064	Collier Manor-Cresthaven(u)	7,202	......
32809	Conway(u)	8,642	......
33134	Coral Gables	42,494	34,793
32536	Crestview	7,952	7,467
33157	Cutler Ridge(u)	17,441	7,005
33004	Dania	9,013	7,065
33314	Davie	5,859	......
*32015	Daytona Beach	45,327	37,395
33441	Deerfield Beach	16,662	9,573
32720	De Land	11,641	10,775
33444	Delray Beach	19,915	12,230
33528	Dunedin	17,639	8,444
33610	East Lake-Orient Park(u)	5,711	......
33940	East Naples(u)	6,152	......
32542	Eglin(u)	7,769	......
33614	Egypt Lake(u)	7,556	......
33533	Englewood(u)	5,108	2,877
32726	Eustis	6,722	6,189
32034	Fernandina Beach	6,955	7,276
33030	Florida City	5,133	4,114
*33310	Fort Lauderdale	139,590	82,648
*33902	Fort Myers	27,351	22,523
33901	Fort Myers Southwest(u)	5,086	
33450	Fort Pierce	29,721	25,256
32548	Fort Walton Beach	19,994	12,147
*32601	Gainesville	64,510	29,701
32960	Gifford(u)	5,772	3,509
33170	Goulds(u)	6,690	5,121
33581	Gulf Gate Estates(u)	5,874	......
33737	Gulfport	9,976	9,730
33844	Haines City	8,956	9,135
33009	Hallandale	23,849	10,483
*33010	Hialeah	102,452	66,972
32805	Holden Heights(u)	6,206	......
32017	Holly Hill	8,191	4,182
*33022	Hollywood	106,873	35,237
33030	Homestead	13,674	9,152
33030	Homestead Base(u)	8,257	......
32937	Indian Harbour Beach	5,371	......
*32201	Jacksonville	528,865	201,030
33156	Kendall(u)	35,497	......
33040	Key West	29,312	33,956
32741	Kissimmee	7,119	6,845
33618	Lake Carroll(u)	5,577	......
32055	Lake City	10,575	9,465
32208	Lake Forest(u)	5,216	......
33803	Lake Holloway(u)	6,227	3,172
*33802	Lakeland	41,550	41,350
33612	Lake Magdalene(u)	9,266	......
33403	Lake Park	6,993	3,589
33853	Lake Wales	8,240	8,346
33460	Lake Worth	23,714	20,758
33460	Lantana	7,126	5,021
33540	Largo	22,031	5,302
33313	Lauderdale Lakes	10,577	......
33313	Lauderhill	8,465	132
32748	Leesburg	11,869	11,172
33614	Leto(u)	8,458	......
33064	Lighthouse Point	9,071	2,453
32060	Live Oak	6,830	6,544
32810	Lockhart(u)	5,809	......
32751	Maitland	7,157	3,570
33063	Margate	8,867	2,646
32446	Marianna	6,741	7,152
*32901	Melbourne	40,236	11,982
33314	Melrose Park(u)	6,111	......
32952	Merritt Island(u)	29,233	3,554
*33152	Miami	334,859	291,688
33139	Miami Beach	87,072	63,145
33153	Miami Shores	9,425	8,865
33166	Miami Springs	13,279	11,229
32570	Milton	5,360	4,108
32754	Mims(u)	8,309	1,307
33023	Miramar	23,997	5,485
32506	Myrtle Grove(u)	16,186	......
33940	Naples	12,042	4,655
33552	New Port Richey 1973	7,137	3,520
32069	New Smyrna Beach	10,580	8,781
33308	North Andrews Terrace(u)	7,082	......
33903	North Fort Myers(u)	8,798	......
33314	North Lauderdale 1974	9,285	......
33161	North Miami	34,767	28,708
33160	North Miami Beach	30,544	21,405
33408	North Palm Beach	9,035	2,684
33169	Norwood(u)	14,973	......
33308	Oakland Park	16,261	5,331
32670	Ocala	22,583	13,598
32548	Ocean City(u)	5,267	......
33054	Opa-Locka 1976	13,729	9,810
32073	Orange Park	7,619	2,624
*32802	Orlando	99,006	88,135
32074	Ormond Beach	14,063	8,658
32074	Ormond By-The-Sea(u)	6,002	3,476
33476	Pahokee	5,663	4,709
32077	Palatka	9,444	11,028
32905	Palm Bay	7,176	2,808
33480	Palm Beach	9,086	6,055
33403	Palm Beach Gardens	6,102	1
33561	Palmetto	7,422	5,556
33619	Palm River-Clair Mel(u)	8,536	......
32401	Panama City	32,096	33,275
33023	Pembroke Pines	15,496	1,429
*32502	Pensacola	59,507	56,752
33157	Perrine(u)	10,257	6,424
32347	Perry	7,701	8,030
32808	Pine Hills(u)	13,882	......
33565	Pinellas Park	22,287	10,848
33566	Plant City	15,451	15,711
33314	Plantation	23,523	4,772
*33060	Pompano Beach	38,587	15,992
33064	Pompano Beach Highlands(u)	5,014	......
33950	Port Charlotte(u)	10,769	3,197
32351	Quincy	8,334	8,874
33156	Richmond Heights(u)	6,663	4,311
33312	Riverland Village-Lauderdale Isles(u)	5,512	......
33404	Riviera Beach	21,401	13,046
32955	Rockledge	10,523	3,481
32084	St. Augustine	12,352	14,734
32769	St. Cloud	5,041	4,353
*33730	St. Petersburg 1976	236,413	181,298
33706	St. Petersburg Beach	8,024	6,268
32771	Sanford	17,393	19,175
*33578	Sarasota	40,237	34,083

ZIP code	Place	1970	1960
33579	Sarasota Southeast(u)	6,885	....
32937	Satellite Beach	6,558	825
33870	Sebring	7,223	6,939
33143	South Miami	11,780	9,846
33157	South Miami Heights(u)	10,395	....
32937	South Patrick Shores(u)	10,313	....
32401	Springfield	5,949	4,628
33304	Sunrise 1972	11,693	....
33614	Sweetwater Creek(u)	19,453	....
*32303	Tallahassee	72,624	48,174
33313	Tamarac 1975	22,614	....
*33602	Tampa	277,753	274,970
33589	Tarpon Springs	7,118	6,768
33617	Temple Terrace	7,347	3,812
33905	Tice(u)	7,254	4,377
32780	Titusville	30,515	6,410
33740	Treasure Island	6,120	3,506
33620	University (Hillsborough)(u)	10,039	....
32580	Valparaiso	6,504	5,975
33595	Venice	6,648	3,444
32960	Vero Beach	11,908	8,849
32960	Vero Beach South(u)	7,330	....
32507	Warrington(u)	15,848	16,752
33505	West Bradenton(u)	6,162	....
32446	West End(u)	5,289	3,124
33144	West Miami	5,494	5,296
*33401	West Palm Beach	57,375	56,208
32505	West Pensacola(u)	20,924	....
33880	West Winter Haven(u)	7,716	5,050
33165	Westwood Lakes(u)	12,811	22,517
33305	Wilton Manors	10,948	8,257
32787	Winter Garden, 1976	6,238	5,513
33880	Winter Haven	16,136	16,277
32789	Winter Park	21,895	17,162

Georgia

ZIP code	Place	1970	1960
*31701	Albany	72,623	55,890
31709	Americus	16,091	13,472
30601	Athens	44,342	31,355
*30304	Atlanta	497,421	487,455
*30901	Augusta	59,864	70,626
31717	Bainbridge	10,887	12,714
31723	Blakely	5,267	3,580
31520	Brunswick	19,585	21,703
31728	Cairo	8,061	7,427
30117	Carrollton	13,520	10,973
30120	Cartersville	10,138	8,668
30125	Cedartown	9,253	9,340
30341	Chamblee	9,127	6,635
31014	Cochran	5,161	4,714
30337	College Park	18,203	23,469
*31902	Columbus	155,028	116,779
31015	Cordele	10,733	10,609
30209	Covington	10,267	8,167
30720	Dalton	18,872	17,868
31742	Dawson	5,383	5,062
*30030	Decatur	21,943	22,026
31520	Dock Junction(u)	6,009	5,417
30340	Doraville	9,157	4,437
31533	Douglas	10,195	8,736
30134	Douglasville	5,472	4,462
31021	Dublin	15,143	13,814
31023	Eastman	5,416	5,118
30344	East Point	39,315	35,633
30635	Elberton	6,438	7,107
31750	Fitzgerald	8,187	8,781
30050	Forest Park	19,994	14,201
31905	Fort Benning(u)	27,495	....
30905	Fort Gordon(u)	15,589	....
30741	Fort Oglethorpe 1974	5,083	2,251
31030	Fort Valley	9,251	8,310
30501	Gainesville	15,459	16,523
31408	Garden City	5,790	5,451
30223	Griffin	22,734	21,735
30354	Hapeville	9,567	10,082
31545	Jesup	9,091	7,304
30728	La Fayette	6,044	5,588
30240	La Grange	23,301	23,632
30245	Lawrenceville	5,115	3,804
*31201	Macon	122,423	69,764
30060	Marietta	27,216	25,565
31034	Midway-Hardwick(u)	14,047	16,909
31061	Milledgeville	11,601	11,117
30655	Monroe	8,071	6,826
31768	Moultrie	14,400	15,764
30263	Newnan	11,205	12,169
31069	Perry	7,771	6,032
30161	Rome	30,759	32,226
30075	Roswell	5,430	2,983
31522	St. Simons(u)	5,346	3,199
31082	Sandersville	5,546	5,425
*31401	Savannah	118,349	149,245
30080	Smyrna	19,157	10,157
30458	Statesboro	14,616	8,356
30747	Summerville	5,043	4,706
30401	Swainsboro	7,325	5,943
30286	Thomaston	10,024	9,336
31792	Thomasville	18,155	18,246
30824	Thomson	6,503	4,522
31794	Tifton	12,179	9,903
30577	Toccoa	6,971	7,303
31601	Valdosta	32,303	30,652
30474	Vidalia	9,507	7,569
31093	Warner Robins	33,491	18,633
31501	Waycross	18,996	20,944
30830	Waynesboro	5,530	5,359
30680	Winder	6,605	5,555
31406	Windsor Forest(u)	7,288	....

Hawaii

ZIP code	Place	1970	1960
96701	Aiea	12,560	11,826
96706	Ewa Beach	7,765	4,627
96701	Halawa Heights	5,809	....
96824	Hickam Housing	7,352	....
96720	Hilo	26,353	25,966
*96813	Honolulu	324,871	294,194
96732	Kahului	8,280	4,223
96734	Kailua	33,783	25,622
96744	Kaneohe	29,903	14,414
96734	Maunawili	5,303	....
96734	Mokapu	7,860	....
96792	Nanakuli	6,506	2,745
96782	Pacific Palisades	7,846	....
96782	Pearl City	19,552	....
96786	Schofield Barracks	13,516	....
96786	Wahiawa	17,598	15,512
96793	Wailuku	7,979	6,969
96797	Waipahu	24,150	....

Idaho

ZIP code	Place	1970	1960
83221	Blackfoot	8,716	7,378
*83708	Boise City	74,990	34,481
83318	Burley 1976	8,773	7,508
83605	Caldwell	14,219	12,230
83814	Coeur D'Alene 1975	17,994	14,291
83401	Idaho Falls 1975	37,126	33,161
83338	Jerome 1974	5,625	4,761
83501	Lewiston	26,068	12,691
83843	Moscow	14,146	11,183
83647	Mountain Home 1974	6,755	5,984
83648	Mountain Home Base (u)	6,038	....
83651	Nampa	20,768	18,897
83661	Payette 1975	5,235	4,451
83201	Pocatello 1975	42,565	28,534
83440	Rexburg 1973	9,761	4,767
83301	Twin Falls	21,914	20,126

Illinois

ZIP code	Place	1970	1960
60101	Addison 1976	28,019	6,741
60658	Alsip 1974	15,694	3,770
62002	Alton 1975	35,741	43,047
*60004	Arlington Heights 1976	71,012	27,878
*60507	Aurora	74,182	63,715
60010	Barrington 1976	9,410	5,434
61607	Bartonville 1976	6,145	7,253
60510	Batavia 1974	10,816	7,496
62618	Beardstown	6,222	6,294
*62220	Belleville	41,699	37,264
60104	Bellwood 1971	21,473	20,729
61008	Belvidere	14,061	11,223
60106	Bensenville 1976	13,876	9,141
62812	Benton	6,833	7,023
60162	Berkeley	6,152	5,792
60402	Berwyn	52,502	54,224
62010	Bethalto 1976	8,373	3,235
60108	Bloomingdale 1975	8,788	1,262
61701	Bloomington 1975	41,409	36,271
60406	Blue Island 1975	21,190	19,618
60439	Bolingbrook 1976	31,143	....
60914	Bourbonnais 1976	10,620	3,336
60915	Bradley 1972	10,631	8,082
60455	Bridgeview 1972	13,495	7,334
60153	Broadview 1971	9,470	8,588
60513	Brookfield	20,284	20,429
60090	Buffalo Grove 1974	18,390	1,492
60459	Burbank 1976	29,448	....
62206	Cahokia	20,649	15,829
62914	Cairo	6,277	9,348
60409	Calumet City 1976	38,761	25,000
60643	Calumet Park	10,069	8,448
61520	Canton	14,217	13,588
62901	Carbondale	22,816	14,670
62626	Carlinville	5,675	5,440
62821	Carmi	6,033	6,152
60187	Carol Stream 1975	8,537	836
60110	Carpentersville 1975	24,869	17,424
62801	Centralia	15,217	13,904
62206	Centreville	11,378	12,769
61820	Champaign	56,532	49,583
61920	Charleston 1975	18,162	10,505
62233	Chester	5,310	4,460
*60607	Chicago	3,366,957	3,550,404
60411	Chicago Heights	40,900	34,331
60415	Chicago Ridge 1974	12,576	5,748

ZIP code	Place	1970	1960
61523	Chillicothe	6,052	3,054
60650	Cicero	67,058	69,130
60514	Clarendon Hills	6,750	5,885
61727	Clinton	7,570	7,355
62234	Collinsville	17,992	14,217
60477	Country Club Hills 1975	12,239	3,421
60525	Countryside 1973	5,434	......
60435	Crest Hill 1973	8,322	5,887
60445	Crestwood 1973	7,557	1,213
61611	Creve Coeur 1973	6,594	6,684
60014	Crystal Lake 1975	16,797	8,314
61832	Danville	42,570	41,856
60559	Darien 1973	9,770	......
*62521	Decatur	90,397	78,004
60015	Deerfield 1972	18,867	11,786
60115	De Kalb	32,949	18,486
*60016	Des Plaines 1973	55,594	34,886
61021	Dixon	18,147	19,565
60419	Dolton 1974	26,321	18,746
60515	Downers Grove 1975	38,776	21,154
62832	Du Quoin	6,691	6,558
62024	East Alton	7,309	7,630
60411	East Chicago Heights 1973	6,405	3,270
60064	North Chicago	47,275	22,938
61611	East Peoria	18,455	12,310
*62201	East St. Louis	69,996	81,712
62025	Edwardsville	11,070	9,996
62401	Effingham 1976	10,772	8,172
60120	Elgin 1976	61,116	49,447
60007	Elk Grove Village 1974	25,303	6,608
60126	Elmhurst	48,887	36,991
60635	Elmwood Park	26,160	23,866
*60204	Evanston	80,113	79,283
60642	Evergreen Park 1971	25,981	24,178
62837	Fairfield	5,897	6,362
62208	Fairview Heights	8,625	......
62839	Flora	5,283	5,331
60422	Flossmoor 1975	8,310	4,624
60130	Forest Park	15,472	14,452
60131	Franklin Park	20,348	18,322
61032	Freeport	27,736	26,628
60030	Gages Lake-Wildwood(u)	5,337	......
61401	Galesburg 1971	34,501	37,243
61254	Geneseo	5,840	5,169
60134	Geneva 1974	9,140	7,646
60022	Glencoe	10,675	10,472
60137	Glendale Heights 1975	15,528	173
60137	Glen Ellyn	21,909	15,972
60025	Glenview 1975	30,551	18,132
60425	Glenwood 1975	10,409	882
62040	Granite City	40,685	40,073
60030	Grayslake 1974	5,062	3,762
60103	Hanover Park 1972	19,609	451
62946	Harrisburg	9,535	9,171
60033	Harvard 1976	5,156	4,248
60426	Harvey	34,636	29,071
60656	Harwood Heights 1971	8,837	5,688
60429	Hazel Crest 1974	13,229	6,205
62948	Herrin	9,623	9,474
60457	Hickory Hills 1974	13,951	2,707
62249	Highland	5,981	4,943
60035	Highland Park	32,263	25,532
60162	Hillside 1971	9,466	7,794
60521	Hinsdale	15,918	12,859
60172	Hoffman Estates 1974	31,549	8,296
60456	Hometown	6,729	7,479
60430	Homewood 1976	19,679	13,371
60942	Hoopeston	6,461	6,606
60143	Itasca 1975	6,148	3,564
62650	Jacksonville	20,553	21,690
62052	Jerseyville 1976	7,432	7,420
*60431	Joliet 1975	74,140	66,780
60458	Justice	9,473	2,803
60901	Kankakee	30,944	27,666
61109	Ken Rock(u)	5,945	......
61443	Kewanee	15,762	16,324
60525	La Grange	17,814	15,285
60525	La Grange Highlands(u)	6,842	......
60525	La Grange Park	15,459	13,793
60044	Lake Bluff	5,008	3,494
60045	Lake Forest	15,642	10,687
60047	Lake Zurich 1975	6,789	3,458
60438	Lansing 1973	28,232	18,098
61301	La Salle	10,736	11,897
62439	Lawrenceville	5,863	5,492
60439	Lemont 1976	5,197	3,397
60048	Libertyville 1976	14,730	8,560
62656	Lincoln	17,582	16,890
60645	Lincolnwood	12,929	11,744
60532	Lisle 1976	9,368	4,219
62056	Litchfield	7,190	7,330
60441	Lockport	9,985	7,560
60148	Lombard 1974	36,839	22,561
61111	Loves Park 1975	12,198	9,086
60534	Lyons	11,124	9,936
60050	McHenry 1976	8,459	3,336
61455	Macomb 1975	23,495	12,135
62060	Madison	7,042	6,861
62959	Marion 1975	13,176	11,274
60426	Markham	15,987	11,704
62258	Mascoutah	5,045	3,625
60443	Matteson 1974	6,086	3,225
61938	Mattoon 1972	19,270	19,088
60153	Maywood	29,019	27,330
*60160	Melrose Park	22,716	22,291
61342	Mendota	6,902	6,154
62960	Metropolis	6,940	7,339
60445	Midlothian 1974	14,241	6,605
61264	Milan 1975	6,036	3,065
61265	Moline	46,237	42,705
61462	Monmouth	11,022	10,372
60450	Morris 1972	8,435	7,935
61550	Morton 1975	13,243	5,325
60053	Morton Grove	26,369	20,533
62863	Mount Carmel	8,096	8,594
60056	Mount Prospect 1975	48,975	18,906
62864	Mount Vernon	16,382	15,566
60060	Mundelein 1974	17,315	10,526
62966	Murphysboro 1976	9,629	8,673
60540	Naperville 1976	30,959	12,933
60648	Niles 1971	32,432	20,393
61761	Normal 1975	32,091	13,357
60656	Norridge 1971	18,043	14,087
60542	North Aurora 1974	5,344	2,088
60062	Northbrook 1974	27,681	11,635
60064	North Chicago	47,275	22,938
60093	Northfield	5,010	4,005
60164	Northlake	14,212	12,318
61111	North Park(u)	15,679	......
60546	North Riverside 1971	7,849	7,989
60521	Oak Brook 1975	5,251	324
60452	Oak Forest 1975	22,220	3,724
*60454	Oak Lawn 1974	62,245	27,471
*60301	Oak Park	62,511	61,093
62269	O'Fallon 1973	10,045	4,018
62450	Olney	8,974	8,780
60462	Orland Park 1975	13,137	2,592
61350	Ottawa	18,716	19,408
60067	Palatine 1976	31,447	11,504
60463	Palos Heights 1973	9,879	3,775
60465	Palos Hills 1972	9,778	3,766
62557	Pana	6,326	6,432
61944	Paris	9,971	9,823
60466	Park Forest	30,638	29,993
60466	Park Forest South 1976	5,832	......
60068	Park Ridge	42,614	32,659
61554	Pekin 1974	32,315	28,146
*61601	Peoria	126,963	103,162
61614	Peoria Heights 1975	8,239	7,064
61354	Peru	11,772	10,460
61764	Pontiac	10,595	8,435
60469	Posen	5,498	4,517
61356	Princeton 1976	7,025	6,250
60070	Prospect Heights(u)	13,333	......
62301	Quincy	45,288	43,793
61866	Rantoul	25,562	22,116
60471	Richton Park 1976	8,016	933
60627	Riverdale	15,806	12,008
60305	River Forest	13,402	12,695
60171	River Grove	11,465	8,464
60546	Riverside	10,432	9,750
60472	Robbins	9,641	7,511
62454	Robinson	7,178	7,226
61068	Rochelle 1974	8,850	7,008
61071	Rock Falls	10,287	10,261
*61125	Rockford	147,370	126,706
61201	Rock Island	50,166	51,863
60008	Rolling Meadows 1974	19,785	10,879
60441	Romeoville 1971	15,336	3,574
60172	Roselle 1976	10,213	3,581
60073	Round Lake Beach 1974	10,525	5,011
60174	St. Charles 1974	15,144	9,269
62881	Salem 1973	6,359	6,165
60548	Sandwich	5,056	3,842
60411	Sauk Village 1974	9,956	4,687
60172	Schaumburg 1976	43,580	986
60176	Schiller Park	12,712	5,687
62225	Scott(u)	7,871	......
61282	Silvis	5,907	3,973
60076	Skokie 1971	68,911	59,364
60473	South Holland 1972	25,220	10,412
60459	South Stickney(u) (see Burbank)		
*62703	Springfield	91,753	83,271
61362	Spring Valley	5,605	5,371
60475	Steger 1973	9,285	6,432
61081	Sterling	16,113	15,688
60402	Stickney	6,601	6,239
60103	Streamwood	18,176	4,821
61364	Streator	15,600	16,868
60501	Summit	11,569	10,374
62221	Swansea 1975	5,473	3,018
60178	Sycamore	7,843	6,961
62568	Taylorville	10,927	8,801
60477	Tinley Park 1974	20,782	6,392
61801	Urbana	32,800	27,294
62471	Vandalia	5,160	5,537
60181	Villa Park 1971	25,546	20,391
61571	Washington 1973	9,466	5,919

ZIP code	Place	1970	1960
62204	Washington Park	9,524	6,601
60970	Watseka	5,294	5,219
60084	Wauconda 1974	5,662	3,227
60085	Waukegan 1975	65,133	55,719
60153	Westchester	20,033	18,092
60185	West Chicago 1975	12,689	6,854
61120	West End(u)	7,554	....
60558	Western Springs 1974	13,728	10,838
62896	West Frankfort	8,854	9,027
60559	Westmont	8,920	5,997
61604	West Peoria(u)	6,873	....
60187	Wheaton 1976	39,360	24,312
60090	Wheeling 1974	18,106	7,169
60091	Wilmette	32,134	28,268
60093	Winnetka	13,998	13,368
60191	Wood Dale 1973	10,494	3,071
60515	Woodridge 1974	16,827	542
62095	Wood River	13,186	11,694
60098	Woodstock	10,226	8,897
60482	Worth 1971	12,153	8,196
60099	Zion 1975	17,511	11,941

Indiana

ZIP code	Place	1970	1960
46001	Alexandria	5,600	5,582
*46011	Anderson	70,787	49,061
46703	Angola	5,117	4,746
46706	Auburn	7,388	6,350
47421	Bedford	13,087	13,024
46107	Beech Grove 1973	14,651	10,973
46408	Black Oak(u)	9,624	....
47401	Bloomington	43,262	31,357
46714	Bluffton	8,297	6,238
47601	Boonville	5,736	4,801
47834	Brazil	8,163	8,853
46112	Brownsburg	5,751	4,478
46032	Carmel 1976	15,181	1,442
46303	Cedar Lake 1976	7,764	....
47111	Charlestown	5,933	5,726
46304	Chesterton	6,177	4,335
47130	Clarksville 1974	14,177	8,088
47842	Clinton	5,340	5,843
47201	Columbus	26,457	20,778
47331	Connersville	17,604	17,698
47933	Crawfordsville	13,842	14,231
46307	Crown Point 1973	13,420	8,443
46733	Decatur	8,445	8,327
46312	East Chicago	46,982	57,669
46405	East Gary	9,858	9,309
46514	Elkhart	43,152	40,274
46036	Elwood	11,196	11,793
*47708	Evansville	138,764	141,543
*46802	Fort Wayne	178,021	161,776
46041	Frankfort	14,956	15,302
46131	Franklin	11,477	9,453
*46401	Gary	175,415	178,320
46933	Gas City	5,742	4,469
46526	Goshen 1976	18,709	13,718
46135	Greencastle	8,852	8,506
46140	Greenfield 1973	10,808	9,049
47240	Greensburg	8,620	7,492
46142	Greenwood 1975	16,097	7,169
46319	Griffith 1974	17,681	9,483
*46320	Hammond	107,885	111,698
47348	Hartford City	8,207	8,053
46322	Highland	24,947	16,284
46342	Hobart	21,485	18,680
46750	Huntington	16,217	16,185
*46206	Indianapolis	746,302	476,258
47546	Jasper	8,641	6,737
47130	Jeffersonville	20,008	19,522
46755	Kendallville	6,838	6,765
46901	Kokomo	44,042	47,197
*47901	Lafayette	44,955	42,330
46350	La Porte	22,140	21,157
46226	Lawrence	16,917	10,103
46052	Lebanon	9,766	9,523
47441	Linton	5,450	5,736
46947	Logansport	19,255	21,106
46356	Lowell 1975	5,305	2,270
47250	Madison	13,081	10,488
46952	Marion	39,607	37,854
46151	Martinsville	9,723	7,525
46410	Merrillville 1973	25,978	....
46360	Michigan City	39,369	36,653
46544	Mishawaka	35,517	33,361
46158	Mooresville	5,800	3,856
47620	Mount Vernon 1974	7,092	5,970
*47302	Muncie	69,082	68,603
46321	Munster 1973	18,894	10,313
47150	New Albany	38,402	37,812
47362	New Castle	21,215	20,349
46774	New Haven	5,728	3,396
46060	Noblesville 1975	10,189	7,664
46962	North Manchester	5,791	4,377
46970	Peru	14,139	14,453
46168	Plainfield	8,211	5,460
46563	Plymouth	7,661	7,558
46368	Portage 1973	20,624	11,822
47371	Portland	7,115	6,999
47670	Princeton	7,431	7,906
47374	Richmond	43,999	44,149
46173	Rushville	6,686	7,264
47167	Salem 1975	5,323	4,546
47274	Seymour	13,352	11,629
46176	Shelbyville	15,094	14,317
*46624	South Bend	125,580	132,445
46224	Speedway	14,649	9,624
47586	Tell City 1974	8,515	6,609
*47808	Terre Haute	70,335	72,500
46072	Tipton	5,313	5,604
46383	Valparaiso 1974	20,544	15,227
47591	Vincennes	19,867	18,046
46992	Wabash	13,379	12,621
46580	Warsaw 1974	9,679	7,234
47501	Washington	11,358	10,846
46408	West Glen Park(u)	5,940	....
47906	West Lafayette 1975	20,372	12,680
46394	Whiting	7,152	8,137
47394	Winchester	5,493	5,742

Iowa

ZIP code	Place	1970	1960
50511	Algona	6,032	5,702
50010	Ames 1975	43,561	27,003
50021	Ankeny 1975	13,212	2,964
50022	Atlantic 1976	7,324	6,890
52722	Bettendorf 1975	24,290	11,534
50036	Boone	12,468	12,468
52601	Burlington	32,366	32,430
51401	Carroll 1976	9,218	7,682
50613	Cedar Falls 1974	33,154	21,195
*52401	Cedar Rapids 1975	108,987	92,035
52544	Centerville	6,531	6,629
50049	Chariton	5,009	5,042
50616	Charles City 1974	9,119	9,964
51012	Cherokee	7,272	7,724
51632	Clarinda	5,420	5,901
50428	Clear Lake City 1973	6,876	6,158
52732	Clinton	34,719	33,589
52240	Coralville	6,130	2,357
51501	Council Bluffs	60,348	55,641
50801	Creston	8,234	7,667
*52802	Davenport 1975	99,836	88,981
52101	Decorah	7,458	6,435
51442	Denison	6,218	4,930
*50318	Des Moines	201,404	208,982
52001	Dubuque 1975	61,728	56,606
51334	Estherville	8,108	7,927
50707	Evansdale	5,038	5,738
52556	Fairfield	8,715	8,054
50501	Fort Dodge	31,263	28,399
52627	Fort Madison	13,996	15,247
50112	Grinnell 1975	8,685	7,367
51537	Harlan 1976	5,251	4,350
50644	Independence	5,910	5,498
50125	Indianola 1975	9,611	7,062
52240	Iowa City 1974	47,744	33,443
50126	Iowa Falls	6,454	5,565
52632	Keokuk	14,631	16,316
50138	Knoxville	7,755	7,817
51031	Le Mars	8,159	6,767
52060	Maquoketa	5,677	5,909
52302	Marion 1974	18,190	10,882
50158	Marshalltown 1975	26,506	22,521
50401	Mason City	30,379	30,642
52641	Mount Pleasant	7,007	7,339
52761	Muscatine	22,405	20,997
50208	Newton	15,619	15,381
50662	Oelwein	7,735	8,282
52577	Oskaloosa	11,224	11,053
52501	Ottumwa	29,610	33,871
50219	Pella	6,668	5,198
50220	Perry	6,906	6,442
51566	Red Oak	6,210	6,421
51601	Shenandoah 1976	6,242	6,567
*51101	Sioux City	85,925	89,159
51301	Spencer	10,278	8,864
50588	Storm Lake 1975	8,589	7,728
50322	Urbandale 1975	16,410	5,821
52353	Washington	6,317	6,037
*50701	Waterloo 1975	73,064	71,755
50677	Waverly 1975	7,351	6,357
50595	Webster City	8,488	8,520
50265	West Des Moines 1975	20,712	11,949
50311	Windsor Heights	6,303	4,715

Kansas

ZIP code	Place	1970	1960
67410	Abilene	6,661	6,746
67005	Arkansas City	13,216	14,262
66002	Atchison	12,565	12,529
67010	Augusta	5,977	6,434
66720	Chanute	10,341	10,849
67337	Coffeyville	15,116	17,382
66901	Concordia	7,221	7,022
67037	Derby	7,947	6,458
67801	Dodge City	14,127	13,520

ZIP code	Place	1970	1960
67042	El Dorado	12,308	12,523
66801	Emporia	23,327	18,190
66205	Fairway	5,133	5,398
66027	Fort Leavenworth(u)	8,060	......
66701	Fort Scott	8,967	9,410
67846	Garden City	14,790	11,811
67735	Goodland	5,510	4,459
67530	Great Bend	16,133	16,670
67601	Hays	15,396	11,947
67060	Haysville	6,483	5,836
67501	Hutchinson	36,885	37,574
67301	Independence	10,347	11,222
66749	Iola	6,493	6,885
66441	Junction City	19,018	18,700
*66110	Kansas City	168,213	121,901
66044	Lawrence	45,698	32,858
66048	Leavenworth	25,147	22,052
66206	Leawood	10,349	7,466
66215	Lenexa	5,242	2,487
67901	Liberal	13,789	13,813
67460	McPherson	10,851	9,996
66502	Manhattan	27,575	22,993
66203	Merriam	10,851	5,084
66222	Mission	8,376	4,626
67114	Newton	15,439	14,877
66442	North Fort Riley(u)	12,469	......
66061	Olathe	17,917	10,987
66067	Ottawa	11,036	10,673
66204	Overland Park	79,034	......
67357	Parsons	13,015	13,929
66762	Pittsburg	20,171	18,678
66208	Prairie Village	28,138	25,356
67124	Pratt	6,736	8,156
66203	Roeland Park	9,974	8,949
67665	Russell	5,371	6,113
67401	Salina	37,714	43,202
*66203	Shawnee	20,482	9,072
*66603	Topeka	125,011	119,484
67152	Wellington	8,072	8,809
*67202	Wichita	276,554	254,698
67156	Winfield	11,405	11,117

Kentucky

ZIP code	Place	1970	1960
41101	Ashland	29,245	31,283
40004	Bardstown	5,816	4,798
41073	Bellevue	8,847	9,336
40403	Berea	6,956	4,302
42101	Bowling Green	36,705	28,338
40218	Buechel(u)	5,359	......
42718	Campbellsville	7,598	6,966
42330	Central City	5,450	3,694
40701	Corbin	7,317	7,119
*41011	Covington	52,535	60,376
41031	Cynthiana	6,356	5,641
40422	Danville	11,542	9,010
41074	Dayton	8,751	9,050
42701	Elizabethtown	11,748	9,641
41018	Elsmere	5,161	4,607
41018	Erlanger	12,676	7,072
41139	Flatwoods	7,380	3,741
41042	Florence	11,661	5,837
42223	Fort Campbell North(u)	13,616	......
40121	Fort Knox(u)	37,608	......
41017	Fort Mitchell	6,982	525
41075	Fort Thomas	16,338	14,896
40601	Frankfort	21,902	18,365
42134	Franklin	6,553	5,319
40324	Georgetown	8,629	6,986
42141	Glasgow	11,301	10,069
40330	Harrodsburg	6,741	6,061
41701	Hazard	5,459	5,958
42420	Henderson	22,976	16,892
42240	Hopkinsville	21,250	19,465
40299	Jeffersontown	9,701	3,431
40033	Lebanon	5,528	4,813
*40511	Lexington	108,137	62,810
*40201	Louisville	361,706	390,639
41016	Ludlow	5,815	6,233
42431	Madisonville	15,332	13,110
42066	Mayfield	10,724	10,762
41056	Maysville	7,411	8,484
40965	Middlesborough	11,878	12,607
40351	Morehead	7,191	4,170
40353	Mount Sterling	5,083	5,370
42071	Murray	13,537	9,303
*41071	Newport	25,998	30,070
40356	Nicholasville	5,829	4,275
40219	Okolona(u)	17,643	......
42301	Owensboro	50,329	42,471
42001	Paducah	31,627	34,479
40361	Paris	7,823	7,791
41501	Pikeville	5,205	4,754
40258	Pleasure Ridge Park(u)	28,566	10,612
42445	Princeton	6,292	5,618
40160	Radcliff	7,881	3,384
40475	Richmond	16,861	12,168
42276	Russellville	6,456	5,861
40207	St. Matthews	13,152	8,738
40216	Shively	19,139	15,155
42501	Somerset	10,436	7,112
40272	Valley Station(u)	24,471	10,533
40383	Versailles	5,679	4,060
40391	Winchester	13,402	10,187

Louisiana

ZIP code	Place	1970	1960
70510	Abbeville	10,996	10,414
71301	Alexandria	41,557	40,279
70714	Baker	8,281	4,823
71220	Bastrop	14,713	15,193
*70821	Baton Rouge	165,963	152,419
70360	Bayou Cane(u)	9,077	3,173
70380	Bayou Vista(u)	5,121	......
70427	Bogalusa	18,412	21,423
71010	Bossier City	41,595	32,776
71322	Bunkie	5,395	5,188
71101	Cooper Road(u)	9,034	......
70433	Covington	7,170	6,754
70526	Crowley	16,104	15,617
70726	Denham Springs	6,752	5,991
70634	De Ridder	8,030	7,188
70346	Donaldsonville	7,367	6,082
70535	Eunice	11,390	11,326
71334	Ferriday	5,239	4,563
70538	Franklin	9,325	8,673
70053	Gretna	24,875	21,967
70401	Hammond	12,487	10,563
70123	Harahan	13,037	9,275
70058	Harvey(u)	6,347	......
70360	Houma 1975	30,562	22,561
70544	Jeanerette	6,322	5,568
70121	Jefferson Heights(u)	16,489	19,353
70546	Jenning	11,783	11,887
71251	Jonesboro	5,072	3,848
70548	Kaplan	5,540	5,267
70062	Kenner	29,858	17,037
70501	Lafayette	68,908	40,400
70501	Lafayette Southwest	5,396	6,682
70601	Lake Charles	77,998	63,392
71254	Lake Providence	6,183	5,781
70068	Laplace(u)	5,953	3,541
71446	Leesville	8,928	4,689
70123	Little Farms(u)	15,713	......
71052	Mansfield	6,432	5,839
70072	Marrero(u)	29,015	......
*70004	Metairie(u)	136,477	......
71055	Minden	13,996	12,785
71201	Monroe	56,374	52,219
70380	Morgan City	16,586	13,540
71457	Natchitoches	15,974	13,924
70560	New Iberia	30,147	29,062
*70113	New Orleans	593,471	627,525
71459	North Fort Polk(u)	7,955	......
71463	Oakdale	7,301	6,618
70570	Opelousas	20,387	17,417
71360	Pineville	8,951	8,636
70764	Plaquemine	7,739	7,689
70767	Port Allen	5,728	5,026
70578	Rayne	9,510	8,634
70084	Reserve(u)	6,381	5,297
71270	Ruston	17,365	13,991
70582	St. Martinville	7,153	6,468
70807	Scotlandville(u)	22,557	......
*71102	Shreveport	182,064	164,372
70458	Slidell	16,101	6,356
71459	South Fort Polk(u)	15,600	......
71075	Springhill	6,496	6,437
70663	Sulphur	14,959	11,429
71282	Tallulah	9,643	9,413
71285	Terry(u)	13,382	......
70301	Thibodaux	15,028	13,403
71373	Vidalia	5,538	4,313
70586	Ville Platte	9,692	7,512
71291	West Monroe	14,868	15,215
70094	Westwego	11,402	9,815
71483	Winnfield	7,142	7,022
71295	Winnsboro	5,349	4,437

Maine

See Note on Page 201

ZIP code	Place	1970	1960
04210	Auburn	24,151	24,449
04330	Augusta	21,945	21,680
04401	Bangor 1975	32,205	38,912
04530	Bath	9,679	10,717
04915	Belfast	5,957	6,140
04005	Biddeford	19,983	19,255
04412	Brewer	9,300	9,009
04011	Brunswick Center(u)	10,867	9,444
.....	*Brunswick*	16,195	15,797
04107	*Cape Elizabeth*	7,873	5,505
04736	Caribou	10,419	12,464
.....	*Fairfield*	5,684	5,829
04105	*Falmouth*	6,291	5,976
.....	*Farmington*	5,657	5,001
04345	Gardiner	6,685	6,897

ZIP code	Place	1970	1960
......	*Gorham*	7,839	5,767
04730	Houlton Center(u)	6,760	5,976
......	*Houlton*	8,111	8,289
......	*Kennebunk*	5,646	551
03904	Kittery Center(u)	7,363	8,051
......	*Kittery*	11,028	10,689
04240	Lewiston	41,779	40,804
04750	*Limestone*	10,360	13,102
04250	*Lisbon*	6,544	5,042
04750	Loring(u)	7,881	....
......	*Madawaska*	5,585	5,507
04462	Millinocket Center(u)	7,558	7,318
......	*Millinocket*	7,742	7,453
04064	Old Orchard Beach Ctr.(u)	5,273	4,431
......	*Old Orchard Beach*	5,404	4,580
04468	Old Town	9,057	8,626
04473	Orono Center(u)	9,146	3,234
......	*Orono*	9,989	8,341
*04101	Portland	65,116	72,566
04769	Presque Isle	11,452	12,886
04841	Rockland	8,505	8,769
04276	Rumford Compact(u)	6,198	7,233
......	*Rumford*	9,363	10,005
04072	Saco	11,678	10,515
04073	Sanford Center(u)	10,457	10,936
......	*Sanford*	15,812	14,962
04074	*Scarborough*	7,845	6,418
04976	Skowhegan Center(u)	6,571	6,667
......	*Skowhegan*	7,601	7,661
04106	South Portland	23,267	22,788
......	*Topsham*	5,022	3,818
04901	Waterville	18,192	19,001
04092	Westbrook	14,444	13,820
04082	*Windham*	6,593	4,498
04901	Winslow Center(u)	5,389	3,640
......	*Winslow*	7,299	5,891
03909	*York*	5,690	4,663

Maryland

ZIP code	Place	1970	1960
21001	Aberdeen	12,375	9,679
21005	Aberdeen Proving Ground(u)	7,403	....
20331	Andrews(u)	6,418	....
*21401	Annapolis	30,095	23,385
21227	Arbutus(u)	22,745	22,402
20853	Aspen Hill(u)	16,823	....
20783	Avenel-Hilandale(u)	19,520	....
21905	Bainbridge Center(u)	5,257	....
*21233	Baltimore	905,759	939,024
21014	Bel Air	6,307	4,300
20705	Beltsville(u)	8,912	....
20014	Bethesda(u)	71,621	56,527
20021	Birchwood City(u)	13,514	....
20710	Bladensburg	7,488	3,103
20715	Bowie	35,028	1,072
21225	Brooklyn(u)	13,896	....
20705	Calverton(u)	6,543	....
21613	Cambridge	11,595	12,239
20031	Camp Springs(u)	22,776	....
20027	Carmody Hills-Pepper Mill(u)	6,335	....
21228	Catonsville(u)	54,812	37,372
20027	Chapel Oaks-Cedar Heights(u)	6,049	....
20785	Cheverly(u)	6,808	5,223
20015	Chevy Chase(u)	16,424	....
20783	Chillum(u)	35,656	....
20904	Colesville(u)	9,455	....
20740	College Park	26,156	18,482
21043	Columbia(u)	8,815	....
20027	Coral Hills(u)	9,058	....
21502	Cumberland	29,724	33,415
21222	Defense Heights(u)	6,775	....
20028	District Heights	7,659	7,524
21222	Dundalk(u)	85,377	82,428
21601	Easton	6,809	6,337
21219	Edgemere(u)	10,352	11,775
21040	Edgewood(u)	8,551	1,670
21921	Elkton	5,362	5,989
*21043	Ellicott(u)	9,435	....
21221	Essex(u)	38,193	35,205
21061	Ferndale(u)	9,929	....
20028	Forestville(u)	16,188	....
20755	Fort Meade(u)	16,699	....
21701	Frederick	23,641	21,744
21532	Frostburg	7,327	6,722
20760	Gaithersburg	8,344	3,847
21061	Glen Burnie(u)	38,608	....
20801	Good Luck(u)	10,584	....
20770	Greenbelt	18,199	7,479
21740	Hagerstown	35,862	36,660
21740	Halfway(u)	6,106	4,256
20852	Halpine(u)	6,118	....
21078	Havre De Grace	9,791	8,510
20031	Hillcrest Heights	24,037	15,295
*20780	Hyattsville	14,998	15,168
21085	Joppatowne(u)	9,092	....
20904	Kemp Mill(u)	10,037	....
20785	Kentland(u)	9,649	....
20785	Landover(u)	5,597	....
20787	Langley Park(u)	11,564	11,510
20801	Lanham-Seabrook(u)	13,244	....
21227	Lansdowne-Baltimore Highlands(u)	17,770	13,134
20810	Laurel	10,525	8,503
20653	Lexington Pk.-Patuxent R.(u)	9,136	....
21090	Linthicum(u)	9,775	....
21093	Lutherville-Timonium(u)	24,055	12,265
20810	Maryland City(u)	7,102	....
21220	Middle River(u)	19,935	10,825
20852	Montrose(u)	5,902	....
20822	Mount Rainier	8,180	9,855
20784	New Carrollton	14,870	3,385
20854	North Potomac(u)	12,784	....
20012	North Takoma Park(u)	7,373	....
21113	Odenton(u)	5,989	1,914
21206	Overlea(u)	13,124	10,795
21117	Owings Mills(u)	7,360	3,810
20021	Oxon Hill(u)	11,974	....
20785	Palmer Park(u)	8,172	....
21234	Parkville(u)	33,589	27,236
21128	Perry Hall(u)	5,446	....
21208	Pikesville(u)	25,395	18,737
20016	Potomac Valley(u)	5,122	....
21227	Pumphrey(u)	6,425	....
21133	Randallstown(u)	33,683	....
20853	Randolph(u)	13,215	....
21136	Reisterstown(u)	12,568	4,216
20840	Riverdale	5,724	4,389
20840	Riverdale Hgts.-E. Pines(u)	8,941	....
21122	Riviera Beach(u)	7,464	4,902
*20850	Rockville	41,821	26,090
21237	Rosedale(u)	19,417	....
21801	Salisbury	15,252	16,302
20027	Seat Pleasant	7,217	5,365
21146	Severna Park	16,358	3,728
*20907	Silver Spring(u)	77,411	66,348
21061	South Gate(u)	9,356	....
20795	South Kensington(u)	10,289	....
20810	South Laurel(u)	13,345	....
20023	Suitland-Silver Hills(u)	30,355	10,300
20012	Takoma Park	18,507	16,799
21204	Towson(u)	77,768	19,090
20601	Waldorf(u)	7,368	1,048
20028	Walker Mill(u)	7,103	....
21157	Westminster	7,207	6,123
20902	Wheaton(u)	66,280	54,635
20903	White Oak(u)	19,769	....
21207	Woodlawn-Woodmoor(u)	28,821	....

Massachusetts

See Note on Page 201

ZIP code	Place	1970	1960
02351	*Abington*	12,334	10,607
01720	*Acton*	14,770	7,238
02743	*Acushnet*	7,767	5,755
01220	Adams Center(u)	11,256	11,949
......	*Adams*	11,772	12,391
01001	*Agawam*	21,717	15,718
01913	Amesbury Center(u)	10,088	9,625
......	*Amesbury*	11,388	10,787
01002	Amherst Center	17,926	10,306
......	*Amherst*	26,331	13,718
01810	*Andover*	23,695	17,134
02174	*Arlington*	53,534	49,953
01721	*Ashland*	8,882	7,779
01331	Athol Center(u)	9,723	10,161
......	*Athol*	11,185	11,637
02703	Attleboro	32,907	27,118
01501	*Auburn*	15,347	14,047
02322	*Avon*	5,295	4,301
*01432	*Ayer*	7,393	14,927
02630	*Barnstable*	19,842	13,465
01730	*Bedford*	13,513	10,969
01007	*Belchertown*	5,936	5,186
02019	*Bellingham*	13,967	6,774
02178	*Belmont*	28,285	28,715
01915	Beverly	38,348	36,108
01821	*Billerica*	31,648	17,867
01504	*Blackstone*	6,566	5,130
*02109	Boston	641,071	697,197
02532	*Bourne*	12,636	14,011
02184	*Braintree*	35,050	31,069
02324	*Bridgewater*	11,829	10,276
*02403	Brockton	89,040	72,813
02146	*Brookline*	58,886	54,044
01803	*Burlington*	21,980	12,852
*02138	Cambridge	100,361	107,716
02021	*Canton*	17,100	12,771
01824	*Chelmsford*	31,432	15,130
02150	Chelsea	30,625	33,749
*01021	Chicopee	66,676	61,553
01510	*Clinton*	13,383	12,848
02025	*Cohasset*	6,954	5,840
01742	*Concord*	16,148	12,517
01226	*Dalton*	7,505	6,436
01923	*Danvers*	26,151	21,926
02714	*Dartmouth*	18,800	14,607
02026	*Dedham*	25,938	23,869
02638	*Dennis*	6,454	3,727

ZIP code	Place	1970	1960
01826	Dracut	18,214	13,674
01570	Dudley	8,087	6,510
02332	Duxbury	7,636	4,727
02333	East Bridgewater	8,347	6,139
01027	Easthampton	13,012	12,326
01028	East Longmeadow	13,029	10,294
02334	Easton	12,157	9,078
02149	Everett	42,485	43,544
02719	Fairhaven	16,332	14,339
*02722	Fall River	96,898	99,942
*02540	Falmouth Center(u)	5,806	3,308
......	Falmouth	15,942	13,037
01420	Fitchburg	43,343	43,021
01433	Fort Devens(u)	12,019	......
02035	Foxborough	14,218	10,136
01701	Framingham	64,048	44,526
02038	Franklin Center(u)	8,863	6,391
......	Franklin	17,830	10,530
01440	Gardner	19,748	19,038
01833	Georgetown	5,290	3,755
01930	Gloucester	27,941	25,789
01519	Grafton	11,659	10,627
01033	Granby	5,473	4,221
01230	Great Barrington	7,537	6,624
01301	Greenfield Center(u)	14,642	14,389
......	Greenfield	18,116	17,690
01450	Groton	5,109	3,904
01834	Groveland	5,382	3,297
01936	Hamilton	6,373	5,488
02339	Hanover	10,107	5,923
02341	Hanson	7,148	4,370
01451	Harvard	12,494	2,563
02645	Harwich	5,892	3,747
01830	Haverhill	46,120	46,346
02043	Hingham	18,845	15,378
02343	Holbrook	11,775	10,104
01520	Holden	12,564	10,117
01746	Holliston	12,069	6,222
01040	Holyoke	50,112	52,689
01748	Hopkinton	5,981	4,932
01749	Hudson Center(u)	14,283	7,987
......	Hudson	16,084	9,666
02045	Hull	9,961	7,055
02601	Hyannis(u)	6,847	5,139
01938	Ipswich(u)	5,022	4,617
......	Ipswich	10,750	8,544
02364	Kingston	5,999	4,302
01523	Lancaster	6,095	3,958
*01842	Lawrence	66,915	70,933
01238	Lee	6,426	5,271
01524	Leicester	9,140	8,177
01240	Lenox	5,804	4,253
01453	Leominster	32,939	27,929
02173	Lexington	31,886	27,691
01773	Lincoln	7,567	5,613
01460	Littleton	6,380	5,109
01106	Longmeadow	15,630	10,565
*01853	Lowell	94,239	92,107
01056	Ludlow	17,580	13,805
01462	Lunenburg	7,419	6,334
*01901	Lynn	90,294	94,478
01940	Lynnfield	10,826	8,398
02148	Malden	56,127	57,676
01944	Manchester	5,151	3,932
02048	Mansfield	9,939	7,773
01945	Marblehead	21,295	18,521
01752	Marlborough	27,936	18,819
02050	Marshfield	15,223	6,748
01754	Maynard	9,710	7,695
02052	Medfield	9,821	6,021
02155	Medford	64,397	64,971
02053	Medway	7,938	5,168
02176	Melrose	33,180	29,619
01844	Methuen	35,456	28,114
02346	Middleborough Center(u)	6,259	6,003
......	Middleborough	13,607	11,065
01757	Milford Center(u)	13,740	13,722
......	Milford	19,352	15,749
01527	Millbury	11,987	9,623
02054	Millis	5,686	4,374
02186	Milton	27,190	26,375
01057	Monson	7,355	6,712
01351	Montague	8,451	7,836
01760	Natick	31,057	28,831
02192	Needham	29,748	25,793
*02741	New Bedford	101,777	102,477
01950	Newburyport	15,807	14,004
02158	Newton	91,066	92,384
01247	North Adams	19,195	19,905
01060	Northampton	29,664	30,058
01845	North Andover	16,284	10,908
*02760	North Attleborough	18,665	14,777
01532	Northborough	9,218	6,687
01534	Northbridge	11,795	10,800
01864	North Reading	11,264	8,331
02060	North Scituate(u)	5,507	3,421
02766	Norton	9,487	6,818
02061	Norwell	7,796	5,207
02062	Norwood	30,815	24,898
01364	Orange	6,104	6,154
01253	Otis(u)	5,596	......
01540	Oxford Center(u)	6,109	6,985
......	Oxford	10,345	9,282
01069	Palmer	11,680	10,358
01960	Peabody	48,080	32,202
02359	Pembroke	11,193	4,919
01463	Pepperell	5,887	4,336
01866	Pinehurst	5,681	1,991
01201	Pittsfield	57,020	57,879
*02360	Plymouth Center(u)	6,940	6,488
......	Plymouth	18,606	14,445
02169	Quincy	87,966	87,409
02368	Randolph	27,035	18,900
02767	Raynham	6,705	4,150
01867	Reading	22,539	19,259
02769	Rehoboth	6,512	4,953
02151	Revere	43,159	40,080
02370	Rockland	15,674	13,119
01966	Rockport	5,636	4,616
01970	Salem	40,556	39,211
02563	Sandwich	5,239	2,082
01906	Saugus	25,110	20,666
02066	Scituate	16,973	11,214
02771	Seekonk	11,116	8,399
02067	Sharon	12,367	10,070
01545	Shrewsbury	19,196	16,622
02725	Somerset	18,088	12,196
02143	Somerville	88,779	94,697
01772	Southborough	5,798	3,996
01550	Southbridge Center(u)	14,261	15,889
......	Southbridge	17,057	16,523
01075	South Hadley	17,033	14,956
01077	Southwick	6,330	5,139
02664	South Yarmouth(u)	5,380	2,029
01562	Spencer Center	5,895	5,593
......	Spencer	8,779	7,838
*01101	Springfield	163,905	174,463
02180	Stoneham	20,725	17,821
02072	Stoughton	23,459	16,328
01776	Sudbury	13,506	7,447
01907	Swampscott	13,578	13,294
02777	Swansea	12,640	9,916
02780	Taunton	43,756	41,132
01468	Templeton	5,863	5,371
01876	Tewksbury	22,755	15,902
01983	Topsfield	5,225	3,351
01376	Turners Falls(u)	5,168	4,917
01569	Uxbridge	8,253	7,789
01880	Wakefield	25,402	24,295
02081	Walpole	18,149	14,068
02154	Waltham	61,582	55,413
01082	Ware Center(u)	6,509	6,650
......	Ware	8,187	7,517
02571	Wareham	11,492	9,461
02172	Watertown	39,307	39,092
01778	Wayland	13,461	10,444
01570	Webster Center(u)	12,432	12,072
......	Webster	14,917	13,680
02181	Wellesley	28,051	26,071
01581	Westborough	12,594	9,599
01583	West Boylston	6,369	5,526
02379	West Bridgewater	7,152	5,061
01085	Westfield	31,433	26,302
01886	Westford	10,368	6,261
02193	Weston	10,870	8,261
02790	Westport	9,791	6,641
01089	West Springfield	28,461	24,924
02090	Westwood	12,750	10,354
02188	Weymouth	54,610	48,177
01588	Whitinsville(u)	5,210	5,102
02382	Whitman	13,059	10,485
01095	Wilbraham	11,984	7,387
01267	Williamstown	8,454	7,322
01887	Wilmington	17,102	12,475
01475	Winchendon	6,635	6,237
01890	Winchester	22,269	19,376
02152	Winthrop	20,335	20,303
01801	Woburn	37,406	31,214
*01613	Worcester	176,572	186,587
02093	Wrentham	7,315	6,685
02675	Yarmouth	12,033	5,504

Michigan

ZIP code	Place	1970	1960
49221	Adrian	20,382	20,347
49224	Albion	12,112	12,749
48101	Allen Park	40,747	37,494
48801	Alma	9,611	8,978
49707	Alpena	13,805	14,682
*48106	Ann Arbor	99,797	67,340
*49016	Battle Creek	38,931	44,169
48706	Bay City	49,449	53,604
48809	Belding	5,121	4,887
49022	Benton Central(u)	8,067	
49022	Benton Harbor	16,481	19,136
48072	Berkley	21,879	23,275

ZIP code	Place	1970	1960
48009	Beverly Hills	13,598	8,633
49307	Big Rapids	11,995	8,686
*48012	Birmingham	26,170	25,525
49601	Cadillac	9,990	10,112
48724	Carrollton(u)	7,300	......
48015	Center Line	10,379	10,164
48813	Charlotte	8,244	7,657
49721	Cheboygan	5,553	5,859
48017	Clawson	17,617	14,795
49036	Coldwater	9,155	8,880
49041	Comstock(u)	5,003	......
49321	Comstock Park(u)	5,766	......
49508	Cutlerville(u)	6,267	......
48423	Davison 1976	6,193	3,761
*48120	Dearborn	104,199	112,007
48127	Dearborn Heights	80,069	......
*48233	Detroit	1,513,601	1,670,144
49047	Dowagiac	6,583	7,208
48020	Drayton Plains(u)	16,462	......
48021	East Detroit	45,920	45,756
49506	East Grand Rapids	12,565	10,924
48823	East Lansing	47,540	30,198
49001	Eastwood(u)	9,682	......
48229	Ecorse	17,515	17,328
49829	Escanaba	15,368	15,391
48024	Farmington	10,329	6,881
48430	Fenton	8,284	6,142
48220	Ferndale	30,850	31,347
48134	Flat Rock	5,643	4,696
*48502	Flint	193,317	196,940
48433	Flushing 1976	8,313	3,761
48026	Fraser	11,868	7,027
48135	Garden City	41,864	38,017
49837	Gladstone	5,237	5,267
48439	Grand Blanc	5,132	1,565
49417	Grand Haven	11,844	11,066
48837	Grand Ledge	6,032	5,165
*49501	Grand Rapids	197,649	177,313
49418	Grandville	10,764	7,975
48838	Greenville	7,493	7,440
48138	Grosse Ile(u)	8,306	......
48236	Grosse Pointe	6,637	6,631
48236	Grosse Pointe Farms	11,701	12,172
48236	Grosse Pointe Park	15,641	15,457
48236	Grosse Pointe Woods	21,878	18,580
48212	Hamtramck	27,245	34,137
48236	Harper Woods	20,186	19,995
49058	Hastings	6,501	6,375
48030	Hazel Park	23,784	25,631
48203	Highland Park	35,444	38,063
49242	Hillsdale	7,728	7,629
49423	Holland	26,479	24,777
48842	Holt(u)	6,980	4,818
49931	Houghton	6,067	3,393
48843	Howell	5,224	4,861
48070	Huntington Woods	8,536	8,746
48141	Inkster	38,595	39,097
48846	Ionia	6,361	6,754
49801	Iron Mountain	8,702	9,299
49938	Ironwood	8,711	10,265
49849	Ishpeming	8,245	8,857
*49201	Jackson	45,484	50,720
49428	Jenison(u)	11,266	......
*49001	Kalamazoo	85,555	82,089
49508	Kentwood 1976	25,731	......
49788	Kincheloe(u)	6,331	......
49801	Kingsford	5,276	5,084
49843	K.I. Sawyer(u)	8,224	......
49015	Lakeview(u)	11,391	10,384
48144	Lambertville(u)	5,711	1,168
*48924	Lansing	131,403	107,807
48446	Lapeer	6,314	6,160
48503	Lapeer Heights(u)	7,130	......
48146	Lincoln Park	52,984	53,933
*48150	Livonia	110,109	66,702
49431	Ludington	9,021	9,421
48071	Madison Heights	38,599	33,343
49660	Manistee	7,723	8,324
49855	Marquette	21,967	19,824
49068	Marshall	7,253	6,736
48040	Marysville	5,610	4,065
48854	Mason	5,468	4,522
48122	Melvindale	13,862	13,089
49858	Menominee	10,748	11,289
48640	Midland	35,176	27,779
48161	Monroe	23,894	22,968
48043	Mount Clemens	20,476	21,016
48858	Mount Pleasant	20,524	14,875
*49440	Muskegon	44,631	46,485
49444	Muskegon Heights	17,304	19,552
49866	Negaunee	5,248	6,126
49120	Niles	12,988	13,842
48167	Northville	5,400	3,967
49441	Norton Shores	22,271	......
48050	Novi	9,668	6,390
48237	Oak Park	36,762	36,632
48864	Okemos(u)	7,770	......
48867	Owosso	17,179	17,006
49770	Petroskey	6,342	6,138
48170	Plymouth	11,758	8,766
*48053	Pontiac	85,279	82,233
49081	Portage	33,590	......
48060	Port Huron	35,794	36,084
48024	Quakertown North(u)	7,101	......
48218	River Rouge	15,947	18,147
48192	Riverview	11,342	7,237
48063	Rochester	7,054	5,431
48066	Roseville	60,529	50,195
*48068	Royal Oak	86,238	80,612
*48605	Saginaw	91,849	98,265
*48083	St. Clair Shores	88,093	76,657
48879	St. Johns	6,672	5,629
49085	St. Joseph	11,042	11,755
48176	Saline 1974	6,050	2,334
49793	Sault Ste. Marie	15,136	18,722
*48075	Southfield	69,285	31,501
48198	Southgate	33,909	29,404
49090	South Haven	6,471	6,149
*48078	Sterling Heights 1976	92,904	......
49091	Sturgis	9,295	8,915
48180	Taylor 1976	77,490	......
49286	Tecumseh	7,120	7,045
49093	Three Rivers	7,355	7,092
49684	Traverse City	18,048	18,432
48183	Trenton	24,127	18,439
48084	Troy	39,419	19,402
49504	Walker 1976	13,349	......
*48089	Warren	179,260	89,246
48184	Wayne	21,054	16,034
48185	Westland	86,749	......
49007	Westwood(u)	9,143	......
48753	Wurtsmith(u)	6,932	......
*48192	Wyandotte	41,061	43,519
49509	Wyoming	56,560	45,829
48197	Ypsilanti	29,538	20,957

Minnesota

ZIP code	Place	1970	1960
56007	Albert Lea	19,418	17,108
56308	Alexandria	6,973	6,713
55303	Anoka	13,295	10,562
55068	Apple Valley 1975	15,315	......
55112	Arden Hills	5,149	3,930
55912	Austin	25,074	27,908
56601	Bemidji	11,490	9,958
55433	Blaine	20,625	7,570
55420	Bloomington 1975	79,119	50,498
56401	Brainerd	11,667	12,898
55429	Brooklyn Center	35,173	24,356
55429	Brooklyn Park 1972	29,945	10,197
55337	Burnsville	19,940	......
55316	Champlin 1972	6,298	1,271
55317	Chanhassen 1971	5,054	244
55318	Chaska 1972	5,398	2,501
55719	Chisholm 1975	6,085	7,144
55720	Cloquet	8,699	9,013
55421	Columbia Heights	23,837	17,533
55433	Coon Rapids	30,505	14,931
55016	Cottage Grove	13,419	......
56716	Crookston	8,312	8,546
55428	Crystal	30,925	24,283
56501	Detroit Lakes	5,797	5,633
*55806	Duluth	100,578	106,884
56721	East Grand Forks 1975	8,397	6,998
55343	Eden Prairie 1975	9,109	......
55424	Edina	44,046	28,501
56031	Fairmont	10,751	9,745
55113	Falcon Heights	5,641	5,927
55021	Fairbault	16,595	16,926
56537	Fergus Falls	12,443	13,733
55421	Fridley	29,233	15,173
55427	Golden Valley	24,246	14,559
55744	Grand Rapids	7,247	7,265
55033	Hastings	12,195	8,965
55746	Hibbing 1976	16,126	17,731
55343	Hopkins	13,428	11,370
55350	Hutchinson	8,031	6,207
56649	International Falls	6,439	6,778
55075	Inver Grove Heights	12,148	......
55044	Lakeville	7,556	924
55355	Litchfield	5,262	5,078
55110	Little Canada 1974	5,977	3,512
56345	Little Falls	7,467	7,551
56001	Mankato	30,895	23,797
55369	Maple Grove 1975	10,039	2,213
55109	Maplewood	25,222	18,519
56258	Marshall	9,886	6,681
55118	Mendota Heights	6,165	5,028
*55401	Minneapolis	434,400	482,872
55343	Minnetonka	35,737	25,037
56265	Montevideo	5,661	5,693
56560	Moorhead	29,687	22,934
56267	Morris	5,366	4,199
55364	Mound	7,572	5,440
55112	Mounds View	10,641	6,146
55112	New Brighton	19,507	6,448
54428	New Hope	23,180	3,552
56073	New Ulm	13,051	11,114

ZIP code	Place	1970	1960
55057	Northfield	10,235	8,707
56001	North Mankato 1975	8,071	5,927
55109	North St. Paul	11,950	8,520
55119	Oakdale	7,304	....
55391	Orono	6,787	5,643
55060	Owatonna	15,341	13,409
56164	Pipestone	5,328	5,324
55427	Plymouth	18,077	9,576
55066	Red Wing	10,441	10,528
55423	Richfield	47,231	42,523
55422	Robbinsdale	16,845	16,381
55901	Rochester	53,766	40,663
55113	Roseville	34,438	23,997
55418	St. Anthony	9,239	5,084
56301	St. Cloud 1975	40,715	33,815
55426	St. Louis Park	48,922	43,310
*55101	St. Paul	309,714	313,411
55071	St. Paul Park	5,587	3,267
56082	St. Peter	8,339	8,484
56379	Sauk Rapids	5,051	4,038
55379	Shakopee	6,876	5,201
55112	Shoreview	10,995	7,157
55075	South St. Paul	25,016	22,032
55432	Spring Lake Park	6,417	3,260
55082	Stillwater	10,191	8,310
56701	Thief River Falls 1975	8,929	7,151
55792	Virginia	12,450	14,034
56093	Waseca 1975	7,804	5,898
55118	West St. Paul	18,799	13,101
55110	White Bear Lake	23,313	12,849
56201	Willmar	12,869	10,417
55987	Winona	26,438	24,895
55119	Woodbury	6,184	....
56187	Worthington	9,916	9,015

Mississippi

ZIP code	Place	1970	1960
39730	Aberdeen	6,507	6,450
38821	Amory	7,236	6,474
39520	Bay St. Louis	6,752	5,073
*39530	Biloxi 1975	46,497	44,053
38829	Booneville	5,895	3,480
39601	Brookhaven	10,700	9,885
39046	Canton	10,503	9,707
38614	Clarksdale	21,673	21,105
38732	Cleveland 1975	14,043	10,172
39056	Clinton 1976	12,100	3,438
39429	Columbia	7,587	7,117
39701	Columbus	25,795	24,771
38834	Corinth	11,581	11,453
39532	D'Iberville(u)	7,288	3,005
38701	Greenville	39,648	41,502
38930	Greenwood	22,400	20,436
38901	Grenada	9,944	7,914
39501	Gulfport	40,791	30,204
39401	Hattiesburg	38,277	34,989
38635	Holly Springs	5,728	5,621
38751	Indianola	8,947	6,714
*39205	Jackson	153,968	144,422
39090	Kosciusko	7,266	6,800
39440	Laurel	24,145	27,889
38756	Leland	6,000	6,295
39560	Long Beach 1975	7,113	4,770
39339	Louisville	6,626	5,066
39648	McComb	11,969	12,020
39301	Meridian 1974	46,087	49,374
39563	Moss Point	19,321	6,631
39120	Natchez	19,704	23,791
38652	New Albany	6,426	5,151
39564	Ocean Springs	9,580	5,025
38655	Oxford City	13,846	5,283
39567	Pascagoula	27,264	17,155
39208	Pearl(u)	9,623	5,081
39465	Petal(u)	6,986	4,007
39350	Philadelphia	6,274	5,017
39466	Picayune	10,467	7,834
38671	Southaven(u)	8,931	....
39759	Starkville	11,369	9,041
38801	Tupelo	20,471	17,221
39180	Vicksburg	25,478	29,143
39501	West Gulfport(u)	6,996	3,323
39773	West Point	8,714	8,550
38967	Winona	5,521	4,282
39194	Yazoo City	11,688	11,236

Missouri

ZIP code	Place	1970	1960
63123	Affton(u)	24,264	....
65605	Aurora	5,359	4,683
63011	Ballwin	10,656	5,710
63137	Bellefontaine Neighbors	14,084	13,650
63133	Bel-Ridge	5,346	4,395
64012	Belton	12,179	4,897
63134	Berkeley	19,743	18,676
64015	Blue Springs	6,779	2,555
65233	Boonville	7,514	7,090
63114	Breckenridge Hills	7,011	6,299
63144	Brentwood	11,248	12,250
63044	Bridgeton	19,992	7,820
64628	Brookfield	5,491	5,694
63701	Cape Girardeau	31,282	24,947
64836	Carthage	11,035	11,264
63830	Caruthersville	7,350	8,643
63834	Charleston	5,131	5,911
64601	Chillicothe	9,519	9,236
63105	Clayton	16,100	15,245
64735	Clinton	7,504	6,925
65201	Columbia	58,812	36,650
63128	Concord(u)	21,217	....
63126	Crestwood	15,123	11,106
63141	Creve Coeur 1976	10,660	5,122
63136	Dellwood	7,137	4,720
63020	De Soto	5,984	5,804
63131	Des Peres, 1975	7,130	4,362
63841	Dexter	6,024	5,519
64024	Excelsior Springs	9,411	6,473
63640	Farmington	6,590	5,618
63135	Ferguson	28,759	22,149
63028	Festus	7,530	7,021
*63033	Florissant	65,908	38,166
65473	Fort Leonard Wood(u)	33,799	....
65251	Fulton	12,248	11,131
64118	Gladstone	23,422	14,502
63122	Glendale	6,981	7,048
64030	Grandview	17,456	6,027
63401	Hannibal	18,698	20,028
64701	Harrisonville	5,052	3,510
*63042	Hazelwood	14,082	6,045
*64051	Independence	111,630	62,328
63755	Jackson	5,896	4,875
65101	Jefferson City	32,407	28,228
63136	Jennings	19,379	19,965
64801	Joplin	39,256	38,958
*64108	Kansas City	507,330	475,539
63857	Kennett	10,090	9,098
63140	Kinloch	5,629	6,501
63501	Kirksville	15,560	13,123
63122	Kirkwood	31,679	29,421
63124	Ladue	10,359	9,466
65536	Lebanon	8,616	8,220
64063	Lee's Summit	16,230	8,267
63125	Lemay(u)	40,516	....
64067	Lexington	5,388	4,845
64068	Liberty	13,704	8,909
63552	Macon	5,301	4,547
63863	Malden	5,374	5,007
63011	Manchester	5,031	2,021
63143	Maplewood	12,785	12,552
65340	Marshall	12,051	9,572
63043	Maryland Heights(u)	8,805	....
64468	Maryville	9,970	7,807
65265	Mexico	11,807	12,889
65270	Moberly	12,988	13,170
65708	Monett	5,937	5,359
64850	Neosho	7,517	7,452
64772	Nevada	9,736	8,416
63121	Normandy	6,236	4,452
64116	North Kansas City 1974	5,046	5,657
63366	O'Fallon	7,018	3,770
63124	Olivette	9,156	8,257
63114	Overland	24,819	22,763
63133	Pagedale	5,044	5,106
63775	Perryville	5,149	5,117
63120	Pine Lawn	5,745	5,943
63901	Poplar Bluff	16,653	15,926
64133	Raytown	33,306	17,083
63117	Richmond Heights	13,802	15,622
63124	Rock Hill	6,815	6,523
65401	Rolla	13,571	11,132
63074	St. Ann	18,215	12,155
63301	St. Charles	31,834	21,189
63114	St. John	8,960	7,342
*64501	St. Joseph	72,691	79,673
*63155	St. Louis	622,236	750,026
63126	Sappington(u)	10,603	....
65301	Sedalia	22,847	23,874
63119	Shrewsbury	5,896	4,730
63801	Sikeston	14,699	13,765
63138	Spanish Lake(u)	15,647	....
*65801	Springfield	120,096	95,865
63080	Sullivan	5,111	4,098
64683	Trenton	6,063	6,262
63084	Union	5,183	3,937
63130	University City	47,527	51,249
64093	Warrensburg	13,125	9,689
63090	Washington	8,499	7,961
64870	Webb City	6,923	6,740
63119	Webster Groves	27,457	28,990
63112	Wellston	7,050	7,979
65775	West Plains	6,893	5,836
65301	Whiteman	5,040	....
63134	Woodson Terrace	5,880	6,048

Montana

ZIP code	Place	1970	1960
59711	Anaconda	9,771	12,054
*59101	Billings	61,581	52,851
59715	Bozeman	18,670	13,361

ZIP code	Place	1970	1960
59701	Butte	23,368	27,877
59701	Floral Park(u)	5,113	4,079
59330	Glendive	6,305	7,058
*59401	Great Falls	60,091	55,244
59501	Havre	10,558	10,740
59601	Helena	22,730	20,227
59901	Kalispell	10,526	10,151
59457	Lewistown	6,437	7,408
59047	Livingston	6,883	8,229
59402	Malmstrom(u)	8,374	......
59301	Miles City 1976	9,622	9,665
59801	Missoula	29,497	27,090
59801	Missoula West(u)	9,148	......
59701	Silver Bow Park(u)	5,524	4,798

Nebraska

ZIP code	Place	1970	1960
69301	Alliance	6,862	7,845
68310	Beatrice	12,389	12,132
68005	Bellevue 1974	21,145	8,831
68008	Blair	6,106	4,931
69337	Chadron	5,921	5,079
68601	Columbus	15,471	12,476
68352	Fairbury	5,265	5,572
68355	Falls City	5,444	5,598
68025	Fremont	22,962	19,698
69341	Gering 1976	6,680	4,585
68801	Grand Island	31,269	25,742
68901	Hastings	23,580	21,412
68949	Holdrege	5,635	5,226
68847	Kearney 1976	19,350	14,210
68128	La Vista 1974	7,840	1,004
68850	Lexington	5,654	5,572
*68501	Lincoln	149,518	128,521
69001	McCook	8,285	8,301
68137	Millard	7,460	1,014
68410	Nebraska City	7,441	7,252
68701	Norfolk	16,607	13,640
69101	North Platte	19,447	17,184
68113	Offutt East(u)	5,195	......
68113	Offutt West(u)	8,445	......
*68108	Omaha	346,929	301,598
68046	Papillion 1974	6,493	2,235
68048	Plattsmouth	6,371	6,244
69361	Scottsbluff	14,507	13,377
68434	Seward	5,294	4,208
69162	Sidney 1976	6,092	8,004
68776	South Sioux City 1976	8,504	7,200
68787	Wayne	5,379	4,217
68467	York	6,778	6,173

Nevada

ZIP code	Place	1970	1960
89005	Boulder City	5,223	4,059
89701	Carson City	15,468	5,163
89112	East Las Vegas(u)	6,501	......
89801	Elko	7,621	6,298
89015	Henderson	16,395	12,525
*89114	Las Vegas	125,787	64,405
89110	Nellis(u)	6,449	......
89030	North Las Vegas	36,216	18,422
89109	Paradise(u)	24,477	......
*89501	Reno	72,863	51,470
89431	Sparks	24,187	16,618
89110	Sunrise Manor(u)	10,886	......
89109	Vegas Creek(u)	8,970	......
89101	Winchester(u)	13,981	......

New Hampshire

See note on page 201

ZIP code	Place	1970	1960
03102	*Bedford*	5,859	3,636
03570	Berlin	15,256	17,821
03743	Claremont	14,221	13,563
03301	Concord	30,022	28,991
03038	Derry Compact(u)	6,090	4,468
03038	*Derry*	11,712	6,987
03820	Dover	20,850	19,131
03824	Durham Compact(u)	7,221	4,688
......	*Durham*	8,869	5,504
03833	Exeter Compact(u)	6,439	5,896
......	*Exeter*	8,892	7,243
03235	Franklin	7,292	6,742
03045	Goffstown	9,284	7,230
03842	Hampton Compact(u)	5,407	3,281
......	*Hampton*	8,011	5,379
03755	Hanover Compact(u)	6,147	5,649
......	*Hanover*	8,494	7,329
03106	*Hookset*	5,564	3,713
03051	*Hudson*	10,638	5,876
03431	Keene	20,467	17,562
03246	Laconia	14,888	15,288
03766	Lebanon	9,725	9,299
03516	*Littleton*	5,290	5,003
03053	*Londonderry*	5,346	2,457
*03101	Manchester	87,754	88,282
03054	*Merrimack*	8,595	2,989
03055	*Milford*	6,622	4,863
03060	Nashua	55,820	39,096
03773	*Newport*	5,899	5,458
03076	*Pelham*	5,408	2,605
03801	Portsmouth	25,717	26,900
03867	Rochester	17,938	15,927
03079	*Salem*	20,142	9,210
03874	*Seabrook* 1974	5,128	2,209
03878	Somersworth	9,026	8,529

New Jersey

ZIP code	Place	1970	1960
08201	Absecon	6,094	4,320
07401	Allendale	6,240	4,092
07712	Asbury Park	16,533	17,366
*08401	Atlantic City	47,859	59,544
07716	Atlantic Highlands	5,102	4,119
08106	Audubon	10,802	10,440
08007	Barrington	8,409	7,943
07002	Bayonne	72,743	74,215
07109	Belleville	37,629	35,005
08030	Bellmawr	15,618	11,853
07719	Belmar	5,782	5,190
07621	Bergenfield	29,000	27,203
07922	Berkeley Hts. Twp.	13,078	8,721
07924	Bernardsville	6,652	5,515
07003	Bloomfield	52,029	51,867
07403	Bloomingdale	7,797	5,293
07603	Bogota	8,960	7,965
07005	Boonton	9,261	7,981
08805	Bound Brook	10,450	10,263
08723	Brick Twp.	35,057	16,299
08302	Bridgeton	20,435	20,966
08203	Brigantine	6,741	4,201
08015	Browns Mills(u)	7,144	......
08016	Burlington	11,991	12,687
07405	Butler	7,051	5,414
07006	Caldwell	8,677	6,942
*08101	Camden	102,551	117,159
08701	Candlewood(u)	5,629	......
07072	Carlstadt	6,724	6,042
07008	Carteret	23,137	20,502
07009	Cedar Grove Twp.	15,582	14,603
07928	Chatham	9,566	9,517
*08002	Cherry Hill Twp.	64,395	31,522
08077	Cinnaminson Twp.	16,962	8,302
07066	Clark Twp.	18,829	12,195
08312	Clayton	5,193	4,711
07010	Cliffside Park	18,891	17,642
07721	Cliffwood-Cliffwood Beach(u)	7,056	......
*07015	Clifton	82,437	82,084
07624	Closter	8,604	7,767
08108	Collingswood	17,422	17,370
07016	Cranford Twp.	27,391	26,424
07626	Cresskill	8,298	7,290
08075	Delran Twp.	10,065	5,327
07627	Demarest	5,133	4,231
07834	Denville Twp.	14,045	10,632
08096	Deptford Twp.	24,232	17,878
07801	Dover	15,039	13,034
07628	Dumont	20,155	18,882
08812	Dunellen	7,072	6,840
08816	East Brunswick Twp.	34,166	19,965
*07019	East Orange	75,471	77,259
07407	East Paterson	20,511	19,344
07073	East Rutherford	8,536	7,769
08520	East Windsor Twp. 1974	19,788	2,298
07724	Eatontown	14,619	10,334
08817	Edison Twp.	67,120	44,799
*07207	Elizabeth	112,654	107,698
07630	Emerson	8,428	6,849
*07631	Englewood	24,985	26,057
07632	Englewood Cliffs	5,938	2,913
08053	Evesham Twp.	13,477	4,548
08618	Ewing Twp.	32,831	26,628
07006	Fairfield	6,884	......
07701	Fair Haven	6,142	5,678
07410	Fair Lawn	37,975	36,421
07022	Fairview	10,698	9,399
07023	Fanwood	8,920	7,963
08518	Florence-Roebling(u)	7,551	......
07932	Florham Park	8,094	7,222
08640	Fort Dix(u)	26,290	......
07024	Fort Lee	30,631	21,815
07417	Franklin Lakes	7,550	3,316
07728	Freehold	10,545	9,140
07026	Garfield	30,797	29,253
07027	Garwood	5,260	5,426
08028	Glassboro	12,938	10,253
07028	Glen Ridge	8,518	8,322
07452	Glen Rock	13,011	12,896
08030	Gloucester City	14,707	15,511
07093	Guttenberg	5,754	5,118
*07602	Hackensack	36,008	30,521
07840	Hackettstown	9,472	5,276
08108	Haddon Twp.	18,192	17,099
08033	Haddonfield	13,118	13,201
08035	Haddon Heights	9,365	9,260
07508	Haledon	6,767	6,161

ZIP code	Place	1970	1960
08037	Hammonton	11,464	9,854
07981	Hanover Twp.	10,700	9,329
07029	Harrison	11,811	11,743
07604	Hasbrouck Heights	13,651	13,046
07506	Hawthorne	19,173	17,735
07730	Hazlet Twp.	22,239	15,334
08904	Highland Park	14,385	11,049
08520	Hightstown	5,431	4,317
07642	Hillsdale	11,768	8,734
07205	Hillside Twp.	21,636	22,304
07030	Hoboken	45,380	48,441
07843	Hopatcong	9,052	3,391
08560	Hopewell Twp. (Mercer)	10,030	7,818
07111	Irvington	59,743	59,379
08527	Jackson Twp.	18,276	5,939
*07303	Jersey City	260,350	276,101
07734	Keansburg	9,720	6,854
07032	Kearny	37,585	37,472
08824	Kendall Park(u)	7,412	......
07033	Kenilworth	9,165	8,379
07735	Keyport	7,205	6,440
07405	Kinnelon	7,600	4,431
07034	Lake Hiawatha(u)	11,389	......
07871	Lake Mohawk(u)	6,262	4,647
07054	Lake Parsippany(u)	7,488	......
08701	Lakewood(u)	17,874	13,004
08879	Laurence Harbor(u)	6,715	......
07605	Leonia	8,847	8,384
07035	Lincoln Park	9,034	6,048
07036	Linden	41,409	39,931
08021	Lindenwold 1973	16,265	7,335
08221	Linwood	6,159	3,847
07424	Little Falls Twp.	11,727	9,730
07643	Little Ferry	9,064	6,176
07739	Little Silver	6,010	5,202
07039	Livingston Twp.	30,127	23,124
07644	Lodi	25,163	23,502
07740	Long Branch	31,774	26,228
07071	Lyndhurst Twp.	22,729	21,867
07940	Madison	16,710	15,122
08049	Magnolia	5,893	4,199
07430	Mahwah Twp.	10,800	7,376
08835	Manville	13,029	10,995
08052	Maple Shade Twp.	16,464	12,947
07040	Maplewood Twp.	24,932	23,977
08402	Margate City	10,576	9,474
07746	Marlboro Twp.	12,273	8,038
08053	Marlton(u)	10,180	......
07747	Matawan	9,136	5,097
07607	Maywood	11,087	11,460
08641	McGuire(u)	10,933	......
08619	Mercerville-Hamilton Sq.(u)	24,465	......
08840	Metuchen	16,031	14,041
08846	Middlesex	15,038	10,520
07748	Middletown Twp.	54,623	39,675
07432	Midland Park	8,159	7,543
07041	Millburn Twp.	21,089	18,799
08850	Milltown	6,470	5,435
08332	Millville	21,366	19,096
07434	Monroe Twp. (Gloucester)	14,071	9,396
*07042	Montclair	44,043	43,129
07645	Montvale	7,327	3,699
07045	Montville Twp.	11,846	6,772
08057	Moorestown-Lenola(u)	14,179	......
07950	Morris Plains	5,540	4,703
07960	Morristown	17,662	17,712
07092	Mountainside	7,520	6,325
08059	Mount Ephraim	5,625	5,447
08060	Mount Holly Twp.	12,713	13,271
07753	Neptune Twp.	27,863	21,487
07753	Neptune City	5,502	4,013
*07102	Newark	381,930	405,220
*08901	New Brunswick	41,885	40,139
08511	New Hanover	27,410	28,528
07646	New Milford	19,149	18,810
07974	New Providence	13,796	10,243
07724	New Shrewsbury	8,395	7,313
07860	Newton	7,297	6,563
07032	North Arlington	18,096	17,477
07047	North Bergen Twp.	47,751	42,387
08902	North Brunswick Twp.	16,691	10,099
07006	North Caldwell	6,733	4,163
08225	Northfield	8,875	5,849
07508	North Haledon	7,614	6,026
07060	North Plainfield	21,796	16,993
07647	Northvale	5,177	2,892
07110	Nutley	31,913	29,513
07755	Oakhurst(u)	5,558	4,374
07436	Oakland	14,420	9,446
08226	Ocean City	10,575	7,618
07757	Oceanport	7,503	4,937
08857	Old Bridge(u)	25,176	......
07649	Oradell	8,903	7,487
*07050	Orange	32,566	35,789
07650	Palisades Park	13,351	11,943
08065	Palmyra	6,969	7,036
07652	Paramus	28,381	23,238
07656	Park Ridge	8,709	6,389
*07055	Passaic	55,124	53,963

ZIP code	Place	1970	1960
*07510	Paterson	144,824	143,663
08066	Paulsboro	8,084	8,121
08110	Pennsauken Twp.	36,394	33,771
08069	Penns Grove	5,727	6,176
08070	Pennsville Center(u)	11,014	......
07440	Pequannock Twp.	14,350	10,553
*08861	Perth Amboy	38,798	38,007
08865	Phillipsburg	17,849	18,502
08021	Pine Hill	5,132	3,939
08854	Piscataway Twp.	36,418	19,890
08071	Pitman	10,257	8,644
*07061	Plainfield	46,862	45,330
08232	Pleasantville	13,778	15,172
08742	Point Pleasant	15,968	10,182
07442	Pompton Lakes	11,397	9,445
08540	Princeton	12,331	11,890
08540	Princeton North(u)	5,488	4,506
07508	Prospect Park	5,176	5,201
*07065	Rahway	29,114	27,699
08057	Ramblewood(u)	5,556	......
07446	Ramsey	12,571	9,527
07970	Randolph Twp.	13,296	7,295
08869	Raritan	6,691	6,137
07701	Red Bank	12,847	12,482
07657	Ridgefield	11,308	10,788
07660	Ridgefield Park	13,990	12,701
*07451	Ridgewood	27,547	25,391
07456	Ringwood	10,393	4,182
07661	River Edge	12,850	13,264
08075	Riverside Twp.	8,591	8,474
07662	Rochell Park Twp.	6,380	6,119
07866	Rockaway	6,383	5,413
07203	Roselle	22,585	21,032
07204	Roselle Park	14,227	12,546
07760	Rumson	7,421	6,405
08078	Runnemede	10,475	8,396
*07070	Rutherford	20,802	20,473
07662	Saddle Brook Twp.	15,975	13,834
08079	Salem	7,648	8,941
08872	Sayreville	32,508	22,553
07076	Scotch Plains Twp.	22,279	18,491
07094	Secaucus	13,228	12,154
08083	Somerdale	6,510	4,839
08244	Somers Point	7,919	4,504
08876	Somerville	13,652	12,458
08879	South Amboy	9,338	8,422
07079	South Orange	16,971	16,175
07080	South Plainfield	21,142	17,879
08882	South River	15,428	13,397
07871	Sparta Twp.	10,819	6,717
08884	Spotswood	7,891	5,788
07081	Springfield Twp.	15,740	14,467
08084	Stratford	9,801	4,308
07747	Strathmore	7,674	......
07901	Summit	23,620	23,677
07666	Teaneck Twp.	42,355	42,085
07670	Tenafly	14,827	14,264
08753	Toms River	7,303	6,062
07512	Totowa	11,580	10,897
*08608	Trenton	104,786	114,167
07083	Union Twp.	53,077	51,499
07735	Union Beach	6,472	5,862
07087	Union City	57,305	52,180
07458	Upper Saddle River	7,949	3,570
08406	Ventnor City	10,385	8,688
07044	Verona	15,067	13,782
08360	Vineland	47,399	37,685
07463	Waldwick	12,313	10,495
07057	Wallington	10,284	9,261
07465	Wanaque	8,636	7,126
07882	Washington	5,943	5,723
07675	Washington Twp. (Bergen)	10,577	6,654
07470	Wayne Twp.	49,141	29,353
07087	Weehawken Twp.	13,383	13,504
07006	West Caldwell	11,913	8,314
*07091	Westfield	33,720	31,447
07764	West Long Branch	6,845	5,337
07480	West Milford Twp.	17,304	8,157
07093	West New York	40,627	35,547
07052	West Orange	43,715	39,895
07424	West Paterson	11,692	7,602
08093	Westville	5,170	4,951
07675	Westwood	11,105	9,046
07885	Wharton	5,535	5,006
08610	White Horse-Yardville(u)	18,680	......
07886	White Meadow Lake(u)	8,499	......
08046	Willingboro Twp. 1973	44,607	11,861
08095	Winslow Twp.	11,202	9,142
07095	Woodbridge Twp.	98,944	78,846
08096	Woodbury	12,408	12,453
07675	Woodcliff Lake	5,506	2,742
07075	Wood-Ridge	8,311	7,964
07481	Wyckoff Twp.	16,039	11,205

New Mexico

ZIP code	Place	1970	1960
88310	Alamogordo	23,035	21,723
*87101	Albuquerque	243,751	201,189
88210	Artesia	10,315	12,000

ZIP code	Place	1970	1960
88101	Cannon(u)	5,461	....
88220	Carlsbad	21,297	25,541
88101	Clovis	28,495	23,713
88030	Deming	8,343	6,764
87401	Farmington	21,979	23,786
87301	Gallup	14,596	14,089
87020	Grants	8,768	10,274
88240	Hobbs	26,025	26,275
88330	Holloman(u)	8,001	....
88001	Las Cruces	37,857	29,367
87701	Las Vegas (city)	7,528	7,790
87701	Las Vegas (town)	6,307	6,028
87544	Los Alamos(u)	11,310	12,584
88260	Lovington	8,915	9,660
87107	North Valley(u)	10,366	....
88130	Portales	10,554	9,695
87740	Raton	6,962	8,146
88201	Roswell	33,908	39,593
87115	Sandia(u)	6,867	....
87501	Santa Fe	41,167	33,394
88061	Silver City	8,557	6,972
87801	Socorro	5,849	5,271
87105	South Valley(u)	29,389	....
88401	Tucumcari	7,189	8,143

New York

ZIP code	Place	1970	1960
*12207	Albany	115,781	129,726
11507	Albertson(u)	6,825	....
14411	Albion	5,122	5,182
11701	Amityville	9,794	8,318
12010	Amsterdam	25,524	28,772
12603	Arlington(u)	11,203	8,317
13021	Auburn	34,599	35,249
*11702	Babylon	12,897	11,062
11510	Baldwin(u)	34,525	30,204
13027	Baldwinsville	6,298	5,985
14020	Batavia	17,338	18,210
14810	Bath	6,053	6,166
11705	Bayport(u)	8,232	....
11706	Bay Shore(u)	11,119	....
11709	Bayville	6,147	3,962
12508	Beacon	13,255	13,922
11710	Bellmore(u)	18,431	12,784
11714	Bethpage(u)	18,555	....
*13902	Binghamton	64,123	75,941
10913	Blauvelt(u)	5,426	....
11716	Bohemia(u)	8,926	....
11717	Brentwood(u)	28,327	15,387
10510	Briarcliff Manor	6,521	5,105
14420	Brockport	7,878	5,256
10708	Bronxville	6,674	6,744
*14240	Buffalo	462,768	532,759
14424	Canadaigua 1971	10,753	9,370
13032	Canastota	5,033	4,896
13617	Canton	6,398	5,046
11514	Carle Place(u)	6,326	....
12414	Catskill	5,317	5,825
11516	Cedarhurst	6,941	6,954
11720	Centereach(u)	9,427	8,524
11722	Central Islip(u)	36,391	....
12065	Clifton Knolls(u)	5,771	....
12047	Cohoes	18,653	20,129
11724	Cold Spring Harbor(u)	5,450	1,705
12205	Colonie	8,701	6,992
11725	Commack(u)	24,138	9,613
10920	Congers(u)	5,928	....
11726	Copiague(u)	19,632	14,081
14830	Corning	15,792	17,085
13045	Cortland	19,621	19,181
10520	Croton-on-Hudson	7,523	6,812
14437	Dansville	5,436	5,460
11729	Deer Park(u)	32,274	16,726
14043	Depew	22,158	13,580
13214	DeWitt(u)	10,032	....
11746	Dix Hills(u)	10,050	....
10522	Dobbs Ferry	10,353	9,260
14048	Dunkirk	16,855	18,205
14052	East Aurora	7,033	6,791
10709	Eastchester(u)	23,750	....
12302	East Glenville(u)	5,898	....
11746	East Half Hollow Hills(u)	9,691	....
11576	East Hills	8,624	7,184
11730	East Islip(u)	6,861	....
11758	East Massapequa(u)	15,926	14,779
11554	East Meadow(u)	46,290	46,036
11743	East Neck(u)	5,221	3,789
11731	East Northport(u)	12,392	8,381
11772	East Patchogue(u)	8,092	....
14445	East Rochester	8,347	8,152
11518	East Rockaway	11,795	10,721
13902	East Vestal(u)	10,472	....
*14901	Elmira	39,945	46,517
11003	Elmont(u)	29,363	30,138
11731	Elwood(u)	15,031	....
13760	Endicott	16,556	18,775
13760	Endwell(u)	15,999	....
13219	Fairmount(u)	15,317	....
14450	Fairport	6,474	5,507
12601	Fairview(u)	8,517	8,626
11735	Farmingdale	9,297	6,128
*11001	Floral Park	18,466	17,499
11010	Franklin Square(u)	32,156	32,483
14063	Fredonia	10,326	8,477
11520	Freeport	40,374	34,419
13069	Fulton	14,003	14,261
11530	Garden City	25,373	23,948
11040	Garden City Park(u)	7,488	....
14454	Geneseo	5,714	3,284
14456	Geneva	16,793	17,286
11542	Glen Cove	25,770	23,817
12801	Glens Falls	17,222	18,580
12078	Gloversville	19,677	21,741
*11022	Great Neck	10,798	10,171
11020	Great Neck Plaza	6,043	4,948
11740	Greenlawn(u)	8,493	5,422
11746	Half Hollow Hills(u)	12,081	....
14075	Hamburg	10,215	9,145
10528	Harrison Town	21,544	19,201
10530	Hartsdale(u)	12,226	....
10706	Hastings-on-Hudson	9,479	8,979
11787	Hauppauge(u)	13,957	....
10927	Haverstraw	8,198	5,771
*11551	Hempstead	39,411	34,641
13350	Herkimer	8,960	9,396
11040	Herricks(u)	9,112	....
11557	Hewlett(u)	6,796	....
*11802	Hicksville(u)	49,820	50,405
10977	Hillcrest(u)	5,357	....
11741	Holbrook-Holtsville(u)	12,103	....
14843	Hornell	12,144	13,907
14845	Horseheads Village	7,989	7,207
12534	Hudson	8,940	11,075
12839	Hudson Falls	7,917	7,752
11743	Huntington(u)	12,601	11,255
11746	Huntington Station(u)	28,817	23,438
13357	Ilion	9,808	10,199
11696	Inwood(u)	8,433	10,362
10533	Irvington	5,878	5,494
11558	Island Park	5,396	3,846
11751	Islip	7,692	....
14850	Ithaca	26,226	28,799
14701	Jamestown	39,795	41,818
10535	Jefferson Valley-Yorktown(u)	9,008	....
11753	Jericho(u)	14,010	10,795
13790	Johnson City	18,025	19,118
12095	Johnstown	10,045	10,390
14217	Kenmore	20,980	21,261
11754	Kings Park(u)	5,555	4,949
11024	Kings Point	5,614	5,410
12401	Kingston	25,544	29,260
14218	Lackawanna	28,657	29,564
11755	Lake Grove 1975	9,359	....
14086	Lancaster	13,365	12,254
10538	Larchmont	7,203	6,789
12110	Latham(u)	9,661	....
11559	Lawrence	6,566	5,907
14482	Le Roy	5,118	4,662
11756	Levittown(u)	65,440	65,276
11757	Lindenhurst	28,359	20,905
13365	Little Falls	7,629	8,935
14094	Lockport	25,399	26,443
11791	Locust Grove(u)	11,626	11,558
11561	Long Beach(u)	33,127	26,473
12211	Loudonville(u)	9,299	....
11563	Lynbrook	23,151	19,881
10541	Mahopac(u)	5,265	1,337
12953	Malone	8,048	8,737
11565	Malverne	10,036	9,968
10543	Mamaroneck	18,909	17,673
11030	Manhasset(u)	8,541	....
11050	Manorhaven	5,488	3,566
11758	Massapequa(u)	26,821	32,900
11762	Massapequa Park	22,112	19,904
13662	Massena	14,042	15,478
13211	Mattydale(u)	8,292	....
12118	Mechanicville	6,247	6,831
14103	Medina	6,415	6,681
11746	Melville(u)	6,641	....
11566	Merrick(u)	25,904	18,789
10940	Middletown	22,607	23,475
11501	Mineola	21,744	20,519
10952	Monsey(u)	8,797	....
12701	Monticello	5,991	5,222
10549	Mt. Kisco	8,172	6,805
*10551	Mount Vernon	72,788	76,010
10954	Nanuet(u)	10,447	....
11767	Nesconset(u)	10,048	1,964
14513	Newark 1975	10,717	12,868
12550	Newburgh	26,219	30,979
11590	New Cassel(u)	8,721	....
10956	New City(u)	27,344	....
11040	New Hyde Park	10,116	10,808
12561	New Paltz	6,058	3,041

ZIP code	Place	1970	1960
*10802	New Rochelle	75,385	76,812
*12550	New Windsor	8,803	4,041
*10001	New York	7,895,563	7,781,984
*10451	Bronx	1,471,701	1,424,815
*11201	Brooklyn	2,602,012	2,627,319
*10001	Manhattan	1,539,233	1,698,281
*(Q)	Queens	1,987,174	1,809,578

(Q) There are 4 P.O.s for Queens; 11101 for L. I. City; 11690 Far Rockaway; 11351 Flushing and 11431 Jamaica.

ZIP code	Place	1970	1960
*10314	Staten Island	295,443	221,991
*14302	Niagara Falls	85,615	102,394
13745	Nimmonsburg-Chenango Br.(u)	5,059	......
12309	Niskayuna(u)	6,186	......
11701	North Amityville(u)	11,936	......
11703	North Babylon(u)	39,526	......
11710	North Bellmore(u)	22,893	19,639
11713	North Bellport(u)	5,903	......
11752	North Great River(u)	12,080	......
11757	North Lindenhurst(u)	11,117	......
11758	North Massapequa(u)	23,123	......
11566	North Merrick(u)	13,650	12,976
11040	North New Hyde Park(u)	18,154	17,929
11772	North Patchogue(u)	5,232	......
10803	North Pelham	5,184	5,326
11768	Northport	7,494	5,972
13212	North Syracuse	8,687	7,412
10591	North Tarrytown	8,334	8,818
14120	North Tonawanda	36,012	34,757
11580	North Valley Stream(u)	14,881	17,239
11793	North Wantagh(u)	15,053	......
13815	Norwich	8,843	9,175
10960	Nyack	6,659	6,062
11769	Oakdale(u)	7,334	......
11572	Oceanside(u)	35,372	30,448
13669	Ogdensburg	14,554	16,122
11804	Old Bethpage(u)	7,084	......
14760	Olean	19,169	21,868
13421	Oneida	11,658	11,677
13820	Oneonta	16,030	13,412
10562	Ossining	21,659	18,662
13126	Oswego	20,913	22,155
11771	Oyster Bay(u)	6,822	......
11772	Patchogue 1975	11,283	8,838
10965	Pearl River(u)	17,146	......
10566	Peekskill	19,283	18,737
10803	Pelham Manor	6,673	6,114
14527	Penn Yan	5,293	5,770
11714	Plainedge(u)	10,759	21,973
11803	Plainview(u)	31,695	27,710
12901	Plattsburgh	18,715	20,172
12903	Plattsburgh Base(u)	7,078	......
10570	Pleasantville	7,110	5,877
10573	Port Chester	25,803	24,960
11777	Port Jefferson 1975	5,800	......
11776	Port Jefferson Station(u)	7,403	1,041
12771	Port Jervis	8,852	9,268
11050	Port Washington(u)	15,923	15,657
13676	Potsdam	10,303	7,765
*12601	Poughkeepsie	32,029	38,330
12144	Rensselaer	10,136	10,506
11901	Riverhead(u)	7,585	5,830
*14603	Rochester	296,233	318,611
11570	Rockville Centre	27,444	26,355
12205	Roessleville(u)	5,476	......
13440	Rome	50,148	51,646
11779	Ronkonkoma(u)	7,284	4,220
11575	Roosevelt(u)	15,008	12,883
11577	Roslyn Heights(u)	7,242	......
12303	Rotterdam(u)	25,214	16,871
10580	Rye	15,869	14,225
11780	St. James(u)	10,500	3,524
14779	Salamanca	7,877	8,480
11754	San Remo(u)	8,302	3,160
12983	Saranac Lake	6,086	6,421
12866	Saratoga Springs	18,845	16,630
11782	Sayville(u)	11,680	......
10583	Scarsdale	19,229	17,968
12301	Schenectady	77,958	81,682
12302	Scotia	7,370	7,625
11579	Sea Cliff	5,890	5,669
11783	Seaford(u)	17,379	14,718
11784	Selden(u)	11,613	1,604
13148	Seneca Falls	7,794	7,439
11733	Setauket-South Setauket(u)	6,857	......
11967	Shirley(u)	6,280	......
4225	Sloan	5,216	5,803
13209	Solvay	8,280	8,732
11735	South Farmingdale(u)	20,464	16,318
11741	South Holbrook(u)	6,700	......
1746	South Huntington(u)	9,115	7,084
4904	Southport(u)	8,685	6,698
1790	South Stony Brook(u)	15,329	......
1581	South Valley Stream(u)	6,595	......
1590	South Westbury(u)	10,978	11,977
0977	Spring Valley	18,112	6,538
1790	Stony Brook(u)	6,391	3,548
10980	Stony Point(u)	8,270	3,330
10901	Suffern	8,273	5,094
11791	Syosset(u)	10,084	......
*13201	Syracuse	197,297	216,038
10983	Tappan(u)	7,424	......
10591	Tarrytown	11,115	11,109
10594	Thornwood(u)	6,874	......
14150	Tonawanda	21,898	21,561
*12180	Troy	62,918	67,492
10707	Tuckahoe	6,236	6,423
11553	Uniondale(u)	22,077	20,041
*13503	Utica	91,340	100,410
10989	Valley Cottage(u)	6,007	......
*11580	Valley Stream	40,413	38,629
11731	Vernon Valley(u)	7,925	5,998
13850	Vestal-Twin Orchards(u)	8,303	......
10901	Viola(u)	5,136	......
12586	Walden	5,277	4,851
11793	Wantagh(u)	21,873	34,172
12590	Wappingers Falls	5,607	4,447
13165	Waterloo	5,418	5,098
13601	Watertown	30,787	33,306
12189	Watervliet	12,404	13,917
14892	Waverly	5,261	5,950
14580	Webster	5,037	3,060
14895	Wellsville	5,815	5,967
11758	West Amityville(u)	6,424	......
11704	West Babylon(u)	12,893	......
11590	Westbury	15,362	14,757
14905	West Elmira(u)	5,901	5,763
10993	West Haverstraw	8,558	5,020
11552	West Hempstead(u)	20,375	......
11795	West Islip(u)	17,374	......
12203	Westmere(u)	6,364	......
10994	West Nyack(u)	5,510	......
11796	West Sayville(u)	7,386	......
13219	Westvale(u)	7,253	......
*10602	White Plains	50,346	50,485
14221	Williamsville	6,835	6,316
11596	Williston Park	9,154	8,255
11598	Woodmere(u)	19,831	14,011
11798	Wyandanch(u)	15,716	......
11980	Yaphank(u)	5,460	......
*10701	Yonkers	204,297	190,634
10598	Yorktown Heights(u)	6,805	2,478

North Carolina

ZIP code	Place	1970	1960
27910	Ahoskie	5,105	4,583
28001	Albemarle	11,126	12,261
27203	Asheboro	10,797	9,449
*28801	Asheville	57,681	60,192
28012	Belmont	5,054	5,007
28607	Boone	8,754	3,686
28712	Brevard	5,243	4,857
27215	Burlington	35,930	33,199
28542	Camp Le Jeune Central(u)	34,549	......
28716	Canton	5,158	5,068
27510	Carrboro	5,058	1,997
27511	Cary 1975	14,677	3,356
27514	Chapel Hill	25,537	12,573
*28202	Charlotte	241,178	201,564
28533	Cherry Point(u)	12,029	......
28021	Cherryville	5,258	3,607
28328	Clinton	7,157	7,461
28025	Concord	18,464	17,799
28334	Dunn	8,302	7,566
*27701	Durham	95,438	78,302
27288	Eden	15,871	......
27909	Elizabeth City	14,069	14,062
*28302	Fayetteville	53,510	47,106
28043	Forest City	7,179	6,556
28307	Fort Bragg(u)	46,995	......
28052	Gastonia	47,142	37,276
27530	Goldsboro	26,810	28,873
27253	Graham	8,172	7,723
*27420	Greensboro	144,076	119,574
27834	Greenville	29,063	22,860
28532	Havelock	5,283	2,433
27536	Henderson	13,896	12,740
28739	Hendersonville	6,443	5,911
28601	Hickory	20,569	19,328
*27260	High Point	63,259	62,063
28540	Jacksonville	16,289	13,491
28081	Kannapolis(u)	36,293	34,647
28086	Kings Mountain	8,465	8,008
28501	Kinston	23,020	24,819
28352	Laurinburg	8,859	8,242
28645	Lenoir	14,705	10,257
27292	Lexington	17,205	16,093
28092	Lincolnton	5,293	5,699
28358	Lumberton	16,961	15,305
28110	Monroe	11,282	10,882
28115	Moorsville	8,808	6,918
28557	Morehead City	5,233	5,583
28655	Morganton	13,625	9,186
27030	Mount Airy	7,325	7,055

ZIP code	Place	1970	1960
28120	Mount Holly	5,107	4,037
28560	New Bern	14,660	15,717
28540	New River Gieger(u)	8,699	......
28658	Newton	7,857	6,658
28012	North Belmont(u)	10,672	8,328
27565	Oxford	7,178	6,978
*27611	Raleigh	123,793	93,931
27320	Reidsville	13,636	14,267
27870	Roanoke Rapids	13,508	13,320
28379	Rockingham	5,852	5,512
27801	Rocky Mount	34,284	32,147
27573	Roxboro	5,370	5,147
28144	Salisbury	22,515	21,297
27330	Sanford	11,716	12,253
27530	Seymour-Johnson(u)	8,172	......
28150	Shelby	16,328	17,698
27577	Smithfield	6,677	6,117
28387	Southern Pines	5,937	5,198
28677	Statesville	20,007	19,844
27886	Tarboro	9,425	8,411
27360	Thomasville	15,230	15,190
27889	Washington	8,961	9,939
28786	Waynesville	6,488	6,159
28025	West Concord(u)	5,347	5,510
27892	Williamston	6,570	6,924
28401	Wilmington	46,169	44,013
27893	Wilson	29,347	28,753
*27102	Winston-Salem	133,683	111,135

North Dakota

ZIP code	Place	1970	1960
58501	Bismarck 1975	38,123	27,670
58301	Devils Lake 1974	7,354	6,299
58601	Dickinson 1975	12,496	9,971
58102	Fargo	53,365	46,662
58237	Grafton 1973	5,931	5,885
58201	Grand Forks(u) 1976	42,581	34,451
58201	Grand Forks Base(u)	10,474	......
58401	Jamestown 1971	15,078	15,163
58554	Mandan 1973	11,400	10,525
58701	Minot 1975	32,823	30,604
58701	Minot Base(u)	12,077	......
58072	Valley City	7,843	7,809
58075	Wahpeton 1975	8,257	5,876
58078	West Fargo 1976	7,919	3,328
58801	Williston	11,280	11,866

Ohio

ZIP code	Place	1970	1960
45810	Ada	5,309	3,918
*44309	Akron	275,425	290,351
44601	Alliance	26,547	28,362
44001	Amherst	9,902	6,750
44805	Ashland	19,872	17,419
44004	Ashtabula	24,313	24,559
45701	Athens	24,168	16,470
44202	Aurora	6,549	4,049
44515	Austintown(u)	29,393	......
44011	Avon	7,214	6,002
45404	Avondale(u)	5,240	......
44012	Avon Lake	12,261	9,403
44203	Barberton	33,052	33,805
44140	Bay Village	18,163	14,489
44122	Beachwood	9,631	6,089
44146	Bedford	17,552	15,223
44146	Bedford Heights	13,063	5,275
43906	Bellaire	9,655	11,502
43311	Bellefontaine	11,255	11,424
44811	Bellevue	8,604	8,286
45714	Belpre	7,189	5,418
44017	Berea	22,465	16,592
43209	Bexley	14,888	14,319
43004	Blacklick Estates(u)	8,351	......
45242	Blue Ash	8,324	8,341
44512	Boardman(u)	30,852	......
43402	Bowling Green	21,760	13,574
44141	Brecksville	9,137	5,435
45211	Bridgetown(u)	13,352	......
44141	Broadview Heights	11,463	6,209
44144	Brooklyn	13,142	10,733
44142	Brook Park	30,774	12,856
44212	Brunswick	15,852	11,725
43506	Bryan	7,008	7,361
44820	Bucyrus	13,111	12,276
43725	Cambridge	13,656	14,562
44405	Campbell	12,577	13,406
*44711	Canton	110,053	113,631
45822	Celina	8,072	7,659
45459	Centerville	10,333	3,490
45211	Cheviot	11,135	10,701
45601	Chillicothe	24,842	24,957
44505	Churchill(u)	7,457	......
*45234	Cincinnati	451,455	502,550
43113	Circleville	11,687	11,059
*44101	Cleveland	750,879	876,050
44118	Cleveland Heights	60,767	61,813
43410	Clyde	5,503	4,826
*43216	Columbus	540,025	471,316
44030	Conneaut	14,552	10,557
43812	Coshocton	13,747	13,106
45238	Covedale(u)	6,639	......
44827	Crestline	5,947	5,521
45341	Crystal Lakes(u)	5,851	1,569
*44222	Cuyahoga Falls	49,678	47,922
*45401	Dayton	242,917	262,332
45236	Deer Park	7,415	8,423
43512	Defiance	16,281	14,553
43015	Delaware	15,008	13,282
45833	Delphos	7,608	6,961
44622	Dover	11,516	11,300
44112	East Cleveland	39,600	37,991
44094	Eastlake	19,690	12,467
43920	East Liverpool(u)	20,020	22,306
43920	East Liverpool North	6,223	......
44413	East Palestine	5,604	5,232
45320	Eaton	6,020	5,034
*44035	Elyria	53,427	43,782
45322	Englewood	7,885	1,515
44117	Euclid	71,552	62,998
45324	Fairborn	32,267	19,453
45014	Fairfield	14,680	9,734
44313	Fairlawn	6,102	......
44126	Fairview Park	21,681	14,624
45840	Findlay	35,800	30,344
45405	Forest Park	15,139	......
45426	Fort McKinley(u)	11,536	......
44830	Fostoria	16,037	15,732
45005	Franklin	10,075	7,91
43420	Fremont	18,490	18,76
43230	Gahanna	12,400	2,71
44833	Galion	13,123	12,65
45631	Gallipolis	7,490	8,77
44125	Garfield Heights	41,417	38,45
44041	Geneva	6,449	5,67
44420	Girard	14,119	12,99
45237	Golf Manor	5,170	4,64
43212	Grandview Heights	8,460	8,27
45218	Greenhills	6,092	5,40
45331	Greenville	12,380	10,58
43123	Grove City	13,911	8,10
*45012	Hamilton	67,865	72,35
43055	Heath	6,768	2,42
44124	Highland Heights	5,926	2,92
43026	Hilliard	8,369	5,63
45133	Hillsboro	5,584	5,47
44425	Hubbard	8,583	7,13
45424	Huber Heights(u)	18,943	......
44839	Huron	6,896	5,19
44131	Independence	7,034	6,86
45243	Indian Hill	5,651	4,52
45638	Ironton	15,030	15,74
45640	Jackson	6,843	6,98
44240	Kent	28,183	17,83
43326	Kenton	8,315	8,74
45236	Kenwood(u)	15,789	......
45429	Kettering	71,864	54,46
44094	Kirtland	5,530	......
45432	Knollwood(u)	5,353	......
44107	Lakewood	70,173	66,15
43130	Lancaster	32,911	29,91
45036	Lebanon	7,934	5,99
*45802	Lima	53,734	51,03
45215	Lincoln Heights	6,099	7,79
43228	Lincoln Village(u)	11,215	......
45215	Lockland	5,288	5,29
43138	Logan	6,269	6,41
43140	London	6,481	6,37
*44052	Lorain	78,185	68,93
44641	Louisville	6,298	5,11
45140	Loveland	7,144	5,00
44124	Lyndhurst	19,749	16,80
44056	Macedonia	6,375	......
45243	Madeira	6,713	6,74
44057	Madison North(u)	6,882	......
*44901	Mansfield	55,047	47,32
44137	Maple Heights	34,093	31,66
45750	Marietta	16,861	16,84
43302	Marion	38,646	37,07
43935	Martins Ferry	10,757	11,9
43040	Marysville	5,744	4,95
45040	Mason	5,677	4,72
44646	Massillon	32,539	31,23
43537	Maumee	15,937	12,06
44124	Mayfield Heights	22,139	13,47
44256	Medina	10,913	8,23
44060	Mentor	36,912	4,35
44060	Mentor-on-the-Lake	6,517	3,29
45342	Miamisburg	14,797	9,89
44017	Middleburg Heights	12,367	7,28
45042	Middletown	48,767	42,11
43938	Mingo Junction	5,278	4,98
45242	Montgomery	5,683	3,07
45231	Mount Healthy	7,446	6,55
43050	Mount Vernon	13,373	13,28
43545	Napoleon	7,791	6,73

ZIP code	Place	1970	1960
055	Newark	41,836	41,790
344	New Carlisle	6,112	4,107
663	New Philadelphia	15,184	14,241
444	Newton Falls	5,378	5,038
446	Niles	21,581	19,545
720	North Canton	15,228	7,727
239	North College Hill	12,363	12,035
070	North Olmsted	34,861	16,290
414	Northridge(u)	10,084	....
039	North Ridgeville	13,152	8,057
133	North Royalton	12,807	9,290
203	Norton	12,308	....
857	Norwalk	13,386	12,900
212	Norwood	30,420	34,580
419	Oakwood City	10,095	10,493
074	Oberlin	8,761	8,198
616	Oregon	16,563	13,319
667	Orrville	7,408	6,511
431	Overlook-Page Manor(u)	19,719	....
056	Oxford	15,868	7,828
077	Painesville	16,536	16,116
077	Painesville Southwest(u)	5,461	....
129	Parma	100,216	82,845
130	Parma Heights	27,192	18,100
124	Pepper Pike	5,382	3,217
551	Perrysburg	7,693	5,519
356	Piqua	20,741	19,219
452	Port Clinton	7,202	6,870
662	Portsmouth	27,633	33,637
266	Ravenna	11,780	10,918
215	Reading	14,617	12,832
068	Reynoldsburg	13,921	7,793
143	Richmond Heights	9,220	5,068
217	Rickenbacker Base(u)	5,623	....
270	Rittman	6,308	5,410
116	Rocky River	22,958	18,097
460	Rossford	5,302	4,406
217	St. Bernard	6,080	6,778
885	St. Marys	7,699	7,737
460	Salem	14,186	13,854
870	Sandusky	32,674	31,989
870	Sandusky South(u)	8,501	4,724
131	Seven Hills	12,700	5,708
947	Shadyside	5,070	5,028
120	Shaker Heights	36,306	36,460
241	Sharonville	11,393	3,890
054	Sheffield Lake	8,734	6,884
875	Shelby	9,847	9,106
415	Shiloh(u)	11,368	....
365	Sidney	16,332	14,663
236	Silverton	6,588	6,682
139	Solon	11,519	6,333
121	South Euclid	29,579	27,569
246	Springdale	8,127	3,556
501	Springfield	81,941	82,723
952	Steubenville	30,771	32,495
224	Stow	19,847	12,194
240	Streetsboro	7,966	....
136	Strongsville	15,182	8,504
471	Struthers	15,343	15,631
560	Sylvania	12,031	5,187
278	Tallmadge	15,274	10,246
883	Tiffin	21,596	21,478
371	Tipp City	5,090	4,267
601	Toledo	383,105	318,003
964	Toronto	7,705	7,780
067	Trenton	5,278	3,064
426	Trotwood	6,997	4,992
373	Troy	17,186	13,685
087	Twinsburg	6,432	4,098
683	Uhrichsville	5,731	6,201
118	University Heights	17,055	16,641
221	Upper Arlington	38,727	28,486
351	Upper Sandusky	5,645	4,941
078	Urbana	11,237	10,461
377	Vandalia	10,796	6,342
891	Van Wert	11,320	11,323
089	Vermilion	9,872	4,785
281	Wadsworth	13,142	10,635
895	Wapakoneta	7,324	6,756
481	Warren	63,494	59,648
122	Warrensville Heights	18,925	10,609
160	Washington	12,495	12,388
692	Wellston	5,410	5,728
968	Wellsville	5,891	7,117
449	West Carrollton	10,748	4,749
081	Westerville	12,530	7,011
145	Westlake	15,689	12,906
213	Whitehall	25,263	20,818
092	Wickliffe	21,354	15,760
890	Willard	5,510	5,457
094	Willoughby	18,634	15,058
094	Willoughby Hills	5,247	4,241
094	Willowick	21,237	18,749
177	Wilmington	10,051	8,915
691	Wooster	18,703	17,046
085	Worthington	15,326	9,239
433	Wright-Patterson(u)	10,151	....

ZIP code	Place	1970	1960
45215	Wyoming	9,089	7,736
45385	Xenia	25,373	20,445
*44501	Youngstown	140,909	166,689
43701	Zanesville	33,045	39,077

Oklahoma

ZIP code	Place	1970	1960
74820	Ada	14,859	14,347
73521	Altus	23,302	21,225
73717	Alva	7,440	6,258
73005	Anadarko	6,682	6,299
73401	Ardmore	20,881	20,184
74003	Bartlesville	29,683	27,893
73008	Bethany	22,694	12,342
74631	Blackwell	8,645	9,588
74012	Broken Arrow	11,787	5,928
73018	Chickasha	14,194	14,866
74017	Claremore	9,084	6,639
73601	Clinton	8,513	9,617
74023	Cushing	7,529	8,619
73115	Del City	27,133	12,934
73533	Duncan	19,718	20,009
74701	Durant	11,118	10,467
73034	Edmond	16,633	8,577
73644	Elk City	7,323	8,196
73036	El Reno	14,510	11,015
73701	Enid	44,986	38,859
73503	Fort Sill(u)	21,217	....
73542	Frederick	6,132	5,879
73044	Guthrie	9,575	9,502
73942	Guymon	7,674	5,760
74437	Henryetta	6,430	6,551
74848	Holdenville	5,181	5,712
74743	Hugo	6,585	6,287
74745	Idabel	5,946	4,967
73501	Lawton	74,470	61,697
74501	McAlester	18,802	17,419
74354	Miami	13,880	12,869
73110	Midwest City	48,212	36,058
73060	Moore	18,761	1,783
74401	Muskogee	37,331	38,059
73064	Mustang, 1976	5,725	198
73069	Norman	52,117	33,412
*73125	Oklahoma City	368,377	324,253
74447	Okmulgee	15,180	15,951
73075	Pauls Valley	5,769	6,856
73077	Perry	5,341	5,210
74601	Ponca City	25,940	24,411
74953	Poteau	5,500	4,428
74361	Pryor	7,057	6,476
74063	Sand Springs	10,565	7,754
74066	Sapulpa	15,159	14,282
74868	Seminole	7,878	11,464
74801	Shawnee	25,075	24,326
74074	Stillwater	31,126	23,965
73086	Sulphur	5,158	4,737
74464	Tahlequah	9,254	5,840
73120	The Village	13,695	12,118
*74101	Tulsa	330,350	261,685
74301	Vinita	5,847	6,027
73132	Warr Acres	9,887	7,135
73096	Weatherford	7,959	4,499
74884	Wewoka	5,284	5,954
73801	Woodward	9,412	7,747
73099	Yukon 1975	12,980	3,076

Oregon

ZIP code	Place	1970	1960
97321	Albany	18,181	12,926
97601	Altamont(u)	15,746	10,811
97520	Ashland	12,342	9,119
97103	Astoria	10,244	11,239
97814	Baker	9,354	9,986
97005	Beaverton	18,577	5,937
97701	Bend	13,710	11,936
97420	Coos Bay	13,466	7,084
97330	Corvallis	35,056	20,669
97424	Cottage Grove	6,004	3,895
97338	Dallas	6,361	5,072
*97401	Eugene	79,028	50,977
97116	Forest Grove	8,275	5,628
97301	Four Corners(u)	5,823	4,743
97027	Gladstone	6,254	3,854
97526	Grants Pass	12,455	10,118
97030	Gresham	10,030	3,944
97303	Hayesville(u)	5,518	4,568
97123	Hillsboro	14,675	8,232
97303	Keizer(u)	11,405	5,288
97601	Klamath Falls	15,775	16,949
97850	La Grande	9,645	9,014
97034	Lake Oswego	14,615	8,906
97355	Lebanon	6,636	5,858
97128	McMinnville	10,125	7,656
97501	Medford	28,454	24,425
97222	Milwaukie	16,444	9,099
97361	Monmouth	5,237	2,229
97132	Newberg	6,507	4,204
97365	Newport	5,188	5,344

ZIP code	Place	1970	1960
97459	North Bend	8,553	7,512
97914	Ontario	6,523	5,101
97045	Oregon City	9,176	7,996
97801	Pendleton	13,197	14,434
*97208	Portland	379,967	372,676
97470	Roseburg	14,461	11,467
97051	St. Helens	6,212	5,022
*97301	Salem	68,480	49,142
97477	Springfield	26,874	19,616
97058	The Dalles	10,423	10,493
97223	Tigard	5,302	......
97068	West Linn	7,091	3,933
97071	Woodburn	7,495	3,120

Pennsylvania

ZIP code	Place	1970	1960
19001	Abington(u)	8,594	......
19018	Aldan	5,001	4,324
15001	Aliquippa	22,277	26,369
*18101	Allentown	109,527	108,347
*16603	Altoona	63,115	69,407
19002	Ambler	7,800	6,765
15003	Ambridge	11,324	13,865
18403	Archbald	6,118	5,642
19003	Ardmore(u)	5,131	......
15068	Arnold	8,174	9,437
15202	Avalon	7,010	6,859
15005	Baden	5,536	6,109
19004	Bala-Cynwyd(u)	6,483	......
15234	Baldwin	26,729	24,489
18013	Bangor	5,425	5,766
15009	Beaver	6,100	6,160
15010	Beaver Falls	14,375	16,240
16823	Bellefonte	6,828	6,088
15202	Bellevue	11,586	11,412
18603	Berwick	12,274	13,353
15102	Bethel Park	34,791	23,650
*18016	Bethlehem	72,686	75,408
18447	Blakely	6,391	6,374
17815	Bloomsburg	11,652	10,655
15104	Braddock	8,795	12,337
16701	Bradford	12,672	15,061
19406	Brandywine Village(u)	11,411	......
15227	Brentwood	13,732	13,706
19405	Bridgeport	5,630	5,306
15017	Bridgeville	6,717	7,112
19007	Bristol	12,085	12,364
19015	Brookhaven 1973	7,262	5,280
19010	Bryn Mawr(u)	5,815	......
16001	Butler	18,691	20,975
15419	California	6,635	5,978
17011	Camp Hill	9,931	8,559
15317	Canonsburg	11,439	11,877
18407	Carbondale	12,808	13,595
17013	Carlisle	18,079	16,623
15106	Carnegie	10,864	11,887
15108	Carnot-Moon(u)	13,093	......
15234	Castle Shannon	11,899	11,836
18032	Catasauqua	5,702	5,062
19095	Cedarbrook-Melrose Park (u)	9,980	......
19428	Cedar Heights(u)	6,326	......
17201	Chambersburg	17,315	17,670
15022	Charleroi	6,723	8,148
19380	Chatwood(u)	7,168	3,621
*19003	Chester	56,331	63,658
15025	Clairton	15,051	18,389
16214	Clarion	6,095	4,958
18411	Clarks Summit	5,376	3,693
16830	Clearfield	8,176	9,270
19018	Clifton Heights	8,348	8,005
19320	Coatesville	12,331	12,971
19023	Collingdale	10,605	10,268
17512	Columbia	11,237	12,075
15425	Connellsville	11,643	12,814
19428	Conshohocken	10,195	10,259
15108	Coraopolis	8,435	9,643
16407	Corry	7,435	7,744
15205	Crafton	8,233	8,418
17821	Danville	6,176	6,889
19023	Darby	13,729	14,059
18519	Dickson City	7,698	7,738
15033	Donora	8,825	11,131
15216	Dormont	12,856	13,098
19335	Downingtown	7,437	5,598
18901	Doylestown	8,270	5,917
15801	Du Bois	10,112	10,667
18512	Dunmore	17,300	18,917
15110	Duquesne	11,410	15,019
18642	Duryea	5,264	5,626
18042	Easton	29,450	31,955
18301	East Stroudsburg	7,894	7,674
15005	Economy 1976	8,379	5,925
15218	Edgewood	5,138	5,124
18704	Edwardsville	5,633	5,711
17022	Elizabethtown	8,072	6,780
16117	Ellwood City	10,857	12,413
18049	Emmaus	11,511	10,262
17522	Ephrata	9,662	7,688

ZIP code	Place	1970	19
*16501	Erie	129,231	138,4
15223	Etna	5,819	5,5
16121	Farrell	11,022	13,7
19031	Flourtown(u)	9,149	.....
19032	Folcroft	9,610	7,0
15221	Forest Hills	9,561	8,7
18704	Forty Fort	6,114	6,4
18015	Fountain Hill	5,384	5,4
17931	Frackville	5,445	5,6
16323	Franklin	8,629	9,5
15143	Franklin Park	5,310	.....
18052	Fullerton(u)	7,908	.....
19004	General Wayne(u)	5,368	.....
17325	Gettysburg	7,275	7,9
15045	Glassport	7,450	8,4
19036	Glenolden	8,697	7,2
19038	Glenside(u)	17,353	.....
15601	Greensburg	17,077	17,3
15220	Green Tree	6,441	5,2
16125	Greenville	8,704	8,7
16127	Grove City	8,312	8,3
17331	Hanover	15,623	15,5
*17105	Harrisburg	68,061	79,6
19040	Hatboro	8,880	7,3
19044	Hatboro West(u)	13,542	.....
18201	Hazelton	30,426	32,0
18055	Hellertown	6,615	6,7
17033	Hershey(u)	7,407	6,8
18042	Highland Park (Northampton)(u)	5,500	.....
16648	Hollidaysburg	6,262	6,4
16001	Homeacre-Lyndora(u)	8,415	.....
15120	Homestead	6,309	7,5
18431	Honesdale	5,224	5,5
16652	Huntingdon	6,987	7,2
15701	Indiana	16,100	13,0
15644	Jeannette	15,209	16,5
15344	Jefferson	8,512	8,2
19401	Jefferson-Trooper(u)	13,022	.....
19046	Jenkintown	5,990	5,0
17740	Jersey Shore	5,322	5,6
18229	Jim Thorpe	5,456	5,9
*15901	Johnstown	42,476	53,9
16735	Kane	5,001	5,3
18704	Kingston	18,325	20,2
16201	Kittanning	6,231	6,7
19444	Lafayette Hills-Plymouth Meeting(u)	8,275	.....
*17604	Lancaster	57,690	61,0
19446	Lansdale	18,451	12,6
19050	Lansdowne	14,090	12,6
18232	Lansford	5,168	5,9
15650	Latrobe	11,749	11,9
17042	Lebanon	28,572	30,0
18235	Lehighton	6,095	6,3
17837	Lewisburg	6,376	5,5
17044	Lewistown	11,098	12,6
17543	Lititz	7,072	5,9
17745	Lock Haven	11,427	11,7
15068	Lower Burrell	13,654	11,9
*15134	McKeesport	37,977	45,4
15136	McKees Rocks	11,901	13,1
17948	Mahanoy City	7,257	8,5
17545	Manheim	5,434	4,7
16335	Meadville	16,573	16,6
17055	Mechanicsburg	9,385	8,1
*19063	Media	6,444	5,8
19066	Merion(u)	5,686	....
17057	Middletown	9,080	11,1
15059	Midland	5,271	6,4
17551	Millersville	6,396	3,8
15209	Millvale	5,815	6,6
17847	Milton	7,723	7,9
17954	Minersville	6,012	6,6
15061	Monaca	7,486	8,3
15062	Monessen	15,216	18,4
15063	Monongahela	7,113	8,3
15146	Monroeville	29,011	22,4
17754	Montoursville	5,985	5,2
19067	Morrisville	11,309	7,7
17851	Mount Carmel	9,317	10,7
17552	Mount Joy	5,041	3,2
15210	Mount Oliver	5,487	5,9
15666	Mount Pleasant	5,895	6,1
15120	Munhall	16,574	17,3
18634	Nanticoke	14,632	15,6
19072	Narberth	5,151	5,1
18064	Nazareth	5,815	6,2
15066	New Brighton	7,637	8,3
*16101	New Castle	38,559	44,7
17070	New Cumberland	9,803	9,2
15068	New Kensington	20,312	23,4
*19401	Norristown	38,169	38,9
18067	Northampton	8,389	8,8
19003	North Ardmore(u)	5,856	....
15104	North Braddock	10,838	13,2
19038	North Hills-Ardsley(u)	13,096	.....
19074	Norwood	7,229	6,7
19126	Oak Lane(u)	6,192	.....

ZIP code	Place	1970	1960
5139	Oakmont	7,550	7,504
9117	Ogontz(u)	5,463	2,254
6301	Oil City	15,033	17,692
8518	Old Forge	9,522	8,928
8447	Olyphant	5,422	5,864
9075	Oreland(u)	9,261	......
8071	Palmerton	5,620	5,942
7078	Palmyra	7,615	6,999
9301	Paoli(u)	5,835	......
7331	Parkville(u)	5,120	4,516
9004	Pencoyo(u)	6,650	......
9401	Penn Sq.-Plymouth Valley(u)	20,238	......
9151	Penn Wynne(u)	6,038	......
8944	Perkasie	5,451	4,650
9104	Philadelphia	1,949,996	2,002,512
9460	Phoenixville	14,823	13,797
5219	Pittsburgh	520,117	604,332
8640	Pittston	11,113	12,407
8705	Plains(u)	6,606	......
5236	Pleasant Hills	10,409	8,573
5239	Plum	21,932	10,241
8651	Plymouth	9,536	10,401
5133	Port Vue	5,862	6,635
9464	Pottstown	25,355	26,144
7901	Pottsville	19,715	21,659
9076	Prospect Park	7,250	6,596
5767	Punxsutawney	7,792	8,805
8951	Quakertown	7,276	6,305
9603	Reading	87,643	98,177
7356	Red Lion	5,645	5,594
5853	Ridgway	6,022	6,387
9078	Ridley Park	9,025	7,387
9001	Roslyn(u)	18,380	......
9046	Rydal(u)	5,083	......
5857	St. Marys	7,470	8,065
8840	Sayre	7,473	7,917
7972	Schuylkill Haven	6,125	6,470
5683	Scottdale	5,818	6,244
8503	Scranton	102,696	111,443
7870	Selinsgrove	5,116	3,948
5143	Sewickley	5,660	6,157
7872	Shamokin	11,719	13,674
6146	Sharon	22,653	25,267
9079	Sharon Hill	7,464	7,123
5215	Sharpsburg	5,453	6,096
6150	Sharpsville	6,126	6,061
7976	Shenandoah	8,287	11,073
9607	Shillington	6,249	5,639
7257	Shippensburg	6,536	6,138
5501	Somerset	6,269	6,347
8964	Souderton	6,366	5,381
7701	South Williamsport	7,153	6,972
5144	Springdale	5,202	5,602
6801	State College	33,778	22,409
7113	Steelton	8,556	11,266
8360	Stroudsburg	5,451	6,070
6323	Sugar Creek	5,944	......
7801	Sunbury	13,025	13,687
9081	Swarthmore	6,156	5,753
5218	Swissvale	13,819	15,089
8704	Swoyersville	6,786	6,751
8252	Tamaqua	9,246	10,173
5084	Tarentum	7,379	8,232
8517	Taylor	6,977	6,148
6354	Titusville	7,331	8,356
5145	Turtle Creek	8,308	10,607
6686	Tyrone	7,072	7,792
5401	Uniontown	16,282	17,942
5690	Vandergrift	7,889	8,742
6365	Warren	12,998	14,505
5301	Washington	19,827	23,545
7268	Waynesboro	10,011	10,427
5370	Wanyesburg	5,152	5,188
9380	West Chester	19,301	15,705
8201	West Hazleton	6,059	6,278
5122	West Mifflin	28,070	27,289
5905	Westmont	6,673	6,573
8643	West Pittston	7,074	6,998
5229	West View	8,312	8,079
7404	West York	5,314	5,526
8052	Whitehall	16,551	16,075
5131	White Oak	9,304	9,047
8701	Wilkes-Barre	58,856	63,551
5221	Wilkinsburg	26,780	30,066
7701	Williamsport	37,918	41,967
9090	Willow Grove(u)	16,494	......
5025	Wilson	8,406	8,465
5963	Windber	6,332	6,994
9610	Wyomissing	7,136	5,044
9050	Yeadon	12,136	11,610
7405	York	50,335	54,504

Rhode Island

See Note on Page 201

ZIP code	Place	1970	1960
2806	*Barrington*	17,554	13,826
2809	*Bristol*	17,860	14,570
02830	*Burrillville*	10,087	9,119
02863	Central Falls	18,716	19,858
02816	*Coventry*	22,947	15,432
02910	Cranston	74,287	66,766
02864	*Cumberland*	26,605	18,792
02818	*East Greenwich*	9,577	6,100
02914	East Providence	48,207	41,955
02814	*Glocester*	5,160	3,397
02833	*Hopkinton*	5,392	4,174
02919	*Johnston*	22,037	17,160
02881	Kingston(u)	5,601	2,616
02865	*Lincoln*	16,182	13,551
02840	*Middletown*	29,290	12,675
02882	*Narragansett*	7,138	3,444
02840	Newport	34,562	47,049
02843	Newport East(u)	10,285	2,643
02852	*North Kingstown*	29,793	18,977
02908	*North Providence*	24,337	18,220
02876	*North Smithfield*	9,349	7,632
02860	Pawtucket	76,984	81,001
02871	*Portsmouth*	12,521	8,251
02904	Providence	179,116	207,498
02857	*Scituate*	7,489	5,210
02917	*Smithfield*	13,468	9,442
02879	*South Kingstown*	16,913	11,942
02878	*Tiverton*	12,559	9,461
02880	Wakefield-Peacedale(u)	6,331	5,569
02885	*Warren*	10,523	8,750
02887	Warwick	83,694	68,504
02891	Westerly Center(u)	13,654	9,698
02891	*Westerly*	17,248	14,267
02893	*West Warwick*	24,323	21,414
02895	Woonsocket	46,820	47,080

South Carolina

ZIP code	Place	1970	1960
29620	Abbeville	5,515	5,436
29801	Aiken	13,436	11,243
29621	Anderson	27,556	41,316
29407	Avondale-Moorland(u)	5,236	......
29902	Beaufort	9,434	6,298
29627	Belton	5,257	5,106
29512	Bennettsville	7,468	6,963
29611	Berea	7,186	......
29020	Camden	8,532	6,842
29033	Cayce	9,967	8,517
29401	Charleston	66,945	65,925
29404	Charleston Base(u)	6,238	......
29408	Charleston Yard(u)	13,565	......
29520	Cheraw	5,627	5,171
29706	Chester	7,045	6,906
29631	Clemson	5,578	1,587
29325	Clinton	8,138	7,937
29201	Columbia	113,542	97,433
29526	Conway	8,151	8,563
29532	Darlington	6,990	6,710
29536	Dillon	6,391	6,173
29640	Easley	11,175	8,283
29501	Florence	25,997	24,722
29206	Forest Acres	6,808	3,842
29340	Gaffney	13,253	10,435
29605	Gantt(u)	11,386	......
29440	Georgetown	10,449	12,261
29602	Greenville 1976	57,849	66,188
29646	Greenwood	21,069	16,644
29651	Greer	10,642	8,967
29410	Hanahan(u) 1974	11,518	......
29550	Hartsville	8,017	6,392
29560	Lake City	6,247	6,059
29720	Lancaster	9,186	7,999
29360	Laurens	10,298	9,598
29571	Marion	7,435	7,174
29662	Mauldin 1973	5,480	1,462
29464	Mount Pleasant	6,879	5,116
29574	Mullins	6,006	6,299
29577	Myrtle Beach	9,035	7,834
29108	Newberry	9,218	8,208
29841	North Augusta	12,883	10,348
29115	Orangeburg	13,252	13,852
29905	Parris Island(u)	8,868	......
29730	Rock Hill	33,846	29,404
29407	St. Andrews(u)	9,202	......
29678	Seneca	6,382	5,227
29150	Shannontown(u)	7,491	7,064
29152	Shaw(u)	5,819	......
29681	Simpsonville 1974	6,209	2,282
29301	Spartanburg	44,546	44,352
29150	Sumter	24,555	23,062
29687	Taylors(u)	6,831	1,071
29379	Union	10,775	10,191
29607	Wade-Hampton(u)	17,152	......
29488	Walterboro	6,257	5,417
29169	West Columbia	7,838	6,410
29745	York	5,081	4,758

South Dakota

ZIP code	Place	1970	1960
57401	Aberdeen	26,476	23,073
57006	Brookings	13,717	10,558
57706	Ellsworth(u)	6,207	......
57350	Huron	14,299	14,180
57754	Lead	5,420	6,211
57042	Madison	6,315	5,420
57301	Mitchell	13,425	12,555
57501	Pierre	9,699	10,088
57701	Rapid City	43,836	42,399
*57101	Sioux Falls	72,488	65,466
57785	Sturgis 1974	5,162	4,639
57069	Vermillion	9,128	6,102
57201	Watertown	13,388	14,077
57078	Yankton	11,919	9,279

Tennessee

ZIP code	Place	1970	1960
37701	Alcoa	7,739	6,395
37303	Athens	11,790	12,103
38008	Bolivar	6,674	3,338
37620	Bristol	20,064	17,582
38012	Brownsville	7,011	5,424
*37401	Chattanooga	119,923	130,009
37040	Clarksville 1975	52,621	22,021
37311	Cleveland	20,651	16,196
38401	Columbia	21,471	17,624
38501	Cookeville 1975	17,070	7,805
38019	Covington	5,801	5,298
38555	Crossville	5,381	4,668
37055	Dickson	5,665	5,028
38024	Dyersburg	14,523	12,499
37801	Eagleton Village(u)	5,345	5,068
37412	East Ridge	21,799	19,570
37643	Elizabethton	12,269	10,896
37334	Fayetteville	7,030	6,804
42223	Fort Campbell South(u)	9,279	......
37064	Franklin 1974	11,298	6,977
37066	Gallatin 1976	14,374	7,901
37075	Greater Hendersonville(u)	11,996	......
37743	Greeneville	13,722	11,759
37748	Harriman	8,734	5,931
37343	Hixson(u)	6,188	......
38343	Humboldt	10,066	8,482
38301	Jackson	39,996	34,376
37760	Jefferson City	5,124	4,550
37601	Johnson City	33,770	31,187
*37662	Kingsport	31,938	26,314
37665	Kingsport North(u)	13,118	......
*37901	Knoxville	174,587	111,827
37766	La Follette	6,902	6,204
37416	Lake Hills-Murray Hills(u)	7,806	......
38464	Lawrenceburg	8,889	8,042
37087	Lebanon	12,492	10,512
37771	Lenoir City	5,324	4,979
37091	Lewisburg	7,207	6,338
38351	Lexington	5,024	3,943
37110	Mc Minnville	10,662	9,013
37355	Manchester	6,208	3,930
38237	Martin	7,781	4,750
37801	Maryville	13,808	10,348
*38101	Memphis	623,530	497,524
38358	Milan	7,313	5,208
38053	Millington	21,177	6,059
37814	Morristown	20,318	21,267
37130	Murfreesboro	26,360	18,991
*37202	Nashville-Davidson	**447,877	170,874
37821	Newport	7,328	6,448
37830	Oak Ridge	28,319	27,169
38242	Paris	9,892	9,325
38478	Pulaski	6,989	6,616
37415	Red Bank	12,715	10,777
37854	Rockwood	5,259	5,345
38372	Savannah	5,576	4,315
37160	Shelbyville	12,262	10,466
37167	Smyrna	5,698	3,612
37379	Soddy-Daisy	7,569	......
37311	South Cleveland(u)	5,070	1,512
38583	Sparta 1975	5,038	4,510
37172	Springfield	9,720	9,221
37388	Tullahoma	15,311	12,242
38261	Union City	11,925	8,837
37398	Winchester	5,256	4,760

***Comprises the Metropolitan Government of Nashville and Davidson County.*

Texas

ZIP code	Place	1970	1960
*79604	Abilene	89,653	90,368
78209	Alamo Heights	6,933	7,552
78332	Alice	20,121	20,861
79830	Alpine	5,971	4,740
77511	Alvin	10,671	5,643
*79105	Amarillo	127,010	137,969
79714	Andrews	8,625	11,13
77515	Angleton	9,770	7,31
78336	Aransas Pass	5,813	6,95
*76010	Arlington	90,032	44,77
75751	Athens	9,582	7,08
75551	Atlanta	5,007	4,07
*78710	Austin	251,808	186,54
75149	Balch Springs	10,464	6,82
77414	Bay City	13,445	11,65
77520	Baytown	43,980	28,15
*77704	Beaumont	117,548	119,17
76021	Bedford	10,049	2,70
78102	Beeville	13,506	13,81
77401	Bellaire	19,009	19,87
76704	Bellmead	7,698	5,12
76513	Belton	8,696	8,16
76126	Benbrook	8,169	3,25
79720	Big Spring	28,735	31,23
75418	Bonham	7,698	7,35
79007	Borger	14,195	20,91
76230	Bowie	5,185	4,56
76825	Brady	5,557	5,33
76024	Breckenridge	5,944	6,27
77833	Brenham	8,922	7,74
77611	Bridge City(u)	8,164	4,67
79316	Brownfield	9,647	10,28
78520	Brownsville	52,522	48,04
76801	Brownwood	17,368	16,97
77801	Bryan	33,719	27,54
76354	Burkburnett	9,230	7,62
76028	Burleson	7,713	2,34
76520	Cameron	5,546	5,64
79015	Canyon	8,333	5,86
78834	Carrizo Springs	5,374	5,69
75006	Carrollton	13,855	4,24
75633	Carthage	5,392	5,26
78213	Castle Hills	5,311	2,62
79201	Childress	5,408	6,39
76031	Cleburne	16,015	15,38
77327	Cleveland	5,627	5,83
77531	Clute City	6,023	4,50
76834	Coleman	5,608	6,37
77840	College Station	17,676	11,3
79512	Colorado City	5,227	6,45
75428	Commerce	9,534	5,78
77301	Conroe	11,969	9,19
76522	Copperas Cove	10,818	4,56
*78408	Corpus Christi	204,525	167,69
75110	Corsicana	19,972	20,34
75835	Crockett	6,616	5,35
78839	Crystal City	8,104	9,10
77954	Cuero	6,956	7,33
79022	Dalhart	5,705	5,16
*75260	Dallas	844,401	679,6
77536	Deer Park	12,773	4,8
78840	Del Rio	21,330	18,6
75020	Denison	24,923	22,7
76201	Denton	39,874	26,8
75115	De Soto	6,617	1,9
77539	Dickinson(u)	10,776	4,7
78537	Donna	7,365	7,5
79029	Dumas	9,771	8,4
75116	Duncanville	14,105	3,7
78852	Eagle Pass	15,364	12,0
78539	Edinburg	17,163	18,7
77957	Edna	5,332	5,0
77437	El Campo	9,332	7,7
*79910	El Paso	322,261	276,6
75119	Ennis	11,046	9,3
76039	Euless	19,316	4,2
78355	Falfurrias	6,355	6,5
75234	Farmers Branch	27,492	13,4
76119	Forest Hill	8,236	3,2
79906	Fort Bliss(u)	13,288	....
76544	Fort Hood(u)	32,597	....
78234	Fort Sam Houston(u)	10,553	....
79735	Fort Stockton	8,283	6,3
*76101	Fort Worth	393,476	356,2
78624	Fredericksburg	5,326	4,6
77541	Freeport	11,997	11,6
77546	Friendswood	5,675	....
76240	Gainesville	13,830	13,0
77547	Galena Park	10,479	10,8
77550	Galveston	61,809	67,1
*75040	Garland	81,437	38,5
78626	Georgetown	6,395	5,2
75647	Gladewater	5,574	5,7
78629	Gonzales	5,854	5,8
76046	Graham	7,477	8,5
75050	Grand Prairie	50,904	30,3
76051	Grapevine	7,023	2,8
75401	Greenville	22,043	19,0
77619	Groves	18,067	17,3
76117	Haltom City	28,127	23,1
78550	Harlingen	33,503	41,2
75652	Henderson	10,187	9,6
79045	Hereford	13,414	7,6

ZIP code	Place	1970	1960
75205	Highland Park	10,133	10,411
76645	Hillsboro	7,224	7,402
77563	Hitchcock	5,565	5,216
78861	Hondo	5,487	4,992
*77013	Houston	1,232,802	938,219
77340	Huntsville	17,610	11,999
76053	Hurst	27,215	10,165
76367	Iowa Park	5,796	3,295
*75061	Irving	97,260	45,985
77029	Jacinto City	9,563	9,547
75766	Jacksonville	9,734	9,590
75951	Jasper	6,251	4,889
79745	Kermit	7,884	10,465
78028	Kerrville	12,672	8,901
75662	Kilgore	9,495	10,092
76541	Killeen	35,507	23,377
78363	Kingsville	28,915	25,297
78236	Lackland(u)	19,141	......
77566	Lake Jackson	13,376	9,651
77568	La Marque	16,131	13,969
79331	Lamesa	11,559	12,438
76550	Lampasas	5,922	5,061
75146	Lancaster	10,522	7,501
77571	La Porte	7,149	4,512
78040	Laredo	69,024	60,678
77573	League City	10,818	......
79336	Levelland	11,445	10,153
75067	Lewisville	9,264	3,956
77575	Liberty	5,591	6,127
79339	Littlefield	6,738	7,236
78644	Lockhart	6,489	6,084
75601	Longview 1975	51,953	40,050
*79408	Lubbock	149,101	128,691
75901	Lufkin	23,049	17,641
78501	McAllen	37,636	32,728
75069	McKinney	15,193	13,763
76661	Marlin	6,351	6,918
75670	Marshall	22,937	23,846
78368	Mathis	5,351	6,075
78570	Mercedes	9,355	10,943
75149	Mesquite	55,131	27,526
76667	Mexia	5,943	6,121
79701	Midland	59,463	62,625
76067	Mineral Wells	18,411	11,053
78572	Mission	13,043	14,081
79756	Monahans	8,333	8,567
75455	Mount Pleasant	9,459	8,027
75961	Nacogdoches	22,544	12,674
77868	Navasota	5,111	4,937
77627	Nederland	16,810	12,036
78130	New Braunfels	17,859	15,631
76118	North Richland Hills	16,514	8,662
*79760	Odessa	78,380	80,338
77630	Orange	24,457	25,605
75801	Palestine	14,525	13,974
79065	Pampa	21,726	24,664
75460	Paris	23,441	20,977
*77501	Pasadena	89,277	58,737
77581	Pearland	6,444	1,497
78061	Pearsall 1976	6,495	4,957
79772	Pecos	12,682	12,728
79070	Perryton	7,810	7,903
78577	Pharr	15,829	14,106
79072	Plainview	19,096	18,735
75074	Plano	17,872	3,695
78064	Pleasanton	5,407	3,467
77640	Port Arthur	57,371	66,676
78374	Portland	7,302	2,538
77979	Port Lavaca	10,491	8,864
77651	Port Neches	10,894	8,696
75475	Randolph(u)	5,329	......
78580	Raymondville	7,987	9,385
75080	Richardson	48,582	16,810
76118	Richland Hills	8,865	7,804
77469	Richmond	5,777	3,668
78582	Rio Grande City(u)	5,676	5,835
77019	River Oaks	8,193	8,444
78380	Robstown	11,217	10,266
77471	Rosenberg	12,098	9,698
76901	San Angelo	63,884	58,815
*78284	San Antonio	654,153	587,718
78586	San Benito	15,176	16,422
78589	San Juan	5,070	4,371
78666	San Marcos	18,860	12,713
78155	Seguin	15,934	14,299
79360	Seminole	5,007	5,737
75090	Sherman	29,061	24,988
77656	Silsbee	7,271	6,277
78387	Sinton	5,563	6,008
79364	Slaton	6,583	6,568
79549	Snyder	11,171	13,850
77587	South Houston	11,527	7,523
76401	Stephenville	9,277	7,359
75482	Sulphur Springs	10,642	9,160
79556	Sweetwater	12,020	13,914
76574	Taylor	9,616	9,434
76501	Temple	33,431	30,419
75160	Terrell	14,182	13,803
78209	Terrell Hills	5,225	5,572
75501	Texarkana	30,497	30,218
77590	Texas City	38,908	32,065
79088	Tulia	5,294	4,410
75701	Tyler	57,770	51,230
78148	Universal City	7,613	......
76308	University Park	23,498	23,202
78801	Uvalde	10,764	10,293
76384	Vernon	11,454	12,141
77901	Victoria	41,349	33,047
77662	Vidor	9,738	......
*76701	Waco	95,326	97,808
75165	Waxahachie	13,452	12,749
76086	Weatherford	11,750	9,759
78596	Weslaco	15,313	15,649
77005	West University Place	13,317	14,628
77488	Wharton	7,881	5,734
76108	White Settlement	13,449	11,513
*76307	Wichita Falls	96,265	101,724
77995	Yoakum	5,755	5,761

Utah

ZIP code	Place	1970	1960
84003	American Fork	7,713	6,373
84010	Bountiful	27,751	17,039
84302	Brigham City	14,007	11,728
84720	Cedar City	8,946	7,543
84015	Clearfield	13,316	8,833
84121	Cottonwood(u)	8,431	......
84109	East Millcreek(u)	26,579	......
84119	Granger-Hunter(u)	9,029	......
84106	Granite Park(u)	9,573	......
84117	Holladay(u)	23,014	......
84037	Kaysville	6,192	3,608
84118	Kearns(u)	17,247	17,172
84041	Layton	13,603	9,027
84321	Logan	22,333	18,731
84044	Magna(u)	5,509	6,442
84047	Midvale	7,840	5,802
84117	Mount Olympus(u)	5,909	......
84107	Murray	21,206	16,806
84404	North Ogden	5,257	2,621
*84401	Ogden	69,478	70,197
84057	Orem	25,729	18,394
84062	Pleasant Grove	5,327	4,772
84501	Price	6,218	6,802
84601	Provo	53,131	36,047
84067	Roy	14,356	9,239
84770	St. George	7,097	5,130
*84101	Salt Lake City	175,885	189,454
84070	Sandy City	6,438	3,322
84403	South Ogden	9,991	7,405
84115	South Salt Lake	7,810	9,520
84660	Spanish Fork	7,284	6,472
84663	Springville	8,790	7,913
84015	Sunset	6,268	4,235
84074	Tooele	12,539	9,133
84403	Washington Terrace	7,241	6,441
74070	White City(u)	6,402	......

Vermont

See Note on Page 201

ZIP code	Place	1970	1960
05641	Barre	10,209	10,387
......	*Barre*	6,509	4,580
05201	*Bennington*	14,586	13,002
......	Bennington	7,950	8,023
05301	Brattleboro Center(u)	9,055	9,315
......	*Brattleboro*	12,239	11,734
05401	Burlington	38,633	35,531
05446	*Colchester*	8,776	4,718
05451	*Essex*	10,951	7,090
05452	Essex Junction	6,511	5,340
05047	*Hartford*	6,477	6,355
05753	*Middlebury*	6,532	5,305
05602	Montpelier	8,609	8,782
05101	*Rockingham*	5,501	5,704
05701	*Rutland*	19,293	18,325
05478	St. Albans	8,082	8,806
05819	St. Johnsbury	8,409	8,869
05401	*South Burlington*	10,032	6,903
05156	Springfield Center(u)	5,632	6,600
......	*Springfield*	10,063	9,934
05401	Williston Road Section(u)	5,376	3,259
05404	Winooski	7,309	7,420

Virginia

ZIP code	Place	1970	1960
*22313	Alexandria	110,927	91,023
22003	Annandale(u)	27,405	......
*22210	Arlington(u)	174,284	163,401
22041	Bailey's Crossroads(u)	7,295	......
24523	Bedford	6,011	5,921
22307	Belleview(u)	8,299	......
24060	Blacksburg	9,384	7,070
24605	Bluefield	5,286	4,235
23235	Bon Air(u)	10,771	......

ZIP code	Place	1970	1960
24201	Bristol	14,857	17,144
24416	Buena Vista	6,425	6,300
*22906	Charlottesville	38,880	29,427
*23320	Chesapeake	89,580	....
23831	Chester(u)	5,556	1,290
24073	Christiansburg	7,857	3,653
24422	Clifton Forge	5,501	5,268
24078	Collinsville(u)	6,015	3,586
23834	Colonial Heights	15,097	9,587
24426	Covington	10,060	11,062
22701	Culpeper	6,056	2,412
22191	Dale City(u)	13,857	....
24541	Danville	46,391	46,577
23847	Emporia	5,300	5,535
22030	Fairfax	21,970	13,585
*22046	Falls Church	10,772	10,192
22060	Fort Belvoir(u)	14,591	....
22308	Fort Hunt(u)	10,415	....
23801	Fort Lee(u)	12,435	....
23851	Franklin	6,880	7,264
22401	Fredericksburg	14,450	13,639
22630	Front Royal	8,211	7,949
24333	Galax	6,278	5,254
22306	Groveton(u)	11,761	....
*23360	Hampton	120,779	89,258
22801	Harrisonburg	14,605	11,916
23075	Highland Springs(u)	7,345	....
23860	Hopewell	23,471	17,895
22303	Huntington(u)	5,559	....
22042	Jefferson(u)	25,432	....
22041	Lake Barcroft(u)	11,605	....
23228	Lakeside(u)	11,137	....
24450	Lexington	7,597	7,537
22312	Lincolnia(u)	10,761	....
22030	Long Branch(u)	21,634	....
*24505	Lynchburg	54,083	54,790
22110	Manassas	9,164	3,555
22110	Manassas Park	6,844	5,342
22030	Mantua(u)	6,911	....
24354	Marion	8,158	8,385
24112	Martinsville	19,653	18,798
22101	McLean(u)	17,698	....
23111	Mechanicsville(u)	5,189	....
*23607	Newport News	138,177	113,662
*23501	Norfolk	307,951	304,869
22151	North Springfield(u)	8,631	....
23803	Petersburg	36,103	36,750
23662	Poquoson	5,441	4,278
*23705	Portsmouth	110,963	114,773
24301	Pulaski	10,279	10,469
22134	Quantico Station(u)	6,213	....
24141	Radford	11,596	9,371
22070	Reston(u)	5,723	....
*23232	Richmond	249,431	219,958
*24001	Roanoke	92,115	97,110
22310	Rose Hill(u)	14,492	....
24153	Salem	21,982	16,058
22044	Seven Corners(u)	5,590	....
24592	South Boston	6,889	5,974
*22150	Springfield(u)	11,613	10,783
24401	Staunton	24,504	22,232
22170	Sterling Park(u)	8,321	....
23434	Suffolk	9,858	12,609
22180	Vienna	17,146	11,440
24179	Vinton	6,347	3,432
*23458	Virginia Beach	172,106	8,091
22980	Waynesboro	16,707	15,694
22152	West Springfield(u)	14,143	....
23185	Williamsburg	9,069	6,832
22601	Winchester	14,643	15,110
22191	Woodbridge-Marumsco(u)	25,412	....
24382	Wytheville	6,069	5,634

Washington

ZIP code	Place	1970	1960
98520	Aberdeen	18,489	18,741
98221	Anacortes	7,701	8,414
98002	Auburn	21,653	11,933
*98009	Bellevue	61,196	12,809
98225	Bellingham	39,375	34,688
98011	Bothell	5,420	2,237
98310	Bremerton	35,307	28,922
98607	Camas	5,790	5,666
98531	Centralia	10,054	8,586
98532	Chehalis	5,727	5,199
99004	Cheney	6,358	3,173
99403	Clarkston	6,312	6,209
99213	Dishman(u)	9,079	....
98020	Edmonds	23,998	8,016
98926	Ellensburg	13,568	8,625
98823	Ephrata	5,255	6,548
*98201	Everett	53,622	40,304
99011	Fairchild(u)	6,754	....
98466	Fircrest	5,651	3,565
98433	Fort Lewis(u)	38,054	....
98550	Hoquiam	10,466	10,762
98626	Kelso	10,296	8,379
99336	Kennewick	15,212	14,244
98031	Kent	16,596	9,017
98033	Kirkland	14,970	6,025
98503	Lacey	9,696	....
98499	Lakes District(u)	48,195	....
98632	Longview	28,373	23,349
98036	Lynwood	16,919	7,297
98438	McChord(u)	6,515	....
98040	Mercer Island	19,047	....
98837	Moses Lake	10,310	11,299
98273	Mount Vernon	8,804	7,921
98277	Oak Harbor	9,167	3,942
*98501	Olympia	23,296	18,273
99214	Opportunity(u)	16,604	12,465
98444	Parkland(u)	21,012	....
99301	Pasco	13,920	14,522
98362	Port Angeles	16,367	12,653
98368	Port Townsend	5,241	5,074
99163	Pullman	20,509	12,957
98371	Puyallup	14,742	12,063
98052	Redmond	11,020	1,426
98055	Renton	25,878	18,453
99352	Richland	26,290	23,548
*98109	Seattle	530,831	557,087
98584	Shelton	6,515	5,651
98290	Snohomish	5,174	3,894
98387	Spanaway(u)	5,768	....
*99210	Spokane	170,516	181,608
98944	Sunnyside	6,751	6,208
*98402	Tacoma	154,407	147,979
98948	Toppenish	5,744	5,667
99268	Town and Country(u)	6,484	....
98502	Tumwater	5,373	3,885
98406	University Place(u)	13,230	....
*98660	Vancouver	41,859	32,464
99362	Walla Walla	23,619	24,536
98801	Wenatchee	16,912	16,726
*98901	Yakima	45,588	43,284

West Virginia

ZIP code	Place	1970	1960
25801	Beckley	19,884	18,642
24701	Bluefield	15,921	19,256
26201	Buckhannon	7,261	6,386
*25301	Charleston	71,505	85,796
26301	Clarksburg	24,864	28,112
25064	Dunbar	9,151	11,006
26241	Elkins	8,287	8,307
26554	Fairmont	26,093	27,477
26354	Grafton	6,433	5,791
*25701	Huntington	74,315	83,627
26726	Keyser	6,586	6,192
25401	Martinsburg	14,626	15,179
26505	Morgantown	29,431	22,487
26041	Moundsville	13,560	15,163
26155	New Martinsville	6,528	5,607
25143	Nitro	8,019	6,894
26105	Parkersburg	44,208	44,797
25550	Point Pleasant	6,122	5,785
24740	Princeton	7,253	8,393
25177	St. Albans	14,356	15,103
25303	South Charleston	16,333	19,180
26101	Vienna	11,549	9,381
26062	Weirton	27,131	28,201
26452	Weston	7,323	8,754
26505	Westover	5,086	4,749
26003	Wheeling	48,188	53,400
25661	Williamson	5,831	6,746

Wisconsin

ZIP code	Place	1970	1960
54301	Allouez(u) 1976	15,159	....
54409	Antigo	9,005	9,691
54911	Appleton	56,377	48,411
54806	Ashland	9,615	10,132
54304	Ashwaubenor(u)	9,323	....
53913	Baraboo	7,931	7,660
53916	Beaver Dam	14,265	13,118
53511	Beloit 1974	35,957	32,846
54923	Berlin	5,338	4,838
53005	Brookfield 1974	33,371	19,812
53209	Brown Deer	12,582	11,280
53105	Burlington	7,479	5,856
53012	Cedarburg	7,697	5,191
54729	Chippewa Falls	12,351	11,708
53110	Cudahy	22,078	17,975
53115	Delavan	5,526	4,846
54115	De Pere 1976	14,626	10,045
54701	Eau Claire	44,619	37,987
53122	Elm Grove	7,201	4,994
54935	Fond Du Lac	35,515	32,719
53538	Fort Atkinson	9,164	7,908
53217	Fox Point	7,939	7,315
53132	Franklin	12,247	10,006
53022	Germantown 1974	8,219	622
53209	Glendale	13,426	9,537
53024	Grafton 1973	7,169	3,748
*54305	Green Bay 1976	88,304	62,888
53220	Greenfield	24,424	17,636

ZIP code	Place	1970	1960
53130	Hales Corners	7,771	5,549
53027	Hartford	6,499	5,627
54016	Hudson 1973	5,322	4,325
53545	Janesville	46,426	35,164
53549	Jefferson	5,429	4,548
54130	Kaukauna	11,308	10,096
53140	Kenosha	78,805	67,899
54136	Kimberly	6,131	5,322
54601	La Crosse 1976	48,864	47,575
54140	Little Chute	5,522	5,099
*53701	Madison 1974	168,671	126,706
53701	Madison town 1975	5,995	4,925
54220	Manitowoc	33,430	32,275
54143	Marinette 1976	12,157	13,329
54449	Marshfield	15,619	14,153
54952	Menasha	14,836	14,647
53051	Menomonee Falls	31,697	18,276
54751	Menomonie	11,275	8,624
53092	Mequon	12,150	8,543
54452	Merrill	9,502	9,451
53562	Middleton	8,286	4,410
*53203	Milwaukee 1975	669,022	741,324
53716	Monona	10,420	8,178
53566	Monroe	8,654	8,050
53150	Muskego	11,573	......
54956	Neenah	22,902	18,057
53151	New Berlin	26,910	15,788
54961	New London	5,801	5,288
53154	Oak Creek 1976	15,510	9,372
53066	Oconomowoc	8,741	6,682
54901	Oshkosh	53,082	45,110
53511	Perry Go Place(u)	5,912	4,475
53818	Platteville	9,599	6,957
53073	Plymouth	5,810	5,128
53901	Portage	7,821	7,822
53074	Port Washington	8,752	5,984
53821	Prairie Du Chien	5,540	5,649
*53401	Racine	95,162	89,144
54501	Rhinelander	8,218	8,790
54868	Rice Lake	7,278	7,303
53581	Richland Center	5,086	4,746
54971	Ripon	7,053	6,163
54022	River Falls	7,238	4,857
53207	St. Francis 1974	9,951	10,065
54166	Shawano	6,488	6,103
53081	Sheboygan	48,484	45,747
53211	Shorewood	15,576	15,990
53172	South Milwaukee	23,297	20,307
54656	Sparta	6,258	6,080
54481	Stevens Point	23,479	17,837
53589	Stoughton	6,096	5,555
54235	Sturgeon Bay 1976	7,764	7,353
53590	Sun Prairie	9,935	4,008
54880	Superior	32,237	33,563
54660	Tomah	5,647	5,321
54241	Two Rivers 1974	13,243	12,393
53094	Watertown	15,683	13,943
53186	Waukesha	39,695	30,004
53963	Waupun	7,946	7,935
54401	Wausau	32,806	31,943
54401	Wausau West(u)	6,399	4,105
53213	Wauwatosa	58,676	56,923
53214	West Allis	71,649	68,157
53095	West Bend	16,555	9,969
53217	Whitefish Bay	17,402	18,390
53190	Whitewater	12,038	6,380
54494	Wisconsin Rapids 1975	18,134	15,042

Wyoming

ZIP code	Place	1970	1960
82601	Casper	39,361	38,930
82001	Cheyenne	40,914	43,505
82414	Cody	5,161	4,838
82716	Gillette	7,194	3,580
82520	Lander	7,125	4,182
82070	Laramie	23,143	17,520
82301	Rawlins	7,855	8,968
82501	Riverton	7,995	6,845
82901	Rock Springs	11,657	10,371
82801	Sheridan	10,856	11,651
82401	Worland	5,055	5,806

1970 Census and Areas of Counties and States

With Names of County Seats or Court Houses
Source: U.S. Bureau of the Census

Alabama

(67 counties, 50,708 sq. mi. land; pop., 3,444,165)

County	Pop. Apr. 1 1970	County seat or court house	Land area sq. mi.
Autauga	24,460	Prattville	599
Baldwin	59,382	Bay Minette	1,578
Barbour	22,543	Clayton	891
Bibb	13,812	Centreville	625
Blount	26,853	Oneonta	639
Bullock	11,824	Union Springs	615
Butler	22,007	Greenville	773
Calhoun	103,092	Anniston	611
Chambers	36,356	Lafayete	597
Cherokee	15,606	Centre	556
Chilton	25,180	Clanton	699
Choctaw	16,589	Butler	911
Clarke	26,724	Grove Hill	1,232
Clay	12,636	Ashland	603
Cleburne	10,996	Heflin	574
Coffee	34,872	Elba	677
Colbert	49,632	Tuscumbia	596
Conecuh	15,645	Evergreen	850
Coosa	10,662	Rockford	650
Covington	34,079	Andalusia	984
Crenshaw	13,188	Luverne	611
Cullman	52,445	Cullman	730
Dale	52,938	Ozark	559
Dallas	55,296	Selma	976
De Kalb	41,981	Fort Payne	778
Elmore	33,661	Wetumpka	624
Escambia	34,912	Brewton	962
Etowah	94,144	Gadsden	555
Fayette	16,252	Fayette	627
Franklin	23,933	Russellville	644
Geneva	21,924	Geneva	577
Greene	10,650	Eutaw	627
Hale	15,888	Greensboro	662
Henry	13,254	Abbeville	554
Houston	56,574	Dothan	575
Jackson	39,202	Scottsboro	1,079
Jefferson	644,991	Birmingham	1,115
Lamar	14,335	Vernon	605
Lauderdale	68,111	Florence	662
Lawrence	27,281	Moulton	685
Lee	61,268	Opelika	612
Limestone	41,699	Athens	546
Lowndes	12,897	Hayneville	715
Macon	24,841	Tuskegee	616
Madison	186,540	Huntsville	803
Marengo	23,819	Linden	978
Marion	23,788	Hamilton	743
Marshall	54,211	Guntersville	571
Mobile	317,308	Mobile	1,240
Monroe	20,883	Monroeville	1,032
Montgomery	167,790	Montgomery	790
Morgan	77,306	Decatur	570
Perry	15,388	Marion	734
Pickens	20,326	Carrollton	887
Pike	25,038	Troy	673
Randolph	18,331	Wedowee	581
Russell	45,394	Phenix City	627
St. Clair	27,956	Ashville & Pell City	640
Shelby	38,037	Columbiana	798
Sumter	16,974	Livingston	915
Talladega	65,280	Talladega	750
Tallapoosa	33,840	Dadeville	704
Tuscaloosa	116,029	Tuscaloosa	1,333
Walker	56,246	Jasper	805
Washington	16,241	Chatom	1,066
Wilcox	16,303	Camden	899
Winston	16,654	Double Springs	615

Alaska

(29 divisions, 566,432 sq. mi. land; pop., 302,173)

Census division	Pop. Apr. 1, 1970	Land area sq. mi.
Aleutian Islands	8,057	14,583
Anchorage	126,385	927
Angoon	503	2,825
Barrow	2,663	57,587

Census Division	Pop. Apr. 1 1970	Land Area sq. mi.
Bethel	7,767	19,642
Bristol Bay Borough	1,147	531
Bristol Bay	3,485	36,565
Cordova-McCarthy	1,857	15,481
Fairbanks	45,864	7,074
Haines	1,504	2,128
Juneau	13,556	1,286
Kenai-Cook Inlet	14,250	12,474
Ketchikan	10,041	1,345
Kobuk	4,434	42,978
Kodiak	9,409	5,375
Kuskokwim	2,306	56,562
Matanuska-Susitna	6,509	25,730
Nome	5,749	24,968
Outer Ketchikan	1,676	3,762
Prince of Wales	2,106	3,485
Seward	2,336	3,727
Sitka	6,106	2,296
Skagway-Yakutat	2,157	8,646
Southeast Fairbanks	4,179	17,713
Upper Yukon	1,684	84,142
Valdez-Chitina-Whittier	3,098	18,619
Wade Hampton	3,917	16,770
Wrangell-Petersburg	4,913	6,178
Yukon-Koyukuk	4,758	73,053

Arizona

(14 counties, 113,417 sq. mi. land; pop. 1,772,482)

County	Pop. Apr. 1 1970	County seat or court house	Land area sq. mi.
Apache	32,304	Saint Johns	11,171
Cochise	61,918	Bisbee	6,256
Coconino	48,326	Flagstaff	18,540
Gila	29,255	Globe	4,748
Graham	16,578	Safford	4,618
Greenlee	10,330	Clifton	1,879
Maricopa	968,487	Phoenix	9,155
Mohave 1974	35,714	Kingman	13,217
Navajo	47,559	Holbrook	9,910
Pima 1975	449,544	Tucson	9,240
Pinal	68,579	Florence	5,364
Santa Cruz	13,966	Nogales	1,246
Yavapai	37,005	Prescott	8.091
Yuma	60,827	Yuma	9,983

Arkansas

(75 counties, 51,945 sq. mi. land; pop. 1,923,295)

County	Pop. Apr. 1 1970	County seat or court house	Land area sq. mi.
Arkansas	23,347	DeWitt & Stuttgart	1,015
Ashley	24,976	Hamburg	928
Baxter	15,319	Mountain Home	537
Benton	50,476	Bentonville	851
Boone	19,073	Harrison	586
Bradley	12,778	Warren	651
Calhoun	5,573	Hampton	629
Carroll	12,301	Berryville and Eureka Sprg.	626
Chicot	18,164	Lake Village	643
Clark	21,537	Arkadelphia	878
Clay	18,771	Corning; Piggott	639
Cleburne	10,349	Heber Springs	554
Cleveland	6,605	Rison	601
Columbia	25,952	Magnolia	768
Conway	16,805	Morrilton	561
Craighead	52,068	Jonesboro and Lake City	716
Crawford	25,677	Van Buren	596
Crittenden	48,106	Marion	608
Cross	19,783	Wynne	625
Dallas	10,022	Fordyce	672
Desha	18,761	Arkansas City	736
Drew	15,157	Monticello	832
Faulkner	31,578	Conway	641
Franklin	11,301	Charleston and Ozark	613
Fulton	7,699	Salem	608
Garland	54,131	Hot Spgs. Nat'l Pk.	658
Grant	9,711	Sheridan	631
Greene	24,765	Paragould	579
Hempstead	19,308	Hope	726
Hot Spring	21,963	Malvern	621
Howard	11,412	Nashville	569
Independence	22,723	Batesville	752
Izard	7,381	Melbourne	574
Jackson	20,452	Newport	629
Jefferson	85,329	Pine Bluff	873
Johnson	13,630	Clarksville	673
Lafayette	10,018	Lewisville	523
Lawrence	16,320	Walnut Ridge	590
Lee	18,884	Marianna	608
Lincoln	12,913	Star City	563
Little River	11,194	Ashdown	486
Logan	16,789	Booneville & Paris	718
Lonoke	26,249	Lonoke	796
Madison	9,453	Huntsville	832
Marion	7,000	Yellville	584
Miller	33,385	Texarkana	623
Mississippi	62,060	Blytheville and Osceola	904
Monroe	15,657	Clarendon	607
Montgomery	5,821	Mount Ida	775
Nevada	10,111	Prescott	616
Newton	5,844	Jasper	822
Ouachita	30,896	Camden	736
Perry	5,634	Perryville	551
Phillips	40,046	Helena	686
Pike	8,711	Murfreesboro	600
Poinsett	26,843	Harrisburg	760
Polk	13,297	Mena	859
Pope	28,607	Russellville	812
Prairie	10,249	Des Arc and De Valls Bluff	661
Pulaski	287,189	Little Rock	765
Randolph	12,645	Pocohontas	647
St. Francis	30,799	Forest City	635
Saline	36,107	Benton	724
Scott	8,207	Waldron	898
Searcy	7,731	Marshall	664
Sebastian	79,237	Fort Smith; Greenwood	527
Sevier	11,272	De Queen	522
Sharp	8,233	Ash Flat	581
Stone	6,838	Mountain View	608
Union	45,428	El Dorado	1,050
Van Buren	8,275	Clinton	699
Washington	77,370	Fayetteville	958
White	39,253	Searcy	1,041
Woodruff	11,566	Augusta	591
Yell	14,208	Danville and Dardanelle	929

California

(58 counties, 156,361 sq. mi. land; pop. 19,953,134)

County	Pop. Apr. 1 1970	County seat or court house	Land area sq. mi.
Alameda	1,073,184	Oakland	733
Alpine	484	Markleeville	727
Amador	11,821	Jackson	583
Butte	101,969	Oroville	1,645
Calaveras	13,585	San Andreas	1,024
Colusa	12,430	Colusa	1,152
Contra Costa	555,805	Martinez	735
Del Norte	14,580	Crescent City	1,007
El Dorado	43,833	Placerville	1,715
Fresno	413,329	Fresno	5,966
Glenn	17,521	Willows	1,314
Humboldt	99,692	Eureka	3,586
Imperial	74,492	El Centro	4,241
Inyo	15,571	Independence	10,130
Kern	329,281	Bakersfield	8,152
Kings	66,717	Hanford	1,396
Lake	19,548	Lakeport	1,261
Lassen	16,796	Susanville	4,561
Los Angeles	7,040,697	Los Angeles	4,069
Madera	41,519	Madera	2,145
Marin	206,758	San Rafael	520
Mariposa	6,015	Mariposa	1,453
Mendocino	51,101	Ukiah	3,511
Merced	104,629	Merced	1,958
Modoc	7,469	Alturas	4,097
Mono	4,016	Bridgeport	3,027
Monterey	247,450	Salinas	3,324
Napa	79,140	Napa	787
Nevada	26,346	Nevada City	973
Orange	1,420,676	Santa Ana	782
Placer	77,632	Auburn	1,431
Plumas	11,707	Quincy	2,566
Riverside	459,074	Riverside	7,176
Sacramento	634,190	Sacramento	975
San Benito	18,226	Hollister	1,396
San Bernardino 1975	696,064	San Bernardino	20,117
San Diego	1,357,854	San Diego	4,261
San Francisco	715,674	San Francisco	45
San Joaquin 1975	299,831	Stockton	1,412
San Luis Obispo	105,690	San Luis Obispo	3,183
San Mateo	556,605	Redwood City	447
Santa Barbara	264,324	Santa Barbara	2,737
Santa Clara	1,066,174	San Jose	1,300
Santa Cruz	123,790	Santa Cruz	440
Shasta	77,640	Redding	3,788
Sierra	2,365	Downieville	958
Siskiyou	33,225	Yreka	6,262
Solano	171,989	Fairfield	823
Sonoma	204,885	Santa Rosa	1,604
Stanislaus	194,506	Modesto	1,511

County	Pop. Apr. 1 1970	County seat or court house	Land area sq. mi.
Sutter	41,935	Yuba City	603
Tehama	29,517	Red Bluff	2,982
Trinity	7,615	Weaverville	3,173
Tulare	188,322	Visalia	4,812
Tuolumne	22,169	Sonora	2,252
Ventura	378,497	Ventura	1,863
Yolo	91,788	Woodland	1,028
Yuba	44,736	Marysville	639

Colorado

(63 counties, 103,766 sq. mi. land; pop. 2,207,259)

County	Pop. Apr. 1 1970	County seat or court house	Land area sq. mi.
Adams	185,789	Brighton	1,237
Alamosa	11,422	Alamosa	719
Arapahoe	162,142	Littleton	797
Archuleta	2,733	Pagosa Springs	1,364
Baca	5,674	Springfield	2,563
Bent	6,493	Las Animas	1,519
Boulder	131,889	Boulder	748
Chaffee	10,162	Salida	1,038
Cheyenne	2,396	Cheyenne Wells	1,772
Clear Creek	4,819	Georgetown	394
Conejos	7,846	Conejos	1,268
Costilla	3,091	San Luis	1,213
Crowley	3,086	Ordway	802
Custer	1,120	Westcliffe	737
Delta	15,286	Delta	1,154
Denver	514,678	Denver	95
Dolores	1,641	Dove Creek	1,026
Douglas	8,407	Castle Rock	843
Eagle	7,498	Eagle	1,681
Elbert	3,903	Kiowa	1,864
El Paso	235,972	Colorado Springs	2,157
Fremont	21,942	Canon City	1,561
Garfield	14,821	Glenwood Springs	2,996
Gilpin	1,272	Central City	148
Grand	4,107	Hot Sulphur Springs	1,854
Gunnison	7,578	Gunnison	3,220
Hinsdale	202	Lake City	1,054
Huerfano	6,590	Walsenburg	1,574
Jackson	1,811	Walden	1,622
Jefferson	235,300	Golden	783
Kiowa	2,029	Eads	1,767
Kit Carson	7,530	Burlington	2,171
Lake	8,282	Leadville	379
La Plata	19,199	Durango	1,683
Larimer	89,900	Fort Collins	2,611
Las Animas	15,744	Trinidad	4,794
Lincoln	4,836	Hugo	2,593
Logan	18,852	Sterling	1,822
Mesa	54,374	Grand Junction	3,301
Mineral	786	Creede	921
Moffat	6,525	Craig	4,743
Montezuma	12,952	Cortez	2,094
Montrose	18,366	Montrose	2,238
Morgan	20,105	Fort Morgan	1,278
Otero	23,523	LaJunta	1,254
Ouray	1,546	Ouray	540
Park	2,185	Fairplay	2,162
Phillips	4,131	Holyoke	680
Pitkin	6,185	Aspen	973
Prowers	13,258	Lamar	1,621
Pueblo	118,238	Pueblo	2,405
Rio Blanco	4,842	Meeker	3,263
Rio Grande	10,494	Del Norte	915
Routt	6,592	Steamboat Spgs.	2,330
Saguache	3,827	Saguache	3,144
San Juan	831	Silverton	391
San Miguel	1,949	Telluride	1,283
Sedgwick	3,405	Julesburg	544
Summit	2,665	Breckenridge	604
Teller	3,316	Cripple Creek	553
Washington	5,550	Akron	2,526
Weld	89,297	Greeley	4,002
Yuma	8,544	Wray	2,379

Connecticut

(8 counties, 4,862 sq. mi. land; pop. 3,032,217)

County	Pop. Apr. 1 1970	County seat or court house	Land area sq. mi.
Fairfield	792,814	Bridgeport	626
Hartford	816,737	Hartford	739
Litchfield	144,091	Litchfield	925
Middlesex	115,018	Middletown	372
New Haven	744,948	New Haven	604
New London	230,654	Norwich	667
Tolland	103,440	Rockville	416
Windham	84,515	Putnam	514

Delaware

(3 counties, 1,982 sq. mi. land; pop. 548,104)

County	Pop. Apr. 1 1970	County seat or court house	Land area sq. mi.
Kent	81,892	Dover	594
New Castle	385,856	Wilmington	438
Sussex	80,356	Georgetown	950

District of Columbia

(61 sq. mi. land; pop. 756,510)

Florida

(67 counties, 54,090 sq. mi. land; pop. 6,789,443)

County	Pop. Apr. 1 1970	County seat or court house	Land area sq. mi.
Alachua	104,764	Gainesville	916
Baker	9,242	Macclenny	585
Bay	75,283	Panama City	747
Bradford	14,625	Starke	294
Brevard	230,006	Titusville	1,011
Broward	620,100	Fort Lauderdale	1,219
Calhoun	7,624	Blountstown	561
Charlotte	27,559	Punta Gorda	703
Citrus	19,196	Inverness	560
Clay	32,059	Green Cove Spgs.	593
Collier	38,040	Naples	2,006
Columbia	25,250	Lake City	784
Dade	1,267,792	Miami	2,042
De Soto	13,060	Arcadia	648
Dixie	5,480	Cross City	692
Duval	528,865	Jacksonville	766
Escambia	205,334	Pensacola	665
Flagler	4,454	Bunnell	487
Franklin	7,065	Apalachicola	536
Gadsden	39,184	Quincy	512
Gilchrist	3,551	Trenton	346
Glades	3,669	Moore Haven	753
Gulf	10,096	Port St. Joe	565
Hamilton	7,787	Jasper	514
Hardee	14,889	Wauchula	629
Hendry	11,859	La Belle	1,187
Hernando	17,004	Brooksville	484
Highlands	29,507	Sebring	997
Hillsborough	490,265	Tampa	1,038
Holmes	10,720	Bonifay	482
Indian River	35,992	Vero Beach	506
Jackson	34,434	Marianna	935
Jefferson	8,778	Monticello	605
Lafayette	2,892	Mayo	549
Lake	69,305	Tavares	961
Lee	105,216	Fort Myers	785
Leon	103,047	Tallahassee	670
Levy	12,756	Bronson	1,083
Liberty	3,379	Bristol	839
Madison	13,481	Madison	703
Manatee	97,115	Bradenton	739
Marion	69,030	Ocala	1,600
Martin	28,035	Stuart	556
Monroe	52,586	Key West	1,034
Nassau	20,626	Fernandina Beach	650
Okaloosa	88,187	Crestview	944
Okeechobee	11,233	Okeechobee	777
Orange	344,311	Orlando	910
Osceola	25,267	Kissimmee	1,313
Palm Beach	348,993	West Palm Beach	2,023
Pasco 1973	108,865	Dade City	742
Pinellas	522,329	Clearwater	265
Polk	228,026	Bartow	1,858
Putnam	36,424	Palatka	779
St. Johns	31,035	Saint Augustine	605
St. Lucie	50,836	Fort Pierce	584
Santa Rosa	37,741	Milton	1,032
Sarasota	120,413	Sarasota	587
Seminole	83,692	Sanford	305
Sumter	14,839	Bushnell	555
Suwannee	15,559	Live Oak	686
Taylor	13,641	Perry	1,051
Union	8,112	Lake Butler	241
Volusia	169,487	De Land	1,062
Wakulla 1974	8,546	Crawfordville	601
Walton	16,087	De Funiak Springs	1,053
Washington	11,453	Chipley	585

Georgia

(159 counties, 58,073 sq. mi. land; pop. 4,589,575)

County	Pop. Apr. 1 1970	County seat or court house	Land area sq. mi.
Appling	12,726	Baxley	513
Atkinson	5,879	Pearson	318
Bacon	8,233	Alma	293
Baker	3,875	Newton	355
Baldwin	34,240	Milledgeville	255
Banks	6,833	Homer	231
Barrow	16,859	Winder	171
Bartow	32,911	Cartersville	461
Ben Hill	13,171	Fitzgerald	255
Berrien	11,556	Nashville	468

County	Pop. Apr. 1 1970	County seat or court house	Land area sq. mi.
Bibb	143,418	Macon	254
Bleckley	10,291	Cochran	219
Brantley	5,940	Nahunta	447
Brooks	13,743	Quitman	491
Bryan	6,539	Pembroke	443
Bulloch	31,585	Statesboro	685
Burke	18,255	Waynesboro	831
Butts	10,560	Jackson	185
Calhoun	6,606	Morgan	289
Camden	11,334	Woodbine	653
Candler	6,412	Metter	250
Carroll	45,404	Carrollton	495
Catoosa	28,271	Ringgold	167
Charlton	5,680	Folkston	796
Chatham	187,816	Savannah	445
Chattahoochee	25,813	Cusseta	253
Chattooga	20,541	Summerville	317
Cherokee	31,059	Canton	415
Clarke	65,177	Athens	116
Clay	3,636	Fort Gaines	200
Clayton	98,126	Jonesboro	149
Clinch	6,405	Homerville	797
Cobb	196,793	Marietta	343
Coffee	22,828	Douglas	612
Colquitt	32,298	Moultrie	563
Columbia	22,327	Appling	290
Cook	12,129	Adel	233
Coweta	32,310	Newnan	442
Crawford	5,748	Knoxville	315
Crisp	18,087	Cordele	292
Dade	9,910	Trenton	168
Dawson	3,639	Dawsonville	211
Decatur	22,310	Bainbridge	575
De Kalb	415,387	Decatur	269
Dodge	15,658	Eastman	498
Dooly	10,404	Vienna	395
Dougherty	89,639	Albany	324
Douglas	28,659	Douglasville	202
Early	12,682	Blakely	524
Echols	1,924	Statenville	425
Effingham	13,632	Springfield	480
Elbert	17,262	Elberton	358
Emanuel	18,357	Swainsboro	686
Evans	7,290	Claxton	186
Fannin	13,357	Blue Ridge	394
Fayette	11,364	Fayetteville	199
Floyd	73,742	Rome	514
Forsyth	16,928	Cumming	219
Franklin	12,784	Carnesville	263
Fulton	607,592	Atlanta	530
Gilmer	8,956	Ellijay	439
Glascock	2,280	Gibson	143
Glynn	50,528	Brunswick	412
Gordon	23,570	Calhoun	358
Grady	17,826	Cairo	466
Greene	10,212	Greensboro	403
Gwinnett	72,349	Lawrenceville	437
Habersham	20,691	Clarkesville	282
Hall	59,405	Gainesville	378
Hancock	9,019	Sparta	478
Haralson	15,927	Buchanan	285
Harris	11,520	Hamilton	465
Hart	15,814	Hartwell	231
Heard	5,354	Franklin	297
Henry	23,724	McDonough	331
Houston	62,924	Perry	380
Irwin	8,036	Ocilla	372
Jackson	21,093	Jefferson	346
Jasper	5,760	Monticello	373
Jeff Davis	9,425	Hazlehurst	331
Jefferson	17,174	Louisville	530
Jenkins	8,332	Millen	351
Johnson	7,727	Wrightsville	313
Jones	12,218	Gray	402
Lamar	10,688	Barnesville	181
Lanier	5,031	Lakeland	177
Laurens	32,738	Dublin	810
Lee	7,044	Leesburg	355
Liberty	17,569	Hinesville	514
Lincoln	5,895	Lincolnton	193
Long	3,746	Ludowici	402
Lowndes	55,112	Valdosta	508
Lumpkin	8,728	Dahlonega	292
McDuffie	15,276	Thomson	253
McIntosh	7,371	Darien	426
Macon	12,933	Oglethorpe	403
Madison	13,517	Danielsville	281
Marion	5,099	Buena Vista	365
Meriwether	19,461	Greenville	499
Miller	6,424	Colquitt	287
Mitchell	18,956	Camilla	510
Monroe	10,991	Forsyth	398
Montgomery	6,099	Mount Vernon	237
Morgan	9,904	Madison	356
Murray	12,986	Chatsworth	342
Muscogee	167,377	Columbus	220
Newton	26,282	Covington	271
Oconee	7,915	Watkinsville	186
Oglethorpe	7,598	Lexington	435
Paulding	17,520	Dallas	318
Peach	15,990	Fort Valley	151
Pickens	9,620	Jasper	225
Pierce	9,281	Blackshear	342
Pike	7,316	Zebulon	230
Polk	29,656	Cedartown	312
Pulaski	8,066	Hawkinsville	253
Putnam	9,394	Eatonton	339
Quitman	2,180	Georgetown	156
Rabun	8,327	Clayton	368
Randolph	8,734	Cuthbert	436
Richmond	162,437	Augusta	323
Rockdale	18,152	Conyers	128
Schley	3,097	Ellaville	162
Screven	12,591	Sylvania	651
Seminole	7,059	Donalsonville	246
Spalding	39,514	Griffin	201
Stephens	20,331	Toccoa	173
Stewart	6,511	Lumpkin	452
Sumter	26,931	Americus	488
Talbot	6,625	Talbotton	390
Taliaferro	2,423	Crawfordville	195
Tattnall	16,557	Reidsville	490
Taylor	7,865	Butler	403
Telfair	11,394	MacRae	440
Terrell	11,416	Dawson	329
Thomas	34,562	Thomasville	541
Tift	27,288	Tifton	266
Toombs	19,151	Lyons	368
Towns	4,565	Hiawassee	166
Treutlen	5,647	Soperton	194
Troup	44,466	La Grange	415
Turner	8,790	Ashburn	293
Twiggs	8,222	Jeffersonville	364
Union	6,811	Blairsville	309
Upson	23,505	Thomaston	334
Walker	50,691	La Fayette	445
Walton	23,404	Monroe	330
Ware	33,525	Waycross	912
Warren	6,669	Warrenton	284
Washington	17,480	Sandersville	674
Wayne	17,858	Jesup	645
Webster	2,362	Preston	195
Wheeler	4,596	Alamo	306
White	7,742	Cleveland	243
Whitfield	55,108	Dalton	281
Wilcox	6,998	Abbeville	383
Wilkes	18,184	Washington	468
Wilkinson	9,393	Irwinton	458
Worth	14,770	Sylvester	579

Hawaii

(4 counties, 6,425 sq. mi. land; pop. 769,913)

County	Pop. Apr. 1 1970	County seat or court house	Land area sq. mi.
Hawaii	63,468	Hilo	4,037
Honolulu	630,528	Honolulu	596
Kauai	29,761	Lihue	619
Maui*	46,156	Wailuku	1,173

*Includes population of Kalawao County (279) shown separately in 1960 but included with Maui County in 1970.

Idaho

(44 counties, 82,677 sq. mi. land; pop. 713,008)

County	Pop. Apr. 1 1970	County seat or court house	Land area sq. mi.
Ada	112,230	Boise	1,043
Adams	2,877	Council	1,371
Bannock	52,200	Pocatello	1,122
Bear Lake	5,801	Paris	984
Benewah	6,230	Saint Maries	788
Bingham	29,167	Blackfoot	2,084
Blaine	5,749	Hailey	2,647
Boise	1,763	Idaho City	1,910
Bonner	15,560	Sandpoint	1,733
Bonneville 1975	58,499	Idaho Falls	1,836
Boundary	5,484	Bonners Ferry	1,275
Butte	2,925	Arco	2,239
Camas	728	Fairfield	1,054
Canyon	61,288	Caldwell	578
Caribou	6,534	Soda Springs	1,746
Cassia	17,017	Burley	2,544
Clark	741	Dubois	1,751
Clearwater	10,871	Orofino	2,521
Custer	2,967	Challis	4,929
Elmore	17,479	Mountain Home	3,048
Franklin	7,373	Preston	664
Fremont	8,710	Saint Anthony	1,864
Gem	9,387	Emmett	555
Gooding	8,645	Gooding	720
Idaho	12,891	Grangeville	8,516
Jefferson	11,740	Rigby	1,096
Jerome	10,253	Jerome	595

County	Pop. Apr. 1 1970	County seat or court house	Land area sq. mi.
ootenai	35,332	Coeur d'Alene	1,249
atah	24,898	Moscow	1,090
emhi	5,566	Salmon	4,580
ewis	3,867	Nezperce	476
incoln	3,057	Shoshone	1,203
adison	13,452	Rexberg	473
inidoka	15,731	Rupert	750
ez Perce	30,376	Lewiston	844
neida	2,864	Malad City	1,191
wyhee	6,422	Murphy	7,641
ayette 1975	14,390	Payette	402
ower	4,864	American Falls	1,413
hoshone 1976	18,938	Wallace	2,609
eton	2,351	Driggs	457
win Falls	41,807	Twin Falls	1,947
alley	3,609	Cascade	3,676
ashington 1976	8,485	Weiser	1,462

Illinois

(102 counties, 55,748 sq. mi. land; pop. 11,113,976)

County	Pop. Apr. 1 1970	County seat or court house	Land area sq. mi.
dams	70,861	Quincy	862
exander	12,015	Cairo	229
ond	14,012	Greenville	378
oone	25,440	Belvidere	283
own	5,586	Mount Sterling	306
ureau	38,541	Princeton	866
alhoun	5,675	Hardin	247
arroll	19,276	Mount Carroll	456
ass	14,219	Virginia	371
hampaign	163,281	Urbana	1,000
hristian	35,948	Taylorville	709
ark	16,216	Marshall	505
ay	14,735	Louisville	464
inton	28,315	Carlyle	434
oles	47,815	Charleston	506
ook	5,493,766	Chicago	954
awford	19,824	Robinson	443
umberland	9,772	Toledo	347
e Kalb	71,654	Sycamore	636
e Witt	16,975	Clinton	399
uglas	18,997	Tuscola	420
Page	490,822	Wheaton	331
gar	21,591	Paris	628
wards	7,090	Albion	225
ingham	24,608	Effingham	481
yette	20,752	Vandalia	703
rd	16,382	Paxton	488
anklin	38,329	Benton	434
lton	41,900	Lewiston	877
llatin	7,418	Shawneetown	328
eene	17,014	Carrollton	543
undy	26,535	Morris	432
milton	8,665	McLeansboro	435
ncock	23,664	Carthage	797
rdin	4,914	Elizabethtown	183
nderson	8,451	Oquawka	376
nry	53,217	Cambridge	826
quois	33,532	Watseka	1,122
kson	55,008	Murphysboro	605
sper	10,741	Newton	495
ferson	31,848	Mount Vernon	573
sey	18,492	Jerseyville	376
Daviess	21,766	Galena	606
nson	7,550	Vienna	345
ne	251,005	Geneva	520
nkakee	97,250	Kankakee	678
ndall	26,374	Yorkville	320
ox	60,939	Galesburg	728
e	382,638	Waukegan	457
Salle	111,409	Ottawa	1,150
vrence	17,522	Lawrenceville	374
	37,947	Dixon	728
ngston	40,690	Pontiac	1,043
an	33,538	Lincoln	622
Donough	36,653	Macomb	582
Henry	111,555	Woodstock	610
Lean	104,389	Bloomington	1,173
con	125,010	Decatur	578
coupin	44,557	Carlinville	872
dison	250,911	Edwardsville	733
ion	38,986	Salem	579
shall	13,302	Lacon	391
son	16,180	Havana	541
sac	13,889	Metropolis	245
ard	9,685	Petersburg	312
cer	17,294	Aledo	556
roe	18,831	Waterloo	382
tgomery	30,260	Hillsboro	705
gan	36,174	Jacksonville	561
ltrie	13,263	Sullivan	326
e	42,867	Oregon	758
ria	195,318	Peoria	623
y	19,757	Pinckneyville	439
	15,509	Monticello	437
	19,185	Pittsfield	828
Pope	3,857	Golconda	381
Pulaski	8,741	Mound City	204
Putnam	5,007	Hennepin	160
Randolph	31,379	Chester	594
Richland	16,829	Olney	364
Rock Island	166,734	Rock Island	424
St. Clair	285,199	Belleville	673
Saline	25,721	Harrisburg	383
Sangamon	161,335	Springfield	879
Schuyler	8,135	Rushville	434
Scott	6,096	Winchester	251
Shelby	22,589	Shelbyville	752
Stark	7,510	Toulon	291
Stephenson	48,861	Freeport	568
Tazewell	118,649	Pekin	652
Union	16,071	Jonesboro	416
Vermilion	97,047	Danville	899
Wabash	12,841	Mt. Carmel	222
Warren	21,595	Monmouth	541
Washington	13,780	Nashville	564
Wayne	17,004	Fairfield	715
White	17,312	Carmi	502
Whiteside	62,877	Morrison	687
Will	247,825	Joliet	847
Williamson	49,021	Marion	429
Winnebago	246,623	Rockford	519
Woodford	28,012	Eureka	528

Indiana

(92 counties, 36,097 sq. mi. land; pop. 5,193,669)

County	Pop. Apr. 1 1970	County seat or court house	Land area sq. mi.
Adams	26,871	Decatur	345
Allen	280,455	Fort Wayne	671
Bartholomew	57,022	Columbus	402
Benton	11,262	Fowler	409
Blackford	15,888	Hartford City	167
Boone	30,870	Lebanon	427
Brown	9,057	Nashville	319
Carroll	17,734	Delphi	374
Cass	40,456	Logansport	415
Clark	75,876	Jeffersonville	384
Clay	23,933	Brazil	364
Clinton	30,547	Frankfort	407
Crawford	8,033	English	312
Daviess	26,602	Washington	430
Dearborn	29,430	Lawrenceburg	306
Decatur	22,738	Greensburg	370
De Kalb	30,837	Auburn	366
Delaware	129,219	Muncie	396
Dubois	30,934	Jasper	433
Elkhart	126,529	Goshen	468
Fayette	26,216	Connersville	215
Floyd	55,622	New Albany	149
Fountain	18,257	Covington	397
Franklin	16,943	Brookville	394
Fulton	16,984	Rochester	368
Gibson	30,444	Princeton	498
Grant	83,955	Marion	421
Greene	26,894	Bloomfield	549
Hamilton	54,532	Noblesville	401
Hancock	35,096	Greenfield	305
Harrison	20,423	Corydon	479
Hendricks	53,974	Danville	417
Henry	52,603	New Castle	400
Howard	83,198	Kokomo	293
Huntington	34,970	Huntington	369
Jackson	33,187	Brownstown	520
Jasper	20,429	Rensselaer	562
Jay	23,575	Portland	386
Jefferson	27,006	Madison	366
Jennings	19,454	Vernon	377
Johnson	61,138	Franklin	315
Knox	41,546	Vincennes	516
Kosciusko	48,127	Warsaw	540
Lagrange	20,890	Lagrange	381
Lake	546,253	Crown Point	513
La Porte	105,342	La Porte	607
Lawrence	38,038	Bedford	459
Madison	138,522	Anderson	453
Marion	793,769	Indianapolis	392
Marshall	34,986	Plymouth	443
Martin	10,969	Shoals	345
Miami	39,246	Peru	377
Monroe	85,221	Bloomington	386
Montgomery	33,930	Crawfordsville	507
Morgan	44,176	Martinsville	406
Newton	11,606	Kentland	413
Noble	31,382	Albion	412
Ohio	4,289	Rising Sun	87
Orange	16,968	Paoli	405
Owen	12,163	Spencer	390
Parke	14,600	Rockville	445
Perry	19,075	Cannelton	384
Pike	12,281	Petersburg	335
Porter	87,114	Valparaiso	425
Posey	21,740	Mount Vernon	412

County	Pop. Apr. 1 1970	County seat or court house	Land area sq. mi.
Pulaski	12,534	Winamac	433
Putnam	26,932	Greencastle	490
Randolph	28,915	Winchester	457
Ripley	21,138	Versailles	442
Rush	20,352	Rushville	409
St. Joseph	245,045	South Bend	466
Scott	17,144	Scottsburg	193
Shelby	37,797	Shelbyville	409
Spencer	17,134	Rockport	396
Starke	19,280	Knox	310
Steuben	20,159	Angola	309
Sullivan	19,889	Sullivan	457
Switzerland	6,306	Vevay	221
Tippecanoe	109,378	Lafayette	500
Tipton	16,650	Tipton	261
Union	6,582	Liberty	168
Vanderburgh	168,772	Evansville	241
Vermillion	16,793	Newport	263
Vigo	114,528	Terre Haute	415
Wabash	35,553	Wabash	398
Warren	8,705	Williamsport	368
Warrick	27,972	Boonville	391
Washington	19,278	Salem	516
Wayne	79,109	Richmond	405
Wells	23,821	Bluffton	368
White	20,995	Monticello	497
Whitley	23,395	Columbia City	337

Iowa

(99 counties; 55,941 sq. mi. land; pop. 2,825,041)

County	Pop. Apr. 1 1970	County seat or court house	Land area sq. mi.
Adair	9,487	Greenfield	569
Adams	6,322	Corning	426
Allamakee	14,968	Waukon	636
Appanoose	15,007	Centerville	523
Audubon	9,595	Audubon	448
Benton	22,885	Vinton	718
Black Hawk	132,916	Waterloo	568
Boone	26,470	Boone	573
Bremer	22,737	Waverly	439
Buchanan	21,762	Independence	568
Buena Vista	20,693	Storm Lake	572
Butler	16,953	Allison	582
Calhoun	14,292	Rockwell City	571
Carroll	22,912	Carroll	574
Cass	17,007	Atlantic	559
Cedar	17,655	Tipton	585
Cerro Gordo	49,223	Mason City	575
Cherokee	17,269	Cherokee	573
Chickasaw	14,969	New Hampton	505
Clarke	7,581	Oscea	429
Clay	18,464	Spencer	580
Clayton	20,606	Elkader	779
Clinton	56,749	Clinton	693
Crawford	19,116	Denison	716
Dallas	26,085	Adel	597
Davis	8,207	Bloomfield	509
Decatur	9,737	Leon	530
Delaware	18,770	Manchester	572
Des Moines	46,982	Burlington	408
Dickinson	12,565	Spirit Lake	380
Dubuque	90,609	Dubuque	612
Emmet	14,009	Estherville	394
Fayette	26,898	West Union	728
Floyd	19,860	Charles City	503
Franklin	13,255	Hampton	586
Fremont	9,282	Sidney	524
Greene	12,716	Jefferson	569
Grundy	14,119	Grundy Center	501
Guthrie	12,243	Guthrie Center	596
Hamilton	18,383	Webster City	577
Hancock	13,506	Garner	570
Hardin	22,248	Eldora	574
Harrison	16,240	Logan	696
Henry	18,114	Mount Pleasant	440
Howard	11,442	Cresco	471
Humboldt	12,519	Dakota City	435
Ida	9,283	Ida Grove	431
Iowa	15,419	Marengo	584
Jackson	20,839	Maquoketa	644
Jasper	35,425	Newton	731
Jefferson	15,774	Fairfield	436
Johnson 1974	75.025	Iowa City	619
Jones	19,868	Anamosa	585
Keokuk	13,943	Sigourney	579
Kossuth	22,937	Algona	979
Lee	42,996	Fort Madison and Keokuk	527
Linn	163,213	Cedar Rapids	717
Louisa	10,682	Wapello	403
Lucas	10,163	Chariton	434
Lyon	13,340	Rock Rapids	588
Madison	11,558	Winterset	564
Mahaska	22,177	Oskaloosa	572
Marion	26,352	Knoxville	498
Marshall	41,076	Marshalltown	5[illegible]
Mills	11,832	Glenwood	4[illegible]
Mitchell	13,108	Osage	4[illegible]
Monona	12,069	Onawa	6[illegible]
Monroe	9,357	Albia	4[illegible]
Montgomery	12,781	Red Oak	4[illegible]
Muscatine	37,181	Muscatine	4[illegible]
O'Brien	17,522	Primghar	5[illegible]
Osceola	8,555	Sibley	3[illegible]
Page	18,537	Clarinda	5[illegible]
Palo Alto	13,289	Emmetsburg	5[illegible]
Plymouth	24,322	Le Mars	8[illegible]
Pocahontas	12,793	Pocahontas	5[illegible]
Polk	286,130	Des Moines	5[illegible]
Pottawattamie	86,991	Council Bluffs	9[illegible]
Poweshiek	18,803	Montezuma	5[illegible]
Ringgold	6,373	Mount Ayr	5[illegible]
Sac	15,573	Sac City	5[illegible]
Scott	142,687	Davenport	4[illegible]
Shelby	15,528	Harlan	5[illegible]
Sioux	27,996	Orange City	7[illegible]
Story	62,783	Nevada	5[illegible]
Tama	20,147	Toledo	7[illegible]
Taylor	8,790	Bedford	5[illegible]
Union	13,557	Creston	4[illegible]
Van Buren	8,643	Keosauqua	4[illegible]
Wapello	42,149	Ottumwa	4[illegible]
Warren	27,432	Indianola	5[illegible]
Washington	18,967	Washington	5[illegible]
Wayne	8,405	Corydon	5[illegible]
Webster	48,391	Fort Dodge	7[illegible]
Winnebago	12,990	Forest City	4[illegible]
Winneshiek	21,758	Decorah	6[illegible]
Woodbury	103,052	Sioux City	8[illegible]
Worth	8,984	Northwood	4[illegible]
Wright	17,294	Clarion	5[illegible]

Kansas

(105 counties, 81,787 sq. mi. land; pop. 2,249,071)

County	Pop. Apr. 1 1970	County seat or court house	Land area sq. mi.
Allen	15,043	Iola	5[illegible]
Anderson	8,501	Garnett	5[illegible]
Atchison	19,165	Atchison	4[illegible]
Barber	7,016	Medicine Lodge	1,1[illegible]
Barton	30,663	Great Bend	8[illegible]
Bourbon	15,215	Fort Scott	6[illegible]
Brown	11,685	Hiawatha	5[illegible]
Butler	38,658	El Dorado	1,4[illegible]
Chase	3,408	Cottonwood Falls	7[illegible]
Chautauqua	4,642	Sedan	6[illegible]
Cherokee	21,549	Columbus	5[illegible]
Cheyenne	4,256	Saint Francis	1,0[illegible]
Clark	2,896	Ashland	9[illegible]
Clay	9,890	Clay Center	6[illegible]
Cloud	13,466	Concordia	7[illegible]
Coffey	7,397	Burlington	6[illegible]
Comanche	2,702	Coldwater	[illegible]
Cowley	35,012	Winfield	1,[illegible]
Crawford	37,850	Girard	[illegible]
Decatur	4,988	Oberlin	8[illegible]
Dickinson	19,993	Abilene	8[illegible]
Doniphan	9,107	Troy	3[illegible]
Douglas	57,932	Lawrence	4[illegible]
Edwards	4,581	Kinsley	6[illegible]
Elk	3,858	Howard	6[illegible]
Ellis	24,730	Hays	9[illegible]
Ellsworth	6,146	Ellsworth	7[illegible]
Finney	19,029	Garden City	1,[illegible]
Ford	22,587	Dodge City	1,[illegible]
Franklin	20,007	Ottawa	[illegible]
Geary	28,111	Junction City	3[illegible]
Gove	2,940	Gove	1,0[illegible]
Graham	4,751	Hill City	8[illegible]
Grant	5,961	Ulysses	5[illegible]
Gray	4,516	Cimarron	8[illegible]
Greeley	1,819	Tribune	[illegible]
Greenwood	9,141	Eureka	1,[illegible]
Hamilton	2,747	Syracuse	[illegible]
Harper	7,871	Anthony	[illegible]
Harvey	27,236	Newton	[illegible]
Haskell	3,672	Sublette	5[illegible]
Hodgeman	2,662	Jetmore	8[illegible]
Jackson	10,342	Holton	6[illegible]
Jefferson	11,945	Oskaloosa	5[illegible]
Jewell	6,099	Mankato	9[illegible]
Johnson	220,073	Olathe	[illegible]
Kearny	3,047	Lakin	[illegible]
Kingman	8,886	Kingman	[illegible]
Kiowa	4,088	Greensburg	[illegible]
Labette	25,775	Oswego	[illegible]
Lane	2,707	Dighton	[illegible]
Leavenworth	53,340	Leavenworth	[illegible]
Lincoln	4,582	Lincoln	[illegible]
Linn	7,770	Mound City	[illegible]
Logan	3,814	Oakley	1,[illegible]

County	Pop. Apr. 1 1970	County seat or court house	Land area sq. mi.
Lyon	32,071	Emporia	841
McPherson	24,778	McPherson	896
Marion	13,935	Marion	945
Marshall	13,139	Marysville	883
Meade	4,912	Meade	979
Miami	19,254	Paola	592
Mitchell	8,010	Beloit	714
Montgomery	39,949	Independence	628
Morris	6,432	Council Grove	697
Morton	3,576	Elkhart	728
Nemaha	11,825	Seneca	708
Neosho	18,812	Erie	587
Ness	4,791	Ness City	1,081
Norton	7,279	Norton	872
Osage	13,352	Lyndon	707
Osborne	6,416	Osborne	886
Ottawa	6,183	Minneapolis	723
Pawnee	8,484	Larned	755
Phillips	7,888	Phillipsburg	897
Pottawatomie	11,755	Westmoreland	820
Pratt	10,056	Pratt	729
Rawlins	4,393	Atwood	1,078
Reno	60,765	Hutchinson	1,260
Republic	8,498	Belleville	718
Rice	12,320	Lyons	725
Riley	56,788	Manhattan	597
Rooks	7,628	Stockton	886
Rush	5,117	LaCrosse	724
Russell	9,428	Russell	867
Saline	46,592	Salina	720
Scott	5,606	Scott City	724
Sedgwick	350,694	Wichita	1,007
Seward	16,062	Liberal	646
Shawnee	155,322	Topeka	548
Sheridan	3,859	Hoxie	893
Sherman	7,792	Goodland	1,055
Smith	6,757	Smith Center	893
Stafford	5,943	Saint John	795
Stanton	2,287	Johnson	676
Stevens	4,198	Hugoton	731
Sumner	23,553	Wellington	1,186
Thomas	7,501	Colby	1,070
Trego	4,436	Wakeeney	901
Wabaunsee	6,397	Alma	792
Wallace	2,215	Sharon Springs	911
Washington	9,249	Washington	891
Wichita	3,274	Leoti	724
Wilson	11,317	Fredonia	574
Woodson	4,789	Yates Center	497
Wyandotte	186,845	Kansas City	152

Kentucky

(120 counties, 39,650 sq. mi. land; pop. 3,219,311)

County	Pop. Apr. 1 1970	County seat or court house	Land area sq. mi.
Adair	13,037	Columbia	370
Allen	12,598	Scottsville	351
Anderson	9,358	Lawrenceburg	206
Ballard	8,276	Wickliffe	259
Barren	28,677	Glasgow	468
ath	9,235	Owingsville	287
ell	31,121	Pineville	370
oone	32,812	Burlington	249
ourbon	18,476	Paris	300
oyd	52,376	Catlettsburg	159
oyle	21,861	Danville	183
racken	7,227	Brooksville	204
reathitt	14,221	Jackson	494
reckinridge	14,789	Hardinsburg	554
ullitt	26,090	Shepherdsville	300
utler	9,723	Morgantown	443
aldwell	13,179	Princeton	357
alloway	27,692	Murray	384
ampbell	88,704	Alexandria	149
arlisle	5,354	Bardwell	195
arroll	8,523	Carrollton	130
arter	19,850	Grayson	397
asey	12,930	Liberty	435
hristian	56,224	Hopkinsville	725
lark	24,090	Winchester	259
lay	18,481	Manchester	474
linton	8,174	Albany	190
rittenden	8,493	Marion	365
umberland	6,850	Burkesville	310
aviess	79,486	Owensboro	462
dmonson	8,751	Brownsville	298
lliott	5,933	Sandy Hook	240
still	12,752	Irvine	260
ayette	174,323	Lexington	280
eming	11,366	Flemingsburg	350
oyd	35,889	Prestonsburg	399
anklin	34,481	Frankfort	211
ilton	10,183	Hickman	203
allatin	4,134	Warsaw	100
arrard	9,457	Lancaster	236
ant	9,999	Williamstown	249
aves	30,939	Mayfield	60
ayson	16,445	Leitchfield	496
Green	10,350	Greensburg	282
Greenup	33,192	Greenup	351
Hancock	7,080	Hawesville	187
Hardin	78,421	Elizabethtown	616
Harlan	37,370	Harlan	469
Harrison	14,158	Cynthiana	308
Hart	13,980	Munfordville	420
Henderson	36,031	Henderson	433
Henry	10,910	New Castle	289
Hickman	6,264	Clinton	246
Hopkins	38,167	Madisonville	553
Jackson	10,005	McKee	337
Jefferson	695,055	Louisville	375
Jessamine	17,430	Nicholasville	177
Johnson	17,539	Paintsville	264
Kenton	129,440	Independence	165
Knott	14,698	Hindman	356
Knox	23,689	Barbourville	373
Larue	10,672	Hodgenville	260
Laurel	27,386	London	446
Lawrence	10,726	Louisa	425
Lee	6,587	Beattyville	210
Leslie	11,623	Hyden	409
Letcher	23,165	Whitesburg	339
Lewis	12,355	Vanceburg	486
Lincoln	16,663	Stanford	340
Livingston	7,596	Smithland	311
Logan	21,793	Russellville	563
Lyon	5,562	Eddyville	216
McCracken	58,281	Paducah	250
McCreary	12,548	Whitley City	418
McLean	9,062	Calhoun	257
Madison	42,730	Richmond	446
Magoffin	10,443	Salyersville	303
Marion	16,714	Lebanon	343
Marshall	20,381	Benton	303
Martin	9,377	Inez	231
Mason	17,273	Maysville	238
Meade	18,796	Brandenburg	305
Menifee	4,050	Frenchburg	210
Mercer	15,960	Harrodsburg	256
Metcalfe	8,177	Edmonton	296
Monroe	11,642	Tompkinsville	334
Montgomery	15,364	Mount Sterling	204
Morgan	10,019	West Liberty	369
Muhlenberg	27,537	Greenville	481
Nelson	23,477	Bardstown	437
Nicholas	6,508	Carlisle	204
Ohio	18,790	Hartford	596
Oldham	14,687	La Grange	184
Owen	7,470	Owenton	351
Owsley	5,023	Booneville	197
Pendleton	9,949	Falmouth	279
Perry	26,259	Hazard	341
Pike	61,059	Pikeville	782
Powell	7,704	Stanton	173
Pulaski	35,234	Somerset	653
Robertson	2,163	Mount Olivet	101
Rockcastle	12,305	Mount Vernon	311
Rowan	17,010	Morehead	290
Russell	10,542	Jamestown	238
Scott	17,948	Georgetown	284
Shelby	18,999	Shelbyville	383
Simpson	13,054	Franklin	239
Spencer	5,488	Taylorsville	193
Taylor	17,138	Campbellsville	277
Todd	10,823	Elkton	376
Trigg	8,620	Cadiz	408
Trimble	5,349	Bedford	146
Union	15,882	Morganfield	340
Warren	57,884	Bowling Green	546
Washington	10,728	Springfield	307
Wayne	14,268	Monticello	440
Webster	13,282	Dixon	339
Whitley	24,145	Williamsburg	459
Wolfe	5,669	Campton	227
Woodford	14,434	Versailles	193

Louisiana

(64 parishes, 44,930 sq. mi. land; pop. 3,643,180)

Parish	Pop. Apr. 1 1970	Parish seat or court house	Land area sq. mi.
Acadia	52,109	Crowley	663
Allen	20,794	Oberlin	774
Ascension	37,086	Donaldsonville	301
Assumption	19,654	Napoleonville	356
Avoyelles	37,751	Marksville	832
Beauregard	22,888	De Ridder	1,181
Bienville	16,024	Arcadia	832
Bossier	63,703	Benton	849
Caddo	230,184	Shreveport	899
Calcasieu	145,415	Lake Charles	1,105
Caldwell	9,354	Columbia	551
Cameron	8,149	Cameron	1,441
Catahoula	11,769	Harrisonburg	742

Parish	Pop. Apr. 1 1970	Parish seat or court house	Land area sq. mi.
Claiborne	17,024	Homer	763
Concordia	22,578	Vidalia	718
De Soto	22,764	Mansfield	894
East Baton Rouge	285,167	Baton Rouge	459
East Carroll	12,884	Lake Providence	436
East Feliciana	17,657	Clinton	454
Evangeline	31,932	Ville Platte	669
Franklin	23,946	Winnsboro	648
Grant	13,671	Colfax	670
Iberia	57,397	New Iberia	589
Iberville	30,746	Plaquemine	627
Jackson	15,963	Jonesboro	582
Jefferson	338,229	Gretna	369
Jefferson Davis	29,554	Jennings	658
Lafayette	111,643	Lafayette	283
Lafourche	68,941	Thibodaux	1,141
La Salle	13,295	Jena	643
Lincoln	33,800	Ruston	469
Livingston	36,511	Livingston	654
Madison	15,065	Tallulah	661
Morehouse	32,463	Bastrop	804
Natchitoches	35,219	Natchitoches	1,292
Orleans	593,471	New Orleans	197
Ouachita	115,387	Monroe	638
Plaquemines	25,225	Pointe a la Hache	1,030
Pointe Coupee	22,002	New Roads	563
Rapides	118,078	Alexandria	1,318
Red River	9,226	Coushatta	406
Richland	21,774	Rayville	576
Sabine	18,638	Many	873
St. Bernard	51,185	Chalmette	514
St. Charles	29,550	Hahnville	294
St. Helena	9,937	Greensburg	420
St. James	19,733	Convent	253
St. John The Baptist	23,813	Edgard	227
St. Landry	80,364	Opelousas	932
St. Martin	32,453	Saint Martinville	736
St. Mary	60,752	Franklin	624
St. Tammany	63,585	Covington	887
Tangipahoa	65,875	Amite	808
Tensas	9,732	Saint Joseph	626
Terrebonne	76,049	Houma	1,368
Union	18,447	Farmerville	885
Vermilion	43,071	Abbeville	1,205
Vernon	53,794	Leesville	1,351
Washington	41,987	Franklinton	665
Webster	39,939	Minden	615
West Baton Rouge	16,864	Port Allen	203
West Carroll	13,028	Oak Grove	356
West Feliciana	11,376	Saint Francisville	405
Winn	16,369	Winnfield	950

Maine

(16 counties, 30,920 sq. mi. land; pop. 993,663)

County	Pop. Apr. 1 1970	County seat or court house	Land area sq. mi.
Androscoggin	91,279	Auburn	474
Aroostook	94,078	Houlton	6,821
Cumberland	192,528	Portland	879
Franklin	22,444	Farmington	1,709
Hancock	34,598	Ellsworth	1,536
Kennebec	95,306	Augusta	872
Knox	29,013	Rockland	369
Lincoln	20,537	Wiscasset	454
Oxford	43,457	South Paris	2,080
Penobscot	125,393	Bangor	3,390
Piscataquis	16,285	Dover-Foxcroft	3,892
Sagadahoc	23,452	Bath	257
Somerset	40,597	Skowhegan	3,894
Waldo	23,328	Belfast	737
Washington	29,859	Machias	2,554
York	111,576	Alfred	1,001

Maryland

(23 cos., 1 ind. city, 9,891 sq. mi. land; pop. 3,922,399)

County	Pop. Apr. 1 1970	County seat or court house	Land area sq. mi.
Allegany	84,044	Cumberland	428
Anne Arundel	298,042	Annapolis	423
Baltimore	620,409	Towson	598
Calvert	20,682	Prince Frederick	217
Caroline	19,781	Denton	321
Carroll	69,006	Westminster	456
Cecil	53,291	Elkton	362
Charles	47,678	La Plata	459
Dorchester	29,405	Cambridge	594
Frederick	84,927	Frederick	665
Garrett	21,476	Oakland	659
Harford	115,378	Bel Air	453
Howard	62,394	Ellicott City	251
Kent	16,146	Chestertown	281
Montgomery	522,809	Rockville	495
Prince Georges	661,082	Upper Marlboro	485
Queen Annes	18,422	Centreville	37
St. Marys	47,388	Leonardtown	37
Somerset	18,924	Princess Anne	33
Talbot	23,682	Easton	26
Washington	103,829	Hagerstown	45
Wicomico	54,236	Salisbury	38
Worcester	24,442	Snow Hill	47
Independent City.			
Baltimore	905,787		7

Massachusetts

(14 counties; 7,826 sq. mi. land; pop. 5,689,170)

County	Pop. Apr. 1 1970	County seat or court house	Land area sq. mi.
Barnstable	96,656	Barnstable	39
Berkshire	149,402	Pittsfield	94
Bristol	444,301	Taunton	55
Dukes	6,117	Edgartown	10
Essex	637,887	Salem	49
Franklin	59,210	Greenfield	70
Hampden	459,050	Springfield	61
Hampshire	123,981	Northampton	52
Middlesex	1,397,465	Cambridge	82
Nantucket	3,774	Nantucket	4
Norfolk	604,854	Dedham	39
Plymouth	333,314	Plymouth	65
Suffolk	735,190	Boston	5
Worcester	637,037	Worcester	1,50

Michigan

(83 counties; 56,817 sq. mi. land; pop. 8,875,083)

County	Pop. Apr. 1 1970	County seat or court house	Land area sq. mi.
Alcona	7,113	Harrisville	67
Alger	8,568	Munising	90
Allegan	66,575	Allegan	82
Alpena	30,708	Alpena	56
Antrim	12,612	Bellaire	47
Arenac	11,149	Standish	36
Baraga	7,789	L'Anse	90
Barry	38,166	Hastings	55
Bay	117,339	Bay City	44
Benzie	8,593	Beulah	31
Berrien	163,940	Saint Joseph	58
Branch	37,906	Coldwater	50
Calhoun	141,963	Marshall	70
Cass	43,312	Cassopolis	49
Charlevoix	16,541	Charlevoix	41
Cheboygan	16,573	Cheboygan	72
Chippewa	32,412	Sault Sainte Marie	1,59
Clare	16,695	Harrison	57
Clinton	48,492	Saint Johns	57
Crawford	6,482	Grayling	56
Delta	35,924	Escanaba	1,17
Dickinson	23,753	Iron Mountain	75
Eaton	68,892	Charlotte	57
Emmet	18,331	Petoskey	46
Genesee	445,589	Flint	64
Gladwin	13,471	Gladwin	50
Gogebic	20,676	Bessemer	1,10
Grand Traverse	39,175	Traverse City	46
Gratiot	39,246	Ithaca	56
Hillsdale	37,171	Hillsdale	60
Houghton	34,652	Houghton	1,01
Huron	34,083	Bad Axe	81
Ingham	261,039	Mason	55
Ionia	45,848	Ionia	57
Iosco	24,905	Iawas City	54
Iron	13,813	Crystal Falls	1,17
Isabella	44,594	Mount Pleasant	57
Jackson	143,274	Jackson	69
Kalamazoo	201,550	Kalamazoo	56
Kalkaska	5,272	Kalkaska	56
Kent	411,044	Grand Rapids	85
Keweenaw	2,264	Eagle River	53
Lake	5,661	Baldwin	57
Lapeer	52,361	Lapeer	65
Leelanau	10,872	Leland	34
Lenawee	81,951	Adrian	75
Livingston	58,967	Howell	57
Luce	6,789	Newberry	90
Mackinac	9,660	Saint Ignace	1,01
Macomb	625,309	Mount Clemens	48
Manistee	20,393	Manistee	55
Marquette	64,686	Marquette	1,82
Mason	22,612	Ludington	49
Mecosta	27,992	Big Rapids	56
Menominee	24,587	Menominee	1,0
Midland	63,769	Midland	52
Missaukee	7,126	Lake City	56
Monroe	119,172	Monroe	5
Montcalm	39,660	Stanton	7
Montmorency	5,247	Atlanta	5
Muskegon	157,426	Muskegon	5
Newaygo	27,992	White Cloud	8
Oakland	907,871	Pontiac	8
Oceana	17,984	Hart	5
Ogemaw	11,903	West Branch	5

County	Pop. Apr. 1 1970	County seat or court house	Land area sq. mi.
ntonagon	10,548	Ontonagon	1,316
sceola	14,838	Reed City	581
scoda	4,726	Mio	563
tsego	10,422	Gaylord	527
ttawa	128,181	Grand Haven	563
esque Isle	12,836	Rogers City	648
oscommon	9,892	Roscommon	521
aginaw	219,743	Saginaw	814
. Clair	120,175	Port Huron	734
t. Joseph	47,392	Centreville	506
anilac	35,181	Sandusky	961
choolcraft	8,226	Manistique	1,181
hiawassee	63,075	Corunna	540
uscola	48,603	Caro	815
an Buren	56,173	Paw Paw	603
ashtenaw	234,103	Ann Arbor	711
ayne	2,670,368	Detroit	605
exford	19,717	Cadillac	559

Minnesota

(87 counties; 79,289 sq. mi. land; pop., 3,805,069)

County	Pop. Apr. 1 1970	County seat or court house	Land area sq. mi.
tkin	11,403	Aitkin	1,828
noka	154,401	Anoka	424
ecker	24,372	Detroit Lakes	1,297
eltrami	26,373	Bemidji	2,507
enton	20,841	Foley	402
g Stone	7,941	Ortonville	490
ue Earth	52,322	Mankato	737
own	28,887	New Ulm	610
arlton	28,072	Carlton	862
arver	28,331	Chaska	359
ass	17,323	Walker	1,998
hippewa	15,109	Montevideo	582
hisago	17,492	Center City	419
lay	46,608	Moorhead	1,045
earwater	8,013	Bagley	1,000
ook	3,423	Grand Marais	1,346
ottonwood	14,887	Windom	636
ow Wing	34,826	Brainerd	995
akota	139,808	Hastings	576
odge	13,037	Mantorville	435
ouglas	22,910	Alexandria	647
aribault	20,896	Blue Earth	711
llmore	21,916	Preston	859
eeborn	38,064	Albert Lea	701
oodhue	34,804	Red Wing	753
ant	7,462	Elbow Lake	546
ennepin	960,080	Minneapolis	567
ouston	17,556	Caledonia	565
ubbard	10,583	Park Rapids	932
anti	16,560	Cambridge	438
sca	35,530	Grand Rapids	2,633
ckson	14,352	Jackson	696
anabec	9,775	Mora	524
andiyohi	30,548	Willmar	783
ttson	6,853	Hallock	1,123
oochiching	17,131	International Falls	3,127
c Qui Parle	11,164	Madison	768
ke	13,351	Two Harbors	2,062
ke of the Woods 1974	4,196	Baudette	1,311
Sueur	21,332	Le Center	440
ncoln	8,143	Ivanhoe	531
on	24,273	Marshall	709
cLeod	27,662	Glencoe	488
ahnomen	5,638	Mahnomen	563
arshall	13,060	Warren	1,789
artin	24,316	Fairmont	703
eeker	18,387	Litchfield	619
lle Lacs	15,703	Milaca	571
orrison	26,949	Little Falls	1,127
ower	43,783	Austin	703
urray	12,508	Slayton	703
ollet	24,518	Saint Peter	432
obles	23,208	Worthington	712
rman	10,008	Ada	885
nstead	84,104	Rochester	656
ter Tail	46,097	Fergus Falls	1,962
nnington 1975	14,589	Thief River Falls	622
ne	16,821	Pine City	1,414
estone	12,791	Pipestone	464
lk	34,435	Crookston	2,013
pe	11,107	Glenwood	669
msey	476,350	Saint Paul	155
d Lake	5,388	Red Lake Falls	432
dwood	20,024	Redwood Falls	874
nville	21,139	Olivia	979
e	41,582	Faribault	496
ck	11,346	Luverne	485
seau	11,569	Roseau	1,676
Louis	220,693	Duluth	6,092
ott	32,423	Shakopee	353
erburne	18,344	Elk River	431
ley	15,845	Gaylord	583
earns	95,400	Saint Cloud	1,342
eele	26,931	Owatonna	425
Stevens	11,218	Morris	558
Swift	13,177	Benson	739
Todd	22,114	Long Prairie	942
Traverse	6,254	Wheaton	568
Wabasha	17,224	Wabasha	522
Wadena	12,412	Wadena	536
Waseca	16,663	Waseca	415
Washington	82,948	Stillwater	386
Watonwan	13,298	Saint James	433
Wilkin	9,389	Breckenridge	752
Winona	44,409	Winona	620
Wright	38,933	Buffalo	674
Yellow Medicine	14,523	Granite Falls	753

Mississippi

(82 counties, 47,296 sq. mi. land; pop., 2,216,912)

County	Pop. Apr. 1 1970	County seat or court house	Land area sq. mi.
Adams	37,293	Natchez	449
Alcorn	27,179	Corinth	405
Amite	13,763	Liberty	729
Attala	19,570	Kosciusko	724
Benton	7,505	Ashland	412
Bolivar	49,409	Cleveland & Rosedale	923
Calhoun	14,623	Pittsboro	575
Carroll	9,397	Carrollton & Vaiden	637
Chickasaw	16,805	Houston & Okolona	506
Choctaw	8,440	Ackerman	417
Claiborne	10,086	Port Gibson	489
Clarke	15,049	Quitman	697
Clay	18,840	West Point	414
Coahoma	40,447	Clarksdale	569
Copiah	24,764	Hazlehurst	780
Covington	14,002	Collins	416
De Soto	35,885	Hernando	476
Forrest	57,849	Hattiesburg	468
Franklin	8,011	Meadville	568
George	12,459	Lucedale	481
Greene	8,545	Leakesville	728
Grenada	19,854	Grenada	431
Hancock	17,387	Bay Saint Louis	482
Harrison	134,582	Gulfport	585
Hinds	214,973	Jackson & Raymond	876
Holmes	23,120	Lexington	769
Humphreys	14,601	Belzoni	421
Issaquena	2,737	Mayersville	414
Itawamba	16,847	Fulton	541
Jackson	87,975	Pascagoula	736
Jasper	15,994	Bay Springs & Paulding	683
Jefferson	9,295	Fayette	521
Jefferson Davis	12,936	Prentiss	414
Jones	56,357	Ellisville & Laurel	702
Kemper	10,233	De Kalb	757
Lafayette	24,181	Oxford	668
Lamar	15,209	Purvis	500
Lauderdale	67,087	Meridian	708
Lawrence	11,137	Monticello	433
Leake	17,075	Carthage	586
Lee	46,148	Tupelo	455
Leflore	42,111	Greenwood	592
Lincoln	26,198	Brookhaven	586
Lowndes	49,700	Columbus	508
Madison	29,737	Canton	727
Marion	22,871	Columbia	550
Marshall	24,027	Holly Springs	710
Monroe	34,043	Aberdeen	769
Montgomery	12,918	Winona	403
Neshoba	20,802	Philadelphia	568
Newton	18,983	Decatur	580
Noxubee	14,288	Macon	695
Oktibbeha	28,752	Starkville	454
Panola	26,829	Batesville & Sardis	693
Pearl River	27,802	Poplarville	828
Perry	9,065	New Augusta	653
Pike	31,813	Magnolia	409
Pontotoc	17,363	Pontotoc	501
Prentiss	20,133	Booneville	418
Quitman	15,888	Marks	412
Rankin	43,933	Brandon	775
Scott	21,369	Forest	615
Sharkey	9,937	Rolling Fork	436
Simpson	19,947	Mendenhall	587
Smith	13,561	Raleigh	642
Stone	8,101	Wiggins	448
Sunflower	37,047	Indianola	694
Tallahatchie	19,338	Charleston & Sumner	644
Tate	18,544	Senatobia	405
Tippah	15,852	Ripley	464
Tishomingo	14,940	Iuka	443
Tunica	11,854	Tunica	458
Union	19,096	New Albany	422
Walthall	12,500	Tylertown	403

County	Pop. Apr. 1 1970	County seat or court house	Land area sq. mi.
Warren	44,981	Vicksburg	581
Washington	70,581	Greenville	734
Wayne	16,650	Waynesboro	827
Webster	10,047	Walthall	416
Wilkinson	11,099	Woodville	674
Winston	18,406	Louisville	606
Yalobusha	11,915	Coffeeville & Water Valley	488
Yazoo	27,314	Yazoo City	938

Missouri

(114 cos., 1 ind. city, 68,995 sq. mi. land; pop., 4,677,399)

County	Pop. Apr. 1 1970	County seat or court house	Land area sq. mi.
Adair	22,472	Kirksville	572
Andrew	11,913	Savannah	436
Atchison	9,240	Rockport	549
Audrain	25,362	Mexico	692
Barry	19,597	Cassville	783
Barton	10,431	Lamar	594
Bates	15,468	Butler	841
Benton	9,695	Warsaw	735
Bollinger	8,820	Marble Hill	621
Boone	80,935	Columbia	685
Buchanan	86,915	Saint Joseph	404
Butler	33,529	Poplar Bluff	715
Caldwell	8,351	Kingston	430
Callaway	25,991	Fulton	835
Camden	13,315	Camdenton	640
Cape Girardeau	49,350	Jackson	574
Carroll	12,565	Carrollton	697
Carter	3,878	Van Buren	506
Cass	39,448	Harrisonville	698
Cedar	9,424	Stockton	496
Chariton	11,084	Keytesville	754
Christian	15,124	Ozark	567
Clark	8,260	Kahoka	506
Clay	123,702	Liberty	412
Clinton	12,462	Plattsburg	420
Cole	46,228	Jefferson City	384
Cooper	14,732	Boonville	566
Crawford	14,828	Steelville	760
Dade	6,850	Greenfield	504
Dallas	10,054	Buffalo	537
Daviess	8,420	Gallatin	563
De Kalb	7,305	Maysville	423
Dent	11,457	Salem	756
Douglas	9,268	Ava	809
Dunklin	33,742	Kennett	543
Franklin	55,127	Union	934
Gasconade	11,878	Hermann	519
Gentry	8,060	Albany	488
Greene	152,929	Springfield	677
Grundy	11,819	Trenton	435
Harrison	10,257	Bethany	720
Henry	18,451	Clinton	734
Hickory	4,481	Hermitage	377
Holt	6,654	Oregon	458
Howard	10,561	Fayette	472
Howell	23,521	West Plains	920
Iron	9,529	Ironton	554
Jackson	654,178	Independence	603
Jasper	79,852	Carthage	642
Jefferson	105,248	Hillsboro	668
Johnson	34,172	Warrensburg	826
Knox	5,692	Edina	512
Laclede	19,944	Lebanon	770
Lafayette	26,626	Lexington	632
Lawrence	24,585	Mount Vernon	619
Lewis	10,993	Monticello	508
Lincoln	18,041	Troy	625
Linn	15,125	Linneus	622
Livingston	15,368	Chillicothe	530
McDonald	12,357	Pineville	540
Macon	15,432	Macon	798
Madison	8,641	Fredericktown	496
Maries	6,851	Vienna	525
Marion	28,121	Palmyra	438
Mercer	4,910	Princeton	455
Miller	15,026	Tuscumbia	600
Mississippi	16,647	Charleston	415
Moniteau	10,742	California	419
Monroe	9,542	Paris	669
Montgomery	11,000	Montgomery City	534
Morgan	10,083	Versailles	592
New Madrid	23,420	New Madrid	679
Newton	32,981	Neosho	629
Nodaway	22,467	Maryville	877
Oregon	9,180	Alton	784
Osage	10,994	Linn	608
Ozark	6,226	Gainesville	732
Pemiscot	26,373	Caruthersville	493
Perry	14,393	Perryville	471
Pettis	34,137	Sedalia	679
Phelps	29,567	Rolla	677
Pike	16,928	Bowling Green	681
Platte	32,081	Platte City	427
Polk	15,415	Bolivar	63
Pulaski	53,967	Waynesville	55
Putnam	5,916	Unionville	51
Ralls	7,764	New London	47
Randolph	22,434	Huntsville	47
Ray	17,599	Richmond	57
Reynolds	6,106	Centerville	81
Ripley	9,803	Doniphan	63
St. Charles	92,954	St. Charles	55
St. Clair	7,667	Osceola	69
St. Francois	36,875	Farmington	45
St. Louis	951,671	Clayton	49
Ste. Genevieve	12,867	Ste. Genevieve	49
Saline	24,837	Marshall	75
Schuyler	4,665	Lancaster	30
Scotland	5,499	Memphis	44
Scott	33,250	Benton	42
Shannon	7,196	Eminence	99
Shelby	7,906	Shelbyville	50
Stoddard	25,771	Bloomfield	82
Stone	9,921	Galena	44
Sullivan	7,572	Milan	65
Taney	13,023	Forsyth	61
Texas	18,320	Houston	1,18
Vernon	19,065	Nevada	83
Warren	9,699	Warrenton	4
Washington	15,086	Potosi	7
Wayne	8,546	Greenville	76
Webster	15,562	Marshfield	59
Worth	3,359	Grant City	26
Wright	13,667	Hartville	68
Independent City			
St. Louis	623,236		6

Montana

(57 counties, 145,587 sq. mi. land; pop., 694,409)

County	Pop. Apr. 1 1970	County seat or court house	Land area sq. mi.
Beaverhead	8,187	Dillon	5,5
Big Horn 1976	10,618	Hardin	5,0
Blaine	6,727	Chinook	4,2
Broadwater	2,526	Townsend	1,1
Carbon	7,080	Red Lodge	2,0
Carter	1,956	Ekalaka	3,3
Cascade	81,804	Great Falls	2,6
Chouteau	6,473	Fort Benton	3,9
Custer 1976	12,979	Miles City	3,7
Daniels	3,083	Scobey	1,4
Dawson	11,269	Glendive	2,3
Deer Lodge	15,652	Anaconda	74
Fallon	4,050	Baker	1,6
Fergus	12,611	Lewistown	4,2
Flathead	39,460	Kalispell	5,1
Gallatin	32,505	Bozeman	2,5
Garfield	1,796	Jordan	4,4
Glacier	10,783	Cut Bank	2,9
Golden Valley	931	Ryegate	1,1
Granite	2,737	Philipsburg	1,7
Hill	17,358	Havre	2,9
Jefferson	5,238	Boulder	1,6
Judith Basin	2,667	Stanford	1,8
Lake	14,445	Polson	1,4
Lewis & Clark	33,281	Helena	3,4
Liberty	2,359	Chester	1,4
Lincoln	18,063	Libby	3,7
McCone	2,875	Circle	2,6
Madison	5,014	Virginia City	3,5
Meagher	2,122	White Sulphur Springs	2,3
Mineral	2,958	Superior	1,2
Missoula	58,263	Missoula	2,6
Musselshell	3,734	Roundup	1,8
Park	11,197	Livingston	2,6
Petroleum	675	Winnett	1,6
Phillips	5,386	Malta	5,2
Pondera	6,611	Conrad	1,6
Powder River	2,862	Broadus	3,2
Powell	6,660	Deer Lodge	2,3
Prairie	1,752	Terry	1,7
Ravalli	14,409	Hamilton	2,3
Richland	9,837	Sidney	2,0
Roosevelt	10,365	Wolf Point	2,3
Rosebud, 1976	9,578	Forsyth	5,0
Sanders	7,093	Thompson Falls	2,7
Sheridan	5,779	Plentywood	1,6
Silver Bow	41,981	Butte	7
Stillwater	4,632	Columbus	1,7
Sweet Grass	2,980	Big Timber	1,8
Teton	6,116	Choteau	2,2
Toole	5,839	Shelby	1,9
Treasure	1,069	Hysham	9
Valley	11,471	Glasgow	4,9
Wheatland	2,529	Harlowton	1,4
Wibaux	1,465	Wibaux	8
Yellowstone	87,367	Billings	2,6
Yellowstone Nat. Park	64		2

Nebraska

(93 counties, 76,483 sq. mi. land; pop., 1,483,791)

County	Pop. Apr. 1 1970	County seat or court house	Land area sq. mi.
Adams	30,553	Hastings	562
Antelope	9,047	Neligh	853
Arthur	606	Arthur	704
Banner	1,034	Harrisburg	738
Blaine	847	Brewster	710
Boone	8,190	Albion	683
Box Butte	10,094	Alliance	1,065
Boyd	3,752	Butte	538
Brown	4,021	Ainsworth	1,216
Buffalo	31,222	Kearney	949
Burt	9,247	Tekamah	483
Butler	9,461	David City	582
Cass	18,076	Plattsmouth	555
Cedar	12,192	Hartington	742
Chase	4,129	Imperial	890
Cherry	6,846	Valentine	5,966
Cheyenne	10,778	Sidney	1,186
Clay	8,266	Clay Center	570
Colfax	9,498	Schuyler	406
Cuming	12,034	West Point	571
Custer	14,092	Broken Bow	2,558
Dakota 1976	15,683	Dakota City	255
Dawes	9,761	Chadron	1,386
Dawson	19,771	Lexington	975
Deuel	2,717	Chappell	436
Dixon	7,453	Ponca	475
Dodge	34,782	Fremont	528
Douglas	389,455	Omaha	335
Dundy	2,926	Benkelman	921
Fillmore	8,137	Geneva	577
Franklin	4,566	Franklin	578
Frontier	3,982	Stockville	962
Furnas	6,897	Beaver City	722
Gage	25,731	Beatrice	858
Garden	2,929	Oshkosh	1,678
Garfield	2,411	Burwell	569
Gosper	2,178	Elwood	464
Grant	1,019	Hyannis	764
Greeley	4,000	Greeley	570
Hall	42,851	Grand Island	537
Hamilton	8,867	Aurora	537
Harlan	4,357	Alma	556
Hayes	1,530	Hayes Center	711
Hitchcock	4,051	Trenton	712
Holt	12,933	O'Neil	2,405
Hooker	939	Mullen	722
Howard	6,807	Saint Paul	564
Jefferson	10,436	Fairbury	577
Johnson	5,743	Tecumseh	377
Kearney	6,707	Minden	512
Keith	8,487	Ogallala	1,032
Keya Paha	1,340	Springview	768
Kimball	6,009	Kimball	953
Knox	11,723	Center	1,107
Lancaster	167,972	Lincoln	845
Lincoln	29,538	North Platte	2,522
Logan	991	Stapleton	570
Loup	854	Taylor	574
McPherson	623	Tryon	856
Madison	27,402	Madison	572
Merrick	8,751	Central City	480
Morrill	5,813	Bridgeport	1,402
Nance	5,142	Fullerton	439
Nemaha	8,976	Auburn	400
Nuckolls	7,404	Nelson	579
Otoe	15,576	Nebraska City	619
Pawnee	4,473	Pawnee City	433
Perkins	3,423	Grant	885
Phelps	9,553	Holdrege	544
Pierce	8,493	Pierce	573
Platte	26,544	Columbus	667
Polk	6,468	Osceola	432
Red Willow	12,191	McCook	686
Richardson	12,277	Falls City	550
Rock	2,231	Bassett	1,009
Saline	12,809	Wilber	575
Sarpy 1974	73,479	Papillion	239
Saunders	17,108	Wahoo	759
Scotts Bluff	36,432	Gering	726
Seward	14,460	Seward	571
Sheridan	7,285	Rushville	2,462
Sherman	4,725	Loup City	567
Sioux	2,034	Harrison	2,063
Stanton	5,758	Stanton	431
Thayer	7,779	Hebron	577
Thomas	954	Thedford	716
Thurston	6,942	Pender	388
Valley	5,783	Ord	569
Washington	13,310	Blair	386
Wayne	10,400	Wayne	443
Webster	5,396	Red Cloud	575
Wheeler	1,051	Bartlett	576
York	13,685	York	577

Nevada

(16 cos., 1ind. city, 109,889 sq. mi. land; pop., 488,738)

County	Pop. Apr. 1 1970	County seat or court house	Land area sq. mi.
Churchill	10,513	Fallon	4,883
Clark	273,288	Las Vegas	7,874
Douglas	6,882	Minden	703
Elko	13,958	Elko	17,162
Esmeralda	629	Goldfield	3,570
Eureka	948	Eureka	4,182
Humboldt	6,375	Winnemucca	9,702
Lander	2,666	Austin	5,621
Lincoln	2,557	Pioche	10,649
Lyon	8,221	Yerington	2,030
Mineral	7,051	Hawthorne	3,765
Nye	5,599	Tonopah	18,064
Pershing	2,670	Lovelock	6,001
Storey	695	Virginia City	262
Washoe	121,068	Reno	6,366
White Pine	10,150	Ely	8,904
Independent City			
Carson City	15,468	Carson City	150

New Hampshire

(10 counties, 9,027 sq. mi. land; pop., 737,681)

County	Pop. Apr. 1 1970	County seat or court house	Land area sq. mi.
Belknap	32,367	Laconia	400
Carroll	18,548	Ossipee	938
Cheshire	52,364	Keene	715
Coos	34,291	Lancaster	1,820
Grafton	54,914	Woodsville	1,732
Hillsborough	223,941	Nashua	887
Merrimack	80,925	Concord	930
Rockingham	138,951	Exeter	691
Strafford	70,431	Dover	376
Sullivan	30,949	Newport	539

New Jersey

(21 counties, 7,521 sq. mi. land; pop. 7,168,164)

County	Pop. Apr. 1 1970	County seat or court house	Land area sq. mi.
Atlantic	175,043	Mays Landing	569
Bergen	897,148	Hackensack	234
Burlington	323,132	Mount Holly	819
Camden	456,291	Camden	221
Cape May	59,554	Cape May Court House	267
Cumberland	121,374	Bridgeton	500
Essex	932,526	Newark	130
Gloucester	172,681	Woodbury	329
Hudson	607,839	Jersey City	47
Hunterdon	69,718	Flemington	423
Mercer	304,116	Trenton	228
Middlesex	583,813	New Brunswick	312
Monmouth	461,849	Freehold	476
Morris	383,454	Morristown	468
Ocean	208,470	Toms River	642
Passaic	460,782	Paterson	192
Salem	60,346	Salem	365
Somerset	198,372	Somerville	307
Sussex	77,528	Newton	527
Union	543,116	Elizabeth	103
Warren	73,960	Belvidere	362

New Mexico

(32 counties, 121,412 sq. mi. land; pop., 1,016,000)

County	Pop. Apr. 1 1970	County seat or court house	Land area sq. mi.
Bernalillo	315,774	Albuquerque	1,169
Catron	2,198	Reserve	6,897
Chaves	43,335	Roswell	6,084
Colfax	12,170	Raton	3,764
Curry	39,517	Clovis	1,403
De Baca	2,547	Fort Sumner	2,356
Dona Ana	69,773	Las Cruces	3,804
Eddy	41,119	Carlsbad	4,167
Grant	22,030	Silver City	3,970
Guadalupe	4,969	Santa Rosa	2,998
Harding	1,348	Mosquero	2,134
Hidalgo	4,734	Lordsburg	3,447
Lea	49,554	Lovington	4,393
Lincoln	7,560	Carrizozo	4,858
Los Alamos	15,198	Los Alamos	108
Luna	11,706	Deming	2,957
McKinley	43,208	Gallup	5,454
Mora	4,673	Mora	1,940
Otero	41,097	Alamogordo	6,638
Quay	10,903	Tucumcari	2,875
Rio Arriba	25,170	Tierra Amarilla	5,843
Roosevelt	16,479	Portales	2,454
Sandoval	17,492	Bernalillo	3,714
San Juan	52,517	Aztec	5,500
San Miguel	21,951	Las Vegas	4,741
Santa Fe	54,774	Santa Fe	1,902
Sierra	7,189	Truth or Consequences	4,166
Socorro	9,763	Socorro	6,603
Taos	17,516	Taos	2,256

County	Pop. Apr. 1 1970	County seat or court house	Land area sq. mi.
Torrance	5,290	Estancia	3,346
Union	4,925	Clayton	3,816
Valencia	40,576	Los Lunas	5,656

New York

(62 counties, 47,831 sq. mi. land; pop., 18,241,266)

County	Pop. Apr. 1 1970	County seat or court house	Land area sq. mi.
Albany	286,742	Albany	526
Allegany	46,458	Belmon	1,047
Bronx	1,471,701	Bronx	41
Broome	221,815	Binghamton	714
Cattaraugus	81,666	Little Valley	1,318
Cayuga	77,439	Auburn	698
Chautauqua	147,305	Mayville	1,081
Chemung	101,537	Elmira	415
Chenango	46,368	Norwich	903
Clinton	72,934	Plattsburgh	1,059
Columbia	51,519	Hudson	645
Cortland	45,894	Cortland	502
Delaware	44,718	Delhi	1,443
Dutchess	222,295	Poughkeepsie	813
Erie	1,113,491	Buffalo	1,058
Essex	34,631	Elizabethtown	1,823
Franklin	43,931	Malone	1,674
Fulton	52,637	Johnstown	498
Genesee	58,722	Batavia	501
Greene	33,136	Catskill	653
Hamilton	4,714	Lake Pleasant	1,735
Herkimer	67,633	Herkimer	1,435
Jefferson	88,508	Watertown	1,294
Kings	2,602,012	Brooklyn	70
Lewis	23,644	Lowville	1,291
Livingston	54,041	Geneseo	638
Madison	62,864	Wampsville	661
Monroe	711,917	Rochester	675
Montgomery	55,883	Fonda	408
Nassau	1,428,838	Mineola	289
New York	1,539,233	New York	23
Niagara	235,720	Lockport	532
Oneida	273,037	Utica	1,223
Onondaga	472,835	Syracuse	794
Ontario	78,849	Canandaigua	651
Orange	221,657	Goshen	833
Orleans	37,305	Albion	396
Oswego	100,897	Oswego	964
Otsego	56,181	Cooperstown	1,013
Putnam, 1975	68,765	Carmel	231
Queens	1,987,174	Jamaica	108
Rensselaer	152,510	Troy	665
Richmond	295,443	Saint George	58
Rockland	229,903	New City	176
St. Lawrence	112,309	Canton	2,768
Saratoga	121,764	Ballston Spa	818
Schenectady	161,078	Schenectady	207
Schoharie	24,750	Schoharie	624
Schuyler	16,737	Watkins Glen	330
Seneca	35,083	Ovid & Waterloo	330
Steuben	99,546	Bath	1,410
Suffolk	1,127,030	Riverhead	929
Sullivan	52,580	Monticello	980
Tioga	46,513	Owego	524
Tompkins	77,064	Ithaca	482
Ulster	141,241	Kingston	1,141
Warren	49,402	Lake George	887
Washington	52,725	Hudson Falls	836
Wayne, 1975	82,194	Lyons	606
Westchester	894,406	White Plains	443
Wyoming	37,688	Warsaw	598
Yates	19,831	Penn Yan	343

North Carolina

(100 counties, 48,798 sq. mi. land; pop., 5,082,059)

County	Pop. Apr. 1 1970	County seat or court house	Land area sq. mi.
Alamance	96,362	Graham	428
Alexander	19,466	Taylorsville	259
Alleghany	8,134	Sparta	225
Anson	23,488	Wadesboro	533
Ashe	19,571	Jefferson	426
Avery	12,655	Newland	245
Beaufort	35,980	Washington	826
Bertie	20,528	Windsor	698
Bladen	26,477	Elizabethtown	883
Brunswick	24,223	Southport	856
Buncombe	145,056	Asheville	657
Burke	60,364	Morganton	511
Cabarrus	74,629	Concord	363
Caldwell	56,699	Lenoir	469
Camden	5,453	Camden	239
Carteret	31,603	Beaufort	536
Caswell	19,055	Yanceyville	428
Catawba	90,873	Newton	394
Chatham	29,554	Pittsboro	709
Cherokee	16,330	Murphy	452
Chowan	10,764	Edenton	173
Clay	5,180	Hayesville	209
Cleveland	72,556	Shelby	468
Columbus	46,937	Whiteville	945
Craven	62,554	New Bern	699
Cumberland	212,042	Fayetteville	654
Currituck	6,976	Currituck	246
Dare	6,995	Manteo	391
Davidson	95,627	Lexington	549
Davie	18,855	Mocksville	265
Duplin	38,015	Kenansville	815
Durham	132,681	Durham	295
Edgecombe	52,341	Tarboro	510
Forsyth	215,118	Winston-Salem	419
Franklin	26,820	Louisburg	491
Gaston	148,415	Gastonia	356
Gates	8,524	Gatesville	337
Graham	6,562	Robbinsville	292
Granville	32,762	Oxford	537
Greene	14,967	Snow Hill	267
Guilford	288,645	Greensboro	655
Halifax	53,884	Halifax	734
Harnett	49,667	Lillington	603
Haywood	41,710	Waynesville	551
Henderson	42,804	Hendersonville	378
Hertford	23,529	Winton	353
Hoke	16,436	Raeford	389
Hyde	5,571	Swanquarter	613
Iredell	72,197	Statesville	572
Jackson	21,593	Sylva	491
Johnston	61,737	Smithfield	797
Jones	9,779	Trenton	467
Lee	30,467	Sanford	256
Lenoir	55,204	Kinston	400
Lincoln	32,682	Lincolnton	297
McDowell	30,648	Marion	436
Macon	15,788	Franklin	513
Madison	16,003	Marshall	450
Martin	24,730	Williamston	455
Mecklenburg	354,656	Charlotte	530
Mitchell	13,447	Bakersville	215
Montgomery	19,267	Troy	488
Moore	39,048	Carthage	704
Nash	59,122	Nashville	544
New Hanover	82,996	Wilmington	185
Northampton	24,009	Jackson	536
Onslow	103,126	Jacksonville	765
Orange	57,707	Hillsboro	400
Pamlico	9,467	Bayboro	338
Pasquotank	26,824	Elizabeth City	228
Pender	18,149	Burgaw	871
Perquimans	8,351	Hertford	246
Person	25,914	Roxboro	401
Pitt	73,900	Greenville	655
Polk	11,735	Columbus	239
Randolph	76,358	Asheboro	798
Richmond	39,889	Rockingham	475
Robeson	84,842	Lumberton	949
Rockingham	72,402	Wentworth	569
Rowan	90,035	Salisbury	523
Rutherford	47,337	Rutherfordton	563
Sampson	44,954	Clinton	945
Scotland	26,929	Laurinburg	319
Stanly	42,822	Albemarle	398
Stokes	23,782	Danbury	457
Surry	51,415	Dobson	536
Swain	8,835	Bryson City	524
Transylvania	19,713	Brevard	382
Tyrrell	3,806	Columbia	390
Union	54,714	Monroe	639
Vance	32,691	Henderson	249
Wake	229,006	Raleigh	858
Warren	15,810	Warrenton	424
Washington	14,038	Plymouth	343
Watauga	23,404	Boone	317
Wayne	85,408	Goldsboro	557
Wilkes	49,524	Wilkesboro	757
Wilson	57,486	Wilson	375
Yadkin	24,599	Yadkinville	336
Yancey	12,629	Burnsville	312

North Dakota

(53 counties, 69,273 sq. mi. land; pop., 617,761)

County	Pop. Apr. 1 1970	County seat or court house	Land area sq. mi.
Adams	3,832	Hettinger	989
Barnes	14,669	Valley City	1,479
Benson	8,245	Minnewaukan	1,403
Billings	1,198	Medora	1,139
Bottineau	9,496	Bottineau	1,677
Bowman	3,901	Bowman	1,170
Burke	4,739	Bowbells	1,119
Burleigh, 1975	46,079	Bismarck	1,625
Cass	73,653	Fargo	1,749
Cavalier 1973	10,977	Langdon	1,512
Dickey	6,976	Ellendale	1,143
Divide	4,564	Crosby	1,300

County	Pop. Apr. 1 1970	County seat or court house	Land area sq. mi.
Dunn	4,895	Manning	1,992
Eddy	4,103	New Rockford	635
Emmons	7,200	Linton	1,503
Foster	4,832	Carrington	645
Golden Valley	2,611	Beach	1,014
Grand Forks	61,102	Grand Forks	1,438
Grant	5,009	Carson	1,666
Griggs	4,184	Cooperstown	710
Hettinger	5,075	Mott	1,134
Kidder	4,362	Steele	1,358
La Moure	7,117	La Moure	1,136
Logan	4,245	Napoleon	1,001
McHenry	8,977	Towner	1,879
McIntosh	5,545	Ashley	992
McKenzie	6,127	Watford City	2,735
McLean	11,251	Washburn	2,065
Mercer	6,175	Stanton	1,042
Morton	20,310	Mandan	1,920
Mountrail	8,437	Stanley	1,819
Nelson	5,807	Lakota	995
Oliver	2,322	Center	721
Pembina	10,728	Cavalier	1,124
Pierce	6,323	Rugby	1,038
Ramsey	12,915	Devils Lake	1,248
Ransom	7,102	Lisbon	861
Renville	3,828	Mohall	886
Richland	18,089	Wahpeton	1,449
Rolette	11,549	Rolla	913
Sargent	5,937	Forman	853
Sheridan	3,232	McClusky	989
Sioux	3,632	Fort Yates	1,103
Slope	1,484	Amidon	1,225
Stark	19,613	Dickinson	1,316
Steele	3,749	Finley	710
Stutsman	23,550	Jamestown	2,264
Towner	4,645	Cando	1,043
Traill	9,571	Hillsboro	861
Walsh	16,251	Grafton	1,286
Ward	58,560	Minot	2,044
Wells	7,847	Fessenden	1,299
Williams	19,301	Williston	2,064

Ohio

(88 counties, 40,975 sq. mi. land; pop., 10,652,017)

County	Pop. Apr. 1 1970	County seat or court house	Land area sq. mi.
Adams	18,957	West Union	587
Allen	111,144	Lima	410
Ashland	43,303	Ashland	424
Ashtabula	98,237	Jefferson	700
Athens	55,747	Athens	504
Auglaize	38,602	Wapakoneta	400
Belmont	80,917	Saint Clairsville	534
Brown	26,635	Georgetown	490
Butler	226,207	Hamilton	471
Carroll	21,579	Carrollton	390
Champaign	30,491	Urbana	432
Clark	157,115	Springfield	402
Clermont	95,887	Batavia	458
Clinton	31,464	Wilmington	410
Columbiana	108,310	Lisbon	534
Coshocton	33,486	Coshocton	562
Crawford	50,364	Bucyrus	404
Cuyahoga	1,720,835	Cleveland	456
Darke	49,141	Greenville	605
Defiance	36,949	Defiance	412
Delaware	42,908	Delaware	450
Erie	75,909	Sandusky	264
Fairfield	73,301	Lancaster	505
Fayette	25,461	Washington C. H.	404
Franklin	833,249	Columbus	538
Fulton	33,071	Wauseon	407
Gallia	25,239	Gallipolis	471
Geauga	62,977	Chardon	407
Greene	125,057	Xenia	415
Guernsey	37,665	Cambridge	528
Hamilton	923,205	Cincinnati	414
Hancock	61,217	Findlay	532
Hardin	30,813	Kenton	467
Harrison	17,013	Cadiz	401
Henry	27,058	Napoleon	416
Highland	28,996	Hillsboro	549
Hocking	20,322	Logan	421
Holmes	23,024	Millersburg	424
Huron	49,587	Norwalk	497
Jackson	27,174	Jackson	419
Jefferson	96,193	Steubenville	411
Knox	41,795	Mount Vernon	531
Lake	197,200	Painesville	231
Lawrence	56,868	Ironton	456
Licking	107,799	Newark	686
Logan	35,072	Bellefontaine	460
Lorain	256,843	Elyria	495
Lucas	483,594	Toledo	343
Madison	28,318	London	463
Mahoning	304,545	Youngstown	415
Marion	64,724	Marion	405
Medina	82,717	Medina	425
Meigs	19,799	Pomeroy	436
Mercer	35,558	Celina	444
Miami	84,342	Troy	407
Monroe	15,739	Woodsfield	456
Montgomery	608,413	Dayton	459
Morgan	12,375	McConnelsville	420
Morrow	21,348	Mount Gilead	403
Muskingum	77,826	Zanesville	651
Noble	10,428	Caldwell	398
Ottawa	37,099	Port Clinton	261
Paulding	19,329	Paulding	417
Perry	27,434	New Lexington	410
Pickaway	40,071	Circleville	504
Pike	19,114	Waverly	443
Portage	125,868	Ravenna	495
Preble	34,719	Eaton	427
Putnam	31,134	Ottawa	486
Richland	129,997	Mansfield	496
Ross	61,211	Chillicothe	687
Sandusky	60,983	Fremont	409
Scioto	76,951	Portsmouth	608
Seneca	60,696	Tiffin	551
Shelby	37,748	Sidney	408
Stark	372,210	Canton	576
Summit	553,371	Akron	408
Trumbull	232,579	Warren	608
Tuscarawas	77,211	New Philadelphia	569
Union	23,786	Marysville	434
Van Wert	29,194	Van Wert	409
Vinton	9,420	McArthur	411
Warren	85,505	Lebanon	408
Washington	57,160	Marietta	641
Wayne	87,123	Wooster	561
Williams	33,669	Bryan	421
Wood	89,722	Bowling Green	619
Wyandot	21,826	Upper Sandusky	406

Oklahoma

(77 counties, 68,782 sq. mi. land; pop., 2,559,253)

County	Pop. Apr. 1 1970	County seat or court house	Land area sq. mi.
Adair	15,141	Stillwell	570
Alfalfa	7,224	Cherokee	868
Atoka	10,972	Atoka	991
Beaver	6,282	Beaver	1,790
Beckham	15,754	Sayre	907
Blaine	11,794	Watonga	917
Bryan	25,552	Durant	889
Caddo	28,931	Anadarko	1,272
Canadian	32,245	El Reno	897
Carter	37,349	Ardmore	830
Cherokee	23,174	Tahlequah	756
Choctaw	15,141	Hugo	778
Cimarron	4,145	Boise City	1,843
Cleveland	81,839	Norman	527
Coal	5,525	Coalgate	526
Comanche	108,144	Lawton	1,084
Cotton	6,832	Walters	651
Craig	14,722	Vinita	764
Creek	45,532	Sapulpa	936
Custer	22,665	Arapaho	980
Delaware	17,767	Jay	707
Dewey	5,656	Taloga	1,018
Ellis	5,129	Arnett	1,242
Garfield	56,343	Enid	1,054
Garvin	24,874	Pauls Valley	814
Grady	29,354	Chickasha	1,096
Grant	7,117	Medford	1,007
Greer	7,979	Mangum	633
Harmon	5,136	Hollis	545
Harper	5,151	Buffalo	1,041
Haskell	9,578	Stigler	602
Hughes	13,228	Holdenville	807
Jackson	30,902	Altus	810
Jefferson	7,125	Waurika	780
Johnston	7,870	Tishomingo	638
Kay	48,791	Newkirk	950
Kingfisher	12,857	Kingfisher	904
Kiowa	12,532	Hobart	1,027
Latimer	8,601	Wilburton	737
Le Flore	32,137	Poteau	1,560
Lincoln	19,482	Chandler	973
Logan	19,645	Guthrie	751
Love	5,637	Marietta	513
McClain	14,157	Purcell	573
McCurtain	28,642	Idabel	1,800
McIntosh	12,472	Eufaula	608
Major	7,529	Fairview	963
Marshall	7,682	Madill	366
Mayes	23,302	Pryor	648
Murray	10,669	Sulphur	423
Muskogee	59,542	Muskogee	818
Noble	10,043	Perry	743
Nowata	9,773	Nowata	537
Okfuskee	10,683	Okemah	637
Oklahoma	527,717	Oklahoma City	700

County	Pop. Apr. 1 1970	County seat or court house	Land area sq. mi.
Okmulgee	35,358	Okmulgee	700
Osage	29,750	Pawhuska	2,272
Ottawa	29,800	Miami	464
Pawnee	11,338	Pawnee	61
Payne	50,654	Stillwater	694
Pittsburg	37,521	McAlester	1,241
Pontotoc	27,867	Ada	714
Pottawatomie	43,134	Shawnee	794
Pushmataha	9,385	Antlers	1,420
Roger Mills	4,452	Cheyenne	1,140
Rogers	28,425	Claremore	685
Seminole	25,144	Wewoka	630
Sequoyah	23,370	Sallisaw	696
Stephens	35,902	Duncan	891
Texas	16,352	Guymon	2,062
Tillman	12,901	Frederick	901
Tulsa	399,982	Tulsa	573
Wagoner	22,163	Wagoner	563
Washington	42,302	Bartlesville	424
Washita	12,141	Cordell	1,009
Woods	11,920	Alva	1,298
Woodward	15,537	Woodward	1,251

Oregon

(36 counties, 96,184 sq. mi. land; pop., 2,091,385)

County	Pop. Apr. 1 1970	County seat or court house	Land area sq. mi.
Baker	14,919	Baker	3,068
Benton	53,776	Corvallis	668
Clackamas	166,088	Oregon City	1,884
Clatsop	28,473	Astoria	805
Columbia	28,790	Saint Helens	639
Coos	56,515	Coquille	1,604
Crook	9,985	Prineville	2,975
Curry	13,006	Gold Beach	1,627
Deschutes	30,442	Bend	3,031
Douglas	71,743	Roseburg	5,063
Gilliam	2,342	Condon	1,208
Grant	6,996	Canyon City	4,530
Harney	7,215	Burns	10,166
Hood River	13,187	Hood River	523
Jackson	94,533	Medford	2,812
Jefferson	8,548	Madras	1,793
Josephine	35,746	Grants Pass	1,625
Klamath	50,021	Klamath Falls	5,970
Lake	6,343	Lakeview	8,231
Lane	215,401	Eugene	4,552
Lincoln	25,755	Newport	986
Linn	71,914	Albany	2,283
Malheur	23,169	Vale	9,859
Marion	151,309	Salem	1,166
Morrow	4,465	Heppner	2,060
Multnomah	554,668	Portland	423
Polk	35,349	Dallas	736
Sherman	2,139	Moro	830
Tillamook	18,034	Tillamook	1,115
Umatilla	44,923	Pendleton	3,227
Union	19,377	La Grande	2,032
Wallowa	6,247	Enterprise	3,178
Wasco	20,133	The Dalles	2,381
Washington	157,920	Hillsboro	716
Wheeler	1,849	Fossil	1,707
Yamhill	40,213	McMinnville	711

Pennsylvania

(67 counties, 44,966 sq. mi. land; pop., 11,793,909)

County	Pop. Apr. 1 1970	County seat or court house	Land area sq. mi.
Adams	56,937	Gettysburg	526
Allegheny	1,605,133	Pittsburgh	728
Armstrong	75,590	Kittanning	652
Beaver	208,418	Beaver	440
Bedford (1973)	43,278	Bedford	1,018
Berks	296,382	Reading	862
Blair	135,356	Hollidaysburg	530
Bradford	57,962	Towanda	1,148
Bucks	416,728	Doylestown	614
Butler	127,941	Butler	794
Cambria	186,785	Ebensburg	692
Cameron	7,096	Emporium	401
Carbon	50,573	Jim Thorpe	404
Centre	99,267	Bellefonte	1,115
Chester	277,746	West Chester	761
Clarion	38,414	Clarion	597
Clearfield	74,619	Clearfield	1,139
Clinton	37,721	Lock Haven	899
Columbia	55,114	Bloomsburg	484
Crawford	81,342	Meadville	1,012
Cumberland	158,177	Carlisle	555
Dauphin	223,713	Harrisburg	518
Delaware	601,715	Media	184
Elk	37,770	Ridgeway	807
Erie	263,654	Erie	813
Fayette	154,667	Uniontown	802
Forest	4,926	Tionesta	419
Franklin	100,833	Chambersburg	754
Fulton	10,776	McConnellsburg	435
Greene	36,090	Waynesburg	578
Huntingdon	39,108	Huntingdon	895
Indiana	79,451	Indiana	825
Jefferson	43,695	Brookville	652
Juniata	16,712	Mifflintown	386
Lackawanna	234,107	Scranton	454
Lancaster	320,079	Lancaster	946
Lawrence	107,374	New Castle	367
Lebanon	99,665	Lebanon	363
Lehigh	255,304	Allentown	348
Luzerne	342,329	Wilkes-Barre	886
Lycoming	113,296	Williamsport	1,216
McKean	51,915	Smethport	992
Mercer	127,225	Mercer	670
Mifflin	45,268	Lewistown	431
Monroe	45,422	Stroudsburg	611
Montgomery	623,956	Norristown	496
Montour	16,508	Danville	130
Northampton	214,545	Easton	376
Northumberland	99,190	Sunbury	453
Perry	28,615	New Bloomfield	551
Philadelphia	1,949,996	Philadelphia	129
Pike	11,818	Milford	542
Potter	16,395	Coudersport	1,092
Schuylkill	160,089	Pottsville	784
Snyder	29,269	Middleburg	327
Somerset	76,037	Somerset	1,078
Sullivan	5,961	Laporte	478
Susquehanna	34,344	Montrose	833
Tioga	39,691	Wellsboro	1,146
Union	28,603	Lewisburg	318
Venango	62,353	Franklin	678
Warren	47,682	Warren	905
Washington	210,876	Washington	857
Wayne	29,581	Honesdale	741
Westmoreland	376,935	Greensburg	1,024
Wyoming	19,082	Tunkhannock	398
York	272,603	York	909

Rhode Island

(5 counties, 1,049 sq. mi. land; pop., 949,723)

County	Pop. Apr. 1 1970	County seat or court house	Land area sq. mi.
Bristol	45,937	Bristol	25
Kent	142,382	East Greenwich	173
Newport	94,228	Newport	115
Providence	581,470	Providence	416
Washington	85,706	West Kingston	321

South Carolina

(46 counties, 30,225 sq. mi. land; pop., 2,590,516)

County	Pop. Apr. 1 1970	County seat or court house	Land area sq. mi.
Abbeville	21,112	Abbeville	506
Aiken	91,023	Aiken	1,087
Allendale	9,783	Allendale	418
Anderson	105,474	Anderson	749
Bamberg	15,950	Bamberg	395
Barnwell	17,176	Barnwell	553
Beaufort	51,136	Beaufort	579
Berkeley	56,199	Moncks Corner	1,110
Calhoun	10,780	Saint Matthews	377
Charleston	247,650	Charleston	939
Cherokee	36,791	Gaffney	394
Chester	29,811	Chester	584
Chesterfield	33,667	Chesterfield	790
Clarendon	25,604	Manning	599
Colleton	27,622	Walterboro	1,049
Darlington	53,442	Darlington	543
Dillon	28,838	Dillon	407
Dorchester	32,276	Saint George	569
Edgefield	15,692	Edgefield	482
Fairfield	19,999	Winnsboro	696
Florence	89,636	Florence	805
Georgetown	33,500	Georgetown	812
Greenville	240,774	Greenville	792
Greenwood	49,686	Greenwood	446
Hampton	15,878	Hampton	562
Horry	69,992	Conway	1,154
Jasper	11,885	Ridgeland	652
Kershaw	34,727	Camden	781
Lancaster	43,328	Lancaster	502
Laurens	49,713	Laurens	711
Lee	18,323	Bishopville	409
Lexington	89,012	Lexington	717
McCormick	7,955	McCormick	360
Marion	30,270	Marion	487
Marlboro	27,151	Bennettsville	483
Newberry	29,273	Newberry	635
Oconee	40,728	Walhalla	654
Orangeburg	69,789	Orangeburg	1,106
Pickens	58,956	Pickens	492
Richland	233,868	Columbia	748
Saluda	14,528	Saluda	458
Spartanburg	173,724	Spartanburg	831
Sumter	79,425	Sumter	672
Union	29,230	Union	514

County	Pop. Apr. 1 1970	County seat or court house	Land area sq. mi.
Williamsburg	34,243	Kingstree	935
York	85,216	York	684

South Dakota

(67 counties, 75,955 sq. mi. land; pop., 666,257)

County	Pop. Apr. 1 1970	County seat or court house	Land area sq. mi.
Aurora	4,183	Plankinton	709
Beadle	20,877	Huron	1,259
Bennett	3,088	Martin	1,181
Bon Homme	8,577	Tyndall	560
Brookings	22,158	Brookings	800
Brown	36,920	Aberdeen	1,674
Brule	5,870	Chamberlain	818
Buffalo	1,739	Gannvalley	482
Butte	7,825	Belle Fourche	2,250
Campbell	2,866	Mound City	732
Charles Mix	9,994	Lake Andes	1,097
Clark	5,515	Clark	964
Clay	12,923	Vermillion	405
Codington	19,140	Watertown	687
Corson	4,994	McIntosh	2,470
Custer	4,698	Custer	1,557
Davison	17,319	Mitchell	432
Day	8,713	Webster	1,030
Deuel	5,686	Clear Lake	639
Dewey	5,170	Timber Lake	2,351
Douglas	4,569	Armour	435
Edmunds	5,548	Ipswich	1,154
Fall River	7,505	Hot Springs	1,743
Faulk	3,893	Faulkton	996
Grant	9,005	Milbank	681
Gregory	6,710	Burke	997
Haakon	2,802	Philip	1,816
Hamlin	5,520	Hayti	511
Hand	5,883	Miller	1,432
Hanson	3,781	Alexandria	430
Harding	1,855	Buffalo	2,682
Hughes	11,632	Pierre	748
Hutchinson	10,379	Olivet	815
Hyde	2,515	Highmore	863
Jackson	1,531	Kadoka	808
Jerauld	3,310	Wessington Spgs.	527
Jones	1,882	Murdo	973
Kingsbury	7,657	De Smet	818
Lake	11,456	Madison	567
Lawrence	17,453	Deadwood	800
Lincoln	11,761	Canton	576
Lyman	4,060	Kennebec	1,683
McCook	7,246	Salem	575
McPherson	5,022	Leola	1,147
Marshall	5,965	Britton	848
Meade	17,020	Sturgis	3,465
Mellette	2,420	White River	1,306
Miner	4,454	Howard	570
Minnehaha	95,209	Sioux Falls	813
Moody	7,622	Flandreau	523
Pennington	59,349	Rapid City	2,779
Perkins	4,769	Bison	2,860
Potter	4,449	Gettysburg	869
Roberts	11,678	Sisseton	1,108
Sanborn	3,697	Woonsocket	570
Shannon	8,198	(Attached to Fall River)	2,100
Spink	10,595	Redfield	1,505
Stanley	2,457	Fort Pierce	1,414
Sully	2,362	Onida	1,004
Todd	6,606	(Attached to Tripp)	1,388
Tripp	8,171	Winner	1,620
Turner	9,872	Parker	612
Union	9,643	Elk Point	452
Walworth	7,842	Selby	718
Washabaugh	1,389	(Attached to Jackson)	1,061
Yankton	19,039	Yankton	519
Zeibach	2,221	Dupree	1,981

Tennessee

(95 counties, 41,328 sq. mi. land; pop., 3,924,164)

County	Pop. Apr. 1 1970	County seat or court house	Land area sq. mi.
Anderson	60,300	Clinton	335
Bedford	25,039	Shelbyville	482
Benton	12,126	Camden	392
Bledsoe	7,643	Pikeville	404
Blount	63,744	Maryville	575
Bradley	50,686	Cleveland	334
Campbell	26,045	Jacksboro	451
Cannon	8,467	Woodbury	271
Carroll	25,741	Huntingdon	596
Carter	42,259	Elizabethton	348
Cheatham	13,199	Ashland City	305
Chester	9,927	Henderson	285
Claiborne	19,420	Tazewell	444
Clay	6,624	Celina	233
Cocke	25,283	Newport	424
Coffee	32,572	Manchester	434
Crockett	14,402	Alamo	269
Cumberland	20,733	Crossville	678
Davidson	447,877	Nashville	508
Decatur	9,457	Decaturville	337
De Kalb	11,151	Smithville	278
Dickson	21,977	Charlotte	485
Dyer	30,427	Dyersburg	529
Fayette	22,692	Somerville	704
Fentress	12,593	Jamestown	498
Franklin	27,289	Winchester	553
Gibson	47,871	Trenton	607
Giles	22,138	Pulaski	619
Grainger	13,948	Rutledge	282
Greene	47,630	Greeneville	613
Grundy	10,631	Altamont	358
Hamblen	38,696	Morristown	155
Hamilton	255,077	Chattanooga	550
Hancock	6,719	Sneedville	230
Hardeman	22,435	Bolivar	656
Hardin	18,212	Savannah	587
Hawkins	33,757	Rogersville	480
Haywood	19,596	Brownsville	519
Henderson	17,360	Lexington	515
Henry	23,749	Paris	567
Hickman	12,096	Centerville	610
Houston	5,853	Erin	201
Humphreys	13,560	Waverly	530
Jackson	8,141	Gainesboro	323
Jefferson	24,940	Dandridge	274
Johnson	11,569	Mountain City	293
Knox	276,293	Knoxville	508
Lake	8,074	Tiptonville	167
Lauderdale	20,271	Ripley	477
Lawrence	29,097	Lawrenceburg	634
Lewis	6,761	Hohenwald	285
Lincoln	24,318	Fayetteville	580
Loudon	24,266	Loudon	237
McMinn	35,462	Athens	432
McNairy	18,369	Selmer	569
Macon	12,315	Lafayette	304
Madison	65,774	Jackson	560
Marion	20,577	Jasper	506
Marshall	17,319	Lewisburg	377
Maury	44,028	Columbia	614
Meigs	5,219	Decatur	191
Monroe	23,475	Madisonville	660
Montgomery	62,721	Clarksville	539
Moore	3,568	Lynchburg	124
Morgan	13,619	Wartburg	539
Obion	30,247	Union City	556
Overton	14,866	Livingston	441
Perry	5,238	Linden	411
Pickett	3,774	Byrdstown	158
Polk	11,669	Benton	434
Putnam	35,487	Cookeville	405
Rhea	17,202	Dayton	312
Roane	38,881	Kingston	350
Robertson	29,102	Springfield	476
Rutherford	59,428	Murfreesboro	612
Scott	14,762	Huntsville	544
Sequatchie	6,331	Dunlap	273
Sevier	28,241	Sevierville	597
Shelby	722,111	Memphis	755
Smith	12,509	Carthage	323
Stewart	7,319	Dover	470
Sullivan	127,329	Blountville	413
Sumner	56,266	Gallatin	534
Tipton	28,001	Covington	459
Trousdale	5,155	Hartsville	114
Unicoi	15,254	Erwin	185
Union	9,072	Maynardville	212
Van Buren	3,758	Spencer	254
Warren	26,972	McMinnville	439
Washington	73,924	Jonesboro	323
Wayne	12,365	Waynesboro	739
Weakley	28,827	Dresden	576
White	16,329	Sparta	382
Williamson	34,423	Franklin	593
Wilson	36,999	Lebanon	567

Texas

(254 counties, 262,134 sq. mi. land; pop., 11,196,730)

County	Pop. Apr. 1 1970	County seat or court house	Land area sq. mi.
Anderson	27,789	Palestine	1,072
Andrews	10,372	Andrews	1,504
Angelina	49,349	Lufkin	738
Aransas	8,902	Rockport	275
Archer	5,759	Archer City	913
Armstrong	1,895	Claude	907
Atascosa	18,696	Jourdanton	1,206
Austin	13,831	Bellville	663
Bailey	8,487	Muleshoe	835
Bandera	4,747	Bandera	763
Bastrop	17,297	Bastrop	890
Baylor	5,221	Seymour	845
Bee	22,737	Beeville	842

County	Pop. Apr. 1 1970	County seat or court house	Land area sq. mi.
Bell	124,483	Belton	1,047
Bexar	830,460	San Antonio	1,246
Blanco	3,567	Johnson City	719
Borden	888	Gail	907
Bosque	10,966	Meridian	990
Bowie	67,813	Boston	891
Brazoria	108,312	Angleton	1,423
Brazos	57,978	Bryan	586
Breaster	7,780	Alpine	6,204
Briscoe	2,794	Silverton	874
Brooks	8,005	Falfurrias	904
Brown	25,877	Brownwood	938
Burleson	9,999	Caldwell	670
Burnet	11,420	Burnet	996
Caldwell	21,178	Lockhart	544
Calhoun	17,831	Port Lavanca	527
Callahan	8,205	Baird	856
Cameron	140,368	Brownsville	896
Camp	8,005	Pittsburg	192
Carson	6,358	Panhandle	900
Cass	24,133	Linden	941
Castro	10,394	Dimmitt	880
Chambers	12,187	Anahuac	616
Cherokee	32,008	Rusk	1,049
Childress	6,605	Childress	699
Clay	8,079	Henrietta	1,102
Cochran	5,326	Morton	783
Coke	3,087	Robert Lee	911
Coleman	10,288	Coleman	1,280
Collin	66,920	McKinney	836
Collingsworth	4,755	Wellington	894
Colorado	17,638	Columbus	949
Comal	24,165	New Braunfels	567
Comanche	11,898	Comanche	944
Concho	2,937	Paint Rock	1,004
Cooke	23,471	Gainesville	985
Coryell	35,311	Gatesville	1,043
Cottle	3,204	Paducah	900
Crane	4,172	Crane	795
Crockett	3,885	Ozona	2,794
Crosby	9,085	Crosbyton	911
Culberson	3,429	Van Horn	3,851
Dallam	6,012	Dalhart	1,494
Dallas	1,327,695	Dallas	859
Dawson	16,604	Lamesa	902
Deaf Smith	18,999	Hereford	1,510
Delta	4,927	Cooper	276
Denton	75,633	Denton	911
Dewitt	18,660	Cuero	910
Dickens	3,737	Dickens	931
Dimmit	9,039	Carrizo Springs	1,344
Donley	3,641	Clarendon	905
Duval	11,722	San Diego	1,814
Eastland	18,092	Eastland	952
Ector	91,805	Odessa	907
Edwards	2,107	Rocksprings	2,076
Ellis	46,638	Waxahachie	940
El Paso	359,291	El Paso	1,057
Erath	18,141	Stephenville	1,085
Falls	17,300	Marlin	764
Fannin	22,705	Bonham	905
Fayette	17,650	La Grange	934
Fisher	6,344	Roby	904
Floyd	11,044	Floydada	993
Foard	2,211	Crowell	676
Fort Bend	52,314	Richmond	869
Franklin	5,291	Mount Vernon	293
Freestone	11,116	Fairfield	865
Frio 1976	12,702	Pearsall	1,116
Gaines	11,593	Seminole	1,489
Galveston	169,812	Galveston	399
Garza	5,289	Post	914
Gillespie	10,553	Fredericksburg	1,055
Glasscock	1,155	Garden City	863
Goliad	4,869	Goliad	871
Gonzales	16,375	Gonzales	1,056
Gray	26,949	Pampa	934
Grayson	83,225	Sherman	940
Gregg	75,929	Longview	282
Grimes	11,855	Anderson	801
Guadalupe	33,554	Seguin	714
Hale	34,137	Plainview	979
Hall	6,015	Memphis	885
Hamilton	7,198	Hamilton	844
Hansford	6,351	Spearman	907
Hardeman	6,795	Quanah	687
Hardin	29,996	Kountze	897
Harris	1,741,912	Houston	1,723
Harrison	44,841	Marshall	894
Hartley	2,782	Channing	1,488
Haskell	8,512	Haskell	877
Hays	27,642	San Marcos	650
Hemphill	3,084	Canadian	904
Henderson	26,466	Athens	943
Hidalgo	181,535	Edinburg	1,543
Hill	22,596	Hillsboro	1,010
Hockley	20,396	Levelland	908

County	Pop. Apr. 1 1970	County seat or court house	Land area sq. mi.
Hood	6,368	Granbury	426
Hopkins	20,710	Sulphur Springs	793
Houston	17,855	Crockett	1,237
Howard	37,796	Big Spring	911
Hudspeth	2,392	Sierra Blanca	4,554
Hunt	47,948	Greenville	826
Hutchinson	24,443	Stinnett	875
Irion	1,070	Mertzon	1,073
Jack	6,711	Jacksboro	945
Jackson	12,975	Edna	850
Jasper	24,692	Jasper	907
Jeff Davis	1,527	Fort Davis	2,259
Jefferson	246,402	Beaumont	951
Jim Hogg	4,654	Hebbronville	1,143
Jim Wells	33,032	Alice	845
Johnson	45,769	Cleburne	740
Jones	16,106	Anson	956
Karnes	13,462	Karnes City	758
Kaufman	32,392	Kaufman	815
Kendall	6,964	Boerne	670
Kenedy	678	Sarita	1,394
Kent	1,434	Jayton	880
Kerr	19,454	Kerrville	1,101
Kimble	3,904	Junction	1,274
King	464	Guthrie	944
Kinney	2,006	Brackettville	1,393
Kleberg	33,166	Kingsville	851
Knox	5,972	Benjamin	851
Lamar	36,062	Paris	984
Lamb	17,770	Littlefield	1,022
Lampasas	9,323	Lampasas	726
La Salle	5,014	Cotulla	1,500
Lavaca	17,903	Hallettsville	975
Lee	8,048	Giddings	637
Leon	8,738	Centerville	1,102
Liberty	33,014	Liberty	1,180
Limestone	18,100	Groesbeck	931
Lipscomb	3,486	Lipscomb	934
Live Oak	6,697	George West	1,055
Llano	6,979	Llano	941
Loving	164	Mentone	648
Lubbock	179,295	Lubbock	893
Lynn	9,107	Tahoka	915
McCulloch	8,571	Brady	1,066
McLennan	147,553	Waco	1,000
McMullen	1,095	Tilden	1,159
Madison	7,693	Madisonville	480
Marion	8,517	Jefferson	380
Martin	4,774	Stanton	911
Mason	3,356	Mason	935
Matagorda	27,913	Bay City	1,157
Maverick	18,093	Eagle Pass	1,289
Medina	20,249	Hondo	1,352
Menard	2,646	Menard	914
Midland	65,433	Midland	939
Milam	20,028	Cameron	1,028
Mills	4,212	Goldthwaite	734
Mitchell	9,073	Colorado City	920
Montague	15,326	Montague	932
Montgomery	49,479	Conroe	1,090
Moore	14,060	Dumas	909
Morris	12,310	Daingerfield	260
Motley	2,178	Matador	980
Nacogdoches	36,362	Nacogdoches	902
Navarro	31,150	Corsicana	1,070
Newton	11,657	Newton	949
Nolan	16,220	Sweetwater	922
Nueces	237,544	Corpus Christi	841
Ochiltree	9,704	Perryton	907
Oldham	2,258	Vega	1,478
Orange	71,170	Orange	359
Palo Pinto	28,962	Palo Pinto	948
Panola	15,894	Carthage	869
Parker	33,888	Weatherford	903
Parmer	10,509	Farwell	859
Pecos	13,748	Fort Stockton	4,740
Polk	14,457	Livingston	1,100
Potter	90,511	Amarillo	898
Presidio	4,842	Marfa	3,892
Rains	3,752	Emory	210
Randall	53,885	Canyon	914
Reagan	3,239	Big Lake	1,132
Real	2,013	Leakey	622
Red River	14,298	Clarksville	1,033
Reeves	16,526	Pecos	2,608
Refugio	9,494	Refugio	774
Roberts	967	Miami	899
Robertson	14,389	Franklin	877
Rockwall	7,046	Rockwall	147
Runnels	12,108	Ballinger	1,058
Rusk	34,102	Henderson	939
Sabine	7,187	Hemphill	456
San Augustine	7,858	San Augustine	473
San Jacinto	6,702	Coldspring	624
San Patricio	47,288	Sinton	685
San Saba	5,540	San Saba	1,120
Schleicher	2,277	Eldorado	1,331

County	Pop. Apr. 1 1970	County seat or court house	Land area sq. mi.
Scurry	15,760	Snyder	904
Shackelford	3,323	Albany	887
Shelby	19,672	Center	778
Sherman	3,657	Stratford	916
Smith	97,096	Tyler	934
Somervell	2,793	Glen Rose	197
Starr	17,707	Rio Grande City	1,211
Stephens	8,414	Breckenridge	899
Sterling	1,056	Sterling City	914
Stonewall	2,397	Aspermont	926
Sutton	3,175	Sonora	1,493
Swisher	10,373	Tulia	896
Tarrant	716,317	Fort Worth	861
Taylor	97,853	Abilene	912
Terrell	1,940	Sanderson	2,391
Terry	14,118	Brownfield	899
Throckmorton	2,205	Throckmorton	920
Titus	16,702	Mount Pleasant	418
Tom Green	71,047	San Angelo	1,500
Travis	295,516	Austin	1,012
Trinity	7,628	Groveton	707
Tyler	12,417	Woodville	919
Upshur	20,976	Gilmer	584
Upton	4,697	Rankin	1,312
Uvalde	17,348	Uvalde	1,588
Val Verde	27,471	Del Rio	3,241
Van Zandt	22,155	Canton	845
Victoria	53,766	Victoria	892
Walker	27,680	Huntsville	790
Waller	14,285	Hempstead	509
Ward	13,019	Monahans	827
Washington	18,842	Brenham	594
Webb	72,859	Laredo	3,306
Wharton	36,729	Wharton	1,076
Wheeler	6,434	Wheeler	914
Wichita	120,563	Wichita Falls	611
Wilbarger	15,355	Vernon	952
Willacy	15,570	Raymondville	591
Williamson	37,305	Georgetown	1,104
Wilson	13,041	Floresville	802
Winkler	9,640	Kermit	887
Wise	19,687	Decatur	922
Wood	18,589	Quitman	721
Yoakum	7,344	Plains	830
Young	15,400	Graham	888
Zapata	4,352	Zapata	957
Zavala	11,370	Crystal City	1,291

Utah

(29 counties, 82,096 sq. mi. land; pop. 1,059,273)

County	Pop. Apr. 1 1970	County seat or court house	Land area sq. mi.
Beaver	3,800	Beaver	2,584
Box Elder	28,129	Brigham City	5,603
Cache	42,331	Logan	1,174
Carbon	15,647	Price	1,476
Daggett	666	Manila	682
Davis	99,028	Farmington	297
Duchesne	7,299	Duchesne	3,255
Emery	5,137	Castle Dale	4,439
Garfield	3,157	Panguitch	5,158
Grand	6,688	Moab	3,682
Iron	12,177	Parowan	3,300
Juab	4,574	Nephi	3,412
Kane	2,421	Kanab	3,904
Millard	6,988	Fillmore	6,793
Morgan	3,983	Morgan	603
Piute	1,164	Junction	754
Rich	1,615	Randolph	1,023
Salt Lake	458,607	Salt Lake City	764
San Juan	9,606	Monticello	7,707
Sanpete	10,976	Manti	1,597
Sevier	10,103	Richfield	1,929
Summit	5,879	Coalville	1,849
Tooele	21,545	Tooele	6,923
Uintah	12,684	Vernal	4,487
Utah	137,776	Provo	2,014
Wasatch	5,863	Heber City	1,191
Washington	13,669	Saint George	2,427
Wayne	1,483	Loa	2,486
Weber	126,278	Ogden	581

Vermont

(14 counties, 9,267 sq. mi. land; pop. 444,732)

County	Pop. Apr. 1 1970	County seat or court house	Land area sq. mi.
Addison	24,266	Middlebury	784
Bennington	29,282	Bennington	672
Caledonia	22,789	Saint Johnsbury	612
Chittenden	99,131	Burlington	533
Essex	5,416	Guildhall	663
Franklin	31,282	Saint Albans	660
Grand Isle	3,574	North Hero	83
Lamoille	13,309	Hyde Park	474
Orange	17,676	Chelsea	690
Orleans	20,153	Newport	715
Rutland	52,637	Rutland	927
Washington	47,659	Montpelier	707
Windham	33,476	Newfane	784
Windsor	44,082	Woodstock	962

Virginia

(96 cos., 38 ind. cities, 39,780 sq. mi. land; pop, 4,648,494)

County	Pop. Apr. 1 1970	County seat or court house	Land area sq. mi.
Accomack	29,004	Accomac	476
Albemarle	37,780	Charlottesville	740
Alleghany	12,461	Covington	444
Amelia	7,592	Amelia, C. H.	366
Amherst	26,072	Amherst	470
Appomattox	9,784	Appomattox	345
Arlington	174,284	Arlington	26
Augusta	44,220	Staunton	986
Bath	5,192	Warm Springs	540
Bedford	26,728	Bedford	727
Bland	5,423	Bland	369
Botetourt	18,193	Fincastle	548
Brunswick	16,172	Lawrenceville	579
Buchanan	32,071	Grundy	508
Buckingham	10,597	Buckingham	582
Campbell	43,319	Rustburg	529
Caroline	13,925	Bowling Green	545
Carroll	23,092	Hillsville	494
Charles City	6,158	Charles City	181
Charlotte	12,366	Charlotte Courthouse	470
Chesterfield	77,045	Chesterfield	442
Clarke	8,102	Berryville	174
Craig	3,524	New Castle	336
Culpeper	18,218	Culpeper	389
Cumberland	6,179	Cumberland	291
Dickenson	16,077	Clintwood	332
Dinwiddie	25,046	Dinwiddie	507
Essex	7,099	Tappahannock	250
Fairfax	455,032	Fairfax	399
Fauquier	26,375	Warrenton	660
Floyd	9,775	Floyd	383
Fluvanna	7,621	Palmyra	288
Franklin	28,163	Rocky Mount	716
Frederick	28,893	Winchester	405
Giles	16,741	Pearisburg	363
Gloucester	14,059	Gloucester	228
Goochland 1976	11,221	Goochland	289
Grayson	15,439	Independence	452
Greene	5,248	Stanardsville	153
Greensville	9,604	Emporia	299
Halifax	30,076	Halifax	796
Hanover	37,479	Hanover	465
Henrico	154,364	Richmond	229
Henry	50,901	Martinsville	381
Highland	2,529	Monterey	416
Isle of Wight	18,285	Isle of Wight	317
James City	17,853	Williamsburg	152
King and Queen	5,491	King and Queen	318
King George	8,039	King George	176
King William	7,497	King William	278
Lancaster	9,126	Lancaster	137
Lee	20,321	Jonesville	438
Loudoun	37,150	Leesburg	517
Louisa	14,004	Louisa	517
Lunenburg	11,687	Lunenburg	442
Madison	8,638	Madison	327
Mathews	7,168	Mathews	89
Mecklenburg	29,426	Boydton	612
Middlesex	6,295	Saluda	130
Montgomery	47,157	Christiansburg	394
*Nansemond	35,166	Suffolk	408
Nelson	11,702	Lovingston	471
New Kent	5,300	New Kent	210
Northampton	14,442	Eastville	220
Northumberland	9,239	Heathsville	190
Nottoway	14,260	Nottoway	308
Orange	13,792	Orange	355
Page	16,581	Luray	316
Patrick	15,282	Stuart	464
Pittsylvania	58,789	Chatham	1,001
Powhatan	7,696	Powhatan	269
Prince Edward	14,379	Farmville	357
Prince George	29,092	Prince George	276
Prince William	111,102	Manassas	347
Pulaski	29,564	Pulaski	328
Rappahannock	5,199	Washington	267
Richmond	6,504	Warsaw	190
Roanoke	67,339	Salem	262
Rockbridge	16,637	Lexington	601
Rockingham	47,890	Harrisonburg	865
Russell	24,533	Lebanon	483
Scott	24,376	Gate City	539
Shenandoah	22,852	Woodstock	507
Smyth	31,349	Marion	435
Southampton	18,582	Courtland	602
Spotsylvania	16,424	Spotsylvania	409
Stafford	24,587	Stafford	270
Surry	5,882	Surry	277
Sussex	11,464	Sussex	494
Tazewell	39,816	Tazewell	522

County	Pop. Apr. 1 1970	County seat or court house	Land area sq. mi.
Warren	15,301	Front Royal	219
Washington	40,835	Abingdon	574
Westmoreland	12,142	Montross	229
Wise	35,947	Wise	412
Wythe	22,139	Wytheville	460
York	33,203	Yorktown	129

*1/1/74 merged with ind. city of Suffolk.

County	Pop. Apr. 1 1970	County seat or court house	Land area sq. mi.
Independent Cities			
Alexandria	110,927		15
Bedford	6,011		7
Bristol	14,857		4
Buena Vista	6,425		3
Charlottesville	38,880		10
Chesapeake	89,580		341
Clifton Forge	5,501		4
Colonial Heights	15,097		8
Covington	10,060		4
Danville	46,391		17
Emporia	5,300		2
Fairfax	21,970		6
Falls Church	10,772		2
Franklin	6,880		4
Fredericksburg	14,450		6
Galax	6,278		7
Hampton	120,779		55
Harrisonburg	14,605		6
Hopewell	23,471		9
Lexington	7,597		3
Lynchburg	54,083		25
Martinsville	19,653		11
Newport News	138,177		69
Norfolk	307,951		53
Norton	4,172		4
Petersburg	36,103		8
Portsmouth	110,963		29
Radford	11,596		5
Richmond	249,431		60
Roanoke	92,115		27
Salem	21,982		14
South Boston	6,889		5
Staunton	24,504		9
Suffolk	9,858		2
Virginia Beach	172,106		259
Waynesboro	16,707		7
Williamsburg	9,069		5
Winchester	14,643		3

Washington

(39 counties, 66,570 sq. mi. land; pop., 3,409,169)

County	Pop. Apr. 1 1970	County seat or court house	Land area sq. mi.
Adams	12,014	Ritzville	1,894
Asotin	13,799	Asotin	633
Benton	67,540	Prosser	1,722
Chelan	41,103	Wenatchee	2,918
Clallam	34,770	Port Angeles	1,753
Clark	128,454	Vancouver	627
Columbia	4,439	Dayton	853
Cowlitz	68,616	Kelso	1,144
Douglas	16,787	Waterville	1,831
Ferry	3,655	Republic	2,202
Franklin	25,816	Pasco	1,253
Garfield	2,911	Pomeroy	709
Grant	41,881	Ephrata	2,675
Grays Harbor	59,553	Montesano	1,910
Island	27,011	Coupeville	212
Jefferson	10,661	Port Townsend	1,805
King	1,159,375	Seattle	2,128
Kitsap	101,732	Port Orchard	393
Kittitas	25,039	Ellensburg	2,317
Klickitat	12,138	Goldendale	1,908
Lewis	45,467	Chehalis	2,423
Lincoln	9,572	Davenport	2,306
Mason	20,918	Shelton	962
Okanogan	25,867	Okanogan	5,301
Pacific	15,796	South Bend	908
Pend Oreille	6,025	Newport	1,402
Pierce	411,027	Tacoma	1,676
San Juan	3,856	Friday Harbor	179
Skagit	52,381	Mount Vernon	1,735
Skamania	5,845	Stevenson	1,672
Snohomish	265,236	Everett	2,098
Spokane	287,487	Spokane	1,758
Stevens	17,405	Colville	2,481
Thurston	76,894	Olympia	714
Wahkiakum	3,592	Cathlamet	261
Walla Walla	42,176	Walla Walla	1,262
Whatcom	81,950	Bellingham	2,126
Whitman	37,900	Colfax	2,153
Yakima	144,971	Yakima	4,268

West Virginia

(55 counties, 24,070 sq. mi. land; pop., 1,744,237)

County	Pop. Apr. 1 1970	County seat or court house	Land area sq. mi.
Barbour	14,030	Philippi	341
Berkeley	36,356	Martinsburg	316
Boone	2,118	Madison	501
Braxton	12,666	Sutton	511
Brooke	29,685	Wellsburg	88
Cabell	106,918	Huntington	279
Calhoun	7,046	Grantsville	281
Clay	9,330	Clay	343
Doddridge	6,389	West Union	319
Fayette	49,332	Fayetteville	663
Gilmer	7,782	Glenville	339
Grant	8,607	Petersburg	478
Greenbrier	32,090	Lewisburg	1,026
Hampshire	11,710	Romney	639
Hancock	39,749	New Cumberland	83
Hardy	8,855	Moorefield	585
Harrison	73,028	Clarksburg	418
Jackson	20,903	Ripley	461
Jefferson	21,280	Charles Town	211
Kanawha	229,515	Charleston	907
Lewis	17,847	Weston	392
Lincoln	18,912	Hamlin	438
Logan	46,269	Logan	456
McDowell	50,666	Welch	533
Marion	61,356	Fairmont	311
Marshall	37,598	Moundsville	304
Mason	24,306	Point Pleasant	433
Mercer	63,206	Princeton	417
Mineral	23,109	Keyser	330
Mingo	32,780	Williamson	423
Monongalia	63,714	Morgantown	365
Monroe	11,272	Union	473
Morgan	8,547	Berkeley Springs	233
Nicholas	22,552	Summersville	642
Ohio	64,197	Wheeling	106
Pendleton	7,031	Franklin	695
Pleasants	7,274	St. Marys	129
Pocahontas	8,870	Marlinton	943
Preston	25,455	Kingwood	645
Putnam	27,625	Winfield	348
Raleigh	70,080	Beckley	605
Randolph	24,596	Elkins	1,036
Ritchie	10,145	Harrisville	452
Roane	14,111	Spencer	486
Summers	13,213	Hinton	350
Taylor	13,878	Grafton	174
Tucker	7,447	Parsons	421
Tyler	9,929	Middlebourne	256
Upshur	19,092	Buckhannon	352
Wayne	37,581	Wayne	513
Webster	9,809	Webster Springs	551
Wetzel	20,314	New Martinsville	363
Wirt	4,154	Elizabeth	235
Wood	86,818	Parkersburg	368
Wyoming	30,095	Pineville	504

Wisconsin

(72 counties, 54,464 sq. mi. land, pop., 4,417,933)

County	Pop. Apr. 1 1970	County seat or court house	Land area sq. mi.
Adams	9,234	Friendship	646
Ashland	16,743	Ashland	1,038
Barron	33,955	Barron	864
Bayfield	11,683	Washburn	1,460
Brown	158,244	Green Bay	524
Buffalo	13,743	Alma	711
Burnett	9,276	Grantsburg	840
Calumet	27,604	Chilton	322
Chippewa	47,717	Chippewa Falls	1,018
Clark	30,361	Neillsville	1,221
Columbia	40,150	Portage	776
Crawford	15,252	Prairie du Chien	568
Dane	290,272	Madison	1,198
Dodge	69,004	Juneau	889
Door	20,106	Sturgeon Bay	492
Douglas	44,657	Superior	1,305
Dunn	29,154	Menomonie	853
Eau Claire, 1975	72,237	Eau Claire	647
Florence	3,298	Florence	487
Fond Du Lac	84,567	Fond du Lac	725
Forest (1973)	8,265	Crandon	1,007
Grant	48,398	Lancaster	1,147
Green	26,714	Monroe	585
Green Lake	16,878	Green Lake	354
Iowa	19,306	Dodgeville	762
Iron	6,533	Hurley	747
Jackson	15,325	Black River Falls	999
Jefferson	60,060	Jefferson	564
Juneau	18,455	Mauston	774
Kenosha	117,917	Kenosha	272
Kewaunee	18,961	Kewaunee	330
La Crosse	80,468	La Crosse	451
Lafayette	17,456	Darlington	643
Langlade	19,220	Antigo	856
Lincoln	23,499	Merrill	892
Manitowoc	82,294	Manitowoc	590
Marathon	97,457	Wausau	1,589
Marinette	35,810	Marinette	1,378

County	Pop. Apr. 1 1970	County seat or court house	Land area sq. mi.
Marquette	8,865	Montello	455
Menominee	2,607	Keshena	360
Milwaukee	1,054,249	Milwaukee	237
Monroe	31,610	Sparta	915
Oconto	25,553	Oconto	1,001
Oneida	24,427	Rhinelander	1,112
Outaramie	119,398	Appleton	634
Ozaukee	54,461	Port Washington	236
Pepin	7,319	Durand	235
Pierce	26,652	Ellsworth	590
Polk	26,666	Balsam Lake	931
Portage	47,541	Stevens Point	806
Pricė	14,520	Phillips	1,260
Racine	170,838	Racine	337
Richland	17,079	Richland Center	583
Rock	131,970	Janesville	721
Rusk	14,238	Ladysmith	906
St. Croix	34,354	Hudson	734
Sauk	39,057	Baraboo	841
Sawyer	9,670	Hayward	1,259
Shawano	32,650	Shawano	919
Sheboygan	96,660	Sheboygan	505
Taylor	16,958	Medford	975
Trempealeau	23,344	Whitehall	735
Vernon	24,557	Viroqua	802
Vilas	10,958	Eagle River	867
Walworth	63,444	Elkhorn	557
Washburn	10,601	Shell Lake	817
Washington	63,839	West Bend	429
Waukesha	231,338	Waukesha	554
Waupaca	37,780	Waupaca	751
Waushara	14,795	Wautoma	627
Winnebago	129,946	Oshkosh	448
Wood	65,362	Wisconsin Rapids	807

Wyoming

(23 counties, 97,203 sq. mi. land; pop., 332,416)

County	Pop. Apr. 1 1970	County seat or court house	Land area sq. mi.
Albany	26,431	Laramie	4,248
Big Horn	10,202	Basin	3,157
Campbell	12,957	Gillette	4,756
Carbon	13,354	Rawlins	7,905
Converse	5,938	Douglas	4,281
Crook	4,535	Sundance	2,882
Fremont	28,352	Lander	9,106
Goshen	10,885	Torrington	2,228
Hot Springs	4,952	Thermopolis	2,022
Johnson	5,587	Buffalo	4,175
Laramie	56,360	Cheyenne	2,703
Lincoln	8,640	Kemmerer	4,085
Natrona	51,264	Casper	5,342
Niobrara	2,924	Lusk	2,614
Park	17,752	Cody	6,959
Platte	6,486	Wheatland	2,086
Sheridan	17,852	Sheridan	2,532
Sublette	3,755	Pinedale	4,851
Sweetwater	18,391	Green River	10,429
Teton	4,823	Jackson	4,000
Uinta	7,100	Evanston	2,086
Washakie	7,569	Worland	2,262
Weston	6,307	Newcastle	2,407

1970 Population of Outlying Areas

Source: U.S. Bureau of the Census

Puerto Rico

ZIP code	Municipios	Pop. April 1	Land area sq. mile
00601	Adjuntas	18,691	66
00602	Aguada	25,658	30
00603	Aguadilla	51,355	36
00607	Aguas Buenas	18,600	30
00609	Aibonito	20,044	31
00610	Anasco	19,416	40
00612	Arecibo	73,468	127
00615	Arroyo	13,033	15
00617	Barceloneta	20,792	34
00618	Barranquitas	20,118	33
00619	Bayamon	156,192	44
00623	Cabo Rojo	26,060	72
00625	Caguas	95,661	58
00627	Camuy	19,922	46
00630	Carolina	107,643	48
00632	Catano	26,459	5
00633	Cayey	38,432	50
00635	Ceiba	18,312	27
00638	Ciales	15,595	66
00639	Cidra	23,892	36
00640	Coamo	26,468	77
00642	Comerio	18,819	28
00643	Corozal	24,545	42
00645	Culebra	732	10
00646	Dorado	17,388	23
00648	Fajardo	23,032	31
00653	Guanica	14,889	37
00654	Guayama	36,249	65
00656	Guayanilla	18,144	42
00657	Guaynabo	67,042	27
00658	Gurabo	18,289	28
00659	Hatillo	21,913	42
00660	Hormigueros	10,827	11
00661	Humacao	36,023	45
00662	Isabela	30,430	56
00664	Jayuya	13,588	39
00665	Juana Diaz	36,270	61
00666	Juncos	21,814	26
00667	Lajas	16,545	60
00669	Lares	25,263	62
00670	Las Marias	7,841	44
00671	Las Piedras	18,112	33
00672	Loiza	39,062	53
00673	Luquillo	10,390	26
00701	Manati	30,559	46
00706	Maricao	5,991	37
00707	Maunabo	10,792	21
00708	Mayaguez	85,857	77
00716	Moca	22,361	51
00717	Morovix	19,059	39
00718	Naguabo	17,996	52
00719	Naranjito	19,913	28
00720	Orocovis	20,201	63
00723	Patillas	17,828	48
00724	Penuelas	15,973	44
00731	Ponce	158,981	116
00742	Quebradillas	15,582	23
00743	Rincon	9,094	14
00745	Rio Grande	22,032	61
00747	Sabana Grande	16,343	37
00751	Salinas	21,837	69
00753	San German	27,990	54
*00936	San Juan	463,242	47
00754	San Lorenzo	27,755	53
00755	San Sebastian	30,157	71
00757	Santa Isabel	16,056	34
00758	Toa Alta	18,964	27
00759	Toa Baja	46,384	24
00760	Tujillo Alto	30,669	21
00761	Utuado	35,494	115
00762	Vega Alta	22,810	28
00763	Vega Baja	35,327	47
00765	Vieques	7,767	52
00766	Villalba	18,733	37
00767	Yabucoa	30,165	55
00768	Yauco	35,103	68
	Total	**2,712,033**	**3,421**

ZIP code	Area	Pop. April 1	Land area sq. mile
	American Samoa		
96920	American Samoa	27,159	76
	Canal Zone		
	Canal Zone	**44,198**	**362**
	Balboa	32,552	222
	Cristobal	11,646	140
	Guam		
96910	**Guam**	**84,996**	**209**
	Agana	2,119	1
	Agana Hts.	3,156	1
	Agat	4,308	10
	Asan	2,629	6
	Barrigada	6,356	9
	Chalan-Pago-Ordot	2,931	6
	Dededo	10,780	30
	Inarajan	1,897	19
	Mangilao	3,228	10
	Merizo	1,529	6
	Mongmong-Too-Maite	6,057	2
	Piti	1,284	7
	Santa Rita	8,109	17
	Sinajana	3,506	1
	Talofofo	1,935	17
	Tamuning	10,218	6
	Umatac	813	6
	Yigo	11,542	35
	Yona	2,599	20
	Virgin Islands		
	St. Croix	31,779	80
00830	St. John	1,729	20
00801	St. Thomas	28,960	32
00801	Charlotte Amalie	12,220	
00820	Christiansted	3,020	
00840	Frederiksted	1,531	
	Total	**62,468**	**132**
	Trust Territory of Pacific Islands		
	Mariana district	9,640	184
	Marshall district	22,888	70
	Palau district	11,210	192
	Ponape district	18,536	176
	Truk district	21,041	49
	Yap district	7,625	46
	Total	**90,940**	**717**

1977: The Year That Women Lost

By Hana Umlauf

Women lost in the courts in 1977. That may seem to be a harsh judgement on a year that did see some gains for women. Yet the anti-women's rights stance of several major Supreme Court rulings, beginning in late 1976, is compelling. In sharp contrast to many previous years, the Burger court dealt several stunning blows to the arguments of women's rights groups.

"It feels as if everything has gone back a decade.... It's so troublesome. You don't know where to pick up the pieces," said Carol H. Arber, co-founder of Lefcourt, Kraft, and Arber, the first all-woman law firm in New York City. Both in the Supreme Court and in lower courts, rulings limited or eliminated specific legal victories women had won over the past few years. Legal experts, who in the past have criticized the Supreme Court's sex discrimination rulings for their ad-hoc nature, feel that was confirmed over the past year. According to Kathleen Willert Peratis, director of the American Civil Liberties Union Women's Rights Project, the court has demonstrated the "lack of a clear standard . . . of a clear guiding principle that can be consistently applied."

Pregnancy Not a Disability

The disappointing year for women's rights advocates began last December 7 when the Supreme Court ruled that exclusion of pregnancy-related disabilities from an employer's disability insurance plan does not discriminate against women. The decision wiped out gains for women under the April 1972 findings of the Equal Employment Opportunity Commission which administers Title VII of the Civil Rights Act. The 1972 guidelines had established pregnancy, miscarriage, abortion, and childbirth as temporary disabilities that should be treated under any health or temporary disability insurance or sick leave plan available at a place of employment. Prior to the court's December ruling, all federal court of appeals rulings had supported the EEOC guidelines. In its ruling, the Supreme Court said, in essence, that pregnancy is a voluntary, unique condition and therefore cannot be classified as a disability. It ruled that the refusal to cover pregnancy was a refusal to cover a special condition, not a refusal to cover people based on sex.

The decision shocked women's organizations. They feel that the claim that pregnancy is voluntary is a false issue. Noreen Connell of Women Office Workers summed up the argument: "Sex discrimination is money. The companies are mainly concerned about what they think it will cost to continue to pay women who are on leave to have babies. I don't think they trust women workers; they say that women will go on disability and then quit."

Of the year's rulings, women's rights advocates felt this decision had the broadest potential impact on rights of women workers. They fear it may now be possible for employers to set up other restrictions involving pregnant employees.

Homemakers' Rights

During 1977, the National Commission on the Observance of International Women's Year released booklets on the legal status of homemakers in the 50 states and District of Columbia. Each booklet delineates the legal rights of homemakers during marriage, at divorce, and at widowhood in each state.

The booklets are available from the Superintendant of Documents, U.S. Government Printing Office, Washington, DC 20402. A summary of homemakers' rights in all the states is also available in *The Good Housekeeping Woman's Almanac* by the editors of *The World Almanac*.

No Medicaid for Abortions

The other major blow came June 20 when the Supreme Court ruled that neither the Constitution or current federal law requires states to spend Medicaid funds for elective abortions. The court went even further, ruling the Constitution did not require cities and towns with public hospitals to provide or even permit elective abortions in those hospitals. Prior to the ruling, Medicaid funds had covered abortions for as many as 300,000 women a year.

As in the case of the pregnancy disability ruling, previous abortion rulings had followed a generally consistent pattern in support of the arguments of women's rights advocates.

In one of its opinions, the court conceded that the ruling would make it difficult, if not impossible, for some women to get abortions. The majority, however, specified that it would stand by its landmark 1973 ruling that states could not make it a crime for doctors to provide abortions. However, it is clear that the decisions will place a severe limitation on that law.

The decision sparked an uproar, especially when President Jimmy Carter voiced his agreement with the Supreme Court. "There are many things in life that are not fair, that wealthy people can afford and poor people can't," Carter stated. The outraged included high-level women in the Carter administration who first voiced their opposition July 18 at a meeting in the office of Midge Constanza, assistant to the president for public liaison. According to one participant, the statement had touched "deep sensitivities" especially among representatives from the anti-poverty agencies. Since that meeting, the administration women have muted their dissent and are at work preparing a memorandum to the president taking issue with his position.

Other Anti-Women's Rights Rulings

In another Supreme Court ruling, a stewardess who claimed that the denial of her seniority claim meant she was still suffering from the effects of sex discrimination lost her case. The stewardess had been fired from her airline when she got married under a policy which was later invalidated. When she was rehired, the stewardess demanded seniority based on her prior experience. She claimed that she would have had it if she hadn't been fired under circumstances later deemed discriminatory. In ruling against her, the Supreme Court said, in effect, that she should have filed her discrimination complaint when she was fired, not years later when she was denied back-dated seniority.

The women's movement suffered another blow when the Supreme Court deadlocked on the issue of sex-segregated schools. The case involved separate college preparatory schools for girls and boys in the Philadelphia, Pa., public school system. In failing to come to a decision, the court affirmed a lower court ruling which had permitted the sex-segregated schools.

Some Legal Gains in 1977

Despite general dismay at court rulings in 1977, women's rights advocates saw several significant cases decided in their favor.

In June, the Supreme Court invalidated an Alabama law that required state prison guards to be at least 5'2" tall and weigh at least 120 pounds. The court ruled that employment height and weight requirements discriminate illegally against women, unless the employer can prove they bear some "bona fide" relation to job requirements. However, the court did uphold a state regulation barring female guards from "contact" jobs in maximum security, all-male penitentiaries.

The court determined that the height/weight requirement would exclude 41% of U.S. women from such jobs as opposed to less than 1% of the male population. The ruling may open up more jobs for women by ending arbitrary eligibility requirements.

Another significant victory for women came in March when the Supreme Court struck down the dependency requirement for men seeking survivors' benefits based on their wives' earnings. The Social Security Act required a man to prove he had been receiving at least half of his support from his wife. No such dependency test was required for widows seeking benefits. The court held that under the arrangement women's Social Security taxes had produced less protection for their spouses than those of male workers. This unconstitutional inequality, the court ruled, was justified by no more than "archaic and overbroad generalizations" and "assumptions as to dependency" reflecting "the role-typing society has long imposed" rather than contemporary reality.

In another Social Security decision, the court deemed constitutional a former section of the Social Security Act which treated retired women more favorably than retired men in determining old age benefits. Congress had specifically formulated this provision to compensate women for past employment discrimination based on sex.

Death Penalty for Rape Struck Down

The Supreme Court struck down imposition of the death penalty for rape of adult women, a move favored by several women's groups that had entered the case. The organizations had argued that the death penalty was an outgrowth of the view that a wife was her husband's property and the crime, consequently, was a crime against a man's property. They had argued further that, because of its severity, the penalty had been applied infrequently and rapes had gone unpunished.

Another boon for women came in February with a $2-million settlement by NBC of a sex-bias suit filed by its women employees. Under the agreement, NBC will make "good faith efforts" to promote women to professional, managerial, and official positions. Specific "affirmative goals" under the agreement call for women to fill 15% of top positions below the vice presidential rank by Dec. 31, 1981. To adjust for past inequities, some 2,600 past and present women employees of NBC will receive cash payments ranging from $500 to $1,000 each. Salaries for promoted women will be adjusted to equal "the average annual salary of men" who have 5 years of NBC service.

America's 25 Most Influential Women in 1977

The following women, listed alphabetically, were chosen by: Dr. Karen Blaker, syndicated columnist for Newspaper Enterprise Association; Marie Burke, women's editor, the New York News; John Mack Carter, editor, *Good Housekeeping*; Charlotte Curtis, associate editor, *The New York Times*; George E. Delury, editor, *The World Almanac*; Lenore Hershey, editor, *The Ladies' Home Journal*; Billie Jean King, tennis star and publisher, *womenSports*; Barbara McDowell, co-editor, *The Good Housekeeping Woman's Almanac*; and Gay Pauley, senior editor, United Press International.

Bella Abzug, former Democratic Congresswoman from New York and 1977 New York City mayoral candidate, is a prominent figure on the national political scene.

Helen Gurley Brown, editor of *Cosmopolitan* since 1965, was an advertising copywriter when she wrote the best-seller, *Sex and the Single Girl*.

Anita Bryant, entertainer, author, and leader of Save Our Children, the group that successfully fought to repeal a Dade County, Fla., ordinance prohibiting discrimination against homosexuals.

Rosalynn Carter, first lady and honorary chairman of the President's Commission on Mental Health, was the president's envoy to Latin America in July 1977.

Charlotte Curtis, associate editor and Op-Ed page editor of *The New York Times*, joined the *Times* in 1961, where as family/style editor she broke the mold of society writing.

Katherine Graham, publisher of the *Washington Post*, also controls the parent company which owns *Newsweek* and radio and television stations.

Ella Grasso, Democratic governor of Connecticut, has served Connecticut as a state representative and secretary of state, and in the U.S. Congress.

Nancy Hanks, chairman of the National Endowment for the Arts and National Council for the Arts since 1969.

Patricia Roberts Harris, secretary of housing and urban development, was the first black woman to reach cabinet rank as well as ambassadorial rank, having served as ambassador to Luxemburg under President Johnson.

Lenore Hershey, editor of *The Ladies' Home Journal*, was influential in the creation of the Advisory Committee on the Economic Role of Women.

Shere Hite, author of the best-selling book, *The Hite Report*, describing in detail the sexual experiences of American women, compiled and edited when Hite was a doctoral candidate at Columbia University.

Barbara Jordan, Democratic Congresswoman from Texas, serves on the Judiciary Committee and, in 1976, ignited the Democratic National Convention with her keynote address.

Billie Jean King, tennis star, 5-time Wimbledon champion, and publisher of *womenSports*, has boosted interest in women's tennis and other sports.

Coretta Scott King, civil rights leader, has become increasingly prominent since the assassination of her husband, Rev. Dr. Martin Luther King, Jr.

Juanita Kreps, secretary of commerce, was formerly vice president of Duke University where she began her teaching career in economics in 1955.

Maggie Kuhn, a retired social worker, at age 64 in 1970 organized the Gray Panthers, a network of highly vocal older people dedicated to improving conditions for senior citizens.

Mary Wells Lawrence, chairman of the board of Wells, Rich, Greene, a New York City advertising agency, has won wide acclaim for her achievements in advertising.

Margaret Mead, anthropologist, has studied 7 cultures, written 17 books, and is a major intellectual force.

Marabel Morgan, a Miami, Fla., housewife and author of *The Total Woman* and *Total Joy*, is a fervent believer in the virtues of middle-class monogamy.

Eleanor Holmes Norton, Equal Employment Opportunity Commission chairman, was formerly New York City Human Rights Commission chairman.

Phyllis Schlafly, author, politician, and housewife, is the chief spokesman for STOP-ERA forces and publishes the monthly *Phyllis Schlafly Report*.

Beverly Sills, one of the finest soprano voices of this century, recounts her life in *Bubbles*, a best-seller.

Eleanor Smeal, president of the National Organization for Women, joined NOW in 1970 and has served as a chapter and state president, and chairman of the board in 1975.

Lila Acheson Wallace, owner and co-founder, with her husband DeWitt Wallace, of the *Reader's Digest*.

Barbara Walters, television anchorwoman, became the first woman to anchor a national evening news program in 1976.

UNITED STATES GOVERNMENT

The Carter Administration

As of Aug. 1, 1977

Terms of office of the president and vice president, from Jan. 20, 1977 to Jan. 20, 1981. No person may be elected president of the United States for more than 2 4-year terms.

PRESIDENT — Jimmy (James Earl) Carter of Georgia. Receives salary of $200,000 a year taxable, and in addition an expense allowance, also taxable, of $50,000 to assist in defraying expenses resulting from his official duties. Also there may be expended not exceeding $100,000, non-taxable, a year for travel expenses and official entertainment. Congress has provided lifetime pensions of $60,000 a year, free mailing privileges, free office space, and up to $90,000 a year for office help for ex-Presidents and $20,000 annually for their widows.

VICE PRESIDENT — Walter F. Mondale of Minnesota, salary $75,000 a year and $10,000 for expenses, all of which is taxable.

For succession to presidency, see Succession in Index.

The Cabinet

(Salaries $66,000 each)

Secretary of State — Cyrus R. Vance, N.Y.
Secretary of Treasury — W. Michael Blumenthal, Mich.
Secretary of Defense — Harold Brown, Cal.
Attorney General — Griffin B. Bell, Ga.
Secretary of Interior — Cecil D. Andrus, Ida.
Secretary of Agriculture — Bob Bergland, Minn.
Secretary of Commerce — Juanita M. Kreps, N.C.
Secretary of Labor — F. Ray Marshall, Tex.
Secretary of Health, Education, and Welfare — Joseph A. Califano Jr., Wash., D.C.
Secretary of Housing and Urban Development — Patricia Roberts Harris, Wash., D.C.
Secretary of Transportation — Brock Adams, Wash.
Secretary of Energy — James R. Schlesinger, Va.

The White House Staff

1600 Pennsylvania Ave. NW 20500

Assistant to the President — Hamilton Jordan.
Press Secretary to the President — Jody Powell.
Counsel to the President — Robert Lipshutz.
Personal Assistant to the President — Susan Clough.
Press Secretary to the First Lady — Mary Finch Hoyt.
Physician to the President — Rear Adm. William M. Lukash, USN.
Chief Usher — Rex W. Scouten.

Executive Agencies

National Security Council — Assistant to the President for Natl. Security Affairs—Zbigniew Brzezinski.
Council of Economic Advisers—Charles Schultze.
Council on Environmental Quality—Charles Warren, chairman.
Central Intelligence Agency—Adm. Stansfield Turner, director.
Office of Management and Budget—Bert Lance, director.
Special Representative for Trade Negotiations—Robert Strauss.

Department of State

2201 C St. NW 20520

Secretary of State — Cyrus R. Vance.
Deputy Secretary — Warren Christopher.
Under Sec. for Political Affairs — Philip C. Habib.
Under Sec. for Security Assistance, Science and Technology — Lucy Wilson Benson.
Under Sec. for Economic Affairs — Richard N. Cooper.
Deputy Under Secretary — vacant (for management).
Ambassadors at Large — Ellsworth Bunker, Elliot L. Richardson, Gerard C. Smith.
Counselor — Matthew Nimetz.
Legal Advisor — Herbert J. Hansell.
Assistant Secretaries for:
Administration — John M. Thomas.
African Affairs — Richard M. Moose Jr.
Congressional Relations — Douglas J. Bennett Jr.
Economic Affairs — Julius L. Katz.
Educational & Cultural Affairs — Joseph D. Duffey.
European Affairs — George S. Vest.
East Asian & Pacific Affairs — Richard Holbrooke.
Internatl. Organization Affairs — Charles William Maynes.
Near-Eastern & S. Asian Affairs — Alfred L. Atherton Jr.
Public Affairs — Hodding Carter 3d.
Bureau of Security & Consular Affairs — Barbara M. Watson, administrator.
Chief of Protocol — Evan S. Dobelle.
Dir. General, Foreign Service — Carol C. Laise.
Dir. of Intelligence & Research — Harold H. Saunders.
Bureau of Oceans and Internatl. Environmental and Scientific Affairs — Assistant Sec. Patsy T. Mink.
Dir. of Politico-Military Affairs — Leslie H. Gelb.
Insp. Gen. Foreign Service — Robert M. Sayre.
Foreign Service Inst. — George S. Springsteen, director.
Agency for Internatl. Development — John J. Gilligan, administrator.
ACTION — Sam Brown.
U.S. Rep. to the UN and Rep. in the Security Council — Andrew Young, ambassador.

Treasury Department

15th St. & Pennsylvania Ave. NW 20220

Secretary of the Treasury — W. Michael Blumenthal.
Deputy Sec. of the Treasury — Robert Carswell.
Under Sec. for Monetary Affairs — Anthony M. Solomon.
Under Sec. — Bette Anderson.
General Counsel — Robert H. Mundheim.
Assistant Secretaries: — Roger C. Altman, C. Fred Bergsten, Daniel H. Brill, William J. Beckham Jr., Joseph Laitin.
Bureaus:
Alcohol, Tobacco, and Firearms — Rex D. Davis, director.
Consolidated Federal Law Enforcement Training Center — Arthur F. Brandstatter, director.
Comptroller of the Currency — Robert Bloom (acting).
Customs — G.R. Dickerson (acting), commissioner.
Engraving & Printing — James A. Conlon, director.
Internal Revenue Service — Jerome Kurtz, commissioner.
Mint — director, vacant.
Public Debt — H. J. Hintgen, commissioner.
Treasurer of the U.S. — Azie Morton.
U.S. Savings Bonds — national director vacant.
U. S. Secret Service — H. Stuart Knight, director.

Department of Defense

The Pentagon 20301

Secretary of Defense — Harold Brown.
Deputy Sec. — Charles Duncan Jr.
Dir. of Def. Research and Engineering — Dr. William J. Perry.
Asst. Secretaries of Defense:
Comptroller — Fred P. Wacker.
Communication, Command, Control & Intelligence — G. P. Dineen.
Health Affairs — Robert Smith.
International Security — David E. McGiffert.
Manpower, Reserve Affairs & Logistics — John P. White.
Public Affairs — Thomas B. Ross.
Program Analysis & Evaluation — Russell Murray II.
General Counsel — Dianne Siemer.
Joint Chiefs of Staff, chairman — Gen. George S. Brown, USAF.

Department of the Army

The Pentagon 20310

Secretary of the Army — Clifford L. Alexander Jr.

Under Secretary — vacant.
Assistant Secretaries for:
Finance Management — Hadlai A. Hull.
Civil Works — vacant.
Installations, Logistics and Financial Management — Alan J. Gibbs.
Research, Development and Acquisition — Percy A. Pierre.
Manpower & Reserve Affairs — Robert L. Nelson.
Chief of Public Affairs — Brig. Gen. Robert B. Solomon.
Chief of Staff — Gen. Bernard C. Rogers.
Comptroller of the Army, General Counsel — Jill Wine-Volner.
Surgeon General — Lt. Gen. Richard R. Taylor.
Adjutant General — Maj. Gen. James C. Pennington.
Inspector General & Auditor General — Lt. Gen. Marvin D. Fuller.
Judge Advocate General — Maj. Gen. Wilton B. Persons Jr.
Deputy Chiefs of Staff:
Logistics — Lt. Gen. Eivind H. Johansen.
Operations & Plans — Lt. Gen. Edward C. Meyer.
Research, Development, Acquisition — Lt. Gen. Howard H. Cooksey.
Personnel — Lt. Gen. DeWitt C. Smith Jr.
Ass't. Chief of Staff, Intelligence — Maj. Gen. Harold R. Aaron.
Chief of Engineers — Lt. Gen. John W. Morris.
Director, Women's Army Corps. — Brig. Gen. Mary E. Clarke.
Chief, Nat. Guard Bureau — Maj. Gen. LaVern E. Weber.
Chief Army Reserve — Maj. Gen. Henry Mohr.
U.S. Army Materiel Development and Readiness Command — Gen. John R. Guthrie.
U.S. Army Forces Command — Gen. Frederick J. Kroesen.
U.S. Army Training and Doctrine Command — Gen. Don A. Starry.
First U.S. Army — Lt. Gen. Jeffrey G. Smith.
Fifth U.S. Army — Lt. Gen. Allen M. Burdette.
Sixth U.S. Army — Lt. Gen. Edward M. Flanagan Jr.
Military Dist. of Washington — Maj. Gen. Kenneth E. Dohleman.
XVIII Airborne Corps. Ft. Bragg, N.C. — Lt. Gen. Volney Warner.
III Corps. and Ft. Hood, Tex. — Lt. Gen. Robert M. Shoemaker.

Department of the Navy

The Pentagon 20360

Secretary of the Navy — W. Graham Claytor Jr.
Under Secretary — R. James Woolsey.
Assistant Secretaries for:
Financial Management — Gary D. Penisten.
Installations & Logistics — vacant.
Manpower & Reserve Affairs — Edward Hidalgo.
Research & Development — Dr. David E. Mann.
Judge Advocate General — R. Adm. W. O. Miller.
Chief of Naval Operations — Adm. J. L. Holloway 3d.
Chief of Naval Materiel — Adm. F. H. Michaelis.
Chief of Information — R. Adm. D. M. Cooney.
Bureau Chiefs:
Medicine & Surgery — V. Adm. W. P. Arentzen.
Naval Personnel — V. Adm. J. D. Watkins.
Military Sealift Command — R. Adm. J. D. Johnson Jr.
U. S. Marine Corps:
Commandant — Gen. Louis H. Wilson.
Asst. Commandant — Gen. Samuel Jaskilka.
Chief of Staff — Lt. Gen. Lawrence F. Snowden.
Commandants, Naval Districts:
1st, Boston — R. Adm. F. F. Palmer.
3d, Brooklyn —
4th, Philadelphia —
5th, Norfolk — R. Adm. W. H. Ellis.
6th, Charleston — R. Adm. R. F. Hoffman.
8th, New Orleans — V. Adm. P. N. Charbonnet Jr.
9th, Great Lakes — R. Adm. A. M. Sackett.
11th, San Diego — R. Adm. W. H. Rogers.
12th, San Francisco — "
13th, Seattle — R. Adm. J. D. Murray Jr.
14th, Pearl Harbor — R. Adm. R. B. Wentworth Jr.
Naval District, Wash., D. C. — R. Adm. R. H. Carnahan.

Department of the Air Force

The Pentagon 20330

Secretary of the Air Force — John C. Stetson.
Under Secretary of the Air Force — Hans Mark.
Assistant Secretaries for:
Financial Management — Everett J. Keech.
Research and Development — John J. Martin (acting).
Installations and Logistics — vacant.
Manpower, Reserve Affairs and Installations — Antonia Handler Chayes.
General Counsel — Peter B. Hamilton.
Director of Information — Brig. Gen. H. J. Dalton Jr.
Director of Space Systems — Brig. Gen. W. L. Shields Jr.
Chief of Staff — Gen. David C. Jones.
Vice Chief of Staff — Gen. William V. McBride.
Chief, National Guard Bureau — Maj. Gen. John T. Guice, USA.
Chief of Air Force Reserves — Maj. Gen. William Lyon.
Surgeon General — Lt. Gen. George E. Schafer.
Judge Advocate — Maj. Gen. H. R. Vague.
Inspector General — Lt. Gen. John T. Flynn.
Deputy Chiefs of Staff:
Systems and Logistics — Lt. Gen. Thomas M. Ryan Jr.
Programs and Resources — Lt. Gen. Abbott C. Greenleaf.
Personnel — Lt. Gen. Bennie L. Davis.
Research and Development — Lt. Gen. Alton D. Slay.
Plans and Operations — Lt. Gen. Andrew B. Anderson.
Major Air Commands:
NORAD/ADCOM — Gen. Daniel James Jr.
AF Logistics Command — Gen. F. Michael Rogers.
AF Systems Command — Gen. Lew Allen Jr.
Air Training Command — Lt. Gen. John W. Roberts
Air University — Lt. Gen Raymond B. Furlong.
Military Airlift Command — Gen. William J. Moore Jr.
Strategic Air Command — Gen. Richard D. H. Ellis.
Tactical Air Command — Gen. Robert J. Dixon.
Alaskan Air Command — Lt. Gen. Marion L. Boswell.
Pacific Air Forces — Lt. Gen. James A. Hill.
USAF Europe — Gen. William J. Evans.
USAF Security Service — Brig. Gen. Kenneth D. Burns.
AF Communications Service — Maj. Gen. Rupert H. Burris.
USAF Academy — Lt. Gen. Kenneth L. Tallman.
USAF Acct. and Finance Center — Maj. Gen. Lucius Theus.

Department of Justice

Constitution Ave. & 10th St. NW 20530

Attorney General — Griffin B. Bell.
Deputy Attorney General — Peter F. Flaherty.
Solicitor General — Wade H. McCree.
Assistant Attorneys General:
Antitrust Division — John H. Shenefield.
Civil Division — Barbara Allen Babcock.
Civil Rights Division — Drew S. Days.
Criminal Division — Benjamin R. Civiletti.
Drug Enforcement Admin. — Peter B. Bensinger.
Land & Natural Resources Division — James W. Moorman (acting).
Legal Counsel — John M. Harmon (acting).
Office of Legislative Affairs — Patricia M. Wald.
Office of Management & Finance — Kevin D. Rooney.
Public Information — Marvin D. Wall, director
Tax Division — M. Carr Ferguson (acting).
Fed. Bureau of Investigation — Clarence M. Kelley.
Board of Immigration Appeals — David L. Mil-Hollan, chairman.
Board of Parole — Curtis C. Crawford (acting).
Bureau of Prisons — Norman A. Carlson.
Community Relations Ser. — Gilbert G. Pompa (acting).
Immigration and Naturalization Service — Leonel J. Castillo, commissioner.
Law Enforcement Assistance Admin. — James M. H. Gregg (acting).
Pardon Attorney — John R. Stanish.

Department of the Interior

C St. between 18th & 19th Sts. NW 20240

Secretary of the Interior — Cecil D. Andrus.
Under Secretary — James A. Joseph.
Assistant Secretaries for:
Fish, Wildlife and Parks — Robert Herbst.
Energy & Minerals — Joan Davenport.
Land and Water Resources — Guy Richard Martin.
Policy, Budget, and Administration — vacant.
Indian Affairs — vacant.
Bureau of Land Management — vacant.
Bureau of Mines — Dr. John D. Morgan (acting).
Bureau of Outdoor Recreation — Chris Delaporte.
Bureau of Reclamation — Keith Higginson.
Bureau of Sport Fisheries & Wildlife — Lynn Greenwalt.
Geological Survey — V.E. McKelvey.
National Park Service — William J. Whalen.

Office of Public Affairs — Chris Carlson.
Office of Water Research and Technology — William S. Butcher, director.
Office of Solicitor — Leo Krulitz.

Department of Agriculture

14th St. & Independence Ave. SW 20250

Secretary of Agriculture — Bob Bergland.
Deputy Secretary — John C. White.
Conservation, Research, & Education — M. Rupert Cutler.
Internat. Affairs & Commodity Programs — Dale E. Hathaway.
Marketing Services — Robert H. Meyer.
Rural Development — Alex P. Mercure.
Agricultural Economics, Policy Analysis, and Budget — Howard W. Hjort.
Congressional & Public Affairs — James C. Webster.
Agric. Stabilization & Converv. Service — Ray Fitzgerald, administrator.
Animal & Plant Health Inspection Ser. — F. J. Mulhern.
Cooperative State Research Ser. — R. J. Aldrich.
Econ. Research Service — Quentin M. West, admin.
Extension Service — W. Neill Schaller, admin.
Farmer Coop. Service — Randall Torgerson, admin.
Farmers Home Admin. — Gordon Cavanaugh, admin.
Fed. Crop Insurance Corp. — James Deal.
Federal Grain Inspection Service — Leland E. Bartlett.
Food & Nutrition Ser. — Lewis B. Straus.
Food Safety and Quality Service — Robert Angelotti.
Foreign Agric. Service — Thomas R. Hughes.
Forest Service — John R. McGuire, chief.
General Counsel — Sara Weddington.
General Sales Manager — Kelley Harrison.
Inspector General — Thomas McBride.
Packers - Stockyards Admin. — Charles Jennings.
Rural Development Service — William J. Nagle.
Rural Electrific. Admin. — David Hamil, admin.
Soil Conservation Service — Ronello M. Davis, admin.
Statistical Reporting Service — William Kibler.

Department of Commerce

14th St. between Constitution & E St. NW 20230

Secretary of Commerce — Juanita M. Kreps.
Under Secretary — Sidney Harman.
Asst Secretaries — Robert J. Blackwell, vacant.
General Counsel — C. L. Haslam.
Maritime Affairs — Robert J. Blackwell.
Science & Technology — Jordan J. Baruch.
Bureau of the Census — Manuel D. Plotkin.
Bureau of Economic Analysis — George Jaszi.
Bureau of Internatl. Commerce — Robert G. Shaw (acting).
Bureau of East-West Trade — Alan A. Reich.
Bureau of Domestic Commerce — John F. Klingenman.
Natl. Oceanic & Atmospheric Admin. — Richard A. Frank, administrator.
Natl. Technical Info. Service — William T. Knox, director.
Economic Develop. Admin. — Robert P. Hall.
Natl. Bureau of Standards — Ernest Ambler (acting).
Office of Minority Business Enterprise — Randolph T. Blackwell, director (designate).
Office of Product Standards — Howard I. Forman.
Office of Telecommunications — John M. Richardson, acting director.
Office of Textiles — Arthur Garel, director.
U.S. Patent Office — C. Marshall Dann.
U.S. Travel Service — Fabian Chavez Jr.

Department of Labor

200 Constitution Ave. NW 20210

Secretary of Labor — F. Ray Marshall.
Under Secretary — Robert Brown.
Executive Assistant-Counselor — Paul Jensen.
Assistant Secretaries for:
- **Employment and Training** — Earnest Green.
- **Labor-Management Relations** — Francis X. Burkhardt.
- **Occupational Safety & Health** — Eula Bingham.
- **Employment Standards** — Donald E. Elisburg.

Women's Bureau — Alexis M. Herman, director.
Asst. Secretary for Policy, Evaluation & Research — Arnold H. Packer.
Solicitor of Labor — Carin A. Clauss.
Bureau of Labor Statistics — Julius Shiskin.
Dep. Under Secy. for Internatl. Affairs — Howard D. Samuel.
Dep. Under Secy. for Legislative Affairs — Nik B. Edes.
Asst. Secretary for Admin. & Management — Alfred Zuk.
Director of Public Affairs & Counselor — John W. Leslie.
Office of Information, Publications & Reports — John W. Leslie.

Department of Health, Education, and Welfare

330 Independence Ave. SW 20201

Secretary of HEW — Joseph A. Califano Jr.
Under Secretary — Hale Champion.
Assistant Secretaries for:
- **Management and Budget** — John D. Young.
- **Public Affairs** — Eileen Shanahan.
- **Health** — Dr. Julius B. Richmond.
- **Planning and Evaluation** — Henry Aaron.
- **Education** — Dr. Mary Berry.
- **Human Development Services** — Arabella Martinez.
- **Legislation** — Richard Warden.
- **Personnel Administration** — Thomas McFee (acting).

General Counsel — Peter Libassi.
Surgeon General, Public Health Ser. — Dr. Julius B. Richmond.
Center for Disease Control — Dr. William H. Foege.
Alcohol, Drug Abuse, and Mental Health Admin. — vacant.
Health Resources Admin. — vacant.
Health Services Admin. — Dr. George I. Lythcott.
Office for Civil Rights — David S. Tatel.
Health Care Financing Admin. — Robert A. Derzon.
Commissioners of:
- **Education** — Ernest Boyer.
- **Social Security** — James B. Cardwell.
- **Food and Drug Admin.** — Donald Kennedy.

National Institutes of Health — Dr. Donald S. Frederickson.
National Institute of Education — Patricia Graham (designate).

Department of Housing and Urban Development

451 7th St. SW 20410

Secretary of Housing & Urban Development — Patricia Roberts Harris.
Under Secretary — Jay Janis.
Assistant Secretaries:
- **Administration** — William A. Medina.
- **Community Planning & Development** — Robert C. Embry.
- **Fair Housing and Equal Opportunity** — Chester C. McGuire.
- **Federal Housing Commissioner** — Lawrence B. Simons.
- **Neighborhoods; Voluntary and Consumer Protection Assns.** — Msgr. Geno Baroni.
- **Policy Development & Research** — Donna E. Shalala.
- **Legislation and Intergovernmental Relations** — Harry K. Schwartz.

President, Govt. Natl. Mortgage Assn. — John Dalton.
Office of Public Affairs — Gerald Huard (Deputy).
Office of International Affairs, — Tila M. DeHancock.
General Counsel — Ruth T. Prokop.
Federal Insurance Administrator — J. Robert Hunter (Deputy)
Fed. Disaster Assistance Admin. — Thomas P. Dunne.
New Communities Admin. — William J. White.
Inspector General — James B. Thomas Jr.

Department of Transportation

400 7th St. SW 20590

Secretary — Brock Adams.
Deputy Secretary — Alan A. Butchman.
Assistant Secretaries — Edward W. Scott Jr., Chester C. Davenport.
General Counsel — Linda H. Kamm.
National Highway Traffic Safety Admin. — Joan Claybrook.
U. S. Coast Guard Commandant — Adm. Owen W. Siler.
Federal Aviation Admin. — Langhorne M. Bond.
Federal Highway Admin. — William M. Cox.
Federal Railroad Admin. — John M. Sullivan.
Urban Mass Transportation Admin. — Dr. Richard S. Page.
St. Lawrence Seaway Development Corp. — David W. Oberlin, administrator.

Department of Energy

Independence Ave. & 10th St. SW 20003

Secretary — James R. Schlesinger.

State Officials, Salaries, Party Membership

Compiled from data supplied by state officials, mid-1977.

Alabama

Governor — George C. Wallace, D., $28,955.
Lt. Gov. — Jere Beasley, D., $50 per legislative day, plus annual salary of $300 per month.
Sec. of State — Mrs. Agnes Baggett, D., $22,959.
Atty. Gen. — Bill Baxley, D., $33,500.
Treasurer — Mrs. Melba Till Allen, D., $22,959.
Auditor — Bettye Frink, D., $22,959.
Legislature: meets annually, first Tuesday in Feb. except in 4th year (2d Tuesday in Jan.), at Montgomery. Members receive $50 per day during legislative sessions, limited to 30 days, plus annual salary of $300 per month.
Senate — Dem., 35; Rep., 0. Total, 35.
House — Dem., 104; Rep., 1. Total, 105.

Alaska

Governor — Jay S. Hammond, R., $50,000.
Lt. Gov. — Lowell Thomas Jr., R., $44,000.
Atty. General — Avrum M. Gross, D., $48,000.
Comm. of Educ. — Marshall L. Lind.
Legislature: meets annually, in January, at Juneau, for as long as may be necessary. First session in odd years. Members receive $14,720 per year plus $48 per day if from out of town, $35 if from Juneau, while in session. Also, $4,000 for stenographic services and other expenses.
Senate — Dem., 12; Rep., 8. Total, 20.
House — Dem., 25; Rep., 15. Total, 40.

Arizona

Governor — Raul H. Castro, D., $40,000.
Sec. of State — Wesley Bolin, D., $22,000.
Atty. Gen. — Bruce Babbitt, D., $35,000.
Treasurer — Bart Fleming, R., $22,500.
Supt. Public Instr. — Carolyn Warner, D., $27,500.
Legislature: meets annually, in January, at Phoenix. Each member receives an annual salary of $6,000.
Senate — Dem., 16; Rep., 14. Total, 30.
House — Dem., 22; Rep., 38. Total, 60.

Arkansas

Governor —David Pryor, D., $35,000.
Lt. Gov. — Joe Purcell, D., $14,000.
Sec. of State — Winston Bryant, D., $22,500.
Auditor — Jimmy Jones, D., $22,500.
Atty. Gen. — Bill Clinton, D., $26,500.
Treasurer — Mrs. Nancy J. Hall, D., $22,500.
General Assembly: meets odd years, in January, at Little Rock. Members receive $7,500 per year, $45 a day while in regular session, plus 13c a mile travel expense.
Senate — Dem., 34; Rep., 1. Total, 35.
House — Dem., 97; Rep., 3. Total, 100.

California

Governor — Edmund G. Brown Jr., D., $49,100.
Lt. Gov. — Mervyn M. Dymally, D., $35,000.
Sec. of State — March Fong Eu, D., $35,000.
Comptroller — Kenneth Cory, D., $35,000.
Atty. Gen. — Evelle J. Younger, R., $42,500.
Treasurer — Jesse M. Unruh, D., $35,000.
Supt. Public Instr. — Wilson Riles, NP, $35,000.
Legislature: meets at Sacramento, in biennial general sessions, unlimited as to duration. Members receive $23,232 per year plus mileage and $30 daily expenses while in session. Daily expenses on interim business: $30.
Senate — Dem., 26; Rep., 14. Total, 40.
Assembly — Dem., 55; Rep., 23; 2 vacancies. Total, 80.

Colorado

Governor — Dick Lamm, D., $40,000.
Lt. Gov. — George Brown, D., $25,000.
Secy. of State — Mary Estill Buchanan, R., $25,000.
Atty. Gen. — J. D. MacFarlane, D., $32,500.
Treasurer — Roy Romer, D., $25,000.
General Assembly: meets annually, in January, at Denver. Members receive $7,600 annually, plus $35 per day for non-session meetings up to a maximum of $1,050 in any calendar year.
Senate — Dem., 17; Rep., 18. Total, 35.
House — Dem., 30; Rep., 35. Total, 65.

Connecticut

Governor — Ella T. Grasso, D., $42,000.
Lt. Gov. — Robert K. Killian, D., $18,000.
Sec. of State — Gloria Schaffer, D., $20,000.
Treasurer — Henry E. Parker, D., $20,000.
Comptroller — J. Edward Caldwell, D., $20,000.
Atty. Gen. — Carl R. Ajello, D., $30,000.
General Assembly: meets annually odd years in January and even years in February at Hartford. Salary $11,000 per 2-year term plus $2,000 per 2-year term for expenses and 12c per mile travel allowance.
Senate — Dem., 22; Rep., 14. Total, 36.
House — Dem., 93; Rep., 58. Total, 151.

Delaware

Governor — Pierre S. duPont 4th, R., $35,000.
Lt. Gov. — James D. McGinnis, D., $12,000.
Sec. of State — Glenn C. Kenton, R., $19,900.
Auditor — Richard T. Collins, R., $18,000.
Atty. Gen. — Richard R. Wier Jr., D., $30,000.
Treasurer — Thomas R. Carper, D., $18,000.
General Assembly: meets annually at Dover, from the 2d Tuesday in January to midnight June 30. Members receive $9,000 base salary.
Senate — Dem., 13; Rep., 8. Total, 21.
House — Dem., 26; Rep., 15. Total, 41.

Florida

Governor — Reubin Askew, D., $50,000.
Lt. Gov. — J. H. Williams, D., $36,000.
Sec. of State — Bruce A. Smathers, D., $40,000.
Comptroller — Gerald Lewis, D., $40,000.
Atty. Gen. — Robert L. Shevin, D., $40,000.
Treasurer — Bill Gunter, D., $40,000.
Comm. of Publ. Educ. — Ralph D. Turlington, $40,000.
Legislature: meets annually, in April, at Tallahassee. Members receive $12,000 per year plus expense allowance while on official business.
Senate — Dem., 30; Rep., 9; Ind., 1. Total, 40.
House — Dem., 92; Rep., 28. Total, 120.

Georgia

Governor — George Busbee, D., $50,000.
Lt. Gov. — Zell Miller, D., $25,000.
Sec. of State — Ben W. Fortson Jr., D., $35,000.
Comptroller General — Johnnie L. Caldwell, D., $35,000.
Atty. Gen. — Arthur K. Bolton, D., $40,000.
Auditor — William M. Nixon, $32,000.
Supt. of Schools — Jack P. Nix, D., $35,000.
General Assembly: meets annually at Atlanta. Members receive $4,200 per year. During session $25 per day for expenses.
Senate — Dem., 52; Rep., 4. Total, 56.
House — Dem., 155; Rep., 24; Ind., 1. Total, 180.

Hawaii

Governor — George R. Ariyoshi, D., $50,000.
Lt. Gov. — Nelson K. Doi, D., $45,000.
Dir., Budg. & Finance — Eileen Anderson, D., $42,500.
Atty. Gen. — Ronald Amemiya, D., $42,500.
Supt. Educ. Dept. — Charles Clark, D., $42,500.
Comptroller — Hideo Murakami, D., $42,500.
Legislature: meets annually, in January, at Honolulu. Members receive $12,000 per year plus allowance for expenses.
Senate — Dem., 18. Rep., 7. Total, 25.
House — Dem., 41. Rep., 10. Total, 51.

Idaho

Governor — John V. Evans, D., $33,000.
Lt. Gov. — William J. Murphy, D., $8,000.
Sec. of State — Pete T. Cenarrusa, R., $21,500.
Treasurer — Marjorie Ruth Moon, D., $21,500.
Atty. Gen. — Wayne L. Kidwell, R., $25,000.
Auditor — Joe R. Williams, D., $21,500.
Supt. Publ. Instr. — Roy Truby, D., $23,000.
Legislature: meets on the Monday after the first day in January, at Boise. Members receive $3,000 per year, plus $25 per day when authorized, plus travel allowances.
Senate — Dem., 15; Rep., 20. Total, 35.
House — Dem., 22; Rep., 48. Total, 70.

Illinois

Governor — James R. Thompson, R., $50,000.
Lt. Gov. — Dave Oneal, R., $37,500.
Sec. of State — Alan J. Dixon, D., $42,500.
Comptroller — Michael J. Bakalis, D., $40,000.
Atty. Gen. — William J. Scott, R., $42,500.
Treasurer — Donald R. Smith, R., $40,000.
General Assembly: meets each year in January, at Springfield. Members receive $20,000 per annum.
Senate — Dem., 34; Rep., 25. Total, 59.
House — Dem., 93; Rep., 83; Ind., 1. Total, 177.

Indiana

Governor — Otis R. Bowen, R., $36,000 plus discretion-

ary expenses.
Lt. Gov. — Robert Orr, R., $23,500; also $6,000 per year as president of Senate, plus $25 per day during legislative sessions.
Sec. of State — Larry Conrad, D., $23,500.
Auditor — Mary Aikins Currie, D., $23,500.
Atty. Gen. — Theodore L. Sendak, R., $27,000.
Treasurer — Jack L. New, D., $23,500.
Supt. Publ. Instr. — Harold Negley, R., $25,000.
General Assembly: meets annually in January. Members receive $6,000 per year, plus $100 each month not in session, plus $25 per day expense allowance when in session. Also, 8c a mile for round trip each week.
Senate — Dem., 28; Rep., 22. Total, 50.
House — Dem., 48, Rep., 52. Total, 100.

Iowa

Governor — Robert D. Ray, R., $40,000, plus $5,000 expenses.
Lt. Gov. — Arthur A. Neu, R., $12,000 plus personal expenses and travel allowances at same rate as for a senator.
Sec. of State — Melvin D. Synhorst, R., $22,500.
Auditor — Lloyd R. Smith, R., $22,500.
Atty. Gen. — Richard C. Turner, R., $29,000.
Treasurer — Maurice E. Baringer, R., $22,500.
Supt. Public Instr. — Robert Benton.
General Assembly: meets annually in January, at Des Moines. Members receive $8,000, plus maximum expense allowance of $20 per day 5 days a week during session, mileage expenses at 15c a mile.
Senate — Dem., 26; Rep., 24. Total, 50.
House — Dem., 59; Rep., 41. Total, 100.

Kansas

Governor — Robert F. Bennett, R., $35,000.
Lt. Gov. — Shelby Smith, R., $10,400.
Sec. of State — Mrs. E. M. Shanahan, R., $20,000.
Atty. Gen. — Curt Schneider, D., $32,500.
Treasurer — Joan Finney, D., $20,000.
Legislature: meets annually in January, at Topeka. Members receive $25 a day plus $44 a day expenses, plus $200 per month while not in session.
Senate — Dem., 19; Rep., 21. Total, 40.
House — Dem., 65; Rep., 60. Total, 125.

Kentucky

Governor — Julian Carroll, D., $35,000.
Lt. Gov. — Thelma Stovall, D., $29,240.
Sec. of State — Drexel Davis, D., $29,240.
Auditor — George Adkins, D., $29,240.
Atty. Gen. — Robert Stephens, D., $29,240.
Treasurer — Francis Mills, D., $29,240.
Supt. Public Instr. — Robert Graham, $29,240.
General Assembly: meets even years, in January, at Frankfort. Members receive $50 per day during session; officers, $65-$75. All members also receive $50 per day and $550 per month for expenses.
Senate — Dem., 30; Rep., 8. Total, 38.
House — Dem., 78; Rep., 22. Total, 100.

Louisiana

Governor — Edwin W. Edwards, D., $50,000.
Lt. Gov. — James E. Fitzmorris Jr., D., $40,000.
Sec. of State — Paul Hardy, D., $35,000.
Atty. Gen. — William J. Guste Jr., D., $35,000.
Treasurer — Mary Evelyn Parker, D., $35,000.
Supt. of Education — Kelly Nix, D., $35,000.
Legislature: meets annually for 60 legislative days, commencing on 3d Monday in April. Members receive $50 per day and mileage at 16c a mile for 8 round trips, plus $1,000 per month expense allowance.
Senate — Dem., 39; Rep., 0. Total, 39.
House — Dem., 102; Rep., 3. Total, 105.

Maine

Governor — James B. Longley, I., $35,000.
Sec. of State — Markham L. Gartley, D., $20,000.
Atty. Gen. — Joseph E. Brennan, D., $25,500.
Auditor — Rodney L. Scribner, D., $17,500.
Treasurer — Leighton Cooney, D., $15,000.
Comm. of Education — H. Sawin Millett Jr., $25,500.
Legislature: meets biennially in January, at Augusta. Members receive $4,500 for regular session, $2,500 for special session plus expenses; presiding officers receive 50% more.
Senate — Dem., 12; Rep., 21. Total, 33.
House — Dem., 88; Rep., 63. Total, 151.

Maryland

Governor — Marvin Mandel, D., $25,000.
Lt. Gov. — Blair Lee 3d, D., $44,856.
Comptroller — Louis L. Goldstein, D., $44,856.
Atty. Gen. — Francis B. Burch, D., $44,856.
Treasurer — William S. James, D., $44,856.
Supt. of Education — David S. Hornbeck, $47,300.
General Assembly: meets 90 days annually on the 3rd Wednesday in January, at Annapolis. Members receive $12,500 per year.
Senate — Dem., 39; Rep., 8. Total, 47.
House — Dem., 126; Rep., 15. Total, 141.

Massachusetts

Governor — Michael S. Dukakis, D., $40,000.
Lt. Gov. — Thomas P. O'Neill 3d, D., $30,000.
Sec. of the Commonwealth — Paul Guzzi, D., $30,000.
Atty. Gen. — Francis X. Belloti, D., $37,500.
Auditor — Thaddeus Buczko, D., $30,000.
Treasurer — Robert Q. Crane, D., $30,000.
General Court (Legislature): meets each January in Boston. Salaries $14,400 per annum.
Senate — Dem., 33; Rep., 7. Total, 40.
House — Dem., 192; Rep., 43; Ind., 3; vacancies, 2. Total, 240.

Michigan

Governor — William G. Milliken, R., $58,000 (by 1978).
Lt. Gov. — James J. Damman, R., $40,000 (by 1978).
Sec. of State — Richard H. Austin, D., $45,000.
Atty. Gen. — Frank J. Kelley, D., $45,000.
Auditor — Albert Lee, Non-Part., $45,000.
Treasurer — Allison Green, Non-Part., $41,800.
Supt. Public Instr. — John Porter, Non-Part., $43,784.
Legislature: meets annually in January, at Lansing. Members receive $24,000 per year (by 1978), plus $4,600 expense allowance.
Senate — Dem., 24; Rep., 14. Total, 38.
House — Dem., 66; Rep., 44. Total, 110.

Minnesota

Governor — Rudy Perpich, DFL., $58,000.
Lt. Gov. — Alec G. Olson, DFL., $36,000.
Sec. of State — Joan Anderson Growe, DFL., $30,000.
Auditor — Robert W. Mattson, DFL., $30,000.
Atty. Gen. — Warren Spannaus, DFL., $49,000.
Treasurer — Jim Lord, DFL., $30,000.
(DFL means Democratic-Farmer-Labor. IR means Independent Republican.)
Legislature: meets for a total of 120 days within every 2 years, at St. Paul. Members receive $8,400 per year plus expense allowance during session.
Senate — DFL., 49; IR, 18. Total, 67.
House — DFL., 103; IR, 31. Total, 134.

Mississippi

Governor — Cliff Finch, D., $43,000.
Lt. Gov. — Evelyn Gandy, D., $15,000 per regular legislative session, plus expense allowance.
Sec. of State — Heber Ladner, D., $28,000.
Auditor — W. H. (Hamp) King, D., $26,000.
Atty. Gen. — A. L. Summer, D., $30,000.
Treasurer — Edwin Lloyd Pittman, D., $26,000.
Supt. Public Educ. — Charles E. Holladay, D., $26,000.
Legislature: meets annually in January, at Jackson. Members receive $8,100 per regular session, plus travel allowance and $210 per month while not in session.
Senate — Dem., 50; Rep., 2. Total, 52.
House — Dem., 119; Rep., 2; Ind., 1. Total, 122.

Missouri

Governor — Joseph P. Teasdale, D., $37,500.
Lt. Gov. — William C. Phelps, R., $16,000.
Sec. of State — James C. Kirkpatrick, D., $25,000.
Atty. Gen. — John Ashcroft, R., $25,000.
Treasurer — James I. Spainhower, D., $20,000.
Comm. of Educ. — Arthur L. Mallory.
General Assembly: meets in Jefferson City annually, first Wednesday after first Monday in January; adjournment in odd-numbered years by June 30, in even-numbered years by May 15. Members receive $8,400 per annum.
Senate — Dem., 22; Rep., 12. Total, 34.
House — Dem., 112; Rep., 51. Total, 163.

Montana

Governor — Thomas L. Judge, D., $30,000.
Lt. Gov. — Ted Schwinden, D., $20,500.
Sec. of State — Frank Murray, D., $18,000.
Auditor — E. V. (Sonny) Omholt, R., $18,000.
Atty. Gen. — Mike Greely, D., $25,000.
Supt. Public Instru. — Georgia Ruth Rice, D., $20,000.
Legislative Assembly: meets biennially in January, at

Helena. Members receive $31.62 per month plus $40 per day for expenses while in session.
Senate — Dem., 25; Rep., 25. Total, 50.
House — Dem., 57; Rep., 43. Total, 100.

Nebraska

Governor — J. James Exon, D., $40,000.
Lt. Gov. — Gerald T. Whelan, D., $25,000.
Sec. of State — Allen J. Beermann, R., $25,000.
Auditor — Ray A. C. Johnson, R., $25,000.
Atty. Gen. — Paul Douglas, R., $32,500.
Treasurer — Frank Marsh, R., $25,000.
Legislature: meets annually in January, at Lincoln. Members receive salary of $4,800 annually plus travelling expenses for one round trip to and from session.
Unicameral body composed of 49 members who are elected on a nonpartisan ballot and are classed as senators.

Nevada

Governor — Mike O'Callaghan, D., $40,000.
Lt. Gov. — Robert Rose, D., $6,000 plus $60 per day when acting as governor and president of the Senate during legislative sessions.
Sec. of State — William D. Swackhamer, D., $25,000.
Comptroller — Wilson McGowen, R., $22,500.
Atty. Gen. — Robert List, R., $30,000.
Treasurer — Michael Mirabelli, D., $22,500.
Supt. Public Instr. — John Gambel.
Legislature: meets odd years in January, at Carson City. All members receive $60 per day for 60 days (20 days for special sessions). All members receive per diem of $40 per day for 60 days (20 days special session). Travel allowance of 10c per mile.
Senate — Dem., 17; Rep., 3. Total, 20.
Assembly — Dem., 35; Rep., 5. Total, 40.

New Hampshire

Governor — Meldrim Thomson, Jr., R., $34,070.
Sec. of State — William M. Gardner, D., $25,216.
Atty. Gen. — David H. Souter, $28,846.
Comptroller — Arthur H. Fowler.
Comm. of Education — Robert L. Brunelle.
Dir. of Accounts — Donald Bernier.
Treasurer — Robert W. Flanders, R., $25,216.
General Court (Legislature): meets odd years, in January, at Concord. Members receive $200; presiding officers $250.
Senate — Dem., 12; Rep., 12. Total, 24.
House — Dem., 180; Rep., 219, vacancies, 1. Total, 400.

New Jersey

Governor — Brendan Byrne, D., $65,000 (returned $5,000).
Sec. of State — George Lee (acting), $43,000.
Atty. Gen. — William F. Hyland, $43,000.
Treasurer — Clifford Goldman, $43,000.
Auditor — George B. Harper, $21,250.
Comm. of Education — Fred G. Burke, $43,000.
Legislature: meets annually, in January, at Trenton. Members receive $10,000 per year, except president of Senate and speaker of Assembly who receive 1/3 more by virtue of their office.
Senate — Dem., 29; Rep., 10; Ind., 1. Total, 40.
Assembly — Dem., 48; Rep. 31; vacancy, 1. Total, 80.

New Mexico

Governor — Jerry Apodaca, D., $35,000*.
Lt. Gov. — Robert E. Ferguson, D., $15,000, $75 per day when presiding over Senate. Acting governor, $75 per day*.
Sec. of State — Ernestine D. Evans, D., $30,000.
Auditor — Max Sanchez, D., $30,000.
Atty. Gen. — Toney Anaya, D., $35,000.
Treasurer — Edward Murphy, D., $30,000.
Legislature: meets in January, at Sante Fe, odd years for 60 days, even years for 30 days. Members receive $24 per day while in session.
Senate — Dem., 33; Rep., 9. Total, 42.
House — Dem., 48; Rep., 22. Total, 70.
*Gov. refused $5,000 increase; Lt. Gov. turned down $15,000 raise.

New York

Governor — Hugh L. Carey, D., $85,000.
Lt. Gov. — Mary Anne Krupsak, D., $60,000.
Sec. of State — Mario M. Cuomo, D., $47,800.
Comptroller — Arthur Levitt, D., $60,000.
Atty. Gen. — Louis J. Lefkowitz, R., $60,000.
Legislature: meets annually, in January, at Albany. Members receive $23,500 per year.
Senate — Dem., 25; Rep., 35. Total, 60.
Assembly — Dem., 89; Rep., 60; Vacancy, 1. Total, 150.

North Carolina

Governor — James B. Hunt, D., $45,000.
Lt. Gov. — James C. Greene, D., $30,000 per year, plus $20 per day not to exceed 120 days per regular session; $4,000 per year expense allowance.
Sec. of State — Thad Eure, D., $32,544.
Auditor — Henry L. Bridges, D., $32,544.
Atty. Gen. — Rufus L. Edmisten, D., $36,708.
Treasurer — Harlan E. Boyles, D., $32,544.
Supt. Public Instr. — Craig Phillips, D., $35,148.
General Assembly: meets odd years in January, at Raleigh. Members receive $4,800 annual salary and $1,200 annual expense allowance plus subsistence and travel allowance while in session.
Senate — Dem., 46; Rep., 4. Total, 50.
House — Dem., 114; Rep., 6. Total, 120.

North Dakota

Governor — Arthur A. Link, D., $27,500.
Lt. Gov. — Wayne Sanstead, D., $5,000.
Sec. of State — Ben Meier, R., $22,500.
Auditor — Robert W. Peterson, R., $22,500.
Atty. Gen. — Allen I. Olson, R., $25,000.
Treasurer — Walter Christensen, $22,500.
Supt. Public Instruction — H. J. Snortland, $22,500.
Legislative Assembly: meets odd years, in January at Bismarck. Members receive $65 per day during session, plus $75 per month.
Senate — Dem., 18; Rep., 22. Total 51.
House — Dem., 50; Rep., 50. Total 100.

Ohio

Governor — James A. Rhodes, R., $50,000.
Lt. Gov. — Richard F. Celeste, D., $30,000.
Sec. of State — Ted W. Brown, R., $38,000.
Atty. Gen. — William J. Brown, D., $38,000.
Auditor — Thomas E. Ferguson, D., $38,000.
Treasurer — Gertrude W. Donahey, D., $38,000.
General Assembly: meets at Columbus on first Monday in January in odd-numbered years; no later than Mar. 15 of following year for 2d session. Members receive $17,500 per annum.
Senate — Dem., 21; Rep., 12. Total, 33.
House — Dem., 62; Rep., 37. Total, 99.

Oklahoma

Governor — David L. Boren, D., $42,500.
Lt. Gov. — George Nigh, D., $24,000.
Sec. of State — Jerome W. Byrd, D., $18,500.
Auditor — Joe Bailey Cobb, D., $18,500.
Atty. Gen. — Larry Derryberry, D., $27,500.
Treasurer — Leo Winters, D., $22,000.
Supt. Public Instr. — Leslie R. Fisher, D., $30,000.
Legislature: meets each year in January, at Oklahoma City. Members receive $12,948.
Senate — Dem., 39; Rep., 9. Total, 48.
House — Dem., 79; Rep., 22. Total, 101.

Oregon

Governor — Robert W. Straub, D., $42,350, plus $1,000 monthly expenses.
Sec. of State — Norma Paulus, R., $35,090.
Atty. Gen. — James A. Redden, R., $35,090.
Treasurer — Clay Meyers, R., $35,090.
Supt. Public Instr. — Verne A. Duncan, N-P, $35,090.
Legislative Assembly: meets odd years, in January, at Salem. Members receive $484 monthly and $39 expenses per day while in session; $175 per month while not in session.
Senate — Dem., 24; Rep., 6; Ind., 1. Total, 31.
House — Dem., 37; Rep., 23. Total, 60.

Pennsylvania

Governor — Milton J. Shapp, D., $60,000.
Lt. Gov. — Ernest P. Kline, D., $45,000.
Sec. of State — C. DeLores Tucker, D., $35,000.
Atty. Gen. — Robert Kane, D., $40,000.
Treasurer — Robert E. Casey, D., $42,500.
General Assembly — meets annually, in January, at Harrisburg. Members receive $18,720 per year plus $10,000 for expenses.
Senate — Dem., 29; Rep., 19; vacancies, 2.
House — Dem., 118; Rep., 84; vacancies, 1. Total, 203.

Rhode Island

Governor — J. Joseph Garrahy, D., $42,500.
Lt. Gov. — Thomas R. DiLuglio, D., $25,500.
Sec. of State — Robert F. Burns, D., $25,500.
Atty. Gen. — Julius C. Michaelson, D., $31,875.
Treasurer — Anthony J. Solomon, D., $25,500.
General Assembly: meets annually, in January, at Providence. Members receive $5 per day for 60 days (the speaker, $10), also travel allowance of 8c per mile.
Senate —Dem., 45; Rep., 5. Total, 50.
House — Dem., 83; Rep., 17. Total, 100.

South Carolina

Governor — James B. Edwards, R., $39,000.
Lt. Gov. — W. Brantley Harvey Jr., D., $16,250.
Sec. of State — O. Frank Thornton, D., $34,000.
Comptroller Gen. — Earle E. Morris Jr., D., $34,000.
Atty. Gen. — Daniel R. McLeod, D., $34,000.
Treasurer — G. L. Patterson Jr., D., $34,000.
Supt. of Educ. — Cyril B. Busbee, D., $34,000.
General Assembly: meets annually in January, at Columbia. Members receive $7,000 per year plus expense allowance of $25 per day and travel and postage allowance.
Senate — Dem., 40; Rep., 6. Total, 46.
House — Dem. 114; Rep., 10. Total, 124.

South Dakota

Governor — Richard F. Kneip, D., $32,000 (as of 1979).
Lt. Gov. — Harvey Wollman, D., $4,500 per 30-day legislative session, $7,500 for 45-day session, plus $40 per legislative day.
Sec. of State — Lorna B. Herseth, D., $22,500.
Treasurer — David Volk, R., $22,500.
Atty. Gen. — William J. Janklow, R., $30,000.
Auditor — Alice Kundert, R., $22,500.
Legislature: meets annually in January, at Pierre. Members receive $3,000 for 45-day session in odd-numbered years, and $2,000 for 30-day session in even-numbered years, plus $25 per legislative day.
Senate — Dem., 11; Rep., 24. Total, 35.
House — Dem., 22; Rep., 48. Total, 70.

Tennessee

Governor — Ray Blanton, D., $50,000.
Lt. Gov. — John S. Wilder, D.
Sec. of State — Gentry Crowell, D., $41,280.
Comptroller — William Snodgrass, D., $38,000.
Atty. Gen. — Brooks McLemore, D., $47,628.
Comm. of Education — Sam Ingram, D.
General Assembly: meets annually in January, at Nashville. Members receive $7,800.96 yearly plus $58.99 expenses for each day in session (not to exceed 105 days).
Senate — Dem., 23; Rep., 9; Ind., 1. Total, 33.
House — Dem., 66; Rep., 32; Ind., 1. Total, 99.

Texas

Governor — Dolph Briscoe, D., $66,800.
Lt. Gov. — Bill Hobby, D., same salary as state senator while presiding over Senate, plus living quarters. Governor's salary when acting as governor.
Sec. of State — Mark W. White, D., $39,900.
Comptroller — Bob Bullock, D., $42,300.
Atty. Gen. — John L. Hill, D., $42,300.
Treasurer — Jesse James, D., $42,300.
Legislature: meets odd years in January, at Austin. Members receive annual salary not exceeding $7,200 plus per diem while in session and travel allowance.
Senate — Dem., 28; Rep., 3. Total, 31.
House — Dem., 132; Rep., 18. Total, 150.

Utah

Governor — Scott M. Matheson, D., $40,000.
Sec. of State/Lt. Gov. — David S. Monson, R., $26,500.
Auditor — Richard Jensen, R., $26,500.
Atty. Gen. — Robert B. Hansen, R., $30,000.
Treasurer — Linn C. Baker, D., $26,500.
Legislature: convenes for 60 days on 2d Monday in January in odd-numbered years; for 20 days in even-numbered years; members receive $25 per day, plus $15 daily expenses, plus mileage.
Senate — Dem., 17; Rep., 12. Total, 29.
House — Dem., 35; Rep., 40. Total, 75.

Vermont

Governor — Richard A. Snelling, R., $36,100.
Lt. Gov. — T. Garry Buckley, R., $15,500.
Sec. of State — James A. Guest, D., $19,600.
Auditor — Alexander V. Acebo, R., $19,600.
Atty. Gen. — M. Jerome Diamond, D., $24,700.
Treasurer — Emory H. Hebard, R., $19,600.
General Assembly: meets odd years, in January, at Montpelier. Members receive $150 weekly, while in session, with a limit of $4,500 for a regular session and $30 per day for special session, with specified expenses.
Senate — Dem., 9; Rep., 21. Total, 30.
House — Dem., 68; Rep., 70; R/D, 4; D/R, 3; I/D, 1; D/I, 3; I, 1. Total, 150.

Virginia

Governor — Mills E. Godwin Jr., R., $50,000.
Lt. Gov. — John N. Dalton, R., $10,525.
Atty. Gen. — Anthony F. Troy, D., $37,500.
Sec. of the Commonwealth — Patricia R. Perkinson, $20,000.
Treasurer — Robert C. Watts Jr., R., $31,800.
Auditor — Charles K. Trible, $27,700.
Supt. Public Instr. — Dr. Walter E. Campbell.
General Assembly: meets every year in January, at Richmond. Members receive $5,475 annually.
Senate — Dem., 34; Rep., 6. Total, 40.
House — Dem., 79; Rep., 17; Ind., 4. Total, 100.

Washington

Governor — Dixy Lee Ray, R., $42,150.
Lt. Gov. — John A. Cherberg, D., $17,800.
Sec. of State — Bruce K. Chapman, R., $21,400.
Auditor — R. V. Graham, D., $24,950.
Atty. Gen. — Slade Gorton, R., $31,500.
Treasurer — Robert S. O'Brien, D., $24,150.
Supt. of Public Instr. — Dr. Frank Brouillet, NP, $31,500.
Legislature: meets odd years in January, at Olympia. Members receive $7,200 annually, plus $40 per day while in session for subsistence and lodging.
Senate — Dem., 30; Rep., 19. Total, 49.
House — Dem., 62; Rep., 36. Total, 98.

West Virginia

Governor — John D. Rockefeller 4th, D., $50,000.
Sec. of State — A. James Manchin, D., $30,000.
Auditor — Glen B. Gainer Jr., D., $32,000.
Atty. Gen. — Chauncey Browning Jr., D., $35,000.
Treasurer — Larry Bailey, D., $35,000.
Comm. of Agric. — Gus R. Douglas, D., $32,500.
Legislature: meets annually in January, at Charleston. Members receive compensation fixed by citizens' commission.
Senate — Dem., 28; Rep., 6. Total, 34.
House — Dem., 91; Rep., 9. Total, 100.

Wisconsin

Governor — Patrick J. Lucey, D., $44,292.
Lt. Gov. — Martin J. Schreiber, D., $28,668.
Sec. of State — Douglas La Follette, D., $13,500.
Treasurer — Charles P. Smith, D., $22,140.
Atty. Gen. — Bronson C. LaFollette, D., $36,450.
Supt. of Public Instr. — Barbara Thompson, NP, $36,450.
Legislature: meets in January, at Madison. Members receive $15,678 annually plus $25 per day expenses.
Senate — Dem., 23; Rep., 10. Total, 33.
Assembly — Dem., 66; Rep., 33. Total, 99.

Wyoming

Governor — Ed Herschler, D., $37,500.
Sec. of State — Mrs. Thyra Thomson, R., $23,000.
Auditor — James B. Griffith, R., $23,000.
Atty. Gen. — V. Frank Mendicino, D., $24,000.
Treasurer — Edwin J. Wirtzenburger, R., $23,000.
Supt. of Public Instr. — Robert G. Schrader, R., $23,000.
Legislature: meets odd years in January, even years in February, at Cheyenne. Members receive $30 per day while in session, plus $36 per day for expenses.
Senate — Dem., 12; Rep., 18. Total, 30.
House — Dem., 29; Rep. 32; Ind. 1. Total, 62.

Puerto Rico

Governor — Carlos Romero-Barcelo, $36,200.
Secretaries (all at $26,200):
Agric. — Heriberto J. Martinez Torres.
Commerce — Juan H. Cintron.
Educ. — Carlos Chardon.
Health — Dr. Jaime Rivera Dueno.
Justice — Miguel Gimenez Munoz.
Labor — Carlos S. Uiros.
Public Works — Manuel A. Pietrantoni.
Social Services — Dr. Jenaro Collazo.
State — Reinaldo Paniagua.
Treasury — Julio Cesar Perez.
All officials belong to the New Progressive party.
Legislative Assembly: composed of a Senate of 27 members and a House of Representatives of 51 members. Meets annually, in January, at San Juan. Members receive $15,000 plus expenses and travel allowances.

Judiciary of the U.S.

Data as of July 15, 1977

Justices of the United States Supreme Court

The Supreme Court comprises the chief justice of the United States and 8 associate justices, all appointed by the president with advice and consent of the Senate. Salaries: chief justice $75,000 annually, associate justice $72,000.

Name; apptd from *Chief Justices in italics*	Service Term	Yrs.	Born	Died
John Jay, N. Y.	1789-1795	5	1745	1829
John Rutledge, S. C.	1789-1791	1	1739	1800
William Cushing, Mass.	1789-1810	20	1732	1810
James Wilson, Pa.	1789-1798	8	1742	1798
John Blair, Va.	1789-1796	6	1732	1800
James Iredell, N. C.	1790-1799	9	1751	1799
Thomas Johnson, Md.	1791-1793	1	1732	1819
William Paterson, N. J.	1793-1806	13	1745	1806
John Rutledge, S. C.	1795(a)	—	1739	1800
Samuel Chase, Md.	1796-1811	15	1741	1811
Oliver Ellsworth, Conn.	1796-1800	4	1745	1807
Bushrod Washington, Va.	1798-1829	31	1762	1829
Alfred Moore, N. C.	1799-1804	4	1755	1810
John Marshall, Va.	1801-1835	34	1755	1835
William Johnson, S. C.	1804-1834	30	1771	1834
Henry B. Livingston, N.Y.	1806-1823	16	1757	1823
Thomas Todd, Ky.	1807-1826	18	1765	1826
Joseph Story, Mass.	1811-1845	33	1779	1845
Gabriel Duval, Md.	1811-1835	22	1752	1844
Smith Thompson, N. Y.	1823-1843	20	1768	1843
Robert Trimble, Ky.	1826-1828	2	1777	1828
John McLean, Oh.	1829-1861	32	1785	1861
Henry Baldwin, Pa.	1830-1844	14	1780	1844
James M. Wayne, Ga.	1835-1867	32	1790	1867
Roger B. Taney, Md.	1836-1864	28	1777	1864
Philip P. Barbour, Va.	1836-1841	4	1783	1841
John Catron, Tenn.	1837-1865	28	1786	1865
John McKinley, Ala.	1837-1852	15	1780	1852
Peter V. Daniel, Va.	1841-1860	19	1784	1860
Samuel Nelson, N. Y.	1845-1872	27	1792	1873
Levi Woodbury, N. H.	1845-1851	5	1789	1851
Robert C. Grier, Pa.	1846-1870	23	1794	1870
Benjamin R. Curtis, Mass.	1851-1857	6	1809	1874
John A. Campbell, Ala.	1853-1861	8	1811	1889
Nathan Clifford, Me.	1858-1881	23	1803	1881
Noah H. Swayne, Oh.	1862-1881	18	1804	1884
Samuel F. Miller, Ia.	1862-1890	28	1816	1890
David Davis, Ill.	1862-1877	14	1815	1886
Stephen J. Field, Cal.	1863-1897	34	1816	1899
Salmon P. Chase, Oh.	1864-1873	8	1808	1873
William Strong, Pa.	1870-1880	10	1808	1895
Joseph P. Bradley, N. J.	1870-1892	21	1813	1892
Ward Hunt, N. Y.	1872-1882	9	1810	1886
Morrison R. Waite, Oh.	1874-1888	14	1816	1888
John M. Harlan, Ky.	1877-1911	34	1833	1911
William B. Woods, Ga.	1880-1887	6	1824	1887
Stanley Matthews, Oh.	1881-1889	7	1824	1889
Horace Gray, Mass.	1881-1902	20	1828	1902
Samuel Blatchford, N.Y.	1882-1893	11	1820	1893
Lucius Q.C. Lamar, Miss.	1888-1893	5	1825	1893
Melville W. Fuller, Ill.	1888-1910	21	1833	1910
David J. Brewer, Kan.	1889-1910	20	1837	1910
Henry B. Brown, Mich.	1890-1906	15	1836	1913
George Shiras Jr., Pa.	1892-1903	10	1832	1924
Howell E. Jackson, Tenn.	1893-1895	2	1832	1895
Edward D. White, La.	1894-1910	16	1845	1921
Rufus W. Peckham, N.Y.	1895-1909	13	1838	1909
Joseph McKenna, Cal.	1898-1925	26	1843	1926
Oliver W. Holmes, Mass.	1902-1932	29	1841	1935
William R. Day, Oh.	1903-1922	19	1849	1923
William H. Moody, Mass.	1906-1910	3	1853	1917
Horace H. Lurton, Tenn.	1909-1914	4	1844	1914
Charles E. Hughes, N.Y.	1910-1916	5	1862	1948
Willis Van Devanter, Wy.	1910-1937	26	1859	1941
Joseph R. Lamar, Ga.	1910-1916	5	1857	1916
Edward D. White, La.	1910-1921	10	1845	1921
Mahlon Pitney, N. J.	1912-1922	10	1858	1924
Jas. C. McReynolds, Tenn.	1914-1941	26	1862	1946
Louis D. Brandeis, Mass.	1916-1939	22	1856	1941
John H. Clarke, Oh.	1916-1922	5	1857	1945
William H. Taft, Conn.	1921-1930	8	1857	1930
George Sutherland, Ut.	1922-1938	15	1862	1942
Pierce Butler, Minn.	1922-1939	16	1866	1939
Edward T. Sanford, Tenn.	1923-1930	7	1865	1930
Harlan F. Stone, N. Y.	1925-1941	16	1872	1946
Charles E. Hughes, N.Y.	1930-1941	11	1862	1948
Owen J. Roberts, Pa.	1930-1945	15	1875	1955
Benjamin N. Cardozo, N.Y.	1932-1938	6	1870	1938
Hugo L. Black, Ala.	1937-1971	34	1886	1971
Stanley F. Reed, Ky.	1938-1957	19	1884	—
Felix Frankfurter, Mass.	1939-1962	23	1882	1965
William O. Douglas, Conn.	1939-1975	36	1898	—
Frank Murphy, Mich.	1940-1949	9	1890	1949
Harlan F. Stone, N.Y.	1941-1946	5	1872	1946
James F. Byrnes, S. C.	1941-1942	1	1879	1972
Robert H. Jackson, N.Y.	1941-1954	12	1892	1954
Wiley B. Rutledge, Ia.	1943-1949	6	1894	1949
Harold H. Burton, Oh.	1945-1958	13	1888	1964
Fred M. Vinson, Ky.	1946-1953	7	1890	1953
Tom C. Clark, Tex.	1949-1967	18	1899	1977
Sherman Minton, Ind.	1949-1956	7	1890	1965
Earl Warren, Cal.	1953-1969	16	1891	1974
John Marshall Harlan, N. Y.	1955-1971	16	1899	1971
William J. Brennan Jr., N.J.	1956 —	—	1906	—
Charles E. Whittaker, Mo.	1957-1962	5	1901	1973
Potter Stewart, Oh.	1958 —	—	1915	—
Byron R. White, Col.	1962 —	—	1917	—
Arthur J. Goldberg, Ill.	1962-1965	3	1908	—
Abe Fortas, Tenn.	1965-1969	4	1910	—
Thurgood Marshall, N.Y.	1967 —	—	1908	—
Warren E. Burger, Va.	1969 —	—	1907	—
Harry A. Blackmun, Minn.	1970 —	—	1908	—
Lewis F. Powell Jr., Va.	1971 —	—	1907	—
William H. Rehnquist, Ariz.	1971 —	—	1924	—
John Paul Stevens, Ill.	1975 —	—	1920	—

(a) Rejected Dec. 15, 1795.

U.S. Court of Customs and Patent Appeals

Washington, D.C. 20439 (Salaries, $57,500)

Chief Judge — Howard T. Markey.

Associate Judges — Giles S. Rich, Phillip B. Baldwin, Donald E. Lane, Jack R. Miller.

U. S. Court of Claims

Washington, D.C. 20005 (Salaries, $57,500)

Chief Judge — vacant.

Associate Judges — Oscar H. Davis, Shiro Kashiwa, Robert L. Kunzig, Marion T. Bennett, Philip Nichols Jr.

U. S. Customs Court

New York, N.Y. 10007 (Salaries, $54,500)

Chief Judge — Edward D. Re.

Judges — Morgan Ford, Scovel Richardson, Frederick Landis, James L. Watson, Herbert N. Maletz, Bernard Newman, Paul P. Rao, Nils A. Boe.

U. S. Tax Court

Washington, D.C. 20217 (Salaries, $54,500)

Chief Judge — Howard A. Dawson Jr.

Judges — Arnold Raum, Irene F. Scott, William M. Fay, William M. Drennen, Theodore Tannenwald Jr., Charles R. Simpson, C. Moxley Featherston, Leo H. Irwin, Samuel B.

Sterrett, William Quealy, William A. Goffe, Cynthia H. Hall, Darrell D. Wiles, Richard C. Wilbur.

U.S. Courts of Appeals

(Salaries, $57,500. CJ means Chief Judge)

District of Columbia — David L. Bazelon, CJ; J. Skelly Wright, Carl McGowan, Edward Allen Tamm, Harold Leventhal, Spottswood W. Robinson III, Roger Robb, George E. MacKinnon, Malcolm Richard Wilkey; Clerk's office, Washington, D.C. 20001.

First Circuit (Me., Mass., N.H., R.I., Puerto Rico) — Frank M. Coffin, CJ; Levin H. Campbell; Clerk's Office, Boston, Mass. 02109.

Second Circuit (Conn., N.Y., Vt.) — Irving R. Kaufman, CJ; Wilfred Feinberg, Walter R. Mansfield, William H. Mulligan, James L. Oakes, William H. Timbers, Murray I. Gurfein, Ellsworth Van Graafeiland, Thomas J. Meskill; Clerk's Office, New York, N.Y. 10007.

Third Circuit (Del., N.J., Pa., Virgin Is.) — Collins J. Seitz, CJ; Ruggero J. Aldisert, Arlin M. Adams, John J. Gibbons, Max Rosenn, James Hunter 3d, Joseph F. Weis Jr., Leonard I. Garth; Clerk's Office, Philadelphia, Pa. 19106.

Fourth Circuit (Md., N.C., S.C., Va., W.Va.) — Clement F. Haynsworth Jr., CJ; Harrison L. Winter, Kenneth K. Hall, John D. Butzner Jr., Donald Stuart Russell, H. Emory Widener Jr.; Clerk's Office, Richmond, Va. 23219.

Fifth Circuit (Ala., Fla., Ga., La., Miss., Tex., Canal Zone) — John R. Brown, CJ; Homer Thornberry, James P. Coleman, Irving L. Goldberg, Robert A. Ainsworth Jr., John C. Godbold, Lewis R. Morgan, Charles Clark, Thomas G. Gee, Paul H. Roney, Gerald B. Tjoflat, James C. Hill, Peter T. Fay; Clerk's Office, New Orleans, La. 70130.

Sixth Circuit (Ky., Mich., Ohio, Tenn.) — Harry Phillips, CJ; Paul C. Weick, George Clifton Edwards Jr., Anthony J. Celebrezze, John W. Peck, Albert J. Engel, Pierce Lively; Clerk's Office, Cincinnati, Oh. 45202.

Seventh Circuit (Ill., Ind., Wis.) — Thomas E. Fairchild, CJ; Luther M. Swygert, Walter J. Cummings, Wilbur F. Pell Jr., Robert A. Sprecher, Philip W. Tone, Harlington Wood Jr., William J. Bauer; Clerk's Office, Chicago, Ill. 60604.

Eighth Circuit (Ark., Ia., Minn., Mo., Neb., N.D., S.D.) — Floyd R. Gibson, CJ; Donald P. Lay, Gerald W. Heaney, Myron H. Bright, Donald R. Ross, Roy L. Stephenson, William H. Webster, J. Smith Henley; Clerk's Office, St. Louis, Mo. 63101.

Ninth Circuit (Ariz., Cal., Ida., Mont., Nev., Ore., Wash., Alaska, Ha., Guam) — James R. Browning, CJ; Walter Ely, Shirley M. Hufstedler, Eugene A. Wright, Ozell M. Trask, Joseph T. Sneed, Herbert Y. C. Choy, J. Clifford Wallace, Alfred T. Goodwin, Anthony M. Kennedy, J. Blaine Anderson; Clerk's Office, San Francisco, Cal. 94101.

Tenth Circuit (Col., Kan., N.M., Okla., Ut., Wy.) — David T. Lewis, CJ; Oliver Seth, William J. Holloway Jr., Robert H. McWilliams, James E. Barrett, William E. Boyle; Clerk's Office, Denver, Col. 80202.

Temporary Emergency Court of Appeals —Edward Allen Tamm, CJ; Clerk's Office, Washington, D.C. 20001.

U. S. District Courts

(Salaries, $54,500. CJ means Chief Judge)

Alabama — Northern: Frank H. McFadden, CJ; Sam C. Pointer Jr., James Hughes Hancock, J. Foy Guin Jr.; Clerk's Office, Birmingham 35203. **Middle:** Frank M. Johnson Jr., CJ; Robert E. Varner; Clerk's Office, Montgomery 36101. **Southern:** Virgil Pittman, CJ; William Brevard Hand; Clerk's Office, Mobile 36602.

Alaska — James A. Von der Heydt, CJ; James M. Fitzgerald; Clerk's Office, Anchorage 99510.

Arizona — Walter Early Craig, CJ; C. A. Muecke, William P. Copple, William C. Frey, Mary Ann Richey; Clerk's Office, Phoenix 85025.

Arkansas — Eastern: Garnett Thomas Eisele, CJ; Terry L. Shell; Clerk's Office, Little Rock 72203. **Western:** Paul X. Williams, CJ; Terry L. Shell; Clerk's Office, Fort Smith 72901.

California—Northern: Robert F. Peckham, CJ; Lloyd H. Burke, Stanley A. Weigel, Robert H. Schnacke, Samuel Conti, Spencer M. Williams, Charles B. Renfrew; William H. Orrick Jr., William H. Schwarzer, William A. Ingraham, Cecil F. Poole; Clerk's Office, San Francisco 94102. **Eastern:** Thomas J. MacBride, CJ; M. D. Crocker, Philip C. Wilkins; Clerk's Office, Sacramento 95814. **Central:** Albert Lee Stephens Jr., CJ; Francis C. Whelan, Irving Hill, A. Andrew Hauk, William P. Gray, Warren J. Ferguson, Manuel L. Real, Harry Pregerson, David W. Williams, Robert J. Kelleher, Wm. Matthew Byrne Jr., Lawrence T. Lydick, Malcolm M. Lucas, Robert Firth, Robert M. Takasugi, Laughlin E. Waters; Clerk's Office, Los Angeles 90012. **Southern:** Edward J. Schwartz, CJ; Howard B. Turrentine, Gordon Thompson Jr., Leland C. Nielsen, William B. Enright; Clerk's Office, San Diego 92101.

Colorado — Fred M. Winner, CJ; Sherman G. Finesilver, Richard P. Matsch; Clerk's Office, Denver 80294.

Connecticut — T. Emmet Clarie, CJ; Robert C. Zampano, Jon O. Newman; Clerk's Office, New Haven 06505.

Delaware — James L. Latchum, CJ; Walter K. Stapleton, Murray M. Schwartz; Clerk's Office, Wilmington 19801.

District of Columbia —William B. Bryant, CJ; George L. Hart Jr., John J. Sirica, Howard F. Corcoran, Oliver Gasch, John Lewis Smith Jr., Aubrey E. Robinson Jr., Joseph C. Waddy, Gerhard A. Gesell, John H. Pratt, June L. Green, Barrington D. Parker, Charles R. Richey, Thomas A. Flannery; Clerk's Office, Washington, D.C. 20001.

Florida—Northern: Winston E. Arnow, CJ; William H. Stafford Jr.; Clerk's Office, Tallahassee 32302. **Middle:** George C. Young, CJ; Ben Krentzman, Howard W. Melton, William Terrell Hodges, John A. Reed Jr.; Clerk's Office, Jacksonville 32201. **Southern:** Charles B. Fulton, CJ; C. Clyde Atkins, Joe Eaton, James Lawrence King, Norman C. Roettger Jr.; Clerk's Office, Miami 33101.

Georgia — Northern: Albert J. Henderson Jr., CJ; William C. O'Kelley, Charles A. Moye Jr., Richard C. Freeman; Clerk's Office, Atlanta 30303. **Middle:** J. Robert Elliott, CJ; Wilbur D. Ownes Jr.; Clerk's Office, Macon 31202. **Southern:** Anthony A. Alaimo, CJ; Alexander A. Lawrence; Clerk's Office, Savannah 31402.

Hawaii — Samuel P. King, CJ; Dick Yin Wong; Clerk's Office, Honolulu 96801.

Idaho — Ray McNichols, CJ; Marion J. Callister; Clerk's Office, Boise 83724.

Illinois — Northern: James B. Parsons, CJ; Hubert L. Will, Bernard M. Decker, Frank J. McGarr, Thomas R. McMillen, Prentice H. Marshall, Joel M. Flaum, Alfred Y. Kirkland, John F. Grady, George N. Leighton, John Powers Crowley; Clerk's Office, Chicago 60604. **Eastern:** Henry S. Wise, CJ; James L. Foreman; Clerk's Office, Danville 61832. **Southern:** Robert D. Morgan, CJ; J. Waldo Ackerman; Clerk's Office, Peoria 61601.

Indiana — Northern: Jesse E. Eschbach, CJ; Allen Sharp, Phil M. McNagny Jr.; Clerk's Office, Hammond 46325. **Southern:** William E. Steckler, CJ; Cale J. Holder, S. Hugh Dillin, James E. Noland; Clerk's Office, Indianapolis 46204.

Iowa — Northern: Edward J. McManus, CJ; William C. Hanson; Clerk's Office, Cedar Rapids 52407. **Southern:** William C. Hanson, CJ; William C. Stuart; Clerk's Office, Des Moines 50309.

Kansas — Wesley E. Brown, CJ; Frank G. Theis, Earl E. O'Connor, Richard Dean Rodgers; Clerk's Office, Wichita 67201.

Kentucky — Eastern: Bernard T. Moynahan Jr., CJ; Howard David Hermansdorfer, Eugene E. Siler Jr.; Clerk's Office, Lexington 40501. **Western:** Rhodes Bratcher, CJ; Charles M. Allen, Eugene E. Siler Jr.; Clerk's Office, Louisville 40202.

Louisiana — Eastern: Frederick J. R. Heebe, CJ; Edward J. Boyle Sr., Lansing L. Mitchell, Fred J. Cassibry, Alvin B. Rubin, R. Blake West, Jack M. Gordon, Morey L. Sear, Charles Schwartz Jr.; Clerk's Office, New Orleans 70130. **Middle:** E. Gordon West; Clerk's Office, Baton Rouge 70801. **Western:** Nauman S. Scott, CJ; Tom Stagg, W. Eugene Davis; Clerk's Office, Shreveport 71161.

Maine — Edward Thaxter Gignoux; Clerk's Office, Portland 04112.

Maryland — Edward S. Northrop, CJ; Frank A. Kaufman, Alexander Harvey 2d, James R. Miller Jr., Joseph H. Young, Herbert F. Murray, C. Stanley Blair; Clerk's Office, Baltimore 21202.

Massachusetts — Andréw A. Caffrey, CJ; W. Arthur Garrity Jr., Frank J. Murray, Frank H. Freedman, Joseph L. Tauro, Walter Jay Skinner; Clerk's Office, Boston 02109.

Michigan — Eastern: Damon J. Keith, CJ; Lawrence Gubow, Cornelia G. Kennedy, John Feikens, Philip Pratt, Robert E. DeMascio, Charles W. Joiner, James Harvey, James P. Churchill, Ralph B. Guy Jr.; Clerk's Office, Detroit 48226. **Western:** Noel P. Fox, CJ; Wendell A. Miles; Clerk's Office, Grand Rapids 49503.

Minnesota — Edward J. Devitt, CJ; Earl R. Larson, Miles W. Lord, Donald D. Alsop; Clerk's Office, St. Paul 55101.

Mississippi — Northern: William C. Keady, CJ; Orma R. Smith; Clerk's Office, Oxford 38655. **Southern:** Dan M. Russell Jr., CJ; William Harold Cox, Walter L. Nixon Jr.; Clerk's Office, Jackson 39205.

Missouri — Eastern: James H. Meredith, CJ; John K. Regan, William R. Collinson, H. Kenneth Wangelin, John F. Nangle; Clerk's Office, St. Louis 63101. **Western:** John W.

Oliver, CJ; William R. Collinson, Elmo B. Hunter, H. Kenneth Wangelin; Clerk's Office, Kansas City 64106.

Montana — Russell E. Smith, CJ; James F. Battin; Clerk's Office, Great Falls 59403.

Nebraska — Warren K. Urbom, CJ; Robert V. Denney, Albert G. Schatz; Clerk's Office, Omaha 68101.

Nevada — Roger D. Foley, CJ; Bruce R. Thompson; Clerk's Office, Las Vegas 89101.

New Hampshire — Hugh H. Bownes; Clerk's Office, Concord 03301.

New Jersey — Lawrence A. Whipple, CJ; George H. Barlow, Clarkson S. Fisher, Frederick B. Lacey, Vincent P. Biunno, Herbert J. Stern, H. Curtis Meanor, John F. Gerry, Stanley S. Brotman; Clerk's Office, Trenton 08605.

New Mexico — H. Vearle Payne, CJ; Howard C. Bratton, Edwin L. Mechem; Clerk's Office, Albuquerque 87103.

New York — **Northern:** James T. Foley, CJ; Howard G. Munson; Clerk's Office, Albany 12201. **Eastern:** Jacob Mishler, CJ; Jack B. Weinstein, Mark A. Costantino, Edward R. Neaher, Thomas C. Platt Jr., Henry Bramwell, George C. Pratt; Clerk's Office, Brooklyn 11201. **Southern:** David N. Edelstein, CJ; Edward Weinfeld, Charles M. Metzner, Lloyd F. MacMahon, John M. Cannella, Charles H. Tenney, Marvin E. Frankel, Constance Baker Motley, Milton Pollack, Morris E. Lasker, Lawrence W. Pierce, Lee P. Gagliardi, Charles L. Brieant, Whitman Knapp, Charles E. Stewart Jr., Thomas P. Griesa, Robert L. Carter, Robert J. Ward, Kevin Thomas Duffy, William C. Conner, Richard Owen, Henry F. Werker, Gerard L. Goettel, Charles S. Haight Jr., Vincent L. Broderick; Clerk's Office, N. Y. City 10007. **Western:** John T. Curtin, CJ; Harold P. Burke, John T. Elfvin; Clerk's Office, Buffalo 14202.

North Carolina — **Eastern:** John D. Larkins Jr., CJ; Franklin T. Dupree Jr.; Clerk's Office, Raleigh 27611. **Middle:** Eugene A. Gordon, CJ; Hiram H. Ward; Clerk's Office, Greensboro 27402. **Western:** Woodrow Wilson Jones, CJ; James B. McMillan; Clerk's Office, Asheville 28802.

North Dakota — Paul Benson, CJ; Bruce M. Van Sickle; Clerk's Office, Bismarck 58501.

Ohio — **Northern:** Frank J. Battisti, CJ; Don J. Young, William K. Thomas, Thomas D. Lambros, Robert B. Krupansky, Nicholas J. Walinski, Leroy J. Contie Jr., John M. Manos; Clerk's Office, Cleveland 44114. **Southern:** Timothy S. Hogan, CJ; Joseph P. Kinneary, Davis S. Porter, Carl B. Rubin, Robert M. Duncan; Clerk's Office, Columbus 43215.

Oklahoma — **Northern:** Allen E. Barrow, CJ; Frederick A. Daugherty, H. Dale Cook; Clerk's Office, Tulsa 74103. **Eastern:** Joseph W. Morris, CJ; Frederick A. Daugherty, H. Dale Cook; Clark's Office, Muskogee 74401. **Western:** Frederick A. Daugherty, CJ; Luther B. Eubanks, H. Dale Cook, Ralph G. Thompson; Clerk's Office, Oklahoma City 73102.

Oregon — Otto R. Scopil Jr., CJ; Robert C. Belloni, James M. Burns; Clerk's Office, Portland 97207.

Pennsylvania — **Eastern:** Joseph S. Lord 3d, CJ; Alfred L. Luongo, A. Leon Higginbotham Jr., John P. Fullam, Charles R. Weiner, E. Mac Troutman, John B. Hannum, Daniel H. Huyett 3d, Donald W. VanArtsdalen, J. William Ditter Jr., Edward R. Becker, James H. Gorbey, Raymond J. Broderick, Clarence C. Newcomer, Clifford Scott Green, Louis Charles Bechtle, Herbert A. Fogel, Joseph L. McGlynn Jr., Edward N. Cahn; Clerk's Office, Philadelphia 19106. **Middle:** William J. Nealon Jr., CJ; R. Dixon Herman, Malcolm Muir; Clerk's Office, Scranton 18501. **Western:** Gerald J. Weber, CJ; Rabe Ferguson Marsh, Edward Dumbauld, William W. Knox, Hubert I. Teitelbaum, Barron P. McCune, Daniel J. Snyder Jr., Maurice B. Cohill Jr.; Clerk's Office, Pittsburgh 15230.

Rhode Island — Raymond J. Pettine, CJ; Edward William Day; Clerk's Office, Providence 02901.

South Carolina — J. Robert Martin Jr., CJ; Robert W. Hemphill, Charles E. Simons Jr., Solomon Blatt Jr., Robert F. Chapman; Clerk's Office, Columbia 29202.

South Dakota — Fred J. Nichol, CJ; Andrew A. Bogue; Clerk's Office, Sioux Falls 57102.

Tennessee — **Eastern:** Frank W. Wilson, CJ; Robert L. Taylor, C. G. Neese; Clerk's Office, Knoxville 37901. **Middle:** Frank Gray Jr., CJ; L. Clure Morton; Clerk's Office, Nashville 37203. **Western:** Bailey Brown, CJ; Robert M. McRae Jr., Harry W. Wellford; Clerk's Office, Memphis 38103.

Texas — **Northern:** Halbert O. Woodward, CJ; William M. Taylor Jr., Eldon B. Mahon, Robert M. Hill, Robert W. Porter, Patrick E. Higginbotham; Clerk's Office, Dallas 75242. **Southern:** Reynaldo G. Garza, CJ; John V. Singleton Jr., Woodrow B. Seals, Carl O. Bue Jr., Owen D. Cox, Robert O'Conor Jr., Ross N. Sterling; Clerk's Office, Houston 77208. **Eastern:** Joe J. Fisher, CJ; William Wayne Justice, William M. Steger; Clerk's Office, Beaumont 77704. **Western:** Adrian A. Spears, CJ; Dorwin W. Suttle, Jack Roberts, William S. Sessions, John H. Wood Jr.; Clerk's Office, San Antonio 78206.

Utah — Willis W. Ritter, CJ; Aldon J. Anderson; Clerk's Office, Salt Lake City 84101.

Vermont — James S. Holden, CJ; Albert W. Coffrin; Clerk's Office, Burlington 05401.

Virginia — **Eastern:** Richard B. Kellam, CJ; Robert R. Merhige Jr., John A. MacKenzie, Albert V. Bryan Jr., D. Dortch Warriner, J. Calvitt Clarke; Clerk's Office, Norfolk 23501. **Western:** James C. Turk, CJ; Glen M. Williams; Clerk's Office, Roanoke 24006.

Washington — **Eastern:** Marshall A. Neill, CJ; Clerk's Office, Spokane 99210. **Western:** Walter T. McGovern; Morell E. Sharp, Donald S. Voorhees; Clerk's Office, Seattle 98104.

West Virginia — **Northern:** Robert Earl Maxwell, CJ; Charles H. Haden 2d; Clerk's Office, Elkins 26241. **Southern:** Dennis Raymond Knapp, CJ; John T. Copenhaver Jr., Charles H. Haden 2d; Clerk's Office, Charleston 25329.

Wisconsin — **Eastern:** John W. Reynolds, CJ; Myron L. Gordon, Robert W. Warren; Clerk's Office, Milwaukee 53202. **Western:** James E. Doyle; Clerk's Office, Madison 53701.

Wyoming — Clarence A. Brimmer; Clerk's Office, Cheyenne 82001.

U.S. Territorial District Courts

Canal Zone — Clerk's Office, Balboa Heights.

Guam — Cristobal C. Duenas; Clerk's Office, P.O. Box 96910, Agana 96910.

Puerto Rico — Jose V. Toledo, CJ; Hernan G. Pesquera, Juan R. Torruella; Clerk's Office, San Juan 00904.

Virgin Islands — Almeric L. Christian, CJ; Warren H. Young; Clerk's Office, Charlotte Amalie, St. Thomas 00801.

The Federal Judicial System

The federal judicial system begins with the District Court. There are 94 of these courts, at least one in each state, in Washington, D.C., and in certain territories. Called courts of general jurisdiction, they have power to determine the facts and pass judgment in criminal cases involving violations of federal law and in civil cases where the amount of the suit is $10,000 or more and the contending parties reside in different states. Other types of cases handled by District Courts include suits in admiralty (maritime matters involving navigational waters), bankruptcy, patents, trademarks, and copyrights.

Equal to the District Courts are special courts which handle only certain issues: the U.S. Customs Court, the Tax Court, and the Court of Claims, which hears suits against the U.S. government.

These trial courts are responsible for finding the facts in a case and for applying the law to the facts found.

The District Courts and special courts are trial courts. Above them are several levels of appellate courts. The U.S. Courts of Appeals, often called circuit courts, sit in 10 judicial circuits and Washington, D.C. They hear appeals from the District Courts and the Tax Court, and will review decisions of federal administrative agencies if it appears that such decisions may be unreasonable or arbitrary. The U.S. Court of Customs and Patent Appeals hears appeals from the Customs Court.

Appellate courts, theoretically, do not review the trial court's findings of fact. The job of the appellate court is to decide whether the trial judge applied the law properly. If an appellate court decides that there was error in the application of the law, it can simply reverse the lower court's decision and end the case there. But it can also send the case back to the lower court for retrial or for other proceedings that may be appropriate.

Ultimately, all decisions of these courts can be reviewed by the U.S. Supreme Court, which is also the first court of appeal from the U.S. Court of Claims. Besides reviewing federal court decisions, the Supreme Court is empowered to hear suits between the states and to review state supreme court decisions if an issue of federal law or the Constitution is involved.

Presidential Election Statistics

Popular and Electoral Vote, 1972 and 1976

	1972				1976					
	Electoral Vote		Republican	Democrat	Electoral Vote		Democrat	Republican	Indep.	Libert.
States	Nixon	McGovern	Nixon	McGovern	Carter	Ford	Carter	Ford	McCarthy	MacBride
Ala.	9		728,701	256,923	9		659,170	504,070		1,481
Alas.	3		55,349	32,967		3	44,058	71,555		6,785
Ariz.	6		402,812	198,540		6	295,602	418,642	19,229	7,647
Ark.	6		445,751	198,899	6		498,604	267,903	639	
Cal.	45		4,602,096	3,475,847		45	3,742,284	3,882,244		56,388
Col.	7		597,189	329,980		7	460,801	584,278	26,047	5,338
Conn.	8		810,763	555,498		8	647,895	719,261		
Del.	3		140,357	92,298	3		122,461	109,780	2,432	
D.C.		3	35,226	127,627	3		137,818	27,873		274
Fla.	17		1,857,759	718,117	17		1,636,000	1,469,531	23,643	
Ga.	12		881,496	289,529	12		979,409	483,743		
Ha.	4		168,865	101,409	4		147,375	140,003		3,923
Ida.	4		199,384	80,826		4	126,549	204,151		3,558
Ill.	26		2,788,179	1,913,472		26	2,271,295	2,364,269	55,939	3,057
Ind.	13		1,405,154	708,568		13	1,014,714	1,185,958		
Ia.	8		706,207	496,206		8	619,931	632,863	20,051	1,452
Kan.	7		619,812	270,287		7	430,421	502,752	13,185	3,242
Ky.	9		676,446	371,159	9		615,717	531,852	6,837	814
La.	10		686,852	298,142	10		661,365	587,446	6,490	3,134
Me.	4		256,458	160,584		4	232,279	236,320	10,874	
Md.	10		829,305	505,781	10		759,612	672,661		
Mass.		14	1,112,078	1,332,540	14		1,429,475	1,030,276	65,637	135
Mich.	21		1,961,721	1,459,435		21	1,696,714	1,893,742	47,905	5,407
Minn.	10		898,269	802,346	10		1,070,440	819,395	35,490	3,529
Miss.	7		505,125	126,872	7		381,329	366,846	4,074	2,609
Mo.	12		1,154,058	698,531	12		998,387	927,443	24,029	
Mon.	4		183,976	120,197		4	149,259	173,703		
Neb.	5		406,298	169,991		5	233,293	359,219	9,383	1,476
Nev.	3		115,750	66,016		3	92,479	101,273		1,519
N.H.	4		213,724	116,435		4	147,645	185,935	4,095	936
N.J.	17		1,845,502	1,102,211		17	1,444,653	1,509,688	32,717	9,449
N.M.	4		235,606	141,084		4	201,148	211,419		1,110
N.Y.	41		4,192,778	2,951,084	41		3,389,558	3,100,791		12,197
N.C.	13		1,054,889	438,705	13		927,365	741,960		2,219
N.D.	3		174,109	100,384		3	136,078	153,684	2,952	256
Oh.	25		2,441,827	1,558,889	25		2,009,959	2,000,626	58,267	8,952
Okla.	8		759,025	247,147		8	532,442	545,708	14,101	
Ore.	6		486,686	392,760		6	490,407	492,120	40,207	
Pa.	27		2,714,521	1,796,951	27		2,328,677	2,205,604	50,584	
R.I.	4		218,290	191,981	4		227,636	181,249		715
S.C.	8		477,044	186,824	8		450,807	346,149		
S.D.	4		166,476	139,945		4	147,068	151,505		1,619
Tenn.	10		813,147	357,293	10		825,879	633,969	5,004	1,375
Tex.	26		2,298,896	1,154,289	26		2,082,319	1,953,300	20,118	
Ut.	4		323,643	126,284		4	182,110	337,908	3,907	2,438
Vt.	3		117,149	68,174		3	77,798	100,387	4,001	
Va.	11*		988,493	438,887		12	813,896	836,554		4,648
Wash.	9		837,135	568,334		8**	717,323	777,732	36,986	5,042
W. Va.	6		484,964	277,435	6		435,864	314,726		
Wis.	11		989,430	810,174	11		1,040,232	1,004,987	34,943	3,814
Wyo.	3		100,464	44,358		3	62,239	92,717	624	89
TOTAL	**520**	**17**	**47,165,234**	**28,168,110**	**297**	**240**	**40,825,839**	**39,147,770**	**680,390**	**171,627**

*One elector in Virginia for John Hospers and Theodora Nathan. **One elector in Washington for Reagan.

Presidential Election Returns by Counties

Compiled from official returns by The World Almanac.

Alabama

County	1972 McGovern (D)	1972 Nixon (R)	1976 Carter (D)	1976 Ford (R)
Autauga	1,593	5,367	4,640	4,512
Baldwin	2,923	15,104	9,191	13,256
Barbour	1,846	4,985	4,730	3,758
Bibb	837	3,332	2,850	1,591
Blount	1,582	6,486	6,645	4,233
Bullock	2,321	2,178	3,536	1,482
Butler	1,401	4,685	4,271	2,909
Calhoun	5,832	20,364	20,466	11,763
Chambers	2,076	8,716	6,164	5,488
Cherokee	1,182	3,179	4,668	1,492
Chilton	1,356	7,349	5,550	4,725
Choctaw	1,934	3,055	3,911	3,033
Clarke	2,031	5,256	4,737	4,126
Clay	507	3,948	2,946	1,883
Cleburne	581	3,420	2,490	1,436
Coffee	2,160	9,076	7,844	4,683
Colbert	4,811	11,215	11,996	4,471
Conecuh	1,042	3,214	3,086	1,812
Coosa	773	2,672	2,533	1,196
Covington	1,547	9,278	7,081	4,977
Crenshaw	1,085	3,129	3,372	1,801
Cullman	3,571	14,390	12,961	6,899
Dale	1,594	8,346	6,346	4,996
Dallas	5,427	8,644	8,866	7,144
DeKalb	3,759	9,434	9,759	6,597
Elmore	1,891	8,461	6,646	6,551
Escambia	1,598	8,883	5,957	4,934
Etowah	7,372	20,851	25,020	10,333
Fayette	836	4,240	4,076	2,165
Franklin	1,840	5,877	6,279	3,345
Geneva	1,049	5,851	5,983	2,663
Greene	3,235	1,404	2,900	903
Hale	1,779	2,859	3,236	2,034
Henry	853	3,414	3,144	2,052
Houston	2,358	12,622	8,787	10,672
Jackson	2,985	6,202	10,989	3,913
Jefferson	57,288	135,095	99,531	113,590
Lamar	766	3,283	3,860	1,739
Lauderdale	5,112	14,410	15,549	7,226
Lawrence	1,416	4,433	6,810	1,415
Lee	3,622	11,571	8,427	9,884
Limestone	2,079	6,188	8,803	2,997
Lowndes	2,559	1,990	3,732	1,621
Macon	3,636	1,931	5,915	1,387
Madison	13,108	38,899	35,497	20,959
Marengo	2,645	5,156	4,731	3,841
Marion	986	5,927	6,244	3,036
Marshall	3,894	12,090	13,696	6,006
Mobile	20,694	62,639	50,264	53,835
Monroe	1,636	5,155	3,669	3,476
Montgomery	12,723	35,353	24,641	29,360
Morgan	5,004	18,100	16,547	9,058
Perry	2,718	2,800	4,486	2,164
Pickens	1,933	4,071	3,776	2,969
Pike	1,624	5,690	5,387	4,363
Randolph	1,330	4,427	3,539	2,286
Russell	2,644	6,034	8,077	4,150
St. Clair	1,859	6,952	5,653	4,877
Shelby	1,538	9,390	7,197	9,035
Sumter	2,737	2,686	3,457	2,191
Talladega	4,567	12,763	10,577	6,425
Tallapoosa	2,113	8,535	7,614	5,237
Tuscaloosa	8,272	21,172	20,275	16,021
Walker	3,724	14,581	16,232	7,389
Washington	1,096	3,282	3,471	2,171
Wilcox	3,254	2,641	3,723	1,824
Winston	779	4,971	4,134	3,710
Totals	**256,923**	**728,701**	**659,170**	**504,070**

Alabama Vote Since 1932

1932 (Pres.), Roosevelt, Dem., 207,910; Hoover, Rep., 34,675; Foster, Com., 406; Thomas, Soc., 2,030; Upshaw, Proh., 13.

1936 (Pres.), Roosevelt, Dem., 238,195; Landon, Rep., 35,358; Colvin, Proh., 719; Browder, Com., 679; Lemke, Union, 549; Thomas, Soc., 242.

1940 (Pres.), Roosevelt, Dem., 250,726; Willkie, Rep., 42,174; Babson, Proh., 698; Browder, Com., 509; Thomas, Soc., 100.

1944 (Pres.), Roosevelt, Dem., 198,918; Dewey, Rep., 44,540; Watson, Proh., 1,095; Thomas, Soc., 190.

1948 (Pres.), Thurmond, States' Rights, 171,443; Dewey, Rep., 40,930; Wallace, Prog., 1,522; Watson, Proh., 1,085.

1952 (Pres.), Eisenhower, Rep., 149,231; Stevenson, Dem., 275,075; Hamblen, Proh., 1,814.

1956 (Pres.), Stevenson, Dem., 290,844; Eisenhower, Rep., 195,694; Independent electors, 20,323.

1960 (Pres.), Kennedy, Dem., 324,050; Nixon, Rep., 237,981; Faubus, States' Rights, 4,367; Decker, Proh., 2,106; King, Afro-Americans, 1,485; scattering, 236.

1964 (Pres.), Dem., 209,848 (electors unpledged); Goldwater, Rep., 479,085; scattering, 105.

1968 (Pres.), Nixon, Rep., 146,923; Humphrey, Dem., 196,579; Wallace, 3d party, 691,425; Munn, Proh., 4,022.

1972 (Pres.), Nixon, Rep., 728,701; McGovern, Dem. 219,108 plus 37,815 Natl. Demo. Party of Alabama; Schmitz, Conservative, 11,918; Munn, Proh., 8,551.

1976 (Pres.), Carter, Dem., 659,170; Ford, Rep., 504,070; Maddox, Am. Ind., 9,198; Bubar, Proh., 6,669; Hall, Comm., 1,954; MacBride, Libertarian, 1,481.

Alaska

County	1972 McGovern (D)	1972 Nixon (R)	1976 Carter (D)	1976 Ford (R)
No. 1	1,526	2,529	1,983	2,994
No. 2	967	1,386	1,022	1,423
No. 3	1,393	1,549	1,152	1,710
No. 4	2,968	4,277	3,214	5,252
No. 5	903	1,689	1,307	2,071
No. 6	849	2,384	1,486	2,882
No. 7	2,854	4,527	2,935	4,105
No. 8	2,454	5,275	3,368	5,412
No. 9	2,501	6,759	1,726	2,561
No. 10	2,854	6,882	2,839	6,837
No. 11	1,337	2,686	3,568	6,588
No. 12	727	1,117	2,700	6,381
No. 13	178	293	2,099	4,057
No. 14	843	1,042	856	1,380
No. 15	1,235	919	538	746
No. 16	1,004	902	876	1,063
No. 17	5,535	7,672	1,149	1,074
No. 18	640	1,202	804	942
No. 19	1,155	1,114	1,415	1,893
No. 20	...	...	6,706	10,306
No. 21	...	...	1,229	749
No. 22	...	...	1,086	1,129
Totals	**32,967**	**55,349**	**44,058**	**71,555**

Alaska Vote Since 1960

1960 (Pres.), Kennedy, Dem., 29,809; Nixon, Rep., 30,953.

1964 (Pres.), Johnson, Dem., 44,329; Goldwater, Rep., 22,930.

1968 (Pres.), Nixon, Rep., 37,600; Humphrey, Dem., 35,411; Wallace, 3d party, 10,024.

1972 (Pres.), Nixon, Rep., 55,349; McGovern, Dem., 32,967; Schmitz, American, 6,906.

1976 (Pres.), Carter, Dem., 44,058; Ford, Rep., 71,555; MacBride, Libertarian, 6,785.

Arizona

County	1972 McGovern (D)	1972 Nixon (R)	1976 Carter (D)	1976 Ford (R)
Apache	3,145	3,394	6,583	3,447
Cochise	6,023	11,706	9,281	9,921
Coconino	6,250	10,611	9,450	11,036
Gila	4,295	5,673	6,440	5,136
Graham	1,863	3,575	3,050	3,659
Greenlee	2,013	1,758	2,601	1,532
Maricopa	95,135	244,593	144,613	258,262
Mohave	2,588	6,755	6,504	7,601
Navajo	4,003	6,999	7,323	6,796
Pima	56,223	73,154	71,214	77,264
Pinal	6,404	10,584	10,595	9,354
Santa Cruz	1,866	2,137	2,265	2,312
Yavapai	3,977	12,277	7,685	12,998
Yuma	4,755	9,596	7,998	9,324
Totals	**198,540**	**402,812**	**295,602**	**418,642**

Arizona Vote Since 1932

1932 (Pres.), Roosevelt, Dem., 79,264; Hoover, Rep., 36,104; Thomas, Soc., 2,030; Foster, Com., 406.

1936 (Pres.), Roosevelt, Dem., 86,722; Landon, Rep., 33,433; Lemke, Union, 3,307; Colvin, Proh., 384; Thomas, Soc., 317.
1940 (Pres.), Roosevelt, Dem., 95,267; Willkie, Rep., 54,030; Babson, Proh., 742.
1944 (Pres.), Roosevelt, Dem., 80,826; Dewey, Rep., 56,287; Watson, Proh., 421.
1948 (Pres.), Truman, Dem., 95,251; Dewey, Rep., 77,597; Wallace, Prog., 3,310; Watson, Proh., 786; Teichert, Soc. Lab., 121.
1952 (Pres.), Eisenhower, Rep., 152,042; Stevenson, Dem., 108,528.
1956 (Pres.), Eisenhower, Rep., 176,990; Stevenson, Dem., 112,880; Andrews, Ind. 303.
1960 (Pres.), Kennedy, Dem., 176,781; Nixon, Rep., 221,241; Haas, Soc. Lab., 469.
1964 (Pres.), Johnson, Dem., 237,753; Goldwater, Rep., 242,535; Haas, Soc. Labor, 482.
1968 (Pres.), Nixon, Rep., 266,721; Humphrey, Dem., 170,514; Wallace, 3d party, 46,573; McCarthy, New Party, 2,751; Halstead, Soc. Worker, 85; Cleaver, Peace and Freedom, 217; Bloman, Soc. Labor, 75.
1972 (Pres.), Nixon, Rep., 402,812; McGovern, Dem., 198,540; Schmitz, American, 21,208; Soc. Worker, 30,945. (Due to ballot peculiarities in 3 counties (particularly Pima), thousands of voters cast ballots for the Socialist Workers Party *and* one of the major candidates. Court ordered both votes counted as official.
1976 (Pres.), Carter, Dem., 295,602; Ford, Rep., 418,642; McCarthy, Ind., 19,229; MacBride, Libertarian, 7,647; Camejo, Soc. Workers, 928; Anderson, American, 564; Maddox, Am. Ind., 85.

Arkansas

County	1972 McGovern (D)	1972 Nixon (R)	1976 Carter (D)	1976 Ford (R)
Arkansas	1,849	5,225	5,640	2,480
Ashley	1,680	5,506	5,253	3,092
Baxter	2,677	6,754	5,766	5,885
Benton	4,083	14,621	11,289	12,670
Boone	1,862	5,484	5,388	3,959
Bradley	1,368	3,218	3,567	1,134
Calhoun	707	1,298	2,014	495
Carroll	1,401	3,565	3,791	2,804
Chicot	1,469	2,858	3,868	1,621
Clark	2,741	4,173	6,641	1,816
Clay	1,933	4,381	5,664	1,893
Cleburne	1,400	2,870	5,726	1,992
Cleveland	734	1,837	2,320	646
Columbia	2,193	5,801	4,708	4,287
Conway	3,009	4,187	6,443	2,177
Craighead	5,843	11,312	13,840	6,213
Crawford	1,520	6,974	5,946	4,764
Crittenden	3,246	7,971	8,249	5,202
Cross	1,221	3,743	4,198	1,909
Dallas	1,402	2,152	3,266	1,012
Desha	1,665	3,385	4,228	1,372
Drew	1,168	3,334	3,750	1,730
Faulkner	4,604	6,746	11,423	3,904
Franklin	1,252	3,678	3,703	1,973
Fulton	960	2,030	2,670	1,038
Garland	5,207	15,602	15,707	10,394
Grant	1,147	2,414	3,797	1,047
Greene	2,263	6,128	7,495	2,690
Hempstead	2,047	4,963	5,397	2,859
Hot Spring	2,872	5,378	7,809	2,187
Howard	1,069	2,682	3,207	1,575
Independence	2,630	5,076	7,116	2,878
Izard	1,108	2,001	3,328	1,394
Jackson	2,092	4,196	6,456	1,783
Jefferson	10,346	16,888	21,001	8,034
Johnson	2,045	4,107	5,044	2,173
Lafayette	952	2,460	2,342	1,467
Lawrence	1,751	3,981	5,167	1,708
Lee	1,907	3,540	3,463	1,574
Lincoln	1,115	2,318	3,045	699
Little River	1,091	2,550	3,142	1,431
Logan	1,956	4,964	5,313	2,909
Lonoke	2,504	5,298	7,761	2,522
Madison	1,889	3,372	2,926	2,502
Marion	1,108	2,331	2,979	2,045
Miller	2,855	8,355	6,821	4,737
Mississippi	3,544	10,931	10,292	6,009
Monroe	1,578	2,897	3,556	1,285
Montgomery	688	1,555	2,420	924
Nevada	1,179	2,513	3,101	1,163
Newton	831	1,924	1,840	1,641
Ouachita	3,931	6,620	8,946	2,753
Perry	810	1,445	2,310	832
Phillips	4,283	6,235	7,774	3,342
Pike	798	2,316	2,822	1,234
Poinsett	1,908	7,010	6,835	2,726
Polk	1,120	3,609	3,505	2,432
Pope	3,302	6,917	8,355	4,348
Prairie	873	2,186	2,836	813
Pulaski	33,611	57,576	63,541	37,690
Randolph	1,525	2,578	4,551	1,571
St. Francis	2,674	5,692	6,851	3,639
Saline	4,503	7,972	12,008	4,123
Scott	771	2,424	2,880	1,427
Searcy	853	3,163	2,067	1,767
Sebastian	5,770	25,219	15,698	17,665
Sevier	1,048	2,526	3,391	1,468
Sharp	1,154	2,677	3,532	2,151
Stone	958	1,989	2,718	1,014
Union	3,531	11,925	8,257	7,918
Van Buren	1,594	2,622	4,004	1,624
Washington	7,108	17,523	15,610	14,132
White	4,161	8,701	11,412	4,756
Woodruff	1,183	1,989	3,040	848
Yell	1,669	3,310	5,785	1,932
Totals	**198,899**	**445,751**	**498,604**	**267,903**

Arkansas Vote Since 1932

1932 (Pres.), Roosevelt, Dem., 189,602; Hoover, Rep., 28,467; Thomas, Soc., 1,269; Harvey, Ind., 1,049; Foster, Com., 175.
1936 (Pres.), Roosevelt, Dem., 146,765; Landon, Rep., 32,039; Thomas, Soc., 446; Browder, Com., 164; Lemke, Union, 4.
1940 (Pres.), Roosevelt, Dem., 158,622; Willkie, Rep., 42,121; Babson, Proh., 793; Thomas, Soc., 305.
1944 (Pres.), Roosevelt, Dem., 148,965; Dewey, Rep., 63,551; Thomas, Soc. 438.
1948 (Pres.), Truman, Dem., 149,659; Dewey, Rep., 50,959; Thurmond, States' Rights, 40,068; Thomas, Soc., 1,037; Wallace, Prog., 751; Watson, Proh., 1.
1952 (Pres.), Eisenhower, Rep., 177,155; Stevenson, Dem., 226,300; Hamblen, Proh., 886; MacArthur, Christian Nationalist, 458; Haas, Soc. Lab. 1.
1956 (Pres.), Stevenson, Dem., 213,277; Eisenhower, Rep., 186,287; Andrews, Ind., 7,008.
1960 (Pres.), Kennedy, Dem., 215,049; Nixon, Rep., 184,508; National States' Rights, 28,952.
1964 (Pres.), Johnson, Dem., 314,197; Goldwater, Rep., 243,264; Kasper, Nat'l. States Rights, 2,965.
1968 (Pres.), Nixon, Rep., 189,062; Humphrey, Dem., 184,901; Wallace, 3d party, 235,627.
1972 (Pres.), Nixon, Rep. 445,751; McGovern, Dem., 198,899; Schmitz, Amer. Party, 3,016.
1976 (Pres.), Carter, Dem., 498,604; Ford, Rep., 267,903; McCarthy, Ind., 639; Anderson, American, 389.

California

County	1972 McGovern (D)	1972 Nixon (R)	1976 Carter (D)	1976 Ford (R)
Alameda	259,254	201,862	235,988	155,280
Alpine	195	366	189	225
Amador	2,705	3,533	4,037	3,699
Butte	18,401	28,819	24,203	28,400
Calaveras	2,268	4,119	3,607	3,695
Colusa	1,810	2,715	2,340	2,733
Contra Costa	111,718	139,044	123,742	126,598
Del Norte	2,156	2,927	2,789	2,481
El Dorado	8,654	11,330	12,763	12,472
Fresno	72,682	79,051	74,958	72,533
Glenn	2,681	4,569	3,501	4,094
Humboldt	21,132	22,345	23,500	18,034
Imperial	7,982	14,178	10,244	10,618
Inyo	2,006	4,873	2,635	3,905
Kern	41,937	71,686	50,567	58,023
Kings	7,274	10,509	8,061	8,263
Lake	4,715	6,477	6,374	5,462
Lassen	3,134	3,618	3,801	3,007
Los Angeles	1,189,977	1,549,717	1,221,893	1,174,926
Madera	6,580	7,835	7,625	6,844
Marin	47,414	54,123	43,590	53,425
Mariposa	1,487	2,122	2,093	2,012
Mendocino	9,435	11,128	10,653	9,784
Merced	13,914	17,737	16,637	14,842
Modoc	1,271	2,085	1,733	1,917
Mono	828	1,872	1,025	1,600
Monterey	32,545	47,004	36,849	40,896
Napa	14,529	23,403	18,048	20,839

	1972 (D)	1972 (R)	1976 (D)	1976 (R)
Nevada	5,693	8,004	7,926	8,170
Orange	176,847	448,291	232,246	408,632
Placer	16,911	18,597	21,026	18,154
Plumas	3,057	2,952	3,429	2,884
Riverside	71,591	108,120	96,228	97,774
Sacramento	137,287	141,218	144,203	123,110
San Benito	2,582	3,961	3,122	3,398
San Bernardino	85,986	144,689	109,636	113,265
San Diego	206,455	371,627	263,654	353,302
San Francisco	170,882	127,461	133,733	103,561
San Joaquin	44,062	61,646	48,733	50,277
San Luis Obispo	20,779	28,566	24,926	27,785
San Mateo	109,745	135,377	102,896	117,338
Santa Barbara	50,609	67,075	55,018	60,922
Santa Clara	208,506	237,334	208,023	219,188
Santa Cruz	32,336	34,799	37,772	31,872
Shasta	17,214	16,618	19,200	17,273
Sierra	658	629	841	680
Siskiyou	6,434	7,563	7,060	7,070
Solano	24,766	31,314	33,682	26,136
Sonoma	43,746	57,697	50,353	50,555
Stanislaus	35,005	39,521	38,448	32,937
Sutter	5,409	10,224	6,966	8,745
Tehama	5,175	6,054	6,990	6,110
Trinity	1,621	1,868	2,172	1,989
Tulare	21,775	36,048	25,551	31,864
Tuolumne	4,596	5,894	6,492	6,104
Ventura	49,307	95,310	68,529	82,670
Yolo	23,694	17,969	23,533	18,376
Yuba	4,435	6,623	6,451	5,496
Totals	**3,475,847**	**4,602,096**	**3,742,284**	**3,882,244**

California Vote Since 1932

1932 (Pres.), Roosevelt, Dem., 1,324,157; Hoover, Rep., 847,902; Thomas, Soc., 63,299; Upshaw, Proh., 20,637; Harvey, Liberty, 9,827; Foster, Com., 1,023.

1936 (Pres.), Roosevelt, Dem., 1,766,836; Landon, Rep., 836,431; Colvin, Proh., 12,917; Thomas, Soc., 11,325; Browder, Com., 10,877.

1940 (Pres.), Roosevelt, Dem., 1,877,618; Willkie, Rep., 1,351,419; Thomas, Prog., 16,506; Browder, Com., 13,586; Babson, Proh., 9,400.

1944 (Pres.), Roosevelt, Dem., 1,988,564; Dewey, Rep., 1,512,965; Watson, Proh., 14,770; Thomas, Soc., 3,923; Teichert, Soc. Lab., 327.

1948 (Pres.), Truman, Dem., 1,913,134; Dewey, Rep., 1,895,269; Wallace, Prog., 190,381; Watson, Proh., 16,926; Thomas, Soc., 3,459; Thurmond, States' Rights, 1,228; Teichert, Soc. Lab., 195; Dobbs, Soc. Wkr., 133.

1952 (Pres.), Eisenhower, Rep., 2,897,310; Stevenson, Dem., 2,197,548; Hallinan, Prog., 24,106; Hamblen, Proh., 15,653; MacArthur, (Tenny Ticket), 3,326; (Kellems Ticket) 178; Haas, Soc. Lab., 273; Hoopes, Soc., 206; Scattered, 3,249.

1956 (Pres.), Eisenhower, Rep., 3,027,668; Stevenson, Dem., 2,420,136; Holtwick, Proh., 11,119; Andrews, Constitution, 6,087; Haas, Soc. Lab., 300; Hoopes, Soc., 123; Dobbs, Soc. Workers, 96; Smith, Christian Nat'l., 8.

1960 (Pres.), Kennedy, Dem., 3,224,099; Nixon, Rep., 3,259,722; Decker, Proh., 21,706; Haas, Soc. Lab., 1,051.

1964 (Pres.), Johnson, Dem., 4,171,877; Goldwater, Rep., 2,879,108; Haas, Soc. Labor, 489; DeBerry, Soc. Worker, 378; Munn, Proh., 305; Hensley, Universal, 19.

1968 (Pres.), Nixon, Rep., 3,467,664; Humphrey, Dem., 3,244,318; Wallace, 3d party, 487,270; Peace and Freedom party, 27,707; McCarthy, Alternative, 20,721; Gregory, write-in, 3,230; Mitchell, Communist, 260; Munn, Prohibition, 59; Blomen, Socialist, 341; Soeters, Defense, 17.

1972 (Pres.), Nixon, Rep., 4,602,096; McGovern, Dem., 3,475,847; Schmitz, Amer., 232,554; Spock, Peace and Freedom, 55,167; Hall, Communist, 373; Hospers, Libertarian, 980; Munn, Prohibition, 53; Fisher, Soc. Labor, 197; Jenness, Soc. Workers, 574; Green, Universal, 21.

1976 (Pres.), Carter, Dem., 3,742,284; Ford, Rep., 3,882,244; MacBride, Libertarian, 56,388; Maddox, Am. Ind., 51,098; Wright, People's, 41,731; Camejo, Soc. Workers, 17,259; Hall, Comm., 12,766; write-in, McCarthy, 58,412; other write-in, 4,935.

Colorado

County	1972 McGovern (D)	1972 Nixon (R)	1976 Carter (D)	1976 Ford (R)
Adams	24,170	40,372	40,551	35,392
Alamosa	1,540	2,916	2,052	2,599
Arapahoe	18,631	52,283	33,685	63,154
Archuleta	300	606	632	768
Baca	527	1,645	1,164	1,303
Bent	787	1,525	1,268	1,156
Boulder	29,494	40,766	33,284	42,830
Chaffee	1,354	2,859	2,064	2,925
Cheyenne	400	815	625	610
Clear Creek	815	1,557	1,069	1,477
Conejos	1,140	1,658	1,698	1,426
Costilla	744	602	1,033	392
Crowley	414	1,094	667	834
Custer	154	495	259	491
Delta	1,903	4,890	3,232	4,980
Denver	98,062	121,995	112,229	105,960
Dolores	166	498	374	343
Douglas	1,048	3,625	2,459	5,078
Eagle	1,306	1,920	1,502	2,963
Elbert	451	1,416	1,068	1,279
El Paso	21,234	53,892	32,911	50,929
Fremont	2,813	6,701	4,886	5,647
Garfield	2,088	4,452	2,852	4,699
Gilpin	362	516	563	451
Grand	685	1,721	910	1,703
Gunnison	1,187	2,231	1,250	2,568
Hinsdale	44	172	83	189
Huerfano	1,341	1,620	1,932	1,182
Jackson	178	623	279	455
Jefferson	31,555	80,082	52,782	87,080
Kiowa	372	849	529	598
Kit Carson	824	2,316	1,647	1,888
Lake	1,263	1,556	1,549	1,575
La Plata	2,830	5,691	3,843	6,228
Larimer	13,731	27,462	19,005	32,169
Las Animas	3,222	3,659	4,459	2,615
Lincoln	685	1,678	1,059	1,276
Logan	2,426	5,352	3,543	4,256
Mesa	6,358	15,527	8,807	17,924
Mineral	96	247	167	235
Moffat	591	1,928	1,451	2,099
Montezuma	1,223	3,391	1,993	3,002
Montrose	1,870	4,571	3,164	4,838
Morgan	2,081	5,365	3,798	4,603
Otero	2,929	6,016	4,118	4,597
Ouray	186	669	333	645
Park	386	1,001	741	1,034
Philips	687	1,480	1,173	1,142
Pitkin	2,531	2,064	2,194	2,955
Prowers	1,860	3,272	2,861	2,578
Pueblo	19,620	25,607	25,841	18,518
Rio Blanco	414	1,586	627	1,439
Rio Grande	1,029	2,787	1,475	2,627
Routt	1,613	2,629	2,130	2,822
Saguache	578	1,062	1,059	1,094
San Juan	140	238	167	221
San Miguel	426	583	674	622
Sedgwick	588	4,129	773	902
Summit	707	1,082	1,087	1,826
Teller	535	1,440	986	1,410
Washington	643	1,837	1,211	1,440
Weld	11,690	24,695	16,501	21,976
Yuma	1,066	2,873	2,025	2,350
Total	**329,980**	**597,189**	**460,353**	**584,367**

Colorado Vote Since 1932

1932 (Pres.), Roosevelt, Dem., 250,877; Hoover, Rep., 189,617; Thomas, Soc., 14,018; Upshaw, Proh., 1,928.

1936 (Pres.), Roosevelt, Dem., 295,081; Landon, Rep., 18,267; Lemke, Union, 9,962; Thomas, Soc., 1,593; Browder, Com., 497; Aiken, Soc. Labor, 336.

1940 (Pres.), Roosevelt, Dem., 265,554; Willkie, Rep., 279,576; Thomas, Soc., 1,899; Babson, Proh., 1,597; Browder, Com., 378.

1944 (Pres.), Roosevelt, Dem., 234,331; Dewey, Rep., 268,731; Thomas, Soc., 1,977.

1948 (Pres.), Truman, Dem., 267,288; Dewey, Rep., 239,714; Wallace, Prog., 6,115; Thomas, Soc., 1,678; Dobbs, Soc. Workers, 228; Teichert, Soc. Lab., 214.

1952 (Pres.), Eisenhower, Rep., 379,782; Stevenson, Dem., 245,504; MacArthur, Constitution, 2,181; Hallinan, Prog., 1,919; Hoopes, Soc., 365; Haas, Soc. Lab., 352.

1956 (Pres.), Eisenhower, Rep., 394,479; Stevenson,

Dem., 263,997; Haas, Soc. Lab., 3,308; Andrews, Ind., 759; Hoopes, Soc., 531.

1960 (Pres.), Kennedy, Dem., 330,629; Nixon, Rep., 402,242; Haas, Soc. Lab., 2,803; Dobbs, Soc. Workers, 572.

1964 (Pres.), Johnson, Dem., 476,024; Goldwater, Rep., 296,767; Haas, Soc. Labor, 302; DeBerry, Soc. Worker, 2,537; Munn, Proh., 1,356.

1968 (Pres.), Nixon, Rep., 409,345; Humphrey, Dem., 335,174; Wallace, 3d party, 60,813; Blomen, Soc., 3,016; Gregory, New-party, 1,393; Munn, Proh., 275; Halstead, Soc. Work., 235.

1972 (Pres.), Nixon, Rep., 597,189; McGovern, Dem., 329,980; Fisher, Soc. Labor, 4,361; Hospers, Libertarian, 1,111; Hall, Com., 432; Jenness, Soc. Wrks., 555; Munn, Proh., 467; Schmitz, American, 17,269; Spock, Peoples, 2,403.

1976 (Pres.), Carter, Dem., 460,353; Ford, Rep., 584,-367; McCarthy, Ind., 26,107; MacBride, Libertarian, 5,330.

Connecticut

County	1972 McGovern (D)	1972 Nixon (R)	1976 Carter (D)	1976 Ford (R)
Fairfield	125,128	233,188	148,353	209,458
Hartford	174,837	194,095	191,257	175,064
Litchfield	27,929	43,478	32,419	40,705
Middlesex	23,573	33,249	29,097	31,115
New Haven	135,132	200,818	157,402	174,342
New London	32,935	58,516	45,908	47,231
Tolland	19,505	25,798	23,079	23,703
Windham	16,459	21,621	20,380	17,643
Totals	**555,498**	**810,763**	**647,895**	**719,261**

Connecticut Vote Since 1932

1932 (Pres.), Roosevelt, Dem., 281,632; Hoover, Rep., 288,420; Thomas, Soc., 22,767.

1936 (Pres.), Roosevelt, Dem., 382,129; Landon, Rep., 278,685; Lemke, Union, 21,805; Thomas, Soc., 5,683; Browder, Com., 1,193.

1940 (Pres.), Roosevelt, Dem., 417,621; Willkie, Rep., 361,021; Browder, Com., 1,091; Aiken, Soc. Lab., 971; Willkie, Union, 798.

1944 (Pres.), Roosevelt, Dem., 435,146; Dewey, Rep., 390,527; Thomas, Soc., 5,097; Teichert, Soc. Lab., 1,220.

1948 (Pres.), Truman, Dem., 423,297; Dewey, Rep., 437,754; Wallace, Prog., 13,713; Thomas, Soc., 6,964; Teichert, Soc. Lab., 1,184; Dobbs, Soc. Workers, 606.

1952 (Pres.), Eisenhower, Rep., 611,012; Stevenson, Dem., 481,649; Hoopes, Soc., 2,244; Hallinan, Peoples, 1,466; Haas, Soc. Lab., 535; write-in, 5.

1956 (Pres.), Eisenhower, Rep., 711,837; Stevenson, Dem., 405,079; scattered, 205.

1960 (Pres.), Kennedy, Dem., 657,055; Nixon, Rep., 565,813.

1964 (Pres.), Johnson, Dem., 826,269; Goldwater, Rep., 390,996; scattered, 1,313.

1968 (Pres.), Nixon, Rep., 556,721; Humphrey, Dem., 621,561; Wallace, 3d party, 76,650; scattered, 1,300.

1972 (Pres.), Nixon, Rep., 810,763; McGovern. Dem., 555,498; Schmitz, Amer. Party, 17,239; scattered, 777.

1976 (Pres.), Carter, Dem., 647,895; Ford, Rep., 719,-261; Maddox, George Wallace Party, 7,101; LaRouche, U.S. Labor, 1,789.

Delaware

County	1972 McGovern (D)	1972 Nixon (R)	1976 Carter (D)	1976 Ford (R)
Kent	10,463	17,712	16,523	12,604
New Castle	70,190	100,681	87,521	80,074
Sussex	11,630	21,964	18,552	17,153
Totals	**92,283**	**140,357**	**122,596**	**109,831**

Delaware Vote Since 1932

1932 (Pres.), Hoover, Rep., 57,074; Roosevelt, Dem., 54,319; Thomas, Soc., 1,376; Foster, Com., 133.

1936 (Pres.), Roosevelt, Dem., 69,702; Landon, Rep. 54,014; Lemke, Union, 442; Thomas, Soc., 179; Browder, Com., 52.

1940 (Pres.), Roosevelt, Dem., 74,559; Willkie, Rep., 61,440; Babson, Proh., 220; Thomas, Soc., 115.

1944 (Pres.), Roosevelt, Dem., 68,166; Dewey, Rep., 56,747; Watson, Proh., 294; Thomas, Soc., 154.

1948 (Pres.), Truman, Dem., 67,813; Dewey, Rep., 69,-688; Wallace, Prog., 1,050; Watson, Proh., 343; Thomas, Soc., 250; Teichert, Soc. Lab., 29.

1952 (Pres.), Eisenhower, Rep., 90,059; Stevenson, Dem., 83,315; Haas, Soc. Lab., 242; Hamblen, Proh., 234; Hallinan, Prog., 155; Hoopes, Soc., 20.

1956 (Pres.), Eisenhower, Rep., 98,057; Stevenson, Dem., 79,421; Oltwick, Proh., 400; Haas, Soc. Lab., 110.

1960 (Pres.), Kennedy, Dem., 99,590; Nixon, Rep., 96,-373; Faubus, States' Rights, 354; Decker, Proh., 284; Haas, Soc. Lab., 82.

1964 (Pres.), Johnson, Dem., 122,704; Goldwater, Rep., 78,078; Haas, Soc. Lab., 113; Munn, Proh., 425.

1968 (Pres.), Nixon, Rep., 96,714; Humphrey, Dem., 89,194; Wallace, 3d party, 28,459.

1972 (Pres.), Nixon, Rep., 140,357; McGovern, Dem., 92,283; Schmitz, Amer. Party, 2,638; Munn, Proh., 238.

1976 (Pres.), Carter, Dem., 122,596; Ford, Rep., 109,-831; McCarthy, non-partisan, 2,437; Anderson, American, 645; LaRouche, U.S. Labor, 136; Bubar, Proh., 103; Levin, Soc. Labor, 86.

District of Columbia

County	1972 McGovern (D)	1972 Nixon (R)	1976 Carter (D)	1976 Ford (R)
Totals	**127,627**	**35,226**	**137,818**	**27,873**

District of Columbia Vote Since 1964

1964 (Pres.), Johnson, Dem., 169,796; Goldwater, Rep., 28,801.

1968 (Pres.), Nixon, Rep., 31,012; Humphrey, Dem., 139,566.

1972 (Pres.), Nixon, Rep., 35,226; McGovern, Dem., 127,627; Reed, Soc. Work., 316; Hall, Comm. 252.

1976 (Pres.), Carter, Dem., 137,818; Ford, Rep., 27,-873; Camejo, Soc. Workers, 545; MacBride, Libertarian, 274; Hall, Comm., 219; LaRouche, U.S. Labor, 157.

Florida

County	1972 McGovern (D)	1972 Nixon (R)	1976 Carter (D)	1976 Ford (R)
Alachua	17,245	22,536	27,895	15,546
Baker	379	1,943	2,985	1,058
Bay	3,914	20,245	14,858	14,208
Bradford	1,217	3,652	3,868	1,680
Brevard	16,854	62,773	46,421	44,470
Broward	74,127	196,528	176,491	161,411
Calhoun	461	2,069	2,487	1,153
Charlotte	3,874	12,888	10,300	12,703
Citrus	2,607	8,848	9,438	7,973
Clay	1,748	10,467	8,410	8,468
Collier	3,201	13,501	8,764	14,643
Columbia	1,664	6,723	6,683	3,947
Dade	177,693	256,529	303,047	211,148
De Soto	852	2,958	2,715	2,000
Dixie	367	1,628	2,169	558
Duval	46,530	122,154	105,912	74,997
Escambia	14,078	56,071	38,279	41,471
Flagler	493	1,409	2,086	1,262
Franklin	490	2,277	1,859	1,054
Gadsden	3,829	5,995	6,798	3,531
Gilchrist	247	1,306	1,807	528
Glades	253	1,019	1,311	624
Gulf	713	2,628	2,641	1,584
Hamilton	626	1,741	2,053	794
Hardee	647	3,563	2,670	2,189
Hendry	739	2,763	2,337	1,843
Hernando	2,110	6,296	7,717	5,793
Highlands	2,458	9,645	7,218	8,317
Hillsborough	45,305	106,956	94,589	78,504
Holmes	309	3,819	3,256	1,850
Indian River	3,316	11,741	8,512	9,818
Jackson	2,220	8,904	7,687	4,795
Jefferson	1,049	2,108	2,310	1,361

	1972 (D)	1972 (R)	1976 (D)	1976 (R)
Lafayette	173	1,060	1,126	523
Lake	4,803	23,079	14,369	19,976
Lee	9,404	36,738	30,567	38,038
Leon	15,555	27,479	28,729	23,739
Levy	862	3,273	4,025	1,965
Liberty	222	1,199	1,137	620
Madison	1,187	3,236	3,218	1,761
Manatee	8,058	32,664	24,342	29,300
Marion	5,397	19,505	16,963	16,163
Martin	2,946	11,296	8,785	11,682
Monroe	4,469	11,688	11,079	8,232
Nassau	1,293	5,078	5,896	3,136
Okaloosa	2,843	23,303	14,210	18,598
Okeechobee	621	2,581	3,184	1,598
Orange	23,840	94,516	58,442	70,451
Osceola	1,875	9,320	6,893	7,062
Palm Beach	40,825	108,670	96,705	98,236
Pasco	11,330	29,249	33,710	28,306
Pinellas	77,197	179,541	141,879	150,003
Polk	16,419	60,748	47,286	44,238
Putnam	2,901	8,741	9,597	5,040
St. Johns	2,549	8,919	7,412	6,660
St. Lucie	4,593	14,258	12,386	11,502
Santa Rosa	1,491	12,669	8,020	9,122
Sarasota	12,235	48,939	26,293	44,157
Seminole	6,503	27,658	19,609	26,655
Sumter	1,107	3,695	4,721	2,212
Suwannee	1,027	4,435	4,718	2,405
Taylor	754	4,109	3,370	1,983
Union	253	1,314	1,480	544
Volusia	21,637	52,656	49,161	37,523
Wakulla	539	2,466	2,353	1,580
Walton	988	6,217	5,196	2,927
Washington	606	3,777	3,566	2,313
Totals	**718,117**	**1,857,759**	**1,636,000**	**1,469,531**

Florida Vote Since 1932

1932 (Pres.), Roosevelt, Dem., 206,307; Hoover, Rep., 69,170; Thomas, Soc., 775.

1936 (Pres.), Roosevelt, Dem., 249,117; Landon, Rep., 78,248; Thomas, Soc., 775.

1940 (Pres.), Roosevelt, Dem., 359,334; Willkie, Rep., 126,158.

1944 (Pres.), Roosevelt, Dem., 339,377; Dewey, Rep., 143,215.

1948 (Pres.), Truman, Dem., 281,988; Dewey, Rep., 194,280; Thurmond, States' Rights, 89,755; Wallace, Prog., 11,620.

1952 (Pres.), Eisenhower, Rep., 544,036; Stevenson, Dem., 444,950; scattered, 351.

1956 (Pres.), Eisenhower, Rep., 643,849; Stevenson, Dem., 480,371.

1960 (Pres.), Kennedy, Dem., 748,700; Nixon, Rep., 795,476.

1964 (Pres.), Johnson, Dem., 948,540; Goldwater, Rep., 905,941.

1968 (Pres.), Nixon, Rep., 886,804; Humphrey, Dem., 676,794; Wallace, 3d party, 624,207.

1972 (Pres.), Nixon, Rep., 1,857,759; McGovern, Dem., 718,117; scattered 7,407.

1976 (Pres.), Carter, Dem., 1,636,000; Ford, Rep., 1,469,531; McCarthy, Ind., 23,643; Anderson, Amer., 21,325.

Georgia

County	1972 McGovern (D)	1972 Nixon (R)	1976 Carter (D)	1976 Ford (R)
Appling	512	2,755	3,585	961
Atkinson	309	924	1,560	347
Bacon	192	1,771	2,395	594
Baker	345	965	1,162	305
Baldwin	1,435	4,826	4,674	3,612
Banks	356	1,336	2,387	330
Barrow	867	3,423	4,756	1,364
Bartow	1,590	4,836	8,166	1,876
Ben Hill	703	2,104	2,449	814
Berrien	371	2,285	3,394	555
Bibb	10,201	27,402	31,902	12,819
Bleckley	377	2,308	2,605	972
Brantley	338	1,587	2,294	358
Brooks	643	2,430	2,653	1,102
Bryan	263	1,409	2,045	761
Bulloch	1,524	5,683	5,199	3,156
Burke	1,058	2,846	3,014	1,565
Butts	727	1,968	2,898	819
Calhoun	495	892	1,394	436
Camden	753	2,380	2,962	995
Candler	238	1,427	1,388	646
Carroll	2,158	8,296	10,050	3,640
Catoosa	894	6,008	6,020	3,799
Charlton	310	1,244	1,750	452
Chatham	15,566	38,079	32,075	24,160
Chattahoochee	121	345	506	178
Chattooga	923	3,188	4,686	1,087
Cherokee	1,159	5,509	6,539	2,609
Clarke	6,090	11,465	11,342	6,610
Clay	283	632	947	295
Clayton	3,740	23,681	21,432	12,905
Clinch	239	1,127	1,414	383
Cobb	7,688	43,977	45,002	34,324
Coffee	607	3,934	4,601	1,417
Colquitt	930	6,900	6,928	2,181
Columbia	946	4,839	4,674	3,423
Cook	525	2,135	2,882	670
Coweta	1,560	5,751	6,195	3,044
Crawford	512	1,167	1,842	378
Crisp	682	3,623	3,747	1,328
Dade	148	2,110	2,263	1,388
Dawson	230	828	1,384	370
Decatur	1,196	4,292	3,736	2,500
DeKalb	30,671	104,750	86,872	67,160
Dodge	884	4,346	5,267	848
Dooly	590	1,904	2,441	655
Dougherty	3,625	12,878	11,461	9,337
Douglas	982	6,610	7,805	3,959
Early	513	2,396	2,405	1,157
Echols	68	404	585	111
Effingham	497	3,175	2,906	1,654
Elbert	884	2,875	4,730	961
Emanuel	916	3,684	4,603	1,493
Evans	375	1,666	1,511	746
Fannin	949	3,873	3,402	2,646
Fayette	450	3,401	3,718	2,837
Floyd	3,372	15,485	15,151	7,713
Forsyth	549	2,968	4,693	1,443
Franklin	435	2,022	4,192	687
Fulton	74,329	96,256	129,849	61,552
Gilmer	768	2,729	2,499	1,261
Glascock	41	578	704	371
Glynn	3,002	9,443	9,459	5,403
Gordon	870	4,344	6,052	1,698
Grady	874	3,732	3,758	1,209
Greene	919	1,679	2,534	652
Gwinnett	2,986	18,181	20,838	13,912
Habersham	172	971	5,120	1,315
Hall	2,440	10,686	12,804	5,093
Hancock	1,502	1,595	2,117	651
Haralson	767	3,460	4,550	1,301
Harris	701	2,617	2,861	1,544
Hart	784	2,308	4,605	860
Heard	276	1,239	1,593	433
Henry	1,460	5,155	5,717	2,622
Houston	2,556	13,576	13,164	5,404
Irwin	335	1,851	2,012	561
Jackson	1,055	4,124	5,931	1,239
Jasper	463	1,289	1,852	689
Jeff Davis	302	1,857	2,405	622
Jefferson	1,184	2,777	3,115	1,309
Jenkins	484	1,769	1,820	563
Johnson	417	2,201	2,210	698
Jones	861	2,483	3,471	1,317
Lamar	666	1,844	2,785	847
Lanier	193	850	1,269	207
Laurens	2,130	7,350	8,617	3,281
Lee	390	1,441	1,727	1,110
Liberty	1,217	2,337	3,328	979
Lincoln	340	1,246	1,583	576
Long	236	764	1,243	222
Lowndes	2,015	7,812	8,830	4,512
Lumpkin	385	1,477	2,301	547
Macon	837	2,005	3,013	638
Madison	572	2,600	3,367	1,115
Marion	164	850	1,314	291
McDuffie	996	2,990	3,024	1,694
McIntosh	833	1,367	1,978	535
Meriwether	1,213	3,420	4,830	1,450
Miller	118	1,269	1,536	476
Mitchell	1,120	2,400	4,495	1,572
Monroe	789	2,181	2,962	1,078
Montgomery	337	1,370	1,610	626
Morgan	668	2,007	2,274	904
Murray	644	2,643	3,511	889
Muscogee	18,234	28,449	24,092	13,496
Newton	1,380	4,647	6,294	2,137
Oconee	464	2,029	2,228	1,184
Oglethorpe	326	1,712	1,854	811
Paulding	1,004	2,814	5,420	1,432
Peach	2,413	3,747	3,989	1,163
Pickens	520	2,101	2,571	973
Pierce	269	1,982	2,628	544
Pike	423	1,432	1,903	776
Polk	1,317	4,929	6,115	1,944
Pulaski	444	1,966	2,318	485
Putnam	604	1,963	2,040	835
Quitman	140	502	677	313
Rabun	366	1,477	2,398	591
Randolph	798	1,603	2,186	747
Richmond	9,219	24,362	24,042	17,893
Rockdale	791	3,560	4,640	2,974
Schley	162	694	783	268

	1972		1976	
	(D)	(R)	(D)	(R)
Screven	575	2,402	2,168	1,176
Seminole	376	1,851	2,074	681
Spalding	1,702	7,183	7,593	3,739
Stephens	871	3,773	5,560	1,340
Stewart	353	1,020	1,632	433
Sumter	1,268	4,533	5,328	2,053
Talbot	508	990	1,634	459
Taliaferro	372	585	748	236
Tattnall	492	2,892	3,556	1,326
Taylor	514	1,580	1,962	504
Telfair	687	2,245	3,534	637
Terrell	686	2,057	2,348	1,168
Thomas	2,171	6,668	6,147	3,263
Tift	816	4,591	5,185	2,162
Toombs	675	4,080	4,047	2,126
Towns	404	1,573	1,786	1,175
Treutlen	210	1,346	1,567	465
Troup	2,056	8,350	7,699	4,422
Turner	437	2,120	2,265	416
Twiggs	1,113	1,363	2,515	513
Union	742	2,317	2,795	1,154
Upson	896	4,892	4,219	2,897
Walker	1,574	8,728	8,007	4,807
Walton	1,140	3,994	5,402	1,687
Ware	1,724	6,578	7,719	2,661
Warren	475	1,175	1,335	720
Washington	1,246	3,901	3,865	1,657
Wayne	733	3,677	4,489	1,499
Webster	108	483	622	165
Wheeler	294	1,093	1,378	344
White	343	1,537	2,125	625
Whitfield	1,955	8,591	10,475	4,498
Wilcox	315	1,863	2,153	346
Wilkes	646	2,195	2,461	1,067
Wilkinson	751	2,196	2,652	837
Worth	542	2,942	2,790	1,156
Totals	**289,529**	**881,496**	**979,409**	**483,743**

Georgia Vote Since 1932

1932 (Pres.), Roosevelt, Dem., 234,118; Hoover, Rep., 19,863; Upshaw, Proh., 1,125; Thomas, Soc., 461; Foster, Com., 23.

1936 (Pres.), Roosevelt, Dem., 255,364; Landon, Rep., 36,942; Colvin, Proh., 660; Lemke, Union, 141; Thomas, Soc., 68.

1940 (Pres.), Roosevelt, Dem., 265,194; Willkie, Rep., 23,934; Ind. Dem., 22,428; total, 46,362; Babson, Proh., 983.

1944 (Pres.), Roosevelt, Dem., 268,187; Dewey, Rep., 56,506; Watson, Proh., 36.

1948 (Pres.), Truman, Dem., 254,646; Dewey, Rep., 76,691; Thurmond, States' Rights, 85,055; Wallace, Prog., 1,636; Watson, Proh., 732.

1952 (Pres.), Eisenhower, Rep., 198,979; Stevenson, Dem., 456,823; Liberty Party, 1.

1956 (Pres.), Stevenson, Dem., 444,388; Eisenhower, Rep., 222,778; Andrews, Ind., write-in, 1,754.

1960 (Pres.), Kennedy, Dem., 458,638; Nixon, Rep., 274,472; write-in 239.

1964 (Pres.), Johnson, Dem., 522,557; Goldwater, Rep., 616,600.

1968 (Pres.), Nixon, Rep., 380,111; Humphrey, Dem., 334,440; Wallace, 3d party, 535,550; write-in, 162.

1972 (Pres.), Nixon, Rep., 881,496; McGovern, Dem., 289,529; Schmitz, Amer. Party, 2,288; scattered.

1976 (Pres.), Carter, Dem., 979,409; Ford, Rep., 483,-743; write-in, 4,306.

Hawaii

	1972		1976	
	McGov-ern	Nixon	Carter	Ford
County	(D)	(R)	(D)	(R)
Hawaii	11,652	16,832	15,960	15,366
Honolulu	76,957	132,844	111,389	108,041
Kauai	5,401	7,571	8,105	6,278
Maui	7,339	11,618	11,921	10,318
Totals	**101,409**	**168,865**	**147,375**	**140,003**

Hawaii Vote Since 1960

1960 (Pres.), Kennedy, Dem., 92,410; Nixon, Rep., 92,-295.

1964 (Pres.), Johnson, Dem., 163,249; Goldwater, Rep., 44,022.

1968 (Pres.), Nixon, Rep., 91,425; Humphrey, Dem., 141,324; Wallace, 3d party, 3,469.

1972 (Pres.), Nixon, Rep., 168,865; McGovern, Dem., 101,409.

1976 (Pres.), Carter, Dem., 147,375; Ford, Rep., 140,-003; MacBride, Libertarian, 3,923.

Idaho

	1972		1976	
	McGov-ern	Nixon	Carter	Ford
County	(D)	(R)	(D)	(R)
Ada	12,687	36,665	21,125	41,135
Adams	293	963	639	809
Bannock	7,840	12,856	10,261	13,172
Bear Lake	716	2,213	960	2,094
Benewah	1,062	1,494	1,549	1,458
Bingham	2,476	6,886	4,347	7,327
Blaine	1,240	2,113	1,604	2,176
Boise	256	676	433	684
Bonner	2,599	4,405	4,065	4,549
Bonneville	4,199	13,134	7,230	15,793
Boundary	860	1,587	1,217	1,458
Butte	387	788	663	751
Camas	95	344	160	288
Canyon	5,630	18,383	9,460	17,263
Caribou	614	2,069	1,110	2,253
Cassias	1,080	4,576	1,881	4,575
Clark	64	339	169	334
Clearwater	1,412	1,590	1,752	1,469
Custer	274	989	516	850
Elmore	1,153	3,078	2,164	2,808
Franklin	611	2,787	1,157	2,720
Freemont	819	2,621	1,445	2,581
Gem	1,069	2,717	1,978	2,401
Gooding	1,030	3,124	1,923	2,909
Idaho	1,622	3,235	2,323	3,185
Jefferson	715	2,983	1,745	3,599
Jerome	888	3,661	1,800	3,188
Kootenai	5,162	9,958	7,225	10,493
Latah	4,548	6,043	5,314	6,846
Lemhi	526	1,812	1,159	1,685
Lewis	635	961	898	824
Lincoln	313	1,120	615	909
Madison	710	3,606	1,320	4,190
Minidoka	1,423	4,097	2,441	3,600
Nez Perce	5,081	6,232	6,324	6,151
Oneida	402	1,204	637	1,065
Owyhee	463	1,630	1,054	1,519
Payette	1,113	3,577	2,195	3,115
Power	625	1,405	1,286	1,374
Shoshone	3,020	3,868	3,216	3,570
Teton	298	932	514	904
Twin Falls	3,344	13,075	6,085	12,659
Valley	537	1,324	897	1,374
Washington	935	2,264	1,693	2,044
Totals	**80,826**	**199,384**	**126,549**	**204,151**

Idaho Vote Since 1932

1932 (Pres.), Roosevelt, Dem., 109,479; Hoover, Rep., 71,312; Harvey, Lib., 4,712; Thomas, Soc., 526; Foster, Com., 491.

1936 (Pres.), Roosevelt, Dem., 125,683; Landon, Rep., 66,256; Lemke, Union, 7,684.

1940 (Pres.), Roosevelt, Dem., 127,842; Willkie, Rep., 106,553; Thomas, Soc., 497; Browder, Com., 276.

1944 (Pres.), Roosevelt, Dem., 107,399; Dewey, Rep., 100,137; Watson, Proh., 503; Thomas, Soc., 282.

1948 (Pres.), Truman, Dem., 107,370; Dewey, Rep., 101,514; Wallace, Prog., 4,972; Watson, Proh., 628; Thomas, Soc., 332.

1952 (Pres.), Eisenhower, Rep., 180,707; Stevenson, Dem., 95,081; Hallinan, Prog., 443; write-in, 23.

1956 (Pres.), Eisenhower, Rep., 166,979; Stevenson, Dem., 105,868; Andrews, Ind., 126; write-in, 16.

1960 (Pres.), Kennedy, Dem., 138,853; Nixon, Rep., 161,597.

1964 (Pres.), Johnson, Dem., 148,920; Goldwater, Rep., 143,557.

1968 (Pres.), Nixon, Rep., 165,369; Humphrey, Dem., 89,273; Wallace, 3d party, 36,541.

1972 (Pres.), Nixon, Rep., 199,384; McGovern, Dem., 80,826; Schmitz, American, 28,869; Spock, Peoples, 903.

1976 (Pres.), Carter, Dem., 126,549; Ford, Rep., 204,-151; Maddox, Amer., 5,935; MacBride, Libertarian, 3,558; LaRouche, U.S. Labor, 739.

Illinois

	1972		1976	
	McGov-ern	Nixon	Carter	Ford
County	(D)	(R)	(D)	(R)
Adams	9,055	20,731	11,926	18,189
Alexander	2,482	3,669	3,246	2,349

	1972		1976	
	(D)	(R)	(D)	(R)
Bond	2,704	4,475	3,682	3,716
Boone	3,131	7,003	4,458	6,470
Brown	1,203	1,780	1,533	1,519
Bureau	6,133	12,786	7,566	10,854
Calhoun	1,299	1,705	1,549	1,364
Carroll	2,571	6,041	3,372	5,059
Cass	2,803	4,414	3,589	3,524
Champaign	24,743	33,700	26,858	34,546
Christian	7,556	10,072	9,306	7,445
Clark	2,965	5,706	4,071	4,506
Clay	2,844	5,283	3,837	3,860
Clinton	4,756	7,931	6,275	7,245
Coles	7,988	13,681	8,639	11,021
Cook	1,063,268	1,234,307	1,180,814	987,498
Crawford	3,477	6,568	5,007	5,522
Cumberland	2,083	3,257	2,752	2,518
DeKalb	12,375	18,910	11,535	18,193
DeWitt	2,672	5,025	3,477	4,137
Douglas	2,656	5,840	3,826	4,635
DuPage	57,043	172,341	72,137	175,055
Edgar	3,889	7,195	5,058	5,842
Edwards	1,055	3,017	1,648	2,379
Effingham	4,431	8,752	5,952	7,194
Fayette	4,192	6,574	5,128	5,059
Ford	1,934	5,656	2,690	4,801
Franklin	8,545	10,121	12,818	7,420
Fulton	7,529	12,328	9,314	9,588
Gallatin	1,844	2,148	2,611	1,499
Greene	2,824	4,673	4,057	3,706
Grundy	3,584	8,725	5,534	7,581
Hamilton	2,006	3,282	3,036	2,433
Hancock	3,592	7,519	4,730	6,043
Hardin	1,140	1,915	1,602	1,393
Henderson	1,744	2,689	2,152	2,210
Henry	8,368	14,796	9,822	12,849
Iroquois	3,723	11,995	5,167	10,129
Jackson	13,146	12,393	12,940	10,152
Jasper	2,114	3,461	2,772	2,794
Jefferson	6,396	9,448	8,989	7,422
Jersey	3,317	5,164	4,625	4,273
JoDaviess	3,318	5,763	3,979	5,478
Johnson	1,293	2,826	2,182	2,417
Kane	27,525	64,546	34,057	59,275
Kankakee	13,434	26,866	18,394	23,003
Kendall	2,525	9,373	4,202	9,011
Knox	9,333	17,315	11,525	14,123
Lake	47,416	92,052	57,741	92,231
LaSalle	21,405	31,190	23,105	25,114
Lawrence	2,818	5,347	4,044	4,345
Lee	4,788	10,636	6,076	8,674
Livingston	5,110	13,217	5,174	10,097
Logan	4,395	10,277	5,686	8,623
Macon	20,296	29,596	28,243	24,893
Macoupin	9,662	13,583	11,910	10,242
Madison	43,289	55,385	56,457	44,183
Marion	6,968	10,755	9,834	8,729
Marshall	2,141	4,452	2,570	4,017
Mason	2,901	4,897	3,947	3,847
Massac	1,831	4,313	3,666	3,226
McDonough	5,143	10,573	5,464	9,683
McHenry	12,090	36,114	16,799	37,115
McLean	14,824	31,060	16,601	28,493
Menard	1,587	3,657	2,301	3,137
Mercer	3,477	5,452	4,090	4,816
Monroe	2,958	6,479	3,984	5,602
Montgomery	6,858	9,025	8,322	7,379
Morgan	5,674	11,103	7,403	8,885
Moultrie	2,350	3,143	3,332	2,803
Ogle	4,743	13,512	6,463	11,073
Peoria	27,264	50,324	34,606	46,526
Perry	4,084	6,968	5,976	5,286
Piatt	2,394	5,057	3,509	4,442
Pike	3,883	5,940	5,006	4,975
Pope	773	1,440	1,070	1,187
Pulaski	1,683	2,485	2,489	1,836
Putnam	1,112	1,665	1,344	1,572
Randolph	6,440	9,761	8,693	8,190
Richland	2,553	5,558	3,485	4,434
Rock Island	32,529	37,548	35,994	34,007
St. Clair	46,636	50,519	59,177	40,333
Saline	5,226	7,660	7,472	5,970
Sangamon	25,720	50,458	38,017	43,309
Schuyler	1,534	2,994	2,014	2,635
Scott	1,145	2,228	1,424	1,789
Shelby	4,389	7,217	6,172	5,234
Stark	993	2,529	1,146	2,191
Stephenson	6,404	13,584	7,192	11,678
Tazewell	15,576	31,937	22,821	28,951
Union	3,428	5,034	5,003	3,531
Vermilion	14,413	24,863	18,438	19,751
Wabash	1,985	4,310	2,781	3,388
Warren	2,969	7,021	3,808	5,822
Washington	2,327	5,179	3,222	4,485
Wayne	2,763	6,400	4,303	5,211
White	3,678	6,052	5,306	4,600
Whiteside	7,909	17,305	11,255	14,308
Will	33,633	65,155	51,103	61,784
Williamson	9,202	14,101	13,600	10,703
Winnebago	35,937	57,682	42,399	52,736
Woodford	3,558	9,622	4,819	8,899
Totals	**1,913,472**	**2,788,179**	**2,271,295**	**2,364,269**

Illinois Vote Since 1932

1932 (Pres.), Roosevelt, Dem., 1,882,304; Hoover, Rep., 1,432,756; Thomas, Soc., 67,258; Foster, Com., 15,582; Upshaw, Proh., 6,388; Reynolds, Soc. Lab., 3,638.

1936 (Pres.), Roosevelt, Dem., 2,282,999; Landon, Rep., 1,570,393; Lemke, Union, 89,439; Thomas, Soc., 7,530; Colvin, Proh., 3,439; Aiken, Soc. Lab., 1,921.

1940 (Pres.), Roosevelt, Dem., 2,149,934; Willkie, Rep., 2,047,240; Thomas, Soc., 10,914; Babson, Proh., 9,190.

1944 (Pres.), Roosevelt, Dem., 2,079,479; Dewey, Rep., 1,939,314; Teichert, Soc. Lab., 9,677; Watson, Proh., 7,411; Thomas, Soc., 180.

1948 (Pres.), Truman, Dem., 1,994,715; Dewey, Rep., 1,961,103; Watson, Proh., 11,959; Thomas, Soc., 11,-522; Teichert, Soc. Lab., 3,118.

1952 (Pres.), Eisenhower, Rep., 2,457,327; Stevenson, Dem., 2,013,920; Haas, Soc. Lab., 9,363; write-in, 448.

1956 (Pres.), Eisenhower, Rep., 2,623,327; Stevenson, Dem., 1,775,682; Haas, Soc. Lab., 8,342; write-in, 56.

1960 (Pres.), Kennedy, Dem., 2,377,846; Nixon, Rep., 2,368,988; Haas, Soc. Lab., 10,560; write-in, 15.

1964 (Pres.), Johnson, Dem., 2,796,833; Goldwater, Rep., 1,905,946; write-in, 62.

1968 (Pres.), Nixon, Rep., 2,174,774; Humphrey, Dem., 2,039,814; Wallace, 3d party, 390,958; Blomen, Soc. Labor, 13,878; write-in, 325.

1972 (Pres.), Nixon, Rep., 2,788,179; McGovern, Dem., 1,913,472; Fisher, Soc. Labor, 12,344; Schmitz, Amer., 2,471; Hall, Communist, 4,541; others, 2,229.

1976 (Pres.), Carter, Dem., 2,271,295; Ford, Rep., 2,364,269; McCarthy, Ind., 55,939; Hall, Comm., 9,250; MacBride, Libertarian, 8,057; Camejo, Soc. Workers, 3,615; Blomen, Soc. Labor, 2,422; La-Rouche, U.S. Labor, 2,018; write-in, 1,968.

Indiana

	1972		1976	
	McGov-ern	Nixon	Carter	Ford
County	(D)	(R)	(D)	(R)
Adams	3,971	7,549	4,908	6,280
Allen	38,621	76,924	44,744	71,321
Bartholomew	6,974	17,365	11,203	14,771
Benton	1,566	3,703	2,071	3,093
Blackford	2,311	3,876	3,174	2,886
Boone	3,235	9,874	5,686	9,214
Brown	1,443	2,737	2,381	2,466
Carroll	2,214	5,885	3,606	4,797
Cass	5,317	12,681	7,610	10,342
Clark	10,838	16,111	16,670	12,732
Clay	3,742	7,146	5,433	5,674
Clinton	4,283	9,849	6,662	8,199
Crawford	1,801	2,623	2,721	2,181
Daviess	3,538	8,490	4,952	6,829
Dearborn	4,137	7,689	6,348	6,176
Decatur	2,994	6,761	4,365	5,555
Dekalb	4,354	8,834	6,151	7,860
Delaware	17,936	32,468	25,151	26,417
Dubois	6,365	6,637	7,385	6,383
Elkhart	12,659	31,009	17,581	27,291
Fayette	3,519	7,273	5,519	5,704
Floyd	9,243	13,198	12,744	11,259
Fountain	2,977	5,979	4,089	4,903
Franklin	2,131	4,324	3,234	3,557
Fulton	2,150	6,170	3,488	5,083
Gibson	5,633	9,115	8,430	7,105
Grant	7,912	20,969	13,468	16,847
Greene	4,450	8,453	7,263	6,442
Hamilton	4,151	20,247	7,857	21,828
Hancock	3,069	11,019	6,191	10,072
Harrison	3,927	5,910	5,685	4,911
Hendricks	4,384	17,699	9,066	16,725
Henry	5,610	14,538	10,137	11,620
Howard	8,083	23,089	14,815	19,571
Huntington	4,908	10,858	6,515	9,182
Jackson	4,984	9,546	7,610	7,615
Jasper	1,920	6,369	3,286	5,398
Jay	3,349	6,090	4,124	4,606
Jefferson	4,267	6,722	6,139	5,573
Jennings	2,903	5,156	4,430	4,505

	1972		1976	
	(D)	(R)	(D)	(R)
Johnson	5,067	17,537	10,075	16,414
Knox	6,089	11,940	9,612	9,100
Kosciusko	4,233	16,216	7,328	14,505
LaGrange	1,658	4,152	2,835	3,876
Lake	88,510	115,480	120,700	90,119
LaPorte	13,222	26,243	18,217	21,989
Lawrence	4,278	10,936	7,908	9,278
Madison	20,921	39,036	29,811	32,437
Marion	102,166	206,065	145,274	177,767
Marshall	4,349	11,908	6,424	9,707
Martin	2,021	3,470	2,827	2,702
Miami	3,889	9,477	6,257	8,263
Monroe	15,241	19,953	16,609	18,938
Montgomery	3,431	10,997	5,320	9,509
Morgan	3,390	11,980	7,181	10,983
Newton	1,252	3,771	2,236	3,204
Noble	4,250	7,916	5,875	6,885
Ohio	922	1,368	1,300	1,027
Orange	2,932	5,715	4,031	4,399
Owen	1,708	3,896	3,103	2,896
Parke	2,207	5,014	3,158	3,929
Perry	4,277	5,204	5,620	4,088
Pike	2,648	4,252	3,938	3,138
Porter	8,943	26,877	16,468	25,489
Posey	3,586	6,771	5,298	5,136
Pulaski	1,863	4,243	2,813	3,586
Putnam	3,339	7,879	5,116	6,063
Randolph	3,409	8,754	5,330	6,891
Ripley	3,601	6,594	4,792	5,293
Rush	1,764	5,965	3,052	4,723
St. Joseph	41,629	64,808	49,156	50,358
Scott	2,785	3,564	4,229	2,657
Shelby	4,028	10,794	7,098	8,918
Spencer	3,867	5,518	4,796	4,166
Starke	2,994	5,520	4,753	4,354
Steuben	2,401	5,636	3,323	5,079
Sullivan	3,624	5,338	5,198	3,747
Switzerland	1,612	1,872	2,150	1,329
Tippecanoe	14,598	31,565	17,850	29,186
Tipton	2,095	5,674	3,428	4,776
Union	765	2,043	1,160	1,631
Vanderburgh	22,163	47,806	34,911	37,975
Vermillion	3,515	4,764	4,791	3,674
Vigo	18,898	29,730	24,684	23,555
Wabash	4,601	10,011	5,704	8,534
Warren	1,164	2,746	1,906	2,377
Warrick	4,296	8,520	7,804	7,200
Washington	3,086	4,758	4,409	3,794
Wayne	7,655	21,610	12,306	16,697
Wells	3,244	6,425	4,250	5,596
White	2,675	7,419	3,963	6,287
Whitley	3,838	7,489	5,445	6,761
Totals	**708,568**	**1,405,154**	**1,014,714**	**1,183,958**

Indiana Vote Since 1932

1932 (Pres.), Roosevelt, Dem., 862,054; Hoover, Rep., 677,184; Thomas, Soc., 21,388; Upshaw, Proh., 10,399; Foster, Com., 2,187; Reynolds, Soc. Lab., 2,070.

1936 (Pres.), Roosevelt, Dem., 943,974; Landon, Rep., 691,570; Lemke, Union, 19,407; Thomas, Soc., 3,856; Browder, Com., 1,090.

1940 (Pres.), Roosevelt, Dem., 874,063; Willkie, Rep., 899,466; Babson, Proh., 6,437; Thomas, Soc., 2,075; Aiken, Soc. Lab., 706.

1944 (Pres.), Roosevelt, Dem., 781,403; Dewey, Rep., 875,891; Watson, Proh., 12,574; Thomas, Soc., 2,223.

1948 (Pres.), Truman, Dem., 807,833; Dewey, Rep., 821,079; Watson, Proh., 14,711; Wallace, Prog., 9,649; Thomas, Soc., 2,179; Teichert, Soc. Lab., 763.

1952 (Pres.), Eisenhower, Rep., 1,136,259; Stevenson, Dem., 801,530; Hamblen, Proh., 15,335; Hallinan, Prog., 1,222; Haas, Soc. Lab., 979.

1956 (Pres.), Eisenhower, Rep., 1,182,811; Stevenson, Dem., 783,908; Holtwick, Proh., 6,554; Haas, 1,334.

1960 (Pres.), Kennedy, Dem., 952,358; Nixon, Rep., 1,175,120; Decker, Proh., 6,746; Haas, Soc. Lab., 1,136.

1964 (Pres.), Johnson, Dem., 1,170,848; Goldwater, Rep., 911,118; Munn, Proh., 8,266; Haas, Soc. Lab., 1,374.

1968 (Pres.), Nixon, Rep., 1,067,885; Humphrey, Dem., 806,659; Wallace, 3d party, 243,108; Munn, Prohibition, 4,616; Halstead, Soc. Worker, 1,293; Gregory, 36.

1972 (Pres.), Nixon, Rep., 1,405,154; McGovern, Dem., 708,568; Reed, Soc. Worker, 5,575; Fisher, Soc. Labor, 1,688; Spock, Peace & Freedom, 4,544.

1976 (Pres.), Carter, Dem., 1,014,714; Ford, Rep., 1,185,958; Anderson, American, 14,048; Camejo, Soc. Worker, 5,695; LaRouche, U.S. Labor, 1,947.

Iowa

	1972		1976	
	McGovern	Nixon	Carter	Ford
County	(D)	(R)	(D)	(R)
Adair	1,642	3,041	2,294	2,326
Adams	1,161	1,814	1,507	1,388
Allamakee	2,271	4,150	2,568	3,648
Appanoose	2,283	4,321	3,424	3,036
Audubon	1,533	2,515	2,104	1,978
Benton	4,282	5,273	5,514	5,014
Black Hawk	21,721	30,929	29,508	30,994
Boone	5,057	6,271	6,595	5,413
Bremer	3,122	6,333	4,203	6,252
Buchanan	3,609	5,277	4,258	4,794
Buena Vista	3,460	5,685	4,227	5,126
Butler	1,682	4,615	2,503	4,207
Calhoun	2,446	3,821	3,001	3,215
Carroll	4,608	4,415	5,333	4,094
Cass	1,923	5,234	2,866	4,589
Cedar	2,465	4,452	3,354	4,308
Cerro Gordo	9,460	11,856	11,189	10,604
Cherokee	2,780	4,726	3,358	3,993
Chickasaw	3,134	3,836	3,503	3,432
Clarke	1,590	2,241	2,333	1,737
Clay	2,887	4,564	3,776	4,548
Clayton	3,366	5,447	3,804	4,826
Clinton	9,895	12,768	11,746	12,401
Crawford	3,018	4,493	3,903	3,879
Dallas	5,085	6,143	6,722	5,308
Davis	1,806	2,287	2,426	1,631
Decatur	1,880	2,638	2,698	1,932
Delaware	2,944	4,848	3,168	4,161
Des Moines	8,869	10,216	11,268	9,023
Dickinson	2,373	3,739	3,074	3,795
Dubuque	18,417	17,272	20,548	17,459
Emmet	1,970	3,436	2,720	2,872
Fayette	4,413	7,263	5,220	6,618
Floyd	3,338	4,726	4,646	4,361
Franklin	1,986	3,643	2,682	3,056
Fremont	1,210	2,642	1,964	2,163
Greene	2,152	3,371	3,094	2,811
Grundy	1,844	4,706	2,410	4,173
Guthrie	2,258	3,655	2,873	2,644
Hamilton	2,913	4,803	3,953	3,932
Hancock	2,349	3,706	2,975	3,127
Hardin	3,516	5,969	4,479	4,682
Harrison	2,369	4,721	3,228	3,489
Henry	2,721	5,066	3,882	3,848
Howard	2,439	2,980	2,917	2,618
Humboldt	2,062	3,622	2,677	3,075
Ida	1,490	2,819	1,868	2,590
Iowa	2,578	4,202	3,367	3,926
Jackson	3,704	4,975	4,467	4,221
Jasper	7,007	9,133	8,783	7,728
Jefferson	2,362	4,628	3,377	3,746
Johnson	20,922	14,823	20,208	16,090
Jones	3,468	4,962	4,245	4,463
Keokuk	2,619	3,831	3,482	2,920
Kossuth	4,393	5,841	5,190	4,653
Lee	7,510	9,748	9,017	8,195
Linn	31,370	36,503	38,252	36,513
Louisa	1,707	2,806	2,089	2,284
Lucas	1,759	2,851	2,733	2,071
Lyon	1,407	3,788	1,870	3,558
Madison	2,234	3,480	3,109	2,681
Mahaska	3,382	6,374	4,838	5,267
Marion	4,643	6,583	6,226	5,429
Marshall	6,618	10,798	8,695	9,562
Mills	1,060	3,531	1,908	2,722
Mitchell	2,449	3,395	2,906	2,887
Monona	2,189	3,237	2,661	2,636
Monroe	1,736	2,357	2,360	1,581
Montgomery	1,559	4,391	2,229	3,673
Muscatine	4,917	8,436	6,567	7,697
O'Brien	2,224	5,159	2,732	4,643
Osceola	1,317	2,262	1,309	1,955
Page	1,790	6,200	2,865	5,343
Palo Alto	2,845	3,141	3,182	2,623
Plymouth	4,033	6,339	4,284	5,590
Pocahontas	2,241	3,138	3,055	2,700
Polk	59,169	70,245	71,917	62,316
Pottawattamie	8,074	19,722	14,754	17,264
Poweshiek	3,718	4,785	4,360	4,194
Ringgold	1,003	2,264	1,739	1,543
Sac	2,452	4,017	2,996	3,347
Scott	23,810	34,135	29,771	35,021
Shelby	2,259	4,052	2,851	3,301
Sioux	2,867	10,721	3,322	9,448
Story	13,972	16,617	15,717	18,394
Tama	3,693	5,058	4,580	4,379
Taylor	1,247	3,042	1,947	2,059
Union	2,112	3,734	2,955	2,873
Van Buren	1,268	2,272	1,807	1,804
Wapello	8,348	9,301	10,249	6,786
Warren	5,143	7,332	7,653	6,099
Washington	2,784	5,187	3,448	4,218
Wayne	1,574	2,681	2,145	1,781
Webster	8,358	11,133	10,543	9,068
Winnebago	2,324	4,300	2,950	3,315
Winneshiek	4,401	5,877	4,158	4,765

	1972		1976	
	(D)	(R)	(D)	(R)
Woodbury	16,974	23,757	19,664	22,853
Worth	2,034	2,564	2,399	1,964
Wright	2,780	4,278	3,637	3,544
Total	**496,206**	**706,207**	**619,931**	**632,863**

Iowa Vote Since 1932

1932 (Pres.), Roosevelt, Dem., 598,019; Hoover, Rep., 414,433; Thomas, Soc., 20,467; Upshaw, Proh., 2,111; Coxey, Farm-Lab., 1,094; Foster, Com., 559.

1936 (Pres.), Roosevelt, Dem., 621,756; Landon, Rep., 487,977; Lemke, Union, 29,687; Thomas, Soc., 1,373; Colvin, Proh., 1,182; Browder, Comm., 506; Aiken, Soc. Lab., 252.

1940 (Pres.), Roosevelt, Dem., 578,800; Willkie, Rep., 632,370; Babson, Proh., 2,284; Browder, Com., 1,524; Aiken, Soc. Lab., 452.

1944 (Pres.), Roosevelt, Dem., 499,876; Dewey, Rep., 547,267; Watson, Proh., 3,752; Thomas, Soc., 1,511; Teichert, Soc. Lab., 193.

1948 (Pres.), Truman, Dem., 522,380; Dewey, Rep., 494,018; Wallace, Prog., 12,125; Teichert, Soc. Lab., 4,274; Watson, Proh., 3,382; Thomas, Soc., 1,829; Dobbs, Soc. Workers, 26.

1952 (Pres.), Eisenhower, Rep., 808,906; Stevenson, Dem., 451,513; Hallinan, Prog., 5,085; Hamblen, Proh., 2,882; Hoopes, Soc., 219; Haas, Soc. Lab., 139; scattering 29.

1956 (Pres.), Eisenhower, Rep., 729,187; Stevenson, Dem., 501,858; Andrews (A.C.P. of Iowa), 3,202; Hoopes, Soc., 192; Haas, Soc. Lab., 125.

1960 (Pres.), Kennedy, Dem., 550,565; Nixon, Rep., 722,381; Haas, Soc. Lab., 230; write-in, 634.

1964 (Pres.), Johnson, Dem., 733,030; Goldwater, Rep., 449,148; Haas, S. L., 182; DeBerry, S. W., 159; Munn, P., 1,902.

1968 (Pres.), Nixon, Rep., 619,106; Humphrey, Dem., 476,699; Wallace, 3d party, 66,422; Munn, Proh., 362; Halstead, Soc. Worker, 3,377; Cleaver, Peace and Freedom, 1,332; Blomen, S. L., 241.

1972 (Pres.), Nixon, Rep., 706,207; McGovern, Dem., 496,206; Schmitz, American, 22,056; Jenness, Soc. Worker, 488; Fisher, Soc. Labor, 195; Hall, Communist, 272; Green, Universal, 199; scattered, 321.

1976 (Pres.), Carter, Dem., 619,931; Ford, Rep., 632,863; McCarthy, Ind., 20,051; Anderson, American, 3,040; MacBride, Libertarian, 1,452.

Kansas

	1972		1976	
	McGovern	Nixon	Carter	Ford
County	(D)	(R)	(D)	(R)
Allen	1,610	3,938	2,746	3,269
Anderson	1,035	2,718	1,886	1,872
Atchison	2,404	5,471	4,108	4,030
Barber	727	2,308	1,494	1,568
Barton	3,481	8,479	5,497	7,311
Bourbon	1,912	4,776	3,237	3,589
Brown	1,038	4,314	1,745	3,407
Butler	4,669	11,045	8,540	8,390
Chase	315	1,184	643	922
Chautauqua	378	1,546	866	1,159
Cherokee	2,806	6,019	5,154	3,957
Cheyenne	399	1,440	758	1,008
Clark	311	1,142	680	761
Clay	887	3,562	1,610	3,085
Cloud	1,806	3,832	2,976	2,954
Coffey	782	2,667	1,549	2,145
Comanche	281	1,052	630	719
Cowley	3,592	10,332	7,095	7,513
Crawford	6,683	9,652	9,021	7,225
Decatur	616	1,707	1,011	1,232
Dickinson	1,957	6,515	3,672	4,759
Doniphan	690	2,856	1,428	2,469
Douglas	11,646	15,316	11,922	14,277
Edwards	757	1,534	1,304	1,001
Elk	428	1,522	865	1,087
Ellis	4,113	5,463	6,280	4,719
Ellsworth	1,028	2,087	1,573	1,618
Finney	2,062	4,335	3,813	3,711
Ford	2,804	6,232	4,934	4,679
Franklin	2,056	6,011	3,607	4,760
Geary	1,708	4,299	2,843	3,230
Gove	466	1,226	848	860
Graham	488	1,440	936	1,112
Grant	476	1,469	1,151	1,226
Gray	511	1,235	1,111	837
Greeley	212	639	479	389
Greenwood	951	3,157	1,737	2,319
Hamilton	394	941	746	560
Harper	729	2,628	1,681	1,777
Harvey	3,555	8,287	6,003	6,624
Haskell	383	1,036	676	761
Hodgeman	331	853	697	576
Jackson	1,191	3,363	2,129	2,725
Jefferson	1,237	3,679	2,470	3,225
Jewell	716	2,242	1,111	1,592
Johnson	24,324	76,161	35,605	75,798
Kearny	325	876	658	674
Kingman	1,107	2,756	2,142	1,839
Kiowa	406	1,559	764	1,180
Labette	3,210	6,399	5,294	4,640
Lane	294	943	646	651
Leavenworth	4,727	10,762	8,022	8,407
Lincoln	476	1,649	985	1,225
Linn	876	2,593	1,681	1,873
Logan	428	1,164	694	957
Lyon	3,720	9,157	5,634	7,062
Marion	1,478	4,373	2,483	3,519
Marshall	1,823	4,127	3,004	3,226
McPherson	2,858	7,457	5,366	6,187
Meade	526	1,712	983	1,109
Miami	2,140	5,234	4,000	3,999
Mitchell	1,030	2,830	1,700	2,095
Montgomery	3,685	11,717	7,157	8,864
Morris	704	2,471	1,337	1,698
Morton	363	1,165	735	738
Nemaha	1,777	3,422	2,586	2,759
Neosho	2,559	5,034	3,842	4,038
Ness	652	1,539	1,106	1,016
Norton	776	2,688	1,337	2,201
Osage	1,522	4,073	2,755	2,945
Osborne	724	2,182	1,190	1,574
Ottawa	705	2,065	1,393	1,629
Pawnee	1,110	2,370	1,959	1,692
Phillips	827	2,919	1,264	2,317
Pottawatomie	1,298	3,947	2,316	3,483
Pratt	1,214	3,253	2,307	2,427
Rawlins	560	1,553	903	1,148
Reno	8,183	15,714	14,620	11,212
Republic	1,059	2,421	1,617	2,294
Rice	1,825	3,843	3,056	2,584
Riley	5,333	11,120	6,540	9,518
Rooks	904	2,457	1,412	1,664
Rush	806	1,629	1,359	1,170
Russell	1,011	3,168	1,453	3,165
Saline	5,406	12,592	8,476	11,218
Scott	449	1,547	919	1,195
Sedgwick	39,220	83,949	63,989	69,828
Seward	989	3,866	1,907	3,604
Shawnee	20,383	43,727	28,578	37,101
Sheridan	552	1,134	793	838
Sherman	785	2,225	1,573	1,671
Smith	818	2,600	1,333	2,009
Stafford	844	2,200	1,659	1,430
Stanton	259	754	489	510
Stevens	408	1,392	901	1,262
Sumner	2,685	6,941	5,385	4,645
Thomas	943	2,300	1,802	2,246
Trego	621	1,369	1,003	1,025
Wabaunsee	622	2,461	1,354	1,921
Wallace	214	782	486	600
Washington	996	3,301	1,564	2,543
Wichita	288	794	614	593
Wilson	1,043	3,568	2,047	2,682
Woodson	550	1,592	904	1,104
Wyandotte	28,206	34,157	37,478	23,141
Totals	**270,287**	**619,812**	**430,421**	**502,752**

Kansas Vote Since 1932

1932 (Pres.), Roosevelt, Dem., 424,204; Hoover, Rep., 349,498; Thomas, Soc., 18,276.

1936 (Pres.), Roosevelt, Dem., 464,520; Landon, Rep., 397,727; Thomas, Soc., 2,766; Lemke, Union, 494.

1940 (Pres.), Roosevelt, Dem., 364,725; Willkie, Rep., 489,169; Babson, Proh., 4,056; Thomas, Soc., 2,347.

1944 (Pres.), Roosevelt, Dem., 287,458; Dewey, Rep., 442,096; Watson, Proh., 2,609; Thomas, Soc., 1,613.

1948 (Pres.), Truman, Dem., 351,902; Dewey, Rep., 423,039; Watson, Proh., 6,468; Wallace, Prog., 4,603; Thomas, Soc., 2,807.

1952 (Pres.), Eisenhower, Rep., 616,302; Stevenson, Dem., 273,296; Hamblen, Proh., 6,038; Hoopes, Soc., 530.

1956 (Pres.), Eisenhower, Rep., 566,878; Stevenson, Dem., 296,317; Holtwick, Proh., 3,048.

1960 (Pres.), Kennedy, Dem., 363,213; Nixon, Rep., 561,474; Decker, Proh., 4,138.

1964 (Pres.), Johnson, Dem., 464,028; Goldwater, Rep., 386,579; Munn, Proh., 5,393; Haas, Soc. Labor, 1,901.

1968 (Pres.), Nixon, Rep., 478,674; Humphrey, Dem., 302,996; Wallace, 3d, 88,921; Munn, Proh., 2,192.
1972 (Pres.), Nixon, Rep., 619,812; McGovern, Dem., 270,287; Schmitz, Cons., 21,808; Munn, Proh., 4,188.
1976 (Pres.), Carter, Dem., 430,421; Ford, Rep., 502,752; McCarthy, Ind., 13,185; Anderson, Amer., 4,724; MacBride, Libertarian, 3,242; Maddox, Cons., 2,118.

Kentucky

	1972		1976	
County	McGovern (D)	Nixon (R)	Carter (D)	Ford (R)
Adair	1,610	3,859	2,366	3,201
Allen	1,259	3,025	2,231	2,508
Anderson	1,302	2,298	2,388	1,682
Ballard	1,411	1,542	2,794	649
Barren	3,384	6,070	5,878	3,797
Bath	1,347	1,919	2,113	938
Bell	3,219	6,518	5,284	5,035
Boone	2,595	7,355	5,602	5,602
Bourbon	1,860	3,180	3,504	2,260
Boyd	6,434	12,812	11,150	9,106
Boyle	2,395	4,317	4,095	3,511
Bracken	873	1,628	1,577	879
Breathitt	2,677	1,346	3,544	1,014
Breckinridge	1,921	3,574	3,347	2,698
Bullitt	2,827	4,517	5,623	3,639
Butler	835	2,941	1,588	2,363
Caldwell	1,345	2,952	3,016	1,808
Calloway	3,468	5,167	8,141	3,171
Campbell	8,585	20,025	12,423	15,798
Carlisle	872	1,169	1,985	435
Carroll	1,308	1,228	2,251	815
Carter	2,591	4,082	3,915	3,185
Casey	913	3,727	1,602	3,379
Christian	4,063	7,414	7,845	4,964
Clark	2,020	4,506	4,575	3,114
Clay	1,709	4,046	1,674	3,652
Clinton	659	2,632	987	2,354
Crittenden	859	2,248	1,715	1,596
Cumberland	686	2,294	853	1,653
Daviess	8,168	17,234	14,114	12,826
Edmonson	722	2,327	1,418	1,976
Elliott	1,499	782	1,987	455
Estill	1,322	3,054	2,034	2,250
Fayette	19,828	42,362	28,012	35,170
Fleming	1,455	2,484	2,317	1,647
Floyd	7,544	6,099	10,151	3,108
Franklin	5,601	7,781	10,475	5,536
Fulton	1,024	1,807	2,370	1,060
Gallatin	612	719	1,164	436
Garrard	1,441	3,143	1,887	2,045
Grant	1,054	2,086	2,336	1,212
Graves	3,701	6,098	8,982	3,195
Grayson	1,839	4,155	3,064	3,658
Green	1,209	2,755	2,085	2,397
Greenup	4,491	6,828	6,880	5,062
Hancock	791	1,583	1,562	1,124
Hardin	4,060	8,740	7,977	6,965
Harlan	4,349	6,527	7,300	4,624
Harrison	1,780	2,732	3,582	1,911
Hart	2,307	3,582	3,189	2,013
Henderson	3,889	6,231	7,916	4,053
Henry	1,688	1,919	2,985	1,192
Hickman	976	1,430	2,035	585
Hopkins	3,129	7,133	7,749	5,115
Jackson	436	5,303	680	2,766
Jefferson	88,143	142,436	122,731	130,262
Jessamine	1,269	3,819	2,795	3,081
Johnson	1,840	4,907	3,683	4,891
Kenton	12,872	28,076	18,833	22,087
Knott	2,774	1,479	4,762	962
Knox	1,805	5,017	3,642	4,931
Larue	1,483	2,449	2,207	1,409
Laurel	2,274	7,276	3,813	6,186
Lawrence	1,529	2,392	2,402	1,838
Lee	744	1,629	1,091	1,449
Leslie	913	3,299	1,478	3,770
Letcher	2,908	4,213	4,590	3,122
Lewis	1,200	3,124	1,929	2,383
Lincoln	1,882	3,623	3,198	2,694
Livingston	1,065	1,673	2,497	878
Logan	2,459	3,573	4,850	2,430
Lyon	687	1,030	1,606	585
McCracken	7,567	11,260	14,956	6,997
McCreary	684	3,203	1,827	3,272
McLean	1,191	2,298	2,346	1,212
Madison	4,328	8,659	7,299	6,581
Magoffin	2,024	2,243	2,451	1,793
Marion	2,351	2,370	3,520	1,723
Marshall	2,806	4,290	6,906	2,578
Martin	661	2,495	1,267	2,120
Mason	2,459	3,529	3,397	2,529
Meade	1,541	2,492	3,030	1,755
Menifee	732	596	1,041	304
Mercer	1,707	3,575	3,411	2,451
Metcalfe	1,308	1,896	1,877	1,356
Monroe	768	3,770	1,412	3,352
Montgomery	1,657	2,868	3,141	2,032
Morgan	1,815	1,535	2,897	973
Muhlenberg	3,246	5,596	7,058	4,292
Nelson	2,828	3,495	4,454	2,804
Nicholas	804	1,076	1,582	738
Ohio	906	2,392	3,508	3,764
Oldham	1,311	3,041	2,819	3,695
Owen	1,161	1,456	2,332	676
Owsley	251	1,328	305	1,053
Pendleton	909	1,966	2,147	1,230
Perry	3,601	5,373	5,633	4,434
Pike	9,513	12,535	14,320	9,178
Powell	1,230	1,766	1,859	1,148
Pulaski	3,080	10,602	5,752	9,226
Robertson	421	456	546	275
Rockcastle	968	3,437	1,408	2,583
Rowan	2,169	3,245	3,541	2,244
Russell	1,169	3,992	1,803	2,882
Scott	1,642	3,255	3,118	2,408
Shelby	2,074	3,893	3,841	2,916
Simpson	1,325	2,285	2,782	1,481
Spencer	481	1,120	1,209	742
Taylor	1,859	4,035	3,456	3,337
Todd	1,222	1,964	2,436	1,095
Trigg	1,514	1,767	2,727	991
Trimble	757	935	1,568	517
Union	1,855	2,701	3,540	1,716
Warren	5,934	12,481	9,657	9,439
Washington	1,552	2,378	2,376	1,765
Wayne	1,853	3,514	2,537	3,243
Webster	1,712	2,396	3,523	1,402
Whitley	2,199	6,788	4,212	6,100
Wolfe	957	936	1,777	659
Woodford	1,268	3,363	2,689	2,646
Totals	**371,159**	**676,446**	**615,717**	**531,852**

Kentucky Vote Since 1932

1932 (Pres.), Roosevelt, Dem., 580,574; Hoover, Rep., 394,716; Upshaw, Proh., 2,252; Thomas, Soc., 3,853; Reynolds, Soc. Lab., 1,396; Foster, Com., 272.
1936 (Pres.), Roosevelt, Dem., 541,944; Landon, Rep., 369,702; Lemke, Union, 12,501; Colvin, Proh., 929; Thomas, S., 627; Aiken, S. L., 294; Browder, Com., 204.
1940 (Pres.), Roosevelt, Dem., 557,222; Willkie, Rep., 410,384; Babson, Proh., 1,443; Thomas, Soc., 1,014.
1944 (Pres.), Roosevelt, Dem., 472,589; Dewey, Rep., 392,448; Watson, Proh., 2,023; Thomas, Soc., 535; Teichert, Soc. Lab., 326.
1948 (Pres.), Truman, Dem., 466,756; Dewey, Rep., 341,210; Thurmond, States' Rights, 10,411; Wallace, Prog., 1,567; Thomas, Soc., 1,284; Watson, Proh., 1,245; Teichert, Soc. Lab., 185.
1952 (Pres.), Eisenhower, Rep., 495,029; Stevenson, Dem., 495,729; Hamblen, Proh., 1,161; Haas, Soc. Lab., 893; Hallinan, Proh., 336.
1956 (Pres.), Eisenhower, Rep., 572,192; Stevenson, Dem., 476,453; Byrd, States' Rights, 2,657; Holtwick, Proh., 2,145; Haas, Soc. Lab., 358.
1960 (Pres.), Kennedy, Dem., 521,855; Nixon, Rep., 602,607.
1964 (Pres.), Johnson, Dem., 669,659; Goldwater, Rep., 372,977; John Kasper, Nat'l. States Rights, 3,469.
1968 (Pres.), Nixon, Rep., 462,411; Humphrey, Dem., 397,547; Wallace, 3d p., 193,098; Halstead, S. W., 2,843.
1972 (Pres.), Nixon, Rep., 676,446; McGovern, Dem., 371,159; Schmitz, Amer., 17,627; Jenness, Soc. Worker, 685; Hall, Comm., 464; Spock, Peoples, 1,118.
1976 (Pres.), Carter, Dem., 615,717; Ford, Rep., 531,852; Anderson, American, 8,308; McCarthy, Ind., 6,837; Maddox, Amer. Independent, 2,328.

Louisiana

	1972		1976	
Parish	McGovern (D)	Nixon (R)	Carter (D)	Ford (R)
Acadia	4,406	9,698	10,814	6,296
Allen	2,029	3,581	5,373	2,080
Ascension	3,324	5,187	9,100	4,435
Assumption	2,065	3,751	4,401	3,117
Avoyelles	3,395	6,225	8,104	4,574

	1972 (D)	1972 (R)	1976 (D)	1976 (R)
Beauregard	1,728	4,955	5,322	3,196
Bienville	1,890	3,384	3,402	2,499
Bossier	2,914	12,856	8,062	12,132
Caddo	15,649	47,215	30,593	42,627
Calcasieu	15,330	24,778	33,980	17,485
Caldwell	508	2,306	1,830	1,890
Cameron	739	1,391	2,432	819
Catahoula	823	2,683	2,547	2,086
Claiborne	1,551	3,432	2,891	3,216
Concordia	2,142	4,521	3,892	3,849
DeSoto	2,596	4,017	4,630	3,601
E. Baton Rouge	23,617	52,648	49,956	51,655
East Carroll	1,661	1,736	2,367	1,681
East Feliciana	1,603	1,992	3,485	1,668
Evangeline	2,919	5,523	7,578	3,715
Franklin	1,272	4,967	3,824	3,947
Grant	859	3,626	3,670	2,280
Iberia	5,143	11,812	9,984	10,392
Iberville	3,650	3,972	7,254	3,822
Jackson	1,477	4,152	3,605	3,310
Jefferson	20,981	75,348	53,257	71,787
Jefferson Davis	2,551	5,903	6,376	3,603
Lafayette	8,740	22,939	19,918	22,805
Lafourche	5,713	13,936	14,131	11,434
LaSalle	651	3,858	2,961	3,161
Lincoln	2,589	6,736	4,971	6,828
Livingston	1,898	7,481	9,875	5,555
Madison	2,249	2,420	4,933	2,096
Morehouse	2,355	5,770	4,017	5,418
Natchitoches	3,180	6,994	6,692	5,248
Orleans	60,790	88,075	93,130	70,925
Ouachita	6,920	24,860	15,738	24,082
Plaquemines	990	6,595	2,614	6,052
Pointe Coupee	3,133	3,192	5,147	2,567
Rapides	8,422	22,306	20,851	17,766
Red River	957	2,245	1,906	1,728
Richland	1,335	4,304	3,495	3,630
Sabine	1,332	4,935	4,555	3,531
St. Bernard	3,189	15,198	12,969	12,707
St. Charles	2,788	5,469	6,872	4,270
St. Helena	943	1,446	2,622	1,046
St. James	2,633	3,112	4,531	2,751
St. John	2,815	3,525	5,700	3,597
St. Landry	7,421	12,510	15,613	9,956
St. Martin	3,202	6,337	7,992	4,112
St. Mary	4,435	11,117	9,401	8,919
St. Tammany	3,949	15,438	14,691	15,822
Tangipahoa	5,227	11,607	14,432	9,242
Tensas	1,568	1,729	2,081	1,553
Terrebonne	4,415	13,753	10,627	12,895
Union	1,465	4,322	3,600	4,139
Vermillion	3,876	8,909	11,246	6,133
Vernon	1,345	6,225	6,202	3,970
Washington	2,947	8,162	10,000	5,677
Webster	2,859	8,829	7,286	7,550
W. Baton Rouge	1,849	2,626	3,809	1,913
West Carroll	571	2,997	2,595	2,407
West Feliciana	1,079	1,001	1,890	990
Winn	1,490	4,235	3,543	3,209
Totals	**298,142**	**686,852**	**661,365**	**587,446**

Louisiana Vote Since 1932

1932 (Pres.), Roosevelt, Dem., 249,418; Hoover, Rep., 18,863.

1936 (Pres.), Roosevelt, Dem., 292,894; Landon, Rep., 36,791.

1940 (Pres.), Roosevelt, Dem., 319,751; Willkie, Rep., 52,446.

1944 (Pres.), Roosevelt, Dem., 281,564; Dewey, Rep., 67,750.

1948 (Pres.), Thurmond, States' Rights, 204,290; Truman, Dem., 136,344; Dewey, Rep., 72,657; Wallace, Prog., 3,035.

1952 (Pres.), Eisenhower, Rep., 306,925; Stevenson, Dem., 345,027.

1956 (Pres.), Eisenhower, Rep., 329,047; Stevenson, Dem., 243,977; Andrews, States' Rights, 44,520.

1960 (Pres.), Kennedy, Dem., 407,339; Nixon, Rep., 230,890; States' Rights (unpledged) 169,572.

1964 (Pres.), Johnson, Dem., 387,068; Goldwater, Rep., 509,225.

1968 (Pres.), Nixon, Rep., 257,535; Humphrey, Dem., 309,615; Wallace, 3d party, 530,300.

1972 (Pres.), Nixon, Rep., 686,852; McGovern, Dem., 298,142; Schmitz, American, 52,099; Jenness, Soc. Worker, 14,398.

1976 (Pres.), Carter, Dem., 661,365; Ford, Rep., 587,446; Maddox, American, 10,058; Hall, Comm., 7,417; McCarthy, Ind., 6,588; MacBride, Libertarian, 3,325.

Maine

County	1972 McGovern (D)	1972 Nixon (R)	1976 Carter (D)	1976 Ford (R)
Androscoggin	19,509	19,406	26,484	16,330
Aroostook	11,474	19,051	15,484	15,550
Cumberland	33,326	51,268	47,007	48,959
Franklin	2,988	5,958	5,140	5,799
Hancock	4,191	11,889	6,725	12,064
Kennebec	16,379	24,617	23,473	22,534
Knox	3,601	8,478	5,922	8,315
Lincoln	2,903	7,580	4,818	7,554
Oxford	6,661	12,114	10,340	10,551
Penobscot	18,552	30,186	24,672	29,016
Piscataquis	2,518	4,617	3,727	4,084
Sagadahoc	3,414	6,463	5,529	5,988
Somerset	5,921	10,079	9,465	8,868
Waldo	2,941	6,480	4,853	6,289
Washington	3,742	7,820	6,644	7,039
York	22,464	30,452	31,996	27,380
Totals	**160,584**	**256,458**	**232,279**	**236,320**

Maine Vote Since 1932

1932 (Pres.), Roosevelt, Dem., 128,907; Hoover, Rep., 166,631; Thomas, Soc., 2,439; Reynolds, Soc. Lab., 255; Foster, Com., 162.

1936 (Pres.), Landon, Rep., 168,823; Roosevelt, Dem., 126,333; Lemke, Union, 7,581; Thomas, Soc., 783; Colvin, Proh., 334; Browder, Com., 257; Aiken, Soc. Lab., 129.

1940 (Pres.), Roosevelt, Dem., 156,478; Willkie, Rep., 165,951; Browder, Com., 411.

1944 (Pres.), Roosevelt, Dem., 140,631; Dewey, Rep., 155,434; Teichert, Soc. Lab., 335.

1948 (Pres.), Truman, Dem., 111,916; Dewey, Rep., 150,234; Wallace, Prog., 1,884; Thomas, Soc., 547; Teichert, Soc. Lab., 206.

1952 (Pres.), Eisenhower, Rep., 232,353; Stevenson, Dem., 118,806; Hallinan, Prog., 332; Haas, Soc. Lab., 156; Hoopes, Soc., 138; scattered, 1.

1956 (Pres.), Eisenhower, Rep., 249,238; Stevenson, Dem., 102,468.

1960 (Pres.), Kennedy, Dem., 181,159; Nixon, Rep., 240,608.

1964 (Pres.), Johnson, Dem., 262,264; Goldwater, Rep., 118,701.

1968 (Pres.), Nixon, Rep., 169,254; Humphrey, Dem., 217,312; Wallace, 3d party, 6,370.

1972 (Pres.), Nixon, Rep., 256,458; McGovern, Dem., 160,584; scattered, 229.

1976 (Pres.), Carter, Dem., 232,279; Ford, Rep., 236,320; McCarthy, Ind., 10,874; Bubar, Proh., 3,495.

Maryland

County	1972 McGovern (D)	1972 Nixon (R)	1976 Carter (D)	1976 Ford (R)
Allegany	10,808	20,687	15,967	15,435
Anne Arundel	26,082	71,707	54,351	61,353
Baltimore	70,309	175,897	118,505	143,293
Calvert	2,232	4,024	4,626	3,439
Caroline	1,567	4,325	3,017	3,114
Carroll	4,408	16,847	9,940	15,661
Cecil	4,113	10,759	8,950	7,833
Charles	4,502	9,665	9,525	7,792
Dorchester	2,136	6,859	4,528	4,768
Frederick	8,235	19,907	14,542	17,941
Garrett	1,510	5,480	3,332	4,640
Harford	8,737	25,141	19,890	24,309
Howard	10,668	19,265	20,533	21,200
Kent	2,168	4,036	3,211	2,821
Montgomery	100,228	133,090	131,098	122,674
Prince George's	79,914	116,166	111,743	81,027
Queen Anne's	1,712	4,380	3,457	3,479
St. Mary's	3,571	7,689	7,227	5,640
Somerset	2,036	4,342	3,472	3,254
Talbot	2,181	6,620	3,715	5,848
Washington	10,039	24,234	15,902	20,194
Wicomico	5,510	13,115	9,412	10,537
Worcester	1,792	5,584	4,076	4,647
BALTIMORE CITY	141,323	119,486	178,593	81,762
Totals	**505,781**	**829,305**	**759,612**	**672,661**

Maryland Vote Since 1932

1932 (Pres.), Roosevelt, Dem., 314,314; Hoover, Rep.,

184,184; Thomas, Soc., 10,489; Reynolds, Soc. Lab., 1,036; Foster, Com., 1,031.
1936 (Pres.), Roosevelt, Dem., 389,612; Landon, Rep., 231,435; Thomas, Soc., 1,629; Aiken, Soc. Lab., 1,305; Browder, Com.,915.
1940 (Pres.), Roosevelt, Dem., 384,546; Wilkie, Rep., 269,534; Thomas, Soc., 4,093; Browder, Com., 1,274; Aiken, Soc. Lab., 657.
1944 (Pres.), Roosevelt, Dem., 315,490; Dewey, Rep., 292,949.
1948 (Pres.), Truman, Dem., 286,521; Dewey, Rep., 294,814; Wallace, Prog., 9,983; Thomas, Soc., 2,941; Thurmond, States' Rights, 2,476; Wright, write-in, 2,294.
1952 (Pres.), Eisenhower, Rep., 499,424; Stevenson, Dem., 395,337; Hallinan, Prog., 7,313.
1956 (Pres.), Eisenhower, Rep., 559,738; Stevenson, Dem., 372,613.
1960 (Pres.), Kennedy, Dem., 565,800; Nixon, Rep., 489,538.
1964 (Pres.), Johnson, Dem., 730,912; Goldwater, Rep., 385,495; write-in, 50.
1968 (Pres.), Nixon, Rep., 517,995; Humphrey, Dem., 538,310; Wallace, 3d party, 178,734.
1972 (Pres.), Nixon, Rep., 829,305; McGovern, Dem., 505,781; Schmitz, American Party, 18,726.
1976 (Pres.), Carter, Dem., 759,612; Ford, Rep., 672,-661.

Massachusetts

County	1972 McGovern (D)	1972 Nixon (R)	1976 Carter (D)	1976 Ford (R)
Barnstable	22,636	36,340	31,268	39,295
Berkshire	35,391	30,380	39,337	27,462
Bristol	103,163	84,390	116,318	69,957
Dukes	2,001	2,312	2,513	2,365
Essex	157,324	138,040	165,710	125,538
Franklin	11,968	16,088	14,985	14,837
Hampden	94,945	86,164	110,028	70,008
Hampshire	28,572	24,529	34,947	22,219
Middlesex	345,343	269,064	359,919	260,044
Nantucket	952	1,418	1,115	1,399
Norfolk	150,232	134,459	155,342	136,628
Plymouth	69,124	76,062	83,663	74,684
Suffolk	166,250	85,272	142,010	80,623
Worcester	144,139	127,560	172,320	105,217
Totals	**1,332,540**	**1,112,078**	**1,429,475**	**1,030,276**

Massachusetts Vote Since 1932

1932 (Pres.), Roosevelt, Dem., 800,148; Hoover, Rep., 736,959; Thomas, Soc., 34,305; Foster, Com., 4,821; Reynolds, Soc. Lab., 2,668; Upshaw, Proh., 1,142.
1936 (Pres.), Roosevelt, Dem., 942,716; Landon, Rep., 768,613; Lemke, Union, 118,639; Thomas, Soc., 5,111; Browder, Com., 2,930; Aiken, Soc. Lab., 1,305; Colvin, Proh., 1,032.
1940 (Pres.), Roosevelt, Dem., 1,076,522; Willkie, Rep., 939,700; Thomas, Soc., 4,091; Browder, Com., 3,806; Aiken, Soc. Lab., 1,492; Babson, Proh., 1,370.
1944 (Pres.), Roosevelt, Dem., 1,035,296; Dewey, Rep., 921,350; Teichert, Soc. Lab., 2,780; Watson, Proh., 973.
1948 (Pres.), Truman, Dem., 1,151,788; Dewey, Rep., 909,370; Wallace, Prog., 38,157; Teichert, Soc. Lab., 5,535; Watson, Proh., 1,663.
1952 (Pres.), Eisenhower, Rep., 1,292,325; Stevenson, Dem., 1,083,525; Hallinan, Prog., 4,636; Hass, Soc. Lab., 1,957; Hamblen, Proh., 886; scattered, 69; blanks, 41,150.
1956 (Pres.), Eisenhower, Rep., 1,393,197; Stevenson, Dem., 948,190; Haas, Soc. Lab., 5,573; Holtwick, Proh., 1,205; others, 341.
1960 (Pres.), Kennedy, Dem., 1,487,174; Nixon, Rep., 976,750; Haas, Soc. Lab., 3,892; Decker, Proh., 1,633; others, 31; blank and void, 26,024.
1964 (Pres.), Johnson, Dem., 1,786,422; Goldwater, Rep., 549,727; Haas, Soc. Lab., 4,755; Munn, Proh., 3,735; scattered, 159; blank, 48,104.
1968 (Pres.), Nixon, Rep., 766,844; Humphrey, Dem., 1,469,218; Wallace, 3d party, 87,088; Blomen, Soc. Labor, 6,180; Munn, Prohibition, 2,369; scattered, 53; blanks, 25,394.
1972 (Pres.), Nixon, Rep., 1,112,078; McGovern, Dem. 1,332,540; Jenness, Soc. Worker, 10,600; Fisher, Soc. Labor, 129; Schmitz, American, 2,877; Spock, Peoples, 101; Hall, Communist, 46; Hospers, Libertarian, 43; scattered, 342.
1976 (Pres.), Carter, Dem., 1,429,475; Ford, Rep., 1,030,276; McCarthy, Ind., 65,637; Camejo, Soc. Workers, 8,138; Anderson, American, 7,555; La Rouche, U.S. Labor, 4,922.

Michigan

County	1972 McGovern (D)	1972 Nixon (R)	1976 Carter (D)	1976 Ford (R)
Alcona	1,195	2,434	2,038	2,328
Alger	1,803	2,035	2,379	1,722
Allegan	7,883	18,407	9,794	19,330
Alpena	5,104	6,513	6,310	6,380
Antrim	2,000	4,068	3,032	4,369
Arenac	1,829	2,588	2,695	2,687
Baraga	1,517	1,905	1,778	1,788
Barry	5,484	10,393	6,967	11,178
Bay	21,712	23,094	25,958	23,174
Benzie	1,310	2,686	1,891	3,085
Berrien	18,597	43,047	25,163	40,835
Branch	4,887	8,388	6,301	8,251
Calhoun	22,154	32,531	25,229	30,390
Cass	4,982	10,398	7,843	9,893
Charlevoix	2,831	4,522	3,953	5,145
Cheboygan	2,985	4,529	3,880	4,894
Chippewa	4,744	7,028	6,022	7,025
Clare	2,434	4,402	4,153	4,879
Clinton	5,770	13,438	7,549	13,475
Crawford	1,143	1,953	1,889	2,359
Delta	8,003	7,647	9,027	7,809
Dickinson	5,339	5,989	6,134	5,922
Eaton	8,986	20,413	12,083	22,120
Emmet	3,081	4,288	4,013	5.910
Genesee	73,896	85,747	88,967	80,004
Gladwin	2,016	3,484	3,719	3,794
Gogebic	4,984	5,631	6,341	3,953
Grand Traverse	5,810	11,421	7,263	13,505
Gratiot	4,370	9,904	5,429	9,526
Hillsdale	3,942	9,261	5,427	9,307
Houghton	6,402	9,053	7,352	8,049
Huron	4,456	9,832	5,721	9,297
Ingham	53,458	63,376	47,890	66,729
Ionia	6,240	10,898	6,820	11,737
Iosco	3,065	5,750	4,875	5,500
Iron	3,512	3,630	4,401	3,224
Isabella	7,446	9,682	7,281	10,577
Jackson	19,350	34,220	24,726	32,873
Kalamazoo	33,324	50,405	33,411	51,462
Kalkaska	924	1,855	1,957	2,280
Kent	67,587	104,041	59,000	126,805
Keweenaw	456	715	658	606
Lake	1,548	1,532	2,179	1,598
Lapeer	5,531	11,615	9,503	12,349
Leelanau	1,855	3,809	2,437	4,240
Lenawee	11,018	19,125	14,610	18,397
Livingston	7,634	16,856	12,415	19,437
Luce	862	1,579	1,099	1,379
Mackinac	1,937	3,096	2,452	3,107
Macomb	82,346	147,777	121,176	132,499
Manistee	3,625	5,070	4,479	5,532
Marquette	11,555	13,249	12,837	12,984
Mason	3,697	6,811	4,541	6,812
Mecosta	3,799	7,158	4,725	7,287
Menominee	4,657	6,060	5,596	5,633
Midland	9,504	16,473	11,959	17,631
Missaukee	924	2,647	1,688	2,943
Monroe	17,726	23,263	23,290	20,676
Montcalm	5,402	9,591	6,684	10,439
Montmorency	914	1,798	1,684	1,882
Muskegon	22,804	36,428	27,013	35,548
Newaygo	3,978	8,254	5,622	8,258
Oakland	129,400	241,613	164,266	244,271
Oceana	2,525	4,992	3,427	5,236
Ogemaw	2,056	3,367	3,545	3,212
Ontonagon	2,140	3,040	3,104	2,462
Osceola	1,706	4,441	2,603	4,467
Oscoda	678	1,561	1,108	1,541
Otsego	1,912	2,854	2,724	3,155
Ottawa	15,119	42,169	16,381	49,196
Presque Isle	2,440	3,372	3,334	3,545
Roscommon	2,187	4,136	3,691	4,608
Saginaw	29,424	47,920	36,280	46,765
St. Clair	15,712	23,471	22,734	26,311
St. Joseph	5,119	18,438	7,306	11,784
Sanilac	3,780	11,031	6,042	10,597
Schoolcraft	1,759	2,310	2,158	1,933
Shiawassee	3,932	15,489	12,202	15,113
Tuscola	5,449	12,198	7,932	12,059
Van Buren	7,159	13,903	10,366	13,615
Washtenaw	55,350	50,535	50,917	56,807

	1972		1976	
	(D)	(R)	(D)	(R)
Wayne	514,913	435,877	548,767	348,588
Wexford	3,048	5,221	4,519	5,670
Totals	**1,459,435**	**1,961,721**	**1,696,714**	**1,893,742**

Michigan Vote Since 1932

1932 (Pres.), Roosevelt, Dem., 871,700; Hoover, Rep., 739,894; Thomas, Soc., 39,025; Foster, Com., 9,318; Upshaw, Proh., 2,893; Reynolds, Soc. Lab., 1,041; Harvey, Lib., 217.

1936 (Pres.), Roosevelt, Dem., 1,016,794; Landon, Rep., 699,733; Lemke, Union, 75,795; Thomas, Soc., 8,208; Browder, Com., 3,384; Aiken, Soc. Lab., 600; Colvin, Proh., 579.

1940 (Pres.), Roosevelt, Dem., 1,032,991; Willkie, Rep., 1,039,917; Thomas, Soc., 7,593; Browder, Com., 2,834; Babson, Proh., 1,795; Aiken, Soc. Lab., 795.

1944 (Pres.), Roosevelt, Dem., 1,106,899; Dewey, Rep., 1,084,423; Watson, Proh., 6,503; Thomas, Soc., 4,598; Smith, America First, 1,530; Teichert, Soc. Lab., 1,264.

1948 (Pres.), Truman, Dem., 1,003,448; Dewey, Rep., 1,038,595; Wallace, Prog., 46,515; Watson, Proh., 13,052; Thomas, Soc., 6,063; Teichert, Soc. Lab., 1,263; Dobbs, Soc. Workers, 672.

1952 (Pres.), Eisenhower, Rep., 1,551,529; Stevenson, Dem., 1,230,657; Hamblen, Proh., 10,331; Hallinan, Prog., 3,922; Haas, Soc. Lab., 1,495; Dobbs, Soc. Workers, 655; scattered, 3.

1956 (Pres.), Eisenhower, Rep., 1,713,647; Stevenson, Dem., 1,359,898; Holtwick, Proh., 6,923.

1960 (Pres.), Kennedy, Dem., 1,687,269; Nixon, Rep., 1,620,428; Dobbs, Soc. Workers, 4,347; Decker, Proh., 2,029; Daly, Tax Cut, 1,767; Haas, Soc. Lab., 1,718; Ind. American 539.

1964 (Pres.), Johnson, Dem., 2,136,615; Goldwater, Rep., 1,060,152; DeBerry, Soc. Workers, 3,817; Haas, Soc. Lab., 1,704; Proh. (no candidate listed), 699; scattering, 145.

1968 (Pres.), Nixon, Rep., 1,370,665; Humphrey, Dem., 1,593,082; Wallace, 3d party, 331,968; Halstead, Soc. Worker, 4,099; Blomen, Soc. Labor, 1,762; Cleaver, New Politics, 4,585; Munn, Prohib., 60; scattering, 29.

1972 (Pres.), Nixon, Rep., 1,961,721; McGovern, Dem., 1,459,435; Schmitz, Amer., 63,321; Fisher, Soc. Labor, 2,437; Jenness, Soc. Worker, 1,603; Hall, Communist, 1,210.

1976 (Pres.), Carter, Dem., 1,696,714; Ford, Rep., 1,893,742; McCarthy, Ind., 47,905; MacBride, Libertarian, 5,406; Wright, People's, 3,504; Camejo, Soc. Workers, 1,804; LaRouche, U.S. Labor, 1,366; Levin, Soc. Labor, 1,148; scattering, 2,160.

Minnesota

	1972		1976	
	McGovern	Nixon	Carter	Ford
County	(D)	(R)	(D)	(R)
Aitkin	2,687	3,241	4,308	2,476
Anoka	28,031	29,546	48,173	27,863
Becker	4,695	6,033	6,597	5,611
Beltrami	5,194	5,947	7,540	5,214
Benton	4,282	4,652	6,235	4,099
Big Stone	2,185	1,748	2,581	1,332
Blue Earth	10,638	12,702	12,930	11,998
Brown	4,347	7,791	5,792	7,479
Carlton	7,116	5,445	9,247	4,371
Carver	4,852	8,546	7,574	8,199
Cass	3,347	4,906	5,424	4,443
Chippewa	3,630	3,787	4,648	3,254
Chisago	4,174	4,718	6,625	3,874
Clay	9,076	11,089	10,876	10,317
Clearwater	1,751	1,819	2,437	1,374
Cook	742	1,047	1,018	1,034
Cottonwood	2,802	4,396	3,813	3,906
Crow Wing	7,328	8,774	10,653	8,072
Dakota	28,479	34,967	44,253	37,542
Dodge	1,921	3,863	3,009	3,446
Douglas	5,501	6,678	7,097	5,910
Faribault	3,519	6,503	5,049	5,577
Fillmore	3,155	7,107	4,758	5,984
Freeborn	7,163	9,747	9,470	8,220
Goodhue	6,147	11,107	8,926	9,967
Grant	2,085	1,899	2,624	1,635
Hennepin	205,943	228,951	257,380	211,892
Houston	2,467	5,186	3,861	4,853
Hubbard	2,136	3,294	3,196	2,985
Isanti	3,660	3,715	6,013	3,159
Itasca	8,683	7,558	12,979	6,646
Jackson	3,304	3,599	4,311	2,870
Kanabec	1,979	2,395	3,188	1,943
Kandiyohi	7,241	6,624	9,992	6,664
Kittson	1,584	1,832	2,008	1,555
Koochiching	3,396	3,681	4,846	2,893
LacQuiParle	2,845	2,773	3,647	2,292
Lake	3,640	2,575	3,973	2,313
Lake O' Woods	672	877	1,105	757
Le Sueur	4,725	5,388	6,556	4,565
Lincoln	2,148	1,881	2,594	1,599
Lyon	5,614	5,820	7,122	5,036
McLeod	4,538	7,820	6,249	6,519
Mahnomen	1,397	1,246	1,590	905
Marshall	2,790	3,264	3,744	2,605
Martin	3,816	7,569	5,672	6,484
Meeker	3,601	5,097	5,295	4,097
Millie Lacs	3,221	4,291	5,172	3,212
Morrison	5,993	5,714	8,176	4,590
Mower	10,286	9,929	12,837	8,163
Murray	2,893	2,959	3,685	2,605
Nicollet	4,680	6,230	5,777	6,071
Nobles	5,464	4,951	6,034	4,503
Norman	2,444	2,536	2,946	1,983
Olmsted	9,817	23,806	14,676	24,030
Otter Tail	7,881	13,519	11,881	12,113
Pennington	2,892	3,548	3,787	3,023
Pine	3,794	3,881	5,442	3,057
Pipestone	2,758	3,543	3,272	3,018
Polk	7,366	8,139	9,078	6,552
Pope	2,910	2,610	3,746	2,251
Ramsey	108,392	95,716	133,682	86,480
Red Lake	1,409	1,052	1,748	737
Redwood	3,177	5,776	4,525	4,926
Renville	4,499	5,329	5,762	4,482
Rice	8,065	9,195	10,590	8,311
Rock	2,089	3,470	2,769	2,892
Roseau	2,396	2,844	3,215	2,382
St. Louis	61,103	41,435	75,040	35,331
Scott	6,745	7,310	9,912	7,154
Sherburne	4,070	4,332	6,678	4,361
Sibley	2,433	4,543	3,752	3,871
Stearns	19,315	18,951	25,027	19,574
Steele	4,010	7,678	6,263	7,053
Stevens	2,870	2,830	3,171	2,484
Swift	3,823	2,673	4,428	2,190
Todd	4,270	5,387	6,530	4,278
Traverse	1,744	1,276	2,020	1,130
Wabasha	3,017	5,158	4,286	4,484
Wadena	2,430	3,408	3,164	3,048
Waseca	2,767	5,064	4,002	4,582
Washington	16,102	19,142	26,454	20,716
Watonwan	2,229	3,960	3,177	3,351
Wilkin	1,739	2,292	2,103	1,882
Winona	8,080	10,910	10,939	10,436
Wright	8,695	9,996	13,379	9,314
Yellow Med	3,462	3,683	4,337	2,946
Totals	**802,346**	**898,269**	**1,070,440**	**819,395**

Minnesota Vote Since 1932

1932 (Pres.), Roosevelt, Dem., 600,806; Hoover, Rep., 363,959; Thomas, Soc., 25,476; Foster, Com., 6,101; Coxey, Farm.-Lab., 5,731; Reynolds, Ind., 770.

1936 (Pres.), Roosevelt, Dem., 698,811; Landon, Rep., 350,461; Lemke, Union, 74,296; Thomas, Soc., 2,872; Browder, Com., 2,574; Aiken, Soc., 961.

1940 (Pres.), Roosevelt, Dem., 644,196; Willkie, Rep., 596,274; Thomas, Soc., 5,454; Browder, Com., 2,711; Aiken, Ind., 2,553.

1944 (Pres.), Roosevelt, Dem., 589,864; Dewey, Rep., 527,416; Thomas, Soc., 5,073; Teichert, Ind. Gov't., 3,176.

1948 (Pres.), Truman, Dem., 692,966; Dewey, Rep., 483,617; Wallace, Prog., 27,866; Thomas, Soc., 4,646; Teichert, Soc. Lab., 2,525; Dobbs, Soc. Workers, 606.

1952 (Pres.), Eisenhower, Rep., 763,211; Stevenson, Dem., 608,458; Hallinan, Prog., 2,666; Haas, Soc. Lab., 2,383; Hamblen, Proh., 2,147; Dobbs, Soc. Workers, 618.

1956 (Pres.), Eisenhower, Rep., 719,302; Stevenson Dem., 617,525; Haas, Soc. Lab. (Ind. Gov.), 2,080; Dobbs, Soc. Workers, 1,098.

1960 (Pres.), Kennedy, Dem., 779,933; Nixon, Rep., 757,915; Dobbs, Soc. Workers, 3,077; Industrial Gov., 962.

1964 (Pres.), Johnson, Dem., 991,117; Goldwater,

Rep., 559,624; DeBerry, Soc. Workers, 1,177; Haas, Industrial Gov., 2,544.

1968 (Pres.), Nixon, Rep., 658,643; Humphrey, Dem., 857,738; Wallace, 3d party, 68,931; scattered, 2,443; Halstead, Soc. Worker, 808; Blomen, Ind. Gov't., 285; Mitchell, Communist, 415; Cleaver, Peace, 935; McCarthy, write-in, 585; scattered 170.

1972 (Pres.), Nixon, Rep. 898,269; McGovern, Dem., 802,346; Schmitz, American, 31,407; Spock, Peoples, 2,805; Fisher, Soc. Labor, 4,261; Jenness, Soc. Worker, 940; Hall, Communist, 662; scattered 962.

1976 (Pres.), Carter, Dem., 1,070,440; Ford, Rep., 819,395; McCarthy, Ind. 35,490; Anderson, American, 13,592; Camejo, Soc. Workers, 4,149; MacBride, Libertarian, 3,529; Hall, Comm., 1,092.

Mississippi

County	1972 McGovern (D)	1972 Nixon (R)	1976 Carter (D)	1976 Ford (R)
Adams	3,697	8,500	6,619	6,431
Alcorn	982	5,732	6,995	3,430
Amite	1,185	2,846	2,574	2,256
Attala	1,103	4,738	4,068	3,146
Benton	701	1,483	2,375	790
Bolivar	3,616	7,397	7,561	5,136
Calhoun	245	3,023	2,724	1,892
Carroll	580	1,777	1,566	1,561
Chickasaw	579	3,753	2,891	2,581
Choctaw	326	2,301	1,520	1,562
Claiborne	2,076	1,521	2,657	1,078
Clarke	954	4,561	2,816	2,935
Clay	1,410	4,035	3,514	3,017
Coahoma	3,708	6,602	6,412	4,269
Copiah	1,803	5,498	4,267	4,108
Covington	642	3,842	2,862	2,591
DeSoto	1,557	7,917	7,756	6,240
Forrest	2,933	14,418	7,914	10,770
Franklin	561	2,361	1,578	1,719
George	270	3,979	3,072	1,957
Greene	513	2,884	2,127	1,538
Grenada	1,471	4,800	3,263	3,569
Hancock	745	5,133	3,855	3,765
Harrison	4,761	28,962	16,569	19,207
Hinds	12,679	49,877	28,748	45,803
Holmes	3,459	3,158	4,616	2,438
Humphreys	892	2,334	2,172	1,445
Issaquena	395	701	567	325
Itawamba	509	4,419	4,480	2,153
Jackson	2,534	22,204	12,533	17,177
Jasper	935	3,597	3,109	2,356
Jefferson	1,457	1,131	2,562	782
Jefferson Davis	1,005	2,830	2,747	1,868
Jones	2,790	16,489	10,139	11,098
Kemper	837	2,748	2,436	1,680
Lafayette	1,545	5,391	4,375	3,735
Lamar	493	5,022	3,109	4,056
Lauderdale	3,453	18,337	9,813	14,273
Lawrence	709	3,394	2,242	2,109
Leake	1,053	4,217	3,415	2,952
Lee	1,632	10,730	8,504	7,366
Leflore	2,038	6,779	6,135	5,872
Lincoln	1,070	7,593	4,043	6,084
Lowndes	2,398	10,098	6,181	8,003
Madison	3,464	5,047	6,240	4,838
Marion	1,693	6,805	5,283	5,300
Marshall	1,875	3,326	6,769	2,242
Monroe	1,279	7,273	6,097	4,737
Montgomery	925	3,210	2,410	2,278
Neshoba	812	6,815	3,891	3,859
Newton	597	5,585	2,741	3,813
Noxubee	1,052	2,239	2,121	1,860
Oktibbeha	1,880	6,160	4,339	5,194
Panola	2,091	5,284	5,517	3,341
Pearl River	901	7,487	5,024	4,332
Perry	446	2,689	1,965	1,527
Pike	2,332	6,542	5,749	5,659
Pontotoc	488	4,476	4,066	2,245
Prentiss	398	4,607	4,431	2,362
Quitman	790	2,524	2,621	1,287
Rankin	1,913	12,187	6,937	11,507
Scott	1,213	5,244	3,643	3,649
Sharkey	655	1,426	1,283	1,024
Simpson	871	5,669	3,600	4,291
Smith	329	4,419	2,434	3,147
Stone	293	2,467	1,648	1,575
Sunflower	1,874	5,389	4,322	3,456
Tallahatchie	835	3,442	2,991	2,146
Tate	1,151	3,966	3,747	2,497
Tippah	569	3,937	4,260	1,887
Tishomingo	443	4,177	3,734	1,969
Tunica	858	1,446	1,695	951
Union	658	5,477	5,021	2,507
Walthall	747	3,110	2,650	2,110
Warren	3,480	10,420	6,299	8,699
Washington	4,623	9,634	9,650	7,474
Wayne	975	4,648	3,306	3,022
Webster	403	3,624	2,218	1,943
Wilkinson	1,409	1,608	2,514	1,273
Winston	1,354	5,155	3,956	3,659
Yalobusha	797	2,944	2,603	1,808
Yazoo	2,008	5,555	4,053	4,255
Totals	**126,782**	**505,125**	**381,309**	**366,846**

Mississippi Vote Since 1932

1932 (Pres.), Roosevelt, Dem., 140,168; Hoover, Rep., 5,180; Thomas, Soc., 686.

1936 (Pres.), Roosevelt, Dem., 157,318; Landon, Rep., Howard faction, 2,760; Rowlands faction, 1,675 total, 4,435; Thomas, Soc., 329.

1940 (Pres.), Roosevelt, Dem., 168,252; Willkie, Ind. Rep., 4,550; Rep., 2,814; total, 7,364; Thomas, Soc., 103.

1944 (Pres.), Roosevelt, Dem., 158,515; Dewey, Rep., 3,742; Reg. Dem., 9,964; Ind. Rep., 7,859.

1948 (Pres.), Thurmond, States' Rights, 167,538; Truman, Dem., 19,384; Dewey, Rep., 5,043; Wallace, Prog., 225.

1952 (Pres.), Eisenhower, Ind. vote pledged to Rep. candidate, 112,966; Stevenson, Dem., 172,566.

1956 (Pres.), Stevenson, Dem., 144,498; Eisenhower, Rep., 56,372; Black and Tan Grand Old Party, 4,313; total, 60,685; Byrd, Independent, 42,966.

1960 (Pres.), Democratic unpledged electors, 116,248; Kennedy, Dem., 108,362; Nixon, Rep., 73,561. Mississippi's victorious slate of 8 unpledged Democratic electors cast their votes for Sen. Harry F. Byrd (D-Va.).

1964 (Pres.), Johnson, Dem., 52,618; Goldwater, Rep., 356,528.

1968 (Pres.), Nixon, Rep., 88,516; Humphrey, Dem., 150,644; Wallace, 3d party, 415,349.

1972 (Pres.), Nixon, Rep., 505,125; McGovern, Dem., 126,782; Schmitz, American, 11,598; Jenness, Soc. Worker, 2,458.

1976 (Pres.), Carter, Dem., 381,309; Ford, Rep., 366,846; Anderson, American, 6,678; McCarthy, Ind., 4,074; Maddox, Ind., 4,049; Camejo, Soc. Workers, 2,805; MacBride, Libertarian, 2,609.

Missouri

County	1972 McGovern (D)	1972 Nixon (R)	1976 Carter (D)	1976 Ford (R)
Adair	2,286	6,157	3,684	5,249
Andrew	1,686	4,180	3,042	3,130
Atchison	1,509	2,927	1,126	1,960
Audrain	3,706	7,197	5,600	5,378
Barry	3,167	7,295	5,046	5,053
Barton	1,140	4,026	2,326	2,708
Bates	3,020	5,314	4,288	3,350
Benton	1,423	3,537	2,684	2,875
Bollinger	1,818	3,069	2,740	2,113
Boone	13,666	17,488	17,674	16,373
Buchanan	11,395	21,850	17,427	16,446
Butler	3,466	9,198	6,759	5,669
Caldwell	1,231	3,167	2,113	2,094
Callaway	3,036	6,313	4,843	5,115
Camden	1,761	4,996	3,975	4,469
Cape Girardeau	6,280	15,693	10,440	12,607
Carroll	1,927	4,100	3,114	2,936
Carter	565	1,257	1,154	842
Cass	3,731	9,242	9,008	7,182
Cedar	1,152	3,520	2,192	2,752
Chariton	1,999	2,812	3,055	2,128
Christian	1,945	6,305	3,830	4,553
Clark	1,403	2,499	1,679	1,582
Clay	14,538	33,017	26,609	24,962
Clinton	1,944	3,924	3,424	2,807
Cole	4,754	16,685	7,949	14,370
Cooper	2,332	5,172	3,087	3,694
Crawford	2,248	4,595	3,565	3,224
Dade	747	2,624	1,681	2,015
Dallas	1,085	3,120	2,453	2,430
Daviess	1,430	2,840	2,250	1,919
DeKalb	1,339	2,766	2,023	1,739
Dent	1,710	3,024	2,931	2,433
Douglas	1,209	3,773	1,981	2,652
Dunklin	2,776	5,926	7,107	3,314
Franklin	7,464	13,785	11,695	12,242
Gasconade	1,226	4,944	1,702	3,925
Gentry	1,642	2,984	2,249	1,772
Greene	20,155	48,348	33,824	37,691
Grundy	1,428	3,969	2,597	2,646

	1972		1976	
	(D)	(R)	(D)	(R)
Harrison	1,383	3,574	2,304	2,478
Henry	3,125	5,802	5,282	4,168
Hickory	622	1,851	1,398	1,403
Holt	1,011	2,578	1,529	1,777
Howard	2,041	2,613	2,769	1,690
Howell	2,795	7,253	5,265	4,692
Iron	1,346	2,203	2,646	1,765
Jackson	92,830	129,989	130,120	101,401
Jasper	7,652	22,482	14,910	17,086
Jefferson	13,787	21,947	25,159	18,261
Johnson	3,044	7,228	5,551	5,513
Knox	1,031	1,986	1,319	1,216
Laclede	2,186	6,152	4,381	4,067
Lafayette	4,063	9,187	6,410	6,823
Lawrence	3,130	8,445	5,315	5,784
Lewis	1,695	2,738	2,486	1,983
Lincoln	2,784	5,127	4,473	3,581
Linn	3,073	4,595	4,092	3,114
Livingston	2,662	5,253	3,819	3,010
McDonald	1,787	4,339	3,111	2,949
Macon	2,844	4,538	4,296	3,360
Madison	1,451	2,837	2,229	1,739
Maries	1,219	2,082	1,796	1,485
Marion	4,171	7,197	6,124	5,501
Mercer	607	1,592	1,177	1,025
Miller	1,598	5,682	2,739	4,095
Mississippi	1,470	2,727	3,366	1,733
Moniteau	1,395	3,963	2,462	3,077
Monroe	2,299	2,141	3,039	1,585
Montgomery	1,691	3,707	2,535	2,665
Morgan	1,685	4,021	2,738	2,831
New Madrid	3,500	4,735	5,319	2,798
Newton	4,291	10,701	7,045	7,142
Nodaway	3,322	5,942	4,875	4,558
Oregon	1,352	2,118	2,564	1,122
Osage	1,485	4,266	2,015	3,224
Ozark	625	2,119	1,341	1,754
Pemiscot	2,017	4,697	4,681	2,541
Perry	1,953	4,736	2,801	4,086
Pettis	5,016	10,065	7,887	7,344
Phelps	3,567	7,598	6,261	6,153
Pike	2,659	4,452	3,770	3,355
Platte	4,183	8,764	8,651	8,103
Polk	2,245	5,409	3,663	3,893
Pulaski	1,903	4,243	4,370	2,865
Putnam	571	2,112	1,097	1,444
Ralls	1,371	1,827	2,318	1,334
Randolph	3,814	5,195	5,839	3,594
Ray	2,844	4,205	5,535	2,853
Reynolds	1,031	1,541	2,143	879
Ripley	1,361	2,810	2,577	1,640
St. Charles	11,034	25,677	22,063	26,105
St. Clair	1,410	2,847	2,271	1,808
St. Francois	4,658	8,812	8,852	7,002
Ste. Genevieve	2,247	2,900	3,091	2,241
St. Louis	160,801	264,147	196,915	246,988
Saline	3,460	6,641	5,890	4,883
Schuyler	991	1,495	1,417	1,193
Scotland	1,269	1,918	1,449	1,286
Scott	3,646	7,316	8,075	5,473
Shannon	1,134	1,623	1,960	989
Shelby	1,569	2,057	2,227	1,453
Stoddard	2,636	6,282	6,097	3,989
Stone	1,094	4,180	2,358	3,457
Sullivan	1,588	2,611	2,313	2,141
Taney	1,435	4,982	3,626	4,696
Texas	2,737	5,104	4,638	3,338
Vernon	3,057	4,892	4,921	3,715
Warren	1,225	3,530	2,164	3,214
Washington	2,229	3,818	3,543	2,526
Wayne	1,746	3,091	2,987	1,963
Webster	2,343	5,095	3,759	3,510
Worth	727	1,170	969	771
Wright	1,368	4,350	2,781	3,397
ST. LOUIS CITY	119,817	72,402	118,703	58,367
Write-in Vote	1,384	206	1,576	1,365
Totals	**698,531**	**1,154,058**	**999,163**	**928,808**

Missouri Vote Since 1932

1932 (Pres.), Roosevelt, Dem., 1,025,406; Hoover, Rep., 564,713; Thomas, Soc., 16,374; Upshaw, Proh., 2,429; Foster, Com., 568; Reynolds, Soc. Lab., 404.

1936 (Pres.), Roosevelt, Dem., 1,111,403; Landon, Rep., 697,891; Lemke, Union, 14,630; Thomas, Soc., 3,454; Colvin, Proh., 908; Browder, Com., 417; Aiken, Soc. Lab., 292.

1940 (Pres.), Roosevelt, Dem., 958,476; Willkie, Rep., 871,009; Thomas, Soc., 2,226; Babson, Proh., 1,809; Aiken, Soc. Lab., 209.

1944 (Pres.), Roosevelt, Dem., 807,357; Dewey, Rep., 761,175; Thomas, Soc., 1,750; Watson, Proh., 1,175; Teichert, Soc. Lab., 221.

1948 (Pres.), Truman, Dem., 917,315; Dewey, Rep., 655,039; Wallace, Prog., 3,998; Thomas, Soc., 2,222.

1952 (Pres.), Eisenhower, Rep., 959,429; Stevenson, Dem., 929,830; Hallinan, Prog., 987; Hamblen, Proh., 885; MacArthur, Christian Nationalist, 302; America First, 233; Hoopes, Soc. 227; Haas, Soc.-Lab., 169.

1956 (Pres.), Stevenson, Dem., 918,273: Eisenhower, Rep., 914,299.

1960 (Pres.), Kennedy, Dem., 972,201; Nixon, Rep., 962,221.

1964 (Pres.), Johnson, Dem., 1,164,344; Goldwater, Rep., 653,535.

1968 (Pres.), Nixon, Rep., 811,932; Humphrey, Dem., 791,444; Wallace, 3d party, 206,126.

1972 (Pres.), Nixon, Rep., 1,154,058; McGovern, Dem., 698,531.

1976 (Pres.), Carter, Dem., 999,163; Ford, Rep., 928,808; McCarthy, Ind., 24,329.

Montana

	1972		1976	
	McGovern	Nixon	Carter	Ford
County	(D)	(R)	(D)	(R)
Beaverhead	775	2,460	1,013	2,461
Big Horn	1,552	2,148	1,962	1,615
Blaine	1,151	1,513	1,356	1,349
Broadwater	411	916	557	820
Carbon	1,292	2,378	1,853	2,121
Carter	218	726	344	558
Cascade	12,899	16,159	14,678	15,289
Chouteau	1,149	2,027	1,568	1,814
Custer	1,875	3,486	2,425	3,120
Daniels	570	973	797	816
Dawson	1,685	3,207	2,201	2,639
Deer Lodge	3,979	2,373	3,859	2,197
Fallon	531	1,034	847	934
Fergus	1,652	4,082	2,470	3,556
Flathead	5,412	10,417	7,827	10,494
Gallatin	5,096	10,663	6,215	11,062
Garfield	173	695	273	625
Glacier	1,469	2,143	1,755	1,892
Golden Valley	170	359	255	302
Granite	422	804	509	746
Hill	3,061	3,759	3,878	3,274
Jefferson	904	1,281	1,210	1,387
Judith Basin	557	961	772	809
Lake	2,260	4,172	3,253	3,809
Lewis & Clark	6,081	10,719	8,118	10,155
Liberty	365	808	506	638
Lincoln	2,402	3,276	3,146	3,017
Madison	669	1,780	870	1,688
McCone	562	854	749	730
Meagher	230	674	364	565
Mineral	659	706	819	679
Missoula	13,784	15,557	15,099	16,350
Musselshell	689	1,202	922	1,117
Park	1,923	3,771	2,364	3,281
Petroleum	87	232	110	211
Phillips	828	1,659	1,117	1,347
Pondera	1,215	1,890	1,413	1,666
Powder River	267	844	429	683
Powell	1,050	1,720	1,302	1,610
Prairie	303	685	415	597
Ravalli	2,480	4,611	3,504	4,894
Richland	1,438	2,645	1,961	2,189
Roosevelt	1,464	2,304	2,061	1,822
Rosebud	777	1,486	1,413	1,538
Sanders	1,197	1,779	1,725	1,738
Sheridan	1,197	1,500	1,560	1,114
Silver Bow	11,704	7,967	11,377	7,506
Stillwater	716	1,698	1,143	1,446
Sweet Grass	350	1,260	502	1,135
Teton	1,121	1,991	1,506	1,730
Toole	897	1,679	1,080	1,469
Treasure	176	377	239	315
Valley	1,973	3,210	2,352	2,520
Wheatland	445	761	535	755
Wibaux	283	390	352	308
Yellowstone	13,602	25,205	18,329	25,201
Totals	**120,197**	**183,976**	**149,259**	**173,703**

Montana Vote Since 1932

1932 (Pres.), Roosevelt, Dem., 127,286; Hoover, Rep., 78,078; Thomas, Soc., 7,891; Foster, Com., 1,775; Harvey, Lib., 1,449.

1936 (Pres.), Roosevelt, Dem., 159,690; Landon, Rep., 63,598; Lemke, Union, 5,549; Thomas, Soc., 1,066; Browder, Com., 385; Colvin, Proh., 224.

1940 (Pres.), Roosevelt, Dem., 145,698; Willkie, Rep., 99,579; Thomas, Soc., 1,443; Babson, Proh., 664; Browder, Com., 489.

1944 (Pres.), Roosevelt, Dem., 112,556; Dewey, Rep., 93,163; Thomas, Soc., 1,296; Watson, Proh., 340.

1948 (Pres.), Truman, Dem., 119,071; Dewey, Rep., 96,770; Wallace, Prog., 7,313; Thomas, Soc., 695; Watson, Proh., 429.
1952 (Pres.), Eisenhower, Rep., 157,394; Stevenson, Dem., 106,213; Hallinan, Prog., 723; Hamblen, Proh., 548; Hoopes, Soc., 159.
1956 (Pres.), Eisenhower, Rep., 154,933; Stevenson, Dem., 116,238.
1960 (Pres.), Kennedy, Dem., 134,891; Nixon, Rep., 141,841; Decker, Proh., 456; Dobbs, Soc. Workers, 391.
1964 (Pres.), Johnson, Dem., 164,246; Goldwater, Rep., 113,032; Kasper, Nat'l States Rights, 519; Munn, Proh., 499; DeBerry, Soc. Worker, 332.
1968 (Pres.), Nixon, Rep., 138,835; Humphrey, Dem., 114,117; Wallace, 3d party, 20,015; Halstead, Soc. Worker, 457; Munn, Prohibition 510; Caton, New Reform, 470.
1972 (Pres.), Nixon, Rep., 183,976; McGovern, Dem., 120,197; Schmitz, American, 13,430.
1976 (Pres.), Carter, Dem., 149,259; Ford, Rep., 173,-703; Anderson, American, 5,772.

Nebraska

County	1972 McGovern (D)	1972 Nixon (R)	1976 Carter (D)	1976 Ford (R)
Adams	3,359	8,841	4,949	7,612
Antelope	851	3,228	1,325	2,488
Arthur	45	236	64	193
Banner	96	404	210	281
Blaine	56	343	133	281
Boone	883	2,406	1,329	2,035
Box Butte	960	3,431	1,516	2,956
Boyd	506	1,419	792	1,004
Brown	330	1,462	557	1,239
Buffalo	2,988	8,587	4,296	8,083
Burt	900	2,937	1,373	2,507
Butler	1,812	2,301	2,336	1,808
Cass	1,805	4,503	3,202	3,800
Cedar	1,807	2,995	2,225	2,415
Chase	307	1,318	724	1,146
Cherry	463	2,610	906	2,197
Cheyenne	950	3,120	1,663	2,285
Clay	861	2,542	1,369	2,254
Colfax	1,107	2,799	1,666	2,363
Cuming	1,019	3,810	1,367	3,298
Custer	1,147	4,836	1,985	3,935
Dakota	1,748	2,879	2,290	2,629
Dawes	711	2,987	1,278	2,435
Dawson	1,424	6,211	2,393	5,411
Deuel	224	1,001	398	775
Dixon	941	2,299	1,286	1,981
Dodge	3,826	9,837	5,276	8,972
Douglas	48,201	101,579	61,692	92,980
Dundy	221	1,003	457	774
Fillmore	1,270	2,511	1,483	2,098
Franklin	599	1,510	941	1,170
Frontier	324	1,315	588	994
Furnas	676	2,282	1,126	1,844
Gage	3,588	6,298	4,506	5,199
Garden	204	1,161	445	928
Garfield	209	903	343	726
Gosper	242	829	332	654
Grant	69	376	116	313
Greeley	760	1,005	877	787
Hall	4,218	10,987	6,077	10,931
Hamilton	907	2,960	1,337	2,737
Harlan	539	1,549	879	1,325
Hayes	123	486	267	411
Hitchcock	364	1,339	786	898
Holt	1,053	4,147	1,751	3,389
Hooker	52	394	98	326
Howard	945	1,691	1,316	1,362
Jefferson	1,476	3,008	2,067	2,628
Johnson	917	1,637	1,115	1,298
Kearney	759	2,203	1,218	1,827
Keith	665	2,513	1,139	2,485
Keya Paha	146	563	245	405
Kimball	437	1,650	696	1,257
Knox	1,289	3,318	1,922	2,610
Lancaster	25,924	42,573	28,193	38,937
Lincoln	3,220	7,502	5,352	7,074
Logan	73	320	195	283
Loup	58	345	140	299
McPherson	42	247	104	221
Madison	2,224	8,580	3,433	7,844
Merrick	887	2,418	1,360	2,229
Morrill	520	1,740	971	1,351
Nance	641	1,413	936	1,119
Nemaha	909	2,600	1,404	2,092
Nuckolls	999	2,089	1,424	1,752
Otoe	1,718	4,815	2,436	3,715
Pawnee	524	1,299	845	990
Perkins	354	1,165	622	98
Phelps	735	3,356	1,166	3,20
Pierce	653	2,451	1,004	2,17
Platte	2,855	7,871	3,681	7,20
Polk	827	2,050	1,190	1,79
Red Willow	931	3,701	1,722	2,97
Richardson	1,508	3,662	2,415	3,11
Rock	138	937	255	73
Saline	2,654	2,828	3,205	2,33
Sarpy	3,904	11,514	7,384	11,91
Saunders	2,501	4,282	3,504	3,84
Scotts Bluff	2,764	8,649	4,297	6,88
Seward	2,087	3,707	2,609	3,21
Sheridan	481	2,386	810	2,00
Sherman	811	1,099	1,078	93
Sioux	129	639	329	53
Stanton	478	1,662	763	1,46
Thayer	978	2,274	1,315	1,99
Thomas	73	397	103	34
Thurston	840	1,565	1,020	1,29
Valley	771	2,011	1,042	1,58
Washington	1,401	4,290	2,233	3,79
Wayne	902	2,659	1,089	2,52
Webster	696	1,631	1,130	1,26
Wheeler	84	361	146	27
York	1,318	4,651	1,655	4,20
Totals	**169,991**	**406,298**	**233,287**	**359,21**

Nebraska Vote Since 1932

1932 (Pres.), Roosevelt, Dem., 359,082; Hoover, Rep 201,177; Thomas, Soc., 9,876.
1936 (Pres.), Roosevelt, Dem., 347,454; Landon, Rep 248,731; Lemke, Union, 12,847.
1940 (Pres.), Roosevelt, Dem., 263,677; Willkie, Rep 352,201.
1944 (Pres.), Roosevelt, Dem., 233,246; Dewey, Rep 329,880.
1948 (Pres.), Truman, Dem., 224,165; Dewey, Rep 264,774.
1952 (Pres.), Eisenhower, Rep., 421,603; Stevenson Dem., 188,057.
1956 (Pres.), Eisenhower, Rep., 378,108; Stevenson Dem., 199,029.
1960 (Pres.), Kennedy, Dem., 232,542; Nixon, Rep 380,553.
1964 (Pres.), Johnson, Dem., 307,307; Goldwate Rep., 276,847.
1968 (Pres.), Nixon, Rep., 321,163; Humphrey, Dem 170,784; Wallace, 3d party, 44,904.
1972 (Pres.), Nixon, Rep., 406,298; McGovern, Dem 169,991; scattered 817.
1976 (Pres.), Carter, Dem., 233,287; Ford, Rep., 359 219; McCarthy, Ind., 9,383; Maddox, Amer. Ind 3,378; MacBride, Libertarian, 1,476.

Nevada

County	1972 McGovern (D)	1972 Nixon (R)	1976 Carter (D)	1976 Ford (R)
Churchill	1,038	2,970	1,800	2,35
Clark	36,807	53,101	51,178	48,23
Douglas	983	2,898	1,934	3,09
Elko	1,467	3,886	1,955	3,29
Esmeralda	127	273	214	18
Eureka	139	371	163	27
Humboldt	713	1,659	1,074	1,38
Lander	468	798	518	56
Lincoln	382	841	642	70
Lyon	959	2,813	1,866	2,06
Mineral	768	2,111	1,361	1,10
Nye	802	1,287	1,261	1,02
Pershing	365	853	633	63
Storey	226	508	310	27
Washoe	17,106	33,539	21,687	29,26
White Pine	1,546	2,446	2,009	1,54
CARSON CITY	2,120	5,396	3,874	5,28
Totals	**66,016**	**115,750**	**92,479**	**101,27**

Nevada Vote Since 1932

1932 (Pres.), Roosevelt, Dem., 28,756; Hoover, Rep 12,674.
1936 (Pres.), Roosevelt, Dem., 31,925; Landon, Rep 11,923.
1940 (Pres.), Roosevelt, Dem., 31,945; Willkie, Rep 21,229.
1944 (Pres.), Roosevelt, Dem., 29,623; Dewey, Rep 24,611.
1948 (Pres.), Truman, Dem., 31,291; Dewey, Rep., 29 357; Wallace, Prog., 1,469.

1952 (Pres.), Eisenhower, Rep., 50,502; Stevenson, Dem., 31,688.
1956 (Pres.), Eisenhower, Rep., 56,049; Stevenson, Dem., 40,640.
1960 (Pres.), Kennedy, Dem., 54,880; Nixon, Rep., 52,387.
1964 (Pres.), Johnson, Dem., 79,339; Goldwater, Rep., 56,094.
1968 (Pres.), Nixon, Rep., 73,188; Humphrey, Dem., 60,598; Wallace, 3d party, 20,432.
1972 (Pres.), Nixon, Rep., 115,750; McGovern, Dem. 66,016.
1976 (Pres.), Carter, Dem., 92,479; Ford, Rep., 101,273; MacBride, Libertarian, 1,519; Maddox, Amer. Ind., 1,497; scattered 5,108.

New Hampshire

County	1972 McGovern (D)	1972 Nixon (R)	1976 Carter (D)	1976 Ford (R)
Belknap	4,610	11,536	6,143	9,876
Carroll	2,395	8,525	3,374	8,561
Cheshire	9,157	13,390	10,388	12,554
Coos	5,829	9,468	7,385	7,094
Grafton	8,388	16,605	8,996	14,430
Hillsborough	34,739	65,274	45,554	53,581
Merrimack	11,737	25,354	14,865	21,853
Rockingham	21,998	38,825	30,051	36,738
Strafford	12,028	16,846	14,566	14,569
Sullivan	5,554	7,901	6,323	6,679
Totals	**116,435**	**213,724**	**147,645**	**185,935**

New Hampshire Vote Since 1932

1932 (Pres.), Roosevelt, Dem., 100,680; Hoover, Rep., 103,629; Thomas, Soc., 947; Foster, Com., 264.
1936 (Pres.), Roosevelt, Dem., 108,640; Landon, Rep., 104,642; Lemke, Union, 4,819; Browder, Com., 193.
1940 (Pres.), Roosevelt, Dem., 125,292; Willkie, Rep., 110,127.
1944 (Pres.), Roosevelt, Dem., 119,663; Dewey, Rep., 109,916; Thomas, Soc., 46.
1948 (Pres.), Truman, Dem., 107,995; Dewey, Rep., 121,299; Wallace, Prog., 1,970; Thomas, Soc., 86; Teichert, Soc. Lab., 83; Thurmond, States' Rights, 7.
1952 (Pres.), Eisenhower, Rep., 166,287; Stevenson, Dem., 106,663.
1956 (Pres.), Eisenhower, Rep., 176,519; Stevenson, Dem., 90,364; Andrews, Const., 111.
1960 (Pres.), Kennedy, Dem., 137,772; Nixon, Rep., 157,989.
1964 (Pres.), Johnson, Dem., 182,065; Goldwater, Rep., 104,029.
1968 (Pres.), Nixon, Rep., 154,903; Humphrey, Dem., 130,589; Wallace, 3d party, 11,173; New Party, 421; Halstead, Soc. Worker, 104.
1972 (Pres.), Nixon, Rep., 213,724; McGovern, Dem., 116,435; Schmitz, American, 3,386; Jenness, Soc. Worker, 368; scattered, 142.
1976 (Pres.), Carter, Dem., 147,645; Ford, Rep., 185,935; McCarthy, Ind., 4,095; MacBride, Libertarian, 936; Reagan, write-in, 388; La Rouche, U.S. Labor, 186; Camejo, Soc. Workers, 161, Levin, Soc. Labor, 66; scattered, 215.

New Jersey

County	1972 McGovern (D)	1972 Nixon (R)	1976 Carter (D)	1976 Ford (R)
lantic	28,203	45,667	41,965	36,733
ergen	147,155	285,458	180,738	237,331
urlington	41,520	70,805	63,309	60,960
amden	75,202	111,935	108,854	82,801
ape May	8,729	22,621	16,489	19,498
umberland	18,692	26,409	29,165	20,535
ssex	161,270	170,036	174,434	133,911
loucester	25,509	44,806	38,726	34,888
udson	89,977	136,895	116,241	92,636
unterdon	9,031	21,282	12,592	19,616
ercer	62,180	69,303	69,621	58,453
iddlesex	88,397	149,033	122,859	113,539
onmouth	63,176	124,830	88,956	110,104
orris	50,937	113,469	63,749	105,921
cean	27,710	77,979	56,413	77,875
assaic	63,302	108,511	76,194	85,102
Salem	8,609	16,371	12,826	11,639
Somerset	26,537	56,524	36,258	51,260
Sussex	8,585	25,977	14,759	23,613
Union	90,482	148,290	106,267	118,019
Warren	10,008	19,301	14,238	15,254
Totals	**1,102,211**	**1,845,502**	**1,444,653**	**1,509,688**

New Jersey Vote Since 1932

1932 (Pres.) Roosevelt, Dem., 806,630; Hoover, Rep., 775,684; Thomas, Soc., 42,998; Foster, Com., 2,915; Reynolds, Soc. Lab., 1,062; Upshaw, Proh., 774.
1936 (Pres.) Roosevelt, Dem., 1,083,549; Landon, Rep., 719,421; Lemke, Union, 9,405; Thomas, Soc., 3,895; Browder, Com., 1,590; Colvin, Proh., 916; Aiken, Soc. Lab., 346.
1940 (Pres.) Roosevelt, Dem., 1,016,404; Willkie, Rep., 944,876; Browder, Com., 8,814; Thomas, Soc., 2,823; Babson, Proh., 851; Aiken, Soc. Lab., 446.
1944 (Pres.) Roosevelt, Dem., 987,874; Dewey, Rep., 961,335; Teichert, Soc. Lab., 6,939; Watson, Nat'l Proh., 4,255; Thomas, Soc., 3,385.
1948 (Pres.) Truman, Dem., 895,455; Dewey, Rep., 981,124; Wallace, Prog., 42,683; Watson, Proh., 10,593; Thomas, Soc., 10,521; Dobbs, Soc. Workers, 5,825; Teichert, Soc. Lab., 3,354.
1952 (Pres.) Eisenhower, Rep., 1,373,613; Stevenson, Dem., 1,015,902; Hoopes, Soc., 8,593; Haas, Soc. Lab., 5,815; Hallinan, Prog., 5,589; Krajewski, Poor Man's, 4,203; Dobbs, Soc. Workers, 3,850; Hamblen, Proh., 989.
1956 (Pres.) Eisenhower, Rep., 1,606,942; Stevenson, Dem., 850,337; Holtwick, Proh., 9,147; Haas, Soc. Lab., 6,736; Andrews, Conservative, 5,317; Dobbs, Soc. Workers, 4,004; Krajewski, American Third Party, 1,829.
1960 (Pres.) Kennedy, Dem., 1,385,415; Nixon, Rep., 1,363,324; Dobbs, Soc. Workers, 11,402; Lee, Conservative, 8,708; Haas, Soc. Lab., 4,262.
1964 (Pres.) Johnson, Dem., 1,867,671; Goldwater, Rep., 963,843; DeBerry, Soc. Workers, 8,181; Haas, Soc. Labor, 7,075.
1968 (Pres.) Nixon, Rep., 1,325,467; Humphrey, Dem., 1,264,206; Wallace, 3d party, 262,187; Halstead, Soc. Worker, 8,667; Gregory, Peace Freedom, 8,084; Blomen, Soc. Labor, 6,784.
1972 (Pres.) Nixon, Rep., 1,845,502; McGovern, Dem., 1,102,211; Schmitz, American, 34,378; Spock, Peoples, 5,355; Fisher, Soc. Labor, 4,544; Jenness, Soc. Worker, 2,233; Mahalchik, Amer. First, 1,743; Hall, Communist, 1,263.
1976 (Pres.) Carter, Dem., 1,444,653; Ford, Rep., 1,509,688; McCarthy, Ind., 32,717; MacBride, Libertarian, 9,449; Maddox, American, 7,716; Levin, Soc. Labor, 3,686; Hall, Comm., 1,662; LaRouche, U.S. Labor, 1,650; Camejo, Soc. Workers, 1,184; Wright, People's, 1,044; Bubar, Proh., 554; Zeidler, Socialist, 469.

New Mexico

County	1972 McGovern (D)	1972 Nixon (R)	1976 Carter (D)	1976 Ford (R)
Bernalillo	48,753	79,993	63,949	76,614
Catron	271	829	517	602
Chaves	4,296	11,493	7,139	10,631
Colfax	1,855	2,663	2,718	2,259
Curry	2,416	8,392	5,004	6,232
De Baca	270	752	597	556
Dona Ana	9,416	14,562	12,036	13,888
Eddy	5,040	9,921	9,073	7,698
Grant	4,081	4,431	5,176	4,095
Guadalupe	1,202	1,297	1,379	1,047
Harding	220	522	285	387
Hidalgo	562	1,051	938	891
Lea	3,429	12,478	6,533	8,773
Lincoln	696	2,528	1,415	2,320
Los Alamos	2,435	5,039	2,890	5,383
Luna	1,560	2,958	2,872	2,966
McKinley	5,124	5,366	6,856	4,617
Mora	1,135	1,165	1,438	904
Otero	2,981	7,033	5,333	5,914
Quay	1,161	3,224	2,095	2,059
Rio Arriba	5,642	4,351	7,125	3,213
Roosevelt	1,612	4,727	3,111	3,269
Sandoval	3,293	3,507	5,072	4,110
San Juan	4,296	30,788	8,615	10,852

	1972		1976	
	(D)	(R)	(D)	(R)
San Miguel	4,663	4,434	5,204	3,162
Santa Fe	10,761	12,211	14,127	11,576
Sierra	934	2,074	1,564	1,665
Socorro	1,994	2,658	2,606	2,265
Taos	3,472	3,617	4,414	3,012
Torrance	908	1,758	1,526	1,462
Union	496	1,545	975	1,146
Valencia	6,110	8,239	8,566	7,851
Totals	**141,084**	**235,606**	**201,148**	**211,419**

New Mexico Vote Since 1932

1932 (Pres.), Roosevelt, Dem., 95,089; Hoover, Rep., 54,217; Thomas, Soc., 11,776; Harvey, Lib., 389; Foster, Com., 135.

1936 (Pres.), Roosevelt, Dem., 105,838; Landon, Rep., 61,710; Lemke, Union, 942; Thomas, Soc., 343; Browder, Com., 43.

1940 (Pres.), Roosevelt, Dem., 103,699; Willkie, Rep., 79,315.

1944 (Pres.), Roosevelt, Dem., 81,389; Dewey, Rep., 70,688; Watson, Proh., 148.

1948 (Pres.), Truman, Dem., 105,464; Dewey, Rep., 80,303; Wallace, Prog., 1,037; Watson, Proh., 127; Thomas, Soc., 83; Teichert, Soc. Lab., 49.

1952 (Pres.), Eisenhower, Rep., 132,170; Stevenson, Dem., 105,661; Hamblen, Proh., 297; Hallinan, Ind. Prog., 225; MacArthur, Christian National, 220; Haas, Soc. Lab., 35.

1956 (Pres.), Eisenhower, Rep., 146,788; Stevenson, Dem., 106,098; Holtwick, Proh., 607; Andrews, Ind., 364; Haas, Soc. Lab., 69.

1960 (Pres.), Kennedy, Dem., 156,027; Nixon, Rep., 153,733; Decker, Proh., 777; Haas, Soc. Lab., 570.

1964 (Pres.), Johnson, Dem., 194,017; Goldwater, Rep., 131,838; Haas, Soc. Labor, 1,217; Munn, Proh., 543.

1968 (Pres.), Nixon, Rep., 169,692; Humphrey, Dem., 130,081; Wallace, 3d party, 25,737; Chavez, 1,519; Halstead, Soc. Worker, 252.

1972 (Pres.), Nixon, Rep., 235,606; McGovern, Dem., 141,084; Schmitz, Amer., 8,767; Jenness, Soc. Worker, 474.

1976 (Pres.), Carter, Dem., 201,148; Ford, Rep., 211,419; Camejo, Soc. Worker, 2,462; MacBride, Libertarian, 1,110; Zeidler, Soc., 240; Bubar, Proh., 211.

New York

County	1972 McGovern (D-L*)	1972 Nixon (R-C**)	1976 Carter (D-L)	1976 Ford (R-C)
Albany	67,297	81,848	71,616	69,592
Allegany	4,812	13,426	6,134	11,769
Broome	37,154	55,736	39,827	50,340
Cattaraugus	10,909	21,906	13,768	19,469
Cayuga	11,907	22,774	13,348	19,775
Chatauqua	26,253	37,158	27,447	33,730
Chemung	12,650	26,200	17,207	20,640
Chenango	5,695	13,770	7,356	12,384
Clinton	9,703	17,048	11,555	15,433
Columbia	7,558	17,995	10,514	15,871
Cortland	5,234	12,885	6,947	11,222
Delaware	5,243	15,136	7,254	12,443
Dutchess	27,872	68,864	37,531	51,312
Erie	218,105	256,462	229,397	220,310
Essex	4,955	11,763	6,556	10,194
Franklin	5,266	10,959	7,248	8,846
Fulton	7,303	15,200	9,323	12,161
Genesee	8,631	17,107	10,803	14,567
Greene	5,260	14,213	7,740	11,370
Hamilton	731	2,597	1,052	2,306
Herkimer	9,487	20,194	12,875	15,362
Jefferson	11,629	23,123	13,503	20,401
Lewis	2,987	6,591	3,764	5,840
Livingston	7,031	15,886	9,629	14,044
Madison	6,241	18,392	8,822	15,674
Monroe	120,031	196,579	134,739	167,303
Montgomery	9,460	16,640	11,271	13,281
Niagara	38,991	54,777	43,667	46,101
Oneida	33,642	78,549	47,779	57,655
Onondaga	61,895	140,039	76,097	115,474
Ontario	11,012	23,828	14,044	21,118
Orange	25,778	63,556	40,362	49,685
Orleans	4,371	10,938	5,927	8,994
Oswego	11,317	29,109	16,332	23,949
Otsego	7,898	17,364	9,787	14,796
Putnam	7,747	21,673	11,963	18,523
Rensselaer	24,019	48,864	28,979	40,229
Rockland	35,771	64,753	48,673	52,087
St. Lawrence	15,286	26,145	17,503	22,249
Saratoga	17,899	40,582	23,768	38,296
Schenectady	29,619	47,529	31,838	40,789
Schoharie	3,730	8,644	5,250	7,154
Schuyler	1,937	4,945	2,885	4,267
Seneca	4,441	9,368	5,745	7,659
Steuben	9,462	28,708	14,685	23,164
Sullivan	9,847	17,035	14,189	13,709
Tioga	5,470	13,396	6,969	11,824
Tompkins	12,344	17,605	12,808	15,463
Ulster	21,371	46,883	30,190	35,353
Warren	5,760	16,649	7,264	14,548
Washington	5,677	16,136	7,262	13,946
Wayne	8,203	23,379	12,061	19,324
Wyoming	4,365	11,184	5,737	9,726
Yates	1,958	6,639	2,903	5,796
Outside N.Y. Metro Area	**1,068,404**	**1,914,829**	**1,281,893**	**1,607,517**
Nassau	252,831	438,723	302,869	329,176
Suffolk	132,441	316,452	208,263	248,908
Westchester	154,412	262,901	173,153	208,527
N.Y. Suburban	**539,684**	**1,018,076**	**684,285**	**786,611**
Bronx	243,345	196,754	238,786	96,842
Kings	387,768	373,903	419,382	190,728
New York	354,326	178,515	337,438	117,702
Queens	328,316	426,015	379,907	244,396
Richmond	29,241	84,686	47,867	56,995
N.Y. City	**1,342,996**	**1,259,873**	**1,423,380**	**706,663**
N.Y. Metro Area	**1,882,680**	**2,277,949**	**2,107,665**	**1,493,274**
D/R total	**2,767,956**	**3,824,642**	**3,244,165**	**2,825,913**
2d Party (Lib/Con)	**83,128**	**368,136**	**145,393**	**274,878**
Totals	**2,951,084**	**4,192,778**	**3,389,558**	**3,100,791**

*Democratic and Liberal **Republican and Conservative

New York Vote Since 1932

1932 (Pres.), Roosevelt, Dem., 2,534,959; Hoover, Rep., 1,937,963; Thomas, Soc., 177,397; Foster, Com., 27,956; Reynolds, Soc. Lab., 10,339.

1936 (Pres.), Roosevelt, Dem., 3,018,298; American Lab., 274,924; total, 3,293,222; Landon, Rep., 2,180,670; Thomas, Soc., 86,879; Browder, Com., 35,609.

1940 (Pres.), Roosevelt, Dem., 2,834,500; American Lab., 417,418; total 3,251,918; Willkie, Rep., 3,027,478; Thomas, Soc., 18,950; Babson, Proh., 3,250.

1944 (Pres.), Roosevelt, Dem., 2,478,598; American Lab., 496,405; Liberal, 329,325; total, 3,304,238 Dewey, Rep., 2,987,647; Teichert, Ind. Gov't., 14,352; Thomas, Soc., 10,553.

1948 (Pres.), Truman, Dem., 2,557,642; Liberal, 222,562; total, 2,780,204; Dewey, Rep., 2,841,163 Wallace, Amer. Lab., 509,559; Thomas, Soc., 40,879 Teichert, Ind. Gov't., 2,729; Dobbs, Soc. Workers 2,675.

1952 (Pres.), Eisenhower, Rep., 3,952,815; Stevenson Dem., 2,687,890, Liberal, 416,711; total, 3,104,601 Hallinan, American Lab., 64,211; Hoopes, Soc. 2,664; Dobbs, Soc. Workers, 2,212; Haas, Ind Gov't., 1,560; scattering, 178; blank and void, 87,813.

1956 (Pres.), Eisenhower, Rep., 4,340,340; Stevenson Dem., 2,458,212; Liberal, 292,557; total, 2,750,769 write-in votes for Andrews, 1,027; Werdel, 492 Haas, 150; Hoopes, 82; others, 476.

1960 (Pres.), Kennedy, Dem., 3,423,909; Liberal, 406,176; total, 3,830,085; Nixon, Rep., 3,446,419; Dobbs Soc. Workers, 14,319; scattering, 256; blank an void, 88,896.

1964 (Pres.), Johnson, Dem., 4,913,156; Goldwater Rep., 2,243,559; Haas, Soc. Labor, 6,085; DeBerry Soc. Workers, 3,215; scattering, 188; blank an void, 151,383.

1968 (Pres.), Nixon, Rep., 3,007,932; Humphrey Dem., 3,378,470; Wallace, 3d party, 358,864 Blomen, Soc. Labor, 8,432; Halstead, Soc. Worker 11,851; Gregory, Freedom and Peace, 24,517 blank, void, and scattering, 171,624.

1972 (Pres.), Nixon, Rep., 3,824,642; Conservative 368,136; McGovern, Dem., 2,767,956; Liberal, 183,128; Reed, Soc. Worker, 7,797; Fisher, Soc. Labor 4,530; Hall, Communist, 5,641; blank, void, or scattered, 161,641.

1976 (Pres.), Carter, Dem., 3,389,558; Ford, Rep 3,100,791; MacBride, Libertarian, 12,197; Hal Comm., 10,270; Camejo, Soc. Worker, 6,996; L

Rouche, U.S. Labor, 5,413; blank, void, or scattered, 143,037.

North Carolina

County	1972 McGovern (D)	1972 Nixon (R)	1976 Carter (D)	1976 Ford (R)
Alamance	6,833	22,046	17,371	12,680
Alexander	2,468	5,865	5,287	4,661
Alleghany	1,304	2,158	2,550	1,532
Anson	2,188	3,551	4,796	1,608
Ashe	3,313	5,784	5,193	4,937
Avery	627	3,510	1,869	3,085
Beaufort	2,901	6,915	5,728	4,677
Bertie	1,819	2,874	4,117	1,332
Bladen	2,201	4,205	6,009	1,546
Brunswick	2,500	6,153	7,377	3,636
Buncombe	12,626	32,091	26,633	22,461
Burke	6,197	14,447	14,254	10,070
Cabarrus	5,336	18,384	12,049	12,455
Caldwell	4,886	12,976	11,894	9,872
Camden	556	909	1,231	562
Carteret	2,805	8,463	7,080	5,786
Caswell	1,922	2,983	3,707	1,761
Catawba	7,744	24,106	16,862	18,696
Chatham	3,624	6,175	6,397	4,279
Cherokee	2,411	4,113	3,571	3,210
Chowan	936	1,906	1,862	1,019
Clay	797	1,545	1,569	1,428
Cleveland	4,994	13,726	14,406	8,106
Columbus	3,305	8,468	11,148	3,184
Craven	2,384	9,372	7,553	5,881
Cumberland	9,853	24,376	24,297	14,226
Currituck	718	1,578	1,999	954
Dare	634	1,986	2,191	1,680
Davidson	7,691	24,875	17,859	18,813
Davie	1,578	5,613	3,635	4,772
Duplin	2,857	7,153	7,696	3,912
Durham	15,566	25,576	22,425	18,945
Edgecombe	4,635	8,244	8,001	4,850
Forsyth	20,928	46,415	39,561	38,886
Franklin	2,341	5,431	5,405	2,630
Gaston	8,462	27,956	22,878	19,727
Gates	1,177	1,264	2,291	722
Graham	1,057	1,699	1,791	1,621
Granville	2,918	6,037	5,244	2,955
Greene	847	2,788	2,740	1,356
Guilford	25,800	61,381	46,826	45,441
Halifax	4,241	8,908	7,892	5,257
Harnett	3,347	10,259	8,992	5,935
Haywood	4,515	8,903	10,692	5,885
Henderson	2,701	12,134	8,155	10,830
Hertford	1,928	2,794	3,986	1,517
Hoke	1,466	1,927	3,186	920
Hyde	403	1,112	1,084	623
Iredell	5,088	16,736	13,295	11,573
Jackson	3,169	4,709	5,223	3,536
Johnston	3,488	14,272	10,301	8,511
Jones	1,093	1,650	2,016	948
Lee	2,024	5,836	5,104	3,691
Lenoir	3,672	11,065	7,650	7,715
Lincoln	5,100	8,597	9,462	6,682
Macon	1,749	4,134	4,406	3,673
Madison	2,039	3,273	3,433	2,446
Martin	1,840	4,188	4,518	1,931
McDowell	2,348	6,570	6,246	4,450
Mecklenburg	33,730	77,546	63,198	61,715
Mitchell	800	4,240	2,031	3,728
Montgomery	2,175	4,417	4,308	2,872
Moore	3,627	9,406	7,373	7,577
Nash	4,503	12,679	8,937	8,477
New Hanover	5,984	19,060	14,504	13,687
Northamptom	3,233	2,997	5,118	1,238
Onslow	2,424	10,343	7,954	5,953
Orange	12,634	11,632	15,755	9,302
Pamlico	919	1,847	2,113	1,068
Pasquotank	2,115	3,906	4,302	2,651
Pender	1,415	3,327	4,422	2,063
Perquimans	723	1,299	1,666	909
Person	2,246	5,941	3,977	3,038
Pitt	5,858	14,406	11,636	9,532
Polk	1,416	3,121	3,155	2,605
Randolph	5,346	18,724	12,714	14,337
Richmond	3,508	5,692	8,793	2,848
Robeson	7,391	11,362	20,695	4,907
Rockingham	5,530	14,519	13,413	9,362
Rowan	6,834	20,735	15,363	14,644
Rutherford	4,140	9,506	10,361	6,718
Sampson	4,888	9,684	8,869	6,968
Scotland	1,938	3,485	4,430	1,932
Stanly	5,218	12,459	9,262	8,845
Stokes	3,254	7,118	6,647	6,029
Surry	4,706	10,497	10,024	7,403
Swain	1,101	2,052	2,151	1,608
Transylvania	2,321	5,860	4,636	4,089
Tyrrell	459	676	900	403
Union	3,886	10,264	10,578	6,184
Vance	3,117	6,491	5,620	3,813
Wake	22,807	56,808	44,005	44,291
Warren	1,698	2,603	3,185	1,427
Washington	1,546	2,559	2,840	1,486
Watauga	3,451	6,017	5,358	5,400
Wayne	5,234	14,352	9,265	9,607
Wilkes	4,634	13,105	10,176	11,768
Wilson	4,166	12,060	8,209	6,795
Yadkin	1,592	6,824	4,497	5,916
Yancey	2,278	3,106	3,932	2,688
Totals	**438,705**	**1,054,889**	**927,365**	**741,960**

North Carolina Vote Since 1932

1932 (Pres.), Roosevelt, Dem., 497,566; Hoover, Rep., 208,344; Thomas, Soc., 5,591.

1936 (Pres.), Roosevelt, Dem., 616,141; Landon, Rep., 223,283; Thomas, Soc., 21; Browder, Com., 11; Lemke, Union, 2.

1940 (Pres.), Roosevelt, Dem., 609,015; Willkie, Rep., 213,633.

1944 (Pres.), Roosevelt, Dem., 527,399; Dewey, Rep., 263,155.

1948 (Pres.), Truman, Dem., 459,070; Dewey, Rep., 258,572; Thurmond, States' Rights, 69,652; Wallace, Prog., 3,915.

1952 (Pres.), Eisenhower, Rep., 558,107; Stevenson, Dem., 652,803.

1956 (Pres.), Eisenhower, Rep., 575,062; Stevenson, Dem., 590,530.

1960 (Pres.), Kennedy, Dem., 713,136; Nixon, Rep., 655,420.

1964 (Pres.), Johnson, Dem., 800,139; Goldwater, Rep., 624,844.

1968 (Pres.), Nixon, Rep., 627,192; Humphrey, Dem., 464,113; Wallace, 3d party, 496,188.

1972 (Pres.), Nixon, Rep., 1,054,889; McGovern, Dem., 438,705; Schmitz, American, 25,018.

1976 (Pres.), Carter, Dem., 927,365; Ford, Rep., 741,-960; Anderson, American, 5,607; MacBride, Libertarian, 2,219; LaRouche, U.S. Labor, 755.

North Dakota

County	1972 McGovern (D)	1972 Nixon (R)	1976 Carter (D)	1976 Ford (R)
Adams	665	1,177	959	940
Barnes	2,804	4,518	3,321	4,011
Benson	1,635	2,050	1,973	1,689
Billings	192	509	285	351
Bottineau	1,369	3,263	1,987	2,638
Bowman	643	1,111	911	1,033
Burke	651	1,446	899	1,087
Burleigh	5,841	13,909	9,188	13,680
Cass	14,073	21,770	17,879	22,583
Cavalier	1,867	2,898	2,178	2,046
Dickey	1,266	2,277	1,612	2,027
Divide	774	1,230	1,057	881
Dunn	644	1,438	1,051	1,041
Eddy	911	1,022	1,123	890
Emmons	1,115	2,194	1,459	1,370
Foster	861	1,352	1,147	1,120
Golden Valley	362	774	479	633
Grand Forks	9,416	13,361	11,545	13,820
Grant	596	1,569	952	1,205
Griggs	901	1,312	1,122	1,086
Hettinger	726	1,511	1,095	1,135
Kidder	557	1,315	936	954
La Moure	1,399	2,110	1,718	1,735
Logan	554	1,408	809	944
McHenry	1,554	2,765	1,994	2,043
McIntosh	521	2,440	912	1,785
McKenzie	937	1,913	1,335	1,595
McLean	1,703	3,575	2,815	2,729
Mercer	784	2,567	1,298	1,982
Morton	3,312	5,494	5,241	4,921
Mountrail	1,391	2,038	2,189	1,430
Nelson	1,358	1,625	1,610	1,336
Oliver	293	669	529	575
Pembina	1,801	3,317	2,274	2,810
Pierce	973	1,970	1,434	1,396
Ramsey	2,384	3,954	3,096	3,293
Ransom	1,355	2,056	1,715	1,696
Renville	702	1,121	1,008	812
Richland	3,367	5,194	4,592	4,991
Rolette	1,803	1,713	2,531	1,094
Sargent	1,331	1,616	1,644	1,344
Sheridan	334	1,460	569	935
Sioux	557	561	697	354
Slope	249	413	347	355
Stark	2,636	5,115	4,076	4,374
Steele	892	1,063	1,066	835
Stutsman	3,589	6,269	4,883	5,653

	1972		1976	
	(D)	(R)	(D)	(R)
Towner	944	1,349	1,216	993
Traill	1,892	3,118	2,352	2,800
Walsh	2,908	3,991	3,555	3,518
Ward	6,706	13,900	9,484	12,751
Wells	1,297	2,519	1,742	1,941
Williams	2,989	4,800	4,189	4,230
Totals	**100,384**	**174,109**	**136,078**	**153,470**

North Dakota Vote Since 1932

1932 (Pres.), Roosevelt, Dem., 178,350; Hoover, Rep., 71,772; Harvey, Lib., 1,817; Thomas, Soc., 3,521; Foster, Com., 830.

1936 (Pres.), Roosevelt, Dem., 163,148; Landon, Rep., 72,751; Lemke, Union, 36,708; Thomas, Soc., 552; Browder, Com., 360; Colvin, Proh., 197.

1940 (Pres.), Roosevelt, Dem., 124,036; Willkie, Rep., 154,590; Thomas, Soc., 1,279; Knuttson, Com., 545; Babson, Proh., 325.

1944 (Pres.), Roosevelt, Dem., 100,144; Dewey, Rep., 118,535; Thomas, Soc., 943; Watson, Proh., 549.

1948 (Pres.), Truman, Dem., 95,812; Dewey, Rep., 115,139; Wallace, Prog., 8,391; Thomas, Soc., 1,000; Thurmond, States' Rights, 374.

1952 (Pres.), Eisenhower, Rep., 191,712; Stevenson, Dem., 76,694; MacArthur, Christian Nationalist, 1,075; Hallinan, Prog., 344; Hamblen, Proh., 302.

1956 (Pres.), Eisenhower, Rep., 156,766; Stevenson, Dem., 96,742; Andrews, American, 483.

1960 (Pres.), Kennedy, Dem., 123,963; Nixon, Rep., 154,310; Dobbs, Soc. Workers, 158.

1964 (Pres.), Johnson, Dem., 149,784; Goldwater, Rep., 108,207; DeBerry, Soc. Worker, 224; Munn, Proh., 174.

1968 (Pres.), Nixon, Rep., 138,669; Humphrey, Dem., 94,769; Wallace, 3d party, 14,244; Halstead, Soc. Worker, 128; Munn, Prohibition, 38; Troxell, Ind., 34.

1972 (Pres.), Nixon, Rep., 174,109; McGovern, Dem., 100,384; Jenness, Soc. Worker, 288; Hall, Communist, 87; Schmitz, American, 5,646.

1976 (Pres.), Carter, Dem., 136,078; Ford, Rep., 153,470; Anderson, American, 3,698; McCarthy, Ind., 2,952; Maddox, Amer. Ind., 269; MacBride, Libertarian, 256; scattering, 371.

Ohio

	1972		1976	
	McGovern	Nixon	Carter	Ford
County	(D)	(R)	(D)	(R)
Adams	2,709	4,980	4,450	4,197
Allen	10,184	26,966	14,627	23,721
Ashland	4,302	12,470	7,205	9,761
Ashtabula	15,052	22,762	20,883	16,885
Athens	9,977	9,735	9,896	8,387
Auglaize	4,617	11,900	5,840	9,772
Belmont	14,800	17,628	21,162	13,550
Brown	3,770	6,772	5,432	4,549
Butler	21,194	50,380	35,123	49,625
Carroll	2,755	5,984	5,006	5,091
Champaign	3,626	8,756	4,748	6,526
Clark	19,725	34,447	26,135	26,745
Clermont	8,276	22,936	14,850	19,616
Clinton	2,709	8,140	4,959	6,597
Columbiana	15,683	27,308	23,096	22,318
Coshocton	3,790	8,082	5,827	6,361
Crawford	5,518	14,632	7,553	10,801
Cuyahoga	317,670	329,493	349,186	255,594
Darke	6,534	13,862	9,901	11,580
Defiance	4,377	8,914	5,850	7,526
Delaware	4,452	12,950	7,058	12,285
Erie	10,889	16,714	13,843	14,742
Fairfield	7,746	21,909	13,361	19,098
Fayette	2,344	6,970	4,477	5,719
Franklin	117,562	219,771	141,624	189,645
Fulton	3,615	8,387	4,850	7,891
Gallia	2,341	6,506	4,971	5,198
Geauga	7,329	15,624	10,449	15,004
Greene	12,736	25,349	20,245	22,598
Guernsey	4,757	9,648	7,573	7,746
Hamilton	119,054	239,212	135,605	211,267
Hancock	6,084	18,111	8,548	15,983
Hardin	3,535	8,713	4,650	6,076
Harrison	2,388	4,554	4,070	3,509
Henry	3,145	8,099	4,592	7,656
Highland	3,464	8,524	6,327	6,853
Hocking	2,874	5,407	5,126	4,114
Holmes	1,507	3,752	2,242	2,870
Huron	5,491	10,942	7,742	9,386
Jackson	3,410	7,351	6,699	5,987
Jefferson	16,198	21,531	22,318	14,839
Knox	5,370	10,705	7,361	9,290
Lake	27,523	42,488	40,734	36,390
Lawrence	7,112	15,125	12,072	10,668
Licking	12,460	28,070	19,247	23,518
Logan	3,786	10,938	5,949	9,092
Lorain	36,634	51,102	52,387	39,459
Lucas	90,142	88,401	103,658	76,069
Madison	2,484	8,372	4,885	7,074
Mahoning	62,428	64,144	75,837	46,314
Marion	7,970	17,197	10,962	13,141
Medina	10,643	21,010	16,251	19,066
Meigs	2,335	5,961	5,262	4,942
Mercer	5,798	8,587	6,724	7,678
Miami	9,121	21,226	13,074	18,686
Monroe	2,483	3,721	4,296	2,728
Montgomery	82,231	120,998	106,468	100,223
Morgan	1,554	3,679	2,727	2,971
Morrow	2,527	6,886	4,870	5,814
Muskingum	10,313	19,897	14,178	15,358
Noble	1,449	3,274	2,612	3,007
Ottawa	6,465	9,772	9,646	8,241
Paulding	2,283	4,553	3,229	3,593
Perry	3,728	6,716	6,268	5,637
Pickaway	2,978	9,661	5,907	7,695
Pike	3,531	5,037	5,734	3,729
Portage	20,769	23,294	24,417	17,927
Preble	3,472	8,993	5,850	6,654
Putnam	3,729	8,185	5,035	7,332
Richland	13,468	31,117	23,065	24,310
Ross	5,879	15,573	10,743	11,477
Sandusky	8,308	15,489	11,202	13,074
Scioto	11,008	19,998	18,019	13,021
Seneca	8,180	13,939	10,074	11,730
Shelby	4,721	9,089	6,414	8,011
Stark	51,565	92,110	70,012	72,607
Summit	108,534	112,419	123,711	80,415
Trumbull	35,278	47,680	53,828	36,469
Tuscarawas	12,255	18,413	16,880	14,279
Union	2,447	8,389	4,377	7,464
Van Wert	3,644	9,545	5,689	8,344
Vinton	1,537	2,725	2,629	2,148
Warren	6,941	20,210	13,349	16,115
Washington	5,814	14,023	8,914	11,513
Wayne	9,260	20,368	13,087	16,976
Williams	4,278	9,083	4,920	7,596
Wood	13,494	21,080	16,926	19,331
Wyandot	2,771	6,414	4,043	5,661
Totals	**1,558,889**	**2,441,827**	**2,011,621**	**2,000,505**

Ohio Vote Since 1932

1932 (Pres.), Roosevelt, Dem., 1,301,695; Hoover, Rep., 1,227,679; Thomas, Soc., 64,094; Upshaw, Proh., 7,421; Foster, Com., 7,221; Reynolds, Soc. Lab., 1,968.

1936 (Pres.), Roosevelt, Dem., 1,747,122; Landon, Rep., 1,127,709; Lemke, Union, 132,212; Browder, Com., 5,251; Thomas, Soc., 117; Aiken, Soc. Lab., 14.

1940 (Pres.), Roosevelt, Dem., 1,733,139; Willkie, Rep., 1,586,773.

1944 (Pres.), Roosevelt, Dem., 1,570,763; Dewey, Rep., 1,582,293.

1948 (Pres.), Truman, Dem., 1,452,791; Dewey, Rep., 1,445,684; Wallace, Prog., 37,596.

1952 (Pres.), Eisenhower, Rep., 2,100,391; Stevenson, Dem., 1,600,367.

1956 (Pres.), Eisenhower, Rep., 2,262,610; Stevenson, Dem., 1,439,655.

1960 (Pres.), Kennedy, Dem., 1,944,248; Nixon, Rep., 2,217,611.

1964 (Pres.), Johnson, Dem., 2,498,331; Goldwater, Rep., 1,470,865.

1968 (Pres.), Nixon, Rep., 1,791,014; Humphrey, Dem., 1,700,586; Wallace, 3d party, 467,495; Gregory, 372; Munn, Prohibition, 19; Blomen, Soc. Labor, 120; Halstead, Soc. Worker, 69; Mitchell, Communist, 23.

1972 (Pres.), Nixon, Rep., 2,441,827; McGovern, Dem., 1,558,889; Fisher, Soc. Labor, 7,107; Hall, Communist, 6,437; Schmitz, American, 80,067; Wallace, Ind., 460.

1976 (Pres.), Carter, Dem., 2,011,621; Ford, Rep., 2,000,505; McCarthy, Ind., 58,258; Maddox, Amer. Ind., 15,529; MacBride, Libertarian, 8,961; Hall, Comm., 7,817; Camejo, Soc. Workers, 4,717; LaRouche, U.S. Labor, 4,335; scattered, 130.

Oklahoma

County	1972 McGovern (D)	1972 Nixon (R)	1976 Carter (D)	1976 Ford (R)
Adair	1,601	4,720	3,183	3,013
Alfalfa	641	3,208	1,725	2,113
Atoka	993	2,905	3,276	1,098
Beaver	522	2,562	1,213	1,801
Beckham	1,608	4,472	4,530	2,351
Blaine	963	3,958	2,297	2,682
Bryan	3,144	5,397	7,410	2,848
Caddo	2,921	7,683	7,382	3,854
Canadian	2,751	11,400	7,288	9,766
Carter	4,577	9,368	8,319	6,668
Cherokee	2,899	7,080	6,006	4,443
Choctaw	1,798	3,399	4,269	1,821
Cimarron	323	1,350	962	872
Cleveland	11,126	25,777	20,054	22,098
Coal	680	1,461	1,774	769
Comanche	4,559	19,759	12,910	13,163
Cotton	798	2,050	1,911	1,127
Craig	1,642	4,163	3,577	2,540
Creek	3,705	12,396	8,964	8,458
Custer	2,298	7,267	4,597	4,847
Delaware	2,135	5,476	4,924	3,642
Dewey	626	2,106	1,540	1,230
Ellis	473	2,059	1,256	1,429
Garfield	4,557	19,348	8,969	14,202
Garvin	2,685	7,245	6,797	3,905
Grady	3,440	7,762	7,155	4,686
Grant	805	2,829	1,853	1,685
Greer	1,004	2,154	2,113	1,164
Harmon	568	1,319	1,371	666
Harper	385	1,976	978	1,303
Haskell	1,408	2,815	3,388	1,401
Hughes	1,787	3,497	4,185	1,715
Jackson	2,054	5,519	4,914	3,189
Jefferson	969	1,709	2,303	956
Johnston	983	2,205	2,765	1,127
Kay	4,246	17,244	9,371	12,441
Kingfisher	912	4,861	2,372	3,443
Kiowa	1,495	3,711	3,403	1,971
Latimer	1,239	2,520	2,661	1,312
Le Flore	3,433	7,932	8,033	4,907
Lincoln	1,919	6,512	4,988	4,429
Logan	2,760	6,543	4,594	4,382
Love	671	1,407	1,923	846
McClain	1,350	4,241	4,048	2,444
McCurtain	2,568	6,441	7,560	3,423
McIntosh	1,686	3,216	4,145	1,822
Major	512	3,203	1,357	2,282
Marshall	1,113	2,273	2,939	1,358
Mayes	2,656	7,535	6,298	5,040
Murray	1,294	2,983	2,932	1,563
Muskogee	7,380	15,161	14,678	10,287
Noble	999	4,085	2,278	2,634
Nowata	1,096	3,293	2,195	2,077
Okfuskee	1,328	2,862	2,663	1,630
Oklahoma	46,986	156,437	87,185	119,120
Okmulgee	4,494	8,706	8,499	5,333
Osage	2,968	9,288	6,832	6,398
Ottawa	3,657	8,348	7,446	4,985
Pawnee	1,135	4,280	3,031	3,111
Payne	5,644	17,019	9,987	13,481
Pittsburg	4,748	9,989	10,743	4,807
Pontotoc	3,160	8,762	7,466	4,895
Pottawatomie	4,822	13,308	11,255	9,090
Pushmataha	1,016	2,456	2,987	1,360
Roger Mills	420	1,696	1,346	873
Rogers	2,607	9,697	7,368	7,318
Seminole	2,746	6,879	5,874	4,237
Sequoyah	2,519	6,842	5,873	3,938
Stephens	3,623	10,309	9,795	7,099
Texas	924	5,726	2,591	3,919
Tillman	1,256	3,331	2,852	1,802
Tulsa	32,779	125,278	65,298	108,653
Wagoner	2,257	6,569	5,879	5,071
Washington	3,658	16,347	6,898	14,560
Washita	1,305	3,578	3,304	2,165
Woods	1,234	4,413	2,530	2,788
Woodward	1,104	5,350	2,807	3,782
Totals	**247,147**	**759,025**	**532,442**	**545,708**

Oklahoma Vote Since 1932

1932 (Pres.), Roosevelt, Dem., 515,468; Hoover, Rep., 188,165.

1936 (Pres.), Roosevelt, Dem., 501,069; Landon, Rep., 245,122; Thomas, Soc., 2,221; Colvin, Proh., 1,328.

1940 (Pres.), Roosevelt, Dem., 474,313; Willkie, Rep., 348,872; Babson, Proh., 3,027.

1944 (Pres.), Roosevelt, Dem., 401,549; Dewey, Rep., 319,424; Watson, Proh., 1,663.

1948 (Pres.), Truman, Dem., 452,782; Dewey, Rep., 268,817.

1952 (Pres.), Eisenhower, Rep., 518,045; Stevenson, Dem., 430,939.

1956 (Pres.), Eisenhower, Rep., 473,769; Stevenson, Dem., 385,581.

1960 (Pres.), Kennedy, Dem., 370,111; Nixon, Rep., 533,039.

1964 (Pres.), Johnson, Dem., 519,834; Goldwater, Rep. 412,665.

1968 (Pres.), Nixon, Rep., 449,697; Humphrey, Dem., 301,658; Wallace, 3d party, 191,731.

1972 (Pres.), Nixon, Rep., 759,025; McGovern, Dem., 247,147; Schmitz, American, 23,728.

1976 (Pres.), Carter, Dem., 532,442; Ford, Rep., 545,-708; McCarthy, Ind., 14,101.

Oregon

County	1972 McGovern (D)	1972 Nixon (R)	1976 Carter (D)	1976 Ford (R)
Baker	2,047	3,441	3,306	3,340
Benton	10,842	14,906	11,887	15,555
Clackamas	32,540	41,767	42,504	47,671
Clatsop	6,017	5,998	6,690	6,178
Columbia	5,997	5,348	8,005	5,226
Coos	11,778	10,370	14,168	9,481
Crook	1,743	2,167	2,536	2,093
Curry	2,108	2,832	3,227	2,962
Deschutes	6,319	7,747	9,480	9,054
Douglas	9,009	15,881	14,965	16,500
Gilliam	335	665	508	612
Grant	932	1,781	1,393	1,640
Harney	1,004	1,693	1,567	1,652
Hood River	2,330	3,152	3,114	3,210
Jackson	14,529	24,003	23,384	24,237
Jefferson	1,229	1,816	1,769	1,810
Josephine	5,090	9,911	9,061	10,726
Klamath	5,719	11,169	9,659	11,649
Lake	777	1,619	1,381	1,575
Lane	46,177	47,739	56,479	46,245
Lincoln	5,117	6,112	6,685	5,755
Linn	11,178	15,079	15,776	14,128
Malheur	1,870	5,908	3,507	5,682
Marion	23,908	36,441	33,781	35,497
Morrow	718	1,059	1,162	1,091
Multnomah	125,470	118,219	129,060	112,400
Polk	5,908	8,985	8,141	8,528
Sherman	330	677	491	567
Tillamook	3,544	4,120	4,456	4,033
Umatilla	6,090	10,470	7,985	9,345
Union	3,272	5,073	4,280	5,111
Wallowa	899	1,909	1,310	1,693
Wasco	3,749	4,537	4,560	4,258
Washington	27,890	43,958	34,847	52,376
Wheeler	267	474	402	355
Yamhill	6,008	9,660	8,881	9,885
Totals	**392,760**	**486,686**	**490,407**	**492,120**

Oregon Vote Since 1932

1932 (Pres.), Roosevelt, Dem., 213,871; Hoover, Rep., 136,019; Thomas, Soc., 15,450; Reynolds, Soc. Lab., 1,730; Foster, Com., 1,681.

1936 (Pres.), Roosevelt, Dem., 266,733; Landon, Rep., 122,706; Lemke, Union, 21,831; Thomas, Soc., 2,143; Aiken, Soc. Lab., 500; Browder, Com., 104; Colvin, Proh., 4.

1940 (Pres.), Roosevelt, Dem., 258,415; Willkie, Rep., 219,555; Aiken, Soc. Lab., 2,487; Thomas, Soc., 398; Browder, Com., 191; Babson, Proh., 154.

1944 (Pres.), Roosevelt, Dem., 248,635; Dewey, Rep., 225,365; Thomas, Soc., 3,785; Watson, Proh., 2,362.

1948 (Pres.), Truman, Dem., 243,147; Dewey, Rep., 260,904; Wallace, Prog., 14,978; Thomas, Soc., 5,051.

1952 (Pres.), Eisenhower, Rep., 420,815; Stevenson, Dem., 270,579; Hallinan, Ind., 3,665.

1956 (Pres.), Eisenhower, Rep., 406,393; Stevenson, Dem., 329,204.

1960 (Pres.), Kennedy, Dem., 367,402; Nixon, Rep., 408,060.

1964 (Pres.), Johnson, Dem., 501,017; Goldwater, Rep., 282,779; write-in, 2,509.

1968 (Pres.), Nixon, Rep., 408,433; Humphrey, Dem., 358,866; Wallace, 3d party, 49,683; write-in, McCarthy, 1,496; N. Rockefeller, 69; others, 1,075.

1972 (Pres.), Nixon, Rep., 486,686; McGovern, Dem., 392,760; Schmitz, Amer., 46,211; write-in, 2,289.

1976 (Pres.), Carter, Dem., 490,407; Ford, Rep., 492,-120; McCarthy, Ind., 40,207; write-in, 7,142.

Pennsylvania

County	1972 McGovern (D)	1972 Nixon (R)	1976 Carter (D)	1976 Ford (R)
Adams	5,529	13,593	8,771	12,133
Allegheny	282,496	371,737	328,343	303,127
Armstrong	10,490	17,557	15,179	13,378
Beaver	31,570	43,637	46,117	33,593
Bedford	3,836	11,243	6,652	9,355
Berks	36,563	66,172	50,994	54,452
Blair	10,023	33,126	18,397	28,290
Bradford	5,204	15,050	7,913	12,851
Bucks	56,784	99,684	79,838	85,628
Butler	14,695	29,665	22,611	26,366
Cambria	27,950	43,825	38,797	32,469
Cameron	828	1,935	1,319	1,616
Carbon	7,774	11,639	10,791	8,883
Centre	13,194	20,683	17,867	21,177
Chester	31,118	72,726	42,712	67,686
Clarion	4,509	10,073	6,585	8,360
Clearfield	9,246	16,780	13,714	13,626
Clinton	4,772	8,205	6,532	5,858
Columbia	7,222	14,187	12,051	11,508
Crawford	9,371	18,393	14,712	15,301
Cumberland	14,562	42,099	23,008	39,950
Dauphin	22,587	54,307	34,342	46,819
Delaware	94,144	175,414	117,252	148,679
Elk	4,710	7,900	6,713	6,159
Erie	42,022	61,542	55,385	49,641
Fayette	22,475	27,288	32,232	20,021
Forest	509	1,374	1,017	1,135
Franklin	9,456	24,093	14,643	20,009
Fulton	1,192	2,515	1,737	2,219
Greene	5,562	7,890	8,769	5,293
Huntingdon	3,394	9,606	5,410	7,843
Indiana	10,833	18,122	14,650	15,786
Jefferson	5,024	11,631	7,456	9,437
Juniata	2,156	4,412	3,105	3,991
Lackawanna	45,465	58,838	57,685	43,354
Lancaster	24,223	81,036	35,533	72,106
Lawrence	17,595	23,712	23,337	18,546
Lebanon	6,683	25,008	11,785	20,880
Lehigh	33,325	58,023	46,620	46,895
Luzerne	51,128	81,358	74,655	60,058
Lycoming	11,999	28,913	18,635	22,648
McKean	4,513	11,958	6,424	10,305
Mercer	18,087	27,961	25,041	22,469
Mifflin	3,667	9,989	6,210	7,698
Monroe	5,619	12,701	9,544	10,228
Montgomery	91,959	173,662	112,644	155,480
Montour	1,755	4,386	2,727	3,259
Northampton	32,335	41,822	42,514	32,926
Northumberland	13,885	25,912	18,939	19,283
Perry	2,731	8,082	4,605	7,454
Philadelphia	431,736	344,096	494,579	239,000
Pike	1,385	4,568	2,775	4,241
Potter	1,710	4,422	2,983	3,828
Schuylkill	26,077	44,071	33,905	31,944
Snyder	1,834	7,308	3,097	6,557
Somerset	8,743	19,739	13,452	15,960
Sullivan	885	1,886	1,347	1,584
Susquehanna	4,154	9,476	6,075	8,331
Tioga	3,733	10,028	5,795	8,417
Union	2,278	6,905	3,405	6,309
Venango	6,302	13,991	8,653	12,270
Warren	4,877	10,018	7,412	8,508
Washington	34,781	42,587	49,317	32,827
Wayne	2,733	8,948	4,244	7,811
Westmoreland	59,322	75,085	74,217	59,172
Wyoming	2,112	6,423	3,628	5,705
York	27,520	63,606	41,281	56,912
Totals	**1,796,951**	**2,714,521**	**2,328,677**	**2,205,604**

Pennsylvania Vote Since 1932

1932 (Pres.), Roosevelt, Dem., 1,295,948; Hoover, Rep., 1,453,540; Thomas, Soc., 91,119; Upshaw, Proh., 11,319; Foster, Com., 5,658; Cox, Jobless, 725; Reynolds, Indust., 659.

1936 (Pres.), Roosevelt, Dem., 2,353,788; Landon, Rep., 1,690,300; Lemke, Royal Oak, 67,467; Thomas, Soc., 14,375; Colvin, Proh., 6,691; Browder, Com., 4,060; Aiken, Ind., Lab., 1,424.

1940 (Pres.), Roosevelt, Dem., 2,171,035; Willkie, Rep., 1,889,848; Thomas, Soc., 10,967; Browder, Com., 4,519; Aiken, Ind. Gov., 1,518.

1944 (Pres.), Roosevelt, Dem., 1,940,479; Dewey, Rep., 1,835,054; Thomas, Soc., 11,721; Watson, Proh., 5,750; Teichert, Ind. Gov., 1,789.

1948 (Pres.), Truman, Dem., 1,752,426; Dewey, Rep., 1,902,197; Wallace, Prog., 55,161; Thomas, Soc., 11,325; Watson, Proh., 10,338; Dobbs, Militant Workers, 2,133; Teichert, Ind. Gov., 1,461.

1952 (Pres.), Eisenhower, Rep., 2,415,789; Stevenson, Dem., 2,146,269; Hamblen, Proh., 8,771; Hallinan, Prog., 4,200; Hoopes, Soc., 2,684; Dobbs, Militant Workers, 1,502; Haas, Ind. Gov., 1,347; scattered, 155.

1956 (Pres.), Eisenhower, Rep., 2,585,252; Stevenson, Dem., 1,981,769; Haas, Soc. Lab., 7,447; Dobbs, Militant Workers, 2,035.

1960 (Pres.), Kennedy, Dem., 2,556,282; Nixon, Rep., 2,439,956; Haas, Soc. Lab., 7,185; Dobbs, Soc. Workers, 2,678; scattering, 440.

1964 (Pres.), Johnson, Dem., 3,130,954; Goldwater, Rep., 1,673,657; DeBerry, Soc. Worker, 10,456; Haas, Soc. Labor, 5,092; scattering, 2,531.

1968 (Pres.), Nixon, Rep., 2,090,017; Humphrey, Dem., 2,259,405; Wallace, 3d party, 378,582; Blomen, Soc. Labor, 4,977; Halstead, Soc. Worker, 4,862; Gregory, 7,821; others, 2,264.

1972 (Pres.), Nixon, Rep., 2,714,521; McGovern, Dem., 1,796,951; Schmitz, American, 70,593; Jenness, Soc. Worker, 4,639; Hall, Communist, 2,686; others 2,715.

1976 (Pres.), Carter, Dem., 2,328,677; Ford, Rep., 2,205,604; McCarthy, Ind., 50,584; Maddox, Constitution, 25,344; Camejo, Soc. Workers, 3,009; Larouche, U.S. Labor, 2,744; Hall, Comm., 1,891; others, 2,934.

Rhode Island

County	1972 McGovern (D)	1972 Nixon (R)	1976 Carter (D)	1976 Ford (R)
Bristol	9,928	12,009	11,228	10,131
Kent	29,004	40,534	35,855	34,131
Newport	12,844	19,142	17,768	15,155
Providence	129,232	129,418	144,805	103,976
Washington	13,637	19,280	17,980	17,856
Totals	**194,645**	**220,383**	**227,636**	**181,249**

Rhode Island Vote Since 1932

1932 (Pres.), Roosevelt, Dem., 146,604; Hoover, Rep., 115,266; Thomas, Soc., 3,138; Foster, Com., 546; Reynolds, Soc. Lab., 433; Upshaw, Proh., 183.

1936 (Pres.), Roosevelt, Dem., 165,238; Landon, Rep., 125,031; Lemke, Union, 19,569; Aiken, Soc. Lab., 929; Browder, Com., 411.

1940 (Pres.), Roosevelt, Dem., 182,182; Willkie, Rep., 138,653; Browder, Com., 239; Babson, Proh., 74.

1944 (Pres.), Roosevelt, Dem., 175,356; Dewey, Rep., 123,487; Watson, Proh., 433.

1948 (Pres.), Truman, Dem., 188,736; Dewey, Rep., 135,787; Wallace, Prog., 2,619; Thomas, Soc., 429; Teichert, Soc. Lab., 131.

1952 (Pres.), Eisenhower, Rep., 210,935; Stevenson, Dem., 203,293; Hallinan, Prog., 187; Haas, Soc. Lab., 83.

1956 (Pres.), Eisenhower, Rep., 225,819; Stevenson, Dem., 161,790.

1960 (Pres.), Kennedy, Dem., 258,032; Nixon, Rep., 147,502.

1964 (Pres.), Johnson, Dem., 315,463; Goldwater, Rep., 74,615.

1968 (Pres.), Nixon, Rep., 122,359; Humphrey, Dem., 246,518; Wallace, 3d party, 15,678; Halstead, Soc. Worker, 383.

1972 (Pres.), Nixon, Rep., 220,383; McGovern, Dem., 194,645; Jenness, Soc. Worker, 729.

1976 (Pres.), Carter, Dem., 227,636; Ford, Rep., 181,249; MacBride, Libertarian, 715; Camejo, Soc. Workers, 462; Hall, Comm., 334; Levin, Soc. Labor, 188.

South Carolina

County	1972 McGovern (D)	1972 Nixon (R)	1976 Carter (D)	1976 Ford (R)
Abbeville	1,347	3,265	4,700	1,791
Aiken	5,745	21,117	14,927	16,011
Allendale	1,383	1,740	2,634	1,064
Anderson	5,241	17,514	19,002	9,496
Bamberg	1,680	2,537	3,330	1,849

	1972		1976	
	(D)	(R)	(D)	(R)
Barnwell	1,560	3,955	4,083	2,569
Beaufort	3,237	5,929	6,049	5,935
Berkeley	4,497	9,345	9,741	6,981
Calhoun	1,148	1,867	2,055	1,382
Charleston	16,856	39,832	34,328	34,010
Cherokee	2,107	7,570	7,765	3,931
Chester	2,352	4,724	5,200	2,982
Chesterfield	2,938	5,230	7,687	2,537
Clarendon	3,276	3,958	5,489	3,040
Colleton	2,376	5,738	5,134	3,324
Darlington	4,414	11,756	10,165	6,678
Dillon	1,604	4,364	5,089	2,527
Dorchester	3,606	8,095	8,046	6,695
Edgefield	1,326	2,812	3,216	1,878
Fairfield	2,491	2,608	4,155	1,817
Florence	7,451	18,107	16,294	13,539
Georgetown	4,446	6,114	7,169	4,068
Greenville	10,163	46,360	35,923	39,099
Greenwood	3,400	9,370	9,976	5,974
Hampton	2,086	2,891	3,923	1,773
Horry	4,437	15,324	15,720	9,339
Jasper	1,203	1,650	2,903	1,221
Kershaw	2,531	8,035	6,211	6,126
Lancaster	2,461	9,016	8,324	4,997
Laurens	2,650	8,141	7,440	5,300
Lee	1,996	3,076	3,869	2,357
Lexington	4,069	25,327	14,339	21,442
Marion	844	1,302	5,927	3,076
Marlboro	2,535	4,719	5,409	1,961
McCormick	2,999	3,838	1,774	640
Newberry	2,035	7,325	5,034	4,931
Oconee	1,739	6,825	8,447	3,805
Orangeburg	7,652	11,711	13,652	8,794
Pickens	2,255	11,776	8,505	8,029
Richland	20,875	38,500	36,855	32,727
Saluda	1,022	3,095	2,715	2,085
Spartanburg	9,723	31,187	27,925	20,456
Sumter	5,795	10,892	10,471	9,332
Union	2,676	8,337	6,363	3,463
Williamsburg	5,213	5,729	8,745	5,275
York	6,374	14,441	14,099	9,843
Totals	**186,824**	**477,044**	**450,807**	**346,149**

South Carolina Vote Since 1932

1932 (Pres.), Roosevelt, Dem., 102,347; Hoover, Rep., 1,978; Thomas, Soc., 82.

1936 (Pres.), Roosevelt, Dem., 113,791; Landon, Rep., Tolbert faction 953, Hambright faction 693, total, 1,646.

1940 (Pres.), Roosevelt, Dem., 95,470; Willkie, Rep., 1,727.

1944 (Pres.), Roosevelt, Dem., 90,601; Dewey, Rep., 4,547; Southern Democrats, 7,799; Watson, Proh., 365; Rep. Tolbert faction, 63.

1948 (Pres.), Thurmond, States' Rights, 102,607; Truman, Dem., 34,423; Dewey, Rep., 5,386; Wallace, Prog., 154; Thomas, Soc., 1.

1952 (Pres.), Eisenhower ran on two tickets. Under State law vote cast for two Eisenhower slates of electors could not be combined. Eisenhower, Ind., 158,289; Rep., 9,793; total 168,082; Stevenson, Dem., 173,004; Hamblen, Proh., 1.

1956 (Pres.), Stevenson, Dem., 136,372; Byrd., Ind., 88,509; Eisenhower, Rep., 75,700; Andrews, Ind., 2.

1960 (Pres.), Kennedy, Dem., 198,129; Nixon, Rep., 188,558; write-in, 1.

1964 (Pres.), Johnson, Dem., 215,700; Goldwater, Rep., 309,048; write-ins: Nixon, 1; Wallace, 5; Powell, 1; Thurmond, 1.

1968 (Pres.), Nixon, Rep., 254,062; Humphrey, Dem., 197,486; Wallace, 3d party, 215,430.

1972 (Pres.), Nixon, Rep., 477,044; McGovern, Dem., 184,559, United Citizens, 2,265; Schmitz, American, 10,075; write-in, 17.

1976 (Pres.), Carter, Dem., 450,807; Ford, Rep., 346,-149; Anderson, American, 2,996; Maddox, Amer. Ind., 1,950; write-in, 681.

South Dakota

	1972		1976	
	McGovern	Nixon	Carter	Ford
County	(D)	(R)	(D)	(R)
Aurora	1,257	1,075	1,269	831
Beadle	4,297	5,922	4,846	4,758
Bennett	476	808	481	610
Bon Homme	2,368	2,116	2,154	1,897
Brookings	4,701	5,182	4,685	5,278
Brown	8,216	8,134	8,888	7,609
Brule	1,665	1,421	1,534	1,175
Buffalo	275	221	240	194
Butte	1,085	2,452	1,366	2,055
Campbell	361	1,169	489	897
Chas. Mix	2,691	2,020	2,593	1,779
Clark	1,336	1,617	1,376	1,449
Clay	2,821	2,518	2,593	2,647
Codington	4,601	4,936	4,680	4,504
Corson	689	975	967	846
Custer	798	1,476	995	1,373
Davison	4,710	3,796	4,510	3,688
Day	2,719	1,971	2,610	1,617
Deuel	1,370	1,357	1,465	1,177
Dewey	699	1,008	706	820
Douglas	887	1,434	975	1,315
Edmunds	1,646	1,567	1,629	1,294
Fall River	1,107	2,374	1,537	2,046
Faulk	986	1,004	1,063	868
Grant	2,231	2,247	2,398	2,051
Gregory	1,555	1,670	1,658	1,475
Haakon	366	1,021	477	812
Hamlin	1,276	1,693	1,402	1,452
Hand	1,307	1,806	1,477	1,510
Hanson	1,022	876	1,005	693
Harding	253	637	459	470
Hughes	2,037	4,231	2,506	3,997
Hutchinson	2,248	3,092	2,062	2,822
Hyde	533	789	572	687
Jackson	261	581	313	532
Jerauld	829	988	845	821
Jones	346	642	374	515
Kingsbury	1,632	2,320	1,762	1,844
Lake	2,886	2,919	2,930	2,530
Lawrence	2,533	4,795	3,102	4,206
Lincoln	2,617	3,201	2,957	3,105
Lyman	744	1,166	831	892
Marshall	1,646	1,500	1,721	1,233
McCook	1,993	1,963	1,822	1,744
McPherson	579	1,950	693	1,662
Meade	1,633	3,146	2,478	3,096
Mellette	433	637	429	508
Miner	1,337	1,059	1,289	839
Minnehaha	22,386	22,447	22,068	23,286
Moody	1,895	1,648	1,942	1,475
Pennington	8,592	13,654	10,058	13,352
Perkins	900	1,691	1,262	1,298
Potter	858	1,389	908	1,136
Roberts	2,976	2,187	2,890	1,915
Sanborn	1,074	1,064	1,025	881
Shannon	1,246	356	756	301
Spink	2,321	2,547	2,650	2,003
Stanley	492	779	548	637
Sully	414	773	505	630
Todd	907	806	826	583
Tripp	1,538	2,592	1,822	1,980
Turner	1,993	3,007	1,906	2,694
Union	2,554	2,271	2,540	2,297
Walworth	1,287	2,416	1,516	2,187
Washabaugh	211	245	276	229
Yankton	3,835	4,366	3,987	4029
Ziebach	378	486	370	369
Totals	**139,945**	**166,476**	**147,068**	**151,505**

South Dakota Vote Since 1932

1932 (Pres.), Roosevelt, Dem., 183,515; Hoover, Rep., 99,212; Harvey, Lib., 3,333; Thomas, Soc., 1,551; Upshaw, Proh., 463; Foster, Com., 364.

1936 (Pres.), Roosevelt, Dem., 160,137; Landon, Rep., 125,977; Lemke, Union, 10,338.

1940 (Pres.), Roosevelt, Dem., 131,862; Willkie, Rep., 177,065.

1944 (Pres.), Roosevelt, Dem., 96,711; Dewey, Rep., 135,365.

1948 (Pres.), Truman, Dem., 117,653; Dewey, Rep., 129,651; Wallace, Prog., 2,801.

1952 (Pres.), Eisenhower, Rep., 203,857; Stevenson, Dem., 90,426.

1956 (Pres.), Eisenhower, Rep., 171,569; Stevenson, Dem., 122,288.

1960 (Pres.), Kennedy, Dem., 128,070; Nixon, Rep., 178,417.

1964 (Pres.), Johnson, Dem., 163,010; Goldwater, Rep., 130,108.

1968 (Pres.), Nixon, Rep., 149,841; Humphrey, Dem., 118,023; Wallace, 3d party, 13,400.

1972 (Pres.), Nixon, Rep., 166,476; McGovern, Dem., 139,945; Jenness, Soc. Worker, 994.

1976 (Pres.), Carter, Dem., 147,068; Ford, Rep., 151,-505; MacBride, Libertarian, 1,619; Hall, Comm., 318; Camejo, Soc. Workers, 168.

Tennessee

County	1972 McGovern (D)	1972 Nixon (R)	1976 Carter (D)	1976 Ford (R)
Anderson	6,713	13,865	13,455	10,494
Bedford	2,565	4,262	7,228	3,023
Benton	1,479	2,614	4,088	1,678
Bledsoe	899	1,952	1,757	1,620
Blount	5,303	16,078	12,096	13,851
Bradley	2,804	10,440	8,776	9,136
Campbell	1,629	4,909	5,206	4,277
Cannon	911	1,615	2,463	908
Carroll	2,290	5,784	5,581	4,031
Carter	2,191	11,102	7,443	8,934
Cheatham	1,321	2,235	4,225	1,376
Chester	961	2,787	2,532	1,949
Claiborne	1,230	3,632	3,461	3,227
Clay	648	982	1,671	982
Cocke	805	5,268	3,141	5,004
Coffee	2,973	6,416	8,017	3,848
Crockett	735	2,642	2,963	1,694
Cumberland	1,482	4,593	4,543	4,119
Davidson	48,869	82,636	99,007	60,662
Decatur	1,187	2,368	2,432	1,637
De Kalb	1,243	2,014	3,222	1,443
Dickson	2,619	3,645	6,551	2,285
Dyer	1,600	6,066	5,937	4,391
Fayette	2,067	3,264	3,853	2,133
Fentress	665	2,154	1,953	1,767
Franklin	2,896	4,136	6,788	2,619
Gibson	3,625	9,900	10,356	5,563
Giles	1,875	2,914	5,225	1,952
Grainger	828	2,842	2,018	2,805
Greene	2,764	9,772	7,070	8,664
Grundy	1,005	1,364	2,850	850
Hamblen	2,563	8,879	7,504	6,989
Hamilton	20,657	58,469	45,348	47,969
Hancock	393	1,813	764	1,309
Hardeman	1,550	3,494	3,934	2,254
Hardin	1,202	4,401	3,438	3,362
Hawkins	2,608	7,791	5,931	6,407
Haywood	1,966	3,123	3,681	1,952
Henderson	1,313	5,122	3,366	4,152
Henry	2,694	4,613	7,162	2,585
Hickman	1,393	1,943	3,590	1,154
Houston	870	800	1,990	407
Humphreys	1,973	2,263	4,021	1,338
Jackson	1,085	956	2,959	591
Jefferson	1,357	5,925	3,995	5,459
Johnson	450	3,362	1,464	2,986
Knox	24,076	64,747	53,034	56,013
Lake	536	1,147	1,933	591
Lauderdale	1,771	3,597	4,747	2,105
Lawrence	2,824	6,438	7,140	4,967
Lewis	1,138	1,056	2,391	617
Lincoln	1,867	3,266	5,732	1,724
Loudon	1,604	5,357	4,683	4,458
McMinn	2,838	7,423	7,020	6,638
McNairy	1,610	4,774	4,293	3,388
Macon	653	2,295	1,951	2,063
Madison	5,203	15,481	12,989	11,364
Marion	1,929	3,711	4,615	2,965
Marshall	1,526	2,593	4,457	1,674
Maury	3,262	7,371	8,747	5,327
Meigs	539	1,052	1,254	975
Monroe	2,870	5,657	5,368	5,335
Montgomery	5,691	7,839	12,310	5,923
Moore	356	608	1,101	331
Morgan	1,084	2,531	2,953	1,949
Obion	2,243	5,800	7,204	2,986
Overton	1,573	1,947	3,897	1,115
Perry	937	900	1,660	520
Pickett	357	957	948	986
Polk	1,431	2,285	3,284	1,835
Putnam	3,738	6,038	8,485	4,079
Rhea	1,312	3,842	3,735	3,449
Roane	3,433	8,742	9,216	7,121
Robertson	2,985	4,175	7,547	2,505
Rutherford	5,811	11,256	14,854	7,921
Scott	679	2,775	2,260	2,432
Sequatchie	629	1,298	1,733	1,065
Sevier	1,128	8,273	3,993	7,608
Shelby	81,089	161,922	147,893	128,646
Smith	1,260	1,812	3,753	1,332
Stewart	1,098	790	2,442	510
Sullivan	10,007	27,593	23,353	22,087
Sumner	4,596	10,020	13,848	7,946
Tipton	1,853	5,542	5,667	3,329
Trousdale	539	663	1,385	332
Unicoi	822	3,877	2,526	3,211
Union	570	1,927	1,631	1,801
Van Buren	364	629	1,085	346
Warren	2,118	3,565	6,666	2,364
Washington	5,284	17,343	13,951	14,770
Wayne	673	2,898	1,891	2,597
Weakley	2,027	5,836	6,605	2,875
White	1,392	2,252	3,874	1,382
Williamson	2,616	7,556	8,183	7,880
Wilson	3,096	6,486	10,537	4,696
Totals	**357,293**	**813,147**	**825,879**	**633,969**

Tennessee Vote Since 1932

1932 (Pres.), Roosevelt, Dem., 259,817; Hoover, Rep., 126,806; Upshaw, Proh., 1,995; Thomas, Soc., 1,786; Foster, Com., 234.

1936 (Pres.), Roosevelt, Dem., 327,083; Landon, Rep., 146,516; Thomas, Soc., 685; Colvin, Proh., 632; Browder, Com., 319; Lemke, Union, 296.

1940 (Pres.), Roosevelt, Dem., 351,601; Willkie, Rep., 169,153; Babson, Proh., 1,606; Thomas, Soc., 463.

1944 (Pres.), Roosevelt, Dem., 308,707; Dewey, Rep., 200,311; Watson, Proh., 882; Thomas, Soc., 892.

1948 (Pres.), Truman, Dem., 270,402; Dewey, Rep., 202,914; Thurmond, States' Rights, 73,815; Wallace, Prog., 1,864; Thomas, Soc., 1,288.

1952 (Pres.), Eisenhower, Rep., 446,147; Stevenson, Dem., 443,710; Hamblen, Proh., 1,432; Hallinan, Prog., 885; MacArthur, Christian Nationalist, 379.

1956 (Pres.), Eisenhower, Rep., 462,288; Stevenson, Dem., 456,507; Andrews, Ind., 19,820; Holtwick, Proh., 789.

1960 (Pres.), Kennedy, Dem., 481,453; Nixon, Rep., 556,577; Faubus, States' Rights, 11,304; Decker, Proh., 2,458.

1964 (Pres.), Johnson, Dem., 635,047; Goldwater, Rep., 508,965; write-in, 34.

1968 (Pres.), Nixon, Rep., 472,592; Humphrey, Dem., 351,233; Wallace, 3d party, 424,792.

1972 (Pres.), Nixon, Rep., 813,147; McGovern, Dem., 357,293; Schmitz, American, 30,373; write-in, 369.

1976 (Pres.), Carter, Dem., 825,879; Ford, Rep., 633,-969; Anderson, American, 5,769; McCarthy, Ind., 5,004; Maddox, Am. Ind., 2,303; MacBride, Libertarian, 1,375; Hall, Comm., 547; LaRouche, U.S. Labor, 512; Bubar, Proh., 442; Miller, Ind., 316; write-in, 230.

Texas

County	1972 McGovern (D)	1972 Nixon (R)	1976 Carter (D)	1976 Ford (R)
Anderson	2,233	5,826	5,499	4,172
Andrews	677	2,615	1,777	2,127
Angelina	4,970	11,453	9,750	7,223
Aransas	844	2,037	2,136	1,985
Archer	632	1,494	1,577	966
Armstrong	177	768	513	506
Atascosa	1,804	3,400	4,565	2,415
Austin	1,043	3,084	2,313	2,686
Bailey	465	1,837	1,356	1,255
Bandera	434	1,796	1,183	1554
Bastrop	1,906	3,097	4,788	2,383
Baylor	598	1,190	1,335	783
Bee	2,067	3,779	3,690	2,953
Bell	6,848	17,525	17,499	15,126
Bexar	91,662	137,572	146,581	121,176
Blanco	460	1,215	923	1,015
Borden	96	330	234	150
Bosque	1,014	2,947	2,954	1,912
Bowie	5,227	14,722	12,445	9,590
Brazoria	11,350	21,045	21,711	19,475
Brazos	5,692	14,243	10,628	15,685
Brewster	904	1,524	1,227	1,368
Briscoe	349	642	823	285
Brooks	1,657	1,117	2,782	641
Brown	2,171	5,990	5,577	4,483
Burleson	1,361	1,762	2,924	1,142
Burnet	1,227	3,438	3,818	2,777
Caldwell	1,974	3,171	3,647	2,235
Calhoun	1,936	3,614	3,642	2,377
Callahan	665	2,223	2,241	1,581
Cameron	13,340	20,816	25,310	16,448
Camp	1,041	1,599	2,146	1,133
Carson	561	1,868	1,542	1,269
Cass	1,981	5,303	5,134	3,712
Castro	751	1,685	2,033	1,007
Chambers	1,206	2,390	2,927	1,835
Cherokee	2,467	5,743	6,509	3,921
Childress	729	1,716	1,578	1,043
Clay	1,023	1,893	2,568	1,200
Cochran	415	1,106	1,031	701
Coke	358	761	844	517
Coleman	721	2,386	2,264	1,669
Collin	4,783	17,667	14,039	21,608
Collingsworth	501	1,250	1,169	629
Colorado	1,502	3,495	3,028	2,991
Comal	1,823	6,761	4,068	6,377
Comanche	1,176	2,608	3,414	1,297
Concho	350	709	715	474
Cooke	1,702	6,317	4,483	4,804
Coryell	1,235	5,077	4,710	4,140

	1972 (D)	1972 (R)	1976 (D)	1976 (R)
Cottle	571	564	1,047	311
Crane	349	1,123	664	963
Crockett	329	851	804	802
Crosby	1,021	1,503	2,176	897
Culberson	238	555	407	373
Dallam	327	1,271	1,029	936
Dallas	129,662	305,112	196,303	263,081
Dawson	846	3,247	2,162	2,474
Deaf Smith	1,240	3,690	2,613	2,776
Delta	581	957	1,563	421
Denton	9,720	19,138	18,887	20,440
DeWitt	1,357	3,755	2,540	2,754
Dickens	534	708	1,222	343
Dimmit	1,078	1,172	1,721	890
Donley	350	1,229	1,095	704
Duval	3,729	623	4,267	661
Eastland	1,630	4,106	4,320	2,340
Ector	5,449	21,386	10,802	18,973
Edwards	109	520	258	412
Ellis	3,839	8,779	9,991	6,996
El Paso	32,435	49,981	45,477	42,697
Erath	1,648	4,777	4,821	2,925
Falls	1,825	3,017	4,277	2,261
Fannin	2,295	3,826	5,845	2,102
Fayette	1,400	3,882	3,428	3,030
Fisher	933	1,207	1,993	573
Floyd	841	2,181	1,991	1,402
Foard	312	369	706	240
Fort Bend	4,541	10,475	11,264	17,354
Franklin	546	1,059	1,636	758
Freestone	1,283	2,459	2,679	1,674
Frio	1,588	1,904	2,598	1,280
Gaines	669	1,923	1,880	1,643
Galveston	22,565	30,936	37,873	25,251
Garza	446	1,153	957	755
Gillespie	526	3,490	1,260	3,541
Glasscock	75	288	190	218
Goliad	464	1,018	875	846
Gonzales	1,164	2,707	3,219	1,789
Gray	1,367	7,968	3,872	6,010
Grayson	6,952	16,769	17,015	11,981
Gregg	5,325	19,927	9,827	17,582
Grimes	1,116	2,243	2,656	1,473
Guadalupe	3,404	8,287	6,054	6,766
Hale	2,135	7,051	5,580	5,390
Hall	607	1,303	1,633	671
Hamilton	685	1,931	1,981	1,176
Hansford	202	1,947	983	1,401
Hardeman	614	1,357	1,403	805
Hardin	2,952	5,190	6,558	4,046
Harris	215,916	365,672	321,897	357,536
Harrison	4,333	9,600	7,796	7,787
Hartley	206	946	774	811
Haskell	950	1,744	2,512	838
Hays	4,068	5,406	7,005	5,714
Hemphill	214	942	707	858
Henderson	2,741	6,263	8,245	4,658
Hidalgo	18,366	22,920	35,021	19,199
Hill	1,882	4,481	5,327	2,680
Hockley	1,625	4,084	3,949	3,137
Hood	949	1,743	3,181	1,857
Hopkins	1,710	3,903	4,992	2,556
Houston	1,844	3,317	3,179	2,229
Howard	2,714	7,343	6,984	4,899
Hudspeth	250	467	479	395
Hunt	3,655	9,535	8,543	6,676
Hutchinson	1,405	7,411	3,691	6,137
Irion	111	363	297	302
Jack	775	1,719	1,814	1,049
Jackson	1,163	2,743	2,524	1,884
Jasper	2,746	4,575	5,422	3,167
Jeff Davis	202	382	309	288
Jefferson	29,909	45,819	47,581	32,451
Jim Hogg	848	765	1,645	429
Jim Wells	4,404	5,283	7,961	3,547
Johnson	3,968	10,042	10,864	7,194
Jones	1,050	3,202	3,318	2,072
Karnes	1,780	2,639	2,996	1,675
Kaufman	2,795	5,100	6,302	3,867
Kendall	484	2,681	1,190	2,543
Kenedy	88	124	139	65
Kent	223	465	474	171
Kerr	1,511	6,039	3,767	6,021
Kimble	266	971	759	846
King	75	143	100	96
Kinney	234	425	516	318
Kleberg	4,481	5,312	5,803	3,771
Knox	638	1,148	1,498	551
Lamar	2,865	7,736	8,601	4,443
Lamb	1,350	3,981	3,374	2,413
Lampasas	688	2,251	2,376	1,563
LaSalle	567	1,073	1,294	677
Lavaca	1,429	3,288	3,458	2,466
Lee	920	1,877	1,937	1,348
Leon	863	1,699	2,085	1,161
Liberty	3,311	6,111	7,086	4,552
Limestone	1,452	2,949	3,825	2,045
Lipscomb	156	1,226	644	911
Live Oak	610	1,745	1,656	1,287
Llano	766	2,164	2,361	1,947
Loving	7	55	35	47
Lubbock	15,353	43,564	24,797	38,478
Lynn	697	1,766	1,575	1,166
Madison	561	1,540	1,885	1,062
Marion	1,106	1,680	1,860	1,291
Martin	287	935	907	698
Mason	369	1,096	814	805
Matagorda	2,473	5,003	4,971	3,679
Maverick	1,710	1,477	2,840	924
McCulloch	753	1,769	1,888	1,300
McLennan	15,947	33,377	30,091	25,370
McMullen	88	304	194	217
Medina	1,507	4,059	3,681	3,252
Menard	273	644	543	441
Midland	4,388	18,905	7,725	19,178
Milam	2,159	3,554	4,871	2,404
Mills	388	1,089	1,012	684
Mitchell	699	1,790	1,730	1,058
Montague	1,286	3,463	4,087	2,182
Montgomery	4,358	15,067	13,718	15,739
Moore	863	3,620	2,767	2,759
Morris	1,162	2,699	3,071	1,843
Motley	230	657	522	428
Nacogdoches	3,656	8,757	6,697	7,315
Navarro	3,246	6,039	6,995	4,012
Newton	1,636	1,946	3,468	1,011
Nolan	1,338	3,634	3,094	2,431
Nueces	33,277	41,682	52,755	32,797
Ochiltree	298	2,861	1,084	2,471
Oldham	173	666	554	354
Orange	7,172	13,234	15,177	9,147
Palo Pinto	2,181	5,058	5,170	2,684
Panola	1,511	4,324	3,731	3,218
Parker	3,184	7,152	8,186	4,692
Parmer	495	2,304	1,914	1,487
Pecos	847	2,419	1,971	2,234
Polk	1,760	3,048	4,384	2,529
Potter	6,264	18,891	11,917	13,819
Presidio	674	785	1,232	687
Rains	532	865	1,339	510
Randall	3,470	18,557	9,074	17,115
Reagan	244	703	563	666
Real	150	483	510	448
Red River	1,361	3,112	3,670	1,852
Reeves	1,510	2,427	2,613	1,711
Refugio	1,060	1,937	2,218	1,537
Roberts	71	467	202	350
Robertson	1,976	1,977	3,741	1,244
Rockwall	610	1,890	1,828	2,087
Runnels	739	2,752	2,068	2,203
Rusk	2,867	8,179	6,063	6,800
Sabine	936	1,333	2,391	904
San Augustine	753	1,508	1,817	1,047
San Jacinto	1,020	1,296	2,406	1,094
San Patricio	5,097	7,179	9,469	5,853
San Saba	567	1,106	1,408	582
Schleicher	250	630	468	516
Scurry	1,223	3,777	2,639	2,797
Shackelford	331	909	764	748
Shelby	1,792	4,292	4,680	2,695
Sherman	169	996	718	679
Smith	8,041	23,671	16,856	22,238
Somervell	284	703	1,054	332
Starr	3,320	2,389	4,646	664
Stephens	678	2,259	1,796	1,621
Sterling	94	286	174	202
Stonewall	394	662	812	252
Sutton	245	705	768	831
Swisher	1,300	1,790	2,811	753
Tarrant	69,187	151,586	122,287	124,433
Taylor	6,024	22,417	14,453	19,822
Terrell	124	467	321	317
Terry	1,099	3,057	2,859	2,113
Throckmorton	348	568	658	356
Titus	1,703	3,671	4,205	2,603
Tom Green	6,082	15,784	11,064	12,316
Travis	54,147	70,561	78,585	71,031
Trinity	826	1,467	2,100	1,042
Tyler	1,321	2,955	3,322	1,965
Upshur	1,879	4,736	4,902	3,272
Upton	256	1,186	686	869
Uvalde	1,438	3,883	2,299	3,103
Val Verde	2,049	4,052	4,603	3,476
Van Zandt	1,939	4,839	6,449	3,385
Victoria	4,226	11,246	7,326	9,594
Walker	2,940	5,082	5,105	4,974
Waller	1,538	2,263	2,828	1,992
Ward	1,049	2,687	2,046	2,123
Washington	1,323	3,862	2,635	3,820
Webb	8,435	6,011	10,362	4,222
Wharton	3,481	6,271	5,914	4,682
Wheeler	502	1,766	1,598	1,273
Wichita	10,948	25,197	22,017	19,024
Wilbarger	1,139	3,183	3,280	2,145
Willacy	1,384	2,317	2,984	1,542
Williamson	3,806	6,998	9,355	7,481
Wilson	2,072	2,953	3,973	1,926
Winkler	602	2,467	1,382	1,842
Wise	1,741	4,230	5,133	2,856
Wood	1,842	4,746	4,107	3,076

	1972		1976	
	(D)	(R)	(D)	(R)
Yoakum	457	1,952	1,181	1,477
Young	1,486	3,353	3,473	2,652
Zapata	768	695	1,216	462
Zavala	1,122	1,288	1,822	735
Totals	**1,154,289**	**2,298,896**	**2,082,319**	**1,953,300**

Texas Vote Since 1932

1932 (Pres.), Roosevelt, Dem., 760,348; Hoover, Rep., 97,959; Thomas, Soc., 4,450; Harvey, Lib., 324; Foster, Com., 207; Jackson Party, 104.

1936 (Pres.), Roosevelt, Dem., 734,485; Landon, Rep., 103,874; Lemke, Union, 3,281; Thomas, Soc., 1,075; Colvin, Proh., 514; Browder, Com., 253.

1940 (Pres.), Roosevelt, Dem., 840,151; Willkie, Rep., 199,152; Babson, Proh., 925; Thomas, Soc., 728; Browder, Com., 212.

1944 (Pres.), Roosevelt, Dem., 821,605; Dewey, Rep., 191,425; Texas Regulars, 135,439; Watson, Proh., 1,017; Thomas, Soc., 594; America First, 250.

1948 (Pres.), Truman, Dem., 750,700; Dewey, Rep., 282,240; Thurmond, States' Rights, 106,909; Wallace, Prog., 3,764; Watson, Proh., 2,758; Thomas, Soc., 874.

1952 (Pres.), Eisenhower, Rep., 1,102,878; Stevenson, Dem., 969,228; Hamblen, Proh., 1,983; MacArthur, Christian Nationalist, 833; MacArthur, Constitution, 730; Hallinan, Prog., 294.

1956 (Pres.), Eisenhower, Rep., 1,080,619; Stevenson, Dem., 859,958; Andrews, Ind., 14,591.

1960 (Pres.), Kennedy, Dem., 1,167,932; Nixon, Rep., 1,121,699; Sullivan, Constitution, 18,169; Decker, Proh., 3,870; write-in, 15.

1964 (Pres.), Johnson, Dem., 1,663,185; Goldwater, Rep., 958,566; Lightburn, Constitution, 5,060.

1968 (Pres.), Nixon, Rep., 1,227,844; Humphrey, Dem., 1,266,804; Wallace, 3d party, 584,269; write-in, 489.

1972 (Pres.), Nixon, Rep., 2,298,896; McGovern, Dem., 1,154,289; Schmitz, American, 6,039; Jenness, Soc. Worker, 8,664; others, 3,393.

1976 (Pres.), Carter, Dem., 2,082,319; Ford, Rep., 1,953,300; McCarthy, Ind., 20,118; Anderson, American, 11,442; Camejo, Soc. Workers, 1,723; write-in, 2,982.

Utah

	1972		1976	
	McGovern	Nixon	Carter	Ford
County	(D)	(R)	(D)	(R)
Beaver	682	1,332	963	1,088
Box Elder	2,134	9,880	3,353	9,319
Cache	4,018	16,538	5,430	16,636
Carbon	3,335	3,956	5,157	3,360
Daggett	50	204	131	217
Davis	7,954	29,706	14,084	31,216
Duchesne	629	2,183	1,110	2,619
Emery	769	1,666	1,771	1,717
Garfield	242	1,290	539	1,163
Grand	560	1,837	931	1,781
Iron	1,098	5,085	1,700	4,757
Juab	691	1,629	1,091	1,290
Kane	218	1,146	330	1,094
Millard	777	2,689	1,224	2,484
Morgan	363	1,456	701	1,356
Piute	102	475	265	377
Rich	120	604	248	541
Salt Lake	64,489	132,066	86,659	144,100
San Juan	677	1,893	1,182	1,856
Sanpete	1,220	3,995	1,925	3,683
Sevier	820	3,700	1,564	3,686
Summit	836	2,209	1,282	2,316
Tooele	2,621	5,641	4,371	4,657
Unitah	716	4,712	1,342	4,017
Utah	10,828	42,179	18,327	49,328
Wasatch	693	2,046	1,092	1,940
Washington	956	5,176	1,893	5,944
Wayne	183	597	334	555
Weber	14,503	37,753	23,111	34,811
Totals	**126,284**	**323,643**	**182,110**	**337,908**

Utah Vote Since 1932

1932 (Pres.), Roosevelt, Dem., 116,750; Hoover, Rep., 84,795; Thomas, Soc., 4,087; Foster, Com., 947.

1936 (Pres.), Roosevelt, Dem., 150,246; Landon, Rep., 64,555; Lemke, Union, 1,121; Thomas, Soc., 432; Browder, Com., 280; Colvin, Proh., 43.

1940 (Pres.), Roosevelt, Dem., 154,277; Willkie, Rep., 93,151; Thomas, Soc., 200; Browder, Com., 191.

1944 (Pres.), Roosevelt, Dem., 150,088; Dewey, Rep., 97,891; Thomas, Soc., 340.

1948 (Pres.), Truman, Dem., 149,151; Dewey, Rep., 124,402; Wallace, Prog., 2,679; Dobbs, Soc. Workers, 73.

1952 (Pres.), Eisenhower, Rep., 194,190; Stevenson, Dem., 135,364.

1956 (Pres.), Eisenhower, Rep., 215,631; Stevenson, Dem., 118,364.

1960 (Pres.), Kennedy, Dem., 169,248; Nixon, Rep., 205,361; Dobbs, Soc. Workers, 100.

1964 (Pres.), Johnson, Dem., 219,628; Goldwater, Rep., 181,785.

1968 (Pres.), Nixon, Rep., 238,728; Humphrey, Dem., 156,665; Wallace, 3d party, 26,906; Halstead, Soc. Worker, 89; Peace and Freedom, 180.

1972 (Pres.), Nixon, Rep., 323,643; McGovern, Dem., 126,284; Schmitz, American, 28,549.

1976 (Pres.), Carter, Dem., 182,110; Ford, Rep., 337,908; Anderson, American, 13,304; McCarthy, Ind., 3,907; MacBride, Libertarian, 2,438; Maddox, Am. Ind., 1,162; Camejo, Soc. Workers, 268; Hall, Comm., 121.

Vermont

	1972		1976	
	McGovern	Nixon	Carter	Ford
County	(D)	(R)	(D&IV)	(R)
Addison	3,262	6,467	4,164	5,726
Bennington	4,804	7,542	5,443	6,712
Caledonia	3,094	6,762	3,511	5,488
Chittenden	16,163	23,063	17,992	22,013
Essex	655	1,441	1,002	1,161
Franklin	3,898	8,109	5,610	6,190
Grand Isle	743	1,259	866	1,004
Lamoille	1,659	4,164	2,016	3,535
Orange	2,332	5,389	3,171	4,768
Orleans	2,793	4,906	3,561	4,075
Rutland	8,261	14,143	7,613	9,867
Washington	7,596	12,421	8,764	10,919
Windham	5,925	9,062	6,794	7,928
Windsor	6,989	12,421	8,282	11,001
Totals	**68,174**	**117,149**	**78,789**	**100,387**

Vermont Vote Since 1932

1932 (Pres.), Roosevelt, Dem., 56,266; Hoover, Rep., 78,984; Thomas, Soc., 1,533; Foster, Com., 195.

1936 (Pres.), Landon, Rep., 81,023; Roosevelt, Dem., 62,124; Browder, Com., 405.

1940 (Pres.), Roosevelt, Dem., 64,269, Willkie, Rep., 78,371; Browder, Com., 411.

1944 (Pres.), Roosevelt, Dem., 53,820; Dewey, Rep., 71,527.

1948 (Pres.), Truman, Dem., 45,557; Dewey, Rep., 75,926; Wallace, Prog., 1,279; Thomas, Soc., 585.

1952 (Pres.), Eisenhower, Rep., 109,717; Stevenson, Dem., 43,355; Hallinan, Prog., 282; Hoopes, Soc., 185.

1956 (Pres.), Eisenhower, Rep., 110,390; Stevenson, Dem., 42,549; scattered, 39.

1960 (Pres.), Kennedy, Dem., 69,186; Nixon, Rep., 98,131.

1964 (Pres.), Johnson, Dem., 107,674; Goldwater, Rep., 54,868.

1968 (Pres.), Nixon, Rep., 85,142; Humphrey, Dem., 70,255; Wallace, 3d party, 5,104; Halstead, Soc. Worker, 295; Gregory, New Party, 579.

1972 (Pres.), Nixon, Rep., 117,149; McGovern, Dem., 68,174; Spock, Liberty Union, 1,010; Jenness, Soc. Worker, 296; scattered, 318.

1976 (Pres.), Carter, Dem., 77,798; Carter, Ind. Vermonter, 991; Ford, Rep., 100,387; McCarthy, Ind., 4,001; Camejo, Soc. Workers, 430; LaRouche, U.S. Labor, 196; scattered, 99.

Virginia

	1972		1976	
	McGovern	Nixon	Carter	Ford
County	(D)	(R)	(D)	(R)
Accomack	2,406	6,496	4,807	4,494
Albemarle	4,303	8,447	7,310	9,084
Alleghany	1,069	2,584	2,462	1,756

	1972 (D)	1972 (R)	1976 (D)	1976 (R)
Amelia	778	1,606	1,715	1,634
Amherst	1,512	4,909	3,675	3,956
Appomattox	684	2,788	1,702	1,964
Arlington	25,877	39,406	32,536	30,972
Augusta	1,766	9,106	5,626	8,452
Bath	462	1,127	1,029	888
Bedford	1,501	5,286	4,766	4,189
Bland	527	1,352	961	1,047
Botetourt	1,519	3,806	4,021	3,343
Brunswick	2,130	3,072	3,071	2,387
Buchanan	3,566	4,801	5,791	3,850
Buckingham	1,186	2,107	2,179	1,487
Campbell	2,055	11,676	4,354	7,442
Caroline	1,814	2,086	3,064	1,648
Carroll	1,583	5,247	4,010	4,820
Charles City	1,177	535	1,455	439
Charlotte	1,182	2,501	2,312	2,023
Chesterfield	3,823	24,934	14,126	27,812
Clarke	715	1,816	1,276	1,440
Craig	425	774	1,103	546
Culpeper	1,316	3,707	2,892	3,659
Cumberland	969	1,371	1,302	1,284
Dickenson	2,711	3,633	4,583	3,471
Dinwiddie	1,901	3,314	3,873	2,413
Essex	808	1,482	1,306	1,380
Fairfax	54,844	112,135	92,037	110,424
Fauquier	2,039	4,654	4,002	4,715
Floyd	708	2,444	1,728	2,071
Fluvanna	637	1,438	1,415	1,296
Franklin	2,273	4,674	6,439	3,532
Frederick	1,604	5,367	3,389	5,162
Giles	1,869	3,671	3,779	2,731
Gloucester	1,292	3,642	3,156	3,025
Goochland	1,254	2,127	2,259	2,104
Grayson	1,603	3,565	3,146	3,021
Greene	318	1,208	895	1,095
Greensville	1,197	1,608	2,413	1,137
Halifax	2,384	5,469	4,352	4,045
Hanover	2,200	11,095	6,069	11,559
Henrico	8,420	52,536	21,729	45,405
Henry	4,042	7,556	9,680	5,612
Highland	206	774	493	629
Isle of Wight	2,305	3,555	4,145	2,718
James City	1,992	3,372	3,000	3,186
King George	658	1,675	1,513	1,383
King and Queen	708	1,033	1,111	778
King William	797	1,839	1,501	1,597
Lancaster	1,009	2,683	1,581	2,381
Lee	2,825	4,957	5,415	4,679
Loudoun	3,941	9,417	7,995	9,192
Louisa	1,338	2,545	2,857	2,151
Lunenburg	1,044	2,464	1,739	1,816
Madison	639	1,864	1,466	1,710
Mathews	730	2,164	1,309	1,908
Mecklenburg	2,804	6,381	4,076	4,423
Middlesex	724	1,697	1,312	1,608
Montgomery	3,692	9,348	7,539	7,971
Nelson	954	2,145	2,426	1,516
New Kent	633	1,370	1,338	1,259
Northampton	1,246	2,587	2,459	2,043
Northumberland	884	2,332	1,814	2,167
Nottoway	1,308	2,979	2,558	2,486
Orange	1,032	2,758	2,309	2,549
Page	1,585	4,326	3,401	3,780
Patrick	942	2,951	2,740	2,349
Pittsylvania	4,429	12,108	7,929	9,173
Powhatan	810	1,751	1,528	2,010
Prince Edward	1,585	3,199	2,448	2,734
Prince George	1,084	2,405	2,630	2,254
Prince William	7,266	20,149	15,215	15,446
Pulaski	2,311	6,281	5,546	4,764
Rappahannock	471	1,055	1,071	881
Richmond	435	1,565	864	1,391
Roanoke	5,318	19,920	13,120	13,587
Rockbridge	956	3,009	2,525	2,157
Rockingham	2,026	10,025	5,349	9,768
Russell	3,367	5,010	6,014	4,287
Scott	2,474	5,125	4,496	4,313
Shenandoah	1,422	7,128	3,364	6,296
Smyth	2,280	6,409	5,246	5,032
Southampton	1,498	3,225	3,399	2,366
Spotsylvania	1,775	3,577	4,210	3,210
Stafford	1,901	5,222	4,900	4,451
Surry	988	1,067	1,829	929
Sussex	1,645	2,120	2,497	1,360
Tazewell	3,181	7,233	7,565	5,565
Warren	1,508	3,718	3,221	2,985
Washington	3,028	8,805	6,547	6,865
Westmoreland	1,113	2,331	2,355	1,909
Wise	4,402	6,739	7,134	5,691
Wythe	1,431	4,553	3,578	4,231
York	2,302	7,745	4,736	5,603
Total	**251,451**	**621,848**	**489,208**	**540,351**
CITIES				
Alexandria	15,409	20,235	19,858	16,880
Bedford	529	1,407	1,122	1,043
Bristol	1,157	2,665	3,343	2,943
Buena Vista	373	990	993	771
Charlottesville	5,240	7,935	6,846	6,673
Chesapeake	7,289	17,722	17,651	12,851
Clifton Forge	575	1,127	993	770
Colonial Heights	541	5,304	2,409	4,291
Covington	948	1,910	1,820	1,173
Danville	4,148	12,463	6,425	10,235
Emporia	565	1,340	899	1,055
Fairfax	2,274	5,063	3,464	4,174
Falls Church	1,895	2,967	2,202	2,323
Franklin	738	1,416	1,116	1,127
Fredericksburg	1,702	3,211	2,550	2,527
Galax	524	1,497	1,218	1,128
Hampton	10,648	21,897	19,202	15,021
Harrisonburg	992	3,626	1,803	3,376
Hopewell	1,485	5,229	3,691	3,764
Lexington	695	1,345	945	1,027
Lynchburg	4,208	13,259	8,227	14,564
Manassas	N.A.	N.A.	1,646	1,992
Manassas Park	N.A.	N.A.	709	444
Martinsville	2,292	3,879	3,491	3,147
Newport News	12,233	27,169	23,058	20,914
Norfolk	25,737	38,385	39,295	28,099
Norton	463	823	811	577
Petersburg	5,156	6,710	7,852	5,041
Poquoson	N.A.	N.A.	1,140	1,461
Portsmouth	13,124	20,090	22,837	12,872
Radford	1,121	2,577	2,240	1,844
Richmond	33,055	46,244	44,687	37,176
Roanoke	9,498	18,541	20,696	14,738
Salem	1,744	5,649	4,404	4,196
South Boston	709	1,865	1,001	1,389
Staunton	1,416	5,531	2,951	4,681
Suffolk	4,827	7,502	9,246	6,066
Virginia Beach	10,373	38,074	25,824	34,593
Waynesboro	1,061	4,163	2,209	3,528
Williamsburg	1,274	1,786	1,468	1,654
Winchester	1,418	4,647	2,346	4,075
Total	**187,436**	**366,645**	**324,688**	**296,203**
Aggregate	**438,887**	**988,493**	**813,896**	**836,554**

Virginia Vote Since 1932

1932 (Pres.), Roosevelt, Dem., 203,979; Hoover, Rep., 89,637; Thomas, Soc., 2,382; Upshaw, Proh., 1,843; Foster, Com., 86; Cox, Ind., 15.

1936 (Pres.), Roosevelt, Dem., 234,980; Landon, Rep., 98,366; Colvin, Proh., 594; Thomas, Soc., 313; Lemke, Union, 233; Browder, Com., 98.

1940 (Pres.), Roosevelt, Dem., 235,961; Willkie, Rep., 109,363; Babson, Proh., 882; Thomas, Soc., 282; Browder, Com., 71; Aiken, Soc. Lab., 48.

1944 (Pres.), Roosevelt, Dem., 242,276; Dewey, Rep., 145,243; Watson, Proh., 459; Thomas, Soc., 417; Teichert, Soc. Lab., 90.

1948 (Pres.), Truman, Dem., 200,786; Dewey, Rep., 172,070; Thurmond, States' Rights, 43,393; Wallace, Prog., 2,047; Thomas, Soc., 726; Teichert, Soc. Lab., 234.

1952 (Pres.), Eisenhower, Rep., 349,037; Stevenson, Dem., 268,677; Haas, Soc. Lab., 1,160; Hoopes, Social Dem., 504; Hallinan, Prog., 311.

1956 (Pres.), Eisenhower, Rep., 386,459; Stevenson, Dem., 267,760; Andrews, States' Rights, 42,964; Hoopes, Soc. Dem., 444; Haas, Soc. Lab., 351.

1960 (Pres.), Kennedy, Dem., 362,327; Nixon, Rep., 404,521; Coiner, Conservative, 4,204; Haas, Soc. Lab., 397.

1964 (Pres.), Johnson, Dem., 558,038; Goldwater, Rep., 481,334; Haas, Soc. Lab., 2,895.

1968 (Pres.), Nixon, Rep., 590,319; Humphrey, Dem., 442,387; Wallace, 3d party, *320,272; Blomen, Soc. Labor, 4,671; Munn, Prohibition, 601; Gregory, Peace and Freedom, 1,680.

*10,561 votes for Wallace were omitted in the count.

1972 (Pres.), Nixon, Rep., 988,493; McGovern, Dem., 438,887; Schmitz, American, 19,721; Fisher, Soc. Labor, 9,918.

1976 (Pres.), Carter, Dem., 813,896; Ford, Rep., 836,554; Camejo, Soc. Workers, 17,802; Anderson, American, 16,686; LaRouche, U.S. Labor, 7,508; MacBride, Libertarian, 4,648.

Washington

County	1972 McGovern (D)	1972 Nixon (R)	1976 Carter (D)	1976 Ford (R)
Adams	1,110	3,083	1,790	2,795
Asotin	2,559	2,911	2,898	2,752
Benton	9,824	18,517	11,306	22,135
Chelan	5,889	10,470	7,623	10,492

	1972		1976	
	(D)	(R)	(D)	(R)
Clallam	5,620	9,372	8,268	9,132
Clark	27,179	28,775	31,080	27,938
Columbia	533	1,445	829	1,153
Cowlitz	12,682	14,431	14,958	12,531
Douglas	2,420	4,512	3,809	4,547
Ferry	560	815	814	776
Franklin	3,867	5,972	4,369	5,671
Garfield	481	1,004	616	892
Grant	5,487	9,370	7,777	9,192
Grays Harbor	11,786	10,839	13,478	9,464
Island	3,149	7,495	5,859	7,804
Jefferson	2,096	2,770	2,913	2,794
King	212,509	298,707	248,743	279,382
Kitsap	17,011	25,831	25,701	23,124
Kittitas	4,299	5,464	4,858	4,765
Klickitat	2,293	3,061	2,890	2,573
Lewis	6,946	12,071	9,026	10,933
Lincoln	1,453	3,647	1,978	2,925
Mason	3,907	4,873	6,060	4,758
Okanogan	3,835	5,796	5,543	5,455
Pacific	3,585	3,349	4,278	2,781
Pend Oreille	1,071	1,746	1,533	1,516
Pierce	56,933	84,265	78,238	74,668
San Juan	906	1,786	1,467	1,998
Skagit	9,233	14,212	12,718	13,060
Skamania	1,153	1,288	1,436	1,102
Snohomish	39,471	60,032	55,623	55,375
Spokane	44,337	74,320	55,660	68,290
Stevens	2,390	4,839	3,824	4,719
Thurston	14,596	22,297	21,247	21,000
Wahkiakum	796	818	942	704
Walla Walla	5,364	12,579	7,012	10,883
Whatcom	15,027	22,585	19,739	20,007
Whitman	6,248	9,548	6,197	8,168
Yakima	19,729	32,240	24,223	29,478
Totals	**568,334**	**837,135**	**717,323**	**777,732**

Washington Vote Since 1932

1932 (Pres.), Roosevelt, Dem., 353,260; Hoover, Rep., 208,645; Harvey, Lib., 30,308; Thomas, Soc., 17,080; Foster, Com., 2,972; Upshaw, Proh., 1,540; Reynolds, Soc. Lab., 1,009.

1936 (Pres.), Roosevelt, Dem., 459,579; Landon, Rep., 206,892; Lemke, Union, 17,463; Thomas, Soc., 3,496; Browder, Com., 1,907; Pellsy, Christian, 1,598; Colvin, Proh., 1,041; Aiken, Soc. Lab., 362.

1940 (Pres.), Roosevelt, Dem., 462,145; Willkie, Rep., 322,123; Thomas, Soc., 4,586; Browder, Com., 2,626; Babson, Proh., 1,686; Aiken, Soc. Lab., 667.

1944 (Pres.), Roosevelt, Dem., 486,774; Dewey, Rep., 361,689; Thomas, Soc., 3,824; Watson, Proh., 2,396; Teichert, Soc. Lab., 1,645.

1948 (Pres.), Truman, Dem., 476,165; Dewey, Rep., 386,315; Wallace, Prog., 31,692; Watson, Proh., 6,117; Thomas, Soc., 3,534; Teichert, Soc. Lab., 1,133; Dobbs, Soc. Workers, 103.

1952 (Pres.), Eisenhower, Rep., 599,107; Stevenson, Dem., 492,845; MacArthur, Christian Nationalist, 7,290; Hallinan, Prog., 2,460; Haas, Soc. Lab., 633; Hoopes, Soc., 254; Dobbs, Soc. Workers, 119.

1956 (Pres.), Eisenhower, Rep., 620,430; Stevenson, Dem., 523,002; Haas, Soc. Lab., 7,457.

1960 (Pres.), Kennedy, Dem., 599,298; Nixon, Rep., 629,273; Haas, Soc. Lab., 10,895; Curtis, Constitution, 1,401; Dobbs, Soc. Workers, 705.

1964 (Pres.), Johnson, Dem., 779,699; Goldwater, Rep., 470,366; Haas, Soc. Labor, 7,772; DeBerry, Freedom Soc., 537.

1968 (Pres.), Nixon, Rep., 588,510; Humphrey, Dem., 616,037; Wallace, 3d party, 96,990; Blomen, Soc. Labor, 488; Cleaver, Peace and Freedom, 1,609; Halstead, Soc. Worker, 270; Mitchell, Free Ballot, 377.

1972 (Pres.), Nixon, Rep., 837,135; McGovern, Dem., 568,334; Schmitz, American, 58,906; Spock, Ind., 2,644; Fisher, Soc. Labor, 1,102; Jenness, Soc. Worker, 623; Hall, Communist, 566; Hospers, Libertarian, 1,537.

1976 (Pres.), Carter, Dem., 717,323; Ford, Rep., 777,732; McCarthy, Ind., 36,986; Maddox, Amer. Ind., 8,585; Anderson, American, 5,046; MacBride, Libertarian, 5,042; Wright, People's, 1,124; Camejo, Soc. Workers, 905; LaRouche, U.S. Labor, 903; Hall, Comm., 817; Levin, Soc. Labor, 713; Zeidler, Socialist, 358.

West Virginia

County	1972 McGovern (D)	1972 Nixon (R)	1976 Carter (D)	1976 Ford (R)
Barbour	2,258	4,432	3,647	3,235
Berkeley	4,523	10,954	8,216	8,935
Boone	5,342	5,985	8,528	3,072
Braxton	2,771	3,155	4,012	1,913
Brooke	5,226	7,544	8,197	4,792
Cabell	14,312	29,582	20,811	19,644
Calhoun	1,528	1,992	2,173	1,283
Clay	1,830	2,168	2,662	1,282
Doddridge	645	2,284	1,245	1,804
Fayette	9,966	11,876	15,496	5,459
Gilmer	1,359	2,056	2,245	1,371
Grant	614	3,556	1,323	2,976
Greenbrier	4,423	8,827	8,291	5,862
Hampshire	1,637	3,084	3,104	2,097
Hancock	6,727	10,634	10,627	6,771
Hardy	1,510	2,690	2,993	1,858
Harrison	12,910	22,196	21,467	15,172
Jackson	3,007	7,226	5,334	5,360
Jefferson	2,782	4,822	5,166	3,864
Kanawha	38,032	65,021	53,602	42,213
Lewis	2,062	5,778	3,960	3,736
Lincoln	3,876	4,673	5,260	2,997
Logan	10,045	9,533	13,122	4,021
Marion	11,864	16,095	17,800	10,391
Marshall	6,378	10,966	8,641	6,705
Mason	4,008	7,129	6,769	5,205
McDowell	7,826	17,846	10,557	4,107
Mercer	3,276	7,157	14,761	10,791
Mineral	5,585	7,484	5,898	5,130
Mingo	10,721	16,758	8,655	3,010
Monongalia	2,114	3,716	16,163	11,827
Monroe	1,118	3,014	3,297	2,750
Morgan	6,811	8,942	1,929	2,369
Nicholas	3,628	5,907	6,235	3,462
Ohio	10,491	18,435	11,817	12,476
Pendleton	1,248	2,207	2,104	1,554
Pleasants	1,207	2,025	1,699	1,608
Pocahontas	1,635	2,391	2,330	1,740
Preston	2,977	7,807	5,595	5,719
Putnam	4,771	8,265	8,226	6,334
Raleigh	10,586	19,150	19,768	10,637
Randolph	3,809	6,923	7,265	4,822
Ritchie	990	3,635	1,941	2,874
Roane	2,386	4,253	3,519	3,216
Summers	2,518	3,895	3,943	2,254
Taylor	2,085	4,385	3,905	2,891
Tucker	1,457	2,163	2,323	1,396
Tyler	1,125	3,362	1,817	2,514
Upshur	1,795	6,449	3,513	4,789
Wayne	6,251	9,775	9,958	6,009
Webster	2,069	2,114	2,931	971
Wetzel	3,276	6,046	5,042	3,793
Wirt	691	1,442	1,182	1,031
Wood	10,886	27,315	17,025	18,348
Wyoming	4,468	7,926	7,775	4,286
Totals	**277,435**	**484,964**	**435,864**	**314,726**

West Virginia Vote Since 1932

1932 (Pres.), Roosevelt, Dem., 405,124; Hoover, Rep., 330,731; Thomas, Soc., 5,133; Upshaw, Proh., 2,342; Foster, Com., 444.

1936 (Pres.), Roosevelt, Dem., 502,582; Landon, Rep., 325,358; Colvin, Prog., 1,173; Thomas, Soc., 832.

1940 (Pres.), Roosevelt, Dem., 495,662; Willkie, Rep., 372,414.

1944 (Pres.), Roosevelt, Dem., 392,777; Dewey, Rep., 322,819.

1948 (Pres.), Truman, Dem., 429,188; Dewey, Rep., 316,251; Wallace, Prog., 3,311.

1952 (Pres.), Eisenhower, Rep., 419,970; Stevenson, Dem., 453,578.

1956 (Pres.), Eisenhower, Rep., 449,297; Stevenson, Dem., 381,534.

1960 (Pres.), Kennedy, Dem., 441,786; Nixon, Rep., 395,995.

1964 (Pres.), Johnson, Dem., 538,087; Goldwater, Rep., 253,953.

1968 (Pres.), Nixon, Rep., 307,555; Humphrey, Dem., 374,091; Wallace, 3d party, 72,560.

1972 (Pres.), Nixon, Rep., 484,964; McGovern, Dem., 277,435.

1976 (Pres.), Carter, Dem., 435,864; Ford, Rep., 314,726.

Wisconsin

County	1972 McGovern (D)	1972 Nixon (R)	1976 Carter (D)	1976 Ford (R)
dams	1,833	2,200	3,089	2,377
shland	3,771	3,478	4,688	3,045
arron	5,376	8,418	8,678	7,393
ayfield	2,736	3,045	3,885	2,624
rown	26,511	37,101	33,572	36,571
uffalo	2,461	3,079	3,448	2,844
urnett	2,389	2,972	3,720	2,573
alumet	4,804	6,446	6,241	6,589
hippewa	8,210	8,451	11,538	8,137
lark	4,617	7,138	7,238	6,095
olumbia	7,083	10,122	9,457	10,075
rawford	2,487	3,705	3,629	3,393
ane	79,567	56,020	82,321	63,466
odge	9,898	17,068	13,643	17,335
oor	3,430	6,503	4,553	6,557
ouglas	11,054	8,419	13,478	6,999
unn	5,681	6,660	7,882	6,751
au Claire	14,300	15,883	18,263	16,388
lorence	757	971	965	922
ond duLac	N.A.	N.A.	16,571	22,226
orest	1,678	1,856	2,574	1,604
rant	6,915	11,873	9,639	12,016
reen	3,634	7,422	5,632	7,085
reen Lake	2,174	5,046	3,411	5,020
wa	3,131	4,387	4,252	4,195
on	1,648	1,723	2,399	1,340
ackson	2,445	3,937	3,735	3,406
efferson	9,303	14,621	12,577	15,528
uneau	2,943	4,833	4,512	4,242
enosha	19,441	24,041	27,585	22,349
ewaunee	3,360	4,802	4,607	4,447
a Crosse	12,152	21,992	16,674	24,188
a Fayette	2,804	4,898	3,839	4,131
anglade	3,011	4,368	4,134	4,630
incoln	4,175	6,206	5,800	5,672
lanitowoc	16,489	16,599	19,819	16,039
larathon	18,500	21,454	24,934	21,898
larinette	5,900	8,740	8,482	8,591
larquette	1,537	2,682	2,516	2,607
lenominee	608	355	766	324
lilwaukee	210,802	191,874	249,739	192,008
lonroe	3,640	7,625	6,465	7,242
conto	4,041	6,511	6,541	6,232
neida	4,262	6,811	7,216	7,347
utagamie	17,477	27,533	23,079	28,363
zaukee	8,503	15,759	11,271	19,817
epin	1,409	1,458	1,955	1,312
ierce	5,611	5,899	8,039	5,676
olk	5,738	6,567	8,485	6,159
ortage	13,564	9,346	15,912	9,520
rice	2,831	3,694	4,028	3,204
acine	27,778	38,490	36,740	37,088
ichland	2,492	5,062	3,634	4,466
ock	21,033	30,361	28,048	28,325
usk	3,075	3,007	4,050	2,724
t. Croix	7,488	8,553	10,601	7,685
auk	6,980	10,285	9,204	9,577
awyer	1,765	3,081	3,055	2,720
hawano	3,940	8,807	6,751	8,505
heboygan	21,114	21,500	24,226	22,332
aylor	2,934	4,125	4,101	3,591
rempealeau	4,232	5,723	6,218	5,341
ernon	3,407	6,836	5,534	6,132
ilas	1,907	4,422	3,209	4,929
Valworth	8,598	17,823	12,418	18,091
Vashburn	2,336	3,220	3,503	2,787
Vashington	10,434	15,338	14,422	18,798
Vaukesha	34,573	59,399	47,487	70,418
Vaupaca	4,418	11,040	6,857	10,849
Vaushara	2,094	4,466	3,485	4,449
Vinnebago	20,450	29,488	24,485	32,149
Vood	10,415	14,806	14,728	15,479
Totals	**810,174**	**989,430**	**1,040,232**	**1,004,987**

Wisconsin Vote Since 1932

932 (Pres.), Roosevelt, Dem., 707,410; Hoover, Rep., 347,741; Thomas, Soc., 53,379; Foster, Com., 3,112; Upshaw, Proh., 2,672; Reynolds, Soc., Lab., 494.

936 (Pres.), Roosevelt, Dem., 802,984; Landon, Rep., 380,828; Lemke, Union, 60,297; Thomas, Soc., 10,-626; Browder, Com., 2,197; Colvin, Proh., 1,071; Aiken, Soc. Lab., 557.

940 (Pres.), Roosevelt, Dem., 704,821; Willkie, Rep., 679,260; Thomas, Soc., 15,071; Browder, Com., 2,394; Babson, Proh., 2,148; Aiken, Soc. Lab., 1,882.

944 (Pres.), Roosevelt, Dem., 650,413; Dewey, Rep., 674,532; Thomas, Soc., 13,205; Teichert, Soc. Lab., 1,002.

948 (Pres.), Truman, Dem., 647,310; Dewey, Rep., 590,959; Wallace, Prog., 25,282; Thomas, Soc., 12,-547; Teichert, Soc.Lab., 399; Dobbs, Soc.Work., 303.

1952 (Pres.), Eisenhower, Rep., 979,744; Stevenson, Dem., 622,175; Hallinan, Ind., 2,174; Dobbs, Ind., 1,350; Hoopes, Ind., 1,157; Haas, Ind., 770.

1956 (Pres.), Eisenhower, Rep., 954,844; Stevenson, Dem., 586,768; Andrews, Ind., 6,918; Hoopes, Soc., 754; Haas, Soc. Lab., 710; Dobbs, Soc. Workers, 564.

1960 (Pres.), Kennedy, Dem., 830,805; Nixon, Rep., 895,175; Dobbs, Soc. Workers, 1,792; Haas, Soc. Lab., 1,310.

1964 (Pres.), Johnson, Dem., 1,050,424; Goldwater, Rep., 638,495; DeBerry, Soc. Worker, 1,692; Haas, Soc. Lab., 1,204.

1968 (Pres.), Nixon, Rep., 809,997; Humphrey, Dem., 748,804; Wallace, 3d party, 127,835; Blomen, Soc. Labor, 1,338; Halstead, Soc. Worker, 1,222; scattered, 2,342.

1972 (Pres.), Nixon, Rep., 989,430; McGovern, Dem., 810,174; Schmitz, American, 47,525; Spock, Ind., 2,701; Fisher, Soc. Labor, 998; Hall, Communist, 663; Reed, Ind., 506; scattered, 893.

1976 (Pres.), Carter, Dem., 1,040,232; Ford, Rep., 1,004,987; McCarthy, Ind., 34,943; Maddox, Amer. Ind., 8,552; Zeidler, Socialist, 4,298; MacBride, Liber., 3,814; Camejo, Soc. Work., 1,691; Wright, People's, 943; Hall, Comm., 749; LaRouche, U.S. Lab., 738; Levin, Soc. Lab., 389; Scattered, 2,839.

Wyoming

County	1972 McGovern (D)	1972 Nixon (R)	1976 Carter (D)	1976 Ford (R)
Albany	4,873	7,021	4,663	6,734
Big Horn	1,049	3,244	1,618	3,117
Campbell	783	2,953	1,620	3,306
Carbon	2,292	4,037	3,010	3,556
Converse	682	2,312	1,150	2,188
Crook	339	1,760	653	1,438
Fremont	3,248	7,359	4,423	6,584
Goshen	1,515	3,629	2,262	2,764
Hot Springs	689	1,678	958	1,413
Johnson	436	2,203	797	2,042
Laramie	7,791	15,010	12,040	14,061
Lincoln	969	2,459	1,555	2,464
Natrona	6,514	15,649	8,640	13,761
Niobrara	289	1,245	427	1,042
Park	1,950	5,890	2,656	5,878
Platte	925	2,200	1,593	1,844
Sheridan	2,874	6,432	3,206	5,382
Sublette	304	1,348	528	1,284
Sweetwater	3,713	5,175	5,575	4,937
Teton	810	2,182	1,204	2,667
Uinta	968	2,011	1,559	2,124
Washakie	825	2,604	1,168	2,361
Weston	520	2,063	934	1,770
Totals	**44,358**	**100,464**	**62,239**	**92,717**

Wyoming Vote Since 1932

1932 (Pres.), Roosevelt, Dem., 54,370; Hoover, Rep., 39,583; Thomas, Soc. 2,829; Foster, Com., 180.

1936 (Pres.), Roosevelt, Dem., 62,624; Landon, Rep., 38,739; Lemke, Union, 1,653; Thoms, Soc., 200; Browder, Com., 91; Colvin, Proh., 75.

1940 (Pres.), Roosevelt, Dem., 59,287; Willkie, Rep., 52,633; Babson, Proh., 172; Thomas, Soc., 148.

1944 (Pres.), Roosevelt, Dem., 49,419; Dewey, Rep., 51,921.

1948 (Pres.), Truman, Dem., 52,354; Dewey, Rep., 47,-947; Wallace, Prog., 931; Thomas, Soc., 137; Teichert, Soc. Lab., 56.

1952 (Pres.), Eisenhower, Rep., 81,047; Stevenson, Dem., 47,934; Hamblen, Proh., 194; Hoopes, Soc., 40; Haas, Soc. Lab., 36.

1956 (Pres.), Eisenhower, Rep., 74,573; Stevenson, Dem., 49,554.

1960 (Pres.), Kennedy, Dem., 63,331; Nixon, Rep., 77,-451.

1964 (Pres.), Johnson, Dem., 80,718; Goldwater, Rep., 61,998.

1968 (Pres.), Nixon, Rep., 70,927; Humphrey, Dem., 45,173; Wallace, 3d party, 11,105.

1972 (Pres.), Nixon, Rep., 100,464; McGovern, Dem., 44,358; Schmitz, American, 748.

1976 (Pres.), Carter, Dem., 62,239; Ford, Rep., 92,717; McCarthy, Ind., 624; Reagan, Ind., 307; Anderson, Amer., 290; MacBride, Libertarian, 89; Brown, Ind., 47; Maddox, Amer. Ind., 30.

Major Parties' Popular and Electoral Vote for President

(F) Federalist; (D) Democrat; (R) Republican; (DR) Democrat Republican; (NR) National Republican; (W) Whig; (P) People's; (PR) Progressive; (SR) States' Rights; (LR) Liberal Republican; Asterisk (*)—See notes.

Year	President Elected	Popular	Elec.	Losing Candidate	Popular	Elec
1789	George Washington (F)	Unknown	69	No opposition		
1792	George Washington (F)	Unknown	132	No opposition		
1796	John Adams (F)	Unknown	71	Thomas Jefferson (DR)	Unknown	68
1800*	Thomas Jefferson (DR)	Unknown	73	Aaron Burr (DR)	Unknown	73
1804	Thomas Jefferson (DR)	Unknown	162	Charles Pinckney (F)	Unknown	14
1808	James Madison (DR)	Unknown	122	Charles Pinckney (F)	Unknown	47
1812	James Madison (DR)	Unknown	128	DeWitt Clinton (F)	Unknown	89
1816	James Monroe (DR)	Unknown	183	Rufus King (F)	Unknown	34
1820	James Monroe (DR)	Unknown	231	John Quincy Adams (DR)	Unknown	[illegible]
1824*	John Quincy Adams (NR)	105,321	84	Andrew Jackson (D)	155,872	99
				Henry Clay (DR)	46,587	37
				William H. Crawford (DR)	44,282	41
1828	Andrew Jackson (D)	647,231	178	John Quincy Adams (NR)	509,097	83
1832	Andrew Jackson (D)	687,502	219	Henry Clay (DR)	530,189	49
1836	Martin Van Buren (D)	762,678	170	William H. Harrison (W)	548,007	73
1840	William H. Harrison (W)	1,275,017	234	Martin Van Buren (D)	1,128,702	60
1844	James K. Polk (D)	1,337,243	170	Henry Clay (W)	1,299,068	105
1848	Zachary Taylor (W)	1,360,101	163	Lewis Cass (D)	1,220,544	127
1852	Franklin Pierce (D)	1,601,474	254	Winfield Scott (W)	1,386,578	42
1856	James C. Buchanan (D)	1,927,995	174	John C. Fremont (R)	1,391,555	114
1860	Abraham Lincoln (R)	1,866,352	180	Stephen A. Douglas (D)	1,375,157	12
				John C. Breckinridge (D)	845,763	72
				John Bell (Const. Union)	589,581	39
1864	Abraham Lincoln (R)	2,216,067	212	George McClellan (D)	1,808,725	21
1868	Ulysses S. Grant (R)	3,015,071	214	Horatio Seymour (D)	2,709,615	80
1872*	Ulysses S. Grant (R)	3,597,070	286	Horace Greeley (D-LR)	2,834,079	...
1876*	Rutherford B. Hayes (R)	4,033,950	185	Samuel J. Tilden (D)	4,284,757	18
1880	James A. Garfield (R)	4,449,053	214	Winfield S. Hancock (D)	4,442,030	15
1884	Grover Cleveland (D)	4,911,017	219	James G. Blaine (R)	4,848,334	18
1888*	Benjamin Harrison (R)	5,444,337	233	Grover Cleveland (D)	5,540,050	16
1892	Grover Cleveland (D)	5,554,414	277	Benjamin Harrison (R)	5,190,802	14
				James Weaver (P)	1,027,329	22
1896	William McKinley (R)	7,035,638	271	William J. Bryan (D-P)	6,467,946	17
1900	William McKinley (R)	7,219,530	292	William J. Bryan (D)	6,358,071	15
1904	Theodore Roosevelt (R)	7,628,834	336	Alton B. Parker (D)	5,084,491	14
1908	William H. Taft (R)	7,679,006	321	William J. Bryan (D)	6,409,106	16
1912	Woodrow Wilson (D)	6,286,214	435	Theodore Roosevelt (PR)	4,216,020	8
				William H. Taft (R)	3,483,922	[illegible]
1916	Woodrow Wilson (D)	9,129,606	277	Charles E. Hughes (R)	8,538,221	25
1920	Warren G. Harding (R)	16,152,200	404	James M. Cox (D)	9,147,353	12
1924	Calvin Coolidge (R)	15,725,016	382	John W. Davis (D)	8,385,586	13
				Robert M. LaFollette (PR)	4,822,856	1
1928	Herbert Hoover (R)	21,392,190	444	Alfred E. Smith (D)	15,016,443	8
1932	Franklin D. Roosevelt (D)	22,821,857	472	Herbert Hoover (R)	15,761,841	5
				Norman Thomas (Socialist)	884,781	...
1936	Franklin D. Roosevelt (D)	27,751,597	523	Alfred Landon (R)	16,679,583	[illegible]
1940	Franklin D. Roosevelt (D)	27,243,466	449	Wendell Willkie (R)	22,304,755	8
1944	Franklin D. Roosevelt (D)	25,602,505	432	Thomas E. Dewey (R)	22,006,278	9
1948	Harry S. Truman (D)	24,105,812	303	Thomas E. Dewey (R)	21,970,065	18
				J. Strom Thurmond (SR)	1,169,021	3
				Henry A. Wallace (PR)	1,157,172	...
1952	Dwight D. Eisenhower (R)	33,936,252	442	Adlai E. Stevenson (D)	27,314,992	8
1956*	Dwight D. Eisenhower (R)	35,585,316	457	Adlai E. Stevenson (D)	26,031,322	7
1960*	John F. Kennedy (D)	34,227,096	303	Richard M. Nixon (R)	34,108,546	21
1964	Lyndon B. Johnson (D)	43,126,506	486	Barry M. Goldwater (R)	27,176,799	5
1968	Richard M. Nixon (R)	31,785,480	301	Hubert H. Humphrey (D)	31,275,166	19
				George C. Wallace (3d party)	9,906,473	4
1972*	Richard M. Nixon (R)	47,165,234	520	George S. McGovern (D)	28,168,110	1
1976*	Jimmy Carter (D)	40,825,839	297	Gerald R. Ford (R)	39,147,770	24

1800— Elected by House of Representatives because of tied electoral vote.

1824— Elected by House of Representatives. No candidate polled a majority.

1872— Greeley died Nov. 29, 1872. His electoral votes were split among 4 individuals.

1876— Fla., La., Ore., and S. C. election returns were disputed. Congress in joint session (Mar. 2, 1877) de clared Hayes and Wheeler elected President and Vice-President.

1888— Cleveland had more votes than Harrison but the 233 electoral votes cast for Harrison against the 16 for Cleveland elected Harrison president.

1956— Democrats elected 74 electors but one from Alabama refused to vote for Stevenson.

1960— Sen. Harry F. Byrd (D-Va.) received 15 electoral votes.

1972— John Hospers of Cal. and Theodora Nathan of Ore. received one vote from an elector of Virginia.

1976— Ronald Reagan of Cal. received one vote from an elector of Washington.

Political Divisions of the U.S. Senate and House of Representatives From 1855 (34th Cong.) to 1977-1979 (95th Cong.)

Source: Clerk of the House of Representatives

Congress	Years	Senate: Number of Senators	Senate: Democrats	Senate: Republicans	Senate: Other parties	Senate: Vacant	House of Representatives: Number of Representatives	House: Democrats	House: Republicans	House: Other parties	House: Vacant
34th	1855-57	62	42	15	5		234	83	108	43	
35th	1857-59	64	39	20	5		237	131	92	14	
36th	1859-61	66	38	26	2		237	101	113	23	
37th	1861-63	50	11	31	7	1	178	42	106	28	2
38th	1863-65	51	12	39			183	80	103		
39th	1865-67	52	10	42			191	46	145		
40th	1867-69	53	11	42			193	49	143		1
41st	1869-71	74	11	61		2	243	73	170		
42d	1871-73	74	17	57			243	104	139		
43d	1873-75	74	19	54		1	293	88	203		2
44th	1875-77	76	29	46		1	293	71	107	3	2
45th	1877-79	76	36	39	1		293	156	137		
46th	1879-81	76	43	33			293	150	128	14	1
47th	1881-83	76	37	37	2		293	130	152	11	
48th	1883-85	76	36	40			325	200	119	6	
49th	1885-87	76	34	41		1	325	182	140	2	1
50th	1887-89	76	37	39			325	170	151	4	
51st	1889-91	84	37	47			330	156	173	1	
52d	1891-93	88	39	47	2		333	231	88	14	
53d	1893-95	88	44	38	3	3	356	220	126	10	
54th	1895-97	88	39	44	5		357	104	246	7	
55th	1897-99	90	34	46	10		357	134	206	16	1
56th	1899-1901	90	26	53	11		357	163	185	9	
57th	1901-03	90	29	56	3	2	357	153	198	5	1
58th	1903-05	90	32	58			386	178	207		1
59th	1905-07	90	32	58			386	136	250		
60th	1907-09	92	29	61		2	386	164	222		
61st	1909-11	92	32	59		1	391	172	219		
62d	1911-13	92	42	49		1	391	228	162	1	
63d	1913-15	96	51	44	1		435	290	127	18	
64th	1915-17	96	56	39	1		435	231	193	8	3
65th	1917-19	96	53	42	1		435	[1]210	216	9	
66th	1919-21	96	47	48	1		435	191	237	7	
67th	1921-23	96	37	59			435	132	300	1	2
68th	1923-25	96	43	51	2		435	207	225	3	
69th	1925-27	96	40	54	1	1	435	183	247	5	
70th	1927-29	96	47	48	1		435	195	237	3	
71st	1929-31	96	39	56	1		435	163	267	1	4
72d	1931-33	96	47	48	1		435	[2]216	218	1	
73d	1933-35	96	59	36	1		435	313	117	5	
74th	1935-37	96	69	25	2		435	322	103	10	
75th	1937-39	96	75	17	4		435	333	89	13	
76th	1939-41	96	69	23	4		435	262	169	4	
77th	1941-43	96	66	28	2		435	267	162	6	
78th	1943-45	96	57	38	1		435	222	209	4	
79th	1945-47	96	57	38	1		435	243	190	1	
80th	1947-49	96	45	51			435	188	246	1	
81st	1949-51	96	54	42			435	263	171	1	
82d	1951-53	96	48	47	1		435	234	199	2	
83d	1953-55	96	46	48	2		435	213	221	1	
84th	1955-57	96	48	47	1		435	232	203		
85th	1957-59	96	49	47			435	234	201		
86th	1959-61	98	64	34			[3]436	283	153		
87th	1961-63	100	64	36			[4]437	262	175		
88th	1963-65	100	67	33			435	258	176		1
89th	1965-67	100	68	32			435	295	140		
90th	1967-69	100	64	36			435	248	187		
91st	1969-71	100	58	42			435	243	192		
92d	1971-73	100	54	44	2		435	255	180		
93d	1973-75	100	56	42	2		435	242	192	1	
94th	1975-77	100	61	37	2		435	291	144		
95th	1977-79	100	61	38	1		435	292	143		

[1]Democrats organized House with help of other parties. [2]Democrats organized House due to Republican deaths. [3]Proclamation declaring Alaska a State issued Jan. 3, 1959. [4] Proclamation declaring Hawaii a State issued Aug. 21, 1959.

The Ninety-Fifth Congress

With 1976 Election Results

The Senate

Terms are for 6 years and end Jan. 3 of the year preceding name. Annual salary $57,500. To be eligible for the U.S. Senate a person must be at least 30 years of age, a citizen of the United States for at least 9 years, and a resident of the state from which he is chosen. The Congress must meet annually on Jan. 3, unless it has, by law, appointed a different day.

Senate officials: President Pro Tempore James O. Eastland; Deputy President Pro Tempore Hubert H. Humphrey; Majority Leader Robert C. Byrd; Majority Whip Alan Cranston; Minority Leader Howard H. Baker Jr.; Minority Whip Ted Stevens.

Dem., 61; Rep., 38; Indep., 1; Total, 100. *Designates senior senator.

Term ends	Senator (Party, home)	1976 Election
	Alabama	
1979	John Sparkman* (D, Huntsville)	
1981	James B. Allen (D, Gadsden)	
	Alaska	
1979	Ted Stevens* (R, Anchorage)	
1981	Mike Gravel (D, Anchorage)	
	Arizona	
1981	Barry M. Goldwater* (R, Scottsdale)	
1983	Dennis DeConcini (D, Tucson)	400,334
	Sam Steiger (R, Prescott)	321,236
	Arkansas	
1979	John L. McClellan* (D, Little Rock)	
1981	Dale Bumpers (D, Charleston)	
	California	
1981	Alan Crantson* (D, Palm Springs)	
1983	S. I. (Sam) Hayakawa (R, Mill Valley)	3,748,973
	John V. Tunney (D, Beverly Hills)	3,502,862
	Colorado	
1979	Floyd K. Haskell* (D, Denver)	
1981	Gary Hart (D, Denver)	
	Connecticut	
1981	Abraham A. Ribicoff* (D, Hartford)	
1983	Lowell P. Weicker Jr. (R, Greenwich)	785,683
	Gloria Schaffer (D, Woodbridge)	561,018
	Delaware	
1979	Joseph R. Biden Jr. (D, Faulkland)	
1983	William V. Roth Jr.* (R, Wilmington)	125,502
	Thomas C. Maloney (D, Wilmington)	98,055
	Florida	
1981	Richard Stone (D, Tallahassee)	
1983	Lawton Chiles* (D, Lakeland)	1,799,518
	John Grady (R, Belle Glade)	1,057,886
	Georgia	
1979	Sam Nunn (D, Perry)	
1981	Herman E. Talmadge* (D, Lovejoy)	
	Hawaii	
1981	Daniel K. Inouye* (D, Honolulu)	
1983	Spark M. Matsunaga (D, Honolulu)	162,305
	William Quinn (R, Honolulu)	122,724
	Idaho	
1979	James A. McClure (R, Payette)	
1981	Frank Church* (D, Boise)	
	Illinois	
1979	Charles H. Percy* (R, Kenilworth)	
1981	Adlai E. Stevenson 3d (D, Chicago)	
	Indiana	
1981	Birch Bayh* (D, Indianapolis)	
1983	Richard G. Lugar (R, Indianapolis)	1,275,833
	Vance Hartke (D, Evansville)	868,522
	Iowa	
1979	Dick Clark* (D, Marion)	
1981	C. Culver (D, Cedar Rapids)	
	Kansas	
1979	James B. Pearson* (R, Prairie Village)	
1981	Robert J. Dole (R, Russell)	
	Kentucky	
1979	Walter Huddleston* (D, Elizabethtown)	
1981	Wendell H. Ford (D, Owensboro)	
	Louisiana	
1979	J. Bennett Johnston Jr. (D, Shreveport)	
1981	Russell B. Long* (D, Baton Rouge)	
	Maine	
1979	William D. Hathaway (D, Auburn)	
1983	Edmund S. Muskie* (D, Waterville)	292,704
	Robert A. G. Monks (R, Cape Elizabeth)	193,489
	Maryland	
1981	Charles C. Mathias* (R, Frederick)	
1983	Paul S. Sarbanes (D, Baltimore)	772,101
	J. Glenn Beall Jr. (R, Frostburg)	530,439
	Massachusetts	
1979	Edward W. Brooke (R, Newton Center)	
1983	Edward M. Kennedy* (D, Boston)	1,726,657
	Michael S. Robertson (R, Berkley)	722,641
	Michigan	
1979	Robert P. Griffin* (R, Traverse City)	
1983	Donald W. Riegle Jr. (D, Flint)	1,831,031
	Marvin L. Esch (R, Ann Arbor)	1,635,087
	Minnesota	
1979	Wendell R. Anderson (D, St. Paul) appointed Dec. 30, 1976 to replace Walter Mondale.	
1983	Hubert H. Humphrey (D, Waverly)	1,290,736
	Jerry Brekke (R)	478,611

Mississippi

erm nds	Senator (Party, home)	1976 Election
979	James O. Eastland* (D, Doddsville)	
983	John C. Stennis (D, DeKalb)	Unopposed

Missouri

erm nds	Senator (Party, home)	1976 Election
981	Thomas F. Eagleton* (D, St. Louis)	
983	John C. Danforth (R, Jefferson City)	1,090,067
	Warren E. Hearnes (D, Charleston)	813,571

Montana

erm nds	Senator (Party, home)	1976 Election
979	Lee Metcalf* (D, Helena)	
983	John Melcher (D, Forsyth)	206,232
	Stanley C. Burger (R, Bozeman)	115,213

Nebraska

erm nds	Senator (Party, home)	1976 Election
979	Carl T. Curtis* (R, Minden)	
983	Edward Zorinsky (D, Omaha)	313,805
	John Y. McCollister (R, Omaha)	279,284

Nevada

erm nds	Senator (Party, home)	1976 Election
981	Paul Laxalt (R, Carson City)	
983	Howard W. Cannon* (D, Las Vegas)	127,295
	David Towell (R, Minden)	63,471

New Hampshire

erm nds	Senator (Party, home)	1976 Election
979	Thomas J. McIntyre* (D, Laconia)	
981	John A. Durkin (D, Manchester)	

New Jersey

erm nds	Senator (Party, home)	1976 Election
979	Clifford P. Case* (R, Rahway)	
983	Harrison A. Williams Jr. (D, Bedminster)	1,681,140
	David F. Norcross (R, Morristown)	1,054,508

New Mexico

erm nds	Senator (Party, home)	1976 Election
979	Pete V. Domenici* (R, Albuquerque)	
983	Harrison "Jack" Schmitt (R, Silver City)	234,681
	Joseph M. Montoya (D, Santa Fe)	176,382

New York

erm nds	Senator (Party, home)	1976 Election
981	Jacob K. Javits* (R,L, New York)	
983	Daniel Patrick Moynihan (D, New York)	3,512,594
	James L. Buckley (R,C, New York)	2,836,633

North Carolina

erm nds	Senator (Party, home)	1976 Election
979	Jesse A. Helms* (R, Raleigh)	
981	Robert Morgan (D, Lillington)	

North Dakota

erm nds	Senator (Party, home)	1976 Election
981	Milton R. Young* (R, LaMoure)	
983	Quentin N. Burdick (D, Fargo)	175,772
	Robert Stroup (R, Hazen)	103,466

Ohio

erm nds	Senator (Party, home)	1976 Election
981	John Glenn* (D, Columbia)	
983	Howard M. Metzenbaum (D, Shaker Heights)	1,941,113
	Robert Taft Jr. (R, Indian Hill)	1,823,774

Oklahoma

erm nds	Senator (Party, home)	1976 Election
979	Dewey F. Bartlett (R, Tulsa)	
981	Henry Bellmon* (R, Red Rock)	

Oregon

erm nds	Senator (Party, home)	1976 Election
979	Mark O. Hatfield* (R, Salem)	
981	Robert W. Packwood (R, Lake Oswego)	

Pennsylvania

Term ends	Senator (Party, home)	1976 Election
1981	Richard S. Schweiker* (R, Worcester)	
1983	H. John Heinz III (R, Pittsburgh)	2,381,891
	William J. Green (D, Philadelphia)	2,126,977

Rhode Island

Term ends	Senator (Party, home)	1976 Election
1979	Claiborne Pell* (D, Newport)	
1983	John H. Chafee (R, Warwick)	230,329
	Richard P. Lorber (D, Providence)	167,665

South Carolina

Term ends	Senator (Party, home)	1976 Election
1979	Strom Thurmond* (R, Aiken)	
1981	Ernest F. Hollings (D, Columbia)	

South Dakota

Term ends	Senator (Party, home)	1976 Election
1979	James Abourezk (D, Rapid City)	
1981	George McGovern* (D, Mitchell)	

Tennessee

Term ends	Senator (Party, home)	1976 Election
1979	Howard H. Baker Jr.* (R, Knoxville)	
1983	James R. Sasser (D, Nashville)	751,180
	Bill Brock (R, Lookout Mountain)	673,231

Texas

Term ends	Senator (Party, home)	1976 Election
1979	John G. Tower* (R, Wichita Falls)	
1983	Lloyd Bentsen (D, Houston)	2,199,956
	Alan Steelman (R, Dallas)	1,636,370

Utah

Term ends	Senator (Party, home)	1976 Election
1981	Jake Garn* (R, Salt Lake City)	
1983	Orrin G. Hatch (R, Salt Lake City)	290,221
	Frank E. Moss (D, Salt Lake City)	223,948

Vermont

Term ends	Senator (Party, home)	1976 Election
1981	Patrick J. Leahy (D, Burlington)	
1983	Robert T. Stafford* (R, Rutland)	94,481
	Thomas P. Salmon (D, Rockingham)	85,682

Virginia

Term ends	Senator (Party, home)	1976 Election
1979	William Lloyd Scott (R, Fairfax)	
1983	Harry F. Byrd Jr.* (I, Winchester)	890,778
	E. R. (Bud) Zumwalt (D, Arlington)	596,009

Washington

Term ends	Senator (Party, home)	1976 Election
1981	Warren G. Magnuson* (D, Seattle)	
1983	Henry M. Jackson (D, Everett)	1,071,219
	George M. Brown (R, Renton)	361,546

West Virginia

Term ends	Senator (Party, home)	1976 Election
1979	Jennings Randolph* (D, Elkins)	
1983	Robert C. Byrd (D, Sophia)	Unopposed

Wisconsin

Term ends	Senator (Party, home)	1976 Election
1981	Gaylord A. Nelson (D, Madison)	
1983	William Proxmire* (D, Madison)	1,396,970
	Stanley York (R, Madison)	521,902

Wyoming

Term ends	Senator (Party, home)	1976 Election
1979	Clifford P. Hansen* (R, Jackson)	
1983	Malcolm Wallop (R, Big Horn)	84,810
	Gale McGee (D, Laramie)	70,558

The House of Representatives

Members' terms to Jan. 3, 1979. Annual salary $57,500; house speaker $75,000. To be eligible for membership, a person must be at least 25, a U.S. citizen for at least 7 years, and a resident of the state from which he is chosen.

House Officials: Speaker Thomas P. O'Neill; Majority Leader James Wright; Majority Whip John Brademas; Minority Leader John J. Rhodes; Minority Whip Robert H. Michel.

Democrats, 292, Republicans, 143. Total 435.
(Those marked * served in the 94th Congress.)
Bold face numbers denote the winner.

Alabama

Dist.	Representative (Party, Home)	1976 Election
1.	Bill Davenport (D, Citronelle)	58,906
	Jack Edwards* (R, Mobile)	**98,257**
2.	J. Carole Keahey (D, Ozark)	66,288
	William L. "Bill" Dickinson* (R, Montgomery)	**90,069**
3.	Bill Nichols* (D, Sylacauga)	**Unopposed**
4.	Tom Bevill* (D, Jasper)	**141,490**
	Leonard Wilson (R, Jasper)	34,531
5.	Ronnie G. Flippo (D, Florence)	**Unopposed**
6.	Mel Bailey (D, Birmingham)	69,384
	John H. Buchanan Jr.* (R, Birmingham)	**92,113**
7.	Walter Flowers* (D, Tuscaloosa)	**Unopposed**

Alaska - At Large

Dist.	Representative (Party, Home)	1976 Election
	Eben Hopson (D, Barrow)	34,194
	Don Young* (R, Fort Yukon)	**83,722**

Arizona

Dist.	Representative (Party, Home)	1976 Election
1.	Patricia M. Fullinwider (D, Tempe)	68,404
	John J. Rhodes* (R, Mesa)	**96,397**
2.	Morris K. Udall* (D, Tucson)	**106,054**
	Laird Guttersen (R, Tucson)	71,765
3.	Bob Stump (D, Tolleson)	**88,854**
	Fred Koory Jr. (R, Glendale)	79,162
4.	Tony Mason (D, Phoenix)	92,435
	Eldon Rudd (R, Scottsdale)	**93,154**

Arkansas

Dist.	Representative (Party, Home)	1976 Election
1.	Bill Alexander* (D, Osceola)	**116,217**
	Harlan "Bo" Holleman (R, Wynne)	52,565
2.	Jim Guy Tucker (D, Little Rock)	**144,780**
	James J. Kelly (R, North Little Rock)	22,819
3.	John Paul Hammerschmidt* (R, Harrison)	**Unopposed**
4.	Ray Thornton* (D, Sheridan)	**Unopposed**

California

Dist.	Representative (Party, Home)	1976 Election
1.	Harold T. (Bizz) Johnson* (D, Roseville)	**160,477**
	James E. Taylor (R, Auburn)	56,539
2.	Oscar Klee (D, Ukiah)	88,829
	Don H. Clausen* (R, Cresent City)	**121,290**
3.	John E. Moss* (D, Sacramento)	**139,779**
	George R. Marsh Jr. (R, Sacramento)	52,075
4.	Robert L. Leggett* (D, Suisun City)	**75,844**
	Albert Dehr (R, Citrus Heights)	75,193
5.	John L. Burton* (D, San Francisco)	**103,746**
	Branwell Fanning (R, Tiburon)	64,008
6.	Phillip Burton* (D, San Francisco)	**86,493**
	Tom Spinosa (R, San Francisco)	35,359
7.	George Miller* (D, Martinez)	**147,064**
	Robert L. Vickers (R, Concord)	45,863
8.	Ronald V. Dellums* (D, Berkeley)	**122,342**
	Philip Stiles Breck Jr. (R, Berkeley)	68,374
9.	Fortney H. (Pete) Stark* (D, Oakland)	**116,398**
	James K. Mills (R, Livermore)	44,607
10.	Don Edwards* (D, San Jose)	**111,992**
	Herb Smith (R, San Jose)	38,088
11.	Leo J. Ryan* (D, Belmont)	**107,618**
	Bob Jones (R, Belmont)	62,435
12.	David Harris (D, Menlo Park)	61,526
	Paul N. "Pete" McCloskey Jr.* (R, Menlo Park)	**130,332**
13.	Norman Y. Mineta* (D, San Jose)	**135,291**
	Ernest L. Konnyu (R, Saratoga)	63,130
14.	John J. McFall* (D, Manteca)	**123,285**
	Roger A. Blain (R, Stockton)	46,674
15.	B.F. Sisk* (D, Fresno)	**92,735**
	Carol Harner (R, Mariposa)	35,700
16.	Leon E. Panetta (D, Carmel Valley)	**104,545**
	Burt Talcott* (R, Salinas)	91,160
17.	John Krebs* (D, Fresno)	**103,898**
	Henry J. Andreas (R, Sanger)	54,270
18.	Dean Close (D, Bakersfield)	56,683
	William M. Ketchum* (R, Bakersfield)	**101,658**
19.	Dan Sisson (D, Santa Barbara)	68,722
	Robert J. Lagomarsino* (R, Ventura)	**124,201**
20.	Patti Lear Corman (D, Encino)	71,193
	Barry Goldwater Jr.*(R, Woodland Hills)	**146,158**
21.	James C. Corman* (D, Van Nuys)	**101,837**
	Erwin "Ed" Hogan (R, Panorama City)	44,094
22.	Robert L. Salley (D, Altadena)	68,543
	Carlos J. Moorhead* (R, Glendale)	**114,769**
23.	Anthony C. Beilenson (D, Los Angeles)	**130,619**
	Thomas F. Bartman (R, Sherman Oaks)	86,434
24.	Henry A. Waxman* (D, Los Angeles)	**108,296**
	David Irving Simmons (R, Los Angeles)	51,478
25.	Edward R. Roybal* (D, Los Angeles)	**57,966**
	Jim Madrid (R, Los Angeles)	17,737
26.	John H. Rousselot* (R, San Marino)	**112,619**
	Bruce Latta (D)	59,093
27.	Gary Familian (D, Marina Del Rey)	94,988
	Robert K. Dornan (R, Los Angeles)	**114,623**
28.	Yvonne Brathwaite Burke* (D, Los Angeles)	**114,612**
	Edward S. Skinner (R, El Monte)	28,303
29.	Augustus F. "Gus" Hawkins* (D, Los Angeles)	**82,515**
	Michael D. Germonprez (R, Los Angeles)	10,352
30.	George E. Danielson* (D, Monterey Park)	**82,767**
	Harry Couch (R, Monterey Park)	28,503
31.	Charles H. Wilson* (D, Hawthorne)	**Unopposed**
32.	Glenn M. Anderson* (D, Harbor City)	**92,034**
	Clifford O. Young (R, Carson)	35,394
33.	Ted Snyder (D, Whittier)	77,807
	Del Clawson* (R, Downey)	**95,398**
34.	Mark W. Hannaford* (D, Lakewood)	**100,988**
	Daniel E. Lungren (R, Long Beach)	98,147
35.	Jim Lloyd* (D, West Covina)	**87,472**
	Louis Brutocao (R, Covina)	76,765
36.	George E. Brown Jr.* (D, Colton)	**90,83**
	Grant Carner (R, Riverside)	49,36
37.	Douglas C. Nilson Jr. (D, Mentone)	49,02
	Shirley N. Pettis* (R, Loma Linda)	**133,63**
38.	Jerry Patterson* (D, Buena Park)	**103,31**
	James (Jim) Combs (R, Costa Mesa)	59,09
39.	William E. "Bill" Farris (D, Orange)	86,74
	Charles E. Wiggins* (R, Fullerton)	**122,65**
40.	Vivian Hall (D, Irvine)	102,13
	Robert E. Badham (R, Newport Beach)	**148,51**
41.	King Golden Jr. (D, San Diego)	94,59
	Bob C. Wilson* (R, San Diego)	**128,78**
42.	Lionel Van Deerlin*(D,Chula Vista)	**103,06**
	Wes Marden (R, Chula Vista)	32,56
43.	Pat Kelly (D, Vista)	93,47
	Clair W. Burgener* (R, La Jolla)	**173,57**

Colorado

Dist.	Representative (Party, Home)	1976 Election
1.	Patricia Schroeder* (D, Denver)	**103,03**
	Don Friedman (R, Denver)	89,38
2.	Timothy E. Wirth* (D, Denver)	**121,34**
	Ed Scott (R, Lakewood)	118,93
3.	Frank E. Evans* (D, Beulah)	**89,30**
	Melvin H. Takaki (R, Pueblo)	82,31

Dist	Representative (party, home)	1976 Election
4.	Daniel M. Ogden Jr. (D, Fort Collins)	76,995
	James P. Johnson* (R, Fort Collins)	**119,458**
5.	Dorothy Hores (D, Littleton)	64,067
	William L. Armstrong* (R, Aurora)	**126,784**

Connecticut

Dist	Representative (party, home)	1976 Election
1.	William R. Cotter* (D, Hartford)	**128,479**
	Lucien P. Di Fazio Jr. (R, Hartford)	94,106
2.	Christopher J. Dodd* (D, North Stonington)	**142,684**
	Richard M. Jackson (R, Willimantic)	74,743
3.	Robert N. Giaimo* (D, North Haven)	**121,623**
	John G. Pucciano (R, Orange)	96,714
4.	Geoffrey G. Peterson (D, Westport)	76,722
	Stewart B. McKinney* (R, Fairfield)	**126,314**
5.	Michael J. Adanti (D, Ansonia)	77,308
	Ronald A. Sarasin* (R, Beacon Falls)	**157,009**
6.	Anthony Toby Moffett* (D, Unionville)	**134,914**
	Thomas F. Upson (R, Watertown)	102,364

Delaware - At Large

Dist	Representative (party, home)	1976 Election
	Samuel L. Shipley (D, Wilmington)	102,431
	Thomas B. Evans Jr. (R, Wilmington)	**110,677**

Florida

Dist	Representative (party, home)	1976 Election
1.	Robert L. F. Sikes* (D, Crestview)	**Unopposed**
2.	Don Fuqua* (D, Altha)	**Unopposed**
3.	Charles E. Bennett* (D, Jacksonville)	**Unopposed**
4.	Bill Chappell Jr.* (D, Ocala)	**Unopposed**
5.	Jo Ann Saunders (D, Orlando)	96,260
	Richard Kelly* (R, Holiday)	**138,371**
6.	Gabriel Cazares (D, Clearwater)	80,821
	C.W. Bill Young* (R, St. Petersburg)	**151,371**
7.	Sam Gibbons* (D, Tampa)	**102,739**
	Dusty Owens (R, Temple Terrace)	53,599
8.	Andy Ireland (D, Winter Haven)	**103,360**
	Bob Johnson (R, Sarasota)	74,794
9.	Joseph A. Rosier (D, Winter Park)	36,630
	Louis Frey Jr.* (R, Winter Park)	**130,509**
10.	Bill Sikes (D, Clewiston)	83,413
	L.A. (Skip) Bafalis*, (R, Fort Myers Beach)	**164,273**
11.	Paul G. Rogers* (D, West Palm Beach)	**199,031**
	C. Adams (A)	19,406
12.	Charlie Friedman (D, Hollywood)	91,749
	J. Herbert Burke* (R, Hollywood)	**107,268**
13.	William Lehman* (D, North Miami Beach)	**127,822**
	Lee Arnold Spiegelman (R, Miami Shores)	35,357
14.	Claude Pepper* (D, Miami)	**82,665**
	Evelio S. Estrella (R, Miami)	30,774
15.	Dante B. Fascell* (D, Miami)	**121,292**
	Paul R. Cobb (R, Miami)	50,941

Georgia

Dist	Representative (party, home)	1976 Election
1.	Bo Ginn* (D, Millen)	**Unopposed**
2.	Dawson Mathis* (D, Albany)	**Unopposed**
3.	Jack Brinkley* (D, Columbus)	**93,174**
	Steven Dugan (R, Warner Robins)	11,829
4.	Elliott H. Levitas* (D, Atlanta)	**110,261**
	George T. Warren II (R, Decatur)	51,140
5.	Andrew Young* (D, Atlanta)	**96,056**
	Edward W. Gadrix (R, Atlanta)	47,998
6.	John J. Flynt Jr. (D, Griffin)	**77,532**
	Newt Gingrich (R, Carrollton)	72,400
7.	Larry P. McDonald* (D, Marietta)	**84,587**
	Quincy Collins (R, Marietta)	68,947
8.	Bill Lee Evans (D, Macon)	**90,559**
	Billy Adams (R, Macon)	39,623
9.	Ed Jenkins (D, Jaspar)	**113,245**
	Louise Wofford (R, Gainesville)	29,954
10.	Doug Barnard (D, Augusta)	**Unopposed**

Hawaii

Dist	Representative (party, home)	1976 Election
1.	Cecil L. Heftel (D, Honolulu)	**60,050**
	Frederick Rohlfing (R, Honolulu)	53,745
2.	Daniel K. Akaka (D, Honolulu)	**124,116**
	Hank Inouye (R, Honolulu)	23,917

Idaho

Dist	Representative (party, home)	1976 Election
1.	Ken Pursley (D, Boise)	79,662
	Steven D. Symms* (R, Caldwell)	**95,833**
2.	Stan Kress (D, Firth)	82,237
	George Hansen* (R, Pocatello)	**84,175**

Illinois

Dist	Representative (party, home)	1976 Election
1.	Ralph H. Metcalfe* (D, Chicago)	**126,632**
	A.A. Rayner Jr. (R, Chicago)	10,147
2.	Morgan F. Murphy* (D, Chicago)	**127,297**
	Spencer Leak (R, Chicago)	23,037
3.	Martin A. Russo* (D, S. Holland)	**115,591**
	Ronald Buikema (R, S. Holland)	79,434
4.	Ronald A. Rodger (D, Tinley Park)	64,924
	Edward Derwinski* (R, Flossmoor)	**124,847**
5.	John G. Fary* (D, Chicago)	**119,336**
	Vincent Krok (R, Chicago)	35,756
6.	Marilyn D. Clancy (D, Oak Park)	69,359
	Henry J. Hyde* (R, Park Ridge)	**106,667**
7.	Cardiss Collins* (D, Chicago)	**88,239**
	Newell Ward (R, Chicago)	15,854
8.	Daniel D. Rostenkowski* (D, Chicago)	**105,595**
	John F. Urbaszewski (R, Chicago)	25,512
9.	Sidney R. Yates* (D, Chicago)	**121,915**
	Thomas J. Wajerski (R, Chicago)	47,054
10.	Abner J. Mikva* (D, Evanston)	**106,804**
	Samuel H. Young (R, Glenview)	106,603
11.	Frank Annunzio* (D, Chicago)	**135,755**
	Daniel C. Reber (R, Chicago)	65,680
12.	Edwin L. Frank (D, Hoffman Estates)	56,644
	Philip M. Crane* (R, Mount Prospect)	**151,899**
13.	James J. Cummings (D, Barrington)	49,777
	Robert McClory* (R, Lake Bluff)	**109,726**
14.	Marie Agnes Fese (D, Elmhurst)	60,505
	John Erlenborn* (R, Glen Ellyn)	**176,076**
15.	Tim L. Hall* (D, Dwight)	87,676
	Tom Corcoran (R, Ottawa)	**102,555**
16.	Stephen Eytalis (D, Rockford)	54,002
	John B. Anderson* (R, Rockford)	**114,324**
17.	Merlin Karlock (D, Momence)	81,220
	George M. O'Brien* (R, Joliet)	**113,145**
18.	Matthew Ryan (D, Washington)	79,102
	Robert H. Michel* (R, Peoria)	**108,028**
19.	John Craver (D, London Mills)	60,967
	Tom Railsback* (R, Moline)	**132,571**
20.	Peter Mack (D, Springfield)	78,634
	Paul Findley* (R, Pittsfield)	**137,223**
21.	Anna Wall Scott (D, Urbana)	46,996
	Edward R. Madigan* (R, Lincoln)	**137,037**
22.	George E. Shipley* (D, Olney)	**129,187**
	Ralph Y. McGinnis (R, Charleston)	81,102
23.	Melvin Price* (D, E. St. Louis)	**128,113**
	Sam P. Drenovac (R, Granite City)	34,825
24.	Paul Simon (D, Carbondale)	**153,344**
	Peter G. Prineas (R, Carbondale)	73,766

Indiana

Dist	Representative (party, home)	1976 Election
1.	Adam Benjamin Jr. (D, Hobart)	**121,155**
	Robert J. Billings (R, Dyer)	48,756
2.	Floyd J. Fithian* (D, Lafayette)	**117,617**
	William W. Erwin (R, Bourbon)	95,605
3.	John Brademas* (D, South Bend)	**101,777**
	Thomas L. Thorson (R, LaPorte)	77,094
4.	J. Edward Roush* (D, Huntington)	88,361
	J. Danforth Quayle (R, Huntington)	**107,762**
5.	William C. Stout (D, Rochester)	78,807
	Elwood Hillis* (R, Kokomo)	**127,194**
6.	David W. Evans* (D, Indianapolis)	**105,773**
	David G. Crane (R, Martinsville)	86,854
7.	John E. Tipton (D, Jasonville)	77,355
	John T. Myers* (R, Covington)	**130,005**
8.	David L. Cornwell (D, Paoli)	**109,013**
	Belden Bell (R, Evansville)	107,013
9.	Lee H. Hamilton* (D, Columbus)	**Unopposed**
10.	Philip R. Sharp* (D, Muncie)	114,559
	William G. Frazier (R, Muncie)	76,890

Dist	Representative (party, home)	1976 Election
11.	Andrew Jacobs Jr.* (D, Indianapolis)	**115,895**
	Lawrence L. Buell (R, Indianapolis)	74,829

Iowa

Dist	Representative (party, home)	1976 Election
1.	Edward Mezvinsky* (D, Iowa City)	101,024
	James A.S. Leach (R, Bettendorf)	**109,694**
2.	Michael T. Blouin* (D, Dubuque)	**102,980**
	Tom Riley (R, Cedar Rapids)	100,344
3.	Stephen J. Rapp (D, Waterloo)	90,981
	Charles E. Grassley* (R, Clear Lake)	**117,957**
4.	Neal Smith* (D, Altoona)	**145,343**
	Charles E. Minor (R, Mitchellville)	65,013
5.	Tom Harkin* (D, Ames)	**135,600**
	Kenneth R. Fulk (R, Clarinda)	71,377
6.	Berkley Bedell* (D, Spirit Lake)	**133,507**
	Joanne D. Soper (R, Sioux City)	62,292

Kansas

Dist	Representative (party, home)	1976 Election
1.	Randy Yowell (D, Hays)	52,459
	Keith G. Sebelius* (R, Norton)	**142,311**
2.	Martha Keys* (D, Manhattan)	**88,645**
	Ross Freeman (R, Topeka)	82,946
3.	Philip S. Rhoads (D, Kansas City)	52,110
	Larry Winn Jr.* (R, Overland Park)	**123,578**
4.	Dan Glickman (D, Wichita)	**90,067**
	Garner E. Shriver* (R, Wichita)	86,832
5.	Virgil Leon Olson (D, Chanute)	65,340
	Joe Skubitz* (R, Pittsburg)	**109,573**

Kentucky

Dist	Representative (party, home)	1976 Election
1.	Carroll Hubbard Jr.*(D, Mayfield)	**118,886**
	Bob Bersky (R, Sturgis)	26,089
2.	William H. Natcher* (D, Bowling Green)	**79,016**
	Walter A. Baker (R, Glasgow)	51,900
3.	Romano L. Mazzoli* (D, Louisville)	**80,496**
	Denzil J. Ramsey (R, Louisville)	58,019
4.	Edward J. Winterberg (D, Covington)	77,009
	Gene Snyder* (R, Brownsboro Farms)	**97,493**
5.	Charles C. Smith (D, Williamsburg)	49,128
	Tim Lee Carter* (R, Tomkinsville)	**100,204**
6.	John B. Breckinridge* (D, Lexington)	**90,695**
7.	Carl D. Perkins* (D, Hindman)	**110,450**
	Granville Thomas (R, London)	40,381

Louisiana

Dist	Representative (party, home)	1976 Election
1.	Robert L. Livingston (R, Algiers) by special election Aug. 27, 1977. Replaced Tonry, who was convicted of campaign violations.	
2.	Lindy (Mrs. Hale) Boggs* (D, New Orleans)	**85,923**
3.	David H. "Pro" Scheuermann Jr. (D, Metairie)	39,728
	David C. Treen* (R, Metairie)	**109,135**
4.	Joe D. Waggonner Jr.* (D, Plain Dealing)	**Unopposed**
5.	Jerry Huckaby (D, Ringgold)	**83,696**
	Frank Spooner (R, Monroe)	75,574
6.	J.D. De Blieux (D, Baton Rouge)	53,212
	W. Henson Moore* (R, Baton Rouge)	**99,780**
7.	John B. Breaux* (D, Crowley)	**117,196**
	Charles F. "Chuck" Huff, (R, Lafayette)	23,414
8.	Gillis W. Long* (D, Alexandria)	**106,285**
	Kent Courtney (I)	6,526

Maine

Dist	Representative (party, home)	1976 Election
1.	Frederick D. Barton (D, Portland)	108,105
	David F. Emery* (R, Augusta)	**145,523**
2.	Leighton Cooney (D, Sabattus)	43,150
	William S. Cohen* (R, Bangor)	**169,292**

Maryland

Dist	Representative (party, home)	1976 Election
1.	Roy Dyson (D, Great Mills)	72,993
	Robert E. Bauman* (R, Easton)	**85,919**
2.	Clarence D. Long* (D, Ruxton)	**139,196**

Dist	Representative (party, home)	1976 Electio
	John M. Seney (R, Towson)	35,25
3.	Barbara A. Mikulski (D, Baltimore)	**107,01**
	Samuel A. Culotta (R, Baltimore)	36,44
4.	Werner Fornos (D, Davidsonville)	69,85
	Marjorie S. Holt* (R, Severna Park)	**95,15**
5.	Gladys Noon Spellman* (D, Laurel)	**77,83**
	John Burcham (R, Lanham)	57,05
6.	Goodloe E. Byron* (D, Frederick)	**126,80**
	Arthur T. Bond (R, Frostburg)	52,20
7.	Parren J. Mitchell* (D, Baltimore)	**94,99**
8.	Lanny Davis (D, Silver Spring)	100,34
	Newton I. Steers Jr. (R, Bethesda)	**111,27**

Massachusetts

Dist	Representative (party, home)	1976 Election
1.	Edward A. McColgan (D, Easthampton)	78,18
	Silvio O. Conte* (R, Pittsfield)	**137,65**
2.	Edward P. Boland* (D, Springfield)	**134,40**
	Thomas P. Swank (R, Springfield)	41,56
3.	Joseph D. Early* (D, Worchester)	**Unoppose**
4.	Robert F. Drinan* (D, Newton)	**109,26**
	Arthur D. Mason (R, Brookline)	100,56
5.	Paul E. Tsongas* (D, Lowell)	**144,21**
	Roger P. Durkin (R, Lowell)	70,03
6.	Michael Harrington* (D, Beverly)	**121,56**
	William E. Bronson (R, Manchester)	91,65
7.	Edward J. Markey (D, Malden)	**162,12**
	Richard W. Daly (R, Melrose)	37,06
8.	Thomas P. O'Neill Jr. * (D, Cambridge)	**133,13**
	William A. Barnstead (R, Arlington)	33,43
9.	Joe Moakley* (D, Boston)	**103,90**
	Robert G. Cunningham (R, Westwood)	34,54
10.	Margaret M. Heckler* (R, Wellesley)	**Unoppose**
11.	James A. Burke* (D, Milton)	**131,78**
	Danielle De Benedictis (I)	59,24
12.	Gerry E. Studds* (D, Cohasset)	**Unoppose**

Michigan

Dist	Representative (party, home)	1976 Election
1.	John Conyers Jr.* (D, Detroit)	**126,16**
	Isaac Hood (R, Detroit)	8,92
2.	Edward C. Pierce (D, Ann Arbor)	95,05
	Carl D. Pursell (R, Plymouth)	**95,39**
3.	Howard Wolpe (D, Kalamazoo)	95,26
	Garry Brown* (R, Schoolcraft)	**99,23**
4.	Richard E. Daugherty (D, Dowagiac)	69,66
	Dave Stockman (R, St. Joseph)	**107,88**
5.	Richard F. Vander Veen* (D, Grand Rapids)	94,97
	Harold S. Sawyer (R, Rockford)	**109,58**
6.	Bob Carr* (D, East Lansing)	**108,90**
	Clifford W. Taylor (R, East Lansing)	96,00
7.	Dale E. Kildee (D, Flint)	**124,26**
	Robin Widgery (R, Flint)	50,30
8.	Bob Traxler* (D, Bay City)	**110,12**
	E. Brady Denton (R. Saginaw)	75,32
9.	Stephen E. Fawley (D, Hudsonville)	61,64
	Guy A. Vander Jagt* (R, Luther)	**146,71**
10.	Donald J. Albosta (D, Charles)	89,98
	Elford A. Cederberg* (R, Midland)	**118,72**
11.	Francis Brouillette (D, Iron Mountain)	97,32
	Philip E. Ruppe* (R, Houghton)	**118,87**
12.	David E. Bonior (D, Clemens)	**94,81**
	David M. Serotkin (R, Clemens)	85,32
13.	Charles C. Diggs Jr.* (D, Detroit)	**83,38**
	Richard A. Golden (R, Detroit)	9,00
14.	Lucien N. Nedzi* (D, Detroit)	**107,50**
	John Edward Getz (R, Grosse Pointe Farms)	52,99
15.	William D. Ford* (D, Taylor)	117,31
	James D. Walaskay (R, Plymouth)	39,17
16.	John D. Dingell* (D, Trenton)	**121,68**
	William E. Rostron (R, Detroit)	36,37
17.	William M. Brodhead* (D, Detroit)	**112,74**
	James W. Burdick (R, Southfield)	60,47
18.	James J. Blanchard* (D, Pleasant Ridge)	**123,11**
	John E. Olsen (R, Huntington Woods)	60,99
19.	Dorthea Becker (D, Birmingham)	64,33
	William S. Broomfield* (R, Birmingham)	**131,79**

Dist	Representative (party, home)	1976 Election
	Minnesota	
1.	Robert C. "Bob" Olson Jr. (D, Kasson)	70,630
	Albert H. Quie* (R, Dennison)	**158,177**
2.	Gloria Griffin (D, Excelsior)	97,488
	Tom Hagedorn* (R, Truman)	**148,322**
3.	Jerome W. Coughlin (D, Brooklyn Park)	72,044
	Bill Frenzel* (R, Golden Valley)	**149,013**
4.	Bruce F. Vento (D, St. Paul)	**133,282**
	Andrew Engerbretson (R, St. Paul)	59,767
5.	Donald M. Fraser* (D, Minneapolis)	**138,213**
	Richard M. Erdall (R, Minneapolis)	50,764
6.	Richard Nolan* (D, Waite Park)	**147,507**
	James "Jim" Anderson (R, Marshall)	99,201
7.	Arlan Strangeland (R, Barnesville) by special election Feb. 22, 1977. Replaced Bergland, who resigned.	
	Bob Bergland* (D, Roseau)	**174,080**
	Bob Leiseth (R, Lake Park)	64,333
8.	James L. Oberstar* (D, Chisholm)	**Unopposed**
	Mississippi	
1.	Jamie L. Whitten* (D, Charleston)	**Unopposed**
2.	David R. Bowen* (D, Cleveland)	**75,092**
	Roland Byrd (R, Louisville)	42,601
3.	G. V. (Sonny) Montgomery* (D, Meridian)	129,088
	Dorothy Colby Cleveland (R, Union)	8,321
4.	Sterling P. Davis (D, Vicksburg)	28,737
	Thad Cochran* (R, Jackson)	**101,132**
5.	Gerald Blessey (D, Biloxi)	48,724
	Trent Lott* (R, Pascagoula)	**104,554**
	Missouri	
1.	William (Bill) Clay* (D, St. Louis)	**87,310**
	Robert L. Witherspoon (R, St. Louis)	45,874
2.	Robert A. Young (D, St. Ann)	**111,568**
	Robert O. Snyder (R, Kirkwood)	106,811
3.	Richard A. Gephardt (D, St. Louis)	**115,109**
	Joseph L. Badaracco (R, St. Louis)	65,623
4.	Ike Skelton (D, Lexington)	**115,955**
	Richard A. King (R, Independence)	91,605
5.	Richard Bolling* (D, Kansas City)	**100,876**
	Joanne M. Collins (R, Kansas City)	41,681
6.	Morgan Maxfield (D, Kansas City)	83,755
	E. Thomas Coleman (R, Kansas City)	**120,969**
7.	Dolan G. Hawkins (D, Springfield)	81,848
	Gene Taylor* (R, Sarcoxie)	**133,656**
8.	Richard H. Ichord* (D, Houston)	**132,386**
	Charles R. Leick (R, Davisville)	60,179
9.	Harold L. Volkmer (D, Hannibal)	**120,325**
	Joe Frappier (R, Forissant)	94,816
10.	Bill D. Burlison* (D, Cape Girardeau)	**131,675**
	Joe Carron (R, Arnold)	51,024
	Montana	
1.	Max Baucus* (D, Missoula)	**111,487**
	W. D. "Bill" Diehl (R, Helena)	56,297
2.	Thomas E. "Tom" Towe (D, Billings)	68,972
	Ron Marlenee (R, Scobey)	**84,149**
	Nebraska	
1.	Pauline F. Anderson (D, Lincoln)	53,699
	Charles Thone* (R, Lincoln)	**146,558**
2.	John J. Cavanaugh (D, Omaha)	**106,296**
	Lee Terry (R, Omaha)	88,352
3.	James Thomas Hansen (D, Gering)	51,012
	Virginia Smith* (R, Chappell)	**150,720**
	Nevada — At Large	
	Jim Santini* (D, Las Vegas)	**153,996**
	Walden Charles Earhart (R, Carson City)	24,124

Dist	Representative (party, home)	1976 Election
	New Hampshire	
1.	Norman E. D'Amours* (D, Manchester)	**107,806**
	John Adams (R, Exeter)	48,087
2.	J. Joseph Grandmaison (D, Nashua)	65,792
	James C. Cleveland* (R, New London)	**100,911**
	New Jersey	
1.	James J. Florio* (D, Camden)	**136,624**
	Joseph I. McCullough Jr. (R, Haddon Heights)	56,363
2.	William J. Hughes* (D, Ocean City)	**141,753**
	James R. Hurley (R, Millville)	87,915
3.	James J. Howard* (D, Spring Lake Heights)	**127,164**
	Ralph A. Siciliano (R, Red Bank)	75,934
4.	Frank Thompson Jr.* (D, Trenton)	**113,281**
	Joseph S. Indyk (R, Jamesburg)	54,789
5.	Frank R. Nero (D, North Plainfield)	64,598
	Millicent H. Fenwick* (R, Bernardsville)	**137,803**
6.	Catherine A. Costa (D, Willingboro)	85,053
	Edwin B. Forsythe* (R, Morristown)	**125,920**
7.	Andrew Maguire* (D, Ridgewood)	**120,526**
	James J. Sheehan (R, Wyckoff)	92,624
8.	Robert A. Roe* (D, Wayne)	**108,841**
	Bessie Doty (R, Haskell)	44,775
9.	Henry Helstoski* (D, Rutherford)	89,723
	Harold C. Hollenbeck (R, E. Rutherford)	**107,454**
10.	Peter W. Rodino Jr.* (D, Newark)	**88,245**
	Tony Grandison (R, Newark)	17,129
11.	Joseph G. Minish* (D, West Orange)	**129,026**
	Charles A. Poekel Jr. (R, Essex Fells)	59,397
12.	Richard A. Buggelli (D, Union)	49,189
	Matthew J. Rinaldo* (R, Union)	**136,973**
13.	Helen S. Meyner* (D, Phillipsburg)	**105,291**
	William E. Schluter (R, Pennington)	100,050
14.	Joseph A. Le Fante (D, Bayonne)	**73,174**
	Anthony Louis Campenni (R, Bayonne)	66,319
15.	Edward J. Patten* (D, Perth Amboy)	**106,170**
	Charles W. Wiley (R, Sayreville)	54,487
	New Mexico	
1.	Raymond Garcia (D, Albuquerque)	61,800
	Manuel Lujan Jr.* (R, Albuquerque)	**162,587**
2.	Harold Runnels* (D, Lovington)	**123,563**
	Donald W. Trubey (R, Portales)	52,131
	New York	
1.	Otis G. Pike* (D, L, Riverhead)	**135,528**
	Salvatore Nicosia (R, Holbrook)	61,671
	Seth C. Morgan (C, Manorville)	10,269
2.	Thomas J. Downey* (D, I, West Islip)	**91,241**
	Peter F. Cohalan (R, C, Bayport)	67,755
	Rochelle Davidson (L, Deer Park)	906
3.	Jerome A. Ambro Jr.* (D, East Northport)	**94,265**
	Howard T. Hogan Jr. (R, C, Lattingtown)	84,824
	Hy York (L, Jericho)	2,350
4.	Gerald P. Halpern (D, L, Freeport)	83,971
	Norman F. Lent* (R, C, East Rockaway)	**106,058**
5.	Allard K. Lowenstein (D, L, Long Beach)	87,868
	John W. Wydler* (R, C, Garden City)	**110,366**
6.	Lester L. Wolff* (D, L, Great Neck)	**112,422**
	Vincent R. Balletta Jr. (R, Port Washington)	60,567
	Nelson J. Gammans (C, Oyster Bay)	8,958
7.	Joseph P. Addabbo* (D, R, L, Ozone Park)	**107,312**
	William H. Whitman (C, Ozone Park)	5,321
8.	Benjamin S. Rosenthal* (D, L, Elmhurst)	**107,295**
	Albert Lemishow (R, C, Flushing)	30,191
9.	James J. Delaney* (D, R, C, Long Island City)	**109,552**
	Alan M. Kluger (L, Flushing)	5,643
10.	Mario Biaggi* (D, R, Bronx)	**106,222**
	John P. Hagan (L, Bronx)	3,872
	Joanne S. Fuchs (C, Bronx)	5,868
11.	James H. Scheuer* (D, Neponsit)	**84,770**
	Arthur Cuccia (R, Brooklyn)	19,203

Dist	Representative (party, home)	1976 Election
	Joseph Rothenberg (L, Rockaway Park)	4,169
	Bryan F. Levinson (C, Howard Beach)	6,316
12.	Shirley Chisholm* (D, L, Brooklyn)	**43,203**
	Horace L. Morancie (R, Brooklyn)	5,336
	Martin S. Shepherd Jr. (C, Brooklyn)	1,093
13.	Stephen J. Solarz* (D, L, Brooklyn)	**110,624**
	Jack Dobosh (R, C, Brooklyn)	21,600
14.	Frederick W. Richmond* (D, L, Brooklyn)	**55,723**
	Frank X. Gargiulo (R, C, Brooklyn)	8,977
15.	Leo C. Zeferetti* (D, C, Brooklyn)	**69,242**
	Ronald J. D'Angelo (R, Brooklyn)	33,641
16.	Elizabeth Holtzman* (D, L, Brooklyn)	**93,995**
	Gladys Pemberton (R, C, Brooklyn)	19,423
17.	John M. Murphy* (D, Staten Island)	**89,126**
	Kenneth J. Grossberger (R, New York)	27,734
	John M. Peters (C, Staten Island)	10,399
	Ned Schneier (L, New York)	8,656
18.	Edward I. Koch* (D, L, New York)	**112,187**
	Sonia Landau (R, New York)	29,728
	James W. McConnell (C, New York)	6,319
19.	Charles B. Rangel* (D, R, L, New York)	**91,672**
	Benton Cole (C, New York)	2,169
20.	Theodore S. Weiss (D, L, New York)	**91,977**
	Denise T. Wiseman (R, New York)	14,114
	Herman Dinsmore (C, New York)	3,323
21.	Herman Badillo* (D, R, L, Bronx)	**41,285**
	Lawrence W. Lindsley Sr. (C, Bronx)	598
22.	Jonathan B. Bingham* (D, L, Bronx)	**92,044**
	Paul Slotkin (R, Bronx)	11,130
	Patrick J. Bonner (C, Bronx)	3,418
23.	J. Edward Meyer (D, L, New Castle)	80,424
	Bruce F. Caputo (R, C, Yonkers)	**93,006**
24.	Richard L. Ottinger* (D, Pleasantville)	**99,761**
	David V. Hicks (R, C, Briarcliff Manor)	81,111
	Edmund D. Assante (L, New Rochelle)	2,140
25.	Minna Post Peyser (D, L, Putnam Valley)	58,216
	Hamilton Fish Jr.* (R, C, Millbrook)	**139,389**
26.	John R. Maloney (D, Nanuet)	60,511
	Benjamin A. Gilman* (R, C, Middletown)	**120,049**
	Eugene R. Victor (L)	3,421
27.	Matthew F. McHugh* (D, L, Ithaca)	**127,048**
	William H. Harter (R, C, Margaretville)	63,626
28.	Samuel S. Stratton* (D, L, Amsterdam)	**170,034**
	Mary A. Bradt (R, C, Schenectady)	44,053
29.	Edward W. Pattison* (D, L, West Sand Lake)	**100,663**
	Joseph A. Martino (R, Ballston Lake)	96,476
	James E. De Young (C)	15,337
30.	Norma A. Bartle (D, L, Oswego)	75,951
	Robert C. McEwen* (R, C, Ogdensburg)	**95,564**
31.	Anita Maxwell (D, L, Newport)	62,032
	Donald J. Mitchell* (R, C, Herkimer)	**123,143**
32.	James M. Hanley* (D, Syracuse)	**101,419**
	George C. Wortley (R, C, Manlius)	81,597
	Earl W. Colvin (L, Syracuse)	2,124
33.	Charles R. Welch (D, Camillus)	48,855
	William F. Walsh* (R, Syracuse)	**125,163**
	Lillian Reiner (L, Syracuse)	2,757
	William C. Elkins (C, Burdett)	5,980
34.	William C. Larsen (D, L, Pittsford)	58,247
	Frank J. Horton* (R, Rochester)	**126,566**
	Thomas D. Cook (C, Pittsford)	7,383
35.	Michael Macaluso Sr. (D, L, Rochester)	67,177
	Barber B. Conable Jr.* (R, C, Alexander)	**120,738**
36.	John J. La Falce* (D, L, Kenmore)	**123,246**
	Ralph J. Argen (R, C, Eggertsville)	61,701
37.	Henry J. Nowak* (D, L, Buffalo)	**100,042**
	Calvin Kimbrough (R, Grand Island)	23,660
	Stephen Grimm (C, Buffalo)	4,249
38.	Peter J. Geraci (D, L, N. Tonawanda)	46,307
	Jack F. Kemp* (R, C, Hamburg)	**165,702**
39.	Stanley N. Lundine* (D, L, Jamestown)	**109,986**
	Richard A. Snowden (R, C, Olean)	68,018

North Carolina

Dist	Representative (party, home)	1976 Election
1.	Walter B. Jones* (D, Farmville)	**98,611**
	Joseph M. Ward (R, Greenville)	29,295
2.	L. H. Fountain* (D, Tarboro)	**Unopposed**
3.	Charles Whitley (D, Mt. Olive)	**77,193**
	Willard J. (Jack) Blanchard (R, Salemburg)	35,089
4.	Ike Andrews* (D, Siler City)	**92,165**
	Johnnie L. Gallemore Jr. (R, Durham)	59,917
5.	Stephen L. (Steve) Neal* (D, Winston-Salem)	**98,783**
	Wilmer (Vinegar Bend) Mizell (R, Winston-Salem)	83,129
6.	Richardson Preyer* (D, Greensboro)	**103,851**
	Carl Wagle (L)	2,137
7.	Charles G. Rose* (D, Fayetteville)	**95,463**
	M. H. (Mike) Vaughan (R, Wilmington)	21,955
8.	W. G. (Bill) Hefner* (D, Concord)	**99,296**
	Carl Eagle (R, Salisbury)	49,094
9.	Arthur Goodman Jr. (D, Charlotte)	70,847
	James G. Martin* (R, Davidson)	**82,297**
10.	John J. (Jack) Hunt (D, Lattimore)	67,190
	James T. (Jim) Broyhill* (R, Lenoir)	**99,882**
11.	Lamar Gudger (D, Asheville)	**93,857**
	Bruce Briggs (R, Mars Hill)	88,752

North Dakota - At Large

Dist	Representative (party, home)	1976 Election
	Lloyd B. Omdahl (D, Grand Forks)	104,263
	Mark Andrews* (R, Mapleton)	**181,018**

Ohio

Dist	Representative (party, home)	1976 Election
1.	William F. Bowen (D, Cincinnati)	56,995
	Willis D. Gradison Jr.* (R, Cincinnati)	**109,789**
2.	Thomas A. Luken (D, Cincinnati)	**88,178**
	Donald D. Clancy* (R, Cincinnati)	83,459
3.	Leonard E. Stubbs Jr. (D, Dayton)	33,873
	Charles W. Whalen Jr.* (R, Dayton)	**100,871**
4.	Clinton G. Dorsey (D, Troy)	51,784
	Tennyson Guyer* (R, Findlay)	**121,173**
5.	Bruce Edwards (D, Bowling Green)	60,304
	Delbert L. Latta* (R, Bowling Green)	**124,910**
6.	Ted Strickland (D, Lucasville)	67,067
	William H. Harsha* (R, Portsmouth)	**107,064**
7.	Dorothy Franke (D, Lucasville)	54,755
	Clarence J. Brown (R, Urbana)	**101,027**
8.	John W. Griffin (D, Miamisburg)	46,424
	Thomas N. Kindness* (R, Hamilton)	**110,775**
9.	Thomas Ludlow Ashley* (D, Maumee)	**91,040**
	Carleton S. Finkbeiner (R, Toledo)	73,919
10.	James A. Plummer (D, Jackson)	57,757
	Clarence E. Miller* (R, Lancaster)	**127,147**
11.	Thomas R. West Jr. (D, Hubbard)	47,548
	J. William Stanton* (R, Painesville)	**120,716**
12.	Francine Ryan (D, Columbus)	89,424
	Samuel L. Devine* (R, Columbus)	**90,987**
13.	Donald J. Pease (D, Oberlin)	**108,061**
	Woodrow W. Mathna (R, Lorain)	49,828
14.	John F. Seiberling* (D, Akron)	**121,652**
	James E. Houston (R, Akron)	39,917
15.	Mike McGee (D, Columbus)	57,741
	Chalmers P. Wylie* (R, Worthington)	**109,630**
16.	John G. Freedom (D, North Canton)	55,671
	Ralph Regula* (R, Navarre)	**116,374**
17.	John C. McDonald (D, Newark)	72,168
	John M. Ashbrook* (R, Johnstown)	**94,874**
18.	Douglas Applegate (D, Steubenville)	**116,901**
	Ralph R. McCoy (R, Woodsfield)	45,735
19.	Charles J. Carney* (D, Youngstown)	**90,386**
	Jack C. Hunter (R, Youngstown)	86,162
20.	Mary Rose Oakar (D, Cleveland)	**98,785**
	Raymond J. Grabow (I)	20,553
21.	Louis Stokes* (D, Warrensville Heights)	**91,903**
	Barbara Sparks (R, Shaker Heights)	12,434
22.	Charles A. Vanik* (D, Euclid)	**128,535**
	Harry A. Hanna (R, Shaker Heights)	42,727
23.	Ronald M. Mottl* (D, Parma)	**130,576**
	Michael T. Scanlon (R, North Olmsted)	47,804

Oklahoma

Dist	Representative (party, home)	1976 Election
1.	James R. Jones* (D, Tulsa)	**100,945**
	James M. Inhofe (R, Tulsa)	84,374

Dist	Representative (party, home)	1976 Election
2.	Theodore M. (Ted) Risenhoover* (D, Tahlequah)	**102,402**
	Bud Stewart (R, Muskogee)	87,341
3.	Wes Watkins (D, Ada)	**151,271**
	Gerald Beasley Jr. (R, Duncan)	31,732
4.	Tom Steed* (D, Shawnee)	**116,425**
	M. C. Stanley (R, Midwest City)	34,170
5.	Tom Dunlap (D, Oklahoma City)	74,752
	Mickey Edwards (R, Oklahoma City)	**78,651**
6.	Glenn English* (D, Cordell)	**137,498**
	Carol McCurley (R, Yukon)	55,953

Oregon

Dist	Representative (party, home)	1976 Election
1.	Les AuCoin* (D, Forest Grove)	**154,844**
	Phil Bladine (R, McMinnville)	109,140
2.	Al Ullman,* (D, Baker)	**173,313**
	Thomas H. Mercer (R, Bend)	67,431
3.	Robert B. Duncan* (D, Portland)	**148,503**
	Martin Simon (I)	28,245
4.	James Weaver (D, Eugene)	**122,475**
	Jerry Lausmann (R, Medford)	85,943

Pennsylvania

Dist	Representative (party, home)	1976 Election
1.	Michael O. Myers (D, Philadelphia)	**117,087**
	Samuel N. Fanelli (R, Philadelphia)	40,191
2.	Robert N. C. Nix* (D, Philadelphia)	**109,855**
	Jesse W. Woods Jr. (R, Philadelphia)	37,907
3.	Raymond F. Lederer (D, Philadelphia)	**98,627**
	Terence J. Schade (R, Philadelphia)	35,491
4.	Joshua Eilberg* (D, Philadelphia)	**144,890**
	James E. Mugford (R, Philadelphia)	69,700
5.	Anthony Campolo (D, St. Davids)	81,299
	Richard T. Schulze* (R, Malvern)	**119,682**
6.	Gus Yatron* (D, Reading)	**133,624**
	Stephen Postupack (R, Tamaqua)	46,103
7.	Robert W. Edgar* (D, Bromall)	**109,436**
	John M. Kenney (R, Swarthmore)	92,788
8.	Peter H. Kostmayer (D, Solebury)	93,855
	John S. Renninger (R, Newton)	92,543
9.	Bud Shuster* (R, Everett)	**Unopposed**
10.	Edward Mitchell (D, Scranton)	74,925
	Joseph M. McDade* (R, Scranton)	**125,218**
11.	Daniel J. Flood* (D, Wilkes-Barre)	**130,175**
	Howard G. Williams (R, Wilkes-Barre)	53,621
12.	John P. Murtha* (D, Johnstown)	**122,504**
	Theodore L. Humes (R, Johnstown)	58,409
13.	Gertrude Strick (D, Jenkintown)	75,435
	Lawrence Coughlin* (R, Villanova)	**130,705**
14.	William S. Moorhead* (D, Pittsburgh)	**114,472**
	John F. Bradley (R, Pittsburgh)	43,308
15.	Fred B. Rooney* (D, Bethlehem)	**108,844**
	Alice B. Sivulich (R, Easton)	57,616
16.	Michael J. Minney (D, Lancaster)	57,836
	Robert S. Walker (R, East Petersburg)	**97,527**
17.	Allen E. Ertel (D, Montoursville)	**86,158**
	H. J. Hepford (R, Harrisburg)	82,370
18.	Douglas Walgren (D, Pittsburgh)	**113,787**
	Robert J. Casey (R, Pittsburgh)	77,594
19.	Richard P. Noll (D, York)	51,686
	William F. Goodling* (R, Jacobus)	**124,098**
20.	Joseph M. Gaydos* (D, McKeesport)	**134,961**
	Joseph P. Kostelac (R, White Oak)	44,432
21.	John H. Dent* (D, Greensburg)	**99,160**
	Robert H. Miller (R, Greensburg)	67,763
22.	Austin J. Murphy (D, Monongahela)	**97,036**
	Roger R. Fischer (R, Washington)	77,030
23.	Joseph S. Ammerman (D, Curwensville)	**95,821**
	Albert W. Johnson* (R, Smethport)	73,641
24.	Joseph P. Vigorito* (D, Erie)	79,937
	Marc L. Marks (R, Sharon)	**101,048**
25.	Eugene V. Atkinson (D, Aliquippa)	78,857
	Gary A. Myers* (R, Butler)	**103,632**

Rhode Island

Dist	Representative (party, home)	1976 Election
1.	Fernand J. St. Germain* (D, Woonsocket)	**116,674**
	John J. Slocum Jr. (R, Newport)	68,080
2.	Edward P. Beard* (D, Cranston)	**154,453**
	Thomas V. Iannitti (R, West Warwick)	45,438

South Carolina

Dist	Representative (party, home)	1976 Election
1.	Mendel J. Davis* (D, Charleston)	**89,891**
	Lonnie Rowell (R, Summerville)	40,598
2.	Clyde Burns Livingston (D, Orangeburg)	60,602
	Floyd D. Spence* (R, Lexington)	**83,426**
3.	Butler C. Derrick* (D, Edgefield)	**Unopposed**
4.	James R. Mann* (D, Greenville)	**91,721**
	Robert L. Watkins (R, Greenville)	32,983
5.	Kenneth L. Holland* (D, Camden)	**66,073**
	Robert C. Richardson Jr. (R, Sumter)	62,095
6.	John W. Jenrette Jr.*(D, North Myrtle Beach)	**75,916**
	Edward L. Young (R, Florence)	60,288

South Dakota

Dist	Representative (party, home)	1976 Election
1.	James V. Guffey (D, Watertown)	29,533
	Larry Pressler* (R, Humboldt)	**121,587**
2.	Grace Mickelson (D, Rapid City)	42,968
	James Abdnor* (R, Kennebec)	**99,601**

Tennessee

Dist	Representative (party, home)	1976 Election
1.	Lloyd H. Blevins (D, Kingsport)	69,507
	James H. (Jimmy) Quillen* (R, Kingsport)	**97,781**
2.	Mike Rowland (D, Knoxville)	69,449
	John J. Duncan* (R, Knoxville)	**117,256**
3.	Marilyn Lloyd* (D, Chattanooga)	**123,872**
	Lamar Baker (R, Chattanooga)	57,116
4.	Albert Gore Jr. (D, Carthage)	**115,392**
	William H. McGlamery (I)	7,320
5.	Clifford Allen* (D, Nashville)	**125,830**
	Bissell (I)	10,292
6.	Ross Bass (D, Pulaski)	64,462
	Robin L. Beard Jr.* (R, Brentwood)	**116,905**
7.	Ed Jones * (D, Yorkville)	**Unopposed**
8.	Harold E. Ford* (D, Memphis)	**100,683**
	A. D. (Andy) Allissandratos (R, Memphis)	63,819

Texas

Dist	Representative (party, home)	1976 Election
1.	Sam B. Hall Jr.*(D, Marshall)	**135,384**
	James Hogan (R, Atlanta)	26,334
2.	Charles Wilson* (D, Lufkin)	**133,910**
	James W. Doyle (A)	6,992
3.	Les Shackelford Jr. (D, Dallas)	60,070
	James M. Collins* (R, Dallas)	**171,343**
4.	Ray Roberts* (D, McKinney)	**105,394**
	Frank S. Glenn (R, Flint)	62,641
5.	Jim Mattox (D, Dallas)	**67,871**
	Nancy Judy (R, Dallas)	56,056
6.	Olin E. Teague* (D, College Station)	**119,025**
	Wes Mowery (R, Fort Worth)	60,361
7.	Bill Archer* (R, Houston)	**Unopposed**
8.	Bob Eckhardt* (D, Houston)	**84,404**
	Nick Gearhart (R, Houston)	54,566
9.	Jack Brooks* (D, Beaumont)	**Unopposed**
10.	J. J. Pickle* (D, Austin)	**160,683**
	Paul MClure (R, Austin)	48,482
11.	W. R. Poage* (D, Waco)	**92,142**
	Jack Burgess (R, Waco)	68,373
12.	Jim Wright* (D, Fort Worth)	**101,814**
	W. R. Durham (R, Fort Worth)	31,941
13.	Jack Hightower* (D, Vernon)	**101,798**
	Bob Price (R, Pampa)	69,328
14.	John Young* (D, Corpus Christi)	**93,589**
	I. Dean Holford (R, Port Lavaca)	58,788
15.	E. (Kika) de la Garza* (D, Mission)	**102,837**
	R. L. (Lendy) McDonald (R, Los Fresnos)	35,446
16.	Richard C. White* (D, El Paso)	**71,876**
	Vic Shackelford (R, Odessa)	52,499
17.	Omar Burleson* (D, Abilene)	**Unopposed**
18.	Barbara Jordan* (D, Houston)	**93,953**
	Sam H. Wright (R, Houston)	15,381
19.	George Mahon* (D, Lubbock)	**87,908**
	Jim Reese (R, Odessa)	72,991

Dist	Representative (party, home)	1976 Election
20.	Henry B. Gonzalez* (D, San Antonio)	**Unopposed**
21.	Robert (Bob) Krueger* (D, New Braunfels)	**149,395**
	Bobby A. Locke (R, San Antonio)	56,211
22.	Bob Gammage (D, Houston)	96,535
	Ron Paul* (R, Lake Jackson)	**96,267**
23.	Abraham (Chick) Kazen Jr.* (D, Laredo)	**Unopposed**
24.	Dale Milford* (D, Grand Prairie)	**82,743**
	Leo Berman (R, Arlington)	47,075
	Utah	
1.	Gunn McKay* (D, Huntsville)	**155,631**
	Joe H. Ferguson (R, American Fork)	106,542
	Harry B. Gerlach (A)	5,358
2.	Allan T. Howe* (D, Salt Lake City)	110,931
	Dan Marriott (R, Salt Lake City)	**144,681**
	Darrell McCarty (I)	20,508
	Vermont — At Large	
	John A. Burgess (D, Montpelier)	60,602
	James M. Jeffords* (R, Rutland)	**124,458**
	Virginia	
1.	Robert E. Quinn (D, Hampton)	70,159
	Paul S. Trible Jr. (R, Tappahannock)	**71,789**
2.	Robert E. (Bob) Washington (D, Norfolk)	41,464
	G. William Whitehurst* (R, Virginia Beach)	**79,381**
3.	David E. Satterfield III* (D, Richmond)	**129,066**
	Alan R. Ogden (I, Richmond)	17,503
4.	J. W. "Billy" O'Brien (D, Chesapeake)	65,982
	Robert W. "Bob" Daniel Jr.* (R, Spring Grove)	**74,495**
5.	W. C. (Dan) Daniel* (D, Danville)	**Unopposed**
6.	M. Caldwell Butler* (R, Roanoke)	**90,830**
	Warren D. Saunders (I, Moneta)	55,115
7.	J. Kenneth Robinson* (R, Winchester)	**115,508**
	James B. Hutt Jr. (I, Warrenton)	25,731
8.	Herbert E. Harris II* (D, Alexandria)	**83,245**
	James R. Tate (R, Fairfax)	68,729
9.	Charles J. Horne (D, Abingdon)	71,439
	William C. Wampler* (R, Bristol)	**96,052**
10.	Joseph L. Fisher* (D, Arlington)	**103,689**
	Vincent F. Callahan Jr. (R, McLean)	73,616
	E. Stanley Rittenhouse (I, Dunn Loring)	12,124
	Washington	
1.	Dave Wood (D, Seattle)	58,006
	Joel Pritchard* (R, Seattle)	**161,354**
2.	Lloyd Meeds* (D, Lake Stevens)	**107,328**
	John Nance Garner (R, Everett)	106,786
3.	Don Bonker* (D, Olympia)	**145,198**
	Chuck Elhart (R, Lacey)	57,517
4.	Mike McCormack* (D, Richland)	**115,364**
	Dick Granger (R, Vancouver)	81,813
5.	Thomas S. Foley* (D, Spokane)	**120,415**
	Duane Alton (R, Spokane)	84,262
6.	Norman D. Dicks (D, Port Orchard)	**137,964**
	Robert M. Reynolds (R, Racoma)	47,539
7.	Brock Adams* (D, Seattle)	**133,673**
	Raymond Pritchard (R, Seattle)	46,448
	West Virginia	
1.	Robert H. Mollohan* (D, Fairmont)	**108,055**
	John F. McCuskey (R, Bridgeport)	78,134
2.	Harley O. Staggers* (D, Keyser)	**145,405**
	Jim Sloan (R, Beverly)	52,230
3.	John M. Slack* (D, Charleston)	**Unopposed**
4.	Nick Joe Rahall II (D, Beckley)	**73,626**
	E. S. (Steve) Goodman (R, Huntington)	28,825
	Hechler (Ind.)	59,067
	Wisconsin	
1.	Les Aspin* (D, Racine)	**136,162**
	William W. Petrie (R, Waterford)	71,427
2.	Robert W. Kastenmeier* (D, Sun Prairie)	**155,158**
	Elizabeth T. Miller (R, Portage)	81,350
3.	Alvin J. Baldus* (D, Menomonie)	**139,083**
	Adolf L. Gundersen (R, LaCrosse)	100,218
4.	Clement J. Zablocki* (D, Milwaukee)	**Unopposed**
5.	Henry S. Reuss* (D, Milwaukee)	**134,935**
	Robert L. Hicks (R, Milwaukee)	36,413
6.	Joseph C. Smith (D, Oshkosh)	80,715
	William A. Steiger* (R, Oshkosh)	**139,541**
7.	David R. Obey* (D, Wausau)	**171,366**
	Frank A. Savino (R, Schofield)	60,952
8.	Robert J. Cornell* (D, DePere)	**115,996**
	Harold V. Froehlich (R, Appleton)	107,048
9.	Lynn M. McDonald (D, Whitefish Bay)	84,706
	Robert W. Kasten Jr.* (R, Theinsville)	**163,791**
	Wyoming At Large	
	Teno Roncalio* (D, Cheyenne)	**85,721**
	Larry Hart (R, Powell)	66,147

Non-Voting Delegates

District of Columbia	Walter E. Fauntroy* (D, D.C.)
Guam	Antonio Borja Won Pat* (D, Agana)
Virgin Islands	Ron De Lugo* (D, Christiansted)

Puerto Rico

Jaime Benitez* (Pop. D, Cayey)	663,160
Baltasar Corrada del Rio (New Prog., San Juan)	**705,162**
Baltasar Quinones Elias (P.R.Ind.)	72,988

95th Congress—Standing Committees and Chairmen

Senate

Agriculture	Frank Church (Ida.)
Appropriations	John McClellan (Ark.)
Armed Services	John Stennis (Miss.)
Banking & Urban	William Proxmire (Wis.)
Budget	Edmund Muskie (Me.)
Conduct (Ethics)	Adlai Stevenson 3d (Ill.)
Commerce, Trnsprtn	Warren Magnuson (Wash.)
Energy, Resources	Henry Jackson (Wash.)
Finance	Russell Long (La.)
Foreign Relations	John Sparkman (Ala.)
Governmentl Affairs	Abraham Ribicoff (Conn.)
Human Resources	Harrison Williams Jr. (N.J.)
Indian Affairs	James Abourezk (S.D.)
Intelligence	Daniel Inouye (Ha.)
Judiciary	James Eastland (Miss.)
Nutrition, Needs	George McGovern (S.D.)
Rules	Howard Cannon (Nev.)
Small Business	Gaylord Nelson (Wis.)
Veterans Affairs	Alan Cranston (Cal.)

House

Agriculture	Thomas Foley (Wash.)
Appropriations	George Mahon (Tex.)
Armed Services	Melvin Price (Ill.)
Banking & Urban	Henry S. Reuss (Wis.)
Budget	Robert Giaimo (Conn.)
Commerce	Harley Staggers (W.Va.)
Conduct (Ethics)	John T. Flint Jr. (Ga.)
Dist. of Columbia	Charles Diggs (Mich.)
Education, Labor	Carl Perkins (Ky.)
Intrntl Relations	Clement Zablocki (Wis.)
Govt Operations	Jack Brooks (Tex.)
Interior, Insular	Morris Udall (Ariz.)
Judiciary	Peter Rodino (N.J.)
Marine, Fisheries	John Murphy (N.Y.)
P.O., Civil Service	Robert Nix (Pa.)
Public Works	Harold Johnson (Cal.)
Rules	James J. Delaney (N.Y.)
Science, Tech.	Olin Teague (Tex.)
Small Business	Neal Smith (Ia.)
Veterans Affairs	Ray Roberts (Tex.)
Ways and Means	Al Ullman (Ore.)

Electoral Votes for President, 1960-76

The Constitution, Article 2, Section 1 (consult index), provides for the appointment of electors, the counting of the elec-
oral ballots and the procedure in the event of a tie. *(See Electoral College.)*

State	1960 R.	1960 D.	1964 R.	1964 D.	1968 R.	1968 D.	1968 3d	1972 R.	1972 D.	1976 R.	1976 D.
la.	...	[1]5	10	...	...	...	10	9	...	...	9
las.	[2]3	...	...	3	...	...	3	...	3	3	...
riz.	4	...	5	...	5	...	...	6	...	6	...
rk.	...	8	...	6	...	...	6	6	...	...	6
al.	32	...	...	40	40	...	...	45	...	45	...
ol.	6	...	...	6	6	...	...	7	...	7	...
onn.	...	8	...	8	...	8	...	8	...	8	...
el.	...	3	...	3	3	...	...	3	...	...	3
.C.	...	...	...	3	...	3	...	...	3	...	3
la.	10	...	...	14	14	...	...	17	...	...	17
a.	...	12	12	...	...	...	12	12	...	...	12
a.	...	[2]3	...	4	...	4	...	4	...	...	4
da.	4	...	...	4	4	...	...	4	...	4	...
l.	...	27	...	26	26	...	...	26	...	26	...
nd.	13	...	...	13	13	...	...	13	...	13	...
a.	10	...	...	9	9	...	...	8	...	8	...
an.	8	...	...	7	7	...	...	7	...	7	...
y.	20	...	...	9	9	...	...	9	...	...	9
a.	...	10	10	...	...	...	10	10	...	...	10
le.	5	...	...	4	...	4	...	4	...	4	...
ld.	...	9	...	10	...	10	...	10	...	...	10
lass.	...	16	...	14	...	14	...	...	14	...	14
lich.	...	20	...	21	...	21	...	21	...	21	...
linn.	...	11	...	10	...	10	...	10	...	...	10
liss.	...	(2)	7	...	...	...	7	7	...	...	7
lo.	...	13	...	12	12	...	...	12	...	...	12
lon.	4	...	...	4	4	...	...	4	...	4	...
Neb.	6	...	...	5	5	...	...	5	...	5	...
Nev.	...	3	...	3	3	...	...	3	...	3	...
N.H.	4	...	...	4	4	...	...	4	...	4	...
N.J.	...	16	...	17	17	...	...	17	...	17	...
N.M.	...	4	...	4	4	...	...	4	...	4	...
N.Y.	...	45	...	43	...	43	...	41	...	...	41
N.C.	...	14	...	13	12	...	(3)	1	...	13	...
N.D.	4	...	...	4	4	...	...	3	...	3	...
Oh.	25	...	...	26	26	...	...	25	...	...	25
Okla.	[1]7	...	...	8	8	...	...	8	...	8	...
Ore.	6	...	...	6	6	...	...	6	...	6	...
Pa.	...	32	...	29	...	29	...	27	...	...	27
R.I.	...	4	...	4	...	4	...	4	...	...	4
S.C.	...	8	8	...	8	...	...	8	...	...	8
S.D.	4	...	...	4	4	...	...	4	...	4	...
Tenn.	11	...	...	11	11	...	...	10	...	...	10
Tex.	...	24	...	25	...	25	...	26	...	...	26
Ut.	4	...	...	4	4	...	...	4	...	4	...
Vt.	3	...	...	3	3	...	...	3	...	3	...
Va.	12	...	...	12	12	...	...	[4]11	...	12	...
Wash.	9	...	...	9	...	9	...	9	...	[5]8	...
W. Va.	...	8	...	7	...	7	...	6	...	...	6
Wis.	12	...	...	12	12	...	...	11	...	...	11
Wy.	3	...	...	3	3	...	...	3	...	3	...
Totals	**219**	**303**	**52**	**486**	**301**	**191**	**46**	**520**	**17**	**240**	**297**
Plurality	...	**[1]84**	...	**434**	**110**	...	...	**[4]503**	...	...	**57**

) In 1960 Sen. Harry F. Byrd (D-Va.) got 15 electoral votes including those of 8 unpledged Miss. Dem. electors, 6 unpledged Ala. Dem., and ne Okla. Rep. (2) First Presidential election. (3) In 1968 in N. C. one Rep. elector cast his ballot for Wallace. (4) In 1972 one Rep. elector in a. cast his ballot for John Hospers. (5) In 1976 one Rep. elector in Wash. cast his ballot for Reagan.

Voter Turnout in Presidential Elections

Source: League of Women Voters

National average of voting age population voting: 1960—63%; 1964—62%; 1968—60%; 1972—55.4%; 1976—56.5%. The harp drop in 1972 reflects the expansion of eligibility with the enfranchisement of 18 to 21 year olds.

	1976 Registered voters voting	1976 Voting age population voting	1972 Voting age population voting
la.	63%	47%	44%
las.	59	53	48
riz.	78	49	52
rk.	71	48	49
al.	79	51	60
ol.	81	61	61
onn.	84	64	66
el.	78	58	64
.C.	59	31	32
la.	77	50	51
a.	64	43	38
a.	85	52	51
da.	68	63	65
l.	76	61	63
nd.	76	61	61
a.	n/a	64	64
an.	86	59	59
Ky.	68	49	48
La.	69	50	45
Me.	n/a	66	63
Md.	74	50	50
Mass.	82	62	62
Mich.	72	59	59
Minn.	77	73	68
Miss.	70	50	46
Mo.	82	58	57
Mon.	75	66	69
Neb.	74	58	56
Nev.	82	49	52
N.H.	71	59	64
N.J.	79	58	60
N.M.	81	55	61
N.Y.	78	52	56
N.C.	66	44	44
N.D.	*	71	70
Oh.	89	56	57
Okla.	n/a	57	57
Ore.	78	62	62
Pa.	80	55	56
R.I.	77	63	62
S.C.	72	52	40
S.D.	71	64	71
Tenn.	69	50	44
Tex.	64	48	45
Ut.	78	70	70
Vt.	73	64	61
Va.	81	49	46
Wash.	77	62	62
W.Va.	69	59	65
Wis.	n/a	65	63
Wyo.	82	60	65

No statewide registration. n/a—not available.

Party Nominees for President and Vice President

Asterisk (*) denotes winning ticket

Year	Democratic President	Democratic Vice President	Republican President	Republican Vice President
916	Woodrow Wilson*	Thomas R. Marshall	Charles E. Hughes	Charles W. Fairbanks
920	James M. Cox	Franklin D. Roosevelt	Warren G. Harding*	Calvin Coolidge
924	John W. Davis	Charles W. Bryan	Calvin Coolidge*	Charles G. Dawes
928	Alfred E. Smith	Joseph T. Robinson	Herbert Hoover*	Charles Curtis
932	Franklin D. Roosevelt*	John N. Garner	Herbert Hoover	Charles Curtis
936	Franklin D. Roosevelt*	John N. Garner	Alfred M. Landon	Frank Knox
940	Franklin D. Roosevelt*	Henry A. Wallace	Wendell L. Willkie	Charles McNary
944	Franklin D. Roosevelt*	Harry S. Truman	Thomas E. Dewey	John W. Bricker
948	Harry S. Truman*	Alben W. Barkley	Thomas E. Dewey	Earl Warren
952	Adlai E. Stevenson	John J. Sparkman	Dwight D. Eisenhower*	Richard M. Nixon
956	Adlai E. Stevenson	Estes Kefauver	Dwight D. Eisenhower*	Richard M. Nixon
960	John F. Kennedy*	Lyndon B. Johnson	Richard M. Nixon	Henry Cabot Lodge
964	Lyndon B. Johnson*	Hubert H. Humphrey	Barry M. Goldwater	William E. Miller
968	Hubert H. Humphrey	Edmund S. Muskie	Richard M. Nixon*	Spiro T. Agnew
972	George S. McGovern	R. Sargent Shriver Jr.	Richard M. Nixon*	Spiro T. Agnew
976	Jimmy Carter*	Walter F. Mondale	Gerald R. Ford	Robert J. Dole

Presidents of the U.S.

No.	Name	Politics	Born	in	Inaug. at age	Died at age
1	George Washington	Fed.	1732, Feb. 22	Va.	1789.... 57	1799, Dec. 14..... 67
2	John Adams	Fed.	1735, Oct. 30	Mass.	1797.... 61	1826, July 4...... 90
3	Thomas Jefferson	Dem.-Rep.	1743, Apr. 13	Va.	1801.... 57	1826, July 4...... 83
4	James Madison	Dem.-Rep.	1751, Mar. 16	Va.	1809.... 57	1836, June 28..... 85
5	James Monroe	Dem.-Rep.	1753, Apr. 28	Va.	1817.... 58	1831, July 4...... 73
6	John Quincy Adams	Dem.-Rep.	1767, July 11	Mass.	1825.... 57	1848, Feb. 23..... 80
7	Andrew Jackson	Dem.	1767, Mar. 15	S.C.	1829.... 61	1845, June 8...... 78
8	Martin Van Buren	Dem.	1782, Dec. 5	N.Y.	1837.... 54	1862, July 24..... 79
9	William Henry Harrison	Whig	1773, Feb. 9	Va.	1841.... 68	1841, Apr. 4...... 68
10	John Tyler	Whig	1790, Mar. 29	Va.	1841.... 51	1862, Jan. 18..... 71
11	James Knox Polk	Dem.	1795, Nov. 2	N.C.	1845.... 49	1849, June 15..... 53
12	Zachary Taylor	Whig	1784, Nov. 24	Va.	1849.... 64	1850, July 9...... 65
13	Millard Fillmore	Whig	1800, Jan. 7	N.Y.	1850.... 50	1874, Mar. 8...... 74
14	Franklin Pierce	Dem.	1804, Nov. 23	N.H.	1853.... 48	1869, Oct. 8...... 64
15	James Buchanan	Dem.	1791, Apr. 23	Pa.	1857.... 65	1868, June 1...... 77
16	Abraham Lincoln	Rep.	1809, Feb. 12	Ky.	1861.... 52	1865, Apr. 15..... 56
17	Andrew Johnson	(1)	1808, Dec. 29	N.C.	1865.... 56	1875, July 31..... 66
18	Ulysses Simpson Grant	Rep.	1822, Apr. 27	Oh.	1869.... 46	1885, July 23..... 63
19	Rutherford Birchard Hayes	Rep.	1822, Oct. 4	Oh.	1877.... 54	1893, Jan. 17..... 70
20	James Abram Garfield	Rep.	1831, Nov. 19	Oh.	1881.... 49	1881, Sept. 19.... 49
21	Chester Alan Arthur	Rep.	1829, Oct. 5	Vt.	1881.... 50	1886, Nov. 18..... 57
22	Grover Cleveland	Dem.	1837, Mar. 18	N.J.	1885.... 47	1908, June 24..... 71
23	Benjamin Harrison	Rep.	1833, Aug. 20	Oh.	1889.... 55	1901, Mar. 13..... 67
24	Grover Cleveland	Dem.	1837, Mar. 18	N.J.	1893.... 55	1908, June 24..... 71
25	William McKinley	Rep.	1843, Jan. 29	Oh.	1897.... 54	1901, Sept. 14.... 58
26	Theodore Roosevelt	Rep.	1858, Oct. 27	N.Y.	1901.... 42	1919, Jan. 6...... 60
27	William Howard Taft	Rep.	1857, Sept. 15	Oh.	1909.... 51	1930, Mar. 8...... 72
28	Woodrow Wilson	Dem.	1856, Dec. 28	Va.	1913.... 56	1924, Feb. 3...... 67
29	Warren Gamaliel Harding	Rep.	1865, Nov. 2	Oh.	1921.... 55	1923, Aug. 2...... 57
30	Calvin Coolidge	Rep.	1872, July 4	Vt.	1923.... 51	1933, Jan. 5...... 60
31	Herbert Clark Hoover	Rep.	1874, Aug. 10	Ia.	1929.... 54	1964, Oct. 20..... 90
32	Franklin Delano Roosevelt	Dem.	1882, Jan. 30	N.Y.	1933.... 51	1945, Apr. 12..... 63
33	Harry S. Truman	Dem.	1884, May 8	Mo.	1945.... 60	1972, Dec. 26..... 88
34	Dwight David Eisenhower	Rep.	1890, Oct. 14	Tex.	1953.... 62	1969, Mar. 28..... 78
35	John Fitzgerald Kennedy	Dem.	1917, May 29	Mass.	1961.... 43	1963, Nov. 22..... 46
36	Lyndon Baines Johnson	Dem.	1908, Aug. 27	Tex.	1963.... 55	1973, Jan. 22..... 64
37	Richard Milhous Nixon (2)	Rep.	1913, Jan. 9	Cal.	1969.... 56	
38	Gerald Rudolph Ford	Rep.	1913, July 14	Neb.	1974.... 61	
39	Jimmy (James Earl) Carter	Dem.	1924, Oct. 1	Ga.	1977.... 52	

(1) Andrew Johnson — a Democrat, nominated vice president by Republicans and elected with Lincoln on National Union ticket. (2 Resigned Aug. 9, 1974.

Presidents, Vice Presidents, Congresses

	President	Service		Vice President	Congress
1	George Washington	Apr. 30, 1789—Mar. 3, 1797	1	John Adams	1, 2, 3, 4
2	John Adams	Mar. 4, 1797—Mar. 3, 1801	2	Thomas Jefferson	5, 6
3	Thomas Jefferson	Mar. 4, 1801—Mar. 3, 1805	3	Aaron Burr	7, 8
	"	Mar. 4, 1805—Mar. 3, 1809	4	George Clinton	9, 10
4	James Madison	Mar. 4, 1809—Mar. 3, 1813		" (1)	11, 12
	"	Mar. 4, 1813—Mar. 3, 1817	5	Elbridge Gerry (2)	13, 14
5	James Monroe	Mar. 4, 1817—Mar. 3, 1825	6	Daniel D. Tompkins	15, 16, 17, 18
6	John Quincy Adams	Mar. 4, 1825—Mar. 3, 1829	7	John C. Calhoun	19, 20
7	Andrew Jackson	Mar. 4, 1829—Mar. 3, 1833		" (3)	21, 22
	"	Mar. 4, 1833—Mar. 3, 1837	8	Martin Van Buren	23, 24
8	Martin Van Buren	Mar. 4, 1837—Mar. 3, 1841	9	Richard M. Johnson	25, 26
9	William Henry Harrison (4)	Mar. 4, 1841—Apr. 4, 1841	10	John Tyler	27
10	John Tyler	Apr. 6, 1841—Mar. 3, 1845			27, 28
11	James K. Polk	Mar. 4, 1845—Mar. 3, 1849	11	George M. Dallas	29, 30
12	Zachary Taylor (4)	Mar. 5, 1849—July 9, 1850	12	Millard Fillmore	31
13	Millard Fillmore	July 10, 1850—Mar. 3, 1853			31,32
14	Franklin Pierce	Mar. 4, 1853—Mar. 3, 1857	13	William R. King (5)	33, 34
15	James Buchanan	Mar. 4, 1857—Mar. 3, 1861	14	John C. Breckinridge	35, 36
16	Abraham Lincoln	Mar. 4, 1861—Mar. 3, 1865	15	Hannibal Hamlin	37, 38
	" (4)	Mar. 4, 1865—Apr. 15, 1865	16	Andrew Johnson	39
17	Andrew Johnson	Apr. 15, 1865—Mar. 3, 1869			39, 40
18	Ulysses S. Grant	Mar. 4, 1869—Mar. 3, 1873	17	Schuyler Colfax	41, 42
	"	Mar. 4, 1873—Mar. 3, 1877	18	Henry Wilson (6)	43, 44
19	Rutherford B. Hayes	Mar. 4, 1877—Mar. 3, 1881	19	William A. Wheeler	45, 46
20	James A. Garfield (4)	Mar. 4, 1881—Sept. 19, 1881	20	Chester A. Arthur	47
21	Chester A. Arthur	Sept. 20, 1881—Mar. 3, 1885			47, 48
22	Grover Cleveland (7)	Mar. 4, 1885—Mar. 3, 1889	21	Thomas A. Hendricks (8)	49, 50
23	Benjamin Harrison	Mar. 4, 1889—Mar. 3, 1893	22	Levi P. Morton	51, 52
24	Grover Cleveland (7)	Mar. 4, 1893—Mar. 3, 1897	23	Adlai E. Stevenson	53, 54
25	William McKinley	Mar. 4, 1897—Mar. 3, 1901	24	Garret A. Hobart (9)	55, 56
	" (4)	Mar. 4, 1901—Sept. 14, 1901	25	Theodore Roosevelt	57
26	Theodore Roosevelt	Sept. 14, 1901—Mar. 3, 1905			57, 58
	"	Mar. 4, 1905—Mar. 3, 1909	26	Charles W. Fairbanks	59, 60
27	William H. Taft	Mar. 4, 1909—Mar. 3, 1913	27	James S. Sherman (10)	61, 62
28	Woodrow Wilson	Mar. 4, 1913—Mar. 3, 1921	28	Thomas R. Marshall	63, 64, 65, 66
29	Warren G. Harding (4)	Mar. 4, 1921—Aug. 2, 1923	29	Calvin Coolidge	67
30	Calvin Coolidge	Aug. 3, 1923—Mar. 3, 1925			68
	"	Mar. 4, 1925—Mar. 3, 1929	30	Charles G. Dawes	69, 70
31	Herbert C. Hoover	Mar. 4, 1929—Mar. 3, 1933	31	Charles Curtis	71, 72

Franklin D. Roosevelt (16)	Mar. 4, 1933—Jan. 20, 1941	32 John N. Garner	73, 74, 75, 76
"	Jan. 20, 1941—Jan. 20, 1945	33 Henry A. Wallace	77, 78
" (4)	Jan. 20, 1945—Apr. 12, 1945	34 Harry S. Truman	79
Harry S. Truman	Apr. 12, 1945—Jan. 20, 1949		79, 80
"	Jan. 20, 1949—Jan. 20, 1953	35 Alben W. Barkley	81, 82
Dwight D. Eisenhower	Jan. 20, 1953—Jan. 20, 1961	36 Richard M. Nixon	83, 84, 85, 86
John F. Kennedy (4)	Jan. 20, 1961—Nov. 22, 1963	37 Lyndon B. Johnson	87, 88
Lyndon B. Johnson	Nov. 22, 1963—Jan. 20, 1965		88
"	Jan. 20, 1965—Jan. 20, 1969	38 Hubert H. Humphrey	89, 90
Richard M. Nixon	Jan. 20, 1969—Jan. 20, 1973	39 Spiro T. Agnew (11)	91, 92, 93
" (12)	Jan. 20, 1973—Aug. 9, 1974	40 Gerald R. Ford (13)	93
Gerald R. Ford (14)	Aug. 9, 1974—Jan. 20, 1977	41 Nelson A. Rockefeller (15)	93, 94
Jimmy (James Earl) Carter	Jan. 20, 1977—	42 Walter F. Mondale	95

) Died Apr. 20, 1812. (2) Died Nov. 23, 1814. (3) Resigned Dec. 28, 1832, to become U.S. Senator. (4) Died in office. (5) Died Apr. , 1853. (6) Died Nov. 22, 1875. (7) Terms not consecutive. (8) Died Nov. 25, 1885. (9) Died Nov. 21, 1899. (10) Died Oct. 30, 1912. 1) Resigned Oct. 10, 1973. (12) Resigned Aug. 9, 1974. (13) First non-elected vice president, chosen under 25th Amendment procere. (14) First non-elected president. (15) 2d non-elected vice president, sworn in Dec. 19, 1974. (16) First president to be inauguted under 20th Amendment, Jan. 20, 1937.

Vice Presidents of the U.S.

The numerals given vice presidents do not coincide with those given presidents, because some presidents had none and me had more than one.

	Name	Birthplace	Year	Residence	Inaug.	Politics	Place of death	Year	Age
1	John Adams	Quincy, Mass.	1735	Mass.	1789	Fed.	Quincy, Mass.	1826	90
2	Thomas Jefferson	Shadwell, Va.	1743	Va.	1797	Rep.	Monticello, Va.	1826	83
3	Aaron Burr	Newark, N.J.	1756	N.Y.	1801	Rep.	Staten Island, N.Y.	1836	80
4	George Clinton	Ulster Co., N.Y.	1739	N.Y.	1805	Rep.	Washington, D. C.	1812	73
5	Elbridge Gerry	Marblehead, Mass.	1744	Mass.	1813	Rep.	Washington, D. C.	1814	70
6	Daniel D. Tompkins	Scarsdale, N. Y.	1774	N. Y.	1817	Rep.	Staten Island, N. Y.	1825	51
7	John C. Calhoun (1)	Abbeville, S. C.	1782	S. C.	1825	Rep.	Washington, D. C.	1850	68
8	Martin Van Buren	Kinderhook, N. Y.	1782	N. Y.	1833	Dem.	Kinderhook, N. Y.	1862	79
9	Richard M. Johnson	Louisville, Ky.	1780	Ky.	1837	Dem.	Frankfort, Ky.	1850	70
10	John Tyler	Greenway, Va.	1790	Va.	1841	Whig.	Richmond, Va.	1862	71
11	George M. Dallas	Philadelphia, Pa.	1792	Pa.	1845	Dem.	Philadelphia, Pa.	1864	72
12	Millard Fillmore	Summerhill, N. Y.	1800	N. Y.	1849	Whig.	Buffalo, N. Y.	1874	74
13	William R. King	Sampson Co., N. C.	1786	Ala.	1853	Dem.	Dallas Co., Ala.	1853	67
14	John C. Breckinridge	Lexington, Ky.	1821	Ky.	1857	Dem.	Lexington, Ky.	1875	54
15	Hannibal Hamlin	Paris, Me.	1809	Me.	1861	Rep.	Bangor, Me.	1891	81
16	Andrew Johnson	Raleigh, N. C.	1808	Tenn.	1865	(2)	Carter Co., Tenn.	1875	66
17	Schuyler Colfax	New York City, N.Y.	1823	Ind.	1869	Rep.	Makato, Minn.	1885	62
18	Henry Wilson	Farmington, N.H.	1812	Mass.	1873	Rep.	Washington, D.C.	1875	63
19	William A. Wheeler	Malone, N.Y.	1819	N.Y.	1877	Rep.	Malone, N.Y.	1887	68
20	Chester A. Arthur	Fairfield, Vt.	1830	N.Y.	1881	Rep.	New York City, N.Y.	1886	56
21	Thomas A. Hendricks	Muskingum Co., Ohio	1819	Ind.	1885	Dem.	Indianapolis, Ind.	1885	66
22	Levi P. Morton	Shoreham, Vt.	1824	N.Y.	1889	Rep.	Rhinebeck, N.Y.	1920	96
23	Adlai E. Stevenson (3)	Christian Co., Ky.	1835	Ill.	1893	Dem.	Chicago, Ill.	1914	78
24	Garret A. Hobart	Long Branch, N.J.	1844	N.J.	1897	Rep.	Paterson, N.J.	1899	55
25	Theodore Roosevelt	New York City, N.Y.	1858	N.Y.	1901	Rep.	Oyster Bay, N.Y.	1919	60
26	Charles W. Fairbanks	Unionville Centre, Ohio	1852	Ind.	1905	Rep.	Indianapolis, Ind.	1918	66
27	James S. Sherman	Utica, N.Y.	1855	N.Y.	1909	Rep.	Utica, N.Y.	1912	57
28	Thomas R. Marshall	N. Manchester, Ind.	1854	Ind.	1913	Dem.	Washington, D.C.	1925	71
29	Calvin Coolidge	Plymouth, Vt.	1872	Mass.	1921	Rep.	Northampton, Mass.	1933	60
30	Charles G. Dawes	Marietta, Ohio	1865	Ill.	1925	Rep.	Evanston, Ill.	1951	85
31	Charles Curtis	Topeka, Kan.	1860	Kan.	1929	Rep.	Washington, D.C.	1936	76
32	John Nance Garner	Red River Co., Tex.	1868	Tex.	1933	Dem.	Uvalde, Tex.	1967	98
33	Henry Agard Wallace	Adair County, Ia.	1888	Iowa	1941	Dem.	Danbury, Conn.	1965	77
34	Harry S. Truman	Lamar, Mo.	1884	Mo.	1945	Dem.	Kansas City, Mo.	1972	88
35	Alben W. Barkley	Graves County, Ky.	1877	Ky.	1949	Dem.	Lexington, Va.	1956	78
36	Richard M. Nixon	Yorba Linda, Cal.	1913	Calif.	1953	Rep.			
37	Lyndon B. Johnson	Johnson City, Tex.	1908	Tex.	1961	Dem.	San Antonio, Tex.	1973	64
38	Hubert H. Humphrey	Wallace, S.D.	1911	Minn.	1965	Dem.			
39	Spiro T. Agnew	Baltimore, Md.	1918	Md.	1969	Rep.			
40	Gerald R. Ford	Omaha, Neb.	1913	Mich.	1973	Rep.			
41	Nelson A. Rockefeller	Bar Harbor, Me.	1908	N.Y.	1974	Rep.			
42	Walter F. Mondale	Ceylon, Minn.	1928	Minn.	1977	Dem.			

(1) John C. Calhoun resigned Dec. 28, 1832, having been elected to the Senate to fill a vacancy. (2) Andrew Johnson — a Democrat nominated by Republicans and elected with Lincoln on the National Union Ticket. (3) Adlai E. Stevenson, 23rd vice president, was grandfather of Democratic candidate for president, 1952 and 1956.

The Continental Congress: Meetings, Presidents

Meeting Places	Dates of Meetings	Congress Presidents	Date Elected
Philadelphia	Sept. 5 to Oct. 26, 1774	Peyton Randolph, Va. (1)	Sept. 5, 1774
"	"	Henry Middleton, S.C.	Oct. 22, 1774
Philadelphia	May 10, 1775 to Dec. 12, 1776	Peyton Randolph, Va.	May 10, 1775
"	"	John Hancock, Mass.	May 24, 1775
Baltimore	Dec. 20, 1776 to Mar. 4, 1777	"	
Philadelphia	Mar. 5 to Sept. 18, 1777	"	
Lancaster, Pa.	Sept. 27, 1777 (one day)	"	
York, Pa.	Sept. 30, 1777 to June 27, 1778	Henry Laurens, S.C.	Nov. 1, 1777(4)
Philadelphia	July 2, 1778 to June 21, 1783	John Jay, N.Y.	Dec. 10, 1778
"	"	Samuel Huntington, Conn.	Sept. 28, 1779
"	"	Thomas McKean, Del.	July 10, 1781
"	"	John Hanson, Md. (2)	Nov. 5, 1781
"	"	Elias Boudinot, N.J.	Nov. 4, 1782
Princeton, N.J.	June 30 to Nov. 4, 1783	Thomas Mifflin, Pa.	Nov. 3, 1783

Meeting Places	Dates of Meetings	Congress Presidents	Date Elected
Annapolis, Md.	Nov. 26, 1783 to June 3, 1784	"	
Trenton, N.J.	Nov. 1 to Dec. 24, 1784	Richard Henry Lee, Va.	Nov. 30, 1784
New York City	Jan. 11 to Nov. 4, 1785	"	
"	Nov. 7, 1785 to Nov. 3, 1786	John Hancock, Mass. (3)	Nov. 23, 1785
"	"	Nathaniel Gorman, Mass.	June 6, 1786
"	Nov. 6, 1786 to Oct. 30, 1787	Arthur St. Clair, Pa.	Feb. 2, 1787
"	Nov. 5, 1787 to Oct. 21, 1788	Cyrus Griffin, Va.	Jan. 22, 1788
"	Nov. 3, 1788 to Mar. 2, 1789	"	

(1) Resigned Oct. 22, 1774. (2) Titled "President of the United States in Congress Assembled," John Hanson is considered by some to be the first U.S. President as he was the first to serve under the Articles of Confederation. He was, however, little more than presiding officer of the Congress, which retained full executive power He could be considered the head of government, but not head of state. (3) Resigned May 29, 1786, without serving, because of illness. (4) Articles of Confederation agreed upon, Nov. 15, 1777; last ratification from Maryland, Mar. 1, 1781.

Cabinets of the U. S.

Secretaries of State

The Department of Foreign Affairs was created by act of Congress July 27, 1789, and the name changed to Department of State on Sept. 15.

President	Secretary	Home	Apptd.
Washington	Thomas Jefferson	Va.	1789
"	Edmund Randolph	"	1794
"	Timothy Pickering	Pa.	1795
J. Adams	"	"	1795
"	John Marshall	Va.	1800
Jefferson	James Madison	"	1801
Madison	Robert Smith	Md.	1809
"	James Monroe	Va.	1811
Monroe	John Quincy Adams	Mass.	1817
J. Q. Adams	Henry Clay	Ky.	1825
Jackson	Martin Van Buren	N.Y.	1829
"	Edward Livingston	La.	1831
"	Louis McLane	Del.	1833
"	John Forsyth	Ga.	1834
Van Buren	"	"	1837
W. H. Harrison	Daniel Webster	Mass.	1841
Tyler	"	"	1841
"	Abel P. Upshur	Va.	1843
"	John C. Calhoun	S. C.	1844
Polk	"	"	1845
"	James Buchanan	Pa.	1845
Taylor	"	"	1849
"	John M. Clayton	Del.	1849
Fillmore	"	"	1850
"	Daniel Webster	Mass.	1850
"	Edward Everett	"	1852
Pierce	William L. Marcy	N.Y.	1853
Buchanan	"	"	1857
"	Lewis Cass	Mich.	1857
"	Jeremiah S. Black	Pa.	1860
Lincoln	"	"	1861
"	William H. Seward	N. Y.	1861
Johnson, A.	"	"	1865
Grant	Elihu B. Washburne	Ill.	1869
"	Hamilton Fish	N. Y.	1869
Hayes	"	"	1877
"	William M. Evarts	"	1877
Garfield	"	"	1881
"	James G. Blaine	Me.	1881
Arthur	"	"	1881
"	F. T. Frelinghuysen	N. J.	1881
Cleveland	"	"	1885
"	Thomas F. Bayard	Del.	1885
B. Harrison	"	"	1889
"	James G. Blaine	Me.	1889
"	John W. Foster	Ind.	1892
Cleveland	Walter Q. Gresham	Ill.	1893
"	Richard Olney	Mass.	1895
McKinley	"	"	1897
"	John Sherman	Oh.	1897
"	William R. Day	"	1898
"	John Hay	D. C.	1898
T. Roosevelt	"	"	1901
"	Elihu Root	N. Y.	1905
"	Robert Bacon	"	1909
Taft	"	"	1909
"	Philander C. Knox	Pa.	1909
Wilson	"	"	1913
"	William J. Bryan	Neb.	1913
"	Robert Lansing	N. Y.	1915
"	Bainbridge Colby	"	1920
Harding	Charles E. Hughes	"	1921
Coolidge	"	"	1923
"	Frank B. Kellogg	Minn.	1925
Hoover	"	"	1929
"	Henry L. Stimson	N.Y.	1929
F. D. Roosevelt	Cordell Hull	Tenn.	1933
"	E. R. Stettinius Jr.	Va.	1944
Truman	"	"	1945
"	James F. Byrnes	S. C.	1945
"	George C. Marshall	Pa.	1947
"	Dean G. Acheson	Conn.	1949
Eisenhower	John Foster Dulles	N. Y.	1953
"	Christian A. Herter	Mass.	1959
Kennedy	Dean Rusk	N. Y.	1961
Johnson, L. B.	"	"	1963
Nixon	William P. Rogers	N. Y.	1969
"	Henry A. Kissinger	D. C.	1973
Ford	"	"	1974
Carter	Cyrus R. Vance	N. Y.	1977

Secretaries of the Treasury

The Treasury Department was organized by act of Congress Sept. 2, 1789.

President	Secretary	Home	Apptd.
Washington	Alexander Hamilton	N. Y.	1789
"	Oliver Wolcott	Conn.	1795
J. Adams	"	"	1797
"	Samuel Dexter	Mass.	1801
Jefferson	"	"	1801
"	Albert Gallatin	Pa.	1801
Madison	"	Pa.	1809
"	George W. Campbell	Tenn.	1814
"	Alexander J. Dallas	Pa.	1814
"	William H. Crawford	Ga.	1816
Monroe	"	"	1817
J. Q. Adams	Richard Rush	Pa.	1825
Jackson	Samuel D. Ingham	"	1829
"	Louis McLane	Del.	1831
"	William J. Duane	Pa.	1833
"	Roger B. Taney	Md.	1833
"	Levi Woodbury	N. H.	1834
Van Buren	"	"	1837
W. H. Harrison	Thomas Ewing	Oh.	1841
Tyler	"	"	1841
"	Walter Forward	Pa.	1841
"	John C. Spencer	N. Y.	1843
Tyler	George M. Bibb	Ky.	1844
Polk	Robert J. Walker	Miss.	1845
Taylor	William M. Meredith	Pa.	1849
Fillmore	Thomas Corwin	Oh.	1850
Pierce	James Guthrie	Ky.	1853
Buchanan	Howell Cobb	Ga.	1857
"	Phillip F. Thomas	Md.	1860
	John A. Dix	N. Y.	1861
Lincoln	Salmon P. Chase	Oh.	1861
"	William P. Fessenden	Me.	1864
	Hugh McCulloch	Ind.	1865
Johnson, A.	"	"	1865
Grant	George S. Boutwell	Mass.	1869
"	William A. Richardson	Mass.	1873
"	Benjamin H. Bristow	Ky.	1874
"	Lot M. Morrill	Me.	1876
Hayes	John Sherman	Oh.	1877
Garfield	William Windom	Minn.	1881
Arthur	Charles J. Folger	N. Y.	1881
"	Walter Q. Gresham	Ind.	1884
"	Hugh McCulloch	"	1884
Cleveland	Daniel Manning	N. Y.	1885

President	Secretary	Home	Apptd.
Cleveland	Charles S. Fairchild	"	1887
B. Harrison	William Windom	Minn.	1889
"	Charles Foster	Oh.	1891
Cleveland	John G. Carlisle	Ky.	1893
McKinley	Lyman J. Gage	Ill.	1897
T. Roosevelt	"	"	1901
"	Leslie M. Shaw	Ia.	1902
"	George B. Cortelyou	N. Y.	1907
Taft	Franklin MacVeagh	Ill.	1909
Wilson	William G. McAdoo	N. Y.	1913
"	Carter Glass	Va.	1918
"	David F. Houston	Mo.	1920
Harding	Andrew W. Mellon	Pa.	1921
Coolidge	"	"	1923
Hoover	"	"	1929
"	Ogden L. Mills	N. Y.	1932
F. D. Roosevelt	William H. Woodin	"	1933
"	Henry Morenthau Jr.	"	1934
Truman	Fred M. Vinson	Ky.	1945
"	John W. Snyder	Mo.	1946
Eisenhower	George M. Humphrey	Oh.	1953
"	Robert B. Anderson	Conn.	1957
Kennedy	C. Douglas Dillon	N. J.	1961
Johnson, L. B.	"	"	1963
"	Henry H. Fowler	Va.	1965
"	Joseph W. Barr	Ind.	1968
Nixon	David M. Kennedy	Ill.	1969
"	John B. Connally	Tex.	1970
"	George P. Shultz	Ill.	1972
"	William E. Simon	N. J.	1974
Ford	"	"	1974
Carter	W. Michael Blumenthal	Mich.	1977

Secretaries of Defense

The Department of Defense, originally designated the National Military Establishment, was created Sept. 18, 1947. It is headed by the secretary of defense, who is a member of the president's cabinet.

The departments of the army, of the navy, and of the air force function within the Department of Defense, and their respective secretaries are no longer members of the president's cabinet.

President	Secretary	Home	Apptd.
Truman	James V. Forrestal	N. Y.	1947
"	Louis A. Johnson	W. Va.	1949
"	George C. Marshall	Pa.	1950
"	Robert A. Lovett	N.Y.	1951
Eisenhower	Charles E. Wilson	Mich.	1953
"	Neil H. McElroy	Oh.	1957
"	Thomas S. Gates Jr.	Pa.	1959
Kennedy	Robert S. McNamara	Mich.	1961
Johnson, L. B.	Robert S. McNamara	Mich.	1963
"	Clark M. Clifford	Md.	1968
Nixon	Melvin R. Laird	Wis.	1969
"	Elliot L. Richardson	Mass.	1973
"	James R. Schlesinger	Va.	1973
Ford	"	"	1974
"	Donald H. Rumsfeld	Ill.	1975
Carter	Harold Brown	Cal.	1977

Secretaries of the Armed Services

Not members of the president's Cabinet

The Department of Defense, created Sept. 18, 1947, consolidated the navy, army, air force into a single department.

Secretary of the Air Force	Appointed
W. Stuart Symington	Sept. 18, 1947
Thomas K. Finletter	Apr. 24, 1950
Harold E. Talbot	Feb. 4, 1953
Donald A. Quarles	Aug. 12, 1965
James H. Douglas	Mar. 26, 1957
Dudley C. Sharpe	Dec. 10, 1959
Eugene M. Zuckert	Jan. 23, 1961
Dr. Harold Brown	July 10, 1965
Robert C. Seamans Jr.	Jan. 20, 1969
John L. McLucas	July 19, 1973
Thomas C. Reed	Jan. 2, 1976
John C. Stetson	1977

Secretary of the Army	Appointed
Kenneth C. Royall	Sept. 18, 1947
Gordon Gray*	June 20, 1949
Frank Pace Jr.	Apr. 12, 1950
Earl D. Johnson (Acting)	Jan. 20, 1953
Robert T. Stevens	Feb. 4, 1953
Wilber M. Brucker	July 21, 1955
Elvis J. Stahr Jr.	Jan. 23, 1961
Cyrus R. Vance	May 21, 1962
Stephen Ailes	Jan. 20, 1964
Stanley R. Resor	June 17, 1965
Robert F. Froehlke	June 15, 1971
Howard H. Callaway	May 2, 1973
Norman R. Augustine (acting)	July 3, 1975
Martin R. Hoffman	Aug. 5, 1975
Clifford L. Alexander Jr.	1977

*In addition, Gordon Gray was acting secretary of the army from Apr. 28, 1949, and under secretary from May 25, 1949, until June 20, 1949.

Secretary of the Navy	Appointed
John L. Sullivan	Sept. 18, 1947
Francis P. Matthews	May 25, 1949
Dan A. Kimball	July 31, 1951
Robert B. Anderson	Feb. 4, 1953
Charles S. Thomas	May 3, 1954
Thomas S. Gates Jr.	Apr. 1, 1957
William B. Franke	June 1, 1958
John B. Connally Jr.	Jan. 23, 1961
Fred Korth	Dec. 11, 1961
Paul H. Nitze	Oct. 14, 1963
John T. McNaughton	June 6, 1967
Paul R. Ignatius	Aug. 4, 1967
John H. Chafee	Jan. 20, 1969
John W. Warner	Apr. 7, 1972
J. William Middendorf 2d.	June 10, 1974
W. Graham Claytor Jr.	1977

Secretaries of War

The War (and Navy) Department was created by act of Congress Aug. 7, 1789, and Gen. Henry Knox was commissioned secretary of war under that act Sept. 12, 1789.

President	Secretary	Home	Apptd.
Washington	Henry Knox	Mass.	1789
"	Timothy Pickering	Pa.	1795
"	James McHenry	Md.	1796
J. Adams	"	"	1797
J. Adams	Samuel Dexter	Mass.	1800
Jefferson	Henry Dearborn	"	1801
Madison	William Eustis	Mass.	1809
"	John Armstrong	N. Y.	1813
Madison	James Monroe	Va.	1814
"	William H. Crawford	Ga.	1815
Monroe	John C. Calhoun	S. C.	1817
J. Q. Adams	James Barbour	Va.	1825
"	Peter B. Porter	N. Y.	1828
Jackson	John H. Eaton	Tenn.	1829
"	Lewis Cass	Oh.	1831
"	Benjamin F. Butler	N. Y.	1837
Van Buren	Joel R. Poinsett	S. C.	1837
W. H. Harrison	John Bell	Tenn.	1841
Tyler	"	"	1841
Tyler	John C. Spencer	N.Y.	1841
"	James M. Porter	Pa.	1843
"	William Wilkins	"	1844
Polk	William L. Marey	N. Y.	1845
Taylor	George W. Crawford	Ga.	1849
Fillmore	Charles M. Conrad	La.	1850
Pierce	Jefferson Davis	Miss.	1853
Buchanan	John B. Floyd	Va.	1857
"	Joseph Holt	Ky.	1861
Lincoln	Simon Cameron	Pa.	1861
"	Edwin M. Stanton	Pa.	1862
Johnson, A.	"	"	1865
"	John M. Schofield	Ill.	1868
Grant	John A. Rawlins	Ill.	1869
"	William T. Sherman	Oh.	1869
"	William W. Belknap	Ia.	1869
"	Alphonso Taft	Oh.	1876
Grant	James D. Cameron	Pa.	1876
Hayes	George W. McCrary	Ia.	1877
"	Alexander Ramsey	Minn.	1879
Garfield	Robert T. Lincoln	Ill.	1881
Arthur	"	"	1881
Cleveland	William C. Endicott	Mass.	1885
B. Harrison	Redfield Proctor	Vt.	1890
"	Stephen B. Elkins	W. Va.	1891
Cleveland	Daniel S. Lamont	N. Y.	1893
McKinley	Russel A. Alger	Mich.	1897
"	Elihu Root	N. Y.	1899
T. Roosevelt	"	"	1901
"	William H. Taft	Oh.	1904
"	Luke E. Wright	Tenn.	1908
Taft	Jacob M. Dickinson	"	1909
"	Henry L. Stimson	N. Y.	1911
Wilson	Lindley M. Garrison	N. J.	1913
"	Newton D. Baker	Oh.	1916
Harding	John W. Weeks	Mass.	1921
Coolidge	"	"	1923
"	Dwight F. Davis	Mo.	1925
Hoover	James W. Good	Ill.	1929

Continued

President	Secretary	Home	Apptd.
Hoover	Patrick J. Hurley	Okla.	1929
F. D. Roosevelt	George H. Dern	Ut.	1933
"	Harry H. Woodring	Kan.	1937
F. D. Roosevelt	Henry L. Stimson	N. Y.	1940
Truman	Robert P. Patterson	N. Y.	1945
"	*Kenneth C. Royall	N. C.	1947

Secretaries of the Navy

The Navy Department was created by act of Congress Apr. 30, 1798.

President	Secretary	Home	Apptd.
J. Adams	Benjamin Stoddert	Md.	1798
Jefferson	"	"	1801
"	Robert Smith	"	1801
Madison	Paul Hamilton	S. C.	1809
"	William Jones	Pa.	1813
"	Benjamin Williams Crowninshield	Mass.	1814
Monroe	"	"	1817
"	Smith Thompson	N. Y.	1818
"	Samuel L. Southard	N. J.	1823
J. Q. Adams	"	"	1825
Jackson	John Branch	N. C.	1829
"	Levi Woodbury	N. H.	1831
"	Mahlon Dickerson	N. J.	1834
Van Buren	"	"	1837
"	James K. Paulding	N. Y.	1838
W. H. Harrison	George E. Badger	N. C.	1841
Tyler	"	"	1841
"	Abel P. Upshur	Va.	1841
"	David Henshaw	Mass.	1843
"	Thomas W. Gilmer	Va.	1844
"	John Y. Mason	"	1844
Polk	George Bancroft	Mass.	1845
"	John Y. Mason	Va.	1846
Taylor	William B. Preston	"	1849
Fillmore	William A. Graham	N. C.	1850
"	John P. Kennedy	Md.	1852
Pierce	James C. Dobbin	N. C.	1853
Buchanan	Isaac Toucey	Conn.	1857

President	Secretary	Home	Apptd.
Lincoln	Gideon Welles	Conn.	1861
A. Johnson	"	"	1865
Grant	Adolph E. Borie	Pa.	1869
"	George M. Robeson	N. J.	1869
Hayes	Richard W. Thompson	Ind.	1877
"	Nathan Goff Jr.	W. Va.	1881
Garfield	William H. Hunt	La.	1881
Arthur	William E. Chandler	N. H.	1882
Cleveland	William C. Whitney	N. Y.	1885
B. Harrison	Benjamin F. Tracy	N. Y.	1889
Cleveland	Hilary A. Herbert	Ala.	1893
McKinley	John D. Long	Mass.	1897
T. Roosevelt	"	"	1901
"	William H. Moody	"	1902
"	Paul Morton	Ill.	1904
"	Charles J. Bonaparte	Md.	1905
"	Victor H. Metcalf	Cal.	1906
"	Truman H. Newberry	Mich.	1908
Taft	George von L. Meyer	Mass.	1909
Wilson	Josephus Daniels	N. C.	1913
Harding	Edwin Denby	Mich.	1921
Coolidge	"	"	1923
"	Curtis D. Wilbur	Cal.	1924
Hoover	Charles Francis Adams	Mass.	1929
F. D. Roosevelt	Claude A. Swanson	Va.	1933
"	Charles Edison	N. J.	1940
"	Frank Knox	Ill.	1940
"	*James V. Forrestal	N. Y.	1944
Truman	"	"	1945

*Last members of Cabinet. The War Department became the Department of the Army and the Navy Department became branches of the Department of Defense, created Sept. 18, 1947.

Attorneys General

The office of attorney general was organized by act of Congress Sept. 24, 1789. The Department of Justice was created June 22, 1870.

President	Attorney General	Home	Apptd.
Washington	Edmund Randolph	Va.	1789
"	William Bradford	Pa.	1794
"	Charles Lee	Va.	1795
J. Adams	"	"	1797
Jefferson	Levi Lincoln	Mass.	1801
"	John Breckenridge	Ky.	1805
Jefferson	Caesar A. Rodney	Del.	1807
Madison	"	"	1809
"	William Pinkney	Md.	1811
"	Richard Rush	Pa.	1814
Monroe	"	"	1817
"	William Wirt	Va.	1817
J. Q. Adams	"	"	1825
Jackson	John McP. Berrien	Ga.	1829
"	Roger B. Taney	Md.	1831
"	Benjamin F. Butler	N. Y.	1833
Van Buren	"	"	1837
"	Felix Grundy	Tenn.	1838
"	Henry D. Gilpin	Pa.	1840
W. H. Harrison	John J. Crittenden	Ky.	1841
Tyler	"	"	1841
"	Hugh S. Legare	S. C.	1841
"	John Nelson	Md.	1843
Polk	John Y. Mason	Va.	1845
"	Nathan Clifford	Me.	1846
"	Isaac Toucey	Conn.	1848
Taylor	Reverdy Johnson	Md.	1849
Fillmore	John J. Crittenden	Ky.	1850
Pierce	Caleb Cushing	Mass.	1853
Buchanan	Jeremiah S. Black	Pa.	1857
"	Edwin M. Stanton	Pa.	1860
Lincoln	Edward Bates	Mo.	1861
"	James Speed	Ky.	1864
A. Johnson	"	"	1865
"	Henry Stanbery	Oh.	1866
"	William M. Evarts	N. Y.	1868
Grant	Ebenezer R. Hoar	Mass.	1869
"	Amos T. Akerman	Ga.	1870
"	George H. Williams	Ore.	1871
"	Edwards Pierrepont	N. Y.	1875
"	Alphonso Taft	Oh.	1876

President	Attorney General	Home	Apptd.
Hayes	Charles Devens	Mass.	1877
Garfield	Wayne MacVeagh	Pa.	1881
Arthur	Benjamin H. Brewster	"	1881
Cleveland	Augustus Garland	Ark.	1885
B. Harrison	William H. H. Miller	Ind.	1889
Cleveland	Richard Olney	Mass.	1893
"	Judson Harmon	Oh.	1895
McKinley	Joseph McKenna	Cal.	1897
"	John W. Griggs	N. J.	1898
"	Philander C. Knox	Pa.	1901
T. Roosevelt	"	"	1901
"	William H. Moody	Mass.	1904
"	Charles J. Bonaparte	Md.	1906
Taft	George W. Wickersham	N. Y.	1909
Wilson	J. C. McReynolds	Tenn.	1913
"	Thomas W. Gregory	Tex.	1914
"	A. Mitchell Palmer	Pa.	1919
Harding	Harry M. Daugherty	Oh.	1921
Coolidge	"	"	1923
"	Harlan F. Stone	N. Y.	1924
"	John G. Sargent	Vt.	1925
Hoover	William D. Mitchell	Minn.	1929
F. D. Roosevelt	Homer S. Cummings	Conn.	1933
"	Frank Murphy	Mich.	1939
"	Robert H. Jackson	N. Y.	1940
"	Francis Biddle	Pa.	1941
Truman	Tom C. Clark	Tex.	1945
"	J. Howard McGrath	R. I.	1949
"	J. P. McGranery	Pa.	1952
Eisenhower	H. Brownell Jr.	N. Y.	1953
"	William P. Rogers	Md.	1957
Kennedy	Robert F. Kennedy	Mass.	1961
L. B. Johnson	"	"	1963
"	N. de B. Katzenbach	Ill.	1965
"	Ramsey Clark	Tex.	1967
Nixon	John N. Mitchell	N. Y.	1969
"	Richard G. Kleindienst	Ariz.	1972
"	Elliot L. Richardson	Mass.	1973
"	William B. Saxbe	Oh.	1974
Ford	"	"	1974
"	Edward H. Levi	Ill.	1975
Carter	Griffin B. Bell	Ga.	1977

Secretaries of the Interior

The Department of Interior was created by act of Congress Mar. 3, 1849

President	Secretary	Home	Apptd.
Taylor	Thomas Ewing	Oh.	1849
Fillmore	Thomas M. T. McKennan	Pa.	1850
Fillmore	Alex H. H. Stuart	Va.	1850
Pierce	Robert McClelland	Mich.	1853

President	Secretary	Home	Apptd.
Buchanan	Jacob Thompson	Miss.	1857
Lincoln	Caleb B. Smith	Ind.	1861
"	John P. Usher	"	1863
A. Johnson	"		1865
"	James Harlan	Ia.	1865
"	Orville H. Browning	Ill.	1866
Grant	Jacob D. Cox	Oh.	1869
"	Columbus Delano	"	1870
"	Zachariah Chandler	Mich.	1875
Hayes	Carl Schurz	Mo.	1877
Garfield	Sam. J. Kirkwood	Ia.	1881
Arthur	Henry M. Teller	Col.	1882
Cleveland	Lucius Q. C. Lamar	Miss.	1885
"	William F. Vilas	Wis.	1888
B. Harrison	John W. Noble	Mo.	1889
Cleveland	Hoke Smith	Ga.	1893
"	David R. Francis	Mo.	1896
McKinley	Cornelius N. Bliss	N. Y.	1897
"	Ethan A. Hitchcock	Mo.	1898
T. Roosevelt	"	"	1901
"	James R. Garfield	Oh.	1907

President	Secretary	Home	Apptd.
Taft	Richard A. Ballinger	Wash.	1909
"	Walter L. Fisher	Ill.	1911
Wilson	Franklin K. Lane	Cal.	1913
	John B. Payne	Ill.	1920
Harding	Albert B. Fall	N. M.	1921
"	Hubert Work	Col.	1923
Coolidge	"	"	1923
	Roy O. West	Ill.	1929
Hoover	Ray Lyman Wilbur	Cal.	1929
F. D. Roosevelt	Harold L. Ickes	Ill.	1933
Truman	"	"	1945
"	Julius A. Krug	Wis.	1946
	Oscar L. Chapman	Col.	1950
Eisenhower	Douglas McKay	Ore.	1953
"	Fred A. Seaton	Neb.	1956
Kennedy	Stewart L. Udall	Ariz.	1961
L. B. Johnson	"	"	1963
Nixon	Walter J. Hickel	Alas.	1969
"	Rogers C. B. Morton	Md.	1971
Ford	"	"	1974
"	Thomas S. Kleppe	N. D.	1975
Carter	Cecil D. Andrus	Ida.	1977

Secretaries of Agriculture

The Department of Agriculture was created by act of Congress May 15, 1862. On Feb. 8, 1889, its commissioner was renamed secretary of agriculture and became a member of the cabinet.

President	Secretary	Home	Apptd.
Cleveland	Norman J. Colman	Mo.	1889
B. Harrison	Jeremiah M. Rusk	Wis.	1889
Cleveland	J. Sterling Morton	Neb.	1893
McKinley	James Wilson	Ia.	1897
T. Roosevelt	"	"	1901
Taft	"	"	1909
Wilson	David F. Houston	Mo.	1913
"	Edward T. Meredith	Ia.	1920
Harding	Henry C. Wallace	Ia.	1921
Coolidge	"	"	1923
"	Howard M. Gore	W. Va.	1924
"	W. M. Jardine	Kan.	1925

President	Secretary	Home	Apptd.
Hoover	Arthur M. Hyde	Mo.	1929
F. D. Roosevelt	Henry A. Wallace	Ia.	1933
"	Claude R. Wickard	Ind.	1940
Truman	Clinton P. Anderson	N. M.	1945
"	Charles F. Brannan	Col.	1948
Eisenhower	Ezra Taft Benson	Ut.	1953
Kennedy	Orville L. Freeman	Minn.	1961
L. B. Johnson		"	1963
Nixon	Clifford M. Hardin	Ind.	1969
"	Earl L. Butz	Ind.	1971
Ford	"	"	1974
Carter	Bob Bergland	Minn.	1977

Secretaries of Commerce and Labor

The Department of Commerce and Labor, created by Congress Feb. 14, 1903, was divided by Congress Mar. 4, 1913, into separate departments of Commerce and Labor. The secretary of each was made a cabinet member.

Secretaries of Commerce and Labor

President	Secretary	Home	Apptd.
T. Roosevelt	Geo. B. Cortelyou	N. Y.	1903
"	Victor H. Metcalf	Cal.	1904
"	Oscar S. Straus	N. Y.	1906
Taft	Charles Nagel	Mo.	1909

Secretaries of Labor

President	Secretary	Home	Apptd.
Wilson	William B. Wilson	Pa.	1913
Harding	James J. Davis	Pa.	1921
Coolidge	"	"	1923
Hoover	"	"	1929
"	William N. Doak	Va.	1930
F. D. Roosevelt	Frances Perkins	N. Y.	1933
Truman	L. B. Schwellenbach	Wash.	1945
"	Maurice J. Tobin	Mass.	1949
Eisenhower	Martin P. Durkin	Ill.	1953
"	James P. Mitchell	N. J.	1953
Kennedy	Arthur J. Goldberg	Ill.	1961
"	W. Willard Wirtz	Ill.	1962
L.B. Johnson	W. Willard Wirtz	Ill.	1963
Nixon	George P. Shultz	Ill.	1969
"	James D. Hodgson	Cal.	1970
"	Peter J. Brennan	N. Y.	1973
Ford	"	"	1974
"	John T. Dunlop	Cal.	1975
"	W. J. Usery Jr.	Ga.	1976
Carter	F. Ray Marshall	Tex.	1977

Secretaries of Commerce

President	Secretary	Home	Apptd.
Wilson	William C. Redfield	N. Y.	1913
"	Josh. W. Alexander	Mo.	1919
Harding	Herbert C. Hoover	Cal.	1921
Coolidge	"	"	1923
"	William F. Whiting	Mass.	1928
Hoover	Robert P. Lamont	Ill.	1929
"	Roy D. Chapin	Mich.	1932
F. D. Roosevelt	Daniel C. Roper	S. C.	1933
"	Harry L. Hopkins	N. Y.	1939
"	Jesse Jones	Tex.	1940
"	Henry A. Wallace	Ia.	1945
Truman	"	"	1945
Truman	W. Averell Harriman	N. Y.	1947
"	Charles Sawyer	Oh.	1948
Eisenhower	Sinclair Weeks	Mass.	1953
"	Lewis L. Strauss	N. Y.	1958
"	Frederick H. Mueller	Mich.	1959
Kennedy	Luther H. Hodges	N. C.	1961
L.B. Johnson	John T. Connor	N. J.	1965
"	Alex B. Trowbridge	N. J.	1967
"	C. R. Smith	N. Y.	1968
Nixon	Maurice H. Stans	Minn.	1969
"	Peter G. Peterson	Ill.	1972
"	Frederick B. Dent	S. C.	1973
Ford	"	"	1974
"	Rogers C. B. Morton	Md.	1975
"	Elliot L. Richardson	Mass.	1976
Carter	Juanita M. Kreps	N. C.	1977

Secretaries of Health, Education, and Welfare

The Department of Health, Education, and Welfare was created by act of Congress Apr. 11, 1953.

President	Secretary	Home	Apptd.
Eisenhower	Oveta Culp Hobby	Tex.	1953
"	Marion B. Folsom	N. Y.	1955
	Arthur S. Flemming	Oh.	1958
Kennedy	Abraham A. Ribicoff	Conn.	1961
"	Anthony J. Celebrezze	Oh.	1962
Johnson, L.B.	"	"	1963
"	John W. Gardner	N. Y.	1965

President	Secretary	Home	Apptd.
Johnson, L. B.	Wilbur J. Cohen	Mich.	1968
Nixon	Robert H. Finch	Cal.	1969
"	Elliot L. Richardson	Mass.	1970
"	Caspar W. Weinberger	Cal.	1973
Ford	"	"	1974
"	Forrest D. Mathews	Ala.	1975
Carter	Joseph A. Califano Jr.	D.C.	1977

Secretaries of Housing and Urban Development

The Department of Housing and Urban Development was created by act of Congress Sept. 9, 1965.

President	Secretary	Home	Apptd.
Johnson, L. B.	Robert C. Weaver	Wash.	1966
"	Robert C. Wood	Mass.	1968
Nixon	George W. Romney	Mich.	1969
"	James T. Lynn	Oh.	1973
Ford	"	"	1974
"	Carla Anderson Hills	Cal.	1975
Carter	Patricia Roberts Harris	D.C.	1977

Secretaries of Transportation

The Department of Transportation was created by act of Congress Oct. 15, 1966.

President	Secretary	Home	Apptd.
Johnson, L. B.	Alan S. Boyd	Fla.	1966
Nixon	John A. Volpe	Mass.	1969
"	Claude S. Brinegar	Cal.	1973
Ford	Claude S. Brinegar	Cal.	1974
"	William T. Coleman Jr.	Pa.	1975
Carter	Brock Adams	Wash.	1977

Secretary of Energy

The Department of Energy was created by federal law Aug. 4, 1977.

President	Secretary	Home	Apptd.
Carter	James R. Schlesinger	Va.	1977

Postmasters General

Congress established the Post Office Department as a branch of the Treasury Sept. 22, 1789. The postmaster general was made a member of the Cabinet Mar. 9, 1829. The Postal Reorganization Act of 1970 replaced the department with the U.S. Postal Service, an independent federal agency. Its head, the postmaster general, is not a member of the Cabinet.

Presidents	Postmaster General	Home	Apptd.
Washington	Samuel Osgood	Mass.	1789
"	Timothy Pickering	Pa.	1791
"	Joseph Habersham	Ga.	1795
J. Adams	"	"	1797
Jefferson	"	"	1801
"	Gideon Granger	Conn.	1801
Madison	"	"	1809
"	Return J. Meigs Jr.	Ohio	1814
Monroe	"	"	1817
"	John McLean	"	1823
J. Q. Adams	"	"	1825
Jackson	William T. Barry	Ky.	1829
"	Amos Kendall	"	1835
Van Buren	"	"	1837
"	John M. Niles	Conn.	1840
W. H. Harrison	Francis Granger	N.Y.	1841
Tyler	"	N.Y.	1841
"	Charles A. Wickliffe	Ky.	1841
Polk	Cave Johnson	Tenn.	1845
Taylor	Jacob Collamer	Vt.	1849
Fillmore	Nathan K. Hall	N.Y.	1850
"	Samuel D. Hubbard	Conn.	1852
Pierce	James Campbell	Pa.	1853
Buchanan	Aaron V. Brown	Tenn.	1857
"	Joseph Holt	Ky.	1859
"	Horatio King	Me.	1861
Lincoln	Montgomery Blair	D.C.	1861
"	William Dennison	Ohio	1864
A. Johnson	"	"	1865
"	Alex W. Randall	Wis.	1866
Grant	John A. J. Creswell	Md.	1869
"	James W. Marshall	Va.	1874
"	Marshall Jewell	Conn.	1874
"	James N. Tyner	Ind.	1876
Hayes	David McK. Key	Tenn.	1877
Hayes	Horace Maynard	Tenn.	1880
Garfield	Thomas L. James	N.Y.	1881
Arthur	Timothy O. Howe	Wis.	1881
"	Walter Q. Gresham	Ind.	1883
"	Frank Hatton	Iowa	1884
Cleveland	William F. Vilas	Wis.	1885
"	Don M. Dickinson	Mich.	1888
B. Harrison	John Wanamaker	Pa.	1889
Cleveland	Wilson S. Bissel	N.Y.	1893
"	William L. Wilson	W. Va.	1895
McKinley	James A. Gary	Md.	1897
"	Charles E. Smith	Pa.	1898
T. Roosevelt	"	"	1901
"	Henry C. Payne	Wis.	1902
"	Robert J. Wynne	Pa.	1904
"	George B. Cortelyou	N.Y.	1905
"	George von L. Meyer	Mass.	1907
Taft	Frank H. Hitchcock	"	1909
Wilson	Albert S. Burleson	Tex.	1913
Harding	Will H. Hays	Ind.	1921
"	Hubert Work	Colo.	1922
"	Harry S. New	Ind.	1923
Coolidge	"	"	1923
Hoover	Walter F. Brown	Ohio	1929
F. D. Roosevelt	James A. Farley	N.Y.	1933
"	Frank C. Walker	Pa.	1940
Truman	Robt. E. Hannegan	Mo.	1945
"	Jesse M. Donaldson	Mo.	1947
Eisenhower	A. E. Summerfield	Mich.	1953
Kennedy	J. Edward Day	Calif.	1961
"	John A. Gronouski	Wis.	1963
L. B. Johnson	"	"	1963
"	Lawrence F. O'Brien	Mass.	1965
"	W. Marvin Watson	Texas	1968
Nixon	Winton M. Blount	Ala.	1969
(Elected) (1)	Elmer T. Klassen	Md.	1971
(Elected) (1)	Benjamin F. Bailar	D.C.	1975

(1) Elected by Postal Service Board of Governors.

Law on Succession to the Presidency

If by reason of death, resignation, removal from office, inability, or failure to qualify there is neither a president nor vice president to discharge the powers and duties of the office of president, then the speaker of the House of Representatives shall upon his resignation as speaker and as representative, act as presi-

dent. The same rule shall apply in the case of the death, resignation, removal from office, or inability of an individual acting as president.

If at the time when a speaker is to begin the discharge of the powers and duties of the office of president there is no speaker, or the speaker fails to qualify as acting president, then the president pro tempore of the Senate, upon his resignation as president pro tempore and as senator, shall act as president.

An individual acting as president shall continue to act until the expiration of the then current presidential term, except that (1) if his discharge of the powers and duties of the office is founded in whole or in part in the failure of both the president-elect and the vice president-elect to qualify, then he shall act only until a president or vice president qualifies, and (2) if his discharge of the powers and duties of the office is founded in whole or in part on the inability of the president or vice president, then he shall act only until the removal of the disability of one of such individuals.

If, by reason of death, resignation, removal from office, or failure to qualify, there is no president pro tempore to act as president, then the officer of the United States who is highest on the following list, and who is not under disability to discharge the powers and duties of president, shall act as president: the secretaries of state, treasury, defense; attorney general; secretaries of interior, agriculture, commerce, labor; health, education and welfare; housing and urban development; transportation.

(Legislation approved July 18, 1947; amended Sept. 9, 1965, and Oct. 15, 1966. See also Constitutional Amendment XXV.)

Wives and Children of the Presidents

Listed in order of presidential administrations.

Name	State	Born	Married	Died	Sons	Daughters
Martha Dandridge Custis Washington	Va.	1732	1759	1802		
Abigail Smith Adams	Mass.	1744	1764	1818	3	2
Martha Wayles Skelton Jefferson	Va.	1748	1772	1782	1	5
Dorothea "Dolley" Payne Todd Madison	N.C.	1768	1794	1849		
Elizabeth Kortright Monroe	N.Y.	1768	1786	1830	(1)	
Louise Catherine Johnson Adams	Md. (2)	1775	1797	1852	3	1
Rachel Donelson Robards Jackson	Va.	1767	1791	1828		
Hannah Hoes Van Buren	N.Y.	1783	1807	1819	4	
Anna Symmes Harrison	N.J.	1775	1795	1864	6	4
Letitia Christian Tyler	Va.	1790	1813	1842	3	4
Julia Gardiner Tyler	N.Y.	1820	1844	1889	5	2
Sarah Childress Polk	Tenn.	1803	1824	1891		
Margaret Smith Taylor	Md.	1788	1810	1852	1	5
Abigail Powers Fillmore	N.Y.	1798	1826	1853	1	1
Caroline Carmichael McIntosh Fillmore	N.J.	1813	1858	1881		
Jane Means Appleton Pierce	N.H.	1806	1834	1863	3	
Mary Todd Lincoln	Ky.	1818	1842	1882	4	
Eliza McCardle Johnson	Tenn.	1810	1827	1876	3	2
Julia Dent Grant	Mo.	1826	1848	1902	3	1
Lucy Ware Webb Hayes	Oh.	1831	1852	1889	7	1
Lucretia Rudolph Garfield	Oh.	1832	1858	1918	4	1
Ellen Lewis Herndon Arthur	Va.	1837	1859	1880	2	1
Frances Folsom Cleveland	N.Y.	1864	1886	1947	2	3
Caroline Lavinia Scott Harrison	Oh.	1832	1853	1892	1	1
Mary Scott Lord Dimmick Harrison	Pa.	1858	1896	1948		1
Ida Saxton McKinley	Oh.	1847	1871	1907		2
Alice Hathaway Lee Roosevelt	Mass.	1861	1880	1884		1
Edith Kermit Carow Roosevelt	Conn.	1861	1886	1948	4	1
Helen Herron Taft	Oh.	1861	1886	1943	2	1
Ellen Louise Axson Wilson	Ga.	1860	1885	1914		3
Edith Bolling Galt Wilson	Va.	1872	1915	1961		
Florence Kling De Wolfe Harding	Oh.	1860	1891	1924		
Grace Anna Goodhue Coolidge	Vt.	1879	1905	1957	2	
Lou Henry Hoover	Ia.	1875	1899	1944	2	
Anne Eleanor Roosevelt Roosevelt	N.Y.	1884	1905	1962	4 (1)	1
Bess Wallace Truman	Mo.	1885	1919			1
Mamie Geneva Doud Eisenhower	Ia.	1896	1916		1 (1)	
Jacqueline Lee Bouvier Kennedy	N.Y.	1929	1953		1 (1)	1
Claudia "Lady Bird" Alta Taylor Johnson	Tex.	1912	1934			2
Thelma Catherine Patricia Ryan Nixon	Nev.	1912	1940			2
Elizabeth Bloomer Warren Ford	Ill.	1918	1948		3	1
Rosalynn Smith Carter	Ga.	1927	1946		3	1

James Buchanan, 15th president, was unmarried. (1) plus one infant, deceased. (2) Born London, father a Md. citizen.

Burial Places of the Presidents

G. Washington	Mt. Vernon, Va.
John Adams	Quincy, Mass.
T. Jefferson	Charlottesville, Va.
James Madison	Montpelier Station, Va.
James Monroe	Richmond, Va.
John Q. Adams	Quincy, Mass.
Andrew Jackson	Nashville, Tenn.
M. Van Buren	Kinderhook, N.Y.
W. H. Harrison	North Bend, Oh.
John Tyler	Richmond, Va.
James Knox Polk	Nashville, Tenn.
Zachary Taylor	Louisville, Ky.
Millard Fillmore	Buffalo, N.Y.
Franklin Pierce	Concord, N.H.
James Buchanan	Lancaster, Pa.
A. Lincoln	Springfield, Ill.
Andrew Johnson	Greeneville, Tenn.
Ulysses S. Grant	New York City
R. B. Hayes	Fremont, Oh.
J. A. Garfield	Cleveland, Oh.
C. A. Arthur	Albany, N. Y.
Grover Cleveland	Princeton, N.J.
B. Harrison	Indianapolis, Ind.
W. McKinley	Canton, Oh.
T. Roosevelt	Oyster Bay, N.Y.
William H. Taft	Arlington Nat'l. Cem'y.
Woodrow Wilson	Washington Cathedral
W. G. Harding	Marion, Oh.
Calvin Coolidge	Plymouth, Vt.
Herbert Hoover	West Branch, Ia.
F. D. Roosevelt	Hyde Park, N.Y.
Harry S. Truman	Independence, Mo.
D. D. Eisenhower	Abilene, Kan.
J. F. Kennedy	Arlington Nat'l. Cem'y.
Lyndon B. Johnson	Stonewall, Tex.

BIOGRAPHIES OF U.S. PRESIDENTS

George Washington

George Washington, first president, was born Friday, Feb. 22, 1732 (Feb. 11, 1731, Old Style), the son of Augustine Washington and Mary Ball, at Wakefield on Pope's Creek, Westmoreland Co., Va. Col. John Washington, George's great-grandfather, came from Northamptonshire in 1657 or 1658; in 1665 he and an associate named Spencer bought 5,000 acres on the Potomac. George's father took the north 2,500 acres near Hunting Creek in 1735 and built a house in which George lived from 3 to 6 years of age; then the family moved to Ferry farm, near Fredericksburg. His father died in 1743 when George was 11. He studied mathematics and surveying and when 16 went to live with his half brother Lawrence, who had inherited the Potomac farm and built Mount Vernon, the original house having burned. George surveyed the lands of William Fairfax on the Shenandoah, keeping a diary. He accompanied Lawrence to Barbados, West Indies, contracted small pox, and was deeply scarred. Lawrence died in 1752 and George acquired his property by inheritance and purchase and added the 2,500 acres held by the Spencers. He valued land and when he died owned 70,000 acres in Virginia and 40,000 acres on the Great Kanawha in what is now West Virginia.

Washington's military service began in 1753 when Gov. Dinwiddie of Virginia made him lieutenant-colonel of militia. He clashed with the French and had to surrender Fort Necessity July 3, 1754. He was an aide to Braddock and helped organize the retreat after the fatal ambuscade of July 9, 1755. He helped take Fort DuQuesne from the French in 1758.

After his marriage to Martha Dandridge Custis, a widow, in 1759, Washington lived at Mount Vernon, bred horses and cattle, raised fruit and practiced crop rotation. During the Stamp Act agitation, 1765, he supported the protesting Virginians. Although not at first for independence, he stood out against British exactions and took charge of the Virginia troops before war broke out. He was made commander-in-chief by the Continental Congress June 15, 1775.

The successful issue of a war filled with hardships was due to his leadership. He was resourceful, a stern disciplinarian, and the one strong, dependable force for unity. He favored a federal government and became chairman of the Constitutional Convention of 1787. He helped get the Constitution ratified and was unanimously elected president by the Electoral College and inaugurated, Apr. 30, 1789, on the balcony of New York's Federal Hall at Broad and Wall Sts., now marked by his statue. He was reelected, again unanimously, in 1792.

Although a Federalist, Washington made Thomas Jefferson secretary of state. He was reelected 1792, but refused to consider a 3d term and retired to Mount Vernon, 1797. He suffered acute laryngitis after a ride in snow and rain around his estate, was bled profusely (an 18th Century medical practice), and died Dec. 14, 1799, aged 67. He was mourned here and abroad as one of the great men of his time. He was buried in a vault at Mount Vernon. (See article on Mount Vernon.)

John Adams

John Adams, 2d president, Federalist, was born in Braintree (Quincy), Mass., Oct. 30, 1735 (Oct. 19, O.S.), the son of John Adams, a farmer, and Susanna Boylston of Brookline. He was a great-grandson of Henry Adams who came from England in 1636. He was graduated from Harvard, 1755, taught school, studied law. In 1765 he argued against taxation without representation before the royal governor. In 1770 he defended the British soldiers who fired on civilians in the "Boston Massacre." He took part in the Provincial Congress of Massachusetts and the Continental Congress, seconded the independence resolution presented by Richard Henry Lee and with his cousin, Samuel Adams, signed the Declaration of Independence. He was a commissioner to France, 1778, with Benjamin Franklin and Arthur Lee; won recognition of the United States by The Hague, 1782; was first American minister to England, 1785-1788, and elected vice president with Washington, 1788 and 1792.

In 1796 Adams was chosen president by the electors, 71 to 68, so that opponents called him "president by 3 votes." The candidate with the second highest number of votes became vice president; this was Thomas Jefferson,his opponent. Intense antagonism to America by France caused agitation for war, led by Alexander Hamilton. Adams, breaking with Hamilton, opposed war but put the navy on a fighting basis. The U.S.S. Constitution, the United States, both 44 guns, and the Constellation, 36 guns, and armed merchantmen bagged 84 French ships in an undeclared war. To fight alien influence and muzzle criticism Adams supported the Alien and Sedition laws of 1798, which led to his defeat for reelection. He died July 4, 1826, on the same day as Jefferson (the 50th anniversary of the Declaration of Independence), and is buried in the First Parish Church in Quincy, Mass.

Adams married Abigail Smith, 1764. They had 2 daughters and 3 sons, one of whom, John Quincy Adams, became the 6th president.

Thomas Jefferson

Thomas Jefferson, 3d president, was born Apr. 13, 1743 (Apr. 2, O. S.), at Shadwell, Va., the son of Peter Jefferson, a civil engineer of Welsh descent who raised tobacco, and Jane Randolph. Jefferson was an agrarian and an expansionist. Because he opposed the Federalists and centralization he was called a Republican, the equivalent of a Democrat in later years. His father died when he was 14, leaving him 2,750 acres and his slaves. Jefferson attended the college of William and Mary, 1760-1762, read classics in Greek and Latin and played the violin. In 1769 he was elected to the House of Burgesses. In 1770 he began building Monticello, near Charlottesville. He was a member of the Virginia Committee of Correspondence and the Continental Congress and denied Britain's right to tax. Named a member of the committee to draw up a Declaration of Independence, he wrote the basic draft, 1776. He was a member of the Virginia House of Delegates, 1776-79, elected governor to succeed Patrick Henry, 1779, reelected 1780, resigned June 1781, amid charges of ineffectual military preparation. During his term he wrote the statute on religious freedom. In the Continental Congress, 1783, he drew up an ordinance for the Northwest Territory, forbidding slavery after 1800; its terms were put into the Ordinance of 1787. He was sent to Paris with Benjamin Franklin and John Adams to negotiate treaties of commerce, 1784; made minister to France, 1785. He made treaties with France and Prussia, studied architecture, gardening, and the French Revolution, whose leaders consulted him.

Washington appointed him secretary of state, 1789. Jefferson's strong faith in the consent of the governed, as opposed to executive control favored by Hamilton, secretary of the treasury, often led to conflict: Dec. 31, 1793, he resigned. He was the Republican candidate for president in 1796; beaten by John Adams, he became vice president. He opposed Adams' alien and sedition laws with the Kentucky and Virginia resolutions, reiterating the basic rights of states. In 1800 Jefferson and Aaron Burr received equal Electoral College votes for president, so the House of Representatives, with Hamilton's help, elected Jefferson, the first president to be inaugurated in Washington. Adams left town before the ceremony, but when Jefferson was reelected in 1804 he voted for him. Jefferson canceled levees and titles and ignored diplomatic precedence. He turned Federalists out of office. He opposed a strong navy. By fighting those who feared to give power to the people he made democracy work. He considered John Marshall's Supreme Court reactionary. Big events of his administration were the Louisiana Purchase, 1803, and the Lewis and Clark Expedition. He established the University of Virginia and designed its buildings. After the Library of Congress was burned by the British he sold Congress some 6,000 vols. for $23,950. He was 6 ft. 2, temperate in debate, a deist in religion. He died July 4, 1826, on the same day as John Adams and was buried at Monticello.

He married Martha Wayles Skelton, a widow, Jan. 1, 1772. They had one son and 5 daughters.

James Madison

James Madison, 4th president, Republican, was born Mar. 16, 1751 (Mar. 5, 1750, O. S.) at Port Conway, King George Co., Va., the first of 12 children of James Madison and Eleanor Rose Conway. His great-grandfather, James Taylor (1674-1729), was also the great-grandfather of Zachary Taylor. Madison was graduated from Princeton, 1771; studied theology, 1772; sat in the Virginia Constitutional Convention, 1776, where his resolution on religious freedom was voted down. He was a member of the Continental Congress and of the Annapolis Convention, 1786, where he and Alexander Hamilton proposed the Constitutional Convention. He was chief recorder at that convention in 1787, and supported ratification in the Federalist papers, written with Hamilton and John Jay. In 1785 he carried Jefferson's statute on religious liberty through the Virginia Assembly. He was elected to the House of Representatives in 1789, helped adopt the Bill of Rights and fought John Adams alien and sedition laws. He favored agrarian policies with Jefferson and in 1801 became Jefferson's secretary of state. In 1803, when the Louisiana Purchase was consummated, he insisted on free navigation of the Mississippi.

Elected president in 1808, Madison was a "strict constructionist," opposed to the free interpretation of the Constitution by the Federalists. He vetoed federal funds for state improvements, but changed in his second term. Madison inherited the conflict with Britain over its orders in council and its impressment of American seamen, which had led to Jefferson's embargo act and injured American commerce. He was reelected in 1812 by the votes of the agrarian South and recently admitted western states. Caught between British and French maritime restrictions, Madison drifted into war, declared June 18, 1812, unaware that Britain had canceled the orders 2 days before. While the war was inconclusive, it opened the way to peaceful negotiations. Madison successfully advocated a tariff to protect industry, a national system of roads and canals, and a strong military organization. Reelected in 1812, he retired in 1817 to his estate at Montpelier in Orange County, Va., built 1760. There he edited his famous papers on the Constitutional Convention. He became rector of the University of Virginia, 1826. He died June 28, 1836, and was buried near his home.

Madison married Dorothea "Dolley" Payne Todd, a widow, Sept. 15, 1794.

James Monroe

James Monroe, 5th president, Republican, was born Apr. 28, 1758, in Westmoreland Co., Va., the son of Spence Monroe and Eliza Jones, who were of Scottish and Welsh descent, respectively. He attended the College of William and Mary, fought in the 3d Virginia Regiment at White Plains, Brandywine, Monmouth, and was wounded at Trenton. He studied law with Thomas Jefferson, 1780, was a member of the Virginia House of Delegates and of Congress, 1783-86. He opposed ratification of the Constitution because it lacked a bill of rights; was U.S. senator, 1790; minister to France, 1794-96, during which he improved relations with France, Spain, and Algiers; 4 times governor of Virginia, 1799-1802, and 1811. Jefferson sent him to France as minister, 1803, to join R. R. Livingston in buying the Isle of New Orleans from France and East and West Florida from Spain. Exceeding instructions, he signed a treaty for all of Louisiana. He was also sent to Madrid, 1804, and London, 1805, to settle disputes. He ran against Madison for president in 1808. He was elected to the Virginia Assembly, 1810-1811; was secretary of state under Madison, 1811-1817; also secretary of war, Sept. 1814-Mar. 1815.

In 1816 Monroe was elected president; in 1820 reelected with all but one Electoral College vote, this being cast for John Quincy Adams by William Plumer Sr. of New Hampshire. Many historians have held that Plumer withheld his vote from Monroe so that only Washington would have been elected unanimously. Monroe's administration became the "Era of Good Feeling." He obtained Florida from Spain; settled boundaries with Canada, and eliminated border forts; supported the anti-slavery position that led to the Missouri Compromise. (In 1801 he had proposed settling Negro slaves in Africa. Monrovia, Liberia, was named for him.) In July, 1823, the U.S. served notice on Russia that it would oppose any Russian colony on this continent, after Russia had prohibited fishing on the northwest coasts. On Dec. 2, 1823, Monroe announced the doctrine that the U. S. would consider its safety endangered if European powers had authority in this hemisphere or attempted colonization. First half had been suggested by George Canning, British foreign minister, to curb Spain; U.S., rejecting proposal for joint declaration, issued it also as warning to Russia. Monroe owned Ash Lawn, 5 mi. from Charlottesville, Va., 1799-1825; inherited Oak Hill, Loudon Co., Va., from his uncle Joseph Jones, 1806. The mansion was designed by Jefferson.

Monroe married Elizabeth Kortright in 1786. They had a son who died in infancy and 2 daughters. Mrs. Monroe died in 1830 and he and the daughters moved to New York, where he died July 4, 1831.

John Quincy Adams

John Quincy Adams, 6th president, independent Federalist, was born July 11, 1767, at Braintree (Quincy), Mass., the son of John and Abigail Adams. His father was the 2d president. He was educated in Paris, Leyden, and Harvard, graduating in 1787. He served as American minister in the Netherlands, Berlin, St. Petersburg, and London and helped draft the War of 1812 peace treaty, signed Dec. 24, 1814. He had served as senator from 1803 to 1808 and his support of the Republican administration alienated the Federalists. President Monroe made him secretary of state, 1817, and he negotiated the cession of the Floridas from Spain, supported exclusion of slavery in the Missouri Compromise, and laid the base for the Monroe Doctrine, of which he, as much as Monroe, was the creator. In 1824 he was elected president by the House after he failed to win an Electoral College majority over Henry Clay and Andrew Jackson. His expansion of executive powers was strongly opposed and he was beaten in 1828 by Jackson. In 1831 he was sent to Congress as representative and served 9 terms with distinction and independence. He fought slavery, opposed the annexation of Texas and the war with Mexico; was responsible for the Smithsonian Institution. He had a stroke in the House and died in the Speaker's Room, Feb. 23, 1848.

Adams married Louisa Catherine Johnson on July 26, 1797. They had 3 sons and a daughter.

Andrew Jackson

Andrew Jackson, 7th president, was a Jeffersonian-Republican, later a Democrat. He was born in the Waxhaws district, New Lancaster Co., S.C., Mar. 15, 1767, the posthumous son of Andrew Jackson, who came from County Antrim, Ireland, with his wife, Elizabeth Hutchinson, and 2 sons, in 1765. At 13 young Andrew joined the militia in the Revolution and was captured; a British officer struck him with his sword when the boy refused to shine his boots.

He read law in Salisbury, N.C., moved to Nashville, Tenn., speculated in land, married, and raised cotton at the Hermitage, originally a log house. In 1796 he helped draft the Constitution of Tennessee and for one year occupied its one seat in the national House. He was in the Senate in 1797, and again in 1823. He defeated the Creek Indians at Horseshoe Bend, Ala., 1814, and, as major general, drove the British out of Pensacola. With 6,000 backwoods fighters he defeated Packenham's 12,000 British troops at Chalmette, outside New Orleans, Jan. 8, 1815, losing only 7 to the British loss of 2,000. In 1818 he briefly invaded Spanish Florida to quell Seminoles and outlaws who harassed frontier settlements. In 1824 he ran for president against John Quincy Adams and won the most votes in the Electoral College, but not a majority; the election was decided by the House, which chose Adams. In 1828 he carried everything, the West rising to support "Old Hickory" and a liberal land policy. He was a noisy debater and a duelist and introduced rotation in office called the "spoils system." He was suspicious of privilege; ruined the Bank of the United States by depositing federal funds with state banks. Though "Let the people rule" was his slogan, he at times supported strict constructionist policies against the expansionist West. He killed the Congressional caucus for nominating presidential candidates and substituted the national convention, 1832, when he was reelected, with Martin Van Buren vice president. When South Carolina refused to collect imports under his protective tariff he ordered army and naval forces to Charleston. Jackson recognized the Republic of Texas, 1836.

In 1791 Jackson married Rachel Donelson Robards who believed she had been divorced by Capt. Lewis Robards. But he did not actually obtain a divorce until 1793, after which the Jacksons were remarried. Mrs. Jackson died in 1828, shortly after Jackson's first election. He died at the Hermitage, June 8, 1845, and is buried there.

Martin Van Buren

Martin Van Buren, 8th president, Democrat, was born Dec. 5, 1782, at Kinderhook, N. Y., the son of Abraham Van Buren, a Dutch farmer, and Mary Hoes. He was surrogate of Columbia County, N.Y., state senator and attorney general and a law partner of Benjamin F. Butler in Albany. He was U. S. senator 1821, reelected, 1827, elected governor of New York, 1828. He helped swing eastern support to Andrew Jackson in 1828 and was his secretary of state 1829-31. In 1832 he was elected vice president. He was a consummate politician, known as "the little magician," and influenced Jackson's policies. In 1836 he defeated William Henry Harrison for president by 170 to 73 electoral votes. He inaugurated the independent treasury system, and was the first advocate of mutual insurance of deposits by banks. He urged tariffs for revenue only and opposed internal improvements at national expense. His refusal to spend land revenues led to his defeat by Harrison in 1840. He lost the Democratic nomination of 1844 to Polk because he opposed annexation of Texas. In 1848 he ran for president on the Free Soil ticket and lost. He died July 24, 1862, at Kinderhook.

Van Buren married Hannah Hoes, a cousin, in 1807; she died in 1819.

William Henry Harrison

William Henry Harrison, 9th president, Whig, who served only 31 days, was born in Berkeley, Charles City Co., Va., Feb. 9, 1773, the third son of Benjamin Harrison, signer of the Declaration of Independence. Educated at Hampden Sydney College, he later studied medicine under Dr. Benjamin Rush. Commissioned by Washington, he fought under Gen. Anthony Wayne at Fallen Timbers, 1794. He was secretary of the Northwest Territory, 1798; its delegate in Congress, 1799; first governor of Indiana Territory, and superintendent of Indian affairs. With 900 men he routed Tecumseh's Indians at Tippecanoe, Nov. 7, 1811. A major general, he defeated British and Indians at Battle of the Thames, Oct. 5, 1813. He served Ohio in Congress, 1816; as senator, 1824; was minister to Colombia. In 1840, when 68, he was elected president with John Tyler, 234 to 60, with a "log cabin and hard cider" slogan. He caught pneumonia during the inauguration and died Apr. 4, 1841. He was buried in North Bend, Oh.

Harrison married Anna Symmes in 1795. They had 6 sons. A grandson, Benjamin Harrison, became the 23d president.

John Tyler

John Tyler, 10th president, Independent Whig, was born Mar. 29, 1790, in Greenway, Charles City Co., Va., son of John Tyler and Mary Armistead. His father was governor of Virginia, 1808-11. Tyler was graduated from William and Mary, 1807; member of the House of Delegates, 1811; in Congress, 1816-21; in Virginia legislature, 1823-25; governor of Virginia, 1825-26; U. S. senator, 1827-36. In 1840 he was elected vice president and, on President Harrison's death, succeeded him. He favored pre-emption, allowing settlers to get government land; rejected a new bank bill and thus alienated Whig supporters except Daniel Webster, his secretary of state; refused to honor the spoils system. He signed the resolution annexing Texas, Mar. 1, 1845. He accepted renomination, 1844, but withdrew before election. He condemned South Carolina's nullification and secession and, as Virginia's commissioner to Buchanan, tried to keep Fort Sumter neutralized. He was president of the peace congress called in Washington by Virginia, 1861. After its failure he supported secession, sat in the provisional Confederate Congress, became a member of the Confederate House, but died, Jan. 18, 1862, before it met. He was buried in Richmond.

Tyler first married Letitia Christian, in 1813; they had 3 sons and 4 daughters; she died in 1842. He married Julia Gardiner, of Gardiner's Is., N.Y., in 1844. They had 5 sons and 2 daughters.

James Knox Polk

James Knox Polk, 11th president, Democrat, was born in Mecklenburg Co., N. C., Nov. 2, 1795, the son of Samuel Polk, farmer and surveyor of Scotch-Irish descent, and Jane Knox. He went to Maury Co., Tenn., 1806; was graduated from the University of North Carolina, 1818; member of the Tennessee state legislature, 1823-25, known as "Napoleon of the Stump." He served in Congress 1825-39 and as speaker 1835-39. He supported Jackson and Van Buren, but was always expansionist. He was governor of Tennessee 1839-41, being defeated 1841 and 1843. In 1844, when both Clay and Van Buren announced opposition to annexing Texas, the Democrats made Polk the first dark horse nominee because he demanded control of all Oregon and annexation of Texas. James Buchanan was his secretary of state. Polk re-established the independent treasury system originated by Van Buren. His expansionist policy was opposed by Clay, Webster, Calhoun; he sent Zachary Taylor and an army to the Mexican border and, when Mexicans attacked, declared war existed. Abraham Lincoln, a Whig in Congress, opposed his war policy. Polk approved the acquisition of California, Utah and New Mexico as part of America's "manifest destiny." He compromised on the Oregon boundary ("54-40 or fight!") by accepting the 49th parallel and giving Vancouver to the British. Polk died in Nashville, June 15, 1849, and was buried on the capitol grounds there.

Polk married Sarah Childress Jan. 1, 1824. They had no children.

Zachary Taylor

Zachary Taylor, 12th president, Whig, who served only 16 months, was born Nov. 24, 1784, in Orange Co., Va., the son of Richard Taylor, later collector of the port of Louisville, Ky., and Sarah Strother. His grandfather and James Madison's paternal grandmother were brother and sister. Taylor enlisted 1806; was commissioned lieutenant by Jefferson, 1808; fought in the War of 1812, the Black Hawk War, 1832, and the Seminole war, 1837. He became known as Old Rough and Ready. He settled on a plantation near Baton Rouge, La. In 1845 Polk sent him with an army to the Rio Grande. When the Mexicans attacked him, Polk declared war. Taylor was successful at Palo Alto and Resaca de la Palma, May 8 and 9, 1846; occupied Monterey. Polk made him major general but sent many of his troops to Gen. Winfield Scott at Veracruz. Taylor, with only 5,000 men, defeated Santa Anna's 20,000 at Buena Vista, Feb. 22, 1847. He defeated Scott at the Whig convention, 1848; was elected president, over Martin Van Buren, with Millard Fillmore vice president. He resumed the spoils system and though once a slave-holder worked to have California admitted as a free state. He died of typhus July 9, 1850, and was buried near Louisville.

Taylor married Margaret Smith in 1810. They had one son and 5 daughters, one of whom, Sarah, married Jefferson Davis in 1835. She died a few months later.

Millard Fillmore

Millard Fillmore, 13th president, Whig, was born Jan. 7, 1800, in a log cabin on a Cayuga Co., N.Y., farm cleared in 1795 by his parents, Nathaniel and Phoebe Miller Fillmore. He was apprenticed to a fuller and dyer; bought his freedom for $30 to study and became a teacher and postmaster in Buffalo, N. Y. He was counselor of the state Supreme Court, 1829; in the state Assembly, 1829-32; in Congress, 1833-35 and again 1837-43. He opposed the entrance of Texas as slave territory and voted for a protective tariff. In 1844 he was defeated for governor of New York. In 1848 he was elected vice president and succeeded as president July 10, 1850, after Taylor's death. Fillmore favored the Compromise of 1850 and signed the Fugitive Slave Law. His policies pleased neither expansionists nor slave-holders and he was not renominated in 1852. In 1856 he was nominated by the American (Know-Nothing) party and accepted by the Whigs, but defeated by Buchanan. He was chancellor of the University of Buffalo. He died in Buffalo, Mar. 8, 1874.

Fillmore first married Abigail Powers, in 1826 and they had one son and one daughter. Abigail died in 1853 and Fillmore married Caroline Carmichael McIntosh, a widow, in 1858. They had no children.

Franklin Pierce

Franklin Pierce, 14th president, Democrat, was born in Hillsboro, N. H., Nov. 23, 1804, the son of Benjamin Pierce, veteran of the Revolution and governor of New Hampshire, 1827. He attended Exeter and was graduated from Bowdoin, 1824. A lawyer, he served in the New Hampshire House, 1829-32; in Congress, supporting Jackson, 1833; U.S. senator, 1837-42. He enlisted in the Mexican War, became brigadier general of volunteers and was wounded at Contreras. In 1852 Pierce was nominated on the 49th ballot over the leading candidates: Lewis Cass, Stephen A. Douglas, and James Buchanan, and defeated Gen. Winfield Scott, Whig. Though against slavery, Pierce was influenced by southern pro-slavery men (Jefferson Davis was his secretary of war) but he ignored the Ostend Manifesto that the U.S. either buy or take Cuba. He approved the Kansas-Nebraska Act, leaving slavery to popular vote ("squatter sovereignty"), 1854, and appointed a pro-slavery governor to Kansas. He signed a reciprocity treaty with Canada and approved the Gadsden Purchase from Mexico, 1853. He supported Commodore Matthew Perry's opening of Japan, 1854. Pierce died at Concord, N.H., Oct. 8, 1869.

Pierce married Jane Means Appleton in 1834. They had 3 children who all died in childhood.

James Buchanan

James Buchanan, 15th president, Federalist, later Democrat, was born of Scottish descent near Mercersburg, Pa., Apr. 23, 1791. He was a volunteer in the War of 1812; graduated from Dickinson, 1809; member, Pennsylvania legislature, 1814-16, Congress, 1820-31; Jackson's minister to Russia, 1831-33; U.S. senator 1834-45. As Polk's secretary of state, 1845-49, he ended the Oregon dispute with Britain, supported the Mexican War and annexation of Texas. As minister to Britain, 1853, he signed the Ostend Manifesto, 1854, urging the U. S. to take Cuba. Nominated by Democrats over Pierce and Stephen A. Douglas, he was elected, 1856, over John C. Fremont (Republican) and Millard Fillmore (American Know-Nothing and Whig tickets). On slavery he favored popular sovereignty and choice by state constitutions; he accepted the pro-slavery Dred Scott decision as binding. He denied the right of states to secede. Buchanan refused demands of South Carolina for Federal property, but also refused to reinforce forts there until too late to help Fort Sumter. A strict constructionist, he desired to keep peace and found no authority for using force. He died at Wheatland, near Lancaster, Pa., June 1, 1868, at age 77.

Buchanan was a bachelor. The mistress of the White House was the daughter of Buchanan's sister Jane, Harriet Lane, whose parents had died when she was a child.

Abraham Lincoln

Abraham Lincoln, 16th president, Republican, was born Feb. 12, 1809, in a log cabin on a farm then in Hardin Co., Ky., now in Larue. He was the son of Thomas Lincoln (1778-1851), a descendant of Samuel Lincoln, who came from Hingham, England, 1637, settled at Salem and Hingham, Mass., and had 11 children. Thomas Lincoln, a carpenter, married Nancy Hanks, June 12, 1806.

Abraham had a sister, Sarah, born 1807, died 1828, and a brother Thomas, who died in infancy.

The Lincolns moved to Spencer Co., Ind., near Gentryville, when Abe was 7. Nancy died Oct. 5, 1818, aged 35. His father married Mrs. Sarah Bush Johnston, 1819; she had a favorable influence on Abe. In 1830 the family moved to Macon Co., Ill., where Abe and a cousin split 3,000 fence rails. In 1831 they moved to Coles Co. In New Salem, 1831-1837, Lincoln lost election to the Illinois General Assembly, 1832, but later won 4 times, beginning in 1834. He enlisted in the militia for the Black Hawk War, 1832. In New Salem he ran a store, 1833; surveyed land, 1834-36, and was postmaster, 1833-36.

In 1837 Lincoln was admitted to the bar and became partner in a Springfield, Ill., law office. He began practice in the 8th Judicial Circuit, 1839. He was a presidential elector, 1839, 1844, 1852, 1856. He failed of nomination for representative, 1843, but was elected to the 30th Congress, 1847. He opposed the Mexican War. He stumped New England for Zachary Taylor, 1848. He refused offices of secretary and governor of Oregon Territory, 1849. He opposed the Kansas-Nebraska Act and extension of slavery, 1854. When elected to the Illinois legislature, 1854, he declined in order to try for the Senate, but failed of election, 1855. He was proposed but not chosen for vice president at the first Republican convention, 1856, and he made 50 speeches for John C. Fremont, presidential nominee.

In 1858 Lincoln had Republican support in the Illinois legislature for the Senate but was defeated by Stephen A. Douglas, Dem., who had sponsored the Kansas-Nebraska Act.

Lincoln was nominated for president by the Republican party on an anti-slavery platform, at Chicago, May 18, 1860. He ran against Douglas, a northern Democrat; John C. Breckinridge, southern pro-slavery Democrat; John Bell, Constitutional Union party. Lincoln got only 40% of the popular votes, but 180 electoral votes; Breckinridge, 72; Bell, 39; Douglas, 12. South Carolina seceded from the Union Dec. 20, 1860, followed in 1861 by 10 southern states.

Lincoln was inaugurated Mar. 4, 1861. Fort Sumter was attacked Apr. 12-14, and surrendered. Lincoln called for 75,000 volunteers Apr. 15, and 500,000 May 3. On Sept. 22, 1862, 5 days after the battle of Antietam, he annnounced that slaves in territory then in rebellion would be free Jan. 1, 1863, date of the Emancipation Proclamation. He reached high degrees of moving eloquence in his Gettysburg and Inaugural Addresses and other speeches.

Lincoln was reelected, 1864, over Gen. Geo. B. McClellan, Democrat. Lee surrendered Apr. 9, 1865. On Apr. 14 (Good Friday) Lincoln was shot by actor John Wilkes Booth in Ford's Theatre, Washington. He died the next day. His body lay in state in New York, Chicago, and other cities before burial in Springfield, Ill. His estate reached $110,974, most of it saved from his annual salary of $25,000. His humanity, lofty concept of office, and generous spirit made him the hero of the common man the world over.

Lincoln married Mary Todd in Springfield, Nov. 4, 1842; they had 4 sons.

Andrew Johnson

Andrew Johnson, 17th president, Democrat, was born in Raleigh, N. C., Dec. 29, 1808, the son of Jacob Johnson, porter at an inn and church sexton, and Mary McDonough Johnson, who had been a maid at the inn. His father died when he was 5. At 10 he was apprenticed to a tailor. At 16 he ran off to Greenville, Tenn. He became an alderman, 1828; mayor, 1830; state representative and senator, 1835-43; member of Congress, 1843-53; governor of Tennessee, 1853-57; U.S. senator, 1857-62. He supported John C. Breckinridge against Lincoln in 1860. He had held slaves, but opposed secession and refused to follow Tennessee out of the Union. In Mar. 1862, Lincoln appointed him military governor of occupied Tennessee. In 1864 he was nominated for vice president with Lincoln on the National Union ticket to win Democratic support. He succeeded Lincoln as president April 15, 1865. In a controversy with Congress over the president's power over the South, he proclaimed, May 26, 1865, an amnesty to all Confederates except certain leaders if they would abolish slavery and ratify the 13th Amendment. States doing so added anti-Negro provisions that enraged Congress, which intended to enfranchise all Negroes and disenfranchise former Confederates. Congress restored military control over the South. When Johnson removed Edwin M. Stanton, secretary of war, without notifying the Senate, thus repudiating the Tenure of Office Act, the House impeached him for this and other reasons. He was tried by the Senate, which voted 35 for conviction, 19 for acquittal, lacking by one the two-thirds necessary to convict, May 26, 1868. He was a candidate before the next Democratic convention, but not nominated. He returned to the Senate in 1875, and in a strong speech defended his course. He supported the Lincoln policies, but his conciliatory attitude toward the South was fought by the radical Republicans. Johnson died July 31, 1875, and was buried at Greenville (now Greeneville), where his log cabin tailor shop and home are museums.

Johnson married Eliza McArdle in 1827. They had 3 sons and 2 daughters.

Ulysses Simpson Grant

Ulysses S. Grant, 18th president, Republican, was born at Point Pleasant, Oh., Apr. 27, 1822, son of Jesse R. Grant, a tanner, and Hannah Simpson Grant. The next year the family moved to Georgetown, Oh. Grant was named Hiram Ulysses, but on entering West Point, 1839, his name was entered as Ulysses Simpson and he adopted it. He was graduated in 1843; and was first lieutenant and captain under Gens. Taylor and Scott in the Mexican War; resigned, 1854; worked in St. Louis until 1860, then went to Galena, Ill., where his father sold leather and hardware. With the start of the Civil War, he was named colonel of the 21st Illinois Vols., 1861, then brigadier general; took Forts Henry and Donelson; was made major general of volunteers; fought at Shiloh. Took Vicksburg, became major general USA, and in March 1864, lieutenant general. He accepted Lee's surrender at Appomattox. In 1866 he was named a full general. President Johnson appointed Grant secretary of war when he suspended Stanton in defiance of the Senate, but Grant was not confirmed. He was nominated for president on the first ballot, May 30, 1868, and elected over Horatio Seymour, Democrat, 214 to 80 electoral votes. The 15th Amendment, amnesty bill, and civil service reform were events of his administration. The Liberal Republicans opposed him with Horace Greeley, also Democratic nominee, 1872, but he was reelected. An attempt by the Stalwarts (Old Guard) to nominate him in 1880 failed. In 1884 the collapse of Grant & Ward, investment house, left him penniless. He began his Personal Memoirs, writing while ill of cancer and completing them 4 days before his death at Mt. McGregor, N.Y., July 23, 1885. The book realized over $450,000. Grant was buried in an imposing tomb on Riverside Drive, New York, where his wife also lies.

Grant married Julia Dent in 1848. They had 3 sons and one daughter.

Rutherford Birchard Hayes

Rutherford B. Hayes, 19th president, Republican, was born in Delaware, Oh., Oct. 4, 1822, the posthumous son of Rutherford Hayes, a farmer, and Sophia Birchard. He was descended from George Hayes, a Scot, who reached Windsor, Conn., in 1680. He was raised by his uncle Sardis Birchard, educated in Norwalk, Oh., and Middletown, Conn., and graduated from Kenyon College, 1842, and Harvard Law School, 1845. He practiced law in Lower Sandusky, Oh., now Fremont; was city solicitor of Cincinnati, 1858-61. In the Civil War, he was major of the 23d Ohio Vols., wounded at South Mountain; became brigadier general and major general by brevet, 1864. He served in Congress 1864-67, supporting Reconstruction and Johnson's impeachment. He was elected governor of Ohio, 1867 and 1869; beaten in the race for Congress, 1872; reelected governor, 1875. He supported the merit principle in appointments, prison reform, and public libraries. In 1876 he was nominated for president over James G. Blaine and believed he had lost to Samuel J. Tilden, Democrat, 184 to 163 electoral votes. But Zachariah Chandler, chairman of the Republican National Committee, relying on Republican domination of the South, urged the validity of contesting 22 electoral returns from Florida, South Carolina, Louisiana, and Oregon. Frauds in Louisiana injuring Tilden were permitted to stand. Promises to withdraw troops from the South were reportedly used to suborn Democrats. An Electoral Commission, appointed by Congress, 8 Republicans and 7 Democrats, awarded all disputed votes to Hayes. The Electoral College vote then became 185 for Hayes, 184 for Tilden. The withdrawal of troops followed, but handicapped Republican rule, and as Hayes proceeded to reform the civil service he alienated political spoilsmen. He advocated repeal of the Tenure of Office Act that had led to Johnson's impeachment. He supported sound money and specie payments. Hayes died in Fremont, Oh., Jan. 17, 1893.

Hayes married Lucy Webb in 1852. They had 7 sons and one daughter.

James Abram Garfield

James A. Garfield, 20th president, Republican, was born Nov. 19, 1831, in a log cabin at Orange, Cuyahoga Co., Oh., the son of Abram and Eliza Ballou Garfield. His father, a canal contractor and farmer from New York, was descended from Edward Garfield, who reached Massachusetts Bay Colony in 1630 and helped found Watertown, Mass. James was the youngest of 4 children. His father died in 1833 and his mother supported them. He worked as a canal bargeman, farmer, and carpenter; attended Western Reserve Eclectic, later Hiram College, and was graduated from Williams in 1856. He became professor of ancient languages and literature at Hiram, then principal. He was in the Ohio Senate in 1859. Anti-slavery and anti-secession, he volunteered for the war, became colonel of the 42d Ohio Infantry and brigadier in 1862. He fought at Shiloh, was chief of staff for Rosecrans and was made major general for gallantry at Chickamauga. He entered Congress as a radical Republican in 1863; supported specie payment as against paper money (greenbacks). On the electoral commission in 1876 he voted for Hayes against Tilden on strict party lines. He was senator-elect in 1880 when he became the Republican nominee for president. He was chosen on the 36th ballot as a compromise over Gen. Grant, James G. Blaine, and John Sherman. This alienated the Grant following but Garfield was elected and Blaine became his secretary of state. On July 2, 1881, Garfield was shot by an unbalanced office-seeker, Charles J. Guiteau, while entering the old Baltimore & Potomac station in Washington. He died Sept. 19, 1881, at Elberon, N.J., and was buried in Cleveland, Oh. Guiteau was hanged June 30, 1882.

Garfield married Lucretia Rudolph in 1858. They had 4 sons and one daughter.

Chester Alan Arthur

Chester A. Arthur, 21st president, Republican, was born at Fairfield, Vt., Oct. 5, 1829, the son of the Rev. William Arthur, from County Antrim, Ireland, and Malvina Stone Arthur, member of a New Hampshire family. He graduated at Union College, 1848, taught school at Pownall, Vt., studied law in New York. In 1853 he argued in a fugitive slave case that slaves transported through N.Y. State were thereby freed; in 1855 he obtained a ruling that Negroes were to be treated the same as whites on street cars. He helped organize the N.Y. State Militia, 1861, was made quartermaster general and equipped troops for the front. He was made collector of the Port of New York, 1871. In 1877 President Hayes, reforming the civil service, ordered Arthur's resignation. He refused because he was not personally culpable, but was removed, 1879. This made Senators Conkling, Platt, and the New York machine stalwarts enemies of Hayes. Arthur and the stalwarts tried to nominate Grant for a third term in 1880. When Garfield was nominated, Arthur received second place in the interests of harmony. On Sept. 19, 1881, Garfield died and Arthur became president. He supported civil service reform and the tariff of 1883; arranged an unratified canal treaty with Nicaragua. He was defeated for renomination by James G. Blaine, 1884, but supported Blaine. He died Nov. 18, 1886, and was buried in Albany, N. Y.

Arthur married Ellen Lewis Herndon in 1859. They had 2 sons and one daughter.

Grover Cleveland

(According to a ruling of the State Dept. Grover Cleveland is both the 22d and the 24th president, because his 2 terms were not consecutive. By individuals, he is only the 22d.)

Grover Cleveland, 22d and 24th president, Democrat, was born in Caldwell, N. J., Mar. 18, 1837, the son of Richard F. Cleveland, a Presbyterian minister, and Ann Neale, daughter of a Baltimore merchant who had come from Ireland. The future president was named Stephen Grover, but dropped the Stephen. He clerked in Clinton and Buffalo, N. Y., taught in the N.Y. City Institution for the Blind; was admitted to the bar in Buffalo, 1859; became assistant district attorney 1863; sheriff 1869; mayor, 1881; governor of New York, 1882. He was an independent, honest administrator who hated corruption. He was nominated for president over Tammany Hall opposition, 1884, defeating Republican James G. Blaine, 219 to 182 Electoral College votes. He enlarged the civil service, vetoed many pension raids on the Treasury. In 1888 he was defeated by Benjamin Harrison, although his popular vote was larger. Reelected over Harrison, 1892, by 277 to 145, electoral votes, he faced a money crisis brought about by lowering of the gold reserve, circulation of paper and exorbitant silver purchases under the Sherman Act; obtained a repeal of the latter and a reduced tariff. An income tax was passed but declared unconstitutional by the Supreme Court, 1895. A severe depression and labor troubles racked his administration but he refused to interfere in business matters and rejected, as crackpot theory, Jacob Coxey's demand for work relief of $20 million monthly. He broke the Pullman strike with troops to move the mail, 1894. He rejected the platform of William Jennings Bryan's silver Democrats, 1896, and supported the gold Democrats. He died in Princeton, N.J., June 24, 1908.

Cleveland married Frances Folsom in the White House, June 2, 1886. They had 2 sons and 3 daughters.

Benjamin Harrison

Benjamin Harrison, 23d president, Republican, was born at North Bend, Oh., Aug. 20, 1833. His great-grandfather, Benjamin Harrison, was a signer of the Declaration of Independence; his grandfather, William Henry Harrison, was 9th president; his father, John Scott Harrison, was a member of Congress, 1853-57. His mother was Elizabeth F. Irwin. He attended school in a log cabin on his father's farm; graduated from Miami University, 1852; was admitted to the bar, 1853, and practiced in Indianapolis. As a second Lieutenant in the Civil War, he raised recruits and became colonel of the 70th Indiana Volunteer Infantry. He fought at Kenesaw Mountain, Peachtree Creek, Nashville, and in the Atlanta campaign. In 1865 he was made a brigadier general by brevet. He failed to be elected governor of Indiana, 1876; but became senator, 1881, and worked for the G. A. R. pensions vetoed by Cleveland. In 1888 he defeated Cleveland for president 233 to 168 Electoral College votes. He expanded the pension list greatly; suppressed the Louisiana lottery; signed the McKinley high tariff bill and the Sherman silver purchase act. He helped the admission of North and South Dakota, Montana, Washington, Idaho, and Wyoming, Republican states. He was defeated for reelection, 1892. He represented Venezuela in a boundary arbitration with Great Britain in Paris, 1899. He died at Indianapolis, Mar. 13, 1901, and was buried there.

Harrison married Caroline Lavinia Scott in 1853; they had one son and one daughter. The first Mrs. Harrison died in 1892 and in 1896 Harrison married her niece, Mary Scott Lord Dimmick, a widow. They had one daughter.

William McKinley

William McKinley, 25th president, Republican, was born in Niles, Oh., Jan. 29, 1843, the son of William McKinley, an iron manufacturer, and Nancy Allison McKinley, and was the 7th of 9 children. His father's family was Scotch-Irish from County Antrim, Ireland; his great-grandfather fought in the American Revolution. McKinley attended school in Poland, Oh., and Allegheny College, Meadville, Pa., and enlisted for the Civil War at 18 in the 23d Ohio, in which Rutherford B. Hayes was a major. He was a commissary sergeant at Antietam. He rose to captain and in 1865 was made major by brevet. He studied law in the Albany, N.Y., law school; opened an office in Canton, Oh., in 1867, and campaigned for Grant and Hayes. From 1876 to 1890, excepting 1882, he served in the House of Representatives and led the fight for a high tariff to protect "infant industries" and reciprocal trade agreements (McKinley Tariff, enacted Oct. 1, 1890). Defeated for reelection on the issue in 1890, he was elected governor of Ohio, 1891 and 1893. He received 182 ballots for president in the Republican convention that nominated Benjamin Harrison in 1892. In 1896 he was elected president on a protective tariff, sound money (gold standard) platform over William Jennings Bryan, Democratic proponent of free silver. McKinley was reluctant to intervene in Cuba but the loss of the battleship Maine at Havana crystallized opinion. He demanded Spain's withdrawal from Cuba; Spain agreed to arbitration and armistice but Congress announced state of war as of Apr. 21. (Peace signed Dec. 10). He was reelected in the 1900 campaign, defeating Bryan's anti-imperialist arguments with the prestige of prosperity, "the full dinner pail" and the vigorous campaigning of Theodore Roosevelt, vice presidential nominee. McKinley was a Methodist, respected for his conciliatory nature, but conservative on business issues. He abhorred violence. On Sept. 6, 1901, while welcoming citizens at the Pan-American Exposition, Buffalo, N.Y., he was shot by Leon Czolgosz, an anarchist. He died Sept. 14. His last words were: "It is God's way. His will, not ours, be done." McKinley, his wife, and infant daughters rest in an imposing tomb in Canton.

McKinley married Ida Saxton in 1871. They had 2 daughters; both died in childhood.

Theodore Roosevelt

Theodore Roosevelt, 26th president, Republican, was born in N.Y. City, Oct. 27, 1858, the son of Theodore Roosevelt, collector of the port, and Martha Bulloch, daughter of Maj. J. S. Bulloch, Roswell, Ga. Roosevelt was descended from Claes Martenszan van Rosenvelt, and his wife Janett, who reached New Netherland from Holland about 1650. Theodore was a fifth cousin of Franklin D. Roosevelt and an uncle of Mrs. Eleanor Roosevelt. His mother was of Scotch-Irish, Huguenot stock and a southern sympathizer. Roosevelt was graduated from Harvard, 1880, attended Columbia Law School briefly; sat in the N.Y. State Assembly, 1882-84; ranched in North Dakota, 1884-86; failed election as mayor of N.Y. City, 1886; member of U.S. Civil Service Commission, 1889; president, N.Y. Police Board, 1895, supporting the merit system; assistant secretary of the Navy under McKinley, Apr. 19, 1897 — May 10, 1898, during which he instituted naval target practice and instructed Commodore George Dewey to take Manila in the event of war with Spain. He organized the 1st U.S. Volunteer Cavalry (Rough Riders) as lieutenant colonel; led the charge up Kettle Hill at San Juan and was made colonel by brevet. Elected governor, New York, 1898-1900, he fought the spoils system and achieved taxation of corporation franchises. Drafted for vice president, 1900, he became nation's youngest president at 42 years, 10 mos., 18 days, when McKinley died at Buffalo, Sept. 14, 1901. As president he fought corruption of politics by big business; dissolved Northern Securities Co. and others for violating anti-trust laws; intervened in coal strike on behalf of the public, 1902; instituted the old Dept. of Commerce and Labor; obtained Elkins Law forbidding rebates to favored corporations, 1903; Hepburn Law regulating railroad rates, 1906; Pure Food and Drugs Act, 1906, Reclamation Act and employers' liability laws. He organized conservation, mediated the peace between Japan and Russia, 1905; won the Nobel Peace Prize. He was the first to use the Hague Court of International Arbitration. By recognizing the new Republic of Panama he made Panama Canal possible, appointed Col. George W. Goethals head commissioner and began canal. He was reelected 1904, with 336 electoral votes, vs. 140.

In 1908 he obtained the nomination of William H. Taft, who was elected. Later, considering Taft inimical to liberal policies, he organized the Progressive Party, June 22, 1912, and ran for president against Taft and Woodrow Wilson, splitting the Republicans and insuring Wilson's election. He was shot during the campaign but recovered. He advocated recall of elected officials, referendum on legislation, and recall of judicial decisions, which alienated conservatives. In 1916 he left the Progressives and supported Charles E. Hughes, Republican. A strong friend of Britain, he fought American isolation. In 1917 President Wilson refused to let him organize a division. He wrote on many topics—his *Winning of the West* is best known—was a naturalist and hunter and traced the River of Doubt in Brazil, 1913-14, now Rio Roosevelt. He died Jan. 6, 1919, at Sagamore Hill, Oyster Bay, N. Y., now a national shrine, and was buried near the Roosevelt bird refuge there.

Roosevelt's first marriage, in 1880, was to Alice Hathaway Lee, who died in 1884; they had one daughter. In 1886, he married Edith Kermit Carow; they had one daughter and 4 sons. All 4 served in World War I; one was killed and 2 wounded. The 3 left all served in World War II; 2 died of natural causes while on active duty.

William Howard Taft

William Howard Taft, 27th president, Republican, was born in Cincinnati, Oh., Sept. 15, 1857, the son of Alphonso Taft and Louisa Maria Torrey. His father was secretary of war and attorney general in Grant's cabinet; minister to Austria and Russia under Arthur. Taft was graduated from Yale, 1878; Cincinnati Law School, 1880; became law reporter for Cincinnati newspapers; was assistant prosecuting attorney, 1881-83; assistant county solicitor, 1885; judge, Superior Court, 1887; U.S. solicitor-general, 1890; federal circuit judge, 1892. In 1900 he became head of the U.S. Philippines Commission and was first civil governor of the Philippines, 1901-04; secretary of war, 1904; provisional governor of Cuba, 1906. He was groomed for president by Theodore Roosevelt as an exemplary public servant and elected over William Jennings Bryan, 1908. His administration dissolved Standard Oil and tobacco trusts; instituted Department of Labor; drafted direct election of senators and income tax amendments. His tariff and conservation policies angered progressives; though renominated he was fought by Theodore Roosevelt; the result was Democrat Woodrow Wilson's election. Taft was president of the League to Enforce Peace, supporting the League of Nations. He was professor of constitutional law, Yale, 1913-21; chief justice of the United States, 1921-30; illness forced him to resign. He died in Washington, Mar. 8, 1930, and was buried in Arlington National Cemetery.

Taft married Helen Herron in 1886; they had 2 sons and a daughter.

Woodrow Wilson

Woodrow Wilson, 28th president, Democrat, was born at Staunton, Va., Dec. 28, 1856, as Thomas Woodrow Wilson, son of a Presbyterian minister, the Rev. Joseph Ruggles Wilson and Janet (Jessie) Woodrow, daughter of a Presbyterian minister. He was a grandson of James Wilson, a Presbyterian of Ulster who reached Philadelphia in 1807, became a printer and in 1808 married an Ulster Presbyterian girl, a shipmate. In his youth Wilson lived in Augusta, Ga., Columbia, S.C., and Wilmington, N.C. He attended Davidson College, 1873-74; was graduated from Princeton, A.B., 1879; A.M., 1882; read law at the University of Virginia, 1881; practiced law, Atlanta, 1882-83; Ph.D., Johns Hopkins, 1886. He taught history and political economy at Bryn Mawr, 1885-88; at Wesleyan, 1888-90; was professor of jurisprudence and political economy at Princeton, 1890-1910; president of Princeton, 1902-1910, during which he tried to introduce innovations of organization that were fought by the graduate dean and alumni; governor of New Jersey, 1911-13, during which he obtained a primary election law, an employers' liability law and other reforms. In 1912 he was nominated for president with the aid of William Jennings Bryan, who sought to block James "Champ" Clark and Tammany Hall. Wilson won the election because the Republican vote for Taft was split by the Progressives under Theodore Roosevelt.

Wilson protected American interests in revolutionary Mexico and fought for American rights on the high seas as the first World War opened. His sharp warnings to Germany led to the resignation of his secretary of state, Bryan, a pacifist, while his protests against British interference with American ships disturbed the Allies. In 1916 he was reelected by a slim margin with the slogan, "He kept us out of war," over Charles Evans Hughes, who was strongly supported by Theodore Roosevelt. Wilson's attempts to mediate in the war failed, Dec. 1916 - Jan. 1917. When the Germans started unrestricted submarine warfare, contrary to pledges, he broke diplomatic relations. After 4 American ships had been sunk he asked a declaration of war against Germany; it was voted Apr. 6, 1917.

Wilson kept tight personal control over all phases of diplomatic and military activity. He relied more on reports of his confidential agent in Europe, Col. E. M. House, than on Secretary of State Robert Lansing and the U.S. ambassadors. However, he backed Gen. John J. Pershing, U.S. commander in chief, Herbert Hoover, food administrator, and others who had his confidence.

Wilson proposed peace Jan. 8, 1918, on the basis of his Fourteen Points, a state paper with worldwide influence. Basic was his doctrine of self-determination, or consent of the governed, in which he opposed handing peoples from one sovereignty to another. He also demanded a league to enforce peace. The Germans overturned their monarchy and a new republic accepted his terms and an armistice, Nov. 11. But at the November elections, the Democrats lost control of Congress.

Wilson went to Paris to help negotiate the peace treaty, the crux of which he considered the League of Nations, also urged by ex-President Taft. In the U.S. Senate, Henry Cabot Lodge, William E. Borah, and Hiram Johnson demanded reservations that would not make the United States subordinate to the votes of other nations in case of war. Wilson refused to consider any reservations and toured the country to get support. At Pueblo, Col., Sept. 25, 1919, he broke down and several days later suffered a stroke. An invalid for months, he clung to his executive powers while his wife and doctor sought to shield him from affairs which would tire him.

He was awarded the 1919 Nobel Peace Prize, but the treaty, embodying the League of Nations, was rejected by the Senate, Mar. 1920, by 49 to 35 (29 being sufficient to kill it). He made a public appearance on the day of Harding's inauguration in 1921, and formed a law partnership with Bainbridge Colby, but did not practice. He died Feb. 3, 1924, and was buried in Washington Cathedral.

Wilson's first marriage, in 1885, was to Ellen Louise Axson, who died in 1914. They had 3 daughters. Wilson married Edith Bolling Galt, a widow, in 1915; they had no children.

Warren Gamaliel Harding

Warren Gamaliel Harding, 29th president, Republican, was born near Corsica, now Blooming Grove, Oh., Nov. 2, 1865, the son of Dr. George Tyron Harding, a country physician, and Phoebe Elizabeth Dickerson. He attended Ohio Central College, Iberia, Oh., 1879-82; worked on the Star, Marion, Oh., 1884 and a few years later bought the paper with a friend's help for a reported $300. He was state senator, 1900-04; lieutenant governor, 1904-06; defeated for governor, 1910; chosen U. S. senator, 1915. He was a regular, "Old Guard" Republican; supported Taft, opposed federal control of food and fuel; voted for anti-strike legislation, woman's suffrage, and the Volstead prohibition enforcement act over President Wilson's veto, and opposed the League of Nations. In 1920 he was nominated for president on the 10th ballot; Calvin Coolidge was named for vice president. The Republicans capitalized on war weariness and fear that Wilson's League of Nations would curtail U.S. sovereignty. They defeated the Democrats, James M. Cox and Franklin D. Roosevelt, 16,152,200 to 9,147,353. Harding stressed a return to "normalcy"; worked for tariff revision and repeal of excess profits law and high income taxes. He obtained a Congressional resolution declaring peace with Germany, Austria, and Hungary July 2, 1921; peace treaties with the 3 were signed in Aug. 1921. His cabinet included Charles Evans Hughes (state); Herbert Hoover (commerce); Andrew S. Mellon (treasury). Two appointees, Albert B. Fall (interior) and Harry Daugherty (attorney general), became involved in the Teapot Dome scandal that embittered Harding's last days. He called the International Conference on Limitation of Armaments, 1921-22. Returning from a trip to Alaska he became ill and died in San Francisco, Aug. 2, 1923. He was buried in Marion, Oh.

In 1891 Harding married Florence Kling De Wolfe, who had divorced her first husband. The Hardings had no children.

Calvin Coolidge

Calvin Coolidge, 30th president, Republican, was born in Plymouth, Vt., July 4, 1872, the son of John Calvin Coolidge, a storekeeper, and Victoria J. Moor, and named John Calvin Coolidge. His paternal ancestors came from England to Watertown, later Cambridge, Massachusetts Bay Colony, in 1630. Coolidge graduated from Amherst, 1895; was admitted to the bar in Northampton, Mass., 1897; became city councilman, 1889; city solicitor, 1900-01; clerk of the courts, 1904; member of the lower Massachusetts house, 1907-08; mayor of Northampton, 1910-11; state senator, 1912-15; Senate president, 1914-15; lieutenant governor, 1916-18; governor, 1919; reelected, 1920. In Sept., 1919, Coolidge attained national prominence by calling out the State Guard in the Boston police strike. He declared: "There is no right to strike against the public safety by anybody, anywhere, anytime." This brought his name before the Republican convention of 1920, where he received 34 votes for president and was nominated for vice president by 674 votes. He succeeded to the presidency on Harding's death, Aug. 2, 1923, the oath being administered by his father, a justice of the peace, in his home in Plymouth, Aug. 3, and again Aug. 17 before Justice A. A. Hoehling of the Supreme Court of the District of Columbia. He opposed the League of Nations; approved the World Court; vetoed the soldiers' bonus bill, which was passed over his veto. In 1924 he was reelected by a huge majority with 15,725,016 over John W. Davis, Democrat, 8,385,586, and Robert M. LaFollette, Progressive, 4,822,856. He reduced the national debt by $2 billion in 3 years. He opposed the McNary-Haugen farm bill, and supported his secretary of state, Frank B. Kellogg, in the Kellogg-Briand treaties outlawing war. His dry, laconic remarks are often quoted. Opposing cuts in Europe's war debt, he said: "They hired the money, didn't they?" With Republicans eager to renominate him he announced, Aug. 2, 1927: "I do not choose to run for president in 1928." He became a life insurance director and wrote syndicated articles. He died of a heart attack in Northampton, Jan. 5, 1933. He was buried on a Plymouth hillside.

Coolidge married Grace Anna Goodhue in 1905. They had 2 sons.

Herbert Hoover

Herbert C. Hoover, 31st president, Republican, was born at West Branch, Ia., Aug. 10, 1874, son of Jesse Clark Hoover, a blacksmith (1847-1880), and Hulda Randall Minthorn (1848-83). Ancestor Andrew Hoover came to Pennsylvania from the West German Palatinate, 1738. Hoover grew up in Indian Territory and Oregon; won his A.B. in engineering at Stanford, 1891. Briefly with U.S. Geological Survey and western mines; then mining engineer in Australia, Asia, Europe, Africa, America. While chief engineer, imperial mines, China, he directed food relief for victims of Boxer Rebellion, 1900. He became a world figure in relief work, distributing over $5 billion worth during 1914-1923. He directed American Relief Committee, London, 1914-15; U.S. Comm. for Relief in Belgium, 1915-1919; was U.S. Food Administrator, 1917-1919; American Relief Administrator, 1918-1923, feeding children in defeated nations; Russian Relief, 1918-1923; Interallied Food Council; Supreme Economic Council. As secretary of commerce, 1921-28, he began regulation of radio and aviation, pushed research program for National Academy of Science; organized 7-state pact for Colorado River irrigation and Hoover (Boulder) Dam. Elected president over Alfred E. Smith, 1928, he started White House Conferences on child health and protection, and housing; supported conservation of forests, oil, resources; initiated Naval Conference, 1930; organized Reconstruction Finance Corp., Home Loan Banks; expanded Farm Loan Banks. He gave his official salary to charities and to underpaid help. President Truman made him coordinator of European Food Program, 1947, chairman of the Commission for Reorganization of the Executive Branch, 1947-49, and chairman of the 2d Commission on Reorganization, 1953-55. He founded the Hoover Institution on War, Revolution, and Peace at Stanford University. He died in N.Y. City, Oct. 20, 1964, and was buried at West Branch, Ia., where his birthplace is now a memorial.

Hoover married Lou Henry in 1899. They had 2 sons.

Franklin Delano Roosevelt

Franklin D. Roosevelt, 32d president, Democrat, was born near Hyde Park, N.Y., Jan. 30, 1882, the son of James Roosevelt (died 1900) and Sara Delano (died 1941). His ancestor, Claes Martenszan van Rosenvelt, came to New Amsterdam from Holland about 1650. Claes' son Nicholas, a New York alderman in 1700 and 1715, had a son Johannes, from whom Theodore Roosevelt was descended, and a son Jacobus, from whom Franklin D. Roosevelt was descended. Franklin was graduated at Harvard, 1904; attended Columbia Law School; was admitted to the bar. He went to the New York Senate from his Dutchess County district, 1910 and 1913. In 1913 President Woodrow Wilson made him assistant secretary of the navy.

Roosevelt ran for vice president, 1920, with James Cox and was defeated. From 1920 to 1928 he was a New York lawyer and vice president of Fidelity & Deposit Co. In Aug., 1921, polio paralyzed his legs. He learned to walk with leg braces and a cane and established the Warm Springs, Ga., Foundation, for helping other victims.

Roosevelt presented the name of Alfred E. Smith to the Democratic conventions of 1924 in New York and 1928 in Houston, calling Smith the Happy Warrior. Smith was nominated in 1928 and defeated. Roosevelt was elected governor of New York, 1928 and 1930. In 1932 at Chicago W. G. McAdoo, pledged to John N. Garner, threw his votes to Roosevelt, who was nominated, alienating Smith. The financial crash, unemployment, and the Democratic promise to repeal prohibition insured his election. He asked emergency powers, proclaimed the New Deal, and put into effect a vast number of administrative changes. Foremost was "pump priming," or use of public funds for relief and public works, resulting in deficit financing. He greatly expanded the controls of the central government over business, and by an excess profits tax and progressive income taxes produced a redistribution of earnings on an unprecedented scale. The Wagner Act gave labor many advantages in organizing and collective bargaining. He was the last president inaugurated on Mar. 4 (1933) and the first inaugurated on Jan. 20 (1937).

Roosevelt was a tremendous worker and traveler despite physical handicaps. He was the first president to use radio for "fireside chats." When the Supreme Court nullified some New Deal laws, he sought power to "pack" the court with additional justices, but Congress refused to give him the authority. Court resignations soon enabled him to replace conservatives who had opposed him. He was the first president to break the "no 3d term" tradition and was elected to a 4th term, 1944, despite failing health. The culminating event of his career was World War II. He was openly hostile to fascist governments before the war and gave Britain substantial support, such as exchanging 50 destroyers for air bases, before the Japanese attack on Pearl Harbor made the U.S. a belligerent. He wrote the principles of fair dealing into the Atlantic Charter, Aug. 14, 1941 (with Winston Churchill), and urged the Four Freedoms (freedom of speech, of worship, from want, from fear) Jan. 6, 1941. He conferred with allied heads of state at Casablanca, Jan., 1943; Quebec, Aug., 1943; Teheran, Nov.-Dec., 1943; Cairo, Dec., 1943; Yalta, Feb., 1945. He died at Warm Springs, Ga., Apr. 12, 1945, aged 63, and was buried on his Hyde Park estate, where his house and library are in the national care.

Roosevelt married Anna Eleanor Roosevelt (a 5th cousin who was a niece of Theodore Roosevelt) in 1905. They had 4 sons and one daughter and a child that died in infancy.

Harry S. Truman

Harry S. Truman, 33d president, Democrat, was born at Lamar, Mo., May 8, 1884, the son of John Anderson Truman and Martha Ellen Young. His 4 grandparents were born in Kentucky and moved to Missouri in the 1840s. The Trumans came from England, the president's mother's grandmother from Northern Ireland, while an ancestor of his maternal grandfather, Solomon Young, came from Germany. A family disagreement on whether Harry Truman's middle name was Shippe or Solomon, after names of two grandfathers, resulted in his using only the middle initial S.

He attended public schools in Independence, Mo., worked for the Kansas City Star, 1901, and as railroad timekeeper, and helper in Kansas City banks up to 1905. He joined the Missouri National Guard, 1905, but was rejected by West Point for defective eyesight. He ran his family's farm, 1906-17. He entered the Field Artillery School at Fort Sill, Okla., 1917; beame first lieutenant, Battery F, and captain, Battery ·, 129th Field Artillery, 35th Div., AEF. He served in he Vosges, Meuse-Argonne, and St. Mihiel actions in Vorld War I and was discharged as major, 1919. After the war he ran a haberdashery, became judge f Jackson Co. Court, 1922-24; attended Kansas City chool of Law, 1923-25. He was defeated, then lected presiding judge.

Truman was elected U.S. senator in 1934; reelected 940. In 1944 with President Roosevelt's backing he vas nominated for vice president and elected. On Roosevelt's death Apr. 12,1945, Truman was sworn in s president by Chief Justice Harlan F. Stone. In 1948 e was elected president although polls had predicted his defeat.

Truman authorized the first uses of the atomic omb (Hiroshima and Nagasaki, Aug. 6 and 9, 1945), ringing World War II to a rapid end. He was responsible for creating NATO, the Marshall Plan (to restore Western Europe economically), and for what ame to be called the Truman Doctrine (to aid nations uch as Greece and Turkey, threatened by Russian or ther communist takeover). He broke a Russian lockade of East Berlin with a massive airlift, 1948-9. When communist North Korea invaded South Korea, June, 1950, he won UN approval for a "police ction" and sent in forces under Gen. Douglas MacArthur. When MacArthur sought to pursue North Koeans into communist China, Truman removed him rom command.

On the domestic front, Truman was responsible or higher-minimum-wage, increased-social-security, nd aid-for-housing laws. His 1952 seizure of the nation's steel mills to avert a strike was ruled illegal by he Supreme Court; a strike followed but was settled n 3 weeks. Truman died Dec. 26, 1972, at his Independence, Mo., home at the age of 88.

He married Elizabeth Virginia Wallace in 1919. They had one daughter, Margaret.

Dwight David Eisenhower

Dwight D. Eisenhower, 34th president, Republican, vas born Oct. 14, 1890, at Denison, Tex., the son of David Jacob Eisenhower and Ida Elizabeth Stover Eisenhower. His paternal grandfather was decended from German Mennonites who left the Rhineland for Pennsylvania in the 1730s, moved to Kansas in 1878. His father met his mother at Lane University, a United Brethren college at Lecompton, Kan. When Dwight was one year old his parents noved to Abilene, Kan. He attended high school and n 1915 graduated from West Point. He was a lieutenant colonel in charge of a tank corps at Camp Colt, Gettysburg, Pa., in 1918. He was on the American Military Mission to the Philippines, 1935-39 and during 4 of those years on the staff of Gen. Douglas MacArthur. He was chief of staff, 3d Army, 1941, as rigadier general. After the Louisiana maneuvers he vas made assistant chief of staff, Operations Div., nd in June, 1942, lieutenant general. He was made ommander of allied forces landing in North Africa Nov. 8, 1942, and advanced to full general in Feb., 943, and commander in chief of allied forces in North Africa. He became supreme commander, allied expeditionary forces Dec. 31, 1943, and as such ed the Normandy invasion June 6, 1944. He was iven the rank of general of the army Dec. 20, 1944, nade permanent in 1946. On May 7, 1945, he received he surrender of the Germans at Rheims. He was in ommand of the U.S. Occupation Force in Germany n 1945, and returned to the U.S. to serve as chief of taff, 1945-1948. From 1948 to 1953, he was president f Columbia University, but took leave of absence Dec. 16, 1950, to serve as supreme allied commander n Europe to organize NATO forces.

Eisenhower resigned from the army in June, 1952, nd was nominated for president by the Republicans t Chicago, July 11, 1952. He defeated Adlai E. Stevenson by 442 to 89 electoral votes, was inaugurated Jan. 20, 1953. He was renominated unaninously in San Francisco, Aug. 22, 1956, and defeated Stevenson by 457 to 74. He called himself a moderate, favored "free market system" vs. government price and wage controls; kept government out of labor disputes; reorganized defense establishment; promoted missile programs, including Polaris. With support of John Foster Dulles, his secretary of state, he continued foreign aid; demanded unification of Germany by free elections; sped end of Korean fighting; supplied planes to anti-communist Guatemalan government; endorsed Taiwan and SE Asia defense treaties; backed UN in condemning Anglo-French raid on Egypt; advocated "open skies" policy of mutual inspection to USSR. He sent U.S. troops into Little Rock, Ark., Sept., 1957, during the segregation crisis and ordered Marines into Lebanon July-Aug., 1958.

In 1948, Eisenhower published *Crusade in Europe*, his war memoirs, which quickly became a best seller. He was an enthusiastic golfer and painter.

During his retirement at his farm near Gettysburg, Pa., Eisenhower took up the role of elder statesman, counseling his 3 successors in the White House. He was hospitalized in early 1968 after his 4th heart attack and died Mar. 28, 1969, in Washington. He was buried in Abilene, Kan.

Eisenhower married Mamie Geneva Doud, July 1, 1916. They had 2 sons; the first died at age 4.

John Fitzgerald Kennedy

John F. Kennedy, 35th president, Democrat, was born May 29, 1917, in Brookline, Mass., the 2d of 9 children of Joseph P. Kennedy, financier, who later became ambassador to Great Britain, and Rose Fitzgerald Kennedy. He entered Harvard, attended the London School of Economics briefly in 1935, received a B.S., *cum laude* from Harvard in 1940. He served in the U. S. Navy, 1941-1945, commanded a PT boat in the Solomons and won the Navy and Marine Corps medal and Purple Heart. He covered the Potsdam Conference and the start of the UN at San Francisco for International News Service. He served as representative in Congress from Massachusetts, 1947-1953, defeated Henry Cabot Lodge for the Senate in 1952, was reelected 1958. He nearly won the vice presidential nomination in 1956.

Kennedy won the Democratic nomination for president at Los Angeles, July 14, 1960; Sen. Lyndon B. Johnson (Tex.), was named for vice president. Kennedy defeated Richard M. Nixon, Republican, by the slim margin of 118,550 popular votes and an electoral vote of 303 to 219. He was the first Roman Catholic to be elected president.

President Kennedy's most important act was his successful demand Oct. 22, 1962, that the Soviet Union dismantle its secret missile bases in Cuba. He established a quarantine of arms shipments to Cuba and continued surveillance by air. He defied Soviet attempts to force the Allies out of Berlin. He made the steel industry rescind a price rise. He backed civil rights, a mental health program, arbitration of railroad disputes, and expanded medical care for the aged. Astronaut flights and satellite orbiting were greatly developed during his less than 3 years tenure. He wrote *Profiles in Courage*, which won a Pulitzer Prize, and *Why England Slept*. He turned the White House spotlight on the cultural arts.

On Nov. 22, 1963, Kennedy was assassinated in Dallas, Tex. On Nov. 25, a day of national mourning, he was buried in Arlington National Cemetery.

Kennedy married Jacqueline Lee Bouvier Sept. 12, 1953. They had one daughter and one son; a second son died a few hours after birth.

Lyndon Baines Johnson

Lyndon B. Johnson, 36th president, Democrat, was born on a farm near Stonewall, Tex., Aug. 27, 1908, son of Sam Ealy and Rebekah Baines Johnson. His father and grandfather had served in the Texas legislature. His family moved to Johnson City in 1913, where he was graduated from the high school in 1924. He received a B.S. degree at Southwest Texas State

Teachers College, 1930, attended Georgetown Univ. Law School, Washington, 1935. He taught public speaking in Houston High School, 1930-32; served as secretary to Rep. R. M. Kleberg, 1932-35. In 1935 President Roosevelt appointed Johnson Texas state administrator of the National Youth Administration. In 1937 Johnson won a contest to fill the vacancy caused by the death of a representative and in 1938 was elected to the full term, after which he returned for 4 terms. A member of the naval reserve, he was a lieutenant commander, U.S. Navy, 1941-42, winning the Silver Star for a flight over Japanese positions at New Guinea. He was elected U.S. senator in 1948 by Texas and in 1954 he was reelected by a large majority. He became Democratic whip, 1951, and leader, 1953. Johnson was Texas' favorite son for the Democratic presidential nomination in 1956 and had strong support in the 1960 convention, where the nominee, John F. Kennedy, asked him to run for vice president. His campaigning helped overcome religious bias against Kennedy in the South.

Johnson took the oath of office as president at 2:30 p.m., CST, on Nov. 22, 1963, 99 min. after the death of President Kennedy. In filling out the Kennedy term Johnson worked hard for welfare legislation and signed civil rights, anti-poverty, and tax reduction laws, and averted strikes on railroads. He was nominated for president and elected Nov. 3, 1964, by 486 electoral votes to 52. Overshadowing other developments during Johnson's first full term in the White House were the expansion of the war in Vietnam, the committing of more than 500,000 American servicemen to conflict, intensive bombing by U.S. planes, and mounting U.S. casualties.

In the face of increasing division in the nation and his own party over his handling of the war, Johnson announced, on Mar. 31, 1968, "I shall not seek, and I will not accept the nomination of my party for another term as your president." Near the end of his tenure, he indicated that he felt his greatest achievement was the passage of the Voting Rights Act of 1965. His biggest disappointment was: "peace has eluded me."

Retiring to his LBJ Ranch near Johnson City, Tex., the former president wrote his memoirs, *The Vantage Point* (1971), and oversaw the construction of the Lyndon Baines Johnson Library on the campus of the University of Texas in Austin. Johnson died of a heart attack on Jan. 22, 1973. He was buried on his ranch.

Johnson married Claudia Alta (Lady Bird) Taylor on Nov. 17, 1934. They had 2 daughters.

Richard Milhous Nixon

Richard M. Nixon, 37th president, Republican, was the only president to resign without completing his elected term. He was born in the small farming community of Yorba Linda, Cal., Jan. 9, 1913, the 2d of 5 sons of Francis Anthony and Hannah Milhous Nixon. In 1922, the family moved to Whittier, Cal., where the future president graduated from Whittier College in 1934. He attended Duke University Law School. After practicing law in Whittier and serving briefly in the Office of Price Administration in 1942, he entered the navy, serving in the South Pacific, and was discharged as a lieutenant commander.

Nixon was elected to the House of Representatives from California's 12th Congressional District in 1946 and 1948. He achieved prominence as the House Un-American Activities Committee member who forced the showdown that resulted in the Alger Hiss perjury conviction. In 1950 Nixon moved to the Senate by defeating Democrat Helen Gahagan Douglas in a bitter campaign in which he accused her of being "soft on communism."

He was elected vice president in the Eisenhower landslides of 1952 and 1956.

With Eisenhower's endorsement, Nixon won the Republican presidential nomination in 1960. He was defeated by Democrat John F. Kennedy, returned to California, and 2 years later was defeated in his race for governor against Democratic incumbent Pa Brown.

Taking the "long hard road" of the presidential pri maries in 1968, he won the presidential nominatio on the first ballot and went on to defeat Democra Hubert H. Humphrey.

The 1969-73 Nixon Administration saw remarkabl developments in international affairs as Nixon be came the first U.S. president to visit China and Rus sia. He and his foreign affairs advisor, Dr. Henry A Kissinger, achieved a detente with China and a par tial strategic arms limitation agreement with th Soviet Union. In addition, Nixon brought an end t the U.S. ground combat role in South Vietnam.

These achievements did not, however, overshado the economic difficulties which confronted the na tion. In Aug., 1971, faced with alarming trade an balance of payments deficits and continuing inflatior Nixon announced a "new economic policy," wit wage and price controls and devaluation of the do lar.

Nixon appointed 4 new Supreme Court justices, in cluding the chief justice, thus altering the court' balance in favor of a more conservative view.

By the summer of 1972, the peace movement ha cooled, the economy showed signs of healthy growt and a period of normal relations among the super powers seemed at hand.

Reelected in a massive landslide that year Nixo soon secured a cease-fire agreement in Vietnam an completed the withdrawal of all U.S. troops in spit of heavy fighting and U.S. bombing in Cambodia an continued sporadic conflict in South Vietnam.

Early in 1973, the Nixon administration ende most wage and price controls and announced a fur ther devaluation of the dollar. Inflation, howeve continued at peak levels and the dollar came unde heavy pressure in the world's markets.

Nixon's 2d term was cut short by "The Watergat Affair," a series of scandals beginning with the espic nage burglary of Democratic party national head quarters in the Watergate office complex on June 1 1972. The break-in was led by employees of Nixon' reelection campaign committee and former Whit House staff members. Investigations and press reve lations exposed the existence of secret wiretappin and political espionage by White House aides datin back to May 1969, as well as an organized attempt t frustrate any investigation of these activities or of th Watergate break-in.

From the beginning, Nixon denied any Whit House involvement in the Watergate break-in. Whe White House personnel were implicated in the sprin of 1973, Nixon denied personal knowledge of eithe that involvement or of the subsequent cover-up.

On July 16, 1973, a White House aide, under ques tioning by a Senate committee, revealed that most o Nixon's office conversations and phone calls ha been recorded on tapes. The ensuing year saw a se vere constitutional confrontation as the presider claimed executive privilege to keep the tapes secre and the courts and Congress sought the tapes for th prosecution of criminal indictments against forme White House aides and for a House inquiry into possi ble impeachment proceedings against Nixon.

The confrontation reached its first climax Oct. 1 1973, in the "Saturday Night Massacre" when Nixo fired the special prosecutor assigned to Watergat matters and accepted the resignations of the attorne general and his deputy when they refused to go alon with the firing. The public outcry which followe caused Nixon to appoint a new special prosecutor an to turn over to the courts a number of subpoenae tape recordings. Public reaction also brought th initiation of a formal inquiry into possible impeach ment by the House of Representatives.

The second climax came on July 24, 1974, when th Supreme Court ruled unanimously that Nixon' claim of executive privilege must fall before the spe cial prosecutor's subpoenas of tapes relevant t criminal trial proceedings. At the same time, th court refused to rule on Nixon's claim that a gran jury erred in naming him an "unindicted co-conspirator" in the Watergate cover-up.

Later the same day, the House Judiciary Committee opened a televised debate on whether to recommend that the full House impeach the president. By July 30, the 38-member committee had recommended House adoption of 3 articles charging obstruction of justice, abuse of power, and contempt of Congress for refusing to respond to committee subpoenas.

On Aug. 5, under urging from his legal counsel, Nixon released transcripts of 3 recordings of conversations held on June 23, 1972, 6 days after the Watergate break-in. These transcripts showed that Nixon had known of, approved, and directed Watergate cover-up activities.

As his defenders in Congress withdrew their support, Nixon's aides and top Republican leaders publicly and privately urged him to resign. He announced his resignation on nationwide television on Aug. 8 and left office at noon on Aug. 9. He retired to San Clemente, Cal. One month later, Sept. 8, his chosen successor, Gerald Ford, granted Nixon an unconditional pardon for all federal crimes he "committed or may have committed" while president.

Nixon married Thelma Catherine Patricia "Pat" Ryan on June 21, 1940. They had 2 daughters.

Gerald Rudolph Ford

Gerald R. Ford, 38th president, Republican, was born July 14, 1913, in Omaha, Neb., son of Leslie and Dorothy Gardner King, and was named Leslie Jr. When he was 2, his parents were divorced and his mother moved with the boy to Grand Rapids, Mich. There she met and married Gerald R. Ford, head of a paint company, who formally adopted the boy and gave him his own name.

In high school, young Gerald became a star football center, named to all-city and all-state teams. At the University of Michigan he played on the undefeated 1932 and 1933 teams and was named most valuable player on the 1934 team. He turned down a Green Bay Packers professional football bid and went to Yale Law School, working part-time as assistant football coach, boxing coach, and professional model. He graduated in the top third of the 1941 law class.

He began practicing law in Grand Rapids, but in 1942, shortly after U.S. entry into World War II, he joined the navy and served 47 months in the Pacific, leaving the service in 1946 as a lieutenant commander.

Back in Grand Rapids, he resumed his law practice and won several Chamber of Commerce awards for community work. Entering the 1948 GOP primary, he upset the incumbent congressman in Michigan's 5th District and won the November election. He continued to win elections, spending 25 years in the House of Representatives, 8 of them as Republican leader. He also served on the Warren Commission, investigating the assassination of President Kennedy, and was co-author of a book on the commission.

As congressman and GOP leader, he was consistently conservative, opposing much social welfare legislation but giving support to final passage of civil rights bills. His colleagues described him as dogged, sincere, a man of modest tastes.

On Oct. 12, 1973, after Vice President Spiro T. Agnew pleaded "no contest" to charges of income tax fraud and resigned his high office, House Minority Leader Ford was nominated by President Nixon to become the new vice president. It was the first use of the procedures set out in the 25th Amendment. The Senate approved the appointment Nov. 27 by a 92-3 vote; The House followed suit, 387-35, on Dec. 6 and Ford was sworn in as the nation's 40th vice president that same day. As vice president, he spent much of his time on speaking tours, seeking to soothe the divisiveness which gripped the nation in the wake of the Watergate scandals.

When President Nixon, facing probable impeachment, resigned Aug. 9, 1974, Ford was sworn in as president, the first to serve without being chosen by the American people in a national election. On Sept. 8 he pardoned Nixon for any federal crimes he might have committed as president. Ford vetoed 48 bills in his first 21 months in office, including aid bills for housing, schools, health, day care, and farms; strip mining curbs, jobs creation, and tax cuts extension, saying most would prove too costly. The Democratic controlled Congress overrode 8 of the vetoes. He sought to solve the energy crisis by urging an end to oil and natural gas price controls. He visited China.

On Oct. 15, 1948, Ford married Elizabeth Bloomer Warren, whose first marriage had ended in divorce. The Fords have 3 sons and one daughter.

Jimmy (James Earl) Carter

Jimmy (James Earl) Carter, 39th president, Democrat, was the first president from the Deep South since before the Civil War. He was born Oct. 1, 1924, at Plains, Ga., where his parents, James and Lillian Gordy Carter, had a farm and several businesses.

After studying at Georgia Institute of Technology, he fulfilled a boyhood dream by going to the Naval Academy at Annapolis. On graduating, he entered the Navy's nuclear submarine program as an aide to Adm. Hyman Rickover, and also studied nuclear physics at Union College, Schenectady.

His father died in 1953 and Carter left the Navy to take over the family businesses — peanut-raising, warehousing, and cotton-ginning. He became a Baptist Church deacon, a Sunday school teacher, and public school board member, was elected to the Georgia state Senate, was defeated for governor in 1966, but was elected in 1970.

As a leader of "the new South," Carter declared at his inauguration as governor: "No poor, rural, weak, or black person should ever have to bear the additional burden of being deprived of the opportunity of an education, a job, or simple justice." He appointed blacks to high state positions and, in 1972, hung a portrait of the Rev. Martin Luther King Jr. in the State Capitol.

As governor, he believed his main achievement was reorganization; he consolidated 300 agencies and departments into 22. He claimed credit for a $166 million surplus when he left office.

In his presidential campaign, Carter said the cure for government ills was abolition of government secrecy, a return to majority control, and a government "as good as the American people."

As an outspokenly religious man, Carter was an unusual politician. He was also the first nuclear physicist elected president.

Carter won a brilliant primary campaign against a dozen opponents and captured the Democratic convention in overwhelming style. But he won only a narrow victory over President Gerald R. Ford, topping his Republican opponent by 40,276,040 to 38,532,630. Carter's main strength came in the South, where he carried all the southern and border states except Virginia, but mostly because of strong support from blacks. The industrial north was equally important to his victory; he got strong support there from labor, black, hispanic, urban, and women voters.

As president, Carter launched a campaign on behalf of worldwide human rights, calling in his inaugural address, Jan. 20, 1977, for people in all nations to join the U.S. in an effort to achieve human freedom and dignity. In later speeches, he declared that the U.S. "and other world powers should help shape a new world of justice, equity, and human rights." His campaign appeared particularly aimed at conditions in Soviet Russia.

At home, there were complaints from some segments which had backed him strongly that he had failed to carry out the hopes and promises of his campaign to befriend the poor, blacks, women, and others.

Carter married Rosalynn Smith, a neighbor, in 1946. They have 3 sons and a daughter.

Presidents Pro Tempore of the Senate

Until 1890, presidents "pro tem" were named "for the occasion only." Beginning with that year, they have served "until the Senate otherwise ordered." Sen. John J. Ingalls, chosen under the old rule in 1887, was again elected, under the new rule, in 1890. Party designations are D, Democrat; R, Republican.

Name	Party	State	Elected
John J. Ingalls	R	Kan.	Apr. 3, 1890
Charles F. Manderson	R	Neb.	Mar. 2, 1891
Isham G. Harris	D	Tenn.	Mar. 22, 1893
Matt W. Ransom	D	N.C.	Jan. 7, 1895
Isham G. Harris	D	Tenn.	Jan. 10, 1895
William P. Frye	R	Me.	Feb. 7, 1896
Charles Curtis	R	Kan.	Dec. 4, 1911
Augustus O. Bacon	D	Ga.	Jan. 15, 1912
Jacob H. Gallinger	R	N.H.	Feb. 12, 1912
Henry Cabot Lodge	R	Mass.	Mar. 25, 1912
Frank R. Brandegee	R	Conn.	May 25, 1912
James P. Clarke	D	Ark.	Mar. 23, 1915
Willard Saulsbury	D	Del.	Dec. 14, 1916
Albert B. Cummins	R	Ia.	May 19, 1919
George H. Moses	R	N.H.	Mar. 6, 1925
Key Pittman	D	Nev.	Mar. 9, 1933
William H. King	D	Ut.	Nov. 19, 1940
Pat Harrison	D	Miss.	Jan. 6, 1941
Carter Glass	D	Va.	July 10, 1941
Kenneth McKellar	D	Tenn.	Jan. 6, 1945
Arthur H. Vandenberg	R	Mich.	Jan. 4, 1947
Kenneth McKellar	D	Tenn.	Jan. 3, 1949
Styles Bridges	R	N.H.	Jan. 3, 1953
Walter F. George	D	Ga.	Jan. 5, 1955
Carl Hayden	D	Ariz.	Jan. 3, 1957
Richard B. Russell	D	Ga.	Jan. 3, 1969
Allen J. Ellender	D	La.	Jan. 22, 1971
James O. Eastland	D	Miss.	July 28, 1972

Speakers of the House of Representatives

Party designations: A, American; D, Democratic; DR, Democratic Republican; F, Federalist; R, Republican; W, Whig. *Served only one day.

Name	Party	State	Tenure
Frederick Muhlenberg	F	Pa.	1789-1791
Jonathan Trumbull	F	Conn.	1791-1793
Frederick Muhlenberg	F	Pa.	1793-1795
Jonathan Dayton	F	N.J.	1795-1799
Theodore Sedgwick	F	Mass.	1799-1801
Nathaniel Macon	DR	N.C.	1801-1807
Joseph B. Varnum	DR	Mass.	1807-1811
Henry Clay	DR	Ky.	1811-1814
Langdon Cheves	DR	S.C.	1814-1815
Henry Clay	DR	Ky.	1815-1820
John W. Taylor	DR	N.Y.	1820-1821
Philip P. Barbour	DR	Va.	1821-1823
Henry Clay	DR	Ky.	1823-1825
John W. Taylor	D	N.Y.	1825-1827
Andrew Stevenson	D	Va.	1827-1834
John Bell	D	Tenn.	1834-1835
James K. Polk	D	Tenn.	1835-1839
Robert M. T. Hunter	D	Va.	1839-1841
John White	W	Ky.	1841-1843
John W. Jones	D	Va.	1843-1845
John W. Davis	D	Ind.	1845-1847
Robert C. Winthrop	W	Mass.	1847-1849
Howell Cobb	D	Ga.	1849-1851
Linn Boyd	D	Ky.	1851-1855
Nathaniel P. Banks	A	Mass.	1856-1857
James L. Orr	D	S.C.	1857-1859
William Pennington	R	N.J.	1860-1861
Galusha A. Grow	R	Pa.	1861-1863
Schuyler Colfax	R	Ind.	1863-1869
*Theodore M. Pomeroy	R	N.Y.	1869-1869
James G. Blaine	R	Me.	1869-1875
Michael C. Kerr	D	Ind.	1875-1876
Samuel J. Randall	D	Pa.	1876-1881
Joseph W. Keifer	R	Oh.	1881-1883
John G. Carlisle	D	Ky.	1883-1889
Thomas B. Reed	R	Me.	1889-1891
Charles F. Crisp	D	Ga.	1891-1895
Thomas B. Reed	R	Me.	1895-1899
David B. Henderson	R	Ia.	1899-1903
Joseph G. Cannon	R	Ill.	1903-1911
Champ Clark	D	Mo.	1911-1919
Frederick H. Gillett	R	Mass.	1919-1925
Nicholas Longworth	R	Oh.	1925-1931
John N. Garner	D	Tex.	1931-1933
Henry T. Rainey	D	Ill.	1933-1935
Joseph W. Byrns	D	Tenn.	1935-1936
William B. Bankhead	D	Ala.	1936-1940
Sam Rayburn	D	Tex.	1940-1947
Joseph W. Martin Jr.	R	Mass.	1947-1949
Sam Rayburn	D	Tex.	1949-1953
Joseph W. Martin Jr.	R	Mass.	1953-1955
Sam Rayburn	D	Tex.	1955-1961
John W. McCormack	D	Mass.	1962-1971
Carl Albert	D	Okla.	1971-1976
Thomas P. O'Neill Jr.	D	Mass.	1977-

National Political Parties

As of June, 1977

Republican Party

National Headquarters—310 First St., SE, Washington, DC 20003.
Chairman—Bill Brock.
Co-Chairman—Mary Crisp.
Vice Chairmen—Ray C. Bliss, Ranny Riecker, Mary H. Boatwright, Clarke Reed, Bernard M. Shanley, Paula F. Hawkins, George P. Stadelman, Jo Anne Gray.
Secretary—June Gibbs.
Treasurer—William T. McManus.
General Counsel—William C. Cramer.
Finance Chairman—Ted H. Welch.

Democratic Party

National Headquarters—1625 Massachusetts Ave., NW, Washington, DC 20036.
Chairman—Kenneth M. Curtis.
Vice Chairpersons—Coleman Young, Carmella G. Lacayo.
Secretary—Dorothy V. Bush.
Treasurer—Joel W. McCleary.
Finance Chairman—Jess Hay.

America's Third Parties

Since 1860, there have been only 4 presidential elections in which all third parties together polled more than 10% of the vote: the Populists (James Baird Weaver) in 1892, the National Progressives (Theodore Roosevelt) in 1912, the La Follette Progressives in 1924, and George Wallace's American Party in 1968. In 1948, the combined third parties (Henry Wallace's Progressives, Strom Thurmond's States' Rights party or Dixiecrats, Prohibition, Socialists, and others) received only 5.75% of the vote. In most elections since 1860, fewer than one vote in 20 has been cast for a third party. The only successful third party in American history was the Republican Party in the election of Abraham Lincoln in 1860.

Major Third Parties

Party	Presidential nominee	Election	Issues	Strength in
nti-Masonic	William Wirt	1832	Against secret societies and oaths	Pa., Vt.
ree Soil	Martin Van Buren	1848	Anti-slavery	New York, Ohio
merican (Know Nothing)	Millard Fillmore	1856	Anti-immigrant	Northeast, South
reenback	Peter Cooper	1876	For "cheap money," labor rights	National
reenback	James B. Weaver	1880		
rohibition	(numerous)	1872	Anti-liquor	National
opulist	James B. Weaver	1892	For "cheap money," end of national banks	South, West
ocialist	Eugene V. Debs	1900-20	For public ownership	National
ocialist	Norman Thomas	1928-48	Liberal reforms	National
rogressive (Bull Moose)	Theodore Roosevelt	1912	Against high tariffs	Midwest, West
nion	William Lemke	1936	Anti "New Deal"	National
rogressive	Robert M. LaFollette	1924	Farmer & labor rights	Midwest, West
tates' Rights	Strom Thurmond	1948	For segregation	South
rogressive	Henry Wallace	1948	Anti-cold war	New York, California
merican	George Wallace	1968	For states' rights	South
merican	John G. Schmitz	1972	For "law and order"	California, Ohio

Other Major Political Organizations

American Party
(PO Box 990, Pigeon Forge, TN 37863)
hairman—Thomas J. Anderson.

Americans For Democratic Action
(1411 K St. NW, Washington, DC 20005)
resident—George McGovern.
ational Director—Leon Shull.
hairperson Exec. Comm.—Cushing Dolbeare.

Comm. on Political Education, AFL-CIO
(AFL-CIO Building, 815 16th St., Wash., DC 20006)
hairman—George Meany.
ecretary-Treasurer—Lane Kirkland.
ational Director—Alexander E. Barken.

Conservative Party of the State of N.Y.
(468 Park Ave. So., New York, NY 10016)
hairman—J. Daniel Mahoney.
xecutive Director—Serphin R. Maltese.
ecretary—Barbara A. Keating.
reasurer—James E. O'Doherty.

Liberal Party of New York State
(1560 Broadway, New York, NY 10036)
hairman—Donald S. Harrington.
irst Vice Chairman—David Dubinsky.
ecretary—Ben Davidson.
reasurer—Bernice Benedick.
xecutive Director—James F. Notaro.

Libertarian Party
(1516 P St. NW, Washington, DC 20005)
Chairman—Edward Crane 3d.
Vice-Chairwoman—Andrea Millen.
Secretary—Gregory Clark.
Treasurer—Francine Youngstein.
Director—Robert Meier.

National States' Rights Party
(P.O. Box 1211, Marietta, GA 30061)
Chairman—J. B. Stoner.
Secretary—Edward R. Fields.
Treasurer—Peter Xavier.

Prohibition National Committee
(P.O. Box 2635, Denver, CO 80201)
National Chairman—Charles Wesley Ewing.
Executive Secretary—Earl F. Dodge.
National Secretary—Roger C. Storms.

Socialist Labor Party
In Minnesota: Industrial Gov't. Party
(914 Industrial Ave., Palo Alto, CA 94303)
National Secretary—Nathan Karp.

Socialist Workers Party
(14 Charles Lane, New York, NY 10014)
National Secretary—Jack Barnes.
Organization Secretary—Barry Sheppard.

The Electoral College

The president and the vice president of the United tates are the only elective federal officials not lected by direct vote of the people. They are elected y the members of the Electoral College, an institu-ion that has survived since the founding of the nation espite repeated attempts in Congress to alter or bolish it. In the elections of 1824, 1876 and 1888 the residential candidate receiving the largest popular ote failed to win a majority of the electoral votes.

On presidential election day, the first Tuesday fter the first Monday in November of every 4th year, ach state chooses as many electors as it has senators nd representatives in Congress. In 1964, for the first ime, as provided by the 23d Amendment to the Con-titution, the District of Columbia voted for 3 elec-ors. Thus, with 100 senators and 435 representatives, here are 538 members of the Electoral College, with majority of 270 electoral votes needed to elect the resident and vice president.

Political parties customarily nominate their lists of lectors at their respective state conventions. An lector cannot be a member of Congress or any per-on holding federal office.

Some states print the names of the candidates for resident and vice president at the top of the Novem-er ballot while others list only the names of the lectors. In either case, the electors of the party receiving the highest vote are elected. The electors meet on the first Monday after the 2d Wednesday in December in their respective state capitals or in some other place prescribed by state legislatures. By long-established custom they vote for their party nominees, although the Constitution does not require them to do so. All of the state's electoral votes are then awarded to the winners. The only Constitutional requirement is that at least one of the persons each elector votes for shall not be an inhabitant of that elector's home state.

Certified and sealed lists of the votes of the electors in each state are mailed to the president of the U.S. Senate. He opens them in the presence of the members of the Senate and House of Representatives in a joint session held on Jan. 6 (the next day if that falls on a Sunday), and the electoral votes of all the states are then counted. If no candidate for president has a majority, the House of Representatives chooses a president from among the 3 highest candidates, with all representatives from each state combining to cast one vote for that state. If no candidate for vice president has a majority, the Senate chooses from the top 2, with the senators voting as individuals.

In 1977, Pres. Carter urged elimination of the electoral system and substitution of a plurality of the national popular vote.

U.S. Government Independent Agencies

Source: General Services Administration

Address: Washington, DC. Location and ZIP codes of agencies in parentheses, as of June, 1977.

ACTION — Sam Brown, dir. (806 Connecticut Ave., NW, 20525).

Administrative Conference of the United States — Robert A. Anthony, chmn. (2120 L St., NW, 20037).

American Battle Monuments Commission — Mark W. Clark, chmn. (Forrestal Bldg., 20314).

Appalachian Regional Commission — Donald W. Whitehead, Federal cochmn.; Gov. Marvin Mandel, states co-chmn. (1666 Connecticut Ave. NW, 20235).

Arms Control & Disarmament Agency — Paul C. Warnke, dir. (Department of State Bldg. 20451).

Central Intelligence Agency — Adm. Stansfield Turner, dir. (Wash., DC 20505).

Civil Aeronautics Board — Chairman: vacancy (1825 Connecticut Ave. NW, 20428).

Civil Service Commission — Georgiana H. Sheldon, chmn. (1900 E. St. NW, 20415).

Commission on Civil Rights — Arthur S. Flemming, chmn. (1121 Vermont Ave. NW, 20425).

Commission of Fine Arts — J. Carter Brown, chmn. (708 Jackson Pl. NW, 20006).

Community Services Administration — Robert C. Chase, dir. (1200 19th St. NW, 20506).

Consumer Product Safety Commission — S. John Byington, chmn. (1111 18th St. NW, 20036).

Energy Research and Development Administration — Robert W. Fri, adm. (Washington, DC 20545).

Environmental Protection Agency — John Quarles, adm. (401 M St., SW, 20460).

Equal Employment Opportunity Commission — chmn.: vacancy (2401 E St., NW, 20506).

Export-Import Bank of the United States — Stephen M. DuBrul Jr., pres. and chmn. (811 Vermont Ave. NW, 20571).

Farm Credit Administration — E. Riddell Lages, chmn. (490 L'Enfant Plaza East SW, 20578).

Federal Communications Commission — Richard Wiley, chmn. (1919 M St. NW, 20554).

Federal Deposit Insurance Corporation — Robert E. Barnett, chmn. (550 17th St. NW, 20429).

Federal Election Commission — Vernon W. Thomson, chmn. (1325 K St. NW, 20463).

Federal Energy Administration — John F. O'Leary, adm. (12th St. and Pennsylvania Ave. NW, 20461).

Federal Home Loan Bank Board — Garth Marston, chmn. (320 First St. NW, 20552).

Federal Maritime Commission — Karl E. Bakke, chmn. (1100 L St. NW, 20573).

Federal Mediation and Conciliation Service — James F. Scearce, dir. (2100 K St. NW, 20427).

Federal Power Commission — Richard L. Dunham, chmn., James G. Watt, vice chmn. (825 N. Capital St. NW, 20426).

Federal Reserve System — Chairman, board of governors: Arthur F. Burns. (20th St. & Constitution Ave. NW, 20551).

Federal Trade Commission — Commissioners: Michael Pertschuk, chmn., Paul Rand Dixon, Elizabeth Hanford Dole, Calvin J. Collier, David A. Clanton, (Pennsylvania Ave. at 6th St. NW, 20580).

Foreign Claims Settlement Comm. of the U.S. — J. Raymond Bell, chmn. (1111 20th St., NW, 20579).

General Accounting Office — Comptroller general of the U.S.; Elmer B. Staats. (441 G St. NW, 20548).

General Services Administration — Joel W. (Jay) Solomon, adm. (18th & F Sts. NW, 20405).

Government Printing Office — Public printer: Thomas F. McCormick (North Capitol and H Sts. NW, 20401).

Indian Claims Commission — Jerome K. Kuykendall, chmn. (1730 K St. NW, 20006).

Inter-American Foundation — Augustin S. Hart Jr., chmn. (1515 Wilson Blvd., Rosslyn, VA 22209).

Interstate Commerce Commission — George M Stafford, chmn. (12th St. and Constitution Ave. NW, 20423).

Library of Congress — Daniel J. Boorstin, Librarian (10 First St. SE, 20540).

National Academy of Sciences — National Academy of Engineering — National Research Council — Institute of Medicine — Presidents: Philip Handler (NAS), Courtland D. Perkins (NA of Eng.), David A. Hamburg, M.D. (Inst. of Med.) (2101 Constitution Ave. NW, 20418).

National Aeronautics and Space Administration — Administrator, vacancy. (400 Maryland Ave., SW 20546).

National Credit Union Administration — C. Austin Montgomery, adm. (2025 M. St. NW, 20456).

National Foundation on the Arts and Humanities — Nacy Hanks, chmn. (arts). vacancy, chmn. (humanities) (806 15th St. NW, 20506).

National Labor Relations Board — John H. Fanning, chmn. (1717 Pennsylvania Ave. NW, 20570).

National Mediation Board — Kay McMurray, chmn. (1425 K St. NW, 20572).

National Science Foundation — Norman Hackerman, dir. (1800 G St. NW, 20550).

National Transportation Safety Board — Webster B. Todd Jr., chmn. (800 Independence Ave. SW, 20594).

Nuclear Regulatory Commission — Marcus A. Rowden, chmn. (1717 H St. NW, 20555).

Occupational Safety and Health Review Commission — Frank R. Barnako, chmn. (1825 K St. NW, 20006).

Overseas Private Investment Corporation — Rutherford U. Poates, pres. (1129 20th St. NW, 20527).

Pennsylvania Avenue Development Corporation — Elwood R. Quesada, chmn. (425 13th St. NW, 20004).

Pension Benefit Guaranty Corporation — Matthew M. Lind, exec. dir. (2020 K St. NW, 20006).

Postal Rate Commission — Clyde S. DuPont, chmn. (2000 L St. NW, 20268).

Railroad Retirement Board — James L. Cowen, chmn. (Rm. 444, 425 13th St. NW, 20004), Main Office (844 Rush St., Chicago, IL 60611).

Renegotiation Board — Rex M. Mattingly, chmn. (2000 M St. NW, 20446).

Securities and Exchange Commission — Commissioners: Roderick M. Hills, chmn.; Irving M. Pollack, Philip Loomis Jr., John R. Evans, one vacancy. (500 N. Capitol St., 20549).

Selective Service System — Byron V. Pepitone, dir. (600 E St. NW, 20435).

Small Business Administration — Administrator: vacancy (1441 L St. NW, 20416).

Smithsonian Institution — S. Dillon Ripley, secy. (1000 Jefferson Dr. SW, 20560).

Tennessee Valley Authority — Chairman, board c directors: Aubrey J. Wagner. 400 Commerce Ave., Knoxville, TN 37902 and Woodward Bldg. 15th and H Sts. NW Washington, D.C. 20444).

United States Information Agency — John E. Reinhardt, dir. (1750 Pennsylvania Ave. NW, 20547).

United States International Trade Commission — Daniel Minchew, chmn. (701 E St. NW, 20436).

United States Postal Service — Benjamin F. Bailar postmaster general (475 L'Enfant Plaza West SW 20260).

Veterans Administration — Max Cleland, adm. (810 Vermont Ave. NW, 20420).

NATIONAL DEFENSE

Data as of Aug., 1977

Chairman, Joint Chiefs of Staff

George S. Brown (USAF)

The Joint Chiefs of Staff consists of the Chairman of the Joint Chiefs of Staff; the Chief of Staff, U.S. Army; the Chief of Naval Operations; and the Chief of Staff, U.S. Air Force. The Marine Corps commandant attends meetings regularly, and sits as a coequal of the other members when matters directly concerning the Marine Corps are being considered.

Army

General of the Army	Date of Rank
Bradley, Omar N.	Sept. 20, 1950

Chief of Staff—Bernard W. Rogers

Generals

Blanchard, George S.	Jul. 1, 1975
Guthrie, John R.	May 1, 1977
Haig Jr., Alexander M.	Mar. 18, 1974
Hennessey, John J.	Nov. 8, 1974
Kerwin Jr., Walter T.	Feb. 1, 1973
Knowlton, William A.	Jun. 1, 1976
Kroesen, Frederick J.	Oct. 1, 1976
Rogers, Bernard W.	Nov. 7, 1974
Starry, Donn A.	Jul. 1, 1977
Vessey Jr., John W.	Nov. 1, 1976

Air Force

Chief of Staff—David C. Jones

Generals

Allen, James R.	Aug. 1, 1977
Allen Jr., Lew	Aug. 1, 1977
Brown, George S.	Aug. 1, 1968
Dixon, Robert J.	Oct. 1, 1973
Dougherty, Russell E.	May 5, 1972
Ellis, Richard H.	Sept. 30, 1973
Evans, William J.	Aug. 30, 1975
Huyser, Robert E.	Sept. 1, 1975
James, Daniel	Aug. 29, 1975
McBride, William V.	Sept. 1, 1974
Moore Jr., William G.	Apr. 1, 1977
Roberts, John W.	Mar. 15, 1977
Rogers, Felix M.	Aug. 31, 1975

Navy

Chief of Naval Operations

Admiral James L. Holloway III (aviation)

Admirals

Bagley, David H.	May 21, 1975
Hayward, Thomas B. (aviation)	Aug. 12, 1976
Kidd, Isaac C.	Dec. 1, 1971
Long, Robert L.J.	July 5, 1977
Michaelis, Frederick H. (aviation)	Apr. 19, 1975
Rickover, Hyman G. (retired)	Nov. 16, 1973
Shear, Harold E.	May 24, 1974
Turner, Stansfield	Sept. 1, 1975
Weinel, John P.	Aug. 2, 1974
Weisner, Maurice F. (aviation)	Sept. 1, 1972

Marine Corps

Corps Commandant, with rank of General

Louis H. Wilson . . . July 1, 1975

Asst. Commandant with rank of General

Samuel Jaskilka . . . July 1, 1975

Coast Guard

Commandant, with rank of Admiral

Owen W. Siler . . . June 1, 1974

Vice Commandant, with rank of Vice Admiral

Ellis L. Perry . . . July 1, 1974

United States Unified and Specified Commands

Atlantic Command—Admiral Isaac C. Kidd, USN
North American Air Defense Command—General Daniel James, USAF
U.S. European Command—General Alexander Haig Jr., USA
Pacific Command—Admiral Maurice Weisner, USN
U.S. Southern Command—General Dennis P. McAuliffe, USA
Strategic Air Command—General Richard H. Ellis, USAF
U.S. Readiness Command—General John J. Hennessey, USA
Military Air Lift Command—General William G. Moore Jr., USAF

North Atlantic Treaty Organization International Commands

Supr. Allied Commander, Europe (SACEUR)—Gen. Alexander Haig Jr., USA
Deputy SACEUR—Gen. Sir Harry Tuzo (UK)
C-in-C Allied Forces, Northern Europe—Gen. Peter Whitely (UK)
C-in-C Allied Forces, Central Europe—Gen. F.J. Schulze, (Germany)
C-In-C Allied Forces, Southern Europe—Adm. L. Tomasulo (Italy) (Acting)
Supr. Allied Commander Atlantic (SACLANT)—Adm. Isaac Kidd, USN
Deputy SACLANT—Adm. James Jungius (UK)
Commander Strike Force South—V. Adm. Harry D. Train II, USN
Allied Commander in Chief, Channel—Adm. Sir Edward Ashmore (UK)

Principal U.S. Military Training Centers

Army

Name, P.O. address	Zip	Nearest city
Aberdeen Proving Ground, MD	21005	Aberdeen
Carlisle Barracks, PA	17013	Carlisle
Fort Belvoir, VA	22060	Alexandria
Fort Benning, GA	31905	Columbus
Fort Bliss, TX	79916	El Paso
Fort Bragg, NC	28307	Fayetteville
Fort Devens, MA	01433	Ayer
Fort Dix, NJ	08640	Trenton
Fort Eustis, VA	23604	Newport News
Fort Gordon, GA	30905	Augusta
Fort Wadsworth, NY	10305	Staten Island
Fort Benjamin Harrison, IN	46216	Indianapolis
Fort Sam Houston, TX	78234	San Antonio
Fort Huachuca, AZ	85613	Sierra Vista
Fort Jackson, SC	29207	Columbia
Fort Knox, KY	40121	Louisville
Fort Leavenworth, KS	66027	Leavenworth
Fort Lee, VA	23801	Petersburg
Fort McClellan, AL	36205	Anniston
Fort Monmouth, NJ	07703	Red Bank
Fort Rucker, AL	36362	Dothan
Fort Sill, OK	73503	Lawton
Fort Leonard Wood, MO	65473	Rolla
Redstone Arsenal, AL	35809	Huntsville
Rock Island Arsenal, IL	61202	Rock Island
The Judge Advocate General School, VA	22901	Charlottesville

Navy

Name, P.O. address	Zip	Nearest city
Great Lakes, IL	60088	Waukegan
San Diego, CA	92133	San Diego
Orlando, FL	32813	Orlando

Marine Corps

Name, P.O. address	Zip	Nearest city
MCB Camp Lejeune, NC	28542	Jacksonville
MCB Camp Pendleton, CA	92055	Oceanside
MCB Camp Butler, Okinawa	FPO Seattle 98773	Futenma, Okinawa
MCB Twentynine Palms, CA	92278	Palm Springs
MCDEC Quantico, VA	22134	Quantico
MCRD Parris Island, SC	29905	Beaufort
MCRD San Diego, CA	92140	San Diego
MCAS Cherry Point, NC	28533	Cherry Point
MCAS El Toro (Santa Ana), CA	92709	Santa Ana
MCAS (Helo) Santa Ana, CA	92709	Santa Ana
MCAS (Helo) New River, NC	28540	Jacksonville
MCAS Iwakuni, Japan	FPO Seattle 98764	Iwakuni
MCAS Kaneohe Bay, Oahu, HI	FPO San Francisco 96615	Kailua
MCAS (Helo) Futenma, Okinawa	FPO Seattle 98764	Futenma
MCAS Beaufort, SC	29902	Beaufort
MCAS Yuma, AZ	85364	Yuma

MCB = Marine Corps Base. MCDEC = Marine Corps Development & Education Command. MCAS = Marine Corps Air Station. Helo = Helicopter.

Air Force

Name	Zip	Nearest city
Chanute AFB, IL	61863	Rantoul
Columbus AFB, MS	39701	Columbus
Craig AFB, AL	36701	Selma
Fairchild AFB, MS	99011	Spokane
Keesler AFB, MS	39534	Biloxi
Lackland AFB, TX	78236	San Antonio
Laughlin AFB, TX	78840	Del Rio
Lowry AFB, CO	80230	Denver
Mather AFB, CA	95655	Sacramento
Maxwell AFB, AL	36112	Montgomery
Moody AFB, GA	31601	Valdosta
Nellis AFB, NV	89191	Las Vegas
Randolph AFB, TX	78148	San Antonio
Reese AFB, TX	79401	Lubbock
Sheppard AFB, TX	76311	Wichita Falls
Vance AFB, OK	73701	Enid
Webb AFB, TX	79720	Big Spring
Williams AFB, AZ	85224	Chandler

Personal Salutes and Honors

The United States national salute, 21 guns, is also the salute to a national flag. The independence of the United States is commemorated by the salute to the union — one gun for each state — fired at noon on July 4 at all military posts provided with suitable artillery.

A 21-gun salute on arrival and departure, with 4 ruffles and flourishes, is rendered to the President of the United States, to an ex-President and to a President-elect. The national anthem or *Hail to the Chief*, as appropriate, is played for the President, and the national anthem for the others. A 21-gun salute on arrival and departure, with 4 ruffles and flourishes also is rendered to the sovereign or chief of state of a foreign country or a member of a reigning royal family; the national anthem of his or her country is played. The music is considered an inseparable part of the salute and will immediately follow the ruffles and flourishes without pause.

Rank	Salute—guns Arrive	Salute—guns Leave	Ruffles, flourishes	Music
Vice President of United States	19		4	Hail Columbia
Speaker of House	19		4	March
American or foreign ambassador	19		4	Nat. anthem of official
Premier or prime minister	19		4	Nat. anthem of official
Secretary of Defense, Army, Navy or Air Force	19	19	4	March
Other Cabinet members, Senate President pro tempore, Governor, or Chief Justice of U.S.	19		4	March
Chairman, Joint Chiefs of Staff	19	19	4	General's or Admiral's March
Army Chief of Staff, Chief of Naval Operations, Air Force Chief of Staff, Marine Commandant	19	19	4	General's or Admiral's March
General of the Army, General of the Air Force, Fleet Admiral	19	19	4	General's or Admiral's March
Generals, Admirals	17	17	4	General's or Admiral's March
Assistant Secretaries of Defense, Army, Navy or Air Force	17	17	4	March
Chairman of a Committee of Congress	17		4	March

Other salutes (on arrival only) include 15 guns for American envoys or ministers and foreign envoys or ministers accredited to the United States; 15 guns for a lieutenant general or vice admiral; 13 guns for a major general or rear admiral (upper half); 13 guns for American ministers resident and ministers resident accredited to the U.S.; 11 guns for a brigadier general or rear admiral (lower half); 11 guns for American charges d'affaires and like officials accredited to U.S.; and 11 guns for consuls general accredited to U.S.

Military Units, U.S. Army and Air Force

Army units. Squad. In infantry usually ten men under a staff sergeant. **Platoon.** In infantry 4 squads under a lieutenant. **Company.** Headquarters section and 4 platoons under a captain. (Company in the artillery is a battery; in the cavalry, a troop.) **Battalion.** Hdqts. and 4 or more companies under a lieutenant colonel. (Battalion size unit in the cavalry is a squadron.) **Brigade.** Hdqts. and 3 or more battalions under a colonel. **Division** Hdqts. and 3 brigades with artillery, combat support, and combat service support units under a major general. **Army Corps.** Two or more divisions with corps troops under a lieutenant general. **Field Army.** Hdqts. and two or more corps with field Army troops under a general.

Air Force Units. Flight. Small components of a squadron organized for special purpose such as medical evacuation flights. **Squadron.** The basic organized unit of the Air Force, used by operational as well as support forces but not limited by numbers of personnel assigned; two to three tactical squadrons are assigned to a tactical wing. **Group.** Terminology used for special tactical forces and for many support elements. They do not necessarily have subordinate units assigned. **Wing.** Used for tactical and support forces. A tactical wing usually has two to three operational squadrons assigned. **Division.** An organizational component of operational numbered Air Forces consisting of two to three wings, also used to designate numerous support and research components. **Air Force.** An intermediate echelon of command directly under the headquarters of a large operational command, usually with four to seven subordinate divisions. **Major command.** A major subdivision of the Air Force that is assigned a major segment of the USAF mission, usually two or four subordinate Air Force elements.

U. S. Army Insignia and Chevrons

Source: Department of the Army

Grade — **Insignia**

General of the Armies

(General John J. Pershing, the only person to have held this rank, was authorized to prescribe his own insignia, but never wore in excess of four stars. The rank originally was established by Congress for George Washington in 1799, and he was promoted to the rank by joint resolution of Congress, approved by Pres. Ford Oct. 19, 1976.

General of the Army . . . Five silver stars fastened together in a circle and the coat of arms of the United States in gold color metal with shield and crest enameled.

Grade	Insignia
General	Four silver stars
Lieutenant General	Three silver stars
Major General	Two silver stars
Brigadier General	One silver star
Colonel	Silver eagle
Lieutenant Colonel	Silver oak leaf
Major	Gold oak leaf
Captain	Two silver bars
First Lieutenant	One silver bar
Second Lieutenant	One gold bar

Warrant officers

Grade Four—Silver bar with 4 enamel black bands.
Grade Three—Silver bar with 3 enamel black bands.
Grade Two—Silver bar with 2 enamel black bands.
Grade One—Silver bar with 1 enamel black band.

Non-commissioned officers

Sergeant Major of the Army (E-9). Same as Command Sergeant Major (below). Also wears distinctive red and white shield on lapel.

Command Sergeant Major (E-9). Three chevrons above three arcs with a 5-pointed star with a wreath around the star between the chevrons and arcs.

Sergeant Major (E-9). Three chevrons above three arcs with a five-pointed star between the chevrons and arcs.

First Sergeant (E-8). Three chevrons above three arcs with a lozenge between the chevrons and arcs.

Master Sergeant (E-8). Three chevrons above three arcs.

Platoon Sergeant or Sergeant First Class (E-7). Three chevrons above two arcs.

Staff Sergeant (E-6). Three chevrons above one arc.

Sergeant (E-5). Three chevrons.

Corporal (E-4). Two chevrons.

Specialists

Specialist Seven (E-7). Three arcs above the eagle device.

Specialist Six (E-6). Two arcs above the eagle device.

Specialist Five (E-5). One arc above the eagle device.

Specialist Four (E-4). Eagle device only.

Other enlisted

Private First Class (E-3). One chevron above one arc.

Private (E-2). One chevron.

Private (E-1). None.

U.S. Army

Source: Department of the Army

Army Military Personnel on Active Duty[1]

June 30[2]	Total strength	Commissioned officers: Total	Commissioned officers: Male	Commissioned officers: Female (3)	Warrant officers: Male (4)	Warrant officers: Female	Enlisted personnel: Total	Enlisted personnel: Male	Enlisted personnel: Female
1940	267,767	17,563	16,624	939	763	—	249,441	249,441	—
1942	3,074,184	203,137	190,662	12,475	3,285	—	2,867,762	2,867,762	—
1943	6,993,102	557,657	521,435	36,222	21,919	0	6,413,526	6,358,200	55,325
1944	7,992,868	740,077	692,351	47,726	36,893	10	7,215,888	7,144,601	71,287
1945	8,266,373	835,403	772,511	62,892	56,216	44	7,374,710	7,283,930	90,780
1946	1,889,690	257,300	240,643	16,657	9,826	18	1,622,546	1,605,847	16,699
1950	591,487	67,784	63,375	4,409	4,760	22	518,921	512,370	6,551
1955	1,107,606	111,347	106,173	5,174	10,552	48	985,659	977,943	7,716
1960	871,348	91,056	86,832	4,224	10,141	39	770,112	761,833	8,279
1965	967,049	101,812	98,029	3,783	10,285	23	854,929	846,409	8,520
1966	1,197,468	106,468	102,347	4,121	11,296	22	1,079,682	1,070,503	9,179
1967	1,440,120	127,393	122,685	4,708	16,090	34	1,296,603	1,286,862	9,741
1968	1,567,900	145,988	140,919	5,069	20,158	27	1,401,727	1,391,016	10,711
1969	1,509,637	148,836	143,699	5,137	23,734	20	1,337,047	1,316,326	10,721
1970	1,319,735	143,704	138,469	5,235	23,005	13	1,153,013	1,141,537	11,476
1971	1,120,822	130,261	125,240	5,021	18,670	19	971,872	960,047	11,825
1972	807,985	105,364	100,961	4,403	15,907	19	686,695	674,346	12,349
1973	798,177	101,194	96,936	4,258	14,990	21	681,972	665,515	16,457
1974	780,464	91,873	87,504	4,369	14,106	19	674,466	648,138	26,328
1975	781,316	89,756	85,184	4,572	13,214	22	678,324	640,621	37,703
1976 (Apr. 30)	766,979	85,515	80,588	4,927	12,748	30	668,686	625,792	42,894
1977 (Mar. 31)	774,664	84,984	79,599	5,385	13,005	36	676,639	631,410	45,229

(1) Represents strength of the active Army, including Philippine Scouts, retired Regular Army personnel on extended active duty, and National Guard and Reserve personnel on extended active duty; excludes U. S. Military Academy cadets, contract surgeons, and National Guard and Reserve personnel not on extended active duty.
(2) Data for 1940 to 1947 include personnel in the Army Air Forces and its predecessors (Air Service and Air Corps).
(3) Includes: women doctors, dentists, and Medical Service Corps officers for 1946 and subsequent years, women in the Army Nurse Corps for all years, and the Women's Army Corps and Women's Medical Specialists Corps (dieticians, physical therapists, and occupational specialists) for 1943 and subsequent years.
(4) Act of Congress approved April 27, 1926, directed the appointment as warrant officers of field clerks still in active service. Includes flight officers as follows: 1943, 5,700; 1944, 13,615; 1945, 31,117; 1946, 2,580.

Army Expenditures for Military Functions

Excludes expenditures for all civil functions as defined in "The Budget of the United States Government." Data for fiscal years to 1947 include all Army Air Force expenditures. (In millions of dollars)

Fiscal year	Amount	Fiscal year	Amount	Fiscal year	Amount	Fiscal year	Amount
1942	14,805	1953	16,337	1963	11,499	1970	24,749
1943	42,573	1954	12,910	1964	12,050	1971	23,077
1944	49,289	1955	8,899	1965	11,600	1972	22,596
1945	49,750	1959	9,468	1966	14,832	1973	20,185
1946	27,176	1960	9,392	1967	21,010	1974	21,395
1947	8,027	1961	10,131	1968	25,223	1975	21,920
1950	3,985	1962	11,427	1969	25,035	1976	21,398

U.S. Navy Insignia

Navy

Stripes and corps device are of gold embroidery.

Stripes

Fleet Admiral . . . . 1 two inch with 4 one-half inch.
Admiral . . . . 1 two inch with 3 one-half inch.
Vice Admiral . . . . 1 two inch with 2 one-half inch.
Rear Admiral . . . . 1 two inch with 1 one-half inch.
Commodore
(War time only) . . . . . 1 two inch.
Captain . . . . 4 one-half inch.
Commander . . . . 3 one-half inch.
Lieut. Commander. . . . 2 one-half inch, with 1 one-quarter inch between.
Lieutenant . . . . 2 one-half inch.
Lieutenant (j.g.). . . . . . . 1 one-half inch with one-quarter inch above.
Ensign . . . . 1 one-half inch.

Warrant Officers — One 1/2'' (1/2''for Warrant officer W-1) broken with 1/2'' intervals of blue as follows:
Chief Warrant Officer W-4—1 break
Chief Warrant Officer W-3—2 breaks, 2'' apart
Chief Warrant Officer W-2—3 breaks, 2'' apart

The breaks are symmetrically centered on outer face of the sleeve.

Enlisted personnel (non-Commissioned petty officers) . . . A rating badge worn on the upper left arm, consisting of a spread eagle, appropriate number of chevrons, and centered specialty mark.

Marine Corps

Marine Corps and Army officer insignia are similar. Marine Corps and Army enlisted insignia, although basically similar, differ in color, design, and fewer Marine Corps subdivisions. The Marine Corps' distinctive cap and collar ornament is a combination of the American eagle, globe, and anchor.

Coast Guard

Coast Guard insignia follow Navy custom, with certain minor changes such as the officer cap insignia. The Coast Guard shield is worn on both sleeves of officers and on the right sleeve of all enlisted men.

U. S. Naval Budget Outlays

Source: Department of the Navy

Fiscal year	Total amount expended	Shipbuilding conversion and modernizations	Aircraft and missile procurement	Military construction	All other expenditures
1940	$885,769	$328,819,394	$24,011,998	$72,503,151	$460,435,251
1945	29,380,421,832	7,228,192,871	3,541,009,589	1,576,096,922	17,035,122,450
1950	4,065,484,778	281,328,056	452,723,233	86,054,932	3,245,378,557
1955	9,637,835	903,303,717	1,834,511,038	238,631,005	6,661,192,075
1960	11,848,690,002	1,380,031,231	2,027,098,025	284,928,383	8,228,632,362
1970	2,501,628,282	2,065,660,211	3,183,464,921	333,271,852	16,919,231,298
1971	22,046,000,000	2,592,000,000	3,273,000,000	327,000,000	15,854,000,000
1972	24,100,000,000	3,010,000,000	3,983,000,000	353,000,000	16,754,000,000
1973	25,425,000,000	2,962,000,000	3,673,000,000	486,000,000	18,122,000,000
1974	26,800,000,000	3,509,000,000	3,744,000,000	612,000,000	18,935,000,000
1975	27,934,000,000	3,111,000,000	3,516,000,000	578,000,000	20,730,000,000
1976	31,480,000,000	3,954,000,000	4,098,000,000	707,000,000	22,721,000,000
1977(Plan)	36,499,000,000	5,474,000,000	4,934,000,000	685,000,000	25,356,000,000

U.S. Navy Personnel on Active Duty

Source: Department of the Navy

June 30	Officers[1]	Nurses	Enlisted[2]	Off. Cand.	Total
1940	13,162	442	144,824	2,569	160,997
1945	320,293	11,086	2,988,207	61,231	3,380,817
1950	42,687	1,964	331,860	5,037	381,538
1955	72,423	2,104	579,864	6,304	660,695
1960	67,456	2,103	544,040	4,385	617,984
1965	75,996	1,870	587,183	6,399	671,448
1970	78,488	2,273	605,899	6,000	692,660
1974	67,200	—	478,700	—	545,900
1975	65,900	—	483,500	—	549,400
1976	63,871	—	457,637	—	521,508
1977	64,384	—	456,608	—	520,992

(1) Nurses are included after 1973. (2) Officer candidates are included after 1973.

Marine Corps Personnel On Active Duty

Yr.	Officers	Enl.	Total	Yr.	Officers	Enl.	Total	Yr.	Officers	Enl.	Total
1955	18,417	186,753	205,170	1965	17,258	172,955	190,213	1975	18,100	174,100	192,20[illegible]
1960	16,203	154,408	170,621	1970	24,941	234,796	259,737	1977	18,552	173,448	192,00[illegible]

The Federal Service Academies

U.S. Military Academy, West Point, N.Y. Founded 1802. Awards B.S. degree and Army commission for a 5-year service obligation. For admissions information, write Admissions Office, USMA, West Point, NY 10996.

U.S. Naval Academy, Annapolis, Md. Founded 1845. Awards B.S. degree and Navy or Marine Corps commission for a 5-year service obligation. For admissions information, write Dean of Admissions, Naval Academy, Annapolis, MD 21402.

U.S. Air Force Academy, Colorado Springs, Colo. Founded 1954. Awards B.S. degree and Air Force commission for a 5-year service obligation. For admissions information, write Registrar, U.S. Air Force Academy, CO 80840.

U.S. Coast Guard Academy, New London, Conn Founded 1876. Awards B.S. degree and Coast Guard commission for a 5-year service obligation For admissions information, write Admissions Office, Coast Guard Academy, New London, CT 06320.

U.S. Merchant Marine Academy, Kings Point, N.Y Founded 1943. Awards B.S. degree, a license as deck or engineer officer, and a U.S. Naval Reserve commission. Service obligations vary according to options taken by the graduating ensign. For admissions information, write Admission Office, U.S Merchant Marine Academy, Kings Point, NY 11024

U. S. Air Force

Source: Department of the Air Force

The Army Air forces were started Aug. 1, 1907, as the Aeronautical Division of the Signal Corps, U.S. Army. The division consisted of one officer and two enlisted men, and it was more than a year before it carried out its first mission in an airplane of its own. When the U.S. entered World War I (April 6, 1917), the Aviation Service, as it was called then, had 55 planes and 65 officers, only 35 of whom were fliers. On the day the Japanese struck at Pearl Harbor (Dec. 7, 1941), the Army Air Forces, as they had been renamed 6 months previously, had 10,329 planes, of which only 2,846 were suited for combat service. But when the Army's air arm reached its peak during World War II (in July, 1944), it had 79,908 of all types of aircraft and (in May, 1945) 43,248 combat aircraft and (in March, 1944) 2,411,294 officers and enlisted men. The Air Force was established under the Armed Services Unification Act of July 26, 1947.

USAF Personnel at Home and Overseas — Officers and Enlisted Men

June 30	Continental U. S.	Overseas	Total	June 30	Continental U. S.	Overseas	Total
1940	40,229	10,936	51,165	1970	531,386	255,819	787,205
1945	1,153,373	1,128,886	2,282,259	1971	528,493	222,586	751,079
1950	317,816	93,461	411,277	1972	529,672	191,776	721,449
1955	689,635	270,311	959,946	1973	515,439	171,399	686,838
1957[1]	651,674	268,161	919,835	1974	472,415	171,380	643,795
1960[2]	607,383	207,369	814,752	1975	457,484	150,853	608,337
1965	635,430	189,232	824,662	1976	443,901	128,646	572,547
1969	566,475	291,936	858,411	1977	451,724	129,232	580,956

(1) Since 1957 continental U.S. includes Air Force Academy Cadets as follows: (1957) 504; (1960) 1,949; (1963) 2,660; (1964) 2,838; (1965) 2,907; (1966) 3,152; (1967) 3,361; (1968) 3,652; (1969) 3,941; (1970) 4,144; (1971) 2,997; (1972) 2,885; (1973) 4,356; (1974) 4,412; (1975) 4,414; (1976) 4,415; (1977) 4,680.

(2) Since 1960 Overseas includes Alaska and Hawaii. All figures include Mobilized Personnel.

USAF Military Personnel

June 30	Officers & airmen	Male commissioned officers: USAF (Reg.) & RA	USAFR & ORC	ANG & NG	AFUS & AUS	Total warrant officers
1955	959,946	23,463	105,587	984	2	3,961
1960	814,752	49,584	72,115	248	3	4,069
1965	824,662	62,076	62,537	280	54	2,532
1970	787,205	63,678	65,852	168	105	639
1973	686,838	60,456	49,568	146	37	114
1974	643,795	60,835	9,425[1]	....	27	67
1975	603,317	57,854	42,131	128	28	39
1976	546,779	56,589	48,062	141	27	19
1977	580,956	56,657	41,557	139	21	9

(1) Selected reserves only.

Female Commissioned Officers, and Enlisted Personnel

June 30	Female commissioned officers: Total	WAF	Nurses	WMSC	Female WO	Enlisted personnel: Total	Male	Female
1960	3,858	679	3,020	159	5	685,063	679,412	5,651
1965	4,099	708	3,185	206	1	690,177	685,436	4,741
1970	4,667	1,072	3,407	188	0	657,402	648,415	8,987
1975	4,981	1,542	3,236	203	0	503,176	477,944	25,232
1976	4,967	1,584	3,126	257	0	481,214	451,979	29,235
1977	5,264	1,849	3,085	330	0	482,573	447,961	34,612

Those Who Served in U.S. Wars

Source: Veterans Administration

Revolution (1775-1784)	
Participants	290,000
Deaths in Service	4,000
Last Veteran Died April 5, 1869	Age 109
War of 1812 (1812-1815)	
Participants	287,000
Deaths in Service	2,000
Last Veteran Died May 13, 1905	Age 105
Mexican War (1846-1848)	
Participants	79,000
Deaths in Service	13,000
Last Veteran Died September 3, 1929	Age 98
Civil War (1861-1865) (Union Forces Only)	
Participants	2,213,000
Deaths in Service	364,511
Last Veteran Died August 2, 1956	Age 109
Indian Wars (Approx. 1817-1898)	
Participants	106,000
Deaths in Service	1,000
Last Veteran Died June 18, 1973	Age 101
Spanish-American War (1898-1902)	
Participants	392,000
Deaths in Service	11,000
Living Veterans	573
World War I (1917-1918)	
Participants	4,744,000
Deaths in Service	116,000
Living Veterans	817,000
World War II (1940-1947)	
Participants	[1]16,535,000
Deaths in Service	406,000
Living Veterans	13,271,000
Korean Conflict (June 27,1950-Jan. 31, 1955)	
Participants	[2]6,807,000
Deaths in Service	55,000
Living Veterans	5,939,000
Service Between Korean Conflict and Vietnam Era (Jan. 31, 1955 — Aug. 5,1964)	
Participants	3,195,000
Deaths in Service	20,000
Living Veterans	3,081,000
Vietnam Era (Active duty service after Aug. 4, 1964)	
Participants	[2]9,834,000
On Active Duty	1,396,000
Deaths in Service	108,000
Living Veterans	8,373,000
America's Wars Total through January 1, 1977	
Participants*	44,482,000
Deaths in Service	1,100,000
Living Veterans	29,731,000

*Persons who served in more than one war period are counted as participants in each.

1. Includes 1,476,000 who served in both World War II and the Korean Conflict.

2. Includes 1,252,000 who served in both the Vietnam Era and the Korean Conflict.

Monthly Pay Scale of the

Commissioned Officers

Pay grade	Army rank	Navy rank	Under 2	Over 2	Over 3	Over 4	Over 6	Over 8
	Rank or pay grade		Cumulative years of service					
0-10[1]	General*	Admiral	$2,943.90	$3,047.40	$3,047.40	$3,047.40	$3,047.40	$3,164.10
0-9	Lieutenant General	Vice Admiral	2,609.10	2,677.80	2,734.50	2,734.50	2,734.50	2,804.10
0-8	Major General	Rear Admiral (up. half)	2,363.10	2,433.90	2,491.80	2,491.80	2,491.80	2,677.80
0-7	Brigadier General	Rear Admiral (low. half)	1,963.50	2,097.30	2,097.30	2,097.30	2,190.90	2,190.90
0-6	Colonel	Captain	1,455.30	1,599.30	1,703.40	1,703.40	1,703.40	1,703.40
0-5	Lieutenant Colonel	Commander	1,164.00	1,367.10	1,461.30	1,461.30	1,461.30	1,461.30
0-4	Major	Lieutenant Comdr	981.30	1,194.30	1,274.70	1,274.70	1,297.80	1,355.70
0-3	Captain	Lieutenant	912.00	1,019.40	1,089.60	1,205.70	1,263.30	1,308.90
0-2	First Lieutenant	Lieutenant (J.G.)	795.00	868.50	1,043.10	1,078.20	1,100.70	1,100.70
0-1	Second Lieutenant	Ensign	690.00	718.50	868.50	868.50	868.50	868.50
Commissioned officers with over 4 years service as enlisted members								
0-3	Captain	Lieutenant	0.00	0.00	0.00	1,205.70	1,263.30	1,308.90
0-2	First Lieutenant	Lieutenant (J.G.)	0.00	0.00	0.00	1,078.20	1,100.70	1,135.50
0-1	Second Lieutenant	Ensign	0.00	0.00	0.00	868.50	927.30	961.80
Warrant Officer								
W-4	Chief Warrant	Comm. Warrant	928.80	996.60	996.60	1,019.40	1,065.90	1,112.70
W-3	Chief Warrant	Comm. Warrant	844.50	916.20	916.20	927.30	938.40	1,007.10
W-2	Chief Warrant	Comm. Warrant	739.50	799.80	799.80	823.20	868.50	916.20
W-1	Warrant Officer	Warrant Officer	616.20	706.50	706.50	765.30	799.80	834.60
Enlisted Personnel[2]								
E-9[3]	Sergeant Major**	Master C.P.O.	0.00	0.00	0.00	0.00	0.00	0.00
E-8[3]	Master Sergeant	Senior C.P.O.	0.00	0.00	0.00	0.00	0.00	885.60
E-7	Sgt. 1st Class	Chief Petty Officer	618.30	667.20	692.10	716.10	741.00	764.10
E-6	Staff Sergeant	Petty Officer 1st Class	534.00	582.30	606.60	631.80	655.50	679.80
E-5	Sergeant	Petty Officer 2nd Cl.	468.90	510.30	534.90	558.30	594.60	618.90
E-4	Corporal	Petty Officer 3rd Cl.	450.60	475.80	503.70	543.00	564.30	564.30
E-3	Private 1st Class	Seaman	433.20	457.20	475.50	494.40	494.40	494.40
E-2	Private	Seaman Apprentice	417.30	417.30	417.30	417.30	417.30	417.30
E-1	Private	Seaman Recruit	374.40	374.40	374.40	374.40	374.40	374.40

The pay scale also applies to: Coast Guard and Marine Corps, National Oceanic and Atmospheric Administration, Public Health Service, National Guard, and the Organized Reserves.

*Basic pay is limited to $3,958.20 by Level V of the Executive Schedule. Four star General or Admiral—personal money allowances of $2,200 per annum, or $4,000 if Chief of Staff of the Army, Chief of Staff of the Air Force, Chief of Naval Operations, Commandant of the Marine Corps, or Commandant of the Coast Guard. Three star General or Admiral — personal money allowance of $500 per annum.

**A new title of Chief Master Sergeant created in 1965 rates E-9 classification.

(1) While serving as Chairman of Joint Chiefs of Staff, Chief of Staff of the Army, Chief of Naval Operations, Chief of Staff of the Air Forces, or Commandant of the Marine Corps, basic pay for this grade is $4,565.10 regardless of years of service.

(2) Air Force enlisted personnel pay grades, E-9, Chief Master Sergeant; E-8, Sr. Master Sergeant; E-7, Master Sergeant; E-6, Technical Sergeant; E-5, Staff Sergeant; E-4, Sergeant; E-3, Airman 1st Class; E-2, Airman; E-1, Basic Airman.

Marine Corps enlisted ranks are as follows: E-9, Sergeant Major and Master Gunnery Sergeant; E-8, First Sergeant and Master Sergeant; E-7, Gunnery Sergeant; E-6, Staff Sergeant; E-5, Sergeant; E-4, Corporal; E-3, Lance Corporal; E-2, Private, First Class Marine; E-1, Private.

Marine Corps and Air Force officer ranks are same as Army.

(3) While serving as Sergeant Major of the Army, Master Chief Petty Officer of the Navy, Chief Master Sergeant of the Air Force, or Sergeant Major of the Marine Corps, basic pay for this grade is $1,652.10 regardless of years of service.

American Military Actions, 1900-1973

1900—Occupation of Puerto Rico (ceded to U.S., 1899).
1900—500 Marines, 1,500 Army troops help relieve Peking in Boxer Rebellion.
1900-1902—Occupation of Cuba.
1900-1902—Guerrilla war in Philippines.
1903—Sailors and Marines from U.S.S. Nashville stop Colombian Army at Panama.
1904—Brief intervention in Dominican Republic.
1906-1909—Intervention in Cuba.
1909—Brief intervention in Honduras.
1910, 1912-1913—Intervention in Nicaragua.
1911—Intervention (to collect customs) in Honduras, Nicaragua, Dominican Republic.
1912-1917—Intervention in Cuba.
1914—Intervention in Dominican Republic.
1914—April 21 to Nov. 23, Marines in Vera Cruz.
1914—Navy and Marines enter Haiti, stay until 1934.
1916—Gen. John J. Pershing and 10,000 into Northern Mexico to stop raids by Pancho Villa, Mar. 15-Nov. 24.
1916-1924—Marines in Dominican Republic.
1917—Apr. 6 to Nov. 11, 1918, War with Germany, Austria-Hungary.
1918-1920—Expeditions into North Russia, Siberia.
1918-1923—Occupation of Germany.
1922-1924—Marines in Nicaragua.
1926-1933—Marines in Nicaragua.
1927—1,000 Marines in China.
1941-1945—War with Japan, Germany, Italy and allies.
1950-1953—U.S. and other UN countries aid the Republic of Korea to repel North Korean invaders; U.S. Navy protects Taiwan.
1956—U.S. Fleet evacuates U.S. nationals during Suez crisis.
1957—U.S. Fleet to Near East during Jordan crisis.
1958—Navy, Marines and Army units support Lebanon.
1960—Navy patrol in Caribbean to protect Guatemala and Nicaragua.
1961—Army units to Vietnam.
1962—Units of Navy on Cuban quarantine duty, Marines in Thailand.
1962-1965—U.S. Military Assistance Command, Vietnam; units of Army, Navy, Air Force, Marine Corps, Coast Guard.
1965—Navy, Marines, Army units to Dominican Republic.
1965—American commanders in Vietnam authorized to send U.S. Armed Force into combat.
1969—President Nixon announces, June 8, first phase of withdrawal of U.S. troops from Vietnam.

Uniformed Services (1977)

Commissioned Officers

Cumulative years of service								Basic allowances for quarters	
Over 10	Over 12	Over 14	Over 16	Over 18	Over 20	Over 22	Over 26	Without dependents	With dependents
$3,164.10	$3,406.80	$3,406.80	$3,650.40	$3,650.40	$3,894.60	$3,894.60	$4,137.30*	$297.00	$371.40
2,804.10	2,920.20	2,920.20	3,164.10	3,164.10	3,406.80	3,406.80	3,650.40	297.00	371.40
2,677.80	2,804.10	2,804.10	2,920.20	3,047.40	3,164.10	3,291.00	3,291.00	297.00	371.40
2,318.40	2,318.40	2,433.90	2,677.80	2,861.70	2,861.70	2,861.70	2,861.70	297.00	371.40
1,703.40	1,703.40	1,761.30	2,040.30	2,144.70	2,190.90	2,318.40	2,514.00	268.80	327.90
1,506.00	1,586.40	1,692.30	1,819.50	1,923.90	1,981.80	2,051.40	2,051.40	249.30	300.30
1,447.80	1,529.40	1,599.30	1,668.90	1,715.40	1,715.40	1,715.40	1,715.40	222.90	269.10
1,379.10	1,447.80	1,483.20	1,483.20	1,483.20	1,483.20	1,483.20	1,483.20	196.80	242.70
1,100.70	1,100.70	1,100.70	1,100.70	1,100.70	1,100.70	1,100.70	1,100.70	171.30	216.90
868.50	868.50	868.50	868.50	868.50	868.50	868.50	868.50	133.80	174.30
1,379.10	1,447.80	1,506.00	1,506.00	1,506.00	1,506.00	1,506.00	1,506.00	196.80	242.70
1,194.30	1,240.50	1,274.70	1,274.70	1,274.70	1,274.70	1,274.70	1,274.70	171.30	216.90
996.60	1,031.40	1,078.20	1,078.20	1,078.20	1,078.20	1,078.20	1,078.20	133.80	174.30

Warrant Officers

1,159.20	1,240.50	1,297.80	1,343.70	1,379.10	1,424.70	1,472.10	1,586.40	215.10	259.50
1,065.90	1,100.70	1,135.50	1,169.40	1,205.70	1,252.20	1,297.80	1,343.70	192.60	237.30
950.70	985.20	1,019.40	1,055.10	1,089.60	1,124.10	1,169.40	1,169.40	168.30	213.60
868.50	904.20	938.40	973.20	1,007.10	1,043.10	1,043.10	1,043.10	152.10	197.10

Enlisted Personnel

1,055.40	1,079.40	1,104.00	1,129.50	1,154.10	1,176.90	1,239.00	1,359.00	162.60	228.60
910.20	934.50	959.10	984.00	1,006.80	1,031.70	1,092.00	1,214.10	150.30	212.40
788.40	813.30	849.90	873.90	898.50	910.20	971.40	1,092.00	128.40	198.30
704.40	741.00	764.10	788.40	800.70	800.70	800.70	800.70	117.00	183.00
643.80	667.20	679.80	679.80	679.80	679.80	679.80	679.80	112.50	168.30
564.30	564.30	564.30	564.30	564.30	564.30	564.30	564.30	99.30	147.90
494.40	494.40	494.40	494.40	494.40	494.40	494.40	494.40	88.50	128.40
417.30	417.30	417.30	417.30	417.30	417.30	417.30	417.30	78.30	128.40
374.40	374.40	374.40	374.40	374.40	374.40	374.40	374.40	73.80	128.40

*Limited under existing law to $3,958.20

Basic Allowances for Subsistence

This allowance, the quarters allowance, and any other allowance are not subject to income tax.

Officers — Subsistence (food) is paid to all officers regardless of rank. . . . . 55.61 per month

Enlisted members: When on leave or authorized to mess separately . . . . . 2.65 per day
When rations in kind are not available . . . . . 2.99 per day
When assigned to duty under emergency conditions where no government messing facilities are available . . . . . 3.97 per day (maximum rate)

Family Separation Allowance

Under certain conditions of family separation of more than 30 days, a member in Pay Grades E-4 (with over 4 years' service) and above will be allowed $30 a month in addition to any other allowances to which he is entitled. When separated from family and required to maintain a home for his family and one for himself, the member is entitled to an additional monthly basic allowance for quarters at the "without dependents" rate for his grade.

1970—Army units participate in Cambodian sanctuary operations, Apr. 29-June 30.

1973—Last U.S. troops leave Vietnam, U.S. Military Assistance Command deactivated, March 29.

1973—End of all U.S. bombing operations over Indochina, Aug. 15.

The Medal of Honor

The Medal of Honor is the highest military award for bravery that can be given to any individual in the United States. The first Army Medals were awarded on March 25, 1863, and the first Navy Medals went to sailors and Marines on April 3, 1863.

The Medal of Honor, established by Joint Resolution of Congress, 12 July 1862 (amended by Act of 9 July 1918 and Act of 25 July 1963) is awarded in the name of Congress to a person who, while a member of the Armed Forces, distinguishes himself conspicuously by gallantry and intrepidity at the risk of his life above and beyond the call of duty while engaged in an action against any enemy of the United States; while engaged in military operations involving conflict with an opposing foreign force; or while serving with friendly foreign forces engaged in an armed conflict against an opposing armed force in which the United States is not a belligerent party. The deed performed must have been one of personal bravery or self-sacrifice so conspicuous as to clearly distinguish the individual above his comrades and must have involved risk of life. Incontestable proof of the performance of service is exacted and each recommendation for award of this decoration is considered on the standard of extraordinary merit.

Prior to World War I, the 2,625 Army Medal of Honor awards up to that time were reviewed to determine which past awards met new stringent criteria. The Army removed 911 names from the list, most of them former members of a volunteer infantry group during the Civil War who had been induced to extend their enlistments when they were promised the Medal.

Since that review Medals of Honor have been awarded in the following numbers:

World War I . . . . 124 Korean War 131
World War II . . . . 431 Vietnam (to date) 235

Strategic Nuclear Armaments: U.S. and USSR

Source: International Institute for Strategic Services, London

United States

Land-based missiles[1]		Range[2] (statute miles)	Estimated warhead yield[3]	Deployed (July 1976)
ICBM	Titan 2	7,250	5-10 MT	54
	Minuteman 2	8,000	1-2 MT	450
	Minuteman 3	8,000	3x170 KT	550
Sea-based missiles				
SLBM (nuclear subs)	UGM-27C Polaris A3	2,880	3x200 KT	160
	UGM-73A Poseidon	2,880	10x50 KT	496

Aircraft[7]		Range[8] (statute miles)	Weapons load (lb)	Deployed (July 1976)
Long-range	B-52D-F	11,500	60,000	387[8]
	B-52G/H	12,500	75,000	
Medium range	FB-111A	3,800	37,500	66
Strike aircraft; land-based	F-105D	2,100	16,500	
	F-4	2,300	16,000	(1,400)[9]
	F-111A/E	3,800	25,000	
	A-7D	3,400	15,000	
Strike aircraft: carrier-based	A-4	2,055	10,000	
	A-6A	3,225	18,000	(1,400)[9]
	A-7A/B/E	3,400	15,000	
	F-4	1,997	1,600	

Soviet Union

Land-based missiles[1]		Range[2] (statute miles)	Estimated warhead yield[3]	Deployed (July 1976)
ICBM	SS-7 Saddler	6,900	5 MT	140
	SS-8 Sasin	6,900	5 MT	19
	SS-9 Scarp	7,500	18-25 MT[4]	252
	SS-11 Sego	6,500	1-2 MT[5]	900
	SS-13 Savage	5,000	1 MT	60
	SS-17	6,500	4x KT	20
	SS-18	7,500	18-25 MT[6]	36
	SS-19	6,500	6x KT	100
Sea-based missiles				
SLBM (nuclear subs)	SS-N-6-Sawfly	1,750	MT	544
	SS-N-8	4,800	MT	220

Aircraft[7]	Range[8] (statue miles)	Weapons load (lb)	Deployed (July 1976)
Tu-95 Bear	7,800	40,000	100
Mya-4 Bison	6,050	20,000	35
Tu-16 Badger	4,000	20,000	750
Backfire B	5,500	20,000	60
Il-28 Beagle	2,500	4,850	
Su-7 Fitter	900	4,500	
Tu-22 Blinder	1,400	12,000	
MiG-21 Fishbed J	1,150	2,000	2,500
MiG-23 Flogger	1,800	2,800	
Su-19A Fencer	1,800	8,000	
Su-17/20 Fitter C	1,100	5,000	

(1) ICBM = intercontinental ballistic missile. IRBM = intermediate-range ballistic missile. MRBM = medium-range missile. SLBM = submarine-launched ballistic missile. SLCM = sub-launched cruise missile. (2) Operation range depends upon the payload carried: use of maximum payload may reduce missile range by up to 25%. (3) MT = megaton range = 1,000,000 tons of TNT equivalent or over; KT = kiloton range = 1,000 tons of TNT equivalent or more, but less than 1 MT. (4) Some SS-9 missiles carry 3 warheads of 4-5 MT each. (5) Some SS-11 missiles may carry 3xKT warheads. (6) Some SS-18 may carry 8xMT warheads. (7) All aircraft listed are dual-capable and many, especially in the categories of strike aircraft, would be more likely to carry conventional than nuclear weapons. (8) Theoretical maximum range, with internal fuel only, at optimum altitude and speed. Ranges for strike aircraft assume no weapons load. Especially in the case of strike aircraft, therefore, range falls sharply for flights at lower altitude, at higher speed, or with full weapons load. (9) Figures in parentheses are estimates.

Women in the Armed Forces

Expansion of military women's programs began in the Department of Defense in fiscal year 1973. The planned end strength for fiscal year 1988 is approximately 204,300 which is 6.2 per cent of the planned end strength of the active forces.

Although women are prohibited by law and directives based on law from serving in combat positions, policy changes in the department have resulted in making possible the assignment of women to almost all other career fields. Career progression for women is now comparable to that for male personnel. Women are routinely assigned to overseas locations formerly closed to female personnel. Test programs have been initiated to place women in pilot training and in command of activities and units which have missions other than administration of women.

Admission of women to the service academies began in the fall of 1976 and will further the goal of increased numbers of women officers. The Academies will provide single track education, allowing only for minor variations in the cadet program based on physiological differences between men and women.

Women's Army Corps —Brig. Gen. M. E. Clark, WAC Director, Dept. of Army, Washington, DC 20310; 5,440 officers, 44,871 enlisted women; wide variety of assignments, world-wide; subsidizes some college training.

Army Nurse Corps — Brig. Gen. M. N. Parks, Chief, Army Nurse Corps, Office of the Surgeon General, Dept. of Army, Washington, DC 20310; 2,829 female officers; nursing and supervision assignments, world-wide; subsidizes some training; corps includes men.

Navy — Fully integrated, no director for women. For information: Commander, Naval Recruiting, Dept. of Navy, Washington, DC 22203; 3,636 officers, 19,122 enlisted women; variety of assignments, world-wide.

Navy Nurse Corps — Rear Adm. Maxine Conder, Director, Navy Nurse Corps, Bureau of Medicine and Surgery, Dept. of Navy, Washington DC 20372; 2,092 female officers; nursing and supervision assignments at U.S. and foreign bases, and shipboard; subsidizes some training; corps includes men.

Air Force — Fully integrated, no director for women. For information: USAF Recruiting Service, Randolph Air Force Base, TX 78148; 5,124 officers, 32,396 enlisted women; variety of assignments, world-wide.

Air Force Nurse Corps — Brig. Gen. Clare M. Garrecht, Chief, Air Force Nurse Corps, Office of the Surgeon General, USAF, Washington, DC 20314; 3,084 female officers; nursing and supervision assignments, world-wide; subsidizes training; corps includes men.

Women Marines — Col. Margaret A. Brewer, Director, Women Marines, Headquarters, Marine Corps, Washington, DC 20380; 426 officers, 3,239 enlisted women.

Coast Guard Women — Fully integrated, no commander, U.S. Coast Guard, Washington, DC 20590; 60 officers, 560 enlisted women.

Casualties in Principal Wars of the U. S.

Data on Revolutionary War casualties is from **The Toll of Independence**, Howard H. Peckham, ed., U. of Chicago Press, 1974.

Data prior to World War I are based upon incomplete records in many cases. Casualty data are confined to dead and wounded personnel and therefore exclude personnel captured or missing in action who were subsequently returned to military control. Dash (—) indicates information is not available.

			Casualties			
Wars	**Branch of service**	**Number serving**	**Battle deaths**	**Other deaths**	**Wounds not mortal[8]**	**Total**
Revolutionary War	**Total**	—	**6,824**	**18,500**	**8,445**	**33,769**
1775-1783	Army	184,000	5,992	—	7,988	13,980
	Navy &	to	—	—	—	—
	Marines	250,000	832	—	457	1,289
War of 1812	**Total**	**[9]286,730**	**2,260**	—	**4,505**	**6,765**
1812-1815	Army	—	1,950	—	4,000	5,950
	Navy	—	265	—	439	704
	Marines	—	45	—	66	111
Mexican War	**Total**	**[9]78,718**	**1,733**	**11,550**	**4,152**	**17,435**
1846-1848	Army	—	1,721	11,550	4,102	17,373
	Navy	—	1	—	3	4
	Marines	—	11	—	47	58
Civil War	**Total**	**[9]2,213,363**	**140,414**	**224,097**	**281,881**	**646,392**
(Union forces only)	Army	2,128,948	138,154	221,374	280,040	639,568
1861-1865	Navy	—	2,112	2,411	1,710	6,233
	Marines	84,415	148	312	131	591
Confederate forces	**Total**	—	**74,524**	**59,297**	—	**133,821**
(estimate)[1]	Army	600,000	—	—	—	—
1863-1866	Navy	to	—	—	—	—
	Marines	1,500,000	—	—	—	—
Spanish-American War	**Total**	**306,760**	**385**	**2,061**	**1,662**	**4,108**
1898	Army[4]	280,564	369	2,061	1,594	4,024
	Navy	22,875	10	0	47	57
	Marines	3,321	6	0	21	27
World War I	**Total**	**4,743,826**	**53,513**	**63,195**	**204,002**	**320,710**
April 6, 1917-	Army[5]	4,057,101	50,510	55,868	193,663	300,041
Nov. 11, 1918	Navy	599,051	431	6,856	819	8,106
	Marines	78,839	2,461	390	9,520	12,371
	Coast Gd.	8,835	111	81	—	192
World War II	**Total**	**16,353,659**	**292,131**	**115,185**	**670,846**	**1,078,162**
Dec. 7, 1941-	Army[6]	11,260,000	234,874	83,400	565,861	884,135
Dec. 31, 1946[2]	Navy[7]	4,183,466	36,950	25,664	37,778	100,392
	Marines	669,100	19,733	4,778	67,207	91,718
	Coast Gd.	241,093	574	1,343	—	1,917
Korean War	**Total**	**5,764,143**	**33,629**	**20,617**	**103,284**	**157,530**
June 25, 1950-	Army	2,834,000	27,704	9,429	77,596	114,729
July 27, 1953[3]	Navy	1,177,000	458	4,043	1,576	6,077
	Marines	424,000	4,267	1,261	23,744	29,272
	Air Force	1,285,000	1,200	5,884	368	7,452
	Coast Gd.	44,143	—	—	—	—
Vietnam (preliminary)[10]	**Total**	**8,744,000**	**46,572**	**10,390**	**153,329**	**210,291**
Aug. 4, 1964-	Army	4,368,000	30,707	7,193	96,811	134,711
Jan. 27, 1973	Navy	1,842,000	1,528	910	4,180	6,618
	Marines	794,000	13,020	1,684	51,399	66,103
	Air Force	1,740,000	1,317	603	939	2,859

(1)Authoritative statistics for the Confederate Forces are not available. An estimated 26,000-31,000 Confederate personnel died in Union prisons.

(2)Data are for the period Dec. 1, 1941 through Dec. 31, 1946 when hostilities were officially terminated by Presidential Proclamation, but few battle deaths or wounds not mortal were incurred after the Japanese acceptance of Allied peace terms on Aug. 14, 1945. Numbers serving from Dec. 1, 1941-Aug. 31, 1945 were: Total—14,903,213; Army—10,420,000; Navy—3,883,520; and Marine Corps—599,693.

(3)Tentative final data based upon information available as of Sept. 30, 1954, at which time 24 persons were still carried as missing in action.

(4) Number serving covers the period April 21-Aug. 13, 1898, while dead and wounded data are for the period May 1-Aug. 31, 1898. Active hostilities ceased on Aug. 13, 1898, but ratifications of the treaty of peace were not exchanged between the United States and Spain until April 11, 1899.

(5) Includes Air Service. Battle deaths and wounds not mortal include casualties suffered by American forces in Northern Russia to Aug. 25, 1919 and in Siberia to April 1, 1920. Other deaths covered the period April 1, 1917-Dec. 31, 1918.

(6) Includes Army Air Forces.

(7) Battle deaths and wounds not mortal include casualties incurred in Oct. 1941 due to hostile action.

(8) Marine Corps data for World War II, the Spanish-American War and prior wars represent the number of individuals wounded, whereas all other data in this column represent the total number (incidence) of wounds.

(9) As reported by the Commissioner of Pensions in his Annual Report for Fiscal Year 1903.

(10) Number serving covers the period Aug. 4, 1964-Jan. 27, 1973 (date of ceasefire). Number of casualties incurred in connection with the conflict in Vietnam from Jan. 1, 1961-Mar. 31, 1977. Includes casualties incurred in Mayaguez Incident. Wounds not mortal exclude 150,375 persons not requiring hospital care.

Veterans Administration Keeps Pace With Change

Source: Max Cleland, Administrator, Veterans Administration, Washington, D.C.

America continues to set a world standard in treatment of its veterans. In ten years, 1969, to 1978, money appropriated for veterans' benefits and services increased over $11 billion, about 149 per cent. The Veterans Administration is the federal agency charged with administering these benefits. Although the agency will spend more than $18 billion and employ a record high 215,000 persons in 1978, its administrative expenses will be held to 3 per cent.

Counting the country's 29.7 million veterans and their dependents, the potential VA clientele totals almost 93 million, nearly half the country's population. To assist persons seeking VA assistance, the agency completed in 1977 a nationwide, toll-free telephone system to allow calls from anywhere in the country to a VA benefits counselor at no cost. (Check local directories for listings.) Subtle adjustments of benefits programs are continually made to meet the changing needs of the diverse veteran population.

Demand for VA health care continues at a high level throughout the veteran population. VA medical funding for 1978 will approach $5 billion. The recent opening of the Loma Linda VA Hospital in California brought the number of VA hospitals to 172, and the added facility plus further refinement of treatment techniques will allow the agency to treat 1.3 million inpatients in 1978. Reflecting modern medicine's emphasis on ambulatory care, VA will activate 8 additional outpatient clinics during the year, bringing the total of these facilities to 227. These resources will provide for a record 17.5 million outpatient visits.

The veteran population is getting older. The average veteran age is 46.3, but the 13.2 million WW II veterans average 56.3 years. There are almost 2.3 million veterans over age 65. To meet the implied adjustment in medical requirements, VA is expanding its nursing home care facilities and refining other programs, such as outpatient care, to better provide treatment for older veterans. In addition, 5 new national cemeteries will be opened in the 3-year period from 1977 to 1979, bringing to 60 the number of VA-administered national cemeteries with available gravesites.

Peak usage of GI Bill educational benefits has passed. The 7 million who went to school or trained under the current program represent about 65 per cent of the Vietnam era's veterans. (Only 50.5 per cent of WW II veterans took advantage of their program.) There will still be, however, some 2 million veterans and survivors in training in 1978, receiving monthly payments estimated to total $3.8 billion.

Income security for disabled veterans, their dependents and the families of deceased veterans continues to be a priority. Monthly compensation payments will be made to some 2.3 million veterans with service-related injuries; 367 thousand survivors of veterans who died from service-connected disabilities will also receive monthly checks. These service-connected payments will total $4.7 billion. Based on financial need, another $3.2 billion will be paid in pensions to about 1 million veterans and 1.3 million survivors.

Veterans, especially those between ages 20 to 24, have been hard hit by unemployment. VA works closely with the Department of Labor to find jobs for veterans, and has increased emphasis on its on-job training programs under the GI Bill.

Veterans are seeking assistance in purchasing housing at a record rate. Guarantees for privately financed mortgates will be provided in 1978 for 360 thousand veterans to purchase homes, and the VA will directly loan housing funds to another 2,630 persons. More than 2.5 million Vietnam era veterans have now received VA-backed home loans and, since the home-loan program began in 1944, VA has helped 9.8 million former servicemen and women to buy a home with a modest interest, no-down-payment loan. Currently the guaranty amount is $17,500, but this amount is regularly used to help secure loans on residential property costing up to $100,000. The guaranty can be used to buy, construct, improve, alter or repair a home or farm residence, or to purchase a condominium or mobile home and/or lot.

The VA has continued to have a large impact on both medical education and medical research in America. To supplement the thousands of individual research projects the agency sponsors yearly, the VA will establish in 1978 a new Rehabilitation Engineering Research and Development Center in Chicago. The Center will apply "space age technology" to a full range of projects designed to restore to injured veterans the mobility or use of bodily functions impaired by injury. Experimental use of space satellites in biomedical communications between some 40 VA hospitals will also be continued. VA hospitals are affiliated with 102 medical schools and 58 dental schools.

Veteran Population

	June 1977
Veterans in civil life, end of month — Total	**29,787,000**
War Veterans — Total	**26,712,000**
Vietnam Era — Total (a)	8,608,000
And service in Korean Conflict	521,000
No service in Korean Conflict	8,087,000
Korean Conflict — Total (includes line 4) (b)	5,923,000
And service in WW II	1,219,000
No service in WW II	4,704,000
World War II (includes line 7)	13,152,000
World War I	769,000
Spanish-American War	468
Service between Korean Conflict (January 31, 1955) and Vietnam (August 5, 1964) only (c)	**3,075,000**

(a) Service after Aug. 4, 1964; (b) includes 2,385,000 veterans who also served after the end of the Korean Conflict Jan. 31, 1955; (c) excludes men who served on active duty for training only.

Pension Cases and Compensation Payments

Fiscal year	Living veteran cases No.	Deceased veteran cases No.	Total cases No.	Total disbursement Dollars	Fiscal year	Living veteran cases No.	Deceased veteran cases No.	Total cases No.	Total disbursement Dollars
1890	415,654	122,290	537,944	106,093,850	1965	3,204,275	1,277,009	4,481,284	3,901,598,010
1900	752,510	241,019	993,529	138,462,130	1969	3,107,162	1,443,367	4,550,529	4,722,489,826
1910	602,622	318,461	921,083	159,974,056	1970	3,127,338	1,487,176	4,614,514	5,113,649,490
1920	419,627	349,916	769,543	316,418,029	1971	3,222,394	1,584,167	4,806,561	5,726,485,000
1930	542,610	298,223	840,833	418,432,808	1972	3,268,826	1,641,370	4,910,196	6,045,214,000
1940	610,122	239,176	849,298	429,138,465	1973	3,256,746	1,654,287	4,911,033	6,426,647,000
1950	2,368,238	658,123	3,026,361	2,009,462,298	1974	3,241,263	1,627,482	4,868,745	6,615,599,000
1955	2,668,786	808,303	3,477,089	2,634,292,537	1975	3,226,701	1,628,146	4,854,847	7,600,000,000
1960	3,008,935	950,802	3,959,737	3,314,761,383	1976	3,235,778	1,630,830	4,866,608	8,074,488,000

American Military Cemeteries and Memorials on Foreign Soil

Administered by the American Battle Monuments Commission, Washington, DC 20314
(Numbers of graves and numbers of commemorated missing in parentheses)
All of the cemeteries are closed to further interments.

World War I Cemeteries

Aisne-Marne, Belleau (Aisne) France (2,288-1,060)
Brookwood (Surrey) England (468-563)
Flanders Field, Waregem, Belgium (368-43)
Meuse-Argonne, Romagne (Meuse), France (14,246-954)
Oise-Aisne, Seringes (Aisne), near Fere-en-Tardenois (Aisne), France (6,012-241)
St. Mihiel, Thiaucourt (M. et M.), France (4,153-284)
Somme, Bony (Aisne), France (1,844-284)
Suresnes (Seine), France (1,541-974). In this cemetery rest also 24 of our unknown dead of World War II. The World War I chapel was, by the addition of two loggias, converted into a shrine to commemorate our dead of both wars. Senior representatives of the American and French governments assemble here on ceremonial occasions to pay homage to our military dead of these wars.

World War II Cemetery Memorials

Ardennes, Neupre (Neuville-en-Condroz), Belgium (5,319-462)
Brittany, St. James (Manche), France (4,410-498)
Cambridge, Cambridge, England, (3,811-5,125)
Epinal, Epinal (Vosges), France (5,255-424)
Florence, Florence (Tuscany), Italy (4,402-1,409)
Henri-Chapelle, Henri-Chapelle, Belgium (7,989-450)
Lorraine, St. Avold (Moselle), France (10,489-444)
Luxembourg, Hamm, Luxembourg (5,076-370)
Manila, Manila, Rep. of the Philippines (17,206-36,279)
Netherlands, Margraten, Holland (8,301-1,722)
Normandy, St. Laurent (Calvados), Fr. (9,386-1,557)
North Africa, Carthage, Tunisia (2,841-3,724)
Rhone, Draguignan (Var), France (861-293)
Sicily-Rome, Nettuno, Italy (7,862-3,094)

World War I Monuments

Audenarde, Belgium.
Bellicourt (Aisne), France.
Brest (Finistere), France.
Cantigny (Somme), France.
Chateau-Thierry (Aisne), Fr.
Gibraltar.
Remmel, Ypres, Belgium.
Montfaucon (Meuse), France.
Montsec (Meuse), France.
Sommepy (Marne), France.
Tours (Indre et Loire), France.

World War II Memorials

To commemorate those who met their deaths in the American coastal waters of the Atlantic and Pacific Oceans the commission has erected a memorial in Battery Park, NYC, on which are inscribed 4,596 names, and at the Presidio of San Francisco, Cal., which carries 412 names. At the Honolulu Cemetery a memorial was erected which records the names of 18,093 missing of World War II and 8,194 missing resulting from the Korean operations.

The commission also maintains a cemetery in Mexico City where the remains of 750 Americans who gave their lives in the Mexican War (1846-1848) are buried.

World War II Merchant Marine Casualties

Source: U. S. Coast Guard

Died from direct causes while serving on American flag ships, 845; died in prisoner-of-war camps, 37; listed as missing, 4,780.

There were 572 released prisoners of war, and one prisoner unaccounted for. Another 500 men died while serving on foreign flag ships under U. S. control.

The number of U. S. flag ships lost was 605 of 6,000,000 deadweight tons.

Debts Owed U.S. Arising from World War I

Source: U.S. Treasury Department (Sept. 30, 1976)

Country	Original indebtedness	Interest thru Sept. 30, 1976	Total	Cumulative payments Principal	Cumulative payments Interest	Total outstanding
Armenia	$11,959,917	$34,118,524	$46,078,442	$32	.....	$46,078,409
Austria[1]	26,843,149	44,059	26,887,208	862,668	.....	26,024,540
Belgium	419,837,630	395,807,720	815,645,351	19,157,630	$33,033,643	763,454,078
Cuba	10,000,000	2,286,751	12,286,752	10,000,000	2,286,752	.....
Czechoslovakia	185,071,023	153,494,337	338,565,360	19,829,914	304,178	318,431,268
Estonia	16,466,013	27,165,683	43,631,695	11	1,248,432	42,383,253
Finland	9,000,000	12,661,578	21,661,578	[2]9,000,000	[2]12,661,578	.....
France	4,089,689,588	4,484,525,892	8,574,215,480	226,039,588	260,036,303	8,088,139,589
Great Britain	4,802,181,642	8,385,206,958	13,187,388,600	434,181,642	1,590,672,656	11,162,534,302
Greece	[3]34,319,844	5,799,222	[3]40,119,065	1,625,578	5,461,560	[10]33,031,927
Hungary[4]	[5]2,051,898	3,540,397	[5]5,592,295	73,996	583,553	4,934,747
Italy	2,042,364,319	509,218,970	2,551,583,290	37,464,319	63,365,561	2,450,753,409
Latvia	6,888,664	11,463,427	18,352,092	9,200	752,349	17,590,543
Liberia	26,000	10,472	36,472	26,000	10,472	.....
Lithuania	6,432,465	10,606,112	17,038,577	234,783	1,003,174	15,800,620
Nicaragua[6]	141,950	26,625	168,576	141,950	26,625	.....
Poland	207,344,297	345,725,449	553,069,747	[7]1,287,297	21,359,000	530,423,449
Romania	68,359,192	68,051,521	136,410,714	[8]4,498,632	292,375	131,619,706
Russia	192,601,297	565,167,779	757,769,077	.....	[9]8,750,312	749,018,765
Yugoslavia	63,577,714	45,776,372	109,354,085	1,952,713	636,059	106,765,314
Totals	**12,195,156,605**	**15,060,697,849**	**27,255,854,453**	**766,385,954**	**2,002,484,582**	**24,486,983,918**

(1) The Federal Republic of Germany has recognized liability for securities falling due between Mar. 12, 1938, and May 8, 1945. (2) $8,480,090 has been made available for educational exchange programs with Finland pursuant to 22 U.S.C. 2455(e). (3) Includes $13,155,921 refunded by the agreement of May 28, 1964, ratified by Congress Nov. 5, 1966. (4) Interest payments from Dec. 15, 1932, to June 15, 1937, were paid in pengo equivalent. (5) Includes $69,352 of principal and $120,535 of interest on the moratorium agreement of May 27, 1932. (6) The indebtedness of Nicaragua was canceled pursuant to the agreement of Apr. 14, 1938. (7) Excludes claim allowance of $1,813,429 dated Dec. 15, 1969. (8) Excludes payment of $100,000 on June 14, 1940, as a token of good faith. (9) Principally proceeds from liquidation of Russian assets in the United States. (10) Includes $12,514,265 on agreement of May 28, 1964.

Major New U.S. Weapons Systems

Source: DMS, Inc., U.S. Defense Department

Item	Description	Estimated total cost (millions)	Estimated unit cost (thousands)	Number to be produced	Major contractors	Comment
F-14 Tomcat	Swing-wing jet fighter, carrier-based, for fleet defense, strike escort.	$10,564.0	$24,400	580	Grumman	In production; 80 sold to Iran
F-15 Eagle	Tactical jet fighter. Air Force.	12,603.4	16,200	729	McDonnell Douglas	In production; 21 for Israel, 68 for Japan
F-16 Condor	Supersonic, day-time fighter; defense. Air Force.	13,833.3	9,200	1,730	General Dynamics	Near production; 348 for NATO, up to 700 others to be sold abroad
F-18 Hornet	All-weather fighter and attack plane. Fleet escort, Marine Corps ground support.	12,815.8	15,800	811 for U.S.	McDonnell Douglas; Northrop	Advanced development; 800 more to be produced for sales abroad
AAH	Attack helicopter: anti-tank, air cavalry, escort. Army.	3,758.1	7,000	536	Bell; Hughes	In development
Trident	Nuclear-powered submarine carries 24 missiles with 4,000-mile range.	21,426.5	Boat= 862,400 missile= 12,000	13 boats; 505 missiles	General Dynamics; Lockheed	Boats in production, missiles in development
SSN-688 Los Angeles	Nuclear-powered attack submarines to destroy enemy shipping, subs.	10,053.0	456,200	90	Newport News; General Dynamics	In production
FFG-7	Guided-missile frigate; anti-sub, anti-aircraft, attack and defense.	13,675.3	146,822	74	Bath; Todd	In production
PCM	Patrol Combatant Missile (hydrofoil boat)	383.0	64.9	6	Boeing	Near production
XM-1 Abrams	Main battle tank. Army.	4,779.4	754	3,312	Chrysler, General Motors	In development
MICV-70	Infantry or Cavalry fighting vehicle (IV or CFV)	1,270.9	527	2,410	FMC Corp.	Advanced development
Copperhead	Cannon-launched, laser-guided projectile; 10-12 mile range. Army and Navy.	1,092.1	9[1] 9[2] 16[3]	100,000 (Army only)	Martin Marietta	In development
Hellfire	Missile for AAH; may be laser-guided.	770.8	10	28,000	Rockwell	In development
Patriot (SAM-D)	Surface-to-air missile for field air defense.	5,943.3[4]	47,000[4]	125 batteries[4]	Martin Marietta, Raytheon	In engineering development
MX	Advanced ICBM to replace Minuteman.	Unknown	Unknown	1,000	Unknown	In development
Cruise missile	ALCM-B, air-to ground (AF) TALCM, anti-ship (Navy) SLCM, sub-launched (Navy) GLCM, ground launched	Unknown	600	Unknown	Boeing Gen. Dynam. Gen. Dynam. Unknown	In development

(1) Per 10,000-round buy. (2) Per 11,000 round buy of semi-active laser variant. (3) Per 2,000 round buy of infrared variant. (4) Batteries consist of 4 firing sections and fire control centers each; $47,000 unit cost is for firing sections and missiles only.

Some comparable costs: Total moon program, $30 billion; Bay Area Rapid Transit system, $1.6 billion; World Trade Center, land acquisition and construction, $1 billion; one manned moon shot, $400 million; February 1976 welfare payments to families with dependent children, $813 million; 1974-75 current elementary and secondary school expenditure in California, $3.6 billion; fiscal 1975 Ohio state budget outlays, $6.8 billion. The cost of one Trident submarine with missiles could pay off the Georgia state debt.

Armed Services Senior Enlisted Adviser

The U.S. Army, Navy and Air Force in 1966-67 each created a new position of senior enlisted adviser whose primary job is to represent the point of view of his services' enlisted men and women on matters of welfare, morale, and any problems concerning enlisted personnel. The senior adviser will have direct access to the military chief of his branch of service and policy-making bodies.

The senior enlisted adviser for each Dept. is:

Army-Sgt. Major of the Army William G. Bainbridge.

Navy-Master Chief Petty Officer of the Navy Robert J. Walker.

Air Force-Chief Master Sgt. of the Air Force Thomas N. Barnes.

Marines-Sgt. Major of the Marine Corps Henry H. Black.

ASSOCIATIONS AND SOCIETIES

Source: World Almanac questionnaire

Arranged according to key words in titles. Founding year of organization in parentheses; last figure after ZIP code indicates membership.

—A—

Aaron Burr Assn. (1946), TremonT, Inca Rd., Linden, VA 22642; 600.

Abortion Federation, Natl. (1976), 110 E. 59th St., Suite 1019, N.Y., NY 10022; 150.

Abortion Rights Action League, Natl. (1969), 706 Seventh St. SE, Wash., DC 20003; 12,000.

Accountants, Amer. Institute of Certified Public (1887), 1211 Ave. of the Americas, N.Y., NY 10036; 103,863.

Accountants, Natl. Assn. of (1919), 919 Third Ave., N.Y., NY 10022; 84,000.

Accountants, Natl. Society of Public (1945), 1717 Pennsylvania Ave., NW, Wash., DC 20006; 16,000.

Acoustical Society of America (1929), 335 E. 45 St., N.Y., NY 10017; 5,300.

Actors' Equity Assn. (1913), 1500 Broadway, N.Y., NY 10036; 21,477.

Actors' Fund of America (1882), 1501 Broadway, N.Y., NY 10036; 4,045.

Actuaries, Society of (1949), 208 S. La Salle St., Chicago, IL 60604; 6,000.

Acupuncture Foundation of America (1972), Box 1424, Nantucket, MA 02554.

Adirondack Mountain Club (1922), 172 Ridge St., Glens Falls, NY 12801; 9,000.

Administrative Management Society (1919), Maryland Rd., Willow Grove, PA 19090; 12,000.

Adult Education Assn. of the U.S.A. (1951), 810 18th St. NW, Wash., DC 20006; 2,600.

Advertisers, Assn. of Natl. (1910), 155 E. 44th St., N.Y., NY 10017; 400 cos.

Advertising Agencies, Amer. Assn. of (1917), 200 Park Ave., N.Y., NY 10017; 420 agencies.

Aeronautic Assn. of the U.S.A., Natl. (1922), 806 15th St. NW, Wash., DC 20005; 150,000.

Aeronautics and Astronautics, Amer. Institute of (1930), 1290 Ave. of the Americas, N.Y., NY 10019; 27,000.

Aerospace Industries Assn. of America (1919), 1725 DeSales St. NW, Wash., DC 20036; 61 cos.

Aerospace Medical Assn. (1929), Washington Natl. Airport, Wash., DC 20001; 3,500.

Afro-American Life and History, Assn. for the Study of (1915), 1401 14th St. NW, Wash., DC 20005; 2,500.

Aging Assn., Amer. (1970), Univ. of Nebraska Medical Center, 42d & Dewey Ave., Omaha, NE 68105; 500.

Agricultural Chemicals Assn., Natl. (1933), 1155 15th St. NW, Wash., DC 20005; 122 cos.

Agricultural Economics Assn., Amer. (1910), Univ. of Kentucky, Lexington, KY 40506; 4,500.

Agricultural Engineers, Amer. Society of (1907), 2950 Niles Rd., St. Joseph, MI 49085; 9,000.

Agricultural History Society (1919), Economic Research Service, NEAD, U.S. Dept. of Agriculture, Wash., DC 20250; 800.

Agronomy, Amer. Society of (1907), 677 S. Segoe Rd., Madison, WI 53711; 8,500.

Ahepa, Order of (1922), 1422 K St. NW, Wash., DC 20005; 26,000

Air, Citizens for Clean (1965), 25 Broad St., N.Y., NY 10004; 3,000.

Air Force Aid Society (1942), 1117 N. 19th St., Arlington, VA 22209; 24,000.

Air Force Assn. (1946), 1750 Pennsylvania Ave. NW, Wash., DC 20006; 150,000.

Air Force Sergeants Assn. (1971), 4235 28th Ave., Marlow Heights, MD 20031; 99,000.

Air Line Employees Assn. (1952), 5600 S. Central Ave., Chicago, IL 60638; 10,000.

Air Line Pilots Assn. (1931), 1625 Massachusetts Ave. NW, Wash., DC 20036; 32,000.

Air Pollution Control Assn. (1907), P.O. Box 2861, Pittsburgh, PA 15230; 6,600.

Air Transport Assn. of America (1936), 1709 New York Ave. NW, Wash., DC 20006; 26 airlines.

Air Transport Assn., Internatl. (1945), P.O. Box 550, Internatl. Aviation Sq., Montreal P.Q., Canada H3A 2R4; 109 airlines.

Aircraft Assn., Experimental (1953), 11311 W. Forest Home Ave., Franklin, WI 53132; 50,000.

Aircraft Owners and Pilots Assn. (1939), 7315 Wisconsin Ave., Bethesda, MD 20014; 201,000.

Airport Operators Council Internatl. (1948), 1700 K St. NW, Wash., DC 20006; 160.

Albert Schweitzer Fellowship (1939), 866 UN Plaza, N.Y., NY 10017.

Albert Schweitzer Friendship House (1966), R.D. 1; Box 7, Hurlburt Rd., Great Barrington, MA 01230; 5,000.

Alcohol Problems, Amer. Council on (1964), 119 Constitution Ave. NE, Wash., DC 20002.

Alcoholics Anonymous, 468 Park Ave. So., N.Y., NY 10017; 1,000,000.

Alcoholism, Natl. Council on (1933), 733 Third Ave., N.Y., NY 10017; 162 affiliates.

All Terrain Vehicle Owners Assn., Natl. (1971), D-2, 1446 Bristol Rd., Corwall Heights, PA 19020; 262.

Allergy, Amer. Academy of (1943), 225 E. Michigan St., Milwaukee, WI 53202; 2,400.

Allied Youth (1936), 933 N. Kenmore St., Arlington, VA 22201; 10,000.

Alpine Club, Amer. (1902), 113 E. 90th St., N.Y., NY 10028; 1,200.

Altrusa Internatl. (1917), 332 S. Michigan Ave., Chicago, IL 60604; 19,800.

Aluminum Assn. (1933), 750 Third Ave., N.Y., NY 10017; 77 companies.

American Federation of Labor & Congress of Industrial Organizations (AFL-CIO) (1955, by merging **American Federation of Labor** estab. 1881 and **Congress of Industrial Organizations** estab. 1935), 815 16th St. NW, Wash., DC 20006; 14,300,000.

Amer. Field Service (1914), 313 E. 43d St., N.Y., NY 10017; 45,000.

Amer. Indian Affairs, Assn. on (1923), 432 Park Ave. So., N.Y., NY 10016; 50,000.

American Legion, The (1919), 700 N. Pennsylvania St., Indianapolis, IN 46206; 2,713,962. **American Legion Auxiliary** (1919), 777 N. Meridian St., Indianapolis, IN 46204; 954,000.

Amer. Veterans of World War II, Korea & Vietnam (AMVETS), (1947), 1710 Rhode Island Ave. NW, Wash., DC 20036; 200,000. **AMVETS Auxiliary** (1946), Saco Rd., Old Orchard Beach, ME 04064; 25,000.

Amputation Foundation, Natl. (1919), 12-45 150th St., Whitestone, NY 11357; 2,000.

Animal Ecologist Society (1977), P.O. Box 160371, Sacramento, CA 95816; 50.

Animal Protection Institute of America (1968), 5894 S. Land Park Dr., P.O. Box 22505, Sacramento, CA 95822; 83,000.

Animal Welfare Institute (1951), P.O. Box 3650, Wash., DC 20007; 5,000.

Animals, Amer. Society for Prevention of Cruelty to (ASPCA) (1866), 441 E. 92d St., N.Y., NY 10028; 3,000.

Animals, Friends of (1957), 11 W. 60th St., N.Y., NY 10023; 70,000.

Animals, The Fund for (1967), 140 W. 57th St., N.Y., NY 10019; 65,000.

Anthropological Assn., Amer. (1902), 1703 New Hampshire Ave. NW, Wash., DC 20009; 10,000.

Anti-Vivisection Society, Amer. (1883), 1903 Chestnut St., Philadelphia, PA 19103; 15,000.

Antiquarian Society, Amer. (1812), 185 Salisbury St., Worcester, MA 01609; 308.

Antique Automobile Club of America (1935), 501 W. Governor Rd., Hershey, PA 17033; 40,000.

Appalachian Mountain Club (1876), 5 Joy St., Boston, MA 02108; 22,500.

Appalachian Trail Conference (1925), Box 236, Harpers Ferry, WV 25425; 10,000.

Appraisers, Amer. Society of (1952), P.O. Box 17265, Dulles Internatl. Airport, Wash., DC 20041; 4,800.

Arbitration Assn., Amer. (1926), 140 W. 51st St., N.Y., NY 10020; 4,140.

Arboriculture, Internatl. Society of (1924), P.O. Box 71, 5 Lincoln Sq., Urbana, IL 61801; 3,200.

Archaeological Institute of America (1879), 260 W. Broadway, N.Y., NY 10013; 6,000.

Archers Assn., Professional (1961), P.O. Box 7609, Flint,

MI 48507; 300.

Archery Assn. of the U.S., Natl. (1879), 1951 Geraldson Dr., Lancaster, PA 17601; 5,000.

Architects, Amer. Institute of (1857), 1735 New York Ave. NW, Wash., DC 20006; 25,000.

Architectural Historians, Society of (1940), 1700 Walnut St., Phila., PA 19103; 4,300.

Archivists, Society of Amer. (1936), P.O. Box 8198, Univ. of Illinois at Chicago Circle, Chicago, IL 60680; 2,800.

Armed Forces Communications and Electronics Assn. (1946), 5205 Leesburg Pike, Falls Church, VA 22041; 13,000.

Army and Navy Union U.S.A. (1886), 1391 Main St., Lakemore, OH 44250; 5,700.

Arthritis Foundation (1948), 475 Riverside Dr., N.Y., NY 10027; 73 chapters.

Artists of America, Allied (1914), 1083 Fifth Ave., N.Y., NY 10028; 350.

Arts, Amer. Federation of (1909), 41 E. 65th St., N.Y., NY 10021; 2,000.

Arts, Associated Councils of the (1969), 570 Seventh Ave., N.Y., NY 10018; 2,000.

Arts, Natl. Endowment for the (1965), 2401 E. St. NW, Wash., DC 20506.

Arts and Letters, Amer. Academy and Institute of (1898), 633 W. 155th St., N.Y., NY 10032; 250.

Arts & Psychology, Assn. for the (1976), P.O. Box 160371, Sacramento, CA 95816.

Arts and Sciences, Amer. Academy of (1780), 165 Allandale St., Jamaica Plain Sta., Boston, MA 02130; 2,300.

Assistance League, Natl. (1935), 5627 Fernwood Ave., Hollywood, CA 90028; 11,346.

Associated Press (1848), 50 Rockefeller Plaza, N.Y., NY 10020; 1,265 newspapers & 3,400 broadcast stations.

Astrologers, Amer. Federation of (1938), P.O. Box 22040, Tempe, AZ 85282; 4,200.

Astronautical Society, Amer. (1953), 6060 Duke St., Alexandria, VA 22304; 700.

Astronomical Society, Amer. (1899), 211 FitzRandolph Rd., Princeton, NJ 08540; 3,400.

Atheist Assn. (1925), P.O. Box 2832, San Diego, CA 92112; 300.

Atheists, Amer. (1963), 4408 Medical Pkwy., Austin, TX 78768; 70,000 families.

Athletic Associations, Natl. Federation of State High School (1920), Federation Pl., Elgin, IL 60120; 61 assns.

Athletic Conference, Eastern College (1938), 1311 Craigville Beach Rd., Centerville, MA 02632; 212 schools.

Athletic Union of the U.S., Amateur (1888), 3400 W. 86th St., Indianapolis, IN 46268; 300,000.

Attorneys General, Natl. Assn. of (1907), P.O. Box 11910, Iron Works Pike, Lexington, KY 40511; 55.

Auctioneers Assn., Natl. (1949), 135 Lakewood Dr., Lincoln, NE 68510; 5,200.

Audubon Society, Natl. (1905), 950 Third Ave., N.Y., NY 10022; 350,000.

Authors and Composers, Amer. Guild of (1931), 40 W. 57th St., N.Y., NY 10019; 2,500.

Authors League of America (1912), 234 W. 44th St., N.Y., NY 10036; 7,200.

Automobile Assn., Amer. (1902), 8111 Gatehouse Rd., Falls Church, VA 22042; 18.6 million.

Automobile Club, Natl. (1924), 65 Battery St., San Francisco, CA 94111; 521,422.

Automobile Dealers Assn., Natl. (1917), 8400 Westpark Dr., McLean, VA 22101; 20,885.

Automobile License Plate Collectors' Assn. (1954), P.O. Box 399, Brattleboro, VT 05301; 1,111.

Automotive Booster Clubs (1921), 605 E. Algonquin Rd., Arlington Heights, IL 60005; 3,000.

Automotive Organization Team (1939), P.O. Box 1742, Midland, MI 48640; 2,700.

Aviation Historical Society, Amer. (1956), P.O. Box 99, Garden Grove, CA 92642; 3,625.

—B—

Backpackers' Assn., Internatl. (1973), P.O. Box 85, Lincoln Center, ME 04458; 4,531.

Badminton Assn., Amer. (1936), P.O. Box 237, Swartz Creek, MI 48473; 1,000.

Banker Assn., Internatl. (1968), 422 Washington Bldg., Wash., DC 20005; 1,500.

Bankers Assn., Amer. (1875), 1120 Connecticut Ave. NW, Wash., DC 20036; 13,700 banks.

Bankers Assn. of America, Independent (1930), 1168 S. Main St., Sauk Centre, MN 56378; 7,328 banks.

Bar Assn., Amer. (1878), 1155 E. 60th St., Chicago, IL 60637; 218,000.

Bar Assn., Federal (1920), 1815 H St. NW, Wash., DC 20006; 15,000.

Barber Shop Quartet Singing in America, Society for the Preservation & Encouragement of (1938), 6315 Third Ave., Kenosha, WI 53140; 38,000.

Baseball Congress, Amer. Amateur (1935), 212 Plaza Bldg., 2855 W. Market St., P.O. Box 5332, Akron, OH 44313.

Baseball Congress of America, Natl. (1930), 338 S. Sycamore, Wichita, KS 67213; 6,750.

Baseball Players of America, Assn. of Professional (1924), 530 E. Wardlow Rd., Long Beach, CA 90807; 8,000.

Basketball Assn., Natl. (1946), 2 Penn Plaza, N.Y., NY 10001; 22 teams.

Baton Twirling Assn. of America & Abroad, Intl. (1967), Box 234, Waldwick, NJ 07463; 1,800.

Battleship Assn., Amer. (1963), P.O. Box 11247, San Diego, CA 92111; 1,200.

Beta Sigma Phi (1931), 1800 W. 91st Pl., Kansas City, MO 64114; 241,570.

Bible Society, Amer. (1816), 1865 Broadway, N.Y., NY 10023; 450,000.

Biblical Literature, Society of (1880), Union Theological Seminary, 3401 Brook Rd., Richmond, VA 23227.

Bibliographical Society of America (1904), P.O. Box 397, Grand Central Sta., N.Y., NY 10017; 1,625.

Bicycle Manufacturers Assn. (1965), 1101 15th St. NW, Wash., DC 20005; 6.

Bide-A-Wee Home Assn. (1903), 410 E. 38th St., N.Y., NY 10016; 8,500.

Big Brothers of America (1946), 220 Suburban Station Bldg., Phila., PA 19103; 100,000.

Biological Chemists, Amer. Society of (1906), 9650 Rockville Pike, Bethesda, MD 20014; 4,100.

Biological Sciences, Amer. Institute of (1947), 1401 Wilson Blvd., Arlington, VA 22209; 10,500.

Blind, Amer. Foundation for the (1921), 15 W. 16th St., N.Y., NY 10011.

Blind, Natl. Federation of the (1940), 218 Randolph Hotel, Des Moines, IA 50309; 50,000.

Blind & Visually Handicapped, Natl. Accreditation Council for Agencies Serving the (1967), 79 Madison Ave., N.Y., NY 10016; 64 agencies and schools.

Blinded Veterans Assn. (1945), 1735 DeSales St. NW, Wash., DC 20036; 2,100.

Blindness, Natl. Society for Prevention of (1908), 79 Madison Ave., N.Y., NY 10016; 315.

Blindness, Research to Prevent (1960), 598 Madison Ave., N.Y., NY 10022; 1,870.

Blizzard Club, January 12th, 1888, (1940), c/o Historian, 4827 Hillside Ave., Lincoln, NE 68506; 100.

Blood Banks, Amer. Assn. of (1948), 1828 L St. NW, Wash., DC 20036; 5,183.

Blue Cross Assn. (1948), 840 N. Lake Shore Dr., Chicago, IL 60611; 74 plans.

Blue Shield Plans, Natl. Assn. of (1946), 211 E. Chicago Ave., Chicago, IL 60611; 70 plans.

Blueberry Council, No. Amer. (1965), 715 N. Shore Rd., Marmora, NJ 08223; 8,000.

B'nai B'rith (1843), 1640 Rhode Island Ave. NW, Wash., DC 20036; 500,000.

Boat Owners Assn. of the U.S. (1966), 5261 Port Royal Rd., Springfield, VA 22151; 33,000.

Book Manufacturers' Institute (1933), 904 Ethan Allen Hwy., Ridgefield, CT 06877; 100 companies.

Booksellers Assn., Amer. (1900), 800 Second Ave., N.Y., NY 10017; 4,200.

Botanical Gardens & Arboreta, Amer. Assn. of (1950), Dept. of Horticulture, P.O. Box 3530, New Mexico State Univ., Las Cruces, NM 88003; 850.

Botanical Society of America (1906), Dept. of Botany, Univ. of Texas, Austin, TX 78703; 4,000.

Bottle Clubs, Federation of Historical (1969), 5001 Queen Ave., No. Minneapolis, MN 55430; 130 clubs.

Bowling Congress, Amer. (1895), 5301 S. 76th St., Greendale, WI 53129; 4.3 million.

Bowling Congress, Women's Internatl. (1916), 5301 S. 76th St., Greendale, WI 53129; 3,695,073.

Boy Scouts of America (1910), North Brunswick, NJ 08902; 3,599,929 scouts, 1,284,153 leaders.

Boys' Brigades of America, United (1893), P.O. Box 8406, Baltimore, MD 21234.

Boys' Clubs of America (1906), 771 First Ave., N.Y., NY 10017; 1,086,000.

Brand Names Foundation (1943), 477 Madison Ave., N.Y., NY 10022; 500.

Brewers Assn., U.S. (1862), 1750 K St., Wash., DC 20006.

Brick Institute of America (1934), 1750 Old Meadow Rd., McLean, VA 22101; 100 companies.
Brith Sholom (1905), 1235 Chestnut St., Phila., PA 19107; 20,000.
Broadcasters, Natl. Assn. of (1922), 1771 N St. NW, Wash., DC 20036; 5,000.
Burroughs Bibliophiles, The (1960), 454 Elaine Dr., Pittsburgh, PA 15236; 480.
Business Bureaus, Council of Better (1970), 1150 17th St. NW, Wash., DC 20036; 650.
Business Clubs, Natl. Assn. of Amer. (1922), 3315 No. Main St., High Point, NC 27260; 5,000.
Business Communciation Assn., Amer. (1935), 317-B David Kinley Hall, Univ. of Illinois, Urbana, IL 61801; 1,200.
Business Education Assn., Natl. (1892), 1906 Association Dr., Reston, VA 22091; 21,500.
Business Law Assn., Amer. (1924), Georgia State Univ., University Plaza, Atlanta, GA 30303; 800.
Business Press Editors, Amer. Society of (1964), 2735 Central St., Evanston, IL 60201; 300.
Business Professional Advertising Assn. (1922), 205 E. 42d St., N.Y., NY 10017; 3,000.
Button Society, Natl. (1938), 353 Stockton St., Hightstown, NJ 08520; 2,125
Byron Society, The (1971 England, 1973 in U.S.), 205 West End Ave., Apt. 1B, N.Y., NY 10023; 225.

—C—

CARE (Cooperative For American Relief Everywhere) (1945), 660 First Ave., N.Y., NY 10016; 25 agencies.
CCCO/An Agency for Military and Draft Counseling (1948), 2016 Walnut St., Phila., PA 19103; 12,000.
Cable Television Assn., Natl. (1952), 918 16th St. NW, Wash., DC 20006; 1,350.
Camp Fire Girls (1910), 4601 Madison Ave., Kansas City, MO 64112; 500,000.
Campers & Hikers Assn., Natl. (1954), 7172 Transit Rd., Buffalo, NY 14221; 52,000 families.
Camping Assn., Amer. (1910), Bradford Woods, Martinsville, IN 46151; 6,500.
Cancer Council, United (1963), 1803 N. Meridian St., Indianapolis, IN 46202; serves 30,000,000 people.
Cancer Society, Amer. (1913), 777 Third Ave., N.Y., NY 10017.
Candy Brokers Assn. of America (1956), P.O. Box 28325, Wash., DC 20005; 300.
Canners Assn., Natl. (1907), 1133 20th St. NW, Wash., DC 20036; 600 companies.
Captive European Nations, Assembly of (1954), 29 W. 57th St., N.Y., NY 10019; 9 national committees.
Carillonneurs in North America, Guild of ((1936), 3718 Settle Rd., Cincinnati, OH 45227; 345.),
Carnegie Hero Fund Commission (1904), 1932 Oliver Bldg., Pittsburgh, PA 15222.
Cartoonists Society, Natl. (1946), 9 Ebony Ct., Brooklyn, NY 11229; 450.
Cat Fanciers' Assn. (1919), P.O. Box 430, 11 Globe Ct., Red Bank, NJ 07701; 550 clubs.
Catch Society of America, The (1968), Dept. of English, SUNY—Fredonia; Fredonia, NY 14063; 300.
Catholic Bishops, Natl. Conference of/U.S. Catholic Conference (1966), 1312 Massachusetts Ave. NW, Wash., DC 20015; 300.
Catholic Charities, Natl. Conference of (1910), 1346 Connecticut Ave. NW, Wash., DC 20036; 3,000.
Catholic Church Extension Society of the U.S.A. (1905), 1307 S. Wabash Ave., Chicago, IL 60605; 70,000.
Catholic Daughters of America (1903), 10 W. 71st St., N.Y., NY 10023; 180,000.
Catholic Educational Assn., Natl. (1904), One Dupont Circle NW, Wash., DC 20036; 14,000.
Catholic Press Assn. (1911), 119 N. Park Ave., Rockville Centre, NY 11570; 400.
Catholic Rural Life Conference, Natl. (1923), 3801 Grand Ave., Des Moines, IA 50312; 4,000.
Catholic War Veterans of the U.S.A. (1935), 2 Massachusetts Ave. NW, Wash., DC 20001; 75,000.
Cemetery Assn., Amer. (1887), 250 E. Broad St., Columbus, OH 43215; 1,100.
Ceramic Society, Amer. (1899), 65 Ceramic Dr., Columbus, OH 43214; 6,800.
Cerebral Palsy Assns., United (1949), 66 E. 34th St., N.Y., NY 10016; 276 affiliates.
Chamber of Commerce of the U.S.A. (1912), 1615 H St. NW, Wash., DC 20062; 67,127.
Chamber Music Players, Amateur (1948), P.O. Box 547, Vienna, VA 22180; 5,000.
Chartered Life Underwritesr, Amer. Society of (1928), 270 Bryn Mawr Ave., Bryn Mawr, PA 19010; 20,100.
Chartered Property & Casualty Underwriters, Society of (1944), Providence & Sugartown Rds., Malvern, PA 19355; 8,800.
Checks Anonymous, New Life Group of (1963), Nebraska Penal and Correctional Complex, 14th and Pioneers Bldg., P.O. Box 81248, Lincoln, NE 68501; 50.
Chemical Engineers, Amer. Institute of (1908), 345 E. 47th St., N.Y., NY 10017; 39,000.
Chemical Society, Amer. (1876), 1155 16th St. NW, Wash., DC 20036; 112,730.
Chemists, Amer. Institute of (1923), 7315 Wisconsin Ave., Wash., DC 20014; 5,400.
Chemists and Chemical Engineers, Assn. of Consulting (1928), 50 E. 41st St., N.Y., NY 10017; 120.
Chess Federation, U.S.A. (1939), 186 Rte. 9W, New Windsor, NY 12550; 50,000.
Chief Warrant and Warrant Officers' Assn., USCG (1929), 955 L'Enfant Plaza No. SW, Wash., DC 20024; 3,092.
Child Study Assn. of America/Wel-Met (1888), 50 Madison Ave., N.Y., NY 10010; 300.
Child Welfare League of America (1920), 67 Irving Pl., N.Y., NY 10003; 387 agencies.
Childbirth Without Pain League (1964), P.O. Box 233, Dana Point, CA 92629; 200.
Children of the Amer. Revolution, Natl. Society (1895), 1776 D St. NW, Wash., DC 20006; 12,500.
Children's Aid Society (1853), 105 E. 22d St., N.Y., NY 10010.
Children's Book Council (1945), 67 Irving Pl., N.Y., NY 10003; 59 publishing houses.
Chinese Women's Assn. (1932), 13541 Emperor Dr., Santa Ana, CA 92705; 520.
Chiropractic Assn., Amer. (1964), 2200 Grand Ave., Des Moines, IA 50312; 12,141.
Chiropractors Assn., Internatl. (1926), 741 Brady St., Davenport, IA 52808; 6,100.
Christian Culture Society (1974), P.O. Box 325, Kokomo, IN 46901; 12,695.
Christian Laity Counseling Board (1970), 5901 Plainfield Dr., Charlotte, NC 28215; 5,001,000.
Christians and Jews, Natl. Conference of (1928), 43 W. 57th St., N.Y., NY 10019; 200,000.
Cincinnati, Society of the (1783), 2118 Massachusetts Ave. NW, Wash., DC 20008; 2,750.
Circulation Managers Assn., Internatl. (1889), 11600 Sunrise Valley Dr., Reston, VA 22070; 1,325.
Circulations, Audit Bureau of (1914), 123 N. Wacker Dr., Chicago, IL 60606; 3,965.
Circus Fans Assn. of America (1926), P.O. Box 69, 4 Center Dr., Camp Hill, PA 17011; 2,500.
Circus Historical Society (1939), 1325 Commercial St., Atchison, KS 66002; 1,300.
Cities, Natl. League of (1924), 1620 Eye St. NW, Wash., DC 20006; 15,000 municipalities.
City Management Assn., Internatl. (1914), 1140 Connecticut Ave. NW, Wash., DC 20036; 7,343.
Civil Engineers, Amer. Society of (1852), 345 E. 47th St., N.Y., NY 10017; 74,000.
Civil Liberties Union, Amer. (1920), 22 E. 40th St., N.Y., NY 10016; 275,000.
Civil Service League, Natl. (1881), 917 15th St. NW, Wash., DC 20005; 1,100.
Civitan Internatl. (1920), P.O. Box 2102, Birmingham, AL 35201; 50,000.
Classical League, Amer. (1919), Miami Univ., Oxford, OH 45056; 2,900.
Clinical Pastoral Education, Assn. for (1967), 475 Riverside Dr., N.Y., NY 10027; 4,000.
Clinical Pathologists, Amer. Society of (1922), 2100 W. Harrison St., Chicago, IL 60612; 20,395.
Clowns of America (1968), 2715 E. Fayette St., Baltimore, MD 21224; 5,200.
Coal Assn., Natl. (1917), 1130 17th St. NW, Wash., DC 20036; 200 companies.
Cocoa Exchange, New York (1925), 127 John St., N.Y., NY 10038; 183.
Collectors Assn., Amer. (1939), 4040 W. 70th St., Minneapolis, MN 55435; 2,600.
College Entrance Examination Board (1900), 888 Seventh Ave., N.Y., NY 10019; 2,412 institutions.
College Physical Education Assn. for Men, Natl. (1897), 108 Cooke Hall, Univ. of Minnesota, Minneapolis, MN 55455; 1,200.
College Placement Council (1956), 65 E. Elizabeth Ave., Bethlehem, PA 18018; 1,700.
Colleges, Assn. of Amer. (1915), 1818 R St. NW, Wash., DC 20009; 600 institutions.

Collegiate Athletic Assn., Natl. (1906), P.O. Box 1906, Shawnee Mission, KS 66222; 831.

Collegiate Schools of Business, Amer. Assembly of (1916), 760 Office Parkway, St. Louis, MO 63141; 650 schools.

Colonial Dames of America (1890), 421 E. 61 St., N.Y., NY 10021; 2,000.

Colonial Dames XVII Century, Natl. Society (1915), 1300 New Hampshire Ave. NW, Wash., DC 20036; 9,000.

Colonial Wars, General Society of (1892), 840 Woodbine Ave., Glendale, OH 45246; 4,200.

Colored Women's Clubs, Natl. Assn. of (1896), 5808 16th St. NW, Wash., DC 20011; 50,000.

Commercial Law League of America (1895), 222 W. Adams St., Chicago, IL 60606; 6,200.

Commercial Travelers of America, Order of United (1888), 632 N. Park St., Columbus, OH 43215, 244,000.

Common Cause (1970), 2030 M St. NW, Wash., DC 20036; 253,000.

Composers/USA, Natl. Assn. of (1975), P.O. Box 49652, Barrington Sta., Los Angeles, CA 90049; 450.

Composers, Authors & Publishers, Amer. Society of (ASCAP) (1914), One Lincoln Plaza, N.Y., NY 10023; 20,000.

Computing Machinery, Assn. for (1947), 1133 Ave. of the Americas, N.Y., NY 10036; 31,000.

Concrete Institute, Amer. (1905), 22400 W. Seven Mile Rd., Detroit, MI 48219; 15,000.

Conference Board, The (1916), 845 Third Ave., N.Y., NY 10022; 4,000.

Conservation Engineers, Assn. of (1961), Missouri Dept. of Conservation, P.O. Box 180, Jefferson City, MO 65101; 161.

Conservation Foundation (1948), 1717 Massachusetts Ave. NW, Wash., DC 20036.

Construction Industry Manufacturers Assn. (1922), 111 E. Wisconsin Ave., Milwaukee, WI 53202; 200 companies.

Construction Specifications Institute (1948), 1150 17th St. NW, Wash., DC 20036; 10,700.

Consumer Credit Assn., Internatl. (1912), 375 Jackson Ave., St. Louis, MO 63130; 45,025.

Consumer Federation of America (1968), 1012 14th St. NW, Wash., DC 20005; 225 organizations.

Consumer Interests, Amer. Council on (1953), 162 Stanley Hall, Univ. of Missouri, Columbia, MO 65201; 3,240.

Consumer Protection Council, Natl. Student (1971), Villanova Univ., Bartley Hall, Villanova, PA 19085; 500.

Consumers League, Natl (1899), 1785 Massachusetts Ave. NW, Wash., DC 20036; 20,000.

Consumers Union of the U.S. (1936), 256 Washington St., Mount Vernon, NY 10550; 1.8 million.

Consumers Unions, Internatl. Organization of (1960), 9 Emmastraat, The Hague, Netherlands; 102 organizations.

Contract Bridge League, Amer. (1937), 2200 Democrat Rd., Memphis, TN 38116; 198,000.

Cooperative League of the U.S.A. (1916), 1828 L St. NW, Wash., DC 20036; 140 co-ops.

Correctional Assn., Amer. (1870), 4321 Hartwick Rd., Suite L-208, College Park, MD 20740; 11,000.

Cosmopolitan Internatl. (1933), 7341 W. 80th St., Overland Park, KS 68204; 3,700.

Cotton Council of America, Natl. (1938), 1918 North Parkway, Memphis, TN 38112; 289.

Country Music Assn. (1958), 7 Music Circle No., Nashville, TN 37203; 4,579.

Credit Management, Nat. Assn. of (1896), 475 Park Ave. So., N.Y., NY 10016; 40,000.

Credit Union Natl. Assn. (1934), 1617 Sherman Ave., Madison, WI 53701; 51 state leagues.

Crime and Delinquency, Natl. Council on (1907), 411 Hackensack Ave., Hackensack, NJ 07601; 60,000.

Criminology, Amer. Assn. of (1953), P.O. Box 1115, North Marshfield, MA 02059; 2,500.

Crop Science Society of America (1955), 677 S. Segoe Rd., Madison, WI 53711; 4,035.

Cryptogram Assn., Amer. (1932), 9504 Forest Rd., Bethesda, MD 20014; 1,000.

Cyprus, Sovereign Order of (1192, 1964 in U.S.), 853 Seventh Ave., N.Y., NY 10019; 421.

—D—

Dairy Council, Natl. (1915), 6300 No. River Rd., Rosemont, IL 60018; 700.

Dairy and Food Industries Supply Assn. (1919), 5530 Wisconsin Ave., Wash., DC 20015; 400 organizations.

Dairy Goat Assn., Amer. (1904), 209 W. Main St., Spindale, NC 28160; 9,000.

Dairy Science Assn., Amer. (1906), 113 N. Neil St., Champaign, IL 61820; 2,761.

Dairylea Cooperative (1919), One Blue Hill Plaza, Pearl River, NY 10965; 6,900.

Data Processing Management Assn. (1951), 505 Busse Highway, Park Ridge, IL 60068; 22,185.

Daughters of the American Revolution, Natl. Society, (1890), 1776 D St.NW, Wash., DC 20006; 204,000.

Daughters of the Confederacy, United (1894), 328 North Blvd., Richmond, VA 23220; 35,000.

Daughters of 1812, Natl. Society, U.S. (1892), 1461 Rhode Island Ave. NW, Wash., DC 20005; 4,350.

Daughters of Union Veterans of the Civil War (1885), 503 S. Walnut St., Springfield, IL 62704; 15,000.

Deaf, Alexander Graham Bell Assn. for the (1890), 3417 Volta Pl. NW, Wash., DC 20007; 7,000.

Deaf, Conference of Executives of Amer. Schools for the (1868), 5034 Wisconsin Ave. NW, Wash., DC 20016; 300.

Deaf, Convention of Amer. Instructors of the (1850), 5034 Wisconsin Ave. NW, Wash., DC 20016; 3,500.

Deaf, Natl. Assn. of the (1880), 814 Thayer Ave., Silver Spring, MD 20910; 17,000.

Defense Preparedness Assn., Amer. (1919), 740 15th St. NW, Wash., DC 20005; 27,336.

Delta Kappa Gamma Society Internatl. (1929), 416 W. 12th St., Austin, TX 78701; 140,000.

Deltiologists of America (1960), 3709 Gradyville Rd., Newton Square, PA 19073; 1,850.

DeMoley, Order of (1919), 201 E. Armour Blvd., Kansas City, MO 64111; 2,800,000.

Dental Assn., Amer. (1859), 211 E. Chicago Ave., Chicago, IL 60611; 127,000.

Dental Assn., Natl. (1913), P.O. Box 197, Charlottesville, VA 22902; 1,500.

Descendants of the Colonial Clergy, Society of the (1933), 255 Madison St., Dedham, MA 02026; 1,100.

Descendants of the Signers of the Declaration of Independence (1907), 1300 Locust St., Phila., PA 19107; 1,050.

Desert Protective Council (1954), Box 4294, Palm Springs, CA 92262; 450.

Diabetes Assn., Amer. (1940), 600 Fifth Ave., N.Y., NY 10020; 3,000.

Dialect Society, Amer. (1889), c/o Dept. of English, Univ. of Western Ontario, London, Ontario N6A 3K7; 800.

Dietetic Assn., Amer. (1917), 430 N. Michigan Ave., Chicago, IL 60611; 31,000.

Ding-A-Ling Club, Natl. (1971), P.O. Box 28, Melrose Park, IL 60161; 2,000.

Direct Mail/Marketing Assn. (1917), 6 E. 43d St., N.Y., NY 10017; 2,900 companies.

Directors Guild of America (1936), 7950 Sunset Blvd., Los Angeles, CA 90046; 4,737.

Disabled Amer. Veterans (1921), 3725 Alexandria Pike, Cold Spring, KY 41076; 550,000.

Disabled Officers Assn. (1919), 1612 K St. NW, Wash., DC 20006; 5,500.

Divorce Reform, U.S. (1961), P.O. Box 243, Kenwood, CA 95452; 6,000.

Dowsers, Amer. Society of (1961), Danville, VT 05328.

Dracula Society, Count (1962), 334 W. 54th St., Los Angeles, CA 90037; 500.

Drug, Chemical and Allied Trades Assn. (1890), 42-40 Bell Blvd., Suite 204, Bayside, NY 11361; 500 companies.

Drum Corps Internatl. (1971), 53 E. Charles Rd., Villa Park, IL 60181.

Ducks Unlimited (1937), P.O. Box 66300, Chicago, IL 60666; 225,000.

Dulcimer Assn., Southern Appalachian (1974), Indian Springs School, Helena, AL 35080; 105.

Duodecimal Society of America (1944), 4728 Cielo Dr., Huntington Beach, CA 92649; 120.

Dutch Setters Soc. of Albany (1924), 1088 Cortland St., Albany, NY 12203; 325.

—E—

Eagles, Fraternal Order of (1898), 2401 W. Wisconsin Ave., Milwaukee, WI 53233; 850,000.

Earth, Friends of the (1969), 124 Spear St., San Francisco, CA 94105; 20,000.

Easter Seal Society for Crippled Children and Adults, Natl. (1919), 2023 W. Ogden Ave., Chicago, IL 60612.

Eastern Star, Order of the (1876), 1618 New Hampshire Ave. NW, Wash. DC 20009; 2,500,000.

Ecological Society of America (1915), c/o Dr. E. J. Kormondy, Evergreen State College, Olympia, WA 98505; 5,700.

Economic Assn., Amer. (1885), 1313 21st Ave. So., Nashville, TN 37212; 23,600.

Economic Development, Committee for (1942), 477 Madison Ave., N.Y., NY 10022; 200.

Edison Electric Institute (1933), 90 Park Ave., N.Y., NY 10016.

Education, Amer. Council on (1918), One Dupont Circle NW, Wash., DC 20036; 1,500 schools.
Education, Council for Advancement & Support of (1974), One Dupont Circle NW, Wash., DC 20036; 1,800 schools.
Education, Council for Basic (1956), 725 15th St. NW, Wash., DC 20005; 5,100.
Education, Natl. Society for the Study of (1902), 5835 Kimbark Ave., Chicago, IL 60637; 4,500.
Education, Society for the Advancement of (1939), 1860 Broadway, N.Y., NY 10023; 3,000.
Education Assn., Natl. (1857), 1201 16th St. NW, Wash., DC 20036; 1,700,000.
Education Society, Comparative and Internatl. (1956), Grad. School of Education, Univ. of California at Los Angeles, Los Angeles, CA 90024; 2,450.
Education of Young Children, Natl. Assn. for the (1926), 1834 Connecticut Ave. NW, Wash., DC 20009; 28,000.
Education Broadcasters, Natl. Assn. of (1925), 1346 Connecticut Ave. NW, Wash., DC 20036; 3,500.
Educational Research Assn., Amer. (1915), 1126 16th St. NW, Wash., DC 20036; 13,000.
Educators for World Peace, Internatl. Assn. of (1969), P.O. Box 3282, Blue Springs Sta., Huntsville, AL 35810; 12,500.
Electric Railroaders Assn. (1934), 4 W. 40th St., N.Y., NY 10018; 4,500.
Electrical and Electronics Engineers, Institute of (1884), 345 E. 47th St., N.Y., NY 10017; 175,000.
Electrical Manufacturers Assn., Natl. (1926), 2101 L St. NW, Wash., DC 20024; 550 companies.
Electrochemical Society (1902), P.O. Box 2071, Princeton, NJ 08540; 4,500.
Electronic Industries Assn. (1924), 2001 Eye St. NW, Wash., DC 20006; 280 firms.
Electronics Technicians, Internatl. Society of Certified (1970), 1715 Expo Lane, Indianapolis, IN 46224; 1,300.
Electroplaters' Society, Amer. (1909), 1201 Louisiana Ave., Winter Park, FL 32789; 8,000.
Elks of the U.S.A., Benevolent and Protective Order of (1868), 2750 N. Lake View Ave., Chicago, IL 60614; 1,611,139.
Engine and Boat Manufacturers, Natl. Assn. of (1904), 666 Third Ave., N.Y., NY 10017; 330 firms.
Engineering, Natl. Academy of (1964), 2101 Constitution Ave. NW, Wash., DC 20418; 685.
Engineering Education, Amer. Society for (1893), One Dupont Circle, Wash., DC 20036; 12,000.
Engineering Technicians, Amer. Society of Certified (1964), 2029 K St. NW, Wash., DC 20006; 7,300.
Engineering Trustees, United (1904), 345 E. 47th St., N.Y., NY 10017.
Engineers, Natl. Society of Professional (1934), 2029 K St. NW, Wash., DC 20006; 72,000.
Engineers Joint Council (1949), 345 E. 47th St., N.Y., NY 10017; 500,000.
English Assn., College (1939), English Dept., Oakland Univ., Rochester, MI 48063; 3,000.
English-Speaking Union (1920), 16 E. 69th St., N.Y., NY 10021; 32,500.
Entomological Society of America (1889), 4603 Calvert Rd., College Park, MD 20740; 7,400.
Environmental Defense Fund (1967), 475 Park Ave. So., N.Y., NY 10016; 45,000.
Epilepsy Foundation of America (1968), 1828 L St. NW, Wash., DC 20036; 161 chapters.
Epsilon Pi Tau (1929), Technology Bldg., Bowling Green State Univ., Bowling Green, OH 43403; 25,000.
Esperanto Assn., Internatl. Catholic (1910), Limbiate, Italy; U.S. rep., 7605 Winona Ln., Sebastopol, CA 95472; 1,600.
Esperanto League for North America (1952), P.O. Box 508, Burlingame, CA 94010; 750.
Evangelicals, Natl. Assn. of (1942), 350 S. Main Pl., Wheaton, IL 60187; 3,500,000.
Evangelism Crusades, Internatl. (1969), 7970 Woodman Ave., Van Nuys, CA 91402; 125,000.
Exchange Club, Natl. (1917), 3050 Central Ave., Toledo, OH 43606; 50,000.
Experiment in Internatl. Living (1932), Kipling Rd., Brattleboro, VT 05301; 60,000.
Eye-Bank Assn. of America (1961), 3195 Maplewood Ave., Winston-Salem, NC 27103; 64.
Eye-Bank for Sight Restoration (1945), 3195 Maplewood Ave., Winston-Salem, NC 27103.

—F—

Fairs & Expositions, Internatl. Assn. of (1919), 1010 Dixie Hwy., Chicago Heights, IL 60411; 463.
Family Physicians, Amer. Academy of (1947), 1740 W. 92d St., Kansas City, MO 64114; 37,000.
Family Service Assn. of America (1911), 44 E. 23d St., N.Y., NY 10010; 300 agencies.
Farm Bureau Federation, Amer. (1919), 225 Touhy Ave., Park Ridge, IL 60068; 2,676,259 families.
Farmer Cooperatives, Natl. Council of (1929), 1129 20th St. NW, Wash., DC 20036; 152 co-ops.
Farmers of America, Future (1928), 5630 Mt. Vernon Hwy., Alexandria, VA 22309; 500,385.
Farmers Educational and Co-Operative Union of America (1902), 12025 E. 45th Ave., Denver, CO 80201; 250,000 families.
Federal Employees, Natl. Federation of (1917), 1016 16th St. NW, Wash., DC 20036; 85,000.
Federal Employees Veterans Assn. (1954), P.O. Box 183, Merion Sta., PA 19066; 1,242.
Federally Employed Women (1968), 1249 Natl. Press Bldg., Wash., DC 20045; 6,000.
Feline Society, Amer. (1938), 41 Union Sq. W., N.Y., NY 10003; 425.
Feminists for Life (1972), P.O.Box 12726, Tucson, AZ 85732.
Fencers League of America, Amateur (1891), 601 Curtis St., Albany, CA 94706; 6,000.
Fiddlers Assn., Amer. Old Time (1965), 6141 Morrill Ave., Lincoln, NE 68507; 5,000.
Film Library Assn., Educational (1943), 17 W. 60 St., N.Y., NY 10023; 1,800.
Financial Analysts Federation (1947), 219 E. 42d St., N.Y., NY 10017; 14,700.
Financial Executives Institute (1931), 633 Third Ave., N.Y., NY 10017; 9,600.
Fire Chiefs, Internatl. Assn. of (1873), 1329 18th St. NW, Wash., DC 20036; 7,332.
Fire Fighters, Internatl. Assn. of (1918), 1750 New York Ave. NW, Wash., DC 20006; 175,000.
Fire Marshals Assn. of No. America (1906), 470 Atlantic Ave., Boston, MA 02210; 1,095.
Fire Protection Assn., Natl. (1896), 470 Atlantic Ave., Boston MA 02210; 32,000.
Fire Protection Engineers, Society of (1950), 60 Batterymarch St., Boston, MA 02110; 2,353.
Fisheries Society, Amer. (1870), 5410 Grosvenor Ln., Bethesda, MD 20014; 7,088.
Fishing Institute, Sport (1949), 608 13th St. NW, Wash., DC 20005; 24,500.
Fishing Tackle Manufacturers Assn., Amer. (1933), 20 No. Wacker Dr., Chicago, IL 60606; 400 companies.
Flag Day Assn., Amer. (1888), P.O. Box 1121, Denver, CO 80201.
Florists, Society of Amer. (1884), 901 N. Washington St., Alexandria, VA 22314; 6,100.
Fluid Power Society (1957), 432 E. Kilbourn Ave., Milwaukee, WI 53202; 3,500.
Folklore Society, Amer. (1888), Center for Folklore & Ethnomusicology — SWB 306, Univ. of Texas, Austin, TX 78712; 2,800.
Food Processing Machinery and Supplies Assn. (1885), 7758 Wisconsin Ave., Wash., DC 20014; 405.
Footwear Industries Assn., Amer. (1869), 1611 N. Kent St., Arlington, VA 22209; 400.
Foreign Policy Assn. (1918), 345 E. 46th St., N.Y., NY 10017.
Foreign Press Assn. (1918), 866 Second Ave., N.Y., NY 10017; 350.
Foreign Relations, Council on (1921), 58 E. 68th St., N.Y., NY 10021; 1,701.
Foreign Student Affairs, Natl. Assn. for (1948), 1860 19th St. NW, Wash., DC 20009; 2,500.
Foreign Study, Amer. Institute for (1964), 102 Greenwich Ave., Greenwich, CT 06830; 110,000.
Foreign Trade Council, Natl. (1914), 10 Rockefeller Center, N.Y., NY 10020; 600 companies.
Forensic Sciences, Amer. Academy of (1948), 11400 Rockville Pike, Rockville, MD 20852; 1,875.
Forest Institute, Amer. (1941), 1619 Massachusetts Ave. NW, Wash., DC 20036; 200 cos., 33,000 farmers.
Forest Products Assn., Natl. (1902), 1619 Massachusetts Ave. NW, Wash., DC 22036; 27.
Forest Products Research Society (1947), 2801 Marshall Ct., Madison, WI 53705; 4,500.
Foresters, Society of Amer. (1900), 5400 Grosvenor Ln., Wash., DC 20014; 21,326.
Forestry Assn., Amer. (1875), 1319 18th St. NW, Wash., DC 20036; 80,000.
Fortean Organization, Internatl. (1965), 7317 Baltimore Ave., College Park, MD 20740; 620.
Foundrymen's Society, Amer. (1896), Golf & Wolf Rds., Des Plaines, IL 60016; 16,000.
4-H Clubs (1901-05), Extension Service, U.S. Dept of Agriculture, Wash., DC 20250; 5.8 million.
Franklin D. Roosevelt Philatelic Society (1963), P.O. Box 150, Clinton Corners, NY 12514; 282.
French Institute (1911), 22 E. 60th St., N.Y., NY 10022;

24,000.

French Legion of Honor, Amer. Society of the (1922), 22 E. 60th St., N.Y., NY 10022; 440.

Friends Service Committee, Amer. (1917), 1501 Cherry St., Phila., PA 19102; 12,000.

Frisbee Assn., Internatl. (1967), P.O. Box 664, Alhambra, CA 91802; 82,000.

—G—

Gamblers Anonymous (1957), P.O. Box 17173, Los Angeles, CA 90017; 5,000.

Game Fish Assn., Internatl. (1939), 3000 E. Las Olas Blvd., Ft. Lauderdale, FL 33316; 10,000.

Garden Club of America (1913), 598 Madison Ave., N.Y., NY 10022; 13,000.

Garden Clubs of America, Men's (1932), 5560 Merle Hay Rd., Des Moines, IA 50323; 10,000.

Garden Clubs, Natl. Council of State (1929), 4401 Magnolia Ave., St. Louis, MO 63110; 432,876.

Gas Appliance Manufacturers Assn. (1935), 1901 N. Ft. Myer Dr., Arlington, VA 22209; 275 companies.

Gas Assn., Amer. (1918), 1515 Wilson Blvd., Arlington, VA 22209; 5,000.

Gay Task Force, Natl. (1973), 80 Fifth Ave., N.Y., NY 10011; 5,500.

Genealogical Society, Natl. (1903), 1921 Sunderland Pl. NW, Wash., DC 20036; 3,000.

General Contractors of America, Associated (1918), 1957 E St. NW, Wash., DC 20006; 8,300.

Genetic Assn., Amer. (1903), 1028 Connecticut Ave. NW, Wash., DC 20036; 1,483.

Geographers, Assn. of Amer. (1904), 1710 16th St. NW, Wash., DC 20009; 6,000.

Geographic Education, Natl. Council for (1914), 115 N. Marion St., Oak Park, IL 60301; 5,000.

Geographic Society, Natl. (1888), 1145 17th St. NW, Wash., DC 20036, 9,700,000.

Geographical Society, Amer. (1852), Broadway at 156th St., N.Y., NY 10032; 2,500.

Geolinguistics, Amer. Society of (1965), Bronx Community College, 120 E. 184th St., Bronx, NY 10453; 75.

Geological Institute, Amer. (1948), 5205 Leesburg Pike, Falls Church, VA 22041; 18 societies.

Geological Society of America (1888), 3300 Penrose Pl. Boulder, CO 80302; 12,569.

Geologists, Assn. of Engineering (1957), 8310 San Fernando Way, Dallas, TX 75218; 2,567.

Geophysical Union, Amer. (1919), 1909 K St. NW, Wash., DC 20036; 11,000.

Geophysicists, Society of Exploration (1930), 3707 E. 51st St., Tulsa, OK 74135; 8,173.

Geriatrics Society, Amer. (1942), 10 Columbus Circle, N.Y., NY 10019; 7,000.

Gideons Internatl. (1899), 2900 Lebanon Rd., Nashville, TN 37214; 55,463.

Gifted Children, Amer. Assn. for (1946), 15 Gramercy Park, N.Y., NY 10003.

Gifted Children, Natl. Assn. for (1954), 217 Gregory Dr., Hot Springs, AR 71901; 2,500.

Girl Scouts of the U.S.A. (1912), 830 Third Ave., N.Y., NY 10022; 3,160,000.

Girls Clubs of America (1945), 133 E. 62d St., N.Y., NY 10021; 200,000.

Gladiolus Council, No. Amer. (1945), 6425 Adams St., Lincoln, NE 68507; 2,000.

Gold Star Mothers, Amer. (1928), 2128 Leroy Pl. NW, Wash., DC 20008; 15,000.

Golf Association, U.S. (1894), Golf House, Far Hills, NJ 07931; 4,750.

Golf Assn., Natl. Amputee (1949), 24 Lakeview Terr., Watchung, NJ 07060; 500.

Goose Island Bird & Girl Watching Society (1960), 301 Arthur Ave., Park Ridge, IL 60068; 891.

Gospel Music Assn. (1964), 38 Music Sq. W., P.O. Box 23201, Nashville, TN 37203; 2,000.

Governmental Research Assn. (1938), P.O. Box 387, Ocean Gate, NJ 08740; 425.

Graduate Schools in the U.S., Council of (1961), One Dupont Circle NW, Wash., DC 20036; 358 institutions.

Grandmother Clubs of America, Natl. Federation of (1938), 203 N. Wabash Ave., Chicago, IL 60601; 13,831.

Grange, Natl. (1867), 1616 H St. NW, Wash., DC 20006; 500,000.

Graphic Artists, Society of Amer. (1915), 1083 Fifth Ave., N.Y., NY 10028; 200.

Graphic Arts, Amer. Insitute of (1914), 1059 Third Ave., N.Y., NY 10021; 1,750.

Grocery Manufacturers of America (1906), 1425 K St. NW, Wash., DC 20005; 150 firms.

Guide Dog Foundation for the Blind (1946), 109-19 72d Ave., Forest Hills, NY 11375; 25,000.

Gyro Internatl. (1912), P.O. Box 489, Painesville, OH 44077; 5,600.

—H—

Hadassah, the Women's Zionist Organization of America (1912), 50 W. 58th St., N.Y., NY 10019; 350,000.

Handball Assn., U.S. (1951), 4101 Dempster St., Skokie, Il 60076; 15,000.

Handicapped, Federation of the (1935), 211 W. 14th St., N.Y., NY 10011; 1,000.

Handicapped, Natl. Assn. of the Physically (1958), 6473 Granville, Detroit, MI 48228; 1,300.

Hang Gliding Assn., U.S. (1971), P.O. Box 66306, 11312½ Venice Blvd., Los Angeles, CA 90066; 16,350.

Health Council, Natl. (1920), 1740 Broadway, N.Y., NY 10019; 83 agencies.

Health Insurance Assn. of America (1956), 1750 K St. NW, Wash., DC 20006; 320 companies.

Health Insurance Institute (1956), 1850 K St. NW, Wash., DC; 325 companies.

Health, Physical Education & Recreation, Amer. Alliance for (1885), 1201 16th St. NW, Wash., DC 20036; 45,000.

Hearing Aid Society, Natl. (1951), 20361 Middlebelt Rd., Livonia, MI 48152; 3,600.

Hearing and Speech Action, Natl. Assn. for (1919), 814 Thayer Ave., Silver Spring, MD 20910; 12,000.

Heart Assn., Amer. (1924), 7320 Greenville Ave., Dallas TX 75231; 115,000.

Heating, Refrigerating & Air Conditioning Engineers, Amer. Society of (1894), 345 E. 47th St., N.Y., NY 10017; 32,000.

Helicopter Assn. of America (1948), 1156 15th St. NW, Wash., DC 20005; 576 companies.

Helicopter Society, Amer. (1943), 1325 18th St. NW, Wash., DC 20036; 3,200.

HIAS (Hebrew Immigrant Aid Society) (1884), 200 Park Ave. So., N.Y., NY 10003; 15,000.

High Twelve Internatl. (1921), 3681 Lindell Blvd., St. Louis, MO 63108; 20,000.

Historians, Organization of Amer. (1907), 112 N. Bryan St., Bloomington, IN 47401; 11,832.

Historians, The Society of Amer. (1939), 610 Fayerweather Hall, Columbia Univ., N.Y., NY 10027; 200.

Historic Preservation, Natl. Trust for (1949), 740-748 Jackson Pl. NW, Wash., DC 20006; 116,000.

Historical Assn., Amer. (1884), 400 A St. SE, Wash., DC 20003; 15,000.

Hockey Assn. of the U.S., Amateur (1937), 10 Lake Circle, Colorado Springs, CO 80906; 11,000 teams.

Hockey League, Natl. (1917), 920 Sun Life Bldg., Montreal, Quebec, Canada H3B 2W2; 18 clubs.

Holiday Institute of Yonkers (1969), 82 Borcher Ave., Yonkers, NY 10704; 32.

Holy Cross of Jerusalem, Order of (1965), 853 Seventh Ave., N.Y., NY 10019; 1,062.

Home Builders, Natl. Assn. of (1942), 15th & M Sts. NW Wash., DC 20005; 85,000 firms.

Home Economics Assn., Amer. (1909), 2010 Massachusetts Ave. NW, Wash., DC 20036; 60,000.

Home Improvement Council, Natl. (1956), 11 E. 44th St. N.Y., NY 10017; 1,750.

Homemakers of America, Future (1945), 2010 Massachusetts Ave. NW, Wash., DC 20036; 450,000.

Homemakers Council, Natl. Extension (1936), Rt. 7, Box 516, Kinston, NC 28501; 566,368.

Horatio Alger Society (1961), 4907 Allison Dr., Lansing, MI 48910; 200.

Horse Show Assn. of America Ltd., Natl. (1883), 527 Madison Ave., N.Y., NY 10022.

Horse Shows Assn., Amer. (1917), 598 Madison Ave., N.Y. NY 10022; 20,000.

Hospital Assn., Amer. (1898), 840 N. Lake Shore Dr. Chicago, IL 60611; 20,000.

Hospital Public Relations, Amer. Society for (1965), 840 N Lake Shore Dr., Chicago, IL 60611; 1,069.

Hot Rod Assn., Natl. (1951), 10639 Riverside Dr., N. Hollywood, CA 91602; 38,000.

Hotel & Motel Assn., Amer. (1910), 888 Seventh Ave., N.Y. NY 10019; 6,500 hotels & motels.

Humane Legislation, Committee for (1967), 910 16th St NW, Wash., DC 20024; 60,000.

Humane Society of the U.S. (1954), 2100 L St. NW, Wash. DC 20037;43,575.

Humanics Foundation, Amer. (1948), 912 Baltimore Ave. Kansas City, MO 64105; 950.

Humanities, Natl. Endowment for the (1965), 806 15th St NW, Wash., DC 20506.

—I—

Iceland Veterans (1948), 2101 Walnut St., Phila., PA 19103; 1,600.

Identification, Internatl. Assn. for (1915), P.O. Box 139, Utica, NY 13503; 2,000.
Illuminating Engineering Society of No. America (1906), 345 E. 47th St., N.Y., NY 10017; 9,500.
Illustrators, Society of (1901), 128 E. 63d St., N.Y., NY 10021; 700.
Immigration and Nationality Lawyers, Assn. of (1946), 50 Court St., Brooklyn, NY 11201; 650.
Imperial Order of the Dragon (1900-1901), P.O. Box 1707, San Francisco, CA 94101.
Indian Rights Assn. (1882), 1505 Race St., Phila., PA 19106; 2,500.
Indoor Sports Club (1930), 1145 Highland St., Napoleon, OH 43545; 2,300.
Industrial Democracy, League for (1905), 275 Seventh Ave., N.Y., NY 10001; 15,000.
Industrial Engineers, Amer. Institute of (1948), 25 Technology Park, Norcross, GA 30092; 30,000.
Industrial Health Foundation (1935), 5231 Centre Ave., Pittsburgh, PA 15232; 140 companies.
Industrial Management Society (1938), 570 Northwest Hwy., Des Plaines, IL 60016.
Infant Death Syndrome (SIDS) Foundation, Natl. Sudden (1962), 310 S. Michigan Ave., Chicago, IL 60604; 20,000.
Infant Survival, Internatl. Council for (1964), 1515 Reisterstown Rd., Baltimore, MD 21208; 750 families.
Information, Freedom of, Center (1958), P.O. Box 858, Columbia, MO 65201; 1,050.
Information Industry Assn. (1968), 4720 Montgomery Ln., Bethesda, MD 20014; 108.
Insurance Assn., Amer. (1866), 85 John St., N.Y., NY 10038; 145 companies.
Intercollegiate Athletics, Natl. Assn. of (1940), 1221 Baltimore Ave., Kansas City, MO 64105; 513 schools.
Interfraternity Confernece, Natl. (1909), P.O. Box 40368, Indianapolis, IN 46240; 47 fraternities.
Interior Designers, Amer. Society of (1975), 730 Fifth Ave., N.Y., NY 10019; 16,550.
International Education, Institute of (1919), 809 United Nations Plaza, N.Y., NY 10017.
Internatl. Educational Exchange, Council on (1947), 777 United Nations Plaza, N.Y., NY 10017; 182 organizations.
International Law, Amer. Society of (1906), 2223 Massachusetts Ave. NW, Wash., DC 20008; 5,500.
Investment Clubs, Natl. Assn. of (1951), 1515 E. Eleven Mile Rd., Royal Oak, MI 48067; 5,900 clubs.
Iron Castings Society, (1975), 20611 Center Ridge Rd., Rocky River, OH 44116; 250 firms.
Iron and Steel Engineers, Assn. of (1907), Three Gateway Center, Pittsburgh, PA 15222; 12,800.
Iron and Steel Institute, Amer. (1908), 1000 16th St. NW, Wash., DC 20036; 2,502.
Italian Historical Society of America (1949), 111 Columbia Heights, Bklyn., NY 11201; 2,300.
Italy-America Chamber of Commerce (1887), 350 Fifth Ave., N.Y., NY 10001; 10,000.
Izaak Walton League of America (1922), 1800 N. Kent St., Arlington, VA 22304; 56,000.

—J—

Jamestowne Society (1936), P.O. Box 7389, Richmond, VA 23221; 1,500.
Japanese Amer. Citizens League (1930), 1765 Sutter St., San Francisco, CA 94115; 30,000.
Jaycees, U.S. (1920), P.O. Box 7, 4 W. 21st St., Tulsa, OK 74102; 325,000.
Jewish Appeal, United (1939), 1290 Ave. of the Americas, N.Y., NY 10019.
Jewish Center Workers, Assn. of (1918), 15 E. 26th St., N.Y., NY 10010; 950.
Jewish Committee, Amer. (1906), 165 E. 56th St., N.Y., NY 10022; 42,000.
Jewish Congress, Amer. (1916), 15 E. 84th St., N.Y., NY 10028; 50,000 families.
Jewish Federations and Welfare Funds, Council of (1932), 575 Lexington Ave., N.Y., NY 10022; 205 agencies.
Jewish Historical Society, Amer. (1892), 2 Thornton Rd., Waltham, MA 02154; 3,100.
Jewish War Veterans of the U.S.A. (1896), 1712 New Hampshire Ave. NW, Wash., DC 20009; 105,000.
Jewish Welfare Board, Natl. (1917), 15 E. 26th St., N.Y., NY 10010; serves 1,000,000.
Jewish Women, Natl. Council of (1896), 15 E. 26th St., N.Y.,NY 10010; 10,000.
Job's Daughters, Internatl. Order of (1921), 1820 Douglas, Masonic Temple, Omaha, NE 68102; 86,500.
Jockey Club (1894), 300 Park Ave., N.Y., NY 10022; 76.
Jogging Assn., Natl. (1968), 1910 K St. NW, Wash., DC 20006; 5,000.
John Birch Society (1958), 395 Concord Ave., Belmont, MA 02178; 60,000 to 100,000.
Journalists, Society of Professional; Sigma Delta Chi (1909), 35 E. Wacker Dr., Chicago, IL 60601; 75,000.
Journalists and Authors, Amer. Society of (1948), 123 W. 43d St., N.Y., NY 10036; 450.
Judaism, Amer. Council for (1943), 309 Fifth Ave., N.Y., NY 10016; 15,000.
Judicature Society, Amer. (1913), 200 W. Monroe, Chicago, IL 60606; 33,000.
Juggler's Assn., Internatl. (1947), 211 Forest St., Arlington, MA 02174; 600.
Junior Achievement (1918), 550 Summer St., Stamford, CT 06901; 1,500,000.
Junior College Athletic Assn., Natl. (1938), 12 E. 2d St., Hutchinson, KS 67501; 923.
Junior Colleges, Amer. Assn. of Community and (1921), One Dupont Circle NW, Wash., DC 20036; 1,485.
Junior Leagues, Assn. of (1921), 825 Third Ave., N.Y., NY 10022; 119,000.

—K—

Kailtone Adventure Society (1907), P.O. Box 233, Dayton, NV 89403; 106.
Kennel Club, Amer. (1884), 51 Madison Ave., N.Y., NY 10010; 400 clubs.
Key Club Internatl. (1925), 101 E. Erie St., Chicago, IL 60611; 80,000.
Kitefliers Assn., Internatl. (1948), 633 Third Ave., N.Y., NY 10017; 30,000
Kiwanis Internatl. (1915), 101 E. Erie St., Chicago, IL 60611; 290,000.
Knights of Columbus (1882), One Columbus Plaza, New Haven, CT 06510; 1,242,647.
Knights of Equity (1895), 16 Southern Pkwy., Rochester, NY 14618; 1,500.
Knights Templar U.S.A., Grand Encampment (1816), 14 E. Jackson Blvd., Chicago, IL 60604; 365,000.

—L—

La Leche League Internatl. (1956), 9616 Minneapolis Ave., Franklin Park, IL 60131; 100,000.
Labor (Law) Reform, Natl. Council for (1963), 407 S. Dearborn St., Chicago, IL 60605.
Lacrosse Foundation (1959), Newton H. White Athletic Ctr., Homewood, Balitmore, MD 21218; 750.
Lambs, The (1874), 131 W. 56th St., N.Y., NY 10019; 400.
Landscape Architects, Amer. Society of (1899), 1750 Old Meadow Rd., McLean, VA 22101; 4,500.
Law Enforcement Officers Assn., Amer. (1976), 4005 Plaza Towers, New Orleans, LA 70113; 55,000.
Law Institute, Amer. (1923), 4025 Chestnut St., Phila., PA 19104; 2,043.
Law Libraries, Amer. Assn. of (1906), 53 W. Jackson Blvd., Chicago, IL 60604; 2,460.
Law and Social Policy, Center for (1969), 1751 N St. NW, Wash., DC 20036.
Lawn Bowls Assn., Amer. (1915), 1033 Cheryl Dr., Sun City, AZ 85351; 9,500.
Learned Societies, Amer. Council of (1919), 345 E. 46th St., N.Y., NY 10017; 42 Societies.
Lefthanders, League of (1975), P.O. Box 89, New Milford, NJ 07646; 300.
Lefthanders International (1975), 3601 SW 29th St., Topeka, KS 66614; 3,000.
Legal Secretaries, Natl. Assn. of (1950), 3005 E. Skelly Dr., Tulsa, OK 74105; 23,000.
Legion of Valor of the U.S.A. (1890), 621 S. Taylor St., Arlington, VA 22204; 859.
Leonard Wood Memorial for the Eradication of Leprosy (1928), 2430 Pennsylvania Ave. NW, Wash., DC 20037.
Leprosy Missions, Amer. (1906), 1262 Broad St., Bloomfield, NJ 07003.
Letter Carriers, Natl. Assn. of (1889), 100 Indiana Ave. NW, Wash., DC 20001; 230,353.
Leukemia Society of America (1949), 211 E. 43d St., N.Y., NY 10017; 1,300 trustees.
Liberty Lobby (1955), 300 Independence Ave. SE, Wash., DC 20003; 25,000.
Libraries Assn., Special (1909), 235 Park Ave. So., N.Y., NY 10003; 10,500.
Library Assn., Amer. (1876), 50 E. Huron St., Chicago, IL 60611; 34,000.

Library Assn., Medical (1898), 919 N. Michigan Ave., Chicago, IL 60611; 4,092.
Life Insurance, Amer. Council of (1976), 1850 K St. NW, Wash., DC 20006; 444 companies.
Life Insurance Marketing & Research Assn. (1916), 170 Sigourney St., Hartford, CT 06105; 546.
Life Office Management Assn. (1924), 100 Park Ave., N.Y., NY 10017; 500.
Life Underwriters, Natl. Assn. of (1890), 1922 F St. NW, Wash., DC 20006; 135,000.
Lifespan (1970), 4274 N. Woodward, Royal Oak, MI 48073; 15,000.
Lighter-Than-Air Society (1952), 1800 Triplett Blvd., Akron, OH 44306; 1,200.
Lions Clubs, Internatl. (1917), 300 22d St., Oak Brook, IL 60521; 1,200,000.
Little League Baseball (1939), P.O. Box 1127, Williamsport, PA 17701; 10,951 leagues.
Log Rolling Assn., Internatl. (1926), 143 S. 4th St., Bayport, MN 55003; 200.
Lone Indian Fellowship (1926), 1010 Huron Ave., Sheboygan WI 53081; 850.
Lubrication Engineers, Amer. Society of (1944), 838 Busse Hwy., Park Ridge, IL 60068; 3,300.
Lung Assn., Amer. (1904), 1740 Broadway, N.Y., NY 10019.
Lutheran Education Assn. (1942), 7400 Augusta St., River Forest, IL 60305; 2,525.

—M—

Macaroni Manufacturers Assn., Natl. (1904), 19 S. Bothwell, Box 336, Palatine, IL 60067; 125 firms.
Magazine Publishers Assn. (1919), 575 Lexington Ave., N.Y., NY 10022; 139 companies.
Magicians, Internatl. Brotherhood of (1926), 28 N. Main St., Kenton, OH 44326; 10,500.
Magicians, Society of Amer. (1902), 66 Marked Tree Rd., Needham, MA 02192; 5,500.
Magicians Guild of America (1944), 20 W. 40th St., N.Y., NY 10018; 86.
Male Nurse Assn., Natl. (1975), 2309 State St. W., Saginaw, MI 48602; 4,396.
Mammalogists, Amer. Society of (1919), c/o Museum, Oklahoma State Univ., Stillwater, OK 74074; 3,700.
Management, Amer. Institute of (1948), 125 E. 38th St., N.Y., NY 10016; 5,000.
Management Assns., Amer. (1923), 135 W. 50th St., N.Y., NY 10020; 58,500.
Management Consultants, Institute of (1968), 347 Madison Ave., N.Y., NY 10017; 775.
Management Engineers, Assn. of Consulting (1933), 347 Madison Ave., N.Y., NY 10017; 45 firms.
Management Systems Information, Society for (1969), 10 W. 31st St., Chicago, IL 60616; 686.
Manufacturers, Natl. Assn. of (1895), 1776 F St. NW, Wash., DC 20006; 13,000 companies.
Manufacturers' Agents Natl. Assn. (1947), 2021 Business Center Dr., P.O. Box 16878, Irvine, CA 92713; 5,000.
Manufacturing Chemists Assn. (1872), 1825 Connecticut Ave. NW, Wash., DC 20009; 200 companies.
Manufacturing Engineers, Society of (1932), 20501 Ford Rd., Dearborn, MI 48128; 44,000.
March of Dimes, Natl. Foundation — (1938), 1275 Mamaroneck Ave., White Plains, NY 10605; 1,600 chapters.
Marijuana Laws, Natl. Organization for the Reform of (NORML) (1970), 2717 M St. NW, Wash., DC 20037; 25,000.
Marine Corps League (1923), 933 N. Kenmore St., Arlington, VA 22201; 15,000.
Marine Surveyors, Natl. Assn. of (1960), P.O. Box 55, Peck Slip Sta., N.Y., NY 10038; 315.
Marine Technology Society (1963), 1730 M St. NW, Wash., DC 20036; 4,000.
Marine Underwriters, Amer. Institute of (1898), 99 John St., N.Y., NY 10038; 296.
Marketing Assn., Amer. (1937), 222 S. Riverside Plaza, Chicago, IL 60606; 17,969.
Masonic Relief Assn. of U.S. and Canada (1885), P.O. Box 468, Sioux Falls, SD 57101.
Masonic Service Assn. of the U.S. (1919), 8120 Fenton St., Silver Spring, MD 20910; 43 Grand Lodges.
Masons, Ancient and Accepted Scottish Rite, Southern Jurisdiction, Supreme Council (1801), 1733 16th St. NW, Wash., DC 20009; 647,500.
Masons, Supreme Council 33°, Ancient and Accepted Scottish Rite, Northern Masonic Jurisdiction, (1813), 33 Marret Rd., Lexington, MA 02173; 507,940.
Masons, Royal Arch, General Grand Chapter (1797), 1084 New Circle Rd. N.E., Lexington KY 40505; 469,729.
Masons of the State of N.Y., Grand Lodge of Free & Accepted (1781), 71 W. 23d St., N.Y., NY 10010; 220,000.
Mathematical Assn. of America (1915), 1225 Connecticut Ave. NW, Wash., DC 20036; 18,500.
Mathematical Society, Amer. (1888), 201 Charles St., Providence, RI 02904; 16,403.
Mathematical Statistics, Institute of (1937), 1367 Laurel, San Carlos, CA 94070; 3,000.
Mathematics, Society for Industrial and Applied (1952), 33 S. 17th St., Phila., PA 19103; 4,400.
Mayflower Descendants, General Society of (1897), P.O. Box 297, Plymouth, MA 02360; 17,413.
Mayors, U.S. Conference of (1933), 1620 Eye St. NW, Wash., DC 20006; 750 cities.
Mechanical Engineers, Amer. Society of (1880), 345 E. 47th St., N.Y., NY 10017; 70,000.
Mechanics, Assn. of Chairmen of Departments of (1969), Virginia Polytechnic Institute and State Univ., Dept. of Engineering and Mechanics, Blackburg, VA 24061; 110.
Mechanics, Junior Order of United Amer. (1853), 170 Railway Rd., Grafton, VA 23692; 3,000.
Mediaeval Academy of America (1926), 1430 Massachusetts Ave., Cambridge, MA 02138; 4,000.
Medical Assn., Amer. (1847), 535 N. Dearborn St., Chicago, IL 60610; 210,000.
Medical Assn., Natl. (1895), 1720 Massachusetts Ave. NW, Wash., DC 20036; 6,400.
Medical Colleges, Assn. of Amer. (1876), One Dupont Circle NW, Wash., DC 20036; 2,149.
Medical Record Assn., Amer. (1928), 875 N. Michigan Ave., Chicago, IL 60611; 20,500.
Medical Technologists, Amer. (1939), 710 Higgins Rd., Park Ridge, IL 60068; 12,632.
Medical Technologists, Amer. College of (1942), 5608 Lane, Raytown, MO 64133; 368.
Medical Women's Assn., Amer. (1915), 1740 Broadway, N.Y., NY 10019; 6,000.
Medicine, New York Academy of (1847), 2 E. 103d St., N.Y., NY 10029.
Memorabilia Americana (1973), 1211 Ave. I, Brooklyn, NY 11230; 2,000.
Men Voters of the U.S., League of (1969), 88 Arbol, Oroville, CA 95965.
Mensa, Amer. (1964), 1701 W. 3d St., Brooklyn, NY 11223; 24,000.
Mental Health, Natl. Assn. for (1909), 1800 N. Kent St., Arlington, VA 22209; 1,000,000.
Mental Health Program Directors, Natl. Assn. of State (1963), 1001 3d St. SW, Wash., DC 20024; 54.
Merchant Marine Library Assn., Amer. (1921), One World Trade Center, Suite 2601, N.Y., NY 10048; 3,720 seamen.
Metal Finishers, Natl. Assn. of (1955), 22 S. Park St., Montclair, NJ 07042; 979 firms.
Metals, Amer. Society for (1913), Metals Park, OH 44073; 40,000.
Meteorological Society, Amer. (1919), 45 Beacon St., Boston, MA 02108; 9,000.
Metric Assn., U.S. (1916), Sugarloaf Star Rte., Boulder, CO 80302; 4,200.
Microbiology, Amer. Society for (1899), 1913 Eye St. NW, Wash., DC 20006; 24,000.
Micrographics Assn., Natl. (1943), 8728 Colesville Rd., Silver Srping, MD 20910; 8,000.
Mideast Educational and Training Services, America—, formerly **Amer. Friends of the Middle East** (1951), 1717 Massachusetts Ave. NW, Wash., DC 20036; 500.
Military Chaplains Assn. of the U.S.A. (1925), 7758 Wisconsin Ave. NW, Wash., DC 20014; 2,500.
Military Engineers, Society of Amer. (1920), 740 15th St. NW, Wash., DC 20005; 22,000.
Military Order of the Loyal Legion of the U.S.A. (1865), 1307 New Hampshire Ave. NW, Wash., DC 20036; 1,200.
Military Order of the Purple Heart (1782, by Gen. George Washington; reactivated Feb. 22, 1932, by President Herbert Hoover and Chief of Staff Douglas MacArthur), 1022 Wilson Blvd., Arlington, VA 22209; 15,000.
Military Order of the World Wars (1920), 1100 17th St. NW, Wash., DC 20036; 11,000.
Military Surgeons of the U.S., Assn. of (1891), 10605 Concord St., Kensington, MD 20795; 11,397.
Mining, Metallurgical and Petroleum Engineers, Amer. Institute of (1871), 345 E. 47th St., N.Y., NY 10017; 59,773.
Mining and Metallurgical Society of America (1910), 299 Park Ave., N.Y., NY 10017; 320.
Ministerial Assn., Amer. (1929), 446 Salem Ave., P.O. Box 1252, York, PA 17405; 18,179.
Model Railroad Assn., Natl. (1936), 7061 Twin Oaks Dr., Indianapolis, IN 46226; 30,157.
Modern Language Assn. of America (1883), 62 Fifth Ave., N.Y., NY 10011; 30,000.

Modern Language Teachers Assns., Natl. Federation of (1916), Dept. of Foreign Languages, Gannon Coll., Erie, PA 16501; 15 assns.
Monopoly Assn., U.S. (1963), 1866 City National Bank Bldg., Detroit, MI 48226; 450.
Moose, Loyal Order of (1888), Mooseheart, IL 60539; 1,221,-587.
Mothers Committee, Amer. (1935), Waldorf Astoria Hotel, 301 Park Ave., N.Y., NY 10022; 2,000.
Mothers-in-Law Club Internatl. (1970), 739R Chestnut St., Cedarhurst, NY 11516; 5,000.
Mothers of Twins Clubs, Natl. Organization of (1960), 5402 Amberwood Ln., Rockville, MD 20853; 8,260.
Motion Picture Arts & Sciences, Academy of (1927), 8949 Wilshire Blvd., Beverly Hills, CA 90211; 4,000.
Motion Picture Assn. of America (1922), 522 Fifth Ave., N.Y., NY 10036.
Motion Picture & Television Engineers, Society of (1916), 862 Scarsdale Ave., Scarsdale, NY 10583; 7,800.
Motion Pictures, Natl. Board of Review of (1909), 210 E. 68th St., N.Y., NY 10021; 200.
Motor Bus Owners, Natl. Assn. of (1926), 1025 Connecticut Ave. NW, Wash., DC 20036; 450.
Motor Vehicle Administrators, Amer. Assn. of (1933), 1201 Connecticut Ave. NW, Wash., DC 20036; 130.
Motor Vehicle Manufacturers Assn. (1913), 320 New Center Building, Detroit, MI 48202; 125.
Motorcyclist Assn., Amer. (1924), P.O. Box 141, 33 Collegeview Ave., Westerville, OH 43081; 130,000.
Multiple Sclerosis Society, Natl. (1946), 205 E. 42d St., N.Y., NY 10017; 250,000.
Municipal Finance Officers Assn. of the U.S. & Canada (1906), 1313 E. 60th St., Chicago, IL 60637; 6,100.
Municipal League, Natl. (1894), 47 E. 68th St., N.Y., NY 10021; 6,200.
Mural Painters, Natl. Society of (1895), 41 E. 65th St., N.Y., NY 10021; 150.
Muscular Dystrophy Assn. (1950), 810 Seventh Ave., N.Y., NY 10019; 81 corporate members.
Museums, Amer. Assn. of (1906), 1055 Thomas Jefferson St. NW, Wash., DC 20007; 4,000.
Music, Natl. Assn. of Schools of (1924), 11250 Roger Bacon Dr., Reston, VA 22090; 455 institutions.
Music Center, Amer. (1940), 250 W. 57th St., N.Y., NY 10019; 1,000.
Music Clubs, Natl. Federation of (1898), 310 S. Michigan Ave., Chicago, IL 60604; 500,000.
Music Conference, Amer. (1947), 150 E. Huron St., Chicago, IL 60611; 850.
Music Council, Natl. (1940), 250 W. 57th St., N.Y., NY 10019; 60.
Music Educators Natl. Conference (1907), 1902 Association Dr., Reston, VA 22091; 62,000.
Music Publishers' Assn., Natl. (1917), 110 E. 59th St., N.Y., NY 10022; 130.
Music Scholarship Assn., Amer. (1956), 1826 Carew Tower, Cincinnati, OH 45202; 1,000.
Music Teachers Natl. Assn. (1876), 408 Carew Tower, Cincinnati, OH 45202; 15,000.
Musicians, Amer. Federation of (1896), 1500 Broadway, N.Y., NY 10036; 330,000.
Musicological Society, Amer. (1934), 201 S. 34th St., Phila., PA 19104; 3,285.
Mutual Savings Banks, Natl. Assn. of (1920), 200 Park Ave., N.Y., NY 10017; 475 banks.
Muzzle Loading Rifle Assn. (1933), P.O. Box 67, Friendship, IN 47021; 19,500.
Mystic Seaport (1929), 30 Greenmanville Ave., Mystic, CT 06355; 14,000.

—N—

NAACP (Natl. Assn. for the Advancement of Colored People) (1909), 1790 Broadway, N.Y., NY 10019; 500,000.
NAAFA (Natl. Assn. to Aid Fat Americans) (1969), P.O. Box 745, Westbury, NY 11590; 1,000.
Name Society, Amer. (1951), English Dept., SUNY-Potsdam, Potsdam, NY 13676; 900.
National Guard Assn. of the U.S. (1878), One Massachusetts Ave. NW, Wash., DC 20001; 47,287.
Nationalities Service, Amer. Council for (1922), 20 W. 40th St., N.Y., NY 10018; 30 agencies.
Natural Science for Youth Foundation (1961), 763 Silvermine Rd., New Canaan, CT 06840; 500.
Naturalists, Assn. of Interpretive (1961), 6700 Needwood Rd., Derwood, MD 20855; 1,000.
Nature Conservancy (1951), 1800 N. Kent St., Arlington, VA 22209; 23,000.
Nature & Natural Resources, Internatl. Union for Conservation of (1948), 1110 Morges, Switzerland; 100 countries.
Nature Study Society, Amer. (1908), 4405 Paulsen St., Savannah, GA 31405; 950.
Naval Architects & Marine Engineers, Society of (1893), One World Trade Center, Suite 1369, N.Y., NY 10048; 11,500.
Naval Engineers, Amer. Society of (1888), 1012 14th St. NW, Wash., DC 20005; 4,000.
Naval Institute, U.S. (1873), U.S. Naval Academy, Annapolis, MD 21402; 64,374.
Naval Reserve Assn. (1954), 910 17th St. NW, Wash., DC 20006; 18,000.
Navigation, Institute of (1945), 815 15th St. NW, Wash., DC 20005; 3,000.
Navy Club of the U.S.A. (1940), 1602 Wells St., Fort Wayne, IN 46801; 3,000. **Navy Club of the U.S.A. Auxiliary** (1940), 216 W. Suttenfield, Fort Wayne, IN 46807; 1,000.
Navy League of the U.S. (1902), 818 18th St. NW, Wash., DC 20006; 40,356.
Navy Wives Clubs of America (1936), P.O. Box 6971, Wash., DC 20032; 3,000.
Needlework Guild of America (1885), 1736 Pine St., Phila., PA 19103; 400,000.
Negro College Fund, United (1944), 500 E. 62d St., N.Y., NY 10021.
Newspaper Editors, Amer. Society of (1922), 1350 Sullivan Trail, Easton, PA 18042; 800.
Newspaper Promotion Assn., Internatl. (1931), 11600 Sunrise Valley Dr., Reston, VA 22091; 1,200.
Newspaper Publishers Assn., Amer. (1887), 11600 Sunrise Valley Dr., Reston, VA 22091; 1,160 newspapers.
Newspaper Publishers Assn., Natl. (1940), 770 National Press Bldg., Wash., DC 20045; 300.
Ninety-Nines (Internatl. Organization of Women Pilots) (1929), P.O. Box 59964; Will Rogers World Airport, Oklahoma City, OK 73159; 5,000.
Non-Commissioned Officers Assn. (1960), 10635 IH 35 No., San Antonio, TX 78233; 150,000.
Notaries, Amer. Society of (1965), 810 18th St. NW, Wash. DC 20006; 7,674.
Nuclear Society, Amer. (1954), 244 E. Ogden Ave., Hinsdale, IL 60521; 12,000.
Numismatic Assn., Amer. (1891), 818 N. Cascade Ave., Colorado Springs, CO 80903; 30,919.
Numismatic Society, Amer. (1858), Broadway at 155th St., N.Y., NY 10032; 1,814.
Nurse Education and Service, Natl. Assn. for Practical (1941), 122 E. 42d St., N.Y., NY 10017; 40,000.
Nurses, Natl. Federation of Licensed Practical (1949), 250 W. 57th St., N.Y., NY 10019; 28,000.
Nurses' Assn., Amer. (1897), 2420 Pershing Rd., Kansas City, MO 64108; 191,499.
Nursing, Natl. League for (1952), 10 Columbus Circle, N.Y., NY 10019; 16,000.
Nutrition, Amer. Institute of (1928), 9650 Rockville Pike, Bethesda, MD 20014; 1,722.

—O—

ORT Federation, Amer. (Org. for Rehabilitation through Training) (1921), 817 Broadway, N.Y., NY 10013; 150,000.
Occupational Therapy Assn., Amer. (1917), 6000 Executive Blvd., Rockville, MD 20852; 25,841
Odd Fellows, Independent Order of (1819), 16 W. Chase St., Baltimore, MD 21201; 1,200,000.
Old Crows, Assn. of (1964), 2361 S. Jefferson Davis Hwy., Arlington, VA 22202; 8,000.
Olympic Committee, U.S. (1921), 57 Park Ave., N.Y., NY 10017.
Optical Society of America (1916), 2000 L St. NW, Wash., DC 20036; 7,441.
Optimist Internatl. (1919), 4494 Lindell Blvd., St. Louis, MO 63108; 118,000.
Optometric Assn., Amer. (1898), 7000 Chippewa St., St. Louis, MO 63119.
Oral Surgeons, Amer. Society of (1918), 211 E. Chicago Ave., Chicago, IL 60611; 3,300.
Order of the Rainbow for Girls, Supreme Assembly Internatl. (1922), 315 E. Carl Albert Pkwy., McAlester, OK 74501; 175,000.
Organists, Amer. Guild of (1896), 630 Fifth Ave., N.Y., NY 10020; 16,000.
Organization of American States (1890), Pan American Union, 17th & Constitution Ave. NW, Wash., DC 20006; 24 nations.
Oriental Society, Amer. (1842), 329 Sterling Memorial Library, Yale Sta., New Haven, CT 06520.
Ornithologists' Union, Amer. (1883), c/o National Museum

of Natural History, Smithsonian Institution, Wash., DC 20560; 4,500.

Osteopathic Assn., Amer. (1897), 212 E. Ohio St., Chicago, IL 60611; 13,000.

Ostomy Assn., United (1962), 1111 Wilshire Blvd., Los Angeles, CA 90017; 29,000.

Over-the-Counter Cos., Natl. Assn. of (1973), Box 110, Jenkintown, PA 19046; 180 companies.

Overeaters Anonymous (1960), 2190 190th St., Torrance, CA 90254; 100,000.

—P—

Paleontological Research Institution (1932), 1259 Trumansburg Rd., Ithaca, NY 14850; 537.

Paper Converters Assn. (1934), 1619 Massachusetts Ave. NW, Wash., DC 20036; 25 companies.

Paper Institute, Amer. (1964), 260 Madison Ave., N.Y., NY 10016; 200 companies.

Parasitologists, Amer. Society of (1924), 1041 New Hampshire St., Box 368, Lawrence, KS 66044; 1,900.

PTA (Parents Teachers Assn.), Natl. (1897), 700 N. Rush St., Chicago, IL 60611; 6.6 million.

Parents Without Partners (1957), 7910 Woodmont Ave. NW, Wash., DC 20014; 145,000.

Parish Clergy, Academy of (1968), 409 Greenfield, Oak Park, IL 60302; 500.

Parking Assn., Natl (1951), 1101 17th St. NW, Wash., DC 20036; 700 companies.

Parkinson's Disease Foundation (1957), Wm. Black Research Bldg., 640 W. 168th St., N.Y., NY 10032.

Parks & Conservation Assn., Natl. (1919), 1701 18th St. NW, Wash., DC 20009; 45,000.

Pathologists & Bacteriologists, Amer. Assn. of (1900), Dept. of Pathology, Box 3712, Duke Univ. Medical Center, Durham, NC 27710; 1,271.

Patroitism, Natl. Committee for Responsible (1967), commodore Hotel, 109 E. 42d St., N.Y., NY 10017; 150.

Pearl Harbor Survivors Assn. (1958), P.O. Box 106, McLean, VA 22101; 7,000.

P.E.N. Amer. Center (1922), 156 Fifth Ave., N.Y., NY 10010; 1,500.

Pen Women, Natl. League of Amer. (1897), 1300 17th St. NW, Wash., DC 20036; 6,234.

Pennsylvania Society (1899), Suite 594, Waldorf Astoria Hotel, 301 Park Ave., N.Y., NY 10022; 2,400.

P.E.O. Sisterhood (1869), 3700 Grand Ave., Des Moines, IA 50312; 187,000.

Performance Improvement, Amer. Society for (1966), 790 Broad St., Newark, NJ 07102; 250.

Personnel Administration, Amer. Society for (1948), 19 Church St., Berea, OH 44017; 16,000.

Personnel & Guidance Assn., Amer. (1952), 1607 New Hampshire Ave. NW, Wash., DC 20009; 40,000.

Petroleum Geologists, Amer. Assn. of (1917), Box 979, 1444 S. Boulder, Tulsa, OK 74101; 18,734.

Petroleum Institute, Amer. (1919), 2101 L St. NW, Wash., DC 20037; 7,600.

Petroleum Landmen, Amer. Assn. of (1955), 2408 Continental Life Bldg., Fort Worth, TX 76102; 6,200.

Pharmaceutical Assn., Amer. (1852), 2215 Constitution Ave. NW, Wash., DC 20037; 54,000.

Philatelic Americans, Society of (1894), 58 W. Salisbury Dr., Wilmington, DE 19809; 8,122.

Philatelic Society, Amer. (1886), P.O. Box 800, 336 S. Fraser St., State College, PA 16801; 41,798.

Philaticians, Society of (1972), Salt Point Tpke., Clinton Corners, NY 12514; 240.

Philharmonic Symphony Society of New York (1842), Avery Fisher Hall, Lincoln Center, Broadway at 65th St., N.Y., NY 10023; 5,000

Philologocal Assn., Amer. (1869), 431-432 N. Burrowes, Pennsylvania State Univ., University Park, PA 16802; 2,900.

Philosophical Assn., Amer. (1900), Univ. of Delaware, Newark, DE 19711; 6,000.

Philosophical Society, Amer. (1743), 104 S. 5th St., Phila., PA 19106; 600.

Photographers of America, Professional (1880), 1090 Executive Way, Des Plaines, IL 60018; 16,000.

Photographic Society of Amer. (1934), 2005 Walnut St., Phila. PA 19103; 18,600.

Physical Society, Amer. (1899), 335 E. 45th St., N.Y., NY 10017; 29,000.

Physical Therapy Assn., Amer. (1921), 1156 15th St. NW, Wash., DC 20005; 26,577.

Physicians, Amer. College of (1915), 4200 Pine St., Phila., PA 19104; 20,000.

Physics, Amer. Institute of (1931), 335 E. 45th St., N.Y., NY 10017; 56,000.

Physiological Society, Amer. (1887), 9650 Rockville Pike, Bethesda, MD 20014; 5,000.

Pilgrim Society (1820), 75 Court St., Plymouth, MA 20360; 700.

Pilgrims of the U.S. (1903), 74 Trinity Pl., N.Y., NY 10006; 1,000.

Pilot Club Internatl. (1921), 244 College St., Macon, GA 31201; 18,500.

Pioneer Women, The Women's Labor Zionist Organization of America (1925), 315 Fifth Ave., N.Y., NY 10016; 50,000.

Planned Parenthood Federation of America (1922), 810 Seventh Ave., N.Y., NY 10019; 189 affiliates.

Planners, Amer. Institute of (1917), 1776 Massachusetts Ave. NW, Wash., DC 20036; 11,838.

Plastic Modelers Society, Internatl. (1964), P.O. Box 2555, Long Beach, CA 90801; 4,600.

Plastics Engineers, Society of (1942), 656 W. Putnam Ave., Greenwich, CT 06830; 18,500.

Plastics Industry, Society of (1937), 355 Lexington Ave., N.Y., NY 10017; 1,400 companies.

Platform Assn., Internatl. (1831), 2564 Berkshire Rd., Cleveland Heights, OH 44106; 6,000.

Podiatry Assn., Amer. (1912), 20 Chevy Chase Circle NW, Wash., DC 20015; 6,800.

Poetry Day Committee, Natl. (1947), 1110 N. Venetian Dr., Miami Beach, FL 33139; 17,000.

Poetry Society of America (1910), 15 Gramercy Park So., N.Y., NY 10003; 750.

Poets, Academy of Amer. (1934), 1078 Madison Ave., N.Y., NY 10028; 93.

Polar Society, Amer. (1934), c/o Secretary, 98-20 62d Dr., Apt. 7H, Rego Park, NY 11374; 2,500.

Police, Internatl. Assn. of Chiefs of (1893), 11 Firstfield Rd., Gaithersburg, MD 20760; 10,800.

Police Reserve Officers Assn., Natl. (1967), 14600 S. Tamiami Trail N.P., Venice, FL 33595; 13,500.

Polish Army Veterans Assn. of America (1921), 19 Irving Pl., N.Y., NY 10003; 9,762.

Polish Cultural Society of America (1940), 55 W. 42d St., N.Y., NY 10036; 46,851.

Polish Legion of American Veterans (1920), 3024 N. Laramie Ave., Chicago, IL 60641; 150,000.

Political Items Collectors, Amer. (1945), 66 Golf St., Newington, CT 06111; 2,500.

Political Science, Academy of (1880), 2852 Broadway, N.Y., NY 10025; 10,500.

Political Science Assn., Amer. (1903), 1527 New Hampshire Ave. NW, Wash., DC 20036; 13,565.

Political & Social Science, Amer. Academy of (1889), 3937 Chestnut St., Phila.. PA 19104; 16,000.

Pollution Control, Internatl. Assn. for (1970), 1625 Eye St. NW, Wash., DC 20006; 500.

Polo Assn., U.S. (1890), 1301 W. 22d St., Oak Brook, IL 60521; 1,500.

Population Assn. of America (1931), 806 15th St. NW, Wash., DC 20005; 2,600.

Portuguese Continental Union of the U.S.A. (1925), 899 Boylston St., Boston, MA 02115; 9,658.

Postmasters of the U.S., Natl. Assn. of (1936), 490 L'Enfant Plaza E., SW, Wash., DC 20024; 33,000.

Postmasters of the U.S., Natl. League of (1904), 955 L'Enfant Plaza SW, Wash., DC 20024; 19,500.

Poultry Science Assn. (1908), Illinois Bldg., Room 311, 113 N. Neil St., Champaign, IL 61820; 1,550.

Powder Metallurgy Institute, Amer. (1959), P.O. Box 2054, 44 Princeton Hightstown Rd., Princeton, NJ 08540; 2,000.

Power Boat Assn., Amer. (1903), 22811 Greater Mack, St. Clair Shores, MI 48080; 6,339.

Power Squadrons, U.S. (1914), P.O. Box 30423, Raleigh, NC 27612; 70,000.

Precancel Collectors, Natl. Assn. of (1950), 5121 Park Blvd., Wildwood, NJ 08260; 5,500.

Press Club, Natl. (1908), 529 14th St. NW, Wash., DC 20045; 4,600.

Press Institute, Internatl. (1951), Lindenplatz 6, 8048 Zurich, Switzerland; 1,900.

Press and Radio Club (1948), P.O. Box 7023, Montgomery, AL 36107; 747.

Press Women, Natl. Federation of (1937), 1105 Main St., P.O. Box 99, Blue Springs, MD 64015; 4,250.

Procrastinators' Club of America (1956), 1111 Broad, Locust Bldg., Phila., PA 19102; 3,120.

Production & Inventory Control Society, Amer. (1957), 2600 Virginia Ave. NW, Wash., DC 20037; 14,750.

Propeller Club of the U.S. (1927), 1730 M St. NW, Wash., DC 20036; 12,103.

Psychiatric Assn., Amer. (1844), 1700 18th St. NW, Wash., DC 20009; 22,000.

Psychical Research, Amer. Society for (1907), 5 W. 73d

St., N.Y., NY 10023; 2,500.
Psychoanalytic Assn., Amer. (1911), One E. 57th St., N.Y., NY 10022; 2,503.
Psychological Assn., Amer. (1892), 1200 17th St. NW, Wash., DC 20036; 45,000.
Psychological Assn. for Psychoanalysis, Natl. (1946), 150 W. 13th St., N.Y., NY 10011; 187.
Psychological Minorities, Society for the Aid of (1953), 42-25 Hampton St., Elmhurst, NY 11373; 500.
Psychotheatrics, Assn. for (1976), P.O. Box 160371, Sacramento, CA 95816; 250.
Psychotherapy Assn., Amer. Group (1942), 1995 Broadway, N.Y., NY 10023; 3,000.
Public Health Assn., Amer. (1872), 1015 18th St. NW, Wash., DC 20036; 25,000.
Public Relations Society of America (1947), 845 Third Ave., N.Y., NY 10022; 8,400.
Public Welfare Assn., Amer. (1930), 1155 16th St. NW, Wash., DC 20036; 7,000.
Publishers, Assn. of Amer. (1970), 1707 L St. NW, Wash., DC 20036; 300.

—Q & R—

Quality Control, Amer. Society for (1946), 161 W. Wisconsin Ave., Milwaukee, WI 53203; 23,000.
Quint-A (1954), 23219 Lincolnshire Dr., Bay Village, OH 44140; 7,014.

Racial Equality, Congress of (CORE) (1942), 200 W. 135th St., N.Y., NY 10030.
Racing Commissioners, Natl. Assn. of State (1934), P.O. Box 4216, Lexington, KY 40504; 650.
Racquetball Assn., U.S. (1973), 4101 Dempster St., Skokie, IL 60076; 18,500.
Radio Free Europe (1949), 1201 Connecticut Ave. NW, Wash., DC 20036.
Radio Relay League, Amer. (1914), 225 Main St., Newington, CT 06111; 145,000.
Radio and Television Society, Internatl. (1939), 420 Lexington Ave., N.Y., NY 10017; 1,200.
Radio Union, Internatl. Amateur (1925), P.O. Box AAA, Newington, CT 06111; 100 societies.
Radiological Society of No. America (1915), One MONY-Plaza, Syracuse, NY 13202; 7,560.
Railroad Passengers, Natl. Assn. of (1967), 417 New Jersey Ave. SE, Wash., DC 20003; 5,500.
Railroads, Assn. of Amer. (1934), 1920 L St. NW, Wash., DC 20036; 158.
Railway Historical Society, Natl. (1937), P.O. Box 2051, Phila., PA 19103; 10,451.
Railway Progress Institute (1908), 801 N. Fairfax St., Alexandria, VA 22314; 145 companies.
Range Management, Society for (1948), 2760 W. 5th Ave., Denver, CO 80204; 5,500.

Real Estate Appraisers, Natl. Assn. of (1967), 853 Broadway, N.Y., NY 10003; 1,000.
Real Estate Investment Trusts, Natl. Assn. of (1960), 1101 17th St. NW, Wash., DC 20036; 141 trusts, 223 associates.
Realtors[R], Natl. Assn. of (1908), 430 N. Michigan Ave., Chicago, IL 60611; 433,182.
Reconciliation, Fellowship of (1915), 523 N. Broadway, Nyack, NY 10960; 23,500.
Recording Industry Assn. of America (1952), One E. 57th St., N.Y., NY 10022; 58.
Records Managers & Administrators, Assn. of (1975), P.O. Box 281, Bradford, RI 02808; 3,900.
Recreation and Park Assn., Natl. (1965), 1601 N. Kent St., Arlington, VA 22209; 17,000.
Red Cross, Amer. Natl. (1881), 17th & D Sts. NW, Wash., DC 20006; 30,044,842.
Red Men, Improved Order of (1765), 1525 West Ave., P.O. Box 683, Waco, TX 76707; 51,000.
Redwoods League, Save-the- (1918), 114 Sansome St., San Francisco, CA 94104; 55,000.
Regional Plan Assn. (1929), 235 E. 45th St., N.Y., NY 10017; 3,000.
Rehabilitation Assn., Natl. (1925), 1522 K St. NW, Wash., DC 20005; 35,000.
Religion, Amer. Academy of (1909), 215 Williams Bldg., Florida State Univ., Tallahassee, FL 32306; 4,200.
Renaissance Society of America (1954), 1161 Amsterdam Ave., N.Y., NY 10027; 3,100.
Rescue Committee, Internatl. (1933), 386 Park Ave. So., N.Y., NY 10016; 70.
Reserve Officers Assn. of the U.S. (1922), One Constitution Ave., NE, Wash., DC 20002; 105,000.

Restaurant Assn., Natl. (1919), Suite 2600, One IBM Plaza, Chicago, IL 60611; 7,000 businesses.

Retail Druggists, Natl. Assn. of (1898), One E. Wacker Dr., Chicago, IL 60601; 32,000.
Retail Grocers, Natl. Assn. of (1893), Reston Internatl. Center, Reston, VA 22091; 38,000.
Retail Merchants Assn., Natl. (1911), 100 W. 31st St., N.Y., NY 10001; 35,000 stores.
Retarded Citizens, Natl. Assn. for (1950), P.O. Box 6109, 2709 Ave. F East, Arlington, TX 76011; 219,000.
Retired Federal Employees, Natl. Assn. of (1926), 1533 New Hampshire Ave. NW, Wash., DC 20036; 260,000.
Retired Officers Assn. (1929), 1625 Eye St. NW, Wash., DC 20006; 221,545; 19,878 Auxiliary.
Retired Persons, Amer. Assn. of (1958), 1909 K St. NW, Wash., DC 20049; 8,500,000.
Retired Teachers Assn., Natl. (1947), 1909 K St. NW, Wash., DC 20049; 500,000.
Retreads (of World War I & II) (1947), 40-07 154th St., Flushing, NY 11354; 1,500.
Revolver Assn., U.S. (1900), 59 Alvin St., Springfield MA 01104, 1,500.

Richard III Society (1924), 534 Hudson Rd., Sudbury, MA 01776; 650.
Rifle Assn. of America, Natl. (1871), 1600 Rhode Island Ave. NW, Wash., DC 20036; 1,000,000.

Road Builders' Assn., Amer. (1902), 525 School St. SW, Wash., DC 20024; 6,000.
Rodeo Cowboys Assn., Professional (1936), 2929 W. 19th Ave., Denver, CO 80204; 4,000.
Roller Skating, U.S. Amateur Confederation of (1973), 7700 A St., Lincoln, NE 68510; 25,000.
Roller Skating Rink Operators Assn. (1937), 7700 A St., Lincoln, NE 68510; 1,300.
Rose Society, American (1889), P.O. Box 30,000, Shreveport, LA 71130; 16,000.
Rosicrucian Fraternity (1614, Germany, 1861 in U.S.), R.D. No. 3, Box 220, Quakertown, PA 18951.
Rosicrucian Order, AMORC (1915), Rosicrucian Park, San Jose, CA 95191; 120,000.
Rosicrucians, Society of (1909), 321 W. 101st St., N.Y., NY 10025.
Rotary Internatl. (1905), 1600 Ridge Ave., Evanston, IL 60201; 803,000.
Round Table Internatl., Knights of the (1911), 61 E. Colorado Blvd., Pasadena, CA 91101; 1,900.

Ruritan Natl. (1928), P.O. Box 487, Dublin, VA 24084; 38,-000.
Russian Orthodox Clubs, Federated (1927), 10 Downs Dr. (Plains), Wilkes-Barre, PA 18705; 5,000.

—S—

Safety Council, Natl. (1913), 444 N. Michigan Ave., Chicago, IL 60611; 15,000.
Safety Engineers, Amer. Society of (1911), 850 Busse Hwy., Park Ridge, IL 60068; 14,500.
St. Dennis of Zante, Sovereign Greek Order of (1096,1953 in U.S.), 739 W. 186th St., N.Y., NY 10033; 816.
St. Paul, Natl. Guild of (1937), 601 Hill 'N Dale, Lexington, KY 40503.
Salt Institute (1914), 206 N. Washington St., Alexandria, VA 22314; 25.
Salvation Army, The (1865, England, 1880 in U.S.), 120 W. 14th St., N.Y., NY 10011; 384,817.
Sane World, A Citizen's Organization for a (1957), 318 Massachusetts Ave. NE, Wash., DC 20002; 20,000.
Savings & Loan League, Natl. (1943), 1101 15th St. NW, Wash., DC 20005; 300.

School Administrators, Amer. Assn. of (1865), 1801 N. Moore St., Arlington, VA 22209; 19,000.
School Boards Assn., Natl. (1940), 1055 Thomas Jefferson St. NW, Wash., DC 20007; 52 boards.
School Counselor Assn., Amer. (1952), 1607 New Hampshire Ave. NW, Wash., DC 20015; 13,000.
Schools of Art, Natl. Assn. of (1944), 11250 Roger Bacon Dr., No. 5, Reston, VA 22090; 85 institutions.
Schools & Colleges, Amer. Council on (1927), 446 Salem Ave., P.O. Box 1252, York, PA 17405; 121 institutions.
Science, Amer. Assn. for the Advancement of (1848), 1515 Massachusetts Ave. NW, Wash., DC 20005; 114,000.
Science Fiction Fantasy and Horror Films, Academy of

(1972), 334 W. 54th St., Los Angeles, CA 90037; 300.
Science Service (1921), 1719 N St. NW, Wash., DC 20036.
Science Teachers Assn., Natl. (1944), 1742 Connecticut Ave. NW, Wash., DC 20009; 40,000.
Science Writers, Natl. Assn. of (1934), Box H, Sea Cliff, NY 11579; 950.
Sciences, Natl. Academy of (1863), 2101 Constitution Ave. NW, Wash., DC 20418; 1,182.
Sciences, New York Academy of (1817), 2 E. 63d St., N.Y., NY 10021; 25,000.
Scientific Apparatus Makers Assn. (1918), 1140 Connecticut Ave. NW, Wash., DC 20036; 222 companies.
Scientists, Federation of Amer. (1946), 307 Massachusetts Ave. NE, Wash., DC 20002; 7,000.
Screen Actors Guild (1933), 7750 Sunset Blvd., Hollywood, CA 90046; 32,000.
Sculpture Society, Natl. (1893), 777 Third Ave., N.Y., NY 10017; 350.

Seamen's Service, United (1942), One World Trade Ctr., N.Y., NY 10048.
Secondary School Principals, Natl. Assn. of (1916), 1904 Association Dr., Reston, VA 22091; 35,000.
Secularists of America, United (1947), 377 Vernon St., Oakland, CA 94610.
Securities Industry Assn. (1972), 20 Broad St., N.Y., NY 10005; 575 firms.
Security Industrial Assn., Natl. (1944), 740 15th St. NW, Wash., DC 20005; 260 corporations.
Seeing Eye, The (1929), Morristown, NJ 07960; 26,000.
Semantics, Institute of General (1938), R.R. 1; Box 215, Lakeville, CT 06039; 500.
Separation of Church & State, Americans United for (1947), 8120 Fenton St., Silver Spring, MD 20910; 100,000.
Sertoma Internatl. (1912), 1900 E. Meyer Blvd., Kansas City, MO 64132; 33,883.
Settlements & Neighborhood Centers, Natl. Federation of (1911), 232 Madison Ave., N.Y., NY 10016; 175 agencies.
Sex Information & Education Council of the U.S. (SIECUS) (1964), 137 N. Franklin St., Hempstead, NY 11550.

Shakespeare Assn. of America (1973), Box 6328, Sta. B, Nashville, TN 37235; 500.
Sheriff's Assn., Natl. (1940), 1250 Connecticut Ave. NW, Wash., DC 20036; 60,000.
Ship Society, World (1946), 3319 Sweet Dr., Lafayette CA 94549; 3,900.
Shipbuilders Council of America (1921), Watergate, 600 New Hampshire Ave. NW, Wash., DC 20037; 40 companies.
Shoe Retailers Assn., Natl. (1912), 200 Madison Ave., N.Y., NY 10016; 2,500.
Shore & Beach Preservation Assn., Amer. (1926), 412 O'Brien Hall, Univ. of California, Berkeley, CA 94720; 1,500.
Shorthand Reporters Assn., Natl. (1899), 2361 S. Jefferson Davis Hwy., Arlington, VA 22202; 11,000.
Showmen's League of America (1913), 300 W. Randolph St., Chicago, IL 60606; 1,650.
Shrine, Ancient Arabic Order of the Nobles of the Mystic (1872), 323 N. Michigan Ave., Chicago, IL 60601; 937,712.
Shut-In Day Society, Natl. (1970), 237 Franklin St., Reading, PA 19602; 5,000.

Sierra Club (1892), 530 Bush St., San Francisco, CA 94108; 160,000.
Silurians, Society of the (1924), 45 John St., N.Y., NY 10038; 750.

Skating Union of the U.S., Amateur (1927), 4423 W. Deming Pl., Chicago, IL 60639; 3,500.
Skeet Shooting Assn., Natl. (1946), P.O. Box 28188, San Antonio, TX 78228; 19,888.
Ski Assn., U.S. (1904), 1726 Champa St., Denver, CO 80202; 100,000.

Small Business, Amer. Federation of (1963), 407 S. Dearborn St., Chicago, IL 60605; 5,800.
Small Business Assn., Natl. (1937), 1225 19th St. NW, Wash., DC 20036; 40,000.
Smoking & Health, Natl. Clearinghouse for (1965), Center for Disease Control, 1600 Clifton Road NE, Atlanta, GA 30333.

Soaring Society of America (1932), 3200 Airport Ave., Santa Monica, CA 90405; 13,755.
Soccer Federation, U.S. (1913), 350 Fifth Ave., N.Y., NY 10001; 40 assns.
Social Biology, Society for the Study of (1926), c/o New York State Psychiatric Institute, 722 W. 168th St., N.Y., NY 10032; 480.
Social Science Research Council (1924), 605 Third Ave., N.Y., NY 10016.
Social Sciences, Natl. Institute of (1912), 622 Third Ave., N.Y., NY 10017; 750.
Social Welfare, Internatl. Council on (1928), 345 E. 46th St., N.Y., NY 10017; 70 natl. committees.
Social Welfare, Natl. Conference on (1873), 22 W. Gay St., Columbus, OH 43215; 5,000.
Social Work Education, Council on (1952), 345 E. 46th St., N.Y., NY 10017; 4,500.
Social Workers, Natl. Assn. of (1955), 1425 H St. NW, Wash., DC 20005; 71,000.
Sociological Assn., Amer. (1905), 1722 N St. NW, Wash., DC 20036; 14,000.
Soft Drink Assn., Natl. (1919), 1101 16th St. NW, Wash., DC 20036; 2,000.
Softball Assn. of America, Amateur (1933), 2801 N.E. 50th St., Oklahoma City, OK 73111.
Softball, Cinderella National (1958), 71 Bridge St., Corning, NY 14830.
Soil Conservation Society of America (1945), 7515 N.E. Ankeny Rd., Ankeny, IA 50021; 15,000.
Soil Science Society of America (1936), 677 S. Segoe Rd., Madison, WI 53711; 4,595.
Sojourners, Natl. (1919), 4600 Duke St., Alexandria, VA 22304; 9,500.
Soldier's, Sailor's and Airmen's Club (1919), 283 Lexington Ave., N.Y., NY 10016.
Sons of the Amer. Legion (1932), 700 N. Pennsylvania St., Indianapolis, IN 46206; 30,000.
Sons of the American Revolution, Natl. Society of (1889), 2412 Massachusetts Ave. NW, Wash., DC 20008; 21,500.
Sons of Confederate Veterans (1896), Southern Sta., P.O. Box 5164, Hattiesburg, MS 39401; 5,000.
Sons of Norway (1895), 1455 W. Lake St., Minneapolis, MN 55408; 100,150.
Sons of Poland, Assn. of the (1903), 655 Newark Ave., Jersey City, NJ 07306; 11,569.
Sons of the Revolution in the State of New York (1876), Fraunces Tavern, 54 Pearl St., N.Y., NY 10004; 1,400.
Sons of St. Patrick, Society of the Friendly (1784), 80 Wall St., N.Y., NY 10005; 1,300.
Sons of Union Veterans of the Civil War (1881), 2913 Main St., P.O. Box 6193, Lawrenceville, NJ 08648.
Soroptimist Internatl. of the Americas (1921), 1616 Walnut St., Phila., PA 19103; 32,000.
Southern Christian Leadership Conference (1957), 334 Auburn Ave. NE, Atlanta, GA 30303; 1,000,000.
Southern Regional Council (1944), 75 Marietta St. NW, Atlanta, GA 30303.

Spanish War Veterans, United (1904), 810 Vermont Ave. NW, Wash., DC 20420; 328.
Speech Communication Assn. (1914), 5205 Leesburg Pike, Falls Church, VA 22041; 6,000.
Speech & Hearing Assn., Amer. (1925), 10801 Rockville Pike, Rockville, MD 20852; 27,500.
Speleological Society, Natl. (1941), Cave Ave., Huntsville, AL 35810; 4,500.
Speleological Society of America (1964), 1124 100th Ave. NE, Bellevue, WA 98004; 1,750.
Sports Car Club of America (1944), 1562 S. Parker Rd., Denver, CO 80231; 19,000.
Sports Philatelists Internatl. (1962), 3604 S. Home Ave., Berwyn, IL 60402; 1,112.

Stamp Dealers' Assn., Amer. (1914), 595 Madison Ave., N.Y., NY 10022; 1,200.
Standards Institute, Amer. Natl. (1918), 1430 Broadway, N.Y., NY 10018; 1,000.
State Communities Aid Assn. (1872), 105 E. 22d St., N.Y., NY 10010; 285.
State Governments, Council of (1933), P.O. Box 11910, Iron Works Pike, Lexington, KY 40511; 50 states.
State High School Assns., Natl. Federation of (1920), 400 Leslie St., Elgin, IL 60120; 50 states, 9 provinces.
State & Local History, Amer. Assn. for (1940), 1400 8th Ave. So., Nashville, TN 37203; 5,000.
Statistical Assn., Amer. (1839), 806 15th St. NW, Wash., DC 20005; 12,500.
Steamship Historical Society of America (1935), 414 Pelton Ave., Staten Island, NY 10310; 2,480.
Steel Construction, Amer. Institute of (1921), 1221 Ave. of the Americas, N.Y., NY 10020; 914.
Steel Founders' Society of America (1903), 20611 Center Ridge Rd., Rocky River, OH 44116; 120 companies.
Steeplechase and Hunt Assn., Natl. (1895), Box 308, Elmont, NY 11003; 3,000.
Sterilization, Assn. for Voluntary (1942), 708 Third Ave., N.Y., NY 10017; 2,000.
Steuben Society of America (1919), 369 Lexington Ave., N.Y., NY 10017.
Stock Car Auto Racing, Natl. Assn. for (NASCAR) (1948), 1801 Speedway Blvd., Daytona Beach, FL 32015; 17,000.

Stock Exchange, American (1911), 86 Trinity Pl., N.Y., NY 10006; 650.
Stock Exchange, New York (1792), 11 Wall St., N.Y., NY 10005; 1,366.
Stock Exchange, Philadelphia-Baltimore-Washington (1790), 17th St., Stock Exchange Pl., Phila., PA 19103; 448.
Structural Stability Research Council (1944), Fritz Engineering Laboratory No. 13, Lehigh Univ., Bethlehem, PA 18015; 275.
Student Assn., Natl. (1947), 2115 S St. NW, Wash., DC 20008; 3,600.
Student Councils, Natl. Assn. of (1931), 1904 Association Dr., Reston, VA 22091; 6,000 secondary schools.
Students of German, Natl. Federation of (1968), 339 Walnut St., Phila., PA 19106; 26,500.
Stuttering Project, Natl. (1976), Box 33, Walnut Creek, CA 94596.

Sugar Brokers Assn., Natl. (1903), 76 Beaver St., N.Y., NY 10005; 250.
Sunbathing Assn., Amer. (1929), 810 N. Mills Ave., Orlando, FL 32803; 20,000.
Sunday League (1933), 279 Highland Ave., Newark, NJ 07104; 25,000.
Surfing Assn., Amer. (1966), 7355 Slater Ave., Huntington Beach, CA 92647; 500 teams.
Surgeons, Amer. College of (1913), 55 E. Erie St., Chicago, IL 60611; 38,500.
Surgeons, Internatl. College of (1937), 1516 N. Lake Shore Dr., Chicago, IL 60610; 12,000.
Surveying & Mapping, Amer. Congress on (1941), 210 Little Falls, Falls Church, VA 22046; 7,450.

Symphony Orchestra League, Amer. (1942), P.O. Box 66, Vienna, VA 22180; 2,563.
Systems Management, Assn. for (1947), 24587 Bagley Rd., Cleveland, OH 44138; 10,000.

—T—

Table Tennis Assn., U.S. (1933), P.O. Box 815, Orange, CT 06477; 4,400.
Tall Buildings and Urban Habitat, Council on (1969), Fritz Engineering Laboratory 13, Lehigh Univ., Bethlehem, PA 18015; 1,312.
Tattoo Club of America (1974), 112 W. First St., Mt. Vernon, NY 10550; 5,500.
Tax Accountants, Natl. Assn. of Enrolled Federal (1960), 6108 N. Harding Ave., Chicago, IL 60659; 500.
Tax Administrators, Federation of (1937), 1313 E. 60th St., Chicago, IL 60637; 51 revenue departments.
Tax Assn.-Natl. Tax Institute of America (1907), 21 E. State St., Columbus, OH 43215; 2,800.
Tax Foundation (1937), 50 Rockefeller Plaza, N.Y., NY 10020; 1,573.

Tea Assn. of the U.S.A. (1899), 230 Park Ave., N.Y., NY 10017; 250.
Teachers, Amer. Federation of (1916), 11 Dupont Circle NW, Wash., DC 20036; 475,000.
Teachers of English, Natl. Council of (1911), 1111 Kenyon Rd., Urbana, IL 61801; 38,000.
Teachers of French, Amer. Assn. of (1927), 57 E. Armory Ave., Champaign, IL 61820; 10,800.
Teachers of German, Amer. Assn. of (1926), 339 Walnut St., Phila., PA 19106; 7,600.
Teachers of Singing, Natl. Assn. of (1944), 250 W. 57th St., N.Y., NY 10019; 3,100.
Teachers of Spanish & Portuguese, Amer. Assn. of (1917), Holy Cross Coll., Worcester, MA 01610; 13,000.
Technical Communication, Society for (1958), 1010 Vermont Ave. NW, Wash., DC 20005; 3,300.
Television Arts & Sciences, Natl. Academy of (1947), 291 S. La Cienega Blvd., Beverly Hills, CA 90211; 11,000.
Television Bureau of Advertising (1954), 1345 Ave. of the Americas, N.Y., NY 10019; 350.
Television & Radio Artists, Amer. Federation of (1937), 1350 Ave. of the Americas; N.Y., NY 10019; 30,000.
Telluride Assn. (1910), 217 West Ave., Ithaca, NY 14850; 69.
Tennis Assn., U.S. (1881), 51 E. 42d St., N.Y., NY 10017; 100,000.
Tennis League, Youth (1968), 1701 Vandalia, Collinsville, IL 62234; 850.
Testing & Materials, Amer. Society for (1898), 1916 Race St., Phila., PA 19103; 26,000.
Textile Assn., Northern (1854), 211 Congress St., Boston, MA 02110; 350.
Textile Manufacturers Institute, Amer. (1949), 2124 Wachovia Ctr., Charlotte, NC 28285; 250 companies.

Theatre & Academy, Amer. Natl. (1935), 245 W. 52d St., N.Y., NY 10019; 1,000.
Theatre Assn., Amer. (1936), 1029 Vermont Ave. NW, Wash., DC 20005; 6,000.
Theatre Organ Society, Amer. (1955), P.O. Box 1002, Middleburg, VA 22117; 6,200 families.
Theatre Owners, Natl. Assn. of (1924), 1501 Broadway, N.Y., NY 10036; 8,000.
Theodore Roosevelt Assn. (1919), P.O. Box 720, Oyster Bay, NY 11771; 500.
Theological Library Assn., Amer. (1947), Lutheran Theological Seminary, 7301 Germantown Ave., Phila., PA 19119; 568.
Theological Schools, Amer. Assn. of (1936), P.O. Box 396, Vandalia, OH 45377; 198 schools.
Theosophical Society (1875), 1926 N. Main St., Wheaton, IL 60187; 5,500.
Thoreau Society (1941), SUNY-Geneseo, Geneseo, NY 14454; 1,100.
Thoroughbred Racing Assn. of North America (1942), 3000 Marcus Ave., Lake Success, NY 11040; 53 racetracks.

Titanic Historical Society (1963), P.O. Box 53, Indian Orchard, MA 01151; 1,575.

Toastmasters Internatl. (1924), 2200 N. Grand Ave., Santa Ana, CA 92711; 62,000
Toastmistress Clubs, Internatl. (1938), 9068 E. Firestone Blvd., Downey, CA 90241; 21,429.
Topical Assn., Amer. (1949), 3306 N. 50th St., Milwaukee, WI 53216; 10,000.
Torch Clubs, Internatl. Assn. of (1924), P.O. Box 81890, Lincoln, NE 68501; 5,000.
Toy Manufacturers of America (1916), 200 Fifth Ave., N.Y., NY 10010; 250.

Trade Relations Council of the U.S. (1885), 1001 Connecticut Ave. NW, Wash., DC 20036; 50 companies.
Traffic and Transportation, Amer. Society of (1946), 547 W. Jackson Blvd., Chicago, IL 60606; 2,800.
Training Corps, Amer. (1961), 107-12 Jamaica Ave., Richmond Hill, NY 11418; 350.
Training & Development, Amer. Society for (1943), P.O. Box 5307, Madison, WI 53705; 12,000.
Transit Assn., Amer. Public (1974), 1100 17th St. NW, Wash., DC 20036; 750.
Transportation Assn. of America (1935), 1100 17th St. NW, Wash., DC 20036; 600 companies.
Transportation Engineers, Institute of (1930), 1815 N. Ft. Meyer Dr., Arlington, VA 22209; 5,745.
Trapshooting Assn., Amateur (1923), 601 W. National Rd., Vandalia, OH 45377; 80,000.
Travel Agents, Amer. Society of (1931), 711 Fifth Ave., N.Y., NY 10022; 15,000.
Travel Organizations, Discover America (1969), 1100 Connecticut Ave. NW, Wash., DC 20036; 950.
Travelers Aid-Internatl. Social Service of America (1972), 345 E. 46th St., N.Y., NY 10017; 1,010 U.S. & foreign agencies.
Trucking Assn., Amer. (1933), 1616 P St. NW, Wash., DC 20036; 51 assns.
True Sisters, United Order (1846), 150 W. 85th St., N.Y., NY 10024; 11,000.

Turners, Amer. (1848), 1550 Clinton Ave. N., Rochester, NY 14621; 17,000.

—U—

UNICEF, U.S. Committee for (1947), 331 E. 38th St., N.Y., NY 10016.
UFOs (Unidentified Flying Objects), Natl. Investigations Committee on (1967), 7970 Woodman Ave., Van Nuys, CA 91402; 1,300.
Uniformed Services, Natl. Assn. for (1968), 956 N. Monroe St., Arlington, VA 22201; 25,000.
United Nations Assn. of the U.S.A. (1923, as **League of Nations Assn.**) 300 E. 42d St., N.Y., NY 10017; 25,000.
United Press Internatl. (1907), 220 E. 42d St., N.Y., NY 10017.
United Service Organizations (USO) (1941), 237 E. 52d St., N.Y., NY 10022.
United States Army, Assn. of the (1950), 1529 18th St. NW, Wash., DC 20036; 84,513.
United Way of America (1932), 801 N. Fairfax St., Alexan-

dria, VA 22314; 1,148.

Universities, Assn. of Amer. (1900), One Dupont Circle NW, Wash., DC 20036; 50 institutions.

Universities & Colleges, Assn. of Governing Boards of (1921), One Dupont Circle NW, Wash., DC 20036; 17,000.

University Extension Assn., Natl. (1915), One Dupont Circle NW, Wash., DC 20036; 230 institutions.

University Foundation, Internatl. (1973), 501 E. Armour Blvd., Kansas City, MO 64109; 692.

University Professors, Amer. Assn. of (1915), One Dupont Circle NW, Wash., DC 20036; 73,064.

University Women, Amer. Assn. of (1882), 2401 Virginia Ave. NW, Wash., DC 20037; 190,000.

Urban Coalition, Natl. (1968), 1201 Connecticut Ave. NW, Wash., DC 20024.

Urban League, Natl. (1910), 500 E. 62d St., N.Y., NY 10021.

Utility Commissioners, Natl. Assn. of Regulatory (1889), 1102 ICC Bldg., P.O. Box 684, Wash., DC 20044; 290.

—V—

Variety Clubs Internatl. (1928), 58 W. 58th St., N.Y., NY 10019; 11,000.

Veteran Motor Car Club of America (1938), Museum of Transportation, 15 Newton St., Brookline, MA 02146; 4,509.

Veterans Committee, Amer. (1948), 1333 Connecticut Ave. NW, Wash., DC 20036; 10,000.

Veterans of Foreign Wars of the U.S. (1899) **& Ladies Auxiliary** (1914), 406 W. 34th St., Kansas City, MO 64111; 1,850,000 & 540,000.

Veterans of World War I of the U.S.A. (1958), 916 Prince St., Alexandria, VA 22314; 115,000.

Veterinary Medical Assn., Amer. (1863), 930 N. Meacham Rd., Schaumburg, IL 60196; 27,500.

Victorian Society in America (1966), The Athenaeum, East Washington Sq., Phila., PA 19106; 3,500.

Vocational Assn., Amer. (1925), 1510 H St. NW, Wash., DC 20005; 55,000.

Volleyball Assn., U.S. (1928), 557 Fourth St., San Francisco, CA 94107; 12,000.

—W—

War of 1812, General Society of the (1814), 1307 New Hampshire Ave. NW, Wash., DC 20036; 1,500

War Mothers, Amer. (1917), 2615 Woodley Pl. NW, Wash., DC 20008; 11,000.

Watch & Clock Collectors, Natl. Assn. of (1943), 514 Popular St., Columbia, PA 17512; 30,500.

Water Pollution Control Federation (1928), 2626 Pennsylvania Ave. NW, Wash., DC 20037; 26,000.

Water Resources Assn., Amer. (1964), St. Anthony Falls Hydraulic Lab, Mississippi River at 3d Ave. SE, Minneapolis, MN 55414; 1,523.

Water Ski Assn., Amer. (1939), State Rte. 550 at Carl Floyd Rd., Winter Haven, FL 33880; 15,000.

Water Well Assn., Natl. (1948), 500 W. Wilson Bridge Rd., Worthington, OH 43085; 5,291.

Water Works Assn., Amer. (1881), 6666 W. Quincy Ave., Denver, CO 80235; 26,000.

Watercolor Society, Amer. (1866), 1083 Fifth Ave., N.Y., NY 10028; 575.

Welding Society, Amer. (1919), 2501 NW 7th St., Miami, FL 33125; 30,560.

Wheelchair Athletic Assn., Natl. (1958), 40-24 62d St., Woodside, NY 11377; 2,500.

Wild Horse Organized Assistance (WHOA!) (1971), 63 Keyston, P.O. Box 555, Reno, NV 89504; 12,000.

Wilderness Society (1935), 1901 Pennsylvania Ave. NW, Wash., DC 20006; 75,000.

Wildlife, Defenders of (1925), 1244 19th St. NW, Wash., DC 20036; 35,000.

Wildlife Federation, Natl. (1936), 1412 16th St. NW, Wash., DC 20036; 3,500,000.

Wildlife Foundation, No. Amer. (1935), 1000 Vermont Ave., NW, Wash., DC 20005.

Wildlife Fund—U.S., World (1961), 1319 18th St. NW, Wash., DC 20036; 50,000.

Wildlife Management Institute (1911), 1000 Vermont Ave. NW, Wash., DC 20005.

Wildlife Society (1937), 7101 Wisconsin Ave. NW, Wash., DC 20014; 7,500.

William Penn Assn. (1886), 429 Forbes Ave., Pittsburgh, PA 15219; 66,902.

Wireless Pioneers, Society of (1967), P.O. Box 530, 3366—15 Mendocino Ave., Santa Rosa, CA 95401; 3,267.

Wizard of Oz Club, Internatl. (1957), Box 95, Kinderhook, IL 62345; 1,628.

Woman's Assn., Amer. (1914), 1271 Ave. of the Americas, N.Y., NY 10020; 250.

Woman's Christian Temperance Union, Natl. (1874), 1730 Chicago Ave., Evanston, IL 60201; 250,000.

Women, Natl. Organization for (NOW) (1966), 425 13th St. NW, Wash., DC 20004; 60,000.

Women Artists, Natl. Assn. of (1889), 41 Union Sq. N.Y., NY 10003; 700.

Women Engineers, Society of (1950), 345 E. 47th St., N.Y., NY 10017; 3,800.

Women Geographers, Society of (1925), 1619 New Hampshire Ave. NW, Wash., DC 20009; 460.

Women Marine Assn. (1960), 5403 Oakhurst Dr. No., Seminole, FL 33542; 28,000.

Women Strike for Peace (1961), 145 S. 13th St., Phil., PA 19107.

Women of the U.S.A., Natl. Council of (1888), 345 E. 46th St., N.Y., NY 10017; 2,000.

Women Voters of the U.S., League of (1920), 1730 M St. NW, Wash., DC 20036; 140,000.

Women World War Veterans (1919), 237 Madison Ave., N.Y., NY 10016; 145,000.

Women's Army Corps Veterans Assn. (1946), 3839-37 Vista Campana So., Oceanside, CA 92054; 1,905.

Women's Clubs, General Federation of (1890), 1734 N St. NW, Wash., DC 20036; 10,000,000.

Women's Clubs, Natl. Federation of Business & Professional (1919), 2012 Massachusetts Ave. NW, Wash., DC 20036; 170,000.

Women's Educational & Industrial Union (1877), 356 Boylston St., Boston, MA 02116; 2,500.

Women's Internatl. League for Peace & Freedom (1915), 1213 Race St., Phila., PA 19118; 10,000.

Women's Overseas Service League (1921), P.O. Box 39033, Friendship Sta., Wash., DC 20016; 5,000.

Women's Veterinary Medical Assn. (1947), c/o Dr. Judith Spurling, 6246 S. Ash Circle E., Littleton, CO 81001.

Woodmen of America, Modern (1883), 1701 First Ave., Rock Island, IL 61201; 500,000.

Woodmen of the World (1890), 1450 Speer Blvd., Denver, CO 80204; 28,954.

Wool Growers Assn., Natl. (1865), 336 Southern Bldg., 805 15th St. NW, Wash., DC 20005; 24 state assns.

Workmen's Circle (1900), 45 E. 33d St., N.Y., NY 10016; 55,000.

World Federalists, World Assn. of (1946), Leliegracht 21, Amsterdam, Netherlands; 40,000.

World Future Society (1966), 4916 St. Elmo Ave., Wash., DC 20014; 24,000.

World Health, Amer. Assn. for (1951), 777 United Nations Plaza, N.Y., NY 10017; 1,031.

Writers, Amer. Society of (1975), 890 National Press Bldg., Wash., DC 20045; 1,300.

Writers of America, Western (1952), 1505 W. D St., North Platte, NE 69101; 325.

Writers Assn. of America, Outdoor (1927), 4141 W. Bradley Rd., Milwaukee, WI 53209; 1,400.

Writers Guild of America, west (1932), 8955 Beverly Blvd., Los Angeles, CA 90048; 4,200.

—Y & Z—

Yeomen F. Natl. (1936), 223 El Camino Real, Vallejo, CA 94590; 800.

Young Americans for Freedom (1960), Woodland Rd., Sterling, VA 22170; 55,000.

Young Men's Christian Assns. of the U.S.A., Natl. Council of (1855), 291 Broadway, N.Y., NY 10007; 8,670,000.

YM-YWHAs of Greater New York, Associated (1957), 130 E. 59th St., N.Y., NY 10022; 60,000.

Young Women's Christian Assn. of the U.S.A. (1858), 600 Lexington Ave., N.Y., NY 10022; 2,456,000.

Youth Hostels, Amer. (1934), Natl. Campus, Delaplane, VA 22025; 70,000.

Zero Population Growth (1968), 1346 Connecticut Ave. NW, Wash., DC 20036; 8,700.

Ziegfeld Club (1936), 55 W. 42d St., NY., NY 10036; 347.

Zionist Organization of America (1897), 4 E. 34th St., N.Y., NY 10016; 120,000.

Zonta Internatl. (1919), 59 E. Van Buren St., Chicago, IL 60605; 25,000.

Zoological Parks & Aquariums, Amer. Assn. of (1924), Oglebay Park, Wheeling, WV 26003; 1,500.

Zoologists, Amer. Society of (1913), Box 2739, California Lutheran College, Thousand Oaks, CA 91360; 4,600.

RELIGIOUS INFORMATION

Census of Religious Groups in the U.S.

Source: World Almanac questionnaire and 1977 Yearbook of American and Canadian churches

Membership figures in the following table are the latest available. Some denominations submitted carefully compiled data while others approached the task more casually. The number of churches is given in parentheses.

Denomination	Members
Adventist Churches:	**541,371**
Advent Christian Church (373)	31,049
Primitive Advent Christian Ch. (10)	530
Seventh-day Adventists (3,446)	509,792
Amana Church Society (7)	**735**
American Rescue Workers (25)	**2,700**
Anglican Orthodox Church (37)	**2,630**
Apostolic Faith (45)	**4,100**
Assemblies of God (9,208)	**898,711**
Baptist Churches:	**26,615,480**
American Baptist Assn. (3,789)	794,864
American Baptist Churches in U.S.A. (5,937)	1,593,574
Baptist General Conference (720)	121,313
Baptist Missionary Assn. of Amer. (1,457)	211,000
Christian Unity Baptist Assn. (5)	345
Conserv. Baptist Assn. of Amer. (1,120)	300,000
Duck River (and Kindred) Assns. of Baptists (86)	8,909
Free Will Baptists (2,419)	227,434
Gen. Assn. of Regular Baptist Chs. (1,528)	234,701
General Baptists (800)	70,000
General Six-Principle Baptist (8)	308
Natl. Baptist Conv. of Amer. (11,398)	2,668,799
Natl. Baptist Conv., U.S.A. (26,000)	5,500,000
Natl. Primitive Baptist Convention (2,198)	1,645,000
N. Amer. Baptist Gen. Conf. (245)	41,437
Progressive Natl. Baptist Conv. (655)	521,692
Regular Bap. Chs., Gen. Assn. of (1,503)	250,000
Separate Baptists in Christ (84)	7,496
Seventh Day Bapt. Gen. Conf. (73)	5,230
Southern Baptist Convention (34,710)	12,513,378
Berean Fundamental Church (50)	**2,350**
Bethel Ministerial Association (25)	**4,000**
Bible Protestant Church (42)	**2,254**
Bible Way Church of Our Lord Jesus Christ World Wide (350)	**30,000**
Brethren (German Baptists):	**232,175**
Brethren Ch. (Ashland, Oh.) (119)	16,279
Brethren Churches, Natl. Fellowship of (243)	33,514
Church of the Brethren (1,042)	178,157
Old German Baptist Brethren (54)	4,225
Brethren, Plymouth (690)	**40,000**
Brethren (River):	**11,132**
Brethren in Christ Church (157)	10,255
United Zion Church (16)	877
Buddhist Churches of America (59)	**100,000**
Christadelphians (850)	**15,800**
Christian & Missionary Alliance (1,236)	**188,053**
Christian Catholic Church (6)	**2,000**
Christian Church (Disciples of Christ) (4,426)	**1,278,734**
Christian Church of N. Amer., Gen. Council (110)	**8,500**
Christian Nation Church, U.S.A. (16)	**2,000**
Christian Union (108)	**5,301**
Church of Christ (Holiness) U.S.A. (159)	**9,289**
Church of Christ, Scientist (2,350) (membership not recorded)	
Church of Christ (32)	**2,400**
The Church of God (2,035)	**75,890**
Church of God in Christ (4,500)	**425,000**
Church of Illumination (14)	**9,000**
Church of the Nazarene (4,727)	**430,128**
Church of Revelation (10)	**750**
Churches of Christ (18,000)	**2,400,000**
Chs. of Christ in Christian Union (245)	**9,786**
Churches of God:	**698,066**
Ch. of God (Anderson, Ind.) (2,239)	161,401
Ch. of God (Cleveland, Tenn.) (4,392)	328,892
Church of God of Prophecy (1,755)	62,743
Ch. of God, Seventh Day (7)	2,000
Ch. of God, Seventh Day (Denver) (98)	5,600

Denomination	Members
Churches of God, Gen. Conference (351)	37,040
The Church of God (2,035)	75,890
The (Original) Ch. of God (70)	20,000
The Church of God by Faith (105)	4,500
Churches of the Living God:	**47,670**
Church of the Living God (276)	45,320
House of God, Which is the Church of the Living God, the Pillar and Ground of the Truth (107)	2,350
Church of New Jerusalem, Gen. (33)	**2,143**
Congregational Christian Churches, Natl. Assn. of (379)	**94,000**
Congregational Holiness Ch. (147)	**4,859**
Conservative Cong. Christian Conf. (127)	**21,975**
Eastern Orthodox Churches:	**4,176,040**
Albanian Orthodox Archdio. in Amer. (15)	40,000
Albanian Orthodox Diocese of Amer. (10)	5,240
American Carpatho-Russian Orthodox Greek Catholic Church (70)	100,000
American Catholic Church (Syro-Antiochian) (3)	495
Antiochian Orthodox Christian Archdio. of North America (108)	130,000
Armenian Apostolic Ch. of America (29)	125,000
Armenian Church of Amer., Diocese of the (58)	372,000
Bulgarian Eastern Orthodox Ch. (11)	3,000
Greek Orthodox Archdio. of N. and S. America (530)	2,000,000
Holy Orthodox Church in America (Eastern Cath. & Apostolic) (4)	260
Holy Ukrainian Autocephalic Orthodox Ch. in Exile (15)	4,800
Orthodox Church in America (325)	1,000,000
Romanian Orthod. Episcopate of Amer. (32)	35,000
Russian Orthodox Church in the U.S.A., Patriarchal Parishes (41)	51,500
Russian Orthodox Church Outside Russia (102)	76,000
Serbian Eastern Orthodox Church (48)	65,000
Syrian Orthodox Church of Antioch (Archdio. of the U.S.A. & Canada) (10)	50,000
Ukrainian Orthodox Ch. in the U.S.A. (107)	87,745
Ukrainian Orthodox Church in Amer. (Ecumenical Patriarchate) (23)	30,000
Ethical Union, American (23)	5,000
Evangelical Congregational Ch. (161)	29,636
Evangelical Covenant Ch. of America (508)	69,960
Evangelical Free Ch. of America (562)	70,490
Evangelistic Associations:	78,200
Apostolic Christian Chs. of Amer. (78)	9,500
Apostolic Christian Ch. (Nazarean) (39)	4,000
The Christian Congregation (495)	59,600
Pillar of Fire (61)	5,100
Free Christian Zion Ch. of Christ (742)	22,260
Friends:	125,432
Evangelical Friends Alliance (254)	25,708
Friends General Conference (375)	26,184
Friends United Meeting (506)	65,933
Religious Society of Friends (Conservative) (26)	1,840
Religious Society of Friends (unaffiliated) (72)	2,771
Holiness Church of God (28)	**927**
Independent Fundamental Churches of Amer. (995)	**129,313**
Internatl. Church of the Foursquare Gospel (741)	**89,215**

Denomination	Members
Jehovah's Witnesses (7,128)	**577,362**
Jewish Congregations:	**3,700,000**
Union of Amer. Hebrew Cong. (720)	1,200,000
Union of Orthodox Jewish Cong. of Amer. (1,000)	1,000,000
United Synagogue of Amer. (820)	1,500,000
Latter-day Saints:	**2,551,042**
Church of Jesus Christ (Bickertonites) (50)	2,463
Church of Jesus Christ of Latter-day Saints (Mormon) (5,489)	2,391,892
Reorganized Church of Jesus Christ of Latter Day Saints (1,039)	156,687
Lutheran Churches:	**8,246,895**
The Lutheran Ch. in America (5,727)	2,977,634
Lutheran Church-Mo. Synod (5,813)	2,769,594
The American Lutheran Church (5,985)	2,853,574
Other Lutheran Churches:	**456,262**
Church of the Lutheran Brethren of Amer. (98)	9,300
Church of the Lutheran Confession (72)	9,790
Evangelical Lutheran Church in America (Eielsen) (9)	2,500
Evangelical Lutheran Synod (Norwegian Synod) (107)	19,571
Free Lutheran Congregations, Assn. of (125)	13,471
Protestant Conference (Lutheran) (7)	2,675
Wis. Evangelical Lutheran Synod (1,081)	398,955
Mennonite Churches:	**175,757**
Beachy Amish Mennonite Ch. (72)	4,297
Ch. of God in Christ (Mennonite) (38)	6,204
Evangelical Mennonite Brethren (32)	3,874
Evangelical Mennonite Church (20)	3,131
Gen. Conference Mennonite Ch. (188)	35,534
Hutterian Brethren (29)	3,405
Mennonite Church (1,059)	96,092
Old Order Amish Church (368)	14,720
Old Order (Wisler) Mennonite Ch. (38)	8,000
Reformed Mennonite Church (12)	500
Methodist Churches:	**12,755,894**
African Meth. Episcopal Ch. (5,878)	1,166,301
African M.E. Zion Church (5,994)	1,024,974
Christian Meth. Episcopal Ch. (2,598)	466,718
Evangelical Methodist Church (145)	11,025
Free Methodist Ch. of N. Amer. (1,059)	68,180
Fundamental Methodist Church (14)	692
The United Methodist Church (39,027)	9,957,710
Primitive Method. Ch. U.S.A. (85)	11,024
Reformed Meth. Union Episc. Ch. (18)	2,192
Reformed Zion Union Apostolic Ch. (50)	16,000
Southern Methodist Church (174)	11,000
Missionary Church, The (273)	20,078
Moravian Churches:	**48,700**
Moravian Ch. in Amer., North Prov. (95)	25,385
Moravian Ch. in Amer., South Prov. (50)	17,173
Unity of the Brethren (32)	6,142
New Apostolic Church of N. Amer. (298)	**22,563**

Denomination	Members
Old Catholic Churches:	**84,333**
American Catholic Church, N.Y. Archdio. (7)	700
N. Amer. Old R.C. Church (121)	60,098
N. Amer. Old R.C. Church (5)	972
Open Bible Standard Churches (275)	**30,000**
Pentecostal Assemblies:	**461,088**
Elim Fellowship (70)	5,000
Internatl. Pentecostal Assemblies (55)	10,000
Pentecostal Church of Christ (45)	1,435
Pentecostal Ch. of God of Amer. (1,200)	90,000
Pentecostal Fire-Baptized Holiness Ch. (41)	545
Pentecostal Free Will Baptist Ch. (128)	10,000
Pentecostal Holiness Church (1,340)	74,108
United Pentecostal Church (2,775)	270,000
Polish Natl. Catholic Ch. of Amer. (162)	**282,411**
Presbyterian Churches:	**3,809,638**
Associate Reformed Presbyt. Church (General Synod) (153)	31,154
Cumberland Presbyterian Ch. (854)	85,738
Orthodox Presbyterian Ch. (123)	14,871
Presbyterian Church in America (260)	41,232
Presbyterian Ch. in the U.S. (4,028)	883,185
Reformed Presbyterian Ch., Evangelical Synod (142)	24,248
Reformed Presbyterian Church of N. Amer. (69)	5,445
United Presbyt. Ch. in the U.S.A. (8,675)	2,723,565
Protestant Episcopal Church (7,177)	**2,857,513**
Reformed Churches:	**657,647**
Christian Reformed Church (782)	288,024
Hungarian Reformed Ch. in Am. (28)	11,679
Reformed Church in America (902)	354,004
Reformed Church in the U.S. (24)	3,940
Reformed Episcopal Church (64)	**6,532**
Roman Catholic Church (24,135)	**48,881,872**
Salvation Army (1,163)	**384,817**
The Schwenkfelder Church (5)	**2,250**
Sikh Dharma Brotherhood (108)	**200,000**
Social Brethren (34)	**1,722**
Spiritualists:	**172,302**
Int. Gen. Assembly of Spiritualists (209)	164,072
Natl. Spiritual Alliance of the U.S.A. (34)	3,230
Natl. Spiritualist Assn. of Chs. (200)	5,000
Triumph the Church and Kingdom of God in Christ (475)	**54,307**
Unitarian Universalist Assn. (1,001)	**191,169**
United Brethren:	**26,757**
United Brethren in Christ (276)	26,335
United Christian Church (12)	422
United Church of Christ (6,528)	**1,801,241**
United Holy Ch. of America (470)	**28,980**
Vedanta Society of New York (13)	**1,000**
Volunteers of America (586)	**31,870**
Wesleyan Church, The (1,828)	**94,215**

Religious Population of the World

Source: The 1977 Encyclopaedia Britannica Book of the Year

Religion	N. America[1]	S. America	Europe[2]	Asia	Africa	Oceania[3]	Totals
Total Christian	228,479,000	161,872,500	358,732,600	86,358,000	98,326,000	17,290,000	951,058,100
Roman Catholic	130,789,000	151,017,000	182,087,000	44,239,500	31,168,500	3,230,000	542,531,000
Eastern Orthodox	4,121,000	55,000	62,145,600	1,786,000	16,335,000	360,000	84,803,200
Protestant[4]	93,569,000	10,800,500	114,500,000	40,332,500	50,822,500	13,700,000	323,724,500
Jewish	6,356,675	675,000	3,960,000	3,186,460	274,760	80,000	14,532,895
Moslem	248,100	197,800	8,277,000	427,035,000	101,889,500	66,000	537,713,400
Zoroastrian	250	—	3,000	224,700	530	—	228,480
Shinto	60,000	92,000	—	61,004,000	—	—	61,156,000
Taoist[5]	16,000	12,000	—	29,256,100	—	—	29,284,100
Confucian[5]	96,100	85,000	25,000	175,440,250	500	42,000	175,688,850
Buddhist	155,000	195,300	220,000	244,212,000	2,000	16,000	244,800,300
Hindu	80,000	547,000	330,000	516,713,500	473,650	650,000	518,794,150
Sikh	—	—	—	10,000,000	—	—	12,000,000
Totals	**235,491,125**	**163,676,600**	**371,547,600**	**1,553,430,010**	**200,966,940**	**13,144,000**	**2,545,256,275**
Population[6]	**347,934,000**	**224,154,000**	**733,454,000**	**2,304,929,000**	**412,183,000**	**21,729,000**	**4,044,433,000**

(1) Includes Central America and the West Indies. (2) Includes the USSR where it is difficult to determine religious affiliation. (3) Includes Australia, New Zealand, and islands of the South Pacific. (4) Protestant figures outside Europe usually include "full members" rather than all baptized persons and are not comparable to those of ethnic religions or churches counting all adherents. (5) Statistics for Confucianism and Taoism are undeterminable in China since the Maoist-Marxist revolution. (6) Continental total populations are United Nations data.

Headquarters, Leaders of U.S. Religious Groups

(year organized in parentheses)

Advent Christian Church (1854) — Pres., Rev. Joe Tom Tate. Exec. v.p., Rev. Adrian B. Shepard, Box 23152, Charlotte, NC 28212.

Adventists, Seventh-day, General Conference of, (1863) — Pres., Robert H. Pierson. Sec., C.O. Franz, 6840 Eastern Ave. NW, Takoma Park, Wash., DC 20012.

African Methodist Episcopal Zion Church (1796) — Senior bishop, Herbert Shaw. Sec., Board of Bishops, Bishop Charles H. Foggie, 1200 Windermere Dr., Pittsburgh, PA 15218.

Antiochian Orthodox Christian Archdiocese (formerly Syrian Antiochian Orthodox Church; merged, 1976, with Antiochian Orthodox Archdiocese of Toledo, Oh.) (1894) — Head of Archdiocese Metropolitan, Archbishop Philip (Saliba), primate; Archbishop Michael Shaheen, auxiliary, 358 Mountain Rd., Englewood, NJ 07631.

Armenian Church of America, Diocese of The (1889) — Primate, Most Rev. Archbishop Torkom Manoogian. Sec., Very Rev. Zaven Arzoumanian, 630 2d Ave., N.Y., NY 10016.

Assemblies of God (1914) — Gen. supt., Thomas F. Zimmerman. Gen. sec., Joseph R. Flower, 1445 Boonville Ave., Springfield, MO 65802.

Augustana Evangelical Lutheran Church. *See The Lutheran Church in America.*

Baha'i Faith — About 5,500 communities, groups and isolated centers in the U.S. Sec., Natl. Spiritual Assembly, Glenford E. Mitchell, 536 Sheridan Rd., Wilmette, IL 60091.

Baptist Association, American (1905) — Pres., Dr. Roy M. Reed. Sec., Dr. L. Chester Guinn, 4605 N. State Line, Texarkana, TX 75501.

Baptist Association of America, Conservative (1947) — Pres., Dr. Lee W. Toms. Sec., Rev. Carl E. Abrahamsen Jr., P.O. Box 66, Wheaton, IL 60187.

Baptist Churches in the U.S.A., American (1907) — Pres., Dr. Charles Z. Smith. Gen. Sec., Rev. Dr. Robert C. Campbell, Valley Forge, PA 19481.

Baptist Churches, General Assn. of Regular (1932) — Nat'l. Rep., Dr. Joseph M. Stowell, 1300 N. Meacham Rd., Schaumburg, IL 60195.

Baptist Churches, Unified Free Will (1964) — Pres., Bishop Caldwell Thomas. Exec. sec., Ernest Leonard, P.O. Box 4255, Newark, NJ 07112.

Baptist Convention, Southern (1945) — Pres., James L. Sullivan. Exec. Sec., Dr. Porter Routh, 460 James Robertson Parkway, Nashville, TN 37219.

Baptist General Conference (1879) — Gen. Sec., Warren Magnuson, 1233 Central St., Evanston, IL 60201.

Baptist General Conference, North American (1865) — Moderator, Dr. Kenneth L. Fischer. Exec. sec., Dr. G. K. Zimmerman, 1 So. 210 Summit Ave., Oakbrook Terrace, Villa Park, IL 60181.

Baptist Missionary Assn. of America (formerly **North American Baptist Assn.**) (1950) — Pres., Rev. Kenneth Bobo, 4930 Park Ave., Memphis, TN 38117.

Baptist, National, Convention of America (1880) — Pres., Dr. James C. Sams, 1724 Jefferson St., Jacksonville, FL 32209.

Baptists, Free Will (1727) — Moderator, Dr. J. D. O'Donnell. Exec. sec., Rufus Coffey, P.O. Box 1088, Nashville, TN 37202.

Baptists, General (1611) — Moderator, Rev. Kenneth Kennedy. Clerk, Vern Whitten, 1629 Stinson Ave., Evansville, IN 47712.

Buddhist Churches of America (1914) — Bishop Kenryu Takashi Tsuji, 1710 Octavia St., San Francisco, CA 94109.

Bulgarian Eastern Orthodox Church (1909) — Most Rev. Joseph, Metropolitan, 312 W. 101st St., N.Y., NY 10025.

Calvary Grace Christian Churches of Faith (1898) — Internatl. gen. supt., Rev. Dr. Herman Keck Jr., 5610 Tennessee Ave., Chattanooga, TN 37409.

Calvary Grace Church of Faith (1874) — Rev. A. C. Spern, Internatl. gen. supt., P.O. Box 333, Rillton, PA 15678.

Christian and Missionary Alliance (1887) — Pres., Dr. Nathan Bailey. Sec., Dr. R. W. Battles, 350 N. Highland Ave., Nyack, NY 10960.

Christian Church (Disciples of Christ) (1809) — Gen. minister and pres., Dr. Kenneth L. Teegarden, Box 1986, Indianapolis, IN 46206.

Christian Endeavor, International Society of (1881) — Pres., Timothy J. Kribs. Gen. sec., Rev. Charles W. Barner, 1221 East Broad St., P.O. Box 1110, Columbus, OH 43216.

Christian Reformed Church (1847) — Stated clerk, Rev. William P. Brink, 2850 Kalamazoo Ave., SE, Grand Rapids, MI 49508.

Church of Christ, Scientist (1879) — The Mother Church, The First Church of Christ, Scientist, in Boston, Mass. Pres., James Spencer. First reader, Grace Channell Wasson. Second reader, Bryan G. Pope. Clerk, Corinne LaBarre, Christian Science Center, Boston, MA 02115.

Church of God (Anderson, Ind.) (1880) — Exec. Sec., W. E. Reed, Box 2420, Anderson, IN 46011.

Church of God, The (1903) — General Overseer, Bishop Voy M. Bullen, 2504 Arrow Wood Dr., SE, Huntsville, AL 35803.

Church of Jesus Christ of Latter-Day Saints (Mormon) (1830) — Pres., Spencer W. Kimball. Pres. of the Council of Twelve Apostles, Ezra Taft Benson, 47 E. South Temple St., Salt Lake City, UT 84111.

Church of Jesus Christ of Latter Day Saints, Reorganized (1830) — Pres., W. Wallace Smith. Public Information Office, Elroy Hanton, P.O. Box 1059, Independence, MO 64051.

Church of the Brethren (1719) — Gen sec., General Board, S. Loren Bowman (after Jan. 1, 1978, Robert W. Neff), 1451 Dundee Ave., Elgin, IL 60120.

Church of the Nazarene (1908) — Gen. Sec., B. Edgar Johnson, 6401 The Paseo, Kansas City, MO 64131.

Churches of Christ — No central organization. B. C. Goodpasture, editor, the Gospel Advocate, 1006 Elm Hill Rd., Nashville, TN 37210.

Churches of God, Gen. Conference (1825) — Pres., Dr. K. E. Boldosser. Sec., Rev. Harry G. Cadamore, 1934 Candlewick Dr., Findlay, OH 45840.

Congregational Christian Churches, General Council. *See United Church of Christ.*

Congregational Christian Churches, Natl. Assn. of (1955) — Moderator, Rev. Walter A. Boring. Exec. sec., Rev. Dr. Erwin A. Britton, P.O. Box 1620, Oak Creek, WI 53154.

Ethical Union, American (Ethical Culture Movement) — Pres., Paul Gellert. Exec. Dir., Jean S. Kotkin, 2 W. 64th St., N.Y., NY 10023. Member of Internatl. Humanist and Ethical Union.

Evangelical Christian Churches (1966) — Pres., Rev. John Wahnert, 2075-A N. John Russell Circle, Elkins Park, PA 19117.

Evangelical Christian Churches, California Synod (1966) — Pres.-Treas., Dr. Richard W. Hart Sr., P.O. Box 399, Huntington Park, CA 90255.

Evangelical Lutheran Synod (Norwegian Synod) (1918) — Pres., Rev. W.W. Petersen. Sec., Rev. Alf Merseth, 106 13th St., S., Northwood, IA 50459.

Evangelical Methodist Church (1946) — Gen. sec., Rev. R. D. Driggers, 3036 N. Meridian, Wichita, KS 67204.

Evangelical and Reformed Church. *See United Church of Christ.*

Finnish Evangelical Lutheran Church (Suomi Synod). *See Lutheran Church in America.*

Foursquare Gospel, International Church of the (1927) — Pres., Dr. Rolf K. McPherson. Sec., Dr. Leland B. Edwards, 1100 Glendale Blvd., Los Angeles, CA 90026.

Friends, General Conference of the Religious Society of (1900) — Chmn., Stephen L. Angell Jr. Gen. sec., Dwight L. Wilson, 1520-B Race St., Philadelphia, PA 19102.

Friends United Meeting (formerly **Five Years Meeting of Friends**) (1902) — Presiding Clerk, J. Binford Farlow. Gen. Sec., Lorton G. Heusel, 101 Quaker Hill Dr., Richmond, IN 47374.

Greek Orthodox Church of North and South America (1864) — Primate, the Most Rev. Archbishop Iakovos Chan., Very Rev. George J. Bacopulos, 10 E. 79th St., N.Y., NY 10021.

Hebrew Congregations, Union of American — Pres., Rabbi Alexander M. Schindler, 838 Fifth Ave., N.Y., NY 10021.

Independent Fundamental Churches of America (1930) — Pres., Rev. Donald Hurlburt. Exec. Dir., Rev. Bryan J. Jones, Box 242, Westchester, IL 60153.

Jehovah's Witnesses (1884) — Chairmanship (rotating) of Governing Body. Watchtower Bible and Tract Society, Pres., Nathan H. Knorr, 124 Columbia Heights, Brooklyn, NY 11201.

Jewish Congregations of America, Union of Orthodox — Pres., Harold M. Jacobs. Exec. v.p., Rabbi Pinchas Stolper, 116 East 27th St., N.Y., NY 10016.

Latter-Day Saints. *See Church of Jesus Christ.*

Lutheran Brethren of America, Church of The (1900) — Pres., Rev. Everald H. Strom, Box 655, Fergus Falls, MN 56537.

Lutheran Church, The American (1961) — Pres., Dr. David W. Preus. Sec., Dr. A. R. Mickelson, 422 S. 5th St., Minneapolis, MN 55415.

Lutheran Church in America (estab. 1962 by consolidation of **Amer. Evangelical Lutheran Ch.** (1874), **Augustana Evangelical Lutheran Ch.** (1860), **Finnish Evangelical Lutheran Ch.** (1890) and **The United Lutheran Ch. in Amer.** (1918) —

Pres., Rev. Robert J. Marshall. Sec., Rev. James R. Crumley Jr., 231 Madison Ave., N.Y., NY 10016.

Lutheran Church-Missouri Synod (1847) — Pres., Dr. J. A. O. Preus. Sec., Rev. Herbert A. Mueller, 500 N. Broadway, St. Louis, MO 63102.

Lutheran Confession, Church of The (1961) — Pres., Rev. Egbert Albrecht, R. 2, Markesan, WI 53946.

Lutheran World Ministries — U.S.A. National Committee/Lutheran World Federation (formed 1967, former National Lutheran Council). — Gen. sec., Rev. Paul A. Wee, 315 Park Ave. South, N.Y., NY 10010.

Mennonite Church (1690) — Moderator, Willis L. Breckbill. Sec. Ivan J. Kauffman, 528 E. Madison St., Lombard, IL 60148.

Methodist Church of North America (1860) — Sec., Board of Bishops, 901 College, Winona Lake, IN 46590.

Methodist Church, The United formed 1968 from union of **The Methodist Church** (1784) and the **Evangelical United Brethren Church** (1767) — Council of Bishops Pres., Bishop W. Kenneth Goodson. Sec., Bishop James K. Mathews, 100 Maryland Ave. NE, Washington, DC 20002.

Moravian Church (Unitas Fratrum) (1740) — **Northern Province:** Hq., 69 W. Church St., P.O. Box 1245, Bethlehem, PA 18018; Pres., Provincial Elders' Conf., Dr. J. S. Groenfeldt. **Southern Province:** Hq., 459 S. Church St., Winston-Salem, NC 27101; Pres., Provincial Elders' Conf., Dr. Richard F. Amos.

New Jersusalem in the U.S.A., General Convention of the (1782) — Pres., Rev. Eric J. Zacharias. Rec. Sec., Mrs. Wilfred G. Rice, 983 Fellsway, Apt. 8, Medford MA 02155.

Open Bible Standard Churches (1919) — Gen. supt., Frank W. Smith, Sec.-treas., O. Ralph Isbill, 2020 Bell Ave., Des Moines, IA 50315.

Orthodox Church in America (formerly **Russian Orthodox Catholic Ch. of Amer.)** (1794) — Primate, Metropolitan Archbishop Ireney. Chancellor, Very Rev. Daniel Hubiak, Rt. 25A, P.O. Box 675, Syosset, NY 11791.

Pentecostal Church of God of America (1919) — Gen. supt., Dr. Roy M. Chappell, 211 Main St., Joplin, MO 64801.

Pentecostal Church, United (1945) — Gen. supt., Stanley W. Chambers. Gen. sec., Robert L. McFarland, 8855 Dunn Rd., Hazelwood, MO 63042.

Presbyterian Church, Cumberland (1810) — Moderator, Hubert Covington. Stated clerk, T. V. Warnick, 1978 Union Ave., Memphis, TN 38104.

Presbyterian Church in the U.S. (1861) — Moderator, Jule C. Spach. Stated clerk, Rev. James E. Andrews, 341 Ponce De Leon Ave., NE, Atlanta, GA 30308.

Presbyterian Church in the U.S.A., The United (formed 1958 through merger of the **Presbyterian Ch. in the U.S.A.** (1706) and the **United Presbyt. Ch. of N. America** (1858) — Moderator, Thelma C. D. Adair. Stated clerk, Ruling Elder William P. Thompson, 475 Riverside Dr., N.Y., NY 10027.

Protestant Episcopal Church, The (1789) — Presiding Bishop, Pres. of Exec. Council, Rt. Rev. John M. Allin, 815 Second Ave., N.Y., NY 10017.

Rabbinical Alliance of America — Pres., Rabbi David B. Hollander, 156 5th Ave., N.Y., NY 10010.

Rabbinical Assembly, The — Pres., Rabbi Stanley Rabinowitz. Exec. v.p., Rabbi W. Kelman, 3080 Broadway, N.Y., NY 10027.

Rabbinical Council of America — Pres., Rabbi Fabian Schonfeld. Exec. v.p., Rabbi Israel Klavan, 220 Park Ave. South, N.Y., NY 10003.

Rabbis, Central Conference of American — Pres., Rabbi Ely E. Pilchik. Exec. v.p., Rabbi Joseph B. Glaser, 790 Madison Ave., N.Y., NY 10021.

Reformed Church in America (1628) — Pres., Rev. Bert Van Soest. Gen. Sec., Rev. Marion de Velder, D.D., 475 Riverside Dr., N.Y., NY 10027.

Reformed Episcopal Church (1873) — Pres. and Presiding Bishop, Rev. Theophilus J. Herter. Sec., Rev. D. Ellsworth Raudenbush, 560 Fountain St., Havre de Grace, MD 21078.

Reformed Presbyterian Church, Evangelical Synod (Apr. 6, 1965, union of the **Reformed Presbyterian Ch., General Synod** and the **Evangelical Presbyterian Ch.)** — Stated clerk, Dr. Paul R. Gilchrist, 107 Hardy Rd., Lookout Mountain, TN 37350.

Roman Catholic Church — National Conference of Catholic Bishops. Pres., Archbishop Joseph L. Bernardin. Sec., Rev. Thomas Kelly, O.P., 1312 Massachusetts Ave. NW, Washington, DC 20005.

Romanian Orthodox Episcopate of America (1929) — Archbishop Valerian D. Trifa. Sec., Rev. Laurence C. Lazar, 2522 Grey Tower Rd., Jackson, MI 49201.

Russian Orthodox Church Outside Russia (1920) — Pres., Council of Bishops, Most Rev. Metropolitan Philaret, 75 East 93rd St., N.Y., NY 10028.

Salvation Army, The (1865 in Eng., 1880 in America) — Natl. Cmdr., Paul S. Kaiser. Natl. chief sec., Col. George Nelting. Natl. Hq., 120-130 W. 14th St., N.Y., NY 10011.

Seamen's Church Institute of N.Y. (1834) — Dir., Rev. James R. Whittemore. Sec., Alfred Lee Loomis 3d, 15 State St., N.Y., NY 10004.

Serbian Eastern Orthodox Church — Diocese for U.S., Canada and Europe. Bishops: Most Rev. Dionisije and Iriney. Sec., Very Rev. Aleksandar Ivanovich, St. Sava Monastery, Libertyville, IL 60048.

Serbian Eastern Orthodox Church in U.S. and Canada — Bishops: Rt. Rev. Bishop Firmilian, Midwest Diocese, 5701 N. Redwood Dr., Chicago, IL 60631. Rt. Rev. Gregory, Western Diocese, 2511 W. Garvey Ave., Alhambra, CA 91803. Rev. Seva, Eastern U.S. and Canadian Diocese, Way Hollow Rd., Edgeworth, PA 15143.

Synagogue Council of America — Pres., Joseph H. Lookstein. Exec. V.P., Rabbi Henry Siegman, 432 Park Ave. South, N.Y., NY 10016.

Ukrainian Orthodox Church of the U.S.A. (1919) — Metropolitan Most Rev. Mstyslav S. Skrypnyk, Box 495, South Bound Brook, NJ 08880.

Unitarian Universalist Assn. (formed 1961 by merger of the **American Unitarian Assn.** (1825) and the **Universalist Church of America** (1793) — Pres., Rev. Robert Nelson West. Moderator, Dr. Joseph L. Fisher. Sec., Russell F. Benson, 25 Beacon St., Boston, MA 02108.

United Church of Chirst (formed 1957 through union of the **General Council of the Congregational Christian Churches** with the **Evangelical and Reformed Ch.)** — Pres., Rev. Joseph H. Evans. Sec. pro tem, Charles H. Lockyear, 297 Park Ave. So., N.Y., NY 10010.

United Sons & Daughters of True Holiness Assn. (1912) — Gen. Sec., Elder B. W. Shoffner, 109 Daniel St., Greensboro, NC 27401.

United Synagogue of America — Pres., Arthur Levine, Exec. Vice Pres., Dr. Benjamin Z. Kreitman, 155 5th Ave., N.Y., NY 10010

Volunteers of America (1896) — Commander-in-chief, Gen. John F. McMahon. Natl. Field Sec., Lt. Colonel Belle Leach. Hq., 340 West 85th St., N.Y., NY 10024.

Wesleyan Church, The (1968) (organized through the merger of the **Pilgrim Holiness Ch.** (1897) and the **Wesleyan Methodist Ch. of America** (1943) — Gen. Superintendents, Dr. Robert W. McIntyre, Dr. M. H. Snyder, Dr. J. D. Abbott, Dr. V. A. Mitchell. Sec., D. Wayne Brown, Box 2000, Marion, IN 46952.

Wisconsin Evangelical Luthern Synod (1850) — Pres., Rev. Oscar Naumann, 3512 W. North Ave., Milwaukee, WI 53208. Sec., Prof. Heinrich J. Vogel, 11757 N. Seminary Drive 65W, Mequon, WI 53092.

World Council of Churches, U. S. Conference for the — Chmn., Dr. Robert J. Marshall. Exec. Sec., Rev. Charles H. Long Jr., 475 Riverside Dr., N.Y., NY 10027.

National Council of Churches

The National Council of the Churches of Christ in the U.S.A. is a cooperative federation of 30 Protestant and Orthodox churches which seeks to advance programs and policies of mutual interest to its members. The NCC was formed in 1950 by the merger of 12 inter-denominational agencies. The Council's member churches now have an aggregate membership totaling approximately 40 million. The NCC is not a governing body and has no control over the policies or operations of any church belonging to it. The work of the Council is divided into 3 divisions — Church and Society, Education and Ministry, Overseas Ministries, and 5 commissions on Faith and Order, Regional and Local Ecumenism, Communication, Stewardship, and Justice, Liberation, and Human Fulfillment. The chief administrative officer of the NCC is Dr. Claire Randall, 475 Riverside Drive, N.Y., NY 10027.

Leading Protestant Denominations in the U.S.

(For number of churches and total members, and address of headquarters, see preceding 4 pages)

Baptists

The Baptist church was formed in England in 1609 as part of the separatist movement from the Church of England.

The first Baptist Church in America was founded in 1638 in Providence, R.I., by Roger Williams. National organization began in 1814, and a Missionary Convention was formed to permit followers to express themselves in terms of missionary activities.

American Baptist Churches in the U.S.A. (formerly Northern Baptist Convention, renamed American Baptist Convention in 1950, and renamed American Baptist Churches in the U.S.A. in 1973) was organized in 1907. Agencies operating under this convention of Baptists include the American Baptist Board of International Ministries, American Baptist Board of National Ministries, American Baptist Board of Educational Ministries, and the Ministers and Missionaries Benefit Board, all at Valley Forge, PA 19481.

National Baptist Convention of America, organized 1880. Consists of the General Organization and 9 others; 1724 Jefferson St., Jacksonville, FL 32290.

National Baptist Convention, U.S.A., Inc., founded in 1880, in Montgomery, Ala., is the oldest and parent convention of Negro Baptists; 915 Spain St., Baton Rouge, LA 70802.

Southern Baptist Convention. In 1845 Southern Baptists withdrew from the General Missionary Convention over the question of slavery and other matters and formed the Southern Baptist Convention, largest of Baptist bodies. Churches in all 50 states are related to the Convention; 2,534 missionaries serve in 77 countries. Boards include Sunday Board, Nashville, Tenn.; Foreign Mission Board, Richmond, Va.; Home Mission Board, Atlanta, Ga.; Annuity Board, Dallas, Tex.

Church of Christ, Scientist

First organized in 1879, under the direction of Mary Baker Eddy, the Christian Science Church took its present form in 1892 as the Mother Church, the First Church of Christ, Scientist, in Boston, Mass. Today there are about 3,200 branches in 54 countries. There are 2,350 Christian Science churches in the U.S. Membership figures are not recorded. Christian Science regards the Bible as its ultimate authority and includes spiritual healing as part of its teachings.

The denomination supports radio and television programs, charitable institutions, and a world-wide Board of Lectureship. It also maintains the Christian Science Publishing Society which publishes the Christian Science Monitor and various religious periodicals. The affairs of the denomination are administered by the Christian Science Board of Directors, Christian Science Center, Boston, MA 02115.

Disciples of Christ

The Christian Church (Disciples of Christ) is an American communion arising out of a concern for Christian unity expressed by Barton W. Stone in 1804 and by Thomas Campbell and his son Alexander in 1809. The first churches were Cane Ridge in Kentucky and Brush Run near Washington, Pa. The "Christians" of Kentucky and the "Disciples" of Pennsylvania and Virginia united in 1832. The first General Convention was held in 1849. The church is thoroughly ecumenical in stance, and is congregational in government. Congregations in the U.S. and Canada number 4,524. The communion is served by the General Office of the Christian Church (Disciples of Christ), 17 general units, 37 regional bodies, and 32 educational institutions.

Evangelical Churches

The Evangelical and Reformed Church. *See United Church of Christ.*

The Evangelical United. Brethren Church. *See United Methodist Church.*

Latter-Day Saints

The churches of the Latter-Day Saints do not consider themselves Protestants because they had no part in the 16th century Protestant Reformation and consider themselves to be the "restored" Church of Jesus Christ.

The Church of Jesus Christ of Latter-Day Saints, often called the "Mormon" church, regards the Bible, the Book of Mormon, the Doctrine and Covenants, and the Pearl of Great Price as the word of God. The church was organized Apr. 6, 1830, at Fayette, N.Y., by Joseph Smith, first president. After settling in Kirtland, Oh., and Independence, Mo., the members located in Nauvoo, Ill., in 1839 to escape persecution. Attacks by a mob led to the fatal shooting of Joseph Smith and his brother Hyrum while they were in the Carthage, Ill., jail for protection from the mob, June 27, 1844. Beginning in 1847 most members, under the leadership of Brigham Young, moved by covered wagons across the Great Plains to Utah.

The church is divided into stakes, wards, branches, and missions. Highest authority is the First Presidency, consisting of the president and 2 counselors, assisted by 12 apostles. Spencer W. Kimball is the 12th and current president.

The Reorganized Church of Jesus Christ of Latter Day Saints was founded Apr. 6, 1830, by Joseph Smith Jr. and reorganized under the leadership of the founder's son, Joseph Smith 3d, in 1860. The church is established in 25 countries, the U.S., and Canada.

Lutherans

The church was started in Europe during the Protestant Reformation by the followers of Martin Luther.

Lutheranism was introduced into the U.S. by Dutch colonists in Manhattan, later by Swedes along the Delaware, by Palatines in Pennsylvania and New York, and by Salzburgers in Georgia.

The American Lutheran Church was organized during a constituting convention at Minneapolis, Minn., in Apr. 1960, merging the American Lutheran Church, The Evangelical Lutheran Church, and United Evangelical Lutheran Church. The merger brought together Lutherans of Danish, German, and Norwegian heritage. A 4th body, The Lutheran Free Church, joined with The American Lutheran Church in Feb. 1963. The 4,822 congregations are divided territorially into districts in the U.S. The foreign mission program involves over 400 missionaries (including wives) on 13 fields in South America, Africa, and Asia. The church's Board of Publication operates the Augsburg Publishing House, 422 S. 5th St., Minneapolis, MN 55415.

Augustana Evangelical Lutheran Church. *See The Lutheran Church in America.*

The Lutheran Church-Missouri Synod was organized in 1847. It is the leader in the conservative group among the Lutherans. The Synod is divided into 40 districts (35 in the U.S., 3 in Canada, 2 in South America). The Synod conducts a world-wide mission program and fosters a system of 16 ministerial and teacher training colleges to staff its congregations and its 1,239 parochial schools. Affiliated are the Lutheran Laymen's League, Lutheran Women's Missionary League, and Walther League (a young people's organization). Valparaiso University, Valparaiso, Ind., is supported and controlled by the Lutheran University Assn. Hq. for the Synod: 500 N. Broadway, St. Louis, MO 63102.

The Lutheran Church in America was organized June 28, 1962, by the consolidation of the American Evangelical Lutheran Church, the Augustana Evangelical Lutheran Church, the Finnish Evangelical Lutheran Church and the United Lutheran Church in America. The body is the largest of the Lutheran churches in the U.S. The Lutheran Church in America is organized in 33 synods in the U.S., Canada, Puerto Rico, and the Virgin Islands. Several agencies are located at 2900 Queen Lane, Philadelphia, Pa.; 327 South LaSalle St., Chicago, Ill.; and 608 2d Ave. S., 2d floor, Minneapolis, Minn.

Wisconsin Evangelical Lutheran Synod was organized in 1850. Formerly the second largest body of the Synodical conference, Wisconsin withdrew from the conference in Aug. 1963.

Methodists

The name Methodist was originally given to Charles and John Wesley and several other Oxford students in 1729. It is thought that the term was selected due to the exact and "methodical" manner in which they performed various engagements which a sense of Christian duty induced them to undertake. The Methodist movement was carried to America in 1760, by emigrants from Ireland.

The United Methodist Church was formed Apr. 23, 1968, in Dallas, Tex., by the union of the Methodist Church and the Evangelical United Brethren Church. The 2 churches shared a common historical and spiritual heritage. The Methodist Church resulted in 1939 from the unification of 3 branches of Methodism — the Methodist Episcopal Church, the Methodist Episcopal Church, South, and the Methodist Protestant Church. The Methodist movement began in 18th century England under the preaching of John Wesley, but the so-called Christmas Conference of 1784 in Baltimore is regarded as the date on which the organized Methodist Church was founded as an ecclesiastical organization. It was there that Francis Asbury was elected the first bishop in this country. The Evangelical United Brethren Church was formed in 1946 with the merger of the Evangelical Church and the Church of the United Brethren in Christ, both of which had their beginnings in Pennsylvania in the evangelistic movement of the 18th and early 19th centuries. Philip William Otterbein and Jacob Albright were early leaders of this movement among German-speaking settlers of the Middle Colonies.

The supreme policy-making body of the United Methodist Church is the quadrennial General Conference. Principal agencies are in the following cities: New York, N.Y.; Evanston, Ill.; Nashville, Tenn.; Washington, D. C.; Dayton, Oh.; and Lake Janaluska, N.C.

The African Methodist Episcopal Church, incorporated 1816 under Pennsylvania laws, is 2d largest of the Methodist bodies. Churches, 4,500, membership, 1,500,000. Pres., Board of Bishops, 951 Old Grove Manor, Jacksonville, FL 32207.

Presbyterians

Presbyterianism is a system of representative churches governed by presbyters, or elders. John Calvin (1509-1564) has been regarded as the founder of Presbyterianism. Presbyterians were among the earliest colonists of America. Their first church was established about 1640 and the first presbytery in 1706.

The United Presbyterian Church in the U.S.A., largest of the Presbyterian bodies, was formed on May 28, 1958, by a merger of the Presbyterian Church in the U.S.A. and the United Presbyterian Church of North America. Offices of the General Assembly, General Assembly's Mission Council, Support Agency, Program Agency, and Vocations Agency are at 475 Riverside Dr., N.Y., NY 10027.

The Presbyterian Church in the United States, which established a separate existence in 1861, is sometimes miscalled the Southern church.

Protestant Episcopal Church

An American religious denomination directly descended from the Church of England. Brought to America by the Jamestown colonists in 1607. Separated from English Church and adopted present name in 1789. Alternate name, "The Episcopal Church," was adopted in 1967.

United Church of Christ

Formed in 1957 by a union of the General Council of the Congregational Christian Church and the Evangelical and Reformed Church. It was the first union in the United States of churches with different forms of church government — congregational and modified presbyterian — and different historical backgrounds. Congregationalism was brought to America by both the Pilgrims of the Mayflower and the Puritans of Massachusetts Bay Colony. Eventually it became the dominant form of church organization in New England. The Evangelical and Reformed Church was started in 1934 with the union of the Evangelical Synod of North America and the Reformed Church in the U.S.

A constitution for the United Church of Christ was declared in force in July 1961. The United Church Board of World Ministries has 251 missionaries and other personnel at work in 30 countries. In the U. S., the United Church of Christ is active in Christian education, church extension, health and welfare, mass communication, race relations, and social action. United Church Board for Homeland Ministries, 287 Park Ave. So., N.Y., NY 10010. United Church Board for World Ministries, 475 Riverside Dr., N.Y., NY 10027.

Leading Protestant Denominations in Canada

Source: Yearbook of American and Canadian Churches and Ontario Bible College

Anglicans

The Anglican Church of Canada was established in the early 1700s, and its first bishop Charles Inglis was appointed in 1787. The General Synod, created in 1893, acts to co-ordinate the various activities of the Church, and usually meets biennially. It is made up of the Church's archbishops and bishops together with the elected clerical and lay representatives from the 28 dioceses and one Episcopal district. Church statistics (1974) show: total parish enrollment 1,048,246; communicants 616,294; congregations 3,228.

Baptists

The two largest Baptist churches are the Federation of Canada and the Fellowship of Evangelical Baptist Churches. The Federation has about 667,245 (1971) members in 4 subdivisions: the Baptist Convention of Ontario and Quebec; the Baptist Union of Western Canada; the United Baptist Convention of the Atlantic Provinces; and the French Baptist Union. Other large Baptist organizations are the Baptist General Conference, the North American Baptist Conference, and the Canadian Southern Baptist Conference.

Lutherans

The first large settlement of Lutherans in Canada was in Halifax in 1749. There are 3 main Lutheran bodies: the Evangelical Lutheran Church of Canada, the Lutheran Church-Canada (Missouri Synod), and the Lutheran Church in America-Canada Section. These bodies cooperate through the Lutheran Council in Canada. Lutherans in Canada 716,000; congregations 1,015.

Presbyterians

The Presbyterian Church in Canada is connected historically to the Church of Scotland. It is organized into 8 synods and 44 presbyteries, and has a membership of 872,335 (1971) and 1,057 congregations.

United Church

The United Church of Canada is the largest Protestant denomination in Canada. It was established in 1925 as a result of a merger among the Methodist Church, the Congregational Churches, and 70% of the Presbyterian Church. The Canada Conference of the Evangelical United Brethren Church joined this union in 1968. The highest policy-making body of the United Church of Canada is the General Council which meets biennially. Total membership, 962,163 (1974).

Headquarters of Religious Groups in Canada

Source: The 1977 Corpus Almanac of Canada and The 1977 Canadian Almanac and Directory

(year organized in parentheses)

Anglican Church of Canada (creation of General Synod 1893) — Primate, Most Rev. E. W. Scott, Gen. Sec. of the General Synod, The Ven. E.S. Light, 600 Jarvis St., Toronto, Ont. M4Y 2J6.

Antiochian Orthodox Christian Church (Syrian) — Rev. Father E. Hanna, 555-575 Jean Talon E., Montreal, P.Q. H2R 1T8.

Apostolic Church in Canada — H. O. 27 Castlefield Avenue, Toronto, Ont. M4R 1G3, Pres., Rev. D. S. Morris, 388 Gerald St., La Salle, P.Q.

Apostolic Church of Pentecost of Canada (Inc. 1921) — H.O. 4-3026 Taylor St., E., Saskatoon, Sask. S7J 4J2. Mod. Rev. D. W. Breen, 14447-104A Ave., Surrey, B.C.

Associated Gospel Churches (1922) — Pres., Rev. W. Sifft; Exec. Sec. Rev. J. L. Hockney, 280 Plains Rd. W., Burlington, Ont. L7T 1G4.

Association of Regular Baptist Churches (Canada) — Pres., Dr. H. C. Slade, 337 Jarvis St., Toronto, Ont. M5B 2C7.

Baha'is of Canada, The National Spiritual Assembly of the (1949) — Gen. Sec. J. D. Martin, 7200 Leslie St., Thornhill, Ont. L3T 2A1.

Baptist Federation of Canada — Pres. David Simmonds, Gen. Sec.-Treasurer, Rev. R. Fred Bullen, 91 Queen St., Box 1298, Brantford, Ont. N3T 5T6.

Baptists, North American, Inc. (Canada) — Sec. Rev. Isador Fraszer, 5010 Dalhousie Dr., N.W., Calgary, Alta. T3A 1B4.

Bible Holiness Movement, The (1949) — Pres. Evangelist Wesley H. Wakefield, Box 223, Stn. A, Vancouver, B.C. V6C 2M3.

Brethren in Christ Church, Canada Conference — Mod. Bishop R. V. Sider, Box 65, Sherkston, Ont.

British Israel World Federation — Office Manager and Secretary, Mrs. S. Cunningham, 313 Sherbourne St., Toronto 2, Ont.

Buddhist Churches of Canada (1945) — Bishop, Rev. Seimoka Kosaka, 918 Bathurst St., Toronto, Ont. M5R 3G5.

Byelorussian Autocephalic Orthodox Church Abroad — Rt. Rev. Bishop Mikalay, 524 St. Clarens Ave., Toronto, Ont. M6H 3W7.

Canadian Council of Churches, The (1938) — Pres. Rev. Dr. Norman Berner, 40 St. Clair Ave. E., Toronto, Ont. M4T 1M9.

Christian and Missionary Alliance in Canada, The (1889) — 2026 Yonge St., Toronto, Ont. M4S 1Z9; Pres., Rev. W. J. Newell, 125 Panin Rd., Burlington, Ont. L7T 1N0.

Christian Church (Disciples of Christ) (All Canada Committee formed 1922) — Pres. Mervin Bailey, Exec. Min. Robert K. Leland; 39 Arkell Rd., R.R. 2, Guelph, Ont. N1H 6H8.

Christian Reformed Churches, The Canadian Council of — Rev. John Van Harmelen, R.R. 8, London, Ont.

Christian Science in Canada — Mr. J. D. Fulton, 696 Yonge St., Ste. 403, Toronto, Ont. M4Y 2A7.

Church Army in Canada, The — Dir. Capt. R. A. Taylor, 397 Brunswick Ave., Toronto, Ont. M5R 2Z2.

Church of Jesus Christ of Latter Day Saints (Mormons), (1830) — Pres. Calgary Stake, L. D. Hanks, 531 Willowbrook Dr. S.E., Calgary, Alta. Pres., Edmonton Stake, Warren S. Wilde, 5108-112 St. Edmonton, Alta. T6H 3J2. Pres., Toronto Stake, J.B. Smith, 79 Alpaca Dr., Scarborough, Ont. Pres., Vancouver Stake, F.E. Berrett, 606 Hawstead Pl., West Vancouver, B.C.

Church of Jesus Christ of Latter-Day Saints, The Reorganized (1830) — Bishop of Canada and Regional Bishop Kenneth G. Fisher; Regional Admin. A. Alex Kahtava, Box 38 Guelph, Ont. N1H 6J6.

Church of the Nazarene (1902) — Dist. Superintendent of Canada Central District, Rev. N. Hightower, 38 Riverhead Dr., Rexdale, Ont.; Chairman of Exec. Board, Dr. Herman L. G. Smith, 2236 Capitol Hill Crescent, N.W., Calgary, Alta. T2M 4B9.

Evangelical Alliance Mission of Canada Inc., The — Gen. Dir. Richard M. Winchell, Admin. Sec. Sam Archer, 70 Froom Cres., Box 980, Regina, Sask. S4P 3B2.

Evangelical Mennonite Brethren Conference — Mod., Rev. Sam Hepp, 33573 Lynn Ave., Abbotsford, B.C., Mod., H. Kornelsen, R.R. 1, Giroux, Man. R0A 0N0.

Fellowship of Evangelical Baptist Churches in Canada (merging of **Union of Regular Baptist Churches of Ontario and Quebec,** and **Fellowship of Independent Baptist Churches)** (1953) — Gen. Sec., Dr. J.H. Watt, 74 Sheppard Ave. W., Willowdale, Ontario.

Free Methodist Church in Canada (1880) — Pres., Bishop D. N. Bastian, H.O. 3 Harrowby Ct., Islington, Ont. M9B 3H3; Sec., Rev. E. A. Bull, 10 Walmsley Pl., Belleville, Ont. K8P 1H3.

Gospel Missionary Union of Canada — Sec., Rev. John Harder, 132 High Park Ave., Toronto, Ont. M6P 2S4.

Greek Orthodox Church — Ninth Archdiocese District, Canada, Titular bishop of Constantia, His Grace Sotirios, 27 Teddington Park Ave., Toronto, Ont. M4N 2C4.

Independent Holiness Church (merger of former **Holiness Movement of Canada** with **The Free Methodist Church** in 1958) — Pres., Rev. R. E. Votary, Gen. Sec. Rev. L. E. Snyder; H.O. 72 Queen St. E., Wellesley, Ont. N0B 2T0.

Italian Pentecostal Church of Canada, The (Inc. 1959) — Gen. Supt. Rev. D. Ippolito, 384 Sunnyside Ave., Toronto, Ont. M6R 2S1.

Jehovah's Witnesses (Branch Office estab. in Winnipeg 1918) — Branch Overseer, Mr. Kenneth A. Little, 150 Bridgeland Ave., Toronto, Ont. M6A 1Z5.

Jewish Congress (1919) — Exec. Vice-Pres., Saul Hayes, Q.C., 1590 McGregor Ave., Montreal 109, Que.

Lutheran Church of Canada, The Evangelical — Pres., Dr. S. T. Jacobson, 212 Wiggins Ave., Saskatoon, Sask. S7N 1K4.

Lutheran Church-Canada (1959) — Pres., Rev. Louis Scholl, 3500 Askin, Windsor, Ont. N9E 3J9.

Lutheran Church in America — Canada Section — Pres., Rev. Donald W. Sjoberg, 9901 - 107 St., Edmonton, Alta. T5K 1G4.

Lutheran Council in Canada — a joint body of the three main churches, Pres. Roger Nostibakken, Gen. Sec. Rev. Earl J. Treusch, 500-365 Hargrave St., Winnipeg, Man. R3B 2K3.

Mennonite Brethren Churches of North America, Canadian Conference (Inc. 1945) — Mod. Frank C. Peters, Wilfrid Laurier Univ., Waterloo, Ont. N2L 3C5.

Mennonite Brethren Conference, Evangelical — Mod. Rev. Sam H. Epp, 33573 Lynn Ave., Abbotsford, B.C.

Mennonite Church, The (Old) — First Mennonite Church, Chmn., Newton L. Gingrich, Tavistock, Ont. N0B

Mennonite Conference, Evangelical — Mod. John Koop, Box 133, MacGregor, Man. R0H 0R0.

Mennonite Mission Conference, Evangelical — Mod. John D. Friesen, 1712 Ave. E., North Saskatoon, Sask. S7L 1V4.

Mennonites in Canada, Conference of — Mod. Jake Harms, 767 Buckingham Rd., Winnipeg, Man. R3R 1C3.

Missionary Church, The — (an Anabaptist body) — Dist. Supt. (Ontario) Rev. Grant Sloss, Ste. 203, Federick St. Plaza, Ktichener, Ont. N2H 2P2.

Moravian Church in America, Northern Province, Canadian District of the — Pres., and Corr. Sec., D. H. Laverty, 5719-114A St., Edmonton, Alta. T6H 3M8.

Northern Canada Evangelical Mission — 58 18th St., Prince Albert, Sask.

Old German Baptist Brethren in Canada — c/o Elder Amos Baker, Gormley, Ont.

Overseas Missionary Fellowship (1865) — Gen. Dr., Mr. Michael C. Griffiths, 1058 Avenue Road, Toronto M5N 2C6, Ont.

Pentecostal Assemblies of Canada, The (incorporated 1919) — Gen. Supt., Rev. Robert W. Taitinger, 10 Overlea Blvd., Toronto, Ont. M4H 1A5.

Pentecostal Holiness Church in Canada — Gen. Supt., Rev. G.H. Nunn, 4 Hobart Dr. S., Willowdale, Ont. M2J 2J5.

Polish National Catholic Church of Canada (1967) — The Rt. Rev. Joseph Nieminski, Bishop of the Canadian Diocese, 186 Cowan Ave., Toronto, Ont. M6K 2N6.

Presbyterian Church in Canada, The (1875) — 50 Wynford Dr., Don Mills, Ont. M3C 1J7; Mod. Rev. David W. Hay, Treasurer, R. R. Merifield, Q.C. Victoria and Grey Trust, 197 Bay St., Toronto, Ont. Clerks of the Gen. Assembly; Rev. D. C. MacDonald, Rev. E.H. Bean, Rev. D. B. Lowry.

Religious Society of Friends (Quakers), (Canadian Yearly Meeting of the Religious Society of Friends formed 1955) — Presiding Clerk, Philip Martin, 544 Fraser Ave., Ottawa, Ont. K2A 2R4; Secretary of Yearly Meeting, Ms. Dorothy Muma, 60 Lowther Ave., Toronto, Ont. M5R 1C7.

Roman Catholic Church in Canada — Apostolic Pro Nuncio, His Excellency the Most Reverend Angelo Palmas; Sec. to the Apostolic Nunciature, Rt. Rev. Andre Simard; Apostolic Nunciature, 724 Manor Ave., Rockcliffe Park, Ottawa, Ont. K1M 0E3.

Salvation Army, The (1882) — Territorial Commander, Commissioner Arnold Brown, 20 Albert St., Toronto, Ont. M5G 1A6.

Seventh-day Adventist Church in Canada — Pres., L. L. Reile, Sec. A.N. How; 1148 King St. E., Oshawa, Ont. L1H 1H8.

Ukrainian Greek Orthodox Church in Canada — Primate, Metropolitan of Winnipeg and of all Canada, His Beatitude Metropolitan Andrew (Metiuk), Winnipeg; Chairman of the Praesidium, V. Rev. D. Luchak; Sec. V. Rev. C. Kiciuk; H.O. 9 St. Johns Ave., Winnipeg, Man. R2W 0T9.

Union of Spiritual Communities of Christ (Orthodox Doukhobors in Canada) (1938) — Honorary Chmn. of the Exec. Comm., John J. Verigin, Box 760, Grand Forks, B.C.

Unitarian Church, Canadian (1842) — Pres. Mrs. Elaine Royer; Admin. Sec. Ms. Barbara C. Arnott, Canadian Unitarian Council, 175 St. Clair Ave. W., Toronto, Ont. M4V 1P7.

United Church of Canada, The (1925) — Mod. Rt. Rev. Wilbur K. Howard; Sec. of General Council, Rev. Donald G. Ray, 85 St. Clair Ave. E., Toronto, Ont. M4T 1M8.

Protestant Episcopal Calendar and Altar Colors

White — from Christmas Day through the Epiphany; First Sunday after Epiphany; Maundy Thursday (at the Eucharist); from the Vigil of Easter to Whitsunday; Trinity Sunday; Feasts of the Lord (except Holy Cross Day); St. Joseph; St. Mary Magdalene, St. Mary the Virgin, and St. Michael and All Angels.

Red — Pentecost (Whitsunday); Holy Cross Day; all feasts of apostles, evangelists, and martyrs.

Violet — Advent, Lent, Ember days, and Holy Innocents' Day. Optional color scheme for Lent: **Lenten White** from Ash Wednesday to Palm Sunday; **Crimson** during Holy Week.

Green — Epiphany season and season after Pentecost.

Black — optional for Good Friday and funerals.

Days, etc.	1977	1978	1979	1980	1981	1982
Golden Number	2	3	4	5	6	7
Sunday Letter	B	A	G	FE	D	C
Sundays after Epiphany*	4	2	5	3(6)	5(8)	4(7)
Septuagesima**	Feb. 6	Jan. 22	Feb. 11	Feb. 3	Feb. 15	Feb. 7
Ash Wednesday	Feb. 23	Feb. 8	Feb. 28	Feb. 20	Mar 4	Feb. 24
First Sunday in Lent	Feb. 27	Feb. 12	Mar. 4	Feb. 24	Mar. 8	Feb. 28
Passion Sunday**	Mar. 27	Mar. 12	Apr. 1	Mar. 23	Apr. 5	Mar. 28
Palm Sunday	Apr. 3	Mar. 19	Apr. 8	Mar. 30	Apr. 12	Apr. 4
Good Friday	Apr. 8	Mar. 24	Apr. 13	Apr. 4	Apr. 17	Apr. 9
Easter Day	Apr. 10	Mar. 26	Apr. 15	Apr. 6	Apr. 19	Apr. 11
Rogation Sunday**	May 15	Apr. 30	May 20	May 11	May 24	May 16
Ascension Day	May 19	May 4	May 24	May 15	May 28	May 20
Whitsunday	May 29	May 14	June 3	May 18	June 7	May 30
Trinity Sunday	June 5	May 21	June 10	May 25	June 14	June 6
Sundays after Trinity***	24	27	24	25(26)	23(24)	24(25)
First Sunday in Advent	Nov. 27	Dec. 3	Dec. 2	Nov. 30	Nov. 29	Nov. 28

In the Protestant Episcopal Church the days of fasting are Ash Wednesday and Good Friday. Other days of abstinence are the 40 days of Lent, the Ember Days, and all Fridays of the year except those in the Christmas and Easter seasons. Ember Days (optional) are days of abstinence and prayer for ordinands and the increase of the ministry. They fall on the Wednesday, Friday, and Saturday after the first Sunday in Lent, the Feast of Pentecost (Whitsunday), Sept. 14, and Dec. 13. Rogation Days (also optional) are the three days before Ascension Day, and are days of solemn supplication for God's blessing upon the fields and harvests of the world.

The Episcopal Church has given first constitutional approval to a revised calendar. If adopted in 1979, the following changes in the foregoing table will obtain: *The number of Sundays after Epiphany will be increased by three. **These Sundays will no longer be listed. ***These Sundays will be identified as "Sundays after Pentecost" and will be one more in number than the former "Sundays after Trinity".

Ash Wednesday and Easter Sunday

Year	Ash Wed.	Easter Sunday	Year	Ash Wed.	Easter Sunday	Year	Ash Wed.	Easter Sunday	Year	Ash Wed.	Easter Sunday
1901...	Feb. 20	Apr. 7	1951...	Feb. 7	Mar. 25	2001...	Feb. 28	Apr. 15	2051...	Feb. 15	Apr. 2
1902...	Feb. 12	Mar. 30	1952...	Feb. 27	Apr. 13	2002...	Feb. 13	Mar. 31	2052...	Mar. 6	Apr. 21
1903...	Feb. 25	Apr. 12	1953...	Feb. 18	Apr. 5	2003...	Mar. 5	Apr. 20	2053...	Feb. 19	Apr. 6
1904...	Feb. 17	Apr. 3	1954...	Mar. 3	Apr. 18	2004...	Feb. 25	Apr. 11	2054...	Feb. 11	Mar. 29
1905...	Mar. 8	Apr. 23	1955...	Feb. 23	Apr. 10	2005...	Feb. 9	Mar. 27	2055...	Mar. 3	Apr. 18
1906...	Feb. 28	Apr. 15	1956...	Feb. 15	Apr. 1	2006...	Mar. 1	Apr. 16	2056...	Feb. 16	Apr. 2
1907...	Feb. 13	Mar. 31	1957...	Mar. 6	Apr. 21	2007...	Feb. 21	Apr. 8	2057...	Mar. 7	Apr. 22
1908...	Mar. 4	Apr. 19	1958...	Feb. 19	Apr. 6	2008...	Feb. 6	Mar. 23	2058...	Feb. 27	Apr. 14
1909...	Feb. 24	Apr. 11	1959...	Feb. 11	Mar. 29	2009...	Feb. 25	Apr. 12	2059...	Feb. 12	Mar. 30
1910...	Feb. 9	Mar. 27	1960...	Mar. 2	Apr. 17	2010...	Feb. 17	Apr. 4	2060...	Mar. 3	Apr. 18
1911...	Mar. 1	Apr. 16	1961...	Feb. 15	Apr. 2	2011...	Mar. 9	Apr. 24	2061...	Feb. 23	Apr. 10
1912...	Feb. 21	Apr. 7	1962...	Mar. 7	Apr. 22	2012...	Feb. 22	Apr. 8	2062...	Feb. 8	Mar. 26
1913...	Feb. 5	Mar. 23	1963...	Feb. 27	Apr. 14	2013...	Feb. 13	Mar. 31	2063...	Feb. 28	Apr. 15
1914...	Feb. 25	Apr. 12	1964...	Feb. 12	Mar. 29	2014...	Mar. 5	Apr. 20	2064...	Feb. 20	Apr. 6
1915...	Feb. 17	Apr. 4	1965...	Mar. 3	Apr. 18	2015...	Feb. 18	Apr. 5	2065...	Feb. 11	Mar. 29
1916...	Mar. 8	Apr. 23	1966...	Feb. 23	Apr. 10	2016...	Feb. 10	Mar. 27	2066...	Feb. 24	Apr. 11
1917...	Feb. 21	Apr. 8	1967...	Feb. 8	Mar. 26	2017...	Mar. 1	Apr. 16	2067...	Feb. 16	Apr. 3
1918...	Feb. 13	Mar. 31	1968...	Feb. 28	Apr. 14	2018...	Feb. 14	Apr. 1	2068...	Mar. 7	Apr. 22
1919...	Mar. 5	Apr. 20	1969...	Feb. 19	Apr. 6	2019...	Mar. 6	Apr. 21	2069...	Feb. 27	Apr. 14
1920...	Feb. 18	Apr. 4	1970...	Feb. 11	Mar. 29	2020...	Feb. 26	Apr. 12	2070...	Feb. 12	Mar. 30
1921...	Feb. 9	Mar. 27	1971...	Feb. 24	Apr. 11	2021...	Feb. 17	Apr. 4	2071...	Mar. 4	Apr. 19
1922...	Mar. 1	Apr. 16	1972...	Feb. 16	Apr. 2	2022...	Mar. 2	Apr. 17	2072...	Feb. 24	Apr. 10
1923...	Feb. 14	Apr. 1	1973...	Mar. 7	Apr. 22	2023...	Feb. 22	Apr. 9	2073...	Feb. 8	Mar. 26
1924...	Mar. 5	Apr. 20	1974...	Feb. 27	Apr. 14	2024...	Feb. 14	Mar. 31	2074...	Feb. 28	Apr. 15
1925...	Feb. 25	Apr. 12	1975...	Feb. 12	Mar. 30	2025...	Mar. 5	Apr. 20	2075...	Feb. 20	Apr. 7
1926...	Feb. 17	Apr. 4	1976...	Mar. 3	Apr. 18	2026...	Feb. 18	Apr. 5	2076...	Mar. 4	Apr. 19
1927...	Mar. 2	Apr. 17	1977...	Feb. 23	Apr. 10	2027...	Feb. 10	Mar. 28	2077...	Feb. 24	Apr. 11
1928...	Feb. 22	Apr. 8	1978...	Feb. 8	Mar. 26	2028...	Mar. 1	Apr. 16	2078...	Feb. 16	Apr. 3
1929...	Feb. 13	Mar. 31	1979...	Feb. 28	Apr. 15	2029...	Feb. 14	Apr. 1	2079...	Mar. 8	Apr. 23
1930...	Mar. 5	Apr. 20	1980...	Feb. 20	Apr. 6	2030...	Mar. 6	Apr. 21	2080...	Feb. 21	Apr. 7
1931...	Feb. 18	Apr. 5	1981...	Mar. 4	Apr. 19	2031...	Feb. 26	Apr. 13	2081...	Feb. 12	Mar. 30
1932...	Feb. 10	Mar. 27	1982...	Feb. 24	Apr. 11	2032...	Feb. 11	Mar. 28	2082...	Mar. 4	Apr. 19
1933...	Mar. 1	Apr. 16	1983...	Feb. 16	Apr. 3	2033...	Mar. 2	Apr. 17	2083...	Feb. 17	Apr. 4
1934...	Feb. 14	Apr. 1	1984...	Mar. 7	Apr. 22	2034...	Feb. 22	Apr. 9	2084...	Feb. 9	Mar. 26
1935...	Mar. 6	Apr. 21	1985...	Feb. 20	Apr. 7	2035...	Feb. 7	Mar. 25	2085...	Feb. 28	Apr. 15
1936...	Feb. 26	Apr. 12	1986...	Feb. 12	Mar. 30	2036...	Feb. 27	Apr. 13	2086...	Feb. 13	Mar. 31
1937...	Feb. 10	Mar. 28	1987...	Mar. 4	Apr. 19	2037...	Feb. 18	Apr. 5	2087...	Mar. 5	Apr. 20
1938...	Mar. 2	Apr. 17	1988...	Feb. 17	Apr. 3	2038...	Mar. 10	Apr. 25	2088...	Feb. 25	Apr. 11
1939...	Feb. 22	Apr. 9	1989...	Feb. 8	Mar. 26	2039...	Feb. 23	Apr. 10	2089...	Feb. 16	Apr. 3
1940...	Feb. 7	Mar. 24	1990...	Feb. 28	Apr. 15	2040...	Feb. 15	Apr. 1	2090...	Mar. 1	Apr. 16
1941...	Feb. 26	Apr. 13	1991...	Feb. 13	Mar. 31	2041...	Mar. 6	Apr. 21	2091...	Feb. 21	Apr. 8
1942...	Feb. 18	Apr. 5	1992...	Mar. 4	Apr. 19	2042...	Feb. 19	Apr. 6	2092...	Feb. 13	Mar. 30
1943...	Mar. 10	Apr. 25	1993...	Feb. 24	Apr. 11	2043...	Feb. 11	Mar. 29	2093...	Feb. 25	Apr. 12
1944...	Feb. 23	Apr. 9	1994...	Feb. 16	Apr. 3	2044...	Mar. 2	Apr. 17	2094...	Feb. 17	Apr. 4
1945...	Feb. 14	Apr. 1	1995...	Mar. 1	Apr. 16	2045...	Feb. 22	Apr. 9	2095...	Mar. 9	Apr. 24
1946...	Mar. 6	Apr. 21	1996...	Feb. 21	Apr. 7	2046...	Feb. 7	Mar. 25	2096...	Feb. 29	Apr. 15
1947...	Feb. 19	Apr. 6	1997...	Feb. 12	Mar. 30	2047...	Feb. 27	Apr. 14	2097...	Feb. 13	Mar. 31
1948...	Feb. 11	Mar. 28	1998...	Feb. 25	Apr. 12	2048...	Feb. 19	Apr. 5	2098...	Mar. 5	Apr. 20
1949...	Mar. 2	Apr. 17	1999...	Feb. 17	Apr. 4	2049...	Mar. 3	Apr. 18	2099...	Feb. 25	Apr. 12
1950...	Feb. 22	Apr. 9	2000...	Mar. 8	Apr. 23	2050...	Feb. 23	Apr. 10	2100...	Feb. 10	Mar. 28

A lengthy dispute over the date for the celebration of Easter was settled by the first Council of the Christian Churches at Nicaea, in Asia Minor, in 325 A.D. The Council ruled that Easter would be observed on the first Sunday following the 14th day of the Paschal Moon, referred to as the Paschal Full Moon. The Paschal Moon is the first moon whose 14th day comes on or after March 21. Dates of the Paschal Full Moon, which are not necessarily the same as those of the real or astronomical full moon, are listed in the table below with an explanation of how to compute the date of Easter.

If the Paschal Full Moon falls on a Sunday, then Easter is the following Sunday. The earliest date on which Easter can fall is March 22; it fell on that date in 1761 and 1818 but will not do so in the 20th or 21st century. The latest possible date for Easter is April 25; it fell on that date in 1943 and will again in 2038.

For western churches Lent begins on Ash Wednesday, which comes 40 days before Easter Sunday, not counting Sundays. Originally it was a period of but 40 hours. Later it comprised 30 days of fasting, omitting all the Sundays and also all the Saturdays except one. Pope Gregory (590-604) added Ash Wednesday to the fast, together with the remainder of that week.

The last seven days of Lent constitute Holy Week, beginning with Palm Sunday. The last Thursday — Maundy Thursday — commemorates the institution of the Eucharist. The following day, Good Friday, commemorates the day of the Crucifixion.

Easter is the chief festival of the Christian year, commemorating the Resurrection of Christ. It occurs about the same time as the ancient Roman celebration of the Vernal Equinox, the arrival of spring. In the second century, A.D., Easter Day among Christians in Asia Minor was the 14th Nisan, the seventh month of the Jewish calendar. The Christians in Europe observed the nearest Sunday.

Date of Paschal Full Moon, 1900-2199

The Golden Number, used in determining the date of Easter, is greater by unity (one) than the remainder obtained upon dividing the given year by 19. For example, when dividing 1978 by 19, one obtains a remainder of 2. Adding 1 gives 3 as the Golden Number for the year 1978. From the table then the date of the Paschal Full Moon is Mar. 23, 1978. This being a Thursday, the date of Easter is the following Sunday Mar. 26.

Golden Number	Date	Golden Number	Date	Golden Number	Date	Golden Number	Date
1	Apr. 14	6	Apr. 18	11	Mar. 25	16	Mar. 30
2	Apr. 3	7	Apr. 8	12	Apr. 13	17	Apr. 17
3	Mar. 23	8	Mar. 28	13	Apr. 2	18	Apr. 7
4	Apr. 11	9	Apr. 16	14	Mar. 22	19	Mar. 27
5	Mar. 31	10	Apr. 5	15	Apr. 10		

Jewish Holy Days, Festivals, and Fasts

Source: Synagogue Council of America

All Jewish holy days, etc., begin at sunset on the day previous. (1) Also observed the following day. (2) Hebrew date varies to avoid conflict with Sabbath.

Festivals and fasts	Hebrew date		1977-1978 (5738)	1978-1979 (5739)	1979-1980 (5740)	1980-1981 (5741)
Rosh Hashana (New Year)[1]	Tishri	1	Sept. 13 Tu	Oct. 2 Mo	Sept. 22 Sa	Sept. 11 Th
Fast of Gedalia	Tishri	3	Sept. 15 Th	Oct. 4 We	Sept. 24 Mo	. . . . .
Fast of Gedalia	Tishri	4	. . . . .	. . . . .	. . . . .	Sept. 14 Su
Yom Kippur (Day of Atonement)	Tishri	10	Sept. 22 Th	Oct. 11 We	Oct. 1 Mo	Sept. 20 Sa
Sukkoth (Feast of Tabernacles), 1st Day[1]	Tishri	15	Sept. 27 Tu	Oct. 16 Mo	Oct. 6 Sa	Sept. 25 Th
Sukkoth, 8th Day of Assembly (Shemini Atzereth)	Tishri	22	Oct. 4 Tu	Oct. 23 Mo	Oct. 13 Sa	Oct. 2 Th
Simchat Torah (Rejoicing of the Law)	Tishri	23	Oct. 5 We	Oct. 24 Tu	Oct. 14 Su	Oct. 3 Fr
Chanukah (Feast of Lights)	Kislev	25	Dec. 5 Mo	Dec. 25 Mo	Dec. 15 Sa	Dec. 3 We
Fast of Tebet[2]	Tebet	10	Dec. 20 Tu	Jan. 9 Tu	Dec. 30 Su	Dec. 17 We
Fast of Esther[2]	Adar	13	. . . . .	Mar. 12 Mo	. . . . .	. . . . .
Fast of Esther[2]	Adar II	13	Mar. 22 We	. . . . .	Feb. 28 Th	Mar. 19 Th
Purim (Feast of Lots)	Adar	14	. . . . .	Mar. 13 Tu	Mar. 2 Su	. . . . .
Purim	Adar II	14	Mar. 23 Tu	. . . . .	. . . . .	Mar. 20 Fr
Pesach (Passover), 1st Day[1]	Nisan	15	Apr. 22 Sa	Apr. 12 Th	Apr. 1 Tu	Apr. 19 Su
Pesach, 7th Day[1]	Nisan	21	Apr. 28 Fr	Apr. 18 We	Apr. 7 Mo	Apr. 25 Sa
Lag B'Omer	Iyar	18	May 25 Th	May 15 Tu	May 4 Su	May 22 Fr
Shavuoth (Feast of Weeks)[1]	Sivan	6	June 11 Su	June 1 Fr	May 21 We	June 8 Mo
Fast of Tammuz[2]	Tammuz	17	July 23 Su	July 12 Th	July 1 Tu	July 19 Su
Tisha B'Av (Fast of Av)[2]	Av	9	Aug. 13 Su	Aug. 2 Th	July 22 Tu	Aug. 9 Su

The months of the Jewish year are: 1) Tishri; 2) Cheshvan (also Marcheshvan); 3) Kislev; 4) Tebet (also Tebeth); 5) Shebat (also Shebhat); 6) Adar; 6a) Adar Sheni (II) added in leap years; 7) Nisan; 8) Iyar; 9) Sivan; 10) Tammuz; 11) Av (also Abh); 12) Elul.

Greek Orthodox Church Calendar, 1978

Date	Holy days
Jan. 1	The Circumcision of Christ: Feast day of St. Basil
Jan. 6	The Epiphany: The Baptism of Jesus Christ—The Sanctification of the Waters
Jan. 7	Feast day of St. John the Baptist
Jan. 30	Feast day of Three Hierarchs: St. Basil, St. Gregory, and St. John Chrysostom
Feb. 2	Presentation of Jesus in the Temple
Mar. 13	Easter Lent begins
Mar. 19	Sunday of Orthodoxy (1st Sun. of Lent)
Mar. 25	The Annunciation of the Virgin Mary
Apr. 23	Palm Sunday
Apr. 23-29	Holy Week
Apr. 28	Good Friday: The Burial of Christ
Apr. 30	Easter Sunday
May 1	Feast day of St. George
June 8	The Ascension
June 18	Sunday of Pentecost
June 29	Feast day of Saints Peter and Paul
June 30	Feast day of the Twelve Holy Apostles
Aug. 6	The Transfiguration
Aug. 15	The Dormition of the Virgin Mary
Aug. 29	Beheading of St. John the Baptist
Sept. 1	Beginning of the Church Year
Sept. 8	Nativity of the Virgin Mary
Sept. 14	The Elevation of the Holy Cross
Oct. 23	The Feast of St. James (Iakovos)
Oct. 26	Feast day of St. Demetrios the Martyr
Nov. 15	Christmas Lent begins
Nov. 21	Presentation of Blessed Virgin Mary
Nov. 30	The Feast of St. Andrew, founder, Ecumenical Patriarchate of Constantinople
Dec. 6	Feast day of St. Nicholas, Bishop of Myra
Dec. 25	Christmas Day: The Birth of Jesus Christ

The dates above are according to the Gregorian Calendar, adopted by the Greek Church in 1923. First Greek Orthodox church in U. S. founded 1864, in New Orleans, La.

Islamic (Moslem) Calendar 1977-1978

The Islamic Calendar, often referred to as Mohammedan, is a lunar reckoning from the year of the *hegira*, 622 A.D., when Mohammed moved to Medina from Mecca. It runs in cycles of 30 years, of which the 2d, 5th, 7th, 10th, 13th, 16th, 18th, 21st, 24th, 26th, and 29th are leap years. Common years have 354 days, leap years 355, the extra day being added to the last month, Zu'lhijjah. Except for this case, the 12 months beginning with Muharram have alternately 30 and 29 days. *1398 — leap year (18th), 30 days.

Year	Name of month	Month begins	Year	Name of month	Month begins
1398	Muharram (New Year)	Dec. 12, 1977	1399	Muharram (New Year)	Dec. 12, 1978
1398	Safar	Jan. 11, 1978	1399	Safar	Jan. 11, 1979
1398	Rabia I.	Feb. 9, 1978	1399	Rabia I.	Feb. 9, 1979
1398	Rabia II.	Mar. 11, 1978	1399	Rabia II.	Mar. 11, 1979
1398	Jumada I	Apr. 9, 1978	1399	Jumada I	Apr. 9, 1979
1398	Jumada II	May 9, 1978	1399	Jumada II	May 9, 1979
1398	Rajab	Jun. 7, 1978	1399	Rajab	June 7, 1979
1398	Shaban	Jul. 7, 1978	1399	Shaban	July 7, 1979
1398	Ramadan	Aug. 5, 1978	1399	Ramadan	Aug. 5, 1979
1398	Shawwai	Sept. 4, 1978	1399	Shawwai	Sept. 4, 1979
1398	Zu'lkadah	Oct. 3, 1978	1399	Zu'lkadah	Oct. 3, 1979
1398	Zu'lhijjah*	Nov. 2, 1978	1399	Zu'lhijjah	Nov. 2, 1979

Roman Catholic Hierarchy

Source: Apostolic Delegation, Washington, D.C.

Supreme Pontiff

At the head of the Roman Catholic Church is the Supreme Pontiff, Paul VI, Giovanni Battista Montini, born at Concesio, Italy, Sept. 26, 1897, ordained priest May 29, 1920, enthroned archbishop of Milan Jan. 6, 1955, proclaimed cardinal Dec. 15, 1958; elected Pope as successor of John XXIII, June 21, 1963; crowned June 30, 1963.

Cardinals

Name	Office	Nationality	Born	Named
Alfrink: Bernard		Dutch	1900	1960
Antonelli: Ferdinando		Italian	1896	1973
Aponte Martinez: Luis	Archbishop of San Juan in Puerto Rico	American	1922	1973
Aramburu: Juan	Archbishop of Buenos Aires	Argentinian	1912	1976
Arns: Paulo	Archbishop of Sao Paulo	Brazilian	1921	1973
Bafile: Corrado	Prefect of the Sacred Congregation for the Causes of Saints	Italian	1903	1976
Baggio: Sebastiano	Prefect of the Sacred Congregation for the Bishops	Italian	1913	1969
Barbieri: Antonio Maria		Uruguayan	1892	1958
Baum: William	Archbishop of Washington	American	1926	1976
Bengsch: Alfred	Archbishop-Bishop of Berlin	German	1921	1967
Beras Rojas: Octavio	Archbishop of Santo Domingo	San Domingan	1906	1976
Bertoli: Paolo		Italian	1908	1969
Brandao Vilela: Avela	Archbishop of Sao Salvador da Bahia	Brazilian	1912	1973
Bueno y Monreal: Jose M	Archbishop of Seville	Spanish	1904	1958
Caggiano: Antonio		Argentinian	1889	1946
Carberry: John	Archbishop of St. Louis	American	1904	1969
Carpino: Francesco		Italian	1905	1967
Casariego: Mario	Archbishop of Guatemala	Guatemalan	1909	1969
Cerejeira: Manuel Goncalves		Portuguese	1888	1929
Cody: John P	Archbishop of Chicago	American	1907	1967
Colombo: Giovanni	Archbishop of Milan	Italian	1902	1965
Confalonieri: Carlo		Italian	1893	1958
Cooke: Terence	Archbishop of New York	American	1921	1969
Cooray: Thomas B		Ceylonese	1901	1965
Cordeiro: Joseph	Archbishop of Karachi	Pakistanian	1918	1973
Darmojuwono: Justin	Archbishop of Semarang	Indonesian	1914	1967
de Araujo Sales: Eugenio	Archbishop of St. Sebastian of Rio de Janeiro	Brazilian	1920	1969
Dearden: John	Archbishop of Detroit	American	1907	1969
de Furstenberg: Maximilian		Belgian	1904	1967
Delargey: Reginald	Archbishop of Wellington	New Zealander	1914	1976
Di Jorio: Alberto		Italian	1884	1958
Duval: Leon-Etienne	Archbishop of Algiers	Algerian	1903	1965
Ekandem: Dominic	Bishop of Ikot Ekpene	Nigerian	1917	1976
Enrique y Tarancon: Vincenzo	Archbishop of Madrid	Spanish	1907	1969
Felici: Pericle	President of Pontifical Commission for the Revision of Code of Canon Law	Italian	1911	1967
Filipiak: Boleslaw		Polish	1901	1976
Flahiff: George	Archbishop of Winnipeg	Canadian	1905	1969
Florit: Ermenegildo	Archbishop of Florence	Italian	1901	1965
Freeman: James	Archbishop of Sydney	Australian	1907	1973
Frings: Joseph		German	1887	1946
Garrone: Gabriele M	Prefect of the Sacred Congregation for Catholic Education	French	1901	1967
Gilroy: Norman		Australian	1896	1946
Gonzalez Martin: Marcelo	Archbishop of Toledo	Spanish	1918	1973
Gouyon: Paul	Archbishop of Rennes	French	1910	1969
Gracias: Valerian	Archbishop of Bombay	Indian	1900	1953
Gray: Gordon	Archbishop of St. Andrews and Edinburgh	Scottish	1910	1969
Guerri: Sergio	Pro-President of the Pontifical Comm. for Vatican City State	Italian	1905	1969
Guyot: Jean	Archbishop of Toulouse	French	1905	1973
Hoffner: Joseph	Archbishop of Cologne	German	1906	1969
Hume: Basil	Archbishop of Westminster	English	1923	1976
Jubany Arnau: Narciso	Archbishop of Barcelona	Spanish	1913	1973
Kim Sou Hwan: Stephan	Archbishop of Seoul	Korean	1922	1969
Knox, James	Prefect of the Sacred Congregations of the Sacraments and of Divine Worship	Australian	1914	1973
Koenig: Franz	Archbishop of Vienna	Austrian	1905	1958
Krol: John	Archbishop of Philadelphia	American	1910	1967
Landazuri: Ricketts Juan	Archbishop of Lima	Peruvian	1913	1962
Leger: Paul		Canadian	1904	1953
Lekai: Laszlo	Archbishop of Esztergom	Hungarian	1910	1976
Lercaro: Giacomo		Italian	1891	1953
Lorscheider: Aloisio	Archbishop of Fortaleza	Brazilian	1924	1976
Luciani: Albino	Patriarch of Venice	Italian	1912	1973
Malula: Joseph	Archbishop of Kinshasa	Congolese	1917	1969

Name	Office	Nationality	Born	Named
Manning: Timothy	Archbishop of Los Angeles	American	1909	1973
Marella: Paolo		Italian	1895	1959
Marty: Francis	Archbishop of Paris	French	1904	1969
Maurer: Jose	Archbishop of Sucre	Bolivian	1900	1967
McCann: Owen	Archbishop of Cape Town	S. African	1907	1965
McIntyre: James		American	1886	1953
Medeiros: Humberto	Archbishop of Boston	American	1915	1973
Miranda y Gomez: Miguel	Archbishop of Mexico	Mexican	1895	1969
Motta: Carlos Carmelo de Vasconcellos	Archbishop of Aparecida	Brazilian	1890	1946
Mozzoni: Umberto		Italian	1904	1973
Munoz Duque: Anibal	Archbishop of Bogota	Colombian	1908	1973
Munoz Vega: Paolo	Archbishop of Quito	Ecuadorian	1903	1969
Nasalli Rocca: Mario		Italian	1903	1969
Nsubuga: Emmanuel	Archbishop of Kampala	Ugandan	1914	1976
O'Boyle: Patrick		American	1896	1967
Oddi: Silvio		Italian	1910	1969
Ottaviani: Alfredo		Italian	1890	1953
Otunga: Maurice	Archbishop of Nairobi	Kenyan	1923	1973
Palazzini: Pietro		Italian	1912	1973
Pappalardo: Salvatore	Archbishop of Palermo	Italian	1918	1973
Parecattil: Joseph	Archbishop of Ernakulam	Indian	1912	1969
Parente: Pietro		Italian	1891	1967
Paupini: Giuseppe	Grand Penitentiary	Italian	1907	1969
Pellegrino: Michele	Archbishop of Turin	Italian	1903	1967
Philippe: Paul	Prefect of the Sacred Congregation for the Oriental Churches	French	1905	1973
Picachy: Lawrence	Archbishop of Calcutta	Indian	1916	1976
Pignedoli: Sergio	President of the Secretariat for Non-Christians	Italian	1910	1973
Pironio: Eduardo	Prefect of the Sacred Congregation for Religious and for Secular Institutes	Argentinian	1920	1976
Poletti: Ugo	Vicar General of His Holiness for the City of Rome	Italian	1914	1973
Poma: Antonio	Archbishop of Bologna	Italian	1910	1969
Primatesta: Francisco	Archbishop of Cordova	Argentinian	1919	1973
Quintero: Jose	Archbishop of Caracas	Venezuelan	1902	1961
Razafimahatratra: Victor	Archbishop of Tananarive	Madagascan	1921	1976
Renard: Alexandre	Archbishop of Lyon	French	1906	1967
Ribeiro: Antonio	Patriarch of Lisbon	Portuguese	1928	1973
Roberti: Francesco		Italian	1889	1958
Rosales: Julio	Archbishop of Cebu	Filipino	1906	1969
Rossi: Angelo	Prefect of the Sacred Congregation for the Evangelization of Peoples	Brazilian	1913	1965
Rossi: Opilio		Italian	1910	1976
Roy: Maurice	Archbishop of Quebec	Canadian	1905	1965
Rugambwa: Laurean		Tanzanian	1912	1960
Salazar Lopez: Jose	Archbishop of Guadalajara	Mexican	1910	1973
Samore: Antonio	Archivist of Holy Roman Church	Italian	1905	1967
Scherer: Alfred	Archbishop of Porto Alegre	Brazilian	1903	1969
Schroffer: Joseph	Titular Archbishop of Volturnum and Secretary of the Sacred Congregation for Catholic Education	German	1903	1976
Sensi: Giuseppe	Titular Archbishop of Sardis	Italian	1907	1976
Seper: Franjo	Prefect of Sacred Congregation for the Doctrine of the Faith	Yugoslav	1905	1965
Shehan: Lawrence		American	1898	1965
Sidarouss: Stephanos	Coptic Patriarch of Alexandria	Egyptian	1904	1965
Silva Henriquez: Raul	Archbishop of Santiago	Chilean	1907	1962
Sin: Jaime	Archbishop of Manila	Filipino	1928	1976
Siri: Giuseppe	Archbishop of Genoa	Italian	1906	1953
Slipyj: Josyf	Ukrainian Archbishop of Lwow	Ukrainian	1892	1965
Staffa: Dino	Prefect of Supreme Tribunal of Apostolic Signatura	Italian	1906	1967
Suenens: Leo	Archbishop of Malines Brussels	Belgian	1904	1962
Taguchi: Paul	Archbishop of Osaka	Japanese	1902	1973
Taofinu'u: Pio	Bishop of Samoa and Tokelau	Samoan	1923	1973
Thiandoum: Hyacinthe	Archbishop of Dakar	Senegalese	1921	1976
Traglia: Luigi		Italian	1895	1960
Trin Nhu Khue: Joseph	Archbishop of Hanoi	Vietnamese	1899	1976
Ursi: Corrado	Archbishop of Naples	Italian	1908	1967
Vagnozzi: Egidio	Pres. of the Prefecture of the Holy See's Economic Affairs	Italian	1906	1967
Villot: Jean	Secretary of State of His Holiness	French	1905	1965
Violardo: Giacomo		Italian	1898	1969
Volk: Hermann	Bishop of Mainz	German	1903	1973
Willebrands: John	President of Secretariat for the Union of Christians Archbishop of Utrecht	Dutch	1909	1969
Wojtyla: Karol	Archbishop of Krakow	Polish	1920	1967
Wright: John	Prefect of the Sacred Congregation for the Clergy	American	1909	1969
Wyszynski: Stefan	Archbishop of Gniezno-Warsaw	Polish	1901	1953
Yu Pin: Paul	Archbishop of Nanking	Chinese	1901	1969
Zoungrana: Paul	Archbishop of Ouagadougou	Upper Voltan	1917	1965

NOTED PERSONALITIES

American Statesmen

(Excluding presidents, vice presidents, Supreme Court justices, and most signers of the Declaration of Independence; listed elsewhere.)

Born	Died	Name
1893	1971	Acheson, Dean
1807	1886	Adams, Charles Francis
1841	1915	Aldrich, Nelson W.
1874	1940	Bankhead, William B.
1870	1965	Baruch, Bernard M.
1782	1858	Benton, Thomas Hart
1830	1893	Blaine, James G.
1835	1899	Bland, Richard P.
1865	1940	Borah, William E.
1821	1875	Breckinridge, John C.
1860	1925	Bryan, William Jennings
1891	1967	Bullitt, William C.
1904	1971	Bunche, Ralph
1887	1966	Byrd, Harry F.
1808	1873	Chase, Salmon P.
1850	1921	Clark, Champ
1777	1852	Clay, Henry
1769	1828	Clinton, DeWitt
1829	1888	Conkling, Roscoe
1877	1963	Connally, Tom
1870	1957	Cox, James M.
1787	1863	Crittenden, John J.
1808	1889	Davis, Jefferson
1902	1971	Dewey, Thomas E.
1896	1969	Dirksen, Everett M.
1892	1976	Douglas, Paul
1813	1861	Douglas, Stephen A.
1888	1959	Dulles, John Foster
1794	1865	Everett, Edward
1808	1893	Fish, Hamilton
1892	1949	Forrestal, James V.
1706	1790	Franklin, Benjamin
1761	1849	Gallatin, Albert
1858	1946	Glass, Carter
1755	1804	Hamilton, Alexander
1737	1793	Hancock, John
1838	1905	Hay, John
1736	1799	Henry, Patrick
1890	1946	Hopkins, Harry L.
1858	1938	House, Edward M.
1793	1863	Houston, Samuel
1871	1955	Hull, Cordell
1866	1945	Johnson, Hiram W.
1903	1963	Kefauver, Estes
1856	1937	Kellogg, Frank B.
1925	1968	Kennedy, Robert F.
1755	1827	King, Rufus
1874	1944	Knox, Frank
1855	1925	La Follette, Robert M.
1850	1924	Lodge, Henry Cabot
1786	1857	Marcy, William L.
1880	1959	Marshall, George C.
1863	1941	McAdoo, William G.
1874	1944	McNary, Charles L.
1891	1967	Morgenthau, Henry Jr.
1752	1816	Morris, Gouverneur
1873	1931	Morrow, Dwight W.
1900	1974	Morse, Wayne
1861	1944	Norris, George W.
1893	1976	Patman, Wright
1757	1824	Pinckney, Charles
1746	1825	Pinckney, Charles C.
1753	1813	Randolph, Edmund
1773	1833	Randolph, John
1721	1775	Randolph, Peyton
1880	1973	Rankin, Jeannette
1882	1961	Rayburn, Sam
1872	1937	Robinson, Joseph T.
1884	1962	Roosevelt, Eleanor
1845	1937	Root, Elihu
1829	1906	Schurz, Carl
1733	1804	Schuyler, Philip J.
1801	1872	Seward, William H.
1873	1944	Smith, Alfred E.
1814	1869	Stanton, Edwin M.
1812	1883	Stephens, Alexander H.
1900	1949	Stettinius, Edward R. Jr.
1900	1965	Stevenson, Adlai E.
1867	1950	Stimson, Henry L.
1889	1953	Taft, Robert A.
1884	1968	Thomas, Norman M.
1814	1886	Tilden, Samuel J.
1890	1961	Tydings, Millard E.
1884	1951	Vandenberg, Arthur H.
1877	1953	Wagner, Robert F.
1782	1852	Webster, Daniel
1892	1961	Welles, Sumner
1882	1975	Wheeler, Burton K.
1892	1944	Willkie, Wendell L.

American Reformers, Socio-Economic Leaders

1860	1935	Addams, Jane
1909	1972	Alinsky, Saul O.
1820	1906	Anthony, Susan B.
1891	1969	Arnold, Thurman W.
1867	1961	Balch, Emily G.
1821	1912	Barton, Clara H.
1818	1895	Bloomer, Amelia J.
1809	1890	Brisbane, Albert
1800	1859	Brown, John
1859	1947	Catt, Carrie Chapman
1855	1926	Debs, Eugene
1802	1887	Dix, Dorothea
1817	1895	Douglass, Frederick
1805	1879	Garrison, Wm. L.
1839	1897	George, Henry
1837	1927	Gerry, Elbridge T.
1850	1924	Gompers, Samuel
1873	1952	Green, William
1887	1975	Hansen, Alvin
1887	1946	Hillman, Sidney
1801	1876	Howe, Samuel G.
1880	1968	Keller, Helen
1929	1968	King, Martin Luther
1855	1925	LaFollette, Robt. M.
1880	1969	Lewis, John L.
1793	1880	Mott, Lucretia
1886	1952	Murray, Phillip
1846	1911	Nation, Carry
1811	1886	Noyes, John H.
1801	1877	Owen, Robt. Dale
1842	1933	Parkhurst, Charles H.
1811	1884	Phillips, Wendell
1849	1914	Riis, Jacob A.
1883	1967	Sanger, Margaret
1797	1874	Smith, Gerrit
1816	1902	Stanton, Eliz. Cady
1818	1893	Stone, Lucy
1867	1960	Townsend, Francis E.
1844	1928	Villard, Helen G.
1893	1955	White, Walter
1931	1973	Wiley, George
1839	1898	Willard, Frances E.
1921	1971	Young, Whitney M.

American Educators and Religious Leaders

Educators

1897	1967	Allport, Gordon
1869	1949	Angell, James R.
1811	1900	Barnard, Henry
1862	1947	Butler, Nich. Murray
1862	1948	Cross, Wilbur
1859	1952	Dewey, John
1851	1931	Dewey, Melvil
1868	1963	DuBois, William E. B.
1834	1926	Eliot, Charles W.
1863	1940	Finley, John H.
1903	1967	Gassner, John W.
1831	1908	Gilman, Daniel C.
1906	1963	Griswold, A. Whitney
1844	1924	Hall, G. Stanley
1856	1906	Harper, William R.
1842	1910	James, William
1882	1974	Kallen, Horace M.
1797	1849	Lyon, Mary
1800	1873	McGuffey, William H.
1796	1859	Mann, Horace
1872	1964	Meiklejohn, Alexander
1818	1901	Muhlenberg, Fred. A.
1869	1946	Neilson, William A.
1827	1908	Norton, Chas. Eliot
1855	1902	Palmer, Alice Freeman
1804	1894	Peabody, Elizabeth P.
1870	1964	Pound, Roscoe
1855	1916	Royce, Josiah
1885	1963	Seymour, Charles
1779	1864	Silliman, Benjamin
1917	1969	Smith, Courtney C.
1840	1910	Sumner, Wm. Graham
1893	1969	Tannenbaum, Frank
1858	1915	Washington, Booker T.
1787	1870	Willard, Emma

Religious Leaders

1835	1922	Abbott, Lyman
1745	1816	Asbury, Francis
1813	1887	Beecher, Henry Ward
1775	1863	Beecher, Lyman
1835	1893	Brooks, Phillips
1780	1842	Channing, Wm. Ellery
1584	1652	Cotton, John
1895	1970	Cushing, Richard
1752	1817	Dwight, Timothy
1821	1910	Eddy, Mary Baker
1703	1758	Edwards, Jonathan
1902	1973	Eisendrath, Maurice N.
1878	1969	Fosdick, Harry E.
1900	1968	Fry, Franklin C.
1834	1921	Gibbons, James
1867	1938	Hayes, Patrick J.
1748	1830	Hicks, Elias
1879	1964	Holmes, John Haynes
1590	1643	Hutchinson, Anne
1883	1968	Jones, Bob
1843	1926	Kohler, Kaufmann
1663	1728	Mather, Cotton
1873	1970	McKay, David O.
1890	1944	McPherson, Aimee Semple
1837	1899	Moody, Dwight L.
1897	1975	Muhammad, Elijah
1711	1787	Muhlenberg, H. M.
1891	1963	Oxnam, G. Bromley
1810	1860	Parker, Theodore
1913	1969	Pike, James A.
1884	1968	Poling, Daniel A.
1729	1796	Seabury, Samuel
1774	1821	Seton, Elizabeth
1886	1969	Sheil, Bernard J.
1882	1968	Shipler, Guy E.
1881	1968	Silver, Eliezer
1805	1844	Smith, Joseph
1876	1972	Smith, Joseph Fielding
1889	1970	Sockman, Ralph W.
1889	1967	Spellman, Francis
1863	1935	Sunday, Wm. (Billy)
1886	1965	Tillich, Paul
1862	1969	Welch, Herbert
1599	1683	Williams, Roger
1874	1949	Wise, Stephen S.
1801	1877	Young, Brigham

American Military Leaders

All Army unless marked (N) Navy; (M) Marine; (AF) Air Force.

Born	Died	Name
1914	1974	Abrams, Creighton
1737	1789	Allen, Ethan
1741	1801	Arnold, Benedict
1886	1950	Arnold, Henry H. (Hap) (AF)
1745	1803	Barry, John (N)
1818	1893	Beauregard, Pierre
1853	1930	Bliss, Tasker H.
1878	1967	Bloch, Claude C. (N)
1817	1876	Bragg, Braxton
1888	1950	Buchanan, Pat (N)
1823	1914	Buckner, Simon B.
1886	1945	Buckner, Simon B. Jr.
1826	1863	Buford, John
1861	1947	Bullard, Robert L.
1824	1881	Burnside, Ambrose
1818	1893	Butler, Benjamin F.
1884	1970	Cates, Clifton B. (M)
1772	1840	Chauncey, Isaac (N)
1842	1914	Chaffee, Adna R.
1890	1958	Chennault, Claire (AF)
1752	1818	Clark, George Rogers
1786	1836	Crockett, David
1819	1893	Crittenden, Thomas L.
1842	1874	Cushing, William B. (N)
1839	1876	Custer, George
1779	1820	Decatur, Stephen (N)
1837	1917	Dewey, George (N)
1857	1927	Dickman, Joseph T.
1879	1951	Drum, Hugh A.
1816	1894	Early, Jubal A.
1890	1969	Eisenhower, Dwight D.
1846	1912	Evans, Robley D. (N)
1817	1872	Ewell, Richard
1801	1870	Farragut, David G. (N)
1806	1863	Foote, Andrew (N)
1821	1877	Forrest, Nathan B.
1865	1917	Funston, Frederick
1728	1806	Gates, Horatio
1805	1877	Goldsborough, L. M. (N)
1822	1885	Grant, Ulysses S.
1742	1786	Greene, Nathanael
1896	1970	Groves, Leslie R.
1815	1872	Halleck, Henry
1883	1959	Halsey, William F. (N)
1818	1902	Hampton, Wade
1728	1777	Herkimer, Nicholas
1825	1865	Hill, Ambrose P.
1892	1966	Hobbs, Leland
1870	1937	Hobson, Richmond (N)
1887	1966	Hodges, Courtney
1814	1879	Hooker, Joseph
1831	1879	Hood, John B.
1773	1843	Hull, Isaac (N)
1824	1863	Jackson, Thomas (Stonewall)
1803	1862	Johnston, Albert S.
1807	1891	Johnston, Joseph
1747	1792	Jones, John Paul (N)
1814	1862	Kearny, Philip
1794	1848	Kearny, Stephen
1879	1956	King, Ernest J. (N)
1781	1813	Lawrence, James (N)
1843	1899	Lawton, Henry
1875	1959	Leahy, William D. (N)
1756	1818	Lee, Henry
1807	1870	Lee, Robert E.
1907	1975	Lincoln, George A.
1821	1904	Longstreet, James
1818	1861	Lyon, Nathaniel
1845	1912	MacArthur, Arthur
1880	1964	MacArthur, Douglas
1898	1975	McAuliffe, Anthony C.
1733	1795	Marion, Francis
1880	1959	Marshall, George C.
1826	1885	McClellan, George B.
1818	1885	McDowell, Irvin
1828	1864	McPherson, James
1815	1872	Meade, George
1839	1925	Miles, Nelson A.
1879	1936	Mitchell, Billy
1887	1947	Mitscher, Marc A. (N)
1736	1775	Montgomery, Richard
1736	1802	Morgan, Daniel
1730	1805	Moultrie, William
1885	1966	Nimitz, Chester (N)
1906	1971	O'Donnell, Emmett (Rosy) (AF)
1896	1959	Parks, Floyd L.
1885	1945	Patton, George S.
1814	1881	Pemberton, J. C.
1794	1858	Perry, Matthew C. (N)
1785	1819	Perry, Oliver H. (N)
1860	1948	Pershing, John J.
1739	1817	Pickens, Andrew
1825	1875	Pickett, George E.
1813	1891	Porter, David D. (N)
1905	1970	Power, Thomas S. (AF)
1809	1867	Price, Stirling
1896	1973	Radford, Arthur (N)
1890	1973	Rickenbacker, Edward (AF)
1819	1892	Rodgers, C. R. P. (N)
1773	1838	Rodgers, John (N)
1819	1898	Rosecrans, William S.
1736	1818	St. Clair, Arthur
1840	1903	Sampson, William T. (N)
1831	1906	Schofield, John
1786	1866	Scott, Winfield
1835	1906	Shafter, William R.
1831	1888	Sheridan, Phillip
1820	1891	Sherman, William T.
1858	1936	Sims, William S. (N)
1882	1967	Smith, Holland M. (M)
1895	1961	Smith, W. Bedell
1891	1974	Spaatz, Carl A. (AF)
1886	1969	Spruance, Raymond (N)
1728	1822	Stark, John
1883	1946	Stilwell, Joseph W.
1726	1783	Stirling, Lord (Alexander)
1890	1969	Stratemeyer, George (AF)
1833	1864	Stuart, J. E. B.
1740	1795	Sullivan, John
1822	1880	Sykes, George
1784	1850	Taylor, Zachary
1827	1890	Terry, Alfred H.
1816	1870	Thomas, George H.
1884	1955	Towers, John H. (N)
1899	1954	Vandenberg, Hoyt (AF)
1883	1953	Wainwright, Jonathan
1732	1799	Washington, George
1745	1796	Wayne, Anthony
1908	1975	Wheeler, Earle
1836	1906	Wheeler, Joseph
1837	1925	Wilson, James H.
1860	1927	Wood, Leonard
1818	1897	Worden, John L. (N)
1820	1899	Wright, Horatio G.
1898	1969	Wyman, Willard G.
1876	1959	Yarnell, Hy. E. (N)

American Explorers, Naturalists

Born	Died	Name
1807	1873	Agassiz, Louis
1864	1926	Akeley, Carl Ethan
1884	1960	Andrews, Roy C.
1785	1851	Audubon, John J.
1875	1946	Bartlett, Robert A.
1850	1941	Beard, Daniel C.
1799	1847	Bent, Charles
1875	1956	Bingham, Hiram
1796	1878	Bonneville, Benjamin
1734	1820	Boone, Daniel
1796	1836	Bowie, James
1849	1926	Burbank, Luther
1837	1921	Burroughs, John
1888	1957	Byrd, Richard E.
1809	1868	Carson, Kit
1770	1838	Clark, William
1775	1813	Colter, John
1865	1940	Cook, Frederick A.
1898	1970	Cruzen, Richard H.
1844	1881	De Long, G. W.
1880	1951	Ellsworth, Lincoln
1799	1854	Fitzpatrick, Thomas
1813	1890	Fremont, John C.
1844	1935	Greely, Adolphus W.
1884	1937	Johnson, Martin
1894	1953	Johnson, Osa
1820	1857	Kane, Elisha K.
1774	1809	Lewis, Meriwether
1902	1974	Lindbergh, Charles A.
1784	1864	Long, Stephen H.
1874	1970	Macmillan, Donald
1838	1914	Muir, John
1856	1920	Peary, Robert E.
1779	1813	Pike, Zebulon M.
1834	1902	Powell, John W.
1793	1864	Schoolcraft, Henry R.
1849	1892	Schwatka, Frederick
1799	1845	Sublette, William L.
1817	1862	Thoreau, Henry D.
1798	1876	Walker, Joseph R.
1802	1847	Whitman, Marcus
1798	1877	Wilkes, Charles
1766	1813	Wilson, Alexander

American Scientists, Physicians, Engineers

Born	Died	Name
1872	1973	Abbot, Charles Greeley
1785	1853	Beaumont, William
1899	1964	Blalock, Alfred
1773	1838	Bowditch, Nath.
1882	1961	Bridgman, Percy W.
1890	1974	Bush, Vannevar
1868	1939	Cabot, Richard C.
1864	1943	Carver, George W.
1892	1962	Compton, Arthur H.
1877	1954	Compton, Karl T.
1869	1939	Cushing, Harvey W.
1927	1961	Dooley, Thomas
1901	1965	Du Mont, Allen
1907	1975	Dunning, John R.
1820	1887	Eads, James B.
1879	1955	Einstein, Albert
1895	1974	Fremont-Smith, Frank
1884	1967	Funk, Casimir
1903	1973	Gibbon, John H.
1839	1903	Gibbs, Josiah W.
1858	1928	Goethals, George W.
1874	1929	Goldberger, Joseph
1854	1920	Gorgas, William C.
1863	1914	Hall, Charles M.
1883	1964	Hess, Victor F.
1905	1973	Kuiper, Gerard
1834	1906	Langley, Samuel P.
1881	1957	Langmuir, Irving
1884	1964	Lanza, Anthony J.
1901	1958	Lawrence, Ernest O.
1815	1878	Long, Crawford
1855	1916	Lowell, Percival
1806	1873	Maury, Matthew F.
1865	1939	Mayo, Charles H.
1898	1968	Mayo, Charles W.
1861	1939	Mayo, William J.
1845	1913	McBurney, Charles
1899	1966	Menninger, William C.
1852	1931	Michelson, Albert A.
1903	1966	Millikan, Clark
1868	1953	Millikan, Robert
1866	1945	Morgan, Thomas H.
1819	1868	Morton, W. T. G.
1890	1967	Muller, Hermann J.
1904	1967	Oppenheimer, J. Robert
1883	1962	Papanicolaou, George N.
1903	1967	Pincus, Gregory
1851	1902	Reed, Walter S.
1846	1927	Remsen, Ira
1871	1910	Ricketts, Howard T.
1806	1869	Roebling, John A.

Born	Died	Name
1879	1970	Rous, Peyton
1745	1813	Rush, Benjamin
1877	1967	Schick, Bela
1885	1972	Shapley, Harlow
1859	1934	Smith, Theobald
1865	1923	Steinmetz, Charles
1915	1974	Sutherland, Earl W.
1898	1964	Szilard, Leo
1899	1972	Theiler, Max
1888	1973	Waksman, Selman
1886	1973	White, Paul Dudley
1894	1964	Wiener, Norbert
1844	1930	Wiley, Harvey W.
1858	1931	Williams, Daniel Hale
1898	1974	Zwicky, Fritz

American Inventors

Born	Died	Name
1891	1954	Armstrong, Edwin
1847	1922	Bell, Alex. Graham
1890	1970	Bell, Herbert A.
1851	1929	Berliner, Emile
1857	1898	Burroughs, William
1906	1968	Carlson, Chester F.
1876	1950	Carrier, Willis
1873	1975	Coolidge, William D.
1874	1961	De Forest, Lee
1862	1938	Duryea, Charles E.
1870	1967	Duryea, J. Frank
1803	1889	Ericsson, John
1743	1798	Fitch, John
1765	1815	Fulton, Robert
1818	1903	Gatling, Richard J.
1882	1945	Goddard, Robert H.
1800	1860	Goodyear, Charles
1803	1855	Gorrie, John
1835	1901	Gray, Elisha
1797	1878	Henry, Joseph
1812	1886	Hoe, Richard M.
1819	1867	Howe, Elias
1866	1945	Lake, Simon
1881	1957	Langmuir, Irving
1826	1886	Loomis, Mahlon
1854	1899	Mergenthaler, Ottmar
1791	1872	Morse, S. F. B.
1811	1861	Otis, Elisha
1831	1897	Pullman, George M.
1894	1974	de Seversky, Alexander P.
1889	1972	Sikorsky, Igor
1894	1970	Spencer, Percy L.
1860	1930	Sperry, Elmer A.
1856	1943	Tesla, Nikola
1853	1937	Thomson, Elihu
1846	1914	Westinghouse, George
1900	1975	Williams, David M.
1871	1948	Wright, Orville
1867	1912	Wright, Wilbur

American Business Leaders, Philanthropists

Born	Died	Name
1884	1966	Arden, Elizabeth
1832	1901	Armour, Phillip D.
1763	1848	Astor, John Jacob
1894	1968	Bache, Harold L.
1816	1890	Belmont, August
1786	1844	Biddle, Nicholas
1821	1905	Cooke, Jay
1791	1883	Cooper, Peter
1807	1874	Cornell, Ezra
1834	1928	Depew, Chauncey M.
1826	1893	Drexel, Anthony J.
1856	1925	Duke, James B.
1739	1817	duPont, Pierre S.
1890	1962	Fairless, Benjamin F.
1835	1906	Field, Marshall
1860	1937	Filene, Edward A.
1894	1970	Folsom, Frank M.
1846	1927	Gary, Elbert H.
1898	1974	Gerber, Daniel
1892	1976	Getty, J. Paul
1885	1966	Gimbel, Bernard F.
1836	1892	Gould, Jay
1834	1916	Green, Henrietta (Hetty)
1828	1905	Guggenheim, Meyer
1874	1940	Harkness, Edward S.
1848	1909	Harriman, Edward H.
1865	1957	Hartford, Geo. L.A.
1882	1975	Hogg, Ima
1795	1873	Hopkins, Johns
1905	1976	Hughes, Howard
1889	1974	Hunt, H.L.
1821	1900	Huntington, C.P.
1888	1969	Kennedy, Joseph P.
1876	1958	Kettering, Charles F.
1879	1948	Knudsen, Wm. S.
1867	1966	Kresge, S. S.
1863	1955	Kress, Samuel H.
1870	1948	Lamont, Thomas W.
1891	1969	Lehman, Robert
1903	1972	Litton, Charles
1831	1902	Mackay, John W.
1855	1937	Mellon, Andrew W.
1899	1970	Mellon, Richard K.
1884	1968	Mennen, William G.
1825	1910	Mills, Darius
1875	1973	Mott, Charles Stewart
1875	1970	Neiman, Abraham
1887	1963	Olds, Irving S.
1795	1869	Peabody, George
1887	1973	Post, Marjorie Merriweather
1906	1975	Revson, Charles
1874	1960	Rockefeller, J. D. Jr.
1862	1932	Rosenwald, Julius
1828	1918	Sage, Margaret Olivia
1740	1785	Salomon, Haym
1847	1920	Schiff, Jacob H.
1845	1912	Straus, Isidor
1848	1931	Straus, Nathan
1839	1903	Swift, Gustavus
1794	1877	Vanderbilt, Cornelius
1843	1899	Vanderbilt, Cornelius
1849	1920	Vanderbilt, Wm. K.
1835	1900	Villard, Henry
1838	1922	Wanamaker, John
1896	1969	Warburg, James P.
1888	1974	Whitney, Richard
1841	1904	Whitney, Wm. C.
1886	1972	Wilson, Charles E.
1890	1961	Wilson, Chas. Erwin
1879	1969	Wood, Robert E.
1852	1919	Woolworth, Frank

Business Hall of Fame

Established and supported by Junior Achievement Inc. Laureates selected by *Fortune* board of editors.

1975

William M. Allen, b. 1900
Andrew Carnegie, 1835-1919
George Eastman, 1854-1932
Thomas A. Edison, 1847-1931
Henry Ford, 1863-1947
Amadeo P. Giannini, 1870-1949
J. Erik Jonsson, b. 1901
Royal Little, b. 1896
Cyrus H. McCormick, 1809-1884
J. Pierpont Morgan, 1837-1913
M. J. Rathbone, b. 1900
John D. Rockefeller, 1839-1947
David Sarnoff, 1891-1971
Alfred P. Sloan Jr., 1875-1966
Alexander T. Stewart, 1803-1876
J. Edgar Thomson, 1808-1874
Theodore N. Vail, 1845-1920
George Washington, 1732-1799
Eli Whitney, 1765-1825

1976

Stephen D. Bechtel Sr., b. 1900
Walter E. Disney, 1901-1966
James J. Hill, 1838-1916
Albert D. Lasker, 1880-1952
Charles E. Merrill, 1885-1956
George S. Moore, b. 1905
James C. Penney, 1875-1971
William C. Procter, 1862-1934
Cyrus R. Smith, b. 1899
Thomas J. Watson Jr., b. 1914

1977

William Blackie, b. 1906
Benjamin Franklin, 1706-1790
Florence Nightingale Graham, 1878-1966
Joyce Clyde Hall, b. 1891
Henry John Kaiser, 1882-1967
John J. McCloy, b. 1895
Robert W. Woodruff, b. 1889

Notable American Fiction Writers

Name	Birthplace	Birthdate
Algren, Nelson	(Detroit, Mich.)	3/28/09
Asimov, Isaac	(Petrovichi, Russia)	1/2/20
Auchincloss, Louis	(Lawrence, N.Y.)	9/27/17
Baldwin, James	(New York, N.Y.)	8/2/24
Barth, John	(Cambridge, Md.)	5/27/30
Barthelme, Donald	(Philadelphia, Pa.)	1931
Bellow, Saul	(Quebec, Canada)	7/10/15
Benchley, Nathaniel	(Newton, Mass.)	11/13/15
Benchley, Peter	(New York, N.Y.)	5/8/40
Berger, Thomas	(Cincinnati, Oh.)	7/20/24
Bishop, Jim	(Jersey City, N.J.)	11/21/07
Bradbury, Ray	(Waukeegan, Ill.)	8/22/20
Breslin, Jimmy	(Jamaica, N.Y.)	10/17/30
Brooks, Gwendolyn	(Topeka, Kan.)	6/7/17
Buckley, William Jr.	(New York, N.Y.)	11/24/25
Caldwell, Erskine	(Coweta Co., Ga.)	12/17/03
Caldwell, Taylor	(London, England)	1900
Calisher, Hortense	(New York, N.Y.)	12/20/11
Capote, Truman	(New Orleans, La.)	9/30/24
Cheever, John	(Quincy, Mass.)	5/27/12
Clavell, James	(England)	10/10/24
Cozzens, James Gould	(Chicago, Ill.)	8/19/03
Crews, Harry	(Alma, Ga.)	6/6/35
Crichton, Michael	(Chicago, Ill.)	10/23/42
De Vries, Peter	(Chicago, Ill.)	2/27/10
Dickey, James	(Atlanta, Ga.)	2/2/23
Didion, Joan	(Sacramento, Cal.)	12/5/34
Doctorow, E. L.	(New York, N.Y.)	1/6/31
Drury, Allen	(Houston, Tex.)	9/2/18
Elkin, Stanley	(New York, N.Y.)	5/11/30

Name	Birthplace	Birthdate
Ellison, Ralph	(Oklahoma City, Okla.)	3/1/14
Farrell, James T.	(Chicago, Ill.)	2/27/04
Fox, Paula	(New York, N.Y.)	11/22/23
Gaddis, William	(New York, N.Y.)	1922
Galbraith, John Kenneth	(Ontario, Canada)	10/15/08
Gann, Ernest K.	(Lincoln, Neb.)	10/13/10
Gardner, John	(Batavia, N.Y.)	7/21/33
Goldman, William	(Chicago, Ill.)	8/12/31
Grau, Shirley Ann	(New Orleans, La.)	7/8/29
Hailey, Arthur	(Luton, England)	4/5/20
Haley, Alex	(Ithaca, N.Y.)	8/11/21
Hawkes, John	(Stamford, Conn.)	8/17/25
Heinlein, Robert	(Butler, Mont.)	7/7/07
Heller, Joseph	(Brooklyn, N.Y.)	5/1/23
Hersey, John	(Tientsin, China)	6/17/14
Himes, Chester	(Jefferson City, Mo.)	7/29/09
Jong, Erica	(New York, N.Y.)	4/26/42
Kantor, MacKinlay	(Webster City, Ia.)	2/4/04
Kazan, Elia	(Constantinople, Turkey)	9/7/09
Kesey, Ken	(La Hunta, Cal.)	9/17/35
Knowles, John	(Fairmont, W. Va.)	9/16/26
L'Amour, Louis	(Jamestown, N.D.)	——
Lee, Harper	(Alabama)	1926
LeGuin, Ursala	(Berkeley, Cal.)	10/21/29
Levin, Ira	(New York, N.Y.)	8/27/29
Lindbergh, Ann Morrow	(Englewood, N.J.)	1906
Loos, Anita	(Sisson, Cal.)	4/26/93
Ludlum, Robert	(New York, N.Y.)	5/25/27
MacDonald, John D.	(Sharon, Pa.)	7/24/16
MacDonald, Ross	(Los Gatos, Cal.)	12/13/15
MacInnes, Helen	(Glasgow, Scotland)	10/7/07
Mailer, Norman	(Long Branch, N.J.)	1/31/23
Malamud, Bernard	(Brooklyn, N.Y.)	4/26/14
Mayer, Martin	(New York, N.Y.)	1/14/28
McCarthy, Mary	(Seattle, Wash.)	6/21/12
McGinley, Phyllis	(Ontario, Ore.)	3/21/05
McMurtry, Larry	(Wichita Falls, Tex.)	6/3/36
Michener, James A.	(New York, N.Y.)	2/3/07
Morris, Willie	(Jackson, Miss.)	11/29/34
Oates, Joyce Carol	(Lockport, N.Y.)	6/16/38
Percy, Walker	(Birmingham, Ala.)	5/28/16
Perelman, S. J.	(Brooklyn, N.Y.)	2/1/04
Porter, Katherine Ann	(Indian Creek, Tex.)	5/15/94
Potok, Chaim	(New York, N.Y.)	2/17/29
Puzo, Mario	(New York, N.Y.)	10/15/20
Pynchon, Thomas	(Glen Cove, N.Y.)	5/8/37
Reed, Ayn	(St. Petersburg, Russia)	1905
Reed, Ishmael	(Chattanooga, Tenn.)	2/22/38
Robbins, Harold	(New York, N.Y.)	5/21/12
Rossner, Judith	(New York, N.Y.)	3/31/35
Roth, Henry	(Austria-Hungary)	2/8/06
Roth, Philip	(Newark, N.J.)	3/19/33
Salinger, J. D.	(New York, N.Y.)	1/1/19
Saroyan, William	(Fresno, Cal.)	8/31/08
Schulberg, Budd	(New York, N.Y.)	3/27/14
Segal, Erich	(Brooklyn, N.Y.)	6/16/37
Shaw, Irwin	(New York, N.Y.)	2/27/13
Shirer, William L.	(Chicago, Ill.)	2/23/04
Singer, Isaac Bashevis	(Radzymin, Poland)	7/14/04
Slaughter, Frank G.	(Washington, D.C.)	2/25/08
Spillane, Mickey	(Brooklyn, N.Y.)	3/9/18
Stafford, Jean	(Covina, Cal.)	7/1/15
Stone, Irving	(San Francisco, Cal.)	7/14/03
Styron, William	(Newport News, Va.)	6/11/25
Tryon, Thomas	(Hartford, Conn.)	1/14/26
Updike, John	(Shillington, Pa.)	3/18/32
Uris, Leon	(Baltimore, Md.)	8/3/24
Vidal, Gore	(West Point, N.Y.)	10/3/25
Vonnegut, Kurt Jr.	(Indianapolis, Ind.)	11/11/22
Wallace, Irving	(Chicago, Ill.)	3/18/16
Wambaugh, Joseph	(East Pittsburgh, Pa.)	1/22/37
Warren, Robert Penn	(Guthrie, Ky.)	4/24/05
Welty, Eudora	(Jackson, Miss.)	4/13/09
Willingham, Calder	(Atlanta, Ga.)	12/23/22
Wolfe, Tom	(Richmond, Va.)	3/2/31
Wouk, Herman	(New York, N.Y.)	5/27/15
Yerby, Frank	(Augusta, Ga.)	9/5/16

American Writers of the Past

Novelists, Poets, Historians, Biographers

Charles Francis Adams, biographer, diplomat, 1807-1886.
Charles Francis Adams, historian, lawyer, 1835-1915.
Henry Adams, historian, philosopher, 1838-1918.
James Truslow Adams, historian, 1878-1949.
George Ade, humorist, dramatist, 1866-1944.
Conrad Aiken, poet, critic, 1889-1973.
Louisa May Alcott, novelist, 1832-1888. Little Women.
Horatio Alger, author of "rags-to-riches" boys books, 1832-1899.
Charlotte Armstrong, mystery writer, 1905-1969.
Gertrude Atherton, novelist, 1857-1948. Black Oxen.
Mary Austin, novelist, playwright, 1868-1934.
Ray Stannard Baker, biographer, historian, 1870-1946.
George Bancroft, historian, diplomat, 1800-1891.
Margaret Ayer Barnes, novelist, 1886-1967. Years of Grace.
Bruce Barton, author, businessman, 1886-1967. The Man Nobody Knows.
Charles A. Beard, historian, 1874-1948.
Mary Ritter Beard, historian, 1876-1958.
Edward Bellamy, novelist, 1850-1898. Looking Backward: 2000-1887.
Stephen Vincent Benet, poet, novelist, 1898-1943.
William Rose Benet, poet, novelist, 1886-1950.
John Berryman, poet, 1914-1972.
Ambrose Bierce, short-story writer, journalist, 1842-1914.
Earl Derr Biggers, novelist, 1884-1933. Created Charlie Chan.
Louise Bogan, lyric poet, 1897-1970.
Anne Bradstreet, poet, 1612-1672.
Louis Bromfield, novelist, essayist, 1896-1956.
Van Wyck Brooks, historian, critic, 1886-1963.
Orestes Brownson, author, editor, clergyman, 1803-1876.
Pearl Buck, author, won the Pulitzer and Nobel Prizes, 1892-1973. The Good Earth.
Ned Buntline, wrote dime novels, 1823-1886. Nicknamed "Buffalo Bill" Cody.
Edgar Rice Burroughs, novelist, 1875-1950. Tarzan of the Apes.
Rachel Carson, marine biologist, author, 1907-1964. Silent Spring.
Willa Cather, novelist, essayist, 1876-1947. O Pioneers!, My Antonia.
Raymond Chandler, wrote detective fiction, 1888-1959. Philip Marlowe series.
Walter Van Tilburg Clark, novelist, 1909-1972. The Ox-Bow Incident.
James Fenimore Cooper, novelist, 1789-1851. Leather-Stocking Tales.
Thomas B. Costain, novelist, journalist, 1885-1965. The Black Rose.
Hart Crane, poet, 1899-1932.
Stephen Crane, novelist, 1871-1900. The Red Badge of Courage.
Countee Cullen, poet, 1903-1946. The Black Christ.
E. E. Cummings, poet, 1894-1962.
Richard H. Dana, author, lawyer, 1815-1882. Two Years Before the Mast.
Bernard De Voto, historian, editor, 1897-1955.
Emily Dickinson, poet, 1830-1886.
J. Frank Dobie, author, educator, 1888-1964.
Hilda Doolittle (H.D.), poet, 1886-1961.
John Dos Passos, author, 1896-1970. U.S.A., Midcentury.
Theodore Dreiser, novelist, 1871-1945. An American Tragedy.
Paul L. Dunbar, poet, novelist, 1872-1906.
Ralph Waldo Emerson, poet, essayist, 1803-1882.
John Erskine, novelist, educator, 1879-1951. The Private Life of Helen of Troy.
Martha Farquharson, author of juveniles, 1828-1909. Elsie Dinsmore series.
William Faulkner, novelist, 1897-1962. Sanctuary, Light in August.
Edna Ferber, novelist, 1885-1968. Show Boat, Saratoga Trunk, Giant.
Eugene Field, poet, journalist, 1850-1895. Little Boy Blue; Wynken, Blynken and Nod.
Louis Fischer, historian, 1896-1970. The Life of Lenin.
Dorothy Canfield Fisher, novelist, writer of juveniles, 1879-1958.
John Fiske, historian, philosopher, 1842-1901.
F. Scott Fitzgerald, novelist, short-story writer, 1896-1940. The Great Gatsby.
John Gould Fletcher, poet, critic, 1886-1950.
Gene Fowler, journalist, author, 1890-1960. Good Night, Sweet Prince.
John W. Fox Jr., novelist, 1863-1919. The Little Shepherd of

Kingdom Come.
Mary E. W. Freeman, short-story writer, 1852-1930.
Philip Freneau, poet, journalist, 1752-1832.
Robert Frost, poet, 1874-1963.
Zona Gale, novelist, dramatist, 1874-1938.
Erle Stanley Gardner, author, lawyer, 1889-1970. Perry Mason series.
Hamlin Garland, novelist, 1860-1940. Main-Traveled Roads.
Ellen Glasgow, novelist, 1873-1945.
Susan Glaspell, novelist, dramatist, 1882-1948.
Zane Grey, writer of western stories, 1875-1939.
Edgar A. Guest, poet, 1881-1959. A Heap of Livin'.
Edward Everett Hale, author, clergyman, 1822-1909. The Man Without a Country.
James Norman Hall, novelist, 1887-1951. Co-author Mutiny on the Bounty.
Dashiell Hammett, writer of detective fiction, 1894-1961. Created Sam Spade.
Joel Chandler Harris, short-story writer, 1848-1908. Uncle Remus series.
Bret Harte, short-story writer, poet, 1836-1902. The Luck of Roaring Camp.
Cameron Hawley, novelist, 1905-1969. Executive Suite.
Nathaniel Hawthorne, novelist, 1804-1864. The Scarlet Letter.
John M. Hay, historian, diplomat, 1838-1905. Abraham Lincoln: A History.
Lafcadio Hearn, author, 1850-1904.
Ben Hecht, novelist, playwright, journalist, 1894-1964.
Ernest Hemingway, novelist, short-story writer, 1899-1961. A Farewell to Arms.
O. Henry (W. S. Porter), short-story writer, 1862-1910. The Gift of the Magi.
Alice Tisdale Hobart, novelist, 1882-1967. Oil for the Lamps of China.
Richard Hofstadter, historian, 1916-1970. The Age of Reform.
Oliver Wendell Holmes, poet, novelist, 1809-1894.
Mark DeWolfe Howe, historian, 1906-1967.
Julia Ward Howe, poet, reformer, 1819-1910. The Battle Hymn of the Republic.
William Dean Howells, novelist, critic, 1837-1920.
Elbert Hubbard, author, editor, 1856-1915. A Message to Garcia.
Langston Hughes, poet, playwright, 1902-1967.
Rupert Hughes, novelist, playwright, 1872-1956.
Fannie Hurst, novelist, 1889-1968. Back Street, Lummox.
Washington Irving, essayist, author, 1783-1859. Rip Van Winkle.
Charles Jackson, novelist, 1887-1968. The Lost Weekend.
Henry James, novelist, critic, 1843-1916. Washington Square.
Robinson Jeffers, poet, dramatist, 1887-1962.
Sarah Orne Jewett, novelist, short-story writer, 1849-1909.
James Weldon Johnson, author, poet, 1871-1938.
Jack Kerouac, author, 1922-1969. On the Road.
Francis Scott Key, poet, 1779-1843. The Star-Spangled Banner.
Frances Parkinson Keyes, author, editor, 1885-1970. Dinner at Antoine's.
Joyce Kilmer, poet, 1886-1918. Trees.
Joseph Wood Krutch, author, naturalist, 1885-1970. The Measure of Man.
Oliver La Farge, novelist, 1901-1963. Laughing Boy.
Rose Wilder Lane, novelist, 1887-1968. Let the Hurricane Roar.
Sidney Lanier, poet, critic, 1842-1881.
Ring Lardner, short-story writer, journalist, 1885-1933.
Emma Lazarus, poet, essayist, 1849-1887. The New Colossus.
William Ellery Leonard, poet, 1876-1944.
Oscar Lewis, author, anthropologist, 1914-1970. La Vida.
Sinclair Lewis, novelist, playwright, 1885-1951. Babbitt, Arrowsmith, Dodsworth.
Ludwig Lewisohn, novelist, critic, 1882-1955.
Willy Ley, science writer, 1906-1969.
Vachel Lindsay, poet, 1879-1931.
Louis Lomax, author, 1922-1970. The Negro Revolt.
Jack London, novelist, journalist, 1876-1916. The Call of the Wild.
Henry Wadsworth Longfellow, poet, 1807-1882. The Wreck of the Hesperus, Evangeline, The Song of Hiawatha.
Amy Lowell, poet, critic, 1874-1925.
James Russell Lowell, poet, editor, 1819-1891.
Edwin Markham, poet, 1852-1940. The Man with the Hoe.
John P. Marquand, novelist, 1893-1960. The Late George Apley.
Edgar Lee Masters, poet, biographer, 1869-1950. Spoon River Anthology.
Carson McCullers, novelist, 1917-1967. The Heart is a Lonely Hunter.
John B. McMaster, historian, 1852-1932.
Herman Melville, novelist, poet, 1819-1891. Moby Dick.
Thomas Merton, poet, religious writer, 1915-1968. Seven Storey Mountain.
Edna St. Vincent Millay, poet, 1892-1950.
Joaquin Miller, poet, 1839-1913.
Max Miller, novelist, 1889-1967. I Cover the Waterfront.
Margaret Mitchell, novelist, 1900-1949. Gone With the Wind.
William Vaughn Moody, poet, dramatist, 1869-1910.
Clement C. Moore, poet, educator, 1779-1863. A Visit from Saint Nicholas.
Marianne Moore, poet, 1887-1972.
John L. Motley, historian, diplomat, 1814-1877.
Willard Motley, novelist, 1912-1966. Knock on Any Door.
Ogden Nash, poet, 1902-1971.
Allan Nevins, historian, biographer, 1890-1971.
Charles B. Nordhoff, novelist, 1887-1947. Co-author Mutiny on the Bounty.
Frank Norris, novelist, journalist, 1870-1902. The Pit.
Kathleen Norris, novelist, 1880-1966.
Edwin G. O'Connor, novelist, 1918-1968. Edge of Sadness, The Last Hurrah.
John O'Hara, novelist, 1905-1970. Butterfield 8, Ten North Frederick.
Thomas (Tom) Paine, author, political theorist, 1737-1809. Common Sense.
Dorothy Parker, poet, short-story writer, 1893-1967.
Francis Parkman, historian, 1823-1893.
James K. Paulding, poet novelist, 1778-1860
John Howard Payne, poet, dramatist, 1791-1852. Home, Sweet Home.
Josephine P. Peabody, poet, dramatist, 1874-1922.
Edgar Allan Poe, poet, short-story writer, critic, 1809-1849. Annabel Lee.
Ernest Poole, journalist, novelist, 1880-1950.
Ezra Pound, poet, 1885-1972.
William H. Prescott, historian, 1796-1859.
James G. Randall, historian, 1881-1953.
Marjorie Kinnan Rawlings, novelist, 1896-1953. The Yearling.
Erich Maria Remarque, novelist, 1898-1970. All Quiet on the Western Front.
Alice Hegan Rice, novelist, 1870-1952. Mrs. Wiggs of the Cabbage Patch.
Conrad M. Richter, novelist, 1890-1968. The Town.
James Whitcomb Riley, poet, 1849-1916.
Mary Roberts Rinehart, mystery writer, 1876-1958. The Circular Staircase, The Bat.
Elizabeth Madox Roberts, poet, novelist, 1886-1941.
Kenneth Roberts, novelist, 1885-1957. Northwest Passage.
Edwin Arlington Robinson, poet, 1869-1935.
Theodore Roethke, poet, 1908-1963.
Robert Ruark, novelist, journalist, 1915-1965. Something of Value.
Damon Runyon, short-story writer, journalist, 1884-1946. Guys and Dolls.
Cornelius Ryan, novelist, 1920-1974. The Longest Day.
Carl Sandburg, poet, biographer, 1878-1967.
George Santayana, poet, essayist, philosopher, 1863-1952.
Alan Seeger, poet, 1888-1916. I Have a Rendezvous with Death.
Gilbert Seldes, author, critic, 1893-1970. The 7 Lively Arts, The Great Audience.
Ernest Thompson Seton, author, naturalist, 1860-1946. Wild Animals I Have Known.
Anne Sexton, poet, won Pulitzer Prize, 1928-1974.
Upton Sinclair, novelist, 1878-1968. The Jungle, Dragon's Teeth.
Betty Smith, novelist, 1896-1972. A Tree Grows in Brooklyn.
Lillian Smith, novelist, 1897-1966. Strange Fruit.
Samuel Francis Smith, poet, clergyman, 1808-1895. America.
Jared Sparks, historian, educator, 1789-1866.
Burt L. Standish (Gilbert Patten), author, 1866-1945. Frank Merriwell series.
Edmund C. Stedman, poet, critic, 1833-1908.
Lincoln Steffens, editor, author, 1866-1936. The Shame of the Cities.
Gertrude Stein, author, 1874-1946. Three Lives.
John Steinbeck, novelist, 1902-1968. Of Mice and Men, The Grapes of Wrath.
Wallace Stevens, poet, 1879-1955.
Frank R. Stockton, novelist, short-story writer, 1834-1902. The Lady or the Tiger?
Rex Stout, mystery novelist, 1886-1975. Created Nero Wolfe.
Harriet Beecher Stowe, novelist, 1811-1896. Uncle Tom's Cabin.
Edward Stratemeyer, author, 1862-1930. Creator of such series as the Rover Boys, Bobbsey Twins, Tom Swift.
Gene Stratton-Porter, novelist, 1863-1924. A Girl of the Limberlost.
Jacqueline Susann, novelist, 1921-1974. Valley of the Dolls.
Genevieve Taggard, poet, 1894-1948.
Ida M. Tarbell, editor, author, 1857-1944. The History of the Standard Oil Company.
Booth Tarkington, novelist, 1869-1946. Seventeen, Alice

Adams.
Sara Teasdale, poet, 1884-1933.
Albert Payson Terhune, novelist, journalist, 1872-1942. Lad: A Dog.
Henry D. Thoreau, essayist, naturalist, 1817-1862. Walden.
James Thurber, humorist, artist, 1894-1961. The New Yorker.
Eunice Tietjens, poet, novelist, 1884-1944.
Charles Hanson Towne, poet, editor, 1877-1949.
Lionel Trilling, literary critic, 1905-1975.
Frederick J. Turner, historian, educator, 1861-1932.
Mark Twain (Samuel Clemens), novelist, humorist, 1835-1910. The Adventures of Huckleberry Finn, Tom Sawyer.
Carl Van Doren, historian, critic, educator, 1885-1950.
Mark Van Doren, poet, author, critic, 1894-1972.
Henry Van Dyke, poet, educator, essayist, 1852-1933.
Lew Wallace, novelist, diplomat, 1827-1905. Ben Hur.
Artemus Ward (Charles F. Browne), humorist, 1834-1867.
Nathanael West, novelist, 1903-1940.
Edith Wharton, novelist, 1862-1937. The Age of Innocence.
Walt Whitman, poet, 1819-1892. Leaves of Grass.
John Greenleaf Whittier, poet, journalist, 1809-1892. Snow-Bound.
Kate Douglas Wiggin, children's author, educator, 1856-1923. Rebecca of Sunnybrook Farm.
Ella Wheeler Wilcox, poet, 1850-1919.
Robert Wilder, novelist, 1901-1974. Written on the Wind.
Ben Ames Williams, novelist, 1889-1953.
William Carlos Williams, poet, physician, 1883-1963.
Edmund Wilson, author, literary and social critic, 1895-1972.
P.G. Wodehouse, novelist, playwright, 1881-1975.
Thomas Wolfe, novelist, 1900-1938. Look Homeward, Angel.
Samuel Woodworth, poet, dramatist, 1784-1842.
Harold Bell Wright, novelist, 1872-1944. The Shepherd of the Hills.
Richard Wright, novelist, 1908-1960. Native Son.
Elinor Wylie, poet, novelist, 1885-1928.
Philip Wylie, author, 1902-1971. Generation of Vipers.

Journalists, Publishers

Franklin P. Adams, journalist, 1881-1960.
Thomas Bailey Aldrich, author, editor, 1836-1907.
Henry M. Alden, editor, 1836-1919. Harper's Magazine.
Stewart Alsop, political columnist, writer, 1914-1974.
Hamilton Fish Armstrong, editor, 1893-1973. Foreign Affairs.
Arthur (Bugs) Baer, humorous columnist, 1886-1969.
John Bartlett, publisher, 1820-1905. Familiar Quotations.
Lucius M. Beebe, journalist, author, 1902-1966. N. Y. Herald Tribune.
Robert C. Benchley, humorist, journalist, 1889-1945.
James Gordon Bennett, journalist, 1795-1872. Founded N. Y. Herald.
James Gordon Bennett Jr., journalist, 1841-1918, N.Y. Herald, Evening Telegram.
William Benton, publisher, 1900-1973. Encyclopaedia Britannica.
Ambrose Bierce, short-story writer, journalist, 1842-1914.
William Cowper Brann, iconoclast, editor, reformer, 1855-1898.
Arthur Brisbane, journalist, 1864-1936. N. Y. Sun, Evening Sun, World.
Heywood Broun, journalist, 1888-1939. N. Y. Tribune, World.
John Mason Brown, drama, literary critic, 1900-1969.
William Cullen Bryant, poet, editor, 1794-1878.
Henry Seidel Canby, editor, critic, 1878-1961. Saturday Review of Literature.
Bob Considine, journalist, syndicated columnist, 1908-1975. "On the Line."
Cyrus H.K. Curtis, magazine, newspaper publisher, 1850-1933.
Charles A. Dana, editor, 1819-1897. New York Sun.
Josephus Daniels, journalist, statesman, 1862-1948. Raleigh News & Observer.
Elmer Davis, journalist, radio commentator, 1890-1958.
Richard Harding Davis, journalist, novelist, 1864-1916.
Orvil E. Dryfoos, newspaper publisher, 1912-1963. New York Times.
James T. Fields, editor, author, 1817-1881. Atlantic Monthly.
F.M. Flynn, president, publisher, N.Y. Daily News, 1903-1975.
Frank E. Gannett, newspaper publisher, 1876-1957. Gannett Newspapers.
Edwin L. Godkin, journalist, 1831-1902. Founded The Nation.
Henry W. Grady, journalist, orator, 1850-1889. Atlanta Constitution.
Horace Greeley, journalist, politician, 1811-1872. N. Y. Tribune.
Abel Green, journalist, editor, 1900-1973. Variety.
Gilbert H. Grosvenor, editor, geographer, 1875-1966. National Geographic.
John Gunther, journalist, author, 1901-1970. Inside U.S.A., Inside Europe, Death Be Not Proud.
Gabriel Heatter, radio commentator, 1890-1972.
William Randolph Hearst, newspaper publisher, 1863-1951.
Burton J. Hendrick, biographer, journalist, 1871-1949.
William M. (Bill) Henry, journalist, radio analyst, 1890-1970. Los Angeles Times.
Ben Hibbs, editor, 1901-1975. Saturday Evening Post.
Marguerite Higgins, journalist, 1920-1966.
Roy W. Howard, newspaper publisher, editor, 1883-1964. Scripps-Howard Newspapers.
Chet Huntley, TV newscaster, 1911-1974.
H. V. Kaltenborn, editor, radio commentator, 1878-1965.
Dorothy Kilgallen, journalist, radio-TV personality, 1913-1965.
Bernard Kilgore, journalist, 1908-1967. Wall Street Journal.
Willard M. Kiplinger, journalist, 1891-1967. Changing Times.
Arthur Krock, journalist, 1887-1974, N. Y. Times.
William M. Laffan, publisher, 1848-1900. New York Sun, N. Y. Evening Sun.
David Lawrence, journalist, founder and editor of U. S. News & World Report, 1888-1973.
Charles Godfrey Leland, author, journalist, 1824-1903.
Fulton Lewis, Jr., radio news commentator, 1903-1966.
Walter Lippmann, dean of American political journalism, 1889-1974.
Henry R. Luce, publisher, 1898-1967. Time, Life, Fortune magazines.
Don Marquis, humorist, journalist, 1878-1937. The Old Soak.
James McClatchy, publisher, editor, 1824-1883. McClatchy Newspapers.
Joseph Medill McCormick, journalist, politician, 1887-1925. Chicago Tribune.
Robert R. McCormick, editor, publisher, 1880-1955. Chicago Tribune.
Ralph E. McGill, editor, publisher, 1898-1969. Atlanta Constitution.
Joseph Medill, journalist, 1823-1899. Chicago Tribune.
Henry L. Mencken, editor, author, philologist, 1880-1956. Baltimore Sun, American Mercury.
Christopher Morley, journalist, novelist, 1890-1957. Kitty Foyle.
Edward R. Murrow, radio-TV commentator, 1908-1965.
Frank B. Noyes, newspaper executive, 1863-1948. Associated Press.
Adolph S. Ochs, newspaper publisher, 1858-1935. The New York Times.
Alicia Patterson, journalist, 1906-1963. Newsday.
Eleanor Medill Patterson, journalist, 1884-1948. Washington Times-Herald.
Joseph Medill Patterson, publisher, 1879-1946. Founded N.Y. Daily News.
Drew Pearson, newspaper columnist, 1897-1969.
Westbrook Pegler, newspaper columnist, 1894-1969.
Joseph Pulitzer, journalist, 1847-1911. St. Louis Post-Dispatch, N. Y. World.
Joseph Pulitzer, journalist, 1885-1955. St. Louis Post-Dispatch.
Ralph Pulitzer, journalist, 1879-1939. St. Louis Post-Dispatch, N.Y. World.
Ernie Pyle, journalist, war correspondent, 1900-1945.
Burton Rascoe, journalist, author, 1892-1957.
Ogden M. Reid, journalist, 1882-1947. N. Y. Herald Tribune.
Whitelaw Reid, journalist, diplomat, 1837-1912. N. Y. Tribune.
Quentin Reynolds, journalist, author, 1902-1965.
Grantland Rice, journalist, 1880-1954.
Roy A. Roberts, journalist, 1887-1967. Kansas City Star.
Max L. Schuster, editor, publisher, 1897-1970. Simon & Schuster.
Edward W. Scripps, newspaper publisher, 1854-1926.
Robert P. Scripps, newspaper publisher, 1895-1938. Scripps-Howard Newspapers.
Vincent Sheean, foreign correspondent, 1899-1975.
Merriman Smith, newspaper correspondent, 1913-1970. UPI.
Frank L. Stanton, poet, journalist, 1857-1927. Mighty Lak'a Rose.
Arthur Hays Sulzberger, publisher, 1891-1968. The New York Times.
Herbert Bayard Swope, journalist, 1882-1958. N. Y. World.
Dorothy Thompson, journalist, author, 1894-1961.
James Thurber, humorist, artist, 1894-1961. The New Yorker.
Hendrik Willem van Loon, historian, journalist, 1882-1944.
Oswald G. Villard, editor, author, 1872-1949. The Nation.
William Allen White, editor, author, 1868-1944. Emporia (Kan.) Gazette.
Walter Winchell, Broadway columnist, 1897-1972.
Alexander Woollcott, journalist, critic, 1887-1943.
John Peter Zenger, journalist, printer, 1697-1746. N. Y. Weekly Journal.

Modern American Playwrights and Some of Their Plays

George Abbott, b. 1887. Co-author Three Men on a Horse, The Boys from Syracuse, Damn Yankees.

Edward F. Albee, b. 1928. Who's Afraid of Virginia Woolf?, Tiny Alice, A Delicate Balance, Seascape.

William Alfred, b. 1922. Hogan's Goat.

Maxwell Anderson (1888-1959). What Price Glory?, Winterset, Saturday's Children, High Tor, Key Largo.

Philip Barry (1886-1949). The Animal Kingdom, Holiday, The Philadelphia Story.

Abe Burrows, b. 1910. Co-author Guys and Dolls, How to Succeed in Business Without Really Trying.

Mary C. Chase, b. 1907. Harvey.

Paddy Chayefsky, b. 1923. Middle of the Night, The Tenth Man, Gideon, The Passions of Josef D.

Marc Connelly, b. 1890. The Green Pastures.

Russell Crouse (1893-1966). Co-author State of the Union, Life With Father, Call Me Madam, The Sound of Music.

Edna Ferber (1885-1968). Co-author Dinner at Eight, Stage Door.

Paul Foster, b. 1932. Tom Paine.

Jack Gelber, b. 1932. The Connection, The Cuban Thing.

William Gibson, b. 1914. Two for the Seesaw, The Miracle Worker.

Frank D. Gilroy, b. 1915. The Subject Was Roses, The Only Game in Town.

Charles Gordone, b. 1925. No Place to Be Somebody.

Paul Green, b. 1894. In Abraham's Bosom, Wilderness Road.

William Hanley, b. 1931. Slow Dance on the Killing Ground.

Lorraine Hansberry (1930-1965). A Raisin in the Sun.

Moss Hart (1904-1961). Co-author Once in a Lifetime, You Can't Take it With You.

Ben Hecht (1894-1964). Co-author The Front Page.

Lillian Hellman, b. 1907. The Children's Hour, The Little Foxes, Watch on the Rhine.

Sidney Howard (1881-1939). The Silver Cord, Yellow Jack, They Knew What They Wanted.

William Inge (1913-1973). Come Back Little Sheba, Picnic, Bus Stop, The Dark at the Top of the Stairs, A Loss of Roses.

LeRoi Jones (Imamu Amini Baraka), b. 1934. Dutchman, The Slave.

George S. Kaufman (1889-1961). Co-author Dinner at Eight, Stage Door, You Can't Take It With You, The Man Who Came to Dinner.

George Kelly (1887-1974). The Show-off, Craig's Wife.

Jean Kerr, b. 1923. Mary, Mary, Poor Richard, Finishing Touches.

Joseph Kesserlring (1902-1967). Arsenic and Old Lace.

Sidney Kingsley, b. 1906. Men in White, The Patriots, Dead End, Darkness at Noon.

Arthur Kopit, b. 1937. Oh Dad, Poor Dad, Mamma's Hung You in a Closet and I'm Feelin' So Sad.

Howard Lindsay (1889-1968). Co-author State of the Union, Life With Father, Call Me Madam, The Sound of Music.

Charles MacArthur (1895-1956). Co-author The Front Page.

Archibald MacLeish, b. 1892. J. B.

Terrence McNally, b. 1939. And Things That Go Bump in the Night, Sweet Eros.

Arthur Miller, b. 1915. All My Sons, Death of a Salesman, The Crucible, View from the Bridge, After the Fall, Incident at Vichy, The Price.

Jason Miller, b. 1940. That Championship Season.

Anne Nichols (1891-1966). Abie's Irish Rose.

Clifford Odets (1906-1963). Waiting for Lefty, Awake and Sing, Golden Boy, The Country Girl.

Eugene O'Neill (1888-1953). The Long Voyage Home, The Emperor Jones, Anna Christie, Desire Under the Elms, Strange Interlude, Mourning Becomes Electra, Ah, Wilderness, The Iceman Cometh, Long Day's Journey Into Night.

John Patrick, b. 1905. The Hasty Heart, Teahouse of the August Moon.

Elmer Rice (1892-1967). The Adding Machine, Street Scene, Counsellor-at-Law, Dream Girl.

Howard Sackler, b. 1930. The Great White Hope.

William Saroyan, b. 1908. My Heart's in the Highlands, The Time of Your Life.

Dore Schary, b. 1905. Sunrise at Campobello.

Murray Schisgal, b. 1926. The Typists and the Tiger, Luv.

Robert Sherwood (1896-1955). Reunion in Vienna, The Petrified Forest, Idiot's Delight, There Shall Be No Night, Abe Lincoln in Illinois.

Neil Simon, b. 1927. Sweet Charity, Plaza Suite, The Odd Couple, Barefoot in the Park, Last of the Red Hot Lovers, The Gingerbread Lady, The Prisoner of Second Avenue, The Sunshine Boys, The Good Doctor.

Samuel A. Taylor, b. 1912. The Happy Time, The Pleasure of His Company, co-author Sabrina Fair and No Strings.

John Van Druten (1901-1957). The Voice of the Turtle; I Remember Mama; Bell, Book and Candle; I Am a Camera.

Thornton Wilder (1897-1975). Our Town, The Skin of Our Teeth, The Matchmaker.

Tennessee Williams, b. 1914. The Glass Menagerie, A Streetcar Named Desire, Cat on a Hot Tin Roof, The Night of the Iguana, The Milk Train Doesn't Stop Here Anymore, Camino Real.

Noted American Cartoonists

Charles Addams, b. 1912. Noted for macabre cartoons.
Peter Arno, 1904-1968. Noted for urban characterizations.
George Baker, 1915-1975. The Sad Sack.
C. C. Beck, b. 1910. Captain Marvel.
Jim Berry, b. 1932. Berry's World.
Herb Block (Herblock), b. 1909. Leading political cartoonist.
Dave Breger, 1908-1970. G. I. Joe.
Clare Briggs, 1875-1930. Mr. & Mrs.
Ernie Bushmiller, b. 1905. Nancy.
Milton Caniff, b. 1907. Terry & the Pirates; Steve Canyon.
Al Capp, b. 1909. Li'l Abner.
Roy Crane, 1901-1977. Captain Easy; Buz Sawyer.
Jay N. Darling (Ding), 1876-1962. Political cartoonist won 2 Pulitzer Prizes.
Billy DeBeck, 1890-1942. Barnie Google.
Rudolph Dirks, 1877-1968. The Katzenjammer Kids.
Walt Disney, 1901-1966. Producer of animated cartoons created Mickey Mouse & Donald Duck.
Alan Dunn, 1900-1974. Cartoonist for *The New Yorker*.
Jules Feiffer, b. 1929. Satirical *Village Voice* cartoonist.
Bud Fisher, 1885-1954. Mutt & Jeff.
Ham Fisher, 1900-1955. Joe Palooka.
James Montgomery Flagg, 1877-1960. Illustrator, created the famous Uncle Sam recruiting poster during WW I.
Hal Foster, b. 1892. Tarzan; Prince Valiant.
Fontaine Fox, 1884-1964. Toonerville Folks.
Rube Goldberg, 1883-1970. Boob McNutt. Famed for cartoons of mechanical contrivances whose humor is derived from their absurd, unnecessary complexity.
Chester Gould, b. 1900. Dick Tracy.
Harold Gray, 1894-1968. Little Orphan Annie.
Jimmy Hatlo, 1898-1963. They'll Do It Everytime, Little Iodine.
John Held Jr., 1889-1958. His cartoons epitomized the spirit of the "jazz age" of the 20s.
George Herriman, 1881-1944. Krazy Kat.
Harry Hershfield, 1885-1974. Raconteur; Abie the Agent.
Burne Hogarth, b. 1911. Tarzan.
Helen Hokinson, 1900-1949. Known for satirical drawings of plump, bewildered suburban matrons and clubwomen.
Walt Kelly, 1913-1973. Pogo.
Hank Ketcham, b. 1920. Dennis the Menace.
Ted Key, b. 1912. Hazel.
Frank King, 1883-1969. Gasoline Alley.
Jack Kirby, b. 1917. Captain America.
Rollin Kirby, 1875-1952. Political cartoonist won 3 Pulitzer Prizes.
Bill Mauldin, b. 1921. Depicted squalid life of the G.I. in WW II.
Winsor McCay, 1872-1934. Little Nemo.
John T. McCutcheon, 1870-1949. Noted for cartoons of midwestern rural life.
George McManus, 1884-1954. Bringing Up Father (Maggie & Jiggs).
Dale Messick, b. 1906. Brenda Starr.
Bob Montana, 1920-1975. Archie.
Willard Mullin, b. 1902. Sports cartoonist created the Dodgers "Bum" and the Mets "Kid".
Thomas Nast, 1840-1902. Political cartoonist, instrumental in breaking the corrupt Boss Tweed ring in N.Y. Created the donkey and elephant to represent the Democratic and Republican parties.
Frederick Burr Opper, 1857-1937. Happy Hooligan.
Richard Outcault, 1863-1928. Yellow Kid; Buster Brown.
Alex Raymond, 1909-1956. Flash Gordon; Jungle Jim.
Art Sansom, b. 1920. The Born Loser.
Charles Schulz, b. 1922. Peanuts.
Elzie C. Segar, 1894-1938. Popeye.
Sydney Smith, 1887-1935. The Gumps.
Otto Soglow, 1900-1975. The Little King; The Canyon Kiddies.
James Swinnerton, 1875-1974. Little Jimmy.
James Thurber, 1894-1961. *New Yorker* cartoonist of the smugly childish line coupled with the sophisticated caption.
Mort Walker, b. 1923. Beetle Bailey.
Russ Westover, 1887-1966. Tillie the Toiler.
Frank Willard, 1893-1958. Moon Mullins.
J. R. Williams, 1888-1957. The Willets Family; Out Our Way.
Gahan Wilson, b. 1930. Cartoonist of the macabre.
Art Young, 1866-1943. Political radical and satirist.
Chic Young, 1901-1973. Blondie.

American Architects and Some of Their Achievements

Max Abramovitz, b. 1908. Avery Fisher Hall at Lincoln Center, N.Y.C.

Henry Bacon (1866-1924), Lincoln Memorial.

Pietro Belluschi, b. 1899. Julliard School of Music, Lincoln Center, N.Y.C.

Marcel Breuer, b. 1902. Whitney Museum of American Art, N.Y.C. (with Hamilton Smith).

Charles Bulfinch (1763-1844), State House, Boston; Capitol, Washington, (part).

Daniel H. Burnham (1846-1912), Union Station, Washington; Flatiron, N.Y.C.

Ralph Adams Cram (1863-1942), Cathedral of St. John the Divine, N.Y.C.; U.S. Military Academy (part).

Alexander J. Davis (1803-1892), Sub-treasury, N.Y.C.; capitols of Ind., N.C., Ill., Oh.

R. Buckminster Fuller, b. 1895. U.S. Pavilion, Expo 67, Montreal (geodesic domes).

Cass Gilbert (1859-1934), Custom House, Woolworth Bldg., N.Y.C.; Capitol, St. Paul.

Bertrand Goldberg, b. 1913. Marina City Towers, Chicago.

Bertram G. Goodhue (1869-1924), Capitol, Lincoln, Neb.; St. Thomas, St. Bartholomew, N.Y.C.

Walter Gropius (1883-1969), Pan Am Building, N.Y.C. (with Pietro Belluschi).

Peter Harrison (1716-1775), Jeshuat Israel Synagogue, Redwood Library, Newport, R.I.

Wallace K. Harrison, b. 1895. Metropolitan Opera House at Lincoln Center, N.Y.C.

Thomas Hastings (1860-1929), Public Library, Frick Mansion, N.Y.C.

James Hoban (1762-1831), The White House.

William Holabird (1854-1923), Crerar Library, City Hall, Chicago.

Raymond Hood (1881-1934), Rockefeller Center, N.Y.C. (part); Daily News, N.Y.C.; Tribune, Chicago.

Richard M. Hunt (1828-1896), Metropolitan Museum, N.Y.C. (part); The Breakers, Newport.

William Le Baron Jenney (1832-1907), Home Insurance, Chicago (demolished).

Philip C. Johnson, b. 1906. N.Y. State Theater at Lincoln Center, N.Y.C.

Albert Kahn (1869-1942), Athletic Club Bldg., General Motors Bldg., N.Y.C.

Louis Kahn (1901-1974), Salk Laboratory, La Jolla, Cal.; Yale Art Gallery.

Christopher Grant LaFarge (1862-1938), Chapel, West Point; Cathedral, Seattle.

Benjamin H. Latrobe (1764-1820), U.S. Capitol (part).

William Lescaze (1896-1969), Philadelphia Savings Fund Society; Borg-Warner Bldg., Chicago.

Theodore C. Link (1850-1923), Union Station, St. Louis.

Charles F. McKim (1847-1909), Public Library, Boston, Columbia Univ., N.Y.C. (part).

Charles M. McKim, b. 1920. KUHT-TV Transmitter Building, Houston; Lutheran Church of the Redeemer, Houston.

Milton B. Medary (1874-1929), Bok Carillon Tower, Mountain Lake, Fla.

Ludwig Mies van der Rohe (1886-1969), Seagram Building, N.Y.C. (with Philip C. Johnson); National Gallery, Berlin.

Robert Mills (1781-1855), Washington Monument.

Richard J. Neutra (1892-1970), Mathematics Park, Princeton; Orange Co. Courthouse, Santa Ana, Cal.

Frederick L. Olmsted (1822-1903), Central Park, N.Y.C.; Fairmount Park, Philadelphia.

Ieoh Ming Pei, b. 1917. Kips Bay Plaza, N.Y.C.; Earth Sciences Building (M.I.T.) Cambridge, Mass.; National Center for Atmospheric Research, Boulder, Col.

William Pereira, b. 1909. Cape Canaveral; Transamerica Bldg., San Francisco.

John Russell Pope (1874-1937), National Gallery.

John Portman, b. 1924. Peachtree Center, Atlanta.

James Renwick Jr. (1818-1895), Grace Church, St. Patrick's Cathedral, N.Y.C.; Smithsonian, Corcoran Galleries, Wash., D.C.

Henry H. Richardson (1838-1886), Trinity Church, Boston.

Kevin Roche, b. 1922. Oakland Cal. Museum; Fine Arts Center, U. of Mass.

James Gamble Rogers (1867-1947), Columbia-Presbyterian Medical Center, N.Y.C.; Northwestern Univ., Chicago.

John Weldon Root, b. 1887. Palmolive Building, Chicago; Hotel Statler, Washington; Hotel Tamanaco, Caracas.

Paul Rudolph, b. 1918. Jewitt Art Center, Wellesley College; Art & Architecture Bldg., Yale.

Eero Saarinen (1910-1961), Gateway to the West Arch, St. Louis; Trans World Flight Center, N.Y.C.

Louis Skidmore (1897-1962), AEC town site, Oak Ridge, Tenn.; Terrace Plaza Hotel, Cincinnati.

Clarence S. Stein, b. 1882. Temple Emanu-El, N.Y.C.

Edward Durell Stone, b. 1902. U.S. Embassy, New Delhi, India; (H. Hartford) Gallery of Modern Art, N.Y.C.

Louis H. Sullivan (1856-1924), Auditorium, Chicago.

Richard Upjohn (1802-1878), Trinity Church, N.Y.C.

Ralph T. Walker (1889-1973), N.Y. Telephone Hdqrs., N.Y.C.; IBM Research Lab., Poughkeepsie, N.Y.

Roland A. Wank (1898-1970), Cincinnati Union Terminal; head architect TVA, 1933-44.

Stanford White (1853-1906), Washington Arch; first Madison Square Garden, N.Y.C.

Frank Lloyd Wright (1869-1959), Imperial Hotel, Tokyo; Guggenheim Museum, N.Y.C.

William Wurster, b. 1895. Ghirardelli Sq., San Francisco; Cowell College, U. Cal., Berkeley.

Minoru Yamasaki, b. 1912. World Trade Center, N.Y.C.

Noted Black Americans

Names of black athletes and entertainers are not included here as they are listed elsewhere in The World Almanac.

Explorers, Settlers

James P. Beckwourth (1798-c. 1867) western fur-trader, scout, after whom Beckwourth Pass in northern California is named.

Jean Baptiste Point du Sable (c.1750-1818) pioneer trader and first settler of Chicago, 1779.

Estevanico explorer led Spanish expedition of 1538 into the American Southwest.

Matthew A. Henson (1866-1955) member of Peary's 1909 expedition to the North Pole; placed U.S. flag at the Pole.

Pedro Alonzo Nino, navigator of the Nina, one of Columbus' 3 ships on his first voyage of discovery to the New World, 1492.

Soldiers, Patriots

Crispus Attucks (c. 1723-1770) agitator led group which precipitated the "Boston Massacre," Mar. 5, 1770.

Lt. Gen. Benjamin O. Davis Jr., b. 1912, West Point (1936), first black Air Force general (1954).

Brig. Gen. Benjamin O. Davis Sr. (1877-1970) first black general, 1940, in U. S. Army.

Isaiah Dorman (19th century), U. S. Army interpreter, killed with Custer, 1876, at Battle of the Little Big Horn.

Henry O. Flipper (1856-1940) first black to graduate, 1877, from West Point.

Vice Adm. Samuel L. Gravely Jr., b. 1922, first black admiral, 1971, served in World War II, Korea, and Vietnam.

(Of 274,937 blacks who served in the U.S. Armed Forces during the Vietnam conflict (1965-1974), 5,681 were killed in combat.)

Gen. Daniel James Jr., b. 1920, first black 4-star general, 1975; Commander-in-Chief, North Atlantic Air Defense Command.

Pvt. Henry Johnson (1897-1929) the first American decorated by France in World War I with the Croix de Guerre.

(Of 367,000 blacks in the Armed Forces in World War I, 100,000 served in France.)

Dorie Miller (1919-1943) Navy hero of Pearl Harbor attack; awarded the Navy Cross.

(More than 1,000,000 blacks served in the U. S. Armed Forces in World War II; all-black fighter and bomber AAF units and infantry divisions gave distinguished service. In 1954 the policy of all-black units was finally abolished.)

Peter Salem, at the Battle of Bunker Hill, June 17, 1775, shot and killed British commander Maj. John Pitcairn.

(About 5,000 blacks served in the Continental Army, mostly in integrated units, some in all-black combat outfits.)

Harriet Tubman (1823-1913) Underground Railroad conductor served as nurse and spy for Union Army in the Civil War.

(Some 200,000 blacks served in the Union Army during the Civil War; 38,000 gave their lives; 22 won the Medal of Honor, the nation's highest award.)

Scientists, Inventors

Benjamin Banneker (1731-1806) inventor, astronomer, mathematician, and gazeteer; served on commission which surveyed and laid out Washington, D. C.

Henry Blair (19th century), obtained patents (believed the first issued to a black) for a corn-planter, 1834, and for a cotton-planter, 1836.

George E. Carruthers, b. 1940, physicist developed the Apollo 16 lunar surface ultraviolet camera/spectograph.

George Washington Carver (1861-1943) botanist, chemurgist, and educator; his extensive experiments in soil building and plant diseases revolutionized the economy of the South.

Dr. Charles Richard Drew (1904-1950) pioneer in development of blood banks; director of American Red Cross blood donor project in World War II.
Dr. William A. Hinton (1883-1959) developed the Hinton and Davies-Hinton tests for detection of syphilis; first black professor, 1949, at Harvard Medical School.
Ernest E. Just (1883-1941) marine biologist studied egg development; author, Biology of Cell Surfaces, 1941.
Lewis H. Latimer (1848-1928) associate of Edison; supervised installation of first electric street lighting in N.Y.C.
Jan Matzeliger (1852-1889) invented lasting machine, patented 1883, which revolutionized the shoe industry.
Norbert Rillieux (1806-1894) invented a vacuum pan evaporator, 1846, revolutionizing the sugar-refining industry.
Dr. Daniel Hale Williams (1858-1931) performed one of first 2 open-heart operations, 1893; founded Provident, Chicago's first Negro hospital; first black elected a fellow of the American College of Surgeons.
Granville T. Woods (1856-1910) invented the third-rail system now used in subways, a complex railway telegraph device that helped reduce train accidents, and an automatic air brake.

Writers, Educators

James Baldwin, b. 1924, author, playwright; Another Country, The Fire Next Time, Blues for Mister Charlie.
Imamu Amiri Baraka, b. LeRoi Jones, 1934; poet, playwright.
Edward Bouchet (1852-1918) first black to earn a Ph.D, Yale, 1876, at a U. S. university; first black to be elected to Phi Beta Kappa.
Gwendolyn Brooks, b. 1917, poet, novelist; first black to win a Pulitzer Prize, 1950, for Annie Allen.
William Wells Brown (1815-1884) novelist, dramatist; first American black to publish a novel.
Charles Waddell Chestnutt (1858-1932) author known primarily for his short stories, including The Conjure Woman.
Countee Cullen (1903-1946) poet, winner of numerous literary prizes.
Frederick Douglass (1817-1895) author, editor, orator, diplomat; edited the abolitionist weekly, The North Star, in Rochester, N.Y.; U.S. Minister and Consul General to Haiti.
William Edward Burghardt Du Bois (1868-1963) historian, sociologist; a founder of the National Association for the Advancement of Colored People (NAACP), 1909, and founder of its magazine The Crisis; author, The Souls of Black Folk.
Paul Laurence Dunbar (1872-1906) poet, novelist; won fame with Lyrics of Lowly Life, 1896.
Ralph Ellison b. 1914, novelist, winner of 1952 National Book Award, for Invisible Man.
Charles Gordone, b. 1925, won 1970 Pulitzer Prize in Drama, with No Place to Be Somebody.
Alex Haley, b. 1921, Pulitzer Prize-winning author; Roots, The Autobiography of Malcolm X.
Jupiter Hammon (c.1720-1800) poet; the first black American to have his works published, 1761.
Lorraine Hansberry (1930-1965) playwright; won N. Y. Drama Critics Circle Award, 1959, with Raisin in the Sun.
Langston Hughes (1902-1967) poet; also author of stories and song lyrics.
James Weldon Johnson (1871-1938) poet, lyricist, novelist; first black admitted to Florida bar; U.S. consul in Venezuela and Nicaragua.
Willard Motley (1912-1965) novelist; Knock on Any Door.
Wilson C. Riles, b. 1917, elected, 1970, California State Superintendent of Public Instruction.
John B. Russwurm (1799-1851) with **Samuel E. Cornish** (1793-1858) founded, 1827, the nation's first black newspaper, Freedom's Journal, in N.Y.C.
Booker T. Washington (1856-1915) founder, 1881, and first president of Tuskegee Institute; author, Up From Slavery.
Phillis Wheatley (c. 1753-1784) poet; 2d American woman and first black woman to have her works published, 1770.
Dr. Carter G. Woodson (1875-1950) historian; founded Assn. for the Study of Negro Life and History, 1915, and Journal of Negro History, 1916.
Richard Wright (1908-1960) novelist; Native Son, Black Boy.
Frank Yerby, b. 1916, most successful of American black novelists; The Foxes of Harrow, Vixen.

Public Officials

Dr. Mary McCleod Bethune (1875-1955) adviser to Presidents F. D. Roosevelt and Truman; division administrator in National Youth Administration, 1935; founder, president of Bethune-Cookman College.
Julian Bond, b. 1940, civil rights leader first elected to the Georgia state legislature, 1965; helped found Student Nonviolent Coordinating Committee.
Thomas Bradley, b. 1917, elected mayor of Los Angeles, 1973.
Andrew F. Brimmer, b. 1926, first black member, 1966, Federal Reserve Board.
Edward W. Brooke, b. 1919, attorney general, 1962, of Massachusetts; first black elected to U.S. Senate, 1967, since 19th century Reconstruction.
Dr. Ralph Bunche (1904-1971) first black to win the Nobel Peace Prize, 1950; undersecretary of the UN, 1950.
Mrs. Shirley Chisholm b. 1924, first black woman elected to House of Representatives (Brooklyn, N. Y., 1968).
William L. Dawson (1886-1970) Illinois congressman, first black chairman of a major House of Representatives committee.
Kenneth Gibson, b. 1932, elected mayor of Newark, N.J., 1970.
William H. Hastie, b. 1904, first black federal judge, appointed 1937; governor of Virgin Islands, 1946-1949; judge, U.S. Circuit Court of Appeals, 1949.
Robert C. Henry, elected mayor of Springfield, Oh., 1965, first black mayor of a moderate-sized city in the 20th century.
Maynard Jackson, b. 1938, elected mayor of Atlanta, 1973.
Barbara Jordan, b. 1936, congresswoman from Texas; member, House Judiciary Committee.
Vernon E. Jordan, b. 1935, executive director, National Urban League, 1972.
Thurgood Marshall, b. 1908, first black U.S. solicitor general 1965; first black justice of the U. S. Supreme Court, 1967; as a lawyer led the legal battery which won the historic decision from the Supreme Court declaring racial segregation of public schools unconstitutional, 1954.
Wade H. McCree Jr., b. 1920, solicitor general of the U.S.
Adam Clayton Powell (1908-1972) early civil rights leader, congressman, 1945-1969; as head of House Committee on Education and Labor, 1960-1967, was responsible for 48 major pieces of social legislation.
Joseph H. Rainey (1832-1887) first black elected to House of Representatives, 1869, from South Carolina.
Charles Rangel, b. 1930, congressman from N.Y.C. 1970; chairman of the Congressional Black Caucus.
Hiram R. Revels (1822-1901), first black U.S. senator, elected in Mississippi, served 1870-1871.
Carl T. Rowan, b. 1925, prize-winning journalist; director of the U.S. Information Agency, 1964, the first black to sit on the National Security Council; U. S. ambassador to Finland, 1963.
Dr. Robert C. Weaver, b. 1907, first black member of the U.S. Cabinet, secretary of the Dept. of HUD, 1966.
Andrew Young, b. 1932, civil rights leader, congressman from Georgia, U.S. Ambassador to the United Nations, 1977.

(As of July, 1977, there were 162 black mayors, 1,560 city officials, 381 county officers, 56 state senators, 238 state representatives, one U.S. senator, and 16 U.S. representatives. There are now 4,311 blacks holding elected office in the United States, an increase of 8% over the previous year, according to a survey by the Joint Center for Political Studies, Washington, D.C.)

Labor, Civil Rights Leaders

The Rev. Dr. Ralph David Abernathy, b. 1926, organizer, 1957, and president, 1968, of the Southern Christian Leadership Conference.
James Farmer, b. 1920, a founder of the Congress of Racial Equality, 1942; asst. secretary, Dept. of HEW, 1969.
Marcus Garvey (1887-1940) founded Universal Negro Improvement Assn., 1911.
The Rev. Jesse Jackson, b. 1941, national director, Operation Bread Basket, and major community leader in Chicago.
The Rev. Dr. Martin Luther King Jr. (1929-1968) led 382-day, Montgomery, Ala., boycott which brought 1956 U.S. Supreme Court decision holding segregation on buses unconstitutional; founder, president of the Southern Christian Leadership Conference, 1957; leader of rights marches; won Nobel Peace Prize, 1964.
Malcolm X (1925-1965) leading spokesman for black pride, founded, 1963, Organization of Afro-American Unity.
Elijah Muhammad (1897-1975) founded the Nation of Islam, or Black Muslims, 1931.
A. Philip Randolph, b. 1889, organized the Brotherhood of Sleeping Car Porters, 1925; organizer of 1941 and 1963 March on Washington movements; vice president, AFL-CIO.
Bayard Rustin, b. 1910, organizer of the 1963 March on Washington; executive director of the A. Philip Randolph Institute.
Bishop Stephen Spottswood (1897-1974) board chairman of NAACP from 1966.
Willard Townsend (1895-1957) organized the United Transport Service Employees, 1935 (redcaps, etc.); vice president of AFL-CIO.
Sojourner Truth (1797-1883) born Isabella Baumfree; preacher, abolitionist; raised funds for Union in Civil War; worked for black educational opportunities.
Nat Turner (1800-1831) leader of the most significant of over 200 slave revolts in U.S. history, in Southhampton, Va.; he and 16 others were hanged.
Walter White (1893-1955) exec. sec., NAACP, 1931-1955.
Roy Wilkins, b. 1901, executive director, NAACP, 1955-1977.
Whitney M. Young Jr. (1921-1971) executive director, 1961, of the National Urban League; author, lecturer, newspaper columnist.

Widely Known Americans of the Present

Statesmen, authors, military men, and other prominent persons not listed in other categories.

Name	Birthplace	Birthdate
Abel, I. W.	(Magnolia, Oh.)	8/11/08
Abernathy, Ralph	(Linden, Ala.)	3/11/26
Abzug, Bella	(New York, N.Y.)	7/24/20
Adams, Brockman	(Atlanta, Ga.)	1/13/27
Agnew, Spiro	(Baltimore, Md.)	11/9/18
Albee, Edward	(Washington, D.C.)	3/12/28
Albert, Carl	(McAlester, Okla.)	5/10/08
Aldrin, Edwin E. Jr. (Buzz)	(Glen Ridge, N.J.)	1/20/30
Alsop, Joseph W. Jr.	(Avon, Conn.)	10/11/10
Anderson, Jack	(Long Beach, Cal.)	10/19/22
Andrus, Cecil	(Hood River, Ore.)	8/25/31
Armstrong, Anne	(New Orleans, La.)	12/27/27
Armstrong, Neil	(Wapakoneta, Oh.)	8/5/30
Askew, Reubin	(Muskogee, Okla.)	9/11/28
Bailey, F. Lee	(Waltham, Mass.)	6/10/33
Baker, Howard	(Huntsville, Tenn.)	11/15/25
Baker, Russell	(Loudoun Co., Va.)	8/14/25
Baldwin, James	(New York, N.Y.)	8/2/24
Ball, George	(Des Moines, Ia.)	12/21/09
Bayh, Birch	(Terre Haute, Ind.)	1/22/28
Beame, Abraham	(London, Eng.)	3/20/06
Bell, Griffin	(Americus, Ga.)	10/31/18
Belli, Melvin	(Sonora, Cal.)	7/29/07
Bentsen, Lloyd	(Mission, Tex.)	2/11/21
Bergland, Bob	(Roseau, Minn.)	7/22/28
Bernstein, Carl	(Washington, D. C.)	2/14/44
Blackmun, Harry	(Nashville, Ill.)	11/12/08
Blumenthal, W. Michael	(Berlin, Germany)	1/3/26
Bok, Derek	(Ardmore, Pa.)	3/22/30
Bond, Julian	(Nashville, Tenn.)	1/14/40
Borman, Frank	(Gary, Ind.)	3/14/28
Bowles, Chester	(Springfield, Mass.)	4/5/01
Bradley, Omar N.	(Clark, Mo.)	2/12/93
Bradley, Thomas	(Calvert, Tex.)	12/29/17
Braun, Wernher von	(Wirsitz, Germany)	3/23/12
Brennan, William J.	(Newark, N.J.)	4/25/06
Brewster, Kingman	(Longmeadow, Mass.)	6/17/19
Brinkley, David	(Wilmington, N.C.)	7/10/20
Brooke, Edward	(Washington, D.C.)	10/26/19
Brooks, Jack	(Crowley, La.)	12/18/22
Brown, Edmund G. Jr.	(San Francisco, Cal.)	4/7/38
Brown, George S.	(Montclair, N.J.)	8/17/18
Brown, Harold	(New York, N.Y.)	9/19/27
Brown, Samuel	(Council Bluffs, Ia.)	7/27/43
Brzinski, Zbigniew	(Warsaw, Poland)	3/28/28
Buchwald, Art	(Mt. Vernon, N.Y.)	10/20/25
Bundy, McGeorge	(Boston, Mass.)	3/30/19
Bunker, Ellsworth	(Yonkers, N.Y.)	5/11/94
Burger, Warren	(St. Paul, Minn.)	9/17/07
Burns, Arthur F.	(Stanislau, Aust.)	4/27/04
Burton, Phillip	(Cincinnati, Oh.)	6/1/26
Bush, George	(Milton, Mass.)	6/12/24
Butz, Earl	(Albion, Ind.)	7/3/09
Byrd, Robert	(N. Wilkesboro, N.C.)	1/15/18
Califano, Joseph A. Jr.	(Brooklyn, N.Y.)	3/15/21
Carey, Hugh	(Brooklyn, N.Y.)	4/11/19
Carter, Amy	(Plains, Ga.)	10/19/67
Carter, Billy	(Plains, Ga.)	3/29/37
Carter, Donnel Jeffrey "Jeff"	(New London, Conn.)	8/18/52
Carter, James Earl III "Chip"	(Honolulu, Ha.)	4/12/50
Carter, Jimmy	(Plains, Ga.)	10/1/24
Carter, John William "Jack"	(Portsmouth, Va.)	7/3/47
Carter, Lillian	(Richland, Ga)	8/15/98
Carter, Rosalynn	(Plains, Ga.)	8/18/27
Case, Clifford	(Franklin Park, N.J.)	4/16/04
Celler, Emmanuel	(Brooklyn, N.Y.)	5/6/88
Chancellor, John	(Chicago, Ill.)	7/14/27
Chandler, Otis	(Los Angeles, Cal.)	11/23/27
Chavez, Cesar	(Yuma, Ariz.)	3/31/27
Chisholm, Shirley	(Brooklyn, N.Y.)	11/30/24
Church, Frank	(Boise, Ida.)	7/25/24
Clark, Ramsey	(Dallas, Tex.)	12/18/27
Clay, Lucius D.	(Marietta, Ga.)	4/23/97
Cleland, J. Maxwell	(Atlanta, Ga.)	8/24/42
Commager, Henry Steele	(Pittsburgh, Pa.)	10/25/02
Commoner, Barry	(Brooklyn, N.Y.)	5/28/17
Conant, James B.	(Dorchester, Mass.)	3/26/93
Connally, John B.	(Floresville, Tex.)	2/28/17
Cooke, Terence Cardinal	(New York, N.Y.)	3/1/21
Cooney, Joan Ganz	(Phoenix, Ariz.)	10/30/29
Cooper, John Sherman	(Somerset, Ky.)	8/23/01
Cosell, Howard	(Winston-Salem, N.C.)	1920
Costanza, Margaret	(Le Roy, N.Y.)	11/28/32
Costle, Douglas M.	(Long Beach, Cal.)	7/27/39
Cousins, Norman	(Union Hill, N.J.)	6/24/12
Cox, Archibald	(Plainfield, N.J.)	5/17/12
Cranston, Alan	(Palo Alto, Cal.)	6/19/14
Cronkite, Walter	(St. Joseph, Mo.)	11/4/16
Davis, Angela	(Birmingham, Ala.)	1/26/44
Denenberg, Herbert	(Omaha, Neb.)	10/20/29
Dole, Robert	(Russell, Kan.)	7/22/23
Doolittle, James H.	(Alameda, Cal.)	12/14/96
Douglas, William O.	(Maine, Minn.)	10/16/98
Dubinsky, David	(Brest-Litovsk, Poland)	2/22/92
Eagleton, Thomas	(St. Louis, Mo.)	9/4/29
Eastland, James O.	(Doddsville, Miss.)	11/28/04
Ehrlichman, John	(Tacoma, Wash.)	3/20/25
Eisenhower, Mamie	(Boone, Ia.)	11/14/96
Eisenhower, Milton S.	(Abilene, Kan.)	9/15/99
Ervin, Sam	(Morganton, N.C.)	9/27/96
Farmer, James	(Marshall, Tex.)	1/12/20
Fischer, Bobby	(Chicago, Ill.)	3/9/43
Fitzsimmons, Frank	(Jeannette, Pa.)	4/7/08
Fong, Hiram	(Honolulu, Ha.)	10/1/07
Ford, Elizabeth (Mrs. Gerald)	(Chicago, Ill.)	4/8/18
Ford, Gerald R.	(Omaha, Neb.)	7/14/13
Friedan, Betty	(Peoria, Ill.)	2/4/21
Friedman, Milton	(Brooklyn, N.Y.)	7/31/12
Fulbright, J. William	(Sumner, Mo.)	4/9/05
Galbraith, John Kenneth	(Ontario, Can.)	10/15/08
Gardner, John	(Los Angeles, Cal.)	10/8/12
Glenn, John	(Cambridge, Oh.)	7/18/21
Goheen, Robert F.	(Vengurla, India)	8/15/19
Goldberg, Arthur J.	(Chicago, Ill.)	8/8/08
Goldwater, Barry M.	(Phoenix, Ariz.)	1/1/09
Goodpaster, Andrew J.	(Granite City, Ill.)	2/12/15
Graham, Billy	(Charlotte, N.C.)	11/7/18
Graham, Katharine	(New York, N.Y.)	6/16/17
Grasso, Ella	(Windsor Locks, Conn.)	5/10/19
Greenspan, Alan	(New York, N.Y.)	3/6/26
Griffin, Robert P.	(Traverse City, Mich.)	11/6/23
Haig, Alexander	(Philadelphia, Pa.)	12/2/24
Hanks, Nancy	(Miami Beach, Fla.)	12/31/27
Harriman, W. Averell	(New York, N.Y.)	11/15/91
Harris, Fred	(Walters, Okla.)	11/13/30
Harris, Patricia Roberts	(Mattoon, Ill.)	5/31/24
Hartz, Jim	(Tulsa, Okla.)	2/3/40
Hatfield, Mark O.	(Dallas, Ore.)	7/12/22
Hayakawa, S. I.	(Vancouver, British Columbia)	7/18/06
Heller, Walter	(Buffalo, N.Y.)	8/27/15
Hellman, Lillian	(New Orleans, La.)	6/20/07
Helms, Richard	(St. Davids, Pa.)	3/30/13
Hesburgh, Theodore	(Syracuse, N.Y.)	5/25/17
Hills, Carla	(Los Angeles, Cal.)	1/3/34
Hiss, Alger	(Baltimore, Md.)	11/11/04
Hughes, Harold	(Ida Grove, Ia.)	2/10/22
Humphrey, Hubert	(Wallace, S.D.)	5/27/11
Inouye, Daniel	(Honolulu, Ha.)	9/7/24
Jackson, Henry	(Everett, Wash.)	5/31/12
Jackson, Jesse	(Greenville, N.C.)	10/8/41
Jackson, Maynard	(Dallas, Tex.)	3/23/38
Javits, Jacob K.	(New York, N.Y.)	5/18/04
Johnson, Lady Bird. (Mrs. Lyndon)	(Karnack, Tex.)	12/22/12
Jordan, Barbara	(Houston, Tex.)	2/21/36
Jordan, Hamilton	(Charlotte, N.C.)	9/21/44
Jordan, Vernon	(Atlanta, Ga.)	8/15/35
Kelley, Clarence M.	(Kansas City, Mo.)	10/24/11
Kennedy, Edward M.	(Brookline, Mass.)	2/22/32
Kennedy, Rose (Mrs. Joseph P.)	(Boston, Mass.)	7/22/90
Kerr, Walter	(Evanston, Ill.)	7/8/13
Kheel, Theodore	(New York, N.Y.)	5/9/14
King, Coretta (Mrs. Martin L.)	(Marion, Ala.)	4/27/27
Kirbo, Charles	(Bainbridge, Ga.)	3/15/17
Kirkland, Lane	(Camden, S.C.)	3/12/22
Kissinger, Henry	(Fuerth, Germany)	5/27/23
Kleindienst, Richard	(Winslow, Ariz.)	8/5/23
Koch, Edward I.	(New York, N.Y.)	12/12/24
Kreps, Juanita M.	(Lynch, Ky.)	1/11/21
Laird, Melvin	(Omaha, Neb.)	9/1/22
Lance, Thomas B.	(Young Harris, Ga.)	6/3/31
Landon, Alfred	(West Middlesex, Pa.)	9/9/87
LeMay, Curtis	(Ohio)	11/15/06
Lemnitzer, Lyman L.	(Honesdale, Pa.)	8/29/99
Levi, Edward	(Chicago, Ill.)	6/26/11

Name	Birthplace	Birthdate
Lindsay, John V.	New York, N.Y.	11/24/21
Lipshutz, Robert J.	Atlanta, Ga.	12/27/21
Lodge, Henry Cabot	Nahant, Mass.	7/5/02
Long, Russell B.	Shreveport, La.	11/3/18
Lowell, Robert	Boston, Mass.	3/1/17
Luce, Clare Boothe	New York, N.Y.	4/10/03
MacLeish, Archibald	Glencoe, Ill.	5/7/92
Maddox, Lester	Atlanta, Ga.	9/30/15
Mansfield, Mike	New York, N.Y.	3/16/03
Marshall, Freddie Ray	Oak Grove, La.	8/22/28
Marshall, Thurgood	Baltimore, Md.	7/2/08
McCarthy, Eugene	Watkins, Minn.	3/29/16
McCormack, John W.	Boston, Mass.	12/21/91
McClellan, John J.	Sheridan, Ark.	2/25/96
McCloskey, Paul	San Bernardino, Cal.	9/29/27
McCree, Wade H. Jr.	Des Moines, Ia.	7/3/20
McGovern, George	Avon, S.D.	7/19/22
McNamara, Robert S.	San Francisco, Cal.	6/9/16
Mead, Margaret	Philadelphia, Pa.	12/16/01
Meany, George	New York, N.Y.	8/16/94
Miller, Arthur	New York, N.Y.	10/17/15
Millett, Kate	St. Paul, Minn.	9/14/34
Milliken, William	Traverse City, Mich.	3/26/22
Mills, Wilbur	Kensett, Ark.	5/24/09
Mitchell, John	Detroit, Mich.	9/15/13
Mondale, Walter F.	Ceylon, Minn.	1/5/28
Morton, Rogers	Louisville, Ky.	9/19/14
Morton, Thruston	Louisville, Ky.	8/19/07
Moses, Robert	New Haven, Conn.	12/18/88
Moynihan, Daniel P.	Tulsa, Okla.	3/16/27
Muskie, Edmund	Rumford, Me.	3/28/14
Nader, Ralph	Winsted, Conn.	2/27/34
Nixon, Julie (Mrs. David Eisenhower)	Wash., D.C.	7/5/48
Nixon, Mrs. Richard	Ely, Nev.	3/16/12
Nixon, Richard	Yorba Linda, Cal.	1/9/13
Nixon, Tricia (Mrs. Edward Cox)	Cal.	2/21/46
Nizer, Louis	London, England	2/6/02
O'Brien, Lawrence F.	Springfield, Mass.	7/7/17
Onassis, Jacqueline	Southampton, N.Y.	7/28/29
O'Neill, Thomas P.	Cambridge, Mass.	12/9/12
Paley, William S.	Chicago, Ill.	9/28/01
Pauling, Linus	Portland, Ore.	2/28/01
Peale, Norman Vincent	Bowersville, Oh.	5/31/98
Percy, Charles H.	Pensacola, Fla.	9/27/19
Powell, Jody	Cordele, Ga.	9/30/43
Powell, Lewis F.	Suffolk, Va.	9/19/07
Proxmire, William	Lake Forest, Ill.	1/11/15
Randolph, A. Philip	Crescent City, Fla.	4/15/89
Ray, Dixy Lee	Tacoma, Wash.	9/3/14
Reagan, Ronald	Tampico, Ill.	2/6/11
Reasoner, Harry	Dakota City, Ia.	4/17/23
Rehnquist, William	Milwaukee, Wis.	10/1/24
Reston, James	Clydebank, Scotland	11/3/09
Rhodes, John	Council Grove, Kan.	9/18/16
Ribicoff, Abe	New Britain, Conn.	4/9/10
Richardson, Elliot L.	Boston, Mass.	7/20/21
Rickover, Hyman	Makowa, Poland	1/27/00
Rockefeller, David	New York, N.Y.	6/12/15
Rockefeller, John D. 3d	New York, N.Y.	3/21/06
Rockefeller, John D. 4th "Jay"	New York, N.Y.	6/18/37
Rockefeller, Laurance S.	New York, N.Y.	5/26/10
Rockefeller, Nelson A.	Bar Harbor, Me.	7/8/08
Rockwell, Norman	New York, N.Y.	2/3/94
Rodino, Peter	Newark, N.J.	6/7/09
Romney, George W.	Chihuahua, Mexico	7/8/07
Roosevelt, Elliot	New York, N.Y.	9/23/10
Roosevelt, Franklin D. Jr.	Canada	8/17/14
Ruckelshaus, William	Indianapolis, Ind.	7/24/32
Rumsfeld, Donald	Chicago, Ill.	7/9/32
Rusk, Dean	Cherokee Co., Ga.	2/9/09
Safire, William	New York, N.Y.	12/17/29
Sagan, Carl	New York, (N.Y.	11/9/34
Salinger, Pierre	San Francisco, Cal.	6/14/25
Salk, Jonas	New York, N.Y.	10/28/14
Samuelson, Paul A.	Gary, Ind.	5/15/15
Schlesinger, Arthur Jr.	Columbus, Oh.	10/15/17
Schlesinger, James R.	New York, N.Y.	2/15/29
Schultze, Charles	Alexandria, Va.	12/22/24
Scott, Hugh	Fredericksburg, Va.	11/11/00
Scranton, William W.	Madison, Conn.	7/19/17
Seaborg, Glenn T.	Ishpeming, Mich.	4/19/12
Sevareid, Eric	Velva, N.D.	11/26/12
Shanker, Albert	New York, N.Y.	9/14/28
Sheen, Fulton J.	El Paso, Ill.	5/8/95
Shirer, William L.	Chicago, Ill.	2/23/04
Shriver, R. Sargent	Westminster, Md.	11/9/15
Shultz, George	New York, N.Y.	12/13/20
Simon, Neil	New York, N.Y.	7/4/27
Simon, William	Paterson, N.J.	1927
Sirica, John J.	Waterbury, Conn.	3/19/04
Smith, Howard K.	Ferriday, La.	5/12/14
Smith, Margaret Chase	Skowhegan, Me.	12/14/97
Snyder, Tom	Milwaukee, Wisc.	5/12/36
Sorensen, Theodore	Lincoln, Neb.	5/8/28
Spock, Benjamin	New Haven, Conn.	5/2/03
Stassen, Harold	West St. Paul, Minn.	4/13/07
Steinem, Gloria	Toledo, Oh.	3/25/34
Stennis, John	Kamper City, Miss.	8/3/01
Stevens, John Paul	Chicago, Ill.	4/20/20
Stevenson 3d, Adlai	Chicago, Ill.	10/10/30
Stewart, Potter	Jackson, Mich.	1/23/15
Stokes, Carl	Cleveland, Oh.	6/21/27
Sulzberger, Arthur Ochs	New York, N.Y.	2/5/26
Symington, Stuart	Amherst, Mass.	6/26/01
Taft, Robert Jr.	Cincinnati, Oh.	2/26/17
Talmadge, Herman	Lovejoy, Ga.	8/9/13
Taylor, Maxwell D.	Keytesville, Mo.	8/26/01
Thomas, Helen	Winchester, Ky.	8/4/20
Thomas, Lowell	Woodington, Oh.	4/6/92
Thurmond, J. Strom	Edgefield, S.C.	12/5/02
Tower, John	Houston, Tex.	9/29/25
Truman, Mrs. Harry	Independence, Mo.	2/13/85
Truman, Margaret (Mrs. Clifton Daniel)	Independence, Mo.	2/17/24
Tuchman, Barbara	New York, N.Y.	1/30/12
Turner, Stansfield	Chicago, Ill.	2/1/33
Udall, Morris K.	St. Johns, Ariz.	6/15/22
Ullman, Al	Great Falls, Mont.	3/9/14
Van Buren, Abigail	Sioux City, Ia.	7/4/18
Vance, Cyrus R.	Clarksburg, W. Va.	3/27/17
Vanderbilt, Alfred G.	London, England	9/22/12
Veeck, Bill	Chicago, Ill.	2/9/14
Vonnegut, Kurt Jr.	Indianapolis, Ind.	11/11/22
Wallace, George	Clio, Ala.	8/25/19
Wallace, Mike	Brookline, Mass.	5/9/18
Walters, Barbara	Boston, Mass.	9/25/31
Warnke, Paul	Webster, Mass.	1/31/20
Washington, Walter E.	Dawson, Ga.	4/15/15
Weicker, Lowell	Paris, France	5/16/31
Westmoreland, William	Spartanburg, S.C.	3/26/14
White, Byron R.	Ft. Collins, Col.	6/8/17
White, Theodore	Boston, Mass.	5/6/15
Wicker, Tom	Hamlet, N.C.	6/18/26
Wilkins, Roy	St. Louis, Mo.	8/30/01
Williams, Edward Bennett	Hartford, Conn.	5/31/20
Williams, Tennessee	Columbus, Miss.	3/26/14
Woodcock, Leonard	Providence, R.I.	2/15/11
Woodward, Bob	Geneva, Ill.	3/26/43
Wright, James C. Jr.	Ft. Worth, Tex.	12/22/22
Wriston, Walter B.	Middletown, Conn.	8/3/19
Wurf, Jerry	New York, N.Y.	5/18/19
Yorty, Sam	Lincoln, Neb.	10/1/09
Young, Andrew	New Orleans, La.	3/12/22
Zumwalt, Elmo	San Francisco, Cal.	11/29/20

The Hall of Fame for Great Americans

The Hall of Fame for Great Americans was founded in 1900 by Dr. Henry Mitchell MacCracken, chancellor of New York University, with funds donated by Mrs. Helen Gould Shepard. It honors persons whose outstanding achievements have influenced the culture and course of the nation. Formerly administered by New York University, the Hall of Fame became a separately incorporated educational institution in 1974, maintaining joint affiliation with New York University and the City University of New York. The Americans honored to date are:

1900

John Adams
John James Audubon
Henry Ward Beecher
William Ellery Channing
Henry Clay
Peter Cooper
Jonathan Edwards
Ralph Waldo Emerson
David Glasgow Farragut
Benjamin Franklin
Robert Fulton
Ulysses Simpson Grant
Asa Gray
Nathaniel Hawthorne

Washington Irving
Thomas Jefferson
James Kent
Robert Edward Lee
Abraham Lincoln
Henry Wadsworth Longfellow
Horace Mann
John Marshall
Samuel Finley Breese Morse
George Peabody
Joseph Story
Gilbert Charles Stuart
George Washington
Daniel Webster
Eli Whitney

1905

John Quincy Adams
James Russell Lowell
Mary Lyon
James Madison
Maria Mitchell
William Tecumseh Sherman
John Greenleaf Whittier
Emma Willard

1910

George Bancroft
Phillips Brooks
William Cullen Bryant
James Fenimore Cooper
Oliver Wendell Holmes
Andrew Jackson
John Lothrop Motley
Edgar Allan Poe
Harriet Beecher Stowe
Frances Elizabeth Willard

1915

Louis Agassiz
Daniel Boone
Rufus Choate
Charlotte Saunders Cushman
Alexander Hamilton
Joseph Henry
Mark Hopkins
Elias Howe
Francis Parkman

1920

Samuel Langhorne Clemens (Mark Twain)
James Buchanan Eads
Patrick Henry
William Thomas Green Morton
Alice Freeman Palmer
Augustus Saint-Gaudens
Roger Williams

1925

Edwin Booth
John Paul Jones

1930

Matthew Fontaine Maury
James Monroe
James Abbott McNeil Whistler
Walt Whitman

1935

Grover Cleveland
Simon Newcomb
William Penn

1940

Stephen Collins Foster

1945

Sidney Lanier
Thomas Paine
Walter Reed
Booker T. Washington

1950

Susan B. Anthony
Alexander Graham Bell
Josiah Willard Gibbs
William Crawford Gorgas
Theodore Roosevelt
Woodrow Wilson

1955

Thomas Jonathan Jackson
George Westinghouse
Wilbur Wright

1960

Thomas A. Edison
Edward A. MacDowell
Henry David Thoreau

1965

Jane Addams
Oliver Wendell Holmes Jr.
Sylvanus Thayer
Orville Wright

1970

Albert Abraham Michelson
Lillian D. Wald

1973

Louis Dembitz Brandeis
George Washington Carver
Franklin Delano Roosevelt
John Philip Sousa

1976

Clara Barton
Luther Burbank
Andrew Carnegie

Entertainment Personalities — Where and When Born

Actors, Actresses, Dancers, Musicians, Producers, Radio-TV Performers, Singers

Name	Birthplace	Born
A		
Abbott, George	Forestville, N.Y.	1887
Abel, Walter	St. Paul, Minn.	1898
Abner (Norris Goff)	Cove, Ark.	1906
Ackermann, Bettye	Cottageville, S.C.	1928
Acuff, Roy	Maynardsville, Tenn.	1903
Adams, Don	New York, N.Y.	1927
Adams, Edie	Kingston, Pa.	1929
Adams, Joey	New York, N.Y.	1911
Adams, Julie	Waterloo, Ia.	1926
Addams, Dawn	Suffolk, England	1930
Adler, Kurt H.	Vienna, Austria	1905
Adler, Larry	Baltimore, Md.	1914
Adler, Luther	New York, N.Y.	1903
Agar, John	Chicago, Ill.	1921
Aherne, Brian	Worcestershire, England	1902
Aimee, Anouk	Paris, France	1932
Akins, Claude	Bedford, Ind.	1918
Albanese, Licia	Bari, Italy	1913
Alberghetti, Anna	Pesaro, Italy	1936
Albert, Eddie	Rock Island, Ill.	1908
Albert, Edward	Los Angeles, Cal.	1951
Albertson, Jack	Malden, Mass.	1910
Albright, Lola	Akron, Oh.	1925
Alda, Alan	New York, N.Y.	1936
Alda, Robert	New York, N.Y.	1914
Alexander, Jane	Boston, Mass.	1939
Alexander, Katherine	Arkansas	1901
Allan, Elizabeth	England	1910
Allbritton, Louise	Oklahoma City, Okla.	1920
Allen, Mel	Birmingham, Ala.	1913
Allen, Steve	New York, N.Y.	1921
Allen, Woody	Brooklyn, N.Y.	1935
Allison, Fran	LaPorte City, Ia.	—
Allyson, June	Lucerne, N.Y.	1923
Alpert, Herb	Los Angeles, Cal.	1935
Altman, Rooert	Kansas City, Mo.	1925
Ameche, Don	Kenosha, Wis.	1908
Ames, Ed	Boston, Mass.	1929
Ames, Leon	Portland, Ind.	1903
Ames, Nancy	Washington, D.C.	1937
Amos (F. F. Gosden)	Richmond, Va.	1904
Amos, John	Newark, N.J.	—
Amsterdam, Morey	Chicago, Ill.	1914
Anderson, Judith	Adelaide, Australia	1898
Anderson, Lynn	Grand Forks, N.D.	1947
Anderson, Marian	Philadelphia, Pa.	1902
Anderson, Mary	Birmingham, Ala.	1922
Anderson, Michael Jr.	London, England	1943
Andersson, Bibi	Stockholm, Sweden	1935
Andress, Ursula	Switzerland	1938
Andrews, Dana	Collins, Miss.	1909
Andrews, Edward	Griffin, Ga.	1915
Andrews, Julie	Walton, England	1935
Andrews, Maxene	Minneapolis, Minn.	1918
Andrews, Patty	Minneapolis, Minn.	1920
Angel, Heather	Oxford, England	1909
Anka, Paul	Ottawa, Ont.	1941
Ann-Margret	Stockholm, Sweden	1941
Annabella	Paris, France	1912
Ansara, Michael	Lowell, Mass.	1927
Archer, John	Osceola, Neb.	1915
Arden, Eve	Mill Valley, Cal.	1912
Arkin, Alan	New York, N.Y.	1934
Arnaz, Desi	Santiago, Cuba	1917
Arnaz, Desi Jr.	Los Angeles, Cal.	1953
Arnaz, Lucie	Hollywood, Cal.	1951
Arness, James	Minneapolis, Minn.	1923
Arnold, Eddy	Henderson, Tenn.	1918
Arrau, Claudio	Chillau, Chile	1903
Arroyo, Martina	New York, N.Y.	1937
Arthur, Beatrice	New York, N.Y.	1926
Arthur, Jean	New York, N.Y.	1908
Ashley, Elizabeth	Ocala, Fla.	1941
Asner, Edward	Kansas City, Kan.	1929
Astaire, Fred	Omaha, Neb.	1899
Astin, John	Baltimore, Md.	1930
Astor, Mary	Quincy, Ill.	1906
Atkins, Chet	Luttrell, Tenn.	1924
Attenborough, Richard	Cambridge, England	1923
Aumont, Jean-Pierre	Paris, France	1913
Autry, Gene	Tioga, Tex.	1907
Avalon, Frankie	Philadelphia, Pa.	1940
Ayres, Lew	Minneapolis, Minn.	1908
Aznavour, Charles	Paris, France	1924

Name	Birthplace	Born
B		
Bacall, Lauren	New York, N.Y.	1924
Backus, Jim	Cleveland, Oh.	1913
Baddeley, Hermione	Shropshire, England	1906
Baer, Max Jr.	Oakland, Cal.	1937
Baez, Joan	Staten Island, N.Y.	1941
Bailey, Pearl	Newport News, Va.	1918
Bailey, Raymond	San Francisco, Cal.	1904
Bain, Barbara	Chicago, Ill.	1934
Baird, Bill	Grand Island, Neb.	1904
Baker, Carroll	Johnstown, Pa.	1931
Baker, Diane	Hollywood, Cal.	1938
Baker, Kenny	Monrovia, Cal.	1912
Baker, Stanley	Glamorgan, Wales	1928
Bakewell, William	Hollywood, Cal.	1908
Balanchine, George	St. Petersburg, Russia	1904
Ball, Lucille	Jamestown, N.Y.	1911
Ballard, Kaye	Cleveland, Oh.	1926
Balsam, Martin	New York, N.Y.	1919
Bampton, Rose	Cleveland, Oh.	1909
Bancroft, Anne	New York, N.Y.	1931
Bannon, Ian	Airdrie, Scotland	1928
Barber, Red	Columbus, Miss.	1908
Bardot, Brigitte	Paris, France	1934
Bari, Lynn	Roanoke, Va.	1917
Barnett, Vincent	Pittsburgh, Pa.	1902
Barrault, Jean-Louis	Le Vesinet, France	1919
Barrie, Mona	London, England	1909
Barrie, Wendy	Hong Kong, China	1913
Barry, Gene	New York, N.Y.	1922
Barry, Jack	Lindenhurst, N.Y.	1918
Barrymore, John Jr.	Beverly Hills, Cal.	1932
Bartholomew, Freddie	London, England	1924
Bartok, Eva	Budapest, Hungary	1929
Basehart, Richard	Zanesville, Oh.	1914
Basie, Count (Wm.)	Red Bank, N.J.	1904
Bassey, Shirley	Cardiff, Wales	1937
Bates, Alan	Allestree, England	1934
Baum, Kurt	Cologne, Germany	1908
Bavier, Frances	New York, N.Y.	1905
Baxter, Anne	Michigan City, Ind.	1923
Beal, John	Joplin, Mo.	1909
Bean, Orson	Burlington, Vt.	1928
Beatty, Robert	Hamilton, Ont.	1909
Beatty, Warren	Richmond, Va.	1938
Becker, Sandy	New York, N.Y.	1922
Bedelia, Bonnie	New York, N.Y.	1948
Beery, Noah Jr.	New York, N.Y.	1916
Belafonte, Harry	New York, N.Y.	1927
Bel Geddes, Barbara	New York, N.Y.	1922
Bellamy, Ralph	Chicago, Ill.	1904
Belmondo, Jean-Paul	Neuilly-sur-Seine, France	1933
Benjamin, Dick	New York, N.Y.	1939
Bennett, Joan	Palisades, N.J.	1910
Bennett, Tony	Astoria, N.Y.	1926
Bennett, Michael	Buffalo, N.Y.	1943
Bentley, John	Warwickshire, England	1916
Bergen, Candice	Beverly Hills, Cal.	1946
Bergen, Edgar	Chicago, Ill.	1903
Bergen, Polly	Knoxville, Tenn.	1930
Berger, Senta	Vienna, Austria	1941
Bergerac, Jacques	Biarritz, France	1927
Bergman, Ingmar	Uppsala, Sweden	1918
Bergman, Ingrid	Stockholm, Sweden	1915
Bergner, Elisabeth	Vienna, Austria	1900
Berle, Milton	New York, N.Y.	1908
Berlinger, Warren	Brooklyn, N.Y.	1937
Berman, Shelley	Chicago, Ill.	1926
Bernardi, Herschel	New York, N.Y.	1923
Bernstein, Elmer	New York, N.Y.	1922
Bernstein, Leonard	Lawrence, Mass.	1918
Berry, Chuck	St. Louis, Mo.	1926
Berry, Ken	Moline, Ill.	—
Bessell, Ted	Flushing, N.Y.	1936
Bikel, Theodore	Vienna, Austria	1924
Birney, David	Washington, D.C.	1940
Bishop, Joey	Bronx, N.Y.	1918
Bisset, Jacqueline	Weybridge, England	1946
Bixby, Bill	San Francisco, Cal.	1934
Black, Karen	Park Ridge, Ill.	1942
Blaine, Vivian	Newark, N.J.	1924
Blair, Janet	Altoona, Pa.	1921
Blair, Linda	Westport, Conn.	1959
Blake, Amanda	Buffalo, N.Y.	1931
Blake, Robert	Nutley, N.J.	1938
Blakeley, Ronee	Idaho	1946
Blakely, Susan	Germany	—
Blanc, Mel	San Francisco, Cal.	1908
Bloch, Ray	Alsace-Lorraine	1902
Blondell, Joan	New York, N.Y.	1912
Bloom, Claire	London, England	1931
Blyth, Ann	Mt. Kisco, N.Y.	1928
Boehm, Karl	Graz, Austria	1894
Bogarde, Dirk	London, England	1921
Bogdanovich, Peter	Kingston, N.Y.	1939
Bolger, Ray	Boston, Mass.	1904
Bologna, Joe	Brooklyn, N.Y.	—
Bondi, Beulah	Chicago, Ill.	1892
Bono, Sonny	Detroit, Mich.	1940
Boone, Pat	Jacksonville, Fla.	1934
Boone, Richard	Los Angeles, Cal.	1917
Booth, Shirley	New York, N.Y.	1909
Borge, Victor	Copenhagen, Denmark	1909
Borgnine, Ernest	Hamden, Conn.	1917
Bosley, Tom	Chicago, Ill.	1927
Bottoms, Timothy	Santa Barbara, Cal.	1951
Bowie, David	London, England	1947
Bowman, Lee	Cincinnati, Oh.	1914
Boyer, Charles	Figeac, France	1899
Boyle, Peter	Philadelphia, Pa.	1933
Bracken, Eddie	Astoria, N.Y.	1920
Brand, Neville	Kewanee, Ill.	1921
Brando, Marlon	Omaha, Neb.	1924
Brasselle, Keefe	Elyria, Oh.	1923
Brazzi, Rossano	Bologna, Italy	1916
Brennan, Eileen	Los Angeles, Cal.	1937
Brenner, David	Philadelphia, Pa.	1945
Brent, George	Dublin, Ireland	1904
Brewer, Teresa	Toledo, Oh.	1931
Brian, David	New York, N.Y.	1914
Bridges, Beau	Hollywood, Cal.	1941
Bridges, Jeff	Los Angeles, Cal.	1950
Bridges, Lloyd	San Leandro, Cal.	1913
Britton, Barbara	Long Beach, Cal.	1923
Brolin, James	Los Angeles, Cal.	1942
Bronson, Charles	Scooptown, Pa.	1921
Brooks, Louise	Cherryvale, Kan.	1906
Brooks, Mel	New York, N.Y.	1926
Brooks, Stephen	Columbus, Oh.	1942
Brown, James	Augusta, Ga.	1934
Brown, Jimmy	St. Simons Island, Ga.	1936
Brown, Les	Reinerton, Pa.	1912
Brown, Tom	New York, N.Y.	1913
Brown, Vanessa	Vienna, Austria	1928
Bruce, Carol	Great Neck, N.Y.	1919
Bruce, Virginia	Minneapolis, Minn.	1910
Bryant, Anita	Barnsdale, Okla.	1940
Brynner, Yul	Sakhalin, Japan	1920
Bubbles, John	Louisville, Ky.	1903
Buchanan, Edgar	Humansville, Mo.	1903
Bucholz, Horst	Berlin, Germany	1933
Bujold, Genevieve	Montreal, Que.	1942
Buono, Victor	Los Angeles, Cal.	1938
Burke, Paul	New Orleans, La.	1926
Burnett, Carol	San Antonio, Tex.	1936
Burns, George	New York, N.Y.	1896
Burr, Raymond	New Westminster, B.C.	1917
Burrows, Abe	New York, N.Y.	1910
Burstyn, Ellen	Detroit, Mich.	1932
Burton, Richard	South Wales	1925
Bushell, Anthony	Kent, England	1904
Buttons, Red	New York, N.Y.	1919
Buzzi, Ruth	Westerly, R.I.	1936
C		
Caan, James	New York, N.Y.	1939
Cabot, Sebastian	London, England	1918
Caesar, Sid	Yonkers, N.Y.	1922
Cagney, James	New York, N.Y.	1899
Caine, Michael	London, England	1933
Caldwell, Sarah	Maryville, Mo.	1929
Caldwell, Zoe	Melbourne, Australia	1933
Calhoun, Rory	Los Angeles, Cal.	1922
Callan, Michael	Philadelphia, Pa.	1935
Callas, Maria	New York, N.Y.	1923
Calloway, Cab	Rochester, N.Y.	1907
Calvert, Phyllis	London, England	1917
Calvet, Corinne	Paris, France	1926
Cameron, Rod	Calgary, Canada	1912
Campbell, Glen	Billstown, Ark.	1936
Canary, David	Elwood, Ind.	1938
Cannon, Dyan	Tacoma, Wash.	1937
Canova, Judy	Jacksonville, Fla.	1916
Cantinflas	Mexico City, Mex.	1917
Cantrell, Lana	Sydney, Australia	1944

Name	Birthplace	Born
Capra, Frank	Palermo, Italy	1897
Cardinale, Claudia	Tunisia	1939
Carey, Macdonald	Sioux City, Ia.	1913
Carey, Phil	Hackensack, N.J.	1925
Carle, Frankie	Providence, R.I.	1903
Carlisle, Kitty	New Orleans, La.	1915
Carlson, Richard	Alberta Lea, Minn.	1914
Carmichael, Hoagy	Bloomington, Ind.	1899
Carmichael, Ian	Hull, England	1920
Carne, Judy	Northampton, England	1939
Carney, Art	Mt. Vernon, N.Y.	1918
Carnovsky, Morris	St. Louis, Mo.	1897
Caron, Leslie	Boulogne, France	1931
Carpenter, Karen	New Haven, Conn.	1950
Carpenter, Richard	New Haven, Conn.	1945
Carr, Vicki	El Paso, Tex.	1942
Carradine, David	Hollywood, Cal.	1937
Carradine, John	New York, N.Y.	1906
Carradine, Keith	San Mateo, Cal.	1950
Carroll, Diahann	Bronx, N.Y.	1935
Carroll, Madeleine	W. Bromwich, England	1906
Carroll, Pat	Shreveport, La.	1927
Carson, Jeannie	Yorkshire, England	1929
Carson, Johnny	Corning, Ia.	1925
Carson, Mindy	New York, N.Y.	1927
Carter, Jack	New York, N.Y.	1923
Carter, Lynda	Texas	—
Casadesus, Gaby	Marseilles, France	1902
Cash, Johnny	Kingsland, Ark.	1932
Cass, Peggy	Boston, Mass.	1926
Cassavetes, John	New York, N.Y.	1929
Cassidy, David	New York, N.Y.	1950
Cassidy, Ted	Pittsburgh, Pa.	1932
Castellano, Richard	New York, N.Y.	1934
Caulfield, Joan	West Orange, N.J.	1922
Cavallaro, Carmen	New York, N.Y.	1913
Cavett, Dick	Gibbon, Neb.	1936
Chamberlain, Richard	Beverly Hills, Cal.	1935
Champion, Gower	Geneva, Ill.	1921
Champion, Marge	Los Angeles, Cal.	1923
Channing, Carol	Seattle, Wash.	1923
Chaplin, Charles	London, England	1889
Chaplin, Geraldine	Santa Monica, Cal.	1944
Chaplin, Sydney	Beverly Hills, Cal.	1926
Charisse, Cyd	Amarillo, Tex.	1923
Charles, Ray	Albany, Ga.	1930
Chase, Chevy	New York, N.Y.	1944
Chase, Ilka	New York, N.Y.	1905
Checker, Chubby	Philadelphia, Pa.	1941
Cher	El Centro, Cal.	1946
Christian, Linda	Tampico, Mexico	1924
Christie, Audrey	Chicago, Ill.	1912
Christie, Julie	Chukur, India	1941
Christopher, Jordon	Youngstown, Oh.	1941
Christy, June	Springfield, Ill.	1925
Cilento, Diane	Queensland, Australia	1933
Claire, Ina	Washington, D.C.	1892
Clapton, Eric	Surrey, England	1945
Clark, Dane	New York, N.Y.	1915
Clark, Dick	Mt. Vernon, N.Y.	1929
Clark, Petula	Ewell, Surrey, England	1934
Clark, Roy	Meherrin, Va.	1933
Clayton, Jan	Tularosa, N. M.	1925
Cliburn, Van	Shreveport, La.	1934
Clooney, Rosemary	Maysville, Ky.	1928
Coburn, James	Laurel, Neb.	1928
Coca, Imogene	Philadelphia, Pa.	1908
Coco, James	New York, N.Y.	1928
Cohen, Myron	Grodno, Poland	1902
Colbert, Claudette	Paris, France	1907
Cole, Dennis	Detroit, Mich.	1943
Cole, Michael	Madison, Wis.	1945
Cole, Tina	Hollywood, Cal.	1943
Collins, Dorothy	Windsor, Ont.	1926
Collins, Joan	London, England	1933
Collins, Judy	Seattle, Wash.	1939
Colonna, Jerry	Boston, Mass.	1903
Comden, Betty	Brooklyn, N.Y.	1919
Como, Perry	Canonsburg, Pa.	1912
Conklin, Peggy	Dobbs Ferry, N.Y.	1912
Conley, Eugene	Lynn, Mass.	1908
Conner, Nadine	Compton, Cal.	1913
Connery, Sean	Edinburgh, Scotland	1930
Conniff, Ray	Attleboro, Mass.	1916
Connors, Chuck	Brooklyn, N.Y.	1921
Connors, Michael	Fresno, Cal.	1925
Conrad, Robert	Chicago, Ill.	1935
Conrad, William	Louisville, Ky.	1920
Conried, Hans	Baltimore, Md.	1917
Constantine, Michael	Reading, Pa.	1927
Converse, Frank	St. Louis, Mo.	1938
Conway, Gary	Boston, Mass.	1938
Conway, Shirl	Franklinville, N.Y.	1916
Conway, Tim	Chagrin Falls, Oh.	1933
Coogan, Jackie	Los Angeles, Cal.	1914
Cook, Barbara	Atlanta, Ga.	1927
Cooke, Alistair	England	1908
Cooper, Alice	Detroit, Mich.	1948
Cooper, Jackie	Los Angeles, Cal.	1922
Coppola, Francis Ford	Detroit, Mich.	1939
Corby, Ellen	Racine, Wis.	1913
Corey, Jeff	New York, N.Y.	1914
Cosby, Bill	Philadelphia, Pa.	1937
Costello, Dolores	Pittsburgh, Pa.	1905
Cotsworth, Staats	Oak Park, Ill.	1908
Cotten, Joseph	Petersburg, Va.	1905
Courtenay, Tom	Hull, England	1937
Crabbe, Buster	Oakland, Cal.	1908
Crain, Jeanne	Barstow, Cal.	1925
Crane, Bob	Waterbury, Conn.	1928
Crawford, Broderick	Philadelphia, Pa.	1911
Crawford, Michael	Salisbury, England	1942
Crenna, Richard	Los Angeles, Cal.	1927
Cristal, Linda	Argentina	1936
Cronyn, Hume	London, Ont.	1911
Crosby, Bing (Harry)	Tacoma, Wash.	1904
Crosby, Bob	Spokane, Wash.	1913
Crowley, Pat	Scranton, Pa.	1929
Cruz, Brandon	Bakersfield, Cal.	1962
Cugat, Xavier	Barcelona, Spain	1900
Cullen, Bill	Pittsburgh, Pa.	1920
Cullum, John	Knoxville, Tenn.	1930
Culp, Robert	Berkeley, Cal.	1930
Cummings, Constance	Seattle, Wash.	1910
Cummings, Robert	Joplin, Mo.	1910
Cummins, Peggy	Prestatyn, N. Wales	1925
Curtin, Phyllis	Clarksburg, W. Va.	1930
Curtis, Ken	Lamar, Col.	1916
Curtis, Tony	New York, N.Y.	1925
Cusack, Cyril	Druban, S. Africa	1910
Cushing, Peter	Surrey, England	1913

D

Name	Birthplace	Born
Dagmar (Egnor)	Huntington, W.Va.	1926
Dahl, Arlene	Minneapolis, Minn.	1927
Dailey, Dan	New York, N.Y.	1917
Dalrymple, Jean	Morristown, N.J.	1910
Dalton, Abby	Las Vegas, Nev.	1935
Daly, James	Wisconsin Rapids, Wis.	1918
Daly, John	Johannesburg, S. Africa	1914
Damita, Lili	Paris, France	1907
Damone, Vic	Brooklyn, N.Y.	1928
Dana, Bill	Quincy, Mass.	1924
Dangerfield, Rodney	Babylon, N.Y.	1921
Daniels, William	Brooklyn, N.Y.	1927
Danilova, Alexandra	Peterhof, Russia	1907
Danner, Blythe	Philadelphia, Pa.	—
Danton, Ray	New York, N.Y.	1931
Darby, Kim	Hollywood, Cal.	1948
Darcel, Denise	Paris, France	1925
Darren, James	Philadelphia, Pa.	1936
Darrieux, Danielle	Bordeaux, France	1917
Darrow, Henry	New York, N.Y.	1933
Da Silva, Howard	Cleveland, Oh.	1909
Dassin, Jules	Middletown, Conn.	1911
Dauphin, Claude	Corbeil, France	1905
Davidson, John	Pittsburgh, Pa.	1941
Davis, Ann B.	Schenectady, N.Y.	1926
Davis, Bette	Lowell, Mass.	1908
Davis, Clifton	Chicago, Ill.	1945
Davis, Mac	Lubbock, Tex.	1942
Davis, Ossie	Cogdell, Ga.	1917
Davis, Sammy Jr.	New York, N.Y.	1925
Dwan, Hazel	Ogden, Ut.	1898
Day, Dennis	New York, N.Y.	1917
Day, Doris	Cincinnati, Oh.	1924
Day, Laraine	Roosevelt, Ut.	1920
Dean, Jimmy	Plainview, Tex.	1928
De Camp, Rosemary	Prescott, Ariz.	1913
De Carlo, Yvonne	Vancouver, B. C.	1924
Dee, Frances	Los Angeles, Cal.	1907
Dee, Joey	Passaic, N.J.	1940
Dee, Ruby	Cleveland, Oh.	1924
Dee, Sandra	Bayonne, N.J.	1942
DeFore, Don	Cedar Rapids, Ia.	1917

Name	Birthplace	Born
DeHaven, Gloria	Los Angeles, Cal.	1925
de Havilland, Olivia	Tokyo, Japan	1916
De Niro, Robert	New York, N.Y.	1945
Del Rio, Dolores	Durango, Mexico	1905
Dell, Gabriel	Brooklyn, N.Y.	1921
Della Chiesa, Vivienne	Chicago, Ill.	1920
Delon, Alain	France	1935
DeLuise, Dom	Brooklyn, N.Y.	1933
Demarest, William	St. Paul, Minn.	1892
De Mille, Agnes	New York, N.Y.	1905
Dempster, Carol	Duluth, Minn.	1901
Deneuve, Catherine	Paris, France	1943
Denning, Richard	Poughkeepsie, N.Y.	1914
Dennis, Sandy	Hastings, Neb.	1937
Denver, Bob	New Rochelle, N.Y.	1935
Denver, John	Roswell, N.M.	1943
Derek, John	Hollywood, Cal.	1926
Dern, Bruce	Chicago, Ill.	1936
Desmond, Johnny	Detroit, Mich.	1921
Devane, William	Albany, N.Y.	1937
Dewhurst, Colleen	Montreal, Que.	1926
Dey, Susan	Pekin, Ill.	1952
Diamond, Neil	Brooklyn, N.Y.	1941
Dickinson, Angie	Kulm, N. D.	1936
Dietrich, Marlene	Berlin, Germany	1901
Diller, Phyllis	Lima, Oh.	1917
Dillman, Bradford	San Francisco, Cal.	1930
Dixon, Ivan	New York, N.Y.	1931
Domingo, Placido	Madrid, Spain	1951
Domino, Fats	New Orleans, La.	1928
Donahue, Troy	New York, N.Y.	1936
Donald, James	Aberdeen, Scotland	1917
Donald, Peter	Bristol, England	1918
Donnelly, Ruth	Trenton, N.J.	1896
Donovan	Glasgow, Scotland	1946
Dors, Diana	Swindon, England	1931
d'Orsay, Fifi	Montreal, Que.	1908
Douglas, Donna	Baywood, La.	1939
Douglas, Kirk	Amsterdam, N.Y.	1918
Douglas, Melvyn	Macon, Ga.	1901
Douglas, Michael	New Brunswick, N.J.	1945
Douglas, Mike	Chicago, Ill.	1925
Downey, Morton	Wallingford, Conn.	1902
Downs, Hugh	Akron, Oh.	1921
Dragonette, Jessica	Calcutta, India	—
Drake, Alfred	Bronx, N.Y.	1914
Drake, Betsy	Paris, France	1923
Drew, Ellen	Kansas City, Mo.	1915
Dreyfuss, Richard	Brooklyn, N.Y.	1949
Dru, Joanne	Logan, W.Va.	1923
Drury, James	New York, N.Y.	1934
Duchin, Peter	New York, N.Y.	1937
Duff, Howard	Bremerton, Wash.	1917
Duke, Patty	New York, N.Y.	1946
Dullea, Keir	Cleveland, Oh.	1936
Dunaway, Faye	Bascom, Fla.	1941
Duncan, Sandy	Henderson, Tex.	1946
Duncan, Todd	Danville, Ky.	1900
Duncan, Vivian	Los Angeles, Cal.	1902
Dunham, Katherine	Chicago, Ill.	1910
Dunne, Irene	Louisville, Ky.	1904
Dunnock, Mildred	Baltimore, Md.	1906
Durante, Jimmy	New York, N.Y.	1893
Durbin, Deanna	Winnipeg, Man.	1922
Duvall, Robert	San Diego, Cal.	1931
Duvall, Shelly	Houston, Tex.	—
Dvorak, Ann	New York, N.Y.	1912
Dylan, Bob	Duluth, Minn.	1941

E

Name	Birthplace	Born
Eastwood, Clint	San Francisco, Cal.	1930
Eaton, Shirley	London, England	1937
Ebsen, Buddy	Belleville, Ill.	1908
Eckstine, Billy	Pittsburgh, Pa.	1914
Edelman, Herb	Brooklyn, N.Y.	1933
Eden, Barbara	Tucson, Ariz.	1934
Edwards, Ralph	Merino, Col.	1913
Edwards, Vincent	Brooklyn, N.Y.	1928
Egan, Richard	San Francisco, Cal.	1923
Eggar, Samantha	London, England	1939
Eggerth, Marta	Budapest, Hungary	1916
Ekberg, Anita	Malmo, Sweden	1931
Ekland, Britt	Stockholm, Sweden	1942
Elam, Jack	Phoenix, Ariz.	—
Eldridge, Florence	Brooklyn, N.Y.	1901
Elgart, Larry	New London, Conn.	1922
Elgart, Les	New Haven, Conn.	1918
Elliott, Bob	Boston, Mass.	1923
Emerson, Faye	Elizabeth, La.	1917
Erickson, Leif	Alameda, Cal.	1911
Esmond, Jill	London, England	1908
Etting, Ruth	David City, Neb.	1896
Evans, Dale	Uvalde, Tex.	1912
Evans, Gene	Holbrook, Ariz.	1924
Evans, Maurice	Dorchester, England	1901
Everett, Chad	South Bend, Ind.	1937
Everly, Don	Brownie, Ky.	1937
Everly, Phil	Brownie, Ky.	1938
Evers, Jason	New York, N.Y.	1927
Ewell, Tom	Owensboro, Ky.	1909

F

Name	Birthplace	Born
Fabares, Shelley	Santa Monica, Cal.	1944
Fabian (Forte)	Philadelphia, Pa.	1943
Fabray, Nanette	San Diego, Cal.	1920
Fadiman, Clifton	Brooklyn, N.Y.	1904
Fairbanks, Douglas Jr.	New York, N.Y.	1909
Falk, Peter	New York, N.Y.	1927
Falkenburg, Jinx	Barcelona, Spain	1919
Farber, Barry	Baltimore, Md.	1930
Farentino, James	Brooklyn, N.Y.	1938
Fargo, Donna	Mt. Airy, N.C.	1945
Farr, Felicia	Westchester, N.Y.	1932
Farrell, Charles	Onset Bay, Mass.	1901
Farrell, Eileen	Willimantic, Conn.	1920
Farrow, Mia	Los Angeles, Cal.	1946
Fawcett-Majors, Farah	Houston, Tex.	1947
Faye, Alice	New York, N.Y.	1915
Feld, Fritz	Berlin, Germany	1900
Feldman, Marty	England	1933
Feldon, Barbara	Pittsburgh, Pa.	1941
Feliciano, Jose	Puerto Rico	1945
Fellini, Federico	Rimini, Italy	1920
Fellows, Edith	Boston, Mass.	1923
Ferrer, Jose	Santurce, P.R.	1912
Ferrer, Mel	Elberon, N.J.	1917
Ferris, Barbara	London, England	1942
Fetchit, Stepin	Key West, Fla.	1902
Fiedler, Arthur	Boston, Mass.	1894
Field, Sally	Pasadena, Cal.	1946
Fields, Gracie	Rochdale, England	1898
Fields, Totie	Hartford, Conn.	1931
Finney, Albert	Salford, England	1936
Firkusny, Rudolf	Napajedla, Czechoslovakia	1912
Fisher, Carrie	Beverly Hills, Cal.	1956
Fisher, Eddie	Philadelphia, Pa.	1928
Fisher, Gail	Orange, N.J.	—
Fitzgerald, Ella	Newport News, Va.	1918
Fitzgerald, Geraldine	Dublin, Ireland	1914
Fitzgerald, Pegeen	Norcatur, Kan.	1910
Fix, Paul	Dobbs Ferry, N.Y.	1902
Flack, Roberta	Black Mountain, N.C.	1939
Flatt, Lester	Overton County, Tenn.	1914
Fleming, Rhonda	Hollywood, Cal.	1923
Fletcher, Louise	Birmingham, Ala.	1935
Foch, Nina	Leyden, Netherlands	1924
Fonda, Henry	Grand Island, Neb.	1905
Fonda, Jane	New York, N.Y.	1937
Fonda, Peter	New York, N.Y.	1939
Fontaine, Frank	Cambridge, Mass.	1920
Fontaine, Joan	Tokyo, Japan	1917
Fontanne, Lynn	London, England	1887
Fonteyn, Margot	Reigate, England	1919
Foran, Dick	Flemington, N.J.	1910
Forbes, Bryan	London, England	1926
Ford (Tenn.), Ernie	Bristol, Tenn.	1919
Ford, Glenn	Quebec, Canada	1916
Ford, Ruth	Hazelhurst, Miss.	1915
Forrest, Steve	Huntsville, Tex.	1925
Forster, Robert	Rochester, N.Y.	1942
Forsythe, John	Penns Grove, N.J.	1918
Fosse, Bob	Chicago, Ill.	1927
Foster, Jodie	Los Angeles, Cal.	1962
Foster, Phil	Brooklyn, N.Y.	1914
Fox, James	London, England	1939
Foxx, Redd	St. Louis, Mo.	1922
Foy, Eddie Jr.	New Rochelle, N.Y.	1905
Frampton, Peter	Kent, England	1950
Francescatti, Zino	Marseilles, France	1904
Franciosa, Anthony	New York, N.Y.	1928
Francis, Arlene	Boston, Mass.	1908
Francis, Connie	Newark, N.J.	1938
Franciscus, James	Clayton, Mo.	1934

Name	Birthplace	Born
Frankenheimer, John	Malba, N.Y.	1930
Franklin, Aretha	Memphis, Tenn.	1942
Franklin, Joe	New York, N.Y.	1926
Franz, Arthur	Perth Amboy, N.J.	1920
Freberg, Stan	Pasadena, Cal.	1926
Freed, Bert	New York, N.Y.	1919
Freeman, Mona	Baltimore, Md.	1926
Froman, Jane	St. Louis, Mo.	1911
Frost, David	Tenterden, England	1939
Frye, David	Brooklyn, N.Y.	1934
Funicello, Annette	Utica, N.Y.	1942
Funt, Allen	New York, N.Y.	1914
Furness, Betty	New York, N.Y.	1916

G

Name	Birthplace	Born
Gabel, Martin	Philadelphia, Pa.	1912
Gabor, Eva	Hungary	1921
Gabor, Zsa Zsa	Hungary	1919
Gahagan, Helen	Boonton, N.J.	1900
Galloway, Don	Brooksville, Ky.	1937
Gam, Rita	Pittsburgh, Pa.	1929
Gambling, John	New York, N.Y.	1930
Garagiola, Joe	St. Louis, Mo.	1926
Garbo, Greta	Stockholm, Sweden	1905
Gardenia, Vincent	Naples, Italy	1922
Gardiner, Reginald	Wimbledon, England	1903
Gardner, Ava	Smithfield, N.C.	1922
Garfunkel, Art	New York, N.Y.	1941
Gargan, William	Brooklyn, N.Y.	1905
Garland, Beverly	Santa Cruz, Cal.	1930
Garner, James	Norman, Okla.	1928
Garner, Peggy Ann	Canton, Oh.	1932
Garrett, Betty	St. Joseph, Mo.	1919
Garroway, Dave	Schenectady, N.Y.	1913
Garson, Greer	Co. Down, N. Ireland	1908
Garver, Kathy	Long Beach, Cal.	1948
Gary, John	Watertown, N.Y.	1932
Gavin, John	Los Angeles, Cal.	1932
Gaye, Marvin	Washington, D.C.	1939
Gaynor, Janet	Philadelphia, Pa.	1906
Gaynor, Mitzi	Chicago, Ill.	1931
Gazzara, Ben	New York, N.Y.	1930
Gedda, Nicolai	Sweden	1925
Geer, Will	Frankfort, Ind.	1902
Geeson, Judy	Sussex, England	1948
Genevieve (G. Auger)	Paris, France	1930
Genn, Leo	London, England	1905
Gennaro, Peter	Metairie, La.	1924
Gentry, Bobby	Chickasaw Co., Miss.	1944
Ghostley, Alice	Eve, Mo.	1926
Gibson, Henry	Germantown, Pa.	1935
Gielgud, John	London, England	1904
Gilford, Jack	New York, N.Y.	1907
Gillespie, Dizzy	Cheraw, N.C.	1917
Gillette, Anita	Baltimore, Md.	1936
Gingold, Hermione	London, England	1897
Gish, Lillian	Springfield, Oh.	1896
Givot, George	Omaha, Neb.	1903
Gleason, Jackie	Brooklyn, N.Y.	1916
Gobel, George	Chicago, Ill.	1919
Godard, Jean Luc	Paris, France	1930
Goddard, Paulette	Great Neck, N.Y.	1911
Godfrey, Arthur	New York, N.Y.	1903
Goldsboro, Bobby	Marianne, Fla.	1941
Goodman, Benny	Chicago, Ill.	1909
Goodman, Dody	Columbus, Oh.	1929
Gordon, Gale	New York, N.Y.	1906
Gordon, Max	New York, N.Y.	1892
Gordon, Ruth	Wollaston, Mass.	1896
Gorin, Igor	Ukraine, Russia	1909
Gorme, Eydie	Bronx, N.Y.	1932
Gorshin, Frank	Pittsburgh, Pa.	1935
Gortner, Marjoe	Long Beach, Cal.	1945
Gosden, Freeman (Amos)	Richmond, Va.	1904
Gould, Elliot	Brooklyn, N.Y.	1938
Gould, Morton	Richmond Hill, N.Y.	1913
Goulding, Ray	Lowell, Mass.	1922
Goulet, Robert	Lawrence, Mass.	1933
Gowdy, Curt	Green River, Wyo.	1919
Grady, Don	San Diego, Cal.	1944
Graham, Martha	Pittsburgh, Pa.	1902
Graham, Virginia	Chicago, Ill.	1913
Grahame, Gloria	Los Angeles, Cal.	1929
Grahame, Margot	Canterbury, England	1911
Granger, Farley	San Jose, Cal.	1925
Granger, Stewart	London, England	1913
Granville, Bonita	New York, N.Y.	1923
Grant, Cary	Bristol, England	1904
Grant, Kathryn	Houston, Tex.	1933
Grant, Lee	New York, N.Y.	1927
Graves, Peter	Minneapolis, Minn.	1926
Gray, Coleen	Staplehurst, Neb.	1922
Gray, Dolores	Chicago, Ill.	1924
Grayson, Kathryn	Winston-Salem, N.C.	1923
Graziano, Rocky	New York, N.Y.	1922
Greco, Buddy	Philadelphia, Pa.	1926
Greco, Jose	Abruzzi, Italy	1918
Greco, Juliette	Paris, France	—
Green, Al	Forest City, Ark.	1946
Green, Adolph	New York, N.Y.	1915
Greene, Lorne	Ottawa, Ont.	1915
Greenwood, Charlotte	Philadelphia, Pa.	1893
Greenwood, Joan	London, England	1921
Greer, Jane	Washington, D.C.	1924
Gregory, Dick	St. Louis, Mo.	1933
Grey, Joel	Cleveland, Oh.	1932
Griffin, Merv	San Mateo, Cal.	1925
Griffith, Andy	Mount Airy, N.C.	1926
Griffith, Hugh	Wales	1912
Grimes, Gary	San Francisco, Cal.	1955
Grimes, Tammy	Lynn, Mass.	1936
Grizzard, George	Roanoke Rapids, N.C.	1928
Guardino, Harry	New York, N.Y.	1925
Guinness, Alec	London, England	1914
Gunn, Moses	St. Louis, Mo.	1929
Guthrie, Arlo	New York, N.Y.	1947

H

Name	Birthplace	Born
Hackett, Buddy	Brooklyn, N.Y.	1924
Hackett, Joan	New York, N.Y.	1933
Hackman, Gene	San Bernardino, Cal.	1931
Hagen, Uta	Gottingen, Germany	1919
Haggard, Merle	Bakersfield, Cal.	1937
Hagman, Larry	Ft. Worth, Tex.	1931
Hale, Barbara	DeKalb, Ill.	1922
Haley, Bill	Detroit, Mich.	1927
Haley, Jack	Boston, Mass.	1899
Hall, Huntz	New York, N.Y.	1920
Hall, Monty	Winnipeg, Man.	1923
Hall, Tom T.	Olive Hill, Ky.	1936
Hamilton, George	Memphis, Tenn.	1939
Hamilton, Margaret	Cleveland, Oh.	1902
Hamilton, Neil	Lynn, Mass.	1899
Hampshire, Susan	London, England	1941
Hampton, Lionel	Birmingham, Ala.	1914
Hampton, Ruth	Throop, Pa.	1932
Harding, Ann	Ft. Sam Houston, Tex.	1904
Harper, Ron	Turtle Creek, Pa.	1935
Harper, Valerie	Suffern, N.Y.	1940
Harrington, Pat Jr.	New York, N.Y.	1929
Harris, Barbara	Evanston, Ill.	1935
Harris, Julie	Grosse Pte. Park, Mich.	1925
Harris, Phil	Linton, Ind.	1906
Harris, Richard	Co. Limerick, Ireland	1933
Harris, Rosemary	Ashby, England	1930
Harrison, George	Liverpool, England	1943
Harrison, Noel	London, England	1933
Harrison, Rex	Huyton, England	1908
Hartman, David	Pawtucket, R.I.	1935
Hartman, Elizabeth	Boardman, Oh.	1943
Hasso, Signe	Stockholm, Sweden	1915
Haver, June	Rock Island, Ill.	1926
Havoc, June	Vancouver, B.C.	1916
Hawn, Goldie	Washington, D.C.	1945
Haworth, Jill	Sussex, England	1945
Hayden, Melissa	Toronto, Ont.	1928
Hayden, Russell	Chico, Cal.	1912
Hayden, Sterling	Montclair, N.Y.	1916
Hayes, Helen	Washington, D.C.	1900
Hayes, Isaac	Covington, Tenn.	1942
Hayes, Peter Lind	San Francisco, Cal.	1915
Haymes, Dick	Buenos Aires, Argentina	1918
Haynes, Lloyd	South Bend, Ind.	1934
Hayward, Louis	Johannesburg, S. Africa	1909
Hayworth, Rita	New York, N.Y.	1918
Healy, Mary	New Orleans, La.	1918
Heatherton, Joey	Rockville Centre, N.Y.	1944
Heckart, Eileen	Columbus, Oh.	1919
Hefner, Hugh	Chicago, Ill.	1926
Heifetz, Jascha	Vilna, Russia	1901
Helpmann, Robert	Mt. Gambier, Australia	1909
Hemmings, David	Guilford, England	1941
Henderson, Florence	Dale, Ind.	1934
Henderson, Marcia	Andover, Mass.	1932

Name	Birthplace	Born
Henderson, Skitch	Halstad, Minn.	1918
Henning, Linda Kaye	Toluca Lake, Cal.	1944
Henreid, Paul	Trieste, Italy	1908
Hepburn, Audrey	Brussels, Belgium	1929
Hepburn, Katharine	Hartford, Conn.	1909
Herbert, Evelyn	Philadelphia, Pa.	1898
Heston, Charlton	Evanston, Ill.	1924
Heywood, Anne	Birmingham, England	1937
Hickman, Darryl	Los Angeles, Cal.	1931
Hickman, Dwayne	Los Angeles, Cal.	1934
Hildegarde	Adell, Wis.	1906
Hill, Arthur	Melfort, Sask.	1922
Hiller, Wendy	Stockport, England	1912
Hines, Earl (Fatha)	Duquesne, Pa.	1905
Hines, Jerome	Hollywood, Cal.	1921
Hines, Mimi	Vancouver, B.C.	1933
Hingle, Pat	Denver, Col.	1924
Hirt, Al	New Orleans, La.	1922
Hitchcock, Alfred	London, England	1899
Ho, Don	Kakaako, Oahu, Ha.	1930
Hobart, Rose	New York, N.Y.	1906
Hoffman, Dustin	Los Angeles, Cal.	1937
Holbrook, Hal	Cleveland, Oh.	1925
Holden, William	O'Fallon, Ill.	1918
Holder, Geoffrey	Trinidad	1930
Holliman, Earl	Delhi, La.	1928
Holloway, Stanley	London, England	1890
Holloway, Sterling	Cedartown, Ga.	1905
Holm, Celeste	New York, N.Y.	1919
Holtz, Lou	San Francisco, Cal.	1893
Homeier, Skip	Chicago, Ill.	1930
Homolka, Oscar	Vienna, Austria	1903
Hooks, Robert	Washington, D.C.	1937
Hope, Bob	London, England	1903
Hopkin, Mary	Wales	1950
Hopkins, Anthony	England	1941
Hopkins, Bo	Greenwood, S.C.	—
Hopper, Dennis	Dodge City, Kan.	1936
Horne, Lena	Brooklyn, N.Y.	1917
Horowitz, Vladimir	Kiev, Russia	1904
Horton, Robert	Los Angeles, Cal.	1924
Houseman, John	Bucarest, Romania	1902
Howard, Clint	Burbank, Cal.	1959
Howard, Ken	El Centro, Cal.	1944
Howard, Ron	Duncan, Okla.	1954
Howard, Trevor	Kent, England	1916
Howes, Sally Ann	London, England	1934
Hudson, Rock	Winnetka, Ill.	1925
Humperdinck, Engelbert	Madras, India	1936
Hunnicutt, Arthur	Gravelly, Ark.	1911
Hunt, Lois	York, Pa.	1925
Hunt, Marsha	Chicago, Ill.	1917
Hunter, Kim	Detroit, Mich.	1922
Hunter, Ross	Cleveland, Oh.	1924
Hunter, Tab	New York, N.Y.	1931
Hussey, Olivia	Buenos Aires, Argentina	1952
Hussey, Ruth	Providence, R.I.	1917
Huston, John	Nevada, Mo.	1906
Hutchinson, Josephine	Seattle, Wash.	1916
Hutton, Betty	Battle Creek, Mich.	1921
Hutton, Ina Ray	Chicago, Ill.	1918
Hutton, Lauren	Charleston, S.C.	1944
Hyde-White, Wilfrid	England	1903
Hyer, Martha	Fort Worth, Tex.	1929
Hyman, Earle	Rocky Mt., N.C.	1926

I

Name	Birthplace	Born
Ian, Janis	New York, N. Y.	1951
Inescort, Frieda	Edinburgh, Scotland	1901
Ingels, Marty	Brooklyn, N.Y.	1936
Ireland, John	Vancouver, B.C.	1915
Iturbi, Jose	Valencia, Spain	1895
Ives, Burl	Hunt, Ill.	1909

J

Name	Birthplace	Born
Jackson, Anne	Allegheny, Pa.	1926
Jackson, Glenda	Cheshire, England	1936
Jackson, Kate	Alabama	1949
Jackson, Michael	Gary, Ind.	1958
Jaeckel, Richard	Long Beach, Cal.	1926
Jaffe, Sam	New York, N.Y.	1891
Jagger, Dean	Columbus Grove, Oh.	1905
Jagger, Mick	Dartford, England	1944
James, Dennis	Jersey City, N.J.	1917
James, Harry	Albany, Ga.	1916
Janssen, David	Naponee, Neb.	1930
Jason, Rick	New York, N.Y.	1926
Jeanmaire, Renee	Paris, France	1925
Jeffreys, Anne	Goldsboro, N.C.	1923
Jeffries, Fran	San Jose, Cal.	1939
Jeffries, Lionel	England	1926
Jennings, Waylon	Littlefield, Tex.	1937
Jens, Salome	Milwaukee, Wis.	1935
Jepson, Helen	Titusville, Pa.	1907
Jessel, George	New York, N.Y.	1898
John, Elton	Middlesex, England	1947
Johns, Glynis	Durban, S. Africa	1923
Johnson, Ben	Foraker, Okla.	1918
Johnson, Richard	Essex, England	1927
Johnson, Van	Newport, R.I.	1916
Johnston, Johnny	St. Louis, Mo.	1916
Jones, Allan	Scranton, Pa.	1907
Jones, Carolyn	Amarillo, Tex.	1933
Jones, Chris	Jackson, Tenn.	1941
Jones, Dean	Morgan Co., Ala.	1935
Jones, Grandpa	Niagara, Ky.	1913
Jones, Henry	Philadelphia, Pa.	1912
Jones, Jack	Hollywood, Cal.	1938
Jones, James Earl	Tate Co., Miss.	1931
Jones, Jennifer	Tulsa, Okla.	1919
Jones, Quincy	Chicago, Ill.	1933
Jones, Shirley	Smithton, Pa.	1934
Jones, Tom	Pontypridd, Wales	1940
Jory, Victor	Dawson, Yukon, Canada	1902
Joslyn, Allyn	Milford, Pa.	1905
Jourdan, Louis	Marseilles, France	1921
Jurado, Katy	Guadalajara, Mexico	1927

K

Name	Birthplace	Born
Kahn, Madeline	Boston, Mass.	—
Kaminska, Ida	Odessa, Russia	1899
Kaplan, Gabe	Brooklyn, N.Y.	1945
Kashi, Aliza	Tel-Aviv, Israel	1940
Kasznar, Kurt	Vienna, Austria	1913
Kaye, Danny	Brooklyn, N.Y.	1913
Kaye, Sammy	Lakewood, Oh.	1913
Kazan, Elia	Constantinople, Turkey	1909
Kazan, Lainie	New York, N.Y.	1940
Keach, Stacy	Savannah, Ga.	1941
Keaton, Diane	Santa Ana, Cal.	1949
Keel, Howard	Gillespie, Ill.	1919
Keeler, Ruby	Halifax, N.S.	1910
Keeshan, Bob	Lynbrook, N.Y.	1927
Keitel, Harvey	Brooklyn, N.Y.	1941
Keith, Brian	Bayonne, N.J.	1921
Keller, Marthe	Switzerland	1946
Kellerman, Sally	Long Beach, Cal.	1937
Kelley, DeForrest	Atlanta, Ga.	1920
Kelly, Emmett	Sedan, Kan.	1898
Kelly, Gene	Pittsburgh, Pa.	1912
Kelly, Grace	Philadelphia, Pa.	1929
Kelly, Jack	Astoria, N.Y.	1927
Kelly, Nancy	Lowell, Mass.	1921
Kelly, Patsy	Brooklyn, N.Y.	1910
Kennedy, Arthur	Worcester, Mass.	1914
Kennedy, George	New York, N.Y.	1926
Kennedy, Madge	Chicago, Ill.	—
Kent, Allegra	Los Angeles, Cal.	1938
Kenyon, Doris	Syracuse, N.Y.	1897
Kerr, Deborah	Helensburgh, Scotland	1921
Kerr, John	New York, N.Y.	1931
Kert, Larry	Los Angeles, Cal.	1930
Keyes, Evelyn	Port Arthur, Tex.	1925
Kiley, Richard	Chicago, Ill.	1922
Kilian, Victor	Jersey City, N.J.	1898
King, Alan	Brooklyn, N.Y.	1927
King, B. B.	Itta Bena, Miss.	1925
King, Carole	Brooklyn, N.Y.	1942
King, Henry	Christianburg, Va.	1896
King, Walter Woolf	San Francisco, Cal.	1899
King, Wayne	Savannah, Ill.	1901
Kirby, Durward	Covington, Ky.	1912
Kirk, Lisa	Brownsville, Pa.	1925
Kirk, Phyllis	Plainfield, N.J.	1930
Kirsten, Dorothy	Montclair, N.J.	1919
Kitt, Eartha	North, S.C.	1928
Klemperer, Werner	Cologne, Germany	1920
Klugman, Jack	Philadelphia, Pa.	1922
Knight, Gladys	Atlanta, Ga.	1944
Knight, Ted	Terryville, Conn.	—
Knotts, Don	Morgantown, W.Va.	1924
Knowles, Patric	Horsforth, England	1911
Knox, Alexander	Strathroy, Canada	1907
Korjus, Miliza	Warsaw, Poland	1912

Name	Birthplace	Born
Korman, Harvey	Chicago, Ill.	1927
Kostelanetz, Andre	St. Petersburg, Russia	1901
Kramer, Stanley	New York, N.Y.	1913
Kristofferson, Kris	Brownsville, Tex.	1936
Kruger, Hardy	Berlin, Germany	1928
Kubelik, Rafael	Bychori, Czechoslovakia	1914
Kubrick, Stanley	Bronx, N.Y.	1928
Kulp, Nancy	Harrisburg, Pa.	1921
Kwan, Nancy	Hong Kong	1939
Kyser, Kay	Rocky Mount, N.C.	1905
L		
Laine, Frankie	Chicago, Ill.	1913
Lamarr, Hedy	Vienna, Austria	1915
Lamas, Fernando	Buenos Aires, Argentina	1915
Lamb, Gil	Minneapolis, Minn.	1906
Lamour, Dorothy	New Orleans, La.	1914
Lancaster, Burt	New York, N.Y.	1913
Lanchester, Elsa	London, England	1902
Landau, Martin	Brooklyn, N.Y.	1934
Landon, Michael	Forest Hills, N.Y.	—
Lane, Abbe	Brooklyn, N.Y.	1932
Lane, Lola	Macy, Ind.	1909
Lane, Priscilla	Indianola, Ia.	1917
Lane, Sara	New York, N.Y.	1949
Lange, Hope	Redding Ridge, Conn.	1933
Langella, Frank	Bayonne, N.J.	1940
Langford, Frances	Lakeland, Fla.	1913
Lansbury, Angela	London, England	1925
Lansing, Robert	San Diego, Cal.	1929
Lanson, Snooky (Roy)	Memphis, Tenn.	1919
LaPlante, Laura	St. Louis, Mo.	1904
La Rosa, Julius	Brooklyn, N.Y.	1930
La Rue, Jack	New York, N.Y.	—
Lasser, Louise	New York, N.Y.	—
Laughlin, Tom	Minneapolis, Minn.	1938
Laurie, Piper	Detroit, Mich.	1932
Lavin, Linda	Portland, Ore.	—
Law, John Philip	Hollywood, Cal.	1937
Lawford, Peter	London, England	1923
Lawrence, Barbara	Carnegie, Okla.	1930
Lawrence, Carol	Melrose Park, Ill.	1934
Lawrence, Marjorie	Victoria, Australia	1909
Lawrence, Steve	Brooklyn, N.Y.	1935
Lawrence, Vicki	Inglewood, Cal.	1949
Leachman, Cloris	Des Moines, Ia.	1926
Lean, David	Croydon, England	1908
Lear, Norman	New Haven, Conn.	1922
Learned, Michael	Washington, D.C.	—
Lederer, Francis	Prague, Czechoslovakia	1906
Lee, Brenda	Atlanta, Ga.	1944
Lee, Christopher	London, England	1922
Lee, Michele	Los Angeles, Cal.	1942
Lee, Peggy	Jamestown, N.D.	1920
Lee, Pinky	St. Paul, Minn.	—
Le Gallienne, Eva	London, England	1899
Legrand, Michel	Paris, France	1932
Leigh, Janet	Merced, Cal.	1927
Leinsdorf, Erich	Vienna, Austria	1912
Lembeck, Harvey	New York, N.Y.	1923
Lemmon, Jack	Boston, Mass.	1925
Lennon, Dianne	Los Angeles, Cal.	1939
Lennon, Janet	Culver City, Cal.	1946
Lennon, John	Liverpool, England	1940
Lennon, Kathy	Santa Monica, Cal.	1934
Lennon, Peggy	Los Angeles, Cal.	1941
Leonard, Sheldon	New York, N.Y.	1907
Leontovich, Eugenie	Moscow, Russia	1894
LeRoy, Mervyn	San Francisco, Cal.	1900
Leslie, Joan	Detroit, Mich.	1925
Lester, Jerry	Chicago, Ill.	1911
Lester, Mark	Richmond, England	1958
Lester, Tom	Jackson, Miss.	1938
Levene, Sam	Russia	1905
Levenson, Sam	New York, N.Y.	1911
Lewis, Jerry	Newark, N.J.	1926
Lewis, Jerry Lee	Ferriday, La.	1935
Lewis, Monica	Chicago, Ill.	1925
Lewis, Robert Q.	New York, N.Y.	1924
Lewis, Shari	New York, N.Y.	1934
Liberace	West Allis, Wis.	1919
Lillie, Beatrice	Toronto, Ont.	1894
Lincoln, Abbey	Chicago, Ill.	1930
Linden, Hal	New York, N.Y.	1931
Lindfors, Viveca	Uppsala, Sweden	1920
Lindsay, Margaret	Dubuque, Ia.	1910
Lindsey, Mort	Newark, N.J.	1923
Linkletter, Art	Saskatchewan, Canada	1912
Lipton, Peggy	Lawrence, N.Y.	1948
Lisi, Virna	Italy	1937
Little, Cleavon	Chickasha, Okla.	1939
Little, Rich	Ottawa, Ont.	1938
Little Richard	Macon, Ga.	1935
Livingston, Barry	Los Angeles, Cal.	1953
Livingston, Stanley	Los Angeles, Cal.	1950
Livingstone, Mary	Seattle, Wash.	1909
Lockhart, June	New York, N.Y.	1925
Lockwood, Margaret	Karachi, India	1916
Loden, Barbara	Marion, N.C.	1937
Loder, John	London, England	1898
Logan, Joshua	Texarkana, Tex.	1908
Lollobrigida, Gina	Subiaco, Italy	1929
Lom, Herbert	Prague, Czechoslovakia	1917
Lombardo, Guy	London, Ont.	1902
London, Julie	Santa Rosa, Cal.	1926
Longet, Claudine	France	1942
Lopez, Trini	Dallas, Tex.	1937
Lord, Jack	New York, N.Y.	—
Loren, Sophia	Rome, Italy	1934
Loring, Gloria	New York, N.Y.	1946
Loudon, Dorothy	Boston, Mass.	1932
Louise, Tina	New York, N.Y.	1934
Love, Bessie	Midland, Tex.	1898
Loy, Myrna	Helena, Mon.	1905
Lucas, Nick	New Jersey	1897
Ludwig, Christa	Berlin, Germany	1928
Luke, Keye	Canton, China	1904
Lulu	Glasgow, Scotland	1948
Lum (Chester Lauck)	Allene, Ark.	1902
Lumet, Sidney	Philadelphia, Pa.	1924
Lund, John	Rochester, N.Y.	1913
Lunt, Alfred	Milwaukee, Wis.	1892
Lupino, Ida	London, England	1918
Lynde, Paul	Mt. Vernon, Oh.	1926
Lynley, Carol	New York, N.Y.	1942
Lynn, Jeffrey	Auburn, Mass.	1909
Lynn, Loretta	Butcher Hollow, Ky.	1932
Lyon, Ben	Atlanta,Ga.	1901
Lyon, Sue	Davenport, Ia.	1946
M		
Maazel, Lorin	Nevilly, France	1930
MacArthur, James	Los Angeles, Cal.	1937
MacGraw, Ali	Pound Ridge, N.Y.	1939
MacKenzie, Gizele	Winnipeg, Man.	1927
MacKay, Jim	Philadelphia, Pa.	1921
MacLaine, Shirley	Richmond, Va.	1934
MacMurray, Fred	Kankakee, Ill.	1908
MacRae, Gordon	East Orange, N.J.	1921
MacRae, Meredith	Houston, Tex.	1945
MacRae, Sheila	London, England	1924
Macy, Bill	Revere, Mass.	1922
Madison, Guy	Bakersfield, Cal.	1922
Majors, Lee	Wyandotte, Mich.	1940
Malbin, Elaine	New York, N.Y.	1932
Malden, Karl	Gary, Ind.	1913
Malone, Dorothy	Chicago, Ill.	1925
Malone, Nancy	New York, N.Y.	1935
Manchester, Melissa	Bronx, N.Y.	1951
Mancini, Henry	Cleveland, Oh.	1924
Mandrell, Barbara	Houston, Tex.	1948
Manilow, Barry	New York, N.Y.	1946
Mann, Herbie	New York, N.Y.	1930
Manning, Irene	Cincinnati, Oh.	1918
Mantovani, Annuzio	Venice, Italy	1905
Marceau, Marcel	France	1923
Margo	Mexico City, Mexico	1918
Margolin, Janet	New York, N.Y.	1943
Markova, Alicia	London, England	1910
Marlowe, Hugh	Philadelphia, Pa.	1914
Marsh, Jean	London, England	1934
Marshall, Brenda	Philippines	1915
Marshall, E. G.	Awatonna, Minn.	1910
Marshall, William	Chicago, Ill.	1917
Martin, Dean	Steubenville, Oh.	1917
Martin, Dick	Detroit, Mich.	1922
Martin, Mary	Weatherford, Tex.	1913
Martin, Ross	Poland	1920
Martin, Strother	Kokomo, Ind.	1919
Martin, Tony	San Francisco, Cal.	1913
Martino, Al	Philadelphia, Pa.	1927
Marvin, Lee	New York, N.Y.	1924
Marx, Herbert (Zeppo)	New York, N.Y.	1901
Marx, Julius (Groucho)	New York, N.Y.	1890

Name	Birthplace	Born
Mason, Jackie	Sheboygan, Wis.	1931
Mason, James	Huddersfield, England	1909
Mason, Marsha	St. Louis, Mo.	—
Mason, Pamela	Westgate, England	1918
Massey, Curt	Midland, Tex.	—
Massey, Raymond	Toronto, Ont.	1896
Massine, Leonide	Moscow, Russia	1896
Mastroianni, Marcello	Italy	1924
Mathieu, Mireille	Avignon, France	1946
Mathis, Johnny	San Francisco, Cal.	1935
Matthau, Walter	New York, N.Y.	1920
Mature, Victor	Louisville, Ky.	1916
May, Billy	Pittsburgh, Pa.	1916
May, Elaine	Philadelphia, Pa.	1932
Mayehoff, Eddie	Baltimore, Md.	1914
Mayo, Virginia	St. Louis, Mo.	1920
Mazurki, Mike	Austria	1909
McArdle, Andrea	Philadelphia, Pa.	1964
McBride, Patricia	Teaneck, N.J.	1942
McCallum, David	Glasgow, Scotland	1933
McCambridge, Mercedes	Joliet, Ill.	1918
McCarthy, Kevin	Seattle, Wash.	1915
McCartney, Paul	Liverpool, England	1942
McClure, Doug	Glendale, Cal.	1935
McCord, Kent	Los Angeles, Cal.	1942
McCoy, Tim	Saginaw, Mich.	1891
McCrary, Tex (John)	Calvert, Tex.	1910
McCrea, Joel	Los Angeles, Cal.	1905
McDowall, Roddy	London, England	1928
McDowell, Malcolm	Leeds, England	1943
McEachin, James	Pennert, N.C.	1930
McFarland, George (Spanky)	Dallas, Tex.	1928
McGavin, Darren	San Joaquin, Cal.	1922
McGee, Fibber	Peoria, Ill.	1896
McGoohan, Patrick	Astoria, N.Y.	1928
McGuire, Dorothy	Omaha, Neb.	1919
McGuire Sisters:		
Christine	Middletown, Oh.	1928
Dorothy	Middletown, Oh.	1930
Phyllis	Middletown, Oh.	1931
McHugh, Frank	Homestead, Pa.	1899
McIntire, John	Spokane, Wash.	1907
McKenna, Siobhan	Belfast, Ireland	1923
McLean, Don	New Rochelle, N.Y.	1945
McLerie, Allyn	Grand Mere, Que.	1926
McMahon, Ed	Detroit, Mich.	1923
McNair, Barbara	Chicago, Ill.	1939
McQueen, Butterfly	Tampa, Fla.	1911
McQueen, Steve	Indianapolis, Ind.	1930
Meadows, Audrey	Wu Chang, China	1924
Meadows, Jayne	Wu Chang, China	1926
Meara, Anne	New York, N.Y.	1929
Medford, Kay	New York, N.Y.	1920
Meeker, Ralph	Minneapolis, Minn.	1920
Melanie	New York, N.Y.	1947
Melton, Sid	Brooklyn, N.Y.	1920
Menuhin, Yehudi	New York, N.Y.	1916
Mercouri, Melina	Athens, Greece	1915
Meredith, Burgess	Cleveland, Oh.	1909
Merkel, Una	Covington, Ky.	1903
Merman, Ethel	Astoria, N.Y.	1909
Merrick, David	Hong Kong	1911
Merrill, Dina	New York, N.Y.	1925
Merrill, Gary	Hartford, Conn.	1915
Merrill, Robert	Brooklyn, N.Y.	1919
Middleton, Ray	Chicago, Ill.	1907
Midler, Bette	New Jersey	1945
Milanov, Zinka	Zagreb, Yugoslavia	1908
Miles, Sarah	Ingatestone, England	1941
Miles, Vera	near Boise City, Okla.	1930
Milland, Ray	Neath, Wales	1908
Miller, Ann	Houston, Tex.	1923
Miller, Cheryl	Sherman Oaks, Cal.	1943
Miller, Jason	Scranton, Pa.	1940
Miller, Mitch	Rochester, N.Y.	1911
Miller, Roger	Erick, Okla.	1936
Mills, Hayley	London, England	1946
Mills, John	Suffolk, England	1908
Mills, Juliet	London, England	1941
Milner, Martin	Detroit, Mich.	—
Milstein, Nathan	Odessa, Russia	1904
Mimieux, Yvette	Hollywood, Cal.	1942
Minnelli, Liza	Los Angeles, Cal.	1946
Mitchell, Cameron	Dallastown, Pa.	1918
Mitchell, Guy	Detroit, Mich.	1925
Mitchell, Joni	Alberta, Canada	1943
Mitchum, Robert	Bridgeport, Conn.	1917
Moffo, Anna	Wayne, Pa.	1934
Montalban, Ricardo	Mexico City, Mexico	1920
Montand, Yves	Monsummano, Italy	1921
Montgomery, Elizabeth	Hollywood, Cal.	1933
Montgomery, George	Brady, Mon.	1916
Montgomery, Robert	Beacon, N.Y.	1904
Moore, Colleen	Port Huron, Mich.	1902
Moore, Constance	Sioux City, Ia.	1922
Moore, Dickie	Los Angeles, Cal.	1925
Moore, Garry	Baltimore, Md.	1915
Moore, Mary Tyler	Brooklyn, N.Y.	1937
Moore, Melba	New York, N.Y.	1945
Moore, Roger	London, England	1928
Moore, Terry	Los Angeles, Cal.	1932
Moreau, Jeanne	Paris, France	1929
Moreno, Rita	Humacao, P.R.	1931
Morgan, Dennis	Prentice, Wis.	1910
Morgan, Harry	Detroit, Mich.	1915
Morgan, Henry	New York, N.Y.	1915
Morgan, Jane	Boston, Mass.	1920
Morgana, Nina	Buffalo, N.Y.	1895
Moriarty, Michael	Detroit, Mich.	1942
Morini, Erika	Vienna, Austria	1910
Morison, Patricia	New York, N.Y.	1915
Morley, Robert	Wiltshire, England	1908
Morris, Greg	Cleveland, Oh.	1934
Morris, Howard	New York, N.Y.	1919
Morrow, Vic	Bronx, N.Y.	1932
Morse, Robert	Newton, Mass.	1931
Moss, Arnold	Brooklyn, N.Y.	1911
Mostel, Zero (Sam)	Brooklyn, N.Y.	1915
Muir, Jean	New York, N.Y.	1911
Mulhall, Jack	Wappingers Falls, N.Y.	1894
Mulhare, Edward	Ireland	1923
Munsel, Patrice	Spokane, Wash.	1925
Murphy, George	New Haven, Conn.	1902
Murray, Anne	Springhill, Nova Scotia	—
Murray, Arthur	New York, N.Y.	1895
Murray, Don	Hollywood, Cal.	1929
Murray, Jan	New York, N.Y.	1917
Murray, Kathryn	Jersey City, N.J.	1906
Murray, Ken	New York, N.Y.	1903
Musante, Tony	Bridgeport, Conn.	1941

N

Name	Birthplace	Born
Nabors, Jim	Sylacauga, Ala.	1933
Natwick, Mildred	Baltimore, Md.	1908
Neal, Patricia	Packard, Ky.	1926
Neff, Hildegarde	Ulm, Germany	1925
Negri, Pola	Lipno, Poland	1899
Nelson, Barry	San Francisco, Cal.	1920
Nelson, David	New York, N.Y.	1936
Nelson, Ed	New Orleans, La.	1928
Nelson, Gene	Seattle, Wash.	1920
Nelson, Harriet (Hilliard)	Des Moines, Ia.	1914
Nelson, Ricky	Teaneck, N.J.	1940
Nero, Peter	New York, N.Y.	1934
Nesbit, Cathleen	Cheshire, England	1889
Newhart, Bob	Oak Park, Ill.	1929
Newley, Anthony	Hackney, England	1931
Newman, Barry	Boston, Mass.	1938
Newman, Paul	Cleveland, Oh.	1925
Newman, Phyllis	Jersey City, N.J.	1935
Newmar, Julie	Los Angeles, Cal.	1935
Newton, Wayne	Roanoke, Va.	1942
Newton-John, Oliva	Cambridge, England	1948
Nicholas, Denise	Detroit, Mich.	—
Nichols, Mike	Berlin, Germany	1931
Nicholson, Jack	Neptune, N.J.	1937
Nielsen, Leslie	Regina, Sask.	1926
Nilsson, Birgit	W. Karop, Sweden	1918
Nimoy, Leonard	Boston, Mass.	1931
Niven, David	Kirriemuir, Scotland	1910
Noble, Ray	Sussex, England	1908
Nolan, Doris	New York, N.Y.	1916
Nolan, Jeannette	Los Angeles, Cal.	1911
Nolan, Kathy	St. Louis, Mo.	1934
Nolan, Lloyd	San Francisco, Cal.	1902
Nolte, Nick	Omaha, Neb.	1940
North, Jay	Hollywood, Cal.	1953
North, John Ringling	Baraboo, Wis.	1903
North, Sheree	Los Angeles, Cal.	1933
Norton, Judy	Santa Monica, Cal.	1958
Novak, Kim	Chicago, Ill.	1933
Nugent, Edward	New York, N.Y.	1904

Name	Birthplace	Born
Nugent, Elliott	Dover, Oh.	1899
Nureyev, Rudolf	Russia	1938
Nuyen, France	Marseilles, France	1939
O		
Oakie, Jack	Sedalia, Mo.	1903
Oakland, Simon	New York, N.Y.	1922
Oberon, Merle	Tasmania, Australia	1911
O'Brian, Hugh	Rochester, N.Y.	1930
O'Brien, Edmond	New York, N.Y.	1915
O'Brien, George	San Francisco, Cal.	1900
O'Brien, Margaret	San Diego, Cal.	1937
O'Brien, Pat	Milwaukee, Wis.	1899
O'Connell, Arthur	New York, N.Y.	1908
O'Connell, Helen	Lima, Oh.	1920
O'Connor, Carroll	New York, N.Y.	1925
O'Connor, Donald	Chicago, Ill.	1925
Odetta	Birmingham, Ala.	1930
O'Driscoll, Martha	Tulsa, Okla.	1922
O'Hara, Jill	Warren, Pa.	1947
O'Hara, Maureen	Dublin, Ireland	1921
O'Herlihy, Dan	Wexford, Ireland	1919
O'Keefe, Walter	Hartford, Conn.	1907
Olivier, Laurence	Dorking, England	1907
O'Malley, J. Pat	Burnley, England	1901
O'Neal, Patrick	Ocala, Fla.	1927
O'Neal, Ryan	Los Angeles, Cal.	1941
O'Neal, Tatum	Los Angeles, Cal.	1963
O'Neill, Jennifer	Brazil	1949
Opatoshu, David	New York, N.Y.	1918
Orbach, Jerry	New York, N.Y.	1935
Orlando, Tony	New York, N.Y.	1944
Ormandy, Eugene	Budapest, Hungary	1899
Osmond, Donny	Ogden, Ut.	1957
Osmond, Marie	Odgen, Ut.	1959
O'Sullivan, Maureen	Boyle, Ireland	1911
O'Toole, Peter	Connemara, Ireland	1934
Owens, Buck	Sherman, Tex.	1929
Owens, Gary	Mitchell, S.D.	1936
P		
Paar, Jack	Canton, Oh.	1918
Pacino, Al	New York, N.Y.	1940
Page, Geraldine	Kirksville, Mo.	1924
Page, Patti	Claremore, Okla.	1927
Paige, Janis	Tacoma, Wash.	1923
Paige, Robert	Indianapolis, Ind.	1910
Palance, Jack	Lattimer, Pa.	1920
Palmer, Betsy	East Chicago, Ind.	1929
Palmer, Lilli	Posen, Germany	1914
Papas, Irene	Greece	1926
Papp, Joseph	Brooklyn, N.Y.	1921
Parker, Eleanor	Cedarville, Oh.	1922
Parker, Fess	Ft. Worth, Tex.	1925
Parker, Frank	New York, N.Y.	1906
Parker, Jean	Deer Lodge, Mon.	1916
Parker, Suzy	New York, N.Y.	1934
Parkins, Barbara	Vancouver, B.C.	1942
Parks, Bert	Atlanta, Ga.	1914
Parsons, Estelle	Lynn, Mass.	1927
Parton, Dolly	Sevierville, Tenn.	1946
Pasternak, Joseph	Hungary	1901
Patterson, Melody	Los Angeles, Cal.	1947
Patterson, Neva	Nevada, Ia.	1922
Paulsen, Pat	South Bend, Wash.	—
Pavan, Marisa	Cagliari, Sardinia	1932
Pavarotti, Luciano	Modena, Italy	1935
Payne, John	Roanoke, Va.	1912
Pearl, Jack	New York, N.Y.	1895
Pearl, Minnie	Centerville, Tenn.	1912
Peck, Gregory	La Jolla, Cal.	1916
Peckinpah, Sam	Fresno, Cal.	1925
Peerce, Jan	New York, N.Y.	1904
Penn, Arthur	Philadelphia, Pa.	1922
Peppard, George	Detroit, Mich.	1928
Perkins, Anthony	New York, N.Y.	1932
Perrine, Valerie	Galveston, Tex.	1943
Persoff, Nehemiah	Jerusalem	1920
Peters, Bernadette	Queens, N.Y.	1944
Peters, Brock	New York, N.Y.	1927
Peters, Jean	Canton, Oh.	1926
Peters, Roberta	New York, N.Y.	1930
Petit, Pascale	France	1937
Pettet, Joanna	London, England	1944
Piazza, Marguerite	New Orleans, La.	1926
Pickens, Jane	Macon, Ga.	—
Pickens, Slim	Kingsberg, Cal.	1919
Pickford, Mary	Toronto, Canada	1894
Picon, Molly	New York, N.Y.	1898
Pidgeon, Walter	E. St. John, N.B.	1898
Pleasance, Donald	Worksop, England	1919
Pleshette, Suzanne	New York, N.Y.	1937
Plimpton, George	New York, N.Y.	1927
Plowright, Joan	Brigg, England	1929
Plummer, Christopher	Toronto, Ont.	1929
Poitier, Sidney	Miami, Fla.	1927
Polanski, Roman	Paris, France	1933
Pollard, Michael	Passaic, N.J.	1939
Ponselle, Carmela	Schenectady, N.Y.	1892
Ponselle, Rosa	Meriden, Conn.	1897
Ponti, Carlo	Milan, Italy	1913
Poston, Tom	Columbus, Oh.	1927
Powell, Eleanor	Springfield, Mass.	1912
Powell, Jane	Portland, Ore.	1929
Powell, William	Pittsburgh, Pa.	1892
Powers, Mala	San Francisco, Cal.	1931
Powers, Stefanie	Hollywood, Cal.	1942
Preminger, Otto	Vienna, Austria	1906
Prentiss, Paula	San Antonio, Tex.	1939
Preston, Robert	Newton, Mass.	1918
Previn, Andre	Berlin, Germany	1929
Price, Leontyne	Laurel, Miss.	1927
Price, Ray	Perryville, Tex.	1926
Price, Roger	Charleston, W. Va.	1920
Price, Vincent	St. Louis, Mo.	1911
Pride, Charlie	Sledge, Miss.	1938
Prima, Louis	New Orleans, La.	1912
Prince, William	Nichols, N.Y.	1913
Provine, Dorothy	Deadwood, S. D.	1937
Prowse, Juliet	Bombay, India	1937
Pryor, Richard	Peoria, Ill.	—
Pyle, Denver	Bethune, Col.	1920
Q		
Qualen, John	Vancouver, B.C.	1899
Quayle, Anthony	Lancashire, England	1913
Quillan, Eddie	Philadelphia, Pa.	1907
Quinn, Anthony	Chihuahua, Mexico	1916
R		
Raffin, Deborah	Los Angeles, Cal.	1953
Raft, George	New York, N.Y.	1895
Rainer, Luise	Vienna, Austria	1912
Raines, Ella	Snoqualmie Falls, Wash.	1921
Raitt, John	Santa Ana, Cal.	1917
Ralston, Esther	Bar Harbor, Me.	1902
Ralston, Vera	Prague, Czechoslovakia	1921
Randall, Tony	Tulsa, Okla.	1920
Rawls, Lou	Chicago, Ill.	1935
Ray, Aldo	Pen Argyl, Pa.	1926
Ray, Johnnie	Dallas, Ore.	1927
Rayburn, Gene	Christopher, Ill.	1917
Raye, Martha	Butte, Mon.	1916
Raymond, Gene	New York, N.Y.	1908
Reddy, Helen	Melbourne, Australia	1941
Redford, Robert	Santa Monica, Cal.	1937
Redgrave, Lynn	London, England	1943
Redgrave, Michael	Bristol, England	1908
Redgrave, Vanessa	London, England	1937
Redman, Joyce	Co. Mayo, Ireland	1918
Reed, Donna	Denison, Ia.	1921
Reed, Jerry	Atlanta, Ga.	1937
Reed, Rex	Ft. Worth, Tex.	1940
Reed, Robert	Highland Park, Ill.	1932
Reese, Della	Detroit, Mich.	1932
Regan, Phil	Brooklyn, N.Y.	1906
Reid, Kate	London, England	1930
Reilly, Charles Nelson	New York, N.Y.	1931
Reiner, Carl	Bronx, N.Y.	1922
Reiner, Rob	Bronx, N.Y.	1945
Remick, Lee	Boston, Mass.	1937
Renaldo, Duncan	Camden, N.J.	1904
Resnik, Regina	New York, N.Y.	1923
Rey, Alejandro	Buenos Aires, Argentina	1930
Reynolds, Burt	Waycross, Ga.	1936
Reynolds, Debbie	El Paso, Tex.	1932
Reynolds, Marjorie	Buhl, Ida.	1921
Reynolds, William	Los Angeles, Cal.	1931
Rhodes, Hari	Cincinnati, Oh.	1932

Name	Birthplace	Born
Rich, Charlie	Forest City, Ark.	1932
Rich, Irene	Buffalo, N.Y.	1897
Richardson, Ralph	Cheltenham, England	1902
Richardson, Tony	Shipley, England	1929
Rickles, Don	New York, N.Y.	1926
Riddle, Nelson	Hackensack, N.J.	1921
Rigg, Diana	Doncaster, England	1938
Ritchard, Cyril	Sydney, Australia	1898
Ritz, Harry	Newark, N.J.	1908
Ritz, Jimmy	Newark, N.J.	1905
Rivera, Chita	Washington, D.C.	1933
Rivers, Joan	Brooklyn, N.Y.	1937
Robards, Jason Jr.	Chicago, Ill.	1922
Robbins, Jerome	New York, N.Y.	1918
Robbins, Marty	Glendale, Ariz.	1925
Robertson, Cliff	La Jolla, Cal.	1925
Robertson, Dale	Oklahoma City, Okla.	1923
Robinson, Jay	New York, N.Y.	1930
Robson, Flora	South Shields, England	1902
Rockwell, Geo. (Doc.)	Providence, R.I.	1889
Rodgers, Jimmie	Camas, Wash.	1933
Rodriquez, Johnny	Sabinal, Tex.	1951
Rogers, Chas. (Buddy)	Olathe, Kan.	1904
Rogers, Ginger	Independence, Mo.	1911
Rogers, Roy	Cincinnati, Oh.	1912
Roland, Gilbert	Juarez, Mexico	1905
Rolle, Esther	Pompano Beach, Fla.	—
Roman, Ruth	Boston, Mass.	1924
Romero, Cesar	New York, N.Y.	1907
Ronstadt, Linda	Tucson, Ariz.	1946
Rooney, Mickey	Brooklyn, N.Y.	1920
Rose Marie	New York, N.Y.	—
Ross, David	St. Paul, Minn.	1924
Ross, Diana	Detroit, Mich.	1944
Ross, Katharine	Hollywood, Cal.	1943
Ross, Lanny	Seattle, Wash.	1906
Roth, Lillian	Boston, Mass.	1910
Roundtree, Richard	New Rochelle, N.Y.	1942
Rowan, Dan	Beggs, Okla.	1922
Rowlands, Gena	Cambria, Wis.	1936
Rubin, Benny	Boston, Mass.	1899
Rubinoff, David	Grodno, Russia	1897
Rubinstein, Arthur	Lodz, Poland	1887
Rudolf, Max	Frankfurt, Germany	1902
Rule, Janice	Norwood, Oh.	1931
Rush, Barbara	Denver, Col.	1930
Russell, Jane	Bemidji, Minn.	1921
Russell, Ken	Southampton, England	1927
Russell, Nipsy	Atlanta, Ga.	1924
Rutherford, Ann	Toronto, Ont.	1924
Ryan, Peggy	Long Beach, Cal.	1924
Rydell, Bobby	Philadelphia, Pa.	1942

S

Name	Birthplace	Born
Sahl, Mort	Montreal, Que.	1927
Saint, Eva Marie	Newark, N.J.	1924
St. James, Susan	Los Angeles, Cal.	1946
St. John, Jill	Los Angeles, Cal.	1940
Sainte-Marie, Buffy	Maine	1941
Sales, Soupy	Franklinton, N.C.	1926
Sand, Paul	Los Angeles, Cal.	1941
Sands, Tommy	Chicago, Ill.	1937
Sargent, Dick	Carmel, Cal.	1933
Sarnoff, Dorothy	New York, N.Y.	1919
Sarrazin, Michael	Quebec City, Que.	1940
Savalas, Telly	Garden City, N.Y.	1927
Saxon, John	Brooklyn, N.Y.	1935
Sayao, Bidu	Rio de Janeiro, Brazil	1908
Schallert, William	Los Angeles, Cal.	1922
Schary, Dore	Newark, N.J.	1905
Scheider, Roy	Orange, N.J.	1934
Schell, Maria	Vienna, Austria	1926
Schell, Maximilian	Vienna, Austria	1930
Schenkel, Chris	Bippus, Ind.	1924
Scherman, Thomas	New York, N.Y.	1917
Schippers, Thomas	Kalamazoo, Mich.	1930
Schneider, Alexander	Vilna, Poland	1908
Schneider, Romy	Austria	1938
Schreiber, Avery	Chicago, Ill.	1935
Schuman, William	New York, N.Y.	1910
Schwarzkopf, Elisabeth	Jarotschin, Poland	1915
Scofield, Paul	Hurst, Pierpont, England	1922
Scott, George C.	Wise, Va.	1927
Scott, Hazel	Trinidad	1920
Scott, Lizabeth	Scranton, Pa.	1923

Name	Birthplace	Born
Scott, Martha	Jamesport, Mo.	1914
Scott, Randolph	Orange Co., Va.	1903
Scourby, Alexander	New York, N.Y.	1913
Sebastian, John	New York, N.Y.	1944
Seberg, Jean	Marshalltown, Ia.	1938
Sedaka, Neil	New York, N.Y.	1939
Seeger, Pete	New York, N.Y.	1919
Segal, George	Great Neck, N.Y.	1934
Segal, Vivienne	Philadelphia, Pa.	1897
Sellers, Peter	Southsea, England	1925
Serkin, Rudolf	Eger, Austria	1903
Severinsen, Doc	Arlington, Ore.	1927
Shankar, Ravi	India	1920
Sharif, Omar	Alexandria, Egypt	1932
Shatner, William	Montreal, Que.	1931
Shaw, Reta	S. Paris, Me.	1912
Shaw, Robert	Red Bluff, Cal.	1916
Shaw, Robert	West Houghton, England	1927
Shaw, Winfred	San Francisco, Cal.	1899
Shawn, Dick	Buffalo, N.Y.	1929
Shearer, Moira	Scotland	1926
Shearer, Norma	Montreal, Que.	1904
Sheen, Martin	Dayton, Oh.	1940
Sheldon, Jack	Jacksonville, Fla.	1931
Shepherd, Cybill	Memphis, Tenn.	1950
Shepherd, Jean	Chicago, Ill.	1929
Sherman, Bobby	Santa Monica, Cal.	1945
Sherwood, Roberta	St. Louis, Mo.	1913
Shirley, Ann	New York, N.Y.	1918
Shore, Dinah	Winchester, Tenn.	1921
Short, Bobby	Danville, Ill.	1936
Sidney, Sylvia	New York, N.Y.	1910
Siepi, Cesare	Milan, Italy	1923
Signoret, Simone	Wiesbaden, Germany	1921
Sills, Beverly	Brooklyn, N.Y.	1929
Silvers, Phil	Brooklyn, N.Y.	1912
Simmons, Jean	London, England	1929
Simon, Carly	New York, N.Y.	1945
Simon, Paul	New York, N.Y.	1940
Simon, Simone	Marseilles, France	1914
Simone, Nina	Tyron, N.C.	1933
Sinatra, Frank	Hoboken, N.J.	1915
Sinatra, Frank Jr.	Jersey City, N.J.	1944
Sinatra, Nancy	Jersey City, N.J.	1940
Skelton, Red (Richard)	Vincennes, Ind.	1913
Skinner, Cornelia Otis	Chicago, Ill.	1903
Slezak, Walter	Vienna, Austria	1902
Slick, Grace	Chicago, Ill.	1939
Smith, Alexis	Penticton, Canada	1921
Smith, Bob	Buffalo, N.Y.	1917
Smith, Connie	Elkhart, Ind.	1941
Smith, Ethel	Pittsburgh, Pa.	1921
Smith, Kate	Greenville, Va.	1909
Smith, Keely	Norfolk, Va.	1935
Smith, Loring	Stratford, Conn.	1900
Smith, Maggie	Ilford, England	1934
Smith, Patti	Chicago, Ill.	1946
Smith, Roger	South Gate, Cal.	1934
Smothers, Dick	New York, N.Y.	1939
Smothers, Tom	New York, N.Y.	1937
Snodgress, Carrie	Park Ridge, Ill.	1945
Snow, Hank	Nova Scotia, Canada	1914
Solti, Georg	Budapest, Hungary	1912
Somes, Michael	nr. Stroud, England	1917
Sommer, Elke	Berlin, Germany	1942
Sorvino, Paul	Brooklyn, N.Y.	1939
Sothern, Ann	Valley City, N.D.	1912
Spacek, Sissy	Quitman, Tex.	1950
Specht, Bobby	Superior, Wis.	1921
Spewack, Bella	Hungary	1899
Spivak, Lawrence	Brooklyn, N.Y.	1900
Stack, Robert	Los Angeles, Cal.	1919
Stafford, Jo	Coalinga, Cal.	1918
Stallone, Sylvester	New York, N.Y.	1946
Stamp, Terence	London, England	1940
Stang, Arnold	Chelsea, Mass.	1925
Stanley, Kim	Tularosa, N.M.	1925
Stanwyck, Barbara	Brooklyn, N.Y.	1907
Stapleton, Jean	New York, N.Y.	1923
Stapleton, Maureen	Troy, N.Y.	1925
Starr, Kay	Dougherty, Okla.	1924
Starr, Ringo	Liverpool, England	1940
Steber, Eleanor	Wheeling, W. Va.	1916
Steele, Bob	Pendleton, Ore.	1907
Steele, Karen	Hawaii	1934
Steele, Tommy	London, England	1937
Steiger, Rod	W. Hampton, N.Y.	1925

Name	Birthplace	Born
Steinberg, David	Winnipeg, Man.	1942
Sterling, Jan	New York, N.Y.	1923
Sterling, Robert	New Castle, Pa.	1917
Stern, Isaac	Kreminisey, Russia	1920
Stevens, Cat	London, England	1947
Stevens, Connie	Brooklyn, N.Y.	1938
Stevens, Kaye	Pittsburgh, Pa.	1935
Stevens, Mark	Cleveland, Oh.	1922
Stevens, Rise	New York, N.Y.	1913
Stevens, Stella	Yazoo City, Miss.	1938
Stevens, Warren	Clark's Summit, Pa.	1919
Stewart, James	Indiana, Pa.	1908
Stewart, Rod	London, England	1945
Stickney, Dorothy	Dickinson, N.D.	1903
Stockwell, Dean	Hollywood, Cal.	1936
Stokowski, Leopold	London, England	1882
Stone, Carol	New York, N.Y.	1916
Stone, Dorothy	Bensonhurst, N.Y.	1905
Stone, Ezra	New Bedford, Mass.	1917
Stone, Milburn	Burton, Kan.	1904
Stone, Paula	New York, N.Y.	1916
Storch, Larry	New York, N.Y.	1925
Storm, Gale	Bloomington, Tex.	1922
Storrs, Suzanne	Salt Lake City, Ut.	1934
Straight, Beatrice	Old Westbury, N.Y.	1918
Strasberg, Susan	New York, N.Y.	1938
Strauss, Peter	New York, N.Y.	1947
Streisand, Barbra	Brooklyn, N.Y.	1942
Stritch, Elaine	Detroit, Mich.	1928
Strode, Woody	Los Angeles, Cal.	1914
Struthers, Sally	Portland, Ore.	1948
Sullivan, Barry	New York, N.Y.	1912
Sumac, Yma	Ichocan, Peru.	1928
Susskind, David	New York, N.Y.	1920
Sutherland, Donald	New Brunswick, Canada	1934
Sutherland, Joan	Sydney, Australia	1926
Suzuki, Pat	Cressey, Cal.	1931
Swanson, Gloria	Chicago, Ill.	1899
Sweet, Blanche	Chicago, Ill.	1896
Swit, Loretta	Passaic, N.J.	—

T

Name	Birthplace	Born
Talbot, Lyle	Pittsburgh, Pa.	1902
Talbot, Nita	New York, N.Y.	1930
Tallchief, Maria	Fairfax, Okla.	1925
Tamblyn, Russ	Los Angeles, Cal.	1935
Tandy, Jessica	London, England	1909
Taylor, Elizabeth	London, England	1932
Taylor, James	Boston, Mass.	1948
Taylor, Kent	Nashua, Ia.	1907
Taylor, Rod	Sydney, Australia	1930
Tebaldi, Renata	Pesaro, Italy	1922
Temple, Shirley	Santa Monica, Cal.	1928
Terris, Norma	Columbus, Kan.	1904
Terry-Thomas	London, England	1911
Thaxter, Phillis	Portland, Me.	1921
Thebom, Blanche	Monessen, Pa.	1919
Thibault, Conrad	Northbridge, Mass.	1898
Thinnes, Roy	Chicago, Ill.	1938
Thomas, B.J.	Houston, Tex.	1942
Thomas, Danny	Deerfield, Mich.	1914
Thomas, Lowell	Woodrington, Oh.	1892
Thomas, Marlo	Detroit, Mich.	1943
Thomas, Richard	New York, N.Y.	1951
Thompson, Marshall	Peoria, Ill.	1926
Thompson, Sada	Des Moines, Ia.	1929
Thulin, Ingrid	Sweden	1929
Tierney, Gene	Brooklyn, N.Y.	1920
Tierney, Lawrence	Brooklyn, N.Y.	1919
Tiffin, Pamela	Oklahoma City, Okla.	1942
Tillis, Mel	Tampa, Fla.	1932
Tillstrom, Burr	Chicago, Ill.	1917
Tiny Tim	New York, N.Y.	—
Tobias, George	New York, N.Y.	1901
Todd, Richard	Dublin, Ireland	1919
Tomlin, Lili	Detroit, Mich.	1939
Tomlinson, David	Scotland	1917
Tompkins, Angel	Albany, Cal.	1943
Toomey, Regis	Pittsburgh, Pa.	1902
Torme, Mel	Chicago, Ill.	1925
Torn, Rip	Temple, Tex.	1931
Totter, Audrey	Joliet, Ill.	1923
Tracy, Arthur	Philadelphia, Pa.	1903
Travers, Mary	Louisville, Ky.	1936
Trevor, Claire	New York, N.Y.	1909
Truffaut, Francois	Paris, France	1932
Tucker, Forrest	Plainfield, Ind.	1919
Tucker, Orrin	St. Louis, Mo.	1911
Tucker, Tanya	Seminole, Tex.	1958
Tucker, Tommy	Souris, N.D.	1907
Turner, Ike	Clarksdale, Miss.	1934
Turner, Lana	Wallace, Ida.	1920
Turner, Tina	Brownsville, Tex.	1941
Tushingham, Rita	Liverpool, England	1942
Twiggy (Leslie Hornby)	London, England	1949
Twitty, Conway	Friar's Point, Miss.	—
Tyrell, Susan	New Canaan, Conn.	1946
Tyson, Cicely	New York, N.Y.	—

U

Name	Birthplace	Born
Uggams, Leslie	New York, N.Y.	1943
Ullmann, Liv	Tokyo, Japan	1939
Umeki, Miyoshi	Hokkaido, Japan	1929
Ustinov, Peter	London, England	1921

V

Name	Birthplace	Born
Vaccaro, Brenda	Brooklyn, N.Y.	1939
Vale, Jerry	New York, N.Y.	1931
Valente, Caterina	Italy	1931
Valentine, Karen	Santa Rosa, Cal.	1947
Vallee, Rudy	Island Pond, Vt.	1901
Valli, Alida	Pola, Italy	1921
Valli, Frankie	Newark, N.J.	1937
Vance, Vivian	Cherryvale, Kan.	1912
Van Cleef, Lee	Somerville, N.J.	1925
Van Doren, Mamie	Rowena, S.D.	1933
Van Dyke, Dick	West Plains, Mo.	1925
Van Dyke, Jerry	Danville, Ill.	1932
Van Fleet, Jo.	Oakland, Cal.	1922
Van Vooren, Monique	Brussels, Belgium	1933
Vandervere, Trish	Tenafly, N.J.	1945
Varnay, Astrid	Stockholm, Sweden	1918
Varsi, Diane	San Francisco, Cal.	1938
Vaughn, Robert	New York, N.Y.	1932
Vaughn, Sarah	Newark, N.J.	1924
Venuta, Benay	San Francisco, Cal.	1911
Vera-Ellen	Cincinnati, Oh.	1926
Verdon, Gwen	Los Angeles, Cal.	1926
Vereen, Ben	Miami, Fla.	1946
Vernon, Jackie	New York, N.Y.	1929
Vidor, King Louis	Galveston, Tex.	1895
Vigoda, Abe	New York, N.Y.	1922
Villella, Edward	Long Island, N.Y.	1936
Vincent, Jan-Michael	Ventura, Cal.	1944
Vinson, Helen	Beaumont, Tex.	1907
Vinton, Bobby	Canonsburg, Pa.	1935
Vogel, Mitch	Alhambra, Cal.	1956
Voight, Jon	Yonkers, N.Y.	1938
Von Furstenberg, Betsy	Westphalia, Germany	1932
Von Sydow, Max	Lund, Sweden	1929
Von Zell, Harry	Indianapolis, Ind.	1906
Voorhees, Donald	Allentown, Pa.	1903

W

Name	Birthplace	Born
Waggoner, Lyle	Kansas City, Kan.	1935
Wagner, Lindsay	Los Angeles, Cal.	1949
Wagner, Robert	Detroit, Mich.	1930
Wagoner, Porter	West Plains, Mo.	1927
Wain, Bea	Bronx, N.Y.	1917
Waite, Ralph	White Plains, N.Y.	1928
Walker, Clint	Hartford, Ill.	1927
Walker, Nancy	Philadelphia, Pa.	1922
Wallace, Mike	Brookline, Mass.	1918
Wallach, Eli	Brooklyn, N.Y.	1915
Wallenstein, Alfred	Chicago, Ill.	1898
Wallis, Hal	Chicago, Ill.	1899
Walston, Ray	New Orleans, La.	1918
Ward, Burt	Los Angeles, Cal.	1946
Ward, Simon	London, England	1941
Warden, Jack	Newark, N.J.	1920
Warfield, William	Helena, Ark.	1920
Warhol, Andy	Cleveland, Oh.	1931
Waring, Fred	Tyrone, Pa.	1900
Warner, David	Manchester, England	1941
Warwicke, Dionne	E. Orange, N.J.	1941
Waters, Ethel	Chester, Pa.	1900
Watts, Andre	Germany	1946
Wayne, David	Traverse City, Mich.	1914
Wayne, John	Winterset, Ia.	1907

Name	Birthplace	Born
Weaver, Dennis	Joplin, Mo.	1924
Weaver, Fritz	Pittsburgh, Pa.	1926
Webb, Jack	Santa Monica, Cal.	1920
Weissmuller, Johnny	Windber, Pa.	1904
Welch, Raquel	Chicago, Ill.	1942
Weld, Tuesday	New York, N.Y.	1943
Welk, Lawrence	nr. Strasburg, N.D.	1903
Welles, Orson	Kenosha, Wis.	1915
Wells, Kitty	Nashville, Tenn.	1919
Werner, Oskar	Vienna, Austria	1922
West, Adam	Walla Walla, Wash.	1929
West, Mae	Brooklyn, N.Y.	1892
Whitaker, Johnny	Van Nuys, Cal.	1959
White, Barry	Galveston, Tex.	1944
White, Jesse	Buffalo, N.Y.	1919
Whiting, Margaret	Detroit, Mich.	1924
Whitman, Stuart	San Francisco, Cal.	1936
Whitmore, James	White Plains, N.Y.	1921
Widmark, Richard	Sunrise, Minn.	1914
Wilcoxon, Henry	British West Indies	1905
Wilde, Cornel	New York, N.Y.	1918
Wilder, Billy	Vienna, Austria	1906
Wilder, Gene	Milwaukee, Wis.	1935
Wilding, Michael	Essex, England	1912
Williams, Andy	Wall Lake, Ia.	1930
Williams, Cindy	Van Nuys, Cal.	—
Williams, Clarence	New York, N.Y.	1946
Williams, Emlyn	Mostyn, Wales	1905
Williams, Esther	Los Angeles, Cal.	1923
Williams, Joe	Cordele, Ga.	1918
Williams, Mason	Abilene, Tex.	1938
Williams, Paul	Omaha, Neb.	1940
Williams, Roger	Omaha, Neb.	1926
Williamson, Fred	Gary, Ind.	1937
Williamson, Nicol	Hamilton, Scotland	1936
Wills, Chill	Seagoville, Tex.	1903
Wilson, Demond	Valdosta, Ga.	—
Wilson, Dolores	Philadelphia, Pa.	1929
Wilson, Don	Lincoln, Neb.	1900
Wilson, Flip	Jersey City, N.J.	1933
Wilson, Julie	Omaha, Neb.	1924
Wilson, Nancy	Chillicothe, Oh.	1937
Winchell, Paul	New York, N.Y.	1922
Windom, William	New York, N.Y.	1923
Winkler, Henry	New York, N.Y.	1945
Winters, Jonathan	Dayton, Oh.	1925
Winters, Shelley	St. Louis, Mo.	1922
Winwood, Estelle	Lee, England	1884
Wiseman, Joseph	Montreal, Que.	1918
Withers, Jane	Atlanta, Ga.	1927
Wonder, Stevie	Saginaw, Mich.	1950
Wood, Helen	Clarksville, Tenn.	1937
Wood, Natalie	San Francisco, Cal.	1938
Wood, Peggy	Brooklyn, N.Y.	1892
Woodward, Joanne	Thomasville, Ga.	1930
Worley, Jo Anne	Lowell, Ind.	1937
Worth, Irene	Nebraska	1916
Wray, Fay	Alberta, Canada	1907
Wright, Martha	Seattle, Wash.	1926
Wright, Teresa	New York, N.Y.	1919
Wrightson, Earl	Baltimore, Md.	1916
Wyatt, Jane	Campgaw, N.J.	1912
Wyler, William	Mulhouse, France	1902
Wyman, Jane	St. Joseph, Mo.	1914
Wynette, Tammy	Red Bay, Ala.	1942
Wynn, Keenan	New York, N.Y.	1916
Wynter, Dana	London, England	1930
Y		
Yarborough, Glenn	Milwaukee, Wis.	1930
Yarrow, Peter	New York, N.Y.	1938
York, Dick	Ft. Wayne, Ind.	1928
York, Michael	Fulmer, England	1942
York, Susannah	London, England	1942
Young, Alan	Northumberland, England	1919
Young, Gig	St. Cloud, Minn.	1917
Young, Loretta	Salt Lake City, Ut.	1913
Young, Robert	Chicago, Ill.	1907
Young, Stephen	Toronto, Ont.	1939
Youngman, Henny	Liverpool, England	1906
Z		
Zanuck, Darryl F.	Wahoo, Neb.	1902
Zimbalist, Efrem	Rostov, Russia	1889
Zimbalist, Efrem Jr.	New York, N.Y.	1923
Zimmer, Norma	Larsen, Ida.	—
Zorina, Vera	Berlin, Germany	1917

Entertainment Personalities of the Past

Born	Died	Name
		A
1896	1974	Abbott, Bud
1872	1953	Adams, Maude
1931	1968	Adams, Nick
1855	1926	Adler, Jacob P.
1898	1933	Adoree, Renee
1909	1964	Albertson, Frank
1885	1952	Alda, Frances
1894	1956	Allen, Fred
1906	1964	Allen, Gracie
1883	1950	Allgood, Sara
1882	1971	Anderson, Gilbert (Bronco Billy)
1886	1954	Anderson, John Murray
1915	1967	Andrews, Laverne
1933	1971	Angeli, Pier
1876	1958	Anglin, Margaret
1887	1933	Arbuckle, Fatty (Roscoe)
1900	1976	Arlen, Richard
1868	1946	Arliss, George
1900	1971	Armstrong, Louis
1890	1956	Arnold, Edward
1905	1974	Arquette, Cliff (Charlie Weaver)
1885	1946	Atwill, Lionel
1845	1930	Auer, Leopold
1905	1967	Auer, Mischa
1900	1972	Austin, Gene
1898	1940	Ayres, Agnes
		B
1864	1922	Bacon, Frank
1903	1951	Bailey, Mildred
1893	1968	Bainter, Fay
1895	1957	Baker, Belle
1906	1975	Baker, Josephine
1898	1963	Baker, Phil
1882	1956	Bancroft, George
1903	1968	Bankhead, Tallulah
1890	1952	Banks, Leslie
1897	1950	Banks, Monty
1890	1955	Bara, Theda
1810	1891	Barnum, Phineas T.
1879	1959	Barrymore, Ethel
1882	1942	Barrymore, John
1878	1954	Barrymore, Lionel
1848	1905	Barrymore, Maurice
1897	1963	Barthelmess, Richard
1890	1962	Barton, James
1873	1951	Bauer, Harold
1893	1951	Baxter, Warner
1880	1928	Bayes, Nora
1904	1965	Beatty, Clyde
1904	1962	Beavers, Louise
1887	1955	Beecher, Janet
1884	1946	Beery, Noah
1889	1949	Beery, Wallace
1901	1970	Begley, Ed.
1854	1931	Belasco, David
1906	1968	Benaderet, Bea
1906	1964	Bendix, William
1905	1965	Bennett, Constance
1873	1944	Bennett, Richard
1894	1974	Benny, Jack
1924	1970	Benzell, Mimi
1867	1944	Beresford, Harry
1899	1966	Berg, Gertrude
1895	1976	Berkeley, Busby
1863	1927	Bernard, Sam
1844	1923	Bernhardt, Sarah
1893	1943	Bernie, Ben
1889	1967	Bickford, Charles
1911	1960	Bjoerling, Jussi
1898	1973	Blackmer, Sidney
1882	1951	Blaney, Charles E.
1900	1943	Bledsoe, Jules
1928	1972	Blocker, Dan
1888	1959	Blore, Eric
1901	1975	Blue, Ben
1899	1957	Bogart, Humphrey
1885	1965	Boland, Mary
1897	1969	Boles, John
1903	1960	Bond, Ward
1833	1893	Booth, Edwin
1796	1852	Booth, Junius Brutus
1894	1953	Bordoni, Irene
1888	1960	Bori, Lucrezia
1867	1943	Bosworth, Hobart
1905	1965	Bow, Clara
1874	1946	Bowes, Maj. Edward
1895	1972	Boyd, William
1893	1939	Brady, Alice
1863	1950	Brady, William A.
1871	1936	Breese, Edmund
1898	1964	Brendel, El
1901	1948	Breneman, Tom
1894	1974	Brennan, Walter
1875	1948	Brian, Donald
1891	1951	Brice, Fanny
1891	1959	Broderick, Helen
1898	1965	Brokenshire, Norman
1904	1951	Bromberg, J. Edward
1892	1973	Brown, Joe E.

Born	Died	Name
1926	1966	Bruce, Lenny
1895	1953	Bruce, Nigel
1891	1957	Buchanan, Jack
1886	1957	Buck, Gene
1904	1965	Bunce, Alan
1863	1915	Bunny, John
1885	1970	Burke, Billie
1912	1967	Burnette, Smiley
1896	1956	Burns, Bob
1902	1971	Burns, David
1882	1941	Burr, Henry
1883	1966	Bushman, Francis X.
1896	1946	Butterworth, Charles
1893	1971	Byington, Spring

C

Born	Died	Name
1905	1972	Cabot, Bruce
1895	1956	Calhern, Louis
1858	1942	Calve, Emma
1933	1976	Cambridge, Godfrey
1865	1940	Campbell, Mrs. Patrick
1892	1964	Cantor, Eddie
1878	1947	Carey, Harry
1876	1941	Carle, Richard
1897	1954	Carney, "Uncle Don"
1880	1961	Carrillo, Leo
1892	1972	Carroll, Leo G.
1905	1965	Carroll, Nancy
1910	1963	Carson, Jack
1862	1937	Carter, Mrs. Leslie
1873	1921	Caruso, Enrico
1876	1973	Casals, Pablo
1894	1969	Castle, Irene
1887	1918	Castle, Vernon
1889	1960	Catlett, Walter
1874	1944	Cavalieri, Lina
1887	1950	Cavanaugh, Hobart
1873	1938	Chaliapin, Feodor
1919	1961	Chandler, Jeff
1883	1930	Chaney, Lon
1906	1973	Chaney Jr., Lon
1893	1940	Chase, Charlie
1893	1961	Chatterton, Ruth
1888	1971	Chevalier, Maurice
1888	1960	Clark, Bobby
1914	1968	Clark, Fred
1887	1950	Clayton, Lou
1920	1966	Clift, Montgomery
1932	1963	Cline, Patsy
1900	1937	Clive, Colin
1892	1967	Clyde, Andy
1911	1976	Cobb, Lee J.
1877	1961	Coburn, Charles
1887	1934	Cody, Lew
1878	1942	Cohan, George M.
1876	1916	Cohan, Josephine
1919	1965	Cole, Nat (King)
1878	1955	Collier, Constance
1866	1944	Collier, William Sr.
1890	1965	Collins, Ray
1891	1958	Colman, Ronald
1908	1934	Columbo, Russ
1907	1944	Compton, Betty
1887	1940	Connolly, Walter
1855	1909	Conried, Henrich
1918	1975	Conte, Richard
1904	1967	Conway, Tom
1901	1961	Cook, Donald
1890	1959	Cook, Joe
1893	1958	Cook, Phil
1901	1961	Cooper, Gary
1891	1971	Cooper, Gladys
1896	1973	Cooper, Melville
1914	1968	Corey, Wendell
1893	1974	Cornell, Katherine
1890	1972	Correll, Charles (Andy)
1876	1951	Cossart, Ernest
1904	1957	Costello, Helene
1906	1959	Costello, Lou
1877	1950	Costello, Maurice
1899	1973	Coward, Noel
1890	1950	Cowl, Jane
1924	1973	Cox, Wally
1847	1924	Crabtree, Lotta
1875	1945	Craven, Frank
1908	1977	Crawford, Joan
1916	1944	Cregar, Laird
1880	1942	Crews, Laura Hope
1880	1974	Crisp, Donald
1943	1973	Croce, Jim
1910	1960	Cromwell, Richard
1897	1975	Cross, Milton
1893	1966	Crouse, Russell
1878	1968	Currie, Finlay
1816	1876	Cushman, Charlotte

D

Born	Died	Name
1924	1965	Dandridge, Dorothy
1869	1941	Danforth, William
1894	1963	Daniell, Henry
1901	1971	Daniels, Bebe
1860	1935	Daniels, Frank
1936	1973	Darin, Bobby
1921	1965	Darnell, Linda
1879	1967	Darwell, Jane
1866	1949	Davenport, Harry
1900	1961	Davies, Marion
1908	1961	Davis, Joan
1931	1955	Dean, James
1881	1950	DeCordoba, Pedro
1905	1968	Dekker, Albert
1898	1965	Demarco, Tony
1881	1959	DeMille, Cecil B.
1891	1967	Denny, Reginald
1902	1974	DeSica, Vittorio
1878	1949	Desmond, William
1878	1930	Destinn, Emmy
1905	1977	Devine, Andy
1942	1972	De Wilde, Brandon
1907	1974	De Wolfe, Billy
1865	1950	De Wolfe, Elsie
1879	1947	Digges, Dudley
1890	1944	Dinehart, Alan
1901	1966	Disney, Walt
1895	1949	Dix, Richard
1856	1924	Dockstader, Lew
1892	1941	Dolly, Jennie
1892	1970	Dolly, Rosie
1905	1958	Donat, Robert
1903	1972	Donlevy, Brian
1907	1959	Douglas, Paul
1889	1956	Draper, Ruth
1881	1965	Dresser, Louise
1869	1934	Dressler, Marie
1820	1897	Drew, Mrs. John
1853	1927	Drew, John (son)
1879	1920	Drew, Sydney
1909	1951	Duchin, Eddy
1940	1971	Duel, Peter
1890	1965	Dumont, Margaret
1877	1927	Duncan, Isadora
1905	1967	Dunn, James
1873	1947	Dupree, Minnie
1907	1968	Duryea, Dan
1859	1924	Duse, Eleanora

E

Born	Died	Name
1894	1929	Eagels, Jeanne
1896	1930	Eames, Clare
1865	1952	Eames, Emma
1901	1967	Eddy, Nelson
1894	1971	Edwards, Cliff
1879	1945	Edwards, Gus
1899	1974	Ellington, Duke
1941	1974	Elliot, Cass
1871	1940	Elliott, Maxine
1891	1967	Elman, Mischa
1881	1951	Errol, Leon
1903	1967	Erwin, Stuart
1888	1976	Evans, Edith
1913	1967	Evelyn, Judith

F

Born	Died	Name
1883	1939	Fairbanks, Douglas
1915	1970	Farmer, Frances
1870	1929	Farnum, Dustin
1876	1953	Farnum, William
1882	1967	Farrar, Geraldine
1904	1971	Farrell, Glenda
1868	1940	Faversham, William
1861	1939	Fawcett, George
1897	1960	Fay, Frank
1895	1962	Fazenda, Louise
1903	1971	Fernandel
1918	1973	Field, Betty
1867	1941	Fields, Lew
1879	1946	Fields, W. C.
1916	1977	Finch, Peter
1902	1975	Fine, Larry
1865	1932	Fiske, Minnie Maddern
1888	1961	Fitzgerald, Barry
1874	1941	Fitzgerald, Cissy
1895	1962	Flagstad, Kirsten
1900	1971	Flippen, Jay C.
1909	1959	Flynn, Errol
1925	1974	Flynn, Joe
1880	1942	Fokine, Michel
1910	1968	Foley, Red
1905	1951	Forbes, Ralph
1853	1937	Forbes-Robertson, J.
1887	1970	Ford, Ed (Senator)
1895	1973	Ford, John
1901	1976	Ford, Paul
1899	1965	Ford, Wallace
1806	1872	Forrest, Edwin
1904	1970	Foster, Preston
1854	1928	Foy, Eddie
1905	1968	Francis, Kay
1893	1966	Frawley, William
1885	1938	Frederick, Pauline
1870	1955	Friganza, Trixie
1890	1958	Frisco, Joe
1860	1915	Frohman, Charles
1851	1940	Frohman, Daniel
1885	1947	Fyffe, Will

G

Born	Died	Name
1901	1960	Gable, Clark
1889	1963	Galli-Curci, Amelita
1877	1967	Garden, Mary
1913	1952	Garfield, John
1922	1969	Garland, Judy
1893	1963	Gaxton, William
1904	1954	George, Gladys
1879	1961	George, Grace
1892	1962	Gibson, Hoot
1890	1957	Gigli, Beniamino
1894	1971	Gilbert, Billy
1897	1936	Gilbert, John
1855	1937	Gillette, William
1867	1943	Gillmore, Frank
1879	1939	Gilpin, Charles
1898	1968	Gish, Dorothy
1886	1959	Gleason, James
1884	1938	Gluck, Alma
1874	1955	Golden, John
1882	1974	Goldwyn, Samuel
1917	1969	Gorcey, Leo
1884	1940	Gordon, C. Henry
1887	1948	Gordon, Vera
1869	1944	Gottschalk, Ferdinand
1829	1869	Gottschalk, Louis
1916	1973	Grable, Betty
1901	1959	Gray, Gilda
1879	1954	Greenstreet, Sydney
1874	1948	Griffith, David Wark
1885	1957	Guitry, Sacha
1912	1967	Guthrie, Woody
1875	1959	Gwenn, Edmund

H

Born	Died	Name
1888	1942	Hackett, Charles
1902	1958	Hackett, Raymond
1870	1943	Haines, Robert T.
1892	1950	Hale, Alan
1847	1919	Hammerstein, Oscar
1895	1960	Hammerstein, Oscar 2d
1879	1955	Hampden, Walter
1924	1964	Haney, Carol
1893	1964	Hardwicke, Sir Cedric
1892	1957	Hardy, Oliver
1883	1939	Hare, T. E. (Ernie)
1911	1937	Harlow, Jean
1872	1946	Harned, Virginia
1844	1911	Harrigan, Edward
1895	1943	Hart, Lorenz
1870	1946	Hart, William S.
1907	1955	Hartman, Grace
1928	1973	Harvey, Laurence
1876	1945	Harwood, John
1910	1973	Hawkins, Jack
1890	1973	Hayakawa, Sessue
1885	1969	Hayes, Gabby
1902	1971	Hayward, Leland
1919	1975	Hayward, Susan
1896	1937	Healy, Ted
1910	1971	Heflin, Van

Born	Died	Name
1879	1936	Heggie, O. P.
1873	1918	Held, Anna
1903	1947	Hellinger, Mark
1885	1955	Hempel, Frieda
1943	1970	Hendrix, Jimi
1913	1969	Henie, Sonja
1879	1942	Herbert, Henry
1887	1951	Herbert, Hugh
1886	1956	Hersholt, Jean
1895	1942	Hibbard, Edna
1865	1929	Hitchcock, Raymond
1914	1955	Hodiak, John
1876	1957	Hofmann, Josef
1894	1973	Holden, Fay
1923	1965	Holliday, Judy
1936	1959	Holly, Buddy
1888	1951	Holt, Jack
1871	1947	Homer, Louise
1902	1973	Hopkins, Miriam
1858	1935	Hopper, DeWolf
1874	1959	Hopper, Edna Wallace
1890	1966	Hopper, Hedda
1916	1970	Hopper, William
1888	1970	Horton, Edward Everett
1874	1926	Houdini, Harry
1881	1965	Howard, Eugene
1867	1961	Howard, Joe
1893	1943	Howard, Leslie
1897	1975	Howard, Moe
1886	1955	Howard, Tom
1886	1949	Howard, Willie
1914	1972	Hudson, Rochelle
1890	1977	Hull, Henry
1886	1957	Hull, Josephine
1907	1967	Hume, Benita
1895	1958	Humphrey, Doris
1895	1945	Hunter, Glenn
1925	1969	Hunter, Jeffrey
1901	1962	Husing, Ted
1884	1950	Huston, Walter

I

Born	Died	Name
1892	1950	Ingram, Rex
1895	1969	Ingram, Rex
1838	1905	Irving, Henry
1871	1944	Irving, Isabel
1872	1914	Irving, Laurence
1862	1938	Irwin, May

J

Born	Died	Name
1875	1942	Jackson, Joe
1911	1972	Jackson, Mahalia
1889	1956	Janis, Elsie
1886	1950	Jannings, Emil
1829	1905	Jefferson, Joseph
1859	1923	Jefferson, Thomas
1900	1974	Jenkins, Allen
1862	1930	Jewett, Henry
1892	1962	Johnson, Chic
1878	1952	Johnson, Edward
1886	1950	Jolson, Al
1899	1940	Jones, Billy
1889	1942	Jones, Buck
1911	1965	Jones, Spike
1943	1970	Joplin, Janis
1897	1961	Jordan, Marian (Molly McGee)
1890	1955	Joyce, Alice

K

Born	Died	Name
1878	1965	Kaltenborn, Hans V.
1910	1966	Kane, Helen
1887	1969	Karloff, Boris
1893	1970	Karns, Roscoe
1811	1868	Kean, Charles
1806	1880	Kean, Mrs. Charles
1787	1833	Kean, Edmund
1895	1966	Keaton, Buster
1858	1929	Keenan, Frank
1830	1873	Keene, Laura
1841	1898	Keene, Thomas W.
1899	1960	Keith, Ian
1894	1973	Kellaway, Cecil
1899	1956	Kelly, Paul
1873	1939	Kelly, Walter C.
1909	1968	Kelton, Pert
1823	1895	Kemble, Agnes
1775	1854	Kemble, Charles
1809	1893	Kemble, Fannie
1848	1935	Kendal, Dame Madge
1843	1917	Kendal, William H.
1926	1959	Kendall, Kay
1890	1948	Kennedy, Edgar
1885	1965	Kennedy, Tom
1886	1945	Kent, William
1880	1947	Kerrigan, J. Warren
1886	1956	Kibbee, Guy
1902	1966	Kiepura, Jan
1888	1964	Kilbride, Percy
1863	1933	Kilgour, Joseph
1894	1944	King, Charles
1897	1971	King, Dennis
1889	1938	Kohler, Fred
1897	1957	Korngold, Erich W.
1919	1962	Kovacs, Ernie
1885	1974	Kruger, Otto
1909	1973	Krupa, Gene

L

Born	Died	Name
1913	1964	Ladd, Alan
1895	1967	Lahr, Bert
1919	1973	Lake, Veronica
1904	1948	Landi, Elissa
1919	1948	Landis, Carole
1904	1972	Landis, Jessie Royce
1884	1944	Langdon, Harry
1856	1929	Langtry, Lillian
1921	1959	Lanza, Mario
1881	1958	Lasky, Jesse L.
1870	1950	Lauder, Harry
1899	1962	Laughton, Charles
1890	1965	Laurel, Stan
1892	1954	Laurie Jr., Joe
1898	1952	Lawrence, Gertrude
1890	1929	Lawrence, Margaret
1907	1952	Lee, Canada
1914	1970	Lee, Gypsy Rose
1848	1929	Lehmann, Lilli
1888	1976	Lehmann, Lotte
1896	1950	Lehr, Lew
1913	1967	Leigh, Vivien
1852	1908	Leighton, Margaret
1922	1976	Leighton, Margaret
1894	1931	Leitzel, Lillian
1831	1905	Lemoyne, W. J.
1870	1941	Leonard, Eddie
1911	1973	Leonard, Jack E.
1906	1972	Levant, Oscar
1881	1955	Levy, Ethel
1902	1971	Lewis, Joe E.
1891	1971	Lewis, Ted
1874	1944	Lhevinne, Josef
1889	1952	Lincoln, Elmo
1820	1887	Lind, Jenny
1889	1968	Lindsay, Howard
1869	1952	Lipman, Clara
1889	1971	Lloyd, Harold
1876	1922	Lloyd, Marie
1891	1957	Lockhart, Gene
1876	1943	Loftus, Cissie (Marie)
1913	1969	Logan, Ella
1909	1942	Lombard, Carole
1927	1974	Long, Richard
1895	1975	Lopez, Vincent
1890	1950	Lord, Pauline
1888	1968	Lorne, Marion
1904	1964	Lorre, Peter
1917	1970	Louise, Anita
1914	1962	Lovejoy, Frank
1892	1971	Lowe, Edmund
1892	1947	Lubitsch, Ernst
1885	1956	Lugosi, Bela
1895	1971	Lukas, Paul
1853	1932	Lupino, George
1893	1942	Lupino, Stanley
1897	1957	Lyman, Abe
1926	1971	Lynn, Diana
1885	1954	Lytell, Bert
1867	1936	Lytton, Henry

M

Born	Died	Name
1907	1965	MacDonald, Jeanette
1902	1969	MacLane, Barton
1909	1973	Macready, George
1861	1946	Macy, George Carleton
1908	1973	Magnani, Anna
1896	1967	Mahoney, Will
1890	1975	Main, Marjorie
1933	1967	Mansfield, Jayne
1857	1907	Mansfield, Richard
1897	1975	March, Fredric
1920	1970	March, Hal
1865	1950	Marlowe, Julia
1890	1966	Marshall, Herbert
1864	1943	Marshall, Tully
1885	1969	Martinelli, Giovanni
1888	1964	Marx, Arthur (Harpo)
1887	1961	Marx, Leonard (Chico)
1862	1951	Maude, Cyril
1922	1972	Maxwell, Marilyn
1879	1948	May, Edna
1885	1957	Mayer, Louis B.
1895	1973	Maynard, Ken
1884	1945	McCormack, John
1907	1962	McCormick, Myron
1888	1931	McCoy, Bessie
1883	1936	McCullough, Paul
1895	1952	McDaniel, Hattie
1924	1965	McDonald, Marie
1913	1975	McGiver, John
1879	1949	McIntyre, Frank J.
1857	1937	McIntyre, James
1879	1937	McKinley, Mabel
1886	1959	McLaglen, Victor
1907	1971	McMahon, Horace
1880	1946	Meek, Donald
1879	1936	Meighan, Thomas
1861	1931	Melba, Nellie
1890	1973	Melchior, Lauritz
1904	1961	Melton, James
1890	1963	Menjou, Adolphe
1902	1966	Menken, Helen
1882	1939	Mercer, Beryl
1880	1946	Merivale, Phillip
1904	1944	Miller, Glenn
1860	1926	Miller, Henry
1898	1936	Miller, Marilyn
1895	1927	Mills, Florence
1939	1976	Mineo, Sal
1903	1955	Minnevitch, Borrah
1917	1955	Miranda, Carmen
1875	1957	Mitchell, Grant
1892	1962	Mitchell, Thomas
1880	1940	Mix, Tom
1845	1909	Modjeska, Helena
1926	1962	Monroe, Marilyn
1912	1973	Monroe, Vaughn
1875	1964	Monteux, Pierre
1824	1861	Montez, Lola
1919	1951	Montez, Maria
1903	1947	Moore, Grace
1885	1955	Moore, Tom
1876	1962	Moore, Victor
1906	1974	Moorehead, Agnes
1882	1949	Moran, George
1884	1952	Moran, Polly
1890	1949	Morgan, Frank
1900	1941	Morgan, Helen
1888	1956	Morgan, Ralph
1901	1970	Morris, Chester
1849	1925	Morris, Clara
1914	1959	Morris, Wayne
1943	1971	Morrison, Jim
1897	1969	Mowbray, Alan
1897	1967	Muni, Paul
1894	1953	Munn, Frank
1906	1955	Munson, Ona
1924	1971	Murphy, Audie
1885	1965	Murray, Mae

N

Born	Died	Name
1897	1970	Nagel, Conrad
1900	1973	Naish, J. Carrol
1898	1961	Naldi, Nita
1888	1950	Nash, Florence
1865	1945	Nash, George
1879	1945	Nazimova, Alla
1846	1905	Neilson, Ada
1848	1880	Neilson, Adelaide
1868	1957	Neilson-Terry, Julia
1907	1975	Nelson, Ozzie
1885	1967	Nesbit, Evelyn
1870	1951	Nethersole, Olga
1905	1956	Newton, Robert
1874	1948	Niblo, Fred
1890	1950	Nijinsky, Vaslav
1893	1974	Nilsson, Anna Q.

Born	Died	Name
1898	1930	Normand, Mabel
1879	1959	Norworth, Jack
1905	1968	Novarro, Ramon
1893	1951	Novello, Ivor

O

Born	Died	Name
1860	1926	Oakley, Annie
1898	1943	O'Connell, Hugh
1881	1959	O'Connor, Una
1878	1945	O'Hara, Fiske
1908	1968	O'Keefe, Dennis
1880	1938	Oland, Warner
1860	1932	Olcott, Chauncey
1885	1942	Oliver, Edna May
1892	1963	Olsen, Ole
1847	1920	O'Neill, James
1887	1949	Ouspenskaya, Maria
1887	1972	Owen, Reginald

P

Born	Died	Name
1860	1941	Paderewski, Ignace
1889	1954	Pallette, Eugene
1894	1958	Pangborn, Franklin
1914	1975	Parks, Larry
1881	1972	Parsons, Louella
1881	1940	Pasternack, Josef A.
1837	1908	Pastor, Tony
1843	1919	Patti, Adelina
1840	1889	Patti, Carlotta
1885	1931	Pavlova, Anna
1899	1973	Paxinou, Katina
1917	1966	Pearce, Alice
1885	1950	Pemberton, Brock
1899	1967	Pendleton, Nat
1904	1941	Penner, Joe
1892	1937	Perkins, Osgood
1893	1956	Peters, Brandon
1915	1963	Piaf, Edith
1893	1957	Pinza, Ezio
1900	1963	Pitts, Zasu
1904	1976	Pons, Lili
1903	1969	Portman, Eric
1904	1963	Powell, Dick
1869	1931	Power, F. Tyrone
1914	1958	Power, Tyrone E.
1872	1935	Powers, Eugene
1935	1977	Presley, Elvis
1900	1964	Price, George E.
1856	1919	Primrose, George
1954	1977	Prinze, Freddie
1879	1956	Prouty, Jed
1871	1942	Pryor, Arthur
1925	1970	Pyne, Joe

R

Born	Died	Name
1906	1946	Ragland, John (Rags)
1890	1967	Rains, Claude
1889	1970	Rambeau, Marjorie
1900	1947	Rankin, Arthur
1892	1967	Rathbone, Basil
1897	1960	Ratoff, Gregory
1883	1953	Rawlinson, Herbert
1891	1943	Ray, Charles
1941	1967	Redding, Otis
1860	1916	Rehan, Ada
1893	1923	Reid, Wallace
1873	1943	Reinhardt, Max
1909	1971	Rennie, Michael
1870	1940	Richman, Charles
1895	1972	Richman, Harry
1872	1961	Ring, Blanche
1888	1958	Risdon, Elizabeth
1907	1974	Ritter, Tex
1905	1969	Ritter, Thelma
1903	1966	Ritz, Al
1898	1976	Robeson, Paul
1878	1949	Robinson, Bill
1893	1973	Robinson, Edward G.
1865	1942	Robson, May
1905	1977	Rochester (E. Anderson)
1897	1933	Rodgers, Jimmy
1894	1958	Rodzinsky, Artur
1879	1935	Rogers, Will
1897	1937	Roland, Ruth
1880	1962	Rooney, Pat
1899	1966	Rose, Billy
1882	1936	Rothafel, S. L. (Roxy)
1878	1953	Ruffo, Titta
1892	1970	Ruggles, Charles

Born	Died	Name
1864	1936	Russell, Annie
1924	1961	Russell, Gail
1861	1922	Russell, Lillian
1911	1976	Russell, Rosalind
1892	1972	Rutherford, Margaret
1902	1973	Ryan, Irene
1909	1973	Ryan, Robert

S

Born	Died	Name
1877	1968	St. Denis, Ruth
1884	1955	Sakall, S.Z.
1885	1936	Sale (Chic), Charles
1906	1972	Sanders, George
1934	1973	Sands, Diana
1896	1960	Savo, Jimmy
1879	1954	Scheff, Fritzi
1892	1930	Schenck, Joe
1895	1964	Schildkraut, Joseph
1865	1930	Schildkraut, Rudolph
1889	1965	Schipa, Tito
1882	1951	Schnabel, Artur
1910	1949	Schumann, Henrietta
1861	1936	Schumann-Heink, E.
1866	1945	Scott, Cyril
1914	1965	Scott, Zachary
1843	1896	Scott-Siddons, Mrs.
1892	1974	Seeley, Blossom
1902	1965	Selznick, David O.
1858	1935	Sembrich, Marcella
1884	1960	Sennett, Mack
1881	1951	Shattuck, Arthur
1860	1929	Shaw, Mary
1891	1972	Shawn, Ted
1868	1949	Shean, Al
1915	1967	Sheridan, Ann
1924	1973	Sherman, Allan
1885	1934	Sherman, Lowell
1918	1970	Shriner, Herb
1883	1953	Shubert, Lee
1755	1831	Siddons, Mrs. Sarah
1882	1930	Sills, Milton
1914	1970	Silvera, Frank
1900	1976	Sim, Alastair
1878	1946	Sis Hopkins (Melville)
1891	1934	Skelly, Hal
1858	1942	Skinner, Otis
1870	1952	Skipworth, Alison
1892	1970	Skulnik, Menasha
1863	1948	Smith, C. Aubrey
1826	1881	Sothern, Edward A.
1859	1933	Sothern, Edward H.
1884	1957	Sothern, Harry
1854	1932	Sousa, John Philip
1884	1957	Sparks, Ned
1876	1948	Speaks, Oley
1890	1970	Spitalny, Phil
1873	1937	Standing, Guy
1871	1956	Stephenson, Henry
1900	1941	Stephenson, James
1883	1939	Sterling, Ford
1882	1928	Stevens, Emily A.
1934	1970	Stevens, Inger
1896	1961	Stewart, Anita
1873	1959	Stone, Fred
1879	1953	Stone, Lewis
1871	1954	Straus, Oskar
1911	1960	Sullavan, Margaret
1902	1974	Sullivan, Ed
1903	1956	Sullivan, Francis L.
1892	1946	Summerville, Slim
1904	1969	Swarthout, Gladys

T

Born	Died	Name
1897	1957	Talmadge, Norma
1917	1968	Talman, William
1900	1972	Tamiroff, Akim
1878	1947	Tanguay, Eva
1899	1934	Tashman, Lilyan
1885	1966	Taylor, Deems
1899	1958	Taylor, Estelle
1887	1946	Taylor, Laurette
1911	1969	Taylor, Robert
1878	1938	Tearle, Conway
1884	1953	Tearle, Godfrey
1892	1937	Tell, Alma
1881	1934	Tellegen, Lou
1864	1942	Tempest, Marie
1910	1963	Templeton, Alec
1848	1928	Terry, Ellen

Born	Died	Name
1874	1940	Tetrazzini, Luisa
1899	1936	Thalberg, Irving
1857	1914	Thomas, Brandon
1892	1960	Thomas, John Charles
1882	1976	Thorndike, Sybil
1869	1936	Thurston, Howard
1896	1960	Tibbett, Lawrence
1887	1940	Tinney, Frank
1909	1958	Todd, Michael
1906	1935	Todd, Thelma
1874	1947	Toler, Sidney
1905	1968	Tone, Franchot
1878	1933	Torrence, Ernest
1867	1957	Toscanini, Arturo
1898	1968	Tracy, Lee
1900	1967	Tracy, Spencer
1903	1972	Traubel, Helen
1894	1975	Treacher, Arthur
1853	1917	Tree, Herbert Beerbohm
1890	1973	Truex, Ernest
1883	1942	Tucker, Richard
1915	1975	Tucker, Richard
1884	1966	Tucker, Sophie
1911	1970	Tufts, Sonny
1874	1940	Turpin, Ben
1908	1959	Twelvetrees, Helen

U

Born	Died	Name
1894	1970	Ulric, Lenore
1933	1975	Ure, Mary

V

Born	Died	Name
1895	1926	Valentino, Rudolph
1870	1950	Van, Billy B.
1894	1943	Veidt, Conrad
1886	1957	Von Stroheim, Erich

W

Born	Died	Name
1887	1969	Walburn, Raymond
1874	1946	Waldron, Charles D.
1904	1966	Walker, June
1919	1951	Walker, Robert
1876	1962	Walter, Bruno
1878	1936	Walthall, Henry B.
1872	1952	Ward, Fannie
1866	1951	Warfield, David
1876	1958	Warner, H. B.
1878	1964	Warwick, Robert
1924	1963	Washington, Dinah
1867	1945	Watson, Billy
1879	1962	Watson, Lucille
1890	1965	Watson, Minor
1896	1966	Webb, Clifton
1867	1942	Weber, Joe
1905	1973	Webster, Margaret
1876	1926	Welch, Ben
1873	1918	Welch, Joe
1896	1975	Wellman, William
1883	1953	Werrenrath, Reinald
1879	1942	Westley, Helen
1895	1968	Wheeler, Bert
1889	1938	White, Pearl
1890	1967	Whiteman, Paul
1882	1943	Whiting, George
1865	1948	Whitty, Dame May
1906	1966	Whorf, Richard
1895	1948	William, Warren
1877	1922	Williams, Bert
1867	1918	Williams, Evan
1923	1953	Williams, Hank
1917	1972	Wilson, Marie
1884	1969	Winninger, Charles
1904	1959	Withers, Grant
1881	1931	Wolheim, Louis
1907	1961	Wong, Anna May
1888	1963	Woolley, Monty
1889	1938	Woolsey, Robert
1881	1956	Wycherly, Margaret
1886	1966	Wynn, Ed
1906	1964	Wynyard, Diana

Y

Born	Died	Name
1891	1960	Young, Clara Kimball
1887	1953	Young, Roland

Z

Born	Died	Name
1869	1932	Ziegfeld, Florenz
1873	1976	Zukor, Adolph

Noted Jazz Artists

Jazz has been called America's only completely unique contribution to Western culture. The following individuals have made major contributions in this field:

Julian "Cannonball" Adderley, (1928-1975): alto sax.
Henry "Red" Allen, (1908-1967): trumpet.
Albert Ammons, (1907-1949): boogie-woogie pianist.
Louis "Satchmo" Armstrong, (1900-1971): trumpet, singer; originated the "scat" vocal.
Mildred Bailey, (1907-1951): blues singer.
Count Basie, b. 1904: orchestra leader, piano.
Sidney Bechet, (1897-1959): early innovator on the soprano sax.
Bix Beiderbecke, (1903-1931): cornet, piano, composer.
Bunny Berigan, (1909-1942): trumpet, singer, "I Can't Get Started With You".
Art Blakey, b. 1919: drums, leader.
Jimmy Blanton, (1921-1942): bass.
Charles "Buddy" Bolden, (1868-1931): cornet; formed the first jazz band in the 1890s.
Big Bill Broonzy, (1893-1958): blues singer, guitar.
Dave Brubeck, b. 1920: piano, combo leader.
Harry Carney, (1910-1975): baritone sax.
Benny Carter, b. 1907: alto sax, trumpet, clarinet.
Sidney Catlett, (1910-1951): drums.
Charlie Christian, (1919-1942): guitar; often given credit for the term "bebop".
Buck Clayton, b. 1911: trumpet, arranger.
Al Cohn, b. 1925: tenor sax, composer.
Cozy Cole, b. 1909: drums.
Ornette Coleman, b. 1930: saxophonist noted for his unorthodox style.
John Coltrane, (1926-1967): tenor sax innovator.
Eddie Condon, (1904-1973): guitar, band leader; promoter of Dixieland.
Miles Davis, b. 1926: trumpet; pioneer of cool jazz.
Buddy De Franco, b. 1933: clarinet.
Paul Desmond, (1924-1977): alto sax.
Warren "Baby" Dodds, (1898-1959): Dixieland drummer.
Johnny Dodds, (1892-1940): clarinet.
Jimmy Dorsey, (1904-1957): clarinet, alto sax; band leader in the swing era.
Tommy Dorsey, (1905-1956): trombone; band leader in swing era.
Roy Eldridge, b. 1911: trumpet, drums, singer.
Duke Ellington, (1899-1974): piano, orchestra leader, composer.
Bill Evans, b. 1929: piano.
Ella Fitzgerald, b. 1918: singer.
Erroll Garner, (1921-1977): piano, composer, "Misty".
Stan Getz, b. 1927: tenor sax.
Terry Gibbs, b. 1924: vibes.
John "Dizzy" Gillespie, b. 1917: trumpet, composer; a developer of bop.
Benny Goodman, b. 1909: clarinet, band and combo leader.
Bobby Hackett, (1915-1976): trumpet, cornet.
Lionel Hampton, b. 1913: vibes, drums, piano, combo leader.
W. C. Handy, (1873-1958): composer, "St. Louis Blues", "Memphis Blues".
Bill Harris, (1916-1973): trombone.
Coleman Hawkins, (1904-1969): tenor sax; 1939 recording of "Body and Soul", a classic.
Fletcher Henderson, (1898-1952): orchestra leader, arranger; first jazz man to use written arrangements pioneering the regimented jazz and dance bands of the 30s.
Woody Herman, b. 1913: clarinet, alto sax, band leader.
Jay C. Higginbotham, (1906-1973): trombone.
Bertha "Chippie" Hill, (1905-1950): blues singer.
Earl "Fatha" Hines, b. 1905: piano, songwriter.
Johnny Hodges, b. 1906: alto sax.
Billie Holiday, (1915-1959): blues singer, "Strange Fruit", "God Bless the Child".
Sam "Lightnin' " Hopkins, b. 1912: blues singer, guitar.
Mahalia Jackson, (1911-1972): gospel singer; and example of the link between the religious and secular roots of jazz.
Milt Jackson, b. 1923: vibes, piano, guitar.
Blind Lemon Jefferson, (1897-1930): blues singer, guitar.
Bunk Johnson, (1879-1949): cornet, trumpet.
James P. Johnson, (1891-1955): piano, composer.
J. J. Johnson, b. 1924: trombone, composer.
Quincy Jones, b. 1933: arranger.
Scott Joplin, (1868-1917): ragtime composer, "Maple Leaf Rag".
Stan Kenton, b. 1912: orchestra leader, composer, piano.
Freddie Keppard, (1899-1933): trumpet.
John Kirby, (1908-1952): major combo leader of the 30s.
Lee Konitz, b. 1927: alto sax.
Gene Krupa, (1909-1973): drums, band and combo leader.
Tommy Ladnier, (1900-1939): trumpet.
Eddie Lang, (1904-1933): guitar.
Huddie Ledbetter (Leadbelly), (1888-1949): blues singer, guitar.
John Lewis, b. 1920: composer, piano, combo leader.
Jimmie Lunceford, (1902-1947): band leader, sax.
Shelly Manne, b. 1920: drums.
Jimmy McPartland, b. 1907: trumpet.
Glenn Miller, (1904-1944): trombone, dance band leader.
Charles Mingus, b. 1922: bass, composer, combo leader.
Thelonious Monk, b. 1920: piano, composer, combo leader; a developer of bop.
Wes Montgomery, (1925-1971): guitar.
Ferdinand "Jelly Roll" Morton, (1885-1941): composer, piano, singer.
Bennie Moten, (1894-1935): piano; an early organizer of large jazz orchestras.
Gerry Mulligan, b. 1927: baritone sax, arranger, leader.
Turk Murphy, b. 1915: trombone, band leader.
Theodore "Fats" Navarro, (1923-1950): trumpet.
Red Nichols, (1905-1965): cornet, combo leader.
Jimmie Noone, (1895-1944): clarinet, leader.
Red Norvo, b. 1908: vibes, band leader.
Anita O'Day, b. 1919: singer.
King Oliver, (1885-1938): cornet, band leader; teacher of Louis Armstrong.
Kid Ory, (1886-1973): trombone, composer, "Muskrat Ramble".
Charlie "Bird" Parker, (1920-1955): alto sax, composer; rated by many as the greatest jazz improviser.
Oscar Peterson, b. 1925: piano, composer, combo leader.
Oscar Pettiford, (1922-1960): a leading bassist in the bop era.
Bud Powell, (1924-1966): piano, composer; modern jazz pioneer.
Gertrude "Ma" Rainey, (1886-1939): first of the great blues singers; teacher of Bessie Smith.
Don Redman, (1900-1964): composer, arranger; pioneer in the evolution of the large orchestra.
Django Reinhardt, (1910-1953): guitar; Belgian gypsy, first European to influence American jazz.
Buddy Rich, b. 1917: drums, band leader.
Max Roach, b. 1925: drums.
Shorty Rogers, b. 1924: composer, trumpet, band leader; a founder of the West coast school of jazz.
Sonny Rollins, b. 1929: tenor sax.
Pete Rugolo, b. 1915: composer, orchestra leader.
Jimmy Rushing, (1903-1972): blues singer.
Pee Wee Russell, (1906-1969): clarinet.
Artie Shaw, b. 1910: clarinet, combo leader; 1939 recording of "Begin the Beguine", a classic.
George Shearing, b. 1919: piano, composer, "Lullaby of Birdland".
Horace Silver, b. 1928: piano, combo leader.
Zoot Sims, b. 1925: tenor, alto sax; clarinet.
Zutty Singleton, (1898-1975): Dixieland drummer.
Bessie Smith, (1894-1937): blues singer.
Clarence "Pinetop" Smith, (1904-1929): piano, singer; pioneer of boogie-woogie.
Joe Smith, (1902-1937): trumpet.
Willie "The Lion" Smith, (1897-1973): stride style pianist.
Muggsy Spanier, (1906-1967): cornet, band leader.
Sonny Stitt, b. 1924: alto, tenor sax.
Art Tatum, (1910-1956): piano; considered one of the great technical virtuosos in jazz.
Billy Taylor, b. 1921: piano.
Jack Teagarden, (1905-1964): trombone, singer.
Dave Tough, (1908-1948): drums.
Lennie Tristano, b. 1919: piano, composer.
Joe Turner, b. 1911: blues singer.
Joe Turner, b. 1907: stride piano.
Sarah Vaughan, b. 1924: singer.
Thomas "Fats" Waller, (1904-1943): piano, singer, composer, "Ain't Misbehavin' ".
Dinah Washington, (1924-1963): singer.
Teddy Weatherford, (1903-1945): piano.
Chick Webb, (1902-1939): band leader, drums; generally credited with laying the foundations for jazz percussion.
Paul Whiteman, (1890-1967): orchestra leader; a major figure in the introduction of jazz to a large audience.
Charles "Cootie" Williams, b. 1908: trumpet, band leader.
Mary Lou Williams, b. 1910: singer.
Teddy Wilson, b. 1912: piano, composer.
Kai Winding, b. 1922: trombone, composer.
Jimmy Yancey, (1894-1951): piano.
Lester "Pres" Young, (1909-1959): tenor sax, composer; a bop pioneer.

Popular American Songs

(m-music; w-words)

After You've Gone: Turner Layton(m); Henry Creamer(w); 1918; popularized by Al Jolson, Sophie Tucker.

Ain't She Sweet: Milton Ager(m); Jack Yellen(w); 1927; introduced by Paul Ash orch., Oriental Theater, Chicago.

Alexander's Ragtime Band: Irving Berlin(m,w); 1911.

Always (I'll Be Loving You): Irving Berlin(m,w); 1925.

April In Paris: Vernon Duke(m); E. Y. Harburg(w); 1932; sung by Evelyn Hoey in revue *Walk a Little Faster.*

April Showers: Louis Silvers(m); Bud De Sylva(w); 1921; introduced by Al Jolson in musical *Bombo.*

As Time Goes By: Herman Hupfield(m,w); 1931, in musical *Everybody's Welcome*, also movie *Casablanca*, in 1942.

Baby Face: Harry Akst(m); Benny Davis(w); 1926; introduced by Jan Garber on RCA Victor record.

The Band Played On: C. B. Ward(m); J. E. Palmer(w); 1895; song owned and promoted by newspaper, New York *World.*

Beer Barrel Polka: J. Vejvoda and Lew Brown(w); 1934(w); music was a Czech popular song.

The Best Things in Life Are Free: Ray Henderson(m); De Sylva and Lew Brown(w); 1927; in musical *Good News.*

Beyond the Blue Horizon: R. A. Whiting(m); Leo Robin(w); 1930, introduced by Jeanette MacDonald in movie *Monte Carlo.*

Blue Skies: Irving Berlin(m,w); 1926; introduced by Belle Baker in musical *Betsy.*

Body and Soul: John Green(m); E. Heyton, R. Sour, F. Eyton(w); 1930; introduced by Gertrude Lawrence on BBC.

Bye, Bye Blackbird: R. Henderson(m); Mort Dixon(w); 1926; popularized by Eddie Cantor.

By the Beautiful Sea: Harry Carroll(m); Harold Atteridge(w); 1914; vaudeville.

By the Light of the Silvery Moon: Gus Edwards(m); Edward Madden(w); 1909; in revue *School Boys and Girls.*

Chicago: Fred Fisher(m,w); 1922; vaudeville.

California, Here I Come: Joseph Meyer(m); Al Jolson, De Sylva(w); 1923; by Al Jolson in road tour of *Bombo.*

Daisy Bell (Bicycle Built for Two): Harry Dacre(m,w); circa 1892; London tune popularized in U.S. by Tony Pastor.

Dancing in the Dark: Arthur Schwartz(m); Howard Dietz(w); 1931; in revue *The Band Wagon.*

Down by the Old Mill Stream: Tell Taylor(m,w); 1910.

Easter Parade: Irving Berlin(m,w); 1933; introduced by Clifton Webb and Marilyn Miller in musical *As Thousands Cheer.*

For Me and My Gal: G. W. Meyer(m); Edgar Leslie, E. R. Goetz(w); 1917; sung by Jolson, Cantor, Sophie Tucker, others.

Give My Regards to Broadway: George M. Cohan(m,w); 1904; in musical *Little Johnny Jones.*

Good Night Irene: Huddie Ledbetter(m,w); 1936; found by John Lomax in Louisiana State Prison, Angola, La.

Hail, Hail, the Gang's All Here: Arthur S. Sullivan(m); T. A. Morse(w), under pseudonym. D. A. Esrom; 1917.

Happy Days Are Here Again: Milton Ager(m); Jack Yellen(w); 1929; introduced on Black Thursday (10-24-29) at Penn Hotel, NYC.

Heartaches: Al Hoffman(m); John Klenner(w); 1931; popularized by Ted Weems.

Home on the Range: Daniel E. Kelly?(m); Brewster (Bruce) Higley (w,m); 1904, called Arizona Home(w) 1873; composer and author uncertain.

Hot Time in the Old Town Tonight: T. M. Metz(m); Joe Hayden(w); 1896; minstrel show.

I Can't Give You Anything But Love: Jimmy McHugh(m); Dorothy Fields(w); 1928; in revue *Delmar's Revels.*

I Could Have Danced All Night: F. Loewe(m); A. J. Lerner (w); 1956; by Julie Andrews in *My Fair Lady.*

I Don't Know Why I Love You Like I Do: F. E. Ahlert(m); Roy Turk(w); 1931.

If You Knew Susie: Bud De Sylva and Joseph Meyer(w,m); 1925; by Al Jolson in *Big Boy.*

I Got Plenty o' Nothin': G. Gershwin(m); I. Gershwin, Dubose Heyward(w); 1935; in *Porgy and Bess.*

I'll Be Seeing You: Sammy Fain(m); Irving Kahal(w); 1938; popularized by Sinatra, Hildegarde, in 1943.

I'll See You in My Dreams: Isham Jones(m); Gus Kahn(w); 1924.

I Love You Truly: Carrie Jacobs Bond(m,w); 1901; originally an art song, later picked up by vaudeville.

I'm in the Mood for Love: J. McHugh(m); Dorothy Fields(w); 1935; by Alice Faye in movie *Every Night at Eight.*

I'm Sitting on Top of the World: Ray Henderson(m); Sam M. Lewis, Joe Young(w); 1925; popularized by Jolson in 1929 movie *The Singing Fool.*

In the Good Old Summertime: George Evans(m); Ren Shields(w); 1902.

In the Shade of the Old Apple Tree: Egbert van Alstyne(m); Harry H. Williams(w); 1905.

I Only Have Eyes for You: Harry Warren(m); Al Dubin(w); 1934; by Dick Powell in movie *Dames.*

It Had To Be You: Isham Jones(m); Gus Kahn(w); 1924.

It's Been a Long, Long Time: Julie Styne(m); Sammy Cahn (w); 1945.

It Was a Very Good Year: Ervin Drake(m,w); 1965; introduced by Kingston Trio on record; popularized by Sinatra in 1965.

I've Got You Under My Skin: Cole Porter(m,w); 1936; by Virginia Bruce in movie *Born to Dance.*

I Want a Girl Just Like the Girl: Harry von Tilzer(m); William Dillion(w); 1911.

I Wonder Who's Kissing Her Now: J.E. Howard, H. Orlob (m); Wm. M. Hough, F.R. Adams (w); 1909.

Jeannie With the Light Brown Hair: Stephen Foster (m,w); 1854.

June Is Busting Out All Over: R. Rodgers (m); O. Hammerstein II (w); 1945; in *Carousel.*

Lazy River: S. Arodin, Hoagy Carmichael (m,w); 1931; on record by Carmichael with band including both Dorseys, Teagarden, Krupa, Goodman, Venuti, and Beiderbecke.

Let Me Call You Sweetheart: Leo Friedman (m); Beth Slater Whitson (w); 1910.

Lover: R. Rodgers(m); Lorenz Hart(w); 1933; by Jeanette MacDonald in movie *Love Me Tonight.*

Lullaby of Broadway: Harry Warren (m); Al Dubin (w); 1935; in movie *Gold Diggers of Broadway.*

Memories: Egbert van Alstyne(m); Gus Kahn(w); 1915.

Moonlight and Roses: Neil Moret, Ben Black(m,w); 1925; music based on Lamare's *Andantino;* sung by Grable in 1943 movie *Tin Pan Alley.*

Moon River: Henry Mancini(m); Johnny Mercer(w); 1961; by Andy Williams under title for movie *Breakfast at Tiffany's.*

Moonlight Bay: Percy Wenrich(m); Edward Madden (w); 1912; vaudeville.

My Blue Heaven: Walter Donaldson(m); George Whiting (w); 1927; Tommy Lyman radio theme song.

Melancholy Baby: Ernie Burnett(m); George A. Norton(w); 1912; vaudeville.

My Wild Irish Rose: Chauncey Olcott(m,w); 1899; in musical *A Romance of Athlone.*

Night and Day: Cole Porter(m,w); 1932; by Fred Astaire and Claire Luce in musical *Gay Divorce;* title of Porter film biography.

Now Is The Hour: Kaihan, Scott, Stewart(m,w); originated in Austria in 1913; American version, 1946.

Oh, What a Beautiful Mornin': R. Rodgers(m) O. Hammerstein II(w); 1943; by Alfred Drake in *Oklahoma!*

Oh! You Beautiful Doll: Nat D. Ayer(m); A. Seymour Brown (w); 1911; vaudeville.

Old Folks at Home (Swanee River): Stephen Foster(m,w); 1851; minstrel show.

Ol' Man River: Jerome Kern(m); O. Hammerstein II(w); 1927; by Jules Bledsoe in *Show Boat.*

On the Sunny Side of the Street: J. McHugh(m); Dorothy Fields(w); 1930; in *International Revue* with Gertrude Lawrence.

Over The Rainbow: Harold Arlen(m); E.Y. Harburg(w); 1939; by fourteen-year-old Judy Garland in *Wizard of Oz.*

Peg O'My Heart: Fred Fisher(m); Alfred Bryan(w); in *Ziegfeld Follies of 1913.*

Pennies From Heaven: Arthur Johnston(m); Johnny Burke (w); 1936; by Bing Crosby in movie of same name.

Pretty Baby: E. van Alstyne, Tony Jackson(m); Gus Kahn(w); 1916; by Dolly Hackett in musical *The Passing Show.*

A Pretty Girl Is Like a Melody: Irving Berlin(m,w); in *Ziegfeld Follies of 1919;* became Follies theme song.

Put On Your Old Gray Bonnett: Percy Wenrich(m); Stanley Murphy(w); 1909.

Put Your Arms Around Me, Honey: Albert von Tilzer(m); Junie McCree(w); 1910; vaudeville.

Rudolph, the Red-Nosed Reindeer: Johnny Marks(m,w); 1949; by Gene Autry on Columbia record.

School Days: Gus Edwards(m); Will D. Cobb(w) 1907; vaudeville.

September Song: Kurt Weill(m); Maxwell Anderson(w); 1938; by Walter Houston in play *Knickerbocker Holiday.*

Shine On Harvest Moon: Nora Bayes, Jack Norworth(m); Norworth(w); introduced by Nora Bayes in *Ziegfeld Follies of 1908.*

Sidewalks of New York: J.W. Blake, C.B. Lawlor(m,w); 1894; by Lottie Gilson at Old London Theatre on the Bowery.

Singing in the Rain: Nacio Herb Brown(m); Arthur Freed(w); 1929; by Cliff Edwards in movie *Hollywood Revue of 1929.*

Smoke Gets in Your Eyes: Jerome Kern(m); Otto Harbach (w); 1933; by Tamara in musical *Roberta.*

Somebody Loves Me: G. Gershwin(m); B. DeSylva, B. MacDonald(w); 1929; *George White's Scandals of 1924.*

Some Enchanted Evening: R. Rodgers(m); O. Hammerstein II(w); 1949; by Ezio Pinza in *South Pacific.*

Stardust: Hoagy Carmichael(m); Michell Parish(w); 1929.

Stormy Weather: Harold Arlen(m); Ted Koehler(w); 1933; popularized by Ethel Waters.

Strike Up the Band: George Gershwin(m); Ira Gershwin(w); 1930; in musical of the same name.
Summertime: George Gershwin(m); DuBose Heyward(w); 1935; by Abbie Mitchell opening *Porgy and Bess.*
Sweet Georgia Brown: Ben Bernie, M. Pinkard, K. Casey (m,w); 1925.
Sweethearts: Victor Herbert(m); R.B. Smith(w); 1913; in musical of the same name.
Take Me Out to the Ball Game: Albert von Tilzer(m); Jack Norworth(w); 1908; vaudeville.
Tea for Two: Vincent Youmans(m); Irving Ceasar(w); 1920; by Louise Groody, John Barker, in *No, No, Nanette.*
Tennessee Waltz: Redd Stewart, Pee Wee King(m,w); 1948; popularized by Patti Page.
Thanks for the Memory: R. Rainger(m); Leo Robin(w); 1937; by Bob Hope in his debut film, *The Big Broadcast of 1938.*
That Old Black Magic: Harold Arlen(m); Johnny Mercer(w); 1942; in movie *Star Spangled Rhythm.*
There's a Long, Long Trail: Z. Elliott(m); Stoddard King(w); 1913; written for their Yale frat, became popular at end of World War I.
Three Little Words: Harry Ruby(m); Bert Kalmar(w); 1930; by Bing Crosby in Amos & Andy movie *Check and Double Check.*
Toot, Toot, Tootsie, Goodbye: Dan Russo(m); Gus Kahn, Ernie Erdman(w); 1922; by Jolson in *Bombo;* later in first talkie *The Jazz Singer.*
When Irish Eyes Are Smiling: Ernest R. Ball(m); C. Olcott, G. Graft(w); 1912; by Olcott in musical *Isle of Dreams.*
When Johnny Comes Marching Home: Louis Lambert (m,w); 1863; Lambert believed to be a pen-name for Patrick S. Gilmore.
When You're Smiling: M. Fisher, J. Goodwin, L. Shay(m,w); 1928.
When You Wish Upon A Star: Leigh Harline(m); Ned Washington(w); 1940; by Cliff Edwards in animated *Pinocchio.*
When You Wore a Tulip: Percy Wenrich(m); Jack Mahoney (w); 1914; vaudeville.
Whispering: John Schonberger, Vincent Rose(m); Richard Coburn(w); 1920; introduced by Paul Whiteman.
White Christmas: Irving Berlin(m,w); 1942; by Bing Crosby in movie *Holiday Inn.*
With a Song in My Heart: R. Rodgers(m); Lorenz Hart(w); 1929; in musical *Spring Is Here.*
Without a Song: Vincent Youmans(m); Billy Rose, E. Eliscu (w); 1929; in musical *Great Day.*
Yellow Rose of Texas: nothing is known of the songwriter but initials "J.K."; 1853; minstrel show.
Yes, Sir, That's My Baby: Walter Donaldson(m); Gus Kahn (w); 1925; popularized by Eddie Cantor.
You and the Night and the Music: Arthur Schwartz(m); Howard Dietz(w); 1934; in musical play *Revenge With Music.*
You Are My Sunshine: Jimmie Davis(m); C. Mitchell(w); 1940; in Tex Ritter movie *Take Me Back to Oklahoma.* Davis governor of Louisiana, 1944-48.
You Made Me Love You: J.V. Monaco(m); Joe McCarthy(w); 1913; by Al Jolson in musical *Honeymoon Express.*

Composers of the Western World

Carl Philipp Emanuel Bach, 1714-1788. (G.) Prussian and Wurtembergian Sonatas.
Johann Christian Bach, 1735-1782. (G.) Concertos; sonatas.
Johann Sebastian Bach, 1685-1750. (G.) St. Matthew Passion, The Well-Tempered Clavichord.
Samuel Barber, b. 1910 (U.S.) Adagio for Strings, Vanessa.
Bela Bartok, 1881-1945. (Hung.) Concerto for Orchestra, The Miraculous Mandarin.
Ludwig Van Beethoven, 1770-1827. (G.) Concertos (Emperor); sonatas (Moonlight, Pastorale, Pathetique); symphonies (Eroica).
Vincenzo Bellini, 1801-1835. (It.) La Sonnambula, Norma, I Puritani.
Alban Berg, 1885-1935. (Aus.) Wozzeck, Lulu.
Hector Berlioz, 1803-1869. (F.) Damnation of Faust, Symphonie Fantastique, Requiem.
Leonard Bernstein, b. 1918. (U.S.) Jeremiah, West Side Story.
Georges Bizet, 1838-1875. (F.) Carmen, Pearl Fishers.
Ernest Bloch, 1880-1959. (Swiss) Schelomo, Voice in the Wilderness, Sacred Service.
Luigi Boccherini, 1743-1805 (It.) Cello Concerto in B Flat, Symphony in C.
Alexander Borodin, 1834-1887. (R.) Prince Ignor, In the Steppes of Central Asia.
Johannes Brahms, 1833-1897. (G.) Liebeslieder Waltzes, Rhapsody in E Flat Major, Opus 119 for Piano, Academic Festival Overture; symphonies; quartets.
Benjamin Britten, 1913-1976. (Br.) Peter Grimes, Turn of the Screw, Ceremony of Carols.
Anton Bruckner, 1824-1896, (Aus.) Symphonies (Romantic), Intermezzo for String Quintet.
Ferruccio Busoni, 1866-1924. (It.) Doctor Faust, Comedy Overture.
Dietrich Buxtehud, 1637-1707. (G.) Cantatas, trio sonatas.
William Byrd, 1543-1623 (Br.) Masses, sacred songs.
Alexis Emmanuel Chabrier, 1841-1894. (Fr.) Le Roi Malgre Lui, Espana.
Gustave Charpentier, 1860-1956. (F.) Louise.
Frederic Chopin, 1810-1849. (P.) Concertos, Polonaise No. 6 in A Flat Major (Heroic); sonatas.
Aaron Copland, b. 1900. (U.S.) Appalachian Spring.
Claude Achille Debussy, 1862-1918. (F.) Pelleas et Mellisande, La Mer, Prelude to the Afternoon of a Faun.
C. P. Leo Delibes, 1836-1891, (F.) Lakme, Coppelia, Sylvia.
Norman Dello Joio, b. 1913. (U.S.), Triumph of St. Joan, Psalm of David.
Gaetano Donizetti, 1797-1848. (It.) Elixir of Love, Lucia de Lammermoor, Daughter of the Regiment.
Paul Dukas, 1865-1935. (Fr.) Sorcerer's Apprentice.
Antonin Dvorak, 1841-1904. (C.) Symphony in E Minor (from the New World).
Edward Elgar, 1857-1934. (Br.) Pomp and Circumstance.
Manuel de Falla, 1876-1946. (Sp.) La Vide Breve, El Amor Brujo.
Gabriel Faure, 1845-1924. (Fr.) Requiem, Ballade.
Friedrich von Flotow, 1812-1883. (G.) Martha.
Cesar Franck, 1822-1890. (Belg.) D Minor Symphony.
George Gershwin, 1898-1937. (U.S.) Rhapsody in Blue, American in Paris, Porgy and Bess.
Umberto Giordano, 1867-1948 (It.) Andrea Chenier.
Alex K. Glazunoff, 1865-1936. (R.) Symphonies, Stenka Razin.
Mikhail Glinka, 1857-1904. (R.) Ruslan & Ludmilla.
Christoph W. Gluck, 1714-1787. (G.) Alceste, Iphigenie en Tauride.
Charles Gounod, 1818-1893. (F.) Faust, Romeo and Juliet.
Edvard Grieg, 1843-1907. (Nor.) Peer Gynt Suite, Concerto in A Minor.
George Frederick Handel, 1685-1759, (G. Br.) Messiah, Xerxes, Berenice.
Howard Hanson, b. 1896. (U.S.) Symphonies No. 1 (Nordic) and 2 (Romantic).
Roy Harris, b. 1898. (U.S.) Symphonies, Amer. Portraits.
Joseph Haydn, 1732-1809. (Aus.) Symphonies (Clock); oratorios; chamber music.
Paul Hindemith, 1895-1963. (U.S.) Mathis Der Maler.
Gustav Holst, 1874-1934. (Br.) The Planets.
Arthur Honegger, 1892-1955. (Swiss) Judith, Le Roi David, Pacific 231.
Alan Hovhaness, b. 1911. (U.S.) Symphonies, Magnificat.
Engelbert Humperdinck, 1854-1921. (G.) Hansel and Gretel.
Charles Ives, 1874-1954. (U.S.) Third Symphony.
Aram Khachaturian, b. 1903. (R.) Gayane (ballet), symphonies.
Zoltan Kodaly, 1882-1967. (Hung.) Hary Janos, Psalmus Hungaricus.
Fritz Kreisler, 1875-1962. (Aus.) Caprice Viennois, Tambourin Chinois.
Rodolphe Kreutzer, 1766-1831. (F.) 40 etudes for violin.
Edouard V. A. Lalo, 1823-1892. (F.) Symphonie Espagnole.
Ruggiero Leoncavallo, 1858-1919, (It.) I Pagliacci.
Franz Liszt, 1811-1886. (Hung.) 20 Hungarian rhapsodies; symphonic poems.
Edward MacDowell, 1861-1908. (U.S.) To a Wild Rose.
Gustav Mahler, 1860-1911. (Aus.) Lied von der Erde.
Pietro Mascagni, 1863-1945. (It.) Cavalleria Rusticana.
Jules Massenet, 1842-1912. (F.) Manon, Le Cid, Thais.
Mendelssohn-Bartholdy, 1809-1847. (G.) Midsummer Night's Dream, Songs Without Words.
Gian-Carlo Menotti, b. 1911. (It.-U.S.) The Medium, The Consul, Amahl and the Night Visitors.
Claudio Monteverdi, 1567-1643. (It.) Opera; masses; madrigals.
Wolfgang Amadeus Mozart, 1756-1791. (Aus.) Magic Flute, Marriage of Figaro; concertos; symphonies, etc.
Modest Moussorgsky, 1835-1881. (R.) Boris Godunov, Pictures at an Exhibition.
Jacques Offenbach, 1819-1880. (F.) Tales of Hoffman.
Karl Orff, b. 1895 (G.) Carmina Burana.
Ignace Paderewski, 1860-1941 (P.) Minuet in G.
Giovanni P. da Palestrina, 1524-1594. (It.) Masses; madrigals.
Amilcare Ponchielli, 1834-1886. (It.) La Gioconda.

Francis Poulenc, 1899-1963. (F.) Dialogues des Carmelites.
Serge Prokofiev, 1891-1953. (R.) Love for Three Oranges, Lt. Kije, Peter and the Wolf.
Giacomo Puccini, 1858-1924. (It.) La Boheme, Manon Lescaut, Tosca, Madame Butterfly.
Sergei Rachmaninov, 1873-1943. (R.) Prelude in C Sharp Minor.
Maurice Ravel, 1875-1937. (Fr.) Bolero, Daphne et Chloe, Rapsodie Espagnole.
Nikolai Rimsky-Korsakov, 1844-1908. (R.) Golden Cockerel, Cappriccio Espagnol, Scheherazade, Russian Easter Overture.
Gioacchino Rossini, 1792-1868. (It.) Barber of Seville, Semiramide, William Tell.
Chas. Camille Saint-Saens, 1835-1921. (F.) Samson and Delilah, Danse Macabre.
Alessandro Scarlatti, 1659-1725. (It.) Cantatas; concertos.
Arnold Schoenberg, 1874-1951. (Aus.) Pelleas and Melisande, Transfigured Night, De Profundis.
Franz Schubert, 1797-1828. (A.) Lieder; symphonies (Unfinished); overtures (Rosamunde).
William Schuman, b. 1910. (U.S.) Credendum, New England Triptych.
Robert Schumann, 1810-1856. (G.) Symphonies, songs.
Aleksandr Scriabin, 1872-1915. (R.) Prometheus.
Dimitri Shostakovich, b. 1906-1975. (R.). Symphonies, Lady Macbeth of Minsk, The Nose.
Jean Sibelius, 1865-1957, (Finn.) Finlandia, Karelia.
Bedrich Smetana, 1824-1884. (C.). The Bartered Bride.
Karlheinz Stockhausen, b. 1928. (G.) Kontrapunkte, Kontakte.
Richard Strauss, 1864-1949. (G.) Salome, Elektra, Der Rosenkavalier, Thus Spake Zarathustra.
Igor F. Stravinsky, 1882-1971. (R.-U.S.) Oedipus Rex, Le Sacre du Printemps, Petrushka.
Peter I. Tchaikovsky, 1840-1893. (R.) Nutcracker Suite, Swan Lake, Eugen Onegin.
Ambroise Thomas, 1811-1896. (F.) Mignon.
Virgil Thomson, b. 1896. (U.S.) Opera, ballet; Four Saints in Three Acts.
Ralph Vaughan Williams, 1872-1958, (Br.) Job, London Symphony, Symphony No. 7 (Antarctica).
Giuseppe Verdi, 1813-1901. (It.) Aida, Rigoletto, Don Carlo, Il Trovatore, La Traviata, Falstaff, Macbeth.
Hector Villa Lobos, 1887-1959. (Brazil) Choros.
Antonio Vivaldi, 1678-1741. (It.) Concerti, The Four Seasons.
Richard Wagner, 1813-1883. (G.) Rienzi, Tannhauser, Lohengrin, Tristan und Isolde.
Karl Maria von Weber, 1786-1826. (G.) Der Freischutz.

Composers of Operettas, Musicals, and Popular Music

Milton Ager, b. 1919. (U.S.) I Wonder What's Become of Sally; Hard Hearted Hannah.
Leroy Anderson, 1908-1975. (U.S.) Syncopated Clock; Blue Tango; Sleigh Ride.
Harold Arlen, b. 1905. (U.S.) Stormy Weather; Over the Rainbow; Blues in the Night; That Old Black Magic.
Burt Bacharach, b. 1928. (U.S.) Raindrops Keep Fallin' on My Head; Walk on By; What the World Needs Now is Love.
Ernest Ball, 1878-1927. (U.S.) Mother Machree; When Irish Eyes are Smiling.
Irving Berlin, b. 1888. (U.S.) *This is the Army; Annie Get Your Gun; Call Me Madam;* God Bless America; White Christmas.
Jerry Bock, b. 1928. (U.S.) *Mr. Wonderful; Fiorello; Fiddler on the Roof; The Rothschilds.*
Carrie Jacobs Bond, 1862-1946. (U.S.) I Love You Truly.
Nacio Herb Brown, 1896-1964. (U.S.) Singing in the Rain; You Were Meant for Me; All I Do Is Dream of You.
Hoagy Carmichael, b. 1899. (U.S.) Stardust; Georgia on My Mind; Old Buttermilk Sky.
George M. Cohan, 1878-1942. (U.S.) Give My Regards to Broadway; You're A Grand Old Flag; Over There.
Walter Donaldson, 1893-1947. (U.S.) My Buddy; Carolina in the Morning; You're Driving Me Crazy; Makin' Whoopee.
Vernon Duke, 1903-1969. (U.S.) April in Paris.
Gus Edwards, 1879-1945. (U.S.) School Days; By the Light of the Silvery Moon; In My Merry Oldsmobile.
Sherman Edwards, b. 1919. (U.S.) See You in September; Wonderful! Wonderful!
Sammy Fain, b. 1902. Wedding Bells Are Breaking Up That Old Gang of Mine; Let a Smile Be Your Umbrella.
Fred Fisher, 1875-1942. (U.S.) Peg O' My Heart; Chicago; Dardenella.
Stephen Collins Foster, 1826-1864. (U.S.) My Old Kentucky Home; Old Folks At Home.
Rudolf Friml, 1879-1972. (naturalized U.S.) *The Firefly; Rose Marie; Vagabond King; Bird of Paradise.*
John Gay, 1685-1732. (Br.) *The Beggar's Opera.*
Edwin F. Goldman, 1878-1956. (U.S.) marches.
Percy Grainger, 1882-1961. (Br.) Country Gardens.
John Green, b. 1908. (U.S.) Body and Soul; Out of Nowhere; I Cover the Waterfront.
Ferde Grofe, 1892-1972. (U.S.) Grand Canyon Suite.
W. C. Handy, 1873-1958. (U.S.) St. Louis Blues.
Ray Henderson, 1896-1970. (U.S.) *George White's Scandals;* That Old Gang of Mine; Five Foot Two, Eyes of Blue.
Victor Herbert, 1859-1924. (Ir.-U.S.) *Mlle. Modiste; Babes in Toyland; The Red Mill; Naughty Marietta; Sweethearts.*
Jerry Herman, b. 1932. (U.S.) *Milk and Honey; Hello Dolly; Mame; Dear World.*
Al Hoffman, 1902-1960. (U.S.) Heartaches, Mairzy Doats.
Scott Joplin, 1868-1917. (U.S.) *Treemonisha.*
John Kander, b. 1927. (U.S.) *Cabaret; Chicago; Funny Lady.*
Jerome Kern, 1885-1945. (U.S.) *Sally; Sunny; Show Boat; Cat and the Fiddle; Music in the Air; Roberta.*
Burton Lane, b. 1912. (U.S.) *Three's a Crowd; Finnian's Rainbow; On A Clear Day You Can See Forever.*
Franz Lehar, 1870-1948. (Hung.) *Merry Widow.*
Mitch Leigh, b. 1928. (U.S.) *Man of La Mancha.*
Frank Loesser, 1910-1969. (U.S.) *Guys and Dolls; Where's Charley?; The Most Happy Fella.*
Frederick Loewe, b. 1901. (Aust.-U.S.) *The Day Before Spring; Brigadoon; Paint Your Wagon; My Fair Lady; Camelot.*
Henry Mancini, b. 1924. (U.S.) Moon River; Days of Wine and Roses; Pink Panther Theme.
Jimmy McHugh, 1894-1969. (U.S.) I Can't Give You Anything But Love; I Feel a Song Coming On.
Joseph Meyer, b. 1894. (U.S.) If You Knew Susie; California, Here I Come; Crazy Rhythm.
Chauncey Olcott, 1858-1932. (U.S.) Mother Machree; My Wild Irish Rose.
Cole Porter, 1893-1964. (U.S.) *Anything Goes; Jubilee; DuBarry Was a Lady; Panama Hattie; Mexican Hayride; Kiss Me Kate; Can Can; Silk Stockings.*
Andre Previn, b. 1929. (U.S.) *Coco.*
Richard Rodgers, b. 1902. (U.S.) *Garrick Gaieties; Connecticut Yankee; America's Sweetheart; On Your Toes; Babes in Arms; The Boys from Syracuse; Oklahoma!; Carousel; South Pacific; The King and I; Flower Drum Song; The Sound of Music.*
Sigmund Romberg, 1887-1951. (Hung.) *Maytime; The Student Prince; Desert Song; Blossom Time.*
Harold Rome, b. 1908. (U.S.) *Pins and Needles; Call Me Mister; Wish You Were Here; Fanny; Destry Rides Again.*
Vincent Rose, 1880-1944. (U.S.) Avalon; Whispering; Blueberry Hill.
Harry Ruby, 1895-1974. (U.S.) Three Little Words; Who's Sorry Now?
Arthur Schwartz, b. 1900. (U.S.) *The Band Wagon; Inside U.S.A.; A Tree Grows in Brooklyn.*
Stephen Sondheim, b. 1930. (U.S.) *A Little Night Music.*
John Philip Sousa, b. 1930. (U.S.) *El Capitan;* Stars and Stripes Forever.
Oskar Straus, 1870-1954. (Aus.) *Chocolate Soldier.*
Johann Strauss, 1825-1899. (Aus.) *Gypsy Baron; Die Fledermaus;* waltzes: Blue Danube, Artist's Life.
Charles Strouse, b. 1928 (U.S.) *Bye Bye, Birdie; All American; Golden Boy; Applause.*
Jule Styne, b. 1905. (b. London-U.S.) *Gentlemen Prefer Blondes; Bells Are Ringing; Gypsy; Funny Girl.*
Arthur S. Sullivan, 1842-1900. (Br.) *H.M.S. Pinafore, Pirates of Penzance; The Mikado.*
Deems Taylor, 1885-1966. (U.S.) *Peter Ibbetson.*
Egbert van Alstyne, 1882-1951. (U.S.) In the Shade of the Old Apple Tree; Memories; Pretty Baby.
James Van Heusen, b. 1913. (U.S.) Moonlight Becomes You; Swinging on a Star.
Albert von Tilzer, 1878-1956. (U.S.) I'll Be With You in Apple Blossom Time; Take Me Out to the Ball Game.
Harry von Tilzer, 1872-1946. (U.S.) Only a Bird in a Gilded Cage; On a Sunday Afternoon.
Harry Warren, b. 1893. (U.S.) You're My Everything; We're in the Money; I Only Have Eyes for You; September in the Rain.
Kurt Weill, 1900-1950. (G.-U.S.) *Three-Penny Opera; Lady in the Dark; Knickerbocker Holiday; One Touch of Venus.*
Percy Wenrich, 1887-1952. (U.S.) When You Wore a Tulip; Moonlight Bay; Put On Your Old Gray Bonnet.
Richard A. Whiting, 1891-1938. (U.S.) Till We Meet Again; Sleepytime Gal; Beyond the Blue Horizon.
Meredith Willson, b. 1902. (U.S.) *The Music Man.*
Vincent Youmans, 1898-1946. (U.S.) *Two Little Girls in Blue; Wildflower; No, No, Nanette; Hit the Deck; Rainbow; Smiles.*

Lyricists

Buddy De Sylva, 1895-1950. (U.S.) When Day Is Done; Look for the Silver Lining; April Showers; The Best Things in Life are Free.

Howard Dietz. b. 1896. (U.S.) Dancing in the Dark; You and the Night and the Music.

Al Dubin, 1891-1945. (U.S.) Tiptoe Through the Tulips; Anniversary Waltz; Lullaby of Broadway.

Dorothy Fields, 1905-1974. (U.S.) On the Sunny Side of the Street; Don't Blame Me; The Way You Look Tonight.

Ira Gershwin, b. 1896. (U.S.) The Man I Love; Fascinating Rhythm; S'Wonderful; Embraceable You.

Wm. S. Gilbert, 1836-1911. (Br.) *The Mikado; H.M.S. Pinafore.*

Oscar Hammerstein II, 1895-1960, (U.S.) Ol' Man River; *Oklahoma; Carousel.*

E. Y. (Yip) Harburg, b. 1898. (U.S.) Brother, Can You Spare a Dime; April in Paris; Over the Rainbow.

Lorenz Hart, 1895-1943. (U.S.) With a Song in My Heart; Isn't It Romantic; Blue Moon; Lover.

DuBose Heyward, 1885-1940. (U.S.) Summertime; A Woman Is a Sometime Thing.

Gus Kahn, 1886-1941. (U.S.) Memories; Ain't We Got Fun; Pretty Baby.

Johnny Mercer, b. 1909 (U.S.) Days of Wine and Roses; Come Rain or Come Shine; Laura; That Old Black Magic.

Jack Norworth, 1879-1959. (U.S.) Take Me Out to the Ball Game; Shine On Harvest Moon.

Jack Yellen, b. 1892. (U.S.) Down by the O-Hi-O; Ain't She Sweet; Happy Days Are Here Again.

Noted Artists and Sculptors of the Past

Artists are painters unless otherwise indicated.

Washington Allston (1779-1842), landscapist. The Deluge.

Albrecht Altdorfer (1480-1538), landscapist. Birth of the Virgin.

Fra Angelico (1387-1455), Renaissance muralist. Madonna of the Linen Drapers' Guild.

Aleksandr Archipenko (1887-1967). Boxing Match, Medranos.

Andrea del Sarto (1486-1530), frescoes, Madonna of the Harpies.

John James Audubon (1785-1851). Birds of America.

Hans Baldun-Grien (1484-1545). Todentanz.

Ernst Barlach (1870-1938), Expressionist sculptor. Man Drawing a Sword.

Frederic-Auguste Bartholdi (1834-1904). Liberty Enlightening the World, Lion of Belfort.

Fra Bartolommeo (1472-1517). Vision of St. Bernard.

Aubrey Beardsley (1872-1898), illustrator. Salome, Lysistrata.

Max Beckmann (1884-1950), Expressionist. The Descent from the Cross.

Gentile Bellini (1426-1507), Renaissance. Procession in St. Mark's Square.

Giovanni Bellini (1428-1516). St. Francis in Ecstasy.

Jacopo Bellini (1400-1470). Crucifixion.

George W. Bellows (1882-1925), sports artist. Stag at Sharkey's.

Thomas Hart Benton (1889-1975), American regionalist. Threshing Wheat, Arts of the West.

Gian Lorenzo Bernini (1598-1680), Baroque reliefs. The Assumption.

Albert Bierstadt (1830-1902), landscapist. The Rocky Mountains, Mount Corcoran.

George Caleb Bingham (1811-1879). Fur Traders Descending the Missouri.

William Blake (1752-1827), engraver. Book of Job, Songs of Innocence, Songs of Experience.

Rosa Bonheur (1822-1899). The Horse Fair.

Pierre Bonnard (1867-1947), Intimist. The Breakfast Room.

Paul-Emile Borduas (1905-1960), Abstractionist. Leeward of the Island, Enchanted Shields.

Gutzon Borglum (1871-1941). Mt. Rushmore Memorial.

Hieronymus Bosch (1450-1516), religious allegories. The Crowning with Thorns.

Sandro Botticelli (1444-1510), Renaissance. Birth of Venus.

Constantin Brancusi (1876-1957), Abstract sculptor. Flying Turtle, The Kiss.

Georges Braque (1882-1963), Cubist. Violin and Palette.

Pieter Bruegel the Elder (1525-1569), Flemish landscapist. The Peasant Dance.

Pieter Bruegel the Younger (1564-1638). Village Fair, The Crucifixion.

Edward Burne-Jones (1833-1898), Pre-Rafaelite artist-craftsman. The Mirror of Venus.

Alexander Calder (1898-1976), sculptor. Lobster Trap and Fish Tail.

Caravaggio (1573-1610), Baroque. The Supper at Emmaus.

Emily Carr (1871-1945), landscapist. Blunden Harbour, Big Raven.

Carlo Carra (1881-1966), Metaphysical school. Lot's Daughters.

Mary Cassatt (1845-1926), Impressionist. Woman Bathing.

George Catlin (1796-1872), American Indian life. Gallery of Indians.

Benvenuto Cellini (1500-1571), Mannerist sculptor, goldsmith. Perseus.

Paul Cezanne (1839-1906), early Cubist. Card Players, Mont-Sainte-Victoire with Large Pine Trees.

Jean-Baptiste-Simeon-Chardin (1699-1779), still lifes. The Kiss, The Grace.

Frederick Church (1826-1900), Hudson River school. Niagara, Andes of Ecuador.

Cimabue (1240-1302), Byzantine mosaicist. Madonna Enthroned with St. Francis.

Claude Lorrain (1600-1682), ideal-landscapist. The Enchanted Castle.

Thomas Cole (1801-1848), Hudson River school. The Ox-Bow.

John Constable (1776-1837), landscapist. Salisbury Cathedral from the Bishop's grounds.

John Singleton Copley (1738-1815), portraitist. Samuel Adams, Watson and the Shark.

Lovis Corinth (1858-1925), Expressionist. Apocalypse.

Jean-Baptiste-Camille Corot (1796-1875), landscapist. Souvenir de Mortefontaine, Pastorale.

Correggio (1494-1534), Renaissance muralist. Mystic Marriage of St. Catherine.

Gustave Courbet (1819-1877), Realist. The Artist's Studio.

Lucas Cranach the Elder (1472-1553), Protestant Reformation portraitist. Luther.

Nathaniel Currier (1813-1888) and **James M. Ives** (1824-1895), lithographers. A Midnight Race on the Mississipi.

Honore Daumier (1808-1879), caricaturist. The Third-Class Carriage.

Jacques-Louis David (1748-1825), Neoclassicist. The Oath of the Horatii.

Arthur Davies (1862-1928), Romantic landscapist. Unicorns.

Edgar Degas (1834-1917). The Ballet Class.

Eugene Delacroix (1798-1863), Romantic. Massacre at Chios.

Paul Delaroche (1797-1859), historical themes. Children of Edward.

Luca Della Robbia (1400-1482), Renaissance terracotta artist. Cantoria (singing gallery), Florence cathedral.

Donato Donatello (1386-1466), Renaissance sculptor. David, Gattamelata.

Raoul Dufy (1877-1953), Fauvist. Chateau and Horses.

Asher Brown Durand (1796-1886), Hudson River school. Kindred Spirits.

Albrecht Durer (1471-1528), Renaissance engraver, woodcuts. St. Jerome in His Study, Melancholia I, Apocalypse.

Thomas Eakins (1844-1916), Realist. The Gross Clinic.

Jacob Epstein (1880-1959), religious and allegorical sculptor. Genesis, Ecce Homo.

Jan Van Eyck (1366-1440), naturalistic panels. Adoration of the Lamb.

Anselm Feuerbach (1829-1880), Romantic Classicism. Judgement of Paris, Iphigeneia.

John Bernard Flannagan (1895-1942), primitive animal sculptor. Triumph of the Egg.

Jean-Honore Fragonard (1732-1806), Rococo. The Swing.

Daniel C. French (1850-1931). The Minute Man of Concord; seated Lincoln, Lincoln Memorial, Washington, D.C.

Caspar Daniel Friedrich (1774-1840), Romantic landscapes. Man and Woman Gazing at the Moon.

Thomas Gainsborough (1727-1788), portraitist. The Blue Boy.

Paul Gauguin (1848-1903), Post-impressionist. The Tahitians.

Lorenzo Ghiberti (1378-1455), Renaissance sculptor. Gates of Paradise baptistry doors, Florence.

Alberto Giacometti (1901-1966), attenuated sculptures of solitary figures. Man Pointing.

Giorgione (1477-1510), Renaissance. The Tempest.

Giotto (1276-1337), Renaissance. Presentation of Christ in the Temple.

Francois Girardon (1628-1715), Baroque sculptor of classical themes. Apollo Tended by the Nymphs.

Vincent van Gogh (1853-1890). The Starry Night, L'Arlesienne.

Arshile Gorky (1905-1948), Surrealist. The Liver Is the Cock's Comb.

Francisco de Goya y Lucientes (1746-1828), The Naked Maya, The Disasters of War (etchings).

El Greco (1541-1614). View of Toledo, Burial of the Count of Orgaz.

Horatio Greenough (1805-1852), Neo-classical sculptor. George Washington.

Mathias Grunewald (1480-1528), mystical religious themes. The Resurrection.

Franz Hals (1580-1666), portraitist. Laughing Cavalier, Gypsy Girl.

Childe Hassam (1859-1935), Impressionist. Southwest Wind.

Edward Hicks (1780-1849), primitive folk painter. The Peacable Kingdom.

Hans Hofmann (1880-1966), early Abstract Expressionist. Spring, The Gate.

William Hogarth (1697-1764), caricaturist. The Rake's Progress.

Katsushika Hokusai (1760-1849), printmaker. Crabs.

Hans Holbein the Elder (1460-1524), late Gothic. Presentation of Christ in the Temple.

Hans Holbein the Younger (1497-1543), portraitist. Henry VIII.

Winslow Homer (1836-1910), marine themes. Maine Coast, High Cliff.

Edward Hopper (1882-1967), realistic urban scenes. Sunlight in a Cafeteria.

Jean-Auguste-Dominique Ingres (1780-1867), Classicist. Valpincon Bather.

George Innes (1825-1894), luminous landscapist. Delaware Water Gap.

Vasily Kandinsky (1866-1944), Abstractionist. Capricious Forms.

Paul Klee (1879-1940), Abstractionist. Twittering Machine.

Kathe Kollwitz (1867-1945), printmaker, social justice themes. The Peasant War.

John La Farge (1835-1910), muralist. Red and White Peonies.

Gaston Lachaise (1882-1935), figurative sculptor. Standing Woman.

Fernand Leger (1881-1955), machine art. The Cyclists, Adam and Eve.

Leonardo da Vinci (1452-1519). Mona Lisa, Last Supper, The Annunciation.

Emanuel Leutz (1816-1868), historical themes. Washington Crossing the Delaware.

Jacques Lipchitz (1891-1973), Cubist sculptor. Harpist.

Filippino Lippi (1457-1504), Renaissance. The Vision of St. Bernard.

Fra Filippo Lippi (1406-1469), Renaissance. Coronation of the Virgin.

Aristide Maillol (1861-1944), sculptor. Night, The Mediterranean.

Edouard Manet (1832-1883), forerunner of Impressionism. Luncheon on the Grass, Olympia.

Andrea Mantegna (1431-1506), Renaissance frescoes. Triumph of Caesar.

Franz Marc (1880-1916), Expressionist. Blue Horses.

John Marin (1870-1953), expressionist seascapes. Maine Island.

Reginald Marsh (1898-1954), satirical artist. Tattoo and Haircut.

Tommaso Masaccio (1401-1428), Renaissance. The Tribute Money.

Henri Matisse (1869-1954), Fauvist, Woman with the Hat.

Michelangelo Buonarroti (1475-1564). Pieta, David, Moses, Battle of Cascina, The Last Judgment.

Carl Milles (1875-1955), expressive rhythmic sculptor. Playing Bears.

Jean-Francois Millet (1814-1875), painter of peasant subjects. The Gleaners, The Man with a Hoe.

David Milne (1882-1953), landscapist. Boston Corner, Berkshire Hills.

Amadeo Modigliani (1884-1920). Reclining Nude.

Piet Mondrian (1872-1944), Abstractionist. Composition.

Claude Monet (1840-1926), Impressionist. The Bridge at Argenteuil, Haystacks.

Gustave Moreau (1826-1898), Symbolist. The Apparition, Dance of Salome.

James Wilson Morrice (1865-1924), landscapist. The Ferry, Quebec; Venice, Looking Over the Lagoon.

Grandma Moses (1860-1961), primitive folk painter. Out for the Christmas Trees.

Edward Munch (1863-1944), Expressionist death themes. The Cry.

Bartolome Murillo (1618-1682), Baroque religious artist. Vision of St. Anthony, The Two Trinities.

Barnett Newman (1905-1970), Abstract Expressionist. Stations of the Cross.

Jose Clemente Orozco (1883-1949), frescoes. House of Tears.

Charles Willson Peale (1741-1827), American Revolutionary portraitist. Washington, Franklin, Jefferson, John Adams.

Rembrandt Peale (1778-1860), post-Revolutionary portraitist. Thomas Jefferson.

Pietro Perugino (1446-1523), Renaissance. Delivery of the Keys to St. Peter.

Pablo Picasso (1881-1973), Guernica, Dove, Head of a Woman.

Piero della Francesca (1420-1492), Renaissance. Duke of Urbino, Flagellation of Christ.

Camille Pissarro (1830-1903), Impressionist. Morning Sunlight.

Jackson Pollock (1912-1956), Abstract Expressionist. Autumn Rhythm.

Nicholas Poussin (1594-1665), Baroque pictorial classicism. St. John on Patmos.

Maurice B. Prendergast (1861-1924), Post-impressionist water-colorist. Umbrellas in the Rain.

Pierre-Paul Prud'hon (1758-1823), Romanticist. Crime pursued by Vengeance and Justice.

Puvis de Chavannes (1824-1898), muralist. The Poor Fisherman.

Raphael (1483-1520), Renaissance. Disputa, School of Athens.

Man Ray (1890-1976), Dadaist. Observing Time, The Lovers.

Odilon Redon (1840-1916), Symbolist lithographer. In the Dream.

Rembrandt van Rijn (1606-1669), The Bridal Couple, The Night Watch.

Frederic Remington (1861-1909), portrayal of the American West. Bronco Buster, Cavalry Charge on the Southern Plains.

Pierre-Auguste Renoir (1841-1919), Impressionist. The Luncheon of the Boating Party.

Ilya Repin (1844-1918), historical canvases. Zaporozhye Cossacks.

Joshua Reynolds (1723-1792), portraitist. Mrs. Siddons as the Tragic Muse.

Diego Rivera (1886-1957), frescoes. The Fecund Earth.

Auguste Rodin (1840-1917). The Thinker, The Burghers of Calais.

Mark Rothko (1903-1970), Abstract Expressionist. Light, Earth and Blue.

Georges Rouault (1871-1958), Expressionist. The Old King.

Henri Rousseau (1844-1910), primitive exotic themes. The Snake Charmer.

Theodore Rousseau (1812-1867), landscapist. Under the Birches, Evening.

Peter Paul Rubens (1577-1640), Baroque. Mystic Marriage of St. Catherine.

Andrey Rublyov (1370-1430), iconographer. Old Testament Trinity.

Albert Pinkham Ryder (1847-1917), seascapes and allegories. Toilers of the Sea.

Augustus Saint-Gaudens (1848-1901), memorial statues. Farragut, Mrs. Henry Adams (Grief).

Andrea Sansovino (1460-1529), Renaissance sculptor. Baptism of Christ.

Jacopo Sansovino (1486-1570), Renaissance sculptor. St. John the Baptist.

John Singer Sargent (1486-1570), Edwardian society portraitist. The Wyndham Sisters, Madam X.

Johann Gottfried Schadow (1764-1850), monumental sculptor. Quadriga, Brandenburg Gate.

Georges Seurat (1859-1891), Pointillist. Sunday Afternoon on the Island of Grande Jatte.

Gino Severini (1883-1891), Futurist and Cubist. Dynamic Hieroglyph of the Bal Tabarin.

Ben Shahn (1898-1969), social and political themes. Sacco and Vanzetti series, Seurat's Lunch, Handball.

Charles Sheeler (1883-1965), Abstractionist. Upper Deck, Rolling Power.

David Alfaro Siqueiros (1896-1974), political muralist. March of Humanity.

John F. Sloan (1871-1951), depictions of New York City. Wake of the Ferry.

David Smith (1906-1965), welded metal sculpture. Hudson River Landscape, Zig, Cubi series.

Gilbert Stuart (1755-1828), portraitist. George Washington.

Thomas Sully (1783-1872), portraitist. Col. Thomas Handasyd Perkins, The Passage of the Delaware.

Yves Tanguy (1900-1955), Surrealist. Rose of the Four Winds.

Thomas J. Thomson (1877-1918), landscapist. Spring Ice.

Giovanni Battista Tiepolo (1696-1770), Rococo frescoes. The Crucifixion.

Tintoretto (1518-1594), Mannerist. The Last Supper.

Titian (1477-1576), Renaissance. Venus and the Lute Player,

The Bacchanal.

Henri de Toulouse-Lautrec (1864-1901). At the Moulin Rouge.

John Trumbull (1756-1843), historical themes. The Declaration of Independence.

J.M.W. Turner (1755-1851), Romantic landscapist. Snow Storm.

Paolo Uccello (1397-1475), Gothic-Renaissance. The Rout of San Romano.

Maurice Utrillo (1883-1955), Impressionist. Sacre-Coeur de Montmartre.

Anthony Van Dyck (1599-1641), Baroque portraitist. Portrait of Charles I Hunting.

John Vanderlyn (1775-1852), Neo-classicist. Ariadne Asleep on the Island of Naxos.

Diego Velazquez (1599-1660), Baroque. Las Meninas, Portrait of Juan de Pareja.

Jan Vermeer (1632-1675), interior genre subjects. Young Woman with a Water Jug.

Paolo Veronese (1528-1588), devotional themes, vastly peopled canvases. The Temptation of St. Anthony.

Andrea del Verrocchio (1435-1488), Florentine sculptor. Colleoni.

Maurice de Vlaminck (1876-1958), Fauvist landscapist. The Storm.

Antoine Watteau (1684-1721), Rococo painter of "scenes of gallantry". The Embarkation for Cythera.

George Frederic Watts (1817-1904), painter and sculptor of grandiose allegorical themes. Hope, Physical Energy.

Benjamin West (1738-1820), realistic historical themes. Death of General Wolfe.

James Abbott McNeill Whistler (1834-1903). Arrangement in Grey and Black, No. 1: The Artist's Mother.

Archibald M. Willard (1836-1918). The Spirit of '76.

Grant Wood (1891-1942), Midwestern regionalist. American Gothic, Daughters of Revolution.

Osip Zadkine (1890-1967), School of Paris sculptor. The Destroyed City, Musicians, Christ.

British

British Statesmen

Born	Died	Name
1852	1928	Asquith, Herbert H.
1883	1967	Atlee, Clement
1867	1947	Baldwin, Stanley
1848	1930	Balfour, Arthur J.
1879	1964	Beaverbrook, Lord
1897	1960	Bevan, Aneurin
1881	1951	Bevin, Ernest
1884	1968	Cadogan, Alexander
1770	1827	Canning, George
1769	1822	Castlereagh, Robert
1864	1958	Cecil, Edgar
1863	1937	Chamberlain, Austen
1836	1914	Chamberlain, Joseph
1869	1940	Chamberlain, Neville
1874	1965	Churchill, Winston
1725	1774	Clive, Robert
1889	1952	Cripps, Stafford
1599	1658	Cromwell, Oliver
1859	1925	Curzon of Kedleston
1804	1881	Disraeli, Benjamin
1906	1963	Gaitskell, Hugh
1809	1898	Gladstone, Wm. E.
1764	1845	Grey, Charles
1862	1933	Grey, Edward
1732	1818	Hastings, Warren
1858	1923	Law, Andrew Bonar
1863	1945	Lloyd George, David
1866	1937	MacDonald, J. Ramsay
1732	1792	North, Frederick
1784	1865	Palmerston, Viscount
1788	1850	Peel, Robert
1759	1806	Pitt, William (Younger)
1708	1778	Pitt, William (Chatham)
1853	1902	Rhodes, Cecil
1792	1878	Russell, John
1830	1903	Salisbury, Robert
1676	1745	Walpole, Robert

British Army (A), Navy (N), Air Force (F), Explorers (E)

Born	Died	Name
1891	1969	Alexander, Harold R. (A)
1861	1936	Allenby, Edmund (A)
1584	1622	Baffin, William (E)
1695	1755	Braddock, Edward (A)
1723	1792	Burgoyne, John (A)
1663	1733	Byng, George (N)
1675	1726	Cadogan, Wm. (A)
1738	1795	Clinton, Henry (A)
1770	1851	Codrington, Ed (N)
1727	1779	Cook, James (E)
1738	1805	Cornwallis, Chas. (A)
1550	1605	Davys, John (E)
1883	1970	Dowding, Hugh C. (F)
1540	1596	Drake, Francis (N)
1841	1920	Fisher, John A. (N)
1535	1594	Frobisher, Martin (E)
1721	1787	Gage, Thomas (A)
1833	1885	Gordon, Chas. G. (A)
1541	1591	Grenville, Richard (N)
1861	1928	Haig, Douglas (A)
1853	1947	Hamilton, Ian (A)
1745	1792	Hearne, Samuel (E)
1726	1799	Howe, Richard (N)
1729	1814	Howe, William (A)
1575	1611	Hudson, Henry (E)
1880	1959	Ironside, Wm. E. (A)
1859	1935	Jellicoe, John (N)
1850	1916	Kitchener, H. H. (A)
1888	1935	Lawrence, T. E. (A)
1650	1722	Marlborough, Duke of (A)
1871	1951	Maurice, Frederick (A)
1867	1948	Milne, George (A)
1887	1976	Montgomery, Bernard (A)
1782	1853	Napier, Charles J. (A)
1810	1890	Napier, Robert C. (A)
1758	1805	Nelson, Horatio (N)
1696	1785	Oglethorpe, James (A)
1895	1968	Robb, James (F)
1719	1792	Rodney, George (N)
1800	1862	Ross, James C. (E)
1868	1912	Scott, Robert F. (E)
1874	1922	Shackleton, Ernest (E)
1841	1904	Stanley, Henry M. (E)
1890	1967	Tedder, Arthur W. (F)
1757	1798	Vancouver, George (E)
1883	1950	Wavell, Archibald (A)
1769	1852	Wellington, Duke of (A)
1727	1759	Wolfe, James (A)

British Scientists, Engineers, Physicians

Born	Died	Name
1813	1898	Bessemer, Henry
1881	1966	Campbell, Donald F.
1731	1810	Cavendish, Henry
1891	1974	Chadwick, James
1905	1967	Cockcroft, John
1832	1919	Crookes, William
1766	1844	Dalton, John
1809	1882	Darwin, Charles
1778	1829	Davy, Humphry
1791	1867	Faraday, Michael
1881	1955	Fleming, Alexander
1849	1945	Fleming, Ambrose
1892	1964	Haldane, J. B. S.
1578	1657	Harvey, William
1792	1871	Herschel, John
1738	1822	Herschel, William
1861	1947	Hopkins, Frederick
1887	1975	Huxley, Julian
1749	1823	Jenner, Edward
1815	1898	Jenner, William
1827	1912	Lister, Joseph
1831	1879	Maxwell, James Clerk
1642	1727	Newton, Isaac
1903	1969	Powell, Cecil F.
1733	1804	Priestley, Joseph
1857	1932	Ross, Ronald
1871	1937	Rutherford, Ernest
1624	1689	Sydenham, Thomas
1824	1907	Thomson, Wm. (Kelvin)
1823	1913	Wallace, Alf. Russell
1892	1973	Watson-Watt, Robert
1736	1819	Watt, James E.
1802	1875	Wheatstone, Chas.

British Religious Leaders

Born	Died	Name
1118	1170	Becket, Thomas a
1685	1753	Berkeley, George
1829	1912	Booth, William B.
1566	1644	Brewster, William
1489	1556	Cranmer, Thos.
1624	1691	Fox, George
1554	1600	Hooker, Richard
1860	1954	Inge, William Ralph
1874	1966	Johnson, Hewlett
1505	1572	Knox, John
1485	1555	Latimer, Hugh
1813	1873	Livingston, David
1808	1892	Manning, Henry E.
1801	1890	Newman, John H.
1492	1536	Tyndale, William
1703	1791	Wesley, John
1714	1770	Whitefield, Geo.
1475	1530	Wolsey, Thomas
1320	1384	Wycliffe, John

British Poets, Dramatists, Essayists, Historians, Novelists

Born	Died	Name
1672	1719	Addison, Joseph
1832	1904	Arnold, Edwin
1822	1888	Arnold, Matthew
1775	1817	Austen, Jane
1561	1626	Bacon, Francis
1214	1294	Bacon, Roger
1860	1937	Barrie, James M.
1584	1616	Beaumont, Francis
673	735	Bede, the Venerable
1872	1956	Beerbohm, Max
1870	1953	Belloc, Hilaire
1867	1931	Bennett, Arnold
1748	1832	Bentham, Jeremy
1869	1951	Blackwood, Algernon
1757	1827	Blake, William
1740	1795	Boswell, James
1844	1930	Bridges, Robert
1816	1855	Bronte, Charlotte
1818	1848	Bronte, Emily
1806	1861	Browning, Elizabeth B.
1812	1889	Browning, Robert

Born	Died	Name
1628	1688	Bunyan, John
1729	1797	Burke, Edmund
1759	1796	Burns, Robert
1788	1824	Byron, Lord Geo. Gordon
1795	1881	Carlyle, Thomas
1832	1898	Carroll, Lewis
1888	1957	Cary, Joyce
1340	1400	Chaucer, Geoffrey
1694	1773	Chesterfield, Earl of
1874	1936	Chesterton, G. K.
1891	1976	Christie, Agatha
1763	1835	Cobbett, William
1772	1834	Coleridge, S. T.
1824	1889	Collins, Wilkie
1670	1729	Congreve, William
1857	1924	Conrad, Joseph
1855	1924	Corelli, Marie
1731	1800	Cowper, William
1908	1973	Creasey, John
1660	1731	Defoe, Daniel
1873	1956	De la Mare, Walter
1785	1859	De Quincey, Thomas
1812	1870	Dickens, Charles
1573	1631	Donne, John
1859	1930	Doyle, Arthur Conan
1631	1700	Dryden, John
1834	1896	du Maurier, Geo. L.
1819	1880	Eliot, George
1888	1965	Eliot, T. S.
1707	1754	Fielding, Henry
1809	1883	Fitzgerald, Edward
1908	1964	Fleming, Ian
1873	1939	Ford, Ford Madox
1889	1966	Forester, C. S.
1879	1970	Forster, E. M.
1867	1933	Galsworthy, John
1685	1732	Gay, John
1737	1794	Gibbon, Edward
1728	1774	Goldsmith, Oliver
1716	1771	Gray, Thomas
1840	1928	Hardy, Thomas
1778	1830	Hazlitt, William
1849	1903	Henley, Wm. Ernest
1591	1674	Herrick, Robert
1588	1679	Hobbes, Thomas
1799	1845	Hood, Thomas
1859	1936	Housman, Alfred E.
1711	1776	Hume, David
1894	1963	Huxley, Aldous
1709	1784	Johnson, Samuel
1573	1637	Jonson, Ben
1795	1821	Keats, John
1819	1875	Kingsley, Charles
1865	1936	Kipling, Rudyard
1775	1834	Lamb, Charles
1885	1930	Lawrence, David H.
1838	1903	Lecky, W. E. H.
1866	1947	LeGallienne, Richard
1894	1957	Lewis, Wyndham
1895	1970	Liddell Hart, Basil
1632	1704	Locke, John
1800	1859	Macaulay, Thomas B.
1863	1947	Machen, Arthur
1888	1923	Mansfield, Katherine
1564	1593	Marlowe, Christopher
1897	1969	Martin, Kingsley
1878	1967	Masefield, John
1874	1965	Maugham, W. Somerset
1828	1909	Meredith, George
1806	1873	Mill, John Stuart
1882	1956	Milne, A. A.
1608	1674	Milton, John
1834	1896	Morris, William
1870	1916	Munro, H. H. (Saki)
1880	1958	Noyes, Alfred
1903	1950	Orwell, George
1839	1894	Pater, Walter
1785	1866	Peacock, Thomas L.
1633	1703	Pepys, Samuel
1688	1744	Pope, Alexander
1900	1969	Potter, Stephen
1664	1721	Prior, Matthew
1863	1944	Quiller-Couch, Arthur T.
1552	1618	Raleigh, Sir Walter
1814	1884	Reade, Charles
1689	1761	Richardson, Samuel
1828	1882	Rossetti, Dante
1819	1900	Ruskin, John
1872	1970	Russell, Bertrand
1886	1967	Sassoon, Siegfried
1771	1832	Scott, Sir Walter
1564	1616	Shakespeare, William
1856	1950	Shaw, G. Bernard
1797	1851	Shelley, Mary W.
1792	1822	Shelley, Percy Bysshe
1751	1816	Sheridan, Richard B.
1554	1586	Sidney, Sir Phillip
1887	1964	Sitwell, Edith
1892	1969	Sitwell, Osbert
1721	1771	Smollett, Tobias
1774	1843	Southey, Robert
1552	1599	Spenser, Edmund
1672	1729	Steele, Richard
1713	1768	Sterne, Laurence
1850	1894	Stevenson, Robert Louis
1880	1932	Strachey, Lytton
1667	1745	Swift, Jonathan
1837	1909	Swinburne, Algernon C.
1809	1892	Tennyson, Alfred
1811	1863	Thackeray, W. M.
1914	1953	Thomas, Dylan
1892	1973	Tolkien, J.R.R.
1889	1975	Toynbee, Arnold
1876	1962	Trevelyan, Geo. M.
1815	1882	Trollope, Anthony
1884	1941	Walpole, Hugh
1593	1683	Walton, Izaak
1851	1920	Ward, Mrs. Humphry
1903	1966	Waugh, Evelyn
1866	1946	Wells, H. G.
1906	1964	White, T. H.
1861	1947	Whitehead, Alfred N.
1856	1900	Wilde, Oscar
1882	1941	Woolf, Virginia
1770	1850	Wordsworth, William
1640	1715	Wycherly, William

Poets Laureate of England

There is no authentic record of the origin of the office of Poet Laureate of England. According to Warton, there was a Versificator Regis, or King's Poet, in the reign of Henry III (1216-1272), and he was paid 100 shillings a year. Geoffrey Chaucer (1340-1400) assumed the title of Poet Laureate, and in 1389 got a royal grant of a yearly allowance of wine. In the reign of Edward IV (1461-1483), John Kay held the post. Under Henry VII (1485-1509), Andrew Bernard was the Poet Laureate, and was succeeded under Henry VIII (1509-1547) by John Skelton. Next came Edmund Spenser, who died in 1599; then Samuel Daniel, appointed 1599, and then Ben Jonson, 1619. Sir William D'Avenant was appointed in 1637. He was a godson of William Shakespeare.

Others were John Dryden, 1670; Thomas Shadwell, 1688; Nahum Tate, 1692; Nicholas Rowe, 1715; the Rev. Laurence Eusden, 1718; Colly Cibber, 1730; William Whitehead, 1757, on the refusal of Gray; Rev. Thomas Warton, 1785, on the refusal of Mason; Henry J. Pye, 1790; Robert Southey, 1813, on the refusal of Sir Walter Scott; William Wordsworth, 1843; Alfred, Lord Tennyson, 1850; Alfred Austin, 1896; Robert Bridges, 1913; John Masefield, 1930; Cecil Day Lewis, 1967; Sir John Betjeman, 1972.

Canadian

Statesmen

Born	Died	Name
1878	1943	Aberhart, William
1804	1858	Baldwin, Robert
1870	1957	Bennett, Richard B.
1833	1912	Blake, Edward
1854	1937	Borden, Robert
1823	1917	Bowell, Mackenzie
1818	1880	Brown, George
1814	1873	Cartier, Georges
1804	1873	Howe, Joseph
1874	1950	King, W. Mackenzie
1841	1919	Laurier, Wilfrid
1815	1891	Macdonald, John A.
1795	1861	Mackenzie, Wm. Lyon
1825	1868	McGee, Thomas D'Arcy
1874	1960	Meighen, Arthur
1897	1972	Pearson, Lester B.
1855	1927	Tupper, Charles H.

Scientists, Industrialists

Born	Died	Name
1859	1942	Adams, Frank D.
1810	1882	Allan, Hugh
1891	1941	Banting, Fredk. G.
1877	1943	Beatty, Edward W.
1889	1966	Hilton, Hugh G.
1798	1875	Logan, William
1876	1935	Macleod, John J. R.
1849	1919	Osler, William
1863	1892	Stairs, Wm. Grant
1894	1976	Thomson, Roy
1902	1967	Zimmerman, Adam

Authors

Born	Died	Name
1868	1952	Bourassa, Henri
1861	1918	Campbell, W. Wilfred
1861	1929	Carman, W. Bliss
1858	1946	Chapais, Thomas
1827	1879	Cremazie, Octave
1866	1944	Dafoe, John Wesley
1895	1958	Dawson, R. MacGregor
1860	1936	Doughty, Arthur G.
1862	1932	Duncan, Sara J.
1864	1922	Edwards, Robert (Bob)
1839	1908	Frechette, Louis H.
1809	1866	Garneau, Francis X.
1860	1937	Gordon, Chas. W. (Ralph Connor)
1878	1967	Groulx, Lionel A.
1871	1948	Grove, Frederick
1796	1865	Haliburton, Thos. C.
1880	1913	Hemon, Louis
1894	1952	Innis, H. A.
1881	1943	Kennedy, W. P. M.
1817	1906	Kirby, William
1862	1913	Johnson, Pauline
1861	1899	Lampman, Archibald
1869	1944	Leacock, Stephen
1909	1957	Lowry, Malcolm
1874	1942	Macdonald, Lucy M.
1862	1933	MacMechan, Archibald
1882	1958	Martin, Chester
1872	1918	McCrae, John
1820	1907	McMullen, John
1865	1944	Miner, John T. (Jack)
1874	1942	Montgomery, Lucy
1803	1885	Moodie, Susanna
1889	1963	Morin, Paul
1879	1941	Nelligan, Emile
1862	1932	Parker, Gilbert
1887	1970	Phelps, Arthur L.
1883	1922	Pickthall, Marjorie

Born	Died	Name
1883	1964	Pratt, Edwin J.
1860	1943	Roberts, Chas. G. D.
1885	1961	Roche, Mazo de la
1839	1920	Routhier, Adolphe B.
1870	1943	Roy, Camille
1858	1913	Roy, Joseph E.
1822	1893	Sangster, Charles
1862	1947	Scott, Duncan C.
1874	1958	Service, Robert W.
1859	1931	Short, Adam
1878	1941	Skelton, O. D.
1823	1910	Smith, Goldwin
1841	1923	Sulte, Benjamin
1860	1948	Wrong, George M.

Anthropologists, Geologists, and Naturalists

Born	Died	Name
1876	1961	Anderson, Rudolph M.
1883	1969	Barbeau, Charles M.
1820	1876	Billings, Elkanah
1846	1925	Dionne, Charles Eusibe
1817	1896	Hale, Horatio
1859	1944	Hill-Tout, Charles
1826	1892	Hunt, Thomas Sterry
1886	1969	Jenness, Diamond
1833	1881	LaRue, Francois A. H.
1798	1875	Logan, Sir William E.
1862	1920	Macoun, James Melville
1831	1920	Macoun, John
1869	1933	Macoun, William Tyrell
1885	1944	Marie-Victorin, frere
1867	1947	Massicotte, Edouard Z.
1820	1892	Provancher, Leon, abbe
1905	1970	Rousseau, Jacques
1891	1957	Rowan, William
1870	1953	Roy, Pierre Georges
1867	1937	Saunders, Sir Charles E.
1836	1914	Saunders, William
1875	1947	Taverner, Percy A.
1858	1957	Tyrrell, Joseph Burr
1872	1924	Waugh, Fredrick W.
1881	1964	Wilson, Alice Evelyn
1876	1941	Wintemberg, William J.

French

French Political Leaders

Born	Died	Name
1884	1966	Auriol, Vincent
1872	1950	Blum, Leon
1862	1932	Briand, Aristide
1841	1929	Clemenceau, Georges
1619	1683	Colbert, Jean-Bapt.
1884	1970	Daladier, Edouard
1759	1794	Danton, Georges
1890	1970	DeGaulle, Charles
1760	1794	Desmoulins, Camille
1620	1698	Frontenac, Louis de
1838	1882	Gambetta, Leon
1872	1957	Herriot, Edouard
1883	1945	Laval, Pierre
1871	1950	Lebrun, Albert
1744	1793	Marat, Jean-Paul
1602	1661	Mazarin, Jules
1749	1791	Mirabeau, Honore
1905	1975	Mollet, Guy
1860	1934	Poincare, Raymond
1911	1974	Pompidou, Georges
1878	1966	Reynaud, Paul
1585	1642	Richelieu, Cardinal de
1758	1794	Robespierre, Max.
1754	1838	Talleyrand, Chas. de

French Military Leaders and Explorers

Born	Died	Name
1769	1821	Bonaparte, Napoleon
1658	1730	Cadillac, Antoine
1753	1823	Carnot, Lazare
1491	1557	Cartier, Jacques
1567	1635	Champlain, Sam'l de
1867	1936	Charcot, Jean B.
1519	1572	Coligny, Gasp. de
1621	1686	Conde, Prince de
1881	1942	Darlan, Jean F.
1722	1788	DeGrasse, Francois
1739	1823	Dumouriez, Chas. F.
1851	1929	Foch, Ferdinand
1879	1949	Giraud, Henri H.
1640	1701	Hennepin, Louis
1852	1931	Joffre, Jos.
1645	1700	Jolliet, Louis
1753	1800	Kleber, Jean-Bapt.
1757	1834	Lafayette, Marquis de
1643	1687	LaSalle, Robt. de
1902	1947	Leclerc, Jacques P.
1637	1675	Marquette, Jacques
1756	1817	Massena, Andre
1712	1759	Montcalm, Louis de
1763	1813	Moreau, Jean V.
1767	1815	Murat, Joachim
1769	1815	Ney, Michel
1856	1951	Petain, Henri Philippe
1725	1807	Rochambeau, Jean-Bapt.
1579	1638	Rohan, Henri
1696	1750	Saxe, Maurice de
1769	1851	Soult, Nicolas J.
1611	1675	Turenne, Vicomte de

French Scientists, Physicians

Born	Died	Name
1775	1836	Ampere, Andre-Marie
1788	1878	Becquerel, A. C.
1852	1908	Becquerel, H. A.
1827	1907	Berthelot, Marcelin
1872	1936	Bleriot, Louis
1873	1944	Carrel, Alexis
1825	1893	Charcot, Jean M.
1867	1934	Curie, Marie
1859	1906	Curie, Pierre
1842	1925	Flammarion, Camille
1778	1850	Gay-Lussac, Joseph
1900	1958	Joliot-Curie, Frederic
1897	1956	Joliot-Curie, Irene
1781	1826	Laennec, Rene
1736	1813	Lagrange, Joseph
1744	1829	Lamarck, Jean B.
1749	1827	Laplace, Pierre S.
1743	1794	Lavoisier, Antoine
1862	1954	Lumiere, Auguste
1864	1948	Lumiere, Louis
1822	1895	Pasteur, Louis
1854	1912	Poincare, Henri
1875	1965	Schweitzer, Albert

French Authors, Dramatists, Historians, Religionists

Born	Died	Name
1079	1142	Abelard, Pierre
1717	1783	Alembert, Jean d'
1885	1969	Allain, Marcel
1880	1918	Apollinaire, Guillaume
1799	1850	Balzac, Honore de
1862	1923	Barres, Maurice
1821	1867	Baudelaire, Charles
1732	1799	Beaumarchais, Pierre
1837	1899	Becque, Henry
1780	1857	Beranger, Pierre
1859	1941	Bergson, Henri
1888	1948	Bernanos, Georges
1636	1711	Boileau, Nicolas
1627	1704	Bossuet, Jacques
1852	1935	Bourget, Paul
1707	1788	Buffon, Georges
1509	1564	Calvin, John
1913	1960	Camus, Albert
1768	1848	Chateaubriand, Francois
1762	1794	Chenier, Andre
1895	1969	Chevallier, Gabriel
1889	1963	Cocteau, Jean
1873	1954	Colette, Sidonie
1447	1511	Comines, Philippe de
1798	1857	Comte, Auguste
1767	1830	Constant, Benjamin
1606	1684	Corneille, Pierre
1840	1897	Daudet, Alphonse
1596	1650	Descartes, Rene
1713	1784	Diderot, Denis
1803	1870	Dumas, Alexandre
1824	1895	Dumas (Fils), Alexandre
1651	1715	Fenelon, Francois de
1821	1880	Flaubert, Gustave
1844	1924	France, Anatole
1333	1400	Froissart, Jean
1811	1872	Gautier, Theophile
1869	1951	Gide, Andre
1882	1944	Giraudoux, Jean
1816	1882	Gobineau, Comte de
1822	1896	Goncourt, Edmond de
1830	1870	Goncourt, Jules de
1787	1874	Guizot, Francois
1857	1915	Hervieu, Paul
1802	1885	Hugo, Victor
1848	1907	Huysmans, Joris-Karl
1412	1431	Joan of Arc
1645	1696	La Bruyere, Jean de
1621	1695	La Fontaine, Jean de
1790	1869	Lamartine, Alphonse de
1846	1870	Lautreamont, Comte de
1853	1914	Lemaitre, Jules
1668	1747	Lesage, Alain-Rene
1850	1923	Loti, Pierre (J. Viaud)
1842	1898	Mallarme, Stephane
1882	1973	Maritain, Jacques
1688	1763	Marivaux, Pierre
1850	1893	Maupassant, Guy de
1885	1967	Maurois, Andre
1803	1870	Merimee, Prosper
1798	1874	Michelet, Jules
1622	1673	Moliere, Jean-Baptiste
1533	1592	Montaigne, Michel de
1689	1755	Montesquieu, Charles de
1810	1857	Musset, Alfred de
1623	1662	Pascal, Blaise
1895	1974	Pagnol, Marcel
1873	1914	Peguy, Charles
1887	1975	Perse, St.-John
1697	1763	Prevost (L'Abbe)
1871	1922	Proust, Marcel
1495	1553	Rabelais, Francois
1639	1699	Racine, Jean
1823	1892	Renan, Ernest
1854	1891	Rimbaud, Arthur
1866	1944	Rolland, Romain
1524	1585	Ronsard, Pierre de
1868	1918	Rostand, Edmond
1712	1778	Rousseau, Jean-Jacques
1610	1703	Saint-Evremond, de
1900	1944	Saint-Exupery, Ant. de
1675	1755	Saint-Simon, Duc de
1804	1869	Sainte-Beuve, Charles A.
1567	1622	Sales (Saint Francois de)
1804	1876	Sand, George (Lucile Dupin)
1831	1908	Sardou, Victorien
1626	1696	Sevigne, (Mme. de)
1875	1959	Siegfried, Andre
1766	1817	Stael, (Mme. de)
1783	1842	Stendhal, (Beyle)
1839	1907	Sully-Prudhomme, Rene
1828	1893	Taine, Hippolyte
1795	1856	Thierry, Augustin
1805	1859	Tocqueville, A. C. de
1871	1945	Valery, Paul
1844	1896	Verlaine, Paul
1828	1905	Verne, Jules
1797	1863	Vigny, Alfred de
1838	1889	Villiers de l'Isle, Adam
1431	1484	Villon, Francois
1694	1778	Voltaire (Arouet)
1840	1902	Zola, Emile

German

German Political and Military Leaders, Economists

Born	Died	Name
1876	1967	Adenauer, Konrad
1856	1921	Bethmann-Hollweg, T. v.
1815	1898	Bismarck, Otto v.
1742	1819	Bluecher, Gebhart v.
1885	1970	Bruning, Heinrich
1780	1831	Clausewitz, Karl v.
1875	1921	Erzberger, Matthias
1760	1831	Gneisenau, August
1893	1946	Goering, Hermann
1847	1934	Hindenburg, Paul v.
1889	1945	Hitler, Adolf
1887	1960	Kesselring, Albert
1871	1919	Liebknecht, Karl
1865	1937	Ludendorff, Erich
1880	1919	Luxemburg, Rosa
1818	1883	Marx, Karl
1800	1891	Moltke, Helmuth v.
1848	1916	Moltke, Helmuth v.
1879	1969	Papen, Franz v.
1867	1922	Rathenau, Walter
1891	1944	Rommel, Erwin
1876	1953	Rundstedt, Karl v.
1877	1970	Schacht, Hjalmar
1865	1939	Scheidemann, Philipp
1878	1929	Stresemann, Gustav
1849	1930	Tirpitz, Alf. v.
1893	1973	Ulbricht, Walter

German Engineers, Naturalists, Scientists, Industrialists

Born	Died	Name
1902	1958	Adler, Kurt
1193	1280	Albertus, Magnus
1844	1929	Benz, Carl
1882	1970	Born, Max
1874	1940	Bosch, Karl
1811	1899	Bunsen, Robert
1834	1900	Daimler, Gottlieb
1858	1913	Diesel, Rudolf
1884	1969	Dornier, Claude
1868	1954	Eckener, Hugo
1854	1915	Ehrlich, Paul
1686	1736	Fahrenheit, Gabriel
1882	1964	Franck, James
1400	1468	Gutenberg, Johann
1834	1919	Haeckel, Ernst
1879	1968	Hahn, Otto
1755	1843	Hahnemann, Samuel
1821	1894	Helmholz, Hermann v.
1857	1894	Hertz, Heinrich
1769	1859	Humboldt, Alex. v.
1571	1630	Kepler, Johannes
1843	1910	Koch, Robert
1812	1887	Krupp, Alfred
1907	1967	Krupp, Alfried
1900	1967	Kuhn, Richard
1646	1716	Leibnitz, Gottfried v.
1734	1815	Mesmer, Franz
1899	1968	Nordhoff, Heinrich
1787	1854	Ohm, Geo. S.
1853	1932	Ostwald, Wilhelm
1858	1947	Planck, Max
1875	1951	Porsche, Ferdinand
1845	1923	Roentgen, Wilhelm
1822	1890	Schliemann, Heinrich
1816	1892	Siemens, Werner v.
1842	1926	Thyssen, August
1821	1902	Virchow, Rudolf
1883	1970	Warburg, Otto
1866	1925	Wassermann, Aug. v.
1838	1917	Zeppelin, Ferd. v.

German Authors, Dramatists, Essayists, Religionists

Born	Died	Name
1898	1956	Brecht, Bertolt
1788	1857	Eichendorff, Josef v.
1820	1895	Engels, Friedrich
1886	1933	Ernst, Paul
1170	1220	Eschenbach, Wolfram v.
1884	1958	Feuchtwanger, Lion
1762	1814	Fichte, Johann G.
1869	1966	Foerster, Friedrich
1819	1898	Fontane, Theodor
1816	1895	Freytag, Gustav
1749	1832	Goethe, Johann W. v.
1785	1863	Grimm, Jakob
1786	1859	Grimm, Wilheim
1890	1941	Hasenclever, Walter
1862	1946	Hauptmann, Gerhart
1813	1863	Hebbel, Friedrich
1770	1831	Hegel, Georg W. F.
1797	1856	Heine, Heinrich
1744	1803	Herder, Johann v.
1877	1962	Hesse, Hermann
1878	1945	Kaiser, Georg
1724	1804	Kant, Immanuel
1896	1966	Kasack, Hermann
1777	1811	Kleist, Heinrich v.
1724	1803	Klopstock, Friedr
1875	1967	Kolb, Annette
1729	1781	Lessing, Gotthold
1881	1948	Ludwig, Emil
1483	1546	Luther, Martin
1871	1950	Mann, Heinrich
1875	1955	Mann, Thomas
1817	1903	Mommsen, Theodor
1844	1900	Nietzsche, Friedrich
1795	1886	Ranke, Leopold, v.
1810	1874	Reuter, Fritz
1763	1825	Richter, (Jean Paul)
1875	1926	Rilke, Rainer Maria
1899	1966	Ropke, Wilhelm
1788	1866	Rueckert, Friedrich
1494	1576	Sachs, Hans
1775	1854	Schelling, Friedrich v.
1759	1805	Schiller, Johann v.
1767	1845	Schlegel, August v.
1772	1829	Schlegel, Friedrich v.
1768	1834	Schleiermacher, Friedrich
1788	1860	Schopenhauer, Arthur
1857	1928	Sudermann, Hermann
1893	1939	Toller, Ernst
1834	1896	Treitschke, Heinrich v.
1787	1862	Uhland, Ludwig
1873	1934	Wassermann, Jakob
1733	1813	Wieland, Chris. M.

Italian

Italian Authors, Dramatists, Poets, Philosophers, Historians

Born	Died	Name
1749	1803	Alfieri, Vittorio
1227	1274	Aquinas, Thomas
1492	1556	Aretino, Pietro
1474	1533	Ariosto, Ludovico
1791	1863	Belli, Giuseppe
1313	1375	Boccaccio, Giovanni
1441	1494	Boiardo, Matteo Maria
1548	1599	Bruno, Giordano
1568	1639	Campanella, Tommaso
1835	1907	Carducci, Giosue
1725	1798	Casanova, Giacomo
1478	1529	Castiglione, Baldassarre
1866	1952	Croce, Benedetto
1863	1938	D'Annunzio, Gabriele
1265	1321	Dante, Alighieri
1909	1967	Emanuelli, Enrico
1842	1911	Fogazzaro, Antonio
1875	1944	Gentile, Giovanni
1809	1850	Giusti, Giuseppe
1713	1786	Gozzi, Gaspare
1483	1540	Guicciardini, Francesco
1798	1837	Leopardi, Giacomo
1836	1909	Lombroso, Cedare
1469	1527	Machiavelli, Niccolo
1898	1957	Malaparte, Curzio
1449	1515	Manuzio, Aldo (Aldus)
1785	1873	Manzoni, Alessandro
1805	1872	Mazzini, Giuseppe
1672	1750	Muratori, Ludovico
1848	1923	Pareto, Vilfredo
1855	1912	Pascoli, Giovanni
1304	1374	Petrarca, Francesco
1867	1936	Pirandello, Luigi
1432	1484	Pulci, Luigi
1901	1968	Quasimodo, Salvatore
1544	1595	Tasso, Torquato
1888	1970	Ungaretti, Giuseppe
1668	1744	Vico, Giambattista

Italian Explorers, Scientists, Political Leaders

Born	Died	Name
1776	1856	Avogadro, Amedeo
1738	1794	Beccaria, Cesare
1835	1900	Beltrami, Eugenio
1476	1507	Borgia, Cesare
1450	1498	Cabot, John (Caboto)
1826	1910	Cannizzaro, Stanislao
1810	1861	Cavour, Camillo Benso
1451	1506	Columbus, Christopher
1830	1903	Cremona, Luigi
1881	1954	De Gasperi, Alcide
1466	1560	Doria, Andrea
1901	1954	Fermi, Enrico
1847	1897	Ferraris, Galileo
1564	1642	Galileo (G. Galilei)
1737	1798	Galvani, Luigi
1807	1882	Garibaldi, Giuseppe
1882	1955	Graziani, Rodolfo
1483	1540	Guicciardini, Francesco
1874	1937	Marconi, Guglielmo
1389	1464	Medici, Cosimo de' (1)
1519	1574	Medici, Cosimo de' (2)
1449	1492	Medici, Lorenzo de'
1846	1910	Mosso, Angelo
1883	1945	Mussolini, Benito
1868	1953	Nitti, Francesco
1254	1324	Polo, Marco
1878	1970	Ruini, Meuccio
1835	1910	Schiaparelli, Giovanni
1818	1878	Secchi, Angelo
1872	1952	Sforza, Carlo
1729	1799	Spallanzani, Lazzaro
1608	1647	Torricelli, Evangelista
1485	1533	Verrazano, Giovanni da
1454	1512	Vespucci, Amerigo
1745	1827	Volta, Alessandro

Russian

Political Leaders

Born	Died	Name
1899	1953	Beria, Lavrenti
1814	1876	Bakunin, Mikhail
1888	1938	Bukharin, Nikolai
1895	1975	Bulganin, Nikolai A.
1875	1946	Kalinin, Mikhail
1883	1936	Kamenev, Lev
1881	1970	Kerensky, Aleksandr

Born	Died	Name
1894	1971	Khrushchev, Nikita
1842	1921	Kropotkin, Pyotr
1870	1924	Lenin, Vladimir
1876	1951	Litvinov, Maxim
1857	1918	Plekhanov, Georgi
1739	1791	Potemkin, Grigori
1772	1839	Speransky, Mikhail
1879	1953	Stalin, Josef
1863	1911	Stolypin, Pyotr
1879	1940	Trotsky, Leon
1849	1915	Witte, Sergei
1883	1936	Zinoviev, Grigori

Military Leaders

Born	Died	Name
1883	1973	Budenny, Semyon
1872	1947	Denikin, Anton
1874	1920	Kolchak, Aleksandr
1897	1973	Konev, Ivan
1870	1918	Kornilov, Lavr
1745	1813	Kutuzov, Mikhail
1902	1974	Kuznetzov, Nikolai
1859	1914	Samsonov, Aleksandr
1729	1800	Suvorov, Aleksandr
1895	1970	Timoshenko, Semyon
1881	1969	Voroshilov, Kliment Y.
1895	1974	Zhukov, Georgi K.

Scientists

Born	Died	Name
1877	1968	Arbuzov, Aleksandr
1898	1967	Balandin, Aleksei
1857	1927	Bekhterev, Vladmir
1863	1945	Krylov, Aleksei N.
1908	1968	Landau, Lev D.
1711	1765	Lomonosov, Mikhail
1909	1967	Maltsev, Anatoli
1834	1907	Mendeleyev, Dmitri
1845	1916	Metchnikov, Elie
1905	1970	Mikoyan, Artem I.
1849	1936	Pavlov, Ivan
1859	1905	Popov, Aleksandr
1907	1966	Sisakian, Norayr M.
1891	1969	Stechkin, Boris S.
1857	1935	Tsiolkovsky, Konstantin E.

Authors

Born	Died	Name
1888	1966	Akhmatova, Anna A.
1791	1859	Aksakov, Sergei
1894	1941	Babel, Isaac
1811	1848	Belinsky, Vissarion
1880	1921	Blok, Aleksandr
1891	1940	Bulgakov, Mikhail
1870	1953	Bunin, Ivan
1860	1904	Chekhov, Anton
1821	1881	Dostoyevsky, Fyodor
1891	1967	Ehrenburg, Ilya G.
1809	1852	Gogol, Nikolai
1812	1891	Goncharov, Ivan A.
1868	1936	Gorky, Maxim
1812	1870	Herzen, Aleksandr
1853	1921	Korolenko, Vladimir
1768	1844	Krylov, Ivan A.
1870	1938	Kuprin, Aleksandr
1814	1841	Lermontov, Mikhail
1831	1895	Leskov, Nikolai
1891	1938	Mandelstam, Osip
1893	1930	Mayakovsky, Vladimir
1821	1877	Nekrasov, Nikolai
1890	1960	Pasternak, Boris
1799	1837	Pushkin, Aleksandr
1820	1879	Soloviev, Sergei
1883	1945	Tolstoy, Alexei
1828	1910	Tolstoy, Lev
1892	1941	Tsvetaeva, Marina
1818	1883	Turgenev, Ivan
1895	1925	Yesenin, Sergei

Additional Foreign Personalities of the Past

S. Y. Agnon, Israeli novelist, 1888-1970.
Emilio Aguinaldo, Filipino revolutionary, 1869-1964.
Roald Amundsen, Norwegian explorer, 1872-1928.
Hans Christian Andersen, Danish author, 1805-1875.
Ivo Andric, Yugoslav novelist, 1892-1975.
Pedro Aramburu, Argentine statesman, 1903-1970.
Sholem Asch, Polish-born Yiddish writer, 1880-1957.
Miguel Angel Asturias, Guatemalan novelist, 1899-1974.
Vasco Nunez de Balboa, Spanish explorer, 1475-1519.
Karl Barth, Swiss theologian, 1886-1966.
Brendan Behan, Irish playwright, 1923-1964.
Eduard Benes, Czech. statesman, 1884-1948.
David Ben-Gurion, first Israeli premier, 1886-1973.
Vitus Bering, Danish explorer, 1680-1741.
Folke Bernadotte, Swedish statesman, 1895-1948.
Vicente Blasco-Ibanez, Spanish novelist, 1867-1928.
Niels Bohr, Danish physicist, 1885-1962.
Louis Botha, South African statesman, 1862-1919.
Emil Brunner, Swiss theologian, 1889-1966.
Martin Buber, Austrian-born Jewish philosopher, 1878-1965.
Guatama Buddha, Indian philosopher, C.563-C.483 B.C.
Karel Capek, Czech. writer, 1890-1938.
Venustiano Carranza, Mexican political leader, 1859-1920.
Roger Casement, Irish revolutionary, 1864-1916.
Humberto Castelo Branco, Brazilian political leader, 1900-1967.
Miguel de Cervantes Saavedra, Spanish novelist, 1547-1616.
Chiang Kai-shek, president of Nationalist China, 1886-1975.
Chou En-lai, prime minister of China, 1898-1976.
Henri Christophe, Haitian revolutionary, 1767-1820.
Confucius, Chinese philosopher, 551-479 B.C.
Nicholas Copernicus, Polish astronomer, 1473-1543.
Hernando Cortes, Spanish conqueror of Mexico, 1485-1547.
Hernando de Soto, Spanish explorer, 1500-1542.
Eamon de Valera, Irish statesman, 1882-1975.
Jean J. Dessalines, Haitian emperor, 1758-1806.
Porfirio Diaz, Mexican statesman, 1830-1915.
Ngo Dinh Diem, South Vietnamese president, 1901-1963.
Isak Dinesen, Danish author, 1885-1962.
Engelbert Dollfuss, Austrian statesman, 1892-1934.
Christian Doppler, Austrian physicist, 1803-1853.
Robert Emmet, Irish nationalist, 1778-1803.
Enver Pasha, Turkish political leader, 1881-1922.
Desiderius Erasmus, Dutch scholar, 1466-1536.
Makik Faisal, King of Saudi Arabia, 1906-1975.
Sigmund Freud, Austrian psychiatrist, 1856-1939.
Vasco da Gama, Portuguese navigator, 1469-1524.
Mohandas K. Gandhi, Indian political leader, 1869-1948.
Lady Augusta Gregory, Irish dramatist, 1859-1932.
Dag Hammarskjold, Swedish statesman, 1905-1961.
Theodor Herzl. Austrian founder of modern Zionism, 1860-1904.
Ho Chi Minh, North Vietnamese president, 1890-1969.
Nicholas Horthy, Hungarian statesman, 1868-1957.
Jan Hus, Czech, religionist, 1369-1415.
Henrik Ibsen, Norwegian playwright, 1828-1906.
James Joyce, Irish author, 1882-1941.
Benito Juarez, Mexican statesman, 1806-1872.
Carl Jung, Swiss psychiatrist, 1875-1961.
Franz Kafka, Czech.-born Austrian author, 1883-1924.
Joseph Kasavubu, Congolese political leader, 1910-1969.
Yasunari Kawabata, Japanese novelist, 1899-1972.
Kemal Ataturk, Turkish statesman, 1881-1938.
Elizabeth (Sister) Kenny, Australian nurse, 1886-1952.
Omar Khayyam, Persian poet, C. 1028-1122.
Thaddeus Kosciusko, Polish general, 1746-1817.
Paul Kruger, South African statesman, 1825-1904.
Par Lagerkvist, Swedish novelist, 1891-1974.
Selma Lagerlof, Swedish author, 1858-1940.
Wanda Landowska, Polish harpsichordist, 1877-1959.
Patrice E. Lumumba, Congolese political leader, 1925-1961.
Francisco I. Madero, Mexican statesman, 1873-1913.
Maurice Maeterlinck, Belgian dramatist, 1862-1949.
Ferdinand Magellan, Portuguese explorer, 1480-1521.
Moses Maimonides, Jewish philosopher, 1135-1204.
Carl Gustav Mannerheim, Finnish statesman, 1867-1951.
Mao Tse-tung, Chinese leader, 1893-1976.
Jose Marti, Cuban patriot, 1853-1895.
Thomas Masaryk, Czech. statesman, philosopher, 1850-1937.
Tom Mboya, Kenyan political leader, 1930-1969.
Lise Meitner, Austrian physicist, 1878-1968.
Gregor J. Mendel, Austrian botanist, 1822-1884.
John Metaxas, Greek statesman, 1871-1941.
Klemens W. N. L. Metternich, Austrian statesman, 1773-1859.
Draja Mikhailovich, Yugoslav soldier, 1893-1946.
Jozef Cardinal Mindszenty, Roman Catholic primate of Hungary, 1892-1975.
Vihelm Moberg, Swedish novelist, 1898-1973.
Ferenc Molnar, Hungarian dramatist, 1878-1952.
George Moore, Irish novelist, 1852-1933.
Thomas Moore, Irish poet, 1779-1852.
Jose M. Morelos y Pavon, Mexican patriot, 1765-1815.
Fridtjof Nansen, Norwegian explorer, 1861-1930.
Jawaharlal Nehru, Indian statesman, 1889-1964.
Florence Nightingale, English nurse, 1820-1910.
Alfred Nobel, Swedish inventor, philanthropist, 1833-1896.
Alvaro Obregon, Mexican statesman, 1880-1928.
Sean O'Casey, Irish dramatist, 1884-1964.
Daniel O'Connell, Irish political leader, 1775-1847.
Thomas P. O'Connor, Irish journalist, 1848-1929.
Omar Khayyam, Persian poet, c. 1028-1122.
Aristotle Onassis, Greek shipping magnate, 1900-1975.
George Papandreou, Greek statesman, 1888-1968.
Charles Stewart Parnell, Irish nationalist, 1846-1891.
Juan Peron, president of Argentina, 1895-1974.
Joseph Pilsudski, Polish statesman, 1867-1935.
Miguel Primo de Rivera, Spanish dictator, 1870-1930.
Casimir Pulaski, Polish soldier, 1748-1779.
Adam Rapacki, Polish statesman, 1910-1970.
Syngman Rhee, South Korean president, 1875-1965.
Antonio de O. Salazar, Portuguese statesman, 1899-1970.
Antonio L. de Santa Anna, Mexican general, 1795-1876.
Eisaku Sato, Japanese statesman, 1901-1975.

Arthur Schnitzler, Austrian dramatist, 1862-1931.
Haile Selassie, Ethiopian emperor, 1891-1975.
Jan C. Smuts, South African statesman, 1870-1950.
Paul Henri Spaak, Belgian statesman, 1899-1972.
Baruch Spinoza, Dutch philosopher, 1632-1677.
Antonio Stradivari, Italian violinmaker, 1644-1737.
August Strindberg, Swedish author, 1849-1912.
Sun Yat-Sen, Chinese statesman, 1866-1925.
Otto Sverdrup, Norwegian explorer, 1855-1930.
Emanuel Swedenborg, Swedish scientist, scholar, 1688-1772.
John M. Synge, Irish dramatist, 1871-1909.
Rabindranath Tagore, Indian poet, 1861-1941.
U Thant, Burmese statesman, 1909-1974.
Hideki Tojo, Japanese political & military leader, 1885-1948.
Rafael L. Trujillo Molina, Dominican dictator, 1891-1961.
Moise K. Tshombe, Congolese leader, 1919-1969.
Sigrid Undset, Norwegian author, 1882-1949.
Eleutherios Venizelos, Greek statesman, 1864-1936.
Hendrik F. Verwoerd, South African prime minister, 1901-1966.
Chaim Weizmann, first Israeli president, 1874-1952.
Franz Werfel, Austrian author, 1890-1945.
William Butler Yeats, Irish poet, 1865-1939.
Emiliano Zapata, Mexican revolutionary, 1879-1919.
Stefan Zweig, Austrian author, 1881-1942.

Ancient Greeks and Latins

B. C. years are in black type; A. D. years in light, Herodotus believed Homer lived c. 850 B.C.

Greeks

Born	Died	Name	Subj.	Born	Died	Name	Subj.	Born	Died	Name	Subj.
389	314	Aeschines	Orat.	450	...	Empedocles	Philos.	582	500	Pythagoras	Philos.
525	456	Aeschylus	Dram.	55	135	Epictetus	Philos.	600	...	Sappho	Poet
...	550	Aesop	Tales	342	270	Epicurus	Philos.	556	469	Simonides	Poet
563	478	Anacreon	Poet	480	406	Euripides	Dram.	469	399	Socrates	Philos.
500	428	Anaxagoras	Philos.	576	480	Heraclitus	Philos.	495	405	Sophocles	Dram.
287	212	Archimedes	Physt.	484	424	Herodotus	Hist.	63	24	Strabo	Geog.
448	380	Aristophanes	Dram.	...	735	Hesiod	Poet	600	540	Thales	Philos.
384	322	Aristotle	Philos.	460	377	Hippocrates	Medic.	460	370	Themistocles	Polit.
...	194	Atenaeus	Antiq.	...	...	Homer	Poet	...	255	Theocritus	Poet
460	370	Democritus	Philos.	342	292	Menander	Dram.	382	287	Theophrastus	Philos.
310	240	Callimachus	Poet	522	443	Pindar	Poet	471	401	Thucydides	Hist.
382	322	Demosthenes	Orat.	429	347	Plato	Philos.	280	...	Timon	Philos.
50	13	Diodorus	Hist.	49	120	Plutarch	Biog.	430	357	Xenophon	Hist.
...	7	Dionysius	Hist.	207	122	Polybius	Hist.	490	...	Zeno	Philos.

Latins

Born	Died	Name	Subj.	Born	Died	Name	Subj.	Born	Died	Name	Subj.
330	390	Ammianus	Hist.	59	17	Livy	Hist.	35	95	Quintilian	Critic
125	200	Apuleius	Satir.	38	65	Lucan	Poet	86	34	Sallust	Hist.
130	175	Aulus Gellius	Satir.	180	103	Lucilius	Satir.	5	65	Seneca	Moral.
475	524	Boethius	Philos.	96	52	Lucretius	Philos.	25	100	Silius	Poet
100	44	Caesar, Julius	States.	43	104	Martial	Poet	61	96	Statius	Poet
234	149	Cato (Elder)	Orat.	100	30	Nepos	Hist.	70	150	Suetonius	Biog.
87	54	Catullus	Poet	43	18	Ovid	Poet	55	117	Tacitus	Hist.
107	43	Cicero	Orat.	34	62	Persius	Satir.	185	159	Terence	Dram.
365	408	Claudian	Poet	254	184	Plautus	Dram.	54	18	Tibullus	Poet
65	8	Horace	Poet	23	79	Pliny	Natur.	70	19	Virgil	Poet
60	140	Juvenal	Satir.	62	113	Pliny (Younger)	Letter	70	16	Vitruvius	Arch.

Rulers of England and Great Britain

Name	England	Began	Died	Age	Rgd
	Saxons and Danes				
Egbert	King of Wessex, won allegiance of all English	829	839	—	10
Ethelwulf	Son, King of Wessex, Sussex, Kent, Essex	839	858	—	19
Ethelbald	Son of Ethelwulf, displaced father in Wessex	858	860	—	2
Ethelbert	2d son of Ethelwulf, united Kent and Wessex	860	866	—	6
Ethelred I	3d son, King of Wessex, fought Danes	866	871	—	5
Alfred	The Great, 4th son, defeated Danes, fortified London	871	899	52	28
Edward	The Elder, Alfred's son, united English, claimed Scotland	899	924	55	25
Athelstan	The Glorious, Edward's son, King of Mercia, Wessex	924	940	45	16
Edmund I	3d son of Edward, King of Wessex, Mercia	940	946	25	6
Edred	4th son of Edward	946	955	32	9
Edwy	The Fair, eldest son of Edmund, King of Wessex	955	959	18	3
Edgar	The Peaceful, 2d son of Edmund, ruled all English	959	975	32	17
Edward	The Martyr, eldest son of Edgar, murdered by stepmother	975	978	17	4
Ethelred II	The Unready, son of Edgar, married Emma of Normandy	978	1016	48	37
Edmund II	Ironside, son of Ethelred II, King of London	1016	1016	27	0
Canute	The Dane, gave Wessex to Edmund, married Emma	1016	1035	40	19
Harold I	Harefoot, natural son of Canute	1035	1040	—	5
Harde Canute	Son of Canute by Emma, Danish King	1040	1042	24	2
Edward	The Confessor, son of Ethelred II (Canonized 1161)	1042	1066	62	24
Harold II	Edward's brother-in-law, last Saxon King	1066	1066	44	0
	House of Normandy				
William I	The Conqueror, defeated Harold at Hastings	1066	1087	60	21
William II	Rufus, 3d son of William I, killed by arrow	1087	1100	43	13
Henry I	Beauclerc, youngest son of William I	1100	1135	67	35
	House of Blois				
Stephen	Son of Adela, daughter of William I, and Count of Blois	1135	1154	50	19
	House of Plantagenet				
Henry II	Son of Goeffrey Plantagenet (Angevin) by Matilda, dau. of Henry I	1154	1189	56	35
Richard I	Coeur de Lion, son of Henry II, crusader	1189	1199	42	10
John	Lackland, son of Henry II, signed Magna Carta, 1215	1199	1216	50	17
Henry III	Son of John, acceded at 9, under regency until 1227	1216	1272	65	56

Edward I	Longshanks, son of Henry III	1272	1307	68	35
Edward II	Son of Edward I, deposed by Parliament, 1327	1307	1327	43	20
Edward III	Of Windsor, son of Edward II	1327	1377	65	50
Richard II	Grandson of Edw. III, minor until 1389, deposed 1399	1377	1400	34	22

House of Lancaster

Henry IV	Son of John of Gaunt, Duke of Lancaster, son of Edw. III	1399	1413	47	13
Henry V	Son of Henry IV, victor of Agincourt	1413	1422	34	9
Henry VI	Son of Henry V, deposed 1461, died in Tower	1422	1471	49	39

House of York

Edward IV	Great-great-grandson of Edward III, son of Duke of York	1461	1483	41	22
Edward V	Son of Edward IV, murdered in Tower of London	1483	1483	13	0
Richard III	Crookback, bro. of Edward IV, fell at Bosworth Field	1483	1485	35	2

House of Tudor

Henry VII	Son of Edmund Tudor, Earl of Richmond, whose father had married the widow of Henry V; descended from Edward III through his mother, Margaret Beaufort via John of Gaunt. By marriage with dau. of Edward IV he united Lancaster and York	1485	1509	53	24
Henry VIII	Son of Henry VII *(See Memorable Dates)*	1509	1547	56	38
Edward VI	Son of Henry VIII, by Jane Seymour, his 3d queen. Ruled under regents. Was forced to name Lady Jane Grey his successor. Council of State proclaimed her queen July 10, 1553. Mary Tudor won Council, was proclaimed queen July 19, 1553. Mary had Lady Jane Grey beheaded for treason, Feb., 1554	1547	1553	16	6
Mary I	Daughter of Henry VIII, by Catherine of Aragon	1553	1558	43	5
Elizabeth I	Daughter of Henry VIII, by Anne Boleyn	1558	1603	69	44

Great Britain

House of Stuart

James I	James VI of Scotland, son of Mary, Queen of Scots. *First to call himself King of Great Britain. This became official with the Act of Union, 1707*	1603	1625	59	22
Charles I	Only surviving son of James I; beheaded Jan. 30, 1649	1625	1649	48	24

Commonwealth, 1649-1660

Council of State, 1649; Protectorate, 1653

The Cromwells	Oliver Cromwell, Lord Protector	1653	1658	59	—
	Richard Cromwell, Lord Protector, resigned May 25, 1659	1658	1712	86	—

House of Stuart (Restored)

Charles II	Eldest son of Charles I, died without issue	1660	1685	55	25
James II	2d son of Charles I. Deposed 1688. Interregnum Dec. 11, 1688, to Feb. 13, 1689	1685	1701	68	3
William III	Son of William, Prince of Orange, by Mary, dau. of Charles I	1689	1702	51	13
and Mary II	Eldest daughter of James II and wife of William III		1694	33	6
Anne	2d daughter of James II	1702	1714	49	12

House of Hanover

George I	Son of Elector of Hanover, by Sophia, grand-dau. of James I	1714	1727	67	13
George II	Only son of George I, married Caroline of Brandenburg	1727	1760	77	33
George III	Grandson of George II, married Charlotte of Mecklenburg	1760	1820	81	59
George IV	Eldest son of George III, Prince Regent, from Feb., 1811	1820	1830	67	10
William IV	3d son of George III, married Adelaide of Saxe-Meiningen	1830	1837	71	7
Victoria	Dau. of Edward, 4th son of George III; married (1840) Prince Albert of Saxe-Coburg and Gotha, who became Prince Consort	1837	1901	81	63

House of Saxe-Coburg and Gotha

Edward VII	Eldest son of Victoria, married Alexandra, Princess of Denmark	1901	1910	68	9

House of Windsor

Name Adopted July 17, 1917

George V	2d son of Edward VII, married Princess Mary of Teck	1910	1936	70	25
Edward VIII	Eldest son of George V; acceded Jan. 20, 1936, abdicated Dec. 11	1936	1972	77	1
George VI	2d son of George V; married Lady Elizabeth Bowes-Lyon	1936	1952	56	15
Elizabeth II	Elder daughter of George VI, acceded Feb. 6, 1952	1952	—	—	—

Rulers of Scotland

The Romans gave the name of Caledonia to present-day Scotland. The Scots, a Celtic race that spoke Gaelic, came from Ireland, then called Scotia.

Kenneth I MacAlpin was the first Scot to rule both Scots and Picts, 846 A. D.

Duncan I was the first general ruler, 1034. Macbeth seized the kingdom 1040, was slain by Duncan's son, Malcolm III Mac Duncan (Canmore), 1057.

Malcolm married Margaret, Saxon princess who had fled from the Normans. Queen Margaret introduced English language and English monastic customs. She was canonized. Her son Edgar, 1097, moved the court to Edinburgh. His brothers Alexander I and David I succeeded. Malcolm IV, the Maiden, 1153, grandson of David I, was followed by his brother, William the Lion, 1165, whose son was Alexander II, 1214. The latter's son, Alexander III, 1249, defeated the Norse and regained the Hebrides. When he died, 1286, his granddaughter, Margaret, child of Eric of Norway and grandniece of Edward I of England, known as the Maid of Norway, was chosen ruler, but died on the way, 1290.

John Baliol, 1292-1296. (Interregnum, 10 years).

Robert Bruce (The Bruce), 1306-1329, victor at Bannockburn, 1314.

David II, only son of Robert Bruce, ruled 1329-1371.

Robert II, 1371-1390, grandson of Robert Bruce, son of Walter, the Steward of Scotland, was called The Steward, first of the so-called Stuart line.

Robert III, son of Robert II, 1390-1406.

James I, son of Robert III, 1406-1437.

James II, son of James I, 1437-1460.

James III, 1460-1488, eldest son of James II.

James IV, 1488-1513, eldest son of James III.

James V, 1513-1542, eldest son of James IV.

Mary, daughter of James V, born 1542, became queen when 1 week old; was crowned 1543. Married, 1558, Francis, son of Henry II of France, who became king 1559, died 1560. Mary ruled Scots 1561 until abdication, 1567. She also married (2) Henry Stewart, Lord Darnley, and (3) James, Earl of Bothwell. Imprisoned by Elizabeth I; beheaded 1587.

James VI, 1567-1625, son of Mary and Lord Darnley, became King of England on death of Elizabeth in 1603. Although the thrones were thus united, the legislative union of Scotland and England was not effected until the Act of Union, May 1, 1707.

Rulers of France: Kings, Queens, Presidents

Caesar to Charlemagne

Julius Caesar subdued the Gauls, native tribes of Gaul (France) 57 to 52 B. C. The Romans ruled 500 years. The Franks, a Teutonic tribe, reached the Somme from the East ca. 250 A. D. By the 5th century the Merovingian Franks ousted the Romans. In 451 A.D., with the help of Visigoths, Burgundians and others, they defeated Attila and the Huns at Chalons-sur-Marne.

Childeric I became leader of the Merovingians 458 A. D. His son Clovis I (Chlodwig, Ludwig, Louis), crowned 481, founded the dynasty. After defeating the Alemanni (Germans) 496, he was baptized a Christian and made Paris his capital. His line ruled until Childeric III was deposed, 751.

The West Merovingians were called Neustrians, the eastern Austrasians. Pepin of Herstal (687-714) major domus, or head of the palace, of Austrasia, took over Neustria as dux (leader) of the Franks. Pepin's son, Charles, called Martel (the Hammer) defeated the Saracens at Tours-Poitiers, 732; was succeeded by his son, Pepin the Short, 741, who deposed Childeric III and ruled as king until 768.

His son, Charlemagne, or Charles the Great (742-814) became king of the Franks, 768, with his brother Carloman, who died 771. He ruled France, Germany, parts of Italy, Spain, Austria and enforced Christianity. Crowned Emperor of the Romans by Pope Leo III in St. Peter's, Rome, Dec. 25, 800 A. D. Succeeded by son, Louis I the Pious, 814. At death, 840, Louis left empire to sons, Lothair (Roman emperor); Pepin I (king of Aquitaine); Louis II (of Germany); Charles the Bald (France). They quarreled and by the peace of Verdun, 843, divided the empire.

A.D. Name and Year of Accession

The Carolingians

840 Charles I (the Bald), Roman Emperor, 875
877 Louis II (the Stammerer), son
879 Louis III (died 882) and Carloman (brothers)
884 Charles II (the Fat), Roman Emperor, 881
888 Eudes (Odo) elected by nobles. Ceded land to
898 Charles III (the Simple), son of Louis II, defeated by
922 Robert, brother of Eudes, killed in war
923 Rodolph (Raoul) Duke of Burgundy
936 Louis IV, son of Charles III
954 Lothair, son, aged 13, defeated by Capet
986 Louis V (the Sluggard), left no heirs

The Capets

987 Hugh Capet, son of Hugh the Great
996 Robert (the Wise), his son
1031 Henry I, his son, last Norman
1060 Philip I (the Fair), son, king at 14
1108 Louis VI (the Fat), son
1137 Louis VII (the Younger), son
1180 Philip II (Augustus), son, crowned at Reims
1223 Louis VIII (the Lion), son
1226 Louis IX, son, crusader; Louis IX (1214-1270) reigned 44 years, arbitrated disputes with English King Henry III; led crusades, 1248 (captured in Egypt 1250) and 1270, when he died of plague in Tunis. Canonized 1297 as St. Louis.
1270 Philip III (the Hardy), son
1285 Philip IV (the Fair), son, king at 17
1314 Louis X (the Headstrong), son. His posthumous son, John I, lived only 7 days
1316 Philip V (the Tall), brother of Louis X
1322 Charles IV (the Fair), brother of Louis X

House of Valois

1328 Philip VI (of Valois), grandson of Philip III
1350 John II (the Good), his son, retired to England
1364 Charles V (the Wise), son
1380 Charles VI (the Beloved), son
1422 Charles VII (the Victorious), son. In 1429 Joan of Arc (Jeanne d'Arc) promised Charles to oust the English, who occupied northern France. Joan won at Orleans and Patay and had Charles crowned at Reims July 17, 1429. Joan was captured May 24, 1430, and executed May 30, 1431, at Rouen for heresy. Charles ordered her rehabilitation, effected 1455.
1461 Louis XI (the Cruel), son, civil reformer
1483 Charles VIII (the Affable), son
1498 Louis XII, great-grandson of Charles V
1515 Francis I, of Angouleme, nephew, son-in-law. Francis I (1494-1547) reigned 32 years, fought 4 big wars, was patron of the arts, aided Cellini, del Sarto, Leonardo da Vinci, Rabelais. Embellished Fontainebleau.
1547 Henry II, son, killed at a joust in a tournament. He was the husband of Catherine de Medicis (1519-1589) and the lover of Diane de Poitiers (1499-1566). Catherine was born in Florence, daughter of Lorenzo de Medicis. By her marriage to Henry II she became the mother of Francis II, Charles IX, Henry III and Queen Margaret (Reine Margot) wife of Henry IV. She persuaded Charles IX to order the massacre of Huguenots on the Feast of St. Bartholomew, Aug. 24, 1572, the day her daughter was married to Henry of Navarre.
1559 Francis II, son of Henry II. In 1548, Mary, Queen of Scots since infancy, was betrothed when 6 to Francis, aged 4. They were married 1558. Francis died 1560, aged 16; Mary ruled Scotland, abdicated 1567.
1560 Charles IX, brother of Francis II
1574 Henry III, brother, assassinated

House of Bourbon

1589 Henry IV, of Navarre, assassinated. Henry IV made enemies when he gave tolerance to Protestants by Edict of Nantes, 1598. He was grandson of Queen Margaret of Navarre, literary patron. He married Margaret of Valois, Catherine de Medicis' daughter; was divorced; in 1600 married Marie de Medicis, who became Regent of France, 1610-17 for her son, Louis XIII, but was exiled by Richelieu, 1631.
1610 Louis XIII (the Just), son, Louis XIII (1610-1643) married Anne of Austria. His ministers were Cardinals Richelieu and Mazarine.
1643 Louis XIV (The Grand Monarch), son. Louis XIV was king 72 years. He exhausted a prosperous country in wars for thrones and territory. By revoking the Edict of Nantes (1685) he caused the emigration of the Huguenots. He said: "I am the state."
1715 Louis XV, great-grandson. Louis XV married a Polish princess, lost Canada to the English. His favorites, Mme. Pompadour and Mme. Du Barry influenced policies. Noted for saying: Apres moi, le deluge. (After me, the deluge).
1774 Louis XVI, grandson; married Marie Antoinette, daughter of Empress Maria Therese of Austria. King and queen beheaded by Revolution, 1793. Their son, called Louis XVII, died in prison, never ruled.

First Republic

1792 National Convention of the French Revolution
1795 Directory, under Barras and others
1799 Consulate, Napoleon Bonaparte, First Consul. In 1802 elected Consul for life.

First Empire

1804 Napoleon I, Emperor. Josephine (de Beauharnais) Empress, 1804-09; Marie Louise, Empress, 1810-1814. Her son, Francois (1811-1832) titular King of Rome, later Duke de Reichstadt and "Napoleon II," never ruled. Napoleon abdicated 1814, died 1821.

Bourbons Restored

1814 Louis XVIII king; brother of Louis XVI.
1824 Charles X, brother; reactionary; deposed by the July Revolution, 1830.

House of Orleans

1830 Louis Philippe, the Citizen King.

Second Republic

1848 Louis Napoleon Bonaparte President, nephew of Napoleon I. He became:

Second Empire

1852 Napoleon III, Emperor, Eugenie (de Montijo) Empress. Lost Franco-Prussian war, deposed 1870. Son, Prince Imperial (1856-79), died in Zulu War. Eugenie died 1920.

Third Republic—Presidents

1871 Thiers, Louis Adolphe (1797-1877)
1873 MacMahon, Marshal Patrice M. de (1808-1893)
1879 Grevy, Paul J. (1807-1891)
1887 Sadi-Carnot, M. (1837-1894), assassinated
1894 Casimir-Perier, Jean P. P. (1847-1907)
1895 Faure, Francois Felix (1841-1899)
1899 Loubet, Emile (1838-1929)
1906 Fallieres, C. Armand (1841-1931)
1913 Poincare, Raymond (1860-1934)
1920 Deschanel, Paul (1856-1922)
1920 Millerand, Alexandre (1859-1943)
1924 Doumergue, Gaston (1863-1937)
1931 Doumer, Paul (1857-1932), assassinated
1932 Lebrun, Albert (1871-1950), resigned 1940
1940 **Vichy govt.** under German armistice: Henri Philippe Petain (1856-1951) Chief of State, 1940-1944.
Provisional govt. after liberation: Charles de Gaulle (1890-1970) Oct. 1944-Jan. 21, 1946; Felix Gouin (1884-) Jan. 23, 1946; Georges Bidault (1899-) June 24, 1946.

Fourth Republic—Presidents

1947 Auriol, Vincent (1884-1966)
1954 Coty, Rene (1882-1962)

Fifth Republic—Presidents

1959 De Gaulle, Charles Andre J. M. (1890-1970)
1969 Pompidou, Georges J. R. (1911-1974)
1974 Giscard d'Estaing, Valery (1926-)

Rulers of Middle Europe; Rise and Fall of Dynasties

Carolingian Dynasty

Charles the Great, or Charlemagne, ruled France, Italy, and Middle Europe; established Ostmark (later Austria); crowned Roman emperor by pope in Rome, 800 A. D. Died 814.

Louis I (Ludwig) the Pious, son; crowned by Charlemagne 814, d. 840.

Louis II, the German, son; succeeded to East Francia (Germany) 843-876.

Charles the Fat, son; inherited East Francia and West Francia (France) 876, reunited empire, crowned emperor by pope, 881, deposed 887.

Arnulf, nephew, 887-899. Partition of empire.

Louis the Child, 899-911, last direct descendant of Charlemagne.

Conrad I, duke of Franconia, first elected German king, 911-918, founded House of Franconia.

Saxon Dynasty; First Reich

Henry I, the Fowler, duke of Saxony, 919-936.

Otto I, the Great, 936-973, son; crowned Holy Roman Emperor by pope, 962.

Otto II, 973-983, son; failed to oust Greeks and Arabs from Sicily.

Otto III, 983-1002, son; crowned emperor at 16.

Henry II, the Saint, duke of Bavaria, 1002-1024, great-grandson of Henry the Fowler.

House of Franconia

Conrad II, 1024-1039, son-in-law of Otto I.

Henry III, the Black, 1039-1056, son; deposed 3 popes; annexed Burgundy.

Henry IV, 1056-1106, son; regency by his mother, Agnes of Poitou. Banned by Pope Gregory VII, he did penance at Canossa.

Henry V, 1106-1125, son; last of Salic House.

Lothair, duke of Saxony, 1125-1137. Crowned emperor in Rome, 1134.

House of Hohenstaufen

Conrad III, duke of Suabia, 1138-1152. In 2d Crusade.

Frederick I, Barbarossa, 1152-1190; Conrad's nephew.

Henry VI, 1190-1196, took lower Italy from Normans. Son became king of Sicily.

Philip of Suabia, 1198-1208, son of Frederick I.

Otto IV, of House of Welf, 1198-1215; deposed.

Frederick II, 1215-1250, son of Henry VI; king of Sicily; crowned king of Jerusalem; in 5th Crusade.

Conrad IV, 1250-1254, son; lost lower Italy to Charles of Anjou.

Conradin, 1252-1268, son, king of Jerusalem and Sicily, beheaded. Last Hohenstaufen.

Interregnum, 1250-1273, Rise of the Electors.

Transition

Rudolph I of Hapsburg, 1273-1291, defeated King Ottocar II of Bohemia. Bequeathed duchy of Austria to eldest son, Albert.

Adolphus, count of Nassau, 1291-1298, killed in war with Albert of Austria.

Albert I, king of Germany, 1298-1308.

Henry VII, of Luxemburg, 1308-1313, crowned emperor in Rome. Seized Bohemia, 1310.

Louis IV of Bavaria (Wittelsbach), 1314-1347. Also elected was Frederick of Austria, 1314-1330 (Hapsburg). Abolition of papal sanction for election of Holy Roman Emperor.

Charles IV, of Luxemburg, 1347-1378, grandson of Henry VII, German emperor and king of Bohemia, Lombardy, Burgundy; took Mark of Brandenburg.

Wenceslaus, 1378-1400, deposed.

Rupert, Duke of Palatine, 1400-1410.

Hungary

Stephen I, house of Arpad, 997-1038. Crowned king by Pope Sylvester II, 1001 A. D., converted Magyars. After several centuries of feuds Charles Robert of Anjou became Charles I, 1308-1342.

Louis I, the Great, 1342-1382, son; joint ruler of Poland with Casimir III, 1370. Defeated Turks.

Mary, daughter, 1382-1395, ruled with husband. Sigismund of Luxemburg, 1387-1437, also king of Bohemia. As bro. of Wenceslaus he succeeded Rupert as Holy Roman Emperor, 1410.

Albert II, 1438-1439, son-in-law of Sigismund; also Roman emperor. *(See under Hapsburg.)*

Ladislas V of Poland, 1440-1444.

Ladislaus V, child. John Hunyadi (Hunyadi Janos) guardian, fought Turks, Czechs; died 1456.

Matthias I (Corvinus) son of Hunyadi, 1458-1490. Shared rule of Bohemia, captured Vienna, 1485, annexed Austria, Styria, Carinthia.

Ladislas II (king of Bohemia), 1490-1516.

Louis II, son, aged 10, 1516-1526. Wars with Suleiman, Turk. In 1527 Hungary was split between Ferdinand I, Archduke of Austria, bro.-in-law of Louis II, and John Zapolya of Transylvania. After Turkish invasion, 1547, Hungary was split between Ferdinand, Prince John Sigismund (Transylvania) and the Turks.

House of Hapsburg

Albert V of Austria, Hapsburg, crowned king of Hungary, Jan. 1438, Roman emperor, March, 1438, as Albert II; died 1439.

Frederick III, cousin, 1440-1493. Fought Turks.

Maximilian I, son, 1493-1519. Assumed title of Holy Roman Emperor (German), 1493.

Charles V, grandson, 1519-1556. King of Spain with mother co-regent; crowned Roman emperor at Aix, 1520. Confronted Luther at Worms; attempted church reform and religious conciliation. Abdicated 1556.

Ferdinand I, king of Bohemia, 1526, of Hungary, 1527; disputed. German king, 1531. Crowned Roman emperor on abdication of Charles V, 1556.

Maximilian II, son, 1564-1576; Rudolph II, son, 1576-1612.

Matthias, brother, 1612-1619, king of Bohemia and Hungary.

Ferdinand II of Styria, king of Bohemia, 1617, of Hungary, 1618, Roman emperor, 1619. Bohemian Protestants deposed him, elected Frederick V of Palatine, starting Thirty Years War.

Ferdinand III, son, king of Hungary, 1625, Bohemia, 1627, Roman emperor, 1637. Peace of Westphalia, 1648, ended war. Leopold I, 1658-1705; Joseph I, 1705-1711; Charles VI, 1711-1740.

Maria Theresa, daughter, 1740-1780, Archduchess of Austria, queen of Hungary; ousted pretender, Charles VII, crowned 1742; in 1745 obtained election of her husband Francis I as Roman emperor and co-regent (d. 1765). Fought Seven Years' War with Frederick II (the Great) of Prussia. Mother of Marie Antoinette, Queen of France.

Joseph II, son, 1765-1790, Roman emperor, reformer; powers restricted by Empress Maria Theresa until her death, 1780. First partition of Poland. Leopold II, 1790-1792.

Francis II, son, 1792-1835. Fought Napoleon. Proclaimed first hereditary emperor of Austria, 1806. Forced to abdicate as Roman emperor, 1806; last use of title. Ferdinand I, son, 1835-1848, abdicated during revolution.

Austro-Hungarian Monarchy

Francis Joseph I, nephew, 1848-1916, emperor of Austria, king of Hungary. Dual monarchy of Austria-Hungary formed, 1867. After assassination of heir, Archduke Francis Ferdinand, June 28, 1914, Austrian diplomacy precipitated World War I.

Charles I, grand-nephew, 1916-1918, last emperor of Austria and king of Hungary. Abdicated Nov. 11-13, 1918, died 1922.

Rulers of Prussia

Nucleus of Prussia was the Mark of Brandenburg. First margrave was Albert the Bear (Albrecht), 1134-1170. First Hohenzollern margrave was Frederick, burggrave of Nuremberg, 1415-1440.

Frederick William, 1640-1688, the Great Elector. Son, Frederick III, 1688-1713, was crowned King Frederick of Prussia, 1701.

Frederick William I, son, 1713-1740.

Frederick II, the Great, son, 1740-1786, annexed Silesia part of Austria.

Frederick William II, nephew, 1786-1797.

Frederick William III, son, 1797-1840. Napoleonic wars.

Frederick William IV, son, 1840-1861. Uprising of 1848 and first parliament and constitution.

Second and Third Reich

William I, 1861-1888, brother. Annexation of Schleswig and Hanover; Franco-Prussian war, 1870-71, proclamation of German Reich, Jan. 18, 1871, at Versailles; William, German emperor (Deutscher Kaiser), Bismarck, chancellor.

Frederick III, son, 1888.

William II, son, 1888-1918. Led Germany in World War I, abdicated as German emperor and king of Prussia, Nov. 9, 1918. Died in exile in Netherlands June 4, 1941. Minor rulers of Bavaria, Saxony, Wurttemberg also abdicated.

Germany proclaimed a republic at Weimar, July 1, 1919.

Presidents: Frederick Ebert, 1919-1925, Paul von Hindenburg-Beneckendorff, 1925, reelected 1932, d. Aug. 2, 1934. Adolf Hitler, chancellor, chosen successor as Leader-Chancellor (Fuehrer & Reichskanzler) of Third Reich. Annexed Austria, March, 1938. Precipitated World War II, 1939-1945. Committed suicide April 30, 1945.

Rulers of Denmark, Sweden, Norway

Denmark

Earliest rulers invaded Britain; King Canute, who ruled in London 1017-1035, was most famous. The Valdemars furnished kings until the 15th century. In 1282 the Danes won the first national assembly, Danehof, from King Erik V.

Most redoubtable medieval character was Margaret, daughter of Valdemar IV, born 1353, married at 10 to King Haakon VI of Norway. In 1376 she had her first infant son Olaf made king of Denmark. After his death, 1387, she was regent of Denmark and Norway. In 1388 Sweden accepted her as sovereign. In 1389 she made her grand-nephew, Duke Erik of Pomerania, titular king of Denmark, Sweden, and Norway, with herself as regent. In 1397 she effected the Union of Kalmar of the three kingdoms and had Erik crowned. In 1439 the three kingdoms deposed him and elected, 1440, Christopher of Bavaria king (Christopher III). On his death, 1448, the union broke up.

Succeeding rulers were unable to enforce their claims as rulers of Sweden until 1520, when Christian II conquered Sweden. He was thrown out 1522, and in 1523 Gustavus Vasa united Sweden. Denmark continued to dominate Norway until the Napoleonic wars, when Frederick VI, 1808-1839, joined the Napoleonic cause after Britain had destroyed the Danish fleet (1807). In 1814 he was forced to cede Norway to Sweden and Helgoland to Britain, receiving Lauenburg. Successors: 1839, Christian VIII; 1848, Frederick VII; 1863, Christian IX; 1906, Frederick VIII; 1912, Christian X; 1947, Frederick IX; 1972, Queen Margrethe II.

Sweden

Early kings ruled at Uppsala, but did not dominate the country. Sverker (1130-1150) united the Swedes and Goths. In 1435 Sweden obtained the Riksdag, or parliament. After the Union of Kalmar, 1379, the Danes either ruled or harried the country until Christian II of Denmark conquered it anew, 1520. This led to a rising under Gustavus Vasa, who ruled Sweden 1523-1560, and established an independent kingdom. Charles IX (1594-1611, crowned 1604), conquered Moscow. Gustavus II Adolphus (1611-1632) was called the Lion of the North. Later rulers, 1632, Christina; 1654, Charles X; 1660, Charles XI; 1697, Charles XII (invader of Russia and Poland, defeated at Poltava, June 28, 1709); 1718, his sister, Ulrika Eleanora, elected queen; 1720, her husband, Frederick I (of Hesse); 1751, Adolphus Frederick; 1771, Gustavus III; 1792, Gustavus IV Adolphus; 1809, Charles XIII (Union with Norway began, 1814). 1818, Charles XIV John. He was Jean Bernadotte, Napoleon's Prince of Ponte Corvo, elected 1810 to succeed Charles XIII. He founded the present dynasty. 1844, Oscar I; 1859, Charles XV; 1872, Oscar II; 1907, Gustavus V; 1950, Gustav VI Adolf; 1973, Carl XVI Gustaf.

Norway

Overcoming many rivals, Harald Haarfager, 872-930, conquered Norway, Orkneys and Shetlands; Olaf, great-grandson, 995-1000, brought Christianity into Norway, Iceland, and Greenland. In 1035 Magnus the Good also became king of Denmark. Haakon V, 1299-1319, had married his daughter to Erik of Sweden. Their son, Magnus, became ruler of Norway and Sweden at 6. His son, Haakon VI, married Margaret of Denmark; their son Olaf IV became king of Norway and Denmark, followed by Margaret's regency and the Union of Kalmar, 1397.

In 1450 Norway became subservient to Denmark. Christian IV, 1588-1648, founded Christiania, now Oslo. After Napoleonic wars, when Denmark ceded Norway to Sweden, a strong nationalist movement forced recognition of Norway as an independent kingdom united with Sweden under the Swedish kings, 1814-1905. In 1905 the union was dissolved and Prince Carl of Denmark became Haakon VII. He died Sept. 21, 1957, aged 85; succeeded by son, Olav V, b. July 2, 1903.

Rulers of the Netherlands and Belgium

The Netherlands (Holland)

William Frederick, Prince of Orange, led a revolt against French rule, 1813, and was crowned King of the Netherlands, 1815. Belgium seceded Oct. 4, 1830, after a revolt, and formed a separate government. The change was ratified by the two kingdoms by treaty Apr. 19, 1839.

1840, William II, son; 1849, William III, son; 1890, Wilhelmina (daughter of William III and his second wife Princess Emma of Waldeck); Wilhelmina abdicated Sept. 4, 1948, in favor of daughter, Juliana.

Belgium

A national congress elected Prince Leopold of Saxe-Coburg King; he took the throne July 21, 1831, as Leopold I. 1865, Leopold II, son; 1909, Albert I, nephew of Leopold II; 1934, Leopold III, son of Albert; 1944, Prince Charles, Regent; Leopold returned, 1950, yielded powers to son Baudouin, Prince Royal, Aug. 6, 1950, abdicated July 16, 1951. Baudouin I took throne July 17, 1951.

For political history prior to 1830 see articles on the Netherlands and Belgium.

Roman Rulers

From Romulus to the end of the Empire in the West. Rulers of the Roman Empire in the East sat in Constantinople and for a brief period in Nicaea, until the capture of Constantinople by the Turks in 1453, when Byzantium was succeeded by the Ottoman Empire.

B.C.	Name
	The Kingdom
753	Romulus (Quirinus)
716	Numa Pompilius
673	Tullus Hostillus
640	Ancus Marcius
616	L. Tarquinius Priscus
578	Servius Tullius
534	L. Tarquinius Superbus
	The Republic
509	Consulate established
509	Quaestorship instituted
498	Dictatorship introduced
494	Plebeian Tribunate created
494	Plebeian Aedileship created
444	Consular Tribunate organized
435	Censorship instituted
366	Praetorship established
366	Curule Aedileship crested
362	Military Tribunate elective
326	Proconsulate introduced
311	Naval Duumvirate elective
217	Dictatorship of Fabius Maximus
133	Tribunate of Tiberius Gracchua

B.C.	Name
123	Tribunate of Gaius Gracchus
82	Dictatorship of Sulla
60	First Triumvirate formed (Caesar, Pompeius, Crassus)
46	Dictatorship of Caesar
43	Second Triumvirate formed (Octavianus, Antonius, Lepidus)
	The Empire
27	Augustus (Gaius Julius Caesar Octavianus)
A.D.	
14	Tiberius I
37	Gaius Caesar (Caliguia)
41	Claudius I
54	Nero
68	Galba
69	Galba; Otho; Vitellius
69	Vespasianus
79	Titus
81	Domitianus
96	Nerva
98	Tralanus
117	Hadrianus

A.D.	Name
138	Antoninus Pius
161	Marcus Aurelius and Lucius Verus
169	Marcus Aurelius (alone)
180	Commodus
193	Pertinax; Julianus I
193	Septimius Severus
211	Caracalla and Geta
212	Caracalla (alone)
217	Macrinus
218	Elagabalus (Heliogabalus)
222	Alexander Severus
235	Maximinusi (the Thracian)
238	Gordianus I and Gordianus II; Pupienus and Balbinus
238	Gordianus III
244	Philippus (the Arabian)
249	Decius
251	Gallus and Volusianus
253	Aemilianus
253	Valerianus and Gallienus
258	Gallienus (alone)
268	Claudius II (the Goth)
270	Quintillus

270 Aurelianus
275 Tacitus
276 Florianus
276 Probus
282 Carus
283 Carinus and Numerianus
284 Diocletianus
286 Diocletianus and Maximianus
305 Galerius and Constantius I
306 Galerius, Maximinus II, Severus I
307 Galerius, Maximinus II, Constantinus I, Licinius, Maxentius
311 Maximinus II, Constantinus I, Licinius, Maxentius
314 Maximinus II, Constantinus I, Licinius
314 Constantinus I and Licinius
324 Constantinus I (the Great)
337 Constantinus II, Constans I, Constantius II
340 Constantius II and Constans I
350 Constantius II
361 Julianus II (the Apostate)
363 Jovianus

West (Rome) and East (Constantinople)

364 Valentinianus I (West) and Valens (East)
367 Valentinianus I with Gratianus (West) and Valens (East)
375 Gratianus with Valentinianus II (West) and Valens (East)
378 Gratianus with Valentinianus II (West) Theodosius I (Dast)
383 Valentinianus II (West) and Theodosius I (East)
394 Theodosius I (the Great)
395 Honorius (West) and Arcadius (East)
408 Honorius (West) and Theodosius II (East)
423 Valentinianus III (West) and Theodosius II (East)
450 Valentinianus III (West) and Marcianus (East)
455 Maximus (West), Avitus (West); Marcianus (East)
456 Avitus (West), Marcianus (East)
457 Majorianus (West), Leo I (East)
461 Severus II (West), Leo I (East)
467 Anthemius (West), Leo I (East)
472 Olybrius (West), Leo I (East)
473 Glycerius (West), Leo I (East)
474 Julius Nepos (West), Leo II (East)
475 Romulus Augustulus (West) and Zeno (East)
476 End of Empire in West; Odovacar, King, drops title of Emperor; murdered by King Theodoric of Ostrogoths 493 A.D.

Rulers of Modern Italy

After the fall of Napoleon in 1814, the Congress of Vienna, 1815, restored Italy as a political patchwork, comprising the Kingdom of Naples and Sicily, the Papal States, and smaller units. Piedmont and Genoa were awarded to Sardinia, ruled by King Victor Emmanuel I of Savoy.

United Italy emerged under the leadership of Camillo, Count di Cavour (1810-1861), Sardinian prime minister. Agitation was led by Giuseppe Mazzini (1805-1872) and Giuseppe Garibaldi (1807-1882), soldier. Victor Emmanuel I abdicated 1821. After a brief regency for a brother, Charles Albert was King 1831-1849, abdicating when defeated by the Austrians at Novara. Succeeded by Victor Emmanuel II, 1849-1861.

In 1859 France forced Austria to cede Lombardy to Sardinia, which gave rights to Savoy and Nice to France. In 1860 Garibaldi led 1,000 volunteers in a spectacular campaign, took Sicily and expelled the King of Naples. In 1860 the House of Savoy annexed Tuscany, Parma, Moderna, Romagna, the Two Sicilies, the Marches, and Umbria. Victor Emmanuel assumed the title of King of Italy at Turin Mar. 17, 1861. In 1866 he joined Prussia and Austria in the Triple Alliance and received Venetia from Austria. On Sept. 20, 1870, his troops under Gen. Raffaele Cardorna entered Rome and took over the Papal States, ending the temporal power of the Roman Catholic Church.

Succession: Umberto I, 1878, assassinated 1900; Victor Emmanuel III, 1900, abdicated 1946, died 1947; Umberto II, 1946, ruled a month. In 1921 Benito Mussolini (1883-1945) formed the Fascist party and became prime minister Oct. 31, 1922. He made the King Emperor of Ethiopia, 1937; entered World War II as ally of Hitler. He was deposed July 25, 1943.

At a plebiscite June 2, 1946, Italy voted for a republic, Premier Alcide de Gasperi became Chief of State June 13, 1946. On June 28, 1946, the Constituent Assembly elected Enrico de Nicola, Liberal, Provisional President of the Republic of Italy. Successive presidents: Luigi Einaudi, elected May 11, 1948; Giovanni Gronchi, Apr. 29, 1955; Antonio Segni, May 6, 1962; Giuseppe Saragat, Dec. 28, 1964; Gióvanni Leone, Dec. 29, 1971.

Rulers of Spain

From 8th to 11th centuries Spain was dominated by the Moors (Arabs and Berbers). The Christian reconquest established small competing kingdoms of the Asturias, Aragon, Castile, Catalonia, Leon, Navarre, and Valencia. In 1474 Isabella (Isabel), b. 1451, became Queen of Castile & Leon. Her husband, Ferdinand, b. 1452, inherited Aragon 1474, with Catalonia, Valcencia, and the Balearic Islands, became Ferdinand V of Castile. By Isabella's request Pope Sixtus IV established the Inquisition, 1478. Last Moorish kingdom, Granada, fell 1492. Columbus opened New World of colonies, 1492. Isabella died 1504, succeeded by her daughter, Juana "the Mad," but Ferdinand ruled until his death 1516.

Charles I, b. 1500, son of Juana and grandson of Ferdinand and Isabella, and of Maximilian I of Hapsburg; succeeded later as Holy Roman Emperor, Charles V, 1520. Abdicated 1556. Philip II, son, 1556-1598, inherited only Spanish throne; conquered Portugal, fought Turks, persecuted non-Catholics, sent Armada vs. England. Was briefly married to Mary I of England, 1554-1558. Succession: Philip III, 1598-1621; Philip IV, 1621-1665; Charles II, 1665-1700, left Spain to Philip of Anjou, grandson of Louis XIV, who as Philip V, 1700-1746, founded Bourbon dynasty. Ferdinand VI, 1746-1759; Charles III, 1759-1788; Charles IV, 1788-1808, abdicated.

Napoleon now dominated politics and made his brother Joseph King of Spain but the Spanish ousted him finally in 1813. Ferdinand VII, 1814-1833, lost American colonies; succeeded by daughter Isabella II, aged 3, with wife Maria Christina of Naples regent until 1843. Isabella deposed by revolution 1868. Prince Amadeo of Savoy, 1870-1873. First republic, 1873-1874. Alphonso XII 1875-1885. His posthumous son was Alphonso XIII, with his mother, Queen Maria Christina regent; Spanish-American war, Spain lost Cuba, gave up Puerto Rico, Philippines, Sulu Is., Marianas. Alphonso took throne 1902, aged 16, married British Princess Victoria Eugenia of Battenberg. The dictatorship of Primo de Rivera, 1923-30, precipitated the revolution of 1931. Alphonso agreed to leave without formal abdication. The monarchy was abolished and the second republic established, with strong socialist backing. Presidents were Niceto Alcala Zamora, to 1936, when Manuel Anzana was chosen.

In July, 1936, the army in Morocco revolted against the government and General Francisco Franco led the troops into Spain. The revolution succeeded by Feb., 1939, when Anzana resigned. Franco became chief of state, with provisions that if he is incapacitated the Regency Council by two-thirds vote may propose a king to the Cortes, which must have a two-thirds majority to elect him.

Alphonso XIII, died in Rome Feb. 28, 1941, aged 54. His property and citizenship had been restored.

A succession law restoring the monarchy was approved in a 1947 referendum. Prince Juan Carlos, son of the pretender to the throne, was designated by Franco and the Cortes in 1969 as the future king and chief of state. Upon Franco's death, Nov. 20, 1975, Juan Carlos was proclaimed King, Nov. 22, 1975.

Leaders in the South American Wars of Liberation

Simon Bolivar (1783-1830), Jose Francisco de San Martin (1783-1850), and Francisco Antonio Gabriel Miranda (1750-1816) are among the heroes of the early 19th century struggles of South American nations to free themselves from Spain. All three, and their contemporaries, operated in periods of intense factional strife, during which soldiers and civilians suffered.

Miranda, a Venezuelan, who had served with the French in the American Revolution and commanded parts of the French Revolutionary armies in the Netherlands, attempted to start a revolt in Venezuela in 1806 and failed. In 1810, with British and American backing, he returned and was briefly a dictator, until the British withdrew their support. In 1812 he was overcome by the royalists in Venezuela and taken prisoner, dying in a Spanish prison in 1816.

San Martin was born in Argentina and during 1789-1811 served in campaigns of the Spanish armies in Europe and Africa. He first joined the independence movement in Argentina in 1812 and then in 1817 invaded Chile with 4,000 men over the high mountain passes. Here he and General Bernardo O'Higgins (1778-1842) defeated the Spaniards at Chacabuco, 1817, and O'Higgins was named Liberator and became first dictator of Chile, 1817-1823. In 1821 San Martin occupied Lima and Callao, Peru, and became Protector of Peru.

Bolivar, the greatest leader of South American liberation from Spain, was born in Venezuela, the son of an aristocratic family. His organizing and administrative abilities were superior and he foresaw many of the political difficulties of the future. He first served under Miranda in 1812 and in 1813 captured Caracas, where he was named Liberator. Forced out next year by civil strife, he led a campaign that captured Bogota in 1814. In 1817 he was again in control of Venezuela and was named dictator. He organized Nueva Granada with the help of General Francisco de Paula Santander (1792-1840). By joining Nueva Granada, Venezuela and the present terrain of Panama and Ecuador, the republic of Colombia was formed with Bolivar president. After numerous setbacks he decisively defeated the Spaniards in the second battle of Carabobo, Venezuela, June 24, 1821.

In May, 1822, Gen. Antonio Jose de Sucre, Bolivar's trusted lieutenant, took Quito. Bolivar went to Guayaquil to confer with San Martin, who resigned as Protector of Peru and withdrew from politics. With a new army of Colombians and Peruvians Bolivar defeated the Spaniards in a saber battle at Juin in 1824 and cleared Peru.

De Sucre organized Charcas (Upper Peru) as Republica Bolivar (now Bolivia) and acted as president in place of Bolivar, who wrote its constitution. De Sucre defeated the Spanish faction of Peru at Ayacucho, Dec. 19, 1824.

Continued civil strife finally caused the Colombian federation to break apart. Santander turned against Bolivar, but the latter defeated him and banished him. In 1828 Bolivar gave up the presidency he had held precariously for 14 years. He became ill from tuberculosis and died Dec. 17, 1830. He was honored as the great liberator and is buried in the national pantheon in Caracas.

Rulers of Russia; Premiers of the USSR

First ruler to consolidate Slavic tribes was Rurik, leader of the Russians who established himself at Novgorod, 862 A. D. He and his immediate successors had Scandinavian affiliations. They moved to Kiev after 972 A. D. and ruled as Dukes of Kiev. In 988 Vladimir was converted and adopted the Byzantine Greek Orthodox service, later modified by Slav influences. Important as organizer and lawgiver was Yaroslav, 1018-1054, whose daughters married kings of Norway, Hungary and France. His grandson, Vladimir II (Monomarchos), 1113-1125, was progenitor of several rulers, but in 1169 Andrew Bogolubski overthrew Kiev and began the line known as Grand Dukes of Vladimir.

Of the Grand Dukes of Vladimir, Alexander Nevsky, 1246-1263, had a son, Daniel, first to be called Duke of Muscovy (Moscow) who ruled 1294-1303. His successors became Grand Dukes of Muscovy. After Dmitri III Donskoi defeated the Tartars in 1380, they also became Grand Dukes of all Russia. Independence of the Tartars and considerable territorial expansion were achieved under Ivan III, 1462-1505.

Tsars of Muscovy—Ivan III was referred to in church ritual as Tsar. He married Sofia, niece of the last Byzantine emperor. His successor, Basil, died in 1533 when Basil's son Ivan was only 3. He became Ivan IV, "the Terrible"; crowned 1547 as Tsar of all the Russians, ruled till 1584. Under the weak rule of his son, Feodor, 1584-1598, Boris Godunov had control. The dynasty died, and after years of tribal strife and intervention by Polish and Swedish armies, the Russians united under 17-year-old Michael Romanov, distantly related to the first wife of Ivan IV. He ruled 1613-1645 and established the Romanov line. Fourth ruler after Michael was Peter I.

Tsars, or Emperors of Russia (Romanovs)—Peter I, 1682-1725, known as Peter the Great, took title of Emperor in 1721. His successors and dates of accession were: Catherine, his widow, 1725, Peter II, his grandson, 1727-1730; Anne, Duchess of Courland, 1730, daughter of Peter the Great's brother, Czar Ivan V; Ivan VI, 1740-1741, great-grandson of Ivan V, child, kept in prison and murdered 1764; Elizabeth, daughter of Peter I, 1741; Peter III, grandson of Peter I, 1761, deposed 1762 for his consort, Catherine II, former princess of Anhalt Zerbst (Germany) who is known as Catherine the Great, 1762-1796; Paul I, her son, 1796, killed 1801, Alexander I, son of Paul, 1801-1825, defeated Napoleon; Nicholas I, his brother, 1825; Alexander II, son of Nicholas, 1855, assassinated 1881 by terrorists; Alexander III, son, 1881-1894.

Nicholas II, son, 1894-1917, last Tsar of Russia, was forced to abdicate by the Revolution that followed defeat by Germany. The Tsar, the Empress, the Tsesarevich (Crown Prince) and the Tsar's 4 daughters were murdered by the Bolsheviks in Ekaterinburg, July 16, 1918.

Provisional Government—Prince Georgi Lvov and Alexander Kerensky, premiers, 1917.

Union of Soviet Socialist Republics

Bolshevik Revolution, Nov. 7, 1917, displaced Kerensky; council of People's Commissars formed, Lenin (Vladimir Ilyich Ulyanov), premier. Lenin died Jan. 21, 1924. Alexei Rykov (executed 1938) and V. M. Molotov held the office, but actual ruler was Joseph Stalin (Joseph Vissarionovich Djugashvili), general secretary of the Central Committee of the Communist Party. Stalin became president of the Council of Ministers (premier) May 7, 1941, died Mar. 5, 1953. Succeeded by Georgi M. Malenkov, as head of the Council and premier and Nikita S. Khrushchev, first secretary of the Central Committee. Malenkov resigned Feb. 8, 1955, became deputy premier, was dropped July 3, 1957. Marshal Nikolai A. Bulganin became premier Feb. 8, 1955; was demoted and Khrushchev became premier Mar. 27, 1958. Khrushchev was ousted Oct. 14-15, 1964, replaced by Leonid I. Brezhnev as first secretary of the party and by Aleksei N. Kosygin as premier.

Governments of China

(Until 221 B.C. and frequently thereafter, China was not a unified state. Where dynastic dates overlap, the rulers or events referred to appeared in different areas of China.)

Hsia	c.1994B.C. - c.1523B.C.
Shang	c.1523 - c.1028
Western Chou	c.1027 - 770
Eastern Chou	770 - 256
Warring States	403 - 222
Ch'in (first unified empire)	221 - 206
Han	202B.C. - 220A.D.
Western Han (expanded Chinese state beyond the Yellow and Yangtze River valleys)	202B.C. - 9A.D.
Hsin (Wang Mang, usurper)	9A.D. - 23A.D.
Eastern Han (expanded Chinese state into Indo-China and Turkestan)	25 - 220
Three Kingdoms (Wei, Shu, Wu)	220 - 265
Chin (western)	265 - 317
(eastern)	317 - 420
Northern Dynasties (followed several short-lived governments by Turks, Mongols, etc.)	386 - 581
Southern Dynasties (capital: Nanking)	420 - 589
Sui (reunified China)	581 - 618
T'ang (a golden age of Chinese culture; capital: Sian)	618 - 906
Five Dynasties (Yellow River basin)	902 - 960
Ten Kingdoms (southern China)	907 - 979
Liao (Khitan Mongols; capital: Peking)	947 - 1125
Sung	960 - 1279
Northern Sung (reunified central and southern China)	960 - 1126
Western Hsai (non-Chinese rulers in northwest)	990 - 1227
Chin (Tartars; drove Sung out of central China)	1115 - 1234
Yuan (Mongols; Kublai Khan made Peking his capital in 1267)	1271 - 1368
Ming (China reunified under Chinese rule; capital: Nanking, then Peking in 1420)	1368 - 1644
Ch'ing (Manchus, descendents of Tartars)	1644 - 1911
Republic (disunity: provincial rulers, warlords)	1912 - 1949
People's Republic of China (Nationalist China established on Taiwan)	1949 - —

Chronological List of Popes

Source: Annuario Pontifici Table lists year of coronation of each Pope.

The Roman Catholic Church names the Apostle Peter as founder of the Church in Rome. He arrived there c. 42, was martyred there c. 67, and raised to sainthood.

The Pope's temporal title is: Sovereign of the State of Vatican City.

The Pope's spiritual titles are: Bishop of Rome, Vicar of Jesus Christ, Successor of St. Peter, Prince of the Apostles, Supreme Pontiff of the Universal Church, Patriarch of the West, Primate of Italy, Archbishop and Metropolitan of the Roman Province and Sovereign of the State of Vatican City.

Anti-Popes are in *Italics*. Anti-Popes were illegitimate claimants of or pretenders to the papal throne.

Year	Name of Pope
See above.	St. Peter
67	St. Linus
76	St. Anacletus or Cletus
88	St. Clement I
97	St. Evaristus
105	St. Alexander I
115	St. Sixtus I
125	St. Telesphorus
136	St. Hyginus
140	St. Pius I
155	St. Anicetus
166	St. Soter
175	St. Eleutherius
189	St. Victor I
199	St. Zephyrinus
217	St. Callistus I
217	*St. Hippolytus*
222	St. Urban I
230	St. Pontian
235	St. Anterus
236	St. Fabian
251	St. Cornelius
251	*Novatian*
253	St. Lucius I
254	St. Stephen I
257	St. Sixtus II
259	St. Dionysius
269	St. Felix I
275	St. Eutychian
283	St. Caius
296	St. Marcellinus
308	St. Marcellus I
309	St. Eusebius
311	St. Melchiades
314	St. Sylvester I
336	St. Mark
337	St. Julius I
352	Liberius
355	*Felix II*
366	St. Damasus I
366	*Ursinus*
384	St. Siricius
399	St. Anastasius I
401	St. Innocent I
417	St. Zozimus
418	St. Boniface I
418	*Eulalius*
422	St. Celestine I
432	St. Sixtus III
440	St. Leo I
461	St. Hilary
468	St. Simplicius
483	St. Felix III or II
492	St. Gelasius I
496	Anastasius II
498	St. Symmachus
498	*Lawrence (501-505)*
514	St. Hormisdas
523	St. John I
526	St. Felix IV or III
530	Boniface II
530	*Dioscorus*
533	John II
535	St. Agapitus
536	St. Silverius
537	Vigilius
556	Pelagius I
561	John III
575	Benedict I
579	Pelagius II
590	St. Gregory
604	Sabinian
607	Boniface III
608	St. Boniface IV
615	St. Deusdedit or Adeodatus
619	Boniface V
625	Honorius I
640	Severinus
640	John IV
642	Theodore I
649	St. Martin I
654	St. Eugene I
657	St. Vitalian
672	Adeodatus II
676	Donus
678	St. Agatho
682	St. Leo II
684	St. Benedict II
685	John V
686	Conon
687	*Theodore*
687	*Paschal*
687	St. Sergius I
701	John VI
705	John VII
708	Sisinnius
708	Constantine
715	St. Gregory II
731	St. Gregory III
741	St. Zachary
752	Stephen II (III)
757	St. Paul I
767	*Constantine*
768	*Philip*
768	Stephen III (IV)
772	Adrian I
795	St. Leo III
816	Stephen IV (V)
817	St. Paschal I
824	Eugene II
827	Valentine
827	Gregory IV
844	*John*
844	Sergius II
847	St. Leo IV
855	Benedict III
855	*Anastasius*
858	St. Nicholas I
867	Adrian II
872	John VIII
882	Marinus I
884	St. Adrian III
885	Stephen V (VI)
891	Formosus
896	Boniface VI
896	Stephen VI (VII).
897	Romanus
897	Theodore II
898	John IX
900	Benedict IV
903	Leo V
903	*Christopher*
904	Sergius III
911	Anastasius III
913	Landus
914	John X
928	Leo VI
928	Stephen VII
931	John XI
936	Leo VII
939	Stephen VIII
942	Marinus II
946	Agapitus II
955	John XII
963	Leo VIII
964	Benedict V
965	John XIII
973	Benedict VI
974	*Boniface VII*
974	Benedict VII
983	John XIV
985	John XV
996	Gregory V
997	*John XVI*
999	Sylvester II
1003	John XVII
1004	John XVIII
1009	Sergius IV
1012	Benedict VIII
1012	*Gregory*
1024	John XIX
1032	Benedict IX
1045	Sylvester III
1045	Benedict IX
1045	Gregory VI
1046	Clement II
1047	Benedict IX
1048	Damasus II
1049	St. Leo IX
1055	Victor II
1057	Stephen IX
1058	*Benedict X*
1059	Nicholas II
1061	Alexander II
1061	*Honorius II*
1073	St. Gregory VII
1080	*Clement III*
1086	Bl. Victor III
1088	Bl. Urban II
1099	Paschal II
1100	*Theodoric*
1102	*Albert*
1105	*Sylvester IV*
1118	Gelasius II
1118	*Gregory VIII*
1119	Callistus II
1124	Honorius II
1124	*Celestine II*
1130	Innocent II
1130	*Anacletus II*
1138	*Victor IV*
1143	Celestine II
1144	Lucius II
1145	Bl. Eugene III
1153	Anastasius IV
1154	Adrian IV
1159	Alexander III
1159	*Victor IV*
1164	*Paschal III*
1168	*Callistus III*
1179	*Innocent III*
1181	Lucius III
1185	Urban III
1187	Gregory VIII
1187	Clement III
1191	Celestine III
1198	Innocent III
1216	Honorius III
1227	Gregory IX
1241	Celestine IV
1243	Innocent IV
1254	Alexander IV
1261	Urban IV
1265	Clement IV
1271	Bl. Gregory X
1276	Bl. Innocent V
1276	Adrian V
1276	John XXI
1277	Nicholas III
1281	Martin IV
1285	Honorius IV
1288	Nicholas IV
1294	St. Celestine V
1294	Boniface VIII
1303	Benedict XI
1305	Clement V
1316	John XXII
1328	*Nicholas V*
1334	Benedict XII
1342	Clement VI
1352	Innocent VI
1362	Bl. Urban V
1370	Gregory XI
1378	Urban VI
1378	*Clement VII*
1389	Boniface IX
1394	*Benedict XIII*
1404	Innocent VII
1406	Gregory XII
1409	*Alexander V*
1410	*John XXIII*
1417	Martin V
1431	Eugene IV
1440	*Felix V*
1447	Nicholas V
1455	Callistus III
1458	Pius II
1464	Paul II
1471	Sixtus IV
1484	Innocent VIII
1492	Alexander VI
1503	Pius III
1503	Julius II
1513	Leo X
1522	Adrian VI
1523	Clement VII
1534	Paul III
1550	Julius III
1555	Marcellus II
1555	Paul IV
1559	Pius IV
1566	St. Pius V
1572	Gregory XIII
1585	Sixtus V
1590	Urban VII
1590	Gregory XIV
1591	Innocent IX
1592	Clement VIII
1605	Leo XI
1605	Paul V
1621	Gregory XV
1623	Urban VIII
1644	Innocent X
1655	Alexander VII
1667	Clement IX
1670	Clement X
1676	Bl. Innocent XI
1689	Alexander VIII
1691	Innocent XII
1700	Clement XI
1721	Innocent XIII
1724	Bennedict XIII
1730	Clement XII
1740	Benedict XIV
1758	Clement XIII
1769	Clement XIV
1775	Pius VI
1800	Pius VII
1823	Leo XII
1829	Pius VIII
1831	Gregory XVI
1846	Pius IX
1878	Leo XIII
1903	St. Pius X
1914	Benedict XV
1922	Pius XI
1939	Pius XII
1958	John XXIII
1963	Paul VI

AWARDS — MEDALS — PRIZES

The Alfred B. Nobel Prize Winners

Alfred B. Nobel, inventor of dynamite, bequeathed $9,000,000, the interest to be distributed yearly to those who had most benefited mankind in physics, chemistry, medicine-physiology, literature, and peace. The first Nobel Prize in Economics was awarded in 1969. No awards given for years omitted. In 1976, each prize was worth $160,000.

Physics

1976 Burton Richter, U.S.
Samuel C.C. Ting, U.S.
1975 James Rainwater, U.S.
Ben Mottelson, U.S.-Danish,
Hage Bohr, Danish
1974 Martin Ryle, British
Antony Hewish, British
1973 Ivar Giaever, U.S.
Leo Esaki, U.S.
Brian D. Josephson, British
1972 John Bardeen, U.S.
Leon N. Cooper, U.S.
John R. Schrieffer, U.S.
1971 Dennis Gabor, British
1970 Louis Neel, French
Hannes Alfven, Swedish
1969 Murray Gell-Mann, U.S.
1968 Luis W. Alvarez, U.S.
1967 Hans A. Bethe, U.S.
1966 Alfred Kastler, French
1965 Richard P. Feynman, U.S.
Julian S. Schwinger, U.S.
Shinichiro Tomanaga, Japanese
1964 Nikolai G. Basov, USSR
Aleksander M. Prochorov, USSR
Charles H. Townes, U.S.
1963 Maria Goeppert-Mayer, U.S.
J. Hans D. Jensen, German
Eugene P. Wigner, U.S.
1962 Lev. D. Landau, USSR
1961 Robert Hofstadter, U.S.
Rudolf L. Mossbauer, German
1960 Donald A. Glaser, U.S.
1959 Owen Chamberlain, U.S.
Emilio G. Segre, U.S.
1958 Paval Cerenkov, Ilya Frank,
Igor J. Tamm, all USSR
1957 Tsung-Dao Lee,
Chen Ning Yang, both U.S.
1956 John Bardeen, U.S.
Walter H. Brattain, U.S.
William Shockley, U.S.
1955 Polykarp Kusch, U.S.
Willis E. Lamb, U.S.
1954 Max Born, British
Walter Bothe, German
1953 Frits Zernike, Dutch
1952 Felix Bloch, U.S.
Edward M. Purcell, U.S.
1951 Sir John D. Cockroft, British
Ernest T. S. Walton, Irish
1950 Cecil F. Powell, British
1949 Hideki Yukawa, Japanese
1948 Patrick M. S. Blackett, British
1947 Sir Edward V. Appleton, British
1946 Percy Williams Bridgman, U.S.
1945 Wolfgang Pauli, U.S.
1944 Isidor Isaac Rabi, U.S.
1943 Otto Sern, U.S.
1939 Ernest O. Lawrence, U.S.
1938 Enrico Fermi, U.S.
1937 Clinton J. Davisson, U.S.
George P. Thomson, British
1936 Carl D. Anderson, U.S.
Victor F. Hess, Austrian
1935 James Chadwick, British
1933 Paul A. M. Dirac, British
Erwin Schrodinger, Austrian
1932 Werner Heisenberg, German
1930 Sir Chandrasekhara V. Raman, Indian
1929 Prince Louis-Victor de Broglie, French
1928 Owen W. Richardson, British
1927 Arthur H. Compton, U.S.
Charles T. R. Wilson, British
1926 Jean B. Perrin, French
1925 James Franck,
Gustav Hertz, both German
1924 Karl M. G. Siegbahn, Swedish
1923 Robert A. Millikan, U.S.
1922 Niels Bohr, Danish
1921 Albert Einstein, Ger.-U.S.
1920 Charles E. Guillaume, French
1919 Johannes Stark, German
1918 Max K. E. L. Planck, German
1917 Charles G. Barkla, British
1915 Sir William H. Bragg, British
William L. Bragg, British
1914 Max von Laue, German
1913 Heike Kamerlingh-Onnes, Dutch
1912 Nils G. Dalen, Swedish
1911 Wilhelm Wein, German
1910 Johannes D. van der Waals, Dutch
1909 Carl F. Braun, German
Guglielmo Marconi, Italian
1908 Gabriel Lippmann, French
1907 Albert A. Michelson, U.S.
1906 Sir Joseph J. Thomson, British
1905 Philipp E. A. von Lenard, Ger.
1904 Rayleigh, Lord (John W. Strutt), British
1903 Antoine Henri Becquerel,
Marie and Pierre Curie, all French
1902 Hendrik A. Lorentz,
Pieter Zeeman, both Dutch
1901 Wilhelm C. Rontgen, German

Chemistry

1976 William L. Lipscomb, U.S.
1975 John Cornforth, Austral.-Brit.,
Vladimir Prelog, Yugo.-Switz.
1974 Paul J. Flory, U.S.
1973 Ernst Otto Fischer, W. German
Geoffrey Wilkinson, British
1972 Christian B. Anfinsen, U.S.
Stanford Moore, U.S.
William H. Stein, U.S.
1971 Gerhard Herzberg, Canadian
1970 Luis A. Leloir, Arg.
1969 Derek H. R. Barton, British
Odd Hassel, Norwegian
1968 Lars Onsager, U.S.
1967 Manfred Eigen, German
Ronald G. W. Norrish, British
George Porter, British
1966 Robert S. Mulliken, U.S.
1965 Robert B. Woodward, U.S.
1964 Dorothy C. Hodgkin, British
1963 Giulio Natta, Italian
Karl Ziegler, German
1962 John C. Kendrew, British
Max F. Perutz, British
1961 Melvin Calvin, U.S.
1960 Willard F. Libby, U.S.
1959 Jaroslav Heyrovsky, Czech
1958 Frederick Sanger, British
1957 Sir. Alexander R. Todd, British
1956 Sir Cyril N. Hinshelwood, British
Nikolai N. Semenov, USSR
1955 Vincent du Vigneaud, U.S.
1954 Linus C. Pauling, U.S.
1953 Hermann Staudinger, German
1952 Archer J. P. Martin, British
Richard L. M. Synge, British
1951 Edwin M. McMillan, U.S.
Glenn T. Seaborg, U.S.
1950 Kurt Adler, German
Otto P. H. Diels, German
1949 William F. Glauque, U.S.
1948 Arne W. K. Tiselius, Swedish
1947 Sir Robert Robinson, British
1946 James B. Sumner, John H. Northrop, Wendell M. Stanley, all U.S.
1945 Arttúri I. Virtanen, Finnish
1944 Otto Hahn, German
1943 Georg de Hevesy, Hungarian
1939 Adolf F. J. Butenandt, German
Leopold Ruzicka, Swiss
1938 Richard Kuhn, German
1937 Walter N. Haworth, British
Paul Karrer, Swiss
1936 Peter J. W. Debye, Dutch
1935 Frederic Joliot-Curie, French
Irene Joliot-Curie, French
1934 Harold C. Urey, U.S.
1932 Irving Langmuir, U.S.
1931 Friedrich Bergius, German
Carl Bosch, German
1930 Hans Fischer, German
1929 Arthur Harden, British
Hans von Euler-Chelpin, Swed.
1928 Adolf O. R. Windaus, German
1927 Heinrich O. Wieland, German
1926 Theodor Svedberg, Swedish
1925 Richard A. Zsigmondy, German
1923 Fritz Pergl, Austrian
1922 Francis W. Aston, British
1921 Frederick Soddy, British
1920 Walther H. Nernst, German
1918 Fritz Haber, German
1915 Richard M. Willstatter, German
1914 Theodore W. Richards, U.S.
1913 Alfred Werner, Swiss
1912 Victor Grignard, French
Paul Sabatier, French
1911 Marie Curie, French
1910 Otto Wallach, German
1909 Wilhelm Ostwald, German
1908 Ernest Rutherford, British
1907 Eduard Buchner, German
1906 Henri Moissan, French
1905 Adolf von Baeyer, German
1904 Sir William Ramsay, British
1903 Svante A. Arrhenius, Swedish
1902 Emil Fischer, German
1901 Jacobus H. van't Hoff, Dutch

Physiology or Medicine

1976 Baruch S. Blumberg, U.S.
Daniel Carleton Gajdusek, U.S.
1975 David Baltimore, Howard Temin, both U.S.; Renato Dulbecco, Ital.-U.S.
1974 Albert Claude, Lux.-U.S.; George Emil Palade, Rom.-U.S.; Christian Rene de Duve, Belg.
1973 Karl von Frisch, Konrad Lorenz, both Ger.; Nikolaas Tinbergen, Brit.
1972 Gerald M. Edelman, U.S.
Rodney R. Porter, British
1971 Earl W. Sutherland Jr., U.S.
1970 Julius Axelrod, U.S.
Sir Bernard Katz, British
Ulf von Euler, Swedish
1969 Max Delbruck,
Alfred D. Hershey,
Salvador Luria, all U.S.
1968 Robert W. Holley,
H. Gobind Khorana,
Marshall W. Nirenberg, all U.S.
1967 Ragnar Granit, Swedish
Haldan Keffer Hartline, U.S.
George Wald, U.S.
1966 Charles B. Huggins,

Francis Peyton Rous, both U.S.
1965 Francois Jacob, Andre Lwoff, Jacquest Monod, all French
1964 Konrad E. Bloch, American
Feodor Lynen, German
1963 Sir John C. Eccles, Australian
Alan L. Hodgkin, British
Andrew F. Huxley, British
1962 Francis H. C. Crick, British
James D. Watson, U.S.
Maurice H. F. Wilkins, British
1961 Georg von Bekesy, U.S.
1960 Sir F. MacFarlane Burnet, Australian
Peter B. Medawar, British
1959 Arthur Kornberg, U.S.
Severo Ochoa, U.S.
1958 George W. Beadle, U.S.
Edward L. Tatum, U.S.
Joshua Lederberg, U.S.
1957 Daniel Bovet, Italian
1956 Andre F. Cournand, U.S.
Werner Forssmann, German
Dickinson W. Richards, Jr., U.S.
1955 Alex H. T. Theorell, Swedish
1954 John F. Enders,
Frederick C. Robbins,
Thomas H. Weller, all U.S.
1953 Hans A. Krebs, British
Fritz A. Lipmann, U.S.
1952 Selman A. Waksman, U.S.
1951 Max Theiler, U.S.
1950 Philip S. Hench,
Edward C. Kendall, both U.S.
Tadeus Reichstein, Swiss
1949 Walter R. Hess, Swiss
Antonio Moniz, Portuguese
1948 Paul H. Muller, Swiss
1947 Carl F. Cori,
Gerty T. Cori, both U.S.
Bernardo A. Houssay, Arg.
1946 Hermann J. Muller, U.S.
1945 Ernst B. Chain, British
Sir Alexander Fleming, British
Sir Howard W. Florey, British
1944 Joseph Erlanger, U.S.
Herbert S. Gasser, U.S.
1943 Henrik C. P. Dam, Danish
Edward A. Doisy, U.S.
1939 Gerhard Domagk, German
1938 Corneille J. F. Heymans, Belg.
1937 Albert Szent-Gyorgyi, U.S.
1936 Sir Henry H. Dale, British
Otto Loewi, U.S.
1935 Hans Spemann, German
1934 George R. Minot, Wm. P. Murphy, G. H. Whipple, all U.S.
1933 Thomas H. Morgan, U.S.
1932 Edgard D. Adrian, British
Sir Charles S. Sherrington, Brit.
1931 Otto H. Warburg, German
1930 Karl Landsteiner, U.S.
1929 Christiaan Eijkman, Dutch
Sir Frederick G. Hopkins, British
1928 Charles J. H. Nicolle, French
1927 Julius Wagner-Jauregg, Aus.
1926 Johannes A. G. Fibiger, Danish
1924 Willem Einthoven, Dutch
1923 Frederick G. Banting, Canadian
John J. R. Macleod, Canadian
1922 Archibald V. Hill, British
Otto F. Meyerhof, German
1920 Schack A. S. Krogh, Danish
1919 Jules Bordet, Belgian
1914 Robert Barany, Hungarian
1913 Charles R. Richet, French
1912 Alexis Carrel, U.S.
1911 Allvar Gullstrand, Swedish
1910 Albrecht Kossel, German
1909 Emil T. Kocher, Swiss
1908 Paul Ehrlich, German
Elie Metchnikoff, French
1907 Charles L. A. Laveran, French
1906 Camillo Golgi, Italian
Santiago Roman y Cajal, Sp.
1905 Robert Koch, German
1904 Ivan P. Pavlov, Russian
1903 Niels R. Finsen, Danish
1902 Sir Ronald Ross, British
1901 Emil A. von Behring, German

Literature

1976 Saul Bellow, U.S.
1975 Eugenio Montale, Ital.
1974 Eyyvind Johnson, Harry Edmund Martinson, both Swedish
1973 Patrick White, Australian
1972 Heinrich Boll, W. German
1971 Pablo Neruda, Chilean
1970 Aleksandr I. Solzhenitsyn, Russ.
1969 Samuel Beckett, Irish
1968 Yasunari Kawabata, Japanese
1967 Miguel Angel Asturias, Guate.
1966 Samuel Joseph Agnon, Israeli
Nelly Sachs, Swedish
1965 Mikhail Sholokhov, Russian
1964 Jean Paul Sartre, French (Prize declined)
1963 Giorgos Seferis, Greek
1962 John Steinbeck, U.S.
1961 Ivo Andric, Yugoslavian
1960 Saint-John Perse, French
1959 Salvatore Quasimodo, Italian
1958 Boris L. Pasternak, Russian (Prize declined)
1957 Albert Camus, French
1956 Juan Ramon Jimenez, Puerto Rican
1955 Halldor K. Laxness, Icelandic
1954 Ernest Hemingway, U.S.
1953 Sir Winston Churchill, British
1952 Francois Mauriac, French
1951 Par F. Lagerkvist, Swedish
1950 Bertrand Russell, British
1949 William Faulkner, U.S.
1948 T. S. Eliot, British
1947 Andre Gide, French
1946 Hermann Hesse, Swiss
1945 Gabriela Mistral, Chilean
1944 Johannes V. Jensen, Danish
1939 Frans E. Sillanpaa, Finnish
1938 Pearl S. Buck, U.S.
1937 Roger Martin du Gard, French
1936 Eugene O'Neill, U.S.
1934 Luigi Pirandello, Italian
1933 Ivan A. Bunin, French
1932 John Galsworthy, British
1931 Erik A. Karlfeldt, Swedish
1930 Sinclair Lewis, U.S.
1929 Thomas Mann, German
1928 Sigrid Undset, Norwegian
1927 Henri Bergson, French
1926 Grazia Deledda, Italian
1925 George Bernard Shaw, British
1924 Wladyslaw S. Reymont, Polish
1923 William Butler Yeats, Irish
1922 Jacinto Benavente, Spanish
1921 Anatole France, French
1920 Knut Hamsun, Norwegian
1919 Carl F. G. Spitteler, Swiss
1917 Karl A. Gjellerup, Danish
Henrik Pontoppidan, Danish
1916 Verner von Heidenstam, Swed.
1915 Romain Rolland, French
1913 Rabindranath Tagore, Indian
1912 Gerhart Hauptmann, German
1911 Maurice Maeterlinck, Belgian
1910 Paul J. L. Heyse, German
1909 Selma Lagerlof, Swedish
1908 Rudolf C. Eucken, German
1907 Rudyard Kipling, British
1906 Giosue Carducci, Italian
1905 Henryk Sienkiewicz, Polish
1904 Frederic Mistral, French
Jose Echegaray, Spanish
1903 Bjornsterne Bjornson, Norw.
1902 Theodor Mommsen, German
1901 Rene F. A. Sully Prudhomme, French

Peace

1975 Andrei Sakharov, USSR
1974 Eisaku Sato, Jap., Sean MacBride, Irish
1973 Henry Kissinger, U.S.
Le Duc Tho, N. Vietnamese (Tho declined)
1971 Willy Brandt, W. German
1970 Norman E. Borlaug, U.S.
1969 Intl. Labor Organization
1968 Rene Cassin, French
1965 U.N. Children's Fund (UNICEF)
1964 Martin Luther King Jr., Am.
1963 International Red Cross, League of Red Cross Societies
1962 Linus C. Pauling, U.S.
1961 Dag Hammarskjold, Swedish
1960 Albert J. Luthuli, South African
1959 Philip J. Noel-Baker, British
1958 Georges Pire, Belgian
1957 Lester B. Pearson, Canadian
1954 Office of the UN High Commissioner for Refugees
1953 George C. Marshall, U.S.
1952 Albert Schweitzer, French
1951 Leon Jouhaux, French
1950 Ralph J. Bunche, U.S.
1949 Lord John Boyd Orr of Brechin Mearns, British
1947 Friends Service Council, Brit.
Amer. Friends Service Com.
1946 Emily G. Balch,
John R. Mott, both U.S.
1945 Cordell Hull, U.S.
1944 International Red Cross
1938 Nansen International Office for Refugees
1937 Viscount Cecil of Chelwood, Brit.
1936 Carlos de Saavedra Lamas, Arg.
1935 Carl von Ossietzky, German
1934 Arthur Henderson, British
1933 Sir Norman Angell, British
1931 Jane Addams, U.S.
Nicholas Murray Butler, U.S.
1930 Nathan Soderblom, Swedish
1929 Frank B. Kellogg, U.S.
1927 Ferdinand E. Buisson, French
Ludwig Quidde, German
1926 Aristide Briand, French
Gustav Stresemann, German
1925 Sir J. Austen Chamberlain, Brit.
Charles G. Dawes, U.S.
1922 Fridtjof Nansen, Norwegian
1921 Karl H. Branting, Swedish
Christian L. Lange, Norwegian
1920 Leon V. A. Bourgeois, French
1919 Woodrow Wilson, U.S.
1917 International Red Cross
1913 Henri La Fontaine, Belgian
1912 Elihu Root, U.S.
1911 Tobias M. C. Asser, Dutch
Alfred H. Fried, Austrian
1910 Permanent International Peace Bureau
1909 Auguste M. F. Beernaert, Belg.
Paul H. B. B. d'Estournelles de Constant, French
1908 Klas P. Arnoldson, Swedish
Fredrik Bajer, Danish
1907 Ernesto T. Moneta, Italian
Louis Renault, French
1906 Theodore Roosevelt, U.S.
1905 Baroness Bertha von Suttner, Austrian
1904 Institute of International Law
1903 Sir William R. Cremer, British
1902 Elie Ducommun,
Charles A. Gobat, both Swiss
1901 Jean H. Dunant, Swiss
Frederic Passy, French

Economics

1976 Milton Friedman, U.S.
1975 Tjalling Koopmans, Dutch-U.S., Leonid Kantorovich, USSR
1974 Gunnar Myrdal, Swed., Friedrich A. von Hayek, Austrian
1973 Wassily Leontief, U.S.

1972 Kenneth J. Arrow, U.S.
John R. Hicks, British
1971 Simon Kuznets, U.S.
1970 Paul A. Samuelson, U.S.
1969 Ragnar Frisch, Norwegian
Jan Tinbergen, Dutch

Pulitzer Prizes in Journalism, Letters, and Music

The Pulitzer Prizes were endowed by Joseph Pulitzer (1847-1911), publisher of The World, New York, N. Y., in a bequest to Columbia University, New York, N. Y., and are awarded annually by the president of the university on recommendation of the Advisory Board on Pulitzer Prizes for work done during the preceding year. Secretary of the Advisory Board is Prof. Richard T. Baker of Columbia Univ. All prizes are $1,000 (originally $500) in each category, except Meritorious Public Service for which a gold medal is given. No awards given for years omitted.

Journalism

Meritorious Public Service

For distinguished and meritorious public service by a United States newspaper.

1918—New York Times. Also special award to Minna Lewinson and Henry Beetle Hough.
1919—Milwaukee Journal.
1921—Boston Post.
1922—New York World.
1923—Memphis (Tenn.) Commercial Appeal.
1924—New York World.
1926—Enquirer-Sun, Columbus, Ga.
1927—Canton (Oh.) Daily News.
1928—Indianapolis Times.
1929—Evening World, New York.
1931—Atlanta (Ga.) Constitution.
1932—Indianapolis (Ind.) News.
1933—New York World-Telegram.
1934—Medford (Ore.) Mail-Tribune.
1935—Sacramento (Cal.) Bee.
1936—Cedar Rapids (Ia.) Gazette.
1937—St. Louis Post-Dispatch.
1938—Bismarck (N. D.) Tribune.
1939—Miami (Fla.) Daily News.
1940—Waterbury (Conn.) Republican and American.
1941—St. Louis Post-Dispatch.
1942—Los Angeles Times.
1943—Omaha World Herald.
1944—New York Times.
1945—Detroit Free Press.
1946—Scranton (Pa.) Times.
1947—Baltimore Sun.
1948—St. Louis Post-Dispatch.
1949—Nebraska State Journal.
1950—Chicago Daily News; St. Louis Post-Dispatch.
1951—Miami (Fla.) Herald and Brooklyn Eagle.
1952—St. Louis Post-Dispatch.
1953—Whiteville (N. C.) News Reporter; Tabor City (N. C.) Tribune.
1954—Newsday (Long Island, N.Y.).
1955—Columbus (Ga.) Ledger and Sunday Ledger-Enquirer.
1956—Watsonville (Cal.) Register-Pajaronian.
1957—Chicago Daily News.
1958—Arkansas Gazette, Little Rock.
1959—Utica (N. Y.) Observer-Dispatch and Utica Daily Press.
1960—Los Angeles Times.
1961—Amarillo (Tex.) Globe-Times.
1962—Panama City (Fla.) News-Herald.
1963—Chicago Daily News.
1964—St. Petersburg (Fla.) Times.
1965—Hutchinson (Kan.) News.
1966—Boston Globe
1967—The Louisvillle Courier-Journal; The Milwaukee Journal.
1968—Riverside (Cal.) Press-Enterprise.
1969—Los Angeles Times.
1970—Newsday (Long Island, N.Y.).
1971—Winston Salem (N.C.) Journal & Sentinel.
1972—New York Times.
1973—Washington Post.
1974—Newsday (Long Island, N.Y.).
1975—Boston Globe.
1976—Anchorage Daily News.
1977—Lufkin (Tex.) News.

Reporting

This category originally embraced all fields, local, national, and international. Later separate categories were created for the different fields of reporting.

1917—Herbert Bayard Swope, New York World.
1918—Harold A. Littledale, New York Evening Post.
1920—John J. Leary, Jr., New York World.
1921—Louis Seibold, New York World.
1922—Kirke L. Simpson, Associated Press.
1923—Alva Johnston, New York Times.
1924—Magner White, San Diego Sun.
1925—James W. Mulroy and Alvin H. Goldstein, Chicago Daily News.
1926—William Burke Miller, Louisville Courier-Journal.
1927—John T. Rogers, St. Louis Post-Dispatch.
1929—Paul Y. Anderson, St. Louis Post-Dispatch.
1930—Russell D. Owens, New York Times. Also $500 to W. O. Dapping, Auburn (N. Y.) Citizen.
1931—A. B. MacDonald, Kansas City (Mo.) Star.
1932—W. C. Richards, D. D. Martin, J. S. Pooler, F. D. Webb, J. N. W. Sloan, Detroit Free Press.
1933—Francis A. Jamieson, Asssociated Press.
1934—Royce Brier, San Francisco Chronicle.
1935—William H. Taylor, New York Herald Tribune.
1936—Lauren D. Lyman, New York Times.
1937—John J. O'Neill, N. Y. Herald Tribune; William L. Laurence, N. Y. Times; Howard W. Blakeslee, A. P.; Gobind Behari Lal, University Service; and David Dietz, Scripps-Howard Newspapers.
1938—Raymond Sprigle, Pittsburgh Post-Gazette.
1939—Thomas L. Stokes, Scripps-Howard Newspaper Alliance.
1940—S. Burton Heath, New York World-Telegram.
1941—Westbrook Pegler, New York World-Telegram.
1942—Stanton Delaplane, San Francisco Chronicle.
1943—George Weller, Chicago Daily News.
1944—Paul Schoenstein, N. Y. Journal-American.
1945—Jack S. McDowell, San Francisco Call-Bulletin.
1946—William L. Laurence, New York Times.
1947—Frederick Woltman, N. Y. World-Telegram.
1948—George E. Goodwin, Atlanta Journal.
1949—Malcolm Johnson, New York Sun.
1950—Meyer Berger, New York Times.
1951—Edward S. Montgomery, San Francisco Examiner.
1952—Geo. de Carvalho, San Francisco Chronicle.

(1) General or Spot; (2) Special or Investigative

1953—(1) Providence (R.I.) Journal and Evening Bulletin; (2) Edward J. Mowery, N.Y. World-Telegram & Sun.
1954—(1) Vicksburg (Miss.) Sunday Post-Herald; (2) Alvin Scott McCoy, Kansas City (Mo.) Star.
1955—(1) Mrs. Caro Brown, Alice (Tex.) Daily Echo; (2) Roland K. Towery, Cuero (Tex.) Record.
1956—(1) Lee Hills, Detroit Free Press; (2) Arthur Daley, New York Times.
1957—(1) Salt Lake Tribune, Salt Lake City, Ut.; (2) Wallace Turner and William Lambert, Portland Oregonian.
1958—(1) Fargo (N. D.) Forum; (2) George Beveridge, Evening Star, Washington, D. C.
1959—(1) Mary Lou Werner, Washington Evening Star; (2) John Harold Brislin, Scranton (Pa.) Tribune, and The Scrantonian.
1960—(1) Jack Nelson, Atlanta Constitution; (2) Miriam Ottenberg, Washington Evening Star.
1961—(1) Sanche de Gramont, N. Y. Herald Tribune; (2) Edgar May, Buffalo Evening News.
1962—(1) Robert D. Mullins, Deseret News, Salt Lake City; (2) George Bliss, Chicago Tribune.
1963—(1) Shared by Sylvan Fox, William Longgood, and Anthony Shannon, N. Y. World-Telegram & Sun; (2) Oscar Griffin, Jr., Pecos (Tex.) Independent and Enterprise.

(1) General Reporting; (2) Special Reporting.

1964—(1) Norman C. Miller, Wall Street Journal; (2) Shared by James V. Magee, Albert V. Gaudiosi, and Frederick A. Meyer, Philadelphia Bulletin.
1965—(1) Melvin H. Ruder, Hungry Horse News (Columbia Falls, Mon.); (2) Gene Goltz, Houston Post.
1966—(1) Los Angeles Times Staff; (2) John A. Frasca, Tampa (Fla.) Tribune.
1967—(1) Robert V. Cox, Chambersburg (Pa.) Public Opinion; (2) Gene Miller, Miami Herald.
1968—Detroit Free Press Staff; (2) J. Anthony Lukas, N. Y. Times.
1969—(1) John Fetterman, Louisville Courier-Journal and Times; (2) Albert L. Delugach, St. Louis Globe Democrat, and Denny Walsh, Life.
1970—(1) Thomas Fitzpatrick, Chicago Sun-Times; (2) Harold Eugene Martin, Montgomery Advertiser & Alabama Journal.
1971—(1) Akron Beacon Journal Staff, (2) William Hugh Jones, Chicago Tribune.
1972—(1) Richard Cooper and John Machacek, Rochester Times-Union; (2) Timothy Leland, Gerard M. O'Neill, Stephen Kurkjian and Anne De Santis, Boston Globe.
1973—(1) Chicago Tribune; (2) Sun Newspapers of Omaha.
1974—(1) Hugh F. Hough, Arthur M. Petacque, Chicago Sun-Times; (2) William Sherman, N.Y. Daily News.

1975—(1) Xenia (Oh.) Daily Gazette; (2) Indianapolis Star.
1976—(1) Gene Miller, Miami Herald; (2) Chicago Tribune.
1977—(1) Margo Huston, Milwaukee Journal; (2) Acel Moore, Wendell Rawls Jr., Philadelphia Inquirer.

Criticism or Commentary

(1) Criticism; (2) Commentary

1970—(1) Ada Louise Huxtable, N. Y. Times; (2) Marquis W. Childs, St. Louis Post-Dispatch.
1971—(1) Harold C. Schonberg, N. Y. Times; (2) William A. Caldwell, The Record, Hackensack, N.J.
1972—(1) Frank Peters Jr., St. Louis Post-Dispatch; (2) Mike Royko, Chicago Daily News.
1973—(1) Ronald Powers, Chicago Sun-Times; (2) David S. Broder, Washington Post.
1974—(1) Emily Genauer, Newsday, (N.Y.); (2) Edwin A. Roberts, Jr., National Observer.
1975—(1) Roger Ebert, Chicago Sun Times; (2) Mary McGrory, Washington Star.
1976—(1) Alan M. Kriegsman, Washington Post; (2) Walter W. (Red) Smith, N.Y. Times.
1977—(1) William McPherson, Washington Post; (2) George F. Will, Wash. Post Writers Group.

National Reporting

1942—Louis Stark, New York Times.
1944—Dewey L. Fleming, Baltimore Sun.
1945—James B. Reston, New York Times.
1946—Edward A. Harris, St. Louis Post-Dispatch.
1947—Edward T. Folliard, Washington Post.
1948—Bert Andrews, New York Herald Tribune; Nat S. Finney, Minneapolis Tribune.
1949—Charles P. Trussell, New York Times.
1950—Edwin O. Guthman, Seattle Times.
1952—Anthony Leviero, New York Times.
1953—Don Whitehead, Associated Press.
1954—Richard Wilson, Cowles Newspapers.
1955—Anthony Lewis, Washington Daily News.
1956—Charles L. Bartlett, Chattanooga Times.
1957—James Reston, New York Times.
1958—Relman Morin, AP; Clark Mollenhoff, Des Moines Register & Tribune.
1959—Howard Van Smith, Miami (Fla.) News.
1960—Vance Trimble, Scripps-Howard, Washington, D. C.
1961—Edward R. Cony, Wall Street Journal.
1962—Nathan G. Caldwell and Gene S. Graham, Nashville Tennessean.
1963—Anthony Lewis, New York Times.
1964—Merriman Smith, UPI.
1965—Louis M. Kohlmeier, Wall Street Journal.
1966—Haynes Johnson, Washington Evening Star.
1967—Monroe Karmin and Stanley Penn, Wall Street Journal.
1968—Howard James, Christian Science Monitor; Nathan K. Kotz, Des Moines Register.
1969—Robert Cahn, Christian Science Monitor.
1970—William J. Eaton, Chicago Daily News.
1971—Lucinda Franks & Thomas Powers, UPI.
1972—Jack Anderson, United Features.
1973—Robert Boyd and Clark Hoyt, Knight Newspapers.
1974—James R. Polk, Washington Star-News; Jack White, Providence Journal-Bulletin.
1975—Donald L. Barlett and James B. Steele, Philadelphia Inquirer.
1976—James Risser, Des Moines Register.
1977—Walter Mears, Associated Press.

International Reporting

1942—Laurence Edmund Allen, Associated Press.
1943—Ira Wolfert, No. Am. Newspaper Alliance.
1944—Daniel DeLuce, Associated Press.
1945—Mark S. Watson, Baltimore Sun.
1946—Homer W. Bigart, New York Herald Tribune.
1947—Eddy Gilmore, Associated Press.
1948—Paul W. Ward, Baltimore Sun.
1949—Price Day, Baltimore Sun.
1950—Edmund Stevens, Christian Science Monitor.
1951—Keyes Beech and Fred Sparks, Chicago Daily News; Homer Bigart and Marguerite Higgins, New York Herald Tribune; Relman Morin and Don Whitehead, AP.
1952—John M. Hightower, Associated Press.
1953—Austin C. Wehrwein, Milwaukee Journal.
1954—Jim G. Lucas, Scripps-Howard Newspapers.
1955—Harrison Salisbury, New York Times.
1956—William Randolph Hearst, Jr., Frank Conniff, Hearst Newspapers; Kingsbury Smith, INS.
1957—Russell Jones, United Press.
1958—New York Times.
1959—Joseph Martin and Philip Santora, N. Y. News.
1960—A. M. Rosenthal, New York Times.
1961—Lynn Heinzerling, Associated Press.
1962—Walter Lippmann, N. Y. Herald Tribune Synd.
1963—Hal Hendrix, Miami (Fla.) News.
1964—Malcolm W. Browne, AP; David Halberstam, N. Y. Times.
1965—J. A. Livingston, Philadelphia Bulletin.
1966—Peter Arnett, AP.
1967—R. John Hughes, Christian Science Monitor.
1968—Alfred Friendly, Washington Post.
1969—William Tuohy, L. A. Times.
1970—Seymour M. Hersh, Dispatch News Service.
1971—Jimmie Lee Hoagland, Washington Post.
1972—Peter R. Kann, Wall Street Journal.
1973—Max Frankel, N.Y. Times.
1974—Hedrick Smith, N.Y. Times.
1975—William Mullen and Ovie Carter, Chicago Tribune.
1976—Sydney H. Schanberg, N.Y. Times.

Correspondence

For Washington or foreign correspondence. Category was merged with those in national and international reporting in 1948.

1929—Paul Scott Mowrer, Chicago Daily News.
1930—Leland Stowe, New York Herald Tribune.
1931—H. R. Knickerbocker, Philadelphia Public Ledger and New York Evening Post.
1932—Walter Duranty, New York Times, and Charles G. Ross, St. Louis Post-Dispatch.
1933—Edgar Ansel Mowrer, Chicago Daily News.
1934—Frederick T. Birchall, New York Times.
1935—Arthur Krock, New York Times.
1936—Wilfred C. Barber, Chicago Tribune.
1937—Anne O'Hare McCormick, New York Times.
1938—Arthur Krock, New York Times.
1939—Louis P. Lochner, Associated Press.
1940—Otto D. Tolischus, New York Times.
1941—Bronze plaque to commemorate work of American correspondents on war fronts.
1942—Carlos P. Romulo, Philippines Herald.
1943—Hanson W. Baldwin, New York Times.
1944—Ernest Taylor Pyle, Scripps-Howard Newspaper Alliance.
1945—Harold V. (Hal) Boyle, Associated Press.
1946—Arnaldo Cortesi, New York Times.
1947—Brooks Atkinson, New York Times.

Editorial Writing

1917—New York Tribune.
1918—Louisville (Ky.) Courier-Journal.
1920—Harvey E. Newbranch, Omaha Evening World-Herald.
1922—Frank M. O'Brien, New York Herald.
1923—William Allen White, Emporia Gazette.
1924—Frank Buxton, Boston Herald, Special Prize. Frank I. Cobb, New York World.
1925—Robert Lathan, Charleston (S. C.) News and Courier.
1926—Edward M. Kingsbury, N. Y. Times.
1927—F. Lauriston Bullard, Boston Herald.
1928—Grover C. Hall, Montgomery Advertiser.
1929—Louis Isaac Jaffe, Norfolk Virginian-Pilot.
1931—Chas. Ryckman, Fremont (Neb.) Tribune.
1933—Kansas City (Mo.) Star.
1934—E. P. Chase, Atlantic (Ia.) News Telegraph.
1936—Felix Morley, Washington Post, George B. Parker, Scripps-Howard Newspapers.
1937—John W. Owens, Baltimore Sun.
1938—W. W. Waymack, Des Moines (Ia.) Register and Tribune.
1939—Ronald G. Callvert, Portland Oregonian.
1940—Bart Howard, St. Louis Post-Dispatch.
1941—Reuben Maury, Daily News, N. Y.
1942—Geoffrey Parsons, New York Herald Tribune.
1943—Forrest W. Seymour, Des Moines (Ia.) Register and Tribune.
1944—Henry J. Haskell, Kansas City (Mo.) Star.
1945—George W. Potter, Providence (R. I.) Journal-Bulletin.
1946—Hodding Carter, Greenville (Miss.) Delta Democrat-Times.
1947—William H. Grimes, Wall Street Journal.
1948—Virginius Dabney, Richmond (Va.) Times-Dispatch.
1949—John H. Crider, Boston (Mass.) Herald, Herbert Elliston, Washington Post.
1950—Carl M. Saunders, Jackson (Mich.) Citizen-Patriot.
1951—William H. Fitzpatrick, New Orleans States.
1952—Louis LaCoss, St. Louis Globe Democrat.
1953—Vermont C. Royster, Wall Street Journal.
1954—Don Murray, Boston Herald.
1955—Royce Howes, Detroit Free Press.
1956—Lauren K. Soth, Des Moines (Ia.) Register and Tribune.
1957—Buford Boone, Tuscaloosa (Ala.) News.
1958—Harry S. Ashmore, Arkansas Gazette.
1959—Ralph McGill, Atlanta Constitution.
1960—Lenoir Chambers, Norfolk Virginian-Pilot.
1961—William J. Dorvillier, San Juan (Puerto Rico) Star.
1962—Thomas M. Storke, Santa Barbara (Cal.) News-Press.
1963—Ira B. Harkey, Jr., Pascagoula (Miss.) Chronicle.
1964—Hazel Brannon Smith, Lexington (Miss.) Advertiser.

1965—John R. Harrison, The Gainesville (Fla.) Sun.
1966—Robert Lasch, St. Louis Post-Dispatch.
1967—Eugene C. Patterson, Atlanta Constitution.
1968—John S. Knight, Knight Newspapers.
1969—Paul Greenberg, Pine Bluff (Ark.) Commercial.
1970—Philip L. Geyelin, Washington Post.
1971—Horance G. Davis, Jr., Gainesville (Fla.) Sun.
1972—John Strohmeyer, Bethlehem (Pa.) Globe-Times.
1973—Roger B. Linscott, Berkshire Eagle, Pittsfield, Mass.
1974—F. Gilman Spencer, Trenton (N.J.) Trentonian.
1975—John D. Maurice, Charleston (W. Va.) Daily Mail.
1976—Philip Kerby, Los Angeles Times.
1977—Warren L. Lerude, Foster Church, and Norman F. Cardoza, Reno (Nev.) Evening Gazette and Nevada State Journal.

Editorial Cartooning

1922—Rollin Kirby, New York World.
1924—Jay N. Darling, New York Herald Tribune.
1925—Rollin Kirby, New York World.
1926—D. R. Fitzpatrick, St. Louis Post-Dispatch.
1927—Nelson Harding, Brooklyn Eagle.
1928—Nelson Harding, Brooklyn Eagle.
1929—Rollin Kirby, New York World.
1930—Charles Macauley, Brooklyn Eagle.
1931—Edmund Duffy, Baltimore Sun.
1932—John T. McCutcheon, Chicago Tribune.
1933—H. M. Talburt, Washington Daily News.
1934—Edmund Duffy, Baltimore Sun.
1935—Ross A. Lewis, Milwaukee Journal.
1937—C. D. Batchelor, New York Daily News.
1938—Vaughn Shoemaker, Chicago Daily News.
1939—Charles G. Werner, Daily Oklahoman.
1940—Edmund Duffy, Baltimore Sun.
1941—Jacob Burck, Chicago Times.
1942—Herbert L. Block, Newspaper Enterprise Assn.
1943—Jay N. Darling, New York Herald Tribune.
1944—Clifford K. Berryman, Washington Star.
1945—Bill Mauldin, United Feature Syndicate.
1946—Bruce Alexander Russell, Los Angeles Times.
1947—Vaughn Shoemaker, Chicago Daily News.
1948—Reuben L. (Rube) Goldberg, N. Y. Sun.
1949—Lute Pease, Newark (N. J.) Evening News.
1950—James T. Berryman, Washington Star.
1951—Reginald W. Manning, Arizona Republic.
1952—Fred L. Packer, New York Mirror.
1953—Edward D. Kuekes, Cleveland Plain Dealer.
1954—Herbert L. Block, Washington Post & Times-Herald.
1955—Daniel R. Fitzpatrick, St. Louis Post-Dispatch.
1956—Robert York, Louisville (Ky.) Times.
1957—Tom Little, Nashville Tennessean.
1958—Bruce M. Shanks, Buffalo Evening News.
1959—Bill Mauldin, St. Louis Post-Dispatch.
1961—Carey Orr, Chicago Tribune.
1962—Edmund S. Valtman, Hartford Times.
1963—Frank Miller, Des Moines Register.
1964—Paul Conrad, Denver Post.
1966—Don Wright, Miami News.
1967—Patrick B. Oliphant, Denver Post.
1968—Eugene Gray Payne, Charlotte Observer.
1969—John Fischetti, Chicago Daily News.
1970—Thomas F. Darcy, Newsday.
1971—Paul Conrad, L. A. Times.
1972—Jeffrey K. MacNelly, Richmond News-Leader.
1974—Paul Szep, Boston Globe.
1975—Garry Trudeau, Universal Press Syndicate.
1976—Tony Auth, Philadelphia Inquirer.
1977—Paul Szep, Boston Globe.

Spot News Photography

1942—Milton Brooks, Detroit News.
1943—Frank Noel, Associated Press.
1944—Frank Filan, AP; Earle L. Bunker, Omaha World-Herald.
1945—Joe Rosenthal, Associated Press, for photograph of planting American flag on Iwo Jima.
1947—Arnold Hardy, amateur, Atlanta, Ga.
1948—Frank Cushing, Boston Traveler.
1949—Nathaniel Fein, New York Herald Tribune.
1950—Bill Crouch, Oakland (Cal.) Tribune.
1951—Max Desfor, Associated Press.
1952—John Robinson and Don Ultang, Des Moines Register and Tribune.
1953—William M. Gallagher, Flint (Mich.) Journal.
1954—Mrs. Walter M. Schau, amateur.
1955—John L. Gaunt, Jr., Los Angeles Times.
1956—New York Daily News.
1957—Harry A. Trask, Boston Traveler.
1958—William C. Beall, Washington Daily News.
1959—William Seaman, Minneapolis Star.
1960—Andrew Lopez, UPI.
1961—Yasushi Nagao, Mainichi Newspapers, Tokyo.
1962—Paul Vathis, Associated Press.
1963—Hector Rondon, La Republica, Caracas, Venezuela.
1964—Robert H. Jackson, Dallas Times-Herald.
1965—Horst Faas, Associated Press.
1966—Kyoichi Sawada, UPI.
1967—Jack R. Thornell, Associated Press.
1968—Rocco Morabito, Jacksonville Journal.
1969—Edward Adams, AP
1970—Steve Starr, AP
1971—John Paul Filo, Valley Daily News & Daily Dispatch of Tarentum & New Kensington, Pa.
1972—Horst Faas and Michel Laurent, AP.
1973—Huynh Cong Ut, AP.
1974—Anthony K. Roberts, AP.
1975—Gerald H. Gay, Seattle Times.
1976—Stanley Forman, Boston Herald American.
1977—Neal Ulevich, Associated Press; Stanley Forman, Boston Herald American.

Feature Photography

1968—Toshio Sakai, UPI.
1969—Moneta Sleet, Jr., Ebony.
1970—Dallas Kinney, Palm Beach Post.
1971—Jack Dykinga, Chicago Sun-Times.
1972—Dave Kennerly, UPI.
1973—Brian Lanker, Topeka Capitol-Journal.
1974—Slava Veder, AP.
1975—Matthew Lewis, Washington Post.
1976—Louisville Courier-Journal and Louisville Times.
1977—Robin Hood, Chattanooga News-Free Press.

Special Citation

1938—Edmonton (Alberta) Journal, bronze plaque.
1941—New York Times.
1944—Byron Price and Mrs. William Allen White. Also to Richard Rodgers and Oscar Hammerstein 2d, for musical, Oklahoma!
1945—Press cartographers for war maps.
1947—(Pulitzer centennial year.) Columbia Univ. and the Graduate School of Journalism, and St. Louis Post-Dispatch.
1948—Dr. Frank Diehl Fackenthal.
1951—Cyrus L. Sulzberger, New York Times.
1952—Max Kase, New York Journal-American.
1953—The New York Times; Lester Markel.
1957—Kenneth Roberts, for his historical novels.
1958—Walter Lippmann, New York Herald Tribune.
1960—Garrett Mattingly, for The Armada.
1961—American Heritage Picture History of the Civil War.
1964—The Gannett Newspapers.
1973—James T. Flexner, for "George Washington," a four-volume biography.
1976—John Hohenberg, for services to American journalism.
1977—Alex Haley, for Roots, $1,000.

Letters

Fiction

For fiction in book form by an American author, preferably dealing with American life.
1918—Ernest Poole, His Family.
1919—Booth Tarkington, The Magnificent Ambersons.
1921—Edith Wharton, The Age of Innocence.
1922—Booth Tarkington, Alice Adams.
1923—Willa Cather, One of Ours.
1924—Margaret Wilson, The Able McLaughlins.
1925—Edna Ferber, So Big.
1926—Sinclair Lewis, Arrowsmith. (Refused prize.)
1927—Louis Bromfield, Early Autumn.
1928—Thornton Wilder, Bridge of San Luis Rey.
1929—Julia M. Peterkin, Scarlet Sister Mary.
1930—Oliver LaFarge, Laughing Boy.
1931—Margaret Ayer Barnes, Years of Grace.
1932—Pearl S. Buck, The Good Earth.
1933—T. S. Stribling, The Store.
1934—Caroline Miller, Lamb in His Bosom.
1935—Josephine W. Johnson, Now in November.
1936—Harold L. Davis, Honey in the Horn.
1937—Margaret Mitchell, Gone With the Wind.
1938—John P. Marquand, The Late George Apley.
1939—Marjorie Kinnan Rawlings, The Yearling.
1940—John Steinbeck, The Grapes of Wrath.
1942—Ellen Glasgow, In This Our Life.
1943—Upton Sinclair, Dragon's Teeth.
1944—Martin Flavin, Journey in the Dark.
1945—John Hersey, A Bell for Adano.
1947—Robert Penn Warren, All the King's Men.
1948—James A. Michener, Tales of the South Pacific.
1949—James Gould Cozzens, Guard of Honor.
1950—A. B. Guthrie Jr., The Way West.

1951—Conrad Richter, The Town.
1952—Herman Wouk, The Caine Mutiny.
1953—Ernest Hemingway, The Old Man and the Sea.
1955—William Faulkner, A Fable.
1956—MacKinlay Kantor, Andersonville.
1958—James Agee, A Death in the Family.
1959—Robert Lewis Taylor, The Travels of Jaimie McPheeters.
1960—Allen Drury, Advise and Consent.
1961—Harper Lee, To Kill a Mockingbird.
1962—Edwin O'Connor, The Edge of Sadness.
1963—William Faulkner, The Reivers.
1965—Shirley Ann Grau, The Keepers of the House.
1966—Katherine Anne Porter, Collected Stories of Katherine Anne Porter.
1967—Bernard Malamud, The Fixer.
1968—William Styron, The Confessions of Nat Turner.
1969—N. Scott Momaday, House Made of Dawn.
1970—Jean Stafford, Collected Stories.
1972—Wallace Stegner, Angle of Repose.
1973—Eudora Welty, The Optimist's Daughter.
1975—Michael Shaara, The Killer Angels.
1976—Saul Bellow, Humboldt's Gift.

Drama

For an American play, preferably original and dealing with American life.

1918—Jesse Lynch Williams, Why Marry?
1920—Eugene O'Neill, Beyond the Horizon.
1921—Zona Gale, Miss Lulu Bett.
1922—Eugene O'Neill, Anna Christie.
1923—Owen Davis, Icebound.
1924—Hatcher Hughes, Hell-Bent for Heaven.
1925—Sidney Howard, They Knew What They Wanted.
1926—George Kelly, Craig's Wife.
1927—Paul Green, In Abraham's Bosom.
1928—Eugene O'Neill, Strange Interlude.
1929—Elmer Rice, Street Scene.
1930—Marc Connelly, The Green Pastures.
1931—Susan Glaspell, Alison's House.
1932—George S. Kaufman, Morrie Ryskind and Ira Gershwin, Of Thee I Sing.
1933—Maxwell Anderson, Both Your Houses.
1934—Sidney Kingsley, Men in White.
1935—Zoe Akins, The Old Maid.
1936—Robert E. Sherwood, Idiot's Delight.
1937—George S. Kaufman and Moss Hart, You Can't Take It With You.
1938—Thornton Wilder, Our Town.
1939—Robert E. Sherwood, Abe Lincoln in Illinois.
1940—William Saroyan, The Time of Your Life.
1941—Robert E. Sherwood, There Shall Be No Night.
1943—Thornton Wilder, The Skin of Our Teeth.
1945—Mary Chase, Harvey.
1946—Russel Crouse and Howard Lindsay, State of the Union.
1948—Tennessee Williams, A Streetcar Named Desire.
1949—Arthur Miller, Death of a Salesman.
1950—Richard Rodgers, Oscar Hammerstein 2d, and Joshua Logan, South Pacific.
1952—Joseph Kramm, The Shrike.
1953—William Inge, Picnic.
1954—John Patrick, Teahouse of the August Moon.
1955—Tennessee Williams, Cat on a Hot Tin Roof.
1956—Frances Goodrich and Albert Hackett, The Diary of Anne Frank.
1957—Eugene O'Neill, Long Day's Journey Into Night.
1958—Ketti Frings, Look Homeward, Angel.
1959—Archibald MacLeish, J. B.
1960—George Abbott, Jerome Weidman, Sheldon Harnick and Jerry Bock, Fiorello.
1961—Tad Mosel, All the Way Home.
1962—Frank Loesser and Abe Burrows, How To Succeed In Business Without Really Trying.
1965—Frank D. Gilroy, The Subject Was Roses.
1967—Edward Albee, A Delicate Balance.
1969—Howard Sackler, The Great White Hope.
1970—Charles Gordone, No Place to Be Somebody.
1971—Paul Zindel, The Effect of Gamma Rays on Man-in-the-Moon Marigolds.
1973—Jason Miller, That Championship Season.
1975—Edward Albee, Seascape.
1976—Michael Bennett, James Kirkwood, Nicholas Dante, Marvin Hamlisch, Edward Kleban, A Chorus Line.
1977—Michael Cristofer, The Shadow Box.

History

For a book on the history of the United States.

1917—J. J. Jusserand, With Americans of Past and Present Days.
1918—James Ford Rhodes, History of the Civil War.
1920—Justin H. Smith, The War with Mexico.
1921—William Sowden Sims, The Victory at Sea.
1922—James Truslow Adams, The Founding of New England.
1923—Charles Warren, The Supreme Court in United States History.
1924—Charles Howard McIlwain, The American Revolution: A Constitutional Interpretation.
1925—Frederick L. Paxton, A History of the American Frontier.
1926—Edward Channing, A History of the U. S.
1927—Samuel Flagg Bemis, Pinckney's Treaty.
1928—Vernon Louis Parrington, Main Currents in American Thought.
1929—Fred A. Shannon, The Organization and Administration of the Union Army, 1861-65.
1930—Claude H. Van Tyne, The War of Independence.
1931—Bernadotte E. Schmitt, The Coming of the War, 1914.
1932—Gen. John J. Pershing, My Experiences in the World War.
1933—Frederick J. Turner, The Significance of Sections in American History.
1934—Herbert Agar, The People's Choice.
1935—Charles McLean Andrews, The Colonial Period of American History.
1936—Andrew C. McLaughlin, The Constitutional History of the United States.
1937—Van Wyck Brooks, The Flowering of New England.
1938—Paul Herman Buck, The Road to Reunion, 1865-1900.
1939—Frank Luther Mott, A History of American Magazines.
1940—Carl Sandburg, Abraham Lincoln: The War Years.
1941—Marcus Lee Hansen, The Atlantic Migration, 1607-1860.
1942—Margaret Leech, Reveille in Washington.
1943—Esther Forbes, Paul Revere and the World He Lived In.
1944—Merle Curti, The Growth of American Thought.
1945—Stephen Bonsal, Unfinished Business.
1946—Arthur M. Schlesinger Jr., The Age of Jackson.
1947—James Phinney Baxter 3d, Scientists Against Time.
1948—Bernard De Voto, Across the Wide Missouri.
1949—Roy F. Nichols, The Disruption of American Democracy.
1950—O. W. Larkin, Art and Life in America.
1951—R. Carlyle Buley, The Old Northwest: Pioneer Period 1815-1840.
1952—Oscar Handlin, The Uprooted.
1953—George Dangerfield, The Era of Good Feelings.
1954—Bruce Catton, A Stillness at Appomattox.
1955—Paul Horgan, Great River: The Rio Grande in North American History.
1956—Richard Hofstadter, The Age of Reform.
1957—George F. Kennan, Russia Leaves the War.
1958—Bray Hammond, Banks and Politics in America—From the Revolution to the Civil War.
1959—Leonard D. White and Jean Schneider, The Republican Era; 1869-1901.
1960—Margaret Leech, In the Days of McKinley.
1961—Herbert Feis, Between War and Peace: The Potsdam Conference.
1962—Lawrence H. Gibson, The Triumphant Empire: Thunder-clouds Gather in the West.
1963—Constance McLaughlin Green, Washington: Village and Capital, 1800-1878.
1964—Sumner Chilton Powell, Puritan Village: The Formation of A New England Town.
1965—Irwin Unger, The Greenback Era.
1966—Perry Miller, Life of the Mind in America.
1967—William H. Goetzmann, Exploration and Empire: the Explorer and Scientist in the Winning of the American West.
1968—Bernard Bailyn, The Ideological Origins of the American Revolution.
1969—Leonard W. Levy, Origin of the Fifth Amendment.
1970—Dean Acheson, Present at the Creation: My Years in the State Department.
1971—James McGregor Burns, Roosevelt: The Soldier of Freedom.
1972—Carl N. Degler, Neither Black Nor White.
1973—Michael Kammen, People of Paradox: An Inquiry Concerning the Origins of American Civilization.
1974—Daniel J. Boorstin, The Americans: The Democratic Experience.
1975—Dumas Malone, Jefferson and His Time.
1976—Paul Horgan, Lamy of Santa Fe.
1977—David M. Potter, The Impending Crisis.

Biography or Autobiography

For a distinguished biography or autobiography by an American author, preferably on an American subject.

1917—Laura E. Richards and Maude Howe Elliott, assisted by Florence Howe Hall, Julia Ward Howe.
1918—William Cabell Bruce, Benjamin Franklin, Self-Revealed.
1919—Henry Adams, The Education of Henry Adams.
1920—Albert J. Beveridge, The Life of John Marshall.

1921—Edward Bok, The Americanization of Edward Bok.
1922—Hamlin Garland, A Daughter of the Middle Border.
1923—Burton J. Hendrick, The Life and Letters of Walter H. Page.
1924—Michael Pupin, From Immigrant to Inventor.
1925—M. A. DeWolfe Howe, Barrett Wendell and His Letters.
1926—Harvey Cushing, Life of Sir William Osler.
1927—Emory Holloway, Whitman: An Interpretation in Narrative.
1928—Charles Edward Russell, The American Orchestra and Theodore Thomas.
1929—Burton J. Hendrick, The Training of an American: The Earlier Life and Letters of Walter H . Page.
1930—Marquis James, The Raven (Sam Houston).
1931—Henry James, Charles W. Eliot.
1932—Henry F. Pringle, Theodore Roosevelt.
1933—Allan Nevins, Grover Cleveland.
1934—Tyler Dennett, John Hay.
1935—Douglas Southall Freeman, R. E. Lee.
1936—Ralph Barton Perry, The Thought and Character of William James.
1937—Allan Nevins, Hamilton Fish: The Inner History of the Grant Administration.
1938—Divided between Odell Shepard, Pedlar's Progress; Marquis James, Andrew Jackson.
1939—Carl Van Doren, Benjamin Franklin.
1940—Ray Stannard Baker, Woodrow Wilson, Life and Letters.
1941—Ola Elizabeth Winslow, Jonathan Edwards.
1942—Forrest Wilson, Crusader in Crinoline.
1943—Samuel Eliot Morison, Admiral of the Ocean Sea (Columbus).
1944—Carleton Mabee, The American Leonardo: The Life of Samuel F. B. Morse.
1945—Russell Blaine Nye, George Bancroft: Brahmin Rebel.
1946—Linny Marsh Wolfe, Son of the Wilderness.
1947—William Allen White, The Autobiography of William Allen White.
1948—Margaret Clapp, Forgotten First Citizen: John Bigelow.
1949—Robert E. Sherwood, Roosevelt and Hopkins.
1950—Samuel Flag Bemis, John Quincy Adams and the Foundations of American Foreign Policy.
1951—Margaret Louise Colt, John C. Calhoun: American Portrait.
1952—Merlo J. Pusey, Charles Evans Hughes.
1953—David J. Mays, Edmund Pendleton, 1721-1803.
1954—Charles A. Lindbergh, The Spirit of St. Louis.
1955—William S. White, The Taft Story.
1956—Talbot F. Hamlin, Benjamin Henry Latrobe.
1957—John F. Kennedy, Profiles in Courage.
1958—Douglas Southall Freeman (decd. 1953), George Washington, Vols. I-VI: John Alexander Carroll and Mary Wells Ashworth, Vol. VII.
1959—Arthur Walworth, Woodrow Wilson: American Prophet.
1960—Samuel Eliot Morison, John Paul Jones.
1961—David Donald, Charles Sumner and The Coming of the Civil War.
1963—Leon Edel, Henry James: Vol. II. The Conquest of London, 1870-1881; Vol. III, The Middle Years, 1881-1895.
1964—Walter Jackson Bate, John Keats.
1965—Ernest Samuels, Henry Adams.
1966—Arthur M. Schlesinger, Jr., A Thousand Days.
1967—Justin Kaplan, Mr. Clemens and Mark Twain.
1968—George F. Kennan, Memoirs (1925-1950).
1969—B. L. Reid, The Man from New York: John Quinn and his Friends.
1970—T. Harry Williams, Huey Long.
1971—Lawrence Thompson, Robert Frost: The Years of Triumph, 1915-1938.
1972—Joseph P. Lash, Eleanor and Franklin.
1973—W. A. Swanberg, Luce and His Empire.
1974—Louis Sheaffer, O'Neill, Son and Artist.
1975—Robert A. Caro, The Power Broker: Robert Moses and the Fall of New York.
1976—R.W.B. Lewis, Edith Wharton: A Biography.
1977—John E. Mack, A Prince of Our Disorder: The Life of T.E.

American Poetry

Before this prize was established in 1922, awards were made from gifts provided by the Poetry Society: **1918**—Love Songs, by Sara Teasdale. **1919**—Old Road to Paradise, by Margaret Widdemer; Corn Huskers, by Carl Sandburg.

1922—Edwin Arlington Robinson, Collected Poems.
1923—Edna St. Vincent Millay, The Ballad of the Harp-Weaver; A Few Figs from Thistles; Eight Sonnets in American Poetry, 1922; A Miscellany.
1924—Robert Frost, New Hampshire: A Poem with Notes and Grace Notes.
1925—Edwin Arlington Robinson, The Man Who Died Twice.
1926—Amy Lowell, What's O'Clock.
1927—Leonora Speyer, Fiddler's Farewell.
1928—Edwin Arlington Robinson, Tristram.
1929—Stephen Vincent Benet, John Brown's Body.
1930—Conrad Aiken, Selected Poems.
1931—Robert Frost, Collected Poems.
1932—George Dillon, The Flowering Stone.
1933—Archibald MacLeish, Conquistador.
1934—Robert Hillyer, Collected Verse.
1935—Audrey Wurdemann, Bright Ambush.
1936—Robert P. Tristram Coffin, Strange Holiness.
1937—Robert Frost, A Further Range.
1938—Marya Zaturenska, Cold Morning Sky.
1939—John Gould Fletcher, Selected Poems.
1940—Mark Van Doren, Collected Poems.
1941—Leonard Bacon, Sunderland Capture.
1942—William Rose Benet, The Dust Which Is God.
1943—Robert Frost, A Witness Tree.
1944—Stephen Vincent Benet, Western Star.
1945—Karl Shapiro, V-Letter and Other Poems.
1947—Robert Lowell, Lord Weary's Castle.
1948—W. H. Auden, The Age of Anxiety.
1949—Peter Viereck, Terror and Decorum.
1950—Gwendolyn Brooks, Annie Allen.
1951—Carl Sandburg, Complete Poems.
1952—Marianne Moore, Collected Poems.
1953—Archibald MacLeish, Collected Poems.
1954—Theodore Roethke, The Waking.
1955—Wallace Stevens, Collected Poems.
1956—Elizabeth Bishop, Poems, North and South.
1957—Richard Wilbur, Things of This World.
1958—Robert Penn Warren, Promises: Poems 1954-1956.
1959—Stanley Kunitz, Selected Poems 1928-1958.
1960—W. D. Snodgrass, Heart's Needle.
1961—Phyllis McGinley, Times Three: Selected Verse from Three Decades.
1962—Alan Dugan, Poems.
1963—William Carlos Williams, Pictures From Breughel.
1964—Louis Simpson, At the End of the Open Road.
1965—John Berryman, 77 Dream Songs.
1966—Richard Eberhart, Selected Poems.
1967—Anne Sexton, Live or Die.
1968—Anthony Hecht, The Hard Hours.
1969—George Oppen, Of Being Numerous.
1970—Richard Howard, Untitled Subjects.
1971—William S. Merwin, The Carrier of Ladders.
1972—James Wright, Collected Poems.
1973—Maxine Winokur Kumin, Up Country.
1975—Gary Snyder, Turtle Island.
1976—John Ashbery, Self-Portrait in a Convex Mirror.
1977—James Merrill, Divine Comedies.

General Non-Fiction

For best book by an American, not eligible in any other category.

1962—Theodore H. White, The Making of the President 1960.
1963—Barbara W. Tuchman, The Guns of August.
1964—Richard Hofstadter, Anti-Intellectualism in American Life.
1965—Howard Mumford Jones, O Strange New World.
1966—Edwin Way Teale, Wandering Through Winter.
1967—David Brion Davis, The Problem of Slavery in Western Culture.
1968—Will and Ariel Durant, Rousseau and Revolution.
1969—Norman Mailer, The Armies of the Night; and Rene Jules Dubos, So Human an Animal: How We Are Shaped by Surroundings and Events.
1970—Eric H. Erikson, Gandhi's Truth.
1971—John Toland, The Rising Sun.
1972—Barbara W. Tuchman, Stilwell and the American Experience in China, 1911-1945.
1973—Frances FitzGerald, Fire in the Lake: The Vietnamese and the Americans in Vietnam; and Robert Coles, Children of Crisis, Volumes II and III.
1974—Ernest Becker, The Denial of Death.
1975—Annie Dillard, Pilgrim at Tinker Creek.
1976—Robert N. Butler, Why Survive? Being Old in America.
1977—William W. Warner, Beautiful Swimmers.

Music

For composition by an American (before 1977, by a composer resident in the U.S.), in the larger forms of chamber, orchestra or choral music or for an operatic work including ballet. A special posthumous award was granted in 1976 to Scott Joplin.

1943—William Schuman, Secular Cantata No. 2, A Free Song.
1944—Howard Hanson, Symphony No. 4, Op. 34.
1945—Aaron Copland, Appalachian Spring.
1946—Leo Sowerby, The Canticle of the Sun.
1947—Charles E. Ives, Symphony No. 3.

1948—Walter Piston, Symphony No. 3.
1949—Virgil Thomson, Louisiana Story.
1950—Gian-Carlo Menotti, The Consul.
1951—Douglas Moore, Giants in the Earth.
1952—Gail Kubil, Symphony Concertante.
1954—Quincy Porter, Concerto for Two Pianos and Orchestra.
1955—Gian-Carlo Menotti, The Saint of Bleecker Street.
1956—Ernest Toch, Symphony No. 3.
1957—Norman Dello Joio, Meditations on Ecclesiastes.
1958—Samuel Barber, Vanessa.
1959—John La Montaine, Concerto for Piano and Orchestra.
1960—Elliott Carter, Second String Quartet.
1961—Walter Piston, Symphony No. 7.
1962—Robert Ward, The Crucible.
1963—Samuel Barber, Piano Concerto No. 1.
1966—Leslie Bassett, Variations for Orchestra.
1967—Leon Kirchner, Quartet No. 3.
1968—George Crumb, Echoes of Time and the River.
1969—Karel Husa, String Quartet No. 3.
1970—Charles W. Wuorinen, Time's Encomium.
1971—Mario Davidovsky, Synchronisms No. 6.
1972—Jacob Druckman, Windows.
1973—Elliott Carter, String Quartet No. 3.
1974—Donald Martino, Notturno. (Special citation) Roger Sessions.
1975—Dominick Argento, From the Diary of Virginia Woolf.
1976—Ned Rorem, Air Music.

Special Awards

Awarded in 1977 unless otherwise designated

Books, Allied Arts

Academy of American Poets Fellow, for distinguished achievement, $10,000: J. V. Cunningham.

American Academy and Institute of Arts and Letters Awards: National Medal for Literature, $10,000: Robert Lowell; Gold Medal for The Novel: Saul Bellow; Award for Distinguished Service to the Arts: James Laughlin; Academy-Institute Awards in Literature: $3,000: A. R. Ammons, Walter J. Bate, Cynthia Macdonald, Joseph McElroy, John McPhee, James Schuyler, Paul Theroux, Anne Tyler, Robert Watson, Charles Wright.

Bancroft Prizes, by Columbia Univ. for American history or diplomacy: Alan Dawley for *Class and Community, the Industrial Revolution in Lynn*; Barry W. Higman for *Slave Population and Economy in Jamaica, 1807-1834*.

Bollingen Prize, by Yale Univ. Library, for an American poet, $5,000: David Ignatow.

Louis Brownlow Award, by National Academy of Public Administration (1976): Louis Fisher for *Presidential Spending Power*.

Caldecott Medal, by American Library Assoc. for children's book illustration: Leo and Diane Dillon for *Ashanti to Zulu: African Traditions*.

Canadian Governor General's Literary Awards, $5,000: Marian Engel for *Bear*; Andre Major for *Les rescapes*; Joe Rosenblatt for *Top Soil*; Alphonse Piche for *Poemes 1946-1968*; Carl Berger for *The Writing of Canadian History*; and Fernand Ouellet for *Le Bas Canada 1791-1840*.

Carey-Thomas Award, administered by Publishers Weekly, for a publishing project: Erwin Glikes, Basic Books for *Berggasse 19*; citations: Patrick O'Connor, Popular Library; Herbert Bailey Jr., Princeton Univ. Press.

Gilbert Chinard Prize, by Society for French Historical Studies (1976): Jonathan Dull for *The French Navy and American Independence*.

Copernicus Award, by Academy of American Poets, $10,000, for lifetime achievement: Muriel Rukeyser.

E. M. Forster Award, by American Academy and Institute of Arts and Letters, $5,000: David Cook.

R. T. French Co. Tastemaker Award, for books on cuisine: best cookbook, $500: *Michel Guerard's Cuisine Minceur*; basic: Carol Cutler for *The Six-Minute Souffle and Other Culinary Delights*; specialty: Nika Hazelton for *The Unabridged Vegetable Cookbook*; entertaining: Diana and Paul von Welanetz for *The Pleasure of Your Company*; health: Barbara Gibbons for *The Slim Gourmet*; soft cover: Mable Hoffman for *Crepe Cookery*.

Goethe House-P.E.N. Translation Prize, from German into English, $500: Douglas Parmee for Siegfried Lenz's *An Exemplary Life*.

Golden Spur Awards, by Western Writers of America (1976): novel: Glendon Swarthout for *The Shootist*; nonfiction: Paul Horgan for *Lamy of Santa Fe*; juvenile novel: Bill and Vera Cleaver for *Dust of the Earth*; juvenile nonfiction: Lynn Haney for *Ride 'Em, Cowgirl*.

Haskins Medal, by Medieval Academy of America (1976): Robert I. Burns for *Islam Under the Crusaders: Colonial Survival in the Thirteenth-Century Kingdom of Valencia*.

Ernest Hemingway Prize, by American P.E.N., for first book of fiction, $6,000: Renata Adler for *Speedboat*.

Illustrators Hall of Fame, new inductees: Robert Peak, Joseph C. Leyendecker, Wallace Morgan.

Association of Jewish Libraries Book Award, for children's literature: Marietta Moskin for *Waiting for Mama*.

National Jewish Book Awards, by Jewish Book Council: juvenile: Chaya Burstein for *Rifka Grows Up*; fiction: Cynthia Ozick for *Bloodshed and Three Novellas*; history: Irving Howe for *World of Our Fathers*; holocaust: Ephraim Oshry for *Sefer Sheelot U-Teshuvot Mi-Maamakim: Part 4*; poetry: Myra Sklarew for *From the Backyard of the Diaspora*; Israel: Howard M. Sachar for *A History of Israel from the Rise of Zionism to Our Time*; Jewish thought: David Hartman for *Maimonides: Torah and Philosophic Quest*; translation: Zvi L. Lampel for *Maimonides' Introduction to the Talmud*.

King Award, by Society of Illustrators: Leo and Diane Dillon for *Ashanti to Zulu: African Traditions*.

Roger Klein Award for Creative Editing: Robert D. Loomis of Random House.

Laetare Medal, by Notre Dame Univ. to a Catholic (1976): Paul Horgan for *Lamy of Santa Fe*.

Lamont Poetry Selection, by Academy of American Poets (1976): Larry Lewis for *The Afterlife*.

Jules F. Landry Award, by Louisiana State Univ. Press, for Southern studies, (1976), $1,000: John Hope Franklin for *A Southern Odyssey: Travelers in the Antebellum North*.

David D. Lloyd Prize, by Harry S. Truman Library (1976) $1,000: Lynn Etheridge Davis for *The Cold War Begins*.

James Russell Lowell Prize, by Modern Language Association of America, $1,000: Joseph Frank for *Dostoevsky: The Seeds of Revolt, 1821-1849*.

Man In His Environment Book Award, by E. P. Dutton & Co.: Richard Leakey and Roger Lewin for *Origins: What New Discoveries Reveal About the Emergence of Our Species and its Possible Future*.

Lenore Marshall Poetry Prize (1976), administered by Book-of-the-Month Club, $3,500: Denise Levertov for *The Freeing of the Dust*.

American Medical Writers Assoc. Award, for sex education (1976): David G. Delvin for *The Book of Love*.

Lucille J. Medwick Memorial Award, by P.E.N., $500: Alice S. Morris of *Harper's Bazaar*.

Frank Luther Mott Award, by Kappa Tau Alpha, for journalism book (1976): Claude-Anne Lopez and Eugenia W. Herbert for *The Private Franklin: The Man and his Family*.

George Jean Nathan Award, for drama criticism, $10,000: Michael Goldman, *The Actor's Freedom: Toward a Theory of Drama*.

National Book Awards, administered by American Academy and Institute of Arts and Letters: contemporary thought: Bruno Bettelheim for *The Uses of Enchantment*; fiction: Wallace Stegner for *The Spectator Bird*; translation: Lili Ch'en for *Master Tung's Western Chamber Romance*; biography: W. A. Swanberg for *Norman Thomas: The Last Idealist*; poetry: Richard Eberhart for *Collected Poems: 1930-1976*; children's literature: Katherine Paterson for *The Master Puppeteer*; history: Irving Howe for *World of Our Fathers*; citation of merit: Alex Haley for *Roots*.

National Book Critics Circle Awards: fiction: John Gardner for *October Light*; poems: Elizabeth Bishop for *Geography III*; nonfiction: Maxine Hong Kingston for *The Woman Warrior: Memoirs of a Girlhood Among Ghosts*; criticism: Bruno Bettelheim for *The Uses of Enchantment: The Meaning and Importance of Fairy Tales*.

Newberry Medal, by the American Library Assoc., for children's literature: Mildred D. Taylor for *Roll of Thunder, Hear My Cry*.

George Orwell Memorial Prize, by Penguin Books: Ludvik Vaculik for *The Guinea Pigs*.

P.E.N. Translation Prize, for book-length translation, $1,000: Gregory Rabassa for Gabriel Garcia Marquez's *The Autumn of the Patriarch*.

Photographic Historical Society of New York Prize, $100: James Borcoman for *Charles Negre 1820-1880*.

Edgar Allen Poe Award, by Academy of American Poets, $5,000: Stan Rice for *Whiteboy*.

Edgar Allen Poe Awards, by Mystery Writers of America: best novel: Robert Parker for *Promised Land*; first novel: James Patterson for *Thomas Berryman Number*; paperback: Gregory McDonald for *Confess, Fletch*; juvenile: Richard Peck for *Are You in the House Alone*; critical/biographical: Chris Steinbrunner and Otto Penzler for *Encyclopedia of Mystery and Detection*; fact crime book: Thomas Thompson for *Blood and Money*; hardcover jacket: *King and Joker*; paperback jacket: *Doors*.

Poetry Society of America Awards: Melville Cane Award, $500: Donald R. Howard for *The Idea of the Canterbury Tales*; Alice Fay di Castagnola Award, $2,000: Naomi Lazard for *Ordinances* and Linda Pastan for *The Five Stages of Grief*; Gustav Davidson Award, $500: Ulrich Troubetzkoy; John Masefield Award, $500: Lynn Sukenick and Frederick Feirstein; Lucille Medwick Award, $500: Peter Klappert; Christopher Morley Award, $500: Darcy Gottlieb; Shelley Award, $3,000: Muriel Rukeyser; other awards: Gary Miranda; Diana Der Hovanessian; Siv Cedering Fox; Joan LaBombard; Isabel Nathaniel; Geraldine Clinton Little; Paul J. Davis; Helen Adam, Darrell H. Bartee.

Rome Prize, by American Academy in Rome, for a poet, $7,180: Daniel Mark Epstein.

Richard and Hinda Rosenthal Foundation Award, by American Academy and Institute of Arts and Letters, $2,000: Spencer Holst for *Spencer Holst Stories*.

Deems Taylor Awards, by ASCAP, $500 each: Geoffrey Stokes for *Starmaking Machinery*; Dan Morgenstern for *Jazz People*; Albert Murray for *Stomping the Blues*; Larry Sandberg and Dick Weissman for *The Folk Music Sourcebook*; Leo Kraft for *Gradus*.

Theatre Library Association Awards: Fred W. Friendly for *The Good Guys, the Bad Guys and the First Amendment*; Gerald Kahan for *Jacques Callot: Artist of the Theatre*; Charles Shattuck for *Shakespeare on the American Stage*.

Walt Whitman Award, by Academy of American Poets, $1,000: Lauren Shakely for *Guilty Bystander*.

Morton Dauwen Zabel Prize, by American Academy and Institute of Arts and Letters, for experimental poetry, $2,500: David Shapiro.

Journalism Awards

Americas Foundation Award: Jack R. Howard, Scripps-Howard Newspapers.

Arthritis Foundation Award (1976), $1,000: Marilyn Gardner, Milwaukee Journal.

Audubon Medal, by National Audubon Society: John B. Oakes, New York Times.

Worth Bingham Award, by White House Correspondents Assoc.: for investigative reporting, $1,000: Morton Mintz, Washington Post.

Howard Blakeslee Awards, by Amer. Heart Assoc.: Al Rossiter, UPI; Donald C. Drake, Philadelphia Inquirer; Daniel A. Koger, Flint (Mich.) Journal.

Willard G. Bleyer Award, by Assoc. for Education in Journalism, for journalism history (1976): Fredrick S. Siebert.

Heywood Broun Award, by Newspaper Guild, $1,000: Acel Moore, Wendell Rawls Jr., Philadelphia Inquirer.

Canadian National Business Writing Awards, by Toronto Press Club: Henry Aubin, Montreal Gazette; Peter Brimelow, Financial Post; Georges Gratton, Montreal La Presse; Josh Freed, Montreal Star, Don McGillivray, Southam News Service; Forbes Rhude, Canadian Press.

Canadian National Newspaper Awards, by Toronto Press Club, $500: spot news: Richard Cleroux, Toronto Globe and Mail; feature: Joe Hall, Toronto Star; enterprise: Henry Aubin, Montreal Gazette; editorial: Cameron Smith, Toronto Globe and Mail; sports: Al Strachan, Montreal Gazette; spot photography: Russell Mant, Ottawa Journal, feature photography: Allan Leishman, Montreal Star; cartooning: Andy Donato, Toronto Sun; criticism: John Fraser, Toronto Globe and Mail.

Raymond Clapper Memorial Awards, for Washington-based reporters, $1,000: Alan Horton, Carl West, Scripps-Howard News Service; second prize, $250: Scott Armstrong, Maxine Cheshire, Washington Post.

Clarion Awards, by Women in Communications: Terry Malone, National Catholic Reporter; Amei Wallach, Newsday; Muriel L. Cohen, Boston Globe; Acel Moore, Wendell Rawls Jr., Philadelphia Inquirer; Charlotte Saikowski, Christian Science Monitor; Dan Rottenberg, Richard Griffin, Chicago Magazine; Loretta Schwartz, Philadelphia Magazine.

Deep Woods Award, by Johnson Wax: Ben Callaway, Philadelphia Daily News; runner-up: Tom Opre, Detroit Free Press.

St. Francis de Sales Award, by Catholic Press Association: A.E.P. Wall, The New World.

Editorial Excellence Awards, by William Allen White Found.: Detroit Free Press, Arlington Heights (Ill.) Herald; North Platte (Neb.) Telegraph; Sheridan (Wyo.) Press; for journalistic merit; Clayton Kirkpatrick, Chicago Tribune.

Engineering Journalism Awards, by National Society of Professional Engineers, $500: George F. Alexander, Los Angeles Times; $300: Richard D. Ralls, Kansas City (Mo.) Times; $200: Polly Lane, Seattle Times.

Fourth Estate Award, by National Press Club (1976): John S. Knight, Knight-Ridder Newspapers.

Front Page Awards, by Newswomen's Club of New York: Grace B. Smith, Bergen (N.J.) Record; Judith Randal, N.Y. Daily News; Susan Lea Page, Karen Wiles, Newsday; Alice Walker, Ms.; Molly Ivins, Mimi Sheraton, N.Y. Times.

Gavel Awards, by American Bar Assoc.: Lakeland (Fla.) Ledger; Oakland (Mich.) Press; Philadelphia Inquirer; Detroit Free Press; Boston Magazine; Newsweek; Gannett News Service.

Golden Quill Award, by International Society of Weekly Newspaper Editors: Rodney Smith, Gretna (Va.) Gazette; **Eugene Cervi Award:** Charles and Virginia Russell, DeWitt County (Ill.) Observer.

James T. Grady Award, by American Chemical Society, $2,000: Patrick Young.

John Hancock Awards for Excellence, for business and financial reporting: Lee Mitgang, Associated Press; Steven Brill, New York Magazine; William Wolman, Philip Osborne, Business Week; Susan Trausch, Laurence Collins, Boston Globe; James Asher, Paul Schweizer, Camden (N.J.) Courier-Post; Judd Cohen, Yonkers (N.Y.) Herald Statesman.

National Headliners Awards: news reporting: Lufkin (Tex.) News, Richmond Times-Dispatch, Paul Meskil, New York News; local column: Bob Greene, Chicago Sun-Times; special column: Susan Trausch, Boston Globe; cartoons: Paul Szep, Boston Globe; sports: Jim Murray, Los Angeles Times; newspaper magazine: Miami Herald; investigative: Anthony R. Dolan, Stamford Advocate; public service: Acel Moore, Wendell Rawls Jr., Philadelphia Inquirer.

Higher Education Writers Award, by Amer. Assoc. of University Professors (1976): William Braden, Andy Shaw, Chicago Sun-Times.

Sidney Hillman Awards, by Amalgamated Clothing Workers: Guy Neal Williams, Philadelphia Magazine; John Seigenthaler, Tennessean.

Roy W. Howard Public Service Awards, by Scripps-Howard Foundation, first prize, $2,500: San Francisco Examiner; second prize, $1,000: Philadelphia Bulletin; Santa Fe Reporter; special mention: Boston Globe, Philadelphia Inquirer. Elyria (Ohio) Chronicle-Telegram, Hartford Courant, Camden (N.J.) Courier Post.

Robert F. Kennedy Award, grand prize, $3,000: Acel Moore, Wendell Rawls, Philadelphia Inquirer.

MacMillan Bloedel Awards, for British Columbia newspapers, $500: Tony Eberts, Vancouver Province; Eli Sopow, Prince George Citizen; runners-up, $250: Ashley Ford, Vancouver Province; Mark Hamilton, Alberni Valley Times.

Edward V. McQuade Award, by Assoc. of Catholic Journalists, $700: Ralph Craib, San Francisco Chronicle; runner-up, $300: Larry Hatfield, San Francisco Examiner; third place, $200: Cathy Castillo, San Jose Mercury-News.

Edward J. Meeman Conservation Awards, by Scripps-Howard Foundation, $2,500: Tom Turner, Arizona Daily Star; first prizes, $2,000: Art Carey, Bucks County (Pa.) Courier Times; Alan McConagha, Minneapolis Tribune; second prizes, $1,000: Charles Patrick, St. Petersburg Times; Tom Roberts, Bethlehem (Pa.) Globe-Times.

Missouri Medals, by Univ. of Mo. School of Journalism: Peter Lisagor, posthumous, Chicago Daily News; Newsday, Newsweek.

Charles Stewart Mott Awards, by Education Writers Assoc.: large circ. series: James Worsham, Marguerite Del Giudice, Boston Globe; investigative: Jean Peters, Akron Beacon Journal; opinion: Davis B. Toryle, Denver Post; feature: Shelley Eichenhorn, Detroit News; breaking news: William Grant, Billy Bowles, Detroit Free Press.

United Negro College Fund citation: United Press International.

New England Woman's Press Assoc. Award, best series: Charlotte Saikowski, Christian Science Monitor.

Overseas Press Club: reporting requiring courage: Robin Wright, Christian Science Monitor; photos requiring courage: Catherine Leroy, Time; daily reporting: Edward Cody, Associated Press; interpretation: Flora Lewis, New York Times; photos: Robert W. Madden, W.E. Garrett, National Geographic; magazine reporting: Newsweek; mag. interpretation: Tad Szulc, New Republic; cartoon: Warren King, New York News; business: Alfred Zanker, U.S. News and World Report; human interest: June Goodwin, Christian Science Monitor.

Penney-Missouri Awards, people and lifestyle, $1,000: Frances Craig, Des Moines Register; Rosemary J. McClure, San Bernardino (Cal.) Sun-Telegram; Carolyn Nolte-Watts, St. Petersburg (Fla.) Times; Marji Kunz, Detroit Free Press.

Amer. Society of Planning Officials Awards: Tulsa World, Port Huron (Mich.) Times Herald, Quincy (Mass.) Patriot Ledger.

American Psychological Foundation National Media Awards: magazine: Alice Lake, Woman's Day; newspaper: Joel Greenberg, Miami Herald.

Ernie Pyle Memorial Awards, by Scripps-Howard Foundation, $1,000: Carol McCabe, Providence Journal-Bulletin; second place, $500: Anne Keegan, Chicago Tribune.

Recycling Industries Awards, $1,000: Gladwin Hill, New York Times; Denise Brookman, Purchasing Magazine.

Religion Newswriters Assoc. Awards, $100: Russell Chandler, Los Angeles Times; Jane Hammond, Niagara (N.Y.) Gazette; Lee Kelly, St. Petersburg Times.

Religious Public Relations Awards: Barbara Stoops, Columbia (S.C.) State; Lori Sturdevant, Minneapolis Tribune; Billie Chaney Speed, Atlanta Journal; William Reed, Bucks County (Pa.) Courier-Times; Frank Deford, Sports Illustrated; National Observer.

Reuben Award, by National Cartoonists Society: Ernie Bushmiller.

Jacob Scher Award, for investigative reporting, by Women in Communications, Chicago: Allan Parachini, Chicago Sun-Times.

Science-in-Society Awards, by National Assoc. of Science Writers (1976), $1,000: Walter Sullivan, New York Times, Stuart Auerbach, Washington Post.

Edward Willis Scripps First Amendment Award, by Scripps-Howard Foundation, $2,500: Honolulu Advertiser; special mention: Winsted (Conn.) Citizen.

Sigma Delta Chi Awards: newspaper reporting: Mike Goodman, George H. Reasons, Los Angeles Times; editorials: George W. Wilson, Philadelphia Inquirer; Washington correspondence: Maxine Cheshire, Scott Armstrong, Washington Post; public service: Wall Street Journal; magazine reporting: Larry DuBois, Laurence Gonzales, Playboy; foreign: Joe Rigert, Minneapolis Tribune; news photo: Bruce Fritz, Madison (Wis.) Capitol Times; cartooning: Paul Szep, Boston Globe; magazine public service: Philadelphia Magazine: First Amendment Award: Great Falls (Mont.) Tribune.

Silurians Awards, New York area papers: spot news: Lynn Groh, Mamaroneck (N.Y.) Times; Robert Thomas, N.Y. Times; feature: Richard Gooding, N.Y. Post; investigative: Thomas Hillstrom, Richard Sisk, UPI; humorous: Russell Baker, N.Y. Times; editorial: Fred Hechinger, N.Y. Times.

Best Sports Stories, by E. P. Dutton: News: Shirley Povich, Washington Post; feature: Jane Gross, Newsday; magazine: Mark Jacobson, New York Magazine; action photo: Charles R. Pugh Jr., Atlanta Journal-Constitution; feature photo: Mike Anderson, Boston Herald American.

Walker Stone Awards for Editorial Writing, by Scripps-Howard Foundation, $1,000: John R. Harrison, Lakeland (Fla.) Ledger; second place, $500: Phil Weck, Russell Cook, Bucks County (Pa.) Courier Times.

Deems Taylor Awards, by ASCAP, for articles on music, $500: John Ardoin, Dallas Morning News; Richard Dyer, Boston Globe; Samuel Lipman, Commentary; Karen Monson, Chicago Daily News; Irving Lowens, Washington Star; Paul Baratta, Songwriter Magazine; Gary Giddins, Village Voice; Maureen Orth, Newsweek.

Weiss Philatelic-Numismatic Awards, $50: coins: Roger Boye, Chicago Tribune; stamps: Jon Rose, San Jose Sunday Mercury News.

Westinghouse Science Writing Awards, by American Assoc. for Advancement of Science, $1,000: Paul G. Hayes, Milwaukee Journal; Don Alan Hall, Corvallis (Ore.) Gazette Times; Jonathan Eberhart, Science News.

John Peter Zenger Award, by Univ. of Arizona: Donald F. Bolles, Arizona Republic.

Broadcasting and Theater Awards

Clarion Awards, by Women in Communications: TV: Patricia Lynch, WNBC-TV, New York, Requiem for Tina Sanchez; KYW-TV, Philadelphia, Impact: The Energy Game; WCAU-TV, Philadelphia, Eye on Ukrainians in America; radio: Barbara Esensten, KFWB, Los Angeles, Growing Old; Rachel Kranz,

KSJN-FM, St. Paul, Drought; Beverly Poppell, WRFM, New York, Glass Door Peephole.

New York Drama Critics Circle Awards: play: Otherwise Engaged; American play: American Buffalo; musical: Annie.

New York Film Critics Circle Awards: picture: All The President's Men; actress: Liv Ullmann, Face to Face; actor: Robert De Niro, Taxi Driver; director: Alan J. Pakula, All The President's Men; supporting actress: Talia Shire, Rocky; supporting actor: Jason Robards, All The President's Men; screen-writing: Paddy Chayefsky, Network.

Sidney Hillman Award, by Amalgamated Clothing Workers: Paul Leaf, Tomorrow Entertainment, NBC.

Roy W. Howard Public Service Award, by Scripps-Howard Foundation: KMOX-TV, St. Louis; runner-up: WRFM Radio, New York.

Elizabeth Hull-Kate Warriner Award, by Dramatists Guild; $7,000: David Rabe, Streamers.

Humanitas Prizes, by Human Family Institute: $25,000: David Seltzer, Green Eyes; $15,000: James Lee, William Blinn, Roots; $10,000: Earl Pomerantz, Mary Tyler Moore Show.

Margo Jones Award: Gordon Davidson, Mark Taper Forum, Los Angeles.

Life Achievement Award, by American Film Institute: Bette Davis.

Missouri Medals, by Univ. of Missouri School of Journalism: ABC Sports; Jerrell Shepherd, KWIX-KRES Radio, Moberly, Mo.

National Artist Award, by Amer. National Theater and Academy: Eva Le Gallienne.

National Board of Review of Motion Pictures Awards: actor: David Carradine, Bound for Glory; actress: Liv Ullmann, Face to Face; supporting actor: Jason Robards, All The President's Men; supporting actress: Talia Shire, Rocky; director: Alan J. Pakula, Rocky.

Overseas Press Club Awards: TV spot news: Mike Lee, CBS; TV interpretation: Daniel O'Connor, John Chancellor, NBC: radio spot news: Jerry King, John Cooley, Bill Blakemore, Charles Glass, ABC, Mike Lee, Doug Tennell, CBS; radio interpretation: Charles Collingwood, CBS.

Sigma Delta Chi Awards: TV public service: KNXT-TV, Los Angeles; TV reporting: KMJ-TV, Fresno; broadcast editorials: Ed Hinshaw, WTMJ, Milwaukee, and WCVB-TV, Needham, Mass.; radio reporting: Mike Lee, Doug Tennell, CBS; radio public service: WCAU-AM, Philadelphia.

Antoinette Perry Awards (Tonys): play: The Shadow Box; musical: Annie; actress: Julie Harris, Belle of Amherst; actor: Al Pacino, Basic Training of Pavlo Hummel; director: Gordon Davidson, Shadow Box; director, musical: Gene Saks, I Love My Wife; book: Thomas Meehan, Annie; score: Martin Charnin, Charles Strouse, Annie; musical actress: Dorothy Louden, Annie; musical actor: Barry Bostwick, Robber Bridegroom; revival: Porgy and Bess; choreographer: Peter Gennaro, Annie; scenic design: David Mitchell, Annie; lighting: Jennifer Tipton, Cherry Orchard; costume: Theoni V. Aldredge, Annie, and Santo Loquasto, Cherry Orchard; featured actor: Jonathan Pryce, Comedians; featured actress: Trazana Beverly, For Colored Girls; featured actor, musical: Lenny Baker, I Love My Wife; featured actress: Dolores Hall, Your Arms Too Short to Box With God.

Miscellaneous Awards

American Academy and Institute of Arts and Letters Awards: Gold Medal for Sculpture: Isamu Noguchi; Arnold W. Brunner Prize for architecture: Henry N. Cobb; Academy-Institute Awards, $3,000: art: Nina Bohlen, Alan Gussow, Paul Resika, Fritz Scholder, Alex Markhoff, Susan Smyly; music: Harold Blumenfeld, Paul Cooper, Paul Lansky, George Perle; Rosenthal Award in art, $2,000: Sigrid Burton; Waite Award in art, $1,500: Kenzo Okada; Ives Scholarships in music, $4,000: Gregory Ballard, Larry Thomas Bell, John Halvor Benson, Matthias Kriesberg, John Lennon, Maurice Wright.

Ballington and Maud Booth Award, by Volunteers of America: Roy Wilkins.

Capezio Dance Award, $1,000: Merce Cunningham.

Conservationist of the Year, by National Wildlife Federation: William E. Towell.

Coty Award Fashion Hall of Fame: Ralph Lauren.

Ditson Conductor's Award, by Columbia Univ., $1,000: Eugene Ormandy.

Academy for Educational Development Award, $5,000: Paul C. Reinert.

Enrico Fermi Award, by Energy Research and Development Admin. $25,000: William L. Russell.

Environmental Protection Award, by Natural Resources Defense Council (1976): Barbara Ward.

Avery Fisher Prizes, by Lincoln Center, $2,500: Andre-Michel Schub, Richard Stoltzman.

Franklin Medal, by Franklin Institute (1976): Mahlon B. Hoagland.

Furness Prize, by Pennsylvania Academy of Fine Arts: Ada Louise Huxtable.

Louisa Gross Horwitz Prize, by Columbia Univ., for genetics: Seymour Benzer, California Inst. of Technology; Charles Yanofsky, Stanford Univ.

Dannie Heinemann Prize, $5,000: Steven Weinberg, Stanford Univ.

Alexander von Humboldt Award, for contributions to agriculture, $10,000: Wendell Roelofs, Cornell Univ. and Harry H. Shorey, Univ. of California at Riverside.

Thomas Jefferson Medal in architecture, by Univ. of Virginia: Ada Louise Huxtable.

Albert Lasker Awards in medicine, $10,000 each (1976): Rosalyn S. Yalow, Bronx Veterans Hosp.; Raymond P. Ahlquist, Medical Coll. of Georgia and James W. Black, University College, London; World Health Org.

Andrew W. Mellon Prize for artists, by Carnegie Inst., $50,000: Pierre Alechinsky.

Montreal International Competition, for singers, $3,750 each: William Parker, Louise Wohlafka.

National Arts Club Medal of Honor (1976): Alistair Cooke.

National Federation of Music Clubs Award (1976): Abram Chasins.

Priestley Medal, by American Chemical Society: George S. Hammond, Univ. of California.

Alice Tyler Ecology Award, by Pepperdine Univ., $150,000: Eugene P. Odum.

Miss Universe 1977: Janelle Commissiong, Trinidad-Tobago; **Miss World:** Cindy Breakspeare, Jamaica.

Miss Black America: Ellen Ford, Tennessee.

Motion Picture Academy Awards (Oscars)

1927-28

Actor: Emil Jennings, The Way of All Flesh.
Actress: Janet Gaynor, Seventh Heaven.
Picture: Wings, Paramount.

1928-29

Actor: Warner Baxter, In Old Arizona.
Actress: Mary Pickford, Coquette.
Picture: Broadway Melody, MGM.

1929-30

Actor: George Arliss, Disraeli.
Actress: Norma Shearer, The Divorcee.
Picture: All Quiet on the Western Front, Univ.

1930-31

Actor: Lionel Barrymore, Free Soul.
Actress: Marie Dressler, Min and Bill.
Picture: Cimarron, RKO.

1931-32

Actor: Fredric March, Dr. Jekyll and Mr. Hyde; Wallace Beery, The Champ (tie).
Actress: Helen Hayes, Sin of Madelon Claudet.
Picture: Grand Hotel, MGM.
Special: Walt Disney, Mickey Mouse.

1932-33
Actor: Charles Laughton, Private Life of Henry VIII.
Actress: Katharine Hepburn, Morning Glory.
Picture: Cavalcade, Fox.
1934
Actor: Clark Gable, It Happened One Night.
Actress: Claudette Colbert, same.
Picture: It Happened One Night, Columbia.
1935
Actor: Victor McLaglen, The Informer.
Actress: Bette Davis, Dangerous.
Picture: Mutiny on the Bounty, MGM.
1936
Actor: Paul Muni, Story of Louis Pasteur.
Actress: Luise Rainer, The Great Ziegfeld.
Picture: The Great Ziegfeld, MGM.
1937
Actor: Spencer Tracy, Captains Courageous.
Actress: Luise Rainer, The Good Earth.
Picture: Life of Emile Zola, Warner.
1938
Actor: Spencer Tracy, Boys Town.
Actress: Bette Davis, Jezebel.
Picture: You Can't Take It With You, Columbia.
1939
Actor: Robert Donat, Goodbye Mr. Chips.
Actress: Vivien Leigh, Gone With the Wind.
Picture: Gone With the Wind, Selznick International.
1940
Actor: James Stewart, The Philadelphia Story.
Actress: Ginger Rogers, Kitty Foyle.
Picture: Rebecca, Selznick International.
1941
Actor: Gary Cooper, Sergeant York.
Actress: Joan Fontaine, Suspicion.
Picture: How Green Was My Valley, 20th Cent.-Fox.
1942
Actor: James Cagney, Yankee Doodle Dandy.
Actress: Greer Garson, Mrs. Miniver.
Picture: Mrs. Miniver, MGM.
1943
Actor: Paul Lukas, Watch on the Rhine.
Actress: Jennifer Jones, The Song of Bernadette.
Picture: Casablanca, Warner.
1944
Actor: Bing Crosby, Going My Way.
Actress: Ingrid Bergman, Gaslight.
Picture: Going My Way, Paramount.
1945
Actor: Ray Milland, The Lost Weekend.
Actress: Joan Crawford, Mildred Pierce.
Picture: The Lost Weekend, Paramount.
1946
Actor: Fredric March, Best Years of Our Lives.
Actress: Olivia de Havilland, To Each His Own.
Picture: The Best Years of Our Lives, Goldwyn, RKO.
1947
Actor: Ronald Colman, A Double Life.
Actress: Loretta Young, The Farmer's Daughter.
Picture: Gentleman's Agreement, 20th Cent.-Fox.
1948
Actor: Laurence Olivier, Hamlet.
Actress: Jane Wyman, Johnny Belinda.
Picture: Hamlet, Two Cities Film, Universal International.
1949
Actor: Broderick Crawford, All the Kings Men.
Actress: Olivia de Havilland, The Heiress.
Picture: All the King's Men, Columbia.
1950
Actor: Jose Ferrer, Cyrano de Bergerac.
Actress: Judy Holliday, Born Yesterday.
Picture: All About Eve, 20th Century-Fox.
1951
Actor: Humphrey Bogart, The African Queen.
Actress: Vivien Leigh, A Streetcar Named Desire.
Picture: An American in Paris, MGM.
1952
Actor: Gary Cooper, High Noon.
Actress: Shirley Booth, Come Back, Little Sheba.
Picture: Greatest Show on Earth, C. B. DeMille, Paramount.
1953
Actor: William Holden, Stalag 17.
Actress: Audrey Hepburn, Roman Holiday.
Picture: From Here to Eternity, Columbia.
1954
Actor: Marlon Brando, On the Waterfront.
Actress: Grace Kelly, The Country Girl.
Picture: On The Waterfront, Horizon-American, Colum.
1955
Actor: Ernest Borgnine, Marty.
Actress: Anna Magnani, The Rose Tattoo.
Picture: Marty, Hecht and Lancaster's Steven Prods., U.A.
1956
Actor: Yul Brynner, The King and I.
Actress: Ingrid Bergman, Anastasia.
Picture: Around the World in 80 Days, Michael Todd, U.A.
1957
Actor: Alec Guinness, The Bridge on the River Kwai.
Actress: Joanne Woodward, The Three Faces of Eve.
Picture: The Bridge on the River Kwai, Columbia.
1958
Actor: David Niven, Separate Tables.
Actress: Susan Hayward, I Want to Live.
Picture: Gigi, Arthur Freed Production, MGM.
1959
Actor: Charlton Heston, Ben-Hur.
Actress: Simone Signoret, Room at the Top.
Picture: Ben-Hur, MGM.
1960
Actor: Burt Lancaster, Elmer Gantry.
Actress: Elizabeth Taylor, Butterfield 8.
Picture: The Apartment, Mirisch Co., U.A.
1961
Actor: Maximilian Schell, Judgment at Nuremberg.
Actress: Sophia Loren, Two Women.
Picture: West Side Story, United Artists.
1962
Actor: Gregory Peck, To Kill a Mockingbird.
Actress: Anne Bancroft, The Miracle Worker.
Picture: Lawrence of Arabia, Columbia.
1963
Actor: Sidney Poitier, Lilies of the Field.
Actress: Patricia Neal, Hud.
Picture: Tom Jones, Woodfall Prod., UA-Lopert Pictures.
1964
Actor: Rex Harrison, My Fair Lady.
Actress: Julie Andrews, Mary Poppins.
Picture: My Fair Lady, Warner Bros.
1965
Actor: Lee Marvin, Cat Ballou.
Actress: Julie Christie, Darling.
Picture: The Sound of Music, 20th Century-Fox.
1966
Actor: Paul Scofield, A Man for All Seasons.
Actress: Elizabeth Taylor, Who's Afraid of Virginia Woolf?
Picture: A Man for All Seasons, Columbia.
1967
Actor: Rod Steiger, In the Heat of the Night.
Actress: Katharine Hepburn, Guess Who's Coming to Dinner.
Picture: In the Heat of the Night.
1968
Actor: Cliff Robertson, Charly.
Actress: Katharine Hepburn, The Lion in Winter, Barbra Streisand, Funny Girl (tie).
Picture: Oliver.
1969
Actor: John Wayne, True Grit.
Actress: Maggie Smith, The Prime of Miss Jean Brodie.
Picture: Midnight Cowboy.
1970
Actor: George C. Scott, Patton (refused).
Actress: Glenda Jackson, Women in Love.
Picture: Patton.
1971
Actor: Gene Hackman, The French Connection.
Actress: Jane Fonda, Klute.
Picture: The French Connection.
1972
Actor: Marlon Brando, The Godfather (refused).
Actress: Liza Minnelli, Cabaret.
Picture: The Godfather.
1973
Actor: Jack Lemmon, Save the Tiger.
Actress: Glenda Jackson, A Touch of Class.
Picture: The Sting.
1974
Actor: Art Carney, Harry and Tonto.
Actress: Ellen Burstyn, Alice Doesn't Live Here Anymore.
Picture: The Godfather, Part II.
1975
Actor: Jack Nicholson, One Flew Over the Cuckoo's Nest.
Actress: Louise Fletcher, same.
Picture: One Flew Over the Cuckoo's Nest.
1976
Actor: Peter Finch, Network.

Actress: Faye Dunaway, same.
Picture: Rocky.
Foreign Film: Black and White in Color, Ivory Coast.
Director: John G. Avildsen, Rocky.
Supporting Actor: Jason Robards, All The President's Men.
Supporting Actress: Beatrice Straight, Network.
Screenplay (original): Paddy Chayefsky, Network; (adapted): William Goldman, All The President's Men.
Cinematography: Haskell Wexler, Bound for Glory.
Editing: Richard Halsey, Scott Conrad, Rocky.
Score (original): Jerry Goldsmith, The Omen; (adapted): Leonard Rosenman, Bound for Glory.
Song: Barbra Streisand, Paul Williams, Evergreen (A Star is Born).
Art Direction: George Jenkins, George Gaines, All The President's Men.
Costumes: Danilo Donati, Fellini's Casanova.
Sound: Arthur Piantadosi, Les Fresholtz, Dick Alexander, Jim Webb.
Short Subject (animated): Leisure, Suzanne Baker; (live): In the Region of Ice, Andre Guttfreund, Peter Werner.
Documentary (feature): Harlan County, U.S.A., Barbara Kopple; (short): Number Our Days, Lynne Littman.
Irving Thalberg Award: Pandro S. Berman.
Special Award, Visual Effects: Carolo Rambaldi, Glen Robinson, Frank Van der Veer, King Kong; L. B. Abbott, Glen Robinson, Matthew Yuricich, Logan's Run.

Canadian Film Awards

Source: Canadian Film Institute

1968
Actor: Gerard Parkes, Isabel
Actress: Genevieve Bujold, Isabel
Picture: A Place to Stand

1969
Actor: Chris Wiggins, The Best Damn Fiddler from Calabogie to Kaladar
Actress: Jackie Burroughs, Dulcima
Picture: The Best Damn Fiddler from Calabogie to Kaladar

1970
Actor: Doug McGrath and Paul Bradley (tied), Goin' Down the Road
Actress: Genevieve Bujold, Act of the Heart
Picture: Psychocratie

1971
Actor: Jean Duceppe, Mon oncle Antoine
Actress: Ann Knox, The Only Thing You Know
Picture: Mon oncle Antoine

1972
Actor: Gordon Pinsent, The Rowdyman
Actress: Micheline Lanctot, Vrai nature de Bernadette
Picture: Wedding in White

1973
Actor: Jacques Godin, O.K. Laliberte
Actress: Genevieve Bujold, Kamouraska
Picture: Slipstream

1974
No awards

1975
Actor: Stuart Gillard, Why Rock the Boat?
Actress: Margot Kidder, Black Christmas and A Quiet Day in Belfast.
Picture: Les Ordres
Film of the Year: The Apprenticeship of Duddy Kravitz

1976
Actor: Andre Melancon, Partis pour la gloire
Actress: Marilyn Lightstone, Lies My Father Told Me
Picture: Lies My Father Told Me

The Spingarn Medal

The Spingarn Medal has been awarded annually since 1914 by the National Association for the Advancement of Colored People for the highest achievement by a black American.

1946—Dr. Percy L. Julian
1947—Channing H. Tobias
1948—Ralph J. Bunche
1949—Charles Hamilton Houston
1950—Mabel Keaton Staupers
1951—Harry T. Moore
1952—Paul R. Williams
1953—Theodore K. Lawless
1954—Carl Murphy
1955—Jack Roosevelt Robinson
1956—Martin Luther King, Jr.
1957—Mrs. Daisy Bates and the Little Rock Nine
1958—Edward Kennedy (Duke) Ellington
1959—Langston Hughes
1960—Kenneth B. Clark
1961—Robert C. Weaver
1962—Medgar Wiley Evers
1963—Roy Wilkins
1964—Leontyne Price
1965—John H. Johnson
1966—Edward W. Brooke
1967—Sammy Davis, Jr.
1968—Clarence M. Mitchell, Jr.
1969—Jacob Lawrence
1970—Leon Howard Sullivan
1971—Gordon Parks
1972—Wilson C. Riles
1973—Damon Keith
1974—Henry (Hank) Aaron
1975—Alvin Ailey
1976—Alex Haley

National Teacher of the Year Award

Awarded by the Council of Chief State School Officers, Encyclopedia Britannina, and the Ladies' Home Journal for service in elementary and secondary schools.

1965—Richard E. Klinck, sixth grade, Reed Street Elementary, Wheat Ridge, Col.
1966—Mona Dayton, first grade, Walter Douglas Elementary, Tucson, Ariz.
1967—Roger Tenney, music, Owatonna Junior-Senior H.S., Owatonna, Minn.
1968—David E. Graf, vocational education & industrial arts, Sandwich Comm. H.S., Sandwich, Ill.
1969—Barbara Goleman, language arts, Miami Jackson H.S., Miami, Fla.
1970—Johnnie T. Dennis, physics, math analysis, Walla Walla H.S., Walla Walla, Wash.
1971—Martha Marion Stringfellow, first grade, Lewisville Elementary, Chester Co., S.C.
1972—James Marshall Rogers, American history & Black studies, Durham H.S., Raleigh, N.C.
1973—John A. Ensworth, sixth grade, Kenwood school, Bend, Ore.
1974—Vivian Tom, social studies, Lincoln H.S., Yonkers, N.Y.
1975—Robert G. Heyer, science, Johanna Junior H.S., St. Paul, Minn.
1976—Ruby S. Murchison, social studies, Washington Drive J.H.S., Fayetteville, N.C.
1977—Myrra Leonore Lee, social studies, Helix H.S., La Mesa, Cal.

The Molson Prize

The Molson Prizes have been given annually to recognize and encourage outstanding contributions in the arts, humanities, or social sciences. They are financed from the interest on a gift to the Canada Council by the Molson Foundation. The value of each prize is $20,000.

1963 Donald Creighton; Alain Grandbois
1964 No awards made.
1965 Jean Gascon; Frank Scott
1966 Rev. Georges-Henri Levesque; H. McLennan
1967 Arthur Erickson; Anne Hebert; Marshall McLuhan
1968 Glenn Gould; Jean Le Moyne
1969 Jean-Paul Audet; Morley Callaghan; Arnold Spohr
1970 Northrop Frye; Duncan Macpherson; Yves Pheriault
1971 Maureen Forrester; Rina Lasnier; Norman McLaren
1972 John Deutsch; Alfred Pellan; George Woodcock
1973 W.A.C.H. Dobson; Celia Franca; Jean-Paul Lemieux
1974 Alex Colville, Margaret Laurence; Pierre Dansereau
1975 Jon Vickers; Denise Pelletier; the Orford String Quartet: Andrew Dawes; Terrence Helmer; Kenneth Perkins and Marcel St-Cyr
1976 John Hirsch; Bill Reid; Jean-Louis Roux

Notable New York Theater Openings, 1976-77 Season

American Buffalo, drama by David Mamet; directed by Ulu Grosbard; with Robert Duvall, Kenneth McMillan, and John Savage.

Anna Christie, revival of the Eugene O'Neill waterfront melodrama; directed by Jose Quintero; with Liv Ullmann.

Annie, musical by Charles Strouse based on the "Little Orphan Annie" comic strip; with Andrea McArdle, Dorothy Loudon, and Reid Shelton.

Caesar and Cleopatra, revival of the Shaw classic; with Rex Harrison and Elizabeth Ashley.

For Colored Girls Who Have Considered Suicide/When the Rainbow is Enuf, play by Ntozake Shange.

Comedians, play by Trevor Griffiths; directed by Mike Nichols; with Milo O'Shea and Jonathan Pryce.

Dirty Linen & New-Found-Land, comedy by Tom Stoppard; with Remak Ramsey and Cecilia Hart.

Fiddler on the Roof, revival of the Jerry Bock/Sheldon Harnick musical; with Zero Mostel.

Gemini, play by Albert Innaurato about an Italian family in South Philadelphia.

Going Up, musical by Louis A. Hirsch and Otto Harbach; with Maureen Brennan and Walter Bobbie.

Guys and Dolls, revival of the Frank Loesser musical with an all-black cast; with Norman Donaldson and Robert Guillaume.

Happy End, revival of the Weill/Brecht musical set in Chicago in 1915.

I Love My Wife, musical-comedy by Cy Coleman and Michael Stewart; with Lenny Baker, James Naughton, Joanna Gleason, and Ilene Graff.

Ladies at the Alamo, drama by Paul Zindel; with Estelle Parsons, Eileen Heckart, and Rosemary Murphy.

No Man's Land, play by Harold Pinter about 2 poets; with John Gielgud and Ralph Richardson.

Oh! Calcutta! revival of the comedy review devised by Kenneth Tynan.

Otherwise Engaged, play by Simon Gray; directed by Harold Pinter; with Tom Courtenay.

Poor Murderer, play by Pavel Kohout; with Laurence Luckinbill, Kevin McCarthy, Maria Schell, and Larry Gates.

Porgy and Bess, revival by the Houston Opera of the Gershwin classic.

Side by Side by Sondheim, musical entertainment devoted to the music and lyrics of Stephen Sondheim; with David Kernan, Bonnie Schon, and Millicent Martin.

Sly Fox, comedy by Larry Gelbart based on Ben Jonson's "Valpone"; with George C. Scott, Trish Van Devere, Bob Dishy, and Jack Gilford.

Something Old, Something New, comedy by Henry Denker; with Molly Picon and Hans Conreid.

Texas Trilogy, 3 full-length plays by Preston Jones; with Diane Ladd, Fred Gwynne, Graham Beckel, and Patricia Roe.

The Basic Training of Pavlo Hummel, revival of the David Rabe play; with Al Pacino.

The Cherry Orchard, adaptation by Jean-Claude van Itallie of the Chekhov classic; with Irene Worth and Raul Julia.

The Eccentricities of a Nightingale, rewrite by Tennessee Williams of his play, "Summer and Smoke"; with Betsy Palmer, David Selby, Shepperd Strudwick, and Nan Martin.

The Innocents, revival of the William Archibald play based on "The Turn of the Screw," by Henry James; with Claire Bloom.

The King and I, revival of the Rodgers and Hammerstein musical; with Yul Brynner and Constance Towers.

The Robber Bridegroom, musical by Robert Waldman and Alfred Uhry; with Barry Bostwick and Rhonda Coullet.

The Shadow Box, play by Michael Cristofer set in a treatment center for the terminally ill; won Pulitzer prize and Tony award as best play.

The Trip Back Down, play by John Bishop; with John Cullum.

Vieux Carre, play by Tennessee Williams; with Sylvia Sidney and Richard Alfieri.

Wheelbarrow Closers, play by Louis La Russo; with Danny Aiello.

Your Arms Too Short to Box With God, musical based on the Book of Matthew; conceived and directed by Vinnette Carroll; music and lyrics by Micki Grant; with Delores Hall.

Record Long Run Broadway Plays *Still Running June 8, 1977

Fiddler on the Roof	3,242
Life With Father	3,224
Tobacco Road	3,182
Hello Dolly	2,844
My Fair Lady	2,717
Man of La Mancha	2,329
*Abie's Irish Rose	2,327
Oklahoma	2,212
*Grease	2,170
Pippin	1,900
Harvey	1,775
Hair	1,742
South Pacific	1,694
Born Yesterday	1,643
Mary, Mary	1,572
Voice of the Turtle	1,557
Barefoot in the Park	1,532
Mame	1,508
Arsenic and Old Lace	1,444
The Sound of Music	1,443
How to Succeed in Business Without Really Trying	1,417
Hellzapoppin	1,404
The Music Man	1,375
Funny Girl	1,348
Oh! Calcutta!	1,316
Angel Street	1,295
Lightnin'	1,291
Promises, Promises	1,281
The King and I	1,246
*Magic Show	1,240
Cactus Flower	1,234
Sleuth	1,222
"1776"	1,217
Guys and Dolls	1,200
Cabaret	1,166
Mister Roberts	1,157
Annie Get Your Gun	1,147
Butterflies Are Free	1,128
Pins and Needles	1,108
Plaza Suite	1,097
*Equus	1,075
Kiss Me Kate	1,070

Plays in London *Still running July 1, 1977

*The Mousetrap	10,218
Black and White Minstrels	4,354
*Oh! Calcutta	2,847
Oliver	2,811
There's a Girl in my Soup	2,547
Pyjama Tops	2,498
Sound of Music	2,385
*No Sex, Please, We're British	2,525
Salad Days	2,283
My Fair Lady	2,281
Sleuth	2,258
Hair	2,239
Chu Chin Chow	2,238
The Man Most Likely To	2,213
The Boy Friend	2,084
Canterbury Tales	2,082
*Jesus Christ Superstar	2,045
Boeing Boeing	2,036
Fiddler on the Roof	2,030
Blithe Spirit	1,997
Worms Eye View	1,745
Me and My Girl	1,646
Reluctant Heroes	1,610
Together Again	1,566
Seagulls over Sorrento	1,551
Oklahoma	1,543
Irma La Douce	1,512
Dry Rot	1,475
Charley's Aunt	1,466
The Secretary Bird	1,463
The Beggar's Opera	1,463
Simple Spymen	1,404
Our Boys	1,362
Knights of Madness	1,361
Maid of the Mountains	1,352
Arsenic and Old Lace	1,337
The Farmer's Wife	1,329
Annie Get Your Gun	1,304
The Little Hut	1,261
A Little Bit of Fluff	1,241
Sailor Beware	1,231
One for the Pot	1,221
Beyond the Fringe	1,184

Symphony Orchestras of the U.S. and Canada

Source: American Symphony Orchestra League

(As of Aug. 19, 1977)

Classifications are based on annual incomes or budgets of orchestras.

Major Symphony Orchestras

		Conductor
Atlanta Symphony	1280 Peachtree St., NE, Atlanta, GA 30309	Robert Shaw
Baltimore Symphony	120 West Mount Royal Ave., Baltimore, MD 21201	Sergiu Comissiona
Boston Symphony	Symphony Hall, Boston, MA 02115	Seiji Ozawa
Buffalo Philharmonic	26 Richmond Ave., Buffalo, NY 14222	Michael Thomas
Chicago Symphony	220 S. Michigan Ave., Chicago, IL 60604	Sir Georg Solti
Cincinnati Symphony	1241 Elm St., Cincinnati, OH 45210	Thomas Schippers
Cleveland Orchestra	11001 Euclid Ave., Cleveland, OH 44106	Lorin Maazel
Dallas Symphony	P.O. Box 26207, Dallas, TX 75226	Edwardo Mata
Denver Symphony	1615 California St., Denver, CO 80202	Brian Priestman
Detroit Symphony	20 Auditorium Dr., Detroit, MI 48226	Antel Doratt
Honolulu Symphony	1000 Bishop St., Honolulu, HA 96813	Robert LaMarchina
Houston Symphony	615 Louisiana, Houston, TX 77002	Lawrence Foster
Indianapolis Symphony	4600 Sunset Ave., Indianapolis, IN 46208	John Nelson
Kansas City Philharmonic	210 W. 10th St., Kansas City, MO 64105	Maurice Peress
Los Angeles Philharmonic	135 North Grand, Los Angeles, CA 90012	Zubin Mehta
Milwaukee Symphony	929 N. Water St., Milwaukee, WI 53202	Kenneth Schermerhorn
Minnesota Orchestra	1111 Nicollet Mall, Minneapolis, MN 55403	S. Skrowaczewski
Montreal Symphony	Place des Arts, Montreal, Que. H2X1Y9	Vacant
National Arts Centre Orchestra	Box 1534, Station B., Ottawa, Ont. KIP5W1	Mario Bernardi
National Symphony	JFK Center for the Performing Arts, Wash., DC 20566	Mstislav Rostropovich
New Jersey Symphony	213 Washington St., Newark, NJ 07101	Thomas Michalak
New Orleans Philharmonic	203 Carondelet St. New Orleans, LA 70130	Leonard Slatkin
New York Philharmonic	Broadway at 65th St., New York, NY 19923	Vacant
North Carolina Symphony	P.O. Box 28026, Raleigh, NC 27611	John Gosling
Philadelphia Orchestra	1420 Locust St., Philadelphia, PA 19102	Eugene Ormandy
Pittsburgh Symphony	600 Penn Ave., Pittsburgh, PA 15222	Andre Previn
Rochester Philharmonic	20 Grove Pl., Rochester, NY 14605	David Zinman
St. Louis Symphony	718 N. Grand Blvd., St. Louis, MO 63103	Jerzy Semkow
San Antonio Symphony	109 Lexington Ave., San Antonio, TX 78205	Vacant
San Francisco Symphony	War Memorial Veterans' Bldg., San Fran., CA 94102	Edo de Waart
Seattle Symphony	305 Harrison St., Seattle, WA 98109	Rainer Miedel
Syracuse Symphony	411 Montgomery St., Syracuse, NY 13202	Christopher Keene
Toronto Symphony	215 Victoria St., Toronto, Ont. M5B1V1	Andrew Davis
Utah Symphony	55 W. 1st So. St., Salt Lake City, UT 84101	Maurice Abravanel
Vancouver Symphony	873 Beatty St., Vancouver, B.C. V6B 2M6	Kazuyoshi Akiyama

Regional Orchestras

Birmingham Symphony	2133 7th Ave. N., Birmingham, AL 35203	Amerigo Marino
Calgary Philharmonic	300-330 9th Ave. SW, Calgary, Alta. T2P1K6	Franz Paul Decker
Columbus Symphony	101 E. Town St., Columbus, OH 43215	Evan Whallon
Florida Philharmonic	150 S.E. 2d Ave., Miami, FL 33131	Brian Priestman
Florida Symphony	320 N. Magnolia, Suite 6-A, Orlando, FL 32801	Pavle Despalj
Hartford Symphony	470 Capitol Ave., Hartford, CT 06106	Arthur Winograd
Hudson Valley Philharmonic	Box 191, Poughkeepsie, NY 12602	Imre Pallo
Louisville Orchestra	333 W. Broadway, Louisville, KY 40202	Jorge Mester
Nashville Symphony	1805 West End Ave., Nashville, TN 37203	Michael Charry
Oakland Symphony	P.O. Box 1619, Oakland, CA 94612	Harold Farberman
Oklahoma Symphony	512 Civic Center Music Hall, Oklahoma City, OK 73102	Ainslee Cox
Oregon Symphony	1119 SW Park Ave., Portland, OR 97205	Lawrence Smith
Phoenix Symphony	6328 N. 7th St., Phoenix, AZ 85014	Eduardo Mata
Richmond Symphony	15 S. Fifth St., Richmond, VA 23219	Jacques Houtmann
Saint Paul Chamber Orchestra	St. Paul Bldg., 5th and Wabasha, St. Paul, MN 55102	Dennis Russell Davies
San Diego Symphony	P.O. Box 3175, San Diego, CA 92103	Peter Eros
San Jose Symphony	170 Park Center Plaza, San Jose, CA 94113	George Cleve
Toledo Symphony	1 Stranahan Sq., Toledo, OH 43604	Serge Fournier
Winnipeg Symphony	555 Main St., Winnipeg, Man. R3B1C3	Piero Gamba

Metropolitan Orchestras

Akron Symphony	Thomas Hall, Hill & Center Sts., Akron, OH 44303	Louis Lane
Albany Symphony	19 Clinton Ave., Albany, NY 12207	Julius Hegyi
Amarillo Symphony	P.O. Box 2552, Amarillo, TX 79105	Thomas Conlin
American Symphony	119 W. 57th St., New York, NY 10019	Kazuyoshi Akiyama
Arkansas Orchestra Society	604 E. 6th St., Little Rock, AR 72202	Kurt Klippstatter
Austin Symphony	1101 Red River St., Austin, TX 78701	Akiro Endo
Baton Rouge Symphony	Box 103, Baton Rouge, LA 70821	James Yestadt
Brooklyn Philharmonia	30 Lafayette Ave., Brooklyn, NY 11217	Lukas Foss
California Chamber Orchestra	6380 Wilshire Blvd., Los Angeles, CA 90048	Henri Temianka
Canton Symphony	1001 Market Ave. N., Canton, OH 44702	Thomas Michalak
Cedar Rapids Symphony	223 Dows Bldg., Cedar Rapids, IA 52401	Richard D. Williams
Charleston Symphony	Box 2292, Charleston, WV 25328	Ronald Dishinger
Charlotte Symphony	110 E. 7th St., Charlotte, NC 28202	Leo Driehuys
Chattanooga Symphony	730 Cherry St., Chattanooga, TN 37402	Richard Cormier
Chautauqua Symphony	Chautauqua Institution, Chautauqua, NY 14722	Sergiu Commissiona
Clarion Music Society	415 Lexington Ave., New York, NY 10017	Newell Jenkins
Colorado Springs Symphony	P.O. Box 1692, Colorado Springs, CO 80901	Charles Ansbacher
Corpus Christi Symphony	P.O. Box 495, Corpus Christi, TX 78403	Cornelius Eberhardt
County Symphony of Westchester	Box 333, Scarsdale, NY 10583	Stephen Simon
Dayton Philharmonic	210 N. Main St., Dayton, OH 45402	Charles Wendelken-Wilson
Des Moines Symphony	702 Employers Mutual Bldg., Des Moines, IA 50309	Yuri Krasnapolsky

Duluth-Superior Symphony	506 W. Michigan St., Duluth, MN 55802	Taavo Virkhaus
Eastern Music Festival	712 Summit Ave., Greensboro, NC 27405	Sheldon Morgenstern
Edmonton Symphony	11712 87th Ave., Edmonton, Alta. T6G0Y3	Pierre Hetu
El Paso Philharmonic	P.O. Box 180, El Paso, TX 79942	Abraham Chavez Jr.
Erie Philharmonic	720 G. Daniel Baldwin Bldg., Erie, PA 16501	Walter Hendl
Evansville Philharmonic	P.O. Box 84, Evansville, IN 47701	Minas Christian
Flint Symphony	1025 E. Kearsley St., Flint, MI 48503	John Covelli
Florida Gulf Coast Symphony	P.O. Box 569, St. Petersburg, FL 33731	Irwin Hoffman
Florida West Coast Symphony	P.O. Box 1107, Sarasota, FL 33578	Paul C. Wolfe
Fort Lauderdale Symphony	1430 N. Federal Hwy., Fort Lauderdale, FL 33304	Emerson Buckley
Fort Wayne Philharmonic	227 E. Washington Blvd., Fort Wayne, IN 46802	Thomas Briccetti
Fort Worth Symphony	4401 Trail Lake Dr., Ft. Worth, TX 76109	John Giordano
Fresno Philharmonic	1362 N. Fresno St., Fresno, CA 93703	Guy Taylor
Glendale Symphony	401 N. Brand Blvd., Glendale, CA 91203	Carmen Dragon
Grand Rapids Symphony	Exhibitors Bldg., Grand Rapids, MI 49502	Theo Alcantara
Hamilton Philharmonic	50 Main St., W. Hamilton, Ont. L8P1H3	Boris Brott
Jackson Symphony	P.O. Box 4584 Jackson, MS 39216	Lewis Dalvit
Jacksonville Symphony	333 Laura St., Jacksonville, FL 32202	Willis Page
Kalamazoo Symphony	426 S. Park St., Kalamazoo, MI 49007	Yoshimi Takeda
Kitchener-Waterloo Symphony	Box 2, Waterloo, Ont. N2J3Z6	Raffi Armenian
Knoxville Symphony	618 Gay St., Knoxville, TN 37902	Arpod Joo
Lansing Symphony	230 N. Washington Sq., Lansing, MI 48933	Dr. A. Clyde Roller
Lexington Philharmonic	P.O. Box 838, Lexington, KY 40501	George Zack
Lincoln Symphony	129 N. 10th St., Lincoln, Neb. 68508	Robert Emile
London Symphony	520 Wellington St., London, Ont. N6A3R2	Clifford Evens
Long Beach Symphony	121 Linden Ave., Long Beach, CA 90802	Alberto Bolet
Long Island Symphony	P.O. Box 315, Huntington, NY 11743	Seymour Lipkin
Los Angeles Chamber Orchestra	1777 N. Vine St., Hollywood, CA 90028	Neville Marriner
Madison Symphony	211 N. Carroll St., Madison, WI 53703	Roland Johnson
Memphis Symphony	1503 Monroe,Memphis, TN 38104	Vincent DeFrank
Miami Beach Symphony	420 Lincoln Rd. Mall, Miami Beach, FL 33139	Barnett Breeskin
Midland Odessa Sym. & Chorale	P.O. Box 6266, Midland, TX 79701	Thomas Hohstadt
Monterey County Symphony	P.O. Box 3965, Carmel, CA 93921	Haymo Taeuber
Music for Westchester Symphony	Box 35, Gedney Station, White Plains, NY 10605	Siegfried Landau
New Haven Symphony	33 Whitney Ave., New Haven, CT 06511	Murry Sidlin
New Mexico Symphony	120 Madeira Dr. NE, Albuquerque, NM 87108	Yoshima Takeda
Norfolk Symphony	P.O. Box 26, Norfolk, VA 23501	Russell Stanger
Northeastern Philharmonic	P.O. Box 71, Avoca, PA 18641	Thomas Michalak
Omaha Symphony	478 Aquila Ct., Omaha NE 68102	Thomas Bricetti
Orchestra da Camera	129 East Dr., N. Massapequa, NY 11758	Herbert Grossman
Palm Beach Symphony	253 Sunrise Ave., Palm Beach, FL 33480	Karl Karapetian
Pasadena Symphony	300 E. Green St., Pasadena, CA 91101	Daniel Lewis
Peoria Symphony	416 N.E. Jefferson, Peoria, IL 61603	Robert Kreis
Portland Symphony	30 Myrtle St., Portland, ME 04111	Bruce Hangen
Puerto Rico Symphony	Box 2350, San Juan, PR 00936	Victor Tevah
Quebec Symphony	745 Blvd., St. Cyrille Ouest, Que. G1S1T3	James De Preist
Queens Symphony	1 Station Sq., Forest Hills, NY 11375	David Katz
Regina Symphony	200 Lakeshore Dr., Regina, Sask. S4S0A4	Timothy Vernon
Rhode Island Philharmonic	334 Westminster Mall, Providence, RI 02903	Francis Madeira
Rockford Symphony	415 N. Church St., Rockford, IL 61103	Crawford Gates
Sacramento Symphony	451 Parkfair Dr., Sacramento, CA 95825	Harry Newstone
Saginaw Symphony	P.O. Box 415, Saginaw, MI 48606	Gideon Grau
Santa Barbara Symphony	210 E. Figueroa, Santa Barbara, CA 93101	Ronald Ondrejka
Savannah Symphony	P.O. Box 9505, Savannah, GA 31402	Christian Badea
Shreveport Symphony	P.O. Box 4057, Shreveport, LA 71104	John Shenaut
South Bend Symphony	215 W. North Shore Drive, South Bend, IN 46617	Herbert Butler
Spokane Symphony	W. 245 Spokane Falls Blvd., Spokane, WA 99201	Donald Thulean
Springfield (Mass.) Symphony	284 State St., Springfield, MA 01105	Robert Gutter
Springfield (Ohio) Symphony	Box 1374, Springfield, OH 45501	John E. Ferritto
Stockton Symphony	Box 4273, Stockton, CA 95204	Kyung-Soo Won
Suffolk Symphonic Orchestra	1 W. Main St., Smithtown, NY 11787	Vacant
Thunder Bay Symphony	P.O. Box 2004, Station P, Thunder Bay, Ont. P7B5E7	Dwight Bennett
Tri-City Symphony	P.O. Box 67, Davenport, IA 52805	James Dixon
Tucson Symphony	443 So. Stone Ave., Tucson, AZ 85701	Gregory Millar
Tulsa Philharmonic	2210 S. Main, Tulsa, OK 74114	Vacant
Vermont Symphony	P.O. Box 548, Middlebury, VT 05753	Efrain Guigui
Victoria Symphony	30-B Centennial Sq., Victoria, BC., V8W1P7	Lazlo Gati
Wheeling Symphony	51 16th St., Wheeling, WV 26003	Jeff Holland Cook
Wichita Symphony	225 W. Douglas, Wichita, KS 67202	Francois Huybrechts
Winston-Salem Symphony	610 Coliseum Dr., Winston-Salem, NC 27106	John Iuele
Youngstown Symphony	260 Federal Plaza West, Youngstown, OH 44503	Franz Bibo

Recordings

Disc and Tape Sales Set Records; Revenues, Volume Both Up

Manufacturers' sales of phonograph records and pre-recorded discs jumped by 15% in 1976 to a new high of $2.74 billion, according to the Recording Industry Association of America. Unit sales rose to 592 million, an increase of 11% over 1975. Sales of long-play albums went up 12% to $1.7 billion; singles rose 16% to $245 million; 8-track cartridge tapes were up 16% to $678 million; cassette tapes jumped 47% to $145 million. Quad tapes and reel-to-reels fell off. The RIAA confers Gold Record Awards on single records which sell one million units, Platinum Awards to those selling 2 million, Gold Awards to L-P albums and their tape equivalents which sell 500,000 units, Platinum Awards to those selling one million. Recordings winning awards in 1976-77 follow (most Platinum Award winners also won Gold Awards):

Artists and Recording Titles

A-album, S-single, G-gold, P-platinum

Aug. 1976

The Manhattans; *Kiss and Say Goodby*; S,P.
George Benson; *Breezin'*; A,P.

David Bowie; *Changesonebowie;* A,G.
Helen Reddy; *Music, Music;* A,G.
Captain & Tennille; *Shop Around;* S,G.
Elton John & Kiki Dee; *Don't Go Breaking My Heart;* S,G.
Loggins & Messina; *Native Sons;* A,G.
Lou Rawls; *You'll Never Find Another Love Like Mine;* S,G.
Seals & Crofts; *Get Closer;* A,G.

Sept. 1976

The Beach Boys; *15 Big Ones;* A,G.
Walter Murphy & the Big Apple Band; *A Fifth of Beethoven;* S,G.
The Brothers Johnson; *Look Out for #1;* A,P.
Chicago; *Chicago X;* A,P.
Parliament; *Mothership Connection;* A,P.
Neil Diamond; *Beautiful Noise;* A,P.
Boz Scaggs; *Silk Degrees;* A,P.
Captain & Tennille; *Song of Joy;* A,P.
Steve Miller Band; *Fly Like an Eagle;* A,P.
Jefferson Starship; *Spitfire;* A,P.
War; *Summer;* S,G.
Bee Gees; *You Should Be Dancing;* S,G.
Tavares; *Heaven Must Be Missing an Angel;* S,G.
Andrea True Connection; *More, More, More;* S,G.
Peter Frampton; *Frampton;* A,G.
Jeff Beck; *Wired;* A,G.
Steely Dan; *Royal Scam;* A,G.
Bachman-Turner Overdrive; *Best of BTO (So Far);* A,G.
Bob Dylan; *Hard Rain;* A,G.

Oct. 1976

Wild Cherry; *Play that Funky Music;* S,P.
John Denver; *Spirit;* A,P.
Earth, Wind, & Fire; *Spirit;* A,P.
Linda Ronstadt; *Hasten Down the Wind;* A,P.
England Dan & John Ford Coley; *I'd Really Love to See You Tonight;* S,G.
Parliament; *Tear the Roof Off the Sucker;* S,G.
Cliff Richard; *Devil Woman;* S,G.
Wings; *Let 'Em In;* S,G.
Chicago; *If You Leave Me Now;* S,G.
Earth, Wind, & Fire; *Getaway;* S,G.
Boz Scaggs; *Lowdown;* S,G.
Daryl Hall & John Oates; *Abandoned Luncheonette;* A,G.
Dave Mason; *Dave Mason;* A,G.
The Manhattans; *The Manhattans;* A,G.
The Spinners; *Happiness Is Being with the Spinners;* A,G.
David Crosby & Graham Nash; *Whistling Down the Wire;* A,G.
Parliament; *The Clones of Dr. Funkenstein;* A,G.
James Taylor; *In the Pocket;* A,G.
O'Jays; *Message in the Music;* A,G.
Barry Manilow; *Barry Manilow I;* A,G.
Blue Oyster Cult; *Agents of Fortune;* A,G.
Boston; *Boston;* A,G.
The Walter Murphy Band; *A Fifth of Beethoven;* A,G.
Gordon Lightfoot; *Summertime Dream;* A,G.
Marlo Thomas & Friends; *Free to Be . . . You and Me;* A,G.
Elton John; *Blue Moves;* A,G.
Robin Trower; *For Earth Below;* A,G.

Nov. 1976

Heart; *Dreamboat Annie;* A,P.
Kiss; *Destroyer;* A,P.
Led Zeppelin; *The Song Remains the Same;* A,P.
Boston; *Boston;* A,P.
Rod Stewart; *A Night on the Town;* A,P.
The Outlaws; *The Outlaws;* A,P.
Red Sovine; *Teddy Bear;* S,G.
Marilyn McCoo & Billy Davis Jr.; *You Don't Have to Be a Star;* S,G.
Rod Stewart; *Tonight's the Night;* S,G.
Firefall; *Firefall;* A,G.
Daryl Hall & John Oates; *Bigger than Both of Us;* A,G.
Foghat; *Rock & Roll Outlaws;* A,G.
Fleetwood Mac; *Mystery to Me;* A,G.
The Mothers; *Over-Nite Sensation;* A.G.
Donna Summer; *Four Seasons of Love;* A,G.
Ted Nugent; *Free for All;* A,G.
Brass Construction; *Brass Construction II;* A,G.
Paul Anka; *Times of Your Life;* A,G.
Jackson Browne; *Jackson Browne;* A,G.
Frank Sinatra; *Ol' Blue Eyes Is Back;* A,G.
Van Morrison; *Moondance;* A,G.
Alice Cooper; *Alice Cooper Goes to Hell;* A,G.
Perry Como; *And I Love You So;* A,G.

Dec. 1976

Rick Dees & His Cast of Idiots; *Disco Duck;* S,P.
Bad Company; *Run with the Pack;* A,P.
The Electric Light Orchestra; *A New World Record;* A,P.
Elton John; *Blue Moves;* A,P.
Brass Construction; *Brass Construction;* A,P.
Eagles; *Hotel California;* A,P.
Wild Cherry; *Wild Cherry;* A,P.
Wings; *Wings over America;* A,P.
Doobie Brothers; *Best of the Doobies;* A,P.
Bee Gees; *Children of the World;* A,P.
Lynyrd Skynyrd; *One More (for) from the Road;* A,P.
Average White Band; *Soul Searching;* A,P.
Captain & Tennille; *Muskrat Love;* S,G.
The Spinners; *The Rubberband Man;* S,G.
Leo Sayer; *You Make Me Feel Like Dancing;* S,G.
Bee Gees; *Love So Right;* S,G.
England Dan & John Ford Coley; *Nights Are Forever;* A,G.
Richard Pryor; *Bicentennial Nigger;* A,G.
Olivia Newton-John; *Don't Stop Believin';* A,G.
Glen Campbell; *That Christmas Feeling;* A,G.
Beach Boys; *Best of the Beach Boys, Vol. 2;* A,G.
Robin Trower; *Long Misty Days;* A,G.
Wings; *Wings over America;* A,G.
Daryl Hall & John Oates; *Daryl Hall & John Oates;* A,G.
Dr. Buzzard's Original Savannah Band; *Dr. Buzzard's Original Savannah Band;* A,G.
Rose Royce; *Car Wash (soundtrack);* A,G.
James Taylor; *James Taylor's Greatest Hits;* A,G.
Bob Seger & the Silver Bullet Band; *Live Bullet;* A,G.
Joni Mitchell; *Hejira;* A,G.
Donny & Marie Osmond; *Donny & Marie, Songs from Their TV Show;* A,G.
George Carlin; *Occupation: Foole;* A,G.
Queen; *A Day at the Races;* A,G.
Leon Russell; *The Best of Leon Russell;* A,G.
Abba; *Greatest Hits;* A,G.

Jan. 1977

Kiss; *Rock and Roll Over;* A,P.
War; *Greatest Hits;* A,P.
Barry Manilow; *This One's for You;* A,P.
Linda Ronstadt; *Greatest Hits;* A,P.
Barbra Streisand & Kris Kristofferson; *A Star Is Born;* A,P.
Lou Rawls; *All Things in Time;* A,P.
The Sylvers; *Hot Line;* S,G.
Kiss; *Beth;* S,G.
Brothers Johnson; *I'll Be Good to You;* S,G.
Barry DeVorzon & Perry Botkin Jr.; Nadia's Theme *(The Young & Restless);* S,G.
Burton Cummings; *Stand Tall;* S,G.
Elton John; *Sorry Seems to Be the Hardest Word;* S,G.
Engelbert Humperdinck; *After the Lovin';* A,G.
Stills & Young Band; *Long May You Run;* A,G.
Al Stewart; *Year of the Cat;* A,G.
Z.Z. Top; *Tejas;* A.G.
George Harrison; *Thirty-Three & 1/3;* A,G.
Ohio Players; *Ohio Players Gold;* A,G.
The Emotions; *Flowers;* A,G.
Norman Connors; *You Are My Starship;* A,G.

Feb. 1977

Rose Royce; *Car Wash;* S,P.
The Jacksons; *Enjoy Yourself;* S,G.
Mary MacGregor; *Torn Between 2 Lovers;* S,G.
Foghat; *Night Shift;* A,G.
George Harrison; *The Best of George Harrison;* A,G.
Jethro Tull; *Chrysalis Songs from the Wood;* A,G.
Bread; *Lost Without Your Love;* A,G.

Crusaders; *Southern Comfort*; A,G.
Marilyn McCoo & Billy Davis Jr.; *I Hope We Get to Love in Time*; A,G.
Quincy Jones; . . . *Roots*; A,G.
Kiss; *Dressed to Kill*; A,G.

Mar. 1977

Fleetwood Mac; *Rumours*; A,P.
Pink Floyd; *Animals*; A,P.
Kansas; *Leftoverture*; A,P.
Al Stewart; *Year of the Cat*; A,P.
Bob Seger & the Silver Bullet Band; *Night Moves*; A,P.
Manfred Mann's Earth Band; *Blinded by the Light*; S,G.
Kenny Nolan; *I Like Dreamin'*; S,G.
The Eagles; *New Kid in Town*; S,G.
Abba; *Dancing Queen*; S,G.
Barbra Streisand; *Evergreen (from A Star Is Born)*; S,G.
Hank Williams; *24 Greatest Hits*; A,G.
Natalie Cole; *Unpredictable*; A,G.
Deniece Williams; *This Is Niecy*; A,G.
Statler Bros.; *The Best of the Statler Bros.*; A,G.
Bad Company; *Burnin' Sky*; A,G.
George Benson; *In Flight*; A,G.
Waylon Jennings; *Dreaming My Dreams*; A,G.
Queen; *Queen*; A,G.
Emerson, Lake, & Palmer; *Works, Vol. I*; A,G.
King Crimson; *In the Court of the Crimson King*; A,G.
John Denver; *John Denver's Greatest Hits, Vol. 2*; A,G.

Apr. 1977

Jackson Browne; *The Pretender*; A,P.
Rufus Featuring Chaka Khan; *Ask Rufus*; A,P.
Daryl Hall & John Oates; *Rich Girl*; S,G.
Alice Cooper; *I Never Cry*; S,G.
David Soul; *Don't Give Up on Us*; S,G.
Natalie Cole; *I've Got My Love on My Mind*; S,G.
10 CC; *The Things We Do for Love*; S,G.
Steve Miller Band; *Fly Like an Eagle*; S,G.
Glen Campbell; *Southern Nights*; S,G.
William Bell; *Tryin' to Love Two*; S,G.
Abba; *Arrival*; A,G.
Manfred Mann's Earth Band; *The Roaring Silence*; A,G.
The Jacksons; *The Jacksons*; A,G.
Captain & Tennille; *Come in from the Rain*; A,G.
Atlanta Rhythm Section; *A Rock and Roll Alternative*; A,G.
The Blackbyrds; *Unfinished Business*; A,G.
Montrose; *Montrose*; A,G.
Bootsy's Rubber Band; *Ahh . . . The Name Is Bootsy Baby*; A,G.
Gordon Lightfoot; *Gord's Gold*; A,G.
Leo Sayer; *Endless Flight*; A,G.
Santana; *Festival*; A,G.

May 1977

Engelbert Humperdinck; *After the Lovin'*; A,P.
Leo Sayer; *When I Need You*; S,G.
The Eagles; *Hotel California*; S,G.
Bruce Springsteen; *The Wild, the Innocent, and the E Street Shuffle*; A,G.
The Beatles; *The Beatles at the Hollywood Bowl*; A,G.
Loggins & Messina; *The Best of Friends*; A,G.
Foreigner; *Foreigner*; A,G.
George Carlin; *Toledo Window Box*; A,G.
Average White Band; *Person to Person*; A,G.
Teddy Pendergrass; *Teddy Pendergrass*; A,G.
Brothers Johnson; *Right on Time*; A,G.

June 1977

Isley Brothers; *Go for Your Guns*; A,P.
Steve Miller Band; *Book of Dreams*; A,P.
Peter Frampton; *I'm in You*; A,P.
Barry Manilow; *Barry Manilow Live*; A,P.
Movie Score, *Rocky*; A,P.
Kiss; *Love Gun*; A,P.
Joe Tex; *Ain't Gonna Bump No More*; S,G.
Kenny Rogers; *Lucille*; S,G.
Alan O'Day; *Undercover Angel*; S,G.
Heart; *Little Queen*; A,G.
Johnny Guitar Watson; *Ain't that a Bitch*; A,G.
Johnny Guitar Watson; *A Real Mother for Ya*; A,G.
Marshall Tucker Band; *Carolina Dreams*; A,G.
Kiss; *Kiss*; A,G.
Parliament; *Parliament Live*; A,G.
Cat Stevens; *Izitso*; A,G.
Waylon Jennings; *Ol' Waylon*; A,G.
Slave; *Slave*; A,G.
Jimmy Buffett; *Changes in Latitudes, Changes in Attitudes*; A,G.
Barbra Streisand; *Superman*; A,G.
Kiss; *Hotter than Hell*; A,G.
Bee Gees; *Bee Gees Live*; A,G.
Melissa Manchester; *Melissa*; A,G.
Crosby, Stills, & Nash; *Crosby, Stills, & Nash*; A,G.

July 1977

Neil Diamond; *Love at the Greek*; A,P.
Hot; *Angel in Your Arms*; S,G.
Shaun Cassidy; *Da Doo Ron Ron*; S,G.
Lou Rawls; *Unmistakably Lou*; A,G.
James Taylor; *J.T.*; A,G.
Berlin Philharmonic Orch.; *Beethoven: The 9 Symphonies*; A,G.
Ted Nugent; *Cat Scratch Fever*; A,G.
Emotions; *Rejoice*; A,G.
The O'Jays; *Travelin' at the Speed of Thought*; A,G.
Supertramp; *Even in the Quietest Moments*; A,G.
Donna Summer; *I Remember Yesterday*; A,G.
Blue Oyster Cult; *On Your Feet or on Your Knees*; A,G.
Movie Soundtrack; *Star Wars*; A,G.
Various Artists; Alleluia — *Praise Gathering for Believers*; A,G.

Best-Selling Books of 1976-77

Listed according to frequency of citation on best seller reports from Sept. 1976 to Aug. 1977.
Numbers in parentheses show rank on top ten list for calendar year 1976, according to Publishers Weekly.

Hardcover Fiction

1. Trinity; Leon Uris (1).
2. The Crash of '79; Paul E. Erdman.
3. Sleeping Murder; Agatha Christie (2).
4. Falconer; John Cheever.
5. Oliver's Story; Erich Segal.
6. The Thorn Birds; Colleen McCullough.
7. Storm Warning; Jack Higgins (4)
8. Slapstick or Lonesome No More!; Kurt Vonnegut (7).
9. Condominium; John D. MacDonald.
10. The Chancellor Manuscript; Robert Ludlum.
11. Illusions: The Adventures of a Reluctant Messiah; Richard Bach.
12. Full Disclosure; William Safire.
13. How to Save Your Own Life; Erica Jong.
14. A Book of Common Prayer; Joan Didion.
15. The Users; Joyce Haber.
16. Voyage: A Novel of 1896; Sterling Hayden.
17. Delta of Venus: Erotica; Anais Nin.
18. Ceremony of the Innocent; Taylor Caldwell.
19. October Light; John Gardner.
20. The Valhalla Exchange; Harry Patterson.
21. The Rich Are Different; Susan Howatch.
22. Blue Skies, No Candy; Gael Greene.
23. Pride of the Peacock; Victoria Holt.
24. Crowned Heads; Thomas Tryon.
25. The Shining; Stephen King.

Hardcover Nonfiction

1. Your Erroneous Zones; Dr. Wayne W. Dyer (3).
2. Passages: The Predictable Crises of Adult Life; Gail Sheehy (4).
3. Roots; Alex Haley (2).
4. The Grass Is Always Greener Over the Septic Tank; Erma Bombeck (6).

5. The Book of Lists; David Wallechinsky, Irving Wallace, Amy Wallace.
6. The Dragons of Eden: Speculations on the Evolution of Human Intelligence; Carl Sagan.
7. Haywire; Brooke Hayward.
8. Changing; Liv Ullmann.
9. The Hite Report: A Nationwide Study of Female Sexuality; Shere Hite (9).
10. Adolf Hitler; John Toland.
11. It Didn't Start with Watergate; Victor Lasky.
12. Looking Out for #1; Robert Ringer.
13. The Gamesman: The New Corporate Leaders; Michael Maccoby.
14. Vivien Leigh: A Biography; Anne Edwards.
15. A Man Called Intrepid: The Secret War; William Stevenson.
16. A Year of Beauty and Health; Beverly and Vidal Sassoon.
17. Majesty: Elizabeth II and the House of Windsor; Robert Lacey.
18. The Camera Never Blinks: Adventures of a TV Journalist; Dan Rather with Mickey Herskowitz.
19. Blood and Money; Thomas Thompson.
20. Howard Hughes: The Hidden Years; James Phelan.
21. The Right and the Power: The Prosecution of Watergate; Leon Jaworski.
22. A Civil Tongue; Edwin Newman.
23. World of Our Fathers; Irving Howe and Kenneth Libo.
24. Five Seasons: A Baseball Companion; Roger Angell.
25. Bubbles: A Self-Portrait; Beverly Sills.

Paperback

1. The Deep; Peter Benchley.
2. Life after Life; Raymond A. Moody Jr.
3. Wicked Loving Lies; Rosemary Rogers.
4. Passages: The Predictable Crises of Adult Life; Gail Sheehy.
5. Audrey Rose; Frank de Felitta.
6. The Lonely Lady; Harold Robbins.
7. Curtain; Agatha Christie.
8. Star Wars: From the Adventures of Luke Skywalker; George Lucas.
9. The Hite Report: A Nationwide Study of Female Sexuality; Shere Hite.
10. Captains and the Kings; Taylor Caldwell.
11. The Warriors; John Jakes.
12. A Stranger in the Mirror; Sidney Sheldon.
13. Once an Eagle; Anton Myrer.
14. The Choirboys; Joseph Wambaugh.
15. The Other Side of Midnight; Sidney Sheldon.
16. Dolores; Jacqueline Susann.
17. Sybil; Flora Rheta Schreiber.
18. Kinflicks; Lisa Alther.
19. Ordinary People; Judith Guest.
20. Carrie; Stephen King.
21. Nightwork; Irwin Shaw.
22. Salem's Lot; Stephen King.
23. The Russians; Hedrick Smith.
24. Children of Dune; Frank Herbert.
25. The Pride of the Peacock; Victoria Holt.

Best Sellers, Calendar Year 1976
Hardcover Fiction:

1. Trinity, Leon Uris.
2. Sleeping Murder, Agatha Christie.
3. Dolores, Jacqueline Susann.
4. Storm Warning, Jack Higgins.
5. The Deep, Peter Benchley.
6. 1876, Gore Vidal.
7. Slapstick or Lonesome No More!, Kurt Vonnegut.
8. The Lonely Lady, Harold Robbins.
9. Touch Not the Cat, Mary Stewart.
10. A Stranger in the Mirror, Sidney Sheldon.

Hardcover Nonfiction

1. The Final Days, Bob Woodward, Carl Bernstein.
2. Roots, Alex Haley.
3. Your Erroneous Zones, Dr. Wayne W. Dyer.
4. Passages: The Predictable Crises of Adult Life, Gail Sheehy.
5. Born Again, Charles W. Colson.
6. The Grass Is Always Greener Over the Septic Tank, Erma Bombeck.
7. Angels; God's Secret Agents, Billy Graham.
8. Blind Ambition: The White House Years, John Dean.
9. The Hite Report: A Nationwide Study of Female Sexuality, Shere Hite.
10. The Right and the Power: The Prosecution of Watergate, Leon Jaworski.

Recent Miss America Winners

1959 Mary Ann Mobley, Brandon, Miss. (21).
1960 Lynda Lee Mead, Natchez, Miss. (20).
1961 Nancy Fleming, Montague, Mich. (18).
1962 Maria Fletcher, Asheville, N.C. (19).
1963 Jacquelyn Mayer, Sandusky, Oh. (20).
1964 Donna Axum, El Dorado, Ark. (21).
1965 Vonda Kay Van Dyke, Phoenix, Ariz. (21).
1966 Deborah Irene Bryant, Overland Park, Kan. (19).
1967 Jane Anne Jayroe, Laverne, Okla. (19).
1968 Debra Dene Barnes, Moran, Kan. (20).
1969 Judith Anne Ford, Belvidere, Ill. (18).
1970 Pamela Anne Eldred, Birmingham, Mich. (21).
1971 Phyllis Ann George, Denton, Tex. (21).
1972 Laurie Lea Schaefer, Columbus, Oh. (22).
1973 Terry Anne Meeuwsen, DePere, Wis. (23).
1974 Rebecca Ann King, Denver, Col. (23).
1975 Shirley Cothran, Fort Worth, Tex. (21).
1976 Tawney Elaine Godin, Yonkers, N.Y. (18).
1977 Dorothy Kathleen Benham, Edina, Minn. (20).
1978 Susan Perkins, Columbus, Oh. (23).

America's Favorite TV Programs

Network Programs, Oct.-Dec. 1976

Program	% of Households	% of Women	% of Men	% of Teens	% of Children
Happy Days	31.1	21.7	18.3	30.6	41.1
Laverne and Shirley	30.2	21.5	17.0	27.5	37.9
Charlie's Angels	27.5	21.2	18.4	24.1	—
M-A-S-H	26.0	20.4	18.9	21.0	—
NBC Monday Night Movie	25.6	21.5	16.6	16.3	—
Bionic Woman	24.3	17.7	—	21.8	29.5
All in the Family	24.3	20.4	16.0	—	—
Baretta	24.1	17.6	16.2	21.5	—

Syndicated Programs
(Average Designated Market Area rating.)

Program	% of Households	% of Women	% of Men	% o Children
Lawrence Welk	16.2	—	—	—
Hollywood Squares	15.0	8.6	—	—
Hee Haw	14.9	9.7	9.2	11.0
Name That Tune	14.2	8.4	5.9	—
Match Game PM	14.1	9.2	6.7	—
Price is Right	13.9	7.7	—	—

(continued)

(continued)

Network Programs, Oct.-Dec. 1976

Program	% of Households	% of Women	% of Men	% of Teens	% of Children
Six Million Dollar Man	24.0	—	17.1	22.7	30.2
The Waltons	23.6	19.7	—	—	17.1
One Day at a Time	23.1	17.6	15.9	19.8	—
Little House on the Prairie	22.1	18.7	—	—	22.2
ABC Sunday Night Movie	22.0	—	17.7	16.9	—
Welcome Back, Kotter	22.0	—	—	20.9	24.2
NFL Monday Night Football	—	—	21.1	—	—
60 Minutes	—	—	19.0	—	—
Captain and Tennille	—	—	—	19.2	21.1
Wonderful World of Disney	—	—	—	—	25.8
Donnie and Marie	—	—	—	—	24.4
What's Happening	—	—	—	—	19.9

Syndicated Programs

(Average Designated Market Area rating.)

Program	% of House-holds	% of Wom-en	% of Men	% of Chil-dren
Candid Camera	13.8	8.2	7.3	—
Wild Kingdom	13.7	6.5	6.9	—
$25,000 Pyramid	13.4	8.4	—	—
Muppets	13.2	8.5	7.0	19.8
Truth or Consequences	12.7	7.1	—	—
Gong Show	12.5	9.5	8.6	10.8
Jacques Cousteau	11.8	7.0	7.7	—
$128,000 Question	11.5	6.6	—	—
My Three Sons	—	7.2	—	12.5
Bart Starr	—	—	6.7	—
Tom Landry	—	—	6.3	—
Brady Bunch	—	—	—	18.6
Wonderama	—	—	—	15.5
Daktari	—	—	—	14.5
Gilligan's Island	—	—	—	13.1

All-time Top Television Programs

Source: A.C. Nielsen (estimates)

Program	Date	Net-work	Per cent TV house-holds tuned
Roots	1/30/77	ABC	51.1
Gone With The Wind, Pt. 1	11/7/76	NBC	47.7
Gone With The Wind, Pt. 2	11/8/76	NBC	47.4
Bob Hope Christmas Show	1/15/70	NBC	46.6
Roots	1/28/77	ABC	45.9
The Fugitive	8/29/67	ABC	45.9
Roots	1/27/77	ABC	45.7
Bob Hope Christmas Show	1/14/71	NBC	45.0
Roots	1/25/77	ABC	44.8
Ed Sullivan	2/9/64	CBS	44.6
Super Bowl XI	1/9/77	NBC	44.4
Super Bowl VI	1/16/72	CBS	44.2
Roots	1/24/77	ABC	44.1
Beverly Hillbillies	1/8/64	CBS	44.0
Roots	1/26/77	ABC	43.8

Network TV Program Ratings

Source: A. C. Nielsen, November, 1976

Program type	TV households Rating	TV households No. (000)	Men % 18-34	Men % 25-54	Men % 55+	Women % 18-34	Women % 25-54	Women % 55+	Women % Working	% Teens 12-17	% Children 6-11
Today (7:30-8)	4.9	3,490	1.1	1.5	5.5	1.8	3.2	5.8	2.4	*	*
CBS Morning News (7:30-8)	2.6	1,850	*	*	2.4	1.0	1.4	2.8	*	*	1.0
Daytime:											
Drama	7.8	5,520	*	1.0	3.4	6.6	6.5	8.0	2.7	1.4	*
Quiz & aud. part.	6.0	4,280	1.3	1.4	4.2	3.4	4.0	5.9	1.7	1.4	1.3
All 10:00-4:30	7.0	4,970	1.2	1.3	3.7	5.2	5.4	6.8	2.2	1.6	1.2
Evening Inform.	13.9	9,900	6.3	7.8	15.9	6.7	8.7	15.7	8.5	3.4	5.2
Evening:											
General drama	19.3	13,720	11.2	12.1	13.6	15.7	16.8	15.5	13.5	9.9	11.9
Susp. & myst. drama	18.5	13,200	11.5	13.7	14.9	13.8	15.0	14.1	13.3	10.0	7.4
Situation comedy	20.2	14,370	12.4	12.9	14.7	15.6	15.8	16.0	15.9	12.8	14.8
Variety	15.5	11,010	8.7	9.7	12.7	10.7	11.7	13.7	11.1	9.7	11.9
Feature film	21.7	15,420	16.1	17.2	14.7	17.3	18.5	13.7	15.5	12.7	10.3
All 7:00-11 p.m.	20.2	14,400	13.8	15.1	15.1	15.4	16.4	14.6	14.7	11.7	11.5

* Less than 1.0 rating

Average TV Viewing Time

Source: A.C. Nielsen estimates, Nov. 1976
(hours: minutes, per week)

		Total	Mon.-Sun. 7:30-11:00pm	Mon.-Sun. 4:30-7:30pm	Mon.-Fri. 7:00am-4:30pm	Sat.-Sun. 7:00am-4:30pm	Mon.-Sun. 11:00pm-7:00am
Total persons		**28:41**	**10:54**	**6:36**	**5:10**	**2:51**	**3:09**
Women	18-24	30:05	10:14	6:01	7:13	2:24	4:13
	25-54	32:14	12:34	6:07	7:06	2:15	4:11
	55+	35:23	12:44	8:08	8:51	2:07	3:32
Men	18-24	21:21	8:32	4:29	1:42	2:47	3:51
	25-54	26:38	11:27	5:36	2:08	2:56	4:32
	55+	32:40	12:25	8:10	5:14	3:16	3:36
Teens	Female	21:05	8:26	5:29	3:10	2:32	1:29
	Male	22:35	9:02	5:39	2:29	3:10	2:16
Children	2-5	29:05	6:59	8:09	8:26	4:57	0:35
	6-11	26:40	9:20	7:44	3:44	4:48	1:04

U.S. Television Sets and Stations

Set Ownership

(Nielsen est. as of Sept. 1976)

Total TV Homes	71,200,000	100%
(est. 9/1/77)	72,900,000	
Homes with:		
Color TV sets	54,870,000	77%
B&W only	16,330,000	23
2 or more sets	31,880,000	45
One set	39,320,000	55
CATV	10,230,000	14

Station Facilities

(FCC as of July, 1977)

Commercial TV		725
	VHF	514
	UHF	211
Educational TV		258
	VHF	101
	UHF	157
Total TV		983

Commercial Broadcast Stations on the Air

Source: Federal Communications Commission (1975)

	Total	AM	FM	TV
United States	**7,584**	**4,336**	**2,539**	**709**
Alabama	222	139	66	17
Alaska	28	17	4	7
Arizona	95	60	24	11
Arkansas	136	82	46	8
California	452	228	170	54
Colorado	113	67	35	11
Connecticut	63	38	20	5
Delaware	17	10	7	-
Dist. of Columbia	23	9	8	6
Florida	325	199	97	29
Georgia	267	173	77	17
Hawaii	40	25	5	10
Idaho	63	43	11	9
Illinois	267	124	121	22
Indiana	190	85	88	17
Iowa	146	74	59	13
Kansas	106	59	35	12
Kentucky	207	111	84	12
Louisiana	162	93	52	17
Maine	63	36	20	7
Maryland	89	49	33	7
Massachusetts	117	65	41	11
Michigan	245	126	98	21
Minnesota	157	90	55	12
Mississippi	168	103	55	10
Missouri	193	109	61	23
Montana	69	41	16	12
Nebraska	90	50	24	16
Nevada	34	19	9	6
New Hampshire	44	27	14	3
New Jersey	71	37	29	5
New Mexico	89	57	24	8
New York	301	161	111	29
North Carolina	304	205	81	18
North Dakota	46	26	8	12
Ohio	267	122	118	27
Oklahoma	120	67	44	9
Oregon	121	79	30	12
Pennsylvania	317	174	120	23
Rhode Island	25	15	8	2
South Carolina	166	105	49	12
South Dakota	56	31	15	10
Tennessee	239	153	69	17
Texas	489	287	146	56
Utah	51	33	15	3
Vermont	29	18	9	2
Virginia	214	133	66	15
Washington	151	94	42	15
West Virginia	99	61	29	9
Wisconsin	201	98	86	17
Wyoming	37	29	5	3
Other areas	**96**	**52**	**34**	**10**
Puerto Rico	85	48	30	7
Guam	3	1	1	1
Virgin Islands	8	3	3	2
Total	**7,680**	**4,388**	**2,573**	**719**

50 Leading U.S. Advertisers, 1976

Reprinted by permission of Advertising Age, Aug. 29, 1977
Copyright© Crain Communications Inc. (1977)

Rank	Company	Ad Costs (000)	Sales (000)	Ads as % sales
	Cars			
2	General Motors Corp.	$287,000	$47,181,000	0.6
7	Ford Motor Co.	162,000	28,839,661	0.5
19	Chrysler Corp.	110,000	15,537,800	0.7
48	Volkswagen of America	60,500	8,900,000	0.7
	Food			
3	General Foods Corp.	275,000	3,641,600	7.6
13	General Mills	131,600	2,909,404	4.5
20	McDonald's Corp.	105,000	3,063,000	3.4
25	Norton Simon Inc.	91,634	1,342,491	6.8
27	Nabisco Inc.	90,100	2,027,300	4.4
31	Ralston Purina Co.	87,780	3,393,800	2.6
33	Kraft Inc.	82,800	4,226,788	2.0
36	Beatrice Foods Co.	76,800	5,288,000	1.5
39	Pillsbury Co.	74,000	1,460,826	5.1
42	Campbell Soup Co.	69,000	1,634,762	4.2
44	Kellogg Co.	67,200	1,385,446	4.9
	Soaps, cleansers (and allied)			
1	Procter & Gamble Co.	445,000	5,300,000	8.4
12	Unilever	135,000	1,226,504	10.7
15	Colgate-Palmolive Co.	$118,000	$3,511,492	3.4
	Tobacco			
9	Philip Morris Inc.	149,000	4,293,782	3.5
11	R. J. Reynolds Industries Inc.	140,276	5,753,568	2.4
32	American Brands	87,000	4,125,800	2.1
34	B.A.T. Industries Ltd.	82,000	2,025,723	4.0
	Drugs and cosmetics			
5	Warner-Lambert Co.	199,000	1,300,000	15.3
6	Bristol-Myers Co.	189,000	1,986,370	9.5
8	American Home Products Corp.	158,000	1,800,000	8.8
16	Richardson-Merrell	115,507	745,877	15.5
24	Gillette Co.	94,000	1,491,506	6.3
41	Sterling Drug Inc.	70,000	638,938	11.0
43	Johnson & Johnson	68,900	1,493,172	4.6
47	Revlon Inc.	61,000	600,000	10.2
49	Chesebrough-Pond's Inc.	60,000	746,986	8.0
50	Schering-Plough Corp.	60,000	871,537	6.9

Rank	Company	Ad Costs (000)	Sales (000)	Ads as % sales
	Liquor			
14	Heublein Inc.	129,143	1,550,902	8.3
45	Seagram Co. Ltd.	66,000	2,048,970	3.2
	Oil			
10	Mobil Corp	146,500	28,046,467	0.5
	Soft drinks			
23	PepsiCo Inc.	95,000	2,727,455	3.5
26	Coca-Cola Co.	91,335	1,698,000	5.3
	Appliances, tv, radio			
21	RCA Corp	100,000	5,363,600	1.9
28	General Electric Co.	90,000	15,697,000	0.6
	Retail chains			
4	Sears, Roebuck & Co.†	245,000	12,535,000	2.0
35	J. C. Penney Co.	81,600	8,353,800	1.0
	Chemicals			
22	American Cyanamid Co.	95,880	732,835	13.0
	Photographic equipment			
37	Eastman Kodak Co.	74,332	4,000,000*	1.9
	Telephone service, equipment			
18	American Telephone & Telegraph Co.	112,763	32,815,000	0.3
30	International Telephone & Telegraph Co.	87,842	11,764,106	0.7
	Miscellaneous			
17	U.S. Government	112,996	—	—
29	Gulf & Western Industries	90,000	3,508,430	2.6
38	Goodyear Tire & Rubber Co.	74,000	5,791,500	1.3
40	CBS Inc.	73,251	1,904,654	3.8
46	Loews Corp.	64,275	2,901,454	2.2

†Percentage shown would be two and a half times more if Sears $285,000,000 in local advertising were added to the $225,000,000 national total. The other retail chain (J. C. Penney) ad total also does not include local advertising.
Note: All add totals are domestic. Whenever possible, AA has reported the company's domestic sales figure in this table, although for some companies only a worldwide sales total was available.

Estimated Advertising Expenditures in the U.S.

Source: Advertising Age; prepared by Robert J. Coen of McCann-Erickson, Inc.

Medium	1974 Dollars (millions)	1974 Per cent of total	1975 Dollars (millions)	1975 Per cent of total	1976 Dollars (millions)	1976 Per cent of total	% change '76 vs. '75
Newspapers							
Total	8,001	29.8	$ 8,442	29.9	$ 9,910	29.6	+17.4
National	1,194	4.5	1,221	4.3	1,502	4.5	+23.0
Local	6,807	25.4	7,221	25.6	8,408	25.1	+16.4
Magazines							
Total	1,504	5.6	1,465	5.2	1,789	5.3	+22.1
Weeklies	630	2.3	612	2.2	748	2.2	+22.2
Women's	372	1.4	368	1.3	457	1.4	+24.0
Monthlies	502	1.9	485	1.7	584	1.7	+20.4
Farm publications	72	0.3	74	0.3	86	0.3	+16.0
Television							
Total	4,851	18.1	5,263	18.6	6,622	19.8	+25.8
Network	2,145	8.0	2,306	8.2	2,857	8.5	+23.9
Spot	1,495	5.6	1,623	5.7	2,125	6.4	+31.0
Local	1,211	4.5	1,334	4.7	1,640	4.9	+23.0
Radio							
Total	1,837	6.9	1,980	7.0	2,277	6.8	+15.0
Network	69	0.3	83	0.3	104	0.3	+25.0
Spot	405	1.5	436	1.5	493	1.5	+13.0
Local	1,363	5.1	1,461	5.2	1,680	5.0	+15.0
Direct mail	3,986	14.9	4,181	14.8	4,754	14.2	+13.7
Business publications	900	3.4	919	3.3	1,035	3.1	+12.6
Outdoor							
Total	309	1.2	335	1.2	383	1.2	+14.2
National	203	0.8	220	0.8	252	0.8	+14.5
Local	106	0.4	115	0.4	131	0.4	+14.0
Miscellaneous							
Total	5,270	19.7	5,571	19.7	6,604	19.7	+18.5
National	2,752	10.3	2,882	10.2	3,453	10.3	+19.8
Local	2,518	9.4	2,689	9.5	3,151	9.4	+17.2
Total							
National	14,725	55.1	15,410	54.6	18,450	55.1	+19.7
Local	12,005	44.9	12,820	45.4	15,010	44.9	+17.1
Grand total	26,730	100.0	28,230	100.0	33,460	100.0	+18.5

Television Network Addresses

American Broadcasting Company (ABC)
1330 Avenue of Americas
New York, NY 10019

Canadian Broadcasting Corp. (CBC)
1500 Bronson Ave.
Ottawa, Ontario, Canada K1G 3J5

Columbia Broadcasting System (CBS)
51 W 52nd St.
New York, NY 10019

Metromedia
277 Park Ave.
New York, NY 10017

National Broadcasting Company (NBC)
30 Rockefeller Plaza
New York, N Y 10020

Public Broadcasting Service (PBS)
15 W. 51st St.
New York, NY 10020

Westinghouse Broadcasting (Group W)
90 Park Ave.
New York, NY 10016

Global Communication

Source: UNESCO; data for 1971-72

Nation	No. of daily newspapers	Copies per 1,000 pop.	No. of radio trans-mitters	Radios per 1,000 pop.	No. of TV trans-mitters[1]	TV sets per 1,000 pop.	No. of film theaters	Theater seats per 1,000 pop.	Avg. visits per year pop.
Algeria	4	18	25	46	13	10	640	14	6
Argentina	180	180	147	424	59	191	1,637	31	2
Australia	58	321	212	220	199	234	1,100	64	3
Austria	31	328	366	287	322	226	835	37	4
Bahrain	3[2]	29	3	341	0	59	9	45	6
Bangladesh	25	N/A	16	N/A	1	N/A	(est 100)	N/A	N/A
Belgium	55	N/A	29	366	17	235	740	41	3
Bolivia	16	33	133	260	1	2	120	13	0.6
Brazil	261	35	994	58	50	66	3,194	19	2
Bulgaria	13	206	26	268	118	150	3,106	82	13
Canada	121	234	729	821	534	334	1,156	30	4
Chile	46	N/A	229	156	25	56	360	27	5
China (P.R.)	N/A	N/A	N/A	19	(est. 20)[4]	0.7	N/A	N/A	N/A
Colombia	36	105	131	130	18	53	378	13	3
Cuba	16	107	110	154	19	66	428	N/A	N/A
Czechoslovakia	27	280	119	266	680	228	3,469	68	7
Denmark	53	364	31	329	25	284	350	28	4
Ecuador	22	43	336	261	14	23	164	18	3
Egypt	14	20	43	144	28	15	246	6	2
Ethiopia	3	2	9	20	6	1	30	1	0.4
Finland	60	425	97	409	70	255	318	21	2
France	106	233	294	312	1,961	244	4,237	39	3
Germany, E.	40	425	106	355	455	283	1,197	21	5
Germany, W.	1,093	330	313	340	958	455	3,171	21	2
Ghana	3	30	23	85	4	2	13	2	0.1
Greece	104	N/A	50	313	17	58	1,034	N/A	15
Guinea	1	1	5	21	—	(no TV)	28	2	N/A
Hungary	27	216	29	244	12	193	3,755	57	7
Iceland	5	439	29	303	59	206	25	44	7
India	821	N/A	137	21	2	0.1	4,716	5	6
Indonesia	120	10	140	114	12	2	490	N/A	N/A
Iran	39	25	38	130	70	33	437	9	0.9
Iraq	7	N/A	21	169	5	25	24	N/A	0.8
Ireland	7	233	12	209	20	168	N/A	N/A	7
Israel	24	183	47	220	21	119	252	59	11
Italy	78	142	1,874	230	1,193	201	10,719	N/A	10
Jamaica	2	69	14	408	11	55	42	21	3
Japan	172	529	889	441	4,991	229	2,673	12	2
Kenya	3	10	18	64	4	2	32	2	0.6
Korea, S.	42	138	123	128	39	28	793	15	4
Kuwait	6	44	14	439	7	165	7	13	4
Lebanon	52	N/A	6	210	8	113	170	30	17
Liberia	1	5	16	255	3	4	8	N/A	0.5
Libya	7	17	12	41	2	0.5	28	9	2
Malaysia	40	77	61	162	18	24	550	31	7
Mexico	200	N/A	590	266	78	57	1,765	28	5
Morocco	6	N/A	35	95	14	14	260	9	1
Netherlands	95	307	34	303	16	245	321	14	2
New Zealand	40	367	58	704	7	249	239	49	N/A
Nigeria	11	N/A	37	23	7	1	183	0.7	1
Norway	79	391	248	313	525	227	450	37	5
Pakistan	98	N/A	22	18	7	2	578	5	0.3
Panama	7	86	114	329	13	82	23	19	3
Paraguay	4	30	37	71	1	20	61+	N/A	N/A
Peru	56	N/A	304	138	19	28	276	N/A	N/A
Philippines	19	17	327	42	15	11	951	N/A	N/A
Poland	44	231	51	177	52	159	2,465	18	3
Portugal	33	N/A	95	146	23	40	485	28	3
Rhodesia	4	15	22	38	3	20	90	9	N/A
Romania	57	173	52	152	111	83	6,244	N/A	9
Saudi Arabia	5	7	11	31	6	19	(no public movies)		
Senegal	1	5	12	67	1	0.4	87	13	1
Singapore	10	193	16	130	2	95	75	29	17
S. Africa	21	47	177	102	N/A	N/A	685	22	N/A
Spain	115	99	463	205	641	169	6,064	129	8
Sri Lanka	17	48	29	66	—	(no TV)	303	10	8
Sweden	108	515	292	367	299	333	1,334	N/A	3
Switzerland	98	390	200	310	446	243	554	32	5
Syria	5	9	11	375	7	22	70	N/A	N/A
Tanzania	7	4	9	11	—	—	36	1	0.4
Thailand	35	24	144	85	30	10	392	12	N/A
Tunisia	4	21	6	49	11	16	104	9	2
Turkey	432	N/A	19	132	7	5	700	N/A	N/A
USSR	639	333	3,034	430	1,466	185	147,200	N/A	19
UK	109	437	396	699	314	299	1,482	25	3
U.S.	1,761	314	6,719	1,695	3,695	472	14,300	48	5
Uruguay	29	269	99	507	17	101	180	42	N/A
Venezuela	42	91	235	182	37	89	429	49	3
Vietnam, S.[5]	56	5	22	319	4	26	143	5	1
Yugoslavia	25	89	463	241	348	120	1,393	23	4
Zaire	6	N/A	27	0.9	2	0.3	57	0.8	0.05
Zambia	2	13	20	55	3	4	29	3	N/A

(1) No. of TV transmitters indicates breadth of coverage; mountainous countries require more transmitters, (2) Bahrain, non dailies, (3) Bolivia, date 1963, 64, 68, (4) Originating stations, (5) Vietnam, S., pre-PRG, N/A-not available.

Movies of the Year (Sept. 1, 1976 to Sept. 1, 1977)

Listed below, alphabetically, are some of the major films rated by the New York Daily News star system: ★★★★ is for excellent, ★★★1/2 very good, ★★★ good, ★★1/2 fair, ★★ mediocre, ★1/2 poor, ★ very poor, 0★ not worth rating.

Kathleen Carroll, N. Y. Daily News Movie Editor and Critic

Movie	Star rating	Stars	Director
Airport '77	★★	Jack Lemmon, Lee Grant	Jerry Jameson
Annie Hall	★★★1/2	Diane Keaton, Woody Allen	Woody Allen
Audrey Rose	★★1/2	Marsha Mason, Anthony Hopkins	Robert Wise
Bad News Bears in Breaking Training	★★1/2	William Devane, Clifton James	Michael Pressman
Black and White in Color	★★★1/2	Jean Carmet, Jacques Spiesser	Jean-Jacques Annaud
Black Sunday	★★★	Bruce Dern, Robert Shaw	John Frankenheimer
Bridge Too Far, A	★★1/2	Robert Redford, Sean Connery	Richard Attenborough
Bound For Glory	★★★	David Carradine, Randy Quaid	Hal Ashby
Bugsy Malone	★★★	Jodie Foster, Scott Baio	Alan Parker
Carrie	★★★	Sissy Spacek, Piper Laurie	Brian De Palma
Car Wash	★★1/2	Ivan Dixon, Richard Pryor	Michael Schultz
Casanova	★★★	Donald Sutherland	Federico Fellini
Cassandra Crossing, The	★★1/2	Burt Lancaster, Sophia Loren	George Pan Cosmatos
Cross of Iron	★★1/2	James Coburn, Max. Schell	Sam Peckinpah
Deep, The	★★★1/2	Robert Shaw, Jacqueline Bisset	Peter Yeats
Domino Principle, The	★★	Gene Hackman, Candice Bergen	Stanley Kramer
Eagle Has Landed, The	★★1/2	Michael Caine, Donald Sutherland	John Sturges
Exorcist II: The Heretic	★	Linda Blair, Richard Burton	John Boorman
Freaky Friday	★★★	Barbara Harris, Jodie Foster	Gary Nelson
Front, The	★★★	Woody Allen, Zero Mostel	Martin Ritt
Fun With Dick and Jane	★★	George Segal, Jane Fonda	Ted Kotchoff
Greased Lightning	★★1/2	Richard Pryor, Beau Bridges	Michael Schultz
Greatest, The	★★★	Muhammed Ali, John Marley	Tom Gries
Harlan County, U.S.A.	★★★1/2	Documentary	Barbara Kopple
I Never Promised You A Rose Garden	★★★1/2	Kathleen Quinlan, Bibi Andersson	Anthony Page
In the Realm of the Senses	★★	Eiko Matsuda, Tatsuya Fuji	Nagisa Oshima
Island of Dr. Moreau, The	★★1/2	Burt Lancaster, Michael York	Don Taylor
Islands in the Stream	★★★	George C. Scott, David Hemmings	F. J. Schaffner
Jabberwocky	★★1/2	Michael Pallin	Terry Gilliam
Jacob The Liar	★★★	Vlastimil Brodsky	Frank Beyer
Jonah Who Will Be 25 in the Year 2000	★★★1/2	Jean-Luc Bideau, Miou-Miou	Alain Tanner
King Kong	★★★1/2	Jeff Bridges, Jessica Lange	John Guillerman
Last Remake of Beau Geste, The	★★1/2	Marty Feldman, Ann-Margret	Marty Feldman
Last Tycoon, The	★★1/2	Robert De Niro, Ingrid Boulting	Elia Kazan
Late Show, The	★★★	Lily Tomlin, Art Carney	Robert Benton
Lumiere	★★1/2	Jeanne Moreau, Francine Racette	Jeanne Moreau
MacArthur	★★1/2	Gregory Peck, Ed Flanders	Joseph Sargent
Man on the Roof	★★★	Carl-Gustaf Lindstedt	Bo Widerberg
Marathon Man	★★★1/2	Dustin Hoffman, Lawrence Olivier	John Schlesinger
Marquise of O . . ., The	★★★1/2	Edith Clever, Bruno Ganz	Eric Rohmer
Matter of Time, A	★	Liza Minnelli, Ingrid Bergman	Vincent Minnelli
Memory of Justice, The	★★1/2	Documentary	Marcel Ophuls
Mikey & Nicky	★★★	Peter Falk, John Cassavetes	Elaine May
Mr. Billion	★★1/2	Valerie Perrine, Jackie Gleason	Jonathan Kaplan
Mohammad	★★1/2	Anthony Quinn, Irene Pappas	Moustapha Akkad
Nasty Habits	★★1/2	Glenda Jackson, Sandy Dennis	Michael Lindsay-Hogg
Network	★★★★	Faye Dunaway, William Holden	Sidney Lumet
New York, New York	★★★★	Robert De Niro, Liza Minnelli	Martin Scorsese
Nickelodeon	★★★1/2	Burt Reynolds, Ryan O'Neal	Peter Bogdanovich
One on One	★★★1/2	Robby Benson, Annette O'Toole	Lamont Johnson
Orca	★★1/2	Richard Harris, Charlotte Rampling	Michael Anderson
Other Side of Midnight, The	★★1/2	Marie-France Pisier, John Beck	Charles Jarrott
Outrageous!	★★★1/2	Craig Russel, Hollis McLaren	Richard Benner
Pink Panther Strikes Again, The	★★★	Peter Sellers, Herbert Lom	Blake Edwards
Providence	★★★1/2	John Gielgud, Dirk Bogarde	Alain Renais
Pumping Iron	★★★	Arnold Schwarzenegger	G. Butler, R. Fiore
Rescuers, The	★★★1/2	Animated	Wolfgang Reitherman
Rocky	★★★★	Sylvester Stallone, Talia Shire	John G. Avildsen
Rollercoaster	★★★	George Segal, Richard Widmark	James Goldstone
Sensual Man, The	★★1/2	Giancarlo Giannini, Rosanna Podesta	Mario Vicario
Seven-Per-Cent Solution, The	★★	Alan Arkin, Nicol Williamson	Herbert Ross
Shout at the Devil	★★1/2	Lee Marvin, Roger Moore	Peter Hunt
Silver Streak	★★	Gene Wilder, Richard Pryor	Arthur Hiller
Slap Shot	★★1/2	Paul Newman, Lindsay Crouse	George Roy Hill
Small Change	★★★★	George Desmouceaux	Francois Truffaut
Smokey and the Bandit	★★1/2	Burt Reynolds, Jackie Gleason	Hal Needham
Sorcerer	★★1/2	Roy Scheider, Amidou	William Friedkin
Spy Who Loved Me, The	★★★	Roger Moore, Barbara Bach	Lewis Gilbert
Star Is Born, A	★★1/2	Barbra Streisand, Kris Kristofferson	Frank Pierson
Star Wars	★★★1/2	Mark Hamill, Carrie Fisher	George Lucas
3 Women	★★★1/2	Shelley Duval, Sissy Spacek	Robert Altman
Twilight's Last Gleaming	★1/2	Burt Lancaster, Charles Durning	Robert Aldrich
Two-Minute Warning	★★1/2	Charlton Heston, John Cassavetes	Larry Peerce
Voyage of the Damned	★★★	Faye Dunaway, Lee Grant	Stuart Rosenberg
Welcome To L.A.	★★1/2	Keith Carradine, Sally Kellerman	Alan Rudolph

Selected U.S. Daily Newspapers' Circulation

Source: Audit Bureau of Circulations' FAS-FAX Report. Average paid circulation for 6 months to Mar. 31, 1977. †3 months. For the 6 months up to Sept. 30, 1976, 1,764 English language dailies in the U.S. (337 morning, 1,409 evening, 18 all day) had an average audited circulation of 61,183,649. Sunday papers included 647 with audited average circulation of 51,538,584. (m) morning; (e) evening; *Mon.-Fri. average. Includes all ABC newspapers with daily circulation over 100,000.

Newspaper	Daily	Sunday
Albany, N.Y. Times-Union (m)	78,250	136,669
Albany, N.Y. Knickerbocker News	61,293	
Akron Beacon Journal (e)	171,305	222,461
Allentown Call (m)	*102,244	155,299
Atlanta Constitution (m)	211,405	
Atlanta Journal (e)	222,814	535,587
Baltimore News-American (e)	*173,891	255,998
Baltimore Sun (m&e)	*349,318	361,380
Bergen Co. (N.J.) Record (e)	†155,039	†203,024
Birmingham News (e)	*186,706	225,385
Birmingham Post-Herald (m)	*70,967	
Boston Globe (m&e)	459,568	630,061
Boston Herald American (m) & Sunday Advertiser	*293,004	421,684
Buffalo Courier-Express (m)	125,082	273,909
Buffalo News (e)	*280,320	298,748
Camden (N.J.) Courier-Post (e)	†127,747	
Charlotte News (e)	56,677	
Charlotte Observer (m)	170,005	233,775
Chicago News (e)	*351,061	
Chicago Sun-Times (m)	*574,587	694,227
Chicago Tribune (m&e)	*757,117	1,155,572
Christian Science Monitor (m)	*170,087	
Cincinnati Enquirer (m)	191,773	291,600
Cincinnati Post (e)	203,103	
Cleveland Plain Dealer (m)	381,082	457,963
Cleveland Press (e)	322,731	
Columbia, S.C. State (m)	103,876	121,471
Columbia, S.C. Record (e)	33,315	
Columbus, Ga. Enquirer (m)	*34,524	68,088
Columbus, Ga. Ledger (e)	*31,991	
Columbus, O. Citizen-Journal (m)	106,355	
Columbus, O. Dispatch (e)	198,750	330,631
Dallas News (m)	272,138	339,232
Dallas Times Herald (e)	*235,237	266,543
Dayton Journal-Herald (m)	100,678	
Dayton News (e)	148,885	220,024
Denver Post (e)	*251,511	339,588
Denver: Rocky Mountain News (m)	246,413	266,414
Des Moines Register (m)	228,360	428,212
Des Moines Tribune (e)	92,039	
Detroit Free Press (m)	*620,153	716,325
Detroit News (e)	*643,792	826,304
Flint Journal (e)	106,322	106,658
Fort Lauderdale News (e)	*109,096	161,187
Ft. Worth Star-Telegram (m&e)	222,338	220,151
Fresno Bee (m)	†121,365	139,063
Grand Rapids Press (e)	125,625	137,643
Hartford Courant (m)	205,546	273,689
Honolulu Advertiser (m)	79,652	
Honolulu Star-Bulletin (e)	120,354	195,388
Houston Chronicle (e) (9/30/76)	*308,096	381,843
Houston Post (m) (3/31/76)	*292,008	353,537
Indianapolis News (e)	†155,492	
Indianapolis Star (m)	†219,632	355,216
Jacksonville Journal (e)	53,326	
Jacksonville: Fla. Times Union (m)	148,163	183,504
Kansas City Star (e)	306,403	406,481
Kansas City Times (m)	332,045	
Knoxville News-Sentinel (e)	106,537	161,513
Little Rock: Ark. Democrat (e)	*61,317	113,514
Little Rock: Ark. Gazette (m)	*126,901	151,535
Long Beach Independent (m)	*62,254	137,509
Long Beach Press-Telegram (e)	*82,827	
Long Island, N.Y. Press (e) (9/30/76)	†265,589	254,379
Long Island, N.Y. Newsday (e)	468,407	452,333
Los Angeles Herald-Examiner (e)	*338,372	336,462
Los Angeles Times (m)	*1,018,563	1,300,260
Louisville Courier-Journal (m)	210,528	351,760
Louisville Times (e)	164,855	
Memphis Commercial Appeal (m)	204,733	283,221
Memphis Press Scimitar (e)	108,437	
Miami Herald (m)	435,424	534,853
Miami News (e)	77,663	
Milwaukee Journal (e)	342,253	532,661
Milwaukee Sentinel (m)	164,617	
Minneapolis Star (e)	246,233	
Minneapolis Tribune (m)	227,336	610,408
Nashville Banner (e)	82,208	
Nashville Tennessean (m)	128,714	217,900
Newark Star-Ledger (m)	*†408,000	588,722
New Haven Register (e)	*101,514	134,586
New Haven Journal-Courier (m)	*29,021	
New Orleans Times-Picayune (m)	†213,024	+318,647
New Orleans States-Item (e)	†*116,264	
New York News (m)	*1,911,565	2,752,739
New York Post (e)	*503,369	
New York Times (m)	*866,904	1,479,862
Norfolk Ledger-Star (e)	†94,479	
Norfolk Virginia-Pilot (m)	+124,709	†190,186
Oakland Tribune (e)	*166,896	196,608
Oklahoma City Oklahoman (m)	*173,775	293,180
Oklahoma City Times (e)	*89,309	
Omaha World-Herald (m&e)	*236,830	282,066
Orange Co. (Cal.) Register (m&e)	*205,199	233,914
Orlando Sentinel-Star (m&e)	*190,315	214,178
Palm Beach Post (m)	*78,177	116,943
Palm Beach Times (e)	*30,495	
Peoria Journal Star (m&e)	105,999	121,674
Philadelphia Bulletin (e)	*556,371	655,520
Philadelphia Inquirer (m)	*411,938	861,600
Philadelphia News (e)	*231,886	
Phoenix Republic (m)	†239,948	†358,249
Phoenix Gazette (e)	†112,384	
Pittsburgh Post Gazette (m)	*190,370	
Pittsburgh Press (e)	*266,537	681,536
Portland, Me. Press-Herald (m)	51,870	
Portland, Me. Express (e) & Maine Sunday Telegram	29,923	110,330
Portland Oregonian (m)	234,266	406,694
Portland: Oregon Journal (e)	*107,818	
Providence Bulletin (e)	*143,468	
Providence Journal (m)	*65,559	212,983
Raleigh News & Observer (m)	†128,147	159,798
Raleigh Times (e)	†32,646	
Richmond News Leader (e)	114,976	
Richmond Times Dispatch (m)	135,965	209,213
Rochester Democrat-Chronicle (m)	127,481	227,294
Rochester Times-Union (e)	130,214	
Sacramento Bee (e)	*178,792	206,956
Sacramento Union (m)	*93,104	92,724
St. Louis Globe-Democrat (m)	*270,073	275,070
St. Louis Post-Dispatch (e)	*261,573	462,372
St. Paul Dispatch (e)	119,410	
St. Paul Pioneer Press (m)	104,053	242,172
St. Petersburg Independent (e)	38,369	
St. Petersburg Times (m)	211,825	264,813
Salt Lake City Tribune (m)	107,042	177,318
Salt Lake City Deseret News (e)	75,485	
San Antonio Express (m)	*80,775	165,898
San Antonio News (e)	*76,050	
San Antonio Light (e)	*126,405	179,365
San Diego Union (m)	†190,732	+311,309
San Diego Tribune (e)	†128,957	
San Francisco Examiner (e)	*155,108	
San Francisco Chronicle (m)	*470,003	664,251
San Jose Mercury (m)	*140,265	240,945
San Jose News (e)	*68,013	
Seattle Post-Intelligencer (m)	*185,669	247,530
Seattle Times (e)	*237,454	327,490
South Bend Tribune (e)	111,399	125,592
Spokane Chronicle (e)	63,653	
Spokane Spokesman-Review (m)	72,728	123,435
Springfield, Ill. State Journal (m&e)	71,856	72,571
Springfield, Mass. Union (m)	74,782	
Springfield, Mass. News (e) & Sunday Republican	79,761	144,673
Syracuse Herald-Journal (e)	122,711	240,983
Syracuse Post-Standard (m)	*84,955	
Tacoma Tribune (e)	100,321	104,215
Toledo Blade (e)	170,681	208,487
Tulsa Tribune (e)	†78,397	
Tulsa World (m)	†119,223	+202,820
Wall St. Journal (m) (total)	*1,484,667	
Washington, D.C. Post (m)	*555,030	766,241
Washington, D.C. Star (e)	*375,383	374,251
Wichita Eagle (m)	121,578	174,944
Wichita Beacon (e)	45,678	
Winston-Salem Journal (m)	71,554	96,256
Winston-Salem Sentinel (e)	40,840	
Youngstown Vindicator (e)	†100,324	†156,657

Circulation of Leading U.S. Magazines

Source: Audit Bureau of Circulations' FAS-FAX Report

General magazines, exclusive of groups and comics. Based on total average paid circulation during the 6 months prior to June 30, 1977. *Indicates circulation for the 6 months prior to Dec. 31, 1976.

TV Guide	19,811,268
Reader's Digest	18,512,453
Natl. Geographic	9,601,727
Woman's Day	*8,582,538
Family Circle	8,328,930
Better Homes & Gar.	8,031,981
McCall's	6,502,027
Ladies' Home Jour.	6,037,616
Good Housekeeping	5,081,173
National Enquirer	5,017,569
Playboy	4,919,977
Redbook	4,687,020
Penthouse	4,604,357
Time	4,364,016
Newsweek	2,991,032
Sr. Scholastic	*2,877,621
American Legion	2,629,169
Cosmopolitan	2,501,983
American Home	2,387,598
Sports Illustrated	2,263,259
People	2,137,872
U.S. News-World Rpt.	2,073,026
Field & Stream	2,001,517
Hustler	*1,964,602
Star	1,903,488
Glamour	1,814,702
Popular Science	1,813,230
Workbasket	1,779,253
Outdoor Life	1,775,407
Today's Education	1,686,580
V.F.W. Magazine	1,663,940
Popular Mechanics	1,653,870
Mechanix Illustrated	1,645,518
Boy's Life	1,621,443
Elks Magazine	1,606,335
Smithsonian	1,575,536
True Story	1,554,156
Parent's Magazine	1,505,241
Seventeen	1,467,322
Midnight	1,461,663
Petersen's Hunting	1,438,500
Southern Living	1,381,033
Sunset	1,357,413
Sport	1,340,541
Ebony	1,280,312
Grit	1,258,825
Nation's Business	1,123,469
Scouting	1,059,948
Oui	1,037,472
House & Garden	1,012,543
Jr. Scholastic	*1,012,087
Esquire	1,004,590
'Teen	939,499
Family Health	919,862
Vogue	909,863
Photoplay	891,852
Sports Afield	890,346
Co-ed	*889,406
Golf Digest	887,642
Mademoiselle	850,019
Moneysworth	849,783
Apartment Life	826,593
Hot Rod	823,708
House Beautiful	801,121
Popular Photo'y	786,457
Business Week	768,187
Playgirl	753,898
Club	752,122
Weight Watchers	745,817
TV Mirror	734,281
Car & Driver	730,741
Money	727,372
1001 Decorat. Ideas	726,323
Decorating & Craft	719,713
Motor Trend	714,642
Gallery	703,100
New Woman	670,442
Forbes	668,406
Scientific American	665,285
Simplicity Home Catalogue	663,193
Gourmet	661,184
Lion Magazine	659,256
Golf	652,110
Signature	651,796
Book Digest	632,479
Family Handyman	631,638
National Lampoon	629,016
Fortune	627,548
Flower & Garden	621,113
Penthouse Forum	618,821
Sphere	616,112
Jet	609,612
American Girl	601,377
Carte Blanche	570,007
Modern Photo'y	553,166
Lutheran	553,082
Essence	550,385
Harper's Bazaar	533,490
Catholic Digest	*526,452
Bon Appetit	516,721
Saturday Review	511,393
Road & Track	509,545
Rolling Stone	501,401
Ms. Magazine	500,374
New Yorker	492,568
Modern Romances	486,153
Workbench	479,876
Sat'day Evening Post	470,166
Modern Screen	465,373
Stereo Review	458,078
Westways	452,304
Rotarian	451,694

Sunday Magazines Weekly Circulation

Family Weekly (328 papers)	11,250,000
Parade (115 papers)	19,781,944

Selected Canadian Daily Newspaper Circulation

Source: Audit Bureau of Circulations' FAS-FAX Report of average paid circulation for 6 months ending Mar. 31, 1977. (†) Indicates 3 month circulation average.

For the 6 months up to Sept. 30, 1976, 118 daily newspapers in Canada (23 morning; 94 evening, 1 all day) had an average audited circulation of 4,857,430; 10 Sunday newspapers had an average circulation of 973,135.

(m) Morning; (e) Evening; *Based on Monday to Friday average; **Sunday.

Newspaper	Daily	Saturday
Calgary Albertan (m)	38,988	....
Calgary Herald (e)	124,120	....
Edmonton Journal (e)	179,192	....
Halifax Chronicle-Herald (m)	69,356	....
Halifax Mail-Star (e)	53,083	....
Hamilton Spectator (e)	†139,318	....
Kingston Whig-Standard (e)	†34,964	....
Kitchener-Waterloo Record (e)	†66,231	....
London Free Press (m & e)	127,248	131,670
Montreal Gazette (m)	*111,540	118,865
Montreal: La Presse (e)	*180,972	281,793
Montreal: Le Devoir (m)	*41,017	37,273
Montreal: Le Journal de Montreal (m)	*171,269	**166,208
Montreal-Matin (m)	*140,916	**116,541
Montreal Star (e)	*166,076	230,932
Ottawa Citizen (e)	*107,251	130,839
Ottawa Journal (e)	*73,173	87,075
Ottawa: Le Droit (e)	*45,834	49,646
Quebec: Le Journal de Quebec (m)	*53,666	48,689
Quebec: Le Soleil (e)	*142,899	148,561
Regina Leader Post (e)	66,251	....
St. Catharines Standard (e)	†41,686	....
St. John's Telegram (e)	*33,175	49,810
Saint John Telegraph-Journal (m)	*32,003	64,877
Saint John Times Globe (e)	*29,625	....
Saskatoon Star-Phoenix (e)	50,512	....
Sherbrooke: La Tribune (e)	*38,237	39,804
Sudbury Star (e)	33,489	....
Sydney: Cape Breton Post (e)	29,704	....
Toronto Globe and Mail (m)	*262,310	268,448
Toronto Star (e)	*495,539	785,722
Toronto Sun (m)	*134,818	**275,625
Trois Rivieres Nouvelliste (e)	*49,504	49,733
Vancouver Province (m)	128,365	....
Vancouver Sun (e)	236,433	....
Victoria Colonist (m)'	39,014	**44,403
Victoria Times (e)	29,874	....
Windsor Star (e)	86,992	....
Winnipeg Free Press (e)	140,057	....
Winnipeg Tribune (e)	95,306	....

(1) Excludes Monday

Circulation of Leading Canadian Magazines

Source: Audit Bureau of Circulations' FAS-FAX Report.

General magazines, exclusive of groups and comics. Statistics based on average paid circulation during the 6 months prior to June 30, 1977. *Indicates average circulation for the 6 months prior to Dec. 31, 1976.

Magazine	Circulation
Reader's Digest (English-French)	1,566,030
Chatelaine (English-French)	1,260,164
Reader's Digest (English)	1,255,580
T.V. Guide (English-French)	1,043,688
Chatelaine (English)	1,003,125
MacLean's Magazine	675,849
Legion Magazine	*450,982
Selection du Reader's Digest	310,450
Time Canada	300,654
T.V. Hebdo	293,724
Chatelaine (French)	259,109
L'Actualite	242,010
Miss Chatelaine	173,787
Canadian Motorist	146,350

Off-Beat News Stories of 1977

There was good news and bad news for a group of San Franciscans trying to end California's prolonged drought. They went to nearby Mount Tamalpais to stage a rain dance. First, the good news: One minute after the music and dancing started, it began raining. The bad news: It rained so hard the dance was called off.

The weather (mostly bad) made other odd news items in 1977. In Buffalo, N.Y., hard hit by blizzard after blizzard, it proved too much for the chief meteorologist of the National Weather Service office when the accumulated white stuff in the streets reached 160 inches. James E. Smith, 56, announced his retirement. And that was only Feb. 8; there was more, much more, to come.

A big snowfall proved to be a windfall for Martha Paquette of South Hadley, Mass. Cartelli Pontiac Co. tried to drum up business during the storm by offering $1 off on used cars for each snowball brought in. Mrs. Paquette, her husband, 3 children, and friends spent 4 hours making snowballs, then packed them into the family car and surprised Mr. Cartelli. She picked out a 1969 Catalina priced at $1,895 and produced 1,834 snowballs, adding a check for the $61 difference. She said she just wasn't up to making any more snowballs.

In a dream come true, Buffalo's Stanley Glowacki had a snowball fight with a friend on the 4th of July, something he'd "always wanted to do." He'd stored enough of the stuff 5 months earlier, during one of those blizzards.

Doctors in the News

What with controversies over malpractice insurance, the medical profession was much in the news. Dr. John Sullivan of Vero Beach, Fla., was sued by a patient; his insurance company wanted to settle; the doctor insisted he hadn't been negligent and refused to settle; the insurance company canceled his insurance. Whereupon, Dr. Sullivan sued the patient and his lawyer, charging malicious legal prosecution. The jury awarded the physician $175,000 in what the judge termed a totally unprecedented case.

Dr. Lydia Emery, 67, who has been charging patients $1 for an office visit and $2 for a house call for the past 31 years, was honored when most of her town of Yoncalla, Ore., turned out at a party for her and her husband, Clifford, who always drives her to house calls. The folks heard what they wanted to hear: Dr. Emery announced she had no plans either to retire or change her fees.

A fictional physician saved a baby's life in London, thanks to a nurse who had been reading an old Agatha Christie whodunit. The baby was dying, despite intensive care, and doctors didn't know why. Nurse Marsha Maitland suggested the symptoms resembled those of a person poisoned by thallium in "The Pale Horse." The doctors tested the baby for traces of the rare metal, found it, applied the right treatment, and cured her.

One or two bottles of beer a day, a doctor reported in a study of 6,000 Japanese Hawaiians, may help prevent heart attacks. The 12-year study, he said, showed 50% fewer of those who knocked off a few beers daily had coronaries. Coffee in moderation brought no increase in the heart attack rate, he added. Reporting all this in the staid New England Journal of Medicine, the doctor quipped, "I'll drink to that!"

Words about Birds

Capistrano has its swallows, Holland has its storks, and Hinkley, Oh., has its buzzards. Hinkley celebrated with its annual Buzzard Sunday festival Mar. 20. A sleet storm cut the usual crowd of buzzard-watchers from the normal 30,000 to 2,000, but it did not deter the big black birds with red faces. The Chamber of Commerce reported folks came from hundreds of miles to watch — and to buy local arts and crafts products including chocolate buzzards, buzzard cookies, and buzzard etchings.

A small green-and-blue parakeet named Fred was credited with giving its life to save its mistress harm. When Irene Ortiz came home to her South Bronx apartment she found the door locked from the inside and heard Fred "screaming his head off." She ran for help. Police caught 2 teen-agers ransacking the apartment. But on the kitchen floor they found Fred dead, in a heap of feathers. Employees of the nearby Aqualand Pet Shop gave Mrs. Ortiz a new parakeet. "It was from our heart," said Diane Pizzaro.

Another bird, an unwitting stool pigeon, helped police in Herretshofen, West Germany. The town postman delivered a pigeon in a cage to a housewife. Inside she found a note threatening the death of her daughter unless she put money in a tiny purse strapped to the bird. The woman called police, who released the bird and followed it in a helicopter to its home. Officers knocked at the door. A 13-year-old boy opened it, burst into tears, and confessed.

On the other hand, police were called by neighbors who reported hearing anguished cries of "Mummy! Mummy!" from a locked apartment. The cops burst in and found a caged parrot which greeted them with a scream: "Mummy!"

The War of the Sexes

Afoul of women's lib is where a local school district in Stark Co., Oh., found itself after issuing rules limiting the length of male students' hair and prohibiting the boys from growing mustaches and beards. Federal officials said this discriminated against the males by not placing the same restrictions on females. So the school board issued an order prohibiting girls from growing beards or mustaches.

Divorced husbands can get the same Social Security benefits as divorced wives, a Federal judge ruled in San Francisco. He ordered benefit payments to begin for Stuart Oliver, 81, noting he had been married to an insured person for 20 years, never remarried and was not himself eligible for retirement benefits, fulfilling all requirements except for being a male.

"You're too pretty to be a cop," is what Mary Ann Graupner said the Freeport, N.Y., police chief told her in rejecting her application to join the all-male 76-man village force. She complained to the state Human Rights Division, pointing out she had placed No. 1 on the Civil Service list for the job.

Reds Caught Red-Handed?

The Soviet Union, as usual, contributed its share to offbeat news. First was an enterprising mechanic in the land where private enterprise is frowned on. Nikolai Vasilivitch Maslovsky of Kazakhstan contrived to turn some farm machinery parts into grain, the grain into fat pigs, and the pigs into money. The money he converted into a new Volga auto, a house full of prized possessions, and a fat bank account. The Anti-Corruption Squad and a local court turned Maslovsky from a free man into a prisoner doing 6 years.

Party Life, a Soviet magazine dealing with THE party, not parties, reported that F. Kuzyaev, chief of planning and economics of the Ministry of Culture, was "reprimanded severely" for using ministry construction workers to remodel his apartment and country home, and hiring his son as chief engineer though he was unqualified.

The year's dumbest bank robber got caught because he was so dumb. He shoved a holdup note, written on a withdrawal slip, at teller Kitty Madden in a Brooklyn, N.Y., bank. She shoved it back at him, saying: "I can't read it. You'll have to make it out again." The 23-year-old would-be robber did the logical, but stupid thing. He went back to the customers counter and started making out another holdup note. Ms. Madden meanwhile rang the silent alarms and guards grabbed the youth. Ms. Madden later responded to praise by saying: "I think I was brave because he looked so very dopey and stupid."

Early Explorers of the Western Hemisphere

The first men to discover the New World or Western Hemisphere are believed to have walked across a "land bridge" from Siberia to Alaska, an isthmus since broken by the Bering Strait. From Alaska, these ancestors of the Indians spread through North, Central, and South America. Anthropologists have placed these crossings at between 18,000 and 14,000 B.C.; but evidence found in 1967 near Puebla, Mex., indicates mankind reached there as early as 35,000-40,000 years ago.

At first, these people were hunters using flint weapons and tools. In Mexico, about 7000-6000 B.C., they founded farming cultures, developing corn, squash, etc. Eventually, they created complex civilizations — Olmec, Toltec, Aztec, and Maya and, in South America, Inca. Carbon-14 tests show men lived about 8000 B.C. near what are now Front Royal, Va., Kanawha, W. Va., and Dutchess Quarry, N.Y. The Hopewell Culture, based on farming, flourished about 1000 B.C.; remains of it are seen today in large mounds in Ohio and other states.

Norsemen (Norwegian Vikings sailing out of Iceland and Greenland) are credited by most scholars with being the first Europeans to discover America, with at least five voyages around 1000 A.D. to areas they called Helluland, Markland, and Vinland—possibly Labrador, Nova Scotia or Newfoundland, and New England.

The remains of a settlement at L'Anse-aux-Meadows, near the northern tip of Newfoundland, were uncovered by Dr. and Mrs. Helge Ingstad, Norwegian archeologists, 1960-63, with the aid of a grant from the National Geographic Society. They identified the settlement as Norse. Carbon-14 tests from hearths and the remains of a smithy indicated the site was occupied about 900 A.D. and during several hundred years before and after.

Christopher Columbus, most famous of the explorers, was born at Genoa, Italy, but made his discoveries sailing for the Spanish rulers Ferdinand and Isabella. Dates of his voyages, places he discovered, and other information follow:

1492—First voyage. Left Palos, Spain, Aug. 3 with 88 men (est.). Discovered San Salvador (Guanahani or Watling Is., Bahamas) Oct. 12. Also Cuba, Hispaniola (Haiti-Dominican Republic); built Fort La Navidad on latter.

1493—Second voyage, first part, Sept. 25, with 17 ships, 1,500 men. Dominica (Lesser Antilles) Nov. 3; Guadeloupe, Montserrat, Antigua, San Martin, Santa Cruz, Puerto Rico, Virgin Islands. Settled Isabela on Hispaniola. **Second part** (Columbus having remained in Western Hemisphere), Jamaica, Isle of Pines, La Mona Is.

1498—Third voyage. Left Spain May 30, 1498, 6 ships. Discovered Trinidad. Saw South American continent Aug. 1, 1498, but called it Isla Sancta (Holy Island). Entered Gulf of Paria and landed, first time on continental soil. At mouth of Orinoco Aug. 14 he decided this was the mainland.

1502—Fourth voyage, 4 caravels, 150 men. St. Lucia, Guanaja off Honduras; Cape Gracias a Dios, Honduras; San Juan River, Costa Rica; Almirante, Portobelo, and Laguna de Chiriqui, Panama.

Year	Explorer	Nationality and employer	Discovery or exploration
1497	John Cabot	Italian-English	Newfoundland or Nova Scotia
1498	John and Sebastian Cabot	Italian-English	Labrador to Hatteras
1499	Alonso de Ojeda	Spanish	South American coast, Venezuela
1500, Feb.	Vicente y Pinzon	Spanish	South American coast, Amazon River
1500, Apr.	Pedro Alvarez Cabral	Portuguese	Brazil (for Portugal)
1500-02	Gaspar Corte-Real	Portuguese	Labrador
1501	Rodrigo de Bastidas	Spanish	Central America
1513	Vasco Nunez de Balboa	Spanish	Pacific Ocean
1513	Juan Ponce de Leon	Spanish	Florida
1515	Juan de Solis	Spanish	Rio de la Plata
1519	Alonso de Pineda	Spanish	Mouth of Mississippi River
1519	Hernando Cortes	Spanish	Mexico
1520	Ferdinand Magellan	Portuguese-Spanish	Straits of Magellan, Tierra del Fuego
1524	Giovanni da Verrazano	Italian-French	Atlantic Coast-New York harbor
1531	Alfonso de Souza	Portuguese	Rio de Janeiro
1532	Francisco Pizarro	Spanish	Peru
1534	Jacques Cartier	French	Canada, Gulf of St. Lawrence
1536	Pedro de Mendoza	Spanish	Buenos Aires
1536	A. N. Cabeza de Vaca	Spanish	Texas coast and interior
1539	Francisco de Ulloa	Spanish	California coast
1539-41	Hernando de Soto	Spanish	Mississippi River near Memphis
1539	Marcos de Niza	Italian-Spanish	Southwest (now U.S.)
1540	Francisco V. de Coronado	Spanish	Southwest (now U.S.)
1540	Hernando Alarcon	Spanish	Colorado River
1540	Garcia de L. Cardenas	Spanish	Grand Canyon of the Colorado
1541	Francisco de Orellana	Spanish	Amazon River
1542	Juan Rodriquez Cabrillo	Portuguese-Spanish	San Diego harbor
1565	Pedro Menendez	Spanish	St. Augustine
1573	Pedro Marquez	Spanish	Chesapeake Bay
1576	Martin Frobisher	English	Frobisher's Bay, Canada
1577-80	Francis Drake	English	California coast
1582	Antonio de Espejo	Spanish	Southwest (named New Mexico)
1584	Amadas & Barlow (for Raleigh)	English	Virginia
1585-87	Sir Walter Raleigh's men	English	Roanoke Is., N.C.
1595	Sir Walter Raleigh	English	Orinoco River
1602	Bartholomew Gosnold	English	Martha's Vineyard and Massachusetts
1603-09	Samuel de Champlain	French	Canadian interior, Lake Champlain
1604	Samuel de Champlain	French	Mt. Desert Island
1607	Capt. John Smith	English	Atlantic coast
1609-10	Henry Hudson	English-Dutch	Hudson River, Hudson Bay
1634	Jean Nicolet	French	Lake Michigan; Wisconsin
1673	Jacques Marquette, Louis Jolliet	French	Mississippi S to Arkansas

(Continued)

1682	Sieur de La Salle	French	Mississippi S to Gulf of Mexico
1789	Alexander Mackenzie	Canadian	Canadian Northwest

Arctic Exploration

Early Explorers

1587 — John Davis (England). Davis Strait to Sanderson's Hope, 72° 12′ N.

1596 — Willem Barents and Jacob van Heemskerck (Holland). Discovered Bear Island, touched northwest tip of Spitsbergen, 79° 49′ N, rounded Novaya Zemlya, wintered at Ice Haven.

1607 — Henry Hudson (England). North along Greenland's east coast to Cape Hold-with-Hope, 73° 30′, then north of Spitsbergen to 80° 23′. Returning he discovered Hudson's Touches (Jan Mayen).

1616 — William Baffin and Robert Bylot (England). Baffin Bay to Smith Sound.

1728 — Vitus Bering (Russia). Proved Asia and America were separate by sailing through strait.

1733-40 — Great Northern Expedition (Russia). Surveyed Siberian Arctic coast.

1741 — Vitus Bering (Russia). Sighted Alaska from sea, named Mount St. Elias. His lieutenant, Chirikof, discovered coast.

1771 — Samuel Hearne (Hudson's Bay Co.). Overland from Prince of Wales Fort (Churchill) on Hudson Bay to mouth of Coppermine River.

1778 — James Cook (Britain). Through Bering Strait to Icy Cape, Alaska, and North Cape, Siberia.

1789 — Alexander Mackenzie (North West Co., Britain). Montreal to mouth of Mackenzie River.

1806 — William Scoresby (Britain). North of Spitsbergen to 81° 30′.

1820-3 — Ferdinand von Wrangel (Russia). Completed a survey of Siberian Arctic coast. His exploration joined that of James Cook at North Cape, confirming separation of the continents.

1845 — Sir John Franklin (Britain) was one of many to seek the Northwest Passage — an ocean route connecting the Atlantic and Pacific via the Arctic. His 2 ships (the Erebus and Terror) were last seen entering Lancaster Sound July 26.

1888 — Fridtjof Nansen (Norway) crossed Greenland's icecap. 1893-96 — Nansen in Fram drifted from New Siberian Is. to Spitsbergen; tried polar dash in 1895, reached Franz Josef Land.

1896 — Salomon A. Andree (Sweden) and companion, in June, made first attempt to reach North Pole by balloon; failed and returned in August. On July 11, 1897, Andree and 2 others started in balloon from Danes Is., Spitsbergen, to drift across pole to America, and disappeared. Over 33 years later, Aug. 6, 1930, Dr. Gunnar Horn (Norway) found their frozen bodies on White Is., 82° 57′ N 29° 52′ E.

1903-06 — Roald Amundsen (Norway) first sailed Northwest Passage.

Discovery of North Pole

Robert E. Peary began exploring in 1886 on Greenland, when he was 30. With his hq. at McCormick Bay he explored Greenland's coast 1891-92, tried for North Pole 1893, returned with large meteorites. In 1900 he reached northern limit of Greenland and 83° 50′ N; in 1902 he reached 84° 06′N; in 1906 he went from Ellesmere Is. to 87° 06′N. He sailed in the Roosevelt, July, 1908, to winter off Cape Sheridan, Grant Land. The dash for the North Pole began Mar. 1 from Cape Columbia, Ellesmere Land. Peary reached the pole, 90° N, Apr. 6, 1909.

Peary had several supporting groups carrying supplies until the last group, under Capt. Robt. A. Bartlett, turned back at 87° 47′N. Peary, Matthew Henson, and 4 eskimos proceeded with dog teams and sleds. They crossed the pole several times, finally built an igloo at 90°, remained 36 hours. Started south Apr. 7 at 4 p.m. for Cape Columbia. Eskimos were Coqueeh, Ootah, Eginwah, and Seegloo. Adm. Peary died Feb. 20, 1920. Henson, a Negro, born Aug. 8, 1866, died in New York, N.Y., Mar. 9, 1955, aged 88. Ootah, the last survivor, died near Thule, Greenland, May, 1955, aged 80.

1914 — Donald Macmillan (U.S.). Northwest, 200 miles, from Axel Hieberg Island to seek Peary's Crocker Land.

1915-17 — Vihjalmur Stefansson (Canada) discovered Borden, Brock, Meighen, and Lougheed Islands.

1918-20 — Amundsen sailed Northeast Passage.

1926 — Richard E. Byrd and Floyd Bennett (U.S.) reached 87° 44′N in attempt to fly to North Pole from Spitsbergen.

1926 — Richard E. Byrd and Floyd Bennett (U.S.) first over North Pole by air, May 9.

1926 — Amundsen, Ellsworth, and Umberto Nobile (Italy) flew from Spitsbergen over North Pole May 12, to Teller, Alaska, in dirigible Norge.

1928 — Nobile crossed North Pole in airship Italia May 24, crashed May 25. Amundsen lost while trying to effect rescue by plane.

1928 — Sir Hubert Wilkins and Eielson flew from Point Barrow to Spitsbergen, 84° N.

North Pole Exploration Records

On Aug. 3, 1958, the Nautilus, under Comdr. William R. Anderson, became the first ship to cross the North Pole beneath the Arctic ice.

On Aug. 12, 1958, the nuclear submarine Skate, Comdr. James F. Calvert, became the second ship to make an underwater crossing of the North Pole.

In March, 1959, the Skate returned to the Arctic and, on its third attempt, broke through at the North Pole, the first time any ship had been on the surface at 90° N.

The nuclear-powered U. S. submarine Seadragon, Comdr. George P. Steele 2d, made the first east-west underwater transit through the Northwest Passage during August, 1960. It sailed from Portsmouth, N.H., headed between Greenland and Labrador through Baffin Bay, then west through Lancaster Sound and McClure Strait to the Beaufort Sea. Traveling submerged for the most part, the submarine made 850 miles from Baffin Bay to the Beaufort Sea in six days. The vessel made a 300-foot dive to sail under an iceberg in Baffin Bay.

In February, 1960, the nuclear submarine Sargo traveled under the Arctic ice pack to and around the North Pole. The Sargo departed from and returned to Honolulu, and spent 31 days and 4 hours under the ice. The submarine successfully smashed its way through ice 3 feet thick.

On Aug. 16, 1977, according to press dispatches from Moscow, the Soviet nuclear icebreaker Arktika reached the North Pole and became the first surface ship to break through the Arctic ice pack to the top of the world.

Antarctic Exploration

Early History

Antarctica has been approached since 1773-75, when Capt. Jas. Cook (Britain) reached 71°10′S. Many sea and landmarks bear names of early explorers. Bellingshausen (Russia) discovered Peter I and Alexander I Islands, 1819-21. Nathaniel Palmer (U.S.) discovered Palmer Peninsula, 60°W, 1820, without realizing that this was a continent. Jas. Weddell (Britain) found Weddell Sea, 74°15′S, 1823.

First to announce existence of the continent of Antarctica was Charles Wilkes (U.S.), who followed the coast for 1,500 mi., 1840. Adelie Coast, 140° E, was found by Dumont d'Urville (France), 1840. Ross Ice Shelf was found by Jas. Clark Ross (Britain), 1841-42.

1895 — Leonard Kristensen, Norwegian whaling

captain, landed a party on the coast of Victoria Land in Jan. 1895. They were the first ashore on the main continental mass. C. E. Borchgrevink, a member of that party, returned in 1899 with a British expedition, first to winter on Antarctica.

1902-04 — Robert F. Scott (Britain) discovered Edward VII Peninsula. In 1902 he reached 82°17'S, 146°33'E from McMurdo Sound.

1908-09 — Ernest Shackleton, in 1908, introduced the use of Manchurian ponies in Antarctic sledging. In 1909 he reached 88°23'S, discovering a route on to the plateau by way of the Beardmore Glacier and pioneering the way to the pole.

Discovery of South Pole

1911 — Roald Amundsen (Norway) with 4 men and dog teams reached the pole Dec. 14, 1911.

1912 — Capt. Scott reached the pole from Ross Island Jan. 18, 1912, with four companions (Dr. E. A. Wilson, Lt. Bowers, Capt. Oates, and Petty Officer Edgar Evans), where they found Amundsen's tent. Of Scott's party, Oates and Evans died first; Scott, Wilson, and Boers died in a tent around March 29. They were found Nov. 12, 1912.

1928 — First man to use an airplane over Antarctica was Hubert Wilkins (Britain).

1929 — Richard E. Byrd (U.S.) established Little America on Bay of Whales. On 1600-mi. airplane flight begun Nov. 28 he crossed South Pole Nov. 29 with pilot Bernt Balchen, a radio operator, and a photographer. Dropped U.S. flag over pole, temp. 16° below zero.

1934-35 — Richard E. Byrd (U.S.) led second expedition to Little America, which explored 450,000 sq. mi. Byrd wintered alone at an advance weather station in 80°08'S.

1934-37 — John Rymill led British Graham Land expedition of 1934-37; discovered that Palmer Peninsula is part of Antarctic mainland.

1935 — Lincoln Ellsworth (U.S.) flew south along Palmer Peninsula's east coast, then crossed continent to Little America, making 4 landings on unprepared terrain in bad weather, a new feat.

1939-41 — U. S. Antarctic Service built West Base on Ross Ice Shelf under Paul Siple, and East Base on Palmer Peninsula under Richard Black. U. S. Navy plane flights discovered about 150,000 sq. miles of new land.

1940 — Richard E. Byrd (U.S.) charted most of coast between Ross Sea and Palmer Peninsula.

1946-47 — U. S. Navy undertook Operation Highjump under Rear Admiral Byrd. Ships were commanded by Rear Admiral Richard H. Cruzen. Expedition included 13 ships and 4,000 men. Twenty-nine land-based flights from Little America and 35 by seaplanes from tenders photomapped coastline and penetrated beyond pole.

1946-48 — Ronne Antarctic Research Expedition, Comdr. Finn Ronne, USNR, determined the Antarctic to be only one continent with no strait between Weddell Sea and Ross Sea; discovered 250,000 sq. miles of land by flights to 79°S Lat., and made 14,000 aerial photographs over 450,000 sq. miles of land. Mrs. Ronne and Mrs. H. Darlington, who accompanied their husbands, were the first women to winter on Antarctica.

1955-57 — U. S. Navy's Operation Deep Freeze led by Adm. Richard E. Byrd. Supporting U. S. scientific efforts for the International Geophysical Year, the operation was commanded by Rear Adm. George Dufek. It established 5 coastal stations fronting the Indian, Pacific, and Atlantic Oceans and also 3 interior stations; explored more than 1,000,000 sq. miles in Wilkes Land. Seven Navy men under Adm. Dufek landed by plane at the Pole Oct. 31, 1956, and landed radar reflectors.

1957-58 — During the International Geophysical year, Jul., 1957, through Dec., 1958, scientists from 12 countries conducted ambitious programs of Antarctic research. A network of some 60 stations on the continent and sub-Arctic islands studied oceanography, glaciology, meteorology, seismology, geomagnetism, the ionosphere, cosmic rays, aurora, and airglow. A party from Ellsworth IGY station (U.S.) south of Weddell Sea under the direction of Captain Finn Ronne explored beyond 1947 flight and delineated Berkner Island imbedded in the Filchner Ice Shelf. Pensacola Mountains, first sighted by Argentines in Oct., 1955, and seen by U. S. Navy in Jan., 1956, were accurately located. New mountain ranges about 11,609 ft. high were discovered in Edith Ronne Land.

Dr. V. E. Fuchs led a 12-man Trans-Antarctic Expedition on the first land crossing of Antarctica. Starting from the Weddell Sea, they reached Scott Station Mar. 2, 1958, after traveling 2,158 miles in 98 days.

1958 — A group of 5 U. S. scientists led by Edward C. Thiel, seismologist, moving by tractor from Ellsworth Station on Weddell Sea, identified a huge mountain range, 5,000 ft. above the ice sheet and 9,000 ft. above sea level. The range, originally seen by a Navy plane, was named the Dufek Massif, for Rear Adm. George Dufek.

1959 — Twelve nations — Argentina, Australia, Belgium, Chile, France, Japan, New Zealand, Norway, South Africa, the Soviet Union, the United Kingdom, and the U. S. — signed a treaty suspending any territorial claims for 30 years and reserving the continent for research.

1960-61 — Scientists at Cape Adare found a wooden building erected in 1899 by the first men (led by C. E. Borchgrevink) to winter on the continent.

1961-62 — Scientists discovered a trough, the Bentley Trench, running from Ross Ice Shelf, Pacific, into Marie Byrd Land, around the end of the Ellsworth Mtns., toward the Weddell Sea, which may be the long-suspected link between the Atlantic and Pacific Oceans.

1962 — First nuclear power plant began operation at McMurdo Sound.

1963 — On Feb. 22 a U. S. plane made the longest nonstop flight ever made in the S. Pole area, covering 3,600 miles in 10 hours. The flight was from McMurdo Station south past the geographical S. Pole to Shackleton Mtns., southeast to the "Area of Inaccessibility" and back to McMurdo Station.

1963 — Three turbine-powered helicopters made the first copter landings on the S. Pole.

1964 — A British survey team was landed by helicopter on Cook Island, the first recorded visit since its discovery in 1775.

1964 — New Zealanders completed one of the last and most important surveys when they mapped the mountain area from Cape Adare west some 400 miles to Pennell Glacier.

1966-67 — Fifteen Antarctic areas set aside as Specially Protected Areas for the conservation of flora and fauna.

Exploring Pre-History

Ancient Kingdom Rivaling Egypt Unearthed

Italian archeologists excavating at Ebla in northern Syria have discovered evidence of a major urban civilization that rose some 4,400 years ago and rivaled the only contemporary cultures, Egypt and Mesopotamia.

A report on the "sensational" find, "one of those rare discoveries that transform our knowledge of ancient man," was presented at the annual meeting of the Archeological Institute of America.

The breakthrough in the excavations which have been under way for more than 10 years came in the fall of 1976 with the discovery of 15,000 tablets in the archives chamber of the royal palace of the old kingdom. The tablets covered with a cuneiform script never seen before, more than tripled the known written record of human activities during that period which witnessed the growth of agricultural villages into cities that became centers of cultural and political power. The tablets cover 150 years from 2400 to 2500 B.C.

Paolo Matthiae, the 36-year-old leader of the excavating team and professor of near east archeology at the University of Rome, appraised the value of the tablets: "In our minds, the tablets represent a sensational discovery. Before, this area was dismissed as merely peripheral between the big centers of Mesopotamia and Egypt."

Matthiae and his colleague, Giovanni Pettinato, a professor of Assyriology and a language expert, believe the tablets reveal the most ancient Semitic language yet found. Pettinato was aided in deciphering the tablets by the discovery of vocabularies matching the language, called Eblait, with Sumerian. Matthiae and Pettinato feel certain the language is similar to the biblical Hebrew spoken 1,500 years later.

The tablets describe a vast commercial and cultural empire that thrived for at least 800 years. They indicate that Ebla alone had a population of 260,000 and that the king, at one time, employed some 11,000 administrators and civil servants. The tablets also detail Ebla's government-run textile manufacturing and metal processing industries, as well as military campaigns and international treaties of the period.

Matthiae and Pettinato also believe the tablets have major biblical significance because they contain accounts of the creation and the flood which are similar to those in the Old Testament and Babylonian literature. "The tablets bring to light a civilization that preceded the arrival of the Hebrews in Palestine. We have found the civilization that was the background of the people of the Old Testament . . . But the tablets reflect the kind of life the Hebrews found when they arrived later in Palestine," Matthiae stated.

Oldest Site of European Man Found?

A cave outside of the village of Petralona in northern Greece may be the oldest site inhabited by man yet found in Europe. Greek anthropologist Dr. Aris N. Poulianos believes the site was occupied by ancestors of modern man for more than 100,000 years beginning about 750,000 years ago.

If confirmed, the age of Petralona man would surpass the only other evidence of early man's presence in Europe — a jawbone known as Heidelberg man. Discovered in Germany in 1908, the jawbone is estimated to be between 500,000 and 700,000 years old. Poulianos contends that the lowest level of habitation excavated to date at Petralona dates to an earlier period than that associated with Heidelberg man.

Poulianos believes his discoveries at the Petralona cave have forced anthropologists to rethink their theories about the origins of modern man. "Southeastern Europe must definitely be included in the zone of homonization, the making of man," Poulianos asserted. "Our ideas up until now are still concentrated on Africa. I don't exclude Africa, I'm just widening the area of man's formation."

Archanthropus europeaus petralonieusis, as Petralona man is technically called, is placed in the same species as *Homo erectus*. Although Petralona man is relatively young in comparison to some of the African finds, Poulianos is stirring controversy with his growing doubt of the theory that man migrated from Africa. He bases his opinions on extensive digging inside the cave and on independent opinions from foreign scientists.

Roots of Writing Pushed Back

A specialist in the ancient uses of clay has suggested recently that the roots of writing can be traced back more than 10,000 years, nearly twice as far into the past as previously accepted.

Archeologists have long believed that the invention of writing came about 5,200 years ago when the ancient Sumerians of Mesopotamia created a system using picture-like symbols, or pictographs, inscribed on clay tablets. The oldest known such writings come from ruins of the Sumerian town of Uruk, also called Warka, in Iraq.

Now, Denise Schmandt-Besserat, assistant director of the University of Texas Center for Middle Eastern Studies, has postulated that certain pictographs that are not obviously pictorial were patterned after abstractly shaped tokens or taken directly from impressions made by the tokens in soft clay. She believes true writing was never invented, but evolved directly from the shapes of the tokens and their use in a system of record-keeping. Each of the variously shaped tokens represented a different object or quantity.

These tokens, found for decades in excavations in the ancient villages of the Middle East, were usually thought to be toys or games pieces. Some archeologists, however, had suggested that the tokens had been used in a method of record-keeping that died out with the invention of writing.

Schmandt-Besserat has documented her theory through numerous physical likenesses between the early tokens and the true writing found at Uruk. "Evidence gathered from extensive research has led me to conclude that the origin of the writing was much earlier than previously assumed. My study indicates that the Warka tablets only represent an evolutionary step in a sophisticated system of recording which had been used in the Middle East since 8500 B.C."

According to Schmandt-Besserat's study of the evolution of writing, the tokens, originally representing commodities traded among villages, came into increasingly sophisticated use, with impressions made in soft clay for duplicate records. Eventually, about 5,200 years ago, when the impressions were generally understood, the tokens were no longer necessary and full-fledged writing appeared. Instead of using tokens as "movable type," styluses were used to inscribe the same symbols. Then, within a few centuries, the picto-graphic writing evolved into more stylized cuneiform or wedge-writing.

Evidence Found for North America-Europe Link

Fossil bones found on Canada's Arctic Ellesmere Island have been put forth as evidence for the theory that a land bridge once linked North America and Europe and the two land masses shared the same animal species until 45 to 48 million years ago.

The fossil evidence, presented by Dr. Mary R. Dawson of the Carnegie Museum of Natural History in Pittsburgh and Dr. Robert M. West of the Milwaukee Public Museum, belongs to the same group of species long known from deposits in France, Montana, and Wyoming. According to West, "The animals that we found are probably representative of a single fauna that extended from western Europe to western United States." The species discovered include snakes, birds, salamanders, turtles, alligators, mice, and several extinct larger species. Of special interest is a dog-sized tapir which closely resembles tapir fossils found in France and the western United States.

The researchers believe that by 45 million years ago, the 2 continents, which had been drifting apart for many million of years, lost their last link and then the animal populations evolved separately.

Oldest American Man Dated

Carbon-14 dating of a fire pit containing mammoth bones and stone tools found in 1975 on Santa Rosa Island off the southern coast of California has put early man in America at least 40,000 years ago, more than twice as early as the generally accepted time of man's entry into North America.

Although evidence suggesting an earlier arrival has been reported previously, the dating of that evidence was based on methods that are not accepted as fully reliable. The carbon-14 method, which is widely accepted, is only effective for dating material within the last 40,000 years.

Dr. Rainer Berger, professor of anthropology at UCLA, who presented the evidence at the 8th annual symposium on archeaometry and archeological prospection at the University of Pennsylvania, described the site as a "big barbecue of a mammoth." The evidence indicates that a group of early hunters killed the mammoth on the site and cooked it.

Steelmaking Linked to Start of Iron Age

Traditional archeological thinking has assumed that mankind took a giant step backward in the Middle East some 3,200 years ago when it abandoned bronze implements and weapons in favor of iron, a softer metal. The discovery of bronze had taken mankind out of the Stone Age. This sudden switch to iron was laid to a hypothetical loss of tin supply which was alloyed with copper to make bronze.

Now, Dr. Robert Maddin, a metallurgist at the University of Pennsylvania, has introduced evidence that ancient metallurgists turned to iron because they had learned to make steel. He theorizes these ancient men learned not only how to produce soft iron, but that, through extended heating, they could give it a hardness far exceeding that of bronze.

The switch to iron also democratized the availability of metal implements. Bronze tools, because of the scarcity of tin and copper ores, were only available to the wealthy; but iron or steel tools, because iron was vastly more plentiful, could be made more cheaply and, consequently, were available to common people. This democratization spurred economic and social changes that changed societies many times over.

Maddin had analyzed some "iron" spearheads from ancient Palestine and found that carbon atoms had penetrated the iron, increasing its hardness. Maddin believes this process, called carburization and used to turn iron into carbon steel, probably came about spontaneously because furnaces were heated with charcoal, a rich source of carbon. "I'm sure the ancient ironmakers didn't know about carbon . . . They just knew that if you heated iron long enough in a charcoal fire, it got harder," Maddin explained. The other requirement in steel-making is quenching of the hot metal in cold water, a process, Maddin believes, ancient ironworkers used automatically to cool dangerously hot objects.

King Tut's Grandmummy Identified

The long-lost mummy of Queen Tiy, King Tutankhamen's grandmother, was identified recently through X-rays of the skulls of Egyptian mummies and analysis of their hair. It was the first discovery of a royal Egyptian mummy since King Tut in 1922.

The royal mummy was unearthed in 1898 by a French archeologist in the tomb of Amenhotep II, but, lacking identification, had been taken for an unimportant woman. Actually, Queen Tiy (1397-1360 B.C.), as the wife of Pharaoh Amenhotep III, was a major figure in the 18th dynasty. Heiroglyphic records of the day indicate that Tiy exchanged letters with a number of foreign rulers. Her son, Ikhnaton, is often described as the first monotheist; he established worship of the sun as the state religion for a brief period after 1360 B.C.

The belated identification of Tiy was made by a scientific team headed by Dr. James E. Harris, a University of Michigan researcher. The first clue came when Dr. Edward F. Wente, an egyptologist at the University of Chicago, suggested that one of 3 unidentified mummies in Amenhotep II's tomb might be Tiy because her arm lay across her chest in a style reserved for persons of high rank.

The mummies were relocated and X-rayed and a sample of the anonymous woman's hair was taken for comparison with a sample in a locket found in King Tut's tomb. The locket bore an inscription saying the hair was from Tiy.

Harris analysed the X-rays using a computer that converts contours of the skull into mathematical descriptions. Comparing the results with the same data from all other royal mummies, Harris concluded that the inherited features of her skull shape fit only one logical point in Egyptian lineages. Then, to strengthen the identification, electron probe analysis of the hairs from the locket showed them to be identical to those cut from the head of the mystery mummy.

Bonhomme Richard Remains Found

The wreck of the Bonhomme Richard, the flagship of John Paul Jones, has been found, according to a British-American expedition, in 180 feet of water where it sank after defeating the British warship Serapis in 1779 in the battle immortalized by Jones' famous words, "I have not yet begun to fight."

The Bonhomme Richard and the Serapis battled off Flamborough Head on the coast of Yorkshire. Both ships were heavily damaged and the Bonhomme Richard, burning finally sank after the British captain had surrendered.

Sidney Wignall, a naval historian, has been conducting the search aboard the Decca Recorder, a highly instrumented survey ship. He used contemporary news accounts and historical records to narrow the area of search. The first real clue came from a retired fisherman who, 19 years ago, fished up an iron muzzle-loading gun with a swivel mount. Additionally, Dutch fishermen had pinpointed a wreck in the area which had been tearing their nets.

The Decca Recorder's sonar located 3 wrecks in the area. Two, shown to be of iron or steel, were assumed to be possible victims of World War I or II. The third however, from magnometer readings, indicated cannon and a beam width of about 30 feet, the size of the Bonhomme Richard.

Final proof of identity is awaiting salvage of one or more cannon or the examination of other preserved features. The descriptions of each such items are known, to varying degrees of accuracy, from Revolutionary records.

New Aztec Theory Raises Harsh Criticism

Dr. Michael Harner, professor of anthropology at the New School for Social research, shocked Aztec specialists last February when he suggested that the Aztecs sacrificed human beings not simply for religious reasons but because they needed the protein for their diet. Citing considerable documentation, Harner stated that most specialists on Aztec culture have "consciously or unconsciously covered up evidence of the extent of cannibalism among the Aztecs.

After Harner's theory was published in *The New York Times*, Feb. 22, 17 scholars specializing in Mesoamerican ancient history sent a telegram to the *Times* declaring, "No reputable anthropologist familiar with Aztec culture would subscribe to his (Harner's) views."

Most sources on Aztec culture note that the Aztecs practiced human sacrifice and cannibalism, but dismiss cannibalism as no more than an occasional religious rite. Harner, however, argues that in the 15th century, just before the arrival of the Spanish conquerors in Mexico, the Aztecs had the most cannibalistic culture known to modern anthropology. Harner bases his nutritional need theory on new estimates of the number of people thought to have been sacrificed by the Aztecs. Estimates by Dr. Woodrow Borah, an authority on the demography of ancient Mexico at the University of California at Berkeley, suggest the Aztecs sacrificed about 250,000 people, or about 1% of the region's population, per year.

Harner believes that conventional food in the spectacular Aztec civilization was not always abundant. He argues that cannibalism, although it may have sprung from religious origins, grew to serve nutritional needs because the Aztecs, unlike nearly all other civilizations, lacked domesticated herbivores, like pigs and cows. The Aztecs never sacrificed their own people. They battled neighboring nations, employing tactics that minimized enemy deaths while maximizing the number of prisoners taken. As documentation for cannibalism, Harner cities contemporary sources — Hernando Cortes and Bernal Diaz who accompanied him — which give abundant evidence that the practice was common indeed.

Harner's critics, on the other hand, turn to other contemporary sources, notably Spanish priests who lived among the Aztecs after Cortes' arrival and who were astounded by the plentifulness of food, particularly game. One of the signers of the telegram to the *Times*, Dr. Nancy Troike, an ethnohistorian at the University of Texas, has stated that the "Aztec diet before the Conquest was an awful lot better than what the Mexicans are eating today."

Volcanoes of the World

Source: The Center for Short-Lived Phenomena, Cambridge, Mass.

Year of last eruption in parentheses.

More than 75 per cent of the world's 850 active volcanoes lie within the "Ring of Fire," a zone running along the west coast of the Americas from Chile to Alaska and down the east coast of Asia from Siberia to New Zealand. Twenty per cent of these volcanoes are located in Indonesia. Other prominent groupings are located in Japan, the Aleutian Islands, and Central America. Almost all active volcanic regions are found at the boundaries of the large moving plates which comprise the earth's surface. The "Ring of Fire" marks the boundary between the plates underlying the Pacific Ocean and those underlying the surrounding continents. Other active volcanic regions, such as the Mediterranean Sea and Iceland, are located on plate boundaries.

Major Historical Eruptions

Approximately 7,000 years ago, Mazama, a 3,000-meter-high volcano in southern Oregon, erupted violently, ejecting about 40 cubic kilometers of ash and lava. The ash spread over the entire northwestern United States and as far away as Saskatchewan, Canada. During the eruption, the top of the mountain collapsed, leaving a caldera 10 kilometers across and about one kilometer deep, which filled with rain water to form what is now called Crater Lake.

In 79 A.D., Vesuvio, a 1281-meter-high volcano overlooking Naples Bay, became active after several centuries of quiescence. On October 26 of that year, a heated mud and ash flow swept down the mountain, engulfing the cities of Pompeii, Herculaneum, and Stabiae with debris up to 15 meters deep. Virtually all residents of the 3 towns were killed.

The largest eruptions in recent centuries have been in Indonesia. In 1883, an eruption similar to the Mazama eruption occurred on the island of Krakatau. On August 27, the 800-meter-high peak of the volcano collapsed to 300 meters below sea level, leaving only a small portion of the island standing above the sea. Ash from the eruption covered nearly 1,000,000 square kilometers and colored sunsets around the world for 2 years. A tsunami ("tidal wave") generated by the collapse killed 36,000 people in nearby Java and Sumatra and eventually reached England. A similar, but even more powerful, eruption had taken place 68 years earlier at Tambora volcano on the Indonesian island of Sumbawa.

Major Eruptions 1976-77

From July 1, 1975 to July 1, 1977, significant eruptive activity reportedly took place at 72 volcanoes around the world. Four volcanoes erupted in Africa, including Nyamuragira and Nyiragongo in Zaire. In the January 10, 1977 eruption of Nyirangongo, more than 20 million cubic meters of lava flowed down the volcano's slopes within an hour and spread over 20 square kilometers.

Volcanic activity in Central and South America was also significant. Arenal in Costa Rica has been very active; during the October 1976 eruption, the summit crater was greatly enlarged and emitted thick block lava flows. In a 1968 eruption at Arenal, hot gases, ash, incandescent rock and lava blocks killed 76 people and caused severe destruction along the volcano's western slopes. Purace, a composite strato volcano in Colombia, erupted in March 1977 for the first time since 1949.

Name	Location	Meters
Africa		
Kilimanjaro	Tanzania	5,895
Cameroon	Cameroons	4,070
Teide (Tenerife) (1909)	Canary Is.	3,713
Nyirangongo (1977)	Zaire	3,465
Nyamuragira (1977)	Zaire	3,056
Ol Doinyo Lengai (1960)	Tanzania	2,886
Fogo (1951)	Cape Verde Is.	2,829
Piton de la Fournaise (1977)	Reunion	2,631
Palma (1971)	Canary Is.	2,423
Karthala (1977)	Comoro Is.	2,361
Erta-Ale (1973)	Ethiopia	615
Antarctica		
Erebus (1975)	Ross Island	3,743
Big Ben (1960)	Heard Island	2,745
Melbourne	Victoria Land	2,590
Darnley (1956)	South Sandwich Islands	1,100
Deception Island (1970)	South Shetland Islands	602
Asia-Oceania		
Klyuchevskaya (1974)	USSR	4,850
Kerintji (1968)	Sumatra	3,805
Fuji	Japan	3,776
Rindjani (1966)	Indonesia	3,726
Semeru (1976)	Java	3,676
Ichinskaya	USSR	3,631
Kronotskaya (1923)	USSR	3,528
Koryakskaya (1957)	USSR	3,456
Slamet (1967)	Java	3,432
Shiveluch (1964)	USSR	3,395
Ardjuno-Welirang	Java	3,339
Raung (1945)	Java	3,332
Dempo (1940)	Sumatra	3,173
Sundoro (1906)	Java	3,150
Agung (1964)	Bali	3,142
Plosky Tolbachik (1976)	USSR	3,085
Tjiremai (1938)	Java	3,078
Ontake	Japan	3,063
Mayon (1968)	Philippines	2,990
Gede (1949)	Java	2,958
Zhupanovsky (1959)	USSR	2,958
Apo	Philippines	2,953
Merapi (1976)	Java	2,911
Marapi (1949)	Sumatra	2,891
Tambora (1913)	Indonesia	2,851
Bezymianny (1977)	USSR	2,800
Ruapehu (1975)	New Zealand	2,796
Peuetsagoe (1921)	Sumatra	2,780
Avachinskaya (1945)	USSR	2,751
Papandajan (1925)	Java	2,665
Balbi	Solomon Is.	2,593
Geureudong	Sumatra	2,590
Asama (1973)	Japan	2,542
Sumbing (1921)	Sumatra	2,508
Canlaon (1969)	Philippines	2,465
Sinabung	Sumatra	2,460
Yake Dake (1963)	Japan	2,455
Tandikat (1914)	Sumatra	2,438
Niigata Yakeyama (1974)	Japan	2,400
Idjen (1936)	Java	2,386
Alaid (1972)	Kuril Is.	2,339
Bromo (1950)	Java	2,329
Ulawun (1973)	New Britain	2,300
Ngauruhoe (1975)	New Zealand	2,291
Guntur	Java	2,249

Name	Location	Meters
Bamus	New Britain	2,248
Chokai (1974)	Japan	2,230
Butak Petarangan (1939)	Java	2,222
Sibajak	Sumatra	2,212
Galunggung (1918)	Java	2,168
Sorikmerapi (1917)	Sumatra	2,145
Amburombu (1969)	Indonesia	2,124
Tangkuban Prahu (1967)	Java	2,084
Tokachi (1962)	Japan	2,077
Tongariro	New Zealand	1,978
Zheltovskaya (1923)	USSR	1,953
Kaba (1941)	Sumatra	1,952
Sangeang Api (1966)	Indonesia	1,949
Manam (1977)	Papua New Guinea	1,830
Tiatia (1973)	Kuril Islands	1,822
Siau (1976)	Indonesia	1,784
Soputan (1968)	Celebes	1,784
Lamington (1952)	Papua New Guinea	1,780
Kelud (1967)	Java	1,731
Batur (1968)	Bali	1,717
Ternate (1963)	Indonesia	1,715
Lewotobi (1935)	Indonesia	1,703
Bagana (1960)	Solomon Islands	1,702
Kirishima (1956)	Japan	1,700
Ili Boleng (1950)	Indonesia	1,659
Lamongan	Java	1,651
Malinao	Philippines	1,657
Keli Mutu (1968)	Indonesia	1,640
Akita Komaga take (1970)	Japan	1,637
Gamkunoro (1949)	Indonesia	1,635
Aso (1977)	Japan	1,592
Lewotobi Laki-Laki (1968)	Indonesia	1,584
Lokon-Empung (1970)	Celebes	1,579
Bulusan (1933)	Philippines	1,559
Me-akan (1966)	Japan	1,503
Karkar (1975)	Papua New Guinea	1,500
Sarycheva (1976)	Kuril Islands	1,497
Karymskaya (1976)	USSR	1,486
Lopevi (1960)	New Hebrides	1,447
Ibu (1911)	Indonesia	1,340
Ambrim (1953)	New Hebrides	1,334
Catarman (1952)	Philippines	1,332
Mahawu	Celebes	1,331
Awu (1968)	Indonesia	1,320
Ili Lewotolo (1920)	Indonesia	1,319
Langila (1973)	New Britain	1,189
Tongkoko	Celebes	1,149
Komaga take (1942)	Japan	1,140
Sakura jima (1976)	Japan	1,118
Dukono (1971)	Indonesia	1,087
Bangum	New Britain	1,052
Ili Werung (1948)	Indonesia	1,018
Lolobau (1905)	New Britain	932
Central America—Caribbean		
Tajumulco	Guatemala	4,220
Tacana	Guatemala	4,092
Acatenango (1972)	Guatemala	3,976
Santiaguito (Santa Maria) (1976)	Guatemala	3,772
Fuego (1977)	Guatemala	3,736
Atitlan	Guatemala	3,537
Irazu (1967)	Costa Rica	3,432
Poas (1976)	Costa Rica	2,704
Pacaya (1976)	Guatemala	2,552
San Miguel (1976)	El Salvador	2,130
Izalco (1966)	El Salvador	1,965
Rincon de la Vieja (1968)	Costa Rica	1,806
El Viejo (San Cristobal) (1976)	Nicaragua	1,745
Ometepe (Concepcion) (1977)	Nicaragua	1,610
Arenal (1977)	Costa Rica	1,552
Pelee (1932)	Martinique	1,397
Conchagua (1947)	El Salvador	1,250
Momotombo (1905)	Nicaragua	1,191
Soutriere (1972)	St. Vincent	1,178
Telica (1976)	Nicaragua	1,010

Name	Location	Meters
South America		
Guallatiri (1960)	Chile	6,060
Cotopaxi (1975)	Ecuador	5,897
El Misti	Peru	5,825
Ubinas (1969)	Peru	5,672
Lascar (1968)	Chile	5,641
Tupungatito (1964)	Chile	5,640
Tolima (1943)	Colombia	5,525
Sangay (1976)	Ecuador	5,230
Tungurahua (1944)	Ecuador	5,016
Pichincha	Ecuador	4,787
Purace (1977)	Colombia	4,600
Reventador (1976)	Ecuador	3,485
Lautaro (1960)	Chile	3,380
Llaima (1957)	Chile	3,124
Villarrica (1971)	Chile	2,840
Hudson (1973)	Chile	2,600
Rinihue	Chile	2,430
Puyehue (1960)	Chile	2,240
Calbuco (1961)	Chile	2,015
Fernandina (1977)	Galapagos Is.	1,546
Alcedo (1954)	Galapagos Is.	1,127
Mid-Pacific		
Mauna Kea	Hawaii	4,206
Mauna Loa (1975)	Hawaii	4,170
Haleakala	Hawaii	3,055
Kilauea (1977)	Hawaii	1,222
Mid-Atlantic Ridge		
Beerenberg (1970)	Jan Mayen Is.	2,277
Tristan da Cunha (1962)	Tristan da Cunha Is.	2,060
Askja (1961)	Iceland	1,510
Hekla (1970)	Iceland	1,491
Faial (1968)	Azores	1,043
Katla (1918)	Iceland	900
Leirhnukur (1975)	Iceland	650
Helgafell (1973)	Iceland	226
Surtsey (1967)	Iceland	174
Europe		
Etna (1977)	Italy	3,290
Vesuvio (1944)	Italy	1,281
Stromboli (1975)	Italy	926
Vulcano	Italy	500
Santorini (1950)	Greece	130
North America		
Citlaltepec	Mexico	5,676
Popocatepetl (1920)	Mexico	5,452
Rainier	Washington	4,395
Wrangell	Alaska	4,320
Colima (1975)	Mexico	3,960
Spurr (1953)	Alaska	3,375
Baker	Washington	3,316
Lassen (1915)	California	3,186
Paricutin (1952)	Mexico	3,170
Redoubt (1966)	Alaska	3,110
Iliamna	Alaska	3,073
Shishaldin (1977)	Aleutian Is.	2,858
Pavlof (1977)	Aleutian Is.	2,715
Veniaminof	Alaska	2,560
Chiginagak	Alaska	2,420
Douglas	Alaska	2,328
Pogromni	Alaska	2,286
Katmai (1931)	Alaska	2,285
Mageik (1912)	Alaska	2,210
Tanaga	Aleutian Is.	2,125
Trident (1963)	Alaska	2,070
Kukak	Alaska	2,046
Makushin	Aleutian Is.	2,036
Martin (1912)	Alaska	1,830
Great Sitkin (1974)	Aleutian Is.	1,750
Cleveland (1951)	Aleutian Is.	1,730
Gareloi	Aleutian Is.	1,627
Korovin	Aleutian Is.	1,480
Kanaga	Aleutian Is.	1,348
Aniakchak	Alaska	1,348
Akutan (1974)	Aleutian Is.	1,293
Kiska (1969)	Aleutian Is.	1,220
Augustine (1976)	Alaska	1,210
Little Sitkin	Aleutian Is.	1,195
Okmok (1945)	Aleutian Is.	1,072

Important Islands and Their Areas

Source: National Geographic Society, Washington, D.C.

Figure in parentheses shows rank among the world's 10 largest islands, some islands have not been surveyed accurately; in such cases estimated areas are shown.

Location-Ownership

Area in square miles

Arctic Ocean

Canadian

Axel Heiberg	16,671
Baffin (5)	195,928
Banks	27,038
Bathurst	6,194
Devon	21,331
Ellesmere (10)	75,767
Melville	16,274
Prince of Wales	12,872
Somerset	9,570
Southampton	15,913
Victoria (9)	83,896

USSR

Franz Josef Land	8,000
Novaya Zemlya (two is.)	35,000
Wrangel	2,800

Norwegian

Svalbard	23,940
Nordaustlandet	5,410
Spitsbergen	15,060

Atlantic Ocean

Anticosti, Canada	3,066
Ascension, UK	34
Azores, Portugal	902
Faial	67
Sao Miguel	291
Bahamas	5,380
Bermuda Is., UK	20
Block, Rhode Island	10
Canary Is., Spain	2,808
Fuerteventura	668
Gran Canaria	592
Tenerife	795
Cape Breton, Canada	3,981
Cape Verde Is.	1,557
Faeroe Is., Denmark	540
Falkland Is., UK	4,618
Fernando de Noronha Archipelago, Brazil	7
Greenland, Denmark (1)	840,000
Iceland	39,768
Long Island, N. Y.	1,396
Macias Nguema Biyogo, Equatorial Guinea	785
Madeira Is., Portugal	307
Marajo, Brazil	15,528
Martha's Vineyard, Mass.	91
Mount Desert, Me.	108
Nantucket, Mass.	46
Newfoundland, Canada	42,031
Prince Edward, Canada	2,184
St. Helena, UK	47
South Georgia, UK	1,450
Tierra del Fuego, Chile and Argentina	17,800
Tristan da Cunha, UK	40

British Isles

Great Britain, mainland (8)	84,186
Channel Islands	75
Guernsey	24
Jersey	45
Sark	2
Hebrides	2,744
Ireland	32,598
Irish Republic	27,136
Northern Ireland	5,462
Man	227
Orkney Is.	390
Scilly Is.	6
Shetland Is.	567
Skye	670
Wight	147

Baltic Sea

Aland Is., Finland	581
Bornholm, Denmark	227
Gotland, Sweden	1,164

Caribbean Sea

Antigua, UK	108
Aruba, Netherlands	75
Barbados	166
Cuba	44,218
Isle of Pines	1,182
Curacao, Netherlands	171
Dominica, UK	290
Guadeloupe, France	687
Hispaniola, Haiti and Dominican Republic	29,530
Jamaica	4,232
Martinique, France	425
Puerto Rico, U. S.	3,435
Tobago	116
Trinidad	1,864
Virgin Is., UK	59
Virgin Is., U.S.	133

Indian Ocean

Andaman Is., India	2,500
Madagascar (4)	226,657
Mauritius	720
Pemba, Tanzania	380
Reunion, France	969
Seychelles	107
Sri Lanka	25,332
Zanzibar, Tanzania	640

Persian Gulf

Bahrain	231

Mediterranean Sea

Balearic Is., Spain	1,936
Corfu, Greece	229
Corsica, France	3,365
Crete, Greece	3,186
Cyprus	3,572
Elba, Italy	86
Euboea, Greece	1,409
Malta	122
Rhodes, Greece	542
Sardinia, Italy	9,262
Sicily, Italy	9,822

Pacific Ocean

Aleutian Is., U. S.	6,821
Adak	289
Amchitka	121
Attu	388
Kanaga	135
Kiska	110
Tanaga	209
Umnak	675
Unalaska	1,064
Unimak	1,600
Canton, U. S., UK*	4
Caroline Is., U. S. trust terr.	463
Christmas, U. S., UK*	94
Diomede, Big, USSR	11
Diomede, Little, U.S.	2
Easter, Chile	68
Fiji	7,055
Vanua Levi	2,242
Viti Levu	4,109
Funafuti, UK, U.S.*	2
Galapagos Is., Ecuador	3,043
Guadalcanal, UK	2,500
Hainan, China	13,000
Hawaiian Is., U.S.	6,450
Hawaii	4,037
Oahu	593
Hong Kong, UK	29
Japan	143,750
Hokkaido	30,100
Honshu (7)	87,804
Iwo Jima	9
Kyushu	14,154
Okinawa	460
Shikoku	7,053
Kodiak, U.S.	3,670
Mariana Is., U.S. trust terr. excluding Guam	182
Guam, U. S.	209
Marquesas Is., France	492
Marshall Is., U.S. trust terr.	69
Bikini*	2
Nauru	8
New Caledonia, France	6,530
New Guinea (2)	305,577
New Hebrides, UK, Fr.	5,700
New Zealand	103,747
Chatham	372
North	44,190
South	58,192
Stewart	674
Philippines	115,830
Leyte	2,787
Luzon	40,880
Mindanao	36,775
Mindoro	3,790
Negros	4,907
Palawan	4,554
Panay	4,446
Samar	5,050
Quemoy, Taiwan	56
Sakhalin, USSR	29,500
Samoa Is.	1,177
American Samoa	76
Tutuila	52
Western Samoa	1,101
Savaii	670
Upolu	429
Santa Catalina, U.S.	72
Tahiti, France	402
Taiwan	13,812
Tasmania, Australia	26,383
Tonga Is.	270
Vancouver, Canada	12,079

East Indies

Bali, Indonesia	2,147
Borneo, Indonesia-Malaysia, UK (3)	280,107
Celebes, Indonesia	69,255
Java, Indonesia	48,763
Madura, Indonesia	2,113
Moluccas, Indonesia	28,766
New Britain, Papua New Guinea	14,050
New Ireland, Papua New Guinea	2,700
Sumatra, Indonesia (6)	182,860
Timor	11,570

*Atolls: Bikini (lagoon area, 230 sq. mi., land area 2 sq. mi.), U.S. Trust Territory of the Pacific Islands; Canton (lagoon 20 sq. mi., land 4 sq. mi.), U.S. and UK; Christmas (lagoon 140 sq. mi., land 94 sq. mi.). U.S. and UK; Funafuti (lagoon 84 sq. mi., land 2 sq. mi.). U.S. and UK.

Australia, often called an island, is a continent. Its mainland area is 2,941,526 sq. mi.

Islands in minor waters; Manhattan (23 sq. mi.) Staten (58 sq. mi.) and Governors (173 acres), all in New York Harbor, U.S.; Isle Royale (209 sq. mi.), Lake Superior, U.S.; Manitoulin (1,068 sq. mi.), Lake Huron, Canada; Pinang (110 sq. mi.), Strait of Malacca, Malaysia; Singapore (224 sq. mi.), Singapore Strait, Singapore.

How Deep Is the Ocean?

Principal ocean depths. **Source:** Defense Mapping Agency Hydrographic Center

Name of area	Location		Depth Meters	Depth Fathoms	Feet	Ship and/or country	Year
Pacific Ocean							
Mariana Trench	11°21′N,	142°12′E.	11,034	6,033	36,198	Vityaz (USSR)	1957
Tonga Trench	23°15.3′S,	174°44.7′W.	10,882	5,950	35,702	Vityaz (USSR)	1957
Kuril Trench	44°15.2′N,	150°34.2′E.	10,542	5,764	34,587	Vityaz (USSR)	1954
Philippine Trench	10°24′N,	126°40′E.	10,539	5,763	34,578	Galathea (Danish)	1951
Izu Trench	30°32′N,	142°31′E.	10,374	5,673	34,033	USS Ramapo	1932
Kermadec Trench	31°52.8′S,	177°20.6′W.	10,047	5,494	32,964	Vityaz (USSR)	1957
Bonin Trench	24°30′N,	143°24′E.	9,156	5,005	30,032	Vityaz (USSR)	1964
New Britain Trench	06°34′S,	153°55′E	9,140	4,998	29,988	Planet (German)	1910
Yap Trench	08°33′N,	138°02′E.	8,527	4,662	27,976	Vityaz (USSR)	1958
Japan Trench	36°08′N,	142°43′E.	8,412	4,597	27,591	Bathymetric Map (USSR)	1964
Palau Trench	07°40′N,	135°04′E.	8,138	4,449	26,693	Stefan (Germany)	1905
Aleutian Trench	50°53′N,	176°23′E.	8,100	4,429	26,574	USCGC Bering Strait	1953
Peru Chile Trench	23°18′S,	71°41′W	8,064	4,409	26,454	R/V Spencer F. Baird	1957
(Atacama Trench)	23°27′S,	71°21′W.	8,064	4,409	26,454	IGY	
New Hebrides Trench	20°36′S,	168°37′E.	7,570	4,138	24,830	Planet (Germany)	1910
Ryukyu Trench	25°15′N,	128°32′E.	7,507	4,105	24,629	Mansyu (Japan)	1925
Mid. America Trench	14°02′N,	93°39′W.	6,669	3,642	21,852	USS Epce	1965
Atlantic Ocean							
Puerto Rico Trench	19°35′N,	68°17′W.	8,648	4,729	28,374	SS Archerfish	1961
Cayman Trench	19°12′N,	80°00′W.	7,535	4,120	24,720	R/V Vema (U.S.)	1960
So. Sandwich Trench	55°14′S,	26°29′W.	8,252	4,512	27,072	USS Eltanin	1963
Romanche Gap	00°16′S,	18°35′W.	7,864	4,300	25,800	R/V Vema (U.S.)	1957
Brazil Basin	09°10′S,	23°02′W.	6,119	3,346	20,076	R/V Vema (U.S.)	1956
Indian Ocean							
Java Trench	10°15′S,	109°E′(approx.)	7,725	4,224	25,344	Natl Geographic	1967
Ob Trench	(no position)		6,874	3,759	22,553	Nat'l Geographic	1967
Vema Trench	(no position)		6,402	3,501	21,004	Nat'l Geographic	1967
Agulhas Basin	(no position)		6,195	3,388	20,325	Nat'l Geographic	1967
Diamantina Trench	35°00′S,	105°35′E.	6,062	3,315	19,800	Nat'l Geographic	1967
Arctic Ocean							
Eurasia Basin	82°23′N,	19°31′E.	5,450	2,980	17,880	Fidor Lithke (USSR)	1955
Mediterranean Sea							
Ionian Basin	36°32′N,	21°06′E.	5,150	2,816	16,896	USS Tanner	1955

Ocean Areas and Average Depths

Four major bodies of water are recognized by geographers and mapmakers. They are: the Pacific, Atlantic, Indian, and Arctic oceans. The Atlantic and Pacific oceans are considered divided at the equator into the No. and So. Atlantic; the No. and So. Pacific. The Arctic Ocean is the name for waters north of the continental land masses in the region of the Arctic Circle.

	Sq. miles	Avg. depth in feet
Pacific Ocean	64,186,300	13,739
Atlantic Ocean	33,420,000	12,257
Indian Ocean	28,350,500	12,704
Arctic Ocean	5,105,700	4,362
South China Sea	1,148,500	4,802
Caribbean Sea	971,400	8,448
Mediterranean Sea	969,100	4,926
Bering Sea	873,000	4,893
Gulf of Mexico	582,100	5,297
Sea of Okhotsk	537,500	3,192
Sea of Japan	391,100	5,468
Hudson Bay	281,900	305
East China Sea	256,600	620
Andaman Sea	218,100	3,667
Black Sea	196,100	3,906
Red Sea	174,900	1,764
North Sea	164,900	308
Baltic Sea	147,500	180
Yellow Sea	113,500	121
Persian Gulf	88,800	328
Gulf of California	59,100	2,375

The Malayan Sea is not considered a geographical entity but a term used for convenience for waters between the South Pacific and the Indian Ocean.

Continental Statistics

Source: National Geographic Society, Washington, D.C.

Continents	Area (sq. mi.)	% of Earth	Population (est.)	% World total	Highest point (in feet)	Lowest point
Asia	16,988,000	29.5	2,391,200,000	58.6	Everest, 29,028	Dead Sea, −1,302
Africa	11,506,000	20.0	423,000,000	10.4	Kilimanjaro, 19,340	Lake Assal, −512
North America	9,390,000	16.3	353,000,000	8.6	McKinley, 20,320	Death Valley, −282
South America	6,795,000	11.8	223,000,000	5.5	Aconcagua, 22,834	Valdes Penin., −131
Europe	3,745,000	6.5	670,800,000	16.4	El'brus, 18,510	Caspian Sea −92
Australia	2,968,000	5.2	13,900,000	0.3	Kosciusko, 7,310	Lake Eyre, −52
Antarctica	5,500,000	9.6	—	—	Vinson Massif, 16,860	Not Known
Est. World Population			**4,083,000,000**			

Highest and Lowest Continental Altitudes

Source: National Geographic Society, Washington, D.C.

Continent	Highest point	Feet elevation	Lowest point	Feet below sea level
Asia	Mount Everest, Nepal-Tibet	29,028	Dead Sea, Israel-Jordan	1,302
South America	Mount Aconcagua, Argentina	22,834	Valdes Peninsula, Argentina	131
North America	Mount McKinley, Alaska	20,320	Death Valley, California	282
Africa	Kilimanjaro, Tanzania	19,340	Lake Assal, Djibouti	512
Europe	Mount El'brus USSR Caucasus Mts.	18,510	Caspian Sea, USSR	92
Antarctica	Vinson Massif	16,860	Unknown	...
Australia	Mount Kosciusko, New South Wales	7,310	Lake Eyre, South Australia	52

Height of Mount Everest

Mt. Everest was considered to be 29,002 ft. tall when Edmund Hillary and Tenzing Norgay scaled it in 1953. This triangulation figure had been accepted since 1850. In 1954 the Surveyor General of the Republic of India set the height at 29,028 ft., plus or minus 10 ft. because of snow. The National Geographic Society accepts the new figure, but many mountaineering groups still use 29,002 ft.

High Peaks in United States, Canada, Mexico

Name	Place	Feet
McKinley	Alas	20,320
Logan	Can	19,850
Citlaltepec (Orizaba)	Mexico	18,700
St. Elias	Alas-Can	18,008
Popocatepetl	Mexico	17,887
Foraker	Alas	17,400
Iztaccihuatl	Mexico	17,343
Lucania	Can	17,147
King	Can	16,971
Steele	Can	16,644
Bona	Alas	16,550
Blackburn	Alas	16,390
Kennedy	Alas	16,286
Sanford	Alas	16,237
South Buttress	Alas	15,885
Wood	Can	15,885
Vancouver	Alas-Can	15,700
Churchill	Alas	15,638
Fairweather	Alas-Can	15,300
Zinantecatl (Toluca)	Mexico	15,016
Hubbard	Alas-Can	15,015
Bear	Alas	14,831
Walsh	Can	14,780
East Buttress	Alas	14,730
Matlalcueyetl	Mexico	14,636
Hunter	Alas	14,573
Alverstone	Alas-Can	14,565
Browne Tower	Alas	14,530
Whitney	Cal	14,494
Elbert	Col	14,433
Massive	Col	14,421
Harvard	Col	14,420
Rainier	Wash	14,410
Williamson	Cal	14,375
Blanca	Col	14,345
La Plata	Col	14,336
Uncompahgre	Col	14,309
Crestone	Col	14,294
Lincoln	Col	14,286
Grays	Col	14,270
Antero	Col	14,269
Torreys	Col	14,267
Castle	Col	14,265
Quandary	Col	14,265
Evans	Col	14,264
Longs	Col	14,256
McArthur	Can	14,253
Wilson	Col	14,246
White	Cal	14,246
North Palisade	Cal	14,242
Shavano	Col	14,229
Belford	Col	14,197
Princeton	Col	14,197
Crestone Needle	Col	14,197
Yale	Col	14,196
Bross	Col	14,172
Kit Carson	Col	14,165
Wrangell	Alas	14,163
Shasta	Cal	14,162
Sill	Cal	14,162
El Diente	Col	14,159
Maroon	Col	14,156
Tabeguache	Col	14,155
Oxford	Col	14,153
Sneffels	Col	14,150
Point Success	Wash	14,150
Democrat	Col	14,148
Capitol	Col	14,130
Liberty Cap	Wash	14,112
Pikes Peak	Col	14,110
Snowmass	Col	14,092
Windom	Col	14,087
Russell	Cal	14,086
Eolus	Col	14,084
Columbia	Col	14,073
Augusta	Alas-Can	14,070
Missouri	Col	14,067
Humboldt	Col	14,064
Bierstadt	Col	14,060
Sunlight	Col	14,059
Split	Cal	14,058
Nauhcampatepetl (Cofre de Perote)	Mexico	14,049
Handies	Col	14,048
Culebra	Col	14,047
Langley	Cal	14,042
Lindsey	Col	14,042
Middle Palisade	Cal	14,040
Little Bear	Col	14,037
Sherman	Col	14,036
Redcloud	Col	14,034
Tyndall	Cal	14,018
Pyramid	Col	14,018
Wilson Peak	Col	14,017
Muir	Cal	14,015
Wetterhorn	Col	14,015
North Maroon	Col	14,014
San Luis	Col	14,014
Huron	Col	14,005
Holy Cross	Col	14,005
Colima	Mexico	14,003
Sunshine	Col	14,001
Grizzly	Col	14,000
Barnard	Cal	13,990
Stewart	Col	13,980
Keith	Cal	13,977
Ouray	Col	13,971
Le Conte	Cal	13,960
Meeker	Col	13,911
Kennedy	Can	13,905

South America

Peak, Country	Feet
Aconcagua, Argentina	22,834
Ojos del Salado, Arg.-Chile	22,572
Bonete, Argentina	22,546
Tupungato, Argentina-Chile	22,310
Pissis, Argentina	22,241
Mercedario, Argentina	22,211
Huascaran, Peru	22,205
Llullaillaco, Argentina-Chile	22,057
El Libertador, Argentina	22,047
Cachi, Argentina	22,047
Yerupaja, Peru	21,709
Galan, Argentina	21,654
El Muerto, Argentina-Chile	21,457
Sajama, Bolivia	21,391
Nacimiento, Argentina	21,302
Illimani, Bolivia	21,201
Coropuna, Peru	21,083
Laudo, Argentina	20,997
Ancohuma, Bolivia	20,958
Ausangate, Peru	20,945
Toro, Argentina-Chile	20,932
Illampu, Bolivia	20,873
Tres Cruces, Argentina-Chile	20,853
Huandoy, Peru	20,852
Parinacota, Bolivia-Chile	20,768
Tortolas, Argentina-Chile	20,745
Ampato, Peru	20,702
Condor, Argentina	20,669
Salcantay, Peru	20,574
Chimborazo, Ecuador	20,561
Huancarhuas, Peru	20,531
Famatina, Arg.	20,505
Pumasillo, Peru	20,492
Solo, Argentina	20,492
Polleras, Argentina	20,456
Pular, Chile	20,423
Chani, Argentina	20,341
Aucanquilcha, Chile	20,295
Juncal, Argentina-Chile	20,276
Negro, Argentina	20,184
Quela, Argentina	20,128
Condoriri, Bolivia	20,095
Palermo, Argentina	20,079
Solimana, Peru	20,068
San Juan, Argentina-Chile	20,049
Sierra Nevada, Arg.-Chile	20,023
Antofalla, Argentina	20,013
Marmolejo, Argentina-Chile	20,013
Chachani, Peru	19,931
Licancabur, Argentina-Chile	19,425

The highest point in the West Indies is in the Dominican Republic, Pico Duarte (10,417 ft.)

Africa, Australia, and Oceania

Peak, country	Feet
Kilimanjaro, Tanzania	19,340
Kenya, Kenya	17,058
Margherita Pk., Uganda-Zaire	16,763
Jaja, New Guinea	16,500
Trikora, New Guinea	15,585
Mandala, New Guinea	15,420
Ras Dashan, Ethiopia	15,158
Meru, Tanzania	14,979
Wilhelm, New Guinea	14,793
Karisimbi, Zaire-Rwanda	14,787
Elgon, Kenya-Uganda	14,178
Batu, Ethiopia	14,131
Guna, Ethiopia	13,881
Gughe, Ethiopia	13,780
Toubkal, Morocco	13,665
Kinabalu, Malaysia	13,455
Kerinci, Sumatra	12,467
Cook, New Zealand	12,349
Teide, Canary Islands	12,198
Semeru, Java	12,060
Kosciusko, Australia	7,310

Europe

Alps

Peak, country	Feet
Mont Blanc, Fr. It.	15,771
Monte Rosa (highest peak of group), Switz.	15,203
Dom, Switz.	14,911
Liskamm, It., Switz.	14,852
Weisshorn, Switz.	14,780
Taschhorn, Switz.	14,733
Matterhorn, It., Switz.	14,690
Dent Blanche, Switz.	14,293
Nadelhorn, Switz.	14,196
Grand Combin, Switz.	14,154
Lenzpitze, Switz.	14,088
Finsteraarhorn, Switz.	14,022
Castor, Switz.	13,865
Zinalrothorn, Switz.	13,849
Hohberghorn, Switz.	13,842
Alphubel, Switz.	13,799
Rimpfischhorn, Switz.	13,776
Aletschorn, Switz.	13,763
Strahlhorn, Switz.	13,747
Dent D'Herens, Switz.	13,686
Breithorn, It., Switz.	13,665
Bishorn, Switz.	13,645
Jungfrau, Switz.	13,642
Ecrins, Fr.	13,461
Monch, Switz.	13,448
Pollux, Switz.	13,422
Schreckhorn, Switz.	13,379
Ober Gabelhorn, Switz.	13,330
Gran Paradiso, It.	13,323
Bernina, It., Switz.	13,284
Fiescherhorn, Switz.	13,283
Grunhorn, Switz.	13,266
Lauteraarhorn, Switz.	13,261
Durrenhorn, Switz.	13,238
Allalinhorn, Switz.	13,213
Weissmies, Switz.	13,199
Lagginhorn, Switz.	13,156
Zupo, Switz.	13,120
Fletschhorn, Switz.	13,110
Adlerhorn, Switz.	13,081
Gletscherhorn, Switz.	13,068
Schalihorn, Switz.	13,040
Scerscen, Switz.	13,028
Eiger, Switz.	13,025
Jagerhorn, Switz.	13,024
Rottalhorn, Switz.	13,022

Pyrenees

Peak, country	Feet
Aneto, Sp.	11,168
Posets, Sp.	11,073
Perdido, Sp.	11,007
Vignemale, Fr., Sp.	10,820
Long, Sp.	10,479
Estats, Sp.	10,304
Montcalm, Sp.	10,105

Caucasus (Europe-Asia)

Peak, country	Feet
El'brus, USSR	18,510
Shkara, USSR	17,064
Dykh Tau, USSR	17,054
Kashtan Tau, USSR	16,877
Dzhangi Tau, USSR	16,565
Kazbek, USSR	16,558

Asia

Peak	Country	Feet
Everest	Nepal-Tibet	29,028
K2 (Godwin Austen)	Kashmir	28,250
Kanchenjunga	India-Nepal	28,208
Lhotse I (Everest)	Nepal-Tibet	27,923
Makalu I	Nepal-Tibet	27,824
Lhotse II (Everest)	Nepal-Tibet	27,560
Dhaulagiri	Nepal	26,810
Manaslu I	Nepal	26,760
Cho Oyu	Nepal-Tibet	26,750
Nanga Parbat	Kashmir	26,660
Annapurna I	Nepal	26,504
Gasherbrum	Kashmir	26,470
Broad	Kashmir	26,400
Gosainthan	Tibet	26,287
Annapurna II	Nepal	26,041
Gyachung Kang	Nepal-Tibet	25,910
Disteghil Sar	Kashmir	25,868
Himalchuli	Nepal	25,801
Nuptse (Everest)	Nepal-Tibet	25,726
Masherbrum	Kashmir	25,660
Nanda Devi	India	25,645
Rakaposhi	Kashmir	25,550
Kamet	India-Tibet	25,447
Namcha Barwa	Tibet	25,445
Gurla Mandhata	Tibet	25,355
Ulugh Muz Tagh	Sinkiang-Tibet	25,340
Kungur	Sinkiang	25,325
Tirich Mir	Pakistan	25,230
Makalu II	Nepal-Tibet	25,120
Minya Konka	China	24,900
Kula Gangri	Bhutan-Tibet	24,784
Changtzu (Everest)	Nepal-Tibet	24,780
Muz Tagh Ata	Sinkiang	24,757
Skyang Kangri	Kashmir	24,750
Communism Peak	USSR	24,590
Jongsang Peak	India-Nepal	24,472
Pobedy Peak	Sinkiang-USSR	24,406
Sia Kangri	Kashmir	24,350
Haramosh Peak	Pakistan	24,270
Istoro Nal	Pakistan	24,240
Tent Peak	India-Nepal	24,165
Chomo Lhari	Bhutan-Tibet	24,040
Chamlang	Nepal	24,012
Kabru	India-Nepal	24,002
Alung Gangri	Tibet	24,000
Baltoro Kangri	Kashmir	23,990
Mussu Shan	Sinkiang	23,890
Mana	India	23,860
Baruntse	Nepal	23,688
Nepal Peak	India-Nepal	23,500
Amne Machin	China	23,490
Gauri Sankar	Nepal-Tibet	23,440
Badrinath	India	23,420
Nunkun	Kashmir	23,410
Lenina Peak	USSR	23,405
Pyramid	India-Nepal	23,400
Api	Nepal	23,399
Pauhunri	India-Tibet	23,385
Trisul	India	23,360
Kangto	India-Tibet	23,260
Nyenchhen Thanglha	Tibet	23,255
Trisuli	India	23,210
Pumori	Nepal-Tibet	23,190
Dunagiri	India	23,184
Lombo Kangra	Tibet	23,165
Saipal	Nepal	23,100
Macha Pucchare	Nepal	22,958
Numbar	Nepal	22,817
Kanjiroba	Nepal	22,580
Ama Dablam	Nepal	22,350
Cho Polu	Nepal	22,093
Lingtren	Nepal-Tibet	21,972
Khumbutse	Nepal-Tibet	21,785
Hlako Gangri	Tibet	21,266
Mt. Grosvenor	China	21,190
Thagchhab Gangri	Tibet	20,970
Damavand	Iran	18,606
Ararat	Turkey	16,946

Antarctica

Peak	Feet
Vinson Massif	16,860
Tyree	16,290
Shinn	15,750
Gardner	15,375
Epperly	15,100
Kirkpatrick	14,855
Elizabeth	14,698
Markham	14,290
Bell	14,117
Mackellar	14,098
Anderson	13,957
Bentley	13,934
Kaplan	13,878
Andrew Jackson	13,750
Sidley	13,720
Ostenso	13,710
Minto	13,668
Miller	13,650
Long Gables	13,620
Dickerson	13,517
Giovinetto	13,412
Wade	13,400
Fisher	13,386
Fridtjof Nansen	13,350
Wexler	13,202
Lister	13,200
Shear	13,100
Odishaw	13,008
Donaldson	12,894
Ray	12,808
Sellery	12,779
Waterman	12,730
Anne	12,703
Press	12,566
Falla	12,549
Rucker	12,520
Goldthwait	12,510
Morris	12,500
Erebus	12,450
Campbell	12,434
Don Pedro Christophersen	12,355
Lysaght	12,326
Huggins	12,247
Sabine	12,200
Astor	12,175
Mohl	12,172
Frakes	12,064
Jones	12,040
Gjelsvik	12,008
Coman	12,000

Principal World Rivers

Source: National Geographic Society, Washington, D.C. (length in miles)

River	Outflow	Lgth
Albany	James Bay	610
Amazon	Atlantic Ocean	4,000
Amu	Aral Sea	1,578
Amur	Tatar Strait	2,700
Angara	Yenisey River	1,151
Arkansas	Mississippi	1,459
Back	Arctic Ocean	605
Brahmaputra	Bay of Bengal	1,800
Bug, Southern	Dnieper River	532
Bug, Western	Wisla River	481
Canadian	Arkansas River	906
Churchill, Man.	Hudson Bay	1,000
Churchill, Que.	Atlantic Ocean	532
Colorado	Gulf of Calif.	1,450
Columbia	Pacific Ocean	1,243
Congo	Atlantic Ocean	2,718
Danube	Black Sea	1,776
Dnieper	Black Sea	1,420
Dniester	Black Sea	877
Don	Sea of Azov	1,224
Drava	Danube River	447
Dvina, North	White Sea	824
Dvina, West	Gulf of Riga	634
Ebro	Mediterranean	565
Elbe	North Sea	724
Euphrates	Persian Gulf	2,235
Fraser	Str. of Georgia	850
Gambia	Atlantic Ocean	700
Ganges	Bay of Bengal	1,560
Garonne	Bay of Biscay	357
Hsi	S. China Sea	1,200
Huang	Yellow Sea	2,900
Indus	Arabian Sea	1,800
Irrawaddy	Bay of Bengal	1,300
Japura	Amazon River	1,750
Jordan	Dead Sea	200
Kootenay	Columbia River	485
Lena	Laptev Sea	2,680
Loire	Bay of Biscay	634
Mackenzie	Arctic Ocean	2,635
Madeira	Amazon River	2,013
Magdalena	Caribbean Sea	956
Marne	Seine River	326
Mekong	S. China Sea	2,600
Meuse	North Sea	580
Mississippi	Gulf of Mexico	2,348
Missouri	Mississippi	2,533
Murray-Darling	Indian Ocean	2,310
Negro	Amazon	1,400
Nelson	Hudson Bay	1,600
Niger	Gulf of Guinea	2,600
Nile	Mediterranean	4,145
Ob-Irtysh	Gulf of Ob	3,460
Oder	Baltic Sea	567
Ohio	Mississippi	1,306
Orange	Atlantic Ocean	1,300
Orinoco	Atlantic Ocean	1,600
Ottawa	St. Lawrence R.	790
Paraguay	Parana River	1,584
Parana	Rio de la Plata	2,500
Peace	Slave River	1,195
Pilcomayo	Paraguay River	1,000
Po	Adriatic Sea	405
Purus	Amazon River	2,100
Red	Mississippi	1,270
Red River of N.	Lake Winnipeg	545
Rhine	North Sea	820
Rhone	Gulf of Lions	505
Rio de la Plata	Atlantic Ocean	150
Rio Grande	Gulf of Mexico	1,885
Rio Roosevelt	Aripuana	400
Saguenay	St. Lawrence R.	434
St. John	Bay of Fundy	418
St. Lawrence	Gulf of St. Law.	800
Salween	Andaman Sea	1,500
Sao Francisco	Atlantic Ocean	1,988
Saskatchewan	Lake Winnipeg	1,205
Seine	English Chan.	482
Shannon	Atlantic Ocean	230
Snake	Columbia River	1,038
Sungari	Amur River	1,150
Syr	Aral Sea	1,370
Tajo, Tagus	Atlantic Ocean	626
Tennessee	Ohio River	652
Thames	North Sea	215
Tiber	Tyrrhenian Sea	252
Tigris	Euphrates	1,180
Tisza	Danube River	600
Tocantins	Para River	1,677
Ural	Caspian Sea	1,575
Uruguay	Rio de la Plata	1,000
Volga	Caspian Sea	2,290
Weser	North Sea	454
Wisla	Bay of Danzig	675
Yangtze	E. China Sea	3,400
Yellow (See Huang)		
Yenisey	Kara Sea	2,566
Yukon	Bering Sea	1,979
Zambezi	Indian Ocean	1,700

Major Rivers in North America

Source: U.S. Geological Survey

River	Source or Upper Limit of Length	Outflow	Miles
Alabama	Gilmer County, Ga.	Mobile River	735
Albany	Lake St. Joseph, Ont., Can.	James Bay	320
Allegheny	Potter County, Pa.	Ohio River	325
Altamaha-Ocmulgee	Junction of Yellow and South Rivers, Newton County, Ga.	Atlantic Ocean	392
Apalachicola-Chattahoochee	Towns County, Ga.	Gulf of Mexico, Fla.	524
Arkansas	Lake County, Col.	Mississippi River, Ark.	1,459
Assiniboine	Eastern Saskatchewan	Red River	450
Attawapiskat	Attawapiskat, Ont., Can.	James Bay	465
Big Black (Miss.)	Webster County, Miss.	Mississippi River	330
Big Horn	Junction of Wind and Popo Agie Rivers, Fremont County, Wyo.	Yellowstone River, Mon.	336
Black (N.W.T.)	Contwoyto Lake	Chantrey Inlet	600
Brazos	Junction of Salt and Double Mountain Forks, Stonewall County, Tex.	Gulf of Mexico	870
Canadian	Las Animas County, Col.	Arkansas River, Okla.	906
Cedar (Iowa)	Dodge County, Minn.	Iowa River, Ia.	329
Cheyenne	Junction of Antelope Creek and Dry Fork, Converse County, Wyo.	Missouri River	290
Churchill	Methy Lake	Hudson Bay	1,000
Cimarron	Colfax County, N. M.	Arkansas River, Okla.	600
Clark Fork-Pend Oreille	Silver Bow County, Mon.	Columbia River, B.C.	505
Colorado (Ariz.)	Rocky Mountain National Park, Col. (90 miles in Mexico)	Gulf of Cal., Mexico	1,450
Colorado (Texas)	West Texas	Matagorda Bay	840
Columbia	Columbia Lake, British Columbia	Pacific Ocean, bet. Ore. and Wash.	1,243
Columbia, Upper	Columbia Lake, British Columbia	To mouth of Snake River	890
Connecticut	Third Connecticut Lake, N.H.	L.I. Sound, Conn.	407
Coppermine (N.W.T.)	Lac de Gras	Coronation Gulf (Atlantic Ocean)	525
Cumberland	Letcher County, Ky.	Ohio River	720
Delaware	Schoharie County, N.Y.	Liston Point, Delaware Bay	390
Fraser	Near Mount Robson (on Continental Divide)	Strait of Georgia	850
Gila	Catron County, N.M.	Colorado River, Ariz.	630
Green (Ut.-Wyo.)	Junction of Wells and Trail Creeks, Sublette County, Wyo.	Colorado River, Ut.	730
Hamilton (Lab.)	Lake Ashuanipi	Atlantic Ocean	600
Hudson	Henderson Lake, Essex County, N.Y.	Upper N.Y. Bay, N.Y.,-N.J.	306
Illinois	St. Joseph County, Ind.	Mississippi River	420
James (N.D.-S.D.)	Wells County, N.D.	Missouri River, S.D.	710
James (Va.)	Junction of Jackson and Cowpasture Rivers, Botetourt County, Va.	Hampton Roads	340
Kanawha-New	Junction of North and South Forks of New River, N.C.	Ohio River	352
Kentucky	Junction of North and Middle Forks, Lee County, K.	Ohio River	259

River	Source or Upper Limit of Length	Outflow	Miles
Klamath	Lake Ewauna, Klamath Falls, Ore.	Pacific Ocean	250
Koyukuk	Endicott Mountains, Alaska	Yukon River	470
Kuskokwim	Alaska Range	Kuskokwim Bay	680
Liard	Southern Yukon, Alaska	Mackenzie River	570
Little Missouri	Crook County, Wyo.	Missouri River	560
Mackenzie	Great Slave Lake	Arctic Ocean	900
Milk	Junction of North and South Forks, Alberta Province	Missouri River, Mon.	625
Minnesota	Big Stone Lake, Minn.	Mississippi River, St. Paul, Minn.	332
Mississippi	Lake Itasca, Minn.	Mouth of Southwest Pass	2,348
Mississippi, Upper	Lake Itasca, Minn.	To mouth of Missouri R.	1,171
Mississippi-Missouri-Red Rock	Source of Red Rock River, Mon.	Mouth of Southwest Pass	3,710
Missouri	Junction of Jefferson, Madison, and Gallatin Rivers, Madison County, Mon.	Mississippi River	2,315
Missouri-Red Rock	Source of Red Rock River, Mon.	Mississippi River	2,533
Mobile-Alabama-Coosa	Gilmer County, Ga.	Mobile Bay	780
Nelson (Manitoba)	Lake Winnipeg	Hudson Bay	410
Neosho	Morris County, Kan.	Arkansas River, Okla.	460
Niobrara	Niobrara County, Wyo.	Missouri River, Neb.	431
North Canadian	Union County, N.M.	Canadian River, Okla.	760
North Platte	Junction of Grizzly and Little Grizzly Creeks, Jackson County, Col.	Platte River, Neb.	618
Ohio	Junction of Allegheny and Monongahela Rivers, Pittsburgh, Pa.	Mississippi River, Ill.-Ky.	981
Ohio-Allegheny	Potter County, Pa.	Mississippi River	1,306
Osage	East-central Kansas	Missouri River, Mo.	500
Ottawa	Lake Capimitchigama	St. Lawrence	696
Ouachita	Polk County, Ark.	Red River, La.	605
Pearl	Neshoba County, Miss.	Gulf of Mexico, Miss.-La.	411
Peace	Stikine Mountains, B.C.	Slave River	1,054
Pecos	Mora County, N.M.	Rio Grande, Tex.	735
Pee Dee-Yadkin	Watauga County, N.C.	Winyah Bay, S.C.	435
Pend Oreille	Near Butte, Mon.	Columbia River	490
Platte	Junction of North and South Platte Rivers, Neb.	Missouri River, Neb.	310
Porcupine	Ogilvie Mountains, Alaska	Yukon River, Alaska	460
Potomac	Garrett County, Md.	Chesapeake Bay	383
Powder	Junction of South and Middle Forks, Wyo.	Yellowstone River, Mon.	375
Red (Okla.-Tex.-La.)	Curry County, N.M.	Mississippi River	1,270
Red River of the North	Junction of Otter Tail and Boise de Sioux Rivers, Wilkin County, Minn.	Lake Winnipeg, Manitoba	545
Republican	Junction of North Fork and Arikaree River, Neb.	Kansas River, Kan.	445
Rio Grande	San Juan County, Col.	Gulf of Mexico	1,885
Roanoke	Junction of North and South Forks, Montgomery County, Va.	Albemarle Sound, N.C.	380
Rock (Ill.-Wis.)	Dodge County, Wis.	Mississippi River, Ill.	300
Sabine	Junction of South and Caddo Forks, Hunt County, Tex.	Sabine Lake, Tex.-La.	380
Sacramento	Siskiyou County, Cal.	Suisun Bay	377
St. Francis	Iron County, Mo.	Mississippi River, Ark.	425
St. Lawrence	Lake Ontario	Gulf of St. Lawrence (Atlantic Ocean)	800
Salmon (Idaho)	Custer County, Ida.	Snake River, Ida.	420
San Joaquin	Junction of South and Middle Forks, Madera County, Cal.	Suisun Bay	350
San Juan	Silver Lake, Archuleta County, Col.	Colorado River, Ut.	360
Santee-Wateree-Catawba	McDowell County, N.C.	Atlantic Ocean, S.C.	538
Saskatchewan, North	Rocky Mountains	Lake Winnipeg	1,100
Saskatchewan, South	Rocky Mountains	Lake Winnipeg	1,205
Savannah	Junction of Seneca and Tugaloo Rivers, Anderson County, S.C.	Atlantic Ocean, Ga.-S.C.	314
Severn (Ontario)	Sandy Lake	Hudson Bay	610
Smoky Hill	Cheyenne County, Col.	Kansas River, Kan.	540
Snake	Teton County, Wyo.	Columbia River, Wash.	1,038
South Platte	Junction of South and Middle Forks, Park County, Col.	Platte River, Neb.	424
Susitna	Alaska Range	Cook Inlet	300
Susquehanna	Otsego Lake, Otsego County, N.Y.	Chesapeake Bay, Md.	444
Tallahatchie	Tippah County, Miss.	Yazoo River, Miss.	301
Tanana	Wrangell Mountains	Yukon River, Alaska	620
Tennessee	Junction of French Broad and Holston Rivers	Ohio River, Ky.	652
Tennessee-French Broad	Bland County, Va.	Ohio River	900
Tombigbee	Prentiss County, Miss.	Mobile River, Ala.	525
Trinity	North of Dallas, Tex.	Galveston Bay, Tex.	360
Wabash	Drake County, Oh.	Ohio River, Ill.-Ind.	529
Washita	Hemphill County, Tex.	Red River, Okla.	500
White (Ark.-Mo.)	Madison County, Ark.	Mississippi River	720
Willamette	Douglas County, Ore.	Columbia River	270
Wisconsin	LeVieux Desert, Vilas County, Wis.	Mississippi River	430
Yellowstone	Park County, Wyo.	Missouri River, N.D.	671
Yukon	Junction of Lewes and Pelly Rivers, Yukon	Bering Sea, Alaska	1,770

Flows of Largest U.S. Rivers

Source: U.S. Geological Survey (average discharges for the period 1941-70)
Ranked according to average discharge in cubic feet per second (cfs) at mouth.

Rank	River	Average discharge	Length[a] (miles)	Drainage area	Most distant source	Maximum discharge at gauging station farthest downstream	Date
1	Mississippi	[b]640,000	[c]3,710	[d]1,247,300	Beaverhead Co., Mont.	2,080,000	2-17-37
2	Columbia	262,000	1,243	258,000	Columbia Lake, B.C.	1,240,000	Jun. 1894
3	Ohio	258,000	1,306	203,900	Potter Co., Pa.	1,850,000	2-1-37
4	St. Lawrence	[e]243,000	—	[e]302,000	—	[f]314,000	May 1870
5	Yukon	[g]240,000	1,770	327,600	Coast Mountain, B.C.	1,030,000	6-22-64
6	[h]Atchafalaya	183,000	135	95,105	Curry Co., N. Mex.	—	—
7	Missouri	76,300	2,533	529,400	Beaverhead Co., Mont.	892,000	Jun. 1844
8	Tennessee	[m]64,000	900	40,910	Bland Co., Va.	500,000	2-17-48
9	Red	[i]62,300	1,270	93,244	Curry Co., N. Mex.	233,000	4-17-45
10	Kuskokwim	62,000	680	49,000	Alaska Range, Alas.	392,000	6-5-64
11	Mobile	61,400	780	43,800	Gilmer, Co., Ga.	—	—
12	Snake	50,000	1,038	109,000	Teton Co., Wyo.	409,000	Jun. 1894
13	Arkansas	45,100	1,459	160,600	Lake Co., Col.	536,000	5-27-43
14	Copper	[j]43,000	280	24,000	Alaska Range, Alas.	265,000	7-15-71
15	Tanana	[k]41,000	620	44,000	Wrangell Mtn., Alas.	186,000	8-18-67
16	Susitna	[l]40,000	300	20,000	Alaska Range, Alas.	173,000	7-1-75
17	Susquehanna	37,190	444	27,570	Otsego Co., N.Y.	1,080,000	6-23-72
18	Willamette	35,660	270	11,200	Douglas Co., Ore.	500,000	12-4-1861
19	Alabama	32,400	735	22,600	Gilmer Co., Ga.	267,000	3-7-61
20	White	32,100	720	28,000	Madison Co., Ark.	343,000	4-17-45
21	Wabash	30,400	529	33,150	Darke Co., Oh.	428,000	3-30-13
22	Pend Oreille	29,900	490	25,820	Near Butte, Mont.	171,300	6-13-48
23	Tombigbee	27,300	525	20,100	Prentiss Co., Miss.	280,000	1874 and 1900
24	Cumberland	[m]26,900	720	18,080	Letcher Co., Ky.	201,000	2-18-50
25	Stikine	[n]26,000	310	20,000	Stikine Range, B.C.	120,000	6-26-55
26	Sacramento	—	377	27,100	Siskiyou Co., Cal.	[o]332,000	12-25-64
27	Apalachicola	24,700	524	19,600	Towns Co., Ga.	293,000	3-20-29
28	Illinois	22,800	420	27,900	St. Joseph Co., Ind.	123,000	May 1943
29	Koyukuk	[p]22,000	470	32,400	Endicott Mtns., Alas.	266,000	6-6-64
30	Porcupine	[q]20,000	460	45,000	Ogilvie Mtns., Alas.	299,000	5-24-73
31	Hudson	19,500	306	13,370	Essex Co., N.Y.	215,000	3-19-36
32	Allegheny	19,290	325	11,700	Potter Co., Pa.	365,000	3-18-36
33	Delaware	[r]17,200	390	11,440	Schoharie Co., N.Y.	329,000	8-20-55

(a) Because river lengths and methods of measurement may change from time to time, the length figures given are subject to revision; (b) about 25 percent of flow occurs in the Atchafalaya River; (c) the length from mouth to source of the Mississippi River in Minnesota is 2,348 miles; (d) at Baptiste Collete Bayou, Louisiana; (e) at international boundary lat. 45°; (f) maximum monthly discharge; (g) period 1957-70; (h) continuation of Red River; (i) flow of Quachita River added; (j) period 1956-69; (k) period 1962-69; (l) based on records of Chilitna, Talkeetna, and Yetna rivers; (m) period 1931-60; (n) period 1954-63; summer records only; (o) discharge of American River not included (p) period 1960-69; (q) period 1964-69; (r) at Liston Point on Delaware Bay.

Famous Waterfalls

Source: National Geographic Society, Washington, D. C.

The earth has thousands of waterfalls, some of considerable magnitude. Their importance is determined not only by height but volume of flow, steadiness of flow, crest width, whether the water drops sheerly or over a sloping surface, and in one leap or a succession of leaps. A series of low falls flowing over a considerable distance is known as a cascade.

Sete Quedas or Guaira is the world's greatest waterfall when its mean annual low (estimated at 470,000 cusecs, cubic feet per second) is combined with height. A greater volume of water passes over Boyoma Falls (Stanley Falls), though not one of its seven cataracts, spread over nearly 60 miles of the Congo River, exceeds 10 feet.

Estimated mean annual flow, in cusecs, of other major waterfalls are: Niagara, 212,200; Paulo Afonso, 100,000; Urubupunga, 97,00[illegible]guazu, 61,000; Patos-Maribondo, 53,000; Victoria, 38,400; and Kaieteur, 23,400.

Height = t[illegible] drop in feet in one or more leaps. † = falls of more than one leap; * = falls that diminish greatly seasonally; ** = falls that reduce to a trickle or are dry for part of each year. If river names not shown, they are same as the falls. R. = river; L. = lake; (C) = cascade type.

Name and location	Ht.
Africa	
Angola	
Duque de Braganca, Lucala R.	344
Ruacana, Cunene R.	406
Ethiopia	
Dal Verme, Dorya R.	98
Fincha	508
Tesissat, Blue Nile R.	140
Lesotho	
*Maletsunyane	630
Rhodesia-Zambia	
*Victoria, Zambezi R.	355
South Africa	
*Augrabies, Orange R.	480
Howick, Umgeni R.	364
† Tugela	2,014
Highest fall	597
Tanzania-Zambia	
*Kalambo	726
Uganda	
Kabalega (Murchison) Victoria Nile R.	130
Asia	
India—*Cauvery	330
*Gokak, Ghataprabha R.	170
*Jog (Gersoppa), Sharavathi R.	830
Japan	
*Kegon, Daiya R.	330
Laos	
Khon Cataracts, Mekong R. (C)	70
Australasia	
Australia	
New South Wales	
† Wentworth	614
Highest fall	360
Wollomombi	1,100
Queensland	
Coomera	210
Tully	885
† Wallaman, Stony Cr.	1,137
Highest fall	937
New Zealand	
Bowen	540
Helena	890
Stirling	505
† Sutherland, Arthur R.	1,904
Highest fall	815
Europe	
Austria—†Gastein	492
Highest fall	280
† *Golling, Schwarzbach R.	250
† Krimml	1,312
France—*Gavarnie	1,385
Great Britain—Scotland	
Glomach	370
Wales	
Cain	150
Rhaiadr	240
Iceland—Detti	144
† Gull, Hvita R.	105

Name and location	Ht.
Italy—Frua, Toce R. (C)	470
Norway	
Mardalsfossen (Northern)	1,535
† Mardalsfossen (Southern)	2,150
† **Skjeggedal, Nybuai R.	1,378
**Skykje	984
Vetti, Morka - Koldedola R.	900
Voring, Bjoreio R.	597
Sweden	
† Handol	427
† Tannforsen, Are R	120
Switzerland	
† Diesbach	394
Giessbach (C)	1,982
Handegg, Aare R.	150
Iffigen	120
Pissevache, Salanfe R	213
† Reichenbach	656
Rhine	79
† Simmen	459
Staubbach	984
† Trummelbach	1,312

North America

Name and location	Ht.
Canada	
Alberta	
Panther, Nigel Cr.	600
British Columbia	
† Della	1,443
†Takakkaw, Daly Glacier	1,650
Hunlen, Atnarks R.	830
Heutcken, Murre R.	450
Bridal Veil, Bridal Cr.	400
Northwest Territories	
Virginia, S. Nahanni R	294
Quebec	
Montmorency	274
Canada—United States	
Niagara: American	193
Horseshoe	186
United States	
California	
*Feather, Fall R.	640
Yosemite National Park	
*Bridalveil	620
*Illilouette	370
*Nevada, Merced R.	594
**Ribbon	1,612
**Silver Strand, Meadow Br.	1,170
*Vernal, Merced R.	317
† **Yosemite	2,425
Yosemite (upper)	1,430
Yosemite (lower)	320
Yosemite (middle) (C).	675
Colorado	
† Seven, South Cheyenne Cr.	300
Hawaii	
Akaka, Kolekole Str.	442
Idaho	
**Shoshone, Snake R	212
Twin, Snake R	120
Kentucky	
Cumberland	68
Maryland	
*Great, Potomac R. (C)	71
Minnesota	
**Minnehaha	53
New Jersey	
Passaic	70
New York	
*Taughannock	215
Oregon	
† Multnomah	620
Highest fall	542
Tennessee	
Fall Creek	256
Washington	
Mt. Rainier Natl. Park	
Narada, Paradise R	168
Sluiskin, Paradise R	300
Palouse	197
**Snoqualmie	268
Wisconsin	
*Big Manitou, Black R. (C)	165
Wyoming	
Yellowstone Natl. Pk. Tower	132
*Yellowstone (upper)	109
*Yellowstone (lower)	308
Mexico	
El Salto	218
**Juanacatlan, Santiago R.	72

South America

Name and location	Ht.
Argentina—Brazil	
Iguazu	230
Brazil	
Glass	1,325
Patos-Maribondo, Grande R.	115
Paulo Afonso, Sao Francisco R.	275
Urubupunga, Parana R.	40
Brazil-Paraguay	
Sete Quedas	
Parana R	130
Colombia	
Catarata de Candelas,	
Cusiana R	984
*Tequendama, Bogota R.	427
Ecuador	
*Agoyan, Pastaza R	200
Guyana	
Kaieteur, Potaro R	741
King George VI, Kamarang R.	1,600
† Marina, Ipobe R	500
Highest fall	300
Venezuela—† *Angel	3,212
Highest fall 2,648	
Cuquenan	2,000

Large Rivers in Canada

Source: "Inland Waters Directorate," Department of Fisheries and the Environment.
(Ranked according to average discharge in cubic feet per second (cfs))

Rank	River	Average discharge	Length (miles)	Drainage area (sq. mi.)
1	St. Lawrence	355,000	1,900	396,000[1]
2	Mackenzie (to head of Finlay)	350,000	2,635	690,000
3	Fraser	128,000	850	89,900[2]
4	Columbia (International Boundary to head of Columbia Lake)	102,000	498	59,700[3]
5	Nelson (to head of Bow)	100,000	1,600	437,000[4]
6	Kokosak (to head of Caniapiscau)	85,500	543	51,500
7	Yukon (International Boundary to head of Nisutlin)	83,000	714	115,000[5]
8	Ottawa	69,000	790	56,500
9	Saguenay (to head of Peribonea)	62,200	434	34,000
10	Skeena	62,100	300	21,200

(1) Including 195,000 sq. mi. in U.S. (2) Including diversion. (3) Including 20,000 sq. mi. in U.S. (4) Including 69,500 sq. mi. in U.S. (5) Including 9,000 sq. mi. in U.S.

Largest Lake in Each Province of Canada

Source: "Inland Waters Directorate" and others.

Province	Largest within:	Largest partly in:	Shared with:	Origin	Area (sq. miles)	Ft. above sea level
Alberta	Claire			Natural	555	700
		Athabasca	Saskatchewan	Natural	3,066	700
British Columbia	Williston			Manmade	640	2,180
Manitoba	Winnipeg			Natural	9,417	713
Newfoundland	Smallwood Reservoir			Manmade	2,520	S.L.
New Brunswick	Grand			Natural	75	60
Northwest Territories	Great Bear			Natural	12,096	512
Nova Scotia	Bras d'Or			Natural	424	Tidal
Ontario	Nipigon			Natural	1,872	1,050
		Huron	U.S.	Natural	15,241	580
Prince Edward Island	Forest Hill Pond			Manmade	.7	50
Quebec	Mistassini			Natural	902	1,220
Saskatchewan	Wollaston			Natural	1,035	1,306
		Athabasca	Alberta	Natural	3,066	700

Largest Lake in Each State of the U.S.

Source: National Geographic Society, Washington, D.C.

*indicates reservoir

State	Largest entirely within state	Largest partly in another state	Shared with	Origin	Total area (square miles)	Feet above sea level	Maximum depth (feet)	Shoreline length (miles)
Ala.	Guntersville			Man-made	108	595	94	962
		Walter F. George	Ga.	Man-made	71	190	90	640
Alas.	Illamna			Natural	1,150	150	1,289	230
Ariz.	Theodore Roosevelt			Man-made	27	2,136	280	88
		Powell	Ut.	Man-made	252	3,700	580	1,800
Ark.	Ouachita			Man-made	63	578	179	690
		Bull Shoals	Mo.	Man-made	71	654	175	740
Cal.	Salton Sea			Natural	360	-235	48	—
		Tahoe	Nev.	Natural	192	6,229	1,644	71
Col.	Blue Mesa*			Man-made	14	7,519	325	95
		Navajo*	N.M.	Man-made	24	6,085	382	150
Conn.	Candlewood			Man-made	8	429	85	75
Del.	Lum's Pond			Man-made	.34	44	22	5
Fla.	Okeechobee			Natural	700	14	15	96
Ga.	Sidney Lanier			Man-made	59	1,070	156	540
		Clark Hill	S.C.	Man-made	109	330	150	1,200
Ha.	Waita*			Man-made	.66	242	—	4
Ida.	Pend Oreille			Natural	136	2,063	1,200	127
Ill.	Carlyle*			Man-made	41	445	40	83
		Michigan	Wis., Ind., Mich.	Natural	22,300	579	923	1,660
Ind.	Monroe*			Man-made	29	556	75	100
		Michigan	Wis., Ill., Mich.	Natural	22,300	579	923	1,660
Ia.	Rathbun*			Man-made	18	904	55	180
Kan.	Tuttle Creek*			Man-made	25	1,079	90	112
Ky.	Cumberland			Man-made	79	760	183	1,255
		Kentucky	Tenn.	Man-made	250	359	90	2,380
La.	Pontchartrain			Natural	621	sea lev.	18	112
Me.	Moosehead			Natural	117	1,042	246	190
Md.	Deep Creek			Man-made	6	2,462	72	62
		Conowingo*	Pa.	Man-made	13	109	110	38
Mass.	Quabbin*			Man-made	39	524	150	104
Mich.	Houghton			Natural	31	1,138	20	30
		Superior	Wis., Mich., Ont.	Natural	31,700	600	1,333	2,980
Minn.	Red			Natural	452	1,172	—	—
		Superior	Wis., Mich., Ont.	Natural	31,700	600	1,333	2,980
Miss.	Grenada			Man-made	100	231	102	282
Mo.	Lake of the Ozarks			Man-made	93	659	148	1,300
Mon.	Fort Peck*			Man-made	375	2,246	220	1,540
Neb.	McConaughty			Man-made	50	3,260	130	105
Nev.	Pyramid			Natural	169	3,789	330	66
		Mead	Ariz.	Man-made	247	1,221	432	550
N.H.	Winnipesaukee			Natural	70	504	169	240
N.J.	Hopatcong			Natural	4	924	58	32
N.M.	Elephant Butte*			Man-made	57	4,450	176	201
N.Y.	Oneida			Natural	80	369	55	63
		Erie	Mich., Pa., Ont., Oh.	Natural	9,910	570	210	856
N.C.	Mattamuskeet			Natural	67	3	5	—
		John H. Kerr*	Va.	Man-made	76	300	99	800
N.D.	Sakakawea			Man-made	575	1,850	180	1,600
		Oahe*	S.D.	Man-made	556	1,617	200	2,250
Oh.	Lake St. Mary's			Man-made	17	869	10	60
		Erie	Mich., Pa., N.Y., Ont.	Natural	9,910	570	210	856
Okla.	Eufaula			Man-made	160	585	87	600
Ore.	Klamath			Natural	143	4,143	50	165
		Goose Lake	Cal.	Natural	194	4,716	24	90
Pa.	Raystown*			Man-made	13	786	185	110
		Erie	Mich., N.Y., Oh., Ont.	Natural	9,910	570	210	856
R.I.	Scituate			Man-made	5	284	94	38
S.C.	Marion			Man-made	173	75	55	300
S.D.	Francis Case			Man-made	159	1,375	140	540
		Oahe*	N.D.	Man-made	556	1,617	200	2,250
Tenn.	Watts Bar			Man-made	61	741	75	783
		Kentucky	Ky.	Man-made	250	359	90	2,380
Tex.	Sam Rayburn*			Man-made	179	164	74	—
		Toledo Bend*	La.	Man-made	284	172	92	—
Ut.	Great Salt Lake			Natural	1,438	4,200	36	334
Vt.	Bomoseen			Natural	4	413	—	—
		Champlain	N.Y., Que.	Natural	437	95	400	379
Va.	Smith Mountain			Man-made	31	795	200	500
		John H. Kerr*	N.C.	Man-made	76	300	99	800
Wash.	F.D. Roosevelt			Man-made	123	1,288	375	325
W. Va.	Summersville			Man-made	4	1,652	267	65
Wis.	Winnebago			Natural	215	747	21	78
		Superior	Minn., Mich., Ont.	Natural	31,700	600	1,333	2,980
Wyo.	Yellowstone			Natural	137	7,733	309	110
		Flaming Gorge*	Utah	Man-made	—	6,040	437	—

Lakes of the World

Source: National Geographic Society, Washington, D.C.

A lake is a body of water surrounded by land. Although some lakes are called seas, they are lakes by definition. The Caspian Sea is bounded by the Soviet Union and Iran and is fed by eight rivers.

Name	Continent	Area sq. mi.	Length mi.	Depth feet	Elev. feet
Caspian Sea	Asia-Europe	143,550	760	3,264	—92
Superior	North America	31,700	350	1,333	600
Victoria	Africa	26,828	250	265	3,720
Aral Sea	Asia	25,300	280	223	174
Huron	North America	23,100	206	750	579
Michigan	North America	22,300	307	923	579
Tanganyika	Africa	12,700	420	4,650	2,534
Great Bear	North America	12,096	192	1,356	512
Baykal	Asia	11,780	395	5,315	1,493
Nyasa	Africa	11,430	360	2,226	1,550
Great Slave	North America	11,031	298	2,015	513
Erie	North America	9,910	241	210	570
Winnipeg	North America	9,417	266	60	713
Ontario	North America	7,550	193	802	245
Ladoga	Europe	6,835	124	738	13
Balkhash	Asia	7,115	376	85	1,115
Chad	Africa	6,300	175	24	787
Maracaibo	South America	5,217	72	115	Sea level
Onega	Europe	3,710	145	328	108
Volta	Africa	3,276	250	....	....
Titicaca	South America	3,200	122	822	12,500
Athabasca	North America	3,064	208	407	700
Nicaragua	North America	3,100	102	230	102
Eyre	Australia	3,600	90	4	—52
Rudolf	Africa	2,473	154	240	1,230
Reindeer	North America	2,568	143	....	1,106
Issyk Kul	Asia	2,355	115	2,303	5,279
Torrens	Australia	2,230	130	....	92
Vanern	Europe	2,156	91	328	144
Winnipegosis	North America	2,075	141	38	830
Albert	Africa	2,075	100	168	2,030
Kariba	Africa	2,050	175	390	1,590
Nettilling	North America	2,140	67	Sea level	95
Nipigon	North America	1,872	72	540	855
Gairdner	Australia	1,840	90	....	112
Manitoba	North America	1,799	140	12	813
Urmia	Asia	1,815	90	49	4,180

The Great Lakes

Source: National Ocean Survey, U.S. Commerce Department

The Great Lakes form the largest body of fresh water in the world and with their connecting waterways are the largest inland water transportation unit. Draining the great North Central basin of the U.S., they enable shipping to reach the Atlantic via their outlet, the St. Lawrence R., and also the Gulf of Mexico via the Illinois Waterway, from Lake Michigan to the Mississippi R. A third outlet connects with the Hudson R. and thence the Atlantic via the N. Y. State Barge Canal System.

Only one of the lakes, Lake Michigan, is wholly in the United States; the others are shared with Canada. Ships carrying grain, lumber and iron ore move from the shores of Lake Superior to Whitefish Bay at the east end of the lake, thence through the Soo (Sault Ste. Marie) locks, through the St. Mary's River and into Lake Huron. To reach the steel mills at Gary, and Port of Indiana and South Chicago, Ill., ore ships move west from Lake Huron to Lake Michigan through the Straits of Mackinac.

Lake Huron discharges its waters into Lake Erie through a narrow waterway, the St. Clair R., Lake St. Clair (both included in the drainage basin figures) and the Detroit R. Lake St. Clair, a marshy basin, is 26 miles long and 24 miles wide at its maximum. A ship channel has been dredged through the lake.

Lake Superior is 600 feet above mean water level at Father Point, Quebec, on the International Great Lakes Datum (1955). From Duluth, Minn., to the eastern end of Lake Ontario is 1,156 mi.

	Superior	Michigan	Huron	Erie	Ontario
Length in miles	350	307	206	241	193
Breadth in miles	160	118	183	57	53
Deepest soundings in feet	1,333	923	750	210	802
Volume of water in cubic miles	2,935	1,180	849	116	393
Area (sq. miles) water surface—U.S.	20,600	22,300	9,100	4,980	3,560
Canada	11,100	.....	13,900	4,930	3,990
Area (sq. miles) entire drainage basin—U.S.	16,900	45,600	16,000	18,000	15,200
Canada	32,400	.....	34,700	4,720	12,100
Total Area (sq. miles) U. S. and Canada	**81,100**	**67,900**	**73,700**	**32,630**	**34,850**
Mean surface above mean water level at Father Point, Quebec, aver. level in feet (112 yrs.)	600.39	578.69	578.69	570.39	244.77
Latitude, North	46° 25′	41° 37′	43° 00′	41° 23′	43° 11′
	49° 00′	46° 06′	46° 17′	42° 52′	44° 15′
Longitude, West	84° 22′	84° 45′	79° 43′	78° 51′	76° 03′
	92° 06′	88° 02′	84° 45′	83° 29′	79° 53′
National boundary line in miles	282.8	None	260.8	251.5	174.6
United States shore line (mainland only) miles	909	1,395	564	424	294

Notable Bridges in North America

Source: State Highway Engineers; Canadian Civil Engineering — ASCE

Asterisk (*) designates Railroad Bridge. Span of a bridge is distance (in feet) between its supports.

Suspension

Year	Bridge	Location	Longest span
1964	Verrazano-Narrows	New York, N.Y.	4,260
1937	Golden Gate	San Fran. Bay, Cal.	4,200
1957	Mackinac	Sts. of Mackinac	3,800
1931	Geo. Washington	Hudson River	3,500
1952	Tacoma	Washington	2,800
1939	Lions Gate	Burrard Inlet, B.C.	2,778
1936	[1]Transbay	San Fran. Bay, Cal.	2,310
1939	Bronx-Whitestone	East R., N.Y.C.	2,300
1970	Quebec Road	Quebec	2,190
1951	Del. Memorial	Wilmington, Del.	2,150
1968	Del. Mem. (new)	Wilmington, Del.	2,150
1957	Walt Whitman	Phila., Pa.	2,000
1929	Ambassador	Detroit-Canada	1,850
1961	Throgs Neck	Long Is. Sound	1,800
1926	Benjamin Franklin	Philadelphia	1,750
1924	Bear Mt., N.Y.	Hudson River	1,632
1952	[2]Wm. Preston Lane Mem.	Sandy Point, Md.	1,600
1903	Williamsburg	East R., N.Y.C.	1,600
1969	Newport	Narragansett Bay, R.I.	1,600
1883	Brooklyn	East R., N.Y.C.	1,595
1930	Mid-Hudson, N.Y.	Poughkeepsie	1,500
1964	Vincent Thomas	Los Angeles Harbor	1,500
1909	Manhattan	East R., N.Y.C.	1,470
1936	Triborough	East R., N.Y.C.	1,380
1931	St. Johns	Portland, Ore.	1,207
1929	Mount Hope	Rhode Island	1,200
1939	Deer Isle	Maine	1,080
1931	Maysville (Ky.)	Ohio River	1,060
1867	Cincinnati	Ohio River	1,057
1971	Dent	Clearwater Co., Ida.	1,050
1900	Miampimi	Mexico	1,030
1849	Wheeling, W. Va.	Ohio River	1,010

Cantilever

Year	Bridge	Location	Longest span
1917	*Quebec (Railway)	Quebec	1,800
1970	Chester, Pa.	Delaware River	1,644
1958	New Orleans, La.	Mississippi R.	1,575
1936	Transbay	San. Fran. Bay	1,400
1968	Baton Rouge, La.	Mississippi R.	1,235
1955	Nyack-Tarrytown	Hudson River	1,212
1930	Longview, Wash.	Columbia River	1,200
1909	Queensboro	East R., N.Y.C.	1,182
1927	Carquinez Strait	California	1,100
1958	Parallel Span	"	1,100
1968	Isaiah D. Hart	Jacksonville, Fla.	1,088
1957	[3] Richmond	San Fran. Bay, Cal.	1,070
1929	Grace Memorial	Charleston, S.C.	1,050
1963	Newburgh-Beacon	Hudson R., N.Y.	1,000
1975	Caruthersville, Mo.	Mississippi R.	920
1969	Ohio River	Pt. Pleasant, W.Va.	900
1940	Natchez	Mississippi R.	875
1938	Blue Water	Pt. Huron, Mich.	871
1972	Vicksburg	Mississippi River	870
1954	Sunshine Skyway	St. Petersburg, Fla.	864
1940	*Baton Rouge	Mississippi R.	848
1899	*Cornwall	St. Lawrence R.	843
1940	Greenville	Mississippi R.	840
1961	Helena, Ark.	Mississippi R.	840
1963	Brent Spence	Covington, Ky.	831
1963	Cincinnati, Oh.	Ohio River	830
1956	Earl C. Clements	Ohio R., Ill.-Ky.	825[6]
1930	*Vicksburg	Mississippi R.	825
1929	Louisville	Ohio River	820
1961	Campbellton-Cross Point	New Brunswick-Quebec	815
1943	Jeff'rson Barr'ks., Mo.	Mississippi R.	804
1950	Maurice J. Tobin	Boston, Mass.	800
1935	Rip Van Winkle	Catskill, N.Y.	800
1938	Cairo	Ohio River, Ill.-Ky.	800
1940	Ludlow Ferry	Potomac R.	800
1932	Washington Mem.	Seattle, Wash.	800
1936	North Bend, Ore.	Coos Bay	793
1936	McCullough	Coos Bay, Ore.	793
1935	[4]Huey P. Long	New Orleans	790
1916	*Memphis (Harahan)	Mississippi R.	790
1892	*Memphis	Mississippi R.	790
1949	Memphis-Arkansas	Mississippi R.	790
1904	*Mingo Jct., W. Va.	Ohio River	769
1910	*Beaver, Pa.	Ohio River	767
1966	[5]S.N. Pearman	Charleston, S.C.	760
1940	Owensboro	Ohio River	750
1911	Sewickley, Pa.	Ohio River	750
1928	Outerbridge, N.Y.-N.J.	Arthur Kill	750
1964	Sunshine, Don'ville	Mississippi, La.	750

Simple Truss

Year	Bridge	Location	Longest span
1917	*Metropolis	Ohio River	720
1929	Irvin S. Cobb	Ohio River-Ill.-Ky.	716
1922	*Tanana River	Nenana, Alaska	700
1933	*Henderson	Ohio River-Ind.-Ky.	665
1967	I-77, Ohio River	Marietta, Oh.	650
1917	MacArthur, Ill.-Mo.	St. Louis	647
1919	Louisville	Ohio River	644
1933	Atchafalaya	Morgan City, La.	608
1924	*Castleton	Hudson River	598
1906	Elizabethtown	Great Miami R., Oh.	586
1889	*Cincinnati	Ohio River	542
1951	Allegheny River	Allegheny Co., Pa.	533
1914	Pittsburgh	Allegheny R.	531
1930	*Martinez	California	528
1967	Tanana River	Alaska	500
1963	216 Nenana River	Rex, Alaska	406

Steel Truss

Year	Bridge	Location	Longest span
1940	Gov. Nice Mem.	Potomac River, Md.	800
1975	I-24	Tenn R., Ky.	720
1938	US-62, Ky.	Green River	700
1952	US-62, Ky.	Cumberland River	700
1940	Jamestown	Jamestown, R.I.	640
1940	Greenville	Mississippi R., Ark.	640
1949	Memphis	Mississippi R., Ark.	621
1938	US-22	Delaware River, N.J.	540
1972	Mississippi River	Muscatine, Ia.	512
1896	Newport	Ohio River, Ky.	511
1931	US-60	Cumberland R., Ky.	500
1958	Lake Oahe	Mobridge, S.D.	500
1958	Lake Oahe	Gettysburg, S.D.	500
1910	McKinley, St. Louis	Mississippi River	500
1963	Millard E. Tydings	Susquehanna R., Md.	490
1955	Four Bears	Missouri R., N.D.	475
1930	Lake Champlain	Lake Champlain, N.Y.	434
1947	Mayo	Suwanee R., Fla.	420
1929	Clarendon	White River, Ark.	400
1931	US-60	Tennessee R., Ky.	400

Continuous Truss

Year	Bridge	Location	Longest span
1966	Astoria, Ore.	Columbia R.	1,232
1966	Marquam	Willamette R., Ore.	1,044
1969	Miss. R.	Dyersburg, Tenn.	900
1969	Irondequoit Bay	Rochester, N.Y.	891
1943	Dubuque, Ia.	Mississippi R.	845
1953	John E. Mathews	Jacksonville, Fla.	810
1957	Kingston-Rhinecliff	Hudson R., N.Y.	800
1918	*Sciotoville	Ohio River	775
1929	Madison-Milton	Ohio River	727
1966	Matthew E. Welsh	Mauckport, Ind.	707[6]
1975	Girard Point	Philadelphia, Pa.	700
1929	Chain of Rocks	Mississippi R.	699
1966	Braga	Taunton R., Mass	682
1938	Port Arthur-Orange	Texas	680
1929	*Cincinnati	Ohio River	675
1928	Cape Girardeau, Mo.	Mississippi R.	672
1946	Chester, Ill.	Mississippi R.	670
1930	Quincy, Ill.	Mississippi R.	628
1934	Bourne	Cape Cod Canal	616
1935	Sagamore	Cape Cod Canal	616
1965	Clarion River	Clarion Co., Pa.	612
1965	Rio Grande Gorge	Taos, N.M.	600
1941	Columbia River	Kettle Falls, Wash.	600
1954	Columbia River	Umatilla, Ore.	600
1954	Columbia River	The Dalles, Ore.	576
1962	W. Br. Feather River	Oroville, Cal.	576
1936	Meredosia	Illinois River	567
1936	Mark Twain Mem.	Hannibal, Mo.	562
1957	Mackinac	Mackinac Straits, Mich.	560
1937	Homestead	Pittsburgh	553
1961	Ship Canal	Seattle, Wash.	552
1932	Pulaski Skyway	Passaic R., N.J.	550
1973	I-95, Thames River	New London, Conn.	540
1927	Ross Island	Portland, Ore.	535

Year	Bridge	Location	Longest span
1936	South Omaha	Missouri R., Neb.-Ia.	525
1932	Savanna, Ill.-Sabula	Mississippi R.	520
1962	Columbia River	Beebe, Wash.	520
1970	Snake River	Central Ferry, Wash.	520
1954	Columbia River	Pasco, Wash.	520
1962	Columbia River	Vantage, Wash.	520
1974	New Lyons Fulton	Mississippi R. (Ia.-Ill.)	500
1958	Stevenson, Ala.	Tennessee R.	500

Continuous Box and Plate Girder

Year	Bridge	Location	Longest span
1953	Neches River	Orange County, Tex.	850
1967	San Mateo-Hayward No. 2	San Fran. Bay, Cal.	750
1963	Gunnison River	Gunnison, Col.	720
1969	San Diego-Coronado	San Diego Bay, Cal.	660[7]
1972	Ship Channel	Houston, Tex.	630
1967	Poplar St.	St. Louis, Mo.	600
1971	Lake Koocanusa	Lincoln Co., Mon.	500
1967	Mississippi R.	LaCrescent, Minn.	450
1972	Sitka Harbor	Sitka, Alaska	450
1974	I-430	Arkansas R.	430
1972	Kansas City	Missouri R., Kan.-Mo.	425
1967	Chattanooga	Tennessee R., Tenn.	420
1975	Yukon River	Taylor Highway, Alaska	410
1972	I-75, Tennessee River	Loudon Co., Tenn.	400
1941	Susquehanna	Susquehanna R., Md.	400
1963	Lake Charles B'Pass	Louisiana	399
1971	St. Croix River	Hudson, Minn.	390
1957	Conn. Turnpike	Quinnipiac R.	387
1960	Route 34	New Haven, Conn.	379
1971	S.H. No. 1	Pendleton, Ark.	377
1960	Tennessee River	Chattanooga, Tenn.	375
1966	I-80, LeClaire, Ia.	Mississippi R.	370
1971	Sacramento R.	Bryte, Cal.	370
1963	I-40, Tennessee River	Benton Co., Tenn.	365
1967	San Mateo Creek	Hillsborough, Cal.	360
1950	US-62, Kentucky Dam	Tennessee R., Ky.	350
1961	Whiskey Creek	Trinity Co., Cal.	350
1972	Franklin Falls	Snoq'lmie Pass, Wash.	350
1971	Don Pedro Reserv.	Tuolumne Co., Cal.	350

Continuous Plate

Year	Bridge	Location	Longest span
1965	New Chain of Rocks	Mississippi R., Ill.	5,411[9]
1973	Great Congress Gty.	Schenectady, N.Y.	1,870
1971	Congress St.	Troy, N.Y.	1,420
1966	I-480	Missouri R., Ia.-Neb.	425
1970	I-435	Missouri R., Mo.	425
1972	I-80	Missouri R., Ia.-Neb.	425
1970	Green River	Hendersonville, N.C.	350
1969	Fort Smith	Arkansas River	340
1971	Audubon Pkwy.	Green R., Ky.	330
1974	Green River Pkwy.	Green R., Ky.	330
1974	Camp Nelson	Kentucky, R.	330
1974	Queen Isabella Cswy.	Port Isabel, Tex.	310

I-Beam Girder

Year	Bridge	Location	Longest span
1941	US-31E	Rolling Fork R., Ky.	340
1948	US-27	Licking River, Ky.	316
1947	US-31E	Green River, Ky.	316
1941	US-62	Rolling Fork, Ky.	240
1942	Licking River	Owingsville, Ky.	240
1954	Fuller Warren	Jacksonville, Fla.	224

Steel Arch

Year	Bridge	Location	Longest span
1931	Bayonne, N.J.	Kill Van Kull	1,652
1972	Fremont	Portland, Ore.	1,255
1964	Port Mann	British Columbia	1,200
1959	Glen Canyon	Colorado River	1,028
1967	Trois-Rivieres	St. Lawrence R., P.Q.	1,100
1962	Lewiston-Queenston	Niagara River, Ont.	1,000
1976	Perrine	Twin Falls, Ida.	993
1917	*Hell Gate	East R., N.Y.C.	977
1941	Rainbow	Niagara Falls	950
1972	I-40, Mississippi R.	Memphis, Tenn.	900[10]
1970	Lake Quinsigamond	Worcester, Mass.	849
1966	Charles Braga	Somerset, Mass.	840
1967	Lincoln Trail	Ohio R., Ind.-Ky.	825
1961	Sherman Minton	Louisville, Ky.	800
1936	Henry Hudson	Harlem River	800
1936	French King	Conn. R. (Rt. 2, Mass.)	782
1931	West End	Pittsburgh	778
1972	Piscataqua R.	I-95, N.H.-Me.	756
1963	Cold Spring Canyon	Santa Barbara, Cal.	700

Year	Bridge	Location	Longest span
1973	I-24, Paducah, Ky.	Ohio River	700

Concrete Arch

Year	Bridge	Location	Longest span
1934	New River	Ripplemead, Va.	1,321[9]
1932	Clark Memorial	Wabash River	1,033[9]
1971	Selah Creek (twin)	Selah, Wash.	549
1968	Cowlitz River	Mossyrock, Wash.	520
1931	Westinghouse	Pittsburgh	425
1923	Cappelen	Minneapolis	400
1930	Jack's Run	Pittsburgh	400
1973	Elwha River	Port Angeles, Wash.	380
1931	Bixby Creek	Monterey Coast, Cal.	330
1953	Arroyo Seco	Pasadena, Cal.	320
1927	Mendota	Ft. Snelling, Minn.	304

Twin Concrete Trestle

Year	Bridge	Location	Longest span
1963	Slidell, La.	L. Pontchartrain	28,547

Concrete Slab Dam

Year	Bridge	Location	Longest span
1927	Conowingo Dam	Maryland	4,611
1952	John H. Kerr Dam	Roanoke River, Va.	2,785
1936	Hoover Dam	Boulder City, Nev.	1,324

Drawbridges

Vertical Lift

Year	Bridge	Location	Longest span
1959	*Arthur Kill	N.Y.-N.J.	558
1935	*Cape Cod Canal	Massachusetts	544
1960	*Delair, N.J.	Delaware River	542
1937	Marine Parkway	New York City	540
1931	Burlington, N.J.	Delaware R.	534
1912	*A-S-B Fratt	Kansas City	428
1945	*Harry S. Truman	Kansas City	427
1932	*M-K-T R.R.	Missouri R.	414
1969	Wilm'gtn Mem.	Wilmington, N.C.	408
1930	Duluth	Minnesota	386
1941	Main St.	Jacksonville, Fla.	386
1962	Burlington	Ontario	370
1922	*Cincinnati	Ohio River	365
1967	Benj. Harrison Mem.	James River, Va.	363
1961	Corpus Christi Harbor	Corpus Christi, Tex.	344[4]
1933	Troy-Menands	Hudson River	341
1962	Sand Island Access	Oahu, Hawaii	340
1941	U.S. 1& 9, Passaic R.	Newark, N.J.	332
1929	Carlton	Bath-Woolwich, Me.	328
1930	*Martinez	California	328
1960	St. Andrews Bay	Panama City, Fla.	327
1929	*Penn-Lehigh	Newark Bay	322
1920	*Chattanooga	Tennessee R.	310
1936	Triboro, N.Y.C.	Harlem River	310
1936	Hardin	Illinois River	309
1960	Sacramento River	Rio Vista, Cal.	306
1957	Claiborne Ave.	New Orleans	305
1927	Cochrane	Mobile, Ala.	300
1928	James River	Newport News	300
1929	San Mateo	California	300
1926	*Missouri Pacific	Kragen, Ark.	300

Bascule

Year	Bridge	Location	Longest span
1926	Fort Madison	Mississippi R.	525[4]
1969	Pearl River	Slidell, La.	482
1916	Keokuk Municipal	Mississippi R., Ia.	377
1917	SR-8, Tennessee River	Chattanooga, Tenn.	306
1940	Lorain, Ohio	Black River	295
1958	Morrison	Portland, Ore.	285
1969	Elizabeth River	Chesapeake, Va.	281
1957	Craig Memorial	I-280, Toledo, Oh.	271
1952	Downtown	Norfolk, Va.	230

Swing Bridges

Year	Bridge	Location	Longest span
1950	Douglass Memorial	Anac'tia R., Wash. D.C.	386
1945	Lord Delaware	Mattaponi River, Va.	252
1957	Eltham	Pamunkey River, Va.	237
1939	Chickahominy River	Route 5, Va.	222
1930	Nansemond River	Route 125, Va.	200

Swing Span

Year	Bridge	Location	Longest span
1908	*Willamette R.	Portland, Ore.	521
1903	*East Omaha	Missouri R.	519
1952	Yorktown	York River, Va.	500
1897	*Duluth, Minn.	St. Louis Bay	486
1899	*C.M.&N.R.R.	Chicago	474
1897	Sioux City, Ia.	Missouri R. (Nebr.-Ia.)	470
1914	*Coos Bay	Oregon	458

Floating Pontoon

Year	Bridge	Location	Longest span
1963	Evergreen Pt.	Seattle, Wash.	7,518
1940	Lacey V. Murrow	Seattle	6,561
1961	Hood Canal	Pt. Gamble, Wash.	6,471

(1) The Transbay Bridge has 2 spans of 2,310 ft. each. (2) A second bridge in parallel will be completed. (3) The Richmond Bridge has twin spans 1,070 ft. each. (4) Railroad and vehicular bridge. (5) Two spans each 760 ft. (6) Two spans each 707 ft. (7) Two spans each 660 ft. (8) Two spans each 825 ft. (9) Total length of bridge. (10) Two spans each 900 ft.

Construction Details of Large and Unusual Bridges

Verrazano-Narrows Bridge, between Staten Island and Brooklyn, N.Y., has a suspension span of 4,260 ft., longest in the world and exceeding the Golden Gate Bridge, San Francisco, by 60 ft. One level in use Nov., 1964, second opened Jun. 28, 1969. The name is a compromise; it spans the Narrows and commemorates a visit to New York Harbor in Apr., 1524, deduced from certain notes left by Giovanni da Verrazano, Italian navigator sailing for Francis I of France.

Allegheny River Bridge (Interstate 80) near Emlenton, Pa., 270 ft. above the water, tallest in eastern U.S., a continuous truss, 688 ft. long, 1968.

Angostura, suspension type, span 2,336 feet, 1967 at Ciudad Bolivar, Venezuela. Total length, 5,507.

Charles Braga Bridge over Taunton River between Fall River and Somerset, Mass. It is 5,780 feet long.

Bendorf Bridge on the Rhine River, 5 mi. n. of Coblenz, completed 1965, is a 3-span cement girder bridge, 3,378 ft. overall length, 101 ft. wide, with the main span 682 ft.

Burro Creek Bridge with 4 spans over Burro Creek on highway 93 near Kingman, Ariz. Main span steel truss 680 ft. Others plate girder, 110 and 2 of 85 ft. 1966.

Champlain Bridge at Montreal crossing the St. Lawrence River was opened 1962. It is 4 miles long.

Chesapeake Bay Bridge-Tunnel, opened Apr. 15, 1964 on US-13, connects Virginia Beach-Norfolk with the Eastern Shore of Virginia. Shore to shore, 17.6 miles. Twelve miles of trestles, 4 man-made islands, 2 mile-long tunnels, and 2 bridges.

Cross Bay Parkway Bridge (N.Y.), 3,000 feet long with 6 traffic lanes, 11 eight foot wide precast, prestressed concrete T girders to support spans 130 feet long each with main span 275 feet.

Delaware Memorial Bridge over Delaware River near Wilmington. A twin suspension bridge paralleling the original 250 ft. upstream has a 2,150-ft. main span suspended from 440-ft. towers.

Eads Bridge across the Mississippi R. between St. Louis and E. St. Louis, built in 1874 has 4 main spans 1,520 ft., 2,502 ft., and 1,118 ft. crossing Miss. R., a railroad and a road.

Evergreen Point Bridge, Wash. consists of 33 floating concrete pontoons weighing 4,700 tons each, held in place by 77 ton crete anchors. Pontoon structure is 6,561 ft. long; with approaches bridge is 12,596 ft. long.

Fremont Bridge. Part of Stadium Freeway, Portland, Ore., crossing Willamette R. 1,255 ft. steel arch span with two 452 ft. flanking steel arch spans. 1971.

Frontenac Bridge, Quebec, suspension, span 2,190 ft., open 1970.

Gladesville Bridge at Sydney, Australia, has the longest concrete arch in the world (1,000 ft. span).

George Washington Bridge, New York City, 4th longest suspension bridge in the world, spans the Hudson River between W. 178th St., Manhattan, and Ft. Lee, N.J.; 4,760 ft. between anchorages, two levels, 14 traffic lanes. Triborough Bridge connects Manhattan, the Bronx, and Queens; project comprises a suspension bridge, a vertical lift bridge, and a fixed bridge, all connected by long viaducts. The famous Brooklyn Bridge over the East River, connecting Manhattan and Brooklyn, was completed in 1883, breaking all previous records by spanning 1,595 ft.

Golden Gate Bridge, crossing San Francisco Bay, has the second longest single span, 4,200 ft.

Hampton Roads Bridge-Tunnel, Va. A crossing completed in 1957 consisting of 2 man-made islands, 2 concrete trestle bridges, and one tunnel, under Hampton Roads with a length of 7,479 ft. A parallel facility with a 7,315 ft. tunnel is now open to traffic.

Hood Canal Floating Bridge, Wash., 23 floating concrete pontoons 4,980 tons each. Roadway is supported on crete T-beam sections mounted on pontoons 20 feet above canal. Floating section is 6,471 ft. long, overall 7,866 ft.

International Bridge, a series of 8 arch and truss bridges crossing St. Mary's and the Soo Locks between Mich. and Ontario. Two-mile toll completed 1962.

Lacy V. Murrow Floating Bridge, Wash., 25 floating pontoons of 4,558 tons each. Bridge with approaches is 8,583 ft.

Lake Pontchartrain Twin Causeway, a twin-span crete trestle bridge and 24-mile link within metropolitan New Orleans that connects the north and south shore. First span opened 1956, second 1969.

Lavaca Bay Causeway, Tex., 2.2 miles long, consisting of one 260 ft. continuous plate girder unit and 194 precast, prestressed concrete spans of 60 ft. length. 1961.

Newport Bridge between Newport and Jamestown, R. I. Total length 11,248 ft., a main suspension span of 1,600 feet, 2 side spans each 688 feet long. It has U.S.A.'s first prefabricated wire strands.

New York City bridges, *see Verrazano-Narrows Bridge and George Washington Bridge above.*

Ogdensburg-Prescott Internat'l Bridge across the St. Lawrence River from Ogdensburg, N.Y., to Johnston, Ont., opened 1970, is 13,510 ft. long with approaches and 7,260 ft. between abutments.

Oland Island Bridge in Sweden was completed in 1972. It is 19,882 feet long, Europe's longest.

Oosterscheldebrug, opened Dec. 15, 1965, is a 3.125-mile causeway for automobiles over a sea arm in Zeeland, the Netherlands. It completes a direct connection between Flushing and Rotterdam.

Poplar St. Bridge over the Mississippi at St. Louis, a 5-span continuous orthotropic deck plate girder bridge, longest span 600 ft. Eight lanes, 2,165 ft. long.

Quebec Road, suspension, span 2,190 feet, 1969, Quebec, Canada.

Rio-Niteroi, Guanabara Bay, Brazil, under construction, will be world's longest continuous box and plate girder bridge, 8 miles, 3,363 feet long, with a center span of 984 feet and a span on each side of 656 feet.

Robert Opie Norris Bridge, Rappahannock R. between Greys Pt. and White Stone, Va. 9,989 ft. long. Main spans are two 144 foot cantilever truss spans with a 360 foot truss span suspended between them.

Rockville Bridge, world's longest 4-track stone arch bridge, 3,810 ft., with 48 arches. Part of the Penn-Central RR system west of Harrisburg, Pa. It contains 440 million lbs. of stone, 100,000 cubic yds. of masonry and crosses the Susquehanna Riv. to Rockville, Pa.

Royal Gorge Bridge, 1,053 ft. above the Arkansas River in Colorado, is the highest bridge above water. Opened Dec. 8, 1929, it is 1,260 ft. long with a main span of 880 ft., width 18 ft.

San Mateo-Hayward Bridge across San Francisco Bay is first major orthotropic bridge in U.S. It is 6.7 miles long, 4.9 mile low-level concrete trestle and 1.8 miles high-level steel bridge.

Seven Mile Bridge is the longest of an expanse of bridges connecting the Florida Keys. It was built by the Florida East Coast Railway between 1904 and 1916, now a state highway.

Shenandoah River Bridges, one spans the south fork, 1,924 ft. long, the other the north fork, 1,090 ft. long, Warren County, Va.

Straits of Mackinac Bridge, completed in 1957, is the longest suspension bridge between anchorages and with approaches extends nearly 5 mi. between Mackinaw City and St. Ignace, Mich.

Sunshine Skyway, a 15-mile-long bridge-causeway with twin roadbeds that crosses Tampa Bay at St. Petersburg, Fla., a system of twin bridges 864 feet long and 4 smaller bridges with 6 causeways.

Tagus River Bridge near Lisbon, Portugal, longest suspension bridge outside the United States, has a 3,323-ft. main span. Opened Aug. 6, 1966, it was named Salazar Bridge for the former premier.

Thomas A. Edison Memorial Bridge (causeway) across Sandusky Bay between Martin Point and Danbury, Oh., is 2.67 miles long. The main bridge is 2,044 feet long.

Thousand Island Bridge, St. Lawrence River. American span 800 ft.; Canadian 750 ft.

Union St. Bridge in Woodstock, Vt., a timber lattice truss with a span of 122 feet built in 1969 using old time procedure of hand drilled holes and wooden pegs.

Vancouver Bridge, Canada's longest railway lift span connecting Vancouver and North Vancouver over Burrard Inlet. It is in 3 sections, the longest 493 ft. Spans are part of a project that includes a 2-mile tunnel under Vancouver Hts.

Woodrow Wilson Memorial Bridge across the Potomac River at Alexandria, Va., is over a mile long.

Zoo Bridge across the Rhine at Cologne, with steel box girders, has a main span of 850 ft.

The Interstate Highway 610 crossing of the Houston Ship Channel in Texas is 6,300 feet in length and consists of various lengths of prestressed concrete beam and slab approach spans and a 1,233 foot main unit of two 471'6" plate girder units and one 290 ft. simple span.

Underwater Vehicular Tunnels in North America

(3,000 feet in length or more)

Name	Location	Waterway	Lgth. Ft.
Bart Trans-Bay Tube (Rapid Transit)	San Francisco, Cal.	S.F. Bay	3.6 miles
Brooklyn-Battery	New York, N.Y.	East River	9,117
Holland Tunnel	New York, N.Y.	Hudson River	8,557
Lincoln Tunnel	New York, N.Y.	Hudson River	8,216
Baltimore Harbor Tunnel	Baltimore, Md.	Patapsco River	7,650
Hampton Roads	Norfolk, Va.	Hampton Roads	7,479
Queens Midtown	New York, N.Y.	East River	6,414
Thimble Shoal Channel	Cape Henry, Va.	Chesapeake Bay	5,738
Sumner Tunnel	Boston, Mass.	Boston Harbor	5,650
Chesapeake Channel	Cape Charles, Va.	Chesapeake Bay	5,450
Louis-Hippolyte Lafontaine Tunnel	Montreal, Que.	St. Lawrence River	5,280
Detroit-Windsor	Detroit, Mich.	Detroit River	5,135
Callahan Tunnel	Boston, Mass.	Boston Harbor	5,046
Midtown Tunnel	Norfolk, Va.	Elizabeth River	4,194
Baytown Tunnel	Baytown, Tex.	Houston Ship Channel	4,111
Posey Tube	Oakland, Cal.	Oakland Estuary	3,500
Downtown Tunnel	Norfolk, Va.	Elizabeth River	3,350
Webster St.	Alameda, Cal.	Oakland Estuary	3,350
Bankhead Tunnel	Mobile, Ala.	Mobile River	3,109
I-10 Twin Tunnel	Mobile, Ala.	Mobile River	3,000

Land Vehicular Tunnels in U.S.

(over 1,000 feet in length.)

Name	Location	Lgth. Ft.
Eisenhower Memorial	Route 70, Col.	8,941
Copperfield	Copperfield, Ut.	6,989
Allegheny (twin)	Penna. Turnpike	6,070
Liberty Tubes	Pittsburgh, Pa.	5,920
Zion Natl. Park	Rte. 1, Utah	5,766
East River Mt. (twin)	Interstate 77, W. Va.-Va.	5,661
Tuscarora (twin)	Penna. Turnpike	5,326
Kittatinny (twin)	Penna. Turnpike	4,727
Lehigh	Penna. Turnpike	4,379
Blue Mountain (twin)	Penna. Turnpike	4,339
Wawona	Yosemite Natl. Park	4,233
Squirrel Hill	Pittsburgh, Pa.	4,225
Big Walker Mt.	Route I-77, Va.	4,200
Fort Pitt	Pittsburgh, Pa.	3,560
Mall Tunnel	Dist. of Columbia	3,400
Caldecott	Oakland, Cal.	3,371
Kalihi	Honolulu, Ha.	2,780
Memorial	W. Va. Tpke. (I-77)	2,669
Cross-Town	178 St. N.Y.C.	2,414
F.D. Roosevelt Dr.	81-89 Sts. N.Y.C.	2,400
Dewey Sq.	Boston, Mass.	2,400
Battery Park	N.Y.C.	2,300
Battery St.	Seattle, Wash.	2,140
Big Oak Flat	Yosemite Natl. Park	2,083
Prudential	Boston, Mass.	1,980
Internatl. Underpass	Los Angeles, Cal.	1,910
Street-Car	Providence, R.I.	1,793
Broadway	San Francisco, Cal.	1,616
9th Street Expy	Washington, D.C.	1,610
F.C. Roosevelt Dr.	42-48 Sts. N.Y.C.	1,600
Lowry Hill	Minneapolis	1,496
Wheeling	Interstate 70, W. Va.	1,490
Mt. Baker Ridge (3)	Seattle, Wash.	1,466
Knowls Creek	Lane County, Ore.	1,430
Mule Pass	Near Bisbee, Ariz.	1,400
Arch Cape	Oregon Coast Hwy. 9	1,228
Queen Creek	Superior, Ariz.	1,200
West Rock	New Haven, Conn.	1,200
Green River	Route I-80, Wyo.	1,135
Nouanu Pali	Koolau Mt. Oahu, Ha.	1,080
Elk Creek	Umpqua Hwy 45, Ore.	1,080
Golden	Clear Cr'k Canyon, Col.	1,068

World's Longest Railway Tunnels

Source: Railway Directory & Year Book. Tunnels over 4 miles in length.

Tunnel	Date	Miles	Yds	Operating railway	Country
Simplon No. I and II	1922	12	559	Swiss Fed. & Italian St.	Switz.-Italy
Apennine	1934	11	892	Italian State	Italy
Cotthard	1882	9	562	Swiss Federal	Switzerland
Lotschberg	1913	9	140	Bern-Lotschberg-Simplon	Switzerland
Hokuriku	1962	8	1,089	Japanese National	Japan
Mont Cenis (Frejus)	1871	8	855	Italian State	France-Italy
Cascade	1929	7	1,397	Great Northern	U.S.
Flathead Tunnel, Mont.	1970	6	1,758	Great Northern	U.S.
Arlberg	1884	6	650	Austrian Federal	Austria
Moffat	1928	6	373	Denver & Rio Grande	U.S.
Shimizu	1931	6	50	Japanese National	Japan
Kvineshei	1943	5	1,112	Norwegian State	Norway
Rimutaka	1955	5	821	New Zealand Gov.	New Zealand
Ricken	1910	5	608	Swiss Federal	Switzerland
Grenchenberg	1915	5	581	Swiss Federal	Switzerland
Otira	1923	5	564	New Zealand Gov.	New Zealand
Tauern	1909	5	551	Austrian Federal	Austria
Haegebostad	1943	5	467	Norwegian State	Norway
Ronco	1889	5	277	Italian State	Italy
Hauenstein (Lower)	1916	5	95	Swiss Federal	Switzerland
Connaught	1916	5	39	Canadian Pacific	Canada
Karawanken	1906	4	1,683	Austrian Federal	Austria-Yugo.
New Tanna	1964	4	1,663	Japanese National	Japan
Somport	1928	4	1,572	French National	France-Spain
Tanna	1934	4	1,493	Japanese National	Japan
Ulrikken	1964	4	1,338	Norwegian State	Norway
Hoosac	1875	4	1,230	Boston & Maine	U.S.
Monte Orso	1927	4	1,230	Italian State	Italy
Lupacino	1958	4	1,178	Italian State	Italy
Vivola	1927	4	1,004	Italian State	Italy
Monte Adone	1934	4	760	Italian State	Italy
Jungfrau	1912	4	750	Jungfrau	Switzerland
Borgallo	1884	4	700	Italian State	Italy
Severn	1886	4	628	Western Region	Great Britain
Lusse (Vosges)	1937	4	474	French National	France

Major World Dams

Source: Bureau of Reclamation, U.S. Interior Department. *Replaces existing dam.
Volume in cubic yards. **Capacity** (gross) in acre feet. Year of completion. **U.C.** under construction.
Type: A—Arch. B—Buttress. E—Earthfill. G—Gravity. R—Rockfill. MA—Multi-arch.

Name of dam	Type	Year	River and basin	Country	Height Feet	Crest Length Feet	Volume (1,000 C.Y.)	Res. cap. (1,000 A.F.)
Afsluitdijk	E	1932	ZuiderZee	Netherlands	62	10,500	82,927	4,864
Akosombo-Main	R	1965	Volta	Ghana	463	2,100	10,400	120,000
Almendra	A	1970	Turmes-Douro	Spain	662	1,860	2,188	2,148
Alpe Gera	G	1965	Comor-Adda-Po	Italy	584	1,710	2,252	53
Bagdad Tailings	E	1973	Maroney Gulch	U.S.	121	2,601	37,304	40
Beas	G	1975	Beas-Indus	India	435	6,400	45,800	6,600
W.A.C. Bennett*	E	1967	Peace-Mackenzie	Canada	600	6,700	57,203	57,006
Bhakra	G	1963	Sutlend-Indus	India	742	1,700	5,400	8,000
Bratsk	GE	1964	Angara	USSR	410	16,864	18,283	137,220
Brouwershavense Gat	E	1972		Netherlands	118	20,341	35,316	466
Castaic	E	1973	Castaic Cr.	U.S.	340	5,200	44,000	432
Charvak	E	1970	Chirchik-Sir Darya	USSR	551	2,483	24,983	1,620
Chirkey	A	1975	Sulak-Caspian Sea	USSR	764	1,109	1,602	2,252
Chivor	R	1975	Bata	Colombia	778	919	14,126	661
Cochiti	E	1975	Rio Grande	U.S.	253	26,891	64,631	513
Copper Cities Tailing 2	E	1973	Tinhorn Wash	U.S.	325	7,598	30,003	4
Cougar	R	1964	S.F. McKenzie	U.S.	519	1,600	13,000	219
Dartmouth	R		Mitta-Mitta	Australia	591	2,264	20,012	5,232
Dneprodzerzhinsk	GE	1964	Dnieper	USSR	112	118,090	28,503	1,994
Don Pedro*	ER	1971	Tuolume-San Joaquin	U.S.	585	1,900	16,760	2,030
Dworshak	G	1974	N. Fork Clearwater	U.S.	717	3,287	6,500	3,453
El Chocon	E	1974	Limay	Argentina	282	7,546	17,004	17,025
Emosson	A	1974	Barberine	Switz	590	1,818	1,400	182
Esperanza Tailings	E	1973	Santa Cruz	U.S.	121	10,600	39,704	5
Fort Peck	E	1940	Missouri	U.S.	250	21,026	125,612	19,133
Fort Randall	E	1956	Missouri	U.S.	165	10,700	50,205	5,701
Gardiner*	E	1968	South Saskatchewan	Canada	223	16,700	85,743	8,000
Garrison	E	1956	Missouri	U.S.	203	11,300	66,506	24,321
Gepatsch	R	1965	Faggenbach-Inn	Austria	500	1,908	9,810	113
Glen Canyon	A	1964	Colorado	U.S.	710	1,560	4,901	27,000
Goscheneralp	E	1960	Goschener	Switz	508	1,771	12,230	61
Grand Coulee	G	1942	Columbia	U.S.	550	4,173	10,585	9,724
Grande Dixence	G	1962	Dixence-Rhone	Switz	935	2,280	7,792	324
Guri	GER	1968	Caroni-Orinoco	Venezuela	348	2,264	4,917	14,349
Haringvliet	E	1970	Haringvliet	Netherlands	79	18,044	26,160	527
High Aswan (Saad-El-Aali)	ER	1970	Nile	Egypt	364	12,565	57,203	137,000
Hirakud	GE	1956	Mahandi	India	202	15,748	25,100	6,600
Hoover	A	1936	Colorado	U.S.	726	1,244	4,400	29,755
Hungry Horse	AG	1953	S. Fork Flathead	U.S.	564	2,115	3,086	3,468
Ilha Solteira	EG	1973	Parana Rio de la Plata	Brazil	295	20,308	29,454	27,730
Irkutsk	GE	1956	Angara	USSR	144	8,989	16,219	37,290
Ivankova	EG	1937	Volga-Caspian S.	USSR	98	31,398	20,207	908
Jari	E	1967	Jari	Pakistan	234	5,700	42,400	400
Daniel Johnson*	MA	1968	Manicougan-St. Lawrence	Canada	703	4,311	2,950	115,000
Kakhovka	EG	1955	Dnieper	USSR	121	5,380	46,617	14,755
Kanev	E	1974	Dnieper	USSR	82	52,950	49,520	2,125
Kapchagay	E	1970	Ili	USSR	164	1,542	5,078	22,813
Kariba	A	1959	Zambesi	Rhodesia-Zambia	420	2,025	1,350	130,000
Keban	RG	1974	First (Euphrates)	Turkey	679	3,881	20,900	25,110
Kiev	E	1964	Dnieper	USSR	72	177,448	57,552	3,021
King Paul (Kremasta)	ER	1965	Acheloos	Greece	541	1,510	10,686	3,850
Kremenchug	EG	1961	Dnieper	USSR	108	39,844	41,192	10,945
Kurobegawa No. 4	A	1964	Kurobe	Japan	610	1,603	1,782	162
Lauwerszee	E	1969	Lauwerszee	Netherlands	75	42,650	46,532	40
Ludington	E	1973	Lake Michigan	U.S.	170	29,301	37,703	83
Luzzone	A	1963	Brenno di Luzzone	Switz	682	1,738	1,739	70
Mangla	E	1967	Jhelum	Pakistan	380	11,000	85,872	5,150
Marimbondo	E	1975	Grande	Brazil	295	12,297	24,328	5,184
Mauvoisin	A	1957	Drance de Bagnes	Switz	777	1,706	2,655	146
Mica	R	1974	Columbia	Canada	794	2,600	42,000	20,000
Mingechaur	E	1953	Kura	USSR	262	5,085	20,400	12,970
Navajo	E	1963	San Juan	U.S.	407	3,648	26,841	1,709
New Bullards Bar	A	1970	North Yuba-Sacramento	U.S.	637	2,200	2,700	960
New Cornelia Tailings	E	1973	Ten Mile Wash, Ariz.	U.S.	98	35,600	274,026	20
New Melones	R	1975	Stanislaus-San Joaquin	U.S.	625	1,600	15,970	2,400
Oahe	E	1963	Missouri	U.S.	245	9,300	92,008	23,591
Okutadami	G	1961	Tadami	Japan	515	1,575	2,145	487
Oroville	E	1968	Feather-Sacramento	U.S.	770	6,920	78,008	3,538
Owen Falls	G	1954	Lake Victoria-Nile	Uganda	100	2,725	n	166,000
Place Moulin	AG	1965	Buthier-Dora Baltea	Italy	502	2,181	1,962	81
Reza Shah Kabir	A	1975	Karoun	Iran	656	1,247	1,570	2,351
Rybinsk	GE	1941	Volga-Caspian S.	USSR	98	2,060	3,329	20,590
Sakuma	G	1956	Tenryu	Japan	510	963	1,465	265
San Luis	E	1967	San Luis-San Joaquin	U.S.	382	18,600	77,666	2,039
Saratov	E	1967	Volga-Caspian S.	USSR	131	37,204	52,843	10,458
Shasta	G	1945	Sacramento	U.S.	602	3,460	8,711	4,552
Swift	E	1958	Lewis-Columbia	U.S.	610	2,100	15,800	756
Tabka	E	1975	Euphrates	Syria	197	14,764	60,168	11,350
Talbingo	R	1971	Tamut	Australia	530	2,300	18,950	747
Tarbela	ER	1975	Indus	Pakistan	486	9,000	186,000	11,100
Trinity	E	1962	Trinity-Klamath	U.S.	537	2,600	29,252	2,448
Tsimlyansk	EG	1952	Don	USSR	128	43,411	44,323	17,715
Tuttle Creek	E	1962	Big Blue-Missouri	U.S.	154	7,500	22,937	413
Twin Buttes	E	1963	Concho-Colorado, Texas	U.S.	134	42,463	21,442	641
Twin Buttes Tailings	E	1973	Santa Cruz	U.S.	239	11,299	38,604	209
Vilyui	ER	1967	Vilyui	USSR	246	2,297	3,793	29,104
Volga-22d congress USSR	ERG	1958	Volga-Caspian S.	USSR	144	13,108	33,020	27,160
Volga-V. I. Lenin	EG	1955	Volga-Caspian S.	USSR	148	12,405	44,298	47,020
Yellowtail	A	1966	Bighorn-Missouri	U.S.	525	1,480	1,456	1,375
Zeya	G	1975	Zeya	USSR	369	2,343	3,139	55,452

Major U.S. Public and Private Dams and Reservoirs

Source: Corps of Engineers, U.S. Army

Heights over 330 feet.

Height—Difference in elevation in feet, between lowest point in foundation and top of dam, exclusive of parapet or other projections. **Length**—Overall length of barrier in feet, main dam and its integral features as located between natural abutments. **Volume**—Total volume in cubic yards of all material in main dam and its appurtenant works. **Year**—Date structure was originally completed for use. (UC) Under construction subject to revision. **River**—Mainstream. **Purpose**— I-Irrigation; C-Flood Control; H-Hydroelectric; N-navigation; S-Water Supply; R-Recreation; D-Debris Control; O-Other. **Parentheses** after name indicate type of dam as follows: (RE)-Earth; (PG)-Gravity; (ER)-Rockfill; (CB)-Buttress; (VA)-Arch; (MV)-Multi-arch; (OT)-Other. ✢Replacing existing dam.

Name of dam	State	River	Ht.	Lgth.	Vol. (1,000)	Purpose	Year
Oroville (RE)	Cal.	Feather River	742	6800	78000	IR	1968
Hoover (VA)	Nev.	Colorado River	726	1242	4400	IHCO	1936
Dworshak (PG)	Ida.	North Fork of Clearwater	717	3287	6500	HCR	1972
Glen Canyon (VA)	Ariz.	Colorado River	710	1560	4901	HCSR	1964
Auburn (PG)	Cal.	North Fork American	680	3500	6000	ISCH	UC
New Bullards Bar (VA)	Cal.	North Yuba River	635	2200	2600	S D	1970
New Melones (ER)	Cal.	Stanislaus River	625	1600	15970	IH	UC
Swift Dam (RE)	Wash.	North Fork Lewis River	610	2100	15800	HR	1958
Mossyrock Dam (VA)	Wash.	Cowlitz River	605	1300	1231	HCR	1968
Shasta (PG)	Cal.	Sacramento River	602	3460	8711	ISHN	1945
Kopperston No. 3 Refuse Bank (DT)	W.Va.	Jones Br of Toney Cr.	580	1100		O	1963
Don Pedro (RE)	Cal.	Tuolumne River	568	1800	16000	H I	1971
Hungry Horse (VA)	Mon.	South Fork of Flathead River	564	2115	3086	IHCN	1953
Grand Coulee (PG)	Wash.	Columbia River	550	4173	10585	IHCN	1942
Ross Dam (VA)	Wash.	Skagit River	540	1235	905	HR	1949
Trinity (RE)	Cal.	Trinity River	537	2600	29410	IHCR	1962
Yellowtail (VA)	Mon.	Bighorn River	525	1480	1546	ICHR	1966
Cougar (ER)	Ore.	South Fork McKenzie River	519	1600	13000	HCIR	1964
Flaming Gorge (VA)	Ut.	Green River	502	1285	987	HCSR	1964
Fontana Dam (PG)	N.C.	Little Tennessee River	480	2365	3576	H	1944
New Exchequer (ER)	Cal.	Merced River	479	1240	5169	H I	1926
Morrow Point (VA)	Col.	Gunnison River	468	741	365	HCRO	1968
Carters Main Dam (ER,RE)	Ga.	Coosawattee River	464	1950	15000	CHR	1974
Detroit (PG)	Ore.	North Santiam River	463	1580	1500	HCRI	1953
Anderson Ranch (RE)	Ida.	South Fork Boise River	456	1350	9653	IHCR	1950
Union Valley (RE)	Cal.	Silver Creek	453	1800	10000	S H	1963
Elmore Mine Refuse Dump (OT)	W.Va.	Tr-Guyandotte River	447	1975		O	1973
Round Butte Dam (RE,ER)	Ore.	Deschutes River	440	1450	9600	HR	1964
Pine Flat Lake (PG)	Cal.	Kings River	440	1840	2400	CIRH	1954
Kopperston No. 4 Dam (OT)	W. Va.	Crane Fork of Clear Fork	435	1100		O	1963
Jocassee (ER)	S.C.	Keowee River	435	1800	11600	H	1973
Mud Mountain Dam (ER)	Wash.	White River	425	700	2300	C	1948
Libby Dam (PG)	Mon.	Kootenai River	420	3055	13760	HC	1973
Owyhee Dam (VA)	Ore.	Owyhee River	417	833	538	ICR	1932
Lower Hell Hole (ER)	Cal.	Rubicon River	410	1550	8315	S D	1966
Mammoth Pool (RE)	Cal.	San Joaquin River	406	820	5355	H S	1960
Navajo (RE)	N.M.	San Juan River	402	3648	26840	IR	1963
Stirrat No. 15 Embankment (OT)	W.Va.	Rockhouse Br. of Island Cr.	400	1200		O	1973
Toxaway Lake (RE)	S.C.	Jocassee River	400	1000		H	1972
Diablo Dam (VA)	Wash.	Skagit River	400	1142	350	HR	1930
Trout Lake Dam (RE)	Col.	Lake Fork San Miguel River	395	870		H	1906
Brownlee Dam (ER)	Ida.	Snake River	395	1380	6700	H	1959
Summersville Dam (ER)	W.Va.	Cauley River	393	2280	13565	CRSO	1965
Blue Mesa (RE)	Col.	Gunnison River	390	785	3093	HCRO	1966
Pyramid (ER)	Cal.	Piru Creek	386	1080	6952	I R	1973
Boundary Dam (VA)	Wash.	Pend Oreille River	385	740	240	HR	1967
San Luis (RE)	Cal.	San Luis Creek	382	18000	77664	ISHR	1967
Green Peter (PG)	Ore.	Middle Santiam River	378	1517	1142	CHRI	1967
Pacoima (VA)	Cal.	Pacoima Creek	365	640	226	C	1929
Yale Dam (RE)	Wash.	Lewis River	357	1600	4200	HR	1952
Abiquiu Dam (RE)	N.M.	Rio Chama	354	1540	11793	CDD	1963
Arrowrock (VA)	Ida.	Boise River	350	1150	636	IC	1915
Pardee (PG)	Cal.	Mokelumne River	345	1337	615	S	1929
Hills Creek (RE)	Ore.	Middle Fork Willamette River	341	2306	10800	CHIS	1962
Folsom (PG)	Cal.	American River	340	10200	8980	ISHC	1956
Whitman Cr. Embankment (OT)	W.Va.	Whitman Cr. of Coopers Fk.	340	625		O	1952
Reservoir No. 22 (VA)	Col.	Boulder Creek	340	1090		S	1953
Gross Dam (PG)	Col.	South Boulder Creek	340	1050	592	S	1955
Castaic (RE)	Cal.	Castaic Creek	340	5200	44000	I R	1973
Casitas (RE)	Cal.	Coyote Creek	334	2000	9112	ISC	1959
Smith Dam (RE)	Ore.	Smith River	333	1150	2500	H	1962
Upper Baker Dam (PG)	Wash.	Baker River	332	1220	628	HR	1961

World's Largest Dams

Source: Bureau of Reclamation, U.S. Interior Department

Based on total volume of structure. All dams listed are predominantly earthfill or rockfill and may contain concrete sections. UC—Under Construction.

Name of dam	Cubic yards	Completed
New Cornelia Tailings, U.S.	274,026,000	1973
Tarbela, Pakistan	186,000,000	1975
Fort Peck, U.S.	125,612,000	1940
Oahe, U.S.	92,008,000	1963
Mangla, Pakistan	85,872,000	1967
Gardiner, Canada	85,743,000	1968
Afsluitdijk, Netherlands	82,927,000	1932
Orville, U.S.	78,008,000	1968
San Luis, U.S.	77,666,000	1967
Garrison, U.S.	66,506,000	1956
Cochiti, U.S.	64,631,000	1975
Tabka, Syria	60,168,000	1975
Kiev, USSR	57,552,000	1964
W.A.C. Bennett, Canada	57,203,000	1967
High Aswan Saad-El-Aili, Egypt	57,203,000	1970
Saratov, U.S.S.R.	52,843,000	1967
Mission Tailings, No. 2, U.S.	52,435,000	1973
Fort Randall, U.S.	50,205,000	1956
Kanev, USSR	49,520,000	1974
Kakhovka, USSR	46,617,000	1955
Volga, V.I. Lenin, USSR	44,298,000	1955
Castaic, U.S.	44,000,000	1971
Jari, Pakistan	42,400,000	1967
Kremenchug, USSR	41,192,000	1961

Superlative U. S. Statistics

Source: National Geographic Society, Washington, D.C.

Area for 50 states	Total Land 3,536,855 sq. mi. — Water 78,267 sq. mi.	3,615,122 sq. mi.
Largest state	Alaska	586,412 sq. mi.
Smallest state	Rhode Island	1,214 sq. mi.
Largest county	San Bernardino County, California	20,117 sq. mi.
Smallest county	New York, New York	23 sq. mi.
Northernmost city	Barrow, Alaska	71° 17′N.
Northernmost point	Point Barrow, Alaska	71° 23′N.
Southernmost city	Hilo, Island of Hawaii	19° 43′N.
Southernmost town	Naalehu, Island of Hawaii	19° 03′N.
Southernmost point	Ka Lae (South Cape), Island of Hawaii	18° 56′N. (155° 41′W.)
Easternmost city	Eastport, Maine	66° 59′02″W.
Easternmost town	Lubec, Maine	66° 58′49″W.
Easternmost point	West Quoddy Head, Maine	66° 57′W.
Westernmost city	Lihue, Island of Kauai, Hawaii	159° 22′W.
Westernmost town	Adak, Aleutians, Alaska	176° 45′W.
Westernmost point	Cape Wrangell, Attu Island, Aleutians, Alaska	172° 27′E.
Highest city	Leadville, Colorado	10,200 ft.
Lowest town	Calipatria, California	—183 ft.
Highest point on Atlantic coast	Cadillac Mountain, Mount Desert Is., Maine	1,530 ft.
Largest and oldest national park	Yellowstone National Park (1872), Wyoming, Montana, Idaho	3,468 sq. mi.
Largest national monument	Glacier Bay, Alaska	4,383 sq. mi.
Highest waterfall	Yosemite Falls—Total in three sections	2,425 ft.
	Upper Yosemite Fall	1,430 ft.
	Cascades in middle section	675 ft.
	Lower Yosemite Fall	320 ft.
Longest river	Mississippi-Missouri	3,710 mi.
Highest mountain	Mount McKinley, Alaska	20,320 ft.
Lowest point	Death Valley, California	—282 ft.
Deepest lake	Crater Lake, Oregon	1,932 ft.
Rainiest spot	Mt. Waialeale, Hawaii	Annual aver. rainfall 460 inches
Largest gorge	Grand Canyon, Colorado River, Arizona	217 miles long, 4 to 18 miles wide, 1 mile deep
Deepest gorge	Hells Canyon, Snake River, Idaho	7,900 ft.
Strongest surface wind	Mount Washington, New Hampshire recorded 1934	231 mph
Biggest dam	New Cornelia Tailings, Ten Mile Wash, Arizona	274,026,000 cu. yds. material used
Tallest building	Sears Tower, Chicago, Illinois	1,454 ft.
Largest building	Boeing 747 Manufacturing Plant, Everett, Washington	205,600,000 cu. ft.; covers 47 acres.
Tallest structure	TV tower, Blanchard, North Dakota	2,063 ft.
Longest bridge span	Verrazano-Narrows, New York	4,260 ft.
Highest bridge	Royal Gorge, Colorado	1,053 ft. above water
Deepest well	Gas well, Washita County, Oklahoma	31,441 ft.

The 49 States, Including Alaska

Area for 49 states	Total Land 3,530,430 sq. mi. — Water 78,242 sq. mi.	3,608,672 sq. mi.

The 48 Contiguous States

Area for 48 states	Total Land 2,963,998 sq. mi. — Water 58,262 sq. mi.	3,022,260 sq. mi.
Largest state	Texas	267,338 sq. mi.
Northernmost town	Angle Inlet, Minnesota	49° 22′N.
Northernmost point	Northwest Angle, Minnesota	49° 23′N.
Southernmost city	Key West, Florida	24° 33′N.
Southernmost mainland city	Florida City, Florida	25° 27′N.
Southernmost point	Key West, Florida	24° 33′N.
Westernmost town	La Push, Washington	124° 38′W.
Westernmost point	Cape Alava, Washington	124° 44′W.
Highest mountain	Mount Whitney, California	14,494 ft.

Note to users: The distinction between cities and towns varies from state to state. In this table the U.S. Bureau of the Census usage was followed.

Geodetic Datum Point of North America

The geodetic datum point of the U.S. is the National Ocean Survey's triangulation station Meades Ranch in Osborne County, Kansas, at latitude 39° 13′26″. 686 N and longitude 98° 32′30″. 506 W. (Frequently this is referred to as the geodetic center of the U.S., which has no meaning.) This geodetic datum point is a fundamental point from which all latitude and longitude computations originate for North America and Central America.

Statistical Information about the U.S.

In the *Statistical Abstract of the United States* the Bureau of the Census, U.S. Dept. of Commerce, annually publishes a summary of social, political, and economic information. A book of more than 1,000 pages, it presents in 32 sections comprehensive data on population, housing, health, education, employment, income, prices, business, banking, energy, science, defense, trade, government finance, foreign country comparison, and other subjects. Special features include an appendix on statistical methodology and reliability and a summary of recent trends. The book is prepared under the direction of William Lerner, Data User Services Division, Bureau of the Census. Supplements to the *Statistical Abstract* are *Pocket Data Book USA, 1976; County and City Data Book, 1972; Congressional District Data Book, 93rd Congress with supplements for the 3 states that redistricted for the 94th Congress; Historical Statistics of the United States, Colonial Times to 1970.* Information concerning these and other publications may be obtained from the Supt. of Documents, Government Printing Office, Wash., D.C. 20402, or from the U.S. Bureau of the Census, Data User Services Division, Wash., D.C. 20233.

Highest and Lowest Altitudes in the U.S. and Territories

Source: Geological Survey, U.S. Interior Department. (Minus sign means below sea level; elevations are in feet.)

State	Highest Point Name	County	Elev.	Lowest Point Name	County	Elev.
Alabama	Cheaha Mountain	Cleburne	2,407	Gulf of Mexico		Sea level
Alaska	Mount McKinley		20,320	Pacific Ocean		Sea level
Arizona	Humphreys Peak	Coconino	12,633	Colorado R.	Yuma	70
Arkansas	Magazine Mountain	Logan	2,753	Ouachita R.	Ashley Union	55
California	Mount Whitney	Inyo-Tulare	14,494	Death Valley	Inyo	—282
Canal Zone	Cerro Galera	Balboa District	1,205	Atlantic Ocean		Sea level
Colorado	Mount Elbert	Lake	14,433	Arkansas R	Prowers	3,350
Connecticut	Mount Frissell	Litchfield	2,380	L. I. Sound		Sea level
Delaware	On Ebright Road	New Castle	442	Atlantic Ocean		Sea level
Dist. of Col.	Tenleytown	N. W. part	410	Potomac R.		1
Florida	West boundary	Walton	345	Atlantic Ocean		Sea level
Georgia	Brasstown Bald	Towns-Union	4,784	Atlantic Ocean		Sea level
Guam	Mount Lamlam	Agat District	1,329	Pacific Ocean		Sea level
Hawaii	Mauna Kea	Hawaii	13,796	Pacific Ocean		Sea level
Idaho	Borah Peak	Custer	12,662	Snake R.	Nez Perce	710
Illinois	Charles Mound	Jo Daviess	1,235	Mississippi R.	Alexander	279
Indiana	Franklin Township	Wayne	1,257	Ohio R.	Posey	320
Iowa	NE of Sibley	Osceola	1,670	Mississippi R.	Lee	480
Kansas	Mount Sunflower	Wallace	4,039	Verdigris R.	Montgomery	680
Kentucky	Black Mountain	Harlan	4,145	Mississippi R.	Fulton	257
Louisiana	Driskill Mountain	Bienville	535	New Orleans	Orleans	—5
Maine	Mount Katahdin	Piscataquis	5,268	Atlantic Ocean		Sea level
Maryland	Backbone Mountain	Garrett	3,360	Atlantic Ocean		Sea level
Massachusetts	Mount Greylock	Berkshire	3,491	Atlantic Ocean		Sea level
Michigan	Mount Curwood	Baraga	1,980	Lake Erie		572
Minnesota	Eagle Mountain	Cook	2,301	Lake Superior		602
Mississippi	Woodall Mountain	Tishomingo	806	Gulf of Mexico		Sea level
Missouri	Taum Sauk Mt.	Iron	1,772	St. Francis R.	Dunklin	230
Montana	Granite Peak	Park	12,799	Kootenai R.	Lincoln	1,800
Nebraska	Johnson Township	Kimball	5,426	S.E. cor. State	Richardson	840
Nevada	Boundary Peak	Esmeralda	13,143	Colorado R.	Clark	470
New Hamp.	Mt. Washington	Coos	6,288	Atlantic Ocean		Sea level
New Jersey	High Point	Sussex	1,803	Atlantic Ocean		Sea level
New Mexico	Wheeler Peak	Taos	13,161	Red Bluff Res.	Eddy	2,817
New York	Mount Marcy	Essex	5,344	Atlantic Ocean		Sea level
North Carolina	Mount Mitchell	Yancey	6,684	Atlantic Ocean		Sea level
North Dakota	White Butte	Slope	3,506	Red R.	Pembina	750
Ohio	Campbell Hill	Logan	1,550	Ohio R.	Hamilton	433
Oklahoma	Black Mesa	Cimarron	4,973	Little R.	McCurtain	287
Oregon	Mount Hood	Clackamas-Hood R.	11,235	Pacific Ocean		Sea level
Pennsylvania	Mt. Davis	Somerset	3,213	Delaware R.	Delaware	Sea level
Puerto Rico	Cerro de Punta	Ponce	4,389	Atlantic Ocean		Sea level
Rhode Island	Jerimoth Hill	Providence	812	Atlantic Ocean		Sea level
Samoa	Lata Mountain	Tau Island	3,160	Pacific Ocean		Sea level
South Carolina	Sassafras Mountain	Pickens	3,560	Atlantic Ocean		Sea level
South Dakota	Harney Peak	Pennington	7,242	Big Stone Lake	Roberts	962
Tennessee	Clingmans Dome	Sevier	6,643	Mississippi R.	Shelby	182
Texas	Guadalupe Peak	Culberson	8,751	Gulf of Mexico		Sea level
Utah	Kings Peak	Duchesne	13,528	Beaverdam Cr.	Washington	2,000
Vermont	Mount Mansfield	Lamoille	4,393	Lake Champlain	Franklin	95
Virginia	Mount Rogers	Grayson-Smyth	5,729	Atlantic Ocean		Sea level
Virgin Islands	Crown Mountain	Is. St. Thomas	1,556	Atlantic Ocean		Sea level
Washington	Mount Rainier	Pierce	14,410	Pacific Ocean		Sea level
West Virginia	Spruce Knob	Pendleton	4,863	Potomac R.	Jefferson	240
Wisconsin	Timms Hill	Price	1,952	Lake Michigan		581
Wyoming	Gannett Peak	Fremont	13,804	B. Fourche R.	Crook	3,100

U. S. Coastline by States

Source: NOAA, U.S. Commerce Department (statute miles)

State	Coastline[1]	Shoreline[2]
Atlantic coast	**2,069**	**28,673**
Connecticut	0	618
Delaware	28	381
Florida	580	3,331
Georgia	100	2,344
Maine	228	3,478
Maryland	31	3,190
Massachusetts	192	1,519
New Hampshire	13	131
New Jersey	130	1,792
New York	127	1,850
North Carolina	301	3,375
Pennsylvania	0	89
Rhode Island	40	384
South Carolina	187	2,876
Virginia	112	3,315
Gulf coast	**1,631**	**17,141**
Alabama	53	607
Florida	770	5,095
Louisiana	397	7,721
Mississippi	44	359
Texas	367	3,359
Pacific coast	**7,623**	**40,298**
Alaska	5,580	31,383
California	840	3,427
Hawaii	750	1,052
Oregon	296	1,410
Washington	157	3,026
Arctic coast, Alaska	**1,060**	**2,521**
United States	**12,383**	**88,633**

(1) Figures are lengths of general outline of seacoast. Measurements were made with a unit measure of 30 minutes of latitude on charts as near the scale of 1:1,200,000 as possible. Coastline of sounds and bays is included to a point where they narrow to width of unit measure, and includes the distance across at such point.

(2) Figures obtained in 1939-40 with a recording instrument on the largest-scale charts and maps then available. Shoreline of outer coast, offshore islands, sounds, bays, rivers, and creeks is included to the head of tidewater or to a point where tidal waters narrow to a width of 100 feet.

International Boundary Lines of the U.S.

The length of the northern boundary of the contiguous U.S. — the U.S.-Canadian border, excluding Alaska — is 3,987 miles according to the U.S. Geological Survey, Dept. of the Interior. The length of the Alaskan-Canadian border is 1,538 miles. The length of the U.S.-Mexican border, from the Gulf of Mexico to the Pacific Ocean, is approximately 1,933 miles (1963 boundary agreement).

States: Settled, Capitals, Entry into Union, Area, Rank

The original 13 states — The 13 colonies that seceded from Great Britain and fought the War of Independence (American Revolution) became the 13 original states. They were:,Delaware, Pennsylvania, New Jersey, Georgia, Connecticut, Massachusetts, Maryland, South Carolina, New Hampshire, Virginia, New York, North Carolina, and Rhode Island. The order for the original 13 states is the order in which they ratified the Constitution.

State	Settled*	Capital	Entered Union Date	Entered Union Order	Extent in miles Long (approx. mean)	Extent in miles Wide (approx. mean)	Area in square miles Land	Area in square miles Inland water	Area in square miles Total	Rank in area
Ala.	1702	Montgomery	Dec. 14, 1819	22	330	190	50,708	901	51,609	29
Alas.	1784	Juneau	Jan. 3, 1959	49	(a)1,480	810	566,432	19,980	586,412	1
Ariz.	1776	Phoenix	Feb. 14, 1912	48	400	310	113,417	492	113,909	6
Ark.	1785	Little Rock	June 15, 1836	25	260	240	51,945	1,159	53,104	27
Cal.	1769	Sacramento	Sept. 9, 1850	31	770	250	156,361	2,332	158,693	3
Col.	1858	Denver	Aug. 1, 1876	38	380	280	103,766	481	104,247	8
Conn.	1635	Hartford	Jan. 9, 1788	5	110	70	4,862	147	5,009	48
Del.	1683	Dover	Dec. 7, 1787	1	100	30	1,982	75	2,057	49
D.C.		Washington			...	...	61	6	67	51
Fla.	1565	Tallahassee	Mar. 3, 1845	27	500	160	54,090	4,470	58,560	22
Ga.	1733	Atlanta	Jan. 2, 1788	4	300	230	58,073	803	58,876	21
Ha.	......	Honolulu	Aug. 21, 1959	50	...	...	6,425	25	6,450	47
Ida.	1842	Boise	July 3, 1890	43	570	300	82,677	880	83,557	13
Ill.	1720	Springfield	Dec. 3, 1818	21	390	210	55,748	652	56,400	24
Ind.	1733	Indianapolis	Dec. 11, 1816	19	270	140	36,097	194	36,291	38
Ia.	1788	Des Moines	Dec. 28, 1846	29	310	200	55,941	349	56,290	25
Kan.	1727	Topeka	Jan. 29, 1861	34	400	210	81,787	477	82,264	14
Ky.	1774	Frankfort	June 1, 1792	15	380	140	39,650	745	40,395	37
La.	1699	Baton Rouge	Apr. 30, 1812	18	380	130	44,930	3,593	48,523	31
Me.	1624	Augusta	Mar. 15, 1820	23	320	190	30,920	2,295	33,215	39
Md.	1634	Annapolis	Apr. 28, 1788	7	250	90	9,891	686	10,577	42
Mass.	1620	Boston	Feb. 6, 1788	6	190	50	7,826	431	8,257	45
Mich.	1668	Lansing	Jan. 26, 1837	26	490	240	56,817	1,399	58,216	23
Minn.	1805	St. Paul	May 11, 1858	32	400	250	79,289	4,779	84,068	12
Miss.	1699	Jackson	Dec. 10, 1817	20	340	170	47,296	420	47,716	32
Mo.	1735	Jefferson City	Aug. 10, 1821	24	300	240	68,995	691	69,686	19
Mon.	1809	Helena	Nov. 8, 1889	41	630	280	145,587	1,551	147,138	4
Neb.	1847	Lincoln	Mar. 1, 1867	37	430	210	76,483	744	77,227	15
Nev.	1850	Carson City	Oct. 31, 1864	36	490	320	109,889	651	110,540	7
N.H.	1623	Concord	June 21, 1788	9	190	70	9,027	277	9,304	44
N.J.	1664	Trenton	Dec. 18, 1787	3	150	70	7,521	315	7,836	46
N.M.	1605	Santa Fe	Jan. 6, 1912	47	370	343	121,412	254	121,666	5
N.Y.	1614	Albany	July 26, 1788	11	330	283	47,831	1,745	49,576	30
N.C.	1650	Raleigh	Nov. 21, 1789	12	500	150	48,798	3,788	52,586	28
N.D.	1766	Bismarck	Nov. 2, 1889	39	340	211	69,273	1,392	70,665	17
Oh.	1788	Columbus	Mar. 1, 1803	17	220	220	40,975	247	41,222	35
Okla.	1889	Oklahoma City	Nov. 16, 1907	46	400	220	68,782	1,137	69,919	18
Ore.	1811	Salem	Feb. 14, 1859	33	360	261	96,184	797	96,981	10
Pa.	1682	Harrisburg	Dec. 12, 1787	2	283	160	44,966	367	45,333	33
R.I.	1636	Providence	May 29, 1790	13	40	30	1,049	165	1,214	50
S.C.	1670	Columbia	May 23, 1788	8	260	200	30,225	830	31,055	40
S.D.	1856	Pierre	Nov. 2, 1889	40	380	210	75,955	1,092	77,047	16
Tenn.	1757	Nashville	June 1, 1796	16	440	120	41,328	916	42,244	34
Tex.	1691	Austin	Dec. 29, 1845	28	790	660	262,134	5,204	267,338	2
Ut.	1847	Salt Lake City	Jan. 4, 1896	45	350	270	82,096	2,820	84,916	11
Vt.	1724	Montpelier	Mar. 4, 1791	14	160	80	9,267	342	9,609	43
Va.	1607	Richmond	June 25, 1788	10	430	200	39,780	1,037	40,817	36
Wash.	1811	Olympia	Nov. 11, 1889	42	360	240	66,570	1,622	68,192	20
W. Va.	1727	Charleston	June 20, 1863	35	240	130	24,070	111	24,181	41
Wis.	1766	Madison	May 29, 1848	30	310	260	54,464	1,690	56,154	26
Wyo.	1834	Cheyenne	July 10, 1890	44	360	280	97,203	711	97,914	9

*First European permanent settlement. (a) Aleutian Islands and Alexander Archipelago are not considered in these lengths.

The Continental Divide

Source: Geological Survey, U.S. Interior Department

Continental Divide: watershed, created by mountain ranges or table-lands of the Rocky Mountains, from which the drainage is easterly or westerly; the easterly flowing waters reaching the Atlantic Ocean chiefly through the Gulf of Mexico, and the westerly flowing waters reaching the Pacific Ocean through the Columbia River, or through the Colorado River, which flows into the Gulf of California.

The location and route of the Continental Divide across the United States may briefly be described as follows:

Beginning at point of crossing the United States-Mexican boundary, near long. 108°45′W., the Divide, in a northerly direction, crosses New Mexico along the western edge of the Rio Grande drainage basin, entering Colorado near long. 106°41′W.

Thence by a very irregular route northerly across Colorado along the western summits of the Rio Grande and of the Arkansas, the South Platte, and the North Platte River basins, and across Rocky Mountain National Park, entering Wyoming near long. 106°52′W.

Thence in a northwesterly direction, forming the western rims of the North Platte, Big Horn, and Yellowstone River basins, crossing the southwestern portion of Yellowstone National Park.

Thence in a westerly and then a northerly direction forming the common boundary of Idaho and Montana, to a point on said boundary near long. 114°00′ W.

Thence northeasterly and northwesterly through Montana and the Glacier National Park, entering Canada near long. 114°04′W.

Chronological List of Territories

Source: National Archives and Records Service

Name of territory	Date of Organic Act	Organic Act effective	Admission as state	Yrs. terr.
Northwest Territory (a)	July 13, 1787	No fixed date	Mar. 1, 1803(b)	16
Territory southwest of River Ohio	May 26, 1790	No fixed date	June 1, 1796(c)	6
Mississippi	Apr. 7, 1798	When president acted	Dec. 10, 1817	19
Indiana	May 7, 1800	July 4, 1800	Dec. 11, 1816	16
Orleans	Mar. 26, 1804	Oct. 1, 1804	Apr. 30, 1812(d)	7
Michigan	Jan. 11, 1805	June 30, 1805	Jan. 26, 1837	31
Louisiana-Missouri (e)	Mar. 3, 1805	July 4, 1805	Aug. 10, 1821	16
Illinois	Feb. 3, 1809	Mar. 1, 1809	Dec. 3, 1818	9
Alabama	Mar. 3, 1817	When Miss. became a state	Dec. 14, 1819	2
Arkansas	Mar. 2, 1819	July 4, 1819	June 15, 1836	17
Florida	Mar. 30, 1822	No fixed date	Mar. 3, 1845	23
Wisconsin	Apr. 20, 1836	July 3, 1836	May 29, 1848	12
Iowa	June 12, 1838	July 3, 1838	Dec. 28, 1846	7
Oregon	Aug. 14, 1848	Date of act	Feb. 14, 1859	10
Minnesota	Mar. 3, 1849	Date of act	May 11, 1858	9
New Mexico	Sept. 9, 1850	On president's proclamation	Jan. 6, 1912	61
Utah	Sept. 9, 1850	Date of act	Jan. 4, 1896	44
Washington	Mar. 2, 1853	Date of act	Nov. 11, 1889	36
Nebraska	May 30, 1854	Date of act	Mar. 1, 1867	12
Kansas	May 30, 1854	Date of act	Jan. 29, 1861	6
Colorado	Feb. 28, 1861	Date of act	Aug. 1, 1876	15
Nevada	Mar. 2, 1861	Date of act	Oct. 31, 1864	3
Dakota	Mar. 2, 1861	Date of act	Nov. 2, 1889	28
Arizona	Feb. 24, 1863	Date of act	Feb. 14, 1912	49
Idaho	Mar. 3, 1863	Date of act	July 3, 1890	27
Montana	May 26, 1864	Date of act	Nov. 8, 1889	25
Wyoming	July 25, 1868	When officers were qualified	July 10, 1890	22
Alaska	May 17, 1884	No fixed date	Jan. 3, 1959	75
Oklahoma	May 2, 1890	Date of act	Nov. 16, 1907	17
Hawaii	Apr. 30, 1900	June 14, 1900	Aug. 21, 1959	59

(a) Included Ohio, Indiana, Illinois, Michigan, Wisconsin, eastern Minnesota; (b) as the state of Ohio; (c) as the state of Tennessee; (d) as the state of Louisiana; (e) organic act for Missouri Territory of June 4, 1812, became effective Dec. 7, 1812.

Geographic Centers, U.S. and Each State

Source: Geological Survey, U. S. Interior Department

United States, including Alaska and Hawaii — South Dakota; Butte County, 17 miles W of Castle Rock, 14 miles E of junction of borders of South Dakota, Montana, and Wyoming. Approx. lat. 44°58′N. long. 103°46′W.

Contiguous U. S. (48 States) — Near Lebanon, Smith Co., Kansas. lat. 39°50′N. long. 98°35′W.

North American continent — The geographic center is in Pierce County, North Dakota, 6 miles W of Balta, latitude 48°10′, longitude 100°10′W.

State—county, locality

Alabama—Chilton, 12 miles SW of Clanton.
Alaska—lat. 63°50′N. long. 152°W. Approx. 60 mi. NW of Mt. McKinley.
Arizona—Yavapai, 55 miles ESE of Prescott.
Arkansas—Pulaski, 12 miles NW of Little Rock.
California—Madera, 38 miles E of Madera.
Colorado—Park, 30 miles NW of Pikes Peak.
Connecticut—Hartford, at East Berlin.
Delaware—Kent, 11 miles S of Dover.
District of Columbia—Near Fourth and "L" Streets, NW
Florida—Hernando, 12 miles NNW of Brooksville.
Georgia—Twiggs, 18 miles SE of Macon.
Hawaii—Hawaii, 20°15′N, 156°20′W, off Maui Island.
Idaho—Custer, at Custer, SW of Challis.
Illinois—Logan, 28 miles NE of Springfield.
Indiana—Boone, 14 miles NNW of Indianapolis.
Iowa—Story, 5 miles NE of Ames.
Kansas—Barton, 15 miles NE of Great Bend
Kentucky—Marion, 3 miles NNW of Lebanon.
Louisiana—Avoyelles, 3 miles SE of Marksville.
Maine—Piscataquis, 18 miles north of Dover.

State—county, locality

Maryland—Prince Georges, 4.5 miles NW of Davidsonville.
Massachusetts—Worcester, north part of city.
Michigan—Wexford, 5 miles NNW of Cadillac.
Minnesota—Crow Wing, 10 miles SW of Brainerd.
Mississippi—Leake, 9 miles WNW of Carthage.
Missouri—Miller, 20 miles SW of Jefferson City.
Montana—Fergus, 12 miles west of Lewistown.
Nebraska—Custer, 10 miles NW of Broken Bow.
Nevada—Lander, 26 miles SE of Austin.
New Hampshire—Belknap, 3 miles E of Ashland.
New Jersey—Mercer, 5 miles SE of Trenton.
New Mexico—Torrance, 12 miles SSW of Willard.
New York—Madison, 12 miles S of Oneida and 26 miles SW of Utica.
North Carolina—Chatham, 10 miles NW of Sanford.
North Dakota—Sheridan, 5 miles SW of McClusky.
Ohio—Delaware, 25 miles NNE of Columbus.
Oklahoma—Oklahoma, 8 miles N of Oklahoma City.
Oregon—Crook, 25 miles SSE of Prineville.
Pennsylvania—Centre, 2.5 miles SW of Bellefonte.
Rhode Island—Kent, 1 mile SSW of Crompton.
South Carolina—Richland, 13 miles SE of Columbia.
South Dakota—Hughes, 8 miles NE of Pierre.
Tennessee—Rutherford, 5 mi. NE of Murfreesboro.
Texas—McCulloch, 15 miles NE of Brady.
Utah—Sanpete, 3 miles N of Manti.
Vermont—Washington, 3 miles E of Roxbury.
Virginia—Buckingham, 5 miles SW of Buckingham.
Washington—Chelan, 10 mi. WSW of Wenatchee.
West Virginia—Braxton, 4 miles E of Sutton.
Wisconsin—Wood, 9 miles SE of Marshfield.
Wyoming—Fremont, 58 miles ENE of Lander.

There is no generally accepted definition of geographic center, and no satisfactory method for determining it. The geographic center of an area may be defined as the center of gravity of the surface, or that point on which the surface of the area would balance if it were a plane of uniform thickness.

No marked or monumented point has been established by any government agency as the geographic center of either the 50 states, the contiguous United States, or the North American continent. A monument was erected in Lebanon, Kan., contiguous U.S. center, by a group of citizens.

Origin of the Names of U.S. States

Source: State officials, the Smithsonian Institution, and the Topographic Division, U.S. Geological Survey.

Alabama—Indian for tribal town, later a tribe (Alabamas or Alibamons), of the Creek confederacy.

Alaska—Russian version of Aleutian (Eskimo) word, alakshak, for "peninsula" or "great lands."

Arizona—Spanish version of Pima Indian word for "little spring place," or Aztec arizuma, meaning "silver-bearing."

Arkansas—French variant of Kansas, a Sioux Indian name for "south wind people."

California—Bestowed by the Spanish conquistadors (possibly by Cortez). It was the name of an imaginary island, an earthly paradise, in "Las Serges de Esplandian," a Spanish romance written by Montalvo in 1510. Baja California (Lower California, in Mexico) was first visited by Spanish in 1533. The present U.S. state was called Alta (Upper) California.

Colorado—Spanish, red, first applied to Colorado River.

Connecticut—From Mohican and other Algonquin words meaning "long river place."

Delaware—Named for Lord De La Warr, early governor of Virginia; first applied to river, then to Indian tribe (Lenni-Lenape), and the state.

District of Columbia—For Columbus, 1791.

Florida—Named by Ponce de Leon on Pascua Florida, "Flowery Easter," on Easter Sunday, 1513.

Georgia—For King George II of England by James Oglethorpe, colonial administrator, 1732.

Hawaii—Possibly derived from native word for homeland, Hawaiki or Owhyhee.

Idaho—Shoshone derivation. State calls it "light on the mountains."

Illinois—French for Illini or land of Illini, Algonquin word meaning men or warriors.

Indiana—Means "land of the Indians."

Iowa—Indian word variously translated as "one who puts to sleep" or "beautiful land."

Kansas—Sioux word for "south wind people."

Kentucky—Indian word variously translated as "dark and bloody ground," "meadow land" and "land of tomorrow."

Louisiana—Part of territory called Louisiana by LaSalle for French King Louis XIV.

Maine—From Maine, ancient French province.

Maryland—For Queen Henrietta Maria, wife of Charles I of England.

Massachusetts—From Indian tribe named after "large hill place" identified by Capt. John Smith as near Milton, Mass.

Michigan—From Chippewa words mici gama meaning "great water," after the lake of the same name.

Minnesota—From Dakota Sioux word meaning "cloudy water" or "sky-tinted water" of the Minnesota River.

Mississippi—Probably Chippewa: mici zibi, "great river" or "gathering-in of all the waters."

Missouri—Indian tribe named after Missouri River, meaning "muddy water."

Montana—Latin or Spanish for "mountainous."

Nebraska—From Omaha or Otos Indian word meaning "broad water" or "flat river," describing the Platte River.

Nevada—Spanish, meaning snow-clad.

New Hampshire—Named 1629 by Capt. John Mason of Plymouth Council for county in England.

New Jersey—The Duke of York, 1664, gave a patent to John Berkeley and Sir George Carteret to be called Nova Caesaria, or New Jersey, after England's Isle of Jersey.

New Mexico—Spaniards in Mexico applied term to land north and west of Rio Grande in the 16th century.

New York—For Duke of York and Albany who received patent to New Netherland from his brother Charles II and sent an expedition to capture it, 1664.

North Carolina—In 1619 Charles I gave a large patent to Sir Robert Heath to be called Province of Carolana, from Carolus, Latin name for Charles. A new patent was granted by Charles II to Earl of Clarendon and others. Divided into North and South Carolina, 1710.

North Dakota—Dakota is Sioux for friend or ally.

Ohio—Iroquois word for "beautiful river."

Oklahoma—Choctaw coined word meaning red man, proposed by Rev. Allen Wright, Choctaw-speaking Indian.

Oregon—Origin unknown.

Pennsylvania—William Penn, the Quaker, who was made full proprietor by King Charles II in 1681, suggested Sylvania, or woodland, for his tract. The king's government owed Penn's father, Admiral William Penn, £16,000, and the land being granted in part settlement, the king added the Penn to Sylvania, against the desires of the modest proprietor, in honor of the admiral.

Puerto Rico—Spanish for Rich Port.

Rhode Island—Named Roode Eylandt by Adriaen Block, Dutch explorer, because of its red clay. Name of Roger Williams' settlement was added to give the small state its long, official title: State of Rhode Island and Providence Plantations.

South Carolina—See North Carolina.

South Dakota—See North Dakota.

Tennessee—From 1784 to 1788 this was the State of Franklin, or Frankland. Tanasi was the name of Cherokee villages on the Little Tennessee River.

Texas—Variant of word used by Caddo and other Indians meaning friends or allies, and applied to them by the Spanish in eastern Texas. Also written texias, tejas, teysas.

Utah—From a Navajo word meaning upper, or higher up, as applied to a Shoshone tribe called Ute. Spanish form is Yutta, English Uta or Utah. Proposed name Deseret, "land of honeybees," from Book of Mormon, was rejected by Congress.

Vermont—From French words Vert, green, and Mont, mountain. The Green Mountains were said to have been named by Samuel de Champlain. The Green Mountain Boys were Gen. Stark's men in the Revolution. When the state was formed, 1777, Dr. Thomas Young suggested combining vert and mont into Vermont.

Virginia—Named by Sir Walter Raleigh, who fitted out the expedition of 1584, in honor of Queen Elizabeth, the Virgin Queen of England.

Washington—Named after George Washington. When the bill creating the Territory of Columbia was introduced in the 32d Congress, the name was changed to Washington because of the existence of the District of Columbia.

West Virginia—So named when western counties of Virginia refused to secede from the United States, 1863.

Wisconsin—An Indian name, spelled Ouisconsin and Misconsing by early chroniclers. Believed to mean "grassy place" in Chippewa. Congress made it Wisconsin.

Wyoming—The word was taken from Wyoming Valley, Pa., which was the site of an Indian massacre and became widely known by Campbell's poem, Gertrude of Wyoming. In Algonquin it means "large prairie place."

Accession of Territory by the U.S.

Source: Statistical Abstract of the United States

Division	Year	Sq. mi.[1]	Division	Year	Sq. mi.[1]	Division	Year	Sq. mi.[1]
Total (1970)		3,628,066	Oregon	**1846**	285,580	American Samoa	**1900**	76
50 states & D.C.		3,615,122	Mexican Cession	**1848**	529,017	Canal Zone[4]	**1904**	553
Territory in 1790[2]		888,685	Gadsden Purchase	**1853**	29,640	Corn Islands[5]	**1914**	4
Louisiana Purchase	**1803**	827,192	Alaska	**1867**	586,412	Virgin Islands, U.S.	**1917**	133
By treaty with Spain:			Hawaii	**1898**	6,450	Trust Territory of		
Florida	**1819**	58,560	The Philippines[3]	**1898**	115,600	the Pacific Is.	**1947**	8,489
Other areas	**1819**	13,443	Puerto Rico	**1899**	3,435	All other[6]	....	42
Texas	**1845**	390,143	Guam	**1899**	212			

(1) Gross area (land and water). (2) Includes drainage basin of Red River on the north, south of 49th parallel sometimes considered a part of the Louisiana Purchase. (3) Area not included in total; became Republic of the Philippines July 4, 1946. (4) Under U.S. jurisdiction by treaty with Panama. (5) Leased from Nicaragua for 99 years but returned Apr. 25, 1971; area not included in total. (6) See index for Outlying Areas, U.S.

Confederate States and Secession

The American Civil War, 1861-1865, grew out of sectional disputes over the continued existence of slavery in the South and the contention of Southern legislators that the states retained many sovereign rights, including the right to secede from the Union.

The principal product of the South was cotton, harvested by slave labor. For 50 years Northern leaders had been trying to curtail slavery, but were checkmated in Congress by Southern legislators. Extreme partisans in the North, called Abolitionists, demanded the immediate end of slavery for moral reasons.

The Southern states argued that the U.S.Constitution was a contract between sovereign states, which could withdraw (secede) when state rights were violated. This has led Southern historians to call the Civil War the War Between the States. Actually the war was not fought by state against state but by one federal regime against another, the Confederate government in Richmond assuming control over the economic, political, and military life of the South, under protest from Georgia and South Carolina.

Early Slavery Laws

Milestone U.S. laws on the slavery issue included the Missouri Compromise of 1820 which admitted Missouri as a slave state but prohibited slavery in the Louisiana Territory north of Arkansas; the Compromise of 1850, which admitted California as a free state, omitted action on slavery in organizing Utah and New Mexico as territories, ended slave trade in the District of Columbia, amended the Fugitive Slave Act to punish any who aided a fugitive, and abolished trial by jury for fugitives; Kansas-Nebraska Act, 1854, which left choice of slavery in Kansas and Nebraska to residents there (squatter sovereignty).

Harriet Beecher Stowe's *Uncle Tom's Cabin*, 1851-1852, intensified feeling against slavery.

Tension increased when the Supreme Court ruled Mar. 6, 1857, that Dred Scott, a Negro, did not become free when taken to a free state and did not have rights as a citizen; also that the Missouri Compromise on slavery was unconstitutional.

John Brown's attempt to arm slaves at Harpers Ferry, Oct. 16-18, 1859, inflamed partisans.

Abraham Lincoln's stand for free soil (no slavery) in new states and territories, and his general condemnation of slavery, caused Southern fanatics to threaten secession if he were elected. Before inauguration Lincoln had Sen. William H. Seward (N.Y.) offer a resolution that the Constitution never be altered to interfere with slavery where established, that the Fugitive Slave Law be amended to include trial by jury, that all states repeal laws contrary to the Constitution. When Sen. Stephen A. Douglas split the Democratic party by his stand against secession, Republican Lincoln's election was assured.

Secession of States

South Carolina voted an ordinance of secession from the Union repealing its 1788 ratification of the U.S. Constitution on Dec. 20, 1860, to take effect Dec. 24. Other states seceded in 1861 and their votes in conventions were:

Mississippi, Jan. 1861, by 84 to 15.

Florida, Jan. 10, 1861, by 62 to 7.

Alabama, Jan. 11, 1861, by 61 to 39.

Georgia, Jan. 19, 1861, by 208 to 89.

Louisiana, Jan. 26, 1861, by 113 to 17.

Texas, Feb. 1, 1861, by 166 to 7, ratified by popular vote Feb. 23, 1861 (for 34,794; against 11,325).

Virginia had delayed action, but when Pres. Lincoln called for troops after Fort Sumter fell (Apr. 14, 1861), it voted for secession Apr. 17, 1861, by 88 to 55, ratified by popular vote May 23, 1861 (for secession, 128,884; against, 32,134).

Arkansas, May 6, 1861, by 69 to 1.

North Carolina, May 21, 1861, voted secession but refused by two-thirds vote to submit it to people for ratification.

Tennessee, May 7, 1861, entered a military league with the Confederacy (popular vote, June 8, for secession, 104,019; against 47,238).

Missouri Unionists stopped secession in the convention at Jefferson City Feb. 28 and at the second session in St. Louis Mar. 9. The legislature condemned secession Mar. 7. Under the protection of Confederate troops, secessionist members of the legislature adopted a resolution of secession at Neosho, Oct. 31, 1861. The Confederate Congress seated the secessionists' representatives.

Kentucky did not secede and its government remained Unionist. In a part occupied by Confederate troops, Kentuckians approved secession and the Confederate Congress admitted their representatives.

The Maryland legislature voted against secession Apr. 27, 53 to 13. Delaware did not secede. Western Virginia held conventions at Wheeling, named a pro-Union governor June 11, 1861; admitted to Union as West Virginia June 30, 1863; its constitution provided for gradual abolition of slavery.

Confederate Government

Forty-two delegates from South Carolina, Georgia, Alabama, Mississippi, Louisiana and Florida met in convention at Montgomery, Ala., Feb. 4, 1861. The Congress adopted a provisional constitution of the Confederate States of America Feb. 8, 1861, and on the next day elected Jefferson Davis (Miss.), provisional president, and Alexander H. Stephens (Ga.), provisional vice president. Davis was inducted into office at Montgomery, Feb. 18, 1861.

A permanent constitution was adopted Mar. 11, 1861. It provided that the president should be elected for a single term of 6 years; it also abolished the African slave trade. The Congress moved to Richmond, Va., July 20, 1861. Jefferson Davis was elected president, October, 1861; inaugurated Feb. 22, 1862.

Jefferson Davis (1808-1889) was a West Point graduate, 1828; served in Black Hawk and Mexican Wars; senator from Mississippi, 1847-1851; secretary of war, 1853-1857; senator, 1857-1861.

The Congress adopted a flag, consisting of a red field with a white stripe in the middle third, and a blue jack with a circle of white stars, going two-thirds of the way down the flag. This flag was unfurled in Montgomery, Mar. 4, 1861. Later the more popular flag was the red field with blue diagonal cross bars that held 13 white stars, designed by Gen. P. G. T. Beauregard. The 13 stars represented the 11 states actually in the Confederacy plus Kentucky and Missouri.

(See also Civil War, U. S., in Index)

Dixie

The name Dixie is popularly associated with the southern states of the U.S. Several possible origins have been suggested.

One is said to be the French word dix (ten) which was printed on $10 bills used in early Louisiana which were called "dixies" by Americans. Louisiana became known as "Dix's Land" or "Land of the Dixies."

Some sources suggest that the name originated from a kind-hearted Dutch farmer, Dixie (Dixye), who unsuccessfully tried to cultivate tobacco in Harlem, N.Y. City, in the late 1700s. When he sold his slaves to a farmer in Piedmont County, S.C., they are said to have longed to return to Dixie's farm and sang of its joys.

In the South many consider Dixie a derivation from the "Mason-Dixon Line" which divided the free and slave states.

Public Lands of the U. S.

Source: Bureau of Land Management, U.S. Interior Department

Acquisition of the Public Domain 1781-1867

Acquisition	Area* (acres) Land	Water	Total	Cost[1]
State Cessions (1781-1802)	233,415,680	3,409,920	236,825,600	[2]$6,200,000
Louisiana Purchase (1803)[3]	523,446,400	6,465,280	529,911,680	23,213,568
Red River Basin[4]	29,066,880	535,040	29,601,920	
Cession from Spain (1819)	43,342,720	2,801,920	46,144,640	6,674,057
Oregon Compromise (1846)	180,644,480	2,741,760	183,386,240	
Mexican Cession (1848)	334,479,360	4,201,600	338,680,960	16,295,149
Purchase from Texas (1850)	78,842,880	83,840	78,926,720	15,496,448
Gadsden Purchase (1853)	18,961,920	26,880	18,988,800	10,000,000
Alaska Purchase (1867)	362,516,480	12,787,200	375,303,680	7,200,000
Total	**1,804,716,800**	**33,053,440**	**1,837,770,240**	**$85,079,222**

*All areas except Alaska were computed in 1912, and have not been adjusted for the recomputation of the area of the United States which was made for the 1950 Decennial Census. (1) Cost data for all except "State Cessions" obtained from U.S. Geological Survey. (2) Paid by federal government for Georgia cession, 1802 (56,689,920 acres). (3) Excludes areas eliminated by Treaty of 1819 with Spain. (4) Basin of the Red River of the North, south of the 49th parallel.

Disposition of Public Lands 1781 to 1970

Disposition by methods not elsewhere classified[1]	Acres
Disposition by methods not elsewhere classified[1]	303,500,000
Granted or sold to homesteaders	287,500,000
Granted to railroad corporations	94,300,000
Granted to veterans as military bounties	61,100,000
Confirmed as private land claims[2]	34,000,000
Sold under timber and stone law[3]	13,900,000
Granted or sold under timber culture law[4]	10,900,000
Sold under desert land law[5]	10,700,000

Granted to states for:	Acres
Support of common schools	77,600,000
Reclamation of swampland	64,900,000
Construction of railroads	37,100,000
Support of misc. institutions[6]	21,700,000
Purposes not elsewhere classified[7]	117,500,000
Canals and rivers	6,100,000
Construction of wagon roads	3,400,000
Total granted to states	**328,300,000**

Grand Total **1,144,200,000**

(1) Chiefly public, private, and preemption sales, but includes mineral entries, script locations, sales of townsites and townlots. (2) The Government has confirmed title to lands claimed under valid grants made by foreign governments prior to the acquisition of the public domain by the United States. (3) The law provided for the sale of lands valuable for timber or stone and unfit for cultivation. (4) The law provided for the granting of public lands to settlers on condition that they plant and cultivate trees on the lands granted. (5) The law provided for the sale of arid agricultural public lands to settlers who irrigate them and bring them under cultivation. (6) Universities, hospitals, asylums, etc. (7) For construction of various public improvements (individual items not specified in the granting act) reclamation of desert lands, construction of water reservoirs, etc.

Land Owned by the Federal Government

(acres)

Agency (June 30, 1975)	Public domain	Acquired	Total
Bureau of Land Management	467,817,798	2,356,519	470,174,318
U.S. Forest Service	160,202,013	27,305,957	187,507,970
U.S. Fish and Wildlife Service	26,251,564	4,029,626	30,281,190
U.S. Park Service	19,765,785	5,318,965	25,084,750
U.S. Army	7,066,789	3,955,894	11,022,683
Bureau of Reclamation	5,659,928	1,891,661	7,551,589
U.S. Air Force	6,921,141	1,415,909	8,337,050
Corps of Engineers	724,851	7,158,999	7,883,850
Bureau of Indian Affairs	4,204,849	763,121	4,967,971
U.S. Navy	2,262,766	1,254,517	3,517,283
Atomic Energy Commission	1,438,510	670,405	2,108,915
Other	550,741	1,426,495	1,977,237
Total	**702,866,735**	**57,548,072**	**760,414,810**

Total land holdings in foreign countries 637,414.4 acres.

The Homestead Act; Sale of Public Land

On October 21, 1976 Congress repealed the Homestead Act of 1862 for all states except Alaska. At the present time the exception for Alaska has little meaning since homesteading along with all disposal laws had been suspended from operation by the Alaska Native Claims Settlement Act. The suspension which was first imposed by Secretarial order in 1969, will remain in effect until all claims for Federal land by Alaska's native Eskimos, Indians, and Aleuts have been satisfied. The Homestead Act is scheduled to expire in Alaska in 1986.

The Homestead Act was repealed because there was no longer any land in the public domain suitable for cultivation. The law had been in effect for 114 years. During that time it had exerted a profound influence on the settlement of the west. Under the authority of the Homestead Act more than 1.6 million settlers claimed more than 270 million acres of public lands. The influx of settlers into the west in persuit of homestead land made such states as Oklahoma, Kansas, Nebraska, and North and South Dakota a reality and brought substantial numbers of settlers into many other western states.

Public Land Sale

From time to time the Bureau of Land Management sells public land to private individuals. Public land is always sold for its fair market value as determined by public auction. The Federal Govt. offers no free land. Persons wishing to purchase public land should contact the Bureau of Land Management, Wash., DC 20240, or one of the Bureau's Land Offices in the public land states.

The Bureau stresses that it is the only authoritative source of information on the sale of land under its jurisdiction.

National Parks, Other Areas Administered by Nat'l Park Service

Figures given are date area was set aside by Congress or proclaimed by president, and area in acres.

National Parks

Acadia, Me. (1916) 38,097. Includes Mount Desert Island, half of Isle au Haut, Schoodic Point on mainland. Highest elevation on Eastern seaboard.

Arches, Ut. (1929) 73,379. Contains giant red sandstone arches and other products of erosion.

Big Bend, Tex. (1935) 708,118. Rio Grande, Chisos Mts.

Bryce Canyon, Ut. (1923) 35,835. Spectacularly colorful and unusual display of erosion effects.

Canyonlands, Ut. (1964). 337,570. At junction of Colorado and Green rivers, extensive evidence of prehistoric Indians.

Capitol Reef, Ut. (1937) 241,866. A 70-mile uplift of sandstone cliffs dissected by high-walled gorges.

Carlsbad Caverns, N.M. (1923) 46,755. Largest known underground caverns, not yet fully explored.

Crater Lake, Ore. (1902) 160,290. Extraordinary blue lake in crater of extinct volcano encircled by lava walls 500 to 2,000 feet high.

Everglades, Fla. (1934) 1,398,800. Largest remaining subtropical wilderness in Continental U.S.

Glacier, Mon. (1910) 1,013,598. Superb Rocky Mountain scenery, numerous glaciers and glacial lakes. Part of Waterton-Glacier International Peace Park established by U.S. and Canada in 1932.

Grand Canyon, Ariz. (1908) 1,218,375. Most spectacular part of Colorado River's greatest canyon.

Grand Teton, Wy. (1929) 310,418. Most impressive part of the Teton Mountains, winter feeding ground of largest American elk herd.

Great Smoky Mountains, N.C.-Tenn. (1926) 517,368. Largest eastern mountain range, magnificent forests.

Guadalupe Mountains, Tex. (1966) 76,293. Extensive Permian limestone fossil reef; tremendous earth fault.

Haleakala, Ha. (1960) 28,072. 10,023 foot dormant volcano on Maui.

Hawaii Volcanoes, Ha. (1916) 229,177. Contains Kilauea and Mauna Loa, active volcanoes.

Hot Springs, Ark. (1832) 5,801. Government supervised bath houses use waters of 45 of the 47 natural hot springs.

Isle Royale, Mich. (1931) 542,429. Largest island in Lake Superior, noted for its wilderness area and wildlife.

Kings Canyon, Cal. (1890) 460,136. Mountain wilderness, dominated by Kings River Canyons and High Sierra; contains giant sequoias.

Lassen Volcanic, Cal. (1907) 106,372. Contains Lassen Peak, most recently active volcano in continental U.S., and other volcanic phenomena.

Mammoth Cave, Ky. (1926) 52,129. 144 miles of surveyed underground passages, beautiful natural formations, river 360 feet below surface.

Mesa Verde, Col. (1906) 52,036. Most notable and best preserved prehistoric cliff dwellings in the United States.

Mount McKinley, Alas. (1917) 1,939,493. Highest mountain in North America, large glaciers, and unusual wildlife.

Mount Rainier, Wash. (1899) 235,404. Greatest single-peak glacial system in the U.S. radiates from this dormant volcano.

North Cascades, Wash. (1968) 504,785. Spectacular mountainous region with many glaciers, lakes.

Olympic, Wash. (1909) 901,216. Mountain wilderness containing finest remnant of Pacific Northwest rain forest, active glaciers, Pacific shoreline, rare elk.

Petrified Forest, Ariz. (1906) 94,493. Extensive petrified wood and Indian artifacts. Contains part of Painted Desert.

Redwood, Cal. (1968) 62,211. Forty miles of Pacific coastline, groves of ancient redwoods.

Rocky Mountain, Col. (1915) 263,793. On the continental divide, includes 107 named peaks over 11,000 feet.

Sequoia, Cal. (1890) 386,823. Groves of giant sequoias, highest mountain in contigious United States — Mount Whitney (14,494 feet).

Shenandoah, Va. (1926) 190,539. Portion of the Blue Ridge Mountains; overlooks Shenandoah Valley.

Virgin Islands, V.I. (1956) 14,488. Covers 75% of St. John Island, lush growth, lovely beaches, Indian relics, evidence of colonial Danes.

Voyageurs, Minn. (1971) 219,128. Abundant lakes, forests, wildlife, canoeing, boating.

Wind Cave, S.D. (1903) 28,060. Limestone Caverns in Black Hills. Extensive wildlife includes a herd of bison.

Yellowstone, Ida., Mon., Wy., (1872) 2,219,823. Oldest and largest national park. World's greatest geyser area has about 3,000 geysers and hot springs; spectacular falls and impressive canyons of the Yellowstone River, grizzly bear, moose, bison, other wildlife are major attractions.

Yosemite, Cal. (1890) 760,917. Yosemite Valley, the nation's highest waterfall, 3 groves of giant sequoias, and mountainous terrain.

Zion, Ut. (1909) 146,547. Unusual shapes and landscapes have resulted from the effects of erosion and faulting activity; Zion Canyon, with sheer walls ranging up to 2,500 feet, is readily accessible.

National Historical Parks

Appomattox Court House, Va. (1930) 995. Where Lee surrendered to Grant.

Boston, Mass. (1974) 35. Includes Faneuil Hall, Old North Church, Bunker Hill, Paul Revere House.

Chalmette, La. (1907) 143. Scene of part of the Battle of New Orleans.

Chesapeake and Ohio Canal, Md.-W. Va.-D.C. (1961) 20,239. 185 mile historic canal; D.C. to Cumberland, Md.

City of Refuge, Ha. (1955) 182. Until 1819, a sanctuary for Hawaiians vanquished in battle, and those guilty of crimes or breaking taboos.

Colonial, Va. (1930) 9,834. Includes most of Jamestown Island, site of first successful English colony; Yorktown site of Cornwallis' surrender to George Washington; Cape Henry Memorial, approximate site of the first landing of the Jamestown colonists; and the Colonial Parkway.

Cumberland Gap, Ky.-Tenn.-Va. (1940) 20,273. Mountain pass of the Wilderness Road which carried the first great migration of pioneers into America's interior.

George Rogers Clark, Vincennes, Ind. (1966) 24. Commemorates American defeat of British in west during Revolution.

Harpers Ferry, Md., W. Va. (1944) 1,910. At the confluence of the Shenandoah and Potomac rivers, the site of John Brown's 1859 raid on the Army arsenal. Scene of several Civil War maneuvers.

Independence, Pa., (1948) 35. Contains several properties in Philadelphia associated with the Revolutionary War and the founding of the U.S.

Klondike Gold Rush, Alas.-Wash. (1976) 13,271.

Minute Man, Mass. (1959) 745. Where the colonial Minute Men battled the British, April 19, 1775. Also contains Nathaniel Hawthorne's home.

Morristown, N.J. (1933) 1,677. Sites of important military encampments during the Revolutionary War; Washington's headquarters 1777, 1779-80.

Nez Perce, Ida. (1965) 2,114. Illustrates the history and culture of the Nez Perce Indian country. 22 separate sites.

San Juan Island, Wash. (1966) 1,752. Commemorates peaceful relations of the U.S., Canada and Great Britain since the 1872 boundary disputes.

Saratoga, N.Y. (1938) 2,432. Scene of a major battle which became a turning point in the War of Independence.

Sitka, Alas. (1910) 108. Scene of last major resistance of the Tlingit Indians to the Russians, 1804.

National Memorial Park

Theodore Roosevelt, N.D. (1947) 70,409. Part of T.R.'s Elkhorn Ranch along the Little Missouri River. Has bison and some original prairie.

Valley Forge, Pa. (1976) 2,466.

National Battlefields

Big Hole, Mon. (1910) 656. Site of major battle with Nez Perce Indians.

Cowpens, S.C. (1929) 824. Revolutionary War battlefield.

Fort Necessity, Pa. (1931) 901. First battle of French and Indian War.

Monocacy, Md. (1976) 633.

Petersburg, Va. (1926) 1,515. Scene of 10-month Union campaign 1864-65.

Stones River, Tenn. (1927) 331. Civil War battle leading to Sherman's "March to the Sea."

Tupelo, Miss. (1929) 1.0 Crucial battle over Sherman's supply line.

Wilson's Creek, Mo. (1960) 1,750. Civil War battle for control of Missouri.

National Battlefield Parks

Kennesaw Mountain, Ga. (1917) 2,884. Two major battles of Atlanta campaign in Civil War.

Manassas, Va. (1940) 3,032. Two early Civil War battles.

Richmond, Va. (1936) 769. Site of battles defending Confederate capital.

National Battlefield Sites

Antietam, Md. (1890) 1,800. End of first Confederate invasion of North.

Brices Cross Roads, Miss. (1929) 1. Civil War battlefield.

National Military Parks

Chickamauga and Chattanooga, Ga.-Tenn. (1890) 8,095. Four Civil War battlefields.

Fort Donelson, Tenn. (1928) 544. Site of first major Union victory.

Fredericksburg and Spotsylvania County, Va. (1927) 5,839. Sites of several major Civil War battles and campaigns.

Gettysburg, Pa. (1895) 3,862. Site of decisive Confederate defeat in North. Gettysburg Address.

Guilford Courthouse, N.C. (1917) 220. Revolutionary War battle site.

Horseshoe Bend, Ala. (1956) 2,040. On Tallapoosa River, where Gen. Andrew Jackson broke the power of the Creek Indian Confederacy.

Kings Mountain, S.C. (1931) 3,945. Revolutionary War battle.

Moores Creek, N.C. (1926) 84. Pre-Revolutionary War battle.

Pea Ridge, Ark. (1956) 4,300. Civil War battle.

Shiloh, Tenn. (1894) 3,753. Major Civil War battle; site includes some well-preserved Indian burial mounds.

Vicksburg, Miss. (1899) 1,741. Union victory gave North control of the Mississippi and split the Confederacy in two.

National Memorials

Arkansas Post, Ark. (1960) 389. First permanent French settlement in the lower Mississippi River valley.

Chamizal, El Paso, Tex. (1966) 55. Commemorates 1963 settlement of 99-year border dispute with Mexico.

Coronado, Ariz. (1952) 2,834. Commemorates first European exploration of the Southwest.

DeSoto, Fla. (1948) 30. Commemorates 16th-century Spanish explorations.

Federal Hall, N.Y. (1939) 0.45. First seat of U.S. government under the Constitution.

Fort Caroline, Fla. (1950) 129. On St. Johns River, overlooks site of second attempt by French Huguenots to colonize North America.

Fort Clatsop, Ore. (1958) 125. Lewis and Clark encampment 1805-06.

General Grant, N.Y. (1958) 0.76. Tombs of Pres. and wife.

Hamilton Grange, N.Y. (1962) 0.71. Home of Alexander Hamilton.

John F. Kennedy Center for the Performing Arts, D.C. (1972) 18.

Johnstown Flood, Pa. (1964) 106. Commemorates tragic flood of 1889.

Lincoln Boyhood, Ind. (1962) 198. Lincoln grew up here.

Lincoln Memorial, D.C. (1911) 164.

Lyndon B. Johnson Grove on the Potomac, D.C. (1973) 17.

Mount Rushmore, S.D. (1925) 1,279. World famous sculpture of 4 presidents.

Perry's Victory and International Peace Memorial, Oh. (1936) 26. American naval victory, War of 1812.

Roger Williams, R.I. (1965) 5. Memorial to founder of Rhode Island.

Thaddeus Kosciuszko, Pa. (1972) 0.02. Memorial to Polish hero of American Revolution.

Theodore Roosevelt Island, D.C. (1947) 89.

Thomas Jefferson Memorial, D.C. (1943) 18.

Washington Monument, D.C. (1848) 106.

Wright Brothers, N.C. (1927) 431. Site of first powered flight.

National Historic Sites

Abraham Lincoln Birthplace, Hodgenville, Ky. (1916) 117.

Adams, Quincy, Mass. (1946) 9. Home of Presidents John Adams, John Quincy Adams, and celebrated descendants.

Allegheny Portage Railroad, Pa. (1964) 760. Part of the Pennsylvania Canal system.

Andersonville, Andersonville, Ga. (1970) 488. Noted Civil War prison.

Andrew Johnson, Greeneville, Tenn. (1935) 17. Home of the President.

Bent's Old Fort, Col. (1960) 178. Old West fur-trading post.

Carl Sandburg Home, N.C. (1968) 247. Poet's farm home.

Christiansted, St. Croix; V.I. (1952) 27. Commemorates Danish colony.

Clara Barton, Md. (1974) 9. Home of founder of American Red Cross.

Edison, West Orange, N.J. (1955) 21. Home and laboratory.

Eisenhower, Gettysburg, Pa. (1967) 493. Home of 34th president. Not open to public.

Eleanor Roosevelt, Hyde Park, N.Y. (1977) 174.

Ford's Theatre, Washington, D.C. (1866) 0.25. Includes theater, now restored, where Lincoln was assassinated, house where he died, and Lincoln Museum.

Fort Bowie, Ariz. (1964) 1,000. Focal point of operations against Geronimo and the Apaches.

Fort Davis, Tex. (1961) 460. Frontier outpost battled Comanches and Apaches.

Fort Laramie, Wy. (1938) 571. Military post on Oregon Trail.

Fort Larned, Kan. (1964) 718. Military post on Sante Fe Trail.

Fort Point, San Francisco, Cal. (1970) 29. Largest West Coast fortification.

Fort Raleigh, N.C. (1941) 160. First English settlement.

Fort Smith, Ark. (1961) 67. Active post from 1817 to 1890.

Fort Union Trading Post, Mon., N.D. (1966) 399. Principal fur-trading post on upper Missouri, 1828-1867.

Fort Vancouver, Wash. (1948) 209. Hdqts. for Hudson's Bay Company in 1825. Early military and political seat.

Golden Spike, Utah (1957) 2,203. Commemorates completion of first transcontinental railroad in 1869.

Grant-Kohrs Ranch, Mon. (1972) 1,528. Ranch house and part of 19th century ranch.

Hampton, Md. (1948) 45. 18th-century Georgian mansion.

Herbert Hoover, West Branch, Ia. (1965) 187. Birthplace and boyhood home of 31st president.

Home of Franklin D. Roosevelt, Hyde Park, N.Y. (1944) 264. Birthplace, home and "Summer White House".

Hopewell Village, Pa. (1938) 848. 19th-century iron making village.

Hubbell Trading Post, Ariz. (1965) 160. Indian trading post.

Jefferson National Expansion Memorial, St. Louis, Mo. (1935) 91. Commemorates westward expansion with park and memorial arch.

John Fitzgerald Kennedy, Brookline, Mass. (1967) .09 Birthplace and childhood home of the President.

John Muir, Martinez, Cal. (1964) 9. Home of early conservationist and writer.

Knife River Indian Villages, N.C. (1974) 1,310. Remnants of 5 Hidatsa villages.

Lincoln Home, Springfield, Ill. (1971) 12. Lincoln's residence when he was elected President, 1860.

Longfellow, Cambridge, Mass. (1972) 2. Longfellow's home, 1837-82, and Washington's hq. during Boston Siege 1775-76. **No federal facilities.**

Lyndon B. Johnson, Johnson City, Tex. (1969) 241. Birthplace and boyhood home of the 36th president.

Mar-A-Largo, Fla. (1969) 17. Mansion expresses the affluent Palm Beach life of the 1920s. Not open to public.

Martin Van Buren, N.Y. (1974) 42. Lindenwald, Home of 8th president, near Kingston.

Ninety Six, S.C. (1976) 1,115.

Puukohola Heiau, Ha. (1972) 77. Ruins of temple built by King Kamehameha.

Sagamore Hill, Oyster Bay, N.Y. (1962) 85. Home of President Theodore Roosevelt from 1885 until his death in 1919.

Saint-Gaudens, Cornish, N.H. (1964) 149. Home, studio and gardens of American sculptor Augustus Saint-Gaudens.

Salem Maritime, Mass. (1938) 9. Only port never seized from the Patriots by the British. Major fishing and whaling port.

San Juan, P.R. (1949) 53. 16th-century Spanish fortifications.

Saugus Iron Works, Mass. (1968) 9. Reconstructed 17th-century colonial ironworks.

Sewall-Belmont House, D.C. (1974) 0.35. National Women's Party headquarters 1929-74.

Springfield Armory, Mass. (1974) 55. Small arms center of world for nearly 200 years.

Theodore Roosevelt Birthplace, N.Y., N.Y. (1962) 0.11.

Theodore Roosevelt Inaugural, Buffalo, N.Y. (1966) 1. Wilcox House where he took oath of office, 1901.

Tuskegee Institute, Ala. (1974) 74. College founded by Booker T. Washington in 1881 for blacks, includes student-made brick buildings.

Vanderbilt Mansion, Hyde Park, N.Y. (1940) 212. Mansion of 19th-century financier.

Whitman Mission, Wash. (1936) 98. Site where Dr. and Mrs. Marcus Whitman ministered to the Indians until slain, 1847.

William Howard Taft, Cincinnati, Oh. (1969) 0.83. Birthplace and early home of the 27th president.

National Capital Parks

District of Columbia — Maryland — Virginia (1790) 7,052. Includes 367 reservations.

White House

Washington, D.C. (1792) 18. Presidential residence since November 1800.

National Seashores

Name	State	Year	Acreage
Assateague Island	Md.-Va.	1965	39,631
Canaveral	Fla.	1975	57,627
Cape Cod	Mass.	1961	44,600
Cape Hatteras	N.C.	1937	30,326
Cape Lookout**	N.C.	1966	28,400
Cumberland Island	Ga.	1972	36,877
Fire Island	N.Y.	1964	19,357
Gulf Island	Fla.-Miss.	1971	139,176
Padre Island	Tex.	1962	133,919
Point Reyes	Cal.	1962	65,300

National Monuments

Name	State	Year	Acreage
Agate Fossil Beds	Neb.	1965	3,054
Alibates Flint Quarries and Texas Panhandle Pueblo Culture	Tex.	1965	93
Aztec Ruins	N.M.	1923	27
Badlands	S.D.	1929	243,302
Bandelier	N.M.	1916	36,971
Biscayne	Fla.	1968	103,701
Black Canyon of the Gunnison	Col.	1933	13,672
Booker T. Washington	Va.	1956	224
Buck Island Reef	V.I.	1961	880
Cabrillo	Cal.	1913	144
Canyon de Chelly	Ariz.	1931	83,840
Capulin Mountain	N.M.	1916	775
Casa Grande Ruins	Ariz.	1892	473
Castillo de San Marcos	Fla.	1924	21
Castle Clinton	N.Y.	1946	1
Cedar Breaks	Ut.	1933	6,155
Chaco Canyon	N.M.	1907	21,510
Channel Islands	Cal.	1938	18,388
Chiricahua	Ariz.	1924	10,648
Colorado	Col.	1911	20,445
Congaree Swamp	S.C.	1976	15,135
Craters of the Moon	Ida.	1924	53,545
Custer Battlefield	Mon.	1879	765
Death Valley	Cal.-Nev.	1933	2,067,795
Devils Postpile	Cal.	1911	799
Devils Tower	Wy.	1906	1,347
Dinosaur	Col.-Ut.	1915	211,054
Effigy Mounds	Ia.	1949	1,475
El Morro	N.M.	1906	1,279
Florissant Fossil Beds**	Col.	1969	5,992
Fort Frederica	Ga.	1936	215
Fort Jefferson	Fla.	1935	47,125
Fort McHenry National Monument & Historic Shrine	Md.	1925	43
Fort Matanzas	Fla.	1924	299
Fort Pulaski	Ga.	1924	5,616
Fort Stanwix	N.Y.	1935	16
Fort Sumter	S.C.	1948	64
Fort Union	N.M.	1954	721
Fossil Butte	Wy.	1972	8,178
G. Washington Birthplace	Va.	1930	456
George Washington Carver	Mo.	1943	210
Gila Cliff Dwellings	N.M.	1907	533
Glacier Bay	Alas.	1925	2,805,270
Grand Portage	Minn.	1951	710
Gran Quivira	N.M.	1909	611
Great Sand Dunes	Col.	1932	36,827
Hohokam Pima*	Ariz.	1972	1,555
Homestead Nat'l. Monument of America	Neb.	1936	195
Hovenweep	Col.-Ut.	1923	785
Jewel Cave	S.D.	1908	1,275
John Day Fossil Beds	Ore.	1974	14,402
Joshua Tree	Cal.	1936	559,960
Katmai	Alas.	1918	2,792,151
Lava Beds	Cal.	1925	46,821
Lehman Caves	Nev.	1922	640
Montezuma Castle	Ariz.	1906	842
Mound City Group	Oh.	1923	68
Muir Woods	Cal.	1908	554
Natural Bridges	Ut.	1908	7,779
Navajo	Ariz.	1909	360
Ocmulgee	Ga.	1934	684
Oregon Caves	Ore.	1909	466
Organ Pipe Cactus	Ariz.	1937	330,689
Pecos	N.M.	1965	365
Pinnacles	Cal.	1908	16,216
Pipe Spring	Ariz.	1923	40
Pipestone	Minn.	1937	282
Rainbow Bridge	Ut.	1910	160
Russell Cave	Ala.	1961	311
Saguaro	Ariz.	1933	83,576
Saint Croix Island**	Me.	1949	35
Scotts Bluff	Neb.	1919	2,988
Statue of Liberty	N.J.-N.Y.	1924	58
Sunset Crater	Ariz.	1930	3,040
Timpanogos Cave	Ut.	1922	250
Tonto	Ariz.	1907	1,120
Tumacacori	Ariz.	1908	10
Tuzigoot	Ariz.	1939	58
Walnut Canyon	Ariz.	1915	2,250
White Sands	N.M.	1933	145,335
Wupatki	Ariz.	1924	35,253
Yucca House*	Col.	1919	10

National Lakeshores

Apostle Islands, Wis. (1970) 42,217. Picturesque islands and coastal portion of Bayfield Peninsula on south shore of Lake Superior.

Name	State	Year	Acreage
Indiana Dunes	Ind.	1966	8,330
Pictured Rocks	Mich.	1966	70,822

Sleeping Bear Dunes, Mich. (1970) 71,105. Notable for its beaches, massive sand dunes, forests, lakes. Benzie and D. H. Day State Parks open to public.

National River

Name	State	Year	Acreage
Buffalo	Ark.	1972	94,146

National Scenic Rivers and Riverways

Name	State	Year	Acreage
Big South Fork	Ky.-Tenn.	1976	122,960
Lower Saint Croix**	Minn.-Wis.	1972	7,845
Obed Wild	Tenn.	1976	6,451
Ozark	Mo.	1964	79,587
Saint Croix**	Minn.-Wis.	1968	62,728

National Recreation Areas

Name	State	Year	Acreage
Amistad	Tex.	1965	62,452
Bighorn Canyon	Mon.-Wy.	1964	120,158
Chickasaw	Okla.	1976	9,656
Coulee Dam	Wash.	1946	100,059
Curecanti	Col.	1965	41,572
Cuyahoga	Oh.	1974	30,020
Delaware Water Gap	N.J.-Pa.	1965	47,676
Gateway	N.Y.-N.J.	1972	26,172
Glen Canyon	Ariz.-Ut.	1958	1,236,880
Golden Gate	Cal.	1972	34,938
Lake Chelan	Wash.	1968	61,890
Lake Mead	Ariz.-Nev.	1936	1,496,601
Lake Meredith	Tex.	1965	45,964
Ross Lake	Wash.	1968	117,574
Shadow Mountain	Col.	1952	19,004
Whiskeytown-Shasta-Trinity	Cal.	1962	42,498

National Scenic Trail

Name	State	Year	Acreage
Appalachian	Me. to Ga.	1968	52,034

* Not open to the public
** No federal facilities

Federal and State Indian Reservations

Source: U. S. Commerce Department (data as of circa Dec., 1972)

State	No. of reservations	Tribally-owned acreage[1]	Alloted acreage[1]	No. of tribes[3]	No. of persons[4]	Avg. unemp. rate%[5]	Major tribes
Alaska	13[2]	(2)	(2)	6	35,817	NA	Eskimo, Tlingit, Haida, Aleut, Athapascan[6]
Arizona	17	23,467,727	892,917	13	173,412	41	Navaho, Apache, Papago, Hopi, Pima
California	76	386,954	67,390	(7)	6,905	45	Quechan, Hoopa, Paiute, mission bands[7]
Colorado	2	888,155	14,425	1	2,144	37	Ute
Connecticut	4	795	—	3	25	NA	Pequot, Mohegan[8]
Florida	5	183,319	—	2	1,511	31	Seminole, Miccosukee[9]
Idaho	4	274,428	36,723	5	4,849	36	Shoshone, Bannock, Nez Perce
Iowa	1	3,476	—	1	561	35	Sac and Fox[10]
Kansas	4	2,436	24,030	5	3,009	10	Potawatomi, Kickapoo, Iowa
Louisiana	1	262	—	1	268	NA	Chitimacha
Maine	3	27,546	—	2	1,077	45	Passamaquoddy, Penobscot
Massachusetts	1	12	—	1	1	0	Hassanamisco-Nipmuk[11]
Michigan	5	4,425	12,210	2	2,069	38	Chippewa, Potawatami
Minnesota	11	682,534	50,935	2	10,739	40	Chippewa, Sioux
Mississippi	1	17,381	209	1	3,294	10	Choctaw
Montana	7	1,792,383	3,279,926	10	24,137	38	Blackfeet, Sioux, Crow, Assiniboine, Cheyenne
Nebraska	3	27,193	45,467	3	2,601	62	Omaha, Winnebago, Santee Sioux
Nevada	23	1,133,529	32,691	3	4,784	46	Paiute, Shoshone, Washoe
New Mexico	24	3,329,270	119,877	7	30,125	43	Keresan, Zuni, Apache, Tanoan, Navajo[12]
New York	9	88,158	—	7	11,616	27	Seneca, Mohawk, Onondaga, Oneida[13]
North Carolina	1	56,573	—	1	4,880	21	Cherokee
North Dakota	4	375,936	996,744	5	16,735	41	Chippewa, Sioux, Mandan, Arikara, Hidatsa
Oklahoma[14]	—	56,741	991,715	27	80,994	24	Cherokee, Creek, Choctaw, Chicasaw, Cheyenne, Arapaho[14]
Oregon	4	495,842	165,778	8	2,718	41	Warm Springs, Wasco, Paiute, Umatilla
South Dakota	8	1,807,623	2,371,427	1	29,119	37	Sioux
Texas	2	4,400	—	3	1,000	30	Tigua (Pueblo), Alabama, Coushatta
Utah	4	1,095,531	48,095	3	1,961	36	Ute, Southern Paiute, Goshute
Virginia	2	925	—	1	110	NA	Algonquian
Washington	22	1,920,850	537,876	20	18,138	45	Yakima, Confederated, Lummi, Quinault
Wisconsin	10	61,911	82,977	6	7,497	38	Chippewa, Oneida, Winnebago
Wyoming	1	1,776,136	109,344	2	4,435	47	Shoshone, Arapaho

(1) Approximations. Ownership of reservation land is very complex. Most tribally-owned land listed here is owned by tribal organizations, but some of it is held in trust by the government and some is leased to or occupied by non-Indians. Government-owned land, even that held for the exclusive use of Indians, and non-Indian land formally included in reservations is not counted here.

Allotted land was land held by Indian individuals or families. The Department of Commerce data is not clear on whether all land listed as alloted is still securely held by Indians.

(2) Alaskan Indian affairs are handled under the Native Claims Settlement Act (Dec. 18, 1971). The act provides for the establishment of regional and village corporations to conduct business for profit. There are 12 regional corporations. Within each regional corporation, village corporations must be organized. These village corporations then receive title to lands previously held in reservations. There were approximately 2.5 million acres in reservations subject to the Settlement Act. Another 86,471 acres remain outside the Act in the Annette Island Reserve. Latest figures show that 5,687 acres have been assigned to village corporations, while an additional 13,490 acres have been surveyed but not yet assigned.

(3) The concept of "tribe" is, in many cases, a white man's invention and, at first, was used to define loosely associated Indians with cultural similarities. Today, "tribe" is a formal status of Indians organized by law. Some present day "tribes", such as the Blackfeet are really confederacies of smaller groups. The Alaskan natives are organized, on paper, into general linguistic groups.

(4) Number of Indians living on or adjacent to reservations. When these figures are compared to 1970 census figures, it appears that nearly 64% of Indians are living on or near reservations.

(5) Unemployment rate of Indian labor force living on or adjacent to reservations.

(6) Aleuts and Eskimos are racially and linguistically related. Athapascans are related to the Navaho and Apache Indians.

(7) Many California Indians are historically associated with groups which settled near Spanish missions where much of the traditional culture was destroyed. Many of these bands, however, still retain some of their Indian language and customs. Excluding the bands, there are 22 tribes represented on California reservations.

(8) The Mohegan or Mohican are a branch of the Pequot.

(9) "Seminole" means "runaways" and these Indians from various tribes were originally refugees from whites in the Carolinas and Georgia. Later joined by runaway slaves, the Seminole were united by their hostility to the United States. Formal peace with the Seminoles in Florida was not achieved until 1934. The Miccosukee are a branch of the Seminole; they retain their Indian religion and have not made formal peace with the U.S.

(10) Once two tribes, the Sac and Fox formed a political alliance in 1734.

(11) Reservation prior to 1728 consisted of 8,000 acres. The land was sold to whites who put the Indians' money in a bank. Over the years the money was "lost" or "borrowed." In 1848, the state granted 11.9 acres to one Indian family of which there are about 20 direct descendants today.

(12) Tanoan, Keresan, and Zuni are all pueblo-dwelling Indians.

(13) These 4 tribes along with the Cayuga and Tuscarora made up the Iroquois League, which ruled large portions of New York, New England, and Pennsylvania and ranged into the Mid-West and South. The Onondaga, who traditionally provide the president of the League, maintain that they are a foreign nation within New York and the U.S.

(14) Indian land status in Oklahoma is unique and there are no reservations in the sense that the term is used elsewhere in the U.S. Likewise, many of the Oklahoma tribes are unique in their high degree of assimilation to the white culture.

Declaration of Independence

The Declaration of Independence as adopted by the Continental Congress in Philadelphia, on July 4, 1776. John Hancock was president of the Congress and Charles Thomson was secretary. A copy of the Declaration, engrossed on parchment, was signed by members of Congress on and after Aug. 2, 1776. On Jan. 18, 1777, Congress ordered that "authenticated copies, with the names of the members of Congress subscribed the same, be sent to each of the United States, and that they be desired to have same put upon record." Authenticated copies were printed in broadside form in Baltimore, where the Continental Congress was then in session. The following text is that of the original printed by John Dunlap at Philadelphia for the Continental Congress.

IN CONGRESS, July 4, 1776.

A DECLARATION

By the REPRESENTATIVES of the

UNITED STATES OF AMERICA,

In GENERAL CONGRESS assembled

When in the Course of human Events, it becomes necessary for one People to dissolve the Political Bands which have connected them with another, and to assume among the Powers of the Earth, the separate and equal Station to which the Laws of Nature and of Nature's God entitle them, a decent Respect to the Opinions of Mankind requires that they should declare the causes which impel them to the Separation.

We hold these Truths to be self-evident, that all Men are created equal, that they are endowed by their Creator with certain unalienable Rights, that among these are Life, Liberty, and the Pursuit of Happiness—That to secure these Rights, Governments are instituted among Men, deriving their just Powers from the Consent of the Governed, that whenever any Form of Government becomes destructive of these Ends, it is the Right of the People to alter or to abolish it, and to institute new Government, laying its Foundation on such Principles, and organizing its Powers in such Form, as to them shall seem most likely to effect their Safety and Happiness. Prudence, indeed, will dictate that Governments long established should not be changed for light and transient Causes; and accordingly all Experience hath shewn, that Mankind are more disposed to suffer, while Evils are sufferable, than to right themselves by abolishing the Forms to which they are accustomed. But when a long Train of Abuses and Usurpations, pursuing invariably the same Object, evinces a Design to reduce them under absolute Despotism, it is their Right, it is their Duty, to throw off such Government, and to provide new Guards for their future Security. Such has been the patient Sufferance of these Colonies; and such is now the Necessity which constrains them to alter their former Systems of Government. The History of the present King of Great-Britain is a History of repeated Injuries and Usurpations, all having in direct Object the Establishment of an absolute Tyranny over these States. To prove this, let Facts be submitted to a candid World.

He has refused his Assent to Laws, the most wholesome and necessary for the public Good.

He has forbidden his Governors to pass Laws of immediate and pressing Importance, unless suspended in their Operation till his Assent should be obtained; and when so suspended, he has utterly neglected to attend to them.

He has refused to pass other Laws for the Accommodation of large Districts of People, unless those People would relinquish the Right of Representation in the Legislature, a Right inestimable to them, and formidable to Tyrants only.

He has called together Legislative Bodies at Places unusual, uncomfortable, and distant from the Depository of their public Records, for the sole Purpose of fatiguing them into Compliance with his Measures.

He has dissolved Representative Houses repeatedly, for opposing with manly Firmness his Invasions on the Rights of the People.

He has refused for a long Time, after such Dissolutions, to cause others to be elected; whereby the Legislative Powers, incapable of Annihilation, have returned to the People at large for their exercise; the State remaining in the mean time exposed to all the Dangers of Invasion from without, and Convulsions within.

He has endeavoured to prevent the Population of these States; for that Purpose obstructing the Laws for Naturalization of Foreigners; refusing to pass others to encourage their Migrations hither, and raising the Conditions of new Appropriations of Lands.

He has obstructed the Administration of Justice, by refusing his Assent to Laws for establising Judiciary Powers.

He has made Judges dependent on his Will alone, for the Tenure of their Offices, and the Amount and payment of their Salaries.

He has erected a Multitude of new Offices, and sent hither Swarms of Officers to harrass our People, and eat out their Substance.

He has kept among us, in Times of Peace, Standing Armies, without the consent of our Legislatures.

He has affected to render the Military independent of and superior to the Civil Power.

He has combined with others to subject us to a Jurisdiction foreign to our Constitution, and unacknowledged by our Laws; giving his Assent to their Acts of pretended Legislation:

For quartering large Bodies of Armed Troops among us:

For protecting them, by a mock Trial, from Punishment for any Murders which they should commit on the Inhabitants of these States:

For cutting off our Trade with all Parts of the World:

For imposing Taxes on us without our Consent:

For depriving us, in many Cases, of the Benefits of Trial by Jury:

For transporting us beyond Seas to be tried for pretended Offences:

For abolishing the free System of English Laws in a neighbouring Province, establishing therein an arbitrary Government, and enlarging its Boundaries, so as to render it at once an Example and fit Instrument for introducing the same absolute Rule into these Colonies:

For taking away our Charters, abolishing our most valuable Laws, and altering fundamentally the Forms of our Governments:

For suspending our own Legislatures, and declaring themselves invested with Power to legislate for us in all Cases whatsoever.

He has abdicated Government here, by declaring us out of his Protection and waging War against us.

He has plundered our Seas, ravaged our Coasts, burnt our towns, and destroyed the Lives of our People.

He is, at this Time, transporting large Armies of foreign Mercenaries to compleat the works of Death, Desolation, and Tyranny, already begun with circumstances of Cruelty and Perfidy, scarcely paralleled in the most barbarous Ages, and totally unworthy the Head of a civilized Nation.

He has constrained our fellow Citizens taken Captive on the high Seas to bear Arms against their Country, to become the Executioners of their Friends and Brethren, or to fall themselves by their Hands.

He has excited domestic Insurrections amongst us, and has endeavoured to bring on the Inhabitants of our Frontiers, the merciless Indian Savages, whose known Rule of Warfare, is an undistinguished Destruction, of all Ages, Sexes and Conditions.

In every stage of these Oppressions we have Petitioned for Redress in the most humble Terms: Our repeated Petitions have been answered only by repeated Injury. A Prince, whose Character is thus marked by every act which may define a Tyrant, is unfit to be the Ruler of a free People.

Nor have we been wanting in Attentions to our British Brethren. We have warned them from Time to Time of Attempts by their Legislature to extend an unwarrantable Jurisdiction over us. We have reminded them of the Circumstances of our Emigration and Settlement here. We have appealed to their native Justice and Magnanimity, and we have conjured them by the Ties of our common Kindred to disavow these Usurpations, which, would inevitably interrupt our Connections and Correspondence. They too have been deaf to the Voice of Justice and of Consanguinity. We must, therefore, acquiesce in the Necessity, which denounces our Separation, and hold them, as we hold the rest of Mankind, Enemies in War, in Peace, Friends.

We, therefore, the Representatives of the UNITED STATES OF AMERICA, in General Congress, Assembled, appealing to the Supreme Judge of the World in the Rectitude of our Intentions, do, in the Name, and by Authority of the good People of these Colonies, solemnly Publish and Declare, That these United Colonies are, and of Right ought to be, Free and Independent States; that they are absolved from all Allegiance to the British Crown, and that all political Connection between them and the State of Great-Britain, is and ought to be totally dissolved; and that as Free and Independent States, they have full Power to levy War, conclude Peace, contract Alliances, establish Commerce, and to do all other Acts and Things which Independent States may of right do. And for the support of this declaration, with a firm Reliance on the Protection of divine Providence, we mutually pledge to each other our lives, our Fortunes, and our sacred Honor.

JOHN HANCOCK, President.

Attest.
CHARLES THOMSON, Secretary.

Signers of the Declaration of Independence

Delegate and state	Vocation	Birthplace	Born	Died
Adams, John (Mass.)	Lawyer	Braintree (Quincy), Mass.	Oct. 30, 1735	July 4, 1826
Adams, Samuel (Mass.)	Political leader	Boston, Mass.	Sept. 27, 1722	Oct. 2, 1803
Bartlett, Josiah (N. H.)	Physician, judge	Amesbury, Mass.	Nov. 21, 1729	May 19, 1795
Braxton, Carter (Va.)	Farmer	Newington, Va.	Sept. 10, 1736	Oct. 10, 1797
Carroll, Chas. of Carrollton (Md.)	Lawyer	Annapolis, Md.	Sept. 19, 1737	Nov. 14, 1832
Chase, Samuel (Md.)	Judge	Princess Anne, Md.	Apr. 17, 1741	June 19, 1811
Clark, Abraham (N. J.)	Surveyor	Elizabeth, N. J.	Feb. 15, 1726	Sept. 15, 1794
Clymer, George (Pa.)	Merchant	Philadelphia, Pa.	Mar. 16, 1739	Jan. 23, 1813
Ellery, William (R. I.)	Judge	Newport, R. I.	Dec. 22, 1727	Feb. 15, 1820
Floyd, William (N. Y.)	Soldier	Brookhaven, N. Y.	Dec. 17, 1734	Aug. 4, 1821
Franklin, Benjamin (Pa.)	Printer, publisher	Boston, Mass.	Jan. 17, 1706	Apr. 17, 1790
Gerry, Elbridge (Mass.)	Merchant	Marblehead, Mass.	July 17, 1744	Nov. 23, 1814
Gwinnett, Button (Ga.)	Merchant	Down Hatherly, England	1732	May 19, 1777
Hall, Lyman (Ga.)	Physician	Wallingford, Conn.	Apr. 12, 1724	Oct. 19, 1790
Hancock, John (Mass.)	Merchant	Braintree (Quincy), Mass.	Jan. 12, 1737	Oct. 8, 1793
Harrison, Benjamin (Va.)	Farmer	Berkeley, Va.	Apr. 5, 1726	Apr. 24, 1791
Hart, John (N. J.)	Farmer	Stonington, Conn.	(1707-1711?)	May 11, 1779
Hewes, Joseph (N. C.)	Merchant	Kingston, N. J.	Jan. 23, 1730	Nov. 10, 1779
Heyward, Thos. Jr. (S. C.)	Lawyer, farmer	St. Luke's Parish, S. C.	July 28, 1746	Mar. 6, 1809
Hooper, William (N. C.)	Lawyer	Boston, Mass.	June 28, 1742	Oct. 14, 1790
Hopkins, Stephen (R. I.)	Judge, educator	Providence, R. I.	Mar. 7, 1707	July 13, 1785
Hopkinson, Francis (N. J.)	Judge, author	Philadelphia, Pa.	Sept. 21, 1737	May 9, 1791
Huntington, Samuel (Conn.)	Judge	Windham County, Conn.	July 3, 1731	Jan. 5, 1796
Jefferson, Thomas (Va.)	Lawyer	Old Shadwell, Va.	Apr. 13, 1743	July 4, 1826
Lee, Francis Lightfoot (Va.)	Farmer	Stratford, Va.	Oct. 14, 1734	Jan. 11, 1797
Lee, Richard Henry (Va.)	Farmer	Stratford, Va.	Jan. 20, 1732	June 19, 1794
Lewis, Francis (N. Y.)	Merchant	Landaff, Wales	Mar., 1713	Dec. 30, 1803
Livingston, Philip (N. Y.)	Merchant	Albany, N. Y.	Jan. 15, 1716	June 12, 1778
Lynch, Thomas Jr. (S. C.)	Farmer	Winyah, S. C.	Aug. 5, 1749	(at sea) 1779
McKean, Thomas (Del.)	Lawyer	New London, Pa.	Mar. 19, 1734	June 24, 1817
Middleton, Arthur (S. C.)	Farmer	Charleston, S. C.	June 26, 1742	Jan. 1, 1787
Morris, Lewis (N. Y.)	Farmer	Morrisania, N. Y. (N.Y.C.)	Apr. 8, 1726	Jan. 22, 1798
Morris, Robert (Pa.)	Merchant	Liverpool, England	Jan. 20, 1734	May 9, 1806
Morton, John (Pa.)	Judge	Ridley, Pa.	1724	Apr., 1777
Nelson, Thos. Jr. (Va.)	Farmer	Yorktown, Va.	Dec. 26, 1738	Jan. 4, 1789
Paca, William (Md.)	Judge	Abingdon, Md.	Oct. 31, 1740	Oct. 23, 1799
Paine, Robert Treat (Mass.)	Judge	Boston, Mass.	Mar. 11, 1731	May 12, 1814
Penn, John (N. C.)	Lawyer	Near Port Royal, Va.	May 17, 1741	Sept. 14, 1788
Read, George (Del.)	Judge	Near North East, Md.	Sept. 18, 1733	Sept. 21, 1798
Rodney, Caesar (Del.)	Judge	Dover, Del.	Oct. 7, 1728	June 29, 1784
Ross, George (Pa.)	Judge	New Castle, Del.	May 10, 1730	July 14, 1779
Rush, Benjamin (Pa.)	Physician	Byberry, Pa. (Philadelphia)	Dec. 24, 1745	Apr. 19, 1813
Rutedge, Edward (S. C.)	Lawyer	Charleston, S. C.	Nov. 23, 1749	Jan. 23, 1800
Sherman, Roger (Conn.)	Lawyer	Newton, Mass.	Apr. 19, 1721	July 23, 1793
Smith, James (Pa.)	Lawyer	Dublin, Ireland	1713	July 11, 1806
Stockton, Richard (N. J.)	Lawyer	Near Princeton, N. J.	Oct. 1, 1730	Feb. 28, 1781
Stone, Thomas (Md.)	Lawyer	Charles County, Md.	1743	Oct. 5, 1787
Taylor, George (Pa.)	Ironmaster	Ireland	1716	Feb. 23, 1781
Thornton, Matthew (N. H.)	Physician	Ireland	1714	June 24, 1803
Walton, George (Ga.)	Judge	Prince Edward County, Va.	1741	Feb. 2, 1804
Whipple, William (N. H.)	Merchant, judge	Kittery, Me.	Jan. 14, 1730	Nov. 28, 1785
Williams, William (Conn.)	Merchant	Lebanon, Conn.	Apr. 23, 1731	Aug. 2, 1811
Wilson, James (Pa.)	Judge	Carskerdo, Scotland	Sept. 14, 1742	Aug. 28, 1798
Witherspoon, John (N.J.)	Educator	Gifford, Scotland	Feb. 5, 1723	Nov. 15, 1794
Wolcott, Oliver (Conn.)	Judge	Windsor, Conn.	Dec. 1, 1726	Dec. 1, 1797
Wythe, George (Va.)	Lawyer	Elizabeth City, Va.	1726	June 8, 1806

Constitution of the United States

The Original 7 Articles

PREAMBLE

We, the people of the United States, in order to form a more perfect Union, establish justice, insure domestic tranquility, provide for the common defense, promote the general welfare, and secure the blessings of liberty to ourselves and our posterity, do ordain and establish this Constitution for the United States of America.

ARTICLE I.

Section 1—Legislative powers; in whom vested:

All legislative powers herein granted shall be vested in a Congress of the United States, which shall consist of a Senate and House of Representatives.

Section 2—House of Representatives, how and by whom chosen. Qualifications of a Representative. Representatives and direct taxes, how apportioned. Enumeration. Vacancies to be filled. Power of choosing officers, and of impeachment.

1. The House of Representatives shall be composed of members chosen every second year by the people of the several States, and the electors in each State shall have the qualifications requisite for electors of the most numerous branch of the State Legislature.

2. No person shall be a Representative who shall not have attained to the age of twenty-five years, and been seven years a citizen of the United States, and who shall not, when elected, be an inhabitant of that State in which he shall be chosen.

3. *(Representatives and direct taxes shall be apportioned among the several States which may be included within this Union, according to their respective numbers, which shall be determined by adding to the whole number of free persons, including those bound to service for a term of years, and excluding Indians not taxed, three-fifths of all other persons.) (The previous sentence was superseded by Amendment XIV, section 2.)* The actual enumeration shall be made within three years after the first meeting of the Congress of the United States, and within every subsequent term of ten years, in such manner as they shall by law direct. The number of Representatives shall not exceed one for every thirty thousand, but each State shall have at least one Representative; and until such enumeration shall be made, the State of New Hampshire shall be entitled to choose three, Massachusetts eight, Rhode Island and Providence Plantations one, Connecticut five, New York six, New Jersey four, Pennsylvania eight, Delaware one, Maryland six, Virginia ten, North Carolina five, South Carolina five, and Georgia three.

4. When vacancies happen in the representation from any State, the Executive Authority thereof shall issue writs of election to fill such vacancies.

5. The House of Representatives shall choose their Speaker and other officers; and shall have the sole power of impeachment.

Section 3—Senators, how and by whom chosen. How classified. Qualifications of a Senator, President of the Senate, his right to vote. President pro tem., and other officers of the Senate, how chosen. Power to try impeachments. When President is tried, Chief Justice to preside. Sentence.

1. The Senate of the United States shall be composed of two Senators from each State. *(chosen by the Legislature thereof,) (The preceding five words were superseded by Amendment XVII, section 1.)* for six years; and each Senator shall have one vote.

2. Immediately after they shall be assembled in consequence of the first election, they shall be divided as equally as may be into three classes. The seats of the Senators of the first class shall be vacated at the expiration of the second year, of the second class at the expiration of the fourth year, and of the third class at the expiration of the sixth year, so that one-third may be chosen every second year; *(and if vacancies happen by resignation, or otherwise, dur-*

Origin of the Constitution

The War of Independence was conducted by delegates from the original 13 states, called the Congress of the United States of America and generally known as the Continental Congress. In 1777 the Congress submitted to the legislatures of the states the Articles of Confederation and Perpetual Union, which were ratified by New Hampshire, Massachusetts, Rhode Island, Connecticut, New York, New Jersey, Pennsylvania, Delaware, Virginia, North Carolina, South Carolina, and Georgia, and finally, in 1781, by Maryland.

The first article of the instrument read: "The stile of this confederacy shall be the United States of America." This did not signify a sovereign nation, because the states delegated only those powers they could not handle individually, such as power to wage war, establish a uniform currency, make treaties with foreign nations and contract debts for general expenses (such as paying the army). Taxes for the payment of such debts were levied by the individual states. The president under the Articles signed himself "President of the United States in Congress assembled," but here the United States were considered in the plural, a cooperating group. Canada was invited to join the union on equal terms but did not act.

When the war was won it became evident that a stronger federal union was needed to protect the mutual interests of the states. The Congress left the initiative to the legislatures. Virginia in Jan. 1786 appointed commissioners to meet with representatives of other states, with the result that delegates from Virginia, Delaware, New York, New Jersey, and Pennsylvania met at Annapolis. Alexander Hamilton prepared for their call by asking delegates from all states to meet in Philadelphia in May 1787 "to render the Constitution of the Federal government adequate to the exigencies of the union." Congress endorsed the plan Feb. 21, 1787. Delegates were appointed by all states except Rhode Island.

The convention met May 14, 1787. George Washington was chosen president (presiding officer). The states certified 65 delegates, but 10 did not attend. The work was done by 55, not all of whom were present at all sessions. Of the 55 attending delegates, 16 failed to sign, and 39 actually signed Sept. 17, 1787, some with reservations. Some historians have said 74 delegates (9 more than the 65 actually certified) were named and 19 failed to attend. These 9 additional persons refused the appointment, were never delegates and never counted as absentees. Washington sent the Constitution to Congress with a covering letter and that body, Sept. 28, 1787, ordered it sent to the legislatures, "in order to be submitted to a convention of delegates chosen in each state by the people thereof."

The Constitution was ratified by votes of state conventions as follows: Delaware, Dec. 7, 1787, unanimous; Pennsylvania, Dec. 12, 1787, 43 to 23; New Jersey, Dec. 18, 1787, unanimous; Georgia, Jan. 2, 1788, unanimous; Connecticut, Jan. 9, 1788, 128 to 40; Massachusetts, Feb. 6, 1788, 187 to 168; Maryland, Apr. 28, 1788, 63 to 11; South Carolina, May 23, 1788, 149 to 73; New Hampshire, June 21, 1788, 57 to 46; Virginia, June 25, 1788, 89 to 79; New York, July 26, 1788, 30 to 27. Nine states were needed to establish the operation of the Constitution "between the states so ratifying the same" and New Hampshire was the 9th state. The government did not declare the Constitution in effect until the first Wednesday in Mar. 1789 which was Mar. 4. After that North Carolina ratified it Nov. 21, 1789, 197 to 77; and Rhode Island May 29, 1790, 34 to 32. Vermont in convention ratified it Jan. 10, 1791, and by act of Congress approved Feb. 19, 1791, was admitted into the Union as the 14th state, Mar. 4, 1791.

ing the recess of the Legislature of any State, the Executive thereof may make temporary appointments until the next meeting of the Legislature, which shall then fill such vacancies.) (The words in parenthesis were superseded by Amendment XVII, section 1.)

3. No person shall be a Senator who shall not have attained to the age of thirty years, and been nine years a citizen of the United States, and who shall not, when elected, be an inhabitant of that State for which he shall be chosen.

4. The Vice President of the United States shall be President of the Senate, but shall have no vote, unless they be equally divided.

5. The Senate shall choose their other officers, and also a President pro tempore, in the absence of the Vice President, or when he shall exercise the office of President of the United States.

6. The Senate shall have the sole power to try all impeachments. When sitting for that purpose, they shall be on oath or affirmation. When the President of the United States is tried, the Chief Justice shall preside: and no person shall be convicted without the concurrence of two-thirds of the members present.

7. Judgment in cases of impeachment shall not extend further than to removal from office, and disqualification to hold and enjoy any office of honor, trust or profit under the United States: but the party convicted shall nevertheless be liable and subject to indictment, trial, judgment and punishment, according to law.

Section 4—Times, etc., of holding elections, how prescribed. One session in each year.

1. The times, places and manner of holding elections for Senators and Representatives, shall be prescribed in each State by the Legislature thereof; but the Congress may at any time by law make or alter such regulations, except as to the places of choosing Senators.

2. The Congress shall assemble at least once in every year, and such meeting shall *(be on the first Monday in December,) (The words in parenthesis were superseded by Amendment XX, section 2)*. unless they shall by law appoint a different day.

Section 5—Membership, quorum, adjournments, rules. Power to punish or expel, Journal. Time of adjournments, how limited, etc.

1. Each House shall be the judge of the elections, returns and qualifications of its own members, and a majority of each shall constitute a quorum to do business; but a smaller number may adjourn from day to day, and may be authorized to compel the attendance of absent members, in such manner, and under such penalties as each House may provide.

2. Each House may determine the rules of its proceedings, punish its members for disorderly behavior, and, with the concurrence of two-thirds, expel a member.

3. Each House shall keep a journal of its proceedings, and from time to time publish the same, excepting such parts as may in their judgment require secrecy; and the yeas and nays of the members of either House on any question shall, at the desire of one-fifth of those present, be entered on the journal.

4. Neither House, during the session of Congress, shall, without the consent of the other, adjourn for more than three days, nor to any other place than that in which the two Houses shall be sitting.

Section 6—Compensation, privileges, disqualifications in certain cases.

1. The Senators and Representatives shall receive a compensation for their services, to be ascertained by law, and paid out of the Treasury of the United States. They shall in all cases, except treason, felony and breach of the peace, be privileged from arrest during their attendance at the session of their respective Houses, and in going to and returning from the same; and for any speech or debate in either House, they shall not be questioned in any other place.

2. No Senator or Representative shall, during the time for which he was elected, be appointed to any civil office under the authority of the United States, which shall have been created, or the emoluments whereof shall have been increased during such time; and no person holding any office under the United States, shall be a member of either House during his continuance in office.

Section 7—House to originate all revenue bills. Veto. Bill may be passed by two-thirds of each House, notwithstanding, etc. Bill, not returned in ten days, to become a law. Provisions as to orders, concurrent resolutions, etc.

1. All bills for raising revenue shall originate in the House of Representatives; but the Senate may propose or concur with amendments as on other bills.

2. Every bill which shall have passed the House of Representatives and the Senate, shall, before it becomes a law, be presented to the President of the United States; if he approves he shall sign it, but if not he shall return it, with his objections to that House in which it shall have originated, who shall enter the objections at large on their journal, and proceed to reconsider it. If after such reconsideration two-thirds of that House shall agree to pass the bill, it shall be sent, together with the objections, to the other House, by which it shall likewise be reconsidered, and if approved by two-thirds of that House, it shall become a law. But in all such cases the votes of both Houses shall be determined by yeas and nays, and the names of the persons voting for and against the bill shall be entered on the journal of each House respectively. If any bill shall not be returned by the President within ten days (Sundays excepted) after it shall have been presented to him, the same shall be a law, in like manner as if he had signed it, unless the Congress by their adjournment prevent its return, in which case it shall not be a law.

3. Every order, resolution, or vote to which the concurrence of the Senate and House of Representatives may be necessary (except on a question of adjournment) shall be presented to the President of the United States; and before the same shall take effect, shall be approved by him, or being disapproved by him, shall be repassed by two-thirds of the Senate and House of Representatives, according to the rules and limitations prescribed in the case of a bill.

Section 8—Powers of Congress.

The Congress shall have power

1. To lay and collect taxes, duties, imposts and excises, to pay the debts and provide for the common defense and general welfare of the United States; but all duties, imposts and excises shall be uniform throughout the United States;

2. To borrow money on the credit of the United States;

3. To regulate commerce with foreign nations, and among the several States, and with the Indian tribes;

4. To establish a uniform rule of naturalization, and uniform laws on the subject of bankruptcies throughout the United States;

5. To coin money, regulate the value thereof, and of foreign coin, and fix the standard of weights and measures;

6. To provide for the punishment of counterfeiting the securities and current coin of the United States;

7. To establish post-offices and post-roads;

8. To promote the progress of science and useful arts, by securing for limited times to authors and inventors the exclusive right to their respective writings and discoveries;

9. To constitute tribunals inferior to the Supreme Court;

10. To define and punish piracies and felonies committed on the high seas, and offenses against the law of nations;

11. To declare war, grant letters of marque and reprisal, and make rules concerning captures on land and water;

12. To raise and support armies, but no appropriation of money to that use shall be for a longer term than two years;

13. To provide and maintain a navy;

14. To make rules for the government and regulation of the land and naval forces;

15. To provide for calling forth the militia to execute the laws of the Union, suppress insurrections and repel invasions;

16. To provide for organizing, arming, and disciplining the militia, and for governing such part of them as may be employed in the service of the United States, reserving to the States respectively, the appointment of the officers, and the authority of training and militia according to the discipline prescribed by Congress;

17. To exercise exclusive legislation in all cases whatsoever, over such district (not exceeding ten miles square)

as may, by cession of particular States, and the acceptance of Congress, become the seat of the Government of the United States, and to exercise like authority over all places purchased by the consent of the Legislature of the State in which the same shall be, for the erection of forts, magazines, arsenals, dockyards, and other needful buildings; — And

18. To make all laws which shall be necessary and proper for carrying into execution the foregoing powers, and all other powers vested by this Constitution in the Government of the United States, or in any department or officer thereof.

Section 9—Provision as to migration or importation of certain persons. Habeas corpus, bills of attainder, etc. Taxes, how apportioned. No export duty. No commercial preference. Money, how drawn from Treasury, etc. No titular nobility. Officers not to receive presents, etc.

1. The migration or importation of such persons as any of the States now existing shall think proper to admit, shall not be prohibited by the Congress prior to the year one thousand eight hundred and eight, but a tax or duty may be imposed on such importation, not exceeding ten dollars for each person.

2. The privilege of the writ of habeas corpus shall not be suspended, unless then in cases of rebellion or invasion the public safety may require it.

3. No bill of attainder or ex post facto law shall be passed.

4. No capitation, or other direct, tax shall be laid, unless in proportion to the census or enumeration herein before directed to be taken. *(Modified by Amendment XVI.)*

5. No tax or duty shall be laid on articles exported from any State.

6. No preference shall be given by any regulation of commerce or revenue to the ports of one State over those of another: nor shall vessels bound to, or from, one State, be obliged to enter, clear, or pay duties in another.

7. No money shall be drawn from the Treasury, but in consequence of appropriations made by law; and a regular statement and account of the receipts and expenditures of all public money shall be published from time to time.

8. No title of nobility shall be granted by the United States: and no person holding any office of profit or trust under them, shall, without the consent of the Congress, accept of any present, emolument, office, or title, of any kind whatever, from any king, prince, or foreign state.

Section 10—States prohibited from the exercise of certain powers.

1. No State shall enter into any treaty, alliance, or confederation; grant letters of marque and reprisal; coin money; emit bills of credit; make anything but gold and silver coin a tender in payment of debts; pass any bill of attainder, ex post facto law, or law impairing the obligation of contracts, or grant any title of nobility.

2. No State shall, without the consent of the Congress, lay any imposts or duties on imports or exports, except what may be absolutely necessary for executing its inspection laws: and the net produce of all duties and imposts, laid by any State on imports or exports, shall be for the use of the Treasury of the United States; and all such laws shall be subject to the revision and control of the Congress.

3. No State shall, without the consent of Congress, lay any duty of tonnage, keep troops, or ships of war in time of peace, enter into any agreement or compact with another State, or with a foreign power, or engage in war, unless actually invaded, or in such imminent danger as will not admit of delay.

ARTICLE II.

Section 1—President: his term of office. Electors of President; number and how appointed. Electors to vote on same day. Qualification of President. On whom his duties devolve in case of his removal, death, etc. President's compensation. His oath of office.

1. The Executive power shall be vested in a President of the United States of America. He shall hold his office during the term of four years, and together with the Vice President, chosen for the same term, be elected as follows

2. Each State shall appoint, in such manner as the Legislature thereof may direct, a number of electors, equal to the whole number of Senators and Representatives to which the State may be entitled in the Congress: but no Senator or Representative, or person holding an office of trust or profit under the United States, shall be appointed an elector.

(The electors shall meet in their respective States, and vote by ballot for two persons, of whom one at least shall not be an inhabitant of the same State with themselves. And they shall make a list of all the persons voted for, and of the number of votes for each; which list they shall sign and certify, and transmit sealed to the seat of the Government of the United States, directed to the President of the Senate. The President of the Senate shall, in the presence of the Senate and House of Representatives, open all the certificates, and the votes shall then be counted. The person having the greatest number of votes shall be the President, if such number be a majority of the whole number of electors appointed; and if there be more than one who have such majority, and have an equal number of votes, then the House of Representatives shall immediately choose by ballot one of them for President; and if no person have a majority, then from the five highest on the list the said House shall in like manner choose the President. But in choosing the President, the votes shall be taken by States, the representation from each State having one vote; a quorum for this purpose shall consist of a member or members from two-thirds of the States, and a majority of all the States shall be necessary to a choice. In every case, after the choice of the President, the person having the greatest number of votes of the electors shall be the Vice President. But if there should remain two or more who have equal votes, the Senate shall choose from them by ballot the Vice President.)

(This clause was superseded by Amendment XII.)

3. The Congress may determine the time of choosing the electors, and the day on which they shall give their votes; which day shall be the same throughout the United States.

4. No person except a natural born citizen, or a citizen of the United States, at the time of the adoption of this Constitution, shall be eligible to the office of President; neither shall any person be eligible to that office who shall not have attained to the age of thirty-five years, and been fourteen years a resident within the United States.

(For qualification of the Vice President, see Amendment XII.)

5. In case of the removal of the President from office, or of his death, resignation, or inability to discharge the powers and duties of the said office, the same shall devolve on the Vice President, and the Congress may by law provide for the case of removal, death, resignation or inability, both of the President and Vice President, declaring what officer shall then act as President, and such officer shall act accordingly, until the disability be removed, or a President shall be elected.

(This clause has been modified by Amendment XX, sections 3 and 4).

6. The President shall, at stated times, receive for his services, a compensation, which shall neither be increased nor diminished during the period for which he shall have been elected, and he shall not receive within that period any other emolument from the United States, or any of them.

7. Before he enter on the execution of his office, he shall take the following oath or affirmation:

"I do solemnly swear (or affirm) that I will faithfully execute the office of President of the United States, and will to the best of my ability, preserve, protect and defend the Constitution of the United States."

Section 2—President to be Commander-in-Chief. He may require opinions of cabinet officers, etc., may pardon. Treaty-making power. Nomination of certain officers. When President may fill vacancies.

1. The President shall be Commander-in-Chief of the Army and Navy of the United States, and of the militia of the several States, when called into the actual service of the United States; he may require the opinion, in writing, of the principal officer in each of the executive departments, upon any subject relating to the duties of their respective offices, and he shall have power to grant reprieves and pardons for offenses against the United States, except

in cases of impeachment.

2. He shall have power, by and with the advice and consent of the Senate, to make treaties, provided two-thirds of the Senators present concur; and he shall nominate, and by and with the advice and consent of the Senate, shall appoint ambassadors, other public ministers and consuls, judges of the Supreme Court, and all other officers of the United States, whose appointments are not herein otherwise provided for, and which shall be established by law: but the Congress may by law vest the appointment of such inferior officers, as they think proper, in the President alone, in the courts of law, or in the heads of departments.

3. The President shall have power to fill up all vacancies that may happen during the recess of the Senate, by granting commissions, which shall expire at the end of their next session.

Section 3—President shall communicate to Congress. He may convene and adjourn Congress, in case of disagreement, etc. Shall receive ambassadors, execute laws, and commission officers.

He shall from time to time give to the Congress information of the state of the Union, and recommend to their consideration such measures as he shall judge necessary and expedient; he may, on extraordinary occasions, convene both Houses, or either of them, and in case of disagreement between them, with respect to the time of adjournment, he may adjourn them to such time as he shall think proper; he shall receive ambassadors and other public ministers; he shall take care that the laws be faithfully executed, and shall commission all the officers of the United States.

Section 4—All civil offices forfeited for certain crimes.

The President, Vice President, and all civil officers of the United States, shall be removed from office on impeachment for, and conviction of, treason, bribery, or other high crimes and misdemeanors.

ARTICLE III.

Section 1—Judicial powers, Tenure. Compensation.

The judicial power of the United States, shall be vested in one Supreme Court, and in such inferior courts as the Congress may from time to time ordain and establish. The judges, both of the Supreme and inferior courts, shall hold their offices during good behavior, and shall at stated times, receive for their services, a compensation, which shall not be diminished during their continuance in office.

Section 2—Judicial power; to what cases it extends. Original jurisdiction of Supreme Court; appellate jurisdiction. Trial by jury, etc. Trial, where.

1. The judicial power shall extend to all cases, in law and equity, arising under this Constitution, the laws of the United States, and treaties made, or which shall be made, under their authority; to all cases affecting ambassadors, other public ministers and consuls; to all cases of admiralty and maritime jurisdiction; to controversies to which the United States shall be a party; to controversies between two or more States; between a State and citizens of another State; between citizens of different States, between citizens of the same State claiming lands under grants of different States, and between a State, or the citizens thereof, and foreign states, citizens or subjects.

(This section is modified by Amendment XI.)

2. In all cases affecting ambassadors, other public ministers and consuls, and those in which a State shall be party, the Supreme Court shall have original jurisdiction. In all the other cases before mentioned, the Supreme Court shall have appellate jurisdiction, both as to law and fact, with such exceptions, and under such regulations as the Congress shall make.

3. The trial of all crimes, except in cases of impeachment, shall be by jury; and such trial shall be held in the State where the said crimes shall have been committed; but when not committed within any State, the trial shall be at such place or places as the Congress may by law have directed.

Section 3—Treason Defined, Proof of Punishment of.

1. Treason against the United States, shall consist only in levying war against them, or in adhering to their enemies, giving them aid and comfort. No persons shall be convicted of treason unless on the testimony of two witnesses to the same overt act, or on confession in open court.

2. The Congress shall have power to declare the punishment of treason, but no attainder of treason shall work corruption of blood, or forfeiture except during the life of the person attainted.

ARTICLE IV.

Section 1—Each State to give credit to the public acts, etc., of every other State.

Full faith and credit shall be given in each State to the public acts, records, and judicial proceedings of every other State. And the Congress may by general laws prescribe the manner in which such acts, records and proceedings shall be proved, and the effect thereof.

Section 2—Privileges of citizens of each State. Fugitives from justice to be delivered up. Persons held to service having escaped, to be delivered up.

1. The citizens of each State shall be entitled to all privileges and immunities of citizens in the several States.

2. A person charged in any State with treason, felony, or other crime, who shall flee from justice, and be found in another State, shall on demand of the Executive authority of the State from which he fled, be delivered up, to be removed to the State having jurisdiction of the crime.

(3. No person held to service or labor in one State, under the laws thereof, escaping into another, shall in consequence of any law or regulation therein, be discharged from such service or labor, but shall be delivered up on claim of the party to whom such service or labor may be due.) (This clause was superseded by Amendment XIII.)

Section 3—Admission of new States. Power of Congress over territory and other property.

1. New States may be admitted by the Congress into this Union; but no new State shall be formed or erected within the jurisdiction of any other State; nor any State be formed by the junction of two or more States, or parts of States, without the consent of the Legislatures of the States concerned as well as of the Congress.

2. The Congress shall have power to dispose of and make all needful rules and regulations respecting the territory or other property belonging to the United States; and nothing in this Constitution shall be so construed as to prejudice any claims of the United States, or of any particular State.

Section 4—Republican form of government guaranteed. Each state to be protected.

The United States shall guarantee to every State in this Union a Republican form of government, and shall protect each of them against invasion; and on application of the Legislature, or of the Executive (when the Legislature cannot be convened) against domestic violence.

ARTICLE V.

Constitution: how amended; proviso.

The Congress, whenever two-thirds of both Houses shall deem it necessary, shall propose amendments to this Constitution, or, on the application of the Legislatures of two-thirds of the several States, shall call a convention for proposing amendments, which, in either case, shall be valid to all intents and purposes, as part of this Constitution, when ratified by the Legislatures of three-fourths of the several states, or by conventions in three-fourths thereof, as the one or the other mode of ratification may be proposed by the Congress; provided that no amendment which may be made prior to the year one thousand eight hundred and eight shall in any manner affect the first and fourth clauses in the Ninth Section of the First Article; and that no State, without its consent, shall be deprived of its equal suffrage in the Senate.

ARTICLE VI.

Certain debts, etc., declared valid. Supremacy of Constitution, treaties, and laws of the United States.

Oath to support Constitution, by whom taken. No religious test.

1. All debts contracted and engagements entered into, before the adoption of this Constitution, shall be as valid against the United States under this Constitution, as under the Confederation.

2. This Constitution, and the laws of the United States which shall be made in pursuance thereof; and all treaties made, or which shall be made, under the authority of the United States, shall be the supreme law of the land; and the judges in every State shall be bound thereby, any thing in the Constitution or laws of any State to the contrary notwithstanding.

3. The Senators and Representatives before mentioned, and the members of the several State Legislatures, and all executive and judicial officers, both of the United States and of the several States, shall be bound by oath or affirmation, to support this Constitution; but no religious test shall ever be required as a qualification to any office or public trust under the United States.

ARTICLE VII.

What ratification shall establish Constitution.

The ratification of the Conventions of nine States, shall be sufficient for the establishment of this Constitution between the States so ratifying the same.

Done in convention by the unanimous consent of the States present the Seventeenth day of September in the year of our Lord one thousand seven hundred and eighty seven, and of the independence of the United States of America the Twelfth. In witness whereof we have hereunto subscribed our names.

George Washington, President and deputy from Virginia.
New Hampshire—John Langdon, Nicholas Gilman.
Massachusetts—Nathaniel Gorham, Rufus King.
Connecticut—Wm. Saml. Johnson, Roger Sherman.
New York—Alexander Hamilton.
New Jersey—Wil: Livingston, David Brearley, Wm. Paterson, Jona: Dayton.
Pennsylvania—B. Franklin, Thomas Mifflin, Robt. Morris, Geo. Clymer, Thos. FitzSimons, Jared Ingersoll, James Wilson, Gouv. Morris.
Delaware—Geo: Read, Gunning Bedford Jun., John Dickinson, Richard Bassett, Jaco: Broom.
Maryland—James McHenry, Daniel of Saint Thomas Jenifer, Danl. Carroll.
Virginia—John Blair, James Madison Jr.
North Carolina—Wm. Blount, Rich'd. Dobbs Spaight, Hugh Williamson.
South Carolina—J. Rutledge, Charles Cotesworth Pinckney, Charles Pinckney, Pierce Butler.
Georgia—William Few, Abr. Baldwin.
Attest: William Jackson, Secretary.

Ten Original Amendments: The Bill of Rights

In force Dec. 15, 1791

(The First Congress, at its first session in the City of New York, Sept. 25, 1789, submitted to the states 12 amendments to clarify certain individual and state rights not named in the Constitution. They are generally called the Bill of Rights.

(Influential in framing these amendments was the Declaration of Rights of Virginia, written by George Mason (1725-1792) in 1776. Mason, a Virginia delegate to the Constitutional Convention, did not sign the Constitution and opposed its ratification on the ground that it did not sufficiently oppose slavery or safeguard individual rights.

(In the preamble to the resolution offering the proposed amendments, Congress said: "The conventions of a number of the States having at the time of their adopting the Constitution, expressed a desire, in order to prevent misconstruction or abuse of its powers, that further declaratory and restrictive clauses should be added, and as extending the ground of public confidence in the government will best insure the beneficent ends of its institution, be it resolved," etc.

(Ten of these amendments now commonly known as one to 10 inclusive, but originally 3 to 12 inclusive, were ratified by the states as follows: New Jersey, Nov. 20, 1789; Maryland, Dec. 19, 1789; North Carolina, Dec. 22, 1789; South Carolina, Jan. 19, 1790; New Hampshire, Jan. 25, 1790; Delaware, Jan. 28, 1790; New York, Feb. 24, 1790; Pennsylvania, Mar. 10, 1790; Rhode Island, June 7, 1790; Vermont, Nov. 3, 1791; Virginia, Dec. 15, 1791; Massachusetts, Mar. 2, 1939; Georgia, Mar. 8, 1939; Connecticut, Apr. 19, 1939. These original 10 ratified amendments follow as Amendments I to X inclusive.

(Of the two original proposed amendments which were not ratified by the necessary number of states, the first related to apportionment of Representatives; the second, to compensation of members.)

AMENDMENT I.

Religious establishment prohibited. Freedom of speech, of the press, and right to petition.

Congress shall make no law respecting an establishment of religion, or prohibiting the free exercise thereof; or abridging the freedom of speech, or of the press; or the right of the people peaceably to assemble, and to petition the Government for a redress of grievances.

AMENDMENT II.

Right to keep and bear arms.

A well-regulated militia, being necessary to the security of a free State, the right of the people to keep and bear arms, shall not be infringed.

AMENDMENT III.

Conditions for quarters for soldiers.

No soldier shall, in time of peace be quartered in any house, without the consent of the owner, nor in time of war, but in a manner to be prescribed by law.

AMENDMENT IV.

Right of search and seizure regulated.

The right of the people to be secure in their persons, houses, papers, and effects, against unreasonable searches and seizures, shall not be violated, and no warrants shall issue, but upon probable cause, supported by oath or affirmation, and particularly describing the place to be searched, and the persons or things to be seized.

AMENDMENT V.

Provisions concerning prosecution. Trial and punishment—private property not to be taken for public use without compensation.

No person shall be held to answer for a capital, or otherwise infamous crime, unless on a presentment or indictment of a Grand Jury, except in cases arising in the land or naval forces, or in the militia, when in actual service in time of war or public danger; nor shall any person be subject for the same offense to be twice put in jeopardy of life or limb; nor shall be compelled in any criminal case to be a witness against himself, nor be deprived of life, liberty, or property, without due process of law; nor shall private property be taken for public use without just compensation.

AMENDMENT VI.

Right to speedy trial, witnesses, etc.

In all criminal prosecutions, the accused shall enjoy the right to a speedy and public trial, by an impartial jury of the State and district wherein the crime shall have been committed, which district shall have been previously ascertained by law, and to be informed of the nature and cause of the accusation; to be confronted with the witnesses against him; to have compulsory process for obtaining witnesses in his favor, and to have the assistance of counsel for his defense.

AMENDMENT VII.

Right of trial by jury.

In suits at common law, where the value in controversy shall exceed twenty dollars, the right of trial by jury shall be preserved, and no fact tried by a jury shall be otherwise reexamined in any court of the United States, than according to the rules of the common law.

AMENDMENT VIII.

Excessive bail or fines and cruel punishment prohibited.

Excessive bail shall not be required, nor excessive fines imposed, nor cruel and unusual punishments inflicted.

AMENDMENT IX.

Rule of construction of Constitution.

The enumeration in the Constitution, of certain rights, shall not be construed to deny or disparage others retained by the people.

AMENDMENT X.

Rights of States under Constitution.

The powers not delegated to the United States by the Constitution, nor prohibited by it to the States, are reserved to the States respectively, or to the people.

Amendments Since the Bill of Rights

AMENDMENT XI.

Judicial powers construed.

The judicial power of the United States shall not be construed to extend to any suit in law or equity, commenced or prosecuted against one of the United States by citizens of another State, or by citizens or subjects of any foreign state.

(This amendment was proposed to the Legislatures of the several States by the Third Congress on March 4, 1794, and was declared to have been ratified in a message from the President to Congress, dated Jan. 8, 1798.

(It was on Jan. 5, 1798, that Secretary of State Pickering received from 12 of the States authenticated ratifications, and informed President John Adams of that fact.

(As a result of later research in the Department of State, it is now established that Amendment XI became part of the Constitution on Feb. 7, 1795, for on that date it had been ratified bv 12 States as follows:

(1. New York, Mar. 27, 1794. 2. Rhode Island, Mar. 31, 1794. 3. Connecticut, May 8, 1794. 4. New Hampshire, June 16, 1794. 5. Massachusetts, June 26, 1794. 6. Vermont, between Oct. 9, 1794, and Nov. 9, 1794. 7. Virginia, Nov. 18, 1794. 8. Georgia, Nov. 29, 1794. 9. Kentucky, Dec. 7, 1794. 10. Maryland, Dec. 26, 1794. 11. Delaware, Jan. 23, 1795. 12. North Carolina, Feb. 7, 1795.

(On June 1, 1796, more than a year after Amendment XI had become a part of the Constitution (but before anyone was officially aware of this), Tennessee had been admitted as a State; but not until Oct. 16, 1797, was a certified copy of the resolution of Congress proposing the amendment sent to the Governor of Tennessee (John Sevier) by Secretary of State Pickering, whose office was then at Trenton, New Jersey, because of the epidemic of yellow fever at Philadelphia; it seems, however, that the Legislature of Tennessee took no action on Amendment XI, owing doubtless to the fact that public announcement of its adoption was made soon thereafter.

(Besides the necessary 12 States, one other, South Carolina, ratified Amendment XI, but this action was not taken until Dec. 4, 1797; the two remaining States, New Jersey and Pennsylvania, failed to ratify.)

AMENDMENT XII.

Manner of choosing President and Vice-President.

(Proposed by Congress Dec. 9, 1803; ratification completed June 15, 1804.)

The Electors shall meet in their respective States and vote by ballot for President and Vice-President, one of whom, at least, shall not be an inhabitant of the same State with themselves; they shall name in their ballots the person voted for as President, and in distinct ballots the person voted for as Vice-President, and they shall make distinct lists of all persons voted for as President, and of all persons voted for as Vice-President, and of the number of votes for each, which lists they shall sign and certify, and transmit sealed to the seat of the Government of the United States, directed to the President of the Senate; the President of the Senate shall, in the presence of the Senate and House of Representatives, open all the certificates and the votes shall then be counted;—The person having the greatest number of votes for President, shall be the President, if such number be a majority of the whole number of Electors appointed; and if no person have such majority, then from the persons having the highest numbers not exceeding three on the list of those voted for as President, the House of Representatives shall choose immediately, by ballot, the President. But in choosing the President, the votes shall be taken by States, the representation from each State having one vote; a quorum for this purpose shall consist of a member or members from two-thirds of the States, and a majority of all the States shall be necessary to a choice. *(And if the House of Representatives shall not choose a President whenever the right of choice shall devolve upon them, before the fourth day of March next following, then the Vice-President shall act as President, as in case of the death of other constitutional disability of the President.) (The words in parentheses were superseded by Amendment XX, section 3.)* The person having the greatest number of votes as Vice-President, shall be the Vice-President, if such number be a majority of the whole number of Electors appointed, and if no person have a majority, then from the two highest numbers on the list, the Senate shall choose the Vice-President; a quorum for the purpose shall consist of two-thirds of the whole number of Senators, and a majority of the whole number shall be necessary to a choice. But no person constitutionally ineligible to the office of President shall be eligible to that of Vice-President of the United States.

THE RECONSTRUCTION AMENDMENTS

(Amendments XIII, XIV, and XV are commonly known as the Reconstruction Amendments, inasmuch as they followed the Civil War, and were drafted by Republicans who were bent on imposing their own policy of reconstruction on the South. Post-bellum legislatures there—Mississippi, South Carolina, Georgia, for example—had set up laws which, it was charged, were contrived to perpetuate Negro slavery under other names.)

AMENDMENT XIII.

Slavery abolished.

(Proposed by Congress Jan. 31, 1865; ratification completed Dec. 18, 1865. The amendment, when first proposed by a resolution in Congress, was passed by the Senate, 38 to 6, on Apr. 8, 1864, but was defeated in the House, 95 to 66 on June 15, 1864. On reconsideration by the House, on Jan. 31, 1865, the resolution passed, 119 to 56. It was approved by President Lincoln on Feb. 1, 1865, although the Supreme Court had decided in 1798 that the President has nothing to do with the proposing of amendments to the Constitution, or their adoption.)

1. Neither slavery nor involuntary servitude, except as a punishment for crime whereof the party shall have been duly convicted, shall exist within the United States or any place subject to their jurisdiction.

2. Congress shall have power to enforce this article by appropriate legislation.

AMENDMENT XIV.

Citizenship rights not to be abridged.

(The following amendment was proposed to the Legisla-

tures of the several states by the 39th Congress, June 13, 1866, and was declared to have been ratified in a proclamation by the Secretary of State, July 28, 1868.

(The 14th amendment was adopted only by virtue of ratification subsequent to earlier rejections. Newly constituted legislatures in both North Carolina and South Carolina (respectively July 4 and 9, 1868), ratified the proposed amendment, although earlier legislatures had rejected the proposal. The Secretary of State issued a proclamation, which, though doubtful as to the effect of attempted withdrawals by Ohio and New Jersey, entertained no doubt as to the validity of the ratification by North and South Carolina. The following day (July 21, 1868), Congress passed a resolution which declared the 14th Amendment to be a part of the Constitution and directed the Secretary of State so to promulgate it. The Secretary waited, however, until the newly constituted Legislature of Georgia had ratified the amendment, subsequent to an earlier rejection, before the promulgation of the ratification of the new amendment.)

1. All persons born or naturalized in the United States, and subject to the jurisdiction thereof, are citizens of the United States and of the State wherein they reside. No State shall make or enforce any law which shall abridge the privileges or immunities of citizens of the United States; nor shall any State deprive any person of life, liberty, or property, without due process of law; nor deny to any person within its jurisdiction the equal protection of the laws.

2. Representatives shall be apportioned among the several States according to their respective numbers, counting the whole number of persons in each State, excluding Indians not taxed. But when the right to vote at any election for the choice of Electors for President and Vice-President of the United States, Representatives in Congress, the executive and judicial officers of a State, or the members of the Legislature thereof, is denied to any of the male inhabitants of such State, being twenty-one years of age, and citizens of the United States, or in any way abridged, except for participation in rebellion, or other crime, the basis of representation therein shall be reduced in the proportion which the number of such male citizens shall bear to the whole number of male citizens twenty-one years of age in such State.

3. No person shall be a Senator or Representative in Congress, or Elector of President and Vice-President, or hold any office, civil or military, under the United States, or under any State, who, having previously taken an oath, as a member of Congress, or as an officer of the United States, or as a member of any State Legislature, or as an executive or judicial officer of any State, to support the Constitution of the United States, shall have engaged in insurrection or rebellion against the same, or given aid or comfort to the enemies thereof. But Congress may by a vote of two-thirds of each House, remove such disability.

4. The validity of the public debt of the United States, authorized by law, including debts incurred for payment of pensions and bounties for services in suppressing insurrection or rebellion, shall not be questioned. But neither the United States nor any State shall assume or pay any debt or obligation incurred in aid of insurrection or rebellion against the United States, or any claim for the loss or emancipation of any slave; but all such debts, obligations and claims, shall be held illegal and void.

5. The Congress shall have power to enforce, by appropriate legislation, the provisions of this article.

AMENDMENT XV.

Race no bar to voting rights.

(The following amendment was proposed to the legislatures of the several States by the 40th Congress, Feb. 26, 1869, and was declared to have been ratified in a proclamation by the Secretary of State, Mar. 30, 1870.)

1. The right of citizens of the United States to vote shall not be denied or abridged by the United States or by any State on account of race, color, or previous condition of servitude.

2. The Congress shall have power to enforce this article by appropriate legislation.

AMENDMENT XVI.

Income taxes authorized.

(Proposed by Congress July 12, 1909; ratification completed Feb. 3, 1913.)

The Congress shall have power to lay and collect taxes on incomes, from whatever sources derived, without apportionment among the several States, and without regard to any census or enumeration.

AMENDMENT XVII.

United States Senators to be elected by direct popular vote.

(Proposed by Congress May 13, 1912; ratification completed Apr. 8, 1913.)

1. The Senate of the United States shall be composed of two Senators from each State, elected by the people thereof, for six years; and each Senator shall have one vote. The electors in each State shall have the qualifications requisite for electors of the most numerous branch of the State Legislatures.

2. When vacancies happen in the representation of any State in the Senate, the executive authority of such State shall issue writs of election to fill such vacancies: Provided, That the Legislature of any State may empower the Executive thereof to make temporary appointments until the people fill the vacancies by election as the Legislature may direct.

3. This amendment shall not be so construed as to affect the election or term of any Senator chosen before it becomes valid as part of the Constitution.

AMENDMENT XVIII.

Liquor prohibition amendment.

(Proposed by Congress Dec. 18, 1917; ratification completed Jan. 16, 1919. Repealed by Amendment XXI, effective Dec. 5, 1933.)

(1. After one year from the ratification of this article the manufacture, sale, or transportation of intoxicating liquors, within, the importation thereof into, or the exportation thereof from the United States and all territory subject to the jurisdiction thereof, for beverage purposes is hereby prohibited.

(2. The Congress and the several States shall have concurrent power to enforce this article by appropriate legislation.

(3. This article shall be inoperative unless it shall have been ratified as an amendment to the Constitution by the Legislatures of the several States, as provided in the Constitution, within seven years from the date of the submission hereof to the States by the Congress.)

(The total vote in the Senates of the various States was 1,310 for, 237 against — 84.6% dry. In the lower houses of the States the vote was 3,782 for, 1,035 against — 78.5% dry.

(The amendment ultimately was adopted by all the States except Connecticut and Rhode Island.)

AMENDMENT XIX.

Giving nationwide suffrage to women.

(Proposed by Congress June 4, 1919; ratification certified by Secretary of State Aug. 26, 1920.)

1. The right of citizens of the United States to vote shall not be denied or abridged by the United States or by any State on account of sex.

2. Congress shall have power to enforce this Article by appropriate legislation.

AMENDMENT XX.

Terms of President and Vice President to begin on Jan. 20; those of Senators, Representatives, Jan. 3.

(Proposed by Congress Mar. 2, 1932; ratification completed Jan. 23, 1933.)

1. The terms of the President and Vice President shall end at noon on the 20th day of January, and the terms of Senators and Representatives at noon on the 3rd day of January, of the years in which such terms would have ended if this article had not been ratified; and the terms of their successors shall then begin.

2. The Congress shall assemble at least once in every year, and such meeting shall begin at noon on the 3rd day of January, unless they shall by law appoint a different day.

3. If, at the time fixed for the beginning of the term of the President, the President elect shall have died, the Vice President elect shall become President. If a President shall not have been chosen before the time fixed for the beginning of his term, or if the President elect shall have failed to qualify, then the Vice President elect shall act as Presi-

dent until a President shall have qualified; and the Congress may by law provide for the case wherein neither a President elect nor a Vice President shall have qualified, declaring who shall then act as President, or the manner in which one who is to act shall be selected, and such person shall act accordingly until a President or Vice President shall have qualified.

4. The Congress may by law provide for the case of the death of any of the persons from whom the House of Representatives may choose a President whenever the right of choice shall have devolved upon them, and for the case of the death of any of the persons from whom the Senate may choose a Vice President whenever the right of choice shall have devolved upon them.

5. Sections 1 and 2 shall take effect on the 15th day of October following the ratification of this article (Oct., 1933).

6. This article shall be inoperative unless it shall have been ratified as an amendment to the Constitution by the Legislatures of three-fourths of the several States within seven years from the date of its submission.

AMENDMENT XXI.

Repeal of Amendment XVIII.

(Proposed by Congress Feb. 20, 1933; ratification completed Dec. 5, 1933.)

1. The eighteenth article of amendment to the Constitution of the United States is hereby repealed.

2. The transportation or importation into any State, Territory, or Possession of the United States for delivery or use therein of intoxicating liquors, in violation of the laws thereof, is hereby prohibited.

3. This article shall be inoperative unless it shall have been ratified as an amendment to the Constitution by conventions in the several States, as provided in the Constitution, within seven years from the date of the submission hereof to the States by the Congress.

AMENDMENT XXII.

Limiting Presidential terms of office.

(Proposed by Congress Mar. 21, 1947; ratification completed Feb. 27, 1951.)

1. No person shall be elected to the office of the President more than twice, and no person who has held the office of President, or acted as President, for more than two years of a term to which some other person was elected President shall be elected to the office of the President more than once. But this Article shall not apply to any person holding the office of President when this Article was proposed by the Congress, and shall not prevent any person who may be holding the office of President, or acting as President, during the term within which this Article becomes operative from holding the office of President or acting as President during the remainder of such term.

2. This article shall be inoperative unless it shall have been ratified as an amendment to the Constitution by the Legislatures of three-fourths of the several States within seven years from the date of its submission to the States by the Congress.

AMENDMENT XXIII.

Presidential vote for District of Columbia.

(Proposed by Congress June 17, 1960; ratification completed Mar. 29, 1961.)

1. The District constituting the seat of Government of the United States shall appoint in such manner as the Congress may direct:

A number of electors of President and Vice President equal to the whole number of Senators and Representatives in Congress to which the District would be entitled if it were a State, but in no event more than the least populous State; they shall be in addition to those appointed by the States, but they shall be considered, for the purposes of the election of President and Vice President, to be electors appointed by a State; and they shall meet in the District and perform such duties as provided by the twelfth article of amendment.

2. The Congress shall have power to enforce this article by appropriate legislation.

AMENDMENT XXIV.

Barring poll tax in federal elections.

(Proposed by Congress Aug. 27, 1962; ratification completed Jan. 23, 1964.)

1. The right of citizens of the United States to vote in any primary or other election for President or Vice President, for electors for President or Vice President, or for Senator or Representative in Congress, shall not be denied or abridged by the United States or any State by reason of failure to pay any poll tax or other tax.

2. The Congress shall have power to enforce this article by appropriate legislation.

AMENDMENT XXV.

Presidential disability and succession.

(Proposed by Congress July 6, 1965; ratification completed Feb. 10, 1967.)

1. In case of the removal of the President from office or of his death or resignation, the Vice President shall become President.

2. Whenever there is a vacancy in the office of the Vice President, the President shall nominate a Vice President who shall take office upon confirmation by a majority vote of both houses of Congress.

3. Whenever the President transmits to the President pro tempore of the Senate and the Speaker of the House of Representatives his written declaration that he is unable to discharge the powers and duties of his office, and until he transmits to them a written declaration to the contrary, such powers and duties shall be discharged by the Vice President as Acting President.

4. Whenever the Vice President and a majority of either the principal officers of the executive departments or of such other body as Congress may by law provide, transmit to the President pro tempore of the Senate and the Speaker of the House of Representatives their written declaration that the President is unable to discharge the powers and duties of his office, the Vice President shall immediately assume the powers and duties of the office as Acting President.

Thereafter, when the President transmits to the President pro tempore of the Senate and the Speaker of the House of Representatives his written declaration that no inability exists, he shall resume the powers and duties of his office unless the Vice President and a majority of either the principal officers of the executive department or of such other body as Congress may by law provide, transmit within four days to the President pro tempore of the Senate and the Speaker of the House of Representatives their written declaration that the President is unable to discharge the powers and duties of his office. Thereupon Congress shall decide the issue, assembling within forty-eight hours for that purpose if not in session. If the Congress, within twenty-one days after receipt of the latter written declaration, or, if Congress is not in session, within twenty-one days after Congress is required to assemble, determines by two-thirds vote of both houses that the President is unable to discharge the powers and duties of his office, the Vice President shall continue to discharge the same as Acting President; otherwise, the President shall resume the powers and duties of his office.

AMENDMENT XXVI.

Lowering voting age to 18 years.

(Proposed by Congress Mar. 23, 1971; ratification completed June 30, 1971.)

1. The right of citizens of the United States, who are 18 years of age or older, to vote shall not be denied or abridged by the United States or any state on account of age.

2. The Congress shall have the power to enforce this article by appropriate legislation.

PROPOSED EQUAL RIGHTS AMENDMENT

(Proposed by Congress Mar. 22, 1972; ratification completed, as of mid-1977, by 35 states, not ratified by 6, defeated in 9; needed total of 38 for adoption before deadline, Mar. 22, 1979.)

1. Equality of rights under the law shall not be denied or abridged by the United States or by any State on account of sex.

2. The Congress shall have the power to enforce, by appropriate legislation, the provisions of this article.

3. This amendment shall take effect two years after the date of ratification.

How the Declaration of Independence Was Adopted

On June 7, 1776, Richard Henry Lee, who had issued the first call for a congress of the colonies, introduced in the Continental Congress at Philadelphia a resolution declaring "that these United Colonies are, and of right ought to be, free and independent states, that they are absolved from allegiance to the British Crown, and that all political connection between them and the state of Great Britain is, and ought to be, totally dissolved."

The resolution, seconded by John Adams on behalf of the Massachusetts delegation, came up again June 10 when a committee of 5, headed by Thomas Jefferson, was appointed to express the purpose of the resolution in a declaration of independence. The others on the committee were John Adams, Benjamin Franklin, Robert R. Livingston, and Roger Sherman.

Drafting the Declaration was assigned to Jefferson, who worked on a portable desk of his own construction in a room at Market and 7th Sts. The committee reported the result June 28, 1776. The members of the Congress suggested a number of changes, which Jefferson called "deplorable." They didn't approve Jefferson's arraignment of the British people and King George III for encouraging and fostering the slave trade, which Jefferson called "an execrable commerce." They made 86 changes, eliminating 480 words and leaving 1,337. In the final form capitalization was erratic. Jefferson had written that men were endowed with "inalienable" rights; in the final copy it came out as "unalienable" and has been thus ever since.

The Lee-Adams resolution of independence was adopted by 12 yeas July 2 — the actual date of the act of independence. The Declaration, which explains the act, was adopted July 4, in the evening.

After the Declaration was adopted, July 4, 1776, it was turned over to John Dunlap, printer, to be printed on broadsides. The original copy was lost and one of his broadsides was attached to a page in the journal of the Congress. It was read aloud July 8 in Philadelphia, Easton, Pa., and Trenton, N. J. On July 9 at 6 p.m. it was read by order of Gen. George Washington to the troops assembled on the Common in New York City (City Hall Park).

The Continental Congress on July 19, 1776, adopted the following resolution:

"Resolved, That the Declaration passed on the 4th, be fairly engrossed on parchment with the title and stile of 'The Unanimous Declaration of the thirteen United States of America' and that the same, when engrossed, be signed by every member of Congress."

Not all delegates who signed the engrossed Declaration were present on July 4. Robert Morris (Pa.), William Williams (Conn.) and Samuel Chase (Md.) signed on Aug. 2, Oliver Wolcott (Conn.), George Wythe (Va.), Richard Henry Lee (Va.) and Elbridge Gerry (Mass.) signed in August and September. Matthew Thronton (N. H.) joined the Congress Nov. 4 and signed later. Thomas McKean (Del.) rejoined Washington's Army before signing and said later that he signed in 1781.

Charles Carroll of Carrollton was appointed a delegate by Maryland on July 4, 1776, presented his credentials July 18, and signed the engrossed Declaration Aug. 2. Born Sept. 19, 1737, he was 95 years old and the last surviving signer when he died Nov. 14, 1832.

Two Pennsylvania delegates who did not support the Declaration on July 4 were replaced.

The 4 New York delegates did not have authority from their state to vote on July 4. On July 9 the New York state convention authorized its delegates to approve the Declaration and the Congress was so notified on July 15, 1776. The 4 signed the Declaration on Aug. 2.

The original engrossed Declaration is preserved in the National Archives Building in Washington.

The Liberty Bell: Its History and Significance

The Liberty Bell, in Independence Hall, Philadelphia, is an object of great reverence to Americans because of its association with the historic events of the War of Independence.

The original Province bell, ordered to commemorate the 50th anniversary of the Commonwealth of Pennsylvania, was cast by Thomas Lister, Whitechapel, London, and reached Philadelphia in Aug. 1752. It bore an inscription from Leviticus XXV, 10: "Proclaim liberty throughout all the land unto all the inhabitants thereof."

The bell was cracked by a stroke of its clapper in Sept. 1752 while it hung on a truss in the State House yard for testing. Pass & Stow, Philadelphia founders, recast the bell, adding 1 1/2 ounces of copper to a pound of the original metal to reduce brittleness. It was found that the bell contained too much copper, injuring its tone, so Pass & Stow recast it again, this time successfully.

In June 1753 the bell was hung in the wooden steeple of the State House, erected on top of the brick tower. In use while the Continental Congress was in session in the State House, it rang out in defiance of British tax and trade restrictions, and proclaimed the Boston Tea Party and the first public reading of the Declaration of Independence.

On Sept. 18, 1777, when the British Army was about to occupy Philadelphia, the bell was moved in a baggage train of the American Army to Allentown, Pa., where it was hidden in the Zion Reformed Church until June 27, 1778. It was moved back to Philadelphia after the British left.

In July 1781 the wooden steeple became insecure and had to be taken down. The bell was lowered into the brick section of the tower. Here it was hanging in July, 1835, when it cracked while tolling for the funeral of John Marshall, chief justice of the United States. Because of its association with the War of Independence it was not recast but remained mute in this location until 1846, the year of the Mexican War, when it was placed on exhibition in the Declaration Chamber of Independence Hall.

In 1876, when many thousands of Americans visited Philadelphia for the Centennial Exposition, it was placed in its old walnut frame in the tower hallway. In 1877 it was hung from the ceiling of the tower by a chain of 13 links. It was returned again to the Declaration Chamber and in 1896 taken back to the tower hall, where it occupied a glass case. In 1915 the case was removed so that the public might touch it. On Jan. 1, 1976, just after midnight to mark the opening of the Bicentennial Year, the bell was moved to a new glass and steel pavilion behind Independence Hall for easier viewing by the larger number of visitors expected during the year.

The measurements of the bell follow: circumference around the lip, 12 ft.; circumference around the crown, 7 ft. 6 in.; lip to the crown, 3 ft.; height over the crown, 2 ft. 3 in.; thickness at lip, 3 in.; thickness at crown, 1 1/4 in.; weight, 2080 lbs.; length of clapper, 3 ft. 2 in.; cost, £60 14s 5d.

Lincoln's Address at Gettysburg, 1863

Fourscore and seven years ago our fathers brought forth on this continent a new nation, conceived in liberty and dedicated to the proposition that all men are created equal.

Now we are engaged in a great civil war, testing whether that nation or any nation so conceived and so dedicated can long endure. We are met on a great battle field of that war. We have come to dedicate a portion of that field, as a final resting-place for those who here gave their lives that that nation might live. It is altogether fitting and proper that we should do this.

But, in a larger sense, we can not dedicate — we can not consecrate — we can not hallow — this ground. The brave men, living and dead, who struggled here, have consecrated it, far above our poor power to add or detract. The world will little note, nor long remember, what we say here, but it can never forget what they did here. It is for us the living, rather, to be dedicated here to the unfinished work which they who fought here have thus far so nobly advanced. It is rather for us to be here dedicated to the great task remaining before us — that from these honored dead we take increased devotion to that cause for which they gave the last full measure of devotion — that we here highly resolve that these dead shall not have died in vain — that this nation, under God, shall have a new birth of freedom — and that government of the people, by the people, for the people, shall not perish from the earth.

History of the Address

President Lincoln delivered his address at the dedication of the military cemetery at Gettysburg, Pa., Nov. 19, 1863. The battle had been fought July 1-3, 1863. He was preceded by Edward Everett, former president of Harvard, secretary of state and senator from Massachusetts, then 69 and one of the nation's great orators. Everett gave a full resume of the battle, Lincoln's speech was so short that the photographer did not get his camera adjusted in time. The report that newspapers ignored Lincoln's address is not entirely accurate; Everett's address swamped their columns, but the greatness of Lincoln's speech was immediately recognized. Everett wrote him: "I should be glad if I could flatter myself that I came as near the central idea of the occasion in 2 hours as you did in 2 minutes."

Five copies of the Gettysburg address in Lincoln's hand are extant. The first and 2d drafts, prepared in Washington and Gettysburg just before delivery, are in the Library of Congress. The 3d draft, written at the request of Everett to be sold at a fair in New York for the benefit of soldiers, was given the Illinois State Historical Library by popular subscription.

The 4th copy was written out by Lincoln for George Bancroft, the historian, and remained in custody of the Bancroft family until 1929, when it was acquired by Mrs. Nicholas H. Noyes, of Indianapolis, Ind. In 1949 Mrs. Noyes presented this copy to the Cornell University Library, Ithaca, N.Y. The 5th copy, usually described as the clearest and best, was also written by Lincoln for George Bancroft, for facsimile reproduction in a volume to be sold for the benefit of soldiers and sailors in Baltimore, where Bancroft lived. It is called the 2d Bancroft copy. It passed to Bancroft's stepchildren, named Bliss, and was sold for $54,000 by the estate of Dr. William J. A. Bliss in New York Apr. 27, 1949, to Oscar B. Cintas, former Cuban ambassador to the United States. He died in May 1957 and willed it to the Lincoln Room of the White House, where it was placed in Mar. 1959. Lincoln's spelling of battle field and can not as separated words in that version is reproduced above.

Sen. John Sherman Cooper (R. Ky.), president of the Lincoln Sesquicentennial Commission, on June 17, 1959, presented a Latin translation of Lincoln's Gettysburg Address to the Apostolic Delegation of the Roman Catholic Church, in Washington, D. C. It was engrossed on vellum and was to be sent to Pope John XXIII for deposit in the Vatican Library. The presentation took place in the presence of government officials and members of the diplomatic corps. The translation was made by the Rt. Rev. Edwin Ryan of White Plains, N. Y. The Latin version was ordered printed in the Congressional Record.

Forms of Address for Persons of Rank and Public Office

In these examples John Smith is used as a representative American name. The salutation Dear Sir is always permissible when addressing a person not known to the writer.

President of the United States

Address: The President, The White House, Washington, D.C. 20500. Also, The President and Mrs. ——.

Salutation: Dear Sir or Mr. President or Dear Mr. President. More intimately: My dear Mr. President. Also: Dear Mr. President and Mrs. ——

The vice president takes the same forms.

Cabinet Officers

Address: Mr. John Smith, Secretary of State, Washington, D.C. or The Hon. John Smith. Similar addresses for other members of the cabinet. Also: Secretary and Mrs. John Smith.

Salutation: Dear Sir, or Dear Mr. Secretary. Also: Dear Mr. and Mrs. Smith.

The Bench

Address: The Hon. John Smith, Chief Justice of the United States. The Hon. John Smith, Associate Justice of the Supreme Court of the United States. The Hon. John Smith, Associate Judge, U. S. District Court.

Salutation: Dear Sir, or Dear Mr. Chief Justice. Dear Mr. Justice. Dear Judge Smith.

Members of Congress

Address: The Hon. John Smith, United States Senate, Washington, D.C. 20510, or Sen. John Smith, etc. Also The Hon. John Smith, House of Representatives, Washington, D.C. 20515, or Rep. John Smith, etc.

Salutation: Dear Mr. Senator or Dear Mr. Smith; for Representative, Dear Mr. Smith.

Officers of Armed Forces

Address: Careful attention should be given to the precise rank, thus: General of the Army John Smith, Fleet Admiral John Smith. The rules for Air Force are same as Army.

Salutation: Dear Sir, or Dear General. All general officers, whatever rank, are entitled to be addressed as generals. Likewise a lieutenant colonel is addressed as colonel and first and second lieutenants are addressed as lieutenant.

Warrant officers and flight officers are addressed as Mister. Chaplains are addressed as Chaplain. A Catholic chaplain may be addressed as Father. Cadets of the United States Military Academy and Air Force Academy are addressed as Cadet. Noncommissioned officers are addressed by their titles. In the U. S. Navy all men from midshipman at Annapolis up to and including lieutenant commander are addressed as Mister.

Ambassador, Governor, Mayor

Address: The Hon. John Smith, followed by his title. He can be addressed either at his embassy, or at the Department of State, Washington, D.C. An ambassador from a foreign nation may be addressed as His Excellency. An American is not to be so addressed.

Salutation: Dear Mr. Ambassador. An ambassador from a foreign nation may be called Your Excellency.

Governors and mayors are often addressed as The Hon. John Smith, Governor of ———, or The Hon. John Smith, Mayor of ———; also Governor John Smith, State House, Albany, N.Y., or Mayor John Smith, City Hall, Erie, Pa.

The Clergy

Address: His Holiness, the Pope, or His Holiness

Pope (name), State of Vatican City, Italy.
Salutation: Your Holiness or Most Holy Father.
Also: His Eminence, John, Cardinal Smith; salutation: Your Eminence. An archbishop or a bishop is addressed The Most Reverend, and the salutation is Your Excellency. A monsignor who is a papal chamberlain is The Very Reverend Monsignor and the salutation is Dear Sir or Very Reverend Monsignor; a monsignor who is a domestic prelate is The Right Reverend Monsignor and salutation is Right Reverend Monsignor. A priest is addressed Reverend John Smith. A brother of an order is addressed Brother —. A sister takes the same form.
A bishop of the Protestant Episcopal Church is The Right Reverend John Smith; salutation is Right Reverend Sir, or Dear Bishop Smith. If a clergyman is a doctor of divinity, he is addressed: The Reverend John Smith, D.D., and the salutation is Reverend Sir, or Dear Dr. Smith. When a clergyman does not have the degree the salutation is Dear Mr. Smith.
A bishop of the Methodist Church is addressed Bishop John Smith with titles following.

Royalty and Nobility

An emperor is to be addressed in a letter as Sir, or Your Imperial Majesty.
A king or queen is addressed as His Majesty (Name), King of (Name), or Her Majesty (Name), Queen of (Name). Salutation: Sir, or Madam, or May it please Your Majesty.
Princes and princesses and other persons of royal blood are addressed as His (or Her) Royal Highness, and saluted with May it please Your Royal Highness.
A duke or marquis is My Lord Duke (or Marquis), a duke is His (or Your) Grace.

The National Anthem — The Star-Spangled Banner

The Star-Spangled Banner was ordered played by the military and naval services by President Woodrow Wilson in 1916. It was designated the National Anthem by Act of Congress, Mar. 3, 1931. It was written by Francis Scott Key, of Georgetown, D. C., during the bombardment of Fort McHenry, Baltimore, Md., Sept. 13-14, 1814. Key was a lawyer, a graduate of St. John's College, Annapolis, and a volunteer in a light artillery company. When a friend, Dr. Beanes, a physician of Upper Marlborough, Md., was taken aboard Admiral Cockburn's British squadron for interfering with ground troops, Key and J. S. Skinner, carrying a note from President Madison, went to the fleet under a flag of truce on a cartel ship to ask Beanes' release. Admiral Cockburn consented, but as the fleet was about to sail up the Patapsco to bombard Fort McHenry he detained them, first on H. M. S. Surprise, and then on a supply ship.
Key witnessed the bombardment from his own vessel. It began at 7 a.m., Sept. 13, 1814, and lasted, with intermissions, for 25 hours. The British fired over 1,500 shells, each weighing as much as 220 lbs. They were unable to approach closely because the Americans had sunk 22 vessels in the channel. Only four Americans were killed and 24 wounded. A British bomb-ship was disabled.

During the bombardment Key wrote a stanza on the back of an envelope. Next day at Indian Queen Inn, Baltimore, he wrote out the poem and gave it to his brother-in-law, Judge J. H. Nicholson. Nicholson suggested the tune, Anacreon in Heaven, and had the poem printed on broadsides, of which two survive. On Sept. 20 it appeared in the Baltimore American. Later Key made 3 copies; one is in the Library of Congress and one in the Pennsylvania Historical Society.

The copy that Key wrote in his hotel Sept. 14, 1814, remained in the Nicholson family for 93 years. In 1907 it was sold to Henry Walters of Baltimore. In 1934 it was bought at auction in New York from the Walters estate by the Walters Art Gallery, Baltimore, for $26,400. The Walters Gallery in 1953 sold the manuscript to the Maryland Historical Society for the same price.
The flag that Key saw during the bombardment is preserved in the Smithsonian Institution, Washington. It is 30 by 42 ft., and has 15 alternate red and white stripes and 15 stars, for the original 13 states plus Kentucky and Vermont. It was made by Mary Young Pickersgill. The Baltimore Flag House, a museum, occupies her premises, which were restored in 1953.

The Star-Spangled Banner

I

Oh, say can you see by the dawn's early light
What so proudly we hailed at the twilight's last gleaming?
Whose broad stripes and bright stars thru the perilous fight.
O'er the ramparts we watched were so gallantly streaming?
And the rocket's red glare, the bombs bursting in air.
Gave proof through the night that our flag was still there.
Oh, say does that star-spangled banner yet wave
O'er the land of the free and the home of the brave?

II

On the shore, dimly seen through the mists of the deep,
Where the foe's haughty host in dread silence reposes,
What is that which the breeze, o'er the towering steep,
As it fitfully blows, half conceals, half discloses?
Now it catches the gleam of the morning's first beam.
In full glory reflected now shines on the stream:
'Tis the star-spangled banner! O long may it wave
O'er the land of the free and the home of the brave!

III

And where is that band who so vauntingly swore
That the havoc of war and the battle's confusion,
A home and a country should leave us no more!
Their blood has washed out their foul footsteps' pollution.
No refuge could save the hireling and slave
From the terror of flight, or the gloom of the grave:
And the star-spangled banner in triumph doth wave
O'er the land of the free and the home of the brave!

IV

Oh! thus be it ever, when freemen shall stand
Between their loved homes and the war's desolation!
Blest with victory and peace, may the heav'n rescued land
Praise the Power that hath made and preserved us a nation.
Then conquer we must, when our cause it is just,
And this be our motto: "In God is our trust."
And the star-spangled banner in triumph shall wave
O'er the land of the free and the home of the brave!

Statue of Liberty National Monument

Since 1886, the Statue of Liberty Enlightening the World ha stood as a symbol of freedom in New York harbor. It also commemorates French-American friendship for it was given by the people of France, designed by Frederic Auguste Bartholdi (1834-1904). A $2.5 million building housing the American Museum of Immigration was opened by Pres. Nixon Sept. 26, 1972, at the base of the statue. It houses a permanent exhibition of photos, posters, and artifacts tracing the history of American immigration. In addition, there is a small immigration library. The Monument is administered by the National Park Service.

Nearby Ellis Island, gateway to America for more than 12 million immigrants between 1892 and 1954, was proclaimed part of the National Monument in 1965 by Pres. Johnson. It can be visited between May and October.

Edouard de Laboulaye, French historian and admirer of American political institutions, suggested that the French present a monument to the United States, the latter to provide pedestal and site. Bartholdi visualized a colossal statue at the entrance of New York harbor, welcoming the peoples of the world with the torch of liberty.

The French approved the idea and formed the Franco-American Union to raise funds, which eventually reached $250,000. Bartholdi began work about 1874 in Paris. He made several models and one, 36 ft. tall, enabled him to compute the statue in sections. Wooden battens were made and sheets of copper 3/32 of an inch thick were hammered into shape by hand. A framework of 4 steel supports was designed by Gustave Eiffel, creator of the Eiffel Tower.

On Washington's birthday, Feb. 22, 1877, Congress approved the use of a site on Bedloe's Island suggested by Bartholdi. This island of 12 acres had been owned in the 17th century by a Walloon named Isaac Bedloe, who came to New Amsterdam in 1639. He died in 1673 and his wife sold the island for £ 80. In later years it was owned by the City of New York and the U.S. Government. It was called Bedloe's until Aug. 3, 1956, when Pres. Eisenhower approved a resolution of Congress changing the name to Liberty Island.

The statue was finished May 21, 1884, and formally presented to U.S. Minister Morton July 4, 1884, by Ferdinand de Lesseps, head of the Franco-American Union, promoter of the Panama Canal, and builder of the Suez Canal.

On Aug. 5, 1884, the Americans laid the cornerstone for the pedestal. This was to be built on the foundations of Fort Wood, which had been erected by the Government in 1811. The American committee had raised $125,000, but when the pedestal was 15 ft. high, this was found to be inadequate. Joseph Pulitzer, owner of the New York World, appealed on Mar. 16, 1885, for general donations. By Aug. 11, 1885, he had raised $100,000. The pedestal was made of concrete with granite facing and steel girders were built into it to connect with framework of the statue.

The statue arrived dismantled, in 214 packing cases, in the steamship Isere, which reached New York from Rouen, France, in June, 1885. The last rivet of the statue was driven Oct. 28, 1886, when Pres. Grover Cleveland dedicated the monument. The total cost of statue and pedestal was estimated at $500,000.

Funds for permanently lighting the statue were raised by the World in 1916 and President Wilson turned on the lights Dec. 2, 1916.

At the celebration of the statue's 50th anniversary, in 1936, Pres. Franklin D. Roosevelt said: "The realization that we are all bound together by hope of a common future rather than by reverence for a common past has helped us to build upon this continent a unity unapproached in any similar area or similar size population in the whole world. For all our millions of people, there is a unity in language and speech, in law and economics, in education and in general purpose which nowhere finds its match.

"It was the hope of those who gave us this statue and the hope of the American people in receiving it that the Goddess of Liberty and the Goddess of Peace were the same."

The statue weighs 450,000 lbs. or 225 tons. The copper sheeting weighs 200,000 lbs. There are 167 steps from the land level to the top of the pedestal, 168 steps inside the statue to the head, and 54 rungs on the ladder leading to the arm that holds the torch. Visitors may enter the head, which holds from 30 to 40 persons, but not the torch. The statue is open daily.

Dimensions of the Statue	Ft.	In.
Height from base to torch (45.3 meters)	151	1
Foundation of pedestal to torch (91.5 meters)	305	1
Heel to top of head	111	1
Length of hand	16	5
Index finger	8	0
Circumference at second joint	3	6
Size of finger nail	13x10 in.	
Head from chin to cranium	17	3
Head, thickness from ear to ear	10	0
Distance across the eye	2	6
Length of nose	4	6
Right arm, length	42	0
Right arm, greatest thickness	12	0
Thickness of waist	35	0
Width of mouth	3	0
Tablet, length	23	7
Tablet, width	13	7
Tablet, thickness	2	0

Emma Lazarus' Famous Poem

A poem by Emma Lazarus is graven on a tablet within the pedestal on which the statue stands:

The New Colossus

Not like the brazen giant of Greek fame,
With conquering limbs astride from land to land;
Here at our sea-washed, sunset gates shall stand
A mighty woman with a torch, whose flame
Is the imprisoned lightning, and her name
Mother of Exiles. From her beacon-hand
Glows world-wide welcome; her mild eyes command
The air-bridged harbor that twin cities frame.
"Keep ancient lands, your storied pomp!" cries she
With silent lips. "Give me your tired, your poor,
Your huddled masses yearning to breathe free,
The wretched refuse of your teeming shore.
Send these, the homeless, tempest-tost to me,
I lift my lamp beside the golden door!"

Code of Etiquette for Display and Use of the U.S. Flag

Although the Stars and Stripes originated in 1777, it was not until 146 years later that there was a serious attempt to establish a uniform code of etiquette for the U.S. flag. The War Department issued Feb. 15, 1923, a circular on the rules of flag usage. These were adopted almost in their entirety June 14, 1923, by a conference of 68 patriotic organizations in Washington. Finally, on June 22, 1942, a joint resolution of Congress codified "existing rules and customs pertaining to the flag for civilians."

When to Display the Flag—The flag should be displayed on all days when the weather permits, especially on legal holidays and other special occasions, on official buildings when in use, in or near polling places on election days, and in or near schools when in session. A citizen may fly the flag at any time he wishes. It is customary to display the flag only from sunrise to sunset on buildings and on stationary flagstaffs in the open. However, it may be displayed at night on special occasions, preferably lighted. In Washington, the flag now flies over the White House both day and night. It flies over the Senate wing of the Capitol when the Senate is in session and over the House wing when that body is in session. It flies day and night over the east and west fronts of the Capitol, without floodlights at night but receiving light from the illuminated Capitol Dome. It flies 24 hours a day at several other places, including the Fort McHenry Nat'l. Monument in Baltimore, where it inspired Francis Scott Key to write The Star Spangled Banner.

How to Fly the Flag—The flag should be hoisted briskly and lowered ceremoniously, and should never be allowed to touch the ground or the floor. When hung over a sidewalk from a rope extending from a building to a pole, the union should be away from the building. When hung over the center of a street it should have the union to the north in an east-west street and to the east in a north-south street. No other flag may be flown above or, if on the same level, to the right of the U.S. flag, except that at the United Nations Headquarters the UN flag may be placed above flags of all member nations and other national flags may be flown with equal prominence or honor with the flag of the U.S. At services by Navy chaplains at sea, the church pennant may be flown above the flag.

When two flags are placed against a wall with crossed staffs, the U.S. flag should be at right—its own right, and its staff should be in front of the staff of the other flag; when a number of flags are grouped and displayed from staffs, it should be at the center and highest point of the group.

Church and Platform Use—In an auditorium, the flag may be displayed flat, above and behind the speaker. If on a staff in a church chancel or on a speaker's platform, it should be in the position of honor at the clergyman's or speaker's right as he faces the congregation or audience. Any other flag in the chancel or on the platform should be displayed at the clergyman's or speaker's left. If elsewhere than in chancel or on platform, the flag should be displayed at the right of the congregation or audience as they face the speaker.

When the flag is displayed horizontally or vertically against a wall, the stars should be at the observer's left.

When to Salute the Flag—All persons present should face the flag, stand at attention and salute on the following occasions: (1) When the flag is passing in a parade or in a review, (2) During the ceremony of hoisting or lowering, (3) When the National Anthem is played and the flag is displayed, and (4) During the Pledge of Allegiance. Those present in uniform should render the military salute. When not in uniform, men should remove the hat with the right hand holding it at the left shoulder, the hand being over the heart. Men without hats should salute in the same manner. Aliens should stand at attention. Women should salute by placing the right hand over the heart.

On Memorial Day, the flag should fly at half-staff until noon, then be raised to the peak.

As provided by Presidential proclamation the flag should fly at half-staff for 30 days from the day of a death of a president or former president; for 10 days from the day of death of a vice president, chief justice or retired chief justice of the U.S., or speaker of the House of Representatives; from day of death until burial of an associate justice of the Supreme Court, cabinet member, former vice president, or Senate president pro tempore, majority or minority Senate leader, or majority or minority House leader; for a U.S. senator, representative, territorial delegate, or the resident commissioner of Puerto Rico, on day of death and the following day within the metropolitan area of the District of Columbia and from day of death until burial within the decedent's state, congressional district, territory or commonwealth; and for the death of the governor of a state, territory, or possession of the U.S., from day of death until burial within that state, territory, or possession.

When used to cover a casket, the flag should be placed so that the union is at the head and over the left shoulder. It should not be lowered into the grave nor touch the ground.

Prohibited Uses of the Flag—The flag should not be dipped to any person or thing. It should never be displayed with the union down save as a distress signal. It should never be carried flat or horizontally, but always aloft and free.

It should not be displayed on a float, motor car or boat except from a staff.

It should never be used as a covering for a ceiling, nor have placed upon it any word, design, or drawing. It should never be used as a receptacle for carrying anything. It should not be used to cover a statue or a monument.

The flag should never be used for advertising purposes, nor be embroidered on such articles as cushions or handkerchiefs, printed or otherwise impressed on boxes or used as a costume or athletic uniform. Advertising signs should not be fastened to its staff or halyard.

The flag should never be used as drapery of any sort, never festooned, drawn back, nor up, in folds, but always allowed to fall free. Bunting of blue, white and red always arranged with the blue above and the white in the middle, should be used for covering a speaker's desk, draping the front of a platform, and for decoration in general.

An Act of Congress approved Feb. 8, 1917, provided certain penalties for the desecration, mutilation or improper use of the flag within the District of Columbia. A 1968 federal law provided penalties of up to a year's imprisonment or a $1,000 fine or both, for publicly burning or otherwise desecrating any flag of the United States. In addition, many states have laws against flag desecration.

How to Dispose of Worn Flags—The flag, when it is in such condition that it is no longer a fitting emblem for display, should be destroyed in a dignified way, preferably by burning in private.

Pledge of Allegiance to the Flag

I pledge allegiance to the flag of the United States of America and to the republic for which it stands, one nation under God, indivisible, with liberty and justice for all.

This, the current official version of the Pledge of Allegiance, has developed from the original pledge, which was first published in the Sept. 8, 1892, issue of the Youth's Companion, a weekly magazine then published in Boston. The original pledge contained the phrase "my flag," which was changed more than 30 years later to "flag of the United States of America." An act of Congress in 1954 added the words "under God."

The authorship of the pledge has been in dispute for many years. The Youth's Companion stated in 1917 that the original draft was written by James B. Upham, an executive of the magazine who died in 1910. A leaflet circulated by the magazine later named Upham as the originator of the draft "afterwards condensed and perfected by him and his associates of the Companion force."

Francis Bellamy, a former member of the Youth's Companion editorial staff, publicly claimed authorship of the pledge in 1923. The United States Flag Assn., acting on the advice of a committee named to study the controversy, upheld in 1939 the claim of Bellamy, who had died 8 years earlier. The Library of Congress issued in 1957 a report attributing the authorship to Bellamy.

The Flag of the U.S.—The Stars and Stripes

The 50-star flag of the United States was raised for the first time officially at 12:01 a.m. on July 4, 1960, at Fort McHenry National Monument in Baltimore, Md. The 50th star had been added for Hawaii; a year earlier the 49th, for Alaska. Before that, no star had been added since 1912, when N. M. and Ariz. were admitted to the Union.

History of the Flag

The true history of the Stars and Stripes has become so cluttered by a volume of myth and tradition that the facts are difficult, and in some cases impossible, to establish. For example, it is not certain who designed the Stars and Stripes, who made the first such flag, or even whether it ever flew in any sea fight or land battle of the American Revolution. Historians disagree on many details of the history of the Stars and Stripes and the flags that preceded it.

One thing all agree on is that the Stars and Stripes originated as the result of a resolution offered by the Marine Committee of the Second Continental Congress at Philadelphia and adopted June 14, 1777. It read:

Resolved: that the flag of the United States be thirteen stripes, alternate red and white; that the union be thirteen stars, white in a blue field, representing a new constellation.

Congress gave no hint as to the designer of the flag, no instructions as to the arrangement of the stars, and no information on its appropriate uses. Historians have been unable to find the original flag law.

The resolution establishing the flag was not even published until Sept. 2, 1777, more than 11 weeks after its passage. Despite repeated requests by the American commander, Gen. George Washington, for the "Standard of the United States" for his army, he did not get the flags until 1783, after the Revolutionary War was over. And there is no certainty that they were the Stars and Stripes.

Early Flags

Although it was never officially adopted by the Continental Congress, many historians consider the first flag of the United States to have been the Grand Union (sometimes called Great Union) flag. This was a modification of the British Meteor flag, which had the red cross of St. George and the white cross of St. Andrew combined in the blue canton. For the Grand Union flag, 6 horizontal stripes were imposed on the red field, dividing it into 13 alternate red and white stripes. On Jan. 1, 1776, when the Continental Army came into formal existence, this flag was unfurled on Prospect Hill, Somerville, Mass. Washington wrote that "we hoisted the Union Flag in compliment to the United Colonies."

One of several flags about which controversy has raged for years is at Easton, Pa. Containing the devices of the national flag in reversed order, this has been in the public library at Easton for over 150 years. Supporters of the movement contend that this flag was actually the first Stars and Stripes, and that it was first displayed on July 8, 1776, on the occasion of the public reading of the Declaration of Independence at the court house in Easton. This flag has 13 red and white stripes in the canton, 13 white stars centered in a blue field.

A flag was hastily improvised from garments by the defenders of Fort Schuyler at Rome, N.Y., Aug. 3-22, 1777, and this has led to the assumption that it was the Stars and Stripes. Historians believe it was the Grand Union Flag.

The Sons of Liberty had a flag of 9 red and white stripes, to signify 9 colonies, when they met in New York in 1765 to oppose the Stamp Tax. By 1775, the flag had grown to 13 red and white stripes, with a rattlesnake on it.

At Concord, Apr. 19, 1775, the minute men from Bedford, Mass., are said to have carried a flag having a silver arm with sword on a red field.

At Cambridge, Mass., the Sons of Liberty used a plain red flag with a green pine tree on it.

In June 1775, Washington went from Philadelphia to Boston to take command of the army, escorted to New York by the Philadelphia Light Horse Troop. It carried a yellow flag which had an elaborate coat of arms — the shield charged with 13 knots, the motto "For These We Strive" — and a canton of 13 blue and silver stripes.

In Feb., 1776, Col. Christopher Gadsden, member of the Continental Congress, gave the South Carolina Provincial Congress a flag "such as is to be used by the commander-in-chief of the American Navy." It had a yellow field, with a rattlesnake about to strike and the words "Don't Tread on Me." Benjamin Franklin's paper, the Pennsylvania Gazette, had suggested sending a cargo of rattlesnakes to London parks to retaliate for British injustice.

At the battle of Bennington, Aug. 16, 1777, patriots used a flag of 7 white and 6 red stripes with a blue canton extending down 9 stripes and showing an arch of 11 white stars over the figure 76 and a star in each of the upper corners. The stars are seven-pointed. This flag is preserved in the Historical Museum at Bennington, Vt.

At the Battle of Cowpens, Jan. 17, 1781, the 3d Maryland Regt. is said to have carried a flag of 13 red and white stripes, with a blue canton containing 12 stars in a circle around one star.

Legends about the Flag

Who Designed the Flag? No one knows for a certainty. Francis Hopkinson, a signer of the Declaration of Independence and designer of seals for the State Department, the Treasury Board, and of a naval flag, declared he also had designed the flag and in 1781 asked Congress to reimburse him for his services. Congress did not do so. Dumas Malone of Columbia Univ. wrote: "This talented man . . . designed the American flag."

Who Called the Flag Old Glory? — The flag is said to have been named Old Glory by William Driver, a sea captain of Salem, Mass. One legend has it that when he raised the flag on his brig, the Charles Doggett, in 1824, he said: "I name thee Old Glory." But his daughter, who presented the flag to the Smithsonian Institution, said he named it at his 21st birthday celebration Mar. 17, 1824, when his mother presented the homemade flag to him.

Washington Coat-of-Arms Legend — The idea that the flag was suggested by Washington's coat of arms was publicized by Martin F. Tupper, an English writer, in a play in the 1870s. It rests on a coincidence and has no validity.

Washington's Invocation Legend — Circulation has been given to this speech attributed to General Washington: "We take the stars from heaven, the red from our mother country, separating it by white stripes, thus showing that we have separated from her, and the white stripes shall go down to posterity representing liberty." There is no proof that Washington ever said this.

The Betsy Ross Legend — The widely publicized legend that Mrs. Betsy Ross made the first Stars and Stripes in June 1776, at the request of a committee composed of George Washington, Robert Morris, and George Ross, an uncle, was first made public in 1870, by a grandson of Mrs. Ross. Historians have been unable to find a historical record of such a meeting or committee. Dr. Milo Milton Quaife wrote: "No record has ever been found of the creation by Mrs. Ross of the first Stars and Stripes." The New Century Cyclopedia of Names (1954) says: "There is documentary evidence that she was paid in May, 1777, for 'making ships' colours, etc.' but no direct documentary evidence has been found to link her with the flag adopted by the Continental Congress on June 14, 1777, as the national emblem, and most historians now doubt if she made it."

Adding New Stars

The flag of 1777 was used until 1795. Then, on the admission of Vermont and Kentucky to the Union, Congress passed and Pres. Washington signed an act that after May 1, 1795, the flag should have 15 stripes, alternate red and white, and 15 white stars on a blue field in the union.

When new states were admitted it became evident that the flag would become burdened with stripes. Congress thereupon ordered that after July 4, 1818, the flag should have 13 stripes, symbolizing the 13 original states; that the union have 20 stars, and that whenever a new state was admitted a new star should be added on the July 4 following admission. No law designates the permanent arrangement of the stars. However, since 1912 when a new state has been admitted, the new design has been announced by executive order. No star is specifically identified with any state.

Mail this card to:

THE WORLD ALMANAC

P.O. Box 91428

Cleveland, Ohio 44101

(Please allow three weeks for delivery)

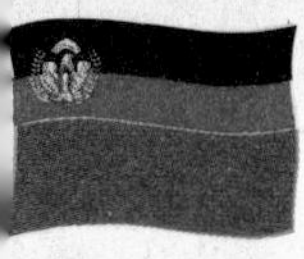
AFGHANISTAN

ALBANIA

ALGERIA

ANDORRA

ANGOLA

ARGENTINA

AUSTRALIA

AUSTRIA

BAHAMAS

BAHRAIN

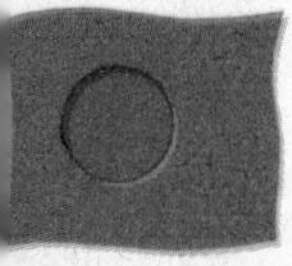
BANGLADESH

BARBADOS

BELGIUM

BENIN

BHUTAN

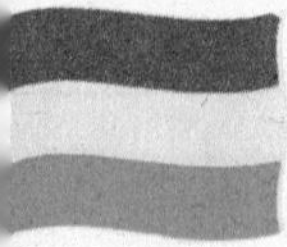
BOLIVIA

BOTSWANA

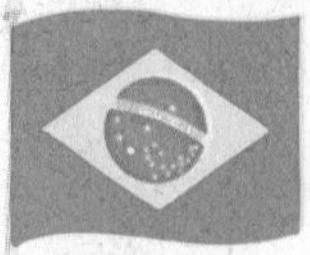
BRAZIL

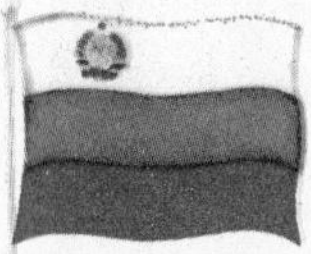
BULGARIA

BURMA

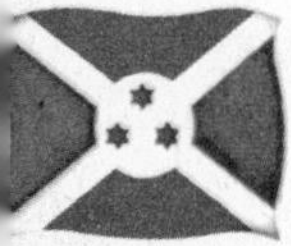
BURUNDI

CAMBODIA

CAMEROON

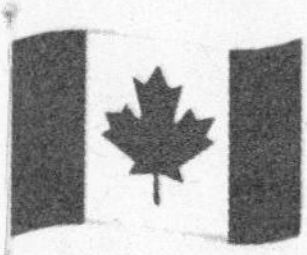
CANADA

CAPE VERDE

ENTRAL AFRICAN EMPIRE

CHAD

CHILE

CHINA (MAINLAND)

CHINA (TAIWAN)

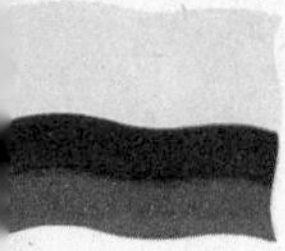
COLOMBIA

COMORO ISLANDS

CONGO

COSTA RICA

CUBA

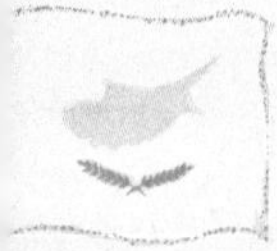
CYPRUS

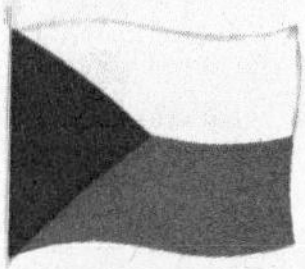
CZECHOSLOVAKIA

DENMARK

DJIBOUTI

DOMINICAN REPUBLIC

Flags shown are *national* flags in common use and vary slightly from official *state* flags, most particularly by omitting coats of arms in some cases.

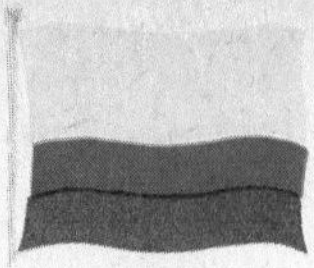
ECUADOR

EGYPT

EL SALVADOR

EQUATORIAL GUINEA

ETHIOPIA

FIJI

FINLAND

FRANCE

GABON

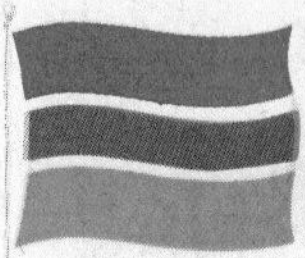
GAMBIA

GERMAN DEM. REP.

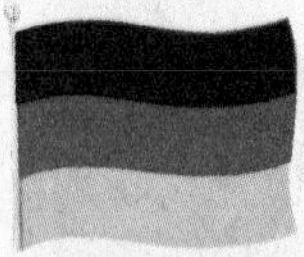
GERMANY, FED. REP. OF

GHANA

GREECE

GRENADA

GUATEMALA

GUINEA

GUINEA-BISSAU

GUYANA

HAITI

HONDURAS

HUNGARY

ICELAND

INDIA

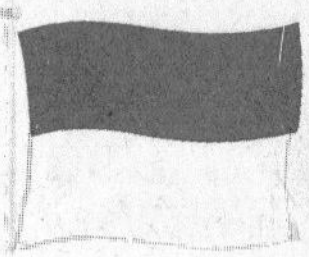
INDONESIA

IRAN

IRAQ

IRELAND

ISRAEL

ITALY

IVORY COAST

JAMAICA

JAPAN

JORDAN

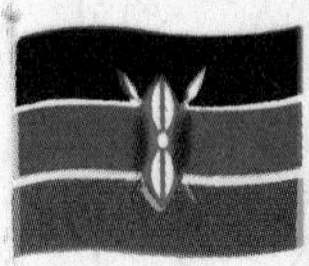
KENYA

KOREA, NORTH

KOREA, SOUTH

KUWAIT

LAOS

LEBANON

LESOTHO

LIBERIA

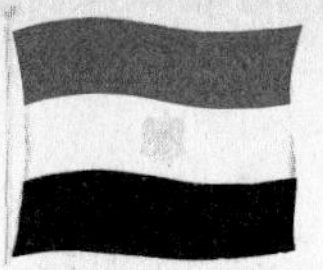
LIBYA

LIECHTENSTEIN

LUXEMBOURG

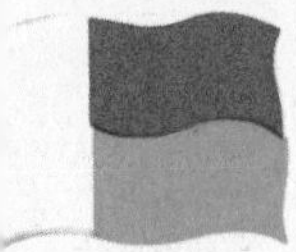
MADAGASCAR

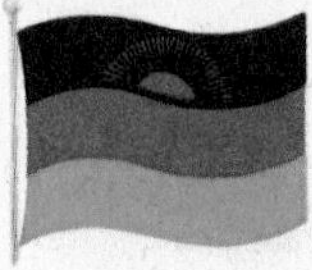
MALAWI

MALAYSIA

MALDIVES

MALI

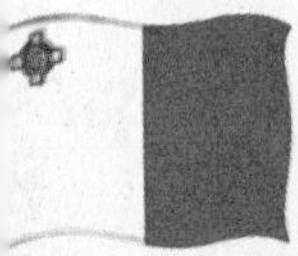
MALTA

MAURITANIA

MAURITIUS

MEXICO

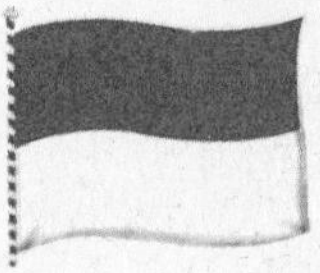
MONACO

MONGOLIA

MOROCCO

MOZAMBIQUE

NAURU

NEPAL

NETHERLANDS

NEW ZEALAND

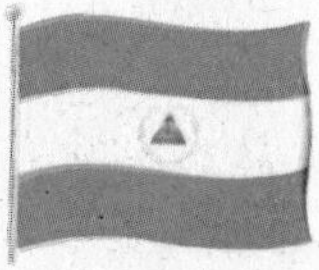
NICARAGUA

NIGER

NIGERIA

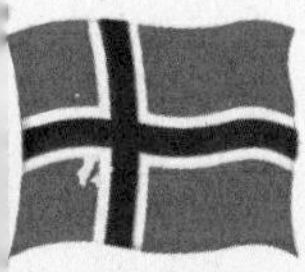
NORWAY

OMAN

PAKISTAN

PANAMA

PAPUA NEW GUINEA

PARAGUAY

PERU

PHILIPPINES

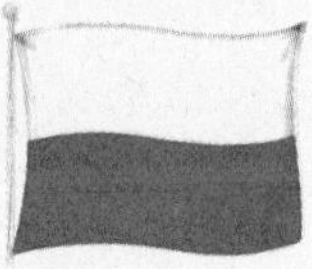
POLAND

PORTUGAL

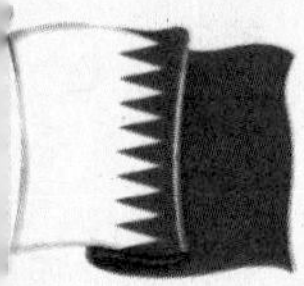
QATAR

RHODESIA

ROMANIA

RWANDA

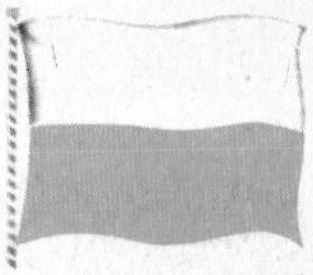
SAN MARINO

SAO TOME & PRINCIPE

SAUDI ARABIA

SENEGAL

SEYCHELLES

SIERRA LEONE

SINGAPORE

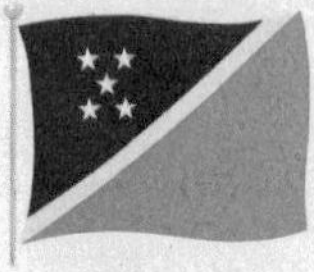
SOLOMON ISLANDS

SOMALIA

SOUTH AFRICA

SPAIN

SRI LANKA

SUDAN

SURINAM

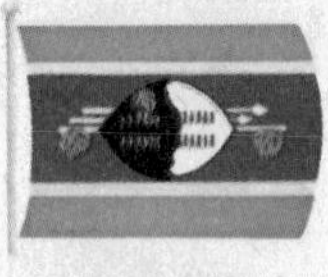
SWAZILAND

SWEDEN

SWITZERLAND

SYRIA

TANZANIA

THAILAND

TOGO

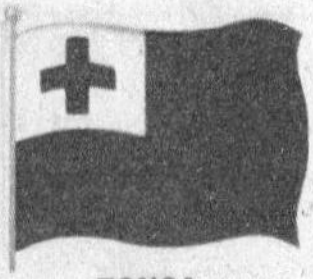
TONGA

TRINIDAD & TOBAGO

TUNISIA

TURKEY

UGANDA

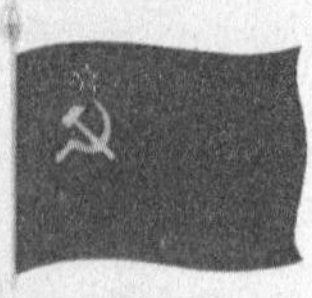
U.S.S.R.

UNITED ARAB EMIRATES

UNITED KINGDOM

UNITED STATES

UPPER VOLTA

URUGUAY

VATICAN CITY

VENEZUELA

VIETNAM

WESTERN SAMOA

YEMEN

YEMEN, P.D.R. OF

YUGOSLAVIA

ZAIRE

ZAMBIA

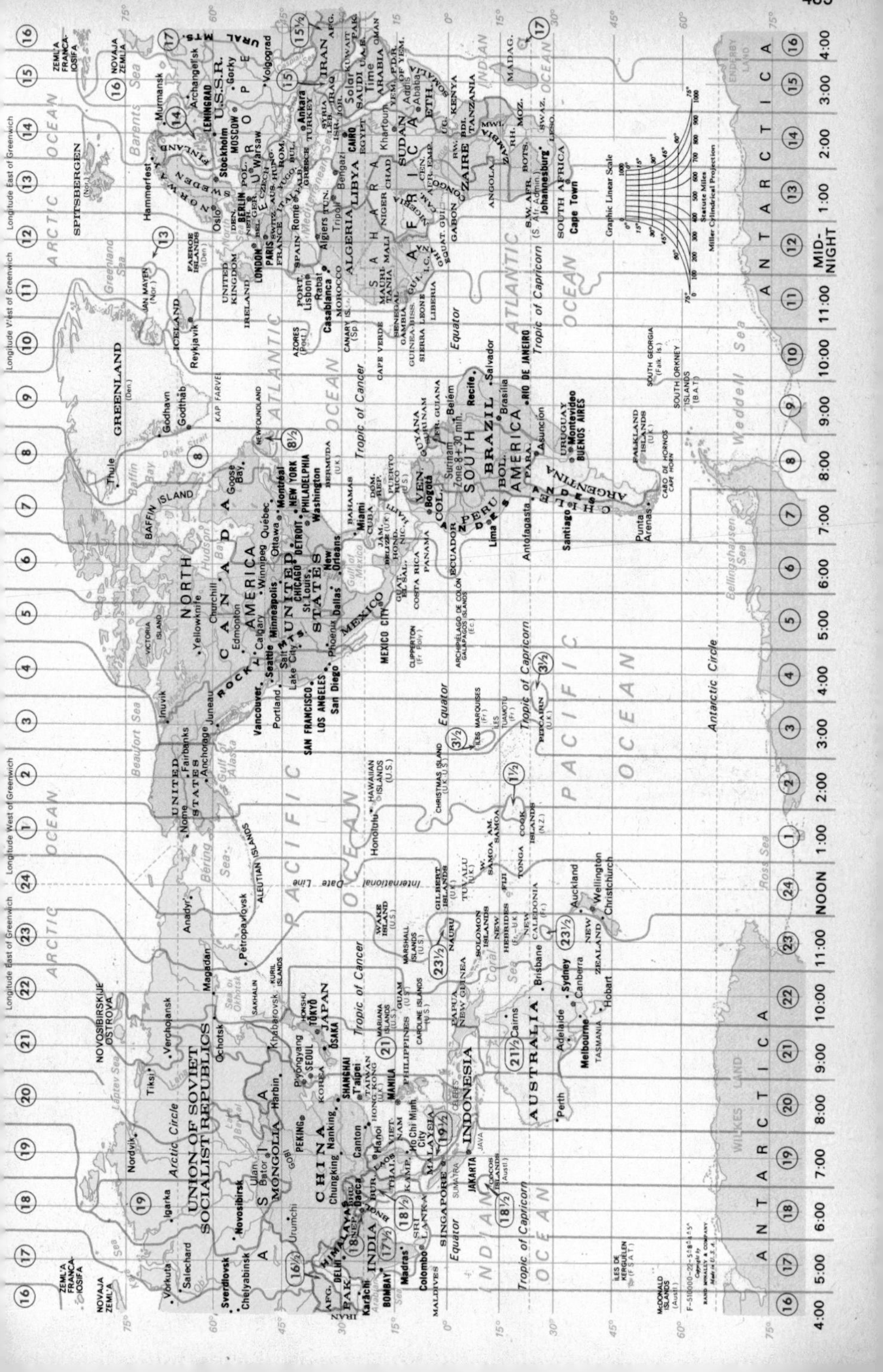
ARCTIC OCEAN
NORTH AMERICA
CANADA
UNITED STATES
SOUTH AMERICA
BRAZIL
AFRICA
EUROPE
U.S.S.R.
UNION OF SOVIET SOCIALIST REPUBLICS
ASIA
CHINA
INDIA
AUSTRALIA
INDONESIA
ANTARCTICA
PACIFIC OCEAN
ATLANTIC OCEAN
INDIAN OCEAN
Tropic of Cancer
Tropic of Capricorn
Equator
Arctic Circle
Antarctic Circle
International Date Line
Longitude East of Greenwich
Longitude West of Greenwich
4:00
5:00
6:00
7:00
8:00
9:00
10:00
11:00
NOON
1:00
2:00
3:00
4:00
5:00
6:00
7:00
8:00
9:00
10:00
11:00
MID-NIGHT
1:00
2:00
3:00
4:00
Graphic Linear Scale
Statute Miles
Miller Cylindrical Projection

North Pole
ARCTIC OCEAN
ASIA
U.S.S.R.
Anadyr'
GREENLAND
(Den.)
ICELAND
Reykjavik
JAN MAYEN
(Nor.)
FAEROE ISLANDS
(Den.)
ELLESMERE ISLAND
Thule
Baffin Bay
BAFFIN ISLAND
Godthåb
Angmagssalik
Labrador Sea
Hudson Strait
Hudson Bay
Beaufort Sea
VICTORIA ISLAND
BANKS ISLAND
MELVILLE ISLAND
UNITED STATES
Nome
Barrow
Fairbanks
Anchorage
Bethel
Valdez
Seward
Gulf of Alaska
KODIAK ISLAND
BERING SEA
Bering Strait
BROOKS RA.
ALASKA PIPELINE
MACKENZIE MTS.
Inuvik
Arctic Circle
Cambridge Bay
Port Radium
Yellowknife
Great Slave Lake
Great Bear Lake
Whitehorse
Skagway
Juneau
Ketchikan
Prince Rupert
QUEEN CHARLOTTE ISLANDS
Pine Point
Uranium City
Repulse Bay
Frobisher Bay
Churchill
CANADA
ROCKY MOUNTAINS
Dawson Creek
Prince George
Edmonton
Calgary
Saskatoon
Regina
Winnipeg
Flin Flon
York Factory
BELCHER ISLANDS
Schefferville
Goose Bay
Fort George
Moosonee
Gander
St. John's
NEWFOUNDLAND
Halifax
Québec
MONTRÉAL
Ottawa
Timmins
Sudbury
VANCOUVER ISLAND
Victoria
Vancouver
Seattle
Portland
Spokane
Great Falls
Bismarck
Fargo
Duluth
Minneapolis
Saint Paul
Boise
Pierre
Milwaukee
Madison
DETROIT
TORONTO
Buffalo
Albany
BOSTON
Providence
NEW YORK
PHILADELPHIA
WASHINGTON
CLEVELAND
Pittsburgh
Baltimore
CHICAGO
Cheyenne
Omaha
Salt Lake City
Sacramento
Reno
SAN FRANCISCO
GREAT BASIN
Denver
Kansas City
Indianapolis
Cincinnati
Norfolk
ST. LOUIS
Louisville
Richmond
Raleigh
Wichita
Nashville
Charlotte
Las Vegas
LOS ANGELES
San Diego
Albuquerque
Santa Fe
Oklahoma City
Little Rock
Memphis
Columbia
Charleston
Atlanta
Birmingham
Savannah
Montgomery
Jacksonville
Phoenix
El Paso
Fort Worth
Dallas
Mobile
Houston
New Orleans
Tampa
Miami
BAHAMAS
Nassau
Tropic of Cancer
Hermosillo
Chihuahua
San Antonio
Laredo
Brownsville
GULF OF MEXICO
Torreón
Monterrey
La Paz
Mazatlán
Tampico
Mérida
Guadalajara
MEXICO CITY
Veracruz
Villahermosa
Acapulco
Oaxaca
Havana
CUBA
WEST INDIES
HAITI
DOM. REP.
San Juan
PUERTO RICO
(U.S.)
Port-au-Prince
JAMAICA
Kingston
BERMUDA
(U.K.)
BELIZE
Belmopan
HONDURAS
Tegucigalpa
Guatemala
San Salvador
EL SALVADOR
NICARAGUA
Managua
Bluefields
Barranquilla
Maracaibo
VENEZUELA
COSTA RICA
San José
Panamá
CANAL ZONE
(U.S.)
PANAMA
Medellín
BOGOTÁ
COLOMBIA
SOUTH AMERICA
CARIBBEAN SEA
ATLANTIC OCEAN
PACIFIC OCEAN
BERING SEA
ALEUTIAN ISLANDS
Kavača
Unalaska
Statute Miles 0 200 400 600 800
Kilometers 0 200 400 600 800 1000 1200
Longitude West of Greenwich
F-520000-21-3-5-3-3
Copyright by RAND McNALLY & COMPANY
Made in U.S.A.

INDEX

INDEX

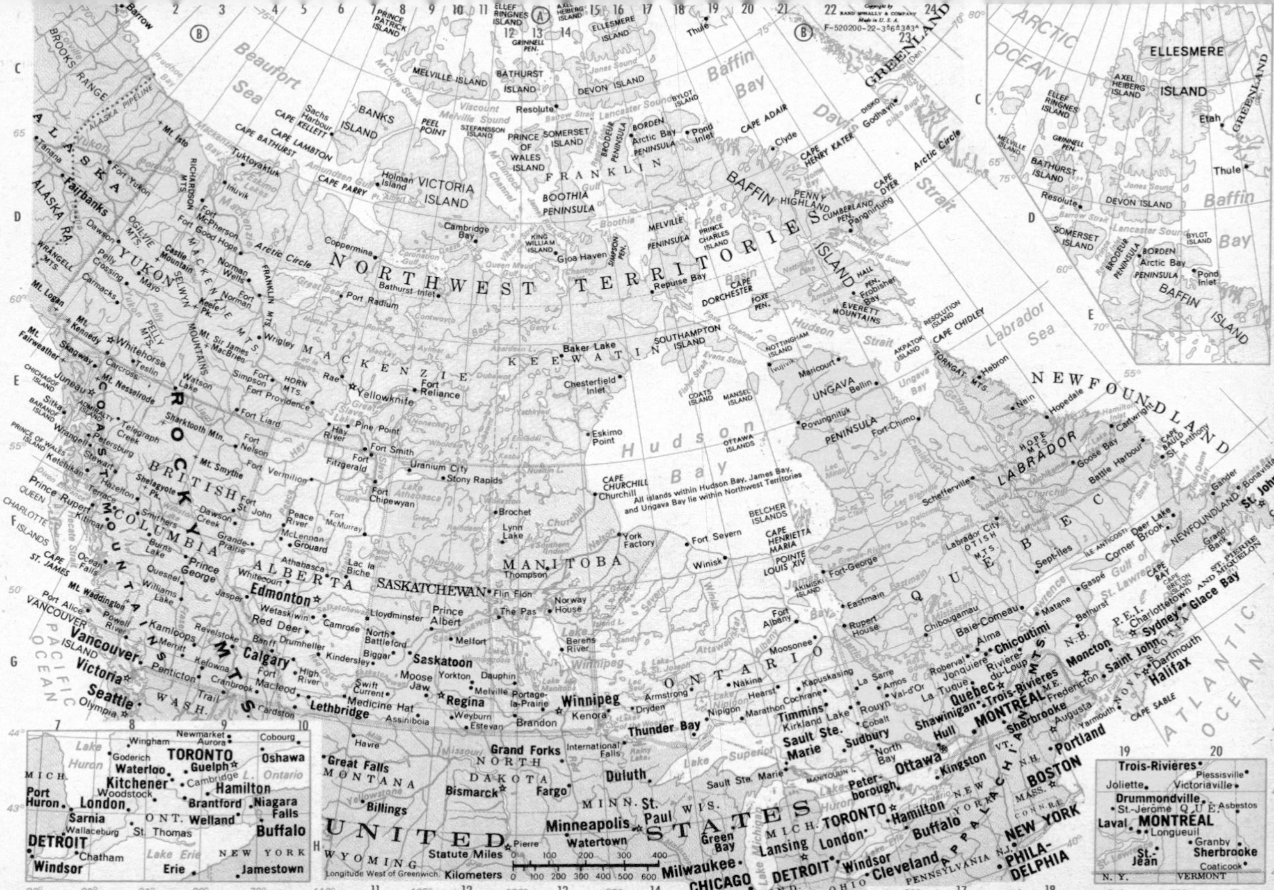

NORTHWEST TERRITORIES
FRANKLIN
KEEWATIN
MACKENZIE
YUKON
ALASKA
BRITISH COLUMBIA
ALBERTA
SASKATCHEWAN
MANITOBA
ONTARIO
QUEBEC
LABRADOR
NEWFOUNDLAND
UNITED STATES
ROCKY MTS.
COAST MOUNTAINS
Hudson Bay
Beaufort Sea
Baffin Bay
Labrador Sea
Davis Strait
Hudson Strait
PACIFIC OCEAN
ATLANTIC OCEAN
ARCTIC OCEAN
GREENLAND (Den.)
VICTORIA ISLAND
BANKS ISLAND
BAFFIN ISLAND
ELLESMERE ISLAND
DEVON ISLAND
SOUTHAMPTON ISLAND
UNGAVA PENINSULA
BOOTHIA PENINSULA
Arctic Circle
All islands within Hudson Bay, James Bay, and Ungava Bay lie within Northwest Territories
Statute Miles
Kilometers
Longitude West of Greenwich
F-520200-22-3-6-3-3

CANADA
BRITISH COLUMBIA
ALBERTA
SASKATCHEWAN
MANITOBA
ONTARIO
QUEBEC
NEW BRUNSWICK
ROCKY MOUNTAINS
APPALACHIAN MOUNTAINS
PACIFIC OCEAN
ATLANTIC OCEAN
GULF OF MEXICO
MEXICO
CUBA
BAHAMAS
WASHINGTON
OREGON
IDAHO
MONTANA
WYOMING
NEVADA
UTAH
COLORADO
ARIZONA
NEW MEXICO
CALIFORNIA
NORTH DAKOTA
SOUTH DAKOTA
NEBRASKA
KANSAS
OKLAHOMA
TEXAS
MINNESOTA
IOWA
MISSOURI
ARKANSAS
LOUISIANA
WISCONSIN
ILLINOIS
MICHIGAN
INDIANA
OHIO
KENTUCKY
TENNESSEE
MISSISSIPPI
ALABAMA
GEORGIA
FLORIDA
SOUTH CAROLINA
NORTH CAROLINA
VIRGINIA
WEST VIRGINIA
PENNSYLVANIA
NEW YORK
MAINE
HAWAIIAN ISLANDS
ALASKA
ALEUTIAN ISLANDS
U.S.S.R.
Longitude West of Greenwich
Statute Miles 0 100 200 300 400
Kilometers 0 100 200 300 400 500
Tropic of Cancer
F-520500-22-5-8-7-2-5-4-4
Copyright by RAND McNALLY & COMPANY
Made in U.S.A.

INDEX

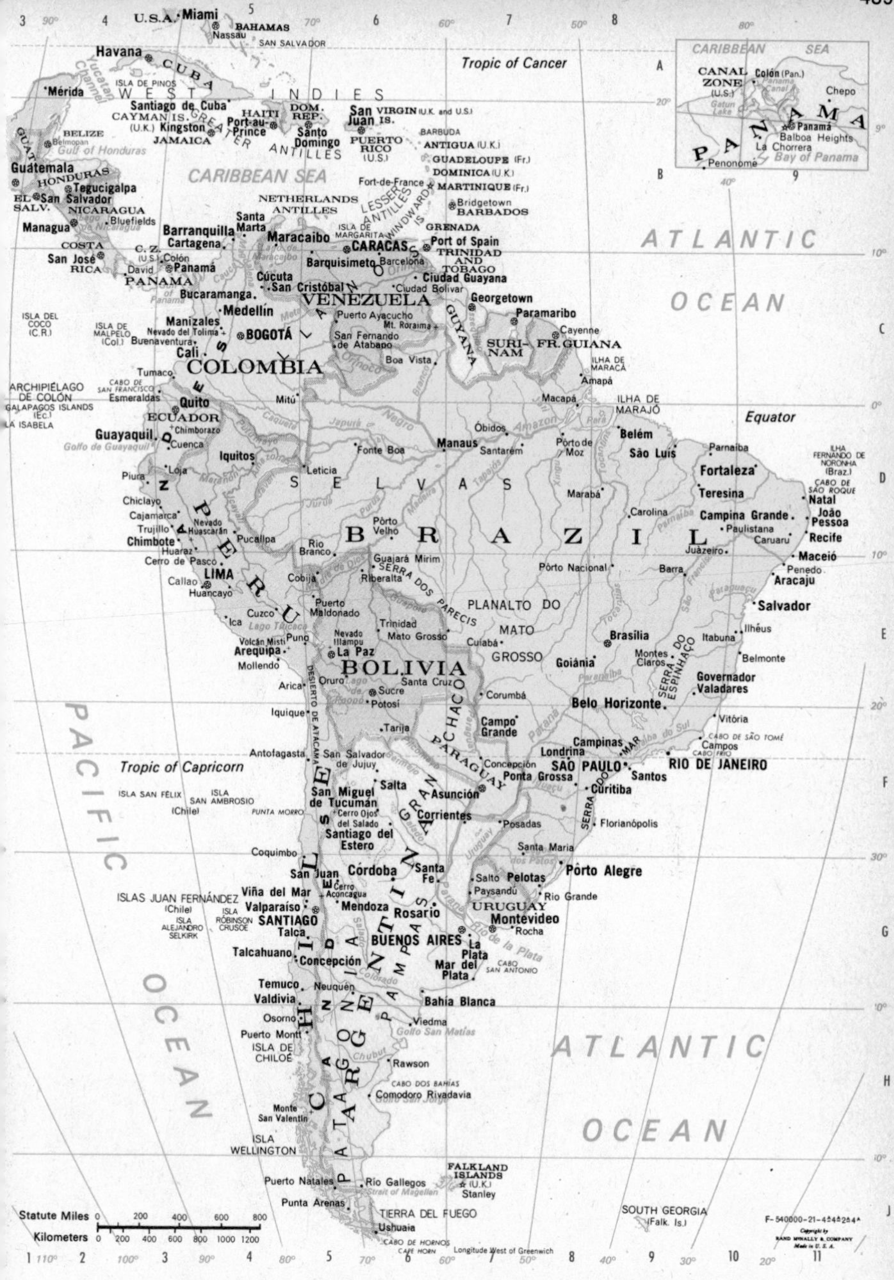

INDEX

ISLANDS

INDEX

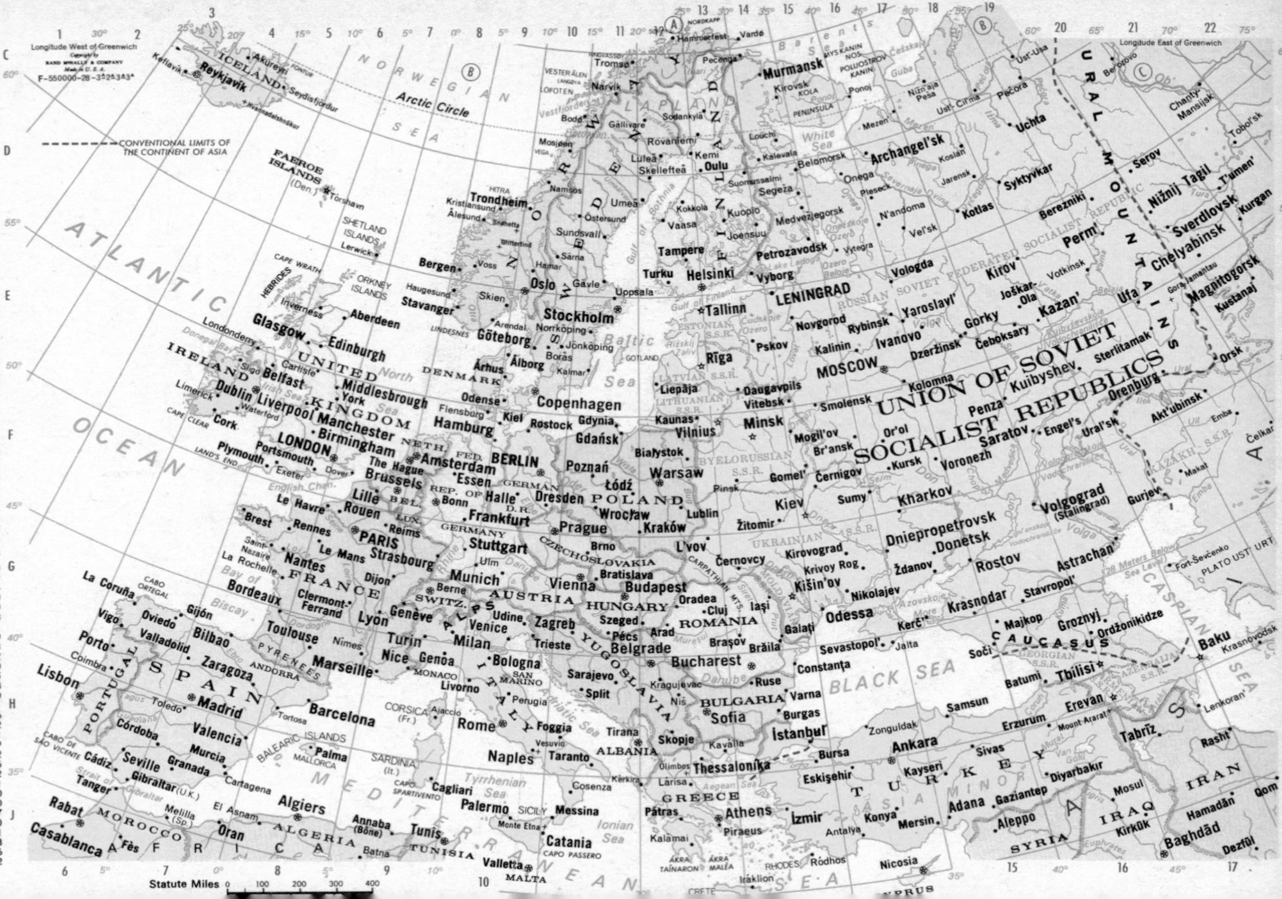
Longitude West of Greenwich
Copyright by RAND McNALLY & COMPANY
Made in U.S.A.
F-550000-28-3-25383
CONVENTIONAL LIMITS OF THE CONTINENT OF ASIA
Longitude East of Greenwich
Statute Miles 0 100 200 300 400

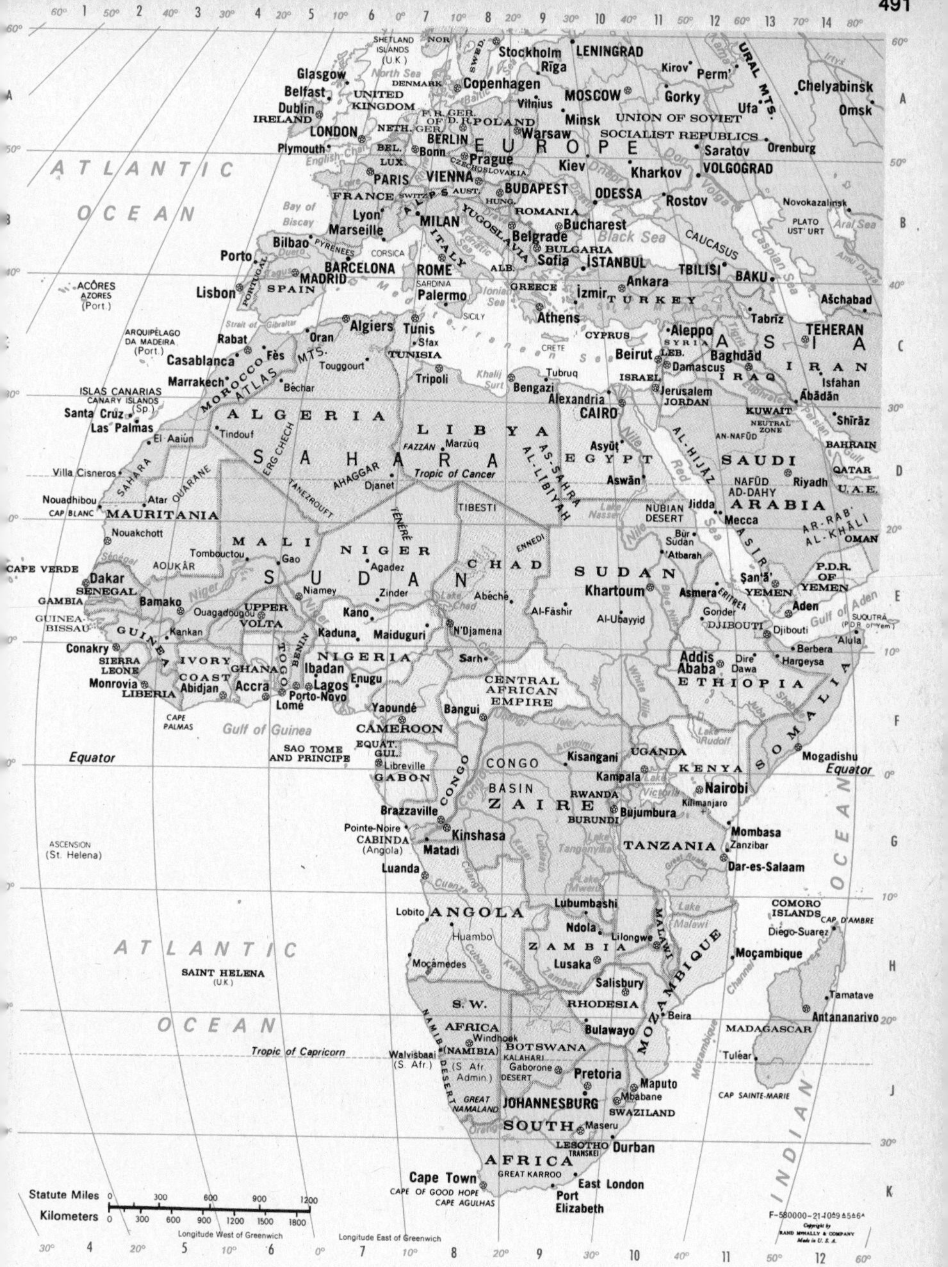

INDEX

COUNTRIES

INDEX

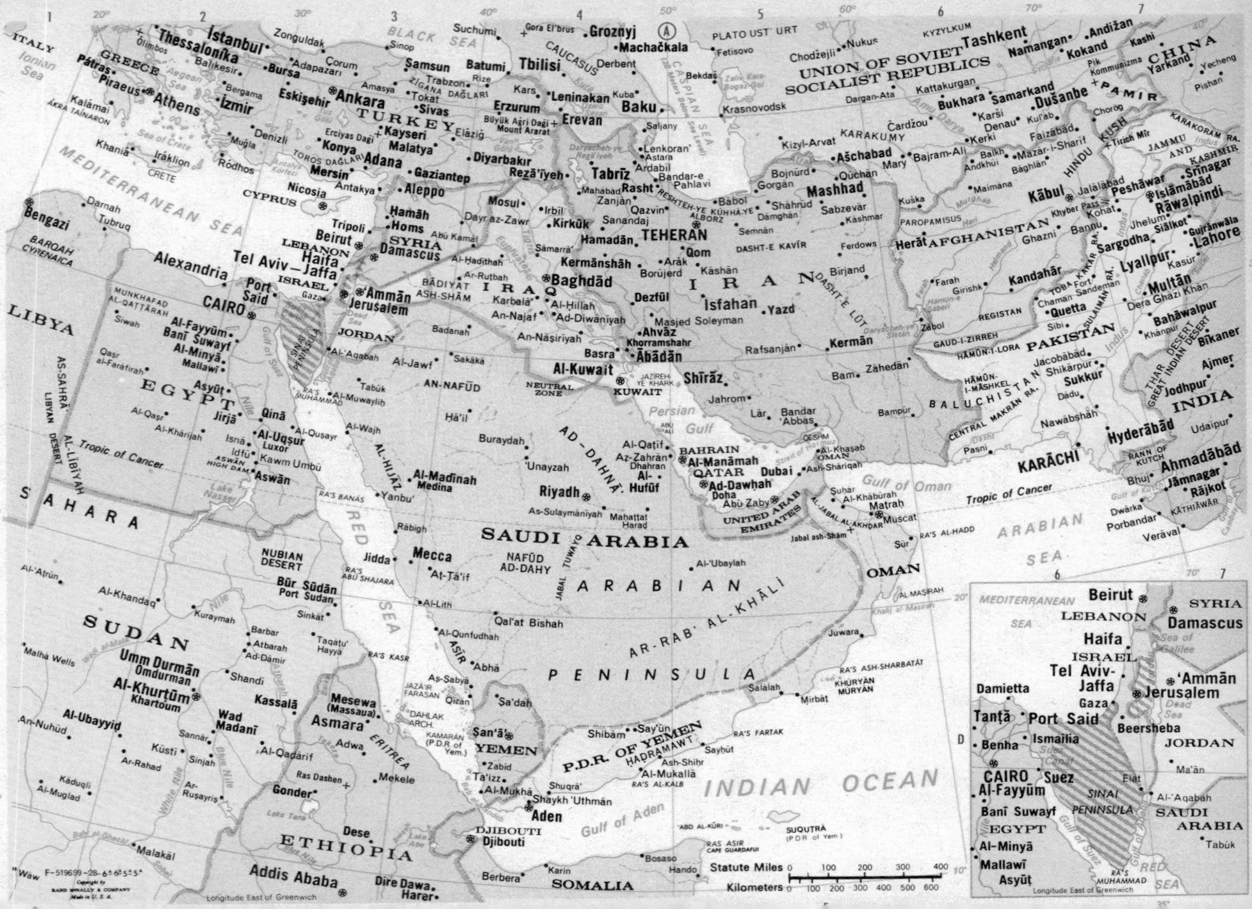
UNION OF SOVIET SOCIALIST REPUBLICS
TURKEY
SYRIA
IRAQ
IRAN
AFGHANISTAN
PAKISTAN
INDIA
CHINA
SAUDI ARABIA
EGYPT
LIBYA
SUDAN
ETHIOPIA
SOMALIA
JORDAN
ISRAEL
LEBANON
CYPRUS
KUWAIT
QATAR
BAHRAIN
UNITED ARAB EMIRATES
OMAN
YEMEN
P.D.R. OF YEMEN
DJIBOUTI
GREECE
ITALY
MEDITERRANEAN SEA
BLACK SEA
CASPIAN SEA
RED SEA
ARABIAN SEA
INDIAN OCEAN
Persian Gulf
Gulf of Oman
Gulf of Aden
ARABIAN PENINSULA
AR-RAB' AL-KHĀLĪ
SAHARA
Tropic of Cancer
Statute Miles
Kilometers
Longitude East of Greenwich
F-519699-28-6-6-5-5
Copyright by RAND McNALLY & COMPANY
Made in U.S.A.

INDEX

UNION OF SOVIET
SOCIALIST REPUBLICS
EUROPE
ASIA
AFRICA
CHINA
MONGOLIA
INDIA
ARCTIC OCEAN
PACIFIC OCEAN
INDIAN OCEAN
ATLANTIC OCEAN
ARABIAN SEA
Bay of Bengal
Tropic of Cancer
Equator
CONVENTIONAL LIMITS OF THE CONTINENT OF ASIA
Statute Miles
Kilometers
Longitude East of Greenwich
Longitude West of Greenwich
F-560000-22-4-4-4-5-5-5
Copyright by RAND McNALLY & COMPANY
Made in U.S.A.

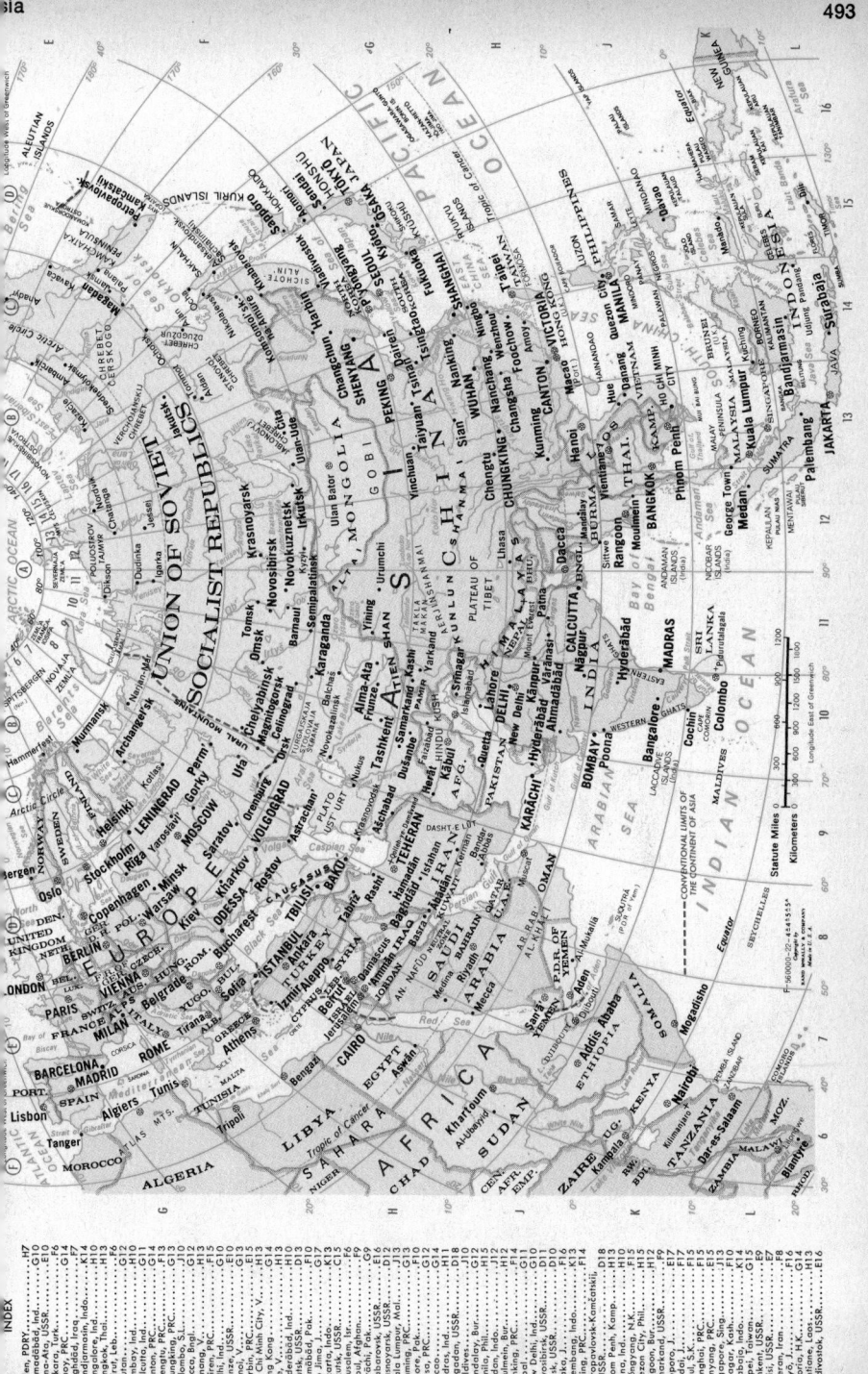

INDEX

MISCELLANEOUS

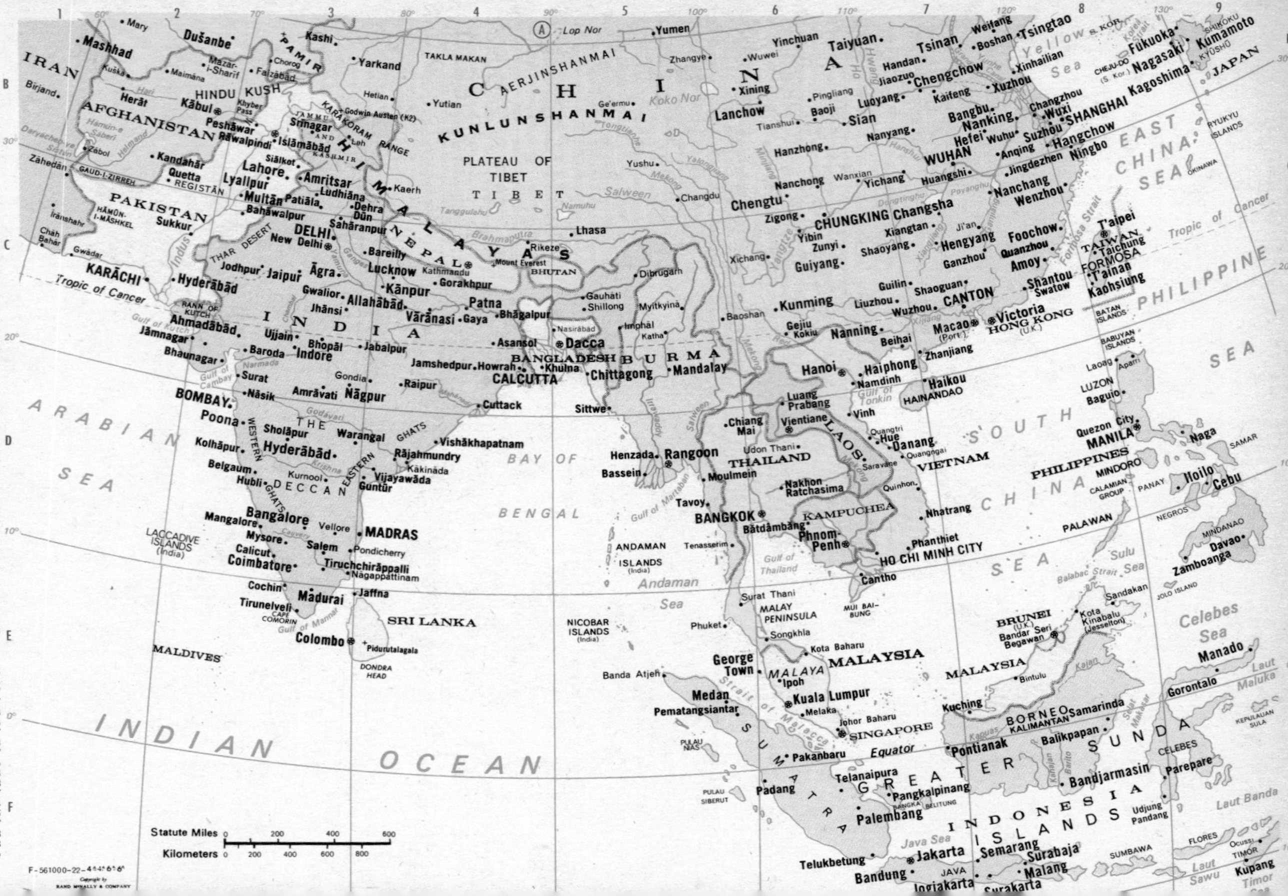

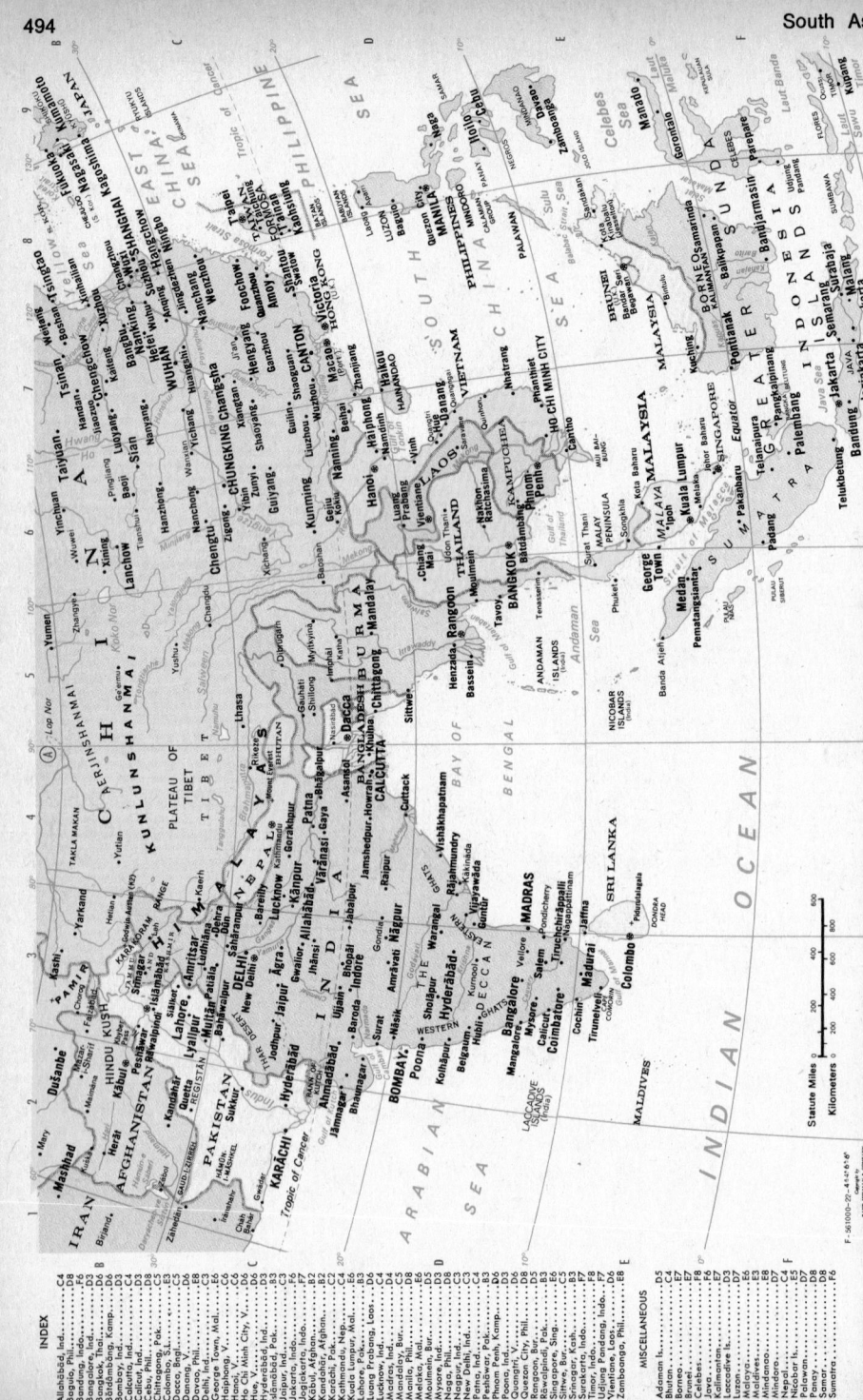

INDEX

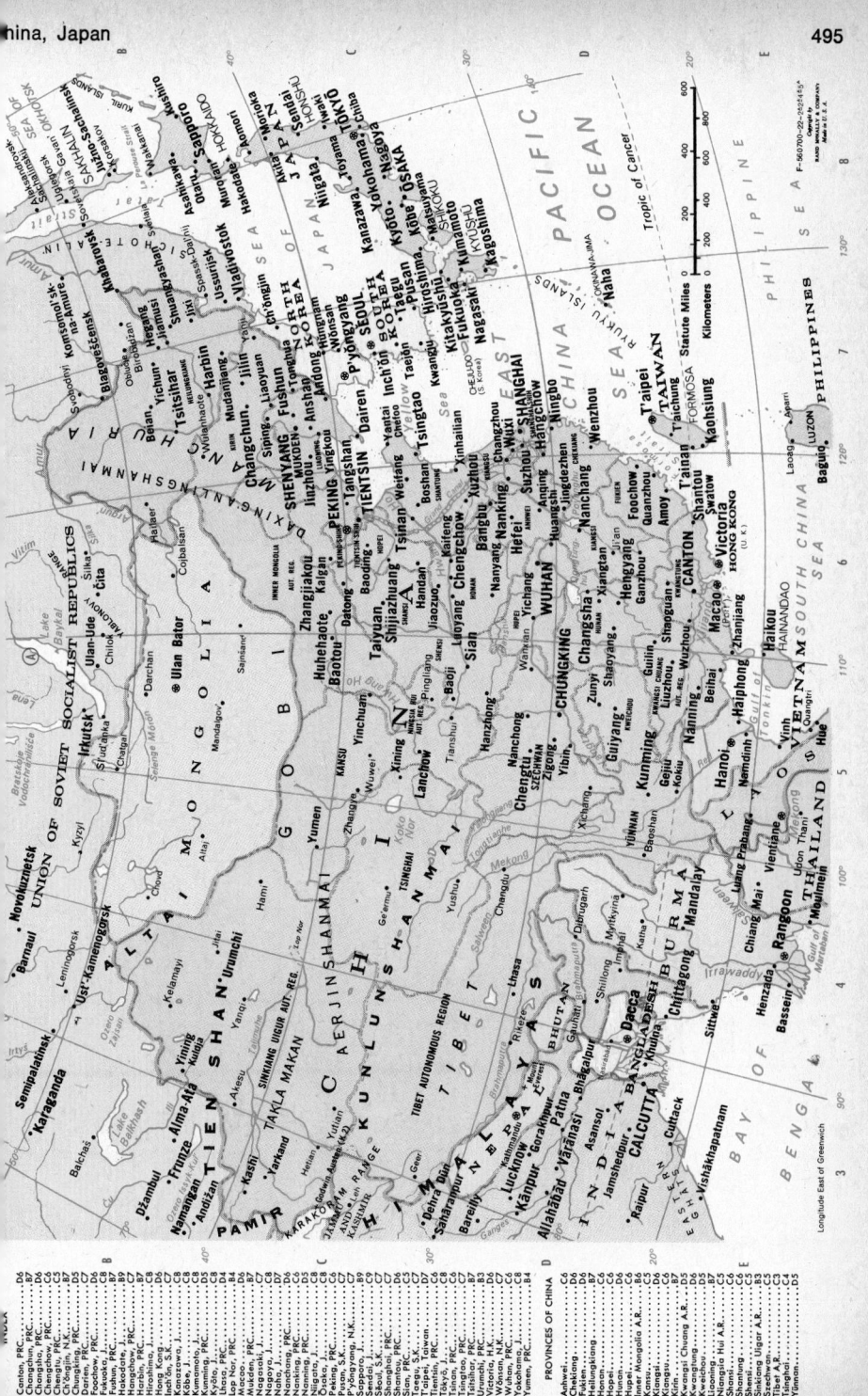

PROVINCES OF CHINA

INDEX

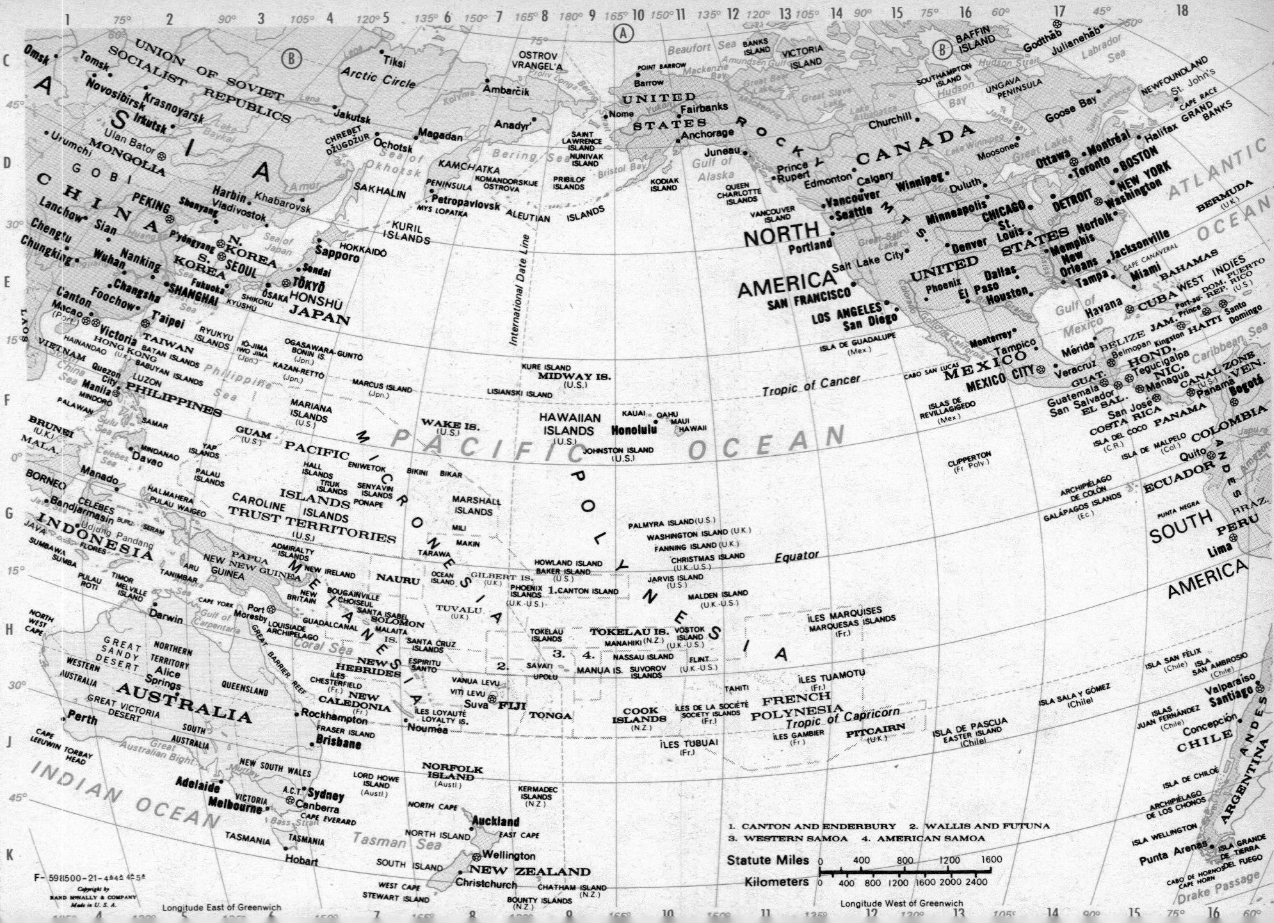

ASIA
UNION OF SOVIET SOCIALIST REPUBLICS
CHINA
MONGOLIA
JAPAN
PHILIPPINES
INDONESIA
AUSTRALIA
NEW ZEALAND
NORTH AMERICA
CANADA
UNITED STATES
MEXICO
SOUTH AMERICA
PACIFIC OCEAN
INDIAN OCEAN
ATLANTIC OCEAN
MICRONESIA
MELANESIA
POLYNESIA
International Date Line
Tropic of Cancer
Equator
Tropic of Capricorn
Arctic Circle
1. CANTON AND ENDERBURY 2. WALLIS AND FUTUNA
3. WESTERN SAMOA 4. AMERICAN SAMOA
Statute Miles 0 400 800 1200 1600
Kilometers 0 400 800 1200 1600 2000 2400
Longitude East of Greenwich
Longitude West of Greenwich
F-598500-21-4444 4454
Copyright by RAND McNALLY & COMPANY Made in U.S.A.

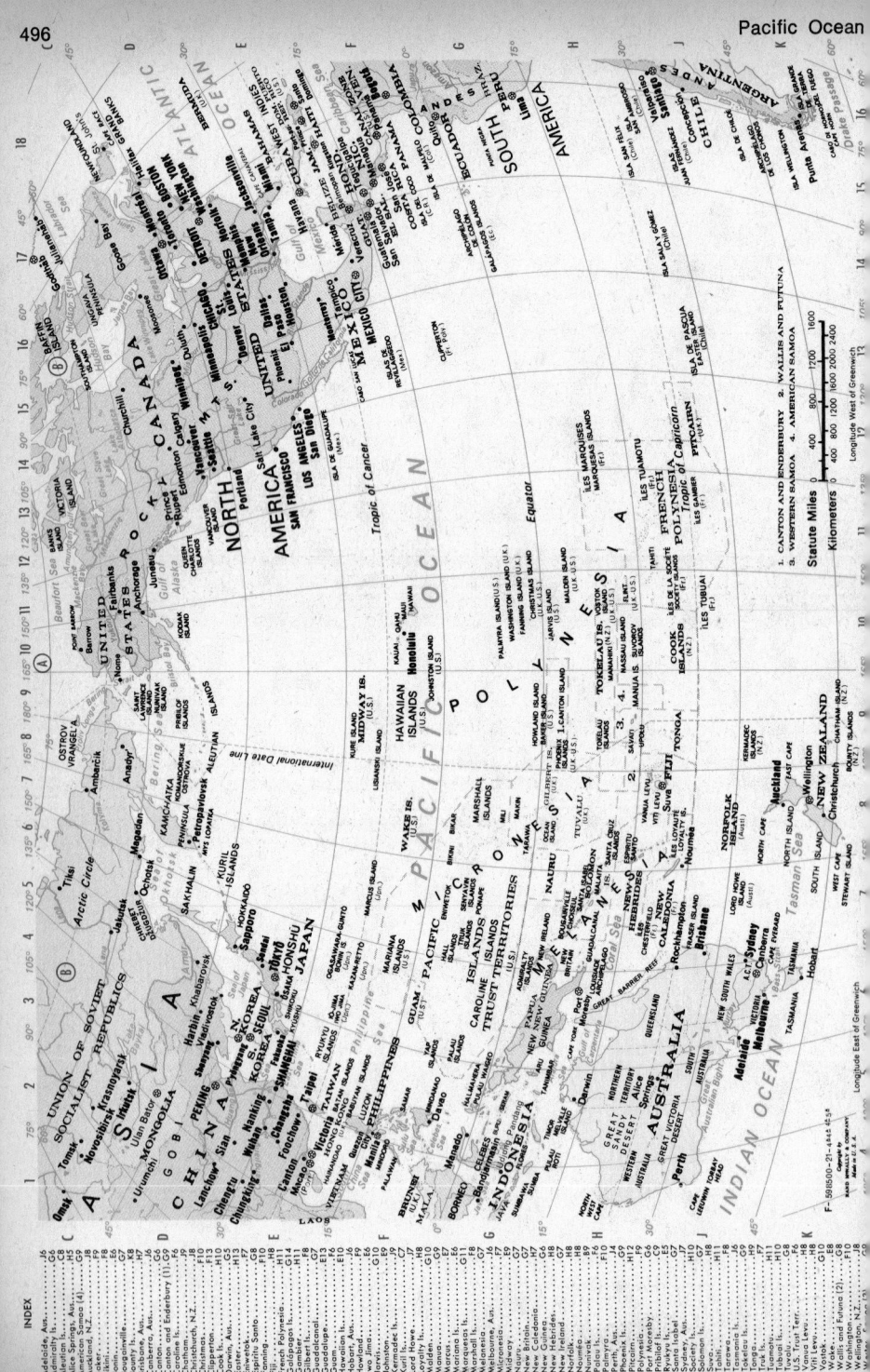

CANADA

See Index for Calgary, Edmonton, Halifax, Hamilton, Kitchener-Waterloo, Lethbridge, Montreal, Ottawa, Quebec, Regina, Saskatoon, Toronto, Vancouver, Windsor, Winnipeg.

Capital: Ottawa. Area: 3,851,809 sq. mi. Population (Govt. est., Jan. 1976): 22,998,000. Monetary unit: Canadian dollar.

Government and Politics

Threat of a great schism hangs ominously over Canada, founded as a nation in 1867. One of its charter provinces, French-speaking Quebec, is moving towards separation. The change would be enormous.

Quebec is the largest of the 10 provinces, occupying 15.4% of Canada's area; it has 27% of Canada's population and contains Canada's largest city, Montreal.

Economically, Quebec ranks 6th in per capita income among the provinces. However, it forms a major part of the industrial heartland of Canada: it is 2d to Ontario in manufacturing output and value of shipments; ranks 4th in farm cash receipts; and is the 3rd mineral producing province in the nation, asbestos being the leading mineral resource, followed by iron ore, copper and zinc.

In terms of its financial contribution to federalism, Quebec accounts for roughly 22% of the number of taxable federal returns and 23% of the total taxable income in Canada, although only 18% of the federal tax is derived from the province.

Quebec is the bastion of French Canadians, the 2d largest ethnic group in the country. About 80% of Quebec's population is of French ethnic origin. This amounts to 77% of Canada's total French population.

For all these reasons the separation of Quebec would drastically alter the size, social composition and economic strength and viability of Canada as a whole.

Quebec's relations with the rest of Canada have always been characterized by controversy, though never of the present magnitude. The existing crisis has been precipitated by the stunning victory of the Parti Quebecois (PQ) in the provincial election held on November 15, 1976. Less than a decade old, the PQ came from behind fast and routed the incumbent Liberal government. Sidestepping the issue of separatism, the PQ capitalized on the growing public dissatisfaction with the aging and corrupt regime of Quebec Premier Robert Bourassa.

PQ leader Rene Levesque, who has become the 27th premier, has been a flamboyant public figure for over 20 years, first as a television personality and then as a politician. Premier Levesque was a provincial Liberal cabinet minister until he quit in 1967 to lead the independence movement.

Quebec's sovereign aspiration is rooted in the resentment of French Canadians against their conquest by the British in 1763.

The Parti Quebecois is dedicated to emancipating the province from what many French Canadians believe is continuing subordination to the English element represented by the federal government. In Premier Levesque's words, "What Quebec wants, is to be able to deal with others as an equal," including the United States as well as Canada. Quebec "needs to be master of its destiny".

To achieve independence, the PQ proposes to hold a provincial referendum which will probably offer an economic association like the European common market with the rest of Canada. The latter, however, will not likely endorse such a choice. The right of a province to secede also raises the baffling constitutional question of whether a province has the legal right to separate.

The Liberal party, which has held power in Ottawa for most of the 20th century only because of Quebec's support, stands in danger of losing its dominance if Quebec secedes. Yet it is likely to be the governing party which will have to negotiate a settlement if the Parti Quebecois wins the referendum. Federal Prime Minister Pierre Trudeau, himself a French Canadian, and Premier Levesque are sparring now, preparing for the show-down.

Foreign Relations

Following an extensive foreign policy review in 1970, Canada adopted in 1972 the so-called "Third Option": a policy of "enlightened self-interest", aimed at reducing Canada's vulnerability to U.S. influence by greatly diversifying its external relations.

Under this policy the Canadian Government has given top priority to establishing firm relations with the European Communities and the countries of the Pacific basin, particularly Japan. The Prime Minister's visits in 1976 to the European Communities and Japan culminated in the signing of a "Framework Agreement for Commercial and Economic Co-operation" between Canada and the European Communities, and a "Framework for Economic Co-operation" between Canada and Japan. The latter also provided for the establishment of the Canada-Japan Joint Economic Committee whose first meeting was in June 1977. Canada seeks a better "mix" of its exports to these countries through easier access to their markets for more Canadian processed and manufactured goods.

High-level visits occurred between the Governments of Canada and Australia and New Zealand to emphasize the importance of these countries to Canada's trade: total Australian-Canadian trade approached $700 million in 1976.

Canada has given support to the goals of the Association of Southeast Asian Nations (ASEAN), formed in 1957, and granted development assistance to the organization. Canada's most extensive relations are with Indonesia, the largest, most influential, and potentially the richest country in the region.

Canada endorses the policy of limitations and reductions in nuclear arms and an effective ban on all nuclear-weapons testing, with a further strengthening of the nuclear-non-proliferation system. Canada changed its nuclear-export policy in 1976, and decided upon a further tightening of the safeguard requirements for the export of Canadian reactors and uranium. Shipments under future contracts will be restricted to countries that ratify the Non-Proliferation Treaty or otherwise accept international safeguards on their entire nuclear programs. Canada will terminate nuclear shipments to any non-nuclear-weapon state that explodes a nuclear device.

The Canadian Government continues to affirm its sovereign right to manage the living resources of the seas in a 200-mile zone adjacent to its shoreline, and has boosted its efforts at control and surveillance in that zone.

The visit of Prime Minister Pierre Trudeau to the United States in 1977, and his address to a joint session of the U.S. Congress were strong affirmations of close Canada-U.S. relations. Canada sells more than

$20-billion worth of goods annually to the United States, the greater part of them either processed or fully finished. Some highly-visible contentious issues exist between Canada and the U.S., the two most important being energy and the 200-mile fishing zone.

The Canadian Government has expressed its abhorrence of the pattern of institutionalized racial discrimination in South Africa. It has denounced South Africa's policy of "Bantustanization", and has rejected the so-called independence of the Transkei.

The Economy

An all time high for production of Canadian minerals was reached during 1976. Based on an estimate prepared by Statistics Canada the total value exceeded $15.3 billion. The metals group accounted for a value of $5.24 billion which is an increase of 9.3% from the previous year; the non-metal group provided a gross value of $1.14 billion, an increase of 21.7%; the fuel sector reached a new peak of $7.99 billion, a recorded increase of 20.3%; and structural materials amounted to $1.02 billion, up 5.8% from 1975. Values of the leading mineral commodities were: crude petroleum, $4.13 billion; natural gas, $2.47 billion; iron ore, $1.24 billion; nickel, $1.23 billion; copper, $1.13 billion; zinc, $862 million.

Total value added by manufacture was $36.1 billion in 1975. Total value of manufacturing shipments rose $7.3% in 1975 to $88.4 billion. Per capita income was $5,838 in 1975.

Leading manufacturing industries include food and beverages, transportation equipment, paper and allied products, primary metal, metal fabricating, petroleum and coal products, chemical and chemical products, electrical products, wood, and machinery.

Value of fisheries in 1976 was $329.4 million, up from $269.3 million the previous year. Value of salmon landings in British Columbia alone made up 22.2% of the total value of fisheries.

Total cash receipts from farming operations for the January-September period of 1976 are estimated at $7.48 million for Canada compared to a level of $7.42 million for the corresponding period in 1975. Total returns during the first nine months of 1976 from the sale of field crops amounted to $3.55 billion compared to $3.67 billion for the same period in 1975. Total cash receipts to farmers from the sale of livestock and livestock products during the first nine months of 1976 amounted to $3.69 billion compared to a level of $3.49 billion for the same months in 1975.

Tourism receipts in Canada in 1976 approximated $9.2 billion, about 5% of the country's gross national product. The tourist industry declined in 1976 with a drop of 5.9% in visitors. The number of visitors from the United States decreased for the third successive year, by 6.8% to 32.2 million. Gross revenues were slightly higher, up to $1.35 billion in 1976 from $1.34 billion the year before.

The Land

Canada is the world's 2d largest country in land size, extending south from the North Pole to the U.S. border and including all the islands of the Arctic from near Greenland to near the Alaskan border. Its seacoast, one of the longest in the world, includes 17,-860 miles of mainland and 41,810 miles of islands.

A great sweep of the nation, stretching across the northern territories and prairies through northern Ontario and Quebec down to the Atlantic provinces, is known as the Canadian Shield, where past ice ages scraped most soil and vegetation off the land. This is the world's oldest surface rock, and it is here that most Canadian mineral discoveries have been made.

Canada's continental climate, while generally temperate, can run to freezing cold and blistering heat. The range is well beyond 100 degrees Fahrenheit.

History

French explorer Jacques Cartier is generally regarded as the founder of Canada. But his 1534 exploration of the Gulf of St. Lawrence followed by 37 years the sighting of Newfoundland in 1497 by English seaman John Cabot. Centuries prior to that, increasing evidence shows, Vikings had reached Newfoundland and Canada's Atlantic coast.

France pioneered Canadian settlement and the French have multiplied to become about 27% of the Canadian population today. Quebec was settled as early as 1608, Montreal in 1642; New France was declared a colony in 1663.

Britain and France clashed in Canada as a result of European rivalries and British expansion in America. Britain acquired Acadia (later Nova Scotia) in 1713, and captured Quebec in 1759, obtaining control of the rest of New France in 1763. The Quebec Act in 1774 gave the French rights to their own language, religion, and civil law. This was one reason why the French-Canadian settlers did not join American colonists in the War of Independence.

During the American Revolution, many former colonials moved north to settle in Canada, proudly calling themselves United Empire Loyalists.

The fur trade and exploration opened up the western plains and led Canadians across the continent to the Pacific. Alexander Mackenzie scrawled on a rock by the Pacific "From Canada, by land, 1793."

In Upper and Lower Canada (later called Ontario and Quebec) and in the Maritimes, legislative assemblies appeared in the 18th century and reformers called for responsible government. But the War of 1812 with the U.S. intervened. The war ended in a stalemate that was symbolic of the end to armed conflict between Canada and the U.S.

In 1837 political agitation for more democratic government culminated in rebellions in Upper and Lower Canada. The British sent Lord Durham to investigate and, in a famous report, he recommended union of the two parts into one colony called Canada. The union lasted until Confederation brought 2 additional colonies, Nova Scotia and New Brunswick, to join the new country in 1867. During the period 1840 to 1867, the Canadian colonies won the right to internal self-government.

The Dominion of Canada was launched on July 1, 1867, by the proclamation of the British North America Act, which became the country's written constitution, establishing a federal system of government on the model of a British parliament and cabinet structure under the crown. Canada was proclaimed a self-governing Dominion within the British Empire in 1931. Empire has now given way to Commonwealth, and Canada remains an independent member.

World War I had much to do with the development of Canadian nationhood. The pride it engendered and the industrial base it created in Canada led to the demand for full sovereignty.

But the achievement of nationhood was dulled by the blight of the Great Depression in the 1930s. It took World War II and Canada's accomplishments in it to revive the country's pride and sense of direction. It also fired the furnaces of industry, converting the country into an urban, industrial state.

Industrial Boom

On the Pacific coast a chain of rivers and lakes was

reversed to flow backwards through the mountains to power electric generators for the huge aluminum smelters at Kitimat. The Columbia and Kootenay Rivers and Arrow Lakes were dammed to provide electricity. Oil wells and mineral strikes led to an El Dorado. Immense iron ore resources were discovered and developed in the wilds of Labrador. Uranium was unearthed in northern Ontario and turned into nuclear power.

Canada joined with the U.S. to build the St. Lawrence River Seaway, and Ottawa shared costs with the provinces to complete the Trans-Canada Highway, the longest in the world. Two million immigrants arrived in Canada in the 2 decades after World War II and the country imported a billion dollars a year of foreign capital to finance a new industrial boom.

Economic System

Canada has a "mixed economy" — a mixture of private and public ownership. Despite a long historical tradition of state aid which has been necessary because of Canada's harsh climate and sparse population, private enterprise has flourished. But like Sweden, with which it vies for the 2d highest standard of living in the world, Canada accepts the idea of state capitalism and collectivism.

Most hydroelectric and many transportation and communication facilities are owned by either federal, provincial, or municipal governments. Air Canada, one of the largest airlines in the world, is a federal crown corporation, while the competing Canadian Pacific airline is privately owned. Canadian National Railways is another crown corporation. Its chief rival is the Canadian Pacific company. The Canadian Broadcasting Corp. is publicly owned, although independently managed. There are also private radio chains and private television networks.

Social Security

Under the British North America Act (1867), the provinces are responsible for welfare programs to benefit their citizens. The federal government helps the provinces bear the cost of welfare programs. Federal payments reimburse up to 50% of the cost of welfare assistance provided by the provinces. Ottawa has also used its fiscal strength to launch the social security system and help bring about a certain uniformity in the existing programs, ensuring a high level of equity in programs among the provinces.

In the mid-1960s the federal government conceived of a universal and compulsory medicare and hospitalization system. Strenuous provincial opposition to the federal government's proposals delayed implementation of a revised plan until 1968.

Following a three-year review of the social security system, the federal government in 1976 proposed a new program for supplementing incomes of the "working poor" by about $1,200 a year for a family of four when the program begins, perhaps in 1978 or 1979. Ottawa's proposal involves a cost-sharing arrangement whereby the federal government will pay two-thirds of the cost of the supplementary program with the rest being paid by the provinces. While Ontario opposed the plan and New Brunswick and Prince Edward Island took no position, even the 7 provinces which agreed in principle were reluctant to give a firm commitment to undertake their share of the cost. Since the provincial governments are trying to cut their spending, they are afraid that if the program is implemented, the cost of supplementary income could escalate and lead to further increases in public expenditure. To overcome provincial opposition, the federal government has threatened to introduce the program unilaterally by assuming the full cost of payments, administering the plan through the tax system rather than through the provincial welfare offices.

The Social Security system in Canada covers several schemes: Family Allowances, Shared Cost Welfare Programs of the Federal and Provincial Governments; Old Age Security; Guaranteed Income Supplement; The Canada Pension Plan; and Veterans Benefits. Payments under almost all of these schemes are adjusted to the cost of living index.

Provinces of Canada

Alberta

CAPITAL: Edmonton. AREA: 255,285 sq. mi., rank 4th. POPULATION: 1,804,000 (est. Jan. 1976). FLOWER: The Wild Rose. ENTERED CONFEDERATION: 1905.

The vast area of Alberta was controlled by the Hudson's Bay Co. until 1870, at which time it was transferred to the Northwest Territories.

Along with Saskatchewan, Alberta is nicknamed the "sunshine" province because of its good weather. The weather is strongly affected by the "chinook," a warm wind blowing eastward over the Rockies. The Rocky Mountains provide such famous tourist attractions as Banff and Jasper parks, Lake Louise and the Columbian ice fields.

Wheat and cattle gave Alberta its start but the economy was transformed by the discovery of huge petroleum and natural gas supplies at Leduc near Edmonton in 1947. Since then the province has become the 3d wealthiest in Canada with per capita income in 1975 of $6,064.

In total value of mineral output, Alberta ranked first, with $6.9 billion in 1976 (up 17.9%) of which $6.8 billion was derived from fuel production. Alberta alone accounts for 85% of total fuel production in Canada. It was first in value of its natural gas, natural gas by-products, and crude petroleum production, and 2d in coal. Alberta produces slightly over 98% of all the elemental sulphur in Canada.

Since 1974 Alberta's farm cash receipts have been the 3d highest in Canada, totalling $1.8 billion in 1976, 2% over the previous year. Alberta is the leading producer of barley, sugar beets, and oats, and ranks 2d in the production of wheat, rye, mixed grain, rapeseed, mustard seed and tame hay.

Alberta has the lowest tax structure in Canada, no sales tax, no succession duties (inheritance taxes), and the highest per capita spending on health and education, with 5 institutions of higher learning.

Premier of Alberta is Peter Lougheed, leader of the Progressive Conservative party in the province. The Conservatives, who gained office in 1971, bringing an end to 36 years of Social Credit rule, were re-elected in 1975 with a healthy 69 to 6 majority.

British Columbia

CAPITAL: Victoria. AREA: 366,255 sq. mi., rank 3d. POPULATION: 2,481,000 (est. Jan. 1976).

FLOWER: The Dogwood. ENTERED CONFEDERATION: 1871.

Canada's most westerly province, British Columbia, on the Pacific coast, has mild winters and moderate summer temperatures which give the province the warmest climate in Canada and make it a haven for tourists and retired people. The interior is a series of rugged mountain ranges.

In 1849 the territory of the province became a British colony. The first significant settlement of the area took place in 1858 with the Fraser River gold rush. The full emergence of British Columbia as a distinct province came about by the union of the two former British colonies of Victoria and British Columbia.

British Columbia's per capita income of $6,272 was 2d in the nation in 1975.

In total value of 1976 mineral production, British Columbia stood 4th with $1.4 billion, an increase of 9.6% over 1975. It was the leading producer of coal, copper, lead, and molybdenum.

Total value of fisheries in 1976 of $117 million ranked first and represented an increase of 48% over the previous year. Salmon accounted for 62.8% of the total value. The province's most lucrative fishing site is the Fraser River.

In the agriculture sector, British Columbia's farm cash receipts in 1976 of $471 million ranked 6th in the country.

British Columbia ranks first in the production of lumber, producing 67% of the total Canadian lumber output.

British Columbia has 8 institutions of higher learning. The largest institution is the University of British Columbia which alone accounts for 62% of the total enrollment in the province.

The premier of British Columbia is William Bennett, leader of the provincial Social Credit party (or Socreds).

Manitoba

CAPITAL: Winnipeg. AREA: 251,000 sq. mi., rank 6th. POPULATION: 1,023,000 (est. Jan. 1976). FLOWER: The Prairie Crocus. ENTERED CONFEDERATION: 1870.

Most easterly of the Prairie provinces, Manitoba is called the "keystone" province because it links the eastern and western halves of the country.

Previously called the Red River Colony, and controlled by the Hudson's Bay Co., the area was purchased by the Dominion of Canada in 1870. The Red River Colony is of great historical importance because it was the site of the Riel rebellion that occurred in 1869. The execution of Riel in 1885 had a dramatic impact on the course of Canadian history.

Estimated gross provincial product for 1976 was $8.2 billion, up 22% from 1975. In 1975 the per capita income was $5,635, 5th in Canada.

In 1976, total value of mineral production declined from the 2 previous years to $478 million. Nickel production, 2d in the nation, accounted for almost 50% of the total value of Manitoba's mineral production.

Manitoba's total farm cash receipts amounted to $897.1 million in 1976 which was below the 1975 value. Manitoba produces the total output of sunflower seed and is the leading producer in Canada of flaxseed. Manitoba ranks 3d in the production of wheat, oats, barley, rye, and mustard seed.

Manitoba has 5 institutions of higher learning.

The New Democratic party under the leadership of Premier Edward Schreyer has established a firm foothold on the government of Manitoba, winning two consecutive elections in 1969 and 1973.

New Brunswick

CAPITAL: Fredericton. AREA: 27,835 sq. mi., rank 8th. POPULATION: 684,000 (est. Jan. 1976). FLOWER: The Purple Violet. ENTERED CONFEDERATION: 1867.

The rectangular Atlantic province has an extensive seacoast and the world's highest tides on the Bay of Fundy.

The gross provincial product for New Brunswick for 1976 has been estimated at $3.8 billion (up 15%). Per capita income in 1975 was $4,498, the 3d lowest in Canada.

In total value of mineral production, New Brunswick contributed $255 million in 1976, roughly 1.6% of the Canada total. The province ranked 2d in lead and zinc production which comprised over 68% of the total value. New Brunswick produces almost all of the antimony and bismuth in Canada.

Farm cash receipts for New Brunswick rose to $113.9 million in 1976. New Brunswick is the 2d leading producer of potatoes after Prince Edward Island.

Total value of fisheries was down to $24.1 million in 1976. Lobster, tuna and herring made up two-thirds of the total value of fisheries.

New Brunswick has 4 institutions of higher learning.

The province is governed by the Progressive Conservative party under Premier Richard Hatfield.

Newfoundland

CAPITAL: St. John's. AREA: 156,185 sq. mi., rank 7th. POPULATION: 554,000 (est. Jan. 1976). FLOWER: The Pitcher-Plant. ENTERED CONFEDERATION: 1949.

Newfoundland consists of 2 parts: an Atlantic island of 43,359 sq. mi. and the 112,826 sq. mi. of Labrador. Both sections are hilly, rugged, and generally barren.

The estimated gross provincial product for Newfoundland has been set at $2.6 billion for 1976 or about 17.5% higher than the year before. Per capita income in 1975 increased to $4,027 but was still the 2d lowest in Canada.

Total value of mineral production in 1976 greatly surpassed previous years, amounting to $756 million, an increase of 37%. Newfoundland is the leading producer of iron ore, which alone made up 85% of the total value of mineral output.

Newfoundland ranks first in cod production. In 1976 total value of cod made up 36.9% of the total value of fisheries, which rose to $58.8 million.

Newfoundland has one institution of higher learning.

The province is governed by the Progressive Conservative party, headed by Premier Frank Moores.

Nova Scotia

CAPITAL: Halifax. AREA: 21,425 sq. mi., rank 9th. POPULATION: 830,000 (est. Jan. 1976). FLOWER: The Trailing Arbutus. ENTERED CONFEDERATION: 1867.

Nova Scotia is called "The Wharf of North America" because of its many excellent harbors, of which Halifax, the capital, is the most extensive and famous.

Of the Canadian provinces, Nova Scotia has the

longest history, beginning with John Cabot's visit to Cape Breton in 1497. The province gained its name in 1621 with the establishment of New Scotland.

Once considered the wealthiest of the British North American colonies, the province has long been looked upon as a "have not" province, because its economy has not kept pace with rapid industrialization. Per capita income was $4,625 in 1975, the 4th lowest in Canada.

Total value of mineral production increased by 15% to $117.2 million in 1976; coal alone accounted for 46.5% of the total value. Nova Scotia is the 3d leading producer of coal.

Value of shipments of manufactured goods reached $1.82 billion in 1975 (up 7.3%). Petroleum and coal products and food and beverage products made up 46% of the shipments.

Fisheries production in 1976 was valued at an estimated $101.9 million, the 2d highest in Canada. Scallops, lobsters, and catfish made up 67% of the total value of fisheries.

The tourist industry took a plunge downwards by 12% in 1976, the number of visitors declining to 149,997 from 170,483 in 1975. The decline reflected a drop in visitors from the United States.

Total farm cash receipts for Nova Scotia were estimated at $124 million in 1976. This was up 6.7% from the $116.2 million reported in 1975.

Nova Scotia has 11 institutions of higher learning.

The Liberal party, headed by premier Gerald Regan, was re-elected in 1974.

Ontario

CAPITAL: Toronto. AREA: 412,582 sq. mi., rank 2d. POPULATION: 8,290,000 (est. Jan. 1976). FLOWER: The White Trillium. ENTERED CONFEDERATION: 1867.

The first big wave of settlers in Ontario consisted of Loyalists forced to flee from the rebelling American colonies. At the time, the area was part of Quebec. Conflict between the English-speaking settlers and the French-speaking inhabitants led to the division of the province. Upper Canada later became Ontario. The vast industrialization of the region following World War II led to the arrival of millions of immigrants. Between 1946 and 1972, Ontario alone received over 60% of all immigrants into Canada, a fact which has drastically altered the ethnic and racial composition of the province.

Ontario occupies the heartland of Canada, stretching from the Great Lakes to Hudson and James Bays in the north.

Ontario ranked second in Canada, after Alberta, in mineral production in 1976, with output valued at $2.59 billion, up from $2.35 billion in the previous year. Metal production in 1976, valued at an estimated $2.15 billion, made up 83% of total mineral production value. Ontario is the leading producer of zinc and nickel and ranks 2d among the provinces in copper production. Also important are salt production (58.4% of Canada's total) and structural materials.

Ontario alone accounts for 50.2% of Canada's value of manufactured shipments, which in 1975 was valued at $44.43 billion (up 7.3%).

In 1976 Ontario continued to rank first in farm cash receipts, which amounted to $2.77 billion. Corn is the principal crop, 91.9% of Canada's total. Ontario is the leading producer of mixed grains and produces all the soybeans.

Preliminary estimates for the year 1976 show that Ontario received 21,640,015 visitors (down 6.4% from the previous year). The drop was due solely to a decline of visitors from the United States, visitors from countries other than the U.S. increased by 20.8%.

Ontario has the largest number of institutions of higher education in Canada, a total of 22, including Canada's largest university, University of Toronto.

Gross provincial product was estimated at $73.9 billion for 1976. Ontario's 1976 per capita income of $6,431 was the highest among the provinces.

The Progressive Conservative party of Ontario formed its second minority government in a row after being re-elected in June 1977. The party has held power continuously since 1943. The incumbent Conservative premier is William Davis who was first elected as premier in 1971. Present party standing in the Ontario legislature is: Progressive Conservatives 58; Liberals 34, and New Democrats 33.

Prince Edward Island

CAPITAL: Charlottetown. AREA: 2,184 sq. mi., rank 10th. POPULATION: 20,000 (est. Jan. 1976). FLOWER: Lady's Slipper. ENTERED CONFEDERATION: 1873.

Prince Edward Island, nicknamed "The Garden of the Gulf" because it is situated in the Gulf of the St. Lawrence, is the smallest province of Canada both in area and population. Per capita income is the lowest in Canada, $4,008 in 1976.

The economy of Prince Edward Island is heavily dependent on agricultural production. In 1976 farm cash receipts were the lowest in Canada, amounting to $104.8 million, but they accounted for 17.7% of the total gross provincial product, $587 millon in 1976. Prince Edward Island is the nation's leading producer of potatoes, producing 23.7% of Canada's total potato output.

Next to agriculture, tourism and fisheries are the prime industries. The tourist industry suffered a serious setback in 1976 when the number of visitors, all from the U.S., declined to 250 from 1,965 in 1975.

Lobster had by far the greatest value among Prince Edward Island fisheries products: Lobster value in 1976 amounted to $8.5 million, 67.5% of the total value of fisheries, $12.6 million.

Manufacturing shipments are the lowest among the Canadian provinces, $108.6 million in 1976 (up 15.3%).

Prince Edward Island has virtually no mineral resources. Total value of minerals is derived solely from the production of sand and gravel, $1.7 million in 1976.

Prince Edward Island has one institution of higher learning.

The Liberals are in office under Premier Alexander Campbell.

Quebec

CAPITAL: Quebec City. AREA: 594,860 sq. mi., rank 1st. POPULATION: 6,224,000 (est. Jan. 1976). FLOWER: The White Garden Lily. ENTERED CONFEDERATION: 1867.

Quebec was founded by Champlain in 1608 as a French colony and continues to struggle today to maintain its French heritage and culture. Quebec City, the provincial capital, dates to about 1625. The commercial and industrial center of the province is located in Montreal, Canada's largest city. Scene of

Expo '67, Montreal was the site of the 1976 Olympic Games.

The rocky and barren Canadian shield spreads over the largest part of the province north of the St. Lawrence River. South of the river, the Appalachian Mountains run east and south to the U.S.A. A fertile agricultural band called the St. Lawrence Lowlands surrounds the western end of the river. Quebec experiences the most severe climatic conditions in Canada. In the north and northwest the winters are long and harsh, the summers short and hot. The upper St. Lawrence Valley has a more moderate climate, but in the lower reaches of the river from Quebec to Gaspe winter arrives early and is followed by a late spring and hot summer.

Quebec, along with Ontario, forms the industrial backbone of Canada. Per capita income in the province of Quebec ranks 6th in Canada and is considerably below the national average. In 1976 per capita income was $5,312 whereas the national per capita income was $5,838. Gross provincial product for Quebec in 1976 has been estimated at $44.8 billion.

Quebec ranked 3d in 1976 in total value of mineral production: $1.52 billion (metals, $766 million, 2d in Canada; non-metals, $439 million, first; structural materials, $316, 2d). In 1976 Quebec ranked first in the production of asbestos, producing 82% of Canada's total output. Quebec is the largest producer of raw asbestos fibre in the non-Communist world. Iron ore, copper and zinc were the largest sources of Quebec's income from minerals.

Quebec's total value of manufactured shipments rose by 7% to $23.97 billion in 1975, the 2nd highest in Canada.

Total farm cash receipts for 1976 were $1.36 billion, slightly below the previous year and the 4th highest in Canada. Principal field crops in Quebec include oats, tame hay and fodder corn.

Cod and lobster catch made up 53.7% of the 1976 value of fisheries in Quebec, $14.9 million.

Foreign visitors to Quebec declined to 3,681,765 in 1976 from the previous year's total of 3,827,854, resulting from a decline in visitors from the U.S.

Quebec has the highest minimum wage in Canada, $3.15 an hour. The Quebec Government has been the only one in North America to introduce an anti-scab law.

Quebec has 7 institutions of higher education.

The new Parti Quebecois government was elected on November 15, 1976, by an overwhelming majority: P.Q. 71; Liberal 26; Union Nationale 11; Social Credit 1; other 1. The new leader of the government is Premier Rene Levesque.

Saskatchewan

CAPITAL: Regina. AREA: 251,700 sq. mi., rank 5th. POPULATION: 929,000 (est. Jan. 1976). FLOWER: The Prairie Lily. ENTERED CONFEDERATION: 1905.

Formerly part of the Northwest Territories, Saskatchewan became a province in 1905. The southern portion is an arable plain devoted to the production of wheat.

Per capita income in Saskatchewan in 1975 was $5,971, the nation's 4th highest.

Saskatchewan's total farm cash receipts in 1976 were estimated at $2.29 billion in 1976, 2d highest in Canada. Saskatchewan ranked first in 1976 in the production of wheat, rye, rapeseed, and mustard seed, and second in the production of oats, barley, flaxseed. Saskatchewan wheat production accounts for 63.4% of Canada's total output.

Saskatchewan mineral value in 1976 increased to $908.5 million from $861.6 million in 1975, and ranked 5th among the provinces. Saskatchewan has very few metal resources, but is the sole Canadian producer of potash, valued at $361.4 million in 1976, 39.7% of the province's total mineral value. In the fuel sector, Saskatchewan is the 3rd largest producer, sustained by petroleum production which is the 2d highest in Canada.

Manufacturing shipments in Saskatchewan rose by 12.6% in 1975 to $1.18 billion over the 1974 figure.

While the number of visitors to most other parts of Canada declined in 1976, the number of visitors to Saskatchewan increased to 235,139, up by 0.4%.

Saskatchewan has 4 institutions of higher learning.

Saskatchewan elected the first democratic socialist government in North America in 1944. Defeated by the Liberals in 1964, the socialists regained office under the New Democratic party label in 1971. Premier of the province is Allan Blakeney.

Approximate Land and Freshwater Areas

Source: Canada Year Book

Province or Territory	Land sq. miles	Freshwater sq. miles	Total sq. miles	Percentage of total area
Newfoundland	143,045	13,140	156,185	4.1
Island of Newfoundland	*41,164*	*2,195*	*43,359*	*1.1*
Labrador	*101,881*	*10,945*	*112,826*	*3.0*
Prince Edward Island	2,184	—	2,184	0.1
Nova Scotia	20,402	1,023	21,425	0.6
New Brunswick	27,835	519	28,354	0.7
Quebec	523,860	71,000	594,860	15.4
Ontario	344,092	68,490	412,582	10.7
Manitoba	211,775	39,225	251,000	6.5
Saskatchewan	220,182	31,518	251,700	6.5
Alberta	248,800	6,485	255,285	6.6
British Columbia	359,279	6,976	366,255	9.5
Yukon Territory	205,346	1,730	207,076	5.4
Northwest Territories	1,253,438	51,465	1,304,903	33.9
Franklin	*541,753*	*7,500*	*549,253*	*14.3*
Keewatin	*218,460*	*9,700*	*228,160*	*5.9*
Mackenzie	*493,225*	*34,265*	*527,490*	*13.7*
Canada	**3,560,238**	**291,571**	**3,851,809**	**100.0**

The Government of Canada

Canada is a constitutional monarchy with a parliamentary system of government. It is also a federal state. The head of state is Queen Elizabeth, represented in Canada, a self-governing member of the Commonwealth of Nations, by a resident Governor-General, appointed by Her Majesty on the advice of the federal cabinet.

The cabinet is drawn from members of the party holding the largest number of seats in the House of Commons. Its members are appointed by the Governor-General on the advice of the prime minister, the leader of the party. The prime minister is the head of the executive branch of government which is composed of the cabinet and the Governor-General, the formal title of the body being "the governor-in-council," also known constitutionally as the Privy Council.

Canada has a bicameral Parliament. The House of Commons, the more important chamber, is composed of 264 members elected at least every 5 years. The prime minister chooses the date within this period.

The upper house is the senate, comprised of 102 Senators who now are appointed to serve until 75. Prime ministers are free to choose appointees, the tradition being that they are party patronage nominations. The British North America Act requires that 30 members come from the Atlantic provinces, 24 from Quebec, 24 from Ontario, and 24 from the 4 western provinces.

Legislation becomes law by receiving 3 "readings" in the Commons, passing in the Senate and obtaining assent from the Governor-General. Financial bills can be introduced only in the Commons.

Each province has a modified version of the Ottawa pattern. Each province has a unicameral legislature. The executive head in the province is referred to usually as the Premier.

Head of State and Cabinet

Queen Elizabeth, succeeded to the throne in 1952, is represented by Governor-General Rt. Hon. Jules Leger, appointed 1974. Titles: Minister unless otherwise stated or *Minister of State.

(listed according to precedence) (Sept. 16, 1977)

Prime Minister — Pierre Elliott Trudeau
President of the Queen's Privy Council for Canada — Allan J. MacEachen
Finance — Jean Chretien
Labor — John Carr Munro
Justice and Attorney General — Stanley R. Basford
Secretary of State for External Affairs — Donald Jamieson
President of Treasury Board — Robert K. Andras
Transport — Otto E. Lang
Supply and Services — Jean-Pierre Goyer
Energy, Mines and Resources — Alastair W. Gillespie
Agriculture — Eugene F. Whelan
Corporate and Consumer Affairs — W. Warren Allmand
Indian Affairs and Northern Development — James H. Faulkner
***Urban Affairs** — Andre Ouellet
Veteran Affairs — Daniel J. MacDonald
***Federal-Provincial Relations** — Marc Lalonde
Communications — Jeanne Sauve
Leader of the Government in the Senate — Raymond J. Perrault
National Defence — Barnett J. Danson
Public Works — J. Judd Buchanan
***Science and Technology** — J. Judd Buchanan
Fisheries and Environment — Romeo LeBlanc
Regional Economic Expansion — Marcel Lessard
Manpower and Immigration — Jack (Bud) Cullen
***Environment** — Leonard S. Marchand
Secretary of State — John Roberts
National Health and Welfare — Monique Begin
Postmaster General — Jean-Jacques Blais
Solicitor General — Francis Fox
***Small Businesses** — Anthony C. Abbott
***Fitness and Amateur Sport** — Iona Campagnolo
National Revenue — Joseph-Philippe Guay
Industry, Trade, and Commerce — Jack H. Horner
***Multiculturism** — Norman Cafik

Governors-General of Canada Since Confederation, 1867

Name	Term
The Viscount Monck of Ballytrammon	1867-1868
The Baron Lisgar of Lisgar and Bailieborough	1869-1872
The Earl of Dufferin	1872-1878
The Marquis of Lorne	1878-1883
The Marquis of Lansdowne	1883-1888
The Baron Stanley of Preston	1888-1893
The Earl of Aberdeen	1893-1898
The Earl of Minto	1898-1904
The Earl Grey	1904-1911
Field Marshal H.R.H. The Duke of Connaught	1911-1916
The Duke of Devonshire	1916-1921
General The Baron Byng of Vimy	1921-1926
The Viscount Willingdon of Ratton	1926-1931
The Earl of Bessborough	1931-1935
The Baron Tweedsmuir of Elsfield	1935-1940
Major General The Earl of Athlone	1940-1946
Field Marshal The Viscount Alexander of Tunis	1946-1952
The Right Hon. Vincent Massey	1952-1959
General The Right Hon. Georges P. Vanier	1959-1967
The Right Hon. Roland Michener	1967-1974
The Right Hon. Jules Leger	1974-

Prime Ministers of Canada

Name	Party	Term
Sir John A. Macdonald	Conservative	1867-1873 1878-1891
Alexander Mackenzie	Liberal	1873-1878
Sir John J. C. Abbott	Conservative	1891-1892
Sir John S. D. Thompson	Conservative	1892-1894
Sir Mackenzie Bowell	Conservative	1894-1896

Name	Party	Term
Sir Charles Tupper	Conservative	1896
Sir Wilfrid Laurier	Liberal	1896-1911
Sir Robert L. Borden	Conservative Unionist	1911-1920
Arthur Meighen	Conservative Unionist	1920-1921
W.L.M. King	Liberal	1921-1926

Name	Party	Term
		1926-1930
		1935-1948
R. B. Bennett	Conservative	1930-1935
Louis St. Laurent	Liberal	1948-1957
John G. Diefenbaker	Prog. Cons.	1957-1963
Lester B. Pearson	Liberal	1963-1968
Pierre Elliott Trudeau	Liberal	1968-

The Political Parties

Canadian parties, from whatever point in the political spectrum they begin, tend to move to the middle of the road where most of the votes lie. They all take much the same kind of moderate line.

The Canadian political spectrum has embraced a plethora of political parties. Since the year of Confederation, 1867, there have been over 45 different party labels in official existence and contesting elections. Most of these parties have never attained any national prominence; indeed, the majority disappeared into oblivion without electing a single candidate.

The four political parties that have dominated Canadian political life are:

Conservatives—The oldest party, they have adopted the prefix "Progressive" and moved to the left, advocating farm support programs and endorsing an extension of social welfare. Their support comes from older voters, Protestants, and English-speaking rural residents.

Liberals—Originally the Canadian equivalent of the American Jacksonian Democrats, favoring strict representation by population and the rural pioneer against the urban elite, they now get most of their electoral support from the middle and upper classes in cities, from ethnic voters, and among French-speaking Canadians. Liberals are cautious about extending the welfare state.

New Democratic Party—Successor to the Cooperative Commonwealth Federation, which combined the agrarian protest movement in western Canada with a democratic socialism of the British Labor Party variety, the N.D.P. was founded in 1961. It now attempts to attract the vote of middle-class Canadians and fuse it with the party's labor support.

Social Credit — Adopting the unorthodox monetary theories of its English founder, Major C. H. Douglas, Social Credit has appealed to the have-nots, especially now in rural Quebec.

Political power in Canada has been completely dominated by the 2 major parties — the Progressive Conservatives and the Liberals. Since 1867 these 2 parties have alternated in forming the government and in monopolizing political power. In the 30 federal elections conducted in Canada, the Conservatives have won 12, holding power for 47 years; the Liberals have gained office in 18 elections, governing the country for 61 years. A noteworthy feature of these 2 parties' political rule has been the tendency for one or the other to remain entrenched in office for a considerable length of time.

Although the Conservatives and the Liberals have been the only 2 parties to form the government of Canada and have clearly dominated Canadian political life, the role of 3d parties in Canadian politics has been significant. Since 1961, 2 minority parties, the New Democratic Party and Social Credit, have exerted some measure of influence on political outcomes. The NDP, Canada's most persistent 3d party, has been the more important of the 2. Pressure from the NDP on the left has pushed the 2 major parties to a position close to the center stream of the political spectrum. Minority party success at the polls has not been particularly spectacular. At best the NDP has succeeded in obtaining 31 seats or 12% with 18% of the popular vote.

In contrast to the NDP, the Social Credit Party is to the extreme right. The SC came into national prominence in the 1962 election following a sudden sweep in the Province of Quebec when the party succeeded in winning 26 of the 75 seats in that province. This victory increased the party's federal strength to 30 seats (12%), the highest it has ever been. In the 1974 election the party received only 11 seats of the total 264 and captured a mere 5% of the popular vote.

Party Representation by Regions, 1949-1974

Canada[1]	1949	1953	1957	1958	1962	1963	1965	1968	1972	1974
Liberal	193	171	105	40	100	129	131	155	109	141
Conservative	41	51	112	208	116	95	97	72	107	95
New Democratic	13	23	25	8	19	17	21	22	31	16
Social Credit	10	15	19	—	30	24	14	14	15	11
Other	5	5	4	—	—	—	2	1	2	1
Ontario										
Liberal	56	51	21	15	44	52	51	64	36	55
Conservative	25	33	61	67	35	27	25	17	40	25
New Democratic	1	1	3	3	6	6	9	6	11	8
Quebec										
Liberal	68	66	62	25	35	47	56	56	56	60
Conservative	2	4	9	50	14	8	8	4	2	3
Social Credit	—	—	—	—	26	20	9	14	15	11
Atlantic										
Liberal	26	27	12	8	14	20	15	7	10	13
Conservative	7	5	21	25	18	13	18	25	22	17
New Democratic	1	1	—	—	1	—	—	—	—	1
Western										
Liberal	43	27	10	1	7	10	9	27	7	13
Conservative	7	9	21	66	49	47	46	25	42	49
New Democratic	11	21	22	5	12	11	12	16	19	6
Social Credit	10	15	19	—	4	4	5	—	—	—

(1) Total seats in 1968, 1972, and 1974 elections include one each for Yukon and Northwest Territories.

Canadian Armed Forces

In Feb., 1968, Canada carried out the unification of its traditionally separate services: the Royal Canadian Navy, the Canadian Army, and the Royal Canadian Air Force. The first step towards a unified force was taken in 1964 when the 3 services were brought together under one control with common logistics and supply and training systems, but retaining their separate legal entities. The positions of Chairman of the Chiefs of Staff and Chiefs of the Navy, Army, and Air Force were abolished and replaced by the Chief of the Defense Staff. On Feb. 1, 1968, the 3 services ceased to exist. They were unified into the Canadian Armed Forces in which all officers, men, and women are managed within a single body, with a common uniform.

Chief of the Defense Staff: Admiral R. H. Falls
Vice Chief of the Defense Staff: Lieut. Gen. R. M. Withers

Maritime Command — Vice Admiral A. L. Collier
Mobile Command — Lieut. Gen. J. J. Paradis
Air Command — Lieut. Gen. W. K. Carr
Communications Command — Brig. Gen. R. N. Senior
Canadian Forces Europe — Maj. Gen. C. H. Belzile

Regular Forces Strength

(as of March 31)

Year	Navy	Army	Air Force	Total
1945	92,529	494,258	174,254	761,041
1955	19,207	49,409	49,461	118,077
1965	19,756	46,264	48,144	114,164
1970	....	....	....	91,433
1971	....	....	....	87,715
1972	....	....	....	82,879
1973	....	....	....	81,443
1974	....	....	....	80,639
1975	....	....	....	78,448
1976	....	....	....	78,394

Canadian Military Participation in Major Conflicts

Northwest Rebellion (1885)[1]
Participants—3,323
Killed—38
Last veteran died at the age of 104 in 1971.
South African War (1899-1902)
Participants—7,368[2]
Killed—89
Living Veterans—less than 50
First World War (1914-1918)
Participants—626,636[3]
Killed—61,332[4]
Living Veterans—96,900
Second World War (1939-1945)
Participants—1,086,343 (inc. 45,423 women)
Killed—37,714 (inc. 8 women)
Living Veterans—801,000
Korean War (1950-1953)
Participants—25,583
Killed—314
Living Veterans—25,000

(1) First battle in history to be fought entirely by Canadian troops. (2) Includes Canadians in the South African constabulary and 8 nursing sisters. (3) Includes 2,854 nursing sisters. (4) Includes 21 nursing sisters and 1,563 airmen serving with the British air forces.

Canadian Peacekeeping Operations

Since World War II Canada has played a vital role in cooperating with the United Nations in its capacity as a peacekeeping agency for the preservation of peace and the promotion of international security. Canadians have participated in almost all UN peacekeeping operations to date — in Egypt, Israel, Syria, Lebanon, Cyprus, Korea, India, Pakistan, West New Guinea, the Congo, Yemen, and Nigeria.

Nearly 900 Canadian soldiers served in the Gaza Strip following the Israeli-Egyptian crisis of 1956 until the force was disbanded in 1967.

In the Congo, a 300-man signals unit provided communications for the UN Force from 1960 to 1964.

Canadian participation in the International Commission for Control and Supervision in Vietnam and Laos began in 1954 and at the high point of participation in 1973, following the U.S. military withdrawal from Vietnam, there were 245 Canadian Forces personnel involved in the supervision of the ceasefire. The Canadian Vietnam supervisory contingent was withdrawn in July 1973 and the Laos mission was withdrawn in the spring of 1974.

Canada's largest peacekeeping commitment at the present time (mid-1977) is in the Middle East where Canadians participate in the United Nations Emergency Force (UNEF), and in the United Nations Disengagement Observer Force (UNDOF). Canada shares with Poland the logistics support role for UNEF in the Sinai and UNDOF in the Golan Heights. Canada's current overall participation in UNEF/UNDOF is approximately 1,000 personnel — about 850 Canadians are serving with UNEF and about 150 with UNDOF.

Th UN Force in Cyprus is another of Canada's large military commitments. Since 1964 Canadian participation included provision of a reduced infantry battalion and a Canadian element in the UN Headquarters — a total of approximately 580 officers and men. However, in July 1974, following the troubles in Cyprus, Canada, at the request of the UN, augmented the Cyprus contingent by an additional force of approximately 480 officers and men and some additional military equipment. About 515 Canadians presently serve in the Peacekeeping Force in Cyprus.

Other Canadian peacekeeping operations in 1977 are as follows:

— 9 Canadian Forces personnel with UN Military Observer Group, India-Pakistan.

— 20 Canadian officers with the UN Truce Supervisory Organization, Israel.

— 2 Canadian Forces personnel in Korea with the UN Military Armistice Commission.

Canadian World War II Winners of the Victoria Cross

The Victoria Cross is Britain's highest military honor. It has been accorded to 94 Canadians since its inception in 1856. The cross was originally cast from metal of a Russian cannon captured during the Crimean War.

Name	Unit	Theater of war & date
Sgt. Mjr. J. R. Osborn	Winnipeg Grenadiers	Hong Kong, Dec. 19, 1941
Lt. Col. C. E. Merritt	S. Sask. Regiment	Dieppe, Aug. 19, 1942
Capt. J. W. Foote	Royal Hamilton Light Infantry	Dieppe, Aug. 19, 1942
Capt. F. T. Peters	Royal Navy	Oran, North Africa, Nov. 8, 1942
Capt. Paul Triquet	Royal 22d Regiment	Casa Berardi, Dec. 14, 1943
Maj. C. F. Hoey	Lincolnshire Regiment	Burma, Feb. 16, 1944
Maj. John K. Mahoney	Westminster Regiment	Melfa River, May 24, 1944
P.O.A.C. Mynarksi	RCAF	Camria, France, June 12, 1944
Flt. Lieut. D. E. Hornell	RCAF	"Northern waters", June 25, 1944
Sqd. Ldr. Ian Bazalgette	RCAF	Trossy St. Maximin, Aug. 4, 1944
Maj. D. V. Currie	South Alberta Regiment	Normandy, Aug. 20, 1944
Pvt. E. A. Smith	Seaforth Highlanders	Savio River, Italy, Oct. 22, 1944
Sgt. Aubrey Cosens	Queen's Own Rifles	Holland, Feb. 26, 1945
Maj. F. A. Tilston	Essex Scottish	Hochwald Forest, Mar. 1, 1945
Cpl. F. G. Topham	1st Canadian Parachute Battalion	Germany, Mar. 24, 1945
Lt. R. H. Gray	Royal Canadian Navy	Pacific, Aug. 9, 1945

Superlative Canadian Statistics

Area	Total: Land 3,560,238 sq. mi.; Water 291,571 sq. mi.	3,851,809 sq. mi.
Largest city in area	Whitehorse	162 sq. mi.
Smallest city in area (east)	Thetford Mines, Que.	7 sq. mi.
Smallest city in area (west)	Prince George, B.C.	17 sq. mi.
Northernmost point	Cape Columbia, N.W.T.	83°07′N.
Northernmost town	Inuvik, N.W.T.	68°21′N.
Southernmost point	Middle Island (Lake Erie), Ont.	42°41′N.
Southernmost town	Kingsville, Ont.	42°02′N.
Westernmost point	Mount St. Elias, Yukon	141°W.
Westernmost town	Dawson, Yukon	139°25′W.
Easternmost point	Cape Spear, Nfld.	52°37′W.
Easternmost town	St. John's, Nfld.	52°43′W.
Highest City	Rossland, B.C. at R.R. Stn. (49°05′N117°47′W)	3,465 ft.
Highest town	Lake Louise, Alta.	5,051 ft.
Highest waterfall	Takakkaw Falls, B.C. (51°30′N116°29′W)	1.650 ft.
Longest river	Mackenzie (from head of Finlay R.)	2,635 mi.
Highest mountain	Mt. Logan	19,850 ft.
Rainiest spot	Henderson Lake, Vancouver Is. yrly avg. rainfall	262.0 inches
Highest lake	Chilco Lake (51°20′N124°05′W) 75.1 sq. mi.	3,842 ft.

Population and Area of Canada by Provinces

Source: Statistics Canada

Province, territory	Capital	Area in square miles: Land	Area in square miles: Fresh water	Area in square miles: Total	Population: 1966 census	Population: 1976 census	Population: April 1977 estimate
Newfoundland	St. John's	143,045	13,140	156,185	493,396	557,725	561,000
Prince Edward Island	Charlottetown	2,184	. . .	2,184	108,645	118,229	120,000
Nova Scotia	Halifax	20,402	1,023	21,425	756,039	828,571	835,000
New Brunswick	Fredericton	27,385	519	28,345	616,788	677,250	685,000
Quebec	Quebec	523,860	71,000	594,860	5,780,845	6,234,445	6,276,000
Ontario	Toronto	344,092	68,490	412,582	6,960,870	8,264,465	8,355,000
Manitoba	Winnipeg	211,775	39,225	251,000	963,066	1,021,506	1,029,000
Saskatchewan	Regina	220,182	31,518	251,700	955,344	921,323	935,000
Alberta	Edmonton	248,800	6,485	255,285	1,463,203	1,838,037	1,890,000
British Columbia	Victoria	359,279	6,976	366,255	1,873,674	2,466,608	2,492,000
Northwest Territories	Yellowknife	1,253,438	51,465	1,304,903	28,738	21,836	43,000
Yukon Territory	Whitehorse	205,345	1,730	207,076	1,382	42,609	22,000
Total		**3,560,238**	**291,571**	**3,851,809**	**20,014,880**	**22,992,604**	**23,243,000**

Canadian Cities with Metropolitan Populations Over 100,000

Source: Statistics Canada

Census Metropolitan Areas. All figures shown are for the 1976 Census.

	Metro Area	City
Toronto, Ontario	2,803,101	633,318
Montreal, Quebec	2,802,485	1,080,546
Vancouver, British Columbia	1,166,348	410,188
Ottawa-Hull, Ontario, Quebec	693,288	304,462
Winnipeg, Manitoba	578,217	560,874
Edmonton, Alberta	554,228	461,361
Quebec, Quebec	542,158	177,082
Hamilton, Ontario	529,371	312,003
Ontario (part) Ontario	521,341	—
Calgary, Alberta	469,917	469,917
St. Catharines-Niagara, Ontario	301,921	123,351
Kitchener, Ontario	272,158	131,870
London, Ontario	270,383	240,392
Halifax, Nova Scotia	267,991	117,882
Windsor, Ontario	247,582	196,526
Victoria, British Columbia	218,250	62,551
Quebec (part) Quebec	171,947	—
Sudbury, Ontario	157,030	97,604
Regina, Saskatchewan	151,191	149,593
St. John's, Newfoundland	143,390	86,576
Oshawa, Ontario	135,196	107,023
Saskatoon, Saskatchewan	133,750	133,750
Chicoutimi-Jonquiere, Quebec	128,643	57,737
Thunder Bay, Ontario	119,253	111,476
Saint John, New Brunswick	112,974	85,956

Immigration to Canada, by Country of Last Permanent Residence

Source: Canadian Statistical Review, May 1977

Year	Total	UK and Ireland	France	Germany	Netherlands	Greece	Italy
1974	218,465	39,748	4,232	3,621	2,103	5,632	5,226
1975	187,881	36,076	3,891	3,469	1,448	4,062	5,078
1976	149,429	22,187	3,251	2,672	1,359	2,487	4,530

Year	Portugal	Other Europe	Asia	Australasia	United States	West Indies	All Other
1974	16,333	11,799	50,566	2,594	26,541	23,670	26,400
1975	8,547	10,327	47,382	2,174	20,155	17,800	27,472
1976	5,344	8,078	44,328	1,886	17,315	14,723	21,269

Immigration to Canada, by Province of Intended Destination

Source: Canadian Statistical Review

Year	Canada	Nfld.	P.E.I.	N.S.	N.B.	Que.	Ont.	Man.	Sask.	Alta.	B.C.	N.W.T. Yukon
1972	122,006	686	175	1,872	1,301	18,592	63,805	5,262	1,511	8,390	20,107	305
1973	184,200	984	273	2,548	1,729	26,871	103,187	6,621	1,866	11,904	27,949	268
1974	218,465	1,036	311	2,601	2,207	33,458	120,115	7,423	2,244	14,289	34,481	300
1975	187,881	1,106	235	2,124	2,093	28,042	98,471	7,134	2,837	16,277	29,272	290
1976	149,429	725	235	1,942	1,752	29,282	72,031	5,509	2,323	14,896	20,484	250

Canadian Population by Mother Tongue, 1971

Source: Statistics Canada

Province	English	French	German	Indian, Eskimo	Italian	Dutch	Polish	Ukrainian	Other
Newfoundland	514,520	3,635	515	1,620	175	120	45	50	1,430
Prince Edward Island	103,105	7,360	140	145	35	280	40	30	510
Nova Scotia	733,560	39,330	2,000	2,710	1,495	1,850	555	435	7,020
New Brunswick	410,400	215,730	1,110	2,725	755	665	155	110	2,905
Quebec	789,185	4,867,250	31,025	21,050	135,455	4,660	15,480	11,385	152,265
Ontario	5,971,570	482,045	184,880	28,590	344,285	77,475	73,985	80,230	460,050
Manitoba	662,720	60,550	82,720	31,665	7,265	10,385	15,900	72,925	44,130
Saskatchewan	685,920	31,605	75,885	26,020	2,045	4,695	7,675	53,385	39,025
Alberta	1,263,935	46,500	92,800	29,920	15,570	20,670	13,730	70,895	73,855
British Columbia	1,807,250	38,035	89,020	18,550	31,030	23,955	7,100	20,055	149,620
Yukon	15,345	450	565	1,030	75	100	55	150	620
Northwest Territories	16,305	1,160	425	15,800	175	80	60	205	595
Total	**12,973,810**	**5,793,650**	**561,085**	**179,825**	**538,360**	**144,920**	**134,780**	**309,855**	**932,020**

Population by Religious Denomination

Source: Statistics Canada

Denomination	1961	1971
Adventist	25,999	28,590
Anglican	2,409,068	2,543,180
Baptist	593,553	667,245
Buddhist	11,611	16,175
Chr. & Miss'nary Alliance	18,006	23,630
Christian Reformed	62,257	83,390

Denomination	1961	1971	Denomination	1961	1971
Ch. of Christ, Disciples	19,512	16,405	Orthodox (3)	239,766	316,605
Confucian	5,089	2,165	Pentecostal	143,877	220,390
Doukhobor	13,234	9,107	Presbyterian	818,588	872,335
Free Methodist	14,245	19,125	Roman Catholic	8,342,826	9,974,895
Hutterite	(1)	13,650	Salvation Army	92,054	119,665
Jehovah's Witnesses	68,018	174,810	Ukrainian Catholic(4)	189,653	227,730
Jewish	254,368	276,025	Unitarian	15,062	20,995
Lutheran	662,744	715,740	United Church	3,664,008	3,768,800
Mennonite(2)	152,452	168,150	Other	277,508	293,240
Mormon	50,016	66,635	No religion	94,763	929,575

(1) Included with Mennonite. (2) Includes Hutterites in 1961. (3) Those churches which observe the Eastern Orthodox rite, including Greek, Russian, Ukrainian, and Syrian Orthodox. (4) Includes other "Greek Catholic."

Canadian Government Budget

Source: Canadian Statistical Review (May 1977)
(millions of Canadian dollars)

Expenditures

Fiscal Year	National defense	Health and welfare	Agriculture	Post Office	Public works	Transport	Veterans affairs	Payments to provinces	Total expenditures
1971-72...	1,895.2	2,706.1	286.1	413.3	336.8	512.4	423.3	1,425.5	14,840.9
1972-73...	1,932.2	2,916.0	322.3	496.5	374.1	598.9	452.3	1,501.4	16,120.7
1973-74...	2,232.0	3,775.0	426.0	591.0	470.0	827.0	538.0	1,874.0	20,056.0
1974-75...	2,509.0	5,199.0	664.0	732.0	524.0	1,303.0	619.0	2,639.0	26,055.0
1975-76...	2,973.0	9,731.0	651.0	913.0	624.0	1,185.0	684.0	2,460.0	33,977.0
1976-77...	3,171.0	10,664.0	583.0	1,071.0	633.0	1,169.0	743.0	2,553.0	37,357.0

Revenues[1]

Fiscal year	Personal income tax	Corporation income tax	Sales tax	Other excise tax[2]	Excise duties	Customs duties	Estate taxes	Post Office	Total budgetary revenues
1971-72...	5,582.0	2,183.1	1,984.7	388.4	606.6	988.6	132.4	403.8	14,226.6
1972-73...	7,172.8	2,653.5	2,288.7	400.4	638.0	1,181.8	61.4	470.1	16,601.6
1973-74...	7,925.0	3,411.0	2,693.0	695.0	686.0	1,385.0	15.0	480.0	19,383.0
1974-75...	10,069.0	4,285.0	2,900.0	2,083.0	748.0	1,809.0	7.0	485.0	24,909.0
1975-76...	12,708.0	5,748.0	3,939.0	1,501.0	817.0	1,887.0	12.0	443.0	29,956.0
1976-77...	15,086.0	5,273.0	4,320.0	1,097.0	858.0	2,057.0	68.0	589.0	32,282.0

(1) This statement includes only receipts relating to revenue. Excluded are non-budgetary revenues such as Old Age Security Fund taxes, Prairie Farm Assistance Act levies, employer and employee contributions to government-held funds.
(2) Beginning in Dec. 1973, this category includes oil export tax.

Assets and Deposits of Chartered Banks in Canada

Source: Supplement to the Canada Gazette, June 1, 1977
(as of April 30, 1977—thousands of Canadian dollars)

Bank	Assets	Deposits
Royal Bank of Canada	32,151,962	29,324,508
Imperial Bank of Commerce	28,965,873	26,498,266
Bank of Montreal	22,921,948	20,934,171
Bank of Nova Scotia	20,777,398	18,765,477
Toronto-Dominion Bank	17,973,047	16,132,283
Banque Canadienne	6,389,182	5,959,265
Banque Provinciale	3,864,969	3,643,777
Mercantile Bank of Canada	1,843,813	1,679,205
Bank of British Columbia	1,025,595	954,924
Unity Bank of Canada	115,524	98,547
Commerc'l & Indust'l Bank	63,533	48,830
Northland Bank	21,935	10,837

Canadian Foreign Trade

Source: Canadian Statistical Review (May 1977)
(millions of Canadian dollars)

Year	Exports including re-exports				Imports			
	All countries	U.S.	UK	All other countries	All countries	U.S.	UK	All other countries
1969	14,931	10,614	1,113	3,204	14,130	10,243	791	3,096
1970	16,820	10,917	1,485	4,404	13,951	9,917	738	3,296
1971	17,744	12,006	1,361	4,377	15,607	10,941	837	3,827
1972	20,140	13,932	1,358	4,780	18,678	12,878	950	4,844
1973	25,419.5	17,129.0	1,604.3	6,686.3	23,323.6	16,502.0	1,005.3	5,816.0
1974	32,441.3	21,399.5	1,928.6	9,113.3	31,692.3	21,356.6	1,126.4	9,209.1
1975	33,103.6	21,652.4	1,789.1	9,661.9	34,635.4	23,559.4	1,222.1	9,854.1

Canadian Consumer Price Index

Source: Statistics Canada
(All items; 1971=100)

Year	Avg.	Year	Avg.	Year	Avg.	Year	Avg.
1962	75.9	1966	83.5	1970	97.2	1974	125.0
1963	77.2	1967	86.5	1971	100.0	1975	138.5
1964	78.6	1968	90.0	1972	104.8	1976	148.9
1965	80.5	1969	94.1	1973	112.7	1977 (May)	159.2

Price Indexes By Item

Source: Canadian Statistical Review, May 1977 (1971:100)

Year and month	All items	Food	Shelter	Clothing	Trans-portation	Health, personal	Recreation, education	Tobacco, alcohol	Total services
1974......	125.0	143.4	120.7	118.0	115.8	119.4	116.4	111.8	120.5
1975......	138.5	161.9	130.9	125.1	129.4	133.0	128.5	125.3	133.4
1976......	148.9	166.2	145.7	132.0	143.3	144.3	136.2	134.3	149.6
1977 Jan...	154.0	168.0	154.0	135.4	150.1	148.8	139.5	138.3	157.8
Apr...	157.9	174.7	156.1	139.5	152.7	152.7	140.7	141.7	160.7

Personal Expenditure on Consumer Goods and Services in Current Dollars

Source: Statistics Canada
(millions of dollars)

	1968	1969	1970	1971	1972	1973	1974	1975
Food, beverage, and tobacco	9,739	10,471	11,217	12,021	13,349	15,499	18,059	20,935
Clothing and footwear	3,671	3,908	4,034	4,382	4,842	5,618	6,588	7,498
Gross rent, fuel and power	7,960	8,742	9,861	10,581	11,412	12,586	12,322	16,539
Furniture, furnishings, household equipment and operation	4,322	4,658	4,785	5,228	6,047	7,183	8,556	9,744
Medical care and health services	1,902	1,912	1,758	1,680	1,858	2,121	2,477	2,796
Transportation and communication	6,458	6,863	6,946	7,805	8,784	10,142	11,572	13,531
Recreation, entertainment, education and cultural services	3,682	4,104	4,467	5,193	5,951	6,863	8,180	9,450
Personal goods and services	6,034	6,683	7,133	8,285	9,159	10,485	12,182	14,000
Net expenditure abroad	-10	151	126	96	129	162	128	525
Total	**43,704**	**47,492**	**50,327**	**55,271**	**61,531**	**70,659**	**82,064**	**95,018**
Durable goods	6,494	6,975	6,799	7,762	9,111	10,872	12,513	14,634
Semi-durable goods	5,953	6,426	6,645	7,224	8,109	9,504	11,270	12,823
Non-durable goods	14,019	15,073	16,186	17,359	19,265	22,300	26,322	30,347
Services	17,238	19,018	20,697	22,926	25,046	27,983	31,959	37,214

Canadian Grain Receipts at Western Grain Centers

Source: Canadian Grain Commission
(thousands of bushels)

Crop year 1974-75

Province	Wheat	Oats	Barley	Rye	Flaxseed	Rapeseed	Total
Western Canada	422,431	40,280	209,224	10,435	10,797	41,217	734,385
Manitoba	49,693	12,535	32,368	1,911	5,028	6,300	107,834
Saskatchewan	280,184	13,486	80,482	3,984	3,880	19,637	401,653
Alberta	92,554	14,258	96,374	4,540	1,890	15,281	224,898

Crop year 1975-76

Province	Wheat	Oats	Barley	Rye	Flaxseed	Rapeseed	Total
Western Canada	525,420	51,458	215,227	12,629	15,549	60,312	880,596
Manitoba	61,091	16,598	29,007	2,953	7,609	9,602	129,321
Saskatchewan	339,556	15,468	73,535	4,990	5,413	28,377	467,340
Alberta	121,773	19,393	112,684	4,686	2,528	22,873	283,936

Canadian Shipping Traffic

Source: Canadian Statistical Review, May, 1977 (thousand short tons)
Total cargo handled includes cargo loaded and unloaded in foreign and coastwise shipping.

Year and month	Halifax	Saint John	Quebec	Montreal	Toronto	Vancouver	All Ports	Coastwise
1971	10,999	7,438	10,811	21,690	4,710	30,813	286,606	122,536
1972	11,355	10,263	14,901	20,431	4,534	29,894	298,076	122,403
1973	13,703	12,181	15,946	21,177	4,170	39,126	320,498	122,436
1974	13,290	9,998	12,943	19,654	4,605	36,761	302,138	118,241
1975	11,743	10,851	12,496	18,633	4,891	35,521	303,098	119,871

Canadian Sea Fish Catch and Exports

Source: Canadian Statistical Review May 1977

(in millions of pounds)

Year	Total Value	Landings of Sea Fish							Exports to[1]			Exports[1]	
		Total	Nfld	P.E.I.	N.S.	N.B.	Que.	B.C.	Total	U.S.	Other	Salmon	Lobste
1971.....	$192,993,000	2,466.1	871.6	97.5	658.1	370.1	240.2	228.7	607.6	438.3	169.3	58.5	22.5
1972.....	219,829,000	2,215.1	649.3	59.9	654.0	394.5	182.1	336.7	642.0	443.6	169.3	77.6	19.8
1973.....	296,288,000	2,190.4	675.9	62.9	615.4	286.1	161.3	388.8	752.6	491.6	211.1	93.1	20.1
1974.....	259,108,000	1,839	517	36	624	353	118	293	551.4	394.6	155.0	78.5	18.2
1975.....	225,423,000	1,518	191	30	582	268	108	252	588.9	397.8	191.1	51.3	19.5
1976.....	300,823,000	831,119	147,288	17,088	355,193	108,448	42,074	161,027	646.4	432.2	194.4	42.5	19.6

(1) Exports include sea and freshwater fish and shellfish products but exclude bait, meal, oils, offal, livers, fish roe, and fishery foods and feeds.

Value of Canadian Fishery Products and By-products

Source: Statistics Canada (C$1,000)

Final sales for the provinces by fish processors, handlers, and fishermen.

Province	1974	1975
Newfoundland	114,612	120,753
Prince Edward Island	20,402	27,760
Nova Scotia	183,644	208,574
New Brunswick	100,581	116,274
Quebec	29,836	30,609
Ontario	19,310	22,104
Manitoba, Saskatchewan, Alberta, Northwest Territories	19,217	22,07
British Columbia[2]	220,452	167,01
Yukon	107	8
Total[1]	**708,161**	**713,33**

(1) The sum of the provincial totals differ from the Canada total as duplications (intershipments between provinces) have been removed from the Atlantic Coast totals. (2) Includes halibut landed in United States ports.

Canadian Source of Electric Energy, by Province, 1976

Source: Statistics Canada

(megawatt hours)

	Net generation				Total imported	Total exported	Total supply available
	Hydro	Thermal: Conventional	Thermal: Nuclear	Total			
Canada	213,088,812	63,892,165	16,430,255	293,411,232	3,513,033	12,800,884	284,123,38
Newfoundland	38,773,517	416,598	—	39,190,115	—	32,104,464	7,085,65
Prince Edward Island	—	444,989	—	444,989	—	—	444,98
Nova Scotia	792,013	4,871,162	—	5,663,175	389,692	16,269	6,036,59
New Brunswick	3,456,633	3,206,819	—	6,663,452	3,825,761	2,956,623	7,532,59
Quebec	77,425,756	271,770	—	77,697,526	32,468,841	15,964,693	94,201,67
Ontario	38,291,644	32,515,058	16,430,235	87,236,957	15,291,275	6,595,918	95,932,31
Manitoba	12,728,648	1,275,461	—	14,004,109	1,174,149	2,872,049	12,306,20
Saskatchewan	2,463,546	5,051,184	—	7,514,730	658,041	794,328	7,378,44
Alberta	1,950,550	13,828,865	—	15,779,415	432,090	118,994	16,092,51
British Columbia	36,694,397	1,849,342	—	38,543,739	1,200,485	3,304,847	36,439,37
Yukon	257,652	48,974	—	306,626	—	—	306,62
Northwest Territories	254,456	111,943	—	366,399	—	—	366,39

Marriages, Divorces in Canada

Source: Statistics Canada

(Rates per 1,000 population)

Year	Marriages No.	Marriages Rate	Divorces No.	Divorces Rate
1940	125,799	10.8	2,416	0.21
1950	125,083	9.1	5,386	0.39
1960	130,338	7.3	6,980	0.39
1965	145,519	7.4	8,974	0.45
1970	188,428	8.8	29,775	1.39
1973	199,064	9.0	36,704	1.66
1974	198,824	8.9	45,019	2.00
1975	197,585	8.7	50,611	2.22

Births and Deaths in Canada by Province

Source: Statistics Canada

Province	Births 1975	Births 1976	Deaths 1975	Deaths 1976
Newfoundland	11,213	11,320	3,208	3,230
Prince Edward Island	1,928	1,900	1,054	1,060
Nova Scotia	13,119	13,200	6,794	6,860
New Brunswick	11,775	12,060	5,121	5,160
Quebec	93,000	95,420	42,800	42,750
Ontario	125,708	124,770	60,482	60,710
Manitoba	17,144	17,240	8,380	8,41
Saskatchewan	15,260	15,570	7,670	7,56
Alberta	31,618	33,000	11,396	11,32
British Columbia	36,277	38,590	19,143	19,10
Total	**357,042**	**363,070**	**166,048**	**166,16**

NATIONS OF THE WORLD

The nations of the world are listed in alphabetical order, except for Canada and the United States (see Index r listings). Initials in the following articles include UN (United Nations), OAS (Org. of American States), ATO (North Atlantic Treaty Org.), EC (European Communities or Common Market), OAU (Org. of African nity). Areas based primarily upon U.S. State Department figures.

See special color section for maps and flags of all nations.

Afghanistan

Republic of Afghanistan

People: Population (1976 est.): 19,800,000. **Pop. density:** per sq. mi. **Ethnic groups:** Pushtuns (Pathans) nearly 60%; jiks nearly 30%; Uzbek over 5%; Hazara, others. **Languages:** ıshtun (Iranian), Dari Persian (spoken by Tajika, Hazaras), bek (Turkic). **Religions:** Moslem, mostly Sunni.

Geography: Area: 253,861 sq. mi., slightly smaller than xas. **Location:** Between Soviet Central Asia and the Indian bcontinent. **Neighbors:** Pakistan on E, S, Iran on W, USSR on (Turkmenistan, Uzbekistan, Tadzhikistan, Kirghizia); the NE touches China (Sinkiang). **Topography:** The country is landked and mountainous, much of it over 4,000 ft. above sea el. The Hindu Kush Mts. tower 16,000 ft. above Kabul and ach a height of 25,000 ft. to the E. Trade with Pakistan flows ough the 35-mile long Khyber Pass. The climate is dry, with treme temperatures, and large desert regions, though moun- n rivers produce intermittent fertile valleys. **Capital:** Kabul. **ties** (1976 est.): Kabul (met.) 587,643, Kandahar 149,361; ghlan 118,269; Herat 116,003; Tagab 113,901.

Government: Head of State: Pres. Mohammad Daoud; in offe: July 19, 1973; **Head of government:** Prime. Min. Mohamad Daoud. **Local divisions:** 26 provinces, each under a vernor. **Armed forces:** regulars 100,000; reserves 160,000.

Economy: Industries: Textiles, carpets, cement, sheepskin ats. **Chief crops:** Cotton, oilseeds, fruits. **Minerals:** Copper, ad, gas, coal, zinc, iron, silver, asbestos. **Other resources:** ool, hides, karacul pelts. **Per capita arable land:** 1.0 acres. **vestock** (1974): 3,550,000 cattle 17,000,000 sheep (7,000,- 0 karacul); **Electricity production** (1972): 439 mln. kwh. **bor force:** 81% agriculture.

Finance: Currency: Afghani (Apr. 1977: 45=$1 US). **Gross mestic product** (est. 1974): $2 bln. **Per capita income** 974): $100. **Imports** (1975): $293 mln.; partners (1972): USSR %, Jap. 15%, U.S. 11%, W. Ger. 9%. **Exports** (1974): $210 n; partners (1972): USSR 29%, Ind. 24%, U.K. 16%, W. Ger. . **Tourists** (1974): 96,200; receipts: $12 million. **International serves** (Feb. 1977): $164.64 mln.

Transport: Motor vehicles: in use (1971): 38,400 passenger rs, 26,100 commercial vehicles.

Communications: Daily newspaper circulation (1973): 90,- 0; 5 per 1,000 pop.

Health: Life expectancy at birth (1970-75): 39.9 male; 40.7 male. **Births** (annual per 1,000 pop. 1970-75): 49.2. **Deaths** nnual per 1,000 pop. 1970-75): 23.8. **Natural increase** nnual 1970-75): 2.54%. **Pop. per hospital bed** (1973): 5,542. **p. per physician** (1973): 15,242. **Infant mortality** (per 1,000 p. under 1 yr. 1973): 182.

Education: Literacy (1973): 8%. **Pop. 5-19:** in school (1973): %; per teacher (1973): 261.

Afghanistan, occupying a favored invasion route since anuity, has been variously known as Ariana or Bactria (in ancient nes) and Khorasan (in the Middle Ages). Foreign empires altered rule with local emirs and kings until the 18th century, when unified kingdom was established. In 1973, a military coup hered in a republic.

Modern Afghanistan has attempted to remain neutral, receivg aid from the U.S., USSR, and China. Largest trade partner is e USSR, with natural gas the chief export.

In recent centuries, isolation has hampered modernization.

Albania

People's Republic of Albania

People: Population (1976 est.): 2,550,000. **Pop. density:** 0 per sq. mi. **Urban** (1971): 33.8%. **Ethnic groups:** Albanians egs in N, Tosks in S) 95%, Greeks 2.5%. **Languages:** Albanian (Tosk is official dialect), Greek. **Religions:** (historically) Moslems 70%, Orthodox 20%, Roman Catholic 10%. All public worship and religious institutions were outlawed in 1967.

Geography: area: 11,100 sq. mi., slightly larger than Maryland. **Location:** On SE coast of Adriatic Sea. **Neighbors:** Greece on S, Yugoslavia on N, E. **Topography:** Apart from a narrow coastal plain, Albania consists of hills and mountains covered with scrub forest, cut by small E-W rivers. **Capital:** Tirana. **Cities** (1976 est.): Tirana 192,300; Shkoder 62,500; Durres 61,000; Vlone 58,400.

Government: Head of state: Pres. Haxhi Lleshi, b. 1913, in office: July 1953; **Head of government:** Chmn. Mehmet Shehu, b. 1913. **Head of Communist Party:** Enver Hoxha, b. 1908, in office: 1944. **Local divisions:** 26 administrative districts. **Armed forces:** regulars 47,000; reserves 100,000.

Economy: Industries: Chem. fertilizers, textiles, electric cables. **Chief crops:** Grain, corn, sugar beets, cotton, tobacco, fruits. **Minerals:** Coal, chromium, copper, bitumen, iron, oil **Crude oil output** (1976): 15,012,000 bbls. **Other resources** Forests. **Per capita arable land:** 0.5 acres. **Livestock** (1974) 397,000 cattle; 117,000 pigs; 1,163,000 sheep. **Fish catch** (1964): 3,600 metric tons. **Electricity production** (1973): 1,603 mln. kwh. **Labor force:** 62% agric.

Finance: currency: Lek (1974: 10.25=$1 US). **Gross domestic product** (est. 1974): $1.7 bln. **Per capita income** (1974): $650. **Imports:** (1974): $250 mln.; partners P. R. China, E. Eur., It. **Exports** (1974): $200 mln.; partners P. R. China, E. Eur., It. **Chief ports:** Durres, Vlone.

Communications: Television sets: 4,000 in use (1973). **Radios:** 172,000 in use (1973). **Daily Newspaper circulation** (1973): 115,000; 49 per 1,000 pop.

Health: Life expectancy at birth (1965-66): 64.9 male; 67.0 female. **Births** (per 1,000 pop. 1971): 33.3. **Deaths** (per 1,000 pop. 1971): 8.1. **Natural increase** (1971): 2.52%. **Pop. per hospital bed** (1973): 162. **Pop. per physician** (1973): 1,175. **Infant mortality** (per 1,000 pop. under 1 yr. 1965): 86.8.

Education: Literacy (1973): 75%. **Pop. 5-19:** in school (1973): 66%; per teacher (1973): 36.

Ancient Illyria was conquered by Romans, Slavs, and Turks (15th century); the latter Islamized the population. Independent Albania was proclaimed in 1912, republic was formed in 1920. Self-styled King Zog I ruled 1925-39, until Italy invaded.

Communist partisans took over in 1944, allied Albania with USSR, then broke with USSR in 1960 over de-Stalinization. Strong political alliance with China followed, leading to substantial Chinese aid, which was curtailed after 1974. China accounts for over half of foreign trade. Relations between the two countries cooled in 1977 after the death of Chinese ruler Mao Tsetung.

In 1971, after years of mistrust, Albania resumed relations with Greece and Yugoslavia, but ties with U.S. and USSR are still rejected.

Industrialization, pressed in 1960s, slowed in 1970s. Large-scale purges of officials occurred 1973-76.

Algeria

Democratic and Popular Republic of Algeria

People: Population (1976 est.): 17,300,000. **Age distrib.** (%): 0-14: 47.2; 15-59: 46.2; 60+: 6.6 **Pop. Density:** 19 per sq. mi. **Urban** (1974): 52.0%. **Ethnic groups:** Arabs 75%, Berbers 25%. **Languages:** Arab, Berber (indigenous language), French (spoken by Arab elite). **Religions:** Sunni Moslem the state religion.

Geography: Area: 919,951 sq. mi., more than 3 times the size of Texas. **Location:** In NW Africa, from Mediterranean Sea into Sahara Desert. **Neighbors:** Morocco on W, Mauritania, Mali, Niger on S, Libya, Tunisia on E. **Topography:** The Tell, located on the coast, comprises fertile plains 50-100 miles wide, with a moderate climate and adequate rain. Two major chains of the Atlas Mts., running roughly E-W, and reaching 7,000 ft., enclose a dry plateau region. Below lies the Sahara, mostly desert with major mineral resources. **Capital:** Algiers. **Cities** (1973 est.): Algiers (met.) 1,200,000; (1966 cen.): Oran 327,493; Constantine 243,558; Annaba 152,006.

Government: Head of state: Pres. Houari Boumedienne, b. 1925, in office: June 19, 1965. **Local divisions:** 31 wilayas (states); governors are responsible to the center. **Armed forces:** regulars 69,300; reserves 100,000.

Economy: Industries: Wine, cigarettes, oil products, iron, steel, textiles, fertilizer, plastics. **Chief crops:** Grains, corn, winegrapes, potatoes, artichokes, flax, olives, tobacco, dates, figs, pomegranates. **Minerals:** Oil, iron, zinc, lead, mercury, coal, copper, natural gas, phosphates. **Crude oil output** (1976): 391 mln. bbls. In 1975, Algeria was world's 14th largest producer. **Other resources:** Cork trees. **Per capita arable land:** 1.0 acres. **Livestock** (1974): 920,000 cattle; 4,000 pigs; 8,850,000 sheep. **Fish catch** (1974): 35,800 metric tons. **Electricity production** (1975): 3,120 mln. kwh. **Labor force:** 50% agric.; 6% manuf.

Finance: Currency: Dinar (Apr. 1977: 4.17 =$1 US). **Gross domestic product** (1973): $7.50 bln. **Per capita income** (1974): $660. **Imports** (1976) $5.311 bln.; partners (1973): Fr. 32%, W. Ger. 14%, It. 8%, U.S. 8%. **Exports** (1976): $5.061 bln.; partners (1973): Fr. 22%, W. Ger. 22%, It. 9%, Sp. 9%. **Tourists** (1972): 196,700; receipts (1973): $13 mln. **Balance of payments.** (1975): $−334 mln. **National budget** (1974): $5.94 bln. revenues; $3.13 bln. expenditures. **International reserves** (Feb. 1977): $2.217 bln. **Consumer prices** (change in 1975): 8.3%.

Transport: Railway traffic (1974): 657 mln. passenger-miles; 1,180 mln. net ton-miles. **Motor vehicles:** in use (1974): 180,000 passenger cars, 95,000 commercial vehicles; assembled (1970): 6,000 passenger cars, (1974) 6,300 commercial vehicles. **Chief ports:** Algiers, Oran.

Communications: Television sets: 260,000 licenses (1973); 32,000 manufactured (1973). **Radios:** 725,000 licenses (1973); 19,000 manufactured (1973). **Telephones in use** (1976): 250,424. **Daily newspaper circulation** (1973): 265,000; 17 per 1,000 pop.

Health: Life expectancy at birth (1970-75): 51.7 male; 54.8 female. **Births** (annual per 1,000 pop. 1970-75): 48.7. **Deaths** (annual per 1,000 pop. 1970-75): 15.4. **Natural increase** (annual 1970-75): 3.33%. **Pop. per hospital bed** (1973): 350. **Pop. per physician** (1973): 8,200. **Infant mortality** (per 1,000 pop. under 1 yr. 1965): 86.3.

Education: Literacy (1973): 26%. **Pop. 5-19:** in school (1973): 45%; per teacher (1973): 79.

Earliest known inhabitants were ancestors of Berbers, followed by Phoenicians, Romans, Vandals, and, finally, Arabs; but 25% still speak Berber dialects. Turkey ruled 1518 to 1830, when France took control.

Large-scale European immigration and French cultural inroads did not prevent an Arab nationalist movement from launching guerrilla war. Peace, and French withdrawal, was negotiated with French Pres. Charles de Gaulle. One million Europeans left.

Ahmed Ben Bella was the victor of infighting, and ruled 1962-65, when an army coup installed Col. Houari Boumedienne as leader. Ben Bella and other opponents remain under house arrest.

In 1967, Algeria declared war with Israel, broke with U.S., and moved toward eventual military and political ties with the USSR. French oil interests were partly seized in 1971, but relations with the West have since improved, based on oil and gas exports; U.S. ties were resumed 1974.

Algeria strongly backs Saharan guerrillas against Morocco and Mauritania.

The one-party Socialist regime faces endemic mass unemployment and poverty, despite land reform and industrialization attempts.

Andorra

Valleys of Andorra

People: Population (1975): 26,558. **Age distrib.** (%): 0−14: 29.2; 15−59: 61.7; 60+: 9.1. **Pop. density:** 148 per sq. mi. **Ethnic groups:** Spanish over 60%, Andorran 30%, French 6%. **Languages:** Catalan (official), Spanish, French. **Religions:** Roman Catholic.

Geography: Area: 180 sq. mi., half the size of New York City. **Location:** In Pyrenees Mtns. **Neighbors:** Spain on S, France c N. **Topography:** High mountains and narrow valleys over th country. **Capital:** Andorra la Vella.

Government: Head of state: Co-Princes are the president France (Valery Giscard d'Estaing) and the bishop of Urgel Spain. **Local divisions:** 6 parishes.

Economy: Industries: Tourism, sheep-raising.

Finance: Currency: Franc, Peseta.

Communications: Television sets: 1,700 in use (1969 **Radios:** 6,100 in use (1973). **Telephones in use** (1976): 3,857

Health: Births (per 1,000 pop. 1974): 20.1. **Deaths** (per 1,0C pop. 1974): 4.6. **Natural increase** (1974): 1.54%.

The present political status, with joint sovereignty by Franc and the bishop of Urgel, dates from 1278.

Tourism, especially skiing, is the economic mainstay. A ne road from France is being built.

Angola

People's Republic of Angola

People: Population (1972 est.): 5,800,000. **Pop. density:** per sq. mi. **Ethnic groups:** Ovimbundu 38%, Kimbundu 23% Bacongo 13%, European 1%; Mesticos 2%. **Languages:** Po tuguese (official), various Bantu languages. **Religions:** Roma Catholic 30%, Protestant 12%, others.

Geography: Area: 481,351 sq. mi., larger than Texas ar California combined. **Location:** In SW Africa on Atlantic coas **Neighbors:** Namibia (SW Africa) on S, Zambia on E, Zaire on N Cabinda, an enclave separated from rest of country by sho Atlantic coast of Zaire, borders Congo Republic. **Topography** Most of Angola consists of a plateau elevated 3,000 to 5,000 fe above sea level, rising from a narrow coastal strip. There is als a temperate highland area in the west-central region, a desert the S, and a tropical rain forest covering Cabinda. **Capita** Luanda. **Cities** (1970 cen.): Luanda (met.) 475,328; Huamb 61,885; Lobito 59,528.

Government: Head of state: Pres. Agostinho Neto, b. 192 in office: Nov. 11, 1975; **Head of government:** Prime Min. Lop do Nascimento. **Local divisions:** 16 provinces. **Armed force** regulars 30,000.

Economy: Industries: Alcohol, cotton goods, fishmea paper, palm oil, footwear. **Chief crops:** Coffee (5% of wor crop), corn, sugar, palm oil, cotton, wheat, tobacco, caeao, sisa wax. **Minerals:** Iron, diamonds (over 2 mln. carats a year), co per, manganese, sulphur, phosphates, oil. **Crude oil outpu** (1976): 46.4 mln. bbls. **Per capita arable land:** 0.3 acres. **Live stock** (1974): 2,900,000 cattle; 350,000 pigs; 195,000 shee **Fish catch** (1974): 469,700 metric tons. **Electricity productio** (1972): 984 mln. kwh. **Labor force** 63% agric.

Finance: Currency: Escudo (1974: 25.4=$1 US). **Gros domestic product** (est. 1974): $3.15 bln. **Per capita incon** (1974): $510. **Imports** (1974): $614 mln.; partners (1973): Po 26%, W. Ger. 13%, U.S. 10%, U.K. 8%. **Exports** (1974): $1.2C mln.; partners (1973): U.S. 28%, Port 25%, Can. 10%, Jap. 9%.

Transport: Railway traffic (1974 est.): 250 mln. passenge miles; 3,390 mln. net ton-miles. **Motor vehicles:** in use (1973 127,300 passenger cars, 35,700 commercial vehicles. **Chi ports:** Lobito, Luanda.

Communications: Radios: 115,000 licenses (1973); 26,0C manufactured (1973). **Daily newspaper circulation** (1973): 87 000; 15 per 1,000 pop.

Health: Life expectancy at birth (1970-75): 37.0 male; 40 female. **Births** (annual per 1,000 pop. 1970-75): 47.2. **Death** (annual per 1,000 pop. 1970-75): 24.5. **Natural increas** (annual 1970-75): 2.31%. **Infant mortality** (per 1,000 pop. und 1 yr. 1972): 24.1.

From the early centuries A.D. to 1500, Bantu tribes penetrate most of the region. Portuguese came in 1583, allied with th Bakongo kingdom in the north, and developed the slave trad Large-scale colonization did not begin until the 20th centu when 400,000 Portuguese immigrated.

A guerrilla war begun in 1961 lasted until 1974, when the ne regime in Portugal offered independence. Violence betwe three factions, the National Front, based in Zaire, the Sovie backed Popular Movement, and the moderate National Unio killed thousands of blacks, drove most whites to emigrate, ar completed economic ruin. Some 15,000 Cuban troops and ma sive Soviet aid helped the Popular Movement win most of th country after independence Nov. 11, 1975. Some units of th her factions continued to resist in 1977. The regime, headed by nites or mulattos, crushed with Cuban help a revolt by black aders within the Popular Movement in May, 1977.

Russian influence, backed by 20-25,000 Cubans, 1-2,000 ast Germans, and Portuguese Communists, is strong in the arxist regime.

Argentina

Argentine Republic

People: Population (1976 est.): 25,720,000. **Age distrib.** 6): 0–14: 28.6; 15–59: 59.6; 60+:11.7. **Pop. density:** 24 per . mi. **Ethnic groups:** Europeans 97% (Spanish, Italian), Inans, Mestizos, Arabs. **Languages:** Spanish. **Religions:** oman Catholic 94%, Protestant 2%, Jewish 2%.

Geography: Area: 1,072,067 sq. mi., 4 times the size of exas, second largest in S. America. **Location:** Occupies most southern S. America. **Neighbors:** Chile on W, Bolivia, Paraay on N, Brazil, Uruguay on NE. **Topography:** The mountains West, are grouped into 4 systems: the Andean, Central, Misnes, and Southern. Aconcagua is the highest peak in the estern hemisphere, altitude 22,834. East of the Andes are eat plains, heavily wooded and called the Gran Chaco in the N, nd the fertile, treeless Pampas in the central region, given over wheat and cattle raising. Patagonia, in the S, is bleak and arid; etroleum and sheep are its main products. Rio de la Plata, 170 140 miles, is mostly fresh water, from 2,500-mi. Paranak and 000-mi. Uruguay. R. **Capital:** Buenos Aires. **Cities** (1974 est.): uenos Aires (met.) 8,925,000; (1970 cen.): Rosario (met.) 810,-40; Cordoba (met.) 798,663; La Plata (met.) 506,287; Mendoza net.) 470,896.

Government: Head of state: Pres. Jorge Rafael Videla, b. ug. 2, 1925, in office: Mar. 24, 1976. **Local divisions:** 22 provces, formerly with elected legislatures and governors; now nder military governors. **Armed forces:** regulars 132,800; reerves 250,000.

Economy: Industries: Meat processing, flour milling, chemials, textiles, machinery, autos. **Chief crops:** Cotton, grains, orn, grapes, linseed, sugar, fruit, tobacco, peanuts. Grains are xported. **Minerals:** Oil, coal, lead, zinc, iron, sulphur, silver, opper, gold. **Crude oil output** (1976): 146 mln. bbls. **Per capita rable land:** 2.2 acres. **Livestock** (1976): 60,500,000 cattle; 000,000 pigs; 36,500,000 sheep; Argentina is a major meat exorter. **Fish catch** (1974): 301,300 metric tons. **Electricity roduction** (1976): 25,404 mln. kwh. **Labor force:** 15% agric.; 0% manuf.

Finance: Currency: Peso (Apr. 1977: 353=$1 US). **Gross omestic product** (mid-1975): $49.6 bln. **Per capita income** 975): $1,885. **Imports** (1976) $3.050 bln.; partners (1973): US 2%, Jap. 11%, W. Ger. 11%, Braz. 9%. **Exports** (1976): $3.895 n.; partners (1973): It. 12%, Braz. 10%, W. Ger. 8%, U.S. 8%. **ourists** (1974): 955,100; receipts: $109 million. **Balance of ayments** (1976): $919 mln. **National budget** (1976): $2.82 bln. venues; $6.88 bln. expenditures. **International reserves** Dec. 1976): $1.608 bln. **Consumer prices** (change in 1976): 36.6%.

Transport: Railway traffic (1974): 8,163 mln. passengeriles; 7,653 mln. net ton miles. **Motor vehicles:** in use (1974): 160,000 passenger cars, 966,000 commercial vehicles; manuctured (1976): 142,000 passenger cars, 39,000 commercial ehicles. **Civil aviation:** 2,586 mln. passenger-miles (1976); 64 ln. freight ton-miles (1976). **Chief ports:** Buenos Aires, Bahia lanca, La Plata.

Communications: Television sets: 3,950,000 in use (1973); 79,000 manufactured (1974). **Radios:** 10,000,000 in use 972). **Telephones in use** (1976): 2,469,250. **Daily newsaper circulation** (1973): 3,988,000.

Health: Life expectancy at birth (1970-75): 65.16 male; 1.38 female. **Births** (per 1,000 pop. 1970): 22.9. **Deaths** (per 000 pop. 1970): 9.4. **Natural increase** (1970): 1.35%. **Pop. er hospital bed** (1973): 181. **Pop. per physician** (1973): 467. **fant mortality** (per 1,000 pop. under 1 yr. 1970): 59.0.

Education: Literacy (1973): 93%. **Pop. 5-19:** in school 973): 60%; per teacher (1973): 25.

Nomadic Indians roamed the Pampas when Spaniards arved, 1515-1516, led by Juan Diaz de Solis. Nearly all the Inans were killed by the late 19th century. The colonists won dependence, 1810-1819, and a long period of disorders ended a strong centralized government.

Large-scale Italian, German, and Spanish immigration in the decades after 1880 spurred modernization, making Argentina the most prosperous, educated, and industrialized of the major Latin American nations. Social reforms were enacted in the 1920s, but military coups prevailed 1930-46, until the election of Gen. Juan Peron as president.

Peron, with his wife Eva Duarte, effected labor reforms, but also suppressed speech and press freedoms, closed religious schools, and ran the country into debt. A 1955 coup exiled Peron, who was followed by a series of military and civilian regimes. Peron returned in 1973, and was once more elected president. He died ten months later, succeeded by his wife, Isabel, who had been elected vice president, and who became the first woman head of state in the Western hemisphere. Terrorist violence of right and left, long a problem, worsened in the 1970s, with 900 killed in 1975 alone; lucrative kidnappings netted tens of millions of dollars.

A military junta ousted Mrs. Peron in 1976 amid charges of corruption. Under a state of siege, the army battled guerrillas and leftists, killed 2,000-5,000 people, and jailed and tortured others.

Gains in Argentina's productive agricultural sector did not prevent catastrophic inflation in the 1970s, and balance of payment problems.

Australia

Commonwealth of Australia

People: Population (1976): 13,640,000. **Age distrib.** (%): 0-14: 28.4; 15-59: 59.2; 60+:12.4. **Pop. density:** 4.6 per sq. mi. **Urban** (1971): 85.6%. **Ethnic groups:** British 95%, other European 3%, aborigines (including mixed) 1.5%. **Languages:** English. **Religions:** Anglican 36%, other Protestant 20%, Roman Catholic 25%.

Geography: Area: 2,965,368 sq. mi., almost as large as the 48 conterminous U.S. states. **Location:** SE of Asia, Indian O. is W and S, Pacific O. (Coral, Tasman Seas) is E; they meet N of Australia in Timor and Arafura Seas; Tasmania lies 150 mi. S of Victoria state, across Bass Strait. **Neighbors:** Nearest island neighbors are Indonesia, Papira New Guinea on N, Solomons, Fiji, and New Zealand on E. **Topography:** An island continent, Australia is bisected by the Tropic of Capricorn. The Great Dividing Range along the E coast has Mt. Kosciusko, 7,316 ft. The W plateau rises to 2,000 ft., with arid areas in the Great Sandy and Great Victoria Deserts. The NW part of Western Australia and Northern Terr. are arid and hot. The NE has heavy rainfall and Cape York Peninsula has jungles. The Murray R. rises in New South Wales and flows 1,600 mi. to the Indian O. **Capital:** Canberra. **Cities** (1973 est.): Sydney (met.) 2,874,380; Melbourne (met.) 2,583,900; Brisbane (met.) 911,000; Adelaide (met.) 868,-000; Perth (met.) 739,200.

Government: Head of state: Queen Elizabeth II, represented by Gov.-gen. Zelman Cowen; **Head of government:** Prime Min. John Malcolm Fraser, b. May 21, 1930, in office: Dec. 22, 1975. **Local divisions:** 6 states, with elected governments and substantial powers; 2 territories. **Armed forces:** regulars 69,400; reserves 26,700.

Economy: Industries: iron, steel, textiles, electrical equip., chemicals, autos, aircraft, ships, machinery. **Chief crops:** Wheat (a leading exporter), sugar, wine, fruit, vegetables. **Minerals:** Major uranium, iron, oil, gas producer; gold, coal, copper, silver, lead, nickel, tin, bauxite. **Crude oil output** (1976): 142 mln. bbls. **Other resources:** Wool (30% of world output). **Per capita arable land:** 8.1 acres. **Livestock** (1976): 33,800,000 cattle; 2,160,000 pigs; 154,500,000 sheep; 31,000,000 poultry. Australia is among world leaders in beef and lamb export. **Fish catch** (1974): 123,500 metric tons. **Electricity production** (1976): 76.-500 mln. kwh. **Labor force:** 7% agric.; 25% manuf.

Finance: Currency: Dollar (Apr. 1977: 1=$1.10 US). **Gross domestic product** (1976): $86.1 bln. **Per capita income** (1975): $6,311. **Imports** (1976) $12.462 bln.; partners (1974): U.S. 20%, Jap. 18%, U.K. 14%, W. Ger. 7%. **Exports** (1976): $13.106 bln; partners (1974): Jap. 29%, U.S. 9%, N.Z. 7%. U.K. 6%. **Tourists** (1973): 543,600; receipts (1974): $260 million. **Balance of payments** (1976): $–350 mln. **National budget** (1976): $22.9 bln. revenues; $28.0 bln. expenditures. **International reserves** (Feb. 1977): $3.483 bln. **Consumer prices** (change in 1976): 13.5%.

Transport: Railway traffic (1974): 17.593 mln. net ton-miles. **Motor vehicles:** in use (1974): 4,769,200 passenger cars, 1,130,800 commercial vehicles; manufactured (1975): 361,000 passenger cars, 94,000 commercial vehicles. **Civil aviation:** 11.036 mln. passenger-miles (1975); 225 mln. freight ton-miles (1975). **Chief ports:** Sydney, Melbourne, Newcastle, Port Kemble, Fremantle, Geelong.

Communications: Television sets: 2,939,000 licenses (1973); 457,000 manufactured (1974). **Radios:** 2,815,000 licenses (1973); 902,000 manufactured (1974). **Telephones in use** (1975): 5,266,843. **Daily newspaper circulation** (1973): 5,126,000; 386 per 1,000 pop.

Health: Life expectancy at birth (1965-67): 67.63 male; 74.15 female. **Births** (per 1,000 pop. 1974): 18.4. **Deaths** (per 1,000 pop. 1974): 8.7. **Natural increase** (1974): 0.97%. **Pop. per hospital bed** (1973): 85. **Pop. per physician** (1973): 821. **Infant mortality** (per 1,000 pop. under 1 yr. 1974): 16.5.

Education: Literacy (1973): 98%. **Pop. 5-19:** in school (1973): 83%; per teacher (1973): 26.

Capt. James Cook explored the east coast of Australia in 1770, when the continent was inhabited by a variety of different tribes. Within decades, Britain had claimed the entire continent, which became a penal colony until immigration increased in the 1850s. The commonwealth was proclaimed Jan. 1, 1901, as a federation of six states and two territories. Their capitals and 1976 census pop.:

	Area (sq. mi.)	Population
New South Wales, Sydney	309,418	4,777,000
Victoria, Melbourne	87,854	3,647,000
Queensland, Brisbane	666,699	2,037,000
South Aust., Adelaide	379,824	1,245,000
Western Aust., Perth	974,843	1,145,000
Tasmania, Hobart	26,171	402,800
Northern Terr., Darwin	519,633	97,000
Aust. Capital Terr., Canberra	926	197,600

The U.S. succeeded Britain as the major ally following two world wars, with Japan as the leading trade and development partner in the 1970s.

Australia's racially discriminatory immigration policies were abandoned in 1973, after 3 million Europeans (half British) had entered since 1945. In 1975 there was a net emigration of 5,000. The 50,000 aborigines and 150,000 part aborigines are mostly detribalized, but there are several preserves in the Northern Territory. They remain economically disadvantaged.

Australia's agricultural success makes it among the top exporters of beef, lamb, wool, and wheat. Major mineral deposits have been developed as well, largely for exports. Industrialization has been completed since 1945.

The National Health Scheme provides free drugs and subsidizes hospital and medical expenses. Australia was a leader in introducing social security provisions. Maternity allowances and child endowment payments continue to age 16.

Australia harbors many plant and animal species not found elsewhere, including the kangaroo, koala bear, platypus, dingo (wild dog), Tasmanian devil (racoon-like marsupial), wombat (bear-like marsupial), and barking and frilled lizards.

Australian External Territories

Norfolk Island was taken over by Australia, 1914. It has an area of 13.5 sq. mi. and a population (1974) of 1,894. The soil is very fertile and is suitable for citrus fruits, bananas, and coffee. Many of the inhabitants are descendants of the Bounty mutineers; some moved to Norfolk in 1856 from Pitcairn Is.

Coral Sea Islands Territory, 1 sq. mi., is administered from Norfolk Is.

Territory of Ashmore and Cartier Islands, area 2 sq. mi., in the Indian Ocean came under the authority of Australia May 1934 and are administered as part of Northern Territory. **Heard** and **McDonald Islands** are administered by the Department of Science.

Cocos (Keeling) Islands, 27 small coral islands in the Indian Ocean 1,300 miles NW of Australia. Pop. (1974): 650; area: 5 sq. mi.

Christmas Island, 52 sq. mi., pop. 2,900 (1974), 230 mi. S of Java, was transferred by Britain in 1958. It has phosphate deposits.

Australian Antarctic Territory was claimed by Australia in 1933, including 2,472,000 sq. mi. of territory S of 60th parallel S Lat. and between 160th-45th meridians E Long.

Austria

Republic of Austria

People: Population (1976): 7,510,000. **Pop. density:** 23 per sq. mi. **Age distrib.** (%): 0-14: 24.0; 15-59: 55.4; 60+: 20.6 **Urban** (1971): 51.9%. **Ethnic groups:** German 98%, Slovene Croatian, Hungarian, Italian. **Languages:** German, Slovene **Religions:** Roman Catholic 90%, Protestant 10%.

Geography: Area: 32,374 sq. mi., slightly smaller than Maine **Location:** In S Central Europe. **Neighbors:** Switzerland, Liechtenstein on W, W. Germany, Czechoslovakia on N, Hungary on E, Yugoslavia, Italy on S. **Topography:** Austria is primarily mountainous, with the Alps and foothills covering the western and southern provinces. The eastern provinces and Vienna are located in the Danube River Basin. **Capital:** Vienna. **Cities** (1971 cen.): Vienna 1,614,841; Graz 248,500; Linz 202,874.

Government: Head of state: Pres. Rudolf Kirchschlaeger, b. Mar. 20, 1915, in office: June 23, 1974; **Head of government** Chancellor Bruno Kreisky, b. Jan. 22, 1911, in office: 1970 **Local divisions:** 9 lander (states), each with a legislature **Armed forces:** regulars 37,300; reserves 112,700.

Economy: Industries: Steel, machinery, autos, electrical and optical equip., glassware, sport goods, paper, textiles, chemicals, cement. **Chief crops:** Grains, corn, potatoes, beets grapes. **Minerals:** Iron ore, oil, magnesite, aluminum, coal, lignite, copper, graphite. **Crude oil output** (1976): 14.2 mln. bbls **Other resources:** Forests, hydro power. **Per capita arable land:** 0.5 acres. **Livestock** (1976): 3,683,000 cattle; 3,683,000 pigs; 169,000 sheep; 12,472,000 poultry. **Electricity production** (1976): 35,040 mln. kwh. **Labor force:** 16% agric.; 29% manuf.

Finance: Currency: Schillings (Apr. 1977: 16.77=$1 US) **Gross domestic product** (1976): $40.6 bln. **Per capita income** (1975): $4,436. **Imports** (1976) $11.516 bln.; partners (1974) W. Ger. 40%, It. 7%, Switz. 7%, U.K. 4%. **Exports** (1976) $8.506 bln.; partners (1974): W. Ger. 20%, Switz. 10%, It. 10% **Tourists** (1974): 10,886,200; receipts: $2.303 billion. **Balance of payments** (1976): $-54 mln. **National budget** (1975): $7.45 bln. revenues; $8.90 bln. expenditures. **International reserves** (Feb. 1977): $3.886 bln. **Consumer prices** (change in 1976) 7.3%.

Transport: Railway traffic (1974): 4,217 mln. passenger miles; 6,978 mln. net ton-miles. **Motor vehicles:** in use (1974) 1,635,900 passenger cars, 435,500 commercial vehicles; manufactured (1976): 1,000 passenger cars, 8,000 commercial vehicles. **Civil aviation:** 511 mln. passenger-miles (1976); 6.1 mln freight ton-miles (1976).

Communications: Television sets: 1,779,000 licenses (1973); 479,000 manufactured (1974). **Radios:** 2,157,000 licenses (1973); 82,000 manufactured (1972). **Telephones in use** (1976): 2,132,758. **Daily newspaper circulation** (1973) 2,296,000; 305 per 1,000 pop.

Health: Life expectancy at birth (1974): 67.4 male; 74.7 female. **Births** (per 1,000 pop. 1975): 12.3. **Deaths** (per 1,000 pop. 1975): 12.7. **Natural increase** (1975): -0.04%. **Pop. per hospital bed** (1973): 93. **Pop. per physician** (1973): 509. **Infant mortality** (per 1,000 pop. under 1 yr. 1975): 20.8.

Education: Literacy (1973): 99%. **Pop. 5-19:** in school (1973): 66%; per teacher (1973): 31.

Rome conquered Austrian lands around 15 B.C. After centuries of invasions by Celts, Goths, Avars, and Magyars, Austria was incorporated into Charlemagne's empire in 788. By 1300 the House of Hapsburg had gained control; they added vast territories in all parts of Europe to their realm in the next few hundred years.

Austrian dominance of Germany was undermined in the 18th century and ended by Prussia by 1866. But the Congress of Vienna, 1815, confirmed Austrian control of a large empire in southeast Europe, conquered from the Turks over centuries of battle, and consisting of Germans, Hungarians, Slavs, Italians and others.

The dual Austro-Hungarian monarchy was established in 1867, giving autonomy to Hungary and 50 years of peace.

World War I, started after the June 28, 1914 assassination of Archduke Ferdinand, the Hapsburg heir, by a Serbian nationalist destroyed the empire. By 1918 Austria was reduced to a small republic, almost entirely German-speaking, with the borders it has today.

Nazi Germany invaded Austria Mar. 13, 1938, after four years of control by right-wing dictators Dollfuss and Schuschnigg. Th public was reestablished in 1948, under allied occupation. Full dependence and neutrality were guaranteed by a 1955 treaty th the major powers.

Austria produces 85% of its food, as well as an array of indusal products. A large part of Austria's economy is controlled by ate enterprises. Socialists have shared or alternated power ith the conservative People's Party, and every president ected since 1945 has been a Socialist.

Economic agreements with the Common Market give Austria ccess to a free-trade area encompassing most of West Europe.

Bahamas

Commonwealth of the Bahamas

People: Population (1976): 210,000. **Age distrib.** (%): 0-14: 3.6; 15-59: 50.9; 60+: 5.5. **Pop. density:** 48 per sq. mi. **Urban** 970): 57.9%. **Ethnic groups:** Negro 85%, Caucasian (British, anadian, U.S.). **Languages:** English. **Religions:** Baptist 29%, nglican 23%, Roman Catholic 22%.

Geography: Area: 4,404 sq. mi., slightly smaller than Conecticut. **Location:** In Atlantic O., E of Florida. **Neighbors:** earest are U.S. on W, Cuba on S. **Topography:** The Bahamas omprise nearly 700 islands (30 inhabited) and over 2,000 islets the western Atlantic. They extend 760 mi. NW to SE. **Capital:** assau. **Cities** (1970 cen.): Nassau (met.) 101,503.

Government: Head of state: Queen Elizabeth II, represented y Gov.-Gen. Sir Milo Boughton Butler; **Head of government:** rime Min. Lynden Oscar Pindling, b. Mar. 22, 1930, in office: an. 10, 1967. **Local divisions:** 18 districts.

Economy: Industries: Tourism, intl. banking, rum, drugs. **hief crops:** Fruits, vegetables. **Minerals:** Salt. **Other reources:** Lobsters. **Per capita arable land:** 0.025 acres. **Livetock** (1974): 4,000 cattle; 15,000 pigs; 28,000 sheep; 729,000 oultry. **Electricity production** (1974): 324 mln. kwh. (New rovidence). **Labor force:** 7% agric.; 5% manuf.

Finance: Currency: Dollar (Apr. 1977: 1=$1 US). **Gross omestic product** (est. 1974): $250 mln. **Per capita income** 1974): $3,000. **Imports** (1975): $2,482 bln.; partners (1974): audi Ar. 26%, Nigeria 17%, Iran 15%, U.S. 12%. **Exports** 1975): $2.216 bln.; partners (1974): U.S. 83%, Puerto Rico 8%, an. 3%, U.K. 1%. **Tourists** (1974): 929,200; receipts: $328 milon. **Balance of payments** (1976): $-6 mln. **National budget** 1976): $134 mln. revenues; $141 mln. expenditures. **International reserves** (Dec. 1976): $47.4 mln. **Consumer prices** change in 1976): 4.2%.

Transport: Motor vehicles: in use (1974): 40,100 passenger ars, 5,500 commercial vehicles. **Chief ports:** Nassau, Freeport.

Communications: Radios: 85,000 in use (1973). **Telephones in use** (1976): 57,201. **Daily newspaper circulation** 1973): 30,000; 155 per 1,000 pop.

Health: Life expectancy at birth (1969-71): 64.0 male; 67.3 emale. **Births** (per 1,000 pop. 1975): 18.1. **Deaths** (per 1,000 op. 1975): 3.9. **Natural increase** (1975): 1.42%. **Infant mortaly** (per 1,000 pop. under 1 yr. 1975): 29.2.

Christopher Columbus first set foot in the New World on San alvador (Watling I.) in 1492, when Arawak Indians inhabited the slands. British settlement began in 1647; the islands became a ritish colony in 1783. Internal self-government was granted in 964, with the election of the first black prime minister in 1967. ull independence within the Commonwealth was attained July 0, 1973.

International banking and investment management has beome a major industry alongside tourism, despite controversy ver financial irregularities.

Bahrain

State of Bahrain

People: Population (1976 est.): 260,000. **Age distrib.** (%): -14: 44.3; 15-59: 51.1; 60+: 4.6. **Pop. density:** 1,126 per sq. ni. **Urban** (1972): 78.1%. **Ethnic groups:** Arabs 88%, Iranians %, Indians, Pakistanis 5%. **Languages:** Arabic, Persian. **Religions:** Sunni Moslem 50%, Shiite Moslem 50%.

Geography: Area: 231 sq. mi., smaller than New York City. **ocation:** In Persian Gulf. **Neighbors:** Nearest are Saudi Arabia n W, Qatar on E. **Topography:** Bahrain Island, and several djacent, smaller islands, are flat, hot and humid, with little rain. **Capital:** Manama. **Cities** (1971 cen.): Manama 88,785; Muharraq 41,143.

Government: Head of state: Amir Shaikh Isa bin Salman al-Khalifa, b. July 3, 1933, in office: Dec. 16, 1961; **Head of government:** Prime Min. Khalifa bin Salman al-Khalifa, b. 1935, in office: 1966. **Local divisions:** 6 towns and cities. **Armed forces:** regulars 1,600.

Economy: Industries: Oil products, aluminum smelting, shipping. **Chief crops:** Fruits, vegetables. **Minerals:** Oil, gas. **Crude oil output** (1976): 21.3 mln. bbls. **Per capita arable land:** 0.005 acres. **Livestock** (1974): 4,000 cattle; 4,000 sheep; 165,000 poultry. **Electricity production** (1973): 330 mln. kwh. **Labor force:** 7% agri.; 14% manuf.

Finance: Currency: Dinar (Apr. 1977: 1=$2.53 US). **Gross domestic product** (est. 1974): $1.1 bln. **Per capita income** (1974): $2,500. **Imports** (1976): $1,664 bln.; partners (1974): U.S. 18%, U.K. 15%, Jap. 13%, P.R. China 6%. **Exports** (1976): $1.346 bln.; partners (1974): Jap. 29%, Australia 13%, Saud Ar. 6%, Sing. 5%. **International reserves** (Feb. 1977): $409.1 mln. **Consumer prices** (change in 1976): 31.1%.

Transport: Motor vehicles: in use (1974): 19,600 passenger cars, 7,200 commercial vehicles. **Chief ports:** Sitra.

Communications: Television sets: 18,000 in use (1973). **Radios:** 80,000 in use (1973). **Telephones in use** (1976): 26,-228.

Long ruled by the Khalifa family, Bahrain was a British protectorate from 1861 to Aug. 14, 1971, when it regained independence.

Pearls, shrimp, fruits, and vegetables were the mainstays of the economy until oil was discovered in 1932. By the 1970s, oil reserves showed signs of depletion.

Bahrain took part in the 1973-74 Arab oil embargo against the U.S. and other nations. The government bought controlling interest in the oil industry in 1975. U.S. Navy base rights were ended in a 1977 agreement.

Bangladesh

People's Republic of Bangladesh

People: Population (1975 est.): 76,820,000. **Pop. density:** 1,394 per sq. mi. **Urban** (1974): 8.8%. **Ethnic groups:** Bengali 98%, Bihari, tribesmen. **Languages:** Bengali, Urdu, English. **Religions:** Moslems 85%, Hindus 14%.

Geography: Area: 55,126 sq. mi., slightly smaller than Wisconsin. **Location:** In S Asia, on N bend of Bay of Bengal. **Neighbors:** India nearly surrounds country on W, N, E; Burma on SE. **Topography:** The country is mostly a low plain cut by the Ganges and Brahmaputra rivers and their delta. The land is alluvial and marshy along the coast, with hills only in the extreme SE and NE. A tropical monsoon climate prevails, among the rainiest in the world. **Capital:** Dacca. **Cities** (1974 cen.): Dacca (met.) 1,730,253; Chittagong (met.) 889,760; Khulna (met.) 437,304.

Government: Head of state: Pres. Ziaur Rahman, b.1936, in office: Apr. 21, 1977. **Local divisions:** 19 districts. **Armed forces:** regulars 63,000.

Economy: Industries: Cement, textiles, jute, fertilizers. **Chief crops:** Jute (most of world output), rice. **Minerals:** Natural gas, offshore oil. **Other resources:** Water. **Per capita arable land:** 0.3 acres. **Livestock** (1974): 26,709,000 cattle; 727,000 sheep; 35,540,000 poultry. **Fish catch** (1975): 640,000 metric tons. **Electricity production** (1975): 1,380 mln. kwh. **Labor force:** 70% agric.

Finance: Currency: Taka (Apr. 1977: 15.53=$1 US). **Gross domestic product** (est. 1974): **$5.5 bln.** Per capita income **(1974):** $70. **Imports** (1976) $865 mln.; partners (1974): U.S. 24%, Austral. 9%, Jap. 7%, India 7%, W. Ger. 7%. **Exports** (1976): $401 mln.; partners (1974): U.S. 20%, U.K. 9%, India 8%, Austral. 5%. **Tourists** (1974): 86,900; receipts: $3 million. **Balance of payments** (1976): $66.2 mln. **International reserves** (Feb. 1977): $279.7 mln.

Transport: Railway traffic (1973): 2,069 mln. passenger-miles; 397 mln. net ton-miles. **Motor vehicles:** in use (1972): 31,700 passenger cars, 24,800 commercial vehicles. **Chief ports:** Chittagong, Chalna.

Communications: Telephones in use (1976): 80,100. **Daily newspaper circulation** (1973): 85,000.

Health: Life expectancy at birth (1970-75): 35.8 male; 35.8

female. **Births** (annual per 1,000 pop. 1970-75): 49.5. **Deaths** (annual per 1,000 pop. 1970-75): 28.1. **Natural increase** (annual 1970-75): 2.14%. **Pop. per hospital bed** (1973): 6,392. **Pop. per physician** (1973): 10,009. **Infant mortality** (per 1,000 pop. under 1 yr. 1973): 132.

Education: Literacy (1973): 22%. **Pop. 5-19:** in school (1973): 29%; per teacher (1973): 149.

Moslem invaders conquered the formerly Hindu area in the 12th century. British rule lasted from the 18th century to 1947, when East Bengal became part of Pakistan.

Charging West Pakistani domination, the Awami League, based in the East, won National Assembly control in 1971. When Assembly sessions were postponed, riots broke out in the East. Pakistani troops attacked Mar. 25; Bangladesh independence was proclaimed the next day. In the ensuing civil war, about one million died, mostly civilians, amid charges of Pakistani atrocities. Ten million fled to India.

War between India and Pakistan broke out Dec. 3, 1971. Pakistan surrendered in the East Dec. 15. Sheik Mujibur Rahman became prime minister. The country moved into the Indian and Soviet orbits, in response to U.S. support of Pakistan, and much of the economy was nationalized.

In 1974, the government took emergency powers to curb widespread violence; Mujibur was assassinated and a series of coups followed.

Chronic destitution among the densely crowded population has been worsened by the decline of jute as a major world commodity. A 1970 cyclone killed 300,000, and 1974 floods, combined with the world oil price hike, caused famine deaths to soar.

A new regime in 1977 restored Islam to a central constitutional role. Relations with India had soured in disputes over Ganges waters and offshore rights.

Barbados

People: Population (1976): 250,000 **Age distrib.** (%): 0-14: 36.3; 15-59: 52.5; 60+: 11.1 **Pop. density:** 1,506 per sq. mi. **Urban** (1970): 3.7%. **Ethnic groups:** Negro 90%, mixed 5%, Caucasian 5%. **Languages:** English. **Religions:** Anglican 70%, Methodist, Pentecostal, Roman Catholic.

Geography: Area: 166 sq. mi. **Location:** In Atlantic, farthest E of W. Indies. **Neighbors:** Nearest are Trinidad, Grenada on SW. **Topography:** The island lies alone in the Atlantic almost completely surrounded by coral reefs. Highest point is Mt. Hillaby, 1,115 ft. **Capital:** Bridgetown. **Cities** (1970 cen.): Bridgetown (met.) 85,000.

Government: Head of state: Queen Elizabeth II, represented by Gov.-Gen. Sir Deighton L. Ward; **Head of government:** Prime Min. J.M.G. Adams, b. Sept. 24, 1931, in office: Sept. 2, 1976. **Local divisions:** 11 parishes, one city.

Economy: Industries: Rum, molasses, tourism. **Chief crops:** Sugar, cotton. **Minerals:** Lime. **Other resources:** Fish. **Per capita arable land:** 0.3 acres. **Livestock** (1974): 21,000 cattle; 34,000 pigs; 47,000 sheep; 371,000 poultry. **Electricity production** (1975): 204 mln. kwh. **Labor force:** 16% agric., 15% manuf.

Finance: Currency: Dollar (Apr. 1977: 2.00=$1 US). **Gross domestic product** (1975): $347 mln. **Per capita income** (1974): $1,133. **Imports** (1976) $236 mln.; partners (1974): U.K. 21%, U.S. 19%, Trin. 12%, Venez. 10%. **Exports** (1976): $87 mln.; partners (1974): U.S. 26%, U.K. 16%, Windward Is. 7%, Trin. 6%. **Tourist** receipts (1973): $70 million. **Balance of payments** (1976): $−19.6 mln. **National budget** (1973): $72.58 mln. revenues; $89.20 mln. expenditures. **International reserves** (1975): $−9.1 mln. **Consumer prices** (change in 1976): 5.1%.

Transport: Motor vehicles: in use (1973): 19,000 passenger cars, 3,000 commercial vehicles. **Chief ports:** Bridgetown.

Communications: Television sets: 35,000 in use (1973); **Radios:** 116,000 in use (1973). **Telephones in use** (1976): 41,535. **Daily newspaper circulation** (1973): 24,000; 99 per 1,000 pop.

Health: Life expectancy at birth (1959-61): 62.74 male; 67.43 female. **Births** (per 1,000 pop. 1974): 19.5. **Deaths** (per 1,000 pop. 1974): 8.4. **Natural increase** (1974): 1.11%. **Infant mortality** (per 1,000 pop. under 1 yr. 1973): 37.7.

Barbados was probably named by Portuguese sailors in reference to bearded fig trees. An English ship visited in 1605, and British settlers arrived on the uninhabited island in 1627. Slaves worked the sugar plantations, but were freed in 1834.

Self-rule came gradually, with full independence proclaimed Nov. 30, 1966. British traditions have remained; literacy is almost universal.

Belgium

Kingdom of Belgium

People: Population (1976 est.): 9,890,000. **Age distrib.** (%) 0–14: 23.4; 15–59: 57.6; 60+: 19. **Pop. density:** 840 per sq. mi. **Urban** (1974): 87.1%. **Ethnic groups:** Flemings 58%, Walloons 41%. **Languages:** Flemish (Dutch), French. **Religions:** Roman Catholic 90%, Protestant.

Geography: Area: 11,779 sq. mi., slightly larger than Maryland. **Location:** In NW Europe, on N. Sea. **Neighbors:** France on W, S, Luxembourg on SE, W. Germany on E, Netherlands on N. **Topography:** Mostly flat, the country is trisected by the Scheldt and Meuse, major commercial rivers. The land becomes hilly and forested in the SE (Ardennes) region. **Capital:** Brussels. **Cities** (1971 est.): Brussels (met.) 1,074,726; Antwerp (met.) 672,703; Liege (met.) 440,447; Ghent (met.) 224,728.

Government: Head of state: King Baudouin, b. Sept. 7, 1930, in office: July 17, 1951; **Head of government:** Prime Min. Leo Tindemans, b. Apr. 16, 1922, in office: Apr. 25, 1974. **Local divisions:** 9 provinces, with elected governments & substantial powers. **Armed forces:** regulars 88, 300; reserves 57,600.

Economy: Industries: Steel, glassware, diamond cutting, textiles, chemicals. **Chief crops:** Grains, potatoes, sugar beets. **Minerals:** Coal. **Other resources:** Forests. **Per capita arable land:** 0.2 acres. **Livestock** (1976): 2,812,000 cattle; 4,648,000 pigs; 88,000 sheep; 31,366,000 poultry. **Fish catch** (1974): 46,400 metric tons. **Electricity production** (1976): 47,352 mln. kwh. **Labor force:** 4% agric.; 32% manuf.

Finance: Currency: Franc (Apr. 1977: 36.06=$1 US). **Gross domestic product** (1976): $67.2 bln. **Per capita income** (1975): $5,851. **Imports** (1976) $34.992 bln.; partners (1974): W. Ger. 22%, Fr. 17%, Neth. 16%, U.S. 7%. **Exports** (1976): $32.781 bln; partners (1974): W. Ger. 22.7, Fr. 20%, Neth. 17%, U.S. 6%. **Tourists** (1974): 7,477,400; receipts (including Luxembourg): $719 million. **Balance of payments** (1976): $−663 mln. **National budget** (1976): $17.23 bln. revenues; $20.68 bln. expenditures. **International reserves** (Feb. 1977): $5.378 bln. **Consumer prices** (change in 1976): 9.2%.

Transport: Railway traffic (1974): 5,142 mln. passenger-miles; 5,652 mln. net ton-miles. **Motor vehicles:** in use (1974): 2,502,200 passenger cars, 287,000 commercial vehicles; assembled (1975): 803,000 passenger cars, 61,000 commercial vehicles. **Civil aviation:** 2,414 mln. passenger-miles (1976): 202 mln. freight ton-miles (1976). **Chief ports:** Antwerp, Zeebrugge, Ghent.

Communications: Television sets: 2,376,000 licenses (1973); 739,000 manufactured (1974). **Radios;** 3,662,000 licenses (1973); 2,156,000 manufactured (1974). **Telephones in use** (1976): 2,776,882. **Daily newspaper circulation** (1973): 2,614,000; 268 per 1,000 pop.

Health: Life expectancy at birth (1968-72): 67.79 male; 74.21 female. **Births** (per 1,000 pop. 1974): 12.7. **Deaths** (per 1,000 pop. 1974): 11.9. **Natural increase** (1974): 0.08%. **Pop. per hospital bed** (1973): 121. **Pop. per physician** (1973): 599. **Infant mortality** (per 1,000 pop. under 1 yr. 1974): 16.2.

Education: Literacy (1973): 98%. **Pop. 5-19:** in school (1973): 71%; per teacher (1973): 22.

Belgium derives its name from the Belgae, the first recorded inhabitants, probably Celts. The land was conquered by Julius Caesar, and was ruled for 1800 years by conquerors, including Rome, the Franks, Burgundy, Spain, Austria, and France. After 1815, Belgium was made a part of the Netherlands, but it became an independent constitutional monarchy in 1830.

Belgian neutrality was violated by Germany in both world wars. King Leopold III surrendered to Germany, May 28, 1940. After the war, he was forced by political pressure to abdicate in favor of his son, King Baudouin.

The Flemings of northern Belgium speak Dutch while French is the language of the Walloons in the south. The language difference has been a perennial source of controversy, particularly as it affects education, with Flemish parents unwilling to have their children taught in French.

Disagreement between the two groups became embittered in 1968 elections. In 1970 and 1974 the government sought to solve the problem through creation of decentralized administrative and cultural communities and regional assemblies.

Belgium lives by its foreign trade; about 40% of its entire production is sold abroad.

Benin
People's Republic of Benin

People: Population (1976 est.): 3,200,000. **Pop. density:** 74 per sq. mi. **Urban** (1975): 13.5%. **Ethnic groups:** Fons, Adjas, Baribas, Yorubas. **Languages:** French is only common language. **Religions:** Christian 15% (south), Moslem 13% (north), others.

Geography: Area: 43,483 sq. mi., slightly smaller than Pennsylvania. **Location:** In W Africa on Gulf of Guinea. **Neighbors:** Togo on W, Upper Volta, Niger on N, Nigeria on E. **Topography:** most of Benin is flat and covered with dense vegetation. The coast is hot, humid, and rainy. **Capitals:** Porto Novo, Cotonou. **Cities** (1975 est.): Cotonou 178,000; Porto-Novo 104,000.

Government: Head of state: Pres. Mathieu Kerekou, b. 1933, in office: Oct. 26, 1972. **Local divisions:** 6 departments. **Armed forces:** regulars 1,650; para-military 1,100.

Chief crops: Palm products, peanuts, cotton, kapok, coffee, tobacco. **Minerals:** Some oil. **Per capita arable land:** 1.2 acres. **Livestock** (1974): 740,000 cattle; 355,000 pigs; 810,000 sheep. **Fish catch** (1974): 32,900 metric tons. **Electricity production** (1971): 50,000 kwh. **Labor force:** 52% agric.

Finance: Currency: CFA Franc (Apr. 1977: 248 = $1 US). **Gross domestic product** (1975): $377 mln. **Per capita income** (1974): $125. **Imports** (1974): $146 mln.; partners (1972): Fr. 40%, U.S. 7%, W. Ger. 6%, Neth. 6%. **Exports** (1974): $34 mln.; partners (1972): Fr. 37%, W. Ger. 16%, Neth. 14%, Nigeria 4%. **Tourists** (1974): 19,100; receipts (1973): $2 million. **Balance of payments** (1974): $0.4 mln. **International reserves** (Jan. 1977): $15.5 mln.

Transport: Railway traffic (1974): 63 mln. passenger-miles; 80 mln. net ton-miles. **Motor vehicles;** in use (1974): 14,000 passenger cars, 8,600 commercial vehicles. **Chief ports:** Cotonou.

Communications: Television sets: 100 licenses (1972). **Radios:** 150,000 licenses (1972). **Daily newspaper circulation** (1972): 2,000; 0.7 per 1,000 pop.

Health: Life expectancy at birth (1970-75): 39.4 male; 42.6 female. **Births** (annual per 1,000 pop. 1970-75): 49.9. **Deaths** (annual per 1,000 pop. 1970-75): 23.0. **Natural increase** (annual 1970-75): 2.69%. **Pop. per hospital bed** (1973): 882. **Pop. per physician** (1973): 30,632. **Infant mortality** (per 1,000 pop. under 1 yr. 1961): 109.6.

Education: Literacy (1973): 20%. **Pop. 5-19:** in school (1973): 18%; per teacher (1973): 214.

The Kingdom of Abomey, rising to power in wars with neighboring kingdoms in the 17th century, came under French domination in the late 19th century, and was incorporated into French West Africa by 1904.

Under the name Dahomey, the country became independent Aug. 1, 1960. The name was changed to Benin in 1975. In the fifth coup since Independence, Maj. Mathieu Kerekou took power in 1972; two years later he declared a socialist state with a "Marxist-Leninist" philosophy.

The drought of 1972-73 damaged agriculture and slowed economic growth.

Bhutan
Kingdom of Bhutan

People: Population (1974 est.): 1,035,000 **Pop. density:** 54 per sq. mi. **Ethnic groups:** Bhotia (Tibetan) 60%, Nepalese, Lepcha (indigenous), Indians **Languages:** Dzongkha Tibetan (official), Nepaleses, **Religions:** Buddhist 75%, Hindu 25%.

Geography: Area: 19,305 sq. mi., the size of Vermont and New Hampshire combined. **Location:** In eastern Himalayan Mts. **Neighbors:** India on W (Sikkim) and S, China on N. **Topography:** Bhutan is comprised of very high mountains in the North, fertile valleys in the center, and thick forests in the Duar Plain in the S. **Capital:** Thimphu. **Cities:** (1971 est.): Thimphu 10,000.

Government: Head of state: King Jigme Singye Wangchuk, b. Nov. 11, 1955, in office: July 21, 1972. **Local divisions:** 4 regions comprised of 15 districts.

Economy: Industries: Cloth. **Chief crops:** Rice, corn, wheat, oranges, cardamon, yak butter, lac, wax. **Other resources:** Elephants, timber. **Per capita arable land:** 0.01 acres.

Finance: Currency: Ngultrum (Indian Rupee also used) (1974: 8.1=$1 US). **Gross domestic product** (est. 1974): $80 mln. **Per capita income** (1974): $60. **Imports** (1974) $5 mln.; partners: India 99%. **Exports** (1974): $1 mln. partners: India 99%.

Health: Life expectancy at birth (1970-75): 42.2 male; 45.0 female. **Births** (annual per 1,000 pop. 1970-75): 43.6. **Deaths** (annual per 1,000 pop. 1970-75): 20.5. **Natural increase** (annual 1970-75): 2.31%.

The region came under Tibetan rule in the 16th century. British influence grew in the 19th century. A monarchy, set up in 1907, became a British protectorate by a 1910 treaty. The country became independent in 1949, with India guiding foreign relations and supplying aid.

Links to India have been strengthened by airline service and a road network. Most of the population engages in subsistence agriculture.

Bolivia
Republic of Bolivia

People: Population (1976 est.): 5,790,000. **Age distrib.** (%): 0-14: 41.9; 15-59: 52.7; 60+: 5.4 **Pop. density:** 14 per sq. mil. **Ethnic groups:** Quechua 30%, Aymara 25%, mestizo (cholo) 25-30%, European 5-15%. **Languages:** Spanish (official) 55%, Quechua, Aymara. **Religions:** Roman Catholic 95%.

Geography: Area: 424,162 sq. mi., the size of Texas and California combined. **Location:** In central Andes Mtns. **Neighbors:** Peru, Chile on W, Argentina, Paraguay on S, Brazil on E and N. **Topography:** The great central plateau, at an altitude of 12,000 ft., over 500 mi. long, lies between two great cordilleras having 3 of the highest peaks in S. America. Lake Titicaca, on Peruvian border, is highest lake in world on which steamboats ply (12,506 ft.). The E central region has semitropical forests; the llanos, or Amazon-Chaco lowlands are in E. **Capitals:** Sucre, La Paz. **Cities** (1975 est.): La Paz 660,700; Cochabamba 184,340; Santa Cruz 149,230.

Government: Head of state: Pres. Hugo Banzer Suares, b. May 10, 1926, in office: Aug. 22, 1971. **Local divisions:** 9 departments headed by prefects, 98 provinces. **Armed forces:** regulars: 22,000.

Economy: Chief crops: Potatoes, sugar, coffee, barley, cocoa, rice, corn, bananas, citrus. **Minerals:** (chief industry): tin (12% of world output), silver, copper, lead, zinc, oil, gas, antimony, bismuth, wolfram, gold, iron, cadmium, borate of lime. **Crude oil output** (1976): 15.5 mln. bbls. **Other resources:** rubber, cinchona bark. **Per capita arable land:** 1.3 acres. **Livestock** (1974): 2,326,000 cattle; 1,104,000 pigs; 7,508,000 sheep. **Electricity production** (1974): 967 mln. kwh. **Labor force:** 58% agric.

Finance: Currency: Peso (Apr. 1977: 20=$1 US). **Gross domestic product** (1975): $2.15 bln. **Per capita income** (1975): $329. **Imports** (1975) $558 mln.; partners (1974): U.S. 26%, Braz. 16%, Arg. 15%, Jap. 14%. **Exports** (1976): $513 mln.; partners (1974): U.S. 19%, Argen. 10%, Jap. 6%, Braz. 5%. **Tourist:** receipts (1974): $13 million. **Balance of payments** (1976): $63.2 mln. **National budget** (1973): $123.9 mln. revenues; $168.4 mln. expenditures. **International reserves** (Nov. 1976): $197.3 mln. **Consumer prices** (change in 1976): 4.6%.

Transport: Railway traffic (1973): 168 mln. passenger-miles; 227 mln. net ton-miles. **Motor vehicles:** in use (1974): 29,600 passenger cars, 33,000 commercial vehicles. **Civil aviation:** 276 mln, passenger-miles (1976): 2.7 mln. freight ton-miles (1976).

Communications: Television sets: 11,000 in use (1972). **Radios:** 1,350,000 in use (1970). **Daily newspaper circulation** (1973): 202,000; 38 per 1,000 pop.

Health: Life expectancy at birth (1970-75): 45.7 male; 47.9 female. **Births** (annual per 1,000 pop. 1970-75): 44.0. **Deaths** (annual per 1,000 pop. 1970-75): 19.1. **Natural increase** (annual 1970-75): 2.49%. **Pop. per hospital bed** (1973): 561. **Pop. per physician** (1973): 2,487. **Infant mortality** (per 1,000 pop. under 1 yr. 1966): 77.3.

Education: Literacy (1973): 45%. **Pop. 5-19:** in school (1973): 48%; per teacher (1973): 50.

The Incas conquered the region from earlier Indian inhabitants in the 13th century. Spanish rule began in the 1530s, and lasted until Aug. 6, 1825. The country is named after Simon Bolivar, independence fighter.

In a series of wars, Bolivia lost its Pacific coast to Chile, the oilbearing Chaco to Paraguay, and rubber-growing areas to Brazil, 1879-1935.

Economic unrest, especially among the militant mine workers, has contributed to continuing political instability. A reformist government under Victor Paz Estenssoro, 1951-64, nationalized tin mines and attempted to improve conditions for the Indian majority, but was overthrown by a military junta. A series of coups and countercoups continued until 1971, when the present regime ousted the leftist regime of Gen. Juan Jose Torres.

In 1974, civilians were dismissed from the cabinet, and political parties and labor unions were banned. Troops occupied the mines during strikes in 1976.

Botswana

Republic of Botswana

People: Population (1976 est.): 690,000 **Age distrib.:** (%): 0-14: 47.5; 15-59: 44.9; 60+: 7.6. **Pop. density:** 3.1 per sq. mi. **Urban** (1974): 12.3%. **Ethnic groups:** Bantus (8 main tribes), Bushmen. **Languages:** English (official), Setswana. **Religions:** Christian 15%, others.

Geography: Area: 219,815 sq. mi., slightly smaller than Texas. **Location:** In southern Africa. **Neighbors:** Namibia (S.W. Africa) on N and W, S. Africa on S, Rhodesia on NE, Botswana claims border with Zambia on N. **Topography:** The Kalahari Desert, supporting nomadic Bushmen and wildlife, spreads over SW; there are swamplands and farming areas in N, and rolling plains in E where livestock are grazed. **Capital:** Gaborone. **Cities** (1971 cen.): Gaborone 17,718.

Government: Head of state: Pres. Seretse M. Khama, b. July 1, 1921, in office: Sept. 10, 1966. **Local divisions:** 9 districts, 4 towns, all with local councils.

Economy: Industries: Tourism. **Chief crops:** Corn, sorghum, beans, peanuts. **Minerals:** Copper, coal, nickel, diamonds. **Other resources:** Big game. **Per capita arable land:** 2.1 acres. **Livestock** (1974): 2,200,000 cattle; 415,000 sheep. **Electricity production** (1972): 32 mln. kwh. **Labor force:** 87% agric.

Finance: Currency: Pula (Nov. 1976: 1=$1.15 US). **Gross domestic product:** (est. 1974): $220 mln. **Per capita income** (1974): $340. **Imports** (1974): $151 mln.; partners: mostly So. Afr.

Transport: Motor vehicles: in use (1974): 3,400 passenger cars, 6,800 commercial vehicles.

Communications: Radios: 117,000 licenses (1972). **Telephones in use:** (1976): 7,947. **Daily newspaper circulation** (1971): 14,000; 21 per 1,000 pop.

Health: Life expectancy at birth (1970-75): 41.9 male; 45.1 female. **Births** (annual per 1,000 pop. 1970-75): 45.6. **Deaths** (annual per 1,000 pop. 1970-75): 23.0. **Natural increase** (annual 1970-75): 22.6%. **Pop. per hospital bed** (1973): 356. **Pop. per physician** (1973): 14,545. **Infant mortality** (per 1,000 pop under 1 yr. 1973): 97.

Education: Literacy (1973): 20%. **Pop. 5-19:** in school (1973): 39%; per teacher (1973): 76.

First inhabited by bushmen, then by Bantus, the region became the British protectorate of Bechuanaland in 1886, halting encroachment by Boers and Germans from the south and southwest. The country became fully independent Sept. 30, 1966, changing its name to Botswana.

Cattle-raising is the chief economic activity. Many workers have become migrant laborers in South Africa, and much of Botswana's chief export, meat, goes to that country.

Brazil

Federative Republic of Brazil

People: Population (1976 est.): 109,180,000. **Age distrib.** (%): 0-14: 41.7; 15-59: 53.2; 60+: 5.1. **Pop. density:** 33 per sq. mi. **Urban** (1975):59.1%. **Ethnic groups:** Portuguese, Africans, and mulattoes make up the vast majority; Italians, Germans, Japanese, Indians, Jews, Arabs. **Languages:** Portuguese. **Religions:** Roman Catholic 89%, Protestant 10%.

Geography: Area: 3,286,470 sq. mi., larger than conterminous 48 U.S. states; largest country in S. America. **Location:** Occupies eastern half of S America. **Neighbors:** French Guiana, Surinam, Guyana, Venezuela on N, Colombia, Peru, Bolivia, Paraguay, Argentina on W. Uruguay on S. **Topography:** Brazil's Atlantic coastline stretches 4,603 miles. In N is the heavily-wooded Amazon basin covering half the country. Its network of rivers navigable for 15,814 mi. The Amazon itself flows 2,093 miles in Brazil, all navigable. The NE region is semiarid scrubland, heavily settled and poor. The S central region, favored by climate and resources, has 45% of the population, produces 75% of farm goods and 80% of industrial output. The narrow coastal belt includes most of the major cities. Almost the entire country has a tropical or semitropical climate. **Capital:** Brasilia. **Cities** (1970 cen.): Sao Paulo (met.) 5,869,966; Rio de Janeiro 4,252,009; Belo Horizonte (met.) 1,228,295; Recife 1,046,454; Salvador (met.) 1,005,216; Porto Alegre 869,795; Fortaleza (met.) 828,763; Belem (met.) 603,267; Curitiba (met.) 583,857; Brasilia 272,002.

Government: Head of state: Pres. Ernesto Geisel, b. Aug. 3, 1908, in office: Mar. 15, 1974. **Local divisions:** 21 states, with individual constitutions and elected governments; the former autonomy has been curbed in recent years; 4 territories, federal district. **Armed forces:** regulars 257,200; para-military 200,000.

Economy: Industries: Textiles, steel, autos, aluminum, chemicals, drugs, plastics, ships, appliances, shoes, paper, glass, machinery. **Chief crops:** Coffee (largest grower), cotton, soybeans, sugar, cocoa, rice, corn, fruits. **Minerals:** Iron (one third world reserve); leader in quartz crystals, beryl, sheet mica, manganese, columbium, titanium, diamonds, chrome; also thorium, gold, nickel, gem stones, coal, tin, tungsten, bauxite, oil. **Crude oil output** (1976): 61 mln. bbls. **Per capita arable land:** 0.6 acres. **Livestock** (1976): 98,160,000 cattle; 47,000,000 pigs; 25,100,000 sheep; 255,462,000 poultry. **Fish catch** (1975): 674,000 metric tons. **Electricity production** (1975): 78,072 mln. kwh. **Labor force:** 44% agric.; 11% manuf.

Finance: Currency: Cruzeiro (Apr. 1977: 13.3=$1 US). **Gross domestic product** (1975): $109 bln. **Per capita income** (1974): $905. **Imports** (1976): $13,623 bln.; partners (1974): U.S. 24%, W. Ger. 12%, Saudi Ar. 10%, Jap. 9%. **Exports** (1976): $10.126 bln.; partners (1974): U.S. 22%, Neth. 8%, Jap. 7%, W. Ger. 6%. **Tourists** (1974): 539,600; receipts: $66 million. **Balance of payments** (1976): $2.62 bln. **National budget** (1976): $15.41 bln. revenues; $15.37 bln. expenditures. **International reserves** (Nov. 1976): $5.139 bln. **Consumer prices** (change in 1976): 41.7%.

Transport: Railway traffic (1973): 6,584 mln. passenger-miles; 26,515 mln. net ton-miles. **Motor vehicles:** in use (1974): 3,679,300 passenger cars, 1,001,900 commercial vehicles; manufactured (1975): 554,000 passenger cars, 370,000. commercial vehicles. **Civil aviation:** 6,438 mln. passenger-miles (1976); 303 mln. freight ton-miles (1976). **Chief ports:** Santos, Rio de Janeiro, Vitoria, Salvador, Rio Grande, Recife.

Communications: Television sets: 6,600,000 in use (1972); 1,683,000 manufactured (1974). **Radios:** 6,250,000 in use (1973); 1,185,000 manufactured (1974). **Telephones in use** (1976): 3,371,284. **Daily newspaper circulation** (1973): 4,058,-000; 40 per 1,000 pop.

Health: Life expectancy at birth (1960-70): 57.61 male; 61.10 female. **Births** (annual per 1,000 pop. 1970-75): 37.1. **Deaths** (annual per 1,000 pop. 1970-75): 8.8. **Natural increase** (annual 1970-75): 2.83%. **Pop. per hospital bed** (1973): 282. **Pop. per physician** (1973): 1,811. **Infant mortality** (per 1,000 pop. under 1 yr. 1973): 94.

Education: Literacy (1973): 66%. **Pop. 5-19:** in school (1973): 50%; per teacher (1973): 51.

Pedro Alvares Cabral, a Portuguese navigator, is generally credited as the first European to reach Brazil, in 1500. The country was thinly settled by various Indian tribes. Only a few have survived to the present, mostly in the Amazon basin, where they have been threatened by genocidal trends.

The first Portuguese governor-general was appointed in 1549. In the next centuries, colonists gradually pushed inland, bringing along large numbers of African slaves. Slavery was not abolished until 1888.

The King of Portugal, fleeing before Napoleon's army, moved the seat of government to Brazil in 1808. Brazil thereupon became a kingdom under Dom Joao VI. After his return to Portugal his son Pedro proclaimed the independence of Brazil, Sept. 7,

1822, and was acclaimed emperor. The second emperor, Dom Pedro II, was deposed in 1889, and a republic proclaimed, called the United States of Brazil. In 1967 the country was renamed the Federative Republic of Brazil.

A military junta took control in 1930, and dictatorial power was assumed by Getulio Vargas. He was elected president in 1933, ruled until a 1945 military coup, was reelected in 1950, but was forced out once more by the military in 1954. A democratic regime prevailed 1956-64, during which time the capital was moved from Rio de Janeiro to Brasilia in the interior.

In 1964, economic and social problems, including runaway inflation, led to political agitation. The elected government of Pres. Joao Goulart was overthrown in a military coup. The 1967 constitution strengthened presidential powers and weakened the congress.

The next four presidents were all military leaders. Censorship was imposed, and much of the opposition was suppressed, amid charges of torture. In 1974 elections, the official opposition party made gains in the chamber of deputies, and some relaxation of censorship occurred, though church liberals, labor leaders, and intellectuals continued to report cases of arrest and torture. In 1977, a series of constitutional changes assured long-term control by the regime.

Close ties with the U.S. were damaged in 1977, when the U.S. criticized the human rights situation in Brazil, and opposed construction of a nuclear fuel reprocessing plant. West Germany had agreed in 1975 to supply Brazil with the technology for a complete nuclear energy industry. Brazil cancelled a 25-year old U.S. military assistance agreement.

Since 1930, successive governments have pursued industrial and agricultural growth and the development of interior areas, with the state sector playing a larger role in recent years. Exploiting vast mineral resources, fertile soil in several regions, and a huge labor force, Brazil became the leading industrial power of Latin America by the 1970s, while agricultural output soared. Education was advanced and illiteracy reduced.

However, income maldistribution remained unaffected by economic growth, and a return of inflation (46% in 1976) aggravated malnutrition, which affected 40% of the population. A huge oil import bill increased the foreign debt.

Bulgaria

People's Republic of Bulgaria

People: Population (1976): 8,760,000. **Age distrib.** (%): 0-14: 22.3; 15-59: 62.3; 60+: 15.5. **Pop. density:** 205 per sq. mi. **Urban** (1975): 58.7% **Ethnic groups:** Bulgarians 85%, Turks 9%, Gypsies 2%. **Languages:** Bulgarian, Turkish, Greek. **Religions:** Orthodox 70%, Moslem 9%.

Geography: Area: 42,829 sq. mi., slightly larger than Tennessee. **Location:** In eastern Balkan Peninsula on Black Sea. **Neighbors:** Romania on N, Yugoslavia on W, Greece, Turkey on S. **Topography:** The Stara Planina (Balkan) Mts. stretch E-W across the center of the country, with the Danubian plain on N, the Rhodope Mts. on SW, and Thracian Plain on SE. **Capital:** Sofia. **Cities** (1974 est.): Sofia 962,500; Plovdiv 305,091; Varna 269,980.

Government: Head of state: Pres. Todor Zhivkov, b. Sept. 7, 1911, in office: July 7, 1971; **Head of government:** Premier Stanko Todorov, b. 1920, in office: July 7, 1971; **Head of Communist Party:** First Sec. Todor Zhivkov, in office: 1954. **local divisions:** 27 provinces, one city. **Armed forces:** regular 164,500; reserves 285,000.

Economy: Industries: Chemicals, machinery, metals, textiles, fur, leather goods, vehicles, wine, processed food. **Chief crops:** Grains, fruits, corn, potatoes, tobacco. **Minerals:** Coal, oil, lead, zinc. **Crude oil output** (1976): 890,000 bbls. **Per capita arable land:** 1.2 acres. **Livestock** (1976): 1,710,000 cattle: 3,900,000 pigs: 9,990,000 sheep: 35,089,000 poultry. **Fish catch** (1974): 115,100 metric tons. **Electricity production** (1976): 27,744 mln. kwh. **Labor force** 42% agric.

Finance: Currency: Lev (1974: 1.65=$1 US). **Gross domestic product** (est. 1974) $15 bln. **Per capita income** (1974): $1,650. **Imports** (1976) $5.626 bln.; partners (1974): USSR 44%, E. Ger. 9%, W. Ger. 7%, Pol. 5%, Czech. 4%. **Exports** (1976): $5.382 bln.; partners (1974): USSR 50%, E Ger. 8%, Pol. 5%, Czech. 4%. **Tourists** (including those in transit) (1974): 3,818,000; receipts: $198 million. **Balance of payments** (1976): -$13.3 mln.

Transport: Railway traffic (1974): 4,628 mln. passenger-miles; 10,749 mln. net ton-miles. **Motor vehicles:** in use (1970): 160,000 passenger cars. **Chief ports:** Burgas, Varna.

Communications: Television sets: 1,383,000 licenses (1973); 113,000 manufactured (1974). **Radios:** 2,266,000 licenses (1973); 110,000 manufactured (1974). **Telephones in use** (1976): 777,127. **Daily newspaper circulation** (1973): 1,856,000; 215 per 1,000 pop.

Health: Life expectancy at birth (1969-71): 68.58 male; 73.86 female. **Births** (per 1,000 pop. 1975): 16.6. **Deaths** (per 1,000 pop. 1975): 10.3. **Natural increase** (1975): 0.63%. **Pop. per hospital bed** (1973): 126. **Pop. per physician** (1973): 490. **Infant mortality** (per 1,000 pop. under 1 yr. 1975): 22.9.

Education: Literacy (1973): 90%. **Pop. 5-19:** in school (1973): 58% per teacher (1973): 35.

Bulgaria was settled by Slavs in the 6th century. Turkic Bulgars arrived in the 7th century, merged with the Slavs, became Christians by the 9th century, and set up powerful empires in the 10th and 12th centuries. The Ottomans prevailed in 1396 and remained for 500 years.

A revolt in 1876 led to autonomy in 1878 and an independent kingdom in 1908. Bulgaria expanded after the first Balkan War but lost its Aegean coastline in World War I, when it sided with Germany. Bulgaria joined the Axis in World War II, but withdrew in 1944. Communists took power with Soviet aid, and the monarchy was abolished Sept. 8, 1946.

Industrialization has advanced. Most trade is with Comecon countries. Bulgaria is Moscow's most loyal supporter in international questions.

Burma

Socialist Republic of the Union of Burma

People: Population (1976 est.): 30,830,000. **Pop. density:** 118 per sq. mi. **Ethnic groups:** Burmans (related to Tibetans) 72%; Karen 7%, Shan 6%, Kachin 2%, Chinese 2%, Indians 3%, others. **Languages:** Burmese (official) 80%, English, others. **Religions:** Buddhist 85%; Hinduism, Islam, Christianity, others.

Geography: Area: 261,789 sq. mi., nearly as large as Texas. **Location:** Between S. and S.E. Asia, on Bay of Bengal. **Neighbors:** Bangladesh, India on W., China, Laos, Thailand on E. **Topography:** Mountains surround Burma on W, N, and E, and dense forests cover much of the nation. N-S rivers provide habitable valleys and communications, especially the Irrawaddy, navigable for 900 miles. The country has a tropical monsoon climate. **Capital:** Rangoon. **Cities** (1973 est.): Rangoon 2,055,365; (1974 est.) Mandalay 417,000; Moulmein 202,000.

Government: Head of state: Pres. Ne Win, b. 1911, in office: Mar. 2, 1962; **Head of government:** Prime Min. Maung Kha, in office: Mar. 29, 1977. **Local divisions:** 7 states and 7 divisions. **Armed forces:** regulars 169,500.

Economy: Chief crops: Rice, cotton, maize, tobacco. **Minerals:** Oil, lead, silver, tin, tungsten, zinc, rubies, sapphires, jade. **Crude oil output** (1976): 8.2 mln. bbls. **Other resources:** Rubber, teakwood. **Per capita arable land:** 1.4 acres. **Livestock** (1974): 7,800,000 cattle; 1,900,000 pigs; 210,000 sheep; 22,100,000 poultry. **Fish catch** (1974): 433,800 metric tons. **Electricity production** (1976): 840 mln. kwh. **Labor force:** 64% agric.

Finance: Currency: Kyat (Feb. 1977: 6.76=$1 US). **Gross domestic product** (1974): $3.06 bln. **Per capita income** (1974): $100. **Imports** (1976) $117 mln.; partners (1973): Jap. 28%, P.R. China 18%, W. Ger. 9%, UK 8%. **Exports** (1976): $186 mln.; partners (1973): Jap. 26%, Sing. 11%, U.K. 10%, W. Ger. 6%, Belg. 6%. **Tourist receipts** (1974): $4 million. **International reserves** (Feb. 1977): $101.9 mln. **Consumer prices** (change in 1976): 23.3%.

Transport: Railway traffic (1974): 1,938 mln. passenger-miles; 245 mln. net ton-miles. **Motor vehicles:** in use (1974): 36,300 passenger cars, 39,300 commercial vehicles. **Civil aviation:** 101 mln. passenger-miles (1975); 745,000 freight ton-miles (1975). **Chief ports:** Rangoon, Sittwe, Bassein, Moulmein, Tavoy.

Communications: Radios: 627,000 licenses (1973); 19,000 manufactured (1973). **Daily newspaper circulation** (1973) 283,000.

Health: Life expectancy at birth (1970-75): 48.6 male; 51.5 female. **Births** (annual per 1,000 pop. 1970-75): 39.5. **Deaths**

(annual per 1,000 pop. 1970-75): 15.8. **Natural increase** (annual 1970-75): 2.37%. **Pop. per hospital bed** (1973): 1,207. **Pop. per physician** (1973): 6,906. **Infant mortality** (per 1,000 pop. under 1 yr. 1952): 195-300.

Education: Literacy (1973): 60%. **Pop. 5-19:** in school (1973): 53%; per teacher (1973): 93.

The Burmese arrived from Tibet before the 9th century, displacing earlier cultures, and a Buddhist monarchy was established by the 11th. Burma was conquered by the Mongol dynasty of China in 1272, then ruled by Shans as a Chinese tributary, until the 16th century.

Britain subjugated Burma in three wars, 1824-84, and ruled the country as part of India until 1937, when it became self-governing. It was overrun by Japan in World War II. Burma became independent outside the Commonwealth, Jan. 4, 1948.

Gen. Ne Win has dominated politics since 1958. He led a Revolutionary Council set up in 1962, which drove out Indians from the civil service and Chinese from commerce. Socialization of the economy was advanced, and isolation from foreign countries enforced. Lagging production and export, and rebellions by communists and Karen and Shan ethnic groups plague the country.

Burundi

Republic of Burundi

People: Population (1976 est.): 3,860,000. **Age distrib.** (%): 0-14: 46.9; 15-59: 47.3; 60+: 5.9. **Pop. density:** 359 per sq. mi. **Urban** (1970): 2.2%. **Ethnic groups:** Hutu 85%, Tutsi 14%, Twa (pygmy) 1%. **Languages:** French, Kirundi (official), Swahili. **Religions:** Roman Catholic 50%, Protestant 4%, others.

Geography: Area: 10,739 sq. mi., the size of Maryland. **Location:** In central Africa. **Neighbors:** Rwanda on N, Zaire on W, Tanzania on E. **Topography:** Much of the country is grassy highland, with mountains reaching 8,900 ft. The southernmost source of the White Nile is located in Burundi. Lake Tanganyika is the second deepest lake in the world. **Capital:** Bujumbura. **Cities** (1970 est.): Bujumbura (met.) 78,810.

Government: Head of state: Pres. Jean-Baptiste Bagaza, b. Aug. 29, 1946, in office: Nov. 1, 1976. **Local divisions:** 8 provinces and capital city.

Economy: Chief crops: Coffee (chief export), cotton, tea. **Minerals:** Nickel. **Per capita arable land:** 0.6 acres. **Livestock** (1974): 761,000 cattle; 203,000 sheep. **Fish catch** (1973): 7,940 metric tons. **Electricity production** (1972): 24 mln. kwh. **Labor force:** 86% agric.

Finance: Currency: Burundi Franc (Apr. 1977: 90=$1 US). **Gross domestic product** (est. 1974): $340 mln. **Per capita income** (1974): $90. **Imports** (1976) $58 mln.; partners (1973): Belg. 24%, Fr. 12%, W. Ger. 9%, Iran 6%. **Exports** (1976): $55 mln.; partners (1973): U.S. 54%, W. Ger. 12%, Belg. 6%, USSR 5%. **Tourists** (1974): 14,500. **National budget** (1975): $40.95 mln. revenues; $41.69 mln. expenditures. **International reserves** (Feb. 1977): $50.77 mln. **Consumer prices** (change in 1976): 6.9%.

Transport: Motor vehicles: in use (1974): 4,200 passenger cars, 1,700 commercial vehicles.

Communications: Radios: 100,000 in use (1973). **Daily newspaper circulation** (1970): 300; 0.1 per 1,000 pop.

Health: Life expectancy at birth (1970-71): 40 male; 43 female. **Births** (annual per 1,000 pop. 1970-71): 42.0. **Deaths** (annual per 1,000 pop. 1970-71): 20.4. **Natural increase** (annual 1970-71): 2.16%. **Pop. per hospital bed** (1973): 746. **Pop. per physician** (1973): 44,750. **Infant mortality** (per 1,000 pop. under 1 yr. 1965): 150.

Education: Literacy (1973): 10%. **Pop. 5-19:** in school (1973): 15%; per teacher (1973): 220.

The pygmy Twa were the first inhabitants, followed by Bantu Hutus, who were conquered in the 16th century by the tall Tutsi (Watusi), probably from Ethiopia. Under German control in 1899, the area fell to Belgium in 1916, which exercised successively a League of Nations mandate and UN trusteeship over Ruanda-Urundi (now two countries).

Independence came in 1962, and the monarchy was overthrown in 1966. An unsuccessful Hutu rebellion in 1972-73 left 10,000 Tutsi and 100,000 Hutu dead. Over 100,000 Hutu fled to Tanzania and Zaire. Michel Micombero, ruler for ten years, was overthrown in a military coup.

Burundi is one of the poorest and most densely populated countries in Africa.

Cambodia

See Kampuchea

Cameroon

United Republic of Cameroon

People: Population (1976 est.): 6,530,000. **Pop. density:** 36 per sq. mi. **Urban** (1970): 20.3%. **Ethnic groups:** Some 200 tribes; largest are Bamileke 30%, Fulani 7%. **Languages:** English, French (both official), 24 others. **Religions:** Roman Catholic 20%, Protestant 15%, Islam (mostly in N) 12%, others.

Geography: Area: 183,568 sq. mi., somewhat larger than California. **Location:** Between W and central Africa. **Neighbors:** Nigeria on NW, Chad, Central African Empire on E, Congo, Gabon, Equatorial Guinea on S. **Topography:** A low coastal plain with rain forests is in S; plateaus in center lead to forested mountains in W, including Mt. Cameroon, 13,000 ft.; grasslands in N lead to marshes around Lake Chad. **Capital:** Yaounde. **Cities** (1974 est.): Douala (met.) 350,000; Yaounde (met.) 250,000.

Government: Head of state: Pres. Ahmadou Ahidjo, b. Aug. 24, 1924, in office: Jan. 1, 1960. **Local divisions:** 7 provinces with appointed governors. **Armed forces:** regulars 5,600; paramilitary 7,000.

Economy: Industries: Aluminum processing, palm products. **Chief crops:** Cocoa, coffee, peanuts, tea, bananas, cotton, tobacco. **Other resources:** Timber, rubber. **Per capita arable land:** 2.5 acres. **Livestock** (1974): 2,500,000 cattle; 370,000 pigs; 2,000,000 sheep. **Fish catch** (1974): 71,600 metric tons. **Electricity production** (1973): 1,130 mln. kwh. **Labor force:** 82% agric.

Finance: Currency: CFA Franc (Apr. 1977: 248=$1 US). **Gross domestic product** (1974): $1.73 bln. **Per capita income** (1974): $260. **Imports** (1975) $599 mln.; partners (1974): Fr. 47%, W. Ger. 9%, U.S. 6%, It. 6%. **Exports** (1975): $448 mln.; partners (1974): Fr. 29%, Neth. 24%, W. Ger. 10%, U.S. 7%. **Tourists** (1974): 96,100; receipts (1972): $19 million. **Balance of payments** (1975): $−59.9 mln. **International reserves** (Oct. 1976): $41.93 mln. **Consumer prices** (change in 1975): 15.2%.

Transport: Railway traffic (1974): 152 mln. passenger-miles; 253 mln. net ton-miles. **Motor vehicles:** in use (1972): 39,100 passenger cars, 37,300 commercial vehicles. **Chief ports:** Douala.

Communications: Radios: 225,000 licenses (1973); 60,000 manufactured (1971). **Daily newspaper circulation** (1973): 18,000; 3 per 1,000 pop.

Health: Life expectancy at birth (1970-75): 39.4 male; 42.6 female. **Births** (annual per 1,000 pop. 1970-75): 40.4. **Deaths** (annual per 1,000 pop. 1970-75): 22.0. **Natural increase** (annual 1970-75): 1.84%. **Pop. per hospital bed** (1973): 323. **Pop. per physician** (1973): 27,000. **Infant mortality** (per 1,000 pop. under 1 yr. 1973): 137.

Education: Literacy (1973): 10%. **Pop. 5-19:** in school (1973): 41%; per teacher (1973): 90.

Portuguese sailors were the first Europeans to reach Cameroon, in the 15th century. The European and American slave trade was very active in the area. German control lasted from 1884 to 1916, when France and Britain divided the territory, later receiving League of Nations mandates and UN trusteeships. French Cameroon became independent Jan. 1, 1960; one part of British Cameroon joined Nigeria in 1961, the other part joined Cameroon. Stability has allowed for development of roads, railways, and agriculture.

Canada

See Index

Cape Verde Islands

Republic of Cape Verde

People: Population (1976 est.): 300,000. **Pop. density:** 193 per sq. mi. **Ethnic groups:** Creole (mulatto) 70%, African 28%, European 1%. **Languages:** Portuguese (official), Crioulo. **Religions:** Roman Catholicism prevails.

Geography: Area: 1,557 sq. mi., a bit larger than Rhode Island. **Location:** In Atlantic O., off western tip of Africa. **Neigh-**

bors: Nearest are Mauritania, Senegal. **Topography:** Cape Verde Islands are 15 in number, volcanic in origin (active crater on Fogo). The landscape is eroded and stark, with vegetation mostly in interior valleys. **Capital:** Praia. **Cities** (1974 est.): Praia 11,000; Mindelo 8,000.

Government: Head of state: Pres. Aristides Pereiro, in office: July 5, 1975; **Head of government:** Premier Pedro Pires, in office: July 5, 1975. **Local divisions:** 24 electoral districts.

Economy: Chief crops: Coffee, fruit, grain. **Minerals:** Salt. **Other resources:** Fish. **Per capita arable land:** 0.3 acres. **Livestock** (1973):18,000 cattle; 17,000 pigs; 3,000 sheep. **Electricity production** (1972): 6 mln. kwh.

Finance: Currency: Escudo (1974: 25.4=$1 US). **Gross domestic product** (est 1974): $79 mln. **Per capita income** (1974): $250. **Imports** (1975) $31 mln.; partners (1973): Port. 53%, U.K. 13%, Ang. 11%, Moz. 4%. **Exports** (1975): $33 mln.; partners (1973): Port. 61%, U.S. 25%. Zaire 3%.

Transport: Motor vehicles: in use (1973): 2,300 passenger cars, 700 commercial vehicles. **Chief ports:** Mindelo, Praia.

Communications: Radios: 5,200 licenses (1972).

Health: Life expectancy at birth (1970-75): 48.3 male; 51.7 female. **Births** (per 1,000 pop. 1974): 29.2. **Deaths** (per 1,000 pop. 1974): 8.8. **Natural increase** (1974): 2.04%. **Infant mortality** (per 1,000 pop. under 1 yr. 1974): 78.9.

The uninhabited Cape Verdes were discovered by the Portuguese in 1456 or 1460. The first Portuguese colonists landed in 1462; African slaves were brought soon after, and most Cape Verdeans descend from both groups. Many of the relatively well-educated Cape Verdeans served as officials in Portuguese African countries. Others led the Guinea-Bissau independence movement. Cape Verde independence came July 5, 1975. The government backs eventual union with Guinea-Bissau.

Central African Empire

People: Population (1974 est.): 2,610,000. **Age distrib.** (%): 0-14: 41.6; 15-59: 53.9; 60+: 4.5. **Pop. density:** 11 per sq. mi. **Ethnic groups:** Banda 47%, Baya 27%, 80 other groups. **Languages:** French (official), Sangho (national). **Religions:** Protestant, Roman Catholic 35-65%, Moslem 8%, others.

Geography: Area: 241,313 sq. mi., slightly smaller than Texas. **Location:** In central Africa. **Neighbors:** Chad on N, Cameroon on W, Congo, Zaire on S, Sudan on E. **Topography:** The country is mostly a rolling plateau, average altitude 2,000 ft., with rivers draining S to the Congo and N to Lake Chad. Open, well-watered savanna covers most of the area, with an arid area in NE, and tropical rainforest in SW. **Capital:** Bangui. **Cities** (1971 est.): Bangui 187,000.

Government: Head of state: Emperor Bokassa I, b. Feb. 22, 1920, in office: Jan. 1, 1966; **Head of government:** Prime Min. Ange Patasse, in office: Sept. 5, 1976. **Local divisions:** 14 prefectures.

Economy: Industries: Textiles, radios. **Chief crops:** Cotton, coffee, peanuts, corn, sorghum. **Minerals:** Diamonds (chief export), uranium, iron, copper. **Other resources:** Timber. **Per capita arable land:** 8.0 acres. **Livestock** (1974): 460,000 cattle; 60,000 pigs; 72,000 sheep. **Electricity production** (1973): 51 mln. kwh. **Labor force:** 87% agric.

Finance: Currency: CFA Franc (Apr. 1977: 248=$1 US). **Gross domestic product** (est. 1974): $310 mln. **Per capita income** (1974): $110. **Imports** (1975): $69 mln.; partners (1973): Fr. 57%, U.S. 9%, W. Ger. 7%, U.K. 4%. **Exports** (1975): $47 mln.; partners (1973): Fr. 41%, U. S. 15%, Isr. 11%, It. 6%. **Tourists** (1974): 4,100; receipts (1973): $3 million. **Balance of payments** (1975): $0.7 mln. **International reserves** (Oct. 1976): $20.91 mln. **Consumer prices** (change in 1976): 10.5%.

Transport: Motor vehicles: in use (1974): 9,100 passenger cars, 3,900 commercial vehicles.

Communications: Radios: 65,000 licenses (1973); 12,000 manufactured (1973). **Daily newspaper circulation** (1972): 500; 0.3 per 1,000 pop.

Health: Life expectancy at birth (1959-60): 33 male; 36 female. **Births** (annual per 1,000 pop. 1970-75): 43.4. **Deaths** (annual per 1,000 pop. 1970-75): 22.5. **Natural increase** (annual 1970-75): 2.09%. **Pop. per hospital bed** (1973): 489. **Pop. per physician** (1973): 28,983. **Infant mortality** (per 1,000 pop. under 1 yr. 1959-60): 190.

Education: Literacy (1973): 8%. **Pop. 5-19:** in school (1973): 33%; per teacher (1973): 145.

Various Bantu tribes migrated through the region for centuries before French control was asserted in the late 19th century, when the region was named Ubangi-Shari. Complete independence was attained Aug. 13, 1960.

All political parties were dissolved in 1960, and the country became a center for Chinese political influence in Africa. Relations with China were severed after a 1965 coup. Elizabeth Domitien, premier 1975-76, was the first woman to hold that post in an African country. Pres. Jean-Bedel Bokassa, ruler since 1965, proclaimed himself emperor of the newly-named Central African Empire December 1976.

The landlocked nation has been unable to develop its large mineral resources.

Chad

Republic of Chad

People: Population (1976 est.): 4,120,000. **Age distrib.** (%): 0-14: 41; 15-59: 55; 60+: 4. **Pop. density:** 8.3 per sq. mi. **Urban** (1974): 13.9%. **Ethnic groups:** Sudanese Arab 30%, Sudanic tribes 25%, Nilotic, Saharan tribes. **Languages:** French (official), Arabic, others. **Religions:** Moslems 40%, Christians 30%, others.

Geography: Area: 495,752 sq. mi., four-fifths the size of Alaska. **Location:** In central N. Africa. **Neighbors:** Libya on N, Niger, Nigeria, Cameroon on W. Central African Empire on S, Sudan on E. **Topography:** Chad has a southern wooded savanna, a steppe, and a desert, part of the Sahara, in the N. Southern rivers flow N to Lake Chad, surrounded by marshland. **Capital:** N'Djamena. **Cities** (1972 est.): N'Djamena (met.) 179,000; Sarh 43,770; Mondon 39,600.

Government: Head of state: Pres. Felix Malloum, b. Sept. 10, 1932, in office: Apr. 16, 1975. **Local divisions:** 14 prefectures with appointed governors. **Armed forces:** regulars 4,700; para-military 6,000.

Economy: Chief crops: Cotton. **Minerals:** Uranium. **Per capita arable land:** 4.0 acres. **Livestock** (1974): 2,800,000 cattle; 2,000,000 sheep. **Fish catch** (1974): 115,000 metric tons. **Electricity production** (1975): 56 mln. kwh. **Labor force:** 91% agric.

Finance: Currency: CFA Franc (Apr. 1977: 248=$1 US). **Gross domestic product** (est. 1974): $390 mln. **Per capita income** (1974): $94. **Imports** (1974): $87 mln.; partners (1973): Fr. 42%, Nigeria 12%, Congo 4%, Camer. 4%. **Exports** (1974): $37 mln.; partners (1973): Nigeria 6%, Congo 5%, Fr. 3%, Cent. Af. Emp. 2%. **Tourists** (1973): 16,700; receipts: $7 million. **Balance of payments** (1975): $−22.7 mln. **International reserves** (Oct. 1976): $11.87 mln. **Consumer prices** (change in 1975): 15.8%.

Transport: Motor vehicles: in use (1973): 5,800 passenger cars, 6,300 commercial vehicles.

Communications: Radios: 70,000 in use (1973). **Telephones in use** (1976): 5,378. **Daily newspaper circulation** (1973): 2,000; 0.5 per 1,000 pop.

Health: Life expectancy at birth (1963-64): 29 male; 35 female. **Births** (annual per 1,000 pop. 1970-75): 44.0. **Deaths** (annual per 1,000 pop. 1970-75): 24.0. **Natural increase** (annual 1970-75): 2.00%. **Pop. per hospital bed** (1973): 656. **Pop. per physician** (1973): 43,483. **Infant mortality** (per 1,000 pop. under 1 yr. 1963-64): 160.

Education: Literacy (1973): 6%. **Pop. 5-19:** in school (1973): 14%; per teacher (1973): 358.

Chad was the site of paleolithic and neolithic cultures before the Sahara advanced. A succession of kingdoms and Arab slave traders dominated Chad until France took control around 1900. Independence came Aug. 11, 1960.

Arab rebels, reportedly aided by Libya, fought government and French troops from 1969; France withdrew its fighting force in 1975, though some troops remain. French aid and influence is strong.

Libya, which reportedly switched some aid from rebels to the regime after it broke ties with Israel, annexed 37,000 sq. mi. of uranium and iron-rich land in northern Chad in 1976, stirring protests by Chad.

Chad was hardest hit among Sahel countries during the 1972-74 drought, whose effects have lingered.

Chile

Republic of Chile

People: Population (1976): 10,450,000. **Age distrib** (%): 0-14: 39.6; 15-59: 53.2; 60+: 7.2. **Pop. density:** 36 per sq. mi. **Urban** (1970): 76.0%. **Ethnic groups:** Mestizo 66%, Spanish 25%, Indian 5%. **Languages:** Spanish. **Religions:** Roman Catholic 90%, Protestants 6%.

Geography: Area: 286,396 sq. mi., larger than Texas. **Location:** Occupies western coast of southern S. America. **Neighbors:** Peru on N, Bolivia on NE, Argentina on E. **Topography:** Andes Mtns. are on E border including some of the world's highest peaks; on W is 2,650-mile Pacific Coast. Width varies between 100 and 250 miles. In N is Atacama Desert, in center are agricultural regions, in S are forests and grazing lands. **Capital:** Santiago. **Cities** (1975 est.): Santiago (met.) 3,262,990; Valparaiso (met.) 591,840; Concepcion (met.) 499,800.

Government: Head of state: Pres. Augusto Pinochet Ugarte, b. Nov. 25, 1915, in office: Sept. 11, 1973. **Local divisions:** 12 regions and Santiago region, comprised of 25 provinces, all headed by presidential appointees. **Armed forces:** regulars 79,-600; reserves 160,000.

Economy: Industries: Steel, textiles, wood products. **Chief crops:** Grain, rice, beans, potatoes, peas, fruits, grapes. **Minerals:** Copper (10% world output), nitrates, iodine (half world output), iron, coal oil, gas, gold, silver, molybdenum, cobalt, zinc, manganese, borate, mica, mercury, salt, sulphur, marble, onyx. **Crude oil output** (1976): 8.4 mln. bbls. **Other resources:** Water, forests. **Per capita arable land:** 1.3 acres. **Livestock** (1976): 3,700,000 cattle; 650,000 pigs; 6,000,000 sheep; 19,500,000 poultry. **Fish catch** (1975): 1,128,000 metric tons. **Electricity production** (1976): 9,432 mln. kwh. **Labor force:** 21% agric.; 16% manuf.

Finance: Currency: Peso (Apr. 1977: 18.97=$1 US). **Gross domestic product** (1975): $7.45 bln. **Per capita income** (1975): $661. **Imports** (1975) $1.911 bln.; partners (1973): U.S. 16%, Arg. 15%, W. Ger. 10%, U.K. 6%. **Exports** (1975): $1.661 bln.; partners (1973): Jap. 18%, W. Ger. 14%, U.K. 10%, U.S. 9%. **Tourists** (1973): 168,700; receipts (1974): $77 million. **Balance of payments** (1976): $459 mln. **National budget** (1975): $1.48 bln. revenues; $ 1.39 bln. expenditures. **International reserves** (Feb. 1977): $455.6 mln. **Consumer prices** (change in 1976): 229.5%.

Transport: Railway traffic (1974): 1,787 mln. passenger-miles; 1,498 mln. net ton-miles. **Motor vehicles:** in use (1974): 197,800 passenger cars, 151,400 commercial vehicles; manufactured (1975): 4,800 passenger cars, 2,600 commercial vehicles. **Civil aviation:** 815 mln. passenger-miles (1975); 37 mln. freight ton-miles (1975). **Chief ports:** Valparaiso, Arica, Antofagasta.

Communications: Television sets: 525,000 in use (1973); 76,000 manufactured (1974). **Radios:** 1,500,000 in use (1973); 121,000 manufactured (1973). **Telephones in use** (1976): 455,-169. **Daily newspaper circulation** (1972): 907,000; 94 per 1,000 pop.

Health: Life expectancy at birth (1969-70): 60.48 male; 66.01 female. **Births** (per 1,000 pop. 1971): 26.0. **Deaths** (per 1,000 pop. 1971): 8.7. **Natural increase** (1971): 1.73%. **Pop. per hospital bed** (1973): 276. **Pop. per physician** (1973): 1,836. **Infant mortality** (per 1,000 pop. under 1 yr. 1971): 77.8.

Education: Literacy (1973): 90%. **Pop. 5-19:** in school (1973): 79%; per teacher (1973): 57.

Northern Chile was under Inca rule before the Spanish conquest, 1536-40. The southern Araucanian Indians resisted until the late 19th century. Independence was gained 1810-18, under Jose de San Martin and Bernardo O'Higgins; the latter, as supreme director 1817-23, sought social and economic reforms until deposed. Chile defeated Peru and Bolivia in 1836-39 and 1879-84, gaining mineral-rich northern land.

After 30 years of intermittent reform attempts, Christian Democrats under Eduardo Frei Montalva came into office in 1964, and instituted social programs and gradual nationalization of foreign-owned mining companies. In 1970, Salvador Allende Gossens, a Marxist, became president with a third of the national vote, despite reported attempts by the U.S. Central Intelligence Agency and the International Telephone & Telegraph Corp. to foment a military coup.

The Allende government furthered nationalizations, and improved conditions for the poor. But illegal and violent actions by extremist supporters of the government, the regime's failure to attain majority support, and poorly planned socialist economic programs led to political and financial chaos and drastic declines in production. Protests by farmers and the urban middle class, some of them reportedly aided by U.S. government and business figures, helped provoke a crisis.

A military junta seized power Sept. 11, 1973, and said Allende killed himself. A few thousand were killed in street fighting and junta reprisals. The junta named a mostly-military cabinet, broke off relations with Cuba, which had been close under Allende, and announced plans to "exterminate Marxism."

Some 15,000 Allende supporters, mostly foreigners, were allowed to leave Chile. According to a 1977 statement of the Conference of Chilean Bishops, about 900 Chilean political prisoners had disappeared since the coup. Torture was still being used by the regime at that time, according to a UN report.

The economy continued to deteriorate under the new regime, thought inflation had been somewhat reduced by 1977.

Tierra del Fuego is the largest (18,800 sq. mi.) island in the archipelago of the same name at the southern tip of South America, an area of majestic mountains, torturous channels, and high winds. It was discovered 1520 by Magellan; he named the island Land of Fire because of its many Indian bonfires. Part of the island is in Chile, part in Argentina. Punta Arenas, on a mainland peninsula in Chile, is a center of sheep-raising and the world's southernmost city (pop. 67,600); Puerto Williams, pop. 949, is the southernmost settlement.

China

People's Republic of China

People: Population (1976 est.): 852,130,000. **Pop. density:** 230 per sq. mi. **Ethnic groups:** Han Chinese 94%, Mongol, Korean, Turkic groups, Manchu, others. **Languages:** Mandarin Chinese (official), Shanghai, Canton, Fukien, Hakka dialects; Tibetan, Vigus (Turkic). **Religions:** Confucianism, Buddism, Taoism, are traditional; Moslems 5%.

Geography: Area: 3,691,502 sq. mi., slightly larger than the U.S. **Location:** Occupies most of the habitable mainland of E. Asia. **Neighbors:** Mongolia on N, USSR on NE and NW, Afghanistan, Pakistan on W, India, Nepal, Bhutan, Burma, Laos, Vietnam on S, N. Korea on NW. **Topography:** Two-thirds of the vast territory is mountainous or desert, and only one-tenth is cultivated. Rolling topography rises to high elevations in the N in the Khinghan Mtns. separating Manchuria and Mongolia; the Tarabagota Mtns. in Sinkiang; the Himalayan and Kunlun Mtns. in the SW and in Tibet. Length is 1,860 mi. from N to S, width E to W is more than 2,000 mi. The eastern half of China is one of the best-watered lands in the world. Three great river systems, the Yangtze, the Hwang (Yellow) and the Xijiang (Si Kianj) provide water for vast farmlands. **Capital:** Peking. **Cities** (1970 est.): Shanghai 10,820,000; Peking 7,570,000; Tientsen 4,280,000, Canton 3,000,000; Shenyang 3,000,000; Wuhan 2,700,000; (1957 est.); Chungking 2,121,000; Harbin 1,552,000; Nanking 1,419,000; Sian 1,310,000; Tsinglao 1,121,000; Chengtu 1,107,000; Taiyuan 1,020,000.

Government: Head of government: Premier Hua Kuo-feng, b. 1921, in office: Feb. 1976; **Head of Communist Party:** Chmn. Hua Kuo-feng, in office: Oct. 1976. **Local divisions:** 21 provinces, 5 ethnic autonomous regions, and 3 cities; local autonomy varies. **Armed forces:** regulars 3,525,000 (army 3,000,000, navy 275,000, air force 250,000).

Economy: Industries: Textile, steel, chemicals, cement, plastics, agricultural implements, trucks. **Chief crops:** Grain, corn, peas, soybeans in N; rice, sugar in S, abutilon, hemp, jute, ramie, flax, cotton, tea. **Minerals:** Coal (3d in world), iron, tin, antimony, tungsten, molybdenum, salt. **Crude oil output** (1976): 646 mln. bbls. **Other resources:** Silk. **Per capita arable land:** 0.3 acres. **Livestock** (1974): 63,409,000 cattle; 238,971,000 pigs; 72,633,000 sheep; 1,250,000,000 poultry. **Fish catch** (1975): 6,880,000 metric tons (3d in world). **Electricity production** (1974): 120.000 mln. kwh. **Labor force:** 67% agric.

Finance: Currency: Yuan (1974: 2=$1 US). **Gross domestic product** (est. 1974): $170 bln. **Per capita income** (1974): $200. **Imports** (1974) $7 bln.; partners (1974): Jap. 32%, U.S. 13%, Can. 7%, W. Ger. 7%. **Exports** (1974): $5.6 bln.; partners (1974): Jap. 21%, Hong Kong 19%, Sing. 5%.

Transport: Railway traffic (1971 est.): 186.921 mln. net ton-miles. **Motor vehicles:** in use (1973): 30,000 passenger cars, 650,000 commercial vehicles. **Chief ports:** Shanghai, Tientsin, Dairen.

Communications: Television sets: 500,000 in use (1973). **Radios:** 12,000,000 in use (1970).

Health: Life expectancy at birth (1970-75): 59.9 male; 63.3 female. **Births** (annual per 1,000 pop. 1970-75): 26.9. **Deaths** (annual per 1,000 pop. 1970-75): 10.3. **Natural increase** (annual 1970-75): 1.66%. **Pop. per hospital bed** (1973): 1,000. **Pop. per physician** (1973): 8,142. **Infant mortality** (per 1,000 pop. under 1 yr. 1973): 55.

Education: Literacy (1973): 95%. **Pop. 5-19:** in school (1973): 63%; per teacher (1973): 47.

History. Remains of various man-like creatures who lived as early as several hundred thousand years ago have been found in many parts of China. Neolithic agricultural settlements dotted the Yellow River basin from about 5,000 B.C. Their language, religion, and art were the sources of later Chinese civilization.

A more developed culture, with the beginnings of literacy and metallurgy, emerged under the Shang Dynasty (c. 1500 B.C.-c.1000B.C.) which ruled much of North China. Its relation to earlier Middle Eastern and Indian civilizations is unknown.

A succession of dynasties and interdynastic warring kingdoms ruled China for the next 3,000 years. They expanded Chinese political and cultural domination to the south and west, and developed a brilliant technologically and culturally advanced society. Rule by foreigners (Mongols in the Yuan Dynasty, 1271-1368, and Manchus in the Ch'ing Dynasty, 1644-1911) did not alter the underlying culture.

A period of relative stagnation left China vulnerable to internal and external pressures in the 19th century. Rebellions left tens of millions dead, and Russia, Japan, Britain, and other powers exercised political and economic control in large parts of the country. China became a republic Jan. 1, 1912, following the Wuchang Uprising inspired by Dr. Sun Yat-sen.

For a period of 50 years, 1894-1945, China was involved in conflicts with Japan. In 1895, China ceded Korea, Taiwan, and other areas. On Sept. 18, 1931, Japan seized the Northeastern Provinces (Manchuria) and set up a puppet state called Manchukuo. The border province of Jehol was cut off as a buffer state in 1933. Japan invaded China proper July 7, 1937. After its defeat in World War II, Japan gave up all seized land.

After the war with Japan ended, Aug. 15, 1945, internal disturbances arose involving the Kuomintang, communists, and other factions. Manchuria was lost by the Kuomintang regime in 1948, and China proper came under domination of Communist armies during 1949-1950. The Kuomintang government moved to Taipei, Taiwan (Formosa), 90 mi. off the mainland, Dec. 8, 1949.

The People's Republic of China was proclaimed in Peking (Peiping) Sept. 21, 1949, by the Chinese People's Political Consultative Conference under Mao Tse-tung, communist leader. Chou En-lai was named premier and foreign minister Oct. 1, 1949.

The communist regime and the USSR signed a 30-year treaty of "friendship, alliance and mutual assistance," Feb. 15, 1950, repudiating the 1945 treaty between the Soviet Union and nationalist China authorized by the Yalta Agreement. Great Britain recognized the People's Republic in 1950 and France did so in 1964. By 1975, over 100 nations had recognized the regime.

The U.S. refused recognition, and after its consular officers met with abuse, withdrew them. On Nov. 26, 1950, the People's Republic sent armies into Korea against U.S. troops and forced a stalemate.

By the 1960s, relations with the USSR deteriorated, with disagreements on borders, ideology and leadership of world communism. The USSR cancelled aid accords, and China, with Albania, launched anti-Soviet propaganda drives.

On Mar. 2, 1969, Chinese and Russian soldiers fought one of a series of clashes on an island in the Ussuri River on the border between the two nations in the Far East. There were later clashes and reports of skirmishes to the west on the Sinkiang-USSR border. In 1970, ambassadors were exchanged for the first time since 1966. Border talks through 1975 were unsuccessful, and minor skirmishes took place on both fronts in 1976.

China has sought to promote revolutionary movements in Africa, Asia and South America. The program suffered serious setbacks, 1965-66. In the 1970s, China was sending a few hundred million dollars a year in military and economic aid to several governments, two-thirds of them in Africa.

On Oct. 25, 1971, the UN General Assembly ousted the Taiwan government from the UN and seated Communist China in its place. The U.S. had supported the mainland's admission but opposed Taiwan's expulsion.

In April 1971, after the U.S. relaxed restrictions on visits by its citizens, a U.S. table tennis team toured the People's Republic.

U.S. Pres. Nixon visited China Feb. 21-28, 1972, on invitation from Premier Chou En-lai, ending years of antipathy between the two nations. They agreed to continue progress toward normalization of relations. China and the U.S. moved close to formal diplomatic relations by opening liaison offices in each other's capitals, May-June 1973. Trade between the two countries neared $1 billion in 1974, largely U.S. grain exports, but declined in subsequent years.

Internal developments. After an initial period of consolidation, 1949-52, industry, agriculture, and social and economic institutions were forcibly molded according to Maoist ideals. However, frequent drastic changes in policy, and violent factionalism have, at times, interfered with economic development, and have prevented the return to stability and national unity lost a century ago.

In 1957, Mao Tse-tung admitted an estimated 800,000 people had been executed 1949-54; opponents claimed much higher figures.

The Great Leap Forward, 1958-60, tried to force the pace of economic development through intensive labor on the huge new rural communes, and through emphasis on ideological purity and enthusiasm. The program caused resistance and severe dislocations, and was largely abandoned; poor weather and suspension of Soviet aid were also blamed for the failure. Serious food shortages developed, and the government was forced to buy grain from Argentina, Mexico, Canada, and Australia. Light industries dependent on agriculture for raw materials were also affected.

Mao and his supporters within the Communist hierarchy launched a movement in 1965 called the Great Proletarian Cultural Revolution, in an attempt to oppose pragmatism and bureaucratic power and instruct a new generation in revolutionary principles. Massive purges took place at the national and local levels. Red Guards, composed largely of students and other youths, helped leftists seize power in many areas, but factional fighting weakened their power. A program of forcibly relocating millions of urban teenagers into the countryside was launched.

By 1968 the movement had run its course. Revolutionary committees that had assumed control were largely dominated by the military. Many purged officials returned to office in subsequent years, and reforms in education and industry that had placed ideology above expertise were gradually weakened.

In the mid-1970s, factional and ideological fighting increased, and emerged into the open after the 1976 deaths of Mao and premier Chou En-lai. Chiang Ching, Mao's widow, and three other leading leftists were purged and placed under arrest, after reportedly trying to seize power. Their opponents charged the "gang of four" with having sparked severe local fighting and disrupting production in many parts of China.

About 750,000 people were killed in 1977 when an earthquake leveled the northern industrial city of Tangshan. Severe drought and transport disruptions reportedly caused food shortages.

Increased army influence was reflected by a series of nuclear test explosions in 1976, including the largest ever in China. The first Chinese atomic bomb was exploded in 1964; the first hydrogen bomb in 1967. There is a growing stockpile of nuclear weapons and intermediate range missiles. Long range missiles have been tested. The Chinese navy has been built into the world's third largest. The first orbiting space satellite was launched in 1970.

Religion. Buddhism had the largest following. Confucianism, which reveres God but stresses ethical and philosophical principles rather than divine revelation, had wide acceptance. Taoism (after Lao Tze, b. 604 B.C.) is more metaphysical and looks to immortality. Islam, at one time, had 50 million followers; there were 3,280,000 Roman Catholics and 700,000 Protestants. On the mainland foreign missionaries and church schools are no longer tolerated.

Manchuria. Home of the Manchus, rulers of China 1644-1911, Manchuria has accommodated millions of Chinese settlers in the 20th century. Under Japanese rule 1931-45, the area became industrialized. China no longer uses the name Manchuria for the region, which is divided into three provinces.

Kwantung is the southernmost part of Manchuria. Russia in 1898 forced China to lease it Kwantung, and built Port Arthur (Lushun) and the port of Dairen (Luda). Japan seized Port Arthur in 1905. It was turned over to the USSR by the 1945 Yalta agreement, but finally returned to China in 1950.

Inner Mongolia was organized by the People's Republic in 1947. Its boundaries have undergone frequent changes, allegedly in order to dilute the minority Mongol population. Only

20% of the 6.2 million inhabitants are Mongol. Capital: Huhehaote (Kweisui).

Sinkiang Uigur Autonomous Region, in Central Asia, comprising Chinese Turkestan, Kulia, and Kashgaria, is 633,802 sq. mi., pop. 7.3 million (75% Uigurs, a Turkic Moslem group, with a heavy Chinese increase in recent years). Capital: Urumchi. It is China's richest region in strategic minerals. Some Uigurs have fled to the USSR, claiming national oppression by China.

Tibet, 470,000 sq. mi., is a thinly populated region of high plateaus and massive mountains, the Himalayas on the S, the Kunluns on the N. High passes connect with India and Nepal; roads lead into China proper. Capital: Lhasa. Average altitude is 15,000 ft. Jiachan, 15,870 ft., is believed to be the highest inhabited town on earth. Agriculture is primitive. Pop. 1.7 million (of whom 500,000 are Chinese). Another four million Tibetans form the majority of the population of vast adjacent areas that have long been incorporated into China.

China ruled all of Tibet from the 18th century, but independence came in 1911. China reasserted control in 1951, and a communist government was installed in 1953, revising the theocratic Lamaist Buddhist rule. Serfdom was abolished, but all land remained collectivized.

A Tibetan uprising within China in 1956 spread to Tibet in 1959. The rebellion was crushed with Chinese troops, and Buddhism was almost totally suppressed. The Dalai Lama and 85,000 Tibetans fled to India. Chinese have taken nearly all major posts in the Tibet Autonomous Region set up in 1965. Revolts continued in 1965-66, and fighting was reported as late as 1976. The International Commission of Jurists charged the Chinese regime with genocide in Tibet in 1961.

China (Taiwan)

Republic of China

People: Population (1975): 16,050,000. **Pop. density:** 1,181 per sq. mi. **Ethnic groups:** Han Chinese 98% (18% from mainland), aborigines (of Indonesian origin) 2%. **Languages:** Mandarin Chinese (official), Taiwan, Hakka dialects, Japanese, English. **Religions:** Buddhism, Taoism, Confucianism prevail, Christians 2.5%.

Geography: Area: 13,592 sq. mi., the size of Maryland and Delaware combined. **Location:** Off SE coast of China, between E. and S. China Seas. **Neighbors:** Nearest is China. **Topography:** A range of mountains forms the backbone of the island, the eastern half is very steep and craggy, the western slope is flat, fertile, and well-cultivated. **Capital:** Taipei. **Cities** (1974 est.): Taipei (met.) 2,000,000; Kaohsiung 1,000,000; Tainau 500,000.

Government: Head of state: Pres. Yen Chai-kan, b. Oct. 23, 1905, in office: Apr. 5, 1975; **Head of government:** Prime Min. Chiang Ching-kuo, b. Mar. 18, 1910, in office: June 1, 1972. **Armed forces:** regulars 470,000; reserves 1,170,000.

Economy: Industries: Textiles, clothing, electrical and electronic equip., processed foods, chemicals, glass, machinery. **Chief crops:** Rice, bananas, pineapples, sugar cane, sweet potatoes, wheat, soybeans, peanuts, jute. **Minerals:** Coal, gold, copper, sulphur, oil. **Crude oil output** (1975): 1.4 mln. bbls. **Per capita arable land:** 0.2 acres. **Livestock** (1976): 240,000 cattle; 2,881,000 pigs; 28,266,000 poultry. **Fish catch** (1974): 698,000 metric tons. **Electricity production** (1974): 20,500 mln. kwh. **Labor force:** 37% agric. 19% manuf.

Finance: Currency: NT Dollar (Apr. 1977: 38=$1 US). **Gross domestic product** (1976): $17.3 bln. **Per capita income** (1976): $800. **Imports** (1976): $7.593 bln.; partners (1974): Jap. 32%, U.S. 24%, W. Ger. 7%, Kuw. 6%. **Exports** (1976): $8.147 bln.; partners (1974): U.S. 37%, Jap. 15%, Hong Kong 6%, W. Ger. 6%. **Tourists** (1973): 824,300. **Balance of payments** (1976): $409 mln. **National budget** (1973): $2.27 bln. revenues; $2.01 bln. expenditures. **International reserves** (Feb. 1977): $1.414 bln. **Consumer prices** (change in 1976): 2.5%.

Transport: Railway traffic (1973): 4,979 mln. passenger-miles; 1.839 mln. net ton-miles. **Motor vehicles:** in use (1973): 95,100 passenger cars, 83,900 commercial vehicles. **Chief ports:** Kaohsiung, Keelung.

Communications: Television sets: 1,500,000 in use (1973); over 4,500,000 manufactured (1973). **Radios:** 3,000,000 in use (1973). **Telephones in use** (1976): 1,117,989. **Daily newspaper circulation** (1974): 1,300,000; 83 per 1,000 pop.

Health: Life expectancy at birth (1972): 66.8 male; 72.0 female. **Births** (per 1,000 pop. 1973): 23.8. **Deaths** (per 1,000 pop. 1973): 4.8. **Natural increase** (1973): 1.90%. **Pop. per hospital bed** (1973): 1,064. **Pop. per physician** (1973): 2,967. **Infant mortality** (per 1,000 pop. under 1 yr. 1973): 18.

Education: Literacy (1973): 85%. **Pop. 5-19:** in school (1973): 66%; per teacher (1973): 53.

Large-scale Chinese immigration began in the 17th century. The island came under mainland control after an interval of Dutch rule, 1620-62. Taiwan (also called Formosa) was ruled by Japan 1895-1945. Two million Kuomintang supporters fled to Taiwan in 1949. Both the Taipei and Peking governments consider Taiwan an integral part of China. The U.S., one of the few nations to maintain formal ties, keeps 1,100 troops on Taiwan.

Land reform, government planning, U.S. aid and investment, and free universal education have brought huge advances in industry, agriculture, and mass living standards.

The Penghus (Pescadores), 50 sq. mi., pop. 120,000, lie between Taiwan and the mainland. **Quemoy** and **Matsu,** civilian pop. 75,000, lie just off the mainland; the last U.S. advisers left in 1976.

Colombia

Republic of Colombia

People: Population (1976 est.): 24,370,000. **Pop. density:** 54 per sq. mi. **Urban** (1974): 64.3%. **Ethnic groups:** Mestizo 58%, Caucasian 20%, Mulatto 14%, Negro 4%, Indian 1%. **Languages:** Spanish. **Religions:** Roman Catholic 95%, Protestant under 1%.

Geography: Area: 455,355 sq. mi., larger than Texas and California combined. **Location:** At the NW corner of S. America. **Neighbors:** Panama on NW, Ecuador, Peru on S, Brazil, Venezuela on E. **Topography:** Three ranges of Andes, the Western, Central, and Eastern Cordilleras, run through the country from N to S. The eastern range consists mostly of high table lands, densely populated. The Magdalena R. rises in Andes, flows N to Carribean, through a rich alluvial plain. Sparsely-settled plains in E are drained by Orinoco and Amazon systems. **Capital:** Bogota. **Cities** (1973 cen.): Bogota 2,855,065; Medellin (met.) 1,417,384; Cali (met.) 923,264; Barranquilla (met.) 726,726.

Government: Head of state: Pres. Alfonso Lopez-Michelson, b. June 30, 1913, in office: Aug. 7, 1974. **Local divisions:** 22 departments with elected legislatures and various special districts. **Armed forces:** regulars 54,300; reserves 250,000.

Economy: Industries: Textiles, rubber goods, hides, steel, paper, cement, chemicals. **Chief crops:** Coffee (2d in exports), rice, tobacco, cotton, cocoa, maize, potatoes, sugar, bananas. **Minerals:** Oil, gas, emeralds (95% world output), gold, silver, copper, lead, mercury, cinnabar, manganese, platinum, coal, iron, nickel, salt. **Crude oil output** (1976): 53.3 mln. bbls. **Other resources:** Rubber, balsam, dye-woods, copaiba, hydro power. **Per capita arable land:** 0.3 acres. **Livestock** (1976): 24,724,-000 cattle; 2,001,000 pigs; 2,016,000 sheep; 45,000,000 poultry. **Fish catch** (1974): 90,500 metric tons. **Electricity production** (1976): 13,620 mln. kwh. **Labor force:** 45% agric.

Finance: Currency: Peso (Mar. 1977: 36.74=$1 US). **Gross domestic product** (1975): $13.4 bln. **Per capita income** (1975): $515. **Imports** (1976) $1.710 bln.; partners (1973): U.S. 40%, W. Ger. 9%, Jap. 8%, Fr. 5%. **Exports** (1976): $1.882 bln.; partners (1973): U.S. 37%, W. Ger. 12%, Sp. 5%, Jap. 4%. **Tourists** (1974): 362,900; receipts, $102 million. **Balance of payments** (1975): $95 mln. **National budget** (1976): $1.39 bln. revenues; $1.26 bln. expenditures. **International reserves** (Feb. 1977): $1.326 bln. **Consumer prices** (change in 1976): 17.4%.

Transport: Railway traffic (1974): 300 mln. passenger-miles; 825 mln. net ton-miles. **Motor vehicles:** in use (1973): 326,900 passenger cars, 107,000 commercial vehicles; assembled (1975): 23,000 passenger cars, 6,500 commercial vehicles. **Civil aviation:** 1,691 mln. passenger-miles (1975); 63 mln. freight ton-miles (1975). **Chief ports:** Buenaventura, Santa Marta, Barranquilla, Cartagena.

Communications: Television sets: 1,200,000 in use (1972); 64,000 manufactured (1972). **Radios:** 2,793,000 in use (1973); 37,000 manufactured (1972). **Telephones in use** (1976): 1,285,670. **Daily newspaper circulation** (1973): 1,299,000.

Health: Life expectancy at birth (1970-75): 59.2 male; 62.7 female. **Births** (annual per 1,000 pop. 1970-75): 40.6. **Deaths** (annual per 1,000 pop. 1970-75): 8.8. **Natural increase** (annual 1970-75): 3.18%. **Pop. per hospital bed** (1973): 505. **Pop. per physician** (1973): 2,184. **Infant mortality** (per 1,000 pop. under 1 yr. 1971): 62.8.

Education: Literacy (1973): 74%. **Pop. 5-19:** in school (1973): 40%; per teacher (1973): 73.

The country, ruled for 300 years by Spain, became independent in 1819 as Greater Colombia. Venezuela and Ecuador broke away in 1829-30, and Panama withdrew in 1903.

One of the few functioning Latin American democracies, Colombia is nevertheless plagued by rural and urban violence, though scaled down from "La Violencia" of 1948-58, which claimed 200,000 lives. Attempts at land and social reform, and progress in industrialization have not yet succeeded in reducing massive social problems aggravated by a very high birth rate.

Comoros

Republic of the Comoros

People: Population (1976 est.): 310,000. **Age distrib.** (%): 0–14: 45.6; 15–59: 46.6; 60+: 7.9. **Pop. density:** 447 per sq. mi. **Ethnic groups:** Arabs, Africans, East Indians. **Languages:** Arabic, French, Swahili. **Religions:** Islam prevails.

Geography: Area: 693 sq. mi., half the size of Rhode Island. **Location:** In the Mozambique Channel between NW Madagascar and SE Africa. **Neighbors:** Nearest are Mozambique on W, Madagascar on E. **Topography:** The islands are of volcanic origin, with an active volcano on Grand Comoro. **Capital:** Moroni. **Cities** (1974 est.): Moroni 12,000.

Government: Head of state: Pres. Ali Soilih, b. 1937, in office: Jan. 2, 1976. **Local divisions:** each of the 4 main islands is a prefecture.

Economy: Industries: Perfume. **Chief crops:** Vanilla, copra, perfume plants, fruits. **Per capita arable land:** 0.7 acres. **Livestock** (1973): 70,000 cattle; 81,000 goats; 6,000 sheep. **Electricity production** (1972): 3 mln. kwh.

Finance: Currency: CFA Franc (Apr. 1977: 248=$1 US). **Gross domestic product** (est. 1974): $50 mln. **Per capita income** (1974): $150. **Imports** (1973) $15 mln.; partners (1973): Fr. 50%, Madag. 15%, Ken. 5%. **Exports** (1973): $5 mln.; partners (1973): Fr. 75%, Madag. 19%, It. 7%.

Transport: Chief port: Dzaoudzi.

Communications: Radios: 35,000 in use (1973).

Health: Life expectancy at birth (1970-75): 40.9 male; 44.1 female. **Births** (annual per 1,000 pop. 1970-75): 46.6. **Deaths** (annual per 1,000 pop. 1970-75): 21.7. **Natural increase** (annual 1970-75): 2.49%. **Infant mortality** (per 1,000 pop. under 1 yr. 1952): 51.7.

The islands were controlled by Moslem sultans until the French acquired them 1841-1909. A 1974 referendum favored independence, with only the Christian island of Mayotte preferring association with France. The French National Assembly decided to allow each of the islands to decide its own fate. The Comoro Chamber of Deputies declared independence July 6, 1975. In a referendum in 1976, Mayotte voted to remain French.

Congo

People's Republic of the Congo

People: Population (1976 est.): 1,390,000. **Pop. density:** 11 per sq. mi. **Ethnic groups:** Bakongo 45%, Bateke 20%, others. **Languages:** French (official), others. **Religions:** Christians 50% (two-thirds Roman Catholic), others.

Geography: Area: 132,046 sq. mi., slightly smaller than Montana. **Location:** In western central Africa. **Neighbors:** Gabon, Cameroon on W, Central African Empire on N, Zaire on E, Angola (Cabinda) on SW. **Topography:** Much of the Congo is covered by thick forests. A coastal plain leads to the fertile Niari Valley. The center is a plateau; the Congo R. basin consists of flood plains in the lower and savanna in the upper portion. **Capital:** Brazzaville. **Cities** (1974 cen.): Brazzaville (met.) 289,700; Pointe-Noire 141,700.

Government: Head of state: Pres. Joachim Yombi Opango, b. 1939, in office: Apr. 3, 1977. **Head of government:** Prime Min. Louis Sylvain Ngoma, in office: Apr. 3, 1977. **Local divisions:** 9 regions and capital district. **Armed forces:** regulars 7,000; para-military 3,900.

Economy: Chief crops: Palm oil and kernels, cocoa, coffee, bananas, peanuts. **Minerals:** Oil, potash, lead, zinc. **Crude oil output** (1976): 14.2 mln. bbls. **Other resources:** Forests (wood products a major export.) **Per capita arable land:** 1.1 acres. **Livestock** (1973): 30,000 cattle; 15,000 pigs; 33,000 sheep. **Electricity production** (1975): 110 mln. kwh. **Labor force** 45% agric.

Finance: Currency: CFA Franc (Apr. 1977: 248=$1 US). **Gross domestic product** (est. 1974): $500 mln. **Per capita income** (1974): $350. **Imports** (1975) $254 mln.; partners (1972): Fr. 54%, W. Ger. 8%, U.S. 6%, P.R. China 5%. **Exports** (1975): $382 mln.; partners (1972): Fr. 16%, W. Ger. 14%, So. Afr. 8%, Neth. 5%. **Tourist** receipts (1974): $2 million. **Balance of payments** (1975): -$10.4 mln. **International reserves** (Oct. 1976): $4.94 mln. **Consumer prices** (change in 1975): 17.4%.

Transport: Railway traffic (1974): 130 mln. passenger-miles; 345 mln. net ton-miles. **Motor vehicles:** in use (1974): 19,000 passenger cars, 10,500 commercial vehicles. **Chief ports:** Pointe-Noire, Brazzaville.

Communications: Television sets: 3,800 in use (1973). **Radios:** 75,000 in use (1973). **Daily newspaper circulation** (1973): 1,000; 1 per 1,000 pop.

Health: Life expectancy at birth (1970-75): 41.9 male; 45.1 female. **Births** (annual per 1,000 pop. 1970-75): 45.1. **Deaths** (annual per 1,000 pop. 1970-75): 20.80. **Natural increase** (annual 1970-75): 2.43%. **Pop. per hospital bed** (1973): 175. **Pop. per physician** (1973): 6,173. **Infant mortality** (per 1,000 pop. under 1 yr. 1960-61): 180.

Education: Literacy (1973): 20%. **Pop. 5-19:** in school (1973): 58%; per teacher (1973): 43.

The Loango Kingdom flourished in the 15th century, as did the Anzico Kingdom of the Batekes; by the late 17th century they had become weakened. France established control by 1885. Independence came Aug. 15, 1960.

After a 1963 coup sparked by trade unions, the country adopted a Marxist-Leninist stance, with the USSR and China vying for influence. Relations with the U.S. were broken in 1965; an agreement to restore ties was reported in 1977. Throughout, France remained the dominant trade partner and source of technical assistance, and French-owned private enterprise retained a major economic role. The 1973 constitution was suspended in 1977 following an unsuccessful coup, in which Pres. Marien Ngouabi was killed.

Costa Rica

Republic of Costa Rica

People: Population (1976): 2,010,000. **Age distrib.** (%): 0–14: 44.1; 15–59: 50.4; 60+: 5.6. **Pop. density:** 102 per sq. mi. **Urban** (1973): 40.6%. **Ethnic groups:** Spanish (with Mestizo minority); Indians 0.4%, Jamaican Negroes 2%. **Languages:** Spanish (official), English. **Religions:** Roman Catholicism prevails.

Geography: Area: 19,653 sq. mi., smaller than W. Virginia. **Location:** In central America. **Neighbors:** Nicaragua on N, Panama on S. **Topography:** Lowlands by the Caribbean are tropical. The interior plateau, with an altitude of about 4,000 ft., is temperate. **Capital:** San Jose. **Cities** (1970 cen.): San Jose (met.) 395,401.

Government: Head of state: Pres. Daniel Oduber Quiros, b. Aug. 25, 1921, in office: May 8, 1974. **Local divisions:** 7 provinces, with presidentially-appointed governors.

Economy: Industries Fiberglass, aluminum, textiles, fertilizers, roofing, cement. **Chief crops:** Coffee (chief export), bananas, sugar, cocoa, cotton, hemp. **Minerals:** Gold, salt, sulphur, iron. **Other resources:** Fish, forests. **Per capita arable land:** 0.3 acres. **Livestock** (1976): 1,894,000 cattle; 230,000 pigs; 4,600,000 poultry. **Electricity production** (1975): 1,536 mln. kwh. **Labor force:** 37% agric.; 12% manuf.

Finance: Currency: Colones (Apr. 1977: 8.57=$1 US). **Gross domestic product** (1975): $1.93 bln. **Per capita income** (1975): $899. **Imports** (1976) $775 mln.; partners (1973): U.S. 35%, Jap. 9%, Guat. 7%, W. Ger. 7%. **Exports** (1976): $558 mln.; partners (1973): U.S. 33%, W. Ger. 13%, Nic. 8%, Guat. 6%. **Tourists** (1973): 246,800; receipts (1974): $44 million. **Balance of payments** (1976): $64.8 mln. **National budget** (1972): $172.3 mln. revenues; $229.2 mln. expenditures. **International reserves** (Feb. 1977): $117.67 mln. **Consumer prices** (change in 1976): 3.7%.

Transport: Railway traffic (1973): 60 mln. passenger-miles; 12 mln. net ton-miles. **Motor vehicles:** in use (1973): 52,100 passenger cars, 34,400 commercial vehicles. **Civil aviation:** 203 mln. passenger-miles (1976); 8.3 mln. freight ton-miles (1976). **Chief ports:** Limon, Puntarenas.

Communications: Television sets: 122,000 in use (1973).

Radios: 140,000 in use (1973). **Telephones in use** (1976): 111,812. **Daily newspaper circulation** (1973): 206,000; 112 per 1,000 pop.

Health: Life expectancy at birth (1962-64): 61.87 male; 64.83 female. **Births** (per 1,000 pop. 1974): 29.5. **Deaths** (per 1,000 pop. 1974): 5.0. **Natural increase** (1974): 2.45%. **Pop. per hospital bed** (1973): 246. **Pop. per physician** (1973): 1,413. **Infant mortality** (per 1,000 pop. under 1 yr. 1974): 37.6.

Education: Literacy (1973): 89%. **Pop. 5-19:** in school (1973): 65%; per teacher (1973): 37.

Guaymi Indians inhabited Costa Rica when Spaniards arrived in 1502. Independence came in 1821. Costa Rica seceded from the Central American Federation in 1838. Since the civil war of 1948-49, there has been no violent social conflict, and free political institutions have been preserved.

Costa Rica, though still a largely agricultural country, has achieved a relatively high standard of living and social services, and land ownership is widespread.

The country has generally followed a pro-U.S. foreign policy.

Cuba

Republic of Cuba

People: Population (1975): 9,330,000. **Age distrib.** (%): 0-14: 37.3; 15-59: 53.6; 60+: 9.1. **Pop. density:** 211 per sq. mi. **Urban** (1971): 60.5%. **Ethnic groups:** Spanish, Negro, and mixtures. **Languages:** Spanish. **Religions:** Roman Catholicism prevailed in past.

Geography: Area: 44,218 sq. mi., nearly as large as Pennsylvania. **Location:** Westernmost of West Indies. **Neighbors:** Nearest are Bahamas, U.S. on N, Mexico on W, Jamaica on S, Haiti on E. **Topography:** The coastline is about 2,500 miles. The N coast is steep and rocky, the S coast low and marshy. Low hills and fertile valleys cover more than half the country. The Sierra Maestra, in the east, is the highest of three mountain ranges. **Capital:** Havana. **Cities** (1970 cen.): Havana (met.) 1,751,216; Santiago de Cuba 277,600; Camaguey 197,720.

Government: Head of state: Pres. Fidel Castro, b. Aug. 13, 1926, in office: Dec. 3, 1976 (formerly Prime Min. since Jan. 1, 1959); Head of Communist Party: Gen. Sec. Fidel Castro, in office: Oct. 2, 1965. **Local divisions:** 14 provinces plus Isle of Pines, 169 municipal assemblies. **Armed forces:** regulars 175,000; reserves 90,000; para-military 100,000.

Economy: Industries: Textiles, wood products, cement, chemicals, cigars. **Chief crops:** Sugar cane (80% of exports), tobacco, coffee, pineapples, bananas, citrus fruit, coconuts. **Minerals:** Iron, copper, manganese, nickel, salt. **Crude oil output** (1976): 775,000 bbls. **Other resources:** Forests. **Per capita arable land:** 0.9 acres. **Livestock** (1974): 7,500,000 cattle; 1,450,000 pigs; 320,000 sheep; 15,700,000 poultry. **Fish catch** (1974): 165,000 metric tons. **Electricity production** (1970): 4,500 mln. kwh. **Labor force:** 30% agric.

Finance: Currency: Peso (1974: 0.829=$1 US). **Gross domestic product** (est. 1974): $5.8 bln. **Per capita income** (1974): $570. **Imports** (1975) $4.001 bln.; partners (1971): USSR 53%, E. Ger. 5%, U.K. 4%, Jap. 4%. **Exports** (1975): $3.680 bln.; partners (1971): USSR 35%, Jap. 12%, E. Ger. 6%, Czech. 5%.

Transport: Railway traffic (1972): 587 mln. passenger-miles; 934 mln. net ton-miles. **Motor vehicles:** in use (1973): 70,000 passenger cars, 33,000 commercial vehicles. **Chief ports:** Havana, Matanzas, Cienfuegos, Santiago de Cuba.

Communications: Television sets: 525,000 in use (1973). **Radios:** 1,790,000 in use (1973); 24,000 manufactured (1973).

Health: Life expectancy at birth (1970): 68.5 male; 71.8 female. **Births** (per 1,000 pop. 1973): 25.4. **Deaths** (per 1,000 pop. 1973): 5.8. **Natural increase** (1973): 1.96%. **Pop. per hospital bed** (1973): 238. **Pop. per physician** (1973): 1,115. **Infant mortality** (per 1,000 pop. under 1 yr. 1973): 28.9.

Education: Literacy (1973): 85%. **Pop. 5-19:** in school (1973): 69%; per teacher (1973): 34.

Some 50,000 Indians lived in Cuba when it was discovered by Columbus in 1492. Its name derives from the Indian Cubanacan. Except for British occupation of Havana, 1762-63, Cuba remained Spanish until 1898. A slave-based sugar plantation economy developed from the 18th century, aided by early mechanization of milling. Sugar remains the chief product and chief export despite government attempts to diversify.

Under Spanish governors Cubans were denied citizenship. A ten-year uprising ended in 1878 with guarantees of rights by Spain, which Spain failed to carry out. A full-scale movement under Jose Marti began Feb. 24, 1895.

The U.S. declared war on Spain in April, 1898, after the sinking of the U.S.S. Maine in Havana harbor, and defeated it in the short Spanish-American War. Spain gave up all claims to Cuba. U.S. troops withdrew in 1902, but under 1903 and 1934 agreements, the U.S. leased a site at Guantanamo Bay in the SE as a naval base. U.S. and other foreign investments acquired a dominant role in the economy.

In 1952, former president Fulgencio Batista seized control and established a dictatorship, which grew increasingly harsh and corrupt. Former student leader Fidel Castro assembled a rebel band in 1956; guerrilla fighting intensified in 1958. Batista fled Jan. 1, 1959, and in the resulting political vacuum Castro took power, becoming premier Feb. 16.

The government, quickly dominated by extreme leftists, began a program of sweeping economic and social changes, without restoring promised liberties. Opponents were imprisoned, and some were executed. Many of Castro's former supporters joined some 700,000 Cubans who emigrated in the years after the Castro takeover, mostly to the U.S.

Cattle and tobacco lands were nationalized, while a system of cooperatives was instituted. By the end of 1960 all banks and industrial companies had been nationalized, including over $1 billion worth of U.S.-owned properties, mostly without compensation.

Soviet, Chinese, and Eastern European economic penetration was extended by trade and credit agreements, including preferential sugar purchases and credits for construction of factories. Cuba is a member of Comecon, the Soviet economic union.

Eventually, poor sugar crops and food shortages resulted in collectivization of farms and stringent labor controls. Rationing of food, clothing, and consumer goods became more or less permanent, despite continued massive aid from the USSR and other Communist countries (over $2.5 million a day by 1977). However, mass health and education services were greatly improved, and social inequalities somewhat mitigated.

The U.S. cut back Cuba's sugar quota in 1960, and imposed a partial export embargo, which became total in 1962, severely damaging the economy. In 1961, some 1,400 Cubans, trained and backed by the U.S. Central Intelligence Agency, unsuccessfully tried to invade and overthrow the regime. It was revealed in 1975 that CIA agents had plotted to kill Castro in 1959 or 1960. Cuba complained of numerous raids by infiltrators, 1964-70.

In the fall of 1962, the U.S. learned that the USSR had brought nuclear missiles to Cuba. After an Oct. 22 warning from Pres. Kennedy, the missiles were removed.

The Organization of American States voted 15-4 in 1964 for mandatory sanctions against Cuba and for cooperation against Cuban revolutionary activities in Latin America. The sanctions were lifted in 1975, with the tacit concurrence of the U.S.

In 1973, Cuba and the U.S. signed an agreement providing for extradition or punishment of hijackers of planes or vessels, and for each nation to bar activity from its territory against the other. In 1977, the two countries signed agreements, to exchange diplomats, without restoring full ties, and to regulate offshore fishing.

But relations were strained by continued Cuban military involvement abroad. In 1975-77, Cuba sent over 20,000 troops to aid one faction in the Angola civil war. Other Cuban troops or military advisers were reported in the Congo, Ethiopia, Equatorial Guinea, Guinea, Guinea-Bissau, Somalia, and Mozambique.

Cyprus

Republic of Cyprus

People: Population (1976 est.): 640,000. **Age distrib.** (%): 0-14: 28.9; 15-59: 57.6; 60+: 13.6. **Pop. density:** 179 per sq. mi. **Urban** (1974): 42.2%. **Ethnic groups:** Greeks 75%, Turks 20%, Armenians, Maronites. **Languages:** Greek, Turkish. **Religions:** Orthodox 76%, Moslems 20%.

Geography: Area: 3,572 sq. mi., smaller than Connecticut. **Location:** In eastern Mediterranean Sea, off Turkish coast. **Neighbors:** Nearest are Turkey on N, Syria, Lebanon on E. **Topography:** Two mountain ranges run E-W, separated by a wide, fertile plain. **Capital:** Nicosia. **Cities** (1973 cen.): Nicosia (met.) 115,700.

Government Head of state: Pres. Spyros Achilles Kyprianou, b. Oct. 28, 1932, in office: Aug. 31, 1977. **Local divisions:** 6 districts.

Economy: Industries: Wine, clothing, shoes, tourism. **Chief crops:** Grains, grapes, carobs, citrus fruits, potatoes, olives. **Minerals:** Copper, iron, asbestos, gypsum, chrome, umber. **Per capita arable land:** 1.3 acres. **Livestock** (1974): 33,000 cattle; 151,000 pigs; 430,000 sheep. **Electricity production** (1976): 804 mln. kwh. **Labor force:** 34% agric.; 14% manuf.

Finance: Currency: Pound (Apr. 1977: 1=$2.43 US). **Gross domestic product** (1976): $753 mln. **Per capita income** (1975): $1,084. **Imports** (1976) $432 mln.; partners (1974): U.K. 21%, W. Ger. 9%, It. 8%, Gr. 7%. **Exports** (1976): $253 mln.; partners (1974): U.K. 38%, USSR 7%, W. Ger. 6%, Libya 5%. **Tourists** (1974): 231,800; receipts: $38 million. **Balance of payments** (1976): $44.9 mln. **National budget** (1974): $135.8 mln. revenues; $203.2 mln. expenditures. **International reserves** (Nov. 1976): $294.3 mln.

Transport: Motor vehicles: in use (1974): 69,100 passenger cars, 17,300 commercial vehicles. **Civil aviation:** 189 mln. passenger-miles (1976); 4.2 mln. freight ton-miles (1976). **Chief ports:** Famagusta, Limassol.

Communications: Television sets: 66,000 licenses (1973). **Radios:** 171,000 licenses (1973). **Telephones in use** (1976): 71,394. **Daily newspaper circulation** (1973): 92,000.

Health: Life expectancy at birth (1970-75): 69.5 male; 73.4 female. **Births** (annual per 1,000 pop. 1970-75): 22.2. **Deaths** (annual per 1,000 pop. 1970-75): 6.8. **Natural increase** (annual 1970-75): 1.54%. **Pop. per hospital bed** (1973): 197. **Pop. per physician** (1973): 1,195. **Infant mortality** (per 1,000 pop. under 1 yr. 1975): 29.2.

Education: Literacy (1973): 76%. **Pop. 5-19:** in school (1973): 55%; per teacher (1973): 50.

Agitation for enosis (union) with Greece increased after World War II, with the Turkish minority opposed, and broke into violence in 1955-56. In 1959, Britain, Greece, Turkey, and Cypriot leaders approved a plan for an independent republic, with constitutional guarantees for the Turkish minority and permanent division of offices on an ethnic basis. Greek and Turkish Communal Chambers dealt with religion, education, and other matters.

Archbishop Makarios, formerly the leader of the enosis movement, was elected president, and full independence became final Aug. 16, 1960.

Further communal strife led the United Nations to send a peace-keeping force in 1964; its mandate has been repeatedly renewed.

Makarios was re-elected in 1968 and 1973 with an overwhelming popular vote.

The Cypriot National Guard, led by officers from the Army of Greece, seized the government July 15, 1974, and named Nikos Sampson, an advocate of union with Greece, president. Makarios fled the country. On July 20, Turkey invaded the island; Greece mobilized its forces but did not intervene. A cease-fire was arranged July 22. On the 23d, Sampson turned over the presidency to Glafkos Clerides (on the same day, Greece's military junta resigned). A peace conference collapsed Aug. 14; fighting resumed. Greek Cypriots and Turks charged each other with massacres and atrocities. By Aug. 16 Turkish forces had occupied the NE 40% of the island, despite the presence of UN peace forces. On Aug. 19 the U.S. ambassador to Cyprus was slain by a Greek Cypriot during a riot in Nicosia. Makarios resumed the presidency in December.

Turkish Cypriots voted overwhelmingly June 8, 1975 to form a separate Turkish Cypriot federated state. A president and assembly were elected in 1976. Some 200,000 Greeks had left the Turkish-controlled area, replaced by thousands of Turks, some from the mainland.

Czechoslovakia

Czechoslovak Socialist Republic

People: Population (1976): 14,920,000. **Age distrib.** (%): 0-14: 22.8; 15-59: 59.9; 60+: 17.3. **Pop. density:** 302 per sq. mi. **Urban** (1974): 66.7%. **Ethnic groups:** Czechs 65%, Slovaks 30%, Hungarians 4%, Germans, Poles, Ukrainians. **Languages:** Czech, Slovak, Hungarian. **Religions:** Roman Catholics were majority, Lutherans, Orthodox.

Geography: Area: 49,371 sq. mi., the size of New York. **Location:** In E central Europe. **Neighbors:** Poland, E. Germany on N, W. Germany on W, Austria, Hungary on S, USSR on E. **Topography:** Bohemia, in W, is a plateau surrounded by mountains; Moravia is hilly, Slovakia, in E, has mountains (Carpathians) in N, fertile Danube plain in S. Vltava (Moldau) and Labe (Elbe) rivers flow N from Bohemia to G. **Capital:** Prague. **Cities** (1974 est.): Prague 1,095,615; Brno 343,860; Bratislava 328,765; Ostrava 292,404.

Government: Head of state: Pres. Gustav Husak, b. Jan. 10, 1913, in office: May 1975; **Head of government:** Prime Min. Lubomir Strougal, b. Oct. 19, 1924, in office: 1970; **Head of Communist Party:** First Sec. Gustav Husak, in office: April 1969. **Local divisions:** Czech and Slovak republics each have an assembly. **Armed forces:** regulars 180,000; reserves 350,000.

Economy: Industries: Machinery, oil products, weapons, steel, glass, chemicals, beer, aircraft, textiles, shoes. **Chief crops:** Wheat, sugar beets, potatoes, rye, hops. **Minerals:** Coal, iron. Jachymov has Europe's greatest pitchblend (for uranium and radium). **Crude oil output** (1976): 890,000 bbls. **Per capita arable land:** 0.9 acres. **Livestock** (1976): 4,560,000 cattle; 6,683,000 pigs; 800,000 sheep; 38,017,000 poultry. **Electricity production** (1976): 62,628 mln. kwh. **Labor force:** 16% agric.; 38% manuf.

Finance: Currency: Koruna (1974: 12=$1 US). **Gross domestic product** (est. 1974): $47 bln. **Per capita income** (1974): $3,000. **Imports** (1976): $9,706 bln.; partners (1973): USSR 30%, E Ger. 13%, Pol. 8%, Hung. 6%. **Exports** (1976): $9.035 bln.; partners (1973): USSR 32%, E. Ger. 11%, Pol. 10%, W. Ger. 6%. **Tourists** (1974): 11,785,700; receipts (1971): $61 million.

Transport: Railway traffic (1974): 11,298 mln. passenger-miles; 42,198 mln. net ton-miles. **Motor vehicles:** in use (1974): 1,328,200 passenger cars, 241,400 commercial vehicles; manufactured (1976): 179,000 passenger cars, 74,000 commercial vehicles. **Civil aviation:** 823 mln. passenger-miles (1976); 11 mln. freight ton-miles (1976).

Communications: Television sets: 3,404,000 licenses (1973); 409,000 manufactured (1974). **Radios:** 3,793,000 licenses (1973); 198,000 manufactured (1974). **Telephones in use** (1976): 2,614,761. **Daily newspaper circulation** (1973): 3,922,000; 269 per 1,000 pop.

Health: Life expectancy at birth (1973): 66.53 male; 73.49 female. **Births** (per 1,000 pop. 1975): 19.5. **Deaths** (per 1,000 pop. 1975): 11.5. **Natural increase** (1975): 0.81%. **Pop. per hospital bed** (1973): 99. **Pop. per physician** (1973): 432. **Infant mortality** (per 1,000 pop. under 1 yr. 1975): 20.9.

Education: Literacy (1973): 98%. **Pop. 5-19:** in school (1973): 57%; per teacher (1973): 33.

Bohemia, Moravia and Slovakia were part of the Great Moravian Empire when overrun by the Magyars 906 A.D. Bohemia and Moravia later became part of the Holy Roman Empire. Under the kings of Bohemia, Prague in the 14th century was the cultural center of Central Europe. In 1526 Ferdinand, brother of Holy Roman Emperor Charles V, became king of Bohemia and Hungary. Later the lands became part of Austria-Hungary.

In 1914-1918 Thomas G. Masaryk and Eduard Benes formed a provisional government with the support of Slovak leaders including Milan Stefanik. They proclaimed the Republic of Czechoslovakia Oct. 30, 1918.

By 1938 Nazi Germany had worked up disaffection among German-speaking citizens in Sudetenland and demanded its cession. Prime Minister Neville Chamberlain of Britain, with the acquiescence of France, signed an agreement with Hitler at Munich, Sept. 30, 1938, agreeing to the cession, with a guarantee of peace by Hitler and Mussolini. Germany occupied Sudetenland Oct. 1-2.

Hitler on Mar. 15, 1939, dissolved Czechoslovakia, made protectorates of Bohemia and Moravia, and supported the autonomy of Slovakia, which was proclaimed independent Mar. 14, 1939, with Josef Tisco president.

Soviet troops with some Czechoslovak contingents entered eastern Czechoslovakia in 1944 and reached Prague in May 1945; Benes returned as president. In May 1946 elections, the Communist Party won 38% of the votes, largest for a single party, and Benes accepted Klement Gottwald, a Communist, as prime minister. Tiso was executed in 1947.

Large numbers of Hungarians were moved out of Slovakia and many Slovaks were moved from Hungary to Slovakia in 1945-46. An estimated 3 million Sudeten Germans were transferred to Germany under the Potsdam Agreement.

In February, 1948, the Communists seized power in advance

of scheduled elections. In May 1948 a new constitution was approved. Benes refused to sign it. On May 30 the voters were offered a one-slate ballot and the Communists won full control. Benes resigned June 7. Gottwald became president and Benes died Sept. 3. A harsh Stalinist period followed, with complete and violent suppression of all opposition. Communist Party head Rudolf Slansky and other leading officials were sentenced to death in 1952 on trumped-up charges of disloyalty.

In Jan. 1968 a liberalization movement spread explosively through Czechoslovakia. Antonin Novotny, long the Stalinist boss of the nation, was deposed as party leader and succeeded by Alexander Dubcek, a Slovak, who declared he intended to make communism democratic. On Mar. 22 Novotny resigned as president and was succeeded by Gen. Ludvik Svoboda. On Apr. 6, Premier Joseph Lenart resigned and was succeeded by Oldrich Cernik, whose new cabinet was pledged to carry out democratization and economic reforms.

In July 1968 the USSR and 4 hard-core Warsaw Pact nations demanded an end to liberalization. On Aug. 20, the Russian, Polish, East German, Hungarian and Bulgarian armies invaded Czechoslovakia.

Despite demonstrations and riots by students and workers, press censorship was imposed, liberal leaders were ousted from office and promises of loyalty to Soviet policies were made by some old-line Communist Party leaders.

On Apr. 17, 1969, Dubcek resigned as leader of the Communist Party and was succeeded by Gustav Husak. In Jan. 1970, Premier Cernik was ousted. Censorship was tightened and the Communist Party expelled a third of its members. In 1972, more than 40 liberals were jailed on subversion charges. In 1973, amnesty was offered to some of the 40,000 who fled the country after the 1968 invasion, but repressive policies remained in force through 1976.

More than 700 leading Czechoslovak intellectuals and former party leaders signed a human rights manifesto in 1977, called Charter 77, prompting a renewed crackdown by the regime.

Czechoslovakia has long been an industrial and technological leader of the eastern European countries, though its relative standing has declined in recent years.

Denmark

Kingdom of Denmark

People: Population (1976): 5,070,000. **Age distrib.** (%): 0-14: 23.0; 15-59: 58.9; 60+: 18.1. **Pop. density:** 298 per sq. mi. **Urban** (1970): 66.9%. **Ethnic groups:** Almost all Scandinavian. **Languages:** Danish. **Religions:** Lutherans 97%.

Geography: Area: 17,028 sq. mi., the size of Massachusetts and New Hampshire combined. **Location:** In northern Europe, separating the North and Baltic Seas. **Neighbors:** W. Germany on S., Norway on NW (across Skagerrak), Sweden on NE (across Kattegat). **Topography:** Denmark consists of the Jutland Peninsula and about 500 islands, 100 inhabited. The land is flat or gently rolling, and is almost all in productive use. **Capital:** Copenhagen. **Cities** (1974 est.): Copenhagen (met.) 1,327,940; Arhus 245,941.

Government: Head of state: Queen Margrethe II, b. Apr. 16, 1940, in office: Jan. 14, 1972; **Head of government:** Prime Min. Anker Jorgensen, b. July 13, 1922, in office: Feb. 13, 1975. **Local divisions:** 14 counties, each with an elected council, and 2 urban communes. **Armed forces:** regulars 34,700, reserves 82,000.

Economy: Industries: Machinery, ships, textiles, furniture, steel. **Chief crops:** Daily products, grains, potatoes. **Crude oil output** (1976): 1.1 mln. bbls. **Per capita arable land:** 1.3 acres. **Livestock** (1976) 3,075,000 cattle; 7,585,000 pigs; 60,000 sheep; 16,124,000 poultry (largest pork exporter, 3d largest meat exporter). **Fish catch** (1975): 2,053,000 metric tons. **Electricity production** (1976): 19,248 mln. kwh. **Labor force:** 10% agric.; 24% manuf.

Finance: Currency: Kroner (Apr. 1977: 5.96=$1 US). **Gross domestic product** (1976): $38.2 bln. **Per capita income** (1975): $6,245. **Imports** (1976): $12,427 bln.; partners (1974): W. Ger. 18%, Swed. 13%, U.K. 10%, U.S. 6%. **Exports** (1976): $9.115 bln.; partners (1974): U.K. 16%, Swed. 15%, W. Ger. 12%, Nor. 6%. **Balance of payments** (1976): $−61 mln. **National budget** (1972): $6.54 bln. revenues; $6.17 bln. expenditures. **International reserves** (Feb. 1977): $1.208 bln. **Consumer prices** (change in 1976): 9.0%.

Transport: Railway traffic (1974): 1,979 mln. passenger-miles; 1,266 mln. net ton-miles. **Motor vehicles:** in use (1974): 1,260,900 passenger cars, 226,000 commercial vehicles; assembled (1973): 12,000 passenger cars, 900 commercial vehicles. **Civil aviation:** 1,497 mln. passenger-miles (1976); 69 mln. freight ton-miles (1976). **Chief ports:** Copenhagen, Alborg, Arhus, Odense.

Communications: Television sets: 1,527,000 licenses (1973); 87,000 manufactured (1974). **Radios:** 1,671,000 licenses (1973); 175,000 manufactured (1974). **Telephones in use** (1976): 2,316,208. **Daily newspaper circulation** (1973): 1,830,000; 364 per 1,000 pop.

Health: Life expectancy at birth (1972-73): 70.8 male; 76.3 female. **Births** (per 1,000 pop. 1974): 14.1. **Deaths** (per 1,000 pop. 1974): 10.2. **Natural increase** (1974): 0.39%. **Pop. per hospital bed** (1973): 120. **Pop. per physician** (1973): 591. **Infant mortality** (per 1,000 pop. under 1 yr. 1973): 11.5.

Education: Literacy (1973): 99%. **Pop. 5-19:** in school (1973): 67%; per teacher (1973): 21.

The origin of Copenhagen dates back to ancient times, when the fishing and trading place named Havn (port) grew up on a cluster of islets, but Bishop Absalon (1128-1201) is regarded as the actual founder of the city. On one of the islets he built a stronghold against the pirating Wends (a Slavic group).

Danes formed a large component of the Viking raiders in the early Middle Ages. The Danish kingdom was a major north European power until the 17th century, when it lost its lands in southern Sweden. Norway was separated in 1815, and Schleswig-Holstein in 1864. Northern Schleswig was returned in 1920.

The **Faeroe Islands** in the North Atlantic, about 300 mi. NE of the Shetlands, and 850 mi. from Denmark proper, 18 inhabited, have an area of 540 sq. mi. and pop. (est. 1975) of 40,000. They are self-governing in most matters.

Greenland

Greenland, a huge island between the North Atlantic and the Polar Sea, is separated from the North American continent by Davis Strait and Baffin Bay. Its total area is 840,000 sq. mi., 705,-234 of which are ice-capped. Most of the island is a lofty plateau 9,000 to 10,000 ft. in altitude. The average thickness of the ice cap is 1,000 ft. The population (est. 1975) is 50,000. The capital is Godthaab. Under the 1953 Danish constitution the colony became an integral part of the realm with representatives in the Folketing. Fish and fur are exported.

Djibouti

Republic of Djibouti

People: Population (1977 est.): 300,000. **Pop. density:** 34 per sq. mi. **Ethnic groups:** Issa (Somali) 47%; Afar 37%; European 8%; Arab 6%. **Languages:** Somali, Afar, French, Arabic. **Religions:** Most are Moslems; Europeans are Roman Catholic.

Geography: Area: 8,800 sq. mi., about the size of Massachusetts. **Location:** On E coast of Africa, separated from Arabian Peninsula by the strategically vital strait of Bab el-Mandeb. **Neighbors:** Ethiopia on N (Eritrea) and W, Somalia on S. **topography:** The territory, divided into a low coastal plain, mountains behind, and an interior plateau, is arid, sandy, and desolate. The climate is generally hot and dry. **Capital:** Djibouti. **Cities** (1970 est.): Djibouti (met.) 62,000.

Government: Capital: Head of state: Pres. Hassan Gouled, b. 1916, in office: June 24, 1977; **Head of government:** Prime Min. Ahmed Dini Ahmed, in office: July 12, 1977. **Local divisions:** 5 cercles (districts).

Economy: Minerals: Salt. **Livestock** (1976): 18,000 cattle; 561,000 goats; 95,000 sheep. **Electricity production** (1973): 46 mln. kwh.

Finance: Per capita income (1974): $980. **Imports** (1974) $117 mln.; partners (1973): Fr. 49%, Eth. 12%, Jap. 6%. **Exports** (1974): $20 mln.; partners (1973): Fr. 84%, Eth. 4%, It. 2%.

Transport: Motor vehicles: in use (1969): 7,400 passenger cars, 1,500 commercial vehicles. **Chief ports:** Djibouti.

Communications: Television sets: 2,300 in use (1973). **Radios:** 10,000 in use (1973).

Health: Births (per 1,000 pop. 1970): 42.0. **Deaths** (per 1,000 pop. 1970): 7.6. **Natural increase** (1970): 3.44%. **Infant mortality** (per 1,000 pop. under 1 yr. 1970): 3.44.

France gained control of the territory in stages between 1862 and 1900.

Ethiopia and Somalia have renounced their claims to the area, but each has accused the other of trying to gain control. There were clashes between Afars (ethnically related to Ethiopians) and Issas (related to Somalis) in 1976. Immigrants from both countries continued to enter the country up to independence, which came June 27, 1977.

Unemployment is about 80%. French aid is the mainstay of the economy.

Dominican Republic

People: Population (1976 est.): 4,840,000. **Age distrib.** (%): 0-14: 47.5; 15-59: 47.5; 60+: 4.9. **Pop. density:** 259 per sq. mi. **Urban** (1973): 43.5%. **Ethnic groups:** Caucasian 16%, mulatto 73%, Negro 11%. **Languages:** Spanish. **Religions:** Roman Catholic 95%, Protestant 2%.

Geography: Area: 18,704 sq. mi., the size of Vermont and New Hampshire combined. **Location:** In West Indies, sharing I. of Hispaniola with Haiti. **Neighbors:** Haiti on W. **Topography:** The Cordillera Central range crosses the center of the country, rising to over 10,000 ft., highest in the Caribbean. The Cibao valley to the N is major agricultural area. **Capital:** Santo Domingo. **Cities** (1970 cen.): Santo Domingo (met.) 817,645; Santiago de Los Caballeros (met.) 245,165.

Government: Head of state: Pres. Joaquin Balaguer, b. Sept. 1, 1907, in office: June 1, 1966. **Local divisions:** 26 provinces and a national district; pres. appoints governors. **Armed forces:** regulars 18,000; para-military 10,000.

Economy: Industries: Molasses, rum, alcohol, cement, textiles, furniture, apparel. **Chief crops:** Sugar, cocoa, coffee, tobacco, corn, peanuts, bananas. **Minerals:** Nickel, gold, copper, iron, salt, chalk, bauxite, marble, amber, kaolin. **Other resources:** Timber. **Per capita arable land:** 0.5 acres. **Livestock** (1976): 1,950,000 cattle; 705,000 pigs; 27,000 sheep; 7,600,000 poultry. **Electricity production** (1972): 1,300 mln. kwh. **Labor force:** 44% agric.; 8% manuf.

Finance: Currency: Peso (Apr. 1977: 1=$1 US). **Gross domestic product** (1975): $3.61 bln. **Per capita income** (1975): $702. **Imports** (1976) $878 mln.; partners (1974): U.S. 68%, Jap. 8%, Can. 5%, W. Ger. 5%. **Exports** (1976): $716 mln.; partners (1974): U.S. 70%, Neth. 8%, Sp. 3%, Algeria 2%. **Tourist receipts** (1974): $54 million. **Balance of payments** (1975): $27.6 mln. **National budget** (1976): $583.9 mln. revenues; $555.2 mln. expenditures. **International reserves** (Feb. 1977): $94.7 mln. **Consumer prices** (change in 1976): 7.9%.

Transport: Motor vehicles: in use (1974): 59,000 passenger cars, 29,000 commercial vehicles. **Chief ports:** Santo Domingo, San Pedro de Macoris, Puerto Plata.

Communications: Television sets: 155,000 in use (1973). **Radios:** 180,000 in use (1973). **Telephones in use** (1976): 108,023. **Daily newspaper circulation** (1973): 164,000.

Health: Life expectancy at birth (1959-61): 57.15 male; 58.59 female. **Births** (annual per 1,000 pop. 1970-75): 45.8. **Deaths** (annual per 1,000 pop. 1970-75): 11.0. **Natural increase** (annual 1970-75): 3.48%. **Pop. per hospital bed** (1973): 326. **Pop. per physician** (1973): 1,926. **Infant mortality** (per 1,000 pop. under 1 yr. 1974): 43.4.

Education: Literacy (1973): 68%. **Pop. 5-19:** in school (1973): 54%; per teacher (1973): 79.

Carib and Arawak Indians inhabited the island of Hispaniola when Columbus landed in 1492. The city of Santo Domingo, founded 1496, is the oldest settlement by Europeans in the hemisphere and has the supposed ashes of Columbus in an elaborate tomb in its ancient cathedral.

The western third of the island was ceded to France in 1697. Santo Domingo itself was ceded to France in 1795. Haitian leader Toussaint L'Ouverture seized it, 1801. Spain returned intermittently 1803-21, as several native republics came and went. Haiti ruled again, 1822-44, and Spanish occupation occurred 1861-63.

The country was occupied by U.S. Marines from 1916 to 1924, when a constitutionally elected government was installed.

In 1930, Gen. Rafael Leonidas Trujillo Molina was elected president. Trujillo remained in power, ruling brutally until his assassination in 1961.

Pres. Joaquin Balaguer, appointed by Trujillo in 1960, resigned under pressure in 1962, and Juan Bosch was elected president in the first free elections in 38 years. Bosch was overthrown in 1963.

On April 24, 1965, a revolt was launched by followers of Bosch and others, including a few communists. Four days later, with fighting continuing, 405 U.S. Marines intervened against the pro-Bosch forces; their numbers grew to 21,000. Token units were later sent by Brazil, Honduras, Nicaragua, Paraguay, and Costa Rica as a peace-keeping force.

A provisional government, approved by all major local groups, supervised a June, 1966 election, in which Balaguer defeated Bosch by a 3-2 margin; there were some charges of election fraud. Balaguer's followers won control of Congress.

The Inter-American Peace Force completed its departure Sept. 20, 1966. Balaguer was reelected, 1970 and 1974, the latter time without real opposition.

In 1971, scores of leftists were reported killed by terrorists. Renewed violence occurred in 1975. A crash in world sugar prices since 1975, combined with the increased oil export bill, ended five years of economic growth.

Ecuador

Republic of Ecuador

People: Population (1976 est.): 7,310,000. **Age distrib.** (%): 0–14: 47.2; 15–59: 48.3; 60+: 4.5. **Pop. density:** 69 per sq. mi. **Urban** (1974): 41.3%. **Ethnic groups:** Indians 40%, mestizos 40%, Caucasians 10%, Negroes 10%. **Languages:** Spanish 93%, Quechua dialects 7%. **Religions:** Roman Catholics 94%, Protestants 6%.

Geography: Area: 105,685 sq. mi., the size of Colorado. **Location:** In NW S. America, on Pacific coast, astride Equator. **Neighbors:** Colombia to N, Peru to E and S. **Topography:** Two ranges of Andes run N and S, splitting the country into 3 zones; hot, humid lowlands on the coast; temperate highlands between the ranges, and rainy, tropical lowlands to the E. **Capital:** Quito. **Cities** (1972 est.): Guayaquil 860,600; Quito 564,900.

Government: Head of state: Pres. Alfredo Poreda Burbano, b. Jan. 24, 1926, in office: Jan. 11, 1976. **Local divisions:** 20 provinces, headed by presidentially-appointed governors. **Armed forces:** regulars 23,550; para-military 5,800.

Economy: Industries: Cement, edible oils, textiles, sugar, chemicals, oil products, paper. **Chief crops:** Bananas (largest exporter), rice, grains, potatoes, fruits, cocoa, coffee, kapok. **Minerals:** Oil, copper, iron, lead, coal, sulphur. **Crude oil output** (1976): 68.5 mln. bbls. **Other resources:** Rubber, bark. **Per capita arable land:** 1.0 acres. **Livestock** (1976): 3,300,000 cattle; 2,700,000 pigs; 2,150,000 sheep. **Fish catch** (1974): 105,-200 metric tons. **Electricity production** (1972): 1,117 mln. kwh. **Labor force:** 54% agric.

Finance: Currency: Sucre (Apr. 1977: 25=$1 US). **Gross domestic product** (1976): $4.95 bln. **Per capita income** (1975): $577. **Imports** (1976) $993 mln.; partners (1973): U.S. 34%, Jap. 14%, W. Ger. 12%, Col. 6%. **Exports** (1976): $1.163 bln.; partners (1973): U.S. 32%, Trin. 12%, Pan. 9%, Peru 6%. **Tourists** (1974): 148,100; receipts; $16 million. **Balance of payments** (1976): $203 mln. **National budget** (1975): $504.7 mln. revenues; $492.4 mln. expenditures. **International reserves** (Feb. 1977): $544.3 mln. **Consumer prices** (change in 1976): 10.6%.

Transport: Railway traffic (1972): 39 mln. passenger-miles; 27 mln. net ton-miles. **Motor vehicles:** in use (1972): 33,000 passenger cars, 51,500 commercial vehicles. **Chief ports:** Guayaquil, Manta, Esmeraldas.

Communications: Television sets: 178,000 in use (1972); 4,000 manufactured (1973). **Radios:** 1,700,000 in use (1972); 26,000 manufactured (1973). **Telephones in use** (1976): 193,-066. **Daily newspaper circulation** (1973): 308,000; 46 per 1,000 pop.

Health: Life expectancy at birth (1961-63): 51.04 male; 53.67 female. **Births** (annual per 1,000 pop. 1970-75): 41.8. **Deaths** (annual per 1,000 pop. 1970-75): 9.5. **Natural increase** (annual 1970-75): 3.23%. **Pop. per hospital bed** (1973): 479. **Pop. per physician** (1973): 3,059. **Infant mortality** (per 1,000 pop. under 1 yr. 1974): 70.2.

Education: Literacy (1973): 68%. **Pop. 5-19:** in school (1973): 48%; per teacher (1973): 59.

Spain conquered the region, which was the northern Inca empire, in 1633. Liberation forces defeated the Spanish May 24, 1822, near Quito. Ecuador became part of the Great Colombia Republic but seceded, May 13, 1830.

Liberals became a dominant force in political life in 1895, but have been unable to end instability and a succession of military coups.

In June 1968 elections, Dr. Jose Maria Velasco Ibarra, who had been elected president 4 times but had been ousted 3 times by coups, was again chosen by the voters. In June 1970, he assumed dictatorial powers. On Feb. 15, 1972, he was ousted by a military junta. A new junta took over in 1976, after strikes, inflation, and other economic problems arose.

Ecuador and Peru have long disputed their Amazon Valley boundary.

The **Galapagos Islands**, 600 mi. to the W, are the home of huge tortoises and other unusual animals.

Egypt

Arab Republic of Egypt

People: Population (1976 est.): 38,070,000. **Pop. density:** 98 per sq. mi. **Urban** (1975): 44.6%. **Ethnic groups:** Egyptians, Bedouins, Nubians. **Languages:** Arabic. **Religions:** Sunni Moslems (state religion) 92%, Christians 7% (mostly Copts).

Geography: Area: 386,872 sq. mi., the size of Texas and New Mexico combined. **Location:** NE corner of Africa. **Neighbors:** Libya on W, Sudan on S, Israel on E. **Topography:** Almost the entire country is desolate and barren, with hills and mountains in E and along Nile. The Nile Valley, where most of the people live, stretches 550 miles in Egypt. **Capital:** Cairo. **Cities** (1974 est.): Cairo 5,715,000; Alexandria 2,259,000; Giza 853,-700; Suez 368,000; Subra-Elkhema 346,000; Port Said 342,000; El Mahalla et Kubra 287,800.

Government: Head of state: Pres. Mohamed Anwar El-Sadat, b. Dec. 25, 1918, in office: Oct. 17, 1970; **Head of government:** Prime Min. Mamdouh Salem, b. Mar. 10, 1918, in office: Nov. 10, 1976. **Local divisions:** 25 governorates; pres. appoints governors. **Armed forces:** regulars 342,500; reserves 515,000; para-military 120,000.

Economy: Industries: Textiles, chemicals, steel, cement, fertilizers, motion pictures. **Chief crops:** Cotton (one of largest producers), grains, vegetables, sugar cane, fruits. **Minerals:** Oil, phosphates, salt, iron, manganese, cement, gold, gypsum, kaolin, titanium. **Crude oil output** (1976): 120 mln. bbls. **Per capita arable land:** 0.2 acres. **Livestock** (1974): 2,160,000 cattle; 16,-000 pigs; 2,080,000 sheep; 29,284,000 poultry. **Fish catch** (1974): 96,200 metric tons. **Electricity production** (1973): 8,104 mln. kwh. **Labor force** 55% agric.

Finance: Currency: Pound (Apr. 1977: 1=$2.56 US). **Gross domestic product** (1974): $10.1 bln. **Per capita income** (1974): $279. **Imports** (1976) $3.807 bln.; partners (1973): U.S. 13%, Fr. 8%, W. Ger. 8%, USSR 7%. **Exports** (1976): $1.406 bln.; partners (1973): USSR 33%, Czech. 6%, Jap. 5%, It. 4%, E. Ger. 4%. **Tourists** (1974): 679,500; receipts (1973): $97 million. **Balance of payments** (1975): $−1.34 bln. **International reserves** (Dec. 1976): $339 mln. **Consumer prices** (change in 1976): 10.4%.

Transport: Railway traffic (1973): 4,507 mln. passenger-miles; 1,590 mln. net ton-miles. **Motor vehicles:** in use (1974): 184,500 passenger cars, 40,200 commercial vehicles; assembled (1975): 11,600 passenger cars, 2,600 commercial vehicles. **Civil aviation:** 909 mln. passenger-miles (1975); 13 mln. freight ton-miles (1975). **Chief ports:** Alexandria, Port Said, Suez.

Communications: Television sets: 600,000 licenses (1973); 68,000 manufactured (1974). **Radios:** 5,100,000 licenses (1973); 157,000 manufactured (1974). **Daily newspaper circulation** (1971): 745,000; 22 per 1,000 pop.

Health: Life expectancy at birth (1960): 51.6 male; 53.8 female. **Births** (per 1,000 pop. 1974): 35.5. **Deaths** (per 1,000 pop. 1974): 12.4. **Natural increase** (1974): 2.31%. **Pop. per hospital bed** (1973): 478. **Pop. per physician** (1973): 1,516. **Infant mortality** (per 1,000 pop. under 1 yr. 1974): 100.4.

Education: Literacy (1973): 26%. **Pop. 5-19:** in school (1973): 42%; per teacher (1973): 88.

Archeological records of ancient Egyptian civilization date back to 4,000 B.C. A unified kingdom arose around 3200 B.C., and extended its way south into Nubia and north as far as Syria. A high culture of rulers and priests was built on an economic base of serfdom, fertile soil, and annual flooding of the Nile banks.

Imperial decline facilitated conquest by Asian invaders (Hyksos, Assyrians). The last native dynasty fell in 341 B.C. to the Persians, who were in turn replaced by Greeks (Alexander and the Ptolemies), Romans, Byzantines, and Arabs, who introduced Islam and the Arabic language. The ancient Egyptian language is preserved only in the liturgy of the Coptic Christians.

Egypt was ruled as part of larger Islamic empires for several centuries. The Mamluks, a military caste of Caucasian origin, ruled Egypt from 1250 until defeat by the Ottoman Turks in 1517.

Under Turkish sultans the khedive as hereditary viceroy had wide authority, but European influence grew along with the beginnings of modernization in the 19th century. Britain intervened in 1882 and took control of administration, though nominal allegiance to the Ottoman Empire continued until 1914.

The country was a British protectorate from 1914 to 1922. A 1936 treaty strengthened Egyptian autonomy, but Britain retained bases in Egypt and a condominium over the Sudan. Britain fought German and Italian armies from Egypt, 1940-42, but Egypt did not declare war against Germany until 1945. In 1951 Egypt abrogated the 1936 treaty. The Sudan became independent in 1956.

Delays in reforms, corruption in public office, and royal extravagance led to an uprising July 23, 1952, led by the Society of Free Officers which named Maj. Gen. Mohammed Naguib commander in chief and forced King Farouk to abdicate. When the republic was proclaimed June 18, 1953, Naguib became its first president and premier. Lt. Col. Gamal Abdel Nasser, the principal influence behind the revolt, removed Naguib and became premier in 1954. In 1956, he was voted president. Nasser died in 1970 and was replaced as president by Vice President Anwar Sadat.

A new constitution was approved Sept. 11, 1971. At the same time, Egypt adopted the name Arab Republic of Egypt, dropping the name United Arab Republic, which it had used since its brief union with Syria, 1958-1961.

A series of decrees in July, 1961, nationalized about 90% of industry and reduced land holdings to 52 acres per family. In 1974 an economic liberalization was begun, with more emphasis on private domestic and foreign investment. Riots over food price increases and severe poverty left scores dead in January, 1977.

In July, 1956, the United States and Great Britain withdrew support for loans to start the Aswan High Dam. President Nasser nationalized the Suez Canal and seized control of the assets of the canal company. Later he obtained credits and technicians from the USSR to build the dam.

The billion-dollar Aswan High Dam project, begun 1960, completed 1971, provided irrigation for more than a million acres of land and a potential of 10 billion kwh of electricity per year. Artesian wells, drilled in the Western Desert, reclaimed 43,000 acres, 1960-66.

When the state of Israel was proclaimed in 1948, Egypt joined other Arab nations invading Israel and was defeated. No peace treaties were made and Egypt later denied Israeli shipping the use of the Suez Canal.

After terrorist raids across its border, Israel invaded Egypt's Sinai Peninsula, Oct 29, 1956. Egypt rejected a cease-fire demand by Britain and France; on Oct. 31 the 2 nations dropped bombs and on Nov. 5-6 landed forces. Egypt and Israel accepted a UN cease-fire, followed by Britain and France; fighting ended Nov. 7.

A UN Emergency Force guarded the 117-mile long border between Egypt and Israel until May 19, 1967, when it was withdrawn at Nasser's demand. Egyptian troops entered the Gaza Strip and the heights at Sharm el Sheikh and 3 days later closed the Strait of Tiran leading into the Gulf of Aqaba to all Israeli shipping. Full-scale war broke out June 5 and before it ended under a UN cease-fire June 10, Israel had captured Gaza and the Sinai Peninsula, controlled the east bank of the Suez Canal and reopened the gulf.

Sporadic fighting with Israel broke out late in 1968. In 1969-70 there were almost daily artillery duels across the Suez Canal, ground forays and air raids in which Israeli planes penetrated deep into Egypt. Military and economic aid was received from the USSR and it was est. in 1971 there were 19,000 or more Soviet military personnel in Egypt. Israel and Egypt agreed, Aug. 7, 1970, to a cease-fire and peace negotiations proposed by the U.S. Negotiations, pressed by the UN and U.S., failed to achieve results, but the cease-fire continued into 1973.

In July 1972 Sadat ordered most of the 20,000 Soviet military advisers and personnel to leave Egypt. They complied, leaving behind bases and equipment they had installed for the Egyptians. Some Soviet military shipments have continued, despite an Egyptian debt of several billion dollars.

In a surprise attack Oct. 6, 1973 Egyptian forces crossed the Suez Canal into the Sinai. (At the same time, Syrian forces attacked Israelis on the Golan Heights.) Egypt was supplied by a USSR military airlift; the U.S. responded with an airlift to Israel. Israel counter-attacked, crossed the canal, surrounded Suez City. A UN cease-fire took effect Oct. 24.

A disengagement agreement was signed Jan. 18, 1974, mainly through the efforts of U.S. Secretary of State Henry Kissinger. Under it, Israeli forces withdrew from the canal's W bank; limited numbers of Egyptian forces occupied a strip along the E bank. A second accord was signed in 1975, with Israel yielding Sinai oil fields.

The U.S. and Egypt resumed, in Feb. 1974, diplomatic relations, severed by Egypt after the 1967 war.

Iran, Saudi Arabia, and Kuwait provided aid of several billion dollars and low interest loans between 1975 and 1977. The U.S. also has provided some $1 billion annually in loans and grants since 1975.

The **Suez Canal**, 103 mi. long, links the Mediterranean and Red Seas. It was built by a French corporation 1859-69, but Britain obtained controlling interest in 1875. The last British troops were removed June 13, 1956. On July 26, Egypt nationalized the canal. French and British stockholders eventually received some compensation.

Egypt had barred Israeli ships and cargoes destined for Israel since 1948, and closed the canal to all shipping after the 1967 Israeli-Arab War. The canal was reopened in 1975, after Israel agreed to withdraw its troops eastward, and Egypt agreed to allow passage to Israeli cargo in third party ships. By 1977, annual tolls, at $500 million, had once more become a major source of government revenue.

El Salvador

Republic of El Salvador

People: Population (1976): 4,120,000. **Age distrib.** (%): 0-14: 46.2; 15-59: 48.4; 60+: 5.4 **Pop. density:** 499 per sq. mi. **Urban** (1974): 38.8%. **Ethnic groups:** Mestizos 89%, Indians 10%, Caucasians 1%. **Languages:** Spanish, Nahuatl (among some Indians). **Religions:** Roman Catholicism prevails.

Geography: Area: 8,260 sq. mi., the size of Massachusetts. **Location:** In Central America. **Neighbors:** Guatemala on W, Honduras on N. **Topography:** A hot Pacific coastal plain in the south rises to a cooler plateau and valley region, densely populated. The N is mountainous, including many volcanoes. **Capital:** San Salvador. **Cities** (1971 cen.): San Salvador 337,171; Santa Ana 172,300.

Government: Head of state: Pres. Carlos Humberto Romero, b. Feb. 29, 1929, in office: July 1, 1977. **Local divisions:** 14 departments; pres. appoints governors. **Armed forces:** regular 7,155; para-military 3,000.

Economy: Industries: Cement, textiles, refined sugar. **Chief crops:** Coffee, cotton, rice, maize, cacao, tobacco, indigo, sugar. **Other resources:** Rubber, forests. **Per capita arable land:** 0.3 acres. **Livestock** (1976): 1,100,000 cattle, 400,000 pigs; 5,000 sheep; 8,643,000 poultry. **Electricity production** (1975): 1,068 mln. kwh. **Labor force:** 47% agric.

Finance: Currency: Colones (Apr. 1977: 2.5=$1 US). **Gross domestic product** (1976): $2.18 bln. **Per capita income** (1974): $382. **Imports** (1976): $705 mln.; partners (1973): U.S. 29%, Guat. 16%, Jap. 10%, W. Ger. 8%. **Exports** (1976): $721 mln.; partners (1973): U.S. 33%, Guat. 18%, W. Ger. 13%, Jap. 10%. **Tourists** (1974): 285,400; receipts: $16 million. **Balance of payments** (1976): $84 mln. **National budget** (1975): $232.3 mln. revenues; $242.2 mln. expenditures. **International reserves** (Feb. 1977): $283.6 mln. **Consumer prices** (change in 1976): 7.1%.

Transport: Motor vehicles: in use (1974): 40,000 passenger cars, 20,000 commercial vehicles. **Chief ports:** La Union, Acajutla.

Communications: Television sets: 110,000 in use (1973); 16,000 manufactured (1974). **Radios:** 350,000 in use (1972). **Telephones in use** (1976): 55,813. **Daily newspaper circulation** (1973): 348,000.

Health: Life expectancy at birth (1960-61): 56.56 male; 60.42 female. **Births** (per 1,000 pop. 1975): 40.1. **Deaths** (per 1,000 pop. 1975): 8.0. **Natural increase** (1975): 3.21%. **Pop. per hospital bed** (1973): 613. **Pop. per physician** (1973): 3,676. **Infant mortality** (per 1,000 pop. under 1 yr. 1975): 58.3.

Education: Literacy (1973): 57%. **Pop. 5-19:** in school (1973): 47%; per teacher (1973): 99.

El Salvador became independent of Spain in 1821, and of the Central American Federation in 1839.

A fight with Honduras in 1969 over the presence of 300,000 Salvadorean workers left 2,000 dead. New clashes occurred in 1970 and 1974.

In 1977, the government faced protests charging election fraud, and an accusation by the national conference of Roman Catholic bishops that the government was "persecuting" priests working with landless peasants.

Equatorial Guinea

Republic of Equatorial Guinea

People: Population (1976 est.): 320,000. **Age distrib.** (%): 0-14: 35.2; 15-59: 57.1; 60+: 7.7. **Pop. density:** 30 per sq. mi. **Ethnic groups:** Fangs 75%, several other groups. **Languages:** Spanish (official), Fang, English. **Religions:** Roman Catholics 60%, Protestants, others.

Geography: Area: 10,832 sq. mi., the size of Maryland. **Location:** Consists of Masie Nguema Biyogo Is. (area 780 sq. mi.) off W. Africa coast in Gulf of Guinea, and Rio Muni, enclave on Mainland. **Neighbors:** Gabon on S, Cameroon on E, N. **Topography:** Masie Nguema Biyogo Island consists of two volcanic mountains and a connecting valley. Rio Muni, with over 90% of the area, has a coastal plain and low hills beyond. **Capital:** Malabo. **Cities** (1973 est.): Bata 50,000; Malabo 23,000.

Government: Head of state: Pres. Masie Nguema Biyogo, b. Jan. 1, 1924, in office: Oct. 12, 1968. **Local divisions:** 2 provinces.

Economy: Chief crops: Cocoa, coffee, bananas, palm oil. **Other resources:** Timber. **Per capita arable land:** 1.8 acres. **Labor force:** 79% agric.

Finance: Currency: Ekpwele (1974: 57.7=$1 US). **Gross domestic product** (est. 1974): $120 mln. **Per capita income** (1974): $350. **Imports** (1973) $36 mln.; partners (1973): Sp. 41%. **Exports** (1973): $32 mln.; partners (1973): Sp. 41%.

Transport: Chief ports: Malabo, Bata.

Communications: Daily newspaper circulation (1967): 1,000; 4 per 1,000 pop.

Health: Life expectancy at birth (1970-75): 41.9 male; 45.1 female. **Births** (annual per 1,000 pop. 1970-75): 36.8. **Deaths** (annual per 1,000 pop. 1970-75): 19.7. **Natural increase** (annual 1970-75): 1.71%. **Pop. per hospital bed** (1973): 154. **Pop. per physician** (1973): 10,000. **Infant mortality** (per 1,000 pop. under 1 yr. 1966): 53.2.

Education: Literacy (1973): 20%. **Pop. 5-19:** in school (1973): 44%; per teacher (1973): 90.

Fernando Po Island was discovered by Portugal in the late 15th century and ceded to Spain in 1778. Independence came Oct. 12, 1968. Riots occurred in 1969 over disputes between the island and the more backward Rio Muni province on the mainland. Masie Nguema Biyogo, himself from the mainland, became president for life in 1972; he ended provincial autonomy in 1973.

Most of the nation's 7,000 Europeans have emigrated, and 45,000 Nigerian workers were evacuated amid charges of a reign of terror. According to reports, slavery has been revived. As many as 50,000 people have been murdered by government forces. The economy has deteriorated.

Relations with Cameroon and Gabon have cooled due to boundary disputes. The U.S. suspended relations in 1976. The USSR, China, and North Korea maintain ties, and Cuba has a military advisory mission.

Ethiopia

People: Population (1976 est.): 28,680,000. **Age distrib.** (%): 0-14: 45.5; 15-44: 42.7; 45+: 11.9. **Pop. density:** 63 per sq. mi. **Urban** (1975): 11.7%. **Ethnic groups:** Galla 33%, Amhara 25%, Tigre 12%, Somali, Afar, Sidama. **Languages:** Amharic, Tigre (Semitic languages); Galla (Hamitic), Arabic, others. **Religions:** Orthodox Christian 40%, Moslem 40%.

Geography: Area: 457,142 sq. mi., four-fifths the size of Alaska. **Location:** In E. Africa. **Neighbors:** Sudan on W, Kenya on S. Somalia, Afars, and Issas on E. **Topography:** A high central plateau, between 6,000 and 10,000 ft. high, rises to higher mountains near the Great Rift Valley, cutting in from the SW. The Blue Nile and other rivers cross the plateau, which descends to plains on both W and SE. **Capital:** Addis Ababa. **Cities** (1975 est.): Addis Ababa 1,161,267; Asmara 317,950; (1977 est.): Dire Dawa (66,570).

Government: Head of state: Chmn. Mengistu Haile Mariam, in office: Feb. 1977. **Local divisions:** 14 regions. **Armed forces:** regulars 50,800; reserves 28,000.

Economy: Industries: Food processing, cement, shoes, textiles. **Chief crops:** Coffee (Ethiopia is reputed birthplace of coffee; yields 50% export earnings), grains, tobacco, sugar. **Minerals:** Coal, iron, platinum, gold, silver, manganese, tin, copper, asbestos, potash, sulphur, mica, cement, salt. **Other resources:** Hydro power potential. **Per capita arable land:** 1.1 acres. **Livestock** (1974): 24,663,000 cattle; 17,322,000 goats; 23,320,000 sheep; 52,900,000 poultry. **Fish catch** (1974): 26,-800 metric tons. **Electricity production** (1975): 456 mln. kwh. **Labor force:** 85% agric.

Finance: Currency: Birr (Feb. 1977: 2.086=$1 US). **Gross domestic product** (1974): $2.68 bln. **Per capita income** (1972): $74. **Imports** (1976): $350 mln.; Partners (1973): It. 15%, Jap. 12%, W. Ger. 12%, U.K. 9%. **Exports** (1976): $278 mln.; partners (1973): U.S. 30%, W. Ger. 9%, It. 8%, Djibouti 7%. **Tourists** (1974): 50,200; receipts: $11 million. **Balance of payments** (1976): $14.4 mln. **National budget** (1974): $295.4 mln. revenues; $350.3 mln. expenditures. **International reserves** (Feb. 1977): $291.6 mln. **Consumer prices** (change in 1976): 28.5%.

Transport: Railway traffic (1974): 59 mln. passenger-miles; 152 mln. net ton-miles. **Motor vehicles:** in use (1972): 41,000 passenger cars, 12,700 commercial vehicles. **Civil aviation:** 325 mln. passenger-miles (1976); 12 mln. freight ton-miles (1976). **Chief ports:** Mesewa, Aseb.

Communications: Television sets: 25,000 in use (1973). **Radios:** 175,000 in use (1973). **Telephones in use** (1976): 68,-894. **Daily newspaper circulation** (1973): 51,000; 2 per 1,000 pop.

Health: Life expectancy at birth (1970-75): 36.5 male; 39.6 female. **Births** (annual per 1,000 pop. 1970-75): 49.9. **Deaths** (annual per 1,000 pop. 1970-75): 25.8. **Natural increase** (annual 1970-75): 2.36%. **Pop. per hospital bed** (1973): 3,124. **Pop. per physician** (1973): 73,750. **Infant mortality** (per 1,000 pop. under 1 yr. 1963): 84.2.

Education: Literacy (1973): 7%. **Pop. 5-19:** in school (1973): 10%; per teacher (1973): 420.

Ethiopian culture was influenced by Egypt and Greece. The ancient monarchy was invaded by Italy in 1880, but maintained its independence until a second Italian invasion in 1936. British forces freed the country in 1941.

The last emperor, Haile Selassie I, established a parliament and judiciary system in 1931, but barred all political parites.

A 1973 famine killed over 100,000 people. An army mutiny, strikes, and student demonstrations led to the dethronement of Selassie in 1974, and the execution of 60 former officials. The ruling junta pledged to form a one-party socialist state, and instituted a successful land reform. The influence of the Coptic Church, embraced in 330 A.D., was curbed, and the monarchy was abolished in 1975. A famine in the east killed thousands in 1975.

The regime, torn by bloody coups, faced uprisings by tribal and political groups in several parts of the country, in part aided by Sudan and Somalia. Ties with the U.S., once a major arms and aid source, deteriorated, while cooperation accords were signed with the USSR in 1977.

Eritrea, an Italian colony since 1890, reverted to Ethiopia in 1952 in accordance with a UN General Assembly vote. Since 1970 secessionist guerrillas, aided by Arab states, have seized most of the country.

Fiji

Dominion of Fiji

People: Population (1976 est.): 580,000. **Age distrib.** (%): 0-14: 40.4; 15-59: 55.3; 60+: 4.3. **Pop. density:** 82 per sq. mi. **Ethnic groups:** Indian 50%, Fijians (Melanesian-Polynesian) 42%, Europeans 2%. **Languages:** English (official), Fijian, Hindi. **Religions:** Most Fijians are Methodist, most Indians are Hindu.

Geography: Area: 7,055 sq. mi., the size of New Jersey. **Location:** In western S. Pacific O. **Neighbors:** Nearest are Solomons on NW, Tonga on E. **Topography:** There are 840 islands (106 inhabited), many of them mountainous, with tropical forests and large fertile areas, Viti Levu, the largest island, has over half the total land area. **Capital:** Suva. **Cities** (1975 est): (met.) 96,000.

Government: Head of state: Queen Elizabeth II, represented by Gov.-Gen. George Cakobau; **Head of government:** Prime Min. Kamisese Mara, b. May 13, 1920, in office Oct. 10, 1970. **Local divisions:** 4 administrative divisions.

Economy: Industries: Cement, shipyards, light industry, molasses, tourism. **Chief crops:** Sugar, coconut products, ginger. **Minerals:** Gold. **Other resources:** Timber. **Per capita arable land:** 0.3 acres. **Livestock** (1974): 165,000 cattle; 30,000 pigs; 530,000 poultry. **Electricity production** (1973): 217 mln. kwh. **Labor force:** 49% agric.

Finance: Currency: Dollar (Apr. 1974: 1=$1.08 US). **Gross domestic product** (1976): $661 mln. **Per capita income** (1974): $958. **Imports** (1976): $261 mln.; partners (1974): Australia 30%, Jap. 18%, N.Z. 11%, U.K. 10%. **Exports** (1976): $137 mln.; partners (1974): U.K. 30%, U.S. 26%, Australia 10%, N.Z. 7%. **Tourists** (1971): 152,200; receipts (1973): $49 million. **Balance of payments** (1976): $−18.9 mln. **National budget** (1975): $130 mln. revenues; $156 mln. expenditures. **International reserves** (Feb. 1977): $111.49 mln. **Consumer prices** (change in 1976): 11.5%.

Transport: Motor vehicles: in use (1974): 19,800 passenger cars, 9,200 commercial vehicles. **Chief ports:** Suva, Lautoka.

Communications: Radios: 53,000 licenses (1972). **Telephones in use** (1976): 29,007. **Daily newspaper circulation** (1973): 20,000; 36 per 1,000 pop.

Health: Life expectancy at birth (1970-75): 68.5 male; 71.7 female. **Births** (annual per 1,000 pop. 1970-75): 25.0. **Deaths** (annual per 1,000 pop. 1970-75): 4.3. **Natural increase** (annual 1970-75): 2.17%. **Infant mortality** (per 1,000 pop. under 1 yr. 1974): 20.6.

A British colony since 1874, Fiji became an independent parliamentary democracy Oct. 10, 1970.

Cultural differences between the majority Indian community, descendants of contract laborers brought to the islands in the 19th century, and the less modernized native Fijians, who by law own 83% of the land in communal villages, have led to political polarization.

Finland

Republic of Finland

People: Population (1976): 4,730,000. **Age distrib.** (%): 0-14: 23.7; 15-59: 61.6; 60+: 14.7. **Pop. density:** 36 per sq. mi. **Urban** (1974): 57.7%. **Ethnic groups:** Finns, Swedes. **Languages:** Finnish 93.5%, Swedish 6.5% (both official). **Religions:** Lutheran 92%, Russian Orthodox 1.3%.

Geography: Area: 130,119 sq. mi., slightly smaller than Montana. **Location:** In northern Baltic region of Europe. **Neighbors:** Norway on N, Sweden on W, USSR on E. **Topography:** South and central Finland are mostly flat areas with low hills and many lakes. The N has mountainous areas, 3,000-4,000 ft. **Capital:** Helsinki. **Cities** (1973 est.): Helsinki (met.) 821,505; Tampere (met.) 231,197; Turku (met.) 227,339.

Government: Head of state: Pres. Urho F. Kekkonen, b. Sept. 3, 1900, in office: Mar. 1, 1956; **Head of government:** Prime Min. Kalevi Sorsa, in office: May 15, 1977. **Local divisions:** 12 laanit (provinces). **Armed forces:** Regulars 35,800; reserves 690,000.

Economy: Industries: Machinery, metal, shipbuilding, textiles, leather, chemicals, tourism. **Chief crops:** Grains, potatoes. **Minerals:** Copper, iron, zinc, nickel, lead. **Other resources:** Forests (55% of exports). **Per capita arable land:** 1.4 acres. **Livestock** (1976): 1,670,000 cattle; 970,000 pigs; 70,000 sheep. **Fish catch** (1974): 100,000 metric tons. **Electricity production** (1976): 29,316 mln. kwh. **Labor force:** 18% agric.; 26% manuf.

Finance: Currency: Markkaa (Apr. 1977: 4.05=$1 US). **Gross domestic product** (1976): $28.5 bln. **Per capita income** (1975): $5,036. **Imports** (1976) $7.393 bln.; partners (1974): Swed. 18%, USSR 18%, W. Ger. 15%, U.K. 9%. **Exports** (1976): $6.342 bln.; partners (1974): U.K. 19%, Swed. 16%, USSR 14%, W. Ger. 9%. **Balance of payments** (1976): −$106 mln. **National budget** (1976): $7.81 bln. revenues; $7.08 bln. expenditures. **International reserves** (Feb. 1977): $446.0 mln. **Consumer prices** (change in 1976): 14.6%.

Transport: Railway traffic (1974): 1,892 mln. passenger-miles; 4,648 mln. net ton-miles. **Motor vehicles:** in use (1974): 936,700 passenger cars, 133,500 commercial vehicles. **Civil aviation:** 857 mln. passenger-miles (1976); 20 mln. freight ton-miles (1976). **Chief ports:** Helsinki, Turku.

Communications: Television sets: 1,224,000 licenses (1973); 174,000 manufactured (1973). **Radios:** 1,944,000 licenses (1973); 148,000 manufactured (1973). **Telephones in use** (1976): 1,833,993.

Health: Life expectancy at birth (1972): 66.57 male; 74.87 female. **Births** (per 1,000 pop. 1975): 14.2. **Deaths** (per 1,000 pop. 1975): 9.4. **Natural increase** (annual 1975): 0.47%. **Pop. per hospital bed** (1973): 72. **Pop. per physician** (1973): 832. **Infant mortality** (per 1,000 pop. under 1 yr. 1974): 10.2.

Education: Literacy (1973): 99%. **Pop. 5-19:** in school (1973): 67%; per teacher (1973): 28.

The early Finns probably migrated from the Ural area at about the beginning of the Christian era. Swedish settlers brought the country into Sweden, 1154 to 1809, when Finland became an autonomous grand duchy of the Russian Empire. Russian exactions created a strong national spirit; on Dec. 6, 1917, Finland declared its independence and in 1919 became a republic. On Nov. 30, 1939, the Soviet Union invaded, and the Finns were forced to cede 16,173 sq. mi., including the Karelian Isthmus, Viipuri, and an area on Lake Ladoga. After World War II, in which Finland tried to recover its lost territory, further cessions were exacted. In 1948, Finland signed a treaty of mutual assistance with the USSR. In 1956 Russia returned Porkkala, which had been ceded as a military base.

Finland is oriented toward the West in trade and culture, but Soviet influence is strong. The governing coalition usually includes the Communist Party.

Aland, constituting an autonomous department, is a group of small islands, 572 sq. mi., in the Gulf of Bothnia, 25 mi. from Sweden, 15 mi. from Finland. It is demilitarized. Mariehamn is the principal port.

France

French Republic

People: Population (1976): 52,920,000. **Age distrib.** (%): 0-14: 23.7; 15-59: 57.6; 70+: 18.7. **Pop. density:** 251 per sq. mi. **Urban** (1968): 70.0%. **Ethnic groups:** A mixture of various European and Mediterranean groups. **Languages:** French; minorities speak Breton, Alsatian German, Flemish, Italian, Basque, Catalan. **Religions:** Roman Catholic 90%, Protestant 1%, Jewish 1%, Moslems 1%.

Geography: Area: 211,000 sq. mi., four-fifths the size of Texas. **Location:** In Western Europe, between Atlantic O. and Mediterranean Sea. **Neighbors:** Spain on S, Italy, Switzerland, W. Germany on E, Luxembourg, Belgium on N. **Topography:** A wide plain covers more than half of the country, in N and W, drained to W by Seine, Loire, Garonne rivers. The Massif Central, is a mountainous plateau in center. In E are Alps (Mt. Blanc is tallest in W. Europe, 15,771 ft.), the lower Jura range, and the forested Vosges. The Rhone flows from Lake Geneva (Lac Leman) to Mediterranean. Pyrenees are in SW, on border with Spain. **Capital:** Paris. **Cities** (1975 cen.): Paris (met.) 9,863,000; (1968 cen.) Lyon (met.) 1,074,823; Marseilles (met.) 964,412; Lille (met.) 881,439; Bordeaux (met.) 555,152; Toulouse (met.) 439,764; Nantes (met.) 393,731; Nice (met.) 392,635; Rouen (met.) 369,793.

Government: Head of state: Pres. Valery Giscard d'Estaing, b. Feb. 2, 1926, in office: May 24, 1974, **Head of government:** Premier Raymond Barre, b. Apr. 12, 1924, in office: Aug. 25, 1976. **Local divisions:** 95 departments, grouped into 22 development regions. **Armed forces:** regulars 512,900; reserves 450,000.

Economy: Industries: Steel, chemicals, autos, textiles, wine, perfume, aircraft, ships, instruments, plastics, electronic equipment. **Chief crops:** Grains, corn, rice, fruits, vegetables. France is largest food producer, exporter, in W. Eur. **Minerals:** Iron, bauxite, coal, asphalt, rock salt, potash. **Crude oil output** (1976): 7.7 mln. bbls. **Other resources:** Forests. **Per capita arable land:** 0.8 acres. **Livestock** (1976): 24,100,000 cattle; 12,030,000 pigs; 10,707,000 sheep; 200,000,000 poultry. **Fish catch** (1975): 806,000 metric tons. **Electricity production** (1976): 191,196 mln. kwh. **Labor force:** 12% agric.; 27% manuf.

Finance: Currency: Franc (Apr. 1977: 4.96=$1 US). **Gross domestic product** (1976): $347 bln. **Per capita income** (1975): $5,639. **Imports** (1976) $64.391 bln.; partners (1974): W. Ger. 19%, Belg. 10%, U.S. 8%, It. 7%. **Exports** (1976): $57.162 bln.; partners (1974): W. Ger. 17%, It. 12%, Belg. 11%, U.K. 7%. **Tourists** (1974): 9,838,000; receipts: $2.666 billion. **Balance of payments** (1975): $3.50 bln. **National budget** (1975): $68.95 bln. revenues; $78.98 bln. expenditures. **International reserves** (Feb. 1977): $9.840 bln. **Consumer prices** (change in 1976): 9.6%.

Transport: Railway traffic (1974): 29,112 mln. passenger-miles; 47,818 mln. net ton-miles. **Motor vehicles:** in use (1974): 15,000,000 passenger cars, 3,565,000 commercial vehicles; manufactured (1976): 3,384,000 passenger cars, 468,000 commercial vehicles. **Civil aviation:** 15,641 mln. passenger-miles (1976); 857 mln. freight ton-miles (1976). **Chief ports:** Marseille, LeHavre, Nantes, Bordeaux, Rouen.

Communications: Television sets: 12,332,000 licenses (1973); 1,694,000 manufactured (1974). **Radios:** 17,034,000 licenses (1972); 3,374,000 manufactured (1974). **Telephones in use** (1976): 13,833,346. **Daily newspaper circulation** (1972): 11,969,000; 231 per 1,000 pop.

Health: Life expectancy at birth (1972): 68.6 male; 76.4 female. **Births** (per 1,000 pop. 1974): 15.2. **Deaths** (per 1,000 pop. 1974): 10.4. **Natural increase** (1974): 0.49%. **Pop. per hospital bed** (1973): 97. **Pop. per physician** (1973): 677. **Infant mortality** (per 1,000 pop. under 1 yr. 1974): 12.1.

Education: Literacy (1973): 99%. **Pop. 5-19:** in school (1973): 70%; per teacher (1973): 24.

Celtic Gaul was conquered by Julius Caesar 58-51 B.C. Romans ruled for 500 years, bequeathing their language, which survived Teutonic invasions. Under Charlemagne, Frankish rule extended over much of Europe. After his death France emerged as one of the successor kingdoms.

The monarchial system was overthrown by the French Revolution (1789-93) and succeeded by the First Republic; thereafter successively followed by the First Empire under Napoleon (1804-15), a monarchy (1814-48), the Second Republic (1848-52), the Second Empire (1852-70), the Third Republic (1871-1946), the Fourth Republic (1946-58), and the Fifth Republic (1958 to present).

France suffered severe losses in manpower and wealth in the first World War, 1914-18, when it was invaded by Germany. By the Treaty of Versailles, France exacted return of Alsace and Lorraine, French provinces seized by Germany in 1871. Germany invaded France again in May, 1940, and signed an armistice with a government based in Vichy. After France was liberated by the allies Sept. 1944, Gen. Charles de Gaulle became head of the provisional government, serving until 1946.

De Gaulle again became premier in 1958, during a crisis over Algeria, and obtained voter approval for a new constitution, ushering in the Fifth Republic. Using strong executive powers, he promoted French economic and technological advances in the context of the European Economic Community, and guarded French foreign policy independence. France has become the world's fifth greatest industrial power.

France had withdrawn from Indochina in 1954, and from Morocco and Tunisia in 1956. Most of its remaining African territories were freed 1958-62, but France retained strong economic and political ties.

France tested atomic bombs in the Sahara beginning in 1960. Land-based and submarine launched strategic missiles were also developed. In 1966, France withdrew all its troops from the integrated military command of NATO, though 60,000 remained stationed in Germany. France continued to attend political meetings of NATO.

In May 1968 rebellious students in Paris and other centers rioted, battled police, and were joined by some 10 million workers who launched nationwide strikes and took over many factories. The government awarded pay increases to the strikers May 26, and dissolved the Assembly four days later. In elections to the Assembly in June, de Gaulle's backers won a landslide victory. Nevertheless, he resigned from office in April, 1969, after losing a nationwide referendum on constitutional reform.

De Gaulle's policies were largely continued after his death in 1970. Independent Republican Valery Giscard d'Estaing, president since 1974, has tried to resist electoral inroads by the Socialist-Communist alliance through moderate economic, social, and educational reforms. The leftist alliance won a majority of local offices in 1976 and 1977 elections.

The island of **Corsica,** in the Mediterranean W of Italy and N of Sardinia, is an official region of France comprising 2 departments. Area: 3,369 sq. mi.; pop.: 220,000. The capital is Ajaccio, birthplace of Napoleon. A militant separatist movement led to violence 1975-76.

Overseas Departments

French Guiana is on the NE coast of South America with Surinam on the W and Brazil on the E and S. Its area is 37,740 sq. mi. population (1975), 55,125. Guiana sends one senator and one deputy to the French Parliament. Guiana has a prefect and a Council General of 15 elected members; capital is Cayenne.

In 1944 France closed the famous penal colony, Devil's Island, and repatriated 2,800 inmates.

Immense forests of rich timber cover 90% of the land. The principal crops are rice, corn, manioc, cacao, bananas, and sugar cane. Placer gold mining is the most important industry. Exports are cocoa, bananas, wood, gold, fish glue, rum, rosewood essence, shrimp and hides.

Guadeloupe, in the West Indies' Leeward Islands, consists of 2 large islands, Basse-Terre and Grande-Terre, separated by the Salt River, plus Marie Galante and the Saintes group to the S and, to the N, Desirade, St. Barthelemy, and over half of St. Martin (the Netherlands portion is St. Maarten). A French possession since 1635, the department is represented in the French Parliament by 2 senators and 3 deputies; administration consists of a prefect (governor) and an elected General Council.

Area of the islands is 687 sq. mi.; population (1975) 334,900, mainly descendants of slaves; capital is Basse-Terre on Basse-Terre Is. The land is fertile; sugar, rum, and bananas are exported; tourism is an important industry.

Martinique, one of the Windward Islands, in the West Indies, has been a possession since 1635, and a Department since March, 1946. It is represented in the French Parliament by 2 senators and 3 deputies. Mt. Pelee, a volcano, erupted May 8, 1902, destroying the city of St. Pierre and 30,000 inhabitants. The island was the birthplace of Napoleon's Empress Josephine.

It has an area of 426 sq. mi. and population (1975) 324,832, mostly descendants of slaves. The capital is Fort-de-France. It is a popular tourist stop. The chief exports are sugar, rum, bananas, pineapples, and cocoa.

Mayotte, formerly part of Comoros, voted in 1976 to become an overseas department of France. An island NW of Madagascar, area is 144 sq. mi., pop. 36,000.

Reunion is an island in the Indian Ocean, about 420 miles east of Madagascar, and has belonged to France since 1665. The area is 969 sq. mi.; the population (1975) 476,675, is 30% of French extraction. Capital: Saint-Denis. The chief products are sugar, rum, corn, perfume essences, vanilla, and spices. It elects 3 deputies, 2 senators to the French Parliament.

St. Pierre and Miquelon, formerly an Overseas Territory, began the transition to department status in 1976. It consists of 2 groups of rocky islands near the SW coast of Newfoundland, inhabited by fishermen. The exports are chiefly fish products. The St. Pierre group has an area of 10 sq. mi.; Miquelon, 83 sq. mi. Total population (1974), 5,840. The capital is St. Pierre. A deputy and a senator are elected to the French Parliament.

Overseas Territories

French Polynesia. Overseas Territory, comprises 130 islands widely scattered among 5 archipelagos in the South Pacific; administered by a governor. Territorial Assembly and a Council with headquarters at Papeete, Tahiti, one of the **Society Islands.** A deputy and a senator are elected to the French Parliament.

Other groups are the **Marquesas Islands,** the **Tuamotu Archipelago,** the **Gambier Islands** and the **Austral Islands.**

Total area of the islands administered from Tahiti is 1,544 sq. mi.; pop. (est. 1974), 130,000, more than half on Tahiti. Tahiti is picturesque and mountainous with a productive coastline bearing coconut, banana and orange trees, sugar cane and vanilla.

Tahiti was visited by Capt. James Cook in 1769 and by Capt. Bligh in the Bounty, 1788-89. Its beauty impressed Herman Melville, Paul Gauguin, Charles Darwin and Robert Louis Stevenson who called Tahitians "God's sweetest works."

New Caledonia and its dependencies, an Overseas Territory, are a group of islands in the Pacific Ocean about 1,115 mi. E of Australia and approx. the same distance NW of New Zealand. Dependencies are the **Loyalty Islands,** the **Isle of Pines, Huon Islands** and the **Chesterfield Islands.**

New Caledonia, the largest, has 6,530 sq. mi. Total area of the territory is 8,548 sq. mi.; population (est. 1975) 138,000, (including 50,000 Europeans). The group was acquired by France in 1853.

The territory is administered by a governor and government council. There is a popularly elected Territorial Assembly. A deputy and a senator are elected to the French parliament. Capital: Noumea.

Mining is the chief industry. New Caledonia is the world's third largest nickel producer. Other minerals found are chrome, cobalt, manganese, antimony, mercury, cinnebar, silver, gold, lead, and copper. Agricultural products include coffee, copra, cotton, manioc (cassava), corn, tobacco, bananas and pineapples.

Wallis and Futuna Islands, 2 archipelagos raised to status of Overseas Territory July 29, 1961, are in the SW Pacific S of the Equator between Fiji and Samoa. The islands have a total area of 106 sq. mi. and population (est. 1974) of 9,000. **Alofi,** attached to Futuna, is uninhabited. Capital: Mata-Utu. Chief products are copra, yams, taro roots, bananas. A senator and a deputy are elected to the French parliament.

French Southern and Antarctic Lands, Overseas Territory, comprises **Adelie Land,** on Antarctica, and 4 island groups in the Indian Ocean. Adelie, discov. 1840, has 2 research bases, a coastline of 185 mi. and tapers 1,240 mi. inland to the South Pole. The US does not recognize national claims in Antarctica. There are 2 huge glaciers, Ninnis, 22 mi. wide, 99 mi. long, and Mentz, 11 mi. wide, 140 mi. long. The Indian Ocean groups are:

Kerguelen Archipelago, discovered 1772, has 300 islands. The chief is 87 mi. long, 74 mi. wide, and has Mt. Ross, 6,429 ft. tall. Principal research station is Port-aux-Francais. Seals often weigh 2 tons; there are blue whales, coal, peat, semi-precious stones. **Crozet Archipelago** (discov. 1772), covers 195 sq. mi. Eastern Island rises to 6,560 ft. **Saint Paul,** in southern Indian Ocean, has warm springs with earth at places heating to 120° to 390° F. **Amsterdam** is nearby; both have temperate climates, produce cod and rock lobster.

The former **French Territory of the Afars and the Issas** became in 1977 the independent nation of Djibouti.

New Hebrides

New Hebrides, a condominium administered since 1906 by France and Great Britain, is a group of 11 main islands and about 69 islets 250 mi. NE of New Caledonia and 500 mi. W. of Fiji. It has 5,790 sq. mi. and population (est. 1975) of 95,000, mostly Melanesian. It has 2 administrations—French and British. Chief products are copra, frozen fish, cocoa, and coffee.

Gabon

Gabonese Republic

People: Population (1976 est.): 530,000. **Age distrib.** (%): 0-14: 25.2; 15-59: 64.9; 60+: 10. **Pop. density:** 5.2 per sq. mi. **Urban** (1970): 32.0%. **Ethnic groups:** Fangs 25%, Bapounon 10%, others. **Languages:** French (official), Fang, Bantu languages. **Religions:** Roman Catholics 25%, Protestants 10%, others.

Geography: Area: 102,317 sq. mi., the size of Colorado. **Location:** On Atlantic coast of central Africa. **Neighbors:** Equatorial Guinea, Cameroon on N, Congo on E, S. **Topography:** Heavily forested, the country consists of coastal low-lands, plateaus in N, E, and S, mountains in N, SE, and center. The Ogooue R. system covers most of Gabon. **Capital:** Libreville. **Cities** (1970 est.): Libreville (met.) 75,000; Port-Gentil 30,000.

Government: Head of state: Pres. Albert-Bernard Bongo, b. Dec. 30, 1935, in office: Dec. 2, 1967. **Head of government:** Prime. Min. Leon Mebiame, in office: Apr. 16, 1975. **Local divisions:** 9 provinces.

Economy: Industries: Oil products. **Chief crops:** Cocoa, coffee, rice, peanuts, palm products, cassava, bananas. **Minerals:** Manganese, oil, uranium, iron, gas. **Crude oil output** (1976): 81.5 mln. bbls. **Other resources:** Timber. **Per capita arable land:** 0.6 acres. **Livestock** (1974): 5,000 cattle; 57,000 sheep; 62,000 goats. **Electricity production** (1976): 240 mln. kwh. **Labor force** 72% agric.

Finance: Currency: CFA Franc (Apr. 1977: 248=$1 US). **Gross domestic product** (1974): $1.55 bln. **Per capita income** (1974): $2,425. **Imports** (1976) $694 mln.; partners (1973): Fr. 59%, W. Ger. 9%, U.S. 9%, U.K. 4%. **Exports** (1976): $896 mln.; partners (1973): Fr. 37%, W. Ger. 10%, Neth. 7%, U.S. 7%. **Tourists** (1973): 62,500; receipts (1974): $10 million. **Balance of payments** (1975): $45.8 mln. **International reserves** (Oct. 1976): $127.25 mln. **Consumer prices** (change in 1975): 28.0%.

Transport: Motor vehicles: in use (1974): 10,100 passenger cars, 7,300 commercial vehicles. **Chief ports:** Libreville, Port-Gentil.

Communications: Television sets: 1,300 licenses (1972).

adios: 90,000 licenses (1973).

Health: Life expectancy at birth (1960-61): 25 male; 45 fe-ıale. **Births** (annual per 1,000 pop. 1970-75): 32.2. **Deaths** annual per 1,000 pop. 1970-75): 22.2. **Natural increase** annual 1970-75): 1.00%. **Pop. per hospital bed** (1973): 98. **'op. per physician** (1973): 5,200. **Infant mortality** (per 1,000 op. under 1 yr. 1960-61): 229.

Education: Literacy (1973): 30%. **Pop. 5-19:** in school 1973): 67%; per teacher (1973): 50.

France established control over the region in the second half f the nineteenth century. Gabon became independent Aug. 17, 960. It is one of the most prosperous black African countries, ıanks to abundant natural resources, foreign private invest-ıent, and government development programs.

Gambia
Republic of the Gambia

People: Population (1976 est.): 540,000. **Age distrib.** (%): -14: 41.4; 15-59: 55.2; 60+: 3.5 **Pop. density:** 135 per sq. mi. **Irban** (1972): 14.2%. **Ethnic groups:** Mandingo 40%, Fula 3%, Wolof 12%, others. **Languages:** English (official), others. **eligions:** Moslems 85%, Christian 4%, others.

Geography: Area: 4,003 sq. mi., smaller than Connecticut. **ocation:** On Atlantic coast near western tip of Africa. **Neigh-ors:** Surrounded on three sides by Senegal. **Topography:** The ountry consists of a narrow strip of land on each side of the ower Gambiak. **Capital:** Banjul. **Cities** (1975 est.): Banjul (met.) 8,333.

Government: Head of state: Pres. Dawda Kairaba Jawara, . May 16, 1924, in office: Apr. 24, 1970. **Local divisions:** 5 divi-ions and Banjul.

Economy: Industries: Tourism. **Chief crops:** Peanuts (main xport), rice. **Per capita arable land:** 1.0 acres. **Livestock** 1974): 292,000 cattle; 8,000 pigs; 90,000 sheep; 92,000 goats. **lectricity production** (1976): 30 mln. kwh. **Labor force:** 84% gric.

Finance: Currency: Dalasi (Apr. 1977: 1=$0.429 US). **Gross omestic product** (1975): $96.3 mln. **Per capita income** 1974): $120. **Imports** (1976): $74 mln.; partners (1973): U.K. 4%, P.R. China 10%, Neth. 6%. **Exports** (1976): $35 mln.; part-ers (1973): U.K. 37%, Fr. 23%, Neth. 17%, Port. 8%. **Tourist** eceipts (1974): $6 million. **Balance of payments** (1976): $6.5 ıln. **National budget** (1972): $11.36 mln. revenues; $13.57 ıln. expenditures. **International reserves** (Feb. 1977): $15.16 ıln. **Consumer prices** (change in 1976): 16.9%.

Transport: Motor vehicles: in use (1973): 3,000 passenger ars, 2,500 commercial vehicles. **Chief ports:** Banjul.

Communications: Radios: 60,000 in use. **Telephones in se** (1976): 2,498.

Health: Life expectancy at birth (1970-75): 38.5 male; 41.6 emale. **Births** (annual per 1,000 pop. 1970-75): 43.3. **Deaths** annual per 1,000 pop. 1970-75): 24.1. **Natural increase** annual 1970-75): 1.92%. **Pop. per hospital bed** (1973): 754. **op. per physician** (1973): 24,500. **Infant mortality** (per 1,000 op. under 1 yr. 1973): 165.

Education: literacy (1973): 10%. **Pop. 5-19:** in school 1973): 19%; per teacher (1973): 160.

The tribes of Gambia were at one time associated with the Vest African empires of Ghana, Mali, and Songhay. The area ecame Britain's first African possession in 1588.

Independence came Feb. 18, 1965; republic status within the Commonwealth was achieved in 1970. Gambia is one of the only ınctioning democracies in Africa.

Germany

Now comprises 2 nations: Federal Republic of Germany (West Germany), German Democratic Republic (East Germany).

Germany, prior to World War II, was a central European nation omposed of numerous states which had a common language nd traditions and which had been united in one country since 871; since World War II it has been split in 2 parts (see below).

History and Government. Germanic tribes were defeated by ulius Caesar, 55 and 53 B. C. but Roman expansion N of the hine was stopped in 9 A.D. Charlemagne, ruler of the Franks, consolidated Saxon, Bavarian, Rhenish, Frankish, and other lands; after him the eastern part became the German Empire. The Thirty Years' War, 1618-1648, split Germany into small principalities and kingdoms. After Napoleon, Austria contended with Prussia for dominance, but lost the Seven Weeks' War to Prussia, 1866. Otto von Bismarck, Prussian chancellor, formed the North German Confederation, 1867.

In 1870 Bismarck maneuvered Napoleon III into declaring war. After the quick defeat of France, Bismarck formed the **German Empire** and on Jan. 18, 1871, in Versailles, proclaimed King Wilhelm I of Prussia German emperor (Deutscher kaiser).

The German Empire reached its peak before World War I in 1914, with 208,780 sq. mi., plus a colonial empire. After that war Germany ceded Alsace-Lorraine to France; Eupen and Malmedy to Belgium; parts of Silesia to Poland and Czechoslovakia; part of Schleswig to Denmark; lost all of its colonies as well as the ports of Memel and Danzig.

Republic of Germany, 1919-1933, adopted the Weimar constitution; met reparation payments and elected Friedrich Ebert and Gen. Paul von Hindenburg presidents.

Third Reich, 1933-1945, Adolf Hitler, born in Austria, 1889, led the National Socialist German Workers' (Nazi) party after World War I. In 1923 he attempted to unseat the Bavarian government and was imprisoned. President von Hindenburg named Hitler chancellor Jan. 30, 1933; on Aug. 3, 1934, the day after Hindenburg's death, the cabinet joined the offices of president and chancellor and made Hitler fuehrer (leader). Hitler abolished freedom of speech and assembly, and began a long series of persecutions climaxed by the murder of millions of Jews and opponents.

Hitler repudiated the Versailles treaty and reparations agreements. He remilitarized the Rhineland 1936 and annexed Austria (Anschluss, 1938). At Munich he made an agreement with Neville Chamberlain, British prime minister, enabling him to annex Czechoslovakia. He signed a non-aggression treaty with the Soviet Union, 1939. He declared war on Poland Sept. 1, 1939, precipitating World War II.

With total defeat near, Hitler committed suicide in Berlin Apr. 1945. The victorious Allies voided all acts and annexations of Hitler's Reich.

Postwar changes. The zones of occupation administered by the Allied Powers and later relinquished gave the Soviet Union Saxony, Saxony-Anhalt, Thuringia, and Mecklenburg, and the former Prussian provinces of Saxony and Brandenburg.

The territory E of the Oder-Neisse line within 1937 boundaries comprising the provinces of Silesia, Pomerania, West Prussia and the southern part of East Prussia, totaling about 41,220 sq. mi., population (1939) 9,600,000, was taken by Poland. Northern East Prussia was taken by the Soviet Union. Several million Germans emigrated from these territories to W. Germany.

The Western Allies ended the state of war with Germany in 1951. The USSR did so in 1955.

There was also created the area of Greater Berlin, within but not part of the Soviet zone, administered by the 4 occupying powers under the Allied Command. In 1948 the Soviet Union withdrew and established its single command in East Berlin. The Communists cut off supplies, whereupon the Allies utilized a gigantic airlift to bring food to West Berlin during 1948-1949. In Aug. 1961 the East Germans built a wall dividing Berlin, after over 3 million E. Germans had emigrated.

East Germany
German Democratic Republic

People: Population (1976): 16,790,000. **Age Distrib.** (%): 0-14: 22.6; 15-59: 55.4; 60+: 22. **Pop. density:** 413 per sq. mi. **Urban** (1975): 75.4%. **Ethnic groups:** Germans, Wends (0.7%). **Languages:** German. **Religions:** Protestant 80%, Roman Catholic 11%.

Geography: Area: 40,646 sq. mi., the size of Virginia. **Location:** In E central Europe. **Neighbors:** W. Germany on W, Czechoslovakia on S, Poland on E. **Topography:** East Germany lies mostly on the North German plains, with lakes in N, Harz Mtns., Elbe Valley, and sandy soil of Brandenburg in center, and highlands in S. **Capital:** East Berlin. **Cities** (1975 est.): Berlin 1,094,496; Leipzig 568,877, Dresden 508,298.

Government: Head of state: Chmn. Erich Honecker, b. Aug. 25, 1912, in office: Oct. 1976; **Head of government:** Chmn. Willi Stoph, b. July 9, 1914, in office: 1964-1973, Oct. 1976; **Head of Communist Party:** Gen. Sec. Erich Honecker, in office: 1971.

Local divisions: 15 administrative districts. **Armed forces:** regulars 157,000; reserves 405,000.

Economy: Industries: Steel, chemicals, cement, textiles, shoes, oil products, machinery. **Chief crops:** Grains, potatoes, sugar beets. **Minerals:** Lignite (largest producer), uranium, cobalt, bismuth, arsenic, antimony. **Crude oil output** (1976): 2.5 mln. bbls. **Per capita arable land:** 0.7 acres. **Livestock** (1976): 5,532,000 cattle; 11,500,000 pigs; 1,888,000 sheep; 45,667,000 poultry. **Fish catch** (1975): 375,000 metric tons. **Electricity production** (1976): 89,148 mln. kwh. **Labor force:** 12% agric.; 38% manuf.

Finance: Currency: Mark (1974: 3.48=$1 US). **Gross domestic product** (est. 1974): $59 bln. **Per capita income** (1974): $3,300. **Imports** (1975): $11,290 bln; partners (1974): USSR 30%, W. Ger. 9%, Czech. 7%, Pol. 7%. **Exports** (1975): $10.088 bln.; partners (1974): USSR 33%, Czech. 10%, W. Ger. 10%, Pol. 9%. **Tourists** (1974): 15,229,400.

Transport: Railway traffic (1974): 12,912 mln. passenger-miles; 33,989 mln. net ton-miles. **Motor vehicles:** in use (1974): 1,702,900 passenger cars, 511,300 commercial vehicles; manufactured (1976): 164,000 passenger cars, 36,000 commercial vehicles. **Chief ports:** Rostock, Wismar, Stralsund.

Communications: Television sets: 4,966,000 licenses (1973); 467,000 manufactured (1974). **Radios:** 6,082,000 licenses (1973); 1,016,000 manufactured (1974). **Telephones in use** (1976): 2,570,113. **Daily newspaper circulation** (1973): 7,527,000; 443 per 1,000 pop.

Health: Life expectancy at birth (1969-70): 68.85 male; 74.19 female. **Births** (per 1,000 pop. 1974): 10.6. **Deaths** (per 1,000 pop. 1974): 13.5. **Natural increase** (1974): −0.30%. **Pop. per hospital bed** (1973): 91. **Pop. per physician** (1973): 580. **Infant mortality** (per 1,000 pop. under 1 yr. 1974): 15.9.

Education: Literacy (1973): 98%. **Pop. 5-19:** in school (1973): 66%; per teacher (1973): 25.

The German Democratic Republic was proclaimed in the Soviet sector of Berlin Oct. 7, 1949. It was proclaimed fully sovereign in 1954, but Soviet troops remained on grounds of security and the 4-power Potsdam agreement.

East Germany negotiated a treaty with Poland placing Poland's boundary at the line formed by the Oder and Neisse Rivers. A pact with Czechoslovakia accepted the expulsion of 3 million Sudeten Germans as "permanent and just."

Coincident with the entrance of West Germany into the European Defense community in 1952, the East German government decreed a prohibited zone three miles deep along its 600-mile border with West Germany and cut Berlin's telephone system in two. Berlin was further divided by erection of a fortified wall in 1961, but the exodus of refugees to the West continued, though on a smaller scale. By 1977, nearly 50,000 had fled to the West since 1961, thousands of retired persons had been allowed to leave, and some 20,000 others held in East German jails were released upon West German payments totalling $250 million.

The government signed a 20-year friendship treaty with the USSR in 1964. The economy has been integrated with other communist nations.

East Germany suffered severe economic problems until the mid-1960s. A "new economic system" was introduced, easing the former central planning controls and allowing factories to make "profits" provided they were reinvested in operations or redistributed to workers as bonuses. By the early 1970s, the economy was highly industrialized, and was the world's ninth greatest industrial power. In May 1972 the few remaining private firms were ordered sold to the government. The nation was credited with the highest standard of living among communist countries. But growth slowed in the late 1970s, due to shortages of natural resources and labor, and a huge debt to lenders in the West.

Travel restrictions between the 2 Germanies were eased in their first formal treaty, in 1972, and millions of West Germans have since visited the GDR. The GDR gained admission to the UN in 1973.

The U.S. and East Germany established diplomatic relations in 1974. East Germany agreed to negotiate claims of U.S. citizens for properties seized under the Nazis.

West Germany

Federal Republic of Germany

People: Population (1976): 61,500,000. **Age distrib.** (%): 0-14: 22.4; 15-59; 57.9; 60+: 19.7. **Pop. density:** 642 per sq. mi. **Urban** (1975): 86%. **Ethnic groups:** Germans, immigrant workers from Spain, Italy, Yugoslavia, Turkey. **Languages:** German. **Religions:** Protestant 49%, Roman Catholic 45%.

Geography: Area: 95,815 sq. mi., the size of Oregon. **Location:** In central Europe. **Neighbors:** Denmark on N, Netherlands, Belgium, Luxembourg, France on W, Switzerland, Austria on S, Czechoslovakia, E. Germany on E. **Topography:** West Germany is flat in N, hilly in center and W, and mountainous in Bavaria (maximum altitude 9,719 ft.). Chief rivers are Elbe, Weser, Ems, Rhine, and Main, all flowing toward North Sea, and Danube, flowing toward Black Sea. **Capital:** Bonn. **Cities** (1974 est.): Berlin 2,047,948; Hamburg 1,751,621; Munich 1,336,576; Cologne 832,396; Essen 674,000; Frankfurt 663,422; Dortmund 632,317; Dusseldorf 628,498; Stuttgart 624,835.

Government: Head of state: Pres. Walter Scheel, b. July 1919, in office: July 1, 1974; **Head of government:** Chanc. Helmut Schmidt, b. Dec. 1918, in office: May 16, 1974. **Local divisions:** West Berlin and 10 lander (states) with substantial powers: Schleswig-Holstein, Hamburg, Lower Saxony, Bremen, North Rhine-Westphalia, Hessen, Rhineland-Palatinate, Baden-Wurttemberg, Bavaria, Saarland. **Armed forces:** regulars 495,-000; reserves 1,181,000.

Economy: Industries: Steel, ships, oil products, autos, machinery, textiles, electrical and electronic equipment, wine. **Chief crops:** Grains, potatoes, sugar beets, fruits, tobacco, nuts. **Minerals:** Coal, lignite, iron, zinc, lead, copper, salt, potash, oil. **Crude oil output** (1976): 40 mln. bbls. **Per capita arable land:** 0.3 acres. **Livestock** (1976): 14,466,000 cattle; 19,865,000 pigs; 1,040,000 sheep; 98,805,000 poultry. **Fish catch** (1975): 442,-000 metric tons. **Electricity production** (1976): 333,648 mln. kwh. **Labor force:** 7% agric.; 39% manuf.

Finance: Currency: Mark (Apr. 1977: 2.36 = $1 US). **Gross domestic product** (1976): $451 bln. **Per capita income** (1975): $6,029. **Imports** (1976): $88.209 bln.; partners (1974): Neth. 14%, Fr. 12%, Belg. 9%, It. 8%. **Exports** (1976): $101.977 bln.; partners (1974): Fr. 12%, Neth. 10%, It. 8%, Belg. 8%. **Tourists** (1974): 6,950,600; receipts: $2.338 billion. **Balance of payments** (1976): $3.37 bln. **National budget** (1976): $56.22 bln. revenues; $68.17 bln. expenditures. **International reserves** (Feb. 1977): $34.547 bln. **Consumer prices** (change in 1976): 4.6%.

Transport: Railway traffic (1974): 25,193 mln. passenger-miles; 42,925 mln. net ton-miles. **Motor vehicles:** in use (1974): 16,879,100 passenger cars, 1,100,000 commercial vehicles; manufactured assembled (1976): 3,552,000 passenger cars, 324,000 commerical vehicles. **Civil aviation:** 9,307 mln. passenger-miles (1976); 682 mln. freight ton-miles (1976). **Chief ports:** Hamburg, Bremen, Lubeck.

Communications: Television sets: 18,486,000 licenses (1973); 4,293,000 manufactured (1974). **Radios:** 20,586,000 licenses (1973); 5,340,000 manufactured (1974). **Telephones in use** (1976): 19,602,606. **Daily newspaper circulation** (1973): 18,667,000; 301 per 1,000 pop.

Health: Life expectancy at birth (1971-73): 67.61 male; 74.09 female. **Births** (per 1,000 pop. 1975): 9.7. **Deaths** (per 1,000 pop. 1975): 12.1 **Natural increase** (1975): -0.24%. **Pop. per hospital bed** (1973): 87. **Pop. per physician** (1973): 532. **Infant mortality** (per 1,000 pop. under 1 yr. 1974): 21.1.

Education: Literacy (1973): 99%. **Pop. 5-19:** in school (1973): 68%; per teacher (1973): 30.

The Federal Republic of Germany was proclaimed May 23, 1949, in Bonn, after a constitution had been drawn up by a consultative assembly formed by representatives of the 11 laender (states) in the French, British, and American zones. Later reorganized into 9 units, the laender numbered 10 with the addition of the Saar Jan. 1, 1957: Schleswig-Holstein, Hamburg, Lower Saxony, Bremen, North Rhine-Westphalia, Hesse, Rhineland-Palatinate, Baden-Wurttemberg, Bavaria, Saarland,. Berlin also was granted land (state) status, but the 1945 occupation agreements placed restrictions on it.

The occupying powers, the U.S., Britain, and France, restored the civil status, Sept. 21, 1949. The U. S. resumed diplomatic relations July 2, 1951. The powers lifted controls and the republic became fully independent May 5, 1955.

Dr. Konrad Adenauer, Christian Democrat, was made chancellor Sept. 15, 1949, re-elected 1953, 1957, 1961. Dr. Ludwig Erhard, Christian Democrat, was elected 1963. Kurt Georg Kiesinger was elected chancellor Dec. 1, 1966, heading a coalition government of Christian Democrats and Social Democrats. Willy Brandt, heading a coalition of Social Democrats and Free Demo-

'ats, became chancellor Oct. 21, 1969.

In 1970 Brandt signed friendship treaties with the USSR and 'oland. In 1971, the U.S., Britain, France, and the USSR signed n agreement on Western access to West Berlin. In 1972 the undestag approved the USSR and Polish treaties and East and Vest Germany signed their first formal treaty, implementing the greement easing access to West Berlin. In 1973 a West Germany-Czechoslovakia pact normalized relations and nullified ne 1938 "Munich Agreement." In 1974 Bonn agreed to extend 350 million yearly in long-term credits to East Germany until 981. Other credits spurred trade with the East European coun-ies.

In May 1974 Brandt resigned, saying he took full responsibility r "negligence" for allowing an East German spy to become a member of his staff. Helmut Schmidt, Brandt's finance minister, ucceeded him.

West Germany has experienced tremendous economic rowth since the 1950s. It is the world's fourth greatest economic ower. Some of the 2.6 million foreigners working in West Germany left during a 1974-75 industrial slowdown. The country eads Europe in provisions for worker participation in the man-gement of industry.

About 214,000 U.S., 55,000 British, and 50,000 French troops re stationed in West Germany.

Helgoland, an island of 130 acres in the North Sea, was taken om Denmark by a British Naval Force in 1807 and later ceded) Germany to become a part of Schleswig-Holstein province in eturn for rights in East Africa. The heavily fortified island was urrendered to Great Britain, May 23, 1945, demilitarized in 1947 nd returned to West Germany, Mar. 1, 1952. It is a free port.

The Saar (Fr. Sarre), 10th land (state) of the Federal Repub-:, is an industrial and mining area N of Lorraine, originally 738 q. mi., now extended to about 991 and population (1973) of 1.1 nillion. Capital: Saarbrucken. After World War II it had semi-au-onomy and economic links to France until it became a German tate again Jan. 1, 1957.

Ghana
Republic of Ghana

People: Population (1976 est.): 10,310,000. **Age distrib.** %): 0-14: 25. 2; 15-59: 64.9; 60+: 10. **Pop. density:** 112 per sq. i. **Urban** (1974): 31.4%. **Ethnic groups:** Akan 44%, Moshi-agomba 16%, Ewe 13%, Ga 8%, others. **Languages:** English official), others. **Religions:** Protestant 29%, Roman Catholic 4%, Moslem 12%, others.

Geography: Area: 92,100 sq. mi., slightly smaller than Ore-on. **Location:** On southern coast of W. Africa. **Neighbors:** ory Coast on W, Upper Volta on N, Togo on E. **Topography:** ost of Ghana consists of low fertile plains and scrubland, cut by vers and by the artificial Lake Volta. **Capital:** Accra. **Cities** 970 cen.): Accra (met.) 738,498; Kumasi (met.) 345,117; akoradi 58,161.

Government: Head of state: Gen. Ignatius Kutu Acheam-ong, b. Sept. 23, 1931, in office: Jan. 13, 1972. **Local divi-ions:** 9 regions. **Armed forces:** regulars 17,600; para-military 000.

Economy: Industries: Aluminum, light industry. **Chief crops:** ocoa (largest producer), coffee, palm products, corn, rice, assava, plantain, peanuts, yams, tobacco. **Minerals:** Industrial amonds, manganese, gold, bauxite. **Other resources:** Timber, are woods, rubber. **Per capita arable land:** 0.2 acres. **Live-tock** (1974): 1,100,000 cattle; 340,000 pigs; 1,600,000 sheep; 0,000,000 poultry. **Fish catch** (1974): 223,500 metric tons. **lectricity production** (1974): 3,984 mln. kwh. **Labor force:** 5% agric.

Finance: Currency: New Cedi. (Mar. 1977: 1=$0.87 US). **ross domestic product** (1974): $1.91 bln. **Per capita income** 974): $394. **Imports** (1975) $791 mln.; partners (1973): U.K. 6%, U.S. 16%, W. Ger. 12%, Jap. 7%, Fr. 6%. **Exports** (1975): 307 mln.; partners (1973): U.K. 19%, U.S. 15%, Neth. 9%, Jap. %. **Tourists** (1974): 30,200; receipts: $1 million. **Balance of ayments** (1976): $−55 mln. **National budget** (1975): $765.2 ln. revenues; $1.069 bln. expenditures. **International re-erves** (Feb. 1977): $109.2 mln. **Consumer prices** (change in 976): 52.4%.

Transport: Railway traffic (1971): 323 mln. passenger-iles; 189 mln net ton-miles. **Motor vehicles:** in use (1972): 40,-00 passenger cars, 31,000 commercial vehicles. **Civil avia-on:** 102 mln. passenger-miles (1975); 2 mln. freight ton-miles (1974). **Chief ports:** Tema, Sekondi-Takoradi.

Communications: Television sets: 25,000 in use (1973); 3,000 manufactured (1972). **Radios:** 775,000 in use (1972); 49,-000 manufactured (1972). **Telephones in use** (1976): 60,707. **Daily newspaper circulation** (1973): 381,000; 41 per 1,000 pop.

Health: Life expectancy at birth (1970-75): 41.9 male; 45.1 female. **Births** (annual per 1,000 pop. 1970-75): 48.8. **Deaths** (annual per 1,000 pop. 1970-75): 21.9. **Natural increase** (annual 1970-75): 2.69%. **Pop. per hospital bed** (1973): 796. **Pop. per physician** (1973): 10,344. **Infant mortality** (per 1,000 pop. under 1 yr. 1960): 156.

Education: Literacy (1973): 25%. **Pop. 5-19:** in school (1973): 44%; per teacher (1973): 58.

Named for an African empire along the Niger River, 800-1076 A.D., Ghana was ruled by Britain for 113 years as the Gold Coast. The UN in 1956 approved merger with the British Togo-land trust territory. Independence came March 6, 1957. Republic status within the Commonwealth was attained in 1960.

President Kwame Nkrumah built hospitals and schools, and promoted development projects like the Volta River hydroelectric and aluminum plants, but ran the country into debt, jailed oppo-nents, and was accused of corruption. In 1964 a referendum gave Nkrumah dictatorial powers and made Ghana a one-party socialist state.

Nkrumah was overthrown by a police-army coup, which ex-pelled Chinese and East German teachers and technicians. Elections were held in 1969, but a second, bloodless coup occur-red in 1972.

In 1972-73 the government pressed a program of agricultural diversification to cut costly food imports.

Greece
Hellenic Republic

People: Population (1976): 9,170,000. **Age distrib.** (%): 0-14: 24.4; 15-59: 58.7; 60+: 16.8. **Pop. density:** 181 per sq. mi. **Urban** (1971): 64.8%. **Ethnic groups:** Greeks 95%, Macedo-nians (Slavic) 1.8%, Turks 1.4%, Albanians 0.6%, Armenians 0.6%. **Languages:** Greek, others. **Religions:** Greek Orthodox 97%, Moslem 1.3%.

Geography: Area: 50,547 sq. mi., the size of New York State. **Location:** Occupies southern end of Balkan Peninsula in SE Eu-rope. **Neighbors:** Albania, Yugoslavia, Bulgaria on N, Turkey on E. **Topography:** About 75% of Greece is non-arable, with moun-tains in all areas. Pindus Mts. run through the country N to S. Total length of the heavily indented coastline is 9,385 mi. Of hun-dreds of islands, 166 are inhabited, among them Crete, Rhodes, Milos, Kerkira (Corfu), Chios, Lesbos, Samos. **Capital:** Athens. **Cities** (1971 cen.): Athens (met.) 2,101,103; Saloniki (met.) 557,360; Piraeus (met.) 439,138.

Government: Head of state: Pres. Constantine Tsatsos, b. July 1, 1899, in office: June 20, 1975; **Head of government:** Prime Min. Constantine Karamanlis, b. Feb. 23, 1907, in office: July 24, 1974. **Local divisions:** 52 prefectures. **Armed forces:** regulars 199,500; reserves 240,000.

Economy: Industries: Textiles, chemicals, aluminum, wine, food processing, cement. **Chief crops:** Grains, corn, rice, cotton, tobacco, olives, citrus fruits, raisins, figs. **Minerals:** Bauxite, iron, emery, lignite, oil, silver, manganese, chromite, nickel, baryte. **Per capita arable land:** 0.8 acres. **Livestock** (1976): 1,300,000 cattle; 750,000 pigs; 8,900,000 sheep; 30,000,000 poultry. **Fish catch** (1974): 95,000 metric tons. **Electricity production** (1976): 16,320 mln. kwh. **Labor force:** 40% agric.; 16% manuf.

Finance: Currency: Drachma (Apr. 1977: 37.1=$1 US). **Gross domestic product** (1976): $21.8 bln. **Per capita income** (1975): $2,208. **Imports** (1976) $4.906 bln.; partners (1974): W. Ger. 16%, U.S. 9%, It. 9%, Fr. 7%. **Exports** (1976): $2.554 bln.; partners (1974): W. Ger. 21%, It. 9%, U.S. 6%, Fr. 6%. **Tourists** (excluding cruises) (1974): 1,956,400; receipts: $437 million. **Balance of payments** (1976): $−128 mln. **National budget** (1976): $4.62 bln. revenues; $5.46 bln. expenditures. **Interna-tional reserves** (Jan. 1977): $923.3 mln. **Consumer prices** (change in 1976): 13.4%.

Transport: Railway traffic (1974): 990 mln. passenger-miles; 560 mln. net ton-miles. **Motor vehicles:** in use (1974): 380,200 passenger cars, 183,800 commercial vehicles. **Civil aviation:** 2,869 mln. passenger-miles (1976); 36 mln. freight ton-miles (1976). **Chief ports:** Piraeus, Thessaloniki, Patrai.

Communications: Television sets: 950,000 in use (1973);

298,000 manufactured (1973). **Radios:** 1,000,000 in use (1972). **Telephones in use** (1976): 2,008,522. **Daily newspaper circulation** (1973): 920,000; 101 per 1,000 pop.

Health: Life expectancy at birth (1960-62): 67.46 male; 70.70 female. **Births** (per 1,000 pop. 1975): 15.6. **Deaths** (per 1,000 pop. 1975): 8.9. **Natural increase** (1975): 0.67%. **Pop. per hospital bed** (1973): 154. **Pop. per physician** (1973): 568. **Infant mortality** (per 1,000 pop. under 1 yr. 1975): 24.1.

Education: Literacy (1973): 84%. **Pop. 5-19:** in school (1973): 67%; per teacher (1973): 47.

The achievements of Ancient Greece in art, architecture, science, mathematics, philosophy, drama, literature, and democracy became legacies for succeeding ages. Greece reached the height of its glory and power, particularly in the Athenian city-state, in the 5th century B.C.

Greece fell under Roman rule in the 2d and 1st centuries B.C. In the 4th century A.D. it became part of the Byzantine Empire and, after the fall of Constantinople to the Turks in 1453, part of the Ottoman Empire.

Greece won its war of independence from Turkey 1821-1829, and became a kingdom. A republic was established 1925; the monarchy was restored, 1935, and George II, King of the Hellenes, resumed the throne. In Oct., 1940, Greece rejected an ultimatum from Italy. Nazi support resulted in the defeat and occupation of Greece by Germans, Italians, and Bulgarians. By the end of 1944 the invaders withdrew. Communist resistance forces were defeated by Royalist and British troops.

A plebiscite recalled King George II. He died Apr. 1, 1947, and was succeeded by his brother, Paul I.

Communists waged guerrilla war 1947-49 against the government but were defeated with the aid of the U.S. (acting under the Truman Doctrine).

A period of reconstruction and rapid development followed, mainly with conservative governments under Premier Constantine Karamanlis. The Center Union led by George Papandreou won elections in 1963 and 1964. King Constantine, who acceded in 1964, forced Papandreou to resign. A period of political maneuvers ended in the military takeover of April 21, 1967, by Col. George Papadopoulos. King Constantine tried to reverse the consolidation of the harsh dictatorship Dec. 13, 1967, but failed and fled to Italy. Papadopoulos was ousted Nov. 25, 1973, in a coup led by rightist Brig. Demetrius Ioannides.

Greek army officers serving in the National Guard of Cyprus staged a coup on the island July 15, 1974. Turkey invaded Cyprus a week later, precipitating the collapse of the Greek junta, which was implicated in the Cyprus coup.

The military turned the government over to Karamanlis, who named a civilian cabinet, freed political prisoners, and sought to solve the Cyprus crisis. In Nov. 1974 elections his party won a large parliamentary majority, though local elections in 1975 showed leftist gains. A Dec. 1974 referendum resulted in the proclamation of a republic.

The new government promoted educational and agricultural reforms, and sought to advance from associate to full membership in the EC.

The **Dodecanese** are a group of 13 islands in the southeastern Aegean Sea. They were seized from Turkey by Italy in 1912. Rhodes is the capital.

After World War II the islands were ceded to Greece at the Paris Conference of Foreign Ministers, June 27, 1946, and annexed Mar. 7, 1948.

Crete, largest Greek island and 5th largest in Mediterranean, original site of Minoan civilization, lies SE of the Peloponnesus peninsula and is 160 mi. long, 35 mi. wide, with area of 3,207 sq. mi. Principal towns: Heraklion (Candia) and Khania (Canea).

Grenada
State of Grenada

People: Population (1976 est.): 100,000. **Pop. density:** 752 per sq. mi. **Ethnic groups:** Negroes over 52%, whites 1%, mulattoes 43% (including some E. Indians), Carib. Indians. **Languages:** English, French-African patois. **Religions:** Roman Catholics, Anglicans.

Geography: Area: 133 sq. mi. **Location:** Southernmost of West Indies, 90 mi. N. of Venezuela. **Topography:** Main island is mountainous; country includes Carriacon and Petit Martinique islands, 13 sq. mi. together. **Capital:** St. George's. **Cities** (1975 est.): St. George's 30,000.

Government: Head of state: Queen Elizabeth II, represented by Leo V. DeGale; **Head of government:** Prime Min. Eric M. Gairy, b. 1923, in office: Feb. 7, 1974. **Local divisions:** 6 parishes.

Economy: Industries: Rum. **Chief crops:** Nutmegs, bananas, cocoa, sugar, mace. **Livestock** (1974): 6,000 cattle; 16,000 pigs; 9,000 sheep; 308,000 poultry. **Electricity production** (1971): 18 mln. kwh. **Labor force:** 26% agric.

Finance: Currency: E. Carib. Dollar (1974: 2.05=$1 US). **Gross domestic product** (est. 1974): $44 mln. **Per capita income** (1974): $390. **Imports** (1976): $26 mln.; partners (1972): U.K. 26%, U.S. 10%. **Exports** (1976): $13 mln.; partners (1972): U.K. 36%, U.S. 7%. **Tourists** (1972): 37,900; receipts: $12 million.

Transport: Motor vehicles: in use (1971): 3,800 passenger cars, 100 commercial vehicles. **Chief ports:** Saint George's.

Communications: Telephones in use (1976): 4,921. **Daily newspaper circulation** (1971): 3,000; 31 per 1,000 pop.

Health: Life expectancy at birth (1959-61): 60.14 male 65.60 female. **Births** (per 1,000 pop. 1974): 26.2. **Deaths** (per 1,000 pop. 1974): 7.5. **Natural increase** (1974): 1.87%. **Infant mortality** (per 1,000 pop. under 1 yr. 1974): 31.5.

First European visitor was Columbus, 1498. First European settlers were French, 1650. The island was held alternately by France and England until final British occupation, 1784. Grenada became fully independent Feb. 7, 1974 during a general strike. It is the smallest independent nation in the Western Hemisphere.

Guatemala
Republic of Guatemala

People: Population (1976): 6,260,000. **Age distrib.** (%): 0-14: 45.1; 15-59: 50.1; 60+: 4.7. **Pop. density:** 149 per sq. mi. **Urban** (1970): 33.8%. **Ethnic groups:** Indians 54%, Mestizos 42%, whites 4%. **Languages:** Spanish, 18 Maya-Quiche dialects. **Religions:** Roman Catholics over 90%; Mayan religion practiced.

Geography: Area: 42,042 sq. mi., the size of Tennessee. **Location:** In Central America. **Neighbors:** Mexico N, W; El Salvador on S, Honduras, Belize on E. **Topography:** The central highland and mountain areas are bordered by the narrow Pacific coast and the lowlands and fertile river valleys on the Caribbean. There are numerous volcanoes in S, more than half a dozen over 11,000 ft. **Capital:** Guatemala City. **Cities** (1973 cen.): Guatemala City 706,920; (1973 est.) Escuintla 68,573; Quezaltenango 65,733.

Government: Head of state: Pres. Kjell Eugenio Laugerud Garcia, b. Jan. 24, 1930, in office: July 1, 1974. **Local divisions:** Guatemala City and 22 departments; pres. appoints governors. **Armed forces:** regulars 10,870; para-military 3,000.

Economy: Industries: Shoes, textiles. **Chief crops:** Coffee (one third of exports), sugar, bananas, cotton. **Minerals:** Zinc, lead, antimony, tungsten, cadmium, silver, copper, nickel, gas. **Other resources:** Rare woods, fish, chicle. **Per capita arable land:** 0.5 acres. **Livestock** (1976): 2,153,000 cattle; 840,000 pigs; 520,000 sheep. **Electricity production** (1972): 910 mln kwh. **Labor force:** 57% agric.; 14% manuf.

Finance: Currency: Quetzales (Apr. 1977: 1=$1 US). **Gross domestic product** (1975): $3.59 bln. **Per capita income** (1974): $470. **Imports** (1976): $982 mln.; partners (1974): U.S 32%, Venez. 12%, El Salv. 10%, Jap. 9%. **Exports** (1975): $641 mln.; partners (1974): U.S. 33%, El Salv. 11%, W. Ger. 11%, Nic 7%. **Tourist receipts** (1974): $57 million. **Balance of payments** (1976): $212 mln. **National budget** (1976): $428 mln. revenues $525 mln. expenditures. **International reserves** (Feb. 1977) $617.6 mln. **Consumer prices** (change in 1976): 10.8%.

Transport: Railway traffic (1970): 66 mln. net ton-miles. **Motor vehicles:** in use (1972): 54,100 passenger cars, 36,900 commercial vehicles. **Civil aviation:** 82 mln. passenger-miles (1976); 4.4 mln. freight ton-miles (1976). **Chief ports:** Puerto Barrios, San Jose.

Communications: Television sets: 105,000 in use (1973) **Radios:** 260,000 in use (1973). **Daily newspaper circulation** (1973): 168,000.

Health: Life expectancy at birth (1963-65): 48.29 male 49.74 female. **Births** (per 1,000 pop. 1973): 42.4. **Deaths** (per 1,000 pop. 1973): 12.6. **Natural increase** (1973): 2.98%. **Pop. per hospital bed** (1973): 374. **Pop. per physician** (1973) 3,957. **Infant mortality** (per 1,000 pop. under 1 yr. 1973): 81.2.

Education: Literacy (1973): 38%. **Pop. 5-19:** in school (1973): 32%; per teacher (1973): 123.

The old Mayan Indian empire flourished in what is today Guatemala for over 1,000 years before the Spanish conquest.

Guatemala was a Spanish colony 1524-1821; briefly a part of Mexico and then of the U.S. of Central America; the republic was established in 1839.

Since 1945 when a liberal government was elected to replace the long-term dictatorship of Jorge Ubico, the country has seen a swing toward socialism, an armed revolt, renewed attempts at social reform and a military coup. Assassinations and political violence from left and right plagued the country. Some 20,000 Guatemalans, mostly liberal or radical opponents of the regime, were killed in the decade up to 1976.

A 1976 earthquake killed 20,000 people and left over 1 million homeless.

Guinea

Republic of Guinea

People: Population (1976 est.): 4,530,000. **Age distrib.** (%): 0-14: 43.7; 15-59: 47; 60+: 9.3. **Pop. density:** 48 per sq. mi. **Ethnic groups:** Fula 40%, Mandingo 25%, Soussous 10%, 15 other tribes. **Languages:** French (official), tribal languages. **Religions:** Moslems 70%, Christians 1%, others.

Geography: Area: 94,925 sq. mi., slightly smaller than Oregon. **Location:** On Atlantic coast of W. Africa. **Neighbors:** Guinea-Bissau, Senegal, Mali on N, Ivory Coast on E, Liberia on S. **Topography:** A narrow coastal belt leads to the mountainous Middle Guinea region, the source of the Gambia, Senegal, and Niger rivers. Upper Guinea, farther inland, is a cooler upland region. The SE is forested. **Capital:** Conakry. **Cities** (1972 est.): Conakry (met.) 525,671.

Government: Head of state: Pres. Ahmed Sekou Toure, b. Jan. 19, 1922, in office: Oct. 2, 1958; **Head of government:** Premier Lansana Beavoqui, in office: Apr. 26, 1972. **Local divisions:** 29 administrative regions. **Armed forces:** regulars 5,850; para-military 8,000.

Economy: Chief crops: Bananas, pineapples, rice, corn, palm nuts, coffee, honey. **Minerals:** Bauxite, iron, diamonds. **Per capita arable land:** 0.8 acres. **Livestock** (1974): 1,880,000 cattle; 520,000 sheep; 570,000 goats. **Electricity production** (1973): 450 mln. kwh. **Labor force:** 83% agric.

Finance: Currency: Sily (1974: 20.5=$1 US). **Gross domestic product** (est. 1974): $590 mln. **Per capita income** (1974): $130. **Imports** (1973): $100 mln.; partners (1973): Fr. 23%, USSR 20%, U.S. 12%, P.R. China 10%. **Exports** (1973): $70 mln.; partners (1973): Nor. 15%, USSR 15%, Sp. 14%, Cameroon 10%.

Transport: Motor vehicles: in use (1972): 10,200 passenger cars, 10,800 commercial vehicles. **Chief ports:** Conakry.

Communications: Radios: 101,000 in use (1973). **Daily newspaper circulation** (1973): 5,000; 1 per 1,000 pop.

Health: Life expectancy at birth (1970-75): 39.4 male; 42.0 female. **Births** (annual per 1,000 pop. 1970-75): 46.6. **Deaths** (annual per 1,000 pop. 1970-75): 22.9. **Natural increase** (annual 1970-75): 2.37%. **Pop. per hospital bed** (1973): 569. **Pop. per physician** (1973): 22,394. **Infant mortality** (per 1,000 pop. under 1 yr. 1955): 216.

Education: Literacy (1973): 10%. **Pop. 5-19:** in school (1973): 20%; per teacher (1973): 111.

Part of the ancient West African empires, Guinea fell under French control 1849-98. Under Sekou Toure, it opted for full independence in 1958, and France withdrew all aid.

Toure turned to Communist nations for support, and set up a militant one-party state. France and Guinea restored ties in 1975, after a 10-year break. Western firms, as well as the Soviet government, have invested in Guinea's vast bauxite mines.

According to reports, thousands of opponents were jailed in the 1970s, in the aftermath of an unsuccessful Portuguese invasion. Many were tortured and killed.

Guinea-Bissau

Republic of Guinea-Bissau

People: Population (1976 est.): 530,000. **Pop. density:** 38 per sq. mi. **Ethnic groups:** Balanta 30%, Fula 20%, Mandyako 14%, other tribes. **Languages:** Portuguese (official), Crioulo, tribal languages. **Religions:** Moslems 30%, Christians 1%, others.

Geography: Area: 13,948 sq. mi. **Location:** On Atlantic coast of W. Africa. **Neighbors:** Senegal on N, Guinea on E, S. **Topography:** A swampy coastal plain covers most of the country; to the east is a low savanna region. **Capital:** Bissau. **Cities** (1973 est.): Bissau 60,000.

Government: Head of state: Pres. Luis de Almeida Cabral, b. 1931, in office: July 22, 1973; **Head of government:** Prime Min. Francisco Mendes, in office: Sept. 24, 1973. **Local divisions:** 12 regions.

Economy: Chief crops: Peanuts, palm oil. **Minerals:** Bauxite, oil. **Per capita arable land:** 1.2 acres. **Livestock** (1974): 253,000 cattle; 165,000 pigs; 68,000 sheep; 178,000 goats. **Electricity production** (1973): 13 mln. kwh. **Labor force:** 86% agric.

Finance: Currency: Escudo (1974: 25.4 = $1 US). **Gross domestic product** (est. 1974): $160 mln. **Per capita income** (1974): $300. **Imports** (1975): $38 mln.; partners (1973): Port. 56%, Sp. 7%, U.K. 5%, Jap. 5%. **Exports** (1975): $12 mln.; partners (1973): Port. 90%, Neth. 3%, Cape Verde 2%.

Communications: Radios: 4,000 licenses (1972). **Daily newspaper circulation** (1973): 6,000; 12 per 1,000 pop.

Health: Life expectancy at birth (1970-75): 37.0 male; 40.1 female. **Births** (annual per 1,000 pop. 1970-75): 40.1 **Deaths** (annual per 1,000 pop. 1970-75): 25.1. **Natural increase** (annual 1970-75): 1.50%. **Infant mortality** (per 1,000 pop. under 1 yr. 1969): 47.1.

Portuguese mariners explored the area in the mid-15th century; the slave trade flourished in the 17th and 18th centuries, and colonization began in the 19th.

Beginning in the 1960s, an independence movement waged a guerrilla war and formed a government in the interior that achieved international support. Full independence came Sept. 10, 1974, after the Portuguese regime was overthrown.

Union with Cape Verde was foreseen in a number of cooperation accords signed in 1975.

Guyana

Cooperative Republic of Guyana

People: Population (1976): 780,000. **Age distrib.** (%): 0-14: 44.2; 15-59: 50.7; 60+: 5. **Pop. density:** 9.4 per sq. mi. **Urban** (1973): 40.0%. **Ethnic groups:** East Indians 55%, Negroes 36%, others (Amerindians, Chinese, Europeans) 10%. **Languages:** English (official), Hindi, Portuguese, Chinese, Negro patois. **Religions:** Christians 57%, Hindus 33%, Moslems 9%, others.

Geography: Area: 83,000 sq. mi., the size of Idaho. **Location:** On N coast of S. America. **Neighbors:** Venezuela on W, Brazil on S, Surinam on E. **Topography:** Dense tropical forests cover much of the land, altough a flat coastal area up to 40 mi. wide, where 90% of the population lives, provides rich alluvial soil for agriculture. A grassy savanna divides the two zones. **Capital:** Georgetown. **Cities** (1970 cen.): Georgetown (met.) 164,039.

Government: Head of state: Pres. Arthur Chung, b. Jan. 10, 1918, in office: Feb. 23, 1970; **Head of government:** Prime Min. Linden Forbes Sampson Burnham, b. Feb. 20, 1923, in office: May 26, 1966. **Local divisions:** 9 districts, 4 counties, 2 municipalities. **Armed forces:** regulars 2,000; para-military 2,250.

Economy: Industries: Cigarettes, rum, clothing, furniture, drugs. **Chief crops:** Sugar, rice, coconuts, coffee, cocoa, citrus and other fruits. **Minerals:** Bauxite (5th largest producer), gold, diamonds. **Other resources:** Timber, shrimp. **Per capita arable land:** 2.5 acres. **Livestock** (1974): 254,000 cattle; 105,000 pigs; 107,000 sheep; 9,000 poultry. **Electricity production** (1975): 384 mln. kwh. **Labor force:** 32% agric.

Finance: Currency: Dollar (Apr. 1977: 2.55=$1 US). **Gross domestic product** (1975): $503 mln. **Per capita income** (1975): $588. **Imports** (1975): $342 mln.; partners (1974): U.S. 26%, Trin. 23%, U.K. 20%, Can. 5%. **Exports** (1975): $357 mln.; partners (1974): U.S. 25%, U.K. 21%, Trin. 7%, Morocco 5%. **Tourist receipts** (1974): $4 mln. **Balance of payments** (1976): $−103.4 mln. **National budget** (1973): $74.47 mln. revenues; $139.1 mln. expenditures. **International reserves** (Jan. 1977): $22.08 mln. **Consumer prices** (change in 1976): 9.1%.

Transport: Railway traffic (1971): 14 mln. passenger-miles. **Motor vehicles:** in use: 24,400 passenger cars (1974), 9,900 commercial vehicles (1973). **Chief ports:** Georgetown.

Communications: Radios: 150,000 licenses (1973). **Tele-**

phones in use (1976): 21,074. **Daily newspaper circulation** (1973): 67,000; 88 per 1,000 pop.

Health: Life expectancy at birth (1959-61): 59.03 male; 63.01 female. **Births** (per 1,000 pop. 1971): 33.4. **Deaths** (per 1,000 pop. 1971): 7.2. **Natural increase** (1971): 2.62%. **Pop. per hospital bed** (1973): 220. **Pop. per physician** (1973): 3,820. **Infant mortality** (per 1,000 pop. under 1 yr. 1971): 42.3.

Education: Literacy (1973): 83%. **Pop. 5-19:** in school (1973): 68%; per teacher (1973): 40.

Guyana became a Dutch possession in the 17th century, but sovereignty passed to Britain in 1815. Indentured servants from India soon outnumbered African slaves.

Guyana became independent May 26, 1966. A Venezuelan claim to the western half of Guyana was suspended in 1970 for 12 years. The Surinam border is also disputed. The government has nationalized most of the economy in recent years.

Haiti

Republic of Haiti

People: Population (1976 est.): 4,670,000. **Age distrib.** (%) 0-14: 42.5; 15-59: 51.2; 60+: 6.3. **Pop. density:** 436 per sq. mi **Urban** (1971): 20.3%. **Ethnic groups:** Negroes 95%, mulattoes 5%. **Languages:** French (official), Creole. **Religions:** Roman Catholics 80%, Protestants 10%; Voodoo widely practiced.

Geography: Area: 10,714 sq. mi., the size of Maryland. **Location:** In West Indies, occupies western third of I. of Hispaniola. **Neighbors:** Dominican Republic on E, Cuba on W (across Windward Passage). **Topography:** About two-thirds of Haiti is mountainous. Much of the rest is semiarid. The coastal areas are warm and moist. **Capital:** Port-au-Prince. **Cities** (1971 est.): Port-au-Prince (met.) 493,932.

Government: Head of state: Pres. Jean Claude Duvalier, b. July 3, 1951, in office: Apr. 22, 1971. **Local divisions:** 5 departments. **Armed forces:** regulars 6,550; para-military 14,900.

Economy: Industries: Rum, molasses, tourism. **Chief crops:** Coffee, sisal, cotton, sugar, bananas, cocoa, tobacco, rice. **Minerals:** Bauxite, copper, gold, silver, cement. **Other resources:** Timber. **Per capita arable land:** 0.2 acres. **Livestock** (1974): 737,000 cattle; 1,690,000 pigs; 77,000 sheep. **Electricity production** (1973): 141 mln. kwh.

Finance: Currency: Gourdes (Apr. 1977: 5 =$1 US). **Gross domestic product** (1975): $922 mln. **Per capita income** (1974): $158. **Imports** (1975): $142 mln.; partners (1973): U.S 43%, Jap. 9%, Can. 8%, Fr. 6%, W. Ger. 6%. **Exports** (1975) $80 mln.; partners (1973): U.S. 62%, Fr. 9%, Belg. 9%, It. 7%. **Tourists** (1974): 47,600; receipts: $19 million. **Balance of payments** (1975): $−7.8 mln. **National budget** (1975): $103.8 mln. revenues; $119.9 mln. expenditures. **International reserves** (Nov. 1976): $25,7 mln. **Consumer prices** (change in 1976): 7.9%.

Transport: Motor vehicles: in use (1973): 11,700 passenger cars, 1,300 commercial vehicles. **Chief ports:** Port-au-Prince, Les Cayes.

Communications: Television sets: 13,000 in use (1973). **Radios:** 90,000 in use (1973). **Daily newspaper circulation** (1973): 82,000; 16 per 1,000 pop.

Health: Life expectancy at birth (1970-75): 49.0 male; 51.0 female. **Births** (Annual per 1,000 pop. 1970-75): 35.8. **Deaths** (annual per 1,000 pop. 1970-75): 16.3. **Natural increase** (annual 1970-75): 1.95%. **Pop. per hospital bed** (1973): 1,253. **Pop. per physician** (1973): 8,640. **Infant mortality** (per 1,000 pop. under 1 yr. 1973): 150.

Education: Literacy (1973): 10%. **Pop. 5-19:** in school (1973): 21%; per teacher (1973): 188.

Haiti, visited by Columbus, 1492, and a French colony from 1677, attained its independence, 1804, following the rebellion led by former slave Toussaint L'Ouverture. Following a period of political violence, 1910-15, the U.S. occupied the country until 1934.

Dr. Francois Duvalier was voted president in 1957; in 1964 he was named president for life. Upon his death in 1971, he was succeeded by his son Jean-Claude. Under the latter's less violent rule, foreign investment and tourism revived. But drought in 1975-77 brought famine, aggravated by erosion caused by the destruction of most trees for charcoal.

Honduras

Republic of Honduras

People: Population (1976 est.): 3,140,000. **Age distrib.** (%): 0-14: 46.8; 15-59: 49.3; 60+: 4. **Pop. density:** 73 per sq. mi. **Urban** (19⁻ 4): 31.1%. **Ethnic groups:** Mestizo 90%, Caucasian, Negroes, Indians. **Languages:** Spanish, English (on N coast). **Religions:** Roman Catholics predominate.

Geography: Area: 43,277 sq. mi., slightly larger than Tennessee. **Location:** In Central America. **Neighbors:** Guatemala on W, El Salvador, Nicaragua on S. **Topography:** The Caribbean coast is 500 mi. long. Pacific coast, on Gulf of Fonseca, is 40 mi. long. Honduras is mountainous, with wide fertile valleys and rich forests. **Capital:** Tegucigalpa. **Cities** (1973 est.): Tegucigalpa (met.) 302,483; San Pedro Sula (met.) 153,307.

Government: Head of state: Gen. Juan Alberto Melgar Castro, in office: Apr. 22, 1975. **Local divisions:** 18 departments; pres. appoints governors. **Armed forces:** regulars 14,200; paramilitary 3,000.

Economy: Industries: Clothing, textiles, cement, chemicals. **Chief crops:** Bananas (chief export), coffee, cotton, sugar, tobacco. **Minerals:** Gold, silver, copper, lead, zinc, iron, antimony, coal. **Other resources:** Timber. **Per capita arable land:** 0.6 acres. **Livestock** (1976): 1,700,000 cattle; 520,000 pigs; 5,000 sheep; 7,700,000 poultry. **Electricity production** (1973): 408 mln. kwh. **Labor force:** 67% agric.

Finance: Currency: Lempira (Apr. 1977: 2 =$1 US). **Gross domestic product** (1976): $1.20 bln. **Per capita income** (1974): $306. **Imports** (1976) $453 mln.; partners (1973): U.S. 41%, Jap. 10%, Venez. 8%, Guat. 6%. **Exports** (1976): $383 mln.; partners (1974): U.S. 57%, W. Ger. 12%, Domin. Rep. 4%, Jap. 3%. **Tourist:** receipts (1974): $8 million. **Balance of payments** (1976): $39 mln. **National budget** (1975): $135.9 mln. revenues; $160 mln. expenditures. **International reserves** (Nov. 1976): $116.18 mln. **Consumer prices** (change in 1976): 4.9%.

Transport: Motor vehicles: in use (1974): 14,700 passenger cars, 22,900 commercial vehicles. **Civil aviation:** 149 mln. passenger-miles (1976); 1.9 mln. freight ton-miles (1975). **Chief ports:** Puerto Cortes, La Ceiba.

Communications: Television sets: 25,000 in use (1972). **Radios:** 155,000 in use (1973). **Telephones in use** (1976): 19,-548. **Daily newspaper circulation** (1973): 116,000.

Health: Life expectancy at birth (1970-75): 52.1 male; 55.0 female. **Births** (annual per 1,000 pop. 1970-75): 49.3. **Deaths** (annual per 1,000 pop. 1970-75): 14.6. **Natural increase** (annual 1970-75): 3.47%. **Pop. per hospital bed** (1973): 604. **Pop. per physician** (1973): 3,523. **Infant mortality** (per 1,000 pop. under 1 yr. 1974): 34.1.

Education: Literacy (1973): 45%. **Pop. 5-19:** in school (1973): 46%; per teacher (1973): 63.

Mayan civilization flourished in Honduras in the 1st millenium A.D. Columbus arrived in 1502.

Honduras became independent after freeing itself from Spain, 1821 and from the Fed. of Central America, 1838.

Gen. Oswaldo Lopez Arellano, president for most of the period 1963-75 by virtue of 1 election and 2 coups, was ousted by the Army in 1975 over charges of pervasive bribery by United Brands Co. of the U.S.

Honduras and El Salvador fought a 5-day war in 1969 over the presence in Honduras of 300,000 Salvadoreans. Further clashes occurred in 1970 and 1976.

Hungary

Hungarian People's Republic

People: Population (1976): 10,600,000. **Age distrib.** (%): 0-14: 20.0; 15-59: 61.9; 60+: 18.1. **Pop. density:** 295 per sq. mi. **Urban** (1974): 49.7%. **Ethnic groups:** Magyar 98%, German 0.5%, Slovak 0.3%, Gypsy 0.3%, Croatian 0.3%. **Languages:** Hungarian (Magyar). **Religions:** Roman Catholics 55%, Calvinist 20%, Lutherans 5%, Jews 1%.

Geography: Area: 35,919 sq. mi., slightly smaller than Indiana. **Location:** In east central Europe. **Neighbors:** Czechoslovakia on N, Austria on W, Yugoslavia on S, Romania, USSR on E. **Topography:** The Danube R. forms the Czech border in the NW, then swings S to bisect the country. The eastern half of Hungary is mainly a great fertile plain, the Alfold, the Wand N are hilly. **Capital:** Budapest. **Cities** (1974 est.): Budapest 2,051,354; Mispolc 194,648; Debrecen 179,755.

Government: Head of state: Pres. Pal Losonczi, b. 1919, in office: Apr. 14, 1967; **Head of government:** Chmn. Gyorgy Lazar, b. 1924, in office: May 15, 1975; **Head of Communist Party:** First Sec. Janos Kadar, b. May 26, 1912, in office: 1956. **Local divisions:** 19 counties, 5 cities with county status. **Armed forces:** regulars 100,000; reserves 148,000.

Economy: Industries: Iron and steel, machinery, chemicals, vehicles, communications equipment, milling, and distilling. **Chief crops:** Grains, vegetables, fruits, grapes. **Minerals:** Bauxite, natural gas. **Crude oil output** (1976): 14.3 mln. bbls. **Per capita arable land:** 1.2 acres. **Livestock** (1976): 1,900,000 cattle; 6,900,000 pigs; 2,000,000 sheep; 52,260,000 poultry. **Fish catch** (1974): 30,200 metric tons. **Electricity production** (1976): 22,044 mln. kwh. **Labor force:** 23% agric.; 36% manuf.

Finance: Currency: Forint (1974: 23.4 =$1 U.S.). **Gross domestic product** (est. 1974): $24.6 bln. **Per capita income** (1974): $2,200. **Imports** (1975) $7.176 bln; partners (1974): USSR 28%, W. Ger. 10%, E. Ger. 9%, Czech. 7%. **Exports** (1975): 6.091 bln.; partners (1974): USSR 32%, E. Ger. 10%, Czech. 9%, W. Ger. 6%. **Tourists** (1974): 4,655,200; receipts: $240 million.

Transport: Railway traffic (1974): 8,621 mln. passenger-miles; 13,956 mln. net ton-miles. **Motor vehicles:** in use (1974): 490,800 passenger cars, 187,100 commercial vehicles; manufactured (1976): 13,000 commercial vehicles.

Communications: Television sets: 2,199,000 licenses (1973); 395,000 manufactured (1974). **Radios:** 2,533,000 licenses (1973); 205,000 manufactured (1974). **Telephones in use** (1976): 1,048,090. **Daily newspaper circulation** (1973): 2,355,000; 226 per 1,000 pop.

Health: Life expectancy at birth (1972): 66.87 male; 72.59 female. **Births** (per 1,000 pop. 1975): 18.4. **Deaths** (per 1,000 pop. 1975): 12.4. **Natural increase** (1975): 0.60%. **Pop. per hospital bed** (1973): 122. **Pop. per physician** (1973): 518. **Infant mortality** (per 1,000 pop. under 1 yr. 1975): 32.6.

Education: Literacy (1973): 98%. **Pop. 5-19:** in school (1973): 52%; per teacher (1973): 32.

Earliest settlers, chiefly Slav and Germanic, were overrun by Huns and Magyars from the east. Stephen I (997-1038) was made king by Pope Sylvester II in 1001 A.D. The country suffered repeated Turkish invasions in the 15th-17th centuries. After the defeats of the Turks, 1686-1697, Austria dominated, but Hungary obtained concessions until it regained internal independence in 1867, with the emperor of Austria as king of Hungary in a dual monarchy with a single diplomatic service. Defeated with the Central Powers in 1918, Hungary lost Transylvania to Romania, Croatia and Bacska to Yugoslavia, Slovakia and Carpatho-Ruthenia to Czechoslovakia, all of which had large Hungarian minorities. A republic under Michael Karolyi and a bolshevist revolt under Bela Kun were followed by a vote for a monarchy in 1920 with Admiral Nicholas Horthy as regent.

Hungary joined Germany in World War II, and was allowed to annex most of its lost territories. Russian troops captured the country, 1944-1945. By terms of an armistice with the Allied powers Hungary agreed to give up territory acquired by the 1938 dismemberment of Czechoslovakia and to return to its borders of 1937.

Hungary declared for a republic Feb. 1, 1946, and elected Zoltan Tildy president. In 1947 the communists forced Tildy out.

Premier Imre Nagy, in office since mid-1953, was ousted for his moderate policy of favoring agriculture and consumer production, April 18, 1955.

In 1956, popular demands for the ousting of Erno Gero, Communist party secretary, and for formation of a government by Nagy, resulted in the latter's appointment Oct. 23; demonstrations against communist rule developed into open revolt. Gero called in Soviet forces. On Nov. 4 Soviet forces launched a massive attack against Budapest with 200,000 troops, 2,500 tanks and armored cars.

Estimates varied from 6,500 to 32,000 dead, and thousands deported. About 200,000 persons fled the country. The U.S. received 38,248 under a refugee emergency program. In the spring of 1963 the regime freed many anti-communists and captives from the revolution in a sweeping amnesty.

Nagy was executed by the Russians. Janos Kadar, sponsored by the USSR, became first secretary of the Hungarian Workers (Communist) party.

Some 40,000 Soviet troops are stationed in Hungary. Hungarian troops participated in the 1968 Warsaw Pact invasion of Czechoslovakia.

Major economic reforms were launched early in 1968, switching from a central planning system to one in which market forces and profit control much of production. Productivity and living standards have improved. By the 1970s, Hungary led the communist states in comparative tolerance for cultural freedoms and small private enterprise. Some 60,000 of the 1956 emigres have returned.

In 1973 Hungary agreed to pay the U.S. $18,900,000 for nationalized U.S. properties in Hungary, but minor disputes have hampered full trade relations.

Iceland

Republic of Iceland

People: Population (1976): 220,000. **Age distrib.** (%): 0-14: 31.0; 15-59: 56.4; 60+: 12.6. **Pop. density:** 5.5 per sq. mi. **Urban** (1974): 86.3%. **Ethnic groups:** Homogeneous, descendants of Norwegians, Celts. **Language:** Icelandic. **Religion:** Lutherans 98%.

Geography: Area: 39,702 sq. mi., the size of Virginia. **Location:** At N end of Atlantic O. **Neighbors:** Nearest is Greenland. **Topography:** Iceland is of recent volcanic origin. Three-quarters of the surface in wasteland: glaciers, lakes, a lava desert. There are geysers and hot springs, and the climate is moderated by the Gulf Stream. **Capital:** Reykjavik. **Cities** (1974 est.): Reykjavik (met.) 98,971.

Government: Head of state: Pres. Kristjan Eldjarn, b. Dec. 6, 1916, in office: Aug. 1, 1968; **Head of government:** Prime Min. Geir Hallgrimsson, b. Dec. 16, 1925, in office: Aug. 28, 1974. **Local divisions:** 23 syslur (counties).

Economy: Industries: Fish products, aluminum, cement, chemicals. **Chief crops:** Potatoes, turnips, hay. **Per capita arable land:** 0.013 acres. **Livestock** (1974): 67,000 cattle; 846,000 sheep; 234,000 poultry. **Fish catch** (1975): 995,000 metric tons. **Electricity production** (1976): 2,424 mln. kwh. **Labor force:** 16% agric., 26% manuf.

Finance: Currency: Kronur (Apr. 1977: 193=$1 US). **Gross domestic product** (1976): $1.4 bln. **Per capita income** (1975): $4,682. **Imports** (1976): $467 mln.; partners (1974): W. Ger. 12%, UK 11%, USSR 10%, Den. 9%. **Exports** (1976): $406 mln.; partners (1974): U.S. 22%, Port. 10%, W. Ger. 9%, U.K. 9%. **Tourists** (1972): 68,000 receipts (1974): $16 million. **Balance of payments** (1976): $15.9 mln. **International reserves** (Feb. 1977): $85.3 mln. **Consumer prices** (change in 1976): 32.9%.

Transport: Motor vehicles: in use (1974): 63,800 passenger cars, 7,500 commercial vehicles. **Civil aviation:** 1,185 mln. passenger-miles (1976); 18.9 mln. freight ton-miles (1976). **Chief port:** Reykjavik.

Communications: Television sets: 46,000 licenses (1973). **Radios:** 64,000 licenses (1973). **Telephones in use** (1976): 91,406. **Daily newspaper circulation** (1971): 96,000; 449 per 1,000 pop.

Health: Life expectancy at birth (1966-70): 70.7 male; 76.3 female. **Births** (per 1,000 pop. 1975): 20.6. **Deaths** (per 1,000 pop. 1975): 6.9. **Natural increase** (1975): 1.38%. **Pop. per hospital bed** (1973): 66. **Pop. per physician** (1973): 656. **Infant mortality** (per 1,000 pop. under 1 yr. 1975): 11.1.

Education: Literacy (1973): 98%. **Pop. 5-19:** in school (1973): 82%; per teacher (1973): 20.

Iceland was an independent republic from 930 to 1262, when it joined with Norway. Its language has maintained its purity, as in the Eddas, for 1,000 years. Danish rule lasted from 1380-1918; the last ties with the Danish crown were severed in 1941. The Althing, or assembly, is the world's oldest surviving parliament.

A four-year dispute with Britain ended in 1976 when the latter accepted Iceland's 200-mile territorial waters claim.

A conservative coalition won power in 1974 and stopped plans to oust U.S. NATO air and naval personnel, which totalled 2,900 in 1975.

India

Republic of India

People: Population (1976 est.): 610,080,000. **Age distrib.** (%): 0-14: 40.1; 15-59: 54.6; 60+: 5.3. **Pop. density:** 496 per sq.

mi. **Urban** (1974): 20.6%. **Ethnic groups:** Indo-Aryan groups 72%, Dravidians 25%, Mongoloids 3%. **Languages:** 14 official languages, including English and Hindi. **Religions:** Hindus 84%, Moslems 10%, Christians 2.6%, Sikhs 1.9%, Buddhists 0.7%, Jains 0.5%, others.

Geography: Area: 1,229,737 sq. mi., one third the size of the U.S. **Location:** Occupies most of the Indian subcontinent in S. Asia. **Neighbors:** Pakistan on W, China, Nepal, Bhutan on N, Burma, Bangladesh on E. **Topography:** The Himalaya Mts., highest in world, stretch across India's northern borders. Below, the Ganges Plain is wide, fertile, and among the most densely populated regions of the world. The area below includes the Deccan Peninsula. Close to one quarter the area is forested. The climate varies from tropical heat in S to near-Arctic cold in N. Rajasthan Desert is in NW; NE Assam Hills get 400 in. of rain a year. **Capital:** New Delhi. **Cities** (1971 cen.): Calcutta (met.) 7,031,382; Bombay 5,970,575; Delhi (met.) 3,647,023; Madras (met.) 3,169,930; Hyderabad (met.), 1,796,339; Ahmedabad (met.) 1,741,522; Bangalore (met.), 1,653,779; Kanpur (met.) 1,275,242; Poona (met.) 1,135,034; Nagpur (met.) 930,459; Lucknow (met.) 813,982.

Government: Head of state: Pres. Neelam Sanjiva Reddy, b. 1913 in office: July 25, 1977; **Head of government:** Prime Min. Morarji Desai, b. Feb. 29, 1896, in office: Mar. 24, 1977. **Local divisions:** 22 states with elected governments and substantial powers, 9 union territories; largest state, Uttar Pradesh, had over 88 million people in 1971. **Armed forces:** regulars 1,055,500 (army 913,000; Navy 42,500; air force 100,000); reserves 240,000; para-military 180,000.

Economy: Industries: Textiles, steel, processed foods, cement, machinery, chemical, fertilizers, consumer appliances, autos. **Chief crops:** Rice, grains, coffee, sugar cane, spices, tea, cashews, cotton, copra, coir, juta, linseed. **Minerals:** Coal, mica, manganese, salt, iron, bauxite, gypsum, oil. **Crude oil output** (1976): 65.3 mln. bbls. **Other resources:** rubber, timber. **Per capita arable land:** 0.6 acres. **Livestock** (1974): 239,900,000 cattle; 6,900,000 pigs; 40,000,000 sheep; 118,000,000 poultry. **Fish catch** (1975): 2,328,000 metric tons. **Electricity production** (1976): 89,208 kwh. **Labor force:** 72% agri. 9% manuf.

Finance: Currency: Rupee (Apr. 1977: 8.82=$1 US). **Gross domestic product** (1974-75): $84.5 bln. **Per capita income** (1974): $136. **Imports** (1976) $4.952 bln.; partners (1975): US 16%, Iran 11%, Jap. 10%, USSR 9%. **Exports** (1976): $4.982 bln.; partners (1975): USSR 13%, U.S. 11%, UK 9%, Jap. 9%. **Tourists** (1974): 423,000; receipts: $96 million. **Balance of payments** (1974): $-453 mln. **National budget** (1975): $8.81 bln. revenues; $10.67 bln. expenditures. **International reserves** (Jan. 1977): $3.2 bln. **Consumer prices** (change in 1976): 7.7%.

Transport: Railway traffic (1973): 84,308 mln. passenger-miles; 76,005 mln net ton-miles. **Motor vehicles:** in use (1974): 704,600 passenger cars, 397,200 commercial vehicles; manufactured (1976): 39,000 passenger cars, 42,000 commercial vehicles. **Civil aviation:** 3,726 mln. passenger-miles (1975); 145 mln. freight ton-miles (1975). **Chief ports:** Calcutta, Bombay, Madras, Cochin, Vishalshapatnam.

Communications: Television sets: 163,000 licenses (1973). **Radios:** 14,034,000 licenses (1973); 2,112,000 manufactured (1974). **Telephones in use** (1976): 1,816,901. **Daily newspaper circulation** (1972): 8,873,000; 16 per 1,000 pop.

Health: Life expectancy at birth (1951-60): 41.89 male; 40.55 female. **Births** (per 1,000 pop. 1973): 34.6. **Deaths** (per 1,000 pop. 1973): 15.5. **Natural increase** (1973): 1.91%. **Pop. per hospital bed** (1973): 1,980. **Pop. per physician** (1973): 4,399. **Infant mortality** (per 1,000 pop. under 1 yr. 1971):122.

Education: Literacy (1973): 34%. **Pop. 5-19:** in school (1973): 39%; per teacher (1973): 58.

India has one of the oldest civilizations in the world. Excavations trace the Indus Valley civilization back for at least 5,000 years. Paintings in the mountain caves of Ajanta, richly carved temples, the Taj Mahal in Agra and the Kutab Minar in Delhi are among relics of the past.

Aryan tribes, speaking Sanskrit (related to Persian and to European languages), invaded from the NW around 1500 B.C., and merged with the earlier inhabitants to create classical Indian civilization.

Asoka ruled most of the Indian subcontinent in the 3rd century B.C., and established Buddhism. But Hinduism revived and eventually predominated. During the Gupta kingdom, 4th-6th century A.D., science, literature, and the arts enjoyed a "golden age."

Arab invaders established a Moslem foothold in the W in the 8th century, and Turkish Moslems gained control of North India by 1200. The Mogul emperors (Moslems from Afghanistan) ruled 1526-1707.

Vasco de Gama established Portuguese trading posts 1498-1503. The Dutch followed. The British East India Co. sent Capt. William Hawkins, 1609, to get concessions from the Mogul emperor for spices and textiles. Operating as the East India Co. the British gained control of most of India. The British parliament assumed political direction; under Lord Bentinck, 1828-35, rule by rajahs was curbed. After the Sepoy troops mutinied, 1857-58, the British supported the native rulers.

Nationalism grew rapidly after World War I. The Indian National Congress and the Moslem League demanded constitutional reform. A leader emerged in Mohandas K. Gandhi (called Mahatma, or Great Soul), born Oct. 2, 1869, assassinated Jan. 30, 1948. A Hindu, trained in law in England, he began advocating self-rule, non-violence, pursuit of native handicrafts, removal of untouchability (which forced millions of poor to remain menials by heredity) in 1919. In 1930 he launched "civil disobedience," including boycott of British goods and rejection of taxes without representation.

In 1935 Britain gave India a constitution providing a bicameral federal congress. Suffrage was granted about 30 million. Mohammed Ali Jinnah, head of the Moslem League, sought creation of a Moslem nation, Pakistan.

Following more than 40 years' active struggle for freedom by both Hindus and Moslems, the British government announced Feb. 20, 1947, its intention to partition India into 2 dominions and set June, 1948, for British withdrawal from India. Aug. 15, 1947, was designated Indian Independence Day. India became a self-governing member of the Commonwealth and a member of the UN. It became a democratic republic, Jan. 26, 1950.

It was estimated that more than 12 million refugees (Hindus and Moslems) crossed the India-Pakistan borders in a mass transferral of some of the two peoples during 1947; about 200,000 were killed in communal fighting.

After Pakistan troops began attacks on Bengali separatists in East Pakistan, Mar. 25, 1971, some 10 million refugees fled into India. On Aug. 9, India and the USSR signed a 20-year friendship pact while U.S.-India relations soured. India and Pakistan went to war Dec. 3, 1971, on both the East and West fronts. Pakistan troops in the East surrendered Dec. 16; Pakistan agreed to a cease-fire in the West Dec. 17.

India and Pakistan signed a pact agreeing to withdraw troops from their borders and seek peaceful solutions, July 3, 1972. In Aug. 1973 India agreed to release 93,000 Pakistanis held prisoner since 1971; the return was completed in Apr. 1974. The two countries resumed full relations in 1976.

Prime Minister Mrs. Indira Gandhi, named Jan. 19, 1966, succeeded Lal Bahadur Shastri, who on June 2, 1964, succeeded India's first prime minister, Jawaharlal Nehru. Mrs. Gandhi, Nehru's daughter, was no relation to Mahatma Gandhi. Nehru, prime minister from the beginning of India's independence in 1947, died May 27, 1964.

Long the dominant power in India's politics, the Congress party lost some of its near monopoly by 1967. The party split into New and Old Congress parties in 1969. Mrs. Gandhi's New Congress party won control of the House.

Threatened with adverse court rulings in a voting law case, an opposition protest campaign and strikes, Gandhi invoked emergency provisions of the constitution June, 1975. Thousands of opponents were arrested and press censorship imposed. Measures to control prices, protect small farmers, and improve productivity were adopted.

The emergency, especially enforcement of coercive birth control measures in some areas, and the prominent extra-constitutional role of Indira Gandhi's son Sanjay, was widely resented. Opposition parties, united in the Janata coalition, scored massive victories in federal and state parliamentary elections in 1977, turning the Congress Party from power.

Severe droughts in northern areas have repeatedly threatened mass starvation and brought large shipments of grain from the U.S. In July 1967 plentiful rains broke the drought; there were bumper crops, 1968-72; the drought and food shortages returned in 1972-75, but a bumper crop in 1976 assured self-sufficiency.

Indian agriculture has made progress with high-yield seeds, fertilizers, irrigation and limited mechanization.

For many years India has had large textile industries with a wide variety of cotton, woolen, and silk products. In the 1960s, other industries, including steel, processed foods, cement, machinery, chemicals, and fertilizers came into prominence, along with many finished products such as sewing machines, typewriters, bicycles, telephones, and transportation equipment.

India's 1st nuclear power plant, built with U.S. help, was dedicated in 1970 near Bombay; Canada helped India build 2 reactors. In May 1974 India exploded a nuclear device underground, assertedly for peaceful development. Canada halted shipments of nuclear equipment and material to India. Restricted shipments from both the U.S. & Canada resumed in 1976. An Indian space satellite was launched by the USSR April 19, 1975.

There are 14 language groups, 12 originating from Sanskrit, and over 1,600 "mother tongues." Hindi is spoken by 30%, with Urdu, the principal Moslem language, spoken by 5%. Hindi became the official language in Jan. 1965 with English the associate official language. Much government work and instruction at universities is done in English. English-language dailies outsell those of any other language.

Sikkim, bordered by Tibet, Bhutan, Nepal and India, formerly British protected, became a protectorate of India in 1950. Area, 2,818 sq. mi.; population 1974, 210,000; capital, Gangtok. In Sept. 1974 India's Parliament voted to make Sikkim an associate Indian state, absorbing it into India. The monarchy was abolished in an April, 1975 referendum.

Kashmir, a predominantly Moslem region in the northwest, has been in dispute between India and Pakistan since 1947 when British rule was ending and Indian and Pakistani troops entered the area. A cease-fire was negotiated by the UN, Jan. 1, 1949; it gave Pakistan control of one-third of the area, in the west and northwest, and India the remaining two-thirds, the Indian state of Jammu and Kashmir, which enjoys internal autonomy. In late Aug. 1965, clashes broke out along the line.

A new truce line, slightly altering the old cease-fire line, was agreed on in Dec. 1972, accommodating changes made during Dec. 1971 fighting.

There were also clashes in April 1965 along the Assam-East Pakistan border and in the **Rann** (swamp) **of Cutch** area along the West Pakistan-Gujarat border near the Arabian Sea. An international arbitration commission on Feb. 19, 1968, awarded 90% of the Rann to India, 10% to Pakistan.

France, 1952-54, peacefully yielded to India its 5 colonies on the Bay of Bengal, former French India, comprising Pondicherry, Kirkal, Mahe, Yanaon, and Chandernagor, totalling 196 sq. mi. and 346,000 pop.

Goa, 1,426 sq. mi. pop., 1971, 857,771, which had been ruled by Portugal since 1505 A.D., was taken by India by military action Dec. 18, 1961, together with 2 other Portuguese enclaves, Daman and Liu, located near Bombay.

Indonesia

Republic of Indonesia

People: Population (1976 est.): 139,620,000. **Age distrib.** (%): 0-14: 44.1; 15-59: 51.5; 60+: 4.4. **Pop. density:** 190 per sq. mi. **Urban** (1974): 18.2%. **Ethnic groups:** Javanese 45%, Sundanese 13.6%, Chinese 2.3%, others. **Languages:** Bahasa Indonesian (Malay) (official), Javanese, other Austronesian languages. **Religions:** Moslems 90%, Christians 5%, Hindus 3%.

Geography: Area: 735,268 sq. mi. **Location:** Archipelago SE of Asia along the Equator. **Neighbors:** Malaysia on N, Papua New Guinea on E. **Topography:** Indonesia comprises 13,000 islands, including Java (one of the most densely populated areas in the world with 1,500 persons to the sq. mi.), Sumatra, Kalimantan (most of Borneo), Sulawesi (Celebes), and West Irian (Irian Jaya, the west half of New Guinea). Among others are Bangka, Billiton, Madura, Bali, Timor. The mountains and plateaus on the major islands have a cooler climate than the tropical lowlands. **Capital:** Jakarta. **Cities** (1971 cen.): Jakarta 4,576,009; Surabaja, 1,556,255; Bandung 1,201,730; Semarang 646,590; Medan 635,562.

Government: Head of state: Pres. Suharto, b. June 8, 1921, in office: May 27, 1968. **Local divisions:** 26 provinces with elected legislatures, appointed governors. **Armed forces:** regulars 246,000; para-military 112,000.

Economy: Industries: Food processing, textiles, light industry. **Chief crops:** Rice, maize, cassava, peanuts, soybeans, tobacco, coffee, pepper, kapok, coconuts, palm oil, tea, sugar, indigo. **Minerals:** Tin, oil, coal, bauxite, manganese, copper, nickel, gold, silver. **Crude oil output** (1976): 550 mln. bbls. **Other resources:** Rubber, cinchona. **Per capita arable land:** 0.3 acres. **Livestock** (1974): 6,682,000 cattle; 4,068,000 pigs; 3,207,000 sheep; 100,317,000 poultry. **Fish catch** (1975): 1,390,000 metric tons. **Electricity production** (1973): 2,932 mln. kwh. **Labor force** 62% agric.; 7% manuf.

Finance: Currency: Rupiah (Apr. 1977: 415=$1 US). **Gross domestic product** (1975): $29.4 bln. **Per capita income** (1974): $158. **Imports** (1976) $5.673 bln.; partners (1974): Jap. 30%, U.S. 16%, W. Ger. 8%, Sing. 7%. **Exports** (1976): $8.547 bln.; partners (1974): Jap. 53%, U.S. 20%, Sing. 7%. **Tourists** (1974): 313,500; receipts (1973): $21 million. **Balance of payments** (1975): $-857 mln. **National budget** (1975): $5.44 bln. revenues; $6.42 bln. expenditures. **International reserves** (Feb. 1977): $1.787 bln. **Consumer prices** (change in 1976): 20.0%.

Transport: Railway traffic (1973): 1,693 mln. passenger-miles; 663 mln. net ton-miles. **Motor vehicles:** in use (1973): 306,700 passenger cars, 173,300 commercial vehicles. **Civil aviation:** 1,892 mln. passenger-miles (1976); 29 mln. freight ton-miles (1976). **Chief ports:** Jakarta, Surabaja, Medan, Palembang, Semarang.

Communications: Television sets: 95,000 in use (1971). **Radios:** 6,000,000 in use licensed (1972); 900,000 manufactured (1973). **Telephones in use** (1976): 305,455. **Daily newspaper circulation** (1973): 1,110,000.

Health: Life expectancy at birth (1960): 47.5 male; 47.5 female. **Births** (annual per 1,000 pop. 1970-75): 42.9. **Deaths** (annual per 1,000 pop. 1970-75): 16.9. **Natural increase** (annual 1970-75): 2.60%. **Pop. per hospital bed** (1973): 1,407. **Pop. per physician** (1973): 24,553. **Infant mortality** (per 1,000 pop. under 1 yr. 1962): 125.

Education: Literacy (1973): 60%. **Pop. 5-19:** in school (1973): 34%; per teacher (1973): 84.

Hindu and Buddhist civilization from India reached the peoples of Indonesia nearly 2,000 years ago, taking root especially in Java. Islam spread along the maritime trade routes in the 15th century, and became predominant by the 16th century. The Dutch replaced the Portuguese as the most important European trade power in the area in the 17th century. They secured territorial control over Java by 1750. The outer islands were not finally subdued until the early 20th century, when the full area of present-day Indonesia was united under one rule for the first time in history.

Following Japanese occupation, 1942-45, nationalists led by Sukarno and Hatta proclaimed a republic. The Netherlands ceded sovereignty Dec. 27, 1949, after four years of intermittent fighting. West Irian, on New Guinea, remained under Dutch control.

After the Dutch in 1957 rejected proposals for new negotiations over West Irian, Indonesia stepped up the seizure of Dutch property. A U.S. mediator's plan was adopted in 1962. In 1963 the UN turned the area over to Indonesia, which promised a plebiscite. In 1969, voting by tribal chiefs favored staying with Indonesia, despite an uprising and widespread opposition.

Sukarno suspended Parliament in 1960, and was named president for life in 1963. Russian-armed Indonesian troops staged raids in 1964 and 1965 into Malaysia, whose formation Sukarno had opposed. Indonesia withdrew from the UN in 1965; anti-American demonstrations were staged.

Indonesia's popular, pro-Peking Communist party tried to seize control in 1965, killing 6 high generals. The army smashed the coup and later intimated that Sukarno had played a role in it. In parts of Java, Communists seized several districts before being defeated; over 300,000 Communists were executed.

Gen. Suharto, head of the Army, was named president for 5 years in 1968, and elected to another term in 1973. A coalition of his supporters won a strong majority in House elections in 1971, the first national vote in 16 years. Moslem opposition parties made gains in 1977 elections. The military retains a predominant political role.

In 1966 Indonesia and Malaysia signed an agreement ending hostility, and Indonesia reentered the UN. After ties with Peking were cut in 1967, there were riots against the economically important ethnic Chinese minority. Riots against Chinese and Japanese also occurred in 1974.

The former Portuguese Timor became Indonesia's 27th province in 1976. It had been seized by Indonesian troops during a local civil war. Thousands of civilians were reportedly killed by the Indonesians.

Oil export earnings, and a decline in the high birth rate, have given hope for future improvements in living conditions.

Iran

Imperial Government of Iran

People: Population (1976 est.): 33,900,000. **Age distrib.** (%): 0-14: 47.2; 15-59: 48; 60+: 4.9. **Pop. density:** 53 per sq. mi. **Urban** (1975): 44.0%. **Ethnic groups:** Iranian groups 66%, Turkish groups 25%, Kurds 5%, Arabs 4%. **Languages:** Persian, Turk, Kurdish, Arabic. **Religions:** Moslems 96% (mostly Shiites), Christians, Jews, Zoroastrians.

Geography: Area: 636,363 sq. mi. **Location:** Between the Middle East and S. Asia. **Neighbors:** Turkey, Iraq on W, USSR on N (Armenia, Azerbaijan, Turkmenistan), Afghanistan, Pakistan on E. **Topography:** Interior highlands and plains are surrounded by high mountains, up to 18,000 ft. Large salt deserts cover much of the area, but there are many oases and forest areas. Most of the population inhabits the N and NW. **Capital:** Teheran. **Cities** (1973 est.): Teheran 4,002,000; Isfahan 605,000; Mashhad 592,000; Tabriz 510,000.

Government: Head of state: Shah Mohammed Reza Pahlavi, b. Oct. 26, 1919, in office: Sept. 17, 1941; **Head of government:** Prime Min. Jamshid Amouzegar, b. 1920, in office: Aug. 7, 1977. **Local divisions:** 14 provinces, 8 governorates. **Armed forces:** regulars 300,000; reserves 300,000.

Economy: Industries: Steel, petrochemicals, cement, auto assembly, sugar refining, carpets. **Chief crops:** Grains, rice, fruits, sugar beets, cotton, grapes. **Minerals:** Oil, gas, chromite, copper, iron, lead, manganese, zinc, barite, sulphur, coal, emeralds, turquoise. **Crude oil output** (1976): 2.16 bln. bbls. Iran is 4th largest producer and 2d largest exporter. **Other resources:** Gums, wool, silk, caviar. **Per capita arable land:** 1.1 acres. **Livestock** (1976): 7,700,000 cattle; 70,000 pigs; 38,000,000 sheep. **Electricity production** (1973): 12,093 mln. kwh. **Labor force:** 42% agric.; 17% manuf.

Finance: Currency: Rial (Apr. 1977: 70.6=$1 US). **Gross domestic product** (1975): $54 bln. **Per capita income** (1974): $1,295. **Imports** (1976) $13,813 bln.; partners (1975): U.S. 20% W. Ger. 18%, Jap. 15%, U.K. 8%. **Exports** (1976): $23,526 bln.; partners (1975): Jap. 20%, Neth. 11%, U.S. 10%, W. Ger. 5%. **Tourists** (1974): 390,000; receipts; $158 million. **Balance of payments** (1975): $110 mln. **National budget** (1973): $6.53 bln. revenues; $7.34 bln. expenditures. **International reserves** (Feb. 1977): $10,142 bln. **Consumer prices** (change in 1976): 11.3%

Transport: Railway traffic (1973): 1,331 mln. passenger-miles; 2,752 mln. net ton-miles. **Motor vehicles:** in use (1972): 393,900 passenger cars, 87,600 commercial vehicles; assembled (1974): 73,000 passenger cars, 35,000 commercial vehicles. **Chief ports:** Khorramshahr, Bushehr, Bandar-e Shahpur, Bandar Abbas.

Communications: Television sets: 1,200,000 in use (1973); 242,000 manufactured (1973). **Radios:** 7,000,000 in use (1972). **Telephones in use** (1976): 688,396. **Daily newspaper circulation** (1972): 750,000; 24 per 1,000 pop.

Health: Life expectancy at birth (1970-75): 50.7 male; 51.3 female. **Births** (annual per 1,000 pop. 1970-75): 45.3. **Deaths** (annual per 1,000 pop. 1970-75): 15.6. **Natural increase** (annual 1970-75): 2.97%. **Pop. per hospital bed** (1973): 745. **Pop. per physician** (1973): 2,953. **Infant mortality** (per 1,000 pop. under 1 yr. 1973): 139.

Education: Literacy (1973): 37%. **Pop. 5-19:** in school (1973): 46%; per teacher (1973): 71.

Iran is the official name of the country long known as Persia. The Iranians, who supplanted an earlier agricultural civilization, came from the E during the 2d millenium B.C.; they were an Indo-European group related to the Aryans of India. The name Iran became widespread in the 1920s.

In 549 B.C. Cyrus the Great united the Medes and Persians in the Persian Empire, conquered Babylonia in 538 B.C, restored Jerusalem to the Jews. Alexander the Great conquered Persia in 333 B.C., but Persians regained their independence in the next century under the Parthians, themselves succeeded by Sassanian Persians in 226 A.D. Arabs brought Islam to Persia in the 7th century, replacing the indigenous Zoroastrian faith. After Persian political and cultural autonomy was reasserted in the 9th century, the arts and sciences flourished for several centuries.

Turks and Mongols ruled Persia in turn from the 11th century to 1502, when a native dynasty reasserted full independence. The British and Russian empires vied for influence in the 19th century, and Afghanistan was severed from Iran by Britain in 1857.

The current dynasty was founded by Reza Khan, a military leader, in 1925. He abdicated as shah in 1941, and was succeeded by his son, Mohammed Reza Pahlavi.

British and Russian forces entered Iran Aug. 25, 1941, withdrawing later. Britain and the USSR signed an agreement Jan. 29, 1942, to respect Iranian integrity and give economic aid. In 1946 a Soviet attempt to take over the Azerbaijan region in the NW was defeated when a puppet regime was ousted by force.

Parliament, under Premier Mohammed Mossadegh, nationalized the oil industry in 1951, leading to a British blockade. Mossadegh was overthrown in 1953. The shah assumed control, and has retained it ever since. Under his rule, Iran has undergone economic and social change, including land reform, the spread of literacy, and gains in women's rights. However, serious political opposition is not tolerated. Thousands were arrested in the 1970s, while hundreds of purported terrorists were executed.

The shah in 1954 signed an agreement with a consortium of British, U.S., Dutch and French companies. In 1973 a new agreement gave the National Iranian Oil Co. control over all operations.

In 1969-74 Iran and Iraq were involved in a dispute over Iran's right to use the Shatt al Arab, a border river estuary. Iraq acceeded to Iran's border claims in a June 13, 1975 pact. In late 1971, Iran occupied 3 islands at the mouth of the gulf, claimed by states of the United Arab Emirates. Iran in the 1970s modernized its military forces, aided by multi-billion dollar purchases from the U.S. Economic aid to Egypt, and military aid against leftist Oman rebels advanced Iran's regional status in the 1970s.

In 1974 Iran invested some of its oil wealth in a multi-billion dollar trade pact with France including nuclear energy facilities: a 25% interest in West Germany's Krupp enterprises, and a $1.2 billion loan to Britain. In 1975, Iran signed an 8-year agreement to facilitate $25 billion in purchases in the U.S., to further Iran's five-year development plan, including 8 large nuclear power plants.

The first Iranian steel mill, near Isfahan, was built by the Soviet Union and paid for by natural gas piped to the USSR.

Iraq

Republic of Iraq

People: Population (1976 est.): 11,510,000. **Age distrib.** (%): 0-14: 48.3; 15-59: 46.5; 60+: 5.3. **Pop. density:** 67 per sq. mi. **Urban** (1975): 63.7%. **Ethnic groups:** Arabs 78%, Kurds 18%, Persians 1.2%, Turks 1.2%, Assyrians 0.5%. **Languages:** Arabic (official), Kurdish, others. **Religions:** Moslems 95% (Shiites two-thirds, Sunnis one-third), Christians 3%.

Geography: Area: 172,000 sq. mi., larger than California. **Location:** In the Middle East, occupying most of historic Mesopotamia. **Neighbors:** Jordan, Syria on W, Turkey on N, Iran on E, Kuwait, Saudi Arabia on S. **Topography:** Iraq is mostly an alluvial plain, including the Tigris and Euphrates rivers, descending from mountains in N to SW of rivers is desert. Persian Gulf region is marshland. **Capital:** Baghdad. **Cities** (1974 est.): Baghdad (met.) 2,760,000; Basra 620,000; Mosul 508,500.

Government: Head of state: Pres. Ahmed Hassan al-Bakr, b. 1912, in office: July 17, 1968. **Local divisions:** 16 provinces. **Armed forces:** regulars 158,000; reserves 250,000.

Economy: Industries: Textiles, food processing, cigarettes, oil refining, cement. **Chief crops:** Grains, rice, dates, cotton, tobacco. **Minerals:** Oil, gas. **Crude oil output** (1976): 800 mln. bbls. **Other resources:** Wool, hides. **Per capita arable land:** 1.1 acres. **Livestock** (1974): 2,134,000 cattle. 15,500,000 sheep. **Electricity production** (1972): 2,358 mln. kwh. **Labor force:** 50% agric.

Finance: Currency: Dinar (Apr. 1977: 1=$3.38 US). **Gross domestic product** (1975): $13.59 bln. **Per capita income** (1974): $951. **Imports** (1976) $4.186 bln.; partners (1973): USSR 9%, U.K. 9%, Fr. 8%, Jap. 7%. **Exports** (1976): $8.854 bln.; partners (1973): It. 25%, Fr. 23%, Braz. 10%, USSR 6%. **Tourists** (1974): 544,800; receipts: $81 million. **Balance of payments** (1975): $−498. **International reserves** (Dec. 1976): $4.600 bln. **Consumer prices** (change in 1976): 10.4%.

Transport: Railway traffic (1973): 393 mln. passenger-miles; 1,060 mln. net ton-miles. **Motor vehicles:** in use (1974): 83,400 passenger cars, 59,000 commercial vehicles. **Civil aviation:** 331 mln. passenger-miles (1975); 4.7 mln. freight ton-miles (1975). **Chief port:** Basra.

Communications: Television sets: 520,000 in use (1973); 4,000 manufactured (1969). **Radios:** 1,250,000 in use (1973). **Telephones in use** (1976): 184,924. **Daily newspaper circulation** (1973): 226,000; 22 per 1,000 pop.

Health: Life expectancy at birth (1970-75): 51.2 male; 54.3 female. **Births** (annual per 1,000 pop. 1970-75): 48.1. **Deaths** (annual per 1,000 pop. 1970-75): 14.6. **Natural increase** (annual 1970-75): 3.35%. **Pop. per hospital bed** (1973): 534. **Pop. per physician** (1973): 2,525. **Infant mortality** (per 1,000 pop. under 1 yr. 1973): 27.5

Education: Literacy (1973): 26%.

Pop. 5-19: in school (1973): 42%; per teacher (1973): 52.

The Tigris-Euphrates valley, formerly called Mesopotamia, was the site of one of the earliest civilizations in the world, the first known to have used writing. The Sumerian city-states of 3,000 B.C. originated the culture later developed by the Semitic Akkadians, Babylonians, and Assyrians.

Mesopotamia ceased to be a separate political or cultural entity after the conquests of the Persians, Greeks, and Arabs. The latter founded Baghdad, from where the caliph ruled a vast empire and presided over a thriving culture in the 8th and 9th centuries.

Mongol and Turkish conquests led to a decline in population, the economy, and cultural life. The irrigation system that had supported Mesopotamian civilizations declined as well.

Britain secured a League of Nations mandate over Iraq after World War I. Independence under a king came in 1932. A leftist, pan-Arab revolution established a republic in 1958, which oriented foreign policy toward the USSR. Most industry has been nationalized, and large land holdings broken up.

A local faction of the international Baath Arab Socialist party has ruled by decree since 1968. Russia and Iraq signed an aid pact in 1972, and arms were sent along with several thousand advisers. In the 1973 Israel-Arab war Iraq sent forces to aid Syria (some units had fought Israel in 1948), but disputes with Syria persisted over sharing of river waters. Iraq has supported terrorist groups within the Palestine Liberation Org.

Several years of border clashes with Iran over navigation rights were ended in a 1975 pact conceding Iranian claims. U.S. trade and diplomatic contacts increased in the 1970s, despite suspension of diplomatic relations in 1967.

Years of battling with the Kurdish minority resulted in total defeat for the Kurds in 1975, when Iran withdrew support. Egyptian Arab immigrants have been settled in Kurdistan, and Iraq was accused in 1977 of using executions and deportations to Arabize Kurdistan.

Ireland

Irish Republic

People: Population (1976): 3,160,000. **Pop. density:** 119 per sq. mi. **Urban** (1971): 52.2%. **Ethnic groups:** Irish, Anglo-Irish minority. **Languages:** English predominates, Irish (Gaelic) spoken by minority. **Religions:** Roman Catholics 94%, Episcopalians 5%.

Geography: Area: 26,600 sq. mi. **Location:** In the Atlantic O. just W of Great Britain. **Neighbors:** United Kingdom (Northern Ireland). **Topography:** Ireland consists of a central plateau surrounded by isolated groups of hills and mountains. The coastline is heavily indented by the Atlantic O. **Capital:** Dublin. **Cities** (1971 cen.): Dublin 566,034; Cork 128,235.

Government: Head of state: Pres. Patrick Hillery, b. May 2, 1923, in office: Dec. 3, 1976; **Head of government:** Prime Min. John Lynch, b. 1917, in office: June 1977. **Local divisions:** 26 counties. **Armed forces:** regulars 14,000, reserves 22,800.

Economy: Industries: Tobacco, food processing, auto assembly, metals, textiles, chemicals, brewing, electrical and non-electrical machinery, tourism. **Chief crops:** Potatoes, grain, sugar beets, fruits, vegetables. **Minerals:** Zinc, lead, silver, gas. **Per capita arable land:** 0.9 acres. **Livestock** (1976): 5,966,000 cattle; 880,000 pigs; 2,503,000 sheep; 10,232,000 poultry. **Fish catch** (1974): 89,500 metric tons. **Labor force:** 25% agric.; 20% manuf.

Finance: Currency: Pound (Apr. 1971: 1=$1.72 US). **Gross domestic product** (1976): $7.97 bln. **Per capita income** (1975): $2,329. **Imports** (1976): $4,185 bln; partners (1974): U.K. 46%, W Ger. 8%, U.S. 6%, Fr. 5%. **Exports** (1976): $1.811 bln.; partners (1974): U.K. 56%, U.S. 9%, W Ger. 6%, Neth. 4%. **Tourists** (1974): 1,266,000; receipts: $254 million. **Balance of payments** (1975): $401 mln. **National budget** (1976): $2.80 bln. revenues; $3.69 bln. expenditures. **International reserves** (Feb. 1977): $1.813 bln. **Consumer prices** (change in 1976): 18.0%.

Transport: Railway traffic (1974): 546 mln. passenger-miles; 356 mln. net ton-miles. **Motor vehicles:** in use (1974): 492,400 passenger cars, 58,100 commercial vehicles; assembled (1976): 43,000 passenger cars, 4,200 commercial vehicles. **Civil aviation:** 924 mln. passenger-miles (1975); 44 mln. freight ton-miles (1975). **Chief ports:** Dublin, Cork.

Communications: Television sets: 532,000 licenses (1973); 84,000 manufactured (1971). **Radios:** 805,000 licenses (1973); 98,000 manufactured (1971). **Telephones in use** (1976): 444,000. **Daily newspaper circulation** (1973): 709,000; 234 per 1,000 pop.

Health: Life expectancy at birth (1965-67): 68.58 male; 72.85 female. **Births** (per 1,000 pop. 1974): 22.3. **Deaths** (per 1,000 pop. 1974): 11.2. **Natural increase** (1974): 1.11%. **Pop. per hospital bed** (1973): 82. **Pop. per physician** (1973): 842. **Infant mortality** (per 1,000 pop. under 1 yr. 1974): 17.1.

Education: Literacy (1973): 98%. **Pop. 5-19:** in school (1973): 65%; per teacher (1973): 30.

Celtic tribes invaded the islands about the 4th century B.C.; their Gaelic culture and literature flourished and spread to Scotland and elsewhere in the 5th century A.D., the same century in which St. Patrick converted the Irish to Christianity. Invasions by Norsemen began in the 8th century, but were ended with defeat of the Danes by the Irish King Brian Boru in 1014. English invasions started in the 12th century; for over 700 years the Anglo-Irish struggle continued with bitter rebellions and savage repressions.

The Easter Monday Rebellion (1916) failed but was followed by guerrilla warfare and harsh reprisals by British troops, the "Black and Tans." The Dail Eireann, or Irish parliament, reaffirmed independence in Jan. 1919. The British offered dominion status to Ulster (6 counties) and southern Ireland (26 counties) Dec. 1921. The constitution of the Irish Free State, a British dominion, was adopted Dec. 11, 1922. Northern Ireland remained part of the United Kingdom.

A new constitution adopted by plebiscite came into operation Dec. 29, 1937. It declared the name of the state Eire in the Irish language and Ireland in the English and declared it a sovereign democratic state.

On Dec. 21, 1948, an Irish law declared the country a republic rather than a dominion and withdrew it from the Commonwealth. In 1949 the British Parliament recognized both actions, but reasserted its claim to incorporate the 6 northeastern counties in the United Kingdom. This claim has not been recognized by Ireland. *See United Kingdom — Northern Ireland.*

First president was William T. Cosgrave, 1922-32. Eamon de Valera, hero of the rebellion, was president 1932-38, 1959-66, 1966-73. He was prime minister 1937-48, 1951-54, 1957-59. He died in 1975.

Following Feb. 28, 1973, elections the Fianna Fail party was ousted from power after 16 years, although it won 69 seats, by a coalition of Fine Gael, 54 seats, and Labor, 19. Independents won 2. The Fianna Fail returned to power in 1977 elections.

Irish governments have favored peaceful unification of all Ireland. Ireland cooperated with England against terrorist groups.

Emigration had been high and for years the population had remained static. Since 1961, however, emigration has decreased and steady population growth has resumed. Industrialization increased after 1962, with over 750 new factories, many with foreign participation. A mining boom has followed the discovery of zinc, lead, and silver deposits.

Although over 90% of the people profess Roman Catholicism, voters in 1972 repealed a constitutional provision giving the Church a "special position." The Irish language is a required study, but English is the native tongue of most.

Israel

State of Israel

People: Population (1976): 3,540,000. **Age distrib.** (%): 0-14: 32.9; 15-59: 55.8; 60+: 11.4. **Pop. density:** 442 per sq. mi. **Urban** (1974): 81.9%. **Ethnic groups:** Jews (half Ashkenazi, half Sephardi), Arabs, Druzes. **Languages:** Hebrew, Arabic (official), Yiddish, various European and West Asian languages. **Religions:** Jews 85%, Moslems 11%, Christians 2.5%, Druzes 1.2%.

Geography: Area: 8,017 sq. mi. (the size of Massachusetts), within 1949 armistice lines, over 30,000 sq. mi. within 1973 cease-fire lines. **Location:** On eastern end of Mediterranean Sea. **Neighbors:** Lebanon on N, Syria, Jordan on E, Egypt on

W. **Topography:** The Mediterranean coastal plain is fertile and well-watered. In the center is the Judean Plateau. A traingular-shaped semi-desert region, the Negev, extends from south of Beersheba to an apex at the head of the Gulf of Aqaba. The eastern border drops sharply into the Jordan Rift Valley, including Lake Tiberias (Sea of Galilee) and the Dead Sea, which is 1,296 ft. below sea level, lowest point on the earth's surface. **Capital:** Jerusalem. **Cities** (1974 est.): Tel Aviv-Yafo (met.) 1,156,800; Haifa (met.) 353,700; Jerusalem 344,200.

Government: Head of state: Pres. Ephraim Katzir, b. May 16, 1916, in office: Apr. 10, 1973; **Head of government:** Prime Min. Menachem Begin, b. July 31, 1913, in office: June 21, 1977. **Local divisions:** 6 administrative districts. **Armed forces:** regulars 158,500; reserves 450,000.

Economy: Industries: Diamond cutting, textiles, electronics, machinery, plastics, tires, drugs, aircraft, munitions, wine. **Chief crops:** Citrus fruit, grains, olives, fruits, grapes, figs, cotton, vegetables. **Minerals:** Limestone, gypsum, copper, iron, phosphates, magnesium, manganese, salt, sulphur, potash. **Crude oil output** (1976): 312,000 bbls. **Per capita arable land:** 0.2 acres. **Livestock** (1976): 306,000 cattle; 195,000 sheep; 14,636,000 poultry. **Fish catch** (1974): 23,800 metric tons. **Electricity production** (1976): 10,344. mln. kwh. **Labor force:** 7% agric.; 24% manuf.

Finance: Currency: Pound (Apr. 1977: 9.24=$1 US). **Gross domestic product** (1976): $12.45 bln. **Per capita income** (1975): $3,038. **Imports** (1976): $5.739 bln.; partners (1974): U.S. 18%, W. Ger. 16%, U.K. 13%, It. 5%, Neth. 5%. **Exports** (1976): $2.406 bln.; partners (1974): U.S. 16%, U.K. 9%, Neth. 8%, W. Ger. 7%. **Tourists** (1974): 569,600 (plus 124,000 to West Bank); receipts: $200 mln. **Balance of payments** (1976): $30 mln. **National budget** (1972): $2.73 bln. ravenues; $3.63 bln. expenditures. **International reserves** (Jan. 1977): $1.397 bln. **Consumer prices** (change in 1976): 31.1%.

Transport: Railway traffic (1974): 201 mln. passenger-miles; 288 mln. net ton-miles. **Motor vehicles:** in use (1974): 271,700 passenger cars, 118,800 commercial vehicles; assembled (1976): 3,900 passenger cars. **Civil aviation:** 2,616 mln. passenger-miles (1976); 82 mln. freight ton-miles (1976). **Chief ports:** Haifa, Ashdod, Eilat.

Communications: Television sets: 370,000 licenses (1972). **Radios:** 680,000 licenses (1972). **Telephones in use** (1976): 796,348.

Health: Life expectancy at birth (1974): 70.13 male; 73.27 female. **Births** (per 1,000 pop. 1975): 28.3 **Deaths** (per 1,000 pop. 1975): 7.2 **Natural increase** (1975): 2.11%. **Pop. per hospital bed** (1973): 183. **Pop. per physician** (1973): 361. **Infant mortality** (per 1,000 pop. under 1 yr. 1975): 22.0.

Education: Literacy (1973): 84%. **Pop. 5-19:** in school (1973): 60%; per teacher (1973): 21.

Occupying the SW corner of the ancient Fertile Crescent, Israel contains some of the oldest known evidence of agriculture and of primitive town life. A more advanced civilization emerged among the Semitic speaking peoples of the area in the 3d millenium B.C. The Hebrews, a nomadic people speaking a language similar to that of the earlier inhabitants, probably arrived early in the 2d millenium B.C. Under King David and his successors (c. 1000 B.C.-597 B.C.) Judaism was developed and secured.

After conquest by Babylonians, Persians, and Greeks, an independent Jewish kingdom was revived, 168 B.C., but Rome took effective control in the next century, suppressed Jewish revolts in 70 A.D. and 135 A.D., and renamed Judea Palestine, after the earlier coastal inhabitants, the Philistines.

Arab invaders conquered Palestine in 636. The Arabic language and Islam prevailed within a few centuries, but a Jewish minority always remained. The land was ruled as a part of larger empires by the Caliphate, the Mamluks, and the Ottomans (with a crusader interval, 1098-1291).

After 4 centuries of Turkish rule, during which the population declined to a low of 250,000, the land was taken in 1917 by Britain, which in the Balfour Declaration that year pledged to support a Jewish national homeland there, as foreseen by the Zionists. In 1920 a British Palestine Mandate was recognized; in 1922 the land east of the Jordan was detached.

Jewish immigration, begun in the late 19th century, swelled in the 1930s with refugees from the Nazis; heavy Arab immigration from Syria and Lebanon also occurred. Arab opposition to Jewish immigration turned violent in 1920, 1921, 1929, and 1936. The UN General Assembly voted in 1947 to partition Palestine into an Arab and a Jewish state. Britain withdrew in May 1948.

Israel was declared an independent state May 14, 1948; the Arabs rejected partition. Egypt, Jordan, Syria, Lebanon, Iraq, and Saudi Arabia invaded, but failed to destroy the Jewish state, which gained territory. Separate armistices with the Arab nations were signed in 1949; Jordan occupied the West Bank, Egypt occupied Gaza, but neither granted Palestinian autonomy. No peace settlement was obtained, and the Arab nations continued policies of economic boycott, blockade in the Suez Canal, and support of guerrillas. Several hundred thousand Arabs left the area of Jewish control; an equal number of Jews left the Arab countries for Israel 1949-53, becoming a majority of the Jewish population.

After persistent terrorist provocations, Israel invaded Egypt's Sinai, Oct. 29, 1956, aided briefly by British and French forces. A UN cease-fire was arranged Nov. 6.

An uneasy truce between Israel and the Arab countries, supervised by a UN Emergency Force, prevailed until May 19, 1967, when the UN force withdrew at the demand of Egypt's President Gamal Abdel Nasser. Egyptian forces rapidly reoccupied the Gaza Strip and closed the Gulf of Aqaba to Israeli shipping. In a full-scale 6-day war that started June 5, the Israelis took the Gaza Strip, occupied the Sinai Peninsula to the Suez Canal, and captured Old Jerusalem, Syria's Golan Heights, and Jordan's West Bank. The fighting was halted June 10 by UN-arranged cease-fire agreements. The USSR and its satellites broke relations with Israel in 1967.

By 1969-70 there were almost daily Egyptian-Israeli artillery duels across the Suez Canal as well as ground forays and air raids with Israeli planes penetrating deep into Egypt. Palestinian guerrilla raids and Israeli reprisals continued across the Jordanian, Syrian, and Lebanese frontiers; there were also encounters with Syrian and Jordanian forces.

It was est. in 1970 there were 10,000 or more Soviet military men in Egypt, and increasing supplies of Soviet planes and anti-aircraft missiles, some of which Israel charged were manned by Russians. In July 1972 most of the Russians, then est. at 20,000, were sent home by Egypt.

In June 1970 the U.S. proposed a 3-month, standstill cease-fire and peace negotiations, Israel, Egypt, and Jordan agreed. Terrorist attacks continued in 1972-73 and Israel made reprisal raids in Lebanon and Syria.

Egypt and Syria attacked Israel, Oct. 6, 1973 (Yom Kippur, most solemn day on the Jewish calendar). Egypt and Syria were supplied by massive USSR military airlifts; the U.S. responded with an airlift to Israel. Israel counter-attacked, driving the Syrians back, and crossing the Suez Canal.

Israel and Egypt agreed to a UN cease-fire which took effect Oct. 24; a UN peace-keeping force went to the area. A disengagement agreement was signed Jan. 18, 1974, following negotiations by U.S. Secretary of State Henry Kissinger. Israel withdrew from the canal's W bank. A second withdrawal was completed in 1976; Israel yielded additional Sinai territory including an oil field. Some 200 unarmed American technicians were stationed to monitor the cease-fire. The U.S. agreed to provide substantial arms aid to Israel.

Israel and Syria agreed to disengage June 1; Israel completed withdrawing from its salient (and a small part of the land taken in the 1967 war) June 25. Nearly all black African nations broke relations with Israel in 1972-74, reportedly at the urging of Libya, despite Israel's technical aid programs.

In the wake of the war, Golda Meir, long Israel's premier, resigned; severe inflation gripped the nation. Palestinian guerrillas staged massacres, killing scores of civilians 1974-75. Israel conducted preventive attacks in Lebanon through 1975. Israel aided Christian forces in the 1975-76 Lebanese civil war. By mid-1974 the USSR had replenished arms and equipment lost by Syria in 1973.

Israeli forces raided Entebbe, Uganda, July 3, 1976, and rescued 103 hostages seized by Arab and German terrorists.

In 1977, the conservative opposition, led by Menachem Begin, was voted into office for the first time.

Israel's economy has grown rapidly, aided by German reparations payments, U.S. aid (mostly since 1970), international loans, and contributions. In 1975, Israel signed agreements with the U.S. to facilitate investments in Israel, and with the Common Market allowing free trade.

Since 1955 total cultivated area has more than doubled, mostly through irrigation. A pipeline was completed in 1964 to carry water from Lake Kinneret (Galilee) to the Negev desert. Desalinization plants have been built.

Israel's first atomic reactor began operations in 1960. The nation launched its first successful solid-fuel rocket in 1961. Israel has denied reports that it has assembled 10-20 atom bombs.

Non-Jewish population (1974): Moslem 392,500; Christian 84,500; Druzes and others 41,600. The last remnant of martial law for the Arab minority was ended in 1966. Druzes are subject to the military draft; Moslems and Christians may volunteer.

Italy

Italian Republic

People: Population (1976): 56,190,000. **Age distrib.** (%): 0-14: 24.3; 15-59: 59.6; 60+: 16.1. **Pop. density:** 483 per sq. mi. **Ethnic groups:** Italians, small minorities of Germans, Slovenes, Albanians, French, Ladins, Greeks. **Languages:** Italian. **Religions:** Roman Catholics 99%.

Geography: Area: 116,303 sq. mi., slightly larger than Arizona. **Location:** In S Europe, jutting into Mediterranean Sea. **Neighbors:** France on W, Switzerland, Austria on N, Yugoslavia on E. **Topography:** Italy occupies a long boot-shaped peninsula, extending SE from the Alps into the Mediterranean, with the islands of Sicily and Sardinia offshore. The alluvial Poe Valley drains most of N. The rest of the country is rugged and mountainous, except for intermittent coastal plains, like the Campajna, S of Rome. Appenine Mts. run down through center of peninsula. **Capital:** Rome. **Cities** (1975 est.): Rome 2,868,248; Milan 1,731,281; Naples 1,223,785; Turin 1,202,215; Genoa 805,855; Palermo 662,567; Bologna 491,330; Florence 465,823; Catania 398,642; Venice 365,208.

Government: Head of state: Pres. Giovanni Leone, b. Nov. 3, 1908, in office: Dec. 24, 1971; **Head of government:** Prime Min. Giulio Andreotti, b. Jan. 14, 1919, in office: July 29, 1976. **local divisions:** 20 regions with some autonomy, 94 provinces. **Armed forces:** regulars 352,000; reserves 737,800.

Economy: Industries: Steel, machinery, autos, textiles, shoes, machine tools, chemicals, oil products, typewriters. **Chief crops:** Grapes, olives, citrus fruits, vegetables, wheat, rice. **Minerals:** Gas, marble, sulphur, mercury, coal. **Crude oil output** (1976): 7.6 mln. bbls. **Per capita arable land:** 0.4 acres. **Livestock** (1976): 8,888,000 cattle; 8,888,000 pigs; 8,050,000 sheep; 110,000,000 poultry. **Fish catch** (1975): 406,000 metric tons. **Electricity production** (1976): 160,560 mln. kwh. **Labor force:** 15% agric.; 31% manuf.

Finance: Currency: Lire (Apr. 1977: 887=$1 US). **Gross domestic product** (1976): $171 bln. **Per capita income** (1975): $2,759. **Imports** (1976) $43.423 bln.; partners (1974): W. Ger. 18%, Fr. 13%, U.S. 8%, Saudi Ar. 7%. **Exports** (1976): $36.960 bln.; partners (1974): W. Ger. 18%, Fr. 13%, U.S. 8%, U.K. 5%. **Tourists** (1974): 12,441,700; receipts: $2.668 billion. **Balance of payments** (1976): $−21 mln. **National budget** (1976): $38.59 bln. revenues; $51.22 bln. expenditures. **International reserves** (Feb. 1977): $6.470 bln. **Consumer prices** (change in 1976): 15.7%.

Transport: Railway traffic (1974): 23,523 mln. passenger-miles; 11,268 mln. net ton-miles. **Motor vehicles:** in use (1974): 14,295,000 passenger cars, 1,549,000 commercial vehicles; manufactured (1976): 1,476 passenger cars, 119,000 commercial vehicles. **Civil aviation:** 6,692 mln. passenger-miles (1976); 267 mln. freight ton-miles (1975). **Chief ports:** Genoa, Venice, Trieste, Taranto, Naples, La Spezia.

Communciations: Television sets: 11,426,000 licenses (1973); 2,330,000 manufactured (1974). **Radios:** 12,448,000 licenses (1973); 1,800,000 manufactured (1974). **Telephones in use** (1976): 14,495,677. **Daily newspaper circulation** (1973): 6,604,000; 120 per 1,000 pop.

Health: Life expectancy at birth (1970-72): 68.97 male; 74.88 female. **Births** (per 1,000 pop. 1974): 15.7. **Deaths** (per 1,000 pop. (1974): 9.5 **Natural increase** (1974): 0.62%. **Pop. per hospital bed** (1973): 96. **Pop. per physician** (1973): 527. **Infant mortality** (per 1,000 pop. under 1 yr. 1974): 22.6.

Education: Literacy (1973): 93%. **Pop. 5-19:** in school (1973): 64%; per teacher (1973): 25.

Rome emerged as the major power in Italy after 500 B.C., dominating the more civilized Etruscans to the N and Greeks to the S. Under the Empire, which lasted until the 5th century A.D., Rome ruled most of Western Europe, the Balkans, the Near East, and North Africa.

After the Germanic invasions, lasting several centuries, a high civilization arose in the city-states of the N, culminating in the Renaissance. But German, French, Spanish, and Austrian intervention prevented the unification of the country. In 1859 Lombardy came under the crown of King Victor Emmanuel II of Sardinia. By plebiscite in 1860, Parma, Modena, Romagna, and Tuscany joined, followed by Sicily and Naples, and by the Marches and Umbria. The first Italian parliament declared Victor Emmanuel king of Italy Mar. 17, 1861. Mantua and Venetia were added in 1866 as an outcome of the Austro-Prussian war. The Papal States were taken by Italian troops Sept. 20, 1870, on the withdrawal of the French garrison. The states were annexed to the kingdom by plebiscite. Italy recognized the State of Vatican City as independent Feb. 11, 1929.

Fascism appeared in Italy Mar. 23, 1919, led by Benito Mussolini, who took over the government at the invitation of the king Oct. 28, 1922. Mussolini acquired dictatorial powers and was called duce (leader). He made war on Ethiopia and proclaimed Victor Emmanuel III emperor, defied the sanctions of the League of Nations, joined the Berlin-Tokyo axis, sent troops to fight for Franco against the Republic of Spain and joined Germany in World War II.

After Fascism was overthrown in 1943, Italy declared war on Germany and Japan and contributed to the Allied victory. It surrendered conquered lands and lost its colonies. Mussolini was killed by partisans Apr. 28, 1945.

Victor Emmanuel III abdicated May 9, 1946; his son Humbert II was king until June 10, when Italy became a republic after a referendum, June 2-3.

Reorganization of the Fascist party is forbidden. The cabinet normally represents a coalition of the Christian Democrats, largest of Italy's many parties, and one or 2 other parties. After June 1976 elections, the Communists were given several important parliamentary posts, and entered into a formal cooperation with the Christian Democrats and other parties in parliament, without entering the government. They also controlled many local and regional governments, alone or in coalition with the Socialists.

The Vatican agreed in 1976 to revise its 1929 concordat with the state, depriving Roman Catholicism of its status as state religion. In 1974 Italians voted by a 3-to-2 margin to retain a 3-year-old law permitting divorce, which was opposed by the church.

Italy has enjoyed an extraordinary growth in industry and living standards since World War II, in part due to membership in the Common Market. But in 1973-74, a fourfold increase in international oil prices helped disrupt the economy. Taxes were boosted in 1974. Western aid helped ease the crisis in 1975, but inflation and decline in confidence continued through 1977. Trade unions agreed to some austerity measures. A wave of left- and right-wing political violence worsened in 1977.

Sicily, 9,927 sq. mi., pop. (1971) 4,680,715, is an island 180 by 120 mi., seat of a region that embraces the island of **Pantelleria,** 32 sq. mi., and the **Lipari** group, 44 sq. mi., pop. 14,000, including 2 active volcanoes: **Vulcano,** 1,637 ft. and **Stromboli,** 3,038 ft. From prehistoric times Sicily has been settled by various peoples; a Greek state had its capital at Syracuse. Rome took Sicily from Carthage 215 B.C. **Mt. Etna,** 10,705 ft. active volcano, is tallest peak.

Sardinia, 9,283 sq. mi., pop. (1971) 1,473,800, lies in the Mediterranean, 115 mi. W of Italy and 7-1/2 mi. S of Corsica. It is 160 mi. long, 68 mi. wide, and mountainous, with mining of coal, zinc, lead, copper. In 1720 Sardinia was added to the possessions of the Dukes of Savoy in Piedmont and Savoy to form the Kingdom of Sardinia. Giuseppe Garibaldi is buried on the nearby isle of Caprera.

Elba, 87 sq. mi., pop. 30,000, lies 6 mi. west of Tuscany. Napoleon I lived in exile on Elba 1814-1815.

Trieste. An agreement was signed Oct. 5, 1954, by Italy and Yugoslavia which gave Italy provisional administration over the northern section and the seaport of Trieste, and Yugoslavia the part of Istrian peninsula it had occupied and provision for emergency access to the port. A formal agreement signed Nov. 10, 1975, confirmed this division as permanent.

Ivory Coast

Republic of Ivory Coast

People: Population (1976 est.): 5,020,000. **Pop. density:** 40 per sq. mi. **Ethnic groups:** Baule 23%, Bete 18%, Senufo 15%, Malinke 11%, others. **Languages:** French (official), tribal languages. **Religions:** Moslems 25%, Christians 12%.

Geography: Area: 124,503 sq. mi., slightly larger than New Mexico. **Location:** On S coast of W. Africa. **Neighbors:** Liberia,

Guinea on W, Mali, Upper Volta on N, Ghana on E. **Topography:** Forests cover the W half of the country, and range from a coastal strip to halfway to the N on the E. A sparse inland plains leads to low mountains in NW. **Capital:** Abidjan. **Cities** (1974 est.): Abidjan (met.) 800,000; Bouake/accent (met.) 200,000.

Government: Head of state: Pres. Felix Houphouet-Boigny, b. Oct. 18, 1905, in office: 1960. **Local divisions:** 25 departments. **Armed forces:** regulars 4,100; para-military 2,800.

Economy: Chief crops: Coffee, cocoa, bananas, cotton, pineapples, rice, oil palms. **Minerals:** Diamonds, manganese. **Other resources:** Tropical woods, rubber. **Per capita arable land:** 3.9 acres. **Livestock** (1974): 480,000 cattle; 195,000 pigs; 950,000 sheep. **Fish catch** (1974): 69,300 metric tons. **Electricity production** (1975): 864 mln. kwh. **Labor force:** 81% agric.

Finance: Currency: CFA franc (Apr. 1977: 248=$1 US). **Gross domestic product** (1975): $3.80 bln. **Per capita income** (1974): $600. **Imports** (1976) $1.296 bln.; partners (1974): Fr. 39%, U.S. 7%, W. Ger. 6%, Iraq 6%. **Exports** (1976): $1.631 bln.; partners (1974): Fr. 26%, Neth. 15%, It. 9%, W. Ger. 9%. **Tourists** (1974): 86,400; receipts (1973): $11 million. **Balance of payments** (1976): $-33 mln. **International reserves** (Jan. 1977): $87 mln. **Consumer prices** (change in 1976): 12.1%.

Transport: Railway traffic (1974): 570 mln. passenger-miles; 329 mln. net ton-miles. **Motor vehicles:** in use (1972): 90,500 passenger cars, 57,400 commercial vehicles. **Chief ports:** Abidjan, Sassandrao.

Communications: Television sets: 40,000 in use (1972). **Radios:** 80,000 in use (1972); 90,000 manufactured (1974). **Telephones in use** (1976): 58,699. **Daily newspaper circulation** (1973): 44,000; 10 per 1,000 pop.

Health: Life expectancy at birth (1970-75): 41.9 male; 45.1 female. **Births** (annual per 1,000 pop. 1970-75): 45.6. **Deaths** (annual per 1,000 pop. 1970-75): 20.6. **Natural increase** (annual 1970-75): 2.50%. **Pop. per hospital bed** (1973): 499. **Pop. per physician** (1973): 13,257. **Infant mortality** (per 1,000 pop. under 1 yr. 1957-58): 138.

Education: Literacy (1973): 20%. **Pop. 5-19:** in school (1973): 39%; per teacher (1973): 110.

Independent of France since 1960, Ivory Coast is the most prosperous of tropical African nations, due to diversification of agriculture for export, close ties to France, and encouragement of foreign investment. About 20% of the population are workers from neighboring countries.

Jamaica

People: Population (1976 est.): 2,060,000. Age distrib. **(%): 0-14: 45.9; 15-59: 45.7; 60+: 8.4.** Pop. density: **467 per sq. mi. urban** (1970): 37.1%. **Ethnic groups:** Negroes 85%, mixed 10%, Chinese, Caucasians, East Indians. **Languages:** English, Jamaican creole. **Religions:** Protestants 75%, Roman Catholics 5%.

Geography: Area: 4,411 sq. mi., slightly smaller than Connecticut. **Location:** In West Indies. **Neighbors:** Nearest are Cuba on N, Haiti on E. **Topography:** The country is four-fifths covered by mountains. **Capital:** Kingston. **Cities** (1970 cen.): Kingston (met.) 475,548.

Government: Head of state: Queen Elizabeth II, represented by Gov.-Gen. Florizel A. Glasspole; **Head of government:** Prime Min. Michael Manley, in office: Mar. 2, 1972. **Local divisions:** 12 parishes and Kingston. **Economy: Industries:** Aluminum, rum, molasses, cigars, oil products, tourism. **Chief crops:** Sugar cane, coffee, bananas, coconuts, ginger, cocoa, pimento, fruits. **Minerals:** Bauxite, marble, silica, gypsum. **Per capita arable land:** 0.3 acres. **Livestock** (1974): 275,000 cattle; 221,000 pigs; 378,000 goats; 3,600,000 poultry. **Fish catch** (1974): 10,100 metric tons. **Electricity production** (1975): 2,328 mln. kwh. **Labor force:** 27% agric.

Finance: Currency: Dollar (Apr. 1977: 1 = $1.1 US). **Gross domestic product (1975);** $2.92 bln. **Per capita income** (1975): $1,273. **Imports** (1976) $936 mln.; partners (1974); U.S. 35%, Venez. 15%, U.K. 12%, Can. 5%. **Exports** (1976): $602 mln.; partners (1974): U.S. 46%, U.K. 15%, Nor. 12%, Can. 5%. **Tourists** (1974): 535,800; receipts: $133 million. **Balance of payments** (1976): $-271.2 bln. **National budget** (1976): $677.9 mln. revenues; $1.113 bln. expenditures. **International reserves** (Feb. 1977): $41.6 mln. **Consumer prices** (change in 1976): 9.9%.

Transport: Railway traffic (1973): 38 mln. passenger-miles; 97 mln. net ton-miles. **Motor vehicles:** in use (1972): 86,400 passenger cars, 21,900 commercial vehicles. **Chief ports:** Kingston, Montego Bay.

Communications: Television sets: 100,000 in use (1975), 7,000 manufactured (1974). **Radios:** 633,000 in use (1973); 10,000 manufactured (1974). **Telephones in use** (1976): 100,000. **Daily newspaper circulation** (1973): 180,000; 91 per 1,000 pop.

Health: Life expectancy at birth (1959-61): 62.65 male; 66.63 female. **Births** (per 1,000 pop. 1974): 30.8 **Deaths** (per 1,000 pop. 1974): 7.2 **Natural increase** (1974): 2.36%. **Pop. per hospital bed** (1973): 241. **Pop. per physician** (1973): 2,750. **Infant mortality** (per 1,000 pop. under 1 yr. 1974): 26.3.

Education: Literacy (1973): 86%. **Pop. 5-19:** in school (1973): 61%; per teacher (1973): 60.

Jamaica was visited by Columbus, 1494, and ruled by Spain (under whom Arawak Indians died out) until seized by Britain, 1655. Jamaica won independence Aug. 6, 1962.

In 1974 Jamaica sought an increase in taxes paid by U.S. and Canadian companies which mine bauxite on the island. The socialist government acquired 50% ownership of the companies' Jamaican interests in 1976, and was reelected that year. Political violence flared 1975-76.

Japan

People: Population (1976): 112,770,000. **Age distrib.** (%): 0-14: 24.3; 15-59: 64.4; 60+: 11.3. **Pop. density:** 785 per sq. mi. **Urban** (1970): 72.1%. **Ethnic groups:** Japanese 99.4%, Korean 0.5%. **Religions:** Buddhism, Shintoism shared by large majority, Christians 0.8%.

Geography: Area: 143,574 sq. mi., slightly smaller than Montana. **Location:** Archipelago off E coast of Asia. **Neighbors:** nearest are USSR on N, S. Korea on W. **Topography:** Japan consists of four main islands: Honshu ("mainland"), 88,952 sq. mi.; Hokkaido, 30,304; Kyushu, 16,191; and Shikoku, 7,240. The coast is deeply indented, measuring 16,654 mi. The northern islands are a continuation of the Sakhalin Mts. The Kunlun range of China continues into southern islands, the ranges meeting in the Japanese Alps. In a vast transverse fissure crossing Honshu E-W rises a group of volcanoes, mostly extinct or inactive, including 12,388 ft. Fuji-San (Fujiyama) near Tokyo. **Capital:** Tokyo. **Cities** (1975 cen.): Tokyo 11,622,651; Osaka 2,780,000; Yokohama 2,620,000; Nagoya 2,080,000; Kyoto 1,460,000; Kobe 1,360,000; Sapporo 1,240,000; Kitakyushu 1,060,000; Kawasaki 1,020,000; Fukuoka 1,000,000; Hiroshima 761,240; Sakai 716,498; Chiba 613,787.

Government: Head of state: Emp. Hirohito, b. Apr. 29, 1901, in office: Dec. 25, 1926; **Head of government:** Prime Min. Takeo Fukuda, b. Jan. 14, 1905, in office: Dec. 23, 1976. **Local divisions:** 47 prefectures. **Armed forces:** regulars 235,000; reserves 39,600.

Economy: Industries: Steel, vehicles, machinery, ships, electronics, precision instruments, chemicals, textiles, ceramics, wood products. **Chief crops:** Rice, grains, potatoes, tobacco, tea, beans, fruits. **Minerals:** Some gold, silver, copper, lead, zinc, chromite, coal, sulphur, salt, oil, but most minerals are imported. **Crude oil output** (1976): 4.9 mln. bbls. **Per capita arable land:** 0.1 acres. **Livestock** (1976): 3,690,000 cattle; 7,955,000 pigs; 11,000 sheep; 258,790,000 poultry. **Fish catch** (1975): 10,508,000 metric tons, largest in world. **Electricity production** (1975): 475,800 mln. kwh. **Labor force:** 19% agric.; 26% manuf.

Finance: Currency: Yen (Apr. 1977: 278=$1 US). **Gross domestic product** (1976): $555 bln. **Per capita income** (1975): $4,038. **Imports** (1976): $64,748 bln.; partners (1974): U.S. 20%, Saudi Ar. 8%, Iran 8%, Indonesia 7%, Australia 6%, Can. 4%. **Exports** (1976): $67,167 bln.; partners (1974): U.S. 23%, S. Kor. 5%, Taiwan 4%, Australia 4%, P.R. China 4%. **Tourists** (excluding excursionists) (1974): 764,200; receipts: $236 million. **Balance of payments** (1976): $3.80 bln. **National budget** (1976): $45.22 bln. revenues; $56.31 bln. expenditures. **International reserves** (Feb. 1977): $17.052 bln. **Consumer prices** (change in 1976): 9.7%.

Transport: Railway traffic (1974): 201,614 mln. passenger-miles; 33,836 mln. net ton-miles. **Motor vehicles:** in use (1974): 15,852,200 passenger cars, 10,497,100 commercial vehicles; manufactured (1976): 5,028,000 passenger cars, 2,556,000 commercial vehicles. **Civil aviation:** 11,871 mln. passenger-miles (1976); 582 mln. freight ton-miles (1976). **Chief ports:** Yokohama, Tokyo, Kobe, Osaka, Nagoya, Chiba, Kawasaki, Hakodate.

Communications: Television sets: 24,797,000 in use (1973); 13,406,000 manufactured (1974). **Radios:** 70,794,000 in use (1972); 18,026,000 manufactured (1974). **Telephones in use** (1976): 45,514,709. **Daily newspaper circulation** (1973): 58,181,000; 537 per 1,000 pop.

Health: Life expectancy at birth (1974): 71.16 male; 76.31 female. **Births** (per 1,000 pop. 1974): 18.6. **Deaths** (per 1,000 pop. 1974): 6.5. **Natural increase** (1974): 1.21%. **Pop. per hospital bed** (1973): 97. **Pop. per physician** (1973): 864. **Infant mortality** (per 1,000 pop. under 1 yr. 1974): 10.8.

Education: Literacy (1973): 99%. **Pop. 5-19:** in school (1973): 70%; per teacher (1973): 30.

The World Almanac is sponsored in Japan by the Mainichi Newspapers. 1-1 Hitotsubashi, Chiyoda-ku, Tokyo 100; phone 03-212-0321. Mainichi founded 1876, Osaka, Japan; circulation 5,174,156 (m), 2,634,758 (e). (Mainichi Daily News, English Language 45,513); president Toshio Hiraoka; vice president, executive editor Jibei Inano.

According to Japanese legend, the empire was founded by Emperor Jimmu, 660 B.C., but earliest records of a unified Japan date from 1,000 years later. Chinese influence was strong in the formation of Japanese civilization. Buddhism was introduced before the 6th century.

A feudal system, with locally powerful noble families and their samurai warrior retainers, dominated Japan from 1192. Central power was held by successive families of shoguns (military dictators), 1192-1867, until recovered by the Emperor Meiji in 1868. The Portuguese and Dutch had minor trade with Japan in the 16th and 17th centuries. U.S. Commodore Matthew C. Perry opened it to U.S. trade in a treaty ratified 1854. Japan fought China, 1894-95, gaining Taiwan. In war with Russia, 1904-05, Russia's fleet was wiped out at Tsushima; Russia ceded S half of Sakhalin and gave concessions in China. Japan annexed Korea 1910. In World War I Japan ousted Germany from Shantung, took over German Pacific islands as mandates from the League of Nations. Japan took Manchuria 1931, started war with China 1932. Japan launched war against the U.S. by attack on Pearl Harbor Dec. 7, 1941. Japan surrendered Aug. 14, 1945.

In a new constitution adopted May 3, 1947, Japan renounced the right to wage war; the emperor was acknowledged as hereditary symbol of the nation, but gave up claims to divinity; the Diet became the sole law-making authority.

The U.S. and 48 other non-communist nations signed a peace treaty and the U.S. a bilateral defense agreement with Japan, in San Francisco Sept. 8, 1951, restoring Japan's sovereignty as of April 28, 1952. Under the treaty, Japan was reduced territorially to the 4 main islands, but it was to have an opportunity eventually to regain the Ryukyu and Bonin Islands. Japan signed separate treaties with Nationalist China, 1952; India, 1952; a declaration with USSR ending a technical state of war, 1956. In Dec. 1965 Japan and South Korea agreed to resume diplomatic relations.

On June 26, 1968, the U.S. returned to Japanese control the Bonin Islands, the Volcano Islands (including Iwo Jima) and Marcus Island. On May 15, 1972, Okinawa, the other Ryukyu Islands and the Daito Islands were returned to Japan by the U.S., but it was agreed the U.S. would continue to maintain large military bases on Okinawa. Japan and the USSR have failed to resolve disputed claims of sovereignty over four of the Kurile Is.

On Sept. 29, 1972, Japan and mainland China agreed to resume diplomatic relations; Japan and Taiwan severed relations.

Industrialization was begun in the late 19th century. After World War II, Japan emerged as the third most powerful economy in the world, and as a leader in technology.

The Liberal Democratic (conservative) party controlled almost every post-war government, but by declining margins. The opposition, composed of Socialists, the Komeito (a Buddhist party), Communists, and independents, won nearly half the seats in 1976 parliamentary elections.

During 1969 the U.S. began turning over 50 military installation sites, a third of its facilities in Japan, to the Japanese. By 1977, U.S. forces had been reduced to 46,000 men and women.

Jordan

Hashemite Kingdom of Jordan

People: Population (1976 est.): 2,780,000. **Age distrib.** (%): 0-14: 47.5; 15-59: 47.5; 60+: 5.0 **Pop. density:** 75 per sq. mi. **Urban** (1974): 42.0%. **Ethnic groups:** Arabs, small minorities of Circassians, Armenians, Kurds. **Languages:** Arabic is universal. **Religions:** Sunni Moslems 93.6%, Christians 6.4%.

Geography: Area: 37,297 sq. mi., slightly larger than Indiana. **Location:** In W Asia. **Neighbors:** Israel on W, Saudi Arabia on S, Iraq on E, Syria on N. **Topography:** About 88% of Jordan is arid. Fertile areas are in W. Only port is on short Aqaba Gulf coast. Country shares Dead Sea (1,296 ft. below sea level) with Israel. **Capital:** Amman. **Cities** (1974 est.): Amman 598,000; Zarba 226,000.

Government: Head of state: King Hussein I, b. Nov. 14, 1935, in office: May 2, 1952; **Head of government:** Prime Min. Zaid al-Rifai, in office: May 26, 1973. **Local divisions:** 8 governorates. **Armed forces:** regulars 67,900; reserves 30,000.

Economy: Industries: Textiles, plastics, cement, food-processing. **Chief crops:** Grains, olives, vegetables, fruits. **Minerals:** Potash, phosphates. **Per capita arable land:** 1.0 acres. **Livestock** (1974): 47,000 cattle; 792,000 sheep. **Electricity production** (1973): 281 mln. kwh. **Labor force:** 39% agric.

Finance: Currency: Dinar (Apr. 1977: 1=$3.03 US). **Gross domestic product** (1975): $1.08 bln. **Per capita income** (1974): $432. **Imports** (1976) $925 mln.; partners (1974): U.S. 11%, W. Ger. 9%, UK 8%, Leb. 5%. **Exports** (1976): $207 mln.; partners (1974): India 13%, Saudi 11%, Leb. 8%, Jap. 8%. **Tourists** (1974): 554,900; receipts: $54 million. **Balance of payments** (1976): $32.5 mln. **National budget** (1976): $334 mln. revenues; $676 mln. expenditures. **International reserves** (Feb. 1977): $531.1 mln. **Consumer prices** (change in 1976): 15.1%.

Transport: Motor vehicles: in use (1974): 26,300 passenger cars, 7,000 commercial vehicles. **Civil aviation:** 442 mln. passenger-miles (1975); 8.4 mln. freight ton-miles (1975). **Chief ports:** Aqaba.

Communications: Television sets: 80,000 licenses (1973). **Radios:** 521,000 licenses (1973). **Daily newspaper circulation** (1973): 48,000; 19 per 1,000 pop.

Health: Life expectancy at birth (1959-63): 52.6 male; 52.0 female. **Births** (annual per 1,000 pop. 1970-75): 47.6. **Deaths** (annual per 1,000 pop. 1970-75): 14.7. **Natural increase** (annual 1970-75): 3.29%. **Pop. per hospital bed** (1973): 706. **Pop. per physician** (1973): 2,822. **Infant mortality** (per 1,000 pop. under 1 yr. 1974): 21.9.

Education: Literacy (1973): 32%. **Pop. 5-19:** in school (1973): 60%; per teacher (1973): 53.

From ancient times to 1922 the lands to the E of the Jordan were culturally and politically united with the lands to the W. Arabs conquered the area in the 7th century; the Ottomans took control in the 16th. Britain's 1920 Palestine Mandate covered both sides of the Jordan. In 1921, Abdullah, son of the ruler of Hejaz in Arabia, was recognized by Britain as amir of an autonomous Transjordan, covering two-thirds of Palestine. An independent kingdom was proclaimed, 1946.

During the 1948 Arab-Israeli war the West Bank and old city of Jerusalem were added to the kingdom, which changed its name to Jordan. All these territories were lost to Israel in the 1967 war, which swelled the number of Arab refugees on the East Bank. A 1974 Arab summit conference designated the Palestine Liberation Organization as the sole representative of Arabs on the West Bank. Jordan accepted the move, and was granted an annual subsidy by Arab oil states. The U.S. has also provided substantial economic and military support.

In 1970 and 1971, Jordan dispersed all PLO commandos, who had raided Israel from bases in Jordan, 1968-70, and who threatened to seize power in Jordan, which they considered part of Palestine.

Kampuchea

Democratic Kampuchea

People: Population (1976 est.): 8,350,000. **Pop. density:** 119 per sq. mi. **Ethnic groups:** Khmers 90%, Vietnamese 4%, Chinese 3%. **Languages:** Cambodian (Khmer), French. **Religions:** Buddhism prevails.

Geography: Area: 69,898 sq. mi., the size of Missouri. **Location:** In Indochina Peninsula. **Neighbors:** Thailand on W, N, Laos on NE, Vietnam on E. **Topography:** The central area, formed by the Mekong River basin and Tonle Sap lake, is level. Hills and mountains are in SE, a long escarpment separates the country from Thailand on NW. Three-fourths of the area is forested. **Capital:** Phnom Penh. **Cities** (1971 est.): Phnom Penh 393,995.

Government: Head of state: Pres. Khieu Samphan, in office: Apr. 14, 1976; **Armed forces:** regulars 80,000.

Economy: Industries Textiles, paper, plywood, oil products. **chief crops:** Rice, corn, pepper, tobacco, cotton, oil seeds, beans, palm sugar. **Minerals:** Iron, copper, manganese, gold. **Other resources:** Forests, rubber, kapok. **Per capita arable land:** 0.5 acres. **Livestock** (1974): 1,800,000 cattle; 950,000 sheep. **Fish catch** (1974): 84,700 metric tons. **Electricity production** (1973): 150 mln. kwh.

Finance: Currency: Riel (1974: 970=$1 US). **Per capita income** (1974): $100. **Imports** (1971) $78 mln. **Exports** (1972): $15 mln. **Tourists** (1973): 16,500; receipts: $2 million.

Transport: Railway traffic (1973): 34-mln. passenger-miles; 6 mln. net ton-miles. **Motor vehicles:** in use: 27,200 passenger cars (1972), 11,000 commercial vehicles (1973). **Chief ports:** Kompong Som.

Communications: Television sets: 26,000 in use (1973). **Radios:** 1,110,000 in use (1973). **Daily newspaper circulation** (1970): 70,000; 10 per 1,000 pop.

Health: Life expectancy at birth (1970-75): 44.0 male; 46.9 female. **Births** (annual per 1,000 pop. 1970-75): 46.7. **Deaths** (annual per 1,000 pop. 1970-75): 19.0. **Natural increase** (annual 1970-75): 2.77%. **Pop. per hospital bed** (1973): 992. **Pop. per physician** (1973): 16,978. **Infant mortality** (per 1,000 pop. under 1 yr. 1973): 127.

Education: Literacy (1973): 59%. **Pop. 5-19:** in school (1973): 40%; per teacher (1973): 145.

Early kingdoms dating from that of Funan in the 1st century A.D. (heavily influenced by Indian culture), culminated in the great Khmer empire which flourished from the 9th century to the 13th, encompassing present-day Thailand, Cambodia, Laos, and southern Vietnam. The peripheral areas were lost to invading Siamese and Vietnamese, and France established a protectorate in 1863. A 1947 constitution modified the monarchy, and independence came in 1953.

Prince Norodom Sihanouk, king 1941-1955 and head of state from 1960, tried to maintain neutrality. Relations with the U.S. were broken in 1965, after South Vietnam planes attacked Vietcong forces within Cambodia. Relations were restored in 1969, after Sihanouk, charged Viet communists with arming Cambodian insurgents.

U.S. bombing raids on North Viet forces, 1969-70, were not revealed until 1973. In 1970, pro-U.S. premier Lon Nol seized power, demanding removal of 40,000 North Viet troops. The monarchy was abolished and the country's name changed to Khmer Republic. Sihanouk formed a government-in-exile in Peking.

The U.S. provided heavy military and economic aid. U.S. troops fought Vietcong forces within Cambodia for two months in 1970.

Khmer Rouge forces captured Phnom Penh April 17, 1975. Over 100,000 people had died in five years of fighting. Sihanouk was renamed head of state, but resigned in 1976. The new government evacuated all cities and towns, and shuffled the rural population, sending virtually the entire population to clear jungle, forest, and scrub, which covered half the country.

The government guarded its international isolation, but repeated reports from refugees indicated that over one million people were killed in executions and enforced hardships.

Relations with Thailand have been strained. China provides some assistance.

Kenya

Republic of Kenya

People: Population (1976 est.): 13,850,000. **Age distrib.** (%): 0-14: 48.4; 15-59: 46.3; 60+: 5.4. **Pop. density:** 62 per sq. mi. **Urban** (1969): 9.9%. **Ethnic groups:** Kikuyu 20%, Tuo 15%, Balhya 13%, Kamba 11%, others, including 280,000 Asians, Arabs, Europeans. **Languages:** Swahili, English both official. **Religions:** Protestants 37%, Roman Catholics 22%, Moslems 3%, others.

Geography: Area: 224,960 sq. mi., slightly smaller than Texas. **Location:** On Indian O. coast of E. Africa. **Neighbors:** Uganda on W, Tanzania on S, Somalia on E, Ethopia, Sudan on N. **Topography:** The northern three-fifths of Kenya is arid. Most economic production is centered in S, a low coastal area and a plateau varying from 3,000 to 10,000 ft. The Great Rift Valley enters the country N-S, flanked by some high mountains. **Capital:** Nairobi. **Cities** (1973 est.): Nairobi (met.) 630,000; Mombasa (met.) 301,000.

Government: Head of state: Pres. Jomo Kenyatta, b. 1890, in office: Dec. 12, 1964. **Local divisions:** Nairobi and 8 rural provinces. **Armed forces:** regulars 7,600; para-military 1,800.

Economy: Industries: Tourism, light industry. **Chief crops:** Coffee, tea, cereals, cotton, sisal. **Minerals:** Gold, limestone, diatomite, salt, barytes, magnesite, felspar, sapphires, fluospar, garnets. **Other resources:** Timber, hides. **Per capita arable land:** 0.3 acres. **Livestock** (1974): 7,400,000 cattle; 65,000 pigs; 3,200,000 sheep; 14,300,000 poultry. **Fish catch** (1974): 29,400 metric tons. **Electricity production** (1976): 1,044 mln. kwh. **Labor force:** 80% agric.

Finance: Currency: Shilling (Apr. 1977: 8.31=$1 US). **Gross domestic product** (1974): $2.67 bln. **Per capita income** (1975): $209. **Imports** (1976): $973 mln.; partners (1974): U.K. 17%, Jap. 11%, Iran 10%, W. Ger. 10%. **Exports** (1976): $790 mln.; partners (1974): Ugan. 13%, Tanz. 9%, U.K. 9%, W. Ger. 8%. **Tourists** (1974): 405,500; receipts: $76 million. **Balance of payments** (1976): $84.5 mln. **National budget** (1976): $606 mln. revenues; $796 mln. **expenditures.** International reserves **(Jan. 1977): $276 mln.** Consumer prices **(change in 1976): 13.6%.**

Transport: Motor vehicles: in use (1974): 130,900 passenger cars, 23,800 commercial vehicles. **Chief ports:** Mombasa.

Communications: Television sets: 36,000 licenses (1973). **Radios:** 508,000 licenses (1973). **Telephones in use** (1976): 121,910. **Daily newspaper circulation** (1973): 97,000; 8 per 1,000 pop.

Health: Life expectancy at birth (1969): 46.9 male; 51.2 female. **Births** (annual per 1,000 pop. 1970-75): 48.7. **Deaths** (annual per 1,000 pop. 1970-75): 16.0. **Natural increase** (annual 1970-75): 3.27%. **Pop. per hospital bed** (1973): 805. **Pop. per physician** (1973): 8,914. **Infant mortality** (per 1,000 pop. under 1 yr. 1973): 51.4.

Education: Literacy (1973): 25%. **Pop. 5-19:** in school (1973): 39%; per teacher (1973): 73.

Arab colonies exported spices and slaves from the Kenya coast as early as the 8th century. Britain obtained control in the 19th century. Kenya won independence Dec. 12, 1963, four years after the end of the violent Mau Mau uprising.

From 1968 on, thousands of Asians with British passports have been ordered to leave Kenya. But a sizeable minority of Asians and Europeans remain.

Kenya has shown steady growth in industry and agriculture under a modified private enterprise system, and has had a relatively free political life. But stability was shaken in 1974-5, with opposition charges of corruption and oppression.

In 1968 ties with Somalia were restored after 4 years of skirmishes. In 1976-77, relations with Uganda deteriorated. Tanzania closed its Kenya border in 1977 in a dispute over the collapse of the East African Community, an economic union of the 2 states and Uganda.

The U.S. agreed in 1976 to sell several jet fighters to Kenya.

North Korea

Democratic People's Republic of Korea

People: Population (1976 est.): 16,250,000. **Pop. density:** 347 per sq. mi. **Ethnic groups:** Korean. **Languages:** Korean. **Religions:** Buddhism, Confucianism, Shamanism, Chondolsyo prevailed before 1945, repressed since.

Geography: Area: 46,768 sq. mi., slightly smaller than Mississippi. **Location:** In northern E. Asia. **Neighbors:** China (Manchuria), U.S.S.R. on N, S. Korea on S. **Topography:** Mountains and hills cover nearly all the country, with narrow valleys and small plains in between. The N and the east coast are the most rugged areas. **Capital:** Pyongyang. **Cities** (1973 est.): Pyongyang 957,000; Hamhung 484,000; Chongjin 306,000.

Government: Head of state: Pres. Kim Il-sung, b.1912, in office: Dec. 28, 1972; **Head of government:** Kim Il, in office: Dec. 28, 1972. **Head of Communist Party:** Gen. Sec. Kim Il-sung, in office: 1945. **Local divisions:** 9 provinces, 4 municipalities, one urban district. **Armed forces:** regulars 495,000; militia 1,800,-000.

Economy: Industries: Textiles, fertilizers, cement. **Chief crops:** Grain, rice. **Minerals:** Tungsten, graphite, magnesite, coal, lead, zinc, iron, copper, gold, phosphate, salt, fluospar. **Per capita arable land:** 0.3 acres. **Livestock** (1974): 771,000 cattle; 1,485,000 pigs; 205,000 sheep. **Fish catch** (1975): 800,000 metric tons. **Electricity production** (1973): 20,000 mln. kwh. **Labor force:** 53% agric.

Finance: Currency: Won (1974: 0.98=$1 US). **Gross domestic product** (est. 1974): $6.1 bln. **Per capita income** (1974): $380. **Imports** (1973): $1 bln.; partners (1973): P.R. China 50%, USSR 30%, Jap. 10%, Fr. 6%. **Exports** (1973): $1 bln.: partners (1973): P.R. China 65%, USSR 18%, Jap. 7%, Fr. 2%.

Chief ports: Chongjin, Hamhung, Nampo.

Health: Life expectancy at birth (1970-75): 58.8 male; 62.5 female. **Births** (annual per 1,000 pop. 1970-75): 35.7. **Deaths** (annual per 1,000 pop. 1970-75): 9.4. **Natural increase** (annual 1970-75): 2.63%. **Pop. per hospital bed** (1973): 1,500. **Pop. per physician** (1973): 2,286. **Infant mortality** (per 1,000 pop. under 1 yr. 1973): 110.

Education: Literacy (1973): 85%. **Pop. 5-19:** in school (1973): 60%; per teacher (1973): 93.

The Democratic People's Republic of Korea was founded May 1, 1948, in the zone occupied by Russian troops after World War II. Its armies tried to conquer the south, 1950. After 3 years of fighting with Chinese and U.S. intervention, a cease-fire was proclaimed.

Korea has maintained ties with both China and Russia.

Korea's attempts to purchase western technology in the 1970s foundered over $1 billion in defaulted loans. Industry, begun by the Japanese during their 1910-45 occupation, and nationalized in the 1940s, had grown substantially, using North Korea's abundant mineral and hydroelectric resources.

The U.S. has no diplomatic ties with North Korea.

South Korea

Republic of Korea

People: Population (1976 est.): 35,860,000. **Age distrib.** (%): 0 14: 39.9; 15 59: 54.5; 60+: 5.6. **Pop. density:** 943 per sq. mi. **Urban** (1975): 48.5%. **Ethnic groups:** Korean. **Languages:** Korean. **Religions:** Buddhism, Confucianism, Shamanism, Chondokyo widespread; Protestants 10%, Roman Catholics 2%.

Geography: Area: 38,031 sq. mi., slightly larger than Indiana. **Location:** In northern E Asia. **Neighbors:** N. Korea on N. **Topography:** The country is mountainous, with a rugged east coast. The western and southern coast are deeply indented, with many islands and harbors. **Capital:** Seoul. **Cities** (1970 cen.): Seoul 5,433,198; Pusan 1,842,259; Taegu 1,063,553; Inchon 634,046; Kwangchu 493,634.

Government: Head of state: Pres. Park Chung Hee, b. Nov. 14, 1917, in office: Nov. 26, 1963; **Head of government:** Prime Min. Choi Kyu-hah, in office: Mar. 1976. **Local divisions:** 9 provinces, 2 special cities. **Armed forces:** regulars 595,000; reserves 1,115,000.

Economy: Industries: Electronics, ships, rubber, glass, chemicals, oil products, steel. **Chief crops:** Rice, grain, tobacco, beans. **Minerals:** Tungsten, coal, iron, bismuth, fluospar, graphite. **Per capita arable land:** 0.1 acres. **Livestock** (1976): 1,642,000 cattle: 1,246,000 pigs; 5,000 sheep; 23,071,000 poultry. **Fish catch** (1975): 2,133,000 metric tons. **Electricity production** (1976): 23,112 mln. kwh. **Labor force:** 50% agric.; 14% manuf.

Finance: Currency: Won (Apr. 1977: 484=$1 US). **Gross domestic product** (1976): $25.3 bln. **Per capita income** (1975): $496. **Imports** (1976) $8,774 bln.; partners (1974): Jap. 38%, US 25%, Saudi Ar. 10%, Kuw. 4%. **Exports** (1976): $7.716 bln; partners (1974): U.S. 33%, Jap. 31%, W. Ger. 5%, Can. 4%. **Tourists** (1974): 517,600; receipts: $154 million. **Balance of payments** (1976): $1.42 bln. **National budget** (1976): $5.69 bln. revenues; $5.58 bln. expenditures. **International reserves** (Jan. 1977): $2.883 bln. **Consumer prices** (change in 1976): 15.6%.

Transport: Railway traffic (1974): 6,540 mln. passenger-miles; 5,462 mln. net ton-miles. **Motor vehicles:** in use (1974): 76,500 passenger cars, 96,900 commercial vehicles; assembled (1976): 27,000 passenger cars, 23,000 commercial vehicles. **Chief ports:** Pusan, Inchon.

Communications: Television sets: 1,182,000 in use (1973); 1,164,000 manufactured (1974). **Radios:** 4,115,000 in use (1972); 3,692,000 manufactured (1974). **Telephones in use** (1976): 1,400,103. **Daily newspaper circulation** (1972): 4,400,000; 136 per 1,000 pop.

Health: Life expectancy at birth (1970): 63 male; 67 female. **Births** (annual per 1,000 pop. 1970-75): 28.8. **Deaths** (annual per 1,000 pop. 1970-75): 8.9. **Natural increase** (annual 1970-75): 1.99%. **Pop. per hospital bed** (1973): 1,723. **Pop. per physician** (1973): 1,983. **Infant mortality** (per 1,000 pop. under 1 yr. 1973): 60.

Education: Literacy (1973): 88%. **Pop. 5-19** in school (1973): 65%; per teacher (1973): 76.

Korea, once called the Hermit Kingdom, has a recorded history since the 1st century B.C. It was united in a kingdom under the Silla Dynasty, 668 A.D. It was at times associated with the Chinese empire; the treaty that concluded the Sino-Japanese war of 1894-95 recognized Korea's complete independence. In 1910 Japan forcibly annexed Korea as Chosun.

At the Potsdam conference, July, 1945, the 38th parallel was designated as the line dividing the Soviet and the American occupation. Russian troops entered Korea Aug. 10, 1945, U.S. troops entered Sept. 8, 1945. The Soviet military organized socialists and communists and blocked efforts to let the Koreans unite their country. *(See Index for Korean War.)*

The South Koreans formed the Republic of Korea in May 1948 with Seoul as the capital. Dr. Syngman Rhee was chosen president July 20 and the republic was formally proclaimed Aug. 15, 1948. A movement spearheaded by college students forced his resignation Apr. 26, 1960.

But in an army coup May 16, 1961, Gen. Park Chung Hee became chairman of the ruling junta. He was formally elected president Oct. 15, 1963; a referendum Nov. 22, 1972, provided more presidential powers and allowed him to be reelected for 6 year terms unlimited times. In 1974 scores of political dissidents were jailed; eight were executed in 1975.

North Korean raids across the border tapered off in 1971, but 2 South Korean soldiers were killed in 1973; in 1974, 2 South Korean boats were sunk and North Koreans fired on a U.S. helicopter south of the neutral zone. In July 1972 South and North Korea agreed on a common goal of reunifying the 2 nations by peaceful means. Red Cross delegates from both nations met to find ways to aid divided families.

The U.S. announced in 1977 that it would withdraw 33,000 ground troops by 1982. Some 12,000 Air Force and logistics troops would remain. Alleged Korean agents were charged in 1976-77 with giving questionable gifts to U.S. congresspersons to promote foreign aid.

Korea achieved major gains in the 1970s toward industrialization and higher living standards.

Kuwait

State of Kuwait

People: Population (1976 est.): 1,030,000. **Age distrib.** (%): 0-14:43.2; 15-59: 54.0; 60+:2.8. **Pop. density:** 132 per sq. mi. **Ethnic groups:** Arabs 85%, Iranians, Indians, Pakistanis 13%. **Languages:** Arabic, others. **Religions:** Moslems (most Sunni) predominate.

Geography: Area: 7,780 sq. mi., the size of Massachusetts. **Location:** In Middle East, at N end of Persian Gulf. **Neighbors:** Iraq on N, Saudi Arabia on S. **Topography:** The country is flat, very dry, and extremely hot. **Capital:** Kuwait. **Cities** (1970 cen.): Kuwait City (met.) 633,153.

Government: Head of state: Amir Sabah al-Salim al-Sabah, b. 1915, in office: Nov. 24, 1965; **Head of government:** Prime Min. Jaber al-Ahmed al-Jaber, b. 1928, in office: Nov. 30, 1965. **Armed forces:** regulars 9,700.

Economy: Industries: Oil products. **Minerals:** Oil, gas. **Crude oil output** (1976): 788 mln. bbls. **Per capita arable land:** 0.002 acres. **Livestock** (1974): 7,000 cattle; 100,000 sheep. **Electricity production** (1975): 4,656 mln. kwh. **Labor force** 2% agriculture; 13% manuf.

Finance: Currency: Dinar (Apr. 1977: 1=$3.48 US). **Gross domestic product** (1974): $11.0 bln. **Per capita income** (1974): $11,063. **Imports** (1975) $2.390 bln.; partners (1974): Jap. 17%, U.S. 14%, W. Ger. 11%, U.K. 8%. **Exports** (1976): $9.857 bln.; partners (1974): Jap. 26%, U.K. 16%, Fr. 10% Sing. 5%. **International reserves** (Feb. 1977): $1.759 bln.

Transport: Motor vehicles: in use (1974): 164,900 passenger cars, 50,700 commercial vehicles. **Civil aviation:** 592 mln. passenger-miles (1975); 15 mln. freight ton-miles (1975). **Chief ports:** Mina al-Ahmadi.

Communications: Televison sets: 180,000 in use (1973). **Radios:** 210,000 in use (1973). **Telephones in use** (1976): 128,751. **Daily newspaper circulation** (1973): 75,000; 85 per 1,000 pop.

Health: Life expectancy at birth (1970): 66.14 male; 71.82 female. **Births** (annual per 1,000 pop. 1970-75): 47.1. **Deaths** (annual per 1,000 pop. 1970-75): 5.3. **Natural increase** (annual 1970-75): 4.18%. **Pop. per hospital bed** (1973): 183. **Pop. per Physician** (1973): 1,035. **Infant mortality** (per 1,000 pop. under 1 yr. 1974): 44.30.

Education: Literacy (1973): 55%. **Pop. 5-19:** in school (1973): 60%; per teacher (1973): 25.

Kuwait is ruled by the Al-Sabah dynasty, founded 1759. Britain ran foreign relations and defense from 1899 until independence in 1961. The majority of the population is non-Kuwaiti, with many Palestinians, and can not vote.

Iraqi troops crossed the Kuwait border in 1973 but soon withdrew. Kuwait has ordered advanced weapons from France and the U.S.

Oil, first exported in 1946, is the fiscal mainstay. Reserves are 15% of the world total. Oil pays for free medical care, education, and social security. There are no taxes, except customs duties.

Laos

Lao People's Democratic Republic

People: Population (1976 est.): 3,380,000. **Pop. density:** 37 per sq. mi. **Urban** (1973): 14.7%. **Ethnic groups:** Lao 50%, Thai 20%, Meo and Yao 15%, others. **Languages:** Lao (official), others. **Religions:** Buddists 90%, animists, Christians 1.5%.

Geography: Area: 91,428 sq. mi., slightly larger than Utah. **Location:** In Indochina Peninsula in SE Asia. **Neighbors:** Burma, China on N, Vietnam on E, Cambodia on S, Thailand on W. **Topography:** Laos is a landlocked country dominated by jungle. High mountains along the eastern border are the source of the E-W rivers which slice across the country to the Mekong R., which defines most of the western border. **Capital:** Vientiane. **Cities** (1971 est.): Vientiane 160,000.

Government: Head of state: Pres. Souphanouvong, b. July 13, 1909, in office: Dec. 2, 1975; **Head of government:** Prime Min. Kaysone Phomvihane, b. Dec. 13, 1920, in office: Dec. 2, 1975; **Head of Communist Party:** Gen. Sec. Kaysone Phomvihane, in office: 1955. **Local divisions:** 13 provinces. **Armed forces:** regulars 42,500.

Economy: Industries: Wood products. **Chief crops:** Rice, corn, tobacco, cotton, opium, citrus fruits, coffee. **Minerals:** Tin. **Other resources:** Forests. **Per capita arable land:** 0.7 acres. **Livestock** (1974): 463,000 cattle; 1,282,000 pigs; 14,000,000 poultry. **Electricity production** (1973): 245 mln. kwh. **Labor force:** 78% agric.

Finance: Currency: Kip (1974: 600=$1 US). **Gross domestic product** (est. 1974): $500 mln. **Per capita income** (1974): $150. **Imports** (1974) $52 mln.; partners (1973): Thai 47%, Jap. 13%, Fr. 10%, U.S. 7%. **Exports** (1974): $10 mln.; partners (1973): Thai, 65%, Malaysia 29%, Hong Kong 2%, Jap. 2%. **Tourists** (1973): 48,400; receipts: $3 million.

Transport: Motor vehicles: in use (1974): 14,100 passenger cars, 2,500 commercial vehicles.

Communications: Radios: 102,000 licenses (1973).

Health: Life expectancy at birth (1970-75): 39.1 male; 41.8 female. **Births** (annual per 1,000 pop. 1970-75): 44.6. **Deaths** (annual per 1,000 pop. 1970-75): 22.8. **Natural increase** (annual 1970-75): 2.18%. **Pop. per hospital bed** (1973): 1,026. **Pop. per physician** (1973): 12,720. **Infant mortality** (per 1,000 pop. under 1 yr. 1973): 123.

Education: Literacy (1973): 20%. **Pop. 5-19:** in school (1973): 30%; per teacher (1973): 133.

Laos became a French protectorate in 1893, but regained independence as a constitutional monarchy July 19, 1949.

Conflicts among neutralist, communist and conservative factions created a chaotic political situation. Although Laos was intended to be neutral, rivalry between the communist Pathet Lao movement in the north led by Prince Souphanouvong, and right-wing and neutralist factions prevented integration of the Pathet Lao into the royalist army. Armed conflict increased after 1960.

The 3 factions formed a coalition government in June 1962, with neutralist Prince Souvanna Phouma as premier. A 14-nation conference in Geneva signed agreements, 1962, guaranteeing neutrality and independence. By 1964 the Pathet Lao had withdrawn from the coalition, and, with aid from N. Vietnamese troops, renewed sporadic attacks. U. S. planes bombed the Ho Chi Minh trail, supply line from N. Vietnam to communist forces in Laos and S. Vietnam. An estimated 2.75 million tons of bombs were dropped on Laos during the fighting.

In 1970 the U.S. stepped up air support and military aid. There were an est. 67,000 North Vietnamese troops in Laos, and some 15,000 Thais financed by the U.S.

After Pathet Lao military gains, Souvanna Phouma in May 1975 ordered government troops to cease fighting, and the Pathet Lao took effective control. The U. S. retained a reduced diplomatic presence. A Lao People's Democratic Republic was proclaimed Dec. 3, 1975.

Lebanon

Republic of Lebanon

People: Population (1976 est.): 2,960,000. **Age distrib.** (%): 0-14: 42.7; 15-59: 49.6; 60+: 7.7. **Pop. density** 737 per sq. mi. **Urban** (1970): 60.1%. **Ethnic groups:** Arabs 93%, Armenians 6%. **Languages:** Arabic, French, Armenian. **Religions:** Moslems (Sunniand Shiite) 57%, Christians (Maronite, Orthodox) 40%, Druze 3%.

Geography: Area: 4,015 sq. mi., smaller than Connecticut. **Location:** On Eastern end of Mediterranean Sea. **Neighbors:** Syria on E. Israel on S. **Topography:** There is a narrow coastal strip, and two mountain ranges running N-S enclosing the fertile Beqaa Valley. The Litani R. runs S through the valley, turning W to empty into the Mediterranean. **Capital:** Beirut. **Cities** (1970 est.): Beirut (met.) 938,940; (1971 est.) Tripoli 175,000.

Government: Head of state: Pres. Elias Sarkis, b. July 20, 1924, in office: Sept. 23, 1976; **Head of government:** Prime Min. Salim al-Huss, b. Dec. 20, 1929, in office: Dec. 9, 1976. **Local divisions:** 5 provinces. **Armed forces:** regulars 18,250 (nominally; the number of effective, loyal forces is probably lower).

Economy: Industries: Trade, food products, textiles, cement, oil products. **Chief crops:** Fruits, olives, tobacco, grapes, vegetables, grains. **Minerals:** Iron. **Per capita arable land:** 0.2 acres. **Livestock** (1974): 84,000 cattle; 229,000 sheep. **Electricity production** (1975): 1,848 mln. kwh. **Labor force:** 18% agriculture; 17% manuf.

Finance: Currency: Pound (1974: 2.32=$1 US). **Gross domestic product** (1972): $2.44 bln. **Per capita income** (1972): $786. **Imports** (1973) $1.291 bln.; partners (1973): U.S. 12%, W. Ger. 11%, Fr. 10%, It. 10%. **Exports** (1973): $613 mln.; partners (1973): Saudi Ar. 15%, Fr. 9%, U.K. 8%, Libya 7%. **Tourists** (1974): 2,261,800; receipts: $415 million. **International reserves** (Mar. 1976): $1.581 bln. **Consumer prices** (change in 1974): 11.2%.

Transport: Railway traffic (1974): 1 mln. passenger-miles; 26 mln. net ton-miles. **Motor vehicles:** in use (1974): 220,200 passenger cars, 23,400 commercial vehicles. **Civil aviation:** 1,101 mln. passenger-miles (1974); 263 mln. freight ton-miles (1974). **Chief ports:** Beirut, Tripoli, Sidon.

Communications: Television sets: 321,000 in use (1973). **Radios:** 605,000 in use (1971). **Daily newspaper circulation** (1973): 280,000; 92 per 1,000 pop.

Health: Life expectancy at birth (1970-75): 61.4 male; 65.1 female. **Births** (annual per 1,000 pop. 1970-75): 39.8. **Deaths** (annual per 1,000 pop. 1970-75): 9.9. **Natural increase** (annual 1970-75): 2.99%. **Pop. per hospital bed** (1973): 278. **Pop. per physician** (1973): 1,330. **Infant mortality** (per 1,000 pop. under 1 yr. 1960): 13.6.

Education: Literacy (1973): 86%. **Pop. 5-19:** in school (1973): 48%; per teacher (1973): 20.

Lebanon was was formed from 5 former Turkish Empire districts and became an independent state Sept. 1, 1920, administered under French mandate 1920-41. French troops withdrew in 1946.

Under the 1943 National Covenant, all public positions were divided among the various religious communities, with Christians in the majority. By the 1970s, Moslems became the majority, and demanded a larger political and economic role.

U. S. Marines intervened, May-Oct. 1958, during a Syrian-aided revolt. Lebanon's efforts to restrain Palestinian commandos caused armed clashes in 1969. Continued raids against Israeli civilians, 1970-75, brought Israeli attacks against guerrilla camps and villages.

An estimated 60,000 were killed and billions of dollars in damage inflicted in a 1975-76 civil war. Palestinian units and leftist Moslems fought against the Maronite militia, the Phalange, and other Christians. Several Arab countries provided political and arms support to the various factions, while Israel aided Christian forces.

Up to 15,000 Syrian troops intervened in 1976, and fought Palestinian groups. Arab League troops from several nations tried to impose a cease-fire. But sporadic fighting, among Palestinian factions and between Palestinians and Christians near Israel continued in 1977.

Lebanon has a free enterprise economy. Literacy and life expectancy are higher than in most Arab lands.

Lesotho

Kingdom of Lesotho

People: Population (1975 est.): 1,040,000. **Age distrib.** (%): 0–14: 39.5; 15–59: 60+: 6.6. **Pop. density:** 89 per sq. mi. **ethnic groups:** Sotho 85% Nguni 15%. **Languages:** English, Lesotho both official. **Religions:** Christians 70%, others.

Geography: Area: 11,716 sq. mi., slightly larger than Maryland. **Location:** In southern Africa. **Neighbors:** Republic of South Africa completely surrounds Lesotho. **Topography:** Landlocked Lesotho is mountainous, with altitudes ranging from 5,000 to 11,000 ft. Agriculture is pursued on the western lowlands. **Capital:** Maseru. **Cities** (1972 est.): Maseru (met.) 29,049.

Government: Head of state: King Moshoeshoe II, b. May 2, 1938, in office: Oct. 4, 1966; **Head of government:** Prime Mln. Leabua Jonathan, b. Oct. 31, 1914, in office: Oct. 4, 1966. **Local divisions:** 10 districts.

Economy: Industries: Diamond polishing. **Chief crops:** Corn, grains, peas, beans. **Other resources:** Wool, mohair. **Per capita arable land:** 0.8 acres. **Livestock** (1974): 490,000 cattle; 79,000 pigs; 1,600,000 sheep. **Labor force:** 95% agric.

Finance: Currency: S. Af. Rand (Apr. 1977: 1=$1.15 US). **gross domestic product** (est. 1974): $118 mln. **Per capita income** (1974): $140. **Imports** (1973) $87 mln.; partners: Mostly So. Afr. **Exports** (1973): $13 mln.; partners: Mostly So. Afr.

Transport: Motor vehicles: in use (1974): 2,300 passenger cars, 2,000 commercial vehicles.

Communications: Radios: 11,000 licenses (1973).

Health: Life expectancy at birth (1970-75): 44.4 male; 47.6 female. **Births** (annual per 1,000 pop. 1970-75): 39.0. **Deaths** (annual per 1,000 pop. 1970-75): 19.7. **Natural increase** (annual 1970-75): 1.93%. **Pop. per hospital bed** (1973): 471. **Pop. per physician** (1973): 21,522. **Infant mortality** (per 1,000 pop. under 1 yr. 1956): 181.

Education: Literacy (1973): 60%. **Pop. 5-19:** in school (1973): 51%; per teacher (1973): 78.

Lesotho (once called Basutoland) became a British protectorate in 1868 when Chief Mohesh sought protection against the Boers. Independence came Oct. 4, 1966. Elections were suspended in 1970. Up to 70% of males work abroad, most in So. Africa.

Liberia

Republic of Liberia

People: Population (1976 est.): 1,750,000. **Age distrib.** (%): 0–14: 41.6; 15–59: 53.1, 60+: 5.3. **Pop. density:** 41 per sq. mi. **Urban** (1971): 27.6%. **Ethnic groups:** Americo-Liberians 2.5%, 16 tribes 97.5%. **Languages:** English (official), 28 tribal languages. **Religions:** Moslems 10-20%, Christians 10%, others.

Geography: Area: 43,000 sq. mi., slightly smaller than Pennsylvania. **Location:** On SW coast of W. Africa. **Neighbors:** Sierra Leone on W, Guinea on N, Ivory Coast on E. **Topography:** The marshy Atlantic coastline rises to low mountains and plateaus in the interior, which is largely forested. Six major rivers flow in parallel courses to the ocean. **Capital:** Monrovia. **Cities** (1970 est.): Monrovia 96,226.

Government: Head of state: Pres. William Richard Tolbert, b. May 13, 1913, in office: July 23, 1971. **Local divisions:** 9 counties. **Armed forces:** regulars 5,220; para-military 21,300.

Economy: Industries: Food processing and other light industry. **Chief crops:** Fibers, palm kernels, rice, cassava, coffee, cocoa, sugar. **Minerals:** Iron, diamonds, gold. **Other resources:** Rubber, timber. **Per capita arable land:** 0.2 acres. **Livestock** (1974): 33,000 cattle; 88,000 pigs; 168,000 sheep; 1,900,000 poultry. **Fish catch** (1974): 23,000 metric tons. **Electricity production** (1973): 846 mln. kwh. **Labor force:** 74% agric.

Finance: Currency: Dollar (Apr. 1977: 1 =$ 1 US). **Gross domestic product** (1975): $855 mln. **Per capita income** (1973): $235. **Imports** (1976) $399 mln.; partners (1974): U.S. 18%, Saudi A. 9%, U.K. 9%, W. Ger. 5%. **Exports** (1976): $460 mln.; partners (1974): U.S. 20%, Belg. 18%, W. Ger. 17%, Neth. 13%. **National budget** (1975): $125.2 mln. revenues; $121.8 mln. expenditures. **International reserves** (Feb. 1977): $45.38 mln. **Consumer prices** (change in 1976): 5.7%.

Transport: Motor vehicles: in use (1974): 12,100 passenger cars, 10,000 commercial vehicles. **Chief ports:** Monrovia, Buchanan.

Communications: Television sets: 8,500 in use (1973). **Radios:** 155,000 in use (1972). **Daily newspaper circulation** 1973): 7,000; 4 per 1,000 pop.

Health: Life expectancy at birth (1971): 45.8 male; 44.0 female. **Births** (per 1,000 pop. 1971): 49.8. **Deaths** (per 1,000 pop. 1971): 20.9. **Natural increase** (1971): 2.89%. **Pop. per hospital bed** (1973): 638. **Pop. per physician** (1973): 12,576. **Infant mortality** (per 1,000 pop. under 1 yr. 1971): 159.2.

Education: Literacy (1973): 10%. **Pop. 5-19:** in school (1973): 26%; per teacher (1973): 92.

Liberia was founded in 1822 by U.S. black freedmen with the aid of colonization societies. It became a republic July 26, 1847, with a constitution modeled on that of the U.S. Descendants of freedmen dominate politics.

Libya

People's Socialist Libyan Arab Public

People: Population (1975 est.): 2,440,000. **Pop. density:** 3.6 per sq. mi. **Urban** (1974): 29.8%. **Ethnic groups:** Arab-Berber 97%, Italian 1.4%, others. **Languages:** Arabic. **Religions:** Sunni Moslems 97%, Christians 2.5%.

Geography: Area: 679,536 sq. mi., larger than Alaska. **location:** On Mediterranean coast of N. Africa. **Neighbors:** Tunisia, Algeria on W, Niger, Chad on S, Sudan, Egypt on E. **Topography:** Desert and semidesert regions cover 92% of the land, with some low mountains in N, and higher mountains in S. A narrow coastal zone and scattered oases contain most of the population and agriculture. **Capital:** Tripoli. **Cities** (1971 est.): Tripoli 247,000; Benghazi 137,000.

Government: Head of state: Sec.-Gen. Muammar el-Qaddafi, b. 1942, in office: Sept. 1, 1969; **Head of government:** Chmn. Abdulati al-Obeidi, b. 1933, in office: Mar. 2, 1977. **Local divisions:** 10 regions. **Armed forces:** regulars 29,700.

Economy: Industries: Carpets, textiles, shoes. **Chief crops:** Dates, olives, citrus and other fruits, grapes, tobacco. **Minerals:** oil, gas. **Crude oil output** (1976): 700,000 bbls. **Per capita arable land:** 2.3 acres. **Livestock** (1974): 121,000 cattle; 3,200,000 sheep. **Electricity production** (1975): 900 mln. kwh. **Labor force:** 43% agric.

Finance: Currency: Dinar (Apr. 1977: 1=$3.38 US). **Gross domestic product** (1974): $12.28 bln. **Per capita income** (1973): $2,599. **Imports** (1976) $3.802 bln.; partners (1973): It. 26%, W. Ger. 10%, Fr. 8%, U.K. 7%. **Exports** (1976): $8.401 bln.; partners (1973): It. 28%, W. Ger. 21%, U. K. 12%, U.S. 8%. **Tourists** (1974): 296,000; receipts: $35 million. **Balance of payments** (1975): $–1.55 bln. **International reserves** (Jan. 1977): $3.222 bln. **Consumer prices** (change in 1976): 9.1%.

Transport: Motor vehicles: in use (1974): 227,500 passenger cars, 104,900 commercial vehicles. **Chief ports:** Tripoli, Bengazi.

Communications: Television sets: 2,500 licenses (1972). **Radios:** 100,000 licenses (1973).

Health: Life expectancy at birth (1970-75): 51.4 male; 54.5 female. **Births** (annual per 1,000 pop. 1970-75): 45.0. **Deaths** (annual per 1,000 pop. 1970-75): 14.7. **Natural increase** (annual 1970-75): 3.03%. **Pop. per hospital bed** (1973): 254. **Pop. per physician** (1973): 1,244. **Infant mortality** (per 1,000 pop. under 1 yr. 1973): 130.

Education: Literacy (1973): 22%. **Pop.** 5-19: in school (1973): 60%; per teacher (1973): 32.

First settled by Berbers, Libya was ruled by Carthage, Rome, the Vandals, the Ottomans, Italy, from 1912, and Britain and France after WW II. It became an independent constitutional monarchy Jan. 2, 1952. In 1969 a junta lead by Col. Muammar el-Qaddafi seized power, instituting socialist policies.

In 1972 Libya and Egypt agreed on a unification plan, which Egypt canceled in 1974, charging a Qaddafi role in the bombing of an Egyptian presidential palace.

In the mid-1970s, it was widely reported that Libya had armed violent revolutionary groups in Egypt and Sudan, and had aided terrorists of various nationalities. In 1970, Libya arranged to buy jets from France. The USSR sold several billion dollars worth of advanced arms after 1975, and established close political ties.

Libya and Egypt fought several air and land battles along their border in July, 1977. Chad charged Libya with military occupation of its uranium-rich northern region in 1977.

Over one third of all workers are foreigners, half of them Egyptians.

Liechtenstein

Principality of Liechtenstein

People: Population (1974 est.): 24,700. **Age distrib.** (%): 0–14: 27.9; 15–59: 60.2; 60+: 11.9. **Pop. density:** 405 per sq. mi. **Ethnic groups:** Germanic. **Languages:** German. **Religions:** Roman Catholics 90%, Protestants 10%.

Geography: Area: 61 sq. mi., the size of Washington, D.C. **Location:** In the Alps. **Neighbors:** Switzerland on W, Austria on E. **Topography:** The Rhine Valley occupies one-third of the country, the Alps cover the rest. **Capital:** Vaduz. **Cities** (1974 est.): Vaduz 7,500.

Government: Head of state: Prince Franz Josef II, b. Aug. 16, 1906, in office: July 26, 1938; **Head of government:** Walter Kieber, b. Feb. 20, 1931, in office: Mar. 27, 1974. **Local divisions:** 11 districts.

Economy: Industries: Machines, textiles, precision instruments, false teeth, drugs, ceramics.

Finance: Currency: Franken, or Swiss Franc.

Communications: Television sets: 2,500 licenses (1968). **Radios:** 4,500 licenses (1968). **Telephones in use** (1976): 15,358. **Daily newspaper circulation** (1972): 6,000; 286 per 1,000 pop.

Health: Births (per 1,000 pop. 1975): 12.6. **Deaths** (per 1,000 pop. 1975): 7.3. **Natural increase** (1975): 0.54%. **Infant mortality** (per 1,000 pop. under 1 yr. 1974): 9.2.

Liechtenstein became sovereign in 1866. Since 1923 Austria has run its posts, customs, and foreign affairs. Taxes are low; many international corporations have headquarters there.

Luxembourg

Grand Duchy of Luxembourg

People: Population (1976): 360,000. **Age distrib.** (%): 0-14: 20.8; 15-59: 60.7; 60+: 18.5. **Pop. density:** 360 per sq. mi. **Urban** (1973): 68.9%. **Ethnic groups:** Mixture of French and Germans predominate, Italians 7%. **Languages:** French, German, Luxembourgish. **Religions:** Roman Catholics 94%, Protestants 1%.

Geography: Area: 999 sq. mi., smaller than Rhode Island. **Location:** In W. Europe. **Neighbors:** Belgium on W, France on S, W. Germany on E. **Topography:** Heavy forests (Ardennes) cover N, S is a low, open plateau. **Capital:** Luxembourg. **Cities** (1974 est.): Luxembourg 78,403.

Government: Head of state: Grand Duke Jean, b. Jan. 5, 1921, in office: Nov. 12, 1964; **Head of government:** Prime Min. Gaston Thorn, in office: June 18, 1974. **Local divisions:** 3 districts, 12 cantons. **Armed forces:** regulars 625.

Economy: Industries: Steel, chemicals, beer, tires, tobacco, metal products, cement. **Chief crops:** Grain, potatoes, roses. **Minerals:** Iron. **Per capita arable land:** 0.4 acres. **Livestock** (1976): 206,000 cattle; 86,000 pigs; 5,000 sheep; 268,000 poultry. **Electricity production** (1976): 1,548 mln. kwh. **Labor force:** 7% agric.; 34% manuf.

Finance: Currency: Belgian Franc (May, 1977: 36.0=$1 US). **Gross domestic product** $2.4 bln. **Per capita income** (1975): $5,435. **Consumer prices** (change in 1976): 9.8%.

Transport: Railway traffic (1974): 179 mln. passenger-miles; 538 mln. net ton-miles. **Motor vehicles:** in use (1974): 127,900 passenger cars, 11,200 commercial vehicles. **Civil aviation:** 83 mln. passenger miles (1974); 142,000 freight ton-miles (1974).

Communications: Television sets: 85,000 licenses (1973); **Radios:** 176,000 licenses (1973). **Telephones in use** (1976): 146,869. **Daily newspaper circulation** (1973): 161,000.

Health: Life expectancy at birth (1971-73): 67.0 male; 73.9 female. **Births** (per 1,000 pop. 1975): 11.2. **Deaths** (per 1,000 pop. 1975): 12.2. **Natural increase** (1975): −0.11%. **Pop. per hospital bed** (1973): 90. **Pop. per physician** (1973): 933. **Infant mortality** (per 1,000 pop. under 1 yr. 1975): 14.8.

Education: Literacy (1973): 98%. **Pop. 5-19:** in school (1973): 70%; per teacher (1973): 27.

Luxembourg, founded about 963, was ruled by Burgundy, Spain, Austria, and France from 1448 to 1815. It left the Germanic Confederation in 1866. Overrun by Germany in two world wars, Luxembourg ended its neutrality in 1948, when a customs union with Belgium and Netherlands was adopted.

Madagascar

Democratic Republic of Madagascar

People: Population (1976 est.): 8,270,000. **Age distrib.** (%): 0-14: 46.5; 15-59: 47.7; 60+: 5.8. **Pop. density:** 36 per sq. mi. **Urban** (1970): 14.1%. **Ethnic groups:** 18 Malayan-Indonesian tribes (Merina 26%), with Arab and African presence. **Languages:** Malagasy spoken in various dialects by all tribes, Merina dialect official. **Religions:** Roman Catholics 20%, Protestant 18%, Moslems 9%, others.

Geography: Area: 226,657 sq. mi., slightly smaller than Texas. **Location:** In the Indian O., off the SE coast of Africa. **Neighbors:** Nearest are Comoro Is., Mozambique (across Mozambique Channel). **Topography:** Madagascar has a humid coastal strip in the E, fertile valleys in the mountainous center plateau region, and a wider coastal strip on the W. **Capital:** Tananarive. **Cities** (1972 est.): Tananarive 366,530; Majunga 67,450; Tamatave 59,503.

Government: Head of state: Pres. Didier Ratsiraka, b. Nov. 4, 1936, in office: Dec. 30, 1975; **Head of government:** Prime Min. Justin Rakotoniaina, b. Dec. 14, 1933, in office: Aug. 12, 1976. **Local divisions:** 6 provinces. **Armed forces:** regulars 4,760; para-military 6,600.

Economy: Industries: Light industry. **Chief crops:** Coffee, cloves, vanilla (80% world supply), rice, sugar, sisal, tobacco, peanuts. **Minerals:** Chromium, graphite. **Per capital arable land:** 0.9 acres. **Livestock** (1974): 9,617,000 cattle; 689,000 pigs; 716,000 sheep; 15,330 poultry. **Fish catch** (1974): 63,900 metric tons. **Electricity production** (1976): 252 mln. kwh. **Labor force:** 86% agric..

Finance: Currency: Franc (Apr. 1977: 248=$1 US). **Gross domestic product** (1973): $1.32 bln. **Per capita income** (1972): $145. **Imports** (1974) $281 mln.; partners (1973): Fr. 49%, W. Ger. 8%, U.S. 7%, Jap. 5%. **Exports** (1974): $244 mln.; partners (1973): Fr. 37%, U.S. 17%, Reunion 9%, Jap. 6%, Malaysia 6%. **Tourist receipts** (1973): $2 million. **Balance of payments** (1974): $−34 mln. **National budget** (1970): $185 mln. revenues); $202 mln. expenditures, **International reserves** (Feb. 1977): $54.2 mln. **Consumer prices** (change in 1976): 5.0%.

Transport: Railway traffic (1974): 158 mln. passenger-miles; 130 mln. net ton-miles. **Motor vehicles:** in use: 55,000 passenger cars (1974), 40,300 commercial vehicles (1971). **Civil aviation:** 154 mln. passenger-miles (1975); 5.6 mln. freight ton-miles (1975). **Chief ports:** Tamatave, Diego-Suarez, Majunga, Tulear.

Communications: Television sets: 7,500 in use (1972). **Radios:** 700,000 in use (1973). **Telephones in use** (1976): 31,370. **Daily newspaper circulation** (1972): 103,000; 15 per 1,000 pop.

Health: Life expectancy at birth (1966): 37.5 male; 38.3 female. **Births** (per 1,000 pop. 1966): 46. **Deaths** (per 1,000 pop. 1966): 25. **Natural increase** (1966): 2.1%. **Pop. per hospital bed** 1973): 382. **Pop. per physician** (1973): 10,568. **Infant mortality** (per 1,000 pop. under 1 yr. 1966): 102.

Education: Literacy (1973): 39%. **Pop.: 5-19:** in school (1973): 42%; per teacher (1973): 109.

Madagascar was settled 2,000 years ago by Malayan-Indonesian people, whose descendants still predominate. The island became a French protectorate, 1885, and a colony 1896. Independence came June 26, 1960.

Discontent with inflation and French domination led to a coup in 1972. The new regime nationalized French-owned financial interests, closed French bases and a U.S. space tracking station, and obtained Chinese aid.

Malawi

Republic of Malawi

People: Population (1976 est.): 5,180,000. **Age distrib.** (%): 0-14: 43.9; 15-59: 50.4; 60+: 5.6. **Pop. density:** 113 per sq. mi. **Urban** (1972): 10.1%. **Ethnic groups:** Chewa, Nyanja, Lonwe, other Bantu tribes. **Languages:** English (official), Chichewa, other Bantu languages. **Religions:** Christians 50% (half Roman Catholic, half Protestant), Moslems 30%.

Geography: Area: 45,747 sq. mi., the size of Pennsylvania. **Location:** In SE Africa. **Neighbors:** Zambia on W. Mozambique on S. E. Tanzania on N. **Topography:** Malawi stretches 560 mi. N-S along Lake Malawi (Lake Nyasa), most of which belongs to Malawi. High plateaus and mountains line the Rift Valley the length of the nation. **Capital:** Lilongwe. **Cities** (1972 est.): Blantyre-Limbe (met.) 160,063; Lilongwe 20,000.

Government: Head of state: Pres. H. Kamuzu Banda, b. 1906, in office: July 6, 1966. **Local divisions:** 24 districts, 3 sub-districts. **Armed forces:** regulars 2,300.

Economy: Industries: Textiles, sugar, farm implements. **Chief crops:** Tea, tobacco, peanuts, cotton, sugar, soybeans, coffee. **Other resources:** Rubber. **Per capita arable land:** 1.4 acres. **Livestock** (1974): 593,000 cattle; 180,000 pigs; 120,000 sheep; 7,500,000 poultry. **Fish catch** (1974): 42,300 metric tons. **Electricity production** (1976): 252 mln. kwh. **Labor force:** 87% agric.

Finance: Currency: Kwacha (Apr. 1977: .907 = $1 US). **Gross domestic product** (1976): $708 mln. **Per capita income** (1974): $128. **Imports** (1976): $206 mln.; partners (1973): So. Afr. 23%, U.K. 23%, Rhod. 13%, Jap. 5%, W. Ger. 5%. **Exports** (1976): $160 mln.; partners (1973): U.K. 31%, U.S. 9%, Rhod. 7%, Neth. 7%. **Balance of payments** (1975): $−18.6 mln. **National budget** (1976): $90 mln. revenues; $139 mln. expenditures. **International reserves** (Feb. 1977): $24.44 mln. **Consumer prices** (change in 1976): 4.5%.

Transport: Railway traffic (1974): 47 mln. passenger-miles; 156 mln. net ton-miles. **Motor vehicles:** in use (1974): 11,200 passenger cars, 9,500 commercial vehicles. **Civil aviation:** 76 mln. passenger-miles (1976); 2.9 mln. freight ton-miles (1976).

Communications: Radios: 112,000 in use (1973). **Telephones in use** (1976): 19,747.

Health: Life expectancy at birth (1970-72): 40.9 male; 44.2 female. **Births** (annual per 1,000 pop. 1970-72): 50.5. **Deaths** (annual per 1,000 pop. 1970-72): 26.5. **Natural increase** (annual 1970-72): 2.40%. **Pop. per hospital bed** (1973): 647. **Pop. per physician** (1973): 68,429. **Infant mortality** (per 1,000 pop. under 1 yr. 1970-72): 142.1.

Education: Literacy (1973): 22%. **Pop. 5-19:** in school (1973): 24%; per teacher (1973): 154.

Bantus came in the 16th century, Arab slavers in the 19th. The area became a British protectorate Nyasaland, in 1891. It became independent July 6, 1964, and a republic in 1966. It has a pro-West foreign policy.

Malaysia

People: Population (1976 est.): 12,300,000. **Age distrib.** (%): 0-14: 45.0; 15-59: 49.8; 60+: 5.2. **Pop. density:** 96 per sq. mi. **Urban** (1970): 26.8%. **Ethnic groups:** Malays 44%, Chinese 36%, Indians 10%, others. **Languages:** Malay (official), English, Chinese, Indian languages. **Religions:** Malays, some Indians are Moslem; Chinese, Indian, and local religions.

Geography: Area: 128,328 sq. mi., slightly larger than New Mexico. **Location:** Occupies the SE tip of Asia, plus the N coast of the island of Borneo. **Neighbors:** Thailand on N, Indonesia on S. **Topography:** Most of West Malaysia is covered by tropical jungle, including the central mountain range than runs N-S through the peninsula. The western coast is marshy, the eastern coast sandy. East Malaysia has a wide, swampy coastal plain, with interior jungles and mountains. **Capital:** Kuala Lumpur. **Cities** (1970 cen.): Kuala Lumpur 451,977; George Town 269,-003; Ipoh 247,953.

Government: Head of state: Paramount Ruler Tuanku Yahya Putra, b. Dec. 10, 1917, in office: Sept. 21, 1975; **Head of government:** Prime Min. Datuk Hussein bin Onn, b. Feb. 12, 1922, in office: Jan. 15, 1976. **Local divisions:** 13 states, each with legislature, chief minister, and titular ruler. **Armed forces:** regulars 62,300; para-military 82,000.

Economy: Industries: Rubber goods, pottery, fertilizers. **Chief crops:** Palm oil, copra, rice, tapioca, sugar, pepper. **Minerals:** Tin (35% world output), iron. **Crude oil output** (1976): 61.6 mln. bbls. **Other resources:** Rubber (35% world output), timber. **Per capita arable land:** 0.2 acres. **Livestock** (1974): 330,000 cattle; 733,000 pigs; 40,000 sheep; 41,600,000 poultry. **Fish catch** (1974): 525,700 metric tons. **Electricity production** (1975): 5,808 mln. kwh. **Labor force:** 50% agric., 8% manuf.

Finance: Currency: Ringgit (Apr. 1977: 2.49=$1 US). **Gross domestic product** (1975): $9.28 bln. **Per capita income** (1974): $659. **Imports** (1976): $3,964 bln.; partners (1974): Jap. 22%, U.S. 10%, U.K. 9%, Sing. 8%. **Exports** (1976): $5.286 bln.; partners (1974): Sing. 22%, Jap. 17%, U.S. 14%, U.K. 7%. **Tourists** (West only) (1974): 1,080,700; receipts: $41 million. **Balance of payments** (1975): $63 mln. **National budget** (1975): $2.10 bln. revenues; $2.57 bln. expenditures. **International reserves** (Oct. 1976): $2.420 bln. **Consumer prices** (change in 1976): 2.6%.

Transport: Railway traffic (1974): 612 mln. passenger-miles; 614 mln. net ton-miles. **Motor vehicles:** in use (1974): 430,400 passenger cars, 140,300 commercial vehicles; assembled (1975): 39,000 passenger cars, 9,300 commercial vehicles. **Civil aviation:** 1,125 passenger miles (1976); 23 mln. freight ton-miles (1976). **Chief ports:** George Town, Kelang, Melaka, Kuching.

Communications: Television sets: 359,000 licenses (1973); 78,000 manufactured (1974). **Radios:** 462,000 licenses (1973). **Telephones in use** (1976): 291,968. **Daily newspaper circulation** (1973): 1,097,000; 95 per 1,000 pop.

Health (most data cover only W. Malaysia): **Life expectancy at birth** (1972): 63.36 male; 68.01 female. **Births** (per 1,000 pop. 1974): 32.1. **Deaths** (per 1,000 pop. 1974): 6.6. **Natural increase** (1974): 2.55%. **Pop. per hospital bed** (1973): 367. **Pop. per physician** (1973): 5,341. **Infant mortality** (per 1,000 pop. under 1 yr. 1974): 35.4.

Education: Literacy (1973): 43%. **Pop. 5-19:** in school (1973): 53%; per teacher (1973): 53.

European traders appeared in the 16th century; Britain established control in 1867. Malaysia was created Sept. 16, 1963. It included Malaya (which had become independent in 1957), plus the formerly-British Singapore, Sabah (N Borneo), and Sarawak (NW Borneo). Singapore was separated in 1965, in order to end tensions between Chinese, the majority in Singapore, and Malays in control of the Malaysian government.

Sabah and Sarawak have a pop. of 1,900,000 (1975).

A monarch is elected by a council of hereditary rulers of the Malayan states every 5 years.

Abundant natural resources have assured prosperity.

Maldives

Republic of Maldives

People: Population (1976 est.): 120,000. **Age distrib.** (%): 0−14: 44.4; 15−59: 52.0; 60+: 3.6. **Pop. density:** 1,043 per sq. mi. **Urban** (1967): 11.3%. **Ethnic groups:** Sinhalese, Dravidian, Arab mixture. **Languages:** Divehi (Sinhalese dialect). **Religions:** Sunni Moslems.

Geography: Area: 115 sq. mi., twice the size of Washington, D.C. **Location:** In the Indian O. SW of India. **Neighbors:** Nearest is India on N. **Topography:** The Maldives comprise 19 atolls with 1,087 islands, 203 inhabited. None of the islands are over 5 sq. mi. in area, and all are nearly flat. **Capital:** Male. **Cities** (1967 cen.): Male 11,760.

Government: Head of state: Pres. Ibrahim Nasir, b. Sept. 2, 1926, in office: Nov. 11, 1968.

Economy: Industries: Fish processing, tourism. **Chief crops:** Coconuts, fruit, millet. **Other resources:** Shells. **Fish catch** (1974): 37,500 metric tons.

Finance: Currency: Rupee (1974: 7.2=$1 US). **Gross domestic product** (est. 1974): $12 mln. **Per capita income** (1974): $100. **Imports** (1974) $3 mln.; **Exports** (1974): $2 mln.; partners (1973): Sri Lanka, Jap.

Transport: Chief port: Male Atoll.

Communications: Radios: 2,300 licenses (1973). **Telephones in use** (1976): 411.

Health: Births (per 1,000 pop. 1965): 50.1. **Deaths** (per 1,000 pop. 1965): 22.9. **Natural increase** (1965): 2.72%.

The islands had been a British protectorate since 1887. The

country became independent July 26, 1965. Britain retained an air base until 1976. Long a sultanate, the Maldives became a republic in 1968.

Mali

Republic of Mali

People: Population (1976 est.): 5,840,000. **Age distrib.** (%): 0–14: 49.1; 15–59: 47.8; 60+: 3.11. **Pop. density:** 13 per sq. mi. **Ethnic groups:** Mande (Bambara, Malinke, Sarakolle) 50%, Peul 17%, Voltaic 12%, Songhai, Tuareg, Moors. **Languages:** French (official), Bambara, others. **Religions:** Moslems 90%, Christians 1%, others.

Geography: Area: 464,873 sq. mi., larger than Texas and California combined. **Location:** In the interior of W. Africa. **Neighbors:** Mauritania, Senegal on W, Guinea, Ivory Coast, Upper Volta on S, Niger on E, Algeria on N. **Topography:** Mali is a landlocked grassy plain in the upper basins of the Senegal and Niger rivers, extending N into the Sahara. **Capital:** Bamako. **Cities** (1972 est.): Bamako (met.) 196,800; (1971 est.) Mopti 32,000.

Government: Head of state: Pres. Moussa Traore, b. Sept. 25, 1936, in office: Nov. 19, 1968. **Local divisions:** 6 regions. **Armed forces:** regulars 4,200; para-military 5,700.

Economy: Chief crops: Millet, rice, peanuts, cotton. **Other resources:** Rubber. **Per capita arable land:** 4.9 acres. **Livestock** (1974): 4,500,000 cattle; 4,100,000 sheep. **Fish catch** (1974): 90,000 metric tons. **Electricity production** (1972): 52 mln. kwh. **Labor force:** 91% agric.

Finance: Currency: Franc (Apr. 1977: 496=$1 US). **Gross domestic product** (1974): $423 mln. **Per capita income** (1974): $73. **Imports** (1975) $188 mln.; partners (1973): Fr. 57% Ivory C. 15%, U.S. 7%, W. Ger. 6%. **Exports** (1975): $72 mln.; partners (1973): Fr. 34%, Ivory C. 28%, Up. Volta 8%, Jap. 6%. **Tourist** receipts (1973): $1 million. **Balance of payments** (1976): $-36.5 mln. **International reserves** (Dec. 1976): $6.9 mln.

Transport: Railway traffic (1973): 59 mln. passenger-miles; 94 mln. net ton-miles. **Motor vehicles:** in use (1969): 4,500 passenger cars, 5,700 commercial vehicles. **Civil aviation:** 53 mln. passenger-miles (1975); 820,000 freight ton-miles (1975).

Communications: Radios: 75,000 in use (1973). **Daily newspaper circulation** (1968): 3,000; 0.6 per 1,000 pop.

Health: Life expectancy at birth (1970-75): 36.5 male; 39.6 female. **Births** (annual per 1,000 pop. 1970-75): 50.1. **Deaths** (annual per 1,000 pop. 1970-75): 25.9. **Natural increase** (annual 1970-75): 2.42%. **Pop. per hospital bed** (1973): 1,281. **Pop. per physician** (1973): 35,867. **Infant mortality** (per 1,000 pop. under 1 yr. 1960-61): 120.

Education: Literacy (1973): 10%. **Pop. 5-19:** in school (1973): 14%; per teacher (1973): 211.

Until the 15th century the area was part of the great Mali Empire. Timbuktu was a center of Islamic study. French rule was secured, 1898. The Sudanese Rep. and Senegal became independent as the Mali Federation June 20, 1960, but Senegal withdrew, and the Sudanese Rep. was renamed Mali.

Mali signed economic agreements with France and, in 1963, with Senegal. In 1968, a coup ended the socialist regime. Famine struck in 1973-74. Loss of livestock and dislocation of Tuareg nomads remained problems.

Malta

People: Population (1975): 318,000. **Age distrib.** (%): 0–14: 26.3; 15–59: 61.1; 60+: 12.6. **Pop. density:** 2,607 per sq. mi. **Urban** (1967): 94.3%. **Ethnic groups:** Italian, Arab, English, and Phoenician mixture. **Languages:** Maltese, English both official. **Religions:** Roman Catholics 98%.

Geography: Area: 122 sq. mi., twice the size of Washington, D.C. **Location:** In center of Mediterranean Sea. **Neighbors:** Nearest is Italy on N. **Topography:** The Island of Malta is 95 sq. mi.; the other islands in the group are Gozo, 26 sq. mi., and Comino, 1 sq. mi. The coastline is heavily indented. Low hills cover the interior. **Capital:** Valletta. **Cities** (1974 est.): Sliema 22,000; Valletta 14,049.

Government: Head of state: Pres. Anton Buttigieg, b. Feb. 19, 1912, in office: Dec. 27, 1976; **Head of government:** Prime Min. Dom Mintoff, b. Aug. 6, 1916, in office: June, 1971. **Local divisions:** 10 electoral districts.

Economy: Industries: Ship repair, textiles, tourism. **Chief crops:** Wheat, potatoes, onions, beans. **Per capita arable land:** 0.1 acres. **Fish catch** (1974): 1,575 metric tons. **Electricity production** (1976): 384 mln. kwh. **Labor force:** 29% manuf.

Finance: Currency: Pound (Apr. 1977: 1 = $2.35 US). **Gross domestic product** (1975): $411 mln. **Per capita income** (1975): $1,558. **Imports** (1976) $423 mln. **Exports** (1976): $228 mln.; partners (1974): Switz., EEC. **Tourists** (1974): 327,800; receipts: $58 million. **Balance of payments** (1976): $94.8 mln. **National budget** (1975): $211 mln. revenues; $203 mln. expenditures. **International reserves** (Feb. 1977): $611.3 mln. **Consumer prices** (change in 1976): 0.6%. **Transport: Motor vehicles:** in use (1974): 51,600 passenger cars, 12,100 commercial vehicles. **Civil aviation:** 212 mln. passenger-miles (1976); 2.4 mln. freight ton-miles (1976). **Chief port:** Valletta.

Communications: Television sets: 61,000 licenses (1973). **Radios:** 129,000 licenses (1973). **Telephones in use** (1976): 55,207.

Health: Life expectancy at birth (1973): 68.1 male; 72.2 female. **Births** (per 1,000 pop. 1975): 18.7. **Deaths** (per 1,000 pop. 1975): 9.7. **Natural increase** (1975): 0.91%. **Pop. per hospital bed** (1973): 91. **Pop. per physician** (1973): 941. **Infant mortality** (per 1,000 pop. under 1 yr. 1975): 18.9.

Education: Literacy (1973): 60%. **Pop. 5-19:** in school (1973): 66%; per teacher (1973): 23.

Malta was ruled by Phoenicians, Romans, Arabs, Normans, the Knights of Malta, France, and Britain (since 1814). It became independent Sept. 21, 1964, with Britain retaining a naval base. Malta became a republic in 1974. In 1972 British base rights were extended for 7 years.

Maltese is a Semitic language, with Italian influences, written in the Latin alphabet. Malta is democratic but nonaligned, and receives aid from Libya and China.

Mauritania

Islamic Republic of Mauritania

People: Population (1975 est.): 1,320,000. **Age distrib.** (%): 0–14: 43.9; 15–59: 50.8; 60+5.3. **Pop. density:** 3.1 per sq. mi. **Urban** (1975): 23.1%. **Ethnic groups:** Arab-Berber 80%, Negroes 20%. **Languages:** French, Hassaniya Arabic, Niger-Congo languages. **Religions:** Moslems 95%, others.

Geography: Area: 419,229 sq. mi., the size of Texas and California combined. **Location:** In W. Africa. **Neighbors:** Morocco on N, Algeria, Mali on E, Senegal on S. **Topography:** The fertile Senegal R. valley in the S gives way to a wide central region of sandy plains and scrub trees. The N is arid and extends into the Sahara. **Capital:** Nouakchott. **Cities** (1975 est.): Nouakchott (met.) 104,000.

Government: Head of state: Pres. Moktar Ould Daddah, b. 1924, in office: Nov. 1960. **Local divisions:** 8 regions, one district. **Armed forces:** regular 4,750, para-military 1,300.

Economy: Chief crops: Dates, grain. **Minerals:** Iron, copper. **Per capita arable land:** 0.5 acres. **Livestock** (1974): 1,800,000 cattle; 2,800,000 sheep. **Fish catch** (1974): 25,600 metric tons. **Electricity production** (1975): 96 mln. kwh. **Labor force:** 85% agric.

Finance: Currency: Ouguiyas (Apr. 1977: 45.6=$1 US). **Gross domestic product** (1973): $293 mln. **Per capita income** (1973): $183. **Imports** (1976) $180 mln.; partners (1972): Fr. 41%, U.S. 11%, U.K. 7%, Senegal 7%. **Exports** (1976): $178 mln.; partners (1972): Fr. 20%, U.K. 18%, It. 14%, Belg. 12%. **Tourists** (1972): 10,300; receipts (1973): $1 million. **Balance of payments** (1976): $11.1 mln. **International reserves** (Feb. 1977): $76.8 mln. **Consumer prices** (change in 1976): 14.4%.

Transport: Railway traffic (1973): 4,228 mln. net ton-miles. **Motor vehicles:** in use (1972): 4,400 passenger cars, 5,000 commercial vehicles. **Chief ports:** Nouakchott, Nouadhibou.

Communications: Radios: 81,000 in use (1973).

Health: Life expectancy at birth (1970-75): 37.0 male; 40.1 female. **Births** (annual per 1,000 pop. 1970-75): 44.8. **Deaths**

(annual per 1,000 pop. 1970-75): 24.9. **Natural increase** (annual 1970-75): 1.99%. **Pop. per hospital bed** (1973): 2,739. **Pop. per physician** (1973): 17,746. **Infant mortality** (per 1,000 pop. under 1 yr. 1964-65): 187.

Education: Literacy (1973): 5%. **Pop. 5-19:** in school (1973): 11%; per teacher (1973): 146.

Mauritania became independent Nov. 28, 1960. It annexed the south of former Spanish Sahara in 1976. Saharan guerrillas stepped up attacks in 1977. Famine struck in 1973-74. France, China, and the U.S. have sent aid.

Mauritius

People: Population (1976): 870,000. **Age distrib.** (%): 0–14: 40.4; 15–59: 53.8, 60+: 5.8. **Pop. density:** 1,105 per sq. mi. **Urban** (1971): 43.9%. **Ethnic groups:** Indians 69%, mulattoes, whites 28%, Chinese 3%. **Languages:** English (official), French, Creole, Hindi, Urdu, Chinese. **Religions:** Hindu 49%, Roman Catholic 32%, Moslems 16%, Protestants 1%.

Geography: Area: 787 sq. mi., smaller than Rhode Island. **Location:** In the Indian O., 500 mi. E of Madagascar. **Neighbors:** Nearest is Madagascar on W. **Topography:** Mauritius in a volcanic island nearly surrounded by coral reefs. A central plateau is encircled by mountain peaks. **Capital:** Port Louis. **Cities** (1977 est.): Port Louis (met.) 141,100.

Government: Head of state: Queen Elizabeth II, represented by Gov.-Gen. Raman Osman; **Head of government:** Prime Min. Seewoosagur Ramgoolam, b. 1900, in office: Mar. 1968. **Local divisions:** 9 administrative divisions.

Economy: Industries: Tourism. **Chief crops:** Sugar cane, tea. **Per capita arable land:** 0.3 acres. **Livestock** (1974): 51,-000 cattle; 430,000 poultry. **Electricity production** (1976): 276 mln. kwh. **Labor force:** 32% agric.

Finance: Currency: Rupee (Apr. 1977: 6.64=$1 US). **Gross domestic product** (1975): $567 mln. **Per capita income** (1975): $629. **Imports** (1975) $332 mln.; partners (1974): U.K. 14%, So. Afr. 9%, Taiwan 8%. **Exports** (1976): $265 mln.; partners (1974): Can. 36%, U.K. 35%, U.S. 8%, Iran 7%. **Tourists** (1973): 68,000; receipts (1974): $20 million. **Balance of payments** (1975): $52.2 mln. **National budget** (1975): $120 mln. revenues; $139 mln. expenditures. **International reserves** (Feb. 1977): $81.8 mln. **Consumer prices** (change in 1976): 13.6%.

Transport: Motor vehicles: in use (1974): 16,100 passenger cars, 8,200 commercial vehicles. **Chief ports:** Port Louis.

Communications: Television sets: 27,000 licenses (1972). **Radios:** 107,000 licenses (1972). **Telephones in use** (1976): 24,900. **Daily newspaper circulation** (1973): 100,000; 115 per 1,000 pop.

Health: Life expectancy at birth (1961-63): 58.66 male; 61.86 female. **Births** (per 1,000 pop. 1975): 25.1. **Deaths** (per 1,000 pop. 1975): 8.1. **Natural increase** (1975): 1.70%. **Pop. per hospital bed** (1973): 252. **Pop. per physician** (1973): 3,192. **Infant mortality** (per 1,000 pop. under 1 yr. 1974): 46.6.

Education: Literacy (1973): 62%. **Pop. 5-19:** in school (1973): 61%; per teacher (1973): 47.

Mauritius was uninhabited when settled in 1638 by the Dutch, who introduced sugar cane. France took over in 1721, bringing African slaves. Britain ruled from 1810 to Mar. 12, 1968, bringing Indian workers for the sugar plantations. Mauritius has a free political life and high literacy and life expectancy.

Mexico

United Mexican States

People: Population (1976 est.): 62,330,000. **Age distrib.** (%): 0-14: 46.4; 15-59: 48.5; 60+ 5. **Pop. density:** 82 per sq. mi. **Urban** (1975): 62.8%. **Ethnic groups:** Mestizo 60%, Indian 30%, Caucasian 10%. **Languages:** Spanish, Indian languages 1.5%, bilingual 6.5%. **Religions:** Roman Catholics 96%, Protestants 2%.

Geography: Area: 761,601 sq. mi., three times the size of Texas. **Location:** In southern N. America. **Neighbors:** U.S. on N, Guatemala, Belize on S. **Topography:** The Sierra Madre Occidental Mts. run NW-SE near the west coast; the Sierra Madre Oriental Mts., run near the Gulf of Mexico. They join S of Mexico City. Between the two ranges lies the dry central plateau, altitude from 5,000 to 8,000 ft., generally rising toward the S, with temperate vegetation. The coastal lowlands are tropical. About 45% of land is arid. **Capital:** Mexico City. **Cities** (1975 est.): Mexico City (met.) 11,339,774; Guadalajara (met.) 1,963,277; Monterrey (met.) 1,637,681; Juarez 520,539; Leon 496,598; Tijuana (met.) 495,657; Pueblade Zaragoza 482,155.

Government: Head of state: Pres. Jose Lopez Portillo, b. June 16, 1920, in office: Dec. 1, 1976. **Local divisions:** Federal district and 31 states, each with governor, elected legislature, and substantial powers. **Armed forces:** regulars 89,500: reserves 250,000.

Economy: Industries: Steel, chemicals, electric goods, textiles, rubber, paper, cement, shoes, glass, handicrafts, tourism. **Chief crops:** Cotton, coffee, sugar cane, tomatoes, wheat, corn, rice, tobacco, beans, cocoa, sisal (50% world supply), bananas. **Minerals:** Silver, gold, copper, lead, zinc, antimony, mercury, arsenic, graphite, molybdenum, sulphur, coal, opal, oil, gas. **Crude oil output** (1976): 327 mln. bbls. Vast reserves have been found. **Per capita arable land:** 1.1 acres. **Livestock** (1976): 28,700,000 cattle; 12,500,000 pigs; 5,300,000 sheep; 160,000,000 poultry. **Fish catch** (1975): 499,000 metric tons. **Electricity production** (1976): 46,272 mln. kwh. **Labor force:** 39% agriculture; 17% manuf.

Finance: Currency: Peso (Apr. 1977: 22.6=$1 US). **Gross domestic product** (1975): $79 bln. **Per capita income** (1970): $632. **Imports** (1976) $6,036 bln.; partners (1973): U.S. 60%, W. Ger. 7%, Jap. 5%, Fr. 3%. **Exports** (1976): $3.319 bln.; partners (1973): U.S. 63%, Jap. 7%, W. Ger. 3%. **Tourists** (1974): 3,360,900; receipts: $2.056 billion. **Balance of payments** (1976): $−693 mln. **National budget** (1974): $7.39 bln. revenues; $9.86 bln. expenditures. **International reserves** (Mar. 1976): $1,501 bln. **Consumer prices** (change in 1976): 16.0%.

Transport: Railway traffic (1974): 2,865 mln. passenger-miles; 19,309 mln. net ton-miles. **Motor vehicles:** in use (1973): 1,737,700 passenger cars, 632,100 commercial vehicles; manufactured assembled (1975): 264,000 passenger cars, 106,000 commercial vehicles. **Civil aviation:** 4,136 mln. passenger-miles (1975); 49 mln. freight ton-miles (1975). **Chief ports:** Veracruz, Tampico, Mazattan, Coatzacoalcos.

Communications: Television sets: 4,339,000 in use (1973); 547,000 manufactured (1974). **Radios:** 16,870,000 in use (1973); 931,000 manufactured (1974). **Telephones in use** (1976): 2,914,531.

Health: Life expectancy at birth (1965-70): 61.03 male; 63.73 female. **Births:** (annual per 1,000 pop. 1970-75): 42.0. **Deaths** (annual per 1,000 pop. 1970-75): 8.6. **Natural increase** (annual 1970-75): 3.34%. **Pop. per hospital bed** (1973): 628. **Pop. per physician** (1973): 1,392. **Infant mortality** (per 1,000 pop. under 1 yr. 1973): 52.0.

Education: Literacy (1973): 76%. **Pop. 5-19:** in school (1973): 54%; per teacher (1973): 56.

Mexico was the site of advanced Indian civilizations before the Spanish conquest. The Mayas, an agricultural people, moved up from Yucatan and built immense stone pyramids and invented a calendar. The Toltecs were overcome by the Aztecs, who founded Tenochtitlan 1325 A.D., now Mexico City. Hernando Cortes, Spanish conquistador, destroyed the Aztec empire, 1519-1521.

After 3 centuries of Spanish rule the people rose, under Fr. Miguel Hidalgo y Costilla (a priest), 1810, Fr. Morelos y Payon (another priest), 1812, and Gen. Agustin Iturbide, who made independence effectual Sept. 27, 1821, but made himself emperor as Agustin I. A republic was declared in 1823.

Mexican territory extended into the present American Southwest and California until Texas revolted and established a republic in 1836; the Mexican legislature refused recognition but was unable to enforce its authority there. After numerous clashes, the U.S.-Mexican War, 1846-48, resulted in the loss by Mexico of the lands north of the Rio Grande.

French arms supported an Austrian archduke on the throne of Mexico as Maximilian I, 1864-67, but pressure from the U.S. forced France to withdraw. A dictatorial rule by Porfirio Diaz, president 1877-80, 1884-1911, led to fighting by rival forces until the new constitution of Feb. 5, 1917 provided social reform. Since then Mexico has developed large-scale programs of social security, labor protection and school improvement. A constitutional provision requires management to share profits with labor.

The Institutional Revolutionary party has been dominant in

politics since 1929. Radical opposition, including some guerrilla activity, has been contained by strong measures. In 1970 the legal voting age was lowered from 21 to 18.

The presidency of Luis Echeverria, 1970-76, was marked by a more leftist foreign policy and domestic rhetoric. Some land redistribution begun in 1976 was reversed under the succeeding administration.

Gains in agriculture, industry, and social services have been achieved since 1940. The land is rich, but the rugged topography and lack of sufficient rainfall are major obstacles. 45% of the land is arid. Crops and farm prices are controlled, as are export and import. Large estates have been expropriated; since 1915 the government has distributed about 160 million acres to small farmers through landholding communities (ejidos). Four million peasants are still without land, and five million others hold minimal plots.

Monaco

Principality of Monaco

People: Population (1976): 30,000. **Age distrib.** (%): 0–14: 13.0; 15–59: 57.0; 60+:30.1. **Ethnic groups;** French 58%, Italian 17%, Monegasque 15%. **Languages:** French (official), Monegasque, Italian, English. **Religions:** Roman Catholics 95%.

Geography: Area: 600 acres. **Location:** On the NW Mediterranean coast. **Neighbors:** France to W, N, E. **Topography:** Monaco-Ville sits atop a high promontory, the rest of the principality rises from the port up the hillside. **Capital:** Monaco.

Government: Head of state: Prince Rainier III, b. May 31, 1923, in office: May 9, 1949; **Head of government:** Min. of State Andre Saint-Mleux, in office: 1970.

Economy: Industries: Tourism, gambling. **Finance: Currency:** French Franc. **Tourists** (excluding excursionists) (1973): 137,100. **Chief ports:** La Condamine.

Communications: Television sets: 6,300 in use (1969). **Radios:** 7,500 in use (1973). **Telephones in use** (1976): 21,-018.

Health: Births (per 1,000 pop. 1974): 8.2. **Deaths** (per 1,000 pop. 1974): 12.3. **Natural increase** (1974): -0.41%. **Infant mortality** (per 1,000 pop. under 1 yr. 1970): 9.3.

An independent principality for over 300 years, Monaco has belonged to the House of Grimaldi since 1297 except during the French Revolution. It was placed under the protectorate of Sardinia in 1815, and under that of France, 1861. The Prince of Monaco was an absolute ruler until a constitution was promulgated in 1911.

Monaco's fame as a tourist resort and international conference city is widespread. It is noted for its mild climate and magnificent scenery. The area has been extended by land reclamation.

Mongolia

Mongolian People's Republic

People: Population (1976 est.): 1,490,000. **Pop. density:** 2.5 per sq. mi. **Urban** (1973): 46.4%. **Ethnic groups:** Khalkha Mongols 76%, other Mongols 8%, Kazakhs 5%, other Turks, Russians, Chinese. **Languages:** Khalkha Mongolian (official, written in Cyrillic letters since 1941), Turkic 7%. **Religions:** Lama Buddhism prevailed, has been curbed.

Geography: Area: 604,247 sq. mi., more than twice the size of Texas. **Location:** In E Central Asia. **Neighbors:** USSR on N, China on S. **Topography:** Much of Mongolia is a high plateau with mountains, salt lakes, and vast grasslands. Arid lands in the S are part of the Gobi Desert. **Capital:** Ulan Bator. **Cities** (1973 est.): Ulan Bator 326,000.

Government: Head of state: Chmn. Yumjaagiyn Tsedenbal, b. Sept. 17, 1916, in office: June 11, 1974; **Head of government:** Chmn. Jambyn Batmunkh, b. Mar. 10, 1926, in office: June, 1974; **Head of Communist Party:** First Sec. Yumjaagiyn Tsedenbal, in office: 1958. **Local divisions:** Capital city and 18 provinces. **Armed forces:** regulars 30,000; reserves 30,000.

Economy: Industries: Food processing, textiles, chemicals, cement. **Chief crops:** Grain. **Minerals:** Coal, tungsten, copper, molybdenum, gold, tin. **Per capita arable land:** 1.3 acres. **Livestock** (1974): 2,235,000 cattle; 14,070,000 sheep. **Electricity production** (1973): 669 mln. kwh. **Labor force:** 62% agric.; 10% manuf.

Finance: Currency: Togrog (1974: 3.33=$1 US). **Gross domestic product** (est. 1974): $750 mln. **Per capita income** (1974): $500. **Imports** (1973) $370 mln.; partners (1973): USSR 90%, Czech. 3%, E. Ger. 2%. **Exports** (1973): $160 mln.; partners (1973): USSR 76%, Czech. 7%, E. Ger. 5%, Pol. 4%.

Transport: Railway traffic (1974): 129 mln. passenger-miles; 1,438 mln. net ton-miles.

Communications: Television sets: 3,000 in use (1973). **Radios:** 166,000 in use (1970). **Telephones in use** (1976): 30,983. **Daily newspaper circulation** (1970): 133,000; 103 per 1,000 pop.

Health: Life expectancy at birth (1970-75): 59.1 male; 62.3 female. **Births** (annual per 1,000 pop. 1970-75): 38.8. **Deaths** (annual per 1,000 pop. 1970-75): 9.3. **Natural increase** (annual 1970-75): 2.95%. **Pop. per hospital bed** (1973): 104. **Pop. per physician** (1973): 504. **Infant mortality** (per 1,000 pop. under 1 yr. 1973): 75.

Education: Literacy (1973): 95%. **Pop. 5-19:** in school (1973): 60%; per teacher (1973): 49.

One of the world's oldest countries, Mongolia reached the zenith of its power in the 13th century when Genghis Khan and his successors conquered all of China and extended their influence as far W as Hungary and Poland. In later centuries, the empire dissolved and Mongolia came under the suzerainty of China.

With the advent of the 1911 Chinese revolution, Mongolia, with Russian backing, declared its independence. A Mongolian Communist regime was established July 11, 1921.

In the early 1970s Mongolia was changing from a nomadic culture to one of settled agriculture and growing industries with aid from the USSR and East European nations.

Mongolia has sided with the Russians in the Sino-Soviet dispute. A Mongolian-Soviet mutual assistance pact was signed Jan. 15, 1966, and thousands of Soviet troops are based in the country. Ties were expanded in a 1976 pact.

Morocco

Kingdom of Morocco

People: Population (1976 est.): 17,830,000. **Age distrib.** (%):0-14: 46.6; 15-59: 49.2; 60+: 4.2 **Pop. density:** 104 per sq. mi. **Urban** (1974): 37.9%. **Ethnic groups:** Arabs 65%, Berbers 33%, Europeans 1%. **Languages:** Arabic, Berber, French. **Religions:** Sunni Moslems 99%.

Geography: Area: 171,953 sq. mi., larger than California. **Location:** on NW coast of Africa. **Neighbors:** Mauritania on S, Algeria on E. **Topography:** Morocco consists of five natural regions: a series of mountain ranges (Riff in the N, Middle Atlas, Upper Atlas, and Anti-Atlas); a series of rich plains in the W; alluvial plains in SW; well-cultivated plateaus in the center; a pre-Sahara arid zone extending from SE. **Capital:** Rabat. **Cities** (1973 est.): Casablanca (met.) 1,753,400; Rabat-Sale (met.) 596,600; Marrakech (met.) 436,300; Fez (met.) 426,000; Meknes (met.) 403,000. **Government: Head of state:** King Hassan II, b. July 11, 1929, in office: Mar. 3, 1961; **Head of government:** Prime Min. Ahmed Osman, in office: Nov. 2, 1972. **Local divisions:** 2 urban prefectures, 19 provinces. **Armed forces:** regulars 73,000; para-military 30,000.

Economy: Industries: Carpets, clothing, leather goods, tourism. **Chief crops:** Grain, fruits, dates, grapes. **Minerals:** Phosphate (largest exporter), cobalt, antimony, manganese, zinc, lead, oil, coal. **Crude oil output** (1976): 35,000 bbls. **Per capita arable land:** 1.0 acres. **Livestock** (1974): 3,400,000 cattle; 11,-000 pigs; 16,000 sheep; 23,000,000 poultry. **Fish catch** (1974): 288,100 metric tons. **Electricity production** (1976): 3,168 mln. kwh. **Labor force:** 61% agric.

Finance: Currency: Dirhams (Apr. 1977: 4.50=$1 US). **Gross domestic product** (1975): $7.38 bln. **Per capita income**

(1975): $440. **Imports** (1976) $2.618 bln.; partners (1973): Fr. 32%, U.S. 11%, W. Ger. 8%, Sp. 5%. **Exports** (1976): $1.261 bln.; partners (1973): Fr. 34%, W. Ger. 10%, It. 7%, U.K. 5%. **Tourists** (1974): 1,338,100; receipts: $349 million. **Balance of payments** (1975): $-21 mln. **National budget** (1974): $1.68 bln. revenues; $2.00 bln. expenditures. **International reserves** (Jan. 1977): $465 mln. **Consumer prices** (change in 1976): 8.5%.

Transport: Railway traffic (1974): 482 mln. passenger-miles; 2,237 mln. net ton-miles. **Motor vehicles:** in use (1974): 303,500 passenger cars, 111,400 commercial vehicles; assembled (1976): 21,000 passenger cars, 12,000 commercial vehicles. **Civil aviation:** 608 mln. passenger-miles (1975); 6.5 mln. freight-miles top-miles (1975). **Chief prts:** Tangier, Casablanca, Kenitra.

Communications: Televison sets: 333,000 licenses (1973). **Radios:** 1,216,000 licenses (1973); 43,000 manufactured (1973). **Telephones in use** (1976): 198,500. **Daily newspaper circulation** (1972): 234,000; 15 per 1,000 pop.

Health: Life expectancy at birth (1970-75): 51.4 male; 54.5 female. **Births** (annual per 1,000 pop. 1970-75): 46.2. **Deaths** (annual per 1,000 pop. 1970-75): 15.7. **Natural increase** (annual 1970-75): 3.05%. **Pop. per hospital bed** (1973): 703. **Pop. per physician** (1973): 13,592. **Infant mortality** (per 1,000 pop. under 1 yr. 1962): 149.

Education: Literacy (1973): 21%. **Pop. 5-19:** in school (1973): 26%; per teacher (1973): 103.

Berbers were the original inhabitants, followed by Carthaginians and Romans. Arabs conquered in 683. In the 11th and 12th centuries, a Berber empire ruled all NW Africa and most of Spain from Morocco.

Part of Morocco came under Spanish rule in the 19th century; in the early 20th France took control of the rest. Tribal uprisings lasted from 1911 to 1933. The country became independent Mar. 2, 1956. Tangier, an internationalized seaport, was turned over to Morocco in 1956. Ifni, a Spanish enclave, was ceded in 1969.

Morocco annexed over 70,000 sq. mi. of phosphate-rich land Apr. 14, 1976, two-thirds of former Spanish Sahara, with the remainder annexed by Mauritania. Spain had withdrawn in February. Polisario, a guerrilla movement, proclaimed the region independent Feb. 27, and launched attacks with Algerian support.

Morocco accepted U.S. military and economic aid. It has agreements with France on economic cooperation. Conservative King Hassan II exercises considerable powers.

Mozambique

People's Republic of Mozambique

People: Population (1976 est.): 9,440,000. **Pop. density:** 31 per sq. mi. **Ethnic groups:** Bantu tribes. **Languages:** Portuguese (official), others. **Religions:** Christians 15%, Moslems 12.5%, others.

Geography: Area: 303,373 sq. mi., larger than Texas. **Location:** On SE coast of Africa. **Neighbors:** Tanzania on N, Malawi, Zambia, Rhodesia on W, South Africa, Swaziland on S. **Topography:** Coastal lowlands comprise nearly half the country with plateaus rising in steps to the mountains along the western border. **Capital:** Maputo. **Cities** (1970 cen.): Maputo (met.) 383,775; Beria 115,000.

Government: Head of state: Pres. Samora Machel, b. Oct. 1933, in office: June 25, 1975; **Head of government:** Prime Min. Joaquim Alberto Chissano, b. 1939, in office: June 25, 1975. **Local divisions:** 10 provinces.

Economy: Industries: Cement, alcohol, textiles. **Chief crops:** Cashews, cotton, sugar, copra, sisal, tea. **Minerals:** Coal, tantalite, copper, iron, bauxite, gold. **Per capita arable land:** 0.7 acres. **Livestock** (1974): 2,250,000 cattle; 280,000 pigs; 250,000 sheep; 6,300,000 poultry. **Electricity production** (1975): 552 mln. kwh. **Labor force:** 74% agric.

Finance: Currency: Escudo (1974: 25.4=$1 US). **Gross domestic product** (est. 1974): $3 bln. **Per capita income** (1974): $300. **Imports** (1974): $467 min.; partners (1973): So. Afr. 20%, Port. 19%, W. Ger. 13%, Fr. 8%. **Exports** (1975): $198 mln.; partners (1973): Port. 36%, U.S. 14%, So. Afr. 9%, U.K. 6%.

Transport: Railway traffic (1973): 246 mln. passenger-miles; 2,111 mln. net ton-miles. **Motor vehicles:** in use (1972): 89,300 passenger cars, 21,500 commercial vehicles. **Chief ports:** Maputo, Beira, Nacala.

Communications: Television sets: 1,000 licenses (1973). **Radios:** 176,000 licenses (1973); 24,000 manufactured (1974). **Telephones in use** (1976): 49,789. **Daily Newspaper circulation** (1973): 42,000; 5 per 1,000 pop.

Health: Life expectancy at birth (1970-75): 41.9 male; 45.1 female. **Births** (annual per 1,000 pop. 1970-75): 43.1. **Deaths** (annual per 1,000 pop. 1970-75): 20.1. **Natural increase** (annual 1970-75): 2.30%. **Infant mortality** (per 1,000 pop. under 1 yr. 1969): 92.5.

The first Portuguese post on the Mozambique coast was established in 1505, on the trade route to the East. Mozambique became independent June 25, 1975, after a ten-year war against Portuguese colonial domination. The 1974 revolution in Portugal paved the way for the orderly transfer of power to Frelimo (Front for the Liberation of Mozambique), which had earlier gained complete control of the independence movement. Frelimo took over local administration Sept. 20, 1974, over the opposition, in part violent, of some blacks and whites. The new government, led by Maoist Pres. Samora Machel, promised a gradual transition to a communist system, beginning with indoctrination to combat "individualism" and capitalist or traditionalist values. All private schools were closed. Rural collective farms were called for in a July 27, 1975, directive. All private homes were nationalized in 1976. Economic problems included the emigration of most of the country's 160,000 whites, a politically untenable economic dependence on white-ruled South Africa, and a large external debt.

Mozambique closed its border with Rhodesia in March 1976. Border clashes intensified, with Rhodesian troops attacking black Rhodesian guerrillas within Mozambique. Soviet arms were sent following a 1977 friendship treaty.

Nauru

Republic of Nauru

People: Population (1975 est.): 7,128. **Age distrib.** (%): 0–14: 40.0; 15–59: 57.8; 60+: 2.3. **Pop. density:** 891 per sq. mi. **Ethnic groups:** Polynesians, Chinese 15%, European 7%. **Languages:** Nauruan, English. **Religions:** Christianity nearly universal.

Geography: Area: 8 sq. mi. **Location:** In western Pacific O. just S of Equator. **Neighbors:** Nearest are Solomon Is. **Topography:** The bulk of the island is a plateau bearing high grade phosphate deposits, surrounded by a coral cliff and a sandy shore in concentric rings. **Capital:** Yaren.

Government: Head of state: Pres. Bernard Dowiyogo, b. Feb. 14, 1946, in office: Dec. 18, 1976.

Finance: Currency: Australian Dollar. **Gross domestic product** (est. 1974): $60 mln. **Per capita income** (1974): $7,000. **Imports** (1974): $14 min.; partners (1974): Australia 58%, Neth. 30%, U.K. 6%, Jap. 5%. **Exports** (1974): $50 mln.; partners (1974): Australia 57%, Jap. 23%, N.Z. 18%.

Communications: Radios: 3,900 in use (1973).

Health: Births (per 1,000 pop. 1968): 32.2. **Deaths** (per 1,000 pop. 1968): 8.3. **Natural increase** (1968): 2.39%. **Infant mortality** (per 1,000 pop. under 1 yr. 1968): 51.8.

The island was discovered in 1798 by the British but was formally annexed to the German Empire in 1886. After World War I, Nauru became a League of Nations mandate administered by Australia. During World War II the Japanese occupied the island and shipped 1,200 Nauruans to the fortress island of Truk as slave laborers.

In 1947 Nauru was made a UN trust territory, administered by Australia on behalf of the 3 trust powers: Australia, Great Britain and New Zealand. Nauru became an independent republic Jan. 31, 1968.

Phosphate exports provide one of the world's highest per capita revenues for the 3,500 native Nauruans (883 Chinese, 627 Europeans and 1,787 Pacific Islanders also live in Nauru, many working in the phosphate industry). The deposits are expected to be nearly exhausted by 1990.

Nepal

Kingdom of Nepal

People: Population (1976 est.): 12,860,000. **Age distrib.** (%): 0–14: 40.6; 15–59: 53.9; 60+: 5.6. **Pop. density:** 237 per sq. mi. **Urban** (1971): 4.0%. **Ethnic groups:** The many tribes are descendants of Indian, Tibetan, and Central Asian migrants. **Languages:** Nepali (official) (an Indic language), Newari, 11 others. **Religions:** Hindus 90%, Buddhists 9%.

Geography: Area: 54,362 sq. mi., the size of North Carolina. **Location:** Astride the Himalaya Mts. **Neighbors:** China on N, India on S. **Topography:** The Himalayas stretch across the N, the hill country with its fertile valleys extends across the center, while the southern border region is part of the flat, subtropical Ganges Plain. **Capital:** Kathmandu. **Cities** (1971 cen.): Kathmandu (met.) 353,756.

Government: Head of state: King Birendra Bir Bikram, b. Dec. 28, 1945, in office: Jan. 31, 1972; **Head of government:** Prime Min. Tulsi Giri, in office: Dec. 1, 1975. **Local divisions:** 14 zones, 75 districts. **Armed forces:** regulars 20,000.

Economy: Industries: Hides, drugs, tourism. **Chief crops:** Jute, rice, grain. **Minerals:** Quartz. **Other resources:** Forests. **Per capita arable land:** 0.4 acres. **Livestock** (1974): 6,500,000 cattle; 310,000 pigs; 2,280,000 sheep; 20,078,000 poultry. **Electricity production** (1972): 101 mln. kwh. **Labor force:** 94% agric; 1% manuf.

Finance: Currency: Rupee (Apr. 1977: 12.5=$1 US). **Gross domestic product** (1974-5): $1.36 bln. **Per capita income** (1974): $96. **Imports** (1976) $166 mln.; partners (1974): India 80%, Jap. 10%, Hong Kong 3%. **Exports** (1976): $103 mln.; partners (1974): India 83%, Jap. 3%, Sing. 2%. **Tourists** (1974): 89,800; receipts: $9 million. **National budget** (1976): $94.6 mln. revenues; $158.5 mln. expenditures. **International reserves** (Jan. 1977): $137.7 mln. **Consumer prices** (change in 1976): -1.8%.

Transport: Motor vehicles: in use (1968): 4,000 passenger cars, 3,000 commercial vehicles.

Communications: Radios: 100,000 in use (1972).

Health: Life expectancy at birth (1970-75): 42.2 male; 45.0 female. **Births** (annual per 1,000 pop. 1970-75): 42.9. **Deaths** (annual per 1,000 pop. 1970-75): 20.3. **Natural increase** (annual 1970-75): 2.26%. **Pop. per hospital bed** (1973): 6,010. **Pop. per physician** (1973): 42,929. **Infant mortality** (per 1,000 pop. under 1 yr. 1973): 169.

Education: Literacy (1973); 9%. **Pop. 5-19:** in school (1973): 16%; per teacher (1973): 99.

Nepal was originally a group of petty principalities, the inhabitants of one of which, the Gurkhas, became dominant about 1769. In 1951 King Tribhubana Bir Bikram, member of the Shah family, ended the system of rule by hereditary premiers of the Ranas family, who had kept the kings virtual prisoners, and established a cabinet system of government.

Virtually closed to the outside world for centuries, Nepal is now linked to India and Pakistan by roads and air service and to Tibet by road. Polygamy, child marriage, and the caste system were officially abolished in 1963.

India has been the largest aid donor and is the chief trade partner, but Nepal has cultivated good relations with China as well.

Students and political opponents were arrested in 1974 following violent protests.

Netherlands

Kingdom of the Netherlands

People: Population (1976): 13,770,000. **Age distrib.** (%): 0–14: 26.8; 15–59: 58.6; 60+: 14.7. **Pop. density:** 970 per sq. mi. **Urban** (1974): 77.2%. **Ethnic groups:** Dutch. **Languages:** Dutch. **Religions:** Roman Catholics 40%, Protestants 40%.

Geography: Area: 14,192 sq. mi., the size of Mass., Conn., and R.I. combined. **Location:** In NW Europe on North Sea. **Topography:** The land is flat, with average altitude of 37 ft. above sea level, with much land below sea level, reclaimed and protected by dikes, of which there are 1,500 miles. Since 1927 the government has been draining the IJsselmeer, formerly the Zuider Zee, converting the reclaimed land into farms. By 1972, 410,000 of a planned 550,000 acres had been drained. Work is also progressing on damming the SW estuaries, into which flow the Rhine, Meuse, and Scheldt rivers. **Capital:** Amsterdam (govt. sits in The Hague). **Cities** (1974 est.): Rotterdam (met.) 1,036,193; Amsterdam (met.) 996,221; Hague (met.) 681,737; Utrecht (met.) 462,305. **Government: Head of state:** Queen Juliana, b. Apr. 30, 1909, in office: Sept. 6, 1948; **Head of government:** Prime Min. Joop den Uyl, b. Aug. 9, 1919, in office: May 11, 1973. **Local divisions:** 11 provinces, with elected executives. **Armed forces:** regulars 112,200; reserves 183,300.

Economy: Industries: Metals, machinery, food products, chemicals, textiles, oil refinery, diamond cutting, pottery, electronics, tourism. **Chief crops:** Grains, potatoes, sugar beets, vegetables, fruits, flowers. **Minerals:** Natural gas, oil. **Crude oil output** (1976): 9.4 mln. bbls. **Per capita arable land:** 0.1 acres. **Livestock** (1976): 4,550,000 cattle; 7,100,000 pigs; 800,000 sheep; 67,895,000 poultry. **Fish catch** (1975): 351,000 metric tons. **Electricity production** (1976): 58,056 mln kwh. **Labor force:** 7% agric.; 25% manuf.

Finance: Currency: Guilders (Apr. 1977: 2.45=$1 US). **Gross domestic product** (1976): $88.3 bln. **Per capita income** (1975): $5,345. **Imports** (1976): $40.702 bln.; partners (1974): W. Ger. 26%, Belg. 14%, Iran 9%, U.S. 9%. **Exports** (1976): $40.073 bln.; partners (1974): W. Ger. 30%, Belg. 13%, Fr. 10%, U.K. 9%. **Tourists** (1974): 2,683,400; receipts: $1.039 billion. **Balance of payments** (1976): $329 mln. **National Budget** (1976): $29.1 bln. revenues; $32.3 bln. expenditures. **International reserves** (Feb. 1977): $7.001 bln. **Consumer prices** (change in 1976): 8.8%.

Transport: Railway traffic (1974): 5,334 mln. passenger-miles; 2,093 mln. net ton-miles. **Motor vehicles:** in use (1974): 3,440,000 passenger cars, 347,000 commercial vehicles; manufactured (1976): 74,000 passenger cars, 12,000 commercial vehicles. **Civil aviation:** 6,289 mln. passenger-miles (1975); 381 mln. freight ton-miles (1975). **Chief ports:** Rotterdam, Amsterdam, IJmuiden.

Communications: Television sets: 3,462,000 licenses (1973). **Radios:** 3,811,000 licenses (1973). **Telephones in use** (1976): 5,047,117. **Daily newspaper circulation** (1973): 4,175,-000; 311 per 1,000 pop.

Health: Life expectancy at birth (1973): 71.2 male; 77.2 female. **Births** (per 1,000 pop. 1975): 13.0. **Deaths** (per 1,000 pop. 1975): 8.3. **Natural increase** (1975): 0.48%. **Pop. per hospital bed** (1973): 84. **Pop. per physician** (1973): 696. **Infant mortality** (per 1,000 pop. under 1 yr. 1975): 10.6.

Education: Literacy (1973): 99%. **Pop. 5-19:** in school (1973): 62%; per teacher (1973): 37.

Julius Caesar conquered the region in 55 B.C., when it was inhabited by Celtic and Germanic tribes.

After the empire of Charlemagne (d. 814) fell apart, the Netherlands (Holland, Belgium, Flanders) split among counts, dukes and bishops, passed to Burgundy and thence to Charles V of Spain. His son, Philip II, tried to check the Dutch drive toward political freedom and Protestantism (1568-1573). William the Silent, prince of Orange, led a confederation of the northern provinces, called Estates, in the Union of Utrecht, 1579. The Estates retained individual sovereignty, but were represented jointly in the States-General, a body that had control of foreign affairs and defense. In 1581 they repudiated allegiance to Spain. The rise of the Dutch republic to naval, economic and artistic eminence came in the 17th Century.

The United Dutch Republic ended 1795 when the French formed the Batavian Republic. Napoleon made his brother Louis king of Holland, 1806; Louis abdicated 1810 when Napoleon annexed Holland. In 1813 the French were expelled. In 1815 the Congress of Vienna formed a kingdom of the Netherlands, including Belgium, under William I. In 1830, the Belgians seceded and formed a separate kingdom.

The constitution, promulgated 1814, and subsequently revised, assures a hereditary constitutional monarchy. The reigning sovereign is Queen Juliana.

The Netherlands maintained its neutrality in World War I, but was invaded and brutally occupied by Germany from 1940 to 1945. After the war, neutrality was abandoned, and the country joined NATO, the Western European Union, the Benelux Union, and, in 1957, became a charter member of the Common Market.

In 1949, after several years of fighting, the Netherlands granted independence to Indonesia, where it had ruled since the 17th century. In 1963, West New Guinea was turned over to Indonesia, after five years of controversy and seizure of Dutch property in Indonesia.

Some 200,000 Indonesians emigrated to the Netherlands. Of them, 35,000 were from the South Moluccan islands. Terrorists demanding independence for South Molucca from Indonesia staged train hijackings and other incidents in the Netherlands in 1975 and 1977.

Surinam, a Dutch associated state on the northern coast of South America, became independent in 1975. About 160,000 Surinamers (most of them E. Indians), one third of the population, emigrated to the Netherlands, adding to problems of unemployment.

Though the Netherlands has been heavily industrialized, its productive small farms export large quantities of pork and dairy foods.

Rotterdam, located along the principal mouth of the Rhine, handles the most cargo of any ocean port in the world. Canals, of which there are 3,478 miles, are important in transportation. The Rhine, Meuse, and Scheldt reach the sea through the Netherlands and carry enormous traffic.

Netherlands Antilles

The **Netherland Antilles**, constitutionally on a level of equality with the Netherlands homeland within the Kingdom, consist of 2 groups of islands in the West Indies. **Curacao, Aruba** and **Bonaire** are near the South American coast; **St. Eustatius, Saba** and the southern part of **St. Maarten** are SE of Puerto Rico. Northern two-thirds of St. Maarten belong to French Guadeloupe; the French call the island St. Martin. Total area of the 2 groups is 395 sq. mi., including; Aruba 70, Bonaire 112, Curacao 180, St. Eustatius 12, Saba 5, St. Maarten (Dutch part) 16.

The Netherlands Antilles population (est. 1976) was 240,000. Willemstad is the capital. Chief products are corn, pulse, salt and phosphate; principal industry is the refining of crude oil from Venezuela. Tourism is an important industry, as are electronics and shipbuilding.

New Zealand

Dominion of New Zealand

People: Population (1976): 3,140,000. **Age distrib.** (%): 0–14: 30.8; 15–59: 56.5; 60+: 12.7. **Pop. density:** 30 per sq. mi. **Urban** (1971): 81.4%. **Ethnic groups:** European (mostly British) 90%, Polynesian (mostly Maori) 9%. **Languages:** English, Maori. **Religions:** Protestants 70%, Roman Catholics 16%.

Geography: Area: 103,736 sq. mi., the size of Colorado. **Location:** In SW Pacific O. **Neighbors:** Nearest are Australia on W, Fiji, Tongo on N. **Topography:** Each of the two main islands (North and South Is.) is mainly hilly and mountainous. The east coasts consist of fertile plains, especially the broad Canterbury Plains on South I. A volcanic plateau is in center of North I. South Island has glaciers and 15 peaks over 10,000 ft. **Capital:** Wellington. **Cities** (1973 est.): Wellington (met.) 346,900; Auckland (met.) 289,650; Christchurch (met.) 285,920.

Government: Head of state: Queen Elizabeth II, represented by Gov.-Gen. Keith Holyoak; **Head of government:** Prime Min. Robert David Muldoon, b. Sept. 1921, in office: Nov. 1975. **Local divisions:** 112 counties, 142 boroughs, town districts. **Armed forces:** regulars 12,500; reserves 12,600.

Economy: Industries: Food processing, paper, steel, aluminum, oil products. **Chief crops:** Grain. **Minerals:** Oil, gas, gold, iron, limestone, diatomite, coal, pumice. **Crude oil output** (1976): 1.4 mln. bbls. **Other resources:** Wool, timber. **Per capita arable land:** 0.6 acres. **Livestock** (1976): 9,650,000 cattle; 505,000 pigs; 56,700,000 sheep; 5,704,000 poultry; meat, wool, and dairy products yield 70% of exports. **Fish catch** (1974): 69,100 metric tons. **Electricity production** (1975): 20,064 mln. kwh. **Labor force:** 12% agric.; 25% manuf.

Finance: Currency: Dollar (Apr. 1977: 1=$0.96 US). **Gross domestic product** (1975): $13.40 bln. **Per capita income** (1975): $3,943. **Imports** (1976): $3,254 bln.; partners (1974): Australia 20%, U.K. 18%, Jap. 15%, U.S. 13%. **Exports** (1976): $2.795 bln.; partners (1974): U.K. 20%, U.S. 14%, Jap. 13%, Australia 11%. **Tourists** (1974—10 mos.): 347,800; receipts: $131 million. **Balance of payments** (1976): $8 mln. **National budget** (1975): $4.18 bln. revenues; $4.94 bln. expenditures. **International reserves** (Feb. 1977): $509 mln. **Consumer prices** (change in 1976): 16.9%.

Transport: Railway traffic (1974): 318 mln. passenger-miles; 2,217 mln. net ton-miles. **Motor vehicles:** in use (1974): 1,122,400 passenger cars, 198,900 commercial vehicles; assembled (1976): 70,000 passenger cars, 11,500 commercial vehicles. **Civil aviation:** 2,347 mln. passenger-miles (1975); 66 mln. freight ton-miles (1975). **Chief ports:** Aukland, Wellington, Lyttleton, Tauranga.

Communications: Television sets: 732,000 licenses (1973); 97,000 manufactured (1974). **Radios:** 2,700,000 licenses (1973); 169,000 manufactured (1974). **Telephones in use** (1976): 1,570,784.

Health: Life expectancy at birth (1970-72): 68.55 male; 74.60 female. **Births** (per 1,000 pop. 1974): 19.6. **Deaths** (per 1,000 pop. 1974): 7.8. **Natural increase** (1974): 1.18%. **Pop. per hospital bed** (1973): 141. **Pop. per physician** (1973): 740. **Infant mortality** (per 1,000 pop. under 1 yr. 1974): 13.8.

Education: Literacy (1973): 98%. **Pop. 5-19:** in school (1973): 83%; per teacher (1973): 28.

The Maoris, a Polynesian group from the eastern Pacific, reached New Zealand before and during the 14th century. The first European to sight New Zealand was the Dutch navigator Abel Janszoon Tasman, but Maoris refused to allow him to land. British Capt. James Cook explored the coasts, 1769-1770.

British sovereignty was proclaimed in 1840, with organized settlement beginning in the same year. Representative institutions were granted in 1853. Maori Wars ended in 1870 with British victory. The colony became a dominion in 1907, and is an independent member of the Commonwealth.

New Zealand fought on the side of the Allies in both world wars, and signed the ANZUS Treaty of Mutual Security with the U.S. and Australia in 1951. It sent 400 men to aid U.S. forces in South Vietnam. New Zealand joined with Australia and Britain in a pact to defend Singapore and Malaysia; New Zealand units are stationed in those two countries.

In 1973, to protest France's testing of nuclear devices above Mururoa Atoll, a New Zealand Navy frigate cruised just outside the French South Pacific island's 12-mile limit but within the test area. In 1974, New Zealand opposed U.S. plans for a military base on Diego Garcia island in the Indian Ocean.

A labor tradition in politics dates back to the 19th century. Private ownership is basic to the economy, but state ownership or regulation affects many industries. Transportation, broadcasting, mining, and forestry are largely state-owned.

The native Maoris numbered an estimated 200,000 in the early 19th century; violence and European diseases cut them to 40,000 by the end of the century. Recently they have increased at 3% annually and totaled over 250,000 in 1976. Four of 87 members of the House of Representatives are elected directly by the Maori people. Thousands of Samoans, Tongans, and other South Pacific islanders live and work in New Zealand.

New Zealand comprises **North Island,** 44,281 sq. mi.; **South Island,** 58,093 sq. mi.; **Stewart Island,** 670 sq. mi.; **Chatham Islands,** 372 sq. mi. Both the North and South Islands slightly exceed 500 mi. in length. Cook Strait, separating the two, is only 16 mi. wide at its narrowest.

In 1965, the **Cook Islands** (pop. 1974, 19,522; area 93 sq. mi.) became self-governing although New Zealand retains responsibility for defense and foreign affairs. **Niue** attained the same status in 1974; it lies 400 mi. to W (pop. 1974, 3,992; area 100 sq. mi.). **Tokelau Is.,** (pop. 1974, 1,574; area 4 sq. mi.) are 300 mi. N of Samoa.

Ross Dependency, administered by New Zealand since 1923, comprises 160,000 sq. mi. of Antarctic territory.

Nicaragua

Republic of Nicaragua

People: Population (1976 est.): 2,230,000. **Age distrib.** (%): 0-14: 48.1; 15-59: 47.2; 60+: 4.7. **Pop. density:** 39 per sq. mi. **Ethnic groups:** Mestizo 70%, Caucasian 17%, Negro 9%, Indian 4%. **Languages:** Spanish, English (on Caribbean coast). **Religions:** Roman Catholics 95%.

Geography: Area: 57,143 sq. mi., slightly larger than Wisconsin. **Location:** In Central America. **Neighbors:** Honduras on N. Costa Rica on S. **Topography:** Both Atlantic and Pacific coasts are over 200 mi long. The Cordillera mountains, including many volcanic peaks, runs NW-SE through the middle of the country. Between this range and a volcanic range to the E lie Lakes Managua and Nicaragua. **Capital:** Managua. **Cities** (1971 cen.): Managua 398,514; (1968 est.): Leon 79,939.

Government: Head of state: Pres. Anastasio Somoza-Debayle, b. 1925, in office: 1967-72; Dec. 1, 1974. **Local divisions:** 16 departments. **Armed forces:** regulars 7,100; para-military 4,000.

Economy: Industries: Oil refining, chemicals, textiles. **Chief crops:** Bananas, cotton, fruit, yucca, coffee, sugar, corn, beans, cocoa, rice, sesame, tobacco, wheat. **Minerals:** Gold, silver, copper, tungsten. **Other resources:** Forests, shrimp. **Per capita arable land:** 0.8 acres. **Livestock** (1976): 2,600,000 cattle; 670,000 pigs. **Electricity production** (1971): 649 mln. kwh. **Labor force:** 46% agric.

Finance: Currency: Cordoba (Apr. 1977: 7.03=$1 US). **Gross domestic product** (1976): $1.84 bln. **Per capita income** (1974): $633. **Imports** (1976) $532 mln.; partners (1974): U.S. 32%, Venez. 9%, Guat. 7%, Jap. 7%, Costa Rica 7%. **Exports** (1976): $542 mln.; partners (1974): U.S. 19%, W. Ger. 19%, Jap. 9%, Costa Rica 9%. **Tourists** (1972): 148,300; receipts (1973): $12 million. **National budget** (1975): $188 mln. revenues; $251 mln. expenditures. **International reserves** (Dec. 1976): $146.75 mln.

Transport: Railway traffic (1972): 17 mln. passenger-miles; 9 mln. net ton-miles. **Motor vehicles:** in use (1973): 32,000 passenger cars, 20,000 commercial vehicles. **Chief ports:** Corinto, Puerto Somoza, San Juan del Sur.

Communications: Television sets: 63,000 in use (1973); 2,000 manufactured (1970). **Radios:** 125,000 in use (1973); 6,000 manufactured (1969). **Telephones in use** (1976): 21,947. **Daily newspaper circulation** (1973): 53,000.

Health: Life expectancy at birth (1970-75): 51.2 male; 54.6 female. **Births** (annual per 1,000 pop. 1970-75): 48.3. **Deaths** (annual per 1,000 pop. 1970-75): 13.9. **Natural increase** (annual 1970-75): 3.44%. **Pop. per hospital bed** (1973): 359. **Pop. per physician** (1973): 1,436. **Infant mortality** (per 1,000 pop. under 1 yr. 1970-75): 46.0.

Education: Literacy (1973): 58%. **Pop. 5-19:** in school (1973): 50%; per teacher (1973): 75.

Nicaragua, inhabited by various Indian tribes, was conquered by Spain in 1552.

After gaining independence from Spain, 1821, Nicaragua was united for a short period with Mexico, then with the United Provinces of Central America, finally becoming an independent republic, 1838.

U.S. Marines occupied the country at times in the early 20th century, the last time from 1926 to 1933.

Gen. Anastasio Somoza Debayle was elected president 1967. He resigned 1972 and was succeeded by a 3-man National Junta. He was elected president again Sept. 1, 1974. The Somozas, richest Nicaraguan family, have dominated politics for four decades.

Martial law was imposed in Dec. 1974, after officials were kidnapped by the Marxist Sandinista guerrillas. The country's Roman Catholic bishops charged in 1977 that the government had tortured, raped, and executed civilians in its anti-guerrilla campaign.

A severe earthquake, Dec. 23, 1972, destroyed much of Managua; about 6,000 died and 200,000 were left homeless. The nation was also hit by severe drought, lasting into 1973.

Niger

Republic of Niger

People: Population (1976 est.): 4,730,000. **Age distrib.** (%): 0-14: 44.5; 15-59: 50.8; 60+: 4.7. **Pop. density:** 9.7 per sq. mi. **Ethnic groups:** Hausas 50%, Djermas 23%, Fulanis 15%, Tuaregs 12%. **Languages:** French (official), Hausa, Djerma, others. **Religions:** Moslems 85%, others.

Geography: Area: 489,206 sq. mi., almost twice the size of Texas. **Location:** In the interior of N. Africa. **Neighbors:** Libya, Algeria on N, Mali, Upper Volta on W, Benin, Nigeria on S, Chad on E. **Topography:** Most of Niger consists of arid desert and mountains. A narrow savanna in the S and the Niger R. basin in the SW contain most of the population. **Capital:** Niamey. **Cities** (1975 est.): Niamey 130,299.

Government: Head of state: Pres. Seyni Kountche, b. 1931, in office: Apr. 17, 1974. **Local divisions:** 7 departments. **Armed forces:** regulars 2,100; para-military 1,800.

Economy: Chief crops: Peanuts, cotton are main cash crops. **Minerals:** Uranium (5th largest reserves in world). **Per capita arable land:** 7.9 acres. **Livestock** (1974): 2,800,000 cattle; 1,800,000 sheep. **Electricity production** (1973): 57 mln. kwh. **Labor force:** 91% agric.

Finance: Currency: CFA Franc (Apr. 1977: 248=$1 US). **Gross domestic product** (est. 1974): $500 mln. **Per capita income** (1974): $100. **Imports** (1975): $87 mln.; partners (1973): Fr. 43%, W. Ger. 8%, U.S. 7%, Nigeria 6%. **Exports** (1975): $85 mln.; partners (1973): Fr. 51%, Nigeria 26%, It. 6%, W. Ger. 5%. **Balance of payments** (1974): −$6.6 mln. **International reserves** (Jan. 1977): $84.7 mln. **Consumer prices** (change in 1976): 23.4%.

Transport: Motor vehicles: in use (1974): 8,600 passenger cars, 9,100 commercial vehicles.

Communications: Radios: 150,000 licenses (1972). **Daily newspaper circulation** (1973): 2,000; 0.5 per 1,000 pop.

Health: Life expectancy at birth (1970-75): 37.0 male; 40.1 female. **Births** (per 1,000 pop. 1970-75): 52.2. **Deaths** (per 1,000 pop. 1970-75): 25.5. **Natural increase** (1970-75): 2.67%. **Pop. per hospital bed** (1973): 1,792. **Pop. per physician** (1973): 43,000. **Infant mortality** (per 1,000 pop. under 1 yr. 1959-60): 200.

Education: Literacy (1973): 5%. **Pop. 5-19:** in school (1973): 6%; per teacher (1973): 543.

European explorers reached the area in the late 18th century. The French colony of Niger was established 1900-22, after the defeat of Tuareg fighters, who had invaded the area from the N a century before. The country became independent Aug. 3, 1960. The next year it signed a bilateral agreement with France retaining close economic and cultural ties, which have continued. Hamani Diori, Niger's first president, was ousted in a 1974 coup. Drought and famine struck in 1973-74, and again in 1975, and half the country's livestock died.

Nigeria

Federal Republic of Nigeria

The World Almanac is sponsored in Nigeria by the Daily and Sunday Times, 3 Kakawa St., Lagos, Nigeria; founded 1925; circulation 190,000 daily, 244,500 Sunday; published by The Daily Times of Nigeria Ltd.

People: Population (1976 est.): 64,750,000. **Pop. density:** 182 per sq. mi. **Ethnic groups:** Yoruba 18%, Ibo 18%, Hausa-Fulani 32%, 250 others. **Languages:** English (official), Hausa, Yoruba, Ibo, others. **Religions:** Moslems 47% (in N), Christians 34% (in S), others.

Geography: Area: 356,669 sq. mi., more than twice the size of California. **Location:** On the S coast of W. Africa. **Neighbors:** Benin on W, Niger on N, Chad, Cameroon on E. **Topography:** Four E-W regions divide Nigeria: a coastal mangrove swamp 10-60 mi. wide, a tropical rain forest 50-100 mi. wide, a plateau of savanna and open woodland, and semidesert in the N. **Capital:** Lagos. **Cities** (1975 est.): Lagos (met.) 1,476,837; Ibadan 847,000; Ogbomosho 432,000; Kano 399,000; Oshogbo 282,000; Ilorin 282,000.

Government: Head of state: Lt. Gen. Olusegun Obasanjo, b. Mar. 5, 1937, in office: Feb. 13, 1976. **Local divisions:** 19 states, with military governors. **Armed forces:** regulars 230,000.

Economy: Industries: Food processing, assembly of vehicles and other equipment. **Chief crops:** Cocoa (main export crop), tobacco, palm products, peanuts, cotton, soybeans. **Minerals:** Oil, gas, coal, iron, limestone, columbium, tin. **Crude oil output** (1976): 756 mln. bbls. (7th largest producer); oil accounts for 90% of exports. **Other resources:** Timber, rubber, hides. **Per capita arable land:** 0.6 acres. **Livestock** (1974): 10,918,000 cattle; 865,000 pigs; 7,545,000 sheep; 81,000,000 poultry. **Fish catch** (1975): 507,000 metric tons. **Electricity production** (1975): 3,216 mln. kwh. **Labor force:** 67% agric.

Finance: Currency: Naira (Apr. 1977: 1=$1.54 US). **Gross domestic product** (1973-4): $13.86 bln. **Per capita income** (1973): $201. **Imports** (1976) $8.199 bln.; partners (1974): U.K. 23%, W. Ger. 15%, U.S. 12%, Jap. 9%. **Exports** (1976): $10.565 bln.; partners (1974): U.S. 27%, U.K. 17%, Neth. 14%, Fr. 10%.

Tourist receipts (1974): $13 million. **Balance of payments** (1976): $-379 mln. **National budget** (1974): 6.80 bln. revenues; $4.29 bln. expenditures. **International reserves** (Feb. 1977): $4.937 bln.

Transport: Railway traffic (1973): 553 mln. passenger-miles; 834 mln. net ton-miles. **Motor vehicles:** in use (1973): 150,000 passenger cars, 82,000 commercial vehicles. **Civil aviation:** 259 mln. passenger-miles (1974); 4.8 mln. freight ton-miles (1974). **Chief ports:** Port Harcourt, Bonny, Lagos.

Communications: Television sets: 85,000 licenses (1973); 7,000 manufactured (1974). **Radios:** 3,500,000 licenses (1973); 102,000 manufactured (1974). **Daily newspaper circulation** (1973): 213,000.

Health: Life expectancy at birth (1965-66): 37.2 male; 36.7 female. **Births** (annual per 1,000 pop. 1970-75): 49.3. **Deaths** (annual per 1,000 pop. 1970-75): 22.7. **Natural increase** (annual 1970-75): 2.66%. **Pop. per hospital bed** (1973): 1,952. **Pop. per physician** (1973): 23,753.

Education: Literacy (1973): 25%. **Pop. 5-19:** in school (1973): 20%; per teacher (1973): 212.

Early cultures in Nigeria date back to at least 700 B.C. From the 12th to the 14th centuries, more advanced cultures developed in the Yoruba area, at Ife, and in the north, where Moslem influence prevailed.

Portuguese and British slavers appeared from the 15th-16th centuries. Britain seized Lagos, 1861, during an anti-slave trade campaign, and gradually extended control inland until 1900. Nigeria became independent Oct. 1, 1960, and a republic Oct. 1, 1963. Its first constitution provided for 4 regions with local autonomy, and a democratic central government.

In 1966 there were 2 military coups and periods of political assassination and inter-tribal strife, ending a long period of coalition governments of the majority Northern Region and other regions.

On May 30, 1967, the Eastern Region seceded, proclaiming itself the Republic of Biafra. The move plunged the country into civil war. Casualties in the war were estimated at over 1 million, including many "Biafrans" (mostly Ibos) who died of starvation despite international efforts to provide relief. The secessionists, after steadily losing ground, capitulated Jan. 12, 1970. Within a few years, the Ibos were reintegrated into national life, but mistrust among the regions persists, putting all census figures in doubt. Nigeria has been redivided into 19 states.

A military coup in 1975, and a presidential assassination in 1976, has prevented a full return to earlier free institutions.

Under "indigenization" programs, various categories of businesses are to be run by Nigerians only by 1978, while others must have local participation. Oil revenues have made possible a massive economic development program, largely using private enterprise.

Nigeria led in the formation of the West African Economic Community, linking 15 French, English, and Portuguese-speaking countries.

Norway

Kingdom of Norway

People: Population (1976): 4,030,000. **Age distrib.** (%): 0-114: 24.1; 15-59: 57.1; 60+: 18.8. **Pop. density:** 32 per sq. mi. **Urban** (1974): 44.8%. **Ethnic groups:** Only minority are Lapps 0.5%. **Languages:** Norwegian, Lapp. **Religions:** Lutherans 95%.

Geography: Area: 125,181 sq. mi., slightly larger than New Mexico. **Location:** Occupies the W part of Scandinavian Peninsula in NW Europe, and extends farther north than any European land. **Neighbors:** Sweden, Finland, USSR on E. **Topography:** A highly indented coast is lined with tens of thousands of islands. Mountains and plateaus cover most of the country, which is only 25% forested. **Capital:** Oslo. **Cities** (1974 est.): Oslo 465,337; Bergen 214,019.

Government: Head of state: King Olav V, b. July 2, 1903, in office: Sept. 21, 1957; **Head of government:** Prime Min. Odvar Nordli, b. Nov. 3, 1927, in office: Jan. 14, 1976. **Local divisions:** Oslo and 19 fylkes (counties). **Armed forces:** regulars 39,000; reserves 170,000.

Economy: Industries: Paper, shipbuilding, engineering, metals, chemicals, food processing, shipping. **Chief crops:** Grains, potatoes, fruits. **Minerals:** Oil, copper, pyrites, nickel, iron, zinc, lead. **Crude oil output** (1976): 102 mln. bbls. (Norway became a net exporter in 1976). **Other resources:** Forests. **Per capita arable land:** 0.5 acres. **Livestock** (1976): 901,000 cattle; 626,000 pigs; 811,000 sheep; 7,404,000 poultry. **Fish catch** (1975): 2,550,000 metric tons. **Electricity production** (1976): 82,188 mln. kwh. **Labor force:** 10% agric.; 25% manuf.

Finance: Currency: Kroner (Apr. 1977: 5.27=$1 US). **Gross domestic product** (1976): $31.3 bln. **Per capita income** (1975): $5,928. **Imports** (1976) $11,108 bln.; partners (1974): Swed. 19%, W. Ger. 14%, U.K. 10%, U.S. 8%. **Exports** (1976): $7.918 bln.; partners (1974): Swed. 18%, U.K. 17%, W. Ger. 10%, Den. 8%. **Balance of payments** (1976): $-30 mln. **National budget** (1975): $6.60 bln. revenues; $6.79 bln. expenditures. **International reserves** (Feb. 1977): $2.112 bln. **Consumer prices** (change in 1976): 9.2%.

Transport: Railway traffic (1974): 1,170 mln. passenger-miles; 1,792 mln. net ton-miles. **Motor vehicles:** in use (1974): 890,400 passenger cars, 153,300 commercial vehicles. **Civil aviation:** 1,975 mln. passenger-miles (1976); 74 mln. freight ton-miles (1976). **Chief ports:** Bergen, Stavenjer, Oslo, Tonsberg.

Communications: Television sets: 986,000 licenses (1973); 90,000 manufactured (1973). **Radios:** 1,255,000 licenses (1973); 111,000 manufactured (1973). **Telephones in use** (1976): 1,406,995. **Daily newspaper circulation** (1973): 1,553,-000; 391 per 1,000 pop.

Health: Life expectancy at birth (1972-73): 71.32 male; 77.60 female. **Births** (per 1,000 pop. 1975): 14.0. **Deaths** (per 1,000 pop. 1975): 9.9. **Natural increase** (1975): 0.41%. **Pop. per hospital bed** (1973): 73. **Pop. per physician** (1973): 639. **Infant mortality** (per 1,000 pop. under 1 yr. 1974): 10.5.

Education: Literacy (1973): 99%. **Pop. 5-19:** in school (1973): 67%; per teacher (1973): 21.

The first supreme ruler of Norway was Harald the Fairhaired who came to power in 872 A.D. Between 800 and 1000, Norway's Vikings raided and occupied widely dispersed parts of Europe. Christianity was introduced in 1030.

The country was united with Denmark 1381-1814, and with Sweden, 1814-1905. In 1905, the country became independent, with Prince Charles of Denmark as King.

Norway remained neutral during World War I. Germany attacked Norway Apr. 9, 1940, and held it until liberation May 8, 1945. The country abandoned its neutrality after the war, and joined the NATO alliance. Norway, a member of the European Free Trade Assoc., rejected membership in the Common Market in a 1972 referendum.

Abundant hydroelectric resources provided the base for Norway's industrialization, producing one of the highest living standards in the world. Future exports from the huge North Sea oil fields, may be limited by government production restrictions.

Despite an almost total lack of unemployment and an increasing labor shortage, Norway has refused to admit more than a small number of foreign workers.

Norway's merchant marine is the world's fourth largest.

Norway and the Soviet Union have disputed their territorial waters boundary in the Barents Sea, north of the two countries' common border. Oil and mineral deposits are believed to exist under the continental shelf.

Svalbard

Svalbard is a group of mountainous islands in the Arctic Ocean, c. 23,957 sq. mi., pop. varying seasonally from 1,500 to 3,000. The largest, West Spitsbergen, c. 15,000 sq. mi., seat of governor, is about 370 mi. N of Norway. By a treaty signed in Paris, 1920, major European powers recognized the sovereignty of Norway, which incorporated it in 1925. Both Norway and the USSR mine rich coal deposits. Mt. Newton (West Spitsbergen) is 5,633 ft. tall.

Oman

Sultanate of Oman

People: Population (1976 est.): 790,000. **Pop. density:** 9.6 per sq. mi. **Ethnic groups:** Arab 88%, Baluchi 4%, Persian 3%, Indian 2%, African 2%. **Languages:** Arabic, Persian, Urdu, others. **Religions:** Ibadi Moslems 50%, Sunni Moslems 25%, some Hindus.

Geography: Area: 82,000 sq. mi., the size of Kansas. **Location:** On SE coast of Arabian Peninsula. **Neighbors:** United Arab Emirates, Saudi Arabia, South Yemen on W. **Topography:** Oman has a narrow coastal plain up to 10 mi. wide, a range of barren mountains reaching 9,900 ft., and a wide, stony, mostly waterless plateau averaging 1,000 ft. in altitude. Oman also rules the tip of the Ruus-al-Jebal peninsula, controlling access to the Persian Gulf. **Capital:** Muscat. **Cities** (1975 est.): Matrah 20,000; Muscat 7,000.

Government: Head of state: Sultan Qabus bin Said, b. Nov. 18, 1940, in office: July 23, 1970. **Local divisions:** 1 province, 9 regions, and districts. **Armed forces:** reserves 14,150.

Economy: Chief crops: Dates, fruits, vegetables, wheat, frankincense. **Minerals:** Oil. **Crude oil output** (1976): 134 mln. bbls. **Per capita arable land:** 0.05 acres. **Fish catch** (1974): 100,000 metric tons. **Electricity production** (1973): 171 mln. kwh. **Labor force:** 73% agric.

Finance: Currency: Rial (1974: 1=$2.90 US). **Gross domestic product** (est. 1974): $1.3 bln. **Per capita income** (1974): $1,600. **Imports** (1975): $668 mln., partners (1973): U.A.E. 23%, U.K. 19%, Jap. 9%, Neth. 9%. **Exports** (1976): $1.575 bln.; partners (1973): Jap. 35%, Sp. 18%, Fr. 12%, U.K. 9%.

Transport: Chief ports: Matrah, Muscat.

Communications:Telephones in use (1976): 3,701.

A long history of rule by other lands, including Portugal in the 16th century, ended with the ouster of the Persians in 1744. By the early 19th century, Muscat and Oman was one of the most important countries in the region, controlling much of the Persian and Pakistan coasts, and ruling far-away Zanzibar, which was separated in 1861 under British mediation.

British influence was confirmed in a 1951 treaty, and Britain helped supress an uprising by traditionally rebellious interior tribes against control by Muscat in the 1950s. Enclaves on the Pakistan coast were sold to that country in 1958.

On July 23, 1970, Sultan Said bin Taimur was overthrown by his son, who became Sultan Qabus bin Said. The new sultan changed the nation's name to Sultanate of Oman. He launched a domestic development program and battled leftist rebels in the southern Dhofar area. The government received arms aid and over 3,500 advisors from Iran, as well as British assistance; the guerrillas reportedly got arms from the USSR, Iraq, and Southern Yemen.

The government claimed it had defeated the rebels, Dec. 1975. The sole British base was closed down in 1977.

Pakistan

Islamic Republic of Pakistan

People: Population (1976 est.): 72,370,000. **Age distrib.** (%): 0–14: 43.4; 15–59: 49.9; 60+: 6.7. **Pop. density:** 211 per sq. mi. **Urban** (1972): 25.5%. **Ethnic groups:** Punjabi 66%, Sindhi 13%, Pushtun (Iranian) 8.5%, Urdu 7.6%, Baluchi 2.5%, others. **Languages:** Urdu, English are both official. **Religions:** Moslems 96%, Christians 1.4%, Hindus 1.5%.

Geography: Area: 342,750 sq. mi., larger than Texas. **Location:** In W part of South Asia. **Neighbors:** Iran on W, Afghanistan, China on N, India on E. **Topography:** The Indus R. rises in the Hindu Kush and Himalaya mtns. in the N (highest is K2, or Godwin Austen, 28, 250 ft., 2d highest in world), then flows over 1,000 mi. through fertile valley, where most Pakistanis live, and empties into Arabian Sea. With its tributaries it supplies reservoirs, canals, and hydroelectric plants. Thar Desert, Eastern Plains flank Indus Valley. **Capital:** Islamabad. **Cities** (1972 cen.): Karachi 3,498,634; Lahore 2,165,372; Lyallpur 822,263; Hyderabad 628,310; Rawalpindi 615,392.

Government: Head of state: Pres. Fazal Elahi Chaudry, b. Jan. 1, 1904, in office: Aug. 10, 1973; **Head of government:** Martial law admin. Gen. Mohammad Zia ul-Haq, b. 1924, in office: July 5, 1977. **Local divisions:** federal capital and 4 provinces with elected legislatures: Punjab, Sind, Baluchistan, and NW Frontier. **Armed forces:** regulars 428,000; reserves 513,000.

Economy: Industries: Textiles, cement, paper, sugar, chemicals, fertilizers, surgical instruments. **Chief crops:** Rice, wheat, cotton, oilseeds, tobacco, sugar. **Minerals:** Sulphur, gypsum, salt, chromite, cement, oil, gas, coal, asbestos, antimony, magnesite, silica. **Crude oil output** (1976): 2.5 mln. bbls. **Other resources:** Wool. **Per capita arable land:** 0.7 acres. **Livestock** (1974): 13,154,000 cattle; 90,000 pigs; 18,087,000 sheep. **Fish catch** (1974): 191,800 metric tons. **Electricity production** (1972): 7,500 mln. kwh. **Labor force:** 57% agric.; 12% manuf.

Finance: Currency: Rupee (Apr. 1977: 9.93 = $1 US). **Gross domestic product** (1975): $11.15 bln. **Per capita income** (1974): $149. **Imports** (1976): $2.128 bln.; partners (1974): U.S. 25%, Jap. 8%, W. Ger. 8%, U.K. 7%. **Exports** (1976): $1.159 bln.; partners (1974): Hong Kong 11%, Indo. 9%, U.K. 7%, Jap. 6%. **Tourists** (1974): 159,500; receipts: $20 million. **Balance of payments** (1975): -$212 mln. **National budget** (1971): $1.54 bln. revenues; $1.68 bln. expenditures. **International reserves** (Feb. 1977): $418 mln. **Consumer prices** (change in 1976): 7.2%.

Transport: Railway traffic (1973): 7,203 mln. passenger-miles; 4,561 mln. net ton-miles. **Motor vehicles:** in use (1973): 177,300 passenger cars, 79,100 commercial vehicles. **Civil aviation:** 1,632 mln. passengers (1975); 81 mln. freight ton-miles (1975). **Chief ports:** Karachi.

Communications: Television sets: 129,000 licenses (1972). **Radios:** 1,033,000 licenses (1973). **Telephones in use** (1976): 239,600.

Health: Life expectancy at birth (1962, including Bangladesh): 53.7 male; 48.8 female. **Births** (per 1,000 pop. 1968): 36. **Deaths** (per 1,000 pop. 1968): 12. **Natural increase** (1968): 2.4%. **Pop. per hospital bed** (1973): 2,153. **Pop. per physician** (1973): 5,284. **Infant mortality** (per 1,000 pop. under 1 yr. 1968): 124.

Education: Literacy (1973): 16%. **Pop. 5-19:** in school (1973): 29%; per teacher (1973): 134.

The land now called Pakistan shares the 5,000-year history of the India-Pakistan sub-continent. At the present day sites of Harappa and Mohenjo Daro, the Indus Valley Civilization, with large cities and elaborate irrigation systems, flourished c. 4,000-2,500 B.C.

Aryan invaders from the NW conquered the region around 1,500 B.C., forging a Hindu civilization that dominated Pakistan as well as India for 2,000 years, and bringing a language whose descendants are spoken by nearly all Pakistanis.

Beginning with the Persians in the 6th century B.C., and continuing with Alexander the Great, and with the Sassanians, successive nations to the west ruled or influenced Pakistan, eventually separating the area from the Indian cultural sphere.

The first Arab invasion, 712 A.D., introduced Islam, which was adopted by the majority after a subsequent invasion two centuries later. Under the Mogul empire (1526-1867), Moslems ruled most of India, later yielding to British encroachment and resurgent Hindus.

After World War I the Moslems of British India began agitation for minority rights in elections.

Mohammad Ali Jinnah (1876-1948) was the principal architect of Pakistan. A lawyer who studied in England, he was a leader of the Moslem League from 1916, and worked for dominion status for India. From 1940 he advocated a separate Moslem state.

When the British withdrew Aug. 14, 1947, the Islamic majority areas of India acquired self-government as Pakistan, with dominion status in the Commonwealth.

Pakistan was divided into 2 sections, West Pakistan and East Pakistan. The 2 areas were nearly 1,000 mi. apart on opposite sides of India.

Pakistan became a republic in 1956. In Oct. 1958, Gen. Mohammad Ayub Khan took power in a coup. He was elected president in 1960 and reelected in 1965. Pakistan had a National Assembly (legislature) with equal membership from East and West Pakistan, and 2 Provincial Assemblies.

As a member of the Central Treaty Organization, along with neighboring Iran, Pakistan had been aligned with the West. Following clashes between India and China in 1962, Pakistan made commercial and aid agreements with Communist China. U.S. aid to both Pakistan and India was suspended during the 1966 war over Kashmir but both economic aid and "nonlethal" military aid were resumed in 1966. The embargo was modified in 1973 and lifted in 1975.

Ayub resigned Mar. 25, 1969, after several months of violent rioting and unrest, most of it in East Pakistan. There were demands for a parliamentary form of government, for direct elections and economic reforms. In East Pakistan, which had about 56% of the population, there were demands for autonomy.

The government was turned over to Gen. Agha Mohammad

Yahya Khan and martial law was declared; Yahya assumed the presidency.

The Awami League, which sought regional autonomy for East Pakistan, won a majority in Dec. 1970 elections to a National Assembly which was to write a new constitution. In March, 1971 Yahya postponed the Assembly. Rioting and strikes broke out in the East.

On Mar. 25, 1971, government troops launched attacks in the East. The Easterners, aided by India, proclaimed the independent nation of Bangladesh. In months of widespread fighting, countless thousands were killed. Some 10 million Easterners fled into India.

Full scale war between India and Pakistan had spread to both the East and West fronts by December 3. Pakistan troops in the East surrendered Dec. 16; Pakistan agreed to a cease-fire in the West Dec. 17.

Zulfikar Ali Bhutto, leader of the Pakistan People's party, which had won the most West Pakistan votes in the Dec. 1970 elections, became president Dec. 20. In 1972 he announced new land reforms and said the government would control management of major industries.

On July 3, 1972, Pakistan and India signed a pact agreeing to withdraw troops from their borders and seek peaceful solutions to all problems.

In Aug. 1973 India agreed to release 93,000 Pakistani prisoners held since 1971. The return was completed in April, 1974. Pakistan agreed to repatriate 200,000 Bengali nationals stranded in Pakistan, and agreed to accept some Biharis (non-Bengalis) unwanted in Bangladesh. India and Pakistan agreed in 1976 to resume full diplomatic relations.

A new constitution adopted Apr. 10, 1973, made Pakistan a federal Islamic republic. Bhutto became prime minister Aug. 14.

Bhutto was overthrown in a military coup July, 1977. Some 300 people had been killed in protests over alleged rigging of parliamentary elections earlier in the year. The new military rulers made concessions to Moslem conservatives.

Panama

Republic of Panama

People: Population (1976 est.): 1,720,000. **Age distrib.** (%): 0-14: 43.6; 15-59: 50.9; 60+: 5.7. **Pop. density:** 60 per sq. mi. **Urban** (1975): 49.6%. **Ethnic groups:** Mestizo 70%, Negro 13%, Caucasian 10%, Indian 6%. **Languages:** Spanish (official), English. **Religions:** Roman Catholics 93%, Protestants 6%.

Geography: Area: 28,753 sq. mi. slightly larger than West Virginia. **Location:** In Central America. **Neighbors:** Costa Rica on W. Colombia on E. **Topography:** Two mountain ranges run the length of the isthmus. Tropical rain forests cover the Caribbean coast and eastern Panama. **Capital:** Panama. **Cities** (1975 est.): Panama 404,190; (1970 cen.): Colon 95,300.

Government: Head of state: Pres. Demetrio Lakas, b. Aug. 29, 1925, in office: Oct. 11, 1972; **Head of government:** Gen. Omar Torrijos Herrera, b. Feb. 13, 1929, in office: Oct. 11, 1972. **Local divisions:** 9 provinces and 1 territory.

Economy: Industries: Oil refining, shipping, international banking. **Chief crops:** Bananas, pineapples, cocoa, coconuts, sugar. **Minerals:** Cement, clay, salt, copper. **Other resources:** Forests (Mahogany), shrimp. **Per capita arable land:** 0.6 acres. **Livestock** (1976): 1,375,000 cattle; 170,000 pigs; 3,790,000 poultry. **Fish catch** (1974): 66,000 metric tons. **Electricity production** (1976): 1,164 mln. kwh. **Labor force:** 38% agric.

Finance: Currency: Balboa (Apr. 1977: 1=$1 US). **Gross domestic product** (1975): $2.27 bln. **Per capita income** (1975): $1,147. **Imports** (1976): $870 mln.; partners (1974): U.S., Jap., Ecuador, Venez. **Exports** (1976): $285 mln.; partners (1974): U.S., Brazil, Neth. **Tourists** (1974): 708,700; receipts: $121 million. **Balance of payments** (1975): −$22.7 mln. **National budget** (1976): $282 mln revenues; $446 mln. expenditures. **International reserves** (Dec. 1974): $39.4 mln. **Consumer prices** (change in 1976): 2.1%.

Transport: Motor vehicles: in use (1974): 62,900 passenger cars, 25,400 commercial vehicles. **Chief ports:** Balboa, Cristobal, Puerto Armuellas.

Communications: Television sets: 200,000 in use (1972). **Radios:** 255,000 in use (1973). **Telephones in use** (1976): 142,159. **Daily newspaper circulation** (1973): 145,000; 92 per 1,000 pop.

Health: Life expectancy at birth (1970): 64.26 male; 67.50 female. **Births** (annual) per 1,000 pop. 1970-75): 36.2. **Deaths** (annual per 1,000 pop. 1970-75): 7.1. **Natural increase** (annual 1970-75): 2.91%. **Pop. per hospital bed** (1973): 320. **Pop. per physician** (1973): 1,340. **Infant mortality** (per 1,000 pop. under 1 yr. 1974): 32.9.

Educational Literacy (1973): 79%. **Pop. 5-19:** In school (1973): 67%; per teacher (1973): 37.

The coast of Panama was sighted by Rodrigo de Bastidas, sailing with Columbus for Spain in 1501, and was visited by Columbus in 1502. Vasco Nunez de Balboa crossed the isthmus and "discovered" the Pacific Ocean Sept. 13, 1513. Spanish colonies were ravaged by Francis Drake, 1572-95, and Henry Morgan, 1668-71. Morgan destroyed the old city of Panama which had been founded in 1519. Freed from Spain, Panama joined Colombia in 1821. Separatist forces in Panama sought to gain independence from Colombia several times.

Panama declared its independence from Colombia Nov. 3, 1903, with U.S. recognition. U.S. Naval forces deterred action by Colombia. On Nov. 18, 1903, Panama granted use, occupation and control of the Canal Zone to the U.S. by treaty, ratified Feb. 26, 1904. *(See also Canal Zone and Panama Canal.)*

Rioting began Jan. 9, 1964, in a dispute over the flying of the U.S. and Panamanian flags and terms of the 1903 treaty. At least 21 Panamanians and 3 U.S. soldiers died in the rioting.

In 1967 new treaties were proposed, but Panama rejected them in 1970. In Feb. 1974 the U.S. and Panama agreed to negotiate a new treaty which would give the U.S. the right to operate and protect the canal for a certain period, with Panama sharing in the revenues, and would also set a date for final transfer of jurisdiction to Panama. Opposition by U.S. Senators stalled the talks.

Panama adopted its 4th constitution in 1972. The Assembly gave Gen. Omar Torrijos powers as head of government. He had been de facto ruler since 1969.

Due to easy Panama ship regulations and strictures in the U.S., merchant tonnage registered in Panama since World War II ranks high in size. Registered number of ships more than 1,000 gross tons each is over 1,300.

Similarly easy financial regulations have made Panama a center for international banking.

Inflation, unemployment, and uncertainty over the Canal have marred a record of economic growth and social improvement from 1950 to 1973.

The U.S. and Panama initialed two treaties in 1977 that would provide for a gradual takeover by Panama of the canal, and withdrawal of U.S. troops, to be completed by 1999. U.S. payments would be substantially increased in the interim. The permanent neutrality of the canal would also be guaranteed. The treaties faced opposition in the U.S. Senate.

Papua New Guinea

People: Population (1976 est.): 2,830,000. **Age distrib.** (%): 0-14: 45.2; 15-59: 51.9; 60+: 2.9. **Pop. density:** 16 per sq. mi. **Urban** (1971): 11.1%. **Ethnic groups:** Papuans (in S and interior), Melanesian (N, E), pygmies, minorities of Chinese, Australians, Polynesians. **Languages:** Melanesian Pidgin, Police Motu, English, 750 local languages. **Religions:** Protestants 33%, Roman Catholic 18%, local religions.

Geography: Area: 178,260 sq. mi., slightly larger than California. **Location:** Occupies eastern half of island of New Guinea. **Neighbors:** Indonesia (West Irian) on W, Australia on S (across Torres Strait). **Topography:** Thickly forested mts. cover much of the center of the country, with lowlands along the coasts. Included are the nearby islands of Bismarck and Solomon groups, including Admiralty Is., New Ireland, New Britain, and Bougainville. **Capital:** Port Moresby. **Cities** (1971 cen.): Port Moresby (met.) 91,761; Rabaul 62,329.

Government: Head of state: Queen Elizabeth II, represented by Gov. Gen. Tore Lokoloko; **Head of government:** Prime Min. Michael Somare, b. 1936, in office: Sept. 16, 1975. **Local divisions:** National capital and 19 provinces with elected legislatures.

Economy: Chief crops: Coffee, coconuts, cocoa. **Minerals:** Copper, gold, silver, gas. **Per capita arable land:** 0.1 acres. **Livestock** (1974): 83,000 cattle; 1,150,000 pigs; 1,040,000 poultry. **Fish catch** (174): 52,700 metric tons. **Electricity production** (1972): 474 mln. kwh. **Labor force:** 82% agric.

Finance: Currency: Kina (1975: 1 = $1.26 US). **Gross domestic product** (est. 1974): $1.57 mln. **Per capita income** (1974): $500. **Imports** (1976) $473 mln.; partners (1973): Australia 54%, Jap. 16%, U.S. 9%, Sing. 4%. **Exports** (1976): $573 mln.; partners (1973): Jap. 35%, W. Ger. 23%, Australia 20%, U.S. 5%.

Transport: Motor vehicles: in use (1974) 17,300 passenger cars, 18,300 commercial vehicles. **Chief ports:** Port Moresby, Lae.

Communications: Telephones in use (1976): 35,604.

Health: Life expectancy at birth (1970-75): 47.7 male; 47.6 female. **Births** (annual per 1,000 pop. 1970-75): 40.6. **Deaths** (annual per 1,000 pop. 1970-75): 17.1 **Natural increase** (annual 1970-75): 2.35%.

Human remains have been found in the interior of New Guinea dating back at least 10,000 years and possibly much earlier. Successive waves of peoples probably entered the country from Asia through Indonesia. Europeans visited in the 15th century, but land claims did not begin until the 19th century, when the Dutch took control of the western half of the island.

The southern half of eastern New Guinea was first claimed by Britain in 1884, and transferred to Australia in 1905. The northern half was claimed by Germany in 1884, but captured in the first World War by Australia, which was granted a League of Nations mandate and then a UN trusteeship over the area. The two territories were administered jointly after 1949, were given self-government Dec. 1, 1973, and became independent Sept. 16, 1975. Australia promised $1 billion in aid for the 5 years starting 1976-77, and pledged assistance in defense and foreign affairs.

The indigenous population consists of a huge number of tribes, many living in almost complete isolation with mutually unintelligible languages.

A secession movement in copper-rich Bougainville led to violence in 1973 and 1976.

Paraguay

Republic of Paraguay

People: Population (1976 est.): 2,720,000. **Age distrib.** (%): 0–14: 46.5; 15–59: 48.6; 60+: 4.9. **Pop. density:** 17 per sq. mi. **Urban** (1972): 37.4%. **Ethnic groups:** Mestizos 95%, small Caucasian, Indian, Negro minorities. **Languages:** Spanish, 75%, Guarani 90%. **Religions:** Roman Catholics 95%, Mennonites.

Geography: Area: 157,047 sq. mi., the size of California. **Location:** One of the two landlocked countries of S. America. **Neighbors:** Bolivia on N, Argentina on S, Brazil on E. **Topography:** Paraguay R. bisects the country. To E are fertile plains, wooded slopes, grasslands. To W is the Chaco plain, with marshes and scrub trees. Extreme W is arid. **Capital:** Asuncion. **Cities** (1972 cen.): Asuncion (met.) 473,013.

Government: Head of state: Pres. Alfredo Stroessner, b. Nov. 3, 1912, in office: Aug. 15, 1954. **Local divisions:** 16 departments. **Armed forces:** regulars 16,600; reserves 5,000.

Economy: Industries: Food processing, wood products. **Chief crops:** Corn, wheat, cotton, beans, peanuts, tobacco, citrus fruits, yerba mate. **Minerals:** Iron, manganese, limestone. **Other resources:** Forests. **Per capita arable land:** 1.0 acres. **Livestock** (1974): 5,814,000 cattle; 659,000 pigs; 347,000 sheep; 6,724,000 poultry. **Electricity production** (1973): 379 mln. kwh. **Labor force:** 53% agric.

Finance: Currency: Guarani (Apr. 1977: 126=$1 US). **Gross domestic product** (1975): $1.51 bln. **Per capita income** (1975): $536. **Imports** (1976) $219 mln.; partners (1974): Argen. 28%, Braz. 18%, U.S. 10%, W. Ger. 9%. **Exports** (1976): $178 mln.; partners (1974): Argen. 23%, W. Ger. 13%, U.S. 11%, Neth. 9%. **Tourist receipts** (1974): $12 million. **Balance of payments** (1976): $36.4 mln. **National budget** (1976): $154 mln. revenues; $146 mln. expenditures. **International reserves** (Feb. 1977): $163.51 mln. **Consumer prices** (change in 1976): 4.6%.

Transport: Railway traffic (1973): 16 mln. passenger-miles; 19 mln. net ton-miles. **Motor vehicles:** in use (1971): 16,000 passenger cars, 14,000 commercial vehicles. **Chief ports:** Asuncion.

Communications: Television sets: 53,000 in use (1973). **Radios:** 175,000 in use (1973). **Telephones in use** (1976): 37,656. **Daily newspaper circulation** (1973): 89,000.

Health: Life expectancy at birth (1970-75): 60.3 male; 63.6 female. **Births** (annual per 1,000 pop. 1970-75): 39.8. **Deaths** (annual per 1,000 pop. 1970-75): 8.9. **Natural increase** (annual 1970-75): 3.09%. **Pop. per hospital bed** (1973): 703. **Pop. per physician** (1973): 1,907. **Infant mortality** (per 1,000 pop. under 1 yr. 1971): 38.6.

Education: Literacy (1973): 79%. **Pop. 5-19:** in school (1973): 55%; per teacher (1973): 52.

The Guarani Indians were settled farmers speaking a common language before the arrival of Europeans.

Visited by Sebastian Cabot in 1527 and settled as a Spanish possession in 1535, Paraguay gained its independence from Spain in 1811. It lost much of its territory to Brazil, Uruguay, and Argentina in the War of the Triple Alliance, 1865-1870. Large areas were won from Bolivia in the Chaco War, 1932-35, but at great human and economic cost.

Gen. Alfredo Stroessner has ruled since 1954. Suppression of the opposition and decimation of small Indian groups has been charged by international rights groups.

The first stages of a large hydroelectric project were completed in 1968-70; a highway to Brazil was completed. In 1974 the two countries agreed to build a 10-million kilowatt hydroelectric plant, largest in the world, at Itaipu on the Parana River.

Organized international smuggling has been an important industry since the 1940s.

Peru

Republic of Peru

People: Population (1976 est.): 16,090,000. **Age distrib.** (%): 0-14: 44.5; 15-59: 50.6; 60+: 4.9. **Pop. density:** 32 per sq. mi. **Urban** (1974): 55.3%. **Ethnic groups:** Indians 46%, Mestizos 43%, Caucasians 11%. **Languages:** Spanish, Quechua both official, Aymara; 30% speak no Spanish. **Religions:** Roman Catholics over 90%.

Geography: Area: 496,222 sq. mi., five-sixths the size of Alaska. **Location:** On the Pacific coast of S. America. **Neighbors:** Ecuador, Colombia on N, Brazil, Bolivia on E, Chile on S. **Topography:** An arid coastal strip, 10 to 100 mi. wide, supports much of the population thanks to widespread irrigation. The Andes cover 27% of land area. The uplands are well-watered, as are the eastern slopes reaching the Amazon basin, which covers half the country with its forests and jungles. **Capital:** Lima. **Cities** (1972 cen.): Lima (met.) 3,302,523; Arequipa 303,316; Callao 296,721.

Government: Head of state: Pres. Francisco Morales Bermudez, b. 1922, in office: Aug. 29, 1975; **Head of government:** Prime Min. Guillermo Arbulu Galliani, in office: July 17, 1976. **Local divisions:** 24 departments. **Armed forces:** regulars 63,000; para-military 20,000.

Economy: Industries: Fish meal, steel. **Chief crops:** Cotton, sugar, coffee, rice, potatoes, beans, corn, barley, tobacco. **Minerals:** Copper, lead, zinc, iron, oil. **Crude oil output** (1976): 27.5 mln. bbls. **Other resources:** Wool, sardines. **Per capita arable land:** 0.4 acres. **Livestock** (1976): 4,300,000 cattle; 1,950,000 pigs; 14,000,000 sheep; 22,000,000 poultry. **Fish catch** (1975): 3,447,000 metric tons (one of world leaders). **Electricity production** (1971): 5,949 mln. kwh. **Labor force:** 47% agriculture; 15% manuf.

Finance: Currency: Sole (Mar. 1977: 74.2=$1 US). **Gross domestic product** (1975): $13.64 bln. **Per capita income** (1975): $518. **Imports** (1975): $2,559 bln.; partners (1974): U.S. 31%, Jap. 12%, W. Ger. 10%, Ecuador 5%. **Exports** (1976): $1.245 bln.; partners (1974): U.S. 36%, Jap. 13%, W. Ger. 8%, P.R. China 5%. **Tourists** (1974): 262,300; receipts: $78 million. **Balance of payments** (1976): −$295 mln. **National budget** (1973): $1.38 bln. revenues; $1.74 bln. expenditures. **International reserves** (Aug. 1976): $329.4 mln. **Consumer prices** (change in 1976): 33.1%.

Transport: Motor vehicles: in use (1970): 230,400 passenger cars, 117,500 commercial vehicles; assembled (1975): 21,000 passenger cars, 13,000 commercial vehicles. **Chief ports:** Callao, Chimbate, Mollendo.

Communications: Television sets: 411,000 in use (1973); 35,000 manufactured (1970). **Radios:** 2,001,000 in use (1973); 88,000 manufactured (1970). **Telephones in use** (1976): over 67,000.

Health: Life expectancy at birth (1960-65): 52.59 male;

55.48 female. **Births** (annual per 1,000 pop. 1970-75): 41.0. **Deaths** (annual per 1,000 pop. 1970-75): 11.9. **Natural increase** (annual 1970-75): 2.91%. **Pop. per hospital bed** (1973): 511. **Pop. per physician** (1973): 1,818. **Infant mortality** (per 1,000 pop. under 1 yr. 1970): 65.1.

Education: Literacy (1973): 72%. **Pop. 5-19:** in school (1973): 56%; per teacher (1973): 51.

The powerful Inca empire had its seat at Cuzco in the Andes (alt. 11,000 ft.), and covered most of Peru, Bolivia, and Ecuador, as well as parts of Colombia, Chile, and Argentina. Building on the achievements of 800 years of Andean civilization, the Incas had a high level of skill in architecture, engineering, textiles, and social organization.

A civil war had weakened the empire when Francisco Pizarro, Spanish conquistador, began raiding Peru for its wealth, 1532. In 1533 he had the ruling Inca, Atahualpa, fill a room with gold, then executed him and enslaved the natives.

Lima was the seat of Spanish viceroys until the Argentine liberator, Jose de San Martin, captured it in 1821; Spain was defeated by Simon Bolivar and Antonio J. de Sucre and recognized Peruvian independence, 1824. Chile defeated Peru and Bolivia, 1879-84, and took Tarapaca, Tacna, and Arica; returned Tacna, 1929.

On Oct. 3, 1968, a military coup ousted Pres. Fernando Belaunde Terry. In 1968-74, the military government converted large farmlands into cooperatives, expropriated several large U.S. companies with compensation, forced foreign mining companies to expand investments, and ordered local industries to turn over 50% of ownership to their workers.

Food shortages, escalating foreign debt, and strikes helped lead to another coup, Aug. 29, 1976, and to a slowdown of socialist programs. Labor protests culminated in a general strike in July, 1977.

Peru is normally the world's top fishing nation; it takes about a sixth of total world tonnage, mostly anchovies from the plankton-rich waters of the coastal Peru current. Most of the take is ground into fish meal for poultry and livestock feed. But in 1972 the industry was crippled by a disappearance of anchovies from offshore waters. In 1973 the government nationalized the crippled industry. In 1974 a shift in the ocean currents brought at least some of the anchovies back.

A severe earthquake hit northern Peru May 31, 1970, destroying many towns and killing 66,794.

Philippines

Republic of the Philippines

People: Population (1976 est.): 43,750,000. **Age distrib.** (%): 0-14: 43.2; 15-59: 51.4; 60+: 5.5. **Pop. density:** 378 per sq. mi. **Urban** (1970): 31.8%. **Ethnic groups:** Malays the large majority, Chinese, Americans, Spanish are minorities. **Languages:** Pilipino (based on Tagalog), Spanish, English all official; 90 others spoken. **Religions:** Roman Catholics 83%, Protestants 9%, Moslems 5%.

Geography: Area: 115,707 sq. mi., slightly larger than Nevada. **Location:** An archipelago off the SE coast of Asia. **Neighbors:** Nearest are Malaysia, Indonesia on S, Taiwan on N. **Topography:** The country consists of some 7,100 islands stretching 1,100 mi. N-S. About 95% of area and population are on 11 largest islands. The largest islands are mountainous, except for the heavily indented coastlines and for the central plain on Luzon. **Capital:** Quezon City (Manila is de facto capital). **Cities** (1975 est.): Manila 1,438,252; Quezon City 994,679; Davao 591,500.

Government: Head of state: Pres. Ferdinand E. Marcos, b. Sept. 11, 1917, in office: Dec. 30, 1965. **Local divisions:** 72 provinces, 61 chartered cities. **Armed forces:** regulars 78,000; reserves 45,000.

Economy: Industries: Food processing, clothing, drugs, paper, appliances. **Chief crops:** Hemp, copra, sugar, rice, corn, pineapple, tobacco. **Minerals:** Gold, silver, gypsum, sulphur, mercury, phosphates, zinc, nickel, copper, iron, coal, chromite, manganese. **Other resources:** Forests (42% of area). **Per capita arable land:** 0.5 acres. **Livestock** (1976): 7,300,000 cattle; 9,700,000 pigs; 2,000 sheep; 51,000,000 poultry. **Fish catch** (1975): 1,342,000 metric tons. **Electricity production** (1976): 10,604 mln. kwh. **Labor force:** 51% agric.; 11% manuf.

Finance: Currency: Peso (Apr. 1977: 7.41=$1 US). **Gross domestic product** (1976): $17.47 bln. **Per capita income** (1975): $325. **Imports** (1976) $3.938 bln.; partners (1974): Jap. 27%, U.S. 24%, Saudi Ar. 11%, Kuw. 5%. **Exports** (1976): $2.513 bln.; partners (1974): U.S. 42%, Jap. 35%, Neth. 6%, W. Ger. 3%. **Tourists** (1974): 418,600; receipts: $58 million. **Balance of payments** (1976): $373 mln. **National budget** (1976): $2.82 bln. revenues; $3.12 bln. expenditures. **International reserves** (Feb. 1977): $1.370 bln. **Consumer prices** (change in 1976): 8.8%.

Transport: Railway traffic (1974): 558 mln. passenger-miles; 43 mln. net ton-miles. **Motor vehicles:** in use (1974): 362,500 passenger cars, 247,300 commercial vehicles; assembled (1976): 34,000 passenger cars, 17,000 commercial vehicles. **Civil aviation:** 1,766 mln. passenger-miles (1975); 65 mln. freight ton-miles (1975). **Chief ports:** Cebu, Manila, Iloilo, Davao.

Communications: Television sets: 450,000 in use (1973); 64,000 manufactured (1974). **Radios:** 1,800,000 in use (1973); 200,000 manufactured (1974). **Telephones in use** (1976): 489,-717. **Daily newspaper circulation** (1971): 785,000; 21 per 1,000 pop.

Health: Life expectancy at birth (1970-75): 56.9 male; 60.0 female. **Births** (annual per 1,000 pop. 1970-75): 43.8. **Deaths** (annual per 1,000 pop. 1970-75): 10.5 **Natural increase** (annual 1970-75): 3.33%. **Pop. per hospital bed** (1973): 776. **Pop. per physician** (1973): 1,490. **Infant mortality** (per 1,000 pop. under 1 yr. 1974): 58.9.

Education: Literacy (1973): 72%. **Pop. 5-19:** in school (1973): 67%; per teacher (1973): 47.

The Malay peoples of the Philippine islands, whose ancestors probably migrated from Southeast Asia, were mostly hunters, fishers, and unsettled cultivators when first visited by Europeans. A few Moslem sultanates in the southern islands were the only direct link to other Asian civilizations.

The archipelago was visited by Magellan, 1521. The Spanish founded Manila, 1571. The islands, named for King Philip II of Spain, were ceded by Spain to the U.S. in the Treaty of Paris, Dec. 10, 1898, following the Spanish-American War. The U.S. paid Spain $20 million for the territory. U.S. troops suppressed a guerrilla uprising in a brutal 6-year war, 1899-1905.

Japan attacked the Philippines Dec. 8, 1941 (Far Eastern time). Japan conquered the islands in May, 1942. It was ousted by Sept. 1945.

On July 4, 1946, independence was proclaimed in accordance with an act passed by the U.S. Congress in 1934, providing for Philippine independence in 1946. A republic was established.

A rebellion by Communist-led Huk guerrillas was put down by 1954. But urban and rural political violence periodically reappears.

The Philippines and the U.S. have treaties for U.S. military and naval bases and a 1951 Mutual Defense Treaty.

President Ferdinand E. Marcos in 1966 concluded a pact reducing U.S. base leases from 99 to 25 years. There were riots by radical youth groups and terrorism by leftist guerrillas and outlaws, increasing from 1970. On Sept. 21, 1972, Marcos declared martial law. Ruling by decree, he ordered some land reform and stabilized prices. But opposition was suppressed, and a high population growth rate aggravated poverty and unemployment. Political corruption was believed to be widespread. On Jan. 17, 1973, Marcos proclaimed a new constitution with himself as president. Diplomatic and trade ties were set with China in 1975 and with the USSR in 1976.

Government troops battled Moslem (Moro) secessionists in 1973-76 in southern Mindanao. Fighting resumed in 1977 after a Libyan-mediated agreement on autonomy was rejected by the region's voters, a majority of whom are Christian. Some 10,000 civilians had been killed in the war.

The archipelago has a coastline of 10,850 mi. Manila Bay, with an area of 770 sq. mi., and a circumference of 120 mi., is the finest harbor in the Far East.

In the late 1960s self-sufficiency in rice production was achieved after introduction of "miracle" high-yield varieties.

In 1972 and 1974 severe floods destroyed crops in central Luzon. In 1974 the first in a series of flood-control dams, built with U.S. aid, was dedicated. Manufacturing has shown steady gains.

All natural resources of the Philippines belong to the state and their exploitation is limited to citizens of the Philippines or corporations and associations of which 60% of the capital is owned by citizens. In 1946 the right to develop natural resources and to own and operate public utilities until 1974 was extended to U.S. citizens.

Poland

Polish People's Republic

People: Population (1976): 34,360,000. **Age distrib.** (%): 0-14: 25.5; 15-59: 61.2; 60+: 13.3. **Pop. density:** 285 per sq. mi. **Urban** (1974): 54.4%. **Ethnic groups:** Polish 98%, Germans, Ukrainians, Byelorussians. **Language:** Polish. **Religions:** Roman Catholics 90%, Protestants 1.5%.

Geography: Area: 120,359 sq. mi. **Location:** On the Baltic Sea in E Central Europe. **Neighbors:** E. Germany on W, Czechoslovakia on S, USSR (Lithuania, Byelorussia, Ukraine) on E. **Topography:** Most of the country consists of lowlands, forming part of the Northern European Plain. The Carpathian Mts. along the southern border rise to 8,200 ft. **Capital:** Warsaw. **Cities** (1974 est.): Warsaw 1,400,000; Lodz 784,000; Cracow 662,900; Wroclaw 565,000; Poznan 502,800.

Government: Head of state: Chmn. Henryk Jablonski, b. Dec. 27, 1909, in office: Mar. 1972; **Head of government:** Prime Min. Piotr Jaroszewicz, b. Oct. 8, 1909, in office: Dec. 1970; **Head of Communist Party:** First Sec. Edward Gierek, b. Jan. 6, 1913, in office: Dec. 1970. **Local divisions:** 49 provinces. **Armed forces:** regulars 290,000; reserves 505,000.

Economy: Industries: Shipbuilding, textiles, chemicals, wood products, metals, autos, aircraft, machinery, cement, aluminum, oil products. **Chief crops:** Grains, potatoes, sugar beets, tobacco, flax. **Minerals:** Coal, zinc, sulphur, salt, cadmium, iron, copper. **Crude oil output** (1976): 3.4 mln. bbls. **Per capita arable land:** 1.1 acres. **Livestock** (1976): 12,762,000 cattle; 21,643,000 pigs; 2,786,000 sheep; 160,000,000 poultry. **Fish catch** (1975): 801,000 metric tons. **Electricity production** (1976): 104,100 mln. kwh. **Labor force:** 35% agric.; 30% manuf.

Finance: Currency: Zloty (1974: 33.2 = $1 US). **Gross domestic product** (est. 1974): $71 bln. **Per capita income** (1974): $2,000. **Imports** (1976): $13,890 bln.; partners (1974): USSR 22%, W. Ger. 12%, E. Ger. 7%, Czech. 6%. **Exports** (1976): $11,050 bln.; partners (1974): USSR 29%, E. Ger. 9%, Czech. 7%, W. Ger. 6%. **Tourists** (1974): 7,893,400; receipts: $146 million.

Transport: Railway traffic (1974): 25,877 mln. passenger-miles; 77,722 mln. net ton-miles. **Motor vehicles:** in use (1974): 920,300 passenger cars, 386,000 commercial vehicles; manufactured (1976): 216,000 passenger cars, 76,000 commercial vehicles. **Civil aviation:** 887 mln. passenger-miles (1976); 8.8 mln. freight ton-miles (1976). **Chief ports:** Gdansk, Gdynia, Szczecin.

Communications: Television sets: 5,687,000 licenses (1973); 895,000 manufactured (1974). **Radios:** 7,811,000 licenses (1973); 1,422,000 manufactured (1974). **Telephones in use** (1976): 2,577,636. **Daily newspaper circulation** (1973): 7,815,000; 234 per 1,000 pop.

Health: Life expectancy at birth (1970-72): 66.83 male; 73.76 female. **Births** (per 1,000 pop. 1975): 19.0. **Deaths** (per 1,000 pop. 1975): 8.7. **Natural increase** (1975): 1.02%. **Pop. per hospital bed** (1973): 132. **Pop. per physician** (1973): 607. **Infant mortality** (per 1,000 pop. under 1 yr. 1975): 24.8.

Education: Literacy (1973): 98%. **Pop. 5-19:** In school (1973) 60%; per teacher (1973): 34.

Slavic tribes in the area were converted to Latin Christianity in the 10th century. Poland was a great power from the 14th to the 17th centuries. In 3 partitions (1772, 1793, 1795) it was apportioned among Prussia, Russia, and Austria. Overrun by the Austro-German armies in World War I, its independence, self-declared on Nov. 11, 1918, was recognized by the Treaty of Versailles, June 28, 1919. Large territories to the east were taken in a war with Russia, 1921.

Nazi Germany and the Soviet Union invaded Poland Sept. 1-27, 1939, and divided the country. During the war, some 6 million Polish citizens were killed by the Nazis, half of them Jews. With Germany's defeat, a Polish government-in-exile in London was recognized by the U.S., but the Soviet Union pressed the claims of a rival group. The election of 1947 was completely dominated by the Communists.

In compensation for 69,860 sq. mi. ceded to the USSR, 1945, Poland received approx. 40,000 sq. mi. of German territory east of the Oder-Neisse line comprising Silesia, Pomerania, West Prussia, and part of East Prussia.

During 12 years of rule by Stalinists, large estates were abolished, industries nationalized, schools secularized, and some Roman Catholic prelates jailed. Farm production fell off. Harsh working conditions caused a riot by workmen in Poznan June 28-29, 1956.

A new Politburo, committed to development of a more independent Polish Communism, was named Oct. 1956, with Wladyslaw Gomulka as first secretary of the Communist Party. Collectivization of farms was ended and many collectives were abolished.

In 1968, Poland joined other Soviet bloc nations in invading Czechoslovakia. In 1970 Poland and West Germany signed a treaty to normalize relations.

In Dec. 1970 workers in port cities rioted because of price rises and new incentive wage rules. On Dec. 20 Gomulka resigned as party leader; he was succeeded by Edward Gierek; the incentive rules were dropped, price rises were revoked. In June 1971 a new 5-year plan was announced, placing more stress on housing and consumer goods production.

Poland was the first Communist state to get most-favored nation trade terms from the U.S. A 10-year W. Germany cooperation pact was signed in 1974.

A law promulgated Feb. 13, 1953, required government consent to high Roman Catholic church appointments. In 1956 Gomulka agreed to permit religious liberty and religious publications, provided the church kept out of politics. In 1961 religious studies in public schools were halted. Government relations with the Church improved in the 1970s. The number of priests and churches was greater in 1971 than in 1939, and 24 seminaries continued to function.

Key industries are state owned and operate under a planned economy. But about 85% of the farms and close to 200,000 small businesses are privately owned. Poland has become the world's 10th largest industrial power. Heavy indebtedness to Western lenders and rising import prices pose economic problems.

Portugal

Republic of Portugal

People: Population (1975): 9,450,000. **Age distrib.** (%): 0-14: 28.3; 15-59: 57.1; 60+: 14.6. **Pop. density:** 267 per sq. mi. **Urban** 26%. **Ethnic groups:** Homogeneous, with small African minority. **Languages:** Portuguese. **Religions:** Roman Catholics 98%.

Geography: Area: 35,340 sq. mi., slightly smaller than Indiana. **Location:** At SW extreme of Europe. **Neighbors:** Spain on N, E. **Topography:** Portugal N of Tajus R, which bisects the country NE-SW, is mountainous, cool, and rainy. To the S there are drier, rolling plains, and a warm climate. **Capital:** Lisbon. **Cities** (1970 est.): Lisbon (met.) 1,611,887; Porto (met.) 1,314,794.

Government: Head of state: Pres. Antonio Ramalho Eanes, b. Jan. 25, 1935, in office: June 27, 1976; **Head of government:** Prime Min. Mario Soares, b. Dec. 7, 1924, in office: July 23, 1976. **Local divisions:** 18 provinces, autonomous districts of Azores, Madeira. **Armed forces:** regulars 59,800; para-military 23,400.

Economy: Industries: Textiles, pottery, shipbuilding, oil products, paper, glassware, tourism. **Chief crops:** Grains, corn, rice, grapes, olives, fruits. **Minerals:** Coal, copper, tin, kaolin, gold, iron, manganese. **Other resources:** Forests (world leader in cork production). **Per capita arable land:** 10 acres. **Livestock** (1976): 1,000,000 cattle; 1,600,000 pigs; 1,950,000 sheep; 15,700,000 poultry. **Fish catch** (1975): 369,000 metric tons. **Electricity production** (1976): 9,600 mln. kwh. **Labor force:** 30% agric.; 22% manuf.

Finance: Currency: Escudo (Apr. 1977: 38.7=$1 US). **Gross domestic product** (1976): $14.6 bln. **Per capita income** (1974): $1,463. **Imports** (1976): $4,221 bln.; partners (1974): W. Ger. 14%, U.K. 9%, U.S. 9%, Ang. 8%. **Exports** (1976): $1.811 bln.; partners (1974): U.K. 23%, U.S. 10%, W. Ger. 8%, Swed. 6%. **Tourists** (1974): 2,621,800; receipts: $513 million. **Balance of payments** (1976): −$964 mln. **National budget** (1973): $1.6 bln. revenues; $1.68 bln. expenditures. **International reserves**

(Jan. 1977): $1.215 bln. **Consumer prices** (change in 1976): 21.0%.

Transport: Railway traffic (1974): 2,827 mln. passenger-miles; 538 mln. net ton-miles. **Motor vehicles:** in use (1974): 854,400 passenger cars, 237,600 commercial vehicles; assembled (1976): 39,000 passenger cars, 47,000 commercial vehicles. **Civil aviation:** 1,945 mln. passenger-miles (1975); 44 mln. freight ton-miles (1975). **Chief ports:** Lisbon, Setubal, Leixoes.

Communications: Television sets: 569,000 licenses (1973); 113,000 manufactured (1973). **Radios:** 1,505,000 licenses (1973); 530,000 manufactured (1973). **Telephones in use** (1976): 1,065,974. **Daily newspaper circulation** (1973): 740,000; 86 per 1,000 pop.

Health: Life expectancy at birth (1974): 65.29 male; 72.03 female. **Births** (per 1,000 pop. 1974): 19.6. **Deaths** (per 1,000 pop. 1974): 11.0. **Natural increase** (1974): 0.86%. **Pop. per hospital bed** (1973): 157. **Pop. per physician** (1973): 973. **Infant mortality** (per 1,000 pop. under 1 yr. 1974): 37.9.

Education: Literacy (1973): 70%. **Pop. 5-19:** in school (1973): 58%; per teacher (1973): 43.

Portugal, an independent state since the 12th century, was a kingdom until a revolution in 1910 drove out King Manoel II and a republic was proclaimed.

From 1932 a strong, repressive government was headed by Premier Antonio de Oliveira Salazar. Illness forced his retirement in Sept. 1968; he was succeeded by Marcello Caetano. Portugal was the last European nation to hold an extensive empire in Africa, maintaining over 140,000 troops there to battle various independence movements.

On Apr. 25, 1974, the government was seized by a military junta led by Gen. Antonio de Spinola, who was named president.

The new government reached agreements providing independence for Guinea-Bissau, Mozambique, Cape Verde Islands, Angola, and Sao Tome and Principe. Up to 1 million refugees fled to Portugal. Spinola resigned Sept. 30, 1974, in face of increasing pressure from leftist officers. Despite a 64% victory for democratic parties in April 1975, the Soviet-supported Communist party increased its influence. Banks, insurance companies, transport, and other industries were nationalized. A counter-coup in November halted this trend. Free elections under the new constitution were held in 1976, with the Socialist party gaining a parliamentary plurality. After three years of turmoil the economy was in disarray, despite aid from the U.S. and West European countries.

Military forces, which totaled over 200,000, have been rapidly demobilized. A 1951 agreement gave the U.S. rights to use defense facilities in the Azores.

Azores Islands, in the Atlantic, 740 mi. W. of Portugal, have an area of 904 sq. mi. and a population (1970) of 291,028. The **Madeira Islands,** 360 mi. off the NW coast of Africa, have an area of 307 sq. mi. and a population (1976) of 270,000. Both groups were offered partial autonomy in 1976.

Portuguese Timor was annexed by Indonesia May 3, 1976, after 9 months of fighting between local factions. Portuguese troops had withdrawn in 1975.

Macao, with an area of 6 sq. mi., is an enclave, a peninsula and 2 small islands, at the mouth of the Canton River in China. Portugal granted broad autonomy in 1976. Population (UN est. 1974): 270,000.

Qatar

State of Qatar

People: Population (1976 est.): 100,000. **Pop. density:** 25 per sq. mi. **Ethnic groups:** Arabs 56%, Iranians 23%, Pakistani 7%, others. **Languages:** Arabic (official), Farsi (Persian). **Religions:** Moslems 98%.

Geography: Area: 4,000 sq. mi., smaller than Connecticut. **Location:** Occupies peninsula on E coast of Persian Gulf. **Neighbors:** Saudi Arabia on W, United Arab Emirates on S. **Topography:** Most of the country is a flat desert, with some limestone ridges, vegetation of any kind is scarce. **Capital:** Doha. **Cities** (1972 est.): Doha 100,000.

Government: Head of state: Emir Khalifa bin Hamad al-Thani, b. 1932, in office: Feb. 22, 1972. **Armed forces:** regular 2,200.

Economy: Crude oil output (1976): 178 mln. bbls.

Finance: Currency: Riyal (Apr. 1977: 1 = $0.253 US). **Gross domestic product** (est. 1974): $2.2 bln. **Per capita income** (1974): $12,500. **Imports** (1976) $817 mln.; partners (1974): Jap. 18%, U.K. 14%, U.S. 10%, Leb. 6%. **Exports** (1976): $2.192 bln.; partners (1974): U.K. 15%, Fr. 10%, U.A.E. 10%, It. 8%. **National budget** (1975): $1.82 bln. revenues; $1.35 bln. expenditures. **International reserves** (Sept. 1976): $128.9 mln.

Transport: Chief ports: Doha, Musayid.

Communications: Telephones in use (1976): 20,908.

Qatar was under Turkish control from 1872 to 1915. In a treaty signed in 1916 Qatar gave Great Britain responsibility for its defense and foreign relations. After Britain announced it would remove its military forces from the Persian Gulf area by the end of 1971, Qatar sought a federation with other British protected States in the area; this failed and Qatar declared itself independent, Sept. 1, 1971.

Qatar's first ruler under independence, Emir Ahmed bin Ali al-Thani, was replaced by his cousin, Khalifa bin Hamad al-Thani, Feb. 22, 1972, in a bloodless coup.

Oil revenues give Qatar a per capita income second only to the United Arab Emirates.

Rhodesia

(Colony of Southern Rhodesia)

People: Population (1976 est.): 6,530,000. **Pop. density:** 43 per sq. mi. **Urban** (1974): 19.4%. **Ethnic groups:** Bantu tribes 96%, Caucasians 3%, Coloreds, Asians 1%. **Languages:** English (official), Shona, Ndebele. **Religions:** Christians and part Christians 75%, Moslems.

Geography: Area: 150,333 sq. mi., nearly as large as California. **Location:** In southern Africa. **Neighbors:** Zambia on N, Botswana on W, S. Africa on S, Mozambique on E. **Topography:** Rhodesia is high plateau country, rising to mountains on eastern border, sloping down on the other borders. **Capital:** Salisbury. **Cities** (1973 est.): Salisbury (met.) 502,000; Bulawayo (met.) 307,000.

Government: Head of state: Pres. James Wrathall, b. Aug. 28, 1913, in office: Dec. 10, 1975; **Head of government:** Prime Min. Ian Douglas Smith, b. Apr. 18, 1919, in office: Apr. 13, 1964. **Local divisions:** 7 provinces. **Armed forces:** regulars 9,200; reserves 13,000; para-military 44,000.

Economy: Industries: Clothing, chemicals, light industries. **Chief crops:** Tobacco, sugar, cotton, corn, tea. **Minerals:** Asbestos, copper, iron, coal, chrome. **Per capita arable land:** 0.7 acres. **Livestock** (1974): 4,150,000 cattle; 150,000 pigs; 490,000 sheep; 8,200,000 poultry. **Electricity production** (1976): 6,744 mln. kwh. **Labor force:** 63% agric.

Finance: Currency: Dollar (1974: 1 = $1.76 US). **Gross domestic product** (1974): $3.15 bln. **Per capita income** (1974): $502. **Imports** (1973): $541 mln.; partners (1965): U.K. 30%, So. Afr. 23%, U.S. 7%, Jap. 6%. **Exports** (1973): $652 mln.; partners (1965): Zamb. 25%, U.K. 22%, So. Afr. 10%, W. Ger. 9%.

Transport: Railway traffic (1974): 3,844 net ton-miles. **Motor vehicles:** in use (1974): 180,000 passenger cars, 70,000 commercial vehicles.

Communications: Television sets: 57,000 in use (1972). **Radios:** 225,000 in use (1973). **Telephones in use** (1976): 182,594. **Daily newspaper circulation** (1972): 84,000; 15 per 1,000 pop.

Health: Life expectancy at birth (1970-75): 49.8 male; 53.3 female. **Births** (annual per 1,000 pop. 1970-75): 47.9. **Deaths** (annual per 1,000 pop. 1970-75): 14.4. **Natural increase** (annual 1970-75): 3.35%. **Pop. per hospital bed** (1973): 324. **Pop. per physician** (1973): 6,556. **Infant mortality** (per 1,000 pop. under 1 yr. 1954): 33.5.

Education: Literacy (1973): 25%. **Pop. 5-19:** in school (1973): 40%; per teacher (1973): 79.

Britain took over the area as Southern Rhodesia in 1923 from the British South Africa Co. (which, under Cecil Rhodes, had conquered the area by 1897) and granted internal self-government. Under a 1961 constitution, voting was restricted to maintain whites in power. On Nov. 11, 1965, Prime Minister Ian D.

Smith announced his country's unilateral declaration of independence. Britain termed the act illegal, and demanded Rhodesia broaden voting rights to provide for eventual rule by the majority Africans.

Urged by Britain, the UN imposed sanctions, including embargoes on oil shipments to Rhodesia, which were backed by most nations including the U.S. Some oil and gasoline reached Rhodesia, however, from South Africa and Mozambique, before the latter became independent in 1975. Some African nations denounced Britain for refusing to use force against the Rhodesian government. In May 1968, the UN Security Council ordered a trade embargo.

Rhodesia claimed the sanctions were ineffective. A new constitution came into effect, Mar. 2, 1970, providing for a republic with a president and prime minister. The election law effectively prevented full black representation through income tax requirements.

A proposed British-Rhodesian settlement was dropped in May 1972 when a British commission reported most Rhodesian blacks opposed it. In 1972-74 there were small clashes between black nationalist guerrillas and Rhodesian security forces. Intermittent negotiations between the government and various black groups failed to prevent increasing skirmishes. By mid-1977, over 3,000 soldiers and civilians had been killed. Rhodesian troops battled guerrillas within Mozambique.

In 1977, the U.S. congress repealed a law that had allowed U.S. import of Rhodesian chrome.

Romania

Socialist Republic of Romania

People: Population (1976): 21,450,000. **Age distrib.** (%): 0–14: 25.2; 15–59: 60.8; 60+: 14.0. **Pop. density:** 234 per sq. mi. **Urban** (1974): 42.7%. **Ethnic groups:** Romanians 85%, Hungarians 9%, Germans 2%, Serbo-Croats, Ukrainians, Greeks, Turks. **Languages:** Romanian, Hungarian. **Religions:** Orthodox 80%, Roman Catholics 9%, Calvinists, Jews, Lutherans.

Geography: Area: 91,699 sq. mi., slightly smaller than Oregon. **Location:** In SE Europe on the Black Sea. **Neighbors:** USSR on E (Moldavia) and N (Ukraine), Hungary, Yugoslavia on W, Bulgaria on S. **Topography:** The Carpathian Mts. encase the north-central Transylvanian plateau. There are wide plains S and E of the mountains, through which flow the lower reaches of the rivers of the Danube system. **Capital:** Bucharest. **Cities** (1974 est.): Bucharest 1,565,872; Chij 218,703.

Government: Head of state: Pres. Nicolae Ceausescu, b. Jan. 26, 1918, in office: Dec. 7, 1967; **Head of government:** Prime Min. Manea Manescu, b. 1916, in office: Mar. 29, 1974; **Head of Communist Party:** Sec.-Gen. Nicolae Ceausescu, in office: 1965. **Local divisions:** Bucharest and 39 districts. **Armed forces:** regulars 181,000; reserves 545,500.

Economy: Industries: Steel, metals, machinery, oil products, chemicals, textiles, shoes, tourism. **Chief crops:** Corn, wheat, sugar beets, grapes, fruits. **Minerals:** Oil, gas, coal, salt, bauxite, manganese, lead, zinc, gold, silver. **Crude oil output** (1976): 109 mln. bbls. **Other resources:** Timber. **Per capita arable land:** 1.1 acres. **Livestock** (1976): 6,126,000 cattle; 8,812,000 pigs; 13,867,000 sheep; 67,672,000 poultry. **Fish catch** (1974): 129,300 metric tons. **Electricity production** (1975): 53,724 mln. kwh. **Labor force:** 40% agric.; 30% manuf.

Finance: Currency: Leu (1974: 14.38=$1 US). **Gross domestic produce** (est. 1974): $28 bln. **Per capita income** (1974): $1,200. **Imports** (1976): $6.584 bln.; partners (1974): W. Ger. 15%, USSR 15%, U.S. 6%, E. Ger. 5%. **Exports** (1976): $8.730 bln.; partners (1974): USSR 17%, W. Ger. 10%, E. Ger. 6%, It. 5%. **Tourists** (1974): 3,825,300.

Transport: Railway traffic (1974): 13,914 mln. passenger-miles; 38,265 mln. net ton-miles. **Motor vehicles:** in use (1972): 125,000 passenger cars, 50,000 commercial vehicles; manufactured (1975): 68,000 passenger cars, 39,000 commercial vehicles. **Civil aviation:** 478 mln. passenger-miles (1976); 6.6 mln. freight ton-miles (1976). **Chief ports:** Constanta, Galati, Beaila.

Communications: Television sets: 2,145,000 licenses (1973); 451,000 manufactured (1974). **Radios:** 3,076,000 licenses (1973); 602,000 manufactured (1974). **Daily newspaper circulation** (1973): 3,736,000; 179 per 1,000 pop.

Health: Life expectancy at birth (1972-74): 66.83 male; 71.29 female. **Births** (per 1,000 pop. 1974): 20.3 **Deaths** (per 1,000 pop. 1974): 9.1. **Natural increase** (1974): 1.12%. **Pop. per hospital bed** (1973): 116. **Pop. per physician** (1973): 817. **Infant mortality** (per 1,000 pop. under 1 yr. 1974): 35.0.

Education: Literacy (1973): 90%. **Pop. 5-19:** in school (1973): 65%; per teacher (1973): 30.

Romania's earliest known people were merged with invading Proto-Thracians, preceding by centuries the Dacians. The Dacian kingdom was occupied by Rome, 106 A.D.-271 A.D.; the people and language were Romanized. The principalities of Wallachia and Moldavia, dominated by Turkey, were united in 1859, became Romania in 1861. In 1877 Romania proclaimed independence from Turkey, became an independent state by the Treaty of Berlin, 1878, and kingdom, 1881, under Carol I. In 1886 Romania became a constitutional monarchy with a bicameral legislature.

Romania helped Russia in its war with Turkey, 1877-78. After World War I it acquired Bessarabia, Bukovina, Transylvania and Banat. In 1940 it ceded Bessarabia and Northern Bukovina to the USSR and part of Southern Dobrudja to Bulgaria.

Marshal Ion Antonescu, leader of a militarist movement, came to power and forced Romania to join Germany against the USSR in World War II in 1941. In 1944 Antonescu was overthrown by King Michael with Soviet help and Romania joined the Allies.

With occupation by Soviet troops the National Democratic Front, headed by the Communist party, displaced the National Peasant party. A People's Republic was proclaimed, Dec. 30, 1947, and Michael was forced to abdicate. Land owners were dispossessed and most banks, factories and transportation units were nationalized.

On Aug. 22, 1965, a new constitution proclaimed Romania a Socialist, rather than a People's Republic. Since 1966, Romania has adopted an independent attitude toward the USSR, a stand pointed up by the visit of U.S. President Nixon in Aug. 1969. Romanian President Nicolae Ceausescu visited the U.S. in 1970 and 1973. The U.S. granted most-favored-nation tariff treatment in 1975, and a 10-year U.S. trade pact was signed in 1976. Since 1959, USSR troops have not been permitted to enter Romania. In 1974, Ceausescu declared Russia was Romania's top ally.

Romania has maintained friendly relations with China, and has refused to sever diplomatic and trade ties with Israel.

Romania has become industrialized, but lags in consumer goods and in personal freedoms. All industry is state owned, and state farms and cooperatives own over 90% of arable land. Romania is one of the few countries in Europe self-sufficient in oil, though reserves have been depleted.

A major earthquake struck Bucharest in March, 1977, killing over 1,300 people and causing extensive damage to housing and industry.

Rwanda

Republic of Rwanda

People: Population (1976 est.): 4,290,000. **Age distrib.** (%): 0-14: 43.8; 15-59: 51; 60+: 5.2. **Pop. density:** 422 per sq. mi. **Urban** (1971): 3.4%. **Ethnic groups:** Hutu 89%, Tutsi 10%, Twa (pygmies) 1%. **Languages:** French, Kinyarwandu (both official), Swahili. **Religions:** Roman Catholics 45%, Protestants 9%, Moslems 1%.

Geography: Area: 10,169 sq. mi., the size of Maryland. **Location:** In E central Africa. **Neighbors:** Uganda on N, Zaire on W, Burundi on S, Tanzania on E. **Topography:** Grassy uplands and hills cover most of the country, with a chain of volcanoes in the NW. The source of the Nile R. has been located in Rwanda. **Capital:** Kigali. **Cities** (1970) est.): Kigali (met.) 54,403.

Government: Head of state: Pres. Juvenal Habyarimana, b. Mar. 8, 1937, in office: July 5, 1973. **Local divisions:** 10 prefectures. **Armed forces:** regulars 3,750; reserves 1,200.

Economy: Chief crops: Coffee, cotton, tea, pyrethrum, tobacco. **Minerals:** Tin, gold, wolframite. **Per capita arable land:** 0.3 acres. **Livestock** (1974): 740,000 cattle; 55,000 pigs; 245,000 sheep. **Fish catch** (1973): 32 mln. metric tons. **Electricity production** (1973): 32 mln. kwh. **Labor force:** 91% agric.

Finance: Currency: Franc (Apr. 1977: 92.8=$1 US). **Gross domestic product** (1973): $272 mln. **Per capita income** (1970): $54. **Imports** (1976): $103 mln.; partners (1974): Belg. 16%, Kenya 10%, Jap. 9%, W. Ger. 9%. **Exports** (1976): $81 mln.; partners (1974): Belg. 13%, U.S. 3%, U.K. 3%, Zaire 1%. **Balance of payments** (1976): $25.1 mln. **National budget** (1972): $20.4 mln. revenues; $29.3 mln. expenditures. **International reserves** (Nov. 1976): $46.09 mln. **Consumer prices** (change in 1975): 30.9%.

Transport: Motor vehicles: in use (1974): 5,900 passenger cars, 4,200 commercial vehicles.

Communications: Radios: 31,000 in use licensed (1972); 7,000 manufactured (1973). **Telephones in use** (1976): 3,378.

Health: Life expectancy at birth (1970-75): 39.4 male; 42.6 female. **Births** (annual per 1,000 pop. 1970-75): 50.0. **Deaths** (annual per 1,000 pop. 1970-75): 23.6. **Natural increase** (annual 1970-75): 2.64%. **Pop. per hospital bed** (1973): 771. **Pop. per physician** (1973): 52,763. **Infant mortality** (per 1,000 pop. under 1 yr. 1970): 132.8.

Education: Literacy (1973): 10%. **Pop. 5-19:** in school (1973): 33%; per teacher (1973): 192.

For centuries, the Tutsi (an extremely tall people) dominated the Hutus (90% of the population). A civil war broke out in 1959 and Tutsi power was ended. A referendum in 1961 abolished the monarchic system.

Rwanda, which had been part of the Belgian UN trusteeship of Rwanda-Urundi, became independent July 1, 1962. The government was overthrown in a 1973 military coup. Rwanda is one of the most densely populated countries in Africa. All available arable land is being used, and is being subject to erosion. The government has carried out economic and social improvement programs.

The source of the Nile River, long sought by explorers and geographers, has been located in the headwaters of the Kagera (Akagera) River, SW of Kigali.

Samoa

People: Population (1975 est.): 160,000. **Age distrib.** (%): 0–14: 51.3; 15–59: 44.5; 60+: 4.1. **Pop. density:** 141 per sq. mi. **Urban** (1974): 21.0%. **Ethnic groups:** Samoans (Polynesians) 88%, Euronesians (mixed) 10%, Europeans, other Pacific Islanders. **Languages:** Samoan, English both official. **Religions:** Protestants 75%, Roman Catholics 20%.

Geography: Area: 1,133 sq. mi., the size of Rhode Island. **Location:** In the S. Pacific O. **Neighbors:** Nearest are Fiji on W, Tonga on S. **Topography:** Comprises main islands, Savai'i (660 sq. mi.) and Upolu (430 sq. mi.), both ruggedly mountainous, and small islands Manono and Apolima. **Capital:** Apia. **Cities:** (1974 est.): Apia (met.) 32,616.

Government: Head of state: King Malietoa Tanumafili II, b. Jan. 4, 1913, in office: Jan. 1, 1962; **Head of government:** Prime Min. Tupuola Efi, b. 1948, in office: Mar. 1976. **Local divisions:** 24 districts.

Economy: Chief crops: Cocoa, coconuts, bananas, taro, coffee, bark cloth. **Other resources:** Hardwoods, fish. **Livestock** (1974): 21,000 cattle; 45,000 pigs; 93,000 poultry. **Electricity production** (1976): 23 mln. kwh. **Labor force:** 67% agric.; 2% manuf.

Finance: Currency: Tala (Apr. 1977: 1=$1.27 US). **Gross domestic product** (est. 1974): $45 mln. **Per capita income** (1974): $280. **Imports** (1976) $29 mln.; partners (1970): N.Z. 33%, Australia 19%, Jap. 12%, U.S. 10%. **Exports** (1976): $7 mln.; partners (1970): N.Z. 47%, W. Ger. 15%, Neth. 11%, U.S. 9%. **Tourist receipts** (1972): $3 million. **Balance of payments** (1976): $–15.3 mln. **National budget** (1970): $6.9 mln. revenues; $7.6 mln. expenditures. **International reserves** (Feb. 1977): $5.43 mln. **Consumer prices** (change in 1976): 5.0%.

Transport: Motor vehicles: in use (1974): 1,300 passenger cars, 1,900 commercial vehicles. **Chief ports:** Apia, Asau.

Communications: Television sets: 2,800 in use (1973). **Radios:** 50,000 in use (1972). **Telephones in use** (1976): 3,165.

Health: Life expectancy at birth (1961-66): 60.8 male; 65.2 female. **Births** (per 1,000 pop. 1974): 36.7. **Deaths** (per 1,000 pop. 1974): 6.6. **Natural increase** (1974): 3.01%. **Infant mortality** (per 1,000 pop. under 1 yr. 1974): 39.9.

Western Samoa was a German colony, 1899 to 1914, when New Zealand landed troops and took over. It became a New Zealand mandate under the League of Nations and, in 1945, a New Zealand UN Trusteeship.

An elected local government took office in Oct. 1959 and the country became fully independent Jan. 1, 1962. New Zealand has continued economic aid and educational assistance.

The country's name was changed to Samoa in 1977.

San Marino

Most Serene Republic of San Marino

People: Population (1976 est.): 20,000. **Age distrib.** (%): 0–14: 25.7; 15–59: 60.0; 60+: 14.3. **Pop. density:** 851 per sq. mi. **Urban** (1970): 92.4%. **Ethnic groups:** Italian. **Languages:** Italian. **Religions:** Roman Catholics predominate.

Geography: Area: 23.5 sq. mi. **Location:** In N central Italy near Adriatic coast. **Neighbors:** Completely surrounded by Italy. **Topography:** The country lies on the slopes of Mt. Titano. **Capital:** San Marino.

Government: Head of state: Capitani Reggenti: Alberto Lonfernini, Antonio Lazzaro Volpinari, in office: Apr. 1, 1977. **Armed forces:** 180-man ceremonial army.

Economy: Industries: Postage stamps, tourism, woolen goods, paper, cement, ceramics.

Finance: Currency: Italian Lira. **Tourists** (1974): 2,202,100.

Communications: Television sets: 3,200 licenses (1973). **Radios:** 4,700 licenses (1973). **Telephones in use** (1976): 5,218.

Health: Births (per 1,000 pop. 1973): 17.4. **Deaths** (per 1,000 pop. 1973): 7.7. **Natural increase** (1973): 0.97%. **Infant mortality** (per 1,000 pop. under 1 yr. 1973): 9.2.

San Marino claims to be the oldest state in Europe and the oldest republic in the world. It has had a treaty of friendship with Italy since 1862.

Sao Tome and Principe

Democratic Republic of Sao Tome and Principe

People: Population (1976 est.): 80,000. **Pop. density:** 215 per sq. mi. **Ethnic groups:** Portuguese-African mixture, African minority (Angola, Mozambique immigrants). **Languages:** Portuguese. **Religions:** Christians 80%.

Geography: Area: 372 sq. mi., slightly larger than New York City. **Location:** In the Gulf of Guinea about 125 miles off W Central Africa. **Neighbors:** Nearest are Gabon, Equatorial Guinea on E. **Topography:** Sao Tome and Principe islands are both part of an extinct volcano chain. They are both covered by lush forests and croplands. **Capital:** Sao Tome. **Cities** (1960 cen.): Sao Tome 5,714.

Government: Head of state: Pres. Manuel Pinto da Costa, in office: July 12, 1975. **Head of government:** Prime Min. Miguel Trovoada, in office: July 12, 1975. **Local divisions:** 2 provinces, 12 counties.

Economy: Chief crops: Coffee, cocoa, coconut products, cinchona. **Electricity production** (1972): 5.4 mln. kwh.

Finance: Currency: Escudo (1974): 25.4=$1 US). **Gross domestic product** (est. 1974): $35 mln. **Per capita income** (1974): $400. **Imports** (1973) $10 mln.; partners (1973): Port. 47%, Angola 23%, Neth. 6%, Fr. 5%. **Exports** (1973): $13 mln.; partners (1973): Port. 36%, Neth. 32%, W. Ger. 12%, U.S. 8%.

Transport: Motor vehicles: in use (1973): 1,600 passenger cars, 400 commercial vehicles. **Chief ports:** Sao Tome, Santo Antonio.

Communications: Radios: 7,500 licenses (1973). **Telephones in use** (1976): 727.

Health: Births (per 1,000 pop. 1972): 45.0. **Deaths** (per 1,000 pop. 1972): 11.2. **Natural increase** (1972): 3.38%. **Infant mortality** (per 1,000 pop. under 1 yr. 1972): 64.3.

The islands were uninhabited when discovered in 1471 by the Portuguese, who brought the first settlers — convicts and exiled

Jews. Sugar planting was replaced by the slave trade as the chief economic activity until coffee and cocoa were introduced in the nineteenth century.

Portugal agreed in 1974 to turn the colony over to the Gabon-based Movement for the Liberation of Sao Tome and Principe, which proclaimed as the first president its East-German-trained leader Manuel Pinto da Costa. Independence came July 12, 1975.

Low cocoa prices, the emigration of most of the 1,000 whites, and the repatriation of Cape Verdean plantation foremen stymied the economy.

Saudi Arabia

Kingdom of Saudi Arabia

People: Population (1976 est.): 9,240,000. **Pop. density:** 11 per sq. mi. **Ethnic groups:** Arab tribes, immigrants from other Arab and Moslem countries. **Languages:** Arabic. **Religions:** Moslems 99%.

Geography: Area: 873,000 sq. mi., one-fourth the size of the U.S. **Location:** Occupies most of Arabian Peninsula in Middle East. **Neighbors:** Kuwait, Iraq, Jordan on N, Yemen, South Yemen, Oman on S, United Arab Emirates, Qatar on E. **Topography:** The highlands on the W, up to 9,000 ft., slope as an arid, barren desert to the Persian Gulf. There are no permanent rivers. **Capital:** Riyadh. **Cities** (1972 est.): Riyadh 400,000; Jiddah 375,000; Mecca 358,000.

Government: Head of state: King Khalid bin Abdul Aziz, b. 1913, in office: Mar. 28, 1975; **Head of government:** Dep. Prime Min. Fahd bin Abdul Aziz, in office: Mar. 28, 1975. **Local divisions:** 6 major and 12 minor provinces. **Armed forces:** regulars 51,500; para-military 26,500.

Economy: Industries: Oil products. **Chief crops:** Dates, wheat, barley, fruit. **Minerals:** Oil, gas, gold, silver, iron. **Crude oil output** (1976): 3.1 bln. bbls. Largest reserves and exports in world. **Per capita arable land:** 0.2 acres. **Livestock** (1974): 310,000 cattle; 3,030,000 sheep. **Fish catch** (1974): 31,300 metric tons. **Electricity production** (1972): 1,000 mln. kwh. **Labor force:** 61% agric.; 2% manuf.

Finance: Currency: Riyal (Apr. 1977: 3.53=$1 US). **Gross domestic product** (1974-75): $38.4 bln. **Per capita income** (1974): $2,484. **Imports** (1976) $11.759 bln.; partners (1972): U.S. 19%, Jap. 14%, Leb. 12%, U.K. 7%. **Exports** (1976): $36.-083 bln; partners (1972): Jap. 17%, It. 11%, Fr. 10%, U.K. 9%. **Tourist receipts** (1974): $469 million. **Balance of payments** (1975): $16.4 bln. **International reserves** (Feb. 1977): $26.855 bln. **Consumer prices** (change in 1975): 34.6%.

Transport: Railway traffic (1973): 38 mln. passenger-miles; 39 mln. net ton-miles. **Motor vehicles:** in use (1970): 64,900 passenger cars, 50,400 commercial vehicles. **Chief ports:** Jidda, Ad-Dammam, Ras Tannurah.

Communications: Television sets: 18,000 in use (1970). **Radios:** 87,000 in use (1972). **Daily newspaper circulation** (1973): 96,000; 11 per 1,000 pop.

Health: Life expectancy at birth (1970-75): 44.2 male; 46.5 female. **Births** (annual per 1,000 pop. 1970-75): 49.5. **Deaths** (annual per 1,000 pop. 1970-75): 20.2 **Natural increase** (annual 1970-75): 2.93%. **Pop. per hospital bed** (1973): 1,046. **Pop. per physician** (1973): 3,870. **Infant mortality** (per 1,000 pop. under 1 yr. 1973): 152.

Education: Literacy (1973): 15%. **Pop. 5-19:** in school (1973): 27%; per teacher (1973): 97.

Arabia was united for the first time by Mohammed, in the early 7th century. His successors conquered the entire Near East and North Africa, bringing Islam and the Arabic language. But Arabia itself soon returned to its former status as political and cultural backwater.

Nejd, long an independent state and center of the Wahhabi sect, fell under Turkish rule in the 18th century, but in 1913 Ibn Saud, founder of the Saudi dynasty, overthrew the Turks and captured the Turkish province of Hasa; took the Hejaz in 1925 and by 1926, most of Asir. The discovery of oil by an American oil company in the 1930s transformed the new country.

Crown Prince Khalid was proclaimed king on Mar. 25, 1975, after the assassination of King Faisal. There is no constitution and no parliament. The king exercises authority together with a Council of Ministers. The Islamic religious code is the law of the land. Alcohol and public entertainments are restricted, and women have an inferior legal status.

Saudi units fought against Israel in the 1948 and 1973 Arab-Israeli wars. Some 12,000 troops are deployed in Syria and Jordan. Billions of dollars of advanced arms have been purchased from Britain, France, and the U.S., including jet fighters and missiles.

Beginning with the 1967 Arab-Israeli war, Saudi Arabia provided large annual financial gifts to Egypt; aid was later extended to Syria, Jordan, and Palestinian guerrilla groups, as well as to other Moslem countries.

Faisal played a leading role in the 1973-74 Arab oil embargo against the U.S. and other nations in an attempt to force them to adopt an anti-Israel policy.

Between 1973 and 1976, Saudi Arabia acquired full ownership of Aramco (Arabian American Oil Co.). Oil had first been discovered by Western companies in the 1930s. A 5-year $140 billion development plan was approved in 1975, calling for the importation of 500,000 workers. Some one million foreigners already lived in the country, whose native population may be less than 6 million.

The Hejaz contains the holy cities of Islam — Medina where the Mosque of the Prophet enshrines, the tomb of Mohammed, who died in the city June 7, 632, and Mecca, his birthplace. More than 600,000 Moslems from 60 nations pilgrimage to Mecca annually.

Senegal

Republic of Senegal

People: Population (1976 est.): 5,110,000. **Pop. density:** 67 per sq. mi. **Urban** (1971): 31.7%. **Ethnic groups:** Wolof 36%, Peuhl 17.5%, Serere 16.5%, Toucouleur 9%, others. **Languages:** French (official), tribal languages. **Religions:** Moslems 90%, Christians 6%.

Geography: Area: 76,124 sq. mi., the size of South Dakota. **Location:** At the western extreme of Africa. **Neighbors:** Mauritania on N, Mali on E, Guinea, Guinea-Bissau on S, Gambia surrounded on three sides. **Topography:** Low rolling plains cover most of Senegal, rising somewhat in the SE. Swamp and jungles are in SW. **Capital:** Dakar. **Cities** (1973 est.): Dakar (met.) 600,-000; Kaolack 96,000; Thies 81,000.

Government: Head of state: Pres. Leopold Senghor, b. Oct. 9, 1906, in office: Sept. 5, 1960; **Head of government:** Prime Min. Abdou Diouf, b. 1935, in office: Feb. 1970. **Local divisions:** 8 regions. **Armed forces:** regulars 5,950; para-military 1,600.

Economy: Industries: Food processing, chemicals, cement. **Chief crops:** Peanuts are chief export; millet, corn, rice. **Minerals:** Phosphates. **Per capita arable land:** 3.1 acres. **Livestock** (1974): 2,266,000 cattle; 190,000 pigs; 1,000,000 sheep. **Fish catch** (1975): 362,000 metric tons. **Electricity production** (1972): 384 mln. kwh. **Labor force:** 76% agric.

Finance: Currency: CFA Francs (Apr. 1977: 248=$1 US). **Gross domestic product** (1976): $1.48 bln. **Per capita income** (1974): $273. **Imports** (1975) $584 mln.; partners (1973): Fr. 46%, U.S. 7%, P.R. China 5%, W. Ger. 5%. **Exports** (1975): $462 mln.; partners (1973): Fr. 49%, Ivory C. 8%, Mauritania 7%. **Tourists** (1974): 147,400; receipts (1973): $21 million. **Balance of payments** (1975): $7.2 mln. **International reserves** (Jan. 1977): $14.6 mln. **Consumer prices** (change in 1976): 6.2%.

Transport: Railway traffic (1974): 137 mln. passenger-miles; 243 mln. net ton-miles. **Motor vehicles:** in use (1974): 44,800 passenger cars, 25,000 commercial vehicles. **Chief ports:** Dakar, Saint-Louis.

Communications: Television sets: 1,700 in use (1973). **Radios:** 285,000 in use (1973). **Telephones in use** (1976): 37,-547. **Daily newspaper circulation** (1973): 25,000.

Health: Life expectancy at birth (1970-75): 38.5 male; 41.6 female. **Births** (annual per 1,000 pop. 1970-75): 47.6. **Deaths** (annual per 1,000 pop. 1970-75): 23.9. **Natural increase** (annual 1970-75): 2.37%. **Pop. per hospital bed** (1973): 755. **Pop. per physician** (1973): 14,739. **Infant mortality** (per 1,000 pop. under 1 yr. 1960-61): 92.9.

Education: Literacy (1973): 10%. **Pop. 5-19:** in school (1973): 27%; per teacher (1973): 169.

Portuguese settlers arrived in the 15th century, but French

control grew from the 17th century. The last independent Moslem state was subdued in 1893. Dakar became the capital of French West Africa.

Independence as part, along with the Sudanese Rep., of the Mali Federation, came June 20, 1960. Senegal withdrew June 20 that year. French political and economic influence is strong.

A long drought brought famine, 1972-73.

Two opposition parties were allowed to form in 1976.

Seychelles

People: Population (1976 est.): 60,000. **Age distrib.** (%): 0-14: 43.6; 15-59: 47.4; 60+: 9.1. **Pop. density:** 560 per sq. mi. **Urban** (1971): 26.1%. **Ethnic groups:** Creoles (mixture of Asians, Africans, and French) predominate. **Languages:** English (official), Creole 94%, French 5%, others. **Religions:** Roman Catholics 90%, Protestants 8%, Hindus, Moslems.

Geography: Area: 107 sq. mi. **Location:** In the Indian O. 700 miles NE of Madagascar. **Neighbors:** Nearest are Madagascar on SW, Somalia on NW. **Topography:** The Seychelles are a group of 86 islands, about half of them composed of coral, the other half granite, the latter predominantly mountainous. **Capital:** Victoria. **Cities** (1971 cen.): Port Victoria (met.) 13,736.

Government: Head of state: Pres. France Albert Rene, in office: June 5, 1977. **Local divisions:** 8 districts.

Economy: Industries: Food processing, brewing. **Chief crops:** Coconut products, cinnamon, vanilla, tea, patchouli. **Other resources:** Guano, shark fins, tortoise shell, fish. **Electricity production** (1973): 353 mln. kwh.

Finance: Currency: Rupee (1974: 5.7=$1 US). **Gross domestic product** (est. 1974): $28 mln. **Per capita income** (1974): $450. **Imports** (1974) $27 mln.; partners (1974): U.K. 29%, Kenya 20%, So. Afr. 10%, Sing. 5%. **Exports** (1974): $3 mln.; partners (1974): Pak. 13%, U.S. 10%, Fr. 9%. **Tourists** (1974): 25,500.

Transport: Motor vehicles: in use (1974): 2,300 passenger cars, 300 commercial vehicles. **Chief ports:** Victoria.

Communications: Radios: 9,000 in use (1973). **Telephones in use** (1976): 3,339. **Daily newspaper circulation** (1973): 4,000; 71 per 1,000 pop.

Health: Life expectancy at birth (1970-72): 61.9 male; 68.0 female. **Births** (per 1,000 pop. 1974): 32.8. **Deaths** (per 1,000 pop. 1974): 8.8. **Natural increase** (1974): 2.40%. **Infant mortality** (per 1,000 pop. under 1 yr. 1974): 39.3.

The islands were occupied by France in 1768, and seized by Britain in 1794. Ruled as part of Mauritius from 1814, the Seychelles became a separate colony in 1903. Several island groups were detached in 1965. The ruling party had opposed independence as impractical, but pressure from the OAU and the UN became irresistible, and independence was declared June 29, 1976. The first president was ousted in a coup a year later.

Sierra Leone

Republic of Sierra Leone

People: Population (1976 est.): 3,110,000. **Pop. density:** 111 per sq. mi. **Ethnic groups:** Temne 30%, Mende 30%, other tribes. **Languages:** English (official), Krio (pidgin), tribal languages. **Religions:** Moslems 25%, Christians 5%, others.

Geography: Area: 27,925 sq. mi., slightly smaller than North Carolina. **Location:** On W coast of W. Africa. **Neighbors:** Guinea on N, E, Liberia on S. **Topography:** The heavily-indented, 210-mi. coastline has mangrove swamps to 60 mi. inland. Behind are wooded hills, rising to a plateau and mountains in the E. **Capital:** Freetown. **Cities** (1974 est.): Freetown 214,443.

Government: Head of state: Pres. Siaka P. Stevens, b. 1906, in office: Apr. 28, 1971; **Head of government:** Prime Min. Christian A. Kamara-Taylor, in office: July, 1975. **Local divisions:** Freetown and 3 provinces. **Armed forces:** regulars 2,145.

Economy: Industries: Wood products. **Chief crops:** Cocoa, coffee, palm kernels, kola nuts, ginger. **Minerals:** Diamonds, iron ore, bauxite. **Per capita arable land:** 2.9 acres. **Livestock** (1974): 280,000 cattle; 3,150,000 poultry. **Fish catch** (1974): 51,300 metric tons. **Electricity production** (1972): 212 mln. kwh. **Labor force:** 73% agric.

Finance: Currency: Leone (Apr. 1977: 1=$0.86 US). **Gross domestic product** (1975): $648 mln. **Per capita income** (1974): $230. **Imports** (1975) $185 mln.; partners (1974): U.K. 21%, Jap. 10%, Nigeria 8%, W. Ger. 7%. **Exports** (1975): $131 mln.; partners (1974): U.K. 61%, Neth. 15%, U.S. 6%, Jap. 5%. **Balance of payments** (1975): $-23.6 mln. **International reserves** (Feb. 1977): $20.7 mln. **Consumer prices** (change in 1976: 17.4%.

Transport: Motor vehicles: in use (1972): 21,200 passenger cars, 11,200 commercial vehicles. **Chief ports:** Freetown, Bonthe.

Communications: Television sets: 6,000 licenses (1973). **Radios:** 60,000 licenses (1973). **Telephones in use** (1976): 10,915. **Daily newspaper circulation** (1970): 45,000; 17 per 1,000 pop.

Health: Life expectancy at birth (1970-75): 41.9 male; 45.1 female. **Births** (annual per 1,000 pop. 1970-75): 44.7. **Deaths** (annual per 1,000 pop. 1970-75): 20.7. **Natural increase** (annual 1970-75): 2.40%. **Pop. per hospital bed** (1973): 954. **Pop. per physician** (1973): 15,706. **Infant mortality** (per 1,000 pop. under 1 yr. 1973): 136.

Education: Literacy (1973): 10%. **Pop. 5-19:** in school (1973): 20%; per teacher (1973): 109.

Freetown was founded in 1787 by the British government as a home for destitute freed slaves. Their descendants, known as Creoles, number more than 80,000.

Successive steps toward independence followed introduction of a constitution in 1951. Full independence arrived Apr. 27, 1961. The People's Party was dominant until a military junta took over in March, 1967. Civilian rule was restored after another coup a year later. Sierra Leone became a republic Apr. 19, 1971.

Singapore

Republic of Singapore

People: Population (1976): 2,280,000. **Age distrib.** (%): 0-14: 35.5; 15-59: 58.3; 60+: 6.3. **Pop. density:** 10,088 per sq. mi. **Ethnic groups:** Chinese 74%, Malays 14%, Indians, Pakistanis 8%. **Languages:** Chinese, Malay, Tamil, English all official. **Religions:** Buddhism, Taoism, Islam, Hinduism, Christianity.

Geography: Area: 226 sq. mi., smaller than New York City. **Location:** Off tip of Malayan Peninsula in S.E. Asia. **Neighbors:** Nearest are Malaysia on N, Indonesia on S. **Topography:** Singapore is a flat, formerly swampy island. The nation includes 40 nearby islets. **Capital:** Singapore. **Government: Head of state:** Pres. Benjamin H. Sheares, b. Aug. 12, 1907, in office: Jan. 1971; **Head of government:** Prime Min. Lee Kuan Yew, b. Sept. 16, 1923, in office: Aug. 9, 1965. **Armed forces:** regulars 31,000; reserves 45,000.

Economy: Industries: Shipbuilding, oil refining, electronics, banking, textiles; food, rubber, lumber processing, tourism. **Per capita arable land:** 0.003 acres. **Livestock** (1974): 1,186,000 cattle; 14,516,000 poultry. **Fish catch** (1974): 19,200 metric tons. **Electricity production** (1974): 3.874 mln. kwh. **Labor forces:** 3% agric.; 20% manuf.

Finance: Currency: Dollar (Apr. 1977: 2.46=$1 US). **Gross domestic product** (1976) $5.97 bln. **Per capita income** (1974): $2,200. **Imports** (1976) $9.071 bln.; partners (1974): Jap. 18%, U.S. 14%, Malaysia 13%, Kuw. 6%. **Exports** (1976): $6.586 bln.; partners (1974): Malaysia 17%, U.S. 15%, Jap. 11%, Hong Kong 6%. **Tourists** (1974): 1,233,900; receipts: $310 million. **Balance of payments** (1976): $291 mln. **National budget** (1976): $1.41 bln. revenues; $1.08 bln. expenditures. **International reserves** (Nov. 1976): $3.353 bln. **Consumer prices** (change in 1976): −1.9%.

Transport: Motor vehicles: in use (1974): 149,000 passenger cars, 41,200 commercial vehicles. **Civil aviation:** 3.949 mln. passenger-miles (1976); 120 mln. freight ton-miles (1976).

Communications: Television sets: 231,000 licenses (1973). **Radios:** 303,000 licenses (1973). **Telephones in use** (1976): 317,932.

Health: Life expectancy at birth (1970): 65.1 male; 70.0 female. **Births** (per 1,000 pop. 1975): 17.8. **Deaths** (per 1,000 pop. 1975): 5.1. **Natural increase** (1975): 1.27%. **Pop. per hospital bed** (1973): 264. **Pop. per physician** (1973): 1,369. **In-**

fant mortality (per 1,000 pop. under 1 yr. 1975): 13.9.

Education: Literacy (1973): 75%. **Pop. 5-19:** in school (1973): 62%; per teacher (1973): 42.

Founded in 1819 by Sir Thomas Stamford Raffles, Singapore was a British colony until 1959 when it became autonomous within the Commonwealth. On Sept. 16, 1963, it joined with Malaya, Sarawak and Sabah to form the Federation of Malaysia.

Tensions between Malayans, dominant in the federation, and ethnic Chinese, dominant in Singapore, led to an agreement under which Singapore became a separate nation, Aug. 9, 1965.

Singapore is the world's 4th largest port. Manufacturing has surpassed shipping, pushing per capita income to second place in Asia, following Japan. Standards in health, education, and housing are high.

Formerly democratic, the government has suppressed opposition in recent years.

Solomon Islands

People: Population (1976 est.): 200,000. **Pop. density:** 17 per sq. mi. **Urban** (1972): 8.8% **Ethnic groups:** A variety of Melanesian groups and mixtures, some Polynesians. **Languages:** Pidgin English, Melanesian, and Papuan languages. **Religions:** Christianity, traditional religions.

Geography: Area: 11,500 sq. mi., slightly larger than Maryland. **Location:** A Melanesian archipelago in the western Pacific O. **Neighbors:** Nearest is Papua New Guinea on W. **Topography:** The Solomons include ten large islands and four groups of smaller ones. The larger islands are volcanic and rugged. **Capital:** Honiara. **Cities** (1970 cen.): Honiara 11,191.

Economy: Industries: Fish canning. **Chief crops:** Coconuts, cocoa, rice, oil palm. **Other resources:** Forests, marine shell. **Fish catch** (1974): 10,940 metric tons. **Electricity production** (1973): 11.5 mln. kwh.

Finance: Currency: Australian Dollar. **Gross domestic product** (est. 1974): $58 mln. **Per capita income** (1974): $290. **Imports** (1973) $16 mln.; partners (1973): Australia 45%, U.K. 13%, Jap. 12%, Sing. 7%. **Exports** (1973): $14 mln.; partners (1973): Jap. 53%, Amer. Samoa 13%, W. Ger. 7%, Australia 7%.

Communications: Radios: 12,000 in use (1972). **Telephones in use** (1976): 1,726.

Health: Births (per 1,000 pop. 1969): 36.1. **Deaths** (per 1,000 pop. 1969): 13.0. **Natural increase** (1969): 2.31%. **Infant mortality** (per 1,000 pop. under 1 yr. 1969): 52.4.

The Solomon Islands were sighted in 1568 by an expedition from Peru. Britain established a protectorate in the 1890s over most of the group. Self-government came Jan. 2, 1976, and independence was set for 1977.

Somalia

Somali Democratic Republic

People: Population (1976 est.): 3,260,000. **Pop. density:** 13 per sq. mi. **Ethnic groups:** Somalis, related tribes 95%, Bantus 3.6%, Arabs 1.1%. **Languages:** Somali (official), Arabic, Italian, English. **Religions:** Sunni Moslems 99%.

Geography: Area: 246,155 sq. mi., slightly smaller than Texas. **Location:** Occupies the eastern horn of Africa. **Neighbors:** Afars and Issas, Ethiopia, Kenya on W. **Topography:** The coastline extends for 1,700 mi. Hills cover the N; the center and S are flat. **Capital:** Mogadishu. **Cities** (1972 est.): Mogadishu 230,000.

Government: Head of state: Pres. Mohamed Siad Barre, b. 1912, in office: Oct. 15, 1969. **Local divisions:** 15 regions. **Armed forces:** regulars 25,000; para-military 3,000.

Economy: Chief crops: Incense, sugar, bananas, sorghum, corn, kapole, gum. **Minerals:** Iron, tin, gypsum, sandstone, bauxite, meerschaum, titanium, uranium. **Per capita arable land:** 0.7 acres. **Livestock** (1974): 2,978,000 cattle; 3,911,000 sheep; 2,300,000 poultry. **Electricity production** (1971): 38 mln. kwh. **Labor force:** 82% agric.

Finance: Currency: Shilling (Apr. 1977: 6.30 = $1 US). **Gross domestic product** (est. 1974): $370 mln. **Per capita income** (1974): $110. **Imports** (1975) $162 mln.; partners (1972): It. 29%, USSR 10%, U.S. 6%, U.K. 6%. **Exports** (1976): $85 mln.; partners (1972): Saudi Ar. 53%, It. 18%, U.S.S.R 6%, Kuwait 6%. **Tourist receipts** (1974): $1 million. **Balance of payments** (1975): $26.6 mln. **International reserves** (Feb. 1977): $76.9 mln. **Consumer prices** (change in 1976): 14.0%.

Transports: Motor vehicles: in use (1972): 8,000 passenger cars, 8,000 commercial vehicles. **Chief ports:** Mogadishu, Berbera.

Communications: Radios: 65,000 in use (1973). **Daily newspaper circulation** (1973): 4,000; 1 per 1,000 pop.

Health: Life expectancy at birth (1970-75): 39.4 male; 42.6 female. **Births** (annual per 1,000 pop. 1970-75): 47.2. **Deaths** (annual per 1,000 pop. 1970-75): 21.7. **Natural increase** (annual 1970-75): 2.55%. **Pop. per hospital bed** (1973): 566. **Pop. per physician** (1973): 15,544. **Infant mortality** (per 1,000 pop. under 1 yr. 1973): 177.

Education: Literacy (1973): 5%. **Pop. 5-19:** in school (1973): 7%; per teacher (1973): 380.

Many of the Somali peoples are nomadic and include large numbers in Kenya and Ethiopia. Arab trading posts developed into coastal sultanates. The Italian Protectorate of Somalia, acquired from 1885 to 1927, extended along the Indian Ocean from the Gulf of Aden to the Juba River. The UN in 1949 approved eventual creation of Somalia as a sovereign state and in 1950 Italy took over the trusteeship held by Great Britain since World War II.

British Somaliland was formed in the 19th century in the northwest. Britain gave it independence June 26, 1960, and on July 1 it joined with the former Italian part to create the independent Somali Republic.

On Oct. 21, 1969, a Supreme Revolutionary Council seized power in a bloodless army and police coup, named a mainly civilian cabinet to aid it, and abolished the Assembly. It made Somali, a Hamitic language spoken by most of the population, the official language, and decreed a standardized spelling using Latin letters. In May, 1970, several foreign companies were nationalized.

A severe drought in 1975 killed tens of thousands, and spurred efforts to resettle nomads on collective farms. The U.S. charged in 1975 that Soviet naval facilities at Berbera included a missile storage site.

Somalia has laid claim to Ogaden, the huge eastern region of Ethiopia, peopled mostly by Somalis. Ethiopia battled Somali rebels and accused Somalia of sending troops and heavy arms in 1977.

South Africa

Republic of South Africa

People: Population (1976 est.): 26,130,000. **Age distrib.** (%): 0-14: 14.8; 15-59: 52.9; 60+: 6.3. **Pop. density:** 55 per sq. mi. **Urban** (1972): 47.9%. **Ethnic groups:** Bantus 70% (of which Zulu 19%. Xhosa 18%, Tawana 8%), whites 17.5%. Colored 9.4%, Asiatic 2.9% **Religions:** Bantu Christian 14.5%, Dutch Reformed 14.3%, Methodist 10.7%, Anglican 8.8%, Roman Catholic 6.7%, other Christian 18.4%, Moslems, Hindus, and Jews 4%. **Languages:** Afrikaans, English, Bantu and Indian languages.

Geography: Area: 471,819 sq. mi., four-fifths the size of Alaska. **Location:** At the southern extreme of Africa. **Neighbors:** Namibia (SW Africa), Botswana, Rhodesia on N, Mozambique, Swaziland on E; surrounds Lesotho. **Topography:** The large interior plateau reaches close to the country's 2,700-mi. coastline. There are few major rivers or lakes; rainfall is sparse in W. more plentiful in E. **Capitals:** Cape Town (legislative). Pretoria (administrative), and Bloemfontein (judicial). **Cities** (1970 cen.): large interior plateau reaches close to the country's 2,700-mi. Durban (met.) 843,327; Pretoria (met.) 561,703; Port Elizabeth (met.) 468,577.

Government: Head of state: Pres. Nicolaas Diederichs, b. Nov. 11, 1903, in office: Apr. 19, 1975; **Head of government:** Prime Min. Balthazar Johannes Vorster, b. Dec. 13, 1915, in office: Sept. 13, 1966. **Local divisions:** 4 provinces with elected councils and some powers: Transvaal, Orange Free State, Cape of Good Hope, Natal. **Armed forces:** regulars 51,500; reserves 173,500.

Economy: Industries: Steel, tires, motors, textiles, plastics. **Chief crops:** Corn, grain, tobacco, sugar, fruit, peanuts, grapes. **Minerals:** Largest world production of gold, gem diamonds, antimony; platinum, chrome, copper, uranium, vanadium, vermiculite, manganese, asbestos, opal, iron, lead, zinc. Annual mineral output exceeds $6 billion. **Other resources:** Wool. **Per capita arable land:** 1.2 acres. **Livestock** (1976): 13,000,000 cattle; 1,550,000 pigs; 34,950,000 sheep; 12,650,000 poultry. **Fish catch** (1975): 1,315,000 metric tons. **Electricity production** (1976): 80,676 mln. kwh. **Labor force:** 28% agric.; 13% manuf.

Finance: Currency: Rand (Apr. 1977: 1=$1.15 US). **Gross domestic product** (1976): $33.4 bln. **Per capita income** (1975): $1,171. **Imports** (1976) $7.295 bln.; partners (1974): W. Ger. 19%, U.K. 17%, U.S. 16%, Jap. 12%. **Exports** (1976): $7.939 bln.; partners (1974): U.K. 29%, Jap. 11%, W. Ger. 9%, U.S. 7%. **Tourists** (1971): 459,500; receipts (1974): $143 million. **Balance of payments** (1976): $-1.06 bln. **National budget** (1976): $7.26 bln. revenues; $9.54 bln. expenditures. **International reserves** (Feb. 1977): $835 mln. **Consumer prices** (change in 1976): 11.1%.

Transport: Railway traffic (1974): 38,413 mln. net ton-miles. **Motor vehicles:** in use (1974): 1,936,000 passenger cars, 671,400 commercial vehicles; assembled (1975): 206,000 passenger cars, 105,000 commercial vehicles. **Civil aviation:** 3,733 mln. passenger-miles (1976); 100 mln. freight ton-miles (1976). **Chief ports:** Durban, Cape Town, East London, Port Elizabeth.

Communications: Radios: 2,350,000 licenses (1972); 313,000 manufactured (1970). **Telephones in use** (1976): 2,072,131. **Daily newspaper circulation** (1973): 1,192,000.

Health: Life expectancy at birth (1970-75): 49.8 male; 53.3 female. **Births** (annual per 1,000 pop. 1970-75): 42.9. **Deaths** (annual per 1,000 pop. 1970-75): 15.5. **Natural increase** (annual 1970-75): 2.74%. **Pop. per hospital bed** (1973): 253. **Pop. per physician** (1973): 2,012. **Infant mortality** (per 1,000 pop. under 1 yr. 1973): 117.

Education: Literacy (1973): 35%. **Pop. 5-19:** in school (1973): 55%; per teacher (1973): 78.

Bushmen and Hottentots were the original inhabitants. Bantu tribes occupied lands in the N and E at about the time Europeans first arrived.

The Cape of Good Hope area was settled by Dutch, beginning in the 17th century. Britain seized the Cape in 1806. Many Dutch trekked north and founded 2 republics, the Transvaal and the Orange Free State. Diamonds were discovered, 1867, and gold, 1886. The Dutch (Boers) resented encroachments by the British and others; the Anglo-Boer War followed, 1899-1902. Britain won and, effective May 31, 1910, created the Union of South Africa, incorporating the British colonies of the Cape and Natal, the Transvaal and the Orange Free State.

After a referendum, the Union became the Republic of South Africa, May 31, 1961, and withdrew from the Commonwealth.

With the election victory of Daniel Malan's National party in 1948, the policy of separate development of the races, or apartheid, already existing unofficially, became official. This called for separate development, separate residential areas and ultimate political independence for the whites, Bantus, Asians, and Coloreds. In 1959 the government passed acts providing the eventual creation of several Bantu nations or Bantustans on 13% of the country's land area, though most Bantu leaders have opposed the plan. In 1963, the Transkei, an area in the SE, became the first of these partially self-governing territories or "Homelands." By 1974 there were 10. Transkei became independent in Oct. 1976, but received no international recognition.

Under apartheid, blacks are severely restricted to certain occupations, and are paid far lower wages than are whites for similar work. Only whites may vote or run for public office, and militant white opposition has been curbed. There is an advisory Indian Council, partly elected, partly appointed. In 1969, a Colored People's Representative Council was created.

At least 600 persons, mostly Bantus, were killed in 1976 riots protesting apartheid. Black protests continued in the face of rising unemployment.

Namibia (South-West Africa)

South-West Africa, a sparsely populated land twice the size of California, became the object of international dispute in 1966. Made a German protectorate in 1884, it was surrendered to South Africa in 1915 and was administered by that country under an old League of Nations mandate. South Africa refused to accept UN authority under the trusteeship system.

Other African nations charged South Africa imposed apartheid, built military bases, and exploited S-W Africa; 36 African states called on the UN to take over the mandate. The UN General Assembly in May 1968 created an 11-nation council to take over administration of S-W Africa and lead it to independence. In April 1968 the council charged that South Africa had blocked its effort to visit S-W Africa.

In 1968 the UN General Assembly gave the area the name Namibia. In Jan. 1970 the UN Security Council condemned South Africa for "illegal" control of the area. In an advisory opinion in June 1971 the International Court of Justice declared South Africa was occupying the area illegally. In 1973, a South Africa-style "homeland," Ovamboland, in the northern area, was given limited self-government.

Most of S-W Africa is a plateau, 3,600 ft. high, with plains in the N. Kalahari Desert to the E, Orange River on the S, the Atlantic on the W. Area is 318,261 sq. mi.; population (Govt. est. 1975) 852,000 including about 100,000 whites; capital, Windhoek.

Products include cattle, sheep, diamonds, copper, lead, zinc, fish. People include Namas (Hottentots), Ovambos (Bantus), Bushmen, and others.

In a 1977 referendum, white voters backed a plan for a multiracial interim government to lead to independence. The Marxist South-West Africa People's Organization has rejected the plan, and has conducted a guerrilla war.

Walvis Bay, the only deepwater port in the country, was turned over to South African administration in 1922. South Africa said in 1977 it would not cede sovereignty.

Spain

Spanish State

People: Population (1976 est.): 35,970,000. **Age distrib.** (%): 0-14: 27.9; 15-59: 58.1; 60+: 14.1. **Pop. density:** 185 per sq. mi. **Ethnic groups:** Spanish (Castilian, Valencian, Andalusian) 72.8%, Catalan 16.4%, Galician 8.2%, Basque 2.3%. **Languages:** Spanish (official), Catalan, Galician, Valencian, Basque all legally recognized. **Religions:** Roman Catholicism nearly universal.

Geography: Area: 194,883 sq. mi., the size of Colorado and Wyoming combined. **Location:** In SW Europe. **Neighbors:** Portugal on W, France on N. **Topography:** The interior is a high, arid plateau broken by mountain ranges and river valleys. The NW is heavily watered, the south has lowlands and a Mediterranean climate. **Capital:** Madrid. **Cities** (1974 est.): Madrid (met.), 3,520,320; Barcelona (met.) 1,809,722; Valencia (met.) 713,026; Seville (met.) 588,784; Zaragoza (met.) 547,317; Bilbao (met.) 457,655; Malaga (met.) 402,978.

Government: Head of state: King Juan Carlos I, b. Jan. 5, 1938, in office: Nov. 22, 1975; **Head of government:** Premier Adolfo Suarez Gonzalez, b. Sept. 25, 1932, in office: July 7, 1976. **Local divisions:** 50 provinces with appointed governors. **Armed forces:** regulars 302,300; reserves 700,000.

Economy: Industries: Machinery, textiles, shoes, paper, autos, ships, cement, tourism. **Chief crops:** Grains, olives, grapes, citrus fruits, onions, almonds, esparto, flax, hemp, pulse, tobacco, cotton, rice. **Minerals:** Lead, iron, copper, zinc, coal, cobalt, mercury, silver, sulphur, phosphates, oil. **Crude oil output** (1976): 14.8 mln. bbls. **Other resources:** Forests (cork). **Per capita arable land:** 1.1 acres. **Livestock** (1976): 4,425,000 cattle; 8,000,000 pigs; 16,519,000 sheep; 43,099,000 poultry. **Fish catch** (1975): 1,533,000 metric tons. **Electricity production** (1976): 90,600 mln. kwh. **Labor force:** 23% agric.; 26% manuf.

Finance: Currency: Peseta (Apr. 1977: 68.8=$1 US). **Gross domestic product** (1975): $101 bln. **Per capita income** (1974): $2,235. **Imports** (1976) $17.474 bln.; partners (1974): U.S. 15%, Saud. Ar. 12%, W. Ger. 11%, Fr. 8%. **Exports** (1976): $8.730 bln.; partners (1974): Fr. 12%, U.S. 11%, W. Ger. 11%, U.K. 9%. **Tourists** (1974): 30,343,000; receipts: $3,209 mln. **Balance of payments** (1976): $-1.03 bln. **National budget** (1976): $13.21 bln. revenues; $13.63 bln. expenditures. **International reserves** (Jan. 1977): $5.061 bln. **Consumer prices** (change in 1976): 17.6%.

Transport: Railway traffic (1974): 9,985 mln. passenger-miles; 7,382 mln. net ton-miles. **Motor vehicles:** in use (1974): 4,309,500 passenger cars, 987,900 commercial vehicles; manufactured (1976): 754,000 passenger cars, 107,000 commercial vehicles. **Civil aviation:** 6,908 mln. passenger-miles (1976); 180 mln. freight ton-miles (1976). **Chief ports:** Barcelona, Bilbao,

Valencia, Cartagena, Gijon.

Communications: Television sets: 5,719,000 in use (1973); 636,000 manufactured (1974). **Radios:** 8,000,000 in use (1973); 636,000 manufactured (1974). **Telephones in use** (1976): 7,835,970. **Daily newspaper circulation** (1973): 3,396,000; 97 per 1,000 pop.

Health: Life expectancy at birth (1970): 69.69 male; 74.96 female. **Births** (per 1,000 pop. 1975): 18.2. **Deaths** (per 1,000 pop. 1975): 8.1. **Natural increase** (1975): 1.01%. **Pop. per hospital bed** (1973): 232. **Pop. per physician** (1973): 726. **Infant mortality** (per 1,000 pop. under 1 yr. 1974): 13.8.

Education: Literacy (1973): 94%. **Pop. 5-19:** in school (1973): 63%; per teacher (1973): 41.

Spain was settled by Iberians, Basques, and Celts, partly overrun by Carthaginians, conquered by Rome c. 200 B.C. The Visigoths, in power by the 5th century A.D., adopted Christianity but by 711 A.D. lost to the Islamic invasion from Africa. Christian reconquest from the N led to a Spanish nationalism. In 1469 the kingdoms of Aragon and Castile were united by the marriage of Ferdinand II and Isabella I, and the last Moorish power broken by the fall of the kingdom of Granada, 1492. Spain became a bulwark of Roman Catholicism.

Spain obtained a colonial empire with the discovery of America by Columbus, 1492, the conquest of Mexico by Cortes and Peru by Pizarro. It also controlled the Netherlands and parts of Italy and Germany. Spain lost its American colonies in the early 19th century. It lost Cuba, the Philippines, and Puerto Rico during the Spanish-American War, 1898.

Primo de Rivera became dictator in 1923. King Alfonso XIII revoked the dictatorship, 1930, but was forced to leave the country 1931. A republic was proclaimed which disestablished the church, curtailed its privileges, and secularized education. A conservative reaction occurred 1933 but was followed by a Popular Front (1936-1939) composed of socialists, communists, republicans, and anarchists.

Army officers headed a revolt against the government, 1936, under Francisco Franco. In a destructive 3-yr. war, in which one million were said to have died, Franco received help from Italy and Germany, while the Soviet Union, France, and Mexico were active on behalf of the republic. War ended Mar. 28, 1939. Franco was named caudillo, or leader of the nation.

Spain was neutral in World War II but its relations with fascist countries caused its exclusion from the UN in 1946. It was admitted in 1955.

In July 1969, Franco and the Cortes designated Prince Juan Carlos, then 31, as the future king and chief of state. After Franco's death, Nov. 20, 1975, Juan Carlos was sworn in as king. He presided over the formal dissolution of the institutions of the Franco regime. In free elections June 1976, moderates and democratic socialists emerged as the largest parties. Concessions were promised to Basques and Catalans seeking autonomy.

Between 1960 and 1975 Spain changed from an agricultural nation to one of the world's important industrial powers.

The **Balearic Islands** in the western Mediterranean, 1,935 sq. mi., are a province of Spain; they include **Majorca** (Mallorca), with the capital, Palma; **Minorca, Cabrera, Ibiza,** and **Formentera.** The **Canary Islands,** 2,807 sq. mi., in the Atlantic W of Morocco, form 2 provinces, including the islands of **Tenerife, Palma, Gomera, Hierro, Grand Canary, Fuerteventura,** and **Lanzarote** with Las Palmas and Santa Cruz thriving ports. **Ceuta** and **Melilla,** small enclaves on Morocco's Mediterranean coast, are part of Metropolitan Spain.

Spain has sought the return of Gibraltar, in British hands since 1704. *(See Index.)*

Sri Lanka

Republic of Sri Lanka

People: Population (1976 est.): 14,270,000. **pop. density:** 563 per sq. mi. **Urban** (1971): 22.4%. **Ethnic groups:** Sinhalese 72%, Ceylon Tamil 11%, Indian Tamil 9.4%, Moor 6.7%. **Languages:** Sinhala (official), Tamil, English. **Religions:** Buddhists 67%, Hindus 18%, Christians 7.7%, Moslems 7.2%.

Geography: Area: 25,332 sq. mi. **Location:** In Indian O. off SE coast of India. **Neighbors:** Nearest is India on NW. **Topography:** The coastal area and the northern half are flat; the S-central area is hilly and mountainous. **Capital:** Colombo. **Cities** (1973 est.): Colombo 618,000; Dahiwala-Mount Lavinia 136,-000.

Government: Head of state: Pres. William Gopallawa, b. Sept. 16, 1897, in office: May 22, 1972. **Head of government:** Prime Min. Junius Richard Jayewardene, b. 1907, in office July 24, 1977. **Local divisions:** 22 districts. **Armed forces:** regulars 13,-600; para-military 16,300.

Economy: Industries: Plywood, paper, glassware, ceramics, cement, chemicals, textiles. **Chief crops:** Tea, coconuts, rice, cacao, cinnamon, citronella, tobacco. **Minerals:** Graphite, limestone, iron, ilmenite, monazite, zircon, quartz, precious and semiprecious stones. **Other resources:** Forests, rubber. **Per capita arable land:** 0.2 acres. **Livestock** (1974): 1,673,000 cattle; 91,000 pigs; 27,000 sheep. **Fish catch** (1974): 110,700 metric tons. **Electricity production** (1972): 995 mln. kwh. **Labor force:** 41% agric.; 8% manuf.

Finance: Currency: Rupee (Mar. 1977: 7.29=$1 US). **Gross domestic product** (1976): $2.99 bln. **Per capita income** (1975): $230. **Imports** (1976) $573 mln.; partners (1973): U.S. 9%, Jap. 9%, Fr. 8%, P.R. China 8%. **Exports** (1976): $565 mln.; partners (1973): U.K. 11%, P.R. China 9%, Pak. 8%, U.S. 7%. **Tourists** (excluding excursionists) (1974): 85,000; receipts: $14 million. **Balance of payments** (1976): $36.3 mln. **National budget** (1976): $650 mln. revenues; $814 mln. expenditures. **International reserves** (Feb. 1977): $101 mln. **Consumer prices** (change in 1976): 1.3%.

Transport: Railway traffic (1974): 1,725 mln. passenger-miles; 201 mln. net ton-miles. **Motor vehicles:** in use (1974) 89,800 passenger cars, 48,200 commercial vehicles. **Civil aviation:** 167 mln. passenger-miles (1975); 1.4 mln. freight ton-miles (1975). **Chief ports:** Colombo, Trincomalee, Galle.

Communications: Radios: 515,000 licenses (1973), 117,000 manufactured (1973). **Telephones in use** (1975): 72,059.

Health: Life expectancy at birth (1967): 64.8 male; 66.9 female. **Births** (per 1,000 pop. 1972): 29.5. **Deaths** (per 1,000 pop. 1972): 7.7. **Natural increase** (1972): 2.18%. **Pop. per hospital bed** (1973): 335. **Pop. per physician** (1973): 3,681. **Infant mortality** (per 1,000 pop. under 1 yr. 1972): 45.1.

Education: Literacy (1973): 76%. **Pop. 5-19:** in school (1973): 65%; per teacher (1973): 40.

The island was known to the ancient world as Taprobane (Greek for copper-colored) and later as Serendip (from Arabic). Colonists from northern Indian subdued the indigenous Veddahs about 543 B.C.; their descendants, the Sinhalese, still form most of the population. Descendants of Tamil immigrants from southern India account for one-fifth of the population, though many are being repatriated. Parts of the maritime areas were occupied in turn by the Portuguese in 1505 and by the Dutch in 1658. The British seized the island in 1796 and it became a Crown colony in 1802.

As Ceylon it became an independent member of the Commonwealth in 1948. On May 22, 1972, Ceylon became the Republic of Sri Lanka.

Prime Minister W. R. D. Bandaranaike was assassinated Sept. 25, 1959. In new elections, the Freedom Party was victorious. Its leader, Mrs. Sirimavo Bandaranaike, widow of the former prime minister, was sworn in to the office.

In April, 1962, the government expropriated service and terminal facilities of one British and 2 U.S. oil companies. In March 1965 elections, the conservative United National Party won the largest number of seats.

In Dec. 1965, the new government agreed to pay compensation for the seized oil companies. The U.S. in Feb. 1966, agreed to resume economic aid.

After May 1970 elections, Mrs. Bandaranaike became prime minister again. In 1971 the nation suffered economic problems and terrorist activities by ultra-leftists, thousands of whom were executed. Unemployment among graduates and food shortages plagued the nation from 1973 to 1976. Massive land reform and nationalization of foreign-owned plantations was undertaken in the mid-1970s. Mrs. Bandaranaike was ousted in 1977 elections.

Sudan

Democratic Republic of the Sudan

People: Population (1976 est.): 16,130,000. **Pop. density:** 17 per sq. mi. **Urban** (1974): 13.2%. **Ethnic groups:** North:

Arabs, Nubians; South; Nilotic, Sudanic, Negro tribes. **Languages:** Arabic 51%, 32 other languages. **Religions:** Moslems 72%, Christians 5%, traditional 20%.

Geography: Area: 967,491 sq. mi., the largest country in Africa, over one-fourth the size of the U.S. **Location:** At the E end of Sahara desert zone. **Neighbors:** Egypt on N, Libya, Chad, Central African Empire on W, Zaire, Uganda, Kenya on S, Ethiopia on E. **Topography:** The N consists of the Libyan Desert in the W, and the mountainous Nubia desert in E, with narrow Nile valley between. The center contains large, fertile, rainy areas with fields, pasture, and forest. The S has rich soil, heavy rain. **Capital:** Khartoum. **Cities** (1971 est.): Khartoum 261,840; Omdurman 258,532; North Khartoum 127,672; Port Sudan 110,091.

Government: Head of state: Pres. Gaafar Mohammed Nimeiri, b. Jan. 1, 1930, in office: Sept. 1971. (previously prime min. since 1969); **Head of government:** Prime Min. el Rashid el Tahir Bakr, b. 1931, in office: Aug. 1976. **Local divisions:** 15 provinces; the southern 3 have a regional government. **Armed forces:** regulars 52,600.

Economy: Industries: Textile, food processing. **Chief crops:** Gum arabic (principal world source), durra (sorghum), cotton (main export), sesame peanuts, rice, coffee, sugarcane, tobacco, wheat, dates. **Minerals:** Chrome, gold, copper, white mica, vermiculite, asbestos. **Other resources:** Mahogany. **Per capita arable land:** 0.9 acres. **Livestock** (1974): 14,000,000 cattle; 11,900,000 sheep; 20,960,000 poultry. **Electricity production** (1971): 259 mln. kwh. **Labor force:** 80% agric.

Finance: Currency: Pound (Apr. 1977: 1=+$2.87 US). **Gross domestic product** (1974): $4.34 bln. **Per capita income** (1974): $143. **Imports** (1976) $980 mln.; partners (1973): U.K. 17%, P.R. China 8%, U.S. 7%, India 7%. **Exports** (1976): $554 mln.; partners (1973): P.R. China 14%, It. 11%, Jap. 11%, W. Ger. 9%. **Tourist:** receipts (1974): $4 million. **Balance of payments** (1976): $-19.3 mln. **International reserves** (Feb. 1977): $26.4 mln. **Consumer prices** (change in 1976): 1.5%.

Transport: Railway traffic (1971): 1,637 mln. net ton-miles. **Motor vehicles:** in use (1972): 29,200 passenger cars, 21,200 commercial vehicles. **Civil aviation:** 193 mln. passenger-miles (1974); 2.8 mln. freight ton-miles (1973). **Chief ports:** Port Sudan.

Communications: Television sets: 100,000 in use (1973). **Radios:** 1,310,000 in use (1972). **Daily newspaper circulation** (1970): 127,000.

Health: Life expectancy at birth (1970-75): 47.3 male; 49.9 female. **Births** (annual per 1,000 pop. 1970-75): 47.8. **Deaths** (annual per 1,000 pop. 1970-75): 17.5. **Natural increase** (annual 1970-75): 3.03%. **Pop. per hospital bed** (1973): 1,083. **Pop. per physician** (1973): 12,528. **Infant mortality** (per 1,000 pop. under 1 yr. 1956): 93.6.

Education: Literacy (1973): 12%. **Pop. 5-19:** in school (1973): 20%; per teacher (1973): 165.

Northern Sudan, ancient Nubia, was settled by Egyptians in antiquity, and was converted to Coptic Christianity in the 6th century. Arab conquests brought Islam in the 15th century.

In the 1820s Egypt took over the Sudan, defeating the last of earlier empires, including the Fung. In the 1880s a revolution was led by Mohammed Ahmed who called himself the Mahdi (leader of the faithful) and his followers, the dervishes.

In 1898 Horatio Kitchener led an Anglo-Egyptian force which crushed the Mahdi's successors.

In Oct. 1951 the Egyptian Parliament abrogated its 1899 and 1936 treaties with Great Britain, and amended the constitution Oct. 16, to provide for a separate Sudanese constitution.

Sudan voted for complete independence effective Jan. 1 1956. A parliamentary government was set up but in 1958 Gen. Ibrahim Abboud took power; he resigned under pressure in 1964.

In May 1969, in a second military coup, a Revolutionary Council took power, but a civilian premier and cabinet were appointed and the new government announced it would create a socialist state. It also announced plans to negotiate an end to guerrilla warfare, which had beset the southern third of the nation for years and decimated its population. The northern 12 provinces are predominantly Arab-Moslem and have been dominant in the central government. The 3 southern provinces are Negro and predominantly pagan, with small Christian and Moslem minorities. A peace agreement, giving the South regional autonomy, was reached in 1972. Renewed flare-ups occurred in 1975.

The government nationalized a number of businesses in May 1970. An attempted communist coup in July 1971 failed, leading to a temporary diplomatic break with the USSR. Soviet arms shipments were announced in 1975, but relations later deteriorated and U.S. ties improved.

Diplomatic relations with the U.S., broken by Sudan during the 1967 Arab-Israeli war, were restored in 1972; locally-owned firms were denationalized and foreign firms compensated.

On Mar. 2, 1973, the U. S. ambassador and the charge d'affaires and a Belgian diplomat were slain in Khartoum by 8 Palestinian terrorists. The 8 were freed and turned over to a Palestinian liberation group in Egypt.

Sudan charged Libya with aiding an unsuccessful coup in Sudan in 1976. Sudan has backed the Eritrean separatist movement in neighboring Ethiopia.

Surinam

People: Population (1976 est.): 440,000. **Pop. density:** 7 per sq. mi. **Ethnic groups** (before independence): East Indians 35%, Creoles (racially mixed descendants of freed slaves) 30%, Javanese 15%, Bush Negroes (descendants of runaway slaves) 10%, Europeans, Chinese, Amerindians. **Languages:** Dutch (official), Sranan Tongo (Creole) universal, English, others. **Religions:** Hindus, Christians, Moslems.

Geography: Area: 63,251 sq. mi., slightly larger than Georgia. **Location:** On N shore of S. America. **Neighbors:** Guyana on W, Brazil on S, French Guiana on E. **Topography:** Most of the population inhabits the flat Atlantic coast, where dikes permit agriculture. Farther inland is a forest belt; to the S, largely unexplored hills cover three-fourths of the country. **Capital:** Paramaribo. **Cities** (1974 est.): Paramaribo 150,000.

Government: Head of state: Pres. Johan H.E. Ferrier, b. May 12, 1910, in office: Nov. 25, 1975; **Head of government:** Prime Min. Henk A.E. Arron, b. Apr. 25, 1936, in office: Nov. 25, 1975. **Local divisions:** 9 districts.

Economy: Industries: Aluminum. **Chief crops:** Rice, sugar, fruits. **Minerals:** Bauxite. **Other resources:** Forests, shrimp. **Per capita arable land:** 0.2 acres. **Livestock** (1974): 43,000 cattle; 13,000 pigs; 850,000 poultry. **Fish catch** (1973): 7,400 metric tons. **Electricity production** (1972): 1,465 mln. kwh. **Labor force:** 27% agric.

Finance: Currency: Guilders (Apr. 1977: 1.79=$1 US). **Gross domestic product** (1974): $487 mln. **Per capita income** (1974): $970. **Imports** (1975) $262 mln.; partners (1972): U.S. 32%, Neth. 24%, Trin. 10%. **Exports** (1975): $277 mln.; partners (1972): U.S. 44%, Neth. 12%, W. Ger. 11%. **Tourist receipts:** $6 million. **Balance of payments** (1976): $18.6 mln. **International reserves** (Feb. 1977): $113.21 mln. **Consumer prices** (change in 1976): 10.1%.

Transport: Motor vehicles: in use (1973): 21,500 passenger cars, 5,600 commercial vehicles. **Chief ports:** Paramaribo, Nieuw-Nickerie.

Communications: Television sets: 31,000 in use (1972) **Radios:** 108,000 in use (1973). **Telephones in use** (1976) 16,873. **Daily newspaper circulation** (1973): 24,000.

Health: Life expectancy at birth (1963): 62.5 male; 66.7 female. **Births** (per 1,000 pop. 1966): 40.9. **Deaths** (per 1,000 pop. 1966): 7.2. **Natural increase** (1966): 3.37%. **Infant mortality** (per 1,000 pop. under 1 yr. 1966): 30.4.

The Netherlands acquired Surinam in 1667 from Britain, in exchange for New Netherlands (New York). The 1954 Dutch constitution raised the colony to a level of equality with the Netherlands and the Netherlands Antilles. In the 1970s the Dutch government pressured for Surinam independence, which came Nov. 25, 1975, despite objections from East Indians and some Bush Negroes. Some 40% of the population emigrated to the Netherlands in the months before independence. The Netherlands promised $1.5 billion in aid for the first decade of independence.

Both Guyana on the W and French Guiana on the E have disputed parts of their Surinam borders.

Swaziland

Kingdom of Swaziland

People: Population (1976 est.): 500,000. **Age distrib.** (%): 0-14: 48.2; 15-59: 47.5; 60+: 4.3. **Pop. density:** 75 per sq. mi.

Urban (1973): 7.9%. **Ethnic groups:** Swazi 90%, Zulu 2.3%, European 2.1%, other African, non-African groups. **Languages:** siSwati (official), English. **Religions:** Christians 60%, others.

Geography: Area: 6,705 sq. mi., slightly smaller than New Jersey. **Location:** In southern Africa, near Indian O. coast. **Neighbors:** South Africa on N, W, S, Mozambique on E. **Topography:** The country descends from W-E in broad belts, becoming more arid in the lowveld region, then rising to a plateau in the E. **Capital:** Mbabane. **Cities** (1973 est.): Mbabane 20,800; Manzini 25,000.

Government: Head of state: King Sobhuza II, b. July 22, 1899, in office: Oct. 21, 1966; **Head of government:** Prime Min. Makhosini Dlamini, b. 1922, in office: 1967. **Local divisions:** 4 districts, 2 municipalities.

Economy: Industries: Wood pulp. **Chief crops:** Corn, cotton, rice, pineapples, sugar, citrus fruits. **Minerals:** Asbestos, iron, coal. **Other resources:** Forests. **Per capita arable land:** 0.8 acres. **Livestock** (1974): 610,000 cattle; 450,000 poultry. **Electricity production** (1973): 121 mln. kwh. **Labor force:** 83% agric.

Finance: Currency: Lilangeni (1974: 1=$1.47 US) **Gross domestic product** (est. 1974): $200 mln. **Per capita income** (1973): $382. **Imports** (1973) $98 mln.; partners (1973): So. Afr., U.K. **Exports** (1973): $108 mln.; partners (1973): U.K. 25%, Jap. 24%, So. Afr. 21%.

Transport: Motor vehicles: in use (1973): 6,500 passenger cars, 4,000 commercial vehicles.

Communications: Radios: 51,000 licenses (1973). **Telephones in use** (1976): 7,426.

Health: Life expectancy at birth (1970-75): 41.9 male; 45.1 female. **Births** (annual per 1,000 pop. 1970-75): 49.0. **Deaths** (annual per 1,000 pop. 1970-75): 21.8. **Natural increase** (annual 1970-75): 2.72%. **Pop. per hospital bed** (1973): 288. **Pop. per physician** (1973): 7,188. **Infant mortality** (per 1,000 pop. under 1 yr. 1973): 149.

Education: Literacy (1973): 36%. **Pop. 5-19:** in school (1973): 56%; per teacher (1973): 85.

The royal house of Swaziland traces back 400 years, and is one of Africa's last ruling dynasties. The Swazis, a Bantu people, were driven to Swaziland from lands to the N by the Zulus in 1820. Their autonomy was later guaranteed by Britain and Transvaal, with Britain assuming control after 1903. Independence came Sept. 6, 1968. In 1973 the king repealed the constitution and assumed full powers.

Fertile lands and mineral resources have aided development. About 8,000 Swazis hold jobs in South Africa, which has a customs union with Swaziland.

Sweden

Kingdom of Sweden

People: Population (1976): 8,220,000. **Age distrib.** (%): 0-14: 20.8; 15-59: 58.7; 60+: 20.5. **Pop. density:** 47 per sq. mi. **Urban** (1970): 81.4%. **Ethnic groups:** Swedish 93%, Finnish 3%, Lapps, European immigrants. **Languages:** Swedish, Finnish. **Religions:** Lutherans (official) 95%, other Protestants 5%.

Geography: Area: 173,665 sq. mi., larger than California. **Location:** On Scandinavian Peninsula in N. Europe. **Neighbors:** Norway on W, Denmark on S (across Kattegat), Finland on E. **Topography:** Mountains along NW border cover 25% of Sweden, flat or rolling terrain covers the central and southern areas, which includes several large lakes. **Capital:** Stockholm. **Cities:** (1974 est.): Stockholm (met.) 1,353,359; Goteborg (met.) 687,624; Malmo (met.) 453,502.

Government: Head of state: King Carl XVI Gustaf, b. Apr. 30, 1946, in office: Sept. 15, 1973; **Head of government:** Prime Min. Thorbjorn Falldin, b. Apr. 24, 1926, in office: Oct. 7, 1976. **Local divisions:** 24 lan (counties). **Armed forces:** regulars 65,400; reserves 635,200.

Economy: Industries: Steel, machinery, instruments, autos, shipbuilding, shipping, paper. **Chief crops:** Grains, potatoes, sugar, beets. **Minerals:** Iron, lead, copper, zinc, gold, silver. **Other resources:** Forests (half the country); yield one fourth exports. **Per capita arable land:** 0.9 acres. **Livestock** (1976): 1,820,000 cattle; 2,470,000 pigs; 360,000 sheep; 11,954,000 poultry. **Fish catch** (1974): 210,700 metric tons. **Electricity production** (1976): 84,312 mln. kwh. **Labor force:** 7% agric.; 28% manuf.

Finance: Currency: Krona (Apr. 1977: 4.33=$1 US). **Gross domestic product** (1976): $74.1 bln. **Per capita income** (1975): $7,557. **Imports** (1976) $19.254 bln.; partners (1974): W. Ger. 19%, U.K. 11%, Den. 7%, Nor. 7%. **Exports** (1976): $18.445 bln.; partners (1974): U.K. 13%, Nor. 10%, W. Ger. 10%, Den. 8%. **Balance of payments** (1976): $-493 mln. **National budget** (1976): $22.5 bln. revenues; $23.1 bln. expenditures. **International reserves** (Feb. 1977): $2.488 bln. **Consumer prices** (change in 1976): 10.4%.

Transport: Railway traffic (1974): 3,311 mln. passenger-miles; 12,170 mln. net ton-miles. **Motor vehicles:** in use (1974): 2,639,000 passenger cars, 170,000 commercial vehicles; manufactured (1976): 306,000 passenger cars, 48,000 commercial vehicles. **Civil aviation:** 2,511 mln. passenger-miles (1976); 107 mln. freight ton-miles (1976). **Chief ports:** Goteborg, Stockholm, Malmo.

Communications: Television sets: 2,758,000 licenses (1973); 311,000 manufactured (1973). **Radios:** 262,000 licenses (1973); 203,000 manufactured (1973). **Telephones in use** (1976): 5,422,795. **Daily newspaper circulation** (1973): 4,592,000; 564 per 1,000 pop.

Health: Life expectancy at birth (1970-74): 72.11 male; 77.51 female. **Births** (per 1,000 pop. 1975): 12.6. **Deaths** (per 1,000 pop. 1975): 10.8. **Natural increase** (1975): 0.18%. **Pop. per hospital bed** (1973): 63. **Pop. per physician** (1973): 690. **Infant mortality** (per 1,000 pop. under 1 yr. 1975): 8.3.

Education: Literacy (1973): 99%. **Pop. 5-19:** in school (1973): 80%; per teacher (1973): 22.

The Swedes have lived in present-day Sweden for at least 5,000 years, longer than nearly any other European people. Gothic tribes from Sweden played a major role in the disintegration of the Roman Empire. Other Swedes helped create the first Russian state in the 9th century.

The Swedes were Christianized from the 11th century, and a strong centralized monarchy developed. A parliament, the Riksdag, was first called in 1435, the earliest parliament on the European continent, with all classes of society having representation.

Swedish independence from rule by Danish kings (dating from 1397) was secured by Gustavus I in a revolt, 1521-23; he built up the government and military and established the Lutheran Church. In the 17th century Sweden was a major European power, gaining most of the Baltic seacoast, but its international position subsequently declined.

The Napoleanic wars, in which Sweden acquired Norway (it became independent 1905), were the last in which Sweden participated. Armed neutrality was maintained in both world wars.

Over 4 decades of Social Democratic rule was ended in 1976 parliamentary elections.

Although over 95% of the economy is in private hands, the government holds a large interest in water power production and the railroads are operated by a public agency. Worker participation in management is expanding.

Consumer cooperatives are in extensive operation, with 1,700,000 member households. Cooperatives also are important in agriculture and housing. Per capita GNP, 1976, was among the highest in the world.

The U. S. and Sweden in 1974 ended a 15-month diplomatic "freeze" and exchanged ambassadors.

Racial tensions between Swedes and the small number of foreign workers flared into prolonged violence in 1977.

Switzerland

Swiss Confederation

People: Population (1976): 6,350,000. **Age distrib.** (%): 0-14: 22.9; 15-59: 60.0; 60+: 17.1. **Pop. density:** 398 per sq. mi. **Urban** (1970): 54.6%. **Ethnic groups:** Defined by mother tongue. **Languages:** German 65%, French 18%, Italian 12%, Romansch 0.8%. **Religions:** Protestant 48%, Roman Catholic 49%, Jews.

Geography: Area: 15,941 sq. mi., as large as Mass., Conn., and R.I. combined. **Location:** In the Alps Mts. in Central Europe. **Neighbors:** France on W, Italy on S, Austria on E, W. Germany on N. **Topography:** The Alps cover 60% of the land area, the Jura, near France, 10%. Running between, from NE to SW, are midlands, 30%. **Capital:** Bern. **Cities** (1975 est.): Zurich (met.) 720,800; Basel (met.) 379,500; Geneva (met.) 323,000; Bern (met.) 288,100.

Government: Head of state: Pres. Kurt Furgler, b. 1924, in office: Jan. 1, 1977 (to Dec. 31, 1977). **Local divisions:** 19 full cantons, 6 half cantons, all with elected legislatures and substantial powers. **Armed forces:** regulars 46,500; reserves 578,-500.

Economy: Industries: Machinery, machine tools, steel, instruments, watches, textiles, foodstuffs (cheese, chocolate), chemicals, drugs, banking, tourism. **Chief crops:** Grains, potatoes, sugar beets, vegetables, tobacco. **Minerals:** Salt. **Other resources:** Hydro power potential. **Per capita arable land:** 0.1 acres. **Livestock** (1976): 1,997,000 cattle; 1,925,000 pigs; 368,-000 sheep; 6,536,000 poultry. **Electricity production** (1976): 34,836 bln. kwh. **Labor force:** 8% agric.; 38% manuf.

Finance: Currency: Franc (Apr. 1977: 2.52=$1 US). **Gross domestic product** (1976): $57.2 bln. **Per capita income** (1975): $7,810. **Imports** (1976): $14.775 bln.; partners (1974): W. Ger. 29%, Fr. 14%, It. 9%, U.S. 7%. **Exports** (1976): $14.834 bln.; partners (1974): W. Ger. 14%, Fr. 9%, It. 8%, U.K. 7%. **Tourists** (1974): 6,221,800; receipts: $1.793 billion. **Balance of payments** (1976): $2.98 bln. **National budget** (1976): $5.51 bln. revenues; $6.07 bln. expenditures. **International reserves** (Feb. 1977): $10.127 bln. **Consumer prices** (change in 1976): 1.7%.

Transport: Railway traffic (1974): 5,141 mln. passenger-miles; 4,338 mln. net ton-miles. **Motor vehicles:** in use (1974): 1,723,000 passenger cars, 176,500 commercial vehicles. **Civil aviation:** 5,276 mln. passenger-miles (1976); 215 mln. freight ton-miles (1976).

Communications: Television sets: 1,627,000 licenses (1973). **Radios:** 2,003,000 licenses (1973). **Telephones in use** (1976): 3,912,971. **Daily newspaper circulation** (1973): 2,478,-000; 385 per 1,000 pop.

Health: Life expectancy at birth (1968-73): 70.29 male; 76.22 female. **Births** (per 1,000 pop. 1975): 12.4. **Deaths** (per 1,000 pop. 1975): 8.8. **Natural increase** (1975): 0.36%. **Pop. per hospital bed** (1973): 89. **Pop. per physician** (1973): 597. **Infant mortality** (per 1,000 pop. under 1 yr. 1974): 12.5.

Education: Literacy (1973): 99%. **Pop. 5-19:** in school (1973): 75%; per teacher (1973): 22.

Switzerland, the Roman province of Helvetia, is a federation of 22 cantons (19 full cantons and 6 half cantons), 3 of which in 1291 created a defensive league and later were joined by other districts. (Voters in the French-speaking Jura approved a breakaway canton in 1974.) In 1648 the Swiss Confederation obtained its independence from the Holy Roman Empire. The cantons were joined under a federal constitution in 1848, with large powers of local control retained by each canton.

Switzerland has maintained an armed neutrality since 1815, and has not been involved in a foreign war since 1515. It is not a member of the UN or NATO. It is, however, a member of several UN agencies and of the European Free Trade Assoc. and has ties with the EC. Switzerland is the seat of many UN and other international agencies.

Switzerland is a leading world banking center; stability of the currency brings funds from many quarters. Some 20% of all workers are foreign residents.

Syria

Syrian Arab Republic

People: Population (1976 est.): 7,600,000. **Age distrib.** (%): 0-14: 49.3; 15-59: 44.3; 60+: 6.4. **Pop. density:** 106 per sq. mi. **Urban** (1974): 45.9%. **Ethnic groups:** Arabs 88%, Kurds 6.3%, Armenians 2.8%, Turks, Circassians, Assyrians. **Languages:** Arabic (official), French, Kurdish, Armenian. **Religions:** Moslems (Sunni, Alawi, Druze) 88%, Christians 12%.

Geography: Area: 71,498 sq. mi., the size of North Dakota. **Location** At eastern end of Mediterranean Sea. **Neighbors:** Lebanon, Israel on W, Jordan on S, Iraq on E, Turkey on N. **Topography:** Syria has a short Mediterranean coastline, then stretches E and S with fertile lowlands and plains, alternating with mountains and large desert areas. **Capital:** Damascus. **Cities** (1970 cen.): Damascus (met.) 923,253; Aleppo 639,428; Homs 215,423.

Government: Head of state: Pres. Hafez al-Assad, b. Mar. 1930, in office: Mar. 12, 1971; **Head of government:** Prime Min. Abdel Rahman Khliefawi, in office: Aug. 7, 1976. **Local divisions:** Damascus and 13 provinces. **Armed forces:** regulars 227,000; reserves 102,500.

Economy: Industries: Oil products, textiles, cement, tobacco, glassware, sugar, brassware. **Chief crops:** Cotton, grain, olives, fruits, vegetables. **Minerals:** Oil, phosphate, gypsum. **Crude oil output** (1976): 70 mln. bbls. **Other resources:** wool. **Per capita arable land:** 1.8 acres. **Livestock** (1974): 524,000 cattle; 5,295,000 sheep. **Electricity production** (1975): 1,668 mln. kwh. **Labor force:** 54% agric.; 11% manuf.

Finance: Currency: Pound (Apr. 1977: 3.95=$1 US). **Gross domestic product** (1976): $5.81 bln. **Per capita income** (1972): $335. **Imports** (1976) $2.365 bln.; partners (1974): W. Ger. 12%, It. 9%, Fr. 9%, Leb. 8%. **Exports** (1976): $1.065 bln.; partners (1974): Gr. 18%, W. Ger. 15%, USSR 14%, U.K. 10%. **Tourists** (1974): 574,500; receipts: $85 million. **Balance of payments** (1976): −$354 mln. **International reserves** (Sept. 1976): $459 mln. **Consumer prices** (change in 1976): 15.2%.

Transport: Railway traffic (1974): 63 mln. passenger-miles; 97 mln. net ton-miles. **Motor vehicles:** in use (1974): 37,300 passenger cars, 23,100 commercial vehicles. **Chief ports:** Latakia, Tartus.

Communications: Television sets: 150,000 in use (1972); 38,000 manufactured (1974). **Radios:** 2,500,000 in use (1972). **Daily newspaper circulation** (1973): 64,000.

Health: Life expectancy at birth (1970): 54.49 male; 58.73 female. **Births** (annual per 1,000 pop. 1970-75): 45.4. **Deaths** (annual per 1,000 pop. 1970-75): 4.8. **Natural increase** (annual 1970-75): 4.06%. **Pop. per hospital bed** (1973): 1,111. **Pop. per physician** (1973): 2,906. **Infant mortality** (per 1,000 pop. under 1 yr. 1972): 21.7.

Education: Literacy (1973): 31%. **Pop. 5-19:** in school (1973): 57%; per teacher (1973): 77.

Syria contains some of the most ancient remains of civilization. It was the center of the Seleucid empire, but later became absorbed in the Roman and Arab empires. Ottoman rule prevailed for 4 centuries, until the end of World War I.

The state of Syria was formed from former Turkish districts, made a separate entity by the Treaty of Sevres 1920 and divided into the states of Syria and Greater Lebanon. Both were administered under a French League of Nations mandate 1920-1941.

Syria was proclaimed a republic by the occupying French Sept. 16, 1941, and exercised full independence effective Jan. 1, 1944. French troops left in 1946. Syria joined in the Arab invasion of Israel in 1948.

Syria joined with Egypt in Feb. 1958 in the United Arab Republic but seceded Sept. 30, 1961. The Socialist Baath party and military leaders seized power in Mar. 1963. The Baath, a pan-Arab organization, became the only legal party. The government has been dominated by members of the minority Alaivite sect.

In the Israeli-Arab war of June 1967, Israel seized and occupied the Golan Heights area inside Syria, from which Israeli settlements had for years been shelled by Syria.

Syria aided Palestinian guerrillas fighting Jordanian forces in Sept. 1970, and, after a renewal of that fighting in July 1971, broke off relations with Jordan. But by 1975 the 2 countries had entered a military coordination pact.

Syria received large shipments of arms from the USSR in 1972-73 and on Oct. 6, 1973, Syria joined Egypt in an attack on Israel. (For details, see article on Israel.) Arab oil states agreed in 1974 to give Syria $1 billion a year to aid anti-Israel moves. Military supplies used or lost in the 1973 war were replaced by the USSR in 1974. U.S. economic aid has been extended. At least 16,000 Syrian troops entered Lebanon in 1976 to mediate in a civil war, and fought Palestinian guerrillas. Syria has charged Iraqi complicity in a series of terrorist attacks.

Tanzania

United Republic of Tanzania

People: Population (1976 est.): 15,610,000. **Age distrib.**

(%): 0-14: 44.4; 15-59: 53; 60+: 2.6. **Pop. density:** 43 per sq. mi. **Urban** (1973): 7.3%. **Ethnic groups:** Sukuma 12.6%, Maleonde 4%, 130 other tribes (most Bantu); Europeans, Arabs, Asians. **Languages:** Swahili, English are official. **Religions:** Moslems 30%, Christians 30%, Traditional 40%.

Geography: Area: 363,708 sq. mi., more than twice the size of California. **Location:** On coast of E. Africa. **Neighbors:** Kenya, Uganda on N, Rwanda, Burundi, Zaire on W, Zambia, Malawi, Mozambique on S. **Topography:** A hot, arid central plateau is surrounded by the lake region in the west, temperate highlands in N and S, and the coastal plains. Mt. Kilimanjaro, 19,340 ft., is highest in Africa. **Capital:** Dar-es-Salaam. **Cities:** (1975 est.): Dar-es-Salaam 517,000.

Government: Head of state: Pres. Julius Nyerere, b. 1922, in office: 1962 (prime min. Dec. 9, 1961); **Head of government:** Prime Min. Edward Sokoine, b. 1939, in office: Feb. 13, 1977. **Local divisions:** 24 regions (4 in Zanzibar). **Armed forces:** regulars 14,600; para-military 35,000.

Economy: Industries: food processing, clothing. **Chief crops:** Sisal, cotton, coffee, tea, tobacco. **Minerals:** Diamonds, gold, salt, tin, mica. **Other resources:** Hides. **Per capita arable land:** 2.3 acres. **Livestock** (1974): 12,044,000 cattle; 2,850,000 sheep; 22,093,000 poultry. **Fish catch** (1974): 167,700 metric tons. **Electricity production** (1975): 564 mln. kwh. **Labor force:** 86% agric.

Finance: Currency: Shilling (Apr. 1977: 8.31 = $1 US). **Gross domestic product** (1974): $2.19 bln. **Per capita income** (1975): $162. **Imports** (1976): $639 mln.; partners (1974): P.R. China 11%, UK. 10%, Jap. 9%, W. Ger. 8%. **Exports** (1976): $490 mln.; partners (1974): U.K. 13%, U.S. 7%, Kenya 6%, Hong Kong 6%. **Tourists** (1973): 120,000; receipts (1974): $13 million. **Balance of payments** (1976): $22.2 mln. **National budget** (1974): $411 mln. revenues; $574 mln. expenditures. **International reserves** (Feb. 1977): $183 mln. **Consumer prices** (change in 1976): 6.9%.

Transport: Motor vehicles: in use (1974): 39,100 passenger cars, 42,300 commercial vehicles. **Chief ports:** Dar-es-Salaam, Tanga.

Communications: Television sets: 4,000 licenses (1970). **Radios:** 230,000 licenses (1973); 195,000 manufactured (1974). **Telephones in use** (1976): 62,583. **Daily newspaper circulation** (1973): 41,000.

Health: Life expectancy at birth (1967): 40-41 (both sexes). **Births** (per 1,000 pop. 1967): 47. **Deaths** (per 1,000 pop. 1967): 22. **Natural increase** (1967): 2.5%. **Pop. per hospital bed** (1973): 625. **Pop. per physician** (1973): 23,967. **Infant mortality** (per 1,000 pop. under 1 yr. 1967): 160-165.

Education: Literacy (1973): 18%. **Pop. 5-19:** in school (1973): 21%; per teacher (1973): 204.

The Republic of Tanganyika in E. Africa and the Republic of Zanzibar, an island in the Indian Ocean off the coast of Tanganyika, joined into a single nation, the United Republic of Tanzania, Apr. 26, 1964. The central government was given jurisdiction over defense, foreign affairs, and public services. Zanzibar retains internal self-government. In 1973 Dodoma, in the country's center, was named the future capital.

Tanganyika. Arab colonization and slaving began in the 8th century A.D.; Portuguese sailors explored the coast by about 1500. Other Europeans followed.

In 1885 Germany established German East Africa of which Tanganyika formed the bulk. It became a League of Nations mandate and, after 1946, a UN trust territory, both under Britain. It became independent Dec. 9, 1961, and a republic within the Commonwealth a year later.

In 1967 the government set on a socialist course; it nationalized all banks and many industries; some of the latter were taken over completely, in others the government took a part interest. The government also ordered that Swahili, not English, be used in all official business. Nine million people have been moved into cooperative villages.

Relations with Kenya and Uganda, former partners in the East African Community, are strained.

Zanzibar, the Isle of Cloves, lies 23 mi. off the coast of Tanganyika; its area is 640 sq. mi. The island of Pemba, 25 mi. to the NE, area 380 sq. mi., is included in the administration. The total population (1976) is 450,000.

Chief industry is the production of cloves and clove oil, of which Zanzibar and Pemba produce the bulk of the world's supply.

Zanzibar was for centuries the center for Arab slave-traders. Portugal ruled for 2 centuries until ousted by Arabs around 1700. The slave trade was suppressed under British influence, and Zanzibar became a British Protectorate in 1890. Independence came Dec. 10, 1963. Revolutionary forces overthrew the Sultan Jan. 12, 1964. The new government ousted American and British diplomats and newsmen, slaughtered thousands of Arabs, and nationalized farms. Union with Tanganyika followed, 1964.

Thailand

Kingdom of Thailand

People: Population (1976 est.): 42,960,000. **Age distrib.** (%): 0-14: 45.1; 15-59: 50.0; 60+: 4.9. **Pop. density:** 216 per sq. mi. **Urban** (1970): 13.2%. **Ethnic groups** Thais 75%, Chinese 14%, Malays 3%, Khmers, Soais, Karens, Indians. **Languages:** Thai, Chinese. **Religions:** Buddhists 94%, Moslems 4%, Christians 0.6%.

Geography: Area: 198,455 sq. mi., three-fourths the size of Texas. **Location:** On Indochinese and Malayan Peninsulas in S.E. Asia. **Neighbors:** Burma on W. Laos on N, Cambodia on E. Malaysia on S. **Topography:** A plateau dominates the NE third of Thailand, dropping to the fertile alluvial valley of the Chao Phraya R. in the center. Forested mountains are in N, with narrow fertile valleys. The southern peninsula region is covered by rain forests. **Capital:** Bangkok. **Cities** (1970 cen.): Bangkok 1,867,297; Thonburi 627,989.

Government: Head of state: King Bhumibol Adulyadej; b. Dec. 5, 1927, in office: June 9, 1946; **Head of government:** Prime Min. Thanin Kraivichien, b. Apr. 5, 1927, in office: Oct. 6, 1977; **Junta chief:** Adm. Sa-ngad Chaloryu, b. Mar. 3, 1915; in office: Oct. 6, 1977. **Local divisions:** 71 provinces. **Armed forces:** regulars 210,000; reserves 350,000.

Economy: Industries: Auto assembly, drugs, textiles, electrical goods. **Chief crops:** Rice (a major export), corn, tapioca, jute, sugar, coconuts, tobacco, pepper, peanuts, beans, cotton. **Minerals:** Tin (5th largest producer), iron, manganese, tungsten, antimony, gas. **Crude oil output** (1976): 57,000 bbls. **Other resources:** Forests (teak is exported), rubber. **Per capita arable land:** 0.7 acres. **Livestock** (1974): 4,800,000 cattle; 4,700,000 pigs; 55,000,000 poultry. **Fish catch** (1975): 1,370,000 metric tons. **Electricity production** (1975): 7,380 mln. kwh. **Labor force:** 78% agric.; 4% manuf.

Finance: Currency: Baht (Apr. 1977: 20.4=$1 US). **Gross domestic product** (1976): $15.94 bln. **Per capita income** (1975): $318. **Imports** (1976) $3.587 bln.; partners (1974): Jap. 31%, U.S. 13%, W. Ger. 7%, Quatar. 6%. **Exports** (1976): $2.985 bln.; partners (1974): Jap. 26%, Neth. 9%, Sing. 8%, U.S. 8%. **Tourists** (1974): 1,114,600; receipts: $210 million. **National budget** (1976): $2.13 bln. revenues; $2.92 bln. expenditures. **International reserves** (Feb. 1977): $1,959 bln. **Consumer prices** (change in 1976): 4.9%.

Transport: Railway traffic (1974): 3,406 mln. passenger-miles; 1,426 net ton-miles. **Motor vehicles:** in use (1971): 171,-200 passenger cars, 170,100 commercial vehicles; assembled (1975): 16,000 passenger cars, 8,600 commercial vehicles. **Civil aviation:** 2,653 mln. passenger-miles (1975); 66 mln. freight ton-miles (1975). **Chief ports:** Bangkok, Sattahip.

Communications: Television sets: 241,000 in use (1972). **Radios:** 3,009,000 in use (1973). **Telephones in use** (1976): 312,312.

Health: Life expectancy at birth (1960): 53.6 male; 58.7 female. **Births** (annual per 1,000 pop. 1970-75): 43.4. **Deaths** (annual per 1,000 pop. 1970-75): 10.8. **Natural increase** (annual 1970-75): 3.26%. **Pop. per hospital bed** (1973): 927. **Pop. per physician** (1973): 8,041. **Infant mortality** (per 1,000 pop. under 1 yr. 1973): 21.8.

Education: Literacy (1973): 70%. **Pop. 5-19:** in school (1973): 46%; per teacher (1973): 64.

Thais began migrating from southern China in the 11th century. Thailand is the only country in SE Asia never taken over by a European power, thanks to King Mongkut and his son King Chulalongkorn who ruled from 1851 to 1910, modernized the country, and signed trade treaties with both Britain and France.

Thailand underwent a bloodless revolution in 1932, which established a limited monarchy.

Japan occupied the country in 1941. After the war, Thailand followed a pro-West foreign policy. Some 11,000 Thai troops fought in South Vietnam, but were withdrawn by 1972. About 15,000 Thai troops, financed by the U.S., returned from Laos in 1974.

Clashes with Laos and especially with Cambodia have continued. Tribal and political rebels have conducted guerrilla fighting in the NE and extreme S, 1965-77.

A military-civilian junta, headed by Gen. Thanom Kittikachorn, took over the government in Nov. 1971. Civilians, led by students, overwhelmed police, Oct. 1973, and forced Thanom to resign as premier. A civilian cabinet was named. After free elections in January 1975, a coalition government was sworn in. The military resumed control in a bloody 1976 coup.

The fertile land yields a rice surplus. Foreign investment has been encouraged.

Togo

Republic of Togo

People: Population (1976 est.): 2,280,000. **Pop. density:** 104 per sq. mi. **Urban** (1973): 15.2%. **Ethnic groups:** Ewe 20%, Mina 6%, Kabye 14%. **Languages:** French (official), others. **Religions:** Roman Catholics 18%, Protestants 6.5%, Moslems 9%, others.

Geography: Area: 21,853 sq. mi., slightly smaller than West Virginia. **Location:** On S coast of W. Africa. **Neighbors:** Ghana on W. Upper Volta on N. Benin on E. **Topography:** A range of hills running SW-NE splits Togo into two savanna plains regions. **Capital:** Lome. **Cities** (1970 cen.): Lome 148,443.

Government: Head of state: Pres. Gnassingbe Eyadema, b. 1932, in office: Jan. 13, 1967. **Local divisions:** 21 circumscriptions. **Armed forces:** regulars 2,250; para-military 1,200.

Economy: Industries: Textiles, shoes. **Chief crops:** Coffee, cocoa, palm kernels, copra, cotton, kapok, peanuts. **Minerals:** Phosphates. **Per capita arable land:** 2.3 acres. **Livestock** (1974): 225,000 cattle; 237,000 pigs; 715,000 sheep. **Electricity production** (1975): 83 mln. kwh. **Labor force:** 75% agric.

Finance: Currency: CFA Franc (Apr. 1977: 248 = $1 US) **Gross domestic product** (1975): $577 mln. **Per capita income** (1972): $151. **Imports** (1975): $174 mln.; partners (1973): Fr. 38%, W. Ger. 10%, U.K. 7%, Neth. 7%. **Exports** (1975): $126 mln.; partners (1973): Neth. 36%, Fr. 31%, W. Ger. 12%, Belg. 5%. **Balance of payments** (1975): $7.3 mln. **International reserves** (Jan. 1977): $66.8 mln. **Consumer prices** (change in 1975): 18.5%.

Transport: Railway traffic (1974): 40 mln. passenger-miles; 14 mln. net ton-miles. **Motor vehicles:** in use (1974): 13,000 passenger cars, 7,000 commercial vehicles. **Chief ports:** Lome.

Communications: Radios: 50,000 licenses (1973). **Daily newspaper circulation** (1973): 13,000; 6 per 1,000 pop.

Health: Life expectancy at birth (1961): 31.6 male; 38.5 female. **Births** (annual per 1,000 pop. 1970-75): 50.6. **Deaths** (annual per 1,000 pop. 1970-75): 23.3. **Natural increase** (annual 1970-75): 2.73%. **Pop. per hospital bed** (1973): 606. **Pop. per physician** (1973): 22,316. **Infant mortality** (per 1,000 pop. under 1 yr. 1961): 127.

Education: Literacy (1973): 10%. **Pop. 5-19:** in school (1973): 37%; per teacher (1973): 109.

The Ewe arrived in southern Togo several centuries ago. The country later became a major source of slaves. Germany took control from 1884 on. France and Britain administered Togoland as UN trusteeships. The French sector became the republic of Togo Apr. 27, 1960.

The population is divided between Bantus in the S and Hamitic tribes in the N.

Tonga

Kingdom of Tonga

People: Population (1976 est.): 90,000. **Age distrib.** (%): 0-14: 46.3; 15-59: 48.9; 60+: 4.9. **Pop. density:** 335 per sq. mi. **Ethnic groups:** Tongans (Polynesians). **Languages:** Tongan, English. **Religions:** Methodism.

Geography: Area: 269 sq. mi., smaller than New York City. **Location:** In western S. Pacific O. **Neighbors:** Nearest is Fiji, on W, New Zealand, on S. **Topography:** Tongo comprises 150 volcanic and coral islands, 45 inhabited. **Capital** Nuku'alofa. **Cities** (1972 est.): Nuku'alofa 22,000.

Government: Head of state: King Taufa'ahau Tupou IV, b. July 4, 1918, in office: July 5, 1967; **Head of government:** Fatafehi Tu'ipelehake, b. Jan. 7, 1922, in office: Dec. 16, 1965. **Local divisions:** 3 island districts.

Economy: Industries: Tourism. **Chief crops:** Coconut products, bananas are exported. **Other resources:** Fish. **Electricity production** (1973): 5.3 mln. kwh.

Finance: Currency: Pa'anga (1974: 1=$1.49 US). **Gross domestic product** (est. 1974): $25 mln. **Per capita income** (1974): $250. **Imports** (1974): $17 mln.; partners (1974): N.Z. 39%, Fiji 24%, Australia 22%, UK. 4%. **Exports** (1974): $7 mln.; partners (1974): Neth. 40%, Australia 29%, N.Z. 22%, Fiji 6%.

Transport: Motor vehicles: in use (1974): 1,000 passenger cars, 400 commercial vehicles. **Chief ports:** Nuku'alofa.

Communications: Radios: 9,100 in use.

Health: Births (per 1,000 pop. 1971): 28.3. **Deaths** (per 1,000 pop. 1971): 3.2. **Natural increase** (1971): 2.51%. **Infant mortality** (per 1,000 pop. under 1 yr. 1971): 16.0.

The islands were first visited by the Dutch in the early 17th century. A series of civil wars ended in 1845 with establishment of the Tupou dynasty. In 1900 Tonga became a British protectorate. On June 4, 1970, Tonga became completely independent and a member of the Commonwealth.

Trinidad and Tobago

People: Population (1975): 1,080,000. **Age Distrib.** (%): 0-14: 39.7; 15-59: 53.9; 60+: 6.4. **Pop. density:** 546 per sq. mi. **Urban** (1970): 12.4%. **Ethnic groups:** Negroes 43%, East Indians 36%, white 2%, Chinese 1%, mixed 16%. **Languages:** English, Hindi. **Religions:** Roman Catholics 36%, Protestants 30%, Hindus 23%, Moslems 6%.

Geography: Area: 1,979 sq. mi., the size of Delaware. **Location:** Off eastern coast of Venezuela. **Neighbors:** Nearest is Venezuela on SW. **Topography:** Three low mountain ranges cross Trinidad E-W, with a well-watered plain between N and Central Ranges. Parts of E and W coasts are swamps. Tobago, 116 sq. mi., lies 20 mi. NE. **Capital:** Port-of-Spain. **Cities** (1975 est.): Port-of-Spain (met.) 250,000; San Fernando 50,000.

Government: Head of state: Pres. Ellis Emmanuel Innocent Clarke, b. Dec. 28, 1917, in office: July 31, 1976. **Head of government:** Prime Min. Eric Eustace Williams, b. 1911, in office: Aug. 31, 1962. **Local divisions:** 8 counties, Ward of Tobago, 3 municipalities.

Economy: Industries: Oil products, rum, cement, tourism. **Chief crops:** Sugar, cocoa, coffee, citrus fruits, bananas. **Minerals:** Asphalt, oil. **Crude oil output** (1976): 82 mln. bbls. **Per capita arable land:** 0.1 acres. **Livestock** (1974): 71,000 cattle; 54,000 pigs; 6,000,000 poultry. **Electricity production** (1975): 1,128 mln. kwh. **Labor force** : 17% agric.

Finance: Currency: Dollar (Apr. 1971: 2.40=$1 US). **Gross domestic product** (1974): $2 bln. **Per capita income** (1974) $1,400. **Imports** (1976): $1,976 bln.; partners (1974): Saudi Ar. 38%, Indo. 18%, U.S. 11%. **Exports** (1976): $2.220 bln.; partners (1974): U.S. 61%, Puerto Rico 7%. **Tourists** (1974): 129,000; receipts: $66 million. **Balance of payments** (1976): $271 mln. **National budget** (1972): $275 mln. revenues; 296 mln. expenditures. **International reserves** (Feb. 1977): $980.5 mln. **Consumer prices** (change in 1976): 10.5%.

Transport: Motor vehicles: in use (1974): 88,800 passenger cars, 22,900 commercial vehicles; assembled (1976): 9,900 passenger cars, 1,600 commercial vehicles. **Civil aviation:** 616 mln. passengers (1975); 1.3 mln. freight ton-miles (1975). **Chief ports:** Port-of-Spain.

Communications: Television sets: 93,000 licenses (1973) **Radios:** 296,000 licenses (1972); 34,000 manufactured (1973) **Telephones in use** (1976): 67,064. **Daily newspaper circulation** (1973): 100,000.

Health: Life expectancy at birth (1970): 64.08 male; 68.11 female. **Births** (per 1,000 pop. 1974): 24.0. **Deaths** (per 1,000 pop. 1974): 6.5. **Natural increase** (1974): 1.75%. **Pop. per hospital bed** (1973): 221. **Pop. per physician** (1973): 2,120. **Infant mortality** (per 1,000 pop. under 1 yr. 1974): 37.6.

Education: Literacy (1973): 89%. **Pop. 5-19:** in school (1973): 60%; per teacher (1973): 46.

Columbus sighted Trinidad in 1498. Second largest of the old British West Indies and a British possession since 1802, Trinidad and Tobago won independence Aug. 31, 1962. It became a republic in 1976. A leftist opposition party gained strength in 1976 elections.

The nation is one of the most prosperous in the Caribbean, but unemployment usually averages 13%. Oil production has increased with offshore finds. Middle Eastern oil is refined and exported, mostly to the U.S.

Tunisia
Republic of Tunisia

People: Population (1976 est.): 5,740,000. **Age distrib.** (%): 0-14: 44.6; 15-59: 48.7; 60+: 6.7. **Pop. density:** 91 per sq. mi. **Ethnic groups:** Arabs, small Berber minority; Europeans 1%. **Languages:** Arabic, French. **Religions:** Islam nearly universal.

Geography: Area: 63,378 sq. mi., slightly larger than Florida. **Location:** On N coast of Africa. **Neighbors:** Algeria on W, Libya on E. **Topography:** The N is wooded and fertile. The central coastal plains are given to grazing and orchards. The S is arid, approaching Sahara Desert. **Capital:** Tunis. **Cities** (1966 cen.): Tunis (met.) 647,640; Sfax 215,836.

Government: Head of state: Pres. Habib Bourguiba, b. Aug. 3, 1903, in office: July 25, 1957; **Head of government:** Prime Min. Hedi Nouira, b. Apr. 5, 1911, in office: Nov. 2, 1970. **Local divisions:** 18 governorates. **Armed forces:** regulars 20,000; para-military 9,000.

Economy: Industries: Food processing, textiles, clothing, leather, oil products, construction materials, tourism. **Chief crops:** Grains, dates, olives, citrus fruits, figs, vegetables, grapes. **Minerals:** Phosphates, iron, oil, lead, zinc. **Crude oil output** (1976): 28.6 mln. bbls. **Per capita arable land:** 1.9 acres. **Livestock** (1974): 690,000 cattle; 8,000 pigs; 3,300,000 sheep; 13,000,000 poultry. **Fish catch** (1974): 42,700 metric tons. **Electricity production** (1976): 1,344 mln. kwh. **Labor force:** 46% agric.

Finance: Currency: Dinar (Apr. 1977: 0.43 = $1 US). **Gross domestic product** (1976): $4.44 bln. **Per capita income** (1975): $714. **Imports** (1976): $1.529 bln.; partners (1974): Fr. 31%, It. 11%, U.S. 8%, W. Ger. 8%. **Exports** (1976): $788 mln.; partners (1974): It. 25%, Fr. 22%, Gr. 10%, Braz. 6%. **Tourists** (1974): 764,000; receipts: $201 million. **Balance of payments** (1975): −$17 mln. **International reserves** (Feb. 1977): $305.9 mln. **Consumer prices** (change in 1976): 5.4%.

Transport: Railway traffic (1974): 332 mln. passenger-miles; 945 mln. net ton-miles. **Motor vehicles:** in use (1974): 97,400 passenger cars, 59,800 commercial vehicles; assembled (1976): 1,700 passenger cars, 2,600 commercial vehicles. **Civil aviation:** 601 mln. passengers (1976): 4.6 mln. freight ton-miles (1976). **Chief ports:** Tunis, Sfax, Bizerte.

Communications: Television sets: 147,000 licenses (1973); 31,000 manufactured (1974). **Radios:** 277,000 licenses (1973); 97,000 manufactured (1974). **Telephone in use** (1976): 126,750. **Daily newspaper circulation** (1973): 120,000; 22 per 1,000 pop.

Health: Life expectancy at birth (1970-75): 52.5 male; 55.7 female. **Births** (annual per 1,000 pop. 1970-75): 40.0. **Deaths** (annual per 1,000 pop. 1970-75): 13.8. **Natural increase** (annual 1970-75): 2.62%. **Pop. per hospital bed** (1973): 401. **Pop. per physician** (1973): 5,460. **Infant mortality** (per 1,000 pop. under 1 yr. 1969): 125.

Education: Literacy (1973): 32%. **Pop. 5-19:** in school (1973): 60%; per teacher (1973): 67.

Site of ancient Carthage, and a former Barbary state under the suzerainty of Turkey, Tunisia became a protectorate of France under a treaty signed May 12, 1881. The nation became independent Mar. 20, 1956, and ended the monarchy the following year. Habib Bourguiba has headed the country since independence.

Although Tunisia is a member of the Arab League, Bourguiba in the 1960s urged negotiations to end Arab-Israeli disputes and was denounced by other members. In 1966 he broke relations with Egypt but resumed them after the 1967 Israeli-Arab war. He again urged negotiations with Israel in June 1973.

Tunisia and Libya announced in Jan. 1974 that the 2 nations would merge, but Bourguiba soon dropped the plan.

Turkey
Republic of Turkey

People: Population (1976 est.): 40,160,000. **Age distrib.** (%): 0-14: 41.8; 15-59: 51.0; 60+: 7.2. **Pop. density:** 133 per sq. mi. **Urban** (1974): 42.6%. **Ethnic groups:** Turks 90%, Kurds 7%, Arabs 1.2%, Circassians, Greeks, Armenians, Georgians, Jews. **Languages:** Turkish, Kurdish. **Religions:** Moslems over 99%.

Geography: Area: 301,380 sq. mi., twice the size of California. **Location:** Occupies Asia Minor, between Mediterranean and Black Seas. **Neighbors:** Bulgaria, Greece on W, USSR (Georgia, Armenia) on N, Iran on E, Iraq, Syria on W. **Topography:** Central Turkey has wide plateaus, with hot, dry summers and cold winters. High mountains ring the interior on all but W, with more than 20 peaks over 10,000 ft. Rolling plains are in W; mild, fertile coastal plains are in S, W. **Capital:** Ankara. **Cities** (1973 est.): Istanbul (met.) 3,135,354; Ankara (met.) 1,553,897; Izmir (met.) 819,276; Bursa (met.) 426,567.

Government: Head of state: Pres. Fahri Koruturk, b. 1903, in office: Apr. 6, 1973; **Head of government:** Prime Min. Suleyman Demirel, b. 1924, in office: July 21, 1977 (and previous terms). **Local divisions:** 67 provinces, with appointed governors. **Armed forces:** regulars 460,000; reserves 825,000.

Economy: Industries: Silk, textiles, steel, shoes, furniture, cement, paper, glassware, appliances. **Chief crops:** Tobacco (6th largest producer), cereals, cotton, olives, figs, nuts, sugar, opium gums. **Minerals:** Antimony, borate, copper, chrome; also manganese, lead, zinc, coal, iron, oil, silver, mercury, sulphur, molybdenum, magnesite, asbestos. **Other resources:** Wool, silk, forests. **Per capita arable land:** 1.5 acres. **Livestock** (1976): 14,420,000 cattle; 16,000 pigs; 40,600,000 sheep; 38,329,000 poultry. **Fish catch** (1975): 259,000 metric tons. **Electricity production** (1976): 18,252 mln. kwh. **Labor force:** 69% agric.; 8% manuf.

Finance: Currency: Lira (Apr. 1977: 17.68=$1 US). **Gross domestic product** (1976): $39.8 bln. **Per capita income** (1973): $553. **Imports** (1976): $5.129 bln.; partners (1974): W. Ger. 18%, U.S. 9%, Iraq 9%, It. 7%. **Exports** (1976): $1.960 bln.; partners (1974): W. Ger. 22%, U.S. 9%, Leb. 7%, Switz. 6%. **Tourists** (excluding excursionists) (1974): 1,110,300; receipts: $194 million. **Balance of payments** (1975): −$888 mln. **National budget** (1975): $7.36 bln. revenues; $8.19 bln. expenditures. **International reserves** (Feb. 1977): $990 mln. **Consumer prices** (change in 1976): 17.4%.

Transport: Railway traffic (1974): 3,573 mln. passenger-miles; 3,986 mln. net ton-miles. **Motor vehicles:** in use (1974): 303,800 passenger cars, 230,800 commercial vehicles; assembled (1975): 75,000 passenger cars, 30,000 commercial vehicles. **Civil aviation:** 1,252 mln. passenger-miles (1976); 11 mln. freight ton-miles (1976). **Chief ports:** Istanbul, Izmir, Mersin, Samsun.

Communications: Television sets: 257,000 licenses (1973); 371,000 manufactured (1974). **Radios:** 4,033,000 licenses (1973); 272,000 manufactured (1974). **Telephones in use** (1976): 1,011,790.

Health: Life expectancy at birth (1966): 53.7 (both sexes). **Births** (per 1,000 pop. 1967): 39.6. **Deaths** (per 1,000 pop. 1967): 14.6. **Natural increase** (1967): 2.50%. **Pop. per hospital bed** (1973): 488. **Pop. per physician** (1973): 2,016. **Infant mortality** (per 1,000 pop. under 1 yr. 1967): 153.0.

Education: Literacy (1973): 51%. **Pop. 5-19:** in school (1973): 49%; per teacher (1973): 69.

Ancient inhabitants of Turkey were among the worlds first agriculturalists. Such civilizations as the Hittites, Phrygian, and Lydian flourished in Asiatic Turkey (Asia Minor), as did much of Greek civilization. After the fall of Rome in the 5th century, Constantinople was the capital of the Byzantine Empire for 1,000 years. It fell in 1453 to Ottoman Turks, who ruled a vast empire for over 400 years.

Just before World War I, Turkey, or the Ottoman Empire, ruled what is now Syria, Lebanon, Iraq, Jordan, Israel, Arabia, Yemen, and islands in the Aegean Sea.

Turkey joined Germany and Austria in World War I and its defeat resulted in loss of much territory and fall of the sultanate. A republic was declared Oct. 29, 1923. The Caliphate (spiritual leadership of Islam) was renounced 1924. Council of Europe and an associate in EC. Communism is outlawed, and many leftist terrorists have been jailed. Martial law, imposed in 1971, was ended in 1973 and political life is active and free.

Long embroiled with Greece over Cyprus, off Turkey's south coast, Turkey invaded the island July 20, 1974, after Greek officers seized the Cypriot government as a step toward unification with Greece. Turkey sought a new government for Cyprus, with Greek Cypriot and Turkish Cypriot zones. In reaction to Turkey's moves, the U.S. Congress cut off military aid in 1975. Turkey, in turn, suspended the use of most U.S. bases. A new base accord was tentatively reached in March, 1976.

In June, 1971 Turkey agreed to stop all opium poppy production, in return for $37.5 million in economic aid from the U.S. In 1974 it announced it would resume opium production, with U.S. and U.N. controls, for medical use only.

Uganda

Republic of Uganda

People: Population (1976 est.): 11,940,000. **Age distrib.** (%): 0-14: 46.2; 15-59: 48; 60+: 5.8. **Pop. density:** 131 per sq. mi. **Urban** (1972): 7.1%. **Ethnic groups:** Bantu, Nilotic, Nilo-Hamitic, Sudanic tribes. **Languages:** English (official), Swahili (national), Luganda, others. **Religions:** Christians 50%, Moslems 6%, others.

Geography: Area: 91,134 sq. mi., slightly smaller than Oregon. **Location:** In E. Central Africa. **Neighbors:** Sudan on N, Zaire on W, Rwanda, Tanzania on S, Kenya on E. **Topography:** Most of Uganda is a high plateau 3,000-6,000 ft. high, with high Ruwenzori range in W (Mt. Margherita 16,750 ft.), volcanoes in SW. NE is arid, W and SW rainy. Lakes Victoria, Edward, Albert form much of borders. **Capital:** Kampala. **Cities** (1969 cen): Kampala (met.) 330,700.

Government: Head of state: Pres. Idi Amin Dada, b. 1925, in office: Jan. 25, 1971. **Local divisions:** 10 provinces. **Armed forces:** regular 21,000.

Economy: Chief crops: Coffee (68% of 1973 export earnings), cotton, tea, corn, peanuts, sisal, oil seeds, tobacco, sugar. **Minerals:** Copper, tin. **Per capita arable land:** 0.8 acres. **Livestock** (1974): 3,840,000 cattle; 758,000 sheep. **Fish catch** (1974): 167,500 metric tons. **Electricity production** (1976): 696 mln. kwh. **Labor force:** 86% agric.

Finance: Currency: Shilling (Mar. 1977: 8.33=$1 US). **Gross domestic product** (est. 1974): $2.3 bln. **Per capita income** (1972): $132. **Imports** (1976) $160 mln.; partners (1974): Kenya 36%, U.K. 17%, W. Ger. 9%, Jap. 6%. **Exports** (1976): $360 mln.; partners (1974): U.S. 23%, U.K. 18%, Jap. 9%, W. Ger. 5%. **Tourists** (1974): 10,300; receipts (1973): $4 million. **Balance of payments** (1976): $8.8 mln. **National budget** (1972): $214 mln. revenues; $342 mln. expenditures. **International reserves** (Dec. 1970): $56.6 mln. **Consumer prices** (change in 1975): 17.3%.

Transport: Motor vehicles: in use (1974): 27,000 passenger cars, 8,900 commercial vehicles.

Communications: Television sets: 15,000 in use (1972). **Radios:** 250,000 in use (1973). **Telephones in use** (1976): 45,397. **Daily newspaper circulation** (1972): 78,000.

Health: Life expectancy at birth (1970-75): 48.3 male; 51.7 female. **Births** (annual per 1,000 pop. 1970-75): 45.2. **Deaths** (annual per 1,000 pop. 1970-75): 15.9. **Natural increase** (annual 1970-75): 2.93%. **Pop. per hospital bed** (1973): 676. **Pop. per physician** (1973): 9,008. **Infant mortality** (per 1,000 pop. under 1 yr. 1959): 160.

Education: Literacy (1973): 25%. **Pop. 5-19:** in school (1973): 21%; per teacher (1973): 154.

Britain obtained a protectorate over Uganda in 1894. The country became independent Oct. 9, 1962, and a republic within the Commonwealth a year later. In 1967, the traditional kingdoms, including the powerful Buganda state, were abolished and the central government strengthened.

Milton Obote, then prime minister, seized full power in 1966. Gen. Idi Amin seized control in 1971. As many as 300,000 of his opponents were reported killed in subsequent years. Amin was named president for life in 1976.

A June 1977 Commonwealth conference condemned the Uganda government for its "disregard for the sanctity of human life."

In 1972 Amin expelled nearly all of Uganda's 45,000 Asians (Indians and Pakistanis), many of them business and professional men. In 1973 the U.S., Canada and Norway ended economic aid programs; and the U.S. withdrew all diplomatic personnel. Amin seized all British firms.

Several hundred Soviet advisers have helped prop up the regime.

A state of economic chaos has been mitigated by the world rise in coffee prices.

Israeli forces raided Entebbe, Uganda, July 1976, and rescued 103 hostages seized by Arab and German terrorists.

Union of Soviet Socialist Republics

People: Population (1977): 257,900,000. **Age distrib.** (%): 0-19: 36.8; 20-59: 50.5; 60+: 12.7. **pop density:** 30 per sq. mi. **Urban** (1974): 60.9%. **Ethnic groups:** Russians 53%, Ukrainians 17%, Uzbeks 4%, Byelorussians 4%, 150 others. **Languages:** Slavic (Russian, Ukrainian, Byelorussian, Polish) 76%, Altaic (Turkish, etc.) 11%, other Indo-European 8%, Uralian 3%, Caucasian 2%. **Religions:** Russian Orthodox 18%, Moslems 9%, other Orthodox, Protestants, Jews, Buddhists.

Geography: Area: 8,647,250 sq. mi., the largest country in the world, nearly 2½ times the size of the U.S. **Location:** Stretches from E. Europe across N Asia to the Pacific O. **Neighbors:** Finland, Poland, Czechoslovakia, Hungary, Romania on W, Turkey, Iran, Afghanistan, China, Mongolia, N. Korea on S. **Topography:** The USSR occupies the northern part of Asia and the eastern half of Europe. Covering one-sixth of the earth's land area, the USSR contains every type of climate except the distinctly tropical, and has a varied topography.

The European portion is a low plain, grassy in S, wooded in N with Ural Mtns. on the E. Caucasus Mts. on the S. Urals stretch N-S for 2,500 mi. The Asiatic portion is also a vast plain, with mountains on the S and in the E; tundra covers extreme N, with forest belt below; plains, marshes are in W, desert in SW (Central Asia). **Capital:** Moscow. **Cities** (1975 est.): Moscow (met.) 7,632,000; Leningrad (met.) 4,311,000; Kiev 1,947,000; Tashkent 1,595,000; Baku (met.) 1,383,000; Kharkov 1,357,000; Gorky (1,283,000); Novsibirsk 1,265,000; Kuibyshev 1,164,000; Minsk 1,147,000; Sverdlovsk 1,147,000; Tbilisi 1,006,000; Odessa 1,002,000.

Government: Head of state: Pres. Leonid I. Brezhnev, b. Dec. 19, 1906, in office: June 16, 1977; **Head of government:** Alexei N. Kosygin, b. Feb. 1904, in office: Oct. 15, 1964; **Head of Communist Party:** Gen. Sec. Leonid I. Brezhnev, in office: Oct. 14, 1964. **Local divisions:** 15 union republics, within which are 20 autonomous republics, 6 krays, 120 oblasts (regions), 8 autonomous oblasts, 10 national areas. **Armed forces:** regulars 3,650,000 (army 1,825,000; navy 450,000; air force 450,000); reserves 6,800,000; para-military 350,000.

Economy: Industries: Steel, machinery, machine tools, vehicles, chemicals, cement, textiles, appliances, paper. **Chief crops:** Grain, cotton, sugar beets, potatoes, vegetables, sunflowers. **Minerals:** Coal (58% world reserves), oil (59%), iron (41%), manganese (88%), potassium salts (54%), phosphates (30%), gold, and significant deposits of most commercial minerals. **Crude oil output** (1976): 3.8 bln bbls. **Other resources:** Forests (25% of world reserve). **Per capita arable land:** 2.2 acres. **Livestock** (1976): 111,000,000 cattle; 57,800,000 pigs; 141,025,000 sheep; 747,654,000 poultry. **Fish catch** (1975): 9,876,000 metric tons. **Electricity production** (1976): 1,110,960 mln. kwh. **Labor force:** 26% agric.; 40% manuf. & constr.

Finance: Currency: Ruble (1974: 0.76=$1 US). **Gross domestic product** (est. 1974): $560 bln. **Per capita income** (1974): $2,010. **Imports** (1976): $38.151 bln.; partners (1974): E. Ger. 11%, Pol. 9%, Czech. 8%, Bulg. 8%. **Exports** (1976): $37.169 bln.; partners (1974): E. Ger. 10%, Pol. 9%, Czech. 7%, Bulg. 7%. **Tourists** (1974): 3,446,900.

Transport: Railway traffic (1974): 190,211 mln. passenger-miles; 1,923,648 mln. net ton-miles. **Motor vehicles:** in use (1974): 3,000,000 passenger cars, 4,000,000 commercial vehicles; manufactured (1976): 1,200,000 passenger cars, 720,000 commercial vehicles. **Civil aviation:** 4,240 mln. passenger-miles (1976); 150 mln. freight ton-miles (1976). **Chief ports:** Leningrad, Odessa, Murmansk, Kaliningrad, Archangelsk, Riga, Vladivostock.

Communications: Television sets: 49,200,000 in use (1973); 6,569,000 manufactured (1974). **Radios:** 110,300,000 in use (1973); 8,753,000 manufactured (1974). **Telephones in use** (1976): 16,129,000. **Daily newspaper circulation** (1973) 93,243,000; 373 per 1,000 pop.

Health: Life expectancy at birth (1971-72): 64 male; 74 female. **Births** (per 1,000 pop. 1975): 18.2. **Deaths** (per 1,000 pop. 1975): 9.3. **Natural increase** (1975): 0.89%. **Pop. per hospital bed** (1973): 86. **Pop. per physician** (1973): 369. **Infant mortality** (per 1,000 pop. under 1 yr. 1974): 27.7.

Education: Literacy (1973): 99%. **Pop. 5-19:** in school

(1973): 66%; per teacher (1973): 29.

The USSR is nominally a federation consisting of 15 union republics, within certain of which are further subdivisions. Four of the union republics contain 20 autonomous Soviet socialist republics and 8 autonomous regions; the largest union republic, the Russian Soviet Federal Socialist Republic, has also 10 national districts. Nationalist agitation has occasionally been reported in several of the republics. Important positions in the republics are filled by centrally chosen appointees, often ethnic Russians.

Beginning in 1939 the USSR by means of military action and negotiation overran contiguous territory and independent republics, including all or part of Lithuania, Latvia, Estonia, Poland, Czechoslovakia, Romania, Germany, Tannu Tuva, and Japan. The union republics are:

Republic	Area, sq. miles	Pop. (est. 1975)
Russian SFSR	6,593,391	133,700,000
Ukrainian SSR	232,046	48,800,000
Kazakh SSR	1,064,092	14,200,000
Uzbek SSR	158,069	13,700,000
Byelorussian SSR	80,154	9,300,000
Azerbaijan SSR	33,436	5,600,000
Georgian SSR	26,911	4,900,000
Moldavian SSR	13,012	3,800,000
Tadzhik SSR	54,019	3,400,000
Lithuanian SSR	26,173	3,300,000
Kirghiz SSR	76,642	3,300,000
Armenian SSR	11,306	2,800,000
Latvian SSR	24,695	2,500,000
Turkmen SSR	188,417	2,500,000
Estonian SSR	17,413	1,400,000

The Russian Soviet Federal Socialist Republic, contains over 50% of the population of the Soviet Union and includes 76% of its territory. Its territories stretch from the old Estonian, Latvian, and Finnish borders and the Byelorussian and Ukrainian lines on the W, to the shores of the Pacific, and from the Arctic on the N to the Black and Caspian Seas and the borders of Kazakh SSR, Mongolia, and Manchuria on the S. Siberia, divided into a number of administrative units, encompasses a large part of the RSFSR area. Capital: Moscow.

Parts of Eastern and Western Siberia have been transformed by steel mills, huge dams, oil and gas industries, electric railroads, and highways.

The Ukraine is the most densely populated of the major constituent republics. It borders on the Black Sea, with Poland, Czechoslovakia, Hungary, and Romania on the W and SW. The population is 75% Ukrainian. Capital: Kiev.

The Ukraine contains the arable black soil belt, the chief wheat-producing section of the Soviet Union. Sugar beets, potatoes, and livestock are important.

The Donets Basin has large deposits of coal, iron and other metals. There are chemical and machine industries and salt mines.

Byelorussia (White Russia). Capital: Minsk. Chief industries include machinery, tools, appliances, tractors, clocks, cameras, steel, cement, textiles, paper, leather, glass. Main crops are grain, flax, potatoes, sugar beets.

Azerbaijan boasts near Baku, the capital, important oil fields. Its natural wealth includes deposits of iron ore, cobalt, etc. Irrigation has boosted cotton production. A high-yield winter wheat also is grown, as are fruits. It produces iron, steel, cement, fertilizers, synthetic rubber, electrical and chemical equipment. It borders on Iran and Turkey.

Georgia, which lies in the western part of Transcaucasia, contains the largest manganese mines in the world. There are rich timber resources and coal mines. Basic industries are food, textiles, iron, steel. Grain, tea, tobacco, fruits, grapes are grown. Capital: Tbilisi (Tiflis). Despite massive party and government purges since 1972, illegal private enterprise and Georgian nationalist feelings persist; attempts to repress them have led to violence.

Armenia is mountainous, sub-tropical, extensively irrigated. Copper, zinc, aluminum, molybdenum, and marble are mined. Instrument making is important. Capital: Erevan.

Uzbekistan, most important economically of the Central Asia republics, produces 67% of USSR cotton, 50% of rice, 33% of silk, 34% of astrakhan, 85% of hemp. Industries include iron, steel, cars, tractors, TV and radio sets, textiles, food. Mineral wealth includes coal, sulphur copper, and oil. Capital: Tashkent.

Turkmenistan in Central Asia, produces cotton, maize, carpets, chemicals. Minerals: oil, coal, sulphur, barite, lime, salt, gypsum. The Kara Kum desert occupies four-fifths of the area. Capital: Ashkhabad.

Tadzhikistan borders on China and Afghanistan. Over half the population are Tadzhiks, mostly Moslems, speaking an Iranian dialect. Chief occupations are farming and cattle breeding. Cotton, grain, rice, and a variety of fruits are grown. Heavy industry, based on rich mineral deposits, coal and hydroelectric power, has replaced handicrafts. Capital: Dushanbe.

Kazakhstan extends from the lower reaches of the Volga in Europe to the Altai Mtns. on the Chinese border. It has vast deposits of coal, oil, iron, tin, copper, lead, zinc, etc. Fish for its canning industry are caught in Lake Balkhash and the Caspian and Aral Seas. The capital is Alma-Ata. About 50% of the population is Russian or Ukrainian, working in the virgin-grain lands opened up after 1954, and in the growing industries. Kazakhstan is third among industrial republics in the USSR.

Kirghizia is in the eastern part of Soviet Central Asia, on the frontier of Sinkiang (western China). The people, once nomadic, breed cattle and horses and grow tobacco, cotton, rice, sugar beets. New industries include machine and instrument making, chemicals. Capital: Frunze.

Moldavia in the SW part of the USSR, is a fertile black earth plain bordering Romania, and includes Bessarabia. It is an agricultural region that grows grains, fruits, vegetables, and tobacco. Textiles, wine, food and electrical equipment industries have been developed. Capital: Kishinev. The region was taken from Romania in 1940; the people speak Romanian.

Lithuania, on the Baltic, produces cattle, hogs, electric motors, and appliances. The capital is Vilnius (Vilna). **Latvia** on the Baltic and the Gulf of Riga, has timber and peat resources estimated at 3 billion tons. In addition to agricultural products it produces rubber goods, dyes, fertilizers, glassware, telephone apparatus, TV and radio sets, railroad cars. The capital is Riga. **Estonia** also on the Baltic, has textiles, shipbuilding, timber, roadmaking and mining equipment industries and a shale oil refining industry. Tallinn is the capital. The 3 Baltic states were provinces of imperial Russia before World War I, were independent nations between World Wars I and II, but were conquered by Russia in 1940. The U.S. has never formally recognized the takeover. Russian immigration was encouraged after the war.

Economy. Almost all legal economic enterprises are state-owned. There were 31,500 collective farms in 1973, along with 17,300 larger state farms. Small private plots, from which farmers may sell produce, produced 61% of potatoes, a third of vegetables, meat, and milk, 43% of eggs, and 21% of wool in 1973. A huge illegal black market plays an important role in distribution; illegal private production and service firms are periodically exposed.

The USSR is incalculably rich in natural resources. Its heavy industry is second only to the U.S. It leads the world in oil and steel production. Consumer industries have lagged comparatively. Agricultural output has expanded, but in poor crop years the USSR has been forced to make huge grain purchases from the West. Shortages and rationing of basic food products periodically occur.

In 1966 many major factories were put on an incentive profit-sharing system, while bonuses to farms and farm workers were introduced to spur food production. In 1973 steps were taken to group factories into "production associations" partly resembling large U.S. corporations.

In 1971 a proposed new 5-year plan stressed growth in consumer goods, but subsequent adjustments restored priority to heavy industry, and reduced overall goals. The 1976-80 plan called for slower growth, emphasizing modernization of plants and higher farm investment.

Exports include petroleum and its products, iron and steel, rolled non-ferrous metals, industrial plant equipment, arms, lumber, cotton, asbestos, gold, manganese, and others. 60% of its trade is with Communist nations, 25% with the West, which supplies advanced technology. The USSR had a $4 billion trade deficit with the West in 1976, financed by gold sales, long-term loans, and a trade surplus with East Europe and underdeveloped countries. Debt to the West reached $14.4 billion by 1977.

History. Slavic tribes began migrating into Russia from the W in the 5th century A.D. The first Russian state, founded by Scandinavian chieftains, was established in the 9th century, centering in Novgorod and Kiev.

In the 13th century the Mongols overran the country. It recovered under the grand dukes and princes of Muscovy, or Moscow, and by 1480 freed itself from the Mongols. Ivan the Terrible was the first to be formally proclaimed Tsar (1547). Peter the Great (1682-1725), extended the domain and in 1721 founded the Russian Empire.

Western ideas and the beginnings of modernization spread through the huge Russian empire in the 19th and early 20th centuries. Industry, agriculture, transport, and education advanced, and Russia attained leadership status in world literature, music, and art. But political evolution failed to keep pace.

Russian military reverses in the 1905 war with Japan and in World War I led to the breakdown of the Tsarist regime. The 1917 Revolution began in March with a series of sporadic strikes for higher wages by factory workers. A provisional democratic government under Prince Georgi Lvov was established but was quickly followed in May by the second provisional government, led by Alexander Kerensky. The Kerensky government and the freely-elected Constituent Assembly were overthrown in a Communist coup led by Vladimir Ilyich Lenin Nov. 7.

Lenin's death Jan. 21, 1924, resulted in an internal power struggle from which Joseph Stalin eventually emerged the absolute ruler of Russia. Stalin secured his position at first by exiling opponents such as Leon Trotsky. But from the 1930s to 1953 he resorted to a series of "purge" trials, mass executions and mass exiles in work camps. These measures, along with forced collectivization of agriculture, resulted in millions of deaths, according to most estimates. In 1975 it was estimated there still were 10,000 political prisoners, mostly in labor camps.

After Stalin died, Mar. 5, 1953, Nikita Khrushchev was elected first secretary of the Central Committee. In 1956 he condemned Stalin. Khrushchev lifted some restrictions, extended trade policies. The names of Stalin, Molotov, Malenkov, and other supporters of Stalin were eliminated from regions, cities, and other sites in 1961-62 after Stalin's body was removed from the Lenin-Stalin tomb in Moscow.

Under Khrushchev the open antagonism of Poles and Hungarians toward domination by Moscow was brutally suppressed in 1956. He advocated peaceful co-existence with the capitalist countries, but continued arming the USSR with nuclear weapons. He aided the Cuban revolution under Fidel Castro but withdrew Soviet missiles from Cuba during confrontation by U.S. President Kennedy, Sept.-Oct. 1962.

The USSR, the U.S., and Great Britain initialed a joint treaty July 25, 1963, banning above-ground nuclear tests.

The co-existence and economic reform policies; as well as border disputes, alienated the leaders of Albania and Communist China.

Khrushchev was suddenly deposed, Oct. 14-15, 1964, and replaced as party first secretary by Leonid I. Brezhnev, 57, and as premier by Aleksei N. Kosygin, 60. Brezhnev was named president in 1977.

Communist China's Premier Chou En-lai visited the new USSR chiefs in Nov. 1964 but the visit failed to heal the growing rift between the 2 Communist powers.

In 1968, the U.S. and USSR joined 59 other nations in signing a treaty to bar spread of nuclear weapons.

In Aug. 1968 Russian, Polish, East German, Hungarian, and Bulgarian military forces invaded Czechoslovakia to put a curb on liberalization policies of the Czech government. The USSR declared it had a duty to intervene in nations where socialism was "imperiled," according to the "Brezhnev Doctrine."

In March 1969 troops of the USSR and Communist China fought the first of a series of clashes on a disputed island in the Ussuri River on the border between the 2 nations in the Far East, north of Vladivostok. In 1970 ambassadors were exchanged, after a lapse; but both nations increased their border forces.

The USSR in 1971 continued heavy arms shipments to Egypt. In July 1972 Egypt ordered most of the 20,000 Soviet military personnel in that country to leave. The USSR then increased arms shipments to Syria. When Egypt and Syria attacked Israel in Oct. 1973, the USSR launched huge arms airlifts to the 2 Arab nations. In 1974, the Soviet replenished the arms used or lost by the Syrians in the 1973 war, and continued some shipments to Egypt.

Massive Soviet military aid to North Vietnam in the late 1960s and early 1970s helped assure Communist victories throughout Indo-China in 1975. Similar aid helped leftist factions gain control of Angola in 1976. Soviet arms aid and advisers were sent to several African countries in the 1970s, including Algeria, Somalia, and Ethiopia. The Soviet navy expanded its deployment in foreign seas.

In 1972, the U.S. and USSR reached temporary agreements to freeze intercontinental missiles at their current levels, to limit defensive missiles to 200 each and to cooperate on health, environment, space, trade, and science.

Meanwhile, under Brezhnev, dissident intellectuals were repressed and purge-type trials resumed. Andrei Sakharov, creator of the USSR hydrogen bomb, and other Soviet dissidents warned Western nations that aid given Russia would be used against them.

On Aug. 1, 1975, 35 countries of Europe and North America signed a European security declaration tacitly approving current boundaries and urging freer movement of people and ideas.

Well over 100,000 Jews and some 30,000 ethnic Germans were allowed to emigrate from the USSR in the 1970s, following pressure from the West. Many leading figures in the arts also left the country.

Government. The Communist Party leadership dominates all areas of national life. A Politburo of 15 full members and several candidate members makes all major political, economic, and foreign policy decisions. Party membership in 1976 was reported to be 15,700,000.

United Arab Emirates

People: Population (1976 est.): 230,000. **Age distrib.** (%): 0-14: 33.8; 15-59: 63.6; 60+: 2.6. **Pop. density:** 7 per sq. mi. **Ethnic groups:** Arabs 72%, Iranians, Pakistanis and Indians 26%. **Languages:** Arabic (official), Persian, Hindu, Urdu. **Religions:** Moslems 96.7%, Christians 1.3%.

Geography: Area: 32,278 sq. mi., the size of Maine. **Location:** On the S shore of the Persian Gulf. **Neighbors:** Qatar on N, Saudi Ar. on W, S, Oman on E. **Topography:** A barren, flat coastal plain gives way to uninhabited sand dunes on the S. Hajar Mtns. are on E. **Capital:** Abu Dhabi. **Cities** (1975 est.): Dubai 66,000; Abu Dhabi 55,000.

Government: Head of state: Pres. Zayed bin Sultan al Nahayyan, b. 1923, in office: Dec. 2, 1972. **Head of government:** Prime Min. Maktoum bin Rashid al-Maktoum, in office: Dec. 10, 1972. **Local divisions:** 7 autonomous emirates: Abu Dhabi, Ajman, Dubai, Fujaira, Ras al-Khaimah, Sharjah, Umm al-Qaiwain. **Armed forces:** regulars 21,400.

Economy: Chief crops: Vegetables. **Minerals:** Oil. **Crude oil output** (1976): 692 mln. bbls. **Per capita arable land:** 0.2 acres. **Fish catch** (1974): 65,000 metric tons.

Finance: Currency: Dirhams (Apr. 1977: 3.94=$1 US). **Gross domestic product** (est. 1974): $6 bln. **Per capita income** (1974): $16,000. **Imports** (1976) $3.329 bln.; partners (1974): Jap. 18%, U.K. 16%, U.S. 13%, W. Ger. 5%. **Exports** (1976): $8.536 bln.; partners (1974): Jap. 33%, Fr. 21%, W. Ger. 15%, U.K. 10%. **International reserves** (Feb. 1977): $1.79 bln.

Transport: Chief ports: Dubai, Abu Dhabi.

Communications: Telephones in use (1976): 44,278.

The 7 "Trucial Sheikdoms" gave Britain control of defense and foreign relations in the 19th century. They merged to become an independent state Dec. 2, 1971.

The Abu Dhabi Petroleum Co. was fully nationalized in 1975. Oil revenues give the UAE the highest per capita GNP in the entire world.

United Kingdom of Great Britain and Northern Ireland

People: Population (1976): 55,930,000. **Age distrib.** (%): 0-14: 23.9; 15-59: 56.8; 60+: 19.3. **Pop. density:** 594 per sq. mi. **Urban** (1973): 77.7%. **Ethnic groups:** English 81.5%, Scottish 9.6%, Irish 2.4, Welsh 1.9%, Ulster 1.8%; West Indian, Indian, Pakistani over 2%; others. **Languages:** English nearly universal, Welsh spoken in western Wales. **Religions:** Church of England 55% (confirmed 20%), Roman Catholics 10%, Presbyterians 3%, Methodist 1%, Jews 1%, other Protestants, Hindus, Moslems.

Geography: Area: 94,209 sq. mi., slightly smaller than Oregon. **Location:** Off the NW coast of Europe, across English Channel, Strait of Dover, and North Sea. **Neighbors:** Ireland to W, France to SE. **Topography:** England is mostly rolling land, rising to Uplands of southern Scotland; Lowlands are in center of Scotland, granite Highlands are in N. Coast is heavily indented, especially on W. Northern Ireland is farming region. British isles have milder climate than N Europe, ample rainfall. Thames, 210 mi., and Severn are longest rivers. **Capital:** London. **Cities** (1973 est.): London 7,281,080; Manchester (met.) 2,389,260;

Birmingham 2,358,980; Leeds 1,735,700; Glasgow 1,727,625; Liverpool 1,226,310; Newcastle 788,130; Belfast 549,139; Sheffield 511,860; Bristol 421,800.

Government: Head of state: Queen Elizabeth II, b. Apr. 21, 1926, in office: Feb. 6, 1952. **Head of government:** Prime Min. James Callaghan, b. Mar. 27,1912, in office: Apr. 5, 1976. **Local divisions:** England and Wales: 53 counties, 6 metro counties, London; Scotland: 9 regions, 3 island areas; N. Ireland: 26 districts. **Armed forces:** regulars 344,200; reserves 237,300.

Economy: Industries: Steel, metals, vehicles, shipbuilding, shipping, banking, insurance, appliances, textiles, chemicals, electronics, aircraft, machinery, scientific instruments, distilling. **Chief crops:** Grains, sugar beets, fruits, vegetables. **Minerals:** Oil, gas, coal, limestone, iron, salt, clay, chalk, gypsum, lead, tin, silica. **Crude oil output** (1976): 89 mln. bbls. **Per capita arable land:** 0.3 acres. **Livestock** (1976): 13,874,000 cattle; 7,653,000 pigs; 19,526,000 sheep; 139,600,000 poultry. **Fish catch** (1975): 965,000 metric tons. **Electricity production** (1976): 276,972 mln. kwh. **Labor force:** 3% agric. 33% manuf.

Finance: Currency: Pound (Apr. 1977: 1=$1.72 US). **Gross domestic product** (1976): $218.4 bln. **Per capita income** (1975): $3,684. **Imports** (1976): $55,978 mln.; partners (1975): U.S. 10%, W. Ger. 8%, Neth. 8%, Fr. 7%. **Exports** (1976): $46,-264 mln.; partners (1975): U.S. 9%, W. Ger. 6%, Fr. 6%, Neth. 6%. **Tourists** (1974): 7,935,000; receipts: $1.956 billion. **Balance of payments** (1976): −$914 mln. **National budget** (1976): $78.5 bln. revenues; $85.5 bln. expenditures. **International reserves** (Feb. 1977): $7.87 bln. **Consumer prices** (change in 1976): 16.8%

Transport: Railway traffic (1974): 22,437 mln. passenger-miles; 4,338 mln net ton-miles. **Motor vehicles:** in use (1974): 13,820,800 passenger cars, 1,860,500 commercial vehicles; manufactured (1976): 1,332,000 passenger cars, 372,000 commercial vehicles. **Civil aviation:** 19,219 mln. passenger-miles (1976); 568 mln. freight ton-miles (1976). **Chief ports:** London, Liverpool, Glasgow, Southampton, Cardiff, Belfast.

Communications: Television sets: 17,294,000 licenses (1973); 2,637,000 manufactured (1974). **Radios:** 39,000,000 licenses (1973); 944,000 manufactured (1974). **Telephones in use** (1976): 21,035,602. **Daily newspaper circulation** (1973): 24,500,000; 438 per 1,000 pop.

Health: Life expectancy at birth (1968-70): 67.8 male; 73.8 female. **Births** (per 1,000 pop. 1974): 13.3. **Deaths** (per 1,000 pop. 1974): 11.9. **Natural increase** (1974): 0.14%. **Pop. per hospital bed** (1973): 106. **Pop. per physician** (1973): 756. **Infant mortality** (per 1,000 pop. under 1 yr. 1974): 16.3.

Education: Literacy (1973): 98%. **Pop. 5-19:** in school (1973): 83%; per teacher (1973): 24.

The United Kingdom of Great Britain and Northern Ireland comprises England, Wales, Scotland and Northern Ireland.

The climate of the British Isles is mild and somewhat warmer than that of the continent because of the Gulf Stream modifying the temperature, which has a mean of 48°. Rainfall averages 41 inches a year.

Queen and Royal Family. The ruling sovereign is Elizabeth II of the House of Windsor, born Apr. 21, 1926, eldest daughter of King George VI. She succeeded to the throne Feb. 6, 1952, and was crowned June 2, 1953. As Princess Elizabeth, she was married Nov. 20, 1947 to Lt. Philip Mountbatten, born June 10, 1921, former Prince of Greece. He was created Duke of Edinburgh Nov. 19, 1947, H.R.H. Prince Philip Nov. 20, 1947, and given the title Prince of the United Kingdom Feb. 22, 1957. They have 4 children. Prince Charles Philip Arthur George, born Nov. 14, 1948, is the Prince of Wales and heir apparent.

Parliament is the legislative governing body for the United Kingdom, with certain powers over dependent units. It consists of 2 Houses. The **House of Lords** includes heriditary and life peers and peeresses, certain judges, 2 archbishops and 21 bishops of the Church of England. Total membership is over 1,000 but daily attendance averages 270. Women became eligible to sit in the House of Lords for the first time in 1958. **The House of Commons** has 635 members, who are elected by direct ballot and divided as follows: England 516; Wales 36; Scotland 71; Northern Ireland 12.

Clergymen of the Church of England, ministers of the Church in Scotland and Roman Catholic clergymen are disqualified from sitting as members, as are certain government officers and sheriffs. Women have had the right to vote since 1918.

A two-tier system of local government controls a large variety of social and economic activity. Reforms occurred in 1974-75.

Resources and Industries. Great Britain's major occupations are manufacturing and trade. Metals and metal-using industries contribute more than 50% of the exports. Of about 60 million acres of land in England, Wales and Scotland, 47 million are farmed, of which 17.4 million are arable, the rest pastures.

Large oil and gas fields have been found in the North Sea. Commercial oil production began in 1975; self-sufficiency is expected by 1980, with projected output of two million barrels a day. There are large deposits of coal; 1975 output was 127 million tons.

There are 150 civil and 50 service airports in Great Britain. The railroads, nationalized since 1948, have been reduced in total length, with a basic network of 11,326 mi. designated for modernization and development. The merchant marine totaled 31,415,000 gross registered tons in Sept. 1975, comprising over 10% of active world shipping. About 2 million tons of shipping were under construction in 1975.

The worlds's first power station using atomic energy to create electricity for civilian use began operation Oct. 17, 1956, at Calder Hall in Cumbria.

The government in 1967 took ownershp of 14 steel companies which comprised 90% of the nation's steel-making industry, paying shareholders over $1.4 billion. Further industry takeovers and intervention were foreseen in 1974 government proposals.

The Labor government raised taxes, 1966-69; devalued the pound to $2.40 in 1967 and took various measures to improve exports and cut imports. The Conservative government put a freeze on prices, wages and rents in 1972 to combat inflation. In 1973 it substituted "restraints." A Labor government, elected in 1974, obtained trade union approval of wage curbs; yet inflation continued, and the pound dropped to record lows in 1976. Unemployment rose to a postwar high in 1977.

Britons backed continued EC membership by a 67% vote in a referendum June 5, 1975.

On Feb. 15, 1971, Britain completed a changeover to decimal currency. By 1975 it had in part converted to the metric system as well.

Britain imports all of its cotton, rubber, sulphur, four-fifths of its wool, half of its food and iron ore, also certain amounts of paper, tobacco, chemicals. Manufactured goods made from these basic materials have been exported since the industrial age began.

Main exports are machinery, chemicals, woolen and synthetic textiles, clothing, autos and trucks, iron and steel, locomotive, ships, jet aircraft, farm machinery, drugs, radio, TV, radar and navigation equipment, scientific instruments, arms, whisky.

Religion and Education. The Church of England is Protestant Episcopal. The queen is its temporal head, with rights of appointments to archbishoprics, bishoprics and other offices. There are 2 provinces, Canterbury and York, each headed by an archbishop. About 50% of the population is baptized into the Church, less than 20% is confirmed. Most famous church is Westminster Abbey (1050-1760), site of coronations, tombs of Elizabeth I, Mary of Scots, kings, poets and of the Unknown Warrior.

Roman Catholic Church membership in the United Kingdom was about 5,500,000 in 1975. There were about 14,000 Methodist churches and 550,000 full members in 1974.

Others: There are an est. 410,000 Jews in Great Britain; 80% of them are Orthodox; more than half live in the London area. There are 187,000 Baptists and 187,000 members of the United Reformed Church (Congregational and Presbyterian). The Calvinistic Methodist (Presbyterian) Church of Wales has 99,000 communicants. The Unitarians have 330 chapels. The Society of Friends has 20,000 members. There are 72,000 Mormons. The Church of Christ Scientist has 302 branches in Great Britain and Ireland. The Presbyterian Church in Ireland has a membership in Northern Ireland of about 140,000. The number of Hindus and Moslems has been growing steadily with immigration.

The Church of Scotland is Presbyterian. It is presided over by a moderator, chosen annually. Members numbered 1,060,000 in 1975.

Education is free and compulsory from 5 to 16. The most celebrated British universities are Oxford and Cambridge, each dating to the 13th century. There are 40 other universities.

History. Britain was part of the continent of Europe until about 6,000 B.C., but migration of peoples across the English Channel continued long afterward. Celts arrived 2,500 to 3,000 years ago. Their language survives in Welsh, Cornish, and Gaelic enclaves. Religious and cultural ties with Celts in Gaul (France) were maintained.

England was added to the Roman Empire in 43 A.D. After the withdrawal of Roman legions in 410, waves of Jutes, Angles and Saxons arrived from German lands. They contended with Danish raiders for control of Great Britain from the 8th through 11th centuries.

The last successful invasion was by French-speaking Normans in 1066, who united the country with their dominions in France. Anglo-Norman nobles began the conquest of Ireland in the next century.

Opposition by nobles to royal authority forced King John to sign the Magna Carta in 1215, a guarantee of rights and the rule of law. In the ensuing decades, the foundations of the parliamentary system were laid.

Wales was subdued and added to the Kingdom of England by 1282.

English dynastic claims to large parts of France led to the Hundred Years War, 1338-1453, and the defeat of England. A long civil war, the War of the Roses, lasted 1455-85, and ended with the establishment of the powerful Tudor monarchy. A distinct English civilization flourished. The economy prospered over long periods of domestic peace unmatched in continental Europe. Religious independence was secured when the Church of England was separated from the authority of the Pope in 1534.

Under Queen Elizabeth I, Britain became a major naval power, leading to the founding of colonies in the new world and the expansion of trade with Europe and the Orient. Scotland was united with England when James VI of Scotland was crowned James I of England in 1603.

A struggle between Parliament and the Stuart kings led to a bloody civil war, 1642-49, and the establishment of a republic under the Puritan Oliver Cromwell. The monarchy was restored in 1660, but the "Glorious Revolution" of 1688 confirmed the sovereignty of Parliament, and a Bill of Rights was granted the following year.

In the 18th century, parliamentary rule was strengthened Technological and entrepeneurial innovations led to the Industrial Revolution. The 13 North American colonies were lost, but replaced by growing empires in Canada and India. Britain's role in the defeat of Napoleon, 1815, strengthened its position as the leading world power.

The extension of the franchise in 1832 and 1867, the formation of trade unions, and the development of universal public education were among the drastic social changes which accompanied the spread of industrialization and urbanization in the 19th century. Large parts of Africa and Asia were added to the empire during the reign of Queen Victoria, 1837-1901.

Though victorious in World War I, Britain suffered huge casualties and economic dislocation. Ireland became independent in 1921, and independence movements became active in India and other colonies.

The first labor government took office in 1924, though some labor reforms and social security measures had been enacted by previous governments.

The country suffered major bombing damage in World War II, but held out against Germany singlehandedly for a year after the fall of France in 1940.

Industrial growth continued in the postwar period, but Britain lost its leadership position to other powers. Labor governments passed socialist programs nationalizing some basic industries and expanding social security. Most of the empire was given independence. Britain joined the NATO alliance and, in 1973, the European Communities (Common Market).

Wales

The Principality of Wales in western Britain has an area of 8,017 sq. mi. and a population (est. 1974) of 2,759,000.

England and Wales are administered as a unit. Less than one fifth the population of Wales speak both English and Welsh; about 32,000 speak Welsh solely. Welsh nationalism is advocated by a segment. The UK government favors creation of an elected Welsh Assembly.

Early Anglo-Saxon invaders drove Celtic peoples into the mountains of Wales, terming them Waelise (Welsh, or foreign). There they developed a distinct nationality. Members of the ruling house of Gwynedd in the 13th century fought England but were crushed, 1283. Edward of Caernarvon, son of Edward I of England, was created Prince of Wales, 1301.

Cardiff is the capital, pop. (1974) 284,700.

Scotland

Scotland, a kingdom now united with England and Wales in Great Britain, occupies the northern 37% of the main British island, and the Hebrides, Orkney, Shetland and smaller islands. Length, 275 mi., breadth approx. 150 mi., area, 30,411 sq. mi., population (est. 1975) 5,206,000.

The Lowlands, a belt of land approximately 60 miles wide from the Firth of Clyde to the Firth of Forth, divide the farming region of the Southern Uplands from the granite Highlands of the north. Only one-tenth of the land area, the Lowlands contain three-quarters of the population and most of the industry. The Highlands, famous for hunting and fishing, have been opened to industry by many hydroelectric power stations.

Edinburgh, pop. (est. 1974) 475,042, is the capital. It lies on the Firth of Forth in the County of Lothian and has notable memorials of its royal and cultural history. Glasgow, pop. (est. 1974) 905,032, is the largest city, 3d largest in Britain (5th largest metro area), and Britain's greatest industrial center. It is a shipbuilding complex on the Clyde and an ocean port. Aberdeen, pop. (est. 1974) 212,237, NE of Edinburgh, is a major port, center of granite industry, fish processing, and North Sea oil exploitation. Dundee, pop. (1974) 196,423, NE of Edinburgh, is an industrial and fish processing center. About 90,000 persons speak Gaelic as well as English.

History. Scotland was called Caledonia by the Romans who battled early Picts and Celtic tribes and occupied southern areas from the 1st to the 4th centuries. The Scots were an Irish tribe from Scotia (an early name for Ireland). Missionaries from Britain introduced Christianity in the 4th century; St. Columba, an Irish monk, converted most of Scotland in the 6th century.

The Kingdom of Scotland was founded in 1018. William Wallace, patriot leader, defeated an English army, 1297, and Robert Bruce defeated another, 1314. John Knox led the Scottish Reformation in the 16th century.

In 1603 James VI of Scotland, son of Mary, Queen of Scots, succeeded to the throne of England as James I, and effected the Union of the Crowns. In 1707 Scotland received representation in the British Parliament, resulting from the union of former separate Parliaments. Its executive in the British cabinet is the Secretary of State for Scotland. The growing Scottish National Party urges independence. The UK government has proposed creation of an elected Scotland Assembly.

There are 8 universities. Memorials of Robert Burns, Sir Walter Scott, John Knox, Mary, Queen of Scots draw many tourists, as do the beauties of the Trossachs, Loch Katrine, Loch Lomond and abbey ruins.

Industries. Engineering products are the most important industry, with growing emphasis on lighter products such as office machinery, autos, electronics and other consumer goods and less dependence on locomotives, ships, boilers, pumps, valves and other industrial machinery. Oil has been discovered offshore in the North Sea, stimulating on-shore support industries.

Scotland produces fine woolens, worsteds, tweeds; silks, fine linens and jute. It is known for its special breeds of cattle and sheep. Fisheries have large hauls of herring, cod, whiting Whisky is the biggest export.

Atomic projects produce plutonium and electrical energy at Dounreay, Chapelcross, Hunterston.

The Hebrides are a group of c. 500 islands, 100 inhabited, off the W coast. The Inner Hebrides include **Skye, Mull,** and **Iona,** the last famous for the arrival of St. Columba, 563 A.D. The Outer Hebrides include **Lewis** and **Harris.** Industries include sheep raising and weaving. **The Orkney Islands,** c. 90, are to the NE. The capital is Kirkwall, on Pomona Is. Fish curing, sheep raising and weaving are occupations. NE of the Orkneys are the 200 **Shetland Islands,** 24 inhabited, home of Shetland pony. The Orkneys and Shetlands have become centers for the North Sea oil industry.

Northern Ireland

Six of the 9 counties of Ulster, the NE corner of Ireland, constitute Northern Ireland, with the parliamentary boroughs of Belfast and Londonderry. The country has an area of 5,451 sq. mi. and a population (1975 est.) 1,537,000. Belfast is the capital and chief industrial center.

Industries. Shipbuilding, including large tankers, has long been an important industry, centered in Belfast, the largest port. Linen manufacture is also important, along with apparel, rope, and twine. Growing diversification has added engineering products, synthetic fibers, and electronics. There are large numbers of cattle, hogs, and sheep; potatoes, poultry, and dairy foods are also produced. There is an agricultural surplus, mostly shipped to England.

Government. An act of the British Parliament, 1920, divided Northern from Southern Ireland, each with a parliament and government. When Ireland became a dominion, 1921, and later a republic, Northern Ireland chose to remain a part of the United Kingdom. It elects 12 members to the British House of Commons.

During 1968-69, large demonstrations were conducted by Roman Catholics who charged they were discriminated against in voting rights, housing, and employment. The Catholics, a minority comprising about a third of the population, demanded abolition of property qualifications for voting in local elections. Violence and terrorism intensified, involving branches of the Irish Republican Army (outlawed in the Irish Republic), Protestant groups, police, and up to 15,000 British troops.

A succession of Northern Ireland prime ministers pressed reform programs but failed to satisfy extremists on both sides. Nearly 1,700 were killed in 8 years of bombings and shootings, some in England itself. Britain suspended the Northern Ireland parliament Mar. 30, 1972, and imposed direct British rule. A coalition government was formed in 1973 when moderates won election to a new one-house Assembly. But a Protestant general strike overthrew the government in 1974. Direct rule continued in 1977, after the failure of a constitutional convention to achieve a settlement.

Education and Religion. Northern Ireland is 2/3 Protestant, 1/3 Roman Catholic. Elementary education is compulsory through age 15. There are 2 universities and 24 technical colleges.

Channel Islands

The Channel Islands, area 75 sq. mi., est. pop. 1974 130,000, off the NW coast of France, the only parts of the one-time Dukedom of Normandy belonging to England, are **Jersey, Guernsey** and the dependencies of Guernsey — **Alderney, Brechou, Great Sark, Little Sark, Herm, Jethou and Lihou.** Jersey and Guernsey have separate legal existences and lieutenant governors named by the Crown. The islands were the only British soil occupied by German troops in World War II.

Isle of Man

The Isle of Man, area 227 sq. mi., est. 1974 pop. 60,000, is in the Irish Sea, 20 mi. from Scotland, 30 mi. from Cumberland. It is rich in lead and iron. The island has its own laws and a lt. gov. appointed by the Crown. The Tynwald (legislature) consists of the Legislative Council, partly elected, and House of Keys, elected. Capital: Douglas. Farming, tourism, fishing (kippers, scallops) are chief occupations. Man is famous for the Manx tailless cat.

Gibraltar

Gibraltar, a dependency on the southern coast of Spain, guards the entrance to the Mediterranean. The width of the strait dividing Europe from Africa varies from 7.75 mi. at the narrowest part to 23.75 at the widest. The Rock has been in British possession since 1704. There is a large harbor and a naval base. The Rock is 2.75 mi. long, 3/4 of a mi. wide and 1,396 ft. in height; a narrow isthmus connects it with the mainland. Est. pop. 1974: 30,000.

In 1966 Spain called on Britain to give "substantial sovereignty" of Gibraltar to Spain and imposed a partial blockade. In 1967, residents voted 12,138 for remaining under Britain, 44 for returning to Spain. A new constitution, May 30, 1969, gave an elected House of Assembly more control in domestic affairs. A UN General Assembly resolution requested Britain to end Gibraltar's colonial status by Oct. 1, 1969. No settlement has been reached.

British West Indies

Swinging in a vast arc from the coast of Venezuela NE, then N and NW toward Puerto Rico are the Windward and Leeward Islands, forming a coral and volcanic barrier sheltering the Caribbean from the open Atlantic. Many of the islands are self-governing British possessions. Universal suffrage was instituted 1951-54; ministerial systems were set up 1956-1960.

Moving northward from the southern end of the arc lie the British **Windward Islands: St. Vincent,** (1973 pop. 100,000, area 150 sq. mi., capital Kingstown), **St. Lucia** (1974 pop. 110,000, area 238 sq. mi., capital Castries) and **Dominica** (1974 pop. 70,000, area 290 sq. mi., capital Roseau).

Futher north, in the **Leeward Islands,** are **Montserrat** (1970 pop. 12,300, area 33 sq. mi., capital Plymouth), **Antigua** (1974 pop. 70,000, area 171 sq. mi., capital St. John's), and **St. Kitts (St. Christopher)-Nevis-Anguilla,** three islands (1974 pop. 70,000, area 138 sq. mi., capital Basseterre on St. Kitts). Nearby are the small **British Virgin Islands.**

Britain granted self-government to 5 of these islands and island groups in 1967-1969; each became an Associated State, with Britain controlling foreign affairs and defense. These were Antigua, Dominica, St. Lucia, the St. Kitts-Nevis-Anguilla Federation, and St. Vincent.

Anguilla declared its independence from St. Kitts June 16, 1967. A 1976 constitution provides for an autonomous elected government. Area is 35 sq. mi., pop. 5,000.

Sugar is the major crop of Antigua and St. Kitts; bananas are the main product of the Windwards; Dominica produces cocoa; Antigua, Montserrat, St. Kitts, and St. Vincent have Sea Island cotton; St. Vincent has arrowroot; Dominica grows citrus fruits. Imports include foods, clothing, machinery. Tourism is growing. Dominica tried in 1975 to suppress leftist terrorists.

The three **Cayman Islands,** a dependency, lie S of Cuba, NW of Jamaica. Population is 11,500 (1974), most of it on Grand Cayman. It is a free port; in the 1970s Grand Cayman became a tax-free refuge for foreign funds and branches of many Western banks were opened there in the 1970s. Total area: 93 sq. mi. Capital: Georgetown.

The **Turks and Caicos Islands,** at the SE end of the Bahama Islands, are a separate British possession. There are about 30 islands, only 6 inhabited, pop. est. 6,000, area 166 sq. mi., capital Grand Turk. Salt, crayfish and conch shells are the main exports.

Bermuda

Bermuda is a British dependency governed by a royal governor and an Assembly, the oldest legislative body among British dependencies. Capital is Hamilton.

It is a group of 360 small islands of coral formation, 20 inhabited, comprising 21 sq. mi. in the western Atlantic, 580 mi. E of North Carolina. Population, 1974, was 60,000 (about 63% of African descent). Density is high.

The Assembly dates from 1620. In elections May 22, 1968, the first on the basis of universal adult suffrage, the predominantly white United Bermuda party won 30 of the 40 Assembly seats (26 of 40 in 1976 elections); 16 of the 40 elected were blacks. A black, Sir Edward Richards, became prime minister in 1971. The Assembly runs local affairs. Bermuda adopted a dollar-decimal currency in 1970.

Gov. Richard Sharples and an aide were slain by gunmen in 1973. The police commissioner was shot to death in 1972.

The U.S. has air and naval bases under long-term lease, and a NASA tracking station.

Bermuda boasts many resort hotels, serving over 320,000 visitors a year. The government raises most revenue from import duties. Exports: lilies, drugs, cosmetics.

Belize

Belize (formerly called British Honduras) is in Central America facing the Caribbean to the E, with Mexico on the N and Guatemala on the W. Population (UN est. 1974) 140,000, area 8,866 sq. mi., capital Belmopan.

Internal self-government was granted by Britain in 1964.

The area has long been claimed by Guatemala, but also was promised independence by Britain. In Apr. 1968, a mediator proposed that British Honduras be made independent but have close association with Guatemala. The proposal was rejected by Belize. Britain moved several hundred troops to Belize in 1977 to counter Guatemalan "bellicosity."

Main export is sugar, along with citrus fruits, mahogany and other hardwoods, chicle, seafood.

South Atlantic

Falkland Islands and Dependencies, a British dependency, lies 300 mi. E of the Strait of Magellan at the southern end of South America.

The Falklands or Islas Malvinas include about 200 islands with an area of 4,618 sq. mi. and pop. (1976) of 1,905. Sheep-grazing is the main industry; wool is the principal export. There are indications of large oil and gas deposits. The islands are also claimed by Argentina. **South Georgia,** area 1,450 sq. mi., and the uninhabited **South Sandwich Islands** are dependencies of the Falklands.

British Antarctic Territory, south of 60° S lat., was made a separate colony in 1962 and comprises mainly the **South Shetland Islands,** the **South Orkneys** and **Graham's Land.** A chain of meteorological stations is maintained.

St. Helena, an island 1,200 mi. off the W coast of Africa and 1,800 E of South America, has 47 sq. mi. and est. pop., 1974 of 4,952. Flax, lace and rope making are the chief industries. After Napoleon Bonaparte was defeated at Waterloo the Allies exiled him to St. Helena, where he lived from Oct. 16, 1815, to his death, May 5, 1821. His remains were transferred to Paris in 1840. Capital is Jamestown.

Tristan da Cunha is the principal of a group of islands of volcanic origin, total area 40 sq. mi., half way between the Cape of Good Hope and South America. The other islands are inaccessible, Gough (or Diego Alvarez) and the 3 Nightingale Is. A volcanic peak 6,760 ft. high erupted in 1961. The 262 inhabitants were removed to England, but most returned in 1963. The islands are dependencies of St. Helena.

Ascension is an island of volcanic origin, 34 sq. mi. in area, 700 mi. NW of St. Helena, through which it is administered. It is a communications relay center for Britain, and has a U. S. satellite tracking center. Est. pop., 1971, was 1,232, half of them communications workers. The island is noted for sea turtles.

Asia and Indian Ocean

Brunei was between 1888 and 1971 a protected sultanate. It is on the N side of the Island of Borneo, between the Malaysian states of Sarawak and Sabah. Its area is 2,226 sq. mi., the size of Delaware, with population (1974 UN est.), 140,000, two-thirds Malay and indigenous races, one-third of Chinese descent.

A 1959 constitution was amended, 1965, to provide for general elections to the Legislative Council, some members of which are appointed. There is a sultan and a British high commissioner. A 1971 agreement gave Brunei full self-government, with Britain responsible for foreign affairs.

Brunei's rich Seria oilfield provides tax revenues well in excess of expenditures. Rubber is also exported. Some of the surplus has been spent on a growing program of schools and social services.

Hong Kong is a Crown Colony at the mouth of the Canton River in China, 90 mi. south of Canton. Its nucleus is Hong Kong Island, 35 1/2 sq. mi., acquired from China 1841, on which is located Victoria, the capital. Opposite is Kowloon Peninsula, 3 sq. mi. and Stonecutters Island, 1/4 sq. mi., added, 1860. An additional 355 sq. mi. known as the New Territories, comprised of a mainland area and islands, were leased from China, 1898, for 99 years. Total area of the colony is 391 sq. mi., with a population, 1975 est., of 4,440,000 including fewer than 20,000 British. From 1949 to 1962 Hong Kong absorbed more than a million refugees from the mainland. The flow of refugees continued, on a lesser scale, into the 1970's.

Hong Kong harbor was long an important British naval station and one of the world's great trans-shipment ports. Britain announced in 1975 a reduction of its garrison to 6,400 men.

Principal industries are textiles and apparel (52% of exports); also tourism, shipbuilding, iron and steel, fishing, cement, and small manufactures. Total exports exceeded $7 billion in 1976.

Spinning mills, among the best in the world, and low wages compete with textiles elsewhere and have resulted in protective measures in some countries. Hong Kong also has a booming electronics industry. The U. S. is the largest market for Hong Kong products.

During 1967 Communist China launched a campaign against British authority in Hong Kong, including demonstrations, strikes, riots, bombings, border incidents and slowdowns in supplying food. The campaign later subsided.

British Indian Ocean Territory was formed Nov. 1965, embracing islands formerly dependencies of Mauritius or Seychelles: the Chagos Archipelago (including Diego Garcia), Aldabra, Farquhar and Des Roches. The latter three were transferred to Seychelles, which became independent in 1976. Population, 558. In 1973 the U. S. Navy established a communications station on Diego Garcia and in 1975 began constructing a naval base. The USSR and Asian nations opposed the step.

Pacific Ocean

Pitcairn Island is in the Pacific, halfway between South America and Australia. The island was discovered in 1767 by Carteret but was not inhabited until 23 years later when the mutineers of the Bounty landed there. The area is 18 sq. mi. and population, 1974, was 78. It is a British colony and is administered by a British Representative in New Zealand and a local Council. The uninhabited islands of **Henderson, Ducie** and **Oeno** are in the Pitcairn group.

The **British Solomon Islands,** a protectorate, were scheduled to become independent in 1977. *(See Index for Solomon Islands.)*

The Gilbert Islands were proclaimed a protectorate in 1892. Self-government was granted in 1971. The dependency includes the **Gilbert Islands** (16), **Phoenix Islands, Ocean Island, Line Islands,** composed of **Fanning, Washington** and **Christmas Islands,** the last the largest atoll in the Pacific (also claimed by the U. S.). The total area is 264 sq. mi. and the population, 1973 census, 52,000. Exports: chiefly copra and phosphates.

Tuvalu, formerly called the Ellice Islands, was separated from Gilbert Islands administration, 1976; its 9 islands have an area of 10 sq. mi., pop. (1976) 7,000.

New Hebrides, a condominium jointly administered since 1906 by Great Britain and France, is a group of 11 main islands and about 69 islets lying 500 mi. W of Fiji, with an aggregate area of 5,790 sq. mi. Population, 1976, 100,000, mostly Melanesian. Chief products are copra, cotton, cocoa, fish and coffee. British and French resident commissioners are joint heads of the administration; representative bodies were elected in 1975. **Banks** (309 sq. mi.) and **Torres** (40 sq. mi.) **Islands,** with pop. of 2,640, are attached to the New Hebrides for administration.

United States

(See Index for listings)

Upper Volta

Republic of Upper Volta

People: Population (1976 est.): 6,170,000. **Pop. density:** 58 per sq. mi. **Ethnic groups:** Voltaic groups (Mossi, Bobo), Mande. **Languages:** French (official), More, Sudanic tribal languages. **Religions:** Moslems 20%, Roman Catholics 5%, others.

Geography: Area: 105,869 sq. mi., the size of Colorado. **Location:** In W. Africa, S of the Sahara. **Neighbors:** Mali on NW, Niger on NE, Benin, Togo, Ghana, Ivory Coast on S. **Topography:** Landlocked Upper Volta is in the savannah region of W Africa. The N is arid, hot, and thinly populated. **Capital:** Ouagadougou. **Cities** (1970 est.): Ouagadougou 110,000; Bobo-Dioulasso 78,478.

Government: Head of state: Pres. Sangoule Lamizana, b. 1916, in office: Jan. 3, 1966. **Local divisions:** 10 departments. **Armed forces:** regulars 3,050; para-military 2,850.

Economy: Chief Crops: Cotton, rice, peanuts, karite, grain, corn. **Minerals:** Manganese, gold, diamonds. **Per capita arable land:** 2.2 acres. **Livestock** (1974): 1,600,000 cattle; 120,000 pigs; 1,000,000 sheep; livestock yields 50% of exports. **Electricity production** (1974): 12.9 mln. kwh. **Labor force:** 89% agric.

Finance: Currency: CFA Franc (Apr. 1977: 248 = $1 US). **Gross domestic product** (est. 1974: $420 mln. **Per capita income** (1974): $67. **Imports** (1975) $151 mln.; partners (1972): Fr. 54%, Ivory C. 17%., W. Ger. 5%, Mali 4%. **Exports** (1975): $44 mln.; partners (1972): Ivory C. 46%, Fr. 19%, It. 7%, Ghana 5%. **Tourists** (1974): 10,700; receipts (1973): $2 million. **Balance of payments** (1974): $15.5 mln. **International reserves** (Jan. 1977): $68.6 mln. **Consumer prices** (change in 1976): 8.1%.

Transport: Motor vehicles: in use (1974): 8,800 passenger cars, 9,300 commercial vehicles.

Communications: Television sets: 6,000 licenses (1972). **Radios:** 100,000 licenses (1973). **Daily newspaper circulation** (1973): 2,000; 0.4 per 1,000 pop.

Health: Life expectancy at birth (1960-61): 32.1 male; 31.1 female. **Births** (annual per 1,000 pop. 1970-75): 48.5. **Deaths** (annual per 1,000 pop. 1970-75): 25.8. **Natural increase** (annual 1970-75): 2.27%. **Pop. per hospital bed** (1973): 1,221. **Pop. per physician** (1973): 59,792. **Infant mortality** (per 1,000 pop. under 1 yr. 1960-61): 182.

Education: Literacy (1973): 5%. **Pop. 5-19:** in school (1973): 5%; per teacher (1973): 515.

The Mossi tribe entered the area in the 11th to 13th centuries. Their kingdoms ruled until defeated by the Mali and Songhai empires.

French control came by 1896, but Upper Volta was not finally established as a separate territory until 1947. Full independence came Aug. 5, 1960, and a pro-French government was elected. A 1966 coup established the current regime.

Several hundred thousand farm workers migrate each year to Ivory Coast and Ghana. A long drought brought famine in 1973-74.

Uruguay

Oriental Republic of Uruguay

People: Population (1976 est.): 3,100,000. **Age distrib.** (%): 0-14: 28; 15-59: 59.3; 60+: 12.7. **Pop. density:** 45 per sq. mi. **Ethnic groups:** Caucasians (Iberians Italians) 90%, mestizos 5-10%, mulatto and Negro 3-5%. **Languages:** Spanish. **Religions:** Roman Catholics 66%, Jews 2%, Protestants 2%. **Geography: Area:** 68,548 sq. mi., the size of Washington State. **Location:** In southern S. America, on the Atlantic O. **Neighbors:** Argentina on W, Brazil on N. **Topography:** Uruguay is composed or rolling, grassy plains and hills, well-watered by rivers flowing W to Uruguay R. **Capital:** Montevideo. **Cities:** (1975 cen.): Montevideo 1,229,748.

Government: Head of state: Pres. Aparicio Mendez, b. 1904, in office: Sept. 1, 1976. **Local divisions:** 19 departments. **Armed forces:** regulars 23,000; para-military 22,000.

Economy: Industries: Meat-packing, metals, textiles, wine, cement, oil products. **Chief Crops:** Corn, wheat, citrus fruits, rice, oats, linseed. **Per capita arable land:** 1.4 acres. **Livestock** (1976): 11,500,000 cattle; 418,000 pigs; 15,000,000 sheep; 7,200,000 poultry; 70% of area is devoted to stock; meat, wool yield most exports. **Fish catch** (1974): 16,000 metric tons. **Electricity production** (1973): 2,500 mln. kwh. **Labor force** 17% agric.

Finance: Currency: Peso (Feb. 1977: 4.21=$1 US). **Gross domestic product** (1975): $3.53 bln. **Per capita income** (1975): $1,091. **Imports** (1975) $556 mln.; partners (1973): Arg. 21%, Braz. 16%, U.S. 9%, Nigeria 7%. **Exports** (1975): $384 mln.; partners (1973): W. Ger. 14%, Sp. 12%, It. 8%, Neth. 7%. **Tourists** (1974): 587,600; receipts: $45 million. **Balance of payments** (1975): $-88.4 mln. **National budget** (1975): $433 mln. revenues; $580 mln. expenditures. **International reserves** (Dec. 1977): $315 mln. **Consumer prices** (change in 1975): 83.4%.

Transport: Railway traffic (1974): 219 mln. passenger-miles; 148 mln. net ton-miles. **Motor vehicles:** in use (1974): 151,600 passenger cars, 85,700 commercial vehicles. **Civil aviation:** 49 mln. passenger-miles (1975); 60,000 freight ton-miles (1975). **Chief ports:** Montevideo.

Communications: Television sets: 305,000 in use (1973). **Radios:** 1,500,000 in use (1973). **Telephones in use** (1976): 249,655. **Daily newspaper circulation** (1973): 960,000.

Health: Life expectancy at birth (1963-64): 65.51 male; 71.56 female. **Births** (per 1,000 pop. 1972): 20.9. **Deaths** (per 1,000 pop. 1972): 9.6. **Natural increase** (1972): 1.13%. **Pop. per hospital bed** (1973): 193. **Pop. per physician** (1973): 879. **Infant mortality** (per 1,000 pop. under 1 yr. 1972): 45.4.

Education: Literacy (1973): 91%. **Pop. 5-19:** in school (1973): 55%; per teacher (1973): 30.

Spanish settlers did not begin replacing the indigenous Charrua Indians until 1624. Portuguese from Brazil arrived later, but Uruguay was attached to the Spanish Viceroyalty of Rio de la Plata in the 18th century. Rebels sought against Spain beginning in 1810. An independent republic was declared Aug. 25, 1825, and recognized by Argentina and Brazil three years later.

Liberal governments adopted socialist measures as far back as 1911. More than a third of the workers are employed by the state, which owns the power, telephone, railroad, cement, oil-refining and other industries. Social welfare programs are among the most advanced in the world.

Uruguay's standard of living was one of the highest in South America, and political and labor conditions among the freest. Economic stagnation, inflation, plus floods, drought and a cold wave in 1967 and a general strike in 1968 brought attempts by the government to strengthen the economy through a series of devaluations of the peso and wage and price controls. But inflation continued. The cost of living rose 1,200% between 1968 and 1976.

Leftist guerrillas, drawn from the upper classes and called Tupamaros, increased terrorist actions in 1970; a U.S. police adviser was slain in Aug. In 1971 the guerrillas kidnaped and, after 8 months, freed the British ambassador. Violence continued and in Feb. 1973 President Juan Maria Bordaberry agreed to military control of his administration. In June he abolished Congress and set up a Council of State in its place. By 1974 the military had apparently defeated the Tupamaros, using severe repressive measures, including mass arrests and torture, according to many reports. The economic decline continued. Bordaberry was removed by the military in a 1976 coup.

Vatican

State of the Vatican City

People: Population (1976 est.): 1,000. **Ethnic groups:** Italians, Swiss. **Languages:** Italian, Latin. **Religions:** Roman Catholicism.

Geography: Area: 108.7 acres. **Location:** In Rome, Italy. **Neighbors:** Completely surrounded by Italy.

Finance: Currency: Italian Lira.

The popes for many centuries, with brief interruptions, held temporal sovereignty over mid-Italy (the so-called Papal States), comprising an area of some 16,000 sq. mi., with a population in the 19th century of more than 3 million. This territory was incorporated in the new Kingdom of Italy, the sovereignty of the pope being confined to the palaces of the Vatican and the Lateran in Rome and the villa of Castel Gandolfo, by an Italian law, May 13, 1871. This law also guaranteed to the pope and his successors a yearly indemnity of over $620,000. This allowance, however, remained unclaimed.

A Treaty of Conciliation, a concordat and a financial convention were signed Feb. 11, 1929, by Cardinal Gasparri and Premier Mussolini. The documents established the independent state of Vatican City, and gave the Catholic religion special status in Italy. The treaty (Lateran Agreement) was made part of the Constitution of Italy (Article 7) in 1947. Italy and the Vatican reached preliminary agreement in 1976 on revisions of the concordat, that would eliminate required religious education in Italian schools.

Vatican City includes St. Peter's, the Vatican Palace and Museum covering over 13 acres, the Vatican gardens, and neighboring buildings between Viale Vaticano and the Church. Thirteen buildings in Rome, outside the boundaries, enjoy extraterritorial rights; these buildings house congregations or officers necessary for the administration of the Holy See.

The legal system is based on the code of canon law, the apostolic constitutions and the laws especially promulgated for the Vatican City by the pope. In cases not covered the Italian law of Rome applies. The Secretariat of State represents the Holy See in its diplomatic relations. By the Treaty of Conciliation the pope is pledged to a perpetual neutrality unless his mediation is specifically requested. This, however, does not prevent the defense of the Church whenever it is persecuted. A total of 84 nations maintain diplomatic representatives in Vatican City. The U.S. does not have an official ambassador.

The present sovereign of the State of Vatican City is the Supreme Pontiff Paul VI, Giovanni Battista Montini, born in Concesio, Italy, Sept. 26, 1897, elected June 21, 1963, in succession to Angelo Giuseppe Roncalli, John XXIII, who died June 3, 1963.

Venezuela

Republic of Venezuela

People: Population (1976 est.): 12,360,000. **Age distrib.** (%): 0-14: 44.6; 15-59: 50.6; 60+: 4.7. **Pop. density:** 35 per sq. mi. **Urban** (1975): 74.4%. **Ethnic groups:** Mestizo 70%, white (Spanish, Portuguese, Italian) 20%, Negro 8%, Indian 2%. **Languages:** Spanish, Indian languages 2%. **Religions:** Roman Catholics 96%, Protestants 2%.

Geography: Area: 352,143 sq. mi., more than twice the size of California. **Location:** On the Caribbean coast of S. America. **Neighbors:** Colombia on W, Brazil on S, Guyana on E. **Topography:** The flat coastal plain and Orinoco Delta are bordered by Andes Mtns. and hills. Plains, called llanos, extend between mountains and Orinoco. Guyana Highlands and plains are S of Orinoco, which stretches 1,700 mi. and drains 80% of Venezuela. **Capital:** Caracas. **Cities** (1971 cen.): Caracas (met.) 2,175,400; Maracaibo 651,574; Valencia 367,171.

Government: Head of state: Pres. Carlos Andres Perez, b. Oct. 27, 1922, in office: Mar. 12, 1974. **Local divisions:** 20

states, 2 federal territories, federal district, all with elected legislators. **Armed forces:** regulars 42,000; para-military 10,000.

Economy: Industries: Steel, oil products, textiles, containers, tobacco, paper, tires, shoes. **Chief crops:** Coffee, cocoa, fruits, sugar. **Minerals:** Oil (5th largest producer), iron (extensive reserves and production), gold, copper, salt, coal, nickel, manganese, asbestos, diamond, mica. **Crude oil output** (1976): 840 mln. bbls., 5th largest producer in 1976. **Per capita arable land:** 0.9 acres. **Livestock** (1976): 9,362,000 cattle; 2,040,000 pigs; 101,000 sheep; 24,606,000 poultry. **Fish catch** (1974): 162,400 metric tons. **Electricity production** (1973): 16,392 mln. kwh. **Labor force:** 20% agric.; 19% manuf.

Finance: Currency: Bolivar (Apr. 1977: 4.29 = $1 US). **Gross domestic product** (1975): $29.0 bln. **Per capita income** (1975): $2,035. **Imports** (1976): $6.698 bln.; partners (1973): U.S. 42%, W. Ger. 13%, Jap. 8%. **Exports** (1976): $8.672 bln.; partners (1973): U.S. 57%, Can. 17%, U.K. 4%. **Tourists** (1974): 614,700; receipts: $176 million. **Balance of payments** (1976): -$286 mln. **National budget** (1974): $9.93 bln. revenues; $9.11 bln. expenditures. **International reserves** (Feb. 1977): $8.590 bln. **Consumer prices** (change in 1976): 7.6%.

Transport: Railway traffic (1971): 26 mln. passenger-miles; 9 mln. net ton-miles. **Motor vehicles:** in use (1971): 601,100 passenger cars, 208,200 commercial vehicles; assembled (1973): 56,000 passenger cars, 3,000 commercial vehicles. **Civil aviation:** 1,408 mln. passenger-miles (1975); 45 mln. freight ton-miles (1975). **Chief ports:** Maracaibo, La Guaira, Puerto Cabello.

Communications: Television sets: 995,000 in use (1973); 86,000 manufactured (1972). **Radios:** 2,000,000 in use (1973); 74,00 manufactured (1972). **Telephones in use** (1976): 649,-603. **Daily newspaper circulation** (1973): 963,000.

Health: Life expectancy at birth (1961): 66.41 (both sexes). **Births** (annual per 1,000 pop. 1970-75): 36.1 **Deaths** (annual per 1,000 pop. 1970-75): 7.0. **Natural increase** (annual 1970-75): 2.90%. **Pop. per hospital bed** (1973): 344. **Pop. per physican** (1973): 925. **Infant mortality** (per 1,000 pop. under 1 yr. 1974): 46.0.

Education: Literacy (1973): 82%. **Pop. 5-19:** in school (1973): 54%; per teacher (1973): 48.

Columbus first set foot on the South American continent on the peninsula of Paria, Aug. 1498. Alonso de Ojeda, 1499, found Lake Maracaibo, called the land Venezuela, or Little Venice, because natives had houses on stilts. Venezuela was under Spanish domination until 1821. The republic was formed after succession from the Colombian Federation in 1830.

Military governments ruled Venezuela for most of the 20th century. They promoted the oil industry; some social reforms were implemented. Since 1959, the country has enjoyed progressive, democratically-elected governments.

Venezuela helped found the Organization of Petroleum Exporting States (OPEC). On Jan. 1, 1976, the government nationalized the oil industry with compensation. Development has begun of the Orinoco tar belt, believed to contain the world's largest oil reserves. Iron ore production was nationalized Jan. 1, 1975.

Construction is booming, including a new $3.8 billion city, Ciudad Guyana, 300 mi. SE of Caracas. Oil profits help finance the extensive industrial development. Government efforts at income redistribution were thwarted by inflation in 1974-5.

Several hundred thousand legal and illegal Columbian migrants work in Venezuela. European immigration has also been high.

Vietnam

Socialist Republic of Vietnam

People: Population (1976 est.): 46,520,000. **Pop. density:** 368 per sq. mi. **Urban** (1973) (South only): 30.4%. **Ethnic groups:** Vietnamese 80%, Khmer, Tais, Montagnards, Tays, Muong, Nung. **Languages:** Vietnamese, others. **Religions:** Buddhism and Taoism most numerous, Roman Catholics 5%, Dao Dai, Hoa Hao.

Geography: Area: 126,436 sq. mi., the size of New Mexico. **Location:** On the E coast of the Indochinese Peninsula in SE Asia. **Neighbors:** China on N, Laos, Cambodia on W. **Topography:** Vietnam is long and narrow, with a 1,400-mi. coast. About 24% of country is readily arable, including the densely settled Red R. valley in the N, narrow coastal plains in center, and the wide, often marshy Mekong R Delta in the S. The rest consists of semi-arid plateaus and barren mountains, with some stretches of tropical rain forest. **Capital:** Hanoi. **Cities** (1973 est.): Saigon 1,825,297; Danang 492,194; (1960 cen.): Hanoi (met.) 643,576; Haiphong (met.) 369,248.

Government: Head of state: Pres. Ton Duc Thang, b. 1888, in office: Sept. 23, 1969; **Head of government:** Premier Pham Van Dong, b. 1906, in office: Sept. 20, 1955; **Head of Communist Party:** First Sec. Le Duan, b. 1907, in office: Sept. 1960. **Local divisions:** 24 provinces. **Armed forces:** Regulars 615,-000; para-military 1,550,000.

Economy: Industries: Food processing, textiles, paper. **Chief crops:** Rice, corn, sugar cane, sweet potatoes, coffee, tea, cotton, manioc, tobacco. **Minerals:** Coal, iron, manganese, bauxite, apatite, chromate, phosphates. **Other resources:** Forests. **Per capita arable land:** 0.3 acres. **Livestock** (1974): 1,753,000 cattle; 12,141,000 pigs; 93,000,000 poultry. **Fish catch** (1972): 678,000 metric tons (in South, the major fishing area). **Electricity production** (1975): 1,320 mln. kwh. **Labor force:** 76% agric.

Finance: Currency: Dong (1974: 2.40 = $1 US). **Per capita income** (1974): $130. **Imports** (1974) $616 mln. **Exports** (1974): $58 mln. **Tourists** (South only) (1973): 79,200; receipts (1974): $16 million.

Transport: Railway traffic (South only) (1973): 106 mln. passenger-miles; 1 mln. net ton-miles. **Motor vehicles:** in use (South only) (1974): 70,000 passenger cars, 100,000 commercial vehicles. **Chief ports:** Saigon, Haiphong, Da Nang, Cam Raph.

Communications: Television sets: 500,000 in use (South only) (1973). **Radios:** 1,550,000 in use (South only) (1973); 87,000 assembled (South only) (1973). **Daily newspaper circulation** (1973) (South only): 412,000; 21 per 1,000 pop.

Health (Most figures are for North only) **Life expectancy at birth** (1970-75): 46.6 male; 49.5 female. **Births** (annual per 1,000 pop. 1970-75): 41.4. **Deaths** (annual per 1,000 pop. 1970-75): 17.9. **Natural increase** (annual 1970-75): 2.35%. **Pop. per hospital bed** (1973): 490. **Pop. per physician** (1973): 11,700. **Infant mortality** (per 1,000 pop. under 1 yr. 1973): 150.

Education: Literacy (1973): 68%. **Pop. 5-19:** in school (1973): 50%; per teacher (1973): 89.

Vietnam's recorded history began in Tonkin before the Christian era. Settled by Viets from central China, Vietnam was held by China, 111 B.C.-939 A.D., and was a vassal state during subsequent periods. Vietnam defeated the armies of Kublai Khan, 1288. Conquest by France began in 1858 and ended in 1884 with protectorate status.

In 1940 Vietnam was occupied by Japan; during the occupation nationalist aims gathered force. A number of groups formed the Vietminh (Independence) League, headed by Ho Chi Minh, communist guerrilla leader. In Aug. 1945 the Vietminh forced out Bao Dai, former emperor of Annam, head of a regime sponsored by Japan. France, seeking to reestablish colonial control, battled communist and nationalist forces, 1946-1954, and was finally defeated at Dienbienphu, May 8, 1954. Meanwhile, on July 1, 1949, Bao Dai had formed a State of Vietnam, with himself as chief of state, with French approval. Communist China backed Ho Chi Minh.

A cease-fire accord signed in Geneva July 21, 1954, divided Vietnam along the Ben Hai River. It provided for a buffer zone, withdrawal of French troops from the North and elections to determine the country's future. Under the agreement the communists gained control of territory north of the 17th parallel, 22 provinces with area of 62,000 sq. mi. and 13 million pop., with its capital at Hanoi and Ho Chi Minh as president. South Vietnam came to comprise the 39 southern provinces with approx. area of 65,000 sq. mi. and pop. of 12 million. Some 900,000 North Vietnamese fled to South Vietnam. Neither South Vietnam nor the U.S. signed the agreement.

On Oct. 26, 1955, Ngo Dinh Diem, premier of the interim government of South Vietnam, proclaimed the Republic of Vietnam and became its first president.

The Democratic Republic of Vietnam, established in the North, adopted a constitution Dec. 31, 1959, based on communist principles and calling for reunification of all Vietnam. President Ho Chi Minh, re-elected July 15, 1960, by unanimous vote of the National Assembly, had held office since 1945. He died Sept. 3, 1969.

North Vietnam sought to take over South Vietnam beginning in 1954. Fighting persisted from 1956, with the communist Vietcong, aided by North Vietnam, pressing war in the South and South Vietnam receiving U.S. aid. Northern aid to Vietcong guerrillas was intensified in 1959, and large-scale troop infiltration began in 1964, with Russian and Chinese arms assistance. Large Northern forces were stationed in border areas of Laos and Cambodia.

A serious political conflict arose in the South in 1963 when Buddhists denounced authoritarianism and brutality. This paved the way for a military coup Nov. 1-2, 1963, which overthrew Diem.

Several military coups followed. In elections Sept. 3, 1967, Chief of State Nguyen Van Thieu was chosen president.

In 1964, the U.S. began air strikes against North Vietnam. Beginning in 1965, the raids were stepped up and U.S. troops became combatants. U.S. troop strength in Vietnam, which reached a high of 543,400 in Apr. 1969, was ordered reduced by U.S. President Nixon in a series of withdrawals, beginning in June 1969. U.S. bombings were resumed in 1972-73.

A ceasefire agreement was signed in Paris Jan. 27, 1973 (EST), by the U.S., North and South Vietnam, and the Vietcong. It was never implemented. U.S. aid was curbed in 1974 by the U.S. Congress. Heavy fighting continued for two years throughout Indochina.

Massive numbers of North Vietnamese troops, aided by tanks, launched attacks against remaining government outposts in the Central Highlands in the first months of 1975. Government retreats turned into a rout, and the Saigon regime surrendered April 30. Conquest of the country was effectively completed within days.

A Provisional Revolutionary Government assumed control, aided by officials and technicians from Hanoi, and first steps were taken to transform society along communist lines. All businesses and farms were to be collectivized by 1979.

The U.S. accepted over 165,000 Vietnamese fleeing the new regime, while tens of thousands more sought refuge in other countries.

The war's toll included — Combat deaths: U.S. 46,079; South Vietnam over 200,000; other allied forces 5,225. Civilian casualties were over a million. Displaced war refugees in South Vietnam totaled over 6.5 million.

After the fighting ended, eight Northern divisions remained stationed in the South, while Southern forces of over 900,000 were demobilized, adding to severe economic problems. Some urban residents were resettled in the countryside, the first of 7 million scheduled for resettlement, according to the government; an unknown number were sent to long-term re-education camps, including thousands of adherents of the Hoa Hao sect. Some military resistance against the new regime was periodically reported.

The first National Assembly representing both parts of the country met June 24, 1976. The country was officially reunited July 2, 1976. The former North Vietnamese capital, flag, anthem, emblem, and currency were applied to the new state.

Nearly all major government posts went to officials of the former Northern government.

The U.S. agreed in 1977 not to bar Vietnam's membership in the UN.

Western Samoa

See Samoa

Yemen

Yemen Arab Republic

People: Population (1976 est.): 6,870,000. **Pop. density:** 91 per sq. mi. **Ethnic groups:** Arabs, some Negroids. **Languages:** Arabic. **Religions:** Sunni Moslems 50%, Shiite Moslems 50%.

Geography: Area: 75,289 sq. mi., slightly smaller than South Dakota. **Location:** On the southern Red Sea coast of the Arabian Peninsula. **Neighbors:** Saudi Arabia on N.E., South Yemen Canada, W. Germany, India, Mauritius, Venezuela to well-watered fertile mountains in interior. **Capital:** Sana. **Cities** (1970 est.): Sana 120,000.

Government: Head of state: Chmn. Ibrahim M. al-Hamadi, b. 1943, in office: June 13, 1974; **Head of government:** Prime Min. Abdulaziz Abdulghani, in office: Jan. 15, 1975. **Local divisions:** 7 provinces. **Armed forces:** Regulars 39,000; para-military 20,000.

Economy: Industries: Textiles, cement. **Chief crops:** Coffee, cotton, gat (narcotic shrub), grain, dates, cotton, sesame, herbs, fruits. **Minerals:** Salt. **Per capita arable land:** 0.4 acres. **Livestock** (1974): 1,000,000 cattle; 3,100,000 sheep. **Electricity production** (1970): 6.2 mln. kwh. **Labor force:** 73% agric.

Finance: Currency: Rial (Apr. 1977: 4.56 = $1 US). **Gross domestic product** (1973): $804 mln. **Per capita income** (1973); $126. **Imports** (1976): $413 mln.; partners (1974): Jap. 15%, P.R. China 7%, W. Ger. 6%, Saudi Ar. 5%. **Exports** (1976): $8 mln.; partners (1974): Jap. 42%, P.R. China 20%, S. Yemen 10%, Somalia 8%. **Balance of payments** (1976): $373 mln. **International reserves** (Feb. 1977): $807.26 mln. **Transport: Chief ports:** Al-Hudaydah, Al-Mukha.

Communications: Daily newspaper circulation (1970): 56,000; 10 per 1,000 pop.

Health: Life expectancy at birth (1970-75): 43.7 male; 45.9 female. **Births** (annual per 1,000 pop. 1970-75): 49.6. **Deaths** (annual per 1,000 pop. 1970-75): 20.6. **Natural increase** (annual 1970-75): 2.90%. **Pop. per hospital bed** (1973): 1,479. **Pop. per physician** (1973): 25,347. **Infant mortality** (per 1,000 pop. under 1 yr. 1973): 152.

Education: Literacy (1973): 10%. **Pop. 5-19:** in school (1973): 9%; per teacher (1973): 470.

Yemen's territory once was part of the ancient kingdom of Sheba, or Saba, a prosperous link in trade between Africa and India. A Biblical reference speaks of its gold, spices and precious stones as gifts borne by the Queen of Sheba to King Solomon.

Yemen became independent in 1918, after years of Ottoman Turkish rule, but remained politically and economically backward. Imam Ahmed ruled 1948-1962. The king was reported assassinated Sept. 26, 1962, and a revolutionary group headed by Brig. Gen. Abdullah al-Salal declared the country to be the Yemen Arab Republic.

The Imam Ahmed's heir, the Imam Mohamad al-Badr, fled to the mountains where tribesmen joined royalist forces; internal warfare between them and the republican forces continued. Egyptian president Nasser sent 70,000 troops to aid the republicans; Saudi Arabia supported the royalists with military aid. About 150,000 people were killed in the fighting.

After Egypt's defeat in the June 1967 Israeli-Arab war, Egypt announced it would withdraw its troops from Yemen; the last of them left Nov. 29, 1967, and Saudi Arabia said it would stop aiding the royalists.

This was accompanied by a bloodless coup Nov. 5, 1967. Fighting continued between the republican and royalist forces. Saudi Arabia announced in Feb. 1968 it was renewing its aid to the royalists, charging that both Russia and Syria, as well as Southern Yemen, were aiding the republicans.

In April 1970 hostilities ended with an agreement between Yemen and Saudi Arabia and appointment of several royalists to the Yemen government.

There were border skirmishes with forces of the People's Democratic Republic of Yemen in 1972-73. The U.S. and Yemen in 1972 resumed diplomatic relations, broken by Yemen after the 1967 Arab-Israeli war.

On June 13, 1974, an Army group, led by Col Ibrahim al-Hamidi, seized the government.

There are periodic droughts. Per capita GNP is among the lowest in the world. A prolonged drought has forced imports of food. The remittances from 400,000 Yemens living in Arab oil countries provide most of foreign earnings.

South Yemen

People's Democratic Republic of Yemen

People: Population (1976 est.): 1,750,000. **Age distrib.** (%): 0-14: 47.8; 15-59: 45.6; 60+: 6.6 **Pop. density:** 16 per sq. mi. **Urban** (1973): 33.3%. **Ethnic groups:** Arabs 75%, Indians 11%, Somalis 8%, others. **Languages:** Arabic. **Religions:** Moslems (Sunni) 91%, Christians 4%, Hindus 3.5%.

Geography: Area: 112,000 sq. mi., the size of Nevada. **Location:** On the southern coast of the Arabian Peninsula. **Neighbors:** Yemen on W, Saudi Arabia on N, Oman on E. **Topography:** The entire country is very hot and very dry. A sandy coast rises to mountains which give way to desert sands. **Capital:** Aden. **Cities** (1973 est.): Aden (met.) 285,373.

Government: Head of state: Chmn. Salem Robaye Ali, b. 1934, in office: June 23, 1969; **Head of government:** Prime Min. Ali Nasser Mohammed Hassani, in office: 1971. **Local divisions:** 6 governorates. **Armed forces:** regulars 21,300.

Economy: Industries: Transshipment. **Chief crops:** Cotton (main export), grains. **Per capita arable land:** 0.4 acres. **Livestock** (1974): 99,000 cattle; 230,000 sheep. **Fish catch** (1974):

133,500 metric tons. **Electricity production** (1973): 174 mln. kwh. **Labor force:** 62% agric.

Finance: Currency: Dinar (Apr. 1977: 1 = $2.90 US). **Gross domestic product** (est. 1974): $250 mln. **Per capita income** (1974): $140. **Imports** (1975): $312 mln.; partners (1972): Kuw.18%, Iran 11%, U.K. 7%, Jap. 7%. **Exports** (1975): $187 mln.; partners (1972): Jap. 12%, U.K. 9%, Thai. 8%, U.A.E. 7%. **Tourist receipts** (1973): $1 million. **Balance of payments** (1974): $-24.3 mln. **National budget** (1975): $40.1 mln. revenues; $74.0 mln. expenditures. **International reserves** (Nov. 1976): $122.93 mln. **Consumer prices** (change in 1976): 3.9%.

Transport: Motor vehicles: in use (1973): 10,600 passenger cars, 7,900 commercial vehicles. **Chief ports:** Aden.

Communications: Television sets: 26,000 in use (1973). **Radios:** 525,000 in use (1973). **Daily newspaper circulation** (1972): 2,000; 1 per 1,000 pop.

Health: Life expectancy at birth (1970-75): 43.7 male; 45.9 female. **Births** (annual per 1,000 pop. 1970-75): 49.6. **Deaths** (annual per 1,000 pop. 1970-75): 20.6. **Natural increase** (annual 1970-75): 2.90%. **Pop. per hospital bed** (1973): 1,114. **Pop. per physician** (1973): 10,400. **Infant mortality** (per 1,000 pop. under 1 yr. 1973): 152.

Education: Literacy (1973): 10%. **Pop. 5-19:** in school (1973): 35%; per teacher (1973): 66.

Aden, mentioned in the Bible, has been a port for trade in incense, spices and silk between the East and West for 2,000 years. British rule began in 1839. Aden provided Britain with a controlling position at the southern entrance to the Red Sea.

A war for independence began in 1963. The National Liberation Front (NLF) and the Egypt-supported Front for the Liberation of Occupied South Yemen, waged a guerrilla war against the British and local dynastic rulers. The 2 groups vied with each other for control. The NLF won out. Independence came Nov. 30, 1967. In 1969, the left wing of the NLF seized power and inaugurated a thorough nationalization of the economy.

The new government broke off relations with the U.S. and nationalized some foreign firms. Aid has been furnished by the USSR and China, with the USSR supplying most military aid.

In 1972-73 there were border skirmishes with forces of the Yemen Arab Republic. South Yemen aided leftist guerrillas in neighboring Oman. Relations with Saudi Arabia have improved.

The Port of Aden is the country's most valuable resource, but with the closing of the Suez Canal after the Israeli-Arab War in June 1967, the port lost much of its business. Local products exported are cotton, fish, coffee, hides. The canal was reopened in 1975.

Socotra, the largest island in the Arabian Sea, Kamaran, an island in the Red Sea near the coast of North Yemen, and Perim, an island in the strait between the Gulf of Aden and the Red Sea, are controlled by South Yemen.

Yugoslavia

Socialist Federal Republic of Yugoslavia

People: Population (1976): 21,560,000. **Age distrib.** (%): 0-14: 26.6; 15-59: 61.0; 60+: 12.5. **Pop. density:** 218 per sq. mi. **Urban** (1971): 38.6%. **Ethnic groups:** Serbs 40%, Croats 23%, Slovenes 8.6%, Macedonians 5.6%, Bosnian Moslems 5%, Albanians 5%, Montenegrin Serbs 2%, Hungarians 2%, Turks 1%. **Languages:** Serbo-Croatian, Macedonian, Slovene all official. **Religions:** Orthodox 50%, Roman Catholics 30%, Moslems 10%, Protestants 1%.

Geography: Area: 98,766 sq. mi., the size of Wyoming. **Location:** On the Adriatic coast of the Balkan Peninsula in SE Europe. **Neighbors:** Italy on W, Austria, Hungary on N, Romania, Bulgaria on E, Greece, Albania on S. **Topography:** The Dinaric Alps run parallel to the Adriatic coast, which is lined by offshore islands. Plains stretch across N and E river basins. S and NW are mountainous. **Capital:** Belgrade. **Cities** (1971 cen.): Belgrade (met.) 774,744; Zagreb 566,224; Skoplje 312,980.

Government: Head of state: Pres. Josip Broz Tito, b. May 25, 1892, in office: Jan. 14, 1953; **Head of government:** Prime Min. Veselin Djuranovic, b. May 17, 1925, in office: Mar. 15, 1977; **Head of Communist Party:** Pres. Josip Broz Tito, in office: 1937. **Local divisions:** 6 republics: Serbia, Croatia, Slovenia, Bosnia-Herzegovina, Macedonia, Montenegro; 2 autonomous provinces: Vojvodina, Kosovo. **Armed forces:** regulars 250,000; reserves 500,000.

Economy: Industries: Steel, chemicals, wood products, cement, textiles. **Chief crops:** Corn, grains, tobacco, hops, fruits, sugar beets, sunflower, tourism. **Minerals:** Coal, iron, copper, chrome, manganese, lead, zinc, mercury, salt, bauxite. **Per capita arable land:** 0.8 acres. **Livestock** (1976): 5,798,000 cattle; 6,539,000 pigs; 7,915,000 sheep; 55,000,000 poultry. **Fish catch** (1974): 54,200 metric tons. **Electricity production** (1976): 43,572 mln. kwh. **Labor force:** 45% agric.; 18% manuf.

Finance: Currency: Dinar (Mar. 1977: 18.2 =$1 US). **Gross domestic product** (1975): $28.2 bln. **Per capita income** (1974): $1,140. **Imports** (1976): $7.366 bln.; partners (1974): W. Ger. 18%, It. 12%, USSR 10%, Austria 5%. **Exports** (1976): $4.878 bln.; partners (1974): USSR 18%, It. 11%, W. Ger. 10%, U.S. 8%. **Tourists** (excluding excursionists) (1974): 5,457,700; receipts: $701 million. **Balance of payments** (1975): -$338 mln. **National budget** (1975): $6.23 bln. revenues; $6.81 bln. expenditures. **International reserves** (Feb. 1977): $1.985 bln. **Consumer prices** (change in 1976): 11.3%.

Transport: Railway traffic (1974): 6,476 mln. passenger-miles; 14,333 mln. net ton-miles. **Motor vehicles:** in use (1974): 1,333,000 passenger cars, 170,800 commercial vehicles; manufactured (1976): 139,000 passenger cars, 20,000 commercial vehicles. **Civil aviation:** 1,334 mln. passenger miles (1976); 13 mln. freight ton-miles (1976). **Chief ports:** Rijeka, Split, Dubrovnik.

Communications: Television sets: 2,544,000 licenses (1973); 418,000 manufactured (1974). **Radios:** 3,685,000 licenses (1973); 155,000 manufactured (1974). **Telephones in use** (1976): 1,301,219. **Daily newspaper circulation** (1973): 1,828; 87 per 1,000 pop.

Health: Life expectancy at birth (1970-72): 65.42 male; 70.22 female. **Births** (per 1,000 pop. 1975): 18.1. **Deaths** (per 1,000 pop. 1975): 8.6. **Natural increase** (1975): 0.95%. **Pop. per hospital bed** (1973): 169. **Pop. per physician** (1973): 873. **Infant mortality** (per 1,000 pop. under 1 yr. 1975): 40.5.

Education: Literacy (1973): 93%. **Pop.: 5-19:** in school (1973): 57%; per teacher (1973): 41.

Serbia, which had since 1389 been a vassal principality of Turkey, was established as an independent kingdom by the Treaty of Berlin, 1878. Montenegro, independent since 1389, also obtained international recognition in 1878. After the Balkan wars Serbia's boundaries were enlarged by the annexation of Old Serbia and Macedonia, 1913.

When the Austro-Hungarian empire collapsed after World War I, the Kingdom of the Serbs, Croats, and Slovenes was formed from the former provinces of Croatia, Dalmatia, Bosnia, Herzegovina, Slovenia, Voyvodina and the independent state of Montenegro. The name was later changed to Yugoslavia.

Nazi Germany invaded in 1941. Many Yugoslav partisan troops continued to operate. Among these were the Chetniks led by Draja Mikhailovich, who fought other partisans led by Josip Broz, known as Marshal Tito. Tito, backed by the USSR and Britain from 1943, was in control by the time the Germans had been driven from Yugoslavia in 1945. Mikhailovich was executed July 17, 1946, by the Tito regime.

A constituent assembly proclaimed Yugoslavia a republic Nov. 29, 1945. It became a federated republic Jan. 31, 1946, and Marshal Tito, a communist, became head of the government. By terms of a treaty with Italy, the greater part of Venezia-Giulia, Zara, Pelagosa, and adjacent islands were ceded to Yugoslavia.

The Stalin policy of dictating to all communist nations was rejected by Tito. He accepted economic aid and military equipment from the U.S. and received aid in foreign trade also from France and Great Britain.

Tito supported the liberal government of Czechoslovakia in 1968 before the Russian invasion, but he paid a friendship visit to Moscow in 1972.

A separatist movement among Croatians, 2d to the Serbs in numbers, brought arrests and a change of leaders in the Crotian Republic in Jan. 1972. Violence by extreme Croatian nationalists and fears of Soviet political intervention have led to restrictions on political and intellectual dissent, which had previously been freer than in other East European countries. Serbians, Montenegrins, and Macedonians use Cyrillic, Croatians and Slovenians use Latin letters. Croatia and Slovenia have been the most prosperous republics.

Most industry is socialized and private enterprise is restricted to small-scale production. Since 1952 workers are guaranteed a basic wage and a share in cooperative profits.

Management of industrial enterprises is handled by workers' councils. Farmland is 85% privately owned but farms are restricted to 25 acres.

Beginning in 1965, reforms designed to decentralize the

administration of economic development and to force industries to produce more efficiently in competition with foreign producers were introduced.

Yugoslavia has developed considerable trade with Western Europe as well as with Eastern Europe. Money earned by Yugoslavs working temporarily in Western Europe helps pay for imports. Unemployment and inflation became serious in 1975.

Zaire

Republic of Zaire

People: Population (1976 est.): 25,630,000. **Pop. density:** 28 per sq. mi. **Urban** (1974): 26.4%. **Ethnic groups:** Mostly Bantus: Luba 18%, Mongo 17%, Kongo 12%, Ruanda 10%, others. **Languages:** French (official), others. **Religions:** Roman Catholics, Protestants, syncretic sects 60%, Moslems 1%, others.

Geography: Area: 905,063 sq. mi., one-fourth the size of the U.S. **Location:** In central Africa. **Neighbors:** Congo on W, Central African Empire, Sudan on N, Uganda, Rwanda, Burundi, Tanzania on E, Zambia, Angola on S. **Topography:** Zaire includes the bulk of the Zaire (Congo) R. Basin. The vast central region is a low-lying plateau covered by rain forest. Mountainous terraces in the W, savannas in the S and SE, grasslands toward the N, and the high Ruwenzori Mtns. on the E surround the central region. A short strip of territory borders the Atlantic O. The Zaire R. is 2,718 mi. long. **Capital:** Kinshasa. **Cities** (1974 est.): Kinshasa 2,008,352; Kananga 601,239; Luluabourg 506,033; Lubumbashi 403,623; Mbuji-Mayi 336,654.

Government: Head of state: Pres. Mobutu Sese Seko, b. Oct. 14, 1930, in office: Nov. 24, 1965; **Head of government:** Prime Min. Mpinga Kasenga, in office: July, 1977. **Local divisions:** 8 regions. **Armed forces:** Regulars 43,400; para-military 20,000.

Economy: Chief Crops: Coffee, cotton, rice, sugar cane, bananas, plantains, coconuts, manioc, mangoes, tea, cacao, palm oil. **Minerals:** Cobalt (two-thirds of world output), copper, cadmium, gold, silver, tin, germanium, zinc, iron, tungsten, manganese, uranium, radium. **Crude oil output** (1976): 9,000 bbls. **Other resources:** Forests, rubber, ivory. **Per capita arable land:** 0.7 acres. **Livestock** (1974): 1,111,000 cattle; 606,000 pigs; 730,000 sheep; 10,474,000 poultry. **Fish catch** (1974): 123,900 metric tons. **Electricity production** (1973): 3,884 mln. kwh. **Labor force:** 78% agric.

Finance: Currency: Zaire (Feb. 1977: 0.87 = $1 US). **Gross domestic product** (1974): $3.53 bln. **Per capita income** (1974): $124. **Imports** (1975) $905 mln.; partners (1973): Belg. 20%, U.S. 17%, W. Ger. 14%, Fr. 11%. **Exports** (1976): $904 mln.; partners (1973): Belg. 48%, It. 13%, Jap. 7%, Fr. 7%. **Tourists** (1974): 163,700; receipts: $8 million. **Balance of payments** (1975): -$143 mln. **National budget** (1975): $864 mln. revenues; $1.421 mln. expenditures. **International reserves** (Dec. 1976): $104.85 mln. **Consumer prices** (change in 1976): 86.2%.

Transport: Railway traffic (1973): 278 mln. passenger-miles; 1,874 mln. net ton-miles. **Motor vehicles:** in use (1974): 84,800 passenger cars, 76,400 commercial vehicles. **Civil aviation:** 429 mln. passenger-miles (1976); 41 mln. freight ton-miles (1976). **Chief ports:** Matadi, Boma.

Communications: Television sets: 7,000 in use (1973). **Radios:** 100,000 in use (1973); 35,000 manufactured (1969). **Daily newspaper circulation** (1973): 70,000.

Health: Life expectancy at birth (1970-75): 41.9 male; 45.1 female. **Births** (annual per 1,000 pop. 1970-75): 45.2. **Deaths** (annual per 1,000 pop. 1970-75): 20.5. **Natural increase** (annual 1970-75): 2.47%. **Pop. per hospital bed** (1973): 343. **Pop. per physician** (1973): 28,802. **Infant mortlity** (per 1,000 pop. under 1 yr. 1955-58): 104.

Education: Literacy (1973): 12%. **School-age pop. 5-19:** in school (1973): 46%; per teacher (1973): 91.

The earliest inhabitants of Zaire may have been the pygmies, followed by Bantus from the E and Nilotic tribes from the N. The large Bantu Bakongo kingdom ruled much of Zaire and Angola when Portuguese explorers visited in the 15th century.

Leopold II, king of the Belgians, formed an international group to exploit the Congo in 1876. In 1877 Henry M. Stanley explored the Congo and in 1878 the king's group sent him back to organize the region and win over the native chiefs. The Conference of Berlin, 1884-85, organized the Congo Free State with Leopold as king and chief owner. Exploitation of native laborers on the rubber plantations caused international criticism and led to granting of a colonial charter, 1908.

Belgian and Congolese leaders agreed Jan. 27, 1960, that the Congo would become independent June 30. In the first general elections, May 31, the National Congolese movement of Patrice Lumumba won 35 of 137 seats in the National Assembly, lower House of Parliament. He was appointed premier June 21, and formed a coalition cabinet.

Widespread violence caused Europeans and others to flee. Pres. Moise Tshombe of Katanga seceded from the republic July 11, but ended the secession in 1963. Katanga was the seat of the Union Miniere copper mines. The UN Security Council Aug. 9, 1960, called on Belgium to withdraw its troops and sent a UN contingent to guard against civil war. President Kasavubu removed Lumumba as premier. Lumumba fought for control backed by Ghana, Guinea and India. On Feb. 12, 1961, Lumumba was murdered.

The last UN troops left the Congo June 30, 1964, and Tshombe became president.

On Sept. 7, 1964, leftist rebels set up a "People's Republic" in Stanleyville. Tshombe hired foreign mercenaries and sought to rebuild the Congolese Army. In Nov. and Dec. 1964 rebels slew scores of white hostages and thousands of Congolese; Belgian paratroops, dropped from U.S. transport planes, rescued hundreds. By July 1965 the rebels had lost their effectiveness.

In 1965 Gen. Joseph D. Mobutu was named president. He later changed his name to Mobutu Sese Seko. In March 1966 Mobutu took over from Parliament all of its legislative powers. On July 1 he renamed Leopoldville, Kinshasa; Stanleyville, Kisangani; and Elisabethville, Lubumbashi.

The Democratic Republic of Congo changed its name to Republic of Zaire on Oct. 27, 1971; the Congo River was changed to Zaire (its traditional name) and in 1972 Zairians with Christian names were ordered to change them to African names.

In 1969-74, political stability under Mobutu was reflected in improved economic conditions. In 1970, he was elected to a 7-year term as president. In 1974 most foreign-owned businesses were ordered sold to Zaire citizens, but in 1977 the government asked the original owners to return. A fall in copper prices in 1975 brought a surge in foreign debt and economic difficulties.

In 1977, a force of Zairians, apparently trained by Cubans, invaded Shaba province (Katanga) from Angola, Zaire repelled the attack, with the aid of 1,500 Moroccan troops flown in by France and Egyptians pilots. The U.S. sent "nonlethal" supplies.

Zambia

Republic of Zambia

People: Population (1976 est.): 5,140,000. **Age distrib.** (%): 0-14: 46.3; 15-59: 50.1; 60+: 3.6. **Pop. density:** 18 per sq. mi. **Urban** (1975): 36.3%. **Ethnic groups:** Africans 99%, mostly Bantu tribes, Europeans and Asians 1%. **Languages:** English (official), 70 others. **Religions:** Christians 15%, traditional religions.

Geography: Area: 290,724 sq. mi., larger than Texas. **Location:** In southern central Africa. **Neighbors:** Zaire on N, Tanzania, Malawi, Mozambique on E, Rhodesia, Namibia on S, Angola on W. **Topography:** Zambia is mostly high plateau country covered with thick forests, and drained by several important rivers, including the Zambezi. **Capital:** Lusaka. **Cities** (1972 est.): Lusaka (met.) 448,000; Kitwe (met.) 331,000; Ndola (met.) 235,000.

Government: Head of state: Pres. Kenneth David Kaunda, b. Apr. 28, 1924, in office: Oct. 24, 1964; **Head of government:** Prime Min. Elijah Mudenda, in office: May 27, 1975. **Local divisions:** 9 provinces. **Armed forces:** regulars 7,800; para-military 2,500.

Economy: Chief crops: Corn, tobacco, peanuts, cotton, sugar. **Minerals:** Copper (most of exports), zinc, cobalt, gold, lead, vanadium, manganese, coal. **Other resources:** Rubber, ivory. **Per capita arable land:** 2.3 acres. **Livestock** (1974): 1,748,000 cattle; 119,000 pigs. **Fish catch** (1974): 37,000 metric tons. **Electricity production** (1975): 6,192 mln. kwh. **Labor force:** 69% agric.

Finance: Currency: Kwacha (Feb. 1977: 1 = $1.25 US). **Gross domestic product** (1976): $2.26 bln. **Per capita income** (1974): $504. **Imports** (1975) $1.138 bln.; partners (1973): U.K. 22%, So. Afr. 12%, U.S. 9%, Jap. 9%. **Exports** (1975): $810 mln.; partners (1973): Jap. 24%, U.K. 20%, It. 12%, W. Ger. 10%. **Tourists** (1974): 44,600; receipts $12 million. **Balance of payments** (1975): $-78 mln. **National budget** (1976): $576 mln. revenues; $863 mln. expenditures. **International reserves**

(Nov. 1976): $86.4 mln. **Consumer prices** (change in 1976): 18.9%.

Transport: Motor vehicles: in use (1974): 85,800 passenger cars, 62,000 commercial vehicles. **Civil aviation:** 213 mln. passenger-miles (1975); 12 mln. freight ton-miles (1975).

Communications: Television sets: 21,000 licenses (1973). **Radios:** 100,000 licenses (1973); 61,000 manufactured (1972). **Telephones in use** (1976): 77,434. **Daily newspaper circulation** (1973): 105,000; 23 per 1,000 pop.

Health: Life expectancy at birth (1970-75): 42.9 male; 46.1 female. **Births** (annual per 1,000 pop. 1970-75): 51.5. **Deaths** (annual per 1,000 pop. 1970-75): 20.3. **Natural increase** (annual 1970-75): 3.12%. **Infant mortality** (per 1,000 pop. under 1 yr. 1950): 259.

As Northern Rhodesia, the country was under the administration of the South Africa Company, 1889 until 1924, when the office of governor was established, and, subsequently, a legislature. The country became an independent republic within the Commonwealth Oct. 24, 1964.

After the white government of Rhodesia declared its independence from Britain Nov. 11, 1965, relations between Zambia and Rhodesia became strained and use of their jointly owned railroad was disputed.

Britain gave Zambia an extra $12 million aid in 1966 after imposing an oil embargo on Rhodesia, and Zambia set up a temporary airlift to carry copper out from its mines and gasoline in. In Aug. 1968 a 1,058-mi. pipeline was completed, bringing oil from Tanzania. In 1973 a truck road to carry copper to Tanzania's port of Dar es Salaam was completed with U. S. aid. A railroad, built with Chinese aid across Tanzania, reached the Zambian border in 1974.

As part of a program of government participation in major industries, a government corporation in 1970 took over 51% of the ownership of 2 foreign-owned copper mining companies, paying with bonds. Privately-held land and other enterprises were nationalized in 1975, as were all newspapers.

United Nations

History

The 32d regular session of the United Nations General Assembly was scheduled to open in September, 1977. *See Chronology for developments at UN sessions during 1977.*

Foundations of the United Nations were laid at the Dumbarton Oaks Conference in Washington between the United States, the United Kingdom, and the Soviet Union, Aug. 21-Sept. 28, 1944, and between the United States, the United Kingdom, and the Republic of China, Sept. 29-Oct. 7, 1944. Proposals to establish an organization of nations for maintenance of world peace led to the United Nations Conference on International Organization at San Francisco, Apr. 25-June 26, 1945, where the charter of the United Nations was drawn up. It was signed June 26 by 50 nations, and by Poland, one of the original 51, on Oct. 15, 1945. The charter came into effect Oct. 24, 1945, when the requisite ratification by the 5 permanent members of the Security Council, China, France, Soviet Union, United Kingdom and United States, and a majority of other signatories had been completed.

United Nations headquarters are located in New York, N.Y., between First Ave. and Roosevelt Drive and E. 42nd St. and E. 48th St. The General Assembly Bldg. (opened 1952), Secretariat, Conference and Library bldgs. are interconnected. A new UN office building-hotel was opened in New York in 1976. The Dag Hammarskjold Library was dedicated in 1961. The UN has a post office originating its own stamps. *See Postal Information.*

A European office at Geneva includes Secretariat and agency staff members. Other offices of UN bodies and related organizations are scattered throughout the world.

Roster of the United Nations

(As of Aug. 1977)

The 149 members of the United Nations, with the years in which they became members.

Member	Year
Afghanistan	1946
Albania	1955
Algeria	1962
Angola	1976
Argentina	1945
Australia	1945
Austria	1955
Bahamas	1973
Bahrain	1971
Bangladesh	1974
Barbados	1966
Belgium	1945
Benin	1960
Bhutan	1971
Bolivia	1945
Botswana	1966
Brazil	1945
Bulgaria	1955
Burma	1948
Burundi	1962
Byelorussia	1945
Cameroon	1960
Canada	1945
Cape Verde	1975
Central Afr. Emp.	1960
Chad	1960
Chile	1945
China[4]	1945
Colombia	1945
Comoros	1975
Congo	1960
Costa Rica	1945
Cuba	1945
Cyprus	1960
Czechoslovakia	1945
Denmark	1945
Djibouti[6]	1977
Dominican Rep.	1945
Ecuador	1945
Egypt[2]	1945
El Salvador	1945
Equatorial Guinea	1968
Ethiopia	1945
Fiji	1970
Finland	1955
France	1945
Gabon	1960
Gambia	1965
Germany, East	1973
Germany, West	1973
Ghana	1957
Greece	1945
Grenada	1974
Guatemala	1945
Guinea	1958
Guinea-Bissau	1974
Guyana	1966
Haiti	1945
Honduras	1945
Hungary	1955
Iceland	1946
India	1945
Indonesia	1950
Iran	1945
Iraq	1945
Ireland	1955
Israel	1949
Italy	1955
Ivory Coast	1960
Jamaica	1962
Japan	1956
Jordan	1955
Kampuchea (Cambodia)	1955
Kenya	1963
Kuwait	1963
Laos	1955
Lebanon	1945
Lesotho	1966
Liberia	1945
Libya	1955
Luxembourg	1945
Madagascar (Malagasy)	1960
Malawi	1964
Malaysia[1]	1957
Maldives	1965
Mali	1960
Malta	1964
Mauritania	1961
Mauritius	1968
Mexico	1945
Mongolia	1961
Morocco	1956
Mozambique	1975
Nepal	1955
Netherlands	1945
New Zealand	1945
Nicaragua	1945
Niger	1960
Nigeria	1960
Norway	1945
Oman	1971
Pakistan	1947
Panama	1945
Papua New Guinea	1975
Paraguay	1945

Member	Year	Member	Year	Member	Year	Member	Year
Peru	1945	Senegal	1960	Tanzania[3]	1961	United Kingdom	1945
Philippines	1945	Seychelles	1976	Thailand	1946	United States	1945
Poland	1945	Sierra Leone	1961	Togo	1960	Upper Volta	1960
Portugal	1955	Singapore[1]	1965	Trinidad & Tob.	1962	Uruguay	1945
Qatar	1971	Somalia	1960	Tunisia	1956	Venezuela	1945
Romania	1955	South Africa[5]	1945	Turkey	1945	Vietnam[6]	1977
Rwanda	1962	Spain	1955	Uganda	1962	Yemen	1947
Samoa (Western)	1976	Sri Lanka	1955	Ukraine	1945	Yemen, South	1967
Sao Tome e Principe	1975	Sudan	1956	Union of Soviet Soc. Repub's	1945	Yugoslavia	1945
Saudi Arabia	1945	Surinam	1975	United Arab Emirates	1971	Zaire	1960
		Swaziland	1968			Zambia	1964
		Sweden	1946				
		Syria[2]	1945				

(1) Malaya joined the UN in 1957. In 1963, its name was changed to Malaysia following the accession of Singapore, Sabah, and Sarawak. Singapore became an independent UN member in 1965.
(2) Egypt and Syria were original members of the UN. In 1958, the United Arab Republic was established by a union of Egypt and Syria and continued as a single member of the UN. In 1961, Syria resumed its separate membership.
(3) Tanganyika was a member of the United Nations from 1961 and Zanzibar was a member from 1963. Following the ratification in 1964 of Articles of Union between Tanganyika and Zanzibar, the United Republic of Tanganyika and Zanzibar continued as a single member of the United Nations, later changing its name to United Republic of Tanzania.
(4) The General Assembly voted in 1971 to expel the Chinese government on Taiwan and admit the Peking government in its place.
(5) The General Assembly rejected the credentials of the South African delegates in 1974, and suspended the country from the Assembly.
(6) Recommended by Security Council for admission by General Assembly.

Organization

The text of the UN Charter may be obtained from the Office of Public Information, United Nations, N.Y.

General assembly, Pres. of 32d Session — Hamilton Shirley Amersasinghe, Sri Lanka.

The General Assembly is composed of representatives of all the member nations. Each nation is entitled to one vote.

The General Assembly meets in regular annual sessions and in special session when necessary. Special sessions are convoked by the Secretary General at the request of the Security Council or of a majority of the members of the UN. A president and seventeen vice presidents are chosen at each regular session.

Any matter within the scope of the charter may be brought before the General Assembly, which may make recommendations on all except issues on the agenda of the Security Council. However, the General Assembly in November, 1950, decided that if the Security Council, because of lack of unanimity of the permanent members, fails to exercise its primary responsibility for the maintenance of international peace and security, the Assembly may recommend collective measures including, in the case of a breach of peace or act of aggression, the use of armed forces. In such cases, the General Assembly may be convened within 24 hours.

On important questions a two-thirds majority of members present and voting is required; on other questions a simple majority is sufficient.

The General Assembly must approve the budget and apportion expenses among members. A member in arrears will have no vote if the amount of arrears equals or exceeds the amount of the contributions due for the preceding two full years. The General Assembly may permit such a member to vote if it is satisfied that the failure is due to conditions beyond control.

A Credentials Committee, appointed at the start of each session, examines and reports on delegates' credentials. Two standing committees, one on administration and budget and one on contributions, operate throughout the year, with 13 members each, chosen to assure wide geographic representation.

Security Council. The Security Council consists of 15 members, 5 with permanent seats. The remaining 10 are elected for 2-year terms by the General Assembly; they are not eligible for immediate reelection.

Permanent members of the Council: China, France, USSR, United Kingdom, United States.

Non-permanent members were Benin, Libya, Pakistan, Panama, Romania (until Dec. 31, 1977), and Canada, W. Germany, India, Mauritius, Venezuela (until Dec. 31, 1978).

The presidency of the Council is held monthly in turn by the member states in English alphabetical order.

The Security Council has the primary responsibility within the UN for maintaining international peace and security. The Council may investigate any dispute that threatens international peace and security. When the Security Council is handling a dispute or situation the General Assembly makes no recommendation unless the Council requests it.

Any member of the UN at UN headquarters may participate in its discussions and a nation not a member of UN may appear if it is a party to a dispute.

Decisions on procedural questions are made by an affirmative vote of 9 members. On all other matters the affirmative vote of 9 members must include the concurring votes of all permanent members; it is this clause which gives rise to the so-called "veto." A party to a dispute must refrain from voting.

The right of individual or collective self-defense is not prohibited by membership in the UN, and if a member nation is attacked it may do what is necessary, reporting this to the Security Council, which may take independent action.

The Security Council directs the various truce supervisory forces deployed in the Middle East, India-Pakistan, and Cyprus.

Economic and Social Council. The Economic and Social Council consists of 54 members elected by the General Assembly for 3-year terms of office. The council is responsible under the General Assembly for carrying out the functions of the United Nations with regard to international economic, social, cultural, educational, health and related matters. The council meets usually twice a year.

Trusteeship Council. The administration of Trust territories is subject to the supervision of the United Nations. Administering authorities are required to render an account of their stewardship to the Trusteeship Council. The only remaining trust territory is the Pacific Islands, administered by the U.S.

Secretariat. The Secretary General is the chief administrative officer of the UN. He may bring to the attention of the Security Council any matter that threatens international peace. He reports to the General Assembly.

Kurt Waldheim (Austria), Secretary General, was relected to a second 5-year term beginning Jan. 1, 1977.

Secretary General Waldheim proposed a 1976-77 program budget of $737,005,000, exclusive of trust funds and special contributions. This does not include expenses for the Specialized or the Related Organizations.

The US contributes 25% of the regular budget, the Soviet Union 12.97%, Japan and W. Germany over 7% each, and France, China, and Britain over 5% each.

For further information, consult the Public Inquiries Unit, Office of Public Information, United Nations, N. Y. Provides pamphlets, study guides, speakers, films; arranges group visits, provides information on UN activities: (212) 754-1234.

International Court of Justice

The International Court of Justice is the principal judicial organ of the United Nations. All members are *ipso facto* parties to the statute of the Court, as are three nonmembers — Liechtenstein, San Marino, and Switzerland. Other states may become parties to the Court's statute on conditions determined in each case by the General Assembly on the recommendation of the Security Council.

The jurisdiction of the Court comprises cases which the parties submit to it and matters especially provided for in the charter or in treaties. The Court gives advisory opinions and renders judgments. Its decisions, which are final, are only binding between the parties concerned and in respect to a particular dispute. If any party to a case fails to heed a judgment of the Court, the other party may have recourse to the Security Council, which may decide what is to be done.

The Court consists of 15 judges elected for 9-year terms by a majority in both the General Assembly and the Security Council. No two of the judges may be nationals of the same state. Retiring judges are eligible for re-election. The Court remains permanently in session, except during the judicial vacations. All questions are decided by majority. The Court sits in The Hague, Netherlands.

Judges

Nine year term in office ending 1985: Taslim Olawala Elias, Nigeria. Hermann Mosier, W. Germany. Shigeru Oda, Japan. Salah El Dine Tarazi, Syria. Manfred Lachs, Poland.

Nine year term in office ending 1982: Isaac Forster, Senegal. Andre Gros, France. Jose Maria Ruda, Argentina. Nagendra Singh, India. Sir Humphrey Waldock, Britain.

Nine year term in office ending 1979: Hardy C. Dillard, U.S. Louis Ignacio-Pinto, Benin. Federico de Castro, Spain. Platon D. Morozov, USSR. Eduardo Jimenez de Arechaga, Uruguay.

The president until 1979 is Eduardo Jimenez de Arechaga, Uruguay, and the vice president is Nagendra Singh, India.

Specialized Agencies

These agencies are autonomous entities with their own memberships and organs which have a functional relationship with the UN.

International Labor Org. (ILO) aims to promote social justice; improve labor conditions and living standards; and promote economic stability. (Geneva, 135 member nations)

Food & Agriculture Org. (FAO) aims to increase production from farms, forests, and fisheries; improve distribution, marketing, and nutrition. (Rome, 136)

United Nations Educational, Scientific, & Cultural Org. (UNESCO) aims to promote collaboration among nations in the fields of education, science, and culture. (Paris, 142)

World Health Org. (WHO) aims to aid the attainment of the highest possible level of health. (Geneva, 150)

International Bank for Reconstruction & Development (World Bank) aims to help in the economic development of members by facilitating investment of capital; promote foreign investment and supplement private investment by providing loans for productive purposes out of its capital funds raised by it and its other resources; and to promote growth of international trade and equilibrium in balance of payments. (Washington, D. C., 129)

International Development Assn. (IDA) aims to further economic development of less developed members by financing on terms bearing less heavily on balance of payments than those of conventional loans. (Washington, D. C., 117)

International Finance Corp. (IFC) aims to further economic development in member countries by encouraging private enterprise, particularly in less developed areas. (Washington, D. C., 106)

International Monetary Fund (IMF) aims to promote international monetary co-operation and currency stabilization. (Washington, D. C., 131)

International Civil Aviation Org. (ICAO) promotes international civil aviation standards and regulations. (Montreal, 138)

Universal Postal Union (UPU) aims to perfect postal services and promote international collaboration. To this end, members agree to handle other members, mail by the best means used for their own mail. (Berne, 154)

International Telecommunication Union (ITU) sets up international regulations of radio, telegraph, telephone and space radio-communications. Allocates radio frequencies. (Geneva, 153)

World Meteorological Org. (WMO) aims to co-ordinate, standardize and improve world meteorological work and weather data exchange. (Geneva, 147)

Intergovernmental Maritime Consultative Org. (IMCO) aims to promote co-operation on technical matters affecting international shipping. (London, 103)

World Intellectual Property Organization (WIPO) seeks to protect, through international cooperation, literary, industrial, scientific, and artistic "intellectual property." (Geneva, 106)

Related Organizations

These autonomous bodies have working agreements with the UN.

International Atomic Energy Agency (IAEA) aims to promote the safe, peaceful uses of atomic energy. (Vienna, 110)

General Agreement on Tariffs and Trade (GATT) was drafted in 1946. It establishes and administers code for orderly conduct of international trade. Aids export promotion in developing countries. (Geneva, 83 members, 3 provisional members, 25 defacto members)

Major International Organizations

The Commonwealth, originally called the British Commonwealth of Nations, is an association of nations and dependencies loosely joined by a common interest based on having been parts of the old British Empire. The British monarch is the symbolic head of the Commonwealth.

There are 36 self-governing independent nations in the Commonwealth, plus various colonies and protectorates. As of June 1977, the members were the United Kingdom of Great Britain and Northern Ireland and ten other nations recognizing the British monarch, represented by a governor-general, as their head of state: Australia, Bahamas, Barbados, Canada, Fiji, Grenada, Jamaica, Mauritius, New Zealand, and Papua New Guinea; and 25 countries with their own heads of state: Bangladesh, Botswana, Cyprus, Gambia, Ghana, Guyana, India, Kenya, Lesotho, Malawi, Malaysia, Malta, Nauru (a special member), Nigeria, Samoa, Seychelles, Sierra Leone, Singapore, Sri Lanka (Ceylon), Swaziland, Tanzania, Tonga, Trinidad and Tobago, Uganda, Zambia. In addition various Caribbean dependencies take part in certain Commonwealth activities.

The Commonwealth facilitates consultation among member states through meetings of prime ministers and finance ministers, and through a permanent Secretariat established in 1949. Members consult on economic, scientific, educational, financial, legal, and military matters, and try to coordinate policies. Population (est. 1977) was nearly one billion in the member nations; total area, over ten million sq. mi.

European Communities (EC) is the collective designation of three organizations with common membership: the European Economic Community (Common Market), the European Coal and Steel Community, and the European Atomic Energy Community. The nine full members are: Belgium, Denmark, France, West Germany, Ireland, Italy, Luxembourg, Netherlands, United Kingdom. The Common Market also includes as associate members Greece, Turkey, Cyprus, Malta, Morocco, and Tunisia. Portugal applied in 1977 for membership. Another 49 nations in Africa, the Caribbean, and the Pacific are affiliated under the Lome Convention. The Common Market also has trade agreements with EFTA members, Israel, and several Arab nations.

A coordinated structure for the communities went into effect July 1, 1967, though the component organizations date back to 1951 and 1957. A Council of Ministers, an expert Commission, a European Parliament and a Court of Justice comprise the permanent structure. The communities aim to integrate their economies, coordinate social developments, and ultimately, bring about political union of the democratic states of Europe.

A 1975 agreement provides that direct elections for the European Parliament would be held in member countries in 1978, and that a uniform Western Europe passport would be issued in that year.

European Free Trade Association (EFTA), consisting of Austria, Iceland, Norway, Portugal, Sweden, Switzerland and associate member Finland, was created by treaty Jan. 4, 1960, effective May 3, to gradually reduce customs duties and quantitative restrictions between members on industrial products. By Dec. 31, 1966, tariffs and restrictions had been eliminated. The United Kingdom and Denmark withdrew to become members of EC Jan. 1, 1973. Other EFTA members joined in an industrial tariff elimination pact with EC in 1972. All industrial customs barriers between the two blocs were removed July 1, 1976.

League of Arab States (The Arab League) was created March 22, 1945, by Egypt, Iraq, Jordan, Lebanon, Saudi Arabia, Syria and Yemen. Joining later were Algeria, Bahrain, Djibouti, Kuwait, Libya, Mauritania, Morocco, Oman, Qatar, Somalia, Southern Yemen, Sudan, Tunisia and United Arab Emirates. The Palestine Liberation Org. has been admitted as a full member. Cairo is headquarters for the secretary-general. The League mediates disputes between Arab states, represents Arab states in certain international negotiations, and coordinates a military, economic, and diplomatic offensive against Israel. The League fosters cultural, economic, and communications ties among the Arab states.

North Atlantic Treaty Org. (NATO) was created April 4, 1949, in a treaty signed in Washington, effective Aug. 24, by Belgium, Canada, Denmark, France, Iceland, Italy, Luxembourg, the Netherlands, Norway, Portugal, the United Kingdom, and the U.S. Greece, Turkey, and West Germany have joined since. The members agreed to settle disputes by peaceful means; to develop their individual and collective capacity to resist armed attack; to regard an attack on one as an attack on all, and to take necessary action to repel an attack under Article 51 of the United Nations Charter.

Armed forces of NATO members include forces assigned to NATO commands, forces earmarked for NATO commands, and forces under national command. The NATO military command has five branches: Allied Command Europe, Allied Command Atlantic, Allied Command Channel, Canada-U.S. Regional Planning Group, and Allied Air Force, Central Europe.

Following announcement in 1966 of nearly total French withdrawal from the military affairs of NATO, the organization moved its headquarters in 1967 from Paris to Brussels. In August, 1974, Greece announced a total withdrawal of armed forces from NATO, in response to Turkish intervention in Cyprus. Nevertheless, Greece has continued to participate in NATO military planning activities.

Organization of African Unity (OAU), formed May 25, 1963 by 30 African countries (48 by 1977) to coordinate cultural, political, scientific and economic policies; to end colonialism in Africa; to promote a common defense of members' independence. It holds annual conferences of heads of state, has a council of foreign ministers meeting at least twice a year, a secretary-general and a mediation-arbitration commission. Hq. is in Addis Ababa, Ethiopia. The OAU has helped formulate common policies on problems of trade, sea law, etc.

Organization of American States (OAS) was formed in Bogota, Colombia, in 1948. Hq. are in Washington, D.C. It has a Permanent Council, Inter-American Economic and Social Council, and Inter-American Council for Education, Science and Culture, a Juridical Committee, and a Commission on Human Rights. The Permanent Council can call meetings of foreign ministers to deal with urgent security matters. A General Assembly meets annually. A secretary general and assistant are elected for 5-year terms. There are 26 members, each with one vote in the various organizations: Argentina, Barbados, Bolivia, Brazil, Chile, Colombia, Costa Rica, Cuba, Dominican Republic, Ecuador, El Salvador, Grenada, Guatemala, Haiti, Honduras, Jamaica, Mexico, Nicaragua, Panama, Paraguay, Peru, Surinam, Trinidad-Tobago, U.S., Uruguay, Venezuela. In 1962, the OAS excluded Cuba from OAS activities but not from membership.

Organization for Economic Cooperation and Development (OECD) was established in 1960 to promote stable economic growth in member countries and the world at large, and to help expand free trade. Nearly all the industrialized "free market" countries belong, with Yugoslavia as an associate member. OECD is active in collecting and disseminating economic and environmental information, and in channeling resources to developing countries. Members in 1977 were: Australia, Austria, Belgium, Canada, Denmark, Finland, France, West Germany, Greece, Iceland, Ireland, Italy, Japan, Luxembourg, Netherlands, New Zealand, Norway, Portugal, Spain, Sweden, Switzerland, Turkey, United Kingdom, United States.

Organization of Petroleum Exporting Countries (OPEC) was created in 1960 at Venezuelan initiative. The group has successfully maintained high oil prices, and has tried to advance members' interests in trade and development dealings with industrialized oil-consuming nations. Members in 1977 were Algeria, Ecuador, Gabon, Indonesia, Iran, Iraq, Kuwait, Libya, Nigeria, Qatar, Saudi Arabia, United Arab Emirates, Venezuela.

Warsaw Treaty Organization (Warsaw Pact) was created May 14, 1955, as a mutual defense alliance by Albania, Bulgaria, Czechoslovakia, East Germany, Hungary, Poland, Romania and the USSR. It provides for a unified military command with headquarters in Moscow; if one member is attacked, the others will aid it with all necessary steps including armed force; joint maneuvers are held; there is a Political Consultative Committee and economic cooperation is advanced. Albania was barred from meetings in 1962, withdrew in 1968.

Ambassadors and Envoys

Envoys to U.S. as of May 1977; envoys from U.S. as of Aug. 1977.
The address of foreign embassies to the United States is Washington, D.C.

Countries	Envoys from United States	Envoys to United States
Afghanistan	Theodore L. Eliot Jr., Amb.	Mohammed Siddiq Saljooque, Charge
Algeria	Ulric St. Clair Haynes Jr., Amb.	Abdelkader Maadini, Charge
Angola[10]		
Argentina	*Vacant*	Jorge A. Aja Espil, Amb.
Australia	Philip H. Alston Jr., Amb.[11]	Alan Philip Renouf, Amb.
Austria	Milton A. Wolf, Amb.	Karl Herbert Schober, Amb.
Bahamas	William B. Schwartz Jr. Amb.[11]	Livingston B. Johnson, Amb.
Bahrain	Wat Tyler Cluverius IV, Amb.	Abdulaziz Abdulrahman Buali, Amb.
Bangladesh	Edward E. Masters, Amb.	Mustafizur Rahman Siddiqi, Amb.
Barbados	Frank V. Ortiz, Amb.	Oliver H. Jackman, Amb.
Belgium	Anne Cox Chambers, Amb.	Willy Van Cauwenberg, Amb.
Benin	*Vacant*	Thomas S. Boya, Amb.
Bolivia	*Vacant*	Alberto Crespo, Amb.
Botswana	Donald R. Norland, Amb.	Bias Mookodi, Amb.
Brazil	John Hugh Crimmins, Amb.	Joao Baptista Pinheiro, Amb.
Bulgaria	Raymond L. Garthoff, Amb.	Lubomir D. Popov, Amb.
Burma	Maurice D. Bean, Amb.[11]	U Tin Lat, Amb.
Burundi	David E. Mark, Amb.	Laurent Nzeyimana, Amb.
Cameroon	Mabel Murphy Smythe, Amb.	Benoit Bindzi, Amb.
Canada	Thomas O. Enders, Amb.	Jack H. Warren, Amb.
Cape Verde	Edward Marks, Amb.[11]	Raul Querido Varela, Amb.
Centr. African Amp.	Anthony C. E. Quainton, Amb.	Christophe Maidou, Amb.
Chad	William G. Bradford, Amb.	Pierre Toura Gaba, Amb.
Chile	*Vacant*	Jorge Cauas, Amb.
China (Taiwan)	Leonard Unger, Amb.	James C. H. Shen, Amb.
China, People's Rep.[2]	Leonard Woodcock, Head of Liaison	Huang Chen
Colombia	*Vacant*	Alfonso Davila, Charge
Congo (Brazzaville)[3]		
Costa Rica	Marvin Weissman, Amb.	Rodolfo Silva Vargas, Amb.
Cuba[4]		
Cyprus	William R. Crawford Jr., Amb.	Nicos G. Dimitriou, Amb.
Czechoslovakia	Thomas R. Byrne, Amb.	Jaromir Johanes, Amb.
Denmark	John Gunther Dean, Amb.	Otto R. Borch, Amb.
Dominican Republic	Robert A. Hurwitch, Amb.	Horacio Vicioso-Soto, Amb.
Ecuador	Richard J. Bloomfield, Amb.	Gustavo Ycaza Borja, Amb.
Egypt	Hermann F. Eilts, Amb.	Ashraf A. Ghorbal, Amb.
El Salvador	*Vacant*	Francisco Bertrand Galindo, Amb.
Equatorial Guinea[9]		
Estonia[5]		Ernst Jaakson, Consul General
Ethiopia	*Vacant*	Ghebeyehou Mekbib, Charge
Fiji	Armistead I. Selden Jr., Amb.	Berenado Vunibobo, Amb.
Finland	Rozanne L. Ridgway, Amb.	Leo Tuominen, Amb.
France	Arthur A. Hartman, Amb.	Jacques Kosciusko-Morizet, Amb.
Gabon	Andrew L. Steigman, Amb.	Guy Rene Kombila, Amb.
Gambia	Herman J. Cohen, Amb.[11]	*Vacant*
Germany, East	David B. Bolen, Amb.	Rolf Sieber, Amb.
Germany, West	Walter J. Stoessel Jr., Amb.	Berndt von Staden, Amb.
Ghana	Robert P. Smith, Amb.	Samuel Ernest Quarm, Amb.
Greece	William E. Schaufile Jr., Amb.	Menelas D. Alexandrakis, Amb.
Grenada	Frank V. Ortiz, Amb.	Marie McIntyre, Amb.
Guatemala	Davis E. Boster, Amb.	Abundio Maldonado, Amb.
Guinea	*Vacant*	Daouda Kourouma, Amb.
Guinea-Bissau	Edward Marks, Amb.[11]	Gil Vicente Vaz Fernandes, Amb.
Guyana	John Richard Burke, Amb.[11]	Laurence E. Mann, Amb.
Haiti	William Bowdoin Jones, Amb.	Georges Salomon, Amb.
Honduras	Mari Luci Jaramillo, Amb.[11]	Roberto Lazarus, Amb.
Hungary	Philip M. Kaiser, Amb.	Ferenc Esztergalyos, Amb.
Iceland	James J. Blake, Amb.	Hans G. Andersen, Amb.
India	Robert F. Goheen	Kewal Singh, Amb.
Indonesia	David D. Newsom, Amb.	Roesmin Nurjadin, Amb.
Iran	William H. Sullivan, Amb.	Ardeshir Zahedi, Amb.
Iraq[6]		
Ireland	William V. Shannon, Amb.	John G. Molloy, Amb.
Israel	Samuel W. Lewis, Amb.	Simcha Dinitz, Amb.
Italy	Richard N. Gardner, Amb.	Roberto Gaja, Amb.
Ivory Coast	Monteagle Stearns, Amb.	Timothee N'Guetta Ahoua, Amb.
Jamaica	Frederick Irving, Amb.	Alfred A. Rattray, Amb.
Japan	Michael J. Mansfield, Amb.	Fumihiko Togo, Amb.
Jordan	Thomas R. Pickering, Amb.	Abdullah Salah, Amb.
Kampuchea[7]		
Kenya	Wilbert John Le Melle, Amb.	John P. Mbogua, Charge
Korea, South	Richard L. Sneider, Amb.	Yong Shik Kim, Amb.
Kuwait	Frank E. Maestrone, Amb.	Khalid M. Jaffar, Amb.
Laos	*Vacant*	Somphong Vanitsaveth, Charge
Latvia[5]		Dr. Anatol Dinbergs, Charge
Lebanon	Richard B. Parker, Amb.	Najati Kabbani, Amb.
Lesotho	Donald R. Norland, Amb.	Thabo R. Makeka, Amb.
Liberia	W. Beverly Carter Jr., Amb.	Francis A. Dennis, Amb.
Libya	*Vacant*	Shaban F. Gashut, Charge
Lithuania[5]		Stasys A. Backis, Charge
Luxembourg	James G. Lowenstein, Amb.	Adrien Meisch, Amb.
Madagascar	*Vacant*	Norbert Rakotomalala, Charge

Countries	Envoys from United States	Envoys to United States
Malawi	Robert A. Stevenson, Amb.	Jacob T. X. Muwamba, Amb.
Malaysia	Robert H. Miller, Amb.	Zain Azraai, Amb.
Maldives, Rep.	W. Howard Wriggins, Amb.[11]	*Vacant*
Mali	Patricia M. Byrne, Amb.	Ibrahima Sima, Amb.
Malta	L. Bruce Laingren, Amb.	Victor Gauci, Charge
Mauritania	Holsey G. Handyside, Amb.	Mohamed Nassim Kochman, Amb.
Mauritius	Robert V. Keeley, Amb.	Pierre Guy Girald Balancy, Amb.
Mexico	Patrick J. Lucey, Amb.	Hugo B. Margain, Amb.
Morocco	Robert Anderson, Amb.	Mustapha El Kasri, Amb.
Mozambique	William A. De Pree, Amb.	
Nauru	Philip H. Alston Jr., Amb.[11]	*Vacant*
Nepal	L. Douglas Heck, Amb.	Padma Bahadur Khatri, Amb.
Netherlands	Robert J. McCloskey, Amb.	Age R. Tammenoms Bakker, Amb.
New Zealand	Armistead I. Selden Jr., Amb.	Lloyd White, Amb.
Nicaragua	Mauricio Solaun, Amb.	Dr. Guillermo Sevilla-Sacasa, Amb.
Niger	Charles A. James, Amb.	Andre Wright, Amb.
Nigeria	Donald B. Easum, Amb.	Edward Olusola Sanu, Amb.
Norway	Louis A. Lerner, Amb.	Soren Christian Sommerfelt, Amb.
Oman	William D. Wolle, Amb.	Ahmed Macki, Amb.
Pakistan	Arthur W. Hummel Jr., Amb.	Sahabzada Yaqub-Khan, Amb.
Panama	William J. Jorden, Amb.	Gabriel Lewis, Amb.
Papua New Guinea	Mary S. Olmsted, Amb.	Paulias Nguna Matane, Amb.
Paraguay	George W. Landau, Amb.	Mario Lopez Escobar, Amb.
Peru	Harry W. Shlaudeman, Amb.	Carlos Garcia-Bedoya, Amb.
Philippines	*Vacant*	Eduardo Z. Romualdez, Amb.
Poland	Richard T. Davies, Amb.	Witold Trampczynski, Amb.
Portugal	Frank C. Carlucci, Amb.	Joao Hall Themido, Amb.
Qatar	Andrew I. Killgore, Amb.[11]	Abdullah Saleh Al-Mana, Amb.
Romania	Harry G. Barnes Jr., Amb.	Nicolae M. Nicolae, Amb.
Rwanda	T. Frank Crigler, Amb.	Bonaventure Ubalijoro, Amb.
Samoa	Armistead I. Selden Jr., Amb.	*Vacant*
Sao Tome and Principe	Andrew L. Steigman, Amb.	
Saudi Arabia	John C. West, Amb.	Ali Abdallah Alireza, Amb.
Senegal	Herman J. Cohan, Amb.[11]	Andre Coulbary, Amb.
Seychelles	Wilbert John Le Melle, Amb.	
Sierra Leone	John A. Linehan, Amb.	Philip J. Palmer, Amb.
Singapore	John H. Holdridge, Amb.	Punch Coomaraswamy, Amb.
Somali, Democratic Rep.	James L. Loughran, Amb.	Dr. Adbullahi Ahmed Addou, Amb.
South Africa	William G. Bowdler, Amb.	Donald B. Sole, Amb.
Spain	Wells Stabler, Amb.	Juan Jose Rovira, Amb.
Sri Lanka (Ceylon)	W. Howard Wriggins, Amb.[11]	Neville Kanakaratne, Amb.
Sudan	Donald C. Bergus, Amb.	Omer Salih Eissa, Amb.
Surinam	J. Owen Zurhellen Jr., Amb.	Roel F. Karamat, Amb.
Swaziland	Donald R. Norland, Amb.	Simon M. Kunene, Amb.
Sweden	Rodney O. Kennedy-Minott, Amb.[11]	Wilhelm Wachtmeister, Amb.
Switzerland	Marvin L. Warner, Amb.	Raymond Probst, Amb.
Syrian Arab Rep.	Richard W. Murphy, Amb.	Sabah Kabbani, Amb.
Tanzania	James W. Spain, Amb.	Paul Bomani, Amb.
Thailand	Charles S. Whitehouse, Amb.	Arun Panupong, Amb.
Togo	Ronald D. Palmer, Amb.	Messanvi Kokou Kekeh, Amb.
Tonga	Armistead I. Selden Jr., Amb.	*Vacant*
Trinidad and Tobago	Richard K. Fox Jr., Amb.	Victor C. McIntyre, Amb.
Tunisia	Edward W. Mulcahy, Amb.	Ali Hedda, Amb.
Turkey	Ronald I. Spiers, Amb.	Melih Esenbel, Amb.
Uganda[7]		Mahmud Musa, Charge
USSR	Malcolm Toon, Amb.	Anatoliy F. Dobrynin, Amb.
United Arab Emirates	Francois M. Dickman, Amb.	Hamad Abdul Rahman Al Madfa, Amb.
United Kingdom	Kingman Brewster, Amb.	Sir Peter Ramsbotham, Amb.
Upper Volta	Pierre R. Graham, Amb.	Telesphore Yaguibou, Amb.
Uruguay	Lawrence A. Pezzullo, Amb.	Jose Perez Caldas, Amb.
Venezuela	Viron P. Vaky, Amb.	Ignacio Iribarren, Amb.
Vietnam[1]		
Yemen, South[8]		
Yemen Arab Rep.	Thomas J. Scotes, Amb.	Yahya M. Al-Mutawakel, Amb.
Yugoslavia	Lawrence S. Eagleburger, Amb.	Dimce Belovski, Amb.
Zaire	Walter L. Cutler, Amb.	Asal B. Idzumbuir, Amb.
Zambia	Steven Low, Amb.	Fidelis F. Bwalya, Amb.

Ambassadors at Large: Elliot L. Richardson, Ellsworth Bunker, Gerald C. Smith.

Special Missions Headed by Ambassadors

U.S. Mission to North Atlantic Treaty Organization, Brussels—W. Tapley Bennett Jr.
U.S. Mission to the European Communities, Brussels—Deane R. Hinton
U.S. Mission to the International Atomic Energy Agency, Vienna—Gerard C. Smith
U.S. Mission to the United Nations, New York—Andrew Young
U.S. Mission to the European Office of the UN & Other Internatl. Organizations, Geneva, William J. vanden Heuvel.
U.S. Mission to the Organization for Economic Cooperation and Development, Paris—Herbert Salzman
U.S. Mission to the Organization of American States, Washington—Gale McGee

(1) U.S. embassy closed in 1975 during Communist takeover. (2) No formal relations; liaison offices. (3) U.S. embassy closed in 1965; West Germany acts as protective power. (4) Relations severed in 1961; limited ties restored in 1977. (5) U.S. does not officially recognize 1940 annexation by USSR. (6) Relations severed in 1967, limited staff returned in 1972; Belgium protects U.S. interests. (7) U.S. embassy closed in 1973; West Germany protects U.S. interests. (8) U.S. embassy closed in 1969; UK serves as protective power. (9) U.S. severed relations in 1976. (10) Post temporarily closed in 1975. (11) Nominated.

U.S. Aid to Foreign Nations

Source: Bureau of Economic Analysis, U.S. Commerce Department

Data shown by country includes the military supplies and services furnished under the Foreign Assistance Act and direct Defense Department appropriations. Data shown includes credits which have been extended to private entities in the country specified.

Grants are largely outright gifts for which no payment is expected or which at most involve an obligation on the part of the receiver to extend aid to the U.S. or other countries to achieve a common objective.

Net grants and credits take into account all known returns to the U.S. government, including reverse grants, returns of grants, and payments of principal. A minus sign (—) indicates that the total of these returns to the U.S. is greater than the total of grants or credits.

Other assistance represents the transfer of U.S. farm products in exchange for foreign currencies, less the government's disbursements of the currencies as grants, credits, or for purchases. The net acquisitions of currencies represents net transfers of resources to foreign currencies in addition to those classified as grants or credits.

Amounts do not include investments in international financial institutions in 1976 as follows: Asian Development Bank, $75 million; Inter-American Development Bank, $255 million; International Development Assn., $757 million; African Development Fund, $15 million.

In millions of dollars or equivalent (*Less than $500,000)

Calendar year 1976	Total	Net grants	Net credits	Net other
TOTAL	$6,838	$3,620	$3,271	$-53
Military grants	**1,354**	**1,354**	—	—
Other grants, credits, ass't.	**5,484**	**2,266**	**3,271**	**-53**
Western Europe	**152**	**42**	**136**	**4**
Austria	2	—	2	—
Belgium-Luxembourg	-2	—	-2	—
Denmark	-4	—	-4	—
Finland	10	—	10	*
France	-41	—	-41	—
Germany, West	22	—	22	*
Iceland	-3	—	-3	—
Ireland	-6	—	-6	—
Italy	-13	1	-14	—
Malta	14	10	4	—
Netherlands	14	—	14	—
Norway	30	—	30	—
Portugal	113	30	83	*
Spain	18	1	17	*
Sweden	11	—	11	—
Switzerland	8	—	8	—
United Kingdom	-18	—	-18	—
Yugoslavia	78	—	74	4
Atomic EC	-5	—	-5	—
Coal-Steel EC	-6	—	-6	—
Other & unspecified	6	*	6	—
Eastern Europe	**166**	**4**	**184**	**-22**
Hungary	*	—	*	—
Poland	142	4	160	-22
Romania	22	—	22	—
Soviet Union	2	—	2	—
Near East & South Asia	**2,397**	**934**	**1,496**	**-34**
Afghanistan	20	9	11	*
Bangladesh	78	8	70	*
Cyprus	21	18	3	*
Egypt	231	49	216	-34
Greece	121	*	121	*
India	120	140	-13	-6
Iran	-109	1	-110	*
Israel	1,405	505	900	*
Jordan	90	71	19	*
Lebanon	7	1	6	—
Nepal	16	7	*	9
Pakistan	252	62	192	-2
Saudi Arabia	-12	—	-12	—
Sri Lanka (Ceylon)	21	6	15	*
Syria	23	2	20	1
Turkey	57	1	58	-2
Yemen (Sana)	8	8	—	—
Other & unspecified	48	46	—	—
East Asia & Pacific	**1,086**	**186**	**901**	**-1**
Australia	-4	—	-46	—
China-Taiwan	145	*	145	*
Hong Kong	6	*	6	—
Indonesia	333	11	322	*
Japan	63	—	63	*
Korea (So.)	344	4	340	*
Malaysia	15	3	12	—
New Zealand	13	—	13	—
Papua New Guinea	-12	*	-12	—
Philippines	109	43	66	—
Singapore	16	1	15	—
Thailand	7	8	-1	—
Trust Terr. Pacific	89	89	—	—
Other & unspecified	23	23	—	—
Africa	**505**	**231**	**274**	*
Algeria	67	3	64	—

Calendar year 1976	Total	Net grants	Net credits	Net other
Benin	7	1	5	—
Botswana	8	4	4	—
Burundi	2	2	—	—
Cameroon	5	5	*	—
Chad	6	6	—	—
Ethiopia	34	10	24	*
Gabon	7	*	7	—
Gambia	2	2	—	—
Ghana	166	11	5	*
Guinea	9	1	6	2
Guinea Bissau	1	1	—	—
Ivory Coast	*	1	1	*
Kenya	17	7	9	—
Lesotho	6	6	—	—
Liberia	15	9	6	—
Madagascar	1	1	—	—
Malawi	5	1	5	—
Mali	5	5	*	*
Mauritania	9	6	3	—
Morocco	105	22	81	2
Mozambique	12	11	1	—
Niger	9	9	*	—
Nigeria	3	4	-1	—
Senegal	8	8	*	*
Sierra Leone	3	3	*	—
Somalia	3	3	*	—
Sudan	-4	1	-4	-1
Swaziland	1	1	*	—
Tanzania	37	28	9	*
Togo	3	3	*	—
Tunisia	13	8	7	-2
Upper Volta	8	8	—	—
Zaire	37	4	32	*
Zambia	8	*	8	—
Other & unspecified	30	29	4	-1
Western Hemisphere	**517**	**232**	**284**	**1**
Argentina	20	*	20	*
Bahamas	-1	—	-1	—
Barbados	2	1	1	—
Bermuda	-8	—	-8	—
Bolivia	30	10	20	*
Brazil	145	8	137	*
Canada	13	—	13	—
Cayman Islands	-1	—	-1	—
Chile	-71	15	-87	1
Colombia	21	17	4	*
Costa Rica	7	3	4	—
Dominican Republic	29	12	17	—
Ecuador	15	5	10	*
El Salvador	9	4	4	—
Guatemala	43	21	22	—
Guyana	7	*	6	—
Haiti	18	12	6	—
Honduras	18	6	13	—
Jamaica	8	2	6	—
Mexico	34	1	33	—
Nicaragua	17	4	13	—
Panama	36	19	17	—
Paraguay	3	3	*	*
Peru	43	11	32	*
Trinidad-Tobago	-4	—	-4	—
Uruguay	5	1	4	—
Venezuela	-22	1	-23	—
Others & unspecified	101	76	26	—
International organizations & unspecified areas	**631**	**637**	**-4**	**-1**

Cost of Living in Various Cities of the World

This comparison of the cost of living in various cities was drawn up in 1977 by the UN Statistical Office, based on prices for goods, services and housing for international officials stationed in these cities. Figures show relative costs, based on about 120 items. New York City was assigned the index figure 100. Thus, while expenditure for certain items might be $1,000 in New York, it would be $1,140 for them in Paris and $870 in Rio de Janeiro. Figures with an asterisk (*) omit cost of housing (rent, utilities, and domestic service) in cities where they are furnished at nominal cost by governments.

Index	City	Index	City	Index	City
*129	Abidjan, Ivory Coast	68	Georgetown, Guyana	*135	Nouakchott, Mauretania
*136	Accra, Ghana	133	The Hague, Netherlands	111	Ouagadougou, Upper Volta
96	Addis Ababa, Ethiopia	84	Havana, Cuba	87	Panama City, Panama
*88	Aden, Yemen (Dem.)	77	Islamabad, Pakistan	114	Paris, France
*112	Algiers, Algeria	112	Jakarta, Indonesia	91	Port-au-Prince, Haiti
91	Amman, Jordan	82	Kabul, Afghanistan	70	Port Louis, Mauritius
80	Ankara, Turkey	*117	Kampala, Uganda	79	Port-of-Spain, Trinidad
*94	Apia, Western Samoa	76	Katmandu, Nepal	81	Quito, Ecuador
80	Asuncion, Paraguay	*132	Kigali, Rwanda	95	Rabat, Morocco
99	Athens, Greece	99	Kingston, Jamaica	87	Rangoon, Burma
79	Baghdad, Iraq	*138	Kinshasa, Zaire	87	Rio de Janeiro, Brazil
115	Bamako, Mali	84	Kuala Lumpur, Malaysia	84	Rome, Italy
77	Bangkok, Thailand	101	Kuwait, Kuwait	100	Sana, Yemen (Rep.)
*142	Bangui, Cen. African Rep.	*124	Lagos, Nigeria	93	San Jose, Costa Rica
90	Belgrade, Yugoslavia	84	La Paz, Bolivia	87	San Salvador, El Salvador
72	Bogota, Colombia	*123	Libreville, Gabon	85	Santiago, Chile
121	Bonn, West Germany	84	Lima, Peru	97	Seoul, South Korea
77	Bratislava, Czechoslovakia	83	London, United Kingdom	102	Singapore, Singapore
*131	Brazzaville, Congo	*97	Lusaka, Zambia	78	Suva, Fiji
88	Bridgetown, Barbados	95	Managua, Nicaragua	101	Sydney, Australia
98	Budapest, Hungary	84	Manila, Philippines	98	Tananarive, Malagasy
67	Buenos Aires, Argentina	75	Mbabane, Swaziland	89	Tegucigalpa, Honduras
75	Cairo, Egypt	58	Mexico City, Mexico	97	Teheran, Iran
92	Caracas, Venezuela	89	Mogadishu, Somalia	*130	Tokyo, Japan
67	Colombo, Sri Lanka	103	Monrovia, Liberia	109	Tripoli, Libya
132	Conakry, Guinea	79	Montevideo, Uruguay	99	Tunis, Tunisia
119	Copenhagen, Denmark	89	Montreal, Canada	*96	Ulan Bator, Mongolia
81	Dacca, Bangladesh	82	Nairobi, Kenya	68	Valetta, Malta
101	Damascus, Syria	73	New Delhi, India	118	Vienna, Austria
*127	N'Djamena, Chad	100	New York, U.S.	79	Warsaw, Poland
*93	Freetown, Sierra Leone	*115	Niamey, Niger	93	Washington, D.C., U.S.
129	Geneva, Switzerland	68	Nicosia, Cyprus	109	Yaounde, Cameroon

Population of World's Largest Urban Areas

City populations often cannot be used to compare urban areas because city limits may fall short of or exceed the built-up or urban area. The problem of comparison is compounded by the difficulty in obtaining reliable population data for a common year. The ranking of urban areas below represents one attempt at comparing the world's largest urban areas, taking into account, where necessary and within the limits of available data, urban development extending outward from the principal city named in the table. Thus, the Tokyo area included Tokyo plus neighboring smaller cities, towns and villages. (Some computations include Yokohama as part of Tokyo's urban population.) New York's urban area in 1970 included part or all the population of 10 New Jersey and 5 New York counties in addition to the 5 boroughs of New York City.

New York, N.Y. (census, 1970)	16,206,841
Tokyo, Japan (est. 1974)	11,622,651
Mexico City, Mexico (est. 1975)	11,339,774
Shanghai, China (est. 1970)	10,820,000
Paris, France (census, 1975)	9,863,000
Buenos Aires, Argentina (est. 1974)	8,925,000
Osaka, Japan (census, 1973)	7,838,722
Sao Paulo, Brazil (est. 1973)	7,693,000
Moscow, USSR (est. 1975)	7,632,000
Peking, China (est. 1970)	7,570,000
London, England (est. 1973)	7,281,000
Calcutta, India (census, 1971)	7,031,382
Chicago, Ill. (est. 1974)	6,971,200
Los Angeles-Long Beach, Cal. (est. 1974)	6,926,100
Bombay, India (census, 1971)	5,970,575
Cairo, Egypt (est. 1974)	5,715,000
Seoul, S. Korea (census, 1970)	5,433,198
Essen (Ruhr-Gebiet), W. Germany (est. 1971)	5,425,000
Philadelphia, Pa. (est. 1974)	4,809,900
Rio de Janeiro, Brazil (est. 1973)	4,658,000
Jakarta, Indonesia (census, 1971)	4,576,009
Detroit, Mich. (est. 1974)	4,434,300
Hong Kong (est. 1975)	4,370,000
Leningrad, USSR (1975)	4,311,000
Tientsin, China (est. 1970)	4,280,000
Teheran, Iran (est. 1973)	4,002,000
Bangkok, Thailand (est. 1973)	3,967,081
Boston, Mass. (est. 1974)	3,918,400
Delhi-New Delhi, India (census, 1971)	3,647,023
Madrid, Spain (est. 1974)	3,520,320
Karachi, Pakistan (census, 1972)	3,498,634
Lima, Peru (census, 1972)	3,302,523
Santiago, Chile (est. 1975)	3,262,990
Madras, India (census, 1971)	3,169,930
Berlin, E. and W. Germany (est. 1974, 1975)	3,142,444
San Francisco-Oakland, Cal. (est. 1974)	3,135,900
Istanbul, Turkey (est. 1973)	3,135,354
Washington, D.C.-Md.-Va. (est. 1974)	3,015,300
Manila, Philippines (est. 1973)	3,000,000
Sydney, Australia (est. 1973)	2,874,380
Rome, Italy (est. 1975)	2,868,248
Bogota, Colombia (census, 1973)	2,855,065
Shenyang (Mukden), China (est. 1970)	2,800,000
Montreal, Quebec (est. 1974)	2,798,000
Toronto, Ontario (est. 1974)	2,741,000
Yokohama, Japan (census, 1975)	2,620,000
Melbourne, Australia (est. 1973)	2,583,900
Wuhan, China (est. 1970)	2,560,000
Athens, Greece (census, 1971)	2,540,000
Dallas-Ft. Worth, Tex. (est. 1974)	2,498,500
Manchester, England (est. 1973)	2,389,260
St. Louis, Mo. (est. 1974)	2,371,400
Birmingham, England (est. 1973)	2,358,980
Pittsburgh, Pa. (est. 1974)	2,333,600
Chungking, China (est. 1970)	2,300,000
Alexandria, Egypt (est. 1974)	2,259,000
Singapore (est. 1975)	2,250,000
Houston, Tex. (est. 1974)	2,222,700
Canton, China (est. 1970)	2,200,000
Caracas, Venezuela (est. 1970)	2,175,400
Lahore, Pakistan (census, 1972)	2,165,372
Baltimore, Md. (est. 1974)	2,140,400
Nagoya, Japan (census, 1975)	2,080,000
Rangoon, Burma (est. 1973)	2,056,118
Budapest, Hungary (est. 1971)	2,027,300
Newark, N.J. (est. 1974)	2,019,200
Minneapolis-St. Paul, Minn. (est. 1974)	2,010,800
Kinshasa, Zaire (est. 1974)	2,008,352
Taipei, China (est. 1974)	2,000,409

U. S. Passport, Visa, and Health Requirements

Source: Passport Office, U.S. State Department and U.S. Public Health Service

Passports are issued by the United States Department of State to citizens and nationals of the United States for the purpose of documenting them for their foreign travel and identifying them as Americans. Some countries require a visa, or stamp of approval, to be affixed to the passport by the consulate of the country to be visited, while others waive this formality. Also some countries, which do not require visas, require tourist cards from visitors making a short stay.

How to Obtain a Passport

An applicant for a passport who has never been previously issued a passport in his own name, must execute an application in person before (1) a Passport agent; (2) a clerk of any federal court or state court of record or a judge or clerk of any probate court, accepting applications; (3) a postal employee designated by the postmaster at a Post Office which has been selected to accept passport applications; or (4) a diplomatic or consular officer of the U.S. abroad. A wife/husband who is to be included in the passport must appear with the applicant and execute the application. Passport Agencies are located at Boston (John F. Kennedy Bldg., Government Center), Chicago (Federal Office Bldg., 230 S. Dearborn); Honolulu (Fed. Bldg., 300 Ala Moana Blvd.); Los Angeles (Hawthorne Fed. Bldg., 15000 Aviation Blvd., Rm. 2W16, Lawndale, Calif.); Miami (Fed. Bldg., 51 S.W. First Ave.); New Orleans (International Trade Mart, 2 Canal Street); New York (630 Fifth Ave.); Philadelphia, (Federal Bldg., 600 Arch Street); San Francisco (Fed. Bldg., 450 Golden Gate Ave.); Seattle (Federal Bldg., 915 Second Ave.); Washington D.C. (Passport Office, 1425 K St., N.W.)

A passport previously issued to the applicant, or one in which he was included, will be accepted as proof of citizenship in lieu of the following documents. A person born in the United States shall present his birth certificate. To be acceptable, the certificate must show the given name and surname, the date and place of birth and that the birth record was filed shortly after birth. The certificate must also be certified with the registrar's signature and the raised, impressed, embossed, or multi-colored seal of his office. Uncertified copies of birth certificates are not acceptable. A delayed birth certificate (a record filed more than one year after the date of birth) is acceptable provided that it shows that the report of birth was supported by acceptable secondary evidence of birth as described below.

If such primary evidence is not obtainable, a notice from the registrar shall be submitted stating that no birth record exists. The notice shall be accompanied by the best obtainable secondary evidence such as a baptismal certificate, a certificate of circumcision, a hospital birth record, affidavits of persons having personal knowledge of the facts of the birth or other documentary evidence such as early census, school or family bible records, newspaper files and insurance papers. Secondary evidence should be created as close to the time of birth as possible.

A person in the U.S. who has been issued a passport in his own name within the last eight years may obtain a new passport by filling out, signing and mailing a passport by mail application together with his previous passport, two identical signed photographs taken within the last 6 months and the established fee to the nearest Passport Agency or to the Passport Office in Wash., D.C. If, however, an applicant is applying for a passport for the first time, if his prior passport was issued before his 18th birthday, if he wishes to include a person other than himself in the passport, or if he is applying for an official, diplomatic, or other no-fee passport, he must execute a passport application in person before a Passport Agent; a clerk of any federal court or state court of record or a judge or clerk of any probate court accepting applications; a postal employee designated by the postmaster at a Post Office which has been selected to accept passport applications; or a diplomatic or consular officer of the U.S. abroad.

A naturalized citizen should present his naturalization certificate. A person born abroad claiming citizenship through either a native-born or naturalized citizen must submit a certificate of citizenship issued by the Immigration and Naturalization Service; or a Consular Report of Birth or Certification of Birth issued by the Dept. of State. If one of the above documents has not been obtained, he must submit evidence of citizenship of the parent(s) through whom citizenship is claimed and evidence which would establish the parent/child relationship. Additionally, if through birth to one American and one alien parent, an affidavit from parent(s) showing periods and places of residence or physical presence in the United States and abroad, specifying periods spent abroad in the employment of the U.S. government, including the armed forces, or with certain international organizations; if through naturalization of parents, evidence of admission to the United States for permanent residence.

Under certain conditions, married women must present evidence of marriage. Special laws govern women married prior to Mar. 3, 1931 and should be discussed with the person executing the application.

The applicant shall establish his identity to the satisfaction of the person executing the application. Proof of identity may be established through a personal knowledge of the applicant by the Clerk or Agent or by an item which contains the signature and either a physical description or photograph of the applicant. The following items of identification are acceptable: previous United States Passport; certificate of naturalization; driver's license (not temporary or learner's license); a governmental (Federal, State, Municipal) identification card or pass.

If the applicant is not able to establish his identity by personal knowledge or by presentation of one of the above acceptable documents, he should be accompanied by an identifying witness who has known him for at least 2 years, and who is a U.S. citizen or a permanent resident alien of the United States. The witness shall be required to establish his own identity to the satisfaction of the person executing the application by one of the above means.

The identifying witness shall sign an affidavit in the presence of the same person who executes the passport application. The affidavit shall show:

The witness resides at a specific address;

The witness knows or has reason to believe that the applicant is a citizen of the United States;

The basis of the witness' knowledge concerning the applicant;

The information set forth in the affidavit is true to the best of his knowledge and belief.

A person included in the passport of another may not use the passport for travel unless he is accompanied by the bearer.

Aliens — An alien leaving the U.S. must request passport facilities from his home government. He must have a permit from his local Collector of Internal Revenue, and if he wishes to return he should request a re-entry permit from the Immigration and Naturalization Service if it is required.

Contract Employees — Persons traveling because of a contract with the Government must submit with their applications letters from their employer stating position, destination and purpose of travel, armed forces contract number, and expiration date of contract when pertinent.

Photographs and Fees

Photographs — Identical photographs taken within six months, both signed by the applicant and which are a good likeness, must accompany the passport application. An individual photograph of the passport bearer is required at all times. An additional photograph must be submitted showing other persons to be included in the passport. Photographs may be in color or in black and white. They must be full face, printed on thin, nonglossy paper on a plain, light background and must be 2x2 inches in size. The image size measured from the bottom of the chin to the top of the head (including hair) shall be not less than 1 inch nor more than 1 3/8 inches. They must also be capable of withstanding a mounting temperature of over 200°F.

Fees — The passport fee is $10. A fee of $3 shall be charged for execution of the application. No execution fee is payable where a passport is applied for by mail. All applicants must pay the passport fee and, where applicable, the execution fee unless specifically exempted by law. If applying in person, service will be expedited by presenting exact fees. An emergency service fee of $10 is charged in addition to all other fees where work must be performed after hours. The only other fees are for special postage. A passport is valid for five years unless otherwise limited.

During the calendar year 1976 the Passport Office, Dept. of State, issued 2,816,683 passports to American citizens.

The loss or theft of a valid passport is a serious matter and should be reported in writing immediately to the Passport Office, Dept. of State, Wash., D.C. 20524, or to the nearest passport agency, or to the nearest consular office of the U.S. when abroad.

Foreign Regulations

A visa is an endorsement or a notation, usually rubber stamped in a passport by a representative of the country to be visited. It certifies that the bearer of the passport is to be permitted to enter that country for a certain purpose and length of time. With the exception of the Iron Curtain countries, no visas are required for brief tourist travel to Western European countries. Authoritative visa information can be obtained by writing directly to foreign consular officials. The locations of foreign consular offices in the U.S. may be obtained by consulting the Congressional Directory available in most libraries. (Check city telephone directories for complete address.)

Health Information

Smallpox —Vaccination is required for travel to many countries. An International Certificate of Vaccination is not required for travel from the United States directly to Europe, Canada, Mexico, Australia, and New Zealand. For travel to more than one country in the Caribbean, a Certificate may be required. A Certificate is required for travel to the United States only if within the preceeding 14 days a traveler has been in a country any part of which is infected. Currently smallpox is limited to Ethiopia and Somalia.

Yellow Fever — A few African countries require a Vaccination Certificate of all travelers. A number of countries require vaccination if travelers arrive from infected or endemic areas. Vaccination is recommended for travel to infected areas, currently parts of Africa and South America. The United States has no vaccination requirement.

Cholera — A few countries require vaccination if travelers arrive from infected areas. The United States has no vaccination requirement.

Plague — Vaccination is not required by any country as a condition of entry. Selective immunization is advisable for travelers to Vietnam, Cambodia and Laos.

Vaccination Information — Yellow fever vaccine must be obtained at an officially designated Yellow Fever Vaccination Center, and the Certificate, valid for 10 years, must be stamped by the Center. Other vaccinations may be obtained from licensed physicians, and sometimes from local health departments. The Smallpox Certificate, valid for 3 years, and the Cholera Certificate, valid for 6 months, may be stamped by the State or local health department.

Vaccinations must be recorded on an approved version of PHS-731, International Certificates of Vaccination, which are available from State and local health departments, passport offices, travel agencies, and the Superintendent of Documents, U.S. Printing Office, Washington, D.C. 20402.

Travelers are advised to contact their local health department 2 weeks prior to departure to obtain the most current information on countries to be visited.

Customs Exemptions and Advice to Travelers

United States residents returning after a stay abroad of at least 48 hours are, generally speaking, granted customs exemptions of $100 each. Each returning resident may bring home free of duty articles totaling $100 in fair retail value in the country of acquisition, subject to limitations on liquors and cigars. These articles must accompany the traveler at the time of his return, must be for his personal or household use, must have been acquired as an incident of his trip, and must be properly declared to Customs. Not more than one quart of alcoholic beverages may be included in the $100 exemption.

If a U.S. resident arrives directly or indirectly from American Samoa, Guam, or the Virgin Islands of the United States, his purchase may be valued up to $200 fair retail value, but not more than $100 of the exemption may be applied to the value of articles acquired elsewhere than in such insular possessions, and one gallon of alcoholic beverages may be included in his exemption, but not more than 1 quart of such beverages may have been acquired elsewhere than in the designated islands.

In either case, the exemption for alcoholic beverages is accorded only when the returning resident has attained 21 years of age at the time of his arrival. One hundred cigars may be included (except Cuban products) in either exemption.

The $100 or $200 exemption may be granted only if the exemption, or any part of it, has not been used within the preceding 30-day period and your stay abroad was for at least 48 hours. The 48-hour absence requirement does not apply if you return from Mexico or the Virgin Islands of the United States.

Bona fide gifts costing no more than $10 fair retail value or $20 from American Samoa, Guam, or Virgin Islands, may be mailed to friends at home duty-free; addressee cannot receive in a single day gifts exceeding the $10 limit.

Air Travel

Effective June 1, 1977, first class passengers on international flights are allowed 2 pieces of luggage. Dimensions of each piece (length plus height plus depth) are limited to 62 inches. Economy class passengers are allowed 2 pieces; neither piece may exceed 62 inches but the total is limited to 106 inches. All passengers are allowed an additional piece of underseat luggage limited in size to 45 inches. A charge is made for extra baggage.

Precautions for Travel

In some cases naturalized United States citizens desiring to visit the countries of their birth, and sometimes their American-born children traveling to those countries, may be subject to military service and other regulations there. The United States Department of State advises such travelers to get specific information from the consulates of the countries concerned before departure.

U.S. Immigration Law

The Immigration and Nationality Act as amended by the Act of October 3, 1965, and the Immigration and Nationality Amendments of 1976 (P.L. 94-571) "marked the final end of an immigration quota system based on nationality." The latter amendments eliminated inequities in the existing law regarding the admission of immigrants from countries in the Western Hemisphere. The seven-category preference system, the 20,000 per-country limit, and the provisions for adjustment of status, all of which were in effect for Eastern Hemisphere countries, were extended to the Western Hemisphere.

The Immigration and Nationality Act, as amended, provides for the numerical limitation of most immigration. Not subject to any numerical limitations are immigrants classified as immediate relatives who are spouses or children of U.S. citizens, or parents of citizens who are 21 years of age or older; returning residents; certain former U.S. citizens; ministers of religion; and certain long-term U.S. government employees.

Numerical Limitation of Immigrants

Immigration to the U.S. is numerically limited to 290,000 per year. This ceiling is subdivided into an annual limitation of 170,000 for the Eastern and 120,000 for the Western Hemisphere. Within each of these ceilings there is an annual limitation of 20,000 for each country. The colonies and dependencies of foreign states are limited to 600 per year, chargeable to the hemisphere in which the area is located and to the per-country limit of the mother country.

Preference Visa Categories

Applicants for immigration are classified as either preference or nonpreference. The preference visa categories are based on certain relationships to persons in the U.S., i.e., unmarried sons and daughters over 21 of U.S. citizens, spouses and unmarried sons and daughters of resident aliens, married sons and daughters of U.S. citizens, brothers and sisters of U.S. citizens 21 or over (first, 2d, 4th, and 5th preference, respectively); members of the professions or persons of exceptional ability in the sciences and arts whose services are sought by U.S. employers (3rd preference); and skilled and unskilled workers in short supply (6th preference); refugees (7th preference). Spouses and children of preference applicants are entitled to the same preference if accompanying or following to join such persons.

Except for refugee status, preference status is based upon approved petitions, filed with the Immigration and Naturalization Service, by the appropriate relative or employer (or in the 3rd preference by the alien himself). Visa numbers for qualified preference applicants are made available in the order of the filing dates of the petitions. Each preference is alloted a certain percentage of the hemisphere total.

Nonpreference Immigrants

Other immigrants not within one of the above-mentioned preference groups may qualify as nonpreference applicants and receive only those visa numbers not needed by preference applicants.

The availability of nonpreference visa numbers is contingent on the level of preference demand and cannot therefore be predicted with real accuracy. However, in some countries and dependent areas the preference categories may utilize the entire numerical limitation, which will prevent any visa numbers from becoming available for persons from such countries or areas in the nonpreference category.

Labor Certification

The Act of October 3, 1965, established new controls to protect the American labor market from an influx of skilled and unskilled foreign labor. Prior to the issuance of a visa, the would-be 3rd, 6th, and nonpreference immigrant must obtain the Secretary of Labor's certification, establishing that there are not sufficient workers in the U.S. at the alien's destination who are able, willing, and qualified to perform the job; and that the employment of the alien will not adversely affect the wages and working conditions of workers in the U.S. similarly employed; or that there is satisfactory evidence that the provisions of that section do not apply to the alien's case.

Extension of Adjustment of Status

The Act of October 3, 1965, excluded Western Hemisphere natives from adjusting their status to permanent residence under Section 245 of the Immigration and Nationality Act which allows a nonimmigrant alien to adjust to permanent resident without leaving the U.S. to secure a visa. The 1976 Amendments restored the adjustment of status provision to Western Hemisphere natives, and declared ineligible for adjustment of status aliens who are not defined as immediate relatives and who accept unauthorized employment prior to filing their adjustment application.

Excludable Aliens

Aliens who are excludable on medical grounds are those who are mentally retarded, insane, psychopathic, mentally defective, sexual deviates, chronic alcoholics, narcotic addicts, and those who are afflicted with any dangerous contagious disease or who have a physical defect impairing the ability to earn a living. Also excludable are paupers, beggars, illiterates, stowaways, prostitutes, persons engaged in commercial vice, narcotics traffickers, persons convicted of crimes involving moral turpitude, persons who obtain or try to obtain a visa by fraud, or who left the U. S. to avoid military service. Those excludable on security grounds include persons who are anarchists, members or affiliates of certain proscribed organizations, and those who teach or advocate overthrow of the U. S. Government by force or violence.

For more detailed information consult the nearest office of the U. S. Immigration & Naturalization Service, or any U. S. Consul abroad.

Naturalization: How to Become an American Citizen

Source: The Federal Statutes

A person who desires to be naturalized as a citizen of the United States may obtain the necessary application form as well as detailed information from the nearest office of the Immigration and Naturalization Service or from the clerk of a court handling naturalization cases.

There are no racial bars to naturalization. Women have the same right as men to become naturalized.

An applicant must be at least 18 years old. He must have been a lawful resident of the United States continuously for 5 years. For husbands and wives of U.S. citizens the period is 3 years in most instances. Special provisons apply to certain veterans of the Armed Forces.

An applicant must have been physically present in this country for at least half of the required 5 years' residence.

Every applicant for naturalization must:

(1) sign the petition in his own handwriting, if physically able to write.

(2) demonstrate an understanding of the English language, including an ability to read, write, and speak words in ordinary usage in the English language (persons physically unable to do so, and persons who were on December 24, 1952 over 50 years of age and had been residing in the United States for 20 years are excepted).

(3) have been a person of good moral character, attached to the principles of the Constitution, and well disposed to the good order and happiness of the United States for five years just before filing the petition or for whatever other period of residence is required in his case and continue to be such a person until admitted to citizenship; and

(4) demonstrate a knowledge and understanding of the fundamentals of the history, and the principles and form of government, of the U.S.

The petitioner also is obliged to have two credible citizen witnesses. These witnesses must have personal knowledge of the applicant.

A person not of good moral character includes a habitual drunkard, an adulterer, a polygamist, a violator of criminal law, a gambler, one who gave false testimony to obtain a benefit under the immigration law, one in prison for 180 days or more, one convicted of murder.

Naturalization is denied to any person who, within 10 years, has been subversive, including communists and others who favor totalitarian government, and who were members of a proscribed organization, unless the petitioner was under 16 or joined under duress.

When the applicant files his petition he pays the court clerk $25. At the preliminary hearing he may be represented by a lawyer or social service agency. There is a 30-day wait. If action is favorable, there is a final hearing before a judge, who administers the following oath of allegiance:

Oath of Allegiance

I hereby declare, on oath, that I absolutely and entirely renounce and abjure all allegiance and fidelity to any foreign prince, potentate, state or sovereignty, to whom or which I have heretofore been a subject or citizen; that I will support and defend the Constitution and laws of the United States of America against all enemies, foreign and domestic; that I will bear true faith and allegiance to the same; that I will bear arms on behalf of the United States when required by the law; that I will perform noncombatant service in the armed forces of the United States when required by the law; that I will perform work of national importance under civilian direction when required by the law; and that I take this obligation freely without any mental reservation or purpose of evasion; so help me God.

Immigrants Admitted from All Countries

Source: Immigration and Naturalization Service, U.S. Justice Department

Year	Number	Year	Number	Year	Number	Year	Number
1820	8,385	1891-1900	3,687,564	1962	283,763	1971	370,478
1821-1830	143,439	1901-1910	8,795,386	1963	306,360	1972	384,685
1831-1840	599,125	1911-1920	5,735,811	1964	292,248	1973	400,063
1841-1850	1,713,251	1921-1930	4,107,209	1965	296,697	1974	394,861
1851-1860	2,598,214	1931-1940	528,431	1966	323,040	1975	386,194
1861-1870	2,314,824	1941-1950	1,035,039	1968	454,448	1976	398,613
1871-1880	2,812,191	1951-1960	2,515,479	1969	358,579		
1881-1890	5,246,613	1961	271,344	1970	373,326	**1820-1976**	**47,497,532**

Passports Issued and Renewed

Source: Passport Office, U.S. State Department

Passports are actual count; other data based on sample.

Item	1960	1970	1971	1972[5]	1973	1974	1975	1976
New and renewed passports	853,087	2,219,159	2,398,968	2,728,021	2,729,104	2,415,003	2,334,359	2,816,683
Object of Travel[1]								
Government	115,910	146,169	98,938	136,901	146,494	206,343	210,399	287,393
Nongovernment	737,177	2,072,990	2,300,030	2,591,120	2,582,610	2,208,660	2,123,960	2,529,290
Personal reasons[2]	321,590	1,791,330	2,156,640	2,042,560	1,245,780	384,930	376,400	602,980
Pleasure[3]	350,897	216,700	109,210	441,010	1,077,240	1,382,100	1,315,600	1,511,060
Business[4]	24,540	39,940	15,570	68,700	154,820	267,980	273,110	272,600
Education	31,240	20,230	16,040	33,290	95,240	153,210	132,490	125,590
Religion	6,780	3,350	1,380	3,980	7,930	16,510	22,450	13,690
Health	1,460	640	130	800	1,140	1,860	1,510	1,500
Other	670	800	1,060	780	460	2,070	2,400	1,870
First area destination:								
Africa	8,440	18,790	14,820	29,750	26,420	32,110	32,930	35,390
Australia and Oceania	35,220	51,210	48,350	78,580	80,670	101,250	96,300	106,540
Europe	669,662	1,910,169	2,139,508	2,244,161	2,181,114	1,714,613	1,611,410	1,990,993
Far East	55,960	116,730	73,250	135,230	139,740	162,130	154,660	180,090
North Central and South America	58,935	72,410	68,630	135,720	189,280	287,260	317,980	347,020
Middle-East	24,670	48,890	54,380	103,870	111,000	117,110	121,010	156,530
World Tour	200	960	30	710	880	530	60	120
Mode of travel — departure:[6]								
Ship	226,245	....	....	....	....	....	....	...
Air	626,842	....	....	....	....	....	....	...
Sex of passport recipients:								
Male	419,615	1,123,620	1,266,770	1,358,530	1,321,050	1,154,940	1,128,050	1,353,610
Female	433,472	1,095,539	1,132,198	1,369,491	1,408,054	1,260,063	1,206,309	1,463,073
Citizenship of passport recipients:								
Native	710,172	2,072,560	2,270,610	2,553,750	2,511,266	2,154,920	2,039,690	2,458,050
Naturalized	142,915	146,599	128,358	174,271	217,838	260,083	294,669	358,633

(1) Data not entirely comparable because of changes in classifications in 1961. (2) Includes "Personal business," "Join husband," "Accompany husband," "Business and pleasure," "Visit family." (3) Includes "Sightsee," "Vacation," "Visit," and "Tourist." (4) Includes applications formerly listed under "Employment" and "Commercial business." (5) Legislation effective Aug. 26, 1968 eliminated passport renewals. (6) Data eliminated. Over 99% of passport recipients indicate departure by air.

NORTH AMERICAN CITIES

Their History, Business and Industry, Educational Facilities, Cultural Advantages, Tourist Attractions and Transportation

Akron, Ohio

The World Almanac is sponsored in the Akron area by the Akron Beacon Journal, 44 E. Exchange Street, Akron,)H 44328; (216) 375-8111; a Knight-Ridder newspaper; founded 1809; circulation 171,305, daily, 222,461 Sun-ay; John S. Knight, editor emeritus; William Ott, president and publisher; Paul Poorman, editor and vice president.

'opulation: 267,000 (city); 697,740 (metro) 5th in tate; total employed, 276,700; 1976 average metro ousehold buying income, $14,623.

.rea: 56 sq. mi. (city), 413 sq. mi. (metro) on Ohio :anal 30 mi. south of Lake Erie; founded 1825; Sum-iit County seat.

ndustry: approx. $2 billion value added by Akron rea mfg. industry in 1976; home plants of Firestone, ;oodyear, Goodrich, General and many smaller rub-er firms employ 34,700, use 40% of entire world ubber supply; other products mfd. in area include uto bodies, salt, clay, matches, rubber toys, road uilding equipment, missile components.

'ransportation: Akron-Canton Airport served by 3 najor carriers; Akron Muni Airport; Conrail covers 9 ormer private rail and trunk lines; birthplace of rucking industry, served by 70 common and 50 con-ract carriers; metro transit system; Greyhound and :ontinental Trailways; city bisected east-west and orth-south by interstate highway systems.

'ommunications: 5 TV, one cablevision, and 5 radio tations; 2 public broadcast TV outlets.

;ew construction: $13 million Northeastern Ohio Jniv. College of Medicine; $16 million Ohio Edison :o. headquarters; $56 million downtown energy ecycle plant; $10 million in additions to the Univ. of kron; $35 million in additions to 2 major hospitals; 140 million in new construction started in 1976.

Federal facilities: $17 million downtown federal office bldg.; Army Reserve Center; Navy-Marine Reserve Center.

Medical facilities: 7 major hospitals including specialized children's treatment center; State of Ohio Fallsview Mental Health Center.

Education: University of Akron and School of Law; Kent State University; Firestone Conservatory of Music.

Sports: NBA Cleveland Cavaliers and WTT Nets play in nearby Richmond Township Coliseum; Firestone Country Club, home of the World Series of Golf, American Golf Classic; 35,000-seat Akron Rubber Bowl; Derby Downs, home of the All-American Soap Box Derby.

Cultural attractions: E. J. Thomas Performing Arts Center; Blossom Music Center, summer home of the Cleveland Orchestra; Stan Hywet mansion; Akron Art Institute; Akron Symphony Orchestra.

Other attractions: Children's Zoo; John Brown Home; Simon Perkins Mansion; Railway Museum.

Accommodations: Nearly 2,500 Class A hotel and motel rooms in the metro area.

Further information: Akron Regional Development Board, Delaware Bldg., or Akron Convention Bureau, 1 Cascade Plaza, both Akron, OH 44308.

Albany, New York

The World Almanac is sponsored in the Albany-Schenectady-Troy area by The Times-Union and Knickerbocker lews-Union Star, 645 Albany-Shaker Road, Albany, NY 12201; (518) 453-5454; Times-Union founded 1856; :nickerbocker News 1843: Union-Star 1855; circulation Times-Union (morn), 80,046, Sunday Times-Union 140,-10, Knickerbocker News-Union Star (aft) 62,585, publisher J. Roger Grier.

'opulation: 115,781 (city), 286,742 (county); total em-loyed 99,047.

.rea: 19.6 sq. mi. on west bank of Hudson River, 150 niles north of New York City; state capital and lbany County seat.

ndustry: chief products are felts, woolen goods, neat products, paper products, iron and brass cast-ngs, drugs and medicines; 295 manufacturing firms.

'ommerce: 5 savings banks, 11 commercial banks.

'ransportation: 2 major freight lines; 4 airlines at lbany County Airport; New York State Thruway, dirondack Northway; Port of Albany.

'ommunications: 5 TV and 11 radio stations.

ledical facilities: 5 major hospital complexes includ-ig a VA installation.

ultural facilities: Albany Symphony Orchestra, art iuseum, 90 church buildings, city libraries.

ducational facilities: Albany Law School, Albany 'ollege of Pharmacy, Albany Medical College, the tate University of New York at Albany, Siena Col-ge, Saint Rose College, Albany Junior College, and Maria College; 24 elementary schools, 1 senior high school, 25 private and parochial schools.

New construction: Albany has completed a major revamping of its downtown area. The $1-billion South Mall includes a 44-story state office tower, 4 large state agency buildings, as well as cultural buildings.

Recreational facilities: municipal golf course, private clubs, 2 large city parks with tennis, baseball, swimming facilities.

Other attractions: Dudley Observatory, Fort Crailo in Rensselaer, Joseph Henry Memorial Building, Ten Broeck Mansion, First Church in Albany (Reformed), Schuyler Mansion, State Capitol.

Government: 2d only to Washington, Albany is the most important governmental city in the U.S.; home city of the governor, state officials, and 30,000 state employees.

History: founded 1609 when Henry Hudson terminated his voyage in the Half Moon at the location where Albany was later settled by the Dutch.

Further information: Albany Chamber of Commerce, 508 Broadway, Albany, NY 12207.

Albuquerque, New Mexico

The World Almanac is sponsored in the Albuquerque area by the Albuquerque Tribune, 717 Silver Avenue SW Albuquerque, NM 87101; (505) 842-2300; founded June 22, 1922 by Carl Magee; a Scripps-Howard Newspap since Sept. 24, 1923; circulation 38,645; editor Ralph Looney; sponsors Tribune Annual Spelling Bee.

Population: 311,900 (city), 376,600 (county), 409,000 (metro area); first in state, 53d in nation; total employed 1977, 158,000.
Area: 81 sq. mi. on Rio Grande and Interstates 40, 25 and U.S. 66. Bernalillo County seat.
Industry: electronics with GTE-Lenkurt, Gulton, Sparton, Sandia Laboratories, General Electric, Digital Equipment Corp.; clothing with Levi Strauss, Pioneer Wear; movie production center.
Commerce: retail sales $1.57 billion; per capita income $5,213; bank resources $1.50 billion in 12 banks.
Transportation: Santa Fe Railway; Amtrak; Continental Trailways and Greyhound bus lines; Albuquerque Int'l Airport, hub for 7 airlines, average 621 air movements daily.
Communications: 5 TV and 21 radio stations.
New Construction: Value of building permits in 1976, $140 million, up 40% from 1975.
Medical facilities: 9 major hospitals.
Cultural facilities: symphony orchestra, 37 art galleries, 5 museums, 8 library branches, 16 legitimat theaters.
Educational facilities: Univ. of New Mexico, Univ. o Albuquerque, 111 public schools.
Recreational facilities: Sandia Peak ski area wit longest tramway in North America; 152 city parks, 1 swimming pools, 9 golf courses, 83 tennis courts Cibola National Forest, Rio Grande Zoo.
Convention facilities: $9.2 million convention cente with underground parking facility and 300-roor hotel; 106 motels and hotels.
Sports: Dukes AAA baseball, Univ. of New Mexic athletic activities.
History: founded Feb. 7, 1706; named for Duke c Alburquerque, viceroy of New Spain.
Further information: Chamber of Commerce, 401 2 NW, Albuquerque, NM 87102.

Allentown, Pennsylvania

The World Almanac is sponsored in the Allentown-Bethlehem-Easton area by Call-Chronicle Newspapers, 10 North 6th Street, Allentown, PA 18105; (215) 820-6500; Call founded 1883, daily circulation 103,000, Sunday 154,000; Chronicle founded 1870, circulation 22,000; publisher Donald P. Miller, executive editor Edward D. Miller sponsors Park & Shop, housing development, newspaper-in-the-classroom, newsprint recycling.

Population: Allentown 109,871; Bethlehem 73,084; Easton 30,256; metro area 545,000, 3d in state; total employed 231,000.
Area: 5,000 sq. mi. (metro) in eastern Pa. at Lehigh and Delaware rivers; Lehigh County seat.
Industry: Bethlehem Steel Corp., 2d largest in U.S.; home offices for Mack Truck Inc., Air Products & Chemicals, New Jersey Zinc Co., Allen Products (ALPO); area leads in textile production; transistor developed in Western Electric here.
Commerce: retail center for east-central Pa.; retail sales (1976) $1.92 billion; average family buying power 16,674.
Transportation: 4 major rail lines, 5 bus lines; 9 federal and state highways intersect area; jet airport averages 400 movements per day on 6 airlines.
Communications: 4 TV and 12 radio stations.
Medical facilities: 6 major hospitals.
Cultural facilities: Allentown Art Museum (including Kress Renaissance and Baroque collection), Bethlehem Bach Choir, Allentown Symphony, 7 theater groups (plus 4 summer); Allentown Band is oldes continuing concert band in U.S.; 10 colleges includin Lehigh Univ., Muhlenberg, Cedar Crest, and Lafayette serve 12,000 students.
Other attractions: center of "Pennsylvania Dutch" area, covered bridges; 1,400-acre park system; 1,170 acre game preserve, pre-Cambrian mountain range access to Appalachian Trail, many historic houses Allentown Fair, folk festivals, Liberty Bell Shrine.
Sports: fishing, small game hunting, auto racing a Pocono Raceway, Allentown Jets basketball, Olympi bicycle velodrome at Trexlertown.
History: settled in 1600s by Germans seeking religious freedom; Allentown founded 1762; hiding plac for Liberty Bell during Revolutionary War; GA founded Flag Day here 1906; Allentown one of 5 Firs Defender Companies in Civil War.
Further information: Chambers of Commerce i Allentown: 462 Walnut Street, 18105; Bethlehem: 1 W. Market Street, 18018; Easton: 157 S. 4th Street 18042.

Amarillo, Texas

The World Almanac is sponsored in the Amarillo area by the Amarillo Globe-News, 900 S. Harrison, Amarillo, TX 79166, (806) 376-4488; a division of the Southwestern Newspapers Corp., and publisher of Daily News, Globe Times and Sunday News-Globe; James L. Whyte, vice president and general manager; Jerry Huff, executive editor.

Population: 150,039 city; 170,418 metro area; 11th in state; total employed 82,140.
Area: 74.96 sq. mi. in central panhandle of Texas at junction of Interstate 40 and 27 in Potter and Randall counties; Potter County seat.
Industry: 3-state hub of $8.5 billion agribusiness market including wheat, beef, and produce, value $1.27 billion; ASARCO, Inc. copper refinery; Santa Fe rail welding plant; Bell Helicopter, Levi Strauss, Iowa Beef Processors, oil and gas, coal burning electricity plants, and Owens Corning Fiberglas plant.
Commerce: wholesale-retail center for 5-state area retail sales $590.52 million; bank resources $866.2 million, 5 savings and loan associations; 104th i wholesale sales among 230 metro areas.
Transportation: served by 4 airlines; 3 railroads, bus lines, 21 truck lines, 2 interstate, 4 federal, an one state highway intersect Amarillo.
Communications: 4 TV, 10 radio stations.

ledical facilities: 5 hospitals including VA facilities n metro area: mental health centers.
:ulture, recreation: Amarillo Symphony, Fine Arts omplex, Civic Center complex, summer musical, 'Texas"; regional history museum, Discovery Cener, 46 parks, 3 colleges, National Helium Monument.
;ports: drag racing, stock car racing, college and high school football, basketball, baseball, hockey; Gold Sox baseball, rodeo.
History: settled 1887 as railroad crew camp, incorporated 1892; named for yellow lake clay.
Further information: Amarillo Chamber of Commerce, Amarillo Bldg., 301 Polk, Amarillo, TX 79101.

Anchorage, Alaska

The World Almanac is sponsored in the Anchorage area by The Anchorage Times, 820 W. 4th Avenue, Anchorige, AK 99510; (907) 279-5622; founded 1915; circulation 47,000; editor-publisher Robert B. Atwood; sponsors ;pelling Bee, Kodak Photo Contest.

'opulation: city, borough unified in 1975. Total popuation of new municipality is 200,000 (1976), almost ıalf of state's population.
ırea: 927 sq. mi. (census district), at head of Cook nlet on south central coast.
ndustry and commerce: business center for most of ılaska; aviation, oil companies, railroading, shiping, and national defense activities are largest elenents in area's economy; headquarters for onstruction of $7 billion trans-Alaska oil pipeline.
'ransportation: Anchorage International Airport is najor refueling stop on transpolar flights; thousands f small planes make city one of country's busiest air raffic centers with 5 airports and 25% of world's sealanes in area; headquarters of Alaska Railroad; $10 nillion port.
:ommunications: 4 TV and 11 radio stations; 2 daily ıewspapers.
ledical facilities: 5 hospitals.
'ederal facilities: Elmendorf AFB, Ft. Richardson.

Cultural facilities: annual Festival of Music; 4 theater groups; fine arts museum; community concert organization, opera company, civic symphony.

Educational facilities: 57 elementary and secondary schools enroll 41,000; Univ. of Alaska, Alaska Methodist Univ.

Recreation: 2 major ski areas; cross-country skiing and bicycling; annual Fur Rendezvous with dogsled races; Iditarod dogsled race to Nome; Chugach National Forest.

Convention facilities: 5 major hotels and motels offer facilities for over 1,000 persons.

History: founded 1915 as headquarters for Alaska Railroad; twice winner of All America city award, for coping with rapid growth, and for swift recovery from catastrophic 1964 earthquake.

Further information: Chamber of Commerce, 612 F Street, Anchorage, AK 99501.

Atlanta, Georgia

'opulation: 445,300 (city), 1,841,200 (metro), first in tate, 18th in nation; total employed, 745,600 (metro, 976); state capital and Fulton County seat.

ırea: 136 sq. mi. in north central Georgia, on Piednont plateau of Blue Ridge foothills, 1,050 ft. above ea level; 4,326 sq. mil in 15-county metro area.

ndustry: 2,200 manufacturers produce more than ,500 commodities; 430 of Fortune 500 firms operate n Atlanta; Ford assembly plant, 2 GM assembly lants, Lockheed-Ga. Co.; home base for Coca-Cola, 'uqua Ind., Delta Air Lines, Equifax, Scripto, Genune Parts, Simmons Co., Gold Kist, Oxford Ind.

:ommerce: financial, retail, wholesale center of ;outheast; massive Merchandise Mart has 2d largest vholesale showroom in U.S. under one roof; 6th 'ederal Reserve District hdqtrs.; 84 banks, 428 ranches with resources of $8.9 billion (15-county netro); 22 savings and loan associations with 150 ranches in metro area with assets of $4.0 billion 1976).

'ransportation: founded as railroad center, now erved by 7 lines of 2 systems; Greyhound and Trailvays bus terminals used by 3 companies with 250 uses in and out daily; 9 passenger airlines, 4 comnuter carriers, one freight-only carrier; more than ,100 scheduled flights daily; nonstop passenger servce to 100 cities from Hartsfield International Airort, 2d busiest in world, over 27 million passengers 1976), and No. 1 commuting point in nation's domesic air route pattern. Metropolitan Atlanta Rapid 'ransit Authority at $2.1 billion, most massive pubicly financed project in Southeast since TVA; under onstruction is 52.9 mi. rapid rail, 8 mi. of rapid busvays coordinated with street bus operations; Southastern hub of 41,000 mi. interstate system with 6 egs of 3 interstate hwys. intersecting 100-acre downown interchange; 63 mi. hwy. encircles city.

Communications: 8 TV stations; 36 radio stations; Protestant Radio and TV Center; largest Bell System toll-free dialing area; one of nation's 5 TV and radio network control centers; 10 daily newspapers.
New construction: $400 million expansion Hartsfield Int. Airport, $77 million federal office bldg., $20 million downtown library, $2.1 billion MARTA rapid transit system; total value city building permits (1976) $86.3 million.
Medical facilities: 56 hospitals with 10,524 beds (metro), VA hospital; national Center for Disease Control of U.S. Pub. Health Dept., National Cancer Center at Emory Univ. Med. School.
Federal facilities: 31,600 federal, non-military employees; Ft. McPherson, hdqtrs. U.S. Army Forces Command; Ft. Gillem; Dobbins AF Base; NAS Atlanta.
Cultural facilities: Memorial Arts Center with museum, symphony orchestra, ballet, School of Art; Civic Center with auditorium-theater-exhibition hall; Callanwolde, new multi-use arts center; 29 degree-granting colleges, including Ga. Tech, Ga. State Univ., Emory Univ., Atlanta Univ. in 5-county central metro area with over 74,000 students.

Sports: NBA Hawks; NFL Falcons; NL Braves; NHL Flames; stadium seats 52,000; Omni arena, 16,500 World championship tennis, college football's Peach Bowl, PGA Atlanta Classic, Peachtree Road Race; road, sports car racing, motocross.

Convention facilities: 631,000 convention delegates in 1976; $35 million Ga. World Congress Center has largest single display room in U.S., equal to 8 football fields; simultaneous translation facilities; 28,000 hotel/motel rooms, most downtown or near.
History: named 1845, chartered 1847; burned by U.S. Gen. Wm. Sherman 1864.
Further information: Chamber of Commerce, 1300 Commerce Bldg., Atlanta, GA 30303.

Augusta, Georgia

The World Almanac is sponsored in the Augusta area by the Chronicle-Herald, 725 Broad Street, Augusta, GA 30903; (404) 724-0851; Chronicle established in 1785, circulation 53,842; Herald 19,405; Sunday, 77,734; William S. Morris III publisher, E.B. Skinner general manager, L.C. Harris editor, David L. Playford managing editor, Herald W.H. Eanes managing editor, Chronicle.

Population: 59,300 (city), 278,700 (metro area); total employed, 106,210 (metro).

Area: 1,713 sq. mi. (metro: Richmond, Columbia counties, Ga.; Aiken County, S.C.) straddling Savannah River; Augusta County seat.

Industry: diversified; Continental Can, Du Pont, Procter & Gamble, Lily-Tulip, Olin, Dymo, Monsanto, Columbia Nitrogen, A.E.C., TRW Corp.

Commerce: wholesale, retail center of 17 counties in 2 states; 1976 retail sales, $1.215 billion; per capita income, $4,045, per family income, $13,185; effective buying income, $1.950 billion; 7 banks, 5 savings-loan assns.; distribution center.

Transportation: 5 railroads, 26 truck lines, 3 airlines at modern airport and in-city field for executive planes; Interstate 20, other federal highways; river shipping.

Communications: 3 TV and 10 radio stations.

Medical facilities: 9 major hospitals, including Eisenhower Memorial at Ft. Gordon, Medical College of Georgia.

Federal facilities: Ft. Gordon and Savannah River (AEC) Plant.

Cultural facilities: Augusta College, Medical College of Ga., Paine College, Univ. of S.C. at Aiken; museum, art gallery, arts council with 25 affiliates; Augusta Symphony.

Recreational facilities: hunting, fishing, boating, camping; 7 golf courses; home of Masters Golf Tournament.

History: founded as fort 1717; named for wife of Prince of Wales 1735; capital of Georgia, 1778.

Further information: Chamber of Commerce of Greater Augusta, 600 Broad Street Plaza, Augusta, GA 30902.

Austin, Texas

The World Almanac is sponsored in the Austin area by The Austin American-Statesman, 308 Guadalupe Street Austin, TX 78701; (512) 397-1212; Statesman founded 1871, American 1914; combined 1924; published by Newspapers, Inc.; circulation, American-Statesman (morn.) 77,020, American-Statesman (aft.) 36,307, American-Statesman (Sunday) 113,327. The Austin American-Statesman, a division of Texas Newspapers Inc. Jim Fain publisher, Bill Meroney general manager, Ray Mariotti editor.

Population: 308,932 (city) 373,275 (metro area), 6th in state, 46th in nation; total employment 188,100.

Area: 91 sq. mi. in mid-Texas on Colorado River; state capital and Travis County seat.

Industry: electronics — Texas Instruments, IBM, Motorola, Tracor, Glastron (Conroy) Boats, Westinghouse Electric; county has 413 manufacturing firms.

Commerce: wholesale, retail center for 10 counties (950,000 pop.) in triangle of Dallas-Fort Worth, San Antonio, Houston; retail sales (1976) $1.1 billion; bank deposits $1.7 billion in 19 banks; 8 savings associations with assets of $861 million; 33 insurance home offices.

Transportation: 4 airlines; 3 railroads, Amtrak; 4 bus lines; 13 motor freight carriers; U.S. Interstate 35, U.S. 290, State 71, 79, 183.

Communications: 4 TV and cable, 13 radio stations.

Medical facilities: 7 hospitals, 1,100 beds; 600 physicians; 232 dentists.

Federal facilities: Bergstrom AFB; Internal Revenue Service center with 3,300 employes.

Cultural facilities: Univ. of Texas System & UT at Austin; Lyndon Baines Johnson Library dedicated 1971; other libraries; Texas Memorial and art museums; 85,000-seat stadium; law and other graduate schools; 4 small colleges; O. Henry home, Laguna Gloria, Elizabet Ney, and French Legation museums; 4 local theater companies, Austin Symphony, 2 ballet companies; city library, branches and mobile service; Austin public school district, 88 schools, 58,000 students.

State facilities: capitol and office building complex; 5 special schools for handicapped; psychiatric hospital, 37,500 employes.

Convention facilities: city auditorium seats 5,000.

Recreational facilities; 2 lakes, 7,000 acres of parks; pools, 6 golf courses, tennis courts; 3 annual fiestas: Aqua (motor boat racing), Laguna Gloria, and Highland Lakes arts and crafts.

Further information: Chamber of Commerce, 901 W Riverside Drive, P.O. Box 1967, Austin, TX 78767.

Bakersfield, California

The World Almanac is sponsored in the Bakersfield and Kern County area by The Bakersfield Californian (eves and Sunday), 1707 Eye Street, Bakersfield, CA 93302; phone (805) 323-7631; founded 1866 as Havilah Courier christened The Bakersfield Californian 1897; circulation: 60,874 daily, 67,292 Sunday; president Berenice Fritts Koerber, publisher Donald H. Fritts, executive director Alfred T. Fritts, managing editor James E. Griffith.

Population: 77,700 city, 197,410 metro, 348,700 Kern County.

Area: approximately 8,060 square miles in Kern County of which Bakersfield is county seat; in California's San Joaquin Valley.

Industry: oil, gas, agriculture, military; oil valuation $834 million; total agriculture production $744.3 million; Edwards AFB and China Lake Naval Test Station in eastern Kern County.

Commerce: retail sales in Kern $1.346 billion; total bank deposits $860 million.

Transportation: 2 railroads, 3 airlines, 2 bus lines, Interstate 5, Highway 99.

Communications: 3 TV and 12 radio stations; cable TV from Los Angeles.

Cultural facilities: symphony orchestra, Cunningham Art Gallery; 4-year state college, city college; community theater.

History: Kern County organized April 2, 1866, from portions of Los Angeles and Tulare counties; discovery of gold on Kern River in 1851 brought influx of settlers; oil discovered in 1865, with major boom in 1909; gold mining town of Havilah first county seat, moved to Bakersfield in 1875.

Baltimore, Maryland

The World Almanac is sponsored in the Baltimore area by The Baltimore News American, 301 E. Lombard Street, altimore, MD 21202; (301) 752-1212; founded in 1773 as the Maryland Journal and Baltimore Advertiser; Baltimore American founded 1799; Baltimore Evening News founded 1872; adopted present name 1964; daily circulation 178,707, Sunday 259,364; publisher, Mark F. Collins; general manager, Roy W. Anderson; executive editor, omas J. White; American Medical Association award, Howard W. Blakeslee and Albert Lasker awards.

pulation: 807,800 (city), 1,334,800 (metro.), first in ate, 7th in U.S.; total employment 302,820 (city), 7,510 (metro.).
rea: 91 sq. mi. (city), 2,225 sq. mi. (metro.) on Patapo River, a tributary of the Chesapeake Bay.
dustry: highly diversified, none dominating; most nportant are steel fabricating, shipbuilding and reairing; manufacture of electrical equipment and od containers; food processing, sugar, petroleum, emicals, copper; added value of manufacturing in 75 was $3.8 billion.
mmerce: metro area consists of city and 5 adjacent unties; estimated buying income $15,280 per avere household; retail sales about $6 billion in 1976, ea has 209 shopping centers with 3,591 stores; me ownership 57%.
ransportation: 3 railroads including Amtrak; altimore-Washington International Airport, served 15 lines, served 2,975,778 passengers in 1976; 150 rtified truck lines, tunnel carries motor traffic rough city under the harbor; buses operated by ate authority carry 374,000 passengers daily.
rt facilities: 120 steamship lines serve port, the naon's 4th largest and the farthest inland on the Atlan c Coast; in 1975, 4,193 ships moved 41 million short ns of international cargo; port was 2d largest coniner cargo port on the Atlantic and Gulf coasts; ading cargos are petroleum products, ores, grain, al, bananas, automobiles.
mmunications: 3 daily newspapers in city, 2 more metro area; 3 VHF TV stations, 2 UHF public oadcast stations; 25 radio stations.
ultural facilities: Enoch Pratt Free Library with 33 encies and 2.2 million volumes, metro county liraries have 28 branches; Baltimore Symphony Orestra, Maryland Ballet Co.; Baltimore Opera Co.; eale Museum, Carroll Mansion, Maryland Academy Sciences, Morris A. Mechanic Theater and Center age.
ducational facilities: 30 colleges and 20 junior colges including: Johns Hopkins Univ. and medical stitutions, Univ. of Md. (downtown and county camses), Loyola, Goucher, and Towson State Univ., organ State Univ., Peabody Conservatory of Music, d. Inst. College of Art, St. Mary's Seminary and Univ.; Ner Israel Rabbinical College.
Medical facilities: 26 general hospitals with 8,664 beds in metro area, including the renowned Johns Hopkins and the Univ. of Md. and its Institute for Emergency Medicine.
Sports: Memorial Stadium, home of football Colts and baseball Orioles; horse racing, including Preakness at Pimlico and the International race at Laurel; Bowie and Timonium tracks nearby. Chesapeake Bay's 1,700 square miles of open water are noted for fishing, boating, and waterfowl hunting; ocean and ski resorts within a 3 hour drive.

Convention facilities: Civic Center, 45 meeting rooms, 87,160 sq. ft. of exhibition space; 7 hotels downtown and over 100 motels in or near the city.

Other attractions: Fort McHenry Historic Shrine where Francis Scott Key wrote "The Star Spangled Banner," U.S. Frigate Constellation; the Flag House; Baltimore and Ohio Transportation Museum; Edgar Allan Poe's home and grave; Babe Ruth's home; annual Preakness Festival Week in May; Mother Seton House. Most of the central business district rebuilt in last 15 years; Inner Harbor project has provided Baltimore with the World Trade Center, Academy of Science Building, and a floating restaurant; presently in the works are an aquarium, marina, new hotels, and the restoration of early 19th century rowhouses; many old neighborhoods are experiencing a revival with early townhouses being preserved.

History: founded 1729 by act of the Provincial Assembly of the Maryland Colony which was established by members of the Calvert family, the Lords of Baltimore; early economy based on shipment of tobacco, grain, flower, and on shipbuilding; privateering in the War of 1812 tempted British to try to capture the American "nest of pirates". When economic growth was threatened by completion of the Erie Canal, the city's business leaders countered by building the nation's first railroad, the Baltimore and Ohio.

Further information: Chamber of Commerce Metro. Baltimore, 22 Light Street; Baltimore Promotion Council, 102 St. Paul Street, both Baltimore, MD 21202.

Baton Rouge, Louisiana

The World Almanac is sponsored in the Baton Rouge area by the Morning Advocate and State-Times, 525 Lafaye Street, Baton Rouge, LA 70821; (504) 383-1111; founded 1842; combined daily circ., 112,000; Sunday, 105,-0; president, Charles P. Manship Jr.; publisher, Douglas L. Manship; director of news and production, Richard almer; bus. mgr., Charles Garvey; executive editor, all newspapers, Jim Hughes; managing editors, Edwin Price . (Morning Advocate), Jack Lord (State-Times).

opulation: 165,963 (city), 392,400 (metro); total 1976 ty-parish employment, 177,425.
rea: city, 42.83 sq. mi.; parish, 407.01 sq. mi.; on east ank of Mississippi River, 80 mi. northeast of New rleans; state capitol, East Baton Rouge Parish seat.
dustry: northern anchor of 100-mi. long petroemical complex along Mississippi River.
ommerce: marketing center for major trade area of 0,000; bank resources, $1.9 billion; 6 banks, 7 savgs and loan associations.
ransportation: major transfer point on southern deral interstate system; 2 airports with 4 airlines; 2 us lines; 4 railroad trunk lines; Port of Baton Rouge, h largest in U.S., handled over 62 million tons in 976.
ommunications: 4 TV and 9 radio stations; 2 daily ewspapers, 2 weeklies.

Cultural facilities: 6 museums, 4 theaters, symphony, planetarium, 5 art galleries; new "Riverside Centroplex" civic center.
Educational facilities: Louisiana State Univ., founded 1860, center of 8-campus system; Southern Univ., largest Negro land-grant college in U.S., center of 3-college system.

Sports: LSU Tigers and Southern Jaguars home stadia, football, basketball, track.

Other attractions: state capitol; city-parish zoo and arboretum; 67 parks; major recreational lakes.

History: first noted by French explorer Iberville in 1699, Baton Rouge (French: red stick) was already occupied by the Istrouma (also translates red stick) Indians; Louisiana's capital since 1836; government structure is a city-parish combination with a mayor-

president and city-parish council.
Further information: Chamber of Commerce, P.O. Box 1868, Baton Rouge, 70821; Louisiana Tourist Commission, P.O. Box 44291, Capitol Station, Baton Rouge, 70804; Baton Rouge Area Convention and Visitors Bureau, P.O. Box 3202, Baton Rouge, 70821.

Billings, Montana

The World Almanac is sponsored in the Billings area by the Billings Gazette, 401 N. Broadway, Billings, MT 59101; telephone (406) 245-3071; founded 1885; member of Lee Enterprises, Inc., since 1960; circulation, daily 58,556; Sunday, 61,150; publisher George Remington, editor William N. Roesgen.

Population: 79,406 (city), 98,000 (metro area), first in state; total employed (non-agri) 45,900.
Area: south central Montana on Yellowstone River, 125 mi. from Yellowstone Park, Yellowstone County seat.
Industry: 3 oil refineries, beet sugar refinery, 2 packing plants, 3d largest livestock auction yards in U.S., center for Northern Great Plains coal industry.
Commerce: wholesale-retail center for eastern Montana, northern Wyoming; retail sales $332 million; bank debits $5.7 billion; 6 banks, 2 savings and loan associations, 160 wholesale firms, 712 retail firms; average spendable family income $12,538.
Transportation: 3 airlines, 1 railroad, 2 bus lines, 98 motor carriers, Interstates 90 and 94.
Communications: 2 TV and 8 radio stations, one weekly, one daily newspaper.
Medical facilities: 2 hospitals, 422 beds, 11 clinics, 150 doctors, 60 dentists, 5 nursing homes, Northern Rockies Regional Cancer Treatment Ctr., Regional Mental Health Center.
Cultural facilities: 4 art galleries, symphony orchestra, 2 western museums, studio theater, liberal arts college, business college, private (church related) college, Metra Civic Center sports and concerts, 4 golf courses, 85 churches, 2 nursing schools, voc-tech program, 30 public schools, 10 parochial schools, Center for Handicapped Children, Migrant Children's Program.
New construction: $1.6 million parking garage; $1.[illegible] million savings & loan; $1.5 million bakery; $1.0 million grocery/drug complex; housing $11.5 million; [illegible] elem. schools $2.5 million; $.6 million college science expansion.
Other attractions: big game hunting, fishing, boating, skiing within hour's drive; snowmobiling, bicycling, saddle clubs; 22 city parks, 1,882 hotel-motel rooms, convention facilities 5,000; Metra capacity 10,000.
History: founded 1882 with arrival of Northern Pacific Railroad; named after Frederic Billings, then NP president; now largest city in 500-mile radius.
Further information: Tourist Information Bureau, Billings Chamber of Commerce, P.O. Box 2519, Billings, MT 59103.

Binghamton, New York

The World Almanac is sponsored in the Binghamton area by The Evening Press and The Sun-Bulletin, Vestal Parkway East, Binghamton, NY 13902; 607-798-1234; circulation: daily 70,802; Sunday 77,365; morning 26,968; Saturday morning and Holidays 75,601; president and publisher Brian J. Donnelly, Press editor George R. Venizelos; Sun-Bulletin editor Michael G. Doll.

Population: 60,500 (city), 302,800 (metro area), 12th in state; total employed 120,200.
Area: 10.98 sq. mi. at junction of Chenango and Susquehanna rivers. Broome County seat.
Industry: GAF, second largest producer of film in country; computers, IBM; electronics & simulators, Singer Co.; shoes, Endicott Johnson Corp.; a major railroad center.
Commerce: wholesale-retail center of area producing $490 million a year; 11 banks; national headquarters of Security Mutual Life Insurance Co. and Columbian Mutual Life Insurance Co.
Transportation: 5 airlines, major being Allegheny, out of Broome County Airport; intersection Interstates 81 & 88 and Route 17; Erie-Lackawanna and Delaware and Hudson freight rail carriers.
Communications: 3 TV and 4 radio stations.
Medical facilities: 4 major hospitals.
Cultural facilities: Roberson Center Arts & Sciences; State Univ. at Binghamton; Broome County College; Tri-Cities Opera Co.; symphony orchestra; public library; civic theater.
Other attractions: municipal parks zoo; major state park on outskirts; Veterans Memorial Arena.
Sports: Dusters pro-hockey team.
History: Settled 1800; became rail center by 1848, with roads replacing old Chenango Canal that fed Erie Canal; named for Philadelphia patriot and multi-millionaire William Bingham.
Further information: Broome County Chamber of Commerce Tourist Information, 84 Court Street, Binghamton, NY 13902.

Birmingham, Alabama

The World Almanac is sponsored in the Birmingham area by The Birmingham Post-Herald, 2200 Fourth Avenue N. Birmingham, AL 35202; telephone (205) 325-2222; Post founded 1921 by Scripps-Howard Newspapers; Herald founded 1887; circulation, 75,630; editor Duard LeGrand, vice president W. H. Metz, managing editor George Cook; major public service projects include Goodfellow Christmas Fund, Alabama Favorite Teacher selection.

Population: 276,273 (city, 1975 est.), 644,688 (county, 1975 est.), 791,073 (metro, 1975 est.), employment 339,700 (metro, 1977).
Area: 89 sq. mi. in north central Alabama; state's largest city; Jefferson County seat.
Industry: heavy manufacturing in metals; U.S. Steel is area's largest employer; U.S. Pipe and Foundry and American Cast Iron Pipe Co. are in top 10 employers; South Central Bell's 5-state headquarters located in city.
Commerce: wholesale-retail center for Alabama; retail sales, (1976) $4.15 billion; bank debits (1976) $70.7 billion; 14 banks (county); 6 bank holding companies; 7 savings and loan assns.
Transportation: 5 major rail freight lines, Amtrak; Greyhound and Continental Trailways bus lines; Eastern, Delta, United, and Southern air lines with modern airport terminal; 75 truck line terminals; 3 interstate highways, I-65, I-59 and I-20 all under construction.
Communications: 2 daily newspapers, 3 commercial TV stations, 16 commercial radio stations, one PBS TV and one PBS radio outlet.
Medical facilities: Univ. of Alabama in Birmingham

edical Center covers 60 sq. blocks; heart surgery am brings patients from all over the world; Veterıs Administration hospital, in same complex, is the se of organ transplant program; Baptist Medical enters have 2 major hospitals; 13 other hospitals.
ıltural facilities: symphony orchestra; Oscar Wells useum of Art with more than $4 million in assets; vic Opera; 4 resident civic theaters; 2 resident balt companies.
lucation: Samford Univ., Birmingham-Southern, iles, and Daniel Payne colleges; Jefferson State and wson State junior colleges.
onvention facilities: civic center with exhibition ıll, theater, music hall, and coliseum; several new onvention hotels and motels in civic center area.
ports: Birmingham Bulls (WHA) moved from oronto in '76; nicknamed "Football Capital of the outh" for Univ. of Alabama and Auburn Univ. games played at municipal stadium, Legion Field.
Other attractions: world's 2d largest cast iron statue, Vulcan, mythical god of the forge, overlooks Birmingham from Red Mountain as a symbol of the steel industry; Arlington Shrine, antebellum home that housed federal troops during Civil War; Botanical Gardens complex with Japanese Garden; Jimmie Morgan Zoo; extensive city park system.
History: chartered 1871; soon became known as the "Magic City" because of its rapid growth brought on by the presence of the 3 ingredients in steelmaking — coal, iron ore, and lime; mining died out in recent years and most iron ore is now imported by ship and barge to Birmingport on Warrior River from South America; coal mining, in decline since the 1940s, is on the upswing.
Further information: Chamber of Commerce, 1914 Sixth Avenue N., Birmingham, AL 35203.

Bismarck, North Dakota

The World Almanac is sponsored in western North Dakota by the Bismarck Tribune, 222 Fourth Street, Bismarck, D 58501; (701) 223-2500; founded 1873 as weekly, became daily 1881; circ. 28,500; publisher A. G. Sorlie, editor ohn O. Hjelle, advertising director J. Joe Miller; major awards include Pulitzer Prize Gold Medal, 1937.

opulation: 42,002 (est. 1977), 3d in state; total emloyed 20,463.

rea: 14 sq. mi. on Missouri River. State capital and urleigh County seat.

ıdustry: agriculture, printing, trucking, farm maninery, state government, electric power, manufacıring, concrete products, railroad, insurance, liveock sales rings, lignite coal.

ommerce: retail trade area radius 100 miles, servıg 150,000 people; retail sales (1976) $178 million; ank deposits (1976) $564 million; 5 banks, 5 building nd loan associations.

ransportation: 2 rail lines, Amtrak; airport, hub for airlines; 13 truck lines; 4 bus lines; U.S. Highways 3 and 83, I-94.

ommunications: one daily newspaper; 3 AM, 2 FM adio stations; 2 TV stations.

ew construction: 1976 building permits, $44.8 milon (867 housing units).

edical facilities: 2 hospitals, 450 bed capacity, rved by 70 M.D.s.

Federal facilities: federal buildings house 20 offices; 14th Radar Bomb Scoring Detachment.

Cultural facilities: Bismarck Junior College; Mary College; 72,000-volume public library; state library; state museum; Elan Gallery; 45 churches.

Recreation: 20 parks with over 1,250 acres; indoor artificial ice arena; 3 golf courses; 5 swimming pools; playgrounds; tennis courts; YMCA; duck and goose hunting; fishing; nearby Fort Lincoln State Park.

Convention facilities: 8,000 seat Civic Center; 1,300 rooms; 5 banquet and meeting facilities for groups of 200-700.

Other attractions: Dakota Zoo; Garrison Dam; United Tribes of North Dakota Educational Technical Center; state capitol.

History: founded 1872 as Edwinton, a rail town; name changed to Bismarck in 1873 to encourage German investment capital.

Further information: Chamber of Commerce, 412 Sixth Street, Bismarck, ND 58501.

Bloomington, Illinois

The World Almanac is sponsored in Bloomington-Normal and central Illinois by The Daily Pantagraph, 301 W. Washington Street, Bloomington, IL 61701; (309) 829-9411; founded 1837 by Jesse W. Fell; circulation 52,259; resident and publisher Davis U. Merwin; editor Harold Liston; general manager William Diesel; managing editor ene F. Smedley.

opulation: 77,367 Bloomington-Normal, 114,192 netro area) McLean County; mid-way between hicago and St. Louis in central Illinois.

ıdustry: over 50 industries in county, ranks 9th in surance cities in U.S., home offices of State Farm, ountry Companies, Union Auto; uniform diversity f non-agricultural employment in all major work orce areas; leads nation in corn and soybean producon with 2,316 farms in county.

ommerce: 1976 metro retail sales $349.5 million; er household income $17,312; per household retail les, $9,268.

ransportation: new terminal at B-N Airport, 3 bus nes, 6 federal and state highways, 4 railroads, Amak, 35 interstate and 23 intrastate motor carriers, zark Airlines.

Communications: 6 radio stations.

Medical facilities: 3 hospitals; Watson-Gailey Foundation Eye Bank.

Cultural facilities: Illinois Wesleyan Univ., 1,650, in Bloomington; Illinois State Univ., 18,000, in Normal; 49 churches; home of American Passion Play; B-N Symphony, community players, amateur musical.

History: incorporated 1850; site of A. Lincoln's "Lost Speech" and David Davis mansion, state historical shrine; city's Stevenson family has produced 3 generations of leadership; vice president Adlai E.; governor, presidential candidate and UN Ambassador, Adlai E. II; and U.S. Senator Adlai E. III.

Further information: Association of Commerce and Industry of McLean County, 210 S. East Street, Bloomington, IL 61701.

Boise, Idaho

The World Almanac is sponsored in the Boise area by the Idaho Statesman, 1200 N. Curtis Road, Boise, II 83704; (208) 376-2121; founded 1864 as Tri-Weekly; daily circulation 60,282; Sunday 68,764; publisher Robert E Miller Jr., general manager C. Ralph Guilieri, managing editor Gary L. Watson; a Gannett newspaper.

Population: 101,200 (city), 139,600 (metro area), first in state, 204th in nation; total employed 75,350.
Area: 1,054 sq. mi. on Boise River at foot of Salmon River Mountains; state capital and Ada County seat.
Industry: mobile home and recreational trailers produced $240 million in 1976; world headquarters Boise Cascade Corp., Morrison-Knudsen Co., and Albertson Food Stores.
Commerce: wholesale and retail center for southwest Idaho; retail sales $433.9 million (1976); bank resources $706.6 million in 6 banks with 27 branches; 4 savings and loan associations, and 7 insurance company offices.
Transportation: 2 major airlines, 2 feeder airlines, one rail freight line, 4 bus lines, 17 common carrier truck lines; Amtrak.
Communications: 4 TV and 9 radio stations.
Medical facilities: 3 major hospital complexes includ ing a Veteran's Administration facility.
Cultural facilities: Boise Philharmonic Orchestra, ar gallery, state museum, Boise Little Theatre, new $1.4 million public library, Boise State University.
Other attractions: 33 parks, Southwestern Idaho Fairgrounds, 2 major recreational lakes, scenic mountain areas; Bogus Basin ski resort offers one of the world's longest illuminated ski runs.
History: founded 1863; name derived from "les bois" (the trees), a description for area used by French fur trappers in 1811.
Further information: Boise Chamber of Commerce P. O. Box 2368, or Department of Commerce & Development, Idaho Statehouse, both Boise, ID 83701.

Boston, Massachusetts

The World Almanac is sponsored in the Boston area by The Boston Herald American, 300 Harrison Avenue Boston, MA, 02106; (617) 426-3000. Herald American established 1972; daily circulation 293,004; Sunday 421,684. Publisher Robert Bergenheim, executive editor William McIlwain, general manager Dennis Mulligan. Pulitze Prize, Sigma Delta Chi distinguished service awards, Heywood Broun award, AP & UPI first place awards.

Population: 636,960 (city); 2,899,000 (metro area of 92 cities and towns around Boston; 5th largest metropolitan area in nation.
Area: 46 sq. mi. on Massachusetts Bay; state capital and Suffolk County seat.
Commerce: northeast center for finance and insurance; home for 50 insurance companies and regional hqs. for most U.S. and foreign companies; banking center for New England with total deposits of $12.264 billion (1972); birthplace of mutual fund, accounts for 35% of the nation's mutual fund holdings; retail center for northern New England; median family income $8,133 (city), $11,449 (metro); major electronics industry and publishing center.
Transportation: terminating point for 2 railroads, Amtrak and Boston & Maine; MBTA (Massachusetts Bay Transportation Authority) provides surface and subway transportation for metropolitan Boston; Massachusetts Port Authority (operates Logan International Airport and the Port of Boston (shipping); 5 interstate highways.
Communications: 2 newspapers, 7 TV and 31 radio stations.
New construction: John Hancock Tower; Blue Cross-Blue Shield, Mass. hqs.; Stone & Webster Engineering hqs.; Federal Reserve Tower; Faneuil Hall market area; National Shawmut Bank; West End residential-office complex, Atlantic Ave. waterfront, 60 State St. Bldg.
Medical facilities: health care is Boston's largest industry in terms of dollars invested; major institutions: Mass. General, Children's, and New England medical centers; Boston City, Beth Israel, Deaconess hospitals; Harvard, Boston Univ., and Tufts medical schools; Lahey Clinic.
Federal facilities: 50 federal agencies employ 45,700 (military facilities not included).
Cultural facilities: the "Athens of America"; Boston Public Library includes capacity for 500,000 books on open shelf, plus large lecture hall; Boston Symphony Orchestra; Boston Pops; opera company; Boston Ballet; Museum of Fine Art; Museum of Science and Hayden Planetarium; New England Aquarium; Isabella Stewart Gardner Museum; Museum of Transportation; Children's Museum.
Educational facilities: 16 degree-granting institution in the city and 47 in the metro area, including Harvard, Boston College, Boston Univ., Tufts, M.I.T Brandeis, Univ. of Mass., Suffolk, Emmanuel, Simmons, and Wentworth Inst.
Recreation: 2,327 acres of city recreation area, includes historic Boston Common and Public Garden Metropolitan District Commission provides extensiv facilities, including beaches and harbor islands.
Convention facilities: 49 hotels equipped to handl conventions; exhibition halls include Commonwealth Pier Exhibition Hall with 168,000 sq. ft. and John B Hynes Veterans Auditorium in Prudential Cente with 154,000 sq. ft. and auditorium seating 5,800.
Sports: pro teams include Red Sox (baseball), Celtic (basketball), New England Patriots (football), Bruins (hockey), Astros (soccer), and Lobsters (tennis).
Other attractions: "The Freedom Trail," a 1 1/2-mil walk through historic Boston; Beacon Hill and Bac Bay historical districts; U.S.S. Constitution, "Ol Ironsides," oldest commissioned ship in U.S. Navy reconstruction of Boston Tea Party ship, the "Bea ver." "Boston 200" — audio-visual perspective on cit (at Prudential Center).
Nicknames: The Hub (of the Universe), Bean Town.
History: capital city of commonwealth, founded 1630 from 1770, Boston was scene of many events leadin to American Revolution, including Boston Tea Part on Dec. 16, 1773; incorporated Feb. 23, 1822.
Further information: Boston Chamber of Commerce 125 High Street, Boston, MA 02110.

Bridgeport, Connecticut

The World Almanac is sponsored in the Bridgeport area by The Bridgeport Post (evening), The Bridgeport Telegram (morning), and The Bridgeport Sunday Post, published by The Post Publishing Co., 410 State Street, Bridge port, CT 06602; (203) 333-0161; circulation Post, 77,463, Telegram, 15,432, Sunday Post, 90,903; John E. Pfriem president and general manager, Leonard E. Gilbert managing editor.

Population: 142,960 (U.S. Census Bureau, est. 1975) largest in state; planning region, 326,800; 9-town district labor force, 146,040.
Area: 17.5 sq. mi. on north shore of Long Island Sound at mouth of the Pequonnock River in Fairfield County.
Industry: "Industrial Capital of Connecticut"; products include tools, metallic cartridges, wiring devices, brass goods, valves, corsets, electrical apparatus and appliances; nearby are Sikorsky Aircraft and Avco Lycoming; General Electric has its corporate headquarters in Fairfield, one mile from city line.
Commerce: retail sales, $384.3 million (1976); downtown renewal includes completed complex with Gimbels and Sears stores, mall, 2,000-car parking garage, U.S. courthouse; also 2 new bank buildings, major addition to another; new state courthouse; construction completed on downtown residential project.
Transportation: $3 million railroad station opened in 1975, to be connected with planned $7 million multi-transportation center with bus terminal, 1,500-car parking garage. City served by Conn. Turnpike (Interstate 95); historic U.S. 1 (Boston Post Road); 2 airlines at municipal Sikorsky Memorial Airport; Conrail; 2 national bus lines; summer ferry to Port Jefferson, L.I.
Medical facilities: 3 general hospitals, state mental health center; new $5.5 million municipal convalescent hospital; major Easter Seal rehabilitation center.
Cultural facilities: Univ. of Bridgeport, Fairfield Univ., Sacred Heart Univ., Housatonic Community College; Museum of Art, Science, Industry; P. T. Barnum museum; symphony orchestra; municipally-supported downtown cabaret theater; American Shakespeare theater in adjoining town of Stratford.
Recreational facilities: "The Park City" has 1,200 acres of parks, including Seaside with 2-mile shoreline; zoo; municipal indoor ice-skating rink; new $16 million jai alai fronton, one of the largest in world.
Further information: Bridgeport Area Chamber of Commerce, 180 Fairfield Avenue, Bridgeport, CT 06604.

Buffalo, New York

The World Almanac is sponsored in the Buffalo area by The Courier-Express, 785 Main Street, Buffalo, NY 14240; (716) 847-5353; founded 1926, as merger of Courier and Express by William J. Conners Sr.; circulation mornings 125,082, Sunday 273,909; publisher William J. Conners III, asst. to publisher William J. Conners IV; treasurer R. C. Lyons, gen. mgr. Donald J. Maul; sponsors hole-in-one tournament, learn to swim program, ski school, Goodfellows.

Population: 1,349,211 (metro area), 462,768 (city); 2d in state; employment 508,000 (metro); hub of broad 8 county area with population of 1,758,000.
Area: 49.6 sq. mi. city, 1,567 sq. mi. metro; at western end of N.Y. State on Lake Erie, Niagara River, and U.S.-Can. boundary; Erie County seat. Metro area includes cities of Niagara Falls, Lockport, Tonawanda, N. Tonawanda, Lackawanna.
Industry: 1,602 manufacturing establishments with $6.3 billion in shipments, highly diversified; headquarters for Carborundum, Buffalo Forge, Trico Products, Fisher-Price Toys; large plants for National Gypsum, Bethlehem Steel, Chevrolet, Ford, Westinghouse, Union Carbide.
Commerce: wholesale and financial center for western N.Y. area; retail sales $3.3 billion (metro); average income per household after taxes (metro), $13,536; distribution center for northeastern U.S. and Canada; $6.5 billion in trade between U.S. and Canada handled each year; 13 commercial banks, 3 savings banks, 8 savings and loans.
Transportation: Greater Buffalo Int. Airport served by 4 scheduled airlines with 3 million passengers, 146,851 scheduled and non-scheduled flights in 1976; 6 major railroads, 10 freight terminals; about 150 motor carriers; highway system includes New York State Thruway. Direct highway and rail service to all parts of Canada; direct water service to entire Great Lakes-St. Lawrence Seaways system, overseas, and Atlantic seaboard.
Communications: 2 Buffalo newspapers, 3 additional dailies and one Sunday in surrounding cities; 5 TV and 19 AM and FM radio stations; 3 cable systems.
Cultural facilities: Buffalo Philharmonic in Kleinhans Music Hall; Albright-Knox Art Gallery; Studio Arena theater; Museum of Science; Historical Museum; Zoological Gardens (23 acres); Shaw Festival at Niagara-on-the-Lake, Ontario; Performing Arts Center (Artpark) in Lewiston.
Educational facilities: State Univ. at Buffalo (now building $650 million new campus), State College at Buffalo, Niagara University, Canisius College; 5 other colleges; several 2-year institutions.
Convention facilities: newly rebuilt Memorial Auditorium seats up to 17,000; new Buffalo convention center now being built; new Niagara Falls Convention Center seats up to 12,000; additional facilities available at several hotels and motels.
Sports attractions: Bills football (NFL), Sabres hockey (NHL), Braves basketball (NBA); Rich Stadium; Breskis pro women's softball, Blazers pro soccer.
Recreation: abundant facilities for all year around sports and activities; near both U.S. and Canada vacationlands.
Other attractions: Niagara Falls and river areas from Buffalo to Lake Ontario; Robert Moses and Adam Beck hydro stations, St. Lawrence Seaway, Welland Canal Locks, Aquarium (Niag. Falls), Our Lady of Victory Basilica (Lackawanna); Old Fort Niagara; Letchworth and Allegany state parks.
Further information: Chamber of Commerce, 238 Main, Buffalo, NY 14202.

Calgary, Alberta, Canada

The World Almanac is sponsored in the Calgary and southern Alberta area by The Calgary Albertan, 830 Tenth Avenue SW, Calgary, Alta., T2R 0B1; (403) 263-7730; founded 1902; circulation 49,180; publisher John Hamilton; managing editor Les Buhasz; business manager Al Vogt.

Population: 482,643.
Area: 212 sq. mi.; elevation 3,440 feet; in foothills of Rocky Mountains, 150 miles north of the Montana-Alberta border.
Industry: over 500 firms directly connected with the oil industry have headquarters in Calgary; also

chemical, fertilizer and supply industries, and older agricultural industries; manufacturing value in 1976, $1.5 billion; manufacturing payroll, 1976, $324 million; trading area population (1977, est.) 931,835; assistance in locating industrial information provided by Bruce McDonald, director, business development, City Hall, Calgary.
Commerce: retail sales volume, 1976, $1.6 billion.
Transportation: 2 railways, Greyhound bus lines, International Airport served by 6 airlines.
Communications: 3 TV and 6 radio stations; 2 local, 4 U.S. cable stations; 2 daily, 3 weekly newspapers.
Medical facilities: 6 major hospital complexes.
New construction: building permits in 1976 totaled $448 million.
Cultural facilities: 2,700-seat auditorium; Glenbow Museum; QR Arts Centre; centennial planetarium; symphony orchestra, live theater.
Federal facilities: Gov't. of Canada building under construction downtown; one armed forces base.
Education: public schools enroll more than 100,000; separate (Catholic) schools enroll 20,000; Univ. of Calgary enrolls more than 12,000; Mount Royal Junior College; Southern Alberta Institute of Technology; Strathcona-Tweedsmuir co-ed private school.
Recreation: 5 public, 5 private golf courses; 11 indoor, 12 outdoor swimming pools; 11 ice arenas; 11 athletic parks.
Convention facilities: Calgary Convention Centre accommodates 2,400 in one large room, 10 smaller rooms accommodate from 18 to 220.
Sports: facilities for hockey, football, and curling; Stampeders of Canadian Football League; Cowboys, WHA.
Other attractions: Calgary Stampede in July; Heritage Park reconstructs pioneer life; Calgary Zoo and Natural History Park; 626 ft. rotating Calgary Tower gives panoramic view of city, seats 200 for dining and 300 in observation area.

History: began as mounted police outpost; in 1885, when railway arrived, had a population of 1,800; discovery of oil in 1914 at Turner Valley contributed to Calgary's present prominence.

Further information: Chamber of Commerce, 273 - One Palliser Square; Tourist and Convention Bureau, Mewata Park, 1300 Sixth Avenue SW, both Calgary, Alta.

Charleston, West Virginia

The World Almanac is sponsored in the Charleston area by The Charleston Gazette, 1001 Virginia Street, East, Charleston, WV 25330; (304) 348-5140; circulation (morn) 57,874, (Sun.) 107,317; founded 1873 as the Kanawha Chronicle, became The Charleston Gazette 1898; W. E. Chilton III publisher; Don Marsh editor; Dallas C. Higbee executive editor.

Population: 65,807 (city), 226,900 (Kanawha County), most populous county in state; county labor force, 85,800.
Area: 29.3 sq. mi. at meeting place of the Elk and Kanawha rivers; state capital.
Industry: diversified industrial complex, with coal and chemicals dominating; center for production of limestone, lumber, salt brines, vitreous clays and natural gas; also glass, petroleum products, alloys.
Commerce: wholesale, retail center for central and southern West Virginia; county retail sales, $694.3 million; average family income, $13,970.
Transportation: 2 rail freight lines, Amtrak, bus lines, state's busiest airport; barge lines, 3 interstate highways.
Communications: 3 TV and 7 radio stations.
Medical facilities: 6 hospitals, 2 of them major complexes.
Cultural facilities: modern civic center and auditorium, Sunrise Cultural and Art Center, symphony orchestra, Community Music Assn., Light Opera Guild, Kanawha Players, State Museum, Morris Harvey College, W. Va. Univ. Graduate Center.
Other attractions: Coonskin Park, Kanawha State Forest, 6 golf courses, public tennis, International League baseball.
History: first settlement, Fort Lee, 1788; Virginia Assembly established Charles Town 1794; named Charleston 1818.
Further information: Charleston Area Chamber of Commerce, 818 Virginia Street, East, Charleston, WV 25301.

Charlotte, North Carolina

The World Almanac is sponsored in the Charlotte area by The Charlotte Observer, 600 S. Tryon Street, Charlotte, NC 28233; (704) 374-7070; founded 1886 as Charlotte Chronicle; changed to Charlotte Daily Observer, March 1892; sold to Knight Newspapers Inc. 1955; circulation 167,508 daily, 226,021 Sunday; president and publisher Rolfe Neill; editor C.A. McKnight; executive editor David Lawrence.

Population: 306,000 (city), 398,000 (Mecklenburg County), 615,000 (Charlotte-Gastonia metro area), 65th in nation; labor force 306,700.
Area: 105 sq. mi. in Piedmont section of N.C., a plateau extending from the Appalachians to the Coastal Plains.
Industry: over 670 manufacturing companies, industrial chemicals, textiles, food products, machinery, printing and publishing.
Commerce: major trucking center, photographic and data processing center, 1,400 wholesale firms with $6.7 billion sales; retail sales $2.8 billion (SMSA 1977) EBI per household $15,399; 16 banks, 11 mortgage banks, 6 building and loan associations.
Transportation: 115 trucking firms; 2 major railway lines; 4 bus lines; 5 airlines with 184 air movements per day.
Communications: 5 TV and 12 radio stations.
Medical facilities: an outstanding center in Southeast, 7 hospitals including 3 large general.
Cultural facilities: Opera Assn.; Charlotte Symphony Orchestra; Oratorio Society; Mint Museum (art); Nature Museum; Spirit Square (facility for all art activities under one roof); over 400 churches; Discovery Place (new museum).
Education: Univ. of N.C.-Charlotte; Davidson College; Johnson C. Smith Univ.; Queens College; Central Piedmont Community College; Kings College; Biscayne-Southern College.
Convention facilities: Charlotte Coliseum-Auditorium; Civic Center; Trade Mart; Merchandise Mart; many private convention facilities.
Sports: Charlotte Motor Speedway (NASCAR) with World 600 and National 500 races; Kemper Open golf tournament; NCNB Tennis Classic; Charlotte Orioles (professional baseball).

Other attractions: 2 major recreational lakes; Carowinds (family theme park); climate — four distinct seasons, avg. daily max. temp. 71.3, yearly avg. temp. 60.5; Festival in the Park; Southern Living Show.

History: incorporated 1768; named for Queen Charlotte of England; played major role in American Revolution; was gold mining capital of country before 1849; U.S. Mint built in 1836 to serve gold mining industry.

Further information: Chamber of Commerce, P.O. Box 1867, Charlotte, NC 28233.

Chattanooga, Tennessee

The World Almanac is sponsored in the Chattanooga area by the Chattanooga News-Free Press, 400 E. 11th Street, Chattanooga, TN 37401, (615) 756-6900; circulation 63,456 daily and 69,014 Sunday; publisher Roy McDonald, president Frank McDonald, senior vice president Everett Allen, vice president and editor Lee Anderson, secretary J. W. Hoback, treasurer Clifford Welch.

Population: 170,046 (city), 391,300 (metro area); 4th in state, 89th in nation; 174,100 employed in labor force.

Area: 2,109.8 sq. mi. metropolitan shopping area at juncture of Tennessee River and North Georgia boundary line; Hamilton County seat.

Industry: over 600 manufacturers employ 57,300; receipts added by manufacture in 1973, $989 million; producing more than 1,500 classified products including principal products of textile, fabricated metals, chemicals, primary metals, food products, machinery, apparel, paper products, and leather goods.

Commerce: Wholesale and retail çenter; wholesale sales (1975), $752 million; bank assets (1976), $1.2 billion; 9 banks, 2 mortgage banks, 4 savings and loan associations, 3 major life insurance companies.

Transportation: 2 major freight lines, 2 bus lines, 13 federal and state highways; modern municipal airport serves 4 airlines.

New construction: 3 savings and loan associations building new headquarters; development of 11-story Krystal office building; facility for various business-oriented organizations; Tennessee Valley Authority Credit Union structure.

Communications: 1 cable TV, 5 TV, 20 radio stations; 2 newspapers.

Medical facilities: speech and hearing rehabilitation center; children and adults rehabilitation and education center; 11 major hospital complexes including psychiatric hospital.

Cultural facilities: Univ. of Tenn. at Chattanooga; 3 liberal arts colleges; state tech community college; state vocational-tech school; symphony orchestra; opera association, civic chorus, community concert association, Boys Choir, conservatory of music, Little Theatre, programs and performances at the Tivoli Theater, Memorial Auditorium, and Miller Park.

Other attractions: multi-million dollar vacation complex, Chattanooga Choo-Choo, in one of the world's largest restaurants, in restored railroad terminal; recreational lakes, mountains, and museums.

History: explored by DeSoto 1540, settled 1828 at Ross's Landing, incorporated 1839.

Futher information: Chattanooga Convention and Visitors Bureau, Memorial Auditorium, Chattanooga, TN.

Chicago, Illinois

The World Almanac is sponsored in the Chicago area by the Chicago Tribune, 435 N. Michigan Avenue, Chicago, IL 60611; (312) 222-3232; founded 1847; circulation daily 757,117, Sunday 1,155,572; publisher Stanton R. Cook; editor Clayton Kirkpatrick; major awards include 8 Pulitzer prizes won by staff members.

Population: est. 3,108,700 (city), 2d largest in nation; est. 7,610,000 (8-county metro area in Illinois and Indiana); est. 1,116,300 households in city and est. 2,511,200 in metro area; total employed 3,401,100.

Area: 227 sq. mi. on SW shore of Lake Michigan in Cook and DuPage counties.

Industry: metro area is leading producer of steel, telephone equipment, radios, TV sets, confectionery products, household products, diesel engines, and frozen and canned foods. Largest industry is primary metals worth $10.6 billion; food and related products follow at $7.6 billion; then come non-electrical machinery, metal products, electrical machinery equipment, chemicals & allied products, petroleum and coal products, printing & publishing, and transportation equipment. Chicago accounts for 4.90% of the gross national product.

Commerce: 14,000 manufacturers have sales of $69 billion in metro area; 35,000 retailers do a $26 billion business; wholesale sales are estimated at $57 billion. Average spendable family income $18,789. Midwest Stock Exchange markets stocks and bonds; 7th Federal Reserve District Bank; world's leading grain futures market; Chicago Board of Trade; Mercantile Exchange.

Transportation: 3 major airports with 29 commercial airlines handled over 43 million passengers in 1976; O'Hare is world's largest and busiest commercial airport. Lake, ocean and river shipping makes city link between Mississippi River and St. Lawrence Seaway; 1976 overseas cargo tonnage totaled nearly 2 million tons. Amtrak rail system headquarters. Over 12 major highways, expressways, tollways.

New construction: total industrial construction, development, and investment for 1976, $696 million; total commercial construction for 1976, $530 million.

Convention facilities: 1,036 trade shows and conventions in 1976 attended by over 2 million people.

Educational facilities: 95 institutions of higher learning, include University of Chicago, Illinois Institute of Technology, Northwestern University; Univ. of Ill. — Circle Campus; 6 medical schools; 3 dental colleges and one college of pharmacy and osteopathy.

Medical facilities: over 123 hospitals.

Recreation: 568 parks with an area of 6,700 acres; 73 swimming pools; baseball diamonds, golf courses, bicycle paths, handball courts, etc.

Cultural facilities: Art Institute; Museum of Contemporary Art; Museum of Science and Industry; Field Museum of Natural History; Shedd Aquarium is largest in world; Adler Planetarium; Lincoln Park and Brookfield Zoos; museums of Academy of Science and Historical Society.

Sports: NFL Bears, American (baseball) League White Sox, National (baseball) League Cubs, NHL Black Hawks, NBA Bulls, N.A. Soccer League Sting, American Soccer League Cats.

History: Indians named area Checagou after area's strong-smelling wild onions; incorporated 1837 with population of 4,170.

Further information: Visitors Bureau and Information Center, Association of Commerce and Industry, 130 South Michigan Avenue, Chicago, IL 60603.

Cincinnati, Ohio

The World Almanac is sponsored in the Cincinnati area by The Post, a Scripps-Howard Newspaper, 800 Broadway, Cincinnati, OH 45202; (513) 721-1111; founded 1881 by Alfred and Walter Wellman; evening circulation 207,596; editor William R. Burleigh, business manager Earl Brown.

Population: 412,546 (city), 1,372,000 (metro area), 3d in state, 21st in nation; total employed 556,000.
Area: 2,150 sq. mi. (metro) in SW Ohio; SE Indiana and 3 north central counties in Ky.; Hamilton County seat.
Industry: home of Proctor and Gamble, Federated Department Stores, Kroger Foods, Armco Steel, U.S. Shoe, Western-Southern Life Insurance, Baldwin Piano and Organ, Cincinnati Milacron; also the home of GM, Ford, and GE plants; production of jet engines, playing cards, cosmetics, chemicals, machine tools, printing and publishing.
Commerce: retail sales $3.9 billion; bank assets $4.2 billion, deposits $3.4 billion; with 41 banks with 180 branches; 71 savings and loan associations in metro area.
Transportation: 7 trunk lines and Amtrak; 125 common motor carriers; Greater Cincinnati Airport with 300 incoming-outgoing flights daily serving 8 airlines; Lunken Airport with 4 hard surface runways and FAA control tower; port of Cincinnati; Ohio River navigable entire year — links Cincinnati with Mississippi River; 5 public water terminals, 23 private; 2 major transcontinental bus lines; city-owned local bus lines; metro freeway.
Communications: 5 TV, 12 AM, 22 FM radio stations; 2 daily newspapers.
New construction: Ft. Square South redevelopment underway, Government Square demolition, redevelopment underway, Stouffer's Inn addition nearing completion in Fall '77, Greyhound Bus Terminal completion Fall '77, Library expansion in planning, UC Library under construction, Riverfront development continuing.
Medical facilities: 27 hospitals with over 9,078 beds; 88.3 physicians per 100,000 population; UC Medical Center where Sabin oral vaccine was discovered; Burn Institute and VA Hospital.
Cultural facilities: Art Museum, Historical Society, symphony orchestra, Krohn Conservatory, Lloyd Library, May Festival, Taft Museum, Summer Opera, Museum of Natural History, Shubert Theater, Contemporary Arts Center, UC Observatory, Playhouse in the Park.
Educational facilities: Cincinnati, Xavier univs.; Edgecliff, Mt. St. Joseph, Hebrew Union, Thomas More, Bible Seminary colleges; 8 technical and 2-year colleges; 47 vocational schools.
Convention facilities: numerous hotels and restaurants, Convention and Exposition Center, Cincinnati Gardens, Emery Auditorium, Taft Auditorium, Riverfront Coliseum, and Music Hall.
Other attractions: zoo, Reds, '76 baseball world champions, Bengals football, Swords and Stingers, ice hockey, Cincinnati Suds softball, Fountain Square Plaza, River Downs Race Track, Kings Island Amusement Park, Delta Queen and New Mississippi Queen travel riverboats.
Further information: Chamber of Commerce, 120 W. Fifth Street, Cincinnati, OH 45202.

Cleveland, Ohio

The World Almanac is sponsored in the Cleveland area by The Cleveland Press, 901 Lakeside Avenue, Cleveland, OH 44114; (216) 623-1111; founded 1878 by E. W. Scripps; circulation 329,867; editor Thomas L. Boardman; managing editor Robert Sullivan; business manager William Holcombe; major awards include Pulitzer Prize, Lasker Award.

Population: 638,793 (city), 1,975,400 (metro area), first in state, total employed 872,200 (non-agricultural).
Area: 1,519 sq. mi., SMSA 4 county area; along southern shore of Lake Erie, east and west of Cuyahoga River.
Industry: city has been described as "an industrial powerhouse;" bills itself "The Best Location in the Nation." Within 500 miles are: more than 50% of populations of the U.S. and Canada, more than 55% of U.S. manufacturing plants, more than 50% of retail sales in the U.S. and more than 60% of U.S. product value. No single industry dominates economy — steel and metal products are mainstays; manufacturing complex occupied essentially with primary metals, fabricated metal products, machinery, tools, automotive products. Important industries include making of electric motors, products of petroleum, rubber, plastic, stone, clay and glass, chemicals, paints, wearing apparel, measuring instruments, electronic components, food products, and publishing-printing. Value of products is $15 billion a year. Retail sales are almost $5 billion with average family spending about $6,000 on retail merchandise. More than 50% of families earn more than $10,000 a year.
Transportation: Hopkins Airport with more than 5 million passengers each year; Burke Lakefront Airport, 5 minutes from Public Square and capable of handling intermediate jets; Port of Cleveland visited by more than 50 overseas steamship lines and Great Lakes fleet; largest city on Lake Erie and 3d largest on Great Lakes. Cleveland is only U.S. city with airport-to-downtown rail service. Ride takes 20 minutes and costs about $10 less than a cab ride. Amtrak train service.
Communications: Cleveland Press, evening daily; Cleveland Plain Dealer, morning daily plus Sunday; numerous foreign language newspapers; 5 TV stations; 12 AM and 14 FM radio stations.
New construction: projects on the drawing boards include a 32-acre complex of offices, stores and apartments, and a gateway and jetport on Lake Erie.
Cultural facilities: Cleveland Orchestra; Play House, nation's oldest and largest resident professional theater; Museum of Art; Karamu House for interracial arts; Western Reserve Historical Society; Health Museum; Natural Science Museum; Cultural Gardens; zoo; Blossom Music Center; Salvador Dali Museum; Garden Center; Sea World; aquarium.
Educational facilities: Case Western Reserve Univ., Baldwin-Wallace College, Cleveland State Univ., Cuyahoga Community College, John Carroll Univ.; Notre Dame and Ursuline colleges.
Sports attractions: NFL Browns, American League Indians, NBA Cavaliers, NHL Barons, and World Team Tennis Nets; also golfing, horse and car racing, boating.
Other attractions: downtown Convention Center is largest city-owned convention facility in U.S.; public library is 5th in size of book collection in U.S. Public Square, hub of city, marked by 52-story Terminal Tower. "The Forest City" is encircled by "Emerald Necklace," 18,000 acres of metropolitan parks. Cleveland Clinic, known for medical research, attracts patients from throughout the world.
History: settlement established in summer, 1796 by Gen. Moses Cleaveland, was capital of the Western

Reserve, became a city in 1836.
Further information: Greater Cleveland Growth Assn., 690 Union Commerce Bldg., Cleveland, OH 44115.

Columbia, South Carolina

The World Almanac is sponsored in the Columbia area by Columbia Newspapers, Inc., P.O. box 1333, Columbia, SC 29202; phone (803) 771-6161; circulation, The State (am) 101,275; The Columbia Record (pm) 32,178; The State (Sun.) 119,420 (ABC 3/31/76); Ambrose G. Hampton, publisher; Ben R. Morris, co-publisher; Arthur D. Cooper, associate publisher, president and general manager; James W. Holton Jr., assistant general manager and advertising director; William E. Rone, editorial page editor (The State); Thomas N. McLean, editor, The Columbia Record.

Population: 113,542 (1970 census), city corporate limits; 2-county metro area (Richland and Lexington) estimated 373,000 (Fed-State Co-op '76).
Area: 105 sq. mi. (Richland County); 1,525 sq. mi. (metro); center of South Carolina, at confluence of Broad and Saluda rivers (at Columbia).
Government: state capital with about 100 agencies (state); 19 (federal) agencies: government employees total more than 25,000; Fort Jackson Military Post numbers over 25,000 personnel.
Industry: more than 50 national firms such as General Electric, Allied Chemical, Continental Can, Burlington, Litton, Bendix, M. Lowenstein, Rockwell Int., Square D, Westinghouse, Colite Ind., Tamper, Shakespeare, Allis-Chalmers; fibres, heavy equipment, electronics, textiles, fertilizer, and cement products.
Commerce: retail sales (metro) over $1 billion ('76); consumer spendable income $1.7 billion; median household income (metro) $15,750; 11 commercial (main) banking institutions.
Transportation: Metropolitan Airport with 4 major airlines and freight service; 3 rail freight lines, Amtrak; 44 motor freight companies; 3 interstate, 6 federal, and 5 state highways.
Communications: 4 TV and 8 radio stations.
Medical facilities: 6 general hospitals, including modern Richland Memorial; William S. Hall Psychiatric Institute; 2 state mental hospitals.
Cultural facilities: Town Theatre, the oldest continuous community theater in nation; 3 other theaters; Museum of Art and Sciences; Gibbes Planetarium; Township Auditorium, home of Artist Series; Dreher Auditorium with Philharmonic Orchestra, City Ballet, Lyric Theatre and Choral Society; Fraser Hall.
Recreation facilities: 13 golf courses; city park system; 2 municipal pools; wide range of hunting activities; Riverbanks Zoological Park, part of 135-acre complex; Lake Murray, water sports.
Sports: Williams-Brice Stadium, home of Univ. of South Carolina Fighting Gamecock football team; Carolina Coliseum for basketball, conventions.
Educational facilities: 25,000-student Univ. of South Carolina; 4 private colleges; Technical Education Center; Lutheran Seminary.
History: established 1786 as state capital; burned in 1865 by Union General Sherman.
Further information: Chamber of Commerce, 1308 Laurel Street, Columbia, SC 29202.

Columbus, Georgia — Phenix City, Alabama

The World Almanac is sponsored in the Columbus, Ga. - Phenix City, Ala., area by the Columbus Enquirer and the Columbus Ledger, 17 W. 12th Street, Columbus, GA 31902; phone (404) 322-8831; combined daily circulation 66,515; Sunday 68,088. Enquirer founded 1828, awarded Pulitzer Prize 1926; Ledger founded 1886, awarded Pulitzer Prize 1955. Published by the R. W. Page Corporation; M. R. Ashworth, president-emeritus; Glenn Vaughn, president and general manager; J. Carrol Dadisman, vice-president and executive editor. Owned by Knight-Ridder Newspapers, Inc.

Population: 162,700 (Columbus); 26,000 (Phenix City); 222,900 (metro); 81,700 employed (metro).
Area: 1,100 sq. miles (metro: Muscogee and Chattahoochee counties, Ga.; Russell County, Ala.) straddling the Chattahoochee River.
Industry: major textile production center: Swift, Fieldcrest, Gomibo U.S.A., Cartersville, Columbus Mills, Bibb Mfg., Reeves Bros., West Point Pepperell. Union Carbide TRW, International hqs. Tom's Foods Ltd. and Burnham Van Lines; lumber products, beverages, concrete, bakery goods, and paper.
Commerce: center of west Georgia—east Alabama finance, agriculture, textiles, hydroelectric power; metro retail sales $621.4 million; avg. household buying income $12,557; 9 banks, 6 savings and loan associations.
Federal facilities: Ft. Benning, world's largest infantry school, $282 million annual disbursements.
Transportation: 2 rail lines, 2 bus lines; Delta, Eastern, Southern airlines; 33 truck lines; Chattahoochee is navigable river.
Communications: 3 TV and 10 radio stations.
New construction: 70,000 sq. ft. convention and trade center, TRW, Westvaco, metro airport expansion; Ft. Benning expansion for One Station Training; Bradley Office Park, Union Carbide, Southern Bell, Georgia Power, West Georgia Correctional Institute.
Medical facilities: 5 hospitals.
Cultural facilities: Museum of Arts and Crafts, Springer Theater (state theater of Georgia), Three Arts Theater, Bradley Memorial Library; Columbus College, Chattahoochee Valley Community College.
Sports: Astros, Southern baseball league.
History: Columbus founded 1828; gained early prominence as shipping center for cotton, fish; birthplace of Coca-Cola formula. Phenix City founded 1883, growing from a Creek Indian trading post.
Further information: Columbus Chamber of Commerce, P.O. Box 1200, Columbus, GA 31902, or Phenix City-Russell County Chamber of Commerce, P.O. Box 1326, Phenix City, AL 36867.

Columbus, Ohio

The World Almanac is sponsored in the Columbus area by the Columbus Citizen-Journal, 34 S. Third Street, Columbus, OH 43216; (614) 461-5000; Citizen founded 1899, Journal 1811; circ. 106,355 a.m. daily except Sun.;

owned by E. W. Scripps Co.; editor Richard R. Campbell, business manager Gregory A. Dembski, managing editor Seymour Raiz.

Population: 605,200 (city), 19th in nation, 1,114,800 (metro area), 1977 ests.; 2d in state, total employed 477,400

Area: 173.9 sq. mi., central Ohio; state capital, Franklin County seat.

Industry: diversified; 1,019 manufacturers including General Motors, Rockwell International, Western Electric, Columbus Products Co., Borden (natl. hqs.); planes, missiles, refrigerators, mining machinery, telephones, glass products, auto parts; est. 1975 production-workers payroll $989 million; home office of Battelle Memorial Institute with world-wide research laboratories.

Commerce: wholesale, retail center for central, southern Ohio, parts of W. Va., Ky. Retail sales, $3.2 billion; financial assets, $9.9 billion; 7 banks, 20 savings & loan assns.; 51 insurance co. home offices, assets $4.6 billion. Per capita income, $5,321. Defense Construction Supply Center, world's largest; 21% of employment is government.

Transportation: 125 truck lines, 3 intercity bus lines, 4 railroads, 8 airlines using Port Columbus International with 750 air movements daily; 8 major highways.

Communications: 4 TV stations, 12 radio stations.

Medical facilities: 18 hospitals, medical centers; Children's Hospital leads nation in children admitted; Ohio State Univ. School of Medicine.

Cultural facilities: Ohio Theatre; symphony orchestra, public library with 22 branches; art museums, Center of Science and Industry, Ohio Historical Center with recreated early 19th century village.

Other attractions: 235 parks, Park of Roses, world's largest; Ohio Railway Museum; zoo, boating.

Educational facilities: Ohio State, Capital, Franklin univs., Ohio Dominican College, Columbus College of Art & Design, Columbus Technical Institute.

Sports: Ohio Stadium and Franklin County Stadium; Clippers (baseball), Owls (hockey), Beulah Park (thoroughbreds), Scioto Downs (harness); Muirfield Memorial golf tournament.

History: founded 1812 as state capital, named for Christopher Columbus.

Further information: Chamber of Commerce, P. O. Box 1527, Columbus, OH 43216.

Corpus Christi, Texas

The World Almanac is sponsored in the Corpus Christi area by The Caller and The Times, P.O. Box 9136, Corpus Christi, TX 78408; Caller (a.m.) founded 1883; Times (p.m.) founded 1911; merged 1929; Caller circ. 61,958, Times 27,343, Sunday 84,767; publisher Edward H. Harte; president Allan P. Johnson III; Caller managing editor John B. Anderson; Times managing editor Bill Duncan.

Population: 218,000 (est.); labor force 99,700.

Area: 328 sq. mi. (226 water), 210 miles SW of Houston on Corpus Christi Bay; Nueces County seat.

Industry: oil refineries; offshore oil rig fabrication; chemical, petrochemical, synthetics, aluminum, and zinc plants.

Commerce: Port of Corpus Christi handled 48.2 million tons in 1976; 72-foot-deep superport proposed for 1979; economic hub of south Texas; farming, ranching, oil and gas production, commercial fishing, tourist trade; 13 banks have deposits in excess of $778 million.

Transportation: 4 airlines, 2 bus lines, 3 railroads but no rail passenger service.

Communications: 2 daily newspapers, 5 TV stations (one public service, one Spanish), 10 radio stations.

New construction: permits issued for $53.7 million in new construction in 1976.

Medical facilities: 9 hospitals, including a children's center, with 1,497 beds.

Federal facilities: Corpus Christi Naval Air Station is headquarters for Naval Air Training Command; Corpus Christi Army Depot is army's only complete helicopter overhaul plant; combined payroll more than $100 million.

Cultural facilities: Corpus Christi Museum, Art Museum of South Texas, Japanese Art Museum; symphony, little theatre, Del Mar College, Corpus Christi State Univ.

Recreation: public beaches and fishing piers on the bay and along Gulf of Mexico on Mustang Island and in 88-mile-long Padre Island National Seashore; surf and charter boat fishing; sailing, city marina with public launching ramps; large public tennis center, 3 private tennis clubs, 5 golf courses, Lone Star baseball league.

History: Spanish explorer Alonzo de Pineda discovered Corpus Christi Bay in 1519; Blas Maria de la Garza Falcon established San Petronilla Ranch on Petronilla Creek about 1765; city grew from a frontier trading post est. in 1839; city incorporated Feb. 16, 1852.

Further information: Corpus Christi Chamber of Commerce, P.O. Box 640, Corpus Christi, TX 78403.

Dallas, Texas

The World Almanac is sponsored in Dallas by The Dallas Morning News, Communications Center, Dallas, TX 75222; telephone (214) 745-8222; published by the oldest business in Texas, the News was founded in 1842 by Samuel Bangs; circulation, 339,232 Sunday, 272,138 daily; president Joe M. Dealey, executive editor Tom J. Simmons. Winner of numerous national awards including Freedoms Foundation and National Headliner. Sponsors Teen-age Citizenship Tribute, Fly-the-Flag program, Spelling Bee, Sports Show, Involved Citizen Award, etc.

Population: city, 869,500 (8th in nation); county 1,514,350; Dallas-Fort Worth metro area, 2,772,900 (10th in nation); total employed, 1,232,900 with 3.5% unemployment.

Area: 900 sq. mi. astride Trinity River in north Texas, in Dallas, Collin, Kaufman, and Rockwall counties, about 75 miles south of Oklahoma border; elevation from 450 to 750 feet.

Industry: banking and insurance capital of the Southwest, Dallas ranks 3d among U.S. cities in the number of million-dollar-net-worth companies with 675 such firms. Manufacturing accounts for one-fourth of employment, about evenly divided between durable (including electronics, aviation, aerospace, and machinery) and non-durable (including food products, apparel, and printing-publishing).

Commerce: a $4.5 billion wholesale market ($9 billion retail), Dallas ranks first nationally in giftware, home furnishing and floor covering wholesaling, 2d in apparel and toys. Metro retail sales totaled $8.3 billion in 1976, while estimated buying income reached $14 billion and bank deposits $16.7 billion.

Transportation: Dallas-Fort Worth Airport is the nation's largest. In 1976, it was the nation's 4th busiest

with 143,862 aircraft departures; 7.9 million passengers enplaned there. City is served by 12 major commercial and 4 commuter air lines, 8 railroads, 2 trans-continental bus lines, 87 motor freight lines, 3 taxicab companies with 464 cabs. Dallas Transit System serves 100,000 people daily on 73 lines, 481 route miles.
Communications: 2 metropolitan daily newspapers, numerous suburban dailies, 4 commercial VHF TV stations, public television, 1 UHF station, 17 AM and 21 FM radio stations, 2 city magazines.
New construction: $870 million in building permits in 1976 ($423 nonresidential); projects include 300-acre, $300 million office park and $210 million Union Terminal area redevelopment.
Medical facilities: 60 hospitals with 9,749 beds, 500 bassinets. Baylor University Medical Center was recently chosen No. 4 among the country's top 13 "super hospitals."
Culture: symphony orchestra, civic opera, summer musicals, civic ballet, Sunday Concert series — among others — offer varied programs; drama at Dallas Theater Center, Theater Three, National Children's Theater, Repertory Theater, and 4 dinner theaters; 7 museums; SMU's Owens Fine Arts Center with a collection of paintings and sculpture; numerous art galleries.
Education: 143,000 students attend 28 colleges and universities within 50 miles of Dallas; Southern Methodist Univ., the Univ. of Texas at Dallas, Univ. of Dallas, North Texas State, Univ. of Texas at Arlington, Baylor Univ. College of Dentistry, Southwestern Medical School; the Dallas Community College system with 55,000 students on 6 campuses and one more under construction.
Convention facilities: 3 major convention centers, including expanded Dallas Convention Center with more combined meeting-exhibit space (611,000 sq. ft.) than any other in U.S.; 26,000 air-conditioned hotel rooms. Dallas ranked first in the nation in number of conventions in 1976 with 851 attended by 1.2 million people.
Sports: professional sports include football, baseball, tennis, golf, hockey, soccer, and rodeo. Cotton Bowl is site of annual New Year's Day football game and SMU home games.
Other attractions: Six Flags Over Texas, Dallas Zoo, Lion Country Safari, Fair Park is home of State Fair of Texas 16 days each October; museums of fine arts, health and science, natural history; Hall of State; Garden Center and Music Hall; excellent lakes, golf courses, parks, luxury hotels, and restaurants.
History: first settler was Tennessee frontiersman John Neely Bryan who established a trading post and plotted the townsite in 1844; incorporated 1856; named for Vice-President George Millifin Dallas. Since 1931, the city has had council-manager form of government. Spectacular population growth began after World War II, when aircraft manufacturing augmented an economy that had been built first on cotton, then on oil, banking, and insurance. Diversified economic expansion fed the growth of the 1960s.
Further information: Dallas Chamber of Commerce, Fidelity Union Tower, Dallas, TX 75201.

Dayton, Ohio

The World Almanac is sponsored in the Dayton area by The Journal Herald, 37 So. Ludlow Street, Dayton, OH 45402; (513) 225-2421; founded as Dayton Repertory; circulation 103,241; editor Dennis Shere, managing editor William Worth, editorial page editor William Wild, "Day" section editor Virginia Hunt.

Population: 205,986 (city), 835,708 (metro), 4th in state, 44th in nation; total employed 346,300.
Area: 43.7 sq. mi. (1977) at junction Mad, Miami, and Stillwater rivers; Montgomery County seat.
Industry: NCR Corp., McCall Printing Co., General Motors Corp. (Delco Moraine, Delco Products, Delco Air, Inland Mfg., and Frigidaire) more than 800 other manufacturing facilities.
Commerce: retail sales $2.5 billion, average effective buying household income, $17,126.
Transportation: 2 airports, 6 airlines, 3 trunk rail systems, 5 bus lines, Dayton Regional Transit Auth.
Communications: 4 TV stations, 10 radio stations.
Medical facilities: 10 hospitals, including Wright Patterson AFB Hospital and a VA facility.
Federal facilities: Wright Patterson AFB headquarters for Air Force Logistics Command and Aeronautical Systems Div.; Defense Electronics Supply Center; Federal Bldg.
Convention facilities: new downtown convention and exhibition center.
New construction: downtown arcade, Gem City Savings Assoc. headquarters, Great Miami River low dam, NCR world headquarters; newly constructed: Stouffers hotel, Courthouse Sq. Plaza, which includes dept. store, bank bldg., utilities bldg., and the Mead Corp; Tower World Headquarters, Univ. of Dayton Law School, Wright State Med. School, State Fidelity Federal Savings and Loan.
Educational facilities: Univ. of Dayton (new law school), Wright State Univ. (new med. school); 2 jr. colleges; Sinclair (downtown campus), Miami-Jacobs (business); United Theological Seminary, Central State Univ., Wilberforce Univ., Antioch College.
Cultural facilities: Dayton Art Institute, Philharmonic Orchestra, opera, ballet, 4 amateur theatrical groups, 2 professional companies; Diehl band shell, Deed's carillon, dinner theatre.
Sports: Dayton Gems (IHL), Amateur Trapshoot Hdqtrs., college sports, Bogie Busters Tourn., Dayton Hydroglobe.
Other attractions: Air Force Museum, Carillon Park, Aviation Hall of Fame, Dayton Air Fair, Old Courthouse Museum, A World A'Fair, Dayton River Corridor Festival, Paul Lawrence Dunbar Home, Wright Bros. Memorial.
History: "Birthplace of Aviation".
Further information: Dayton Area Chamber of Commerce, 111 W. First Street, Dayton, OH 45402.

Denver, Colorado

The World Almanac is sponsored in the Denver area by the Rocky Mountain News, 400 W. Colfax Avenue, Denver, CO 80201, (303) 892-5000; founded 1859 by William N. Byers; circulation daily 246,413, Sunday 266,414; editor Michael Balfe Howard, business manager William W. Fletcher; sponsors Colorado-Wyoming spelling bee, Golden Wedding party, Huck Finn Day, Showagon.

Population: 530,600 (city), 1,574,000 (metro area), first in state, 26th in nation; total employed 700,000.
Area: 116.4 sq. mi. on S. Platte River at edge of Great Plains near Rocky Mountains. State capital and Denver County seat.
Industry: Gates Rubber Co. is world's largest maker of v-belts and hose, 6th largest U.S. rubber company; Samsonite Corp. is world's largest luggage manufacturer, also makes furniture; Adolph Coors Co. is nation's 4th largest brewer of beer; center for smoke-

less industry with 1,500 manufacturing firms.
Commerce: largest distribution center in region embracing one-third of U.S. geographical area; retail sales, $9 billion (1975); bank deposits $4.7 billion, 94 banks, 16 savings and loan associations and 45 insurance company home offices; per capita income, $4,800.
Transportation: 6 major rail freight lines, Amtrak; Continental and Greyhound bus lines; 3 interstate highways intersect city; Stapleton International Airport is nation's 8th largest, with 680 daily flights, hub for 6 trunk airlines; Frontier Air Lines; United Air Lines Flight Training Center.
Communications: 5 TV and 32 radio stations.
Medical facilities: largest medical center between Kansas City and San Francisco; one of 17 regional comprehensive cancer centers; Univ. of Colorado Medical Center, National Jewish Hospital, Children's Asthma Research Institute and Hospital (CARIH); 22 major hospitals.
Federal facilities: largest complex of federal offices outside Washington, D.C., with 37,700 federal employes; site of Energy Research and Development Administration's Rocky Flats plant, U.S. Mint, Lowry AFB, Air Force Accounting and Finance Center, Fitzsimons Army Medical Center, Army's Rocky Mountain Arsenal.
Cultural facilities: symphony orchestra, 3 nonprofessional orchestras, 3 choral groups, Denver Art Museum, 9 theater companies; 3-sq.-block convention center; 12,000-seat Red Rocks outdoor theater.
Educational facilities: Univ. of Colorado, Univ. of Denver, Colorado School of Mines; Colorado Women's, Metropolitan State, Loretto Heights, and Regis colleges; Univ. of Colorado School of Medicine, Iliff School of Theology.
Recreational facilities: 150 parks, 8,030 acres of mountain parks, 40 golf courses in metro area. City Park Zoo, 2 amusement parks; many ski areas.
Sports: pro teams include Broncos, NFL; Bears, baseball, American Assn.; Nuggets, NBA; Rockies, NHL.
Other attractions: Museum of Natural History, Botanic Gardens, State Historical Museum.
History: founded 1858 with discovery of gold, fast became supply center for mountain mining camps; named for territorial governor.
Further information: Denver Chamber of Commerce, 1301 Welton Street, Denver, CO 80204; Hospitality Center, 280 14th Street, Denver, CO 80202.

Des Moines, Iowa

The World Almanac is sponsored in Iowa by the Des Moines Register and Tribune, 715 Locust Street, Des Moines, IA 50304; (515) 284-8000; founded 1849; circulation evening Tribune 97,300, morning Register 237,621, Sunday Register 446,110; president and publisher David Kruidenier, editor Michael Gartner, business manager Louis Norris; sales director J. Robert Hudson. Major awards include 12 Pulitzer Prizes.

Population: 201,404 (city, 1970), 331,900 (1976 SMSA).
Area: 66 sq. mi., at juncture of Raccoon and Des Moines rivers, south central Iowa. State capital and Polk County seat.
Industry: considered to be 2d largest insurance center in nation (56 home companies) and 2d largest tire center with Firestone, Armstrong plants; publishing center — Meredith Co., Better Homes and Gardens, Wallace-Homestead, others; farm implements — North American headquarters and plant of Massey-Ferguson, John Deere; lawn and garden equipment, sporting goods, food products, cosmetics, dental equipment, automotive accessories, concrete forms, nozzles, tools; 700 wholesale and jobbing firms; Standard Oil credit card center, bulk mail center.
Commerce: retail sales in metro area, $1.165 billion (1976); per capita income, $6,201 (1976); average household income, $17,697.
Transportation: newly enlarged in-city airport, 4 major airlines; 4 bus lines; 6 railroads; 69 truck lines, Interstate Highways 80 and 35.
New construction: civic theater, major hospital additions, 2 state office bldgs., telephone bldg., office bldgs., insurance co. addition, $100 million total.
Communications: 13 radio, 4 TV, cablevision.
Medical facilities: 11 hospitals with 2,700 beds.
Cultural facilities: art center, Center of Science and Industry, community playhouse, drama workshop, Drake University, symphony orchestra; Grand View Junior, Area Community, and 2 bible colleges; College of Osteopathic Medicine and Surgery, ballet.
Recreation: 1,400 acres of parks, 9 public golf courses, 11 public pools, tennis, YMCA; new $96 million reservoir at north edge of city.
Other attractions: AAA baseball, Drake Relays, Missouri Valley and Big Eight (Iowa State U.) conferences; 15,000-seat auditorium; boys and girls state basketball tournaments, State Fair, Living History Farm, Children's Zoo, 36-story Ruan Center, tallest in Iowa, Terrace Hill (Governor's Mansion), state capitol and state historical bldg.
History: founded 1843 as a fort to protect rights of Indians; incorporated 1853, became Iowa capital 1857.
Further information: Chamber of Commerce, 8th and High Streets, Des Moines, IA 50309.

Detroit, Michigan

The World Almanac is sponsored in the Detroit area by The Detroit News, 615 Lafayette, Detroit, MI 48231, (313) 222-2000; founded 1873 by James E. Scripps; circulation (D) 643,702 (S) 826,304; president and publisher Peter B. Clark Sr., v.p. R. M. Spitzley, exec. v.p. J. T. Dorris, v.p. and editor W. E. Giles; major awards won include Pulitzer Prize, Nat'l Headliners; 95 community projects include NCAA Indoor Track Championships, Policeman and Fire Fighter of the Month, Science Fair, Scholastic Writing and Art Awards, Spelling Bee.

Population: 1,500,000 (city), 4,250,000 (metro area), (1972); first in state, 5th in U.S.
Area: 139.6 sq. mi. on the Detroit River, a Great Lakes connecting link and the world's busiest inland waterway; Wayne County seat.
Industry: "The Motor City"; area plants produce 25% of the nation's cars and trucks, employing more than 200,000. Nonautomotive manufacturing and nonmanufacturing firms employ more than 1.4 million; other products are machine tools, iron products, metal stampings, hardware, industrial chemicals, drugs, paint, wire products.
Commerce: total metro personal income per household was $14,111 (1971); area retail sales were $8.6 billion.
Transportation: served by 5 railroads, over 200 intercity truck lines, 19 airlines, and 31 scheduled steamship lines serving more than 40 countries.
Communications: 9 TV and 18 radio stations.
New construction: $500 million riverfront development, Renaissance Center, is located on east side riverfront area, incorporating living units, business offices, and the Plaza Hotel; other projects include 660 acre, $284 million downtown residential develop-

ments, and a 235 acre, $500 million mid-town medical center.
Cultural facilities: symphony orchestra, International Institute, Meadow Brook music and drama programs, Institute of Arts, concert band, and the annual Freedom Festival, celebrating Canada's Dominion Day, July 1, and U.S. Independence Day, July 4.
Educational facilities: 11 colleges and universities are located in the metro area, including Wayne State Univ., Univ. of Detroit, and branches of the Univ. of Michigan and Michigan State Univ.
Convention facilities: 75 acre, $100 million Civic Center, including Cobo Hall and Convention Arena with 400,000 sq. ft. of exhibit space, more than 25,000 rooms in 250 hotels and motels.
Sports: Tigers baseball (American League), NFL Lions, NHL Red Wings, NBA Pistons; 6 winter skiing areas within short driving distance.
Other attractions: Chrysler, Ford, and General Motors auto plants; Henry Ford Museum and Greenfield Village historical displays, Cranbrook Institute (science museum and arts), Belle Isle (1,000 acre park), zoo, public library, historical museum, and Fort Wayne Military Museum.
History: founded 1701 by the Frenchman Cadillac as a strategic frontier fort and trading post, ceded to the British in 1763 and turned over to the U.S. in 1796 as a village of 2,500; reoccupied by the British for a year in the War of 1812. Completion of the Erie Canal in 1825 opened a cheap water transport route from New York to the Northwest and made Detroit an important commercial center. R. E. Olds built Detroit's first auto factory in 1899; and Henry Ford, who handbuilt his first car in 1896, formed his first company in 1899, and the present Ford Motor Co. in 1903. The area's industries made it the "Arsenal of Democracy" in World War II.
Further information: Greater Detroit Chamber of Commerce, 150 Michigan Avenue; Cities Reporting and Information Dept., City-County Bldg.; Detroit Convention Bureau, 1400 Book Bldg., all Detroit, MI 48226.

Edmonton, Alberta, Canada

The World Almanac is sponsored in central and northern Alberta by the Edmonton Journal, 10006 - 101 Street, Edmonton, Alberta, T5J 2S6; telephone (403) 425-9120; founded November 11, 1903. A division of Southam Press Limited; circulation 182,000; publisher J. Patrick O'Callaghan; editor Andrew Snaddon. Sponsor Learn to Ski, curl, play golf, tennis, and Shape Up Fitness programs; Literary Awards, Newspaper in Education.

Population: (est.) 471,474 (city), 564,000 (metro), capital of Alberta, largest Alberta city, 5th in Canada; total metro employed 379,844 (June 30, 1977).
Area: 123.34 sq. mi. on North Saskatchewan River.
Industry: 2d largest refining center in Canada, 7,000 producing wells; petrochemical industries include plastics, fertilizers, man made fibers, steel tube mills; 2d largest meat processing center in Canada; prosperous mixed farming.
Commerce: major supply center for Northwest Territories, Yukon, northeastern B.C., and Canadian Arctic; originating terminus of 5 oil and natural gas pipelines east and west from Alberta, Alaska, and the Canadian north; retail sales (est. '76) $2.53 billion, mfg. shipments (est. '76) $1.95 billion; trading area population (est.) 1,100,000.
Transportation: Alaska and Mackenzie highways; Canadian National, Canadian Pacific; Northern Alberta, Great Slave, and Alberta Resources railroads; 4 airports, 6 airlines, 195,956 itinerant movements in '76.
Communications: 8 radio stations including one French station, 4 TV including one French station, 3 cable TV
Medical facilities: 5 general and 5 auxiliary hospitals, 2 rehabilitation centers, 9 nursing homes.
Cultural facilities: Edmonton Symphony Orchestra, Edmonton Art Gallery, Centennial Library, Provincial Museum and Archives, Univ. of Alberta, Northern Alberta Institute of Technology, Grant McEwan Community College, Alberta and Edmonton ballet companies. Canada's most active professional theatre, now housed in the new $6 million Citadel Theatre complex. Edmonton Opera, Northern Alberta Jubilee Auditorium, Queen Elizabeth Planetarium, Muttart Conservatory.

Other attractions: Klondike Days, annual celebration of the 1898 Yukon gold rush is held in mid-July; Valley Zoo, Fort Edmonton, Hawrelak Park; Alberta Game Farm, Elk Island Park, and many lakes nearby.

Sports: CFL Edmonton Eskimos, WHA Edmonton Oilers, Western Major Fastball League Monarchs; 16,000 seat Coliseum opened in 1974; 45,000 seat sport complex and $8.5 million aquatic centre are being built for the 1978 Commonwealth Games; Kinsmen Field House indoor track seats 4,000.

History: Fort Edmonton built in 1795, named after town now a borough of London, England; oil discovered at Leduc (20 miles south) in 1947 rocketed the city into prominence as one of the world's leading petrochemical centers.

El Paso, Texas

The World Almanac is sponsored in the El Paso area by the El Paso Herald-Post, 401 Mills Avenue, El Paso, TX 79901, phone (915) 747-6700; Herald founded 1881, Post 1922, merged (under Scripps-Howard) 1931; circulation 36,135. Robert W. Lee, editor; Robert McBrinn, managing editor.

Population: 385,000 (city); with twin city, Juarez, Mexico, 1,288,000; 4th in state, 33d in nation; total employed, 140,500.
Area: 161.109 sq. mi. western tip of Texas where Rio Grande cuts boundaries of Texas, New Mexico, and Mexico at foot of the Rockies (including Franklin Mtns.); El Paso County seat.
Industry: manufacturing payroll, $215.3 million in 1976, manufacturing employment, 28,575; clothing largest employer, including Farah, Levi Straus, Mann, Hicks-Ponder, Billy the Kid. Juarez-El Paso border in-bond industries at 85 and 25,000 employed, including electronic and other, such as RCA, GTE Sylvania, General Instruments, American Hospital Supply, and Allen Bradley; home of El Paso Natural Gas, ASARCO, Inc., Peyton Packing, Tony Lama Boots, Phelps Dodge, Standard and Texaco refineries, Old El Paso (Pet Foods) and Ashley's of Texas canned Mexican foods; nut processing, cattle, pecans, cotton, and other agriculture.
Commerce: wholesale-retail center for west Texas, New Mexico, northern Mexico; retail sales in 1976 $1.5 billion; 1976 bank deposits, $1.2 billion; bank clearings, $8.1 billion; 20 banks, 6 savings and loan associations. Value added in 1976, $380.6 million including $215.3 million in labor. Exports in 1976, $579.7 million, with $666.9 million in imports.
Transportation: 4 major rail lines, Amtrak; 6 bus lines, 31 truck lines, 5 major highways; gateway to Mexico, busiest crossing point on U.S. border with 56

million crossings in 1976; International Airport, 4 airlines with 192,966 flights in 1976 and 1,171,258 passengers, 13,043 tons of freight.
Communications: 5 TV and 13 radio stations.
New construction: 1976 buildings permits totaled $147.3 million.
Medical facilities: 17 hospitals with 2,904 beds; area cancer treatment center; Univ. of Texas System School of Nursing.
Federal facilities: Ft. Bliss (U.S. Army Air Defense Center, Allied Students Missile Center, Sgts. Major Academy). William Beaumont Army Medical Center, and nearby McGregor Range, White Sands Missile Range, and Holloman AFB in New Mexico.
Cultural facilities: Univ. of Texas at El Paso, El Paso Community College, El Paso Symphony, Museum of Art with Kress Collection, University Ballet, opera companies, theater groups, and Chamizal National Memorial theater; $20 million civic-convention center; public libraries.
Other attractions: annual year-end Sun Carnival and Sun Bowl football game; Tigua Indian community arts and crafts center, missions that pre-date those of the Californias, horse racing in nearby New Mexico, horse and dog racing in Juarez; zoo, Cavalry Museum, Wilderness Park Museum, Guadalupe Mountains and Big Bend National Parks within 300 miles; exotic Juarez, Mexico, and Pancho Villa country.
Further information: Convention and Visitors Bureau, Five Civic Center Plaza, El Paso, TX 79901.

Erie, Pennsylvania

The World Almanac is sponsored in the Erie area by The Erie Daily Times, 205 W. 12th Street, Erie, PA 16501; (814) 456-8531; founded in 1888; circulation 74,000 daily, 92,000 Sunday; Edward M. Mead, Michael Mead, co-publishers; executive editor Joseph Meagher, managing editor Len Kholos.

Population: 125,600 (city), 187,500 (metro area), 3d in state; total employed, 56,800.
Area: 19.53 sq. mi. at tip of northwestern Pa.; Erie County seat.
Commerce: Erie County, pop. 220,000, produces $133 million in exports, highest per capita export in U.S.; tourism — 5 miles of beaches, good fishing, boating, winter sports; seaport — 60 or more oceangoing vessels each year; over 506 industrial plants producing machinery and parts; iron and steel forgings, hardware, meters, plastics, paper (Hammermill), furniture, and toys; General Electric producing Amtrak passenger trains.
New construction: main street transformed into pedestrian walkway; 200-room Hilton Hotel; "Mid City Towers," a 14-story apt. bldg.; $36 million Hamot Medical Center building project; Millcreek shopping mall, $80 million, largest single-design shopping center under one roof in U.S.; National Fuel Gas Co. office bldg.; addition to Alpine Manor Convalescent Home.
Special awards: All America City through 1974.
Transportation: 4 railroads, Boston-Chicago Amtrak line; airport; 35 trucking companies, 4 bus lines.
Cultural facilities: Penn State Univ. extension, Gannon, Mercyhurst, and Villa Maria colleges; Philharmonic Society, Council of the Arts, theater groups; new field house for plays, entertainment, sports.
History: Named after Eriez Indians; site of building of ship Niagara with which Oliver Hazard Perry defeated British in 1813 in Lake Erie battle.
Further information: Chamber of Commerce, 1006 State, Erie, PA 16501.

Evansville, Indiana

The World Almanac is sponsored in southwestern Indiana, western Kentucky, and southeastern Illinois by the Evansville Press, 201 N.W. Second Street, Evansville, IN 47701; (812) 424-7711; founded July 2, 1906, by E. W. Scripps and J. C. Harper; circulation, 46,000; editor, William W. Sorrels; managing editor, Paul Knue.

Population: 133,566 (city), 286,700 (metro area), 4th in state.
Area: 47 sq. mi. at bend of Ohio River in southwest corner of state; Vanderburgh County seat.
Industry: Whirlpool Corp. plants (refrigeration and air conditioning); Mead Johnson & Co. (pharmaceutical division of Bristol-Myers Co.); Alcoa Warrick Operations (aluminum) just east of city; 283 manufacturing firms.
Commerce: retail sales, $888 million (1976); effective buying income per household, $13,870 (1976); home offices of CrediThrift of America, Inc.; 5 banks, 7 savings and loan associations.
Transportation: world headquarters of Atlas Van Lines; 4 railroads; 5 commercial barge lines; 4 interstate bus lines; Allegheny, Delta, Eastern air lines.
Communications: 2 daily newspapers; 4 TV and 6 radio stations.
Medical facilities: 4 general and mental hospitals; branch of Indiana University Medical School.
Cultural facilities: Philharmonic Orchestra, Museum of Arts and Science, Mesker Zoo, Univ. of Evansville, Indiana State Univ., Evansville; national headquarters of Phi Mu Alpha music fraternity. Abraham Lincoln boyhood home nearby.
Sports: Evansville Triplets baseball of American Assn. (AAA), farm team of Detroit Tigers.
Further information: Chamber of Commerce, Southern Securities Building, Evansville, IN 47708.

Fort Wayne, Indiana

The World Almanac is sponsored in The Fort Wayne area by the Journal-Gazette, 600 W. Main Street, Fort wayne, IN 46802 (219) 423-3311; established June 14, 189? by consolidation of The Journal and The Daily Gazette; circulation daily 62,059, Sundays 102,298; president-publisher Richard G. Inskeep; secretary-treasurer Naomi Erb; editor Larry W. Allen.

Population: 190,200 (city); 374,900 (metro area); total employed 169,800.
Area: 51.96 sq. mi. at confluence of St. Joseph, St. Mary's, and Maumee rivers in NE Ind.; Allen County seat. Allen County is largest of Indiana's 92 counties (671 sq. mi.), and has greatest number of farms in state, 2,011.
Industry: General Electric and International Harvester largest employers; Magnavox, Essex International, and Central Soya home offices; several firms manufacture about 85% of world's diamond wire dies.
Commerce: wholesale and retail center for northeastern Indiana, southeastern Michigan, northwestern Ohio; retail sales (metro) over $1.306 billion; bank deposits $1,677 billion; 5 banks, 4 savings-and-

loan assns.; E. B. I. per household (metro) $16,604; 6 life insurance companies, including Lincoln National Life, based here.
Transportation: 2 major rail freight lines; Amtrak; 56 motor freight lines including home-based North American Van, Elway Express, Scott, and Transport Motor; I-69 connects city with Indianapolis and Indiana Toll Road; U.S. 30 dual lane to Chicago; municipal airport; hq. for 122d Tactical Fighter Wing, Indiana Air National Guard; United, Delta, Air Wisconsin Airlines.
Communications: 10 radio, 3 TV stations.
Medical facilities: 4 hospitals including VA.
Cultural facilities: Philharmonic Orchestra; Fine Arts and Performing Arts complex; 9 universities and colleges; 3 museums; Foellinger outdoor theater.
Sports: Komet hockey team (IHL) plays at Allen Co. War Memorial Coliseum; annual Mad Anthony celebrities golf tournament.
Other attractions: replica of 3d Fort Wayne (1815); children's zoo; 88 parks and playgrounds; 19 golf courses; 37 shopping centers.
History: first white settlement in Indiana (circa 1692).
Further information: Chamber of Commerce, 826 Ewing Street, Ft. Wayne, IN 46802.

Fort Worth, Texas

The World Almanac is sponsored in the Fort Worth area by the Fort Worth Star-Telegram, 400 West Seventh, Fort Worth, TX 76101; phone (817) 336-9271; circulation (morn.) 85,048, (eve.) 137,290, (Sun.) 220,151. Established in 1906, Publisher Amon G. Carter Jr.; executive editor Jack Tinsley; vice-president and general manager Phil J. Meek.

Population: 410,279 (city, 1977 est.); Ft. Worth/Dallas metro area 2.7 million (1977 est.); 4th largest Texas city; work force of 367,330 (1976 avg.), unemployment average 3.9%.
Area: 233 sq. mi. on the Trinity River in north central Texas; Tarrant County seat.
Commerce: all types of manufacturing; wholesale and retail center for large area including west Texas; retail sales $2.9 billion (1977 est.); effective buying income $4.4 billion (1976 est.); bank deposits $3.5 billion (47 Tarrant County banks); over 60 mortgage institutions, insurance companies and savings and loans associations.
Transportation: Dallas-Fort Worth Regional Airport, 17 miles from downtown; Meacham Field, general aviation airport, many smaller airports; 9 railroads; Amtrak, 38 motor carriers, and 5 bus companies.
Communications: 2 TV and 18 area radio stations; 1 daily newspaper; weekly and monthly publications.
Medical facilities: over 20 hospitals.
Federal facilities: 14 federal agencies and Carswell AFB; reserve training centers.
Cultural facilities: Casa Manana, America's first permanent musical arena theater; symphony, opera; Van Cliburn Piano Competition; museums include Kimball Art Museum, Amon Carter Museum of Western Art, Fort Worth Museum of Science & History, and Fort Worth Art Center.
Educational facilities: 3 campuses of Tarrant County Junior College; Texas Christian Univ., Univ. of Texas at Arlington, Texas Wesleyan College, Southwestern Baptist Seminary, Texas Woman's Univ., and other technical and vocational schools.
Recreation: 6 Flags Over Texas, Forest Park and Fort Worth Zoological Park; several other parks.
Convention facilities: Tarrant County Convention Center, Will Rogers Memorial Center.
Sports attractions: Texas Rangers baseball; Fort Worth Texans in hockey; Colonial National Golf Tournament; TCU football, other college and semi-pro teams.
Other attractions: Fat Stock Show and Rodeo; Miss Texas Pageant.
History: founded 1849 as a frontier Army post on the Chisholm Trail; became major railhead.
Further information: Chamber of Commerce, 700 Throckmorton Street, Fort Worth, TX 76102.

Fresno, California

The World Almanac is sponsored in the Fresno area by The Fresno Bee, 1626 E Street, Fresno, CA 93721; phone (209) 268-5221; founded 1922; circulation daily 121,365, Sunday 136,334; president Eleanor McClatchy, editor C. K. McClatchy, managing editor George Gruner.

Population: 186,900 (city), 463,700 (county); total employed 200,500.
Area: one of largest counties in the state, 3,819,456 acres; located in geographical center of the state; Fresno County seat.
Agriculture: leading county in U. S. in annual value of agricultural production; state's leading county in production of field and seed crops, grapes, cantaloupes, barley, tomatoes, turkeys; 2d leading county in plums, peaches, sugar beets, cotton, cattle and calves, fruit and nuts, vegetable crops.
Industry: 475 diversified manufacturing establishments; food processing is major industry; 2d in importance is production of beverages, primarily wine, brandy and spirits; metro retail sales (1976) over $1.5 billion.
Transportation: airports, daily service by 5 airlines; freeways connect to all major metropolitan areas in California; served by 23 common truck carriers, 2 interstate bus lines and 2 mainline railroads with freight handling facilities.
Communications: 5 TV and 16 radio stations.
Medical facilities: 6 general hospitals, including a Veterans' Administration installation.
Cultural facilities: Community and Convention Center; community philharmonic, opera, ballet, and theater; California State Univ.-Fresno, Pacific College, 3 community colleges.
Recreation: golf courses; tennis courts; swimming pools; 3 national parks; Yosemite, Sequoia, and Kings Canyon with groves of giant Sequoia trees plus facilities for boating, sailing, hunting, fishing, skiing, hiking, pack trips and camping.
Other attractions: city zoo, nationally famous rodeo, county fair, underground gardens, Kearney Museum; downtown malls with one of the best outdoor art displays in the West.
History: area explored by the Spaniards in the early 1800s and visited by fur trappers before 1840; settlement began when gold miners came in the 1850s; county created Apr. 19, 1856, from parts of Mariposa, Merced, and Tulare counties.

Halifax, Nova Scotia, Canada

The World Almanac is sponsored in Nova Scotia by The Chronicle-Herald and The Mail-Star, 1650 Argyle Street, Halifax; phone (902) 426-2811; circulation Chronicle (morning) 69,356, Mail-Star (aft.) 53,083; publisher and president Graham W. Dennis, chairman of the board Ira B. MacCallum, general-manager Fred G. Mounce, managing editor Bill Smith, secretary-treasurer W. D. Coleman.

Population: 117,882 (1976); labor force 57,305; employed 53,170.
Area: 24.19 sq. mi. of land, on the southeast coast of the province; capital city.
Industry: leading industrial area in Atlantic provinces; establishments include oil refineries, electronic equipment manufacturers, ship yards, car assembly plants, plastic fabricators, metal works, breweries, and fish processing; 3d largest and one of Canada's most diversified scientific research centers.
Commerce: financial center of region, regional head offices for all major banks and investment houses; retail sales over $379.5 million annually in Halifax County; average family income $16,203 (1976); all 3 levels of government constitute employment for 18,000; armed forces have over 14,000 stationed in city.
Transportation: 2 major passenger-freight rail lines, 8 container lines call regularly at eastern-most commercial port on mainland North America; only Canadian container port with 3 sea-shore cranes; handled 143,000, 20-foot equivalent containers' (1975), over 620,000 tons break bulk general cargo; international airport.
Communications: 5 radio and 2 TV stations.
New construction: building permits issued for $46.7 million worth of construction last year.
Education: 6 degree-granting universities, 48 common and 3 private schools, one technical institute.
Medical facilities: 9 hospitals (3 teaching).
Cultural facilities: Atlantic Symphony Orchestra, 1 professional live theatre and 2 amateur, 2 public libraries.
Parks: 3 major parks (403 acres).
Sports: home of Halifax Voyageurs of the AHL.
History: founded in 1749; meeting place of first legislative assembly in Canada (1758).

Hamilton, Ontario, Canada

The World Almanac is sponsored in Hamilton and the Niagara Peninsula by The Spectator (a division of Southam Press Ltd.), 44 Frid Street., Hamilton, Ontario; (416) 526-3333; founded in 1846; circulation 140,000; publisher John D. Muir, business manager Gordon Bullock, executive editor John Doherty, managing editor Alex Beer.

Population: 312,162 (city), 529,371 (metro area); 7th in Canada, 2d in province; work force 253,00 (metro).
Area: 54.4 sq. mi. (city), 426 sq. mi. (Hamilton-Wentworth region) at the west end of Lake Ontario.
Industry: 62% of Canada's steel is produced at the Steel Company of Canada Ltd., Dominion Foundries and Steel Ltd., and Slater Steel Ltd., 678 plants in the metro area manufacturing iron and steel products, electrical appliances, agricultural equipment, tires, wire, food products, heavy machinery, chemicals, and textiles.
Commerce: retail sales (1976) $1.4 billion or 2.5% of Canadian total sales; average weekly wage $240.72; average total income (1975) $10,578, 15th in Canada in total income.
Transportation: Hamilton Street Railway, Canadian National and Canadian Pacific railways as well as Toronto, Hamilton, and Buffalo line; western terminus for GO Transit (provincial rapid transit system); provincial highways through Toronto to Windsor and Buffalo pass through region; city airport 9 miles south at Mount Hope.
Communications: one TV station, one community programming cable station; 4 radio stations.
New construction: new 420-room hotel planned to accompany $16 million convention centre slated for 1978; second phase of Jackson Square downtown shopping mall completed with 120 stores.
Medical facilities: 5 major hospitals including medical centre at McMaster Univ.; Hamilton Psychiatric Hospital; St. Peter's Centre for chronically ill.
Educational facilities: McMaster Univ., Mohawk College of Applied Arts and Technology.
Cultural facilities: Hamilton Place theatre-auditorium; new $5.5 million art gallery collection rated 4th in Canada; Hamilton Philharmonic Orchestra; Hamilton Players Guild; Multicultural Centre.
Convention facilities: convention centre slated for 1978 will have 17 meeting rooms, banquet space for up to 2,300 people in one room, 15-story office tower.
Other attractions: Dundurn Castle, restored prime minister's residence circa 1850; Whitehearn, restored Victorian home; Canadian Football Hall of Fame; Royal Botanical Gardens; one of the largest park systems per capita in Canada; Hess Village boutiques and restaurants in old restored homes; hiking on Bruce Trail winding through region along Niagara Escarpment.
Sports: Hamilton Tiger-Cats football; two municipal golf courses; Royal Hamilton Yacht Club.
History: explorer Sieur de la Salle discovered Hamilton area in 1669; city takes name from George Hamilton, who laid out streets on part of the farm he bought in 1813.
Further information: Hamilton and District Visitors and Convention Bureau, 58 Jackson Street W. Hamilton; District Chamber of Commerce, 155 James Street South.

Hartford, Connecticut

Population: (1976 est.): 153,000 (city); 826,200 (county); total employed in greater Hartford: 345,000.
Area: 17.2 sq. miles in Hartford County.
Industry: "Insurance City," headquarters for 38 insurance firms employing 35,000. East Hartford is the home office of United Technologies, manufacturers of Pratt & Whitney jet engines, employing 46,000 in the state.
Commerce: total retail sales (county, 1975) $2.59 billion; per household spendable income (1975) $15,529.
Transportation: intersection of Interstates 84 and 91; Amtrak, Conrail; Bradley International Airport with 8 scheduled airlines and freight service; Brainard Airport in city with charter service.
Communications: 4 AM radio stations, 8 FM stations, 3 commercial TV stations, 1 educational TV station.
Educational facilities: Trinity College, Univ. of Hartford, Graduate Center of Rensselaer Polytechnic Institute, St. Joseph College, Greater Hartford Community College, Univ. of Connecticut Law School, School of Social Work, and Hartford Branch.
Cultural facilities: Wadsworth Atheneum, the oldest public art museum in America; Mark Twain House; symphony orchestra; Connecticut Opera Association; Hartford Stage Co., Hartford Ballet; Mark Twain Masquers.

Convention facilities: Hartford Civic Center complex completed January 1975, including retail arcade, 20-story Sheraton Hotel, 10,000-seat coliseum, 70,000 square foot exhibition hall and 17,000 square foot assembly hall.
Sports: Greater Hartford Open (golf), Aetna World Cup Tennis, New England Whalers (hockey).

History: Founded by Dutch in 1633; settled by Thomas Hooker and company from Newtown (Cambridge), Mass., 1636; named sole state capital, a distinction previously shared with New Haven, in 1875.

Further information: Chamber of Commerce, 250 Constitution Plaza, Hartford, CT 06103.

Honolulu, Hawaii

The World Almanac is sponsored in Hawaii by The Honolulu Advertiser, P.O. Box 3110, Honolulu, HI 96802; (808) 537-2977; founded July 2, 1856, as Pacific Commercial Advertiser by Henry M. Whitney; circulation 76,196 mornings, 184,528 Sunday; president and publisher Thurston Twigg-Smith, editor-in-chief George Chaplin, executive editor Buck Buchwach, managing editor Mike Middlesworth; awards from American Political Science Assn., American Assn. for the Advancement of Science, others.

Population: 718,400 (metro); 81% of state population; total employed, 290,000.
Area: 595 sq. mi., encompassing Oahu Island; state capital and Honolulu County seat.
Commerce: major destination for U.S., Japanese tourists; persons staying a night or more, 3.2 million in 1976, up from 835,000 a decade earlier; average daily visitor census, 78,000 in 1976; tourist spending, $1.4 billion in 1976, up from $280 million in 1966; visitors dollars top military spending, $1.0 billion in 1976; sugarcane and pineapple major agriculture export crops; retail sales (statewide), $3.7 billion; total income, $6.1 billion; per capita income, $6,969; Pacific basin business and financial center.
Transportation: dependent on ships, planes for most goods; passengers arrive mostly by air; 18 airlines serve airport: 8 domestic carriers, 8 foreign, 2 inter-island; inter-island hydrofoil.
Communications: 5 TV, 33 radio stations; 2 major daily newspapers.
Medical facilities: 16 hospitals, including Tripler Army Medical Center; Univ. of Hawaii School of Medicine.
Federal facilities: 7 major military bases, including Pearl Harbor Naval Base.
Cultural facilities: 10-campus, University of Hawaii with 45,000 students; main campus at Manoa in Honolulu, 21,356 students in 1976; university stresses oceanography, tropical environment problems and resources, tsunami research, volcanology, interrace relations; East-West Center, Inc., at Manoa, public education corp. funded by federal government, attracts international students and researchers; Bernice Pauahi Bishop Museum is center for studies of Pacific cultures, houses artifacts, maintains floating square-rigger Falls of Clyde, plus branch museum in Waikiki; Polynesian Cultural Center showcases native dances, music, arts; Honolulu Academy of Arts.
Recreation: surfing, swimming, sailing, fishing, football, basketball, baseball.

Other attractions: Waikiki Beach, extinct volcano Diamond Head, Arizona Memorial, balmy weather, tradewinds, multi-racial population, cultural diversity, Polynesian heritage.

History: Honolulu ("sheltered bay" in Hawaiian) was a small village when first Westerners called aboard 2 British ships in 1786, 8 years after Capt. James Cook became first known European to discover Hawaiian Islands.

Further information: Hawaii Visitors Bureau, 2270 Kalakaua Avenue, Honolulu, HI 96815.

Houston, Texas

The World Almanac is sponsored in the Southwest by The Houston Post, 4747 Southwest Freeway, Houston, TX 77001. Phone: (713) 621-7000; founded 1836; Oveta Culp Hobby, chairman of the board and editor; William P. Hobby, president. Circulation: daily 293,805; Saturday 330,878; Sunday 355,396; awards include Pulitzer Prize, Grand Prix, Editor & Publisher; community events sponsored: Educational Services, Science Engineering Fair, Spring Art Festival, travel shows, Houston Post Family Night at the Shrine Circus, the Rodeo, the Ice Capades.

Population: (city) 1,501,000; 5th in nation; (SMSA) 2,571,000; total employed (SMSA) 1,132,500; total wages and salaries (SMSA) $15.2 billion.
Area: 507 sq. mi. (city) on upper center Gulf Coast prairies, 41 ft. above sea level; Harris County seat; connected to Gulf of Mexico by 50-mile inland waterway, the Ship Channel.
Industry: nation's 9th largest mfg. area; supplies nation with 66% petrochemicals, 80% synthetic rubber, 25% natural gas; 9 refineries, 200 chemical plants, 3,500 mfg. plants; produces $2 billion annually in steel, 10 million board feet of lumber monthly, 33% nation's rice; 250 firms in underwater, offshore and oceanographic markets; exports chemicals, oilfield equip., machinery, food supplies.
Commerce: metro retail sales, $8.9 billion; average spendable family income, $14,020; 195 metro banks with resources of $17.3 billion and deposits of $14.3 billion; 8 foreign banks.
Transportation: Port of Houston (nation's 3d in tonnage) connects with 250 world ports by 120 steamship lines, hosts 4,000 ships yearly; 12 major airlines, 2 airports; 6 major rail systems; 34 common carrier truck lines; 200-mile freeway system; bus transit system.
Communications: 2 daily newspapers; 30 radio stations; 5 commercial, one educational TV station.
New construction: non-residential contracts awarded in 1976 $1.2 billion; residential units completed value $960.5 million (1976).
Medical facilities: Texas Medical Center includes 35 buildings on 260 acres, 11 hospitals plus medical, dental, nursing schools, employs 17,000 with annual budget of $388 million; Harris County total, 58 hospitals (including VA) with 14,447 beds.
Federal facilities: Lyndon B. Johnson Space Center, $202 million manned-spacecraft center; Ellington AFB.
Cultural facilities: 11 theatrical organizations perform at $3 million Alley Theatre & Miller Outdoor Theatre; Houston Symphony Orchestra, Grand Opera Assn., Houston Ballet Foundation perform in $7.5 million Jones Hall for Performing Arts; 30 major art galleries including Museum of Fine Arts (permanent

collection valued at $14 million) and Contemporary Arts Museum; 28-branch library.
Education: 24 major universities including Rice, Univ. of Houston, Texas Southern; 2 major medical schools including Baylor College of Medicine, and Univ. of Texas Health Science Center (8 branches). Houston Independent School District, 7th largest in nation; total enrollment 210,025; 22 school districts in Harris County, total enrollment 462,193; private and parochial school enrollment 30,000.
Recreational facilities: 260 parks; 5 municipal golf courses; 38 municipal swimming pools; 3 tennis centers with 54 courts and 85 neighborhood courts; Astroworld 60-acre amusement park; botanical garden, arboretum, Herman Park & Zoo; 50 community centers; 28 county parks; 70 miles of Gulf beaches in one hour's drive.
Convention facilities: 266 major conventions held in Houston in 1976 with 530,800 delegates attending; hotels and motels have 26,000 rooms. The Astrodome can seat 60,000 for conventions; Astrohall has 795,000 sq. ft.; downtown locations include Albert Thomas Convention Center, 300,000 sq. ft.; Sam Houston Coliseum, 50,000 sq. ft.; Music Hall seats 3,036; Exposition Hall, 83,000 sq. ft. exhibit area.
Sports: pro teams Astros baseball, Oilers football, Aeros hockey, Rockets basketball; sports events centers are Astrodome and Summit.
Climate: temperatures moderated by winds from Gulf of Mexico, abundant rainfall; average daily temp. 65.8; total yearly precip. 54.62 inches.
Scientific facilities: 9th among nation's science centers; research in petroleum, chemicals, medicine, earth sciences, aerospace, oceanography; $214 million spent on science and research (1972).
History: founded 1836 by J. K. and A. C. Allen; city eventually encompassed Old Harrisburgh which was an 1826 townsite laid out by John Harris; named for Gen. Sam Houston, commander of the Texas Army, which won independence from Mexico for the Republic of Texas Apr. 21, 1836; Houston was first president of the Republic, later governor of the state of Texas; both Houston and Harrisburg were for brief periods capitals of the Republic.
Further information: Houston Convention & Visitor Council, 10006 Main; Houston Chamber of Commerce, 1100 Milam, both Houston, TX 77002.

Huntington, West Virginia

The World Almanac is sponsored in the Huntington-Ashland-Ironton area by The Herald-Dispatch (morn.), and The Huntington Advertiser (aft.), Huntington Publishing Company, 946 Fifth Avenue, Huntington, WV 25720, member of the Gannett Group; circulation 62,934, Sunday 54,918. Publisher and president Harold E. Burdick, business manager James D. Hoffman, managing editors, C. Donald Hatfield (Advertiser), and Bill Southerland (Herald-Dispatch).

Population: 74,315 (city), 297,200 (5-county metro area); largest city in the state. Cabell County seat.
Area: 15.86 sq. mi., on Ohio River near where West Virginia, Ohio, and Kentucky meet. Cabell County seat.
Industry: center for coal transport and for handcrafted glass; leading industries are Ashland Oil, Armco Steel Co., Huntington Alloys, Inc., division of International Nickel Co.
Commerce: largest port for inland vessels in U.S. handles nearly 20 million tons of materials per year, moved by 7 freight companies; 1975 total retail sales in metro area, $750.1 million.
Transportation: Tri-State Airport, with the longest runway in the state, is served by 2 airlines, 500 air movements a month; 18 truck lines; urban bus transport system; 2 interstate bus lines.
Communications: 4 TV and 11 radio stations.
Cultural facilities: Marshall University; Ashland Community College (University of Kentucky); The Huntington Galleries of Art.
Medical facilities: 5 general hospitals with 1,076 total beds; 3 specialty hospitals including a VA hospital.
New construction: $32 million renewal program calls for large shopping mall, riverfront marina, civic center (to be finished in 1977), and additional convention facilities.
Further information: Chamber of Commerce, 522 Ninth Street, Huntington, WV 25701.

Indianapolis, Indiana

The World Almanac is sponsored in the Indianapolis area by The Indianapolis Star, The Indianapolis News, 307 N. Pennsylvania Street, Indianapolis, IN 46206; phone (317) 633-1240. News founded 1869; Star 1903; circulation daily Star, 221,170; News, 158,847; Sunday Star, 353,977; publisher-Eugene S. Pulliam; president-William A. Dyer Jr.; Star editor-Frank Crane; News editor-Dr. Harvey Jacobs; Pulitzer Prizes-News, Star; Nat'l. Headliners first prize-Star.

Population: 745,739 (consolidated city 1970), nation's 11th largest; 1,111,173 (metro 1970); total employed 518,000.
Area: 379.4 sq. mi.; geographic center of state; state capital and Marion County seat.
Industry: over 1,400 diversified manufacturers including plane and auto engines and parts, electronics, pharmaceuticals, machinery; 1976 manufacturing payroll over $1.5 billion.
Commerce: commercial center for Indiana; retail sales $3.9 billion; per capita personal income $5,600; 6 banks with resources over $5.5 billion; home offices of over 60 insurance companies.
Transportation: 7 airlines; 5 rail freight lines; Amtrak; 3 interstate bus lines; 67 truck lines; 7 interstate freeway routes.
New construction: projects totalling over $229.3 million under construction in 1977.
Communications: 6 TV stations and 18 radio stations.
Medical facilities: 17 hospitals, over 6,800 beds.
Federal facilities: Fort Harrison incl. Army Finance and Acctng. Center, U.S.A. Admin. Center.
Cultural facilities: Museum of Art and Oldfields Museum of Decorative Arts; Indiana State Museum; Indianapolis Zoo; Children's Museum; Conner Prairie Pioneer Settlement and Museum of Indiana Heritage; Clowes Hall, home of symphony orch.; Civic Theatre, oldest U.S. amâteur theatrical group; repertory theatre.
Education facilities: Butler Univ., Indiana Central Univ., Marian College, Christian Theological and St. Mauer's seminaries, Indiana Univ., Purdue Univ. at Indianapolis, with nation's largest medical center.
Convention facilities: Indiana Convention-Exposition

Center, Indiana State Fairgrounds.
Recreational facilities: 13,000 park acres, 16 municipal swimming pools, 12 golf courses; pro basketball and hockey in 18,000-seat domed sports arena, home of the Pacers NBA; Racers WHA; Loves WTA; minor league baseball.

Other attractions: Indianapolis 500; Yankee 300; annual National Drag Racing championships.
History: sesquicentennial in 1971; important before Civil War, with nation's first union railway station (1853); home of James Whitcomb Riley, Booth Tarkington and President Benjamin Harrison.
Additional information: Indianapolis Chamber of Commerce, 320 N. Meridian Street, Indianapolis, IN 46204, (317) 635-4747.

Jacksonville, Florida

The World Almanac is sponsored in the Jacksonville area by the Florida Times-Union and the Jacksonville Journal, One Riverside Avenue, Jacksonville, FL 32202; phone (904) 791-4111; circulation, Times-Union 148,163, Journal 53,326, combined Sunday 183,504, publisher J. J. Daniel, president John A. Tucker, executive editor John S. Walters; Journal won Pulitzer Prize for photography in 1967.

Population: 579,661 (1976); total employment, 238,500 (1976).
Area: 840 sq. mi., includes nearly all of Duval Co. in northeast Fla.; largest incorporated developed area in Western Hemisphere.
Industry: 592 industries, added value total of $505 million annually; Offshore Power Systems investing $250 million in floating nuclear power plant production facility to employ 10,000 when completed.
Commerce: emphasis on finance, distribution; home or regional headquarters for 34 insurance companies; 1975 retail sales, $1.8 billion; effective buying income per household in 1975, $12,104.
Transportation: 3 major railroads and Amtrak; 16 major truck lines; 7 airlines averaging 126 air movements daily; 2 interstate bus lines; port handled 15 million tons in 1974.
Communications: 4 TV and 20 radio stations.
New construction: $154.7 million in building permits issued in 1976.
Medical facilities: 11 general hospitals and one naval hospital with total of 3,358 beds.
Federal facilities: 2 naval air stations, one naval station add $400 million yearly to economy.
Cultural facilities: Cummer Art Gallery, Jacksonville Art Museum, Children's Museum; Jacksonville Symphony, Ballet Guild, 4 community theaters.
Education: Univ. of North Florida, Jacksonville Univ., Edward Waters College, Florida Jr. College.
Sports: Gator Bowl; Tournament Players Championship Golf Tournament, $300,000 purse.

Other attractions: Civic Auditorium, Coliseum, Jacksonville Zoo, Fort Caroline, Kingsley Plantation; 8 miles of public beaches.

History: founded in 1822 by Isaiah Hart, named for Andrew Jackson; fire in 1901 destroyed 2,368 buildings, left 10,000 homeless; city and county governments merged in 1968 after referendum.

Further information: Chamber of Commerce, 604 Hogan Street, or Convention & Visitors Bureau, Hemming Park, Jacksonville, FL 32202.

Kalamazoo, Michigan

The World Almanac is sponsored in the Kalamazoo area by The Kalamazoo Gazette, 401 S. Burdick, Kalamazoo, MI 49003; telephone (616) 345-3511, founded 1833; circulation daily 58,128, Sunday 64,238, owned and operated by Booth Newspapers Inc.; president James E. Sauter, editor Daniel M. Ryan, manager Ralph H. Bastien Jr.

Population: 85,800 (city), 207,700 (county); total employed (Kalamazoo-Portage SMSA) 117,800.
Area: located equidistant to the 3d and 5th largest metro areas in nation — Chicago and Detroit, 140 miles away.
Industry: paper-making is the traditional industry, with 5 large plants. Checker Motors Corp. manufactures cars; large Fisher Body Division body stamping plant; Upjohn Company, pharmaceuticals.
Commerce: shopping center for large part of southwestern Michigan. In 1959, city became first in country to close downtown streets and create a pedestrian mall; now known as "Mall City." Retail sales (1976) $802 million; 4 banks had combined assets in 1976 of $801 million, 2 savings and loan associations have assets of over $200 million.
Transportation: 2 railroads provide freight service, Amtrak passenger service; 34 general carriers provide trucking services; airport with freight and passenger service; 3 bus lines.

Cultural facilities: 5 auditoriums offering music and theatrical performances, 6 live arts theaters, an art center, symphony orchestra, Kalamazoo Civic Players.

Educational facilities: 3 colleges and one university with combined student enrollment over 30,000.

Other attractions: Kalamazoo Nature Center, 83 lakes (county), National Junior Tennis Championships, 2 major hospitals, Kalamazoo Hilton Convention Center, IHL Kalamazoo Wings (hockey).

Further information: Kalamazoo County Chamber of Commerce, 500 W. Crosstown, Kalamazoo, MI 49008, telephone (616)381-4000.

Kansas City, Missouri

Population: 527,766 (city); 1,302,900 (metro area), 28th in nation; total employed, 565,600
Area: 3,341 sq. mi., SMSA, at confluence of Missouri and Kansas rivers in Jackson, Clay, and Platte counties.
Industry: 2d in nation in automotive assembly; first in production of envelopes and greeting cards, farm equipment distribution, frozen food storage and distribution, foreign trade zone space, underground storage space, and hard winter wheat marketing. Top employers: U.S. government, General Motors, TWA, Bendix, Western Electric, Ford. Presently Kansas City is a leading hard wheat center, stocker and feeder market, and is among the top 5 cities in flour

production and grain elevator capacity.
Commerce: total retail sales in 1975, $4.158 billion; the center of a 7-county metro area: Jackson, Clay, Platte, Cass, and Ray counties in Missouri; Johnson and Wyandotte counties in Kansas.
Transportation: 9 airlines with 400 scheduled arrivals and departures daily at Kansas City International Airport; 169 truck lines and 4 barge companies; city is one of the nation's major rail centers.
New construction: $350 million Crown Center business and apartment complex covers 25 square blocks; new medical center of University of Missouri and Univ. of Kansas; American Royal Arena; Mercantile Bank Building; United Missouri Bank headquarters; 30-story office and retail building downtown; 27 story IBM bldg.; H. Roe Bartle exposition hall; Worlds of Fun recreation center. More than 6 large hotels and several hospital additions.
Cultural facilities: Starlight Theater, nation's 2d largest outdoor theater; William Rockhill Nelson Gallery of Art, among the 10 top American museums with the 3d largest Oriental collection outside China; Performing Arts Foundation formed in 1965 to present festival events; University of Missouri at Kansas City; Rockhurst College; Kansas City Art Institute; University of Kansas Medical Center. Within commuting distance are University of Kansas, Park College, William Jewell College, Truman Library in Independence. Linda Hall Library of Science and Technology is one of the largest privately endowed technical reference libraries in the nation.
Recreational facilities: more than 100 parks cover 5,345 acres, including Swope Park, 2d largest in nation, with fine zoo.
Sports: The American Royal Livestock and Horse Show each fall attracts entries from throughout the country; home of the Chiefs of the NFL, Royals, American League baseball, Kings, NBA.
History: Kansas City's beginnings can be traced to a trading post of French fur trappers about 1826. It became an important trade and transportation center as the overland routes of the Oregon and Santa Fe trails spread westward. As agricultural production boomed, it became an important market and distribution center for crops from throughout the middle west.
Further information: Chamber of Commerce of Greater Kansas City, 920 Main, Kansas City, MO.

Kitchener-Waterloo, Ontario, Canada

The World Almanac is sponsored in the Kitchener-Waterloo area by the Kitchener-Waterloo Record, 225 Fairway Road, Kitchener, Ont.; phone (519) 579-2231: founded 1878; circulation 67,884, president and publisher K. A. Baird.

Population: 131,801 (Kitchener) and 49,972 (Waterloo), 291,194 (metro area); total employed 127,300.
Area: 51.74 sq. mi. (Kitchener) and 25.47 sq. mi. (Waterloo), 65 miles west of Toronto.
Industry: highly diversified industry (487 companies), rubber, plastics, electronics, metal fabrication, brewing, distilling, meat packing, footwear, furniture, food processing, automotive components; Budd Automotive Co., largest autoframe manufacturer in Canada; Deilcraft furniture plant is the largest under one roof in North America. Annual gross product exceeds $1 billion.
Agricultural: hog and dairy area; Waterloo County's 1,976 farms accounted for $100 million production in 1976.
Commerce: wholesale and retail center for area; metro retail sales (1975) $526.3 million; 8 banks, 62 branches; 9 trust companies, 21 branches; 41 life insurance offices, 29 other insurance offices; Waterloo, "The Hartford of Canada," head office for 6 insurance companies.
Transportation: 2 major rail lines, 34 truck lines, on Ontario's key highway 401; Waterloo-Wellington Airport; 45 mi. from Toronto International.
Communications: one TV and 4 radio stations; one daily, one weekly newspaper.
Medical facilities: 2 major hospitals.
Cultural facilities: symphony orchestra, Kitchener-Waterloo Art Gallery, Doon Pioneer Village; 28 mi. from famed Stratford Festival Theatre.
Educational facilities: Univ. of Waterloo, Wilfrid Laurier Univ., Conestoga College.
Other attractions: nationally-known farmers market; Canada's largest annual Oktoberfest celebration; Woodside, national historic park, boyhood of W. L. Mackenzie King, Canadian prime minister 22 years.
History: founded 1807 by German settlers; retains strong Germanic flavor.
Further information: Kitchener Chamber of Commerce, 67 King East; Waterloo Chamber of Commerce, 5 Bridgeport Road W.

Knoxville, Tennessee

The World Almanac is sponsored in the Knoxville area by The Knoxville News-Sentinel, 204 West Church Avenue, Knoxville, TN 37901. Sentinel founded in 1886; News in 1921 by Scripps-Howard Newspapers; Sentinel purchased by Scripps-Howard in 1926 and combined with News. Circulation 104,948 daily; 160,922 Sunday; president and general manager Roger A. Daley; editor Ralph L. Millett Jr.; managing editor Harold E. Harlow.

Population: 180,767 (city), 316,147 (county), 461,880 (metro area), 3d in state; total employed metro area 180,500.
Area: city 77.6 sq. mi., county 528 sq. mi., located almost in exact center of that portion of United States lying east of the Mississippi Rover and south of Great Lakes; Knox County seat.
Industry: major manufacturing industries are primary metals and chemicals; nearly 500 plants representing 51 diversified major industries (coal and zinc mining, marble quarrying, meat packing, electronics, steel fabrication, industrial controls eqpt., furniture, auto safety eqpt., refuse eqpt., apparel), with Aluminum Co. of America, Union Carbide Corp. Nuclear Div. at Oak Ridge, included in area market.
Commerce: wholesale and retail trade center of a multi-county area in east Tennessee, Virginia, Kentucky, and N. Carolina; county retail sales (1976) $1.2 billion.
Transportation: 2 rail lines, 5 airlines, 2 interstate bus lines, 25 motor freight carriers; Interstate Highways I-40 and I-75 intersect in heart of city, Tennessee River barges.
New construction: continuance of downtown redevelopment program, over $112 million expended since 1972; in progress 30-story bank bldg., University of Tennessee College of Veterinary under way, Neyland Stadium (football) enlarged to seat 81,000.
Cultural facilities: Univ. of Tennessee, Knoxville Col-

lege, Knoxville Symphony Orchestra, 10 museums, art gallery, auditorium-coliseum, city-county library (612,684 book volume), Zoological Park, university community theater, choral society, opera workshop, Lamar House-Bijou Theater.
Sports: Univ. of Tennessee (all major collegiate sports); Knoxville Sox, Chicago White Sox farm club.
Other attractions: Great Smoky Mountains National Park, 39 miles from Knoxville, offers year-round scenic beauty, skiing in season; within 30 miles of Knoxville, 6 TVA lakes, 2,320 miles of shoreline providing fishing, boating, swimming. Oak Ridge, known for its nuclear developments, 22 miles from Knoxville; American Museum of Atomic Energy and Oak Ridge National Lab; Doogwood Arts Festival held each April.

Further information: Chamber of Commerce, 301 E. Church Avenue, or Tourist Bureau, 811 Henley Street, both Knoxville, TN 37902.

Las Vegas, Nevada

The World Almanac is sponsored in the Las Vegas area by the Las Vegas Review-Journal, P.O. Box 70, 1111 W. Bonanza, Las Vegas, NV 89101; phone (702) 385-4241; founded as a weekly in 1909; purchased 1956 by Donald W. Reynolds, present publisher; member Donrey Media Group; circulation 71,157 weekdays, 76,523 Sundays; general manager Wm. Wright; editor Don Digilio.

Population: 359,720 greater Las Vegas (1976), 1976 total employment 156,800.
Area: southern Nevada, Clark County seat; 7,927 sq. miles; 283 miles NW of Phoenix, 289 miles NE of Los Angeles.
Industry: 24 hour tourism; hotel/gaming/recreation, payroll $453 million, 1976 tourist volume, 9.8 million; convention and tourist revenue, $2.5 billion; gaming revenue, $846 million.
Commerce: 6 banks, total resources over 1.2 billion, 6 savings and loans, total savings $668 million; retail sales over 2 billion; average spendable family income $16,334.
Transportation: McCarran Int'l Airport, total passengers in 1976, 7.6 million; 7 major airlines plus foreign carriers, charters, commuter, and 3d level carriers; 3 bus lines; daily auto traffic entering area, 11.7 thousand.
Communications: 5 TV stations, 15 radio stations, 3 newspapers.
Medical facilities: 8 major hospitals, 23 clinics, 15 convalescent homes, acupuncture clinics.
Federal facilities: Nellis AFB; 8,100 military, 1,300 civilian personnel; over $105 million annual federal payroll.
Education: Univ. of Nevada, Las Vegas; Clark County Community College; 16 libraries and 107 public schools in the area.
Cultural facilities: Las Vegas Art League and Museum, Reed Shipple Cultural Arts Center, Judy Bayley Theatre, Artemus W. Ham Concert Hall, Las Vegas Civic Symphony, Nevada Dance Theatre, University of Nevada museums and collections, Lost City Museum of Archeology, Southern Nevada Museum and Cultural Center, Las Vegas Valley Zoo.
Recreation: Lake Mead, Lake Mojave, Hoover Dam, Tule Springs, Valley of Fire, Red Rock, Tolyabe National Forest (Mt. Charleston), Rogers Springs, Colorado River, skiing, boating, fishing, swimming, hiking, camping.

Sports: amateur and professional competition in tennis, golf, auto racing, bowling, basketball, boccie ball, boxing, soccer, UNLV sports competitions, Mint 400 Off Road race, Sahara Invitational Golf Tournament, Alan King Tennis Classic, WCT Challenge Cup, Pizza Hut Basketball Invitational, home of the Quicksilvers (North American Soccer League).

History: first recorded group to enter the Las Vegas Valley was Antonio Armijo's party in early 1839. Las Vegas, Spanish for "The Meadows," first settled by Europeans in June of 1855, by a 30 man Mormon group under William Bringhurst; city of Las Vegas founded May 15, 1905, as a result of public land auction by the railroad.

Further information: Las Vegas Chamber of Commerce, 2301 East Sahara Avenue, Las Vegas, NV 89104. Telephone (702) 457-4664.

Lethbridge, Alberta, Canada

The World Almanac is sponsored in the Lethbridge area by The Lethbridge Herald, 504 7th Street S., Lethbridge, Alberta; phone (403) 328-4411; founded as a daily in 1907; circulation, weekdays 26,750; Saturdays, 28,160; editor and publisher Cleo W. Mowers, general manager Donald Doram; managing editor Don H. Pilling.

Population: 48,966
Area: 23 square miles; located on Oldman River, 60 miles north of Montana border, 130 miles south of Calgary.
Industry: heavily dependent on agriculture; federally inspected packing plants slaughtered 30% of cattle slaughtered in Alberta in 1976; large dryland grain growing, ranching area, and extensive irrigation district; brewery, distillery, flour mill, foundry, oilseed processing, mobile home construction.
Commerce: 1976 retail sales of $290 million: 11% more than 1974; 5 banks, 4 trust companies, 11 finance companies.
Transportation: CP Rail; 2 bus lines; depots for 50 trucking firms; regional airline flies out of Lethbridge Airport.
Communications: one newspaper, 2 TV, 2 radio stations.
New construction: building permits valued at $60.8 million in 1976, compared with $43.6 million in 1975.
Medical facilities: 2 general hospitals, one long-term care hospital, 4 nursing homes for the aged.
Cultural facilities: Canada agriculture research station, Univ. of Lethbridge, Lethbridge Community College, Alexander Galt Museum, Nikka Yuko Centennial Japanese Garden, symphony orchestra and chorus, local theater groups, Bowman Arts Centre, Yates Memorial Centre.
Other attractions: 4 major parks, 5 artificial ice arenas, 3 golf courses.
Sports: Dodgers, Los Angeles Dodgers farm team; Broncos, Western Canada Hockey League.
History: early coal-mining town, named Lethbridge Oct. 16, 1885, after a coal executive. A whisky traders' depot, Fort Whoop-Up, was booming, 5 miles southwest of what is now Lethbridge, in the 1860's; first settlers in area came 15 years later, many from the United States.

Little Rock, Arkansas

The World Almanac is sponsored in Arkansas by the Arkansas Gazette, 112 West Third Street, Little Rock, AR 72203, phone (501) 376-6161; founded 1819 at Arkansas Post, A. T., by Wm. E. Woodruff, moved to Little Rock 1821; circulation 121,135 daily, 143,635 Sunday; Hugh B. Patterson Jr., publisher and president; J. O. Powell, editorial director; Robert R. Douglas, managing editor; J. R. Williamson, executive vice president-general manager.

Population: 175,000 (city), 375,000 (metro); 152,300 employed.
Area: 110 sq. mi. at point where Ozarks-Ouachita highlands meet central coastal plain at geographical center of state. State capital and Pulaski County seat.
Industry: 378 manufacturing plants, employing 31,500 persons, including Allis-Chalmers, Armstrong Rubber Co., Timex, AMF Cycle Division, Remington Arms, Jacuzzi Bros., Teletype, Westinghouse, CPC, International, and General Electric.
Commerce: retail sales (estimated 1976) $1.2 billion; bank resources (Jan., 1977) $1.3 billion; building permits (1975) $74 million; 11 banks, 6 building & loan associations, 4 old line insurance companies.
Transportation: 3 Amtrak passenger service trunkline railroads, 6 federally certified airlines, 8 bus lines, 14 common carrier barge lines.
Communications: 3 commercial TV, one ETV, 17 radio stations; 2 daily, 1 weekly newspaper.
Medical facilities: 10 hospitals including UA Medical Sciences campus, 2 VA hospitals, and Ark. State Hospital for Nervous Diseases.
Federal facilities: Little Rock AFB, Military Airlift (MAC) Command; Camp Joseph T. Robinson, Arkansas National Guard headquarters and training center; U.S. National Guard Bureau's Non-Commissioned Officers Institute.
Cultural facilities: Univ. of Arkansas at Little Rock with Schools of Law, Medicine, Nursing, and Pharmacy; UA School of Graduate Technology; Philander Smith, Shorter, and Arkansas Baptist colleges; Arkansas State Symphony, Arkansas Arts Center, 3 major public libraries, convention center-auditorium-hotel; Arkansas territorial restoration, and Museum of Science & Natural History.

History: French explorer Bernard de la Harpe noted "le petit roche" on his map of the Arkansas River Valley in 1722.

Further information: Metropolitan Chamber of Commerce, One Spring Street; Arkansas Parks & Tourist Dept., State Capitol — both Little Rock, AR 72201.

Los Angeles, California

Population: 2.7 million (city), 6.9 million (county), (Jan. '76); 5-county urban area 11.3 million (Jan. '77); first in state, 2d county in nation, 3d urban area; total civilians employed 3.1 million (county, June '77); labor force 3.3 million (county, Mar. '77).
Area: 463.7 sq. mi. on Pacific, 418 mi. south of San Francisco, 145 mi. north of Mexico. Los Angeles County seat; one of 79 cities in county.
Industry: leading aerospace industry with 7 of the top 10 defense contractors in the nation located in the area; center of entertainment industry with more than 600 firms in movie and television entertainment work. Women's clothing, sportswear, electronics, rubber tires, printing, furniture, paper, autos, auto parts, chemicals, manufacturing. Work force (county, June '77) 825,100; agriculture 18,900; oil and mining 11,600; construction 105,600; transport, utilities, and communication 178,100; trade 747,300 (237,900 wholesale, 509,400 retail.); finance, insurance, and real estate 196,800; services and misc. 680,800; government 497,200. Among top 20 counties in U.S. in agricultural production; farm income $174.1 million (county '76); livestock (dairy, eggs, meat) production $47.2 million; sea fish harvested 589.6 million pounds (county '76).
Commerce: total taxable retail sales $27.4 billion (county '76) $10.2 billion (city '76); median family income $13,205; personal income $43.9 billion (county '76). 79 banks, 1,088 branches, more than 65 savings and loans with 565 branches; bank deposits $27.5 billion (June '76); S&L savings $25.9 billion (Mar. '77).
Transportation: Sante Fe, Union Pacific, Southern Pacific railroads; Amtrak; Continental, Greyhound bus lines; Southern California Rapid Transit District serving 4,150 mi. with 2,064 buses plus other local and intercity bus lines; Airport Transit Bus and Grey Line tours; 4.3 million vehicles (county, June '77), one of largest concentrations in nation — 3.5 million autos, 638,841 trucks, 165,563 motorcycles, 217,343 trailers; 156.6 mi. freeway (city) 491.2 (county) (June '77); airlines (36 scheduled, 13 charter, 4 commuter) serving Los Angeles International airport, 482,587 takeoffs and landings, 25.9 million passengers, 1.5 billion pounds cargo ('76); 9 other airports; more than 46 miles of commercial waterfront in Los Angeles-Long Beach Harbor, 5,407 ships, 61.7 million tons cargo (Los Angeles 30.3 million, Long Beach 31.4 million) in '76.
Communications: 13 TV stations (7 UHF, 6 VHF), approx. 75 radio stations, 60 commercial; more than 45 newspapers in English and foreign languages, more than 25 publishing daily (county).
New construction: building permits $845.5 million, including $324.4 million for 3,816 residential units (city, fiscal '76) plus $425.6 million in county building permits.
Medical facilities: 813 hospitals and clinics with 76,086 beds, including 178 general care hospitals, 34,654 beds, 24 psychiatric, 2,497 beds, 410 nursing homes, 38,570 beds (county, June '77).
Educational facilities: 1,208 elementary, 208 jr. high, 168 sr. high, 89 continuation, 80 adult, 36 special; approx. 800 private all levels (county '77); 62 libraries (city) plus 177 others in the county; UCLA, Univ. Southern Cal., California Institute of Technology; Loyola, Marymount, Pepperdine universities; Claremont, Woodbury, Occidental, Whittier, Mt. St. Mary colleges; 21 community colleges; campuses of California State University-Los Angeles, Long Beach, Northridge, Dominguez Hills.
Cultural facilities: 1,838 churches, Huntington Art Gallery and Library, Hollywood Bowl, Greek Theater, Music Center, Mark Taper Forum, Ahmanson Theater, Huntington Hartford Theater, Griffith Park Planetarium, Mt. Wilson and Mt. Palomar observatories; Los Angeles Museum, County Art Museum, UCLA Botanical Gardens, La Brea Tar Pits and natural history museum, Southwest Museum.
Recreational facilities: 273 city parks and playgrounds, plus 122 county parks; 5 public golf courses, 15 public beaches within 35 miles of city center; ocean, mountains, desert, lakes, forests; Disneyland, Marineland, Knott's Berry Farm, Lion Country Safari, Universal Movie Studio tour.
Convention facilities: approx. 20,000 hotel rooms (city), 50,000 (county); large convention center.
Sports: collegiate sports, including Rose Bowl; pro teams in baseball (Dodgers), basketball (Lakers), tennis (Strings), hockey (Kings), soccer (Aztecs, Skyhawks).
History: discovered 1542 by Portuguese navigator Juan Rodriguez Cabrillo; Mission San Gabriel founded Sept., 1771; city formally founded Sept. 4, 1781 by Spanish colonial governor as El Pueblo de Nuestra Senora la Reina de los Angeles de Porciuncula; inc. April 4, 1850.
Further information: Chamber of Commerce, P.O. Box 3696, Terminal Annex, Los Angeles, CA 90051.

Louisville, Kentucky

The World Almanac is sponsored in Kentucky and southern Indiana by The Courier-Journal and The Louisville Times, 525 West Broadway, Louisville, KY 40202, (502), 582-4011; Courier-Journal founded 1868; Times 1884; Courier circulation 210,528, Times 164,855, Sunday 351,760; chairman of the board Barry Bingham Sr., editor and publisher Barry Bingham Jr.; major awards include 6 Pulitzer prizes.

Population: 330,522 (city), 927,784 (metro area); first in state; total employed 363,600.
Area: 65.2 sq. mi. (city), 1,392 sq. mi. (metro); on southern bank of Ohio River.
Industry and Commerce: 10th in total industrial shipments; famous for baseball bats, cigarettes, railroad repair shops, electrical appliances, farm machinery, motor vehicles, plumbing fixtures, and whiskey; 997 manufacturing firms in area; estimated retail sales (Jefferson County, 1976) $2.460 billion.
Transportation: 6 trunk-line railroads, 1 terminal railroad, 90 inter-city truck lines; 5 barge lines; 4 bus lines; 7 airlines, and 2 municipal airports.
Communications: 14 radio and 4 TV stations, 2 educational.
Medical facilities: 18 hospitals, 5,732 total beds.
Cultural facilities: Louisville Orchestra, Kentucky Opera Association, Art Center Association, J.B. Speed Art Museum. 20 private art galleries, Macauley Theatre, Actors Theatre, The Children's Theatre, Louisville Civic Ballet, Louisville-Jefferson County Youth Orchestra, The Louisville Free Public Library (23 branches); 681 churches, 48 denominations.
Education: 10 colleges and universities, 3 business colleges and technical schools in area.
Recreation: 158 public parks, covering more than 7,000 acres.
Convention facilities: Kentucky Fair & Exposition Center, largest ground-level exhibit hall and auditorium complex in North America with 650,000 sq. ft., 20,000-plus seating, parking for 27,000 cars; new 100,000 sq. ft. Commonwealth Convention Center in downtown Louisville; Louisville Gardens, downtown, handles up to 7,000.
Sports: Kentucky Derby, held annually at Churchill Downs since 1875; Louisville Downs harness racing.
Other: Belle of Louisville excursion steamboat; Churchill Downs Museum; Louisville Zoo, American Printing House for the Blind; Kentucky Railway Museum; Museum of Natural History and Science.
History: founded by explorer George Rogers Clark, in 1778; named after King Louis XVI of France.
Further information: Louisville Area Chamber of Commerce, 300 West Liberty, Louisville, KY 40202.

Lubbock, Texas

The World Almanac is sponsored in the Lubbock area by the Lubbock Avalanche-Journal, 8th Street and Avenue J, Lubbock, TX 79408; (806) 762-8844; founded 1900 as Leader, became Avalanche 1908, daily 1921; Plains Journal weekly founded 1923; consolidated 1926; circulation (morn) 56,565, (eve) 15,103, (Sat) 65,824, (Sun) 77,308; member Southwestern Newspaper Corp.; general manager Robert R. Norris; editor Jay Harris.

Population: 177,920 (city), 201,200 (metro area), 8th in state; total employed 79,770.
Area: 82.2 sq. mi.; center of South Plains territory of northwest Texas; Lubbock County seat.
Industry: vegetable oils, cotton seed flour, grain sorghum, livestock, petroleum, sand and gravel; 228 manufacturing companies.
Commerce: wholesale and retail center for west Texas and eastern New Mexico; retail sales $499 million; bank resources: $679 million; 8 banks.
Transportation: 12 motor freight carriers; 2 major railroads, and 3 bus lines; Lubbock Regional Airport, 3 major airlines averaging 60 flights per day, 2 intrastate airlines; 6 major federal and state highways.
Communications: 4 TV and 9 radio stations.
Medical facilities: 8 hospitals, Lubbock State School for Mentally Retarded; medical school being constructed on Texas Tech campus, county teaching hospital under construction.
Federal facilities: Reese AFB, federal building, Federal Aviation Admin., and National Weather Service, U.S. Customs port of entry.
Cultural facilities: symphony orchestra, Theatre Centre; Museum of Texas Tech Univ., Moody Planetarium; Ranching Heritage Center (authentic ranch houses dating to 1835), Lubbock Christian College; Texas Tech Univ., Lubbock Cultural Affairs Council, and Lubbock Garden & Arts Center.
Recreational facilities: 39 city parks, 1,750 acres; Mackenzie State Park, state's largest, with Prairie Dog Town, Buffalo Lakes; Municipal Auditorium, 3,200 seats; Municipal Coliseum, 10,000 capacity; annual Panhandle South Plains Fair; Lubbock Memorial Civic Center, modern convention facility with 300,000 sq. ft. including 44,000 sq. ft. exhibit hall with banquet facilities for 1,500, auditorium seating 1,400.
Sports: Texas Tech, and Christian College sports; Tech Jones Stadium; indoor rodeos.
Further information: Chamber of Commerce, P.O. Box 561, Lubbock, TX 79408.

Macon, Georgia

The World Almanac is sponsored in the Macon area by The Macon Telegraph & News, 120 Broadway, Macon, GA 31208; phone (912) 743-2621; acquired by Knight-Ridder Newspapers, Inc., 1969; circulation (morn.) 51,701, News (eve.) 24,146, Sat. 66,232, Sun. 83,637; general manager Bert Struby, executive editor Frank Caperton, Telegraph editor Billy Watson, News editor Joseph Parham.

Population: 124,000 (city), 235,500 (metro). 3d in state; labor force, 99,510.
Area: 52 sq. mi., 6 miles northwest of geographic center of Georgia; Bibb County seat.
Industry: textiles; Bibb Company, longtime industry leader, headquartered in area; textile-related are YKK Zipper Co. of Japan and Texprint. Armstrong Cork Co. acoustical tile plant and Allied Chemical automotive products plant are area's largest; Ga. Kraft container board manufacturer; Keebler Co. cracker manufacturing plant. Kaolin deposits are mined in area and processed in numerous ways; Brown & Williamson Tobacco Corp.; Government Employees Insurance Co. regional office.
Federal facilities: Warner Robins Air Logistics Center and Robins AFB, 16 miles from Macon, are area's largest employers.
Educational Facilities: Wesleyan College, nation's oldest college for women, and Mercer University with law school; Macon Jr. College.
Other attractions: Ocmulgee National Monument displays archeological remains of 3 prehistoric Indian civilizations; $4.5 million coliseum seats 10,000.
History: Settled when U.S. established Fort Hawkins in 1806; chartered in 1823, named for Nathaniel Macon of North Carolina.
Further information: Macon Chamber of Commerce, 305 Coliseum Drive, Macon, GA 31201.

Madison, Wisconsin

The World Almanac is sponsored in Madison by Madison Newspapers, Inc., publisher of The Capital Times and the Wisconsin State Journal, 1901 Fish Hatchery Road, Madison, WI 53713; (608) 252-6100; circulation, Wisconsin State Journal (m) 74,082, The Capital Times (eve) 40,414, combined daily 115,015, Sunday Wisconsin State Journal 118,615.

Population: 168,671 (city), 290,272 (county), 2d in state; metro work force 150,200.
Area: 52 sq. mi. (city), 1,194 sq. mi. (county), in south central Wisconsin, state capital and Dane County seat.
Commerce: home office of 29 insurance firms; 375 industrial firms, 26 banks, 7 savings and loans, retail sales $1.1 billion; average effective buying income $16,700.
Transportation: Dane County regional airport, 3 airlines, 3 railroads, Amtrak (within county), major Interstate highway system, 3 bus lines, 30 common carriers, city owned bus system.
Communications: 4 TV, 2 cable, 6 AM and 10 FM radio stations.
Medical facilities: 9 hospitals, including U.W. and VA; 20 major clinics, approx. 600 physicians.
Federal facilities: Forest Products Laboratory.
Cultural facilities: Dane County Coliseum; Madison Civic Center, 2 art centers, ballet company, dinner playhouse, 11 drama groups, 8 music organizations, 15 Catholic, 150 Protestant, and one Greek Orthodox Church, 2 synagogues.
Education: University of Wisconsin, (39,100 enrolled), 35 elementary, 10 middle, 5 high schools; 15 parochial, one vocational-technical; Madison Area Technical College, Madison Business College, and Edgewood College, and 7 city and 32 university libraries.
Recreation: 5 lakes with total of 18,000 acres of water surface, and 4,676 acres of parks.
Convention facilities: Dane County coliseum, 5 major convention-size hotels, 55 supper clubs.
Sports: Blues, hockey; University of Wisconsin in Big Ten. Football, basketball, and other major sports; national 1977 hockey champions.
Other attractions: U. of W. Arboretum, Vilas Zoo, numerous political organizations, weekly Farmer's Market (May-Sept.), World Dairy Exposition headquarters.
Further information: Greater Madison Chamber of Commerce, 615 E. Washington Avenue, Madison, WI 53701.

Memphis, Tennessee

The World Almanac is sponsored in the Memphis area by The Memphis Press-Scimitar, 495 Union Avenue, Memphis, TN 38101; phone (901) 526-2141; Scimitar founded 1880 by G. P. M. Turner; Press 1906 by Scripps-McRae League, predecessor of Scripps-Howard Newspapers; circulation 111,957; editor Milton R. Britten, managing editor Van Pritchartt Jr.

Population: 667,500 (city), 885,950 (metro area); first in state, 17th in nation; 339,900 employed.
Area: 290 sq. mi., Shelby County seat, on east bank of the Mississippi River.
Industry: extensive cotton marketing-warehousing and processing of cotton seed into vegetable oil products; headquarters of Holiday Inns Inc., Cook Industries (cotton and grain), and Conwood Corp. (tobacco and food products). Other large industries include Schering-Plough (drugs), International Harvester (cotton pickers, hay balers), and Firestone (tires).
Commerce: wholesale-retail center for large parts of Tennessee, Arkansas, and Mississippi; retail sales (1975) $2.7 billion; bank deposits $2.6 billion; 12 banks, 6 savings-loan assns. Per capita personal income $5,162 (1974).
Transportation: 11 airlines; 8 trunk line railroads, 82 motor freight lines, 7 barge lines; river port handled 11.6 million tons of freight in 1975.
Communications: 4 TV and 19 radio stations.
Medical facilities: Univ. of Tennessee Center for Health Sciences and a VA hospital in complex with public hospital; 3 private hospitals and St. Jude Hospital, research center for childhood illnesses, particularly leukemia.
Federal facilities: Naval Air Station, Naval Air Technical Training Center, Defense Depot Memphis, and Air Force's 164th Air Transport Group.
Cultural facilities: Memphis Symphony Orchestra, opera theater, Theatre Memphis, Brooks Art Gallery, Chucalissa Indian Village & Museum, Memphis Museum; annual performances of Metropolitan Opera.
Educational facilities: Memphis State Univ., Southwestern College, LeMoyne-Owen College, Christian Brothers College, U-T Center for Health Sciences, Shelby State Community College, State Technical Institute, Southern College of Optometry, Mid-South Bible College.
Recreational facilities: Meeman-Shelby Forest state park, 12,500 acres; 137 other parks.
Convention facilities: $27 million Cook Convention Center, 1.3 million sq. ft., seating 16,500.
Sports: Liberty Bowl, home of Memphis State University football, site of Liberty Bowl game; Mid-South Coliseum, home of MSU basketball team; Memphis Blues, International Baseball League (AAA); Danny Thomas Memphis Classic golf tournament.
Other attractions: Cotton Carnival each May; Mid-South Fair each September; Beale Street, home of the blues, where composer W. C. Handy lived; Mid-America Mall; Libertyland.
History: DeSoto, exploring Mississippi River, stopped here in 1541; Ft. Adams established in 1797; Memphis incorporated in 1826; Yellow fever in 1878 nearly depopulated city, but its population grew back to 64,589 in 1890.
Further information: Memphis Area Chamber of Commerce 42 S. 2d Street, Memphis, TN 38103.

Mexico City (Ciudad de Mexico), Mexico

Population: 8,299,209 (UN est. 1974).
Area: about 53 sq. mi. within the 573 sq. mi. Federal District (Distrito Federal; population, 1976 est. 11 million); in central Mexico at an altitude of 7,349 ft.
Industry and commerce: capital of Mexico; the political and economic hub of the nation; manufactures include steel, automobiles, appliances, textiles, rubber goods, furniture, and electrical equipment; marketing center of Mexico.
Transportation: center of modern highway and rail system; 25-mi. subway system; served by most international air lines, Mexico City is 4 hrs. by jet from New York and 3 hrs. from Los Angeles.
Communications: major media center for Mexico and parts of Latin America; major film center.
Cultural facilities: Palace of Fine Arts and Ballet Folklorico; National Palace (Diego Rivera murals); National University with over 90,000 students; National Museum of Anthropology; Polyforum Cultural Siqueiros, containing world's largest mural; city itself is an architectural exhibit of Aztec ruins, baroque cathedrals, and ultra-modern buildings.
Other attractions: Xochimilco with the "floating gardens" and gondolas; Chapultepec Castle, palace of the French-supported Emperor and Empress of Mexico, Maximilian and Carlota; 22-ton Aztec Calen-

dar Stone; 2 volcanoes, Popocatepetl (17,887 ft.) and Iztaccihuatl (17,343 ft.); sports centers.
History: traditionally founded 1321 by Aztecs, city was called Tenochtitlan; captured by Spanish under Cortez in 1519 and again in 1521; occupied by the U.S. in 1847 and by the French from 1863 to 1867.
Further information: Mexican National Tourist Council, Mariano Escobedo 726, Mexico, D.F., or 405 Park Avenue, NY 10022; or 9701 Wilshire Boulevard, Beverly Hills, CA 90212.

Miami, Florida

The World Almanac is sponsored in the Miami area by The Miami Herald, 1 Herald Plaza, Miami, FL 33101; phone (305) 350-2111; founded Dec. 1, 1910 by Frank B. Shutts; circulation 401,643 daily, 495,002 Sunday; chairman James L. Knight, executive editor John McMullan, editor Don Shoemaker, managing editor Bob Ingle; newspaper or staff writers have won or shared in 5 Pulitzer prizes, the latest in 1976, and numerous other honors.

Population: 354,000 (city), 1,442,000 (metro); first in state, 24th in nation; total employed in metro area, 683,500.
Area: 53.8 sq. mi., land and water, on Biscayne Bay at mouth of Miami River in southeast Florida; largest of 27 municipalities in Dade County; Dade County seat.
Industry: 4,900 light manufacturing plants; tourism and aviation are mainstays of economy; 851 hotels and motels handle 13.8 million visitors a year; aviation hub with Eastern (largest industrial employer) and National headquarter bases; winter agriculture center.
Commerce: center of Pan-American finance and commerce with 97 banks, 16 savings and loan associations, Federal Reserve Bank branch; retail sales (1976) $4 billion; Port of Miami busy in waterborne commerce as well as Caribbean cruise center with 15 cruise liners based at Port.
Transportation: Miami International, served by 109 air carriers, handled more than 12 million travelers in 1976; Seaboard Coast Line, Amtrak, and all-freight Fla. East Coast Railroads operate in Miami, as do Greyhound and Trailways buses; 65 truck lines.
Communications: 6 commercial and 5 educational or closed-circuit TV stations, 36 radio stations.
New construction: work being completed on $75 million Omni International, Miami "megastructure" of shops, restaurants, theaters, and a hotel.
Medical facilities: 39 hospitals, 11,796 beds; 5,362 beds at 39 nursing homes in metro area; 2,966 members of Dade County Medical Association; VA hospital, Jackson Memorial Hospital one of area's leading research facilities.
Federal facilities: Homestead AFB south of Miami with 7,922 Air Force, Army, and Navy personnel; Federal Aviation Administration; Coast Guard bases; 2 federal hospitals; oceanographic center; 11,700 U.S. employes.
Cultural facilities: Philharmonic, Opera Guild, and other musical groups perform regularly; 18 auditoriums, resident and touring theatrical productions, 6 major art museums, 29 public libraries; 12 playhouses and 55 night clubs and theater restaurants, some in major hotels.
Educational facilities: 8 colleges and universities, plus 3 campuses of Miami-Dade Community College, total enrollment, 62,000; Univ. of Miami is largest independent institution of higher learning in southeast; Florida International Univ.; public school system has 240,636 students, is nation's 6th largest school system.
Recreational facilities: 14 miles of public beach on ocean and bay; 362 parks and playgrounds; 11 stadiums and grandstands; 45 golf courses; 57 marinas with 37,000 boats registered; 95 movie houses; 100 miles of bikeways; 31 bowling alleys.
Convention facilities: newly expanded Miami Beach Convention Hall can handle largest conventions; 187 conventions brought 93,500 delegates to Miami in 1976; 660 conventions brought 385,000 delegates to Miami Beach during the year.
Sports: pro football Miami Dolphins and U. of Miami play in Orange Bowl, which seats 80,050; stadium also hosts Orange Bowl game, Orange Blossom Classic; Miami Stadium is spring home for Baltimore Orioles; Miami Toros, pro soccer; parimutuel wagering at 5 horse and greyhound tracks, jai-alai fronton.
Other attractions: balmy subtropical climate with mean annual temperature of 75.3 degrees; 532 Protestant, 49 Catholic churches, and 41 Jewish synagogues; city is bilingual with 490,000 Latin American residents; one of nation's largest Jewish communities; marine stadium features powerboat and regatta racing; Everglades National Park, 40 miles south of Miami, is virgin wilderness.
History: American's newest big city, Miami had only 3 houses in 1895 in a community called Fort Dallas. Julia Tuttle persuaded Henry M. Flagler to extend his railroad south from West Palm Beach to stimulate Miami development. City was incorporated in 1896, when railroad arrived.
Further information: Miami-Metro Department of Publicity and Tourism, 499 Biscayne Boulevard, Miami, FL 33132.

Milwaukee, Wisconsin

The World Almanac is sponsored in the Milwaukee area by The Milwaukee Journal, Journal Square, Milwaukee, WI 53201; telephone (414) 224-2000; founded 1882 by Lucius W. Nieman; circulation 342,253 daily, 532,661 Sunday; chairman of the board Donald B. Abert; publisher Warren J. Heyse; president of The Journal Co. Thomas J. McCollow; editor Richard H. Leonard; major awards include 2 Pulitzer prizes to the newspaper and 3 to staff members.

Population: 666,400 (city); 1,438,200 (SMSA); city 12th and metro area 20th in U.S.; total employment 615,900 (metro area).
Area: 95.8 sq. mi. on shore of Lake Michigan, Milwaukee County seat.
Industry: largest U.S. producer of diesel and gasoline engines, outboard motors, motorcycles, tractors, padlocks, beer; 4th largest U.S. automaking center; graphic arts and food processing are largest nondurable goods employers; location for 11 "Fortune 500" industries.
Commerce: wholesale and retail trade center for Wisconsin, upper Michigan; total retail sales $4.3 billion (SMSA); wholesale trade $8.2 billion (SMSA). Average household spendable income $16,153 (SMSA); 79 banks with $5.2 billion deposits; 49 savings and loan associations home offices in the (SMSA), with deposits of over $3.3 billion.
Transportation: 5 major rail lines; Amtrak, 6 airlines provide direct service to East and West coasts, south, southeast, southwest, and Florida for 2 million users of Gen. Mitchell field with has new International air arrivals facility; 30 U.S. and foreign-flag ship lines use Milwaukee's St. Lawrence Seaway port, handling nearly 3.6 million tons annually including 553,000 tons overseas cargo; port of Milwaukee gateway for 350 cities in 31 states and overseas ports. Wisconsin ranks 11th in foreign trade-exports and imports; Milwaukee SMSA 4th largest U.S. machinery exporter and 14th largest exporter all products; 4 inter-city

bus lines, 70 motor freight carriers; I-94, 5 federal and 14 state highways intersect Milwaukee.
Communications: morning, evening, and Sunday metropolitan newspaper; 4 commercial, 2 educational TV stations; 28 AM and FM radio stations.
Medical facilities: 21 major hospitals and medical centers, including 600 bed VA hospital.
Cultural facilities: Milwaukee Symphony, Repertory Theater, opera and operetta companies; Mid-America Ballet; Milwaukee Art Center, $5 million addition opened 1977; Milwaukee museum, 4th largest in U.S.; University of Wisconsin-Milwaukee, Marquette University, Medical College of Wisconsin, 8 other colleges and vocational schools enroll over 45,000 annually; 3-theater Performing Arts Center; $15.9 million exhibition addition to convention-arena-auditorium complex; Mitchell Park Conservatory; Milwaukee County Stadium, and Milwaukee County Zoo are parts of 13,000 acre county park system.
Sports: baseball, Brewers (American League); basketball, Bucks (NBA), Marquette Univ., Univ. Wisconsin-Milwaukee; football, Green Bay Packers (NFL) play 5 of 11 home games in Milwaukee.
History: founded by Solomon Juneau, (1818), one of many French trappers in area in early 1800s; incorporated as town 1837; as city 1846.
Further information: Metropolitan Milwaukee Association of Commerce, 828 N. Broadway, Milwaukee, WI 53202.

Minneapolis, Minnesota

Population: 363,800 (city), 1,227,900 (metro); first in state, 31st in nation; total employed (city, 1976) 230,168.
Area: 59 sq. mi. (city), 4,000 sq. mi. (10-county metro area) around St. Anthony Falls near junction of Minnesota and Mississippi rivers; Hennepin County seat.
Industry: diverse; major electronics-computer manufacturing center, including Honeywell, Control Data, Medtronics; headquarters for nation's 4 largest grain millers, including General Mills, Pillsbury, and International Multifoods.
Commerce: $14,680 median household income; $3.8 billion total retail sales metro area (1976); 24 commercial banks, 6 savings and loan assns.; headquarters for Ninth Federal Reserve District; world trade center, 12th among U.S. metro areas in exports.
Transportation: Amtrak regional terminal, 5 trunk railroads; 150 trucking firms; 5 major barge lines headquartered in city; Mpls.-St. Paul International Airport, averaging 350 flights daily.
Communications: 4 commercial, 2 educational TV stations; 39 radio stations.
Medical facilities: 21 hospitals, including a leading heart hospital at Univ. of Minn.
Federal facilities: Farm Credit Administration regional office; FBI regional office; EPA district office, area headquarters HUD.
Cultural facilities: Minnesota Orchestra, 7 art galleries-museums, Tyrone Guthrie Theatre, Walker Art Center, Univ. of Minnesota.
Sports: Minnesota Twins (American League), Minnesota Vikings (NFL), Minnesota North Stars (NHL), Minnesota Kicks (NASL).
Other attractions: 153 parks, 22 lakes; 57-story IDS Tower; Mpls. Aquatennial celebration in July; average yearly snowfall, 41 inches.
History: first visited in 1680s by Fr. Louis Hennepin who discovered and named St. Anthony Falls on the Mississippi River; French fur traders used the area in 18th century; incorp. 1871. Falls became power source for lumber and milling operations in 19th century.
Further information: Greater Minneapolis Chamber of Commerce Information, 15 S. 5th Street, Minneapolis, MN 55402.

Mobile, Alabama

The World Almanac is sponsored in the Mobile area by The Mobile Press Register, 304 Government Street, 36630; phone (205) 433-1551; circulation, Register (morn.) 48,117, Press (eve.) 56,562, Sunday, 98,595; Register founded 1813, Press 1928; William J. Hearin publisher and president, Fallon Trotter executive editor, John Fay associate executive editor.

Population: 196,600 (city), 400,600 (metro), 2d city in state, 65th in nation; total employed (metro), 158,000.
Area: 142 sq. mi., at head of Mobile Bay; Mobile County seat.
Industry: home of Alabama State Docks, a $300 million complex where 33 ocean-going ships can be docked at one time; over $1.9 billion is invested in diversified industry, including paper and paper products, forest products, shipbuilding, chemicals, roofing, paints, alumina, oil, aircraft engines, and metals.
Commerce: wholesale-retail center for large portion of southwest Alabama and southeast Mississippi; Mobile County retail sales (1976), $921 million.
Transportation: served by 4 major railroads, one of the great river systems, 3 major airlines, 55 truck lines and about 100 steamship lines.
Communications: 2 TV and 12 radio stations.
Medical facilities: Univ. of South Alabama Medical College and 5 modern hospitals.
Cultural facilities: Municipal Auditorium-Theater complex seats 16,000; art gallery, museum, amateur dramatic theater, public library and branches; Univ. of South Alabama; Spring Hill, Mobile colleges, and Bishop State Junior College.
Annual attractions: America's Junior Miss Pageant, Senior Bowl football game, and Mardi Gras.
History: founded in 1702 by Jean Baptiste Le Moyne; 6 flags have flown over the city since then.
Further information: Chamber of Commerce, Commercial Guaranty Bank Bldg., Mobile, AL.

Montgomery, Alabama

The World Almanac is sponsored in the Montgomery area by the Advertiser-Journal, 200 Washington Street, Montgomery, AL 36102; phone: (205) 262-1611; Advertiser founded 1828, Journal 1881; circulation Advertiser (morn) 51,184; Journal (eve) 25,959; combined Sunday 75,446; publisher Harold Martin, managing editor Ben R. Davis.

Population: 162,000 (city), 259,000 (metro); 147th in nation; total employed, 102,300.
Area: 50.94 sq. mi. (city), 442 sq. mi. (county).
Industry: machinery manufacture, glass products, textiles, refrigeration equipment, axles, furniture, food products, paper, and fertilizers; over 250 industries.
Commerce: wholesale-retail center for 13 counties in central Alabama; retail trade area sales (1974), $1 billion; 7 banks, 3 savings & loans associations, 6 insurance company home offices; state capital.
Transportation: 5 railroads, 3 airlines, 2 national bus lines, one city bus line; Interstates 65 and 85 intersect in the city; Alabama River navigable to the Gulf of Mexico.
Medical facilities: 4 general hospitals and a VA hospi-

tal; over 1,449 beds.
Military: home of Maxwell AFB, The Air University, and Gunther Field.
Cultural facilities: art guild, civic ballet, little theater, and a community concert series; Museum of Fine Arts; 5 major colleges and universities; new $14 million civic center opened in Dec. '76.
Sports: Rebels, farm team of Detroit; Blue-Gray Football Classic; Southeastern Championship Rodeo; George Lindsey Celebrity Golf Tournament.
History: incorporated 1819; Jefferson Davis inaugurated president of the Confederate States of America, Feb. 18, 1861, in Montgomery.
Other attractions: a riverboat, accommodating 300 passengers, makes regular-scheduled excursions on the now navigable Alabama River; state capitol housed Confederate offices. White House of Confederacy, home of Jefferson Davis, open to public. Nearby Lownesboro — antebellum town with many colonial mansions and churches.

Montreal, Quebec, Canada

The World Almanac is sponsored in Montreal area by The Gazette, a Southam newspaper, 1000 St. Antoine Street, Montreal H3C 3R7, Quebec, Canada: phone (514) 861-1111; founded 1778 by Fleury Mesplet; circulation 116,006 daily; publisher Ross Munro, general manager Robert McConnell, editor Mark Harrison, managing editor Geoff Stevenson, editorial page editor Tom Sloan; sponsors Christmas fund; 10 National Newspaper awards in last 5 years.

Population: 1,214,300 (city), 2,761,000 (metro); after Paris, the 2d largest French-speaking city in the world, 67% French origin, 12% Anglo-Saxon, 21% other origins; Canada's largest urban center.
Area: 68 sq. mi. on an island of 190 sq. mi. in the St. Lawrence River where the Ottawa and Richelieu rivers flow into it at the head of the St. Lawrence Seaway; metro area extends over 1,000 sq. mi.; the 769 ft. Mount Royal dominates the Island which averages 100 ft. above sea level.
Industry: Canada's industrial hub ($7 billion, value of shipments of goods of own manufacture).
Commerce: retail sales of $5 billion, headquarters of many of Canada's largest financial institutions, home of the Montreal and Canadian Stock Exchanges, about 75% of countries have consulates or representatives in Montreal.
Transportation: $1 billion St. Lawrence Seaway, Port of Montreal; 14 miles long, 42 miles of harbour with 140 berths; $500 million Mirabel jetport opened in 1975 with multi-million electric train link to downtown planned for early 1980's; existing 14 mile Metro to expand to 46 miles by 1981; world headquarters of International Civil Aviation Organization and International Air Transport Association serving 2 major airports; headquarters of Canadian National and Canadian Pacific railways.
Communications: 4 TV stations, 18 radio stations, 6 daily newspapers; headquarters for Bell Canada, CN-CP Telecommunications.
Educational facilities: Concordia University, McGill University, Universite de Montreal, Universite de Quebec; enrollment 78,000; faculty 5,500.
Cultural facilities: Place des Arts with 3,000 seat hall and 2 theaters, attracting the finest forms of artistic, cultural, and musical entertainment; the Montreal Museum of Fine Arts, the Musee de l'Art Contemporain; some of the world's most beautiful churches, including the Mary Queen of The World Basilica, a half-size replica of St. Peter's in Rome.
Sports: $1 billion Olympic complex; including a 56,000 permanent seat stadium, home of the National Baseball League Expos and the Canadian Football League Alouettes; 7,200 seat Velodrome, 2 50-meter pools, 25-meter diving pool, and a scuba diving pool — 15-meter depth; the Montreal Forum, home of the National Hockey League Canadiens.
Recreational facilities: within an hour of the Laurentien and Eastern townships skiing, hunting, and fishing resort areas; over 5,000 restaurants of all lands; over 100 cinemas, 19 museums, 13 city libraries, the Montreal Botanical Gardens, St. Helen's Island Park, Dow Planetarium, Montreal Municipal Golf Course.
Convention facilities: over 15,000 hotel and motel rooms with 5,000 plus under construction; full facilities for conventions.
Medical facilities: over 80 hospitals with 26,000 beds, including the renowned Montreal Neurological Institute, and the Montreal Children's Hospital.
History: Montreal was first visited by Jacques Cartier in 1535; founded under the name of Ville Marie in 1642; Old Montreal, some 1,000 acres in all, is the largest such restoration in North America and retains the general atmosphere of the 18th century.
Further information: Convention and Visitor's Bureau of Greater Montreal, 1270 Sherbrooke Street W., H3G 1H7; The Montreal Tourist Bureau, 85 Notre Dame Street East, Montreal, Quebec.

Nashville, Tennessee

The World Almanac is sponsored in Nashville by The Tennessean, 1100 Broadway, Nashville, TN 37202; phone (615) 255-1221; founded as The Tennessean in 1907 but incorporated publications date to 1812; circulation daily 134,700, Sunday 236,400; president Amon Carter Evans, publisher John Seigenthaler; 3 Pulitzer prizes, 8 Headliner awards, 3 Sigma Delta Chi awards.

Population: 486,000 ('77 est.) in unified metro government. 2d in state; labor force 268,000.
Area: 533 sq. mi., straddling Cumberland River, in north central part of state.
Industry: music (52% of U.S. singles are recorded in 40 studio complexes); clothing, headquarters of Genesco, world's largest and most diversified clothing and footwear manufacturer; insurance, 2 of largest U.S. companies located here; world's largest glass plant; chemicals, printing (especially religious materials), aerostructures, tires, air conditioning, heating equipment.
Commerce: retail center for middle Tennessee, south Kentucky; retail sales (1976) $2.1 billion; bank resources, over $3.6 billion in 8 banks, 108 branches.
Transportation: 9 U.S. highways and 6 branches of the interstate system radiate from Nashville; 9 commercial airlines with 190 daily flights; 2 railroads, Amtrak; bus service, 73 motor freight lines.
Communications: 5 TV stations (one public), and 22 AM and FM radio stations.
Medical facilities: 18 hospitals (6,019 beds), 2 medical schools, VA hospital, speech-hearing center.
Cultural: symphony orchestra; replica of Parthenon with art gallery; public and state libraries; botanic garden and fine arts center, 3 community theaters.
Educational facilities: 19 colleges and universities; 137 public schools, 39 private schools.
Convention facilities: 10,000-seat auditorium; Opryland convention center.
Other attractions: Grand Ole Opry, Opryland U.S.A. ($32 million theme park featuring music); Country Music Hall of Fame; Hermitage (home of Andrew Jackson); Belle Meade antebellum mansion.
Recreation facilities: water sports, outdoor activity on Old Hickory and Percy Priest lakes.
History: settled in 1780 as a fort in then western

North Carolina; incorporated, 1784, with first written charter west of Alleghenies.

Further information: Chamber of Commerce, 161 4th Avenue N., Nashville, TN 37219.

New Haven, Connecticut

The World Almanac is sponsored in the greater New Haven area by the New Haven Register (founded 1812) and the New Haven Journal-Courier (founded 1755); circulation Register (eve.) 101,416, Sunday 130,535; Journal-Courier (morn.) 30,923; president and publisher Lionel S. Jackson, vp and general manager Donald A. Spargo, vp and treasurer Lionel S. Jackson Jr., vp and editor Robert J. Leeney.

Population: 135,500 (city), 360,400 (metro); 3d in state.
Area: 21.1 sq. mi. southern coast of Conn. on north shore of Long Island Sound; county seat.
Industry: 1,000 firms in immediate area; principal products are guns, hardware, rubber goods, paper products, machinery, and tools.
Commerce: wholesale-retail center for southern Conn.; total retail sales (preliminary, 1976), $2.4 billion; serves 850,000 people within a radius of 25 miles; busy harbor, particularly oil tankers.
Transportation: Conrail, Amtrak Cosmopolitan turbotrain; 25 major truck lines: 14 federal and state highways; Tweed-New Haven Airport served by 2 airlines; limo service to N. Y. airports, bus line.
Communications: VHF, 2 UHF TV stations, and 6 radio stations.
Medical facilities: Yale Medical Center; Yale-New Haven Hospital; Hospital of St. Raphael.
Cultural facilities: Yale Univ. Library with over 6 million books one of the world's largest collections; Yale's Peabody Museum of Natural History, art gallery, and Beinecke Rare Book Library; The Yale Center for British Art (Paul Mellon $10 million gallery opened in 1977). New Haven Historical Society; Cultural Center; 2 legitimate theaters, and the New Haven Symphony.
Educational facilities: Yale Univ. and graduate schools; Albertus Magnus, Southern Conn. State, South Central Community, Quinnipiac colleges; Univ. of New Haven.
Recreational facilities: Yale Bowl, Woolsey Hall, Ingalls Rink, the Coliseum, 15 parks, including Frederick Brewster's estate, East and West Rock scenic drives, 50 playgrounds, West Rock Nature Center; 7 golf courses, 30 tennis courts, 6 skating rinks.
Convention facilities: Coliseum-convention center with a 19-story hotel nearby.
Sports: AHL Nighthawks; West Haven Yankees (baseball); NASL Connecticut Bicentennials.
History: founded 1638 by Puritans; named after Newhaven in England; incorporated 1638, became a part of Conn. 1662; first mayor was Roger Sherman, signer of Declaration of Independence.
Further information: New Haven Chamber of Commerce, 152 Temple Street, New Haven, CT 06510.

New Orleans, Louisiana

The World Almanac is sponsored in New Orleans by The States-Item, 3800 Howard Ave., New Orleans, LA 70140; phone (504) 586-3560; founded June 11, 1877, circulation 116,575 daily, 106,591 Saturday; editor Walter G. Cowan, associate editor Charles A. Ferguson, city editor William U. Madden; sponsors Football Fund for Underprivileged.

Population: 562,011 (city), 1,109,694 (metro area); first in state; total employed, 436,100 (non-agricultural, Apr., 1977).
Area: 363.5 sq. mi. of which 199.4 are land.
Industry: Port of New Orleans, 2d largest in nation, handled 37 million tons of cargo valued at $8.6 billion in 1976.
Commerce: trade center for lower Mississippi Valley; bank resources $5.5 billion, 1976; retail sales $3.1 billion, 1975; spendable household income median $12,981, 1975.
Transportation: rail hub with direct lines north, east, and west; Amtrak passenger service to Chicago, Los Angeles; Southern railway to New York. New Orleans International Airport serves airlines, Lakefront Airport commercial aviation; cruise ships to Mexico and Caribbean.

New construction: $500 million Canal Place and $250 million Hilton hotel complexes; tallest building, 50-story One Shell Square.
Communications: 4 commercial TV stations and educational channel; 20 radio stations.

Medical facilities: major medical center with 2 schools of medicine; Charity Hospital 2nd largest in nation; Ochsner Medical Institutions.

Cultural facilities: Theater for the Performing Arts seats 2,317 for operas, concerts; Municipal Auditorium seats up to 8,000 for special events; museums include New Orleans Museum of Art, Louisiana State Museum, Historic New Orleans Collection, and many small galleries.
Educational facilities: Tulane Univ., Univ. of New Orleans, Loyola Univ., Dillard, Southern Univ. in New Orleans, Xavier, St. Mary's Dominican.

Other attractions: Louisiana Superdome seats 75,000; French Quarter is historic tourist attraction.

Sports: New Orleans Saints (NFL), New Orleans Jazz (NBA), New Orleans Pelicans (AA baseball); Sugar Bowl game on New Year's day.

History: named after the Duke of Orleans, founded in swamp within crescent of the Mississippi River 100 miles from Gulf of Mexico by Jean Baptiste Le Moyne, Sieur de Bienville, in 1718; became capital of Louisiana Territory in 1722, when Adrien de Pauger laid out what is now the French Quarter; became part of U.S. with Louisiana Purchase in 1803.

Further information: Chamber of Commerce of New Orleans Area, 301 Camp Street; Greater New Orleans Tourist and Convention Commission, 334 Royal Street, both New Orleans, LA 70130.

New York City, New York

The World Almanac is sponsored in the greater New York City metropolitan area by The New York Daily News, 220 E. 42d Street, New York, NY 10017, phone (212) 949-1234; New York News Inc., founded June 26, 1919 by Joseph Medill Patterson; circulation daily 1,911,565; Sunday 2,752,739; president and publisher W. H. James, vice president and editor Michael J. O'Neill, vice president and managing editor William J. Brink, treasurer Robert C. Schneider, secretary and general manager Valfrid E. Palmer; Pulitzer Prizes for editorial writing, news photography, cartoon, international and local investigative reporting; sponsors Golden Gloves, National Spelling Bee championships for New York City, Long Island, Westchester, and other major school athletic, cultural, and educational events as community service programs.

Population: 7,477,563 (city), 10,927,837 (consolidated area, N.Y. City, Westchester, Nassau, Suffolk coun-

ties); first in state and nation; total employed 3,159,500 (1977); per capita personal income $6,453.
Area: 300 sq. mi. at mouth of Hudson River; embraces 5 boroughs — Manhattan, Bronx, Brooklyn, Queens, and Staten Island.
Industry: nation's leader in manufacturing and service industries; produces 25.2% of America's apparel, 15.7% of printing and publishing; 20,960 manufacturing establishments (Oct. 1976).
Commerce: nation's richest port, handling annual 177.8 million tons of maritime cargo; Wall Street, world's largest financial center, with New York and American Stock exchanges; wholesale-retail center for New York, New Jersey and southwestern Connecticut, retail sales $16.2 billion (1976); 35 commercial banks, resources $162.8 billion (1977); 43 savings banks, resources $55.6 billion (1977); World Trade Center, twin 110-story towers, cost $850 million.

Transportation: Kennedy International Airport handles 41% of nation's overseas air travel and 56.5% of export-import air tonnage, served by 56 scheduled air carriers; LaGuardia Airport served by 15 domestic airlines; 5 heliports. Penn Central Railroad, Amtrak; 2 major rail terminals, Pennsylvania and Grand Central stations; 40 interstate bus lines; subway network covers every borough except Staten Island; ferry and the 4,260-ft. Verrazano-Narrows Bridge (world's longest suspension span) link Staten Island to Manhattan and Brooklyn; 18 bridges connect Manhattan with other boroughs, George Washington Bridge over the Hudson connects New Jersey; 5 tunnels under the Hudson and East rivers.

Communications: 17 TV stations (6 commercial, 4 educational, 1 municipal, 2 Spanish, 4 CATV); 38 AM and FM radio stations; WPIX-TV and WPIX-FM are broadcast affiliates of The News.

Medical facilities: 104 hospitals, (16 municipal, 28 private, 60 voluntary non-profit); 5 major medical research centers specialize in cancer, heart diseases, sickle cell anemia, and other research; Sloan-Kettering Institute for Cancer Research; 4 VA hospitals.

Federal facilities: Fort Wadsworth, Staten Island; Governors Island, many federal agencies represented in buildings at Federal Plaza and 90 Church St.
Educational facilities: 6 universities, 23 colleges, including 5 medical colleges, 4 law schools, 3 colleges of pharmacy, 2 colleges of dentistry, 2 institutes of art and architecture; 994 schools in the public school system; more than 1,000 private schools; public libraries total 193.
Cultural facilities: Lincoln Center for the Performing Arts (Philharmonic, Ballet Company, Metropolitan Opera, and other theatrical arts), Carnegie Hall, Brooklyn Academy of Music. Broadway and Off-Broadway alliance for varied theatrical productions; outdoor Delacorte Theatre in Central Park; 65 museums including American Museum of Natural History, Metropolitan Museum of Art, Museum of the Performing Arts, Museum of Modern Art, Whitney Museum, and South Street Seaport Museum.
Other attractions: United Nations; botanic gardens in the Bronx and Brooklyn; Central Park and Prospect Park; Bronx Zoo and 4 other zoos; 13 municipal golf courses, 535 tennis courts, 37 outdoor swimming pools.
Sports: NBA Knicks, Nets; NHL Rangers, Islanders; NL Mets and NFL Jets play in Shea Stadium; AL Yankees play in Yankee Stadium; NFL Giants and NASL Cosmos play in Giants Stadium in nearby E. Rutherford, N.J.; tennis WTT Apples.
History: discovered by Giovanni da Verrazano in 1524; in 1626 Peter Minuit bought the island from the Manhattan Indians for about $24 in goods and trinkets; settlement named New Amsterdam. In 1664, British troops occupied city without resistance and named it New York in honor of the Duke of York, brother of the King. On Jan. 1, 1898, Manhattan and large areas to the NE, E, and S were consolidated into one city of New York.
Further information: Department of Commerce and Industry, 225 Broadway; Convention and Visitors Bureau, 90 East 42d Street both New York, NY.

Newark, New Jersey

Population: 378,670; first in state, swells on weekdays with non-residents working and attending school; 2,011,800 (metro area) including Essex, Morris, Somerset, and Union counties; 136,042 employed (city).
Area: 25.4 sq. mi. (city), 15 miles SW of New York City; Essex County seat.
Industry: wide diversity of manufacturers, fine craftsmanship; major beer, chemicals, and plastics industries; more than 10,000 businesses, major banking and insurance center; headquarters for several national firms.
Transportation: international airport; major port; 5 railroads; world's largest privately owned bus system; one of world's largest truck terminals; world's largest containerized shipping center.
Communications: 5 radio stations, one VHF public TV station and 2 UHF TV stations.
Medical facilities: 6 major hospitals with new home of the College of Medicine and Dentistry to be completed in 1978; Beth Israel Medical Center.
Federal facilities: new federal building; old federal courthouse.
Cultural facilities: museum, library, New Jersey Historical Society, New Jersey Symphony Orchestra, New Jersey Opera, Garden State Ballet, Newark Community Center of the Arts, and Symphony Hall.
Educational facilities: New Jersey College of Medicine and Dentistry; Rutgers Univ.; Seton Hall Univ. Law School; New Jersey Institute of Technology; Essex County College.
Recreational facilities: parks cover 870 acres; 7 pools, 74 playgrounds, one ice rink, 2 lakes.
Convention facilities: large hotel and 3 motor inns.
Other attractions: Annual Cherry Blossom Festival; 7 famous works of sculpture, including "John F. Kennedy" by Jacques Lipchitz and a seated Abraham Lincoln by Gutzon Borglum; Sacred Heart, one of the largest Gothic cathedrals in the world, and the historic Plume House, built in 1710.
History: founded in 1666, incorporated 1836; British troops ravaged the town during the Revolution.
Further information: Greater Newark Chamber of Commerce, 50 Park Place, Newark, NJ 07102.

Norfolk, Virginia

The World Almanac is sponsored in the Norfolk metro area by The Virginian-Pilot and Ledger-Star, 150 W. Brambleton Avenue, Norfolk, VA 23501; phone (804) 446-2000; Va. founded 1865, Ledger, 1876; circulation: LS (eve.) 95,545; VP (morn.) 126,035; VP (Sun.) 197,578; Perry Morgan publisher, Richard F. Barry III president & general manager, Robert H. Mason VP editor, George J. Hebert LS editor.

Population: 285,500 (city), 784,500 (metro); first in state; civilian employed, 282,375; military pop., 85,000.
Area: 915 sq. mi. in SE Virginia.
Industry: General Electric, Ford Motor Co., Norfolk Shipbuilding & Drydock Corp.
Commerce: retail sales (1975) $2.2 billion; aver. household income, $15,624 (1976 effective buying income)
Transportation: Port of Hampton Roads, world's finest natural harbor, ranks first in export tonnage (43,367,404 tons handled 1975) among Atlantic ports;

biggest coal port in world; International Airport, 4 major airlines; Chesapeake Bay Bridge-Tunnel supplies direct north highway route; 7 trunk line railroads, 50 trucking companies, 2 bus companies.
Communications: 5 TV, 13 AM, 12 FM radio stations.
Medical facilities: 12 hospitals including oldest and 2d largest naval hospital in U.S.
Federal facilities: greatest concentration of naval installations in world; approx. 36 major commands include Atlantic Fleet, Second Fleet, NATO Supreme Allied Command Atlantic (SACLANT), Armed Forces Staff College, and Commandant 5th Naval Dist.
Cultural facilities: symphony orchestra, Feldman Chamber Quartet, repertory theater, dinner and little theaters, civic and univ. ballet; Chrysler Museum collection; Va. Opera Assoc.; Festival of the Arts.
Educational facilities: Old Dominion Univ., Norfolk State, Virginia Wesleyan, Tidewater Community colleges; Eastern Va. Medical School.
Recreational facilities: General Douglas MacArthur Memorial, Adam Thoroughgood House (1636), Gardens-by-the-sea; Dismal Swamp located in Chesapeake; resort city of Virginia Beach offers 38 mi. of swimming, fishing, and surfing; camping at Seashore State Park; Hermitage Foundation Museum.
Convention facilities: Scope, $30 million cultural and convention center.
Sports: Tidewater Tides, International League baseball.
Climate: Average temp. 70° to 52°.
Further information: Chamber of Commerce, 475 St. Paul Boulevard, Norfolk, VA 23501.

Oakland, California

Population: 338,000; employed in Oakland, 179,050.
Area: 53.4 sq. mi.; Alameda County seat.
Industry: food processing, fabricated metal products, transportation equipment, chemicals and paint; Port of Oakland is 2d in containerized cargo; home base for Kaiser Industries.
Commerce: 8,350 retail outlets with taxable sales (1977) of $1.2 billion; median income for family, $10,-799 per annum.
Transportation: western terminus for Southern Pacific, Santa Fe, and Western Pacific railroads; International Airport is major airfreight terminal and center for supplemental air carriers; headquarters for Bay Area Rapid Transit, underground, underwater 75-mile subway connecting 15 communities.
Medical facilities: 9 hospitals include Children's Hospital Medical Center, Kaiser Foundation, and the Veterans Administration.
New construction: Pacific Telephone Bldg., Wells Fargo Bldg., Clorox Bldg.; 16 square block city center project, and major downtown garage under construction.
Cultural facilities: museum, half garden, half gallery design, has divisions of natural science, history, and art; symphony, Chinese Community Cultural Center.
Educational facilities: Univ. of California at Berkeley, Mills College, College of Holy Names, Cal. State, Hayward, Chabot, California College of Arts and Crafts, Peralta Community College.
Recreational facilities: 26,000 acre Regional Park System serving the East Bay; zoo in 100-acre Knowland State Park has large collection of gibbons and aerial tram; Lake Merritt Park includes botanical garden, wildfowl refuge, natural science center, and Children's Fairyland.
Sports: Raiders (football), Athletics (baseball), Golden State Warriors (basketball).
Other attractions: Oakland Coliseum, over 50,000 capacity, for theatrical entertainment, exhibits, conventions, and circus; Jack London Square.
History: area explored in 1772, settled in 1850; incorporated as town in 1852, as city in 1854.
Further information: Chamber of Commerce, 1320 Webster Street, Oakland, CA 94612.

Oklahoma City, Oklahoma

The World Almanac is sponsored in the Oklahoma City area by The Daily Oklahoman and Oklahoma City Times, Oklahoma City, OK 73125; phone (405) 232-3311; The Oklahoman founded in 1894; Times in 1888; Oklahoma Publishing Co. acquired The Oklahoman 1903 and the Times 1916; circulation Oklahoman 171,583; Times 90,874; Sunday, 300,681; editor and publisher E. L. Gaylord, executive editor Charles L. Bennett.

Population: (1977 est.) 393,000 (city), 798,700 (metro); largest in state; labor force 351,400.
Area: city area, among nation's largest, is 649 sq. mi.; metro area, 3,491 sq. mi.; located in state's center on Canadian River in Oklahoma, Cleveland, Canadian, McClain, and Pottawatomie counties.
Industry: oil, with about 1,500 producing wells in metro area, employs about 13,000; Tinker AFB, one of world's largest air depots, employs 17,200 civilians and 3,500 military on $100 million installation; FAA and other aviation employ some 30,000, with annual payroll of $300 million; agricultural and ranching area; manufactured goods include aircraft, telecommunications equipment, computers, oil field machinery, oil and greases, building materials, feed, flour, meat, and tires.
Commerce: regional, national, and international marketing center; median household E.B.I., $11,703 (metro), consumer sales near $2.6 billion (metro).
Transportation: 5 passenger airlines; 4 primary federal and 3 major state highways, with I-40 and I-35 intersecting the city; fully planned urban expressway system, major bus, truck, and rail lines.
Medical facilities: Oklahoma Univ. Health Sciences Center and 25 hospitals and clinics.
Cultural facilities: symphony and junior symphony; Oklahoma Art Ctr.; Lyric Theater at Oklahoma City Univ.; Oklahoma Theater Ctr.; Southwest Repertory Theater, Univ. of Oklahoma.
Education: Univ. of Oklahoma, Oklahoma City Univ., Central State Univ, Oklahoma State Univ.
Convention facilities: $23 million Myriad Convention Center, seating 15,000 in the center of a downtown redevelopment project, hosts 350 conventions yearly with more than 284,000 delegates.
Other attractions: National Cowboy Hall of Fame; 130 municipal parks; major college sports; pro sports: Oklahoma City 89ers, American Assn. baseball; International Softball headquarters.
History: founded by land run, Apr. 22, 1889.
Further information: Chamber of Commerce, 1 Santa Fe Plaza, Oklahoma City, OK 73102.

Omaha, Nebraska

The World Almanac is sponsored in Nebraska by The Omaha World-Herald, World-Herald Square, Omaha, NE 68102; phone (402) 444-1000; Evening World, founded 1885 by G. M. Hitchcock, acquired Daily Herald, founded 1865; adopted present name 1889; circulation 235,740 daily, 279,821 Sunday; president Harold W. Andersen, executive editor Louis G. Gerdes; 3 Pulitzer Prizes; sponsors Midwest Spelling Bee, Newspaper in Education, Music in the Parks, Show Wagon, Good Fellows charities, college scholarships, Consumer Preference Studies.

Population: (1977 est.) 377,000, city; 580,000, metro; first in state, 69th in U.S.; 258,000 work force.
Area: eastern Nebraska, 83 sq. mi. of rolling hills on west bank of Missouri River; Douglas County seat.
Industry: manufacturing shipments $3.5 billion annually; 600 plants employ 34,000; food processing center; 4th largest livestock market in salable receipts.
Commerce: major trade center; 1,000 wholesale firms, $1.8 billion retail sales, 45th in median income per household, $15,831; 40 banks, $2 billion deposits; 14 savings and loans, $2 billion assets; 4th largest insurance center in U.S. (36 home offices, including Mutual of Omaha). Also headquarters Union Pacific, Northern Natural Gas, Northwestern Bell, ConAgra.
Transportation: 7 major airlines; 4th largest rail center, served by 8 major railroads, Amtrak, 122 truck lines, Interstates 80 and 29, 2 intercity bus, 3 barge lines; 2.8 million tons carried on Missouri River annually; port of entry, foreign trade zone.
Communications: Nebraska's largest daily newspaper, 6 TV, 17 radio stations.
Medical facilities: 16 hospitals 4,766 beds; 2 medical schools (Nebraska U., Creighton U.), 8 nursing schools, Eppley Institute for Cancer Research.
Federal facilities: Strategic Air Command's global headquarters, U.S. Army Corps of Engineers.
Cultural facilities: Orpheum performing arts center, symphony orchestra, opera company, ballet society; 10 live theater groups, 22 art galleries, 16 museums, Joslyn Art Museum's $20 million collection.
Educational facilities: 3 universities, 5 colleges educate 30,000 students; 30 adult education schools.
Recreation: 5,000 acres of public parks include 120 tennis courts, 25 pools, 16 golf courses, ice rinks.
Sports: Omaha Royals AAA baseball, Ak-Sar-Ben horse racing, NCAA College World Series.
Other attractions: 1,300-acre Fontenelle Forest, Henry Doorly Zoo, Boys Town; Pres. Ford birthsite, Gen. Dodge House, Aerospace Museum, Ranked 10th among 50 largest U.S. cities in quality of life.
History: Lewis and Clark, 1804; Indian trading post, 1825; Mormon settlement, 1846; Omaha (named after Indian tribe) laid out when Nebraska Territory opened, 1854; chartered as city, 1867.
Further information: Chamber of Commerce, 1620 Dodge Street, Omaha, NE 68102.

Orange County, California

The World Almanac is sponsored in Orange County by The Register, 625 N. Grand Avenue, Santa Ana, CA, 92711; telephone (714) 835-1234; circulation combined daily morning and evening 207,658, Sunday 237,034; founded 1905, purchased in 1935 by the late R. C. Hoiles, founder of Freedom Newspapers Inc., a 26-daily newspaper group. Son Clarence H. Hoiles, chairman of the board of Freedom Newspapers and co-publisher of The Register; son Harry Hoiles, Register co-publisher and president of Freedom Newspapers; Richard Wallace, general manager; Jim Dean, executive editor; Mike Maloney, managing editor; Jim Lyons Sr., research and promotion director.

Population: 1,768,000 (Jan., 1977 est.) 2d most populous county in the state; up 22% since 1970; increase average 20 new residents per day in past year; compares to 212,364 in 1950, 2.5 million projected for 1990. County encompasses 26 cities: largest, Anaheim, 200,100 population, (Jan., 1977 est.); county seat Santa Ana, 182,000 (Jan., 1977 est.); unincorporated areas, 227,900 (Jan. 1977 est.).
Area: 511,040 acres in S. Cal. from Pacific Ocean inland 25 miles to Cleveland National Forest; 42-mile coastline stretches from Long Beach past Huntington Beach surfing, Newport Beach yacht harbor, Laguna Beach art colony, Dana Point small-craft harbor, to San Clemente and Camp Pendleton.
Commerce and Industry: median family income (1976) $17,780, 1977 est. $19,420; total personal income 1977 est. $15 billion; taxable retail sales (1976) $6.9 billion, first quarter 1977 at $1.9 billion; automobiles ranked highest segment of retail sales with $1.5 billion, eating and drinking estab. 2d highest at $1.2 billion; employment (1976 average) 825,000, with 159,800 in manufacturing, 146,600 in trades, 114,700 in services, 96,400 in government, 32,800 in insurance, real estate, finance, 10,600 in agriculture; unemployment rate (1976 average) 5.9%. Largest manufacturing employer, Rockwell International's Autonetics, missiles, electronic calculators, sewing and reading machines; Hughes Aircraft Co., 2d; McDonald-Douglas Astronautics, 3d; other employers include corporate or major unit headquarters for such international firms as Fluor Corp., Beckman Instruments, Philco-Ford Aeronutronics, AMF-Voit, Hunt-Wesson Foods; county is center for such industries as tourism, sailboat construction, fiberglas products, glass containers, food processing, computers, and agriculture, a $153.5 million industry in 1976, with nursery stock and cut flowers 1976 top crop at $59.8 million, followed by strawberries $29.5 million, chicken eggs $8.7 million, valencia oranges $7.8 million.
New construction: 30,511 new housing units built in 1976, up 97.6% over 1975; total $1.67 billion in new construction (1976), first 4 months 1977 total new valuation $649.6 million, up 79.7% over same period 1976; average price new home (1976) $81,000, first use of lottery to sell houses, with 3,000 prospective buyers signing up for chance at 221 available homes.
Transportation: 8 major freeways, including main Los Angeles-San Diego artery; transit district with countywide routes served by 369 buses, including freeway commuter buses and Dial-A-Ride in some areas; nation's 2d busiest airport with 627,199 tower operations in 1976.
Communications: local UHF-TV station, 7 VHF-TV stations regionally; over 40 radio stations.
Federal facilities: Marine Corps Air Station at El Toro, Los Alamitos Naval Air Station, Seal Beach Naval Weapons Station, Santa Ana Marine Corps Lighter-Than-Air Station (now used for helicopters, once for dirigibles), federal building in Santa Ana, general services administration building-national archives center in Laguna Niguel, Cleveland National Forest, Marine Corps Camp Pendleton nearby in San Diego County.
Medical facilities: Univ. of Cal. medical school at Irvine, 65 hospitals and convalescent hospitals.
Recreation: 781 acres of beaches, over 13,000 acres regional parks, 141 scenic sea cliffs, 3 yacht basins, 3 fishing lakes, wilderness campgrounds, 35 golf courses, 21-mile equestrian and bicycle trail along Santa Ana River.
Other attractions: Disneyland, Knott's Berry Farm amusement park, Lion Country Safari, Movieland Wax Museum, Los Alamitos racetrack, motorcycle park, auto raceway, mid-summer Laguna Beach Arts Festival-Pageant of Masters, Santa Ana zoo, air and car museums, Anaheim Stadium.
Convention facilities: Anaheim Convention Center, hotels in Anaheim, Buena Park, Costa Mesa, Irvine, Newport Beach, Santa Ana.
Sports: AL Angels, school sports.
Cultural, Educational facilities: 2 major tax-supported universities, 4 private liberal arts colleges, 7 community colleges, multiple trade and special interest schools, 607 tax-supported K-12 schools with 1976 enrollment of 500,000, 71 private and church K-12 schools; city and county libraries, symphony orchestra society; 2 master chorales, 6 ballet companies, 32 community theater groups, 4 art museums.
History: first Spanish expedition 1769 by Capt. Gaspar de Portola, who recorded first reported earthquake in the state; county formed March 11,

1889 from Los Angeles Co.; Glenn Martin tested his first plane near Santa Ana; Madame Modjeska resided in local forest hideaway; Toastmasters International founded in Santa Ana 1924; Howard Hughes set world's speed record in Santa Ana 1935 with 351 mph airplane flight. Swallows traditionally return each year to Mission San Juan Capistrano on March 19.
Further information: Anaheim Visitor and Convention Bureau, 800 W. Katella Avenue, Anaheim CA; Orange County Chamber of Commerce, One City Boulevard W., Orange., CA.

Orlando, Florida

The World Almanac is sponsored in the Orlando area by the Sentinel Star, 633 N. Orange Avenue, Orlando, FL 32802; phone (305) 420-5000; Sentinel and Evening Star founded as dailies in 1913; merged 1931; acquired by Tribune Company of Chicago in 1965; combined to create "all day" newspaper in 1973; circulation, 190,315 weekdays, 183,461 Saturday, 214,178 Sunday; president and chief executive officer Charles T. Brumback, editor James Squires.

Population: 118,000 (city, July '76), 640,000 (metro, April '77); 211,400 employed (metro) average for year of '76; 1975 estimated buying income per household, $13,586.
Area: 30.1 sq. mi. (city), 2,528 sq. mi. (metro) in east central Florida; 52 lakes inside city limits; av. temperature 72.5; Orange County seat.
Industry: center of citrus belt; 6 regional home and 10 national home insurance company offices; Martin Marietta Co., aerospace division; General Electric plant; Westinghouse Electric Co., minicomputer division; 16 industrial parks; naval training center, 30,000 recruits graduated annually, total civilian and military staff of 14,000, trains all Navy's women recruits, Navy's basic nuclear orientation school.
Commerce: 24 main commercial banks (excluding branches) in metro area: total metro deposits (year end '76), $925 million; 6 savings and loan assns. based in metro area, 55 savings and loan branches; 30 major shopping centers with 4 regional malls; retail sales (metro), $2.6 billion in 1976.
Transportation: 4 major commercial airlines serving Orlando International Airport, 1976 passenger total (in and out) 3.7 million, new $100 million terminal to open around 1980; Seaboard Coastline Railroad, Amtrak, 9 intercity bus lines, 195 common carrier truck lines, and 7 freight forwarding services; every major Florida market less than 4 hours by highway.
Communications: 16 radio and 6 TV stations.
Medical facilities: 14 hospitals in metro area.
Cultural facilities: Florida Symphony Orchestra, Loch Haven Art Center, John Young Museum and Planetarium, Central Florida Civic Theater, Orlando Public Library with 12 community libraries and approximately 700,000 volumes; Rollins College, Florida Tech Univ., Valencia (3 campuses), and Seminole Community Colleges.
Other attractions: Walt Disney World, destination resort 18 miles from downtown Orlando visited annually by 13 million people; Sea World, attendance 2 million; $10 million Barnum & Bailey Circus World; Church Street Station, renovated area in downtown Orlando; Stars Hall of Fame, wax museum; Wet and Wild, $3.5 million attraction.
Convention facilities: metro area ranks 6th in world in number of hotel rooms; 30,409 rooms; approximately 1,168 conventions attended by some 327,301 in 1976.

Sports: Minnesota Twins spring training site; Tangerine Bowl sports week; 2 PGA tournaments, National PGA team championship at Walt Disney World, $200,000 Florida Citrus Open, Feb. 27-March 5 in 1978; Ben White Raceways, training ground for trotters; Seminole Harness Raceway; Sanford-Orlando Kennel Club; Jai-Alai Fronton.

Additional Information: Orlando Area Chamber of Commerce, P.O. Box 1913, Orlando FL 32802.

Ottawa, Ontario, Canada

Population: 304,462 (city), 693,288 (metro region including greater Ottawa 521,341 and Hull, Que. 171,47); Canada's 8th largest city, linked with neighboring city of Hull (pop. 61,039) by 5 bridges.
Area: 30,481 acres (city), 1,100 sq. mi. (region) on Ontario-Quebec border at the Chaudiere Falls on the Ottawa River.
National Capital Region: Ottawa and Hull, occupying 1,800 square miles of eastern Ontario and western Quebec, form the National Capital Region of Canada, administered by the National Capital Commision (NCC), created by Parliament in 1959, which deals directly with 2 provincial governments, 2 regional governments, and 57 municipal jurisdictions, all of which exercise their own proper authority.
Industry: major employer is the federal government; E.B. Eddy Co. largest private employer.
Commerce: capital city of Canada with a large tourist business and developing convention capacity; present convention capacity exists for 5,000; 3,100 hotel rooms (motels not included), exhibit space: 60,000 sq. ft. in 3 major hotels, 120,000 sq. ft. in the Civic Centre and 75,700 sq. ft. in the Nepean Sportsplex.
Transportation: Ottawa International Airport, 15 minutes from downtown Ottawa, ranks as the nation's 6th busiest, more than 85 scheduled flights daily by 4 airlines; surface transportation provided by Canadian Pacific and Canadian National railways and intercity bus service.
Communications: 3 daily, (one in French) 2 weekly newspapers; 4 TV and 9 radio stations.
Educational facilities: Carleton Univ., and Univ. of Ottawa — a bilingual univ.
Medical facilities: 11 hospitals, many include a public psychiatric unit; bed capacity over 4,000.
Cultural facilities: $45 million National Arts Centre with 2,300-seat opera house-concert hall, and an 800-seat theater; Ottawa Little Theatre.
National museums: National Gallery of Canada, Museum of Man, Museum of Natural Sciences, Museum of Science and Technology, Canadian War Museum, National Aeronautical Collection.
Other attractions: Gothic-style Parliament buildings, housing Canada's House of Commons and Senate; during the summer, Changing of the Guard ceremony 2 militia regiments; Peace Tower, memorial to Canada's war dead; Central Canada Exhibition; Ottawa's oldest building, the Bytown Museum; Royal Mint; Rideau Canal provides boating facilities in summer, the longest skating rink in the world: 5 miles of the Rideau Canal from downtown Ottawa to Carleton Unv.; the Experimental Farm, 1,200 working acres in the heart of Ottawa; Winter Fair; 80 camping and trailer parks, 7 city beaches; mountain lake recreation facilities; Gatineau Park (88,218 acres).
Sports: Ottawa Rough Riders, CFL; Ottawa 67's, hockey.
History: founded 1827 as Bytown, incorporated as Ottawa 1855; named after Outaouac (or Outaouais Indian tribe); chosen as Canada's capital in 1857 by Queen Victoria.
Further information: Canada's Capital Visitors and Convention Bureau, 251 Laurier Avenue West, Ottawa, Ont., K1P-5J6.

Pensacola, Florida

The World Almanac is sponsored in the Pensacola area by the Pensacola News-Journal, One News Journal Plaza, Pensacola FL 32501; (904) 433-0041; predecessor The Floridian founded in 1821, first daily News 1899, Journal 1898; merged 1924; combined circulation daily 80,461, Sunday 70,684; member Gannett Group; publisher James H. Jesse, editor J. Earle Bowden.

Population: 61,916 (city), 253,965 (county), 308,520 (Metro area).
Area: Southern end of 759 sq. mi. Escambia County at westernmost edge of Florida panhandle.
Industry: Monsanto Corporation, St. Regis Pulp & Paper Co., Vanity Fair, American Cyanamid, Armstrong Cork, Westinghouse, Air Products, Reichhold Chemicals.
Labor force: civilian labor force 110,200, military labor force 13,000.
Commerce: retail sales $884 million; average family income $11,731; effective buying income over $1 billion.
Transportation: 2 airlines, 2 railroads, 2 bus lines, 16 truck lines, intercoastal waterway, interstate 10, 3 U.S. Highways.
Communications: 2 TV, 10 radio stations.
New construction: Interstate 110 spur, County Judicial Building, State Office Building, Regional Sewage Plant, West Campus of Pensacola Junior College, addition to Mutual Federal Savings & Loan Assoc.
Medical facilities: Baptist Hospital, University Hospital, West Florida Hospital, U.S. Naval Hospital, Sacred Heart Hospital.
Federal facilities: Naval Air Station, Corry Field, Saufley Field, Whiting Field, Ellyson Field.
Cultural facilities: public library, Historical Museum, T. T. Wentworth Museum, Hispanic Museum, Transportation Museum, Museum of Naval Aviation, Saenger Theater, Art Association, Arts Council, Inc., Oratorio Society.
Educational facilities: Univ. of West Florida, Pensacola Junior College.
Recreation facilities: Pensacola Beach.
Sports: The Pensacola Open, American Amateur Golf Classic, Virginia Slims tennis, intercollegiate sports.
Further information: Pensacola Area Chamber of Commerce, 117 West Garden Street, Pensacola, FL 32593; phone (904) 438-4081.

Philadelphia, Pennsylvania

The World Almanac is sponsored in the Philadelphia area by the Philadelphia Inquirer, 400 N. Broad Street, Philadelphia, PA 19101; phone (215) 854-2000; established 1829, lineage traced to Pennsylvania Packet, founded 1771; circulation 415,522 daily, 849,649 Sunday; Pulitzer prizes 1975, 1976, 1977; published by Philadelphia Newspaper, Inc.; president Sam S. McKeel; vice president and general manager David Gelsanliter; executive editor Eugene L. Roberts Jr.; editor Edwin Guthman; managing editor Gene Foreman; sponsors Delaware Valley Science Fair, Book & Author Luncheons, Old Newsboys Day. PNI also publishes the Philadelphia Daily News, an afternoon tabloid, at same address; founded 1925; circulation 238,339; editor F. Gilman Spencer; managing editor Zachary Stalberg; sponsors Secret Witness rewards, sports clinics.

Population: 1.8 million (city/co.); 4.7 million (8-co. metro); 5.9 million (14-co. RTA); 6.9 million (19-co. ADI); employment: 1.8 million (metro).
Area: 130 sq. mi. (city); 3,575 sq. mi. (metro area); city located in southeastern Pa. on Delaware and Schuylkill rivers; 90 mi. from N.Y.C., 136 mi. from Wash., D.C., 60 mi. from Atlantic City; Philadelphia County seat.
Industry: diversified, with over 90% of all U.S. basic industries represented; major center for textiles and apparel, food processing, petroleum (largest oil refining region on East Coast), printing and publishing, instruments, chemicals and pharmaceuticals; companies headquartered in metro area include Sun Oil, Campbell Soup, American Stores, Scott Paper, Leeds & Northrup, Smithkline, Rohm & Haas, Food Fair, Crown Cork & Seal, Pennwalt.
Commerce: 24 comm. banks (RTA), over $21 billion deposits; 4 mutual savings banks (city), $7.8 billion; retail sales (metro), $14.6 billion; average household income (metro), $17,983.
Transportation: biggest fresh-water port in world (50 mi. waterfront); leader in shipping vol. among N. Atl. American ports (75.9 millon tons in 1976); 2 modern marine terminals for containerized cargo; rail service by Conrail (Penn Central, Reading), Chessie Syst. (B&O), and Amtrak; over 250 truck lines, vast highway network, 6 bridges in metro area for motor traffic between Pa. and N.J.; Int. Airport terminal, expanded at cost of $174 million, handled 8.1 million passengers in 1976; Cargo City, $50 million air freight facility; area transit (SEPTA) conveyed 284.6 million passengers on subway, el, rail commuter, bus, and streetcar lines in 1976.
Communications: 3 major daily newspapers: Inquirer, Bulletin, and News; 33 AM, 15 FM, 6 commercial TV stations; cable TV.
New construction: Market St. East, $360 million reconstruction of major retail area plus construction of RR commuter tunnel; Franklin Town, privately financed $280 million redevelopment of 50-acre midcity site (will provide 4,000 residential units, employment for 20,000); Penn's Landing, $120 million waterfront development.
Medical facilities: 96 hospitals, 22,000 beds.
Federal facilities: Phila. Naval Base; Defense Industrial Supply Ctr.; Defense Personnel Support Ctr.; U.S. Navy Aviation Supply Office Compound; U.S. Mint; Ft. Dix and McGuire AFB (metro).
Cultural facilities: Phila. Orchestra; Pa. Ballet; Opera Co. of Phila.; Acad. of Music; Museum of Art; Franklin Inst.; Pa. Acad. of the Fine Arts; Rodin Museum; University Museum; Acad. of Natural Sciences; Barnes Fdtn.; Robin Hood Dells (East and new West); Walnut St. Theater (oldest in America); Shubert, Forrest, and New Locust theaters; community and summer theaters.
Educational facilities: 54 colleges and universities within 25 mi. of City Hall; 6 medical schools in city; University City Science Center.
Convention facilities: Civic Ctr., 381,000 sq. ft. of exhibit space, over 50 rms., 11,500-seat Convention Hall; over 500 motels/hotels (metro) with 18,250 first-class rooms.
Recreational facilities: over 8,000 acres of parks incl. 4,079-acre Fairmount Park; hundreds of playgrounds, swimming pools, golf courses, tennis courts, ice-skating rinks; close to seashore, mountains.
Sports: NL Phillies and NFL Eagles (Veterans Stadium); NBA 76ers and NHL Flyers (Spectrum); NAHL Firebirds (Civic Ctr.); Penn Relays (Franklin Field); Army-Navy football (J.F. Kennedy Stadium); sculling races (Schuylkill R.); area horse racing (Keystone, Liberty Bell, Atlantic City, Brandywine, Delaware Park).
Other attractions: old city district and Benjamin Franklin Parkway centers of interest; many historic bldgs. preserved, restored or reconstructed; Liberty

Bell in new pavilion; history comes to life on giant IMAX screen (70'x100') and other multi-media exhibits in $11.6 million Living History Museum; Afro-American Historical and Cultural Museum; City Hall; Elfreth's Alley; Franklin Court; Society Hill; Fairmount Park mansions; Zoo (America's first); Mummers Parade (Jan. 1); Freedom Week (climaxed by July 4th celebration); nearby attractions incl. Valley Forge, Longwood Gardens, Great Adventure.
History: Wm. Penn founded his "Greene Countrie Towne" as Quaker colony in 1682; gave it name that means "City of Brotherly Love"; national capital 1790-1800; historical shrines incl. Independence Hall, Liberty Bell, Carpenters' Hall, Franklin's grave, Betsy Ross House, Gloria Dei Church, Christ Church, USS Olympia, Fort Mifflin.
Further information: City Representative, 1660 Municipal Services Bldg., Phila., PA 19107; Phila. Tourist Bureau, 1525 J. F. Kennedy Boulevard, Phila., PA 19102.

Phoenix, Arizona

The World Almanac is sponsored in the Phoenix area by The Phoenix Gazette, 120 East Van Buren Street, Phoenix, AZ 85004; phone (602) 271-8000; founded Oct. 28, 1880, as Arizona Gazette by Charles H. McNeil; circulation 104,273; publisher Mrs. Eugene C. Pulliam, assistant publisher Mason Walsh, managing editor Alan D. Moyer; sponsors Christmas Fund Drive, Music Memory Programs, Family Symphony Concerts, Phoenix Giants' Bat Boy contest, Tennis Clinic, Cactus Show, and other events.

Population: 696,000 (city), 1,352,000 (metro); capital and largest city in state, 14th (city) in nation; total employed 530,500.
Area: 276.6 sq. mi. (city), 9,226 sq. mi. (metro), in south central Arizona.
Industry: electronic equipment manufacturers, Honeywell Information Systems, and Motorola, Inc. each employ more than 2,500; aircraft and parts manufacturers, AiResearch, a division of The Garrett Corp., and Sperry Flight Systems each employ more than 2,500; other major employers are E. L. Gruber (apparel), Goodyear Aerospace, General Electric, Western Electric Cable, Reynolds Metals, Marathon Steel, Arizona Public Service, Salt River Project, Mountain Bell, Siemens Corp., Amerco, Greyhound, American Express, and Phoenix Newspapers.
Commerce: wholesale-retail center for state; retail sales (1976) $4.8 billion; effective household buying income, $15,398; bank and S&L assets $10.6 billion; 13 banks with 226 area offices, 7 S&Ls with 101 offices in metro area.
Transportation: transportation center of the Southwest; Sky Harbor International Airport served by 9 airlines, 4.4 million passengers (1976); 2 railroads; 2 transcontinental bus lines; 10 transcontinental truck lines; 25 transcontinental heavy equipment haulers; 34 interstate and 39 intrastate truck lines.
Communications: 6 TV and 32 radio stations.
New construction: In 1976, 13,567 new residential building units were permitted; total value all types of building permits, $590 million.
Medical facilities: Barrow Neurological Institute; 21 general care hospitals, Veterans' Hospital; other special service facilities.
Cultural facilities: art museum, public library, symphony orchestra, Indian museums, zoo, botanical gardens, community and professional theaters; Civic Plaza convention center; Gammage Auditorium.
Educational facilities: Arizona State Univ., American Graduate School of International Management; 4 community colleges; Maricopa Technical College (vocational); 56 public and parochial high schools.
Sports: 50 golf courses and $200,000 Phoenix Open; inland surfing beach; ice skating rinks; amusement park; pro basketball, baseball teams; auto, greyhound, and horse racing; annual Fiesta Bowl (holiday football game).
Other attractions: Frank Lloyd Wright's Taliesin West; Paolo Soleri's Arcosanti; Firebird Festival of the Arts; Dons' Club guided tours of Arizona; full calendar of events including state and county fairs and rodeos, horse shows, regattas, polo tournaments.
History: founded 1870, on site of ancient Indian settlement; the Hohokam tribe, which flourished ca. 500-1200 A.D., developed an intricate system of irrigation canals which form the base of the canal system in use today.
Further information: Phoenix and Valley of the Sun Convention and Visitors Bureau, 2701 E. Camelback Road, Phoenix AZ 85016.

Pittsburgh, Pennsylvania

The World Almanac is sponsored in the Pittsburgh area by The Pittsburgh Press, 34 Boulevard of the Allies, Pittsburgh, PA 15222; phone (412) 263-1100; founded June 23, 1884, as Evening Penny Press by Thomas J. Keehan; circulation 265,114 daily, 667,297 Sunday; editor John Troan, business manager Robert Hartmann, executive editor Leo Koeberlein, managing editor Ralph Brem; sponsors Press Old Newsboys Fund for Children's Hospital which raised $1,380,671 in 1976.

Population: 458,651 (city), 2,383,000 (4-county metro area), 2d in state and 28th in nation; metro area labor force of 991,000 is 6th in nation.
Area: 55.5 sq. mi. at juncture of Allegheny and Monongahela rivers which form Ohio River; Allegheny County seat; altitude, 702 feet.
Industry: one-fifth of nation's steelmaking capacity concentrated in metro area; western Pennsylvania mines produce 44 million tons of bituminous coal annually; 6,000 different products made in area; home of world's first full-scale nuclear power plant, world's largest manufacturers of aluminum, steel rolls, rolling mill machinery, air brakes, plate and window glass, and safety equipment; 3d largest headquarters city in nation.
Commerce: retail sales (1975) $6.2 billion; exports abroad of products manufactured here totaled $842,768,000 (1976); average household effective buying income (Allegheny County) $14,008.
Transportation: 7 scheduled airlines handled 8,182,063 passengers on 123,466 flights at International Airport (1976); 19 railroads; Continental Trailways and Greyhound bus lines; over 400 common carriers; Port Authority Transit vehicles carried 105.1 million passengers (1976) over 165 routes, 5 trolley lines; 9 major highways serve the city; rapid and mass transit plan under development.
Communications: 2 daily newspapers; 5 TV (including country's first educational station) and 27 radio stations.
New construction: $32 million, 140,000 sq. ft. convention center underway for completion in 1978.

Medical facilities: 21 hospitals include Univ. of Pittsburgh Health and Medical complex where Dr. Jonas Salk developed polio vaccine; VA installation.
Federal facilities: Federal Building contains scores of U.S. government offices (information center: 412/644-3456); Army base at Oakdale; Air Force base.
Cultural facilities: Heinz Hall is home of the opera co., ballet, civic light opera, youth symphony and symphony orchestra; 3 community theaters, one legitimate theater; Frick Art Museum; Carnegie Museum and Art Gallery, home of the new Pittsburgh International series, a biennial one-man art show starting in 1977 and offering a $55,000 prize; American Wind Symphony.
Educational facilities: Univ. of Pittsburgh, Duquesne Univ.; Point Park, Chatham, Carlow, Robert Morris, and La Roche colleges; Carnegie-Mellon Univ., Community College of Allegheny Co.; 18 Carnegie public libraries, 3 bookmobiles, community libraries.
Sports: NL Pirates, NFL Steelers, NHL Penguins.
Other attractions: Highland Park Zoo, children's zoo, Twilight Zoo, aquarium, aviary, Buhl Planetarium, Allegheny Observatory, Phipps Conservatory, Fort Pitt Museum; 4 amusement parks; 2 operating passenger inclines; folk festival; Three Rivers Arts Festival every June; harness racing; river cruises; Civic Arena; Three Rivers Stadium.
History: first hunters and trappers came through in 1714; city dates from Nov. 25, 1758, when English forces under Brig. Gen. John Forbes occupied the ruins of Fort Duquesne, which French soldiers had burned and abandoned, and built a new and bigger fortress called Fort Pitt. When incorporated in 1816, it already had a reputation as a "Smoky City" from factories and coal-burning homes. Massive "Renaissance Plan" has cleared the skies and rebuilt the heart of the city during the past 25 years.
Further information: Chamber of Commerce, 411 Seventh Avenue; Convention and Visitors Bureau, 3001 Jenkins Arcade; both Pittsburgh, PA 15222.

Portland, Maine

The World Almanac is sponsored in the Portland area by the Maine Sunday Telegram, 390 Congress, Portland, ME 04104; phone (207) 775-5811; published by Guy Gannett Publishing Co., founded 1921; circulation 109,125; president Jean Gannett Hawley; editor John K. Murphy; also publishes morning Press Herald, circulation 53,378, and Evening Express, 30,120.

Population: 66,500 (city), 230,000 (metro area), first in state; total employed, 27,500 (1975).
Area: 21.6 sq. mi.; peninsula on Casco Bay; Cumberland County seat.
Industry: Atlantic Coast's 2d busiest oil shipping center, east terminus Montreal pipeline; fishing fleet base, seafood shipping center; landbased products: printed materials, clothing, metal, processed food, electronic parts, wooden goods.
Commerce: tourist center, regional retail-wholesale hub, large shopping complex, 1,000 retail, 350 wholesale, 600 service enterprises; retail sales (1975), $225 million; median family income (1976), $12,200.
Transportation: municipal jetport, Delta airline; 3 rail freight lines, integrated bus system, Greyhound, Continental bus terminals, 25 truck lines; Maine Turnpike, Interstate 95 and 295 highways connect to all New England; deep water anchorage, auto cruise ferries year round to Yarmouth, Nova Scotia.
Communications: 3 TV, 5 AM, 4 FM stations.
New construction: housing for elderly, parking garage, sewage treatment system.
Medical facilities: medical center, 2 hospitals.
Cultural facilities: symphony orch., Kotzschmar organ, one of world's largest; public, historical libraries; Victorian, art museums; Henry Longfellow home (1785); branch Univ. of Maine, Westbrook College, art, vocational, and business schools; Portland Headlight, oldest lighthouse in country.
Recreation: 18-hole municipal golf course, 9 others in area; scenic cruises; swimming, tennis, fishing within easy travel; scenic parks.
Convention facilities: civic center, 3 large assembly halls, meeting rooms in modern hotels and motels.
Further information: Tourist Bureau, 142 Free Street, Portland, ME.

Portland, Oregon

The World Almanac is sponsored in the Portland area by The Oregon Journal, 1320 SW Broadway, Portland, OR. 97201; phone (503) 221-8275; founded Mar. 1902; circulation 107,039; editor Donald J. Sterling Jr.; managing editor Edward F. O'Meara.

Population: 375,700 (city), 1,094,300 (metro), first in state; 34th in nation; total employed, 483,900.
Area: 80 sq. mi., at juncture of Columbia and Willamette rivers.
Industry: electrical and electronic industries along with lumber and wood products, food, and paper; ranks first in manufacture of logging, lumbering equipment; home of Georgia-Pacific, Louisiana-Pacific (forest products), Tektronix (oscilloscopes), Omark (saw cutting chain), Hyster (lifts, hoists, lumber handling), White Stag, Pendleton, Jantzen (clothing).
Commerce: wholesale-retail center for large part of Oregon, SW Washington; retail sales metro area (1975), $3.34 billion. There are 11 banks, 11 savings and loan associations.
Transportation: 4 major rail freight lines, Amtrak; Greyhound, Trailways buses; 10th largest freshwater port in U.S., with 27-mile frontage, 29 marine berths; 18 million tons of cargo pass over docks annually; more than 1,000 ships visit annually, most active harbor in U.S.; hub for 9 airlines, flights to all parts of world.
Communications: 5 TV and 22 radio stations.
Medical facilities: 17 major hospitals, Univ. of Oregon Medical School, VA hospital.
Cultural facilities: art museum, Oregon Symphony Orchestra, Opera Association, Oregon Historical Society, Portland State Univ., Univ. of Portland, and Lewis & Clark, Reed, and Concordia colleges.
Other attractions: annual Rose Festival, Rose Show; park system includes Washington Park, Hoyt Arboretum International Rose Test Garden, Portland Zoo, Oregon Museum of Science and Industry; Forest Park is largest forest area in a U.S. city's limits.
Sports: NBA champion Trail Blazers play at the Memorial Coliseum.
History: chartered 1851 with population of 821; named after Portland, Me., rather than Boston, Mass., on flip of coin by 2 early citizens.
Further information: Chamber of Commerce, 824 SW 5th, Portland, OR 97204.

Providence, Rhode Island

The World Almanac is sponsored in the Providence area by The Providence Journal-Bulletin, 75 Fountain Street, Providence, RI 02902; phone (401) 277-7000; Journal founded 1829, Bulletin 1863, Sunday Journal 1883; circulation, Journal (morn) 66,501, Bulletin (eve) 143,211, Sunday Journal 208,026; publisher John C. A. Watkins, president Michael P. Metcalf, v.p. and asst. publ. Edwin P. Young, v.p.-admin. Charles P. O'Donnell, v.p. and exec. editor Charles McC Hauser.

Population: 168,000 (city), 875,100 (metro); total employed 109,435.
Area: 18.91 sq. mi., at the head of Narragansett Bay in Providence County; state capital.
Industry: jewelry, silverware, plated ware, costume jewelry are largest industries; Textron is based in Providence, 1,327 manufacturing companies in the city.
Commerce: wholesale-retail center for entire state; retail sales $2.7 billion (metro); consumer spendable income per household $15,303 (metro); Allendale Insurance, world's largest mutual insurer of industrial firms, is based outside of city in Johnston; home of Narragansett Capital, largest small business investment company in nation; 2 savings and loan assns., 2 mutual savings banks, one cooperative bank, 6 commercial banks.
Transportation: Amtrak, passenger service between Boston, Providence, New York, and Washington; 5 bus lines; 45 locally-based common carriers and contract truckers; 9 major highways link Providence to every corner of R.I.; 6 major airlines out of T. F. Green Airport in Warwick (15 min. away); port is 3d largest in New England with 25 wharves and docks, 10.5 miles of commercial waterfront on the bay.
Communications: 3 TV and 8 radio stations.
Medical facilities: 7 hospitals; one VA hospital.
Cultural facilities: Trinity Square Repertory Co., R. I. Philharmonic, R. I. School of Design Museum; R. I. Historical Society.
Education: Brown University, founded 1764, is 7th oldest college in nation; 7-year M.D. program inaugurated 1973; Providence and R. I. colleges, and R.I. School of Design.
Recreation: one of America's most attractive recreational areas centers around Providence: 69 salt water beaches, 25 fresh water beaches, 50 golf and country clubs, 4 ski areas, 29 yacht clubs, 27 parks, all within 45 minutes of city.
Convention facilities: R.I. Civic Center (seats 12,000).
Sports: America's Cup races since 1930; Newport-Bermuda race starts at Newport every other year; Reds (hockey), Oceaneers (soccer).
Other attractions: largest collection of original early American homes of any city; located along Benefit St., they have been preserved by the Providence Preservation Society.
History: founded 1636 by Roger Williams; incorporated 1832; official state name is "Rhode Island and Providence Plantations."
Further information: Chamber of Commerce, 10 Dorrance Street, Providence, RI 02903.

Quebec City, Quebec, Canada

Population: 186,088 (city), 480,500 (metro); oldest city in Canada (1608) and the capital city of the province of Quebec.
Area: 30 sq. mi.; natural citadel on north shore of St. Lawrence River at confluence with St. Charles River; 400 miles from Gulf of St. Lawrence; 167 miles east of Montreal; older part is built on a cliff 360 ft. above the St. Lawrence.
Industry: some 300 industrial firms, ranging from primary industry products to a variety of consumer products, employ over 16,000 people; food and beverage, leather footwear and leather products, textiles, apparel, wood products, pulp and paper, printing and publishing, iron and steel products, non-ferrous metal and chemical products.
Commerce: Quebec harbor, one of the busiest seaports of Canada, accommodates the largest ocean-going vessels with year-round facilities, an important container terminal on the North Atlantic coast; Provincial Government, with more than 15,000 employees, is the largest single employer and consumer in the city.
Transportation: Canadian Pacific and Canadian National railroads; Air Canada, Quebecair, Nordair; major bus center.
Communications: 3 TV stations (2 French, 1 bilingual); 6 radio stations (French), 2 newspapers (French).
Medical facilities: 5 large general hospitals, many smaller ones.
Cultural facilities: historic character, cultural appeal and natural beauty make tourism important area of economic activity; annual "Carnaval" in Feb. is internationally known; annual summer festival (July) changes the city into an open theater for numerous artistic events; Expo-Quebec, an annual provincial exhibition (industrial, commercial, and agricultural), draws over 500,000 people a year.
Educational facilities: Laval University, the first in North America; Quebec University; 3 colleges for general and vocational training, numerous private schools.
Sports: home of WHA Nordiques.
Other attractions: only walled city in North America with fortifications standing today as they were 125 years ago; the Citadel, built from 1823-1832, contains within its walls 25 buildings, including the summer residence of Governor-General of Canada, Parliament buildings (1886), Quebec Museum, Battlefield Park, Ursulines Museum, Seminary (1663), Talon cellars, Notre Dame des Victoires Church, and Tresor Street.
History: founded 1608 by French explorer Samuel de Champlain; cradle of French civilization in America; once the key to the interior of the North American continent.

Raleigh, North Carolina

The World Almanac is sponsored in eastern North Carolina by The News and Observer and The Raleigh Times, 215 S. McDowell Street, Raleigh, NC 27602, (919) 821-1234; circulation N&O (morn) 130,134; Times (eve) 33,351; N&O Sunday 162,169; publisher Frank Daniels Jr., editorial director Claude Sitton, editor Times A. C. Snow, managing editor N&O Bob Brooks, Times Mike Yopp.

Population: 155,000 (city), 275,000 (county), 500,000 (metro); 3d in state; 230,900 employed (metro).
Area: 49 square miles in the geographical center of state where piedmont joins coastal plain; alt. 363 ft.; temperate climate; state capital and Wake County seat.
Industry: major industry is government, employing 25 percent of work force; also electrical machinery, foods, and textiles.
Commerce: financial, retail center of eastern N.C. retail sales $1.25 billion (1976); 15 banks with $58.5 billion in debits (county); average annual income per household $16,145 (county).
Education: 6 colleges; N.C. State Univ. largest, with

Univ. of N.C. (Chapel Hill) and Duke Univ. (Durham) within 30 mi. form Research Triangle; 5,000 Triangle Park employs 12,000 in drug, fiber, biomedical, environmental, engineering, and humanities research; meto area has more Ph.Ds per capita than anywhere in world.
Transportation: 3 rail and 5 bus lines; Amtrak; 39 motor freight companies serve city; airport has 4 airlines and 46 flights daily; one interstate, 4 U.S., and 2 state highways into city; city mass transit.
Communications: 4 TV and 13 radio stations; 2 daily newspapers and one community weekly.
New construction: $58.7 million (1976).
Medical facilities: 3 hospitals (920 beds), 2 are building new facilities; major state mental hospital; private psychiatric hospital under construction; 350 doctors.
Convention facilities: 30 motels, 4,000 rooms; new Civic Center seats 10,000, Dorton Arena 9,111, Memorial Auditorium 3,000, and Reynolds Coliseum 12,000.
Cultural facilities: 3 museums, state fairgrounds; state symphony; community, college, and professional theater groups.
Recreation: 4,200-acre Umstead Park; Carter Stadium; 100 city parks; first Green Survival City in U.S.
Sports: pro golf meet; pro tennis meet; annual powerboat regatta; college sports.
History: founded 1792; Andrew Johnson birthplace; Oakwood Historic District preserves large Victorian neighborhood.
Further information: Chamber of Commerce, 411 S. Salisbury Street, Raleigh, NC 27602, (919) 833-3005.

Regina, Saskatchewan, Canada

The World Almanac is sponsored in southern Saskatchewan by The Leader-Post, 1964 Park St., Regina, Sask., S4P 3GA, phone (306) 527-8511; founded 1883 by Nicholas Flood Davin; circulation 66,251; president Michael Sifton, Toronto; executive vice-president Max Macdonald; editor W. Ivor Williams; managing editor C.E.W. Bell; business manager William Duffus; advertising manager George Crawford; MacLaren Trophy for editorial page reproduction excellence.

Population: 151,191, first in province, 17th in nation; labor force, 77,000.
Area: 34.5 sq. mi., 100 miles north of Canada-U.S. border; provincial capital.
Industry: over 281 manufacturing industries; gross production value (1976) $345 million, 36% of Saskatchewan total.
Commerce: service center for oil, potash; grain production area; retail sales (1976) $497.9 million, 24% of province.
Transportation: 2 rail lines, 2 airlines, 3 bus lines, and 125 trucking companies; main Trans-Canada highway bisects; city-run transit system, including Telebus, hybrid system with demand/response taxi service and mass transit, provides to-and-from service to user's home.
Communications: 3 TV and 6 radio stations.
Medical facilities: 4 major hospitals, 1,391 beds.
Cultural facilities: Saskatchewan Centre of Arts, multi-purpose theater-convention center with: Jubilee theater (seats 450) stage, ballroom, reception hall and dining room; Centennial theater (seats 2,029); Hanbidge Hall convention area, 12,200 square feet, 9 meeting rooms, seats 1,600. Regina Symphony; Globe Repertory; Museum Natural History; Norman Mackenzie Art Gallery; RCMP Museum.
Educational facilities: Regina University;13 collegiates; 89 elementary: Wascana Institute of Applied Arts and Sciences.
Recreation facilities: Saskatchewan Roughriders (Canadian pro football); 137 parks and playgrounds; 8 golf courses; 6 swimming pools; 8 indoor ice rinks.
Other attractions: Wascana Centre, 2,000-acre development, with man-made lake, public buildings, parks, recreation in heart of city; home of Canadian Western Agribition, Canada's major international livestock show.
History: founded 1882, and since that time headquarters for RCMP training depot. Will mark 75th anniversary of incorporation as a city in 1978.
Further information: Regina Chamber of Commerce, 2145 Albert Street, Regina, Sask.

Reno, Nevada

The World Almanac is sponsored in the northern Nevada area by the Nevada State Journal and Reno Evening Gazette, 401 West Second Street, Post Office Box 280, Reno, NV 89520; phone 702/786-8989. Journal founded 1870, Gazette founded 1876, combined daily circulation, 50,362, Sunday 40,678; publisher, Warren L. Lerude.

Population: est. 1976 pop. 93,804 (city), 162,097 (county), including Sparks; 2d largest in the state, 1976 labor force 86,793.
Area: 36.8 square miles (including Stead annexation) in northwestern part of the state at the eastern foot of the Sierra Nevada; Washoe County seat.
Industry: gross gaming revenue for county, $211.6 million (1976) netted state taxes of $16.6 million; 87,779 delegates attended 191 conventions. Warehousing continued to grow because of Nevada's liberal free port law with est. 13 million square feet in the country; marriages (34,251) outnumbered divorces (3,788).
Commerce: taxable sales in metro area (including Sparks) for 1976, $810 million, assessed valuation (city) $96.5 million; median household income $13,971; bank resources $2.2 billion.
Transportation: 12 motor freight lines, 3 freight railroads, Amtrak, 3 commercial bus lines; airport handled (1976) 1.1 million passengers as U.S. port of entry; U.S. 395 and Interstate 80.
Communications: 3 TV, 10 radio, one CATV.
New construction: 159 commercial, 1,541 residential units totaling $185.1 million, new assessed valuation (1976 includes county).
Medical facilities: 3 hospitals, including VA.
Educational facilities: Univ. of Nevada, Reno, 8,700 enrollment (1976); community college 8,000; public schools 31,700; private/parochial schools 700.
Cultural facilities: 1,428 seat Pioneer Theater Auditorium, Atmospherium Planetarium, and 280,000 volume library; national air races; Nevada Historical Society; Nevada Opera Guild, Reno Philharmonic Orchestra; Nevada Art Gallery.
Recreation: 21 ski resorts within a 2-hour drive; Lake Tahoe and Pyramid Lake offering fishing, boating, swimming, sun-bathing, medium game-hunting, camping; historic Virginia City mining town and tourist attraction within 1/2 hour drive.
Sports: Silver Sox minor league baseball.
History: established 1868 with public auction of land by Central Pacific Railroad Company, known prior as Lake's Crossing; named after Civil War hero General Jesse L. Reno.
Further information: Chamber of Commerce, P.O. Box 3499, Reno, NV 89505; Marketing Department, Reno Newspapers, Inc., P.O. Box 280, Reno, NV 89520.

Richmond, Virginia

The World Almanac is sponsored in the Richmond area by the Richmond Times-Dispatch and News Leader, 333 E. Grace Street, Richmond, VA 23213; (804) 649-6000; Times-Dispatch founded 1950 by James A. Cowardin, circulation 135,965 daily, 209,213 Sunday; News Leader founded 1896 by Joseph Bryan, circulation 114,976; publisher D. Tennant Bryan; president Alan S. Donnahoe, executive editor John E. Leard, Times-Dispatch managing editor Alf Goodykoontz, News Leader managing editor J. A. Finch.

Population: 227,200 (city), 581,600 (metro area), total employed (non-agricultural) 290,304.
Area: 62.5 sq. mi. (city), located at fall line of James River, 90 miles from Atlantic Ocean; Richmond County seat.
Industry: tobacco, with 10,000 workers, and chemicals, with 8,200 are leaders in employment; Philip Morris cigarette plant which began production in 1974 is world's largest and most modern; printing, publishing, manufacture of paper and allied products, and food.
Commerce: wholesale-retail center for central Virginia; retail sales $1.8 billion in 1976, per capita income $6,222, $14,194 median family effective buying income, total income $3.2 billion.
Transportation: 4 major railroads, 5 intercity bus lines, 3 commercial air lines, one commuter air line, 50 motor truck lines; 3 interstate, 6 U. S., and 9 state highways; deepwater terminal accessible to ocean-going ships.
Communications: 4 TV, 16 radio stations.
Medical facilities: Medical College of Virginia known worldwide for heart and kidney transplants, medical research; 21 other hospitals, including McGuire VA Hospital.
Federal facilities: Defense General Supply Center, Fifth Federal Reserve Bank, U. S. Fourth Circuit Court, Ft. Lee (Quartermaster Corps).
Cultural facilities: Va. Museum and Theater with professional artists make city a center for dramatic, other performing arts; variety of other drama groups; symphony orchestra.
Educational facilities: Virginia Commonwealth Univ. has state's largest enrollment; Univ. of Richmond, Virginia Union Univ., Union Theological Seminary (Presbyterian), Randolph-Macon College.
Recreational facilities: Coliseum for athletic, entertainment events; city-owned Mosque auditorium, Parker Field, City Stadium, numerous parks.
Convention facilities: large downtown hotels near Mosque and Coliseum.
Sports: Braves (IL baseball), national ranked track and tennis events.
Other attractions: St. John's Church, scene of Patrick Henry's "Liberty or Death" speech; Virginia Capitol, designed by Thomas Jefferson; White House of the Confederacy; Civil War battlefields.
History: exploration here in 1607 by Capt. John Smith, first settlement 1609, incorporated as town 1742, made Va. capital 1780, Confederate Capital 1861-65; burned 1781 by Benedict Arnold, and 1865 when cotton, tobacco stockpiles fire set by fleeing Confederates spread to city; damaged by floods 1771, 1969, 1972.
Further information: Chamber of Commerce, 201 E. Franklin Street, Richmond, VA 23219.

Roanoke, Virginia

The World Almanac is sponsored in the Roanoke area by Roanoke Times and World-News, 201-203 Campbell Avenue, Roanoke, VA 24010, telephone (703) 981-3000; Times founded 1886, World-News founded 1889; Robert Benson, president; Barton W. Morris Jr., publisher; circulation combined daily, 113,247; Sunday 112,486.

Population: 109,500 (city, Jan. 1, 1977), 217,000 (metro area); labor force 109,740.
Area: 43.25 sq. mi.; Metro SMSA includes Roanoke City, Salem City; Roanoke, Craig, Botetourt counties; located at southern extremity of Shenandoah Valley midway between Maryland and Tennessee.
Industry: 22.5% of work force in manufacturing. Leading firms are General Electric, Eaton Corp., ITT, Singer, Burlington Industries, Mohawk Rubber, Ingersoll Rand.
Commerce: headquarters Shenandoah Life Ins. Co., Estate Life Ins. Co., Appalachian Power Co., Advance Stores, Mick or Mack Groceries; Regional Allstate Ins. Co. offices; Kroger (central warehouse); retail sales metro area (1976) $753 million; average spendable family income, $13,647 (metro area); retail center for 20 counties and parts of W. Va. and N.C.
Transportation: Norfolk & Western Railway Co. headquarters. 2 airlines; Trailways and Greyhound buses; Amtrak north-south Washington, D.C.-West Va.; 30 interstate trucking firms with terminals; Highways Interstate 81, Spur 581, US 11, US 460, US 220, US 221, Blue Ridge Parkway.
Communications: 3 TV and 13 radio stations.
Medical facilities: 4 general, 4 specialty hospitals, VA facility; state hospital.
Cultural facilities: 2 civic centers with auditorium, coliseums and exhibit halls, symphony orchestra, art center, theaters, Roanoke College, Hollins College, Virginia Western Community College, National Business College; commuting distance from Va. Polytechnic Inst. and State Univ.; concert and lecture series.
Other attractions: Mill Mt. Park rising 1,000 ft. in center of city; children's zoo; Transportation and Historical Museum; Smith Mt.; Fairy Stone and Claytor Lakes state parks; Natural Bridge, Dixie Caverns, Peaks of Otter.
Sports: baseball; school sports, winter skiing nearby, public recreation and parks programs.
History: formerly named Big Lick, Roanoke, an Indian word for shell money, became a city in 1884 with the linking of the Shenandoah Valley Railroad with Norfolk and Western Railroad.
Further information: Roanoke Valley Chamber of Commerce, 14 West Kirk Avenue, P.O. Box 20, Roanoke, VA 24001.

Rochester, New York

The World Almanac is sponsored in the Rochester area by Gannett Rochester Newspapers, 55 Exchange Street, Rochester, NY 14614; phone (716) 232-7100; circulation, Democrat and Chronicle (morn.) 128,096; Times-Union (eve.) 130,880; Democrat and Chronicle (Sun.) 221,840; publisher Eugene C. Dorsey; executive editor Stuart Dunham; director of advertising Peter Stegner. Times-Union reporters awarded a 1972 Pulitzer Prize.

Population: 5 county metro area 978,700 (est.); 413,700 employed; unemployment 7.3%.
Area: 675 sq. mi. (Monroe County), straddling Genesee River, on Lake Ontario; 2,966 sq. mi. (metro); Monroe County seat.
Industry: world leader in production of photographic, optical, and scientific instruments, with Eastman Kodak (48,000 employees) Xerox (14,000),

and Bausch & Lomb (5,000), all founded in Rochester, the most prominent; other fields include machinery, food products, apparel, printing and publishing; industrial wage increase, 41% since 1969.
Commerce: retail sales (1975 est.) over $2 billion; 20 commercial and savings banks, with assets of $5.8 billion; 1976 median household income (Monroe County) $13,601 (metro area) $17,598.
Transportation: Monroe County Airport, with 3 major airlines and several freight companies; rail freight service by 4 lines, Amtrak, port of Rochester; over 75 motor freight firms.
Communications: 4 TV and 15 radio stations.
New construction: First Federal Bldg., 22 story office tower.
Medical facilities: one of the nation's most advanced health care centers; 8 general hospitals, including Strong Memorial Hospital.
Cultural facilities: Eastman Theater, part of Univ. of Eastman School of Music, and home of the Philharmonic Orchestra; Memorial Art Gallery; Museum and Science Center, including Strasenburgh Planetarium; George Eastman House of Photography; 3 resident theater companies.
Educational facilities: 8 private and 2 public 4-year colleges; 3 community colleges.
Recreational facilities: Finger Lakes area, with 13 parks, summer and winter sports, golf, tennis, bowling; 16-park Monroe County System, including Seneca Park Zoo, Highland Park, Lilac Festival.
Convention facilities: 2d largest used site in NY; War Memorial, 7,500 cap., Dome Arena, 5,000 cap.; 4,600 rms. available.
Sports: International League Red Wings, top Baltimore Orioles farm team; AHL Amerks, North American Soccer League Lancers, thoroughbred racing and Finger Lake race track (Canandaigua).
Further information: Chamber of Commerce, 55 St. Paul Street, 14604 or Convention and Publicity Bureau, 100 Exchange Street, 14614.

Rockford, Illinois

The World Almanac is sponsored in the Rockford area by the Rockford Newspapers, Inc., 97 E. State Street, Rockford, IL 61105, phone (815) 987-1200, publisher of the Morning Star, Register-Republic and Sunday Register-Star; combined daily circulation 80,000; Sunday 80,000. Publisher James Graham, managing editor Gene Cryer; member of the Gannett Group.

Population: 140,000 (city), 241,900 (county), 116,860 work force (county).
Area: 36.4 sq. mi. (city) on Rock River in extreme north central Illinois; Winnebago County seat; 519 sq. mi. (county).
Industry: 575 manufacturing establishments; products include machine tools (Sundstrand, Ingersoll Milling Machine, Barber-Colman, Greenlee Bros.), screws and bolts (Rockford Products, Elco, Camcar, National Lock), pharmaceuticals (Warner-Lambert, American Chicle) and paints (Valspar). Chrysler Corp. assembly plant is in nearby Belvidere.
Commerce: retail "magnet" for northern Illinois and southern Wisconsin; 25 shopping centers and districts including CherryVale Mall (over 90 stores); retail sales (1976) $569.1 million (city); 15 commercial banks, resources (1976) $793.1 million; 4 savings and loan associations, resources (1976) $405.8 million.
Transportation: Amtrak Chicago connection; 4 rail freight lines; 3 bus lines; 50 truck lines; Ozark Air Lines (Denver, Detroit connections); U.S. 51, U.S. 20, and Interstate 90.
Communications: 3 TV, 8 radio stations; 2 cable TV operations; 7 weekly, 2 daily newspapers.
Medical facilities: 3 hospitals; 2 public supported extended care facilities.
Cultural facilities: symphony orchestra; concert band; civic theatre; 2 male and one mixed choral organizations; Rock Valley, Rockford colleges.
Education: (1976-77 school year) 76 public schools (K-12); 19 parochial and private schools (K-12); Rockford College (4 years, liberal arts); Rock Valley College (2 years, liberal arts); UI-Rockford School of Medicine.
Recreation: 20 forest preserves; over 100 parks totaling 3,000 acres; 1 state park; 4 public golf courses; 4 country club courses; 61 public, 7 private tennis courts; 2 indoor tennis facilities; 3 public swimming pools; 7 private swim clubs; 76 baseball diamonds; Riverview Ice House (indoor skating); Wagon Wheel ski area (snow skiing).
Agriculture: 210,475 acres tilled farmland (estimated value $210.5 million); 3,119 people on 977 farms in county.
Other attractions: Children's Farm; Time Museum; Tinker Swiss Cottage; Rockford Museum; John Erlander Home; Burpee Natural History Museum; Burpee Art Museum.
History: founded in 1834 by Germanicus Kent and Thatcher Blake beside fording place across Rock River; incorporated in 1852.
Further information: Rockford Area Chamber of Commerce, 815 E. State Street, Rockford, IL 61101.

Sacramento, California

The World Almanac is sponsored in the Sacramento area by The Sacramento Bee, 21st & Q, Sacramento, CA 95816; telephone (916) 442-5011; founded 1857; circulation daily 172,786, Sunday 202,183; president Eleanor McClatchy, editor C. K. McClatchy, managing editor Frank McCulloch.

Population: 261,900 (city), 706,300 (county), 909,100 (metro); total employed (metro) 367,300.
Area: 94 sq. mi. (city), 997 sq. mi. (county) in Sacramento Valley, 85 mi. northeast of San Francisco; Sacramento County seat.
Industry: 475 manufacturing plants including Campbell Soup, Procter and Gamble, Libby McNeil and Libby, California Almond Growers Exchange, Del Monte, Teichert Construction, and Aerojet-General.
Commerce: state capital; wholesale-retail center for large area of Sacramento Valley; retail sales (metro), $3 billion.
Transportation: 3 county operated airports, including metropolitan airport, plus numerous private airports; $55-million Port of Sacramento gives access to the Pacific; 2 mainline transcontinental rail carriers; junction 4 major highways.
Communications: 6 TV and 21 radio stations.
New construction: downtown Mall; Old Sacramento being restored as state and federal historical project; Rancho Seco Atomic Power Plant; regional sewage treatment plant; 2 major hotels, 2 department stores.
Medical facilities: 10 major hospitals, Univ. of California Medical School in nearby Davis.
Federal facilities: 2 large Air Force bases, Army depot, many regional federal offices.
Cultural facilities: Sacramento Earl Warren Community Center complex; Eagle Theater; symphony orchestra; ballet; Civic Theater; Crocker Art Gallery; California State Univ., Sacramento; McGeorge College of Law; Lincoln Univ. Law School, and 3 community colleges.
Other attractions: zoo, 95 public parks; 74 playgrounds; 12 public and 4 private golf courses, Sutter's Fort, State Capitol, Stanford Home, Pony Express Terminal, Fairytale Town, and Governor's Mansion; fishing, hunting, boating, camping, hiking, and skiing in nearby high Sierras; annual State Fair at Cal Expo.

History: founded by John Augustus Sutter Jr. in 1839; James Marshall discovered gold at Sutter's Mill, in 1848, 35 miles northeast, gateway to Mother Lode Country; Pony Express and Central Pacific Railroad which crossed the Sierra Nevada were part of early history.

St. Louis, Missouri

The World Almanac is sponsored in the St. Louis area by the Post-Dispatch, 900 N. 12th Boulevard, St. Louis, MO 63101; telephone (314) 621-1111; founded Dec. 12, 1878 by Joseph Pulitzer; circulation 274,307 daily, 460,-251 Sunday; editor and publisher Joseph Pulitzer Jr., managing editor Evarts A. Graham Jr., general manager Alex T. Primm, director of promotion and public affaris William J. Isam; major awards include 5 Pulitzer Prizes to the newspaper and 11 to staff members.

Population: 534,100 (city), 963,900 (county), 2,369,500 (metro), 10th in nation in payroll employment (915,-421 in April 1977).
Area: 4,935 sq. mi. (metro) just south of confluence of Missouri and Mississippi rivers.
Industry: 2d to Detroit in auto and truck assembly with Ford, GM, and Chrysler plants; McDonnell Douglas headquarters, aerospace manufacturer; other headquarters include nation's largest shoe company, Interco; Anheuser-Busch, world's largest brewer; Monsanto, General Dynamics, Ralston-Purina, Pet, Inc., Chromalloy American, Consolidated Aluminum, Emerson Electric, Brown Group; grain market with 81.6 million bushel annual yield; 3,106 manufacturing concerns employing 247,903 persons.
Commerce: $6.5 billion retail sales (1976 metro); $13,975 median family income; 192 banking institutions, total deposits $9.7 billion (1976).
Transportation: 10 major airlines with 6.8 million passenger movements (1976); 2d largest rail center in nation, 15 trunk line railroads; largest inland river port in nation; 9 major highways; 14 motor-bus lines; 350 motor freight lines.
Communications: 6 TV and 27 radio stations.
New construction: industrial and commercial contracts totaled $231 million (1976); residential $376 million; Mercantile Center, $150 million office, store and hotel complex; IBM, Equitable, First National Bank, $40 million; rail-to-barge coal terminal, $20 million; Sheraton Convention Center hotel, $12 million.
Medical facilities: 56 hospitals with 16,560 beds; Washington Univ. and St. Louis Univ. medical schools and affiliated hospitals provide specialized treatment in many areas.
Federal facilities: Military Personnel Records Center, Defense Mapping Agency Aerospace Center, Army Troop Support Command, Scott AFB.
Cultural facilities: Art Museum; Museum of Science and Natural History; restored historic homes; symphony orchestra; Mississippi River Festival near Edwardsville in summer; Municipal Theatre (Muny Opera) offers Broadway shows in big outdoor theater in Forest Park.
Educational facilities: 4 major universities: Washington, St. Louis, Univ. of Missouri at St. Louis, and Southern Illinois Univ. at Edwardsville; 5 private colleges; 3-branch junior college system.
Recreational facilities: Jefferson National Expansion Memorial with 630-foot Gateway Arch on riverfront; 1,326-acre Forest Park with 3 golf courses, ball fields, floral displays, zoo, McDonnell Planetarium, and Jefferson Memorial displaying Lindbergh trophies; National Museum of Transport; Six Flags Over Mid-America with world's tallest roller coaster; Grant's Farm with President Grant's cabin and animal displays; Missouri Botanical Garden with floral displays and advanced research display greenhouse, the Climatron.
Convention facilities: 12,632 hotel rooms; 90,000 sq. ft. exhibit space in Kiel Auditorium; 240,000 sq. ft. exhibit space in new Gateway Convention Center.
Sports: Busch Stadium home of the Cardinals baseball and football teams; St. Louis Blues (NHL); soccer Stars.
Other attractions: climate has 4 distinct seasons; spring and autumn warm, winters mild, summers hot with 90-degree temperatures; average temperature 55.9 degrees; average precipitation 35.9 inches; downtown area contains significant architecture including Eads Bridge, Old Post Office, Old Courthouse, Old Cathedral, Spanish International Pavilion which now contains a hotel tower; Louis Sullivan's Wainwright Building that is being refurbished, and restoration of Laclede's Landing area on riverfront adjoining Gateway Arch.
History: named for French King Louis IX by fur trapper Pierre Laclede whose trading post became major fur market and gateway to the West; starting point of Lewis and Clark expedition and other explorations.
Further information: Convention and Visitors Bureau, 500 N. Broadway, or Regional Commerce and Growth Assn., 10 S. Broadway, both St. Louis, Mo.

St. Paul, Minnesota

The World Almanac is sponsored in the St. Paul area by the St. Paul Dispatch and Pioneer Press, 55 E. 4th Street, St. Paul, MN 55101; phone (612) 222-5011; founded 1849 as Minnesota Pioneer by James Goodhue; circulation, Pioneer Press (morn) 102,128, Dispatch (eve) 119,433, Sunday Pioneer Press 240,044. Bernard H. Ridder Jr., president, Ridder Pub., Inc. and vice-chairman Knight-Ridder Newspapers, Inc.; publisher Thomas L. Carlin, executive editor John R. Finnegan, editor William G. Sumner. First newspaper published in Minnesota.

Population: 273,000 (city); 795,700 (metro), 2d in state, 47th in nation; total employed (city, 1976), 152,-137.
Area: 55 sq. mi. in eastern Minnesota on banks of Mississippi River close to Minnesota and Wisconsin vacationlands; state capital and Ramsey County seat.
Industry: West Publishing, world's largest law book publisher; international center for electronics and computer technology; Union Stockyards is largest livestock center in nation (3.2 million head in 1976). Headquarters 3M Co., Am. Hoist & Derrick Co., Burlington Northern RR, Univac, Brown & Bigelow, Whirlpool, Economics Laboratory, Hoerner-Waldorf Corp., St. Paul Companies (insurance).
Commerce: retail sales (1976) $2.1 billion; median household income, $15,093; 25 banks and 6 savings and loan associations.
Transportation: 5 major and 2 regional rail lines, Amtrak; 21 intercity truck firms, 37 terminals; 3 interstate bus lines; 730-mile public transit system; metropolitan airport, hub of 8 commercial airlines, headquarters for Northwest and North Central airlines, averages 350 air movements per day; Downtown Airport; 60 firms operate barges on Mississippi River, using a 9-foot channel downtown.
Communications: 4 commercial and 2 educational TV stations; 29 radio stations.
Medical facilities: 12 private hospitals; a 611 bed community hospital and research center: St. Paul-Ramsey Hospital.

Federal facilities: Ft. Snelling; area headquarters for HEW; district headquarters for IRS, FCC, Immigration and Naturalization Service; U.S. District Court.
Cultural facilities: Minnesota Symphony Orchestra; Univ. of Minnesota Institute of Agriculture, Hamline Univ., St. Thomas, St. Catherine, Bethel, Concordia, and Macalester colleges, and William Mitchell College of Law; $66 million city school system with 80 public schools and 61 private schools.
Recreational facilities: more than 900 lakes in metro area, 438 tennis courts, 148 swimming beaches, 513 parks, 50 golf courses, 27 ski centers; 52 neighborhood recreation centers, 35 miles of parkways, 100 miles of hiking and biking trails.
Convention facilities: Civic Center with 101,000 sq. ft. exhibit space, seating for 35,000 in 4 main buildings, 15 meeting halls; 50 hotels and motels.
Other attractions: Winter Carnival in Jan., Minnesota State Fair, Como Park Zoo and Conservatory; onyx statue of Indian God of Peace in City Hall, Minnesota Historical Society Museums, Arts & Science Center, Fort Snelling State Park.
History: once called "Pig's Eye" for first settler, Pierre "Pig's Eye" Parrant; changed to St. Paul when Father Lucien Galtier built St. Paul's Chapel 1841; became town 1847, city 1854.
Further information: St. Paul Area Chamber of Commerce, Osborn Bldg., St. Paul, MN 55102.

St. Petersburg, Florida

The World Almanac is sponsored in Florida's Suncoast area by The St. Petersburg Times and Evening Independent, 490 1st Avenue S., St. Petersburg, FL 33701; phone (813) 893-8111. Times founded 1884, Independent 1906; circulation, Times (morn) 193,189; Independent (evening) 35,252; Sunday Times 242,278. Nelson Poynter, chairman of the board, The Times Publishing Co.; Eugene C. Patterson, editor of The Times and president of The Times Publishing Co.; Robert Stiff, editor, The Independent; John B. Lake, executive vice president and publisher, The Times Publishing Co.

Population: 237,700 (city), 687,300 (Pinellas County), 1,427,100 (metro); Pinellas County March 1977 employment 212,900; unemployment 6.8%.
Industry and Commerce: tourism, over 3 million visited county in 1976, spending about $1.3 billion; industries include General Electric, Honeywell, Sperry, Milton Roy Co., Eckerd Drugs, Jim Walter Research, All-State Insurance regional office, U.S. Homes headquarters, Morgan Yacht. County 1976 retail sales $2.47 billion.
Transportation: U.S. 19, 41, and 98 link city to rest of Gulf Coast Florida; Interstates 275, 75, and 4 link St. Petersburg with Tampa, Orlando, and east coast; Tampa International Airport 25 minutes from downtown St. Petersburg; other airports are St. Petersburg-Clearwater International and Albert Whitted. Amtrak, Seaboard Coast Line railroads; Greyhound and Trailways bus lines.
Communications: 6 TV and 46 radio stations.
Convention and Tourist facilities: over 52,000 units can house 160,000 visitors; Bayfront Center seats 8,250 in arena, 2,250 in auditorium; Pinellas restaurants can serve 111,007 people at one time. Disney World 2 hours away.
Medical facilities: 13 major hospitals; Bay Pines veterans complex to be greatly expanded adding 1,150 new beds; All Children's Hospital.
Cultural facilities: Museum of Fine Arts, Gulf Coast Symphony, Historical Museum, community theatres, Eckerd College Free Institutions Forums, varied musical, theatrical, and dance events at Bayfront Center Complex.
Educational facilities: Univ. of South Florida's downtown Bayboro Campus to expand enrollment from 1,700 to 7,500; first building phase of $5 million is underway; Stetson College of Law, Eckerd College, St. Petersburg Junior College.
Recreational facilities: 76 parks on 1,800 acres, many with recreational buildings, pools, tennis courts, boat ramps, and picnic areas; municipal and private marinas; deep sea fishing, golf courses, baseball fields.
Sports: St. Louis Cardinals and New York Mets spring training; spectator sports include greyhound racing, baseball, jai alai, horse racing, NFL football, basketball, pro tennis, boat racing, soccer.
Additional information: St. Petersburg Chamber of Commerce, 225 4th Street S., St. Petersburg, FL 33701.

Salem, Oregon

The World Almanac is sponsored in the Salem area by the Statesman Journal Newspapers, 280 Church Street NE, P.O. Box 13009, Salem, OR 97309, (503) 399-6611; publisher of the morning Oregon Statesman and the evening Capital Journal; combined daily circulation 64,271; Sunday 54,372. N.S. Hayden, publisher; John H. McMillan, executive editor.

Population: 80,000 (city), 214,700 (metro)
Area: 32 sq. mi. on the Willamette River in the center of the bountiful Willamette Valley 50 miles south of Portland; 61 miles from Pacific Ocean; state capital and Marion County seat.
Industry: government (over 12,000 state employees), agriculture (over 100 crops), food processing — 2d in nation for fruit, berries, and vegetables; over 16 canneries produced over 16 million cases of canned goods and 260 million pounds of frozen foods; lumber and lumber products; manufacturing (batteries, radios, metal products, feeds, paints, textiles, food processing cans); pulp and paper mill.
Commerce: retail sales (1975) $540 million; avg. household income (1975) $12,342; 6 commercial banks, deposits (1976) $376 million; 7 savings & loan associations, deposits (1976) $335 million.
Transportation: 2 rail freight lines, Amtrak; Greyhound, Trailways bus lines, 11 truck lines, United Airlines.
Communications: one public TV, 6 radio stations, 2 daily newspapers, 1 farm weekly newspaper.
Medical facilities: hospital with 2 units, General and Memorial.
Cultural facilities: symphony orchestra, art association, little theatre, Bush House museum, Deepwood, Mission Mill museum, Northwest History collection, Willamette Univ., $10.5 million Civic Center.
Education: metro area includes 107 public schools — 87 elementary, 12 junior highs, 18 high schools, and 15 parochial schools; State Schools for the Blind and Deaf, Chemeketa Community College, Willamette Univ., Western Baptist Bible College, and Oregon College of Education.
Recreation: back-packing, fishing, golf, snow and water skiing, camping, 44 parks in 5 mile radius; hunting for deer, elk, and fowl; Bush Pasture Park; within one hour drive Mt. Hood, Detroit Lake, Oregon Coast, Mt. Jefferson; 9 golf courses in 15 mile radius; 70 tennis courts in area.
Sports: baseball-Salem Senators, Northwest League.
History: founded in 1840 by Methodist missionary, Jason Lee.
Further information: Chamber of Commerce, P.O. Box 231, Salem, OR 97308.

Salt Lake City, Utah

The World Almanac is sponsored in the Salt Lake City area by The Salt Lake Tribune, 143 S. Main Street, Salt Lake City, UT 84111; phone (801) 524-4545; founded Apr. 15, 1871; circulation, 109,151 daily, 178,885 Sunday; publisher John W. Gallivan; executive editor, Arthur C. Deck; 1957 Pulitzer Prize; civic projects: statewide civic beautification awards; Sub for Santa program; Community Christmas Tree; Arbor Day Tree Plantings; Spring Garden Festival ; Ski Race; No Champs Tennis Tournament.

Population: (1976 est.) 172,000 (city); 518,383 (county); 791,600 (metro); first in state; 48th in nation; 52% of state pop. lives within 30 miles; state capital and Salt Lake County seat.

Area: nestled in a vast valley (elev. 4,327 ft.) surrounded by Wasatch and Oquirrh mountains.

Industry: labor force 247,500; effective buying income, $3.5 billion (1976); per family income, $13,734; 46% of state construction in county; total construction value $355.7 million; employers are Hill AFB (30 miles north), local defense industries, and Kennecott Copper Corp., Utah Mining Division; metro area becoming major center for electronics; apparel manufacturing, mining, smelting, refining, distribution, warehousing center of Mountain West.

Transportation: 6 air lines, customs office, free trade zone, International Airport; geographic center of 11 western states; hub of central transcontinental highway system; 3 railroads, all major western truck, bus lines.

Communications: 2 daily newspapers; 3 commercial, 3 cable TV, one public TV, and 18 radio stations.

New construction: Bicentennial Center for the Cultural Arts; Sheraton Hotel; Empire State Bank; high-rise addition to Little America Motel; 2 major office buildings, small park.

Medical facilities: 10 hospitals, including Univ. of Utah Medical Center, major research in transplant surgery.

Educational facilities: Univ. of Utah; Westminster College; Utah Technical College.

Cultural facilities: Utah Symphony Orchestra among 12 best in U.S.; Mormon Tabernacle Choir, Ballet West, Utah Opera Co., Ririe-Woodbury Co., Repertory Dance Theatre, 2 cultural arts halls.

Other attractions: Temple Square, home of 3.5 million-member Church of Jesus Christ of Latter Day Saints (Mormon); Salt Palace Civic Auditorium; 700 acres in 22 parks, 25 playgrounds, 10 golf courses, 85 tennis courts; near Great Salt Lake (7 times more salty than ocean); Hogle Zoological Gardens, Kennecott Copper's Bingham mine; 4 well-defined seasons, mean annual temperature 51.0 degrees F.

Sports: 9 major ski resorts; Golden Eagles (Central Hockey League), Salt Lake Gulls, Triple A baseball; Bonneville Salt Flats.

History: founded July 24, 1847, by Brigham Young and contingent of pioneers.

Further information: Chamber of Commerce, 19 E. 2d So.; Utah Travel Council, Council Hall; Salt Lake Valley Visitors and Convention Bureau, all Salt Lake City, UT.

San Antonio, Texas

The World Almanac is sponsored in the San Antonio area by the S. A. Express (morning) and S. A. News (evening), P.O. Box 2171, San Antonio, TX 78297; tel. (512) 225-7411; circulation daily, Express 80,775, News 76,050, Sunday Express-News 165,898; chairman K. Rupert Murdoch, publisher and editor Charles O. Kilpatrick; Express-News Corp. is a division of News America, Inc.

Population: 797,197 city; 918,549 Bexar County; total employed, 355,750.

Area: Bexar County, 1,247 sq. mi., 2 1/2 hours from Gulf Coast and Mexican border.

Industry: 5 military bases include Kelly AFB, largest employer; fast-growing medical industry; diverse manufacturing, tourism, construction, trade, and service industries.

Commerce: center for 100 mile radius retail trade area, truck crops, livestock production; retail sales (1976), $4.6 billion.

Federal facilities: Kelly AFB, hq. AF Air Security Service; Randolph AFB, hq. AF Air Training Command & AF Personnel Center; Brooks AFB, hq. AF Aerospace Medical Division; Lackland AFB with Wilford Hall USAF Medical Center; Fort Sam Houston, hq. Fifth Army, & Army Health Services Command, Brooke Army Medical Center.

Medical facilities: University of Texas Medical, Dental, Nursing schools; Audie Murphy VA Hospital; Southwest Research Institute; Southwest Foundation of Research and Education.

Transportation: International Airport, 6 major airlines; 3 rail freight, 2 Amtrak lines.

Education facilities: Univ. of Texas at San Antonio; Trinity, St. Mary's, and Our Lady of the Lake universities; Incarnate Word College; 2 jr. colleges, San Antonio College, St. Philip's College; permanent extension of National University of Mexico.

Convention facilities: Convention Center with large arena, theater, exhibit, meeting space.

Cultural facilities: symphony orchestra; Institute of Texan Cultures, Mexican Cultural Institute, Witte Museum, McNay Art Institute.

Other attractions: historic Alamo, old Spanish missions of San Jose, Concepcion, Capistrano, Espada; Hemis Fair Plaza with 622-foot observation tower-restaurant; downtown River Walk; zoo; annual events: Fiesta San Antonio, Livestock Show & Rodeo, Folklife Festival; pro sports: Spurs (NBA); minor league baseball, Dodgers.

Further information: Greater San Antonio Chamber of Commerce, 602 E. Commerce, P. O. Box 1628, San Antonio, TX 78296.

San Bernardino, California

The World Almanac is sponsored in the San Bernardino area by the Sun-Telegram, 399 North D Street, San Bernardino, CA 92401, phone (714) 889-9666; Telegram founded 1873, Sun 1894; daily circulation 74,039, Sunday 80,671; member Gannett chain; editor-publisher James Geehan, advertising director William Ridenour, managing editor Kent Freeland.

Population: 103,600 (city), 1,262,900 (2-county metro area); 43d in state, 148th in nation; total employed 41,221.

Area: 47.22 sq. mi. at base of Cajon Pass, 58 miles east of Los Angeles; San Bernardino County seat.

Industry: 168 business and industrial firms including Culligan, Edginton Oil, Fleetwood Enterprises, Hanford Foundry, Knudsen Dairy, Lifetime Foam, Mode O'Day, Pepsi Cola and Seven-Up bottling plants, Santa Fe Railway, TRW Systems.

Commerce: trading center for 20,189 sq. mi. San Bernardino county, largest in the nation; retail sales (1976) $624 million; 7 banks, 22 branches; 11 savings and loan assns.; 2 major shopping center complexes, each parking over 5,000 cars.

Transportation: Santa Fe, Southern Pacific, and Union Pacific rail lines, Amtrak; Greyhound and

Continental bus lines; major interstate highways leading from Mexico to Canada and West to East Coast; municipal airport and nearby Ontario International Airport, over 1.4 million passengers (1976).
Communications: 15 radio and one VHF educational TV station; access to 5 Los Angeles channels.
Medical facilities: 3 major hospitals with 995 beds; major research and training center for heart surgery and hip and knee replacement surgery.
Federal facilities: Norton Air Force Base.
Cultural facilities: symphony orchestra, Civic Light Opera, nearby Redlands Bowl (summer concerts); National Orange Show with orange festival every spring; Convention Center-Exhibit Hall complex.
Educational facilities: California State College, junior college, 3 major universities nearby.
History: founded 1852 by Mormons who purchased land from Spanish grant holders.
Further information: Chamber of Commerce, 546 West 6th Street, San Bernardino, CA 92401.

San Diego, California

The World Almanac is sponsored in San Diego by The San Diego Union and Evening Tribune (Copley Newspapers), P.O. Box 191, San Diego, CA 92112; (714) 299-3131; Union founded 1868 (pioneer daily of Southwest); circulation, Union (morn) 190,732, Tribune (eve) 128,957, Sunday Union 311,309; publisher Helen K. Copley, general manager Al De Bakcsy, Union editor Gerald L. Warren, Tribune editor Fred Kinne.

Population: 797,207 (1977, city); 1,656,756 (county); 11th in U.S. (official state estimate); total civilian employment, 577,000.
Area: (county) 4,255 sq. mi.; 70 mi. Pacific Coast, San Clemente to Mexican border.
Industry: tourism, manufacturing, military, and agriculture; manufactured products earn $3 billion a year; non-military payroll $4.1 billion, military $875.2 million; tourist spending over $600 million; corporations with bases or divisions include Bendix, Burroughs, Control Data, Cubic, General Dynamics, Gulf, Honeywell, International Harvester's Solar division, NCR Corp., Pacific Southwest Airlines, Rohr, Sea World, Teledyne Ryan, TraveLodge, Wickes Van Camp sea food, Foodmaker (Jack-in-the-Box); aerospace, rapid transit design and manufacture, oceanography, nuclear energy, medicine important; also shipbuilding, tuna fishing, clothing, ocean shipping; among top 20 counties in farm products (avocados, cut flowers, eggs); Marine Corps Recruit Depot, Naval Training Center, North Island and Miramar Naval Air Stations, Naval Electronics Lab and Undersea Center, Marine Corps base at Camp Pendleton.
Transportation: Freeway system, state's 2d largest; urban transit service, 35-cent fare, Mexican border to 35 miles north; Amtrak, 9 airlines, bus lines; primary airport Lindbergh Field.
Communications: Some 30 TV and radio stations.
Medical facilities: Salk Institute for Biological Studies, Scripps Clinic & Research Foundation; Naval Hospital; many hospitals.
Educational and Cultural facilities: San Diego State Univ., U.S. International Univ., Univ. of San Diego, Univ. of California, San Diego (3 colleges and Scripps Institution of Oceanography), Point Loma College; symphony; Old Globe Theatre (functioning reproduction of Shakespeare's Globe Theatre); opera; ballet; Fine Arts and Timken Galleries; La Jolla Museum of Contemporary Art.
Other attractions: world famous zoo and wild animal park; Balboa Park, central 1,400 acres containing museums, zoo, Fleet Space Theatre (computerized planetarium), many other attractions; Mission Bay Park includes Sea World; "Old San Diego" State Historical Park; "Star of India" ship-museum; visits to neighboring Mexico (Tijuana); 70 miles of beaches.
Sports: NFL Chargers, NL Padres, WHA Mariners; tennis, soccer, volleyball teams; racing at Del Mar, Caliente.
History: area discovered 1542 by Cabrillo, founded in 1769 by Father Serra.
Other attractions: climate sunny; summer and winter resort; average temp. 68° in summer, 57° in winter, rainfall mainly December to March; famous "place names" include La Jolla (part of city of San Diego); 70 golf courses, including Torrey Pines; large convention facilities; off-shore "whale watching."
Further information: San Diego Chamber of Commerce, 233 A Street, San Diego, CA 92101.

San Francisco, California

The World Almanac is sponsored in the San Francisco-Oakland area by The San Francisco Examiner, P.O. Box 3100, Rincon Annex, San Francisco, CA 94119; (415) 781-2424; founded June 12, 1865; circulation daily Examiner, 151,447; Sunday Examiner & Chronicle, 641,112; president, R. A. Hearst; editor and publisher, Reg Murphy; general manager, Frank Huntress; major awards: Pulitzer Prize, Freedoms Foundation; Examiner sponsors Examiner Games, Golden Gloves, Distinguished Ten, Bay to Breakers Race.

Population: 661,100, 4th in state, 13th in nation; total employed: 250,000.
Area: 44.6 sq. mi. on the northern tip of a peninsula. San Francisco County seat.
Industry: food products, printing, publishing, fabricated metal products; west's financial capital and administrative center for many of the nation's leading corporations; West Coast operations' headquarters for a majority of the federal agencies; finance, insurance, and real estate; chief port of the Pacific Coast.
Commerce: wholesale-retail trade employment, 92,900; services 111,300; manufacturing 48,100; total retail outlets 21,978, taxable sales $3 billion; 40 banks with 157 branches; 25 savings and loans with 39 branches; total deposits in banks $19.2 billion.
Transportation: 25 major airlines serve the Bay Area; International Airport processed 18.7 million passengers, 677 million lbs. of freight (1976); Municipal Railway (intra-city); AC-Transit and Bay Area Rapid Transit System (BART) to East Bay cities; Greyhound bus and Southern Pacific Railroad to Peninsula areas; Golden Gate Bridge District bus and ferry service to Marin County; Port of San Francisco services available: LASH, BULK, general cargo, containerization and barge service.
Communications: 2 major newspapers; 118 others serving the Bay Area; 45 radio stations, 7 TV channels received directly, one TV cable system.
Medical facilities: 21 general hospitals with over 6,516 total beds; and 5 specialty hospitals with over 1,935 beds; 3,033 physicians/surgeons and 772 dentists; Univ. of Cal. Medical Center, with 42 buildings, is a general teaching and research institute and is the largest kidney transplant center in the world.
Cultural facilities: San Francisco Opera, Spring Opera, Western Opera Theater, symphony, ballet, Civic Light Opera, American Conservatory Theater, Japanese Cultural Center, Chinese Cultural Center, International Film Festival, 3 museums, 29 libraries, and 540 churches.
Educational facilities: 103 public elementary schools with a total enrollment of 35,439 and 11 junior high and 18 high schools with a combined enrollment of

38,859 students; Univ. of California, San Francisco; California State Univ., Univ. of San Francisco, Lone Mountain College, and City College of San Francisco.
Recreational facilities: 120 parks and many mini-parks, 78 playgrounds, 6 golf courses, numerous tennis courts, 10 swimming pools, 5 1/2 miles of ocean beach, one lake, one fishing pier, Marina small craft harbor and 3 yacht clubs.
Convention facilities: 124 hotels and motels with over 20,000 rooms.
Sports: Candlestick Park, home of the NL Giants and the NFL 49ers.
Other attractions: zoo and 1,013-acre Golden Gate Park containing the California Academy of Sciences, De Young Museum, Japanese Tea Garden, and Arboretum; cable cars, Fisherman's Wharf, Chinatown, the Ferry Building, Coit Tower, the Palace of Fine Arts, and Grace Cathedral.
History: San Francisco Bay discovered 1769 by Sgt. Jose Ortega; pueblo of Yerba Buena established 1834, renamed San Francisco on January 3, 1847; incorporated April 15, 1850.
Further information: Chamber of Commerce, 465 California Street, San Francisco, CA 94104.

San Jose, California

The World Almanac is sponsored in the San Jose area by The Mercury and News, 750 Ridder Park Drive, San Jose, CA 95190; (408) 289-5000; Mercury founded June 20, 1851; News July 23, 1883; combined daily circulation 202,590: Sunday Mercury News; 231,446; publisher P. Anthony Ridder; editor Larry Jinks; president Joseph B. Ridder.

Population: 575,100 (city), 1,202,065 (metro area coextensive with Santa Clara County); total employed 529,000 (metro, Dec. '76).
Area: broad alluvial 832,256-acre valley at south end of San Francisco Bay.
Industry: largest county in northern Cal. for manufacturing employment and total wages; called "Silicone Valley" due to high technology semi-conductor and other electronics firms; IBM, Fairchild Semi-conductor, Hewlett-Packard, Varian Associates, Intel Corp., National Semi-conductor; diversity shown by Ford Motor Co., Lockheed Missiles & Space, FMC Corp., Syntex Laboratories; county a major producer of cut flowers.
Commerce: leading retail trade center of northern Cal., $3.62 billion in sales; 137 shopping centers; 4th nationally in median household income among U.S. metro areas with 2 million and over population, 76% of households earn $10,000 and over annually, 58% earn $15,000 & over annually (metro).
Transportation: Municipal Airport served by 13 airlines; highway system interconnected with interstate in north-south, east-west directions; Southern Pacific and Western Pacific railroads.
Education: San Jose State, Santa Clara, and Stanford universities, plus community colleges have total enrollments of 128,256; 37% of adult pop. is college educated (metro).
Cultural facilities: symphony, First State Capital Museum, Rosicrucian Egyptian Temple, Science Museum and Planetarium, De Saisset Gallery & Museum, Villa Montalvo estate and arboretum, City Gallery, Triton Museum of Art, New Almaden Museum.
Sports: Earthquakes (soccer); Missions, farm club for Oakland A's; Sunbirds, women's professional softball; 8 reservoirs with boat ramps, 2 with camping; outlet to S.F. Bay for ocean sports.
Other attractions: Japanese Tea Gardens, Lick Observatory, Winchester Mystery House.
History: founded 1777, first civil settlement in Cal.; county is one of the original 27 in Cal.; first public school in state, San Jose Granary, 1795; first state capitol, Dec. 15, 1849.
Further information: Chamber of Commerce Metro-San Jose, One Paseo de San Antonio, San Jose, CA 95113, (408) 998-7000.

San Juan, Puerto Rico

The World Almanac is sponsored in Puerto Rico by the San Juan Star, GPO Box 4187, San Juan, PR 00936; telephone (809) 782-4200; founded Nov. 2, 1959; circulation 42,000 daily, 43,000 Sunday; president and general manager John A. Zerbe Jr.; vice president and editor Andrew T. Viglucci; major awards include 1961 Pulitzer Prize for editorial writing; APME citations 1960, 1965; staff awards include 1970 LAPA Mergenthaler Award, 1972 Overseas Press Club Award; National Spelling Bee 1975 champion.

Population: 512,300 (city), 1,027,222 (metro area) first in commonwealth.
Area: 47 sq. mi. in Caribbean, capital city.
Industry: seat of Puerto Rico's tourism industry with 19 luxury hotels and several dozen high rise condominiums. City is also the commercial and shipping hub of the island and is a major stop for cruise ships plying the Caribbean. Major industries are electronics, pharmaceuticals, and an expanding petrochemical industry serviced by 3 major refineries. Petrochemical industry represents $1.5 billion in investments. Center of island's rum industry with the Bacardi distillery on San Juan Bay, the largest in the world. More than 75 per cent of all rum sold in U.S. is Puerto Rican rum.
Transportation: San Juan International Airport handles more than 500,000 passengers monthly with 3 major U.S. airlines and 10 foreign lines. Isla Grande Airport handles small aircraft traffic.
Education: seat of the Rio Piedras campus of the University of Puerto Rico, the public university system, InterAmerican University, College of the Sacred Heart, UPR Medical Sciences campus and UPR Law School, World University, and several junior and regional colleges.
Federal facilities: Ft. Buchanan army base with 9-hole golf course on grounds.
Cultural facilities and events: The Casals Festival, guided for 15 years by the late Maestro Casals, is an annual June event bringing together some of the world's finest musicians; annual San Juan Carnival, last week in June; the Puerto Rico Institute of Culture is housed in a restored Dominican convent; El Morro, the Spanish-built fortress that guards the entrance to San Juan Harbor; numerous art museums in Old San Juan; the Puerto Rico Symphony Orchestra in concerts spread over the year; the capitol building and governor's mansion.
Convention facilities: new Condado Convention Center built by state government seats 5,000 for meetings, 3,000 for meals.
New construction: Old City restoration program, Ramada Inn; banking district located in Hato Rey, Melia Puerto Rico Hotel in Isla Verde. Expansion of Plaza las Americas shopping center to house Sears Roebuck, Inc.; new Banco de San Juan multi-story office bldg.
Sports: Hiram Bithorn Stadium, winter baseball, track, and outdoor events; Roberto Clemente Coliseum, basketball, boxing, and indoor events; soccer, cockfighting arenas (legal); 1979 PanAm Games.
History: discovered by Columbus on his 2d voyage to the New World in 1493, colonized by Juan Ponce de Leon, Puerto Rico's first Spanish governor; since

1952 a commonwealth freely associated with the United States. Free market with U.S. and same currency, common citizenship.

Further information: Chamber of Commerce, 100 Tetuan Street, Old San Juan; Dept. of Tourism, Banco de Ponce Bldg., Hato Rey, PR.

Santa Ana, California

See Orange County, California

Saskatoon, Saskatchewan, Canada

The World Almanac is sponsored in northern Saskatchewan by the Saskatoon Star-Phoenix, 204 Fifth Avenue North, Saskatoon, Sask., S7K 2P1; (306) 652-9200; Daily Star and Phoenix, founded in 1906 and 1902 respectively, merged in 1928 into the Star-Phoenix; circulation daily, 50,491; publisher Michael C. Sifton, executive vice president James K. Struthers.

Population: 136,000, 2d in prov., 15th in nation.

Area: 38.5 sq. mi. land, 1.5 sq. mi. water, on S. Sask. River, center of agricultural province.

Commerce: retail, wholesale, service, distribution hub for 400,000 in 100-mi. radius trading area; world's richest, largest potash reserves; meat packing, grain milling dominant; garment and electronics newest; base for northern mineral explorations; retail sales (1976) $496 million.

Transportation: 2 railways, 2 airlines, 2 bus lines, air and bus terminals on Yellowhead Highway, easiest access through Rockies from prairies to West Coast ports.

Communications: One daily, 2 TV, 5 radio stations, one farm weekly, one community weekly.

Medical facilities: 3 major hospitals, 6 nursing homes; Univ. hospital known for kidney transplants, open-heart surgery; $26 million expansion under way.

Cultural facilities: $7 million, 2,000-seat Centennial Auditorium, convention facilities for over 1,800; Mendel Art Gallery/Civic Conservatory; Western Development Museum houses N. America's largest display of antique cars, farm implements and 1910 Pioneer Village; theme pavilion for summer fair.

Education: Univ. of Sask. (17,500 students), famed for agriculture, space, Arctic, physics, medicine, veterinary college; Kelsey Institute for Applied Arts and Science (4,700 students); School for Deaf.

Recreation: 1,456 acres parkland; wild animal farm; man-made ski mountain; camping, fishing.

History: founded 1883 as temperance colony; incorporated 1906; battle sites of 1885 Riel Rebellion

Further information: Board of Trade, Bessborough Hotel, Saskatoon, Sask. S7K 3GB.

Savannah, Georgia

The World Almanac is sponsored in the Savannah area by the Savannah News-Press, 111 West Bay Street, Savannah, GA 31401, phone (912) 236-9511, publisher of the Savannah Morning News and Evening Press; combined circulation 79,682 daily, Sunday 72,000. Donald E. Harwood, general manager; Wallace M. Davis Jr., executive editor, Michael Boisclair, advertising director.

Population: 118,240 (city), 203,092 (metro).

Area: 37 sq. mi. on Savannah River, 18 mi. from Atlantic Ocean; Chatham County seat.

Industry: world's largest pulp-to-paper container plant owned by Union Camp Corp.; Savannah Sugar Refining Corp. nation's 3d largest seller; jet aircraft manufacturer (Grumman American Aviation); tea packaging (Tetley), fertilizer materials, ship repair, titanium dioxide production (American Cyanamid).

Commerce: hub of "Coastal Empire" economic center of 8 Georgia and 3 South Carolina counties; The city's economic lifeline is Georgia's gateway to world trade and the Southeast's leading foreign trade port between Baltimore and New Orleans; served by 83 steamship lines, 43 deep water terminals; retail sales (1975) $817 million, 7 commercial banks, 3 savings and loan associations.

Transportation: 2 rail freight lines, Seaboard Coastline, and Southern; Amtrak; Greyhound, Trailways bus lines, 74 truck lines; Delta, National airlines.

Communications: Savannah News-Press Inc. (daily and Sunday); 3 weekly papers The Herald, The Tribune, and Savannah Journal; 5 TV and 14 radio stations; 138,315 telephones in service in Savannah area in 1975.

New construction: Candler Hospital, Truman Parkway, Riverfront Restoration, Broughton Street Revitalization, Savannah Beach Restoration, Ga. Port Authority's implementation of $52 million port expansion program.

Medical facilities: 7 hospitals.

Federal facilities: Fort Stewart/Hunter assigned the 24th Infantry Division, 17,000 troops; Fort Stewart is located on one of the largest military reservations in the country and the largest east of the Mississippi, some 280,000 acres 35 mi. south of Savannah.

Cultural facilities: symphony orchestra, ballet guild, dance theater, Telfair Academy of Arts and Sciences; maritime museum Fort Pulaski National Monument, science museum, military museum, $10.4 million Civic Center.

Education facilities: Armstrong State College and Savannah State College, both units of Univ. system of Georgia, 4-year institutions; 60 public, 3 vocational-tech, 18 parochial, 10 private, 3 business schools.

Recreation: 14 theaters; 6 golf courses; 33 public tennis courts; 32 squares, park and playgrounds; 3 sports fields; 2 recreation centers; 2 stadiums.

Sports: Savannah Braves baseball, Southern League; Savannah Speedway.

Annual events: St. Patrick's Day parade, Oktober Festival, Blessing of the Fleet, Night in Old Savannah, Tour of Homes, Camellia Show, arts festival.

History: mother city of Georgia, last of 13 original colonies; founded Feb. 2, 1733 by James Oglethorpe and a band of 120 followers; America's first planned city; much of old city is a national historic landmark, largest in country.

Further information: Chamber of Commerce, P.O. Box 530, Savannah, GA 31402.

Schenectady, New York

Population: 77,958; total employed, 38,000.

Area: 11.3 sq. mi., 13 miles northwest of Albany, Schenectady County seat.

Industry: General Electric, employing about 27,000, is largest employer. Other firms manufacture industrial chemicals, pollution control and measuring devices, and military vehicles.

Commerce: there are 2,100 retail establishments with net sales of over $200 million; 9 banks with total deposits over $500 million.

Cultural facilities: Union College, Schenectady Com-

munity College, 66 homes and buildings built between 1700-1850; the Schenectady Museum and County Historical Society.
Other attractions: 5 hospitals, 87-acre Industrial Park; 65 schools; 175 churches; 25 parks, 5 golf courses, 30 tennis courts, 18 playgrounds.
Further information: Schenectady Chamber of Commerce, 101 State Street, Schenectady, NY 12305.

Seattle, Washington

The World Almanac is sponsored in the Seattle area by The Seattle Times, Fairview Avenue N. & John Street, P.O. Box 70, Seattle, WA 98111; phone (206) 464-2111; founded 1896 by Alden J. Blethen; circulation 237,454 daily, 327,490 Sunday; publisher John A. Blethen; president W. J. Pennington; vice president and general manager Harold G. Fuhrman.

Population: 504,400 (city), 1,431,500 (metro); first in state, 23d in nation; total employed (metro) 653,800.
Area: 91.6 sq. mi. between Puget Sound and Lake Washington; King County seat.
Industry: headquarters for Boeing, 48,000 employes, world's largest manufacturer of commercial jet aircraft; Port of Seattle has $800 million current value of properties and facilities including Seattle-Tacoma airport; nation's 4th largest containerized-shipping seaport; area has 2,313 employer units; major industries are transportation products, retail trade, shipbuilding, wood products, and food products.
Commerce: business center for western Wash. and Alaska; major import-export center for Far East; total retail sales (1976) $5.24 billion; per capita income (1976) $6,160; 29 commercial banks.
Transportation: 3 transcontinental railroads, Amtrak; International Airport served by 12 scheduled airlines, 6 commuter airlines, handled 6.8 million passengers (1976); ferries serve Puget Sound, Canada, and Alaska.
Communications: 4 daily newspapers in metro area; 6 TV, 26 AM and 20 FM stations.
Medical facilities: 26 hospitals, including Univ. of Wash. Health Sciences Center and Fred Hutchinson Cancer Research Center.
Educational facilities: Three 4-year colleges: Univ. of Wash., Seattle Univ., and Seattle Pacific Univ.; 7 community colleges.
Federal facilities: 13th Naval Dist. Hdqts.; Pacific Marine center, National Oceanic & Atmospheric Admin.
Cultural facilities: symphony orchestra, opera association, art museum and 10 other museums, 2 professional theater companies.
Recreation: major boating center; several nearby ski areas; Mt. Rainier, North Cascades, and Olympic National parks within 2-hour drive.
Sports: NBA SuperSonics; WTT Sea-Port Cascades (tennis); Kingdome, concrete-dome stadium, home of NFL Seahawks, American League Mariners, and North American Soccer League Sounders.
Other attractions: $50 million Seattle Center, site of 1962 world's fair, has 14,000-seat coliseum, opera house, playhouse, arena, Space Needle, and Pacific Science Center.
History: settled 1851, named for an Indian chief who befriended the settlers; virtually destroyed by fire in 1889, quickly rebuilt; Alaska Gold Rush of 1897 spurred growth and propelled Seattle toward its status as the Northwest's principal city.
Further information: Chamber of Commerce, 215 Columbia Street, Seattle, WA 98104, or Convention and Visitors Bureau, 1815 7th Avenue, 98101.

Shreveport, Louisiana

The World Almanac is sponsored in the Shreveport area by the Shreveport Journal (eves. except Sunday), 222 Lake Street, Shreveport, LA 71130; phone (318) 424-0373; founded 1895 as The Judge, given present name in 1897; circulation 38,000; publisher Charles T. Beaird, editor Stanley R. Tiner.

Population: 195,783 (1975); total employed approximately 130,000.
Area: 85 sq. mi., on Red River in Caddo Parish, northwest Louisiana.
Industry: oil, gas, timber, agriculture, largest manufacturer of telephones in the world, steel products, glassware, car batteries; Barksdale Air Force Base across Red River in Bossier Parish.
Commerce: wholesale-retail center for Ark.-La.-Tex. area; retail sales (1975) over one billion dollars; total bank deposits $1.4 billion; 11 banks, 2 savings and loan companies.
Transportation: 6 railroads, 4 airlines, one bus line, 16 motor-freight lines; Interstate Hwy. 20; north-south toll road and Red River barge traffic proposed for 1980s.
Communications: 3 TV and 9 radio stations.
Cultural facilities: State Exhibit Museum and Planetarium, 2 art galleries; Norton Arts Gallery and Barnwell Memorial Garden and Arts Center, symphony orchestra, civic opera, 5 colleges, 5 community theaters, headquarters for the American Rose Society, garden center, Men's Camellia Club.
Other attractions: Shreve Square, restoration project downtown on riverfront; Louisiana State Fair; Holiday-in-Dixie spring festival; 12 hospitals, LSU Medical School, speech and hearing center.
Sports: college basketball (Centenary College); Louisiana Downs race track across Red River in Bossier Parish, 7 golf courses, Cross Lake 8,960 acres, boating-fishing waters, skiing, and yacht club.
History: founded 1836 as Shreve Town, named for Capt. Henry M. Shreve who cleared massive logjam on river; starting point for the Texas Trail during westward expansion; Louisiana capital for 2 years during Civil War; 3d largest city in Louisiana.

Sioux Falls, South Dakota

The World Almanac is sponsored in the Sioux Falls area by the Sioux Falls Argus-Leader, 200 S. Minnesota Avenue, Sioux Falls, SD 57102, tel. (605) 336-1130; a Gannett newspaper; founded 1885; circulation 46,930 daily, 54,628 Sunday; publisher Dean C. Smith, managing editor Larry Fuller.

Population: 85,000 (city), 112,000 (metro area) according to city planning dept. est.; largest in state.
Area: 37 square miles in southeastern South Dakota at junction of interstates 29 and 90; Minnehaha County seat.
Federal facilities: Earth Resources Observation Systems Data Center of the U.S. Dept. of Interior.
Industry & Commerce: located in the nation's breadbasket, Sioux Falls Stockyards is the 3d largest public market in the U.S. John Morrell & Co. is the

largest of 170 manufacturers. There are 27 banks with clearings in excess of 1.76 billion in 1976, and 5 savings and loan associations. Wholesale and retail center for South Dakota, parts of Minnesota and Iowa; yearly retail sales over $390 million, wholesale over $750 million; average spendable family income is $9,222, average family income $15,467.
Transportation: served by 3 major rail lines, 2 bus lines, 5 major highways. Joe Foss Field with modern terminal is within 2 miles of business district, has 3 major airlines offering 34 daily flights.
Medical facilities: 4 hospitals including Royal C. Johnson Veterans Hospital and Crippled Children's Hospital and School.
Communications: 2 TV and 12 radio stations.
Culture & Education: public library, convention center, Civic Fine Arts Center, Sioux Falls Symphony, Community Playhouse. Augustana College, Sioux Falls College, North American Baptist Seminary, the South Dakota School for the Deaf, a vocational school, 2 business colleges, 2 nurses training schools, 3 high schools, 29 public, 9 parochial schools, 91 churches.
Further information: Chamber of Commerce, 101 W. 9th, Sioux Falls, SD 57102.

Springfield, Illinois

The World Almanac is sponsored in the Springfield area by The State Journal-Register (morn. and eve.), oldest newspaper in Illinois, 313 S. 6th Street, P.O. Box 219, Springfield, IL 62705; (217) 544-5711; circulation, 72,643; John P. Clarke, publisher; Edward H. Armstrong, editor; Patrick Coburn, managing editor.

Population: 97,250 (city), 181,600 (metro), 4th in state; total employed, 86,800.
Area: 42.23 square miles on Sangamon River in center of state; state capital and Sangamon County seat.
Commerce: state and federal offices; 11 banks, 8 savings and loan assns; 8 insurance company home offices; 130 national, regional, and state assns.; 32 civic clubs; 53 social service orgs.; 275 women's organizations; annual retail sales of $566 million.
Transportation: 4 railroads; 41 truck carriers; one airport; nearby barge facilities.
Communications: one TV station and 7 radio stations.
Medical facilities: 3 hospitals with 1,434 beds, 296 doctors, 28 clinics, 20 nursing homes; Springfield Regional Trauma Center.
Cultural facilities: municipal band, opera, symphony, chorus; Theatre Guild; state museum; Lincoln historical sites; New Salem State Park; Old State Capitol; art assns.; summer theater; Illinois Country Opry; Clayville renovated stagecoach stop; arts & crafts festivals; Oliver Parks Telephone Museum; Saddle Tramp Gap western ranch; new Lincoln Library; Lincoln Memorial Garden; Nelson Recreation Center; Henson Robinson Children's Zoo; convention center under construction.
Education: Sangamon State Univ.; Lincoln Land Community College; Springfield College in Illinois; Southern Illinois Univ. School of Medicine; new Capital Area Vocational School.
Recreation: 33 parks; swimming, boating, skiing at 5 parks on Lake Springfield; public golf, tennis.
Special events: Ill. State Fair; Old Capitol Art Fair; NCAA college division world series; International Carillon Festival; Midwest Charity Horse Show; The LPGA Rail Muscular Dystrophy Golf Classic.

Springfield, Massachusetts

The World Almanac is sponsored in the Springfield area by The Springfield Union, Sunday Republican, and Daily News, 1860 Main Street, Springfield, MA 01101; phone (413) 787-2411. Union founded 1864; Republican 1824; Daily News 1880; circulation, Union, 75,002; Republican 140,026; Daily News, 79,188; president, Sidney R. Cook; publisher, David Starr; Union-Repbulican editor Arnold S. Friedman; Daily News editor Richard C. Garvey.

Population: 168,785 (city); 536,898 (metro); 3d in state (city), 4th in New England, 84th in U.S. 65,665 employed in city.
Area: 33.1 sq. mi. in SW part of state; I-91 skirts city; Hampden County seat.
Industry: 235 manufacturing plants produce boxes, children's games, wallets, auto tires, handguns, plastics, envelopes, hair shampoo, chemicals, paper; major employers Monsanto, Milton Bradley, Smith & Wesson, Breck.
Commerce: metro retail sales, $1.55 billion; avg. household spendable income $14,980; Mass Mutual Life Ins. Co., number 10 in U.S.; Baystate West, a combined highrise shopping mall, office-hotel complex.
Transportation: Amtrak, 2 rail lines, 5 bus lines, Bradley International Airport (Hartford-Springfield) 18 miles south, major truck depot.
Communications: 3 TV, 9 radio stations.
Medical facilities: 6 major hospital complexes.
Educational facilities: college belt of N.E.; North Adams State, Williams, Smith, Hampshire, Amherst, Univ. of Massachusetts at Amherst, Mount Holyoke, Our Lady of the Elms, American International, Springfield, Western New England and Law School, Westfield State, Greenfield, and Holyoke community colleges, Springfield Technical Community College.
Cultural facilities: Stage West Theater; quadrangle complex, 2 museums of art; library, natural history museum including planetarium; 146 churches and 7 synagogues; Tanglewood Festival, 155 parks; civic center.
Sports: Indians (AHL) hockey; Basketball Hall of Fame.
History: founded 1636 by William Pynchon; first U.S. musket developed at city's armory (now a U.S. landmark) 1795; Springfield rifle developed in 1903 and produced here as was the Garand M-1 rifle.
Further information: Chamber of Commerce, 1500 Main Street, Springfield, MA 01101.

Syracuse, New York

The World Almanac is sponsored in the Syracuse area by the Herald-Journal, Clinton Square, Syracuse, NY, 13201; telephone (315) 473-7700; founded Jan. 15, 1877, by Arthur Jenkins; circulation 123,583 daily, 245,507 Sunday Herald-American Post-Standard; publisher, Stephen Rogers; editor, William D. Cotter; sponsors camp scholarships and Christmas toy fund.

Population: 197,297 (city), 636,507 (metro), 5th in state, 66th in nation; 260,000 employed.
Area: 25.82 sq. mi. near center of state; interstate routes 90 and 81 intersect at Syracuse.

Industry: some 500 manufacturing plants produce electrical and non-electrical machinery, primary metals, food, transportation equipment, chemicals, pharmaceuticals, paper, candles, china; new $100 million Schlitz brewery, world's largest ever built at one time, opened in 1975 in suburban Lysander as did major Miller brewery north of city; major employers: General Electric, Carrier Corp., Crucible Steel, Crouse-Hinds, Allied Chemical.
Commerce: retail sales (1976 est.) $2.1 billion; average household spendable income (1976 est.) $13,730.
Transportation: 2 rail freight lines, Amtrak; 3 bus lines, 160 truck lines; 4 airlines.
Communications: 4 TV, 14 radio stations.
Medical facilities: 4 major hospital complexes.
Cultural facilities: Syracuse Univ., State Univ. College of Environmental Science and Forestry, and Le Moyne, Maria Regina, and Onondaga community colleges; Everson Museum of Art; symphony; $22 million county office-cultural center.
Sports: Syracuse Univ. football; Chiefs (baseball).
History: first explored 1615 by French; salt deposits led to area development, known as "Salt City;" "crossroads" since Indian days; became city 1847.
Further information: Chamber of Commerce, One MONY Plaza, Syracuse, NY 13202.

Tallahassee, Florida

The World Almanac is sponsored in the north Florida-south Georgia Panhandle area by The Tallahassee Democrat, 227 N. Magnolia Drive, Tallahassee, FL 32302; (904) 599-2100, founded 1905; circulation 42,082 (eve), 47,492 Sunday; member Knight-Ridder Newspapers, Inc., W. H. Harwell Jr. president and general manager; Malcolm B. Johnson, vice president and editor, Richard Oppel, executive editor.

Population: 83,400 (city) 145,000 (metro); total employment 65,000.
Area: 26.14 sq. mi. between Gulf of Mexico and Georgia line; state capital and Leon County seat.
Commerce: 44% of economic base is state and local government; small manufacturers; agriculture only 1.1% of economic base; retail-wholesale center serving 17 county area; 2 shopping malls and 10 shopping centers containing 232 outlets; retail sales (1976) $515 million; effective buying income per household is $15,346, 3d highest in state; 15 commercial banks (resources, $349 million) and 3 savings & loan (resources $260 million).
Transportation: 3 major airlines, 2 commuter flight services, one railroad, 5 motor carriers.
Communications: 11 radio, 10 TV stations by cable.
Medical facilities: major hospital, retardation hospital, university hospital.
Recreational facilities: 5 recreation centers, 10 playgrounds, 45 ball fields, 21 tennis courts; salt water fishing in Gulf of Mexico, bass fishing in Lake Jackson; deer, dove, quail, duck, geese hunting; 4 golf courses, PGA Tallahassee Open Invitational.

Other attractions: college athletic events at Florida State Univ., and Florida A&M; symphony, ballet, repertory theater, opera, touring plays, and art exhibits; 1845 historic capitol and 22-story capitol tower; Apalachicola National Forest; Junior Museum; Wakulla Springs, Maclay Gardens State Park, LeMoyne Art Gallery, Natural Bridge State Historic Memorial, Florida State Univ. "Flying High" Circus.

History: established as state capital 1823; Tallahassee means "old town" or "deserted fields" in Creek; area prospered with large plantations and antebellum mansions, many still standing.
Further information: Chamber of Commerce, P.O. Box 1639, Tallahassee, FL 32302. (904) 224-8116.

Tampa, Florida

The World Almanac is sponsored in the Tampa Bay area by The Tampa Tribune and The Tampa Times, 202 S. Parker Street, Tampa, FL 33606; (813) 272-7711; Times founded 1893, Tribune 1894; combined ciruculation 194,144; D. T. Bryan, chairman of board, A. S. Donnahoe, president; J. S. Bryan III, executive vice president; R. F. Pittman Jr., vice president/general manager; J. Clendinen, chairman of editorial board; J. Urbanski, business manager; P. Hogan, Tribune managing editor; B. Witwer, Times managing editor.

Population: 293,300 (city), 602,500 (county); total employed in county, 203,100 (civilian, non-agricultural employment).
Area: 84.45 sq. mi., halfway between the northern edge of Florida and southern tip; Hillsborough County seat.
Industry: Tampa port activity ranking 8th in nation for exports; principal export cargo, phosphate; Ybor City section well known for cigar manufacturing; beer breweries, Anheuser-Busch and Joseph Schlitz.
Commerce: retail sales (1975) $1.788 billion; 42 banks, resources $2.698 billion, 9 savings & loan assns.
Transportation: 21 freight lines, Amtrak, 5 bus lines; city-owned bus system expanding into county, 48 truck lines, junction of I-75 & I-4, Int'l Airport, 9 major airlines.
Communications: 6 TV and 21 radio stations.
New construction: Univ. of So. Fla. continuing expansion; Tampa Medical Center; expansion of Busch Gardens; Westinghouse Electric; Tampa's state regional office bldg.; Royster & Co./office and ammonia terminal; U.S. Homes support div.; phosphate mining & processing operation; Metropolitan Bank financial bldg.; waterfront revitalization; city hall expansion (Quad Block); Ybor City Square; Tampa Wholesale Co., waste water treatment plant. Florida State fairgrounds expansion; port, county expressway expansion.
Medical facilities: 6 major hospitals.
Federal facilities; MacDill AFB, Federal Bldg.
Cultural facilities: Florida Gulf Coast Symphony; 2 museums; $2.4 million library; 5 local community theaters, Gasparilla Art Fair.
Education: Univ. of South Florida, Univ. of Tampa, Florida College, and Hillsborough Community College with 2 campuses.

Other attractions: Lowry Park Zoo; Busch Gardens; Ybor City (Latin Quarter); 26 parks, 11 picnic areas; annual Gasparilla Pirate Invasion; site for Florida State Fair.

Sports: pro-football Tampa Bay Buccaneers with 71,500 capacity seat stadium; NASL (Soccer) Tampa Bay Rowdies, Tampa Tarpons (baseball farm team for the Cincinnati Reds); Cincinnati Reds spring training headquarters; greyhound racing, jai-alai.
History: Fort Brooke est. 1824 on site of present Tampa; incorporated 1885.
Further information: Greater Tampa Chamber of Commerce, 801 E. Kennedy Blvd., Tampa, FL 33602, (813) 228-7777.

Toledo, Ohio

The World Almanac is sponsored in the Toledo area by The Blade, 541 Superior Street, Toledo, OH 43660; phone (419) 259-6000; founded 1835; circulation, 172,734 daily, 206,747 Sunday; publishers Paul Block Jr. and William Block; associate publisher John D. Willey; editor Bernard Judy; executive editor Joseph O'Conor; managing editor William Rosenberg.

Population: 389,700 (city), 780,100 (metro), 5th in state, 48th in nation; total employed, 332,700.
Area: 85.3 sq. mi. at juncture of Maumee River and Lake Erie, in northwestern Ohio; Lucas County seat.
Industry: glass, headquarters for Owens-Illinois, Owens Corning & Libbey-Owens-Ford; automotive parts, largest producer in nation, home of American Motors Jeep, Toledo Scale, and Haughton Elevator; largest petroleum refining center between Chicago and the East Coast.
Commerce: Port of Toledo is one of the prime bulk shipping ports on the Great Lakes, handling vast quantities of grain, coal, iron ore, and petroleum products; ranks 4th on Great Lakes and 23d in U.S.; total retail sales $2.62 billion; spendable income per household: $16,650.
Transportation: 9 railroads, 4 major airlines, 120 motor freight lines, 2 interstate bus lines; 13 major highways converge here, permitting the rapid flow of goods to almost 60% of the nation's consumers.
Communications: 4 TV, 15 radio stations and one cablevision company.
Medical facilities: 12 major hospital complexes, including the Medical College of Ohio Hospital.
Cultural facilities: Museum of Art with largest display of antique glass in the world; Peristyle used for the performing arts; symphony, opera society.
Education: Univ. of Toledo and its Community and Technical College; Michael J. Owens Technical College; Bowling Green State Univ.
Other attractions: Municipal Zoo among top 10 in the nation; modern 2,500 seat Masonic Auditorium with a Great Hall annex.
Sports: Mud Hens, farm club of the Cleveland Indians, at the Lucas County Recreation Center.
History: founded in 1836; took its name from sister city, Toledo, Spain.
Further information: Convention and Visitors Bureau, 218 Huron, Toledo, OH 43604.

Toronto, Ontario, Canada

The World Almanac is sponsored in the metropolitan Toronto area by The Toronto Star, One Yonge Street, Toronto, Ontario, M5E 1E6. (416) 367-2000; established 1892, Joseph E. Atkinson, publisher, 1899-1948; circulation daily 493,582; Saturday, 779,063; chairman, Beland H. Honderich; president, William A. Dimma; vice-president, Lionel C. Mohr; editor-in-chief, Martin Goodman. Canada's largest newspaper in circulation, display, and classified advertising lineage; winner of 34 national newspaper awards and sponsor of the Santa Claus Fund and Fresh Air Fund.

Population: 633,318 (city), 2,803,101 (metro); largest city in Canada, 12th in North America; labor force 1.3 million.
Area: 241 sq. mi. on northwest shore of Lake Ontario; provincial capital.
Industry: Canada's leading commercial and industrial center; 6300 manufacturing establishments; value of 1976 factory shipments: $14 billion; principal industries: slaughtering and meat packing, clothing, printing and publishing, machinery, electrical goods, furniture, food products, rubber goods, sheet metal products.
Commerce: retail sales (1977 est.) $8.1 billion; headquarters for Eaton's and Simpson's, Canada's largest department stores; head offices of 10 trust companies and 3 of 9 federally chartered banks; value of cheques cashed (1976), $1040 billion; Toronto Stock Exchange, 4th in North America, traded shares worth $5 billion in 1976; per capita disposable incomes, $6,500.
Transportation: 10 railway lines carry 340 freight and passenger trains daily; 10,900 trucks use 12 major highways; Transit Commission carries 350 million passengers annually on 716 miles of routes including 31 miles of subway; 1.9 million tons of cargo from 26 nations unloaded (1976) at this major Great Lakes port; 24 airlines handle 10.8 million passengers annually at International Airport.
Communications: 6 TV stations including educational and French-language channels; 10 AM and 5 FM radio stations; 3 daily newspapers; 42 foreign language newspapers.
New construction: value of building permits (1976) $840.5 million; $200-million Eaton Centre with 300 shops to be completed 1979; $7 million community center for the deaf; $80 million downtown housing-commercial development will include concert hall.
Medical facilities: 26 active-treatment hospitals including renowned Hospital for Sick Children; special treatment centers: Clark Institute for Psychiatry, Addiction Research Centre, Ontario Crippled Children's Centre.
Cultural facilities: 37 local groups offer alternate theatre; National Ballet of Canada and Canadian Opera Company perform in 3,200-seat O'Keefe Centre; symphony orchestra and Mendelssohn Choir at Massey Hall; touring shows at Royal Alexandra Theatre; 71 public libraries; Royal Ontario Museum; Henry Moore sculptures housed in first of 2 new additions to Art Gallery of Ontario.
Educational facilities: 2 universities, York and Toronto, Canada's largest (1976-77 enrollment: 45,-938); Ryerson Polytechnical Institute, 4 colleges of applied arts and technology, 2 teachers' colleges, Royal Conservatory of Music, Ontario College of Art, Osgoode Hall Law School.
Recreational facilities: Canadian National Exhibition, world's biggest annual fair; Ontario Place, 100 acres of offshore islands with restaurants, marina and 1,000-seat Cinesphere for film showings; Toronto Islands have 3 yacht clubs, 560 acres of beaches and picnic grounds; Harborfront, 86-acre sports, arts, and entertainment park.
Convention facilities: Canada's top convention center; 212,502 visitors attended 479 conventions in 1976 and spent $50 million; total rooms, 18,981.
Sports: 9 public golf courses; thoroughbred and harness racing; NHL Maple Leafs play in 16,435-seat Gardens; Toronto Blue Jays play AL baseball and Argonauts play Canadian Football League games in 54,000-seat Exhibition Stadium.
Other attractions: Ontario Science Centre, designed for participation and involvement; Black Creek Pioneer Village, living displays of upper Canada; McMichael Conservation collection of works by Canada's famed Group of Seven painters; Metro Zoo has 500 species roaming 5 continental areas covering 700 acres; CN Tower, world's tallest free-standing structure, has revolving restaurant, sightseeing decks.
History: town of York founded 1793 on site of French fort as capital of British Colony of upper Canada; incorporated as city 1834 and named Toronto from Indian word for meeting place.
Further information: Convention and Tourist Bureau, Toronto Eaton Centre, Toronto, Ontario, M5B 2H1.

Troy, New York

Population: 62,918.
Area: 9.8 sq. mi., 8 miles northeast of Albany, Rensselaer County seat.
Industry: known for manufacture of collars and shirts; military equipment, precision machines, automobile parts, abrasive materials, metals.
Commerce: 7 banks.
Cultural facilities: Rensselaer Polytechnic Institute Fieldhouse (seating 7,500); Troy Music Hall, Junior Museum, Historical Society.
Other attractions: 21 playgrounds, 3 hospitals, Russell Sage College, Hudson Valley Community College, Emma Willard School for Girls, 31 public and parochial schools.
Further information: Greater Troy Chamber of Commerce, 28 Second Street, Troy, NY 12180.

Tucson, Arizona

The World Almanac is sponsored in the Tucson area by The Arizona Daily Star, 4850 S. Park Ave., Tucson, AZ 85726; (602) 294-4433; founded 1877 as a weekly, Michael E. Pulitzer, editor and publisher; William J. Woestendiek, executive editor; Frank E. Johnson, managing editor; Stephen E. Auslander, editorial page editor; Frank Delehanty, business manager; William Waters, public affairs editor; sponsors Sportsmen's Fund for less-chance youngsters.

Population: 330,700 within city limits, 360,000 in Pima County (Special Census 1975) 157,600 employed in county, out of total civilian labor force of 168,700.
Area: Sonoran Desert of southern Arizona, elev. 2,500 ft.; Santa Catalina Mts. immediately N and E reach 9,000 ft.; Pima County seat.
Industry: Hughes Aircraft, various aircraft-reclamation plants handling surplus craft from Davis-Monthan AFB; electronics, light manufacturing, and tourism; center of the "copper circle" — hundreds of millions of development dollars have been invested in the area by Anaconda, Duval, American Smelting and Refining, Kennecott, Magma, Pima and other mining operations.
Transportation: International Airport served by AeroMexico and Hughes AirWest (to and from Mexico), most major airlines nationally and Cochise Airlines within Arizona; 3 smaller airports; 2 national, one local bus line; Southern Pacific Railroad; trucks.
Communications: 2 newspapers; 5 TV and 18 radio stations.
Medical facilities: 10 hospitals, including Arizona Medical Center, which has teaching hospital.
Climate: mild, dry; rare freezing temperatures in winter; summer brings some rain, mostly after July 1, and temperatures of about 100° F.
Culture: Univ. of Arizona; Tucson Museum of Art; Tucson Symphony; Arizona Civic Theater; Tucson Civic Ballet; many musical, drama, and dance groups; Tucson Boys Chorus, Los Changuitos Feos mariachi group provide local flavor.
Convention facilities: convention center accommodates 10,000 theater-style in arena; sit-down functions 5,000; meeting-rooms 1,000 theater-style; music hall, 2,300; contiguous exhibit space 64,000 sq. ft.
Sports: Toros, farm club of Texas Rangers; Cleveland Indians spring training site; Tucson Open golf tournament; collegiate athletics.
History: Presidio of Tucson est. 1775; Mission San Xavier del Bac founded nearby by Rev. Eusebio Francisco Kino, S. J., who first visited area in 1692.
Further information: Tucson Chamber of Commerce, P.O. Box 991, Tucson, AZ 85702.

Tulsa, Oklahoma

The World Almanac is sponsored in the Tulsa area by The Tulsa Tribune, 315 So. Boulder, Tulsa, OK 74102; phone (918) 582-1101; founded 1904 as The Tulsa Democrat, renamed the Tulsa Tribune in 1920; circulation, 88,210; editor Jenkin Lloyd Jones; managing editor Gordon Fallis; executive editor Jenkin Lloyd Jones Jr.

Population: 350,200 (city), 492,200 (metro); 254,700 employed.
Area: 175 sq. mi., on Arkansas River at 96th meridian in Tulsa, Osage, and Rogers counties.
Industry: petroleum, 30,000 employed by 825 oil and oil-related firms with $185 million annual payroll, Sun Oil and Texaco refineries; aviation, 15,000 in aviation and aerospace industries, including Rockwell International, McDonnell Douglas, and American Airlines; world's largest manufacturer of industrial heaters and winches; 1,200 diversified manufacturing plants.
Commerce: retail sales (1976) $1.527 billion; 17 banks (resources $1,914 billion), 10 savings and loan assns.; per capita income, $4,565.
Transportation: Tulsa Port of Catoosa, nation's most inland port, head of Arkansas-Verdigris navigation channel, total 1976 barge tonnage, 745,600; 4 rail freight lines; 3 bus lines; 32 truck lines; 6 airlines with 1,516,543 passenger movements (1976).
Communications: 2 daily newspapers, 3 TV and 15 radio stations.
New construction: building permits valued at $192.3 million (1976).
Medical facilities: 5 hospitals, 2,250 beds; Osteopathic College, Univ. of Oklahoma medical school branch.
Federal facilities: District Corps of Engineers, 1,200 employees; hq. Southwestern Power Administration.
Cultural facilities: Univ. of Tulsa, Oral Roberts Univ., American Christian and Tulsa junior colleges, Philharmonic, opera, civic ballet, 2 art museums, including Thomas Gilcrease Institute of American History and Art.
Convention facilities: Assembly Center seats 10,000; 370 conventions with 145,525 attendance (1976).
Sports: Tulsa Oilers, St. Louis Cardinals farm team; pro hockey in Central Hockey League; intercollegiate athletics; 4 public and 7 country club golf courses.
Further information: Metropolitan Tulsa Chamber of Commerce, 616 S. Boston Avenue, Tulsa, OK 74127.

Vancouver, British Columbia, Canada

The World Almanac is sponsored in the Vancouver area by The Vancouver Sun, 2250 Granville Street, Vancouver, B.C., V6H 3G2; phone (604) 732-2111; founded 1886; circulation 236,433; publisher Stu Keate, editorial director Bruce Hutchison; sponsors world's largest free Salmon Derby, Sun Family Pops Concerts, Sun Tournament of

Soccer Champions and many other community services.

Population: 410,188 (city), 1,805,242 (metro area), first in province, 3d in Canada.
Area: 44 sq. mi. on the Pacific coast at the mouth of the north arm of the Fraser River; scenic beauty of the city accented by the towering, snowcapped Coast Mountains to the north and rich greenery of agricultural land to the east and south.
Industry: 98 miles of waterfront, stretching up Burrard Inlet, the largest cargo port on the Pacific and Canada's 2d busiest, with 40.9 million tons handled in 1976; major cargos: grain, lumber, coal, mineral ore, chemicals, and manufactured goods; tourism a major industry with an estimated 6.9 million visitors bringing in $600 million in 1976.
Commerce: retail sales: 3.2 billion in 1976; value of shares traded on the Vancouver stock exchange $328.3 million in 1976.
Transportation: western terminus of Canada's 2 national railways: Canadian National Railway and Canadian Pacific; headquarters of provincially operated British Columbia Railway, which is linked to the U.S. by Amtrak along the Burlington Northern Railway right-of-way; 3 major long-distance bus carriers; Provincial Stage Lines, Trailways, and Greyhound; International Airport served by 7 major airlines handled more than 5.1 million passengers in 1976.
Communications: 11 AM—5 FM radio and 4 local TV stations; also 5 U.S. network TV outlets.
Medical facilities: General and St. Paul's are largest hospitals; also Royal Columbian in New Westminster, Burnaby General, Lion's Gate in North Vancouver and Riverview Psychiatric Hospital.
Cultural facilities: symphony orchestra, opera association, several professional theatre groups, Centennial and Maritime Museums and Art Gallery. Queen Elizabeth Theatre and The Orpheun are the major arts facilities.
Other attractions: Pacific National Exhibition, Gastown, Chinatown, the H.R. MacMillan Planetarium, Bloedel Conservatory, aquarium, 1,000 acre Stanley Park, zoo, 18 golf courses, Grouse Mountain, Cypress Bowl and Mount Seymour ski areas, Univ. of British Columbia, Simon Fraser Univ. and 18 beaches.
Sports: professional teams; B.C. Lions (CFL football); Canucks (NHL hockey); Whitecaps (NASL soccer); Exhibition Park racetrack (thoroughbreds); Cloverdale Raceway (harness racing), and several amateur teams and sports activities.
History: discovered by Spaniards; first mapped 1791; taken possession by Capt. George Vancouver for British 1792; Hudson's Bay Company post established early 1800s; city incorporated 1886.

Washington, District of Columbia

The World Almanac is sponsored in the Washington, D.C., area by the Washington Star, 225 Virginia Avenue SE, Washington, DC 20061; phone (202) 484-5000; founded Dec. 16, 1852; chairman of the board Joe L. Allbritton; editor James Bellows; managing editor Sidney Epstein; awards received by newspaper and staff include 8 Pulitzer Prizes.

Population: (1976) 705,100 (city), 3,056,500 (metro area including D.C. and parts of Md. and Va.).
Area: 67 sq. mi. (city), 2,812 (metro) at head of tidewater of Potomac R., 30 miles from Chesapeake Bay, 130 miles from Atlantic O., 240 miles from NYC.
Industry: U.S. Capital, federal government employs 410,000 civilian and military personnel (1976), total labor force 1,456,000 (1976); government related activity, law, journalism, professional and trade associations, unions, lobbying groups, and scientists provide another large portion of employment base; tourism a major industry.
Commerce: metro area average household spendable income, $21,149 (1976); metro area retail sales for 1976, $10.4 billion.
Transportation: circumferential highway; 100-mile rapid rail transit system to be completed 1982 with 18 miles in city and nearby suburbs now open; Metroliner to New York; long distance rail and bus service; National, Dulles, and Baltimore-Washington International airports; National Visitors Center at Union Station; Concorde service at Dulles.
Communications: several national magazines; news bureaus of major newspapers, wire services, and TV networks; 17 FM, 19 AM radio stations; 7 TV stations; 2 daily metropolitan newspapers, over 40 weekly newspapers.
Educational facilities: American, Catholic, District of Columbia, Georgetown, George Washington, and Howard universities, and Gaulladet College; nearby Univ. of Maryland and George Mason Univ.
Medical facilities: major medical research center; National Institutes of Health, Walter Reed Hospital, Bethesda Naval Medical Center; about 40 general hospitals and 3 teaching hospitals.
Cultural facilities: Kennedy Center with 3 performance halls and Wolf Trap Farm Park in nearby Vienna, Va., present major concerts, ballet, opera; Arena Stage, Ford's Theatre, National Theater, many community theater groups; Smithsonian Institution; Corcoran Gallery of Art, Library of Congress; D.C. Public Library with 23 branches.
Sports: pro sports include football (Redskins), basketball (Bullets), hockey (Capitals), soccer (Diplomats).
History: named for George Washington and Christopher Columbus; Georgetown in the District of Columbia first settled 1665, then annexed by the city when D.C. created as seat of federal government by Act of Congress 1790; governed by elected mayor and city council with budget controlled by Congress.
Further information: Convention and Visitors Bureau, 1129 20th Street NW, Washington, DC 20036.

West Palm Beach, Florida

The World Almanac is sponsored in Palm Beach County, Florida, by Palm Beach Newspapers, Inc., 2751 S. Dixie Highway, West Palm Beach, FL 33405, phone (305) 833-7411; publisher of the Palm Beach Times; combined daily circulation 108,672; Sunday, The Palm Beach Post-Times, 116,943.

Population: (1976) 65,368 (city), 543,548 (metro); total labor force: 198,100.
Area: 43.5 sq. mi. (city), 2,023 sq. mi. (metro); southeast Fla., 8th largest county east of the Mississippi; 2d largest county in Fla., Palm Beach County seat, on top of Fla.'s "Gold Coast."
Industry: Pratt & Whitney Aircraft, IBM, RCA, U.S. Sugar Corp., Atlantic Sugar Assn., Osceola Farms Co., Sugar Cane Growers Cooperative of Fla., Gulf & Western Food Products Co., American Foods Inc. farms, Duda & Sons Cooperative Assoc. farms, Rinker Materials Corp., Solitron Devices Inc., NCI Inc., Perry Oceanographics Inc., and tourism.
Commerce: 48 general service banks, 14 savings and loans, total assets $3.8 billion (1976); retail sales $2.2 billion (1976); per capita income $6,940 (1975).
Transportation: 2 rail freight lines, Amtrak; Greyhound, Trailways bus lines, Palm Beach County Transportation Authority (bus); Eastern, National, United, Mackey airlines; 15 truck lines; Port of Palm

Beach ship freight.
Communications: 2 TV, 13 radio stations, cable TV; 3 daily newspapers, 1 winter-season daily, 6 weeklies, society journal magazine, 7 special publications.
Medical facilities: 12 hospitals, 2,108 beds.
Cultural facilities: Society of Four Arts, Henry Morrison Flagler Museum, Norton Gallery of Art, Science Museum and Planetarium, 4 community theaters, 1 legitimate theater, 3 college theaters, West Palm Beach Auditorium, Lion Country Safari, Florida Atlantic Univ., Palm Beach Junior College, Palm Beach Atlantic College.
Sports: West Palm Beach Expos minor league baseball; Atlanta Braves spring training; greyhound racing, jai-alai fronton, Gold Coast Barracudas semi-pro football team, 74 golf courses, 2 polo fields, county fairgrounds, auto race track, tennis, water sports.
History: founded late 1800s by workers and business people associated with the construction of the famed Royal Poinciana Hotel in Palm Beach by Henry Morrison Flagler who set aside 48 homesites on the western shore of Lake Worth; inc. 1894.
Further information: Area Planning Board of Palm Beach County, 2300 Palm Beach Lakes Boulevard, West Palm Beach, FL 33407; Chamber of Commerce, 501 N. Flagler Drive, West Palm Beach, FL 33401.

Wichita, Kansas

The World Almanac is sponsored in the Wichita area by the Wichita Eagle and Beacon Publishing Co., Inc., 825 East Douglas, Wichita, KS 67202; phone (316) 268-6000; founded 1872 as weeklies; became dailies 1884; consolidated 1961; circulation: Eagle (morn) 122,057, Beacon (eve) 44,622, Sunday Eagle and Beacon 177,187 Britt Brown, chairman; Eugene Lambert, president and publisher; W. Davis Merritt Jr., executive editor; Joe Harper, managing editor.

Population: Jan., 1976, (city) 265,455, first in state; (SMSA) 383,312, first in state; SMSA employment (Dec. 1975) 191,300.
Area: (city) 95.98 sq. mi. in Sedgwick County at juncture of Big and Little Arkansas rivers; Sedgwick County seat. Elevation 1,280 feet, average rainfall 30.06; Mean temp.; Jan.—31.5, July—80.3.
Industry: 60% of all U.S. general aviation aircraft is manufactured in Wichita. Aircraft employment: Beech (city) 6,390 (total) 7,927; Cessna 11,500; Gates Learjet 2,200; Boeing 6,500. Other fields: meat processing, flour milling, grain storage, petroleum refining, natural gas, chemicals; largest non-aero manufacturer Coleman Co.
Commerce: wholesale-retail center for large part of Kansas and northern Oklahoma; metro (SMSA) retail sales (1976) $1.5 billion; bank resources (15 city banks) $1.6 billion; median household income $12,-650.
Transportation: 4 major rail freight lines, Amtrak; Continental bus lines; 54 truck lines; 8 major highways; Mid-Continent Airport, 5 airlines, averages 622 air movements per day; National Flying Farmers headquarters.
Communications: 4 TV, 7 AM and 6 FM radio stations.
Medical facilities: world's largest speech and hearing rehabilitation center (Institute of Logopedics); 5 hospital complexes including VA installation.
Federal facility: McConnell Air Force Base.
Educational facilities: Wichita State University and WSU Medical Branch; Friends University; Kansas Newman College.
Cultural facilities: Wichita Symphony Orchestra; Omnisphere (Planetarium); Wichita Art Museum; Wichita Art Association (museum) and Children's Theater; Century II auditorium and convention complex; community theater; city library; 443 churches. Mid-America All Indian Center.
Other attractions: city-county zoo; 67 parks; recreation lakes; Cow Town (restoration of 1872 Wichita); Historical Museum; National Junior Livestock Show.
Sports: Aeros, Chicago Cubs farm team. National Baseball Congress (semi-pro) headquarters and tournaments.
History: founded 1870, became railhead (shipping point) for cattle herds driven up Chisholm Trail; named after Wichita Indians.
Further information: Chamber of Commerce, 350 West Douglas, Wichita, KS 67202.

Wilmington, Delaware

The World Almanac is sponsored in Delaware by The News-Journal Co., 831 Orange Street, Wilmington, DE 19899, (302) 573-2000, publisher of The Morning News, Evening Journal, and Saturday News Journal, circulation: 135,764 and The Sunday News Journal, circulation: 72,601. President and publisher, Andrew Fisher; executive vice president and general manager, Frederick Walter; vice president and executive editor, Frederick W. Hartmann; editor of the editorial page, James E. O'Brien.

Population: 73,000 (Wilmington); 419,000 (New Castle County); 535,000 (metro); Wilmington is largest city in state.
Area: 15.1 sq. mi. at the confluence of the Brandywine, Christina, and Delaware rivers.
Industry: one of the largest chemical and petrochemical centers in the U.S., autos, utilities, steel, about 400 manufacturing firms, offices for many insurance firms and holding companies.
Commerce: port is major auto importing center; retail sales (SMSA 1976) $1.9 billion, est. 1977 personal income in SMSA $4.6 billion, est. personal income per household $26,228; state has 12 state-chartered commercial banks, 19 state-chartered savings and loans, 5 national banks, 2 mutual savings banks, 2 federally chartered savings and loans.
Transportation: 2 major railway lines, 3 bus lines, 35 motor freight carriers, airport.
Communications: 1 public TV station; 6 radio stations.
Medical facilities: Wilmington Medical Center (4 divisions); 2 private hospitals; Alfred I. du Pont Institute.
Cultural attractions: Grand Opera House; Winterthur Museum; Hagley Museum; Old Brandywine Village; Fort Christina Park; Wilmington Symphony Orchestra; Wilmington Opera Society; Wilmington Drama League; Museum of Natural History; Univ. of Delaware (Newark); Delaware State College (Dover); Delaware Technical and Community College.
Sports: Delaware Park; Brandywine Raceway; Dover Downs (Dover); Harrington Raceway (Harrington); Univ. of Delaware football.
Other attractions: Rehoboth Beach; Longwood Gardens and Brandywine River Museum (both in nearby Pa.); several state parks and recreational areas; historic old New Castle; Hillendale Museum.
History: founded as Fort Christina in 1638; named for Queen of Sweden; name changed to Willington in 1731 and then to Wilmington in 1739 in honor of the Earl of Wilmington; it is the first city in the first state of the union.
Further information: Delaware State Chamber of Commerce, 1102 West Street, Wilmington, DE 19801.

Windsor, Ontario, Canada

The World Almanac is sponsored in Windsor and a large part of southwestern Ontario including Essex, Kent, and Lambton counties, by The Windsor Star (Cir. 86,992), 167 Ferry Street, Windsor, Ontario, N9A 4M5; a division of Southam Press Limited; published daily since 1890 (present name since 1957); publisher R. M. Pearson; general manager A. H. Fast; editor G.C. Morgan.

Population: 196,325 (city); 247,582 (metro); 543,400 (tri-county); 13th in province; total employed 99,000.
Area: 50 sq. mi., one-half mile across Detroit River from Detroit, Mich.; largest Canadian city on U.S.-Canada border.
Industry: autos and feeder plants, more than 25% national production (Chrysler, Ford, GM); tool and die shops; alcoholic beverages (home office Hiram Walker and Sons); food processing (H. J. Heinz, Green Giant); pharmaceutical supplies (Wyeth Ltd., G. E. Jamieson Ltd.); salt mining; zinc and plastic diecasting; agriculture (rich producer early vegetables) tomatoes, corn, soybeans, peaches, tobacco; tourism (largest port of entry in nation for U.S. visitors).
Commerce: retail sales $693.8 million; personal disposable income $1,645.8 million; average weekly income $229.37; 6 banks, 73 branches; 9 trust companies; 11 loan companies.
Transportation: 6 rail lines; 2 airlines; linked to Detroit by suspension bridge and underwater tunnel; western terminus Highway 401; major harbor terminal (deep water port); private marinas, yacht club; municipal bus line.
Communications: 6 radio, 1 TV outlet; access to Detroit's 50 radio and 6 TV outlets; 1 monthly magazine; 1 daily newspaper.
New construction: in 1976 $63.5 million.
Cultural facilities: University of Windsor, enrollment 7,500; St. Clair Community College, enrollment 4,250; Light Opera Association; Art Gallery of Windsor; Windsor Symphony Orchestra; Hiram Walker Museum; Fort Malden National Historic Park and Museum, Amherstburg; public libraries; Cleary Auditorium and Convention Centre.

Other attractions: 96 parks and playgrounds; sunken gardens; close access to Great Lakes resort areas; site of International Freedom Festival; access to Detroit Ethnic Festival.

Further information: Chamber of Commerce, 500 Riverside Drive West; Tourist Information, 135 Ouellette Avenue, both Windsor, Ontario.

Winnipeg, Manitoba, Canada

The World Almanac is sponsored in the Winnipeg area by the Winnipeg Free Press, 300 Carlton Street, Winnipeg, Man., Canada: phone (204) 943-9331; founded 1872; daily circulation 140,000; publisher Richard C. Malone; president R. H. Shelford; editor Peter McLintock; managing editor Don Nicol; the newspaper and its staff have received numerous awards for outstanding journalism.

Population: 560,874.
Area: 220 sq. mi., junction Red and Assiniboine rivers, near center of North America; capital of province of Manitoba.
Industry: manufacturing is single largest source of jobs; 800 establishments; 40,700 employees; value of factory shipments $1.2 billion.
Commerce: retail sales over $1.5 billion in 1976; Winnipeg Commodity Exchange only gold futures market in Canada; headquarters Canada Grains Council, Canadian Grain Commission, Canadian Wheat Board.
Transportation: International Airport served by 7 airlines; 2 national railways and one rail line to U.S.; 5 national and regional bus lines; major trucking hub.
Communications: 6 TV and 12 radio stations.
New Construction: valued at $347.5 million in 1976 compared with $220.6 million in 1975.
Medical facilities: one of Canada's largest medical teaching centers; research in immunology, transplant-tissue rejection, cancer, blood diseases, endrocrinology, respiratory diseases, neo-natal, prenatal medicine; of Manitoba's 85 active treatment hospitals, 13 are in Winnipeg, including 2 major teaching centers plus University of Manitoba Rh Inst.
Federal facilities: passport office, Canada Mint.
Cultural facilities: art gallery, Royal Winnipeg Ballet, contemporary dancers, Winnipeg Symphony Orchestra, Manitoba Chamber Orchestra, Manitoba Theatre Centre, Manitoba Opera Assoc., Cercle Moliere, Museum of Man and Nature, Rainbow Stage, Manitoba Theatre Workshop, plus over 20 amateur theatre groups.
Educational facilities: Univ. of Manitoba with 4 affiliated colleges, Univ. of Winnipeg, and Red River Community College.
Sports: Blue Bombers (Canadian Football League), Winnipeg Jets (WHA); Assiniboia Downs race track.
Convention facilities: Winnipeg Convention Centre in downtown, facilitates up to 5,000 delegates.
Other attractions: major zoo, Manisphere exhibition, multi-cultural Folklorama festival in summer; French Canadian winter carnival in St. Boniface; planetarium
History: first colony, Lord Selkirk Settlers, 1812; incorporated Nov. 8, 1873; on Jan. 1, 1972 amalgamation of city government, replacing 7 cities, 4 urban municipalities, one town and a metropolitan government.
Additional information: Chamber of Commerce, 177 Lombard Avenue; Tourist Information, 101 Legislative Bldg., and Tourist and Convention Assn. of Manitoba, 400-365 Hargrave Street.

Winston-Salem, North Carolina

The World Almanac is sponsored in the Piedmont Triad area by the Winston-Salem Journal and The Sentinel, 416-420 N. Marshall Street, Winston-Salem, NC 27102, phone 919-727-7211; Sentinel founded 1856; Journal 1897; brought under one ownership in 1927; now an affiliate of Media General, Inc.; general manager, Thomas E. Waldrop.

Population: 140,000 (city), 225,000 (Forsyth County); 1977 est.
Area: 61.34 square miles (city); 419 square miles (county); in north central North Carolina; Forsyth County seat.
Industry: R.J. Reynolds Industries with diversified interests in tobacco, food, shipping, oil, packaging; Western Electric Co.; Jos. Schlitz Brewery; Westinghouse, Hanes Corp., Hanes Dye and Finishing Co., Brenner Industries, Bahnson, Graveley Corp., Dennis, Inc., Wachovia Corp.
Commerce: Total retail sales (county, 1976) nearly

$1.1 billion, part of the Piedmont Triad which, with Greensboro and High Point, comprise a rapidly growing industrial and business area.
Transportation: headquarters for Piedmont Airlines at Smith Reynolds Airport, city also served by regional airport with 4 airlines; 2 bus lines; 54 motor freight carriers.
Communications: 4 TV, 10 radio stations.
Medical facilities: Bowman Gray School of Medicine of Wake Forest Univ.; Baptist, Forsyth Memorial, Medical Park, and other treatment centers and clinics.
Cultural facilities: one of the nation's first arts councils, formed in 1949; N.C. School of the Arts; Wake Forest Univ.; Salem College; Winston-Salem State Univ.; Old Salem, restoration of colonial town as it was between 1766 and 1830.
Convention facilities: Hyatt House hotel complex sits across from the Benton Convention Center; hotels and motels offer 2,400 rooms.
Recreation: more than 50 public parks; 10 community centers; 10 swimming centers; fishing and boating in Winston and Salem lakes; 17 golf courses including Tanglewood where the 1974 PGA was held.
Sports: Red Sox, Carolina League farm club of Boston Red Sox; stock car racing; Wake Forest football at Groves stadium; Atlantic Coast Conference basketball at Memorial Coliseum.
History: Salem founded 1766 by members of the Moravian Church; Winston, 1849; merged in 1913.
Further Information: Chamber of Commerce, 2640 N. Marshall Street, Winston-Salem, NC 27102.

Yakima, Washington

The World Almanac is sponsored in the Yakima area by the Yakima Herald-Republic (morning and evening Mon.-Fri.) (mornings Sat.-Sun.), 114 North Fourth Street, Yakima, WA. 98907; phone (509) 248-1251; founded in 1903 as the Yakima Republic, given present name in 1970; circulation 37,471 daily and 42,410 Sunday; publisher James E. Tonkin, editorial page editor J. M. (Tom) Thomas, managing editor Stephen M. Kent.

Population: 51,100 (1977 est.); average monthly work force 46,000.
Area: Yakima County seat, latitude 46° 34′ north, longitude 120° 32′ west, altitude 1,052 feet; located in southcentral Washington, an area of rich volcanic soil, 11.78 sq. mi. in area; 142 miles southeast of Seattle, 146 miles south of Canadian border.
Industry: agriculture, timber, first in the nation in production of apples, hops, mints; first in number of fruit trees.
Commerce: (1976) retail sales $321 million, EBI per capita $4,965, bank deposits $11.9 billion, postal receipts $3.2 million, bank debits $11.9 billion.
Transportation: Hughes Airwest and Cascade Airways, Burlington Northern, Union Pacific railroads; Amtrak, Greyhound; Interstate 82, Highways 12 and 97.
Communications: one daily, one weekly newspaper; 4 TV, 8 radio stations.
New construction: 1,145 building permits totalling over $24 million issued in 1976.
Medical facilities: 3 hospitals with 460 beds, 150 physicians, 11 osteopaths, 64 dentists, 13 optometrists.
Federal facilities: U.S. Army Firing Center, 409 permanent personnel trains active and reserve units on 263,131 acres, U.S. Army, Marine, and Navy reserve facilities, U.S. Postal Service regional center.
Cultural facilities: Yakima Valley Museum, Yakima Valley Regional Library, Allied Arts Council, Yakima Symphony and Chorus, Little Theater, Capitol Theater; over 95 churches.
Education: Yakima Valley College, J.M. Perry Institute, Yakima Business College; 7 public school districts in and around city; 5 parochial schools; St. Elizabeth Health Sciences Library.
Sports and Recreation: 6 theaters, 6 drive-ins, 2 historic trolleys, hunting and fishing, skiing in Cascade Mountains 45 minutes from city, golf, 30 tennis courts, 9 swimming pools, 31 parks, auto racing, horse racing, youth baseball, softball, Central Washington Fair.
Convention facilities: Yakima Center, over 1,400 motel units.
History: Founded Jan. 27, 1886 as North Yakima on route of Northern Pacific Railroad.
Further information: Greater Yakima Chamber of Commerce, P.O. Box 1498, Yakima, WA 98907.

Youngstown, Ohio

The World Almanac is sponsored in the Youngstown area by The Vindicator, Vindicator Square, Youngstown, OH, 44501; phone (216) 747-1471; founded 1863 by J. H. Odell; Wm. F. Maag began daily Sept. 25, 1889; daily circulation 100,324, Sunday 156,657; president, publisher, general manager William J. Brown; advertising manager William Mittler; managing editor Ann N. Przelomski.

Population: 140,909 (city) Ohio's 7th largest; 536,836 (metro) 63d largest in U.S.; Mahoning County seat.
Area: 35 sq. mi. in northeastern Ohio at juncture of Ohio Turnpike, I-80, and Ohio Rt. 11.
Industry: historically a strong iron and steel center, still important producer with Youngstown Sheet & Tube, Republic Steel, and U.S. Steel; local steel supplied to big nearby plants of General Motors Packard Electric Div. in Warren and GMAD plant in Lordstown, where Chevrolet Monzas, vans, and other GM models are assembled; GF Business Equipment sells office furnishings world wide; Commercial Shearing does world-wide tunnel frame and hydraulics business; other fabricators use local steel, rubber.
Commerce: wholesale-retail center for large area of northeast Ohio, western Penna.; retail sales of metro area (est) over $1.6 billion; (est) value added by manufacturing $2.1 billion; average spendable family income $15,916.
New construction: $71.9 million in 1976.
Transportation: truck transport center with 95 motor freight terminals; rail lines; airport served by 2 major airlines, headquarters for Beckett Aviation, largest fleet of executive aircraft in U.S.
Communications: 4 TV stations, all major networks and PBS; 9 radio stations.
Medical facilities: Northeastern Ohio Universities College of Medicine, 6 large hospitals in area.
Federal facilities: U.S. Air Force Reserve base flying tactical fighters at airport; new regional post office; army and navy reserve centers.
Cultural facilities: symphony orchestra with downtown bldg., ballet guild, Youngstown Playhouse in own modern bldg., Butler Institute of American Art.
Educational facilities: Youngstown State Univ. with over 15,500 students and graduate program; Penn-Ohio Junior College; Youngstown College of Business and Professional Drafting; 55 public and parochial schools; branches of Kent State Univ. in nearby Warren, Salem, and East Liverpool.
Recreational facilities: in city, 10 parks, 44 playgrounds, golf course; 6 swimming pools; Mill Creek Park with 2,383 acres; 4 large reservoirs in area for recreation, many golf courses.
Further information: Youngstown Area Chamber of Commerce, 200 Wick Bldg., Youngstown, OH 44503.

Washington, Capital of the U.S.

The Capitol

The Capitol (building) since 1961 has presented an entirely new east central front, the central portion having been reconstructed and extended. It was moved forward 32 1/2 ft. The former facade of Virginia sandstone was reproduced in Georgia marble, the original wall becoming an interior wall. The new section added 78 offices and other important facilities. The cost of the extension project was $11.4 million; improved illumination and other work brought the total to $24 million.

The original plan for the Capitol was drawn by Dr. William Thornton, of Tortola, West Indies, and accepted April 5, 1793. It had a central section, nearly square, a low dome and rectangular buildings north and south, 126 by 120 ft. The southeast cornerstone of the north section was laid by President Washington with Masonic ceremonies Sept. 18, 1793. Sandstone from Aquia Creek, Va., was used. The northern wing was completed first. The Congress occupied it in Nov. 1800. The Supreme Court met there in Feb. 1801, and other local courts also used the Capitol. In charge of early construction were architects Stephen H. Hallet, Geo. Hadfield, and James Hoban, who was architect of the White House. Benjamin H. Latrobe was architect of the South or House wing which was occupied in 1807, but not completed until 1811. All the interiors were burned by the British in 1814. Latrobe had charge of the rebuilding until 1818 when Charles Bulfinch became the architect for 11 years. Congress reoccupied the Capitol in 1819 and the central rotunda area was finished in 1829.

The present Senate and House wings were designed and constructed under the architect Thomas U. Walter from 1851 to 1863. The House moved in Dec. 16, 1857; the Senate Jan. 4, 1859. The wing extensions are white marble from Lee, Mass., and the columns are from Maryland. Daniel Webster spoke at the laying of the cornerstone.

In 1860 the Supreme Court moved into the former Senate Chamber, and in 1864 the old Hall of the House was designated Statuary Hall. The court moved into its own building in 1935.

The original dome of the Capitol, wood covered with copper, was replaced, 1856, by the present dome of cast iron, completed 1865. Its greatest exterior diameter is 135 ft. 5 in. The rotunda is 96 ft. in diameter; height from floor to base of lantern is 180 ft. 3 in. In the "eye" of the dome is a fresco by Constantino Brumidi, the "Apotheosis of Washington." Below the dome runs a 300-ft. frieze in fresco, portraying American history from Columbus, 1492, to Kitty Hawk, 1903. Brumidi painted part of it by 1880. Costaggini added panels by 1888. Allyn Cox completed the frieze in 1953 and it was dedicated in 1954.

The Statue of Freedom on the dome, 19 1/2 ft. tall, is of bronze and weighs 14,985 pounds. At its base are the words "E Pluribus Unum" (Out of Many One). It was modeled in plaster by Thomas Crawford in Rome and cast in bronze. It cost $23,796, exclusive of erection.

Inaugurations of presidents and vice presidents are usually held on a platform erected over the great steps on the east front. The oath of office of the president is usually given by the chief justice of the United States.

Prayer Room

A nondenominational room where members of Congress may pray and meditate is located off the rotunda. Dominating the room is a stained glass window of George Washington kneeling in prayer at Valley Forge. Beneath it is an altar of white oak on which stands an open Bible. Flanking either side is a floor candelabra, each with the traditional seven lights.

National Statuary Hall

Statuary Hall was created in 1864 to occupy the former Hall of the House of Representatives. States were invited to contribute not more than two statues of distinguished persons judged worthy of national commemoration by the States. In 1933 the number of statues in Statuary Hall was limited to one statue from each state, others to be placed in other parts of the Capitol. Early in 1976 it became necessary to rearrange the statues again. To date 91 statues have been contributed by 50 states. The statues in Statuary Hall:

Alabama—Gen. Jos. Wheeler, U.S.A., C.S.A.
Arizona—John C. Greenway, U.S.A.
Arkansas—Uriah M. Rose, jurist.
California—Junipero Serra, mission founder.
Colorado—Dr. Florence Rena Sabin, scientist.
Florida—Dr. John Gorrie, inventor.
Georgia—Alex H. Stephens, statesman.
Hawaii—King Kamehameha I, uniter of islands.
Idaho—Geo. L. Shoup, first governor.
Illinois—Frances E. Willard, WCTU head.
Indiana—Lew Wallace, U.S.A., author.
Iowa—Saml. J. Kirkwood, governor.
Kansas—John J. Ingalls, senator.
Kentucky—Henry Clay, statesman.
Louisiana—Huey P. Long, senator.
Maine—Hannibal Hamlin, vice president.
Michigan—Lewis Cass, statesman.
Minnesota—Henry M. Rice, senator.
Mississippi—Jefferson Davis, statesman.
Missouri—Thos. H. Benton, senator.
Montana—Charles Marion Russell, artist.
Nebraska—Wm. Jennings Bryan, statesman.
Nevada—Patrick A. McCarran, senator.
New Hampshire—Daniel Webster, statesman.
North Carolina—Zebulon B. Vance, governor.
North Dakota—John Burke, U.S. treasurer.
Ohio—William Allen, senator, governor.
Oklahoma—Sequoya, Cherokee leader.
Oregon—Rev. Jason Lee, pioneer.
Pennsylvania—Robert Fulton, inventor.
South Dakota—Gen. W.H.H. Beadle, educator.
Tennessee—John Sevier, first governor.
Texas—Sam Houston, pioneer leader.
Utah—Brigham Young, Mormon leader.
Vermont—Ethan Allen, revolutionary leader.
Virginia—Robt. E. Lee, U.S.A., C.S.A.
Washington—Dr. Marcus Whitman, pioneer.
West Virginia—Francis H. Pierpont, statesman.
Wisconsin—Robt. M. La Follette Sr., statesman.
Wyoming—Esther Hobart Morris, suffragette.

Under the dome in the **Great Rotunda** are statues of Washington (Va.), Andrew Jackson (Tenn.), James A. Garfield (Ohio).

Adjoining it, the **South Small Rotunda** has statues of George Clinton (N.Y.), Stephen F. Austin (Tex.), and John Peter Muhlenberg (Pa.). The corridor leading from Statuary Hall to the House has statues of Jonathan Trumbull (Conn.), Wm. King (Me.), Father Jacques Marquette (Wis.), Wade Hampton (S.C.), Will Rogers (Okla.), E. L. "Bob" Bartlett (Alaska), and Dr. John McLoughlin (Ore.).

In the foyer of the old Senate Chamber are statues of John Stark (N.H.), Dennis Chavez (N.M.), and in the corridor leading to the Senate wing are statues of Dr. Ephraim McDowell (Ky.), eminent physician and surgeon, John Hanson (Md.), 9th president of the Continental Congress, and John M. Clayton (Del.), secretary of state, Wm. E. Borah (Ida.), Edward D. White (La.), and Maria L. Sanford (Minn.).

In the **Hall of Columns** on the first floor, House wing, are statues of E. Kirby Smith (Fla.), Zachariah Chandler (Mich.), Jas. Harlan (Ia.), Francis P. Bair Jr. (Mo.), Gen. Philip Kearny (N.J.), Gen. Jas. Shields (Ill.), John Winthrop (Mass.), Oliver P. Morton (Ind.), J. Sterling Morton (Neb.), Rev. Thos. Starr King (Cal.), J. L. M. Curry (Ala.), J. P. Clarke (Ark.), Geo. W. Glick (Kan.), Jas. Z. George (Miss.), Roger Williams (R.I.), Jacob Collamer (Vt.), John E. Kenna (W. Va.), Joseph Ward (S.D.), Eusebio F. Kino, S. J. (Ariz.), and Father Damien (Ha.).

In the **Main Hall** on the first floor are statues of Roger Sherman (Conn.), Caesar Rodney (Del.), Dr. Crawford W. Long (Ga.), Samuel Adams (Mass.), Charles Carroll of Carrollton (Md.), Richard Stockton (N.J.), Robert R. Livingston (N.Y.), Charles B. Aycock (N.C.), Nathanael Greene, and John C. Calhoun (S.C.).

Office Buildings for Members

Members of Congress meet constituents and transact other business in five office buildings on Capitol Hill, two for the Senate and three for the House.

The original Senate building, now named the Richard Brevard Russell Office Building, was completed in 1909, enlarged in 1933; the second Senate building, now named the Everett McKinley Dirksen Office Building, was constructed in 1958. A subway connects both with the Capitol.

The original House building (1908) was named for former Speaker Joseph G. Cannon (R. Ill.), the second (1933) for former Speaker Nicholas Longworth (R. Oh.), and the third (1964) for former Speaker Sam Rayburn (D. Tex.). The Rayburn Building has underground transportation to the Capitol.

Also on Capitol Hill is the bell tower and statue memorial to Sen. Robert A. Taft of Ohio (1889-1953). It was erected by popular subscription and dedicated Apr. 14, 1959, by President Eisenhower.

Hours for Visiting

The Capitol is normally open from 9 a.m. to 4:30 p.m. daily. The Capitol is closed Christmas, New Year's Day, and Thanksgiving Day. Should either the House or the Senate remain in session beyond closing time, the wing of the Capitol in use stays open until the session closes.

Tours through the Capitol, including the House and Senate Galleries, are conducted from 9 a.m. to 4 p.m. without charge. It is not necessary to take a tour to see the Capitol. Visitors desiring to hear debate in either chamber for a longer period than the tour allows must obtain a visitor's card from their Senator or Representative.

The White House

The White House, the president's residence, stands on 18 acres on the south side of Pennsylvania Avenue, between the Treasury and the Executive Office Building. The main building 168 by 85-1/2 ft., has 6 floors, with the East Terrace, 135 by 35 ft., leading to the East Wing, a 3-story building, 139 by 82 ft., used for offices and as an entrance for official functions. The West Terrace, 174 by 35 ft., contains offices and new press facilities above the boarded over swimming pool, and leads to the Executive Office, 3 stories high, 148 by 98 ft., erected in 1902 and enlarged several times since.

The White House was designed by James Hoban, an Irish-born architect, in a competition that paid $500. The main facade resembles the Duke of Leinster's house in Dublin. President Washington chose the site, which was included on the plan of the Federal City prepared by the French engineer, Major Pierre L'Enfant. The cornerstone was laid Oct. 13, 1792. President Washington never lived in the house. President John Adams entered in Nov. 1800, and Mrs. Adams hung her washing in the uncompleted East Room.

The walls are of sandstone, quarried at Aquia Creek, Va. The exterior walls were painted during the course of construction, causing the building to be termed the "White House." For many years, however, it was generally referred to as the "President's House" or the "President's Palace." Thos. Jefferson developed the east and west terraces and built one-story offices, woodsheds, and a wine cellar. On Aug. 24, 1814, during Madison's administration, the house was burned by the British. James Hoban completed rebuilding by Dec. 1817, and President Monroe moved in.

The south portico was added in 1824 and the north portico in 1829. In 1948 President Truman had a second-floor balcony built into the south portico. In 1948 he had Congress authorize complete rebuilding because the White House was unsafe. During its reconstruction he lived in Blair House, 1651 Pennsylvania Ave.

Reconstruction cost $5,761,000. The interior was completely removed, new underpinning 24 ft. deep was placed under the outside walls and a steel frame was built to support the interior.

The Green Room, used for informal receptions, is in American Sheraton style, with green silk moire on the walls, a white marble fireplace, and white enamel wainscoting and door trim. On the west wall hangs a portrait of Benjamin Franklin, painted in 1767. Most of the furniture now in the room was made in New York City about 1815-1825 by Duncan Phyfe or his contemporaries.

The Blue Room, an oval drawing room, is the main reception room. The parquet floor is covered by an oval Chinese rug; the walls are covered with wallpaper reproduced from a French document of 1800. Portraits of Washington, Adams, Jefferson, Jackson, Monroe, and Tyler, as well as two seascapes by Fitz Hugh Lane of Boston harbor and Baltimore harbor decorate the walls. Seven chairs and a French clock from Monroe's original 1817 furnishings remain in the room.

The Red Room, used as a parlor, is furnished in the American Empire style, hung in red twill satin with gold scroll borders. There are a Savonnerie carpet of the period and a marble-topped gueridon labeled by Charles Honore Lannuier. There are portraits of Pierce, Polk, Van Buren, Dolley Madison, Angelica Van Buren, Audubon, and Alexander Hamilton in the room. Also there is a marble bust of Martin Van Buren by Hiram Powers.

The State Dining Room has a large chief table. Other tables are brought in for large dinners but do not remain there. Centerpiece of the main table is a French bronze-dore plateau purchased by Monroe in 1817. China in use was ordered during the Lyndon B. Johnson Administration. Chairs are in Queen Anne style. The room is paneled in oak with Corinthian pilasters, painted white.

The Family Dining Room, used for breakfasts and luncheons, has a portrait of Mrs. Theodore Roosevelt by Theobold Chartran.

The President's Dining Room is on the second floor. It is furnished with American Federal furniture, an 18th Century chandelier, and blue silk window hangings. There is a mahogany sideboard once owned by Daniel Webster.

The Diplomatic Reception Room, an oval room on the ground floor, is used as the entrance to the mansion at state functions. It has scenic wallpaper based on 1820 engravings, and a new Aubusson style rug with seals of the 50 states, installed in June 1971.

The Library, on the ground floor, has the painted decor of an early 19th Century American room. In Aug. 1963, 2,780 titles were selected to be placed in the library. All but a few are by American authors. They were chosen by a committee headed by the late James T. Babb, librarian emeritus of Yale University.

The Map Room, on the ground floor, a top-secret war room during World War II, was redecorated in 1970 at the request of President and Mrs. Nixon. Furnished in American Chippendale style, it contains 4 American landscape paintings and a portrait of Benjamin Franklin which was taken from Franklin's Philadelphia home by a British officer quartered there during the American Revolution.

The Lincoln Bedroom which contains an ornately carved bed and furniture of his period, is at the east end of the second floor. It served as Lincoln's cabinet room and in it he signed the Emancipation Proclamation of Jan. 1, 1863. A portrait of Jackson, admired by Lincoln, hangs there today. Seven pieces of furniture have Lincoln associations. The bed was used in the State Bedroom during the Lincoln administration. In the room is a copy of the **Gettysburg Address,** written out by Lincoln.

The Treaty Room, one door removed from Lincoln's cabinet room, was used by Andrew Johnson as his cabinet room, and was so used until 1902, when it became a sitting room. Here in 1899 was signed the peace protocol, a forerunner to the final treaty of peace with Spain. It is now a waiting or meeting room for the President and contains some of the original Victorian furniture. There are portraits of Presidents A. Johnson, Grant, and Taylor and paintings of McKinley observing the signing of the protocol, and of Lincoln and Grant in conference during the Civil War.

The Queen's Bedroom is assigned to distinguished women guests, and has sheltered five queens — Queen Mother Elizabeth and Queen Elizabeth II of Britain, Wilhelmina and Juliana of the Netherlands, Queen Mother Frederika of Greece. The English overmantel mirror was presented by Princess Elizabeth in 1951.

The Yellow Oval Room, directly above the Blue Room is used as a private sitting room by the president and first lady.

The President's Office, oval in form, is in the West Wing and looks out on the rose garden. The office was added in

1909 to the West Wing, which had been built 7 years earlier by Theodore Roosevelt. The West Wing also contains the Roosevelt Room and the Cabinet Room.

Visiting Hours

The White House is open from 10 a.m. to 12 noon, Tuesday through Friday, except on holidays. Also Saturdays, 10 a.m. to 2 p.m. Jun. 1 through Labor Day, and 10 a.m. to noon Labor Day through May 31. Only the public rooms on the ground floor and state floor may be visited. No permit is required.

President's Guest House

Blair House, the President's Guest House, fronts on Pennsylvania Ave., northwest of the White House grounds. It is supervised by the Dept. of State and is the official residence of heads of state who visit Washington. Built 1824, it was the home of Francis Preston Blair (1791-1876), political leader and Lincoln advisor. President Truman lived there 1948-1952 during rebuilding of the White House, and 2 Puerto Rican fanatics tried to shoot their way in Nov. 1, 1950, killing one guard and wounding 2 others.

Restoration and refurnishing began in 1963 and the house was reopened Jan. 14, 1964, on the occasion of the visit of President Antonio Segni of the Italian Republic. The Blair House Fine Arts Committee continues to provide for the house.

Other Centers of Interest

Arlington National Cemetery

Arlington National Cemetery, on the former Custis-Lee estate in Virginia, is the site of the **Tomb of the Unknown Soldier** and the final resting place of John Fitzgerald Kennedy, president of the United States, who was buried there Nov. 25, 1963. A torch burns day and night over his grave. The remains of his brother Sen. Robert F. Kennedy (N.Y.) were interred on June 8, 1968, in an area adjacent. Many other famous Americans also are buried at Arlington, as well as American soldiers from every major war.

Arlington National Cemetery, administered by the Department of the Army, was established June 15, 1864, on land originally the estate of George Washington Parke Custis. The land was part of the District of Columbia from 1791 until 1847, when Arlington County was returned to Virginia.

The Unknown Soldier of World War I was entombed on the east front of the Arlington Memorial Amphitheater Nov. 11, 1921, in the presence of President Warren G. Harding. The tomb is inscribed: *Here rests in honored glory an American soldier known but to God.* The body had been chosen at Chalons-sur-Marne from unidentified dead in Europe. On Memorial Day, May 30, 1958, two unidentified servicemen, one of whom died in World War II and one in the Korean War, were placed in crypts beside the first, in ceremonies led by President Eisenhower and Vice President Nixon. The president placed the Medal of Honor on each of the two coffins.

As of Mar. 31, 1977, a total of 170,473 interments had been made in Arlington National Cemetery. Among the unknown dead are 2,111 who died on the battlefields of Virginia in the Civil War and 167 who lost their lives when the battleship Maine was blown up in Havana Harbor Feb. 15, 1898. The total of unknown dead interred in Arlington National Cemetery is 4,724.

Arlington House, The Robert E. Lee Memorial

On a hilltop above the cemetery, stands Arlington House, the Robert E. Lee Memorial, which from 1955 to 1972 was officially called the Custis-Lee Mansion. The house has a portico 60 ft. wide, with 8 Doric columns, and faces the Potomac. With its two wings the house extends 140 ft. It was built by George Washington Parke Custis, grandson of Martha Washington and father of Mary Ann Randolph Custis, who married Lee in this house in 1831. Here Lee wrote his resignation from the U.S. Army, Apr. 20, 1861. The house became a military hq. and was confiscated by the government. The U.S. Supreme Court restored it to the legal heir, George Washington Custis Lee, grandson of the builder, who sold the entire estate (including the mansion) to the Government in 1883 for $150,000.

The mansion and grounds are administered by the National Park Service of the Dept. of the Interior.

U.S. Marine Corps War Memorial

North of the National Cemetery, approximately 350 yards, stands the bronze statue of the raising of the United States flag on Iwo Jima, executed by Felix de Weldon from the photograph by Joe Rosenthal, and presented to the nation by members and friends of the U.S. Marine Corps, at a cost of $850,000. It was dedicated Nov. 10, 1954, and is under the administration of the Dept. of the Interior, National Park Service.

Folger Shakespeare Library

The Folger Shakespeare Library on Capitol Hill, Washington, D. C., is a research institution devoted to the advancement of learning in the background of Anglo-American civilization in the 16th and 17th centuries and in most aspects of the continental Renaissance. It has the largest collection of Shakespeareana in the world with 79 copies of the First Folio. Its collection of English books printed before 1640 is the largest in the Western Hemisphere. It also has extensive source materials for the history of theater and drama from the Middle Ages to the end of the 19th century, both English and American. The library owns approximately 250,000 books and manuscripts, about half of them rare.

The library was founded and endowed by Henry Clay Folger, a former president of the Standard Oil Co. of New York, and his wife, Emily Jordan Folger. He left its administration to the trustees of his alma mater, Amherst College. The exhibition gallery and replica Elizabethan Theatre are open free 10 a.m. to 4:30 p.m. daily; closed federal holidays and on Sundays after Labor Day to April 15.

Library of Congress

Established by and for Congress in 1800, the Library of Congress has extended its services over the years to other Government agencies and other libraries, to scholars, and to the general public, and it now serves as the national library. Two buildings, an ornate Italian Renaissance structure, the Library of Congress Building, (1897) and a modern annex, the Thomas Jefferson Building, (1939), cover 6 acres of the $15^2/_3$-acre library site and contain 35 acres of floor space. In addition the library occupies 10 other buildings dispersed throughout the Metropolitan area. In Oct. 1965 Congress passed a law authorizing construction of a third library building, the James Madison Memorial Building; completion is expected in 1980.

Dr. Daniel J. Boorstin became the 12th Librarian of Congress on November 12, 1975.

The library had over 3,000 volumes when it was destroyed in the burning of the Capitol, Aug. 24-25, 1814. In Jan. 1815 Congress bought Thomas Jefferson's library of some 6,000 volumes. In 1851 fire destroyed about half the collections. In 1866 the science library of the Smithsonian Institution was transferred to the library, and in 1870 the library became the repository for materials deposited for copyright. Today the library's collections contain more than 73 million items, including more than 18 million volumes and pamphlets.

In addition to providing a variety of reference and bibliographic services to other government agencies, the Library of Congress serves as a cataloging and bibliographic center for libraries throughout the country. Its cataloging data is available on printed cards (a service offered since 1901), on magnetic tapes for libraries using computers, and in book catalogs. A program called Cataloging in Publication makes cataloging information available in books themselves so that they can be processed and put into circulation almost immediately after their delivery to libraries.

The library's exhibit halls are open to the public. Guided tours are given every hour from 9 a.m. through 8 p.m. Monday through Friday; and at 9 a.m. through 5 p.m. Saturday, Sunday and holidays. Arrangements for groups should be made in advance with the Tour Coordinator. Many of the library's treasures are on permanent exhibit and changing exhibits feature interesting selections from the library's collection of photographs, rare books, music, maps, and manuscripts. These are sometimes seen outside Washington as well, as traveling exhibits circulated by the Library of Congress to libraries and museums elsewhere in the country. The library's resources are also made available to the public through publication of guides, bibliographies, catalogs, and facsimiles. An annual list of **Publications in Print** is available free of charge from Central Services Division, Library of Congress, Washington, DC 20540. A monthly **Calendar of Events** listing exhibits currently on view, literary programs, chamber music, and concerts scheduled is also available from the same address. Information about the Library of Congress, publications, posters, color slides, and greeting and postal cards are available at the Information Counter, in the west entrance ground floor lobby of the Library of Congress Building.

Thomas Jefferson Memorial

The Thomas Jefferson Memorial stands on the south shore of the Tidal Basin in West Potomac park. It is a circular stone structure, with Vermont marble on the exterior and Georgia white marble inside and combines architectural elements of the dome of the Pantheon in Rome and the rotunda designed by Jefferson for the University of Virginia. The central circular chamber, 86 1/4 ft. in diameter, is dominated by a 19-ft. tall full-length figure of Thomas Jefferson by the American sculptor Rudulph Evans. The architects were John Russell Pope and his associates Otto R. Eggers and Daniel P. Higgins. The Memorial was dedicated by President F. D. Roosevelt Apr. 13, 1943, the 200th anniversary of Jefferson's birth.

On the pediment over the portico is a sculptured group by Adolph A. Weinman showing Jefferson standing before the committee appointed by the Continental Congress to draft the Declaration of Independence. On the interior walls are four panels with inscriptions from Jefferson's writings. On the frieze of the main entablature are Jefferson's lines: "I have sworn upon the altar of God eternal hostility against every form of tyranny over the mind of man."

The memorial is open daily from 8 a.m. to midnight, except Christmas Day. An elevator and curb ramps for the handicapped are in service.

John F. Kennedy Center

John F. Kennedy Center for the Performing Arts, designated by Congress as the National Cultural Center and the official memorial in Washington to President Kennedy, was opened September 8, 1971. The white marble building, designed by Edward Durell Stone, houses a 2,300-seat Opera House, a 2,750-seat Concert Hall, the 1,150-seat Eisenhower Theater, the 224-seat American Film Institute Theater, a soon-to-be-completed 600-seat studio theater, and 3 restaurants. All facilities are in full operation throughout the year. Tours are available daily, free of charge, between 10:00 a.m. and 1:15 p.m.

Lincoln Memorial

The Lincoln Memorial in West Potomac Park, on the axis of the Capitol and the Washington Monument, consists of a large marble hall enclosing a heroic statue of Abraham Lincoln in meditation sitting on a large armchair. It was dedicated on Memorial Day, May 30, 1922. The Memorial was designed by Henry Bacon. The statue was made by Daniel Chester French. Murals and ornamentation on the bronze ceiling beams are by Jules Guerin.

The memorial, built on bedrock, is of white Colorado-Yule marble. There are 2 Doric columns at the entrance and 36 others in the colonnade. The frieze above the 36 columns bears the names of the 36 states existing at the time of Lincoln's death. On the attic parapet are recorded names of the 48 states existing in 1922.

Inside are 3 memorials to Lincoln. The seated figure of Lincoln is 19 ft. from head to foot and the classic armchair is 12 1/2 ft. tall. Over the back of the chair a flag is draped in marble. The statue was fashioned out of 28 blocks of Georgia white marble. On the north wall is inscribed the Second Inaugural Address. On the south wall is the Gettysburg Address.

The walls of the interior are Indiana limestone. The panels between the overhead girders are of Alabama marble saturated with melted beeswax to produce translucency. The interior floor and the wall base are of pink Tennessee marble. The cost of the Memorial was $2,957,000 and of the statue $88,400.

The memorial is open daily from 8 a.m. to midnight, except Christmas Day. A new elevator for the handicapped is in service.

Mount Vernon

Mount Vernon on the south bank of the Potomac, 16 miles below Washington, D. C., is part of a large tract of land in northern Virginia which was originally included in a royal grant made to Lord Culpepper, who in 1674 granted 5,000 acres to Nicholas Spencer and John Washington. The division between Spencer and Washington put John Washington's son Lawrence in possession of the Washington half in 1690. Later it became the property of Lawrence Washington's son Augustine, the father of George Washington.

The present house is an enlargement of one apparently built on the site of an earlier one by Augustine Washington, who lived there 1735-1738. His son Lawrence came there in 1743, when he renamed the plantation Mount Vernon in honor of Admiral Vernon under whom he had served in the West Indies. Lawrence Washington died in 1752 and was succeeded as proprietor of Mount Vernon by his half-brother, George Washington.

To Mount Vernon in 1759 Washington brought his wife, Martha Dandridge Custis, having previously enlarged the house from 1-1/2 to 2-1/2 stories. Just before the Revolution he planned additions, and when he was called away to war his kinsman Lund Washington supervised the work, which was completed after Washington returned in 1783. During the Revolution Washington visited Mount Vernon only twice, on the way to and from Yorktown in 1781. In 1789 he left to become president and lived in New York and Philadelphia, with brief visits to the plantation. He came back in 1797 and died in Mount Vernon Dec. 14, 1799. He was buried in the old family vault. He had made plans for a new burial vault and this was built in 1831. Both his remains and those of Martha, who died in 1802, were transferred there.

Mount Vernon was left to Washington's nephew, U.S. Supreme Court Justice Bushrod Washington, and by him to his nephew, John Augustine Washington, whose son, John A. Washington Jr., was the last private owner. In 1853 Miss Ann Pamela Cunningham of South Carolina organized the Mount Vernon Ladies' Assn., which bought the mansion and 200 acres, since extended to just under 500 acres. The Association reassembled original Washington furniture and repaired the buildings. It restored the kitchen garden, flower garden, and experimental botanical garden, reconstructed the greenhouse, and built a museum. Several trees planted by Washington still exist, and the boxwood dates from 1798.

The Association preserves house and tomb with the visitor's fee. The regent of the Mount Vernon Ladies' Association is Mrs. John H. Guy Jr. About 30 states are represented by vice regents. The Resident Director is Harrison M. Symmes.

National Arboretum

The National Arboretum, established in 1927 for the study of trees and plants, has become one of Washington's great show places. Occupying 415 acres of rolling land along the Anacostia River in the northeastern section of the city, it is administered by the secretary of agriculture through the Northeast Region of the Agricultural Research Service.

The Arboretum is open every day of the year except Christmas. The visiting hours are as follows: April through October—8 a.m. to 7 p.m. Monday through Friday; 10 a.m.

to 7 p.m. Saturdays and Sundays. November through March —8 a.m. to 5 p.m. Monday through Friday; 10 a.m. to 5 p.m. Saturdays and Sundays.

National Archives

The Declaration of Independence, the Constitution of the United States, and the Bill of Rights are on permanent display in the National Archives Exhibition Hall. They are sealed in glass-and-bronze cases filled with inert helium gas. They can be lowered 20 feet at a moment's notice into a large shockproof and fireproof safe.

The National Archives holds the permanently valuable federal records of the United States government, 1774 to the present. As a research institution, it is designed to preserve these records and make them available to government agencies, scholars, students, writers, and the general public.

The National Archives and Records Service is a part of the General Services Administration. Through the Presidential Libraries Office it administers the Franklin D. Roosevelt Library at Hyde Park, N. Y., the Harry S. Truman Library at Independence, Mo., the Dwight D. Eisenhower Library at Abilene, Kan., the Herbert Hoover Library at West Branch, Iowa, the Lyndon Baines Johnson Library at Austin, Tex., and the John Fitzgerald Kennedy Library, temporarily at Waltham, Mass., and the Gerald Ford Library to be built in Ann Arbor, Mich., and museum to stand in Grand Rapids.

The National Archives and Records Service is headed by Dr. James B. Rhoads, archivist of the United States, Pennsylvania Ave. and 8th St. N.W. For research information, call 202-523-3218. For visitor information, call 202-523-3000.

National Gallery of Art

The National Gallery of Art, situated in an area bounded by Constitution Avenue and the Mall, between Third and Seventh Streets, was established by Joint Resolution of Congress Mar. 24, 1937, and opened Mar. 17, 1941. Although technically a bureau of the Smithsonian Institution, the gallery is an autonomous organization governed by its own board of trustees. The chairman of the board is the chief justice of the United States. Other members are the secretaries of state and of the treasury, the secretary of the Smithsonian Institution, and five distinguished private citizens.

The collections comprise gifts of over 300 donors (none of the works were acquired with Government funds) and cover the American and various European schools of art from the 13th century to the present.

The building was erected with funds given by Andrew W. Mellon, who also gave his collection of 126 paintings and 26 pieces of sculpture, which included such masterpieces as Raphael's Alba Madonna, the Niccolini-Cowper Madonna, and St. George and the Dragon, van Eyck's Annunciation, Botticelli's Adoration of the Magi, and 9 Rembrandts. Twenty-one paintings came from the Hermitage in Leningrad. Also in this collection are the Vaughan Portrait of George Washington, by Gilbert Stuart, and The Washington Family, by Edward Savage.

The Samuel H. Kress Collection includes the great tondo of the Adoration of the Magi by Fra Angelico and Fra Filippo Lippi, the Laocoon by El Greco, and fine examples by Giorgione, Titian, Grunewald, Durer, Memling, Bosch, Juan de Flandes, Francois Clouet, Poussin, Watteau, Chardin, Boucher, Fragonard, David, and Ingres. Also included are a number of masterpieces of sculpture, especially of the Italian and French schools.

The Widener Collection of over 100 paintings includes 14 Rembrandts, 8 Van Dycks, 2 Vermeers, and examples of Italian, Spanish, English, and French painting, and Italian and French sculpture and decorative arts.

The Chester Dale Collection includes masterpieces by Manet, Cezanne, Renoir, Toulouse-Lautrec, Monet, Modigliani, Pissarro, Degas, van Gogh, Gauguin, Matisse, Picasso, Braque, and such American artists as Gilbert Stuart, Childe Hassam, and George Bellows.

Several major works of art by some of the most important artists of the last hundred years, including Picasso, Cezanne, Gauguin, and the American painter Walt Kuhn, have been given to the gallery by the W. Averell Harriman Foundation in memory of Marie N. Harriman.

The Collection of Edgar William and Bernice Chrysler Garbisch includes more than 300 American naive paintings and watercolors covering the eighteenth and nineteenth centuries. Among them are Edward Hicks' Cornell Farm, Winthrop Chandler's portraits of Captain Samuel Chandler and Mrs. Samuel Chandler, and Linton Park's Flax Scutching Bee.

Pictures to round out the collection have been bought with funds provided by the late Ailsa Mellon Bruce, daughter of Andrew W. Mellon. Preeminent among them is the portrait of Ginevra de' Benci, the only generally acknowledged painting by Leonardo da Vinci outside Europe; Georges de la Tour's Repentant Magdalen, one of the rarest paintings of the 17th Century; and Pablo Picasso's Nude Woman, the key work of the artist's analytical cubist period. Among others are: Rubens' Daniel in the Lions' Den; Claude Lorrain's Judgment of Paris; Saint George and the Dragon, attributed to van der Weyden; and a number of American paintings, including Cole's second set of The Voyage of Life.

Cezanne's great early portrait of his father and 351 paintings by George Catlin, mostly of North and South American Indians, are among recent acquisitions given by Paul Mellon, president of the gallery and son of Andrew Mellon. A fine collection of French impressionist pictures are on loan to the gallery from Mr. and Mrs. Mellon.

Among other works donated to the gallery's collection are Vermeer's A Lady Writing, given by Harry Waldron Havemeyer and Horace Havemeyer Jr., in memory of their father, Horace Havemeyer; Copley's Watson and the Shark, given by Ferdinand Lammot Belin; Goya's Victor Guye, given by William Nelson Cromwell; and Mondrian's Lozenge in Red, Yellow and Blue, given by Herbert and Nannette Rothschild.

The National Gallery's rapidly expanding graphic arts holdings number about 62,000 items and date from the twelfth century to the present. Almost half of these works were the gift of Lessing J. Rosenwald, who had gathered one of the world's great collections of prints and drawings.

The Index of American Design contains over 17,000 watercolor renderings and 500 photographs of American crafts and folk arts from before 1700 until 1900.

The gallery's Education Department gives daily talks on the gallery's collection. The Extension Service lends films and slide programs to schools, colleges, and civic groups in more than 4000 communities in the United States and Canada. Nearly all of the gallery's services are available to the public free of charge.

The National Gallery is in the process of moving into its new East Building, which adjoins the original West Building. Funds for the new construction have come from Mr. Paul Mellon, the late Ailsa Mellon Bruce, and The Andrew W. Mellon Foundation. The architect is I. M. Pei. The gallery segment of the East Building, which is scheduled to open in 1978, provides space for temporary exhibitions and the gallery's growing collection of 20th century paintings and sculpture. Alongside the gallery segment is the administrative and research segment, which will house the Center for Advanced Study in the Visual Arts together with a greatly expanded library, photographic archive, and office facilities. Already open to the public is an underground concourse connecting the East and West Buildings and containing a major new restaurant complex, the Cafe/Buffet.

Open daily except Christmas and New Year's, from 10 a.m. to 5 p.m. Monday through Saturday and noon to 9 p.m. Sunday. During the summer open Monday through Saturday 10 a.m. to 9 p.m., noon to 9 p.m. Sunday.

National Geographic Society

The National Geographic Society, founded in 1888 "for the increase and diffusion of geographic knowledge," is the world's largest nonprofit scientific and educational institution. The Society produces the illustrated monthly *National Geographic*, books, maps, globes, atlases, other educational materials, and television programs. Its activities are supported by the dues of 9,750,000 members.

The society's 10-story headquarters building in Washington, D. C., was dedicated by President Lyndon B.

Johnson in 1964. It attracts many thousands of visitors, including members of the society from all over the world. Explorers Hall offers exhibits, artifacts, and mementos depicting the organization's research and exploration activities.

In 1968 the society occupied its new Membership Center Building on a 100-acre tract near Gaithersburg, Md. The building accommodates 1,200 employees charged with handling membership files, correspondence, changes of address, and other clerical operations.

Executive officers are: Robert E. Doyle, president; Owen R. Anderson, vice president and secretary; Gilbert M. Grosvenor, vice president and editor; Melvin M. Payne, chairman of the board; Melville Bell Grosvenor, chairman emeritus and editor emeritus; Thomas W. McKnew, advisory chairman of the board; Hilleary F. Hoskinson, treasurer.

The Pentagon

The Pentagon, headquarters of the Department of Defense, is the world's largest office building, twice as large as the Merchandise Mart in Chicago and with 3 times the floor space of the Empire State Building in New York. Situated on the Virginia side of the Potomac River, it houses 22,000 employees in offices that occupy 3,707,745 sq. ft.

The Pentagon was completed Jan. 15, 1943, at a cost of about $83,000,000. It covers 34 acres and has 204 acres of lawns and terraces. It is 5 stories high and consists of 5 rings of buildings connected by 10 corridors, with a 5-acre pentagonal court in the center. Each of the outer-most sides of the building is 921 ft. long and the perimeter is seven-eighths of a mile. Total length of corridors is 17 1/2 miles. There is a partial mezzanine below the first floor and a partial basement below that.

Tours are available Monday through Friday (excluding federal holidays), and start every 30 minutes at the Concourse. The first tour begins at 9 a.m. and the last at 3:30 p.m. Walk-ins are welcome. During the summer tourist season, tours are conducted every 15 minutes.

Smithsonian Institution

The Smithsonian Institution is one of the world's great historical, scientific, educational, and cultural establishments. It comprises numerous facilities, mostly in the metropolitan Wash., D.C., area. It was founded by an Act of Congress in 1846, pursuant to a bequest of James Smithson, a British scholar-scientist, to the United States to found at Washington "an establishment for the increase and diffusion of knowledge among men." The Smithsonian, ever since its founding, has been a center for basic scientific research; it engages in programs of education and it is also the largest museum-gallery complex in the world. About 20 million persons visit its halls annually. S. Dillon Ripley became the 8th secretary of the Smithsonian Feb. 1, 1964.

The Anacostia Neighborhood Museum, the first of its kind in the nation, opened in 1967 in a low-income urban community. The museum develops and presents exhibits on topics of interest to the residents of the community as well as the greater Washington area. The staff also conducts independent research in the areas of Afro-American history, minority and ethnic studies, and the history of the Anacostia community and Washington, D.C. Independent programs and activities, such as teacher workshops, seminars, and a circulating library of children's books on African and Afro-American history serve the local school community.

The Arts and Industries Building reopened in May 1976 with an exhibit entitled "1876: A Centennial Exhibition" which displays actual items from the Centennial exhibition in Philadelphia as well as others of the same era. The four halls are devoted to various subjects including machinery, with a large number of the machines in operation; items from the military, U.S. Treasury and the Patent Office; manufactured articles; and displays from many of the 37 states in existence in 1876 and from the foreign countries represented in the Philadelphia exhibition.

The Freer Gallery of Art, the gift of Detroit industrialist Charles Lang Freer, is an outstanding museum and research center in art of the Far and Near East. The gallery also houses the Whistler Peacock Room and his etchings and paintings.

The Hirshhorn Museum and Sculpture Garden, opened in 1974, houses works in the Joseph H. Hirshhorn collection which were donated in 1966 to the people of the United States. Primary emphasis is on art of the 20th century although the sculpture section ranges from antiquity to works of the most significant European and American contemporaries.

The National Museum of History and Technology has exhibits illustrating American culture, civil and military history, and the history of science and technology. The museum consists of 3 floors of exhibitions, and food facilities for its visitors. In the rotunda the visitor will find the original Star-Spangled Banner and a Foucault pendulum demonstrating the earth's rotation. "A Nation of Nations" is a museum within a museum tracing the peopling of America through 6,000 objects. Other major exhibits feature gowns of the first ladies, the Petroleum Hall, the history of transportation, American political and military history, numismatics, philately, ceramics and glass, musical instruments, timekeeping, physical and medical sciences, graphic arts, electricity, photography, and news reporting. National treasures on display include the desk on which Thomas Jefferson drafted the Declaration of Independence and Samuel Morse's first telegraph. A popular attraction is an authentic 19th century country store-post office where mail is hand-stamped with a "Smithsonian Station" postmark.

The National Museum of Natural History serves as a national and international center for the natural sciences. It maintains the largest reference collection in the nation and conducts a broad program of basic research on man, plants, animals, fossil organisms, rocks, minerals, and materials from outer space. Exhibits show aspects of life and cultures in Asia, Africa, the Pacific, and North and South America. Other exhibits include fossil plants and invertebrate animals, mammals, fishes, amphibians, dinosaurs, and primitive reptiles. There are halls of North American archeology, osteology, and physical anthropology. Also on view are geology exhibits on the earth, the moon, and meteorites as well as a Hall of Minerals and Gems which includes the 45 1/2-carat blue Hope diamond and the largest gem emerald on public exhibit, the 858-carat Gachala emerald. The World of Mammals, the Hall of Birds, the Fenykovi Elephant, and the Insect Zoo are additional major exhibits.

The National Air and Space Museum, which opened in a newly constructed building July 1, 1976, houses exhibits on space exploration, air travel and related scientific and technical topics. Its Milestones of Flight Gallery exhibits 'famous firsts' of air and space development such as the Wright Flyer, Lindbergh's "Spirit of St. Louis," John Glenn's Mercury capsule, the Friendship 7 craft, the Apollo 11 command module Columbia, and a moon rock. Aspects of space exploration and air travel are displayed in galleries titled the Space Hall, Hall of Air Transportation, Satellites and Sounding Rockets, Vertical Flight, and Life in the Universe. Other exhibit galleries focus on balloons and airships, flight technology, sea-air operations, and various kinds of military aviation. There is a giant screen theater with presentations related to air and space travel and the Albert Einstein Spacearium presents programs of sky and space simulation.

The National Collection of Fine Arts presents a panorama of American painting, sculpture, and graphic art from the 18th century to today with 18,000 works in its collections and approximately 25 special exhibitions each year. It is housed in the historic Old Patent Office Building; its Lincoln Gallery was the site of Abraham Lincoln's second inaugural reception. **The Renwick Gallery,** a curatorial department of the National Collection of Fine Arts, is a national showcase for American creativity in design, crafts, and the decorative arts. In addition to special temporary exhibitions, two rooms refurnished in the late 19th century period can be seen.

The National Portrait Gallery, also located in the Old Patent Office Bldg., exhibits the likenesses of persons who have made significant contributions to the history, development, and culture of the people of the United States. The gallery's temporary exhibitions are based on a variety of historical themes.

The National Zoological Park is noted for its outstanding collections including two giant pandas from China. Its research includes investigation in animal behavior, ecology, nutrition and reproduction physiology, pathology, and clinical medicine. Conservation-oriented studies cover maintenance of wild population and long-term captive breeding and care of endangered species.

The Smithsonian Associates was founded to stimulate interest and active participation in the Smithsonian's work. Its membership programs for adults and young people include seminars, lectures, workshops, demonstrations, concerts, theater, exhibition previews, dramas, films, tours, and field and camping trips. *Smithsonian*, a monthly magazine of the arts, sciences, and history, is available to members of the Associates.

The Smithsonian Institution Traveling Exhibition Service (SITES) organizes and circulates exhibitions for art and science museums, colleges, and other educational institutions around the United States and Canada. More than 200 exhibitions are on continuous tour, with 75 or 80 openings of these shows occurring monthly across the country.

Washington Monument

The Washington Monument is a tapering shaft or obelisk of white marble, 555 ft., 5-1/8 inches in height and 55 ft., 1-1/2 inches square at base. Eight small windows, 2 on each side, are located at the 500-ft. level, where Washington points of interest are indicated.

The capstone weighs 3,300 lbs. and was placed Dec. 6, 1884. The monument was dedicated Feb. 21, 1885, and opened Oct. 9, 1888. It weighs 81,120 tons. It is dressed with white Maryland marble in 2-ft. courses. The first 150 ft. are backed by rubble masonry. From that point to 452 ft. Maine granite was used as backing, and above 452 ft. marble was used. The face of the monument is primarily marble from Maryland. Set into the interior wall are 190 memorial stones from states, foreign countries, and organizations. An iron stairway has 50 landings and 898 steps. A modern elevator takes sightseers to the 500-ft. level in one minute, compared with 12 "precarious minutes" in 1888.

The erection of the monument by the Washington National Monument society with funds obtained by popular subscription was authorized by Congress in 1848. The cornerstone was laid July 4 of the same year. Work progressed slowly until 1854 when $300,000 had been subscribed and 152 ft. of the shaft erected. In that year the enterprise became controversial and contributions ceased. Work was resumed in 1880 at government expense by the Corps of Engineers.

The Monument is open 7 days a week, 9 a.m. to 5 p.m. Extended summer hours are 8 a.m. to 12 midnight. It is closed Christmas Day.

Famous Churches

The National Shrine of the Immaculate Conception, at Fourth St. and Michigan Ave. NE, Washington, D. C. is the largest Catholic church in the United States and one of the largest in the world. Built by all the bishops and Catholics of the U. S., it honors the Blessed Virgin Mary as Patroness of the United States. The Shrine is impressive not only in size but also in beauty, its blue and gold dome and soaring bell-tower having become Washington landmarks. Open daily from 7 a.m. to 8 p.m., Sunday masses, 7:30, 9:00, 10:30 a.m., 12 noon, 1:30 and 4 p.m. (5:15 p.m. Sat. eve.). Free guided tours 9 a.m. to 5 p.m. daily; Sunday tours 2 p.m. to 4 p.m. Carillon concerts on Sundays and preceding organ and choral concerts. Organ recitals every Sun. at 7:00 p.m. (June through August) and 4th Friday organ recitals (Sept. through May).

Washington Cathedral, Massachusetts and Wisconsin Aves. NW, is atop Mt. Saint Alban, the highest point in Washington, D.C. It is the seat of the Presiding Bishop of the Episcopal Church and of the Bishop of Washington. Started in 1907, the cathedral is nearly complete. The nave was finished and opened in 1976, with a festive dedicatory ceremony July 8, marking the visit of Queen Elizabeth to the nation's capital. The west facade is under construction. It is the 6th largest cathedral in the world. Notables buried in the cathedral include Woodrow Wilson, Adm. George Dewey, Cordell Hull, and Frank B. Kellogg. The cathedral is considered one of the finest examples of Gothic architecture in the country.

Several Protestant churches commemorate the association of presidents with their congregations. **St. John's Episcopal Church,** across Lafayette Sq. from the White House, designed by Benj. Latrobe in 1815, was regularly attended by Madison, F. D. Roosevelt, Ford and at times by other presidents. **New York Ave. Presbyterian Church,** 1313 New York Ave. NW, established in 1803, preserves the pew in which Lincoln sat, also an original manuscript of the first draft of his first proposal to abolish slavery. The church was rebuilt on same site in 1950-51.

The National Presbyterian Church, on a 13-acre tract, at Nebraska Ave. and Van Ness St. NW, was dedicated on May 10, 1970. The Church traces its origin to a group of stonemasons who met in a carpenter's shop in the grounds of the White House in 1795, later becoming the First Presbyterian Church in the District of Columbia. The Church of the Covenant, founded in 1883, united with the original Presbyterian body in 1930 to become the congregation of the National Presbyterian Church. President Eisenhower was baptized by the pastor, Dr. Edward L. R. Elson, and became a member of the Church on Feb. 1, 1953. He laid the cornerstone of the new Church on his 77th birthday, Oct. 14, 1967, and the Chapel of the Presidents is dedicated to him. The Chapel of the Presidents contains the Eisenhower pew, and pews representing 16 additional presidents who worshipped with the congregation. The oldest president's pew, occupied by Jackson, Polk, Pierce, Buchanan, and Cleveland, is on view together with much historic memorabilia.

The Islamic Center, 2551 Massachusetts Ave. NW, a magnificent monument of Islamic culture and outstanding landmark for visitors, a mosque for worship, and an institute for study of Islamic culture.

Cherry Blossom Time

Cherry blossom time in Washington is looked upon as the opening of spring. The famous cherry trees encircle the Tidal Basin in West Potomac Park and for 2 miles line the roadside in East Potomac Park. A gift by the Mayor of Tokyo to the city of Washington, the original 3,000 trees were propagated from the trees on the Arawaka River in a suburb of Tokyo. The first trees were planted by Mrs. William Howard Taft, wife of the president, and by Viscountess Chinda, wife of the Japanese Ambassador, Mar. 27, 1912. Today many of the 650 trees around the Tidal Basin have white blossoms, while some have pink; deep pink blossoms are in East Potomac Park. The trees usually are in full blossom the first week in April, but no precise date can be given earlier than 10 days prior to full blossom, which lasts about one week.

Other Points of Interest

Pan American Union Building, 17th St. and Constitution Ave., NW, houses the General Secretariat of the Organization of American States, the oldest major international organization in the world, representing 26 countries of the western hemisphere. Of traditional Spanish architecture with a tropical garden courtyard, the building is one of the more gracious sights in Washington. It contains the Hall of the Americas assembly room, art exhibitions, the Columbus Memorial Library, and behind the building, the Aztec Gardens, and the Museum of Modern Art of Latin America.

National Society, Daughters of the American Revolution, established in 1890, stands on a block bounded by 17th and 18th Sts., and C and D Sts. NW.

American National Red Cross, 17th and D Sts. NW, occupies 3 white marble buildings of neoclassic design, embellished with a Corinthian portico, colonnades, and bronze doors. The Red Cross Museum is in the east building.

Federal Reserve Building, Constitution Ave., between 20th and 21st Sts. NW, is a 4-story white marble building of Georgian design, with formal gardens and fountains, and tasteful but relatively simple interiors, built 1937. An annex, the William McChesney Martin Building, was occupied in 1974.

The Corcoran Gallery of Art, 17th St. between New York Ave., and E St. NW, Washington, was donated by William Wilson Corcoran in 1859. Other donors, including Sen. W. A. Clark, have augmented its collection. The gallery is open 11 a.m. to 5 p.m., Tuesday through Sunday; closed Mondays, and on Jan. 1, July 4, Thanksgiving, and Dec. 24, 25, and 31. Admission is $1.50; free on Tues. and Wed. and at all times to senior citizens, children under 12 accompanied by an adult, and members.

N.Y. City Places of Interest

Museums, Zoos, Libraries, Churches, Historic Sites, Buildings, Other Attractions

See Index for Statue of Liberty

The New York Aquarium, in Coney Island, exhibits marine life from all climes, with over 3,000 live specimens including whales, sharks, seals, sea lions, fish, penguins; whale and dolphin training sessions.

The New York Botanical Garden covers 250 acres in the Bronx. It offers seasonal botanical and educational exhibits and concerts. There are specialized gardens, a museum of plant evolution and uses, a botanical library, and a plant and book shop.

The Frick Collection, 1 E. 70th St., was founded by Henry Clay Frick (1849-1919). The principal part of the collection consists of 14th-19th century paintings as well as sculpture and Chinese and French enamels.

The Solomon R. Guggenheim Museum, 5th Ave. and 89th St.; permanent collection contains over 3,000 paintings, drawings, sculptures, and graphic works by 19th and 20th Century artists. The museum's spiral building was designed by Frank Lloyd Wright.

The Hayden Planetarium, facing 81st St. near Central Park W., presents changing sky shows with a Zeiss projector in the world's largest planetarium dome; "Astronomia," an exhibit of astronomy fact and fantasy throughout history; Guggenheim Space Theater shows, and a "Hall of the Sun," depicting the role of the sun in our lives.

The Hispanic Society of America is a free public museum and reference library devoted to the art and literature of Spain and Portugal. It is on Audubon Terrace, between 155th and 156th Sts., west of Broadway. Collections run from ancient to modern.

The Jewish Museum, 5th Ave. at 92d St., offers exhibitions of Jewish art and ceremonial objects and exhibits of Jewish interest. The permanent collection of Judaica is considered the most comprehensive in the world. There are lectures, guided tours, and a book and print shop.

The Metropolitan Museum of Art, 5th Ave. at 82d St. With over 1 million works of art, the museum's collection is the largest of its kind in the Western Hemisphere. Great masters of all the ages of art are included in the collections; Egyptian, Greek, Roman, Ancient Near Eastern, Islamic, Far Eastern, Medieval, Arms and Armor, European, Pre-Columbian, American, Contemporary Arts, Musical Instruments, Costume Institute, and Junior Museum. A new American Bicentennial Wing is to be completed in 1978.

The Cloisters, in Manhattan's Fort Tryon Park, is a branch of the Metropolitan devoted to Medieval art and architecture in 5 cloisters and other early European structures.

The Museum of the American Indian, Heye Foundation, Broadway at 155th St., maintains the world's largest collection of American Indian materials, extensive archeological and ethnological displays from North, Central, and South America, as well as study and photographic facilities.

The Museum of Modern Art, 11 W. 53d St., presents 20th century painting, sculpture, drawings, prints, architectural and industrial design, photography, and film. A library contains about 30,000 vols. and a reference collection of more than 100,000 photographs. The film department has more than 12 million ft. of film. Bookstore, restaurant, and gift shop.

The American Museum of Natural History occupies a group of buildings at Central Park West between 77th and 81st Sts. There are large exhibits of man and beast from the most primitive times to the present, with extensive reconstruction of fossilized remains, dioramas of men and animals in their natural settings, dinosaurs, birds, Indians, Eskimos, and glass models of protozoa, rotifers, and coelenterates. The collections of gems, mollusks, meteorites, and ocean life are famous. Live shows include dance, drama, music, crafts, audience participation programs.

The Museum of the City of New York on 5th Ave. at 103d St., illustrates the history and life of the city. Its collections include dioramas, paintings, prints, maps, photographs, portraits, miniatures, fire engines, ship models, costumes, silver, furniture, theatrical and musical memorabilia, toys, and rare books.

The New-York Historical Society, founded 1804, is at 170 Central Park W. between 76th and 77th Sts. The society maintains a museum devoted to Americana; a large gallery of American portrait, landscape, and genre paintings; a reference library of American, and especially New York, history; manuscripts from all periods of the nation's past; maps, prints, broadsides, and photographs. Of special interest are the original watercolor drawings by John James Audubon for his *Birds of America*. Also, fire engine, carriage, toy collections.

The American Numismatic Society, founded 1858, maintains a museum of coins and other currency, ancient and modern medals, and decorations at Broadway and 156th St.

The New York Public Library: In 1976, its resources were placed at more than 34.5 million items of which over 9 million were books, over 10 million manuscripts, over 6 million pictures, 3.5 million posters, photographs, and broadsides, 6 million pamphlets, scrapbooks, and clippings. Of this total, 4 million books and the pictures are in the collections of the Branch Libraries which are maintained by N.Y. City and which operate 82 branch libraries in Manhattan, the Bronx and Staten Island and 3 bookmobiles. The Research Libraries, based at 5th Ave. and 42d St., include the Performing Arts Research Center, in Lincoln Center, and the Schomburg Center for Research in Black Culture, 103 W. 135th St.

Seamen's Church Institute, 15 State St., facing Manhattan's Battery Park, has dining room, cafeteria, collections of ships' bells and models, marine paintings, gym, sauna, and showers, all open to public.

South Street Seaport Museum, on the East River waterfront in lower Manhattan, is a growing restoration of earlier eras of New York's port. At piers off South St. at Fulton, the museum has 8 ships, including an iron-hulled windjammer, one of the world's longest square-riggers, and the original Ambrose Lightship. Ashore on Fulton St. are museum galleries, a printing museum, and a bookshop. Features include puppet and craft shows, songfests, plays for children and adults, and seminars on nautical subjects. Restorations will include 100 early buildings with art shops, apartments, offices, restaurants.

The Staten Island Institute of Arts and Sciences, founded 1881, has a museum of art, natural science, conservation, and Indian life at 75 Stuyvesant Pl., St. George, S.I., and library at 51 Stuyvesant Pl. It offers lectures, nature walks, for children and adults.

Whitney Museum of American Art, Madison Ave. at 75th St., holds exhibitions of group and individual artists, historical and contemporary. Comprehensive permanent collection of American art. Has downtown branch at 55 Water St.

Zoos. One of the world's largest zoos is the N.Y. Zoological Society Park (the Bronx Zoo), Pelham Parkway and Southern Blvd., the Bronx. About 3,000 mammals, birds, reptiles are displayed in its 252 acres, including African Plains exhibit, World of Birds, Children's Zoo, 40 acres of "Wild Asia," and nocturnal animals in World of Darkness. The city's Parks and Recreation Dept. runs the Central Park Zoo and the adjoining Children's Zoo at 5th Ave. and 64th St. in Manhattan, the Prospect Park Zoo and Children's Farmyard in Brooklyn, and the Queens Zoo and Children's Farm in Flushing Meadows-Corona Park, Queens. The Staten Island Zoological Society operates the Staten Island Zoo and Children's Zoo in Barrett Park, West New Brighton.

Brooklyn Centers

Brooklyn Academy of Music, 30 Lafayette Ave., presents a Sept.-through-May program of music, dance, theater, and film.

Brooklyn Botanic Garden, Eastern Parkway, Washington and Flatbush Aves., has 50 acres of gardens, including rose, rock, bonsai, herb, wild flower, Japanese, a fragrance garden for the blind, and conservatory.

The Brooklyn Museum, Eastern Parkway and Washington Ave., estab. 1825, has comprehensive exhibitions in all major fields of art. An Outdoor Sculpture Garden contains ornaments from razed N.Y. area buildings.

The Brooklyn Public Library occupies the Ingersoll Building, Grand Army Plaza, and 59 branches. The Ingersoll Building has 7 major-subject divisions and a children's room, and telephone reference service.

Houses of Worship

Central Synagogue (Reform), Lexington Ave. at 55th St., is the oldest Jewish house of worship in N.Y. City (1872), and combines 2 earlier congregations founded in 1839 and 1846. Its modern community house, 123 E. 55th St., includes a religious school, chapel, meeting rooms. Since 1934, the synagogue has presented the weekly Message of Israel program on a nationwide radio network.

John Street United Methodist Church, 44 John St., erected 1841, on site of Wesley Chapel of 1768, "first Methodist preaching-house in America," houses oldest Methodist Society, formed 1766. Has noontime services for office workers, and a museum.

Marble Collegiate Church (Collegiate Reformed Protestant Dutch), 5th Ave. and W. 29th St., erected 1854, is notable for the preaching by Dr. Norman Vincent Peale.

Mormon Visitors Center, 2 Lincoln Sq. (B'way at 65th St.), opened 1975. There are a meeting house, sports and drama facilities, genealogy research library, displays of Mormon history, open to public.

Plymouth Church of the Pilgrims (Congregational), Orange and Hicks Sts., Brooklyn, is a Nat'l. Historic Site, built 1847, present structure 1849. Has windows illustrating Puritan influence on America and pew where Lincoln sat to hear Henry Ward Beecher, the first minister. In 1860 Beecher raised funds at an auction here to purchase the freedom of a slave girl, Pinky.

Riverside Church (Interdenominational), Riverside Drive and W. 122d St. The chief donor was John D. Rockefeller Jr. The tower, reminiscent of Chartres, is 100 ft. square, rises 392 ft.; it has the world's largest carillon, with 74 bells, and is open to public.

Russian Orthodox Cathedral of the Transfiguration (Orthodox Church in America), 228 N. 12th St., Brooklyn, is of a design similar to Moscow's Cathedral of the Assumption, with 5 onion-shaped domes. A screen of icons includes one from the 13th century.

Cathedral of St. John the Divine on Morningside Heights, Amsterdam Ave. and W. 112th St. (Episcopal), is one of the world's largest cathedrals. It was begun 1892 as a Romanesque building; the design was changed to Gothic. The church is 603 ft. long, 146 ft. wide at nave, and will be 330 ft. wide at transept. Two front towers will rise to nearly 300 ft.

St. Mark's-in-the-Bowery (Episcopal), 2d Ave. and E. 10th St., originally a chapel built on the farm of Director General Peter Stuyvesant in 1660, rebuilt in 1799. A statue of Stuyvesant in the churchyard was presented by Netherlands Queen Wilhelmina in 1915. The church has a theater, dance, and poetry center.

St. Patrick's Cathedral (Roman Catholic) occupies a block facing 5th Ave., between E. 50th and E. 51st Sts., opposite Rockefeller Center. It was begun in 1858 in granite and marble in a Gothic revival style designed by James Renwick. It was opened in part in 1877 and dedicated May 25, 1879. It has 2 spires, 330 ft. tall, and a 26-ft. rose window. St. Patrick's is the cathedral church of the Archdiocese of N.Y.

St. Paul's Chapel of Trinity Parish (Episcopal), Broadway and Vesey St., is the oldest public building in continuous use in Manhattan. It was opened Oct. 30, 1766. Much of the interior decoration was by L'Enfant, who laid the plans for Washington, D.C. There is a unique collection of 14 Waterford Irish cut glass chandeliers.

St. Peter's Church (Roman Catholic), Barclay and Church Sts., has the form of a Greek temple with large porch, wide steps, granite pillars, erected 1836-38 to replace the original church of 1785 of the first Catholic parish of New York.

St. Thomas Church (Episcopal), 5th Ave. at 53d St., is the 4th church building, consecrated 1916, of a parish founded in 1823. The limestone Gothic edifice was designed by architects Bertram G. Goodhue and Ralph Adams Cram. It has 2 organs; recitals are given Thursdays at noon. It also has the only church-affiliated boys boarding choir school in the U.S.; choir recitals are given Wednesdays at noon.

St. Vartan Armenian Cathedral (Armenian Church of America), 2d Ave. and 35th St. In 5th-7th century style, it is the cathedral church of the Eastern North America Diocese.

Temple Emanu-El, 5th Ave. and 65th St., was erected 1929 by Congregation Emanu-El (Reform), which dates from 1845. It was built of limestone in early Romanesque style, its auditorium 77 ft. wide by 150 ft. long and 103 ft. high, one of the largest temples in the world. Noteworthy are the high arch at the entrance, the rose window, mosaics, and 6 bronze doors.

Trinity Church (Episcopal) faces Broadway at the head of Wall St. It was built 1841-46 of brown sandstone in perpendicular Gothic, designed by Richard Upjohn, is 78 ft. wide by 202 ft. long. The first church was completed in 1697. In the churchyard are buried Alexander Hamilton, Robert Fulton, Capt. James Lawrence, and Revolutionary soldiers who died in British prisons.

Historic Sites

Castle Clinton, Battery Park, lower Manhattan, is an 1811 fort, restored 1975; historical exhibits.

Edgar Allan Poe Cottage, Grand Concourse and Kingsbridge Rd., Bronx, is a restored cottage, built 1812, in which Poe lived 1846-49, and in which his wife, Virginia Clem, died, 1847.

Federal Hall National Memorial, Wall and Nassau Sts., is a Greek Revival structure of 1842, originally the Custom House, later the U.S. Sub-Treasury. The site was first occupied by the Colonial City Hall and next by Federal Hall, where the Stamp Act Congress, Continental, and U.S. Congresses met, and George Washington took the oath of office as president.

Fraunces Tavern, Broad and Pearl Sts., was erected 1719 as the DeLancey mansion, acquired 1762 by Samuel Fraunces and operated as the Queen's Head Tavern. The Long Room was the scene of Washington's farewell to his officers, Dec. 4, 1783. It was restored by the Sons of the Revolution in the State of New York and is their headquarters. It contains a Revolutionary War museum and art gallery, free to the public.

General Grant National Memorial (Grant's Tomb), Riverside Dr. and W. 122d St., is a formal Roman-style mausoleum, 165 ft. tall, where Gen. U.S. Grant, 18th president, and Mrs. Grant are buried.

The Morris-Jumel Mansion and Museum, W. 160th St. and Edgecombe Ave., is a 3-story Georgian mansion with 4-pillared portico built in 1765 by retired British Lt. Col. Roger Morris. From Sept. 14-Oct. 18, 1776, it was the headquarters of Gen. George Washington. In 1810 Stephen Jumel bought 36 of the original 100 acres of the property. In 1833, the widowed Eliza Jumel married Aaron Burr in the mansion's front parlor.

Washington Square, at the foot of 5th Ave., is the best known landmark of **Greenwich Village,** a colorful community and tourist attraction. Facing the lower end of 5th Ave. is the marble **Washington Arch,** designed by Stanford White to mark the centennial of the first inauguration and completed in 1895.

Important Buildings

Battery Park City. On a mile-long, 100-acre site reclaimed from the Hudson River, running north from Battery Park in lower Manhattan, buildings will provide 16,000 housing units, 6 million sq. ft. of office space, a hotel, and entertainment, cultural, shopping, and recreational facilities. Occupancy to begin in 1979.

City Hall, headquarters of the mayor, the City Council, and the Board of Estimate of the City of New York, is in City Hall Park (the original Common), bounded by Broadway, Park Row, and Chambers St. Erected 1803-1812, it is an adaptation of French Renaissance with clock cupola surmounted by a figure of Justice.

The Coliseum, facing Columbus Circle between W. 58th and W. 60th Sts., is New York's principal center for national and international exhibitions. Opened in 1956, it cost about $35 million. The Coliseum has over 320,000 sq. ft. of exhibition space.

Empire State Building, 5th Ave., between W. 33d and 34th Sts., is one of the world's tallest buildings (see also World Trade Center, below), 1,250 ft. high plus a 222-ft. television and FM radio transmitting tower. The building was completed May 1, 1931. More than 1.5 million persons annually visit the 86th and 102d floor observatories. On a clear day viewers can see a distance of 80 mi. It also has the Guinness World Records Exhibit Hall.

Lincoln Center for the Performing Arts opened 1962 with a concert in Philharmonic (later renamed Avery Fisher) Hall. The center lies between W. 62d and 66th Sts., Amsterdam and Columbus Aves. It is a private, nonprofit, tax-exempt corporation of 8 constituent organizations. The New York State Theater opened in 1964; the Vivian Beaumont Theater, which includes the Mitzi E. Newhouse Theater, and the Library-museum of the Performing Arts, 1965; the Metropolitan Opera House, 1966; the Juilliard School of Music, including Alice Tully Hall, 1969.

Madison Square Garden Center, Pennsylvania Plaza (7th-8th Aves., 31st-33d Sts.). The huge development, above the modernized underground Pennsylvania RR station, includes a 29-story office building and the Sports and Entertainment Center which has the Garden Arena seating over 20,000, the 5,000-seat Felt Forum, 48 bowling lanes, the National Art Museum of Sport, and an Exposition Rotunda for trade and walk-around shows.

Pan Am Building, north of Grand Central Station, is one of the world's largest commercial office buildings. It has 59 floors rising 808 ft., with provision for a rooftop heliport, and was erected over the tracks of Grand Central Terminal. It covers an area of 3 1/2 acres. Estimated office population is 17,000.

Rockefeller Center, the largest privately-owned business and entertainment center in America was started Sept., 1931. Its area includes the 3 blocks from 48th to 51st Sts. between 5th Ave. and the Ave. of the Americas, a large portion of the 51st-52d St. block and 4 blockfronts on the west side of the Ave. of the Americas between 47th and 51st Sts. There are 21 buildings. It has 175,000 daily visitors; over 66,000 work there.

The surface area of Rockefeller Center covers 24 acres; almost one half are leased for a long period from Columbia University. Rockefeller Center pays Columbia an annual rental of nearly $4 million. The lease with options for renewal runs until 2069.

The part of Rockefeller Center comprising theaters and radio and television studios is often referred to as Radio City. Studios of the National Broadcasting Co. are located in the 70-story RCA building (850 ft. tall). There is an observation roof on the 70th floor.

Radio City Music Hall, Ave. of the Americas and W. 50th St., largest indoor movie theater in the world, seats 6,000 people. Its stage, 144 ft. wide by 67 ft. deep, has a proscenium arch 60 ft. high and 100 ft. wide. Has first-run films and stage spectacles with the Rockettes, Symphony Orchestra, and guest artists, plus concerts and other special events.

New York Stock Exchange, visitors' entrance 20 Broad St., has visitors' gallery, films, guided tours, Mon. through Fri., 10 a.m. to market closing.

American Stock Exchange, visitors' entrance 78 Trinity Pl., has visitors' gallery, guides, multi-media shows, and other exhibits, Mon. through Fri., 9:45 a.m. to 3 p.m.

United Nations Headquarters occupies over 16 acres between 1st Ave. and F.D.R. (East River) Drive, E. 42d and E. 48th Sts. Most unusual is the Secretariat Bldg., 505 ft. high at front entrance, 286 ft. long and only 72 ft. wide. The 2 sides have 5,400 windows; the end walls are of 2,000 tons of Vermont marble. General Assembly Bldg. has a hall 165 ft. long, 115 ft. wide. Conference Bldg. houses 3 Council chambers, etc. There are guided tours daily.

World Trade Center, dedicated Apr. 4, 1973, on Manhattan's lower west side, has twin towers of 110 stories, 1,350 ft. each (2d in height to Chicago's Sears Tower) and 3 low-rise buildings, with total of 9 million sq. ft. of office space. In 1976, over 35,000 of an eventual 50,000 persons worked in the North and South Towers. Atop the South Tower is the world's highest observation deck. Construction of this office complex for international trade, a Port Authority of N.Y. and N.J. facility, was to be completed in 1977.

A Guide to Avenue and Street Addresses in N.Y. City

To find the location of a number on the following avenues of Manhattan, cancel the last figure of the number, divide the remainder by 2 and add the given key number. Thus: Where is 596 7th Ave.? Divide 59 by 2 equals 30, plus 12 equals 42d St.

Ave. A	add	4	Up to 600	add	18	8th Ave.	add	9	Lenox Ave.	add	110
Ave. B	add	3	Up to 775	add	20	9th Ave.	add	13	Lexington Ave.	add	22
Ave. C	add	3	From 775 to 1286			10th Ave.	add	13	Madison Ave.	add	27
Ave. D	add	3	see exception below:			11th Ave.	add	15	Manhattan Ave.	add	100
1st Ave.	add	4	Up to 1500	add	45	Amsterdam Ave.	add	59	Park Ave.	add	34
2d Ave.	add	3	Above 2000	add	24	Audubon Ave.	add	165	Pleasant Ave.	add	101
3d Ave.	add	10	Ave. of Americas (6th Ave.)			Columbus Ave.	add	60	St. Nicholas Ave.	add	110
4th Ave.	add	8		subtract	12 or 13	Convent Ave.	add	127	Wadsworth Ave.	add	175
5th Ave. to 200	add	13	7th Ave.	add	12	Edgecomb Ave.	add	134	West End Ave.	add	59
Up to 400	add	16	Above 1800	add	20	Ft. Wash. Ave.	add	158			

Exceptions

Broadway: Up to 754 below East 8th St.
Above 754, apply above rule but deduct following key numbers:
From 754 to 858 deduct 29.
From 857 to 958 deduct 25.
Above 1000 deduct 31.

Riverside Drive: Below 567, drop last figure, add 75, do not divide by 2.
Above 577, drop last figure, add 78.

Central Park West: Drop last figure, add 60.

5th Ave.: From 775 to 1286, drop last figure and deduct 18 from remainder.

Street Addresses

North of the Washington Square area, most Manhattan streets are numbered. Each street has about 100 building numbers on each block. These building numbers rise east and west from Fifth Ave. Even building numbers are on the south sides of streets, odd numbers on the north sides.

Notable Tall Buildings in North American Cities

Height from sidewalk to roof, including penthouse and tower if enclosed as integral part of structure; actual number of stories beginning at street level. Asterisks (*) denote buildings still under construction Jan. 1978.

City	Hgt. ft.	Stories
Akron, Oh.		
First National Tower Bldg.	330	28
Cascade, 10 W. Bowery	316	24
Edison Tower, 76 S. Main St.	280	19
Albany, N.Y.		
Office Tower, So. Mall	589	44
State Office Building	388	34
Agency (four bldgs.), So. Mall	310	23
University Towers	286	22
Atlanta, Ga.		
Peachtree Center Plaza Hotel	723	71
First National Bank, 2 Peachtree	556	44
Equitable Building, 100 Peachtree	453	34
101 Marietta Tower, 101 Marietta St.	446	36
National Bank of Georgia, 34 Peachtree	439	32
Peachtree Summit No. 1	406	31
Tower Place, 3361 Piedmont Road	401	29
*Richard B. Russell, Federal Bldg.	383	26
Atlanta Hilton Hotel	383	32
Peachtree Center Harris Bldg.	382	31
Southern Bell Telephone	380	...
Trust Company Bank	377	28
Coastal States Insurance, 260 Peachtree	377	27
Peachtree Center Cain Building	376	30
Peachtree Center Building, 230 Peachtree	374	31
Life of Georgia Tower	371	29
Peachtree Center South, 225 Peachtree	332	27
Gas Light Tower, 235 Peachtree	331	27
Hyatt Regency Hotel, 265 Peachtree	330	23
100 Colony Square, 1175 Peachtree	328	25
Georgia Power Building, 270 Peachtree	318	22
Colony Square Hotel, 180 14th St.	310	28
400 Colony Square, 1201 Peachtree	308	23
Atlanta Center Building, 260 Piedmont Ave.	301	23
Merchandise Mart, 240 Peachtree	300	22
Austin, Tex.		
Austin National Bank	328	26
American Bank	313	21
State Capitol	309	...
Univ. of Texas Admin. Bldg.	307	29
J. Frank Dobie Univ. Center	299	29
Westgate Bldg.	261	24
Baltimore, Md.		
U.S. Fidelity & Guaranty Co.	529	40
Maryland National Bank Bldg.	509	34
World Trade Center Bldg.	405	32
Saint-Paul Apartments Bldg.	385	37
Arlington Federal Savings and Loan Assn. Bldg.	370	28
Blaustein Bldg.	370	30
Charles Plaza Apts. So.	350	31
Charles Center South	330	26
Tower Bldg.	330	16
Baltimore Arts Tower	319	15
First National Bank of Maryland	315	22
Lord Baltimore Hotel	315	24
Mercantile-Safe Deposit and Trust Co.	315	21
Charles Plaza Apts. No.	315	28
Baltimore Hilton Hotel	302	29
One Charles Center Bldg.	301	24
Baltimore Gas and Electric Co. Bldg.	300	22
Chesapeake & Potomac Telephone Co.	300	16
Baton Rouge, La.		
State Capitol	460	34
American Bank Bldg.	310	25
Hilton Hotel	290	28
La. National Bank Bldg.	277	21
Birmingham, Ala.		
First Natl. Southern Natural Bldg.	390	30
South Central Bell Hdqts. Bldg.	390	30
City Federal Bldg.	325	27
Cabana Motel	287	21
Daniel Bldg.	283	20
Boston, Mass.		
John Hancock Tower	790	60
Prudential Tower	750	52
Federal Reserve Bldg.	604	32
Employers Commercial Union Co's	603	40
Boston Co. Bldg., Court St.	601	41
First National Bank of Boston	591	37
Shawmut Bank Bldg.	520	38
Sixty State St.	509	38
New England Merch. Bank Bldg.	500	40
U.S. Custom House	496	32
John Hancock Bldg.	495	26
State St. Bank Bldg.	477	34
One Hundred Summer St.	450	33
McCormack Bldg.	401	22
Keystone Custodian Funds	400	32
Saltonstall Office Bldg.	396	22
Harbor Towers (2 bldgs.)	396	40
Suffolk County Courthouse	390	19
John F. Kennedy Bldg.	387	24
Longfellow Towers (2 bldgs.)	380	38
Federal Bldg. & Post Office	345	22
Sheraton-Boston Hotel	310	29
State Service Center	300	23
Buffalo, N.Y.		
Marine Midland, Main St.	529	40
City Hall	378	32
Rand Bldg., not incl. 40-ft. beacon	351	29
Erie County Savings Bank, Main St.	350	26
Manuf. & Trades Trust Co.	317	21
Liberty Bank	305	23
Electric Tower	294	18
Calgary, Alta.		
Calgary Tower	626	...
Norcen Tower	508	33
Scotia Centre	504	38
Oxford Square North	463	34
Shell Tower	460	34
Oxford Square South	449	33
Three Bow Valley Square	432	35
Sun Oil Bldg.	397	34
Western Centre	385	40
Two Bow Valley Square	380	39
Mobil Tower	369	29
One Palliser Square	350	28
Mount Royal House	330	34
Standard Life Bldg.	327	25
Place Concorde (twin towers)	321	36
Penthouse Towers	310	32
International Hotel	301	34
Two Calgary Place	300	24
Charlotte, N.C.		
NCNB Plaza, 101 S. Tryon	503	40
Jefferson First Union Tower	433	32
Wachovia Center, 400 S. Tryon	420	32
Southern National Center, 1200 S. College	300	22
NCNB Bldg., 200 S. Tryon	299	18
Bank of NC Bldg., 112 S. Tryon	280	20
Chicago, Ill.		
Sears Tower (world's tallest)	1,454	110
Standard Oil (Indiana)	1,136	80
John Hancock Center	1,127	100
Water Tower Plaza (a)	859	74
First Natl. Bank	850	60
IBM Bldg.	695	52
Civic Center (city hall)	662	31
Lake Point Towers	645	70
Board of Trade, incl. 81 ft. statue	605	44
Prudential Bldg., 130 E. Randolph	601	41
Antenna tower, 311 ft., makes total	912	...
1000 Lake Shore Plaza Apts.	590	55
Marina City Apts., 2 buildings	588	61
Mid Continental Plaza	580	50
Pittsfield, 55 E. Washington St.	557	38

City	Hgt. ft.	Stories
Kemper Insurance Bldg.	555	45
Newberry Plaza, State & Oak	553	56
Harbor Point	550	54
LaSalle Natl. Bank, 135 S. LaSalle St.	535	44
One LaSalle Street	530	49
111 E. Chestnut St.	529	56
River Plaza, Rush & Hubbard	524	56
Pure Oil, 35 E. Wacker Drive	523	40
United Ins. Bldg., 1 E. Wacker Dr.	522	41
Lincoln Tower, 75 E. Wacker Dr.	519	42
Carbide & Carbon, 230 N. Mich.	503	37
Walton Colonnade	500	44
LaSalle-Wacker, 221 N. LaSalle St.	491	41
Amer. Nat'l. Bank, 33 N. LaSalle St.	479	40
Bankers, 105 W. Adams St.	476	41
Brunswick Bldg.	475	37
Continental Companies	475	45
American Furniture Mart	474	24
Sheraton Hotel, 505 N. Mich. Ave.	471	42
Playboy Bldg., 919 N. Mich. Ave.	468	37
188 Randolph Tower	465	45
Tribune Tower, 435 N. Mich. Ave.	462	36
*Chicago Marriott, Mich. & Ohio Sts.	460	45
Equitable Life, 401 N. Michigan	457	35
Roanoke, 11 S. LaSalle St.	452	37
Edgewater Beach Apts., 5445 Sheridan	449	39

(a) World's tallest reinforced concrete bldg.

Cincinnati, Oh.

City	Hgt. ft.	Stories
Carew Tower	574	48
Central Trust Tower	495	34
Dubois Tower, 5th & Walnut	423	32
Kroger Bldg.	345	25
Stouffer's Cincinnati Tower	324	33
U. of Cinn., Sander Hall	297	27
Terrace Hilton Hotel	273	19

Cleveland, Oh.

City	Hgt. ft.	Stories
Terminal Tower	708	52
Erieview Plaza Tower	529	40
Justice Center, 1250 Ontario	420	26
Federal Bldg.	419	32
Cleveland Trust Tower No. 1	383	29
Ohio-Bell Telephone	365	22
Park Centre	320	26
Central Natl. Bank Bldg.	305	23
Diamond Shamrock Bldg.	300	23
CEI Bldg.	300	22
Union Commerce Bldg.	289	21
Standard Bldg.	282	21
East Ohio Bldg.	275	21
Bond Court, 1300 E. 9th	270	20

Columbus, Oh.

City	Hgt. ft.	Stories
State Office Tower, 30 E. Broad	624	41
LeVeque-Lincoln Tower, 50 W. Broad	555	47
Nationwide Plaza	485	40
Borden Bldg., 180 E. Broad	438	34
Columbus Center, 100 E. Broad	357	20
Ohio Bell Bldg., 150 E. Gay St.	348	26
88 E. Broad St.	324	20
BancOhio Plaza, 155 E. Broad	317	25
Motorists Bldg., 471 E. Broad	297	21
Midland Bldg., 250 E. Broad	278	21

Dallas, Tex.

City	Hgt. ft.	Stories
First International Bldg.	710	56
First National Bank	625	52
Republic Bank Tower	598	50
Southland Life Tower	550	42
2001 Bryan St.	512	40
Republic Bank Bldg., not incl. 150-ft. ornamental tower	452	36
One Main Place	445	34
Ling-Tempco-Vought Tower	434	31
Mercantile Natl. Bank Bldg., not incl. 115-ft. weather beacon	430	31
Mobil Bldg.	430	31
Fidelity Union Tower	400	33
Southwestern Bell Toll Bldg.	372	22
Court House & Fedl. Office Bldg.	362	16
Mercantile Dallas Bldg.	360	22
Sheraton Hotel	352	38
*Hyatt Hotel, 303 Reunion Blvd.	343	30
Elm Place, 1005-09 Elm St.	341	22
Main Tower	336	26
Park Central No. 3	327	20
Adolphus Tower	327	27
Bell Telephone Bldg.	326	23
Davis Bldg.	323	21
Manor House, Bank of Service & Trust	319	26
Preston Tower	316	29
Tower Petroleum Bldg.	315	23
Adolphus Hotel	312	25
Fairmont Hotel	308	24
Baptist Annuity Center	303	17
Life Bldg.	302	22
Santa Fe Bldg. (1st unit)	300	20

Dayton, Oh.

City	Hgt. ft.	Stories
Winters Bank Bldg.	404	30
Mead Tower, 10 W. 2d St.	365	28
Centre City Office Bldg.	297	21
Hulman Bldg.	295	23
Grant-Deneau Bldg.	290	22

Denver, Col.

City	Hgt. ft.	Stories
Brooks Towers, 1020 15th St.	504	42
First of Denver Plaza	415	32
Colorado Nat'l. Bank, 17th & Curtis	389	26
First National Bank	385	28
Security Life Bldg.	384	33
Lincoln Center	367	30
Western Fed. Savings	354	27
Colorado State Bank	352	27
Brooks Tower Annex	350	30
Mountain Bell, 17th & Curtis	330	21
D&F Tower	330	20
Prudential Tower Plaza	322	26
Denver Club Bldg.	277	23

Des Moines, Iowa

City	Hgt. ft.	Stories
Ruan Center	457	36
Financial Center, 7th & Walnut	345	25
Equitable Bldg.	318	19
State Capitol	275	4

Detroit, Mich.

City	Hgt. ft.	Stories
Detroit Plaza Hotel	748	70
City Natl. Bank Bldg., 637 Griswold	557	47
Guardian, 500 Griswold	485	40
Renaissance Center (4 bldgs.)	479	39
Book Tower, 1227 Wash. Blvd.	472	35
Cadillac Tower, 51 Cadillac Sq.	437	40
David Stott, 1150 Griswold	436	38
Mich. Cons. Gas Co. Bldg.	430	32
Fisher, W. Grand Blvd. & 2d St.	420	28
J. L. Hudson Bldg.	397	28
McNamara Federal Office Bldg.	393	27
Detroit Bank & Trust Bldg.	370	28
Walker Cisler	365	25
David Broderick Tower	358	34
Buhl, 535 Griswold	350	26
Michigan Bell Telephone	340	19
1st Federal Savings & Loan	338	23
Pontchartrain Motor Hotel	336	23
Commonwealth Bldg.	325	25
1300 Lafayette East	325	30
First National Bldg.	319	25
City-County Bldg.	317	20
The Executive Plaza, 1200 6th Ave.	313	21
Sheraton Cadillac Hotel	310	28
Mich. Blue Cross/Blue Shield	307	22
The Jeffersonian	305	29

Edmonton, Alta.

City	Hgt. ft.	Stories
AGT Tower, 10020-100 St.	441	34
T-D Bank Tower	390	30
CN Tower, 1004-104 Ave.	365	26
Royal Trust Tower	325	25
Edmonton House	315	34

Fort Wayne, Ind.

City	Hgt. ft.	Stories
Ft. Wayne Natl. Bank	339	26
Lincoln Natl. Bank	312	23

Fort Worth, Tex.

City	Hgt. ft.	Stories
Ft. Worth Natl. Bank	454	37
Continental Natl. Bank Bldg.	380	30
First National Bank, 500 W. 7th	300	21
Continental Life Ins. Bldg.	282	23
Electric Service Bldg., 800 Main St.	275	20
W. T. Waggoner Bldg.	270	22
Service Life Center	270	19

Halifax, N.S.

City	Hgt. ft.	Stories
Fenwick Towers	300	31

Harrisburg, Pa.

City	Hgt. ft.	Stories
State Capitol	272	6
Presbyterian Apts., 322 N. 2nd Ave.	260	23

Hartford, Conn.

City	Hgt. ft.	Stories
Travelers Ins. Co. Bldg.	527	34
Hartford Plaza	420	22
Hartford Natl. Bank & Trust	360	26
One Financial Plaza, 755 Main	335	26

Honolulu, Ha.

City	Hgt. ft.	Stories
Ala Moana Hotel	390	38
Pacific Trade Center	360	30
Discovery Bay	350	42
Hyatt Regency Waikiki	350	39
*Mehelani Waikiki Lodge	350	43
Hemmeter Center	350	39
Regency Tower, 2525 Date St.	350	42
Yacht Harbor Towers	350	40
*Canterbury Place	350	40
*Iolani Towers	350	38
*Diamond Head Tower	350	38
*Ala Wai Sunset	350	44
*Century Center	350	41
*Pacific Beach Hotel	350	43
*Waikiki Ala Wai Waterfront	350	43
*Waikiki Lodge II	350	43
Chateau Waikiki	349	39
Rainbow Plaza	348	37
*Waikiki Beach Tower	347	39
2121 Ala Wai Blvd.	347	41
Royal Kuhio	346	39
Waipuna	343	38
*Waikiki Banyon	341	36
*Waikiki Sunset Makai	341	37
The Villa on Eaton Square	335	37
Kukui Plaza	333	33
The Skyrise	333	38
Diamond Head Vista	322	35
Ke Aloha at Waikiki	330	35
Reed & Martin Apt. Bldg.	321	36

Houston, Tex.

City	Hgt. ft.	Stories
One Shell Plaza (not incl. 285 ft. TV tower)	714	50
One Houston Center	678	47
1100 Milam Bldg.	651	47
Exxon Bldg.	606	44
2 Houston Center	570	40
Dresser Tower	550	40
Pennzoil, 700 Milam	523	36
*Two Allen Center	521	36
Entex Bldg.	518	35
Tenneco Bldg.	502	33
Conoco Bldg.	465	32
One Allen Center	452	34
Summit Tower East	441	32
Gulf Bldg.	428	37
First City Natl. Bank	410	32
Houston Lighting & Power	410	27
Neils Esperson Bldg.	409	31
Hyatt Regency Houston	401	34
Houston Natural Gas Bldg.	386	28
Bank of the Southwest	369	24
Sheraton-Lincoln Hotel	352	28
Two Shell Plaza	341	26
American General Life	337	25
Transco	333	25
609 Fannin Bldg.	325	22
Holiday Inn	325	30
Capital Natl. Bank	320	21
Post Oak Central	318	25
St. Luke's Hospital	316	26
500 Jefferson Bldg.	316	21
Marathon Manufacturing Co. Bldg.	313	21
Sterling Bldg.	312	22
Melrose Bldg.	308	21
Chamber of Commerce Bldg.	306	22
Control Data Center	303	22
First National Life Bldg.	302	22
Prudential Bldg.	300	21
Kellogg Bldg.	300	22

Indianapolis, Ind.

City	Hgt. ft.	Stories
Indiana Natl. Bank Tower	504	37
City-County Bldg.	377	26
Indiana Bell Telephone	320	20
Blue Cross-Blue Shield Bldg.	302	18
Riley Towers (2 bldgs.)	294	30
Indiana Bell "220" Bldg.	284	20
Monument Circle	284	...
Market Square Office Bldg.	283	20
Merchants Plaza Office Bldg./ Regency Hyatt Hotel	271	17

Jacksonville, Fla.

City	Hgt. ft.	Stories
Independent Life & Accident Ins. Co.	535	37
Gulf Life Ins. Co. Bldg.	432	28
Prudential Ins. Co. of America	295	22
Blue Cross-Blue Shield	287	20
Atlantic National Bank	278	19

Jersey City, N.J.

Medical Center (5 bldgs.; 332 ft., 294 ft., 274 ft., (2) 273 ft.)

Kansas City, Mo.

City	Hgt. ft.	Stories
Kansas City Power and Light Bldg.	476	32
City Hall	443	29
Federal Office Bldg.	413	35
Commerce Tower	402	32
Southwest Bell Telephone Bldg.	394	27
Pershing Road Associates, 2333 Grand	352	28
A. T. & T. Long Line Bldg.	331	20
Bryant Bldg.	319	26
Federal Reserve Bldg.	311	21
City Center Square, 1100 Main	302	30
Holiday Inn	300	28

Las Vegas, Nev.

City	Hgt. ft.	Stories
Las Vegas Hilton	375	30
MGM Grand	362	26
Landmark Hotel	356	31
Sahara Hotel	294	24
Dunes Hotel	277	24
Mint Hotel	275	26
Union Plaza Hotel	272	22

Little Rock, Ark.

City	Hgt. ft.	Stories
First National Bank	454	33
Worthen Bank & Trust	375	28
Union National Bank	331	24
Tower Bldg.	300	18

Los Angeles, Cal.

City	Hgt. ft.	Stories
United Cal. Bank	858	62
Security Pacific Natl. Bank	738	55
Atlantic Richfield Plaza (2 bldgs.)	699	52
Crocker-Citizen Plaza	620	42
Century Plaza Towers (2 bldgs.)	571	44
Union Bank Square	516	41
City Hall	454	28
Equitable Life Bldg.	454	34
Occidental Life Bldg.	452	32
Mutual Benefit Life Ins. Bldg.	435	31
Broadway Plaza	414	33
1900 Ave. of Stars	398	27
1 Wilshire Bldg.	395	28
Bonaventure Hotel, 404 S. Figueroa	367	34
Cal. Fed. Savings & Loan Bldg.	363	28
Century City Office Bldg.	363	24
Bunker Hill Towers	349	32
International Industries Plaza	347	24
City Natl. Bank Bldg.	344	24
Wilshire West Plaza	327	24

Louisville, Ky.

City	Hgt. ft.	Stories
First Natl. Bank	512	40
Citizen's Plaza	420	30
Galt House	325	25
Louisville Trust Bldg.	312	24
800 Apartments Bldg.	290	29

Memphis, Tenn.

City	Hgt. ft.	Stories
100 N. Main Bldg.	430	37
Commerce Square	396	31
Sterick Bldg.	365	31
Clark, 5100 Poplar	365	32
First Natl. Bank Bldg.	332	25
Hyatt Regency	329	28
Lowenstein's Towers	296	25
Lincoln American Life Tower	290	22
White Station Tower	280	24

Miami, Fla.

City	Hgt. ft.	Stories
One Biscayne Corp.	456	40
First Federal Savings & Loan	375	32
Dade County Court House	357	28
Ferre Bldg.	340	30
Flagler Center Bldg.	318	25
*Omni International Hotel	296	29
Brickell Bay Club	286	29
Palm Bay Club	279	24

Milwaukee, Wis.

City	Hgt. ft.	Stories
First Wis. Center & Office Tower	625	42
City Hall	350	9

City	Hgt. ft.	Stories
Wisconsin Telephone Co.	313	19
Marine Plaza Bldg.	288	22
Allen-Bradley Co.	280	17
Marshall & Ilsley Bank	277	21
Regency House Apts.	274	27
Prospect Towers Apts.	268	23
Juneau Village Apts.	265	28
Marc Plaza Hotel	265	24
Carl Sandburg Dorm. (U. of Wis.)	264	26
Locust Court Apts.	262	24
Minneapolis, Minn.		
IDS Center	772	57
Foshay Tower, not including 163-ft. antenna tower	447	32
Hennepin County Government Center	403	24
First Natl. Bank Bldg.	366	28
Municipal Building	355	14
North Western Bell Telephone	350	26
Cedar-Riverside	337	39
Dain Tower	311	26
Midwest Federal Savings & Loan	276	20
Montreal, Que.		
Place Victoria	624	47
Place Ville Marie	616	42
Canadian Imperial Bank of Commerce	604	43
Le Complexe Desjardins		
La Tour du Sud	498	40
La Tour du L'Est	428	32
La Tour du Nord	355	27
La Tour Laurier	425	36
C.I.L. House	429	32
Chateau Champlain Hotel	420	38
Port Royal Apts.	400	33
Royal Bank Tower	397	22
Sun Life Bldg.	390	26
Banque Canadienne National	390	32
Place du Canada	372	33
Hydro Quebec	360	27
Alexis Nihon Plaza	331	33
Bell Telephone	324	22
Le Cartier Apts.	320	32
Nashville, Tenn.		
Natl. Life & Acc. Ins. Co.	452	31
Nashville Life & Casualty Tower	409	30
First American Natl. Bank	354	28
Hyatt Regency	300	28
Third Natl. Bank Bldg.	292	20
Andrew Jackson State Office Bldg.	286	17
Newark, N.J.		
National Newark & Essex Bank	465	36
Raymond-Commerce	448	36
Prudential Corporate Bldg.	369	27
Western Electric Bldg.	359	31
Gateway 1, tower	355	30
Prudential Insurance Company	353	21
American Insurance Company	326	21
N. J. Bell Telephone Co.	275	21
Gateway 2, Western Electric	272	20
Mutual Benefit Life Ins. Co.	271	18
New Haven, Conn.		
Knights of Columbus Hqs.	319	23
New Orleans, La.		
One Shell Square	697	51
Plaza Tower	531	45
Marriott Hotel	450	42
Bank of New Orleans	438	31
Int'l. Trade Mart Bldg.	407	33
225 Baronne St.	362	28
Hyatt-Regency Hotel, Poydras Plaza	360	25
Hibernia Bank Bldg.	355	23
New Orleans Hilton, Intl. River Center	340	29
American Bank Bldg.	330	23
Canal LaSalle Bldg.	288	24
Charity Hospital of Louisiana	279	19
Lykes Center, 300 Poydras	276	22
New York, N.Y.		
World Trade Center (2 towers)	1,350	110
Empire State, 34th St. & 5th Ave.	1,250	102
TV tower, 222 ft., makes total	1,472	..
Chrysler, Lexington Ave. & 43d St.	1,046	77
60 Wall Tower, 70 Pine St.	950	67
40 Wall Tower	927	71
RCA, Rockefeller Center	850	70

City	Hgt. ft.	Stories
1 Chase Manhattan Plaza	813	60
Pan Am Bldg., 200 Park Ave.	808	59
Woolworth, 233 Broadway	792	60
1 Penn Plaza	764	57
Exxon, 1251 Ave. of Americas	750	54
1 Liberty Plaza	743	50
Citibank	741	57
One Astor Plaza	730	54
Union Carbide Bldg., 270 Park Ave.	707	52
General Motors Bldg.	705	50
Metropolitan Life, 1 Madison Ave.	700	50
500 5th Ave.	697	60
9 W. 57th St.	688	50
Chem. Bank, N.Y. Trust Bldg.	687	50
55 Water St.	687	53
Chanin, Lexington Ave. & 42d St.	680	56
Gulf & Western Bldg., 15 Columbus Circle	679	44
Marine Midland Bldg., 140 Bway.	677	52
McGraw Hill, 1221 Ave. of Am.	674	51
Lincoln, 60 E. 52d Street	673	53
1633 Broadway	670	48
American Brands, 245 Park Ave.	648	47
Irving Trust, 1 Wall St.	640	50
345 Park Ave.	634	44
Grace Plaza, 1114 Ave. of Am.	630	50
1 New York Plaza	630	50
Home Insurance Co. Bldg.	630	44
1 Dag Hammarskjold Plaza	628	50
Waldorf-Astoria, 301 Park Ave.	625	47
Burlington House, 1345 Ave. of Am.	625	50
Olympic Tower, 643 5th Ave.	620	50
10 E. 40th St.	620	48
General Electric, Lexington Ave.	616	50
New York Life, 51 Madison Ave.	615	40
Penney Bldg., 1301 Ave. of Am.	609	46
560 Lexington Ave.	600	46
Celanese Bldg., 1211 Ave. of Am.	592	45
U.S. Court House, 505 Pearl St.	590	37
Federal Bldg., Foley Square	587	41
Time & Life, 1271 Ave. of Am.	587	47
Cooper Bregstein Bldg., 1250 Bway.	580	40
1185 Ave. of Americas	580	42
Municipal, Park Row & Centre St.	580	34
1 Madison Square Plaza	576	42
Westvaco Bldg., 299 Park Ave.	574	42
Socony Mobil Bldg., East 42d St.	572	45
Sperry Rand Bldg., 1290 Ave. of Am.	570	43
600 3d Ave.	570	42
N.Y. General, 230 Park Ave.	565	35
1 Bankers Trust Plaza	565	40
30 Broad St.	562	48
Sherry-Netherland, 5th Ave. & 59th St.	560	40
Continental Can, 633 3d Ave.	557	39
Sperry & Hutchinson, 330 Madison	555	39
Galleria, 117 E. 57th St.	552	57
Interchem Bldg., 1133 Ave. of Am.	552	45
919 3d Ave.	550	47
Burroughs Bldg., 605 3d Ave.	550	44
Bankers Trust, 33 E. 48 St.	547	41
Transportation Bldg., 225 Bway.	546	45
Equitable Life, 1285 Ave. of Am.	540	42
Ritz Tower, Park Ave. & 57th St.	540	41
Bankers Trust, 6 Wall St.	540	39
1166 Ave. of Americas	540	44
Equitable, 120 Broadway	538	42
1700 Broadway	533	41
Downtown Athletic Club, 19 West St.	530	45
Nelson Towers, 7th Ave. & 34th St.	525	45
Hotel Pierre, 5th Ave. & 61st St.	525	44
House of Seagram, 375 Park Ave.	525	38
Random House, 825 3d Ave.	522	40
3 Park Ave.	522	42
Du Mont Bldg., 515 Madison Ave.	520	42
26 Broadway	520	31
Newsweek Bldg., 444 Madison Ave.	518	43
Sterling Drug. Bldg., 90 Park Ave.	515	41
First National City Bank	515	41
Bank of New York, 48 Wall St.	513	32
Navarre, 512 7th Ave.	513	43
Williamsburg Savings Bank, Bklyn.	512	42
ITT—American, 437 Madison Ave.	512	40
International, Rockefeller Center	512	41
1407 Broadway Realty Corp.	512	44
United Nations, 405 E. 42 St.	505	39
2 New York Plaza	504	40
22 E. 40th St.	503	43
60 Broad St.	503	39
Americana Hotel	501	51

City	Hgt. ft.	Stories
World Apparel Center, 1411 Bway	501	42
Oakland, Cal.		
Ordway Bldg., 2150 Valdez St	404	28
Kaiser Bldg.	390	28
Clorox Bldg.	330	24
City Hall	319	15
Tribune Tower	305	21
United Cal. Bank Bldg.	297	18
Blue Cross Bldg.	296	21
Telephone Bldg.	289	15
565 Bellevue Apts.	270	25
Oklahoma City, Okla.		
Liberty Tower	500	36
First National Bank	493	33
City National Bank Tower	440	32
Kerr-McGee Center	393	30
Fidelity Plaza	310	15
Southwestern Bell Telephone	303	15
Hotel Oklahoma	298	24
The Regency Tower	288	25
Omaha, Neb.		
Woodmen Tower	469	30
Northwestern Bell Telephone Hdqrs	334	16
Masonic Manor	320	22
First Natl. Bank	295	22
Mutual of Omaha	269	13
Ottawa, Ont.		
Place de Ville, tower C	368	29
Place Bell Canada	318	26
DBS Tower	308	26
Holiday Inn	308	28
Parliament Bldgs., Peace Tower	291	...
Skyline Hotel	286	25
L'Esplanade Laurier (2 towers)	285	22
Philadelphia, Pa.		
City Hall Tower, incl. 37-ft. statue of Wm. Penn	548	7
1818 Market St.	500	40
Fidelity Mutual Life Ins. Bldg.	490	38
Phila. Saving Fund Society	490	39
Central Penn Natl. Bank	490	36
Centre Square	490	38, 40
Industrial Valley Bank Bldg.	482	32
Philadelphia National Bank	475	25
2000 Market St. Bldg.	435	29
Fidelity Bank Bldg.	410	30
Two Girard Plaza	404	30
Lewis Tower, 15th & Locust	397	33
Fifteen Hundred Locust	390	44
Philadelphia Electric Co.	384	27
Penn Mutual Life	375	20
The Drake, 15th & Spruce	375	33
Medical Tower, 255 So. 17th	364	33
State Bldg., 1400 Spring Garden	351	18
United Engineers, 17th & Ludlow	344	20
Packard, 15th & Chestnut	340	25
Inquirer Building	340	18
Dorchester	339	32
Transportation Centre	336	18
Land Title, Broad & Chestnut	331	22
Suburban Station Bldg.	330	21
Phoenix, Ariz.		
Valley National Bank	483	40
Arizona Bank Downtown	407	31
First National Bank	372	27
First Federal Savings Bldg.	341	26
Regency Apts.	297	21
Hyatt-Regency Hotel	281	21
Del Webb TowneHouse	280	23
United Bank Square	272	20
Del Webb Bldg.	271	17
Pittsburgh, Pa.		
U.S. Steel Bldg.	841	64
Gulf, 7th Ave. and Grant St.	582	44
University of Pittsburgh	535	42
Mellon Bank Bldg.	520	41
1 Oliver Plaza	511	39
Grant, Grant St. at 3rd Ave.	485	40
Koppers, 7th Ave. and Grant	475	34
Equibank Bldg.	445	34
Pittsburgh National Bldg.	424	30
Alcoa Bldg., 425 Sixth Ave.	410	30
Westinghouse Bldg.	355	23
Oliver, 535 Smithfield St.	347	25

City	Hgt. ft.	Stories
Gateway Bldg. No. 3	344	24
Smithfield Plaza	341	26
Federal Bldg., 1000 Liberty Ave.	340	23
Bell Telephone, 416 7th Ave.	339	21
Hilton Hotel	333	22
Frick, 437 Grant St.	330	20
301 Fifth Ave.	322	24
Washington Plaza Apts.	300	23
Commonwealth, 316 Fourth Ave.	300	21
Portland, Ore.		
First Natl. Bank of Oregon	538	41
Georgia Pacific Bldg.	367	27
Providence, R.I.		
Industrial National Bank	420	26
Rhode Island Hospital Trust Tower	410	30
40 Westminster Bldg.	301	24
Richmond, Va.		
First & Merchants Natl. Bank	313	26
City Hall	310	18
Central National Bank Bldg.	282	24
First National Bank Bldg.	262	19
Fidelity Bankers Life	261	23
Rochester, N.Y.		
Xerox Tower	443	30
Lincoln First Tower	390	26
Eastman Kodak Bldg.	360	19
First Federal Bank Plaza	305	22
Marine Midland Bank Bldg.	280	22
St. Louis, Mo.		
Gateway Arch	630	...
*1st National Bank/IBM	560	40
Mercantile Trust Bldg.	485	35
Laclede Gas. Bldg., 8th & Olive	400	30
S. W. Bell Telephone Bldg.	398	31
Civil Courts	387	13
Queeny Tower	321	24
Counsil House Plaza	320	30
Park Plaza Hotel	310	30
Pierre Laclede Tower	309	24
Stauffer's Riverfront Inn, 3rd St.	301	22
Riverfront Holiday Inn	290	22
Mansion House	285	22
500 Broadway	282	22
Inn of the Spanish Pavilion	280	22
St. Paul, Minn.		
First Natl. Bank Bldg., incl. 100-ft. sign	517	32
Osborn Bldg.	368	20
Kellogg Square Apts.	366	32
Northwestern Bell Telephone Bldg.	340	15
American National Bank Bldg.	335	25
St. Paul Cathedral	307	...
U.S. Post Office Bldg.	274	12
St. Paul Hilton Hotel	273	24
Salt Lake City, Ut.		
L.D.S. Church Office Bldg.	420	30
Beneficial Life Tower	351	27
City & County Bldg.	290	...
State Capitol	285	...
Univ. Club Bldg.	277	24
Kennecott Bldg.	267	18
San Antonio, Tex.		
Tower of the Americas	622	...
Tower Life	404	30
Nix Professional Bldg.	375	23
Natl. Bank of Commerce	310	24
First Natl. Bank Tower	302	20
Frost Bank Tower	300	21
Alamo National Bldg.	288	23
Milam Bldg.	280	20
San Diego, Cal.		
California First Bank	388	27
Crocker Natl. Bank Bldg.	340	25
Financial Square	339	24
Central Federal	320	22
Union Bank	320	22
Little America Westgate Hotel	303	19
San Diego Gas & Electric Bldg.	293	21
Charter Oil Bldg.	281	23
Security Pacific Natl. Bank Bldg.	278	18
Home Tower	278	18

City	Hgt. ft.	Stories
San Francisco, Cal.		
Transamerica Pyramid	853	48
Bank of America	778	52
Security Pacific Bank	569	45
One Market Plaza, Spear St.	565	43
Wells Fargo Bldg.	561	43
Standard Oil, 575 Market St.	551	39
Aetna Life	529	38
First & Market Bldg.	529	38
Metropolitan Life	524	38
Hilton Hotel	493	46
Pacific Gas & Electric	492	34
Union Bank	487	37
Pacific Insurance	476	34
Bechtel Bldg., Fremont St.	475	33
Hartford Bldg.	465	33
Mutual Benefit Life	438	32
Russ Bldg.	435	31
Pacific Telephone Bldg.	435	26
*Embarcadero Center, No. 3	412	31
Levi Strauss	412	31
Calif. State Automobile Assn.	399	29
Alcoa Bldg.	398	27
St. Francis Hotel	395	32
Shell Bldg.	386	29
Del Monte	378	28
Great Western Savings	359	26
Union Square Hyatt House Hotel	355	35
Equitable Life Bldg.	355	25
Fox Plaza	354	29
International Bldg.	350	22
450 Sutter Street	343	26
Cathedral Apts.	340	21
Royal Towers	330	24
Fairmont Hotel	330	29
Bechtel Bldg., Beale St.	327	23
Standard Oil Bldg.	327	22
California First Bank	324	23
Seattle, Wash.		
Seattle-1st Natl. Bank Bldg.	609	50
Space Needle	605	..
Bank of Cal., 900 4th Ave.	536	42
Rainer Bank Tower, 4th & Univ.	536	40
L. C. Smith Bldg.	500	42
Federal Office Bldg.	487	37
1600 Bell Plaza	480	33
Washington Plaza Hotel	397	40
Financial Center	389	30
Safeco Ins. Co. of America	325	22
Northern Life Tower	314	27
Norton Bldg.	310	21
Pacific Bldg.	298	22
Washington Bldg.	289	21
Exchange Bldg.	275	23
IBM Bldg.	272	20
Park Place	270	21
Plaza 600	270	20
Springfield, Mass.		
Valley Bank Tower	370	29
Chestnut Towers	290	34
Syracuse, N.Y.		
State Tower	315	22
Mony Office Bldg.	268	19
Carrier Tower	268	19
Tampa, Fla.		
First Financial Tower	458	36
Exchange Natl. Bldg.	280	22
Toledo, Oh.		
Owens-Corning Fiberglas Tower	400	30
Owens Illinois Bldg.	368	27
Toledo Trust Bldg.	288	21
Toronto, Ont.		
CN Tower, world's tallest self-supporting structure	1815	..
First Bank Tower, First Canadian Place	951	72
Commerce Court West	784	57
Toronto-Dominion Tower (TD Centre)	758	56
Royal Trust Tower (TD Centre)	600	46
Royal Bank Plaza—South Tower	589	41
Manulife Centre	542	52
Two Bloor St. West	478	34
Commerce Court North	476	34
Simpson Tower	473	33
390 Bay St.	452	33
Sheraton Centre	443	43
Two Bloor East	442	35
Harbour Castle Hotel	438	38
Commercial Union Tower (TD Centre)	420	32
Royal York Hotel	407	28
Harbour Square Apts.	403	34
Leaside Towers Apts.	387	43
100 Bloor St. West	370	29
Hyatt Regency Hotel	365	31
York Centre	360	27
Carltoncourt	355	29
Summerhill Square Apts.	354	37
Hotel Toronto	350	32
MacDonald Block	349	24
Sutton Place Hotel	340	32
Richmond-Adelaide Centre	340	26
Tulsa, Okla.		
Bank of Oklahoma Tower	667	52
1st National Tower	516	41
4th Natl. Bank of Tulsa	412	33
320 South Boston Bldg.	400	24
Cities Service Bldg.	388	28
Univ. Club Tower	377	32
Philtower	343	24
Vancouver, B.C.		
Harbour Centre	581	32
Royal Bank Tower	468	37
Scotiabank Tower	451	36
T-D Bank Tower	410	31
200 Granville Square	403	30
Sheraton-Landmark Hotel	394	41
First Bank Tower	386	30
Hyatt Regency Vancouver	357	36
Hotel Vancouver	352	22
Oceanic Plaza	342	26
Board of Trade Tower	342	26
MacMillan-Bloedel Bldg.	340	28
Guinness Tower	328	23
Marine Bldg.	321	21
Four Seasons Hotel	311	30
Martello Tower	300	31
Wilmington, Del.		
Hercules Tower	287	23
American Life Ins. Co. Bldg.	282	21
Winnipeg, Man.		
Richardson Bldg., 1 Lombard Place	439	34
55 Nassau St.	354	39
North Star Inn	300	30
1 Evergreen Place	294	32
Winston-Salem, N.C.		
Wachovia Bldg.	410	30
Reynolds Bldg.	315	21

Tall Buildings in Other Cities

Figures denote number of stories. Height in feet is in parentheses.

Cape Canaveral, Fla., Vehicle Assembly Bldg., 40 (552); Albuquerque, N.M., National Bldg., 18 (272); Allentown, Pa., Power & Light Bldg., 23 (320); Amarillo, Tex., American Natl. Bank, 33 (374); Bethlehem, Pa., Martin Tower, 21 (332); Charleston, W. Va., Kanawha Valley Bldg., 20 (384); Cuyahoga Falls, Oh., Cathedral Tower Restaurant, 60 (554); El Paso, Tex., State Natl. Bank Bldg., 21 (286); Frankfort, Ky., Capital Plaza Office Tower, 28 (338); Galveston, Tex., American National Ins., 20 (358); Greenville, S.C., Daniel Bldg., 22 (305); Knoxville, Tenn., United American Bank, 30 (400); Lansing, Mich., Michigan Natl. Tower, 25 (300, not including antenna tower); Lincoln, Neb., State Capitol (432); Long Beach, Cal., International Tower, 27 (277); Mobile, Ala., First Natl. Bank, 33 (420); Niagara Falls, Ont., Skylon, (520); Norfolk, Va., Va. Natl. Bank, 23 (304); Reading, Pa., Berks County Courthouse (280); So. Bend, Ind., American National Bank Bldg., 25 (312); Tacoma, Wash., Washington Plaza, 23 (290); Tallahassee, Fla., State Capitol Tower, 22 (345).

STATES AND OTHER AREAS OF THE U.S.

Their Resources, Histories, Industries, Agriculture, Mineral Products, Tourist Attractions, Nicknames, State Symbols

Areas of the states are total land and water areas reported by the Geography Division, Bureau of the Census; populations are July 1, 1976, estimates by the Bureau of the Census, including armed forces personnel in each state but excluding such personnel stationed overseas; agricultural figures are based on reports of the Department of Agriculture; mineral statistics are those reported by the Bureau of Mines; manufacturing statistics are from the Bureau of the Census. Per capita income figures are preliminary from the Department of Commerce, Bureau of Economic Analysis.

Alabama

Heart of Dixie, Cotton State

Area: 51,609 sq. mi.; ranks, 29th. **Population** (U.S. est. 1976: 3,665,000; rank, 21st. **Capital:** Montgomery. **Motto:** We Dare Defend Our Rights. **Flower:** Camellia. **Bird:** Yellowhammer. **Tree:** Southern pine. **Song:** Alabama. **Entered Union:** Dec. 14, 1819; rank, 22d.

Alabama lies in the cotton belt of the Old South but introduction of new and diversified industries has given the state a more balanced economy. Natural wealth includes coal, underlying about 7,000 sq. mi. in the north; iron, bauxite, timber, oil, and gas wells.

Alabama ranks 2d behind Arkansas in production of bauxite and is a large producer of asphalt and mica. But bituminous coal accounts for over 50% of the value of its total mineral production, which in 1976 rose to an estimated $1 billion. Also important are cement, stone and petroleum.

Abundant water for hydroelectric power and river shipping has contributed to the growth of Alabama's economy. Three Tennessee Valley Authority dams and a large nuclear power plant are in the northern part of the state. Alabama Power Co. has 13 hydroelectric dams. Historic sites, fishing and hunting are among Alabama's attractions.

With two-thirds of the state's land area in timber, Alabama is a leading producer of pulp, paper, plywood, and paperboard. It ranks second in pulp and third in paper.

Iron and steel production is the most important of Alabama's manufacturing industries; there is also a large segment of manufacturing devoted to primary metal products of wide diversity, particularly structural steel. Other important industry groupings include chemicals and fertilizers, textile mill products and apparel, processing of foods, stone-clay-glass products, and transportation equipment. Value added by manufacture is over $5 billion a year.

Industrial growth in 1976 saw $1.6 billion invested in 1,228 new or expanded plants, providing 12,225 new jobs. Per capita personal income was $5,105 in 1976 (U.S. average was $6,441).

Birmingham, center of the steel industry, has long been known as "the Pittsburgh of the South."

At Huntsville is the George C. Marshall Space Flight Center of NASA.

Agriculture remains a vital part of the economy. Cotton has been dethroned by soybeans as king among Alabama's crops and is rivaled by corn, pecans, and peanuts. Among the states, Alabama ranked 4th in production of pecans in 1975, 2d in peanuts. Also important are potatoes, watermelons, tobacco, and peaches.

Livestock, especially poultry, has grown in importance. Alabama was 4th among the states in number of chickens in 1977. Farm receipts for livestock and livestock products in 1976 totaled $892 million; for crops, the total was $635 million. Forest product sales totaled $122 million.

There are 56 institutions of higher education. Per pupil expenditure in public schools in 1975-76 was $1,199, 6th lowest among the states.

Earliest traces of mankind in the area date to 10,000 years ago. First Europeans were Spanish explorers in the early 1500's. The French made the first permanent settlement, on Mobile Bay, 1701-02; later, English settled in the northern areas. France ceded the entire region to England at the end of the French and Indian War, 1763, but Spanish Florida claimed the Mobile Bay area until U. S. troops took it, 1813. Gen. Andrew Jackson broke the power of the Creek Indians, 1814, and they were removed to Oklahoma.

The Confederate States were organized at Montgomery, Feb. 4, 1861, and Jefferson Davis took the oath as president at State Capitol there, Feb. 18, Davis' "first White House" now is a state shrine; also notable are the house in Tuscumbia where Helen Keller was born June 27, 1880, and the Statue of Vulcan near Birmingham.

Tourists spend an estimated $993 million in Alabama annually.

At Russell Cave National Monument, near Bridgeport, may be seen a detailed record of occupancy by humans from about 7000 B.C. to 1650 A.D., including tools, weapons and pottery.

The George Washington Carver Museum at Tuskegee Institute, Tuskegee, contains records of the famous black scientist's contributions to agronomy, and dioramas of achievements by blacks.

The University of Alabama Museum of Natural History, in Tuscaloosa, displays Alabama fossils, shells and aboriginal materials and collections. Mound State Monument, Moundville, an adjunct of the museum, shows aboriginal burials.

Famous Alabamians include Gov. George Wallace, Hank Aaron, Tallulah Bankhead, Nat King Cole, Hank Williams, Jesse Owens, Helen Keller, Harper Lee, Joe Louis, George Washington Carver, Hugo L. Black, William C. Handy, Booker T. Washington, William C. Gorgas.

(See also Index for Birmingham, Mobile, Montgomery, Phenix City.)

Alaska

No official nickname

Area: 586,412 sq. mi.; rank, 1st. **Population:** 382,000; (U.S. est. 1976); rank, 50th. **Capital:** Juneau. **Flower:** Forget-me-not. **Bird:** Willow ptarmigan. **Tree:** Sitka spruce. **Song:** Alska's Flag. **Fish:** King salmon. **Motto:** North to the Future. **Entered Union:** Jan. 3, 1959; rank, 49th.

Alaska became the 49th state Jan. 3, 1959. Largest political division of the U.S., it is two and one-fifth times the size of Texas. Alaska occupies the NW part of North America, separated from the rest of the continental U.S. by Canada's British Columbia. Alaska's general coastline runs 6,640 mi.; including all its islands, 33,904 mi. It has mountain ranges, volcanoes, fjords and glaciers.

About one-sixth of the population are Eskimos and Indians.

Pt. Barrow in Arctic Alaska is the northernmost spot in the state. The Yukon River flows E to W 1,200 mi. from the Canadian border to the Bering Sea. In south central Alaska stands Mt. McKinley, 20,320 ft., highest point in North America.

In west central Alaska, off the tip of the Seward Peninsula, lies Little Diomede Is., only 2.4 mi. from the Big Diomede Is., owned by the USSR. The Alaska Peninsula and the Aleutian Islands into which it tapers, extends SW and W for 1,200 mi., with numerous volcanoes; at the base of the peninsula is Katmai National Monument, containing the Valley of 10,000 Smokes, scene of a 1912 volcanic eruption.

Alaska's Panhandle stretches SE; it is a narrow strip of mainland and islands, with fjords and Glacier

Bay National Monument (containing the Muir Glacier, 2 mi. wide and 250 ft. high), facing the Pacific, W of British Columbia.

Vitus Bering, a Danish explorer working for Russia, was the first European to land in Alaska, 1741. Alexander Baranov, first governor of Russian America, set up headquarters at Archangel, near present Sitka, in 1799. Secretary of State William H. Seward in 1867 bought Alaska from Russia for $7.2 million, a bargain which some called "Seward's Folly." In 1896, gold was discovered and the famed Gold Rush was on. Many of the fortune hunters settled in Alaska as farmers or traders.

Resources and Industries. Principal income is from fisheries, minerals (esp. oil), wood products, tourism and furs. Salmon, halibut, herring, cod, and shellfish are frozen or canned; Alaska is a leader in value of its commercial catch, about $227 million in 1976.

Processing of fish and other foods is the largest manufacturing industry, followed by forest products.

Spruce, yellow cedar, and hemlock are plentiful; there also are red cedar, and birch. Commercial timberland of Alaska's vast forest totals 28 million acres. The forest products industry in SE is expanding as pulp mills increase. Timber products value is over $134 million yearly.

Furs produced are those of the seal, sable, ermine, wolverine, land otter, muskrat, beaver, mink, red fox, blue fox, lynx, marten. Wildlife includes the gray wolf, moose, caribou, and 5 kinds of bear: black, grizzly, polar, Kodiak, and glacier. There are plenty of sea fowl, but whales, walrus, sea lion, and sea otter have diminished.

The seal herd on the Pribilof Islands is owned by the federal government and seal harvesting is managed by the U.S. Commerce Dept. Reindeer herds are multiplying and their meat is marketed.

Oil production, mainly from offshore fields in Cook Inlet, had an est. value of $353 million in 1976. Total mineral production value was est. at $524 million.

Sale of leases for the vast North Slope oil discovery area at Prudhoe Bay brought the state $900 million in 1969. After long delay caused by ecological controversy, Congress in Nov. 1973 authorized construction of a $6-billion, 796-mi., trans-Alaska pipeline to carry oil from Prudhoe Bay to the south Alaska port of Valdez. Oil started flowing June 20, 1977.

The value of gold production in 1976 was $2.6 million. Alaska also has natural gas, tin, bituminous coal and mercury.

Principal ports are in the Panhandle where Juneau, the capital, is on the mainland shore; N of it is Skagway, historic entry to Klondike gold fields via Chilkoot Pass and White Pass. Sitka, Wrangell, and Ketchikan (center of salmon industry), are on islands of the Alexander group.

At the head of Cook Inlet, in S Central Alaska, is the state's largest city, Anchorage. Seward, S of Anchorage, is government-terminus for the government-owned Alaska Railroad, which runs N to Fairbanks. Nine domestic airlines serve Alaska. International lines flying via Arctic routes make stops; Fairbanks has the northern most international airport. Nearby is Eielson AFB. Ships transport 90% of the goods and foods to and from Alaska, linking some 50 Alaskan ports with Seattle, etc.

More than 235,000 tourists visit Alaska annually, spending some $299 million.

There are 2 motor routes to Alaska. The newer is by way of Marine Highway, a 450-mile ferry route from Prince Rupert, B.C., to Skagway. Motorists leaving the ferry at Haines may drive to Fairbanks, Anchorage, etc., with part of the route passing through Canada. The older route is the Alaska Highway, from British Columbia.

There are 9 institutions of higher education.

Pay of public school teachers, $16,906 in 1975, is the highest in the 50 states. Average per capita income was $10,178 in 1976, highest in the U.S. The Alaskan cost of living was also the highest in the U.S.

The Alaska State Museum in Juneau features Eskimo and Indian exhibits, mounted wildlife specimens, rocks and minerals and historical exhibits.

The University of Alaska Museum, in College, near Fairbanks, maintains cultural and natural history collections for research and for the public.

Famous Alaskans include pioneer pilot Carl Eielson, prospector Joe Juneau, painter Sydney Laurence, former Gov. Ernest Gruening, Congressman James Wickersham.

(See also Index for Anchorage.)

Arizona

Grand Canyon State

Area: 113,909 sq. mi.; rank 6th. **Population** (U.S. est. 1976): 2,270,000; rank, 32d. **Capital:** Phoenix. **Motto:** Ditat Deus, God Enriches. **Flower:** Giant cactus or saguaro. **Bird:** Cactus wren. **Tree:** Paloverde. **Song:** Arizona. **Entered Union:** Feb. 14, 1912, rank, 48th.

Arizona leads the nation in copper production with half of the total U.S. output, but its rapidly-growing manufacturing industries, such as machinery, aerospace, and electronics, form the largest source of income. Agriculture and tourism are also important.

Sunshine and a wealth of scenic attractions give Arizona a mounting tourist business; out-of-state visitors spent an est. $807 million in 1974.

The climate is dry in southern regions and the northern plateau, but high mountains and forests in central areas have heavy snows in winter. Highest point is Humphreys Peak, 12,633 ft. Over 44% of the land is owned by the U.S. government.

The only point in the U.S. at which 4 states meet is the juncture of Arizona, Utah, Colorado and New Mexico.

Arizona is noted for the Grand Canyon of the Colorado, an immense, vari-colored fissure 217 mi. long, 4 to 13 mi. wide at the brim, 4,000 to 5,500 ft. deep. Nature has given Arizona the Painted Desert, extending for 30 mi. along U.S. 66; the Petrified Forest; Canyon Diablo, 225 ft. deep and 500 ft. wide, and Meteor Crater, 4,150 ft. across, 570 ft. deep, made by a prehistoric meteor. The state has 17 national monuments, 2 national parks. Rodeos and historic sites of Indian and Spanish eras are other attractions.

The 1976 est. value of the state's copper production was $1.4 billion. Arizona also ranks high among the states in pumice, silver, molybdenum and gold. Total value of mineral production in 1976 was est. at $1.7 billion.

Cotton is a major crop; Arizona's harvest ranked 4th among the states in 1976. Cash receipts for all crops in 1976 were $754 million; receipts from livestock and livestock products, $534 million. The state ranks 10th in number of sheep. Fruit production is important; Arizona ranks high in lemons, oranges, grapefruit, and grapes. Lettuce, melons, and alfalfa are valuable crops.

Manufacturing has expanded in recent years. Value added by manufacture is over $2.6 billion a year. Electrical machinery, including electronic components, accounts for $340 million of this total.

Federal spending on defense contracts, construction projects, air bases, etc., is an important factor in Arizona's economy. Per capita personal income was $5,817 in 1976.

Schools include the Univ. of Arizona at Tucson, Arizona State Univ. at Tempe, and Northern Arizona Univ. at Flagstaff. The new observatory of the National Science Foundation is located on Kitt Peak near Tucson. Taliesin West is the Frank Lloyd Wright architectural school near Phoenix. There are 22 institutions of higher education.

Marcos de Niza, a Franciscan, and Estevan, a black slave, explored the Arizona area in 1539. Eusebio Francisco Kino, Jesuit missionary, taught Indians Christianity and farming, 1690-1711, and left a chain of missions. Spain ceded Arizona to Mexico, 1821. The U. S. took over at the end of the Mexican War, 1848. The area below the Gila River was obtained from

Mexico in the Gadsden Purchase, 1854. Long Apache wars did not end until 1886, with Geronimo's surrender.

Museums include Arizona State Museum, Tucson, which stresses the archeology and ethnology of the Southwest. The Museum of Northern Arizona, 3 mi. N of Flagstaff, has exhibits illustrating the geology and paleontology of the area.

The Southwestern Arboretum, on U.S. 60 and 70 near Superior, has over 6,000 plants and trees from arid regions of the world, from lowly cactus to lofty boojum tree. The Phoenix Zoo is one of the nation's largest. The Arizona-Sonora Desert Museum, near Tucson, displays animals and plants of the desert.

Famous Arizonans include Cochise, Geronimo, Helen Jacobs, Zane Grey, Barry Goldwater, Percival Lowell, Stewart Udall, Frank Lloyd Wright, William H. Pickering, George W. P. Hunt, Morris Udall.

(See also Index for Phoenix and Tucson.)

Arkansas

Land of Opportunity

Area: 53,104 sq. mi.; rank, 27th. **Population** (U.S. est. 1976): 2,109,000; rank, 33d. **Capital:** Little Rock. **Motto:** Regnat Populus, Let the People Rule. **Flower:** Apple blossom. **Bird:** Mockingbird. **Tree:** Pine. **Song:** Arkansas. **Entered Union:** June 15, 1836; rank, 25th.

Arkansas is an important agricultural state with growing industries and has valuable mineral production. It has thermal springs and is popular with sportsmen.

First European explorers were Hernando de Soto, 1541; Louis Jolliet, 1673; La Salle, 1682. First settlement was by the French under Henri de Tonty, 1686, at Arkansas Post. In 1762 the area was ceded by France to Spain, then back again in 1800 and was part of the Louisiana Purchase by the U. S. in 1803. Arkansas seceded from the Union in 1861, only after the Civil War began, and many Arkansans (over 10,000) fought on the Union side. The state rejoined the Union in 1868.

Manufacturing is growing in importance with a 64% increase in employees in a 10-year period. New and expanded factories provided 13,000 new jobs in 1974. Per capita income was $5,073 in 1976. Lumber, petroleum, bauxite, and cotton are major products.

The $1.2 billion Arkansas River program, involving navigation, flood control, and power developments and construction of 17 dams and locks in Arkansas and Oklahoma, was completed to Catoosa, near Tulsa, Okla., in 1971 and provided an important boost to the area's economy.

The state has 18.5 million acres of oak, hickory, gum, cypress, and pine, and forest industries have a $500 million annual payroll. Cotton accounts for 48% of farm income and Arkansas ranked first among the states in rice production in 1976, and 5th in cotton production. It was 3d in number of chickens, 4th in turkeys. Farm receipts for 1976 totaled $2.4 billion.

Arkansas produces by far the greatest amount of bauxite (aluminum ore) produced in the U.S. It has the only diamond field in the U.S. and ranks 1st in bromine and vanadium.

But petroleum is the state's main mineral product; 1976 output was valued at $163 million; that of bauxite was $22 million. Natural gas and stone were also important. Total value of mineral production was est. at $480 million, up $44 million from the record 1975 figure.

Arkansas has 29 institutions of higher learning. It has the lowest per pupil expenditure in all the state's school systems, $1,045 annually.

Fresh-water fishing, duck-hunting in southeast lowlands, and recreation areas in 21 state parks and 3 national forests attract visitors. There are several reservoir-recreation areas, as at Norfork, Bull Shoals, Nimrod and Dardanelle, and others are being created. There are 47 hot springs in government-operated Hot Springs National Park, which entirely surrounds the city of Hot Springs, about 50 mi. SW of Little Rock. Spring water ranges from 95° to 147°F. and is piped in insulated conduits for baths and drinking. Blanchard Caverns, near Mountain View, are among the nation's largest.

Out-of-state visitors spent more than $535 million in Arkansas in 1974. There are 93 airports.

Historic attractions in Little Rock include the Territorial Capital Restoration, a block of 13 original frame and brick buildings, including the governor's home, furnished as in 1820-36, and an early print shop of the Arkansas Gazette, oldest newspaper west of the Mississippi. The Old State House in Little Rock was the state capitol 1836-1912; it houses many historical exhibits.

The Little Rock Museum of Science and Natural History occupies the building where Gen. Douglas MacArthur was born; also in MacArthur Park is the Arkansas Museum of Fine Arts.

Famous Arkansans include Hattie Caraway, "Dizzy" Dean, Orval Faubus, James W. Fulbright, Douglas MacArthur, John L. McClellan, Winthrop Rockefeller, Edward Durell Stone, Thyra Samter Winslow, Opie Read, Archibald Yell.

(See also Index for Little Rock.)

California

Golden State

Area: 158,693 sq. mi.; rank 3d. **Population** (U.S. est. 1976): 21,520,000; rank, 1st. **Capital:** Sacramento. **Motto:** Eureka, I Have Found It. **Flower:** California poppy. **Bird:** Valley quail. **Tree:** Redwood. **Song:** I Love You, California. **Entered Union:** Sept. 9, 1850; rank 31st.

California is the leading state in agriculture, manufacturing, and population.

Third largest in area, California also has, within only 85 mi. of each other, the highest and lowest points in the conterminous 48 states; Mt. Whitney, 14,494 ft., and Death Valley, 282 ft. below sea level.

The U.S. Bureau of the Census estimated California's population as of July 1, 1964, at 18,084,000 and New York's at 17,915,000, giving California 1st place; New York had been in 1st place from 1820 through the census of 1960. In the 1970 census, New York had 18,241,266; California, 19,953,134. California also has the most dogs and cats — an est. 50 million.

Among scenic regions are the Yosemite Valley, Lassen and Sequoia-Kings Canyon national parks, Lake Tahoe, the Mojave and Colorado deserts, San Francisco Bay, and Monterey Peninsula. National forests cover one-fifth of the state.

Oldest living things on earth are believed to be a stand of Bristlecone pines in the Inyo National Forest, est. to be 4,600 years old.

The world's tallest tree, the Howard Libbey redwood, 362 ft. with a girth of 44 ft., stands on Redwood Creek, Humboldt County.

California's huge fruit and vegetable production is fed by large irrigation systems. Receipts from crops in 1976 totaled $6.3 billion (tops in U.S.); from livestock, $3 billion (3d in U.S.); total receipts were $9.3 billion (most in U.S.)

The state ranked 1st in numbers of chickens, 3d in turkeys, 3d in sheep, 7th in cattle, as of Jan. 1, 1977.

California produces the most apricots, avocados, grapes and raisins, peaches, persimmons, pomegranates, plums, prunes, lemons, nectarines, olives, dates, almonds, walnuts, and sugar beets. Its total vegetable crop is the largest; it ranks 2d to Florida in oranges and was also 2d in grapefruit, cotton, and barley, 3d in rice.

It was 2d to Alaska in commercial fishing in 1976 with a catch valued at $185 million.

The state's giant aerospace industries employ a third of all its manufacturing employees. Value added by manufacture is over $36.7 billion (1973); transportation equipment, especially aircraft and missiles, lead; food products, particularly frozen and canned foods, were 2d; electrical machinery, including electronic components, was 3d followed by ordnance, other machinery, metal products. Per capita income was $7,164 in 1976, 7th highest in the U.S.

Gold, discovered at Sutter's sawmill Jan. 24, 1848, set off the historic Gold Rush and gave initial impetus to California's development, but petroleum is the leading mineral product today.

Oil output in 1976 was valued at an est. $2.2 billion, over half the state's total mineral production value, $3.6 billion, up 13% and 3d highest in the U.S. after Texas and Louisiana. California is a leader in output of asbestos, cement, boron, gypsum, and tungsten.

The Oroville Dam, main unit in the world's largest water project — the $2.8 billion Feather River Project — was dedicated May 4, 1968.

Tourists spend about $7.3 billion a year in California.

There are some 252 institutions of higher learning. Public school expenditures per pupil total $1,440. Three of the world's largest observatories are located on Palomar Mtn., Mt. Hamilton, and Mt. Wilson.

The Tournament of Roses and the Rose Bowl football game at Pasadena are held annually on Jan. 1. Winter sports are featured in many mountain areas.

Vandenberg AFB, 170 mi. NW of Los Angeles, is center of an interservice missile range.

First European visitors were Juan Rodriguez Cabrillo, 1542, and Francis Drake, 1579. First settlement was the Spanish Alta California mission at San Diego, 1769, first in a string founded by Franciscan Father Junipero Serra. U. S. traders and settlers arrived in the 19th century and staged the abortive Bear Flag Revolt, 1846; the Mexican War began later in 1846 and U.S. forces occupied California; Mexico ceded the province to the U.S. in 1848, the same year the Gold Rush began.

Among museums the Pasadena Art Museum has collections of modern German painting, American painting, Oriental art and prints. The Santa Barbara Museum of Art has exhibits of Greek and Roman sculpture, Oriental art, old master and modern paintings, primitive arts, American paintings, and old and modern European drawings. The Santa Barbara Historical Society Museum displays and interprets objects of state and local history and operates the Gledhill Library for historical research. In Sacramento, the Crocker Art Gallery has collections of paintings, drawings, prints, sculpture, and crafts representing all European schools, American glass, and pottery from 5th century B.C. to contemporary American.

The J. Paul Getty Museum in Malibu opened in 1974 with collections of Greek and Roman antiquities, 18th Century French furniture and Western European paintings.

Famous Californians include Luther Burbank, W. R. Hearst, Joe DiMaggio, Jack London, Richard Nixon, Herbert Hoover, William Saroyan, Earl Warren, John Steinbeck, Gertrude Atherton, Bret Harte.

(See also Index for Bakersfield, Fresno, Los Angeles, Oakland, Orange County, Sacramento, San Bernardino, San Diego, San Francisco, San Jose, Santa Ana.)

Colorado

Centennial State

Area: 104,247 sq. mi.; rank, 8th. **Population** (U.S. est. 1976): 2,583,000; rank, 28th. **Capital:** Denver. **Motto:** Nil Sine Numine, Nothing Without Deity. **Flower:** Columbine. **Bird:** Lark bunting. **Tree:** Colorado blue spruce. **Animal:** Big horn sheep. **Song:** Where the Columbines Grow. **Entered Union:** Aug. 1, 1876; rank, 38th.

Once primarily a mining and grazing state, Colorado now draws the largest segment of its income from manufacturing, followed by agriculture, tourism, and mining. Its snow-capped peaks, ski centers, ghost towns and health spas make it a popular vacation-recreation area.

Early civilization centered around Mesa Verde 2,000 years ago. The U. S. acquired eastern Colorado in the Louisiana Purchase, 1803; Lt. Zebulon M. Pike explored the area, 1806, discovering the peak that bears his name. After the Mexican War, 1846-48, U.S. immigrants settled in the east, former Mexicans in the south.

The total of value added by Colorado's varied manufacturing industries is over $2.7 billion yearly. Important industry groups are processing of meat, dairy and other food products, as well as machinery, electronics, metals, and stone-clay-glass products. Research and aerospace industries are growing. Per capita income was $6,503 in 1976.

Farm receipts in 1976 totaled $1.9 billion, about 70% from livestock and livestock products. Colorado ranked 4th among the states in the number of sheep in 1977, 11th in cattle. Its sugar beet crop is the 4th largest in the U.S. Other important crops are wheat, corn, barley, alfalfa, potatoes, apples, peaches, pears.

Gold was discovered on the Platte in 1858 and at Leadville in 1860.

Climax, near Leadville, now produces most of the world's molybdenum. Colorado produces a rich variety of minerals and is a leader among the states in output of tin, vanadium, tungsten, carbon dioxide, uranium, lead, zinc, and pyrites. Total 1976 mineral production was valued at $1.07 billion, up 12% from 1975; petroleum accounted for $377 million of the total, up 10%.

With Utah and Wyoming, Colorado shares the world's richest oil shale deposits, still to be developed.

Colorado is the highest state in the Union, with an average altitude of 6,800 ft. It has 54 of the nation's highest mountains and 1,500 peaks over 10,000 ft. Highest is Mt. Elbert, 14,433 ft. Frozen Lake, altitude 12,940 ft., is the highest lake in the 48 contiguous states.

Six major rivers—the Colorado, Rio Grande, Arkansas, North Platte, South Platte, and Republican — rise in Colorado, supply water to 19 states. The western rivers have cut great canyons; the Black Canyon of the Gunnison and the Royal Gorge of the Arkansas, 1,000 to 1,500 ft. deep. One of the world's highest bridges crosses the Arkansas 1,053 ft. above the river at Royal Gorge.

The federal government owns 36.4% of the land, including 2 national parks, 6 monuments, 2 recreation areas, 12 forests, 2 Indian reservations, 7 major military reservations.

Colorado has 39 institutions of higher education.

Attractions for an annual 8 million tourists include Rocky Mountain National Park, Garden of the Gods, Great Sand Dunes and Dinosaur national monuments, Pikes Peak and Mt. Evans highways, Mesa Verde National Park (pre-historic cliff dwellings). The Grand Mesa tableland comprises Grand Mesa Forest, 659,584 acres, with 200 lakes stocked with trout. Other attractions include the U.S. Air Force Academy near Colorado Springs, Denver Western Stock Show, Colorado State Fair, horse, dog, and auto races, rodeos, and pioneer celebrations. Thirty-one major ski areas operate from November to May. Tourists spend some $1.5 billion a year.

Big game include deer, bear, elk, mountain lion, gray wolf, coyote. There are thousands of miles of trout streams and 2,000 fishing lakes.

The old mining towns of Aspen and Central City have become cultural centers.

Museums include the Colorado Springs Fine Arts Center which has paintings, prints, and drawings by contemporary artists, exhibits of the cultural history of the SW and Latin America, and the John F. Huckel collection of 112 Navajo sand painting reproductions. The University of Colorado Museum, in Boulder, has more than a million objects in its exhibits of rocks, plants, and early peoples as well as an art gallery.

Famous Coloradans include Lowell Thomas, Paul Whiteman, William N. Byers, Frederick Bonfils, Harry Tammen, Jack Dempsey, Douglas Fairbanks, Ralph Edwards, Byron R. White, M. Scott Carpenter.

(See also Index for Denver.)

Connecticut

Constitution State, Nutmeg State

Area: 5,009 sq. mi.; rank 48th. **Population** (U.S. est. 1976): 3,117,000; rank, 24th. **Capital:** Hartford. **Motto:** Qui Transtulit, Sustinet; He Who Transplanted, Still Sustains. **Flower:** Mountain laurel. **Bird:** American robin. **Tree:** White oak. Fifth of the 13 original states to ratify the Constitution, Jan. 9, 1788.

Connecticut's heavily industrialized cities are in sharp contrast to its picturesque New England villages and scenic countryside. Despite its small size, the state has large and diverse manufacturing industries, mainly of high-value specialty products. Per capita income was $7,373 in 1976, 2d only to Alaska.

It is a leading maker of jet engines, helicopters, nuclear subs, pins and needles, silverware, hardware, cutlery, and ball bearings. Ranking 48th in area, it is 16th in value added by manufacturing, a total of over $7.9 billion annually. Its factories employ over 30% of the non-farm work force. Hartford is headquarters for many of the nation's largest insurance companies. The Greenwich-Stamford area has one of the world's highest concentrations of multinational corporation headquarters.

Poultry and dairy products account for the largest part of farm receipts, which totaled $234 million in 1976. Much of the soil is stony, but tobacco, potatoes, fruits, and vegetables are grown. Greenhouse, nursery, and forest products are valued at over $21 million annually.

The vacation-recreation industry is important. Attractions include historic sites, charming villages, the American Shakespeare Theatre in Stratford, famed museums, boating on Long Island Sound, and winter sports.

There are 88 state parks, 30 state forests, recreation areas, and historic sites, covering 170,000 acres.

Tourism brings Connecticut about $550 million a year from out-of-state vacationers.

Mineral production is mostly of sand, stone, and gravel for construction of roads and buildings. Total value for 1976 was $32 million.

Adriaen Block, Dutch explorer, was the first European visitor, 1614. By 1633, settlers from Plymouth Bay started colonies along the Connecticut River and in 1637 defeated the Pequot Indians, opening the area to more settlements. In the Revolution, Connecticut men fought in most major campaigns and beat off British raids on Danbury and other towns. Connecticut privateers captured British merchant ships; the state was nicknamed "The Provision State" for the large amount of food and armaments it furnished the Continental Army.

Free public schools were established in New Haven, 1642; Hartford, 1643. Compulsory education in elementary schools was established in 1650. Per pupil public school expenditures total $1,741.

There are 46 institutions of higher education.

Museums include the P. T. Barnum Museum, Bridgeport; American Clock and Watch Museum, Bristol; trolley museums, East Haven and Warehouse Point; Hill-Stead Museum, a country house with paintings by famous impressionists, Farmington; Museum of American Art, New Britain; Lyman Allyn Museum, New London; Bruce Museum, Greenwich; Wadsworth Atheneum and Museum of Connecticut History in Hartford.

In New Haven, museums include the Winchester Gun Museum, with 5,000 items from the 15th century to present. The Yale University Art Gallery's collections range from ancient to modern. The Peabody Museum at Yale has collections in paleontology, mineralogy, zoology and, archeology.

Mystic Seaport, Mystic, is a recreated 19th century village, including smithy, chapel, and schoolhouse. At the docks lie the wooden whaleship, Charles W. Morgan, the squarerigger, Joseph Conrad, and the Gloucester fishing schooner, L. A. Dunton.

Famous "Nutmeggers" include Phineas T. Barnum, Ethan Allen, Walter Camp, Samuel Colt, Nathan Hale, Isaac Hull, J. Pierpont Morgan, Abraham Ribicoff, Harriet Beecher Stowe, Mark Twain, Noah Webster, Emma Hart Willard, Katharine Hepburn, Jonathan Edwards, Israel Putnam, William Gillette.

(See also Index for Bridgeport, Hartford, New Haven.)

Delaware

First State, Diamond State

Area: 2,057 sq. mi.; rank, 49th. **Population:** (U.S. est. 1976): 582,000; rank, 47th. **Capital:** Dover. **Motto:** Liberty and Independence. **Flower:** Peach blossom. **Bird:** Blue hen chicken. **Tree:** American holly. **Song:** Our Delaware. First of original 13 states to ratify the Constitution, Dec. 7, 1787.

Delaware occupies part of the Delmarva Peninsula, so-called because Delaware and parts of Maryland and Virginia share the peninsula separating Delaware and Chesapeake Bays. Delaware is 96 mi. long and from 9 to 35 mi. wide. The land slopes from rolling hills (442 ft. highest elevation) in the N to a near sea-level plain.

Second smallest of the states in area, Delaware has the 3d highest per capita income in the U.S., $7,290 in 1976. It has large chemical and other industries, the hqs. of many large corporations, prosperous farms, and important shellfish production.

Important in Delaware's total of value added by manufacture are canned and frozen foods, leather and metal products, textiles and machinery. Total value added by manufacture is over $1.5 billion.

Broiler chickens are the largest item of farm income. Farm receipts for 1976 were $270 million.

Mineral production is mainly sand, gravel, and stone used for construction. Total value in 1976 was est. at $1.7 million. There is also a sizable commercial fishing catch, valued at $1.8 million in 1976.

Delaware's major tourist attractions include several famed beaches, racetracks, and historic sites and museums. Annual value of tourism is about $158 million.

The Dutch first settled in Delaware near present Lewes, 1631, but were wiped out by Indians. Swedes settled at present Wilmington, 1638; Dutch settled anew, 1651, near New Castle and seized the Swedish settlement, 1655, only to lose all Delaware and New Netherland to the British, 1664. Delaware troops served in Washington's New Jersey campaigns and at the Brandywine, near home, where Washington suffered defeat. Delaware troops also fought in the southern campaigns and, finally, at Yorktown. In the Civil War, over 10% of Delaware's total population served in the Union Army.

Fort Christina Monument marks the site of founding of New Sweden. Holy Trinity (Old Swedes) Church erected 1698 is the oldest Protestant church in the U.S. still in use. Center New Castle comprises a unique survival of a colonial capital nearly in its late 18th century form. The home of John Dickinson, "Penman of the Revolution," and drafter of the Articles of Confederation, has been restored near Dover.

Museums include the Delaware Art Center in Wilmington which has collections of Pre-Raphaelite English paintings and American paintings. The Henry Francis du Pont Winterthur Museum, at Winterthur near Wilmington, has 100 American period rooms from 17th to early 19th centuries (reservations are required to visit some of them). The Hagley Museum at Wilmington includes many of the old du Pont powder mills and other exhibits illustrating the development of American industry. The Delaware Museum of Natural History is in Greenville.

The Delaware State Museum, Dover, has varied exhibits on Delaware history and life and a collection on the development of the Victor Talking Machine and related sound recording.

Delaware has 10 institutions of higher education.

Famous Delawareans include E. I. du Pont, Caesar Rodney, Howard Pyle, Henry Seidel Canby, John P. Marquand.

(See also Index for Wilmington.)

Florida

Sunshine State

Area: 58,560 sq. mi.; rank 22d. **Population** (U.S. est. 1976): 8,421,000; rank, 8th. **Capital:** Tallahassee. **Motto:** In God We Trust. **Flower:** Orange blossom. **Bird:** Mockingbird. **Tree:** Sabal palm. **Song:** Old Folks at Home. **Entered Union:** Mar. 3, 1845; rank 27th.

Florida's many miles of beaches and other resort areas offer fun in the sun to millions of vacationers. The state also has a tremendous agricultural output, producing 80% of the nation's citrus fruits and ranking 2d only to California in production of vegetables. Its growing and diversified manufacturing industries provide even more income than its agriculture. Per capita income was $6,108 in 1976 (U.S. average: $6,441).

The Florida peninsula juts southward 500 mi. between the Atlantic and the Gulf of Mexico; Cuba is only 90 mi. from its southern tip. It has some 30,000 lakes; Okeechobee, covering 700 sq. mi., is the 4th largest natural lake inside the U.S. The land is flat or rolling; highest point is 345 ft. in the NW.

First European to see Florida was Ponce de Leon, 1513. France established a colony, Fort Caroline, on the St. Johns River, 1564; Spain settled St. Augustine, 1565, and Spanish troops massacred most of the French. Britain's Francis Drake burned St. Augustine, 1586. Britain held the area briefly, 1763-83, returning it to Spain. After Andrew Jackson led a U.S. invasion, 1818, Spain ceded Florida to the U.S., 1819. The Seminole War, 1835-42, resulted in removal of most Indians to Oklahoma. Florida seceded from the Union, 1861, was readmitted, 1868.

Tourism is a major industry; about 29 million visitors spend some $10 billion annually in Florida. It offers a wide variety of tourist attractions in addition to climate, resorts, and water sports. Many tourists have become permanent residents.

Major tourist objectives are metropolitan Miami, with the nation's greatest concentration of luxury hotels at Miami Beach; Palm Beach; St. Augustine, oldest city in U.S.; Daytona Beach, Fort Lauderdale, all on the E coast; Sarasota, Tampa, Key West, St. Petersburg on the W; Walt Disney World, an entertainment and vacation development near Orlando, visited by 13.1 million persons in 1976.

Everglades National Park, 3d largest of U.S. national parks, preserves the beauty of the vast Everglades swamp. Castillo de San Marcos (St. Augustine), Fort Matanzas, Fort Jefferson (Dry Tortugas), De Soto National Memorial (Bradenton), and Fort Caroline (Jacksonville) are national monuments.

The John F. Kennedy Space Center is another big tourist attraction. From it the nation's first earth satellite was launched Jan. 31, 1958; first U.S. manned space flight, May 5, 1961; first manned orbital flight, Feb. 20, 1962 (Col. John H. Glenn), as well as the first man-on-the-moon launch, July 16, 1969.

Key West became the 1st U.S. city to get its fresh water from the sea when a desalting plant, capable of producing 3.5 million gallons a day, opened 1967.

Florida produces most of the nation's oranges and grapefruit; 1976 output was $562 million worth of oranges and $111 million worth of grapefruit, both several times the amount produced by California. Florida is also first in sugarcane. It produces vegetables, avocados, watermelons, limes, tangerines, peanuts, cotton, tobacco, strawberries.

Florida ranks high in chickens. The cattle industry has grown in importance. Crop and livestock receipts for 1976 totaled $2.7 billion.

Manufacturing has made great gains and provides payrolls totaling $3 billion. Leading industries, in terms of value added by manufacturing, are food processing, chemicals, electrical equipment, transportation equipment, metal products, paper. Total added in 1973 was $6.5 billion.

Florida leads the U.S. in production of phosphate rock and is 2d to New York in titanium. Total mineral production value in 1976 was $1.7 billion, 9th largest among the states.

The commercial catch of fish and shellfish is worth over $88 million a year, high among the states.

Florida has 17 airports with scheduled service, 62 scheduled airlines, and 5 major railroads. There are 14 deepwater ports which handle domestic and foreign trade valued at $1.8 billion a year.

Florida has 73 institutions of higher learning.

Museums include the Florida State Museum in Gainesville, with exhibits in archeology, ethnology, paleontology, ornithology, history, and industry. Castillo de San Marcos in St. Augustine is a Spanish fort built 1672-1696 which is now a national monument. Marineland of Florida, 18 mi. S of St. Augustine, has some 2,500 marine specimens ranging from sharks and porpoises to tiny tropical fish; trained porpoises and pilot whales perform in shows. Miami's Seaquarium and Orlando's Sea World have similar shows.

At Pensacola is the Naval Aviation Museum, with exhibits tracing flight development into the space age; Fort Pickens, built 1829, where Geronimo was imprisoned; the T. T. Wentworth Museum, with exhibits of local historical interest; the Pensacola Historical Museum.

At Lake Wales are the 205-ft. Singing Tower with a carillon of 53 bells (the largest weighs 11 tons) and Mountain Lake Sanctuary, with trails and picnic area, given "to the American people" by publisher Edward Bok in thanks for "the successful life they gave" him.

In Sarasota, the John and Mable Ringling Museum of Art, willed to the state, contains works by Rembrandt, Rubens, Hals, Tiepolo, Velasquez, Murillo, Gainsborough, Reynolds, and other masters. The Ringling Museum of the Circus includes elaborately decorated wagons, costumes, and printed bills showing performers at fairs and circuses from the 16th to 20th centuries; the Asolo Theater presents operas.

Also in Sarasota, the Circus Hall of Fame gives circus acts and puppet shows, displays mementos such as a coach given Tom Thumb by Queen Victoria, a sleigh P. T. Barnum gave Jenny Lind.

Famous Floridians include Henry M. Flagler, Rex Beach, Irving Bacheller, James Weldon Johnson, Marjorie Kinnan Rawlings, MacKinlay Kantor, Gen. Joseph W. Stilwell, Henry B. Plant.

(See also Index for Jacksonville, Miami, Orlando, Pensacola, St. Petersburg, Tallahassee, Tampa, West Palm Beach.)

Georgia

Empire State of the South, Peach State

Area: 58,876 sq. mi.; rank, 21st. **Population** (U.S. est. 1976): 4,970,000 rank, 14th. **Capital:** Atlanta. **Motto:** Wisdom, Justice, Moderation. **Flower:** Cherokee rose. **Bird:** Brown thrasher. **Tree:** Live oak. **Song:** Georgia. Fourth of the 13 original states to ratify the Constitution, Jan. 2, 1788.

Largest in area of the states east of the Mississippi, Georgia is rich in a number of natural resources and in its growing, diversified industries.

There are large deposits of marble in the mountainous N, along with fertile plains and industry centers in the NW. The central Georgia Piedmont plateau boasts rich farmlands and a flourishing textile industry. The SE coastal plain produces pecans and peanuts and its forests yield a wealth of pulpwood and turpentine. Islands off its 100-mi. Atlantic coast provide resort havens. The state also has large deposits of clay, limestone, and talc.

Okefenokee in the SE is one of the largest swamps in the U.S., a wetland wilderness and peat bog covering 660 sq. mi. A large part of it is a National Wildlife Refuge, a home for wild birds, alligators, bear, deer.

Highest point in the state is Brasstown Bald in the NE, 4,784 ft.; Stone Mtn., near Atlanta, is 1,686 ft.

Manufacturing has grown many times over since World War II, but the textile industry remains the largest, both in terms of number of workers and value added by manufacture. Also of great importance are paper products, transportation equipment, apparel, food products, and chemicals.

Value added by manufacture totals over $8.6 billion a year. Per capita income was $5,571 in 1976.

Georgia ranks high among the states in forest products, particularly in pulpwood and turpentine.

Georgia is by far the nation's largest producer of peanuts, harvesting 780,000 tons in 1976, three times that of any other state. It is among the leading growers of pecans, peaches, and rye.

It ranked 2d among the states in numbers of chickens, about 35 million in 1976, and also had a large hog production. Farm receipts totaled over $2.3 billion in 1976, more than half from livestock.

Georgia is also a leader in production of marble, zirconium, bauxite, and kyanite. Total value of mineral production in 1976 was an est. $389 million.

Savannah and Brunswick are the main ports. The state is served by 6 major railroads and 10 airlines.

Notable among attractions are the Little White House in Warm Springs where Pres. Franklin D. Roosevelt died Apr. 12, 1945, the 2,500-acre Callaway Gardens, Jekyll Island State Park, the restored 1850s farming community of Westville; Dahlonega, site of America's first gold rush; Helen, a mountain village with Alpine motif, Stone Mountain and Six Flags over Georgia.

Georgia has also become a sports center, with professional baseball, basketball, football, hockey.

Andersonville Prison Park and National Cemetery are on the site of the Confederate prison camp in which a total of 50,000 Union soldiers were confined, Feb. 1864 to Apr. 1865.

There are 67 institutions of higher learning.

Gen. James Oglethorpe established the first settlements, 1733, for poor and religiously-persecuted Englishmen. Oglethorpe defeated a Spanish army from Florida at Bloody Marsh, 1742. In the Revolution, Georgians seized the Savannah armory, 1775, and sent the munitions to the Continental Army. Led by Light-Horse Harry Lee, Elijah Clarke, Andrew Pickens and Anthony Wayne, Georgians fought see-saw campaigns with Cornwallis' British troops, twice liberating Augusta and forcing final evacuation by the British from Savannah, 1782.

Famous Georgians include Jimmy (James Earl) Carter, Ty Cobb, Margaret Mitchell, the Rev. Dr. Martin Luther King Jr., Erskine Caldwell, Joel Chandler Harris, Laurence Stallings, John C. Fremont, James Bowie, Joseph Wheeler, Lucius D. Clay.

(See also Index for Atlanta, Augusta, Columbus, Macon, Savannah.)

Hawaii

Aloha State

Area: 6,450 sq. mi.; rank, 47th. **Population** (U.S. est. 1976): 887,000; rank, 40th. **Capital:** Honolulu. **Motto:** The Life of the Land Is Perpetuated in Righteousness. **Flower:** Hibiscus. **Bird:** Nene (Hawaiian goose). **Tree:** Kukui (candlenut). **Song:** Hawaii ponoi. **Entered Union:** Aug. 21, 1959, rank, 50th.

Hawaii, prosperous paradise of the Pacific, became the 50th state Aug. 21, 1959, and the 50-star U. S. flag became official the following July 4.

The Hawaiian Islands lie in the North Pacific, 2,397 mi. from San Francisco (5 hrs. by commercial jet). They consist of 8 major islands (7 inhabited) and 124 minor islands.

The principal islands are Hawaii, the largest; Oahu, on which are Honolulu and Pearl Harbor; Lanai, Maui, Molokai, Kauai, Niihau and Kahoolawe.

The islands are volcanic. Highest point is Mauna Kea, on Hawaii, an extinct volcano 13,796 ft. above sea level. Its twin is Mauna Loa, about 100 ft. lower but an active volcano. Average annual rainfall is 22.9 inches at Honolulu Airport, 133.57 inches in Hilo, and 486 inches atop Waialeale, a mountain on Kauai. Honolulu is subtropical (all-time range, 57° to 88°) but Mauna Kea is often snowcapped.

Lake Waiau, at 13,020 ft. near the summit of Mauna Kea, is one of the highest lakes in the U.S.

Ka Lae, or South Cape, on the island of Hawaii, is the southernmost point in the 50 states.

Polynesians from islands 2,000 mi. to the south settled the Hawaiian Islands, probably about 700 A.D. First European visitor was British Capt. James Cook, 1778. Missionaries arrived, 1820, taught religion, reading and writing. King Kamehameha III and his chiefs created the first Constitution and a Legislature which set up a public school system. Sugar production began in 1835; it became the dominant industry. In 1893, Queen Liliuokalani was deposed, followed, 1894, by a republic headed by Sanford B. Dole. Annexation by the U.S. came in 1898.

Hawaii has a very heterogeneous population with Americans of Polynesian, Asian, European, and African extraction.

Many of the Polynesians intermarried with the other racial groups, which arrived mainly in the 19th Century.

The 1970 Census gave as racial origins: Japanese, 28.3%; Caucasian, 39.2%; the remainder, Hawaiian, Chinese, Filipino, Korean, etc., with many of mixed racial descent.

Major sources of income are tourism, defense expenditures, sugar and pineapple production, in that order. Visitors totaled 3.2 million in 1976, with an average 78,540 present daily. Tourists spend about $1.5 billion each year.

Value added by manufacturing, led by food processing, was $410 million in 1973. There were 4,270 farms, with a total of 2.3 million acres; farm receipts for 1976 were $375 million. The commercial fishing catch was valued at $7.5 million in 1976.

Mineral production, mostly cement and stone for construction, was valued at $43 million in 1976.

Per capita income was $6,969 in 1976.

More than 1,600 ships put into Honolulu in 1975. Honolulu International Airport has an average of over 319,000 arrivals and departures annually.

The bicentennial of Capt. Cook's arrival in the islands will be observed in 1978.

There are 11 institutions of higher education.

Eminent Islanders include Duke Kahanamoku, Don Ho, Patsy Mink, Daniel K. Inouye, Father Joseph Damien, Bette Midler, Hiram L. Fong, George R. Ariyoshi.

(See also Index for Honolulu.)

Idaho

Gem State

Area: 83,557 sq. mi.; rank, 13th. **Population** (U.S. est. 1976): 831,000; rank, 41st. **Capital:** Boise. **Motto:** Esto Perpetua, Let It Be Forever. **Flower:** Lewis mock orange (syringa). **Bird:** Mountain bluebird. **Tree:** Western white pine. **Song:** Here We Have Idaho. **Entered Union:** July 3, 1890; rank, 43d.

A land of rugged grandeur, Idaho nevertheless ranks high in agricultural production.

Exploration of the Idaho area began with Lewis and Clark, 1805; they returned through Idaho, 1806. Next came fur traders, setting up posts, 1809-34, and missionaries, establishing missions, 1830s-1850s. Mormons made their first permanent settlement at Franklin, 1860. Idaho's Gold Rush began that same year, and brought thousands of permanent settlers. Strangest of the Indian Wars was the 1,300-mi. trek in 1877 of Chief Joseph and the Nez Perce tribe, pursued by troops that caught them a few miles short of the Canadian border. By 1890, Idaho adopted a progressive Constitution and became a state that year.

The Snake River runs through Hells Canyon, which averages 5,510 ft. in depth for 40 mi., at one point 7,900 ft., exceeding Grand Canyon, and is 10 mi. from rim to rim at widest point. The Snake has several noted waterfalls: Shoshone, Twin, American.

Idaho is the nation's leading potato producer, growing about 85 million cwt. annually. It ranks high in sugar beets, barley, wheat, hops, and apples.

It is an important wool producer and was 9th

among the states in number of sheep in 1977 with 503,000. Farm receipts in 1976 totaled $1.3 billion, two-thirds from crops, the rest from livestock.

Manufacturing gains have been mainly in processing of potatoes and other foods, phosphates, paper, etc. Value added by manufacturing was est. at over $976 million. Per capita income was $5,726 in 1976.

Discovery of silver in 1884 at Coeur d'Alene caused a stampede; Idaho still leads the nation in production of that metal. It also ranks high among the states in antimony, lead, cobalt, garnet, phosphate rock, vanadium, zinc, and mercury. Total mineral production in 1976 was estimated at $219 million.

With 39% of its area in forests, Idaho produces much lumber with the world's largest white pine lumber mill at Lewiston. Yellow pine, Douglas fir, white spruce, larch, hemlock abound; the DeVoto Grove has cedars 1,000 years old. Total value of forest products is more than $255 million a year.

Hells Canyon, Brownlee, and Oxbow Dams are 3 recent hydro-electric projects on the Snake River. The National Reactor Testing Station of the AEC on Upper Snake River Plains has more than a score of reactors in operation.

Tourism brings in an est. $358 million annually, making it an important industry.

The state offers excellent hunting and fishing and Lake Pend Oreille, which has a 111-mile shoreline, is home of the world's largest trout, Kamloop rainbow.

Craters of the Moon National Monument, 18 mi. W of Arco, is a jagged landscape; lava covers the area.

The Nez Perce National Historic Park, in northern Idaho, includes many sites visited by the Lewis and Clark Expedition. The State Historical Museum in Boise has displays of early Idaho Indian life, the fur trade, mining, farm and pioneer mementos. The Intermountain Science Experience Center is at Idaho Falls.

There are 9 institutions of higher education.

Famous Idahoans include William E. Borah, Fred T. Dubois, Chief Joseph and Sacajawea, woman guide for Lewis and Clark.

(See also Index for Boise.)

Illinois

The Inland Empire

Area: 56,400 sq. mi.; rank, 24th. **Population:** U.S. est. 1976): 11,229,000; rank, 5th. **Capital:** Springfield. **Motto:** State Sovereignty, National Union. **Flower:** Native violet. **Bird:** Cardinal. **Tree:** White oak. **Song:** Illinois. **Slogan:** Land of Lincoln. **Entered Union:** Dec. 3, 1818; rank, 21st.

Illinois ranks high among the states as both an agricultural and industrial empire. It has large coal and oil reserves and highly developed rail, water, and air transportation facilities. The soil is rich and level.

Fur traders were the first Europeans in Illinois, followed shortly, 1673, by Louis Jolliet and Father Jacques Marquette, and, 1680, La Salle, who built a fort near present Peoria. First settlements were French, at Fort St. Louis on the Illinois River, 1692, and Kaskaskia, 1700. France ceded the area to Britain, 1763, and in 1778 American Gen. George Rogers Clark took it from the British without a shot. Defeat of Indian tribes in Black Hawk War, 1832, inspired new immigration, as did railroads in 1850s.

Illinois ranks 4th highest among the states in terms of value added by manufacture with a total of close to $30 billion. Manufacturing payrolls total $14.3 billion.

Major manufacturing lines are machinery (particularly construction and farm), processing of food products (especially grain, beverages and bakery), electrical machinery (communications, electronic components and appliances), primary metals (mainly iron and steel), transportation equipment and chemicals. Rockford is one of the nation's machine-tool centers; Peoria is a construction machinery and distilling center. Illinois was the birthplace of Pullman and refrigerator cars, barbed wire, the steel plow and grain reapers. Per capita income was $7,432 in 1976 (U.S. average: $6,441).

In 1976 Illinois ranked 2d to California in receipts from farm crops, $4.4 billion. It stood 7th in receipts for livestock and livestock products and was 4th in total cash farm receipts, $6.3 billion.

Illinois and Iowa vie closely with each other for the largest corn crop. Illinois produces the most soybeans; in 1977 it ranked 2d to Iowa in number of hogs and stood high in cattle and milk cows.

The state has large coal and oil reserves. It ranks high among the states in annual bituminous coal production, est. at $915 million in 1976. Petroleum production, 2d in value to coal, was est. to be worth $278 million. The state is a leader in output of fluorspar, tripoli, stone, and peat. Total 1976 minerals were valued at $1.6 billion.

A major research and development installation of the Atomic Energy Commission is the Argonne National Laboratory, Lemont, Ill., directed by the Univ. of Chicago, which also operates the Argonne Cancer Research Hospital in Chicago. At Batavia, W of Chicago, the AEC completed the nation's largest atom-smasher in 1971.

Illinois has 149 institutions of higher education.

The Illinois State Fair is held annually in August in Springfield. Attendance is over 700,000.

State forests, parks, and conservation areas cover 283,430 acres. Some are associated with the history of the Middle West, including Lincoln's home and tomb in Springfield; the restored Fort de Chartres, seat of French 18th century authority; old settlements such as Kaskaskia; prehistoric mound cities.

The Illinois State Museum in Springfield has large collections of local art and archeology, art of the ancient Near East, and antique furnishings.

Located in Springfield is a state memorial including Abraham Lincoln's tomb and the Lincoln home which the family occupied 1844-1860. The Old State Capitol Building has been restored.

New Salem State Park, 20 mi. NW of Springfield, contains the restored pioneer village of New Salem where Lincoln lived as storekeeper, surveyor, and postmaster, 1831-37. Annual performances are staged of Robert Sherwood's Abe Lincoln in Illinois.

Famous Illinoisans include Abraham Lincoln, William Jennings Bryan, Jane Addams, Adlai Stevenson, Carl Sandburg, Mary Garden, Ernest Hemingway, James T. Farrell, Frank Lloyd Wright.

(See also Index for Bloomington, Chicago, Rockford, Springfield.)

Indiana

Hoosier State

Area: 36,291 sq. mi.; rank, 38th. **Population:** (U.S. est. 1976): 5,302,000; rank, 12th. **Capital:** Indianapolis. **Motto:** Cross-roads of America. **Flower:** Peony. **Bird:** Cardinal. **Tree:** Tulip (yellow poplar). **Song:** On the Banks of the Wabash. **Entered Union:** Dec. 11, 1816; rank, 19th.

Indiana is heavily industrialized, yet is also important among the states for its agricultural output. It ranks among the top states in production of both steel and corn; it quarries much of the building limestone used in the U.S. and is a large producer of coal.

Pre-historic Indian Mound Builders of 1,000 years ago were the earliest known inhabitants. French explorer La Salle visited the present South Bend area, 1679 and 1681. A French trading post was built, 1731-32, at Vincennes. France ceded the area to Britain, 1763. During the Revolution, American Gen. George Rogers Clark captured Vincennes, 1778, and defeated British forces 1779; at war's end Britain ceded the area to the U.S. Miami Indians defeated U.S. troops twice, 1790, but were beaten, 1794, at Fallen Timbers by Gen. Anthony Wayne. At Tippecanoe, 1811, Gen. William H. Harrison defeated Tecumseh's Indian confederation.

There are sand dunes and lakes in the N, a level plain through most of the central area, and hills in the S.

The Calumet region in the state's NW corner, including Gary, Hammond, East Chicago, and Whiting, has one of the world's greatest concentrations of heavy industry, especially steel, cement, and oil-refining plants. Gary was a sand dune in 1906 when U.S. Steel began constructing mills there; in 1973 it had a pop. of 177,925.

Per capita income was $6,257 in 1976.

Another vast steel complex has been developed further E along Lake Michigan, including a deep-water port at Burns Harbor in the famed Dunes area, a large plant of the Midwest Steel Div. of the National Steel Corp., plus Bethlehem Steel Corp. works.

While steel and other metal industries are responsible for $2.2 billion of the $14 billion in value added annually by manufacture, electrical machinery, including television sets and household appliances, has risen to $2.3 billion. Auto parts, aircraft and other transportation equipment is next, with $1.9 billion; farm and other machinery, 4th; chemicals, 5th; processing of food products, 6th. Spending by out-of-state tourists is est. at $910 million a year.

Indiana is a leader in production of pre-fabricated wood products, mobile homes, and band instruments. Furniture is manufactured in over 40 cities.

Corn is the principal crop and much of it goes to fatten the hogs. Among the states, Indiana ranks 3d in hogs and corn, 7th in chickens. Farm marketing receipts for 1976 totaled $3.2 billion, 8th highest among the states.

Coal accounts for about half of the value of mineral production which in 1976 totaled $575 million. Portland cement, petroleum, limestone, clay, and gypsum are also important.

Indiana limestone, from vast quarries in the southern part of the state, sheathes tens of thousands of buildings, including the Empire State, Rockefeller Center, the United Nations, the Pentagon, the National Cathedral and many federal and state buildings.

Indiana has 28 state parks and recreation areas, including Dunes State Park on Lake Michigan; prehistoric Indian mounds; over 1,000 lakes; French Lick and other mineral spas; Wyandotte Cave, 3d largest in the U.S.; the Indianapolis 500-mile auto race, and the famous post office, Santa Claus.

Lincoln's boyhood home in Spencer County and the grave of his mother, Nancy Hanks Lincoln, are part of the Lincoln Boyhood National Memorial. State memorials commemorate the capture of Vincennes by George Rogers Clark in the Revolution, the defeat of Indian forces at Tippecanoe, and the Rappite and Robert Owen communities at New Harmony.

Spring Mill, Conner Prairie, and Billie Creek are restored pioneer settlements. The restored Whitewater Canal is at Brookville.

There are 64 institutions of higher education.

Famous "Hoosiers" include Wendell L. Willkie, Wilbur Wright, Lew Wallace, Cole Porter, Hoagy Carmichael, James Whitcomb Riley, Ernie Pyle, Booth Tarkington, Gene Stratton Porter, George Jean Nathan, George Ade, Eugene V. Debs, Theodore Dreiser.

(See also Index for Evansville, Fort Wayne, Indianapolis.)

Iowa

Hawkeye State

Area: 56,290 sq. mi.; rank, 25th. **Population:** (U.S. est. 1976): 2,870,000; rank, 25th. **Capital:** Des Moines. **Motto:** Our Liberties We Prize and Our Rights We Will Maintain. **Flower:** Wild rose. **Bird:** Eastern goldfinch. **Tree:** Oak. **Song:** Iowa. **Entered Union:** Dec. 28, 1846; rank, 29th.

Iowa, the heart of the rich Midwest farm belt, is one of the nation's wealthiest agricultural states, but its industrial growth has been so great that the value of its manufacturing output has become more than twice that of its farms.

Many industries process farm products or produce farm implements. However, the fast-growing industrial economy includes a wide variety of manufacturing plants, with electronic items, home appliances, tires, railway equipment, furnaces, automobile accessories, chemicals and fertilizers, vending machines, office furniture, and gypsum wallboard among the diversified products. Value added by manufacture is over $5.6 billion a year. Per capita income was $6,439 in 1976 ($2 below U.S. average).

Iowa's broad plains contain some of the finest soil in the world. Its huge harvests support the nation's richest livestock industry. Iowa had by far the most hogs, 12.6 million in 1976, twice as many as Illinois, the next largest raiser. In cattle, with 7.5 million, Iowa was 2d only to Texas. It also had large numbers of chickens, turkeys, and sheep.

In field crops, Iowa ranked 2d in corn, soybeans, and oats.

Receipts for livestock and livestock products totaled $4 billion in 1976, tops in the nation. In receipts for crops, Iowa stood 3d. Its total farm receipts were $7 billion, 2d only to California.

Iowa's forests produce hardwood lumber.

Mineral production was valued at $205 million in 1976. Products, in order of value, were cement, limestone, sand and gravel, gypsum, and coal.

Visitors from other states add more than $530 million to Iowa's economy annually.

Tourist attractions include the Herbert Hoover birthplace and library near West Branch, tulip festivals at Pella and Orange City in May, Iowa State Fair at Des Moines in August, several rodeos, the National Hot Air Balloon Races. The Little Brown Church in the Vale, near Nashua, inspired a well-known hymn. There are 95 state parks and other recreation areas. Effigy Mounds National Monument at Marquette is a prehistoric Indian burial site.

The Davenport Municipal Art Gallery has a collection of paintings and memorabilia of the Iowa painter Grant Wood, as well as other American, Mexican, Haitian, and European paintings. The State Historical Building, Des Moines, has Indian artifacts.

In Decorah, the Norwegian-American Museum preserves homes of pioneers from Norway.

Waterloo's Museum of History and Science has exhibits on Iowa history, pioneer life, Indian lore, and earth sciences, and a planetarium.

Iowa has 61 institutions of higher education. Pay of public school teachers was $10,598 in 1975.

A thousand years ago several groups of pre-historic Indian Mound Builders dwelt on Iowa's fertile plains. Father Jacques Marquette and Louis Jolliet gave France its claim to the area, 1673. It became U.S. territory through the 1803 Louisiana Purchase. Indian tribes were moved into the area from states further east, but by mid-19th century were forced to move on to Kansas. Before and during the Civil War, Iowans strongly supported Abraham Lincoln and became traditional Republicans.

Famous Iowans include Herbert Hoover, Buffalo Bill Cody, Billy Sunday, Susan Glaspell, Harry Hansen, Marquis Childs, James Norman Hall, Carl Van Vechten, Grant Wood, Henry Wallace, James A. Van Allen, Meredith Willson.

(See also Index for Des Moines.)

Kansas

Sunflower State

Area: 82,264 sq. mi.; rank, 14th. **Population:** (U.S. est. 1976); 2,310,000; rank, 31st. **Capital:** Topeka. **Motto:** Ad Astra per Aspera, To the Stars through Difficulties. **Flower:** Sunflower. **Bird:** Western meadowlark. **Tree:** Cottonwood. **Song:** Home on the Range. **Entered Union:** Jan. 29, 1861; rank, 34th.

Rolling fields of wheat, clusters of oil well derricks, great herds of cattle, and towering grain storage elevators feature the landscape of Kansas, the geographical center of the 48 contiguous states. The land rises from broad plains in the east, 680 ft. above sea level, to slightly over 4,000 ft. in the west.

Manufacturing, farming, and mining (especially petroleum and natural gas) are major factors in the Kansas economy. Large industry fields include transportation equipment, food processing, machinery, and chemicals. Value added by manufacture is $3.3 billion a year. Per capita income was $6,495 in 1976.

Most of the land of Kansas is devoted to agriculture, and much of that to growing wheat. Kansas ranked first among the states in its wheat crop in 1976, 2d in sorghum, 4th in cattle. Total farm receipts for 1976 were $3.8 billion, 7th highest in the U.S. Forest products, particularly walnut lumber, are valued at about $14 million a year.

Wichita ranks first in the nation in production of general aircraft.

Kansas stands high in petroleum production and has large reserves of natural gas. It ranks first among the states in helium production.

Petroleum production in 1976 was valued at an est. $616 million, over half the total mineral production value, $1.07 billion, up $99 million. Also important are natural gas and salt.

Coronado marched through the Kansas area, 1541; French explorers came next. The U.S. took over in the Louisiana Purchase, 1803. In the pre-war North-South struggle over slavery, so much violence swept the area it was called Bleeding Kansas; it was deeply involved in the Civil War. Railroad construction after the war made Abilene and Dodge City terminals of large cattle drives from Texas. Sale of alcoholic beverages was prohibited from 1880 to 1948.

In Abilene, the boyhood home of the late Pres. Dwight D. Eisenhower, is the Eisenhower Center, with the Eisenhower Home, Museum, and Library. Near them, in a chapel named "Place of Meditation," the 34th president was buried Apr. 2, 1969.

The Agricultural Hall of Fame and National Center, 14 mi. W of Kansas City, Kan., displays farm equipment of the past such as a wooden-wheeled corn planter, anvils, wheat drills, etc. In Dodge City are extensive reproductions of the original Front Street, saloons, and Boot Hill cemetery.

The Wichita Art Museum has works by many modern artists. The Kansas State Historical Society in Topeka has displays and period rooms of Midwest history.

In Lawrence, the Univ. of Kansas has a Museum of Natural History which presents a panorama of North American mammals from the Arctic to the tropics; a Museum of Art, with European and American painting and sculpture and European and Oriental decorative arts; and the Snow Entomological Museum, with over 2 million insects.

It is estimated that tourists spend over $520 million a year in the state.

Kansas has 52 institutions of higher learning.

Kansas has developed an extensive recreation system around its reservoirs, lakes, and roadside parks.

Famous Kansans include John Brown, Dwight D. Eisenhower, Gen. Hugh Johnson, Walter P. Chrysler, Amelia Earhart, Osa Johnson, Brock Pemberton, Walter Johnson, Alf M. Landon.

(See also Index for Wichita.)

Kentucky

Blue Grass State

Area: 40,395 sq. mi.; rank, 37th. **Population:** (U.S. est. 1976): 3,428,000; rank, 23d. **Capital:** Frankfort. **Motto:** United We Stand, Divided We Fall. **Flower:** Goldenrod. **Bird:** Cardinal. **Song:** My Old Kentucky Home. **Tree:** Kentucky coffee tree. **Entered Union:** June 1, 1792; rank, 15th.

Kentucky was the first area west of the Alleghenies settled by American pioneers. First permanent settlers, led by James Harrod, founded Harrodsburg, 1774. Daniel Boone blazed the Wilderness Trail through the Cumberland Gap and founded Boonesboro, 1775. Indian attacks, spurred by the British, were unceasing until, during the Revolution, Gen. George Rogers Clark, leading Kentucky volunteers, captured British forts in Indiana and Illinois, 1778; Boone, captured by Indians, escaped and warned Boonesboro of a coming Indian attack, which was repulsed. In 1792, after Virginia dropped its claims to the region, Kentucky became the 15th state.

Kentucky rises from an elevation of less than 260 ft., at the Mississippi, to over 4,000 ft. in the Cumberland and Pine mountains. Over 42% of the state is forested, and lumbering, particularly of hardwoods, is an important industry. Forest products are valued at over $50 million a year.

Tobacco is the principal crop, 2d only to that of North Carolina. Corn, soybeans, wheat, fruit, hogs, and cattle, especially milk cows, are also important. Farm receipts in 1976 totaled $669 million from livestock, $883 million from crops.

In 1976 Kentucky produced more coal than West Virginia but its value totaled less. It also produced important amounts of petroleum, natural gas, fluorspar, clay, and stone. But coal accounts for 95% of the total mineral value, est. at $2.9 billion for 1976.

In 1966 Kentucky enacted a law requiring surface and strip miners of coal to restore and regrade earth removed by their operations, but problems have remained.

Manufacturing has shown needed growth and diversity. Leading fields are food processing and beverages (including liquor), tobacco products, machinery, chemicals, transportation equipment, and apparel. Value added by manufacture is over $6.5 billion a year. Per capita income was $5,423 in 1976 (U.S. average: $6,441).

Tourists bring in an est. $798 million a year. There are 48 state and national parks and shrines.

Two of the largest man-made lakes in the world, Kentucky Lake and Lake Barkley, parallel each other in western Kentucky, creating a 170,000-acre isthmus called the Land Between the Lakes National Recreation Area.

Lexington, heart of the Bluegrass country, has the University of Kentucky and Transylvania, oldest college west of the Alleghenies (1780), and a large tobacco market, and holds annual trotting and running races and a horse show. The Kentucky Derby is run annually at Churchill Downs, Louisville.

Fort Knox, repository of the nation's gold reserve, also contains the George S. Patton Jr. Military Museum of World War II equipment.

Mammoth Cave, 40 mi. from Bowling Green, is in a national park. Discovered 1799, it has 150 mi. of passageways, rooms with 200-ft. ceilings, blind fish, and Echo River 360 ft. below ground.

Old Fort Harrod State Park, Harrodsburg, contains the reconstructed fort with stockade, blockhouses, the log cabin in which Thomas Lincoln and Nancy Hanks, Abraham Lincoln's parents, were married, and a museum with relics of Shakertown, Ky.

Abraham Lincoln Birthplace National Historic Site, 3 mi. from Hodgenville, contains the original Thomas Lincoln farm and cabin.

My Old Kentucky Home, one mi. E of Bardstown, was the home of John Rowan, senator and state chief justice. Stephen Foster, a relative, visited the Rowan family in 1852 and is said to have written My Old Kentucky Home on a desk preserved in the house.

Kentucky has 38 institutions of higher learning. Public school per pupil expenditure is the third lowest in the nation, $1,093.

Famous Kentuckians include Abraham Lincoln, Adlai Stevenson and Alben Barkley, Henry Clay, Jefferson Davis, Louis D. Brandeis, Kit Carson, Irvin S. Cobb, Elizabeth Madox Roberts, John Fox Jr., Robert Penn Warren, Mary Anderson.

(See also Index for Louisville.)

Louisiana

Pelican State

Area: 48,523 sq. mi.; rank 31st. **Population** (U.S. est. 1976): 3,841,000; rank 20th. **Capital:** Baton Rouge. **Motto:** Union, Justice, Confidence. **Flower:** Southern magnolia. **Bird:** Eastern brown pelican. **Song:** Give Me Louisiana. **Tree:** Bald cypress. **Entered Union:** Apr. 30, 1812; rank, 18th.

Louisiana blends a wealth of historic charm, rich natural resources, and giant modern industries. Fertile soil, huge mineral deposits and over 7,500 mi. of navigable waterways linking the nation's heart with deepsea ports are factors basic to the state's wealth.

Mardi Gras and other festivals, the beat of Dixieland jazz in its birthplace, and relics of French and Spanish rule and the prosperous pre-Civil War era are among the attractions which bring Louisiana an est. $850 million a year in tourist revenues.

In total value of its 1976 mineral output, $8.6 billion, Louisiana was 2d only to Texas among the 50 states. It was first in value of its salt production, 2d in petroleum, natural gas, and sulphur. Much of the oil and sulphur comes from offshore deposits.

The lush Louisiana land produces one of the nation's largest crops of sweet potatoes. It is 4th in rice, 3d in sugarcane. Also important are pecans, soybeans, cotton, and corn.

Farm receipts in 1976 included $855 million from crops, $380 million from livestock.

Total value added by manufacture is over $4.8 billion annually. Per capita income was $5,386 in 1976.

Leading manufacturing industries include chemicals, food processing, petroleum and coal products (especially oil refining), paper (particularly paperboard), lumber and wood products, transportation equipment, stone clay-glass products, apparel.

Louisiana supplies most of the nation's muskrat fur; there are also opossum, raccoon, mink, otter and game birds. The annual catch of fresh and salt water fish, shrimp, and oyster is valued at about $136 million. Lake Pontchartrain covers 630 sq. mi.

Much of the land is a rich alluvial plain; there are also rolling hills, bluffs on the Mississippi, and coastal marshes. The elevation ranges from 5 ft. below sea level, protected by vast levees, to 535 above.

Louisiana is rich in historical relics and traditions. The area was first visited, 1530, by Cabeza de Vaca and Panfilo de Narvaez. The region was claimed for France by LaSalle, 1682. First permanent settlement was by French at Fort St. Jean Baptiste (now Natchitoches), 1717. France ceded the region to Spain, 1762, took it back, 1800, and sold it to the U.S., 1803, in the Louisiana Purchase. During the Revolution, Spanish Louisiana aided the Americans. Admitted to statehood, 1812, Louisiana was the scene of the Battle of New Orleans, 1815. The state seceded from the Union, 1861, was readmitted, 1868.

Louisiana Creoles are descendants of early French and/or Spanish settlers. About 4,000 Acadians, French settlers in Nova Scotia, Canada, were forcibly transported by the British to Louisiana in 1755 (an event commemorated in Longfellow's Evangeline) and settled near Bayou Teche; their descendants became known as Cajuns. Another group, the Islenos, were descendants of Canary Islanders brought to Louisiana by a Spanish governor in 1770. Traces of Spanish and French survive in local dialects.

Louisiana has 31 institutions of higher education.

Famous Louisianians include Zachary Taylor, Leonidas K. Polk, Braxton Bragg, Judah P. Benjamin, Pierre Beauregard, Huey Long, Grace King.

(See also Index for Baton Rouge, New Orleans, Shreveport.)

Maine

Pine Tree State

Area: 33,215 sq. mi.; rank, 39th. **Population** (U.S. est. 1976): 1,070,000; rank, 38th. **Capital:** Augusta. **Motto:** Dirigo, I Direct. **Flower:** Pine cone and tassel. **Bird:** Chickadee. **Tree:** Eastern white pine. **Song:** State of Maine Song. **Entered Union:** Mar. 15, 1820; rank, 23d.

Maine is noted for its scenic and vacation attractions, lobsters, potatoes, poultry, forest products, fishing and hunting.

Largest of the 6 New England states, it is the farthest east and borders on only one other state, New Hampshire. Its rugged coast, because of deep indentations, measures 3,478 mi. Tides are often high; in Passamaquoddy Bay they average 20 ft.

Mt. Cadillac, on Mt. Desert Is., 1,532 ft., is the highest Atlantic seacoast point N of Brazil; West Quoddy Head, Long. 66° 57′ W, is the farthest east point on the U.S. Atlantic coast. Lubec is the most easterly town on the U.S. mainland.

Maine's rocky coast was explored by John and Sebastian Cabot, 1498-99. French settlers arrived, 1604, at the St. Croix River; English, 1607, on the Kennebec. In 1691, Maine was made part of Massachusetts. Joining that colony's protests against Britain, Maine staged its own Tea Party at York. In the Revolution, a Maine regiment fought at Bunker Hill; a British fleet destroyed Falmouth (now Portland), 1775, but the British ship Margaretta was captured near Machiasport. In 1820, Maine broke off from Massachusetts, became a separate state.

Maine's coastal waters produce an annual 20 million lbs. of lobsters, 75% of the nation's total, and 50% of its soft-shelled clams. The state, 1st in sardines, packs over 150 million cans a year. The fish and shellfish catch is valued at $53 million annually.

Maine grows about 12% of the nation's potatoes, trailing Idaho, Washington, and Oregon, and is the leading supplier of seed potatoes. It produces 90% of the nation's low bush blueberries. Also grown are apples, sweet corn, peas, beans. Farm income totaled $431 million in 1976, with poultry and eggs the largest item.

With more than 80% of its area forested, Maine turns out wood products ranging from boats to toothpicks, paper, lumber, and Christmas trees. Over 98% of the forest land is privately owned. Forest products are valued at over $700 million a year. Spruce, white pine, and birch are the most important woods. Also vital to Maine's economy are processed foods, shoes, and textiles. Boatyards build fishing and sailing craft.

Per capita income was $5,385 in 1976 (U.S. average: $6,441).

Granite, cement, and feldspar account for much of the 1976 value of mineral products, $36 million.

Maine's scenic seacoast, beaches, lakes, mountains, and resorts make it a popular vacationland; tourism produces $596 million a year. There are 28 state parks, including Baxter, where Mt. Katahdin, tallest of the state's 10 mountains over 4,000 ft., rises 5,268 ft. Maine has over 2,500 lakes, 1,300 wooded islands and 5,000 streams. Moosehead Lake is 40 mi. long and 2 to 10 mi. wide. Deer, grouse, black bear abound; game fish include salmon, tuna, trout, bass. There are 23 major public skiing facilities. Acadia National Park and Bar Harbor are on Mt. Desert Island.

Museums include the Bowdoin College Museum, Brunswick, which has portraits by American masters; also Assyrian, Greek, and Roman sculpture.

The Colby College Art Museum, Waterville, has paintings by classic and contemporary Europeans and Americans.

The Farnsworth Library and Museum, Rockland, has 19th and 20th century American fine art.

The Portland Museum of Art comprises the Sweat Museum of American Art and the Sweat Mansion, a Federal-style house built in 1800. Other historic homes in Portland are the Tate House, 1755, and the Victoria Mansion, 1859.

There are 25 institutions of higher learning.

Famous "Down Easters" include Longfellow, Kenneth Roberts, Edna St. Vincent Millay, Kate Douglas Wiggin, Ben Ames Williams, James G. Blaine, Hiram and Hudson Maxim, Cyrus H. K. Curtis.

(See also Index for Portland.)

Maryland

Old Line State, Free State

Area: 10,577 sq. mi.; rank, 42d. **Population** (U.S. est. 1976): 4,144,000; rank 18th. **Capital:** Annapolis.

Motto: Fatti Maschi, Parole Femine; Manly Deeds, Womanly Words. **Flower:** Black-eyed Susan. **Bird:** Baltimore oriole. **Tree:** White oak. **Song:** Maryland, My Maryland. Seventh of the original 13 states to ratify Constitution; Apr. 28, 1788.

Maryland stretches from the Atlantic Ocean to the Allegheny Mountains with 2 major interruptions, Chesapeake Bay, and the District of Columbia. Both contribute importantly to the state's economy.

The bay cuts off the low coastal plain of the Eastern Shore from the rest of the state, provides both commercial and sports fishing and leads to the port of Baltimore, which handles some $3 billion in imports and exports a year. The 7.11-mi. Chesapeake Bay Highway Bridge spans the bay near Annapolis.

The national capital area provides a market for much of Maryland's produce, and large-scale employment in federal offices, as well as adding to the crowds which enjoy its recreational facilities.

Virginia's Capt. John Smith first explored Maryland, 1608. William Claiborne set up a trading post on Kent Is. in Chesapeake Bay, 1631. Britain granted land to Lord Baltimore (Cecilius Calvert), 1632; his brother Leonard Calvert led 200 settlers to St. Marys River, 1634. An informal Maryland Convention, 1774, headed pre-Revolutionary agitation. The bravery of Maryland troops in the Revolution, as at the Battle of Long Island, won the state its nickname, The Old Line State. In the War of 1812, when a British fleet tried to take Fort McHenry, Marylander Francis Scott Key wrote The Star-Spangled Banner.

Maryland has a diversified economy. Leading industries in number of workers are wholesale and retail trade, government, services, manufacturing. Value added by manufacture totals over $4.7 billion annually. Important manufacturing industries are food products, primary metals, electrical equipment, printing and publishing, apparel, machinery. Per capita income was $7,036 in 1976, 9th highest in the U.S.

Almost half of the land area is covered with forests. About 40% of timber cut is softwood. Stone and cement are leading mineral products; mineral output was valued at $174 million in 1976.

Seafood is an important industry. In a typical year, the fish and shellfish catch has a value of about $31 million. Striped bass is the principal contributor to the fin fish revenues, while oysters account for about 57% of the shellfish, followed by soft-shelled clams.

Most of Maryland's farms are fertile though not extensive. The state's largest cash crops are tobacco, corn, soybeans, apples, and tomatoes. Commercial broilers and dairy products are important. Farm receipts in 1976 totaled $672 million.

The first U.S. steam locomotive, Peter Cooper's Tom Thumb, was built in Baltimore and made its first run on the tracks of the Baltimore & Ohio RR, 1830.

There are 52 institutions of higher education.

Famous racing events include the Preakness, at Pimlico track, Baltimore; the International at Laurel Race Course, and John B. Campbell Handicap at Bowie. Annapolis is a center for yacht races. Ocean City is a popular summer resort.

Famous historic sites include restored Fort McHenry, Baltimore, near which Francis Scott Key wrote the Star-Spangled Banner in 1814; Antietam Battlefield near Hagerstown (1862); South Mountain Battlefield (1862); Edgar Allan Poe house, Baltimore. The State House, Annapolis (1772), is the oldest still in use in the U.S.

The U.S. Frigate Constellation, which was launched at Baltimore in 1797, has been made a National Historic Landmark in Baltimore.

The Chesapeake Bay Maritime Museum in St. Michael's exhibits the last surviving oyster sloop, a cottage-type lighthouse and models of Baltimore clippers, log canoes, bugeyes, and skipjacks.

Tourism is valued at $1.2 billion a year.

Famous Marylanders include Upton Sinclair, H. L. Mencken, James M. Cain, Benjamin Banneker.

(See also Index for Baltimore.)

Massachusetts

Bay State, Old Colony

Area: 8,257 sq. mi.; rank, 45th. **Population** (U.S. est. 1976): 5,809,000; rank, 10th. **Capital:** Boston. **Motto:** Ense Petit Placidam sub Libertate Quietem: By the Sword We Seek Peace, but Peace Only under Liberty. **Flower:** Mayflower. **Bird:** Chickadee. **Tree:** American elm. **Song:** All Hail to Massachusetts. Sixth of the original 13 states to ratify Constitution, Feb. 6, 1788.

Massachusetts has played important roles in the political, intellectual, and economic development of the U.S.

The Pilgrims, seeking religious freedom, made their first settlement at Plymouth, 1620; the following year they gave thanks for their survival with the first Thanksgiving Day. Indian opposition reached a high point in King Philip's War, 1675-76, won by the colonists. Demonstrations against British restrictions set off the "Boston Massacre," 1770, and Boston "tea party," 1773. First bloodshed of the Revolution was at Lexington, 1775.

In Massachusetts ports, a great shipping industry, including the famed China trade, developed, along with large whaling and fishing interests. Abundant waterpower helped create a variety of industries.

Religious freedom, at first restricted by the Puritans, was eventually achieved. In 1867, Mary Baker Eddy founded Christian Science in Lynn. Heavy immigration of Irish, Italians, Poles, Czechs, and French Canadians increased the number of Catholics.

The first free American public school, the Mather, was founded in Dorchester (Boston) in 1639. The state has 119 institutions of higher learning including Harvard and Mass. Institute of Technology.

Commercial fishing, in the rich waters off Massachusetts and the Grand Banks off Newfoundland, was one of the area's earliest industries. Whalers sailed the oceans around the world. Modern trawlers with huge nets help bring in a catch valued at about $97 million in 1976, ranking high among the states.

Massachusetts was a pioneer in the manufacture of textiles and shoes and in creation of specialized machinery for them. The Bay State remains one of the top producers of shoes. A power loom, perfected by Francis Cabot Lowell in 1822, launched cotton manufacturing in Lowell.

Production of electrical machinery, including electronics and communications equipment, has become the leading manufacturing division, in terms of numbers of employees and value added by manufacture. Also important are apparel, metal and food products, and plastics. The state is a leader in production of medical instruments and mini-computers.

Total value added by manufacture is over $19 billion a year, placing Massachusetts, despite its relatively small size, 11th among the states. A third of the state's workers are employed in manufacturing. Per capita income was $6,585 in 1976 (U.S. average: $6,441).

Massachusetts' cranberry crop is the nation's 2d largest. Also important are dairy and poultry products, apples, peaches, maple syrup. Farm receipts totaled $219 million in 1976. Mineral production for that year was valued at an est. $59 million, mostly of stone, sand, and gravel.

Because of the state's numerous recreational areas and historic landmarks, tourism has become an important factor in the economy of the state. Tourists generate an est. $1.5 billion annually.

Cape Cod has summer theaters, sports, and an artists' colony at Provincetown. Tanglewood, in the Berkshires, has the summer concerts of the Boston Symphony Orchestra.

In New Bedford, the Old Dartmouth Historical Society and Whaling Museum has a large and unique collection of whaling implements, scrimshaw, and logbooks as well as furniture, costumes, and firearms. In Old Deerfield are Memorial Hall (1799), Hall Tavern (1765), Parson Ashley House (1732).

In Pittsfield, the Berkshire Athenaeum has

memorabilia of Herman Melville, who lived there while writing Moby Dick; a scrimshaw and whaling collection, and a large library. The Berkshire Museum, Pittsfield, has paintings by Rubens, Van Dyck, Reynolds, Murillo, the Hudson River artists, etc.; mineral and animal rooms; one of the sledges with which Robert E. Peary reached the North Pole.

In Plymouth, Pilgrim Hall contains relics of the Mayflower Pilgrims, including swords of Myles Standish, Bibles of Gov. William Bradford and John Alden, and the cradle of Peregrine White, first child born in the colony.

Old Sturbridge Village, in Sturbridge, is a re-created early New England village of 35 authentic homes and shops, shown functioning.

The Sterling and Francine Clark Art Institute, Williamstown, displays 14th-17th century European paintings, a large collection of Impressionists, sculpture, silver, and drawings.

The Worcester Art Museum presents a survey of art through 50 centuries, stressing early American painting, pre-Columbian, and contemporary arts. Also in Worcester, the John W. Higgins Armory displays medieval armor, and the American Antiquarian Society has a collection of early printing.

Famous "Bay Staters" include Samuel, John, and John Quincy Adams, Hancock, Revere, Bryant, Emerson, Hawthorne, Holmes, Whittier, Poe, Thoreau, Alger, James, Emily Dickinson, Louisa May Alcott, Lucy Stone, Clara Barton, Whistler, Sargent, Homer, Morse, Elias Howe.

(See also Index for Boston, Springfield.)

Michigan

Great Lake State, Wolverine State

Area: 58,216 sq. mi.; rank, 23d. **Population** (U.S. est. 1976): 9,104,000; rank, 7th. **Capital:** Lansing. **Motto:** Si Quaerie Peninsulam Amoenam Circumspice, If You Seek A Pleasant Peninsula, Look About You. **Flower:** Apple blossom. **Bird:** Robin. **Tree:** White pine. **Song** (unofficial): Michigan, My Michigan. **Entered Union:** Jan. 26, 1837; rank 26th.

Bordering on 4 of the 5 Great Lakes, Michigan is divided into an Upper and Lower Peninsula by the Straits of Mackinac, which link Lakes Michigan and Huron. The 2 parts of the state are connected by the Mackinac Bridge, which has the 3d longest suspension span in the U. S. To the N, separating Michigan from Canada, is the Sault Ste. Marie (Soo) Ship Canal, one of the world's most heavily used waterways.

Rich orchards near the shores of Lake Michigan grow large fruit crops; the Upper Peninsula produces important amounts of iron, copper, and other minerals, and the state's lakes and forests make it a highly popular vacationland.

While Michigan has the world's greatest concentration of motor vehicle manufacturers, it is also a leader in many other lines including prepared cereals, pickles, machine tools, hardware, steel springs, furniture, padding and upholstering, industrial patterns, nonferrous castings, industrial leather belts, paperboard mills, and gray iron foundries.

The state ranked 5th in the U.S. in terms of value added by manufacture, $27.2 billion. Motor vehicles and equipment accounted for $8.3 billion of that and also provided the most jobs, almost 310,000. Other major industry groups were primary metals and metal products, machinery, food, and chemicals. Per capita income was $6,994 in 1976.

Tourist attractions are many and visitors spend $3.9 billion annually, 7th highest among the states. The state has 36,000 mi. of streams, over 11,000 lakes and the longest freshwater shoreline (facing 4 of the Great Lakes). Water sports, music festivals, skiing, winter carnivals, fishing, and hunting are among attractions.

There are 4 national forests, 80 state parks and recreational areas, and numerous canoe trails.

Farm receipts in 1976 totaled $1.7 billion, more than half from crops. The state ranked 6th in the U.S. in number of milk cows. It grew the most tart and sweet cherries and ranked high in apples, pears, grapes, and sugar beets. Truck farm vegetables were valued at $160 million; forest products at $1.75 billion.

Iron ore is the largest source of Michigan's income from minerals. With continued depletion of high-grade iron ore deposits, production of high-grade pellets from low-grade taconite iron ore has increased, amounting to over 85% of the ore total.

Michigan was 2d only to Minnesota among the states in value of iron ore output, $393 million in 1976. It was also a leading producer of gypsum, peat, iodine, bromine, salt, magnesium compounds, lime, gravel, cement. Total output was est. at $1.4 billion up 14%.

There are 94 institutions of higher education.

French fur traders and missionaries visited the region, 1616, set up a mission at Sault Ste. Marie, 1641, and a settlement there, 1668. The whole region went to Britain, 1763. During the Revolution, the British led attacks from the area on American settlements to the south until Anthony Wayne defeated their Indian allies at Fallen Timbers, Ohio, 1794. The British returned, 1812, seized Fort Mackinac and Detroit. Oliver H. Perry's Lake Erie victory and William H. Harrison's troops, who carried the war to the Thames River in Canada, 1813, freed Michigan once more.

Famous Michiganders include Gerald Ford, Henry Ford, Robert Ingersoll, Thomas Dewey, Milton A. McRae, James Oliver Curwood, Stewart Edward White, Paul de Kruif, Gen. George Custer, Edgar Guest, Ellen Burstyn, Betty Hutton, Diana Ross, Mike Marshall, Danny Thomas.

(See also Index for Detroit and Kalamazoo.)

Minnesota

North Star State, Gopher State

Area: 84,068 sq. mi.; rank, 12th. **Population** (U.S. est. 1976): 3,965,000; rank, 19th. **Capital:** St. Paul. **Motto:** L'Etoile du Nord, Star of the North. **Flower:** Showy lady's-slipper. **Bird:** Loon. **Tree:** Red (Norway) pine. **Song:** Hail! Minnesota. **Entered Union:** May 11, 1858; rank, 32d.

Minnesota is a land rich in natural resources. Its fertile prairies support large crops and an important dairy industry, its mines yield most of the iron ore produced in the U.S., its forests produce mountains of pulpwood, its manufacturing is varied and vigorous, its thousands of lakes and other attractions lure millions of sportsmen and vacationers.

Known as the "land of 10,000 lakes," Minnesota actually has 12,034 over 10 acres in size. Lake Itaska is the source of the Mississippi River. Two-thirds of the state is rolling prairie. Highest point is Eagle Mt. in the NE, 2,301 ft.

Fishing, hunting, water sports, and winter sports are among attractions for more than 6.7 million vacationers who spend some $1.1 billion yearly. There are numerous state parks and recreation areas.

Minnesota produces about 62% of the iron ore mined in the U.S., despite depletion of the high-grade ore in the famed Mesabi and other ranges in the NE part of the state. Lost production from the huge open pit and underground mines is being replaced by high-grade pellets refined from low-grade taconite iron ore. By 1975, shipments of taconite pellets comprised about 78% of the total iron ore value.

Settlement was reached in 1977 of a pollution problem involving Reserve Mining Co. dumping of taconite waste in Lake Superior. The company agreed to switch to inland dumping by 1980.

Iron ore production in 1976 was valued at $1.11 billion, the major part of the total mineral production.

Manufacturing has grown and diversified. Largest industries are food processing and non-electrical machinery. Also important are electrical machinery, chemicals, paper, stone-clay-glass products, apparel, lumber, fabricated metal products. Value added by manufacture is $6.7 billion.

Per capita income was $6,153 in 1976.

Much of the land is richly fertile. With $3.9 billion in farm receipts for 1976, Minnesota ranked 6th among the states. About 55% of that income was from livestock products, the rest from crops. Ranking 3d in number of milk cows in 1976, the state was the leader in butter, turkeys, and non-fat dry milk.

Minnesota's farms grew the most oats and it ranked among the top states in spring wheat, corn, rye, alfalfa, and sugar beets.

Forest products have a yearly estimated value of $487 million, most of it in pulpwood.

Nationally known is the Mayo Clinic at Rochester, founded by Drs. William J. and Charles H. Mayo.

Minnesota has 65 institutions of higher learning.

The Minnesota Orchestra, the Tyrone Guthrie Theater in Minneapolis, and the St. Olaf College Choir in Northfield are widely known.

Other attractions are the St. Paul Winter Carnival, Minneapolis Aquatennial, and State Fair. Minnehaha Falls in Minneapolis became famous in Longfellow's "Song of Hiawatha." A new Minnesota zoo is to open in Apple Valley in 1977.

Fur traders and missionaries from French Canada opened the region in the 17th century. Britain took the area east of the Mississippi, 1763. The U.S. took over that portion after the Revolution and in 1803 bought the western area as part of the Louisiana Purchase. The U.S. built present Fort Snelling, 1820, bought lands from the Indians, 1837. In the Civil War, Minnesota was first to offer troops to the Union. Sioux Indians staged a bloody uprising, 1862, and were driven from the state.

Famous Minnesotans include Hubert Humphrey, Walter F. Mondale, Charles Lindbergh, Sinclair Lewis, F. Scott Fitzgerald, Thorstein Veblen, Cass Gilbert, Paul Manship, E. G. Marshall, Blanche Yurka.

(See also Index for Minneapolis and St. Paul.)

Mississippi

Magnolia State

Area: 47,716 sq. mi.; rank, 32d. **Population** (U.S. est. 1976): 2,354,000; rank, 29th. **Capital:** Jackson. **Motto:** Virtute et Armis, By Valor and Arms. **Flower:** Magnolia. **Tree:** Magnolia. **Bird:** Mockingbird. **Song:** Go, Mississippi! **Entered Union:** Dec. 10, 1817; rank, 20th.

Mississippi's economy, long based on one crop, "King Cotton," has become balanced and diversified, thanks to promotion of industry, other crops, tourism, and federal agency installations.

The land slopes from the NE hills, where the high point is Woodall Mt. (806 ft.), to the Delta, a cotton-producing alluvial plain in the W and NW lying between the Yazoo River and the Mississippi, which flows along the state's western border. The land also slopes to the S where the sandy beaches on the Gulf of Mexico have created a popular vacationland.

Hernando de Soto explored the area, 1540, discovered the Mississippi River, 1541. La Salle traced the river from Illinois to its mouth and claimed the entire valley for France, 1682. First settlement was the French Fort Maurepas, near Ocean Springs, 1699. The area was ceded to Britain, 1763; American settlers followed. During the Revolution, Spain seized part of the area and refused to leave even after the U.S. acquired title at the end of the Revolution, finally moving out, 1798. Mississippi seceded 1861. Union forces captured Corinth and Vicksburg and destroyed Jackson and much of Meridian.

Soybeans have taken over as Mississippi's largest crop; the state ranks 3d in cotton production. Other important farm products include pecans, sweet potatoes, rice, and sugarcane. Poultry and eggs are also important. Farm receipts totaled $1.7 billion in 1976.

Biloxi has a large seafood industry, operating deep-sea trawlers for shrimp and oysters. Value of the catch is over $15 million a year. Home-pond catfish production was valued at $28 million in 1974.

With more than 50% of the land classified as forest, timber products yielded over $1 billion in 1974. The state produces the most hardwood pulpwood, much hardwood lumber, and slashpine products, including fiberboard, kraft paper, newsprint.

Petroleum production was valued at $309 million for 1976. Natural gas output was valued at $25 million; total value of mineral production was est. at $426 million.

Mississippi has achieved considerable industrial expansion. The main fields have been lumber, along with furniture and paper, food processing, apparel, chemicals, electronics, machinery.

Per capita income was $4,575 in 1976, lowest in the nation. Annual pay for public school teachers was $8,338 in 1975, also the nation's lowest.

A $250 million NASA space installation is used as a center for International Earth Sciences by NOAA and NASA.

There are 45 institutions of higher learning.

Mississippi became the last state to abandon prohibition, adopting a local-option law May 21, 1966.

Tourism is of growing economic importance. It is estimated that out-of-state tourists spend over $398 million a year in the state.

Gulfport holds an annual yacht regatta and a fishing rodeo in July, Biloxi has a Mardi Gras, Pass Christian has a tarpon rodeo. A dozen cities sponsor pilgrimages each spring featuring visits to ante-bellum mansions.

In Vicksburg National Military Park, visitors may see remains of forts, trenches, and other works of the 1863 siege of the city.

The Old Court House Museum in Vicksburg, built in 1858 by slave labor, has a museum with relics of the siege of Vicksburg, including flags, weapons, newspapers printed on the back of wallpaper, etc.

The Lauren Rogers Library and Museum of Art in Laurel contains works of 19th and early 20th century Americans and Europeans, local artifacts, and an unusual basket collection (about half of them Indian). Pre-historic Indian mounds include one covering 8 acres 12 mi. NE of Natchez.

Famous Mississippians include Jefferson Davis, James Street, William Faulkner, Eudora Welty, Dana Andrews, B. B. King, Bobby Gentry, Elvis Presley, and Leontyne Price.

Missouri

Show Me State

Area: 69,686 sq. mi.; rank, 19th. **Population** (U.S. est. 1976): 4,778,000; rank, 15th. **Capital:** Jefferson City. **Motto:** Salus Populi Suprema Lex Esto, The Welfare of the People Shall Be the Supreme Law. **Flower:** Hawthorn. **Bird:** Eastern bluebird. **Tree:** Dogwood, **Song:** Missouri Waltz. **Entered Union:** Aug. 10, 1821; rank, 24th.

The gateway through which the pioneers passed on their way West, Missouri today is a leading manufacturing state, with aerospace and a wide variety of other industries; it is the nation's largest producer of lead; it ranks high among the states in agricultural products; its areas of scenic and historic interest attract over 28 million vacationers each year.

Gently rolling hills in the N and W produce large crops, and support cattle, sheep, and hogs. The Ozark highlands in the S are famed for fishing, hunting, and rugged scenery, including numerous caves and springs. The "delta" area in the SE produces soybeans, cotton, and melons.

The Mississippi forms the state's boundary on the E; the Missouri forms part of the boundary in the W, then flows across the state to join the Mississippi above St. Louis.

Manufacturing, paced by the state's large aerospace industries, is the top income producer and employs more persons than any other segment of the economy. Value added by manufacture is over $9.1 billion yearly. Transportation equipment, including space capsules, rocket engines, aircraft, and auto assemblies, ranks first, followed by food processing, esp. meat packing, grain milling, beer, and other beverages. Also important are chemicals, printing, metal products, machinery, shoes. Corncob pipes and charcoal are well-known products.

Agriculture is also an important income producer. Farm receipts in 1976 totaled $2.8 billion, 60% from livestock products. Missouri ranked 4th among the states in hogs, 5th in cattle, 6th in turkeys. It has large soybean, corn, and clover crops. Also important are winter wheat, tobacco, apples, peaches, alfalfa, popcorn.

Missouri is rich in minerals. Its output of lead, valued at $233 million for 1976, was the largest in the U.S. Total mineral production value was worth $764 million. It was also a leader in barite and lime. Other products include cement, coal, iron ore, copper, zinc, asphalt.

Per capita income was $6,005 in 1976.

Tourism, described as the 3d largest industry, produces $1.3 billion annually. There is a wide variety of vacation facilities; large resort areas include Lake of the Ozarks, Lake Taneycomo and Table Rock Lake.

Missouri has endeared itself to generations of Americans with its river lore, folk tales, and especially the writings of Mark Twain (Samuel L. Clemens). Statues of 2 of his creations, Tom Sawyer and Huckleberry Finn, stand in Hannibal, his boyhood home. His birthplace near Florida, Mo., has been enshrined in Mark Twain State Park.

The farm birthplace of notorious bandit Jesse James (1847-1882) is near Excelsior Springs. A log cabin built by U.S. Grant is near St. Louis. Near Diamond, the farm where George Washington Carver, agricultural scientist, was born is now a National Monument. The Harry S. Truman Library, near Independence, contains presidential papers and memorabilia. Mr. Truman is buried in the library courtyard.

The St. Joseph Museum in St. Joseph stresses the natural history and wildlife of the region and has exhibits on Indian tribes from Alaska to Florida. Also in St. Joseph is the Pony Express Museum.

There are 83 institutions of higher learning. The nation's first Journalism School, founded 1908, is at the University of Missouri in Columbia.

DeSoto visited the area, 1541. French hunters and lead miners made the first settlement, c. 1735, at Ste. Genevieve. The U.S. acquired Missouri as part of the Louisiana Purchase, 1803. The fur trade and the Santa Fe Trail provided prosperity and adventure; St. Louis became the "jump-off" point for pioneers on their way West. Pro- and anti-slavery forces battled each other there during the Civil War.

Famous Missourians include Harry Truman, John J. Pershing, Omar Bradley, Mark Twain, Zoe Akins, Sara Teasdale, T. S. Eliot, Luman H. Long, George Washington Carver, Shelley Winters, Gladys Swarthout, Helen Traubel, Thomas Hart Benton, Ken Holtzman, Mel Stottlemyre, Bernarr Macfadden.

(See also Index for Kansas City and St. Louis.)

Montana

Treasure State

Area: 147,138 sq. mi.; rank, 4th. **Population** (U.S. est. 1976): 753,000; rank, 43d. **Capital:** Helena. **Motto:** Oro y Plata, Gold and Silver. **Flower:** Bitterroot. **Tree:** Ponderosa pine. **Bird:** Western meadowlark. **Song:** Montana. **Entered Union:** Nov. 8, 1889; rank, 41st.

The Rocky Mountains, with snow-capped peaks, forested slopes, broad valleys, and many lakes, cover the western 40% of Montana; the rest is High Plains country devoted to grazing and farming. Montana is rich in minerals, hydroelectric power, and impressive scenery. Highest mountain is Granite Peak, 12,799 ft.

Agriculture plays a vital role in Montana's economy, along with manufacturing, mining, tourism, recreation. Per capita income was $5,600 in 1976.

Oceans of grain cover much of Montana's plains; it ranks high among the states in wheat and barley output. Also grown are rye, oats, flaxseed, sugar beets, and potatoes. Montana ranks 6th in sheep and high in cattle. Farm receipts totaled over $972 million in 1976, more than half from crops.

Manufacturing industries have grown, with value added by manufacture over $515 million a year. Processing of forest products and primary metal industries are most important and have the most employees, followed by food processing. Wood products include pulp, plywood, and lumber. The state ships more than 3 million Christmas trees annually.

Total mineral production for 1976 was est. at $670 million, with petroleum accounting for $276 million and copper $148 million. Other products include silver, gold, natural gas. Increasing amounts of coal are strip-mined: 14 million tons in 1974, 26 million in 1976.

Out-of-state tourists spend an est. $398 million annually. Tourist attractions include hunting, fishing, skiing, dude ranching.

Hunters annually take about 100,000 deer, 17,000 antelope, 10,000 elk, 1,100 black bear, 500 moose, 600 mountain goats.

Glacier National Park, on the Continental Divide, is a scenic and recreational wonderland, with 60 glaciers, 200 lakes, and many trout streams.

Flathead Lake, in the NW, covers 189 sq. mi. Fort Peck Reservoir, in the NE, covers 382.8 sq. mi.

French explorers, the Verendrye brothers, visited the region, 1742. The U.S. acquired the area partly through the Louisiana Purchase, 1803, and partly through the explorations of Lewis and Clark, 1805-06. Fur traders and missionaries established posts in the early 19th century. Indian uprisings hit their highwater mark in the Battle of the Little Big Horn, in which Col. George Custer and his 264 men were wiped out, 1876. The coming of the Northern Pacific Railway, 1883, spurred farming, cattle raising, and mining and brought population growth.

Important historical site is Custer Battlefield National Cemetery, in Big Horn County (near Hardin).

There are 7 Indian reservations, covering over 5 million acres; tribes are Blackfeet, Crow, Confederated Salish & Kootenai, Assiniboine, Gros Ventre, Sioux, Northern Cheyenne, Chippewa, Cree. Population of the reservations is approximately 25,500.

The Museum of the Plains Indian, on the Blackfeet Reservation near Browning, features exhibits of historic and contemporary arts and crafts of the Northern Plains Indians and an Indian craft shop. Butte has an unusual mining museum.

The Historical Society of Montana, in Helena, has paintings, dioramas, and other exhibits of Montana's Indian and buffalo days, mining camps, frontier settlements, cattle roundups. Outstanding is the collection of nearly 100 Charles M. Russell paintings.

There are 12 colleges and universities.

Famous Montanans include Gary Cooper, Myrna Loy, Mike Mansfield, Chet Huntley, Charles M. Russell, Will James, Jeannette Rankin.

(See also Index for Billings.)

Nebraska

Cornhusker State

Area: 77,227 sq. mi.; rank, 15th. **Population** (U.S. est. 1976): 1,553,000; rank, 35th. **Capital:** Lincoln. **Motto:** Equality Before the Law. **Flower:** Goldenrod. **Tree:** Cottonwood. **Bird:** Western meadowlark. **Song:** Beautiful Nebraska. **Entered Union:** Mar. 1, 1867; rank, 37th.

Fields of corn, wheat, and sorghum cover the Nebraska plain, which slopes gently toward the Missouri River, the eastern border of the state; vast herds of cattle roam the grassy sandhills which rise to the W and end in the broken tablelands marking the foothills of the Rockies.

With more than 23 million acres under cultivation, Nebraska is an agricultural stronghold, an important grain and livestock producer. Many of its manufacturing industries are agriculture-related.

But manufacturing has expanded and diversified, broadening the state's economic base. Firms making electronic components, auto accessories, pharmaceuticals, and other sophisticated products have joined the older industries.

Processing of meat, grain, and dairy products is by far the largest manufacturing field and employs the largest number of workers, accounting for more than a third of the total value added by manufacture, which is estimated at almost $2 billion.

Other important manufacturing fields are electrical machinery and other machinery, especially farm equipment; chemicals, metal products, transportation equipment, instruments, and related products, per capita income was $6,240 in 1976 ($201 below the U.S. average).

Nebraska ranked 5th among the states in total farm receipts for 1976; $3.9 billion, with the larger part coming from livestock products. Its cattle herds ranked 3d among the states; it had 6.5 million cattle in 1977. It ranked 6th in hogs. Nebraska was also a leader in sorghum, winter wheat, corn, and rye. Also important are soybeans, sugar beets, and oats.

Mineral production in Nebraska was valued at $127 million for 1976. Oil continued to be the most important product, valued at $58 million. Other products included cement, line, pumice, sand, and gravel.

Nebraska has a unicameral or one-house legislature with 49 members elected on a non-partisan ballot. All electric power facilities are publicly or member owned.

Nebraska has 29 institutions of higher education.

Tourists spend over $550 million a year.

Arbor Lodge State Park at Nebraska City is a memorial to J. Sterling Morton, founder of Arbor Day, which is observed as a legal holiday on his birthday, Apr. 22. Boys Town is just west of Omaha.

The Sheldon Memorial Art Gallery at the Univ. of Nebraska, Lincoln, in a building designed by Philip Johnson, has works by many leading modern artists.

The Joslyn Art Museum, Omaha, has works by Titian, El Greco, Rembrandt, Goya, Renoir, etc.; exhibits of furniture, the early West, fur trade, Indian art.

Pioneer Village, Minden, has some 30,000 items of Americana displayed in a rural schoolhouse, depot, general store, fort, fire house, sod house, Pony Express station, etc. The Stuhr Museum of the Prairie Pioneer has 57 original 19th century buildings near Grand Island.

The House of Yesterday, Hastings, has exhibits of pioneer days and natural science and the J. M. McDonald Planetarium. The Strategic Aerospace Museum is in Bellevue. Prominent landmarks include Scotts Bluff National Monument and Chimney Rock Historic Site.

Spanish and French explorers and fur traders visited the area prior to the 1803 Louisiana Purchase. Lewis and Clark passed through, 1804-06. First permanent settlement was Bellevue, near Omaha, 1823. Many Civil War veterans settled under free land terms of the 1862 Homestead Act; struggles followed between homesteaders and ranchers. Under Gov. Charles W. Bryan, farm mortgage moratoriums were declared, 1933, during the Depression.

Famous Nebraskans include William Jennings and Charles W. Bryan, the Rev. Edward J. Flanagan, Willa Cather, Mignon Eberhart, Rollin Kirby, Clare Briggs, Gen. Alfred Gruenther, Roscoe Pound, Darryl Zanuck, Susette (Bright Eyes) La Flesche, Harold Lloyd, Marlon Brando, Henry Fonda, Loren Eiseley, George Norris, Malcolm X.

(See also Index for Omaha.)

Nevada

Sagebrush State, Battle Born State

Area: 110,540 sq. mi.; rank, 7th. **Population** (U.S. est. 1976): 610,000; rank, 46th. **Capital:** Carson City. **Motto:** All for Our Country. **Flower:** Sagebrush. **Bird:** Mountain bluebird. **Tree:** Singleleaf pinon. **Song:** Home Means Nevada. **Entered Union:** Oct. 31, 1864; rank, 36th.

Nevada lies mostly in the Great Basin, a rugged plateau region broken by mountain chains running N-S. It is enclosed on the E by the Rockies and the Wasatch Range in Utah, and on the W by California's Sierra Nevada and Cascade Ranges which rob the clouds of moisture, making Nevada's climate extremely dry.

One of the smallest states in population, Nevada has attracted large numbers of outsiders, starting with the famed rush to the Comstock Lode (1859) and other gold and silver mines. Today, the attractions are legalized gambling, highly-developed entertainment and recreation facilities, and lenient divorce laws requiring only 6-weeks residence. New floods of visitors were attracted in the 1970s by lenient marriage laws.

Spending by visitors, $950 million a year, is the biggest factor in Nevada's economy. More than 12 million from out of state, about 50 times the state population, visit annually.

Tourist-connected industries—hotels, casinos, amusement and recreation facilities—make up the largest employment category. Per capita income was $7,337 in 1976.

State collections from gaming were $80,278,392 in 1975-76, up $7,823,104 from 1974-75. This income provides about 45% of the state's revenue. Gross gambling receipts for 1976 were $1.26 billion. Nevada officials state that Florida, California, and New York have higher gambling revenues from parimutuel race betting.

There are big resort areas, with skiing as well as sunbathing, near Lake Tahoe, Reno, Las Vegas. Ghost towns, rodeos, trout fishing, water skiing, and deer hunting are other attractions.

Large recreation areas include those at Pyramid Lake, wholly within the state; Lake Tahoe, partly in California; Lake Mead, formed by Hoover Dam, and Lake Mohave, formed by Davis Dam, both in Lake Mead National Recreation Area, shared with Arizona.

Mineral production value for 1976 was est. at $211 million with copper accounting for $97 million. Nevada is also a leader in gold, mercury, lithium, barite, and silver. With rising prices, old gold mines have been reopened.

Nevada is the largest manufacturer of gaming devices. Also important are electronic devices, chemicals, forest products, suntan lotion, stone-clay-glass products. About $161 million is the est. value added annually by growing manufacturing industries. Warehousing has become a major industry; the state has no inventory tax on goods not sold in Nevada.

Farm receipts totaled $155 million for 1976, more than 80% from livestock products. The dry climate makes much of the state more suitable for grazing than for crops, although large-scale irrigation has expanded the growing areas.

The Nevada Test Site, NW of Las Vegas, is a proving ground for various atomic devices.

There are 6 state institutions of higher learning.

The Nevada State Museum, Carson City, occupies a former U.S. Mint, and exhibits coins, habitat groups of mammals and birds of the Great Basin area, Indian baskets, full-scale replicas of underground mining operations, and thousands of arrowheads.

Nevada was first explored by Spaniards in 1776. Fur trader Peter Skene Ogden trapped the region, 1825 and 1828; Jedediah Smith, another trader, crossed the state, 1826 and 1827. The area was acquired by the U.S., 1848, at the end of the Mexican War. First settlement, Mormon Station, now Genoa, was established 1849. In the early 20th century, Nevada adopted progressive measures such as the initiative, referendum, recall and woman suffrage.

Famous Nevadans include Dr. Robert C. Lynch, Sarah Winnemucca Hopkins, Pat McCarran, Walter Van Tilburg Clark.

(See also Index for Las Vegas, Reno.)

New Hampshire

Granite State

Area: 9,304 sq. mi.; rank, 44th. **Population** (U.S. est. 1976): 822,000; rank, 42d. **Capital:** Concord. **Motto:** Live Free or Die. **Flower:** Purple lilac. **Bird:** Purple finch. **Tree:** Paper (white) birch. **Song:** Old New Hampshire. Ninth of the original 13 states to ratify the Constitution, June 21, 1788.

One of the 6 New England states, New Hampshire is a land of impressive mountains, picturesque lakes, swift rivers, and, in the north, thick forests. Mountain slopes provide excellent ski trails. Numerous lakes and streams afford fishing for trout, bass, pickerel, perch, whitefish.

Abundant water power early turned New Hampshire into an industrial state, and manufacturing is still the principal source of income. Soil and climate have curtailed agricultural growth, but scenic and recreation resources have been developed and the tourist-vacation business, over $430 million a year, ranks 2d in its contribution to the state's economy. Per capita income was $5,973 in 1976.

In 1964, to raise funds to support education, the state ran the first legal sweepstakes lottery in the U.S. since 1894 (in that year, a lottery in Louisiana was outlawed). Profits from the state lottery are turned over to local school districts.

Most important industrial products are shoes, electrical and other machinery, leather goods, and paper products. Most factories are concentrated along the Merrimack and Connecticut Rivers, and in the seacoast area. Manufacturing employs about 100,000 workers. Value added by manufacture is $1.5 billion a year.

Farm receipts for 1976 totaled $77 million, about 55% from dairy and poultry products. Crops include apples, peaches, hay, corn, and maple syrup.

Mineral products, mainly sand, gravel, and stone for construction, were valued at $18 million for 1976.

Recreation and vacation attractions include Lake Winnipesaukee, largest of 1,300 lakes and ponds; the White Mountains, with skiing and scenic beauty; beaches on the Atlantic Coast, and historic sites.

One-third of the state is over 2,000 ft. above sea level. Highest land in northeast U.S. is the Presidential Range of the White Mountains, with Mt. Washington, 6,288 ft. (first cog railway in world opened 1869). National forests cover 677,559 acres; 142 state forests and parks, 63,805 acres.

State-owned parks include areas in Crawford and Franconia Notches; the latter includes the Old Man of the Mountains, described by Nathaniel Hawthorne as the Great Stone Face.

Portsmouth is the state's only port. Manchester is the largest city.

First explorers to visit the New Hampshire area were England's Martin Pring, 1603, and Samuel Champlain, 1605. First settlement was Little Harbor, near Rye, 1623. Indian raids were halted, 1759, by Robert Rogers' Rangers. Before the Revolution, New Hampshire men seized a British fort at Portsmouth, 1774, and drove the royal governor out, 1775. Three regiments served in the Continental Army and scores of privateers raided British shipping.

New Hampshire shared the educational pioneering of Massachusetts Bay from 1642; it established its first free public library at Dublin, 1822.

There are 24 institutions of higher education.

The MacDowell colony at Peterborough, established in 1908 in honor of Edward MacDowell, is a summer haven for writers, composers, artists.

The Currier Gallery of Art, Manchester, exhibits silver by Paul Revere, textiles, hooked rugs, pewter, and glass, and works by old and modern masters.

The New Hampshire Historical Society, Concord, has a museum displaying New Hampshire furniture, silver, pewter, glass, china, quilts, costumes, etc.

Famous men and women included Daniel Webster, Salmon P. Chase, Franklin Pierce, Robert Frost, Charles A. Dana, Horace Greeley, Sarah Buell Hale, Mary Baker Eddy, Ralph Adams Cram, Daniel Chester French, Augustus Saint-Gaudens.

New Jersey

Garden State

Area: 7,836 sq. mi.; rank, 46th. **Population** (U.S. est. 1976): 7,336,000; rank, 9th. **Capital:** Trenton. **Motto:** Liberty and Prosperity. **Flower:** Purple violet. **Bird:** Eastern goldfinch. **Tree:** Red oak. Third of the original 13 states to ratify the Constitution, Dec. 18, 1787.

Smallest of the Middle Atlantic states, New Jersey has the most people (953.1) per sq. mi. of the 50 states, ranks near the top in manufacturing, is rich in poultry and vegetable production, and has a flourishing resort industry. About 63% of the state's land area is in farms and forests.

There are vast shipping facilities, and New Jersey divides authority over important airports, harbors, tunnels, and bridges with the Port Authority of N.Y. and N. J. and the states of Delaware and Pennsylvania.

New Jersey has a heavy concentration of factories, highways, railroads, and farms, and is a leader in many fields.

Highly industrialized, New Jersey ranks 7th among the states in value added by manufacture, over $17.7 billion annually. It ranks 1st among the states in chemical products, having large pharmaceutical, synthetics, basic chemical, and paint industries.

Per capita income was $7,269 in 1976, 5th highest in the U.S.

It is also a leader in other manufacturing lines: apparel, food processing, electrical and other machinery, stone-clay-glass products, printing, rubber and plastics, petroleum products, leather products. It has a large concentration of research installations.

New Jersey also ranks high in the U. S. in gross income per farm acre. Chief crops are tomatoes, corn, asparagus, apples, cranberries, peaches, spinach. Poultry and dairy products are also important.

Total farm receipts in 1976 were $345 million, two-thirds from crops.

Mineral production is mostly stone, sand, and gravel, mainly for construction work. Zinc, peat, and clays are among other products. Total value was $123 million in 1976.

Large refineries, which process oil from out of state, have a total crude capacity of more than 500,000 barrels a day.

The commercial fishing catch is valued at over $19 million a year.

There are 65 institutions of higher learning. Per pupil public school expenditures are $2,076 annually, 3d highest in the nation.

Atlantic City, Ocean City, Cape May, Asbury Park, Point Pleasant, Wildwood, are among more than 100 resorts. The tourist industry generates over $1.2 billion in business annually, expected to increase in 1978 with the start of legal casino gambling in Atlantic City. There are 40 state parks with 55,717 acres. The 10 state forests comprise 176,652 acres.

Legal casino gambling was to be established in Atlantic City in 1977.

In Camden, the Walt Whitman House, home of the poet from 1884 until his death, Mar. 26, 1892, contains books, mementos, and furnishings used by Whitman. The U. S. Army Signal Corps Museum, Fort Monmouth, contains communications equipment from the earliest visual methods to modern satellites.

The Montclair Art Museum exhibits art of many periods and lands, emphasizing the American. The Newark Museum is a museum of art, science and industry, including American paintings and sculpture; Chinese, Japanese and Tibetan art; collections of birds, insects, minerals, shells, glass, ceramics, and jewelry. The New Jersey Historical Society Museum, Newark, has old New Jersey rooms and collections of New Jersey furniture, paintings, china, costumes, etc.

The Garden State Arts Center is an amphitheater for concerts and stage shows at Telegraph Hill Park.

The Johnston Historical Museum, adjacent to the

national hq. of the Boy Scouts of America, New Brunswick, depicts Scouting history, has a weather station, ham radio station, and 22-acre Outdoor Museum of Nature and Conservation.

The Edison National Historic Site, West Orange, displays Thomas Alva Edison's chemical laboratory, machine shop, and library; a reproduction of the "Black Maria," Edison's first movie studio; originals or replicas of his phonograph, incandescent lamp, and movie camera. In South Orange, the New Jersey Fire Museum displays 19th Century hand-pumpers, hose carts, helmets, etc.

In Trenton, the New Jersey State Museum displays the state's achievements in the arts, sciences, history, technology, and industry, and has a planetarium.

The New Jersey Meadowlands, lying close to the state's northeastern metropolitan centers, are the target of new development plans, including a New Jersey Sports Complex with a football stadium and race track. The Football Giants (formerly N.Y. Giants) play in the stadium.

The state's network of modern highways gives New Jersey more miles of roads per sq. mi. of area than any other state. There are 16 airlines and 17 railroads. New Jersey has the most rail trackage per sq. mi. in the U.S.

The Lenni Lenape (Delaware) Indians had mostly peaceful relations with European colonists who arrived after the explorers Verrazano, 1524, and Henry Hudson, 1609. The Dutch were first. When the British took New Netherland, 1664, the area between the Delaware and Hudson Rivers was given to Lord John Berkeley and Sir George Carteret. New Jersey was the scene of nearly 100 battles, large and small, during the Revolution, including Trenton, 1776, Princeton 1777, Monmouth, 1778. The state abolished slavery, 1846.

.Famous New Jerseyites include Cleveland, Wilson, Hamilton, Paine, Burr, Molly Pitcher, Gen. George McClellan, Edison, Whitman, James Fenimore Cooper, George Inness, Paul Robeson, Alexander Woolcott, Joyce Kilmer, Stephen Crane.

(See also Index for Newark.)

New Mexico

Land of Enchantment

Area: 121,666 sq. mi.; rank, 5th. **Population** (U.S. est. 1976): 1,168,000; rank, 37th. **Capital:** Santa Fe. **Motto:** Crescit Eundo, It Grows as it Goes. **Flower:** Yucca. **Bird:** Roadrunner. **Tree:** Pinon (nut pine). **Songs:** O, Fair New Mexico, Asi Es Nuevo Mejico. **Entered Union:** Jan. 6, 1912; rank, 47th.

New Mexico is a land of contrasts, presenting remnants of old Indian and Spanish cultures along with nuclear and space research centers; mountains over 13,000 ft., and a cavern 829 ft. below ground; ski slopes, and desert vistas.

Vast areas are made fertile by irrigation through dams and reservoirs on the Rio Grande, San Juan, Pecos, Canadian, Cimarron, Gila, and San Francisco Rivers.

The climate is dry and invigorating; annual rainfall is 7″ to 16″; mean temperature is 50°, reaching 100° on the plains in summer.

National forests cover 14,370 sq. mi. Douglas fir, Ponderosa pine, and spruce are cut for timber. Almost 33% of the land is federally owned.

Minerals are New Mexico's richest natural resource, and the state leads the U.S. in output of uranium, perlite, and potassium salts.

Mineral production reached a total value of $2.34 billion in 1976, up 13%. Petroleum accounted for the largest single part of this, $823 million, followed by natural gas, $616 million, and copper, $179 million. New Mexico ranks high among the states in carbon dioxide (dry ice) production. Its rich variety of minerals also includes gold, silver, zinc, lead, molybdenum.

Farm receipts accounted for $730 million for 1976, more than two-thirds from livestock products. New Mexico ranked 8th among the states in number of sheep. Cotton, pecans, and sorghum are the most important field crops. Also grown are corn, peanuts, beans, onions, and lettuce.

Manufacturing industries have grown and diversified. Principal lines are food products, chemicals, ordnance, transportation equipment, lumber, electrical machinery, stone-clay-glass products. Value added by manufacture is over $416 million annually.

Federal government activities, especially nuclear and space research and testing, have played a large role in New Mexico's economic growth. Nuclear and space centers are at Los Alamos, White Sands, Holloman, Kirtland, and Sandia.

Per capita income was $5,213 in 1976.

New Mexico's most awe-inspiring natural wonder, Carlsbad Caverns, had 790,000 visitors in 1975. A national park, the caverns are on 3 levels and have the largest natural cave "room" in the world, 1,500 by 300 ft., 300 ft. high.

There are 19 Pueblo, 4 Navajo, and 2 Apache reservations. Acoma, the "sky city," is built atop a 357-ft. mesa. There are pueblo ruins from 1000 A.D. in Chaco Canyon.

Skiing, hunting, fishing, ghost towns, and dude ranches help tourism show steady gains. Visitors spend more than $700 million in the state annually.

Franciscan Marcos de Niza and a black slave Estevan explored the area, 1539, seeking gold. First settlements were at San Juan Pueblo, 1598, and Santa Fe, 1610. Settlers alternately traded and fought with the Apaches, Comanches and Navajos. Trade on the Santa Fe Trail to Missouri started 1821. Before the Mexican War, Gen. Stephen Kearney took Santa Fe, 1846. In the 1870s, cattlemen staged the famed Lincoln County War in which Billy (the Kid) Bonney played a leading role. Pancho Villa raided Columbus, 1916.

Santa Fe is the 2d oldest city in the U.S. It and Taos have large artist colonies. Albuquerque (1706) is the state's largest city.

There are 17 institutions of higher education.

Wheelwright Museum, Santa Fe, housed in a modernized version of a ceremonial hogan, has over 600 sandpaintings, recordings of 2,000 Navajo chants; books, manuscripts, baskets, blankets, a replica of a trading post.

The Museum of New Mexico, Santa Fe, maintains the oldest public building in the U.S., the Palace of the Governors (built 1610), a hall of modern Indian culture, collected works of artists of the SW, folk art exhibits.

The Roswell Museum and Art Center, Roswell, has 19th and 20th century art collections, archeology and geology exhibits, the Robert H. Goddard rocket collection.

Famous New Mexicans include Kit Carson, Archbishop John Lamy, Billy (the Kid) Bonney, Pat Garrett, Lew Wallace, Peter Hurd, Bill Mauldin, Kim Stanley.

(See also Index for Albuquerque.)

New York

Empire State

Area: 49,576 sq. mi.; rank, 30th. **Population** (U.S. est. 1976): 18,084,000; rank, 2d. **Capital:** Albany. **Motto:** Excelsior, Ever Upward. **Flower:** Rose. **Bird:** Bluebird. **Tree:** Sugar maple. Eleventh of the original 13 states to ratify the Constitution, July 26, 1788.

New York is the nation's leading manufacturing state and within its borders are the financial capital of the nation, the largest city and port, the headquarters of the United Nations, the head offices of many of the greatest national corporations and insurance companies, and a great variety of industries.

New York's manufacturing industries outrank those of all other states in number, employees, and payrolls, but are 2d to California in value added by manufacture ($33.6 billion, 1973).

Value added by manufacture in New York exceeded that of every other state in apparel ($3.2 billion), printing and publishing ($4.4 billion), instruments ($4.2 billion), and in the miscellaneous group, which includes jewelry, silverware, toys and sporting goods, pens and pencils, etc. ($1.2 billion).

The state produces more than 34% of the nation's instruments, 22% of apparel, 20% of printing and publishing, 17% of the miscellaneous category. It is one of the largest producers of both leather and paper products.

Average non-farm employment for 1976 was 6.7 million. Wages and salaries totaled over $60 billion.

The bi-state Port Authority of New York and New Jersey handled 18% of the nation's foreign trade (by value) in 1976 by U.S. Commerce Dept. figures. The 3 Customs Districts (New York, Buffalo, and Ogdensburg) handled 24% of U.S. exports and imports by value in 1976.

Kennedy International Airport in N.Y. City handled about 50% of the nation's overseas air travel and is the nation's largest air cargo center, handling half of export-import air tonnage (by value).

The state Barge Canal System is 800 mi. long. There are 26 railroads and 535 landing facilities, including 27 seaplane bases and 79 heliports. The Verrazano-Narrows Bridge has the world's longest suspension span.

Rich, rolling farmlands support a large agricultural output. New York usually ranks 1st among the states in production of timothy, maple syrup, cottage cheese; it is 2d to Washington in apples and 2d to California in grapes (it has large wine and grape juice industries).

It is also a leader in milk production, with the 2d largest number of milk cows in the U.S., and is high in vegetables, melons, cherries, and other fruit; it is 8th among the states in potatoes, 9th in hay. Also important are corn, oats, wheat, peaches. Poultry and egg production is also high. Farm production supports large canning and freezing industries in the state.

Farm receipts for 1976 were est. at $1.7 billion, with more than two-thirds of the total from livestock and dairy products. Commercial fishing produced $32 million in 1976.

The state has a rich and varied mineral industry, normally ranking 1st in the U.S. in zinc, talc, titanium, emery, abrasive garnet, and wollastonite, and among the leaders in salt. Other products include lead, gypsum, petroleum, clay, stone, iron. Total value for 1976 was $408 million.

Per capita income was $7,100 in 1976, (national average: $6,441).

There are 287 institutions of higher education, most in any state. Expenditure per pupil in public schools is $2,360; pay of teachers is $16,000; both were topped in 1975 only by Alaska.

New York was the nation's most populous state from 1820 through 1964. As of July 1, 1964, the U.S. Census Bureau estimated California's pop. reached 18,084,000, New York's 17,915,000 (including Armed Forces stationed in the 2 states; without them, New York still led 17,870,000 to 17,749,000). By July 1, 1965, the Bureau estimated California led in both categories. In the 1970 Census, California had 19,953,134; New York had 18,241,266.

In 1609 Henry Hudson discovered the river that bears his name and Samuel de Champlain explored the lake, far upstate, which was named for him. In 1614 and 1624, the Dutch built posts near Albany; in 1626 they settled Manhattan. A British fleet seized New Netherland, 1664. In New York, 92 of the 300 or more engagements of the Revolution were fought, including the Battle of Bemis Heights-Saratoga, a turning point of the war.

Tourism and business travel provide $4.6 billion a year to businesses in the state. Major vacation areas include the Adirondack and Catskill Mtns., Finger Lakes, Great Lakes, Thousand Islands, Long Island, N.Y. City, and Niagara Falls. The 145 state parks are visited annually by over 45 million persons.

Sunnyside, the home of Washington Irving, "as full of angles and corners as an old cocked hat," is in Tarrytown. The Dutch Church of Sleepy Hollow (1697), North Tarrytown, overlooks a bridge commemorating Irving's story of the "headless horseman;" Irving is buried close by in Sleepy Hollow Cemetery. Also in Tarrytown is Lyndhurst, 19th century mansion of Jay Gould, maintained by the National Trust for Historic Preservation.

The Franklin D. Roosevelt National Historic Site, in Hyde Park, includes the graves of President and Mrs. Roosevelt, the home occupied by the Roosevelt family from 1867, greenhouse, etc. The Roosevelt Library has historic papers, trophies, and ship models.

In Cooperstown are the National Baseball Hall of Fame and Museum with a wide collection of mementos of the national game; nearby is Abner Doubleday Field, said to be where baseball originated in 1839. Near Cooperstown are Fenimore House, hq. of the State Historical Society, with collections including James Fenimore Cooper memorabilia and an art gallery; the Farmers' Museum; the Village Crossroads, with blacksmith shop, etc; the Carriage and Harness Museum.

The restored Fort Ticonderoga, overlooking the waters connecting Lakes George and Champlain, has relics of the French and Indian War and the Revolution in which the fort played important roles.

A new N.Y. State Museum, "Man and Nature in N.Y.," was opened in Albany in 1976.

The Corning Glass Center, Corning, has a museum and the Steuben factory, where visitors may see crystal glass formed and engraved. Also in the Finger Lakes area are the Curtiss Museum of aviation and the Wine Museum at Hammondsport and several wineries which offer tours to visitors. In Binghamton, the Roberson Center for the Arts and Sciences has art and historical collections.

Philipsburg Manor, in North Tarrytown, a trading center of the early 1700s, includes the restored Frederick Philipse home, a dam, and grist mill. Van Cortlandt Manor, Croton-on-Hudson, has the restored Van Cortlandt home and ferry house.

In Kingston, the Senate House, seat of the first Senate of the state, exhibits early historical objects; its museum has works by John Vanderlyn, local historical painter. In Newburgh, Washington's Hq., the Jonathan Hasbrouck House has Revolutionary relics.

The Suffolk Museum and Carriage House, Stony Brook, L.I., has early American paintings and furniture, apothecary shop, tavern, Wells Fargo, Conestoga, and gypsy wagons, etc.

The Remington Art Memorial Museum, Ogdensburg, has paintings and bronzes by Frederic Remington (1861-1909), born in nearby Canton.

Famous New Yorkers include Van Buren, Fillmore, Theodore and Franklin Roosevelt, Alfred E. Smith, Charles Evans Hughes, Julia Ward Howe, Elizabeth Cady Stanton, Melville, Whitman, Henry and William James, Peter Cooper, George Eastman.

(See also index for Albany, Binghamton, Buffalo, N.Y. City, Rochester, Schenectady, Syracuse, Troy.)

North Carolina

Tar Heel State, Old North State

Area: 52,586 sq. mi.; rank, 28th. **Population** (U.S. est. 1976): 5,469,000; rank, 11th. **Capital:** Raleigh. **Motto:** Esse Quam Videri; To Be, Rather Than to Seem. **Flower:** Dogwood. **Bird:** Cardinal. **Tree:** Pine. **Song:** The Old North State. Twelfth of the original 13 states to ratify the Constitution, Nov. 21, 1789.

From a low coastal plain, with Capes Hatteras, Lookout, and Fear jutting into the Atlantic, North Carolina rises to a central Piedmont plateau region and, in the W, to the scenic Blue Ridge and Great Smoky Mountains. Mt. Mitchell, 6,684 ft., is the highest peak E of the Mississippi.

Modernization of production methods has brought North Carolina increasing prosperity from its factories. Per capita personal income was $5,409 in 1976, $1,032 below U.S. average.

The state leads the U.S. in production of textiles, bricks, household furniture, and cigarettes.

In 1976, 124 new industrial plants opened and 911 expanded their facilities, creating an est. 19,700 new jobs through an investment of $1.06 billion.

About 757,700 workers are employed in factories. The textile industry is the state's largest, with shipments valued at about $23.8 billion annually.

North Carolina ranks 1st among the states in tobacco production; in 1976 it was valued at $997 million. It was also first in sweet potatoes, 4th in peanuts. Other large crops are cotton, corn, and soybeans. Also grown are wheat, oats, barley, peaches, apples. In crop receipts, the state ranked 7th in 1976 with $1.7 billion; it was also 11th in total crop and livestock receipts, $2.8 billion. The state ranked 2d in turkeys, 5th in chickens in 1977.

Mineral production value was est. at $160 million for 1976. North Carolina ranked 1st in mica, feldspar, and lithium; it was also a leader in talc and asbestos.

Tourism is important; in 1976 travelers spent an est. $1.28 billion in the state. Sports include golfing, skiing at mountain resorts, fishing and hunting.

Among attractions are the Great Smoky Mtns. (half in Tennessee), the Blue Ridge Parkway and the Cape Hatteras and Cape Lookout National Seashores.

Other attractions include the restored Fort Raleigh National Historic Site, Roanoke Is., where Virginia Dare, first child of English parents in the New World, was born Aug. 18, 1587; Wright Brothers National Memorial near Kitty Hawk with aviation exhibits and a reproduction of the plane in which Wilbur and Orville Wright made their first flights, 1903; Guilford Court House and Moore's Creek parks, sites of Revolutionary battles. The battleship North Carolina, a war memorial, is berthed at Wilmington.

In Asheville is one of the world's largest rayon plants as well as Biltmore Industries, native craft plants set up by Mrs. George W. Vanderbilt in 1901 to continue handweaving traditions of the area. Just S of Asheville is the 19th century Biltmore mansion of the Vanderbilts, which has a large collection of paintings, antiques, and Ming china. Also in Asheville, the Thomas Wolfe Memorial was the home of the author.

Bennett Place, 6 mi. NW of Durham, is the site where Gen. Joseph E. Johnston surrendered the last Confederate army to Gen. William Sherman.

The Mint Museum of Art, Charlotte, has collections of paintings, sculpture, and ceramics. The North Carolina Museum of Art, Raleigh, exhibits American and European paintings, sculpture and decorative art. Tryon Palace, New Bern, is the reconstructed colonial capitol of 1770-1794.

Old Salem, in Winston-Salem, includes buildings erected by the Moravians from 1766 on.

There are 116 institutions of higher education.

The first English colony in America was the first of 2 established by Sir Walter Raleigh on Roanoke Is., 1585 and 1587. The first group returned to England; the second, the "Lost Colony," disappeared without trace. Permanent settlers came from Virginia, c. 1660. Roused by British repressions, the colonists drove out the royal governor, 1775; the province's Congress was the first to vote for independence. Ten regiments were furnished to the Continental Army. Cornwallis' forces were defeated at Kings Mountain, 1780, and forced out after Guilford Courthouse, 1781.

Famous men and women included James K. Polk, Dolley Madison, Gaylord and Jim Perry, Jim (Catfish) Hunter, and Enos Slaughter.

(See also Index for Charlotte, Raleigh, and Winston-Salem.)

North Dakota

Sioux State, Flickertail State

Area: 70,665 sq. mi.; rank, 17th. **Population** (U.S. est. 1976): 643,000; rank, 45th. **Capital:** Bismarck. **Motto:** Liberty and Union, Now and Forever, One and Inseparable. **Flower:** Wild prairie rose. **Bird:** Western meadowlark. **Tree:** American elm. **Song:** North Dakota Hymn. **Entered Union:** Nov. 2, 1889; rank, 39th or 40th, with South Dakota.

The eastern plains of North Dakota are rich in grain and support large numbers of livestock, in sharp contrast to the rough, colorful Badlands in the west which have elements of scenic beauty and include Theodore Roosevelt National Memorial Park.

North Dakota's economy is based on agriculture and mining; but manufacturing industries, especially processing of food, have grown in number and size. Most of the usable land is in farms and ranches.

North Dakota led the other states in production of spring and durum wheat, barley, and flaxseed in 1975 and was 2d to Kansas in total wheat. It was also a leader in rye, oats, sugar beets, pinto and navy beans, and potatoes. Farm receipts for 1976 totaled $2 billion. In 1977 there were 2.3 million cattle in the state.

Mineral production in 1976 was valued at $240 million, up 19% from 1975. The larger part of this was from petroleum. Other products include natural gas, natural gas liquids, coal (lignite), salt, peat.

Per capita income was $5,400 in 1976.

Tourism brings in over $269 million a year.

There are 65 state parks and historic sites. The International Peace Garden, on a 2,200-acre tract extending across the border into Manitoba, commemorates the friendly relations between the U.S. and Canada. The state is known for its waterfowl, grouse, and deer hunting, bass, trout, and northern pike fishing. Lake Sakakawea, formed by the Garrison Dam across the Missouri River, is 609 sq. mi. in area.

A museum with exhibits of pioneer life, the Northern Plains Indians and natural history of the area, is maintained by the State Historical Society on the State Capitol grounds, Bismarck.

Pierre La Verendrye was the first (1738) French fur trader in the area, followed later by English traders. The U.S. acquired half the territory in the Louisiana Purchase, 1803. Lewis and Clark built Fort Mandan, spent the winter of 1804-05 there. In 1818, American ownership of the other half was confirmed by agreement with Britain. First permanent settlement was at Pembina, 1812. Missouri River steamboats reached the area, 1832; the first railroad, 1873, bringing many homesteaders. The state was first to hold a presidential primary, 1912; other progressive measures were the referendum and recall.

There are 15 institutions of higher learning.

Famous North Dakotans include Vilhjalmur Stefansson, Maxwell Anderson, Eric Sevareid, Lawrence Welk, Peggy Lee, Dorothy Stickney, Roger Maris, Angie Dickinson, Louis L'Amour.

(See also Index for Bismarck.)

Ohio

Buckeye State

Area: 41,222 sq. mi.; rank, 35th. **Population** (U.S. est. 1976): 10,690,000; rank, 6th. **Capital:** Columbus. **Motto:** With God, All Things Are Possible. **Flower:** Scarlet carnation. **Bird:** Cardinal. **Tree:** Ohio buckeye. **Song:** Beautiful Ohio. **Entered Union:** Mar. 1, 1803; rank, 17th.

Ohio is the nation's 3d greatest industrial state; it ranks among the wealthier states in livestock and crop receipts, and is a leader in output of lime, coal, and coke.

Ohio leads the U.S. in a wide variety of products: tires, machine tools, playing cards, business machines, glassware, cutlery, dishwashers, clay.

Per capita income was $6,432 in 1976, $9 below national average.

Total value added by manufacture was $31.1 billion. Of this, autos, aircraft, boats, and parts accounted for $2.9 billion; iron, steel, and other metals, $2.9 billion; machinery, especially industrial, $3.4 billion; electrical machinery, especially household appliances, $2.4 billion. Also important are metal products, chemicals, rubber and plastic products, food processing.

Farm receipts for 1976 totaled over $2.8 billion, 10th among the states, with three-fourths of it from livestock products. Ohio has large numbers of milk cows, hogs, and sheep; it ranks high in milk production. It is also a large producer of corn, grapes, clover, popcorn, oats, soybeans, and other crops.

Mineral production was valued at a total $1.4 billion for 1976, with the largest item being bituminous coal. Ohio was the top state in lime production and one of the leaders in clays, salt, gypsum sand, and gravel. Other important products include petroleum, cement, gypsum, and natural gas.

It was estimated that the value of the tourist industry was more than $1.9 billion for 1976.

There are 64 state parks, over 300 roadside parks, and many historic memorials, including Fallen Timbers Battlefield, prehistoric Indian mounds, and the restored first settlement, Schoenbrunn (1772).

The National Rifle and Pistol Matches are held at Camp Perry and the Grand American Trapshoot at Vandalia.

Unusual museums include the Air Force Museum and Paul Lawrence Dunbar House, Dayton; Dental Museum, Bainbridge; Auto-Aviation Museum, Cleveland; Ohio Historical Museum, Columbus; Neil Armstrong Air and Space Museum, Wapakoneta.

In Canton, the Pro Football Hall of Fame has a museum and daily movies; the Stark County Historical Society has industry and historical museums.

The state is served by 27 railroads and 21 scheduled airlines. It has busy ports on Lake Erie.

There are 131 institutions of higher education.

LaSalle visited the Ohio area, 1669; American fur-traders arrived, beginning 1685; the French and Indians sought to drive them out. During the Revolution, Virginians defeated the Indians, 1774, but hostilities were renewed, 1777. The region became U.S. territory after the Revolution. First organized settlement was at Marietta, 1788. Indian warfare ended with Anthony Wayne's victory at Fallen Timbers, 1794. In the War of 1812, Oliver H. Perry's victory on Lake Erie and William H. Harrison's invasion of Canada, 1813, ended British incursions.

Famous Ohioans include Grant, Hayes, Garfield, William H. and Benjamin Harrison, McKinley, Taft, Harding, Sherman, Rickenbacker, Edison, Orville Wright, George Bellows, Ambrose Bierce, Paul Laurence Dunbar, Sherwood Anderson, John D. Rockefeller Sr. and Jr., Bob Hope, John Glenn.

(See also index for Akron, Cincinnati, Cleveland, Columbus, Dayton, Toledo, Youngstown.)

Oklahoma

Sooner State

Area: 69,919 sq. mi.; rank, 18th. **Population** (U.S. est. 1976): 2,766,000; rank, 27th. **Capital:** Oklahoma City. **Motto:** Labor Omnia Vincit, Labor Conquers All Things. **Flower:** Mistletoe. **Bird:** Scissortailed flycatcher. **Tree:** Redbud. **Song:** Oklahoma! **Entered Union:** Nov. 16, 1907; rank, 46th.

Most of Oklahoma is a great, rolling plain sloping S and E with a mean altitude of 1,300 ft. There are 4 mountainous areas; the Ozark Plateau in the NE, the Ouachitas in the SE, the Arbuckles in the S central and the Wichitas in the SW. In the western Panhandle, the land rises toward the Rockies with Black Mesa, 4,973 ft., the highest point.

Oil, wheat, and cattle are the basic ingredients of Oklahoma's economy, but manufacturing industries have gained increasing importance. Per capita income was $5,657 in 1976, up $661 over 1975.

The $1.2 billion Arkansas River Navigation System, involving shipping, flood control, and power dams, was completed to Catoosa, near Tulsa, in 1971. It made Catoosa a "seaport," with barge shipping to the Mississippi and beyond.

The state's output of petroleum was valued at $1.4 billion for 1976, accounting for much of the total value of mineral production, $2.7 billion. The state is one of the leaders in the U.S. in petroleum production, and in total mineral production.

Natural gas was the 2d most important mineral with production valued at $859 million. Other minerals include helium, in which the state is a leader, gypsum, zinc, cement, coal, copper, silver.

Oklahoma's rich plains produced the nation's 2d largest winter wheat crop in 1975 as well as large crops of sorghum, broomcorn, other grains, and peanuts. Its cattle herd was the 6th largest in the U.S. Total farm receipts were $2 billion, more than half from livestock products.

While much of Oklahoma's manufacturing industry is based on processing of the state's own meat, wheat, and oil, other lines have become important rivals. Value added by manufacture exceeds $2.6 billion annually. Important lines include food processing, machinery (especially construction and oil equipment), transportation equipment, metal products, petroleum, and coal products.

There are 44 institutions of higher education.

Total tourist revenues are estimated at more than $1 billion annually. Attractions include 30 state parks, large lakes and reservoirs such as Eufaula (102,500 acres) and Lake Texoma (93,080 acres); Ouachita National Forest (176,000 acres), rodeos, Indian powwows, the National Cowboy Hall of Fame in Oklahoma City, bass fishing, and quail hunting.

The Will Rogers Memorial, Claremore, has collections of the great humorist's saddles and ropes, as well as trophies; his tomb is also there. In Anadarko, the Southern Plains Indian Museum and Crafts Center exhibits Indian arts and has a crafts sales shop. The Woolaroc Museum near Bartlesville has 55,000 exhibits in a panorama of New World history, and a collection of paintings of the West.

The Fort Gibson Stockade, restored with many of the original buildings, near Muskogee, was established 1824 and was the army's largest outpost in the Indian lands.

Near Tahlequah is the Cherokee Cultural Center with a restored 1700 Cherokee village.

The first permanent white settlement in the area was made in 1796 by Maj. Jean Pierre Chouteau on the site of present-day Salina, Okla.

Part of the Louisiana Purchase, 1803, Oklahoma was known as Indian Territory (but was not given territorial government) after it became the home of the "Five Civilized Tribes"—Cherokee, Choctaw, Chickasaw, Creek, and Seminole—1828-1846. The land was also used by Comanche, Osage, and other Plains Indians. As white settlers pressed west, land was opened for homesteading by runs and lottery, a run being a race for a claim at a specific time. The first run took place Apr. 22, 1889; the most famous was the run to the Cherokee Outlet, 1893. The portion thus opened was organized as a Territory; this and Indian Territory were joined by Congress in the State of Oklahoma, admitted to the Union Nov. 16, 1907.

Famous Oklahomans include Will Rogers, Gen. Patrick J. Hurley, Jim Thorpe, Maria Tallchief, Kay Starr, Mickey Mantle, Allie Reynolds, Johnny Bench, Wiley Post, Roger Miller, Woodie Guthrie.

(See also Index for Oklahoma City and Tulsa.)

Oregon

Beaver State

Area: 96,981 sq. mi.; rank, 10th. **Population** (U.S. est. 1976): 2,329,000; rank, 30th. **Capital:** Salem. **Motto:** The Union. **Flower:** Oregon grape. **Bird:** Western meadowlark. **Animal:** Beaver. **Tree:** Douglas fir. **Song:** Oregon, My Oregon. **Entered Union:** Feb. 14, 1859; rank, 33d.

Oregon is rich in timber, fish and wildlife, water power, and scenic beauty, with lofty mountain ranges, deep river gorges, and broad, fertile valleys.

Half of Oregon, or about 30 million acres, is thickly forested and the state leads the nation in value of forest products, over $3 billion a year. Production of lumber, furniture, paper, and other forest products provides jobs for about 75,000 workers and is a major factor in the state's economy.

Also important are food processing, transportation equipment, machinery, fabricated metal. Total value added by manufacture is over $4.3 billion a year.

Per capita income was $6,331 in 1976.

Oregon's agriculture is rich and varied. While farmers grow fair-sized crops of wheat, oats, potatoes, and other staples, the state is a leader in production of berries, pears, cherries, filberts, walnuts, vegetables. It also ranks high in number of turkeys and of sheep. Farm receipts for 1976 were over $1 billion, two-thirds from crops, the rest livestock.

Stone, nickel, cement, lime are important in mineral production, valued at $106 million for 1976.

Hydroelectric power, from both privately-owned and publicly-owned utilities, is abundant. A federal agency, the Bonneville Power Administration, sells electric power, much of it from a series of great dams across the Columbia River, to many of the utilities and to large industrial plants. Among users are plants for the refining and processing of metals from out of state, including aluminum.

The Columbia River brings ocean shipping to Portland, 100 mi. inland but one of the Pacific Coast's principal ports, and to other river ports.

The commercial fish catch, including salmon, tuna, halibut, sole, cod, and shellfish, was worth over $48 million in 1976.

Tourism is an important industry, est. at over $891 million annually. There are 237 state parks, and both state and national forests. Crater Lake, a national park, is a body of sapphire blue water in a former volcano, 6 mi. in diameter and 1,932 ft. deep—deepest lake in the U.S. Oregon Dunes National Recreation Area was created in 1972.

Mt. Hood, which rises 11,235 ft., is the highest point in the state: nearby are scenic recreation areas.

Fort Clatsop National Memorial includes a replica of the fort in which the Lewis and Clark expedition spent the winter of 1805-06. Oregon Caves National Monument contains stone waterfalls. Skiing and the annual Pendleton Round-Up are other attractions.

A summer Shakespearean Festival is staged annually in Ashland.

Oregon has 43 institutions of higher education.

The Univ. of Oregon in Eugene has a Museum of Art with oriental, Pacific Northwest, and other art collections. It also has a Museum of Natural History.

American Capt. Robert Gray discovered and sailed into the Columbia River, 1792; Lewis and Clark, traveling overland, wintered at the mouth of the river, 1805-06. Fur traders followed. Settlers arrived in the Willamette Valley, 1834. In 1843 the first large wave of settlers arrived via the Oregon Trail. Early in the 20th century, the "Oregon System," reforms which included the initiative, referendum, recall, direct primary, and woman suffrage, was adopted.

Famous Oregonians include Dr. John McLoughlin, Ernest Haycox, Stewart Holbrook, John Reed, Childe Hassam, Ernest Bloch, Mrs. Ruth Tooze, Chief Joseph, Joaquin Miller, Jane Powell, Maurine Neuberger, Sally Struthers, Mickey Lolich.

(See also Index for Portland, Salem.)

Pennsylvania

Keystone State

Area: 45,333 sq. mi.; rank, 33d. **Population** (U.S. est. 1976): 11,862,000; rank, 4th. **Capital:** Harrisburg. **Motto:** Virtue, Liberty and Independence. **Flower:** Mountain laurel. **Bird:** Ruffed grouse. **Tree:** Eastern hemlock. Second of the original 13 states to ratify the Constitution, Dec. 12, 1787.

Pennsylvania has extensive mineral resources and fertile farmlands, is a leader in manufacturing, and boasts a wealth of historic landmarks and scenic attractions.

Roughly rectangular in shape, Pennsylvania has prosperous farmlands in the SE and the W. Through the center, running NE-SW, are parallel mountain ridges with valleys between. Highest point is Mt. Davis in the SW, 3,213 ft.

Many of the nation's largest steel plants are in Pennsylvania, with the greatest concentration in the Pittsburgh area. Pennsylvania ranks 1st among the states in steel wire and structural metal.

Mill and factory products are many and varied; value added by manufacture is over $26.8 billion. Primary metals (mainly steel) are the most important, over $4.7 billion. Other large lines are machinery and electrical machinery, food processing, chemicals, metal products, women's dresses, and men's suits.

Per capita income was $6,466 in 1976, $25 above the national average.

Pennsylvania produces almost all of the nation's anthracite coal; it ranked 3d in 1976 in output of bituminous coal. Also important are cement, stone, petroleum, lime, clays, zinc, iron. Mineral production value, 1976, was $3.1 billion, up 6.4%.

Prosperous farms, such as those in the Pennsylvania Dutch country in the SE, brought in total livestock and crop receipts for the state of $1.8 billion in 1976, much of it from dairy and poultry products. The state ranked high in number of cows, chickens, turkeys.

The state ranks high in its output of grapes, peaches, apples, and cherries. It claims 1st place in scrapple, pretzels, mushrooms, and plantation-grown Christmas trees. It also ranks high in ice cream. Forest products are valued at over $7 billion annually.

Pennsylvania is among the leading states in hunting, fishing, golf, and winter sports. Tourism reportedly produces sales of $2.29 billion a year, 7th highest in the U.S.

There are more than 100 state and federal parks, recreation areas, and historic sites. Scenic attractions include the Delaware Water Gap in the east and the 1,000-ft. deep Pine Creek Gorge in the north. Folk festivals, country fairs, and fall foliage in the Poconos draw many visitors.

Washington Crossing State Park, where Continental troops crossed the Delaware to attack Hessian-British forces in Trenton, Christmas Night 1776, has restored buildings and picnic areas.

Longwood Gardens, near Kennett Square, include conservatories and rock, heather, flower, and water gardens; arboretum, illuminated fountains, open-air theater; open every day of the year.

Lancaster County and nearby areas in the southeast are known as Pennsylvania Dutch Country. Descendants of early German, Swiss, and Dutch settlers, many of them Amish or Mennonites, still maintain many of the early customs and "old world" culture which make their farms, festivals, and market places attractive to tourists.

The William Penn Memorial Museum, Harrisburg, has collections of folk art, ironwork, glass, pewter, china, textiles, stage coaches, sleighs; replicas of artisans' shops, period rooms; fine arts, planetarium.

There are 179 institutions of higher learning.

First settlers were Swedish, 1643, on Tinicum Is. In 1655 the Dutch seized the settlement but lost it to the British, 1664. The region was given by Charles II to William Penn, 1681. Philadelphia (brotherly love) was the capital of the colonies during most of the Revolution, and of the U.S., 1790-1800. Pennsylvanians aided in the siege of Boston; Philadelphia was taken by the British, 1777; Washington's troops encamped at Valley Forge in the bitter winter of 1777-78. The Declaration of Independence, 1776, and the Constitution, 1787, were signed in Philadelphia.

Famous Pennsylvanians include Betsy Ross, Benjamin Franklin, Robert E. Peary, Andrew Carnegie, George C. Marshall, Stephen Foster, Marion Anderson, Mary Roberts Rinehart, Maxwell Anderson.

(See also Index for Allentown, Erie, Philadelphia, Pittsburgh.)

Rhode Island

Little Rhody, Ocean State

Area: 1,214 sq. mi.; rank, 50th. **Population** (U.S. est. 1976): 927,000; rank, 39th. **Capital:** Providence. **Motto:** Hope. **Flower:** Violet. **Bird:** Rhode Island red (hen). **Tree:** Red maple. **Song:** Rhode Island. Thirteenth of original 13 states to ratify the Constitution, May 29, 1790.

Rhode Island is the smallest of the 50 states but has the longest official name: State of Rhode Island and Providence Plantations. It is not an island, although its Narragansett Bay, extending from the Atlantic 37 mi. inland, contains many islands, the largest of which is named Rhode Is.

Tiny Rhode Island is densely populated and highly industrialized. It is 2d to New Jersey in population density. The 1970 Census showed New Jersey averaging 953.1 persons per sq. mi.; Rhode Island 905.5.

Industries show more than $1.9 billion in value added annually by manufacturing. Until 1940, textile mills, dating back to a 1793 cotton mill, employed more workers than all other Rhode Island industries put together. Employment in the mills fell off sharply but jobs in other fields increased.

The state also pioneered in the manufacture of jewelry and silverware and remains tops in the U. S. Other leading industry groups are primary metal processing, metal products, machinery, rubber, and plastics, food processing, chemicals, apparel. The tourist industry produces over $150 million annually.

Per capita income was $6,498 in 1976; U.S. average was $6,441.

Only 1% of the labor force is engaged in farming, and farm receipts in 1976 totaled $28 million. Dairy and poultry (notably Rhode Island reds) are the most important lines; potatoes and apples are principal crops. The fish and shellfish catch is valued at over $20 million annually.

There are 12 institutions of higher education.

Rhode Island is distinguished historically for its battle for freedom of conscience and action, begun by Roger Williams, founder of Providence, who was exiled from Massachusetts Bay Colony in 1636, and Anne Hutchinson, exiled in 1638. The first Baptist church in the U.S. was founded in Providence in 1638. Rhode Island gave protection to Quakers in 1657 and to Jews from Holland in 1658.

The colonists broke the power of the Narragansett Indians in the Great Swamp Fight, 1675, the decisive battle in King Philip's War. British trade restrictions angered the colonists and they burned the British revenue cutter Gaspee, 1772. The colony declared its independence May 4, 1776. Gen. John Sullivan and Lafayette won a partial victory, 1778, but failed to oust the British.

The Rhode Island Historical Society in Providence occupies the historic John Brown House, with rooms containing furniture by 18th century cabinet makers. Also in Providence, the Rhode Island School of Design has collections of classic art, 18th century American furniture, 19th century paintings, etc.

Providence is a major manufacturing and educational center, and a port handling over 9 million tons of cargo per year.

Newport became famous as the summer capital of society in the mid-19th century. Touro Synagogue (1763) is the oldest in the U.S., a national historic site.

The Newport Historical Society has a marine museum; extensive exhibits of silver, furniture, china, etc.; a grist mill, several forts, a Seventh Day Baptist meeting house built 1729.

In Pawtucket, the Old Slater Mill Museum is a restored 1793 cotton mill, considered the first to spin yarn successfully in this country; it has demonstrations of hand spinning and weaving.

Famous Rhode Islanders include Nathanael Greene, Gilbert Stuart, Oliver and Matthew C. Perry, Jabez Gorham, George M. Cohan, Nelson Eddy, Ambrose Burnside, Oliver and Christopher La Farge.

(See also Index for Providence.)

South Carolina

Palmetto State

Area: 31,055 sq. mi.; rank, 40th. **Population** (U.S. est. 1976): 2,848,000; rank, 26th. **Capital:** Columbia. **Motto:** Dum Spiro, Spero, While I Breathe, I Hope; and Animis Opibusque Parati, Prepared in Mind and Resources. **Flower:** Carolina (yellow) jessamine. **Bird:** Carolina wren. **Song:** Carolina. **Tree:** Palmetto. Eighth of the original 13 states to ratify the Constitution, May 23, 1788.

In South Carolina, the land slopes from the Blue Ridge Mountains in the NW, through thick pine forests and fertile farmlands with great fields of tobacco and cotton, to semi-tropic beaches and busy ports on the Atlantic. Deep-sea and inland fishing, hunting, antebellum houses, public gardens, and famed shore resorts are among the state's attractions.

Efforts to diversify industry and expand foreign trade and tourism have been highly successful. Per capita income was $5,216 in 1976.

Manufacturing is by far the major source of income; value added by manufacture is over $5 billion annually. The textile industry is still the most important, comprising about 40% of the value of all manufactured products, and employing the most workers. The mills rank high in cotton goods, and are a major producer of synthetic and woolen goods.

Other important manufacturing lines are chemicals, apparel, paper, lumber, food processing, machinery, and stone-clay-glass products.

In 1976, new industrial investment was valued at $488 million; it was estimated this would provide 9,532 new jobs. Major areas of expansion were in chemical, textile, and metal-working fields.

Farms have become fewer but larger. South Carolina grows more peaches than any other state except California; it ranks 4th in tobacco. Also grown are cotton, peanuts, sweet potatoes, pecans, etc. Poultry and eggs are important revenue producers; the state has large sales of chickens and turkeys.

Total farm receipts for 1976 were $845 million.

The state's mineral production value for 1976 was est. at $127 million. It is a leader in production of vermiculite, used in insulation, and of kyanite and kaolin used in ceramics. Also produced are mica, cement, and stone, including Winnsboro blue granite. Lumber for pulp and saw-timber is a major resource, especially the loblolly pine.

Income from tourism has risen; 33 million out-of-state visitors spent an est. $911 million in 1975.

Attractions include state parks, famed gardens, historic sites, coastal islands, shore resorts such as Myrtle Beach, fishing, and quail hunting.

There are many historic churches and white-pillared houses in Charleston, Columbia, and Beaufort. Gardens near Charleston include Middleton Place, Magnolia, and Cypress; Brookgreen, south of Myrtle Beach, has 340 outdoor statues; other gardens are Edisto, at Orangeburg; Glencairn, at Rock Hill.

Fort Sumter National Monument is in Charleston Harbor. Charleston Museum, estab. 1773, has exhibits of interior paneling, furniture, arts, crafts, and utensils from early South Carolina days.

The first English colonists settled, 1670, on the Ashley River, moved to the site of Charleston, 1680. The colonists seized the government, 1775, and the royal governor fled. In 1780 the British took Charleston, but British troops were defeated at Kings Mountain that year, and at Cowpens and Eutaw Springs, 1781. In the 1830s, South Carolinians, angered by Federal protective tariffs, adopted the Nullification Doctrine, holding a state can void an act of Congress. The state was the first to secede and, in 1861, Confederate troops fired on and forced the surrender of U. S. troops at Fort Sumter, in Charleston Harbor, launching the Civil War.

There are 56 institutions of higher education. Public school per pupil expenditures were $1,177 in 1976, 4th lowest in the U.S.

Famous South Carolinians include Andrew Jackson, John C. Calhoun, Francis Marion, James F. Byrnes, Julia Peterkin, DuBose Heyward.

(See also Index for Columbia.)

South Dakota

Coyote State, Sunshine State

Area: 77,047 sq. mi.; rank, 16th. **Population** (U.S.

est. 1976); 686,000; rank, 44th. **Capital:** Pierre. **Motto:** Under God, the People Rule. **Flower:** American pasque. **Bird:** Ringnecked pheasant. **Song:** Hail, South Dakota. **Tree:** Black Hills spruce. **Entered Union:** Nov. 2, 1889; rank, 39th or 40th (entered at same time as North Dakota).

South Dakota is a rectangle split down the middle by the Missouri R. and a chain of huge lakes formed behind dams on the river. In the E are rich farmlands which produce large crops of rye, oats, and other grains. In the W are rolling grasslands which support millions of cattle and sheep, as well as vast acreages of wheat. In the far W are the Black Hills with Harney Peak, 7,242 ft., the highest point E of the Rockies.

With more than 43,000 farms and ranches, occupying most of the land area, agriculture is South Dakota's basic industry. Its livestock and livestock products account for three-quarters of farm income. Mining and lumbering are large natural resource industries. Per capita income was $4,796 in 1976, $1,645 below U.S. average.

The state normally ranks high in the U.S. in size of its rye crop and high in spring wheat, flaxseed, oats, and barley. In 1977 South Dakota ranked 5th in sheep, 10th in cattle, and 10th in hogs. Total farm receipts for 1976 were $1.8 billion.

Large areas are reclaimed by irrigation and plans were under way for additional hundreds of thousands of acres to be fed from the Oahe Reservoir.

South Dakota leads the nation in gold production; the Homestake Mine in Lawrence County is the largest in the U. S. Gold accounted for $40 million of the state's total mineral production value which was $100 million for 1976. The state was also a leader in production of beryllium. Other products include silver, petroleum, uranium, cement.

Processing of foods produced by farms and ranches is the largest of South Dakota's manufacturing industries. Also important are lumber and wood products, and machinery, including farm equipment. Total value added by manufacture is over $330 million.

South Dakota has 8,400 sq. mi. of Indian reservations. The Indians, mostly Sioux, are est. at 32,365.

There are 17 institutions of higher education and 12 state parks, 35 recreation areas, and 49 roadside parks. Pheasant, duck, and geese are abundant. There are large herds of deer and elk and about 5,000 bison in state and private herds.

Mount Rushmore, in the Black Hills, has an altitude of 6,200 ft. Sculptured on its granite face are the heads of Washington, Jefferson, Lincoln, and Theodore Roosevelt. These busts by Gutzon Borglum are proportionate to men 465 ft. tall. Rushmore is visited by about 2 million persons annually.

Other tourist attractions include Custer State Park, with the world's largest herd of bison; the Black Hills Passion Play at Spearfish; Badlands National Monument, 170 sq. mi. of barren, eroded "moonscape."

The "Great Lakes of South Dakota" are 4 reservoirs created behind Oahe, Big Bend, Fort Randall, and Gavins Point Dams on the Missouri River with total water surface area of 571,000 acres.

Nine million out-of-state tourists, it is estimated, spend $258 million a year in South Dakota.

Fort Sisseton State Park, 18 mi. SE of Britton, is a restored army frontier post of 1864. The Sioux Indian Museum in Rapid City features historic and contemporary arts of the Sioux, and an Indian craft shop.

The French Verendrye brothers explored the region, 1742-43. Lewis and Clark passed through the area, 1804, and recrossed it on their return from the Pacific, 1806. First American settlement was at Sioux Falls, 1857, but there were few other settlements until after gold was discovered, 1874, on the Sioux Reservation. Miners rushed in; the U.S. first tried to stop them, then relaxed its opposition. Custer's defeat by the Sioux followed, and in 1877 the Sioux relinquished the land and the "great Dakota Boom" began. Miners and settlers poured in. A new Indian uprising came in 1890, climaxed by the massacre of Indian families at Wounded Knee.

Famous South Dakotans include Sakajawea, Sitting Bull, Crazy Horse, Dr. Ernest O. Lawrence.

(See also Index for Sioux Falls.)

Tennessee

Volunteer State

Area: 42,244 sq. mi.; rank, 34th. **Population** (U.S. est. 1976): 4,214,000; rank, 17th. **Capital:** Nashville. **Motto:** Agriculture, Commerce. **Flower:** Iris. **Bird:** Mockingbird. **Tree:** Tulip poplar. **Song:** Tennessee Waltz. **Entered Union:** June 1, 1796; rank, 16th.

Eastern Tennessee is rugged country with the Great Valley separating the Great Smoky Mtns., on the state's E border, from the Cumberland Mtns.; the Central Basin is a rolling area containing the famed Bluegrass country; from there the state slopes W to the bottom lands of the Mississippi.

Manufacturing has taken top place in Tennessee's economy: Among important products are chemicals (especially plastic fibers), textiles, apparel, electrical machinery. Other lines are food processing, furniture, lumber, paper, metal products, leather.

Value added by manufacture is over $8.8 billion annually. Per capita income was $5,432 in 1976 (U.S. average: $6,441).

There are 24 research centers including Oak Ridge, TVA, and Arnold Engineering Development Center for rocket research.

Tennessee ranks 5th among the states in tobacco production. Farm receipts for 1976 totaled $1.3 billion, more than half of it from livestock, the rest from crops. It has large numbers of hogs and cattle.

Forest products are also important, providing full-time jobs to 40,000 persons and contributing over $500 million annually to the economy. The state is known as the U.S. hardwood flooring center.

Tennessee produces a wide range of minerals and is a leader in production of zinc and pyrites. Other products include silver, copper, coal. Total mineral production was valued at $444 million for 1976.

Tourism is of increasing importance; tourists spend about $1.3 billion annually in Tennessee. "Country and Western" music and the "Nashville sound" have made that city a leading recording center.

With 6 other states, Tennessee shares in federal reservoir developments on the Tennessee and Cumberland River systems. The Tennessee Valley Authority built Norris Dam on the Clinch River and operates a number of other dams in the state. Their reservoirs cover 653,413 acres.

Tennessee has a number of natural wonders—Reelfoot Lake, the reservoir basin of the Mississippi River formed by an earthquake (1811); Lookout Mountain, a rock-faced promontory carved by the currents of the Tennessee River and overlooking Moccasin Bend at Chattanooga; Fall Creek Falls, 256 ft. high; and the west half of Great Smoky Mountains National Park.

The American Museum of Atomic Energy in Oak Ridge has displays, models, lectures. The Hermitage, 13 mi. E of Nashville, home of Andrew Jackson, contains personal effects of the 7th president. The Ancestral Home of James K. Polk, in Columbia, has various articles used by Pres. Polk in the White House. The home, tailor shop, and grave of Pres. Andrew Johnson are a national monument at Greeneville. The Parthenon, in Centennial Park, Nashville, is a replica of the Parthenon of Athens. There are 26 state parks.

There are 67 institutions of higher education. Public school per pupil expenditures in 1976 were $1,18[illegible], 5th lowest in the U.S.

Spanish explorers first visited the area, 1541. English traders crossed the Great Smokies from the east while France's Marquette and Jolliet sailed down the Mississippi on the west, 1673. First permanent settlement was by Virginians on the Watauga River, 1769. During the Revolution, these colonists helped win the Battle of Kings Mountain, N.C., 1780, and joined other eastern campaigns. In the Civil War, hundreds of engagements were fought in the state. It seceded from the Union 1861, but of a total of 145,000 Tennessean soldiers, 30,000 fought for the Union.

Famous Tennesseans include Jackson, Johnson, Polk, Crockett, Houston, Farragut, Cordell Hull, Grace Moore, Pat Boone, Dinah Shore.

(See also Index for Chattanooga, Knoxville, Memphis, Nashville.)

Texas

Lone Star State

Area: 267,338 sq. mi.; rank, 2d. **Population** (U.S. est. 1976): 12,487,000; rank, 3d. **Capital:** Austin. **Motto:** Friendship (from Indian word, Tejas—Friends). **Flower:** Bluebonnet. **Tree:** Pecan. **Bird:** Mockingbird. **Song:** Texas, Our Texas. **Entered Union:** Dec. 29, 1845; rank, 28th.

Texas leads all other states in many categories, among them oil, cattle, sheep, and cotton. While these are basic to the Texas economy, manufacturing, as measured in terms of value added, makes a greater contribution than either mineral output or farm receipts. It is 2d only to Alaska in area.

Texas normally produces a third of the nation's total petroleum output. The state's 1976 petroleum production was valued at $10 billion, more than twice that of Louisiana, its nearest rival. Texas is also the top producer of asphalt, sulphur, graphite, natural gas, natural gas liquids, and magnesium chloride; Louisiana and Texas are the leading producers of natural gas. Texas ranks 2d among the states in output of salt, helium, and bromine, and 3d in cement.

The total value of the state's annual mineral production is by far the greatest of any state, $18 billion in 1976, a 13% increase over 1975.

Texas ranked 4th in 1976 in cash receipts for crops, $3 billion; 2d for livestock products, $3.5 billion; 3d in total farm receipts, $6.4 billion.

It led all states in 1977 in number of cattle, 15.8 million (giving the state more cattle than people), and in sheep, 2.5 million; it ranked 5th in turkeys and 9th in chickens. It grew the largest crops of pecans, sorghum, and cotton, the second largest of rice, the 3d largest of peanuts, and 5th of sweet potatoes. It also grows large amounts of vegetables and melons; its varied output includes oranges, grapefruit, peaches, winter wheat, and roses. Irrigation has reclaimed large arid areas.

The largest of its many livestock expositions are held annually in Fort Worth, San Antonio, Houston, and El Paso; its largest cattle auction in Amarillo.

Manufacturing industries have shown tremendous growth. Value added by manufacture was over $17.7 billion a year. About 20% of the total value is in chemicals, the largest manufacturing industry. Other important lines are petroleum refining, processing of foods, transportation equipment, machinery, primary metals. Per capita income was $6,243 in 1976, $198 below U.S. average.

Texas ranks high among the states in commercial fishing with the 1976 catch valued at $127 million.

About 22 million tourists spend over $3.2 billion dollars annually in Texas. There are 70 state parks, recreation areas, and historic sites; Big Bend and Guadalupe Mtns. National Parks, Padre Is. National Seashore, and Fort Davis National Historic Site. Named for Pres. Lyndon B. Johnson are a National Historic Site, a National Park, and a State Park, marking his birthplace, boyhood home, and ranch, all near Johnson City, and a library in Austin.

Texas lists 376 museums; included are renowned art and historical collections.

Texas has 146 institutions of higher education.

It is the only state that was an independent republic, recognized by the U.S., before annexation. Over it have flown the flags of Spain, France, Mexico, the Lone Star Flag of the Republic, the Confederate States, and the U.S.

Alonso de Pineda sailed along the Texas coast, 1519; Cabeza de Vaca and Coronado visited the interior, 1541. Spaniards made the first settlement at Ysleta, near El Paso, 1682. Americans moved into the vast, empty land early in the 19th century. Mexico, of which Texas was a part, won independence from Spain, 1821; Santa Anna became dictator, 1835; Texans rebelled, Santa Anna wiped out defenders of the Alamo, 1836; Sam Houston's Texans defeated Santa Anna at San Jacinto and independence was proclaimed the same year. In 1845, Texas was admitted to the Union; it seceded, 1861.

Famous Texans include Dwight D. Eisenhower, Stephen Austin, Sam Houston, James Bowie, J. Frank Dobie, Katharine Ann Porter, Lyndon Johnson, Chester Nimitz, Frank Robinson, Howard Hughes, Mary Martin.

(See also Index for Amarillo, Austin, Corpus Christi, Dallas, El Paso, Fort Worth, Houston, Lubbock, San Antonio.)

Utah

Beehive State

Area: 84,916 sq. mi.; rank, 11th. **Population** (U.S. est. 1976): 1,228,000; rank, 36th. **Capital:** Salt Lake City. **Motto:** Industry. **Flower:** Sego lily. **Bird:** California gull. **Tree:** Blue spruce. **Emblem:** Beehive. **Song:** Utah, We Love Thee. **Entered Union:** Jan. 4, 1896; rank, 45th.

Wrested from the wilderness by Mormon settlers in the mid-19th century, Utah is for the most part a mountainous area, broken by fertile irrigated valleys, several deserts and 2 large lakes, Great Salt Lake in the N and Lake Powell in the S.

Great Salt Lake is 4,200 ft. above sea level, but has no known outlet. Its salt density varies from 20% to 25%, 2d only to that of the Dead Sea; it covers more than 1,500 sq. mi.; it is crossed by a 13-mi., rock-fill railroad causeway.

Manufacturing has become the state's major industry, well ahead of mining, agriculture, and tourism. Value added by manufacture in 1975 was an est. $1.2 billion. Transportation equipment was the most important line, followed by food products, machinery, metal products, printing-publishing, and electrical equipment. Per capita income was $5,482 in 1976.

Utah is an important center for research on, and production of, missiles, rocket engines, solid fuel propellants, supersonic engines, aircraft navigational systems, and military computer components.

Utah is a rich storehouse of a wide variety of minerals. Among the states, it is a leading producer of copper, gold, silver, ashphalt, molybdenum, lead, vanadium, beryllium, sodium sulphate, and potassium salts.

Copper and petroleum have by far the greatest value among Utah's mineral products. In 1976, copper production was valued at $260 million, 2d only to Arizona's, and petroleum was worth $306 million; total mineral production value was $1 billion.

The nation's largest open-pit copper mine at Bingham Canyon, normally employs about 7,000 persons and produces about 20% of the newly-mined copper in the U.S. There are large smelters and refineries.

With Colorado and Wyoming, Utah shares what may be the world's richest oil shale deposits.

Utah ranked 7th among the states in number of sheep in 1977 with 580,000. It also raises large flocks of turkeys. It is a leader in apricots and cherries. Other crops include barley, sugar beets, alfalfa, winter wheat, potatoes. Farm receipts for 1976 included $261 million from livestock, $94 million from crops.

Over 66% of the land is owned by the U.S.

Tourists spend about $630 million a year in Utah.

Utah is a great recreational area, with 11,000 mi. of fishing streams and 147,000 acres of lakes and reservoirs, numerous winter sports areas, and camp grounds. Natural wonders may be seen at Zion, Canyonlands, Bryce Canyon, Arches, and Capitol Reef National Parks, and Dinosaur, Rainbow Bridge, Timpanogas Cave and Natural Bridges National Monuments. The Lake Powell Recreation Area and Flaming Gorge Dam are other attractions.

Works by Utah artists, and archeological, botanical, mineral, and fossil collections may be seen at the

Brigham Young University Collections in Provo. There are 14 institutions of higher learning.

In 1776, when the American colonies were declaring independence, 2 Spanish Franciscans visited the Utah area, the first white men to do so. American fur traders followed. Permanent settlement began with the arrival of the Mormons, 1847. They made the arid land bloom and created a prosperous economy; in 1849 they organized the State of Deseret and asked admission to the Union. This was not achieved until 1896, after a long period of controversy over the Mormon Church's doctrine of polygamy, which it discontinued in 1890.

Mormons comprise 72% of the population.

Famous Utahans include Brigham Young, George Romney, Ivy Baker Priest, Philo Farnsworth, Maude Adams, Laraine Day, Loretta Young.

(See also Index for Salt Lake City.)

Vermont

Green Mountain State

Area: 9,609 sq. mi.; rank, 43d. **Population** (U.S. est. 1976): 476,000; rank, 48th. **Capital:** Montpelier. **Motto:** Freedom and Unity. **Flower:** Red clover. **Tree:** Sugar maple. **Bird:** Hermit thrush. **Song:** Hail, Vermont. **Entered Union:** Mar. 4, 1791; rank, 14th.

Vermont, first state to join the Union after the original 13, was the home of the Green Mountain Boys of the American Revolution. They took their name from the Green Mountains which form the N-S backbone of the state. There are rich marble quarries in the western part of the state and large granite beds in the E. The Connecticut River runs along the E boundary, Lake Champlain forms much of the W line; among the many lakes is Memphremagog which lies partly in Canada to the N. Seven peaks rise over 4,000 ft. with Mt. Mansfield, 4,393 ft., the highest.

Vermont has long been known for its stonework-ing, forest, and dairy industries. Per capita income was $5,480 in 1976.

Principal manufactured goods are machine tools, computer components, stone and clay products, lumber, furniture, and paper. Value added by manufacture is over $688 million a year.

Large milk and butter production accounts for most of the total value of farm receipts which was $259 million for 1976. For its small size, Vermont has a large number of milk cows.

The state ranks high in output of marble, granite, limestone; it is a leader in asbestos and talc.

Tourism is important; the accent is on recreation. Visitors spend more than $320 million a year. Skiing has experienced a tremendous growth. There are more than 95 miles of ski lifts in the state.

Vermont has 74 state parks and forests covering 141,000 acres. The Long Trail is popular for hiking and camping. There is fishing for trout, salmon, bass, muskellunge; hunting for deer and game birds.

The Shelburne Museum, 7 mi. S of Burlington, preserves 35 early American buildings; stagecoach inn; covered bridge, side-wheeler, old trains, folk art, etc.; Webb gallery of paintings by Rembrandt, Goya, Corot, Manet, Cassatt.

The Bennington Museum displays early American glass, furniture, pottery, and what is said to be the oldest Stars and Stripes flag in existence.

Champlain explored the lake that bears his name and separates Vermont from New York, 1609. First American settlement was Fort Dummer, 1724, near Brattleboro. With the Revolution, Ethan Allen and Benedict Arnold captured Fort Ticonderoga and Seth Warner took Crown Point, both in N.Y., 1775. Britain's Burgoyne recaptured them, 1777, but John Stark defeated part of Burgoyne's forces near Bennington. In the War of 1812, Thomas MacDonough defeated a British fleet on Champlain off Plattsburgh, 1814. In the Civil War, Confederate soldiers, operating from Canada, robbed St. Albans banks.

Vermont has 23 institutions of higher learning.

Famous Vermonters include Chester Arthur, Calvin Coolidge, Stephen A. Douglas, Adm. George Dewey, Dorothy Canfield Fisher, John Dewey.

Virginia

Old Dominion

Area: 40,817 sq. mi.; rank, 36th. **Population** (U.S. est. 1976): 5,032,000; rank, 13th. **Capital:** Richmond. **Motto:** Sic Semper Tyrannis, Thus Ever to Tyrants. **Flower:** American dogwood. **Bird:** Cardinal. **Tree:** American dogwood. **Song:** Carry Me Back to Old Virginia. Tenth of the original 13 states to ratify the Constitution, June 25, 1788.

The Commonwealth of Virginia is famed for its colonial heritage, for the statesmen it produced, its historic homes and estates, and great battlefields on which the fate of the nation was decided in both the 18th and 19th centuries.

Virginia's coastal plain, the Tidewater, consists mostly of 4 peninsulas formed by Chesapeake Bay and the Potomac, Rappahannock, York, and James Rivers. The central Piedmont plateau rises westward to the Blue Ridge Mtns. Beyond the Blue Ridge and between them and the Alleghenies on the W border lies the Shenandoah Valley, a rich farming region.

Virginia's manufacturing industries have grown and diversified. They provide jobs for 366,500, over 5 times the number employed in agriculture. Total value added by manufacture is $7 billion, with payrolls totalling over $3 billion; value of shipments was estimated at $14.7 billion.

Largest lines were chemicals, textiles, food products, and clothing. Other important lines were lumber, furniture, paper, electrical machinery, transportation equipment, cigarettes, metal products, stone-clay-glass products, shipbuilding.

The federal government is a major employer with large military installations at Hampton Roads and many U.S. agencies near Washington, D.C.

Per capita income was $6,276 in 1976.

Hampton Roads, a large natural harbor at the mouth of the James, is the major port, a leader in bulk export tonnage.

Agriculture remains a vital factor in the economy. Virginia ranks among the leaders in the U.S. in its crops of tobacco, peanuts, apples, and sweet potatoes. Other important crops are corn, vegetables, barley, peaches. It has large numbers of turkeys; its Smithfield hams are famous. Farm receipts for 1976 totaled $1 billion, more than half from crops.

Coal is Virginia's leading mineral commodity and usually accounts for about 70% of the value of total mineral production, which was $1.5 billion in 1976. Also important are lime, zinc, stone.

The fish catch was worth $43 million in 1976.

With its wealth of historical attractions and recreational facilities, such as Shenandoah National Park in the Blue Ridge Mts. and Virginia Beach, on the Atlantic, the state drew 28 million out-of-state travelers who spent about $1.6 billion in 1976.

Virginia was the birthplace of 8 presidents. It has many historic shrines, including Washington's birthplace, Wakefield; his home and grave at Mount Vernon; Jefferson's Monticello, near Charlottesville, and the Univ. of Virginia he designed; Robert E. Lee's birthplace, Stratford Hall, and grave at Lexington.

Colonial Williamsburg is a restoration of the 18th century buildings and living conditions in what was the capital of Virginia when Washington, Jefferson, Patrick Henry, and George Mason were young men. There are over 800 buildings.

At Jamestown, first permanent English settlement, are foundations and ruins of early buildings, relics, statues and monuments.

At Yorktown, where the surrender of British Gen. Cornwallis to American and French forces virtually ended the American Revolution, may be seen colonial buildings, earthworks and cannons.

In Fredricksburg, the James Monroe Law Office and Museum is the original building in which Pres. Monroe practiced law in the 1780s, containing the desk at which he signed the Monroe Doctrine.

Appomattox Court House National Monument includes the rebuilt Wilmer McLean house in which Gen. Lee surrendered to Gen. Grant, Apr. 9, 1865.

Fort Monroe Casement Museum has relics of the imprisonment in the fort of Jefferson Davis and Chief Black Hawk, and of the battle between the Monitor and Merrimac. The Quartermaster Museum, Fort Lee, exhibits clothing, saddles, etc., of American soldiers from the Revolution on. The War Memorial Museum of Virginia, in Newport News, displays World War I and II weapons and equipment.

In Lexington are Washington and Lee University and Virginia Military Institute, both closely linked with leaders and action in the Civil War. Also in Lexington is the George C. Marshall Research Library and Museum with displays of the life of the famed World War II general and statesman.

At Staunton is the Woodrow Wilson birthplace, with memorabilia of his family. The Gen. Douglas MacArthur Memorial in Norfolk contains the general's sarcophagus, flags of 30 units he commanded, documents, and murals of events in his life.

English settlers founded Jamestown, 1607. Virginians took over much of the government from royal Gov. Dunmore in 1775, forcing him to flee. Virginians under George Rogers Clark freed the Ohio-Indiana-Illinois area of British forces. Benedict Arnold burned Richmond and Petersburg, for the British, 1781. That same year, Britain's Cornwallis was trapped at Yorktown and surrendered.

Though a slave state, Virginia was one of the last to secede, 1861. It was the scene of major Civil War battles, ending with Robert E. Lee's surrender at Appomattox.

There are 73 institutions of higher education.

Famous Virginians include Washington, Jefferson, Madison, Monroe, William Harrison, Tyler, Taylor, Wilson, Patrick Henry, John Marshall, Joseph E. Johnston, Poe, Cabell, Cather, Ellen Glasgow, Booker T. Washington, Lewis and Clark, Richard E. Byrd.

(See also Index for Norfolk, Richmond, Roanoke.)

Washington

Evergreen State

Area: 68,192 sq. mi.; rank, 20th. **Population** (U.S. est. 1976): 3,612,000; rank, 22d. **Capital:** Olympia. **Motto:** Al-Ki, By and By. **Flower:** Coast rhododendron. **Tree:** Western hemlock. **Bird:** Willow goldfinch. **Song:** Washington, My Home. **Entered Union:** Nov. 11, 1889; rank, 42d.

The state of Washington in the Pacific Northwest is a leader in many ways — in lumber, in fruit and other crops, and in aircraft production; its ports on Puget Sound are gateways to Alaska and the Far East; the great dams on the Columbia River provide power for production of aluminum and irrigation for the rich Columbia Basin.

The lofty Cascade Range splits the state, running N-S. To the W, the Puget Sound lowlands support dairy, poultry, and truck-farming. On the E slopes of the Cascades are great fruit orchards; further E, plateau country provides sheep and cattle lands and a rich wheat belt.

The Columbia River cuts a zig-zag course across Washington from the NE, then flows W along the Oregon border to the Pacific.

Puget Sound has many deep harbors beside which Seattle, Tacoma, Everett, and other great cities have grown. Foreign trade, mainly with Japan and Canada, has increased greatly in the last 20 years. The state ranks 7th in foreign trade volume.

Manufacturing industries employ 244,000 workers with payrolls of $2.6 billion and value added by manufacture over $5.7 billion a year. Transportation equipment, mostly aircraft, but including ships and trucks, accounts for $1.5 billion. Other important manufacturing lines are lumber, food processing, paper, metal products, chemicals, machinery. The Atomic Energy Commission plant at Hanford produces nuclear fuels and electricity. Per capita income was $6,772 in 1976 (U.S. average: $6,441).

Washington's large production of fruits, berries, and other crops places it first among the states in apples, blueberries, hops, and red raspberries; it is among the top producers of potatoes, winter wheat, pears, grapes, apricots, filberts, cranberries, cherries, asparagus, strawberries. It ranks 3d in winter wheat. Farm receipts for 1976 totaled $1.7 billion, three-fourths from crops, the rest from livestock.

The commercial fishing catch is valued at $80 million a year. Salmon accounts for half the total, followed by halibut, and bottomfish.

Mineral production in 1976 was valued at an est. $177 million. Sand and gravel, silver, cement, zinc, and lead were the most important products.

Large aluminum reduction plants, using refined ore from out-of-state and hydro-electric power, have expanded. Aluminum output is 25% of U.S. total.

A series of great dams on the Columbia, including the massive Grand Coulee in the NE, and Bonneville on the Oregon border, provide power and irrigation.

More than half the state is in forests; one-sixth of the nation's standing sawtimber is in Washington. Towering Douglas firs and Ponderosa pines, western hemlocks, and red cedars are among commercially important trees; income, $1.4 billion a year.

There are 48 institutions of higher education.

Spain's Bruno Hezeta sailed the coast, 1775. American Capt. Robert Gray sailed up the Columbia River, 1792. Canadian fur traders set up Spokane House, 1810; Americans under John Jacob Astor established a post at Fort Okanogan, 1811. Missionary Marcus Whitman settled near Walla Walla, 1836. Final agreement on the border of Washington and Canada was made with Britain, 1846, and gold was discovered in the state's northeast, 1855, bringing new settlers. The 2 World Wars brought great industrial expansion.

The state has 3 national parks, Mt. Rainier, North Cascades, and Olympic National Park. Its state parks and national forests of nearly 10 million acres have large hunting, fishing, and recreation areas.

The Washington State Historical Society, Tacoma, has exhibits of the fur trade, Indian, and Eskimo arts, and pioneer cabins, schoolhouse, and covered wagon.

Tourists, it has been estimated, spend about $1 billion annually in the state.

Famous Washingtonians include Bing Crosby, Patrice Munsel, Eric Johnston, Guthrie McClintic, Upton Close, Dr. Marcus Whitman.

(See also Index for Seattle, Yakima.)

West Virginia

Mountain State

Area: 24,181 sq. mi.; rank, 41st. **Population** (U.S. est. 1976): 1,821,000; rank, 34th. **Capital:** Charleston. **Motto:** Montani Semper Liberi, Mountaineers Always Free. **Flower:** Rhododendron maximum. **Bird:** Cardinal. **Tree:** Sugar maple. **Songs:** The West Virginia Hills, This Is My West Virginia, and West Virginia, My Home, Sweet Home. **Entered Union:** June 20, 1863; rank, 35th.

West Virginia's fortunes have long been based on those of the bituminous coal industry; the state produces 17% of the U.S. total, 2d only to Kentucky. Increased output of coal and natural gas, plus growth in the chemical, steel, glass, and tourist industries, have aided the economy.

The terrain is mountainous, with the Alleghenies running NE-SW in the eastern half of the state; the western half is a plateau sloping down to the Ohio River which forms most of the boundary on the W.

Early explorers included George Washington, 1753, and Daniel Boone. The area became part of Virginia and often objected to rule by the eastern part of the state. When Virginia seceded, 1861, the Wheeling Conventions repudiated the act and created a new state, Kanawha, subsequently changed to West Virginia. It was admitted to the Union as such, 1863. In the late 19th and early 20th centuries, the state was torn by industrial warfare. In recent years, it has had serious economic troubles.

Coal accounts for 94% of the total value of mineral production. In 1976 total production was valued at an est. $3.5 billion.

West Virginia produces and markets more natural gas than any other state east of the Mississippi. Also important are petroleum, salt, stone, cement, lime.

Production of a wide variety of chemicals, based on the state's resources of salt brine, gas, oil, and coal, and including synthetic fibers and plastics, dominates the manufacturing field, accounting for about 36% of the $7.3 billion in value added annually by manufacture. Large plants are in the Ohio and Kanawha valleys, where electric power is abundant. The state is also a major producer of steel, glass, pottery.

Farm receipts totaled $150 million for 1976; the hilly terrain is not conducive to large-scale agriculture. Poultry, dairy products, cattle, and sheep accounted for most receipts. Apples and peaches are profitable. About 79% of the state is forested.

Per capita income was $5,394 in 1976; national average was $6,441.

Tourism is being promoted and an est. 10 million visitors spend over $540 million annually. More than a million acres have been set aside for recreation in 34 state parks, 9 state forests, and Monongahela, George Washington, and part of Jefferson national forests.

Attractions include Harpers Ferry National Historical Park, mineral water resorts at White Sulphur and Berkeley Springs, trout fishing, turkey, deer, and bear hunting.

Part of the town of Harpers Ferry has been restored to its condition in 1859, when John Brown seized the U.S. Armory. Still standing is the fire-engine house in which Brown and a score of followers were besieged and captured by a force of U.S. Marines under Robert E. Lee, then a U.S. colonel.

The Science and Culture Center in Charleston displays local relics and artifacts from prehistoric cultures (as early as 8,000 B.C.), Indians, and pioneers.

The Huntington Galleries, Huntington, has collections of 19th and 20th century European and American paintings, furniture, and decorative arts. The Oglebay Mansion-Museum displays colonial furniture and 19th century glassware.

There are 28 institutions of higher education.

Famous West Virginians include Stonewall Jackson, Dwight Morrow, Michael Owens, John W. Davis, Newton D. Baker, Pearl Buck, Eleanor Steber.

(See also Index for Charleston, Huntington.)

Wisconsin

Badger State

Area: 56,154 sq. mi.; rank, 26th. **Population** (U.S. est. 1976): 4,609,000; rank, 16th. **Capital:** Madison. **Motto:** Forward. **Flower:** Butterfly violet. **Bird:** Robin. **Tree:** Sugar maple. **Animal:** Badger. **Fish:** Muskellunge. **Song:** On, Wisconsin! **Entered Union:** May 29, 1848; rank, 30th.

Known as America's Dairyland, Wisconsin produces more milk and cheese than any other state and agriculture is a vital part of the state's economy. However, manufacturing, including processing of foods, has become the state's largest employer and biggest income producer.

Reforestation has kept the paper and wood product industries important. There are 14 ports on Lakes Michigan and Superior. Per capita income was $6,293 in 1976.

The state has an abundance of recreation resources; water and winter sports, hunting and fishing are among its attractions. Vacationers, it is estimated, spend $1.4 billion a year.

Wisconsin's rolling pasturelands and large crops support the nation's largest herd of milk cows, about 1.8 million; 80% of its farms are dairy farms.

The state produces the most milk, cheese, hay, and alfalfa in the U.S. It ranks 3d in oats, 7th in corn. It is also a leading producer of butter, corn, cranberries, and maple syrup. In addition to cattle, it also has large numbers of hogs and turkeys.

Farm receipts for 1976 totaled $3 billion, 9th highest among the states, four-fifths of it from livestock.

About 40% of income produced in Wisconsin comes from manufacturing and, with over 500,000 factory employees, the state ranks among the top 12. Value added by manufacturing is over $10.8 billion a year.

Most important products, in terms of value added, are: machinery, especially engines, turbines, industrial, and construction; food products, including dairy, meat and beer; transportation equipment, especially motor vehicle parts and equipment, and mobile homes; iron and steel, metal products, paper.

Wisconsin is the top producer of motorcycles, beer, and canned vegetables.

Mineral production for 1976 was valued at $121 million. Zinc, lime, cement, and stone are important. Iron mining ceased in 1965 except for an open-pit taconite operation which by 1976 had increased production to over a half million tons of pellets. Large zinc and copper deposits have been discovered recently.

Most of Wisconsin's timber production goes into pulp and paper, but the state is also a leading producer of hardwood plywood and veneer.

Wisconsin borders Lake Superior to the north and Lake Michigan to the east. It has over 8,500 lakes, of which Winnebago is the largest. Water sports, ice-boating and fishing for trout, bass, and muskellunge are popular, as are skiing and hunting for deer, bear and wildfowl. Public parks and forests take up one-seventh of the land area; there are 49 state parks, 9 state forests, 2 national forests. Wisconsin produces 900,000 mink pelts per year, one-third the U.S. total.

Other attractions include small towns which preserve Swiss, Scandinavian, German, and other European cultures, visits to breweries and cheese factories, Indian festivals, and the Dells (scenic gorges) of the Wisconsin River.

The Circus World Museum in Baraboo has over 100 circus wagons and other displays, and presents circus shows daily, early May-early Sept.

There are 58 institutions of higher learning and the State University system has the 4th largest enrollment in the U.S.

Jean Nicolet was the first European to see the Wisconsin area, arriving in Green Bay, 1634. French missionaries and fur traders followed; the British took over, 1763. Thanks to the Revolution, the U.S. won the land but the British were not ousted until after the War of 1812. Lead miners came next and then farmers. Railroads were started in 1851, serving growing wheat harvests and iron mines. In the 20th Century, Wisconsin became an industrial state and also took the lead in dairy products.

Famous Wisconsinites include Robert and Philip LaFollette, Joseph R. McCarthy, Marc Mitscher, Thorstein Veblen, Thornton Wilder, Edna Ferber, Alfred Lunt, Frank Lloyd Wright, Harry Houdini.

(See also Index for Madison, Milwaukee.)

Wyoming

Equality State

Area: 97,914 sq. mi.; rank, 9th. **Population** (U.S. est. 1976): 390,000; rank, 49th. **Capital:** Cheyenne. **Motto:** Equal Rights. **Flower:** Indian paintbrush. **Bird:** Western meadowlark. **Tree:** Plains cottonwood. **Song:** Wyoming State Song. **Entered Union:** July 10, 1890; rank, 44th.

Wyoming's towering mountains and rolling plains provide spectacular scenery, grazing ranges for sheep and cattle, and a wealth of mineral resources. Ranges of the Rockies cover the western two-thirds of the state; the eastern third is Great Plains country.

The most important industry is mining, particularly of oil and natural gas. Agriculture, especially livestock, runs 2d. Tourism and manufacturing are growing. Per capita income was $6,723 in 1976 (U.S. average: $6,441).

Wyoming has large reserves of coal, oil, gas, oil shale, iron ore, and gypsum.

Production of petroleum in 1976 was valued at $984 million. Total mineral production value for the year was est. at $1.8 billion. The state ranked first in the U.S. in sodium carbonate and bicarbonate production, 2d in uranium. Also important are coal, natural gas, clays, and iron ore.

Wyoming is 2d among the states in wool production, and in 1977 its sheep numbered 1.2 million, exceeded only by Texas; it also had 1.6 million cattle. Principal crops include wheat, oats, sugar beets, corn, potatoes, barley, and alfalfa. Livestock receipts for 1976 totaled $285 million; crops, $133 million.

Much of Wyoming's manufacturing is based on its mining and agricultural products. Leading lines include petroleum and coal products, including coke; processed foods, timber and wood, construction materials, food service equipment, pocket transits, iron and steel, electronic components. Value added by manufacture is about $171 million annually.

Wyoming is a source of 3 important river systems: the Missouri, Colorado, and Columbia. Both power and irrigation are provided by a growing number of dams and reservoirs. Tourism produces an est. annual $311 million.

The French explorers, Francois and Louis Verendrye, were the first European visitors, 1743. John Colter, American, was first to traverse Yellowstone Park, 1807-08. Trappers and fur traders followed in the 1820s. Forts Laramie and Bridger became important stops on the pioneer trail to the West Coast. Indian wars followed massacres of army detachments in 1854 and 1866. Population grew after the Union Pacific crossed the state, 1869. Women won the vote, for the first time in the U.S., from the Territorial Legislature, 1869.

Yellowstone National Park, 3,472 sq. mi. carved from the NW corner of Wyoming and the adjoining edges of Montana and Idaho, is the oldest of U.S. national parks, established 1872. It has some 10,000 geysers, plus hot springs, mud volcanoes, fossil forests, a volcanic glass (obsidian) mountain, the 1,000-ft.-deep canyon and 308-ft.-high waterfall of the Yellowstone River, and a wide variety of animals living free in their natural habitat.

Grand Teton National Park, with mountains 13,000 ft. high, comprises 299,326 acres; the National Elk Refuge covers 25,000 acres. Devils Tower, a cluster of rock columns 865 ft. high, became the first National Monument in the U.S. in 1906. Fort Laramie, partly preserved, partly restored, is a National Historic Site. The annual Cheyenne Frontier Days Celebration, last full week in July, is the state's largest rodeo. Hunting, fishing, and skiing are other attractions.

The Buffalo Bill Historical Center in Cody has a museum with personal effects of William F. Cody (Buffalo Bill), as well as the Whitney Gallery of Modern Art with Indian art and paintings by Frederic Remington, Charles M. Russell, George Catlin, etc.

The Bradford Brinton Memorial Ranch, near Big Horn, has collections of western painting and sculpture, antiques, Indian arts, hunting trophies.

There are 8 institutions of higher education.

Famous Wyomingites include Jim Bridger, Nellie Tayloe Ross, Buffalo Bill Cody.

District of Columbia

Area: 67 sq. mi. **Population** (U.S. est. 1976): 702,000; **Motto:** Justitia omnibus, Justice for all. **Flower:** American beauty rose. **Tree:** Scarlet oak. **Bird:** Wood thrush. The city of Washington is coextensive with the District of Columbia.

The District of Columbia is the seat of the federal government of the United States. It lies on the west central edge of Maryland on the Potomac River, opposite Virginia. Its area was originally 100 sq. mi. taken from the sovereignty of Maryland and Virginia. Virginia's portion south of the Potomac was given back to that state in 1846.

The 23d Amendment, ratified in 1961, granted residents of the District the right to vote for president and vice president for the first time and gave them 3 members in the Electoral College. Residents cast the first such votes in Nov. 1964.

Congress, which has legislative authority over the District under the Constitution, experimented with various forms of municipal government until 1878 when it established a government of 3 commissioners appointed by the president. The Reorganization Plan of 1967 substituted a single commissioner (also called mayor) and assistant, and a 9-member City Council; funds were still appropriated by Congress; residents had no vote in local government (except to elect school board members).

In Sept. 1970, Congress approved legislation giving the District one delegate to the House of Representatives. The delegate could vote in committee but not on the House floor. The first was elected 1971.

In May 1974 voters approved a charter giving them the right to elect their own mayor and a 13-member city council in Nov. 1974. The first mayor and council took office Jan. 2, 1975. The district won the right to levy its own taxes but Congress retained power to kill council actions.

Proposals for a "federal town" for the deliberations of the Continental Congress were made in 1783, 4 years before the adoption of the Constitution that gave the Confederation a national government. Rivalry between northern and southern delegates over the site appeared in the First Congress, meeting in New York in 1789. John Adams, presiding officer of the Senate, cast the deciding vote of that body for Germantown, Pa. In 1790 Congress compromised by making Philadelphia the temporary capital for 10 years. The Virginia members of the House wanted a capital on the eastern bank of the Potomac; they were defeated by the Northerners, while the Southerners defeated the Northern attempt to have the nation assume the war debts of the 13 original states, the Assumption Bill fathered by Alexander Hamilton. Hamilton and Jefferson arranged a compromise: the Virginia men voted for the Assumption Bill, and the Northerners conceded the capital to the Potomac. President Washington chose the site in Oct. 1790 and persuaded landowners to sell their holdings to the government at £25, then about $66, an acre. The capital was named Washington.

Washington appointed Pierre Charles L'Enfant, a French engineer who had come over with Lafayette, to plan the capital on an area not over 10 mi. square. The L'Enfant plan was considered grandiose, for streets 100 to 110 feet wide and one avenue 400 feet wide and a mile long on the Potomac pastures seemed foolhardy. But Washington endorsed his plans. When L'Enfant ordered a wealthy landowner to remove his new manor house because it obstructed a vista, and demolished it when the owner refused, Washington stepped in and dismissed L'Enfant. The official map was completed by Andrew Ellicott and Benjamin Banneker.

On Sept. 18, 1793, Pres. Washington laid the cornerstone of the north wing of the Capitol. The occasion was expected to drum up sales of city lots, but there were few purchasers. Washington bought several lots. In the next few years Robert Morris and others invested. By 1799 the Senate wing of the Capitol had been roofed, the walls of the president's house were up and the Treasury building was ordered. On June 3, 1800, Pres. John Adams moved to Washington and on June 10, Philadelphia ceased to be the temporary capital. The City of Washington was incorporated in 1802; the District of Columbia was created as a municipal corporation in 1871, embracing Washington, Georgetown, and Washington County.

(See also Index for Washington, D. C.)

Outlying U. S. Areas

Commonwealth of Puerto Rico

Estado Libre Asociado de Puerto Rico

Area: 3,435 sq. mi. **Population** (1976 est.): 3,210,000. **Capital:** San Juan. **Song:** La Borinquena. **Tree:** Ceiba. **Bird:** Reinita. **Flower:** Maga.

Puerto Rico is a hilly, tropical island lying between the Atlantic to the N and the Caribbean to the S; it is the easternmost of the West Indies group called the Greater Antilles, of which Cuba, Hispaniola and Jamaica are the larger units. It lies about 1,600 mi. SE of New York, 500 mi. N of Venezuela. It is roughly rectangular, 105 mi. long by 35 wide. Numerous small islands include Vieques, Culebra, and Mona.

The soil of the coast plain is fertile and there are many lush valleys, but there are dry areas in the S which need irrigation and an extensive system has been constructed by the government. The climate is mild, with a mean temperature of 76°; the mean maximum is 82°, and the mean minimum 73°. Highest point is Cerro de Punta, 4,389 ft.

Pres. Truman, on Aug. 5, 1947, signed an act giving Puerto Rico the right to choose its chief executive by popular vote. An act of 1950, affirmed by special election, June 4, 1951, permitted Puerto Rico to draft its own constitution. One similar to that of the U. S. was approved in a convention Feb. 4, 1952, and ratified by a popular vote March 3, 1952. Pres. Truman signed, July 3, 1952, a Congressional resolution approving the new constitution, elevating Puerto Rico to the status of a free commonwealth associated with the U.S., effective July 25, 1952.

In a July 23, 1967, referendum, Puerto Ricans strongly favored continuation of commonwealth status over statehood or independence. But on Nov. 2, 1976, Carlos Romero Barcelo, who favored statehood, was elected governor.

The Legislative Assembly consists of a Senate and House of Representatives, elected by direct vote every 4 years. Eight senatorial districts elect 2 senators each; 40 representative districts one member each; also 11 senators and 11 representatives at large. Puerto Rico's directly elected resident commissioner in the U.S. Congress has only committee voting privileges. Puerto Ricans were granted American citizenship under the Organic Act of 1917. They do not vote for president unless they move to the U.S., where they come under local laws.

Executive power is vested in a governor elected by direct vote. There are 12 executive departments each headed by a secretary. The judiciary consists of a Supreme Court and lower courts.

The Commonwealth's "Operation Bootstrap" program for economic development has radically raised the standard of living per capita income for 1976 was $1,989, up $1,078 from 1965.

Puerto Rico derives its largest income from manufacturing, $2 billion in 1976. Products include textiles and apparel, electrical and electronic equipment, plastics, chemicals, petrochemicals, petroleum products, processed foods, metal, leather.

Gross capital investment in 1976 reached $1.69 billion; gross product was $7.49 billion.

Mineral production is mainly of construction materials, with cement accounting for a large part of the value; total value for 1976 was $120 million.

Agriculture, a large source of income, rose in 1976 to $333 million. Income from dairy and livestock products has surpassed that from sugar. Also important are tobacco, coffee, pineapples, coconuts, fruits, garden truck, rum, molasses.

Off island trade is chiefly with the United States.

	Imports	*Exports*
1975	$4,950,700,000	$2,138,400,000
1976	$5,432,000,000	$3,346,000,000

The flow of migrants to mainland U.S. after 1945 was reversed in 1963. In 1976 38,758 more persons moved to Puerto Rico than departed. These changes are caused mainly by employment conditions, mainland and Puerto Rican. Unemployment on the island is usually over 12%; it reached 20% in 1976.

San Juan, with its international airport and resort hotels, is the center of the tourism industry. Visitors totaled 1,339,000 in 1975, down from 1,441,002 in 1974, but their spending rose to $375 million, up from $360.3 million.

Spanish is the official language but most persons also speak English. Public school education is free and compulsory at the elementary school level; English is taught as a secondary language and is compulsory in all 8 grades. There are 23 institutions of higher education. Chief religion is Roman Catholicism.

Puerto Rico (or Borinquen, after the original Arawak Indian name Boriquen) was discovered by Columbus, Nov. 19, 1493. Ponce de Leon conquered it for Spain, 1509, and established the first settlement at Caparra, across the bay from San Juan.

Sugarcane was introduced, 1515, and slaves were imported 3 years later. Gold mining petered out, 1570. Spaniards fought off a series of British and Dutch attacks; slavery was abolished, 1873. The U.S. took the island during the Spanish-American War, 1898, without any major battle.

Famous Puerto Ricans include Luis Munoz Marin, Dona Felisa Rincon de Gantier, Pablo Casals, Roberto Clemente, Orlando Cepeda, Jose Ferrer, Rita Moreno, Jose Feliciano, Adm. Horatio Rivero.

(See also Index for San Juan.)

Canal Zone and Panama Canal

For Panama Canal cargo traffic see Index.

The Canal Zone has been, in effect, a U. S. Government reservation. It is a strip of land extending 5 mi. on each side of the axis of the Canal, under jurisdiction of the U.S. by treaty with the Republic of Panama in 1903.

Efforts to change its status neared fruition, 1977.

The canal connects the Caribbean with the Bay of Panama on the Pacific. Because of the geographic loop made by the Isthmus of Panama, the Caribbean end of the canal, which could be called the eastern end, is actually further west than the Pacific end.

The zone has an area of 647 sq. mi. of which 372 are land. Population (1976 est.) was 41,800. About 9,100 U.S. army, air force, and navy personnel are normally stationed in the zone. Government headquarters is Balboa Heights.

The Canal Zone government and the Panama Canal Co. are the 2 operating agencies, both headed by an individual who acts as governor of the Canal Zone and president of the company. The governor is appointed by the president of the U.S. As governor he reports directly to the secretary of the army; as president of the company he reports to its board of directors, appointed by the secretary of the army. The Canal Zone government maintains civil government. The company operates the canal, the Panama Railroad, terminals, employee services, and utilities.

A French company under Ferdinand de Lesseps failed to complete a canal, 1880-89, and a second French company failed in 1899. The U. S. bought their rights for $40 million, paid private owners $4 million, and offered Colombia compensation for a canal zone, but Colombia failed to ratify the treaty, Oct. 1903. Panama declared itself independent of Colombia Nov. 3, 1903, and was recognized by Pres. Theodore Roosevelt Nov. 6. American naval forces discouraged action by Colombia. On Nov. 18 Panama granted the canal strip to the U.S. by treaty, ratified Feb. 26, 1904, compensation $10 million, with annual payments of $250,000 after 9 years; and a guarantee of Panama's independence.

Under terms of the 1903 treaty, Panama granted the U.S. perpetual sovereignty over the Canal Zone.

The canal was opened to traffic Aug. 15, 1914. In

1922, Colombia accepted $25 million from the U. S. plus special land transportation privileges, and agreed to recognize Panama. The U. S. increased its annual payment to Panama to $430,000 and withdrew its guarantee of independence.

A further treaty regulating relations between the U. S. and Panama was signed Jan. 25, 1955, increasing the annuity paid Panama to $1.9 million (actually increasing it to $2.3 million because of devaluation of the U.S. dollar.) In addition, the U. S. gave Panama $28 million worth of real estate and buildings. U. S. citizen and non-citizen employees were guaranteed equality of pay and opportunity. In addition, the U. S. agreed to build a high level bridge over the Pacific entrance to the canal. The bridge was opened Oct. 12, 1962, as a link in the Inter-American Highway.

Negotiations for a new treaty began after Panamanian riots protesting the 1903 and 1955 treaties caused the death of 20 Panamanians and 4 U.S. soldiers, Jan. 9, 1964. Preliminary agreement was reached in 1967, but in 1970, after a change of government, Panama rejected the proposal.

Negotiations resumed in Feb. 1977 and in Aug. agreement was reached on a proposed treaty under which the U.S. would retain primary responsibility for defense and administration of the canal until the year 2000, but with Panama assuming an increasing role in both until the final turnover date, Dec. 31, 1999. The Panama Canal Co. would be replaced at an early date with a new U.S. agency with a board of 9, including 5 Americans and 4 Panamanians. Until 1990 the chief administrator would be American and his deputy Panamanian; in 1990 the positions would be reversed.

On the day the treaty, if ratified by both nations, took effect, the U.S. would turn over some 65% of the zone to Panamanian jurisdiction. Times for withdrawal of U.S. troops and disposal of bases would be up to the U.S. The U.S. would pay Panama $50 to $70 million a year from canal revenues and $50 million a year in military assistance for 10 years, plus various loans.

Virgin Islands

Capital: Charlotte Amalie, on St. Thomas Is. **Area:** 133 sq. mi. **Population:** (1975 est.) 100,000. **Flower:** Yellow cedar.

The Virgin Islands of the United States, an unincorporated territory under the jurisdiction of the Interior Department, lie to the E of Puerto Rico at the western end of the Lesser Antilles, 1,629 mi. SE of New York. There are about 100 islands in the Virgins, of which more than 50 islands and islets in the western area belong to the U.S.; the remainder are the British Virgin Islands.

The 3 largest and most populous of the U.S. islands are St. Croix, St. Thomas, and St. John. Formerly the Danish West Indies, the islands were purchased by the U.S. from Denmark for $25 million (effective Mar. 31, 1917) for defense purposes. The islands were discovered by Columbus in 1493. About 80% of the population is of Negro descent.

Mean winter temperature is 78°; summer, 82° Virgin Islands National Park occupies about three-fourths of St. John, smallest of the 3 principal islands.

The inhabitants have been citizens of the U.S. since 1927. Legislation originates in a unicameral house of 15 senators, elected for 2 years.

The governor, formerly appointed by the president of the U.S., was popularly elected for the first time in Nov. 1970 and took office Jan. 4, 1971, for a 4-year term. In 1972 a U.S. law gave the Virgin Islands one delegate to the U.S. House of Representatives; the delegate may vote in committee but not in the House.

Tourism is the largest industry, but it was hurt by a series of murders in 1973 and early 1974. Principal exports are watch movements, jewelry, rum, wool textile products, thermometers, bay rum.

Minor Caribbean Islands

Quita Suena Bank, Roncador Cay, and Serrana Bank lie in the Caribbean between Nicaragua and Jamaica. They are uninhabited. They were to be turned over to Colombia under a 1972 agreement, but this still awaited U.S. Senate action.

Navassa lies between Jamaica and Haiti, covers about 2 sq. mi., is reserved by the U.S. for a lighthouse and is uninhabited.

American Samoa

Capital: Fagotogo, Island of Tutuila. **Area:** 76 sq. mi. **Population:** (1975 est.) 31,000. **Motto:** Samoa Muamua Le Atua - In Samoa, God Is First. **Song:** Amerika Samoa. **Flower:** Paogo (Ula-fala). **Plant:** Ava.

Blessed with spectacular scenery and delightful South Seas climate, American Samoa is the most southerly of all lands under U. S. ownership. It is an unincorporated territory consisting of 6 small islands of the Samoan group: **Tutuila, Aunuu,** the **Manua Islands (Tau, Olosega and Ofu),** and **Rose.** Also administered as part of American Samoa is **Swain's Is.,** 210 mi. to the NW, acquired by the U.S. in 1925. The islands are 2,600 mi. SW of Honolulu.

American Samoa became U. S. territory by a treaty with the United Kingdom and Germany in 1899. The islands were ceded by local chiefs in 1900 and 1904. Pago Pago had been a U.S. navy coaling station under an 1872 commercial treaty.

Samoa (Western), comprising the larger islands of the Samoan group, was a New Zealand mandate and UN Trusteeship until it became an independent nation Jan. 1, 1962. (*See Index.*)

Tutuila has an area of 52 sq. mi. Tau has an area of 17 sq. mi., and the islets of Ofu and Olosega, 5 sq. mi. with a population of a few thousand. Swain's Island has nearly 2 sq. mi. and a population of about 100.

About 70% of the land is forest. Chief products and exports are fish products, copra, and handicrafts. Taro, bread-fruit, yams, coconuts, pineapples, oranges, and bananas are also produced.

Formerly under jurisdiction of the Navy, since July 1, 1951, it has been under the Interior Department, which appoints a governor and a lieutenant governor. It has a bicameral legislature and an elected delegate to appear before U.S. agencies in Washington.

The American Samoans are of Polynesian origin. They are nationals of the U.S.; there are some 15,000 in Hawaii and 75,000 on the U.S. West Coast.

Wake, Midway, Other Islands

Wake Island, and its sister islands, **Wilkes** and **Peale,** lie in the Pacific Ocean on the direct route from Hawaii to Hong Kong, about 2,000 mi. W of Hawaii and 1,290 mi. E of Guam. The group is 4.5 mi. long, 1.5 mi. wide, and totals less than 3 sq. mi. Population (1970 census) was 1,647.

The U.S. flag was hoisted over Wake Island, July 4, 1898. Formal possession was taken Jan. 17, 1899; Wake has been administered by the U.S. Air Force since 1972.

The **Midway Islands,** acquired in 1867, consist of 2, **Sand** and **Eastern,** in the North Pacific 1,150 mi. NW of Hawaii, with area of about 2 sq. mi., administered by the Navy Dept. Population (1975 est.) was 2,256.

Johnston Atoll, SW of Hawaii, area 1 sq. mi., pop. 1,007 (1970 census), is under Air Force control, and **Kingman Reef,** S of Hawaii, is under Navy control.

Howland, Jarvis, and **Baker Islands** south of the Hawaiian group, uninhabited since World War II, are under the Interior Dept.

Palmyra is an atoll SW of Hawaii, 4 sq. mi. Privately owned, it is under the Interior Dept.

Guam

The World Almanac is sponsored on Guam by the Pacific Daily News, 90 O'Hara St., Agana, GU 96910; phone 777-9711; successor in 1970 to Guam Daily News; circulation throughout Micronesia, 20,350; a

Gannett newspaper; president and publisher Robert E. Udick, editor Joe Murphy, managing editor George Blake.

Capital: Agana. **Area:** 209 sq. mi. **Population:** (1974 est.) 100,000.

Guam, the largest of the Mariana Islands, is an unincorporated U.S. territory. It was ceded to the U.S. by Spain in the treaty of Paris, Dec. 10, 1898. It is 30 mi. long and 4 to 8.5 mi. wide. Distance from Manila, 1,499 mi.; from San Francisco, 5,053 mi. Mean annual temp. is 81°, average annual rainfall, July to Sept., 70 in. The island is volcanic and mountains rise 700 to 1,329 ft. Highest peak is Mt. Lamlam.

Magellan arrived in the Marianas Mar. 6, 1521, and called them the Ladrones (thieves). They were colonized in 1668 by Spanish missionaries who renamed them the Mariana Islands in honor of Maria Anna, queen of Spain.

When Spain ceded Guam to the U. S., it sold the other Marianas to Germany. Japan obtained a League of Nations mandate over the German islands in 1919; in Dec. 1941 it seized Guam; the island was retaken by the U.S. in July 1944. Guam has U.S. Navy and Air Force bases.

Guam is under the jurisdiction of the Department of the Interior. It is administered under the Organic Act of 1950, which provides for a governor, a 21-member unicameral legislature, elected biennially by the residents, who are American citizens but do not vote for president.

Beginning in Nov. 1970, Guamanians elected their own governor, previously appointed by the U.S. president. He took office in Jan. 1971. In 1972 a U.S. law gave Guam one delegate to the U.S. House of Representatives; the delegate may vote in committee but not on the House floor.

School attendance is compulsory. There is a University of Guam. English is the official language. Chief religion is Roman Catholicism.

The Guamanians are of primarily Chamorro (Micronesian) stock, with some of mixed Spanish or Filipino descent.

Copra, fish, and handicraft products are exported. Tourism has become a major aspect of Guam's economy. Over 125,000 tourists, most from Japan, visit annually.

Islands Under Trusteeship

The U. S. Trust Territory of the Pacific Islands, also called Micronesia, includes 3 major archipelagoes: the **Caroline Islands, Marshall Islands,** and **Mariana Islands** (except **Guam:** see above). There are 2,141 islands, 98 of them inhabited; land area total 687 sq. mi. but the islands are scattered over 3 million sq. mi. of Micronesia in the western Pacific N of the Equator and E of the Philippines. Pop. est. (1974) at 115,000.

The Marianas

In process of becoming a U.S. commonwealth in 1977 were the Northern Mariana Islands, which since 1947 had been part of the Trust Territory of the Pacific Islands, assigned to U.S. administration by the United Nations. The Northern Marianas comprise all the Marianas except Guam, stretching N-S in a 500-mi. arc of tropical islands east of the Philippines and southeast of Japan.

Residents of the islands on June 17, 1975, voted 78% in favor of becoming a commonwealth of the U.S. rather than continuing with the Carolines and Marshalls in the U.S.-UN Trusteeship. On March 24, 1976, U.S. Pres. Ford signed a Congressionally-approved commonwealth covenant giving the Marianas control of domestic affairs and giving the U.S. control of foreign relations and defense, and the right to maintain military bases on the islands.

Establishment of the commonwealth awaited adoption of a constitution and acceptance of the change in status by the UN Security Council.

Ferdinand Magellan was the first European to visit the Marianas, 1521. Spain, Germany, and Japan held the islands in turn until World War II when the U.S. seized them in bitter battles on 2 of the main islands, Saipan and Tinian.

Population in 1976 was 14,335, mostly on Saipan. English is the official language; Roman Catholicism is the major religion. The people are descendants of the early Chamorros, Spanish, Japanese, Filipinos, and Mexicans. Land area is 181.9 sq. mi.

Tourism is an important industry; visitors are mostly from Japan. Crops include sugar, cotton, coconuts, maize, rice, tobacco, coffee, and breadfruit.

The Carolines and Marshalls

In 1885, many of the Carolines, Marshalls, and Marianas were claimed by Germany. Others, held by Spain, were sold to Germany at the time of the Spanish-American War, 1898. After the outbreak of World War I, Japan took over the 3 archipelagoes and, following that war, League of Nations mandates over them were awarded to Japan.

After World War II, the United Nations assigned them (1947) as a Trust Territory to be administered by the U.S. They were placed under administration of the U.S. Interior Dept. in 1951.

There is a high commissioner, appointed by the U.S. president. Saipan is the headquarters of the administration. The Congress of Micronesia, an elected legislature with limited powers, held its first meeting in 1965. It has a Senate of 12 members and a House of Representatives of 21.

In 1969, a commission of the Congress of Micronesia recommended that Micronesia be given internal self-government in free association with the U.S.

A U.S. offer of commonwealth status was rejected by Micronesian leaders in 1970.

In 1974 talks, tentative agreement was reached on parts of a U. S. plan for self-government for the Marshalls and Carolines in free association with the U. S. (which would control foreign affairs and defense).

Among the noted islands are the former Japanese strongholds of **Palau, Peleliu, Truk,** and **Yap** in the Carolines; **Bikini** and **Eniwetok,** where U.S. nuclear tests were staged, and **Kwajalein,** another World War II battle scene, all in the Marshalls.

Many of the islands are volcanic with luxuriant vegetation; others are of coral formation. Only a few are self-sustaining. Principal exports are copra, trochus shells, fish products, handicrafts, and vegetables.

Disputed Pacific Islands

In the central Pacific, S and SW of Hawaii, lie 25 islands claimed by the U.S.; 18 of them are also claimed by the United Kingdom, and 7 by New Zealand. All are S of the Equator except Christmas Is.

Those claimed by the UK are:

The **Line Islands,** S of Hawaii, including Christmas, Flint, Malden, Starbuck, Vostok, and Caroline; only Christmas is inhabited. All administered by the UK.

Also, the **Phoenix Islands,** SW of Hawaii, including Canton and Enderbury; and Birnie, Gardner, Hull, McKean, Sydney, and Phoenix. All are inhabited and administered by the UK except for Canton and Enderbury which are under joint U.S. and UK admin-

Also, the **Tuvalu (Ellice) Islands,** further to the SW, including Funafuti, Nukufetau, Nukulailai, and Nurakita; all inhabited; all administered by the UK.

Those claimed by New Zealand are:

The **Tokelau (Union) Islands,** S of the Phoenix group, including Nukunono, Atafu, and Fakaofu. All are inhabited and administered by New Zealand.

Also, the **Northern Cook Islands,** E of the Tokelaus, including Danger, Manahiki, Rakahanga, and Penrhyn (Tongareva). All are inhabited and administered by New Zealand.

MEMORABLE DATES

B.C. or B.C.E.
Before Christ or Before Common Era

3000

Indus Valley civilization sites at Mohenjo-Daro and Harappa in West Pakistan. Civilization had complex form of government, elaborate irrigation and drainage system, writing, well planned streets, houses of several stories. Ended about **1500 B. C.**

Pyramids begun by kings of Egypt at Sakkara. Cheops built great pyramid at Giza. Sphinx built about **2900 B.C.**

c. 1792-1750

Hammurabi ruled Semitic kingdom of Babylon; wrote extensive code of laws. Ruled Canaan in days of Abraham.

c. 1450 or c. 1275

Moses led the Israelites out of Egypt.

1360

Ikhnaton introduced monotheistic worship of Aton, or sun, in Egypt. A successor, Tutankhamen, revived polytheistic orthodoxy **1350 B. C.** Tutankhamen buried at Thebes **1344 B.C.**; tomb opened by Howard Carter and Lord Carnarvon **1923-24 A. D.**

1184

Troy (Ilium) fell to Greeks after 10-year siege, according to Homer's Iliad. Excavations show numerous battles were waged on site, NW corner of Asia Minor, 3 mi. from Hellespont (Dardanelles).

In **1871 A. D.** Heinrich Schliemann, German archeologist, excavated site of Troy on hill of Hissarlik and found layered remains of 7 cities. Dorpfeld found 2 more. Schliemann identified 2d city with Homer's Troy, but objects found in 6th city correspond better with Greek remains of **1200 to 1100 B. C.** found at Agamemnon's Mycenae in Greece.

1000

On death of King Saul c. 1000 B. C. David became king of Israel, but for 7 1/2 years ruled only the southern kingdom of Judah. Thereafter he ruled all Israel, made Jerusalem capital. Solomon, son of David and Bathsheba, ruled **c. 973-933 B. C.**

753

Romulus founded Rome, according to legend.

612

Babylonians destroyed Nineveh, Assyrian capital. Nebuchadnezzar's Babylonians defeated Egyptians at Carchemish **605 B.C.** Built famed hanging gardens. Destroyed Solomon's temple **589 B. C.**

563

Gautama (Sakyamuni) Buddha, "the Enlightened," born near Himalayas; died **483 B. C.**, aged 80. Taught that pain in life is caused by desire; if desire is overcome, pain ends.

551

Confucius (Latinized form of K'ung-fu-tze) Chinese social philosopher, born; died **478 B. C.**

490

King Darius' Persian army landed at Marathon to march on Athens. Athenian infantry (10,000) routed 30,000 Persians.

484-480

Persian King Xerxes assembled a large army at Sardis to invade Greece. His Phoenicians and Egyptians built 2 ship bridges across Hellespont from Abydos (Nagara) to Sestos, 2,000 yds. long. One bridge of planks and dirt rested on 360 ships; the other on 314. Herodotus reported army crossing took 7 days and 7 nights.

At Thermopylae Pass, 480 B.C., Leonidas and 300 Spartans, supported by 700 Thespians and 400 Thebans, held off Persians until overcome. Persians took Athens and Attica. Athenians under Themistocles destroyed Persian fleet at Salamis under eyes of Xerxes, won land battle. Rallying 70,000 from Greek states, they routed Persians at Plataea **479 B. C.**

438

Parthenon completed at Athens; Ictinus and Callicrates, designers; Phidias, chief sculptor.

431

Peloponnesian Wars began between Athens and Sparta. Wars ended **404 B.C.** with Sparta victorious.

399

Socrates, Greek philosopher, condemned by Athenian state, drank poison hemlock. Plato, his student, recorded 35 dialogues, famed philosophical work. Xenophon, another student, recorded memorabilia.

356

Alexander "The Great" of Macedon born. Ruthless and energetic military leader, defeated Persians at Granicus, Issus, Arbela; conquered Asia Minor and Egypt, burned Persian capital, Persepolis, carried war to the Punjab in India. Founded Alexandria in Egypt. Died of fever at Babylon **323 B. C.**

300

Invention of Mayan calendar in Yucatan (approximate date) giving solar year 365.24 days and lunar month 29.52 days. Now considered more exact than older calendars of Babylon, Assyria, Egypt, Greece.

264

Rome began first Punic War against Carthage, rich commercial seaport on Bay of Tunis. In **241 B. C.** Carthage ceded Sicily and Lipari Islands; in **239 B. C.** Rome annexed Sardinia and Corsica.

218-146

Hannibal, Carthaginian general, in a campaign against Rome during 2d Punic War, crossed from Spain to Italy via the Alps with 20,000 infantry, 6,000 cavalry, and about 40 elephants. Defeated Romans at Lake Trasimene **217 B. C.** and Cannae **216 B. C.** Victories nullified by Fabius, "the delayer," hence "Fabian tactics." War closed with defeat of Carthage in Africa by Publius Scipio **202 B. C.** Hannibal, after career in Asia Minor, committed suicide in Bithynia upon betrayal to Romans, c. **183 B.C.**

Third Punic War 149-146 B. C., ended with total destruction of Carthage. Later, Roman colony built there; eventually destroyed by Saracens **698 A. D.**

60-27

Julius Caesar formed political triumvirate with Pompey and Crassus **60 B.C.**; defeated Helvetia, Belgae, **58-57 B. C.**; entered Britain **55** and **54 B. C.** Crossed Rubicon River into Italy, despite Senate orders, **49 B.C.**; defeated Pompey at Pharsalus **48 B.C.** Defeated Pharnaces at Zela, Asia Minor, **47 B.C.** Lived with Cleopatra, queen of Egypt, in Rome **46-44 B.C.** Was dictator but refused crown.

Caesar assassinated in Roman Senate by group led by Cassius and Brutus **44 B. C.** Caesar's will made his grand-nephew, Gaius Octavius, successor; he formed new triumvirate, Octavius ruling West, Mark Antony East and Lepidus Africa. At Philippi **42 B. C.** Antony defeated Cassius and Brutus, both committed suicide. Antony joined Cleopatra in Alexandria; they had 3 sons. Octavius defeated their fleet at Actium **31 B. C.**; they committed suicide. Octavius received title of Augustus (venerated) **27 B. C.**, called first Roman emperor. Roman advance into northern Europe ended **9 A. D.** when Germans under Arminius defeated Varus. Augustus died **14 A. D.**

4

Birth of Jesus Christ in Bethlehem.

1 B. C. and 1 A. D.

The year **1 B. C.** *is the first year before the beginning of the Christian era. The year* **1 A. D.** *is the first year of the Christian era.* **Jan. 1, 1 B. C.** *is just one year before* **Jan. 1, 1 A. D.** *The elapsed number of years between a date B. C. and the same date A. D. is one less than the sum of the years. The Christian era was calculated by the monk Dionysius Exiguus in the 6th century after Christ. He placed Jesus' birth on* **Dec. 25** *in the year* **753** *of Rome and decided* **754** *should be the first year of the Christian era. Biblical scholars find his calculations in error and place the birth of Jesus in the Roman year* **750** *(4 B. C.) or earlier.*

A.D.

The Christian or Common Era

30

Crucifixion of Jesus in reign of Roman emperor Tiberius; Pontius Pilate procurator in Judea. The Roman Catholic church gives the date of the crucifixion as **April 7.**

43

Roman Emperor Claudius subdued Britons; occupation of 300 years begun.

64

Persecution of Christians by Nero; burning of Rome. Apostles Paul and Peter martyred c. **67.**

70

Jerusalem destroyed by Titus. Christians persecuted, worship in catacombs of Rome.

79

Pompeii, Herculaneum, and Stabiae destroyed by eruption of Mt. Vesuvius.

180

Death of Marcus Aurelius; onset of Roman decline.

311

Emperor Galerius, on deathbed, agreed to tolerance of Christians, Emperor Constantine **313** promulgated Edict of Milan, made Christianity legal.

325

Council of Nicaea called by Constantine in Bithynia, Asia Minor, to get churchmen to define orthodox Christian belief. Divinity of Christ and Holy Trinity endorsed; minority view of Arius rejected.

330

Constantine dedicated Byzantium capital of Eastern Empire, henceforth called Constantinople, now Istanbul. Baptized a Christian on his deathbed by Eusebius **337.**

380

Theodosius, Roman emperor, made Christianity based on Nicene creed official religion, banned worship of old pagan gods.

410

Rome sacked by Alaric, the Goth; by Genseric, the Vandal, **455.**

432

Bishop (later Saint) Patrick, was missionary to Ireland; labored 30 years, converting inhabitants to Christianity. In **563** Irish missionary (later Saint) Columba founded church on Iona, Scottish island. In **597** St. Augustine founded church at Canterbury reviving Christian church in England.

449

Anglo-Saxon migrations from continent to Britain.

483

Justinian I, Byzantine emperor, born; died **565.** During reign had Tribonian prepare Justinian Code (Corpus Juris Civilis) which became basic Roman law used later as a model by many European nations.

570

Mohammed born in Mecca; left Mecca for Medina (hegira); **July 16, 622** is beginning of Moslem calendar. Saracens crossed to Spain **711,** established Moorish kingdom, lasted until **1492.**

731

Great period of **Mayan empire** began; ended **987.**

732

Charles Martel, Frankish ruler, defeated 90,000 Moors at Tours, France; high-water mark of Moslem invasion of Western Europe.

800

Charlemagne, king of Franks, proclaimed Holy Roman Emperor by Pope Leo III on Christmas Day in St. Peter's. Charlemagne fought Saxons, Lombards, Saracens 30 years to Christianize them; extended empire from Atlantic to eastern boundaries of Hungary. Died **814,** aged 72, was buried in Aix cathedral.

1000

Leif Ericsson's Norsemen reach Vinland (land of grape vines). Variously identified as Labrador, New England coast and Martha's Vineyard.

1014

Brian Boru, Irish king, defeated Danes at Clontarf.

1027

Second Maya empire in Yucatan. Disintegrated **1480.** Destruction of Tayasal, Guatemala, Itza capital, by Spanish governor of Yucatan in **1697** ended Mayan millennium.

1054

Final break between Eastern (Orthodox) and Western (Roman) church came when Pope Leo IX excommunicated Michael Cerularius and his followers. Eastern Orthodox Church became established religion of Russia under the Czars.

1066

William of Normandy conquered England at Hastings **Oct. 14;** Harold, last Saxon king of England, slain.

1096

First crusade, preached by Peter of Amiens, supported by Pope Urban II, raised 100,000 men. Captured Jerusalem **1099,** Acre, **1104. Second, 1146,** lost Jerusalem to Saladin, a Kurd. **Third, 1189,** Richard I of England took Jaffa. **Fourth, 1200,** besieged Constantinople **1204. Fifth, 1216,** achieved 10-year truce. **Sixth, 1238,** lost ground. **Seventh, 1245,** led by Louis IX (St. Louis) of France who was captured **1250. Eighth, 1270,** led by Louis, who died near Tunis **1270. Children's crusade, 1212,** 50,000 children (est.); most died of disease and hunger or were sold as slaves in North Africa.

1162

Genghis Khan, Mongol chief, born; died **1227.** Captured Peking **1215,** defeated Russians **1223,** conquered most of Central Asia and massacred population of Herat, Afghanistan. By **1241** Mongols under Batu had burned Moscow and Kiev and invaded Poland, Hungary, and the Danube Valley.

1215

Magna Carta, great charter of England, agreed to by King John at Runnymede at insistence of 2,000 English barons who refused to fight on foreign soil and demanded end of illegal levies by king. Charter guaranteed privileges of nobility, church free from secular interference, right of freemen to legal protection. Freemen were privileged class; common people were villein farmers, practically serfs. But 400 years later Edward Coke and Puritans demanded protection for the common people under these rights of freemen. Also invoked Clause 39, out of which trial by jury developed. It reads: *No freeman shall be taken or imprisoned, or dispossessed, or outlawed, or banished, or in any way destroyed, nor will we go upon him, nor send upon him, except by the legal judgment of his peers or by the law of the land.*

1271

Marco Polo started with father and uncle for Cathay (China), Mongol kingdom of Kublai Khan. Served under Khan, returned to Venice **1295.** Wrote Travels.

1274

Thomas Aquinas, scholastic philosopher, died.

1300

Dante and Giotto flourished; dawn of Renaissance.

1309

Clement V, French pope, made Avignon seat of church; Urban V returned to Rome **1367,** warfare caused him to return to Avignon, **1370.** Gregory XI finally reentered St. Peter's **1377.** During the Great Schism, **1378-1417,** French and Italian factions chose popes for Avignon and Rome; breach healed by Martin V **1417.**

1346

Battle of Crecy. France, **Aug. 26.** Edward III of England defeated larger French force of Philip VI; first use of English longbow in continental warfare.

1348

Black Death (bubonic plague) reached Venice, rapidly spreading to rest of Europe by **1349.** An estimated one-fourth of European population killed.

1382

John Wycliffe, English forerunner of Reformation, directed translation of Vulgate Bible into English vernacular. Supported bill in Parliament declaring it sinful for clergy to hold property. By elevating Scriptures above church authority he anticipated Lutheran doctrine by 150 years.

1415

John Huss, Bohemian preacher, follower of Wycliffe, agitator of ecclesiastic reforms, burned at stake in Konstanz, Germany, **July 6** for heresy after Emperor Sigismund revoked his safe-conduct.

1429

Joan of Arc, Maid of Orleans, obeying "voices" of saints, rallied French against English, raised siege of Orleans, effected coronation of Charles VII at Rheims. Through carelessness or treachery she was captured by Burgundians **May 24, 1430,** and sold to English for 10,000 livres. Placed on trial before bishop of Beauvais at Rouen for magic, disobeying parents, wearing male attire, and heresy, she made a retraction (which she later revoked), but was given life imprisonment. Tricked to resume male attire, she was condemned to death by a French court and burned at Rouen by the English **May 30, 1431.**

1453

Constantinople captured by Ottoman Turks.

End of 100-years' war between England and France, begun **1338.** England lost all French land except Calais which the French captured **1558.**

1456

Johann Gutenberg of Mainz completed first Bible printed from movable type. Printing took 5 years.

1457

Johann Fust and Peter Schoeffer of Mainz produced a psalter, the first dated book printed in colors.

1475

William Caxton printed first book in English, translation of a French history of Troy, at Bruges. He moved to Westminster, London, where he printed the first dated book in England **1477.**

1492

Christopher Columbus, Genoese navigator, gained support of Spain's Queen Isabella for westward voyage. Left Palos de la Frontera **Aug. 3** with Santa Maria, 100 tons, 52 men; Pinta 50 tons, 18 men; Nina, 40 tons, 18 men. On **Oct. 12** at 2 a.m., Rodrigo de Triana on Pinta discovered land. Columbus landed on Guanahani (Watling Is.), Bahamas, called it San Salvador. Discovered Cuba and Hispaniola (Haiti or San Domingo); built first fort, La Navidad, there. *For later voyages see Index.*

1497

John Cabot, Venetian employed by English, reached Canada. His son Sebastian joined 2d voyage **1498.** English claim to Canada was based on their discoveries.

Amerigo Vespucci, Italian-born Spanish navigator, asserted he reached American mainland (New World) a year before Columbus.

1498

Savonarola, who decried luxury and power of clergy, burned as heretic in Florence **May 23.**

Vasco da Gama, Portuguese navigator, reached India, discovering all-sea, around-Africa route from W. Europe.

1506

Pope Julius II (della Rovere) started new St. Peter's; employed Michelangelo, Bramante, Raphael.

1509

Henry VIII became king of England. Defeated Scots at **Flodden Field 1513.** Named Defender of the Faith by Pope Leo X for attacking Luther **1521.** When pope refused to annul his marriage to **Catherine of Aragon** for lack of male issue, Henry divorced Catherine, married **Anne Boleyn 1533.** Act of Supremacy abrogated pope's authority, made king head of church in England **1534.** He ordered monasteries closed **1536.**

1517

Martin Luther, Augustinian monk, preached faith over works, attacked abuse of selling papal indulgences, posted 95 theses (propositions) on Wittenberg church door **Oct. 31.** Diet of Worms, under Charles V **Jan. 1521** ordered recantation. Luther, backed by German princes, refused; put Scriptures above papal authority. Translated Greek New Testament into German **1522.** Became head of German evangelical movement, broke with Rome, married a former nun. Augsburg Confession, basic Lutheran creed, presented to Diet there by Melanchthon **1530.**

1519

Hernando Cortes began conquest of Mexico.

1520

Ferdinand Magellan discovered Strait of Magellan; killed in Philippines **1521.** His crew completed first circumnavigation of the world arriving in Spain **Sept. 6, 1522.** Voyage proved the world round, showed large proportion of water to land, and revealed the Americas to be a "New World."

1524

Giovanni da Verrazano, Italian, explored New England coast for French, visited New York Bay.

1526

William Tyndale produced in Cologne first printed version of New Testament in English, suppressed in England. Tyndale executed for heresy **Oct. 6, 1536,** at Vilvarde, near Brussels.

1529

Turks failed in siege of Vienna; 2d siege, **1683,** was broken by Polish King John Sobieski's landmark victory.

1531-35

Francisco Pizarro conquered Peru for Spain.

1534

John Calvin, French-born religious reformer, published his Institutes of the Christian Religion, influential Protestant doctrine. Rejected Lutheran doctrine of consubstantiation; believed in religious base of citizenship, original sin, infant damnation. Influence extended to Scottish Presbyterians, English and New England Puritans.

Jacques Cartier, sent by Francis I of France, in 2 voyages **1534-36** discovered St. Lawrence River and site of Montreal, gave France claims to Canada.

1535

Miles Coverdale published first complete Bible in English. Also worked on first authorized Bible, "The Great Bible," completed **1539.** Other editions: Whittingham's New Testament, with Calvin's introduction **1557;** Geneva Bible **1560;** Bishop's Bible **1568.**

1540

Francisco Coronado, searching for gold and "Seven Cities of Cibola," explored Southwest north of Rio Grande with 70 horse and 30 foot soldiers. Hernando de Alarcon discovered Colorado River. Don Garcia Lopez de Cardenas discovered Grand Canyon.

1541

Hernando de Soto discovered Mississippi River.

1543

Nicholas Copernicus published revolutionary doctrine that earth moved around sun, not vice versa.

1545

Council of Trent, in Austrian Tyrol, urged on Pope Paul III by Emperor Charles V, to define Catholic dogma and remedy ecclesiastical abuses, opened **Dec. 13;** continued intermittently until **1563;** reiterated papal authority, outlined Roman Catholic faith.

1555

Bishops Ridley and Latimer burned at Oxford **Oct. 16;** Archbishop Cranmer of Canterbury burned **Mar. 21, 1556;** 277 other religious leaders burned in attempt of Queen Mary Tudor (Bloody Mary) to restore Catholic authority. Elizabeth I became queen **1558,** made Anglican communion official church.

1560

Some 1,200 Huguenots hanged at Amboise. Catherine de Medicis, regent of France for son, Charles IX, by **Edict of Jan. 1562,** granted Huguenots right to worship outside walled towns. Infraction of edict led to massacre of Huguenots at Vassy **Mar. 1, 1562,** beginning of 8 religious wars. Massacre of St. Bartholomew **Aug. 24, 1572,** encouraged by Charles IX on marriage of sister, Marguerite de Valois to Henry of Navarre (non-Catholic). Henry III, who caused assassination of Catholic leaders Duc de Guise and

Cardinal of Lorraine, was himself murdered **Aug. 1, 1589.** Henry IV (of Navarre) first Bourbon king, promulgated **Edict of Nantes Apr. 13, 1598,** giving Huguenots and Catholics equality before law. Henry converted to Catholicism; assassinated **May 14, 1610.** Revocation of edict by Louis XIV **Oct. 23, 1685,** led to large Huguenot emigration to England and America.

1564

William Shakespeare born; traditional date **Apr. 23;** baptismal record **Apr. 26.**

1565

St. Augustine, Fla. founded by Pedro Menendez, Spaniard. Razed by Francis Drake **1586.**

1579

Francis Drake claimed California for Britain. Left metal plate found in Marin Co. **1936.**

1582

First Catholic New Testament in English issued at Rheims; Old Testament translated at Douai **1609.**

1587

Mary, Queen of Scots, executed on charge of treason against Elizabeth I.

Virginia Dare, first child born of English parents in the New World, on Roanoke Is., N.C., **Aug. 18,** 7 days after **Sir Walter Raleigh's** 2d expedition with 117 persons landed. (First, **1585,** returned to England **1586.**) By **1590** all trace of settlement had vanished except for a tree inscribed enigmatically "Croatoan."

1588

Spanish Armada, 132 ships, 33,000 soldiers, sent by Philip II of Spain against England, destroyed by Drake's attacks and storms **July 21-29.** Only 50 ships returned to Spain. Fading of Spanish power, flourishing of Elizabethan England followed.

1590

Edmund Spenser began The Faerie Queen. First Shakespeare poem, Venus and Adonis, registered **1593.** First play to appear in quarto, Titus Andronicus registered **1594.** Romeo and Juliet performed **1597.**

1600

Shakespeare's most productive decade opened. He retired to Stratford-on-Avon **1610;** died **Apr. 23, 1616,** the same date **Cervantes** died.

1605

Gunpowder Plot of Guy Fawkes to blow up King James I and Parliament foiled when 36 barrels of gunpowder were found in Parliament's cellar **Nov. 4-5.**

1607

Capt. John Smith and 105 cavaliers in 3 ships landed on Virginia coast and started first permanent English settlement in New World at Jamestown **May 13.**

1609

Henry Hudson, English explorer of Northwest Passage, employed by Dutch East India Co.; sailed sloop Half Moon into New York harbor **Sept.** and up river to Albany. A few miles further north, Samuel de Champlain, French, was exploring the lake which bears his name.

Spaniards settled Santa Fe, N.M., erected presidio.

1611

King James version of English Bible published; ordered by James I in **1604** it reconciled earlier versions and became basic Protestant Bible.

1618

Thirty Years' War began in Bohemia between Catholic and Protestant armies; ended **1648** with Peace of Westphalia; Alsace given to France. Holland and Switzerland received independence.

1619

House of Burgesses, first representative assembly in New World, elected by popular vote **July 30** at Jamestown, Va., establishing principle of self-government for royal colony.

First Negro laborers—indentured servants—in English N. American colonies, landed by Dutch at Jamestown, Va., in **Aug.**

1620

Plymouth Pilgrims, Puritan separatists from Church of England, some living in Leyden, Holland, since **1609,** left Plymouth, England, **Sept. 16** on Mayflower, 101 passengers, 48 crew. Original destination Virginia, they reached Cape Cod **Nov. 9-19,** explored coast, landed **Dec. 21** (Dec. 11, Old Style) at Plymouth, so named for Plymouth, England. Mayflower Compact, signed shipboard, was agreement to form a local government and abide by its laws; elected own first governor, John Carver. Started first house **Dec. 25.** Half of colony perished during hard winter.

1624

Dutch left 8 men from ship, New Netherland, on Manhattan in **May.** Rest proceeded to Albany.

1626

Peter Minuit bought Manhattan from Man-a-hat-a Indians **May 6** for trinkets valued at $24.

1636

Harvard College founded **Oct. 28,** now oldest in U.S.

1642

Great Rebellion of the Puritan Parliament against the civil and religious policies of Charles I of England began **July** after Charles rejected Parliament's demands for control of militia and church affairs and for right to appoint and dismiss the king's ministers.

Oliver Cromwell led army of Roundheads for Parliament, defeated Charles' Cavaliers at **Marston Moor 1644** and **Naseby 1645.** Charles was delivered to Parliament by the Scots **1648.** Beheaded **1649.**

Galileo died, **Newton** was born (100 years after **Copernicus** published heliocentric theory.) In **1616** the Inquisition at Rome declared the assertion of earth's motion to be heretical and placed works of Copernicus, Kepler, and Galileo on the Index of Forbidden Books.

1648

Taj Mahal outside Agra, India, completed by Mogul Emperor Shah Jehan in memory of his favorite wife Mumtaz Mahal. Begun in **1630.**

1649

Commonwealth ruled by Commons and Council of State with Cromwell at head. Cromwell made protector for life (actually dictator), **1653.**

Cromwell died 1658. His son Richard resigned rule. Puritan government collapsed and Parliament called Charles II to rule the nation.

1660

Restoration under Charles II, "Merry Monarch." Charles' Cavalier Parliament restored Anglican church and refused freedom of worship to "dissenters."

1664

King Charles II ordered Col. Nicolls and 300 men to seize New Netherland from Dutch, granted territory to his brother James, Duke of York. Peter Stuyvesant, Dutch director-general, yielded peacefully; province of New Netherland and city of New Amsterdam became New York. The Dutch recaptured both **Aug. 9, 1673,** but ceded all by treaty to Britain **Nov. 10, 1674.**

1665

Great Plague in London killed 68,000. In **1666** great fire destroyed 13,200 houses, 89 churches.

1676

Nathaniel Bacon led planters, oppressed by taxes, against British Gov. Berkeley, burned Jamestown, Va. Bacon died suddenly; 23 followers executed.

Bloody Indian war in New England ended **Aug. 12.** King Philip, Wampanog chief, and many Narragansett Indians killed.

1682

Robert Cavelier, Sieur de La Salle, claimed lower Mississippi River country for Louis XIV, called it Louisiana **Apr. 9.** Had built French outposts in Illinois, established fort at Lavaca, Tex., **1684** with 400 men; killed by his own men in a mutiny on Trinity River, Tex., **Mar. 19, 1687.**

1683

William Penn signed treaty with Indians.

1689

King William's War, British in America vs. French and Indians, began; ended **1697.**

1692

Witchcraft delusion at Salem (now Danvers, Mass.), inspired by preaching; 19 persons hanged, 1 man crushed to death. Executions in Europe of women for witchcraft between **1484** and **1782** believed to have reached 300,000. Last in England **1716**, in Scotland **1722**.

1696

Capt. William Kidd, American, hired by British king and nobles to fight pirates and take booty, became pirate. Returned to New York with treasure **1698**, buried it on Gardiner's Island. Arrested and sent to England for trial. He was hanged **1701**.

1704

Indians attacked Deerfield, Mass., Feb. 28-29, killed 40, carried off 100.

Gibraltar taken by Britain from Spain **July 24**; formally ceded by Spain in Treaty of Utrecht **1713**.

Boston News Letter, first regular newspaper, started by John Campbell, postmaster. (Publick Occurences was suppressed after one issue **1690.**)

1709

British-Colonial troops captured French fort, Port Royal, Nova Scotia, in Queen Anne's War **1701-13**. France yielded Nova Scotia by treaty **1713**.

1712

Slaves revolted in New York Apr. 6. Six committed suicide, 21 were executed. Second rising, **1741**; 13 slaves hanged, 13 burned, 71 deported.

1720

"**Mississippi Bubble.**" John Law, a Scot, comptroller of finance in France, issued paper currency without security to back trading scheme. On basis of wild stories of gold in Louisiana, shares reached $4,000 value before collapse; provoked large immigration to Louisiana.

1728

Pennsylvania Gazette founded by Samuel Keimer in Philadelphia. Benjamin Franklin bought interest **1729**.

1735

Freedom of the press recognized in New York by acquittal of **John Peter Zenger**, editor Weekly Journal, on charge of libeling British Gov. Cosby by criticizing his conduct in office.

1740-1741

Capt. Vitus Bering, Dane employed by Russians, discovered Alaska.

1743

King George's War. British and colonials vs. French. Siege of Louisburg, Cape Breton Is., was led by Gov. William Shirley of Massachusetts. It surrendered **June 17, 1745.** Returned to France by Treaty of Aix la Chapelle **1748**.

1746

English defeated Scots at Culloden Moor, near Inverness, **Apr. 16**, routing Stuart pretender, Prince Charles. The last battle fought on British soil, it terminated attempts of Stuarts to recover the English throne.

1751

Publication of the Encyclopedie, great popularizer of the Enlightenment, began in France.

1752

Benjamin Franklin, flying kite in thunderstorm, proved lightning is electricity **June 15**.

Gregorian calendar adopted by Great Britain and American colonies, dropping 11 days after Sept. 2; next day Sept. 14.

1754

French and Indian War (in Europe called 7 Years War, started 1756) started after French occupied uncompleted British post, called it Ft. Duquesne (site of Pittsburgh). Col. George Washington with Virginia troops clashed with French at Great Meadows, dug in at Ft. Necessity; capitulated and withdrew **July 3, 1754.** Boston's 3,000 provincial troops took French forts in Nova Scotia **June 16, 1755.** French and Indians ambushed Gen. Edward Braddock's expedition 10 mi. from Ft. Duquesne (now Braddock, Pa.) **July 9**; Braddock fatally wounded, 714 killed. Gen. Sir William Johnson defeated French and Indians under Baron Dieskau at Lake George **Sept. 8.** British moved Acadian French from Nova Scotia to Louisiana **Nov.** Britain formally declared war **May 18, 1756.** Surrendered Ft. William Henry (Lake George) to Montcalm. Montcalm at Ft. Ticonderoga, N.Y., repulsed 17,000 British **July 8, 1758.** British took Louisburg, Ft. Frontenac, Ft. Duquesne in **1758**; Niagara, Ticonderoga, Crown Point in **1759.** British captured Quebec **Sept. 18, 1759** in battles in which Montcalm and Gen. James Wolfe (Br.) died. Peace signed **Feb. 10, 1763.** French lost Canada and American Midwest.

Samuel Johnson published his English Dictionary.

1756

Black Hole of Calcutta. Nawab of Bengal, attacking British East India Co., threw 146 British prisoners into room less than 20 ft. square **June 20**; only 23 survived overnight. Lord Robert Clive with 3,000 troops routed the nawab's force of 50,000 **June 23, 1757.**

First Partition of Poland by Austria, Prussia, and Russia. Second and third partitions of **1793** and **1795** erased Poland from map of Europe, not to re-emerge until after World War I.

1776-1783 American Revolution
See Article, Pages 718-719

1781

Bank of North America incorporated in Philadelphia **May 26.** First chartered bank, Bank of Pennsylvania **Mar. 1, 1780** operated **1782-1784.**

1783

Massachusetts Supreme Court outlawed slavery in that state, noting the words in the state Bill of Rights "all men are born free and equal."

1784

First successful daily newspaper, Pennsylvania Packet & General Advertiser, published **Sept. 21.**

1785

First steamboat experiment by John Fitch. Fitch demonstrated 3 mph steamboat with 12 mechanical oars on Delaware River **Aug. 22, 1787.** He operated steamboat between Trenton and Philadelphia **1790.**

1786

Delegates from 5 states at Annapolis asked Congress to call convention in Philadelphia to write practical constitution for the 13 states.

1787

Shays rebellion in Massachusetts, led by Capt. Daniel Shays; attempt to seize U. S. Arsenal in Springfield failed **Jan. 25.**

Northwest Ordinance adopted **July 13** by Continental Congress made effective Ordinance of 1784 drafted by Jefferson. Determined government of **Northwest Territory** north of Ohio River, west of New York; 5,000 male voters could establish legislature; 60,000 inhabitants could get statehood. Guaranteed freedom of religion, support for schools, no slavery.

James Rumsey, encouraged by George Washington, ran steamboat with power pump on Potomac **Dec. 3** and **11.** Patented **1791.**

Constitutional convention opened at Philadelphia **May 14** with George Washington presiding. Constitution adopted by delegates **Sept. 17**; ratification by 9th state, New Hampshire, **June 21, 1788**, meant adoption; declared in effect **Mar. 4, 1789.**

1788

First British settlement in Australia, a penal colony at Port Jackson, now Sydney.

1789

George Washington chosen president by all electors voting (73 eligible, 69 voting, 4 absent); John Adams, vice president, 34 votes, **Feb.** First U. S. Congress called **Mar. 4**, at Federal Hall, N. Y. City; regular sessions began **Apr. 6.** Washington inaugurated there **Apr. 30.** Supreme Court created by Federal Judiciary Act **Sept. 24.**

The French Revolution began **June 20** when the delegates to the Third Estate (Commons) met on a tennis court and took an oath not to disband until the king had granted France a constitution; Paris mob stormed the Bastille **July 14** to capture ammunition;

released 7 non-political prisoners. France was declared a limited monarchy under Louis XVI; the king and family were arrested **June 21, 1791**; Revolutionary Tribunal set up on **Aug. 19, 1792**; National Convention opened **Sept. 17, 1792**, a republic was established on **Sept. 22**. Louis was beheaded **Jan. 21, 1793**; the Reign of Terror began **May 31, 1793**; Charlotte Corday killed Marat **July 13, 1793**; Queen Marie Antoinette was beheaded **Oct. 16, 1793**; Danton **Apr. 5, 1794**; Robespierre **July 28, 1794**. Revolutionary Tribunal abolished **Dec. 15, 1794**. Moderate Directory of 5 men established to rule France **1795**.

1791

Continued attacks on settlements north of Ohio River by Indians armed by British, led Washington to send Gen. Arthur St. Clair and Gen. Wilkinson to area with 1,400 men. St. Clair was surprised near Wabash River in Ohio **Nov. 4**, lost 630 killed.

1792-94

Gen. "Mad" Anthony Wayne made commander in Ohio-Indiana area, trained "American Legion"; established string of forts. Routed Indians (Ottawas, Shawnees, Miamis, Iroquois) at Fallen Timbers on Maumee River **Aug. 20, 1794**, checked British at Ft. Miami, Oh.

Whiskey Rebellion, west Pennsylvania farmers protesting "discriminatory" liquor tax of **1791**, was suppressed by 15,000 militiamen **Sept. 1794**. Alexander Hamilton used incident to establish authority of the new federal government in enforcing its laws.

1795

Gen. Wayne signed peace with Indians at Fort Greenville.

U. S. bought peace from Algiers and Tunis by paying $800,000, supplying a frigate and annual tribute of $25,000 **Nov. 28**. (See 1801.)

1796

Washington's Farewell Address as president delivered **Sept. 19**. Gave strong warnings against permanent alliances with foreign powers, partiality toward favorite nations, big public debt, large military establishment and devices of "small artful, enterprising minority" to control or change government; praised reciprocal checks of Constitution; stressed need for enlightened public opinion; declared "religion and morality lead to political prosperity."

Vaccination discovered by Edward Jenner **May 14**; laid foundation for modern immunology.

1797

U. S. frigate United States launched at Philadelphia **July 10**; Constellation at Baltimore **Sept. 7**; Constitution (Old Ironsides) at Boston **Sept. 20**.

American Revolution and War of Independence;

Great Britain, after acquiring Canada from France in **1763**, tightened up colonial administration in North America. The 13 colonies, used to self-government, resented duties on commerce and objected to paying for troops now quartered among them. **The Sugar Act of 1764** placed duties on lumber, foodstuffs, molasses and rum. **The Stamp Act of 1765** required revenue stamps to help defray cost of royal troops. The colonists formed Sons of Liberty groups and rejected British goods. Nine colonies, led by New York and Massachusetts at **Stamp Act Congress** in New York **Oct. 7-25, 1765**, adopted Declaration of Rights opposing taxation without representation in Parliament and trial without jury by admiralty courts. In the Virginia House of Burgesses, Patrick Henry warned King George III of consequences declaring, "If this be treason make the the most of it." Parliament repealed Stamp Act on **Mar. 17,1766**.

Townshend Acts of 1767 levied taxes on glass, painter's lead, paper and tea imports. In 1770 all duties except tax on tea were repealed, but principle of right to tax was maintained. British troops fired into a mob **Mar. 5, 1770**, killed 5 including Crispus Attucks, a Negro, reportedly leader of the group; later called the **Boston Massacre**. Tea ships of East India Co., turned back at Boston, New York, Philadelphia in **May 1773**. Cargo ship burned at Annapolis **Oct. 14**. cargo thrown overboard at **Boston Tea Party Dec. 16**. Parliament ordered port closed until tea was paid for, sent 4 regiments to Boston, suppressed town meetings and elective representation in Massachusetts.

Samuel Adams, in Boston, began uniting patriot leaders by Committees of Correspondence. Virginia called for first **Continental Congress** in Philadelphia **Sept. 5-Oct. 26, 1774**. On **Mar. 23, 1775**, Patrick Henry addressed revolutionary convention, Richmond, Va., with famous exclamation: "Give me liberty or give me death!"

Battles of 1775

Paul Revere and **William Dawes** on night of **Apr. 18**, rode to alert Samuel Adams and John Hancock at Lexington and others that 700 British were on way to **Concord** to destroy arms. At **Lexington, Mass., Apr. 19** Minutemen lost 8 killed, 10 wounded. On return from Concord the harassed British lost 273.

Col. Ethan Allen (joined by Col. Benedict Arnold) captured **Ft. Ticonderoga**, N. Y., **May 10**; also Crown Point. Colonials headed for Bunker Hill, fortified Breed's Hill, Charlestown, Mass., repulsed British under Gen. William Howe twice before retreating **June 17**; British casualties 1,000; called **Battle of Bunker Hill**. Continental Congress **June 15** named George Washington commander-in-chief; he took command in Cambridge **July 3**. Maj. Gen. Richard Montgomery led troops against Canada via New York, captured **Montreal Nov. 13**, Col. Arnold marched via Maine wilderness attacked **Quebec Dec. 30-31**; Montgomery killed. Colonials returned to New York State **June 1776**.

Declaration of Independence

Virginia voted for independence May 15. In Continental Congress **June 7, 1776**, Richard Henry Lee (Va.) moved "that these united colonies are and of right ought to be free and independent states." Resolutions adopted **July 2**. **Declaration of Independence July 4**. *See Index for article.*

Col. Moultrie's batteries at Charleston, S.C., repulsed British sea attack **June 28**. Washington, with 10,000 men lost **Battle of Long Island** to Gen. William (Lord) Howe and Gen. Sir Henry Clinton with 15,000 **Aug. 27**, evacuated New York.

Nathan Hale, 21, executed as spy, without trial, by British **Sept. 22**.

Washington repulsed Howe at **Harlem Heights Sept. 16**, retreated to White Plains, N.Y. Brig. Gen. Arnold's Lake Champlain fleet was defeated at **Valcour Oct. 11**, but British returned to Canada. Howe failed to destroy Washington's army at **White Plains Oct. 28**. Hessians captured **Ft. Washington**, Manhattan, and 3,000 men **Nov. 16; Ft. Lee**, N.J., **Nov. 18**.

Washington in Pennsylvania, recrossed Delaware River **Dec. 25-26**, defeated 1,400 Hessians at **Trenton**, N. J., **Dec. 26**.

Brandywine and Saratoga, 1777

Washington defeated Lord Cornwallis at **Princeton Jan. 3**. Continental Congress adopted Stars and Stripes **June 14**. *See Flag article*. Maj. Gen. John Burgoyne with 8,000 from Canada captured Ft. Ticonderoga **July 6**. Brig. Gen. Nicholas Herkimer, to raise St. Leger's siege of **Ft. Stanwix**, routed Indians at **Oriskany**, N. Y. **Aug. 6**. Burgoyne's Hessians defeated by Brig. Gen. John Stark and the Green Mountain

France ordered capture of all neutral ships carrying British cargoes.

1798

War with France threatened over French raids on U. S. shipping and rejection of U. S. diplomats. Congress voided all treaties with France, ordered Navy to capture French armed ships. Navy (45 ships) and 365 privateers captured 84 French ships. U. S. Constellation took French warship Insurgente **1799.** Napoleon stopped French raids after becoming First Consul.

Napoleon invaded Egypt and won Battle of the Pyramids **July 1798;** British Adm. Nelson destroyed French fleet **Aug. 1-2** in Aboukir Bay. Napoleon fled secretly to France **1799,** became First Consul **Nov. 9-10, 1799,** after coup d'etat. Rosetta stone, found in Egypt by one of Napoleon's officers **1799,** contained 3 identical inscriptions in ancient Egyptian hieroglyphics, demotic (common) Greek, and classical Greek. Jean Champollion, a young French scholar, compared these writings and deciphered ancient Egypt's hieroglyphics.

1801

Tripoli declared war June 10 against U. S., which refused added tribute to commerce-raiding Arab corsairs. U. S. frigate Philadelphia captured in Tripoli harbor **Oct. 1803** burned by Stephen Decatur **Feb. 16, 1804,** to block harbor. Land force under William Eaton forced Tripoli to conclude peace **June 4, 1805.**

1803

Robert Emmet convicted of treason by British in Ireland; executed in Dublin **Sept. 19.**

Louisiana Purchase. Pres. Jefferson sent James Monroe to Paris to join Robert R. Livingston, U. S. minister, in offering up to $10 million for the Isle of Orleans (New Orleans) and West Florida. Napoleon, who had recovered Louisiana from Spain by secret treaty, offered all of Louisiana, stretching to Canadian border, for $11,250,000 in bonds, plus $3,750,000 indemnities to American citizens with claims against France. U. S. took title **Dec. 20.**

1804

Lewis and Clark expedition ordered by Pres. Jefferson to explore what is now northwest U. S. Started from St. Louis **May 14;** ended **Sept. 23, 1806.** Sacajawea, an Indian woman, served as guide.

Alexander Hamilton (ex-Sec. of the Treasury) and Vice Pres. Aaron Burr, after years of bitter political rivalry, fought a duel **July 11** on the Hudson Palisades, Weehawken, N.J. Hamilton was mortally wounded, died **July 12.**

Origins, Battles, Results, 1763-1783

Boys near **Bennington,** Vt. **Aug. 16.** Arnold raised siege of Ft. Stanwix.

Howe defeated Washington near **Brandywine Creek,** Pa., **Sept. 11** and occupied Philadelphia. Congress moved to Lancaster, Pa. Inconclusive battle of **Germantown,** Pa., **Oct. 4.** Washington's army wintered at **Valley Forge.**

Americans massed at **Bemis Heights,** near Saratoga, under Maj. Gen. Horatio Gates, attacked by Burgoyne **Sept. 19.** At nearby **Freeman's Farm,** Gen. Arnold and Col. Daniel Morgan's riflemen repulsed British, inflicted great losses. Gen Clinton took **Fts. Clinton** and **Montgomery** below West Point **Oct. 6,** but did not support Burgoyne. Americans beat back Burgoyne at Bemis Heights **Oct. 7** and cut off British escape route. Burgoyne surrendered 5,000 men at **Saratoga,** N. Y., **Oct. 17.**

Marquis de la Fayette (Lafayette), aged 20, made major general.

Articles of Confederation and Perpetual Union adopted by Continental Congress **Nov. 15.**

Help from France

France recognized independence of 13 Colonies, signed treaty of aid with Benjamin Franklin, Silas Deane, Arthur Lee on **Feb. 6, 1778.** Sent fleet under Adm. d'Estaing. British evacuated Philadelphia in consequence **June 18.** Washington harassed British at **Monmouth Court House,** N. J., **June 28.** Wyoming Massacre **July 3** in Pa. by British and Indian force. British overran Georgia in December.

George Rogers Clark who took **Cahokia** and **Kaskaskia** (Ill.) **1778,** took **Vincennes Feb. 1779.** Maj. Gen. Anthony Wayne **July 15** stormed **Stony Point,** on Hudson, but withdrew after victory.

John Paul Jones on the Bonhomme Richard defeated Serapis in British North Sea waters **Sept. 23, 1779.** French fleet and Maj. Gen. Benjamin Lincoln's men were repulsed at Savannah **Oct. 9.**

Benedict Arnold's Treason

Three Continental soldiers, Paulding, Williams and Van Wart, captured Major John Andre, adjutant general of the British army, in disguise at Tarrytown, N. Y., **Sept. 23, 1780,** finding papers betraying West Point, signed by Gen. Arnold, in his socks. He had lost his way after rendezvous with Arnold at Haverstraw, N.Y. Arnold, informed of Andre's capture, escaped from headquarters in Highlands, near present Garrison, N. Y., by barge to British sloop Vulture off Verplanck's Point.

Andre was found guilty by board of American officers at Tappan, N. Y., hanged as spy **Oct. 2.** Washington refused to intercede. Arnold made brigadier general in British army; burned New London, Conn., **1781.** His wife, Peggy Shippen of Philadelphia, adjudged innocent by Washington, since proved implicated. Arnold died in London. Andre's body removed to Westminster Abbey **1821.**

Road to Yorktown

Charleston, S. C., fell to the British **May 12, 1780,** but a segment of Lord Cornwallis' forces led by Maj. Patrick Ferguson was defeated near **Kings Mountain,** N. C., **Oct. 7** by militiamen commanded by Cols. John Sevier, Isaac Shelby, William Campbell and Benjamin Cleveland. Operations in South under Cornwallis and Col. Banastre Tarleton in **1781** were checked by Maj. Gen. Nathanael Greene and Brig. Gen. Daniel Morgan. **Cowpens,** S. C., **Jan. 17** was a victory, but **Guilford Court House,** N. C., **Mar. 15** was a British gain. Greene's harassments caused Cornwallis to retire to Wilmington, N. C., and thence to **Yorktown, Va.**

While Lafayette waited near Yorktown, Adm. De Grasse landed 3,000 French and stopped Adm. Thomas Graves' British fleet in Hampton Roads. Adm. Barras joined De Grasse. Washington and Rochambeau joined forces and left 2,000 men to mislead Sir Henry Clinton in New York, marched to Annapolis, and took boats to James River near Williamsburg, arriving **Sept. 26.** When siege of Cornwallis began **Oct. 6,** British had 6,000, Americans 8,846, French 7,800. Clinton decided too late to relieve Cornwallis. Graves sailed from New York with 7,000 **Oct. 17** too late to reach Cornwallis who surrendered **Oct. 19, 1781.**

Independence, 1782

A new British cabinet agreed to recognize independence **March 1782.** Preliminary agreement signed in Paris **Nov. 30;** treaty **Sept. 3, 1783.** Congress ratified it **Jan. 14, 1784.** Washington ordered army disbanded **Nov. 3, 1783.** British evacuated N.Y. City **Nov. 25.** Washington bade farewell to his officers at Fraunces Tavern, N.Y. City, **Dec. 4;** resigned **Dec. 23,** retired to Mount Vernon, Va. *For casualties of war see Index.*

Code Napoleon systematized French law under Napoleon Bonaparte. It became model for many countries.

John Stevens, of Hoboken, N.J., ran experimental steamboat with twin-screw propellers for 9 mi.

1805

Napoleon, emperor since **May 18, 1804,** defeated Austrians at Ulm **Oct. 17;** Russo-Austrians at Austerlitz, "masterpiece of battles," **Dec. 2.** Dissolved Holy Roman Empire. Made brothers Joseph, king of Naples, Louis, king of Holland.

Lord Nelson defeated French-Spanish fleet at Cape Trafalgar **Oct. 21;** lost his own life.

1806

Napoleon defeated Prussians at Jena **Oct. 14.** In **1807** he defeated Russians at Eylau; signed peace of Tilsit with Czar Alexander I. Made brother Jerome king of Westphalia; allotted Finland to Russia.

1807

Robert Fulton made first practical steamboat trip on Clermont (open boat, 140 by 13 ft., 7 ft. draft, side paddle wheels). Left N.Y. City **Aug. 17,** reached Albany, 150 mi., in 32 hrs.

Aaron Burr was tried for treason in Richmond, Va., **May 22.** Charged with "assembling an armed force . . . to seize the city of New Orleans . . . and to separate the western from the Atlantic states," he was acquitted **Sept. 1.** Chief Justice John Marshall sitting as U.S. Circuit Court judge ruled that treason must be attested to by 2 witnesses. After trial Burr went to Europe to avoid prosecution on Hamilton murder charge.

1808-09

French occupied Madrid in March; Rome in April; Napoleon made brother Joseph king of Spain in Peninsular War begun by British **1808,** continued until **1814.** Napoleon defeated Austrians at Wagram **July 6, 1809;** annexed Papal States.

Phoenix, world's first ocean-going steamboat, built by John Stevens, left N.Y. City for Philadelphia **June 8, 1809.**

1811

William Henry Harrison, governor of Indiana Territory, defeated Indians under the Prophet,

War of 1812 Between U.S. and Great Britain

The War of 1812, coming only 30 years after the end of the Revolution, had 3 major causes: (1) Britain, blockading France, seized American ships trading with France; (2) Britain, refusing to recognize naturalized American sailors, seized 4,000 by 1810 and impressed two-thirds into British service; (3) Britain armed Indians who raided western border. Under Pres. Jefferson U.S., **1807** and **1809,** stopped trade with Europe. This ruined U.S. shippers. Under Pres. Madison **1810** trade with Britain only was stopped.

War might have been averted. The British raised the blockade for American ships **June 16, 1812,** but the news did not reach U. S. by **June 18** when Congress by a small majority voted a declaration of war. Congress voted to raise army from 11,744 to 44,500 and to use militia. The navy had 20 major ships of 500 guns. The West favored war; New England opposed it. The British were handicapped by war with France.

War on Land

Americans made many blunders due to poor leadership and refusal of regulars to work with militia. Brig. Gen. William Hull surrendered Detroit **Aug. 16, 1812.** Maj. Gen. Stephen Van Rensselaer with 2,300 took Queenston Heights, Ont., **Oct. 13,** but retired when regulars did not support him. Brig. Gen. William H. Harrison had 1,000 casualties near Ft. Malden, Ont. (near Detroit). Brig. Gen. Zebulon M. Pike took York (Toronto) **Apr. 27, 1813,** died in explosion. Gen. Henry Dearborn **May 27** took Ft. George and Queenston Heights aided by amphibious assault led by Col. Winfield Scott and Master Commandant Oliver Hazard Perry. British defeated 2,000 Americans a few days later.

Battle of the Thames, Ontario, **Oct. 5, 1813.** Harrison with 3,500 men took Ft. Malden, pursued British 85 mi. Cavalry charge by Kentucky riflemen routed British and Indians, killing Shawnee chief, Tecumseh. Detroit frontier was safe for U. S. Both Brig. Gen. Wade Hampton with 4,000 and Maj. Gen. James Wilkinson with 6,000 mismanaged attempts to invade Canada. British recaptured Fts. George and Niagara, burned Buffalo; Americans burned Newark and Queenston.

Battle of Lundy's Lane. Brig. Gen. Winfield Scott led attack on British at Lundy's Lane, on road to Burlington, Ont., **July 25, 1814;** result a draw with heavy losses. Scott was wounded.

Burning of Washington. In **Aug.,** British landed 4,000 men under Adm. Sir George Cockburn and Maj. Gen. Robert Ross. At Bladensburg, Md., **Aug. 24, 1814,** Ross routed 5,000 hastily assembled U. S. troops, then burned Capitol and White House; Maryland militia stopped British **Sept. 12** from reaching Baltimore; Ross was killed.

Battle of New Orleans. Maj. Gen. Andrew Jackson, who had defeated the Creek Indians at Horseshoe Bend on the Tallapoosa **Mar. 27, 1814,** and captured British base at Pensacola, Fla., in **Nov.;** on **Dec. 23** engaged 2,000 British east of New Orleans. **Jan. 8, 1815,** 5,300 British under Maj. Gen. Sir Edward Pakenham attacked American entrenchments at Chalmette. Jackson had 3,500, a reserve of 1,000, 20 guns and an armed schooner. British had over 2,000 casualties. Pakenham was killed; Americans lost 71. British withdrew and left by sea **Jan. 18.** On **Feb. 8** they took Mobile. News came **Feb. 14** that a treaty of peace had been signed at Ghent **Dec. 24, 1814.** U.S. ratified it **Feb. 17, 1815.**

War at Sea

Brilliant American gunnery brought naval victories. USS Essex captured Alert **Aug. 13, 1812.** USS Constitution, 44 guns, Capt. Isaac Hull, destroyed Guerriere **Aug. 19;** thereafter, Constititution was called **Old Ironsides.** USS Wasp took Frolic **Oct. 18.** USS United States, Capt. Stephen Decatur, defeated Macedonian off Azores **Oct. 25.** Constitution beat Java **Dec. 29, 1812.** USS Chesapeake captured by Shannon **June 1, 1813;** Capt. James Lawrence, dying, called out: "Don't give up the ship!" USS Enterprise took Boxer **Sept. 5.**

Battle of Lake Erie. Commodore Oliver H. Perry defeated British fleet near Put-in-Bay **Sept. 10, 1813.** Perry sent message to Harrison: "We have met the enemy and they are ours: 2 ships, 2 brigs, 1 schooner, 1 sloop."

USS Essex, Capt. David Porter, captured 9 British ships, was defeated off Valparaiso, Chile, **Mar. 28, 1814** by 2 British ships.

Bombardment of Ft. McHenry, Baltimore, for 25 hours, **Sept. 13-14, 1814,** by British fleet failed. Francis Scott Key wrote words to Star Spangled Banner.

Battle of Lake Champlain. Commodore Thomas Macdonough defeated fleet of Sir George Prevost near Plattsburg **Sept. 11, 1814** while Brig. Gen. Thomas Macomb held 4,500 ready to oppose 11,000. British withdrew to Canada.

U. S. frigate President was captured **Jan. 1815.** Constitution captured Cyane and Levant **Feb. 20, 1815.** U.S. sloop Hornet captured Penguin **Mar. 23.**

The War of 1812 gave recognition to westerners, made Andrew Jackson a political power.

brother of Tecumseh, in battle of Tippecanoe **Nov. 7.**

1812

Napoleon invaded Russia June 22 with first modern conscript army of 500,000 men; Russian army, outnumbered 3 to 1, retreated and used "scorched earth" policy. Napoleon's army defeated Russians at Borodino **Sept. 7**; took Moscow **Sept. 14.** Moscow destroyed by fire; lacking shelter and supplies, Napoleon ordered retreat **Oct. 19.** Army suffered from cold, starvation and Cossack attacks; only 30,-000 survived.

1813

Napoleon with 180,000 French decisively defeated at Leipzig by 200,000 allied Prussians, Austrians, Russians, under Austrian Gen. Schwartzenberg in Battle of the Nations **Oct. 16-19.**

1814

Allies entered Paris Mar. 21; Napoleon abdicated **Apr. 11**; Louis XVIII restored to throne, **May 3**; Congress of Vienna opened **Nov. 3.** Napoleon exiled to Elba.

1815

Napoleon re-entered France Mar. 1, assumed command for the "Hundred Days," **Mar. 20-June 22.** Defeated at Waterloo, Belgium, **June 18,** by Duke of Wellington (British), Count von Blucher (Prussian), and allies. Deported to St. Helena; died there **May 5, 1821.**

Holy Alliance, formed by Russia, Austria, and Prussia; signed in Paris **Sept. 26.**

1817

Rush-Bagot treaty signed **Apr. 28-29** limited U. S., Canadian naval armaments on the Great Lakes.

1819

American steamship Savannah made first part steam-powered, part sail-powered crossing of Atlantic, Savannah, Ga., to Liverpool, Eng., 29 days.

1820

Henry Clay's Missouri Compromise bill passed by Congress **Mar. 3.** Slavery was allowed in Missouri, but not elsewhere west of the Mississippi River north of 36° 30′ latitude (the southern line of Missouri). Repealed **1854.**

1822

Brazil proclaimed independence from Portugal **Sept. 7.** Dom Pedro, son of Portugal's King John VI, was crowned emperor **Dec. 1**; abdicated **1831**; succeeded by his son. A republic proclaimed **1888.**

Mexico separated from Spain, made Iturbide emperor **May**; formed republic **Oct. 1823.**

1823

Monroe Doctrine declared **Dec. 2.**

Mississippi River first ascended by steamboat, the Virginia, as far as Fort Snelling, Minn., **Apr. 21-May 10,** 729 mi.

1824

Simon Bolivar liberator of Venezuela, Colombia, Ecuador, Peru broke Spanish power in South America.

1825

Great Britain repeals laws against trade unions.

First railroad to use steam locomotive (on level grade only) Stockton & Darlington RR opened in England **Sept. 27** with Stephenson's engine "Locomotion." First public railroad to use steam exclusively for passenger and freight traffic, Liverpool & Manchester, opened **Sept. 15, 1830.**

Erie Canal opened; first boat left Buffalo **Oct. 26,** reached N.Y. City **Nov. 4.** Canal cost $7 million but cut travel time by one-third, shipping costs to one-tenth; opened Great Lakes area, made N. Y. City chief Atlantic port.

First iron steamboat built in America, the Codorus, at York, Pa., by John Elgar.

John Stevens, of Hoboken, N.J., built and operated first steam locomotive in U.S.

1827

Slavery in N.Y. State abolished **July 4.**

Steamship Curacao, first European-built oceanic vessel to use steam power only, crossed the Atlantic **April** from Antwerp to Paramaribo, Dutch Guiana. The Royal William launched in Montreal **Apr. 29, 1831,** left there **Aug. 18, 1833,** crossed to Europe in 25 days using only steam.

1828

First passenger railroad in U. S., Baltimore & Ohio, was begun **July 4,** first 14 mi. opened to horsedrawn railcar traffic **May 24, 1830.**

1830

Mormon church organized by Joseph Smith in Fayette, N. Y., **Apr. 6.**

Revolution in France. Charles X abdicated **Aug. 2** and was succeeded by the duke of Orleans as Louis Philippe I. There were revolts in Brunswick, Saxony and Belgium. Belgium became independent kingdom.

First regularly scheduled passenger train service in U.S. using steam power began at Charleston on South Carolina RR **Dec. 25** with U.S.-built locomotive, Best Friend of Charleston.

1831

Nat Turner, Negro slave in Virginia, led slave rebellion, killed 57 whites, in **Aug.** Army called in, Turner captured, tried and hanged.

1832

Black Hawk War (Ill.-Wis.) **Apr. - Sept.** pushed Sac & Fox Indians west across Mississippi.

South Carolina convention passed **Ordinance of Nullification Nov. 1832** against permanent tariff protection policy, declaring that if the federal government attempted to enforce the tariff the state would consider itself no longer a member of the Union. Congress **Feb. 1833** passed a compromise tariff act, whereupon South Carolina repealed its act.

British Reform Bill; middle class enfranchised; step toward political democracy **Mar. 23.**

1833

Slavery in British Empire outlawed **Aug. 28** as of **Aug. 1, 1834.** About 700,000 were liberated at cost of £20 million. (Slavery was abolished in Britain **June 22, 1772.** Slave trade was suppressed **1807.)**

Oberlin College, first in U.S. to adopt coeducation; refused to bar students for race, **1835.**

1835

Texas proclaimed independence from Mexico in convention **Nov. 1,** provisional government formed. Stephen Austin and Sam Houston leaders.

Gold discovered on Cherokee land in Georgia. Indians forced to cede lands **Dec. 20** and to cross Mississippi.

1836

Texans besieged in Alamo (San Antonio) by Mexicans under Santa Anna **Feb. 23-Mar. 6**; garrison, including William Travis, Jim Bowie, and David Crockett, died defending the fort. At San Jacinto **Apr. 21** Sam Houston and 800 Texans defeated 3,000 Mexicans. Santa Anna signed treaties ending hostilities, promised to recognize Texan independence but Mexican Congress repudiated treaties.

Marcus Whitman, H. H. Spaulding and wives reached Fort Walla Walla on Columbia River, Oregon. First white women to cross plains.

Seminole Indians in Florida under Osceola began attacks **Nov. 1, 1836,** protesting forced removal. The unpopular 8-year war ended **Aug. 14, 1842;** Indians sent to Oklahoma. War cost the U.S. 1,500 soldiers, $30 million.

1838

First to cross the Atlantic under steam power only, the British ship Sirius left Queenstown **Apr. 4,** reached N.Y. City **Apr. 22.** (See 1819.)

1839

Belgium and the Kingdom of the Netherlands were separated by treaties signed by those 2 countries and by Great Britain, France, Austria, Prussia, and Russia at London **Apr. 19.** To the treaties was annexed a document declaring Belgium independent and perpetually neutral (called "scrap of paper" by Germany in World War I when it invaded Belgium.)

Opium War broke out between China and Britain. China tried to prohibit opium trade in Canton. British resisted and took Canton. War ended **Aug. 1842.**

1840

Antarctic was found to be a continent by Comdr. Charles Wilkes of first U. S. exploring expedition; named Wilkes Land **Jan.-Feb.**

1841

First emigrant wagon train for California, 47 persons, left Independence, Mo., **May 1,** reached Stanislaus River, Cal., **Nov. 4.**

First passenger train on Erie RR **June 30.**

1842

First use of anesthetic (sulphuric ether gas) by Dr. Crawford W. Long in Jefferson, Ga. Dr. William T. G. Morton, dentist, used ether for painless extraction of tooth **Sept. 30, 1846;** administered ether in tumor operation **Oct. 16, 1846** at Massachusetts General Hospital, Boston.

1844

First message over first telegraph line sent from U.S. Supreme Court room **May 24** to Baltimore by inventor **Samuel F. B. Morse:** "What hath God wrought!"

Joseph Smith, founder of Mormons, and brother Hyrum killed in Carthage, Ill., jail by mob **June 27.**

1845

Texas voted for annexation to U. S. **July 4.** Congress admitted Texas as 28th state **Dec. 29.**

1846

Mexican War. Pres. James K. Polk ordered **Gen. Zachary Taylor** to seize disputed Texan land settled by Mexicans. After border clash, U. S. declared war **May 13;** Mexico **May 23.**

Bear flag of Republic of California raised by American settlers at Sonoma **June 14.** Gen. John C. Fremont took charge **July 5.** Commodore J. S. Sloat took Monterey **July 7,** declared California annexed to U. S. Commodore Robert Stockton succeded Sloat, was ordered to recognize Gen. Kearny as governor and commander-in-chief in California. Kearny was defeated by Mexicans **Dec. 6,** retreated to San Diego.

Gen. Taylor defeated Mexicans at Buena Vista **Feb. 23, 1847.** Gen. Winfield Scott with 12,000 troops (est.) took Vera Cruz **Mar. 27;** Mexico City **Sept. 14,** captured dictator Santa Anna. By treaty, **Feb. 1848** Mexico ceded claims to Texas, California, Arizona, New Mexico, Nevada, Utah, part of Colorado. U. S. assumed **$3 million** American claims and paid Mexico **$15 million.**

Treaty with Great Britain June 15, set boundary in Oregon Territory at 49th parallel (extension of existing line). Water boundary settled 1873. Expansionists in U. S. seeking boundary farther North used slogan "54°40′ or fight!"

Mormons, after violent clashes with settlers over polygamy, left Nauvoo, Ill., for West under Brigham Young, settled **July 1847** at Salt Lake City, Utah.

1847

First adhesive U. S. postage stamps on sale **July 1;** Benjamin Franklin 5c, Washington 10c.

1848

Gold discovered Jan. 24 by James W. Marshall, who was erecting sawmill in partnership with Capt. John A. Sutter on American River, branch of the Sacramento, near Coloma, Cal.

Louis Philippe dethroned in France; Second Republic set up **Feb. 26.**

In Austria **Ferdinand I** abdicated **Dec. 2** in favor of his nephew Franz Josef. In Hungary, freedom was briefly declared under Louis Kossuth; revolts in Ireland, Lombardy, Venice, Denmark, and Schleswig-Holstein.

Communist Manifesto written by Karl Marx (1818-1883) and Friedrich Engels (1820-1895).

1850

Sen. Henry Clay's Compromise of 1850 approved; admitted California as 31st state **Sept. 9,** slavery forbidden; made Utah and New Mexico territories without decision on slavery; amended Fugitive Slave Law punishing those who aided fugitives and abolished jury trial for fugitives, ended slave trade in Dist. of Columbia.

Jenny Lind's first American concert at Castle Garden, N.Y. City, **Sept. 11;** P. T. Barnum manager.

Taiping Rebellion, led by Hung Hsiu-ch'uan, began in Kwangsi province, China. One of the largest civil wars in history, it resulted in death of 20 to 40 million, devastated entire provinces, and nearly toppled the Manchu dynasty. The Taiping movement, aimed at foreign exploitation, was finally suppressed **1864** by Tseng Kuo-fan with the help of the "Ever Victorious Army" of Gen. Charles G. (Chinese) Gordon.

1851

New York & Hudson River RR, New York to Albany, opened in **Oct.**

1852

Louis Napoleon crowned emperor of the French.

Uncle Tom's Cabin, by Harriet Beecher Stowe, published.

1853

Commodore Matthew C. Perry, U.S.N., received by Lord of Toda, Japan, **July 14;** negotiated treaty to open Japan to U.S. ships. Ratified **Mar. 8, 1854.**

Crimean War. A dispute between Greek Orthodox and Roman monks over holy places held by Turkey in Palestine led Russian Czar Nicholas I to extend protection to Greeks. Russia occupied Turkish-held Moldavia and Wallachia. Turkey declared war **Oct. 4, 1853.** Britain and France, fearing Russian expansion declared war on Russia **May 28, 1854.** Fighting concentrated in the Crimea and included famous **Charge of the Light Brigade** at Balaklava **Oct. 25, 1854;** 400 of 607 killed; Russian defeat at Inkerman **Nov. 5, 1854;** fall of Sevastopol **Sept. 11, 1855. Florence Nightingale** established first dressing stations. By Treaty of Paris **Mar. 30, 1856,** Russia ceded part of Bessarabia to Moldavia, freed Danube for navigation. Black Sea closed to warships (later repudiated).

1854

Republican party formed at Ripon, Wis., **Feb. 28;** first state organization, Jackson, Mich., **July 6.** Opposed Kansas-Nebraska Act (became law May 30) which left issue of slavery in Kansas and Nebraska to vote of settlers.

Henry D. Thoreau wrote Walden.

1855

Walt Whitman published Leaves of Grass; **Henry W. Longfellow** wrote Song of Hiawatha.

1856

First railroad train crossed Mississippi on the river's first bridge, **Rock Island, Ill.-Davenport, Ia., Apr. 21.**

Republican party's first nominee for president, John C. Fremont **June-Nov.,** defeated by Democrat James Buchanan. Abraham Lincoln made 50 speeches for Fremont.

Lawrence, Kan., sacked May 21 by slavery party; abolitionist John Brown led anti-slavery men against Missourians at Osawatomie, Kan., **Aug. 30.**

1857

Dred Scott decision by U. S. Supreme Court held, 6-3, that a Negro slave did not become free when taken into a free state and had no rights as a citizen. Abraham Lincoln denounced decision. Minnesota outlawed slavery.

Great Mutiny in India (Sepoy Rebellion) began in Merrut **May 10** when Indian soldiers revolted against British officers; crushed **1858.** British East India Co. abolished and India placed under crown rule as a result of mutiny.

John D. Lee, a Mormon, led raid against wagon train at Mountain Meadows **Sept. 11,** killed 120, spared only 17 children under 7; U. S. Army supplies burned. Government sent 6,000 troops to suppress "rebellion." Mormon Church unjustly accused.

1858

First Atlantic cable completed by Cyrus W. Field **Aug. 5.** Queen Victoria and President Buchanan exchanged greetings, but cable failed **Sept. 1.** Field tried again in 1865, succeeded in 1866.

Lincoln-Douglas debates in Illinois **Aug. 21-Oct. 15.**

1859

Dixie, composed by Daniel D. Emmett, was first performed by him with Bryant's Minstrels at Mechanics Hall, N.Y. City **Apr. 4.**

First commercially productive oil well, drilled near Titusville, Pa., by Edwin L. Drake **Aug. 27.**

Abolitionist John Brown with 21 men seized U.S. Armory at Harpers Ferry (then Va.) **Oct. 16.** U.S. Marines under Lt. Col. Robert E. Lee captured raiders, killing 11. One Marine and 5 civilians also killed. Brown and 5 were hanged for treason by Virginia **Dec. 2** at Charleston (now Charles Town, W. Va.).

Charles Darwin published Origin of Species, expounding theory of evolution by natural selection.

1860

Abraham Lincoln, Republican, elected president by 1,866,352 popular and 180 electoral votes; Stephen A. Douglas had 1,375,157 and 12; John C. Breckinridge, 845,763 and 72; John Bell 589,581 and 39. Lincoln took office **Mar. 4, 1861.**

First Pony Express between Sacramento, Cal., and St. Joseph, Mo., 1,980 mi. apart, started from each place at 5 p.m., **Apr. 3;** 80 men used 429 horses, changed every 10 mi. There were 190 relay stations. The service ended **Oct. 24, 1861,** when first transcontinental telegraph line was completed.

Giuseppe Garibaldi led 1,000 volunteers to Sicily in **May** to unify Italy by force; deposed Francis II of Naples; named Victor Emmanuel king of Italy.

1861-65—Civil War.
See Article, Pages 724-725

1861

Emancipation of Russian serfs by Alexander II.

1863

Draft riots in N.Y. City killed an estimated 1,000, including Negroes who were hung by mobs **July 13-16;** protested provision allowing money payment in place of military service. Property loss about $1.5 million. Payment in place of service ended **1864.**

1864

Sand Creek massacre of Cheyenne and Arapaho indians by Col. John M. Chivington **Nov. 29** in a raid by 900 cavalrymen who killed between 150-500 men, women, and children; 9 soldiers died. The tribes were awaiting surrender terms when attacked.

1866

Ku Klux Klan formed secretly in South to terrorize Negroes who voted. Disbanded **1869-1871.** A 2d Ku Klux Klan was organized **1915.**

First post of the Grand Army of the Republic formed at Decatur, Ill., **Apr. 6.** First national encampment met **Nov. 2** in Indianapolis. For years this Union veterans organization was a political force in the nation. Last encampment held **Aug. 31, 1949,** in Indianapolis; 6 of the 16 surviving veterans attended.

1867

Alaska sold to U.S. by Russia for $7.2 million (less than 2 cents an acre) **Mar. 30** through efforts of Secretary of State William H. Seward.

Emperor Maximilian of Mexico executed by Juarez supporters **June 19.** He was an Austrian archduke placed on throne **Apr. 10, 1864,** by French.

Dominion of Canada established **July 1.**

Abolition of the Shogunate and restoration of the Mikado marked beginning of Meiji reforms that industrialized and modernized Japan; feudalism abolished **1871;** constitution promulgated **1889.**

1868

The World Almanac, a publication of the New York World, appeared for the first time.

Thomas D'Arcy McGee, a "Father of Confederation," shot in first Canadian political assassination.

Pres. Andrew Johnson, blocked by Senate in attempt to remove Edwin M. Stanton, secretary of war, for opposing his policies, was impeached for violation of Tenure of Office Act by House; tried by Senate and acquitted **March-May.** Stanton resigned.

1869

Financial "Black Friday" in New York **Sept. 24;** caused by attempt to "corner" gold.

Transcontinental railroad completed; golden spike driven at Promontory, Utah **May 10** marking the junction of Central Pacific and Union Pacific.

Woman suffrage law passed in Territory of Wyoming **Dec. 10.**

1870

Franco-Prussian War. Napoleon III, French emperor, tricked into declaring war on Prussia by Bismarck, Prussian chancellor, over Spanish succession issue; surrendered with large army at Sedan **Sept. 4.** Nationalists declared republic **Sept. 4.**

The troops of Victor Emmanuel II, under Gen. Cadorna, took possession of Rome Sept. 20 in the name of the kingdom of Italy. Rome and the rest of the Papal States then were annexed after a plebiscite taken **Oct. 2.**

1871

William I of Hohenzollern proclaimed German emperor (kaiser) at Versailles **Jan. 18.** Paris "Red Republicans" organized commune **Mar. 18-May 29;** burned Hotel de Ville, Tuileries palace, executed 67 hostages. Communards overcome by French army; deaths est. 20,000. (See 1870.)

Treaty of Frankfort ended Franco-Prussian War **May 23.** France ceded Alsace, most of Lorraine, paid 5 billion francs indemnity.

The Law of Guarantees, passed by the Italian Parliament **May 13,** granted the pope and his successors possession of the Vatican, the Lateran and the villa of Castel Gandolfo and a yearly 3,225,000 lire, or about $645,000. The money was not claimed.

Great fire destroyed Chicago Oct. 8-11; loss est. at $196 million. Supposedly started in Mrs. O'Leary's barn, 558 DeKoven St., by cow upsetting lantern.

Henry M. Stanley sent by James Gordon Bennett, owner of New York Herald, to find David Livingstone, missionary; greeted him **Nov. 10** at Ujiji in Central Africa, now Tanzania, with "Dr. Livingstone, I presume?"

1872

Amnesty Act restored civil rights to citizens of the South **May 22** except 500 Confederate leaders.

1873

Banks failed, panic began in N.Y. City **Sept. 20.**

First U. S. postal card issued **May 1.**

1874

"Boss" William Tweed of N. Y. City convicted of fraud **Nov. 19** and sentenced to 12 years in prison; the court released him from Blackwells Island prison **June 1875** on a technicality; he was committed to Ludlow St. jail in a civil suit, escaped **Dec. 4, 1875,** and went to Cuba, then to Spain; brought back to N.Y. City **Nov. 1876;** died in jail **Apr. 12, 1878.**

1875

Congress passed first Civil Rights Act. Mar. 1 which guaranteed equal rights to Negroes in public accommodations and jury duty. Act invalidated in **1883** by Supreme Court ruling that the federal government can protect only political, not social, rights.

First Kentucky Derby held **May 17,** at Churchill Downs, Louisville, Ky.

Mary Baker Eddy published "Science and Health"

1876

Samuel J. Tilden, Democrat, received majority of 250,807 popular votes for president over Rutherford B. Hayes, Republican, and had 184 electoral votes against 163, with returns from South Carolina, Florida, Louisiana, and Oregon, 22 electoral votes, in dispute. Bitter contest for delegates with charges of corruption; issue left to Congress, which appointed electoral commission, 8 Republicans, 7 Democrats; Hayes given presidency by strict party vote.

Col. George A. Custer and 264 soldiers of the 7th Cavalry killed **June 25** in "last stand," Battle of the Little Big Horn, Mont., in Sioux Indian War, by Indian tribes united by Sitting Bull; fighting led by Chiefs Gall and Crazy Horse.

James Butler (Wild Bill) Hickok, shot dead from behind by Jack McCall, a desperado, in Deadwood, S.D., **Aug. 2.** A vigilance committee acquitted McCall but the U.S. Court in Yankton, S.D., found him guilty and he was hanged.

1877

Molly Maguires, Irish terrorist society in Scranton,

Pa., mining areas, broken up by hanging of 11 leaders for murders of mine officials and police.

1878

First commercial telephone exchange opened, New Haven, Conn., **Jan. 28, 1878.** First private exchange, used by physicians, reported in use **July 1877** at Hartford, Conn.

1879

F. W. Woolworth opened his first five-and-ten store in Utica, N.Y., **Feb. 22.**

Henry George published Progress & Poverty, advocating single tax on land.

1881

Pres. James A. Garfield shot in Washington, D.C., **July 2;** died in Elberon, N.J., **Sept. 19.**

Federation of Organized Trades and Labor Unions formed **Aug. 2** at Terre Haute, Ind.; later joined with 25 independent unions to form the American Federation of Labor at Columbus, Oh., **Dec. 1886.**

1883

Brooklyn Bridge opened May 24; panic on it **May 30,** 12 trampled to death.

1884

Financial panic in N.Y. City **May 5-7.**

Major Events of Civil War, 1861-1865;

For origins of the Civil War see Index for Confederate States and Secession.

South Carolina, Georgia, Alabama, Mississippi, Louisiana, and Florida formed the Confederate States of America **Feb. 8, 1861,** chose Jefferson Davis provisional president; were joined later by Texas, North Carolina, Arkansas, Virginia, and Tennessee.

First Year of War — 1861

Gen. Pierre Beauregard, on Confederate Government orders, demanded surrender of Ft. Sumter in Charleston, S.C., harbor **Apr. 11;** Maj. Robert Anderson, USA, refused. Bombardment started at 4:30 a.m. **Apr. 12.** Anderson surrendered **Apr. 14.**

Pres. Lincoln called for 75,000 militia from states by quotas **Apr. 15.**

Battle of Bull Run or Manassas. Brig. Gen. Irvin McDowell attacked Beauregard's forces on the Warrenton Road **July 21,** pushed them back to Henry House hill. Gen. Joseph E. Johnston's army from Winchester, including forces commanded by Brig. Gen. Thomas J. Jackson and Gen. E. Kirby Smith reinforced Confederates, and with help of Gen. Jubal Early's brigade routed Federals. Brig. Gen. B. E. Bee, CSA, said: "Look, there is Jackson standing like a stone wall!" McDowell had 28,455 troops, 18,500 engaged, 2,708 casualties; Confederates had 32,072 available, 18,000 engaged, 1,967 casualties. Congress **July 22** authorized an army of 500,000.

Events of 1862

Forts Henry and Donelson — Brig. Gen. U.S. Grant with 17,000 attacked **Ft. Henry** on Tennessee River; it fell **Feb. 6.** Grant rushed troops across 10 mi. of bogs to **Ft. Donelson** on the Cumberland, sent his "unconditional surrender" message to Brig. Gen. Simon B. Buckner, CSA, who gave up with 11,500 **Feb. 16.**

Shiloh — Gen. Albert S. Johnston, CSA, with 40,000 men surprised Grant at **Shiloh Church** near **Pittsburg Landing,** Tenn. **Apr. 6;** Johnston was killed. Gen. Beauregard retreated **Apr. 7** after Brig. Gen. Don Carlos Buell reinforced Grant with about 20,000 men. U.S. had 44,895 engaged, with 1,734 killed of 13,047 total casualties; CSA, 1,728 killed of 10,699 casualties.

New Orleans — Fighting ships and gunboats under Flag Officer David G. Farragut took New Orleans Apr. 25. Farragut made rear admiral.

Monitor and Merrimack — Confederates rebuilt scuttled U.S. frigate Merrimack into ironclad Virginia. Sank Cumberland, USN, destroyed Congress, USN, at Hampton Roads, Va., **Mar. 8.** Three other U.S. ships ran aground including Minnesota. Monitor, flat-decked ironclad, 900 tons, 172 ft. long with revolving turret and 2 11-in. guns, built by John Ericsson at $275,000 cost; Lt. John L. Worden commander, crew of 58, badly damaged Virginia **Mar. 9.** After Union took Virginia's base, Confederates scuttled ship **May 11.**

Peninsular Campaign — McClellan moved Army of the Potomac by sea to Fort Monroe, Va., 70 mi. from Richmond. Confederates sent Stonewall Jackson up Shenandoah Valley to divert U.S. troops; Jackson lost at **Kernstown,** Va., but routed U.S. troops at **McDowell, Front Royal, Winchester, Cross Keys, Port Republic, Mar. 23-June 9.** McClellan's advance troops clashed with Maj. Gen. James Longstreet at **Williamsburg May 5.** On **May 25,** 2 U.S. corps crossed to south side of Chickahominy leaving 3 on north side. Gen. Joseph E. Johnston attacked south side **May 30. Battle of Fair Oaks** or **Seven Pines,** was repulsed. Johnston was wounded and Lee took over Army of Northern Virginia.

Gen. Lee started **Seven Days' Battles** at Mechanicsville, Va. **June 26.** McClellan withdrew to **Gaines Mill** (1st Cold Harbor) where Lee with 57,000 assaulted Brig. Gen. Fitz-John Porter's 34,000 **June 29. Frayser's Farm** or Glendale **June 30;** stopped Stonewall Jackson at **White Oak Swamp June 30.** At **Malvern Hill July 1** Confederates had 5,500 casualties, mostly from U.S. artillery; Union casualties were 2,000. Despite this success McClellan withdrew army to Harrison's Landing. With over 115,000 men available against Confederates' 95,000, McClellan from **June 25-July 1** had 1,734 killed, 8,062 wounded, 6,053 missing; CSA had 3,478 killed, 16,261 wounded, 875 missing. McClellan's army was sent to join Gen. John Pope's in northern Virginia.

Second Bull Run (Manassas). Stonewall Jackson and Maj. Gen. A. P. Hill, CSA, attacked Maj. Gen. Nathaniel P. Banks (part of Pope's Army of Virginia) at Cedar Mountain, Va. **Aug. 9.** Jackson destroyed Pope's supplies at **Manassas Aug. 26.** Major battle was fought **Aug. 30.** Pope was checked by Jackson and Longstreet, withdrew; was relieved.

Antietam (Sharpsburg). Lee with 50,000 crossed Potomac **Sept. 4** to Frederick, Md., moved across South Mountain to Hagerstown, Md. McClellan, fought Longstreet and D. H. Hill at **South Mountain Sept. 14,** Lee dropped back to Antietam Creek near Sharpsburg, Md., **Sept. 15;** Jackson took **Harpers Ferry** where only 1,300 cavalry of 12,000 USA escaped. McClellan attacked **Sept. 17;** stopped Lee, but failed to use reserve and let Lee withdraw across Potomac. U.S. had 70,000 engaged, 13,000 casualties; CSA had 50,000 engaged, 13,000 casualties.

Fredericksburg, Va. Lincoln relieved McClellan, gave Army of the Potomac to Maj. Gen. Ambrose E. Burnside. Burnside crossed Rappahannock, made frontal attacks on Marye's Heights above Fredericksburg **Dec. 13.** Lee, Longstreet and Jackson with 75,000 repulsed him. USA lost 12,653; CSA 5,377.

Preliminary proclamation, **Sept. 22,** by President Lincoln announced that **Jan. 1, 1863,** slaves would be declared free in territory then in rebellion.

Events of 1863

Lincoln's Emancipation Proclamation Jan. 1 declared free forever the slaves in Arkansas, Texas, Louisiana (certain parishes already occupied excepted); Mississippi, Alabama, Florida, Georgia, South Carolina, North Carolina, Tennessee, and Virginia (West Virginia and other portions excepted) About 3 million slaves were thus declared free.

Chancellorsville, Va. — Maj. Gen. Joseph E. Hooker succeeded Burnside and with 90,000 avail-

1885

Gen. Charles G. (Chinese) Gordon, British governor of the Sudan, sent there to aid Egyptian troops, was slain **Jan. 26** by a Moslem soldier, at Khartoum. Several thousand whites were massacred by troops of the Mahdi, Sudanese leader. Gen. Kitchener defeated the Mahdi's army **Sept. 2, 1898.**

First electric street railway in U.S. opened in Baltimore by Leo Daft **Aug. 10.**

Canadian rebel Louis Riel hanged for treason at Regina, following crushing of Northwest Rebellion.

Last spike driven Nov. 7 in Canadian Pacific Railway at Craigellachie, British Columbia, completed Canadian transcontinental railway.

1886

Haymarket riot, evening of **May 4,** followed bitter labor battles for 8-hour day in Chicago, attacks on strike-breakers, police violence, and attempts of anarchists to incite workers. A bomb killed 7 police and wounded 66. Eight anarchists found guilty. Gov. John P. Altgeld denounced trial as unfair.

Geronimo, Apache Indian, surrendered **Mar. 27** to U.S. Gen. George Crook in Sonora, Mex., but fled the next day and finally surrendered **Sept. 4** to U. S. Gen.

Emancipation and Lincoln's Assassination

able, attempted to envelop Lee **May 2.** Jackson led 32,000 around U.S. Army, drove in right of Maj. Gen. O. O. Howard. Jackson wounded by own troops **May 2** died **May 10;** succeeded by Maj. Gen. J. E. B. Stuart. Maj. Gen. John Sedgwick forced Confederates out of Marye's Heights; was pushed back May 4. Hooker overruled his advisers and withdrew across Rappahannock. U.S. casualties 17,197; CSA 13,000. Lincoln called for 100,000 men for 6 months June 15.

Gettysburg — Lee with 76,224 and 272 guns, invaded Penn. Army of the Potomac had 115,256, about 90,000 effective, 362 guns. Lincoln gave Maj. Gen. George G. Meade top command June 28. 1st U.S. Cavalry under Gen. John Buford pushed back at Gettysburg by Lt. Gen. A. P. Hill, CSA, **July 1.** Lt. Gen. Richard S. Ewell, CSA, forced U.S. back to Cemetery Hill; U.S. took Culp's Hill, extended line to Round Top. Lee's attacks checked **July 2.** On **July 3** Maj. Gen. George E. Pickett, Maj. Gen. Isaac Trimble, and Brig. Gen. James J. Pettigrew with 15,000 made assault on foot from Seminary Ridge vs. U.S. center held by Gen. W. S. Hancock; were repulsed with 4,500 casualties. Lee retreated into Virginia; Meade did not pursue. Losses: U.S. 3,155 killed, 14,529 wounded, 5,365 missing; CSA, 3,903 killed, 12,709 wounded, 5,425 missing. Many of the missing were prisoners. Total casualties estimated at 23,049 USA, 20,451 CSA.

Vicksburg — Gen. William T. Sherman took **Jackson, Miss., May 14.** Lt. Gen. John C. Pemberton, CSA, commanding 30,000 men, was defeated at **Champion's Hill** and **Black River Bridge,** and besieged in Vicksburg by Grant. He surrendered **July 4;** Grant paroled prisoners. Gen. Nathaniel Banks with 15,000 captured **Port Hudson July 8,** giving U.S. control of Mississippi River.

Tennessee — Maj. Gen. William S. Rosecrans, USA took **Chattanooga Sept. 9.** Braxton Bragg CSA, drove him back to **Chickamauga** but Maj. Gen. George H. Thomas checked Bragg **Sept. 18-20;** was called "Rock of Chickamauga." Hooker took **Lookout Mt.,** fought "Battle Above the Clouds" **Nov. 24.** Sherman and Thomas dislodged Bragg at **Missionary Ridge Nov. 25.** Bragg retreated to Georgia.

Events of 1864

Grant made general-in-chief Mar. 12. Sherman succeeded him in West. Draft for 500,000 men to serve 3 yrs. or duration begun **Mar. 10;** 20,000 more **Mar. 14.**

Rear Adm. David G. Farragut won naval battle of **Mobile Bay Aug. 5.**

Wilderness, Spotsylvania — Bloody battles followed when Grant crossed the Rapidan and was attacked by Lee in the "Wilderness," tangled woods west of Fredericksburg, **May 5.** Grant attacked Lee at **Spotsylvania Court House May 10** (2d Wilderness). Maj. Gen. Francis C. Barlow USA took Spotsylvania salient, including **Bloody Angle May 12** (3d Wilderness). U.S. killed and wounded May 5-12 est. 26,813, missing 4,183. Maj. Gen. Philip H. Sheridan's cavalry defeated Maj. Gen. J.E.B. Stuart at **Yellow Tavern, Va., May 11;** Stuart was fatally wounded, died **May 12** in Richmond.

Cold Harbor — Lee took strong position near the Chickahominy. Grant made frontal attacks **June 3,** lost 7,000 casualties in 30 minutes, 11,000 June 1-3.

USS Kearsarge — Capt. John A. Winslow defeated CSS Alabama, Capt. Raphael Semmes, off Cherbourg, France, **June 19;** Alabama surrendered and sank.

Early vs. Sheridan — Lee sent Maj. Gen. Jubal A. Early to hold Shenandoah Valley. Sheridan defeated Early at **Winchester Sept. 19, Fisher's Hill Sept. 22.** Early surprised Gen. Horatio Wright at **Cedar Creek Oct. 19;** Sheridan's famous ride from Winchester rallied troops, brought victory.

Sherman's Campaign for Atlanta — Sherman defeated J. E. Johnston at **Resaca, Ga., May 14-15.** Johnston repulsed Sherman at **Kenesaw Mtn. June 27** (U.S. casualties 3,000, CSA 600), but told Jefferson Davis he could not annihilate Sherman's large forces, was superseded by Gen. J. B. Hood, CSA, **July 17.** Lt. Gen. William J. Hardee, CSA, defeated at **Peach Tree Creek July 20.** Hardee defeated in battle of **Atlanta July 22** by Gen. J. B. McPherson who was killed. Sherman occupied Atlanta **Sept. 2,** burned it **Nov. 15,** started **March to the Sea,** reached **Savannah Dec. 21.** Thomas defeated Hood at **Nashville,** Tenn.

Events of 1865

Confederates evacuated Columbia, S.C., and **Charleston, S.C., Feb. 17,** lost Cape Fear River forts **Feb. 20-21.** Brig. Gen George A. Custer defeated Early at **Waynesboro, Va., Mar. 2.** Confederates evacuated **Petersburg** and **Richmond Apr. 2-3.** Lee surrendered 27,805 to Grant at **Appomattox Court House, Va., Apr. 9.** J. E. Johnston surrendered 31,243 to Sherman at **Durham Station,** N.C., **Apr. 18.**

Murder of Lincoln

Lincoln was shot by John Wilkes Booth, an actor, in Ford's Theatre, in Washington, D.C., **April 14,** died **April 15.** Booth died of a bullet wound **April 26,** in burning barn, on a farm near Bowling Green, Va. Hanged for complicity in Lincoln's assassination were Mrs. Mary E. Surratt, David E. Herold, George A. Atzerodt, and Lewis Payne (Powell) **July 7.** Also convicted of conspiracy were Dr. Samuel A. Mudd, who set Booth's broken ankle, Samuel Arnold, Michael O'Laughlin, and Edward Spangler. All were sentenced to life imprisonment except Spangler, who received a 6-year sentence. They were sent to Dry Tortugas prison, off Key West, where O'Laughlin died during an 1867 outbreak of yellow fever. Dr. Mudd's unselfish services as a physician during the outbreak won him a pardon; Arnold and Spangler were freed with Dr. Mudd in 1869. John H. Surratt, son of Mary E., fled to Europe, was brought back, tried and freed. Booth's body was buried under the stone floor of a naval prison in Washington, D. C., later reburied in the Booth family plot in Baltimore.

Slavery was abolished by adoption of the 13th amendment to the U.S. Constitution **Dec. 18.**

Nelson A. Miles in Arizona.

1887

Flood in Hwang-ho River, China; 900,000 persons perished.

1888

Great blizzard in eastern U. S. **Mar. 11-14;** 400 deaths.

1889

Crown Prince Rudolf of Austria and Baroness Maria Vetsera found slain in his hunting lodge, Mayerling, near Vienna **Jan. 29.**

Johnstown, Pa., flood May 31; 2,200 lives lost.

Universal Exhibition in Paris **May 6-Nov. 6.** Eiffel Tower (984.25 ft.) opened. First automobile exhibited, a Benz.

Dom Pedro II, emperor of Brazil, forced off throne by planters after he freed slaves. Died in Paris **1891;** last emperor on American soil.

1890

First execution by electrocution; William Kemmler **Aug. 6** at Auburn Prison, Auburn, N. Y., for murder.

Battle of Wounded Knee, S. D., **Dec. 29,** the last major conflict between Indians and U. S. troops, occurred when a band of Sioux were captured and brought to Wounded Knee Creek where Col. J. W. Forsyth ordered them disarmed. Some Indians resisted, sparking the battle which killed about 200 Indian men, women, and children; 29 soldiers died, 33 wounded. (See 1973, 1974.)

Castle Garden closed as immigration depot and Ellis Island opened Dec. 31; closed 1954.

1892

Homestead, Pa., strike at Carnegie steel mills, near Pittsburgh; conflict between 300 Pinkerton guards and strikers; 7 guards and 11 strikers and spectators shot to death, many wounded **July 6.**

1894

Chinese-Japanese War began **July 25;** Battle of Yalu **Sept. 17;** Treaty of Shimonoseki **April 17, 1895** gave Japan the Liaotung Peninsula, Formosa (Taiwan) and the Pescadores.

Jacob S. Coxey led 500 unemployed from the Midwest into Washington, D. C., **Apr. 29.** Coxey was arrested for trespassing on the Capitol grounds. **Strike of employees of Pullman Co.,** South Chicago, Ill., June, led Eugene V. Debs to call sympathetic strike of American Railway Union. Pres. Cleveland called out Federal troops over protest of Gov. Altgeld (Ill.). Debs and 3 others were imprisoned 6 months for contempt of court. Strike ended **Aug. 7.**

Thomas A. Edison's kinetoscope (invented 1887) given first public showing at 1155 Broadway, N.Y. City **Apr. 14,** was patented **1891** for U. S. only.

Capt. Alfred Dreyfus found guilty of betraying French army secrets **Dec. 22** in sensational frame-up; real culprit, Major Esterhazy, acquitted; Dreyfus condemned to Devil's Island, off French Guiana. Recalled for second trial by efforts of Emile Zola and Georges Clemenceau; again condemned **Sept. 9, 1899.** Public clamor led to pardon **Sept. 19.** Further proofs of innocence led to complete exoneration **1906.** He served as a lieutenant colonel in World War I.

1895

Cuban Revolution resumed **Feb. 20;** Gen. Antonio Maceo, leader of the insurrection, killed **Dec. 7, 1896.**

X-rays discovered by Wilhelm Konrad Roentgen, a German physicist; Nobel prize winner **1901.**

Sigmund Freud began publishing revolutionary theories on mental ills.

1896

Guglielmo Marconi received first wireless (radio) patent from Britain **June 2.**

William Jennings Bryan delivered "Cross of Gold" speech at Democratic National Convention in Chicago **July 8.** Bryan nominated for president but defeated by Republican William McKinley.

1897

Eugene V. Debs formed Social Democratic party.

1898

Radium discovered by Pierre Curie, his wife, Marie, and G. Bemont in Paris.

1898—Spanish-American War
See Article page 727

1899

South African (Boer) War began **Oct. 11;** Ladysmith relieved **Feb. 28, 1900;** Pretoria fell **June 5, 1900;** war ended **May 31, 1902** with loss of independence of Boer republics, Transvaal and Orange Free State, now in Republic of South Africa. British losses: 5,773 killed; 16,171 dead of wounds or disease; 22,829 wounded. Boers engaged est. 65,000; losses unknown.

Filipino insurgents (est. 12,000 under arms) unable to get recognition of independence from U. S. started guerrilla war **Feb. 4.** Crushed with capture **Mar. 23, 1901** of leader, Emilio Aguinaldo, by Brig. Gen. Frederick Funston.

Open Door Policy of U. S. Secy. of State John Hay supported by 6 nations. Policy was to make China an open market for international commerce and to preserve its integrity as a nation.

Boxer anti-foreign uprising started in China: Westerners and westernized Chinese murdered.

1900

Carry Nation, Kansas anti-saloon agitator, began raiding with hatchet.

Boxers in China killed German minister **June 20.** Foreigners besieged in Peking legations. Relief expedition of 18,000 American, British, French, Japanese, and Russian troops took Tientsin **July 13;** Peking **Aug. 14.** U. S. had 2,500 men under Maj. Gen. A. R. Chaffee. Germans arrived and Field Marshal Count Alfred von Waldersee led army of occupation. Russia refused to yield parts of Manchuria. Dowager empress of China accepted allied terms **Sept. 1901.** All except U. S. exacted large concessions and indemnity of $333 million payable in 39 years. U.S. used half its $25 million share to provide Chinese students scholarships.

Campaign to wipe out yellow fever in Cuba begun **June 26** by Drs. Walter Reed, Aristides Agramonte, Jesse Lazear, and James Carroll.

1901

Pres. William McKinley was shot at the Pan-American Exposition in Buffalo, N. Y., **Sept. 6** by Leon Czolgosz, anarchist; died **Sept. 14.** Theodore Roosevelt, 42, became youngest U. S. president.

Marconi signalled letter "S" by wireless telegraph across Atlantic from Cornwall, England, to Newfoundland **Dec. 12.**

1902

Cuban Republic inaugurated. American occupation under Gen. Leonard Wood ended **May 20.**

First International Arbitration Court opened in The Hague, Holland, **October.**

1903

First automobile trip across U. S. from San Francisco to New York **May 23-Aug. 1.**

Treaty between U. S. and Colombia to have U. S. dig Panama Canal signed **Jan. 22, 1903,** rejected by Colombia. Panama declared independence **Nov. 3;** recognized by Pres. Theodore Roosevelt **Nov. 6.**

First successful flight in heavier-than-air mechanically propelled airplane by **Orville Wright** (1871-1948) **Dec. 17, 1903,** rising from base of Kill Devil Hill, 4 miles south of Kitty Hawk, N. C., 120 ft. in 12 sec. Fourth flight same day by **Wilbur Wright** (1867-1912), 852 ft., in 59 sec. Plane patented **May 22, 1906.**

1904

Russo-Japanese War began **Feb. 6.** Port Arthur surrendered to Japanese **Jan. 2, 1905.** Peace treaty signed in Portsmouth, N. H., **Sept. 5, 1905.**

New York subway opened **Oct. 27.**

1905

Russian revolution crushed by Czar Nicholas II. Resulted in creation of Duma (parliament) to placate iberals. First meeting **May 10;** dissolved in **July.**

Norway dissolved union with Sweden.

1906

San Francisco earthquake and fire **Apr. 18-19.** Dead: 452. Loss: $350 million.

Harry K. Thaw, Pittsburgh millionaire, shot and killed architect Stanford White on roof of Madison Square Garden, N.Y. (26th and Madison) **June 25** on ground of avenging honor of wife Evelyn Nesbit.

1907

Financial panic in the U.S.

Standard Oil of Indiana fined $29,240,000 by Judge K. M. Landis in U. S. Court, Chicago, for accepting freight rebates **Apr. 3.** Set aside **July 22, 1908.** Railroads found guilty of giving rebates.

First round-world cruise of U.S. "Great White Fleet"; 16 battleships, 12,000 men.

1909

Adm. Robert E. Peary reached North Pole **Apr. 6** on 6th attempt, accompanied by Matthew Henson, a black, and 4 Eskimos.

Louis Bleriot flew across the English Channel from Calais to Dover, 31 mi. in 37 min., **July 25.**

1910

Boy Scouts of America founded **Feb. 8.**

Glenn H. Curtiss won $10,000 offered by the New York World for first continuous flight, Albany to N.Y. City, 137 mi., 152 min., **May 29.**

Dynamite explosion at Los Angeles Times **Oct. 1** caused fire killing 21 in labor dispute.

1911

Italian-Turkish war began **Sept. 29.** Italians made first combat use of aircraft in warfare; Libya acquired by Italy.

First transcontinental airplane flight (with numerous stops) by C. P. Rodgers, New York to Pasadena, **Sept. 17-Nov. 5;** time in air 82 hr., 4 min.

Capt. Roald Amundsen, Norwegian explorer, reached South Pole **Dec. 14.**

Mexican Revolution. Porfirio Diaz, president of Mexico since **1877** (except **1880-84**),resigned **May 25** after successful revolt by Francisco L. Madero who succeeded him. People living in poverty wanted restoration of communal lands (ejidos), better conditions. In **1912** Madero, supported by Gen. Huerta, put down revolts. In **Feb. 1913** Huerta helped depose Madero; Madero, his brother, and Vice Pres. Suarez were murdered. Pres. Wilson refused recognition to Huerta and "government by assassination." Venustiano Carranza, rallying Maderos, was opposed by Gen. Francisco (Pancho) Villa in north. When American sailors were arrested at Tampico **Apr. 9, 1914,** the U.S. sent Atlantic fleet to Veracruz. Huerta resigned **July 14, 1914,** Carranza occupied Mexico City **Aug. 20.** Villa, supported by Zapata, warred on Carranza. U.S. recognized Carranza **Oct. 19, 1915,** placed embargo on arms to other generals. Villa raided Santa Isabel, Mexico, **Jan. 10, 1916,** killed several Americans; raided Columbus, N. M., **Mar. 9, 1916,** killed 17. Gen. John J. Pershing with 12,000 sent into Mexico **Mar. 15.** Fight at Parral and Chihuahua **Apr. 12.** Carranza's troops attacked **June 21.** U. S. troops withdrawn **Feb. 4, 1917.** Carranza called constitutional convention, **Feb. 15, 1917,** became legal president **May 1, 1917.** He restored some of the land, nationalized coal and oil, expropriated some foreign holdings. Discontent caused new uprising and he was ambushed and killed. Obregon became president **Dec. 1, 1920.** Villa was killed in ambush at Parral **July 20, 1923.**

Chinese Revolution led by Sun Yat-sen overthrew Manchu dynasty. Republic formed **Feb. 12, 1912.**

Parliament Act of 1911 reduced the power of British House of Lords to a suspensory veto which could delay but not kill bills.

1912

Capt. Robert F. Scott and 4 companions reached South Pole **Jan. 17;** all 5 died on return journey.

White Star liner Titanic wrecked on maiden trip, from Southampton to N.Y. City; hit iceberg off New-

Spanish-American War of 1898; U.S. Becomes Naval Power

Spanish misrule in Cuba led to repeated attempts by Cuban patriots to gain rights of citizenship, abolition of slavery, and finally independence. When South America broke from Europe in the 1820s proslavery influence in the U.S. blocked movements to free Cuba and Puerto Rico. But in 1852, Pres. Fillmore refused to join Great Britain and France in guaranteeing Spanish authority in Cuba. In 1854, the Ostend Manifesto, written largely by James Buchanan, urged the U.S. to buy Cuba or seize it to abolish oppression. Grant's administration offered to buy Cuba, but Spain rejected the offer.

In Cuba revolts led by Narciso Lopez and Joaquin de Aguero, 1848-1851, were suppressed and the leaders executed. In 1868, a major revolt was led by Carlos de Cespedes and Manuel de Quesada; it lasted 10 years. In 1873, the Virginius expedition, flying the American flag, was seized by the Spaniards, and Americans and Cubans aboard were shot. This did not stop supplying of arms from the U.S. In 1895, the insurrection had spread so widely under Generals Calixto Garcia, Maximo Gomez, and Antonio Macea that Spain landed 150,000 troops, but by 1896 over half of the island was in the hands of the patriots. The U.S. offered to mediate but was repulsed. The country was laid waste by Spanish troops and the accounts of suffering increased sentiment in the U.S. in favor of a free Cuba.

The U.S. battleship Maine, sent to Havana in **Jan.** on goodwill tour, was blown up **Feb. 15, 1898;** 264 men, 2 officers killed. U.S. inquiry blamed external explosion **Mar. 2.** Spanish inquiry **Mar. 28** blamed internal explosion. Congress **Mar. 9** voted $50 million for defense. President McKinley **Mar. 27** demanded Spain grant armistice for negotiation with Cuba via U.S., end relocation of noncombatants in special military enclaves. Spain **Mar. 31** offered to arbitrate Maine charges, end relocation, but wanted Cubans to ask for armistice. After appeal by foreign ministers Spain granted armistice **Apr. 9.** McKinley **Apr. 11** asked Congress for authority to intervene in Cuba. Congress **Apr. 20-25** debated joint resolution recognizing independence of Cuba, asked Spain to withdraw and empowered president to enforce it; adopted it with statement war existed since **Apr. 21.** Spain declared war **Apr. 24.**

Commodore George Dewey, with 6 warships, destroyed the Spanish fleet (10 ships) in Manila Bay **May 1,** occupied Cavite. Spain, 167 dead; U.S., 7 wounded. Marines landed at Guantanamo **May 11.** Maj. Gen. William R. Shafter landed 10,000 men at Daiquiri and Siboney, including 1st U.S. Volunteer Cavalry (Rough Riders) recruited by Lt. Col. Theodore Roosevelt. El Caney and San Juan Hill were captured **July 1.**

Admiral Cervera's fleet left Santiago harbor **July 3,** was destroyed by ships of acting Rear Adm. Sampson and Commodore Winfield S. Schley; 353 Spaniards killed, 151 wounded; one American killed. Santiago surrendered **July 17.** Maj. Gen. Nelson A. Miles took Puerto Rico **July 25-28.** Armistice signed **Aug. 12.** Peace treaty signed in Paris **Dec. 10** eliminated Spain from lands discovered by Columbus. U.S. acquired Puerto Rico, Guam and Philippines, paying $20 million for all Spanish claims in latter; guaranteed Cuban independence (ratified **Feb. 6, 1899.**) U.S. had treaty rights in Cuba until 1934; granted Philippines independence **July 4, 1946.**

foundland **Apr. 14-15**; U. S. reported 1,517 lost; British reported 1,503 lost. There were 2,307 persons aboard. Ship was 882 1/2 ft. long, cost $7.5 million.

War in Balkans against Turkey by Montenegro, Bulgaria, Serbia, and Greece **Oct. 8-Dec. 3**. Turks driven from Europe except for Constantinople (Istanbul) area.

1913

Sixteenth Amendment effective **Feb. 25** empowered Congress to levy and collect income taxes.

Albert Einstein began publishing his theory of relativity.

1914

Ford Motor Co. raised basic wage rates from $2.40 for 9-hr. day to $5 for 8-hr. day, **Jan. 5.**

First ship passed through Panama Canal **Aug. 15.**

Second International: Brussels meeting of International Socialist Bureau **July.** Members included 5 men later heads of governments: Lenin (Russia); Ebert (German Republic); Stauning (Denmark); Branting (Sweden); MacDonald (Britain).

1915

First telephone talk, New York to San Francisco, **Jan. 25** by Alexander Graham Bell and Thomas A. Watson.

First successful wireless from moving Lackawanna train to station, **Feb. 7.**

Twenty-one Demands presented by Japan to China; called for almost complete control of China.

1916

Gregory Rasputin, confessor to czarina, killed in Petrograd (Leningrad) **Dec.**

Bomb exploded during San Francisco Preparedness Day Parade **July 22,** killed 10, wounded 40. Thomas J. Mooney, 33, labor organizer; Warren K. Billings, shoe worker, were convicted of murder. Mooney was sentenced to death, Billings to life imprisonment. Pres. Wilson interceded for Mooney, who got life imprisonment 1918. Mooney was pardoned by Gov. C. L. Olson **Jan. 7, 1939;** Billings freed **Oct. 16, 1939.**

Principal Events of World War I,

Origins. Since the defeat of France by Prussia in 1870-71 major powers of Europe had kept peace by diplomatic negotiations and a balance of power. Triple Alliance, of Germany, Austria and Italy was defensive, with reservations; Triple Entente was an understanding between Britain, France and Russia. Nationalist aspirations in the Balkans had resulted in several wars and Italy had fought with Turkey and Ethiopia; Austria annexed Bosnia, Herzegovina, former Turkish Balkan provinces, in 1908. Russia backed Serbia's efforts to get a port on the Adriatic. Germany's industrial expansion led to building of powerful navy, which Britain matched 2 for one. Germany's universal military service led France to adopt 3-year training.

On **June 28, 1914,** Archduke Francis Ferdinand, heir to Austrian throne, was assassinated, with his wife, by Gavrillo Princip, Bosnian Serb terrorist, in Sarajevo, Bosnia. Austria-Hungary, through Count Berchthold, foreign minister, made 10 demands on Serbia for suppression of anti-Austrian agitation. Serbia conceded all but 2, which called for Austrian enforcement police inside Serbia. It asked reference to The Hague peace tribunal. Austria demanded all or nothing.

Russia supported Serbia. Germany backed Austria. Britain, France, Italy proposed mediation; Sir Edward Grey, British foreign minister, **July 26** proposed conference of 4 major powers; Germany refused.

Austria declared war on Serbia **July 28.** Germany, citing Russian mobilization, declared war on Russia **Aug. 1;** on France **Aug. 3.** Germans entered Belgium in violation of treaty, of which Britian was cosigner. Britain asked Germany to guarantee neutrality of Belgium by midnight **Aug. 4;** Germany refused; British declared war **Aug. 4.** Italy, declaring German aggression made Triple Alliance inoperative, proclaimed neutrality. Japan declared war on Germany **Aug. 23** because of Anglo-Japanese treaty on Far East. Turkey joined Central Powers **Nov. 23.**

Lord Kitchener became British sec. for war. Belgian forts at Liege stopped Germans until **Aug. 7,** delayed German schedule. Germans entered Brussels **Aug. 20;** pushed back British Expeditionary Force (Sir John French) at Mons **Aug. 23-24;** burned most of Louvain **Aug. 25.** Von Hindenburg and Ludendorff defeated Russians at **Tannenberg,** East Prussia, **Aug. 26-31;** at **Masurian Lakes Sept. 5-10.**

In first Battle of the Marne, Sept. 5-10, French under Joseph Joffre, Ferdinand Foch and Joseph Gallieni, stopped German advance of Von Kluck and Von Bulow toward Paris; forced them back to Aisne where trench warfare began. Belgians lost Antwerp **Oct. 9.** British repulsed Germans at **Ypres Oct. 16-Nov. 24.** Russians forced Austrians back in Galicia. Austrians took and lost Belgrade **Dec. 2-15.**

British bombarded Dardanelles forts **Nov. 3;** declared war on Turkey, annexed Cyprus **Nov. 5.** Japan took German-leased Tsingtao **Nov. 6.**

1915—Submarine War Begins

In 1915 the war became a desperate battle of attrition on land and sea. British sank German cruiser Bluecher **Jan. 24.** Germany ordered submarine blockade of Britain to start **Feb. 18.** U. S. held Germany to "strict accountability" for American losses. Germans used liquid fire in Vosges **Mar. 3.** Roving German cruiser Dresden sunk in Pacific **Mar. 15.** Three British, French battleships sunk at Dardanelles **Mar. 18.** Turks sank British battleship Lord Nelson **Apr. 6.** Germans introduced poison gas at **Ypres Apr. 22,** Canadians saved the line. Allies landed at **Gallipoli Apr. 25.** Germans torpedoed Gulflight, U.S. tanker, **Apr. 30,** 2 Americans lost.

German sub sank Cunard liner **Lusitania** off Old Head of Kinsale, Ireland, **May 7;** of 1,959 aboard, including 702 crew, 1,198, including 124 Americans, died. This started a series of protests by U.S. to Germany. Secy. of State William J. Bryan resigned **June 8;** considered Wilson's Lusitania note too severe. After sinking Arabic **Aug. 19** Germans agreed not to sink liners without warning, but U.S. considered promises inadequate. U.S. dismissed Austrian Ambassador Dumba and Germans Boy-Ed and Von Papen for illegal activities.

South Africans under Gen. Botha captured German S. W. Africa. Italy declared war on Austria-Hungary **May 23,** on Turkey **Aug. 20,** on Germany **Aug. 27.** Bulgaria declared war on Serbia **Oct. 14;** Allies against Bulgaria **Oct. 15-19.** Germans occupied Russian Baltic ports, took Vilna; Austrians occupied Serbia. Allies landed at Salonika **Oct. 5.** Sir John French replaced by Sir Douglas Haig on British front **Dec. 15.** Allies began evacuation of Gallipoli (Dardanelles) **Dec. 19.**

1916—Vast Battles

Germany announced Feb.10 that armed merchant ships would be considered warships and sunk without warning. U.S. retorted **Feb. 15** international law permitted self-defense of commercial ships. Germans

1917

The 18th (Prohibition) Amendment to the Constitution was submitted to the states by Congress **Dec. 18.** On **Jan. 16, 1919,** the 36th state (Nebraska) ratified it, whereupon, by proclamation of the sec. of state, it became effective **Jan. 16, 1920.** The **Volstead (Prohibition Enforcement) Act** was passed by Congress **Oct. 1919,** was vetoed by Pres. Wilson, passed over his veto **Jan. 17, 1920.** Franklin D. Roosevelt, as 1932 presidential candidate, endorsed repeal; 21st Amendment repealed 18th; ratification completed **Dec. 5, 1933.**

Balfour Declaration Nov. 2 favored establishment of a national homeland in Palestine for Jews.

1918

Romanovs killed. Czar Nicholas II of Russia, the Empress Alexandra; their daughters, Olga, Tatiana, Marie, Anastasia; their son, Alexis, and aides were shot by Bolshevist orders in Ekaterinburg **July 16;** in Perm **July 12** the Bolshevists assassinated the Czar's brother, Grand Duke Michael.

Influenza epidemic killed estimated 20 million throughout world, 548,000 in U.S.

1919

Rosa Luxemburg and Karl Liebknecht, leading German socialists and founders of the Spartacan party, shot and killed **Jan.** by soldiers who were taking them to prison.

Peace conference opened in Paris **Jan. 18;** treaty, including U.S. Pres. Wilson's proposed League of Nations, signed in palace at Versailles **June 28** between German representatives and Allied powers. Wilson submitted treaty to Senate **July 10;** ratified by Germany, Britain, Italy, France, Japan. Not signed by China. Rejected by U.S. Senate **Nov. 19** which considered American sovereignty not properly safeguarded in League of Nations.

First Transatlantic Flight U.S. Navy seaplane NC-4, commanded by Lt. Com. Albert Cushing Read, left Rockaway, N.Y., **May 8;** stopped at Trepassey, Newfoundland; left **May 16,** reached Azores **May 17;** Lisbon **May 27;** Plymouth, England, **May 31;** covered

1914-1918; Why U.S. Intervened

made huge effort vs. Verdun **Feb. 21,** took Ft. Douaumont **Feb. 25.** Germany declared war on Portugal **Mar. 8.** Russians invaded Persia **Mar. 10.** Wilson threatened **Apr. 18-19** to break relations unless Germany revised sub warfare; Germany met most of U.S. demands.

Uprising in Ireland Apr. 24-May 1. Patrick Pearse et al, executed; Sir Roger Casement hanged **Aug. 3.** Britain adopted conscription **May 24. Jutland** naval battle **May 31-June 1:** British Admirals Jellicoe and Beatty lost 5 major cruisers, 8 destroyers, 6,091 men; German Admirals Scheer and von Hipper lost 2 major ships, also cruisers, destroyers, 2,545 men. **Battle of Ypres June 2.** Lord Kitchener was lost when Hampshire disappeared at sea in **June. Battle of the Somme July 1-10;** second battle **July 11-Aug. 3.** Romania joined Allies **Aug. 16** was defeated by **Jan., 1917.** U.S., **Nov. 29,** protested deportation of Belgian workers into Germany.

Germany and its allies called for peace negotiations **Dec. 12, 1916** to halt bloodshed. Germany told the Vatican it was fighting for the integrity of its frontiers and development in peaceful competition. On **Dec. 18, 1916,** Pres. Wilson asked the belligerents to state their aims and terms; in order to end rival alliances he asked formation of a League of Nations and protection of "weak peoples." The Allies called the German offer "empty and insincere." They also told Pres. Wilson they wanted "restorations, reparations, indemnities."

1917—U. S. Enters War

When **Germany began unrestricted submarine war,** the U.S. **Feb. 3** broke relations, refused negotiations until order was rescinded. Wilson **Feb. 26** asked Congress to order arming of merchant ships; when Senate refused Wilson armed them by executive order **Mar. 12.** Intercepted note of German Foreign Sec. **Zimmerman to** German minister in Mexico suggested Mexico be asked to enter war to recover U.S. Southwest **Feb. 28.** U.S. declared war on Germany **Apr. 6,** adopted selective conscription **May 18,** registered men aged 21-30 **June 5.** First of American Expeditionary Force (AEF) landed in France **June 26;** Gen. John J. Pershing, commander-in-chief, Adm. William S. Sims, chief Naval Operations, Europe. U.S. declared war on Austria-Hungary **Dec. 7.**

Collapse of Russian Empire. When navy and army revolted **Mar. 11-15** Czar Nicholas II abdicated. Provisional govt. made **Kerensky** premier **July 20.** Offensive in Galicia failed. In **April** Germans moved **Lenin** and associates from Switzerland to Russia via Sweden to disrupt war. Bolshevists overthrew **Kerensky Nov. 7,** formed socialist republic of workers and peasants with Lenin president of Council of Commissars; made peace with Germany, Austria-Hungary, Bulgaria and Turkey at **Brest-Litovsk Mar. 3, 1918.** Russians withdrew from Lithuania, Estonia, Latvia, Ukraine, Poland, Finland.

Other Fronts. Huge losses by Allies at Vimy, Arras, Cambrai, Passchendaele, Verdun. Petain succeeded Nivelle as French commander-in-chief. British took Jaffa, Baghdad, Jerusalem. Germans forced Italians back to Piave River.

1918—Victory for U. S. and Allies

German submarine war, Feb. 1, 1917-Feb. 1, 1918, cost U. S. 69 ships (171,061 tons); U. S. seized 686,494 German-Austrian tonnage. British lost 1,169 ships. Allies & neutrals lost 6,617,000 tons.

Pres. Wilson presented his **14 points** for peace to Congress **Jan. 8.** Asked open diplomacy; freedom of seas; restoration of Alsace-Lorraine to France; independence for Poland and Austrian minorities; "a general association of nations" to guarantee political and economic independence.

Collapse of Russian front released German troops for powerful thrusts on West front. **Battle of the Somme, Mar. 21-Apr. 6.** Gen. Foch made supreme commander **Mar. 26. Battle of the Aisne May 27-June 5;** AEF took Cantigny **May 28.** Germans reached Marne. AEF fought at **Chateau Thierry, Belleau Woods.** German retreat began **July 19.** AEF took **St. Mihiel** salient **Sept. 12-20,** fought at **Meuse-Argonne Sept. 20-Nov. 11.** British broke **Hindenburg line Sept. 27.**

Bulgaria gave up **Sept. 30;** Czar Ferdinand abdicated. Turkish armistice **Oct. 30.** Italians defeated Austrians at **Vittorio Veneto,** Austria and Hungary formed separate republics **Nov. 1,** Austria surrendered **Nov. 4.**

Germans accepted Pres. Wilson's terms and recalled submarines **Oct. 20;** U. S. troops reached Sedan **Nov. 7;** revolution in Kiel and Hamburg **Nov. 7;** Bavaria proclaimed a republic **Nov. 8;** Kaiser abdicated **Nov. 9,** fled to Holland. Armistice signed in Marshal Foch's railway coach, near Compiegne, France, took effect **Nov. 11;** bugles sounded "cease firing" at **11 a.m.** German fleet surrendered to British **Nov. 21;** AEF entered Mainz **Dec. 6;** crossed Rhine **Dec. 13.**

4,500 mi. **John Alcock** and **A. W. Brown** made **June 14-15,** a non-stop air flight from Newfoundland to Ireland. A British dirigible, R-34, left Scotland **July 2** and descended in Mineola, N. Y., **July 6.** It left for England **July 10** and arrived there **July 13.** A round-trip transcontinental air race, New York - San Francisco, was won by **Lt. W.B. Maynard** and **Lt. Alex Pearson Oct. 8-18**.

1920

League of Nations held first meeting at Geneva, Switzerland, **Jan. 10;** was dissolved **Jan. 10, 1946.**

The 19th (Woman Suffrage) Amendment, having been adopted by Congress, 1918-1919, and ratified by Tennessee (36th state to do so) Aug. 18, 1920, was proclaimed adopted **Aug. 26.** It had been first introduced in Congress in 1878; by 1918, women had won the vote under laws of 15 states. The amendment gave women full, nationwide voting rights.

Nicola Sacco, 29, shoe factory employee and radical agitator, and **Bartolomeo Vanzetti,** 32, fish peddler and anarchist, accused of killing 2 men in payroll holdup at South Braintree, Mass., **Apr. 15.** Found guilty **1921** they became objects of 6-year campaign for release on grounds of want of conclusive evidence and prejudice of court. Appeals failing, they were executed at Charlestown, Mass., prison **Aug. 22, 1927.** Trial sharply criticized by Wickersham Commission on law procedure.

Wall St., N.Y. City, bomb explosion killed 30, injured 100; did $2 million damage **Sept. 16.**

1921

Joint Congressional resolution declaring peace with Germany, Austria, and Hungary signed **July 2** by Pres. Harding, treaties were signed in **Aug.**

Limitation of Armaments Conference met in Washington **Nov. 12, 1921—Feb. 6, 1922.** U.S., Britain, France, Italy, Japan agreed to curtail naval construction. Nine powers outlawed poison gas and restricted submarine attack on merchantmen. U.S., Britain, France, Japan agreed on integrity of China. Ratified **Aug. 5, 1925.**

1922

Violence during coal-mine strike at Herrin, Ill., **June 22-23** cost 36 lives, 21 of them non-union miners.

Fascist march on Rome Oct. 30; Mussolini took power in Italy.

1923

Occupation of Ruhr by French and Belgian troops to enforce reparations began **Jan. 11.**

First sound-on-film moving picture "Phonofilm" was shown by Lee de Forest at Rivoli Theatre, N.Y. City, beginning **Apr.**

Beer Hall Putsch in Munich led by Gen. Ludendorff and Adolf Hitler **Nov. 8-9.** Several supporters killed in street clashes. Ludendorff was arrested and paroled; Hitler was wounded. He was arrested **Nov. 12** and imprisoned at Landsberg where he wrote Mein Kampf (served 9 months of 5-year sentence).

1924

Dawes Reparation Plan accepted by Allies and Germany in London **Aug. 16.** French troops began evacuation of the Ruhr **Aug. 18.**

Nellie Tayloe Ross elected governor of Wyoming **Nov. 9** after death of her husband **Oct. 2;** installed **Jan. 5, 1925,** first woman governor. Miriam (Ma) Ferguson was elected governor of Texas **Nov. 9;** installed **Jan. 20, 1925.**

1925

John T. Scopes was found guilty of having taught evolution in Dayton, Tenn., high school and was fined $100 and costs **July 24.** The last state law prohibiting teaching evolution in public schools was ruled unconstitutional by the Mississippi Supreme Court **Dec. 2, 1970.**

By Treaty of Locarno Oct. 16 Germany agreed to demilitarization of Rhineland and security of Franco-German and Belgo-German frontiers.

1926

Dr. Robert H. Goddard demonstrated practicality of rockets **Mar. 16** at Auburn, Mass., with first liquid fuel rocket flight; rocket traveled 184 ft. in 2.5 secs.

General strike paralyzed Britain **May 3-12.** Parliament passed act making general strike illegal.

Germany admitted to League of Nations Sept. 8.

1927

About 1,000 U.S. Marines landed in China **Mar. 5** to protect property in civil war. U.S. and British consulates looted by nationalists **Mar. 24.**

Capt. Charles A. Lindbergh, U.S. air mail pilot, left Roosevelt Field, N. Y., at 7:52 a.m., **May 20** alone in monoplane, Spirit of St. Louis, competing for Raymond Orteig's offer of $25,000 for first New York-Paris non-stop flight. Reached Le Bourget airfield, Paris, 5:21 p.m. (10:21 p.m. Paris time) **May 21,** 3,610 mi. in 33 hrs. 29 min., 30 sec. Returned on U.S. cruiser Memphis with plane; given rank of colonel. Tremendous ticker tape parade, N. Y. City **June 13.**

The Jazz Singer, with Al Jolson, demonstrated part-talking pictures in N.Y. City **Oct. 6.**

1928

First all-talking picture, Lights of New York, presented at Strand, N.Y. City, **July 6.**

Kellogg-Briand Peace Pact signed **Aug. 27** by 62 nations; condemned the use of war as an instrument of national policy.

Dirigible Graf Zeppelin, Capt. Hugo Eckener, with 20 passengers and 38 crew, flew from Friedrichshafen, Germany to Lakehurst, N.J., **Oct. 11-15;** returned **Oct. 29-31.** Made round-the-world trip from Friedrichshafen with 20 passengers **Aug. 14-Sept. 4, 1929,** via Tokyo, Los Angeles, Lakehurst.

Stalin issued **first 5-year plan:** rapid, ruthless industrialization of Russian economy.

1929

"**St. Valentine's Day massacre**" in Chicago **Feb. 14;** gangsters killed 7 rivals.

The Papal State, extinct since **1870,** revived as State of Vatican City, at Rome **June 7.**

Albert B. Fall, former sec. of the interior, was convicted of accepting a bribe of $100,000 from Edward L. Doheny in the leasing of the Elk Hills **(Teapot Dome)** naval oil reserve. He was sentenced **Nov. 1** to $100,000 fine and a year in prison.

Stock Market crash Oct. 29 marked end of postwar prosperity as stock prices plummeted. Decline in value estimated at $15 billion by end of 1929; stock losses for 1929-1931 estimated at $50 billion; worst American depression began.

1930

London Naval Reduction Treaty signed by U.S., Britain, Italy, France and Japan **Apr. 22;** in effect **Jan. 1, 1931.** Set proportional reductions of the navies of each country. Its terms expired **Dec. 31, 1936.**

1931

British Parliament gave legal status to declaration of Imperial Conference of 1926 proclaiming Britain and the dominions, including Canada, completely equal and "in no way subordinate one to another."

Mukden Incident occurred **Sept. 18** when Japanese troops attacked Mukden garrison and then overran Manchuria. China protested to League of Nations.

1932

Japan sends troops into China Jan. 27 following murder of Japanese Buddhist priest in Shanghai.

Manchuria became Manchukuo (Japanese puppet state) **Feb. 18;** Henry Pu Yi, Manchu emperor who abdicated in 1912, installed as ruler **Mar. 9.**

Charles Lindbergh Jr. kidnaped **Mar. 1,** found dead, **May 12.**

Bonus March on Washington **May 29** by World War I veterans demanding Congress pay their bonus in full. Army, under Gen. Douglas MacArthur, disbanded the marchers on Pres. Hoover's orders.

1933

Adolf Hitler became German chancellor **Jan. 30.**

German Reichstag building in Berlin was destroyed **Feb. 27** by fire believed set by Nazis, although Marinus van der Lubbe, Dutch communist, was found guilty; beheaded **Jan. 10, 1934.**

All banks in the U.S. were ordered closed by Pres. Roosevelt **Mar. 6.**

Gold standard dropped by U.S.; announced by Pres. Roosevelt on **Apr. 19** and ratified by Congress **June 5.**

Spain, by parliamentary edict, May 17 disestablished the Roman Catholic church.

Germany quit the League of Nations **Oct. 14.**

Pres. Roosevelt accorded diplomatic recognition to the Soviet Union **Nov. 16.**

Prohibition ended in the U.S. as Utah, 36th state, ratified 21st Amendment to Constitution **Dec. 5,** repealing 18th (Prohibition) Amendment.

1934

The Dionne sisters, first quintuplets to survive beyond infancy, were born **May 28** in Callender, Ont., Canada, to Mr. and Mrs. Oliva Dionne.

Pres. von Hindenburg of Germany died **Aug. 2. Adolf Hitler** consolidated offices of president and chancellor, became "fuehrer."

Long March by Chinese Communists started **Oct.** Mao Tse-tung led 100,000 in 6,000-mi. trek from south to north China; only 20,000 completed journey and reached Yenan **Oct. 1935.**

1935

Hitler renounced Versailles Treaty, ordered conscription in Germany **Mar. 10.**

Will Rogers, 56, comedian, and Wiley Post, 36, aviator, were killed **Aug. 15** in Alaskan plane crash.

Social Security Act passed by Congress **Aug. 14.**

Ethiopia appealed to League of Nations after Italy invaded Ethiopia **Oct. 2-4.**

Economic sanctions against Italy went into effect **Nov. 18** supported by 52 nation-members of the League of Nations, and by one non-member, Egypt. The sanctions ended **July 15, 1936.**

1936

British King George V, 70, died Jan. 20 and was succeeded by his eldest son, Prince of Wales, 42, who took the title of King Edward VIII. He abdicated **Dec. 11, 1936,** and was succeeded by his brother, the Duke of York, who became King George VI. The ex-ruler was created Duke of Windsor with the title of "His Royal Highness." He gave up the throne, he said, because he could not marry "the woman I love," Mrs. Wallis Warfield of Baltimore, Md., who obtained a divorce **Oct. 27** in Ipswich, England, from Ernest A. Simpson, an insurance agent. Edward and "Wally" were married **June 3, 1937** in Monts, France.

Reoccupation of demilitarized Rhineland zone begun by German troops **May 7.**

Emperor Haile Selassie of Ethiopia escaped Italian advance by boarding British cruiser **May 1.** Premier Mussolini of Italy announced end of war **May 5,** proclaimed annexation of Ethiopia with King Victor Emmanuel emperor. Haile Selassiè restored 1941; deposed Sept. 12, 1974.

Revolt against Spain's republican government began **July 17** in Morocco and spread to Spain, included much of the army and air force and half of the navy; Gen. Francisco Franco proclaimed head of the nationalist (insurgent) government **Oct. 1;** seige of Madrid begun by insurgents **Oct. 21;** Loyalist government moved to Valencia, **Nov. 6.**

Japan and Germany signed an anti-Comintern pact **Nov. 25.** Italy joined **Nov. 6, 1937.**

1937

Spanish insurgents took Malaga **Feb. 8.** Warships of Great Britain, France, Italy and Germany **March 13** began to police the coasts of Spain under a 27-nation neutrality agreement, effectively blockading the Loyalists, but not the insurgents (Nationalists), from receiving supplies. An est. 70,000 Italian troops and several thousand Germans were aiding Nationalists. Loyalists shifted government to Barcelona **Oct. 28.**

Fighting in China, west of Peking, was renewed by Japanese; **July 29** they bombed Tientsin destroying Nankai Univ.; **Aug. 9** they took formal possession of Peking; **Aug. 11** they shelled Nankow; other eastern cities were hit by Japanese planes **Oct. 23.** Chinese forces abandoned Shanghai and Japanese took control **Nov. 8.** Premier Chiang Kai-shek moved to Hankow **Dec. 12.**

Japanese bombs sank the U. S. gunboat Panay **Dec. 12** with loss of 2 lives, and several American oil carriers (the captain of one died) on the Yangtze River. The Japanese apologized and paid indemnity.

Hitler repudiated war guilt clause of Versailles Treaty **Jan. 30.** (Treaty blamed Germany for World War I.) Hitler stated that Germany was free from obligations imposed upon her by the treaty.

Amelia Earhart Putnam, aviator, and co-pilot Fred Noonan lost **July 2** near Howland Is. in the Pacific.

Italy gave notice Dec. 11 of withdrawal from the League of Nations.

1938

Insurgent air raids killed 1,000 in Barcelona **Mar. 7;** Insurgents took Lerida, cut Spain in half, **Apr. 15.**

Hitler invaded Austria Mar. 11. After resignation of Chancellor Kurt von Schuschnigg and Pres. Wilhelm Miklas **Mar. 13** the new chancellor, Arthur Seyss-Inquart, proclaimed the union of Germany and Austria. This was ratified by a popular vote, excluding Jews, in Austria **Apr. 10.**

At a conference in Munich, Britain and France yielded **Sept. 30** to Nazi demands for the cession of the Sudetenland to Germany by Czechoslovakia, thus ending a 15-day international crisis during which British Prime Minister Neville Chamberlain made 2 flying visits to Hitler. Mussolini backed Hitler's territorial demands. Hitler signed a "peace declaration" with Britain **Sept. 30,** occupied Sudetenland **Oct. 1-10.** Eduard Benes, president of Czechoslovakia, resigned **Oct. 5.**

1939

The Loyalist Spanish government surrendered Barcelona to the insurgents **Jan. 26.** Madrid surrendered **Mar. 24;** war ended **Mar. 29** with Franco victor.

The Republic of Czechoslovakia was dissolved **Mar. 14;** Hungarian troops seized Carpatho-Ukraine **Mar. 14;** Nazis occupied Bohemia and Moravia which became German protectorates **Mar. 16.**

Japanese troops in Manchukuo and Soviet and Mongol troops near Lake Bor began 6-month border fight **May 11;** 20,000 killed.

Germany and Italy signed military pact **May 22.**

Germany and Soviet Union signed a non-aggression treaty **Aug. 24;** Germany invaded Poland **Sept. 1;** USSR invaded Poland **Sept. 17;** Britain and France declared war on Germany **Sept. 3.**

N. Y. World's Fair opened **Apr. 30,** closed **Oct. 31;** reopened **May 11, 1940** and finally closed **Oct. 21.**

Pres. Roosevelt proclaimed a limited national emergency **Sept. 8,** an unlimited emergency **May 27, 1941.** Both ended by Pres. Truman **Apr. 28, 1952.**

Russia invaded Finland Nov. 30.

1939-1945 World War II
See Article Pages 732-733.

1940

Estonia, Latvia, and Lithuania annexed by Soviet Russia **July 14.**

1941

The Four Freedoms termed essential by Pres. Roosevelt in a speech to Congress **Jan. 6:** freedom of speech and expression, freedom of worship, freedom from want, and freedom from fear.

The Atlantic Charter, an 8-point joint U.S.-British declaration of principles, issued by Pres. Roosevelt and Prime Minister Churchill **Aug. 14** after conference aboard battleship off Newfoundland.

Japan attacked U.S. fleet at Pearl Harbor **Dec. 7** as first act of war. *(See World War II.)*

Hitler ordered policy of genocide as the "final solution" to the Jewish "problem." By end of war an estimated 6 million Jews had been killed in Nazi concentration camps. Other religious, ethnic, and political groups were also persecuted and some 4 to 6 million members were murdered by Nazis.

1942

Fire swept through Cocoanut Grove, a Boston night club, **Nov. 28,** killing 491 and injuring scores.

First nuclear chain reaction (fission of uranium isotope, U-235) at Univ. of Chicago, under physicists Arthur Compton, Enrico Fermi, et al., **Dec. 2.**

1943

Pres. Roosevelt signed **June 10** the pay-as-you-go income tax bill. Starting **July 1** wage and salary earners were subject to a paycheck withholding tax.

Race riot in Detroit June 21; 34 dead, 700 injured. Riot in Harlem section of N.Y. City; 6 Negroes killed.

1945

Yalta Conference met in the Crimea, USSR, **Feb. 3-11.** Roosevelt, Churchill and Stalin agreed Russia would enter war against Japan.

Pres. Roosevelt, 63, died of cerebral hemorrhage in Warm Springs, Ga. **Apr. 12.**

Mussolini caught by partisans near Dongo while trying to flee to Switzerland; executed **Apr. 28.**

Hitler committed suicide in ruined chancellery, Berlin, **Apr. 30,** with wife Eva Braun. Goebbels and wife poisoned children, committed suicide.

United Nations Conference on International

Principal Events of World War II, 1939-1945

Major Belligerents — German army invaded Poland **Sept. 1, 1939;** Norway and Denmark **April 9, 1940;** the Netherlands, Belgium, and Luxemburg **May 10, 1940; invaded France, reaching Paris June 14.** Occupied France (Vichy) signed an armistice with Germany **June 22, 1940.** Germany invaded Russia **June 22, 1941,** unoccupied France. **Nov. 11, 1942.** Surrendered unconditionally May 7, 1945 **(May 6 EST).** War with Germany formally declared ended by Britain, France, Australia, New Zealand on **July 9, 1951;** by U.S. **Oct. 19, 1951.**

Great Britain declared war on Germany **Sept. 3, 1939,** as did Australia and New Zealand. Union of South Africa declared war **Sept. 6; Canada Sept. 10.** Britain declared war on Italy **June 11, 1940;** on Finland, Hungary, and Romania, **Dec. 7, 1941;** on Japan **Dec. 8, 1941;** on Bulgaria **Dec. 13, 1941;** on Thailand **Jan. 25, 1942.**

France declared war on Germany **Sept. 3, 1939;** on Italy **June 11, 1940.** Free French (de Gaulle) declared war on Japan **Dec. 8, 1941.**

Italy (under Benito Mussolini) declared war on Great Britain and France **June 10, 1940;** on the U.S. **Dec. 11, 1941.** Surrendered unconditionally **Sept. 8, 1943.** Declared war against Germany **Oct. 13, 1943,** against Japan **July 14, 1945.** Signed treaty of peace **Feb. 10, 1947,** in Paris, with Britain, France, U.S. and USSR.

Japan invaded French Indochina **Sept. 22, 1940;** attacked Pearl Harbor naval station and the Philippines by air **Dec. 7, 1941** and declared war on the U.S., Great Britain, Australia, Canada, New Zealand and the Union of South Africa **Dec. 7, 1941;** on the Netherlands **Jan. 11, 1942.** Japan accepted the Allied terms unconditionally **Aug. 14, 1945;** signed surrender terms **Sept. 1, 1945 (Sept. 2,** Tokyo time) on board USS Missouri; signed treaty of peace with all big powers (except USSR) and a total of 49 nations at San Francisco **Sept. 8, 1951.**

Union of Soviet Socialist Republics (Russia) signed non-aggression pact with Germany **Aug., 1939;** invaded Poland, **Sept. 17, 1939,** and Finland, **Nov. 30, 1939.** Signed peace with Finland **Mar. 12, 1940.** Russia was invaded by Germany and Romania **June 22, 1941.** Finland declared war on Russia **June 25, 1941.** Armistice with Finland **Sept. 19, 1944,** peace treaty **Feb. 10, 1947.** Declared war on Japan **Aug. 8, 1945,** effective **Aug. 9.** Signed treaties of peace with Italy, Hungary, Romania, Bulgaria and Finland **Feb. 10, 1947.**

U.S. declared war on Japan Dec. 8, 1941. Germany and Italy declared war on U.S. **Dec. 11, 1941.** A few hours later U.S. declared war on Germany and Italy; also Bulgaria, Hungary and Romania **June 5, 1942;** signed peace treaties with Italy, Bulgaria, Hungary and Romania **Feb. 10, 1947;** with Japan **Sept. 8, 1951.**

German Blitzkrieg forces outflanked the Maginot Line **May 13, 1940,** and quickly occupied northern France.

Retreat from Dunkirk by British Expeditionary Force took place **May 26-June 4, 1940,** when 900 vessels took 338,226 troops across the English Channel, 26,175 of them French.

Nazi bombing of Britain began **July 10, 1940,** and reached its height **Sept. 7, Oct. 15.** and **Dec. 29.** Coventry was destroyed **Nov. 14;** Birmingham was hit **Nov. 19-22.** Many London churches were burned **Dec. 29.** Desperate attacks on German aircraft by RAF stopped threat of invasion. Of this defense Prime Minister Churchill said: "Never in the field of human conflict was so much owed by so many to so few."

Pearl Harbor. Some 360 Japanese planes attacked Hickam and Wheeler Fields and U. S. Pacific fleet (86 ships) anchored at Pearl Harbor, Hawaii on **Dec. 7, 1941.** (7:55 a.m. Hawaiian time; 1:25 p.m. EST.) Totally destroyed: battleship Arizona. Severely damaged: battleships Oklahoma, Nevada, California, West Virginia, 3 destroyers, 1 target ship, 1 minelayer. Damaged and repaired: battleships Pennsylvania, Maryland, Tennessee; cruisers Helena, Honolulu, Raleigh. Casualties: navy and marines, 2,086 officers and men killed, 749 wounded; army, 194 officers and men killed, 360 wounded.

Planes over Tokyo. Lt. Col. James H. Doolittle, with 16 B-25s and 79 pilots and crewmen, took off **Apr. 18, 1942,** from carrier Hornet, 688 mi. from Tokyo; 13 dropped 500-lb. bombs on Tokyo, 2 on Nagoya, Kobe. Eight airmen were captured off China coast; 3 were shot, others imprisoned. Total dead, 9. One plane landed near Vladivostok and was interned by Russians; the crew escaped to Iran.

Loss and recapture of Philippines. Manila and Cavite taken by Japan **Jan. 2, 1942.** U.S. forces in Bataan were attacked by 200,000 Japanese **Jan. 10.** Gen. Douglas MacArthur ordered to leave Philippines, reached Australia **Mar. 17,** vowed, "I shall return." Maj. Gen. Jonathan M. Wainwright defended Bataan until **Apr. 8, 1942.** Japan took 35,000 U.S. and Filipino troops prisoner, including 5,000 Marines, forced them into prison via the "Death March" of Bataan. Wainwright surrendered **Corregidor May 6** with 11,574 troops. Gen. MacArthur returned to the Philippines near Palo on Leyte, **Oct. 20, 1944.** U.S. returned to Luzon **Jan. 9, 1945.** Manila was taken **Feb. 3:** Corregidor reoccupied **Feb. 16-Mar. 1.**

Germany attacked the Soviet Union June 22, 1941; took Minsk, Smolensk, Kiev, Kharkov, Orel; besieged Leningrad, fought a long battle in the ruins of Stalingrad **Aug. 1942** and extended the German lines to the Caucasus Mts.; tide turned in **Nov. 1942;** the Russians encircled Stalingrad and the Nazi army there surrendered **Jan. 31, 1943.** Russian army reached the Oder River, the German border, **Feb. 1945.**

North African Campaign began **Aug. 6, 1941,** when Marshal Graziani led Italian forces against the British with some success. The first counteroffensive in **Dec.** relieved Tobruk, where British had held out 8 months. The British pushed the Germans under Rommel back to El Agheila but Rommel regained the lost ground. He captured Tobruk with its garrison of 25,000 British **June 21, 1942,** and pushed the British back to within 70 mi. of Alexandria. On **Oct. 23,** the British, heavily reinforced and under Lt. Gen. Bernard L. Montgomery, attacked Rommel at El Alamein, Egypt, and inflicted heavy losses on the Germans and Italians, driving them back over 1,000 mi. to Tunisia.

Organization of 46 nations, San Francisco, opened **Apr. 25;** closed **June 26** with address by Pres. Truman and adoption of UN charter.

Potsdam, Germany, conference of Truman, Stalin, and Churchill **July 17-Aug. 2.** After **July 25** Clement Atlee, new prime minister, replaced Churchill.

First atomic bomb, produced at Los Alamos, N. M., exploded at Alamogordo, N. M., **July 16.** Bomb dropped on Hiroshima **Aug. 6,** on Nagasaki **Aug. 9.**

U.S. forces entered Korea south of 38th parallel to displace Japanese **Sept. 8.**

Gen. Douglas MacArthur took over supervision of Japan **Sept. 9.**

Vidkun Quisling, pro-Nazi premier of Norway, executed by a firing squad in Oslo **Oct. 23.**

1946

William Joyce, "Lord Haw Haw," broadcaster for Nazis, hanged in London for treason **Jan. 3.**

The first General Assembly of the United Nations opened in London **Jan. 10.**

League of Nations in Geneva, Switzerland, transfered physical assets to the United Nations **Apr. 18.**

Philippines given independence by U.S. **July 4;** Manuel Roxas elected first president of new republic.

Summary of Aerial Naval and Military Actions

North African Invasion by U.S. and Britain landed 150,000 American and 140,000 British troops in French Algeria **Nov. 8, 1942** (Nov. 7 EST), with Lt. Gen. Dwight D. Eisenhower in command; Axis forces were driven from Africa by **May 12, 1943.** U.S. 7th Army under Maj. Gen. George S. Patton Jr. and British-Canadian 8th Army landed on Sicily **July 10.** Mussolini was forced to resign **July 25** and escaped to German lines **Sept. 12.** The Italian mainland was invaded and Italy surrendered **Sept. 8, 1943,** but heavy fighting with Germans followed and they were not dislodged until spring of **1945.**

Battle of the Coral Sea on **May 7-8, 1942,** took heavy toll of ships and planes on both sides, was first battle fought by naval planes from ships that had neither sight nor range of enemy. U.S. lost carrier (Lexington), 66 planes, 543 men; Japan lost 80 planes, 900 men. **Battle of Midway June 3-6, 1942,** U. S. lost 1 carrier (Yorktown), 1 destroyer, 150 planes, 307 men; Japan lost 4 carriers, 253 planes, 3,500 men. The Japanese navy halted its advance toward Australia and withdrew northward.

Guadalcanal, in the southern Solomon Islands, assaulted by U. S. Marines **Aug. 7, 1942,** in one of the most costly Allied Pacific campaigns, finally won by the Allies in **Jan. 1943.**

U.S. Return to Philippines: battle for Leyte Gulf, biggest naval action ever fought, **Oct. 22-27, 1944,** in 3 engagements destroying Japanese naval power. Battles were fought in Surigao Strait, off Samar and off Cape Engano. Ships engaged: U.S. 166, Japanese 65. Airplanes, U.S. 1,280; Japanese 716. Losses for Philippine campaign — Japan: 3 large carriers, 3 light carriers, one escort carrier, 4 battleships, 14 cruisers, 32 destroyers, 11 submarines, total 68. U. S.: one light carrier, 3 escort carriers, 6 destroyers, 3 destroyer escorts, one high-speed transport, 7 submarines, total 21. U.S. lost one ship to a kamikaze (suicide) plane at Leyte and 5 in subsequent actions. Total plane losses for Philippine campaign from **Oct., 1944-Jan. 1945:** Japan (est.) 7,000, including 722 kamikaze; U. S. 967.

D-Day: Invasion of France — Invasion of France by Allies **June 6, 1944.** About 1,000 planes and gliders dropped paratroopers on Cotentin Peninsula near Normandy, 5 a.m. London time. About 1,000 RAF, 1,400 U.S. bombers attacked installations. First assault troops landed 6:30 a.m. on beaches along line Carentan-Bayeux-Caen; U.S. on west, British-Canadians on east. Total Allied strength available 2,876,439, including 17 British divisions of which 3 Canadian; 20 U. S. divisions, one French, one Polish. Gen. Dwight D. Eisenhower was Supreme Commander of Allied Expeditionary Forces.

British took Bayeux June 7; Carentan fell **June 13,** U.S. took Cherbourg **June 27;** British-Canadians took Caen **July 9** after desperate fighting. Lt. Gen. George S. Patton Jr. with 3d U.S. Army attacked south and west of St. Lo **Aug. 1.** Canadians took Falaise **Aug 16.** German army routed **Aug. 23** in the Argentan-Falaise gap by U.S.-Canadian armies and Allied aircraft. Allies were then free to overrun northern France and liberate Paris **Aug. 25.**

Allies invaded southern France **Aug. 14-15, 1944,** east of the Rhone River, with 1,000 ships(641 U.S., 316 British).

The Ardennes Bulge was a violent counterattack by 15 German divisions (Gen. von Rundstedt commander-in-chief) launched **Dec. 16, 1944.** By **Dec. 19,** the 1st U. S. Army was pushed out of Germany and the Germans penetrated 60 mi. west of Celles, Belgium. Patton's 3d U.S. Army rescued besieged Americans at Bastogne, Belgium, **Dec. 26** and Nazi drive was stopped by **Dec. 28.** Near Malmedy, Belgium, Germans shot captured American soldiers with machine guns and left them dead on the field. U. S. casualties estimated at 80,000; Germans lost 220,000 dead and prisoners.

Rhine Crossing — On **Mar. 7, 1945,** the 9th Armored Div., 3d Corps, First Army, found Ludendorff Bridge at Remagen on the Rhine intact; Gen. Eisenhower ordered Gen. Omar N. Bradley to put 5 divisions across.

Iwo Jima assaulted by U. S. joint expeditionary force **Feb. 19, 1945,** with land action by U. S. Marines; invasion used 495 ships, including 17 aircraft carriers and 1,170 planes. U. S. troops engaged, 111,308 of which 75,144 were assault troops. Island was conquered by **Mar. 16.** U. S. lost 4,590 killed; Japanese deaths est. over 20,000.

Okinawa, principal Japanese base in the Ryukyu group, was invaded **Apr. 1, 1945,** in the final land campaign in the Far East. U.S. used 1,300 vessels, including airplane carriers. After 83 days of fighting the end was marked by the formal suicide of the 2 Japanese generals. U. S. men engaged up to **June 30, 1945,** reached 176,491 army, 88,500 marines, 18,000 navy. Japanese strength was 77,199, plus reinforcements. U. S. losses were 49,151 of which 12,520 were killed or missing, 36,631 wounded. The Japanese lost 110,071 killed, wounded and 7,400 prisoners.

U. S. lost 763 aircraft; Japan lost 7,830 of which 1,020 were destroyed on the ground. U. S. lost 36 ships sunk, 369 damaged; Japan lost 16 sunk. The Yamato, world's largest battleship, full load displacement 72,809 tons, 861 ft. long, 3,333 personnel, was sunk by 10 aerial torpedoes; 300 survived.

V-E Day — German armies began surrendering **May 4, 1945.** Unconditional surrender signed **May 7** at 2:41 a.m., French time, in Rheims Hq., designating cessation of operations **May 9** at 12:01 a.m., London time **(May 8,** 6:01 p.m., Eastern U.S. War Time). Surrender also signed in Berlin. **May 8** celebrated as V-E Day.

Atomic bombs — First atomic bomb ever used in war was dropped by U. S. plane **Aug. 6, 1945,** on Hiroshima, Japan (pop. 343,969). Second U. S. bomb dropped on Nagasaki (pop. 252,630) **Aug. 9, 1945.** Estimates of dead from bombs and radiation exposure vary: Hiroshima, 80,000 to over 200,000; Nagasaki, 39,000 to 74,000. Japan surrendered **Aug. 14.** Formal surrender aboard USS Missouri **Sept. 2, 1945,** Far Eastern Time, celebrated as V-J Day.

Consult Index for additional listings under World War II.

Twenty-two Nazi leaders convicted of war crimes **Sept. 30** by International Tribunal in Nuremberg. Eleven Nazis were sentenced to death by hanging **Oct. 1.** Hermann Goering committed suicide by poison in Nuremberg Prison, 2 hours before he was scheduled to be hanged **Oct. 15.** The 10 other top Nazis were hanged individually. They were: Hans Frank, Wilhelm Frick, Col. Gen. Alfred Jodl, Gestapo Chief Ernst Kaltenbrunner, Field Marshal Wilhelm Keitel, Alfred Rosenberg, Fritz Sauckel, Arthur Seyss-Inquart, Julius Streicher, Foreign Minister Joachim von Ribbentrop.

Others executed for war crimes: Gen. Anton Dostler, Nazi, hanged in Rome **Dec. 1, 1945,** for shooting 15 U.S. soldiers without trial; Joseph Kramer, "Beast of Belsen" and 10 others hanged **Dec. 14,** by British for atrocities at Belsen and Auschwitz concentration camps; Gen. Yamashita, Japanese commander in Philippines, hanged **Feb. 23, 1946;** Lt. Gen. Homma, who ordered Bataan death march, shot near Manila **Apr. 3, 1946;** Marshal Ion Antonescu, dictator of Romania, hanged **June 1, 1946;** Karl Hermann Frank, Nazi ruler in Czechoslovakia, hanged in Prague **May 22** for ordering massacre at Lidice; 48 Nazi officers and guards hanged by the U.S. Army at Landsberg, Germany, **May, 1947,** for mass murders at Mauthausen camp.

1947

British Labor government took ownership of coal mines, cables and wireless communications **Jan. 1.**

Truman Doctrine. Pres. Truman asked Congress to appropriate $400 million for aid to Greece and Turkey to combat Communist terrorism **Mar. 12.** Approved **May 15.**

The United Nations Security Council voted unanimously **Apr. 2** to place under U. S. trusteeship the Pacific islands formerly mandated to Japan.

Taft-Hartley Labor Act approved by U.S. Senate **May 13.** The House concurred **June 4.** The measure was vetoed by Pres. Truman **June 20,** but Congress overrode the veto.

Proposals known later as the Marshall Plan, under which the U.S. would extend financial aid to all European countries "willing to assist in the task of recovery," were made by Sec. of State George C. Marshall **June 5.** Congress authorized the spending in the next 3 1/2 years of some $12 billion on Marshall Plan aid, which was credited with restoring economic health to free Europe and halting spread of communism.

Hindu India and Moslem Pakistan, formerly parts of British India, gained independence **Aug. 15.**

1948

British Labor government nationalized railways **Jan. 1.**

Mohandas K. Gandhi, Hindu spiritual leader and champion of freedom for India, was shot and killed by a Hindu fanatic in New Delhi **Jan. 30.**

Czechoslovakia joined the communist block in Eastern Europe after Pres. Benes yielded **Feb. 25** to an ultimatum to install a pro-Soviet cabinet. He resigned **June 7;** succeeded by Klement Gottwald, communist. Benes died **Sept. 3.** Communists reported Jan Masaryk, foreign minister, killed himself **Mar. 10.**

A land blockade of Berlin's Allied sectors was started **Apr. 1** by the Soviet military, which refused to permit U.S. and British supply trains to pass through the Soviet zone of Germany. This blockade and a Western counter-blockade were lifted **Sept. 30, 1949,** after British and U.S. planes had airlifted 2,343,315 tons of food and coal into West Berlin.

Charter of the Organization of American States signed **Apr. 30** at 9th International Conference of American States at Bogota, Colombia.

The Free State of Israel was proclaimed in Tel Aviv **May 14** as the British evacuated Palestine. First de facto recognition came from the U.S. **May 14.** Soviet Russia granted recognition **May 17.**

The Cominform (Communist Information Bureau) at a Prague meeting **June 28,** denounced Marshal Tito and other leaders of the Yugoslav Communist party as deserters from the Marxist-Leninist doctrine.

Alger Hiss, former State Department official, was indicted **Dec. 15** on 2 perjury charges after he had denied passing secret documents to Whittaker Chambers, a former magazine editor, for transmission to a communist spy ring. A jury failed to reach an agreement **July 8, 1949.** His second trial **Nov. 17, 1949-Jan. 21, 1950** ended with conviction on 2 counts and a sentence of 5 years in federal prison. He was released **Nov. 27, 1954,** his term shortened for good conduct.

Former Premier Hideki Tojo and 6 other Japanese war leaders were hanged **Dec. 23** as war criminals.

Joseph Cardinal Mindszenty, Roman Catholic primate of Hungary, arrested by Communist government in Budapest on charges of treason **Dec. 27.** Convicted, given life imprisonment **Feb. 8, 1949.** All persons taking part in the cardinal's prosecution were excommunicated by Pope Pius XII. Mindszenty freed **Oct. 31, 1956.** After 15 years in U.S. Embassy in Budapest the cardinal left Hungary **Sept. 28, 1971,** for West Europe. He died **May 6, 1975,** in Vienna.

1949

Mildred E. (Axis Sally) Gillars was convicted by a federal jury in N.Y. City **Mar. 10** of treason in broadcasting Nazi propaganda during war. She received 10 to 30 years in prison. Freed **1961.**

North Atlantic Treaty Organization (NATO) established **Mar. 18** by U.S., Canada and 10 Western European nations, agreeing that "an armed attack against one or more of them in Europe and North America shall be considered an attack against all."

Ireland severed last ties with Britain by leaving Commonwealth **Apr. 18.**

End of American A-bomb monopoly revealed by Pres. Truman's announcement **Sept. 23** that an atomic explosion had been set off in the USSR.

Mrs. I. Toguri D'Aquino, (Tokyo Rose) of Japanese wartime broadcasts, was sentenced in San Francisco **Oct. 7** to 10 years in prison for treason. Paroled **1956,** pardoned **1977.**

Eleven leaders of U.S. Communist party convicted **Oct. 14,** after 9-month trial in N.Y. City, of advocating violent overthrow of U.S. Government. Federal Judge Harold R. Medina **Oct. 21** sentenced 10 defendants to 5 years in prison each and the 11th, a war veteran, to 3 years. Supreme Court upheld the convictions **June 4, 1951.** Seven surrendered **July 2, 1951;** of the other 4, hunted as fugitives, one, Gus Hall, was captured **Oct. 8, 1951,** and given 3 additional years. Robert G. Thompson was captured **Aug. 27, 1953.** Five defense lawyers, cited for contempt during the trial, received sentences ranging from one to 6 months **Apr. 24, 1952.**

Nationalist China's government fled to Formosa (Taiwan) **Dec. 7.** Chinese Communists took Yunnan and Kunming as Nationalists left.

1950

Great Britain recognized Communist China Jan. 6 one day after breaking diplomatic relations with Chiang Kai-shek's nationalist Chinese regime.

U.S. Jan. 14 recalled all consular officials from Communist China after the latter seized the American consulate general in Peking.

Masked bandits robbed Brink's Inc., Boston express office, **Jan. 17** of $2,775,395.12, of which $1,218,211.29 was in cash. Case solved 1956 by FBI; 8 men sentenced to life.

Pres. Truman authorized AEC to produce the hydrogen bomb (H-bomb), **Jan. 31.**

Dr. Klaus J. E. Fuchs, German-born atomic research physicist at Harwell, England, pleaded guilty **Mar. 1** to violating the Official Secrets Act and received 14 years in prison. He had communicated atomic information to Russian agents since 1942. Released **June 23, 1959,** went to E. Germany.

The Army seized all railroads Aug. 27, on orders of Pres. Truman to prevent a general strike after unions had rejected terms of an 18-cents-an-hour raise for yardmen but none for trainmen. Roads returned to owners **May 23, 1952** after new contract.

In an attempt to kill Pres. Truman, 2 members of a

Puerto Rican nationalist movement attacked Blair House in Washington, **Nov. 1.** *(See Assassinations).*

U. S. Dec. 8 banned shipments to Communist China and to Asiatic ports trading with it.

1951

Ilse Koch was sentenced to life by a German court in Frankfurt **Jan. 15** for inciting murder.

With Sen. Estes Kefauver (D. Tenn.) as chairman, the Senate Committee to Investigate Organized Crime in Interstate Commerce exposed nationwide criminal organizations that reaped huge illegal profits, used these funds to enter legitimate businesses, influenced politicians, and bought protection. Preliminary report **Feb. 28** said gambling take was over $20 billion a year.

Julius Rosenberg, his wife, Ethel, and Morton Sobell, all U.S. citizens, were found guilty **Mar. 29** of conspiracy to commit wartime espionage. Rosenbergs sentenced to death, Sobell to 30 years; appeals denied. David Greenglass, brother of Mrs. Rosenberg and a state witness, received 15 years in prison. Rosenbergs executed at Sing Sing prison, Ossining, N.Y., **June 19, 1953.** Sobell released **Jan. 14, 1969.**

European Coal and Steel Plan proposed by French Foreign Minister Robert Schuman **May 9.** France, West Germany, Italy, Belgium, Netherlands, and Luxembourg agreed to conference. Ratified **June 16, 1952.**

UN General Assembly voted arms embargo against Communist China **May 18.**

Tariff concessions by the U.S. to the Soviet Union, Communist China, and all communist-dominated lands were suspended **Aug. 1.**

Transcontinental television inaugurated **Sept. 4** with Pres. Truman's address at the Japanese Peace Treaty Conference in San Francisco.

Japanese Peace Treaty signed in San Francisco **Sept. 8** by U.S. and 48 other nations.

1952

Queen Elizabeth II proclaimed queen of United Kingdom and Canada **Feb. 6,** marking first time monarch was specifically enthroned in name of Canada.

U.S. seizure of nation's steel mills was ordered by Pres. Truman **Apr. 8** to avert a strike by 600,000 CIO United Steelworkers. Seizure was ruled illegal by the Supreme Court **June 2.** Strike followed **June 3,** was settled **July 24.**

First jetliner passenger service opened **May 2,** British DeHavilland Comet, London to Johannesburg.

Peace contract between West Germany, U.S., Great Britain, and France was signed in Bonn **May 26.** Allied high commissions abolished.

Puerto Rico became an "associated free state" or commonwealth of the U.S. **July 25** after Pres. Truman gave approval to a new constitution.

West Germany agreed Sept. 10 to pay Israel and Jews $822 million over 12 to 14 years as indemnity for damages inflicted by Nazis.

Britain successfully completed its first atomic test off northwest Australia **Oct. 3** detonating a bomb aboard a naval vessel.

First hydrogen device explosion Nov. 1 at AEC Eniwetok proving grounds in Pacific reported by witnesses but not officially confirmed for more than a year. Pres. Eisenhower told Congress **Feb. 2, 1954,** that the 1952 test was "the first full-scale thermonuclear explosion in history."

Alan Nunn May, British scientist who gave atom secrets to the USSR, was released from prison **Dec. 29,** after serving 6 yr. 8 mo. of his 10-yr. term.

1953

Joseph Stalin died **Mar. 5.** By 1955, Nikita Khrush-

Korean War and U.S. Intervention

Republic of Korea was invaded June 25, 1950 (June 24 EST) by over 60,000 North Korean troops spearheaded by over 100 Russian-built tanks. UN Security Council demanded cessation of hostilities and withdrawal to 38th parallel (Russia not present, having staged "walkout" from Council). On **June 27,** Council asked UN members to help carry out its demand. Pres. Truman **June 27,** ordered Gen. of the Army Douglas MacArthur to aid South Korea, and the U.S. 7th Fleet to protect Taiwan against possible aggression and keep the Chinese Nationalist forces from attacking the mainland. Requested by the UN to name a commander, the president designated Gen. MacArthur **July 8, 1950.**

North Korean forces took Seoul, South Korean capital **June 29.** U.S. ground forces entered the conflict **June 30.** Truman termed the intervention a "police action."

The war had 3 phases:

(1) The North Korean drive as checked by U.S. and allied troops, with help of a brilliant landing by U.S. Marines at **Inchon Sept. 15. Pyongyang,** North Korean capital, was taken **Oct. 20.** U.S. 7th Div. reached Manchurian border **Nov. 20.**

(2) Counter-attack by 200,000 Chinese Communist "volunteers," who crossed Yalu River **Nov. 26,** forced evacuation of 105,000 UN troops and 91,000 Korean civilians at Hungnam **Dec. 24.** The Chinese pushed across 38th parallel, drove 70 mi. into South Korea. The UN General Assembly **Feb. 1, 1951,** named Communist China the aggressor in Korea. UN troops pushed Chinese back across parallel **Apr. 3,** stopped offensive by 600,000 Chinese **Apr. 22-30.**

(3) Removal of Gen. MacArthur from command **Apr. 11, 1951,** and start of negotiations for truce along 38th parallel **July 10, 1951.**

Pres. Truman removed Gen. MacArthur from all Far East commands and replaced him with Gen. Matthew B. Ridgway, commander of 8th Army. MacArthur had wished to pursue Chinese across Yalu River to their air depots in Manchuria and on **Mar. 25** had threatened Communist China with air and naval attack. He had been warned to clear all announcements of policy through Washington. The president opposed his views. Senate inquiry **May 3-June 27, 1951,** found that MacArthur was not charged with insubordination, but had disregarded the president's order to clear policy statements through the Defense Department.

Cease-fire and armistice talks began **July 1951** and dragged on with numerous breakdowns until **July 27, 1953** (July 26, EST) when armistice was signed; fighting ended 12 hrs. later. A military armistice commission supervised truce; 10 joint UN-Communist teams policed demilitarized zone; Neutral Nations Supervisory Commission watched military movements in ports; voluntary repatriation of prisoners was provided and Communists won privilege of interviewing prisoners refusing repatriation.

Prisoner repatriation began Aug. 6, 1953, at Panmunjom, ended **Sept. 6, 1953.** UN turned over 75,790 prisoners (70,150 North Koreans and 5,640 Chinese). Communists released 12,760, including 7,850 South Koreans, 3,597 Americans, 945 Britons, 228 Turks.

The Supervisory Commission, made up of members from Czechoslovakia, Poland, Sweden, and Switzerland, was reduced one-half in **Sept. 1955** on repeated complaints that the communist members were spying in South Korea. Repeated reports indicated that the North Koreans had violated many terms of the armistice, built numerous airfields and received naval vessels. The UN Command expelled the commission from South Korea in **June 1956,** on grounds that its Czech and Polish members and the North Korean government had frustrated the operation of the armistice agreement. The UN Command announced in **June 1957,** that it could no longer be bound by armistice provisions controlling importation of military equipment into Korea, but would modernize UN forces "to restore the relative balance of military strength that the armistice was intended to preserve."

chev emerged as dominant political leader of USSR.

Mau Mau or "Hidden Ones" of Kenya's Kikuyu tribe, formed to force whites from Kenya and to regain ancestral lands, climaxed sporadic violence **Mar. 26**, by murdering 71 and wounding 100 fellow Kikuyus who remained loyal to colonial government. Jomo Kenyatta, tribal leader, found guilty **Apr. 8** of organizing Mau Mau, sentenced to 7 years on **Dec. 12. 1963**. Kenya became independent and Jomo Kenyatta became president **Dec. 12, 1964**.

Mount Everest was conquered May 29 by Edmund P. Hillary of New Zealand and Tenzing Norgay, a Nepalese living in India.

Demonstration by workers in East Berlin against increased work quotas **June 16** erupted into an anti-communist riot by 20,000 to 50,000 persons **June 17.** Soviet troops quelled disturbances, killed 16.

Lavrenti P. Beria, chief of Soviet secret police, was dismissed **July 10** as an enemy of the people. He was executed **Dec. 23** along with 6 of his aides.

First USSR announcement of H-bomb explosion **Aug. 20;** AEC reported explosion occurred **Aug. 12.**

1954

Nautilus, first atomic-powered submarine, was launched at Groton, Conn., **Jan. 21.**

Five members of Congress were wounded in the House **Mar. 1** by 4 Puerto Ricans, one a woman, who fired pistols at random from a spectators' gallery, shouting for Puerto Rican independence. The wounded recovered; the attackers were imprisoned.

Dien Bien Phu, French military outpost in NW Vietnam, fell to the Vietminh army of Ho Chi Minh **May 7.**

Racial segregation in public schools was unanimously ruled unconstitutional by the Supreme Court **May 17.**

Southeast Asia Treaty Organization (SEATO) formed by collective defense pact signed in Manila **Sept. 3** by the U.S., Britain, France, Australia, New Zealand, Philippines, Pakistan, and Thailand.

Agreement signed in Paris Oct. 23 provided for West German sovereignty, rearmament and entrance into NATO and the Western European Union.

Condemnation of Sen. Joseph R. McCarthy (R. Wis.) voted by Senate, 67-22, **Dec. 2** for contempt of a Senate elections subcommittee, for abuse of its members and for insults to the Senate during investigation **Apr. 22-June 17** of charges brought by the Dept. of the Army against him growing out of his investigation of alleged subversive activities.

1955

Afro-Asian conference of 29 nations met in Bandung, Indonesia, **Apr.** Conference gave expression to the new nationalism of developing nations.

Federal Republic of West Germany became a sovereign state **May 5.** Pres. Eisenhower signed an order ending U. S. occupation but troops remained on a contractual basis.

The Warsaw Pact, a 20-yr. mutual defense treaty, was signed at Warsaw **May 14** by USSR, Albania, Bulgaria, Czechoslovakia, Hungary, Poland, Romania, and East Germany. Albania was barred from meetings **1963;** withdrew from pact **1968.**

A meeting of heads of state "at the summit" proposed by U. S., Great Britain, and France to the USSR, took place **July 18-23** in Geneva, Switzerland, with Pres. Eisenhower representing the U.S.

Juan D. Peron, president and dictator of Argentina, was deposed **Sept. 19** after a revolt begun **June 16** by naval and marine corps units.

Rosa Parks refused **Dec. 1** to give her seat to a white man on a bus in Montgomery, Ala. Bus segregation ordinance declared unconstitutional by a federal court following boycott and NAACP protest.

Merger of America's 2 largest labor organizations was effected **Dec. 5** under the name American Federation of Labor and Congress of Industrial Organizations. George Meany became president, Walter Reuther became vice president in charge of the industrial department. The merged AFL-CIO had a membership estimated at 15 million.

1956

At 20th Congress of Soviet Communist party in Moscow **Feb. 14-25** party chief Nikita S. Khrushchev and other leaders denounced Joseph Stalin, repudiated cruelties of Stalinism, and proclaimed a policy of peaceful coexistence with the West. This alienated Chinese communists and hastened Sino-Soviet split.

Workers in Poznan, Poland, revolted June 28; uprising crushed with 44 killed, many wounded.

Egypt seized Suez Canal July 26 under nationalization decree after Pres. Gamal Abdel Nasser denounced Western withdrawal of proposed Aswan Dam financing.

Polish Communist leaders Oct. 19-21 defied Kremlin leadership and elected Wladyslaw Gomulka to head more independent government.

Hungarian revolt against Soviet-dominated regime began **Oct. 23,** was crushed **Nov. 4** by Soviet Army.

Israel invaded Egypt's Sinai Peninsula **Oct. 29,** saying an Arab attack was imminent. France and Britain invaded Egypt **Nov. 5-6.** U.S. condemned attack, supported cease-fire demand by UN.

UN established first international police force **Nov. 5** to supervise truce in Middle East.

1957

Britain set off its first hydrogen bomb in Pacific test **May 15.**

Soviet Union announced Aug. 26 that it had successfully tested an intercontinental ballistic missile.

Sen. Strom Thurmond (D. S.C.) held Senate floor for 24 hrs., 18 min., **Aug. 28-29,** eclipsing filibuster record of Sen. Wayne Morse (D. Ore.) in 1953.

First underground nuclear explosion set off by Atomic Energy Commission in Nevada **Sept. 19.**

A federal-state controversy over admission of Negroes to the previously all-white Central High School in Little Rock, Ark., reached a showdown **Sept. 4** when National Guardsmen, called out by Gov. Orval Faubus (D), barred 9 Negro students from entering the school. A conference between Faubus and Pres. Eisenhower brought no result but Faubus complied **Sept. 21** with a federal court order to remove the National Guardsmen. The Negroes entered school **Sept. 23** but were ordered to withdraw by local authorities because of fear of mob violence. Pres. Eisenhower sent federal troops to Little Rock **Sept. 24** to enforce the court's order and the school began operation on an integrated basis.

First man-made satellite, Sputnik I, was launched by Soviet scientists **Oct. 4.** The 184-lb. sphere circled the earth about every 1-1/2 hours in an elliptical orbit at altitudes ranging from some 140 to 560 mi. above earth. The Russians **Nov. 3** launched Sputnik II, weighing 1,120 lbs., carrying a live dog, Laika, as the world's first space passenger and orbiting the earth about every 103.7 minutes at altitudes ranging from some 160 mi. to about 1,062 mi. Soviet authorities announced the dog's death **Nov. 10.**

1958

First U. S. earth satellite to go into orbit, Explorer I, launched by Army **Jan. 31** at Cape Canaveral, Fla.

Gen. Charles de Gaulle became French premier **June 1** averting threatened civil war; de Gaulle constitution, increasing power of executive, overwhelmingly adopted **Sept. 28.** De Gaulle elected **Dec. 21** as first president of 5th Republic.

Arab nationalist rebels seized Iraqi government **July 14,** killed King Faisal II, proclaimed republic. Pres. Eisenhower sent U.S. marines to Lebanon **July 15** to forestall alleged effort by Soviet Union and United Arab Republic (Egypt and Syria) to engineer overthrow of Lebanon regime. Withdrawal of U.S troops began **Aug. 12.**

Jet airliner passenger service across Atlantic was opened **Oct. 4** by British Overseas Airways Corp.

First domestic jet airline passenger service in U.S. opened by National Airlines **Dec. 10** between New York and Miami.

1959

Fidel Castro seized power in Cuba following collapse of Fulgencio Batista's government **Jan. 1.**

St. Lawrence Seaway opened **Apr. 25.**

The George Washington, first U.S. ballistic-missile submarine, launched at Groton, Conn., **June 9.**

N.S. Savannah, world's first atomic-powered merchant ship, launched **July 21** at Camden, N.J.

Soviet Premier Khrushchev paid unprecedented visit to U.S. **Sept. 15-27,** made transcontinental tour.

1960

A wave of sit-ins began **Feb. 1** when 4 Negro college students in Greensboro, N. C., refused to move from a Woolworth lunch counter when they were denied service. By **Sept. 1961** more than 70,000 students, whites and blacks, had participated in sit-ins.

First French nuclear test explosion set off **Feb. 13** in Sahara Desert.

A U-2 reconnaissance plane of the U.S., piloted by Francis Gary Powers, was shot down in the Soviet Union **May 1.** Soviet Premier Khrushchev refused to participate in the Paris summit conference scheduled for **May 16** unless Pres. Eisenhower apologized for U-2 flights over the USSR; the Big Four leaders went to Paris but the conference did not take place. Powers

Vietnam War and U.S. Intervention

American combat involvement in Vietnam for about 12 years made the Vietnam War the longest in U.S. history. U.S. interest in the area began when Pres. Harry S. Truman June 27, 1950, sent a 35-man military advisory team to aid the French in their fight against communist forces in North Vietnam.

After the French stronghold of Dien Bien Phu fell to communist forces **May 8, 1954,** France and North Vietnam agreed at the Geneva Conference on Indochina, **May 8** to **July 21,** to partition Vietnam pending reunification elections. Pres. Eisenhower offered South Vietnam economic aid **Oct. 24, 1954,** and agreed to help train the South Vietnamese army **Feb. 12, 1955.** In July, the South Vietnamese government refused a North Vietnamese request to prepare for reunification elections on grounds that free elections would be impossible in North Vietnam.

North Vietnam announced **Dec. 1960** the formation of the National Liberation Front (Vietcong) of South Vietnam; terrorism in the South increased. The number of U.S. military advisers in South Vietnam rose from about 2,000 in Dec. 1961 to over 15,000 by the end of 1963.

Ngo Dinh Diem, South Vietnam president since 1955, was assassinated during a military coup **Nov. 1, 1963.** Stable government did not return to South Vietnam until **June, 1965,** when Gen. Nguyen Van Thieu assumed command of a military government.

The major American commitment in Vietnam began after the U.S. destroyers Maddox and C. Turner Joy were reportedly attacked **Aug. 2, 1964,** by North Vietnamese torpedo boats in the Gulf of Tonkin. The U.S. Congress **Aug. 7** passed the Gulf of Tonkin Resolution giving the president power to "take all necessary measures to repel any armed attack against the forces of the U.S. and to prevent further aggression." In **Feb. 1965,** Pres. Johnson ordered continuous bombing raids over North Vietnam below the 20th parallel.

U.S. commanders were authorized to commit 23,000 advisers to combat **June 8, 1965.** U.S. army, navy, air and marine forces committed in Vietnam reached 184,300 men by year's end. The U.S. began bombing strikes in the Hanoi-Haiphong area **June 29, 1966.** By **Dec. 31, 1966,** U.S. forces in Vietnam reached 385,300 men, not including some 60,000 men in the U.S. fleet and some 33,000 men stationed in Thailand.

As the fighting and American casualties escalated, large-scale protests against the war erupted in the U.S. Thousands of war protesters marched **Oct. 21-22, 1967,** in Washington, D.C., and hundreds were arrested when they stormed the Pentagon. Nevertheless, American troop strength climbed to 474,300 men in **Dec.,** 1,500 more than peak U.S. strength in Korea during the Korean War.

In the "Tet offensive" Jan. 30, 1968, the Vietcong and North Vietnamese attacked 30 provincial capitals in South Vietnam. The city of Hue was held by the Vietcong for 25 days, with bitter street fighting ending **Feb. 24.** Saigon was heavily attacked and the U.S. Embassy was occupied for 6 hrs. Record casualties were suffered on both sides. Pres. Johnson **Mar. 31** announced a bombing halt over 90% of North Vietnam and asked Hanoi for a peaceful response.

While the fighting continued, preliminary peace talks between the U.S. and North Vietnam opened in Paris **May 10.** In Chicago, police and troops clashed with 10,000-15,000 anti-war demonstrators during the Democratic National Convention **Aug. 26-29.**

Expanded peace talks, including representatives from South Vietnam and the Vietcong, opened in Paris **Jan. 18, 1969.** American forces in South Vietnam reached a final peak of 543,400 men in **Apr. 1969.** U.S. battle deaths **Apr. 3** totaled 33,641 men, surpassing by 12 those killed in the Korean War. Withdrawal of U.S. combat troops began **July 8, 1969,** and on **Nov. 3** Pres. Nixon announced a Vietnamization policy which would transfer the fighting to South Vietnamese forces.

Protests in the U.S. continued, however, as hundreds of thousands of Americans demonstrated opposition to the Vietnam War **Oct. 15** in a nationwide "moratorium." Some 250,000 demonstrators gathered in Washington, D.C., **Nov. 15** in the largest anti-war protest in U.S. history.

As the Paris talks continued, U.S. and South Vietnamese forces invaded neutral Cambodia **Apr. 30, 1970,** to destroy communist supply bases in border area sanctuaries. On **May 4** at Kent State Univ. in Ohio, 4 students were slain and 9 wounded when National Guardsmen opened fire during a demonstration against the Cambodian incursion; 100 U.S. colleges were closed down to protest the Cambodian invasion and Kent State killings. A year later, during massive anti-war protests in Washington, D.C., between **May 3-5,** police arrested some 12,614 people, at least 7,000 of them on the first day — a record high for arrests in a civil disturbance in U.S. history.

Pres. Nixon revealed **Jan. 25, 1972,** that secret peace negotiations had been conducted since the previous June by presidential adviser Henry A. Kissinger. In the biggest communist attack since 1968, North Vietnamese forces **Mar. 30** launched an offensive against South Vietnam through the demilitarized zone (DMZ) between the 2 Vietnams. Bombing of North Vietnam resumed **Apr. 15,** the first intensive bombing of North since 1968. Quang Tri, capital city of South Vietnam's northernmost province, fell to Hanoi troops **May 1.** The mining of Haiphong and other North Vietnamese ports was ordered by Pres. Nixon **May 8.** After setbacks, South Vietnamese troops brought the invasion to a halt.

The last U.S. combat troops left Vietnam **Aug. 11.** Hanoi announced **Oct. 26** that secret talks had achieved a tentative agreement. But the peace talks broke down and, on **Dec. 18** Pres. Nixon ordered the heaviest bombing of the war against North Vietnam. B-52 bombers were used for the first time against targets in Hanoi; some 15 were shot down by Hanoi's surface-to-air missiles.

Peace talks resumed **Jan. 8, 1973,** and Pres. Nixon ordered a halt to all offensive military operations against North Vietnam **Jan. 15.** Peace pacts were formally signed in Paris **Jan. 27** by the U.S., North and South Vietnam, and the Vietcong. A cease-fire began in Vietnam on **Jan. 28.** Between **Feb. 12** and **Apr. 1,** 590 American POWs were released by North Vietnam. Some 1,359 Americans were reported missing in Indochina. The last American troops left Vietnam **Mar. 29,** officially ending any direct U.S. military role. U.S. combat deaths were counted at 46,079 as of **Aug. 25, 1973.** Total dead were estimated at some 2 million. Last American civilians were evacuated **Apr. 29, 1975.**

was freed **Feb. 10, 1962**, in exchange for convicted Soviet spy Rudolf Abel, who was serving a 30-year term imposed by U. S. in 1957.

Adolf Eichmann's capture in Argentina by Israeli agents announced **May 22**; former Nazi SS general accused of playing a major role in killing of millions of Jews. After 4-month trial in Jerusalem, Eichmann was convicted by Israeli court **Dec. 15, 1961**, hanged for crimes against humanity **May 31, 1962**.

1961

The U. S. severed diplomatic and consular relations with Cuba **Jan. 3**.

Maj. Yuri Gagarin of the Soviet Union became **Apr. 12** the first human orbital traveler; he was launched into orbit from Siberia in a spacecraft called Vostok I and returned to earth after one circuit of the globe.

Invasion of Cuba "Bay of Pigs" **Apr. 17** by Cuban exiles attempting to overthrow the regime of Premier Fidel Castro was repulsed.

Commander Alan B. Shepard Jr. was rocketed from Cape Canaveral, Fla., 116.5 mi. above the earth in a Mercury capsule **May 5** in the first U. S.-manned sub-orbital space flight; he landed safely in the Atlantic 302 mi. away.

East Germany closed the border between East and West Berlin **Aug. 12-13** to stop the exodus of East Germans to the West; the East Germans built a wall dividing the city.

Dag Hammarskjold, sec. general of the UN, was killed in a plane crash near Ndola, Northern Rhodesia, **Sept. 18**.

Nuclear blasts of 25 megatons and over 50 megatons, largest man-made explosions to date, were set off by the Soviet Union **Oct. 23** and **Oct. 30**.

1962

Lt. Col. John H. Glenn Jr. became the first American in orbit **Feb. 20** when he circled the earth 3 times in the Mercury capsule Friendship 7.

A truce agreement Mar. 18 ended the 7-yr. Moslem revolt against French rule in Algeria. Algerians cast an overwhelming vote for independence **July 1** and French Pres. de Gaulle declared the country independent **July 3**.

The largest cash robbery to date in U. S. history occurred **Aug. 14** when a gang held up a U. S. mail truck near Plymouth, Mass., and stole $1,551,277.

A Soviet offensive buildup in Cuba was revealed to the American people **Oct. 22** by Pres. Kennedy, who ordered a naval and air quarantine on shipment of offensive military equipment to the island. Pres. Kennedy and Soviet Premier Khrushchev reached agreement **Oct. 28** on a formula to end the crisis. Kennedy announced **Nov. 2** that Soviet missile bases in Cuba were being dismantled.

1963

The first woman space traveler, Soviet **Jr. Lt. Valentina V. Tereshkova**, was launched into orbit in Vostok VI **June 16**; landed **June 19** after 48 orbits.

U.S. Supreme Court ruled, 8-1, **June 17** that laws requiring recitation of the Lord's Prayer or Bible verses in public schools were unconstitutional.

A limited nuclear test-ban treaty was agreed upon **July 25** by the U. S., the Soviet Union, and Britain, barring all nuclear tests except underground.

The biggest robbery to date occurred **Aug. 8** when an armed holdup gang stole more than $7 million (£2.5 million) in currency from a mail train near Cheddington, England. Some of the money was recovered and a dozen men were sentenced to prison.

Washington demonstration by 200,000 persons **Aug. 28** in support of Negro demands for equal rights. Highlight was speech in which Dr. Martin Luther King said: "I have a dream that this nation will rise up and live out the true meaning of its creed, 'We hold these truths to be self evident: that all men are created equal."

Pres. John F. Kennedy was shot and fatally wounded by an assassin **Nov. 22** as he rode in a motorcade through downtown Dallas, Tex. **Gov. John B. Connally Jr. of Texas**, riding in the same car, was also shot but not fatally injured. Vice Pres. Lyndon B. Johnson was inaugurated president shortly afterward in Dallas. **Lee Harvey Oswald** was arrested and charged with the murder of the president. Oswald was shot and fatally wounded **Nov. 24** by **Jack Ruby**, 52, a Dallas nightclub owner, who was convicted of murder **Mar. 14, 1964**, and was sentenced to death. The murder conviction was reversed by the Texas Court of Criminal Appeals. Ruby died of natural causes **Jan. 3, 1967** while awaiting re-trial.

1964

Pope Paul VI toured the Holy Land **Jan. 4-6**, the first pope to visit there since Christianity began, and the first to leave Italy in over 150 years.

Three civil rights workers were reported missing in Mississippi **June 22**. The bodies of Michael Schwerner, Andrew Goodman and James E. Chaney were found buried near Philadelphia, Miss., **Aug. 4**. Twenty-one white men were arrested. On **Oct. 20, 1967**, an all-white federal jury convicted 7 of conspiracy in the slayings.

The Warren Commission released **Sept. 27** a report concluding that Lee Harvey Oswald was solely responsible for the Kennedy assassination.

Soviet Premier Khrushchev was ousted as premier and Soviet Communist party chief **Oct. 14-15**. Aleksei N. Kosygin replaced him as premier and Leonid I. Brezhnev took over the party leadership.

Communist China conducted a successful test explosion of its first atomic bomb **Oct. 16**.

1965

A Selma to Montgomery, Ala., civil rights march was led by Dr. Martin Luther King Jr., **Mar. 21-25**. The march started with 3,200 and swelled to 25,000. They were guarded along the way by 4,000 troops dispatched by Pres. Johnson.

U.S. armed forces sent to Dominican Republic to protect U.S. citizens and prevent a revolution **Apr. 28**. The Organization of American States **May 23** set up a peace-keeping force to maintain order.

Los Angeles riot by discontented blacks living in Watts area resulted in death of 35 persons and property damage est. at $200 million **Aug. 11-16**.

Pope Paul VI visited N.Y. City **Oct. 4** and delivered a personal appeal for peace to the UN. It was the first time a pope had come to America.

Massive electric power failure blacked out most of northeastern U.S., parts of 2 Canadian provinces the night of **Nov. 9-10**. Approximately 80,000 sq. mi. with a population of 30 million were affected. In N.Y. City over 800,000 were trapped in the subways for hours.

Independence from Britain proclaimed in Rhodesia by minority white regime **Nov. 11**.

1966

Kwame Nkrumah, president of Ghana since independence in 1957, was overthrown **Feb. 24**.

France withdrew all its armed forces from the integrated NATO military alliance **July 1**.

Medicare, government program to pay part of the medical expenses of citizens over 65, began **July 1**.

Edward Brooke (R, Mass.) elected **Nov. 8** as first Negro U.S. senator in 85 years.

1967

Rep. Adam Clayton Powell (D, N.Y.) was denied **Mar. 1** his seat in 90th Congress because House of Representatives charged him with misuse of government funds and nepotism. Reelected in 1968, he was seated by the 91st Congress but was fined $25,000 and stripped of his 22 years' congressional seniority.

In 6-day Israeli-Arab war June 5-10, Israel smashed armed forces of United Arab Republic (Egypt), Syria and Jordan; Israel captured territory 4 times its own area. **A U.S. communications ship, the U.S.S. Liberty**, was attacked by Israeli planes and torpedo boats **June 8** in international waters off the Sinai Peninsula. Thirty-four U.S. crewmen were killed and 75 wounded. Israel apologized for the attack, which it called accidental.

Pres. Johnson and Soviet Premier Aleksei Kosygin met **June 23 and 25** at Glassboro State College in N.J.; agreed not to let any crisis push them into war.

Black riots in Newark, N.J., July 12-17 killed some 26, injured 1,500; over 1,000 arrested. In Detroit, Mich., **July 23-30** at least 40 died, 2,000 injured, and 5,000 left homeless by rioting, looting, burning in city's black ghetto. Quelled by 4,700 federal paratroopers and 8,000 National Guardsmen.

Thurgood Marshall sworn in **Oct. 2** as first black U.S. Supreme Court Justice. **Carl B. Stokes** (D, Cleveland) and **Richard G. Hatcher** (D, Gary, Ind.), elected first black mayors of major U.S. cities **Nov. 7.**

Dr. Christiaan Barnard, Capetown, South Africa, performed first successful human heart transplant **Dec. 3** on Louis Washkansky, who lived for 18 days.

1968

U.S.S. Pueblo and 83-man crew seized in Sea of Japan **Jan. 23** by North Koreans; 82 men released **Dec. 22.**

White racism cited as chief cause of black violence in Kerner Commission report on civil disorders **Feb. 29.**

Pres. Johnson said Mar. 31 he would not seek or accept the Democratic nomination for president.

The Rev. Dr. Martin Luther King Jr., 39, assassinated **Apr. 4** in Memphis, Tenn. Riots in Washington, D.C., caused Pres. Johnson to call out troops. By **Apr. 14** racial violence erupted in 125 cities in 29 states. James Earl Ray, an escaped convict, pleaded guilty to the slaying, was sentenced to 99 years.

Six New Left students' protest at Univ. of Nanterre, France, **May 2** grew into nearly a month of civil violence and by **May 24** 10 million strikers paralyzed country. De Gaulle saved regime with broad reforms.

Sen. Robert F. Kennedy, 42 (D, N.Y.), shot **June 5** in Hotel Ambassador, Los Angeles, after celebrating Cal. and S.D. presidential primary victories. Died **June 6.** Sirhan Bishara Sirhan, a Jordanian Arab living in Los Angeles, convicted of murder.

Soviet Union and other Warsaw Pact nations invaded Czechoslovakia **Aug. 20-21** to crush Alexander Dubcek's liberal regime.

1969

Unarmed U.S. reconnaissance plane, with 31 aboard, shot down by North Korean jets **Apr. 15** in the Sea of Japan about 100 mi. from the mainland. No survivors found.

Charles de Gaulle resigned as president of France **Apr. 28** after narrowly losing a referendum.

A car driven by Sen. Edward M. Kennedy (D, Mass.) plunged off a bridge into a tidal pool on Chappaquiddick Is., Martha's Vineyard, Mass., **July 18.** The body of Mary Jo Kopechne, a 28-year-old secretary, was found drowned, in the car.

U.S. astronaut Neil A. Armstrong, 38, commander of the Apollo 11 mission, became the first man to set foot on the moon **July 20.** After stepping onto the moon Armstrong said: "That's one small step for a man, one giant leap for mankind." Air Force **Col. Edwin E. Aldrin Jr.** accompanied Armstrong.

1970

The 31-month Nigerian civil war ended with the surrender **Jan. 12** of secessionist Biafra after a loss of about 2 million lives.

A federal jury Feb. 18 found the defendants in the turbulent 21-week trial of the "Chicago 7" innocent of conspiring to incite riots during the 1968 Democratic National Convention. However, 5 were convicted of crossing state lines with intent to incite riots.

The U.S. cast its first veto in the UN Security Council **Mar. 17** when it joined Britain in rejecting a resolution calling on UN members to cut all communications with Rhodesia.

Millions of Americans participated in anti-pollution demonstrations **Apr. 22** to mark the first Earth Day.

The first women generals in U.S. history were named by Pres. Nixon **May 15.** He promoted Col. Elizabeth Hoisington, Women's Army Corps director, and Col. Anna Mae Hays, chief of the Army Nurse Corps, to the rank of brig. gen.

The Norwegian explorer Thor Heyerdahl and a multi-national crew of 7 set sail from Morocco **May 17** in a frail papyrus boat, the Ra II, in an attempt to prove that ancient Egyptians could have reached the new world. The craft sailed into Bridgetown Harbor, Barbados, **July 12.**

A postal reform measure was signed by Pres. Nixon **Aug. 12,** creating an independent U.S. Postal Service, thus relinquishing governmental control of the U.S. mails after almost 2 centuries.

Egypt's Pres. Gamal Abdel Nasser, 52, most powerful leader in Arab world, died **Sept. 28.**

Salvador Allende Gossens, 62, first democratically elected Marxist head of government in the world, was sworn in as Chile's president **Nov. 3.**

Charles de Gaulle, 79, died of a heart attack in Colombey-les-Deux Eglises **Nov. 9.**

1971

Charles Manson, 36, and 3 of his followers were found guilty **Jan. 26** of first-degree murder in the 1969 slaying of actress Sharon Tate and 6 others.

A treaty prohibiting installation of nuclear weapons on the seabed beyond any nation's 12-mi. coastal zone was signed by 63 nations **Feb. 11.**

A Constitutional Amendment lowering the voting age to 18 in all elections was approved in the Senate by a vote of 94-0 **Mar. 10.** The proposed 26th Amendment received House approval by a 400-19 vote **Mar. 23;** Ohio ratified it on **June 30** making it law.

Civil war between East and West Pakistan beginning **Mar. 25** brought death from war and starvation to hundreds of thousands and caused 9 million refugees to pour into India.

A court-martial jury of 6 officers **Mar. 29** after 13 days deliberation, convicted Lt. William L. Calley Jr. of premeditated murder of 22 South Vietnamese men, women and children at Mylai on **Mar. 16, 1968.** He was sentenced to life imprisonment **Mar. 31.** Sentence reduced to 20 years **Aug. 20, 1971,** by Lt. Gen. Albert O. Conner.

Haiti's Francois (Papa Doc) Duvalier, 64, died **Apr. 21.** His son Claude, 19, succeeded him **Apr. 22.**

Amtrak, the nation's new rail passenger system, went into operation **May 1** with the goal to "get people back on trains."

Publication of classified Pentagon papers on the U.S. involvement in Vietnam was begun **June 13** by the New York Times. In a 6-3 vote, the U.S. Supreme Court **June 30** upheld the right of the Times and the Washington Post to publish the documents under the protection of the First Amendment. Daniel Ellsberg, admitted leaker of the 47-volume Pentagon analysis, was arraigned **June 28** on charges of unauthorized possession of secret documents.

Pres. Nixon began a sweeping new economic program **Aug. 15** imposing a 90-day wage, price and rent freeze. He also devalued the dollar by cutting its tie with gold.

More than 1,000 N.Y. State troopers and police stormed the Attica State Correctional Facility where 1,200 inmates held 38 guards hostage **Sept. 13,** ending a 4-day rebellion in the maximum-security prison; 9 hostages, 28 convicts killed in the assault.

Chile virtually expropriated the Anaconda and Kennecott copper mines **Sept. 28** when Pres. Allende subtracted $774 million from proposed compensation for the U.S. owners. He claimed the deduction was for "excess profits" by the U.S. firms over 16 years.

Communist China was granted UN membership when the General Assembly by a vote of 76 to 35, with 17 abstentions, adopted an Albanian resolution **Oct. 25** to seat Mao Tse-tung's communists and oust Chiang Kai-shek's nationalists.

India invaded Pakistan Dec. 3 in defense of splinter nation of Bangladesh, formerly East Pakistan. Following India's victory in the 14-day war, Shiek Mujibur Rahman, the father of the secessionist rebellion, became the prime minister of Bangladesh **Jan. 12.**

Pres. Nixon announced Dec. 18 an 8.57% devaluation of the U.S. dollar to allow American goods to be more competitive in the world market, while raising the price of certain imports; the devaluation was accomplished by a $3 increase in the price of gold, from $35 an ounce to $38.

1972

Pres. Nixon arrived in Peking Feb. 21 for an 8-day visit to China, which he called a "journey for peace." The unprecedented visit ended with a joint communique pledging that both powers would work for "a normalization of relations".

By a vote of 84 to 8, the Senate approved **Mar. 22** a Constitutional Amendment banning legal discrimination against women because of their sex and sent the measure to the states for ratification.

Britain imposed direct rule over North Ireland **Mar. 30,** ending 51 years of semi-autonomous rule by the North Ireland government.

Alabama Gov. George C. Wallace, campaigning at a Laurel, Md., shopping center **May 15,** was shot and seriously wounded as he greeted a large crowd. Arthur H. Bremer, 21, was sentenced **Aug. 4** to 63 years for shooting Wallace and 3 bystanders.

In the first visit of a U.S. president to Moscow, Pres. Nixon arrived **May 22** for a week of summit talks with Kremlin leaders which culminated in a landmark arms pact aimed at a standoff between the missile forces of the 2 nuclear giants.

The Environmental Protection Agency announced **June 14** a near-total ban on agricultural and other uses of the pesticide DDT, to be effective **Dec. 31.**

Five men were arrested June 17 for breaking into the offices of the Democratic National Committee in the Watergate office complex in Washington, D.C.

The White House announced July 8 that the U.S. would sell the Soviet Union at least $750 million of American wheat, corn and other grains over a period of 3 years. But the USSR bought most of it in 1st year.

Less than 2 weeks after Sen. Thomas F. Eagleton received the Democrats' nomination for vice-president, he confirmed **July 25** reports that he had undergone electroshock treatment on 2 occasions in the 1960s. Eagleton withdrew as nominee **July 31.** R. Sargent Shriver was named as vice presidential candidate **Aug. 8.**

By a vote of 88 to 2, the Senate **Aug. 3** ratified the strategic arms treaty limiting the U.S. and Russia to 2 antiballistic missile sites each. In White House ceremonies **Oct. 3** Pres. Nixon and Soviet Foreign Min. Andrei Gromyko signed and exchanged the final documents implementing the accords, which also limited the 2 powers' land-based and submarine-borne nuclear missile forces.

Eight Arab guerrillas, members of the Black September terrorist group, invaded the Israeli dormitory in the Olympics village in Munich early **Sept. 5** killing 2 members of the Israeli squad. Twenty-three hours later, after terrorists and hostages were moved by helicopter to a nearby airport, West German police attacked, killing 5 terrorists. All 9 hostages and a policeman were killed.

Life ended publication with its **Dec. 29** issue after 36 years as the leading weekly pictorial magazine.

1973

All mandatory wage and price controls were ended by Pres. Nixon **Jan. 11.**

All state laws that limited a woman's right to an abortion during the first 3 months of pregnancy were overturned **Jan. 22** by the U.S. Supreme Court, 7-2.

The end of the military draft was announced **Jan. 27** by Defense Sec. Melvin R. Laird.

U. S. Sec. of the Treasury George P. Shultz announced **Feb. 12** a 10% devaluation of the U.S. dollar against nearly all major world currencies.

Some 200-300 members of the militant American Indian Movement **Feb. 27** seized the trading post and church at historic Wounded Knee on the Oglala Sioux Reservation in South Dakota. The insurgents demanded that the U.S. Senate Foreign Relations Committee hold hearings on treaties made with Indians, and that the Senate start a "full-scale investigation" of government treatment of Indians. After numerous negotiation failures both sides signed an agreement **May 5** stipulating removal of government armored personnel carriers and concurrent surrender of weapons by the insurgent Indians. The hamlet was evacuated **May 8.**

Palestinian terrorists invaded a reception **Mar. 1** at the Saudi Arabian embassy in Khartoum, Sudan, and held 6 diplomats hostage. After a breakdown of negotiations between the gunmen and Sudanese government officials, the 8 Palestinians **Mar. 2** tortured and executed 2 U.S. envoys and a Belgian charge d'affaires. Terrorists arrested; later freed.

James W. McCord, a key figure in the Watergate conspiracy, said **Mar. 23** in a letter to the court that he and others had been under "political pressure" to plead guilty and remain silent. He said there were others involved who had escaped indictment.

Pres. Nixon responded to the Watergate crisis in an address over radio and television **Apr. 30.** Although he himself had not played a role in the Watergate case, he said, he accepted, as "top man in the organization," full responsibility for those "people whose zeal exceeded their judgment." Earlier the same day 3 of his top aides resigned: chief of staff H. R. Haldeman, domestic affairs assistant John D. Ehrlichman and presidential counsel John W. Dean 3d. Atty. Gen. Richard G. Kleindienst also resigned.

The West German Bundestag ratified a treaty **May 11** establishing formal relations with the German Democratic Republic in East Germany.

Presiding Judge William M. Byrne dismissed **May 11** all government charges of espionage, theft, and conspiracy against Daniel Ellsberg and Anthony J. Russo Jr., the defendants in the 89-day Pentagon Papers trial. The decision precluded a retrial, but did not vindicate the defendants nor resolve the major constitutional issues in the controversial case. The crucial revelation leading to dismissal of the case came **Apr. 27** when Judge Byrne released a Justice Dept. memorandum stating that 2 of the convicted Watergate defendants, E. Howard Hunt and G. Gordon Liddy, had broken into the office of Ellsberg's psychiatrist with the intention of stealing Ellsberg's medical records. Byrne released E. Howard Hunt's grand jury testimony **May 14** in which Hunt stated that the White House had conceived the plot and supervised and paid for the break-in.

Hearings by the Senate Select Committee on Presidential Campaign Activities into the Watergate scandal opened in Washington, D.C., **May 17** chaired by Sam J. Ervin (D.,N.C.).

Pres. Nixon released a statement **May 22** in which he asserted that he made legitimate efforts to restrict investigation into some matters related to the Watergate affair because they impinged on national security. The president further stated that his concern over foreign policy leaks and the publication of the Pentagon Papers led to the establishment in 1971 of a small White House investigative unit, the "plumbers," supervised by John D. Ehrlichman.

Pres. Nixon set a freeze June 13 on retail prices The freeze included prepared-food prices but excluded rents, interest, dividends, and raw food.

The U.S. and USSR signed 9 agreements during Soviet Communist party Gen. Sec. Leonid I. Brezhnev's **June 16-25** visit to the U. S. One agreement obliged the 2 nations to enter into immediate consultations if relations between them or between one of them and some other country "appear to involve risk of nuclear conflict."

Former Pres. Juan D. Peron returned **June 20** to Argentina after almost 20 years of exile. He was reelected president of Argentina **Sept. 23,** but died 9 months later, July 1, 1974.

John Dean, former presidential counsel, **June 25** testified to a widespread cover-up of the Watergate conspiracy. He said the cover-up had spread from the White House staff and the Committee to Re-elect the President to the Justice Dept. and to the "Oval Office" of the president.

The Federal Trade Commission July 9 charged 8 of

the largest U.S. oil companies with conspiracy to monopolize the refining of petroleum products. The commission said the 23-year conspiracy had led to shortages of gasoline, forcing "substantially higher prices" on American consumers, and caused some independent petroleum marketers to close down.

The Senate Armed Services Committee July 16 began a probe into allegations that the U.S. Air Force had made 3,500 secret B-52 raids into Cambodia in 1969 and 1970.

Herbert Kalmbach, formerly attorney and fund raiser for Pres. Nixon, told the Senate Watergate Committee **July 16** that he had raised $220,000 for the 7 defendants in the Watergate trial, believing the money was intended for legal fees and support of the defendant's families.

White House tape recording of all conversations in the president's offices since Mar. 1971 was revealed by Alexander P. Butterfield, former presidential deputy assistant, in a surprise appearance before the Senate Watergate Committee **July 16.** On **July 23,** citing separation of powers and executive privilege, Pres. Nixon refused to release any tapes to Senate investigators.

The U. S. officially ceased bombing in Cambodia at midnight **Aug. 14** in accord with a June Congressional action. The bombing halt was preceded by several days of intensive bombing around Phnom Penh.

Forty-six years of civilian rule in Chile ended **Sept. 11** when a 4-man military junta overthrew Pres. Salvador Allende Gossens' Marxist government.

Henry A. Kissinger's nomination as Sec. of State was confirmed **Sept. 21.**

Pres. Nixon's 1972 campaign finance aides revealed **Sept. 28** that campaign fund raisers had collected a record $60.2 million.

The 4th and biggest Arab-Israeli War in 25 years erupted **Oct. 6** along the 103-mile-long Suez Canal and on the Golan Heights. The war began on the afternoon of Yom Kippur, the Jewish Holy Day of Atonement, and was marked by heavy troop and materiel losses on both sides. UN observers in the Middle East reported that Egyptian forces had crossed the Suez Canal at 5 points and that Syrian forces had attacked at 2 points on the Golan Heights. By **Oct. 11** the Egyptian army had established a bridgehead of about 60,000 men in the Sinai. The Egyptian army's advance was greatly aided by use of new Russian SAM-6 missiles which stymied the Israeli air offensive against the bridgehead.

After losing ground on both fronts, Israel counterattacked. Israel claimed **Oct. 12** that its forces had pushed to within 18 mi. of Damascus, despite the arrival of Iraqi and Jordanian forces on the Syrian front. Israel **Oct. 16** said it had sent a task force across the Suez Canal to attack Egyptian forces and missile sites on the west side. By **Oct. 24,** the Israelis had isolated the Suez city and the Egyptian 3d Army in Sinai.

The UN Security Council **Oct. 22** passed, 14-0, a U.S.-USSR sponsored resolution calling for a cease-fire in place. Fighting continued until a 2d cease-fire went into effect **Oct. 24** with UN supervision.

A total ban on oil exports to the U.S. was imposed by Arab oil-producing nations **Oct. 19-21.** The ban was lifted Mar. 18, 1974.

The U. S. Oct. 25 placed its military forces on a world-wide "precautionary alert" because of reported USSR plans to send a Russian "peace-keeping" force to the Middle East. The crisis ended when the USSR and U.S. joined in a Security Council vote barring the superpowers from participation in a peace-keeping force. A 7,000-man UN peace-keeping force was approved **Oct. 27.**

Vice Pres. Spiro T. Agnew Oct. 10 resigned and pleaded "nolo contendere" (no contest) to charges of tax evasion on payments made to him by Maryland contractors. Agnew was sentenced to 3 years probation and fined $10,000.

Atty. Gen Elliot Richardson resigned, and his deputy William D. Ruckelshaus and Watergate Special Prosecutor Archibald Cox were fired by Pres. Nixon **Oct. 20** when Cox threatened to secure a judicial ruling that Pres. Nixon was violating a court order to turn tapes over to Judge John Sirica.

Leon Jaworski, conservative Texas Democrat, was named **Nov. 1** by the Nixon administration to be special prosecutor to succeed Archibald Cox, with the understanding Jaworski would have "complete freedom" to investigate administrative wrongdoing.

Congress overrode Nov. 7 Pres. Nixon's veto of the war powers bill which curbed the president's power to commit armed forces to hostilities abroad without Congressional approval.

The U.S. and Egypt announced **Nov. 7** they would renew diplomatic relations.

Sentencing 6 Watergate break-in defendants **Nov. 9,** Federal Judge John J. Sirica dealt E. Howard Hunt 2 1/2-8 years and a $10,000 fine; James W. McCord Jr. 1-5 years; Frank A. Sturgis, Eugenio R. Martinez, and Virgilio R. Gonzalez 1-4 years; Bernard L. Barker 18 months to 6 years. The 7th defendant, G. Gordon Liddy, had already been sentenced to 20 years, reflecting his refusal to cooperate with the prosecution.

Watergate Special Prosecutor Archibald Cox's firing, **Oct. 20,** was ruled illegal by Washington, D.C., Federal Court **Nov. 14.**

Alaska pipeline bill, permitting construction of 789-mi. pipe from Alaska's North Shore oilfield to port of Valdez, signed by Pres. Nixon **Nov. 16.**

Greek Pres. and dictator George Papadopoulos was deposed **Nov. 25** in bloodless military coup after student-worker riots.

Egil Krogh Jr., former head of the "plumbers," White House investigative unit, pleaded guilty **Nov. 30** to violating civil rights of Daniel Ellsberg's psychiatrist, Dr. Lewis J. Fielding, in burglary of Fielding's office. Krogh drew 6 months, **Jan. 24, 1974.**

Gerald Rudolph Ford was sworn in **Dec. 6** as 40th vice president, the first who was not elected, under XXVth Amendment procedures.

Pres. Nixon disclosed his financial records **Dec. 8,** showing large income tax deductions based on gift of his vice presidential papers to the National Archives. He said he would let a joint Congressional committee decide if he owed more taxes.

Allocations for fuel oil and gasoline were announced by energy chief William Simon **Dec. 12,** giving priorities to essential services.

A 3-day work week was ordered by British government **Dec. 13** because of Arab oil embargo and coal miners' slowdown.

Arab nations doubled oil prices and said they would increase oil flow to some nations by 10%, but would continue embargo against U.S., the Netherlands and Denmark, after meetings **Dec. 23-25.**

1974

U.S. oil companies reported huge profits for the 4th quarter of 1973, during the Arab oil embargo, in their **Jan. 1974** reports. Exxon profits were up 59% over the same period of 1972; Mobil, 68%; Texaco, 70%; Ashland, 52%.

A disengagement agreement was reached by Israel and Egypt **Jan. 17** with U.S. aid. Egyptian forces occupied a narrow strip on the east side of the Suez Canal; a UN-patrolled buffer zone separated them from Israeli forces further east; Israelis withdrew from west of the canal.

Alexander Solzhenitsyn, Nobel Prize-winning author, was deported by Soviet Russia to West Germany **Feb. 13.** He had exposed the Soviet prison camp system in Gulag Archipelago, published in Paris.

Herbert W. Kalmbach, Pres. Nixon's personal lawyer and fundraiser, pleaded guilty **Feb. 25** to promising a contributor an ambassadorship for a $100,000 contribution. Sentenced **June 17,** he got 6 to 8 months and a $10,000 fine.

Arab nations ended their oil embargo against the U.S. **Mar. 18** but continued it against Denmark and the Netherlands, designating them "unfriendly."

Pres. Nixon said Apr. 3 he would pay $432,787.13 in back taxes plus interest for 1969 through 1972, after

Joint Congressional Committee, acting on request from Nixon, found him liable.

Lt. Gov. Ed Reinecke of California was indicted **Apr. 3** for lying to the Senate Judiciary Committee. Convicted **July 27**, he resigned and received an 18-month suspended sentence.

W. A. Boyle, deposed United Mine Workers president, was convicted **Apr. 11** of murder for ordering the slayings of union rival Joseph A. Yablonski and Yablonski's wife and daughter. The conviction carried a mandatory life sentence.

Arab guerrillas killed 18, mostly women and children, in attack on Qiryat Shemona, Israel, **Apr. 11.**

Charging Soviet Russia was trying to influence Egyptian actions by putting off requests for more arms, Pres. Anwar Sadat said **Apr. 18** Egypt would end its reliance on Soviet arms aid.

Portugal's Premier Marcello Caetano was ousted **Apr. 25** by a military group pledging democracy and peace for Portugal's African territories.

Former Atty. Gen. John N. Mitchell and former Commerce Sec. Maurice H. Stans were acquitted **Apr. 28** in N.Y. City Federal Court of attempting to impede an official probe of financier Robert L. Vesco in return for a $200,000 cash donation to the 1972 Nixon re-election campaign.

Impeachment hearings were opened **May 9** against Pres. Nixon by the House Judiciary Committee.

Arab terrorists seized 90 students in the Israeli town of Maalot **May 15** after murdering a family of 3. Israeli troops freed the hostages, but 21 students, one Israeli soldier, and the 3 terrorists died.

Ex-Atty. Gen. Richard G. Kleindienst pleaded guilty **May 16** to a misdemeanor charge that he did not testify accurately and fully before a Congressional committee probing handling of an ITT anti-trust settlement. He received 30 days and a $100 fine, both suspended, **June 7.**

India exploded a nuclear device May 18, becoming the 6th nation with nuclear bomb capability.

Jeb Stuart Magruder, former deputy director of the Committee to Re-elect the President, was sentenced **May 21** to 10 months to 4 years for his role in the Watergate break-in and cover-up.

Northern Ireland's Protestant-Catholic coalition government collapsed after a strike; the British government took over direct rule of Ulster **May 29.**

Israel and Syria signed a disengagement agreement **May 31.** Israel gave up some of the Golan Heights territory she had taken in 1967 and 1973; forces on both sides were limited in strips separated by a UN-patrolled buffer zone.

Charles W. Colson, ex-counsel to the president, pleaded guilty **June 3** to attempting to obstruct justice; he was sentenced **June 21** to 1 to 3 years and fined $5,000.

Mrs. Alberta Williams King, 69, mother of slain civil rights leader Dr. Martin Luther King Jr., was shot and killed **June 30**, along with a church deacon, in Atlanta's Ebenezer Baptist Church. Marcus Wayne Chenault, 23, of Dayton, Oh., was convicted **Sept. 12.**

Pres. Juan Domingo Peron of Argentina, 78, died **July 1**; he was succeeded by his vice president and wife, Maria Estela (Isabel) Martinez de Peron.

Turkey announced July 1 it would again allow the growth and sale of opium, but under strict control; in 1971 Turkey had promised the U.S. to outlaw the trade; the U.S. had agreed to give Turkey $35.7 million over 4 years.

John D. Ehrlichman and 3 White House "plumbers" were found guilty **July 12** of conspiring to violate the civil rights of Dr. Lewis Fielding, formerly psychiatrist to Daniel Ellsberg, by breaking into his Beverly Hills, Cal., office. **On July 31,** Ehrlichman, Nixon domestic aide, drew 20 mos. to 5 yrs.; G. Gordon Liddy got 1 to 3 years.; Bernard L. Barker and Eugenio Martinez won suspended sentences.

Turkey invaded Cyprus July 20. Earlier, 650 Greek officers, **July 15,** led the Cypriot National Guard in a violent coup, overthrowing Pres. Makarios, who fled to London. Negotiations brought a promise from Greece to replace gradually the 650 Greek officers but she refused to recall them immediately. The Turkish invasion followed, ostensibly to protect the Turkish minority, 18% of the Cyprus population.

Greece's military government resigned July 23: former Premier Constantine Karamanlis returned from exile to become chief of state. On Cyprus, fighting continued until Turkey, in possession of the NE third of the island, declared a cease-fire **Aug. 16.**

The U.S. Supreme Court ruled, 8-0, **July 24** that Pres. Nixon had to turn over 64 tapes of White House conversations sought by Watergate Special Prosecutor Leon Jaworski.

The House Judiciary Committee, in televised hearings **July 24-30**, recommended 3 articles of impeachment against Pres. Nixon. The first, voted 27-11, **July 27,** charged Nixon with taking part in a criminal conspiracy to obstruct justice in the Watergate cover-up. The second, voted 28-10, **July 29,** charged he "repeatedly" failed to carry out his constitutional oath in a series of alleged abuses of power. The third, voted 27-17, **July 30,** accused him of unconstitutional defiance of committee subpoenas. The House of Representatives **Aug. 20,** without debate, voted 412-3 to accept the committee report, which included the recommended impeachment articles.

Ex-presidential counsel John W. Dean 3d was sentenced **Aug. 2** to 1 to 3 years, on his plea of guilty to conspiracy to obstruct justice.

Pres. Richard M. Nixon resigned and Vice Pres. Gerald R. Ford was sworn in as president **Aug. 9.** Nixon's support in the Watergate struggle began eroding **Aug. 5** when Nixon released 3 tapes, admitting he originated plans to have the FBI stop its probe of the Watergate break-in for political as well as national security reasons. Supporters in both House and Senate said, **Aug. 6-7,** they would vote for his impeachment.

Former N.Y. Gov. Nelson A. Rockefeller was nominated to be vice president by Pres. Ford **Aug. 20.** He became the second non-elected vice president **Dec. 19.**

Portugal began dissolving its African empire **Aug. 26,** signing an agreement to free Portuguese Guinea **Sept. 10;** the new nation became Guinea-Bissau.

The U.S. and East Germany established diplomatic relations **Sept. 4.**

An unconditional pardon to ex-Pres. Nixon for all federal crimes that he "committed or may have committed" while president was issued by Pres. Gerald Ford **Sept. 8,** one month after Nixon resigned. Ford's press secretary, J. F. terHorst resigned in protest. The administration also announced a **Sept. 6** agreement under which the ex-president's papers and tapes would be held for 3 years; after that Nixon could destroy the tapes.

Ethiopian Emperor Haile Selassie, 82, was peacefully deposed **Sept. 12** by armed forces leaders who had been strengthening their power since Feb.

Conditional amnesty to Vietnam era draft evaders and deserters who would be willing to work up to 2 years in public service jobs was proposed by Pres. Ford **Sept. 16.** Organized exiles condemned the program and few took advantage of it.

Charges against Wounded Knee defendants Dennis J. Banks and Russell C. Means, Indian leaders, were dismissed **Sept. 16** by Federal Judge Fred J. Nichol in the 1973 takeover of the South Dakota village. Nichol said that during the trial the FBI had been shown to lie and suborn perjury.

The court martial conviction of Lt. William L. Calley Jr. in the 1968 massacre of civilians in Mylai South Vietnam, was overturned **Sept. 25** by Federal Court Judge J. Robert Elliott in Columbus, Ga.

The provisional president of Portugal, Gen. Antonio de Spinola, resigned **Sept. 30** with several associates, accused of a right-wing plot; the government was left chiefly in the hands of leftist officers and civilians.

A temporary restraining order, barring the Ford administration from carrying out its Sept. 6 agreement on returning Nixon's tapes, was issued **Oct. 21** by Federal Judge Charles Richey.

Leaders of 20 Arab nations declared Palestine Liberation Organization leader Yasir Arafat the "sole legitimate representative" of Palestinian Arabs **Oct. 28.** The UN General Assembly had voted **Oct. 14** to give the PLO a voice at its meetings.

Ex-Pres. Nixon underwent surgery for a blood clot **Oct. 29,** suffered internal bleeding and shock, but recovered in Long Beach, Cal. hospital.

Nixon's ex-attorney, Edward L. Morgan, pleaded guilty **Nov. 8** to backdating documents falsely to give Nixon a $576,000 tax deduction.

South Africa was suspended from taking part in the UN General Assembly session **Nov. 12.**

Ex-Pres. Nixon underwent surgery for phlebitis and suffered vascular shock in a Long Beach, Cal. hospital in **Nov.**

Dominated by Arab and Communist nations, the UN General Assembly welcomed Palestine Liberation Organization leader Yasir Arafat **Nov. 13** and backed his demands for a sovereign Palestine state.

A limit of 2,400 ICBMs each for the U.S. and USSR was tentatively agreed on by Pres. Ford and Soviet leader Leonid Brezhnev **Nov. 24** at Vladivostok.

A second heart was placed in the chest of a 58-year-old man to help his own heart **Nov. 18** by Dr. Christiaan Barnard in Capetown, South Africa.

The Irish Republican Army was outlawed by the British House of Commons **Nov. 19;** police powers were strengthened.

Democracy returned to Greece as a newly-elected Parliament met after 7-year hiatus, **Dec. 9.**

Court-ordered busing for desegregation was rejected, 3-2, by the Boston School Committee **Dec. 16;** 3 members were fined for contempt of court.

Charges that the CIA abused its powers by massive domestic operations were published **Dec. 21.**

1975

Found guilty of Watergate cover-up charges Jan. 1 were ex-Attorney General John N. Mitchell, ex-presidential advisers H.R. Haldeman and John D. Ehrlichman, all for perjury, conspiracy and obstruction of justice, and attorney Robert C. Mardian, for conspiracy to obstruct justice. Mardian's conviction was upset on appeal, **Oct. 1976.** The others got 2 1/2 to 8 years.

A budget deficit of $51.9 billion, largest in the nation's peacetime history, was projected in the $349.4 billion budget Pres. Ford offered Congress **Feb. 3.**

A separate nation, in the part of Cyprus occupied by Turkish troops, was proclaimed **Feb. 13** by Turkish Cypriots.

Senate filibuster rules were reformed **Mar. 7;** vote of 3/5 of Senate, rather than previous 2/3, made sufficient to invoke cloture and end a filibuster.

Saudi Arabian King Faisal, 70, shot dead **Mar. 25** in Riyadh by a nephew, who was beheaded **June 18.**

Tax cuts, individual rebates, and bonuses for some retirees, along with an end to depletion allowances for large oil companies and extended unemployment insurance were approved by Congress **Mar. 26.**

Warfare between Lebanese Moslems and Christians, which would last more than a year, broke out **Apr. 13.**

Cambodian government surrendered to the Communist Khmer Rouge **Apr. 16,** ending 5 years of warfare.

South Vietnam government surrendered to the Communist Vietcong and North Vietnamese **Apr. 30,** shortly after evacuation of last Americans and many South Vietnamese refugees.

Maurice H. Stans, chief fund-raiser for the Nixon reelection campaign, was fined $5,000 **May 14** after admitting 5 violations of federal campaign laws.

U.S. merchant ship Mayaguez and crew of 39 seized by Cambodian forces in Gulf of Siam **May 12.** In rescue operation, U.S. Marines attacked Tang Is., planes bombed air base; Cambodia surrendered ship and crew; U.S. losses were 15 killed in battle and 23 dead in a helicopter crash.

Congress voted $405 million for South Vietnam refugees **May 16;** 140,000 were flown to U.S., 130,000 were resettled in U.S.

Gulf Oil Corp. admitted May 16 it had paid $5 million in illegal gifts to foreign politicians; many other large U.S. corporations admitted making gifts and bribes to do business in foreign countries.

The Suez Canal was reopened June 5 to all but Israeli ships, 8 years after Egypt closed it during the 1967 Arab-Israeli war. It was cleared of debris mainly by the U.S.

U.S. unemployment reached 9.2%, high point of the year, the Labor Dept. reported **June 6.**

Illegal CIA operations, including records on 300,000 persons and groups, infiltration of agents into black, anti-war and political movements, monitoring of overseas phone calls, mail surveillance, and drug-testing, were described by a "blue-ribbon" commission headed by Vice Pres. Rockefeller **June 10.** Information on assassination plots against foreign leaders was ordered withheld by Pres. Ford. The commission recommended a Congressional oversight committee.

N.Y. City default on notes was avoided **June 10** by creation of a state Municipal Assistance Corp. (Big MAC) to refinance $3 billion in loans.

A U.S. Apollo and a USSR Soyuz linked together 140 mi. above the Atlantic **July 17.** The crews exchanged visits and shared meals in the 2 crafts.

Large U.S. grain companies were indicted July 21 and **Aug. 7** for conspiring to steal grain from foreign shipments.

James R. Hoffa, Teamsters ex-president, disappeared **July 30.** The FBI entered the search **Aug. 3.**

The Helsinki Agreement, a non-binding security and cooperation document was signed by 33 European nations, Canada and the U.S. **Aug. 1** at Helsinki. It froze postwar European borders; the nations agreed to broaden detente, renounce force and aid to terrorists, respect human freedoms, aid families to unite across borders, reduce forces and tension in the Mediterranean.

Communist Pathet Lao completed takeover of Laos **Aug. 23.**

Second-stage Sinai agreement was signed by Israel and Egypt **Sept. 4,** providing for new Israeli withdrawals from oil wells and strategic passes in the Sinai. Egypt to permit nonmilitary shipments to and from Israel through the Suez Canal, and a team of 200 U.S. civilians to operate an early-warning system at the passes.

Two assassination attempts against Pres. Ford, by women in California, failed. Lynette Alice (Squeaky) Fromme, a Charles Manson follower, pointed a pistol at him **Sept. 5** in Sacramento, but a Secret Service agent grabbed the gun. Sara Jane Moore, a political activist, fired a revolver at the president **Sept. 22** in San Francisco, but bystander Oliver Sipple deflected the gun.

William L. Calley's court-martial conviction for the murder of 22 Vietnamese, overturned in lower courts, was reinstated by the U.S. Court of Appeals in New Orleans, **Sept. 10.**

Mother Elizabeth Bayley Seton was canonized the Catholic Church's first U.S.-born saint, by Pope Paul VI **Sept. 14.**

FBI agents captured Patricia (Patty) Hearst, kidnaped Feb. 4, 1974, in San Francisco **Sept. 18** with others. She was indicted for bank robbery; a San Francisco Jury convicted her **Mar. 20, 1976.**

Oil prices were raised 10% by the Organization of Petroleum Exporting Countries **Oct. 1.**

Price controls on domestic oil were temporarily restored in a compromise between Pres. Ford and Congress **Sept. 25.** Controls extension had been vetoed by Ford earlier.

A 5-year grain agreement under which the U.S. would sell and the USSR would purchase 6 to 8 million tons of grain per year was announced **Oct. 20.**

Pres. Ford refused federal loan guarantees to N.Y. City to save it from threatened bankruptcy, **Oct. 29,**

claiming such guarantees would be "a bailout."

Generalissimo Francisco Franco, 82, dictator of Spain for 36 years, died **Nov. 20.** Prince Juan Carlos, 37, was proclaimed King Juan Carlos I, **Nov. 22.**

The Senate Committee on Intelligence reported **Nov. 20** that the CIA had instigated death plots against Cuba's Fidel Castro, Patrice Lumumba of the Congo (now Zaire), South Vietnam's Ngo Dinh Diem, the Dominican Republic's Rafael Trujillo, and Gen. Rene Schneider, Chile's chief of staff. All but Castro were killed but the committee said there was no evidence the deaths resulted from the CIA plots.

Short-term loans to New York City were asked of Congress by Pres. Gerald Ford **Nov. 26** to help the city meet cash flow needs. Ford had said **Oct. 29** he would veto any Congressional "bailout" of the city.

The Communist-led Pathet Lao abolished Laos' coalition government, ended its constitutional monarchy, and established a People's Republic, **Dec. 3.**

A liberal Spanish cabinet, which promised to broaden civil liberties, was appointed **Dec. 11.**

An end of covert military aid to factions in the Angolan civil war backed by the U.S. was voted **Dec. 19** by the U.S. Senate after revelations that the U.S. had sent $25 million in arms aid to the groups. The Soviet-backed faction claimed victory in the war **Feb. 12, 1976.**

Pro-Palestinian terrorists raided the Vienna conference of the mostly-Arab Organization of Petroleum Exporting Countries **Dec. 21,** killing 3 persons, wounding 6. The killers flew to Algiers.

1976

Reports that the CIA gave $6 million to anti-Communist Italian politicians brought denials from the alleged recipients but also was followed by resignation, **Jan. 7,** of the coalition government of Christian Democrat Aldo Moro.

China's Prime Minister Chou En-lai, 78, died Jan. 8. Hua Kuo-feng succeeded him **Apr. 7.** Communist Party Chairman Mao Tse-tung, 82, like Chou in power since 1949, died **Sept. 9.**

A House Intelligence Committee report, leaked to the press **Jan. 20,** revealed CIA violation of a bar against secret funds to universities, illegal buggings of phone calls by the National Security Agency, and unwarranted markups in equipment purchases by the FBI.

Daniel P. Moynihan resigned as U.S. ambassador to the UN **Feb. 2.** He quit after charging that the State Department undercut his policy of replying to anti-U.S. votes and statements in the UN; his policy also brought criticism from British UN Ambassador Ivor Richard who likened Moynihan to Wyatt Earp.

Payments abroad of $22 million in bribes by Lockheed Aircraft Corp. to sell its planes were revealed **Feb. 4** by a Senate subcommittee. Lockheed admitted payments in Japan, Turkey, Italy, and Holland.

Isabel Martinez de Peron was ousted as president of Argentina and put in "protective custody" in a coup by armed forces leaders **Mar. 24.** Gen. Jorge Rafael Videla was named junta president; Peronist politicians and union leaders were arrested.

The U.S. vetoed a UN Security Council resolution rapping Israeli policies in occupied territories, **Mar. 25.** Earlier, **Jan. 26,** the U.S. vetoed another Council resolution demanding establishment of a Palestinian state.

The U.S. and Turkey reached a new accord on aid and bases **Mar. 26.** Congress had banned military aid to Turkey after that nation invaded Cyprus; Turkey replied by closing 25 U.S. bases in Turkey; Congress partially lifted the ban in Oct. 1975.

A mechanical respirator that had been keeping Karen Anne Quinlan, 22, alive for 11 months could be turned off, the New Jersey Supreme Court ruled **Mar. 31;** her parents had asked the ruling so that Karen might die "with grace and dignity." The respirator was disconnected but Karen did not die.

Multi-millionaire Howard Hughes, 70, died Apr. 5 en route by plane to a hospital. An autopsy blame kidney failure.

The Senate Intelligence Committee charged in report **Apr. 26** that U.S. intelligence agencies ha investigated too many people for no good reason an used "illegal or questionable" methods includin burglary, mail opening, informers, and electroni surveillance.

Cadet cheating on exams at West Point was mor widespread than previously reported, the U.S. Mili tary Academy admitted **May 23,** involving possibly 7 to 90 cadets in addition to the 50 convicted **Apr. 22.**

British and French supersonic Concordes flew t Dulles Airport, Washington, D.C. from London an Paris **May 24,** taking less than 4 hours. On **Mar. 11,** th Port Authority of N.Y. and N.J. had banned SS flights in the N.Y. City area.

Israeli commandos rescued 103 hostages held i the Entebbe, Uganda, airport by pro-Palestinian ter rorists. Flying 2,500 miles from Tel Aviv, the Israeli liberated the 91 passengers and 12 crew members o a hijacked Air France plane **July 3,** killing all 7 ter rorists (who included 5 Arabs and 2 West Germans) and 20 of the Ugandan troops on guard (it wa charged the troops, under orders from Uganda Pres. Idi Amin, helped hold the kidnap victims mostly Israelis, prisoners). Also killed in the fightin were 3 Israeli hostages and the commando com mander. One Israeli woman, Dora Bloch, disap peared before the raid. An est. 11 Ugandan Russia MIGs were destroyed.

The U.S. celebrated its Bicentennial July 4, mark ing the 200th anniversary of its independence wit festivals, parades, and N.Y. City's Operation Sail, gathering of tall sail ships from around the worl viewed by 6 million persons.

Jimmy (James Earl) Carter, former governor o Georgia, was nominated for president of the U.S., an Minnesota Sen. Walter F. Mondale was nominated fo vice president at the 37th Democratic National Con vention **July 12-15,** in N.Y. City.

Mario Soares, Portugal's Socialist party leader, wa sworn in **July 23** as prime minister of the nation' first consitutional government since the 1974 over throw of its longtime rightist dictatorship.

Pres. Gerald R. Ford was nominated to succee himself and Kansas Sen. Robert J. Dole was nomi nated for vice president of the U.S. at the 31st Repub lican National Convention **Aug. 16-19** in Kansas City Kan.

Two U.S. officers were slain by axe-wielding Nort Korean soldiers **Aug. 18** while U.S. and South Korea soldiers were on a routine mission in the demilita rized zone near Panmunjom. The U.S. replied with show of force **Aug. 21** and North Korean Pres. Kim I Sung said the slayings were "regretful." A nev agreement was signed removing 4 North Korea posts near the scene.

A mystery ailment killed 29 persons who attende an American Legion convention, **July 21-24,** in Phila delphia. It was not until **Jan. 18, 1977,** that the na tional Center for Disease Control at Atlanta, Ga., wa able to announce the cause, a bacterium. On **Mar. 25 1977,** the center said erythromycin, an antibiotic, wa most effective in treating "legionnaire's disease."

Unemployment rose for 3 months in a row, th Labor Department reported **Sept. 3,** reaching 7.9% i August.

The Viking II lander set down on Mars' Utopi Plains **Sept. 3,** following the successful landing b Viking I **July 20.** Photographs and other reports sen to earth by the unmanned craft showed rocks, red dish soil, light blue skies, evidence of possible biologi cal activity, and that Mars' north polar cap was froze water.

Rhodesia accepted a proposal by U.S. Secretary o State Henry A. Kissinger for immediate biracial gov ernment in Rhodesia and black majority rule withi 2 years, Prime Minister Ian Smith announced th agreement **Sept. 24.**

A nationwide program of swine flu vaccination

was halted **Oct. 12** following the deaths of several persons after receiving the shots. The program had been launched **Mar. 24** by Pres. Gerald R. Ford after government scientists warned of a possible recurrence of the flu pandemic of 1918-19.

A peace plan to end Lebanon's long civil war between Christians and Moslems was agreed on by Arab leaders under prodding from Saudi Arabia **Oct. 18**; it ended most of the fighting. Earlier, **June 16**, unidentified gunmen killed U.S. Ambassador Francis E. Meloy Jr., aide Robert O. Waring, and their Lebanese chauffeur. The U.S. Navy evacuated about 140 Americans from Beirut **June 20**, and 308 persons, including 160 Americans **July 27**. Syrian peace-keeping troops **Sept. 29** dislodged Palestine Liberation Organization forces from mountain areas near Beirut after PLO leader Yasir Arafat refused to withdraw them.

For events of 1977 and late 1976, see Chronology.

100 Years Ago

"Ahoy-ahoy" was the cry of subscribers to the nation's first commercial telephone switchboard exchange which opened in New Haven, Conn., on Jan. 28, 1878. That nautical shout over a distance must have seemed more appropriate to the telephone's early users than today's quiet "hello." The first telephone directory was published the following month. It listed some 50 names.

The new Greenback Labor Party, the successor to the Greenback Party of 1874, convened in Toledo, Ohio, in January. The 800 delegates from 28 states passed a platform calling for repeal of specie payments, the free coinage of silver, shorter work days, and limitations on Chinese immigration. In the fall congressional elections, the new party sent 14 members to Congress and the Republicans lost control of both houses for first time since 1858.

Silver Issue Ignites the West

Silver was a volatile issue that year. Under pressure from Western silver mining interests, Congress overrode the veto of Pres. Rutherford B. Hayes and passed the Bland-Allison Act, which resumed coinage of silver as legal tender. The bill required the treasury to buy up to $4 million in silver each month to be converted into silver dollars. Farmers and labor had also lobbied for the bill with the hope that an increased circulation of money would raise farm prices and wages.

In July, President Hayes lashed out against the Republican political machine's control of the civil service. He suspended future president Chester A. Arthur as New York port collector of customs. Arthur had been one of the "Big Four" who ran New York State politics. Entrenched Senate Republicans had blocked previous attempts to separate the civil service from political influence, but Hayes acted after Congress had adjourned. His new appointments were approved later by the new Democratic majority in Congress.

That year, Congress also set up a 3-member commission to govern the District of Columbia. That form of government continues to rule the district to this day.

Russo-Turkish War Ends

In Europe, the Russo-Turkish War of 1877-78 ended on Mar. 3 with the signing of the Treaty of San Stefano. The Turks had capitulated at Shipka Pass on Jan. 9 and had appealed for an armistice. The treaty, imposed by Russia, virtually ended Turkish control over the Balkans. The European powers, outraged by the treaty, met at the Congress of Berlin June 13 to consider the Eastern question. The Congress, in the form of the Treaty of Berlin, imposed limits on the Russian gains under the San Stefano treaty. Russia's influence near Britain's Mediterranean route to India was decreased, Turkey was sustained an European power, and the influence of Austria-Hungary in the Balkans was increased. The crisis abated, but Russia was left humiliated and the aspirations of the Balkan peoples were ignored, leading the way to future crises in the area.

To Italy, deaths made headline news. King Victor Emanuel died on Jan. 9 and was succeeded by his son Humbert. On Feb. 7, Pope Pius IX died. He was succeeded by Leo XIII.

The U.S. broadened its commercial relations with the Pacific and Asia, signing commercial treaties with Japan on July 25 and with Samoan chieftains on Jan. 17. The Samoan treaty gave the U.S. rights to a naval base at Pago Pago on Tutuila island. On Oct. 4, the first Chinese embassy to Washington, D.C., was established.

New Inventions Abound

The year 1878 saw countless minor and major technological innovations. The German firearms designer Ferdinand Mannlicher invented the repeating rifle. David Hughes invented the microphone. The German engineer Karl Benz built a motorized tricycle. Its top speed was 7 miles per hour. Col. Albert Augustus Pope manufactured the first U.S. bicycles. U.S. patent no. 200,521 was issued Feb. 19 to Thomas A. Edison for his phonograph.

Great Britain established the Criminal Investigation Division (Scotland Yard) after a police corruption scandal. Its crime-fighting task was made easier by the appearance of electric street lighting in London. In the U.S., John Wanamaker installed the first electric lights in a store in his "Grand Depot" establishement in Philadelphia, Pa.

The first flight of a modern dirigible took place July 3. The airship, designed by Caesar Spiegler, was cigar-shaped and supported a wicker-cage partition with a door and window.

Eadweard J. Muybridge took the first "moving" pictures in 1878. His subject was a race horse in action. He took consecutive pictures with a series of electrically operated cameras placed in a row.

First Woman Telephone Operator Hired

In a first for women, Miss Emma M. Nutt broke the male monopoly of telephone operator jobs on Sept. 1. She went to work for the Telephone Despatch Co. in Boston, Mass.

In the world of arts, 1878 saw the publication of Thomas Hardy's *The Return of the Native* and the production of Gilbert and Sullivan's *H.M.S. Pinafore*. Paris welcomed travelers to its World Exhibition and Jean Louis Charles Garnier designed the casino at Monte Carlo. In the U.S., the Hungarian-born journalist Joseph Pulitzer purchased the St. Louis Dispatch and merged it with his St. Louis Post to create the present day Post-Dispatch. Pulitzer and his newspapers were eventually to become one of the most constructive forces in American journalism.

In the sporting world, Providence center fielder Paul Hines, on May 8, made the first unassisted triple play in organized baseball. His team beat Boston, 3 to 2, that day.

Births of coming lights in the world were plentiful in 1878. They included English poet John Masefield (died 1967), American poet Carl Sandburg (died 1967), American author and reformer Upton Sinclair (died 1968), and philosopher Martin Buber (died 1965). William Cullen Bryant died in June in New York City.

Some Notable Marine Disasters Since 1865

(Figures Indicate Estimated Lives Lost)

1865, Apr. 27—Sultana; a Mississippi River steamer blew up near Memphis, Tenn., 1,400.

1869, Oct. 27—Stonewall; steamer burned on Mississippi River below Cairo, Ill.; 200.

1870, Jan. 28—City of Boston; American steamer of Inman Line vanished between New York and Liverpool; 191.

1872, Nov. 7—Mary Celeste; American half-brig sailed from New York for Genoa; found abandoned in Atlantic 4 weeks later in mystery of sea; crew never heard from; loss of life unknown.

1873, Jan. 22—Northfleet; British steamer foundered off Dungeness, England; 300.

1873, Apr. 1—Atlantic; British (White Star) steamer wrecked off Nova Scotia; 547.

1873, Nov. 23—Ville de Havre; French steamer, New York to Havre, sank after collision with Loch Earn; 230.

1875, Nov. 7—Schiller; German mail steamer wrecked off Scilly Islands; 200.

1875, Nov. 4—Pacific; American steamer sank after collision off Cape Flattery; 236.

1878, Sept. 3—Princess Alice; British steamer sank after collision in Thames; 700.

1878, Dec. 18—Byzantin; French steamer sank after Dardanelles collision; 210.

1880, Nov. 24—Uncle Joseph; French steamer sank in collision off Spezzia, Greece; 250.

1881, May 24—Victoria; steamer capsized in Thames River, Canada; 200.

1883, Jan. 19—Cambria; German steamer hit iceberg in North Sea; 389.

1887, Nov. 15—Wah Yeung; British steamer burned at sea; 400.

1890, Feb. 17—Duburg; British steamer wrecked, China Sea; 400.

1890, Sept. 19—Ertogrul; Turkish frigate foundered off Japan; 540.

1891, Mar. 17—Utopia; British steamer sank in collision off Gibraltar; 574.

1895, Jan. 30—Elbe; German steamer sank in collision with British steamer Crathie in North Sea; 335.

1895, Mar. 11—Reina Regenta; Spanish cruiser foundered near Gibraltar; 400.

1898, Feb. 15—Maine; U.S. battleship blown up in Havana Harbor; 266.

1898, July 4—La Bourgogne, Cromartyshire; French steamer and British sailing ship collided off Nova Scotia; 560.

1904, June 15—General Slocum; excursion steamer burned in East River, New York City; 1,030.

1904, June 28—Norge; steamer wrecked on Rockall Reef off Scotland; 590.

1906, Aug. 4—Sirio; Italian steamer wrecked off Cape Palos, Spain; 350.

1908, Mar. 23—Matsu Maru; Japanese steamer sank in collision near Hakodate, Japan; 300.

1909, Aug. 1—Waratah; British steamer, Sydney to London, vanished; 300.

1910, Feb. 9—General Chanzy; French steamer wrecked off Minorca, Spain; 200.

1911, Sept. 25—Liberte; French battleship exploded at Toulon; 285.

1912, Mar. 5—Principe de Asturias; Spanish steamer wrecked off Spanish coast; 500.

1912, Apr. 14-15—Titanic; British (White Star) liner hit iceberg in North Atlantic; 1,517.

1912, Sept. 28—Kichemaru; Japanese steamer sank off Japanese coast; 1,000.

1914, May 29—Empress of Ireland; Canadian steamer sank after collision with collier in St. Lawrence River; 1,024.

1915, May 7—Lusitania; British (Cunard Line) steamer torpedoed by German submarine, sank off Ireland; 1,198.

1915, July 24—Eastland, excursion steamer capsized in Chicago River; 812.

1916, Feb. 26—Provence; French cruiser sank in Mediterranean; 3,100.

1916, Aug. 29—Hsin Yu; Chinese steamer sank off Chinese coast; 1,000.

1917, Dec. 6—Mont Blanc, Imo; French ammunition ship and Belgian steamer collided in Halifax Harbor; 1,600.

1918, Apr. 25—Kiang-Kwan Chinese steamer sank in collision off Hankow; 500.

1918, July 12—Kawachi; Japanese battleship blew up in Tokayama Bay; 500.

1918, Oct. 25—Princess Sophia; Canadian steamer sank off Alaskan coast; 398.

1919, Jan. 17—Chaonia; French steamer lost in Straits of Messina, Italy; 460.

1919, Sept. 9—Valbanera; Spanish steamer lost off Florida coast; 500.

1921, Mar. 18—Hong Kong; steamer wrecked in South China Sea; 1,000.

1922, Aug. 26—Niitaka; Japanese cruiser sank in storm off Kamchatka, USSR; 300.

1923, Apr. 23—Mossamedes; Portuguese mail steamer went aground at Cape Frio, Africa; 220.

1924, Jan. 10—L-24; British submarine in collision off Portland, England; 48.

1924, Mar. 19—No. 43; Japanese submarine in collision off Sasebo, Japan; 49.

1925, Sept. 25—S-51; American submarine in collision with steamer City of Rome off Block Island, R. I.; 34.

1925, Nov. 11—M-1; British submarine in English Channel collision; 69.

1927, Oct. 25—Principessa Mafalda; Italian steamer blew up, sank off Porto Seguro, Brazil; 314.

1927, Dec. 17—S-4; American submarine in collision off Provincetown, Mass.; 40.

1934, Sept. 8—Morro Castle; American steamer, Havana to New York, burned off Asbury Park, N. J.; 125.

1939, May 23—Squalus; American submarine sank off Portsmouth, N. H.; 26.

1939, June 1—Thetis; British submarine, sank in Liverpool Bay; 99.

1941, June 16—O-9; American submarine lost in test dive off Maine; 33.

1942, Feb. 18—Truxton and Pollux; American destroyer and cargo ship ran aground, sank off Newfoundland; 204.

1942, Oct. 2—Curacao; British cruiser sank after collision with liner Queen Mary; 335.

1947, Jan. 19—Himera; Greek steamer hit a mine off Athens; 392.

1947, Apr. 16—Grandcamp; French freighter exploded in Texas City, Tex., Harbor, starting fires; 510.

1950, Jan. 12—Truculent; British submarine in Thames collision; 65.

1951, Apr. 16—Affray; British submarine lost in English Channel; 75.

1952, Apr. 26—Hobson and Wasp; American destroyer and aircraft carrier collided in Atlantic; 176.

1952, Sept. 24—La Sibylle; French submarine lost off Toulon; 48.

1953, Jan. 31—Princess Victoria; British ferry foundered off northern Irish coast; 134.

1954, Sept. 26—Toya Maru; Japanese ferry sank in Tsugaru Strait, Japan; 1,172.

1956, July 26—Andrea Doria and Stockholm; Italian liner and Swedish liner collided off Nantucket; 51.

1957, July 14—Eshghabad; Soviet ship ran aground in Caspian Sea; 270.

1961, Apr. 8—Dara; British liner burned in Persian Gulf; 212.

1961, July 8—Save; Portuguese ship ran aground off Mozambique; 259.

1963, Apr. 10—Thresher; U.S. Navy atomic submarine sank in North Atlantic; 129.

1964, Feb. 10—Voyager, Melbourne; Australian destroyer sank after collision with Australian aircraft carrier Melbourne off New South Wales; 82.

1968, Jan. 25—Dakar; Israeli submarine vanished in Mediterranean; 69.

1968, Jan. 27—Minerve; French submarine vanished in Mediterranean; 52.

1968, May 21—Scorpion; U.S. nuclear submarine sank in Atlantic near Azores; 99.

1969, June 2—Evans; U.S. destroyer cut in half by Australian carrier Melbourne, S. China Sea; 74.

1970, Mar. 4—Eurydice; French submarine sank in Mediterranean near Toulon; 57.

1970, Dec. 15—Namyong-Ho; South Korean ferry sank in Korea Strait; 308.

1973, May 5— Three river boats collided near Dacca, Bangladesh; c. 250.

1973, Dec. 24— Ferry capsized off coast of Ecuador; nearly 200.

1974, May 1— Motor launch capsized off Bangladesh coast; 250.

1974, Sept. 26— Soviet destroyer burned and sank in Black Sea; est. 200.

1975, Aug. 9— Two Chinese riverboats collided and sank near Canton; c. 500.

Major Earthquakes

Sources: National Earthquake Information Service, U.S. Geological Survey, and historical records

Magnitude of earthquakes (Mag.), distinct from deaths or damage caused, is measured on the Richter scale, on which each higher number represents a tenfold increase in energy measured in ground motion. Adopted in 1935, the scale has been applied in the following table to earthquakes as far back as reliable seismograms are available.

Date		Place	Deaths	Mag.
526	May 20	Syria, Antioch	250,000	N.A.
856	....	Greece, Corinth	45,000	"
1057	....	China, Chihli	25,000	"
1268	....	Asia Minor, Cilicia	60,000	"
1290	Sept. 27	China, Chihli	100,000	"
1293	May 20	Japan, Kamakura	30,000	"
1531	Jan. 26	Portugal, Lisbon	30,000	"
1556	Jan. 24	China, Shensi	830,000	"
1667	Nov.	Caucasia, Shemaka	80,000	"
1693	Jan. 11	Italy, Catania	60,000	"
1730	Dec. 30	Japan, Hokkaido	137,000	"
1737	Oct. 11	India, Calcutta	300,000	"
1755	June 7	Northern Persia	40,000	"
1755	Nov. 1	Portugal, Lisbon	60,000	8.75*
1783	Feb. 4	Italy, Calabria	30,000	N.A.
1797	Feb. 4	Ecuador, Quito	41,000	N.A.
1811	Dec. 16	Missouri, New Madrid		7.2*
1822	Sept. 5	Asia Minor, Aleppo	22,000	N.A.
1828	Dec. 28	Japan, Echigo	30,000	"
1868	Aug. 13-15	Peru and Ecuador	40,000	"
1875	May 16	Venezuela, Colombia	16,000	"
1896	June 15	Japan, sea wave	27,120	"
1906	Apr. 18-19	Cal., San Francisco	452	8.3
1906	Aug. 16	Chile, Valparaiso	20,000	8.6
1908	Dec. 28	Italy, Messina	83,000	7.5
1915	Jan. 13	Italy, Avezzano	29,980	7.5
1920	Dec. 16	China, Kansu	100,000	8.6
1923	Sept. 1	Japan, Tokyo	99,330	8.3
1927	May 22	China, Nan-Shan	200,000	8.3
1932	Dec. 26	China, Kansu	70,000	7.6
1933	Mar. 2	Japan	2,990	8.9
1934	Jan. 15	India, Bihar-Nepal	10,700	8.4
1935	May 31	India, Quetta	30,000	7.5
1939	Jan. 24	Chile, Chillan	28,000	8.3
1939	Dec. 26	Turkey, Erzincan	30,000	7.9
1946	May 31	Eastern Turkey	1,300	6.0
1946	Dec. 21	Japan, Honshu	2,000	8.4
1948	June 28	Japan, Fukui	5,131	7.3
1949	Aug. 5	Ecuador, Pelileo	6,000	6.8
1950	Aug. 15	India, Assam	1,530	8.7
1953	Mar. 18	NW Turkey	1,200	7.2
1954	Sept. 9-12	Northern Algeria	1,250	6.8
1956	June 10-17	" Afghanistan	2,000	7.7
1957	July 2	Northern Iran	2,500	7.4
1957	Dec. 13	Western Iran	2,000	7.1
1960	Feb. 29	Morocco, Agadir	12,000	5.8
1960	May 21-30	Southern Chile	5,000	8.3
1962	Sept. 1	Northwestern Iran	12,230	7.1
1963	July 26	Yugoslavia, Skopje	1,100	6.0
1964	Mar. 27	Alaska	114	8.5
1966	Aug. 19	Eastern Turkey	2,520	6.9
1968	Aug. 31	Northeastern Iran	12,000	7.4
1970	Mar. 28	Western Turkey	1,086	7.4
1970	May 31	Northern Peru	66,794	7.7
1972	Apr. 10	Southern Iran	5,057	6.9
1972	Dec. 23	Nicaragua	5,000	6.2
1974	Dec. 28	Pakistan (9 towns)	5,200	6.3
1975	Sept. 6	Turkey (Lice, etc.)	2,312	6.8
1976	Feb. 4	Guatemala	22,778	7.5
1976	May 6	Northeast Italy	946	6.5
1976	June 26	New Guinea, Irian Jaya	443	7.1
1976	July 14	Indonesia, N. Bali	500	5.6
1976	July 28	China, Tangshan	655,235	8.2
1976	Aug. 17	Philippines, Mindanao	8,000	7.8
1976	Nov. 24	Eastern Turkey	4,000	7.9
1977	Mar. 4	Romania, Bucharest, etc.	1,541	7.5

(*) estimated from earthquake intensity.
(N.A.) not available.

Floods, Tidal Waves

Date		Location	Deaths
1887	...	Hwang-ho River, China	900,000
1889	May 31	Johnstown, Pa.	2,200
1900	Sept. 8	Galveston, Tex.	5,000
1903	June 15	Heppner, Ore.	325
1911	....	Yangtze River, China	100,000
1913	Mar. 25-27	Ohio, Indiana	732
1915	Aug. 17	Galveston, Tex.	275
1927	....	Mississippi River Valley	214
1928	Mar. 13	Collapse of St. Francis Dam, Santa Paula, Cal.	450
1928	Sept. 13	Lake Okeechobee, Fla.	2,000
1931	Aug.	Hwang-ho River, China	3,700,000
1937	Jan. 22	Ohio, Miss. Valleys	250
1939	....	Northern China	200,000
1947	....	Honshu Island, Japan	1,900
1951	Aug.	Manchuria	1,800
1953	Jan. 31	Western Europe	2,000
1954	Aug. 17	Farahzad, Iran	2,000
1955	Oct. 7-12	India, Pakistan	1,700
1959	Nov. 1	Western Mexico	2,000
1959	Dec. 2	Frejus, France	412
1960	Oct. 10	Bangladesh	6,000
1960	Oct. 31	Bangladesh	4,000
1962	Feb. 17	German North Sea coast	343
1962	Sept. 27	Barcelona, Spain	445
1963	Oct. 9	Dam collapse, Vaiont, Italy	1,800
1966	Nov. 4-6	Florence, Venice, Italy	113
1967	Jan. 18-24	Eastern Brazil	894
1967	Mar. 19	Rio de Janeiro, Brazil	436
1968	Aug. 7-14	Gujarat State, India	1,000
1968	Oct. 7	Northeastern India	780
1969	Mar. 17	Mundau Valley, Alagoas, Brazil	218
1969	Aug. 25	Western Virginia	189
1969	Sept. 15	South Korea	250
1969	Oct. 1-8	Tunisia	500
1970	May 20	Central Romania	160
1970	July 22	Himalayas, India	500
1971	Feb. 26	Rio de Janeiro, Brazil	130
1972	June 9	Rapid City, S.D.	236
1972	Aug. 7	Luzon Is., Philippines	454
1974	Mar. 29	Tubaro, Brazil	1,000
1974	Aug. 12	Monty-Long, Bangladesh	2,500
1975	Jan. 11	Southern Thailand	131
1976	June 5	Teton Dam Collapse, Ida.	11
1976	July 31	Big Thompson Canyon, Col.	130

Some Major Tornadoes Since 1925

Source: National Climatic Center, NOAA, U. S. Commerce Department

Date			Place	Deaths
1925	Mar.	18	Mo., Ill., Ind.	689
1926	Nov.	25	Belleville to Portland, Ark.	53
1927	Apr.	12	Rock Springs, Tex.	74
1927	May	9	Arkansas, Poplar Bluff, Mo.	92
1927	Sept.	29	St. Louis, Mo.	72
1929	Apr.	25	SE-Central Ga.	40
1930	May	6	Hill & Ellis Co., Tex.	41
1932	Mar.	21	Ala. (series of tornadoes)	268
1936	Apr.	5	Tupelo, Miss.	216
1936	Apr.	6	Gainesville, Ga.	203
1938	Sept.	29	Charleston, S.C.	32
1942	Mar.	16	Central to NE Miss.	75
1942	Apr.	27	Rogers & Mayes Co., Okla.	52
1944	June	23	Oh., Pa., W. Va., Md.	150
1945	Apr.	12	Okla.-Ark.	102
1947	Apr.	9	Tex., Okla. & Kan.	169
1948	Mar.	19	Bunker Hill & Gillespie, Ill.	33
1949	Jan.	3	La. & Ark.	58
1952	Mar.	21	Ark., Mo., Tenn. (series)	208
1953	May	11	Waco, Tex.	114
1953	June	8	Flint to Lakeport, Mich.	116
1953	June	9	Worcester and vicinity, Mass.	90

Date			Place	Deaths
1953	Dec.	5	Vicksburg, Miss.	38
1955	May	25	Udall, Kan.	80
1957	May	20	Williamsburg, Kan., to Ruskin Heights, Mo.	48
1958	June	4	Northwestern Wisconsin	30
1959	Feb.	10	St. Louis, Mo.	21
1960	May	5, 6	SE Oklahoma, Arkansas	30
1965	Apr.	11	Ind., Ill., Mich., Wis.	271
1966	Mar.	3	Jackson, Miss.	57
1966	Mar.	3	Mississippi, Alabama	61
1967	Apr.	21	Illinois	33
1968	May	15	Arkansas	34
1969	Jan.	23	Mississippi	32
1971	Feb.	21	Mississippi delta	110
1973	May	26-7	South, Midwest (series)	47
1974	Apr.	3-4	Ala., Ga., Tenn., Ky., Oh.	350
1977	Apr.	1	Southeast Bangladesh	600
1977	Apr.	4	Ala., Miss., Ga.	22

Number of U. S. Tornadoes Since 1934, Deaths

Year	No.	Deaths	Year	No.	Deaths	Year	No.	Deaths	Year	No.	Deaths
1934	147	47	1945	121	210	1956	503	83	1967	929	114
1935	180	70	1946	106	78	1957	856	191	1968	660	131
1936	151	552	1947	165	313	1958	563	66	1969	608	66
1937	147	29	1948	183	140	1959	604	58	1970	652	72
1938	213	183	1949	249	212	1960	616	47	1971	889	156
1939	152	87	1950	199	70	1961	698	51	1972	741	*27
1940	124	65	1951	264	34	1962	658	28	1973	†1109	87
1941	118	53	1952	240	230	1963	461	31	1974	945	361
1942	167	384	1953	422	515	1964	703	73	1975	920	60
1943	152	58	1954	550	36	1965	901	296	1976	835	44
1944	169	275	1955	595	126	1966	585	99			

*Record low; †Record high.

Hurricanes, Typhoons, Blizzards, Other Storms

Names of hurricanes and typhoons in italics—H.—hurricane T.—typhoon

Date	Location	Deaths
1888 Mar. 11-14	Blizzard, Eastern U.S.	400
1900 Sept. 8	H., Galveston, Tex.	6,000
1926 Sept. 16-22	H., Fla., Ala.	372
1926 Oct. 20	H., Cuba	600
1928 Sept. 12-17	H., W. Indies, Fla.	4,000
1930 Sept. 3	H., San Domingo	2,000
1938 Sept. 21	H., New England	600
1942 Oct. 15-16	H., Bengal, India	11,000
1944 Sept. 12-16	H., N.C. to New Eng.	389
1953 Sept. 25-27	T., Vietnam, Japan	1,300
1954 Aug. 30	H. *Carol*, Northeast U.S.	68
1954 Oct. 12-16	H. *Hazel*, Eastern U.S., Haiti	347
1955 Aug. 12-13	H. *Connie*, Carolinas, Va., Md.	43
1955 Aug. 18-19	H. *Diane*, Eastern U.S.	400
1955 Sept. 19	H. *Hilda*, Mexico	200
1955 Sept. 22-28	H. *Janet*, Caribbean	500
1956 Feb. 1-29	Blizzard, Western Europe	1,000
1957 June 27-30	H. *Audrey*, La., Tex.	430
1958 Feb. 15-16	Blizzard, NE U.S.	171
1959 Sept. 17-19	T. *Sarah*, Far East	2,000
1959 Sept. 26-27	T. *Vera*, Honshu, Japan	4,466
1960 Sept. 4-12	H. *Donna*, Caribbean, E. U. S.	148
1961 Oct. 31	H. *Hattie*, Br. Honduras	400
1962 Feb. 17	Flooding, German Coast	343
1962 Sept. 27	Flooding, Barcelona, Spain	445
1963 May 28-29	Windstorm, Bangladesh	22,000
1963 Oct. 4-8	H. *Flora*, Cuba, Haiti	6,000
1964 Oct. 4-7	H. *Hilda*, La., Miss., Ga.	38
1964 June 30	T. *Winnie*, N. Philippines	107
1964 Sept. 5	T. *Ruby*, Hong Kong and China	735
1964 Sept. 14	Flooding, central S. Korea	563
1964 Nov. 12	Flooding, S. Vietnam	7,000
1965 May 11-12	Windstorm, Bangladesh	17,000
1965 June 1-2	Windstorm, Bangladesh	30,000
1965 Sept. 7-10	H. *Betsy*, Fla., Miss., La.	74
1965 Dec. 15	Windstorm, Bangladesh	10,000
1966 June 4-10	H. *Alma*, Honduras, SE U. S.	51
1966 Sept. 24-30	H. *Inez*, Carib., Fla., Mex.	293
1967 July 9	T. *Billie*, Japan	347
1967 Sept. 5-23	H. *Beulah*, Carib., Mex., Tex.	54
1967 Dec. 12-20	Blizzard, Southwest, U.S.	51
1968 Nov. 18-28	T. *Nina*, Philippines	63
1969 Aug. 17-18	H. *Camille*, Miss., La.	258
1970 July 30-Aug 5	H. *Celia*, Cuba, Fla., Tex.	31
1970 Aug. 20-21	H. *Dorothy*, Martinique	42
1970 Sept. 15	T. *Georgia*, Philippines	300
1970 Oct. 14	T. *Sening*, Philippines	583
1970 Oct. 15	T. *Titang*, Philippines	526
1970 Nov. 13	Cyclone, Bangladesh (est.)	300,000
1971 Aug. 1	T. *Rose*, Hong Kong	130
1972 June 19-29	H. *Agnes*, Fla. to N. Y.	118
1972 Dec. 3	T. *Theresa*, Philippines	169
1973 June-Aug.	Monsoon rains in India	1,217
1974 June 11	Storm *Dinah*, Luzon Is., Philip.	71
1974 July 11	T. *Gilda*, Japan, S. Korea	108
1974 Sept. 19-20	H. *Fifi*, Honduras	2,000
1974 Dec. 25	Cyclone leveled Darwin, Aus.	50
1975 Sept. 13-27	H. *Eloise*, Caribbean—NE U.S.	71
1976 May 20	T. *Olga*, floods, Philippines	215

Record Oil Spills, 1967-1977

Source: Conservation Division, U.S. Geological Survey, U.S. Interior Department

Date			Name and Place	Cause of Spill	Gallons
1967	Mar.	18	Tanker Torrey Canyon; off England	Grounding	29,400,000
1967	Sept.	6	Tanker R.C. Stoner, Wake Is.	Grounding	6,006,000
1967	Oct.	15	Pipeline; West Delta, La.	Dragging anchor	6,720,000
1968	May	5	Tanker Andron; off W. Africa	Sinking	4,914,000
1968	June	13	Tanker World Glory; off S. Africa	Hull failure	13,524,000
1969	Jan.	3	Offshore oil rig, Santa Barbara, Cal.	Leakage	235,000
1969	Nov.	4	Storage tank; Sewaren, N.J.	Tank rupture	8,400,000
1969	Nov.	5	Tanker Keo; off Massachusetts	Hull failure	8,820,000
1971	Nov.	30	Tanker; off Japan	Ship broke in half	6,258,000
1976	May	12	Tanker Urquiola; LaCoruna, Spain	Grounding, explosion	21,941,000
1976	June	23	Barge; St. Lawrence Seaway, N.Y.	Grounding	300,000
1976	Oct.	14	Tanker Boehlen; Brest, France	Sunk in storm	3,134,460
1976	Dec.	15	Tanker Argo Merchant; Nantucket Is., Mass.	Grounding	7,700,000
1976	Dec.	17	Tanker Sansinena; Los Angeles	Explosion	5,000
1976	Dec.	30	Tanker Olympic Games; Delaware River	Grounding	133,500
1977	Jan.	17	Tanker Irenes Challenger; near Midway Is.	Broke in half	3,150,000
1977	Feb.	4	Barge; Hudson River, Bear Mtn., N.Y.	Hit rock	420,000
1977	Feb.	10	Freighter; San Francisco Bay	Valve removed	15,540
1977	Feb.	24	Tanker Hawaiian Patriot; W. of Hawaii	Explosion	30,000,000
1977	Mar.	3	Tanker Borag; off Taiwan	Hit reef	3,134,460
1977	Mar.	20	Tanker Claude Conway; off N. Carolina	Explosion	536,000
1977	Apr.	22	Ekofisk oil field; North Sea	Oil well blowout	8,200,000

Explosions

Date	Location	Deaths
1910 Oct. 1	Los Angeles Times Bldg.	21
1913 Mar. 7	Dynamite, Baltimore harbor	55
1915 Sept. 27	Gasoline tank car, Ardmore, Okla.	47
1917 Apr. 10	Munitions plant, Eddystone, Pa.	133
1917 Dec. 6	Halifax Harbor, Canada	1,654
1918 July 2	Explosives, Split Rock, N. Y.	50
1918 Oct. 4	Shell plant, Morgan Station, N.J.	64
1919 May 22	Food plant, Cedar Rapids, Ia.	44
1920 Sept. 16	Wall Street, New York, bomb	30
1924 Jan. 3	Food plant, Pekin, Ill.	42
1937 Mar. 18	New London, Tex., school	294
1940 Sept. 11	Hercules Powder, Kenvil, N. J.	51
1942 June 5	Ordnance plant, Elwood, Ill.	49
1944 Apr. 14	Bombay, India, harbor	700
1944 July 17	Port Chicago, Cal., pier	322
1944 Oct. 21	Liquid gas tank, Cleveland	135
1947 Apr. 16	Texas City, Tex., pier	561
1948 July 28	Farben works, Ludwigshafen, Ger.	184
1950 May 19	Munitions barges, S. Amboy, N. J.	30
1956 Aug. 7	Dynamite trucks, Cal., Colombia	1,100
1958 Apr. 18	Sunken munitions ship, Okinawa	40
1958 May 22	Nike missiles, Leonardo, N. J.	10
1959 Apr. 10	World War II bomb, Philippines	38
1959 June 2	Gas truck, Pa. Turnpike	10
1959 June 28	Rail tank cars, Meldrin, Ga.	25
1959 Aug. 7	Dynamite truck, Roseburg, Ore.	13
1959 Nov. 2	Jamuri Bazar, India, explosives	46
1959 Dec. 13	Dortmund, Ger., 2 apt. bldgs.	26
1960 Mar. 4	Belgian munitions ship, Havana	100
1960 Oct. 25	Gas, Windsor, Ont., store	11
1962 Jan. 16	Gas pipeline, Alberta, Canada	19
1962 Mar. 3	Gasoline truck, Syria	31
1962 Oct. 3	Telephone Co. office, N. Y. City	23
1963 Jan. 2	Packing plant, Terre Haute, Ind.	16
1963 Mar. 9	Dynamite plant, S. Africa	45
1963 Mar. 9	Steel plant, Belecke, W. Germany	19
1963 Aug. 13	Explosives dump, Gauhiti, India	32
1963 Oct. 31	State Fair Coliseum, Indianapolis	73
1964 July 23	Bone, Algeria, harbor munitions	100
1965 Mar. 4	Gas pipeline, Natchitoches, La.	17
1965 Aug. 9	Missile silo, Searcy, Ark.	53
1965 Oct. 21	Bridge, Tila Bund, Pakistan	80
1965 Oct. 30	Cartagena, Colombia	48
1965 Nov. 24	Armory, Keokuk, Ia.	20
1966 Oct. 13	Chemical plant, La Salle, Que.	11
1967 Feb. 17	Chemical plant, Hawthorne, N.J.	11
1967 Dec. 25	Apartment bldg., Moscow	20
1968 Apr. 6	Sports store, Richmond, Ind.	43
1970 Apr. 8	Subway construction, Osaka, Japan	73
1971 June 24	Tunnel, Sylmar, Cal.	17
1971 June 28	School, fireworks, Pueblo, Mex.	13
1971 Oct. 21	Shopping center, Glasgow, Scot.	20
1973 Feb. 10	Liquified gas tank, Staten Is., N.Y.	40
1975 Dec. 27	Chasnala, India, mine	431
1976 Apr. 13	Lapua, Finland, munitions works	45

Fires

Date	Location	Deaths
1845 May	Theater, Canton, China	1,670
1871 Oct. 8	Chicago, $196 million loss	250
1871 Oct. 9	Peshtigo, Wis., forest fire	1,182
1876 Dec. 5	Brooklyn (N.Y.), theater	295
1877 June 20	St. John, N. B., Canada	100
1881 Dec. 8	Ring Theater, Vienna	850
1887 May 25	Opera Comique, Paris	200
1887 Sept. 4	Exeter, England, theater	200
1894 Sept. 1	Hinckley, Minn., forest fire	413
1897 May 4	Charity bazaar, Paris	150
1900 June 30	Hoboken, N. J., docks	326
1902 Sept. 20	Church, Birmingham, Ala.	115
1903 Dec. 30	Iroquois Theater, Chicago	602
1908 Jan. 13	Rhoads Thea., Boyertown, Pa.	170
1908 Mar. 4	School, Collinwood, Oh.	176
1911 Mar. 25	Triangle factory, N. Y. City	145
1913 Oct. 14	Colliery, Mid Glamorgan, Wales	439
1918 Apr. 13	Norman, Okla., state hospital	38
1918 Oct. 12	Cloquet, Minn., forest fire	400
1919 June 20	Mayaguez Theater, San Juan	150
1923 May 17	School, Camden, S. C.	76
1924 Dec. 24	School, Hobart, Okla.	35
1929 May 15	Clinic, Cleveland, Oh.	125
1930 Apr. 21	Penitentiary, Columbus, Oh.	320
1931 July 24	Pittsburgh, Pa., home for aged	48
1938 May 16	Atlanta, Ga., Terminal Hotel	35
1940 Apr. 23	Dance hall, Natchez, Miss.	198
1942 Nov. 28	Cocoanut Grove, Boston	491
1943 Sept. 7	Gulf Hotel, Houston	55
1944 July 6	Ringling Circus, Hartford	168
1946 June 5	LaSalle Hotel, Chicago	61
1946 Dec. 7	Winecoff Hotel, Atlanta	119
1946 Dec. 12	New York, ice plant, tenement	37
1949 Apr. 5	Hospital, Effingham, Ill.	77
1950 Jan. 7	Davenport, Ia., Mercy Hospital	41
1953 Mar. 29	Largo, Fla., nursing home	35
1953 Apr. 16	Chicago, metalworking plant	35
1957 Feb. 17	Home for aged, Warrenton, Mo.	72
1958 Mar. 19	New York City loft building	24
1958 Dec. 1	Parochial school, Chicago	95
1958 Dec. 16	Store, Bogota, Colombia	83
1959 June 23	Resort hotel, Stalheim, Norway	34
1960 Mar. 12	Pusan, Korea, chemical plant	68
1960 July 14	Mental hospital, Guatemala City	225
1960 Nov. 13	Movie theater, Amude, Syria	152
1961 Jan. 6	Thomas Hotel, San Francisco	20
1961 May 15	Tenement, Hong Kong	25
1961 Dec. 8	Hospital, Hartford, Conn.	16
1961 Dec. 17	Circus, Niteroi, Brazil	323
1963 May 4	Theater, Diourbel, Senegal	64
1963 Nov. 18	Surfside Hotel, Atlantic City, N.J.	25
1963 Nov. 23	Rest home, Fitchville, Oh.	63
1963 Dec. 29	Roosevelt Hotel, Jacksonville, Fla.	22
1964 May 8	Apartment building, Manila	30
1964 Dec. 18	Nursing home, Fountaintown, Ind.	20
1965 Mar. 1	Apartment, LaSalle, Canada	28
1965 Dec. 20	Jewish center, Yonkers, N. Y.	12
1966 Mar. 11	Numata, Japan, 2 ski resorts	31
1966 Aug. 13	Melbourne, Australia, hotel	29
1966 Sept. 12	Anchorage, Alaska, hotel	14
1966 Oct. 17	N. Y. City bldg. (firemen)	12
1966 Dec. 7	Erzurum, Turkey, barracks	68
1967 Feb. 7	Restaurant, Montgomery, Ala.	25
1967 May 22	Store, Brussels, Belgium	322
1967 July 16	State prison, Jay, Fla.	37
1968 Jan. 9	Brooklyn, N. Y., tenement	13
1968 Feb. 26	Shrewsbury, England, hospital	22
1968 May 11	Vijayawada, India, wedding hall	58
1968 Nov. 18	Glasgow, Scotland, factory	24
1969 Jan. 26	Victoria Hotel, Dunnville, Ont.	13
1969 Dec. 2	Nursing home, Notre Dame, Can.	54
1970 Jan. 9	Nursing home, Marietta, Oh.	27
1970 Mar. 20	Hotel, Seattle, Wash.	19
1970 Nov. 1	Dance hall, Grenoble, France	145
1970 Nov. 5	Nursing home, Pointe-aux-Trembles, Que.	17
1970 Dec. 20	Hotel, Tucson, Arizona	28
1971 Mar. 6	Psychiatric clinic, Burghoezli, Switzerland	28
1971 Apr. 20	Hotel, Bangkok, Thailand	24
1971 Oct. 19	Nursing home, Honesdale, Pa.	15
1971 Dec. 25	Hotel, Seoul, So. Korea	162
1972 May 13	Osaka, Japan, nightclub	116
1972 July 5	Sherborne, England, hospital	30
1973 Feb. 6	Paris, France, school	21
1973 Nov. 6	Fukui, Japan, train	28
1973 Nov. 29	Kumamoto, Japan, department store	107
1973 Dec. 2	Seoul, Korea, theater	50
1974 Feb. 1	Sao Paulo, Brazil, bank building	189
1974 June 30	Port Chester, N.Y., discotheque	24
1974 Nov. 3	Seoul, So. Korea, hotel discotheque	88
1975 Dec. 12	Mina, Saudi Arabia, Tent City	138
1976 Oct. 24	Bronx, N.Y., social club	25
1977 Feb. 25	Rossiya Hotel, Moscow	45
1977 May 28	Southgate, Ky., nightclub	164
1977 June 26	Columbia, Tenn., jail	42

Major U.S. Railroad Wrecks

Source: Office of Safety, Federal Railroad Administration

Date		Location	Deaths
1876	Dec. 29	Ashtabula, Oh.	92
1880	Aug. 11	Mays Landing, N. J.	40
1887	Aug. 10	Chatsworth, Ill.	81
1888	Oct. 10	Mud Run, Pa.	55
1896	July 30	Atlantic City, N. J.	60
1903	Dec. 23	Laurel Run, Pa.	53
1904	Aug. 7	Eden, Col.	96
1904	Sept. 24	New Market, Tenn.	56
1906	Mar. 16	Florence, Col.	35
1906	Oct. 28	Atlantic City, N.J.	40
1906	Dec. 30	Washington, D. C.	53
1907	Jan. 2	Volland, Kan.	33
1907	Jan. 19	Fowler, Ind.	29
1907	Feb. 16	New York City	22
1907	Feb. 23	Colton, Cal.	26
1907	July 20	Salem, Mich.	33
1907	Sept. 15	Canaan, N. H.	24
1910	Mar. 1	Wellington, Wash.	96
1910	Mar. 21	Green Mountain, Ia.	55
1911	Aug. 25	Manchester, N. Y.	29
1912	July 4	East Corning, N. Y.	39
1912	July 5	Ligonier, Pa.	23
1913	Sept. 2	North Haven, Conn.	21
1914	Aug. 5	Tipton Ford, Mo.	43
1914	Sept. 15	Lebanon, Mo.	28
1916	Mar. 29	Amherst, Oh.	27
1917	Feb. 27	Mount Union, Pa.	20
1917	Sept. 28	Kellyville, Okla.	23
1917	Dec. 20	Shepherdsville, Ky.	46
1918	June 22	Ivanhoe, Ind.	68
1918	July 9	Nashville, Tenn.	101
1918	Nov. 2	Brooklyn, N.Y., Malbone St. Tunnel	97
1919	Jan. 12	South Byron, N. Y.	22
1919	July 1	Dunkirk, N. Y.	12
1919	Dec. 20	Onawa, Maine	23
1921	Feb. 27	Porter, Ind.	37
1921	Dec. 5	Woodmont, Pa.	27
1922	Aug. 5	Sulphur Spring, Mo.	34
1922	Dec. 13	Humble, Tex.	22
1923	Sept. 27	Lockett, Wy.	31
1925	June 16	Hackettstown, N. J.	50
1925	Oct. 27	Victoria, Miss.	21
1926	Sept. 5	Waco, Col.	30
1928	Aug. 24	I.R.T. subway, Times Sq., N.Y.	18
1938	June 19	Saugus, Mont.	47
1939	Aug. 12	Harney, Nev.	24
1940	Apr. 19	Little Falls, N. Y.	31
1940	July 31	Cuyahoga Falls, Oh.	43
1943	Aug. 29	Wayland, N. Y.	27
1943	Sept. 6	Frankford Junction, Philadelphia, Pa.	79
1943	Dec. 16	Between Rennert and Buie, N.C.	72
1944	July 6	High Bluff, Tenn.	35
1944	Aug. 4	Near Stockton, Ga.	47
1944	Sept. 14	Dewey, Ind.	29
1944	Dec. 31	Bagley, Utah	50
1945	Aug. 9	Michigan, N. D.	34
1946	Apr. 25	Naperville, Ill.	45
1947	Feb. 18	Gallitzin, Pa.	24
1950	Feb. 17	Rockville Centre, N. Y.	31
1950	Sept. 11	Coshocton, Oh.	33
1950	Nov. 22	Richmond Hill, N. Y.	79
1951	Feb. 6	Woodbridge, N. J.	84
1951	Nov. 12	Wyuta, Wyo.	17
1951	Nov. 25	Woodstock, Ala.	17
1953	Mar. 27	Conneaut, Oh.	21
1956	Jan. 22	Los Angeles, Cal.	30
1956	Feb. 28	Swampscott, Mass.	13
1956	Sept. 5	Springer, N. M.	20
1957	June 11	Vroman, Col.	12
1958	Sept. 15	Elizabethport, N. J.	48
1960	Mar. 14	Bakersfield, Cal.	14
1962	July 28	Steelton, Pa.	19
1966	Dec. 28	Everett, Mass.	13
1971	June 10	Salem, Ill.	11
1972	Oct. 30	Chicago, Ill.	45
1977	Jan. 4	Chicago, Ill., elevated train	11

World's worst train wreck occurred Dec. 12, 1917, Modane, France, passenger train derailed, 543 killed.

Some Notable Aircraft Disasters Since 1937

Date		Aircraft	Site of accident	Death
1937	May 6	German zeppelin Hindenburg	Burned at mooring, Lakehurst, N. J.	36
1944	Aug. 23	U.S. Air Force B-24	Hit school, Freckelton, England	76[1]
1945	July 28	U.S. Army B-25	Hit Empire State bldg., N.Y.C.	14[1]
1949	Nov. 1	Eastern Air Lines DC-4	Rammed by Bolivian P-38, Wash., D.C.	55
1952	Dec. 20	U. S. Air Force C-124	Fell, burned, Moses Lake, Wash.	87
1953	Mar. 3	Canadian Pacific Comet Jet	Karachi, Pakistan	11[2]
1953	June 18	U. S. Air Force C-124	Crashed, burned near Tokyo	129
1955	Nov. 1	United Air Lines DC-6B	Exploded, crashed near Longmont, Col.	44[3]
1956	June 20	Venezuelan Super-Constellation	Crashed in Atlantic off Asbury Park, N. J.	74
1956	June 30	TWA Super-Const., United DC-7	Collided over Grand Canyon, Arizona	128
1960	Dec. 16	United DC-8 jet, TWA Super-Const.	Collided over N.Y. City	134[4]
1962	Mar. 4	Br. Caledonian Airlines DC-7C	Crashed near Douala, Cameroon	111
1962	Mar. 16	Flying Tiger Super-Const.	Vanished in Western Pacific	107
1962	June 3	Air France Boeing 707 jet	Crashed on takeoff from Paris	130
1962	June 22	Air France Boeing 707 jet	Crashed in storm, Guadeloupe, W. I.	113
1963	June 3	Chartered Northw. Airlines DC-7	Crashed in Pacific off British Columbia	101
1963	Nov. 29	Trans-Canada Airlines DC-8F	Crashed after takeoff from Montreal	118
1965	May 20	Pakistani Boeing 720-B	Crashed at Cairo, Egypt, airport	121
1966	Jan. 24	Air India Boeing 707 jetliner	Crashed on Mont Blanc, France-Italy	117
1966	Feb. 4	All-Nippon Boeing 727	Plunged into Tokyo Bay	133
1966	Mar. 5	BOAC Boeing 707 jetliner	Crashed on Mount Fuji, Japan	124
1966	Dec. 24	U. S. military-chartered CL-44	Crashed into village in So. Vietnam	129[1]
1967	Mar. 9	TWA DC-9, Beechcraft	Collided in air at Urbana, Oh.	26
1967	Apr. 20	Swiss Britannia turboprop	Crashed at Nicosia, Cyprus	126
1967	July 19	Piedmont Boeing 727, Cessna 310	Collided in air, Hendersonville, N. C.	82
1968	Apr. 20	S. African Airways Boeing 707	Crashed on takeoff, Windhoek, SW Africa	122
1968	May 3	Braniff International Electra	Crashed in storm near Dawson, Tex.	85
1969	Mar. 16	Venezuelan DC-9	Crashed after takeoff from Maracaibo, Venezuela	155[5]
1969	Mar. 20	United Arab Ilyushin-18	Crashed at Aswan airport, Egypt	87
1969	June 4	Mexican Boeing 727	Rammed into mountain near Monterrey, Mexico	79
1969	Nov. 20	Nigerian VC-10	Crashed near Iju, Nigeria	87
1969	Dec. 8	Olympia Airways DC-6B	Crashed near Athens in storm	93
1970	Feb. 15	Dominican DC-9	Crashed into sea on takeoff from Santo Domingo	102
1970	July 3	British chartered jetliner	Crashed near Barcelona, Spain	112
1970	July 5	Air Canada DC-8	Crashed near Toronto International Airport	108
1970	Aug. 9	Peruvian turbojet	Crashed after takeoff from Cuzco, Peru	101[1]
1970	Oct. 2	Chartered Martin 404	Crashed in Rocky Mts. near Silver Plume, Col.	30[6]
1970	Nov. 14	Southern Airways DC-9	Crashed in mountains near Huntington, W. Va.	75[7]
1970	Dec. 31	Soviet Aeroflot Ilyushin-18	Crashed on takeoff, Leningrad	90

1971	July 30	All-Nippon Boeing 727 and Japanese Air Force F-86	Collided over Morioka, Japan	162[8]
1971	Aug. 11	Soviet Aeroflot Tupolev-104	Crashed at Irkutsk airport, USSR	97
1971	Sept. 4	Alaska Airlines Boeing 727	Crashed into mountain near Juneau, Alaska	111
1972	Mar. 14	Danish Airliner	Crashed near Dubai, United Arab Emirates	112
1972	Aug. 14	E. German Ilyushin-62	Crashed on take-off East Berlin	156
1972	Oct. 13	Aeroflot Ilyushin-62	E. German airline crashed near Moscow	176
1972	Dec. 4	Chartered Spanish airliner	Crashed on take-off, Canary Islands	155
1972	Dec. 29	Eastern Airlines Lockheed Tristar	Crashed on approach to Miami Int'l. Airport	100
1973	Jan. 22	Chartered Boeing 707	Burst into flames during landing, Kano Airport, Nigeria	176
1973	Apr. 10	British Vanguard turboprop	Crashed during snowstorm at Basel, Switzerland	104
1973	June 3	Soviet Supersonic TU-144	Exploded in air near Goussainville, France	14[9]
1973	July 11	Brazilian Boeing 707	Crashed on approach to Orly airport, Paris	122
1973	July 31	Delta Airlines jetliner	Crashed, landing in fog at Logan Airport, Boston	89
1973	Aug. 13	Spanish Caravelle jet	Exploded and crashed near La Coruna, Spain	85
1973	Dec. 23	French Caravelle jet	Crashed in Morocco	106
1974	Jan. 31	Pan American Boeing 707 jet	Crashed in Pago Pago, American Samoa	96
1974	Mar. 3	Turkish DC-10 jet	Crashed at Ermenonville near Paris	346
1974	Apr. 23	Pan American 707 jet	Crashed in Bali, Indonesia	107
1974	Sept. 8	TWA 707 jet	Crashed in Ionian Sea off Greece, after bomb explosion; Arab guerrilla group claimed responsibility	80
1974	Dec. 1	TWA-727	Crashed in storm, Upperville, Va.	92
1974	Dec. 4	Dutch-chartered DC-8	Crashed in storm near Colombo, Sri Lanka	191
1975	Apr. 4	Air Force Galaxy C-58	Crashed near Saigon, So. Vietnam, after takeoff with load of orphans	172
1975	June 24	Eastern Airlines 727 jet	Crashed in storm, JFK Airport, N.Y. City	113
1975	Aug. 3	Chartered 707	Hit mountainside, Agadir, Morocco	188
1976	Sept. 10	British Airways Trident, Yugoslav DC-9	Collided near Zagreb, Yugoslavia	176
1976	Sept. 19	Turkish 727	Hit mountain, southern Turkey	155
1976	Oct. 6	Cuban DC-8	Crashed near Barbados after bomb explosion	73
1976	Oct. 12	Indian Caravelle jet	Crashed after takeoff, Bombay airport	95
1976	Oct. 13	Bolivian 707 cargo jet	Crashed in Santa Cruz, Bolivia	100[10]
1977	Mar. 27	KLM 747, Pan American 747	Collided on runway, Tenerife, Canary Islands	581

(1) Including those on the ground and in buildings. (2) First fatal crash of commercial jet plane. (3) Caused by bomb planted by John G. Graham in insurance plot to kill his mother, a passenger. (4) Including all 128 aboard the planes and 6 on ground. (5) Killed 84 on plane and 71 on ground. (6) Including 13 members of Wichita State U. football team. (7) Including 43 Marshall U. football players and coaches. (8) Airliner-fighter crash, pilot of fighter parachuted to safety, was arrested for negligence. (9) First supersonic plane crash killed 6 crewmen and 8 on the ground; there were no passengers. (10) Crew of 3 killed; 97, mostly children, killed on ground.

Principal U.S. Mine Disasters

Source: Bureau of Mines, U.S. Interior Department

Note: Prior to 1968, only disasters with losses of 50 or more lives are listed; for 1968-72, all disasters in which 5 or more men are killed are listed. Only fatalities to mining company employees are included. All Bituminous-coal mines unless otherwise noted.

Date	Location	Deaths
1855 Mar.	Coalfield, Va.	55
1867 Apr. 3	Winterpock, Va.	69
1869[1] Sept. 6	Plymouth, Pa.	110
1883 Feb. 16	Braidwood, Ill.	69
1884 Jan. 24	Crested Butte, Col.	59
1884 Mar. 13	Pocahontas, Va.	112
1891 Jan. 27	Mount Pleasant, Pa.	109
1892 Jan. 7	Krebs, Okla.	100
1895 Mar. 20	Red Canyon, Wy.	60
1896[1] June 28	Pittston, Pa.	58
1900 Jan. 1	Scofield, Ut.	200
1902 May 19	Coal Creek, Tenn.	184
1902 July 10	Johnstown, Pa.	112
1903 June 30	Hanna, Wy.	169
1904 Jan. 25	Cheswick, Pa.	179
1905 Feb. 20	Virginia City, Ala.	112
1907 Jan. 29	Stuart W. Va.	84
1907 Dec. 6	Monongah, W. Va.	361
1907 Dec. 16	Yolande, Ala.	57
1907 Dec. 19	Jacobs Creek, Pa.	239
1908 Mar. 28	Hanna, Wy.	59
1908 Nov. 28	Marianna, Pa.	154
1908 Dec. 29	Switchback, W. Va.	50
1909 Jan. 12	Switchback, W. Va.	67
1909 Nov. 13	Cherry, Ill.	259
1910 Jan. 31	Primero, Col.	75
1910 May 5	Palos, Ala.	90
1910 Oct. 8	Starkville, Col.	56
1910 Nov. 8	Delagua, Col.	79
1911 Apr. 7	Throop, Pa.	72
1911 Apr. 8	Littleton, Ala.	128
1911 Dec. 9	Briceville, Tenn.	84
1912 Mar. 20	McCurtain, Okla.	73
1912 Mar. 26	Jed, W. Va.	83
1913 Apr. 23	Finleyville, Pa.	96
1913 Oct. 22	Dawson, N.M.	263
1914 Apr. 28	Eccles, W. Va.	181
1914 Oct. 27	Royalton, Ill.	52
1915 Mar. 2	Layland, W. Va.	112
1917 Apr. 27	Hastings, Col.	121
1917[2] June 8	Butte, Mon.	163
1917 Aug. 4	Clay, Ky.	62
1919[1] June 5	Wilkes-Barre, Pa.	92
1922 Nov. 6	Spangler, Pa.	77
1922 Nov. 22	Dolomite, Ala.	90
1923 Feb. 8	Dawson, N.M.	120
1923 Aug. 14	Kemmerer, Wy.	99
1924 Mar. 8	Castle Gate, Ut.	171
1924 Apr. 28	Benwood, W. Va.	119
1925 Feb. 20	Sullivan, Ind.	52
1925 May 27	Coal Glen, N.C.	53
1925 Dec. 10	Acmar, Ala.	53
1926 Jan. 13	Wilburton, Okla.	91
1926[2] Nov. 3	Ishpeming, Mich.	51
1927 Apr. 30	Everettville, W. Va.	97
1928 May 19	Mather, Pa.	195
1929 Dec. 17	McAlester, Okla.	61
1930 Nov. 5	Millfield, Oh.	79
1932 Dec. 23	Moweagua, Ill.	54
1940 Jan. 10	Bartley, W. Va.	91
1940 Mar. 16	St. Clairsville, Oh.	72
1940 July 15	Portage, Pa.	63
1942 May 12	Osage, W. Va.	56
1943 Feb. 27	Washoe, Mon.	74
1944 July 5	Belmont, Oh.	66
1947 Mar. 25	Centralia, Ill	111
1951 Dec. 21	West Frankfort, Ill.	119
1968[3] Mar. 6	Calumet, La.	21
1968 Aug. 7	Greenville, Ky.	9
1968 Nov. 20	Farmington, W. Va.	78
1970 Dec. 30	Hyden, Ky.	38
1971[3] Apr. 12	Rosiclare, Ill.	7
1972[2] May 2	Kellogg, Ida	91
1972 July 22	Blacksville, W. Va.	9
1972 Dec. 16	Itmann, W. Va.	5
1976 Mar. 9, 11	Oven Fork, Ky.	26
1977 Mar. 9	Tower City, Pa.	9

(1) Anthracite mine. (2) Metal mine. (3) Nonmetal mine.

World's worst mine disaster killed 1,549 workers in Honkeiko Colliery in Manchuria Apr. 25, 1942.

Historic Assassinations Since 1865

1865—Apr. 14. U. S. Pres. Abraham Lincoln, shot in Washington, D. C.; died Apr. 15.

1881—Mar. 13. Alexander II, of Russia—July 2. U.S. Pres. James A. Garfield, Washington; died Sept. 19.

1900—July 29. Umberto I, king of Italy.

1901—Sept. 6, U.S. Pres. William McKinley in Buffalo, N.Y., died Sept. 14. Leon Czolgosz executed for the crime Oct. 29.

1913—Feb. 23. Mexican Pres. Francisco, I, Madero and Vice Pres. Jose Pino Suarez.—Mar. 18. George, king of Greece.

1914—June 28. Archduke Francis Ferdinand of Austria-Hungary and his wife in Sarajevo, Bosnia (later part of Yugoslavia), by Gavrillo Princip.

1916—Dec. 30. Grigori Rasputin, politically powerful Russian monk.

1918—July 12. Grand Duke Michael of Russia, at Perm.—July 16. Nicholas II, abdicated as czar of Russia; his wife, the Czarina Alexandra, their son, Czarevitch Alexis, and their daughters, Grand Duchesses Olga, Tatiana, Marie, Anastasia, and 4 members of their household were executed by Bolsheviks at Ekaterinburg.

1920—May 20. Mexican Pres. Gen. Venustiano Carranza in Tlaxcalantongo.

1922—Aug. 22. Michael Collins, Irish revolutionary.

1923—July 20. Gen. Francisco "Pancho" Villa, ex-rebel leader, in Parral, Mexico.

1928—July 17. Gen. Alvaro Obregon, president-elect of Mexico, in San Angel, Mexico.

1933—Feb. 15. In Miami, Fla., Joseph Zangara, anarchist, shot at Pres.-elect Franklin D. Roosevelt, but a woman seized his arm, and the bullet fatally wounded Mayor Anton J. Cermak, of Chicago, who died Mar. 6. Zangara was electrocuted on Mar. 20, 1933.

1934—July 25. In Vienna, Austrian Chancellor Engelbert Dollfuss by Nazi, in the chancellery. Otto Planetta convicted and hanged.

1935—Sept. 8. U. S. Sen. Huey P. Long, shot in Baton Rouge, La., by Dr. Carl Austin Weiss, who was slain by Long's bodyguards.

1940—Aug. 20. Leon Trotsky (Lev Bronstein), 63, exiled Russian war minister, near Mexico City. Killer identified as Ramon Mercador del Rio, a Spaniard, served 20 years in Mexican prison.

1948—Jan. 30. Mohandas K. Gandhi, 78, shot in New Delhi, India, by Nathuran Vinayak Godse, 36—Sept. 17. Count Folke Bernadotte, UN mediator for Palestine, ambushed in Jerusalem.

1951—July 20. King Abdul ibn Hussein of Jordan.

1956—Sept. 21. Pres. Anastasio Somoza of Nicaragua, in Leon; died Sept. 29.

1957—July 26. Pres. Carlos Castillo Armas of Guatemala, in Guatemala City by one of his own guards, who then committed suicide.

1958—July 14. King Faisal of Iraq; his uncle, Crown Prince Abdul Illah, and July 15, Premier Nuri as-Said, by rebels in Baghdad.

1959—Sept. 25. Prime Minister S.W.R.D. Bandaranaike of Ceylon, by Buddhist monk in Colombo.

1961—Jan. 17. Ex-Premier Patrice Lumumba of the Congo, in Katanga Province—May 30. Dominican dictator Rafael Leonidas Trujillo Molina shot to death by assassins near Ciudad Trujillo.

1963—Jan. 13. Pres. Sylvanus Olympio of Togo, by ex-soldiers at Lome.—June 12. Medgar W. Evers, NAACP's Mississippi field secretary, in Jackson, Miss. — Nov. 12. Pres. Ngo Dinh Diem of the Republic of Vietnam and his brother, Ngo Dinh Nhu, in a military coup. — Nov. 22. U.S. Pres. John F. Kennedy fatally shot in Dallas, Tex.; accused Lee Harvey Oswald murdered while awaiting trial.

1965—Jan. 21. Iranian premier Hassan Ali Mansour fatally wounded by assassin in Teheran; 4 executed.—Feb. 21. Malcolm X, Negro nationalist, fatally shot in N. Y. City; 3 sentenced to life.

1966—Sept. 6. Prime Minister Hendrik F. Verwoerd of South Africa stabbed to death in parliament at Capetown by drifter later ruled insane.

1968—Apr. 4. Rev. Dr. Martin Luther King Jr. fatally shot in Memphis, Tenn.; James Earl Ray sentenced to 99 years.—June 5. Sen. Robert F. Kennedy (D-N.Y.) fatally shot in Los Angeles; Sirhan Sirhan, resident alien, convicted of murder.

1969—July 5. Tom Mboya, Kenya's minister of economic planning and development, in Nairobi.—Oct. 17. Pres. A. A. Shermarke of Somalia, at Las Anos, Somalia.

1971—Nov. 28. Jordan Prime Minister Wasfi Tal, in Cairo, by Palestinian guerrillas.

1973—Mar. 2 U.S. Ambassador Cleo A. Noel Jr., U.S. Charge d'Affaires George C. Moore and Belgian Charge d'Affaires Guy Eid tortured and killed by Palestinian guerrillas in Khartoum, Sudan.

1974—Aug. 15. Mrs. Park Chung Hee, wife of president of So. Korea, hit by bullet meant for her husband. Police said plot was organized in No. Korea.—Aug. 19. U. S. Ambassador to Cyprus, Rodger P. Davies, killed by sniper's bullet in Nicosia.

1975—Feb. 11. Pres. Richard Ratsimandrava, 43, of Madagascar, machine-gunned in Tananarive.—Mar. 25. King Faisal of Saudi Arabia shot by nephew Prince Musad Abdel Aziz, 31, in royal palace, Riyadh.

1975—May 21. U.S. Col. Paul R. Shaffer Jr. and U.S. Lt. Col. John H. Turner slain by 3 Iranian terrorists in Teheran.

1975—Aug. 15. Bangladesh Pres. Sheik Mujibur Rahman and wife and son killed in army coup.

1976—Feb. 13. Nigerian head of state, Gen. Murtala Ramat Mohammed, slain by self-styled "young revolutionaries." Several arrests were made.

1977—Mar. 18. Congo Pres. Marien Ngouabi shot in Brazzaville.

Assassination Attempts

1910—Aug. 6. N. Y. City Mayor Wm. J. Gaynor shot and seriously wounded by discharged city employee.

1912—Oct. 14. Former U. S. President Theodore Roosevelt shot and seriously wounded by demented man in Milwaukee.

1950—Nov. 1. In an attempt to assassinate President Truman, 2 men identified as members of a Puerto Rican nationalist movement — Griselio Torresola and Oscar Collazo — tried to shoot their way into Blair House. Torresola was killed, and a guard, Pvt. Leslie Coffelt was fatally shot. Collazo, wounded, recovered and was tried and convicted Mar. 7, 1951 for the murder of Coffelt. His death sentence was commuted to life imprisonment by President Truman.

1970—Nov. 27. Pope Paul VI unharmed by knife-wielding assailant dressed as priest who attempted to attack him in Manila airport. Benjamin Mendoza, Bolivian, charged with attempted murder.

1972—May 15. Alabama Gov. George Wallace shot in Laurel, Md.; seriously crippled.

1972—Dec. 7. Mrs. Ferdinand E. Marcos, wife of the Philippine president, was stabbed and seriously injured in Pasay City, Philippines.

See also Chronology and Memorable Dates.

Major Kidnapings

Edward A. Cudahy Jr., 16, in Omaha, Neb., **Dec. 18, 1900.** Returned Dec. 20 after $25,000 paid. Pat Crowe confessed.

Robert Franks, 13, in Chicago, **May 22, 1924**, by 2 youths, Richard Loeb and Nathan Leopold, who killed boy. Demand for $10,000 ignored. Loeb died in prison, Leopold paroled 1958, freed 1963.

Charles A. Lindbergh Jr., 20 mos. old, in Hopewell, N.J., **Mar. 1, 1932**; found dead May 12. Ransom of $50,000 was paid to man identified as Bruno Richard Hauptmann, 35, paroled German convict who entered U.S. illegally. Hauptmann passed ransom bill and $14,000 marked money was found in his garage. He was convicted after spectacular trial at Flemington, and electrocuted in Trenton, N.J., prison, Apr. 3, 1936.

William A. Hamm Jr., 39, in St. Paul, **June 15, 1933.** $100,000 paid. Alvin Karpis given life, paroled in 1969.

Charles F. Urschel, in Oklahoma City, **July 22, 1933.** Released July 31 after $200,000 paid. George (Machine Gun) Kelly and 5 others given life.

George Weyerhaeuser, 9, in Tacoma, Wash., **May 24, 1935.** Returned home June 1 after $200,000 paid. Kidnapers given 20 to 60 years.

Charles Mattson, 10, in Tacoma, Wash., **Dec. 27, 1936.** Found dead Jan. 11, 1937. Kidnaper asked $28,000, failed to contact.

Arthur Fried, in White Plains, N. Y., **Dec. 4, 1937.** Body not found. Two kidnapers executed.

Robert C. Greenlease, 6, son of a Kansas City, Mo., motor car dealer, taken from school **Sept. 28, 1953**, and held for $600,000. Body found Oct. 7, when Mrs. Bonnie Brown Heady and Carl A. Hall were arrested. They pleaded guilty and were executed Dec. 18.

Peter Weinberger, 32 days old, Westbury, N.Y., **July 4, 1956**, for $2,000 ransom, not paid. Child found dead. Angelo John LaMarca, 31, convicted, executed.

Cynthia Ruotolo, 6 wks. old, taken from carriage in front of Hamden, Conn. store **Sept. 1, 1956.** Body found in lake.

Lee Crary, 8 in Everett, Wash., **Sept. 22, 1957.** $10,000 ransom, not paid. He escaped after 3 days, led police to George E. Collins, who was convicted.

Eric Peugeot, 4, taken from playground at St. Cloud golf course, Paris, **Apr. 12, 1960.** Released unharmed 3 days later after payment of undisclosed sum to kidnaper who had demanded $100,000. Two sentenced to prison.

Frank Sinatra Jr., 19, from hotel room in Lake Tahoe, Cal., **Dec. 8, 1963.** Released **Dec. 11** after his father paid $240,000 ransom. John W. Irwin, Barry W. Keenan and Joseph C. Amsler sentenced to prison; most of ransom recovered.

Barbara Jane Mackle, 20, abducted **Dec. 17, 1968**, from Atlanta, Ga., motel, was found unharmed 3 days later, buried in a coffin-like wooden box 18 inches underground, after her father had paid $500,000 ransom; Gary Steven Krist sentenced to life, Ruth Eisenmann-Schier to 7 years; most of ransom recovered.

Mrs. Roy Fuchs, 35, and 3 children held hostage 2 hours, **May 14, 1969**, in Long Island, N.Y., released after her husband, a bank manager, paid kidnapers $129,000 in bank funds; 4 men arrested, ransom recovered.

C. Burke Elbrick, U.S. ambassador to Brazil, kidnaped by revolutionaries in Rio de Janeiro **Sept. 4, 1969**; released 3 days later after Brazil yielded to kidnapers' demands to publish manifesto and release 15 political prisoners.

Sean M. Holly, U.S. diplomat, in Guatemala **Mar. 6, 1970**; freed 2 days later upon release of 3 terrorists from prison.

Lt. Col. Donald J. Crowley, U.S. air attache, in Dominican Republic **Mar. 24, 1970**; released after government allowed 20 prisoners to leave the country.

Count Karl von Spreti, W. German ambassador to Guatemala, **Mar. 31, 1970**; slain after Guatemala refused demands for $700,000 and release of 22 prisoners.

Pedro Eugenio Arambaru, former Argentine president, by terrorists **May 29, 1970**; body found July 17.

Ehrenfried von Holleben, W. German ambassador to Brazil, by terrorists **June 11, 1970**; freed after release of 40 prisoners.

Daniel A. Mitrione, U.S. diplomat, **July 31, 1970**, by terrorists in Montevideo, Uruguay; body found Aug. 10 after government rejected demands for release of all political prisoners.

Aloysio Dias Gomide, Brazilian vice consul, in Montevideo, **July 31, 1970**; released Feb. 21, 1971, after wife paid ransom estimated at over $250,000.

James R. Cross, British trade commissioner, **Oct. 5, 1970**, by French Canadian separatists in Quebec; freed Dec. 3 after 3 kidnapers and relatives flown to Cuba by government.

Pierre Laporte, Quebec Labor Minister, by separatists **Oct. 10, 1970**; body found Oct. 18.

Eugen Beihl, W. German businessman, by Basque separatists, in San Sebastian, Spain, **Dec. 1, 1970**; released Dec. 25 unharmed.

Giovanni E. Bucher, Swiss ambassador **Dec. 7, 1970**, by revolutionaries in Rio de Janeiro; freed Jan. 16, 1971, after Brazil released 70 political prisoners.

Geoffrey Jackson, British ambassador, in Montevideo, **Jan. 8, 1971**, by Tupamaro terrorists. Held as ransom for release of imprisoned terrorists, he was released Sept. 9, after the prisoners escaped.

Four U.S. airmen, in Ankara, by Turkish leftist terrorists on **Mar. 4, 1971.** $400,000 ransom was not paid, but the 4 were released unharmed Mar. 8.

Ephraim Elrom, Israel consul general in Istanbul, **May 17, 1971.** Held as ransom for imprisoned terrorists, he was found dead May 23.

Mrs. Virginia Piper, 49, abducted **July 27, 1972**, from her home in suburban Minneapolis; found unharmed near Duluth 2 days later after her husband paid $1 million ransom to the kidnapers.

Victor E. Samuelson, Exxon executive, **Dec. 6, 1973**, in Campana, Argentina, by Marxist guerrillas, freed Apr. 29, 1974, after payment of record $14.2 million ransom.

J. Paul Getty 3d, 17, grandson of the U.S. oil mogul, released by kidnapers **Dec. 15, 1973**, in southern Italy after family paid $2.8 million ransom. Kidnapers had severed his right ear, sent it with ransom demand.

Patricia (Patty) Hearst, 19, taken from her Berkeley, Cal., apartment **Feb. 4, 1974.** Symbionese Liberation Army demanded her father, Randolph A. Hearst, publisher, give millions to poor. Hearst offered $2 million in food; the Hearst Corp. offered $4 million worth. Kidnapers objected to way food was distributed. Patricia, in message, said she had joined SLA; she was identified by FBI as taking part in a San Francisco bank holdup, **Apr. 15**; she claimed, in message, she had been coerced. Again identified by FBI in a store holdup, **May 16**, she was classified by FBI as "an armed, dangerous fugitive." **FBI, Sept. 18, 1975**, captured Patricia and others in San Francisco; they were indicted on various charges, Patricia for bank robbery. A San Francisco jury convicted her, **Mar. 20, 1976.** William and Emily Harris were indicted, 1976, for the Hearst kidnaping.

J. Reginald Murphy, 40, an editor of Atlanta (Ga.) Constitution, kidnaped **Feb. 20, 1974**, freed **Feb. 22** after payment of $700,000 ransom by the newspaper. Police arrested William A. H. Williams, a contractor; most of the money was recovered.

J. Guadalupe Zuno Hernandez, 83, father-in-law of Mexican President Luis Echeverria Alvarez, seized by 4 terrorists **Aug. 28, 1974**; government refused to negotiate; he was released **Sept. 8.**

E. B. Reville, Hepzibah, Ga., banker, and wife Jean kidnaped **Sept. 30, 1974.** Ransom of $30,000 paid. He was found alive; Mrs. Reville was found dead of carbon monoxide fumes in car trunk **Oct. 2.**

Jack Teich, Kings Point, N.Y., steel executive, seized **Nov. 12, 1974**; released **Nov. 19** after payment of $750,000.

Samuel Bronfman, 21, heir to Seagram liquor fortune, abducted **Aug. 9, 1975**, in Purchase, N.Y.; $2.3 million ransom paid by father, Edgar. FBI and N.Y.C. police rescued Samuel **Aug. 17** in Brooklyn, N.Y., apartment, recovered ransom, and arrested Mel Patrick Lynch, a city fireman, and Dominic Byrne, a limousine operator. Two found not guilty of kidnap, but convicted of extortion after they claimed young Bronfman masterminded ransom plot.

Richard O. Hall, seized **Feb. 8, 1977**, shotgun wired to his neck, by Anthony Kiritsis in Indianapolis in dispute with Hall's mortgage company. After negotiations with officials, Kiritsis surrendered; Hall was unharmed.

One hundred and thirty-four hostages were seized **Mar. 8, 1977**, by 12 Hanafi Muslim gunmen in 3 Washington, D.C., buildings. A reporter was killed and 19 persons injured. On **Mar. 11**, hostages were released, gunmen surrendered, after their demand that 5 Black Muslims, jailed in killing of 7 Hanafi Muslims, be delivered to them was refused by authorities. One hostage, wounded, died later of a heart attack.

ASTRONOMY AND CALENDAR

Edited by Dr. Kenneth L. Franklin, Astronomer
American Museum-Hayden Planetarium

Celestial Events Highlights, 1978

(All times are Greenwich Mean Time)

Planet watchers will have a very good year. Mars is in opposition in January, being a reddish jewel in the usually lackluster Cancer. Saturn, just to the east near Regulus, is in opposition in February. Jupiter was in opposition just before last Christmas and is still very much in evidence for the first few months. If you keep track of Jupiter, you may find Venus 1°.6 away from it in May, and Mercury 1°.8 away in June.

Make certain you know how to find Regulus, the alpha star of Leo, for a lot of planet action occurs around this prominent star, which rests almost exactly on the ecliptic. On June 5, Mars passes about 0°.1 from Saturn, then in the next week moves to 0°.8 north of Regulus. The three objects make a fine trio very similar in brightness, if not color. Next, Venus enters the scene, it, too, passing 0°.1 from Saturn on July 10, and 1°.1 from Regulus the next day. On July 28, even Mercury approaches to within 3° from Regulus, although you may have to use binoculars to pick it out of the bright western sky. Watch Venus, for it will first pass 1°.2 from faint Mars August 14, and then approach Spica, coming as close as 0°.3 on August 31.

Another continuing event this year is the series of occultations of Aldebaran, the brightest star of Taurus. An occultation occurs when the moon passes between us and a more distant object. For many months one station or another on the earth will witness the occultation of this bright star.

In the predictions for each month below and in the listing of planetary configurations on page 760, look for the Greenwich Mean Time of the event, and correct it for your time zone, changing the date if necessary. In the calendar tables for the date, note if the moon is above your horizon, calculating the rise and set times if necessary. The shadow this year may fall north of you, but you will witness a close pass of the moon past the star. If it is daylight, you will have to use a telescope.

January

Mercury is in the morning sky, passing 3° south of the moon on the 7th.

Venus is too close to the sun to be seen, passing through superior conjunction on the 22nd, 159 million miles from the earth.

Mars is nearest the earth on the 19th, 60.7 million miles away, and at opposition on the 22d, having receded to 60.8 million miles. It appears as a reddish star of magnitude −1.1 in the sparse constellation of Cancer, southeast of Pollux in Gemini.

Jupiter appears as a −2.3 magnitude star north of Orion, following its opposition on the 23rd of last month. It is 5° north of the gibbous moon on the 21st.

Saturn is 1°.1 north of Regulus and is the brighter of the two. The planet is 776 million miles away from us now, but the star is 84 light-years distant.

Moon is at perigee on the 8th, 222,100 miles away, and at apogee on the 21st, 252,300 miles away. It passes Mercury on the 7th, occults Aldebaran on the 19th, and passes Jupiter on the 21st, Mars on the 24th, and Saturn on the 26th.

Jan. 1 — Earth at perihelion, 91.41 million miles from the sun.

Jan. 4 — Quadrantid meteors may be seen in the morning hours in spite of a waning crescent moon.

Jan. 11 —Mercury at greatest western elongation, 23° from the sun.

Jan. 19 — Mars nearest the earth; the moon occults Aldebaran; the sun enters Capricornus.

Jan. 20 — Saturn passes 1°.1 north of Regulus.

Jan. 22 — Mars in opposition; Venus in superior conjunction.

February

Mercury, in superior conjunction the 27th, 116 million miles from earth, is almost impossible to see.

Venus remains too close to the sun for sighting.

Mars is still in retrograde motion and 3° south of Pollux on the 17th, and 9° north of the moon on the 19th.

Jupiter ends its retrograde mode in Taurus on the 20th and is 5° north of the moon on the 17th.

Saturn is in opposition 766 million miles from us on the 16th, appearing like a +0.3 magnitude star in Leo.

Moon is at perigee on the 5th, 224,500 miles away, and at apogee on the 17th, 251,700 miles away. It occults Aldebaran on the 16th, and passes Jupiter on the 17th, Mars on the 19th, and Saturn on the 22d.

Feb. 16 — Moon occults Aldebaran; Saturn is in opposition; sun enters Aquarius.

Feb. 17 — Mars is 3° south of Pollux.

Feb. 20 — Jupiter is stationary.

Feb. 27 — Mercury in superior conjunction.

March

Mercury is 1°.3 north of Venus on the 12th, but a telescope may be required to find this conjunction because the two planets are still only 12° from the sun. Mercury is 4° north of Venus on the 28th at an elongation of 16°, a wider configuration. It is at greatest eastern elongation (19°) on the 24th.

Venus is in conjunction with Mercury twice this month (see Mercury) on the 12th and the 28th.

Mars is stationary on the 2d, resuming its eastward motion in Gemini, passing 4° south of Pollux on the 17th, 8° north of the moon on the 19th.

Jupiter is 5° north of the moon on the 16th.

Saturn is 5° north of the moon on the 21st.

Moon is at perigee on the 5th, 228,000 miles away, at apogee on the 17th, 251,300 miles away, and again at perigee on the 31st, 230,000 miles away. It passes Venus on the 10th; occults Aldebaran on the 15th; passes Jupiter on the 16th, Mars on the 19th, and Saturn on the 21st; and is totally eclipsed on the 24th.

Mar. 11 — Sun enters Pisces.

Mar. 12 — Conjunction of Mercury with Venus.

Mar. 15 — Moon occults Aldebaran.

Mar. 17 — Mars passes 4° south of Pollux.

Mar. 20 — Vernal Equinox at 23:24 GMT (18:24 EST). Spring begins in the northern hemisphere.

Mar. 24 — Total lunar eclipse; Mercury at greatest eastern elongation, 19° from the sun.

Mar. 28 — Conjunction of Mercury with Venus.

April

Mercury is at inferior conjunction on the 11th, 55

million miles away, and thus invisible most of the month.

Venus is beginning to be visible in clear evening twilight, passing 3° north of the two-day crescent moon on the 9th (the evening of the 8th in North America).

Mars is now moving eastward through Cancer, passing 7° north of the moon on the 16th.

Jupiter moves into Gemini this month, passing 5° north of the moon on the 13th.

Saturn passes 5° north of the moon on the 18th, and is stationary in Leo on the 15th, resuming its eastward motion.

Moon is at apogee on the 14th, 251,300 miles away, and at perigee on the 26th, 227,400 miles away. It partially eclipses the sun on the 7th, passes Venus on the 9th, occults Aldebaran on the 11th.

Apr. 7 — Partial solar eclipse.

Apr. 11 — Mercury at inferior conjunction; the moon occults Aldebaran.

Apr. 18 — Sun enters Aries.

Apr. 25 — Saturn stationary.

May

Mercury is 2° south of the thin crescent moon on the 5th, and in greatest western elongation on the 9th, 26° from the sun.

Venus is 6° north of the moon on the 9th, and 1°.6 north of Jupiter on the 29th.

Mars is 6° north of the moon on the 14th, in Leo.

Jupiter is 5° north of the moon on the 11th.

Saturn is 5° north of the moon on the 15th, in Leo.

Moon is at apogee on the 12th, 251,800 miles away, and at perigee on the 24th, 224,300 miles away. It passes Mercury on the 5th, occults Aldebaran on the 9th (8th in North America).

May 4 — Eta Aquarids, a weak meteor shower, may be visible since the moon is mostly out of the way.

May 5 — Uranus in opposition.

May 9 — Occultation of Aldebaran; Mercury at greatest western elongation.

May 13 — Sun enters Taurus.

May 29 — Venus in conjunction with Jupiter.

June

Mercury is invisible most of this month, being in superior conjunction on the 14th, 123 million miles away. It will be 1°.8 north of Jupiter on the 24th. It will be 5° south of Pollux on the 29th, looking like a star of −0 .7 magnitude, brighter than Pollux.

Venus is 7° north of the moon on the 8th, and 5° south of Pollux on the 11th.

Mars is in conjunction with Saturn on the 5th (4th in North America), passing only 0°.1 south of Saturn. It passes 4° north of the moon and 0°.8 north of Regulus on the 12th.

Jupiter passes 5° north of the moon on the 8th.

Saturn is 0°.1 north of Mars on the 5th (4th in North America), and 5° north of the moon on the 11th.

Moon is at apogee on the 8th, 252,300 miles away, and at perigee on the 21st, 222,200 miles away. It passes Jupiter and Venus on the 8th, Saturn on the 11th, and Mars on the 12th.

June 4 — Pallas in opposition.

June 5 — Vesta in opposition, brighter than 6th magnitude; Mars and Saturn in conjunction, 0°.1 apart in Leo.

June 8 — Neptune in opposition.

June 14 — Mercury in superior conjunction.

June 20 — Sun enters Gemini.

June 21 — Summer solstice at 18:10 GMT (13:10 EST).

June 24 — Mercury in conjunction with Jupiter.

July

Mercury is in the evening sky, passing 5° north of the moon on the 7th; at greatest eastern elongation on the 22nd, 27° from the sun; 3° south of Regulus on the 28th; and 5° south of Saturn on the 31st.

Venus is 4° north of the bright crescent moon on the 9th, 0°.1 north of Saturn on the 10th, and 1°.1 north of Regulus on the 11th.

Mars is 2° north of the moon on the 10th.

Jupiter is in conjunction on the 10th.

Saturn passes 0°.1 south of Venus on the 10th, and 1°.0 north of Regulus on the 19th.

Moon is at apogee on the 6th, 252,600 miles away, and at perigee on the 19th, 221,900 miles away. It occults Aldebaran on the 2d; passes Mercury on the 7th, Venus and Saturn on the 9th, and Mars on the 10th; and occults Aldebaran on the 29th.

July 2 — Occultation of Aldebaran.

July 5 — Earth at aphelion, 94.51 million miles away from the sun.

July 9 — Ceres in opposition.

July 10 — Jupiter in conjunction, 579 million miles from earth; Venus in conjunction with Saturn, 0°.1 apart in Leo.

July 11 — Venus is 1°.1 north of Regulus.

July 19 — Saturn is 1°.0 north of Regulus.

July 20 — Sun enters Cancer.

July 22 — Mercury in greatest eastern elongation, 27° from the sun.

July 24 — Juno in opposition.

July 28 — Mercury 3° south of Regulus.

July 29 — Occultation of Aldebaran.

July 31 — Mercury in conjunction with Saturn, 5° apart.

August

Mercury is again in conjunction with Saturn on the 4th, 5° south of Saturn. It passes 2° south of the moon on the 5th and 5° south of Regulus on the 10th, and is at inferior conjunction on the 18th, 57 million miles from earth.

Venus is occulted by the moon on the 8th (evening of the 7th in North America); in conjunction with Mars on the 14th, 1°.2 separating them.

Mars is occulted by the moon on the 8th.

Jupiter passes 5° north of the moon on the 2d, 7° south of Pollux on the 7th, and 5° north of the moon on the 30th.

Saturn is 5° north of Mercury on the 4th, 4° north of the moon on the 5th, and in conjunction on the 27th.

Moon is at apogee on the 2d, 252,500 miles away, at perigee on the 17th, 223,200 miles away and at apogee again on the 29th, 252,000 miles away. It passes Jupiter on the 2d and Mercury and Saturn on the 5th, occults Venus and Mars on the 8th and Aldebaran on the 26th, and passes Jupiter again on the 30th.

Aug. 4 — Mercury in conjunction with Saturn.

Aug. 8 — The moon occults Venus and Mars.

Aug. 10 — Sun enters Leo.

Aug. 10-14 — Perseid meteor shower with no interference from the first quarter moon.

Aug. 14 — Venus in conjunction with Mars, 1°.2 apart.

Aug. 18 — Mercury at inferior conjunction.

Aug. 26 — Occultation of Aldebaran.

Aug. 27 — Saturn in conjunction.

Aug. 29 — Venus in greatest eastern elongation, 46° from the sun.

Aug. 31 — Venus passes 0°.3 south of Spica.

September

Mercury is 2° north of the moon on the 1st; at greatest western elongation on the 4th, 18° from the sun; passes 0°.5 north of Regulus on the 9th and 0°.1 north of Saturn on the 13th; and is in superior conjunction on the 30th, 130 million miles from us.

Venus is 6° south of the moon the 6th.

Mars is 2° north of the moon on the 5th.

Jupiter, in Cancer, is 5° north of the moon on the 27th.

Saturn is 0°.1 south of Mercury on the 13th, east of Regulus, and 3° north of the moon on the 29th.

Moon is at perigee on the 14th, 226,000 miles away, and at apogee on the 26th, 251,400 miles away. It passes Mercury on the 1st, Mars on the 5th, and Venus on the 6th; is eclipsed totally on the 16th; occults Aldebaran on the 22d; and passes Jupiter on the 27th and Saturn on the 29th.

Sept. 4 — Mercury at greatest western elongation, 18° from the sun.

Sept. 8 — Mars passes 2° north of Spica.

Sept. 9 — Mercury passes 0°.5 north of Regulus.

Sept. 13 — Mercury in conjunction with Saturn, 0°.1 apart.

Sept. 16 — Sun enters Virgo; total lunar eclipse.

Sept. 22 — Occultation of Aldebaran.

Sept. 23 — Autumnal Equinox at 09:26 GMT (04:26 EST). Autumn begins in the north.

Sept. 30 — Mercury in superior conjunction.

October

Mercury, too close to the sun for easy sighting, is 5° north of Venus on the 27th.

Venus, at greatest brilliancy on the 3rd, is approaching inferior conjunction. This is an excellent time to view it with binoculars or a telescope. People are often surprised at the very thin crescent exhibited at this time.

Mars is 4° south of the moon on the 4th and 7° north of Venus on the 20th.

Jupiter is 4° north of the last quarter moon on the 24th.

Saturn is 3° north of the moon on the 27th.

Moon is at perigee on the 11th, 229,100 miles away, and at apogee on the 24th, 251,200 miles away. It produces a partial solar eclipse on the 2d; passes Mars on the 4th and Venus on the 5th; occults Aldebaran on the 19th; and passes Jupiter on the 24th and Saturn on the 27th.

Oct. 2 — Partial solar eclipse.

Oct. 3 — Venus at greatest brilliancy.

Oct. 10 — Pluto in opposition.

Oct. 19 — Occultation of Aldebaran.

Oct. 20 — Venus in conjunction with Mars.

Oct. 21 — Orionid meteors are difficult to see because of a bright, gibbous moon.

Oct. 27 — Venus in conjunction with Mercury.

Oct. 30 — Sun enters Libra.

November

Mercury passes 7° south of the moon on the 2d, 1°.9 south of Mars on the 5th, 2° north of Antares on the 10th, and reaches greatest eastern elongation on the 16th, 23° from the sun.

Venus is at inferior conjunction on the 7th, 25 million miles from the earth, and passes 3° south of the moon on the 28th.

Mars, too close to the sun for viewing, nevertheless passes 5° south of the moon on 2d, 1°.9 north of Mercury on the 5th, 4° north of Antares on the 14th, and 0°.1 south of Mercury on the 29th.

Jupiter is 4° north of the moon on the 21st, and begins its retrograde motion on the 26th.

Saturn is 3° north of the moon on the 24th.

Moon is at perigee on the 5th, 229,300 miles away and at apogee on the 20th, 251,500 miles away. It passes Mercury and Mars on the 2d; occults Aldebaran on the 16th; and passes Jupiter on the 21st, Saturn on the 24th, and Venus on the 28th.

Nov. 5 — Mercury in conjunction with Mars.

Nov. 7 — Venus in inferior conjunction.

Nov. 9 — Uranus in conjunction.

Nov. 16 — Mercury at greatest eastern elongation, 23° from the sun; occultation of Aldebaran.

Nov. 22 — Sun enters Scorpius.

Nov. 26 — Jupiter stationary in Cancer.

Nov. 29 — Sun enters Ophiuchus; Mercury is in conjunction with Mars.

December

Mercury is in inferior conjunction on the 5th, 63 million miles from earth, and is 3° south of the moon on the 28th.

Venus is at greatest brilliancy on the 14th.

Mars is approaching the sun, with conjunction to come next month.

Jupiter is 4° north of the moon on the 18th.

Saturn is 3° north of the moon on the 21st.

Moon is at perigee on the 2d, 226,000 miles away, at apogee on the 18th, 252,000 miles away, and again at perigee on the 30th, 223,000 miles away. It occults Aldebaran on the 13th; passes Jupiter on the 18th and Saturn on the 21st; occults Venus on the 26th.

Dec. 5 — Mercury at inferior conjunction.

Dec. 10 — Neptune in conjunction.

Dec. 13 — Occultation of Aldebaran; Geminid shower gets too much competition from the nearly full moon.

Dec. 14 — Venus at greatest brilliancy.

Dec. 16 — Sun enters Sagittarius.

Dec. 22 — Winter Solstice at 05:21 GMT (00:21 EST).

Dec. 26 — Occultation of Venus.

Astronomical Signs and Symbols

☉ The Sun	⊕ The Earth	♅ Uranus	□ Quadrature
☾ The Moon	♂ Mars	♆ Neptune	☍ Opposition
☿ Mercury	♃ Jupiter	♇ Pluto	☊ Ascending Node
♀ Venus	♄ Saturn	☌ Conjunction	☋ Descending Node

Two heavenly bodies are in "conjunction" (☌) when they are due north and south of each other, either in Right Ascension (with respect to the north celestial pole) or in Celestial Longitude (with respect to the north ecliptic pole). If the bodies are seen near each other, they will rise and set at nearly the same time. They are in "opposition" (☍) when their Right Ascensions differ by exactly 12 hours, or their Celestial Longitudes differ by 180°. One of the two objects in opposition will rise while the other is setting. "Quadrature" (□) refers to the arrangement when the coordinates of two bodies differ by exactly 90°. These terms may refer to the relative positions of any two bodies as seen from the earth, but one of the bodies is so frequently the sun that mention of the sun is omitted; otherwise both bodies are named. The geocentric angular separation between sun and object is termed "elongation." Elongation is limited only for Mercury and Venus; the "greatest elongation" for each of these bodies is noted in the appropriate tables and is approximately the time for longest observation. When a planet is in its "ascending" (☊) or "descending" (☋) node, it is passing northward or southward, respectively, through the plane of the earth's orbit, across the celestial circle called the ecliptic. The term "perihelion" means nearest to the sun, and "aphelion," farthest from the sun. An "occultation" of a planet or star is an eclipse of it by some other body, usually the moon.

Planets and the Sun

The planets of the solar system, in order of their distance from the sun, are Mercury, Venus, Earth, Mars, Jupiter, Saturn, Uranus, Neptune and Pluto. Uranus, Neptune and Pluto are not included in the celestial list because they are too faint to be seen without optical aid. Both Uranus and Neptune are visible through good field glasses, but Pluto is so distant and so small that only large telescopes or long exposure photographs can make it visible.

Since Mercury and Venus are nearer to the sun than is the earth, their motions about the sun are seen from the earth as wide swings first to one side of the sun and then to the other, although they are both passing continuously around the sun in orbits that are almost circular. When their passage takes them either between the earth and the sun, or beyond the sun as seen from the earth, they are invisible to us. Because of the laws which govern the motions of planets about the sun, both Mercury and Venus require much less time to pass between the earth and the sun than around the far side of the sun, so their periods of visibility and invisibility are unequal.

The planets that lie farther from the sun than does the earth may be seen for longer periods of time and are invisible only when they are so located in our sky that they rise and set about the same time as the sun when, of course, they are overwhelmed by the sun's great brilliance. None of the planets has any light or radiant heat of its own but each shines only by reflecting sunlight from its surface. Mercury and Venus, because they are between the earth and the sun, show phases very much as the moon does. The planets farther from the sun are always seen as full, although Mars does occasionally present a slightly gibbous phase — like the moon when not quite full.

The planets move rapidly among the stars because they are very much nearer to us. The stars are also in motion, some of them at tremendous speeds, but they are so far away that their motion does not change their apparent positions in the heavens sufficiently for anyone to perceive that change in a single lifetime. The very nearest star is about 7,000 times as far away as the most distant planet.

Visible Planets of the Solar System

Mercury, Venus, Mars, Jupiter and Saturn

Mercury

Mercury, nearest planet to the sun, is also the smallest of the nine planets known to be orbiting the sun. Its diameter is 3,100 miles and its mean distance from the sun is 36,000,000 miles.

Mercury moves with great speed in its journey about the sun, averaging about 30 miles a second to complete its circuit in 88 of our days. Mercury rotates upon its axis over a period of nearly 59 days, thus exposing all of its surface periodically to the sun. It is believed that the surface passing before the sun may have a temperature of about 800° F., while the temperature on the side turned temporarily away from the sun does not fall as low as might be expected. This night temperature has been described by Russian astronomers as "room temperature" — possibly about 70°. This would contradict the former belief that Mercury did not possess an atmosphere, for some sort of atmosphere would be needed to retain the fierce solar radiation that strikes Mercury. A shallow but dense layer of carbon dioxide would produce the "greenhouse" effect, in which heat accumulated during exposure to the sun would not completely escape at night. The actual presence of a carbon dioxide atmo-sphere is in dispute.

This uncertainty about conditions upon Mercury and its motion arise from its short angular distance from the sun as seen from the earth, for Mercury is always too much in line with the sun to be observed against a dark sky, but is always seen during either morning or evening twilight.

Mariner 10 made three passes by Mercury in 1974 and 1975. A large fraction of the surface was photographed from varying distances, revealing a degree of cratering similar to that of the moon. An atmosphere of hydrogen and helium may be made up of gases of the solar wind temporarily concentrated by the presence of Mercury. The discovery of a weak but permanent magnetic field was a surprise. It has been held that both a fluid core and rapid rotation were necessary for the generation of a planetary magnetic field. Mercury may demonstrate these conditions to be unnecessary, or the field may reveal something about the history of Mercury.

Venus

Venus is slightly smaller than the earth. Its diameter is about 200 miles less than the earth's diameter. Venus moves about the sun at a mean distance of 67,000,000 miles in 225 of our days. Its synodical revolution — its return to the same relationship with the earth and the sun, which is a result of the combination of its own motion and that of the earth — is 584 days. Every 19 months, then, Venus will be nearer to the earth than any other planet of the solar system. The planet is covered with a dense, white, cloudy atmosphere that conceals whatever is below it. This same cloud reflects sunlight efficiently so that when Venus is favorably situated, it is the third brightest object in the sky, exceeded only by the sun and the moon.

Spectral analysis of sunlight reflected from Venus' cloud tops has shown features that can best be explained by identifying the material of the clouds as sulphuric acid (oil of vitriol). Infrared spectroscopy from a balloon-borne telescope nearly 20 miles above the earth's surface gave indications of a small amount of water vapor present in the same region of the atmosphere of Venus. In 1956, a breakthrough in our knowledge came from radio astronomers at the Naval Research Laboratories in Washington, D. C. Their observations indicated a temperature for Venus of about 600° F., in marked contrast to minus 125° F., previously found at the cloud tops. Subsequent radio work confirmed a high temperature and produced evidence for this temperature to be associated with the solid body of Venus. With this peculiarity in mind, space scientists devised experiments for the U.S. space probe Mariner 2 to perform when it flew by in 1962. Mariner 2 confirmed the high temperature and the fact that it pertained to the ground rather than to some special activity of the atmosphere. In addition, Mariner 2 was unable to detect any radiation belts similar to the earth's so-called Van Allen belts. Nor was it able to detect the existence of a magnetic field even as weak as 1/100,000 of that of the earth.

An international scientific drama occurred in 1967 when a Russian space probe, Venera 4, and the American Mariner 5 arrived at Venus within a few hours of each other. Venera 4 was unique in that it was designed to allow an instrument package to land gently on the planet's surface via parachute. It ceased transmission of information after 75 minutes when the temperature it read went above 500° F. After considerable controversy, it was agreed that it still had 20 miles to go to reach the surface. The U.S. probe, Mariner 5, went around the dark side of Venus at a distance of about 6,000 miles. Again, it detected no significant magnetic field, but its radio signals passed to earth through Venus' atmosphere twice — once on the night side and once on the day side. The results are startling. Venus' atmosphere is nearly all carbon dioxide and must exert a pressure at the planet's surface of up to 100 times the earth's normal sea-level pressure of one atmosphere. Since the earth and Venus are about the same size, and were presumably formed at the same time by the same general process, from the same mixture of chemical elements, one is faced with the question: which is the planet with the unusual history — earth or Venus?

In the last several years, astronomers using powerful transmitters as well as sensitive receivers and computers have succeeded in determining the rotation period of Venus. It turns out to be 243 days clockwise — in other words, contrary to the spin of most of the other planets and to its own motion around the sun. If it were exactly 243.16 days, Venus would always present the same face toward the earth at every inferior conjunction. This rate and sense of rotation allows a "day" on Venus of 117.4 earth days. Any part of Venus will receive sunlight on its clouds for over 58 days and will be in darkness for 58 days.

Mariner 10 passed Venus before traveling on to Mercury. The carbon dioxide molecule found in such abundance in the atmosphere is rather opaque to certain ultraviolet wavelengths, enabling sensitive television cameras to take pictures of the Venusian cloud cover. Photos radioed to earth show a spiral pattern in the clouds from equator to the poles. Long-lived features in the clouds have been detected moving at speeds of the order of a hundred miles per hour or more. If this is a typical wind speed, it can account for the transfer of heat to the night side in spite of the low rotation rate of the planet.

Recent radar observations have shown surface features below the clouds. Large craters have been identified. Before the end of 1977, we should have radar-derived pictures of Venus that are as revealing as ordinary telescopic views of our moon taken by earth-based telescopes.

Mars

Mars is the first planet beyond the earth, away from the sun. Mars' diameter is about 4,200 miles, although a determination of the radius and mass of Mars by the space-probe, Mariner 4, which flew by Mars on July 14, 1965 at a distance of less than 6,000 miles, indicated that these dimensions were slightly larger than had been previously estimated. While Mars' orbit is also nearly circular, it is somewhat more eccentric than the orbits of many of the other planets, and Mars is more than 30 million miles farther from the sun in some parts of its year than it is at others. Mars takes 687 of our days to make one circuit of the sun, traveling at about 15 miles a second. Mars rotates upon its axis in almost the same period of time that the earth does — 24 hours and 37 minutes. Mars' mean distance from the sun is 141 million miles, so that the temperature on Mars would be lower than that on the earth even if Mars' atmosphere were about the same as ours. The atmosphere is not, however, for Mariner 4 reported that atmospheric pressure on Mars is between 1% and 2% of the earth's atmospheric pressure. This thin atmosphere appears to be largely carbon dioxide. No evidence of free water was found.

There appears to be no magnetic field about Mars. This would eliminate the previous conception of a dangerous radiation belt around Mars. The same lack of a magnetic field would expose the surface of Mars to an influx of cosmic radiation about 100 times as intense as that on earth.

Deductions from years of telescopic observation indicate that 5/8ths of the surface of Mars is a desert of reddish rock, sand, and soil. The rest of Mars is covered by irregular patches that appear generally green in hues that change through the Martian year. These were formerly held to be some sort of primitive vegetation, but with the findings of Mariner 4 of a complete lack of water and oxygen, such growth does not appear possible. The nature of the green areas is now unknown. They may be regions covered with volcanic salts whose color changes with changing temperatures and atmospheric conditions, or they may be gray, rather than green. When large gray areas are placed beside large red areas, the gray areas will appear green to the eye.

Mars' axis of rotation is inclined from a vertical to the plane of its orbit about the sun by about 25° and therefore has seasons as does the earth, except that the Martian seasons are longer because Mars' year is longer. White caps form about the winter pole of Mars, growing through the winter and shrinking in summer. These polar caps are now believed to be both water ice and carbon dioxide ice. It is the carbon dioxide that is seen to come and go with the seasons. The water ice is apparently in many layers with dust between them, indicating climatic cycles.

The canals of Mars have become more of a mystery than they were before the voyage of Mariner 4. Markings forming a network of fine lines crossing much of the surface of Mars have been seen there by men who have devoted much time to the study of the planet, but no canals have shown clearly enough upon previous photographs to be universally accepted. A few of the 21 photographs sent back to earth by Mariner 4 covered areas crossed by canals. The pictures show faint, ill-defined, broad, dark markings, but no positive identification of the nature of the markings.

Mariners 6 & 7 in 1969 sent back many more photographs of higher quality than those of the pioneering Mariner 4. These pictures showed cratering similar to the earlier views, but in addition showed two other types of terrain. Some regions seemed featureless for many square miles, but others were chaotic, showing high relief without apparent organization into mountain chains or craters.

Mariner 9, the first artificial body to be placed in an orbit about Mars, has transmitted over 10,000 photographs covering 100% of the planet's surface. Preliminary study of these photos and other data shows that Mars resembles no other planet we know. Using terrestrial terms, however, scientists describe features that seem to be clearly of volcanic origin. One of these features is Nix Olympica, apparently a caldera whose outer slopes are over 300 miles in diameter. Some features may have been produced by cracking (faulting) of the surface and the sliding of one region over or past another. Many craters seem to have been produced by impacting bodies such as may have come from the nearby asteroid belt. Features near the south pole may have been produced by glaciers that are no longer present. Flowing water, non-existent on Mars at the present time, probably carved canyons, one 10 times longer and 3 times deeper than the Grand Canyon.

Although the Russians landed a probe on the Martian surface, it transmitted for only 20 seconds. In 1976, the U.S. landed 2 Viking spacecraft on the Martian surface. The landers have devices aboard to perform chemical analyses of the soil in search of evidence of life. So far, the results have been inconclusive. The 2 Viking orbiters have returned the best pictures yet of Martian topographic features. Many features can be explained only if Mars once had large quantities of flowing water.

Mars' position in its orbit and its speed around that orbit in relation to the earth's position and speed bring Mars fairly close to the earth on occasions about two years apart and then move Mars and the earth too far apart for accurate observation and photography. Every 15-17 years, the close approaches are especially favorable to close observation.

Mars has 2 satellites, discovered in 1877 by Asaph Hall. The outer satellite, Deimos, revolves around

Mars in about 31 hours. The inner satellite, Phobos, whips around Mars in a little more than 7 hours, making 3 trips around the planet each Martian day. Mariner and Viking photos show these bodies to be irregularly shaped and pitted with numerous craters. Phobos also shows a system of linear grooves, each about 1/3-mile across and roughly parallel. Phobos measures about 8 by 12 miles and Deimos about 5 by 7.5 miles in size.

Jupiter

Jupiter is the largest of the planets. Its equatorial diameter is 88,000 miles, 11 times the diameter of the earth. Its polar diameter is about 6,000 miles shorter. This is an equilibrium condition resulting from the liquidity of the planet and its extremely rapid rate of rotation: a Jupiter day is only 10 earth hours long. For a planet of this size, this rotational speed is amazing, and it moves a point on Jupiter's equator at a speed of 22,000 miles an hour, as compared with 1,000 miles an hour for a point on the earth's equator. Jupiter is at an average distance of 480 million miles from the sun and takes almost 12 of our years to make one complete circuit of the sun.

The only directly observable chemical constituents of Jupiter's atmosphere are methane (CH_4) and ammonia (NH_3), but it is reasonable to assume the same mixture of elements available to make Jupiter as to make the sun. This would mean a large fraction of hydrogen and helium must be present also, as well as water (H_2O). The temperature at the tops of the clouds may be about minus 260° F. The clouds are probably ammonia ice crystals, becoming ammonia droplets lower down. There may be a space before water ice crystals show up as clouds; in turn, these become water droplets near the bottom of the entire cloud layer. The total atmosphere may be only a few hundred miles in depth, pulled down by the surface gravity (= 2.64 times earth's) to a relatively thin layer. Of course, the gases become denser with depth until they may turn into a slush or a slurry. Perhaps there is no surface — no real interface between the gaseous atmosphere and the body of Jupiter. Pioneers 10 and 11 provided evidence for considering Jupiter to be almost entirely liquid hydrogen. Long before a rocky core about the size of the earth is reached, hydrogen mixed with helium becomes a liquid metal at very high temperature. Jupiter's cloudy atmosphere is a fairly good reflector of sunlight and makes it far brighter than any of the stars.

Jupiter has 14 known satellites, although the last one discovered by Kowal at the Hale Observatory is so faint that it has been lost. Four of the moons are large and bright, rivaling our own moon and the planet Mercury in diameter, and may be seen through a field glass. They move rapidly around Jupiter and their change of position from night to night is extremely interesting to watch. The other satellites are much smaller and in all but one instance much farther from Jupiter and cannot be seen except through powerful telescopes. The 4 outermost satellites are revolving around Jupiter clockwise as seen from the north, contrary to the motions of the great majority of the satellites in the solar system and to the direction of revolution of the planets around the sun. The reason for this retrograde motion is not known, but one theory is that Jupiter's tremendous gravitational power may have captured 4 of the minor planets or asteroids that move about the sun between Mars and Jupiter, and that these would necessarily revolve backward. At the great distance of these bodies from Jupiter — some 14 million miles — direct motion would result in decay of the orbits, while retrograde orbits would be stable. Jupiter's mass is more than twice the mass of all the other planets put together, and accounts for Jupiter's tremendous gravitational field and so, probably, for its numerous satellites and its dense atmosphere.

In December, 1973, Pioneer 10 passed about 80,000 miles from the equator of Jupiter and was whipped into a path taking it out of our solar system in about 50 years. In December, 1974, Pioneer 11 passed within 30,000 miles of Jupiter, moving roughly from south to north, over the poles. Photographs from both encounters reveal much detail in the clouds, including what appear to be cyclonic storms. The Great Red Spot shows a spiral nature suggesting it is a long lived hurricane-like feature. The magnetic field is eccentric and tilted. It is stronger than was thought and of the opposite sign to that of the earth. The action of the trapped particles — the Jovian Van Allen Belts — is too violent to let man pass through in present spacecraft without serious radiation injury. Both Pioneers contain a pictorial message for extra-solar system finders of the derelicts.

Saturn

Saturn, last of the planets visible to the unaided eye, is almost twice as far from the sun as Jupiter, almost 900 million miles. It is second in size to Jupiter but its mass is much smaller. Saturn's specific gravity is less than that of water. Its diameter is about 71,000 miles at the equator; its rotational speed spins it completely around in a little more than 10 hours, and its atmosphere is much like that of Jupiter, except that its temperature at the top of its cloud layer is at least 100° colder. At about 300° F. below zero, the ammonia would be frozen out of Saturn's clouds. The theoretical construction of Saturn resembles that of Jupiter; it is either all gas, or it has a small dense center surrounded by a layer of liquid and a deep atmosphere.

Saturn has 10 satellites, the 10th having been discovered by the French astronomer Audouin Dollfus in December, 1966. The newly found satellite is a few thousand miles outside Saturn's ring system.

Saturn's ring system begins about 7,000 miles above the visible disk of Saturn, lying above its equator and extending about 35,000 miles into space. The diameter of the ring system, including Saturn itself, is about 170,000 miles; the rings are estimated to be no thicker than 10 miles. In 1973, radar observation showed the ring particles to be large chunks of material averaging a meter on a side.

The rings cannot be seen except in a telescope of at least 3-inch aperture. Because of Saturn's inclination, as stated above, there are two periods during Saturn's journey around the sun when the rings are presented to us edge-on. At these times, the rings disappear. Nothing that is only 10 miles wide can be seen from a distance of nearly 900 million miles. The rings are receding from a favorable position to be seen. They were edge-on in 1966 and reached maximum visibility again in 1973.

Pioneer 11 was guided to pass Jupiter in such a way that Jupiter will swing Pioneer 11 into an orbit that will bring it near Saturn in 1979. If the space craft is functioning adequately at that time, it will send us the photos and physical data possible only from a close fly-by. This will complete man's initial on-site inspection of the classical planets.

Greenwich Sidereal Time for 0^h GMT, 1978

(Equivalent to Right Ascension of Mean Sun)

Date	h	m	Date	h	m	Date	h	m	Date	h	m	Date	h	m	Date	h	m
Jan. 1	12	41.2	Mar. 2	22	37.7	May 1	2	34.3	July 10	7	10.3	Sept. 8	11	06.8	Nov. 7	15	03.4
11	19	20.6	12	23	17.1	11	3	13.7	20	7	49.7	18	11	46.2	17	15	42.8
21	20	00.0	22	23	56.6	21	3	53.1	30	8	29.1	28	12	25.7	27	16	22.2
31	20	39.4	Apr. 1	0	36.0	31	4	32.6	Aug. 9	9	08.5	Oct. 8	13	05.1	Dec. 7	17	01.6
Feb. 10	21	18.9	11	1	15.4	June 10	5	12.0	19	9	48.0	18	13	44.5	17	17	41.1
20	21	58.3	21	1	54.8	20	5	51.4	29	10	27.4	28	14	23.9	27	18	20.5
						30	6	30.8									

Planetary Configurations, 1978

Greenwich Mean Time (0 designates midnight; 12 designates noon)

Date		h.	m.		
Jan.	1	23	-		⊕ at perihelion
	7	13	-	☌☿☽	☿ 3° S
	11	09	-		☿ gr. elong. W (23°)
	19	03	-		♂ nearest ⊕
	19	19	-	☌*☽	Aldebaran 1° S; occultation
	20	12	-	☌♄*	♄ 1°.1 N of Regulus
	21	07	-	☌♃☽	♃ 5° N
	22	00	-	☍♂☉	
	22	05	-	☌♀☉	superior
	24	06	-	☌♂☽	♂ 9° N
	26	12	-	☌♄☽	♄ 5° N
Feb.	16	02	-	☌*☽	Aldebaran 0°.9 S; occultation
	16	04	-	☍♄☉	
	17	06	-	☌♂*	♂ 3° S of Pollux
	17	11	-	☌♃☽	♃ 5° N
	19	20	-	☌♂☽	♂ 9° N
	20	02	-		♃ stationary
	22	14	-	☌♄☽	♄ 5° N
	27	03	-	☌☿☉	superior
Mar.	2	21	-		♂ stationary
	10	01	-	☌♀☽	♀ 2° S
	12	22	-	☌♀☿	☿ 1°.3 N
	15	10	-	☌*☽	Aldebaran 1°.3 S; occultation
	16	21	-	☌♃☽	♃ 5° N
	17	05	-	☌♂*	♂ 4° S of Pollux
	19	06	-	☌♂☽	♂ 8° N
	20	23	34		**Vernal Equinox; Spring begins**
	21	19	-	☌♄☽	♄ 5° N
	24	16	-	☍☽☉	Total lunar eclipse
	24	17	-		☿ gr. elong. E (19°)
	28	19	-	☌☿♀	☿ 4° N
Apr.	7	15	-	☌☽☉	Partial solar eclipse
	9	03	-	☌♀☽	♀ 3° N
	11	17	-	☌☿☉	Inferior
	11	18	-	☌*☽	Aldebaran 0°.8 S; occultation
	13	11	-	☌♃☽	♃ 5° N
	16	07	-	☌♂☽	♂ 7° N
	18	02	-	☌♄☽	♄ 5° N
	25	19	-		♄ stationary
May	5	02	-	☌☿☽	☿ 2° S
	9	02	-	☌*☽	Aldebaran 0°.9 S; occultation
	9	11	-	☌♀☽	♀ 6° N
	9	15	-		☿ gr. elong. W (26°)
	11	05	-	☌♃☽	♃ 5° N
	14	15	-	☌♂☽	♂ 6° N
	15	11	-	☌♄☽	♄ 5° N
	29	02	-	☌♀♃	♀ 1°.6 N
June	5	00	-	☌♂♄	♂ 0°.1 S
	8	00	-	☌♃☽	♃ 5° N
	8	23	-	☌♀☽	♀ 7° N
	11	00	-	☌♀*	♀ 5° S of Pollux
	11	21	-	☌♄☽	♄ 5° N
	12	03	-	☌♂☽	♂ 4° N
	12	17	-	☌♂*	♂ 0°.8 N of Regulus
	14	12	-	☌☿☉	superior
	21	18	10		**Summer Solstice; Summer begins**
	24	08	-	☌☿♃	☿ 1°.8 N
	29	10	-	☌☿*	☿ 5° S of Pollux
July	2	15	-	☌*☽	Aldebaran 0°.8 S; occultation
	5	00	-		⊕ at aphelion
	7	14	-	☌☿☽	☿ 5° N
	9	05	-	☌♀☽	♀ 4° N
	9	08	-	☌♄☽	♄ 4° N
	10	11	-	☌♃☉	
	10	12	-	☌♀♄	♀ 0°.1 N
	10	16	-	☌♂☽	♂ 2° N
	11	08	-	☌♀*	♀ 1°.1 N of Regulus
	19	06	-	☌♄*	♄ 1°.0 N of Regulus
	22	00	-		☿ gr. elong. E (27°)
	28	02	-	☌☿*	☿ 3° S of Regulus
	29	20	-	☌*☽	Aldebaran 0°.7 S; occultation
	31	22	-	☌☿♄	☿ 5° S
Aug.	2	14	-	☌♃☽	♃ 5° N
	4	05	-	☌☿♄	☿ 5° S
	5	19	-	☌☿☽	☿ 2° S
	5	20	-	☌♄☽	♄ 4° N
	7	14	-	☌♃*	♃ 7° S of Pollux
	8	01	-	☌♀☽	♀ 0°.4 S; occultation
	8	06	-	☌♂☽	♂ 0°.004 N; occultation
	10	22	-	☌☿*	☿ 5° S of Regulus
	14	15	-	☌♀♂	♀ 1°.2 S
	18	20	-	☌☿☉	inferior
	26	03	-	☌*☽	Aldebaran 0°.5 S; occultation
	27	15	-	☌♄☉	
	29	20	-		♀ gr. elong. E (46°)
	30	08	-	☌♃☽	♃ 5° N
	31	09	-	☌♀*	♀ 0°.3 S of Spica
Sept.	1	05	-	☌☿☽	☿ 2° N
	4	21	-		☿ gr. elong. W (18°)
	5	21	-	☌♂☽	♂ 2° S
	6	10	-	☌♀☽	♀ 6° S
	8	21	-	☌♂*	♂ 2° N of Spica
	9	08	-	☌☿*	☿ 0°.5 N of Regulus
	13	15	-	☌☿♄	☿ 0°.1 N
	16	19	-	☍☽☉	Total Lunar Eclipse
	22	11	-	☌*☽	Aldebaran 0°.4 S; occultation
	23	09	26		**Autumnal Equinox; Autumn begins**
	27	02	-	☌♃☽	♃ 5° N
	29	23	-	☌♄☽	♄ 3° N
	30	15	-	☌☿☉	superior
Oct.	2	07	-	☌☽☉	Partial solar eclipse
	3	22	-		♀ gr. brilliancy
	4	14	-	☌♂☽	♂ 4° S
	5	04	-	☌♀☽	♀ 10° S
	19	20	-	☌*☽	Aldebaran 0°.5 S; occultation
	20	08	-	☌♀♂	♀ 7° S
	24	17	-	☌♃☽	♃ 4° N
	27	04	-	☌☿♀	☿ 5° N
	27	13	-	☌♄☽	♄ 3° N
Nov.	2	05	-	☌☿☽	☿ 7° S
	2	09	-	☌♂☽	♂ 5° S
	5	08	-	☌☿♂	☿ 1°.9 S
	7	21	-	☌♀☉	inferior
	10	06	-	☌☿*	☿ 2° N of Antares
	14	06	-	☌♂*	♂ 4° N of Antares
	16	02	-		☿ gr. elong. E (23°)
	16	05	-	☌*☽	Aldebaran 0°.6 S; occultation
	21	05	-	☌♃☽	♃ 4° N
	24	01	-	☌♄☽	♄ 3° N
	26	03	-		♃ stationary
	28	03	-	☌♀☽	♀ 3° S
	29	19	-	☌☿♂	☿ 0°.1 N
Dec.	5	21	-	☌☿☉	inferior
	13	12	-	☌*☽	Aldebaran 0°.6 S; occultation
	14	05	-		♀ gr. brilliancy
	18	10	-	☌♃☽	♃ 4° N
	21	11	-	☌♄☽	♄ 3° N
	22	05	21		**Winter Solstice; Winter begins**
	26	13	-	☌♀☽	♀ 0°.8 S; occultation
	28	06	-	☌☿☽	☿ 3° S

Planetary Configurations, 1979

As a service to those who wish to consult the planetary configurations for early 1979 in the preceding fall, The World Almanac publishes the configurations for January, February, March, and April, 1979.

Jan.	4	22	-		⊕ at perihelion
	18	06	-		♀ gr. elong. W (47°)
	20	12	-	☌♂☉	
	24	15	-	☍♃☉	
Feb.	9	06	-	☌☿☉	superior
Mar.	1	18	-	☍♄☉	
	8	01	-		☿ gr. elong. E (18)
	21	05	22		**Vernal Equinox; Spring begins**
	24	14	-	☌☿☉	inferior
Apr.	1	22	-	☌☿♂	☿ 3° N
	21	13	-		☿ gr. elong. W (27°)

Rising and Setting of Planets, 1978

Greenwich Mean Time (0 designates midnight)

Venus, 1978

Date	20° N. Latitude Rise	Set	30° N. Latitude Rise	Set	40° N. Latitude Rise	Set	50° N. Latitude Rise	Set	60° N. Latitude Rise	Set
Jan. 1	6:16	17:08	6:38	16:46	7:05	16:19	7:43	15:41	8:52	14:32
15	6:34	17:32	6:54	17:12	7:19	16:47	7:54	16:12	8:55	15:12
Feb. 1	6:49	18:01	7:04	17:46	7:23	17:26	7:50	17:00	8:33	16:17
15	6:54	18:23	7:04	18:13	7:17	18:01	7:34	17:44	8:00	17:17
Mar. 1	6:54	18:44	6:58	18:40	7:03	18:35	7:09	18:29	7:19	18:19
15	6:52	19:03	6:51	19:04	6:48	19:07	6:45	19:10	6:40	19:15
Apr. 1	6:50	19:26	6:41	19:35	6:30	19:46	6:14	20:02	5:50	20:26
15	6:52	19:46	6:37	20:01	6:19	20:20	5:53	20:46	5:11	21:28
May 1	7:00	20:12	6:40	20:32	6:14	20:58	5:38	21:34	4:34	22:38
15	7:13	20:35	6:50	20:58	6:21	21:27	5:38	22:10	4:18	23:30
June 1	7:36	20:58	7:12	21:21	6:43	21:50	6:00	22:33	4:39	23:55
15	7:56	21:10	7:36	21:31	7:10	21:57	6:32	22:34	5:26	23:40
July 1	8:18	21:15	8:03	21:31	7:43	21:50	7:18	22:15	6:32	23:11
15	8:34	21:12	8:24	21:22	8:12	21:35	7:54	21:52	7:27	22:19
Aug. 1	8:48	21:02	8:45	21:05	8:42	21:09	8:37	21:14	8:29	21:22
15	8:56	20:50	9:00	20:47	9:03	20:43	9:08	20:38	9:16	20:31
Sept. 1	9:02	20:32	9:12	20:21	9:24	20:09	9:41	19:52	10:08	19:26
15	9:01	20:13	9:17	19:57	9:36	19:38	10:02	19:11	10:46	18:28
Oct. 1	8:48	19:43	9:09	19:23	9:34	18:57	10:11	18:21	11:14	17:17
15	8:15	19:02	8:38	18:40	9:07	18:11	9:48	17:29	11:04	16:13
Nov. 1	6:50	17:44	7:11	17:23	7:37	16:56	8:14	16:19	9:20	15:13
15	5:17	16:29	5:33	16:13	5:52	15:53	6:19	15:27	7:03	14:43
Dec. 1	3:59	15:25	4:11	15:14	4:25	15:00	4:43	14:41	5:13	14:11
15	3:25	14:52	3:36	14:41	3:50	14:27	4:08	14:09	4:37	13:40

Mars, 1978

Date	20° N. Latitude Rise	Set	30° N. Latitude Rise	Set	40° N. Latitude Rise	Set	50° N. Latitude Rise	Set	60° N. Latitude Rise	Set
Jan. 1	19:33	8:45	19:13	9:05	18:47	9:30	18:11	10:06	17:07	11:10
15	18:16	7:34	17:54	7:55	17:26	8:23	16:46	9:03	15:34	10:16
Feb. 1	16:33	5:56	16:09	6:20	15:39	6:50	14:55	7:34	13:31	8:59
15	15:20	4:45	14:56	5:10	14:25	5:41	13:40	6:26	12:12	7:54
Mar. 1	14:19	3:44	13:55	4:08	13:25	4:38	12:40	5:23	11:14	6:50
15	13:30	2:52	13:06	3:15	12:37	3:45	11:54	4:28	10:32	5:49
Apr. 1	12:41	1:59	12:19	2:21	11:51	2:49	11:11	3:29	9:58	4:42
15	12:02	1:26	11:47	1:41	11:21	2:07	10:44	2:44	9:39	3:50
May 1	11:35	0:41	11:16	1:00	10:53	1:23	10:20	1:56	9:24	2:52
15	11:09	0:09	10:53	0:25	10:32	0:46	10:03	1:14	9:15	2:02
June 1	10:40	23:30	10:27	23:44	10:10	0:01	9:47	0:24	9:09	1:02
15	10:18	23:00	10:07	23:11	9:54	23:24	9:35	23:43	9:05	0:13
July 1	9:54	22:25	9:47	22:33	9:37	22:42	9:24	22:56	9:03	23:16
15	9:34	21:55	9:29	22:00	9:23	22:06	9:15	22:14	9:02	22:27
Aug. 1	9:11	21:19	9:10	21:20	9:08	21:22	9:06	21:24	9:02	21:28
15	8:53	20:51	8:55	20:49	8:57	20:47	9:00	20:44	9:04	20:39
Sept. 1	8:32	20:17	8:38	20:11	8:45	20:05	8:54	19:55	9:08	19:41
15	8:17	19:51	8:26	19:42	8:37	19:31	8:51	19:17	9:14	18:54
Oct. 1	8:01	19:24	8:13	19:11	8:29	18:56	8:49	18:35	9:22	18:03
15	7:49	19:02	8:04	18:46	8:23	18:28	8:49	18:02	9:31	17:20
Nov. 1	7:36	18:39	7:55	18:20	8:17	17:58	8:49	17:26	9:43	16:32
15	7:27	18:23	7:48	18:03	8:13	17:37	8:49	17:01	9:52	15:59
Dec. 1	7:18	18:09	7:39	17:47	8:07	17:19	8:46	16:40	9:56	15:30
15	7:09	17:59	7:31	17:37	7:59	17:09	8:39	16:29	9:51	15:17

Jupiter, 1978

Date	20° N. Latitude Rise	Set	30° N. Latitude Rise	Set	40° N. Latitude Rise	Set	50° N. Latitude Rise	Set	60° N. Latitude Rise	Set
Jan. 1	16:35	5:52	16:14	6:14	15:46	6:42	15:06	7:21	13:55	8:33
15	15:33	4:50	15:11	5:12	14:44	5:39	14:04	6:19	12:52	7:31
Feb. 1	14:20	3:37	13:58	3:59	13:30	4:26	17:51	5:06	11:39	6:18
15	13:22	2:40	13:01	3:02	12:33	3:29	11:53	4:09	10:41	5:21
Mar. 1	12:28	1:45	12:06	2:07	11:38	2:35	10:59	3:15	9:46	4:27
15	11:36	0:54	11:14	1:16	10:46	1:43	10:06	2:23	8:54	3:36
Apr. 1	10:36	23:54	10:14	0:16	9:47	0:44	9:06	1:24	7:53	2:37
15	9:49	23:07	9:27	23:29	9:00	23:57	8:19	0:37	7:06	1:51
May 1	8:58	22:16	8:36	22:38	8:08	23:06	7:28	23:46	6:15	0:59
15	8:14	21:32	7:53	21:54	7:25	22:22	6:45	23:02	5:32	0:15
June 1	7:23	20:40	7:01	21:02	6:34	21:29	5:54	22:09	4:42	23:21
15	6:41	19:58	6:20	20:19	5:53	20:46	5:14	21:25	4:03	22:36
July 1	5:54	19:09	5:33	19:30	5:07	19:57	4:28	20:35	3:20	21:44
15	5:13	18:27	4:53	18:48	4:27	19:14	3:49	19:51	2:43	21:58
Aug. 1	4:24	17:35	4:04	17:56	3:38	18:21	3:02	18:57	1:58	20:01
15	3:42	16:52	3:23	17:12	2:58	17:37	2:23	18:12	1:22	19:13
Sept. 1	2:51	15:59	2:32	16:18	2:08	16:42	1:35	16:42	0:37	18:18
15	2:08	15:14	1:49	15:32	1:26	15:55	0:54	16:28	23:58	17:24
Oct. 1	1:17	14:21	0:59	14:39	0:37	15:01	0:05	15:32	23:12	16:26
15	0:30	13:33	0:13	13:50	23:51	14:12	23:21	14:43	22:29	15:34
Nov. 1	23:31	12:32	23:14	12:49	22:53	13:11	22:23	13:41	21:33	14:30
15	22:39	11:40	22:23	11:57	22:02	12:18	21:32	12:48	20:43	13:37
Dec. 1	21:37	10:38	21:20	10:55	20:59	11:16	20:29	11:46	19:40	12:35
15	20:40	9:41	20:23	9:58	20:01	10:20	19:31	10:49	18:41	11:40

Saturn, 1978

Date	20° N. Latitude Rise	Set	30° N. Latitude Rise	Set	40° N. Latitude Rise	Set	50° N. Latitude Rise	Set	60° N. Latitude Rise	Set
Jan. 1	21:08	9:51	20:57	10:02	20:42	10:16	20:23	10:36	19:52	11:07
15	20:10	8:54	19:58	9:05	19:44	9:20	19:24	9:40	18:56	10:08
Feb. 1	18:58	7:43	18:46	7:55	18:31	8:10	18:10	8:31	17:37	9:04
15	17:58	6:44	17:46	6:57	17:30	7:12	17:09	7:34	16:35	8:08
Mar. 1	16:54	5:42	16:41	5:54	16:25	6:10	16:03	6:32	15:28	7:08
15	15:54	4:43	15:41	4:56	15:25	5:13	15:02	5:35	14:26	6:12
Apr. 1	14:44	3:33	14:30	3:47	14:14	4:03	13:50	4:26	13:13	5:04
15	13:47	2:37	13:33	2:50	13:16	3:07	12:53	3:30	12:15	4:08
May 1	12:44	1:34	12:30	1:47	12:13	2:04	11:50	2:27	11:12	3:05
15	11:50	0:40	11:37	0:53	11:20	1:10	10:57	1:33	10:20	2:10
June 1	10:47	23:36	10:34	23:49	10:18	0:05	9:55	0:28	9:18	1:04
15	9:56	22:44	9:44	22:57	9:28	23:12	9:06	23:35	8:30	0:10
July 1	9:00	21:46	8:47	21:58	8:32	22:13	8:11	22:34	7:37	23:08
15	8:11	20:55	7:59	21:07	7:45	21:22	7:24	21:42	6:52	22:15
Aug. 1	7:13	19:55	7:02	20:06	6:48	20:20	6:29	20:39	5:58	21:10
15	6:25	19:06	6:15	19:16	6:02	19:30	5:43	19:48	5:14	20:17
Sept. 1	5:28	18:06	5:18	18:16	5:06	18:28	4:49	18:45	4:22	19:12
15	4:40	17:16	4:31	17:26	4:19	17:37	4:03	17:53	3:38	18:19
Oct. 1	3:46	16:20	3:37	16:29	3:26	16:39	3:11	16:54	2:48	17:18
15	2:57	15:30	2:49	15:38	2:39	15:48	2:25	16:02	2:03	16:25
Nov. 1	1:58	14:28	1:50	14:36	1:40	14:46	1:27	15:00	1:06	15:20
15	1:07	13:37	1:00	13:44	0:51	13:53	0:38	14:06	0:18	14:26
Dec. 1	0:08	12:37	0:01	12:44	23:52	12:53	23:40	13:05	23:21	13:24
15	23:15	11:43	23:08	11:50	22:59	11:59	22:47	12:11	22:28	12:30

The Planets and the Solar System

Planet	Mean daily motion	Orbital velocity miles per sec.	Sidereal revolution days	Synodical revolution days	Dist. from sun in millions of mi. Max.	Min.	Dist. from Earth in millions of mi. Max.	Min.	Light at' perihelion	aphelion
Mercury	14732.420	29.75	87.9693	115.9	43.403	28.597	136	50	10.58	4.59
Venus	5767.668	21.76	224.7009	583.9	67.726	66.813	161	25	1.94	1.89
Earth	3548.192	18.51	365.2564	—	94.555	91.445	—	—	1.03	0.97
Mars	1886.519	14.99	686.9796	779.9	154.936	128.471	248	35	0.524	0.360
Jupiter	299.160	8.12	4332.1248	398.9	507.046	460.595	600	368	0.0408	0.0336
Saturn	119.713	5.99	10825.863	378.1	937.541	838.425	1031	745	0.01230	0.00984
Uranus	42.248	4.23	30676.15	369.7	1859.748	1699.331	1953	1606	0.00300	0.00250
Neptune	21.632	3.38	59911.13	367.5	2821.686	2760.386	2915	2667	0.00114	0.00109
Pluto	14.269	2.95	90824.2	366.7	4551.386	2756.427	4644	2663	0.00114	0.00042

Light at perihelion and aphelion is solar illumination in units of mean illumination at Earth.

Planet	Mean longitude of:* ascending node °	'	"	perihelion °	'	"	Inclination* of orbit to ecliptic °	'	"	Mean distance*	Eccentricity* of orbit	Mean longitude at the epoch* °	'	"
Mercury	48	04	24	77	07	01	7	00	15	0.387099	0.205630	140	21	38
Venus	76	29	02	131	15	54	3	23	40	0.723332	0.006783	53	33	00
Earth	-	-	-	102	33	59	-	-	-	1.000000	0.016718	189	59	26
Mars	49	23	23	335	39	31	1	50	59	1.523691	0.093385	151	57	50
Jupiter	100	12	56	14	06	30	1	18	20	5.202432	0.0479396	94	04	19
Saturn	113	29	27	94	24	11	2	29	12	9.578194	0.0575851	143	31	43
Uranus	74	00	01	168	51	55	0	46	17	19.17824	0.0480776	219	32	34
Neptune	131	32	51	59	34	17	1	46	19	29.96499	0.0111899	256	54	39
Pluto	109	53	12	223	08	54	17	08	13	39.54322	0.2493373	228	30	29

*Consistent for the standard Epoch: 1978 Apr. 2.0 Ephemeris Time

Sun and planets	Semi-diameter at unit distance "	at mean least dist. "	in miles mean s.d.	Volume ⊕=1.	Mass. ⊕=1.	Density ⊕=1.	Axial rotation d.	h.	m.	s.	Gravity at surface ⊕=1.	Reflecting power Pct.	Probable temperature °F.
Sun	15 59.63		432000	1300000.	332000.	0.26	24	16	48		27.9		+10,000
Mercury	3.34	5.45	1505	0.056	0.0543	0.68	59				0.38	0.07	+ 600
Venus	8.41	30.40	3805	0.910	0.8136	0.94	243	(R)			0.88	0.76	+ 100
Earth			3959	1.000	1.000	1.00		23	56	4	1.00	0.39	+ 50
Moon	2.44	932.58	1080	0.020	0.0120	0.60	27	7	43	12	0.16	0.07	+ 215
Mars	4.68	8.94	2070	0.150	0.1069	0.71		24	37	23	0.39	0.15	+ 0
Jupiter	1 35.19	22.60	43450	1312.	318.35	0.24		9	50		2.65	0.51	- 150
Saturn	1 18.95	9.24	35750	763.	95.3	0.12		10	14		1.17	0.50	- 250
Uranus	34.28	1.88	14750	53.	14.54	0.28		10	45	(R)	1.05	0.66	- 350
Neptune	36.56	1.26	15750	65.	17.2	0.26		15	48		1.23	0.62	400

The planet Pluto was located by C. W. Tombaugh of Lowell Observatory Mar. 13, 1930. Its mass is about 0.11 of the mass of the Earth. It rotates on its axis in 6 days 9 hours. Its average distance from the sun is 3,664,000,000 miles. On Apr. 5 at 11 hours, GMT, it is in opposition in Virgo at right ascension 13 hrs. 22 mins. 21 secs. and declination, North 10 degrees 24 minutes 34 seconds, west of Epsilon Virginis. Pluto will then have a magnitude of about 14. (R) Venus and Uranus are in retrograde motion, rotating in opposite direction from other planets.

Four Eclipses in 1978

Greenwich Mean Time

First Eclipse

A total eclipse of the moon, March 24. The beginning of the umbral phase is visible in the extreme northwestern part of North America, most of the Pacific Ocean, New Zealand, Australia, part of Antarctica, Asia except the western part, and most of the Indian Ocean. The end is visible in New Zealand, Australia, Asia, part of Antarctica, the western part of the Pacific Ocean, the Indian Ocean, Africa except the extreme western part, and Europe except the western part. The magnitude is 1.457.

Circumstances of the Eclipse

Moon enters penumbra.	March 24, 13:28.2
Moon enters umbra....	24, 14:32.8
Total eclipse begins....	24, 15:36.7
Middle of eclipse.......	24, 16:22.4
Total eclipse ends......	24, 17:08.0
Moon leaves umbra....	24, 18:12.0
Moon leaves penumbra.	24, 19:16.4

Second Eclipse

A partial eclipse of the sun, April 7. This partial solar eclipse is visible in the south Atlantic, extreme southern South America, South Africa, and part of the Antarctic. The greatest obscuration is visible from Antarctica where 78.8% of the solar dimension will be covered by the moon.

Circumstances of the Eclipse

Eclipse begins.........	April 7, 13:01.9
Greatest eclipse.......	7, 15:03.3
Eclipse ends..........	7, 17:04.4

Third Eclipse

A total eclipse of the moon, September 16. The beginning of the umbral phase is visible in New Zealand, Australia, part of Antarctica, the western half of the Pacific Ocean, Asia, the Indian Ocean, the eastern half of Africa, and the eastern half of Europe. The end of the umbral phase is visible in western Australia, part of Antarctica, the Indian Ocean, Asia except the northeastern part, Africa, Europe, the eastern part of Atlantic Ocean, and the extreme northeastern part of South America. The magnitude of this eclipse is 1.333.

Circumstances of the Eclipse

Moon enters penumbra.	Sept. 16, 16:20.8
Moon enters umbra....	16, 17:20.2
Total eclipse begins....	16, 18:24.4
Middle of eclipse.......	16, 19:04.2
Total eclipse ends......	16, 19:43.9
Moon leaves umbra....	16, 20:48.1
Moon leaves penumbra.	16, 21:47.7

Fourth Eclipse

A partial eclipse of the sun, October 2. This partial solar eclipse is visible over most of Scandanavia at dawn, all of Siberia, most of China, and in Taiwan and Japan. A maximum of 69.1% of the sun's diameter will be covered by the moon.

Circumstances of the Eclipse

Eclipse begins.........	Oct. 2, 04:30.9
Greatest eclipse.......	2, 06:27.9
Eclipse ends..........	2, 08:25.1

Morning and Evening Stars, 1978

Greenwich Mean Time

	Morning	Evening
Jan.	Mercury Venus (to Jan. 22) Mars (to Jan. 22) Saturn	Venus (from Jan. 22) Mars (from Jan. 22) Jupiter
Feb.	Mercury (to Feb. 27) Saturn (to Feb. 16)	Mercury (from Feb. 22) Venus Mars Jupiter Saturn (from Feb. 16)
Mar.		Mercury Venus Mars Jupiter Saturn
Apr.	Mercury (from Apr. 11)	Mercury (to Apr. 11) Venus Mars Jupiter Saturn
May	Mercury	Venus Mars Jupiter Saturn
June	Mercury (to June 14)	Mercury (from June 14) Venus Mars Jupiter Saturn
July	Jupiter (from July 10)	Mercury Venus Mars Jupiter (to July 10) Saturn
Aug.	Mercury (from Aug. 18) Jupiter Saturn (from Aug. 27)	Mercury (to Aug. 18) Venus Mars Saturn (to Aug. 27)
Sept.	Mercury (to Sept. 30) Jupiter Saturn	Mercury (from Sept. 30) Venus Mars
Oct.	Jupiter Saturn	Mercury Venus Mars
Nov.	Venus (from Nov. 7) Jupiter Saturn	Mercury Venus (to Nov. 7) Mars
Dec.	Mercury (from Dec. 5) Venus Jupiter Saturn	Mercury (to Dec. 5) Mars

Astronomical Constants; Speed of Light

The following astronomical constants were adopted in 1968, in accordance with the resolutions and recommendations of the International Astronomical Union (Hamburg 1964): Velocity of light, 299,792.5 kilometers per second, or about 186,282.3976 statute miles per second; solar parallax, 8″.794; constant of nutation, 9″.210; and constant of aberration, 20″.496.

Star Tables, 1978

These tables include stars of visual magnitude 2.5 and brighter. Co-ordinates are for the epoch Jan. 0.705, 1978. Where no parallax figures are given, the trigonometric parallax figure is smaller than the margin for error and the distance given is obtained by indirect methods. Stars of variable magnitude designated by V.

To find the time when star is on meridian, subtract R.A.M.S. of the sun table on page 759 from the star's right ascension, first adding 24h to the latter, if necessary. Mark this result P.M., if less than 12h; but if greater than 12, subtract 12h and mark the remainder A.M.

Star	Magnitude	Parallax "	Light yrs.	Right ascen. h. m.	Declination ° '
α Andromedae (Alpheratz)	2.06	0.02	90	0 07.2	+28 58
β Cassiopeiae	2.26	0.07	45	0 08.0	+59 02
α Phoenicis	2.39	0.04	93	0 25.2	-42 26
α Cassiopeiae (Schedir)	2.16	0.01	150	0 39.2	+56 25
β Ceti	1.02	0.06	57	0 45.5	-18 06
γ Cassiopeiae	2.13v	0.03	96	0 55.4	+60 36
β Andromedae	2.02	0.04	76	1 08.5	+35 30
α Eridani (Achernar)	0.51	0.02	118	1 36.9	-57 21
γ Andromedae	2.14		260	2 02.5	+42 13
α Arietis	2.00	0.04	76	2 05.9	+23 22
α Ursae Min. (Pole Star)	1.99v		680	2 10.0	+89 10
ο Ceti	2.00v	0.01	103	2 18.2	-3 05
β Persei (Algol)	2.06v	0.03	105	3 06.7	+40 52
α Persei	1.80	0.03	570	3 22.7	+49 47
α Tauri (Aldebaran)	0.86v	0.05	68	4 34.7	+16 28
β Orionis (Rigel)	0.14v		900	5 13.5	-8 14
α Aurigae (Capella)	0.05	0.07	45	5 15.1	+45 59
γ Orionis (Bellatrix)	1.64	0.03	470	5 24.0	+6 20
β Tauri (El Nath)	1.65	0.02	300	5 24.9	+28 35
δ Orionis	2.20v		1500	5 30.9	-0 19
ε Orionis	1.70		1600	5 35.1	-1 13
ζ Orionis	1.79	0.02	1600	5 39.6	-1 57
κ Orionis	2.06		2100	5 46.7	-9 41
α Orionis (Betelgeuse)	0.41v		520	5 54.0	+7 24
β Aurigae	1.86	0.04	88	5 57.9	+44 57
β Canis Majoris	1.96	0.01	750	6 21.7	-17 57
α Carinae (Canopus)	-0.72	0.02	98	6 23.5	-52 41
γ Geminorum	1.93	0.03	105	6 36.4	+16 25
α Canis Majoris (Sirius)	-1.42	0.38	8.7	6 44.2	-16 41
ε Canis Majoris	1.48		680	6 57.8	-28 56
δ Canis Majoris	1.85		2100	7 07.5	-26 21
η Canis Majoris	2.46		2700	7 23.2	-29 16
α Geminorum (Castor)	1.97	0.07	45	7 33.2	+31 56
α Canis Minoris (Procyon)	0.37	0.29	11.3	7 38.2	+5 17
β Geminorum (Pollux)	1.16	0.09	35	7 44.0	+28 05
ζ Puppis	2.23		2400	8 02.8	-39 56
γ Velorum	1.88		520	8 08.9	-47 16
ε Carinae	1.97		340	8 22.1	-59 26
δ Velorum	1.95	0.04	76	8 44.1	-54 38
γ Velorum	2.24	0.02	750	9 07.2	-43 21
β Carinae	1.67	0.04	86	9 13.0	-69 38
ι Carinae	2.25		750	9 16.5	-59 11
κ Velorum	2.45	0.01	470	9 21.4	-54 55
α Hydrae	1.98	0.02	94	9 26.5	-8 34
α Leonis (Regulus)	1.36	0.04	84	10 07.2	+12 05
γ Leonis	1.99	0.02	90	10 18.8	+19 57
β Ursae Majoris (Merak)	2.37	0.04	78	11 00.5	+56 30
α Ursae Majoris (Dubhe)	1.81	0.03	105	11 02.4	+61 52
β Leonis (Denebola)	2.14	0.08	43	11 47.9	+14 42
γ Ursae Majoris (Phecda)	2.44	0.02	90	11 52.7	+53 49
α Crucis	1.39		370	12 25.4	-62 59
γ Crucis	1.69		220	12 29.9	-56 59
γ Centauri	2.17		160	12 40.3	-48 50
β Crucis	1.28		490	12 46.4	-59 34
ε Ursae Majoris (Alioth)	1.79	0.01	68	12 53.1	+56 05
ζ Ursae Majoris (Mizar)	2.26	0.04	88	13 23.0	+55 02
α Virginis (Spica)	0.91v	0.02	220	13 24.0	-11 03
ε Centauri	2.33		570	13 38.5	-53 21
η Ursae Majoris (Alkaid)	1.87		210	13 46.7	+49 25
β Centauri	0.63	0.02	490	14 02.3	-60 16
θ Centauri	2.04	0.06	55	14 05.4	-36 16
α Bootis (Arcturus)	0.06	0.09	36	14 14.7	+19 18
η Centauri	2.39v		390	14 34.1	-42 04
α Centauri	0.01	0.75	4.4	14 38.1	-60 45
α Lupi	2.32		430	14 40.5	-47 18
ε Bootis	2.37	0.01	103	14 44.0	+27 10
β Ursae Minoris	2.04	0.03	105	14 50.8	+74 15
α Coronae Borealis	2.23v	0.04	76	15 33.8	+26 47
δ Scorpii	2.34		590	15 59.0	-22 34
α Scorpii (Antares)	0.92v	0.02	520	16 28.1	-26 23
α Trianguli Australis	1.93	0.02	82	16 46.3	-68 59
ε Scorpii	2.28	0.05	66	16 48.7	-34 15
η Ophiuchi	2.46	0.05	69	17 09.1	-15 42
λ Scorpii	1.60		310	17 32.1	-37 05
α Ophiuchi	2.09	0.06	58	17 33.9	+12 34
θ Scorpii	1.86	0.02	650	17 35.7	-42 59
κ Scorpii	2.39		470	17 41.0	-39 01
γ Draconis	2.21	0.02	108	17 56.1	+51 29
ε Sagittarii	1.81	0.02	124	18 22.7	-34 24
α Lyrae (Vega)	0.04	0.12	26.5	18 36.2	+38 46
σ Sagittarii	2.12		300	18 53.9	-26 20
α Aquilae (Altair)	0.77	0.20	16.5	19 49.7	+8 49
γ Cygni	2.22		750	20 21.4	+40 11
α Pavonis	1.95		310	20 23.9	-56 48
α Cygni (Deneb)	1.26		1600	20 40.7	+45 12
ε Cygni	2.46	0.04	75	20 45.3	+33 53
α Cephei	2.44	0.06	52	21 18.1	+62 30
ε Pegasi	2.31		780	21 43.1	+9 46
α Gruis	1.76	0.05	64	22 0.69	-47 04
β Gruis	2.17v		280	22 41.4	-47 00
α Piscis Austrinis (Fomalhaut)	1.19	0.14	22.6	22 56.4	-29 44
β Pegasi	2.50v	0.02	210	23 02.7	+27 58
α Pegasi	2.50	0.03	109	23 03.7	+15 05

Aurora Borealis and Aurora Australis

The Aurora Borealis, also called the Northern Lights, is a broad display of rather faint light in the northern skies at night. The Aurora Australis, a similar phenomenon, appears at the same time in southern skies. The aurora appears in a wide variety of forms. Sometimes it is seen as a quiet glow, almost foglike in character; sometimes as vertical streamers in which there may be considerable motion; sometimes as a series of luminous expanding arcs. There are many colors, with white, yellow, and red predominating.

The auroras are most vivid and most frequently seen at about 20 degrees from the magnetic poles, along the northern coast of the North American continent and the eastern part of the northern coast of Europe. They have been seen as far south as Key West and as far north as Australia and New Zealand, but such occasions are rare.

While the cause of the auroras is not known beyond question, there does seem to be a definite correlation between auroral displays and sun-spot activity. It is thought that atomic particles expelled from the sun by the forces that cause solar flares speed through space at velocities of 400 to 600 miles per second. These particles are entrapped by the earth's magnetic field, forming what are termed the Van Allen belts. The encounter of these clouds of the solar wind with the earth's magnetic field weakens the field so that previously trapped particles are allowed to impact the upper atmosphere. The collisions between solar and terrestrial atoms result in the glow in the upper atmosphere called the aurora. The glow may be vivid where the lines of magnetic force converge near the magnetic poles.

The auroral displays appear at heights ranging from 50 to about 600 miles and have given us a means of estimating the extent of the earth's atmosphere.

The auroras are often accompanied by magnetic storms whose forces, also guided by the lines of force of the earth's magnetic field, disrupt electrical communication.

Comet Table 1978-1986

Name	Year of first known perihelion	Due to return		Period in years	Peri-helion dist.	Aphe-lion dist.	Inclina-tion to ecliptic degree	Long. of ascend. node degree	From asc. node to perihelion degree
Temple I	1867	Jan.	1978	5.50	1.50	4.74	10	68	179
Arend-Rigaux	1950	Jan.	1978	6.84	1.44	5.76	18	122	329
Temple II	1873	Jan.	1978	5.26	1.36	4.68	12	119	191
Wolf-Harrington	1924	Feb.	1978	6.55	1.62	5.38	18	254	187
Whipple	1933	Mar.	1978	7.47	2.48	5.16	10	188	190
DeVico-Swift	1844	Mar.	1978	6.31	1.62	5.20	4	24	325
Tsuchinshan I	1965	Apr.	1978	6.64	1.49	5.57	10	96	23
Comas-Sola	1927	Apr.	1978	8.55	1.77	6.60	13	63	40
Daniel	1909	May	1978	7.09	1.66	5.72	20	68	11
Ashbrook-Jackson	1948	July	1978	7.43	2.28	5.33	12	2	349
Tsuchinshan II	1965	Aug.	1978	6.80	1.78	5.40	7	288	203
Clark*	1969	Dec.	1978	5.52	1.56	4.68	10	59	209
Van Biesbroeck	1954	Dec.	1978	12.41	2.41	8.30	7	149	134
Tuttle-Giacobini-Kresak	1858	Dec.	1978	5.56	1.15	5.13	14	105	39
Jackson-Neujmin	1936	Dec.	1978	8.39	1.42	6.83	14	163	196
Shajn-Schaldach	1949	Jan.	1979	7.27	2.23	5.27	6	167	215
Giacobini-Zinner	1900	Jan.	1979	6.52	0.99	5.98	32	195	172
Holmes	1892	Jan.	1979	7.05	2.16	5.20	19	328	23
Honda-Mrkos-Pajdusakova	1969	Mar.	1980	5.28	0.58	5.48	13	233	185
Wirtanen	1947	Apr.	1980	5.84	1.26	5.25	12	84	35
Kohoutek*	1975	Aug.	1980	5.67	1.56	4.80	5	274	169
Forbes	1929	Sept.	1980	6.40	1.53	5.36	5	25	260
Brooks II	1889	Oct.	1980	6.88	1.84	5.39	6	176	198
Harrington	1953	Oct.	1980	6.80	1.58	5.59	9	119	233
Reinmuth I	1928	Nov.	1980	7.63	2.00	5.75	8	121	9
Encke	1786	Dec.	1980	3.30	0.34	4.02	12	334	186
Tuttle	1790	Jan.	1981	13.77	1.02	10.47	54	270	207
Reinmuth II	1947	Jan.	1981	6.74	1.94	5.20	7	296	45
Borrelly	1905	Jan.	1981	6.76	1.32	5.84	30	75	353
Halley	240 B.C.	May	1986	76.1	0.59	35.3	162	58	112

*One appearance only.

Most of the comets in the table will not be seen except by professional astronomers or by well-equipped amateurs. At any given time, these observers may be able to follow about a half dozen comets of which the public is unaware. An easily seen comet is rare, one or two every ten to fifteen years.

Comets are named for their discoverers, up to three independent observers being so honored. If a comet becomes unusual, it may be well-known by these names. Usually, however, a preliminary designation is used: the year followed by a letter of the alphabet assigned in the order of discovery during that year. About two years later, after any likely late discoveries, comets are given their permanent designation which states the year of their perihelion passage and a Roman numeral giving the order of passage during that year. Well-known periodic comets receive these designations at each appearance, but the literature and the Comet Table will continue to identify them by their discoverers' names.

Largest Telescopes Are in Northern Hemisphere

Most of the world's major astronomical installations are in the northern hemisphere, while many of astronomy's major problems are found in the southern sky. This imbalance has long been recognized and is being remedied.

In the northern hemisphere the largest reflector is the 236-inch mirror at the Special Astrophysical Observatory in the Caucasus in the Soviet Union. The largest reflectors in the U.S. include 3 in California: at Palomar Mtn., 200 inches; at Lick Observatory, Mt. Hamilton, 120 inches; and at Mt. Wilson Observatory, 100 inches. Also in the U.S. are a 158 inch reflector at Kitt Peak, Arizona, dedicated in June 1973, and a 107-inch telescope at the McDonald Observatory on Mt. Locke in Texas. A telescope at the Crimean Astrophysical Observatory in the Soviet Union has a 104-inch mirror.

Placed in service in 1975 were three large reflectors for the southern hemisphere. Associated Universities for Research in Astronomy (AURA), the operating organization of Kitt Peak National Observatory, dedicated the 158-inch reflector (twin of the telescope on Kitt Peak) at Cerro Tololo International Observatory, Chile; the European Southern Observatory has a 141-inch reflector at La Silla, Chile; and the Anglo-Australian telescope, 152 inches in diameter, is at Siding Spring Observatory in Australia.

Optical Telescopes

Optical astronomical telescopes are of two kinds, refracting and reflecting. In the first, light passes through a lens which brings the light rays into focus, where the image may be examined after being magnified by a second lens, the eye-piece, or directly photographed.

The reflector consists of a concave parabolic mirror, generally of Pyrex or now of a relatively heat insensitive material, cervit, coated with silver or aluminum, which reflects the light rays back toward the upper end of the telescope, where they are either magnified and observed by the eye-piece or, as in the case of the refractors, photographed. In most reflecting telescopes, the light is reflected again by a secondary mirror and comes to a focus after passing through a hole in the side of the telescope, where the eye-piece or camera is located, or after passing through a hole in the center of the primary mirror.

World's Largest Refractors

Location and diameter in inches

Yerkes Obs., Williams Bay, Wis.	40
Lick Obs., Mt. Hamilton, Cal.	36
Astrophys. Obs., Potsdam, E. Germany	32
Paris Observatory, Meuden, France	32
Allegheny Obs., Pittsburgh, Pa.	30
Univ. of Paris, Nice, France	30
Royal Greenwich Obs., Herstmonceux, England	28
Union Obs., Johannesburg, South Africa	26.5
Universitats-Sternwarte, Vienna, Austria	26.5
University of Virginia	26
Obs., Academy of Sciences, Pulkova, USSR	26
Astronomical Obs., Belgrade, Yugoslavia	26
Leander McCormick Obs., Charlottesville, Va.	26
Obs. Mitaka, Tokyo-to, Japan	26
US Naval Obs., Washington, D.C.	26
Mt. Stromlo Obs., Canberra, Australia	26

World's Largest Reflectors

Special Astrophysical Obs., Zelenchukskaya, USSR	236
Hale Obs., Palomar Mtn., Cal.	200, 100, 60
Kitt Peak National Obs., Tucson, Ariz.	158, 84, 60
Cerro Tololo, Chile	158, 60
Siding Spring, Australia	153
La Silla, Chile	141, 60
Lick Obs., Mt. Hamilton, Cal.	120
McDonald Obs., Fort Davis, Tex.	107, 82
Crimean Astrophys. Obs., Nauchny, USSR	104
Byurakan Obs., Armenia S.S.R.	102
Royal Greenwich Obs., Herstmonceux, England	98
Steward Obs., Tucson, Ariz.	90
Mauna Kea Obs., Univ. of Hawaii, Ha.	88, 84
Shemakha Astroph. Obs., Azerbaijan S.S.R.	79
Saint Michel l'Observatoire, (Basses Alpes), Fr.	77
Haute Provence, France	76, 60
Tokyo Obs., Japan	74
Mt. Stromlo, Australia	74
David Dunlap Obs., Ont., Canada	74
Helwan Obs., Helwan, Egypt	74
Astrophys. Obs., Kamogata, Okayama-ken, Japan	74
Sutherland, South Africa	74
Dominion Astrophys. Obs., Victoria, B.C.	73
Perkins Obs., Flagstaff, Ariz.	72
Obs., Padua Univ., Asiago, Italy	72
Agassiz Station Harvard Obs., Cambridge, Mass.	61
National Obs., Bosque Alegre Sta., Argentina	61
U.S. Naval Obs., Flagstaff, Ariz.	61
Catalina Mtn., Ariz.	61
Arizona Univ. Obs., Tucson, Ariz.	60
Boyden Obs., Bloemfontein, South Africa	60
Mt. Haleakala, Ha.	60
Mt. Hopkins (SAO), Ariz.	60
Figl Astroph. Obs., Vienna, Austria	60
Mt. Wilson Obs., Pasadena, Cal.	60

Major U.S. Planetariums

Academy Planetarium, U.S. Air Force Academy.
Adler Planetarium, Chicago, Ill.
American Museum-Hayden Planetarium, N.Y.C.
Buhl Planetarium, Pittsburgh, Pa.
Charles Hayden Planetarium, Boston, Mass.
Einstein Spacearium, Washington, D.C.
Fels Planetarium, Philadelphia, Pa.
Fernbank Science Center Planetarium, Atlanta, Ga.
Griffith Planetarium, Los Angeles, Cal.
La. Arts and Science Planetarium, Baton Rouge, La.
McDonnell Planetarium, St. Louis, Mo.
Morehead Planetarium, Chapel Hill, N.C.
Morrison Planetarium, San Francisco, Cal.
Robert T. Longway Planetarium, Flint, Mich.
Strassenburgh Planetarium, Rochester, N.Y.

The Sun

The sun, the controlling body of our solar system, is a star whose dimensions cause it to be classified among stars as average in size, temperature, and brightness. Its proximity to the earth makes it appear to us as tremendously large and bright. A series of thermo-nuclear reactions involving the atoms of the elements of which it is composed produces the heat and light that make life possible on the earth.

The sun has a diameter of 864,000 miles and is distant, on the average, 92,900,000 miles from the earth. It is 1.41 times as dense as water. The light of the sun reaches the earth in 499.012 seconds or slightly more than 8 minutes. The average solar surface temperature has been measured by several indirect methods which agree closely on a value of 6,000° Kelvin or about 10,000° F. The interior temperature of the sun is about 35,000,000 F.°.

When sunlight is analyzed with a spectroscope, it is found to consist of a continuous spectrum composed of all the colors of the rainbow in order, crossed by many dark lines. The "absorption lines" are produced by gaseous materials in the atmosphere of the sun. More than 60 of the natural terrestrial elements have been identified in the sun, all in gaseous form because of the intense heat of the sun.

Spheres and Corona

The radiating surface of the sun is called the **photosphere**, and just above it is the **chromosphere**. The chromosphere is visible to the naked eye only at times of total solar eclipses, appearing then to be a pinkish-violet layer with occasional great prominences projecting above its general level. With proper instruments the chromosphere can be seen or photographed whenever the sun is visible without waiting for a total eclipse. Above the chromosphere is the **corona**, also visible to the naked eye only at times of total eclipse. Instruments also permit the brighter portions of the corona to be studied whenever conditions are favorable. The pearly light of the corona surges millions of miles from the sun. Iron, nickel, and calcium are believed to be principal contributors to the composition of the corona, all in a state of extreme attenuation and high ionization that indicates temperatures on the order of a million degrees Fahrenheit.

Sunspots

There is an intimate connection between sunspots and the corona. At times of low sunspot activity, the fine streamers of the corona will be much longer above the sun's equator than over the polar regions of the sun, while during high sunspot activity, the corona extends fairly evenly outward from all regions of the sun, but to a much greater distance in space. Sunspots are dark, irregularly-shaped regions whose diameters may reach tens of thousands of miles. The average life of a sunspot group is from two to three weeks, but there have been groups that have lasted for more than a year, being carried repeatedly around as the sun rotated upon its axis. The record for the duration of a sunspot is 18 months. Sunspots reach a low point every 11.3 years, with a peak of activity occurring irregularly between two successive minima.

The sun is 400,000 times as bright as the full moon and gives the earth 6 million times as much light as do all the other stars put together. Actually, most of the stars that can be easily seen on any clear night are brighter than the sun.

The Moon

The moon completes a circuit around the earth in a period whose mean or average duration is 27 days 7 hours 43.2 minutes. This is the moon's sidereal period. Because of the motion of the moon in common with the earth around the sun, the mean duration of the lunar month — the period from one new moon to the next new moon — is 29 days 12 hours 44.05 minutes. This is the moon's synodical period.

The mean distance of the moon from the earth according to the American Ephemeris is 238,857 miles. Because the orbit of the moon about the earth is not circular but elliptical, however, the maximum distance from the earth that the moon may reach is 252,710 miles and the least distance is 221,463 miles. All distances are from the center of one object to the center of the other.

The moon's diameter is 2,160 miles. If we deduct the radius of the moon, 1,080 miles, and the radius of the earth, 3,963 miles from the minimum distance or perigee, given above, we shall have for the nearest approach of the bodies' surfaces 216,420 miles.

The moon rotates on its axis in a period of time exactly equal to its sidereal revolution about the earth — 27.321666 days. The moon's revolution about the earth is irregular because of its elliptical orbit. The moon's rotation, however, is regular and this, together with the irregular revolution, produces what is called "libration in longitude" which permits us to see first farther around the east side and then farther around the west side of the moon. The moon's variation north or south of the ecliptic permits us to see farther over first one pole and then the other of the moon and this is "libration in latitude." These two libration effects permit us to see a total of about 60% of the moon's surface over a period of time. The hidden side of the moon was photographed in 1959 by the Soviet space vehicle Lunik III. Since then many excellent pictures of nearly all of the moon's surface have been transmitted to earth by Lunar Orbiters launched by the U.S.

The tides are caused mainly by the moon, because of its proximity to the earth. The ratio of the tide-raising power of the moon to that of the sun is 11 to 5.

Harvest Moon and Hunter's Moon

The Harvest Moon, the full moon nearest the Autumnal Equinox, ushers in a period of several successive days when the moon rises soon after sunset. This phenomenon gives farmers in temperate latitudes extra hours of light in which to harvest their crops before frost and winter come. The 1978 Harvest Moon falls on Sept. 16. Harvest moon in the south temperate latitudes falls on Mar. 24.

The next full moon after Harvest Moon is called the Hunter's Moon, accompanied by a similar phenomenon but less marked; — Oct. 16, northern hemisphere; Apr. 23, southern hemisphere.

Moon's Perigee and Apogee, 1978

Perigee

Day		Hour GMT	Hour EST	Day		Hour GMT	Hour EST
Jan.	8	12	07	July	19	21	16
Feb.	5	21	16	Aug.	17	06	01
Mar.	5	17	12	Sept.	14	10	05
Mar.	31	05	00	Oct.	11	16	11
Apr.	26	08	03	Nov.	5	12	07
May	24	05	00	Dec.	2	16	11
June	21	12	07	Dec.	30	22	17

Apogee

Day		Hour GMT	Hour EST	Day		Hour GMT	Hour EST
Jan.	21	02	21*	Aug.	2	03	22*
Feb.	17	18	13	Aug.	29	13	08
Mar.	17	14	09	Sept.	26	06	01
Apr.	14	10	05	Oct.	24	01	20*
May	12	04	23*	Nov.	20	22	17
June	8	18	15	Dec.	18	16	11
July	6	00	19*	Jan.	15	03	22

*Previous date.

The Zodiac

The sun's apparent yearly path among the stars is known as the **ecliptic.** The zone 16° wide, 8° on each side of the ecliptic, is known as the **zodiac.** Inside of this zone are the apparent paths of the sun, moon, earth, and major planets. Beginning at the point on the ecliptic which marks the position of the sun at the vernal equinox, and thence proceeding eastward, the zodiac is divided into twelve signs of 30° each, as shown herewith.

These signs are named from the twelve constellations of the zodiac with which the signs coincided in the time of the astronomer Hipparchus, about 2,000 years ago. Owing to the precession of the equinoxes; that is to say, to the retrograde motion of the equinoxes along the ecliptic, each sign in the zodiac has, in the course of 2,000 years, moved backward 30° into the constellation west of it; so that the sign Aries is now in the constellation Pisces, and so on. The vernal equinox will move from Pisces into Aquarius about the middle of the 26th century. The signs of the zodiac with their Latin and English names are as follows:

Spring	1.♈ Aries.	The Ram.
	2.♉ Taurus.	The Bull.
	3.♊ Gemini.	The Twins.
Summer	4.♋ Cancer.	The Crab.
	5.♌ Leo.	The Lion.
	6.♍ Virgo.	The Virgin.
Autumn	7.♎ Libra.	The Balance.
	8.♏ Scorpio.	The Scorpion.
	9.♐ Sagittarius.	The Archer.
Winter	10.♑ Capricorn.	The Goat.
	11.♒ Aquarius.	The Water Bearer.
	12.♓ Pisces.	The Fishes.

The Earth: Size, Computation of Time, Seasons

Size and Dimensions

The earth is the fifth largest planet and the third from the sun. Its mass is 6 sextillion, 588 quintillion short tons. Using the parameters of an ellipsoid adopted by the International Astronomical Union in 1964 and recognized by the International Union of Geodesy and Geophysics in 1967, the length of the equator is 24,901.55 miles, the length of a meridian is 24,859.82 miles, the equatorial diameter is 7,926.41 miles, and the area of this reference ellipsoid is approximately 196,938,800 square miles.

The earth is considered a solid, rigid mass with a dense core of magnetic, probably metallic material. The outer part of the core is probably liquid. Around the core is a thick shell or mantle of heavy crystalline rock which in turn is covered by a thin crust forming the solid granite and basalt base of the continents and ocean basins. Over broad areas of the earth's surface the crust has a thin cover of sedimentary rock such as sandstone, shale, and limestone formed by weathering of the earth's surface and deposition of sands, clays, and plant and animal remains.

The temperature in the earth increases about 1°F. with every 100 to 200 feet in depth, in the upper 100 kilometers of the earth, and the temperature near the core is believed to be near the melting point of the core materials under the conditions at that depth. The heat of the earth is believed to be derived from radioactivity in the rocks, pressures developed within the earth, and original heat (if the earth in fact was formed at high temperatures).

Atmosphere of the Earth

The earth's atmosphere is a blanket composed of nitrogen, oxygen, and argon, in amounts of about 78, 21, and 1% by volume. Also present in minute quantities are carbon dioxide, hydrogen, neon, helium, krypton, and xenon.

Water vapor displaces other gases and varies from nearly zero to about 4% by volume. The height of the **ozone** layer varies from approximately 12 to 21 miles above the earth. Traces exist as low as 6 miles and as high as 35 miles. Traces of methane have been found.

The atmosphere rests on the earth's surface with the weight equivalent to a layer of water 34 ft. deep. For about 300,000 ft. upward the gases remain in the proportions stated. Gravity holds the gases to the earth. The weight of the air compresses it at the bottom, so that the greatest density is at the earth's surface. Pressure, as well as density, decreases as height increases because the weight pressing upon any layer is always less than that pressing upon the layers below.

The temperature of the air drops with increased height, until the **tropopause** is reached. This may vary from 25,000 to 60,000 ft. The atmosphere below the tropopause is the **troposphere**; the atmosphere for about twenty miles above the tropopause is the **stratosphere,** where the temperature generally increases with height except at high latitudes in winter. A temperature maximum near the 30-mile level is called the **stratopause.** Above this boundary is the **mesosphere** where the temperature decreases with height to a minimum, the **mesopause,** at a height of 50 miles. Extending above the mesosphere to the outer fringes of the atmosphere is the **thermosphere,** a region where temperature increases with height to a value measured in thousands of degrees Fahrenheit. The lower portion of this region, extending from 50 to about 400 miles in altitude, is characterized by a high ion density, and is thus called the **ionosphere.** The outer region is called **exosphere;** this is the region where gas molecules traveling at high speed may escape into outer space, above 600 miles.

Latitude, Longitude

Position on the globe is measured by means of meridians and parallels. Meridians, which are imaginary lines drawn around the earth through the poles, determine **longitude.** The meridian running through Greenwich, England, is the **prime meridian of longitude,** and all others are either east or west. Parallels, which are imaginary circles parallel with the equator, determine **latitude.** The length of a degree of longitude varies as the cosine of the latitude. At the equator a degree is 69.171 statute miles; this is gradually reduced toward the poles. Value of a longitude degree at the poles is zero.

Latitude is reckoned by the number of degrees north or south of the equator, an imaginary circle on the earth's surface everywhere equidistant between the two poles. According to the IAU Ellipsoid of 1964, the length of a degree of latitude is 68.708 statute miles at the equator and varies slightly north and south because of the oblate form of the globe; at the poles it is 69.403 statute miles.

Computation of Time

The earth rotates on its axis and follows an elliptical orbit around the sun. The rotation makes the sun appear to move across the sky from East to West. It determines day and night and the complete rotation, in relation to the sun, is called the **apparent** or **true solar day.** This varies but an average determines the **mean solar day** of 24 hours.

The mean solar day is in universal use for civil purposes. It may be obtained from apparent solar time by correcting observations of the sun for the equation of time, but when high precision is required, the mean solar time is calculated from its relation to sidereal time. These relations are extremely complicated, but for most practical uses, they may be considered as follows:

Sidereal time is the measure of time defined by the diurnal motion of the vernal equinox, and is determined from observation of the meridian transits of stars. One complete rotation of the earth relative to the equinox is called the **sidereal day.** The **mean sidereal day** is 23 hours, 56 minutes, 4.091 seconds of mean solar time.

The **Calendar Year** begins at 12 o'clock precisely local clock time, on the night of Dec. 31-Jan. 1. The day and the calendar month also begin at midnight by the clock. The interval required for the earth to make one absolute revolution around the sun is a **sidereal year;** it consisted of 365 days, 6 hours, 9 minutes, and 9.5 seconds of mean solar time (approximately 24 hours per day) in 1900, and is increasing at the rate of 0.0001-second annually.

The **Tropical Year,** on which the return of the seasons depends, is the interval between two consecutive returns of the sun to the vernal equinox. The tropical year consisted of 365 days, 5 hours; 48 minutes, and 46 seconds in 1900. It is decreasing at the rate of 0.530 seconds per century.

In 1956 the unit of time interval was defined to be identical with the second of **Ephemeris Time,** 1/31,556,925.9747 of the tropical year for 1900 January 0d 12th hour E.T. A physical definition of the second based on a quantum transition of cesium (atomic second) was adopted in 1964. The atomic second is equal to 9,192,631,770 cycles of the emitted radiation. In 1967 this atomic second was adopted as the unit of time interval for the Intern'l System of Units.

The Zones and Seasons

The five zones of the earth's surface are torrid, lying between the Tropics of Cancer and Capricorn; North Temperate, between Cancer and the Arctic Circle; South Temperate, between Capricorn and the Antarctic Circle; the Frigid Zones, between the polar Circles and the Poles.

The inclination or tilt of the earth's axis with respect to the sun determines the seasons. These are commonly marked in the North Temperate Zone, where spring begins at the vernal equinox, summer at the summer solstice, autumn at the autumnal equinox and winter at the winter solstice.

In the South Temperate Zone, the seasons are reversed. Spring begins at the autumnal equinox, summer at the winter solstice, etc.

If the earth's axis were perpendicular to the plane of the earth's orbit around the sun there would be no change of seasons. Day and night would be of nearly constant length and there would be equable conditions of temperature. But the axis is tilted 23° 27′ away from a perpendicular to the orbit and only in March and September is the axis at right angles to the sun.

The points at which the sun crosses the equator are the equinoxes, when day and night are most nearly equal. The points at which the sun is at a maximum distance from the equator are the solstices. Days and nights are then most unequal.

In June the North Pole is tilted 23° 27′ toward the sun and the days in the northern hemisphere are longer than the nights, while the days in the southern hemisphere are shorter than the nights. In December the North Pole is tilted 23° 27′ away from the sun and the situation is reversed.

The Seasons in 1978

In 1978 the 4 seasons will begin as follows: add one hour to EST for Atlantic Time; subtract one hour for Central, two hours for Mountain, 3 hours for Pacific, 4 hours for Yukon, 5 hours for Alaska-Hawaii and six hours for Bering Time. Also shown in Greenwich Mean Time.

		Date	GMT	EST
Vernal Equinox	**Spring**	Mar. 20	23:34	18:34
Summer Solstice	**Summer**	June 21	18:10	13:10
Autumnal Equinox	**Autumn**	Sept. 23	09:26	04:26
Winter Solstice	**Winter**	Dec. 22	05:21	00:21

Poles of The Earth

Source: National Oceanic and Atmospheric Admn.

The geographic (rotation) poles, or points where the earth's axis of rotation cuts the surface, are not absolutely fixed in the body of the earth. The pole of rotation describes an irregular curve about its mean position.

Two periods have been detected in this motion: (1) an annual period due to seasonal changes in barometric pressure, load of ice and snow on the surface and to other phenomena of seasonal character; (2) a period of about 14 months due to the shape and constitution of the earth.

In addition there are small but as yet unpredictable irregularities. The whole motion is so small that the actual pole at any time remains within a circle of 30 or 40 feet in radius centered at the mean position of the pole.

The pole of rotation for the time being is of course the pole having a latitude of 90° and an indeterminate longitude.

Magnetic Poles

The **north magnetic pole** of the earth is that region where the magnetic force is vertically downward and the **south magnetic pole** that region where the magnetic force is vertically upward. A compass placed at the magnetic poles experiences no directive force.

There are slow changes in the distribution of the earth's magnetic field. These changes were at one time attributed in part to a periodic movement of the magnetic poles around the geographical poles, but later evidence refutes this theory and points, rather, to a slow migration of "disturbance" foci over the earth.

There appear shifts in position of the magnetic poles due to the changes in the earth's magnetic field. The center of the area designated as the north magnetic pole was estimated to be in about latitude 70.5° N and longitude 96° W in 1905; from recent nearby measurements and studies of the secular changes, the position in 1970 is estimated as latitude 76.2° N and longitude 101° W. Improved data rather than actual motion account for at least part of the change.

The position of the south magnetic pole in 1912 was near 71° S and longitude 150° E; the position in 1970 is estimated at latitude 66° S and longitude 139.1° E.

The direction of the horizontal components of the magnetic field at any point is known as magnetic north at that point, and the angle by which it deviates east or west of true north is known as the magnetic declination, or in the mariner's terminology, the **variation of the compass.**

A compass without error points in the direction of magnetic north. (In general this is *not* the direction of the magnetic north pole.) If one follows the direction indicated by the north end of the compass, he will travel along a rather irregular curve which eventually reaches the north magnetic pole (though not usually by a great-circle route). However, the action of the compass should not be thought of as due to any influence of the distant pole, but simply as an indication of the distribution of the earth's magnetism at the place of observation.

Rotation of The Earth

The speed of rotation of the earth about its axis has been found to be slightly variable. The variations may be classified as:

(A) **Secular.** Tidal friction acts as a brake on the rotation and causes a slow secular increase in the length of the day, about 1 millisecond per century.

(B) **Irregular.** The speed of rotation may increase for a number of years, about 5 to 10, and then start decreasing. The maximum difference from the mean in the length of the day during a century is about 5 milliseconds. The accumulated difference in time has amounted to approximately 44 seconds since 1900. The cause is probably motion in the interior of the earth.

(C) **Periodic.** Seasonal variations exist with periods of one year and six months. The cumulative effect is such that each year the earth is late about 30 milliseconds near June 1 and is ahead about 30 milliseconds near Oct. 1. The maximum seasonal variation in the length of the day is about 0.5 millisecond. It is believed that the principal cause of the annual variation is the seasonal change in the wind patterns of the Northern and Southern Hemispheres. The semiannual variation is due chiefly to tidal action of the sun, which distorts the shape of the earth slightly.

The secular and irregular variations were discovered by comparing time based on the rotation of the earth with time based on the orbital motion of the moon about the earth, and of the planets about the sun. The periodic variation was determined largely with the aid of quartz-crystal clocks. The introduction of the cesium-beam atomic clock in 1955 made it possible to determine in greater detail than before the nature of the irregular and periodic variations.

Astronomical Twilight—Meridian of Greenwich

Date 1978	20° Begin	20° End	30° Begin	30° End	40° Begin	40° End	50° Begin	50° End	60° Begin	60° End
	h m	h m	h m	h m	h m	h m	h m	h m	h m	h m
Jan. 1	5 16	6 50	5 30	6 35	5 45	6 21	6 00	6 07	6 18	5 49
11	5 19	6 56	5 33	6 43	5 46	6 30	6 00	6 17	6 15	6 01
21	5 21	7 01	5 32	6 51	5 43	6 40	5 55	6 30	6 06	6 18
Feb. 1	5 21	7 07	5 29	6 58	5 38	6 51	5 45	6 44	5 51	6 38
11	5 18	7 11	5 24	7 05	5 29	7 01	5 32	6 59	5 32	7 01
21	5 13	7 15	5 17	7 12	5 17	7 12	5 16	7 14	5 09	7 23
Mar. 1	5 08	7 18	5 08	7 19	5 06	7 21	4 59	7 29	4 44	7 45
11	5 00	7 21	4 58	7 24	4 50	7 32	4 38	7 46	4 12	8 12
21	4 52	7 24	4 45	7 32	4 33	7 44	4 14	8 04	3 37	8 43
Apr. 1	4 42	7 28	4 31	7 39	4 14	7 57	3 47	8 25	2 53	9 21
11	4 32	7 32	4 18	7 47	3 56	8 09	3 20	8 47	2 03	10 10
21	4 23	7 36	4 04	7 54	3 37	8 23	2 52	9 11	0 37	11 47
May 1	4 14	7 41	3 52	8 04	3 19	8 37	2 22	9 39		
11	4 08	7 46	3 41	8 13	3 03	8 53	1 49	10 09		
21	4 02	7 52	3 32	8 22	2 48	9 07	1 13	10 46		
June 1	3 58	7 58	3 26	8 30	2 36	9 20	0 21	11 52		
11	3 56	8 03	3 22	8 36	2 29	9 30				
21	3 57	8 06	3 22	8 40	2 28	9 35				
July 1	3 59	8 07	3 25	8 41	2 30	9 35				
11	4 03	8 06	3 30	8 39	2 40	9 30				
21	4 08	8 03	3 39	8 33	2 52	9 18	1 12	11 23		
Aug. 1	4 15	7 56	3 48	8 23	3 09	9 01	1 49	10 20		
11	4 20	7 50	3 56	8 13	3 22	8 46	2 21	9 46		
21	4 24	7 41	4 05	8 01	3 34	8 27	2 47	9 15		
Sept. 1	4 29	7 31	4 14	7 46	3 51	8 08	3 13	8 43	1 40	10 02
11	4 32	7 20	4 20	7 33	4 02	7 50	3 33	8 16	2 36	9 12
21	4 35	7 11	4 26	7 19	4 14	7 31	3 52	7 52	3 11	8 31
Oct. 1	4 38	7 02	4 33	7 05	4 25	7 13	4 10	7 28	3 41	7 54
11	4 40	6 53	4 40	6 53	4 35	6 58	4 26	7 05	4 07	7 23
21	4 43	6 47	4 45	6 44	4 45	6 43	4 41	6 46	4 32	6 55
Nov. 1	4 46	6 41	4 52	6 34	4 56	6 30	4 58	6 27	4 56	6 27
11	4 50	6 38	4 59	6 28	5 06	6 21	5 13	6 14	5 17	6 08
21	4 55	6 36	5 06	6 25	5 16	6 15	5 26	6 04	5 37	5 52
Dec. 1	5 00	6 37	5 13	6 24	5 25	6 11	5 38	5 58	5 53	5 42
11	5 06	6 40	5 20	6 26	5 34	6 12	5 48	5 57	6 06	5 38
21	5 11	6 45	5 25	6 30	5 39	6 16	5 55	6 00	6 15	5 40
31	5 15	6 50	5 30	6 35	5 44	6 21	6 00	6 06	6 18	5 48

Latitude, Longitude, and Altitude of North American Cities

Source: National Oceanic and Atmospheric Administration, U.S. Commerce Department for geographic positions.

Source for Canadian cities: Geodetic Survey of Canada, Dept. of Energy, Mines, and Resources.

Altitudes U.S. Geological Survey and various sources. *Approx. altitude at downtown business area U.S.; in Canada at tower of major airport.

City	Lat. N ° ′ ″	Long. W ° ′ ″	Alt. feet
Abilene, Tex.	32 27 05	99 43 51	1710
Akron, Oh.	41 05 00	81 30 44	874
Albany, N.Y.	42 39 01	73 45 01	20
Albuquerque, N.M.	35 05 01	106 39 05	4,945
Allentown, Pa.	40 36 11	75 28 06	255
Alert, N.W.T.	82 29 50	62 21 15	95
Altoona, Pa.	40 30 55	78 24 03	1,180
Amarillo, Tex.	35 12 27	101 50 04	3,685
Anchorage, Alas.	61 10 00	149 59 00	118
Ann Arbor, Mich.	42 16 59	83 44 52	880
Asheville, N.C.	35 35 42	82 33 26	1,985
Ashland, Ky.	38 28 36	82 38 23	536
Atlanta, Ga.	33 45 10	84 23 37	1,050
Atlantic City, N.J.	39 21 32	74 25 53	10
Augusta, Ga.	33 28 20	81 58 00	143
Augusta, Me.	44 18 53	69 46 29	45
Austin, Tex.	30 16 09	97 44 37	505
Bakersfield, Cal.	35 22 31	119 01 18	400
Baltimore, Md.	39 17 26	76 36 45	20
Bangor, Me.	44 48 13	68 46 18	20
Baton Rouge, La.	30 26 58	91 11 00	57
Battle Creek, Mich.	42 18 58	85 10 48	820
Bay City, Mich.	43 36 04	83 53 15	595
Beaumont, Tex.	30 05 20	94 06 09	20
Belleville, Ont.	44 09 30	77 22 30	280
Bellingham, Wash.	48 45 02	122 28 36	60
Berkeley, Cal.	37 52 10	122 16 17	40
Bethlehem, Pa.	40 37 16	75 22 34	235
Billings, Mon.	45 47 00	108 30 04	3,120
Biloxi, Miss.	30 23 48	88 53 00	20
Binghamton, N.Y.	42 06 03	75 54 47	865
Birmingham, Ala.	33 31 01	86 48 36	600
Bismarck, N.D.	46 48 23	100 47 17	1,674
Bloomington, Ill.	40 28 58	88 59 36	800
Boise, Ida.	43 37 07	116 11 58	2,704
Boston, Mass.	42 21 24	71 03 25	21
Bowling Green, Ky.	36 59 41	86 26 33	510
Brattleboro, Vt.	42 51 06	72 33 48	300
Brandon, Man.	49 51 00	99 57 00	1,265
Brantford, Ont.	43 07 30	80 15 30	705
Bridgeport, Conn.	41 10 49	73 11 22	10
Brockton, Mass.	42 05 02	71 01 25	130
Brownsville, Tex.	25 54 07	97 29 58	35
Buffalo, N.Y.	42 52 52	78 52 21	585
Burlington, Ont.	43 18 30	79 46 30	875
Burlington, Vt.	44 28 34	73 12 46	110
Butte, Mon.	46 01 06	112 32 11	5,765
Calgary, Alta.	51 02 46	114 03 24	3,557
Cambridge, Mass.	42 22 01	71 06 22	20
Camden, N.J.	39 56 41	75 07 14	30
Canton, Oh.	40 47 50	81 22 37	1,030
Carson City, Nev.	39 10 00	119 46 00	4,680
Cedar Rapids, Ia.	41 58 01	91 39 53	730
Central Islip, N.Y.	40 47 24	73 12 00	80
Champaign, Ill.	40 07 05	88 14 48	740
Charleston, S.C.	32 46 35	79 55 53	9
Charleston, W.Va.	38 21 01	81 37 52	601
Charlotte, N.C.	35 13 44	80 50 45	720
Charlottetown, P.E.I.	46 14 00	63 07 45	181
Chattanooga, Tenn.	35 02 41	85 18 32	675
Cheyenne, Wy.	41 08 09	104 49 07	6,100
Chicago, Ill.	41 52 28	87 38 22	595
Churchill, Man.	58 45 15	94 10 00	94
Cincinnati, Oh.	39 06 07	84 30 35	550
Cleveland, Oh.	41 29 51	81 41 50	660
Colorado Springs	38 50 07	104 49 16	5,980
Columbia, Mo.	38 57 03	92 19 46	730
Columbia, S.C.	34 00 02	81 02 00	190
Columbus, Ga.	32 28 07	84 59 24	265
Columbus, Oh.	39 57 47	83 00 17	780
Concord, N.H.	43 12 22	71 32 25	290
Corpus Christi, Tex.	27 47 51	97 23 45	35
Dallas, Tex.	32 47 09	96 47 37	435
Dartmouth, N.S.	44 38 39	63 34 34	476
Davenport, Ia.	41 31 19	90 34 33	590
Dawson, Yukon	64 03 30	139 26 00	1,211
Dayton, Oh.	39 45 32	84 11 43	574
Daytona Beach, Fla.	29 12 44	81 01 10	7
Decatur, Ill.	39 50 42	88 56 47	682
Denver, Col.	39 44 58	104 59 22	5,280
Des Moines, Ia.	41 35 14	93 37 00	805
Detroit, Mich.	42 19 48	83 02 57	585
Dodge City, Kan.	37 45 17	100 01 09	2,480
Dubuque, Ia.	42 29 55	90 40 08	620
Duluth, Minn.	46 46 56	92 06 24	610
Durham, N.C.	36 00 00	78 54 45	405
Eau Claire, Wis.	44 48 31	91 29 49	790

City	Lat. N ° ′ ″	Long. W ° ′ ″	Alt.* feet
Edmonton, Alta.	53 32 45	113 29 15	2,373
El Paso, Tex.	31 45 36	106 29 11	3,695
Elizabeth, N.J.	40 39 43	74 12 59	21
Enid, Okla.	36 23 40	97 52 35	1,240
Erie, Pa.	42 07 15	80 04 57	685
Eugene, Ore.	44 03 16	123 05 30	422
Eureka, Cal.	40 48 08	124 09 46	45
Evansville, Ind.	37 58 20	87 34 21	385
Fairbanks, Alas.	64 48 00	147 51 00	448
Fall River, Mass.	41 42 06	71 09 18	40
Fargo, N.D.	46 52 30	96 47 18	900
Flagstaff, Ariz.	35 11 36	111 39 06	6,900
Flint, Mich.	43 00 50	83 41 33	750
Ft. Smith, Ark.	35 23 10	94 25 36	440
Fort Wayne, Ind.	41 04 21	85 08 26	790
Fort Worth, Tex.	32 44 55	97 19 44	670
Fredericton, N.B.	45 57 40	66 38 30	67
Fresno, Cal.	36 44 12	119 47 11	285
Gadsden, Ala.	34 00 57	86 00 41	555
Gainesville, Fla.	29 38 56	82 19 19	175
Gallup, N.M.	35 31 30	108 44 30	6,540
Galveston, Tex.	29 18 10	94 47 43	5
Gary, Ind.	41 36 12	87 20 19	590
Grand Junction, Col.	39 04 06	108 33 54	4,590
Grand Rapids, Mich.	42 58 03	85 40 13	610
Great Falls, Mon.	47 29 33	111 18 23	3,340
Green Bay, Wis.	44 30 48	88 00 50	590
Greensboro, N.C.	36 04 17	79 47 25	839
Greenville, S.C.	34 50 50	82 24 01	966
Guelph, Ont.	43 32 30	80 15 30	1,075
Gulfport, Miss.	30 22 04	89 05 36	20
Halifax, N.S.	44 38 39	63 34 34	476
Hamilton, Ont.	43 15 17	79 52 28	776
Hamilton, Oh.	39 23 59	84 33 47	600
Harrisburg, Pa.	40 15 43	76 52 59	365
Hartford, Conn.	41 46 12	72 40 49	40
Helena, Mon.	46 35 33	112 02 24	4,155
Hilo, Hawaii	19 43 30	155 05 24	40
Holyoke, Mass.	42 12 29	72 36 36	115
Honolulu, Ha.	21 18 22	157 51 35	21
Houston, Tex.	29 45 26	95 21 37	40
Hull, Que.	45 26 00	75 44 00	225
Huntington, W.Va.	38 25 12	82 26 33	565
Huntsville, Ala.	34 44 18	86 35 19	640
Indianapolis, Ind.	39 46 07	86 09 46	710
Iowa City, Ia.	41 39 37	91 31 53	685
Jackson, Mich.	42 14 43	84 24 22	940
Jackson, Miss.	32 17 56	90 11 06	298
Jacksonville, Fla.	30 19 44	81 39 42	20
Jersey City, N.J.	40 43 50	74 03 56	20
Johnstown, Pa.	40 19 35	78 55 03	1,185
Joplin, Mo.	37 05 26	90 42 11	990
Juneau, Alas.	58 18 12	134 24 30	50
Kalamazoo, Mich.	42 17 29	85 35 14	755
Kansas City, Kan.	39 07 04	94 38 24	750
Kansas City, Mo.	39 04 56	94 35 20	750
Kenosha, Wis.	42 35 43	87 50 11	610
Key West, Fla.	24 33 30	81 48 12	5
Kingston, Ont.	44 13 30	76 30 00	310
Kitchener, Ont.	43 26 59	80 29 17	1,031
Knoxville, Tenn.	35 57 39	83 55 07	890
Lafayette, Ind.	40 25 11	86 53 39	550
Lancaster, Pa.	40 02 25	76 18 29	355
Lansing, Mich.	42 44 01	84 33 15	830
Laredo, Tex.	27 30 22	99 30 30	440
La Salle, Que.	45 25 30	73 38 30	100
Las Vegas, Nev.	36 10 20	115 08 37	2,030
Laval, Que.	45 35 30	73 45 30	100
Lawrence, Mass.	42 42 16	71 10 08	65
Lethbridge, Alta.	49 41 30	112 49 00	2,990
Lexington, Ky.	38 02 50	84 29 46	955
Lihue, Ha.	21 58 48	159 22 30	210
Lima, Oh.	40 44 35	84 06 20	865
Lincoln, Neb.	40 48 59	96 42 15	1,150
Little Rock, Ark.	34 44 42	92 16 37	286
London, Ont.	42 59 00	81 15 00	912
Long Beach, Cal.	33 46 14	118 11 18	35
Lorain, Oh.	41 28 05	82 10 49	610
Los Angeles, Cal.	34 03 15	118 14 28	340
Louisville, Ky.	38 14 47	85 45 49	450
Lowell, Mass.	42 38 25	71 19 14	100
Lubbock, Tex.	33 35 05	101 50 33	3,195
Macon, Ga.	32 50 12	83 37 36	335
Madison, Wis.	43 04 23	89 22 55	860

City	Lat. N ° ′ ″	Long. W ° ′ ″	Alt.* Feet
Manchester, N.H.	42 59 28	71 27 41	175
Marshall, Tex.	32 33 00	94 23 00	410
Memphis, Tenn.	35 08 46	90 03 13	275
Meriden, Conn.	41 32 06	72 47 30	190
Mexico City, Mexico	19 25 45	99 07 00	7,347
Miami, Fla.	25 46 37	80 11 32	10
Milwaukee, Wis.	43 02 19	87 54 15	635
Minneapolis, Minn.	44 58 57	93 15 43	815
Minot, N.D.	48 14 09	101 17 38	1,550
Mississauga, Ont.	43 33 00	79 35 00	260
Mobile, Ala.	30 41 36	88 02 33	5
Moline, Ill.	41 30 31	90 30 49	585
Moncton, N.B.	46 05 30	64 47 30	75
Montgomery, Ala.	32 22 33	86 18 31	160
Montpelier, Vt.	44 15 36	72 34 41	485
Montreal, Que.	45 30 30	73 33 20	117
Moose Jaw, Sask.	50 23 30	105 32 30	1,810
Muncie, Ind.	40 11 28	85 23 16	950
Nashville, Tenn.	36 09 33	86 46 55	450
Natchez, Miss.	31 33 48	91 23 30	210
Newark, N.J.	40 44 14	74 10 19	55
New Bedford, Mass.	41 38 13	70 55 41	15
New Britain, Conn.	41 40 08	72 46 59	200
New Haven, Conn.	41 18 25	72 55 30	40
New Orleans, La.	29 56 53	90 04 10	5
New York, N.Y.	40 45 06	73 59 39	55
Niagara Falls, N.Y.	43 05 34	79 03 26	570
Niagara Falls, Ont.	43 05 30	79 03 30	585
Nome, Alas.	64 30 00	165 25 00	25
Norfolk, Va.	36 51 10	76 17 21	10
North Bay, Ont.	46 18 30	79 27 30	925
Oakland, Cal.	37 48 03	122 15 54	25
Ogden, Ut.	41 13 31	111 58 21	4,295
Oklahoma City	35 28 26	97 31 04	1,195
Omaha, Neb.	41 15 42	95 56 14	1,040
Orlando, Fla.	28 32 42	81 22 38	70
Oshawa, Ont.	43 54 00	78 52 00	350
Ottawa, Ont.	45 25 40	75 42 45	374
Paducah, Ky.	37 05 13	88 35 56	345
Pasadena, Cal.	34 08 44	118 08 41	830
Paterson, N.J.	40 55 01	74 10 21	100
Pensacola, Fla.	30 24 51	87 12 56	15
Peoria, Ill.	40 41 42	89 35 33	470
Peterborough, Ont.	44 18 00	78 19 30	685
Philadelphia, Pa.	39 56 58	75 09 21	100
Phoenix, Ariz.	33 27 12	112 04 28	1,090
Pierre, S.D.	44 22 18	100 20 54	1,480
Pittsburgh, Pa.	40 26 19	80 00 00	745
Pittsfield, Mass.	42 26 53	73 15 14	1,015
Pocatello, Ida.	42 51 38	112 27 01	4,460
Port Arthur, Tex.	29 52 30	93 56 15	10
Portland, Me.	43 39 33	70 15 19	25
Portland, Ore.	45 31 06	122 40 35	77
Portsmouth, N.H.	43 04 30	70 45 24	20
Portsmouth, Va.	36 50 07	76 18 14	10
Prince Rupert, B.C.	54 19 00	130 19 00	125
Providence, R.I.	41 49 32	71 24 41	80
Provo, Ut.	40 14 06	111 39 24	4,550
Pueblo, Col.	38 16 17	104 36 33	4,690
Quebec City, Que.	46 48 46	71 12 20	239
Racine, Wis.	42 43 49	87 47 12	630
Rapid City, S.D.	44 04 52	103 13 11	3,230
Raleigh, N.C.	35 46 38	78 38 21	365
Reading, Pa.	40 20 09	75 55 40	265
Regina, Sask.	50 27 02	104 36 30	1,894
Reno, Nev.	39 31 27	119 48 40	4,490
Richmond, Va.	37 32 15	77 26 09	160
Roanoke, Va.	37 16 13	79 56 44	905
Rochester, Minn.	44 01 21	92 28 03	990
Rochester, N.Y.	43 09 41	77 36 21	515
Rockford, Ill.	42 16 07	89 05 48	715
Sacramento, Cal.	38 34 57	121 29 41	30
Saginaw, Mich.	43 25 52	83 56 05	595
St. Catharines, Ont.	43 09 30	79 14 30	362
Saint John, N.B.	45 16 00	66 04 30	80
St. Cloud, Minn.	45 34 00	94 10 24	1,040
St. John's, Nfld.	47 34 00	52 43 30	200
St. Joseph, Mo.	39 45 57	94 51 02	850
St. Louis, Mo.	38 37 45	90 12 22	455
St. Paul, Minn.	44 57 19	93 06 07	780
St. Petersburg, Fla.	27 46 18	82 38 19	20
Salem, Ore.	44 56 24	123 01 59	155

City	Lat. N ° ′ ″	Long. W ° ′ ″	Alt.* Feet
Salina, Kan.	38 50 36	97 36 46	1,229
Salt Lake City, Ut.	40 45 23	111 53 26	4,390
San Angelo, Tex.	31 27 39	100 26 03	1,845
San Antonio, Tex.	29 25 37	98 29 06	650
San Bernardino, Cal.	34 06 30	117 17 28	1,080
San Diego, Cal.	32 42 53	117 09 21	20
San Francisco, Cal.	37 46 39	122 24 40	65
San Jose, Cal.	37 20 16	121 53 24	90
San Juan, P.R.	18 27 00	66 04 15	35
Santa Barbara, Cal.	34 25 18	119 41 55	100
Santa Cruz, Cal.	36 58 18	122 01 18	20
Santa Fe, N.M.	35 41 11	105 56 10	6,950
Sarasota, Fla.	27 20 05	82 32 30	20
Saskatoon, Sask.	52 07 50	106 39 41	1,653
Sault Ste. Marie, Ont.	46 31 30	84 20 00	650
Savannah, Ga.	32 04 42	81 05 37	20
Schenectady, N.Y.	42 48 42	73 55 42	245
Scranton, Pa.	41 24 32	75 39 46	725
Seattle, Wash.	47 36 32	122 20 12	10
Sheboygan, Wis.	43 45 03	87 42 52	630
Sherbrooke, Que.	45 24 00	71 53 30	625
Sheridan, Wy.	44 47 55	106 57 10	3,740
Shreveport, La.	32 30 46	93 44 58	204
Sioux City, Ia.	42 29 46	96 24 30	1,110
Sioux Falls, S.D.	43 32 35	96 43 35	1,395
Somerville, Mass.	42 23 15	71 06 07	13
South Bend, Ind.	41 40 33	86 15 01	710
Spartanburg, S.C.	34 57 03	81 56 06	875
Spokane, Wash.	47 39 32	117 25 33	1,890
Springfield, Ill.	39 47 58	89 38 51	610
Springfield, Mass.	42 06 21	72 35 32	85
Springfield, Mo.	37 13 03	93 17 32	1,300
Springfield, Oh.	39 55 38	83 48 29	980
Stamford, Conn.	41 03 09	73 32 24	35
Steubenville, Oh.	40 21 42	80 36 53	660
Stockton, Cal.	37 57 30	121 17 16	20
Sudbury, Ont.	46 28 30	80 58 30	917
Superior, Wis.	46 43 14	92 06 07	630
Sydney, N.S.	46 08 30	60 11 00	50
Syracuse, N.Y.	43 03 04	76 09 14	400
Tacoma, Wash.	47 14 59	122 26 15	110
Tallahassee, Fla.	30 26 30	84 16 56	150
Tampa, Fla.	27 56 58	82 27 25	15
Terre Haute, Ind.	39 28 03	87 24 26	496
Texarkana, Tex.	33 25 48	94 02 30	324
Thunder Bay, Ont.	48 25 00	89 14 00	650
Toledo, Oh.	41 39 14	83 32 39	585
Topeka, Kan.	39 03 16	95 40 23	930
Toronto, Ont.	43 39 12	79 23 00	532
Trenton, N.J.	40 13 14	74 46 13	35
Trois-Rivieres, Que.	46 21 00	72 33 00	115
Troy, N.Y.	42 43 45	73 40 58	35
Tucson, Ariz.	32 13 15	110 58 08	2,390
Tulsa, Okla.	36 09 12	95 59 34	804
Urbana, Ill.	40 06 42	88 12 06	...
Utica, N.Y.	43 06 12	75 13 33	415
Vancouver, B.C.	49 16 30	123 07 30	388
Victoria, B.C.	48 25 40	123 21 45	...
Waco, Tex.	31 33 12	97 08 00	405
Walla Walla, Wash.	46 04 08	118 20 24	936
Washington, D.C.	38 53 51	77 00 33	25
Waterbury, Conn.	41 33 13	73 02 31	260
Waterloo, Ia.	42 29 40	92 20 20	850
West Palm Beach, Fla.	26 42 36	80 03 07	15
Wheeling W. Va.	40 04 03	80 43 20	650
Whitehorse, Yukon	60 43 15	135 03 15	2,305
White Plains, N.Y.	41 02 00	73 45 48	220
Wichita, Kan.	37 41 30	97 20 16	1,290
Wichita Falls, Tex.	33 54 34	98 29 28	945
Wilkes-Barre, Pa.	41 14 32	75 53 17	640
Wilmington, Del.	39 44 46	75 32 51	135
Wilmington, N.C.	34 14 14	77 56 58	35
Windsor, Ont.	42 19 50	83 03 00	590
Winnipeg, Man.	49 53 56	97 08 20	765
Winston-Salem, N.C.	36 05 52	80 14 42	860
Worcester, Mass.	42 15 37	71 48 17	475
Yakima, Wash.	46 36 09	120 30 39	1,060
Yellowknife, N.W.T.	62 28 15	114 22 00	674
Yonkers, N.Y.	40 55 55	73 53 54	10
York, Pa.	39 57 35	76 43 36	370
Youngstown, Oh.	41 05 57	80 39 02	840
Yuma, Ariz.	32 42 54	114 37 24	160
Zanesville, Oh.	39 56 18	82 00 30	720

World Cities

City	Lat.	Long.	Alt.
London, UK (Greenwich)	51 30 00N	0 0 0	245
Paris, France	48 50 14N	2 20 14E	300
Berlin, Germany	52 32 00N	13 25 00E	110
Rome, Italy	41 53 00N	12 30 00E	95
Warsaw, Poland	52 15 00N	21 00 00E	360
Moscow, USSR	55 45 00N	37 42 00E	394
Athens, Greece	37 58 00N	23 44 00E	300
Jerusalem, Israel	31 47 00N	35 13 00E	2,500
Johannesburg, So. Afr.	26 10 00S	28 02 00E	5,740
New Delhi, India	28 38 00N	77 12 00E	770
Peking, China	39 54 00N	116 28 00E	600
Rio de Janeiro, Brazil	22 53 43S	43 13 22W	30
Tokyo, Japan	35 45 00N	139 45 00E	30
Sydney, Australia	33 52 00S	151 12 00E	25

Calendar Adjustment Tables

The tables below will allow you to determine the approximate time of the rise or set of the sun and moon at your specific location. It will be necessary to consider only the latitude adjustment for the sun, but rise and set times of the moon for your location can be more than one-half hour later than the times given on the following pages.

A. Find your latitude and longitude or that of a nearby city in the tables on pages 770-771. Mark the appropriate rows in tables A and B. Now, find the times of the event in the calendar table in the columns for the latitude to your south and to your north. Subtract the southern time from the northern time. Find the nearest tens of minutes to your answer in a column head in Table A. Run down the column to the latitude row you have marked. Add (or subtract, if your answer is negative) to the southern time the number you find there.

B. Find the time of the event for the next day at the southern latitude. Subtract the time for the present day from the time for the next day. In Table B, find the column headed by the nearest tens of this answer. Run down the column to the longitude row you have marked. Add this number to your previous answer.

C. To determine the clock time, subtract the nearest time zone meridian used in your state from your longitude. (These are: Atlantic, 60°; Eastern, 75°; Central, 90°; Mountain, 105°; Pacific, 120°; Alaska-Hawaii, 150°.) Change this to degrees and decimals of a degree (divide the minutes by 60) and multiply by 4. Write this number on this page for future use and add it (or subtract, if minus) to your answer from Table B. Watch out for Daylight Time.

Example: Find the approximate time of moonset for April 1 in San Francisco, latitude: 37°46′; longitude: 122°25′, or 122°.4. A resident there should mark rows 7°40′ in Table A and 120° in Table B.

A. Calendar time for 40°—	11:59	
Calendar time for 30°—	12:18	12:18
Difference: North minus South—	-19 min.	-15
Table A: 20 min. and 7°40′—	15	12:03
B. Calendar time for Apr. 2, 30°—	13:20	
Calendar time for Apr. 1, 30°—	12:18	12:03
Difference: Apr. 2 minus Apr. 1=	62 min.	+20
Table B: 60 min. and 120° 20′—	20 min.	12:23
C. SF longitude—	122.4	
PST longitude—	-120.0	12:23
2°.4x4 min. per degree=	9.6 min.	+10
PST of moon set Apr. 1 in SF		12:33

Table A: Latitude Adjustment

Lat. \ Diff. in Min.	10	20	30	40	50	60	70	80	90	100	110	120
0°20	0	1	1	1	2	2	2	3	3	3	4	4
40	1	1	2	3	3	4	5	5	6	7	7	8
1 00	1	2	3	4	5	6	7	8	9	10	11	12
20	1	3	4	5	7	8	9	11	12	13	15	16
40	2	3	5	7	8	10	12	13	15	17	18	20
2 00	2	4	6	8	10	12	14	16	18	20	22	24
20	2	5	7	9	12	14	16	19	21	23	26	28
40	3	5	8	11	13	16	19	21	24	27	29	32
3 00	3	6	9	12	15	18	21	24	27	30	33	36
20	3	7	10	13	17	20	23	27	30	33	37	40
40	4	7	11	15	18	22	26	29	33	37	40	44
4 00	4	8	12	16	20	24	28	32	36	40	44	48
20	4	9	13	17	22	26	30	35	39	43	48	52
40	5	9	14	19	23	28	33	37	42	47	51	56
5 00	5	10	15	20	25	30	35	40	45	50	55	60
20	5	11	16	21	27	32	37	43	48	53	59	64
40	6	11	17	23	28	34	40	45	51	57	62	68
6 00	6	12	18	24	30	36	42	48	54	60	66	72
20	6	13	19	25	32	38	44	51	57	63	70	76
40	7	13	20	27	33	40	47	53	60	67	73	80
7 00	7	14	21	28	35	42	49	56	63	70	77	84
20	7	15	22	29	37	44	51	59	66	73	81	88
40	8	15	23	31	38	46	54	61	69	77	84	92
8 00	8	16	24	32	40	48	56	64	72	80	88	96
20	8	17	25	33	42	50	58	67	75	83	92	100
40	9	17	26	35	43	52	61	69	78	87	95	104
9 00	9	18	27	36	45	54	63	72	81	90	99	108
20	9	19	28	37	47	56	65	75	84	93	103	112
40	10	19	29	39	48	58	68	77	87	97	106	116

Table B: Longitude Adjustment

Long. \ Diff. in Min.	10	20	30	40	50	60	70	80	90	100	110	120
50°	1	3	4	6	7	8	10	11	12	14	15	17
55	2	3	5	6	8	9	11	12	14	15	17	18
60	2	3	5	7	8	10	12	13	15	17	18	20
65	2	4	5	7	9	11	13	14	16	18	20	22
70	2	4	6	8	10	12	14	16	18	19	21	23
75	2	4	6	8	10	12	15	17	19	21	23	25
80	2	4	7	9	11	13	16	18	20	22	24	27
85	2	5	7	9	12	14	16	19	21	24	26	28
90	2	5	8	10	12	15	18	20	22	25	28	30
95	3	5	8	11	13	16	18	21	24	26	29	32
100	3	6	8	11	14	17	19	22	25	28	31	33
105	3	6	9	12	15	18	20	23	26	29	32	35
110	3	6	9	12	15	18	21	24	28	31	34	37
115	3	6	10	13	16	19	22	26	29	32	35	38
120	3	7	10	13	17	20	23	27	30	33	37	40
125	4	7	10	14	17	21	24	28	31	35	38	42
130	4	7	11	14	18	22	25	29	32	36	40	43
135	4	8	11	15	19	22	26	30	34	38	41	45
140	4	8	12	16	19	23	27	31	35	39	43	47
145	4	8	12	16	20	24	28	32	36	40	44	48
150	4	8	12	17	21	25	29	33	38	42	46	50
155	4	9	13	17	22	26	30	34	39	43	47	52
160	4	9	13	18	22	27	31	36	40	44	49	53
165	5	9	14	18	23	28	32	37	41	46	50	55
170	5	9	14	19	24	28	33	38	42	47	52	57

1st Month January, 1978 31 Days

Greenwich Mean Time

NOTE: Light figures indicate Sun. **Dark** figures indicate **Moon.** *Degrees are North Latitude.*

CAUTION: Must be converted to local time. For instruction see page 772.

Day of month week year	Sun on meridian **Moon phase**	20° Rise Sun **Moon**	20° Set Sun **Moon**	30° Rise Sun **Moon**	30° Set Sun **Moon**	40° Rise Sun **Moon**	40° Set Sun **Moon**	50° Rise Sun **Moon**	50° Set Sun **Moon**	60° Rise Sun **Moon**	60° Set Sun **Moon**
	h m s	h m	h m	h m	h m	h m	h m	h m	h m	h m	h m
1 Su	12 03 30	6 35	17 32	6 56	17 11	7 22	16 45	7 59	16 09	9 02	15 05
1		**23 36**	**11 08**	**23 38**	**11 07**	**23 41**	**11 07**	**23 45**	**11 07**	**23 51**	**11 06**
2 Mo	12 03 58	6 35	17 32	6 56	17 12	7 22	16 46	7 59	16 10	9 02	15 06
2	**12 07** ☾		**11 49**		**11 45**		**11 40**		**11 33**		**11 23**
3 Tu	12 04 26	6 36	17 33	6 57	17 12	7 22	16 47	7 58	16 11	9 01	15 08
3		**0 31**	**12 32**	**0 37**	**12 24**	**0 44**	**12 15**	**0 54**	**12 02**	**1 10**	**11 42**
4 Wed	12 04 54	6 36	17 33	6 57	17 13	7 22	16 48	7 58	16 12	9 01	15 09
4		**1 28**	**13 18**	**1 38**	**13 07**	**1 50**	**12 53**	**2 06**	**12 35**	**2 33**	**12 05**
5 Th	12 05 21	6 36	17 34	6 57	17 14	7 22	16 49	7 58	16 13	9 00	15 11
5		**2 28**	**14 09**	**2 41**	**13 55**	**2 57**	**13 37**	**3 20**	**13 13**	**3 56**	**12 35**
6 Fr	12 05 48	6 36	17 35	6 57	17 15	7 22	16 50	7 58	16 14	8 59	15 13
6		**3 30**	**15 05**	**3 46**	**14 49**	**4 06**	**14 28**	**4 33**	**14 00**	**5 18**	**13 14**
7 Sa	12 06 14	6 36	17 36	6 57	17 16	7 22	16 51	7 57	16 15	8 58	15 15
7		**4 34**	**16 06**	**4 51**	**15 48**	**5 13**	**15 20**	**5 43**	**14 50**	**6 33**	**14 06**
8 Su	12 06 40	6 37	17 36	6 57	17 16	7 22	16 52	7 57	16 17	8 57	15 16
8		**5 37**	**17 09**	**5 54**	**16 52**	**6 16**	**16 31**	**6 46**	**16 02**	**7 35**	**16 24**
9 Mo	12 07 05	6 37	17 37	6 57	17 17	7 22	16 53	7 56	16 18	8 56	15 18
9	**04 00** ●	**6 37**	**18 14**	**6 53**	**17 59**	**7 13**	**17 41**	**7 40**	**17 15**	**8 24**	**16 33**
10 Tu	12 07 29	6 37	17 38	6 57	17 18	7 22	16 54	7 56	16 19	8 55	15 20
10		**7 33**	**19 18**	**7 46**	**19 07**	**8 03**	**18 52**	**8 25**	**18 32**	**9 00**	**17 59**
11 We	12 07 54	6 37	17 39	6 57	17 19	7 22	16 55	7 55	16 20	8 54	15 22
11		**8 25**	**20 20**	**8 34**	**20 12**	**8 46**	**20 02**	**9 03**	**19 48**	**9 28**	**19 27**
12 Th	12 08 17	6 37	17 39	6 57	17 20	7 21	16 56	7 55	16 22	8 52	15 24
12		**9 12**	**21 19**	**9 18**	**21 15**	**9 25**	**21 10**	**9 35**	**21 03**	**9 50**	**20 52**
13 Fr	12 08 40	6 38	17 40	6 57	17 20	7 21	16 57	7 54	16 23	8 51	15 27
13		**9 56**	**22 16**	**9 58**	**22 16**	**10 01**	**22 15**	**10 04**	**22 15**	**10 09**	**22 15**
14 Sa	12 09 02	6 38	17 40	6 57	17 21	7 20	16 58	7 54	16 25	8 49	15 29
14		**10 38**	**23 10**	**10 36**	**23 13**	**10 34**	**23 18**	**10 31**	**23 24**	**10 27**	**23 33**
15 Su	12 09 24	6 38	17 41	6 57	17 22	7 20	16 59	7 53	16 26	8 48	15 31
15		**11 19**		**11 13**		**11 07**		**10 58**		**10 45**	
16 Mo	12 09 45	6 38	17 42	6 57	17 23	7 20	17 00	7 52	16 28	8 46	15 33
16	**03 03** ☽	**11 59**	**0 02**	**11 50**	**0 09**	**11 40**	**0 18**	**11 25**	**0 30**	**11 03**	**0 49**
17 Tu	12 10 05	6 38	17 42	6 57	17 24	7 19	17 01	7 51	16 29	8 45	15 36
17		**12 40**	**0 53**	**12 28**	**1 04**	**12 14**	**1 17**	**11 54**	**1 34**	**11 24**	**2 02**
18 We	12 10 24	6 38	17 43	6 56	17 25	7 19	17 02	7 51	16 31	8 43	15 38
18		**13 22**	**1 44**	**13 08**	**1 57**	**12 50**	**2 13**	**12 27**	**2 36**	**11 49**	**3 12**
19 Th	12 10 43	6 38	17 43	6 56	17 26	7 18	17 03	7 50	16 32	8 42	15 41
19		**14 05**	**2 34**	**13 49**	**2 49**	**13 30**	**3 08**	**13 03**	**3 34**	**12 19**	**4 17**
20 Fr	12 11 01	6 38	17 44	6 56	17 27	7 18	17 04	7 49	16 34	8 40	15 43
20		**14 51**	**3 23**	**14 34**	**3 39**	**14 13**	**4 00**	**13 44**	**4 29**	**12 56**	**5 16**
21 Sa	12 11 18	6 38	17 45	6 56	17 28	7 17	17 05	7 49	16 36	8 38	15 45
21		**15 38**	**4 11**	**15 21**	**4 28**	**15 00**	**4 49**	**14 30**	**5 19**	**13 41**	**6 08**
22 Su	12 11 35	6 38	17 45	6 55	17 29	7 17	17 06	7 47	16 37	8 36	15 48
22		**16 26**	**4 58**	**16 10**	**5 15**	**15 50**	**5 35**	**15 27**	**6 04**	**14 35**	**6 51**
23 Mo	12 11 50	6 37	17 46	6 55	17 29	7 16	17 08	7 45	16 39	8 34	15 50
23		**17 16**	**5 43**	**17 01**	**5 59**	**16 43**	**6 18**	**16 18**	**6 44**	**15 36**	**7 27**
24 Tu	12 12 05	6 37	17 46	6 54	17 30	7 16	17 09	7 44	16 40	8 32	15 53
24	**07 55** ◯	**18 07**	**6 27**	**17 54**	**6 40**	**17 39**	**6 57**	**17 17**	**7 20**	**16 43**	**7 56**
25 We	12 12 19	6 37	17 47	6 54	17 31	7 15	17 10	7 43	16 42	8 30	15 55
25		**18 57**	**7 09**	**18 48**	**7 20**	**18 36**	**7 33**	**18 19**	**7 52**	**17 54**	**8 20**
26 Th	12 12 33	6 37	17 48	6 54	17 32	7 14	17 11	7 42	16 44	8 28	15 58
26		**19 49**	**7 50**	**19 42**	**7 57**	**19 34**	**8 07**	**19 23**	**8 20**	**19 07**	**8 40**
27 Fr	12 12 45	6 37	17 49	6 53	17 33	7 13	17 12	7 41	16 45	8 26	16 00
27		**20 40**	**8 29**	**20 37**	**8 34**	**20 34**	**8 40**	**20 29**	**8 47**	**20 21**	**8 58**
28 Sa	12 12 57	6 36	17 49	6 53	17 33	7 13	17 14	7 39	16 47	8 24	16 03
28		**21 32**	**9 09**	**21 33**	**9 10**	**21 34**	**9 11**	**21 36**	**9 13**	**21 38**	**9 15**
29 Su	12 12 08	6 36	17 50	6 52	17 34	7 12	17 15	7 38	16 48	8 22	16 05
29		**22 26**	**9 49**	**22 30**	**9 46**	**22 36**	**9 43**	**22 44**	**9 39**	**22 56**	**9 32**
30 Mo	12 13 18	6 36	17 51	6 52	17 35	7 11	17 16	7 37	16 50	8 20	16 08
30		**23 21**	**10 31**	**23 29**	**10 24**	**23 39**	**10 17**	**23 53**	**10 06**		**9 51**
31 Tu	12 13 27	6 36	17 51	6 51	17 35	7 10	17 17	7 36	16 52	8 18	16 11
31	**23 51** ☾		**11 15**		**11 05**		**10 53**		**10 37**	**0 15**	**10 11**

2d Month — February, 1978 — 28 Days

Greenwich Mean Time

NOTE: Light figures indicate Sun. **Dark** figures indicate **Moon.** *Degrees are North Latitude.*

CAUTION: Must be converted to local time. For instruction see page 772.

Day of month / week / year	Sun on meridian / **Moon phase** (h m s)	20° Rise Sun / **Moon** (h m)	20° Set Sun / **Moon** (h m)	30° Rise Sun / **Moon** (h m)	30° Set Sun / **Moon** (h m)	40° Rise Sun / **Moon** (h m)	40° Set Sun / **Moon** (h m)	50° Rise Sun / **Moon** (h m)	50° Set Sun / **Moon** (h m)	60° Rise Sun / **Moon** (h m)	60° Set Sun / **Moon** (h m)
1 We	12 13 36	6 36	17 52	6 51	17 37	7 09	17 18	7 34	16 54	8 15	16 13
32		**0 18**	**12 02**	**0 30**	**11 49**	**0 44**	**11 33**	**1 04**	**11 11**	**1 36**	**10 37**
2 Th	12 13 43	6 35	17 52	6 50	17 37	7 08	17 20	7 33	16 55	8 13	16 16
33		**1 17**	**12 54**	**1 31**	**12 38**	**1 49**	**12 19**	**2 14**	**11 53**	**2 55**	**11 10**
3 Fr	12 13 50	6 35	17 53	6 50	17 38	7 07	17 21	7 31	16 57	8 10	16 18
34		**2 18**	**13 50**	**2 34**	**13 33**	**2 55**	**13 12**	**3 23**	**12 42**	**4 11**	**11 54**
4 Sa	12 13 56	6 35	17 53	6 49	17 39	7 06	17 22	7 30	16 59	8 08	16 21
35		**3 18**	**14 49**	**3 36**	**14 32**	**3 57**	**14 11**	**4 27**	**13 41**	**5 17**	**12 51**
5 Su	12 14 02	6 35	17 54	6 48	17 40	7 05	17 23	7 28	17 01	8 05	16 24
36		**4 18**	**15 52**	**4 35**	**15 36**	**4 56**	**15 16**	**5 24**	**14 48**	**6 11**	**14 03**
6 Mo	12 14 06	6 34	17 54	6 47	17 41	7 04	17 24	7 27	17 02	8 03	16 26
37		**5 16**	**16 56**	**5 30**	**16 42**	**5 48**	**16 26**	**6 13**	**16 02**	**6 54**	**15 24**
7 Tu	12 14 10	6 34	17 55	6 47	17 42	7 03	17 26	7 25	17 04	8 00	16 29
38	**14 54 ●**	**6 09**	**17 59**	**6 21**	**17 49**	**6 35**	**17 36**	**6 55**	**17 19**	**7 26**	**16 51**
8 We	12 14 13	6 33	17 55	6 46	17 43	7 02	17 27	7 24	17 05	7 58	16 31
39		**6 59**	**19 00**	**7 07**	**18 54**	**7 17**	**18 46**	**7 31**	**18 35**	**7 52**	**18 19**
9 Th	12 14 15	6 33	17 56	6 45	17 44	7 01	17 28	7 22	17 07	7 55	16 34
40		**7 46**	**19 59**	**7 50**	**19 57**	**7 55**	**19 54**	**8 02**	**19 50**	**8 13**	**19 44**
10 Fr	12 14 16	6 32	17 57	6 44	17 45	7 00	17 29	7 20	17 09	7 52	16 37
41		**8 30**	**20 56**	**8 30**	**20 58**	**8 31**	**21 00**	**8 31**	**21 03**	**8 32**	**21 07**
11 Sa	12 14 17	6 32	17 57	6 43	17 46	6 59	17 30	7 18	17 11	7 50	16 39
42		**9 13**	**21 51**	**9 09**	**21 57**	**9 05**	**22 03**	**8 59**	**22 12**	**8 50**	**22 27**
12 Su	12 14 17	6 31	17 58	6 43	17 46	6 57	17 32	7 17	17 12	7 47	16 42
43		**9 54**	**22 44**	**9 47**	**22 53**	**9 38**	**23 04**	**9 27**	**23 19**	**9 09**	**23 43**
13 Mo	12 14 16	6 31	17 58	6 42	17 47	6 56	17 33	7 15	17 14	7 45	16 44
44		**10 36**	**23 36**	**10 26**	**23 48**	**10 13**		**9 56**		**9 29**	
14 Tu	12 14 14	6 30	17 59	6 41	17 48	6 55	17 34	7 13	17 16	7 42	16 47
45	**22 11 ☽**	**11 18**		**11 05**		**10 49**	**0 03**	**10 28**	**0 23**	**9 53**	**0 55**
15 We	12 14 11	6 29	17 59	6 40	17 49	6 54	17 35	7 11	17 18	7 39	16 50
46		**12 02**	**0 27**	**11 47**	**0 41**	**11 28**	**0 59**	**11 02**	**1 23**	**10 21**	**2 03**
16 Th	12 14 08	6 29	18 00	6 39	17 50	6 52	17 36	7 09	17 19	7 36	16 52
47		**12 46**	**1 17**	**12 30**	**1 33**	**12 10**	**1 52**	**11 42**	**2 20**	**10 56**	**3 05**
17 Fr	12 14 04	6 28	18 00	6 39	17 50	6 51	17 38	7 08	17 21	7 34	16 55
48		**13 33**	**2 05**	**13 16**	**2 22**	**12 55**	**2 43**	**12 26**	**3 12**	**11 38**	**4 00**
18 Sa	12 13 59	6 28	18 01	6 38	17 51	6 49	17 39	7 06	17 22	7 31	16 57
49		**14 21**	**2 53**	**14 04**	**3 09**	**13 44**	**3 30**	**13 15**	**3 59**	**12 28**	**4 47**
19 Su	12 13 54	6 27	18 01	6 37	17 52	6 48	17 40	7 04	17 24	7 28	17 00
50		**15 10**	**3 39**	**14 55**	**3 55**	**14 36**	**4 14**	**14 09**	**4 42**	**13 26**	**5 26**
20 Mo	12 13 48	6 26	18 01	6 36	17 53	6 47	17 41	7 02	17 26	7 25	17 03
51		**16 00**	**4 23**	**15 47**	**4 37**	**15 30**	**4 55**	**15 07**	**5 19**	**14 31**	**5 58**
21 Tu	12 13 41	6 26	18 02	6 35	17 53	6 46	17 42	7 00	17 28	7 22	17 05
52		**16 51**	**5 06**	**16 41**	**5 18**	**16 27**	**5 32**	**16 09**	**5 52**	**15 40**	**6 24**
22 We	12 13 34	6 25	18 02	6 34	17 54	6 44	17 44	6 59	17 29	7 20	17 08
53		**17 43**	**5 47**	**17 35**	**5 57**	**17 26**	**6 08**	**17 13**	**6 23**	**16 53**	**6 46**
23 Th	12 13 26	6 25	18 03	6 33	17 54	6 43	17 45	6 57	17 31	7 17	17 10
54	**01 26 ○**	**18 35**	**6 28**	**18 31**	**6 34**	**18 26**	**6 41**	**18 19**	**6 51**	**18 08**	**7 05**
24 Fr	12 13 17	6 24	18 03	6 32	17 55	6 42	17 46	6 55	17 33	7 14	17 13
55		**19 28**	**7 08**	**18 27**	**7 11**	**19 27**	**7 14**	**19 26**	**7 17**	**19 25**	**7 23**
25 Sa	12 13 08	6 23	18 03	6 31	17 56	6 40	17 47	6 53	17 35	7 11	17 16
56		**20 22**	**7 49**	**20 25**	**7 48**	**20 29**	**7 46**	**20 35**	**7 44**	**20 43**	**7 40**
26 Su	12 12 58	6 22	18 04	6 30	17 57	6 39	17 48	6 51	17 36	7 08	17 18
57		**21 17**	**8 31**	**21 24**	**8 26**	**21 32**	**8 20**	**21 44**	**8 11**	**22 03**	**7 59**
27 Mo	12 12 47	6 22	18 04	6 29	17 57	6 37	17 49	6 49	17 38	7 06	17 21
58		**22 13**	**9 14**	**22 24**	**9 06**	**22 37**	**8 55**	**22 55**	**8 41**	**23 23**	**8 19**
28 Tu	12 16 37	6 21	18 06	6 28	17 58	6 36	17 50	6 47	17 39	7 03	17 23
59		**23 11**	**10 00**	**23 25**	**9 49**	**23 41**	**9 34**		**9 14**		**8 43**

3d Month | **March, 1978** | **31Days**

Greenwich Mean Time

NOTE: Light figures indicate Sun. **Dark** figures indicate **Moon.** *Degrees are North Latitude.*
CAUTION: Must be converted to local time. For instruction see page 772.

Day of month week year	Sun on meridian **Moon phase**	20° Rise Sun **Moon**	20° Set Sun **Moon**	30° Rise Sun **Moon**	30° Set Sun **Moon**	40° Rise Sun **Moon**	40° Set Sun **Moon**	50° Rise Sun **Moon**	50° Set Sun **Moon**	60° Rise Sun **Moon**	60° Set Sun **Moon**
	h m s	h m	h m	h m	h m	h m	h m	h m	h m	h m	h m
1 We	12 12 25	6 20	18 05	6 27	17 59	6 34	17 51	6 45	17 41	7 00	17 26
60			**10 50**		**10 35**		**10 17**	**0 05**	**9 53**	**0 42**	**9 13**
2 Th	12 12 13	6 19	18 05	6 26	18 00	6 33	17 52	6 43	17 43	6 57	17 29
61	**08 34** ☾	**0 10**	**11 43**	**0 26**	**11 27**	**0 45**	**11 06**	**1 13**	**10 38**	**1 58**	**9 52**
3 Fr	12 12 01	6 18	18 06	6 25	18 00	6 31	17 53	6 41	17 45	6 54	17 31
62		**1 09**	**12 40**	**1 26**	**12 23**	**1 47**	**12 01**	**2 17**	**11 32**	**3 06**	**10 43**
4 Sa	12 11 48	6 18	18 06	6 23	18 01	6 30	17 55	6 38	17 46	6 51	17 34
63		**2 07**	**13 39**	**2 24**	**13 23**	**2 45**	**13 02**	**3 15**	**12 34**	**4 03**	**11 46**
5 Su	12 11 35	6 17	18 07	6 22	18 01	6 28	17 56	6 36	17 48	6 48	17 36
64		**3 04**	**14 40**	**3 19**	**14 26**	**3 39**	**14 08**	**4 05**	**13 42**	**4 48**	**13 01**
6 Mo	12 11 21	6 16	18 07	6 21	18 02	6 27	17 57	6 34	17 50	6 45	17 39
65		**3 57**	**15 42**	**4 10**	**15 30**	**4 26**	**15 15**	**4 49**	**14 55**	**5 24**	**14 23**
7 Tu	12 11 07	6 15	18 07	6 20	18 03	6 25	17 58	6 32	17 52	6 42	17 41
66		**4 48**	**16 43**	**4 57**	**16 34**	**5 10**	**16 24**	**5 26**	**16 10**	**5 52**	**15 48**
8 We	12 10 53	6 14	18 07	6 19	18 03	6 24	17 59	6 30	17 53	6 39	17 44
67		**5 35**	**17 42**	**5 41**	**17 38**	**5 49**	**17 32**	**5 59**	**17 25**	**6 15**	**17 14**
9 Th	12 10 38	6 14	18 08	6 17	18 04	6 22	18 00	6 28	17 55	6 36	17 46
68	**02 36** ●	**6 20**	**18 40**	**6 22**	**18 40**	**6 25**	**18 39**	**6 29**	**18 39**	**6 35**	**18 38**
10 Fr	12 10 23	6 13	18 08	6 16	18 04	6 21	18 01	6 26	17 56	6 33	17 49
69		**7 04**	**19 36**	**7 02**	**19 40**	**7 00**	**19 44**	**6 58**	**19 50**	**6 54**	**19 59**
11 Sa	12 10 07	6 12	18 08	6 15	18 05	6 19	18 02	6 24	17 58	6 30	17 51
70		**7 46**	**20 31**	**7 41**	**20 38**	**7 34**	**20 47**	**7 26**	**20 59**	**7 13**	**21 18**
12 Su	12 09 51	6 11	18 08	6 14	18 06	6 17	18 03	6 22	18 00	6 27	17 54
71		**8 29**	**21 25**	**8 20**	**21 35**	**8 09**	**21 48**	**7 55**	**22 06**	**7 33**	**22 34**
13 Mo	12 09 35	6 10	18 09	6 13	18 07	6 16	18 04	6 20	18 01	6 24	17 56
72		**9 12**	**22 17**	**9 00**	**22 30**	**8 46**	**22 46**	**8 26**	**23 09**	**7 55**	**23 45**
14 Tu	12 09 19	6 10	18 09	6 11	18 07	6 14	18 05	6 17	18 03	6 21	17 59
73		**9 55**	**23 08**	**9 41**	**23 23**	**9 24**	**23 42**	**9 00**		**8 22**	
15 We	12 09 02	6 09	18 10	6 10	18 08	6 13	18 06	6 15	18 04	6 18	18 01
74		**10 40**	**23 58**	**10 24**		**10 05**		**9 38**	**0 08**	**8 54**	**0 51**
16 Th	12 08 45	6 08	18 10	6 09	18 09	6 11	18 07	6 13	18 06	6 15	18 04
75	**18 21** ☽	**11 26**		**11 10**	**0 14**	**10 49**	**0 35**	**10 20**	**1 03**	**9 33**	**1 50**
17 Fr	12 08 28	6 07	18 10	6 08	18 10	6 09	18 08	6 11	18 08	6 12	18 06
76		**12 14**	**0 46**	**11 57**	**1 03**	**11 36**	**1 23**	**11 27**	**1 52**	**10 20**	**2 40**
18 Sa	12 08 10	6 06	18 10	6 07	18 10	6 08	18 09	6 09	18 09	6 09	18 09
77		**13 02**	**1 32**	**12 47**	**1 49**	**12 27**	**2 09**	**11 59**	**2 37**	**11 15**	**3 22**
19 Su	12 07 53	6 06	18 11	6 05	18 11	6 06	18 11	6 06	18 11	6 06	18 11
78		**13 52**	**2 17**	**13 38**	**2 32**	**13 20**	**2 51**	**12 56**	**3 16**	**12 16**	**3 57**
20 Mo	12 07 35	6 05	18 11	6 04	18 11	6 05	18 12	6 04	18 12	6 03	18 14
79		**14 42**	**3 00**	**14 30**	**3 13**	**14 16**	**3 29**	**13 56**	**3 51**	**13 23**	**4 25**
21 Tu	12 07 17	6 04	18 11	6 03	18 12	6 03	18 13	6 02	18 14	6 00	18 16
80		**15 34**	**3 42**	**15 25**	**3 53**	**15 14**	**4 05**	**14 58**	**4 22**	**14 35**	**4 49**
22 We	12 06 59	6 03	18 11	6 02	18 13	6 01	18 14	6 00	18 16	5 57	18 18
81		**16 26**	**4 23**	**16 20**	**4 31**	**16 13**	**4 39**	**16 04**	**4 51**	**15 49**	**5 09**
23 Th	12 06 41	6 02	18 12	6 01	18 13	6 00	18 15	5 58	18 17	5 54	18 21
82		**17 19**	**5 04**	**17 17**	**5 08**	**17 14**	**5 13**	**17 11**	**5 19**	**17 06**	**5 28**
24 Fr	12 06 23	6 01	18 12	5 59	18 14	5 58	18 16	5 55	18 19	5 51	18 23
83	**16 20** ○	**18 13**	**5 45**	**18 15**	**5 45**	**18 17**	**5 45**	**18 20**	**5 46**	**18 25**	**5 46**
25 Sa	12 06 04	6 00	18 13	5 58	18 14	5 57	18 17	5 53	18 20	5 48	18 26
84		**19 09**	**6 27**	**19 15**	**6 24**	**19 21**	**6 19**	**19 31**	**6 13**	**19 46**	**6 04**
26 Su	12 05 46	5 59	18 13	5 57	18 15	5 55	18 18	5 51	18 22	5 45	18 28
85		**20 06**	**7 11**	**20 15**	**7 04**	**20 27**	**6 55**	**20 43**	**6 43**	**21 08**	**6 24**
27 Mo	12 05 28	5 58	18 13	5 56	18 16	5 53	18 19	5 49	18 24	5 42	18 30
86		**21 05**	**7 57**	**21 17**	**7 47**	**21 33**	**7 33**	**21 55**	**7 15**	**22 29**	**6 47**
28 Tu	12 05 09	5 57	18 13	5 55	18 16	5 52	18 20	5 47	18 25	5 39	18 33
87		**22 05**	**8 47**	**22 20**	**8 33**	**22 39**	**8 16**	**23 05**	**7 53**	**23 48**	**7 16**
29 We	12 04 51	5 57	18 14	5 53	18 17	5 50	18 21	5 44	18 27	5 36	18 35
88		**23 04**	**9 39**	**23 21**	**9 24**	**23 42**	**9 04**		**8 37**		**7 52**
30 Th	12 04 33	5 56	18 14	5 52	18 17	5 49	18 22	5 42	18 28	5 33	18 38
89			**10 35**		**10 18**		**9 57**	**0 11**	**9 28**	**0 58**	**8 39**
31 Fr	12 04 15	5 55	18 14	5 51	18 18	5 47	18 23	5 40	18 30	5 30	18 40
90	**15 11** ☾	**0 03**	**11 34**	**0 20**	**11 17**	**0 41**	**10 56**	**1 10**	**10 27**	**1 59**	**9 39**

4th Month April, 1978 30 Days

Greenwich Mean Time

NOTE: Light figures indicate Sun. **Dark** figures indicate **Moon.** *Degrees are North Latitude.*

CAUTION: Must be converted to local time. For instruction see page 772.

Day of month week year	Sun on meridian **Moon phase** h m s	20° Rise Sun **Moon** h m	20° Set Sun **Moon** h m	30° Rise Sun **Moon** h m	30° Set Sun **Moon** h m	40° Rise Sun **Moon** h m	40° Set Sun **Moon** h m	50° Rise Sun **Moon** h m	50° Set Sun **Moon** h m	60° Rise Sun **Moon** h m	60° Set Sun **Moon** h m
1 Sa	12 03 57	5 54	18 14	5 50	18 36	5 45	18 24	5 38	18 31	5 27	18 42
91		**0 59**	**12 33**	**1 15**	**12 18**	**1 35**	**11 59**	**2 02**	**11 32**	**2 47**	**10 49**
2 Su	12 03 39	5 53	18 14	5 49	18 19	5 44	18 25	5 36	18 33	5 24	18 45
92		**1 52**	**13 33**	**2 06**	**13 20**	**2 23**	**13 04**	**2 47**	**12 42**	**3 25**	**12 07**
3 Mo	12 03 21	5 52	18 15	5 47	18 20	5 42	18 26	5 33	18 34	5 21	18 47
93		**2 42**	**14 32**	**2 53**	**14 23**	**3 07**	**14 11**	**3 25**	**13 54**	**3 54**	**13 29**
4 Tu	12 03 04	5 52	18 15	5 46	18 20	5 41	18 27	5 31	18 36	5 18	18 50
94		**3 29**	**15 31**	**3 37**	**15 25**	**3 46**	**15 17**	**3 59**	**15 07**	**4 18**	**14 52**
5 We	12 02 46	5 51	18 15	5 45	18 21	5 39	18 28	5 29	18 37	5 15	18 52
95		**4 14**	**16 28**	**4 18**	**16 26**	**4 22**	**16 23**	**4 29**	**16 20**	**4 39**	**16 14**
6 Th	12 02 29	5 50	18 15	5 44	18 22	5 37	18 29	5 27	18 39	5 12	18 55
96		**4 57**	**17 24**	**4 57**	**17 25**	**4 57**	**17 28**	**4 57**	**17 31**	**4 58**	**17 36**
7 Fr	12 02 12	5 49	18 16	5 43	18 22	5 36	18 30	5 25	18 40	5 09	18 57
97	**15 15 ●**	**5 39**	**18 19**	**5 36**	**18 24**	**5 31**	**18 31**	**5 25**	**18 41**	**5 16**	**18 55**
8 Sa	12 01 56	5 49	18 16	5 41	18 23	5 34	18 31	5 23	18 42	5 06	19 00
98		**6 22**	**19 13**	**6 14**	**19 22**	**6 05**	**19 33**	**5 54**	**19 48**	**5 35**	**20 12**
9 Su	12 01 39	5 48	18 17	5 40	18 23	5 33	18 32	5 21	18 43	5 03	19 02
99		**7 04**	**20 06**	**6 54**	**20 18**	**6 41**	**20 33**	**6 24**	**20 53**	**5 57**	**21 26**
10 Mo	12 01 23	5 47	18 17	5 39	18 24	5 31	18 33	5 19	18 45	5 00	19 05
100		**7 48**	**20 58**	**7 35**	**21 12**	**7 19**	**21 30**	**6 57**	**21 55**	**6 22**	**22 35**
11 Tu	12 01 07	5 46	18 17	5 38	18 25	5 29	18 34	5 17	18 47	4 57	19 07
101		**8 33**	**21 49**	**8 18**	**22 05**	**7 59**	**22 25**	**7 33**	**22 52**	**6 51**	**23 38**
12 We	12 00 51	5 45	18 17	5 37	18 25	5 26	18 35	5 15	18 48	4 54	19 10
102		**9 19**	**22 38**	**9 02**	**22 55**	**8 42**	**23 16**	**8 14**	**23 45**	**7 28**	
13 Th	12 00 35	5 44	18 18	5 36	18 26	5 26	18 36	5 12	18 50	4 51	19 12
103		**10 06**	**23 26**	**9 49**	**23 42**	**9 28**		**8 59**		**8 11**	**0 33**
14 Fr	12 00 20	5 43	18 18	5 35	18 26	5 25	18 37	5 10	18 51	4 48	19 15
104		**10 54**		**10 38**		**10 18**	**0 03**	**9 50**	**0 31**	**9 03**	**1 18**
15 Sa	12 00 06	5 42	18 18	5 34	18 27	5 23	18 38	5 08	18 53	4 45	19 17
105	**7 39 ☽**	**11 43**	**0 11**	**11 28**	**0 27**	**11 10**	**0 46**	**10 44**	**1 13**	**10 02**	**1 56**
16 Su	11 59 51	5 41	18 18	5 33	18 28	5 22	18 39	5 06	18 55	4 42	19 19
106		**12 33**	**0 55**	**12 20**	**1 08**	**12 04**	**1 26**	**11 42**	**1 49**	**11 06**	**2 26**
17 Mo	11 59 37	5 41	18 19	5 32	18 28	5 20	18 40	5 04	18 56	4 39	19 22
107		**13 23**	**1 37**	**13 13**	**1 48**	**13 00**	**2 02**	**12 43**	**2 21**	**12 15**	**2 52**
18 Tu	11 59 23	5 40	18 19	5 30	18 29	5 19	18 41	5 02	18 58	4 36	19 24
108		**14 14**	**2 18**	**14 07**	**2 26**	**13 58**	**2 37**	**13 46**	**2 51**	**13 27**	**3 13**
19 We	11 59 10	5 40	18 20	5 29	18 29	5 17	18 42	5 00	18 59	4 33	19 27
109		**15 06**	**2 58**	**15 03**	**3 03**	**14 58**	**3 10**	**14 52**	**3 19**	**14 43**	**3 32**
20 Th	11 58 57	5 39	18 20	5 28	18 30	5 16	18 43	4 58	19 01	4 30	19 29
110		**16 00**	**3 38**	**16 00**	**3 40**	**16 00**	**3 42**	**16 00**	**3 45**	**16 01**	**3 50**
21 Fr	11 58 44	5 38	18 20	5 27	18 31	5 15	18 44	4 56	19 03	4 27	19 32
111		**16 56**	**4 20**	**16 59**	**4 18**	**17 04**	**4 16**	**17 11**	**4 12**	**17 21**	**4 08**
22 Sa	11 58 32	5 37	18 20	5 26	18 31	5 13	18 45	4 54	19 04	4 24	19 34
112		**17 53**	**5 03**	**18 01**	**4 58**	**18 10**	**4 51**	**18 23**	**4 41**	**18 44**	**4 27**
23 Su	11 58 20	5 37	18 21	5 25	18 32	5 12	18 46	4 52	19 06	4 22	19 37
113	**4 11 ○**	**18 53**	**5 49**	**19 04**	**5 40**	**19 18**	**5 28**	**19 37**	**5 13**	**20 08**	**4 49**
24 Mo	11 58 09	5 36	18 21	5 24	18 32	5 10	18 47	4 50	19 07	4 19	19 39
114		**19 54**	**6 38**	**20 08**	**6 26**	**20 26**	**6 10**	**20 50**	**5 49**	**21 31**	**5 15**
25 Tu	11 57 58	5 35	18 21	5 23	18 33	5 09	18 48	4 48	19 09	4 16	19 42
115		**20 55**	**7 31**	**21 12**	**7 16**	**21 32**	**6 57**	**22 00**	**6 31**	**22 47**	**5 49**
26 We	11 57 48	5 34	18 21	5 22	18 34	5 08	18 49	4 46	19 10	4 13	19 44
116		**21 56**	**8 28**	**22 13**	**8 11**	**22 35**	**7 50**	**23 04**	**7 21**	**23 54**	**6 33**
27 Th	11 57 38	5 34	18 22	5 21	18 34	5 06	18 50	4 44	19 12	4 10	19 47
117		**22 54**	**9 27**	**23 11**	**9 10**	**23 32**	**8 49**		**8 19**		**7 30**
28 Fr	11 57 29	5 33	18 22	5 21	18 35	5 05	18 51	4 43	19 13	4 08	19 49
118		**23 49**	**10 27**		**10 11**		**9 52**	**0 00**	**9 24**	**0 47**	**8 38**
29 Sa	11 57 20	5 33	18 23	5 20	18 35	5 03	18 52	4 41	19 15	4 05	19 52
119	**21 02 ☾**		**11 28**	**0 04**	**11 14**	**0 22**	**10 57**	**0 48**	**10 33**	**1 28**	**9 55**
30 Su	11 57 12	5 32	18 23	5 19	18 36	5 02	18 53	4 39	19 16	4 02	19 54
120		**0 40**	**12 27**	**0 52**	**12 17**	**1 07**	**12 03**	**1 28**	**11 45**	**2 00**	**11 16**

5th Month May, 1978 31 Days

Greenwich Mean Time

NOTE: Light figures indicate Sun. **Dark** figures indicate **Moon.** *Degrees are North Latitude.*

CAUTION: Must be converted to local time. For instruction see page 772.

Day of month week year	Sun on meridian **Moon phase** h m s	20° Rise Sun **Moon** h m	20° Set Sun **Moon** h m	30° Rise Sun **Moon** h m	30° Set Sun **Moon** h m	40° Rise Sun **Moon** h m	40° Set Sun **Moon** h m	50° Rise Sun **Moon** h m	50° Set Sun **Moon** h m	60° Rise Sun **Moon** h m	60° Set Sun **Moon** h m
1 Mo	11 57 04	5 31	18 23	5 18	18 37	5 01	18 54	4 37	19 18	3 59	19 57
121		**1 28**	**13 25**	**1 37**	**13 18**	**1 47**	**13 09**	**2 02**	**12 57**	**2 25**	**12 38**
2 Tu	11 56 57	5 31	18 24	5 17	18 38	5 00	18 55	4 35	19 19	3 57	19 59
122		**2 12**	**14 22**	**2 18**	**14 18**	**2 24**	**14 14**	**2 32**	**14 08**	**2 45**	**13 59**
3 We	11 56 51	5 30	18 24	5 16	18 38	4 58	18 56	4 34	19 21	3 54	20 02
123		**2 55**	**15 17**	**2 56**	**15 17**	**2 58**	**15 18**	**3 01**	**15 18**	**3 04**	**15 20**
4 Th	11 56 45	5 30	18 25	5 15	18 39	4 57	18 57	4 32	19 22	3 52	20 04
124		**3 37**	**16 11**	**3 34**	**16 15**	**3 31**	**16 20**	**3 28**	**16 27**	**3 22**	**16 38**
5 Fr	11 56 39	5 29	18 25	5 14	18 40	4 56	18 58	4 30	19 24	3 49	20 07
125		**4 18**	**17 04**	**4 12**	**17 12**	**4 05**	**17 22**	**3 55**	**17 35**	**3 40**	**17 55**
6 Sa	11 56 34	5 28	18 25	5 13	18 41	4 55	18 59	4 28	19 25	3 46	20 09
126		**5 00**	**17 57**	**4 51**	**18 08**	**4 39**	**18 22**	**4 24**	**18 40**	**4 00**	**19 10**
7 Su	11 56 30	5 28	18 26	5 12	18 41	4 54	19 00	4 27	19 27	3 44	20 12
127	**04 47 ●**	**5 43**	**18 50**	**5 30**	**19 03**	**5 15**	**19 20**	**4 55**	**19 43**	**4 23**	**20 21**
8 Mo	11 56 26	5 27	18 26	5 12	18 42	4 52	19 01	4 25	19 28	3 41	20 14
128		**6 27**	**19 41**	**6 12**	**19 57**	**5 54**	**20 16**	**5 30**	**20 43**	**4 50**	**21 27**
9 Tu	11 56 23	5 27	18 27	5 11	18 42	4 51	19 02	4 08	19 30	3 39	20 17
129		**7 12**	**20 31**	**6 56**	**20 48**	**6 36**	**21 09**	**6 09**	**21 37**	**5 24**	**22 25**
10 We	11 56 21	5 26	18 27	5 10	18 43	4 50	19 03	4 22	19 31	3 36	20 19
130		**7 59**	**21 20**	**7 42**	**21 36**	**7 21**	**21 57**	**6 52**	**22 27**	**6 04**	**23 15**
11 Th	11 56 19	5 26	18 27	5 09	18 44	4 49	19 04	4 21	19 33	3 34	20 21
131		**8 47**	**22 06**	**8 31**	**22 22**	**8 10**	**22 42**	**7 41**	**23 10**	**6 53**	**23 56**
12 Fr	11 56 17	5 25	18 28	5 09	18 44	4 48	19 05	4 19	19 34	3 31	20 24
132		**9 36**	**22 50**	**9 20**	**23 05**	**9 01**	**23 23**	**8 33**	**23 48**	**7 49**	**-**
13 Sa	11 56 16	5 25	18 28	5 08	18 45	4 47	19 06	4 18	19 36	3 29	20 26
133		**10 25**	**23 32**	**10 11**	**23 45**	**9 54**		**9 30**		**8 51**	**0 29**
14 Su	11 56 16	5 24	18 29	5 08	18 45	4 46	19 07	4 16	19 37	3 26	20 29
134		**11 15**		**11 03**		**10 49**	**0 01**	**10 29**	**0 22**	**9 58**	**0 56**
15 Mo	11 56 16	5 24	18 29	5 07	18 46	4 45	19 08	4 15	19 39	3 24	20 31
135	**07 39 ☽**	**12 05**	**0 13**	**11 56**	**0 23**	**11 45**	**0 36**	**11 31**	**0 52**	**11 08**	**1 18**
16 Tu	11 56 17	5 24	18 29	5 06	18 47	4 44	19 09	4 14	19 40	3 22	20 33
136		**12 55**	**0 53**	**12 50**	**1 00**	**12 43**	**1 08**	**12 34**	**1 20**	**12 20**	**1 37**
17 We	11 56 18	5 23	18 30	5 06	18 47	4 43	19 10	4 12	19 42	3 19	20 35
137		**13 47**	**1 33**	**13 45**	**1 36**	**13 43**	**1 40**	**13 40**	**1 46**	**13 36**	**1 55**
18 Th	11 56 20	5 23	18 30	5 05	18 48	4 43	19 10	4 11	19 43	3 17	20 38
138		**14 41**	**2 13**	**14 43**	**2 13**	**14 45**	**2 12**	**14 48**	**2 12**	**14 54**	**2 12**
19 Fr	11 56 23	5 22	18 31	5 05	18 48	4 42	19 11	4 09	19 45	3 14	20 40
139		**15 37**	**2 54**	**15 42**	**2 50**	**15 50**	**2 46**	**15 59**	**2 39**	**16 15**	**2 30**
20 Sa	11 56 26	5 22	18 31	5 04	18 49	4 41	19 12	4 08	19 46	3 12	20 42
140		**16 35**	**3 38**	**16 45**	**3 31**	**16 56**	**3 22**	**17 13**	**3 09**	**17 39**	**2 50**
21 Su	11 56 29	5 22	18 31	5 04	18 50	4 40	19 13	4 07	19 47	3 10	20 44
141		**17 36**	**4 26**	**17 49**	**4 15**	**18 05**	**4 01**	**18 27**	**3 43**	**19 03**	**3 14**
22 Mo	11 56 33	5 22	18 32	5 03	18 50	4 39	19 14	4 06	19 48	3 08	20 46
142	**13 17 ○**	**18 39**	**5 18**	**18 54**	**5 03**	**19 14**	**4 46**	**19 41**	**4 22**	**20 25**	**3 44**
23 Tu	11 56 38	5 21	18 32	5 03	18 51	4 39	19 15	4 04	19 50	3 06	20 49
143		**19 42**	**6 14**	**19 59**	**5 57**	**20 20**	**5 37**	**20 50**	**5 09**	**21 39**	**4 23**
24 We	11 56 43	5 21	18 33	5 02	18 51	4 38	19 16	4 03	19 51	3 04	20 51
144		**20 44**	**7 14**	**21 01**	**6 56**	**21 22**	**6 35**	**21 52**	**6 05**	**22 41**	**5 15**
25 Th	11 56 48	5 21	18 33	5 02	18 52	4 37	19 17	4 02	19 52	3 02	20 53
145		**21 42**	**8 16**	**21 58**	**7 59**	**22 17**	**7 38**	**22 44**	**7 09**	**23 28**	**6 21**
26 Fr	11 56 54	5 21	18 33	5 02	18 53	4 36	19 18	4 01	19 53	3 00	20 55
146		**22 36**	**9 19**	**22 50**	**9 04**	**23 06**	**8 45**	**23 28**	**8 19**		**7 37**
27 Sa	11 57 01	5 21	18 34	5 01	18 53	4 36	19 19	4 00	19 54	2 58	20 57
147		**23 26**	**10 20**	**23 36**	**10 08**	**23 49**	**9 53**		**9 33**	**0 04**	**9 00**
28 Su	11 57 08	5 20	18 34	5 01	18 54	4 35	19 19	4 00	19 56	2 57	20 59
148			**11 20**		**11 11**		**11 01**	**0 05**	**10 47**	**0 31**	**10 24**
29 Mo	11 57 16	5 20	18 35	5 00	18 54	4 35	19 20	3 59	19 57	2 55	21 01
149	**03 30 ☾**	**0 12**	**12 17**	**0 19**	**12 13**	**0 27**	**12 07**	**0 37**	**11 59**	**0 54**	**11 47**
30 Tu	11 57 24	5 20	18 35	5 00	18 55	4 34	19 21	3 58	19 58	2 53	21 03
150		**0 56**	**13 13**	**0 58**	**13 12**	**1 02**	**13 11**	**1 06**	**13 10**	**1 13**	**13 08**
31 We	11 57 32	5 20	18 35	5 00	18 56	4 34	19 22	3 57	19 58	2 52	21 05
151		**1 37**	**14 07**	**1 36**	**14 10**	**1 35**	**14 14**	**1 33**	**14 19**	**1 31**	**14 26**

6th Month — June, 1978 — 30 Days

Greenwich Mean Time

NOTE: Light figures indicate Sun. **Dark** figures indicate **Moon.** *Degrees are North Latitude.*

CAUTION: Must be converted to local time. For instruction see page 772.

Day of month week year	Sun on meridian Moon phase h m s	20° Rise Sun Moon h m	20° Set Sun Moon h m	30° Rise Sun Moon h m	30° Set Sun Moon h m	40° Rise Sun Moon h m	40° Set Sun Moon h m	50° Rise Sun Moon h m	50° Set Sun Moon h m	60° Rise Sun Moon h m	60° Set Sun Moon h m
1 Th	11 57 41	5 20	18 36	5 00	18 56	4 33	19 22	3 56	20 00	2 50	21 07
152		2 18	15 00	2 13	15 07	2 08	15 15	2 00	15 26	1 48	15 43
2 Fr	11 57 50	5 20	18 36	5 00	18 57	4 33	19 23	3 56	20 01	2 49	21 08
153		2 59	15 52	2 51	16 02	2 41	16 15	2 28	16 31	2 07	16 58
3 Sa	11 58 00	5 20	18 37	4 59	18 57	4 32	19 23	3 55	20 02	2 47	21 10
154		3 41	16 44	3 30	16 57	3 16	17 13	2 57	17 35	2 28	18 10
4 Su	11 58 10	5 20	18 37	4 59	18 58	4 32	19 24	3 54	20 03	2 46	21 12
155		4 24	17 36	4 10	17 51	3 53	18 09	3 30	18 35	2 53	19 17
5 Mo	11 58 20	5 20	18 37	4 59	18 58	4 32	19 25	3 54	20 04	2 45	21 13
156	19 01 ●	5 08	18 26	4 53	18 42	4 33	19 03	4 07	19 31	3 23	20 18
6 Tu	11 58 31	5 20	18 38	4 59	18 59	4 32	19 25	3 53	20 05	2 44	21 15
157		5 55	19 15	5 38	19 32	5 17	19 53	4 48	20 23	4 01	21 11
7 We	11 58 42	5 20	18 38	4 58	18 59	4 31	19 26	3 53	20 05	2 42	21 16
158		6 42	20 02	6 25	20 19	6 04	20 40	5 35	21 08	4 46	21 56
8 Th	11 58 54	5 20	18 39	4 58	19 00	4 31	19 26	3 52	20 06	2 41	21 18
159		7 31	20 47	7 14	21 03	6 54	21 22	6 26	21 49	5 39	22 32
9 Fr	11 59 05	5 20	18 39	4 58	19 00	4 31	19 27	3 52	20 07	2 40	21 19
160		8 20	21 30	8 05	21 44	7 46	22 01	7 21	22 24	6 39	23 01
10 Sa	11 59 17	5 20	18 39	4 58	19 00	4 31	19 28	3 52	20 08	2 39	21 20
161		9 09	22 11	8 56	22 23	8 41	22 36	8 19	22 55	7 44	23 25
11 Su	11 59 29	5 20	18 39	4 58	19 01	4 31	19 28	3 51	20 08	2 39	21 21
162		9 58	22 51	9 48	22 59	9 36	23 10	9 19	23 23	8 52	23 45
12 Mo	11 59 42	5 20	18 40	4 58	19 01	4 30	19 29	3 51	20 09	2 38	21 22
163		10 48	23 30	10 41	23 35	10 33	23 41	10 21	23 50	10 03	
13 Tu	11 59 54	5 20	18 40	4 58	19 02	4 30	19 29	3 50	20 09	2 38	21 23
164	22 44 ☽	11 38		11 35		11 30		11 25		11 16	0 02
14 We	12 00 06	5 20	18 40	4 58	19 02	4 30	19 30	3 50	20 10	2 37	21 24
165		12 30	0 09	12 30	0 10	12 30	0 12	12 30	0 15	12 31	0 19
15 Th	12 00 19	5 20	18 40	4 58	19 02	4 30	19 30	3 50	20 10	2 37	21 25
166		13 23	0 48	13 27	0 46	13 32	0 44	13 38	0 41	13 48	0 36
16 Fr	12 00 32	5 20	18 40	4 59	19 02	4 30	19 31	3 50	20 11	2 36	21 25
167		14 19	1 30	14 26	1 24	14 36	1 17	14 49	1 08	15 09	0 54
17 Sa	12 00 45	5 21	18 40	4 59	19 03	4 31	19 31	3 50	20 11	2 36	21 26
168		15 17	2 14	15 28	2 05	15 42	1 54	16 01	1 38	16 32	1 15
18 Su	12 00 58	5 21	18 41	4 59	19 03	4 31	19 32	3 50	20 12	2 35	21 27
169		16 18	3 03	16 33	2 50	16 50	2 35	17 15	2 14	17 55	1 40
19 Mo	12 01 11	5 21	18 41	4 59	19 03	4 31	19 32	3 50	20 12	2 35	21 27
170		17 21	3 56	17 38	3 41	17 58	3 22	18 27	2 56	19 15	2 14
20 Tu	12 01 24	5 21	18 41	4 59	19 03	4 31	19 32	3 50	20 12	2 35	21 27
171	20 30 ○	18 25	4 55	18 42	4 38	19 04	4 16	19 34	3 47	20 24	2 59
21 We	12 01 37	5 21	18 41	4 59	19 04	4 31	19 32	3 50	20 12	2 35	21 27
172		19 27	5 57	19 43	5 40	20 04	5 18	20 33	4 48	21 20	3 58
22 Th	12 01 50	5 22	18 42	5 00	19 04	4 32	19 33	3 51	20 13	2 36	21 28
173		20 25	7 01	20 40	6 45	20 58	6 25	21 23	5 57	22 03	5 11
23 Fr	12 02 03	5 22	18 42	5 00	19 05	4 32	19 33	3 51	20 13	2 36	21 28
174		21 19	8 06	21 30	7 52	21 45	7 35	22 04	7 12	22 35	6 34
24 Sa	12 02 15	5 22	18 42	5 00	19 05	4 32	19 33	3 51	20 13	2 36	21 28
175		22 08	9 09	22 16	8 59	22 26	8 46	22 40	8 29	23 00	8 01
25 Su	12 02 28	5 22	18 42	5 00	19 05	4 32	19 33	3 51	20 13	2 37	21 28
176		22 54	10 09	22 58	10 03	23 03	9 55	23 10	9 44	23 21	9 28
26 Mo	12 02 41	5 22	18 42	5 00	19 05	4 33	19 33	3 52	20 13	2 38	21 28
177		23 37	11 07	23 37	11 05	23 38	11 02	23 38	10 58	23 39	10 52
27 Tu	12 02 53	5 23	18 43	5 01	19 05	4 33	19 33	3 52	20 13	2 38	21 27
178	11 44 ☾		12 03		12 04		12 06		12 09	23 57	12 13
28 We	12 03 06	5 23	18 43	5 01	19 05	4 34	19 33	3 53	20 13	2 39	21 27
179		0 19	12 56	0 15	13 02	0 11	13 08	0 06	13 17		13 31
29 Th	12 03 18	5 23	18 43	5 01	19 05	4 34	19 33	3 53	20 13	2 40	21 27
180		1 00	13 49	0 53	13 58	0 44	14 09	0 33	14 24	0 15	14 47
30 Fr	12 03 30	5 23	18 43	5 01	19 05	4 34	19 33	3 54	20 13	2 41	21 26
181		1 41	14 41	1 31	14 53	1 18	15 07	1 02	15 27	0 35	15 59

7th Month July, 1978 31 Days

Greenwich Mean Time

NOTE: Light figures indicate Sun. **Dark** figures indicate **Moon.** *Degrees are North Latitude.*
CAUTION: Must be converted to local time. For instruction see page 772.

Day of month week year	Sun on meridian **Moon phase** h m s	20° Rise Sun **Moon** h m	20° Set Sun **Moon** h m	30° Rise Sun **Moon** h m	30° Set Sun **Moon** h m	40° Rise Sun **Moon** h m	40° Set Sun **Moon** h m	50° Rise Sun **Moon** h m	50° Set Sun **Moon** h m	60° Rise Sun **Moon** h m	60° Set Sun **Moon** h m
1 Sa	12 03 42	5 24	18 43	5 02	19 05	4 35	19 33	3 55	20 13	2 42	21 25
182		**2 23**	**15 32**	**2 10**	**15 46**	**1 55**	**16 04**	**1 33**	**16 29**	**0 59**	**17 08**
2 Su	12 03 54	5 24	18 44	5 02	19 05	4 35	19 32	3 55	20 12	2 43	21 25
183		**3 07**	**16 23**	**2 52**	**16 38**	**2 33**	**16 58**	**2 08**	**17 26**	**1 27**	**18 11**
3 Mo	12 04 05	5 25	18 44	5 03	19 05	4 36	19 32	3 56	20 12	2 44	21 24
184		**3 52**	**17 12**	**3 36**	**17 29**	**3 15**	**17 50**	**2 47**	**18 19**	**2 01**	**19 07**
4 Tu	12 04 16	5 25	18 44	5 03	19 05	4 36	19 32	3 57	20 12	2 45	21 23
185		**4 39**	**18 00**	**4 22**	**18 16**	**4 01**	**18 38**	**3 31**	**19 07**	**2 43**	**19 55**
5 We	12 04 27	5 25	18 44	5 04	19 05	4 37	19 32	3 58	20 11	2 46	21 22
186	**09 50 ●**	**5 27**	**18 45**	**5 10**	**19 02**	**4 50**	**19 22**	**4 21**	**19 49**	**3 33**	**20 34**
6 Th	12 04 37	5 26	18 44	5 04	19 05	4 37	19 32	3 59	20 11	2 48	21 21
187		**6 16**	**19 29**	**6 00**	**19 44**	**5 41**	**20 02**	**5 14**	**20 26**	**4 30**	**21 06**
7 Fr	12 04 47	5 26	18 43	5 05	19 04	4 38	19 31	3 59	20 10	2 49	21 19
188		**7 05**	**20 11**	**6 52**	**20 23**	**6 35**	**20 38**	**6 11**	**20 59**	**5 34**	**21 31**
8 Sa	12 04 57	5 27	18 43	5 05	19 04	4 38	19 31	4 00	20 10	2 51	21 18
189		**7 55**	**20 51**	**7 44**	**21 01**	**7 30**	**21 12**	**7 11**	**21 28**	**6 41**	**21 53**
9 Su	12 05 06	5 27	18 43	5 06	19 04	4 39	19 31	4 01	20 09	2 52	21 17
190		**8 44**	**21 30**	**8 36**	**21 37**	**8 26**	**21 44**	**8 12**	**21 55**	**7 51**	**22 11**
10 Mo	12 05 15	5 27	18 43	5 06	19 04	4 40	19 31	4 02	20 08	2 54	21 16
191		**9 34**	**22 08**	**9 29**	**22 12**	**9 23**	**22 15**	**9 15**	**22 20**	**9 02**	**22 28**
11 Tu	12 05 23	5 27	18 43	5 07	19 04	4 40	19 30	4 03	20 07	2 55	21 14
192		**10 24**	**22 47**	**10 22**	**22 47**	**10 21**	**22 46**	**10 18**	**22 45**	**10 15**	**22 44**
12 We	12 05 31	5 28	18 43	5 07	19 03	4 41	19 30	4 04	20 07	2 57	21 13
193		**11 15**	**23 27**	**11 17**	**23 23**	**11 20**	**23 18**	**11 24**	**23 11**	**11 30**	**23 01**
13 Th	12 05 39	5 28	18 43	5 08	19 03	4 41	19 29	4 05	20 06	2 58	21 11
194	**10 49 ☽**	**12 08**		**12 14**		**12 21**	**23 52**	**12 31**	**23 39**	**12 47**	**23 20**
14 Fr	12 05 45	5 28	18 43	5 08	19 03	4 42	19 29	4 06	20 05	3 00	21 10
195		**13 03**	**0 08**	**13 13**	**0 01**	**13 25**		**13 41**		**14 06**	**23 42**
15 Sa	12 05 52	5 28	18 43	5 09	19 03	4 43	19 28	4 07	20 04	3 02	21 08
196		**14 01**	**0 53**	**14 14**	**0 43**	**14 30**	**0 29**	**14 52**	**0 11**	**15 27**	
16 Su	12 05 58	5 29	18 43	5 09	19 02	4 44	19 28	4 08	20 03	3 04	21 06
197		**15 02**	**1 43**	**15 17**	**1 29**	**15 36**	**1 12**	**16 03**	**0 48**	**16 47**	**0 10**
17 Mo	12 06 03	5 29	18 42	5 10	19 02	4 44	19 27	4 09	20 02	3 06	21 05
198		**16 04**	**2 37**	**16 21**	**2 21**	**16 42**	**2 01**	**17 12**	**1 33**	**18 01**	**0 48**
18 Tu	12 06 08	5 30	18 42	5 10	19 01	4 45	19 27	4 10	20 01	3 08	21 03
199		**17 07**	**3 36**	**17 24**	**3 19**	**17 45**	**2 57**	**18 15**	**2 27**	**19 04**	**1 38**
19 We	12 06 12	5 30	18 42	5 11	19 01	4 46	19 26	4 11	20 00	3 10	21 01
200		**18 07**	**4 39**	**18 23**	**4 22**	**18 43**	**4 01**	**19 10**	**3 32**	**19 54**	**2 43**
20 Th	12 06 16	5 30	18 42	5 12	19 01	4 47	19 25	4 12	19 59	3 12	20 59
201	**03 05 ○**	**19 04**	**5 44**	**19 18**	**5 29**	**19 34**	**5 10**	**19 57**	**4 44**	**20 33**	**4 02**
21 Fr	12 06 19	5 31	18 41	5 12	19 00	4 48	19 24	4 14	19 58	3 14	20 57
202		**19 57**	**6 49**	**20 07**	**6 37**	**20 20**	**6 22**	**20 36**	**6 02**	**21 02**	**5 29**
22 Sa	12 06 22	5 31	18 41	5 13	19 00	4 49	19 24	4 15	19 56	3 16	20 54
203		**20 46**	**7 53**	**20 52**	**7 45**	**21 00**	**7 34**	**21 10**	**7 20**	**21 26**	**6 58**
23 Su	12 06 24	5 32	18 40	5 13	18 59	4 50	19 23	4 17	19 55	3 18	20 52
204		**21 32**	**8 54**	**21 34**	**8 50**	**21 37**	**8 45**	**21 41**	**8 37**	**21 46**	**8 26**
24 Mo	12 06 25	5 32	18 40	5 14	18 59	4 51	19 22	4 18	19 54	3 20	20 50
205		**22 16**	**9 53**	**22 14**	**9 52**	**22 12**	**9 52**	**22 09**	**9 52**	**22 05**	**9 51**
25 Tu	12 06 26	5 32	18 40	5 15	18 58	4 52	19 21	4 19	19 53	3 22	20 48
206		**22 58**	**10 49**	**22 53**	**10 53**	**22 46**	**10 57**	**22 37**	**11 04**	**22 23**	**11 13**
26 We	12 06 27	5 33	18 40	5 15	18 58	4 53	19 20	4 20	19 52	3 25	20 46
207	**22 31 ☾**	**23 40**	**11 43**	**23 31**	**11 51**	**23 20**	**12 00**	**23 06**	**12 12**	**22 43**	**12 32**
27 Th	12 06 27	5 33	18 39	5 16	18 57	4 53	19 19	4 22	19 50	3 27	20 43
208			**12 36**		**12 47**	**23 56**	**13 00**	**23 36**	**13 18**	**23 05**	**13 47**
28 Fr	12 06 26	5 34	18 39	5 16	18 57	5 54	19 18	4 23	19 49	3 30	20 41
209		**0 23**	**13 28**	**0 11**	**13 42**		**13 58**		**14 21**	**23 31**	**14 58**
29 Sa	12 06 24	5 34	18 39	5 17	18 56	4 55	19 17	4 24	19 48	3 32	20 39
210		**1 06**	**14 19**	**0 52**	**14 34**	**0 34**	**14 53**	**0 10**	**15 20**		**16 03**
30 Su	12 06 22	5 34	18 38	5 18	18 55	4 56	19 16	4 25	19 46	3 34	20 37
211		**1 51**	**15 09**	**1 35**	**15 25**	**1 15**	**15 46**	**0 48**	**16 14**	**0 03**	**17 02**
31 Mo	12 06 20	5 35	18 38	5 18	18 54	4 57	19 15	4 27	19 45	3 37	20 34
212		**2 37**	**15 57**	**2 20**	**16 14**	**1 59**	**16 35**	**1 30**	**17 04**	**0 42**	**17 52**

8th Month August, 1978 31 Days

Greenwich Mean Time

NOTE: Light figures indicate Sun. **Dark** figures indicate **Moon.** *Degrees are North Latitude.*

CAUTION: Must be converted to local time. For instruction see page 772.

Day of month week year	Sun on meridian **Moon phase**	20° Rise Sun **Moon**	20° Set Sun **Moon**	30° Rise Sun **Moon**	30° Set Sun **Moon**	40° Rise Sun **Moon**	40° Set Sun **Moon**	50° Rise Sun **Moon**	50° Set Sun **Moon**	60° Rise Sun **Moon**	60° Set Sun **Moon**
	h m s	h m	h m	h m	h m	h m	h m	h m	h m	h m	h m
1 Tu	12 06 17	5 35	18 37	5 19	18 54	4 57	19 14	4 28	19 43	3 39	20 32
213		**3 24**	**16 43**	**3 07**	**17 00**	**2 47**	**17 20**	**2 17**	**17 48**	**1 29**	**18 34**
2 We	12 06 13	5 36	18 37	5 19	18 53	4 58	19 13	4 30	19 42	3 42	20 29
214		**4 13**	**17 28**	**3 57**	**17 43**	**3 37**	**18 02**	**3 09**	**18 27**	**2 24**	**19 09**
3 Th	12 06 09	5 36	18 36	5 20	18 52	4 59	19 12	4 31	19 40	3 44	20 27
215		**5 02**	**18 11**	**4 48**	**18 24**	**4,30**	**18 40**	**4 05**	**19 02**	**3 25**	**19 36**
4 Fr	12 06 04	5 36	18 35	5 21	18 51	5 00	19 11	4 32	19 38	3 46	20 24
216	**01 01 ●**	**5 51**	**18 51**	**5 39**	**19 02**	**5 25**	**19 15**	**5 04**	**19 32**	**4 31**	**19 59**
5 Sa	12 05 58	5 37	18 35	5 21	18 50	5 01	19 10	4 34	19 37	3 49	20 22
217		**6 41**	**19 31**	**6 32**	**19 39**	**6 20**	**19 48**	**6 05**	**20 00**	**5 40**	**20 19**
6 Su	12 05 52	5 37	18 34	5 22	18 50	5 02	19 09	4 35	19 35	3 51	20 19
218		**7 31**	**20 10**	**7 25**	**20 14**	**7 17**	**20 19**	**7 07**	**20 26**	**6 52**	**20 37**
7 Mo	12 05 45	5 38	18 34	5 22	18 49	5 03	19 07	4 37	19 34	3 54	20 17
219		**8 21**	**20 48**	**8 18**	**20 47**	**8 15**	**20 50**	**8 11**	**20 51**	**8 04**	**20 53**
8 Tu	12 05 38	5 38	18 33	5 23	18 48	5 04	19 06	4 38	19 32	3 56	20 14
220		**9 11**	**21 27**	**9 12**	**21 24**	**9 14**	**21 21**	**9 15**	**21 17**	**9 18**	**21 10**
9 We	12 05 30	5 38	18 32	5 24	18 47	5 05	19 05	4 40	19 30	3 58	20 11
221		**10 03**	**22 07**	**10 08**	**22 01**	**10 13**	**21 54**	**10 21**	**21 43**	**10 33**	**21 28**
10 Th	12 05 21	5 38	18 32	5 24	18 46	5 06	19 04	4 41	19 28	4 01	20 08
222		**10 57**	**22 50**	**11 05**	**22 41**	**11 15**	**22 29**	**11 29**	**22 13**	**11 50**	**21 48**
11 Fr	12 05 12	5 39	18 31	5 25	18 46	5 07	19 02	4 43	19 27	4 03	20 06
223	**20 06 ☽**	**11 52**	**23 36**	**12 03**	**23 24**	**12 18**	**23 08**	**12 37**	**22 47**	**13 08**	**22 13**
12 Sa	12 05 02	5 39	18 31	5 25	18 45	5 08	19 01	4 44	19 25	4 06	20 03
224		**12 50**		**13 04**		**13 22**	**23 53**	**13 46**	**23 27**	**14 26**	**22 45**
13 Su	12 04 52	5 39	18 30	5 26	18 44	5 09	19 00	4 46	19 23	4 08	20 00
225		**13 49**	**0 27**	**14 05**	**0 11**	**14 25**		**14 54**		**15 40**	**23 27**
14 Mo	12 04 41	5 39	18 29	5 27	18 43	5 10	18 59	4 47	19 21	4 10	19 57
226		**14 49**	**1 21**	**15 06**	**1 05**	**15 28**	**0 44**	**15 57**	**0 15**	**16 47**	
15 Tu	12 04 30	5 40	18 29	5 27	18 42	5 11	18 57	4 49	19 19	4 13	19 54
227		**15 49**	**2 21**	**16 06**	**2 04**	**16 26**	**1 42**	**16 55**	**1 12**	**17 42**	**0 23**
16 We	12 04 18	5 40	18 28	5 28	18 41	5 12	18 56	4 50	19 18	4 15	19 52
228		**16 47**	**3 23**	**17 02**	**3 07**	**17 20**	**2 47**	**17 45**	**2 19**	**18 26**	**1 33**
17 Th	12 04 05	5 41	18 28	5 28	18 40	5 13	18 54	4 52	19 16	4 18	19 49
229		**17 42**	**4 28**	**17 54**	**4 14**	**18 08**	**3 57**	**18 28**	**3 33**	**19 00**	**2 55**
18 Fr	12 03 52	5 41	18 27	5 29	18 39	5 14	18 53	4 53	19 14	4 20	19 46
230	**10 14 ○**	**18 33**	**5 32**	**18 42**	**5 22**	**18 52**	**5 09**	**19 05**	**4 51**	**19 26**	**4 23**
19 Sa	12 03 39	5 41	18 26	5 30	18 38	5 15	18 52	4 55	19 12	4 22	19 43
231		**19 22**	**6 35**	**19 26**	**6 29**	**19 31**	**6 21**	**19 38**	**6 10**	**19 49**	**5 53**
20 Su	12 03 25	5 41	18 25	5 30	18 37	5 16	18 50	4 56	19 10	4 25	19 40
232		**20 08**	**7 36**	**20 08**	**7 34**	**20 08**	**7 31**	**20 08**	**7 27**	**20 09**	**7 21**
21 Mo	12 03 10	5 42	18 25	5 31	18 35	5 17	18 49	4 58	19 08	4 27	19 38
233		**20 52**	**8 35**	**20 48**	**8 37**	**20 43**	**8 39**	**20 37**	**8 42**	**20 28**	**8 47**
22 Tu	12 02 55	5 42	18 24	5 31	18 34	5 18	18 47	4 59	19 06	4 30	19 35
234		**21 35**	**9 32**	**21 78**	**9 38**	**21 19**	**9 45**	**21 07**	**9 54**	**20 48**	**10 09**
23 We	12 02 40	5 42	18 23	5 32	18 33	5 19	18 46	5 01	19 04	4 32	19 32
235		**22 19**	**10 27**	**22 08**	**10 36**	**21 55**	**10 48**	**21 37**	**11 03**	**21 10**	**11 28**
24 Th	12 02 24	5 42	18 22	5 32	18 32	5 20	18 45	5 02	19 02	4 34	19 29
236		**23 02**	**11 21**	**22 49**	**11 33**	**22 33**	**11 48**	**22 10**	**12 09**	**21 35**	**12 42**
25 Fr	12 02 08	5 42	18 21	5 33	18 31	5 21	18 43	5 04	19 00	4 37	19 26
237	**12 18 ☾**	**23 47**	**12 13**	**23 32**	**12 27**	**23 13**	**12 45**	**22 47**	**13 10**	**22 05**	**13 51**
26 Sa	12 01 51	5 43	18 21	5 33	18 30	5 21	18 42	5 05	18 57	4 39	19 23
238			**13 04**		**13 20**	**23 56**	**13 40**	**23 28**	**14 07**	**22 42**	**14 53**
27 Su	12 01 34	5 43	18 20	5 34	18 29	5 22	18 40	5 07	18 55	4 42	19 20
239		**0 33**	**13 53**	**0 17**	**14 09**		**14 30**		**14 59**	**23 26**	**15 47**
28 Mo	12 01 17	5 43	18 19	5 34	18 28	5 23	18 39	5 08	18 53	4 44	19 17
240		**1 20**	**14 40**	**1 04**	**14 56**	**0 43**	**15 17**	**0 14**	**15 45**		**16 32**
29 Tu	12 00 59	5 43	18 18	5 35	18 27	5 24	18 37	5 10	18 51	4 46	19 14
241		**2 09**	**15 25**	**1 52**	**15 41**	**1 32**	**16 00**	**1 04**	**16 26**	**0 18**	**17 09**
30 We	12 00 41	5 43	18 17	5 35	18 26	5 25	18 36	5 11	18 49	4 49	19 11
242		**2 57**	**16 08**	**2 43**	**16 22**	**2 24**	**16 39**	**1 58**	**17 02**	**1 17**	**17 39**
31 Th	12 00 23	5 44	18 17	5 36	18 24	5 26	18 34	5 13	18 47	4 51	19 08
243		**3 47**	**16 50**	**3 34**	**17 01**	**3 18**	**17 15**	**2 56**	**17 34**	**2 21**	**18 04**

9th Month September, 1978 30 Days

Greenwich Mean Time

NOTE: Light figures indicate Sun. **Dark** figures indicate **Moon.** *Degrees are North Latitude.*

CAUTION: Must be converted to local time. For instruction see page 772.

Day of month week year	Sun on meridian **Moon phase** h m s	20° Rise Sun **Moon** h m	20° Set Sun **Moon** h m	30° Rise Sun **Moon** h m	30° Set Sun **Moon** h m	40° Rise Sun **Moon** h m	40° Set Sun **Moon** h m	50° Rise Sun **Moon** h m	50° Set Sun **Moon** h m	60° Rise Sun **Moon** h m	60° Set Sun **Moon** h m
1 Fr	12 00 04	5 44	18 16	5 36	18 23	5 27	18 33	5 14	18 41	4 54	19 05
244		**4 37**	**17 30**	**4 26**	**17 39**	**4 14**	**17 49**	**3 57**	**18 03**	**3 36**	**18 25**
2 Sa	11 59 45	5 44	18 15	5 37	18 22	5 28	18 31	5 16	18 43	4 56	19 02
245	**16 09** ●	**5 27**	**18 10**	**5 20**	**18 15**	**5 11**	**18 22**	**4 59**	**18 30**	**4 45**	**18 44**
3 Su	11 59 26	5 44	18 14	5 38	18 21	5 29	18 29	5 17	18 41	4 58	18 59
246		**6 17**	**18 48**	**6 13**	**18 50**	**6 09**	**18 53**	**6 02**	**18 56**	**5 55**	**19 01**
4 Mo	11 59 06	5 44	18 13	5 38	18 20	5 30	18 28	5 19	18 39	5 01	18 56
247		**7 08**	**19 28**	**7 08**	**19 26**	**7 08**	**19 24**	**7 07**	**19 22**	**7 07**	**19 18**
5 Tu	11 58 47	5 45	18 12	5 39	18 18	5 31	18 26	5 20	18 36	5 03	18 53
248		**8 00**	**20 08**	**8 03**	**20 03**	**8 08**	**19 57**	**8 13**	**19 48**	**8 20**	**19 35**
6 We	11 58 77	5 45	18 11	5 39	18 17	5 32	18 25	5 22	18 34	5 06	18 50
249		**8 53**	**20 50**	**9 00**	**20 41**	**9 09**	**20 31**	**9 20**	**20 17**	**9 34**	**19 55**
7 Th	11 58 06	5 45	18 10	5 40	18 16	5 33	18 23	5 23	18 32	5 08	18 47
250		**9 48**	**21 35**	**9 58**	**21 23**	**10 11**	**21 09**	**10 28**	**20 49**	**10 49**	**20 18**
8 Fr	11 57 46	5 45	18 09	5 41	18 15	5 34	18 21	5 24	18 30	5 10	18 44
251		**10 44**	**22 23**	**10 57**	**22 08**	**11 14**	**21 51**	**11 36**	**21 26**	**12 04**	**20 47**
9 Sa	11 57 25	5 46	18 08	5 41	18 14	5 35	18 20	5 26	18 28	5 12	18 41
252		**11 41**	**23 15**	**11 57**	**22 58**	**12 16**	**22 38**	**12 43**	**22 10**	**13 16**	**21 25**
10 Su	11 57 04	5 46	18 08	5 42	18 12	5 35	18 18	5 27	18 25	5 15	18 38
253	**03 20** ☽	**12 40**		**12 56**	**23 53**	**13 17**	**23 32**	**13 47**	**23 03**	**14 23**	**22 14**
11 Mo	11 56 43	5 47	18 07	5 42	18 11	5 36	18 17	5 29	18 23	5 17	18 35
254		**13 88**	**0 10**	**13 55**		**14 16**		**14 45**		**15 21**	**23 16**
12 Tu	11 56 22	5 47	18 06	5 43	18 10	5 37	18 15	5 30	18 21	5 19	18 32
255		**14 34**	**1 10**	**14 50**	**0 53**	**15 09**	**0 32**	**15 36**	**0 04**	**16 09**	
13 We	11 56 01	5 47	18 05	5 44	18 09	5 38	18 13	5 31	18 19	5 21	18 29
256		**15 29**	**2 11**	**15 42**	**1 56**	**15 59**	**1 38**	**16 21**	**1 12**	**16 48**	**0 30**
14 Th	11 55 40	5 47	18 04	5 44	18 08	5 38	18 11	5 33	18 17	5 24	18 26
257		**16 21**	**3 14**	**16 31**	**3 02**	**16 43**	**2 47**	**17 00**	**2 26**	**17 19**	**1 53**
15 Fr	11 55 18	5 48	18 03	5 45	18 06	5 39	18 10	5 34	18 14	5 26	18 23
258		**17 10**	**4 16**	**17 16**	**4 07**	**17 24**	**3 57**	**17 34**	**3 43**	**17 46**	**3 20**
16 Sa	11 54 57	5 48	18 02	5 45	18 05	5 39	18 08	5 36	18 12	5 29	18 20
259	**19 01** ○	**17 56**	**5 17**	**17 59**	**5 13**	**18 01**	**5 07**	**18 05**	**5 00**	**18 09**	**4 48**
17 Su	11 54 36	5 48	18 01	5 45	18 04	5 40	18 06	5 37	18 10	5 31	18 17
260		**18 42**	**6 17**	**18 40**	**6 17**	**18 38**	**6 17**	**18 35**	**6 16**	**18 32**	**6 16**
18 Mo	11 54 14	5 48	18 04	5 46	18 03	5 41	18 04	5 39	18 08	5 33	18 14
261		**19 26**	**7 16**	**19 21**	**7 20**	**19 14**	**7 24**	**19 04**	**7 31**	**18 54**	**7 41**
19 Tu	11 53 53	5 48	18 02	5 46	18 01	5 43	18 03	5 40	18 06	5 36	18 11
262		**20 10**	**8 13**	**20 01**	**8 20**	**19 50**	**8 30**	**19 35**	**8 43**	**19 18**	**9 03**
20 We	11 53 31	5 49	18 01	5 47	18 00	5 44	18 01	5 42	18 03	5 38	18 07
263		**20 55**	**9 09**	**20 43**	**9 19**	**20 28**	**9 33**	**20 08**	**9 51**	**19 44**	**10 21**
21 Th	11 53 10	5 49	17 59	5 47	17 58	5 46	18 00	5 43	18 01	5 41	18 04
264		**21 41**	**10 03**	**21 26**	**10 16**	**21 08**	**10 33**	**20 44**	**10 56**	**20 14**	**11 34**
22 Fr	11 52 49	5 49	17 57	5 48	17 57	5 47	17 58	5 45	17 59	5 43	18 01
265		**22 27**	**10 55**	**22 11**	**11 11**	**21 51**	**11 30**	**21 24**	**11 57**	**20 50**	**12 40**
23 Sa	11 52 28	5 49	17 56	5 49	17 56	5 48	17 56	5 47	17 57	5 45	17 58
266		**23 14**	**11 46**	**22 58**	**12 02**	**22 37**	**12 23**	**22 08**	**12 51**	**21 33**	**13 38**
24 Su	11 52 07	5 49	17 55	5 49	17 55	5 49	17 55	5 48	17 55	5 48	17 55
267	**05 07** ☾		**12 34**	**23 46**	**12 51**	**23 25**	**13 11**	**22 57**	**13 40**	**22 22**	**14 28**
25 Mo	11 51 46	5 50	17 54	5 50	17 53	5 50	17 53	5 50	17 52	5 50	17 52
268		**0 02**	**13 20**		**13 36**		**13 56**	**23 50**	**14 23**	**23 17**	**15 08**
26 Tu	11 51 26	5 50	17 53	5 50	17 52	5 51	17 52	5 51	17 50	5 53	17 49
269		**0 51**	**14 04**	**0 36**	**14 19**	**0 16**	**14 37**		**15 01**		**15 41**
27 We	11 51 05	5 50	17 52	5 51	17 51	5 52	17 50	5 53	17 48	5 55	17 46
270		**1 40**	**14 47**	**1 27**	**14 59**	**1 10**	**15 14**	**0 46**	**15 35**	**0 18**	**16 07**
28 Th	11 50 45	5 50	17 51	5 52	17 50	5 53	17 48	5 55	17 46	5 57	17 43
271		**2 30**	**15 27**	**2 19**	**15 37**	**2 05**	**15 49**	**1 46**	**16 05**	**1 23**	**16 30**
29 Fr	11 50 25	5 50	17 50	5 52	17 49	5 54	17 46	5 56	17 44	6 00	17 40
272		**3 20**	**16 07**	**3 11**	**16 14**	**3 01**	**16 22**	**2 47**	**16 32**	**2 31**	**16 49**
30 Sa	11 50 05	5 51	17 50	5 53	17 46	5 55	17 45	5 58	17 41	6 02	17 37
273		**4 10**	**16 46**	**4 05**	**16 49**	**3 59**	**16 53**	**3 50**	**16 59**	**3 41**	**17 07**

10th Month — October, 1978 — 31 Days

Greenwich Mean Time

NOTE: Light figures indicate Sun. **Dark** figures indicate **Moon.** *Degrees are North Latitude.*

CAUTION: Must be converted to local time. For instruction see page 772.

Day of month week year	Sun on meridian **Moon phase** h m s	20° Rise Sun **Moon** h m	20° Set Sun **Moon** h m	30° Rise Sun **Moon** h m	30° Set Sun **Moon** h m	40° Rise Sun **Moon** h m	40° Set Sun **Moon** h m	50° Rise Sun **Moon** h m	50° Set Sun **Moon** h m	60° Rise Sun **Moon** h m	60° Set Sun **Moon** h m
1 Su	11 49 46	5 51	17 49	5 53	17 46	5 56	17 44	5 59	17 39	6 05	17 34
274		**5 01**	**17 26**	**5 00**	**17 25**	**4 58**	**17 25**	**4 55**	**17 25**	**4 52**	**17 24**
2 Mo	11 49 27	5 51	17 48	5 54	17 45	5 57	17 42	6 01	17 37	6 07	17 31
275	**06 41** ●	**5 54**	**18 06**	**5 56**	**18 02**	**5 58**	**17 57**	**6 02**	**17 51**	**6 08**	**17 41**
3 Tu	11 49 08	5 51	17 47	5 54	17 44	5 58	17 40	6 02	17 35	6 09	17 28
276		**6 47**	**18 48**	**6 53**	**18 41**	**7 00**	**18 32**	**7 10**	**18 19**	**7 25**	**18 01**
4 We	11 48 50	5 51	17 46	5 55	17 43	5 59	17 39	6 04	17 33	6 12	17 25
277		**7 42**	**19 33**	**7 52**	**19 22**	**8 03**	**19 09**	**8 19**	**18 51**	**8 44**	**18 23**
5 Th	11 48 31	5 52	17 45	5 55	17 41	6 00	17 37	6 05	17 31	6 14	17 22
278		**8 39**	**20 20**	**8 51**	**20 07**	**9 07**	**19 50**	**9 28**	**19 27**	**10 02**	**18 50**
6 Fr	11 48 14	5 52	17 44	5 56	17 40	6 01	17 36	6 07	17 29	6 17	17 19
279		**9 37**	**21 11**	**9 52**	**20 56**	**10 10**	**20 36**	**10 36**	**20 09**	**11 19**	**19 25**
7 Sa	11 47 56	5 52	17 43	5 56	17 39	6 02	17 34	6 08	17 27	6 19	17 16
280		**10 35**	**22 06**	**10 51**	**21 49**	**11 12**	**21 28**	**11 41**	**20 59**	**12 29**	**20 10**
8 Su	11 47 39	5 52	17 42	5 57	17 38	6 03	17 32	6 10	17 25	6 21	17 13
281		**11 33**	**23 03**	**11 50**	**22 46**	**12 11**	**22 25**	**12 40**	**21 56**	**13 29**	**21 08**
9 Mo	11 47 22	5 53	17 41	5 58	17 37	6 04	17 31	6 11	17 23	6 24	17 10
282	**09 38** ☽	**12 29**		**12 45**	**23 47**	**13 05**	**23 28**	**13 33**	**23 01**	**14 18**	**22 17**
10 Tu	11 47 06	5 53	17 41	5 58	17 35	6 05	17 29	6 13	17 20	6 26	17 07
283		**13 22**	**0 03**	**13 37**		**13 54**		**14 18**		**14 57**	**23 35**
11 We	11 46 50	5 54	17 40	5 59	17 34	6 06	17 28	6 14	17 18	6 29	17 04
284		**14 13**	**1 03**	**14 25**	**0 50**	**14 39**	**0 34**	**14 58**	**0 11**	**15 28**	
12 Th	11 46 35	5 54	17 39	6 00	17 33	6 07	17 26	6 16	17 16	6 31	17 01
285		**15 02**	**2 03**	**15 10**	**1 54**	**15 19**	**1 41**	**15 32**	**1 24**	**15 53**	**0 58**
13 Fr	11 46 20	5 54	17 38	6 01	17 32	6 08	17 24	6 18	17 14	6 33	16 58
286		**15 48**	**3 03**	**15 52**	**2 57**	**15 57**	**2 50**	**16 04**	**2 39**	**16 14**	**2 23**
14 Sa	11 46 06	5 54	17 37	6 01	17 31	6 09	17 23	6 19	17 12	6 36	16 55
287		**16 33**	**4 02**	**16 33**	**4 00**	**16 33**	**3 58**	**16 33**	**3 54**	**16 34**	**3 48**
15 Su	11 45 52	5 55	17 37	6 02	17 30	6 10	17 21	6 21	17 10	6 38	16 53
288		**17 17**	**5 01**	**17 13**	**5 02**	**7 09**	**5 05**	**17 02**	**5 08**	**16 53**	**5 13**
16 Mo	11 45 39	5 55	17 36	6 02	17 29	6 11	17 20	6 22	17 08	6 41	16 50
289	**06 09** ○	**18 01**	**5 58**	**17 54**	**6 04**	**17 44**	**6 11**	**17 32**	**6 21**	**17 13**	**6 36**
17 Tu	11 45 26	5 55	17 35	6 03	17 28	6 12	17 18	6 24	17 06	6 43	16 47
290		**18 46**	**6 54**	**18 35**	**7 04**	**18 22**	**7 15**	**18 04**	**7 31**	**17 36**	**7 56**
18 We	11 45 14	5 55	17 34	6 04	17 27	6 13	17 17	6 26	17 04	6 45	16 44
291		**19 32**	**7 50**	**19 18**	**8 02**	**19 01**	**8 18**	**18 38**	**8 39**	**18 02**	**9 13**
19 Th	11 45 03	5 56	17 34	6 04	17 26	6 14	17 15	6 27	17 02	6 48	16 41
292		**20 18**	**8 44**	**20 03**	**8 58**	**19 43**	**9 17**	**19 17**	**9 42**	**18 34**	**10 24**
20 Fr	11 44 52	5 56	17 33	6 05	17 25	6 15	17 14	6 29	17 00	6 50	16 39
293		**21 06**	**9 36**	**20 49**	**9 52**	**20 29**	**10 12**	**20 00**	**10 41**	**19 13**	**11 27**
21 Sa	11 44 42	5 57	17 33	6 05	17 24	6 16	17 12	6 30	16 58	6 53	16 36
294		**21 54**	**10 26**	**21 37**	**10 43**	**21 17**	**11 04**	**20 47**	**11 33**	**20 00**	**12 21**
22 Su	11 44 32	5 57	17 32	6 06	17 23	6 17	17 11	6 32	16 56	6 55	16 33
295		**22 43**	**11 14**	**22 27**	**11 30**	**22 07**	**11 51**	**21 39**	**12 19**	**20 54**	**13 05**
23 Mo	11 44 24	5 57	17 31	6 07	17 22	6 18	17 10	6 34	16 54	6 58	16 30
296		**23 32**	**11 59**	**23 18**	**12 14**	**23 00**	**12 33**	**22 35**	**12 59**	**21 54**	**13 41**
24 Tu	11 44 16	5 58	17 31	6 08	17 21	6 19	17 09	6 35	16 52	7 00	16 27
297	**00 34** ☾		**12 42**		**12 55**	**23 54**	**13 12**	**23 33**	**13 34**	**22 59**	**14 10**
25 We	11 44 08	5 58	17 30	6 08	17 20	6 21	17 07	6 37	16 51	7 03	16 25
298		**0 22**	**13 23**	**0 09**	**13 34**		**13 47**		**14 05**		**14 34**
26 Th	11 44 02	5 59	17 30	6 09	17 19	6 22	17 06	6 38	16 49	7 05	16 22
299		**1 11**	**14 03**	**1 01**	**14 11**	**0 49**	**14 20**	**0 33**	**14 34**	**0 07**	**14 54**
27 Fr	11 43 56	5 59	17 29	6 10	17 18	6 23	17 05	6 41	16 47	7 08	16 19
300		**2 01**	**14 42**	**1 54**	**14 46**	**1 46**	**14 52**	**1 35**	**15 00**	**1 18**	**15 12**
28 Sa	11 43 51	5 59	17 28	6 11	17 17	6 24	17 04	6 43	16 47	7 11	16 16
301		**2 51**	**15 21**	**2 48**	**15 22**	**2 44**	**15 24**	**2 39**	**15 26**	**2 31**	**15 29**
29 Su	11 43 46	6 00	17 28	6 11	17 16	6 25	17 02	6 44	16 47	7 13	16 13
302		**3 43**	**16 01**	**3 44**	**15 58**	**3 44**	**15 56**	**3 45**	**15 52**	**3 46**	**15 46**
30 Mo	11 43 43	6 00	17 27	6 12	17 15	6 26	17 01	6 46	16 48	7 16	16 11
303		**4 36**	**16 42**	**4 41**	**16 36**	**4 46**	**16 29**	**4 53**	**16 19**	**5 04**	**16 04**
31 Tu	11 43 40	6 01	17 27	6 12	17 14	6 27	16 59	6 47	16 48	7 18	16 08
304	**20 06** ●	**5 32**	**17 27**	**5 40**	**17 17**	**5 49**	**17 05**	**6 03**	**16 50**	**6 24**	**16 25**

11th Month — November, 1978 — 30 Days

Greenwich Mean Time

NOTE: Light figures indicate Sun. **Dark** figures indicate **Moon.** *Degrees are North Latitude.*

CAUTION: Must be converted to local time. For instruction see page 772.

Day of month week year	Sun on meridian **Moon phase** h m s	20° Rise Sun **Moon** h m	20° Set Sun **Moon** h m	30° Rise Sun **Moon** h m	30° Set Sun **Moon** h m	40° Rise Sun **Moon** h m	40° Set Sun **Moon** h m	50° Rise Sun **Moon** h m	50° Set Sun **Moon** h m	60° Rise Sun **Moon** h m	60° Set Sun **Moon** h m
1 We	11 43 38	6 01	17 26	6 13	17 13	6 28	16 58	6 49	16 38	7 21	16 05
305		**6 29**	**18 14**	**6 40**	**18 01**	**6 54**	**17 46**	**7 14**	**17 24**	**7 45**	**16 51**
2 Th	11 43 37	6 02	17 25	6 14	17 12	6 29	16 57	6 51	16 36	7 24	16 03
306		**7 28**	**19 05**	**7 42**	**18 50**	**8 00**	**18 31**	**8 24**	**18 05**	**9 04**	**17 23**
3 Fr	11 43 36	6 02	17 25	6 15	17 12	6 30	16 56	6 52	16 35	7 26	16 00
307		**8 28**	**20 00**	**8 44**	**19 43**	**9 04**	**19 22**	**9 33**	**18 53**	**10 19**	**18 05**
4 Sa	11 43 37	6 03	17 24	6 15	17 11	6 32	16 55	6 31	16 33	7 29	15 58
308		**9 27**	**20 57**	**9 44**	**20 40**	**10 06**	**20 19**	**10 35**	**19 49**	**11 25**	**19 00**
5 Su	11 43 38	6 03	17 24	6 16	17 11	6 33	16 54	6 55	16 32	7 31	15 55
309		**10 25**	**21 57**	**10 42**	**21 41**	**11 02**	**21 21**	**11 31**	**20 53**	**17 19**	**20 06**
6 Mo	11 43 40	6 04	17 23	6 17	17 10	6 34	16 53	6 57	16 30	7 34	15 53
310		**11 20**	**22 58**	**11 35**	**22 43**	**11 54**	**22 26**	**12 19**	**22 02**	**13 01**	**21 22**
7 Tu	11 43 43	6 04	17 23	6 18	17 09	6 35	16 52	6 59	16 28	7 37	15 51
311	**16 18 ☽**	**12 11**	**23 58**	**12 24**	**23 46**	**12 39**	**23 33**	**13 00**	**23 14**	**13 33**	**22 43**
8 We	11 43 46	6 05	17 23	6 19	17 08	6 36	16 51	7 00	16 27	7 39	15 48
312		**13 00**		**13 09**		**13 20**		**13 35**		**13 59**	
9 Th	11 43 51	6 05	17 22	6 19	17 08	6 38	16 50	7 02	16 25	7 42	15 46
313		**13 45**	**0 57**	**13 51**	**0 49**	**13 58**	**0 40**	**14 07**	**0 27**	**14 20**	**0 07**
10 Fr	11 43 56	6 06	17 22	6 20	17 07	6 39	16 49	7 03	16 24	7 44	15 43
314		**14 29**	**1 54**	**14 31**	**1 51**	**14 33**	**1 46**	**14 36**	**1 40**	**14 40**	**1 31**
11 Sa	11 44 02	6 06	17 22	6 21	17 06	6 40	16 48	7 05	16 22	7 47	15 41
315		**15 12**	**2 51**	**15 10**	**2 52**	**15 07**	**2 52**	**15 04**	**2 53**	**14 58**	**2 53**
12 Su	11 44 09	6 07	17 22	6 22	17 06	6 41	16 47	7 07	16 21	7 49	15 39
316		**15 55**	**3 47**	**15 49**	**3 52**	**15 42**	**3 57**	**15 32**	**4 04**	**15 17**	**4 15**
13 Mo	11 44 17	6 07	17 21	6 23	17 05	6 42	16 46	7 09	16 19	7 52	15 36
317		**16 39**	**4 43**	**16 29**	**4 51**	**16 18**	**5 01**	**16 02**	**5 14**	**15 38**	**5 35**
14 Tu	11 44 25	6 08	17 21	6 24	17 05	6 44	16 45	7 10	16 18	7 54	15 34
318	**20 00 ◯**	**17 24**	**5 38**	**17 11**	**5 49**	**16 56**	**6 03**	**16 35**	**6 22**	**16 02**	**6 53**
15 We	11 44 35	6 08	17 20	6 25	17 04	6 45	16 44	7 12	16 24	7 57	15 31
319		**18 10**	**6 32**	**17 55**	**6 46**	**17 36**	**7 04**	**17 11**	**7 28**	**16 31**	**8 06**
16 Th	11 44 45	6 09	17 20	6 26	17 04	6 46	16 43	7 14	16 15	7 59	15 29
320		**18 57**	**7 26**	**18 41**	**7 42**	**18 20**	**8 01**	**17 52**	**8 29**	**17 06**	**9 14**
17 Fr	11 44 56	6 10	17 20	6 27	17 04	6 47	16 42	7 16	16 14	8 02	15 27
321		**19 46**	**8 17**	**19 29**	**8 34**	**19 07**	**8 55**	**18 32**	**9 24**	**17 50**	**10 12**
18 Sa	11 45 08	6 10	17 19	6 28	17 03	6 48	16 42	7 17	16 13	8 04	15 25
322		**20 35**	**9 06**	**20 18**	**9 23**	**19 57**	**9 44**	**19 28**	**10 14**	**18 41**	**11 02**
19 Su	11 45 21	6 11	17 19	6 28	17 03	6 49	16 41	7 19	16 12	8 07	15 23
323		**21 24**	**9 53**	**21 09**	**10 09**	**20 49**	**10 29**	**20 23**	**10 57**	**19 39**	**11 41**
20 Mo	11 45 35	6 11	17 19	6 29	17 02	6 50	16 41	7 20	16 11	8 09	15 21
324		**22 13**	**10 37**	**22 00**	**10 52**	**21 43**	**11 09**	**21 20**	**11 34**	**20 42**	**12 13**
21 Tu	11 45 50	6 12	17 19	6 30	17 02	6 51	16 40	7 22	16 10	8 12	15 19
325		**23 02**	**11 19**	**22 51**	**11 31**	**22 38**	**11 46**	**22 19**	**12 07**	**21 49**	**12 39**
22 We	11 46 05	6 13	17 19	6 31	17 02	6 53	16 39	7 23	16 09	8 14	15 17
326	**21 24 ☾**	**23 52**	**11 59**	**23 44**	**12 08**	**23 33**	**12 20**	**23 20**	**12 36**	**22 58**	**13 00**
23 Th	11 46 21	6 13	17 19	6 32	17 01	6 54	16 38	7 24	16 08	8 16	15 16
327			**12 38**		**12 44**		**12 52**		**13 02**		**13 18**
24 Fr	11 46 38	6 14	17 19	6 32	17 01	6 55	16 38	7 26	16 07	8 19	15 14
328		**0 41**	**13 16**	**0 36**	**13 19**	**0 30**	**13 23**	**0 22**	**13 27**	**0 10**	**13 35**
25 Sa	11 46 56	6 14	17 19	6 33	17 00	6 56	16 38	7 28	16 06	8 21	15 13
329		**1 31**	**13 55**	**1 30**	**13 54**	**1 28**	**13 53**	**1 26**	**13 53**	**1 23**	**13 51**
26 Su	11 47 14	6 15	17 19	6 34	17 00	6 57	16 37	7 29	16 05	8 23	15 11
330		**2 23**	**14 35**	**2 25**	**14 31**	**2 28**	**14 26**	**2 32**	**14 19**	**2 38**	**14 08**
27 Mo	11 47 34	6 16	17 19	6 35	17 00	6 58	16 37	7 30	16 04	8 25	15 09
331		**3 17**	**15 17**	**3 23**	**15 09**	**3 30**	**15 00**	**3 41**	**14 47**	**3 57**	**14 27**
28 Tu	11 47 54	6 16	17 19	6 36	17 00	6 59	16 36	7 32	16 03	8 27	15 08
332		**4 13**	**16 03**	**4 23**	**15 52**	**4 35**	**15 38**	**4 51**	**15 19**	**5 17**	**14 50**
29 We	11 48 14	6 17	17 19	6 36	17 00	7 00	16 36	7 33	16 03	8 30	15 06
333		**5 12**	**16 53**	**5 25**	**16 39**	**5 41**	**16 21**	**6 03**	**15 57**	**6 39**	**15 19**
30 Th	11 48 36	6 17	17 19	6 37	17 00	7 01	16 35	7 35	16 02	8 32	15 05
334	**08 19 ●**	**6 13**	**17 47**	**6 28**	**17 31**	**6 48**	**17 10**	**7 14**	**16 42**	**7 59**	**15 57**

12th Month December, 1978 31 Days

Greenwich Mean Time

NOTE: Light figures indicate Sun. **Dark** figures indicate **Moon.** *Degrees are North Latitude.*
CAUTION: Must be converted to local time. For instruction see page 772.

Day of month week year	Sun on meridian **Moon phase** h m s	20° Rise Sun **Moon** h m	20° Set Sun **Moon** h m	30° Rise Sun **Moon** h m	30° Set Sun **Moon** h m	40° Rise Sun **Moon** h m	40° Set Sun **Moon** h m	50° Rise Sun **Moon** h m	50° Set Sun **Moon** h m	60° Rise Sun **Moon** h m	60° Set Sun **Moon** h m
1 Fr	11 48 53	6 18	17 19	6 38	17 00	7 02	16 35	7 36	16 01	8 34	15 03
335		**7 14**	**18 45**	**7 31**	**18 28**	**7 53**	**18 06**	**8 22**	**17 36**	**9 12**	**16 47**
2 Sa	11 49 21	6 19	17 19	6 39	17 00	7 03	16 35	7 37	16 01	8 36	15 02
336		**8 15**	**19 46**	**8 32**	**19 30**	**8 54**	**19 08**	**9 24**	**18 39**	**10 13**	**17 50**
3 Su	11 49 44	6 19	17 19	6 40	17 00	7 04	16 35	7 38	16 01	8 38	15 01
337		**9 13**	**20 49**	**9 29**	**20 34**	**9 49**	**20 15**	**10 17**	**19 48**	**11 01**	**19 05**
4 Mo	11 50 08	6 20	17 20	6 40	17 00	7 05	16 35	7 40	16 00	8 40	15 00
338		**10 08**	**21 51**	**10 21**	**21 38**	**10 38**	**21 23**	**11 01**	**21 02**	**11 38**	**20 28**
5 Tu	11 50 32	6 20	17 20	6 41	17 00	7 06	16 35	7 41	15 59	8 42	14 59
339		**10 58**	**22 51**	**11 09**	**22 42**	**11 22**	**22 31**	**11 39**	**22 16**	**12 06**	**21 53**
6 We	11 50 57	6 21	17 20	6 42	17 00	7 07	16 35	7 42	15 59	8 44	14 58
340		**11 45**	**23 50**	**11 52**	**23 45**	**12 01**	**23 39**	**12 12**	**23 30**	**12 29**	**23 17**
7 Th	11 51 23	6 22	17 20	6 43	17 00	7 08	16 35	7 43	15 59	8 46	14 57
341	**00 34** ☽	**12 30**		**12 33**		**12 36**		**12 41**		**12 49**	
8 Fr	11 51 49	6 23	17 21	6 43	17 00	7 09	16 35	7 44	15 59	8 47	14 56
342		**13 13**	**0 47**	**13 12**	**0 46**	**13 11**	**0 45**	**13 09**	**0 43**	**13 07**	**0 40**
9 Sa	11 52 15	6 26	17 21	6 44	17 01	7 09	16 35	7 46	15 58	8 49	14 56
343		**13 55**	**1 43**	**13 50**	**1 45**	**13 44**	**1 49**	**13 37**	**1 54**	**13 25**	**2 01**
10 Su	11 52 42	6 24	17 22	6 44	17 01	7 10	16 35	7 47	15 58	8 50	14 55
344		**14 37**	**2 37**	**14 29**	**2 44**	**14 19**	**2 52**	**14 05**	**3 03**	**13 44**	**3 21**
11 Mo	11 53 10	6 25	17 22	6 45	17 01	7 11	16 35	7 48	15 58	8 52	14 54
345		**15 20**	**3 31**	**15 09**	**3 41**	**14 55**	**3 54**	**14 36**	**4 11**	**14 06**	**4 38**
12 Tu	11 53 37	6 26	17 22	6 46	17 01	7 12	16 35	7 49	15 58	8 53	14 54
346		**16 05**	**4 25**	**15 51**	**4 38**	**15 33**	**4 54**	**15 10**	**5 16**	**14 32**	**5 52**
13 We	11 54 05	6 26	17 22	6 47	17 01	7 13	16 35	7 50	15 58	8 54	14 54
347		**16 51**	**5 18**	**16 35**	**5 33**	**16 15**	**5 52**	**15 48**	**6 19**	**15 04**	**7 01**
14 Th	11 54 34	6 27	17 23	6 47	17 02	7 13	16 36	7 50	15 58	8 56	14 53
348	**12 31** ○	**17 39**	**6 10**	**17 22**	**6 27**	**17 01**	**6 47**	**16 31**	**7 16**	**15 43**	**8 04**
15 Fr	11 55 02	6 27	17 23	6 48	17 02	7 14	16 36	7 51	15 58	8 57	14 53
349		**18 28**	**7 00**	**18 11**	**7 17**	**17 49**	**7 38**	**17 20**	**8 08**	**16 31**	**8 57**
16 Sa	11 55 31	6 28	17 23	6 49	17 02	7 15	16 36	7 52	15 58	8 58	14 53
350		**19 17**	**7 48**	**19 01**	**8 05**	**18 41**	**8 25**	**18 13**	**8 54**	**17 26**	**9 41**
17 Su	11 56 00	6 28	17 24	6 49	17 02	7 16	16 36	7 53	15 58	8 59	14 53
351		**20 07**	**8 33**	**19 52**	**8 49**	**19 34**	**9 08**	**19 09**	**9 34**	**18 28**	**10 16**
18 Mo	11 56 30	6 29	17 24	6 50	17 03	7 16	16 37	7 54	15 59	9 00	14 53
352		**20 56**	**9 16**	**20 43**	**9 29**	**20 28**	**9 46**	**20 07**	**10 08**	**19 34**	**10 44**
19 Tu	11 56 59	6 29	17 25	6 50	17 03	7 17	16 37	7 54	15 59	9 00	14 54
353		**21 45**	**9 57**	**21 35**	**10 07**	**21 23**	**10 21**	**21 07**	**10 39**	**20 42**	**11 07**
20 We	11 57 29	6 30	17 25	6 51	17 04	7 17	16 38	7 55	16 00	9 01	14 54
354		**22 34**	**10 35**	**22 27**	**10 43**	**22 19**	**10 53**	**22 08**	**11 06**	**21 52**	**11 26**
21 Th	11 57 59	6 30	17 26	6 51	17 04	7 18	16 38	7 56	16 00	9 02	14 54
355		**23 23**	**11 13**	**23 19**	**11 18**	**23 16**	**11 24**	**23 11**	**11 31**	**23 03**	**11 43**
22 Fr	11 58 28	6 31	17 26	6 52	17 05	7 18	16 38	7 56	16 01	9 02	14 55
356	**17 41** ☾		**11 51**		**11 52**		**11 54**		**11 56**		**11 59**
23 Sa	11 58 58	6 31	17 27	6 52	17 05	7 19	16 39	7 57	16 01	9 03	14 55
357		**0 12**	**12 29**	**0 13**	**12 27**	**0 14**	**12 24**	**0 14**	**12 20**	**0 16**	**12 15**
24 Su	11 59 28	6 32	17 27	6 53	17 06	7 19	16 39	7 57	16 02	9 03	14 56
358		**1 04**	**13 09**	**1 08**	**13 03**	**1 13**	**12 56**	**1 20**	**12 47**	**1 31**	**12 32**
25 Mo	11 59 58	6 32	17 28	6 53	17 06	7 20	16 40	7 58	16 02	9 04	14 56
359		**1 57**	**13 53**	**2 05**	**13 43**	**2 15**	**13 31**	**2 28**	**13 16**	**2 48**	**12 52**
26 Tu	12 00 28	6 33	17 28	6 54	17 07	7 20	16 40	7 58	16 03	9 04	14 57
360		**2 53**	**14 39**	**3 05**	**14 26**	**3 18**	**14 11**	**3 38**	**13 50**	**4 08**	**13 16**
27 We	12 00 58	6 33	17 29	6 54	17 08	7 20	16 41	7 58	16 04	9 04	14 58
361		**3 52**	**15 30**	**4 07**	**15 15**	**4 24**	**14 56**	**4 49**	**14 30**	**5 29**	**13 48**
28 Th	12 01 27	6 34	17 29	6 55	17 08	7 21	16 42	7 58	16 05	9 04	14 59
362		**4 54**	**16 26**	**5 10**	**16 09**	**5 30**	**15 48**	**5 59**	**15 19**	**6 46**	**14 31**
29 Fr	12 01 57	6 34	17 30	6 55	17 09	7 21	16 42	7 59	16 05	9 03	15 01
363	**19 36** ●	**5 56**	**17 27**	**6 13**	**17 10**	**6 35**	**16 48**	**7 05**	**16 18**	**7 55**	**15 27**
30 Sa	12 02 26	6 35	17 30	6 56	17 09	7 22	16 43	7 59	16 06	9 03	15 02
364		**6 57**	**18 31**	**7 14**	**18 14**	**7 35**	**17 54**	**8 04**	**17 26**	**8 52**	**16 39**
31 Su	12 02 55	6 35	17 31	6 56	17 10	7 22	16 44	7 59	16 07	9 03	15 03
365		**7 56**	**19 35**	**8 11**	**19 21**	**8 29**	**19 04**	**8 55**	**18 40**	**9 36**	**18 01**

The Julian Period

How many days have you lived? To determine this, you must multiply your age by 365, add the number of days since your last birthday until today, and account for all the leap years. Chances are your answer would be wrong. Astronomers, however, find it convenient to express dates and long time intervals in days rather than in years, months and days. This is done by placing events within the Julian period.

The Julian period was devised in 1582 by Joseph Scaliger and named after his father Julius (not after the Julian calendar). Scaliger had Julian Day (JD) #1 begin at noon, Jan. 1, 4713 B. C., the most recent time that three major chronological cycles began on the same day — 1) the 28-year solar cycle, after which dates in the Julian calendar (e.g., Feb. 11) return to the same days of the week (e.g., Monday); 2) the 19-year lunar cycle, after which the phases of the moon return to the same dates of the year; and 3) the 15-year indiction cycle, used in ancient Rome to regulate taxes. It will take 7980 years to complete the period, the product of 28, 19 and 15.

Noon of Dec. 31, 1977, marks the beginning of JD 2,443,509; that many days will have passed since the start of the Julian period. The JD at noon of any date in 1978 may be found by adding to this figure the day of the year for that date, which is given in the left hand column in the chart below. Simple JD conversion tables are used by astronomers.

Lunar Calendar, Chinese New Years, Vietnamese Tet

The ancient Chinese lunar calendar is divided into 12 months of either 29 or 30 days (compensating for the fact that the mean duration of the lunar month is 29 days, 12 hours, 44.05 minutes). The calendar is synchronized with the solar year by the addition of extra months at fixed intervals.

The Chinese calendar runs on a sexagenary cycle, i.e., 60 years. The cycles 1864-1923 and 1924-1983, with the years grouped under their twelve animal designations, are printed below. The Year 1978 is found in the seventh column, under Horse, and is known as a "Year of the Horse." Readers can find the animal name for the year of their birth, marriage, etc., in the same chart. (Note: the first 3-7 weeks of each of the western years belong to the previous Chinese year and animal designation.)

Both the western (Gregorian) and traditional lunar calendars are used publicly in China, and two New Year's celebrations are held. On Taiwan, in overseas Chinese communities, and in Vietnam, the lunar calendar has been used only to set the dates for traditional festivals, with the Gregorian system in general use.

The four-day Chinese New Year, Hsin Nien, and the three-day Vietnamese New Year festival, Tet, begin at the first new moon after the sun enters Aquarius. The day may fall, therefore, between Jan. 21 and Feb. 19 of the Gregorian calendar. Feb. 7, 1978 marks the start of the new Chinese year. The date is fixed according to the date of the new moon in the Far East. Since this is west of the International Date Line the date may be one day later than that of the new moon in the United States.

Rat	Ox	Tiger	Hare (Rabbit)	Dragon	Snake	Horse	Sheep (Goat)	Monkey	Rooster	Dog	Pig
1864	1865	1866	1867	1868	1869	1870	1871	1872	1873	1874	1875
1876	1877	1878	1879	1880	1881	1882	1883	1884	1885	1886	1887
1888	1889	1890	1891	1892	1893	1894	1895	1896	1897	1898	1899
1900	1901	1902	1903	1904	1905	1906	1907	1908	1909	1910	1911
1912	1913	1914	1915	1916	1917	1918	1919	1920	1921	1922	1923
1924	1925	1926	1927	1928	1929	1930	1931	1932	1933	1934	1935
1936	1937	1938	1939	1940	1941	1942	1943	1944	1945	1946	1947
1948	1949	1950	1951	1952	1953	1954	1955	1956	1957	1958	1959
1960	1961	1962	1963	1964	1965	1966	1967	1968	1969	1970	1971
1972	1973	1974	1975	1976	1977	1978	1979	1980	1981	1982	1983

Days Between Two Dates

Table covers period of two ordinary years. Example—Days between Feb. 10, 1977 and Dec. 15, 1978; subtract 41 from 714; answer is 673 days. For leap year, such as 1976, one day must be added after Feb. 28.

Date	Jan.	Feb.	Mar.	April	May	June	July	Aug.	Sept.	Oct.	Nov.	Dec.
1	1	32	60	91	121	152	182	213	244	274	305	335
2	2	33	61	92	122	153	183	214	245	275	306	336
3	3	34	62	93	123	154	184	215	246	276	307	337
4	4	35	63	94	124	155	185	216	247	277	308	338
5	5	36	64	95	125	156	186	217	248	278	309	339
6	6	37	65	96	126	157	187	218	249	279	310	340
7	7	38	66	97	127	158	188	219	250	280	311	341
8	8	39	67	98	128	159	189	220	251	281	312	342
9	9	40	68	99	129	160	190	221	252	282	313	343
10	10	41	69	100	130	161	191	222	253	283	314	344
11	11	42	70	101	131	162	192	223	254	284	315	345
12	12	43	71	102	132	163	193	224	255	285	316	346
13	13	44	72	103	133	164	194	225	256	286	317	347
14	14	45	73	104	134	165	195	226	257	287	318	348
15	15	46	74	105	135	166	196	227	258	288	319	349
16	16	47	75	106	136	167	197	228	259	289	320	350
17	17	48	76	107	137	168	198	229	260	290	321	351
18	18	49	77	108	138	169	199	230	261	291	322	352
19	19	50	78	109	139	170	200	231	262	292	323	353
20	20	51	79	110	140	171	201	232	263	293	324	354
21	21	52	80	111	141	172	202	233	264	294	325	355
22	22	53	81	112	142	173	203	234	265	295	326	356
23	23	54	82	113	143	174	204	235	266	296	327	357
24	24	55	83	114	144	175	205	236	267	297	328	358
25	25	56	84	115	145	176	206	237	268	298	329	359
26	26	57	85	116	146	177	207	238	269	299	330	360
27	27	58	86	117	147	178	208	239	270	300	331	361
28	28	59	87	118	148	179	209	240	271	301	332	362
29	29	—	88	119	149	180	210	241	272	302	333	363
30	30	—	89	120	150	181	211	242	273	303	334	364
31	31	—	90	—	151	—	212	243	—	304	—	365

Date	Jan.	Feb.	Mar.	April	May	June	July	Aug.	Sept.	Oct.	Nov.	Dec.
1	366	397	425	456	486	517	547	578	609	639	670	700
2	367	398	426	457	487	518	548	579	610	640	671	701
3	368	399	427	458	488	519	549	580	611	641	672	702
4	369	400	428	459	489	520	550	581	612	642	673	703
5	370	401	429	460	490	521	551	582	613	643	674	704
6	371	402	430	461	491	522	552	583	614	644	675	705
7	372	403	431	462	492	523	553	584	615	645	676	706
8	373	404	432	463	493	524	554	585	616	646	677	707
9	374	405	433	464	494	525	555	586	617	647	678	708
10	375	406	434	465	495	526	556	587	618	648	679	709
11	376	407	435	466	496	527	557	588	619	649	680	710
12	377	408	436	467	497	528	558	589	620	650	681	711
13	378	409	437	468	498	529	559	590	621	651	682	712
14	379	410	438	469	499	530	560	591	622	652	683	713
15	380	411	439	470	500	531	561	592	623	653	684	714
16	381	412	440	471	501	532	562	593	624	654	685	715
17	382	413	441	472	502	533	563	594	625	655	686	716
18	383	414	442	473	503	534	564	595	626	656	687	717
19	384	415	443	474	504	535	565	596	627	657	688	718
20	385	416	444	475	505	536	566	597	628	658	689	719
21	386	417	445	476	506	537	567	598	629	659	690	720
22	387	418	446	477	507	538	568	599	630	660	691	721
23	388	419	447	478	508	539	569	600	631	661	692	722
24	389	420	448	479	509	540	570	601	632	662	693	723
25	390	421	449	480	510	541	571	602	633	663	694	724
26	391	422	450	481	511	542	572	603	634	664	695	725
27	392	423	451	482	512	543	573	604	635	665	696	726
28	393	424	452	483	513	544	574	605	636	666	697	727
29	394	—	453	484	514	545	575	606	637	667	698	728
30	395	—	454	485	515	546	576	607	638	668	699	729
31	396	—	455	—	516	—	577	608	—	669	—	730

PERPETUAL CALENDAR

The number shown for each year indicates which Gregorian calendar to use. For 1583-1799, or for Julian calendar, see page 788.

1800....4	1826....1	1852....12	1878....3	1904....13	1930....4	1956....8	1982....6	2008....10	2034....1
1801....5	1827....2	1853....7	1879....4	1905....1	1931....5	1957....3	1983....7	2009....5	2035....2
1802....6	1828....10	1854....1	1880....12	1906....2	1932....13	1958....4	1984....8	2010....6	2036....10
1803....7	1829....5	1855....2	1881....7	1907....3	1933....1	1959....5	1985....3	2011....7	2037....5
1804....8	1830....6	1856....10	1882....1	1908....11	1934....2	1960....13	1986....4	2012....8	2038....6
1805....3	1831....7	1857....5	1883....2	1909....6	1935....3	1961....1	1987....5	2013....3	2039....7
1806....4	1832....8	1858....6	1884....10	1910....7	1936....11	1962....2	1988....13	2014....4	2040....8
1807....5	1833....3	1859....7	1885....5	1911....1	1937....6	1963....3	1989....1	2015....5	2041....3
1808....13	1834....4	1860....8	1886....6	1912....9	1938....7	1964....11	1990....2	2016....13	2042....4
1809....1	1835....5	1861....3	1887....7	1913....4	1939....1	1965....6	1991....3	2017....1	2043....5
1810....2	1836....13	1862....4	1888....8	1914....5	1940....9	1966....7	1992....11	2018....2	2044....13
1811....3	1837....1	1863....5	1889....3	1915....6	1941....4	1967....1	1993....6	2019....3	2045....1
1812....11	1838....2	1864....13	1890....4	1916....14	1942....5	1968....9	1994....7	2020....11	2046....2
1813....6	1839....3	1865....1	1891....5	1917....2	1943....6	1969....4	1995....1	2021....6	2047....3
1814....7	1840....11	1866....2	1892....13	1918....3	1944....14	1970....5	1996....9	2022....7	2048....11
1815....1	1841....6	1867....3	1893....1	1919....4	1945....2	1971....6	1997....4	2023....1	2049....6
1816....9	1842....7	1868....11	1894....2	1920....12	1946....3	1972....14	1998....5	2024....9	2050....7
1817....4	1843....1	1869....6	1895....3	1921....7	1947....4	1973....2	1999....6	2025....4	2051....1
1818....5	1844....9	1870....7	1896....11	1922....1	1948....12	1974....3	2000....14	2026....5	2052....9
1819....6	1845....4	1871....1	1897....6	1923....2	1949....7	1975....4	2001....2	2027....6	2053....4
1820....14	1846....5	1872....9	1898....7	1924....10	1950....1	1976....12	2002....3	2028....14	2054....5
1821....2	1847....6	1873....4	1899....1	1925....5	1951....2	1977....7	2003....4	2029....2	2055....6
1822....3	1848....14	1874....5	1900....2	1926....6	1952....10	1978....1	2004....12	2030....3	2056....14
1823....4	1849....2	1875....6	1901....3	1927....7	1953....5	1979....2	2005....7	2031....4	2057....2
1824....12	1850....3	1876....14	1902....4	1928....8	1954....6	1980....10	2006....1	2032....12	2058....3
1825....7	1851....4	1877....2	1903....5	1929....3	1955....7	1981....5	2007....2	2033....7	2059....4

1 — 1978

JANUARY

S	M	T	W	T	F	S
1	2	3	4	5	6	7
8	9	10	11	12	13	14
15	16	17	18	19	20	21
22	23	24	25	26	27	28
29	30	31				

FEBRUARY

S	M	T	W	T	F	S
			1	2	3	4
5	6	7	8	9	10	11
12	13	14	15	16	17	18
19	20	21	22	23	24	25
26	27	28				

MARCH

S	M	T	W	T	F	S
			1	2	3	4
5	6	7	8	9	10	11
12	13	14	15	16	17	18
19	20	21	22	23	24	25
26	27	28	29	30	31	

APRIL

S	M	T	W	T	F	S
						1
2	3	4	5	6	7	8
9	10	11	12	13	14	15
16	17	18	19	20	21	22
23	24	25	26	27	28	29
30						

MAY

S	M	T	W	T	F	S
	1	2	3	4	5	6
7	8	9	10	11	12	13
14	15	16	17	18	19	20
21	22	23	24	25	26	27
28	29	30	31			

JUNE

S	M	T	W	T	F	S
				1	2	3
4	5	6	7	8	9	10
11	12	13	14	15	16	17
18	19	20	21	22	23	24
25	26	27	28	29	30	

JULY

S	M	T	W	T	F	S
						1
2	3	4	5	6	7	8
9	10	11	12	13	14	15
16	17	18	19	20	21	22
23	24	25	26	27	28	29
30	31					

AUGUST

S	M	T	W	T	F	S
		1	2	3	4	5
6	7	8	9	10	11	12
13	14	15	16	17	18	19
20	21	22	23	24	25	26
27	28	29	30	31		

SEPTEMBER

S	M	T	W	T	F	S
					1	2
3	4	5	6	7	8	9
10	11	12	13	14	15	16
17	18	19	20	21	22	23
24	25	26	27	28	29	30

OCTOBER

S	M	T	W	T	F	S
1	2	3	4	5	6	7
8	9	10	11	12	13	14
15	16	17	18	19	20	21
22	23	24	25	26	27	28
29	30	31				

NOVEMBER

S	M	T	W	T	F	S
			1	2	3	4
5	6	7	8	9	10	11
12	13	14	15	16	17	18
19	20	21	22	23	24	25
26	27	28	29	30		

DECEMBER

S	M	T	W	T	F	S
					1	2
3	4	5	6	7	8	9
10	11	12	13	14	15	16
17	18	19	20	21	22	23
24	25	26	27	28	29	30
31						

2 — 1979

JANUARY

S	M	T	W	T	F	S
	1	2	3	4	5	6
7	8	9	10	11	12	13
14	15	16	17	18	19	20
21	22	23	24	25	26	27
28	29	30	31			

FEBRUARY

S	M	T	W	T	F	S
				1	2	3
4	5	6	7	8	9	10
11	12	13	14	15	16	17
18	19	20	21	22	23	24
25	26	27	28			

MARCH

S	M	T	W	T	F	S
				1	2	3
4	5	6	7	8	9	10
11	12	13	14	15	16	17
18	19	20	21	22	23	24
25	26	27	28	29	30	31

APRIL

S	M	T	W	T	F	S
1	2	3	4	5	6	7
8	9	10	11	12	13	14
15	16	17	18	19	20	21
22	23	24	25	26	27	28
29	30					

MAY

S	M	T	W	T	F	S
		1	2	3	4	5
6	7	8	9	10	11	12
13	14	15	16	17	18	19
20	21	22	23	24	25	26
27	28	29	30	31		

JUNE

S	M	T	W	T	F	S
					1	2
3	4	5	6	7	8	9
10	11	12	13	14	15	16
17	18	19	20	21	22	23
24	25	26	27	28	29	30

JULY

S	M	T	W	T	F	S
1	2	3	4	5	6	7
8	9	10	11	12	13	14
15	16	17	18	19	20	21
22	23	24	25	26	27	28
29	30	31				

AUGUST

S	M	T	W	T	F	S
			1	2	3	4
5	6	7	8	9	10	11
12	13	14	15	16	17	18
19	20	21	22	23	24	25
26	27	28	29	30	31	

SEPTEMBER

S	M	T	W	T	F	S
						1
2	3	4	5	6	7	8
9	10	11	12	13	14	15
16	17	18	19	20	21	22
23	24	25	26	27	28	29
30						

OCTOBER

S	M	T	W	T	F	S
	1	2	3	4	5	6
7	8	9	10	11	12	13
14	15	16	17	18	19	20
21	22	23	24	25	26	27
28	29	30	31			

NOVEMBER

S	M	T	W	T	F	S
				1	2	3
4	5	6	7	8	9	10
11	12	13	14	15	16	17
18	19	20	21	22	23	24
25	26	27	28	29	30	

DECEMBER

S	M	T	W	T	F	S
						1
2	3	4	5	6	7	8
9	10	11	12	13	14	15
16	17	18	19	20	21	22
23	24	25	26	27	28	29
30	31					

3

JANUARY

S	M	T	W	T	F	S
		1	2	3	4	5
6	7	8	9	10	11	12
13	14	15	16	17	18	19
20	21	22	23	24	25	26
27	28	29	30	31		

FEBRUARY

S	M	T	W	T	F	S
					1	2
3	4	5	6	7	8	9
10	11	12	13	14	15	16
17	18	19	20	21	22	23
24	25	26	27	28		

MARCH

S	M	T	W	T	F	S
					1	2
3	4	5	6	7	8	9
10	11	12	13	14	15	16
17	18	29	20	21	22	23
24	25	26	27	28	29	30
31						

APRIL

S	M	T	W	T	F	S
	1	2	3	4	5	6
7	8	9	10	11	12	13
14	15	16	17	18	19	20
21	22	23	24	25	26	27
28	29	30				

MAY

S	M	T	W	T	F	S
			1	2	3	4
5	6	7	8	9	10	11
12	13	14	15	16	17	18
19	20	21	22	23	24	25
26	27	28	29	30	31	

JUNE

S	M	T	W	T	F	S
						1
2	3	4	5	6	7	8
9	10	11	12	13	14	15
16	17	18	19	20	21	22
23	24	25	26	27	28	29
30						

JULY

S	M	T	W	T	F	S
	1	2	3	4	5	6
7	8	9	10	11	12	13
14	15	16	17	18	19	20
21	22	23	24	25	26	27
28	29	30	31			

AUGUST

S	M	T	W	T	F	S
				1	2	3
4	5	6	7	8	9	10
11	12	13	14	15	16	17
18	19	20	21	22	23	24
25	26	27	28	29	30	31

SEPTEMBER

S	M	T	W	T	F	S
1	2	3	4	5	6	7
8	9	10	11	12	13	14
15	16	17	18	19	20	21
22	23	24	25	26	27	28
29	30					

OCTOBER

S	M	T	W	T	F	S
		1	2	3	4	5
6	7	8	9	10	11	12
13	14	15	16	17	18	19
20	21	22	23	24	25	26
27	28	29	30	31		

NOVEMBER

S	M	T	W	T	F	S
					1	2
3	4	5	6	7	8	9
10	11	12	13	14	15	16
17	18	19	20	21	22	23
24	25	26	27	28	29	30

DECEMBER

S	M	T	W	T	F	S
1	2	3	4	5	6	7
8	9	10	11	12	13	14
15	16	17	18	19	20	21
22	23	24	25	26	27	28
29	30	31				

4

JANUARY

S	M	T	W	T	F	S
			1	2	3	4
5	6	7	8	9	10	11
12	13	14	15	16	17	18
19	20	21	22	23	24	25
26	27	28	29	30	31	

FEBRUARY

S	M	T	W	T	F	S
						1
2	3	4	5	6	7	8
9	10	11	12	13	14	15
16	17	18	19	20	21	22
23	24	25	26	27	28	

MARCH

S	M	T	W	T	F	S
						1
2	3	4	5	6	7	8
9	10	11	12	13	14	15
16	17	18	19	20	21	22
23	24	25	26	27	28	29
30	31					

APRIL

S	M	T	W	T	F	S
		1	2	3	4	5
6	7	8	9	10	11	12
13	14	15	16	17	18	19
20	21	22	23	24	25	26
27	28	29	30			

MAY

S	M	T	W	T	F	S
				1	2	3
4	5	6	7	8	9	10
11	12	13	14	15	16	17
18	19	20	21	22	23	24
25	26	27	28	29	30	31

JUNE

S	M	T	W	T	F	S
1	2	3	4	5	6	7
8	9	10	11	12	13	14
15	16	17	18	19	20	21
22	23	24	25	26	27	28
29	30					

JULY

S	M	T	W	T	F	S
		1	2	3	4	5
6	7	8	9	10	11	12
13	14	15	16	17	18	19
20	21	22	23	24	25	26
27	28	29	30	31		

AUGUST

S	M	T	W	T	F	S
					1	2
3	4	5	6	7	8	9
10	11	12	13	14	15	16
17	18	19	20	21	22	23
24	25	26	27	28	29	30
31						

SEPTEMBER

S	M	T	W	T	F	S
	1	2	3	4	5	6
7	8	9	10	11	12	13
14	15	16	17	18	19	20
21	22	23	24	25	26	27
28	29	30				

OCTOBER

S	M	T	W	T	F	S
			1	2	3	4
5	6	7	8	9	10	11
12	13	14	15	16	17	18
19	20	21	22	23	24	25
26	27	28	29	30	31	

NOVEMBER

S	M	T	W	T	F	S
						1
2	3	4	5	6	7	8
9	10	11	12	13	14	15
16	17	18	19	20	21	22
23	24	25	26	27	28	29
30						

DECEMBER

S	M	T	W	T	F	S
	1	2	3	4	5	6
7	8	9	10	11	12	13
14	15	16	17	18	19	20
21	22	23	24	25	26	27
28	29	30	31			

5

JANUARY

S	M	T	W	T	F	S
				1	2	3
4	5	6	7	8	9	10
11	12	13	14	15	16	17
18	19	20	21	22	23	24
25	26	27	28	29	30	31

FEBRUARY

S	M	T	W	T	F	S
1	2	3	4	5	6	7
8	9	10	11	12	13	14
15	16	17	18	19	20	21
22	23	24	25	26	27	28

MARCH

S	M	T	W	T	F	S
1	2	3	4	5	6	7
8	9	10	11	12	13	14
15	16	17	18	19	20	21
22	23	24	25	26	27	28
29	30	31				

APRIL

S	M	T	W	T	F	S
			1	2	3	4
5	6	7	8	9	10	11
12	13	14	15	16	17	18
19	20	21	22	23	24	25
26	27	28	29	30		

MAY

S	M	T	W	T	F	S
					1	2
3	4	5	6	7	8	9
10	11	12	13	14	15	16
17	18	19	20	21	22	23
24	25	26	27	28	29	30
31						

JUNE

S	M	T	W	T	F	S
	1	2	3	4	5	6
7	8	9	10	11	12	13
14	15	16	17	18	19	20
21	22	23	24	25	26	27
28	29	30				

JULY

S	M	T	W	T	F	S
			1	2	3	4
5	6	7	8	9	10	11
12	13	14	15	16	17	18
19	20	21	22	23	24	25
26	27	28	29	30	31	

AUGUST

S	M	T	W	T	F	S
						1
2	3	4	5	6	7	8
9	10	11	12	13	14	15
16	17	18	19	20	21	22
23	24	25	26	27	28	29
30	31					

SEPTEMBER

S	M	T	W	T	F	S
		1	2	3	4	5
6	7	8	9	10	11	12
13	14	15	16	17	18	19
20	21	22	23	24	25	26
27	28	29	30			

OCTOBER

S	M	T	W	T	F	S
				1	2	3
4	5	6	7	8	9	10
11	12	13	14	15	16	17
18	19	20	21	22	23	24
25	26	27	28	29	30	31

NOVEMBER

S	M	T	W	T	F	S
1	2	3	4	5	6	7
8	9	10	11	12	13	14
15	16	17	18	19	20	21
22	23	24	25	26	27	28
29	30					

DECEMBER

S	M	T	W	T	F	S
		1	2	3	4	5
6	7	8	9	10	11	12
13	14	15	16	17	18	19
20	21	22	23	24	25	26
27	28	29	30	31		

6

JANUARY

S	M	T	W	T	F	S
					1	2
3	4	5	6	7	8	9
10	11	12	13	14	15	16
17	18	19	20	21	22	23
24	25	26	27	28	29	30
31						

FEBRUARY

S	M	T	W	T	F	S
	1	2	3	4	5	6
7	8	9	10	11	12	13
14	15	16	17	18	19	20
21	22	23	24	25	26	27
28						

MARCH

S	M	T	W	T	F	S
	1	2	3	4	5	6
7	8	9	10	11	12	13
14	15	16	17	18	19	20
21	22	23	24	25	26	27
28	29	30	31			

APRIL

S	M	T	W	T	F	S
				1	2	3
4	5	6	7	8	9	10
11	12	13	14	15	16	17
18	19	20	21	22	23	24
25	26	27	28	29	30	

MAY

S	M	T	W	T	F	S
						1
2	3	4	5	6	7	8
9	10	11	12	13	14	15
16	17	18	19	20	21	22
23	24	25	26	27	28	29
30	31					

JUNE

S	M	T	W	T	F	S
		1	2	3	4	5
6	7	8	9	10	11	12
13	14	15	16	17	18	19
20	21	22	23	24	25	26
27	28	29	30			

JULY

S	M	T	W	T	F	S
				1	2	3
4	5	6	7	8	9	10
11	12	13	14	15	16	17
18	19	20	21	22	23	24
25	26	27	28	29	30	31

AUGUST

S	M	T	W	T	F	S
1	2	3	4	5	6	7
8	9	10	11	12	13	14
15	16	17	18	19	20	21
22	23	24	25	26	27	28
29	30	31				

SEPTEMBER

S	M	T	W	T	F	S
			1	2	3	4
5	6	7	8	9	10	11
12	13	14	15	16	17	18
19	20	21	22	23	24	25
26	27	28	29	30		

OCTOBER

S	M	T	W	T	F	S
					1	2
3	4	5	6	7	8	9
10	11	12	13	14	15	16
17	18	19	20	21	22	23
24	25	26	27	28	29	30
31						

NOVEMBER

S	M	T	W	T	F	S
	1	2	3	4	5	6
7	8	9	10	11	12	13
14	15	16	17	18	19	20
21	22	23	24	25	26	27
28	29	30				

DECEMBER

S	M	T	W	T	F	S
			1	2	3	4
5	6	7	8	9	10	11
12	13	14	15	16	17	18
19	20	21	22	23	24	25
26	27	28	29	30	31	

7 1977

JANUARY

S	M	T	W	T	F	S
						1
2	3	4	5	6	7	8
9	10	11	12	13	14	15
16	17	18	19	20	21	22
23	24	25	26	27	28	29
30	31					

FEBRUARY

S	M	T	W	T	F	S
		1	2	3	4	5
6	7	8	9	10	11	12
13	14	15	16	17	18	19
20	21	22	23	24	25	26
27	28					

MARCH

S	M	T	W	T	F	S
		1	2	3	4	5
6	7	8	9	10	11	12
13	14	15	16	17	18	19
20	21	22	23	24	25	26
27	28	29	30	31		

APRIL

S	M	T	W	T	F	S
					1	2
3	4	5	6	7	8	9
10	11	12	13	14	15	16
17	18	19	20	21	22	23
24	25	26	27	28	29	30

MAY

S	M	T	W	T	F	S
1	2	3	4	5	6	7
8	9	10	11	12	13	14
15	16	17	18	19	20	21
22	23	24	25	26	27	28
29	30	31				

JUNE

S	M	T	W	T	F	S
			1	2	3	4
5	6	7	8	9	10	11
12	13	14	15	16	17	18
19	20	21	22	23	24	25
26	27	28	29	30		

JULY

S	M	T	W	T	F	S
					1	2
3	4	5	6	7	8	9
10	11	12	13	14	15	16
17	18	19	20	21	22	23
24	25	26	27	28	29	30
31						

AUGUST

S	M	T	W	T	F	S
	1	2	3	4	5	6
7	8	9	10	11	12	13
14	15	16	17	18	19	20
21	22	23	24	25	26	27
28	29	30	31			

SEPTEMBER

S	M	T	W	T	F	S
				1	2	3
4	5	6	7	8	9	10
11	12	13	14	15	16	17
18	19	20	21	22	23	24
25	26	27	28	29	30	

OCTOBER

S	M	T	W	T	F	S
						1
2	3	4	5	6	7	8
9	10	11	12	13	14	15
16	17	18	19	20	21	22
23	24	25	26	27	28	29
30	31					

NOVEMBER

S	M	T	W	T	F	S
		1	2	3	4	5
6	7	8	9	10	11	12
13	14	15	16	17	18	19
20	21	22	23	24	25	26
27	28	29	30			

DECEMBER

S	M	T	W	T	F	S
				1	2	3
4	5	6	7	8	9	10
11	12	13	14	15	16	17
18	19	20	21	22	23	24
25	26	27	28	29	30	31

8

JANUARY

S	M	T	W	T	F	S
1	2	3	4	5	6	7
8	9	10	11	12	13	14
15	16	17	18	19	20	21
22	23	24	25	26	27	28
29	30	31				

FEBRUARY

S	M	T	W	T	F	S
			1	2	3	4
5	6	7	8	9	10	11
12	13	14	15	16	17	18
19	20	21	22	23	24	25
26	27	28	29			

MARCH

S	M	T	W	T	F	S
				1	2	3
4	5	6	7	8	9	10
11	12	13	14	15	16	17
18	19	20	21	22	23	24
25	26	27	28	29	30	31

APRIL

S	M	T	W	T	F	S
1	2	3	4	5	6	7
8	9	10	11	12	13	14
15	16	17	18	19	20	21
22	23	24	25	26	27	28
29	30					

MAY

S	M	T	W	T	F	S
		1	2	3	4	5
6	7	8	9	10	11	12
13	14	15	16	17	18	19
20	21	22	23	24	25	26
27	28	29	30	31		

JUNE

S	M	T	W	T	F	S
					1	2
3	4	5	6	7	8	9
10	11	12	13	14	15	16
17	18	19	20	21	22	23
24	25	26	27	28	29	30

JULY

S	M	T	W	T	F	S
1	2	3	4	5	6	7
8	9	10	11	12	13	14
15	16	17	18	19	20	21
22	23	24	25	26	27	28
29	30	31				

AUGUST

S	M	T	W	T	F	S
			1	2	3	4
5	6	7	8	9	10	11
12	13	14	15	16	17	18
19	20	21	22	23	24	25
26	27	28	29	30	31	

SEPTEMBER

S	M	T	W	T	F	S
						1
2	3	4	5	6	7	8
9	10	11	12	13	14	15
16	17	18	19	20	21	22
23	24	25	26	27	28	29
30						

OCTOBER

S	M	T	W	T	F	S
	1	2	3	4	5	6
7	8	9	10	11	12	13
14	15	16	17	18	19	20
21	22	23	24	25	26	27
28	29	30	31			

NOVEMBER

S	M	T	W	T	F	S
				1	2	3
4	5	6	7	8	9	10
11	12	13	14	15	16	17
18	19	20	21	22	23	24
25	26	27	28	29	30	

DECEMBER

S	M	T	W	T	F	S
						1
2	3	4	5	6	7	8
9	10	11	12	13	14	15
16	17	18	19	20	21	22
23	24	25	26	27	28	29
30	31					

9

JANUARY

S	M	T	W	T	F	S
	1	2	3	4	5	6
7	8	9	10	11	12	13
14	15	16	17	18	19	20
21	22	23	24	25	26	27
28	29	30	31			

FEBRUARY

S	M	T	W	T	F	S
				1	2	3
4	5	6	7	8	9	10
11	12	13	14	15	16	17
18	19	20	21	22	23	24
25	26	27	28	29		

MARCH

S	M	T	W	T	F	S
					1	2
3	4	5	6	7	8	9
10	11	12	13	14	15	16
17	18	19	20	21	22	23
24	25	26	27	28	29	30
31						

APRIL

S	M	T	W	T	F	S
	1	2	3	4	5	6
7	8	9	10	11	12	13
14	15	16	17	18	19	20
21	22	23	24	25	26	27
28	29	30				

MAY

S	M	T	W	T	F	S
			1	2	3	4
5	6	7	8	9	10	11
12	13	14	15	16	17	18
19	20	21	22	23	24	25
26	27	28	29	30	31	

JUNE

S	M	T	W	T	F	S
						1
2	3	4	5	6	7	8
9	10	11	12	13	14	15
16	17	18	19	20	21	22
23	24	25	26	27	28	29
30						

JULY

S	M	T	W	T	F	S
	1	2	3	4	5	6
7	8	9	10	11	12	13
14	15	16	17	18	19	20
21	22	23	24	25	26	27
28	29	30	31			

AUGUST

S	M	T	W	T	F	S
				1	2	3
4	5	6	7	8	9	10
11	12	13	14	15	16	17
18	19	20	21	22	23	24
25	26	27	28	29	30	31

SEPTEMBER

S	M	T	W	T	F	S
1	2	3	4	5	6	7
8	9	10	11	12	13	14
15	16	17	18	19	20	21
22	23	24	25	26	27	28
29	30					

OCTOBER

S	M	T	W	T	F	S
		1	2	3	4	5
6	7	8	9	10	11	12
13	14	15	16	17	18	19
20	21	22	23	24	25	26
27	28	29	30	31		

NOVEMBER

S	M	T	W	T	F	S
					1	2
3	4	5	6	7	8	9
10	11	12	13	14	15	16
17	18	19	20	21	22	23
24	25	26	27	28	29	30

DECEMBER

S	M	T	W	T	F	S
1	2	3	4	5	6	7
8	9	10	11	12	13	14
15	16	17	18	19	20	21
22	23	24	25	26	27	28
29	30	31				

10

JANUARY

S	M	T	W	T	F	S
		1	2	3	4	5
6	7	8	9	10	11	12
13	14	15	16	17	18	19
20	21	22	23	24	25	26
27	28	29	30	31		

FEBRUARY

S	M	T	W	T	F	S
					1	2
3	4	5	6	7	8	9
10	11	12	13	14	15	16
17	18	19	20	21	22	23
24	25	26	27	28	29	

MARCH

S	M	T	W	T	F	S
						1
2	3	4	5	6	7	8
9	10	11	12	13	14	15
16	17	18	19	20	21	22
23	24	25	26	27	28	29
30	31					

APRIL

S	M	T	W	T	F	S
		1	2	3	4	5
6	7	8	9	10	11	12
13	14	15	16	17	18	19
20	21	22	23	24	25	26
27	28	29	30			

MAY

S	M	T	W	T	F	S
				1	2	3
4	5	6	7	8	9	10
11	12	13	14	15	16	17
18	19	20	21	22	23	24
25	26	27	28	29	30	31

JUNE

S	M	T	W	T	F	S
1	2	3	4	5	6	7
8	9	10	11	12	13	14
15	16	17	18	19	20	21
22	23	24	25	26	27	28
29	30					

JULY

S	M	T	W	T	F	S
		1	2	3	4	5
6	7	8	9	10	11	12
13	14	15	16	17	18	19
20	21	22	23	24	25	26
27	28	29	30	31		

AUGUST

S	M	T	W	T	F	S
					1	2
3	4	5	6	7	8	9
10	11	12	13	14	15	16
17	18	19	20	21	22	23
24	25	26	27	28	29	30
31						

SEPTEMBER

S	M	T	W	T	F	S
	1	2	3	4	5	6
7	8	9	10	11	12	13
14	15	16	17	18	19	20
21	22	23	24	25	26	27
28	29	30				

OCTOBER

S	M	T	W	T	F	S
			1	2	3	4
5	6	7	8	9	10	11
12	13	14	15	16	17	18
19	20	21	22	23	24	25
26	27	28	29	30	31	

NOVEMBER

S	M	T	W	T	F	S
						1
2	3	4	5	6	7	8
9	10	11	12	13	14	15
16	17	18	19	20	21	22
23	24	25	26	27	28	29
30						

DECEMBER

S	M	T	W	T	F	S
	1	2	3	4	5	6
7	8	9	10	11	12	13
14	15	16	17	18	19	20
21	22	23	24	25	26	27
28	29	30	31			

11

JANUARY

S	M	T	W	T	F	S
			1	2	3	4
5	6	7	8	9	10	11
12	13	14	15	16	17	18
19	20	21	22	23	24	25
26	27	28	29	30	31	

FEBRUARY

S	M	T	W	T	F	S
						1
2	3	4	5	6	7	8
9	10	11	12	13	14	15
16	17	18	19	20	21	22
23	24	25	26	27	28	29

MARCH

S	M	T	W	T	F	S
1	2	3	4	5	6	7
8	9	10	11	12	13	14
15	16	17	18	19	20	21
22	23	24	25	26	27	28
29	30	31				

APRIL

S	M	T	W	T	F	S
			1	2	3	4
5	6	7	8	9	10	11
12	13	14	15	16	17	18
19	20	21	22	23	24	25
26	27	28	29	30		

MAY

S	M	T	W	T	F	S
					1	2
3	4	5	6	7	8	9
10	11	12	13	14	15	16
17	18	19	20	21	22	23
24	25	26	27	28	29	30
31						

JUNE

S	M	T	W	T	F	S
	1	2	3	4	5	6
7	8	9	10	11	12	13
14	15	16	17	18	19	20
21	22	23	24	25	26	27
28	29	30				

JULY

S	M	T	W	T	F	S
			1	2	3	4
5	6	7	8	9	10	11
12	13	14	15	16	17	18
19	20	21	22	23	24	25
26	27	28	29	30	31	

AUGUST

S	M	T	W	T	F	S
						1
2	3	4	5	6	7	8
9	10	11	12	13	14	15
16	17	18	19	20	21	22
23	24	25	26	27	28	29
30	31					

SEPTEMBER

S	M	T	W	T	F	S
		1	2	3	4	5
6	7	8	9	10	11	12
13	14	15	16	17	18	19
20	21	22	23	24	25	26
27	28	29	30			

OCTOBER

S	M	T	W	T	F	S
				1	2	3
4	5	6	7	8	9	10
11	12	13	14	15	16	17
18	19	20	21	22	23	24
25	26	27	28	29	30	31

NOVEMBER

S	M	T	W	T	F	S
1	2	3	4	5	6	7
8	9	10	11	12	13	14
15	16	17	18	19	20	21
22	23	24	25	26	27	28
29	30					

DECEMBER

S	M	T	W	T	F	S
		1	2	3	4	5
6	7	8	9	10	11	12
13	14	15	16	17	18	19
20	21	22	23	24	25	26
27	28	29	30	31		

12

JANUARY

S	M	T	W	T	F	S
				1	2	3
4	5	6	7	8	9	10
11	12	13	14	15	16	17
18	19	20	21	22	23	24
25	26	27	28	29	30	31

FEBRUARY

S	M	T	W	T	F	S
1	2	3	4	5	6	7
8	9	10	11	12	13	14
15	16	17	18	19	20	21
22	23	24	25	26	27	28
29						

MARCH

S	M	T	W	T	F	S
	1	2	3	4	5	6
7	8	9	10	11	12	13
14	15	16	17	18	19	20
21	22	23	24	25	26	27
28	29	30	31			

APRIL

S	M	T	W	T	F	S
				1	2	3
4	5	6	7	8	9	10
11	12	13	14	15	16	17
18	19	20	21	22	23	24
25	26	27	28	29	30	

MAY

S	M	T	W	T	F	S
						1
2	3	4	5	6	7	8
9	10	11	12	13	14	15
16	17	18	19	20	21	22
23	24	25	26	27	28	29
30	31					

JUNE

S	M	T	W	T	F	S
		1	2	3	4	5
6	7	8	9	10	11	12
13	14	15	16	17	18	19
20	21	22	23	24	25	26
27	28	29	30			

JULY

S	M	T	W	T	F	S
				1	2	3
4	5	6	7	8	9	10
11	12	13	14	15	16	17
18	19	20	21	22	23	24
25	26	27	28	29	30	31

AUGUST

S	M	T	W	T	F	S
1	2	3	4	5	6	7
8	9	10	11	12	13	14
15	16	17	18	19	20	21
22	23	24	25	26	27	28
29	30	31				

SEPTEMBER

S	M	T	W	T	F	S
			1	2	3	4
5	6	7	8	9	10	11
12	13	14	15	16	17	18
19	20	21	22	23	24	25
26	27	28	29	30		

OCTOBER

S	M	T	W	T	F	S
					1	2
3	4	5	6	7	8	9
10	11	12	13	14	15	16
17	18	19	20	21	22	23
24	25	26	27	28	29	30
31						

NOVEMBER

S	M	T	W	T	F	S
	1	2	3	4	5	6
7	8	9	10	11	12	13
14	15	16	17	18	19	20
21	22	23	24	25	26	27
28	29	30				

DECEMBER

S	M	T	W	T	F	S
			1	2	3	4
5	6	7	8	9	10	11
12	13	14	15	16	17	18
19	20	21	22	23	24	25
26	27	28	29	30	31	

13

JANUARY

S	M	T	W	T	F	S
					1	2
3	4	5	6	7	8	9
10	11	12	13	14	15	16
17	18	19	20	21	22	23
24	25	26	27	28	29	30
31						

FEBRUARY

S	M	T	W	T	F	S
	1	2	3	4	5	6
7	8	9	10	11	12	13
14	15	16	17	18	19	20
21	22	23	24	25	26	27
28	29					

MARCH

S	M	T	W	T	F	S
		1	2	3	4	5
6	7	8	9	10	11	12
13	14	15	16	17	18	19
20	21	22	23	24	25	26
27	28	29	30	31		

APRIL

S	M	T	W	T	F	S
					1	2
3	4	5	6	7	8	9
10	11	12	13	14	15	16
17	18	19	20	21	22	23
24	25	26	27	28	29	30

MAY

S	M	T	W	T	F	S
1	2	3	4	5	6	7
8	9	10	11	12	13	14
15	16	17	18	19	20	21
22	23	24	25	26	27	28
29	30	31				

JUNE

S	M	T	W	T	F	S
			1	2	3	4
5	6	7	8	9	10	11
12	13	14	15	16	17	18
19	20	21	22	23	24	25
26	27	28	29	30		

JULY

S	M	T	W	T	F	S
					1	2
3	4	5	6	7	8	9
10	11	12	13	14	15	16
17	18	19	20	21	22	23
24	25	26	27	28	29	30
31						

AUGUST

S	M	T	W	T	F	S
	1	2	3	4	5	6
7	8	9	10	11	12	13
14	15	16	17	18	19	20
21	22	23	24	25	26	27
28	29	30	31			

SEPTEMBER

S	M	T	W	T	F	S
				1	2	3
4	5	6	7	8	9	10
11	12	13	14	15	16	17
18	19	20	21	22	23	24
25	26	27	28	29	30	

OCTOBER

S	M	T	W	T	F	S
						1
2	3	4	5	6	7	8
9	10	11	12	13	14	15
16	17	18	19	20	21	22
23	24	25	26	27	28	29
30	31					

NOVEMBER

S	M	T	W	T	F	S
		1	2	3	4	5
6	7	8	9	10	11	12
13	14	15	16	17	18	19
20	21	22	23	24	25	26
27	28	29	30			

DECEMBER

S	M	T	W	T	F	S
				1	2	3
4	5	6	7	8	9	10
11	12	13	14	15	16	17
18	19	20	21	22	23	24
25	26	27	28	29	30	31

14

JANUARY

S	M	T	W	T	F	S
						1
2	3	4	5	6	7	8
9	10	11	12	13	14	15
16	17	18	19	20	21	22
23	24	25	26	27	28	29
30	31					

FEBRUARY

S	M	T	W	T	F	S
		1	2	3	4	5
6	7	8	9	10	11	12
13	14	15	16	17	18	19
20	21	22	23	24	25	26
27	28	29				

MARCH

S	M	T	W	T	F	S
			1	2	3	4
5	6	7	8	9	10	11
12	13	14	15	16	17	18
19	20	21	22	23	24	25
26	27	28	29	30	31	

APRIL

S	M	T	W	T	F	S
						1
2	3	4	5	6	7	8
9	10	11	12	13	14	15
16	17	18	19	20	21	22
23	24	25	26	27	28	29
30						

MAY

S	M	T	W	T	F	S
	1	2	3	4	5	6
7	8	9	10	11	12	13
14	15	16	17	18	19	20
21	22	23	24	25	26	27
28	29	30	31			

JUNE

S	M	T	W	T	F	S
				1	2	3
4	5	6	7	8	9	10
11	12	13	14	15	16	17
18	19	20	21	22	23	24
25	26	27	28	29	30	

JULY

S	M	T	W	T	F	S
						1
2	3	4	5	6	7	8
9	10	11	12	13	14	15
16	17	18	19	20	21	22
23	24	25	26	27	28	29
30	31					

AUGUST

S	M	T	W	T	F	S
		1	2	3	4	5
6	7	8	9	10	11	12
13	14	15	16	17	18	19
20	21	22	23	24	25	26
27	28	29	30	31		

SEPTEMBER

S	M	T	W	T	F	S
					1	2
3	4	5	6	7	8	9
10	11	12	13	14	15	16
17	18	19	20	21	22	23
24	25	26	27	28	29	30

OCTOBER

S	M	T	W	T	F	S
1	2	3	4	5	6	7
8	9	10	11	12	13	14
15	16	17	18	19	20	21
22	23	24	25	26	27	28
29	30	31				

NOVEMBER

S	M	T	W	T	F	S
			1	2	3	4
5	6	7	8	9	10	11
12	13	14	15	16	17	18
19	20	21	22	23	24	25
26	27	28	29	30		

DECEMBER

S	M	T	W	T	F	S
					1	2
3	4	5	6	7	8	9
10	11	12	13	14	15	16
17	18	19	20	21	22	23
24	25	26	27	28	29	30
31						

Julian and Gregorian Calendars; Leap Year

Calendars based on the movements of sun and moon have been used since ancient times, but none has been perfect. The Julian calendar, under which western nations measured time until 1582 A. D., was authorized by Julius Caesar in 46 B.C., the year 709 of Rome. His expert was a Greek, Sosigenes. The Julian calendar, on the assumption that the true year was 365 1/4 days long, gave every fourth year 366 days. The Venerable Bede, an Anglo-Saxon monk, announced in 730 A.D. that the 365-day Julian year was 11 min., 14 sec. too long, making a cumulative error of about a day every 128 years, but nothing was done about it for over 800 years.

By 1582 the accumulated error was estimated to have amounted to 10 days. In that year Pope Gregory XIII decreed that the day following Oct. 4, 1582, should be called Oct. 15, thus dropping 10 days.

However, with common years 365 days and a 366-day leap year every fourth year, the error in the length of the year would have recurred at the rate of a little more than 3 days every 400 years. So 3 of every 4 centesimal years (ending in 00) were made common years, not leap years. Thus 1600 was a leap year, 1700, 1800 and 1900 were not, but 2000 will be. Leap years are those divisible by 4 except centesimal years, which are common unless divisible by 400.

The Gregorian calendar was adopted at once by France, Italy, Spain, Portugal and Luxembourg. Within 2 years most German Catholic states, Belgium and parts of Switzerland and the Netherlands were brought under the new calendar, and Hungary followed in 1587. The rest of the Netherlands, along with Denmark and the German Protestant states made the change in 1699-1700 (German Protestants retained the old reckoning of Easter until 1776).

The British Government imposed the Gregorian calendar on all its possessions, including the American colonies, in 1752. The British decreed that the day following Sept. 2, 1752, should be called Sept. 14 a loss of 11 days. All dates preceding were marke O.S., for Old Style. In addition New Year's Day wa moved to Jan. 1 from Mar. 25. (e.g., under the ol reckoning, Mar. 24, 1700 had been followed by Mar 25, 1701.) George Washington's birth date, which wa Feb. 11, 1731, O.S., became Feb. 22, 1732, N.S. In 175 Sweden too went Gregorian, retaining the old Easte rules until 1844.

In 1793 the French Revolutionary Governmen adopted a calendar of 12 months of 30 days each wit 5 extra days in September of each common year an a 6th extra day every 4th year. Napoleon reinstate the Gregorian calendar in 1806.

The Gregorian system later spread to non-European regions, first in the European colonies, then i the independent countries, replacing traditiona calendars at least for official purposes. Japan in 1873 Egypt in 1875, China in 1912 and Turkey in 191 made the change, usually in conjunction with political upheavals. In China, the republican governmen began reckoning years from its 1911 founding — e.g. 1948 was designated the year 37. After 1949, th Communists adopted the Common, or Christian Er year count, even for the traditional lunar calendar.

In 1918 the revolutionary government in Russia decreed that the day after Jan. 31, 1918, Old Style would become Feb. 13, 1918, New Style. Greece followed in 1923. (In Russia the Orthodox Church has retained the Julian calendar, as have various Middl Eastern Christian sects.) For the first time in history all major cultures have been brought under on calendar.

To change from the Julian to the Gregorian calendar, add 10 days to dates Oct. 5, 1582, through Feb 28, 1700; after that date add 11 days through Feb. 28 1800, 12 days through Feb. 28, 1900, and 13 day through Feb. 28, 2100.

Julian Calendar

To find which of the 14 calendars printed on pages 786-787 applies to any year under the Julian system, fin the century for the desired year in the three left-hand columns below; read across. Then find the year in th four top rows; read down. The number in the intersection is the calendar designation for that year.

				Year (last two figures of desired year)						
				01 02 03 04	05 06 07 08	09 10 11 12	13 14 15 16	17 18 19 20	21 22 23 24	25 26 27 2
				29 30 31 32	33 34 35 36	37 38 39 40	41 42 43 44	45 46 47 48	49 50 51 52	53 54 55 5
				57 58 59 60	61 62 63 64	65 66 67 68	69 70 71 72	73 74 75 76	77 78 79 80	81 82 83 8
Century			00	85 86 87 88	89 90 91 92	93 94 95 96	97 98 99			
0	700	1400	12	7 1 2 10	5 6 7 8	3 4 5 13	1 2 3 11	6 7 1 9	4 5 6 14	2 3 4 1
100	800	1500	11	6 7 1 9	4 5 6 14	2 3 4 12	7 1 2 10	5 6 7 8	3 4 5 13	1 2 3 1
200	900	1600	10	5 6 7 8	3 4 5 13	1 2 3 11	6 7 1 9	4 5 6 14	2 3 4 12	7 1 2 1
300	1000	1700	9	4 5 6 14	2 3 4 12	7 1 2 10	5 6 7 8	3 4 5 13	1 2 3 11	6 7 1
400	1100	1800	8	3 4 5 13	1 2 3 11	6 7 1 9	4 5 6 14	2 3 4 12	7 1 2 10	5 6 7
500	1200	1900	14	2 3 4 12	7 1 2 10	5 6 7 8	3 4 5 13	1 2 3 11	6 7 1 9	4 5 6 1
600	1300	2000	13	1 2 3 11	6 7 1 9	4 5 6 14	2 3 4 12	7 1 2 10	5 6 7 8	3 4 5 1

Gregorian Calendar

Pick desired year from table below or on page 786 (for years 1800 to 2059). The number shown with eac year shows which calendar to use for that year, as shown on pages 786-787. (The Gregorian calendar was inau gurated Oct. 15, 1582. From that date to Dec. 31, 1582, use calendar 6.)

1583-1799

1583...7	1603...4	1623...1	1643...5	1663...2	1683...6	1703...2	1723...6	1743...3	1763...7	1783...
1584...8	1604..12	1624...9	1644..13	1664..10	1684..14	1704..10	1724..14	1744..11	1764...8	1784..1
1585...3	1605...7	1625...4	1645...1	1665...5	1685...2	1705...5	1725...2	1745...6	1765...3	1785...
1586...4	1606...1	1626...5	1646...2	1666...6	1686...3	1706...6	1726...3	1746...7	1766...4	1786...
1587...5	1607...2	1627...6	1647...3	1667...7	1687...4	1707...7	1727...4	1747...1	1767...5	1787...
1588..13	1608..10	1628..14	1648..11	1668...8	1688..12	1708...8	1728..12	1748...9	1768..13	1788..1
1589...1	1609...5	1629...2	1649...6	1669...3	1689...7	1709...3	1729...7	1749...4	1769...1	1789...
1590...2	1610...6	1630...3	1650...7	1670...4	1690...1	1710...4	1730...1	1750...5	1770...2	1790...
1591...3	1611...7	1631...4	1651...1	1671...5	1691...2	1711...5	1731...2	1751...6	1771...3	1791...
1592..11	1612...8	1632..12	1652...9	1672..13	1692..10	1712..13	1732..10	1752..14	1772..11	1792...
1593...6	1613...3	1633...7	1653...4	1673...1	1693...5	1713...1	1733...5	1753...2	1773...6	1793...
1594...7	1614...4	1634...1	1654...5	1674...2	1694...6	1714...2	1734...6	1754...3	1774...7	1794...
1595...1	1615...5	1635...2	1655...6	1675...3	1695...7	1715...3	1735...7	1755...4	1775...1	1795...
1596...9	1616..13	1636..10	1656..14	1676..11	1696...8	1716..11	1736...8	1756..12	1776...9	1796..1
1597...4	1617...1	1637...5	1657...2	1677...6	1697...3	1717...6	1737...3	1757...7	1777...4	1797...
1598...5	1618...2	1638...6	1658...3	1678...7	1698...4	1718...7	1738...4	1758...1	1778...5	1798...
1599...6	1619...3	1639...7	1659...4	1679...1	1699...5	1719...1	1739...5	1759...2	1779...6	1799...
1600..14	1620..11	1640...8	1660..12	1680...9	1700...6	1720...9	1740..13	1760..10	1780..14	....
1601...2	1621...6	1641...3	1661...7	1681...4	1701...7	1721...4	1741...1	1761...5	1781...2	....
1602...3	1622...7	1642...4	1662...1	1682...5	1702...1	1722...5	1742...2	1762...6	1782...3	....

Standard Time Differences — North American Cities

At 12 o'clock noon, Eastern Standard Time, the standard time in N.A. cities is as follows:

Akron, Oh.	12.00 Noon
Albuquerque, N.M.	10.00 A.M.
Atlanta, Ga.	12.00 Noon
Austin, Tex.	11.00 A.M.
Baltimore, Md.	12.00 Noon
Birmingham, Ala.	11.00 A.M.
Bismarck, N. D.	11.00 A.M.
Boise, Ida.	10.00 A.M.
Boston, Mass.	12.00 Noon
Buffalo, N.Y.	12.00 Noon
Butte, Mon.	10.00 A.M.
Calgary, Alta.	10.00 A.M.
Charleston, S.C.	12.00 Noon
Charleston, W. Va.	12.00 Noon
Charlotte, N.C.	12.00 Noon
Charlottetown, P.E.I.	1.00 P.M.
Chattanooga, Tenn.	12.00 Noon
Cheyenne, Wy.	10.00 A.M.
Chicago, Ill.	11.00 A.M.
Cleveland, Oh.	12.00 Noon
Colorado Spr., Col.	10.00 A.M.
Columbus, Oh.	12.00 Noon
Dallas, Tex.	11.00 A.M.
*Dawson, Yuk.	8.00 A.M.
Dayton, Oh.	12.00 Noon
Denver, Col.	10.00 A.M.
Des Moines, Ia.	11.00 A.M.
Detroit, Mich.	12.00 Noon
Duluth, Minn.	11.00 A.M.
El Paso, Tex.	10.00 A.M.
Erie, Pa.	12.00 Noon
Evansville, Ind.	11.00 A.M.
Fairbanks, Alas.	7.00 A.M.
Flint, Mich.	12.00 Noon
*Fort Wayne, Ind.	12.00 Noon
Fort Worth, Tex.	11.00 A.M.
Frankfort, Ky.	12.00 Noon
Galveston, Tex.	11.00 A.M.
Grand Rapids, Mich.	12.00 Noon
Halifax, N.S.	1.00 P.M.
Hartford, Conn.	12.00 Noon
Helena, Mon.	10.00 A.M.
*Honolulu, Ha.	7.00 A.M.
Houston, Tex.	11.00 A.M.
*Indianapolis, Ind.	12.00 Noon
Jacksonville, Fla.	12.00 Noon
Juneau, Alas.	9.00 A.M.
Kansas City, Mo.	11.00 A.M.
Knoxville, Tenn.	12.00 Noon
Lexington, Ky.	12.00 Noon
Lincoln, Neb.	11.00 A.M.
Little Rock, Ark.	11.00 A.M.
Los Angeles, Cal.	9.00 A.M.
Louisville, Ky.	12.00 Noon
*Mexico City	11.00 A.M.
Memphis, Tenn.	11.00 A.M.
Miami, Fla.	12.00 Noon
Milwaukee, Wis.	11.00 A.M.
Minneapolis, Minn.	11.00 A.M.
Mobile, Ala.	11.00 A.M.
Montreal, Que.	12.00 Noon
Nashville, Tenn.	11.00 A.M.
New Haven, Conn.	12.00 Noon
New Orleans, La.	11.00 A.M.
New York, N.Y.	12.00 Noon
Nome, Alas.	6.00 A.M.
Norfolk, Va.	12.00 Noon
Okla. City, Okla.	11.00 A.M.
Omaha, Neb.	11.00 A.M.
Peoria, Ill.	11.00 A.M.
Philadelphia, Pa.	12.00 Noon
*Phoenix, Ariz.	10.00 A.M.
Pierre, S. D.	11.00 A.M.
Pittsburgh, Pa.	12.00 Noon
Portland, Me.	12.00 Noon
Portland, Ore.	9.00 A.M.
Providence, R.I.	12.00 Noon
*Regina, Sask.	11.00 A.M.
Reno, Nev.	9.00 A.M.
Richmond, Va.	12.00 Noon
Rochester, N.Y.	12.00 Noon
Sacramento, Cal.	9.00 A.M.
St. John's, Nfld.	1.30 P.M.
St. Louis, Mo.	11.00 A.M.
St. Paul, Minn.	11.00 A.M.
Salt Lake City, Ut.	10.00 A.M.
San Antonio, Tex.	11.00 A.M.
San Diego, Cal.	9.00 A.M.
San Francisco, Cal.	9.00 A.M.
Santa Fe, N.M.	10.00 A.M.
Savannah, Ga.	12.00 Noon
Seattle, Wash.	9.00 A.M.
Shreveport, La.	11.00 A.M.
Sioux Falls, S. D.	11.00 A.M.
Spokane, Wash.	9.00 A.M.
Tampa, Fla.	12.00 Noon
Toledo, Oh.	12.00 Noon
Topeka, Kan.	11.00 A.M.
Toronto, Ont.	12.00 Noon
*Tucson, Ariz.	10.00 A.M.
Tulsa, Okla.	11.00 A.M.
Vancouver, B.C.	9.00 A.M.
Washington, D.C.	12.00 Noon
Wichita, Kan.	11.00 A.M.
Wilmington, Del.	12.00 Noon
Winnipeg, Man.	11.00 A.M.

*Cities with an asterisk do not observe daylight savings time. During much of the year, it is necessary to add one hour to the cities which do observe daylight savings time to get the proper time relation.

Standard Time Differences — World Cities

The time indicated in the table is fixed by law and is called the legal time, or, more generally, Standard Time. Use of Daylight Saving Time varies widely. *Indicates morning of the following day. At 12.00, Eastern Standard Time, the standard time (in 24-hour time) in foreign cities is as follows:

Alexandria	19 00
Amsterdam	18 00
Athens	19 00
Auckland	5 00*
Baghdad	20 00
Bangkok	0 00
Belfast	17 00
Berlin	18 00
Bogota	12 00
Bombay	22 30
Bremen	18 00
Brussels	18 00
Bucharest	19 00
Budapest	18 00
Buenos Aires	14 00
Calcutta	22 30
Cape Town	19 00
Caracas	13 00
Copenhagen	18 00
Dacca	23 00
Delhi	22 30
Djakarta	0 00
Dublin	17 00
Gdansk	18 00
Geneva	18 00
Havana	12 00
Helsinki	19 00
Hong Kong	1 00*
Istanbul	19 00
Jerusalem	19 00
Johannesburg	19 00
Karachi	22 00
Le Havre	18 00
Leningrad	20 00
Lima	12 00
Lisbon	18 00
Liverpool	17 00
London	17 00
Madrid	18 00
Manila	1 00*
Melbourne	3 00*
Montevideo	14 00
Moscow	20 00
Nagasaki	2 00*
Oslo	18 00
Paris	18 00
Peking	1 00*
Prague	18 00
Rangoon	23 30
Rio De Janeiro	14 00
Rome	18 00
Saigon	1 00*
Santiago (Chile)	13 00
Seoul	2 00*
Shanghai	1 00*
Singapore	12 30*
Stockholm	18 00
Sydney (Australia)	3 00*
Tashkent	23 00
Teheran	20 30
Tel Aviv	19 00
Tokyo	2 00*
Valparaiso	13 00
Vladivostok	3 00*
Vienna	18 00
Warsaw	18 00
Wellington (N.Z.)	5 00*
Yokohama	2 00*
Zurich	18 00

Chronological Eras, 1978

The year 1978 of the Christian Era comprises the latter part of the 202d and the beginning of the 203d year of the independence of the United States of America.

Era	Year	Begins in 1978
Byzantine	7487	Sept. 14
Jewish	5739	Oct. 2 (sunset)
Olympiads (Second year of Olympiad 689)	2754	July 1
Roman (Ab Urbe Condita)	2731	Jan. 14
Nabonassar (Babylonian)	2727	Apr. 29
Japanese	2638	Jan. 1
Grecian (Seleucidae)	2290	Sept. 14 or Oct. 14
Diocletian	1695	Sept. 11
Indian (Saka)	1900	Mar. 22
Mohammedan (Hegira)	1399	Dec. 2

Chronological Cycles, 1978

Dominical Letter	A
Epact	21
Golden Number (Lunar Cycle)	III
Solar Cycle	27
Roman Indiction	I
Julian Period (year of)	6691

Standard Time, Daylight Saving Time, and Others

Source: Defense Mapping Agency Hydrographic Center; Department of Transportation; National Bureau of Standards; U.S. Naval Observatory

Standard Time

Standard time is reckoned from Greenwich, England, recognized as the Prime Meridian of Longitude. The world is divided into 24 zones, each 15° of arc, or one hour in time apart. The Greenwich meridian (0°) extends through the center of the initial zone, and the zones to the east are numbered from 1 to 12 with the prefix "minus" indicating the number of hours to be subtracted to obtain Greenwich Time.

Westward zones are similarly numbered, but prefixed "plus" showing the number of hours that must be added to get Greenwich Time. While these zones apply generally to sea areas, it should be noted that the Standard Time maintained in many countries does not coincide with zone time. A graphical representation of the zones is shown on the Standard Time Zone Chart of the World published by the Defense Mapping Agency Hydrographic Center, Washington, DC 20390.

The United States and possessions are divided into eight Standard Time zones, as set forth by the Uniform Time Act of 1966, which also provides for the use of Daylight Saving Time therein. Each zone is approximately 15° of longitude in width. All places in each zone use, instead of their own local time, the time counted from the transit of the "mean sun" across the Standard Time meridian which passes near the middle of that zone.

These time zones are designated as Atlantic, Eastern, Central, Mountain, Pacific, Yukon, Alaska-Hawaii, and Bering, and the time in these zones is basically reckoned from the 60th, 75th, 90th, 105th, 120th, 135th, 150th, 165th meridians west of Greenwich. The line wanders to conform to local geographical regions. The time in the various zones is earlier than Greenwich Time by 4, 5, 6, 7, 8, 9, 10, and 11 hours respectively.

High Precision Time and Frequency are broadcast by U.S. Navy Stations which are maintained on frequency with the aid of Atomic Clocks (cesium beam and hydrogen masers). The stations are as follows: NSS: NLK: NAA: NPM/NMO: NWC: NPN: NDT: Omega (U.S. Coast Guard navigational system).

Loran-C Navigational Transmissions at 100 kHz of the East Coast U.S.A., West Coast U.S.A., North Atlantic, North Pacific, Central Pacific, Mediterranean, Northwest Pacific and the Norwegian sea chains may be used for time and frequency comparisons.

Standard Frequency Stations

The National Bureau of Standards (NBS) radio stations WWV at Fort Collins, Colorado, and WWVH on the island of Kauai, Hawaii, broadcast a number of technical services continuously night and day. These services are: 1. standard radio frequencies, 2.5, 5, 10, and 15 MHz (WWV) and 2.5, 5, 10, and 15 MHz (WWVH); 2. standard time voice announcements (WWV—male, 7.5 seconds before the minute; WWVH — female, 15 seconds before the minute); 3. standard time intervals of one second and one minute; 4. corrections to adjust atomic time to astronomical time; 5. standard audio frequencies of 500 and 600 Hz on alternate minutes and a 440 Hz tone (the musical pitch A above middle C) once each hour; 6. a slow time code at 100 Hz giving the day, hour, and minute in binary coded decimal form; 7. geophysical alerts on events in process and summaries of solar and geophysical events of the last 24 hours (WWV only); and 8. storm warnings; 9. Omega Polar Cap Disturbance warnings. The NBS also broadcasts time and frequency signals from its low frequency station (60kHz). WWVB, also located at Fort Collins, Colorado.

Each hour there are periods with no tone modulation during which the carrier frequency, seconds pulses, time announcements, and 100 Hz BCD time code continue.They occur from 45 to 51 minutes after each hour on WWV and from 8 to 11 and 15 to 20 minutes after each hour on WWVH.

The National Research Council of Canada continually transmits precision time signals from Ottawa over station CHU on 3 frequencies, 3330, 7335, and 14670 kHz.

Storm warnings cover the waters of the Atlantic and eastern North Pacific from WWV and the eastern and central North Pacific from WWVH and are given at the 8th, 9th, and 10th minute of each hour from WWV and at the 48th, 49th, and 50th minute of each hour from WWVH. Times of issue are 0500, 1100, 1700, and 2300 UTC from WWV, and 0000, 0600, 1200, and 1800 UTC from WWVH.

The time and frequency broadcasts are controlled by the NBS atomic frequency standards, which realize the internationally defined cesium resonance frequency with an accuracy of 1 part in 10^{13}. (The Cesium atom invariably resonates at a little over 9 billion oscillations per second.)

The atomic time scale is uniform and does not reflect the variable rotational speed of the earth. The time signals are adjusted by introducing a leap second about once a year (at the end of June or December) so that the broadcast time never departs more than nine-tenths of a second from mean solar time, determined by the rotational position of the earth.

Special Publication 432 describes in detail the standard frequency and time service of the National Bureau of Standards. Single copies may be obtained upon request from the National Bureau of Standards, Boulder, CO 80302. Quantities may be obtained from the Superintendent of Documents, U.S. Gov. Printing Office, Wash., DC 20402, at 60c per copy.

24-Hour Time

24-hour time is widely used in scientific work throughout the world. In the United States it is used also in operations of the Armed Forces. In Europe it is used in preference to the 12-hour a.m. and p.m. system. With the 24-hour system the day begins at midnight and hours are numbered 0 through 23.

International Date Line

The Date Line is a zig-zag line that approximately coincides with the 180th meridian, and it is where each calendar day begins. The date must be advanced one day when crossing in a westerly direction and set back one day when crossing in an easterly direction.

The line is deflected between north latitude 48° and 75°, so that all Asia lies to the west of it.

Daylight Saving Time

Daylight Saving Time is achieved by advancing the clock one hour. Under the Uniform Time Act, which became effective in 1967, all states, the District of Columbia, and U. S. possessions were to observe Daylight Saving Time beginning at 2 a.m. on the last Sunday in April and ending at 2 a.m. on the last Sunday in October. Any state could, by law, exempt itself; a 1972 amendment to the act authorized states split by time zones to take that into consideration in exempting themselves. Arizona, Hawaii, Puerto Rico, the Virgin Islands, American Samoa, and part of Indiana are now exempt. Some local zone boundaries in Kansas, Texas, Florida, and Michigan have been modified in the last several years by the Dept. of Transportation, which oversees the act. To conserve energy Congress put most of the nation on year-round Daylight Saving Time for two years effective Jan. 6, 1974 through Oct. 26, 1975; but a further bill signed in October, 1974, restored Standard Time from the last Sunday in that month to the last Sunday in February, 1975.

Legal or Public Holidays, 1978

Technically there are no national holidays in the United States: each state has jurisdiction over its holidays, which are designated by legislative enactment or executive proclamation. In practice, however, most states observe the federal legal public holidays, even though the President and Congress can legally designate holidays only for the District of Columbia and for federal employees.

Federal legal public holidays are: New Year's Day, Washington's Birthday, Memorial Day, Independence Day, Labor Day, Columbus Day, Veterans Day, Thanksgiving, and Christmas.

Chief Legal or Public Holidays

When a holiday falls on a Sunday or a Friday it is usually observed on the following Monday or preceding Friday. For some holidays, government and business closing practices vary. In most states, the office of the Secretary of State can provide details of holiday closings.

Jan. 1 (Sunday) — New Year's Day. All the states. (Most states will celebrate on Jan. 2, 1978.)

Feb. 12 (Sunday) — Lincoln's Birthday. Ariz., Cal., Col., Conn., Ill., Ind., Ia., Me., Md., Mo., Mon., Neb., N.J., N.Y., Pa., Ut., Vt., Wash., W. Va. In Del., Ida., and Ore., celebrated Feb. 6 in 1978.

Feb. 20 (3d Monday in Feb.) — Washington's Birthday. All the states except Fla., Kan., La., N.M., N.C. In several states, the holiday is called Presidents' Day or Washington-Lincoln Day.

Mar. 24 — Good Friday. Observed in all the states. A legal holiday in Conn., Del., Ha., Ind., Ky., La., Md., N.J., N.D., Tenn., W. Va. Partial holiday in Nev., N.M. and Wis.

May 29 (last Monday in May) — Memorial Day. All the states except Ala., Miss., S.C., (Confederate Memorial Day in Va.). Observed May 30 in Ill., Md., N.H., N.M., N.Y., Vt., W.Va.

July 4 (Tuesday) — Independence Day. All the states. (July 3 in Nev.)

Sept. 4 (1st Monday in Sept.) — Labor Day. All the states.

Oct. 9 (2d Monday in Oct.) — Columbus Day. All the states except Alas., Ark., Fla., Ia., Kan., La., Mich., Miss., N.C., N.D., Ore., S.C., S.D., Wash. Observed Oct. 12 in Md. (Discoverer's Day in Hawaii; Pioneer Day in S.D.).

Nov. 7 (1st Tuesday after 1st Monday in Nov.) — General Election Day. In Ariz., Del., Ha., Ill., Ind., La., Md., Mo., Mont., Neb., N.H., N.J., N.Y., Pa., R.I., S.C., Tenn., Tex., Va., W. Va., Wis. Half-day holiday in Nev., Oh. (Observed usually only when presidential or general elections are held. Primary election days are observed as holidays or part holidays in some states.)

Nov. 11 (Saturday) — Armistice Day (Veterans Day). All the states (Utah observes on 4th Monday in Oct.). Most states will also observe on Friday, Nov. 10.

Nov. 23 (4th Thursday in Nov.) — Thanksgiving Day. All the states. The day after Thanksgiving is observed as a full or partial holiday in Ark., Fla., Ga., Ill., Ia., Ky., La., N.C., Wash., W. Va.

Dec. 25 (Monday) — Christmas. All the states.

Other Legal or Public Holidays

Dates are for 1978 observance, when known.

Jan. 8 — Battle of New Orleans. In La.

Jan. 15 — Martin Luther King Birthday. Conn., Ky., Md., Mass., N.Y. Many schools and black groups in other states also observe the day.

Jan. 16 (3d Monday in Jan.) — Robert E. Lee's Birthday. Ala., Miss., S.C. Lee-Jackson Day in Va.

Jan. 19 — Robert E. Lee's Birthday. Ark., Fla., Ga., Ky., La., N.C. Confederate Heroes' Day in Tex.

Jan. 20 — Inauguration Day. In the District of Columbia; observed every fourth year.

Jan. 30 — Franklin D. Roosevelt's Birthday. In Ky.

Feb. 7 — Mardi Gras (Shrove Tuesday). Ala., La., and some Fla. counties.

Feb. 14 — Admission Day. In Ariz.

Mar. 2 — Texas Independence Day. In that state.

Mar. 7 — Town Meeting Day (1st Tuesday in Mar.). In Vt.

Mar. 17 — Evacuation Day. In Boston and Suffolk County, Mass.

Mar. 25 — Maryland Day. In that state.

Mar. 27 — Kuhio Day. In Ha.

Mar. 27 — Easter Monday. In N.C.

Mar. 28 — Seward's Day. In Alas.

Apr. 12 — Halifax Independence Day. In N.C.

Apr. 13 — Thomas Jefferson's Birthday. In Ala.

Apr. 17 — Patriot's Day (3d Monday in Apr.). Me. and Mass.

Apr. 21 — San Jacinto Day. In Tex.

Apr. 22 — Arbor Day. In Neb.

Apr. 24 — Fast Day (4th Monday in Apr.). In N.H.

Apr. 24 — Confederate Memorial Day (4th Monday in Apr.). Ala., Fla., and Miss.

Apr. 26 — Confederate Memorial Day. In Ga.

Apr. 28 — Arbor Day (last Friday in Apr.). In Ut.

May 8 — Harry Truman's Birthday. In Mo.

May 10 — Confederate Memorial Day. In N.C., S.C.

May 20 — Mecklenburg Day. In N.C.

June 3 — Birthday of Jefferson Davis. Fla., Ga., Ky., La., S.C.; in Ala., Miss., observed on first Monday in June.

June 3 — Confederate Memorial Day. In Ky., La.

June 12 — Kamehameha Day. In Ha.

June 14 — Flag Day. Observed in all states; a legal holiday in Pa. Observed June 11 in N.Y.

June 17 — Bunker Hill Day. In Boston and Suffolk County, Mass.

July 24 — Pioneer Day. In Ut.

Aug. 7 — Colorado Day (1st Monday in Aug.). In that state.

Aug. 14 — VJ Day (2d Monday in Aug.). In R.I.

Aug. 16 — Bennington Battle Day. In Vt.

Aug. 18 — Admission Day (3d Friday in Aug.). In Ha.

Aug. 27 — Lyndon Johnson's Birthday. In Tex.

Aug. 30 — Huey Long's Birthday. In La.

Sept. 9 — Admission Day. In Cal.

Sept. 12 — Defenders' Day. In Md.

Oct. 16 — Alaska Day. In that state.

Oct. 31 — Nevada Day. In that state.

Dec. 10 — Wyoming Day. Commemorates woman's suffrage in that state.

Days Usually Observed

All Saints' Day, Nov. 1. A public holiday in Hawaii, Louisiana.

American Indian Day (Sept. 22 in 1978). Always fourth Friday in September.

Arbor Day. Tree-planting day. First observed April 10, 1872, in Nebraska. Now observed in every state in the Union except Alaska (often on the last Friday in April). A legal holiday in Utah (always last Friday in April), and in Nebraska (April 22).

Armed Forces Day (May 20 in 1978). Always third Saturday in that month, by presidential proclamation. Replaced Army, Navy, and Air Force Days.

Bill of Rights Day, Dec. 15. By Act of Congress. Bill of Rights took effect Dec. 15, 1791.

Bird Day. Often observed with Arbor Day.

Child Health Day (Oct. 2 in 1978). Always first Monday in October, by presidential proclamation.

Citizenship Day, Sept. 17. President Truman, Feb. 29, 1952, signed bill designating Sept. 17 as annual Citizenship Day. It replaced I Am An American Day, formerly 3rd Sunday in May and Constitution Day, formerly Sept. 17.

Easter Monday (Mar. 27 in 1978). A statutory day in Canada.

Easter Sunday (Mar. 26 in 1978).

Elizabeth Cady Stanton Day, Nov. 12. Birthday of pioneer leader for equal rights for women.

Farmers' Day (Oct. 9 in 1978). In Florida.

Father's Day (June 18, in 1978). Always third Sunday in that month.

Flag Day, June 14. By presidential proclamation. It is a legal holiday in Pennsylvania.

Forefathers' Day, Dec. 21. Landing on Plymouth Rock, in 1620. Is celebrated with dinners by New England societies, especially "Down East."

Nathan Bedford Forrest's Birthday, July 13. Observed in Tennessee to honor the Civil War general.

Four Chaplains Memorial Day, Feb. 3.

Gen. Douglas MacArthur Day, Jan. 26. A memorial day in Arkansas.

Gen. Pulaski Memorial Day, Oct. 11. Native of Poland and Revolutionary War hero; died (Oct. 11, 1779) from wounds received at the siege of Savannah, Ga. Observed officially in Indiana.

Gen. von Steuben Memorial Day, Sept. 17. By presidential proclamation.

Georgia Day, Feb. 12. Observed in that state. Commemorates landing of first colonists in 1733.

Groundhog Day, Feb. 2. A popular belief is that if the groundhog sees his shadow this day, he returns to his burrow and winter continues 6 weeks longer.

Halloween, Oct. 31. The evening before All Saints or All-Hallows Day. Informally observed in the U.S. with masquerading and pumpkin-decorations. Traditionally an occasion for children to play pranks.

Andrew Jackson's Birthday, Mar. 15. Observed in Tennessee.

Leif Ericsson Day, Oct. 9. Observed in Minnesota, Wisconsin.

Loyalty Day, May 1. By act of Congress.

May Day. Name popularly given to May 1st. Celebrated as Labor Day in most of the world, and by some groups in the U.S. Observed in many schools as a Spring Festival.

Minnesota Day, May 11. In that state.

Mother's Day (May 14 in 1978). Always second Sunday in that month. First celebrated in Philadelphia in 1908. Mother's Day has become an international holiday.

National Aviation Day, Aug. 19. By presidential proclamation.

National Day of Prayer. By presidential proclamation each year on a day other than a Sunday.

National Freedom Day, Feb. 1. To commemorate the signing of the Thirteenth amendment, abolishing slavery, Feb. 1, 1865. By presidential proclamation.

National Maritime Day, May 22. First proclaimed 1935 in commemoration of the departure of the SS Savannah, from Savannah, Ga., on May 22, 1819, on the first successful transatlantic voyage under steam propulsion. By presidential proclamation.

Pan American Day, Apr. 14. In 1890 the First International Conference of American States, meeting in Washington, was held on that date. A resolution was adopted which resulted in the creation of the organization known today as the Pan American Union. By presidential proclamation.

Primary Election Day. Observed usually only when presidential or general elections are held.

Reformation Day, Oct. 31. Observed by Protestant groups.

Sadie Hawkins Day (Nov. 18 in 1978). First Saturday after November 11.

St. Patrick's Day, Mar. 17. Observed by Irish Societies, especially with parades.

St. Valentine's Day, Feb. 14. Festival of a martyr beheaded at Rome under Emperor Claudius. Association of this day with lovers has no connection with the saint and probably had its origin in an old belief that on this day birds begin to choose their mates.

Senior Citizens' Day (Sept. 24 in 1978). Celebrated in Indiana on the fourth Sunday in September.

Susan B. Anthony Day, Feb. 15. Birthday of a pioneer crusader for equal rights for women.

United Nations Day, Oct. 24. By presidential proclamation, to commemorate founding of United Nations.

Verrazano Day, Apr. 17. Observed by New York State, to commemorate the probable discovery of New York harbor by Giovanni da Verrazano in April, 1524.

Victoria Day (May 22 in 1978). Birthday of Queen Victoria, a statutory day in Canada, celebrated the first Monday before May 25.

Frances Willard Day, Sept. 28. Observed in Minnesota to honor the educator and temperance leader.

Will Rogers Day, Nov. 4. In Oklahoma.

World Poetry Day, Oct. 15.

Wright Brothers Day, Dec. 17. By presidential designation, to commemorate first successful flight by Orville and Wilbur Wright, Dec. 17, 1903.

Youth Honor Day, Oct. 31. Iowa day of observance.

Other Holidays, Anniversaries, Events — 1978

Jan. 6, 1878	— Carl Sandburg born.
Jan. 7, 1953	— U.S. announces hydrogen bomb.
Jan. 15 (Sun.)	— Superbowl game.
Feb. 14 (Tues.)	— St. Valentine's Day.
Feb. 18, 1678	— Bunyan's *Pilgrim's Progress* published.
Feb. 19, 1878	— Edison gets phonograph patent.
Mar. 5, 1953	— Joseph Stalin dies.
Mar. 20, 1828	— Henrik Ibsen born.
Mar. 20 (Mon.)	— Spring begins, 6:34 P.M. EST.
Mar. 26, 1953	— Jonas Salk announces polio vaccine.
Apr. 1 (Sat.)	— April Fool's Day.
Apr. 14, 1828	— Noah Webster's *Dictionary* published.
Apr. 22 (Sat.)	— Earth Day.
Apr. 28, 1878	— Lionel Barrymore born.
May 1 (Mon.)	— Law Day.
May 6 (Sat.)	— Kentucky Derby.
May 25, 1878	— *H.M.S. Pinafore* premieres.
May 28 (Sun.)	— Indianapolis 500 auto race.
May 29, 1953	— Hillary and Norgay at Everest peak.
May 30, 1778	— Voltaire dies.
June 2, 1953	— Queen Elizabeth II crowned.
June 19, 1903	— Lou Gehrig born.
June 21 (Wed.)	— Summer begins, 1:10 P.M. EST.
June 28, 1778	— Molly Pitcher mans cannon.
July 1 (Sat.)	— Dominion Day, or Canada Day.
July 2, 1778	— Jean-Jacques Rousseau dies.
July 4, 1878	— George M. Cohan born.
July 9, 1228	— Francis of Assisi canonized.
July 14 (Fri.)	— Bastille Day.
July 27, 1953	— Korean armistice signed.
Aug. 27, 1928	— Kellogg-Briand Pact to end all war signed.
Aug. 28, 1828	— Leo Tolstoy born.
Sept. 6, 1628	— Settlers land at Salem, Mass.
Sept. 16 (Sat.)	— Mexican Independence Day.
Sept. 23 (Sat.)	— Autumn begins, 4:26 A.M. EST.
Nov. 18, 1903	— Panama-U.S. canal treaty signed.
Dec. 17, 1903	— Orville Wright flies heavier-than-air machine.
Dec. 22 (Fri.)	— Winter begins, 12:21 A.M., EST.

Tides and Their Causes

Source: National Oceanic and Atmospheric Administration, U. S. Commerce Department

The tides are a natural phenomenon involving the alternating rise and fall in the large fluid bodies of the earth caused by the combined gravitational attraction of the sun and moon. The combination of these two variable force influences, as modified by certain factors such as depth of the water, configuration of the shoreline, and geographic location produce the complex recurrent cycle of the tides. Tides may occur in both oceans and seas, to a limited extent in large lakes, the atmosphere, and, to a very minute degree, in the earth itself. The period between succeeding tides varies as the result of many factors and force influences.

The tide-generating force represents the difference between (1) the centrifugal force produced by the revolution of the earth around the common center-of-gravity of the earth-moon system and (2) the gravitational attraction of the moon acting upon the earth's overlying waters. Similar tide-producing forces exist in the earth-sun system. Since, on the average, the moon is only 238,857 miles from the earth compared with the sun's much greater distance of 93,000,000 miles, this closer distance outranks the much smaller mass of the moon compared with that of the sun, and the moon's tide-raising force is, accordingly, 2¹/₅ times that of the sun.

The effect of the tide-generating forces of the moon and sun acting tangentially to the earth's surface (the so-called "tractive force") tends to cause a maximum accumulation of the waters of the oceans at two diametrically opposite positions on the surface of the earth and to withdraw compensating amounts of water from all points 90° removed from the positions of these tidal bulges. The presence of the continents, as well as other factors, prevents the total free movement of water. However, as the earth rotates beneath the maxima and minima of these tide-generating forces, a sequence of two high tides, separated by two low tides, ideally is produced each day.

Twice in each lunar month, when the sun, moon, and earth are directly aligned, with the moon between the earth and the sun (at new moon) or on the opposite side of the earth from the sun (at full moon), the sun and the moon exert their gravitational force in a mutual or addititive fashion. Higher high tides and lower low tides are produced. These are called *spring* tides. At two positions 90° in between, the gravitational forces of the moon and sun — imposed at right angles—tend to counteract each other to the greatest extent, and the range between high and low tides is reduced. These are called *neap* tides. This semi-monthly variation between the spring and neap tides is called the *phase inequality*.

The inclination of the moon's orbit to the equator also produces a difference in the height of succeeding high tides and in the extent of depression of succeeding low tides which is known as the *diurnal inequality*. In extreme cases, this phenomenon can result in only one high tide and one low tide each day. The changing distance of the moon from the earth in each lunar month due to the elliptical orbit of the moon produces a difference in the height of the tides known as the *lunar parallactic* inequality. The changing distance of the earth from the sun during the earth's annual revolution around the sun similarly introduces the *solar parallactic inequality*.

The actual amount of the uplift of the waters in the deep ocean may amount to only one or two feet. However, as this tide approaches shoal waters and its effects are augmented the tidal range may be greatly increased. In Nova Scotia along the narrow channel of the Bay of Fundy, the range of tides or difference between high and low waters, may reach 43 1/2 feet or more (under spring tide conditions) due to resonant amplification.

At New Orleans, the periodic rise and fall of the tide varies with the state of the Mississippi, being about 10 inches at low stage and zero at high. The Canadian Tide Tables for 1972 gave a maximum range of nearly 50 feet at Leaf Basin, Ungava Bay.

In every case, actual high or low tide can vary considerably from the average due to weather conditions such as strong winds, abrupt barometric pressure changes, or prolonged periods of extreme high or low pressure.

The Average Rise and Fall of Tides

Places	Ft.	In.	Places	Ft.	In.	Places	Ft.	In.
Baltimore, Md.	1	1	Mobile, Ala.	1	6	San Diego, Cal.	4	1
Boston, Mass.	9	6	New London, Conn.	2	7	Sandy Hook, N.J.	4	7
Charleston, S.C.	5	2	Newport, R.I.	3	6	San Francisco, Cal.	4	0
Colon, Panama	1	1	New York, N.Y.	4	6	Savannah, Ga.	7	5
Eastport, Me.	18	2	Old Pt. Comfort, Va.	2	6	Seattle, Wash.	7	7
Galveston, Tex.	1	5	Philadelphia, Pa.	5	11	Tampa, Fla.	2	10
Halifax, N.S.	4	5	Portland, Me.	9	0	Vancouver, B.C.	10	6
Key West, Fla.	1	4	St. John's, Nfld.	2	7	Washington, D.C.	2	11

Wind Chill Table

Source: National Oceanic and Atmospheric Administration, U. S. Commerce Department

Both temperature and wind cause heat loss from body surfaces. A combination of cold and wind makes a body feel colder than the actual temperature. The table shows, for example, that a temperature of 20 degrees Fahrenheit, plus a wind of 20 miles per hour, causes a body heat loss equal to that in minus 10 degrees with no wind. In other words, the wind makes 20 degrees feel like minus 10.

Top line of figures shows actual temperatures in degrees Fahrenheit. Column at left shows wind speeds.

MPH	35	30	25	20	15	10	5	0	−5	−10	−15	−20	−25	−30	−35	−40	−45
5	33	27	21	19	12	7	0	−5	−10	−15	−21	−26	−31	−36	−42	−47	−52
10	22	16	10	3	−3	−9	−15	−22	−27	−34	−40	−46	−52	−58	−64	−71	−77
15	16	9	2	−5	−11	−18	−25	−31	−38	−45	−51	−58	−65	−72	−78	−85	−92
20	12	4	−3	−10	−17	−24	−31	−39	−46	−53	−60	−67	−74	−81	−88	−95	−103
25	8	1	−7	−15	−22	−29	−36	−44	−51	−59	−66	−74	−81	−88	−96	−103	−110
30	6	−2	−10	−18	−25	−33	−41	−49	−56	−64	−71	−79	−86	−93	−101	−109	−116
35	4	−4	−12	−20	−27	−35	−43	−52	−58	−67	−74	−82	−89	−97	−105	−113	−120
40	3	−5	−13	−21	−29	−37	−45	−53	−60	−69	−76	−84	−92	−100	−107	−115	−123
45	2	−6	−14	−22	−30	−38	−46	−54	−62	−70	−78	−85	−93	−102	−109	−117	−125

(Wind speeds greater than 45 mph have little additional chilling effect.)

National Weather Service Watches and Warnings

Source: National Weather Service, NOAA, U.S. Commerce Department

National Weather Service forecasters issue a Tornado Watch for a specific area where it is reasonably possible that tornadoes may occur during the valid time of the watch. A Watch is to alert people to watch for tornado activity and listen for a Tornado Warning. A Tornado Warning means that a tornado has been sighted or indicated by radar, and that safety precautions should be taken at once. A Hurricane Watch means that an existing hurricane poses a threat to coastal and inland communities in the area specified by the Watch. A Hurricane Warning means hurricane force winds and/or dangerously high water and exceptionally high waves are expected in a specified coastal area within 24 hours.

Definitions

Tornado—A violent rotating column of air pendant from a thundercloud, usually recognized as a funnel-shaped vortex accompanied by a loud roar. With rotating winds est. up to 300 mph., it is the most destructive storm. Tornado paths have varied in length from a few feet to nearly 300 miles (avg. 5 mi.); diameter from a few feet to over a mile (average 220 yards); average forward speed, 25-40 mph.

Cyclone—An atmospheric circulation of winds rotating counterclockwise in the northern hemisphere and clockwise in the southern hemisphere. Tornadoes, hurricanes, and the Lows shown on weather maps are all examples of cyclones having various sizes and intensities. Cyclones are usually accompanied by precipitation or stormy weather.

Hurricane—A severe cyclone originating over tropical ocean waters and having winds 74 miles an hour or higher. (In the western Pacific, such storms are known as typhoons.) The area of strong winds takes the form of a circle or an oval, sometimes as much as 500 miles in diameter. In the lower latitudes hurricanes usually move toward the west or northwest at 10 to 15 mph. When the center approaches 25° to 30° North Latitude, direction of motion often changes to northeast, with increased forward speed.

Blizzard—A severe weather condition characterized by low temperatures and by strong winds bearing a great amount of snow (mostly fine, dry snow picked up from the ground). The National Weather Service specifies, for blizzard, a wind of 35 miles an hour or higher, temperatures 20°F. or lower, and sufficient falling and/or blowing snow to reduce visibility to less than 1/4 of a mile. For "severe blizzard" wind speeds of 45 mph or more, temperature near or below 10°F., and visibility reduced by snow to near zero.

Monsoon—A name for seasonal winds (derived from Arabic "mausim," a season). It was first applied to the winds over the Arabian Sea, which blow for six months from northeast and six months from southwest, but it has been extended to similar winds in other parts of the world. The monsoons are strongest on the southern and eastern sides of Asia.

Flood—The condition that occurs when water overflows the natural or artificial confines of a stream or other body of water, or accumulates by drainage over low-lying areas.

National Weather Service Marine Warnings and Advisories

Source: National Weather Service, NOAA, U.S. Commerce Department

Small Craft Advisory: A Small Craft Advisory alerts mariners to sustained (exceeding two hours) weather and/or sea conditions either present or forecast, potentially hazardous to small boats. Hazardous conditions may include winds of 18 to 33 knots and/or dangerous wave or inlet conditions. It is the responsibility of the mariner, based on his experience and size or type of boat, to determine if the conditions are hazardous. When a mariner becomes aware of a Small Craft Advisory, he should immediately obtain the latest marine forecast to determine the reason for the Advisory. The visual signal is a red pennant by day, a red over white light at night.

Gale Warning: Two red pennants displayed by day and a white light above a red light at night to indicate that winds within the range 34 to 47 knots are forecast for the area.

Storm Warning: A single square red flag with a black center displayed during daytime and two red lights at night to indicate that winds 48 knots and above, no matter how high the speed, are forecast for the area. However, if the winds are associated with a tropical cyclone (hurricane), the storm warning display indicates that winds within the range 48 to 63 knots are forecast.

Hurricane Warning: Displayed only in connection with a hurricane or typhoon. Two square red flags with black centers displayed by day and a white light between two red lights at night to indicate that winds 64 knots and above are forecast for the area.

Visual signals are scheduled to be discontinued Nov. 1, 1977.

Primary sources of dissemination are commercial radio, TV, U.S. Coast Guard Radio stations, and NOAA VHF-FM broadcasts. These broadcasts on 162.40 and 162.55 MHz can usually be received 20-40 miles from the transmitting antenna site, depending on terrain and quality of the receiver used. Where transmitting antennas are on high ground, the range is somewhat greater, reaching 60 miles or more.

The frequencies 162.55 and 162.40 MHz require narrow band FM receivers of +5 kilohertz deviation. In selecting a suitable receiver, special attention should be paid to the manufacturer's rating of the receiver's sensitivity. Generally speaking, a receiver with a sensitivity of one microvolt or less should pick up a broadcast at a distance of about 40-50 miles depending upon antenna height and terrain.

Dissemination is also made by means of visual displays (flags, pennants, and lights). These are indicated under each warning and advisory category.

Hurricane Names in 1978

The National Weather Service has used girls' names to identify hurricanes in the Atlantic, Caribbean, and Gulf of Mexico since 1953. A semi-permanent list of 10 sets of names in alphabetical order was established in 1971. Hurricane season begins June 1 and ends Nov. 30.

Names assigned to hurricanes in 1978: Amelia, Bess, Cora, Debra, Ella, Flossie, Greta, Hope, Irma, Juliet, Kendra, Louise, Martha, Noreen, Ora, Paula, Rosalie, Susan, Tanya, Vanessa, Wanda.

Hurricanes and typhoons in the Eastern North Pacific are also identified by girls' names: 1978 — Aletta, Blanca, Connie, Dolores, Eileen, Francesca, Gretchen, Helga, Ione, Joyce, Kirsten, Lorraine, Maggie, Norma, Orlene, Patricia, Rosalie, Selma, Toni, Vivian, Winona.

Monthly Normal Temperature and Precipitation

Source: National Oceanic and Atmospheric Administration, U.S. Commerce Department

These normals are based on records for the 30-year period 1941 to 1970 inclusive. See explanation on page 800. For stations that did not have continuous records from the same instrument site for the entire 30 years, the means have been adjusted to the record at the present site.

Airport station; * city office stations. T, temperature in Fahrenheit; P, precipitation in inches; L, less than .05 inch.

Station	Jan.		Feb.		Mar.		Apr.		May		June		July		Aug.		Sept.		Oct.		Nov.		Dec.	
	T.	P.	T.	P.	T.	P.	T.	P.	T.	P.	T.	P.	T.	P.	T.	P.	T.	P.	T.	P.	T.	P.	T.	P.
Albany, N. Y.	22	2.2	24	2.1	33	2.6	47	2.7	58	3.3	68	3.0	72	3.1	70	2.9	62	3.1	51	2.6	40	2.8	26	2.9
Albuquerque, N. M.	35	0.3	40	0.4	46	0.5	56	0.5	65	0.5	75	0.5	79	1.4	77	1.3	70	0.8	58	0.8	45	0.3	36	0.5
Anchorage, Alas.	12	0.8	18	0.8	24	0.6	35	0.6	46	0.6	55	1.1	58	2.1	56	2.3	48	2.4	35	1.4	21	1.0	13	1.1
Asheville, N. C.	38	3.4	39	3.6	46	4.7	56	3.5	64	3.3	71	4.0	74	4.9	73	4.5	67	3.6	57	3.3	46	2.9	39	3.6
Atlanta, Ga.	42	4.3	45	4.4	51	5.8	61	4.6	69	3.7	76	3.7	78	4.9	78	3.5	72	3.2	62	2.5	51	3.4	44	4.2
Baltimore, Md.	42	2.9	44	2.8	53	3.7	65	3.1	75	3.6	83	3.8	87	4.1	85	4.2	79	3.1	68	2.8	56	3.1	44	3.3
Barrow, Alas.	-15	0.2	-19	0.2	-15	0.2	-1	0.2	19	0.2	33	0.4	39	0.9	38	1.0	30	0.6	15	0.6	-1	0.3	-12	0.2
Birmingham, Ala.	44	4.8	47	5.3	53	6.2	63	4.6	71	3.6	77	4.0	80	5.2	79	4.3	74	3.6	63	2.6	52	3.7	45	5.2
Bismarck, N. D.	8	0.5	14	0.4	25	0.7	43	1.4	54	2.2	64	3.6	71	2.2	69	2.0	58	1.3	47	0.8	29	0.6	16	0.5
Boise, Ida.	29	1.5	36	1.2	41	1.0	49	1.1	57	1.3	65	1.1	75	0.2	72	0.3	63	0.4	52	0.8	40	1.3	32	1.4
Boston, Mass.	29	3.7	30	3.5	38	4.0	49	3.5	59	3.5	68	3.2	73	2.7	71	3.5	65	3.2	55	3.0	45	4.5	33	4.2
Buffalo, N. Y.	24	2.9	24	2.6	32	2.9	45	3.2	55	3.0	66	2.2	70	2.9	68	3.5	62	3.3	52	3.0	40	3.7	28	3.0
Burlington, Vt.	17	1.7	19	1.7	29	1.9	43	2.6	55	3.0	65	3.5	70	3.5	67	3.7	59	3.1	49	2.7	37	2.9	23	2.2
Caribou, Me.	11	2.0	13	2.1	24	2.2	37	2.4	50	3.0	60	3.4	65	4.0	62	3.8	54	3.5	44	3.3	31	3.5	16	2.6
Charleston, S. C.	49	2.9	51	3.3	57	4.8	65	3.0	72	3.8	78	6.3	80	8.2	80	6.4	75	5.2	66	3.1	56	2.1	49	3.1
Chicago, Ill.	24	1.9	27	1.6	37	2.7	50	3.8	60	3.4	71	4.0	75	4.1	74	3.1	66	3.0	55	2.6	40	2.2	29	2.1
Cincinnati, Oh*	32	3.4	34	3.0	43	4.1	55	3.9	64	4.0	73	3.9	76	4.0	75	3.0	68	2.7	58	2.2	45	3.1	34	2.9
Cleveland, Oh.	27	2.6	28	2.2	36	3.1	48	3.5	58	3.5	68	3.3	71	3.5	70	3.0	64	2.8	54	2.6	42	2.8	30	2.4
Columbus, Oh.	28	2.9	30	2.3	39	3.4	51	3.7	61	4.1	70	4.1	74	4.2	72	2.9	65	2.4	54	1.9	42	2.7	31	2.4
Dallas, Tex.	45	2.0	49	2.6	56	3.0	66	4.7	74	4.9	82	3.3	86	1.8	86	2.4	78	3.3	68	3.2	56	2.6	48	2.3
Denver, Col.	30	0.6	33	0.7	37	1.2	48	1.9	57	2.6	66	1.9	73	1.8	72	1.3	63	1.1	52	1.1	39	0.8	33	0.4
Des Moines, Ia.	19	1.1	24	1.1	34	2.3	50	2.9	61	4.2	71	4.9	75	3.3	73	3.3	64	3.1	54	2.1	38	1.4	25	1.1
Detroit, Mich.	26	1.9	27	1.8	35	2.3	48	3.1	58	3.4	69	3.0	73	3.0	72	3.0	75	2.3	54	2.5	41	2.3	30	2.2
Dodge City, Kan.	31	0.5	35	0.6	41	1.1	54	1.7	64	3.1	74	3.3	79	3.1	78	2.6	69	1.7	58	1.7	43	0.6	33	8.5
Duluth, Minn.	9	1.2	12	0.9	24	1.8	39	2.6	49	3.4	59	4.4	66	3.7	64	3.8	54	3.1	45	2.3	28	1.7	14	1.4
Eureka, Cal.*	47	7.4	48	5.2	48	4.8	50	3.0	53	2.1	55	0.7	56	0.1	57	0.3	57	0.7	54	3.2	52	5.8	49	6.6
Fairbanks, Alas.	-12	0.6	-3	0.5	10	0.5	29	0.3	47	0.7	59	1.4	61	1.9	55	2.2	44	1.1	25	0.7	3	0.7	-10	0.7
Ft. Worth, Tex.	45	1.8	49	2.4	55	2.5	65	4.3	73	4.5	81	3.1	85	1.8	85	2.3	78	3.2	68	2.7	56	2.0	48	1.8
Fresno, Cal.	45	1.8	50	1.7	54	1.6	60	1.2	67	0.3	74	0.1	81	L	78	L	74	0.1	64	0.4	54	1.2	46	1.7
Galveston, Tex.*	54	3.0	56	2.7	61	2.6	69	2.6	76	3.2	81	4.1	83	4.4	83	4.4	80	5.6	73	2.8	64	3.2	57	3.7
Grand Junction, Col.	27	0.6	34	0.6	41	0.8	52	0.8	62	0.6	71	0.6	79	0.5	75	1.1	67	0.8	55	0.9	40	0.6	30	0.6
Gr. Rapids, Mich.	23	1.9	25	1.5	33	2.5	47	3.4	57	3.2	67	3.4	72	3.1	70	2.5	62	3.3	52	2.6	39	2.8	27	2.2
Helena, Mon.	18	0.6	25	0.4	31	0.7	43	0.9	52	1.8	59	2.4	68	1.0	66	1.0	56	1.0	45	0.6	32	0.6	23	0.6
Honolulu, Ha.	72	4.4	72	2.5	73	3.2	75	1.4	77	1.0	79	0.3	80	0.6	81	0.8	80	0.7	79	1.5	77	3.0	74	3.7
Houston, Tex.	52	3.6	55	3.5	61	2.7	69	3.5	76	5.1	81	4.5	83	4.1	83	4.4	79	4.7	71	4.1	61	4.0	55	4.0
Huron, S. D.	13	0.4	18	0.8	29	1.1	46	2.0	57	2.8	67	3.8	74	2.2	72	2.0	61	1.8	50	1.5	32	0.7	19	0.5
Indianapolis, Ind.	28	2.9	31	2.4	40	3.8	52	3.9	62	4.1	72	4.2	75	3.7	73	2.8	66	2.9	56	2.5	42	3.1	31	2.7
Jacksonville, Fla.	55	2.8	56	3.6	61	3.6	68	3.1	74	3.2	79	6.3	81	7.4	81	7.9	78	7.8	71	4.5	61	1.8	55	2.6
Juneau, Alas.	24	3.9	28	3.4	32	3.6	39	3.8	47	3.3	53	2.9	56	4.7	54	5.0	49	6.9	42	7.9	33	5.5	27	4.5
Kansas City, Mo.	28	1.3	33	1.3	41	2.6	55	3.5	65	4.3	74	5.6	79	4.4	77	3.8	69	4.2	59	3.2	44	1.5	32	1.5
Knoxville, Tenn.	41	4.7	43	4.7	50	4.9	60	3.6	68	3.3	76	3.6	78	4.7	77	3.2	72	2.8	61	2.7	49	3.6	42	4.5
Lander, Wyo.	20	0.5	26	0.7	31	1.2	43	2.4	53	2.6	61	1.9	71	0.6	69	0.4	58	1.1	47	1.2	32	0.9	23	0.5
Little Rock, Ark.	40	4.2	43	4.4	50	4.9	62	5.3	70	5.3	78	3.5	81	3.4	81	3.0	73	3.6	62	3.0	50	3.9	42	4.1
Los Angeles, Cal.*	57	3.0	48	2.8	59	2.2	62	1.3	65	0.1	68	L	73	L	74	L	73	0.2	68	0.3	63	2.0	58	2.2
Louisville, Ky.	33	3.5	36	3.5	44	5.1	56	4.1	65	4.2	73	4.1	77	3.8	76	3.0	69	2.9	58	2.4	45	3.3	36	3.3
Marquette, Mich.*	18	1.5	20	1.5	27	1.9	40	2.6	50	2.9	60	3.4	66	3.1	66	3.0	57	3.5	49	2.4	34	3.0	24	2.0
Memphis, Tenn.	41	4.9	44	4.7	51	5.1	63	5.4	71	4.4	79	3.5	82	3.5	80	3.3	74	3.0	63	2.6	51	3.9	43	4.7
Miami, Fla.	67	2.2	68	2.0	71	2.1	75	3.6	78	6.1	81	9.0	82	6.9	83	6.7	82	8.7	78	8.2	72	2.7	68	1.6
Milwaukee, Wis.	19	1.6	23	1.1	31	2.2	45	2.8	54	2.9	65	3.6	70	3.4	69	2.7	61	3.0	51	2.0	37	2.0	24	1.8
Minneapolis, Minn.	12	0.7	17	0.8	28	1.7	45	2.0	57	3.4	67	3.9	72	3.7	70	3.1	60	2.7	50	1.8	32	1.2	19	0.9
Mobile, Ala.	51	4.7	54	4.8	59	7.1	68	5.6	75	4.5	80	6.1	82	8.9	82	6.9	78	6.6	69	2.6	59	3.4	53	5.9
Moline, Ill.	22	1.7	26	1.3	36	2.6	51	3.8	61	3.9	71	4.4	75	4.6	73	3.4	65	3.8	54	2.7	39	1.9	27	1.8
Nashville, Tenn.	38	4.8	41	4.4	49	5.0	60	4.1	69	4.1	77	3.4	80	3.8	79	3.2	72	3.1	61	2.2	48	3.5	40	4.5
Newark, N. J.	31	2.9	33	3.0	41	3.9	52	3.4	62	3.6	71	3.0	76	4.0	75	4.3	68	3.4	58	2.8	46	3.6	35	3.5
New Haven, Conn.	29	3.2	30	3.1	37	4.0	48	3.7	57	3.7	67	2.7	72	3.1	71	3.8	65	3.1	55	3.1	44	4.3	32	4.1
New Orleans, La.	53	4.5	56	4.8	61	5.5	69	4.2	75	4.2	80	4.7	82	6.7	82	5.3	78	5.6	70	2.3	60	3.9	55	5.1
New York, N. Y.*	32	2.9	33	3.1	41	4.0	52	3.6	62	3.4	72	2.9	77	3.9	75	4.5	68	3.2	58	3.0	47	3.8	35	3.6
Nome, Alas.	6	0.9	5	0.8	7	0.8	19	0.7	35	0.7	46	1.0	50	2.4	49	3.6	42	2.4	29	1.4	16	1.0	4	0.7
Norfolk, Va.	41	3.4	41	3.3	48	3.4	58	2.7	67	3.3	76	3.6	78	5.7	77	5.9	72	4.2	62	3.1	52	2.9	42	3.1
Okla. City, Okla.	37	1.1	41	1.3	48	2.1	60	3.5	68	5.2	77	4.2	82	2.7	81	2.6	73	3.6	62	2.6	49	1.4	40	1.3
Omaha, Neb.	23	0.8	28	1.0	37	1.6	52	3.0	63	4.1	72	4.9	77	3.7	76	4.0	66	3.3	56	1.9	40	1.1	28	0.8
Parkersburg, W. Va.*	33	3.1	35	2.8	43	3.8	55	3.5	64	3.6	72	4.0	75	4.3	74	3.3	67	2.8	57	2.1	45	2.5	35	2.8
Philadelphia, Pa.	34	3.9	34	3.0	47	3.5	53	6.7	60	4.1	75	7.9	78	2.4	79	2.0	71	3.4	59	2.2	48	0.6	39	6.3
Phoenix, Ariz.	51	0.1	58	1.4	57	1.7	67	0.1	81	0.1	88	L	94	1.3	93	L	85	L	74	L	61	1.4	55	L
Pittsburgh, Pa.	30	2.0	29	1.8	48	3.9	49	4.7	56	5.9	71	3.1	73	2.2	73	3.4	67	3.6	56	4.5	44	2.7	33	2.2
Portland, Me.	23	2.6	23	2.6	38	2.6	46	9.9	51	6.3	64	4.9	71	1.7	71	3.5	58	2.2	49	3.4	38	2.4	34	9.6
Portland, Ore.	39	3.7	45	1.9	48	2.5	52	1.3	59	1.4	64	1.5	70	0.1	66	1.4	64	3.3	54	3.1	44	11.6	45	10.0
Providence, R. I.	28	3.5	29	3.5	37	4.0	47	3.7	57	3.5	66	2.7	72	2.9	70	3.9	63	3.3	54	3.3	43	4.5	32	4.1
Raleigh, N. C.	41	3.2	42	3.3	49	3.4	60	3.1	67	3.3	74	3.7	78	5.1	77	4.9	71	3.8	60	2.8	50	2.8	41	3.1
Rapid City, S. D.	22	0.5	26	0.6	31	1.0	45	2.1	55	2.8	64	3.7	73	2.1	72	1.5	61	1.2	50	0.9	35	0.5	27	0.4
Reno, Nev.	32	1.2	37	0.9	40	0.7	47	0.5	55	0.7	62	0.4	69	0.3	67	0.2	60	0.2	50	0.4	40	0.7	33	1.1
Richmond, Va.	38	2.9	39	3.0	47	3.4	58	2.8	67	3.4	74	3.5	78	5.6	76	5.1	70	3.6	59	2.9	49	3.2	39	3.2
St. Louis, Mo.	31	1.9	35	2.1	48	3.0	57	3.9	66	3.9	75	4.4	79	3.7	77	2.9	70	2.9	59	2.8	45	2.5	35	2.0
Salt Lake City, Ut.	20	1.5	32	0.9	42	2.7	48	1.6	62	1.7	70	0.2	77	1.1	77	1.2	62	4.1	54	0.7	41	2.5	33	2.3
San Antonio, Tex.	51	1.7	55	2.1	61	1.5	70	2.5	76	3.1	82	2.8	84	1.7	85	2.4	79	3.7	71	2.8	60	1.8	53	1.5
San Diego, Cal.	56	1.7	60	1.6	58	2.3	62	0.1	63	L	68	L	69	L	71	L	69	L	67	L	61	1.6	58	0.2
San Francisco, Cal.	48	4.4	51	3.0	53	2.5	55	1.6	58	0.4	62	0.1	63	L	63	0.0	64	0.2	61	1.0	55	2.3	50	4.0
San Juan, P. R.	75	3.7	75	2.5	76	2.0	78	3.4	79	6.5	81	5.6	81	6.4	81	7.0	81	6.1	81	5.6	79	5.5	77	4.7
Sault Ste. Marie, Mich.*	14	1.9	15	1.5	24	1.7	38	2.2	49	3.0	59	3.3	64	2.6	63	3.1	55	3.9	46	2.9	33	3.3	20	2.4
Savannah, Ga.	50	2.9	52	2.9	58	4.4	66	2.9	73	4.2	79	5.9	81	7.9	81	6.5	76	5.6	67	2.8	57	1.9	50	3.3
Sea.-Tac., Wash.	38	5.8	42	4.2	44	3.6	49	2.5	55	1.7	60	1.5	65	0.7	64	1.1	60	2.0	52	3.9	45	5.9	41	5.9
Spokane, Wash.	25	2.5	32	1.7	38	1.5	46	1.1	55	1.5	62	1.4	70	0.4	68	0.6	60	0.8	48	1.4	36	2.2	29	2.4
Springfield, Mo.	33	1.7	37	2.2	44	3.0	57	4.3	65	4.9	74	4.7	78	3.6	77	2.9	69	4.1	59	3.4	46	2.3	36	2.5
Syracuse, N. Y.	24	2.7	25	2.8	33	3.0	47	3.1	57	3.0	67	3.1	72	3.1	70	3.5	63	2.7	53	3.1	41	3.3	28	3.1
Tampa, Fla.	60	2.3	62	2.9	66	3.9	72	2.1	77	2.4	81	6.5	82	8.4	82	8.0	81	6.4	75	2.5	67	1.8	62	2.2
Trenton, N. J.*	32	2.8	33	2.7	41	3.8	52	3.2	62	3.4	71	3.2	76	4.7	74	4.2	67	3.2	57	2.5	46	3.3	35	3.3
Vicksburg, Miss.*	48	4.9	51	5.3	57	0.5	66	5.4	73	4.2	79	3.3	82	3.6	81	3.0	76	2.8	67	2.3	56	4.1	50	5.5
Washington, D. C.	36	2.6	37	2.5	45	3.3	56	2.9	66	3.7	75	3.5	79	4.1	77	4.7	71	3.1	60	2.7	48	2.9	37	3.0
Wilmington, Del.	32	2.9	34	2.8	42	3.7	52	3.2	62	3.4	71	3.2	76	4.3	74	4.0	68	3.4	57	2.6	46	3.5	35	3.3

Annual Climatological Data

Source: National Oceanic and Atmospheric Administration, U. S. Commerce Department

Station 1976		Temperature°F				Precipitation¹			Sleet or snow			Wind Fastest		No. of days			
	Elev. ft.	Highest	Date	Lowest	Date	Total (in.)	Greatest in 24 hrs.	Date	Total (in.)	Greatest in 24 hrs.	Date	MPH	Date	Clear*	Cloudy*	Prec. .01 in. or more	Snow, sleet .1 in. or more
Albany, N.Y.	275	92	4/19	-16	1/19	42.54	2.70	10/8-9	47.7	10.0	3/16-17	50	2/2	63	199	143	13
Albuquerque, N.M.	5311	97	6/20	-7	11/29	5.19	0.57	6/29	4.3	2.4	11/27	46	4/30	179	70	53	1
Anchorage, Alas.	114	78	7/9	-13	2/10	14.54	1.2	9/20	84.1	14.4	3/18-19	29	1/30	51	255	117	25
Asheville, N.C.	2140	90	7/24	2	1/19	47.23	4.65	5/28-29	5.5	3.0	2/1-2	32	11/8	128	132	109	2
Atlanta, Ga.	1010	94	7/25	9	1/9	45.96	5.09	3/15-16	T	T	3/14	47	2/18	106	149	101	0
Baltimore, Md.	148	94	6/28	5	1/19	43.44	4.92	9/15-16	13.4	7.8	3/9	50	3/13	128	151	102	2
Barrow, Alas.	31	62	7/29	-41	2/26	2.88	0.31	9/2	22.1	1.6	11/13	32	11/27	47	188	87	5
Birmingham, Ala.	620	98	7/25	10	1/9	55.15	3.52	5/13-14	T	T	12/31	50	3/20	102	167	109	0
Bismarck, N.D.	1647	105	7/24	-29	1/4	11.17	1.36	9/18	28.2	6.1	12/31-1/1	47	2/2	109	132	82	8
Boise, Ida.	2838	103	7/16	3	2/5	12.20	1.74	9/11-12	18.2	3.7	2/29	46	3/22	125	137	80	10
Boston, Mass.	15	95	6/24	-4	1/23	36.72	2.32	7/29-30	45.4	11.9	1/11-12	46	12/10	109	151	125	13
Buffalo, N.Y.	705	89	6/14	-11	1/23	46.52	2.93	9/17-18	141.9	19.0	11/30	50	3/27	44	230	178	35
Burlington, Vt.	332	94	7/6	-24	1/19	40.08	1.62	5/11-12	94.1	8.2	1/27-28	37	3/27	45	241	184	27
Charleston, S.C.	40	95	7/25	16	1/19	48.50	5.78	5/23-24	0.4	0.4	1/17	37	2/1	107	153	103	0
Charleston, W. Va.	939	94	6/18	2	1/19	40.78	2.92	7/11-12	34.4	3.8	1/3-4	39	3/5	85	166	150	13
Chicago, Ill.	607	100	7/10	-11	2/2	33.98	4.64	6/13	36.1	4.8	1/13	40	6/13	123	141	110	13
Cincinnati, Oh.	869	95	6/14	-2	12/31	30.29	2.15	8/13-14	12.4	4.1	1/7-8	46	1/13	113	155	112	3
Cleveland, Oh.	777	92	7/11	-11	12/31	34.81	2.05	2/16-17	62.5	5.4	2/5	49	2/18	69	207	160	19
Columbus, Oh.	812	94	7/15	-5	12/31	31.85	2.60	8/6-7	22.9	4.9	1/7-8	51	7/15	88	174	115	9
Concord, N.H.	342	95	4/19	-30	1/19	32.51	2.04	10/20-21	62.1	9.7	3/2	37	5/3	82	168	124	17
Dallas, Tex.	551	102	8/9	11	1/8	35.63	4.05	8/31	5.0	4.8	11/13-14	37	3/4	143	127	85	1
Denver, Col.	5283	98	7/10	-4	1/3	13.41	1.78	8/1	44.3	6.3	10/26	53	1/30	128	126	89	11
Des Moines, Ia.	938	97	7/9	-12	12/31	30.01	3.08	4/17-18	19.0	10.5	2/20-21	46	6/14	114	135	75	3
Detroit, Mich.	633	99	7/14	-18	1/18	29.09	1.75	5/6	40.8	6.2	3/1	49	3/5	91	157	135	12
Dodge City, Kan.	2582	104	6/28	-9	1/8	16.80	2.32	4/19-20	14.5	5.7	2/21	63	2/21	168	100	59	4
Duluth, Minn.	1428	95	9/7	-30	1/17	20.67	1.68	6/14-15	67.1	8.5	1/1-2	42	3/2	116	165	111	20
Fairbanks, Alas.	436	90	8/1	-44	2/9	7.32	2.22	10/23-24	40.1	3.9	10/23-24	27	5/12	86	192	92	18
Fresno, Cal.	328	105	6/28	20	1/2	11.04	1.55	10/1-2	T	T	2/5	35	4/15	201	82	37	0
Galveston, Tex.	7	93	8/7	24	1/8	42.06	3.47	7/8-9	0.0	0.0	. .	36	5/26	N/A	N/A	94	0
Grand Rapids, Mich.	784	94	8/27	-14	12/31	30.57	2.84	5/5-6	67.5	5.1	1/13	66	3/20	87	177	132	26
Helena, Mont.	3828	95	6/30	-20	3/3	10.07	1.18	9/17-18	29.1	5.1	3/1	45	6/30	81	177	86	9
Honolulu, Ha.	7	91	9/24	53	2/2	12.90	2.94	2/5-6	0.0	0.0	. . .	38	2/15	71	99	105	0
Houston, Tex.	96	100	8/7	19	11/30	54.62	8.16	4/18	T	T	11/28	30	4/15	104	158	101	0
Huron, S. D.	1281	104	9/6	-27	1/4	10.97	1.87	6/23-24	44.0	7.4	3/4-5	54	4/16	128	138	65	15
Indianapolis, Ind.	792	94	6/14	-9	12/31	33.82	4.72	8/5-6	12.0	2.2	3/16	37	3/30	110	160	97	4
Jackson, Miss.	310	97	8/25	15	1/9	57.39	2.70	5/27	0.2	0.2	11/28	37	8/1	131	143	105	0
Jacksonville, Fla.	26	97	7/16	24	1/18	50.87	4.06	5/7-8	0.0	0.0	. . .	42	9/3	98	141	113	0
Juneau, Alas.	12	84	7/31	-3	1/13	56.41	1.84	1/18	123	9.6	12/9-10	39	10/26	23	307	241	36
Kansas City, Mo.	1014	104	8/10	-11	12/31	23.68	2.67	12/23-24	12.9	2.5	1/6-7	50	12/28	146	112	78	8
Lander, Wyo.	5563	97	7/10	-21	2/6	11.01	1.06	10/25-26	65.0	9.2	10/25-26	45	5/28	112	113	70	23
Little Rock, Ark.	257	101	8/14	9	1/8	43.04	3.00	6/24-25	1.0	1.0	11/14	46	2/21	137	140	99	1
Los Angeles, Cal.	97	99	6/24	36	1/2	9.25	1.45	9/10	0.0	0.0	. . .	N/A	N/A	157	87	37	0
Louisville, Ky.	477	96	7/24	2	12/31	34.15	2.20	2/17-18	6.0	1.6	11/28	41	1/13	107	151	97	1
Marquette, Mich.	677	98	8/27	-9	12/29	24.28	1.61	5/15-16	189.9	15.3	3/12-13	42	1/18	N/A	N/A	163	60
Memphis, Tenn.	258	97	7/26	9	12/31	45.50	4.08	9/3-4	2.1	1.2	11/14	35	7/29	152	138	102	1
Miami, Fla.	7	93	8/8	40	1/18	55.90	3.70	8/18-19	0.0	0.0	. . .	30	5/23	58	132	126	0
Milford, Ut.	5028	102	7/10	-13	3/5	8.01	0.86	10/1-2	46.8	7.9	2/5-6	57	6/10	181	98	61	17
Milwaukee, Wis.	672	99	7/10	-10	1/8	31.42	3.11	4/24-25	37.5	5.9	2/21	49	7/30	121	150	111	11
Minneapolis, Minn.	834	100	7/13	-23	12/31	16.50	1.98	6/17-18	44.7	8.3	3/4-5	37	3/12	116	149	97	16
Mobile, Ala.	211	100	7/23	22	1/9	58.50	5.27	3/26-27	T	T	12/22	26	7/30	124	148	116	0
Moline, Ill.	582	99	7/14	-12	12/7	24.97	2.23	4/23-24	21.1	6.0	11/26-27	65	6/13	137	124	92	8
Nashville, Tenn.	590	96	7/24	4	12/31	49.57	4.45	8/24-25	6.4	23	2/2	29	2/21	142	145	108	2
New Orleans, La.	4	95	8/25	25	12/1	47.38	2.72	12/14-15	0.0	0.0	. . .	35	5/27	105	148	97	0
New York, N.Y.	132	96	4/18	-1	1/23	41.28	4.25	8/9-10	20.1	4.2	3/9-10	30	1/22	N/A	N/A	113	10
Nome, Alas.	13	77	7/13	-39	2/8	10.44	2.99	8/14-15	41.7	3.4	3/2-3	37	3/7	106	182	113	14
Norfolk, Va.	24	95	7/29	16	1/18	32.36	2.27	7/29-30	1.0	1.0	12/8	35	12/7	129	144	100	1
Oklahoma City, Okla.	1285	103	8/13	3	1/8	18.06	1.28	5/26	0.6	0.3	11/13-14	41	12/30	159	113	64	0
Omaha, Neb.	977	103	7/9	-15	12/30	18.37	1.69	5/22-23	17.8	4.1	2/1-2	58	4/16	125	136	73	7
Philadelphia, Pa.	5	94	4/18	6	1/23	33.27	1.94	6/1-2	19.2	6.9	3/9	50	3/21	117	158	110	6
Phoenix, Ariz.	1112	113	6/27	26	1/2	7.96	1.03	7/24-25	T	T	3/3	86	7/7	229	229	32	0
Pittsburgh, Pa.	1137	88	7/15	-7	12/3	31.78	1.52	3/3-4	44.4	8.2	1/7-8	42	3/27	75	190	145	17
Portland, Me.	43	93	6/24	-20	1/11	41.39	2.58	8/9	70.0	14.3	12/29-30	51	12/11	97	168	129	18
Portland, Ore.	21	92	7/15	22	11/28	26.71	1.57	2/26-27	T	T	5/31	40	2/24	67	221	127	0
Providence, R.I.	51	98	4/19	-13	1/23	46.32	4.83	7/29-30	38.6	9.1	1/21-22	46	12/13	101	147	129	13
Raleigh, N.C.	434	100	7/24	5	1/19	33.71	2.75	9/10	0.4	0.4	1/17	32	5/29	126	137	98	0
Rapid City, S.D.	3162	101	7/12	-18	1/8	15.20	3.61	6/14-15	29.9	9.5	12/31-1/1	57	5/12	123	143	96	13
Reno, Nev.	4404	100	8/31	3	1/2	5.06	0.64	8/30-31	27.1	5.1	2/4	52	3/24	158	124	38	9
Richmond, Va.	164	100	7/15	5	1/19	34.76	2.16	9/15-16	3.9	1.7	12/8	34	3/13	110	155	103	3
Rochester, N.Y.	547	91	6/15	-14	1/23	34.32	1.91	10/9	87.6	7.9	3/16	46	2/19	48	217	159	31
St. Louis, Mo.	535	99	7/23	-10	12/31	23.46	2.10	5/30-31	19.3	4.8	3/15-16	40	3/12	143	115	80	6
Salt Lake City, Ut.	4220	103	7/11	-2	1/1	12.34	1.62	4/25	47.8	6.8	3/11	49	4/25	127	128	73	18
San Antonio, Tex.	788	96	8/10	17	1/8	39.13	3.71	5/6-7	T	T	12/31	43	4/7	99	147	95	0
San Diego, Cal.	13	97	11/4	37	1/2	11.23	1.82	2/8-9	0.0	0.0	. . .	32	4/15	156	113	34	0
San Francisco, Cal.	8	97	6/27	31	1/2	10.02	2.69	12/29-30	T	T	3/1	41	4/15	156	106	40	0
San Juan, P.R.	13	94	8/24	66	2/7	47.20	4.25	9/4-5	0.0	0.0	. . .	42	12/10	65	76	208	0
Sault Ste. Marie, Mich.	721	95	9/8	-25	2/2	25.70	1.81	3/26-27	188.0	7.2	3/12-13	45	12/10	75	208	181	67
Savannah, Ga.	46	97	7/16	20	1/19	63.74	5.67	5/30-31	T	T	1/17	42	3/16	97	168	112	0
Seattle, Wash.	400	86	9/20	24	3/4	26.70	1.33	1/13-14	0.7	0.3	2/28	38	3/24	51	231	131	0
Sioux City, Ia.	1095	102	9/6	-17	12/8	14.33	1.58	5/20-22	16.6	6.0	3/4	N/A	N/A	130	129	66	3
Spokane, Wash.	2356	95	7/17	5	2/5	11.22	0.77	2/13-14	30.9	6.7	1/3-4	44	3/24	70	215	101	10
Springfield, Mo.	1268	97	7/25	-6	12/31	31.29	3.41	8/14-15	4.0	1.2	12/6	35	12/9	155	119	80	1
Syracuse, N.Y.	410	88	6/15	-18	1/23	58.17	2.85	4/15-10	117.9	8.1	1/27-28	48	4/21	58	235	198	42
Tampa, Fla.	19	94	7/20	28	1/19	42.29	4.10	5/14-15	0.0	0.0	. . .	35	8/11	90	161	115	0
Trenton, N.J.	56	93	8/22	3	1/23	31.18	2.15	8/8-9	19.7	4.4	3/9	47	2/2	112	138	115	10
Washington, D.C.	10	95	6/28	11	2/2	38.07	5.13	9/15-16	3.2	0.9	2/2	50	7/15	125	156	101	0
Williston, N.D.	1899	102	8/23	-31	1/8	9.16	1.12	6/23	39.0	8.4	12/31-1/1	44	2/1	85	161	91	12
Wilmington, Del.	74	92	8/22	3	1/19	33.59	2.29	5/1	16.2	6.1	3/9-10	40	2/2	113	162	120	6

*To get partly cloudy days deduct the total of clear and cloudy days from 365 (1 yr.). T—trace. (1) Date shown is the starting date of the storm (in some cases it lasted more than one day).

Normal Temperatures, Highs, Lows, Precipitation

Source: National Oceanic and Atmospheric Administration, U. S. Commerce Department

These normals are based on records for the thirty-year period 1941-1970. (See explanation on page 800.) The extreme temperatures (through 1975) are listed for the stations shown and may not agree with the states' records shown on page 798.

Airport stations; * designates city office stations. The minus (−) sign indicates temperatures below zero. Fahrenheit thermometer registration.

State	Station	Normal temperature: January Max.	January Min.	July Max.	July Min.	Extreme temperature: Highest	Lowest	Normal annual precipitation (inches)
Alabama	Mobile	61	41	91	73	102	8	66.98
Alabama	Montgomery	59	38	92	72	102	5	50.69
Alaska	Juneau	29	18	64	48	86	−22	54.67
Arizona	Phoenix	65	38	105	78	116	19	7.05
Arkansas	Little Rock	50	29	93	70	108	−4	48.52
California	Los Angeles*	67	47	83	64	110	28	14.05
California	San Francisco	55	41	71	54	106	24	19.53
Colorado	Denver	44	16	87	59	103	−25	15.51
Connecticut	New Haven (1)	37	22	81	63	100	−8	46.02
Delaware	Wilmington	40	24	86	66	102	−4	40.25
Dist. of Col.	Washington	44	28	88	69	101	3	38.89
Florida	Jacksonville	65	45	90	72	105	12	54.47
Florida	Key West	74	65	87	79	95	46	39.99
Florida	Miami	76	59	89	76	96	34	59.80
Georgia	Atlanta	51	33	87	69	98	−3	48.34
Hawaii	Honolulu	79	65	87	73	92	53	22.90
Idaho	Boise	36	21	91	59	111	−23	11.50
Illinois	Chicago-Midway	32	17	84	65	101	−16	34.44
Indiana	Indianapolis	36	20	85	65	99	−20	38.74
Iowa	Des Moines	28	11	85	65	104	−24	30.85
Iowa	Dubuque	27	11	84	62	97	−28	35.71
Kansas	Wichita	42	22	92	69	113	−12	28.41
Kentucky	Louisville	42	25	87	66	101	−20	43.11
Louisiana	New Orleans	62	44	90	73	100	14	56.77
Maine	Portland	31	12	79	57	100	−39	40.80
Maryland	Baltimore	42	25	87	66	102	−7	40.46
Massachusetts	Boston	36	23	81	65	99	−4	42.52
Michigan	Detroit-City	32	19	83	63	105	−16	30.96
Michigan	Sault Ste. Marie*	22	6	75	53	98	−28	31.70
Minnesota	Minn.-St. Paul	21	3	82	61	101	−34	25.94
Mississippi	Vicksburg (2)	57	41	90	73	101	2	49.50
Missouri	St. Louis	40	23	88	69	106	−11	35.89
Montana	Helena	28	8	84	52	105	−38	11.38
Nebraska	Omaha	33	12	89	66	110	−22	30.18
Nevada	Winnemucca	40	15	92	50	106	−34	8.63
New Hampshire	Concord	31	10	83	57	102	−29	36.17
New Jersey	Atlantic City	43	27	84	66	106	−8	42.36
New Mexico	Albuquerque	47	24	92	65	105	−17	7.77
New Mexico	Roswell	55	21	95	62	110	−8	11.62
New York	Albany	30	13	84	60	98	−28	33.36
New York	New York-La Guardia	38	26	84	69	107	−2	41.61
No. Carolina	Charlotte	51	34	89	70	100	2	43.38
No. Carolina	Raleigh	51	30	88	67	98	0	42.54
No. Dakota	Bismarck	19	−3	84	57	109	−43	16.16
Ohio	Cincinnati-Abbe	40	24	87	66	109	−17	40.03
Ohio	Cleveland	33	20	82	61	98	−19	34.99
Oklahoma	Oklahoma City	48	26	93	70	108	−1	31.37
Oregon	Portland*	44	33	79	55	107	−3	37.61
Pennsylvania	Harrisburg	39	24	87	65	107	−8	37.65
Pennsylvania	Philadelphia	40	24	87	67	104	−5	39.93
Rhode Island	Block Island	38	26	76	63	91	−4	40.45
So. Carolina	Charleston	60	37	89	71	103	8	52.12
So. Dakota	Huron	23	2	87	61	112	−39	19.44
So. Dakota	Rapid City	34	10	86	59	110	−27	17.12
Tennessee	Nashville	48	29	90	69	103	−6	46.00
Texas	Amarillo	50	24	94	67	104	−9	19.67
Texas	Galveston*	59	48	87	79	101	8	42.20
Texas	Houston	63	42	94	73	101	19	48.19
Utah	Salt Lake City	37	18	93	61	107	−18	15.17
Vermont	Burlington	26	8	81	59	98	−27	32.54
Virginia	Norfolk	49	32	87	70	103	8	44.68
Washington	Seattle-Tacoma	43	33	75	54	99	6	38.79
Washington	Spokane	31	20	84	55	108	−25	17.42
West Virgina	Parkersburg*	41	24	86	65	106	−27	38.44
Wisconsin	Madison	26	9	82	60	98	−30	30.16
Wisconsin	Milwaukee	27	11	80	59	99	−24	29.07
Wyoming	Cheyenne	37	14	85	55	98	−27	15.06
Puerto Rico	San Juan	81	67	87	74	96	60	64.21

(1) Closed June 14, 1969. (2) Closed December 1966.

Mean Annual Snowfall (inches) based on record through 1972: Boston, Mass. 42.8; Sault Ste. Marie, Mich., 108.2; Albany, N.Y., 67.3; Rochester, N.Y. 86.3; Burlington, Vt., 79; Cheyenne, Wyo., 51.7; Juneau, Alas. 106.3.

Wettest Spot: Mount Waialeale, Ha., on the island of Kauai, is the rainiest place in the world, according to the National Geographic Society, with an average annual rainfall of 460 inches.

Highest Temperature: A temperature of 136° F. observed at Azizia, Tripolitania in Northern Africa on Sept. 13, 1922, is generally accepted as the world's highest temperature recorded under standard conditions.

The record high in the United States was 134° in Death Valley, Cal., July 10, 1913.

Lowest Temperature: A record low temperature of —126.9° F. (—88.3° C.) was recorded at the Soviet Antarctic station Vostok on Aug. 24, 1960.

The record low in the United States was —80° at Prospect Creek, Alas., Jan. 23, 1971.

The lowest official temperature on the North American continent was recorded at 81 degrees below zero in February, 1947, at a lonely airport in the Yukon called Snag.

These are the meteorological champions—the official temperature extremes—but there are plenty of other claimants to thermometer fame. However, sun readings are unofficial records, since meteorological data to qualify officially must be taken on instruments in a sheltered and ventilated location.

Record Temperatures by States Through 1976

Source: National Oceanic and Atmospheric Administration, U.S. Commerce Department

State	Lowest °F	Highest	Latest date	Station	Approximate elevation in feet
Alabama	-27		Jan. 30, 1966	New Market	725
		112	*Sept. 5, 1925*	*Centerville*	*345*
Alaska	-79.8		Jan. 23, 1971	Prospect Creek Camp	1,100
		100	*June 27, 1915*	*Fort Yukon*	**419*
Arizona	-40		Jan. 7, 1971	Hawley Lake	8,180
		127	*July 7, 1905*	*Parker*	*345*
Arkansas	-29		Feb. 13, 1905	Pond	1,250
		120	*Aug. 10, 1936*	*Ozark*	*396*
California	-45		Jan. 20, 1937	Boca	5,532
		134	*July 10, 1913*	*Greenland Ranch*	*-178*
Colorado	-60		Feb. 1, 1951	Taylor Park	9,206
		118	*July 11, 1888*	*Bennett*	*5,484*
Connecticut	-32		Jan. 22, 1961	Coventry	480
		105	*July 22, 1926*	*Waterbury*	*409*
Delaware	-17		Jan. 17, 1893	Millsboro	535
		110	*July 21, 1930*	*Millsboro*	*20*
Dist. of Col.	-15		Feb. 11, 1899	Washington	112
		106	*July 20, 1930*	*Washington*	*112*
Florida	-2		Feb. 13, 1899	Tallahassee	193
		109	*June 29, 1931*	*Monticello*	*207*
Georgia	-17		Jan. 27, 1940	CCC Camp F-16	1,000
		112	*July 24, 1952*	*Louisville*	*337*
Hawaii	18		Feb. 20, 1962	Mauna Loa Slope Obs	11,146
		100	*Apr. 27, 1931*	*Pahala*	*850*
Idaho	-60		Jan. 18, 1943	Island Park Dam	6,285
		118	*July 28, 1934*	*Orofino*	*1,027*
Illinois	-35		Jan. 22, 1930	Mount Carroll	817
		117	*July 14, 1954*	*E. St. Louis*	*410*
Indiana	-35		Feb. 2, 1951	Greensburg	954
		116	*July 14, 1936*	*Collegeville*	*672*
Iowa	-47		Jan. 12, 1912	Washta	1,157
		118	*July 20, 1934*	*Keokuk*	*614*
Kansas	-40		Feb. 13, 1905	Lebanon	1,812
		121	*July 24, 1936*	*Alton (near)*	*1,651*
Kentucky	-34		Jan. 28, 1963	Cynthiana	719
		114	*July 28, 1930*	*Greensburg*	*581*
Louisiana	-16		Feb. 13, 1899	Minden	194
		114	*Aug. 10, 1936*	*Plain Dealing*	*268*
Maine	-48		Jan. 19, 1925	Van Buren	510
		105	*July 10, 1911*	*North Bridgton*	*450*
Maryland	-40		Jan. 13, 1912	Oakland	2,461
		109	*July 10, 1936*	*Cumberland and Frederick*	*623-325*
Massachusetts	-34		Jan. 18, 1957	Birch Hill Dam	840
		107	*Aug. 2, 1975*	*Chester and New Bedford*	*120-640*
Michigan	-51		Feb. 9, 1934	Vanderbilt	785
		112	*July 13, 1936*	*Mio*	*963*
Minnesota	-59		Feb. 16, 1903	Pokegama Dam	1,280
		114	*July 6, 1936*	*Moorhead*	*940*
Mississippi	-19		Jan. 30, 1966	Corinth	420
		115	*July 29, 1930*	*Holly Springs*	*600*
Missouri	-40		Feb. 13, 1905	Warsaw	700
		118	*July 14, 1954*	*Warsaw*	*687*
Montana	-70		Jan. 20, 1954	Rogers Pass	5,470
		117	*July 5, 1937*	*Medicine Lake*	*1,950*
Nebraska	-47		Feb. 12, 1899	Camp Clarke	3,700
		118	*July 24, 1936*	*Minden*	*2,169*
Nevada	-50		Jan. 8, 1937	San Jacinto	5,200
		122	*June 23, 1954*	*Overton*	*1,240*
New Hampshire	-46		Jan. 8, 1968	Mt. Washington	6,262
		106	*July 4, 1911*	*Nashua*	*125*
New Jersey	-34		Jan. 5, 1904	River Vale	70
		110	*July 10, 1936*	*Runyon*	*18*
New Mexico	-50		Feb. 1, 1951	Gavilan	7,350
		116	*July 14, 1934*	*Orogrande*	*4,171*
New York	-52		Feb. 9, 1934	Stillwater Reservoir	1,670
		108	*July 22, 1926*	*Troy*	*35*
North Carolina	-29		Jan. 30, 1966	Mt. Mitchell	6,525
		109	*Sept. 7, 1954*	*Weldon*	*81*
North Dakota	-60		Feb. 15, 1936	Parshall	1,929
		121	*July 6, 1936*	*Steele*	*1,857*
Ohio	-39		Feb. 10, 1899	Milligan	800
		113	*July 21, 1934*	*Gallipolis (near)*	*673*
Oklahoma	-27		Jan. 18, 1930	Watts	958
		120	*July 26, 1943*	*Tishmoningo*	*670*
Oregon	-54		Feb. 10, 1933	Seneca	4,700
		119	*Aug. 10, 1898*	*Pendleton*	*1,074*
Pennsylvania	-42		Jan. 5, 1904	Smethport	1,469
		111	*July 10, 1936*	*Phoenixville*	*100*
Rhode Island	-23		Jan. 11, 1942	Kingston	100
		104	*Aug. 2, 1975*	*Providence*	*51*
South Carolina	-13		Jan. 26, 1940	Longcreek (near)	1,631
		111	*June 28, 1954*	*Camden*	*170*
South Dakota	-58		Feb. 17, 1936	McIntosh	2,277
		120	*July 5, 1936*	*Gannvalley*	*1,750*

State	Lowest °F	Highest	Latest date	Station	Approximate elevation in feet
Tennessee	-32		Dec. 30, 1917	Mountain City	2,471
		113	*Aug. 9, 1930*	*Perryville*	*377*
Texas	-23		Feb. 8, 1933	Seminole	3,275
		120	*Aug. 12, 1936*	*Seymour*	*1,291*
Utah	-50		Jan. 5, 1913	Strawberry Tunnel	7,650
		116	*June 28, 1892*	*Saint George*	*2,880*
Vermont	-50		Dec. 30, 1933	Bloomfield	915
		105	*July 4, 1911*	*Vernon*	*310*
Virginia	-29		Feb. 10, 1899	Monterey	3,008
		110	*July 15, 1954*	*Balcony Falls*	*725*
Washington	-48		Dec. 30, 1968	Mazama	2,120
	-48		Dec. 30, 1968	Winthrop	1,755
		118	*Aug. 5, 1961*	*Ice Harbor Dam*	*475*
West Virginia	-37		Dec. 30, 1917	Lewisburg	2,200
		112	*July 10, 1936*	*Martinsburg*	*435*
Wisconsin	-54		Jan. 24, 1922	Danbury	908
		114	*July 13, 1936*	*Wisconsin Dells*	*900*
Wyoming	-63		Feb. 9, 1933	Moran	6,770
		114	*July 12, 1900*	*Basin*	*3,500*

Canadian Normal Temperatures, Highs, Lows, Precipitation

Source: Atmospheric Environment Service, Department of Fisheries and the Environment

These normals are based on varying periods of record over the thirty-year period 1941 to 1970 inclusive. Extreme temperatures are based on varying periods of record for each station through 1970. Airport station; * designates city office stations. The minus (—) sign indicates temperatures below zero. Fahrenheit thermometer registration.

Province	Station	Temperature Normal January Max.	Min.	July Max.	Min.	Extreme Highest	Lowest	Precipitation normal annual (inches)
Alberta	Calgary	23	2	74	49	97	−49	17.21
Alberta	Edmonton (Industrial Airport)	14	3	74	53	94	−55	17.58
British Columbia	Prince George	19	2	72	46	94	−58	24.43
British Columbia	Victoria	43	32	71	52	97	4	33.72
British Columbia	Vancouver	41	31	72	55	92	0	42.05
Manitoba	Churchill	−11	−25	63	45	91	−49	15.61
Manitoba	Winnipeg	8	−10	79	56	105	−49	21.06
Newfoundland	Gander	28	14	71	52	96	−17	42.45
Newfoundland	St. John's	31	19	68	51	87	−10	59.50
New Brunswick	Fredericton	25	7	78	55	98	−35	41.74
New Brunswick	Moncton	26	9	76	55	99	−26	43.27
New Brunswick	Saint John	28	9	72	53	91	−34	55.13
Nova Scotia	Halifax	29	14	74	55	93	−14	54.94
Nova Scotia	Sydney	31	17	74	55	95	−13	52.78
Ontario	Ottawa	21	4	80	59	100	−33	33.50
Ontario	Sudbury	17	−1	77	55	97	−36	32.87
Ontario	Toronto	28	13	81	58	101	−24	29.61
Ontario	Windsor	31	18	82	62	101	−15	32.91
Prince Edward Island	Charlottetown	27	13	75	58	98	−23	41.69
Quebec	Montreal	22	6	79	61	96	−36	37.05
Quebec	Quebec City	19	3	77	56	96	−33	42.85
Quebec	Val-d'Or	12	− 9	74	52	94	−47	35.52
Saskatchewan	Prince Albert	5	−17	77	51	100	−58	15.31
Saskatchewan	Regina	10	− 9	79	53	110	−58	15.66
Northwest Territories	Alert*	−19	−33	44	34	68	−57	6.15
Northwest Territories	Yellowknife	−12	−27	69	53	90	−60	9.84
Yukon Territory	Dawson*	−13	−26	72	48	95	−73	12.81
Yukon Territory	Whitehorse*	6	− 9	68	47	94	−62	10.24

Low and High Temperature Records Through 1970

Source: Atmospheric Environment Service, Department of Fisheries and the Environment

Province	Lowest °F	Highest	Latest date	Station	Approximate elevation in feet
Alberta	—78		Jan. 11, 1911	Fort Vermilion	915
		108	*July 12, 1886*	*Medicine Hat*	*2,365*
British Columbia	—74		Jan. 31, 1947	Smith River	2,208
		112	*July 17, 1941*	*Chinock Cove*	*1324*
		112	*July 17, 1941*	*Lillooet*	*950*
		112	*July 17, 1941*	*Lytton*	*600*
Manitoba	—63		Jan. 9, 1899	Norway House	720
		112	*July 12, 1936*	*Emerson*	*792*
Newfoundland	—56		Mar. 7, 1968	Twin Falls	1,499
		107	*Aug. 11, 1914*	*Northwest River*	*200*
New Brunswick	—53		Feb. 1, 1955	Sisson Dam	915
		103	*Aug. 19, 1935*	*Rexton*	*20*
Nova Scotia	—42		Jan. 31, 1920	Upper Stewiacke	75
		101	*Aug. 19, 1935*	*Collegeville*	*250*
Ontario	—73		Jan. 23, 1935	Iroquois Falls	800
		108	*July 13, 1936*	*Fort Frances*	*1,160*
Prince Edward Island	—35		Jan. 26, 1884	Kilmahumaig	20
		98	*Aug. 19, 1935*	*Charlottetown*	*74*
Quebec	—66		Feb. 5, 1923	Doucet	1,236
		104	*Aug. 15, 1928*	*Bark Lake*	*1,195*
Saskatchewan	—70		Feb. 1, 1893	Prince Albert	1,432
		113	*July 5, 1937*	*Midale*	*1,908*
		113	*July 5, 1937*	*Yellow Grass*	*1,899*
North West Territories	—71		Dec. 26, 1917	Fort Smith	665
		103	*July 18, 1941*	*Fort Smith*	*680*
Yukon Territory	—81		Feb. 3, 1947	Snag	1,925
		95	*June 18, 1950*	*Mayo*	*1,625*

Canadian Normal Temperature and Precipitation

Source: Atmospheric Environment Service, Department of Fisheries and the Environment

Normal refers to the mean daily temperature and total monthly precipitation based on varying periods of record over the thirty-year period 1941 to 1970 inclusive. In most cases no adjustment factor was used.

Airport station; *designates city office stations.

T, temperature in Fahrenheit; P, precipitation in inches; L, less than .05 inch.

Station	Jan. T.	Jan. P.	Feb. T.	Feb. P.	Mar. T.	Mar. P.	Apr. T.	Apr. P.	May T.	May P.	June T.	June P.	July T.	July P.	Aug. T.	Aug. P.	Sept. T.	Sept. P.	Oct. T.	Oct. P.	Nov. T.	Nov. P.	Dec. T.	Dec. P.
Calgary, Alta.	12	0.7	19	0.8	24	0.8	38	1.2	49	2.0	56	3.6	62	2.7	59	2.2	51	1.4	42	0.7	27	0.6	18	0.6
Charlottetown, P.E.I.	20	3.8	20	3.2	27	3.0	37	2.9	49	3.1	58	3.1	66	2.9	65	3.5	58	3.6	48	3.9	39	4.5	26	3.9
Churchill, Man.	-17	0.6	-16	0.5	- 5	0.7	12	0.9	28	1.1	43	1.6	54	1.9	53	2.3	42	2.0	30	1.6	10	1.6	- 7	0.8
Dawson, Yukon*	-20	0.8	- 9	0.6	7	0.5	29	0.4	46	0.9	57	1.5	60	2.1	55	2.0	44	1.1	26	1.1	2	1.0	-14	1.0
Edmonton, Alta.	6	1.0	13	0.8	22	0.7	39	0.9	52	1.4	58	2.9	63	3.2	61	2.8	52	1.4	42	0.7	24	0.7	13	0.8
Fredericton, N.B.	16	3.7	17	3.6	28	2.7	39	2.9	51	3.2	61	3.1	67	3.4	64	3.4	56	3.2	46	3.4	35	4.3	21	4.4
Frobisher Bay, N.W.T.	-15	0.9	-13	1.1	- 8	0.8	7	0.8	26	0.9	38	1.4	46	2.0	44	2.2	36	1.7	23	1.6	9	1.4	- 5	1.0
Halifax, N.S.	21	5.3	20	5.0	28	4.0	37	4.2	48	3.8	58	3.1	64	3.1	64	4.2	57	3.7	48	4.6	39	6.4	27	7.0
Hamilton, Ont.*	25	2.2	26	2.3	33	2.7	45	2.7	56	3.0	67	2.3	72	2.9	71	2.9	62	2.4	52	2.5	40	2.3	29	2.3
Kitchener, Ont.*	20	2.3	21	2.1	30	2.8	44	2.7	54	3.2	65	3.2	69	3.5	68	3.0	60	2.8	49	2.8	37	3.0	25	2.9
London, Ont.	21	3.0	22	2.5	31	2.8	44	3.0	54	2.9	65	3.1	69	3.2	67	2.8	60	3.1	50	2.9	38	3.2	26	3.4
Moncton, N.B.	18	4.2	18	3.9	27	3.6	38	3.3	49	3.1	59	3.5	65	3.1	64	3.1	56	2.8	46	3.5	36	4.4	22	4.2
Montreal, Que.	14	2.9	16	2.7	28	2.7	43	2.9	55	2.6	65	3.2	70	3.3	68	3.4	59	3.1	49	2.9	36	3.4	20	3.4
Ottawa, Ont.	12	2.3	15	2.2	26	2.4	42	2.6	54	2.7	65	2.8	69	3.2	67	3.2	58	3.1	48	2.6	34	3.0	18	3.0
Quebec City, Que.	11	3.3	13	3.0	24	2.7	38	2.9	51	3.1	61	4.0	67	4.2	64	4.0	56	4.1	45	3.2	32	3.9	17	3.9
Regina, Sask.	1	0.7	6	0.6	17	0.7	38	0.9	51	1.6	59	3.2	66	2.2	64	1.9	53	1.4	41	0.7	23	0.7	9	0.6
Saint John, N.B.	19	5.7	18	5.1	27	4.1	37	4.4	48	4.0	56	3.7	62	3.5	61	3.8	54	4.0	46	4.3	37	6.0	24	6.1
St. John's Nfld.	25	5.7	24	6.1	28	5.2	34	4.4	42	3.9	51	3.4	59	3.2	60	4.5	54	4.4	45	5.4	38	6.3	30	6.6
Saskatoon, Sask.	- 2	0.7	5	0.7	16	0.6	38	0.8	51	1.3	60	2.2	66	2.0	63	1.7	52	1.3	41	0.7	22	0.7	7	0.7
Sault Ste. Marie, Ont.	13	3.2	11	2.1	23	2.2	38	2.2	48	3.3	58	3.4	64	2.8	62	2.6	56	3.7	47	3.1	34	4.1	20	3.7
Toronto, Ont.	21	2.1	22	1.9	30	2.3	43	2.5	54	2.8	65	2.4	69	2.9	68	2.8	60	2.4	50	2.3	38	2.4	26	2.2
Vancouver, B.C.	36	5,8	40	4.5	42	3.6	48	2.4	54	1.8	59	1.7	63	1.1	63	1.4	58	2.4	50	4.8	43	5.5	39	6.5
Victoria, B.C.	37	5.7	40	3.8	42	2.7	47	1.7	53	1.2	58	1.1	61	0.7	61	0.9	57	1.4	50	3.4	43	5.0	40	5.7
Whitehorse, Yukon	- 2	0.7	8	0.5	18	0.5	32	0.4	45	0.5	54	1.1	57	1.3	54	1.4	46	1.1	33	0.7	16	0.8	4	0.7
Windsor, Ont.	24	2.1	26	2.0	34	2.6	47	3.2	57	3.2	68	3.2	72	3.2	70	3.2	63	2.3	53	2.4	40	2.4	28	2.5
Winnipeg, Man.	- 1	0.9	4	0.7	17	1.0	38	1.4	51	2.2	62	3.1	67	3.1	66	2.9	55	2.0	44	1.3	24	1.0	7	0.9
Yellowknife, N.W.T.	-19	0.5	-14	0.4	-1	0.4	18	0.4	39	0.5	54	0.6	61	1.3	57	1.4	44	1.1	30	1.2	6	0.9	-11	0.7

Canadian Annual Climatological Data

Source: Atmospheric Environment Service, Department of Fisheries and the Environment

Station		Temperature				Precipitation						Wind Fastest		No. of Days	
1976	Elev. ft.	Highest	Date D./Mo.	Lowest	Date D./Mo.	Total (in.)	Greatest in 24 hrs.	Date D./Mo.	Total (in.)	Greatest in 24 hrs.	Date D./Mo.	MPH	Date D./Mo.	Prec. .01 in. or more	Snow, sleet 1 in. or more
Calgary, Alta.	3540	87	22/8	-27	7/1	15.95	1.18	20/5	39.5	4.0	29/11	53	11/5	98	42
Charlottetown, P.E.I.	186	90	22/8	-13	11/1	50.24	1.96	22/2	126.2	9.9	8/1	52	3/2	184	77
Churchill, Man.	115	91	3/7	-38	5/1	14.11	0.74	4/10	83.7	7.2	4/10	49	4/10	151	109
Dawson, Yukon	1062	90	30/7	-54	11/1	10.51	0.71	14/7	58.8	7.0	20/4	26	21/1	129	74
Edmonton, Alta.	2358	87	16/7	-34	7/1	16.38	2.36	1/8	42.5	4.7	6/12	40	17/11	113	57
Fredericton, N.B.	74	95	22/8	-24	19/1	51.07	2.42	25/6	140.2	15.4	17/12	41	2/2	162	67
Frobisher Bay, N.W.T.	68	59	13/9	-40	17/12	16.94	0.81	24/1	103.8	8.1	24/1	51	2/3	144	112
Halifax, N.S.	461	89	24/6	- 4	12/1	56.1	3.33	30/8	58.1	4.2	18/2	48	2/2	165	54
Hamilton, Ont.	808	88	10/6	-18	18/1	35.77	1.41	17/9	74.8	7.4	13/1	40	8/2	146	62
London, Ont.	912	86	27/6	-23	18/1	43.62	1.91	6/5	99.3	6.7	13/1	41	5/3	175	85
Moncton, N.B.	248	92	22/8	-24	12/1	51.91	2.91	13/7	146.5	20.0	17/3	48	17/3	148	49
Montreal, Que.	98	87	15/6	-24	24/1	42.72	1.40	9/10	103.2	5.6	3/1	49	2/2	197	81
Ottawa, Ont.	413	91	5/7	-25	23/1	33.3	1.26	20/5	101.6	7.9	21/2	31	5/5	170	93
Quebec City, Que.	245	88	6/7	-29	11/1	58.49	1.70	1/4	177.3	11.4	7/12	46	2/2	164	77
Regina, Sask.	1884	99	23/8	-35	8/1	15.70	3.07	12/6	42.5	4.0	1/3	55	14/10	97	56
Saint John, N.B.	352	94	22/8	-24	24/1	60.03	2.84	24/7	127.5	11.0	17/12	62	2/2	135	45
Saint John's, Nfld.	463	82	13/8	2	10/12	59.45	1.42	12/6	123.1	1.39	12/3	58	19/10	203	86
Saskatoon, Sask.	1645	95	22/8	-35	8/1	11.36	1.17	4/6	36.1	2.9	2/3	46	17/11	106	57
Sault Ste. Marie, Ont.	620	96	31/7	-26	22/1	27.90	1.42	5/9	110.9	7.9	8/2	38	sev.	159	75
Thunder Bay, Ont.	644	92	19/8	-36	13/12	19.58	1.01	15/6	88.0	6.8	9/12	33	14/12	122	73
Toronto, Ont.	578	89	10/6	-24	23/1	32.54	1.44	6/5	58.3	5.9	13/1	44	5/3	153	60
Vancouver, B.C.	16	77	25/7	20	4/3	39.71	1.50	24/3	15.0	5.3	1/3	35	15/4	174	10
Victoria, B.C.	67	80	20/9	24	3/3	22.13	1.40	14/1	2.6	0.7	29/2	36	8/12	139	6
Waterloo-Wellington, Ont.	1125	88	8/9	-24	18/1	37.18	2.12	2/3	79.7	6.4	13/1	44	5/5	166	82
Whitehorse, Yukon	2289	88	31/7	-47	7/1	8.61	0.55	21/8	60.7	3.7	2/1	26	sev.	110	65
Windsor, Ont.	637	95	14/7	- 6	18/1	33.11	1.37	17/9	44.2	5.2	13/1	41	5!3	87	26
Winnipeg, Man.	786	97	24/8	-32	6/1	16.81	1.13	25/6	47.7	7.6	2/3	38	20/3	108	57
Yellowknife, N.W.T.	682	84	4/7	-46	5/1	10.17	0.91	2/9	34.7	2.7	29/11	29	19/10	120	72

sev.—several

Explanation of Normal Temperatures

Normal temperatures listed in the tables on pages 795 and 797 are based on records of the National Weather Service for the 30-year period from 1941-1970 inclusive.

To obtain the average maximum temperature for any month, the daily maximum temperatures are added; the total is then divided by the number of days in that month. The average minimum temperature for the month is obtained by adding the daily minimum temperatures during that month and dividing by the number of days in that month.

The normal maximum temperature for January, for example, is obtained by adding the average maximums for January, 1941, January, 1942, etc., through January, 1970. The total is then divided by 30. The normal minimum temperature is obtained in a similar manner by adding the average minimums for each January in the 30-year period and dividing by 30. The normal temperature for January is one half of the sum for the normal maximum and minimum temperatures for that month. The mean temperature for any one day is one-half the total of the maximum and minimum temperatures for that day.

Speed of Winds in the U.S.

Source: National Oceanic and Atmospheric Administration, U.S. Commerce Department

Miles per hour — average through 1976. High through 1976. Wind velocities in true values.

Station	Avg.	High	Station	Avg.	High	Station	Avg.	High
Albuquerque, N.M.	9.0	90	Helena, Mont.	7.9	73	New York, N. Y.(c)	9.4	70
Anchorage, Alas.	6.7	61	Honolulu, Ha.	11.6	67	Omaha, Neb.	10.9	109
Atlanta, Ga.	9.1	70	Jacksonville, Fla.	8.5	82	Pensacola, Fla.	8.3	(b)59
Bismarck, N.D.	10.6	72	Key West, Fla.	11.3	122	Philadelphia, Pa.	9.6	73
Boston, Mass.	12.6	61	Knoxville, Tenn.	7.3	73	Pittsburgh, Pa.	9.4	58
Buffalo, N. Y.	12.3	91	Little Rock, Ark.	8.2	65	Portland, Ore.	7.8	88
Cape Hatteras, N. C.	11.6	(b)110	Louisville, Ky.	8.4	61	Rochester, N.Y.	9.7	73
Chattanooga, Tenn.	6.3	82	Memphis, Tenn.	9.2	57	St. Louis, Mo.	9.5	(b)91
Chicago, Ill.	10.4	60	Miami, Fla.	9.1	(a)74	Salt Lake City, Ut.	8.7	71
Cincinnati, Oh.	7.1	49	Minneapolis, Minn.	10.5	92	San Diego, Cal.	6.7	51
Cleveland, Oh.	10.8	74	Mobile, Ala.	9.2	(b)63	San Francisco, Cal.	10.5	58
Denver, Col.	9.1	56	Montgomery, Ala.	6.8	60	Savannah, Ga.	8.1	66
Detroit, Mich.	10.2	46	Mt. Washington, N.H.	35.2	231	Spokane, Wash.	8.7	59
Fort Smith, Ark.	7.6	58	Nashville, Tenn.	7.9	73	Toledo, Oh.	9.5	72
Galveston, Tex.	11.0	(d)100	New Orleans, La.	8.4	(b)98	Washington, D.C.	9.3	78

(a) Highest velocity ever recorded in Miami area was 132 mph, at former station in Miami Beach in September, 1926. (b) Previous location. (c) Data for Central Park, Battery Place data through 1960, avg. 14.5, high 113. (d) Recorded before anemometer blew away. Estimated high 120.

Speed of Winds in Canada

Source: Atmospheric Environment Service, Department of Fisheries and the Environment

Miles-per-hour average in most cases is for the period of record 1955 to 1972. High is based on varying periods of record dependent on the origin of the station through 1972.

Station	Avg.	High	Station	Avg.	High	Station	Avg.	High
Calgary, Alta.	13.3	65	London, Ont.	10.2	63	Sault Ste. Marie, Ont.	9.5	55
Charlottetown, P.E.I.	12.0	64	Moncton, N.B.	11.6	62	Thunder Bay, Ont.	8.8	50
Churchill, Man.	14.7	78	Montreal, Que.	9.8	51	Toronto, Ont.	10.7	56
Dawson, Yukon	4.2	32	Ottawa, Ont.	9.4	54	Vancouver, B.C.	7.5	55
Edmonton, Alta.	9.2	44	Quebec City, Que.	10.4	68	Victoria, B.C.	11.0	68
Fredericton, N.B.	8.8	50	Regina, Sask.	13.4	60	Whitehorse, Yukon	9.4	50
Frobisher Bay, N.W.T.	10.3	80	Saint John, N.B.	11.8	60	Windsor, Ont.	10.6	57
Halifax, N.S.	11.4	60	Saint John's, Nfld.	15.1	85	Winnipeg, Man.	12.0	56
Hamilton, Ont.	7.9	41	Saskatoon, Sask.	11.2	65	Yellowknife, N.W.T.	10.0	45

Wind Guide

The National Weather Service classifies winds according to their strength, measured in miles per hour, with official descriptive names or designations, shown in the table below. A similar classification is the Beaufort Scale, in which winds are designated as Force 1, Force 2, etc.

Name	MPH	Beau	Name	MPH	Beau	Name	MPH	Beau	Name	MPH	Beau
Calm	less than 1	0	Moderate breeze	13-18	4	Near gale	32-38	7	Storm	55-63	10
Light air	1-3	1	Fresh breeze	19-24	5	Gale	39-46	8	Violent storm	64-73	11
Light breeze	4-7	2	Strong breeze	25-31	6	Strong gale	47-54	9	Hurricane	74 and up	12
Gentle breeze	8-12	3									

The Beaufort Scale further classifies 74-82 mph as Force 12; 83-92, Force 13; 93-103, Force 14; 104-114, Force 15; 115-124, Force 16; 125-136, Force 17.

Temperature-Humidity (Discomfort) Index

The temperature-humidity index, THI, is a measure of summertime human discomfort resulting from the combined effects of temperature and humidity. (The THI may be calculated by adding wet-bulb and dry-bulb temperatures, multiplying the sum by 0.4 and adding 15.)

The following chart shows the combinations of temperature degrees and humidity percentages which produce discomfort for most persons (the equivalent of a THI value of 75) and those which produce acute discomfort for almost everyone (equivalent to a THI of 80).

Discomfort temp.-humid.	Acute discomfort temp.-humid.	Discomfort temp.-humid.	Acute discomfort temp.-humid.	Discomfort temp.-humid.	Acute discomfort temp.-humid.
75°—100%	81°—100%	82°—49%	88°—54%	90°—14%	96°—20%
76°— 91%	82°— 93%	83°—43%	89°—49%	91°—10%	97°—16%
77°— 82%	83°— 86%	84°—38%	90°—43%	92°— 7%	98°—13%
78°— 75%	84°— 78%	85°—33%	91°—38%	93°— 5%	99°—11%
79°— 68%	85°— 71%	86°—29%	92°—34%	94°— 3%	100°— 8%
80°— 61%	86°— 65%	87°—25%	93°—30%	95°— 1%	101°— 6%
81°— 55%	87°— 59%	88°—20%	94°—26%	96°— 1%	102°— 3%
		89°—17%	95°—23%	97°— 1%	103°— 1%

From 95 degrees up there is discomfort at any humidity. When the temperature is over 102 degrees there is acute discomfort at any humidity.

The Meaning of "One Inch of Rain"

An acre of ground contains 43,560 square feet. Consequently, a rainfall of 1 inch over 1 acre of ground would mean a total of 6,272,640 cubic inches of water. This is equivalent of 3,630 cubic feet.

As a cubic foot of pure water weighs about 62.4 pounds, the exact amount varying with the density, it follows that the weight of a uniform coating of 1 inch of rain over 1 acre of surface would be 226,512 pounds, or about 113 short tons. The weight of 1 U.S. gallon of pure water is about 8.345 pounds. Consequently a rainfall of 1 inch over 1 acre of ground would mean 27,143 gallons of water.

WEIGHTS AND MEASURES

Source: National Bureau of Standards, U.S. Commerce Department

U.S. Moving, Inch by 25.4 Mm, to Metric System

The U.S. is the only industrial country in the world which is not on the metric system and is not yet involved in an official changeover program.

On July 2, 1971, following the report of a metric conversion study committee, Commerce Secy. Maurice H. Stans recommended a gradual U.S. changeover during a 10-year period at the end of which the U.S. would be predominantly, but not exclusively, on the metric system. Proposals to that effect are now pending in Congress.

The International System (Metric)

Two systems of weights and measures exist side by side in the United States today, with roughly equal but separate legislative sanction: the U.S. Customary System and the International (Metric) System. Throughout U.S. history, the Customary System (inherited from, but now different from, the British Imperial System) has been, as its name implies, customarily used; a plethora of federal and state legislation has given it, through implication, standing as our primary weights and measures system. However, the Metric System (incorporated in the scientists' new SI or Systeme International d'Unites) is the only system that has ever received specific legislative sanction by Congress. The "Law of 1866" reads:

It shall be lawful throughout the United States of America to employ the weights and measures of the metric system; and no contract or dealing, or pleading in any court, shall be deemed invalid or liable to objection because the weights or measures expressed or referred to therein are weights or measures of the metric system.

Over the last 100 years, the Metric System has seen slow, steadily increasing use in the United States and, today, is of importance nearly equal to the Customary System.

On Feb. 10, 1964, the National Bureau of Standards issued the following bulletin:

Henceforth it shall be the policy of the National Bureau of Standards to use the units of the International System (SI), as adopted by the 11th General Conference on Weights and Measures (October 1960), except when the use of these units would obviously impair communication or reduce the usefulness of a report.

What had been the Metric System became the International System (SI), a more complete scientific system.

Seven units have been adopted to serve as the base for the International System as follows: **Length**—meter; **Mass**—kilogram; **Time**—second; **Electric Current**—ampere; **Thermodynamic Temperature**—kelvin; **Amount of Substance**—Mole; and **Light Intensity**—Candela.

Prefixes

The following prefixes, in combination with the basic unit names, provide the multiples and submultiples in the International System. For example, the unit name "meter," with the prefix "kilo" added, produces "kilometer," meaning "1,000 meters."

Prefix	Symbol	Multiples and submultiples	Equivalent
tera	T	10^{12}	trillionfold
giga	G	10^{9}	billionfold
mega	M	10^{6}	millionfold
kilo	k	10^{3}	thousandfold
hecto	h	10^{2}	hundredfold
deka	da	10	tenfold
deci	d	10^{-1}	tenth part
centi	c	10^{-2}	hundredth part
milli	m	10^{-3}	thousandth part
micro	mu	10^{-6}	millionth part
nano	n	10^{-9}	billionth part
pico	p	10^{-12}	trillionth part
femto	f	10^{-15}	quadrillionth part
atto	a	10^{-18}	quintillionth part

Tables of Metric Weights and Measures

Linear Measure

10 millimeters (mm)	= 1 centimeter (cm)
10 centimeters	= 1 decimeter (dm) = 100 millimeters
10 decimeters	= 1 meter (m) = 1,000 millimeters
10 meters	= 1 dekameter (dam)
10 dekameters	= 1 hectometer (hm) = 100 meters
10 hectometers	= 1 kilometer (km) = 1,000 meters

Area Measure

100 square millimeters (mm^2)	= 1 square centimeter (cm^2)
10,000 square centimeters	= 1 square meter (m^2) = 1,000,000 square millimeters
100 square meters	= 1 are (a)
100 ares	= 1 hectare (ha) = 10,000 square meters
100 hectares	= 1 square kilometer (km^2) = 1,000,000 square meters

Volume Measure

10 milliliters (mL)	= 1 centiliter (cL)
10 centiliters	= 1 deciliter (dL) = 100 milliliters
10 deciliters	= 1 liter (L) = 1,000 milliliters
10 liters	= 1 dekaliter (daL)
10 dekaliters	= 1 hectoliter (hL) = 100 liters
10 hectoliters	= 1 kiloliter (kL) = 1,000 liters

Cubic Measure

1,000 cubic millimeters (mm^3)	= 1 cubic centimeter (cm^3)
1,000 cubic centimeters	= 1 cubic decimeter (dm^3) = 1,000,000 cubic millimeters
1,000 cubic decimeters	= 1 cubic meter (m^3) = 1 stere = 1,000,000 cubic centimeters = 1,000,000,000 cubic millimeters

Weight

10 milligrams (mg)	= 1 centigram (cg)
10 centigrams	= 1 decigram (dg) = 100 milligrams
10 decigrams	= 1 gram (g) = 1,000 milligrams
10 grams	= 1 dekagram (dag)
10 dekagrams	= 1 hectogram (hg) = 100 grams
10 hectograms	= 1 kilogram (kg) = 1,000 grams
1,000 kilograms	= 1 metric ton (t)

Table of U.S. Customary Weights and Measures

Linear Measure

12 inches (in)	=1 foot (ft)
3 feet	=1 yard (yd)
5-1/2 yards	=1 rod (rd), pole, or perch (16 1/2 feet)
40 rods	=1 furlong (fur)=220 yards =660 feet
8 furlongs	=1 statute mile (mi) =1,760 yards = 5,280 feet
3 miles	=1 league = 5,280 yards =15,840 feet
6076.11549 feet	=1 International Nautical Mile

Liquid Measure

When necessary to distinguish the liquid pint or quart from the dry pint or quart, the word "liquid" or the abbreviation "liq" should be used in combination with the name or abbreviation of the liquid unit.

4 gills	=1 pint (pt) = 28.875 cubic inches
2 pints	=1 quart (qt) = 57.75 cubic inches
4 quarts	=1 gallon (gal) =231 cubic inches=8 pints=32 gills

Area Measure

Squares and cubes of units are sometimes abbreviated by using "superior" figures. For example, ft^2 means square foot, and ft^3 means cubic foot.

144 square inches	=1 square foot (ft^2)
9 square feet	=1 square yard (yd^2)=1,296 square inches
30 1/4 square yards	=1 square rod (rd^2)=272 1/4 =square feet
160 square rods	=1 acre=4,840 square yards =43,560 square feet
640 acres	=1 square mile (mi^2)
1 mile square	=1 section (of land)
6 miles square	=1 township=36 sections=36 square miles

Cubic Measure

30 1/4 square yards	=1 square rod (rd^2)=262 1/4(in^3)
1 cubic foot (ft^3)	
27 cubic feet	=1 cubic yard (yd^3)

Gunter's or Surveyors' Chain Measure

7.92 inches (in)	=1 link
100 links	=1 chain (ch)=4 rods=66 feet
80 chains	=1 statute mile (mi)=320 rods =5,280 feet

Troy Weight

24 grains	=1 pennyweight (dwt)
20 pennyweights	=1 ounce troy (oz t)=480 grains
12 ounces troy	=1 pound troy (lb t)=240 pennyweights=5,760 grains

Dry Measure

When necessary to distinguish the dry pint or quart from the liquid pint or quart, the word "dry" should be used in combination with the name or abbreviation of the dry unit.

2 pints (pt)	=1 quart (qt)=(67.2006 cubic inches)
8 quarts	=1 peck (pk)=(537.605 cubic inches) =16 pints
4 pecks	=1 bushel (bu)=(2,150.42 cubic inches) =32 quarts

Avoirdupois Weight

When necessary to distinguish the avoirdupois ounce or pound from the troy ounce or pound, the word "avoirdupois" or the abbreviation "avdp" should be used in combination with the name or abbreviation of the avoirdupois unit.

(The "grain" is the same in avoirdupois and troy weight.)

27 11/32 grains	=1 dram (dr)
16 drams	=1 ounce (oz)=437 1/2 grains
16 ounces	=1 pound (lb)=256 drams =7,000 grains
100 pounds	=1 hundredweight (cwt)°
20 hundredweights	=1 ton=2,000 pounds°

In "gross" or "long" measure, the following values are recognized:

112 pounds	=1 gross or long hundredweight°
20 gross or long hundredweights	=1 gross or long ton=2,240 pounds°

°When the terms "hundredweight" and "ton" are used unmodified, they are commonly understood to mean the 100-pound hundredweight and the 2,000-pound ton, respectively: these units may be designated "net" or "short" when necessary to distinguish them from the corresponding units in gross or long measure.

Tables of Equivalents

When the name of a unit is enclosed in brackets thus, [1 hand], this indicates (1) that the unit is not in general current use in the United States, or (2) that the unit is believed to be based on "custom and usage" rather than on formal definition.

Equivalents involving decimals are, in most instances, rounded off to the third decimal place except where they are exact, in which cases these exact equivalents are so designated.

Lengths

Angstrom (A)	0.1 nanometer (exactly); 0.000 1 micron (exactly); 0.000 000 1 millimeter (exactly); 0.000 000 004 inch
1 cable's length	120 fathoms; 720 feet; 219.456 meters (exactly)
1 centimeter (cm)	0.3937 inch
1 chain (ch) (Gunter's or surveyors)	66 feet; 20.1168 meters (exactly)
1 chain (engineers)	100 feet; 30.48 meters (exactly)
1 decimeter (dm)	3.937 inches
1 dekameter (dam)	32.808 feet
1 fathom	6 feet; 1.8288 meters (exactly)
1 foot (ft)	0.3048 meters (exactly)
1 furlong (fur)	10 chains (surveyors); 660 feet; 220 yards; 1/8 statute mile; 201.168 meters
[1 hand]	4 inches
1 inch (in)	2.54 centimeters (exactly)
1 kilometer (km)	0.621 mile; 3,280.8 feet
1 league (land)	3 statute miles; 4.828 kilometers
1 link (Gunter's or surveyors)	7.92 inches; 0.201 meter
1 link (engineers)	1 foot; 0.305 meter
1 meter (m)	39.37 inches; 1.094 yards
1 micron (u) [the Greek letter mu]	0.001 millimeter (exactly); 0.000 039 37 inch
1 mil	0.001 inch (exactly); 0.025 4 millimeter (exactly)
1 mile (mi) (statute or land)	5,280 feet; 1.609 kilometers
1 international nautical mile (INM)	1,852 kilometers (exactly); 1.150779 statute miles; 6,076.11549 feet
1 millimeter (mm)	0.039 37 inch
1 nanometer (nm)	0.001 micron (exactly); 0.000 000 039 37 inch (exactly)
1 point (typography)	0.013 837 inch (exactly); 0.351 millimeter
1 rod (rd), pole, or perch	16 1/2 feet; 5 1/2 yards; 5.029 meters
1 yard (yd)	0.9144 meter (exactly)

Areas or Surfaces

1 acre	43,560 square feet; 4,840 square yards; 0.405 hectare
1 are (a)	119.599 square yards; 0.025 acre

(continued)

1 hectare (ha)	2.471 acres
[1 square (building)]	100 square feet
1 square centimeter (cm^2)	0.155 square inch
1 square decimeter (dm^2)	15.500 square inches
1 square foot (ft^2)	929.030 square centimeters
1 square inch (in^2)	6.452 square centimeters
1 square kilometer (km^2)	247.105 acres 0.386 square mile 1.196 square yards
1 square meter (m^2)	10.764 square feet
1 square mile (mi^2)	258.999 hectares
1 square millimeter (mm^2)	0.002 square inch
1 square rod (rd^2) sq. pole, or sq. perch	25.293 square meters
1 square yard (yd^2)	0.836 square meter

Capacities or Volumes

1 barrel (bbl) liquid	31 to 42 gallons°

°There are a variety of "barrels," established by law or usage. For example: federal taxes on fermented liquors are based on a barrel of 31 gallons; many state laws fix the "barrel for liquids" as 31 1/2 gallons; one state fixes a 36-gallon barrel for cistern measurement; federal law recognizes a 40-gallon barrel for "proof spirits"; by custom, 42 gallons comprise a barrel of crude oil or petroleum products for statistical purposes, and this equivalent is recognized "for liquids" by 4 states.

1 barrel (bbl), standard, for fruits, vegetables, and other dry commodities except dry cranberries	7,056 cubic inches 105 dry quarts 3.281 bushels, struck measure
1 barrel (bbl), standard, cranberry	5,826 cubic inches $86^{45}/_{64}$ dry quarts 2.709 bushels, struck measure
1 bushel (bu) (U.S.) (struck measure)	2,150.42 cubic inches (exactly) 35.238 liters
[1 bushel, heaped (U.S.)]	2,747.715 cubic inches 1.278 bushels, struck measure°

°Frequently recognized as 1 1/4 bushels, struck measure.

[1 bushel (bu) (British Imperial) (struck measure)]	1.032 U.S. bushels, struck measure 2,219.36 cubic inches
1 cord (cd) firewood	128 cubic feet
1 cubic centimeter (cm^3)	0.061 cubic inch
1 cubic decimeter (dm^3)	61.024 cubic inches
1 cubic inch (in^3)	0.554 fluid ounce 4.433 fluid drams 16.387 cubic centimeters
1 cubic foot (ft^3)	7.481 gallons 28.317 cubic decimeters
1 cubic meter (m^3)	1.308 cubic yards
1 cubic yard (yd^3)	0.765 cubic meter
1 cup, measuring	8 fluid ounces 1/2 liquid pint
[1 dram, fluid (fl dr) (British)]	0.961 U.S. fluid dram 0.217 cubic inch 3.552 milliliters
1 dekaliter (dal)	2.642 gallons 1.135 pecks
1 gallon (gal) (U.S.)	231 cubic inches 3.785 liters 0.833 British gallon 128 U.S. fluid ounces
[1 gallon (gal) British Imperial]	277.42 cubic inches 1.201 U.S. gallons 4.546 liters 160 British fluid ounces
1 gill	7.219 cubic inches 4 fluid ounces 0.118 liter
1 hectoliter (hl)	26.417 gallons 2.838 bushels
1 liter (l)	1.057 liquid quarts 0.908 dry quart 61.024 cubic inches
1 milliliter (ml) (1 cu cm exactly)	0.271 fluid dram 16.231 minims 0.061 cubic inch
1 ounce, liquid (U.S.)	1.805 cubic inches 29.573 milliliters 1.041 British fluid ounces
[1 ounce, fluid (fl oz) (British)]	0.961 U. S. fluid ounce 1.734 cubic inches 28.412 milliliters
1 peck (pk)	8.810 liters
1 pint (pt), dry	33.600 cubic inches 0.551 liter
1 pint (pt) liquid	28.875 cubic inches (exactly) 0.473 liter
1 quart (qt) dry (U.S.)	67.201 cubic inches 1.101 liters 0.969 British quart
1 quart (qt) liquid (U.S.)	57.75 cubic in (exactly) 0.946 liter 0.833 British quart
[1 quart (qt) (British)]	69.354 cubic inches 1.032 U.S. dry quarts 1.201 U.S. liquid quarts
1 tablespoon	3 teaspoons° 4 fluid drams 1/2 fluid ounce
1 teaspoon	1/3 tablespoon° 1 1/3 fluid drams°

°The equivalent "1 teaspoon — 1 1/3 fluid drams" has been found by the bureau to correspond more closely with the actual capacities of "measuring" and silver teaspoons than the equivalent "1 teaspoon — 1 fluid dram" which is given by many dictionaries.

Weights or Masses

1 assay ton°° (AT)	29.167 grams

°°Used in assaying. The assay ton bears the same relation to the milligram that a ton of 2,000 pounds avoirdupois bears to the ounce troy; hence the weight in milligrams of precious metal obtained from one assay ton of ore gives directly the number of troy ounces to the net ton.

1 carat (c)	200 milligrams 3.086 grains
1 dram avoirdupois (dr avdp) gamma, see microgram	$27^{11}/_{32}$ (=27.344) grains 1.722 grams
1 grain	64.799 milligrams
1 gram	15.432 grains 0.035 ounce, avoirdupois
1 hundredweight, gross or long°°° (gross cwt)	112 pounds 50.802 kilograms
1 hundredweight, net or short (cwt. or net cwt.)	100 pounds 45.359 kilograms
1 kilogram (kg)	2.205 pounds
1 microgram (γ [the Greek letter gamma])	0.000001 gram (exactly)
1 milligram (mg)	0.015 grain
1 ounce, avoirdupois (oz avdp)	437.5 grains (exactly) 0.911 troy ounce 28.350 grams
1 ounce, troy (oz t)	480 grains 1.097 avoirdupois ounces 31.103 grams
1 pennyweight (dwt)	1.555 grams
1 pound, avoirdupois (lb avdp)	7,000 grains 1.215 troy pounds 453.592 37 grams (exactly)
1 pound, troy (lb t)	5,760 grains 0.823 avoirdupois pound 373.242 grams
1 ton, gross or long°°° (gross ton)	2,240 pounds 1.12 net tons (exactly) 1.016 metric tons

°°°The gross or long ton and hundredweight are used commercially in the United States to only a limited extent, usually in restricted industrial fields. These units are the same as British "ton" and "hundredweight."

1 ton, metric (t)	2,204.623 pounds 0.984 gross ton 1.102 net tons
1 ton, net or short (sh ton)	2,000 pounds 0.893 gross ton 0.907 metric ton

Tables of Interrelation of Units of Measurement

Bold face type indicates exact values

Units of Length

Units	Inches	Links	Feet	Yards	Rods	Chains	Miles	Cm	Meters
1 inch =	**1**	0.126 263	0.083 333	0.027 778	0.005 051	0.001 263	0.000 016	**2.54**	**0.025 4**
1 link =	**7.92**	**1**	**0.66**	**0.22**	**0.04**	**0.01**	**0.000 125**	20.117	**0.201 168**
1 foot =	**12**	1.515 152	**1**	0.333 333	0.060 606	0.015 152	0.000 189	**30.48**	**0.304 8**
1 yard =	**36**	4.545 45	**3**	**1**	0.181 818	0.045 455	0.000 568	**91.44**	**0.914 4**
1 rod =	**198**	**25**	**16.5**	**5.5**	**1**	**0.25**	**0.003 125**	**502.92**	**5.029 2**
1 chain =	**792**	**100**	**66**	**22**	**4**	**1**	**0.012 5**	**2011.68**	**20.116 8**
1 mile =	**63 360**	**8000**	**5280**	**1760**	**320**	**80**	**1**	**160 934.4**	**1609.344**
1 cm =	0.3937	0.049 710	0.032 808	0.010 936	0.001 988	0.000 497	0.000 006	**1**	**0.01**
1 meter =	39.37	4.970 970	3.280 840	1.093 613	0.198 839	0.049 710	0.000 621	**100**	**1**

Units of Area

Units	Sq. inches	Sq. links	Sq. feet	Sq. yards	Sq. rods	Sq. chains
1 sq. inch =	**1**	.015 942 3	0.006 944	0.00 771 605	0.000 025 5	0.000 001 594
1 sq. link =	62.726 4	**1**	**0.435 6**	**0.0484**	**0.0016**	**0.000 1**
1 sq. foot =	**144**	2.295 684	**1**	0.111 111 1	0.003 673 09	0.000 220 568
1 sq. yard =	**1296**	20.661 16	**9**	**1**	0.033 057 85	0.002 066 12
1 sq. rod =	**39 204**	**625**	**272.25**	**30.25**	**1**	**0.062 5**
1 sq. chain =	**627 264**	**10 000**	**4 356**	**484**	**16**	**1**
1 acre =	**6 272 640**	**100 000**	**43 560**	**4 840**	**160**	**10**
1 sq. mile =	**4 014 489 600**	**64 000 000**	**27 878 400**	**3 097 600**	**102 400**	**6400**
1 sq. cm =	0.155 000 3	0.002 471 05	0.001 076	0.000 119 599	0.000 003 954	0.000 000 247
1 sq. meter =	1550.003	24.710 54	10.763 91	1.195 990	0.039 536 86	0.002 471 054
1 hectare =	15 500 031	247.105	107 639.1	11 959.90	395.368 6	24.710 54

Units	Acres	Sq. miles	Sq. cm	Sq. meters	Hectares
1 sq. inch =	0.000 000 159 423	0.000 000 000 249 10	**6.451 6**	**0.000 645 16**	0.000 000 065
1 sq. link =	**0.000 01**	**0.000 000 015 625**	**404.685 642 24**	0.040 468 56	0.000 004 047
1 sq. foot =	0.000 022 956 84	0.000 000 035 870 06	**929.030 4**	**0.092 903 04**	0.000 009 290
1 sq. yard =	0.000 206 611 6	0.000 000 322 830 6	**8 361.273 6**	**0.836 127 36**	0.000 083 613
1 sq. rod =	**0.006 25**	**0.000 009 765 625**	**252 928.526 4**	**25.292 852 64**	0.002 529 285
1 sq. chain =	**0.1**	**0.000 156 25**	4 046 856	**404.685 642 24**	0.040 468 564
1 acre =	**1**	**0.001 562 5**	40 468 564	**4046.856 422 4**	0.404 685 642
1 sq. mile =	**640**	**1**	25 899 881 103	2 589 988.11	258.998 811 034
1 sq. cm =	0.000 000 024 711	0.000 000 000 038 610	**1**	**0.000 1**	**0.000 000 01**
1 sq. meter =	0.000 247 105 4	0.000 000 386 102 2	**10 000**	**1**	**0.0001**
1 hectare =	2.471 054	0.003 861 022	**100 000 000**	**10 000**	**1**

Units of Mass Not Greater than Pounds and Kilograms

Units	Grains	Pennyweights	Avdp drams	Avdp ounces
1 grain =	**1**	0.041 666 67	0.036 571 43	0.002 285 71
1 pennyweight =	**24**	**1**	0.877 714 3	0.054 857 14
1 dram avdp =	**27.343 75**	1.139 323	**1**	**0.062 5**
1 ounce avdp =	**437.5**	18.229 17	**16**	**1**
1 ounce troy =	**480**	**20**	17.554 29	1.097 143
1 pound troy =	**5760**	**240**	210.651 4	13.165 71
1 pound avdp =	**7000**	291.666 7	**256**	**16**
1 milligram =	0.015 432	0.000 643 015	0.000 564 383	0.000 035 274
1 gram =	15.432 36	0.643 014 9	0.564 383 4	0.035 273 96
1 kilogram =	15 432.36	643.014 9	564.383 4	35.273 96

Units	Troy ounces	Troy pounds	Avdp pounds	Milligrams	Grams	Kilograms
1 grain =	0.002 083 33	0.000 173 611	0.000 142 857	**64.798 91**	**0.064 798 91**	0.000 064 799
1 pennyw't. =	**0.05**	0.004 166 667	0.003 428 571	**1555.173 84**	**1.555 173 84**	0.001 555 174
1 dram avdp =	0.056 966 15	0.004 747 179	0.003 906 25	1771.845 195	1.771 845 195	0.001 771 845
1 oz avdp =	0.911 458 3	0.075 954 86	**0.062 5**	**28 349.523 125**	**28.349 523 125**	0.028 349 52
1 oz troy =	**1**	0.083 333 333	0.068 571 43	**31 103.476 8**	**31.103 476 8**	0.031 103 48
1 lb troy =	**12**	**1**	0.822 857 1	**373 241.721 6**	**373.241 721 6**	0.373 241 722
1 lb avdp =	14.583 33	1.215 278	**1**	**453 592.37**	**453.592 37**	**0.453 592 37**
1 milligram =	0.000 032 151	0.000 002 679	0.000 002 205	**1**	**0.001**	**0.000 001**
1 gram =	0.032 150 75	0.002 679 229	0.002 204 623	**1000**	**1**	**0.001**
1 kilogram =	32.150 75	2.679 229	2.204 623	**1000 000**	**1000**	**1**

Units of Mass Not Less than Avoirdupois Ounces

Units	Avdp oz	Avdp lb	Short cwt	Short tons	Long tons	Kilograms	Metric tons
1 oz av	**1**	**0.0625**	**0.000 625**	**0.000 031 25**	0.000 027 902	0.028 349 523	0.000 028 350
1 lb av	**16**	**1**	**0.01**	**0.000 5**	0.000 446 429	**0.453 592 37**	0.000 453 592
1 sh cwt	**1 600**	**100**	**1**	**0.05**	0.044 642 86	**45.359 237**	**0.045 359 237**
1 sh ton	**32 000**	**2000**	**20**	**1**	0.892 857 1	**907.184 74**	**0.907 184 74**
1 long ton	**35 840**	**2240**	**22.4**	**1.12**	**1**	**1016.046 908 8**	1.016 046 909
1 kg	35.273 96	2.204 623	0.022 046 23	0.001 102 311	0.000 984 207	**1**	**0.001**
1 metric ton	35 273.96	2204.623	22.046 23	1.102 311	0.984 206 5	**1000**	**1**

(continued)

(Continued)

Units of Volume

Units	Cubic inches	Cubic feet	Cubic yards	Cubic cm	Cubic dm	Cubic meters
1 cubic inch=	1	0.000 578 704	0.000 021 433	**16.387 064**	0.016 387	0.000 016 387
1 cubic foot=	**1728**	1	0.037 037 04	**28 316.846 592**	28.316 847	0.028 316 847
1 cubic yard=	**46 656**	**27**	1	**764 554.857 984**	764.554 858	0.764 554 858
1 cubic cm=	0.061 023 74	0.000 035 315	0.000 001 308	1	**0.001**	**0.000 001**
1 cubic dm=	61.023 74	0.035 314 67	0.001 307 951	**1 000**	1	**0.001**
1 cubic meter	61 023.74	35.314 67	1.307 951	**1 000 000**	**1000**	1

Units of Capacity (Liquid Measure)

Units	Minims	Fluid drams	Fluid ounces	Gills	Liquid pt
1 minim=	1	0.016 666 7	0.002 083 33	0.000 520 833	0.000 130 208
1 liquid dram=	**60**	1	**0.125**	**0.031 25**	**0.007 812 5**
1 liquid ounce=	**480**	**8**	1	**0.25**	**0.062 5**
1 gill=	**1920**	**32**	**4**	1	**0.25**
1 liquid pint=	**7680**	**128**	**16**	**4**	1
1 liquid quart=	**15 360**	**256**	**32**	**8**	**2**
1 gallon=	**61 440**	**1024**	**128**	**32**	**8**
1 cubic inch=	265.974	4.432 900	0.554 112 6	0.138 528 1	0.034 632 03
1 cubic foot=	459 603.1	7660.052	957.506 5	239.376 6	59.844 16
1 milliliter=	16.230 73	0.270 512 18	0.033 814 02	0.008 453 506	.002 113 376
1 liter=	16 230.73	270.512 18	33.814 02	8.453 506	2.113 376

Units	Liquid quarts	Gallons	Cubic inches	Cubic feet	Liters
1 minim=	0.000 065 104 17	0.000 016 276 04	0.003 759 766	0.000 002 175 790	0.000 061 611 52
1 liq. dram=	**0.003 906 25**	**0.000 976 562 5**	0.225 585 9	0.000 130 547 4	.003 696 691
1 liquid oz=	**0.031 25**	**0.007 812 5**	1.804 687 5	0.001 044 379	0.029 573 53
1 gill=	**0.125**	**0.031 25**	**7.218 75**	**0.004 177 517**	**0.118 294 118 25**
1 liquid pt=	**0.5**	**0.125**	**28.875**	0.016 710 07	**0.473 176 473**
1 liquid qt=	1	**0.25**	**57.75**	0.033 420 14	**0.946 352 946**
1 gallon=	**4**	1	**231**	0.133 680 6	**3.785 411 784**
1 cubic in.=	0.017 316 02	0.004 329 004	1	0.000 578 703 7	**0.016 387 064**
1 cubic foot=	29.922 08	7.480 519	**1728**	1	**28.316 846 592**
1 liter=	1.056 688	0.264 172 05	61.023 74	0.035 314 67	1

Units of Capacity (Dry Measure)

Units	Dry pints	Dry quarts	Pecks	Bushels	Cubic in.	Liters
1 dry pint=	1	**0.5**	**0.062 5**	**0.015 625**	**33.600 312 5**	550 610 47
1 dry quart=	**2**	1	**0.125**	**0.031 25**	**67.200 625**	1.101 220 9
1 peck=	**16**	**8**	1	**0.25**	**537.605**	8.809 767 5
1 bushel=	**64**	**32**	**4**	1	**2150.42**	35.239 07
1 cubic inch=	**0.029 761 6**	0.014 880 9	0.001 860 10	0.000 465 025	1	**0.016 387 064**
1 liter=	1.816 166	0.908 083	0.113 510 37	0.028 377 59	61.023 74	1

Temperature Conversion Table

The numbers in **bold face type** refer to the temperature either in degrees Celsius or Fahrenheit which are to be converted. If converting from degrees Fahrenheit to Celsius, the equivalent will be found in the column on the left, while if converting from degrees Celsius to Fahrenheit the answer will be found in the column on the right.

For temperatures not shown. To convert Fahrenheit to Celsius subtract 32 degrees and multiply by 5, divide by 9; to convert Celsius to Fahrenheit, multiply by 9, divide by 5 and add 32 degrees.

Celsius		Fahrenheit	Celsius		Fahrenheit	Celsius		Fahrenheit
—273.2	**—459.7**	....	— 17.8	**0**	32	35.0	**95**	203
—184	**—300**	....	— 12.2	**10**	50	36.7	**98**	208.4
—169	**—273**	—459.4	— 6.67	**20**	68	37.8	**100**	212
—157	**—250**	—418	— 1.11	**30**	86	43	**110**	230
—129	**—200**	—328	4.44	**40**	104	49	**120**	248
—101	**—150**	—238	10.0	**50**	122	54	**130**	266
— 73.3	**—100**	—148	15.6	**60**	140	60	**140**	284
— 45.6	**— 50**	— 58	21.1	**70**	158	66	**150**	302
— 40.0	**— 40**	— 40	23.9	**75**	167	93	**200**	392
— 34.4	**— 30**	— 22	26.7	**80**	176	121	**250**	482
— 28.9	**— 20**	— 4	29.4	**85**	185	149	**300**	572
— 23.3	**— 10**	14	32.2	**90**	194			

Water boils at 212° Fahrenheit at sea level. For every 550 feet above sea level, boiling point of water is lower by about 1° Fahrenheit. Methyl alcohol boils at 148° Fahrenheit. Average human oral temperature, 98.6° Fahrenheit. Water freezes at 32° Fahrenheit. Although "Centigrade" is still frequently used, the International Committee on Weights and Measures and the National Bureau of Standards have recommended since 1948 that this scale be called "Celsius."

World Weights and Measures

Source: National Bureau of Standards, U.S. Commerce Department

Unit	Where used	U.S. equiv.
Almude	Portugal	4.423 gal
Ardeb	Egypt	5.6189 bu
Arratel (Libra)	Portugal	1.012 lb
Arroba	Argentina	25.32 lb
"	Brazil	32.38 lb
"	Cuba	25.36 lb
"	Paraguay	25.32 lb
"	Venezuela	25.40 lb
" (liquid)	Cuba, Spain, and Venezuela	4,263 gal
Arshine	USSR	28 in
" (sq)	"	5.44 sq ft
Artel	Morocco	1.12 lb
Baril	Argentina	20.077 gal
"	Mexico	20.0787 gal
Barile (wine)	Malta	11.2 gal
Berkovets	USSR	361.128 lb
Bongkal	Malaysia	832 grains
Bouw	Sumatra	1.75 acres
Bu	Japan	0.12 inch
Bushel (Brit.)	various	1.03205 U.S. bu
Caballeria	Cuba	33.162 acres
Caban (cavan)	Philippines	2.13 bu
		19.8 gal
Caffiso	Malta	5.40 gal
Candy	Bombay	560 lb
"	India (Madras)	500 lb
Cantaro	Malta	175 lb
Carat (metric)	World	3.086 grains
Catty	China	$1.333\frac{1}{3}$ lb
"	Japan (see Kin)	
"	Java, Malacca	1.36 lb
"	Thailand	$2\frac{2}{3}$ lb
" (stand)	Thailand	1.32 lb
"	Sumatra	2.12 lb
Centaro	Central America	4.2631 gal
Centner	Brunswick	117.5 lb
"	Bremen	127.5 lb
"	Denmark, Norway	110.23 lb
"	Germany	113.44 lb
"	Sweden	93.7 lb
Chetvert	USSR	5.957 bu
Ch'ih	China	12.60 in
" (metric)	China	39.37 in=1 meter
Cho	Japan	2.451 acres
Coomb	England	4.1282 bu
Coyan	Thailand	2,645.5 lb
Cuadra	Argentina	4.2 acres
"	Paraguay	94.71 yd
" (sq)	Paraguay	1.85 acres
"	Uruguay	1.82 acres
Cwt. (Brit.)	various	112 lb
Dessiatine	USSR	2.6997 acres
Drachma	Greece	49.38 grains
Dunam	Israel	0.22239 acre
Fanega (dry)	Ecuador, El Salv.	1.5745 bu
"	Chile	2.75268 bu
" (dry)	Guatemala, Spain	1.57744 bu
"	Mexico	2.57716 bu
" (dry)	Spain	1.57501 bu
" (liquid)	Spain	16 gal
" (dry)	Trinidad & Tobago	110 lb
" (double)	Uruguay	7.776 bu
" (single)	Uruguay	3.888 bu
"	Venezuela	3.334 bu
Feddan	Egypt	1.04 acres
Frail (raisins)	Spain	50 lb
Frasco	Argentina	2.51 liq qt
Frasila	Zanzibar	35 lb
Fuder	Luxembourg	264.18 gal
Funt	USSR	0.9028 lb
Gallon (Brit.)	various	1.20094 U.S. gal
Garniec	Poland	1.0567 gal
Jerib	Iran	2.471 acres
Joch	Austria	1.422 acres
"	Hungary	1.067 acres
Kantar	Egypt	99.05 lb
"	Morocco	112 lb
"	Turkey	124.45 lb
Ken	Japan	5.97 feet
Kin	Japan	1.32 lb
Klafter	Austria	2.074 yd
Klafter	Germany	1.90 yd
Koku	Japan	5.119 bu
Kwan	Japan	8.2673 lb
Last	Belgium, Holland	85.134 bu
"	England	82.56 bu
"	Germany	2 metric tons
"	Prussia	112.29 bu
League (land)	Paraguay	4.633 acres
Li	China	1890 ft
"	China	0.01260 in =(1/1000 ch'ih)
Libra (lb)	Argentina	1.0128 lb
"	Cent. Amer., Chile	1.014 lb
"	Cuba	1.0143 lb
"	Mexico	1.01467 lb
"	Peru, Venezuela	1.0143 lb
"	Uruguay	1.0127 lb
Load, timber	England	50 cu ft
Manzana	Nicaragua	1.742 acres
"	Costa Rica, El Salv.	1.727 acres
Marco	Bolivia	0.507 lb
Maund	Bengal	$82\frac{2}{7}$ lb
Mil	Denmark	4.68 miles
Milla	Nicaragua	1.1594 miles
"	Honduras	1.1493 miles
Mina	Greece	0.95 lb
Morgen	Germany	0.63 acre
Oka (Oke)	Greece	2.82 lb
Oke	Egypt	2.7514 lb
"	Turkey	2.826 lb
Pic	Egypt	22.83 inches
Picul	Borneo, Celebes	135.64 lb
"	China	$133\frac{1}{3}$ lb
"	Java	136.16 lb
"	Philippines	139.44 lb
Pie	Argentina	0.9471 ft
"	Spain	0.91416 ft
Pik	Turkey	27.9 inches
Pood	USSR	36,113 lb
Pund (lb)	Denmark	1.102 lb
Quart (Brit.)	various	1.20094 liq qt
	"	1.03205 dry qt
Quarter	"	8.256 bu
Quintal	Argentina	101.3 lb
"	Brazil	129.54 lb
"	Castile, Peru, Chile	101.43 lb
"	Mexico	101.47 lb
Rotl	Israel	6.35 lb
Sagene	USSR	7 feet
Salm	Malta	8.26 bu
Se	Japan	0.02451 acre
Seer	India	2 2/35 lb
Shaku	Japan	11.9303 in
Sho	"	1.91 liq qt
Skalpund	Sweden	0.937 lb
Stone (Brit.)	various	14 lb
Sun	Japan	1.193 inches
Tael (Kuping)	China	575.64 grs (troy)
Tan	Japan	0.25 acre
To	Japan	2.05 pecks
Tonde (cereal)	Denmark	3.9480 bu
Tonde (land)	Denmark	1.36 acres
Tonne	France	2,204.62 lb
Tsubo	Japan	35.58 sq ft
Ts'un	China	1.26 inches
Tunna (wheat)	Sweden	4.16 bu
Tunnland	"	1.22 acres
Vara	Argentina	34.0944 inches
"	Costa Rica, El Salv.	32.913 inches
"	Guatemala	32.909 inches
"	Honduras	32.874 inches
"	Nicaragua	33.057 inches
"	Chile, Peru	32.913 inches
"	Cuba	33.386 inches
"	Mexico	32.992 inches
Vedro	USSR	3.249 gal
Verst	"	0.663 mile
Vloka	Poland	41.50 acres
Wey	Scotland, Ireland	40 bu

The metric carat of 200 milligrams is now very generally in use. The word carat also is used to denote the proportion of alloy in a metal. Thus, pure gold is 24 carats fine.

Squares, Square Roots, Cubes and Cube Roots of Nos. 1 to 100

Square and cube roots are approximate

No.	Sq.	Cube	Sq. root	Cube root
1	1.000	1.000	1.000	1.000
2	4	8	1.414	1.259
3	9	27	1.732	1.442
4	16	64	2.000	1.587
5	25	125	2.236	1.710
6	36	216	2.449	1.817
7	49	343	2.645	1.913
8	64	512	2.828	2.000
9	81	729	3.000	2.080
10	100	1000	3.162	2.154
11	121	1331	3.316	2.224
12	144	1728	3.464	2.289
13	169	2197	3.605	2.351
14	196	2744	3.741	2.410
15	225	3375	3.873	2.466
16	256	4096	4.000	2.519
17	289	4913	4.123	2.571
18	324	5832	4.242	2.620
19	361	6859	4.358	2.668
20	400	8000	4.472	2.714
21	441	9261	4.582	2.758
22	484	10648	4.690	2.802
23	529	12167	4.795	2.843
24	576	13824	4.899	2.884
25	625	15625	5.000	2.924
26	676	17576	5.099	2.962
27	729	19683	5.196	3.000
28	784	21952	5.291	3.036
29	841	24389	5.385	3.072
30	900	27000	5.477	3.107
31	961	29791	5.567	3.141
32	1024	32768	5.656	3.174
33	1089	25937	5.744	3.207
34	1156	39304	5.831	3.239
35	1225	42875	5.916	3.271
36	1296	46656	6.000	3.301
37	1369	50653	6.082	3.332
38	1444	54872	6.164	3.362
39	1521	59319	6.245	3.391
40	1600	64000	6.324	3.420
41	1681	68921	6.403	3.448
42	1764	74088	6.480	3.476
43	1849	79507	6.557	3.503
44	1936	85184	6.633	3.530
45	2025	91125	6.708	3.556
46	2116	97336	6.782	3.583
47	2209	103823	6.855	3.608
48	2304	110592	6.928	3.634
49	2401	117649	7.000	3.659
50	2500	125000	7.071	3.684
51	2601	132651	7.141	3.708
52	2704	140608	7.211	3.732
53	2809	148877	7.280	3.756
54	2916	157464	7.348	3.779
55	3025	166375	7.416	3.803
56	3136	175616	7.483	3.825
57	3249	185193	7.549	3.848
58	3364	195112	7.615	3.870
59	3481	205379	7.681	3.893
60	3600	216000	7.746	3.914
61	3721	226981	7.810	3.936
62	3844	238328	7.874	3.957
63	3969	250047	7.937	3.979
64	4096	262144	8.000	4.000
65	4225	274625	8.062	4.020
66	4356	287496	8.124	4.041
67	4489	300763	8.185	4.061
68	4624	314432	8.246	4.081
69	4761	328509	8.306	4.101
70	4900	343000	8.366	4.121
71	5041	357911	8.426	4.140
72	5184	373248	8.485	4.160
73	5329	389017	8.544	4.179
74	5476	405224	8.602	4.198
75	5625	421875	8.660	4.217
76	5776	438976	8.717	4.235
77	5929	456533	8.775	4.254
78	6084	474552	8.831	4.272
79	6241	493039	8.888	4.290
80	6400	512000	8.944	4.308
81	6561	531441	9.000	4.326
82	6724	551368	9.055	4.344
83	6889	571787	9.110	4.362
84	7056	592704	9.165	4.379
85	7225	614125	9.219	4.396
86	7396	636056	9.273	4.414
87	7569	658503	9.327	4.431
88	7744	681472	9.380	4.448
89	7921	704969	9.434	4.464
90	8100	729000	9.486	4.481
91	8281	753571	9.539	4.497
92	8464	778688	9.591	4.514
93	8649	804357	9.643	4.530
94	8836	830584	9.695	4.546
95	9025	857375	9.746	4.562
96	9216	884736	9.798	4.578
97	9409	912673	9.848	4.594
98	9604	941192	9.899	4.610
99	9801	970299	9.949	4.626
100	10000	1000000	10.000	4.641

Square Roots and Cube Roots, 1000 to 2000

No.	Square root	Cube root
1000	31.62	10.00
1005	31.70	10.02
1010	31.78	10.03
1020	31.94	10.07
1025	32.02	10.08
1030	32.09	10.10
1035	32.17	10.12
1045	32.33	10.15
1050	32.40	10.16
1060	32.56	10.20
1065	32.63	10.21
1075	32.79	10.24
1080	32.86	10.26
1085	32.94	10.28
1090	33.02	10.29
1095	33.09	10.31
1100	33.17	10.32
1105	33.24	10.34
1110	33.32	10.35
1115	33.39	10.37
1120	33.47	10.38
1125	33.54	10.40
1130	33.62	10.42
1135	33.69	10.43
1140	33.76	10.45
1145	33.84	10.46
1150	33.91	10.48
1155	33.99	10.49
1160	34.06	10.51
1165	34.13	10.52
1170	34.21	10.54
1175	34.28	10.55
1180	34.35	10.57
1185	34.42	10.58
1190	34.50	10.60
1195	34.57	10.61
1200	34.64	10.63
1205	34.71	10.64
1210	34.79	10.66
1215	34.86	10.67
1220	34.93	10.69
1225	35.00	10.70
1235	35.14	10.73
1245	35.28	10.76
1255	35.43	10.79
1260	35.50	10.80
1265	35.57	10.82
1275	35.71	10.84
1280	35.78	10.86
1285	35.85	10.87
1290	35.92	10.89
1300	36.06	10.91
1305	36.12	10.93
1315	36.26	10.96
1320	36.33	10.97
1330	36.47	11.00
1335	36.54	11.01
1340	36.61	11.02
1345	36.67	11.04
1350	36.74	11.05
1355	36.81	11.07
1360	36.88	11.08
1365	36.95	11.09
1370	37.01	11.11
1375	37.08	11.12
1380	37.15	11.13
1385	37.22	11.15
1390	37.28	11.16
1395	37.35	11.17
1400	37.42	11.19
1405	37.48	11.20
1410	37.55	11.21
1415	37.62	11.23
1420	37.68	11.24
1425	37.75	11.25
1430	37.82	11.27
1435	37.88	11.28
1440	37.95	11.29
1445	38.01	11.31
1450	38.08	11.32
1455	38.14	11.33
1460	38.21	11.34
1465	32.28	11.36
1470	38.34	11.37
1475	38.41	11.38
1480	38.47	11.40
1490	38.60	11.42
1500	38.73	11.45
1510	38.86	11.47
1515	38.92	11.49
1520	38.99	11.50
1530	39.12	11.52
1535	39.18	11.54
1540	39.24	11.55
1545	39.31	11.56
1555	39.43	11.59
1560	39.50	11.60
1570	39.62	11.62
1575	39.69	11.63
1585	39.81	11.66
1590	39.87	11.67
1595	39.94	11.68
1600	40.00	11.70
1605	40.06	11.71
1610	40.12	11.72
1615	40.19	11.73
1620	40.25	11.74
1625	40.31	11.76
1630	40.37	11.77
1635	40.44	11.78
1640	40.50	11.79
1645	40.56	11.80
1650	40.62	11.82
1655	40.68	11.83
1660	40.74	11.84
1665	40.80	11.85
1670	40.87	11.86
1675	40.93	11.88
1680	40.99	11.89
1685	41.05	11.90
1690	41.11	11.91
1695	41.17	11.92
1700	41.23	11.93
1705	41.29	11.95
1710	41.35	11.96
1715	41.41	11.97
1720	41.47	11.98
1725	41.53	11.99
1730	41.59	12.00
1735	41.65	12.02
1745	41.77	12.04
1755	41.89	12.06
1765	42.01	12.09
1770	42.07	12.10
1775	42.13	12.11
1785	42.25	12.13
1790	42.31	12.14
1795	42.37	12.15
1800	42.43	12.16
1810	42.54	12.19
1815	42.60	12.20
1825	42.72	12.22
1830	42.78	12.23
1840	42.90	12.25
1845	42.95	12.26
1850	43.01	12.28
1855	43.07	12.29
1860	43.13	12.30
1865	43.19	12.31
1870	43.24	12.32
1875	43.30	12.33
1880	43.36	12.34
1885	43.42	12.35
1890	43.47	12.36
1895	43.53	12.37
1900	43.59	12.39
1905	43.65	12.40
1910	43.70	12.41
1915	43.76	12.42
1920	43.82	12.43
1925	43.87	12.44
1930	43.93	12.45
1935	43.99	12.46
1940	44.05	12.47
1945	44.10	12.48
1950	44.16	12.49
1955	44.22	12.50
1960	44.27	12.51
1965	44.33	12.53
1970	44.38	12.54
1975	44.44	12.55
1980	44.50	12.56
1985	44.55	12.57
1990	44.61	12.58
1995	44.67	12.59
2000	44.72	12.60

Chemical Elements, Discoverers, Atomic Weights

Atomic weights, based on the exact number 12 as the assigned atomic mass of the principal isotope of carbon, carbon 12, are provided through the courtesy of the International Union of Pure and Applied Chemistry and Butterworth Scientific Publications.

For the radioactive elements, with the exception of uranium and thorium, the mass number of either the isotope of longest half-life (*) or the better known isotope (**) is given.

Chemical element	Symbol	Atomic number	Atomic weight	Year discov.	Discoverer
Actinium	Ac	89	227*	1899	Debierne
Aluminum	Al	13	26.9815	1825	Oersted
Americium	Am	95	243*	1944	Seaborg, et al.
Antimony	Sb	51	121.75	1450	Valentine
Argon	Ar	18	39.948	1894	Rayleigh, Ramsay
Arsenic	As	33	74.9216	13th c.	Albertus Magnus
Astatine	At	85	210*	1940	Corson, et al.
Barium	Ba	56	137.34	1808	Davy
Berkelium	Bk	97	249**	1949	Thompson, Ghiorso, Seaborg
Beryllium	Be	4	9.0122	1798	Vanquelin
Bismuth	Bi	83	208.980	15th c.	Valentine
Boron	B	5	10.811a	1808	Davy
Bromine	Br	35	79.904b	1826	Balard
Cadmium	Cd	48	112.40	1817	Stromeyer
Calcium	Ca	20	40.08	1808	Davy
Californium	Cf	98	249**	1950	Thompson, et al.
Carbon	C	6	12.01115a	B.C.	
Cerium	Ce	58	140.12	1803	Klaproth
Cesium	Cs	55	132.905	1861	Bunsen, Kirchhoff
Chlorine	Cl	17	35.453b	1774	Scheele
Chromium	Cr	24	51.996b	1797	Vanquelin
Cobalt	Co	27	58.9332	1735	Brandt
Copper	Cu	29	63.546b	B.C.	
Curium	Cm	96	247*	1944	Seaborg, et al.
Dysprosium	Dy	66	162.50	1886	Boisbaudran
Einsteinium	Es	99	254*	1952	Ghiorso, et al.
Erbium	Er	68	167.26	1843	Mosander
Europium	Eu	63	151.96	1901	Demarcay
Fermium	Fm	100	257*	1953	Ghiorso, et al.
Fluorine	F	9	18.9984	1771	Scheele
Francium	Fr	87	223*	1939	Perey
Gadolinium	Gd	64	157.25	1886	Marignac
Gallium	Ga	31	69.72	1875	Boisbaudran
Germanium	Ge	32	72.59	1886	Winkler
Gold	Au	79	196.967	B.C.	
Hafnium	Hf	72	178.49	1923	Coster, Hevesy
Hahnium	Ha	105	262*	1970	Ghiorso, et al.
Helium	He	2	4.0026	1895	Ramsay
Holmium	Ho	67	164.930	1879	Cleve
Hydrogen	H	1	1.00797a	1766	Cavendish
Indium	In	49	114.82	1863	Reich, Richter
Iodine	I	53	126.9044	1811	Courtois
Iridium	Ir	77	192.2	1804	Tennant
Iron	Fe	26	55.847b	B.C.	
Krypton	Kr	36	83.80	1898	Ramsay, Travers
Lanthanum	La	57	138.91	1839	Mosander
Lawrencium	Lr	103	260*	1961	Ghiorso, T. Sikkeland, A.E. Larsh, and R. M. Latimer
Lead	Pb	82	207.19	B.C.	
Lithium	Li	3	6.939	1817	Arfvedson
Lutetium	Lu	71	174.97	1907	Welsbach, Urbain
Magnesium	Mg	12	24.312	1830	Liebig, Bussy
Manganese	Mn	25	54.9380	1774	Gahn
Mendelevium	Md	101	258*	1955	Ghiorso, et al.
Mercury	Hg	80	200.59	B.C.	
Molybdenum	Mo	42	95.94	1782	Hjelm
Neodymium	Nd	60	144.24	1885	Welsbach
Neon	Ne	10	20.183	1898	Ramsay, Travers
Neptunium	Np	93	237*	1940	McMillan, Abelson
Nickel	Ni	28	58.71	1751	Cronstedt
Niobium[1]	Nb	41	92.906	1801	Hatchett
Nitrogen	N	7	14.0067	1772	Rutherford
Nobelium	No	102	259*	1958	Ghiorso, et al.
Osmium	Os	76	190.2	1804	Tennant
Oxygen	O	8	15.9994a	1774	Priestley, Scheele
Palladium	Pd	46	106.4	1803	Wollaston
Phosphorus	P	15	30.9738	1669	Brandt
Platinum	Pt	78	195.09	1735	Ulloa
Plutonium	Pu	94	242**	1940	Seaborg, et al.
Polonium	Po	84	210**	1898	P. and M. Curie
Potassium	K	19	39.102	1807	Davy
Praseodymium	Pr	59	140.907	1885	Welsbach
Promethium	Pm	61	147**	1945	Glendenin, Marinsky
Protactinium	Pa	91	231*	1917	Hahn, Meitner
Radium	Ra	88	226*	1898	P. & M. Curie, Bemont
Radon	Rn	86	222*	1900	Dorn
Rhenium	Re	75	186.2	1925	Noddack, Tacke
Rhodium	Rh	45	102.905	1803	Wollaston
Rubidium	Rb	37	85.47	1861	Bunsen, Kirchhoff
Ruthenium	Ru	44	101.07	1845	Claus

Chemical element	Symbol	Atomic number	Atomic weight	Year discov.	Discoverer
Rutherfordium	Rf	104	261*	1969	Ghiorso, et al.
Samarium	Sm	62	150.35	1879	Boisbaudran
Scandium	Sc	21	44.956	1879	Nilson
Selenium	Se	34	78.96	1817	Berzelius
Silicon	Si	14	28.086a	1823	Berzelius
Silver	Ag	47	107.868b	B.C.	
Sodium	Na	11	22.9898	1807	Davy
Strontium	Sr	38	87.62	1790	Crawford
Sulfur	S	16	32.064a	B.C.	
Tantalum	Ta	73	180.948	1802	Eckeberg
Technetium	Tc	43	99**	1937	Perrier and Segre
Tellurium	Te	52	127.60	1782	Von Reichenstein
Terbium	Tb	65	158.924	1843	Mosander
Thallium	Tl	81	204.37	1861	Crookes
Thorium	Th	90	232.038	1828	Berzelius
Thulium	Tm	69	168.934	1879	Cleve
Tin	Sn	50	118.69	B.C.	
Titanium	Ti	22	47.90	1789	Gregor
Tungsten (Wolfram)	W	74	183.85	1783	d'Elhujar
Uranium	U	92	238.03	1789	Klaproth
Vanadium	V	23	50.942	1830	Sefstrom
Xenon	Xe	54	131.30	1898	Ramsay, Travers
Ytterbium	Yb	70	173.04	1878	Marignac
Yttrium	Y	39	88.905	1794	Gadolin
Zinc	Zn	30	65.37	B.C.	
Zirconium	Zr	40	91.22	1789	Klaproth

(1) Formerly Columbium. (a) Atomic weights so designated are known to be variable because of natural variations in isotopic composition. The observed ranges are: hydrogen±0.0001; boron±0.003; carbon±0.0005; oxygen±0.0001; silicon±0.001; sulfur±0.003. (b) Atomic weights so designated are believed to have the following experimental uncertainties: chlorine±0.001; chromium±0.001; iron±0.003; bromine±0.001; silver±0.001; copper±0.001.

Density of Gases and Vapors

Source: National Bureau of Standards (kilograms per cubic meter)

Gas	Wgt.	Gas	Wgt.	Gas	Wgt.
Acetylene	1.171	Ethylene	1.260	Methyl fluoride	1.545
Air	1.293	Fluorine	1.696	Mono methylamine	1.38
Ammonia	.759	Helium	.178	Neon	.900
Argon	1.784	Hydrogen	.090	Nitric oxide	1.341
Arsene	3.48	Hydrogen bromide	3.50	Nitrogen	1.250
Butane-iso	2.60	Hydrogen chloride	1.639	Nitrosyl chloride	2.99
Butane-n	2.519	Hydrogen iodide	5.724	Nitrous oxide	1.997
Carbon dioxide	1.977	Hydrogen selenide	3.66	Oxygen	1.429
Carbon monoxide	1.250	Hydrogen sulfide	1.539	Phosphine	1.48
Carbon oxysulfide	2.72	Krypton	3.745	Propane	2.020
Chlorine	3.214	Methane	.717	Silicon tetrafluoride	4.67
Chlorine monoxide	3.89	Methyl chloride	2.25	Sulfur dioxide	2.927
Ethane	1.356	Methyl ether	2.091	Xenon	5.897

Medical Signs and Abbreviations

Source: American Medical Association

℞ (Lat. Recipe) .... take
ʒ .... drachm
fʒ .... fluid drachm
℥ .... ounce
f℥ .... fluid ounce
℥ss .... half an ounce
℥i .... one ounce
℥iss ... one ounce and a half
℥ii .... 2 ounces
m .... minim, or drop
o .... pint
aa .... of each
a.c. .... before meals
ad .... to, up to
ad libitum ..... at pleasure
agit .... shake
aqua .... water

b.i.d. .... twice daily
cap .... capsule
cum, or c .... with
e.m.p. .... as directed
fiant (ft) .... make
gargarisma .... a gargle
Gm .... gram
gr. .... grain
gtt. .... drops
h.s. .... at bedtime
inject .... injection
lb .... pound
m .... mix
mg. .... milligram
ml .... milliliter

non. rep. or n.r. ...... do not repeat
p.c. .... after meals
p.r.n. ..... as circumstances may require
pulvis .... powder
q. 3 h .... every 3 hours
q.i.d. .... 4 times daily
q.s. as much as is sufficient
sig. .... sign, write
solutio .... a solution
ss .... one-half
stat .... at once
tab. .... tablet
t.i.d. .... 3 times daily
ung. .... ointment
ut dict .... as directed

Weight of Water

1	cubic inch	.0360	pound	1	imperial gallon	10.0	pounds
12	cubic inches	.433	pound	11.2	imperial gallons	112.0	pounds
1	cubic foot	62.4	pounds	224	imperial gallons	2240.0	pounds
1	cubic foot	7.48052	U.S. gal	1	U.S. gallon	8.33	pounds
1.8	cubic feet	112.0	pounds	13.45	U.S. gallons	112.0	pounds
35.96	cubic feet	2240.0	pounds	269.0	U.S. gallons	2240.0	pounds

Mathematical Formulas

To find the CIRCUMFERENCE of a:

Circle — Multiply the diameter by 3.14159265 (usually 3.1416).

To find the AREA of a:

Circle — Multiply the square of the diameter by 785398 (usually .7854).

Rectangle — Multiply the length of the base by the height.

Sphere (surface) — Multiply the square of the radius by 3.1416 and multiply by 4.

Square — Square the length of one side.

Trapezoid — Add the two parallel sides, multiply by the height and divide by 2.

Triangle — Multiply the base by the height and divide by 2.

To find the VOLUME of a:

Cone — Multiply the square of the radius of the base by 3.1416, multiply by the height, and divide by 3.

Cube — Cube the length of one edge.

Cylinder — Multiply the square of the radius of the base by 3.1416 and multiply by the height.

Pyramid — Multiply the area of the base by the height and divide by 3.

Rectangular Prism — Multiply the length by the width by the height.

Sphere — Multiply the cube of the radius by 3.1416, multiply by 4 and divide by 3.

Common Fractions Reduced to Decimals

8ths	16ths	32ds	64ths	
			1	.015625
		1	2	.03125
			3	.046875
	1	2	4	.0625
			5	.078125
		3	6	.09375
			7	.109375
1	2	4	8	.125
			9	.140625
		5	10	.15625
			11	.171875
	3	6	12	.1875
			13	.203125
		7	14	.21875
			15	.234375
2	4	8	16	.25
			17	.265625
		9	18	.28125
			19	.296875
	5	10	20	.3125
			21	.328125
		11	22	.34375

8ths	16ths	32ds	64ths	
			23	.359375
3	6	12	24	.375
			25	.390625
		13	26	.40625
			27	.421875
	7	14	28	.4375
			29	.453125
		15	30	.46875
			31	.484375
4	8	16	32	.5
			33	.515625
		17	34	.53125
			35	.546875
	9	18	36	.5625
			37	.578125
		19	38	.59375
			39	.609375
5	10	20	40	.625
			41	.640625
		21	42	.65625
			43	.671875
	11	22	44	.6875

8ths	16ths	32ds	64ths	
			45	.703125
		23	46	.71875
			47	.734375
6	12	24	48	.75
			49	.765625
		25	50	.78125
			51	.796875
	13	26	52	.8125
			53	.828125
		27	54	.84375
			55	.859375
7	14	28	56	.875
			57	.890625
		29	58	.90625
			59	.921875
	15	30	60	.9375
			61	.953125
		31	62	.96875
			63	.984375
8	16	32	64	1.

Playing Cards and Dice Chances

Poker Hands

Hand	Number possible	Odds against
Royal flush	4	649,739 to 1
Other straight flush	36	72,192 to 1
Four of a kind	624	4,164 to 1
Full house	3,744	693 to 1
Flush	5,108	508 to 1
Straight	10,200	254 to 1
Three of a kind	54,912	46 to 1
Two pairs	123,552	20 to 1
One pair	1,098,240	4 to 3 (1.37 to 1)
Nothing	1,302,540	1 to 1
Total	**2,598,960**	

Dice

(probabilities on 2 dice)

Total	Odds against (Single toss)	Total	Odds against (Single toss)
2	35 to 1	8	31 to 5
3	17 to 1	9	8 to 1
4	11 to 1	10	11 to 1
5	8 to 1	11	17 to 1
6	31 to 5	12	35 to 1
7	5 to 1		

Dice

(Probabilities of consecutive winning plays)

No. consecutive wins	By 7, 11, or point	No. consecutive wins	By 7, 11 or point
1	244 in 495	6	1 in 70
2	6 in 25	7	1 in 141
3	3 in 25	8	1 in 287
4	1 in 17	9	1 in 582
5	1 in 34		

Pinochle Auction

(Odds against finding in "widow" of 3 cards)

Open places	Odds against	Open places	Odds against
1	5 to 1	4	3 to 2 for
2	2 to 1	5	2 to 1 for
3	Even		

Bridge

The odds—against suit distribution in a hand of 4-4-3-2 are about 4 to 1, against 5-4-2-2 about 8 to 1, against 6-4-2-1 about 20 to 1, against 7-4-1-1 about 254 to 1, against 8-4-1-0 about 2,211 to 1, and against 13-0-0-0 about 158,753,389,899 to 1.

Simple Interest Table

	Time	4%	5%	6%	7%	8%
$1.00	1 month	$.003	$.004	$.005	$.005	$.006
..	2 months	.007	.008	.010	.011	.013
..	3	.010	.013	.015	.017	.020
..	6	.020	.025	.030	.035	.040
..	12	.040	.050	.060	.070	.080
$100.00	1 day	.011	.013	.016	.019	.022
..	2 days	.022	.027	.032	.038	.044
..	3	.033	.041	.050	.058	.067

	Time	4%	5%	6%	7%	8%
$100.00	4 days	$.045	$.053	$.066	$.077	$.889
..	5	.056	.069	.082	.097	.111
..	6	.067	.083	.100	.116	.133
..	1 month	.334	.416	.500	.583	.667
..	2 months	.667	.832	1.000	1.166	1.333
..	3	1.000	1.250	1.500	1.750	2.000
..	6	2.000	2.500	3.000	3.500	4.000
..	12	4.000	5.000	6.000	7.000	8.000

Inventions and Scientific Discoveries

Invention	Date	Inventor	Nation.
Adding machine	1642	Pascal	French
Adding machine	1885	Burroughs	U.S.
Addressograph	1892	Duncan	U.S.
Aerosol spray	1941	Goodhue	U.S.
Air brake	1868	Westinghouse	U.S.
Air conditioning	1911	Carrier	U.S.
Air pump	1650	Guericke	German
Airplane, automatic pilot	1929	Green	U.S.
Airplane, experimental	1896	Langley	U.S.
Airplane jet engine	1939	Ohain	German
Airplane with motor	1903	Wright bros.	U.S.
Airplane, hydro	1911	Curtiss	U.S.
Airship	1852	Giffard	French
Airship, rigid dirigible	1900	Zeppelin	German
Arc tube	1923	Alexanderson	U.S.
Autogyro	1920	de la Cierva	Spanish
Automobile, differential gear	1885	Benz	German
Automobile, electric	1892	Morrison	U.S.
Automobile, exp'mtl.	1875	Marcus	Austrian
Automobile, gasoline	1887	Daimler	German
Automobile, gasoline	1892	Duryea	U.S.
Automobile, magneto	1897	Bosch	German
Automobile muffler	...	Maxim, H.P.	U.S.
Automobile self-starter	1911	Kettering	U.S.
Automobile, steam	1889	Roper	U.S.
Babbitt metal	1839	Babbitt	U.S.
Bakelite	1907	Baekeland	Belg., U.S.
Balloon	1783	Montgolfier	French
Barometer	1643	Torricelli	Italian
Bicycle, modern	1884	Starley	English
Bifocal lens	1780	Franklin	U.S.
Block signals, railway	1867	Hall	U.S.
Bomb, depth	1916	Tait	U.S.
Bottle machine	1903	Owens	U.S.
Braille printing	1829	Braille	French
Burner, gas	1855	Bunsen	German
Calculating machine	1823	Babbage	English
Camera—see also Photography			
Camera, Kodak	1888	Eastman, Walker	U.S.
Camera, Polaroid Land	1948	Land	U.S.
Car coupler	1873	Janney	U.S.
Carburetor, gasoline	1876	Daimler	German
Card time recorder	1894	Cooper	U.S.
Carding machine	1797	Whittemore	U.S.
Carpet sweeper	1876	Bissell	U.S.
Cash register	1879	Ritty	U.S.
Cathode ray tube	1878	Crookes	English
Cellophane	1911	Brandenberger	Swiss
Celluloid	1870	Hyatt	U.S.
Cement, Portland	1845	Aspdin	English
Chronometer	1735	Harrison	English
Circuit breaker	1925	Hilliard	U.S.
Clock, pendulum	1657	Huygens	Dutch
Coaxial cable system	1929	Affel, Espenschied	U.S.
Coke oven	1893	Hoffman	Austrian
Compressed air rock drill	1871	Ingersoll	U.S.
Comptometer	1887	Felt	U.S.
Computer, automatic sequence	1939	Aiken et al.	U.S.
Condenser microphone (telephone)	1920	Wente	U.S.
Corn, hybrid	1917	Jones	U.S.
Cotton gin	1793	Whitney	U.S.
Cream separator	1880	DeLaval	Swedish
Cultivator, disc	1878	Mallon	U.S.
Cystoscope	1877	Nitze	German
Dental plate, rubber	1855	Goodyear	U.S.
Diesel engine	1895	Diesel	German
Dynamite	1866	Nobel	Swedish
Dynamo, continuous current	1860	Picinotti	Italian
Dynamo, hydrogen cooled	1915	Schuler	U.S.
Electric battery	1800	Volta	Italian
Electric fan	1882	Wheeler	U.S.
Electrocardiograph	1903	Einthoven	Dutch
Electroencephalograph	1929	Berger	German
Electromagnet	1824	Sturgeon	English
Electron spectrometer	1944	Deutsch, Elliott, Evans	U.S.
Electron tube multigrid	1913	Langmuir	U.S.
Electroplating	1805	Brugnatelli	Italian
Electrostatic generator	1929	Van de Graff	U.S.
Elevator brake	1852	Otis	U.S.
Elevator, push button	1922	Larson	U.S.
Engine, automobile	1879	Benz	German
Engine, coal-gas 4-cycle	1877	Otto	German
Engine, compression ignition	1883	Daimler	German
Engine, electric ignition	1880	Benz	German
Engine, gas, compound	1926	Eickemeyer	U.S.
Engine, gasoline	1872	Brayton, Geo.	U.S.
Engine, gasoline	1886	Daimler	German
Engine, steam, piston	1705	Newcomen	English
Engine, steam, piston	1769	Watt	Scottish
Engraving, half-tone	1893	Ives	U.S.
Filament, tungsten	1915	Langmuir	U.S.
Flanged rail	1831	Stevens	U.S.
Flatiron, electric	1882	Seeley	U.S.
Furnace (for steel)	1861	Siemens	German
Galvanometer	1820	Sweigger	German
Gas discharge tube	1922	Hull	U.S.
Gas lighting	1792	Murdoch	Scottish
Gas mantle	1885	Welsbach	Austrian
Gasoline (lead ethyl)	1922	Midgely	U.S.
Gasoline, cracked	1913	Burton	U.S.
Gasoline, high octane	1930	Ipatieff	Russian
Geiger counter	1913	Geiger	German
Glass, laminated safety	1909	Benedictus	French
Glider	1853	Cayley	English
Gun, breechloader	1811	Thornton	U.S.
Gun, Browning	1916	Browning	U.S.
Gun, magazine	1875	Hotchkiss	U.S.
Gun, silencer	1909	Maxim, H. P.	U.S.
Guncotton	1846	Schoenbein	German
Gyrocompass	1911	Sperry	U.S.
Gyroscope	1852	Foucault	French
Harvester-thresher	1888	Matteson	U.S.
Helicopter	1939	Sikorsky	U.S.
Hydrometer	1768	Baume	French
Ice-making machine	1851	Gorrie	U.S.
Iron lung	1928	Drinker, Slaw.	U.S.
Kaleidoscope	1817	Brewster	English
Kinetoscope	1887	Edison	U.S.
Lacquer, nitrocellulose	1921	Flaherty	U.S.
Lamp, arc	1879	Brush	U.S.
Lamp, incandescent	1879	Edison	U.S.
Lamp, incand., frosted	1924	Pipkin	U.S.
Lamp, incand., gas	1916	Langmuir	U.S.
Lamp, Klieg	1911	Kliegl, A.&J.	U.S.
Lamp, mercury vapor	1912	Hewitt	U.S.
Lamp, miner's safety	1816	Davy	English
Lamp, neon	1915	Claude	French
Lathe, turret	1845	Fitch	U.S.
Launderette	1934	Cantrell	U.S.
Lens, achromatic	1758	Dollond	English
Lens, fused bifocal	1908	Borsch	U.S.
Leydenjar (condenser)	1745	von Kleist	German
Lightning rod	1752	Franklin	U.S.
Linoleum	1860	Walton	English
Linotype	1885	Mergenthaler	U.S.
Lock, cylinder	1865	Yale	U.S.
Locomotive, electric	1851	Vail	U.S.
Locomotive, exp'mtl.	1801	Trevithick	English
Locomotive, exp'mtl.	1812	Fenton et al	English
Locomotive, exp'mtl.	1813	Hedley	English
Locomotive, exp'mtl.	1814	Stephenson	English
Locomotive practical	1829	Stephenson	English
Locomotive, 1st U.S.	1830	Cooper, P.	U.S.
Loom, power	1785	Cartwright	English
Loudspeaker, dynamic	1924	Rice, Kellogg	U.S.
Machine gun	1861	Gatling	U.S.
Machine gun, improved	1872	Hotchkiss	U.S.
Machine gun (Maxim)	1883	Maxim, H.S.	U.S., Eng.
Magnet, electro	1828	Henry	U.S.
Mantle, gas	1885	Welsbach	Austrian
Mason jar	1858	Mason, J.	U.S.
Match, friction	1827	John Walker	English
Mercerized textiles	1843	Mercer, J.	English

Invention	Date	Inventor	Nation.
Meter, induction	1888	Shallenberger.	U.S.
Metronome	1816	Malzel	Austrian
Micrometer	1636	Gascoigne	English
Microphone	1877	Berliner	U.S.
Microscope, compound	1590	Janssen	Dutch
Microscope, electronic	1931	Knoll, Ruska	German
Microscope, fieldion	1951	Mueller	Germany
Monitor, warship	1861	Ericsson	U.S.
Monotype	1887	Lanston	U.S.
Motor, AC	1892	Tesla	U.S.
Motor, induction	1887	Tesla	U. S.
Motorcycle	1885	Daimler	German
Movie machine	1894	Jenkins	U. S.
Movie, panoramic	1952	Waller	U. S.
Movie, talking	1927	Warner Bros.	U. S.
Mower, lawn	1868	Hills	U. S.
Mowing machine	1831	Manning	U. S.
Neoprene	1930	Carothers	U. S.
Nylon synthetic	1930	Carothers	U. S.
Nylon	1937	Du Pont lab.	U. S.
Oil cracking furnace	1891	Gavrilov	Russian
Oil filled power cable	1921	Emanueli	Italian
Oleomargarine	1868	Mege-Mouries	French
Ophthalmoscope	1851	Helmholtz	German
Paper machine	1809	Dickinson	U. S.
Parachute	1785	Blanchard	French
Pen, ballpoint	1888	Loud	U. S.
Pen, fountain	1884	Waterman	U. S.
Pen, steel	1780	Harrison	English
Pendulum	1581	Galileo	Italian
Percussion cap	1814	Shaw	U. S.
Phonograph	1877	Edison	U. S.
Photo, color	1892	Ives	U. S.
Photo film, celluloid	1887	Goodwin	U. S.
Photo film, transparent	1878	Eastman, Goodwin	U.S.
Photoelectric cell	1895	Elster	German
Photographic paper	1898	Baekeland	U. S.
Photography	1835	Talbot	English
Photography	1837	Daguerre	French
Photography	1839	Niepce	French
Photophone	1880	Bell	U. S.
Phototelegraphy	1925	Bell lab	U. S.
Piano	1709	Cristofori	Italian
Piano, player	1863	Fourneaux	French
Pin, safety	1849	Hunt	U. S.
Pistol (revolver)	1835	Colt	U. S.
Plow, cast iron	1797	Newbold	U. S.
Plow, disc	1896	Hardy	U. S.
Pneumatic hammer	1890	King	U. S.
Powder, smokeless	1863	Schultze	German
Printing press, rotary	1846	Hoe	U. S.
Printing press, web	1865	Bullock	U. S.
Propeller, screw	1804	Stevens	U. S.
Propeller, screw	1837	Ericsson	Swedish
Punch card accounting	1884	Hollerith	U. S.
Radar	1922	Taylor, Young	U.S.
Radio amplifier	1907	De Forest	U. S.
Radio beacon	1928	Donovan	U. S.
Radio crystal oscillator	1918	Nicolson	U. S.
Radio receiver, cascade tuning	1913	Alexanderson	U. S.
Radio receiver, heterodyne	1913	Fessenden	U. S.
Radio transmitter triode modulation	1914	Alexanderson	U. S.
Radio tube-diode	1905	Fleming	English
Radio tube oscillator	1915	De Forest	U. S.
Radio tube triode	1907	De Forest	U. S.
Radio, signals	1895	Marconi	Italian
Radio, magnetic detector	1902	Marconi	Italian
Radio FM 2-path	1929	Armstrong	U. S.
Rayon	1883	Swan	English
Razor, electric	1931	Schick	U. S.
Razor, safety	1895	Gillette	U. S.
Reaper	1834	McCormick	U. S.
Record, cylinder	1887	Bell, Tainter	U. S.
Record, disc	1887	Berliner	U. S.
Record, long playing	1948	Goldmark	U. S.
Record, wax cylinder	1888	Edison	U. S.
Refrigerants, low-boiling fluorine compound	1930	Midgely and co-workers	U.S.
Refrigerator car	1868	David	U. S.

Invention	Date	Inventor	Nation.
Resin, synthetic	1931	Hill	English
Rifle, repeating	1860	Spencer	U. S.
Rocket engine	1929	Goddard	U.S.
Rubber, vulcanized	1839	Goodyear	U. S.
Saw, band	1808	Newberry	English
Saw, circular	1777	Miller	English
Searchlight, arc	1915	Sperry	U. S.
Sewing machine	1846	Howe	U. S.
Shoe-sewing machine	1860	McKay	U. S.
Shrapnel shell	1784	Shrapnel	English
Shuttle, flying	1733	Kay	English
Sleeping-car	1858	Pullman	U. S.
Slide rule	1620	Oughtred	English
Soap, hardwater	1928	Bertsch	German
Spectroscope	1859	Kirchoff, Bunsen	German
Spectroscope (mass)	1918	Dempster	U. S.
Spinning jenny	1767	Hargreaves	English
Spinning mule	1779	Crompton	English
Steamboat, exp'mtl.	1783	Jouffroy	French
Steamboat, exp'mtl.	1785	Fitch	U. S.
Steamboat, exp'mtl.	1787	Rumsey	U. S.
Steamboat, exp'mtl.	1788	Miller	Scottish
Steamboat, exp'mtl.	1803	Fulton	U. S.
Steamboat, exp'mtl.	1804	Stevens	U. S.
Steamboat, practical	1802	Symington	Scottish
Steamboat, practical	1807	Fulton	U. S.
Steam car	1770	Cugnot	French
Steam turbine	1884	Parsons	English
Steel	1856	Bessemer	English
Steel alloy	1891	Harvey	U. S.
Steel alloy, high-speed	1901	Taylor, White	U. S.
Steel, electric	1900	Heroult	French
Steel, manganese	1884	Hadfield	English
Steel, stainless	1916	Brearley	English
Stereoscope	1838	Wheatstone	English
Stethoscope	1819	Laennec	French
Stethoscope, binaural	1840	Cammann	U. S.
Stock ticker	1870	Edison	U. S.
Storage battery, electric	1812	Ritter	German
Stove, electric	1896	Hadaway	U. S.
Submarine	1891	Holland	U. S.
Submarine, even keel	1894	Lake	U. S.
Submarine, torpedo	1776	Bushnell	U. S.
Tank, military	1914	Swinton	English
Tape recorder, magnetic	1899	Poulsen	Danish
Telegraph, magnetic	1837	Morse	U. S.
Telegraph, quadruplex	1874	Edison	U. S.
Telegraph, railroad	. . .	Woods	U.S.
Telegraph, wireless, high frequency	1896	Marconi	Italian
Telephone	1876	Bell	U.S.-Can.
Telephone amplifier	1912	De Forest	U. S.
Telephone, automatic	1891	Stowger	U.S.
Telephone, radio	1902	Poulsen, Fessenden	U. S.
Telephone, radio	1906	De Forest	U. S.
Telephone, radio, l. d.	1915	AT&T	U. S.
Telephone, recording	1898	Poulson	Danish
Telephone, wireless	1899	Collins	U. S.
Telescope	1608	Lippershey	Neth.
Telescope	1609	Galileo	Italian
Telescope, astronomical	1611	Kepler	German
Teletype	1928	Morkrum, Kleinschmidt	U. S.
Television, iconoscope	1923	Zworykin	U.S.
Television, electronic	1927	Farnsworth	U.S.
Television, (mech. scanner)	1926	Baird	Scottish
Thermometer	1593	Galileo	Italian
Thermometer	1710	Reaumur	French
Thermometer, mercury	1714	Fahrenheit	German
Time recorder	1890	Bundy	U. S.
Time, self-regulator	1918	Bryce	U. S.
Tire, double-tube	1845	Thompson	English
Tire, pneumatic	1888	Dunlop	Irish
Toaster, automatic	1918	Strite	U. S.
Tool, pneumatic	1865	Law	English
Torpedo, marine	1804	Fulton	U. S.
Tractor, crawler	1900	Holt	U. S.
Transformer A.C.	1885	Stanley	U. S.
Transistor	1947	Shockley, Brattain, Bardeen	U. S.
Trolley car, electric	1884-87	Van Depoel, Sprague	U. S.

Invention	Date	Inventor	Nation.
Tungsten, ductile	1912	Coolidge	U. S.
Turbine, gas	1899	Curtis, C.G.	U. S.
Turbine, hydraulic	1849	Francis	U. S.
Turbine, steam	1896	Curtis, C.G.	U. S.
Type, movable	1450	Gutenberg	German
Typewriter	1868	Soule, Glidden	U. S.
Vacuum cleaner, electric	1907	Spangler	U. S.
Washer, electric	1907	Hurley Co.	U. S.
Welding, atomic hydrogen	1924	Langmuir, Palmer	U. S.
Welding, electric	1877	Thomson	U. S.
Wind tunnel	1923	Munk	U. S.
Wire, barbed	1874	Glidden	U. S.
Wire, barbed	1875	Haisn	U. S.
X-ray tube	1913	Coolidge	U. S.
Zipper	1891	Judson	U. S.

Discoveries and Innovations: Chemistry, Physics, Biology, Medicine

	Date	Discoverer	Nation.
Acetylene gas	1892	Wilson	U.S.
ACTH	1949	Armour & Co.	U.S.
Adrenalin	1901	Takamine	Japan
Aluminum, electrolytic process	1886	Hall	U.S.
Aluminum, isolated	1825	Oersted	Danish
Analine dye	1856	Perkin	English
Anesthesia, ether	1842	Long	U.S.
Anesthesia, local	1885	Koller	Austria
Anesthesia, spinal	1898	Bier	German
Anti-rabies	1885	Pasteur	French
Antiseptic surgery	1867	Lister	English
Antitoxin, diphtheria	1891	Von Behring	German
Argyrol	...	Barnes	U.S.
Arsphenamine	1910	Ehrlich	German
Aspirin	1889	Dresser	German
Atabrine	...	Mietzsch, et al	German
Atomic numbers	1913	Moseley	English
Atomic theory	1803	Dalton	English
Atomic time clock	1947	Libby	U.S.
Atom-smashing theory	1919	Rutherford	English
Aureomycin	1948	Duggar	U.S.
Bacitracin	1945	Johnson, et al	U.S.
Bacteria (described)	1676	Leeuwenhoek	Dutch
Barbital	1903	Fischer	German
Bleaching powder	1798	Tennant	English
Blood, circulation	1628	Harvey	English
Bordeaux mixture	1885	Millardet	French
Bromine from sea	1924	Edgar, Kramer	U.S.
Calcium carbide	1888	Wilson	U.S.
Calculus	1670	Newton	English
Camphor synthetic	1896	Haller	French
Canning (food)	1804	Appert	French
Carbomycin	1952	Tanner	U.S.
Carbon oxides	1925	Fisher	German
Chlorine	1810	Davy	English
Chloroform	1831	Guthrie, S.	U.S.
Chloromycetin	1947	Burkholder	U.S.
Classification of plants and animals	1735	Linnaeus	Swedish
Cocaine	1860	Niermann	German
Combustion explained	1777	Lavoisier	French
Conditioned reflex	1914	Pavlov	Russian
Conteban	1950	Belmisch, Mietzsch, Domagk	German
Cortisone	1936	Kendall	U.S.
Cortisone, synthesis	1946	Sarett	U.S.
Cosmic rays	1910	Gockel	Swiss
Cyanimide	1905	Frank, Caro	German
Cyclotron	1930	Lawrence	U.S.
DDT (not applied as insecticide until 1939)	1874	Zeidler	German
Deuterium	1932	Urey, Brickwedde, Murphy	U.S.
DNA (structure)	1951	Crick	English
		Watson	U.S.
		Wilkins	English
Electric resistance (law)	1827	Ohm	German
Electric waves	1888	Hertz	German
Electrolysis	1852	Faraday	English
Electromagnetism	1819	Oersted	Danish
Electron	1897	Thomson, J.	English
Electron diffraction	1936	Thomson, G.	English
		Davisson	U.S.
Electroshock treatment	1938	Cerletti, Bini	Italy
Erythromycin	1952	McGuire	U.S.
Evolution, natural selection	1858	Darwin	English
Falling bodies, law	1590	Galileo	Italian
Gases, law of combining volumes	1808	Gay-Lussac	French
Geometry, analytic	1619	Descartes	French
Gold (cyanide process for extraction)	1887	MacArthur, Forest	British
Gravitation, law	1687	Newton	English
Holograph	1948	Gabor	British
Human heart transplant	1967	Barnard	S. Africa
Indigo, synthesis of	1880	Baeyer	German
Induction, electric	1830	Henry	U.S.
Insulin	1922	Banting, Best, MacLeod	Canada
Intelligence testing	1905	Binet, Simon	French
Isniazid	1952	Hoffman-La-Roche	U.S.
		Domagk	German
Isotopes, theory	1912	Soddy	English
Laser (light amplification by stimulated emission of radiation)	1958	Townes,Schawlow	U.S.
Light, velocity	1675	Roemer	Danish
Light, wave theory	1690	Huygens	Dutch
Lithography	1796	Senefelder,	Bohemia
Lobotomy	1935	Egas Moniz	Portugal
LSD-25	1943	Hoffman	Swiss
Mendelian laws	1866	Mendel	Austrian
Mercator projection (map)	1568	Mercator (Kremer)	Flemish
Methanol	1925	Patard	French
Milk condensation	1853	Borden	U.S.
Molecular hypothesis	1811	Avogadro	Italian
Motion, laws of	1687	Newton	English
Neomycin	1949	Waksman, Lechevalier	U.S.
Neutron	1932	Chadwick	English
Nitric acid	1648	Glauber	German
Nitric oxide	1772	Priestley	English
Nitroglycerin	1846	Sobrero	Italian
Oil cracking process	1891	Dewar	U.S.
Oxygen	1774	Priestley	English
Ozone	1840	Schonbein	German
Paper, sulfite process	1867	Tilghman	U.S.
Paper, wood pulp, sulfate process	1884	Dahl	German
Penicillin	1929	Fleming	English
Practical use	1941	Florey, Chain	English
Periodic law and table of elements	1869	Mendelyev	Russian
Planetary motion, laws	1609	Kepler	German
Plutonium fission	1940	Kennedy, Wahl, Seaborg, Segre	U.S.
Polymixin	1947	Ainsworth	English
Positron	1932	Anderson	U.S.
Proton	1919	Rutherford	English
Psychoanalysis	1900	Freud	Austrian
Quantum theory	1900	Planck	German
Quasars	1963	Matthews, Sandage	U.S.

	Date	Discoverer	Nation.
Quinine-synthetic	1918	Rabe	German
Radioactivity	1896	Becquerel	French
Radium	1898	Curie, Pierre	French
		Curie, Marie	Pol.-Fr.
Relativity theory	1905	Einstein	German
Reserpine	1949	Jal Vaikl	India
Salvarsan (606)	1910	Ehrlich	German
Schick test	1913	Schick	U.S.
Silicon	1823	Berzelius	Swedish
Streptomycin	1945	Waksman	U.S.
Sulfadiazine	1940	Roblin	U.S.
Sulfanilamide	1934	Domagk	German
Sulfanilamide theory	1908	Gelmo	German
Sulfapyridine	1938	Ewins, Phelps	English
Sulfathiazole	...	Fosbinder, Walter	U.S.
Sulfuric acid	1831	Phillips	English
Sulfuric acid, lead	1746	Roebuck	English
Terramycin	1950	Finlay, et al	U.S.
Tuberculin	1890	Koch	German
Uranium fission (theory)	1939	Hahn, Strassmann	German
		Bohr	Danish
		Fermi	Italian
		Einstein, Pegram	U.S.
		Wheeler	U.S.
Uranium fission Atomic reactor	1942	Fermi Szilard	U.S.
Vaccine, measles	1954	Enders, Peebles	U.S.
Vaccine, polio	1953	Salk	U.S.
Vaccine, polio, oral	1955	Sabin	U.S.
Vaccine, rabies	1885	Pasteur	French
Vaccine, smallpox	1796	Jenner	English
Vaccine, typhus	1909	Nicolle	French
Van Allen belts, radiation	1958	Van Allen	U.S.
Vitamin A	1913	McCollum, Davis	U.S.
Vitamin B	1916	McCollum	U.S.
Vitamin C	1912	Holst, Froelich	Norway
Vitamin D	1922	McCollum	U.S.
Wassermann test	1906	Wassermann	German
Xerography	1938	Carlson	U.S.
X-ray	1895	Roentgen	German

Electrical Units

The **watt** is the unit of power (electrical, mechanical, thermal, etc.). Electrical power is given by the product of the voltage and the current.

Energy is sold by the **joule**, but in common practice the billing of electrical energy is expressed in terms of the **kilowatt-hour**, which is 3,600,000 joules or 3.6 megajoules.

The **horsepower** is a non-metric unit sometimes used in mechanics. It is equal to 746 watts.

The **ohm** is the unit of electrical resistance and represents the physical property of a conductor which offers a resistance to the flow of electricity, permitting just 1 ampere to flow at 1 volt of pressure.

Breaking the Sound Barrier; Speed of Sound

The prefix Mach is used to describe supersonic speed. It derives from Ernst Mach, a Czech-born German physicist, who contributed to the study of sound. When a plane moves at the speed of sound it is Mach 1. When twice the speed of sound it is Mach 2. When it is near but below the speed of sound its speed can be designated at less than Mach 1, for example, Mach .0. Mach is defined as "in jet propulsion, the ratio of the velocity of a rocket or a jet to the velocity of sound in the medium being considered."

When a plane passes the sound barrier—flying faster than sound travels—listeners in the area hear thunder-claps, but pilots do not hear them.

Sound is produced by vibrations of an object and is transmitted by alternate increase and decrease in pressures that radiate outward through a material media of molecules-somewhat like waves spreading out on a pond after a rock has been tossed.

The frequency of sound is determined by the number of times the vibrating waves undulate per second, and is measured in cycles per second. The slower the cycle of waves, the lower the sound. As frequencies increase, the sound is higher.

Sound is audible to human beings only if the frequency falls within a certain range. The human ear is usually not sensitive to frequencies of less than 20 vibrations per second, or more than about 20,000 vibrations per second-although this range varies among individuals. Anything at a pitch higher than the human ear can hear is termed ultrasonic.

Intensity or loudness is the strength of the pressure of these radiating waves, and is measured in decibels. The human ear responds to intensity in a range from zero to 120 decibels. Any sound with pressure over 120 decibels is painful.

The speed of sound is generally placed at 1,088 ft. per second at sea level at 32°F. It varies in other temperatures and in different media. Sound travels faster in water than in air, and even faster in iron and steel. If in air it travels a mile in 5 seconds, it does a mile under water in 1 second, and through iron in 1/3 of a second. It travels through ice cold vapor at approximately 4,708 ft. per sec., ice-cold water. 4,938; granite, 12,960; hardwood, 12,620; brick, 11,-960; glass, 16,410 to 19,690; silver, 8,658; gold, 5,717.

Colors of the Spectrum

Color, an electromagnetic wave phenomenon, is a sensation produced through the excitation of the retina of the eye by rays of light. The colors of the spectrum may be produced by viewing a light beam refracted by passage through a prism, which breaks the light into its wave lengths.

Customarily, the primary colors of the spectrum are thought of as those 6 monochromatic colors which occupy relatively large areas of the spectrum: red, orange, yellow, green, blue, and violet. However, Sir Isaac Newton named a 7th, indigo, situated between blue and violet on the spectrum. Aubert estimated (1865) the solar spectrum to contain approximately 1,000 distinguishable hues of which according to Rood (1881) 2 million tints and shades can be distinguished; Luckiesh stated (1915) that 55 distinctly different hues have been seen in a single spectrum.

By many physicists only 3 primary colors are recognized: red, yellow, and blue (Mayer, 1775); red, green, and violet (Thomas Young, 1801); red, green, and blue (Clerk Maxwell, 1860).

The color sensation of black is due to complete lack of stimulation of the retina, that of white to complete stimulation. The infra-red and ultra-violet rays, below the red (long) end of the spectrum and the violet end (short end) respectively, are invisible. Heat is the principal effect of the infra-red rays and chemical action that of the ultra-violet rays.

Copyright Law of the U.S.

Source: Copyright Office, Library of Congress

Original works of authorship fixed in any tangible medium of expression are entitled to protection under the copyright law (Title 17 of the United States Code) in accordance with a complete revision of the statute which was signed by President Gerald R. Ford on October 19, 1976 (Public Law 94-553, 90 Stat. 2541). When the new law becomes fully effective on January 1, 1978, it will take the place of the Act of 1909, as amended. Prior to the 1976 Act, there had been only three general revisions of the original copyright law of 1790, namely those of 1831, 1870, and 1909.

Categories of Works

Copyright protection under the new law extends to original works of authorship fixed in any tangible medium of expression, now known or later developed, from which they can be perceived, reproduced, or otherwise communicated, either directly or with the aid of a machine or device. Works of authorship include books, periodicals and other literary works, musical compositions with accompanying lyrics, dramas and dramatico-musical compositions, pantomimes and choreographic works, motion pictures and other audiovisual works, and sound recordings.

The owner of a copyright will be given the exclusive right to reproduce the copyrighted work in copies or phonorecords and distribute them to the public by sale, rental, lease, or lending. The owner of a copyright will also enjoy the exclusive right to make derivative works based upon the copyrighted work, to perform the work publicly if it be a literary, musical, dramatic, or choreographic work, a pantomime, motion picture, or other audiovisual work, and in the case of literary, musical, dramatic, and choreographic works, pantomimes, and pictorial, graphic, or sculptural works, including the individual images of a motion picture or other audiovisual work, to display the copyrighted work publicly. All of these rights are subject to certain specified exceptions, including the so-called judicial doctrine of "fair use," part of the new statute.

Also included in the new act are special provisions permitting compulsory licensing for the recording and distribution of phonorecords of nondramatic musical compositions, non-commercial transmissions by public broadcasters of published musical and graphic works, performances of copyrighted nondramatic music by means of jukeboxes, and the secondary transmission of copyrighted works on cable television systems.

Single National System

Under the present 1909 law, unpublished works are entitled to protection under the common law before they are published and under the Federal statute after publication has occurred. The new law will establish a single system of statutory protection for all copyrightable works fixed in tangible form, whether published or unpublished.

Registration of a claim to copyright in any work, whether published or unpublished, may be made voluntarily at any time during the copyright term by the owner of the copyright or of any exclusive right in the work. Registration will not be a condition of copyright protection, but will be a prerequisite to an infringement suit. Subject to certain exceptions, the remedies of statutory damages and attorney's fees will not be available for those infringements occurring before registration. Even if registration is not made, copies or phonorecords of works published in the U.S. with notice of copyright are required to be deposited for the collections of the Library of Congress. This deposit requirement is not a condition of protection, but does render the copyright owner subject to penalties for failure to deposit after a demand by the Register of Copyrights.

Duration of Copyright

For works created on or after January 1, 1978, copyright will subsist from their creation for a term consisting of the life of the author and 50 years after the author's death. For works made for hire, and for anonymous and pseudonymous works (unless the author's identity is revealed in Copyright Office records), the new term will be 75 years from publication or 100 years from creation, whichever is shorter.

The new law retains for works already under statutory protection, the present term of copyright of 28 years from first publication (or from registration in some cases), renewable by certain persons for a second term of protection, but it increases the length of the second or renewal period to 47 years. Copyrights in their first 28-year term on January 1, 1978, will still have to be renewed in order to be protected for the full new maximum term of 75 years, but copyrights that have already been renewed and are in their second term at any time between December 31, 1976, and December 31, 1977, inclusive, are automatically extended to last for a total term of 75 years from the date they were originally secured.

For unpublished works already in existence on January 1, 1978, but that are not protected by statutory copyright and have not yet entered the public domain, the new Act will generally provide automatic Federal copyright protection for the same life-plus-50 or 75/100-year terms provided for newly created works. However, all works in this category are guaranteed at least 25 years of statutory protection. The law specifies that copyright in a work of this kind will not expire before December 31, 2002, and if the work is published before that date the term is extended by another 25 years, through the end of the year 2027.

Notice of Copyright

The presence of a notice of copyright on the published copies of a work is a mandatory condition of copyright protection under the present 1909 Act. However, although the new law also requires a notice on published copies, omissions or errors will not immediately result in forfeiture of the copyright, and can be corrected within prescribed time limits. Moreover, innocent infringers misled by an omission or error will be shielded from liability.

The notice of copyright required on all visually perceptible copies published in the U.S. or elsewhere under the 1976 Act consists of the symbol © (the letter C in a circle), the word "Copyright," or the abbreviation "Copr.," and the year of first publication of the work, and the name of the owner of copyright in the work. Example:

© 1978 JOHN DOE

The notice must be affixed in such manner and location as to give reasonable notice of the claim of copyright.

The notice of copyright prescribed for all published phonorecords of sound recordings consists of the symbol ℗ (the letter P in a circle), the year of first publication of the sound recording, and the name of the owner of copyright in the sound recording, placed on the surface of the phonorecord, or on the phonorecord label or container in such manner and location as to give reasonable notice of the claim of copyright. Example:

℗ 1978 DOE RECORDS, INC.

Manufacturing Requirements

Certain works must now be manufactured in the U.S. to have copyright protection under U.S. law. The new act would terminate this requirement completely after July 1, 1982. For the period between January 1, 1978 and July 1, 1982, the law narrows the coverage of the manufacturing provisions, permits the importation of 2,000 copies manufactured abroad instead of the present limit of 1,500 copies, and will equate manufacture in Canada with manufacture in the U.S.

The requirements of the 1976 act apply to works in the English language consisting preponderantly of nondramatic literary material, and would not thus extend to: dramatic, musical, pictorial, or graphic works; foreign-language, bilingual, or multilingual works; public domain material; or works consisting preponderantly of material that is not subject to the manufacturing requirement.

Under the new statute, compliance with the manufacturing requirements will no longer constitute a condition of copyright, but, in cases where the requirements are not satisfied, the rights with respect to reproduction and the distribution of copies are limited as against certain infringers. The special "ad interim" time limits and registration requirements of the present law are done away with by the 1976 Act. Even if copies are imported or distributed in violation of the new law, there would be no effect on the copyright owner's right to make and distribute phonorecords of the work, to make derivative works including dramatizations and motion pictures, and to perform or display the work publicly.

International Protection

The U.S. has copyright relations with more than 70 countries, under which works of American authors are protected in those countries, and the works of their authors are protected in the U.S. The basic feature of this protection is "national treatment," under which the alien author is treated by a country in the same manner that it treats its own authors. Relations exist by virtue of bilateral agreements or through the Buenos Aires Convention or the Universal Copyright Convention. U.S. legislation implementing the latter convention, which became effective September 16, 1955, gives the works of foreign authors the benefit of exemptions from the manufacturing requirements of the U.S. copyright law, provided the works are first published abroad with a copyright notice including the symbol ©, the name of the copyright owner and the year date of first publication, and that the work either is by an "author" who is a citizen or subject of a foreign country which belongs to the Convention or is first published in a foreign member country. Conversely, works of U.S. authors are exempt from certain burdensome requirements in particular foreign member countries.

Works published on or after January 1, 1978, are subject to protection under the new copyright statute if, on the date of first publication, one or more of the authors is a national or domiciliary of the U.S., or is a national, domiciliary, or sovereign authority of a foreign nation that is a party to a copyright treaty to which the United States is also a party, or is a stateless person, regardless of domicile, or if the work is first published either in the U.S. or in a foreign nation that, on the date of first publication is a party to the Universal Copyright Convention.

A U.S. citizen may obtain copyright protection in all countries that are members of the Universal Copyright Convention (UCC), provided the copyright notice appears on all copies from the date of first publication includes the symbol ©, together with the name of the copyright owner and the year date of publication. Example:

© JOHN DOE 1978

Further information and application forms may be obtained free of charge by writing to the Copyright Office, The Library of Congress, Washington, D. C. 20559.

Trademarks: How to Obtain and Protect Them

A trademark, as defined by Act of congress, "includes any word, name, symbol, or device, or any combination thereof, adopted and used by a manufacturer or merchant to identify his goods and distinguish them from those manufactured or sold by others." Rights in trademarks are acquired by use, which must continue if those rights are to be preserved. In order to be eligible for registration a mark must be in use in commerce which may be lawfully regulated by Congress.

Trademarks are registered on the Principal Register and the Supplemental Register of the U.S. Patent and Trademark Office. "Coined, arbitrary, fanciful or suggestive marks, usually called technical marks, if otherwise qualified," may be registered on the Principal Register. A trademark that is merely descriptive of goods, or their regional origin, or is primarily a surname, is placed on the Supplemental Register.

The Trademark Act of 1946 provides that "For the purposes of registration on the supplemental register, a mark may consist of any trademark, symbol, label package, configuration of goods, name, word, slogan, phrase, surname, geographical name, numeral, or device, or any combination of any of the foregoing, but such mark must be capable of distinguishing the applicant's goods or services."

A trademark cannot be registered if it comprises immoral, deceptive or scandalous matter, or matter that may disparage or falsely suggest a connection with persons living or dead, institutions, beliefs, or national symbols. It cannot use the flag or coat of arms or other insignia of the United States, any state, municipality or foreign nation. It cannot use a portrait, signature or name of a living individual without his consent, or those of a deceased President of the United States without consent of his widow.

An application for registration must be filed in the name of the owner of the mark, who may submit his case or be represented by an attorney at law, or other person authorized to practice in trademark matters. A complete application comprises a written application, a drawing of the mark, five specimens or facsimiles and the filing fee.

The Patent and Trademark Office publishes a pamphlet, General Information Concerning Trademarks, which describes the way applications and drawings are to be prepared and gives sample forms for applications. The Patent and Trademark Office, upon request, will supply forms for the registration of a trademark in the name of (1) an individual, (2) a firm, and (3) a corporation. If facilities permit, the Office will make drawings from the applicant's direction and at his expense. If the application is allowed, the trademark will be published in the Trademark Official Gazette so that anyone who considers that he will be damaged by the new mark may file his opposition in 30 days.

The Trademark Act of 1946 also provides for the registration of service marks, certification marks and collective marks. A service mark is a title, symbol or name used in sale or advertising of services to identify them. A certification mark is used by others than the owner to certify origin or quality, such as work by a union. A collective mark is used by members of a cooperative, an association or other group and indicates membership in a union or other organization. A digest of registered trademarks may be inspected at the Patent and Trademark Office.

A trademark is registered for 20 years and may be renewed for periods of 20 years if still in use in commerce regulated by Congress, or if nonuse is due to special circumstances which excuse nonuse and is not due to any intention to abandon the mark. The fee for the original application is $35, and for the renewal is $25, with lesser fees for other services.

The pamphlet, General Information Concerning Trademarks, is a general guide. Inquiries may be addressed to the Supt. of Documents, Government Printing Office, Washington, D.C. 20402.

Patents and How to Apply for Them

A patent for an invention is granted by the U.S. Patent and Trademark Office to the inventor of any new and useful process, machine, manufacture, or composition of matter, or any new and useful improvements in these categories. The grant to the patentee is of "the right to exclude others from making, using or selling the invention throughout the U.S." for 17 years. A patent is also granted for certain distinct and new varieties of plants, also for 17 years.

Patents for new, original and ornamental designs for articles of manufacture may be obtained for 3 1/2, 7, and 14 years, as requested by the inventor. The filing fee on each design application is $20; the issue fee is $10 for a 3 1/2-yr. term, $20 for 7 years and $30 for 14 years.

Except in special circumstances, an application must be made by the inventor; if 2 are associated in the invention both must apply; if the inventor is mentally ill or dead, application may be made by the guardian or administrator of the estate. The specification must include a written description of the invention and of the manner and process of making and using it, and is required to be in such full, clear, concise, and exact terms as to enable any person skilled in the art to which the invention pertains, or with which it is most nearly connected, to make and use the same. The claims are full descriptions of the subject matter of the invention. A drawing is required by the statute in all cases which admit of drawings. The filing fee is $65, with $2 additional for each claim in excess of 10, and $10 additional for each claim in independent form in excess of one.

The Patent and Trademark Office examines the application to determine whether the invention is new and useful and whether the application otherwise complies with the law. If the application is allowed, a notice is sent the applicant and the final fee of $100, plus $10 for each page or portion thereof of specification as printed and $2 for each sheet of drawing, is due within 3 months. The terms "patent applied for" and "patent pending" have no legal significance but false usage is punishable by a fine.

If the Patent and Trademark Office rejects an application, the applicant may appeal to the Board of Appeals of the Patent and Trademark Office, and if rejected there, may go to the Court of Customs and Patent Appeals or file a civil action in a U.S. District Court.

Under certain conditions a license must be obtained before an application for a patent can be filed in a foreign country. The Commissioner of Patents and Trademarks may order an invention kept secret if publication would hurt the national safety or defense. Copies of the Patent Laws, Regulations (37 Code of Federal Regulations) and General Information Concerning Patents, can be obtained from the Superintendent of Documents, Government Printing Office, Washington, D.C. 20402.

Delegates from over 40 nations took part in Washington May 25-June 19, 1970, in a diplomatic conference on a Patent Cooperation Treaty. It was unanimously approved and was signed by representatives of 20 governments, including the United States, Great Britain, Germany, Canada, and Japan. The treaty will simplify the filing of patent applications on the same invention in different countries.

SPORTS OF 1977

Olympic Games Records

The modern Olympic Games, first held in Athens, Greece, in 1896, were the result of efforts by Baron Pierre de Coubertin, a French educator, to promote interest in education and culture, also to foster better international understanding through the universal medium of youth's love of athletics.

His source of inspiration for the Olympic Games was the ancient Greek Olympic Games, most notable of the four Panhellenic celebrations. The games were combined patriotic, religious, and athletic festivals held every four years. The first such recorded festival was that held in 776 B.C., the date from which the Greeks began to keep their calendar by "Olympiads," or four-year spans between the games.

The first Olympiad is said to have consisted merely of a 200-yard foot race near the small city of Olympia, but the games gained in scope and became demonstrations of national pride. Only Greek citizens — amateurs — were permitted to participate. Winners received laurel, wild olive, and palm wreaths and were accorded many special privileges. Under the Roman emperors, the games deteriorated into professional carnivals and circuses. Emperor Theodosius banned them in 394 A.D.

Baron de Coubertin enlisted 9 nations to send athletes to the first modern Olympics in 1896; now more than 100 nations compete. Winter Olympic Games were started in 1924.

Sites and Unofficial Winners of Games

1896 Athens (U.S.)
1900 Paris (U.S.)
1904 St. Louis (U.S.)
1906 Athens (U.S.)*
1908 London (U.S.)
1912 Stockholm (U.S.)
1920 Antwerp (U.S.)
1924 Paris (U.S.)
1928 Amsterdam (U.S.)
1932 Los Angeles (U.S.)
1936 Berlin (Germany)
1948 London (U.S.)
1952 Helsinki (U.S.)
1956 Melbourne (USSR)
1960 Rome (USSR)
1964 Tokyo (U.S.)
1968 Mexico City (U.S.)
1972 Munich (USSR)
1976 Montreal (USSR)
1980 Moscow (scheduled)

*Games not recognized by International Olympic Committee. Games 6 (1916), 12 (1940), and 13 (1944) were not celebrated. East and West Germany began competing separately in 1968.

Olympic Games Champions, 1896—1976

(*Indicates Olympic Record)

Track and Field — Men

60-Meter Run

1900	Alvin Kraenzlein, United States	7s*
1904	Archie Hahn, United States	7s*

100-Meter Run

1896	Thomas Burke, United States	12s
1900	Francis W. Jarvis, United States	10.8s
1904	Archie Hahn, United States	11s
1908	Reginald Walker, South Africa	10.8s
1912	Ralph Craig, United States	10.8s
1920	Charles Paddock, United States	10.8s
1924	Harold Abrahams, Great Britain	10.6s
1928	Percy Williams, Canada	10.8s
1932	Eddie Tolan, United States	10.3s
1936	Jesse Owens, United States	10.3s
1948	Harrison Dillard, United States	10.3s
1952	Lindy Remigino, United States	10.4s
1956	Bobby Morrow, United States	10.5s
1960	Armin Hary, Germany	10.2s
1964	Bob Hayes, United States	10.0s
1968	Jim Hines, United States	9.9s*
1972	Valeri Borzov, USSR	10.14s
1976	Hasely Crawford, Trinidad	10.06s

200-Meter Run

1900	Walter Tewksbury, United States	22.2s
1904	Archie Hahn, United States	21.6s
1908	Robert Kerr, Canada	22.4s
1912	Ralph Craig, United States	21.7s
1920	Allan Woodring, United States	22s
1924	Jackson Scholz, United States	21.6s
1928	Percy Williams, Canada	21.8s
1932	Eddie Tolan, United States	21.2s
1936	Jesse Owens, United States	20.7s
1948	Mel Patton, United States	21.1s
1952	Andrew Stanfield, United States	20.7s
1956	Bobby Morrow, United States	20.6s
1960	Livio Berruti, Italy	20.5s
1964	Henry Carr, United States	20.3s
1968	Tommie Smith, United States	19.8s*
1972	Valeri Borzov, USSR	20.00s
1976	Donald Quarrie, Jamaica	20.23s

400-Meter Run

1896	Thomas Burke, United States	54.2s
1900	Maxey Long, United States	49.4s
1904	Harry Hillman, United States	49.2s
1908	Wyndham Halswelle, Great Britain, walkover	50s
1912	Charles Reidpath, United States	48.2s
1920	Bevil Rudd, South Africa	49.6s
1924	Eric Liddell, Great Britain	47.6s
1928	Ray Barbuti, United States	47.8s
1932	William Carr, United States	46.2s
1936	Archie Williams, United States	46.5s
1948	Arthur Wint, Jamaica, B W I	46.2s
1952	George Rhoden, Jamaica, B W I	45.9s
1956	Charles Jenkins, United States	46.7s
1960	Otis Davis, United States	44.9s
1964	Michael Larrabee, United States	45.1s
1968	Lee Evans, United States	43.8s*
1972	Vincent Matthews, United States	44.66s
1976	Alberto Juantorena, Cuba	44.26s

800-Meter Run

1896	Edwin Flack, Great Britain	2m. 11s
1900	Alfred Tysoe, Great Britain	2m. 1.4s
1904	James Lightbody, United States	1m. 56s
1908	Mel Sheppard, United States	1m. 52.8s
1912	James Meredith, United States	1m. 51.9s
1920	Albert Hill, Great Britain	1m. 53.4s
1924	Douglas Lowe, Great Britain	1m. 52.4s
1928	Douglas Lowe, Great Britain	1m. 51.8s
1932	Thomas Hampson, Great Britain	1m. 49.8s
1936	John Woodruff, United States	1m. 52.9s
1948	Mal Whitfield, United States	1m .49.2s
1952	Mal Whitfield, United States	1m. 49.2s
1956	Thomas Courtney, United States	1m. 47.7s
1960	Peter Snell, New Zealand	1m. 46.3s
1964	Peter Snell, New Zealand	1m. 45.1s
1968	Ralph Doubell, Australia	1m. 44.3s
1972	Dave Wottle, United States	1m .45.9s
1976	Alberto Juantorena, Cuba	1m. 43.50s*

1,500-Meter Run

1896	Edwin Flack, Great Britain	4m. 33.2s
1900	Charles Bennett, Great Britain	4m. 6s
1904	James Lightbody, United States	4m. 5.4s
1908	Mel Sheppard, United States	4m. 3.4s
1912	Arnold Jackson, Great Britain	3m. 56.8s
1920	Albert Hill, Great Britain	4m. 1.8s
1924	Paavo Nurmi, Finland	3m. 53.6s
1928	Harry Larva, Finland	3m.53.2s
1932	Luigi Beccali, Italy	3m. 51.2s
1936	Jack Lovelock, New Zealand	3m. 47.8s
1948	Henri Eriksson, Sweden	3m. 49.8s
1952	Joseph Barthel, Luxemburg	3m. 45.2s
1956	Ron Delany, Ireland	3m. 41.2s
1960	Herb Elliott, Australia	3m. 35.6s
1964	Peter Snell, New Zealand	3m. 38.1s
1968	Kipchoge Keino, Kenya	3m. 34.9s*
1972	Pekka Vasala, Finland	3m. 36.3s
1976	John Walker, New Zealand	3m. 39.17s

3,000-Meter Steeplechase

1920	Percy Hodge, Great Britain	10m. 2.4s
1924	Willie Ritola, Finland	9m. 33.6s

1928	Toivo Loukola, Finland	9m. 21.8s
1932	Volnari Iso-Hollo, Finland (About 3450 mtrs. extra lap by error)	10m. 33.4s
1936	Volnari Iso-Hollo, Finland	9m. 3.8s
1948	Thure Sjoestrand, Sweden	9m. 4.6s
1952	Horace Ashenfelter, United States	8m. 45.4s
1956	Chris Brasher, Great Britain	8m. 42.2s
1960	Zdzislaw Krzyszkowiak, Poland	8m. 34.2s
1964	Gaston Roelants, Belgium	8m. 30.8s
1968	Amos Biwott, Kenya	8m. 51s
1972	Kipchoge Keino, Kenya	8m. 23.6s
1976	Anders Garderud, Sweden	8m. 08.2s*

5,000-Meter Run

1912	Hannes Kolehmainen, Finland	14m. 36.6s
1920	Joseph Guillemot, France	14m. 55.6s
1924	Paavo Nurmi, Finland	14m. 31.2s
1928	Willie Ritola, Finland	14m. 38s
1932	Lauri Lehtinen, Finland	14m. 30s
1936	Gunnar Hockert, Finland	14m. 22.2s
1948	Gaston Reiff, Belgium	14m. 17.6s
1952	Emil Zatopek, Czechoslovakia	14m. 6.0s
1956	Vladimir Kuts, USSR	13m. 39.6s
1960	Murray Halberg, New Zealand	13m. 43.4s
1964	Bob Schul, United States	13m. 48.8s
1968	Mohamed Gammoudi, Tunisia	14m. 05.0s
1972	Lasse Viren, Finland	13m. 26.4s
1976	Lasse Viren, Finland	13m. 24.76s*

Cross-Country

1912	Hannes Kolehmainen, Finland	45m. 11.6s

5-Mile Run

1908	Emil Voigt, Great Britain	25m. 11.2s*

10,000-Meter Run

1912	Hannes Kolehmainen, Finland	31m. 20.8s
1920	Paavo Nurmi, Finland	31m. 45.8s
1924	Willie Ritola, Finland	30m. 23.2s
1928	Paavo Nurmi, Finland	30m. 18.8s
1932	Janusz Kusocinski, Poland	30m. 11.4s
1936	Ilmari Salminen, Finland	30m. 15.4s
1948	Emil Zatopek, Czechoslovakia	29m. 59.6s
1952	Emil Zatopek, Czechoslovakia	29m. 17.0s
1956	Vladimir Kuts, USSR	28m. 45.6s
1960	Pytor Bolotnikov, USSR	28m. 32.2s
1964	Billy Mills, United States	28m. 24.4s
1968	Naftali Temu, Kenya	29m. 27.4s
1972	Lasse Viren, Finland	27m. 38.4s*
1976	Lasse Viren, Finland	27m. 40.38s

Marathon

1896	Spyros Loues, Greece	2h. 55m. 20s
1900	Michael Teato, France	2h. 59m. 45s
1904	Thomas Hicks, United States	3h. 28m. 53s
1908	John J. Hayes, United States	2h. 55m. 18.4s
1912	Kenneth McArthur, South Africa	2h. 36. 54.8s
1920	Hannes Kolehmainen, Finland	2h. 32m. 35.8s
1924	Albin Stenroos, Finland	2h. 41m. 22.6s
1928	El Ouafi, France	2h. 32m. 57s
1932	Juan Zabala, Argentina	2h. 31m. 36s
1936	Kitei Son, Japan	2h. 29m. 19.2s
1948	Delfo Cabera, Argentina	2h. 34m. 51.6s
1952	Emil Zatopek, Czechoslovakia	2h. 23m. 03.2s
1956	Alain Mimoun, France	2h. 25m.
1960	Abebe Bikila, Ethiopia	2h. 15m. 15.2s
1964	Abebe Bikila, Ethiopia	2h. 12m. 11.2s
1968	Mamo Wolde, Ethiopia	2h. 20m. 26.4s
1972	Frank Shorter, United States	2h. 12m. 19.8s
1976	Waldemer Cierpinski, E. Germany	2h. 09m. 55s*

10,000-Meter Cross-Country

1920	Paavo Nurmi, Finland	27m. 15s*
1924	Paavo Nurmi, Finland	32m. 54.8s

10,000-Meter Walk

1912	George Goulding, Canada	46m. 28.4s
1920	Ugo Frigerio, Italy	48m. 6.2s
1924	Ugo Frigerio, Italy	47m. 49s
1948	John Mikaelsson, Sweden	45m. 13.2s
1952	John Mikaelsson, Sweden	45m. 02.8s*

20,000-Meter Walk

1956	Leonid Spirine, USSR	1h. 31m. 27.4s
1960	Vladimir Golubnichy, USSR	1h. 34m. 7.2s
1964	Kenneth Mathews, Great Britain	1h. 29m. 34.0s
1968	Vladimir Golubnichy, USSR	1h. 35m. 58.4s
1972	Peter Frenkel, E. Germany	1h. 26m. 42.4s
1976	Daniel Bautista, Mexico	1h. 24m. 40.6s*

50,000-Meter Walk

1932	Thomas W. Green, Great Britain	4h. 50m. 10s
1936	Harold Whitlock Great Britain	4h. 30m. 41.4s
1948	John Lundgren, Sweden	4h. 41m. 52s
1952	Giuseppe Bordoni, Italy	4h. 28m. 07.8s
1956	Norman Read, New Zealand	4h. 30m. 42.8s
1960	Donald Thompson, Great Britain	4h. 25m. 30s
1964	Abdon Pamich, Italy	4h. 11m. 11.2s
1968	Christoph Hohne, E. Germany	4h. 20m. 13.6s
1972	Bern Kannenberg, W. Germany	3h. 56m. 11.6s*

110-Meter Hurdles

1896	Thomas Curtis, United States	17.6s
1900	Alvin Kraenzlein, United States	15.4s
1904	Frederick Schule, United States	16s
1908	Forrest Smithson, United States	15s
1912	Frederick Kelly, United States	15.1s
1920	Earl Thomson, Canada	14.8s
1924	Daniel Kinsey, United States	15s
1928	Sydney Atkinson, South Africa	14.8s
1932	George Saling, United States	14.6s
1936	Forrest Towns, United States	14.2s
1948	William Porter, United States	13.9s
1952	Harrison Dillard, United States	13.7s
1956	Lee Calhoun, United States	13.5s
1960	Lee Calhoun, United States	13.8s
1964	Hayes Jones, United States	13.6s
1968	Willie Davenport, United States	13.3s
1972	Rod Milburn, United States	13.24s*
1976	Guy Drut, France	13.30s

200-Meter Hurdles

1900	Alvin Kraenzlein, United States	25.4s
1904	Harry Hillman, United States	24.6s*

400-Meter Hurdles

1900	J. W. B. Tewksbury, United States	57.6s
1904	Harry Hillman, United States	53s
1908	Charles Bacon, United States	55s
1920	Frank Loomis, United States	54s
1924	F. Morgan Taylor, United States	52.6s
1928	Lord Burghley, Great Britain	53.4s
1932	Robert Tisdall, Ireland	51.8s
1936	Glenn Hardin, United States	52.4s
1948	Roy Cochran, United States	51.1s
1952	Charles Moore, United States	50.8s
1956	Glenn Davis, United States	50.1s
1960	Glenn Davis, United States	49.3s
1964	Rex Cawley, United States	49.6s
1968	Dave Hemery, Great Britain	48.1s
1972	John Akii-Bua, Uganda	47.82s
1976	Edwin Moses, United States	47.64s*

Standing High Jump

1900	Ray Ewry, United States	5ft. 5 in.
1904	Ray Ewry, United States	4ft. 11 in.
1908	Ray Ewry, United States	5ft. 2 in.
1912	Platt Adams, United States	5ft. 4 1-4 in.*

Running High Jump

1896	Ellery Clark, United States	5ft. 11 1-4 in.
1900	Irving Baxter, United States	6ft. 2 4-5 in.
1904	Samuel Jones, United States	5ft. 11 in.
1908	Harry Porter, United States	6ft. 3 in.
1912	Almer W. Richards, United States	6ft. 4 in.
1920	Richard Landon, United States	6ft. 4 3-8 in.
1924	Harold Osborn, United States	6ft. 6 in.
1928	Robert W. King, United States	6ft. 4 3-8 in.
1932	Duncan McNaughton, Canada	6ft. 5 5-8 in.
1936	Cornelius Johnson, United States	6ft. 7 15-16 in.
1948	John L. Winter, Australia	6ft. 6 in.
1952	Walter Davis, United States	6ft. 8.32 in.
1956	Charles Dumas, United States	6ft. 11 1-4 in.
1960	Robert Shavlakadze, USSR	7ft. 1in.
1964	Valery Brumel, USSR	7ft. 1 7-8 in.
1968	Dick Fosbury, United States	7ft. 4 1-4 in.
1972	Yuri Tarmak, USSR	7ft. 3 3-4 in.
1976	Jacek Wszola, Poland	7ft. 4 1-2 in.*

Standing Broad Jump

1900	Ray Ewry, United States	10ft. 6 2-5 in.
1904	Ray Ewry, United States	11ft. 4 7-8 in.*
1908	Ray Ewry, United States	10ft. 11 1-4 m.
1912	Constantin Tsicilitras, Greece	11ft. 3-4 in.

Long Jump

1896	Ellery Clark, United States	20ft. 9 3-4 in.
1900	Alvin Kraenzlein, United States	23ft. 6 7-8 in.
1904	Myer Prinstein, United States	24ft. 1in.

1908	Frank Irons, United States	24ft. 6 1-2 in.
1912	Albert Gutterson, United States	24ft. 11 1-4 in.
1920	Wm. Petterssen, Sweden	23ft. 5 1-2 in.
1924	DeHart Hubbard, United States	24ft. 5 1-8 in.
1928	Edward B. Hamm, United States	25ft. 4 3-4 in.
1932	Edward Gordon, United States	25ft. 3-4 in.
1936	Jesse Owens, United States	26ft. 5 5-16 in.
1948	William Steele, United States	25ft. 8 in.
1952	Jerome Biffle, United States	24ft. 10.03 in.
1956	Gregory Bell, United States	25ft. 8 1-4 in.
1960	Ralph Boston, United States	26ft. 7 3-4 in.
1964	Lynn Davies, Great Britain	26ft. 5 3-4 in.
1968	Bob Beamon, United States	29ft. 2 1-2 in.*
1972	Randy Williams, United States	27ft. 1-2 in.
1976	Arnie Robinson, United States	27 ft. 4 1/2 in.

400-Meter Relay

1912	Great Britain	42.4s
1920	United States	42.2s
1924	United States	41s
1928	United States	41s
1932	United States	40s
1936	United States	39.8s
1948	United States	40.3s
1952	United States	40.1s
1956	United States	39.5s
1960	Germany (U.S. disqualified)	39.5s
1964	United States	39.0s
1968	United States	38.2s
1972	United States	38.19s*
1976	United States	38.33s

1,600-Meter Relay

1908	United States	3m. 27.2s
1912	United States	3m. 16.6s
1920	Great Britain	3m. 22.2s
1924	United States	3m. 16s
1928	United States	3m. 14.2s
1932	United States	3m. 8.2s
1936	Great Britain	3m. 9s
1948	United States	3m. 10.4s
1952	Jamaica, B.W.I.	3m. 03.9s
1956	United States	3m. 04.8s
1960	United States	3m. 02.2s
1964	United States	3m. 00.7s
1968	United States	2m. 56.1s*
1972	Kenya	2m. 59.8s
1976	United States	2m. 58.65s

Pole Vault

1896	William Hoyt, United States	10ft. 9 3-4 in.
1900	Irving Baxter, United States	10ft. 9.9 in.
1904	Charles Dvorak, United States	11ft. 6 in.
1908	A. C. Gilbert, United States Edward Cook Jr., United States	12ft. 2 in.
1912	Harry Babcock, United States	12ft. 11 1-2 in.
1920	Frank Foss, United States	13ft. 5 in.
1924	Lee Barnes, United States	12ft. 11 1-2 in.
1928	Sabin W. Carr, United States	13ft. 9 1-2 in.
1932	William Miller, United States	14ft. 1 7-8 in.
1936	Earle Meadows, United States	14ft. 3 1-4 in.
1948	Guinn Smith, United States	14ft. 1 1-4 in.
1952	Robert Richards, United States	14ft. 11 1-4 in.
1956	Robert Richards, United States	14ft. 11 1-2 in.
1960	Don Bragg, United States	15ft. 5 1-8 in.
1964	Fred Hansen, United States	16ft. 8 1-2 in.
1968	Bob Seagren, United States	17ft. 8 1-2 in.
1972	Wolfgang Nordwig, E. Germany	18ft. 1-2 in.*
1976	Tadeusz Slusarski, Poland	18ft. 1-2 in.*

16-lb. Hammer Throw

1900	John Flannagan, United States	167ft. 4 in.
1904	John Flannagan, United States	168ft. 1 in.
1908	John Flannagan, United States	170ft. 4 1-4 in.
1912	Matt McGrath, United States	179ft. 7 1-8 in.
1920	Pat Ryan, United States	172ft. 5 5-8 in.
1924	Fred Tootell, United States	174ft. 10 1-8 in.
1928	Patrick O'Callaghan, Ireland	168ft. 7 3-8 in.
1932	Patrick O'Callaghan, Ireland	176ft. 11 1-8 in.
1936	Karl Hein, Germany	185ft. 4 3-16 in.
1948	Imre Nemeth, Hungary	183ft. 11 1-2 in.
1952	Jozsef Csermak, Hungary	197ft. 11.67 in.
1956	Harold Connolly, United States	207ft. 3 1-2 in.
1960	Vasily Rudenkov, USSR	220ft. 2 in.
1964	Romuald Klim, USSR	228ft. 9 1-2 in.
1968	Gyula Zsivotsky, Hungary	240ft. 8 in.
1972	Anatoli Bondarchuk, USSR	248ft. 8 in.
1976	Yuri Sedyh, USSR	254ft. 3 3-4 in.*

Discus Throw

1896	Robert Garrett, United States	95ft. 7 1-2 in.
1900	Rudolf Bauer, Hungary	118ft. 2.9-10in.
1904	Martin Sheridan, United States	128ft. 10 1-2 in.
1908	Martin Sheridan, United States	134ft. 2 in.
1912	Armas Taipale, Finland	148ft. 4 in.
	Both hands—Armas Taipale, Finland	271ft. 10 1-4 in.
1920	Elmer Niklander, Finland	146ft. 7 1-4 in.
1924	Clarence Houser, United States	151ft. 5 1-8 in.
1928	Clarence Houser, United States	155ft. 3 in.
1932	John Anderson, United States	162ft. 4 7-8 in.
1936	Ken Carpenter, United States	165ft. 7 3-8 in.
1948	Adolfo Consolini, Italy	173ft. 2 in.
1952	Sim Iness, United States	180ft. 6.85 in.
1956	Al Oerter, United States	184ft. 11 in.
1960	Al Oerter, United States	194ft. 2 in.
1964	Al Oerter, United States	200ft. 1 1-2 in.
1968	Al Oerter, United States	212ft. 6 1-2 in.
1972	Ludik Danek, Czechoslovakia	211 ft. 3 in.
1976	Mac Wilkins, United States	221ft. 5.4 in.*

Standing Hop, Step, and Jump

1900	Ray Ewry, United States	34ft. 8 1-2 in.*
1904	Ray Ewry, United States	34ft. 7 1-4 in.

Triple Jump

1896	James Connolly, United States	45 ft.
1900	Myer Prinstein, United States	47ft. 4 1-4 in.
1904	Myer Prinstein, United States	47 ft.
1908	Timothy Ahearne, Great Britain	48ft. 11 1-4 in.
1912	Gustaf Lindblom, Sweden	48ft. 5 1-8 in.
1920	Vilho Tuulos, Finland	47ft. 7 in.
1924	Archie Winter, Australia	50ft. 11 1-4in.
1928	Mikio Oda, Japan	49ft. 11 in.
1932	Chuhei Nambu, Japan	51ft. 7 in.
1936	Naoto Tajima, Japan	52ft. 5 7-8 in.
1948	Arne Ahman, Sweden	50ft. 6 1-4 in.
1952	Adhemar de Silva, Brazil	53ft. 2.59 in.
1956	Adhemar de Silva, Brazil	53ft. 7 1-2 in.
1960	Jozef Schmidt, Poland	55ft. 1 3-4 in.
1964	Jozef Schmidt, Poland	55ft. 3 1-2 in.
1968	Viktor Saneev, USSR	57ft. 3-4 in.*
1972	Viktor Saneev, USSR	56ft. 11 in.
1976	Viktor Saneev, USSR	56 ft. 8 3-4 in.

16-lb. Shot Put

1896	Robert Garrett, United States	36ft. 2 in.
1900	Robert Sheldon, United States	46ft. 3 1-8 in.
1904	Ralph Rose, United States	48ft. 7 in.
1908	Ralph Rose, United States	46ft. 7 1-2 in.
1912	Pat McDonald, United States	50ft. 4 in.
	Both hands—Ralph Rose, United States	90ft. 5 1-2 in.
1920	Ville Porhola, Finland	48ft. 7 1-8 in.
1924	Clarence Houser, United States	49ft. 2 3-8 in.
1928	John Kuck, United States	52ft. 3-4 in.
1932	Leo Sexton, United States	52ft. 6 3-16 in.
1936	Hans Woelke, Germany	53ft. 1 13-16 in.
1948	Wilbur Thompson, United States	56ft. 2 in.
1952	Parry O'Brien, United States	57ft. 1.43 in.
1956	Parry O'Brien, United States	60ft. 11 in.
1960	William Nieder, United States	64ft. 6 3-4 in.
1964	Dallas Long, United States	66ft. 8 1-2 in.
1968	Randy Matson, United States	67ft. 4 3-4 in.
1972	Wladyslaw Komar, Poland	69 ft. 6 in.
1976	Udo Beyer, E. Germany	69 ft. 6.7 in.*

Discus Throw—Greek Style

1908	Martin Sheridan, United States	124ft. 8 in.*

Javelin Throw

1908	Erik Lemming, Sweden	178ft. 7 1-2 in.
	Held in middle—Erik Lemming, Sweden	179ft. 10 1-2 in.
1912	Erik Lemming, Sweden	198ft. 11 1-4 in.
	Both hands, Julius Saaristo, Finland	358ft. 11 7-8 in.
1920	Jonni Myrra, Finland	215ft. 9 3-4 in.
1924	Jonni Myrra, Finland	206ft. 6 3-4 in.
1928	Eric Lundquist, Sweden	218ft. 6 1-8 in.
1932	Matti Jarvinen, Finland	238ft. 7 in.
1936	Gerhard Stoeck, Germany	235ft. 8 5-16 in.
1948	Kaj T. Rautavaara, Finland	228ft. 10 1-2 in.
1952	Cy Young, United States	242ft. 0.79 in.
1956	Egil Danielsen, Norway	281ft. 2 1-4 in.
1960	Viktor Tsibulenko, USSR	277ft. 8 3-8 in.
1964	Pauli Nevala, Finland	271ft. 2 1-2 in.
1968	Yanis Lusis, USSR	295ft. 7 1-4 in.
1972	Klaus Wolferman, W. Germany	296ft. 10 in.
1976	Miklos Nemeth, Hungary	310 ft. 4 1/2 in.*

Decathlon

1912	Hugo Wieslander, Sweden	7,724.49 pts.
1920	Helge Loveland, Norway	6,804.35 pts.
1924	Harold Osborn, United States	7,710.775 pts.
1928	Paavo Yrjola, Finland	8,056.20 pts.
1932	James Bausch, United States	8,462.23 pts.
1936	Glenn Morris, United States	7,900 pts.
1948	Robert Mathias, United States	7,139 pts.
1952	Robert Mathias, United States	7,887 pts.
1956	Milton Campbell, United States	7,937 pts.
1960	Rafer Johnson, United States	8,392 pts.
1964	Willi Holdorf, Germany	7,887 pts.
1968	Bill Toomey, United States	8,193 pts.
1972	Nikola Avilov, USSR	8,454 pts.
1976	Bruce Jenner, United States	8,618 pts.*

Former point systems used prior to 1964.

Track and Field—Women

100-Meter Run

1928	Elizabeth Robinson, United States	12.2s
1932	Stella Walsh, Poland	11.9s
1936	Helen Stephens, United States	11.5s
1948	Francina Blankers-Koen, Netherlands	11.9s
1952	Marjorie Jackson, Australia	11.5s
1956	Betty Cuthbert, Australia	11.5s
1960	Wilma Rudolph, United States	11.0s*
1964	Wyomia Tyus, United States	11.4s
1968	Wyomiá Tyus, United States	11.0s*
1972	Renate Stecher, E. Germany	11.07s
1976	Annegret Richter, W. Germany	11.01s*

200-Meter Run

1948	Francina Blankers-Koen, Netherlands	24.4s
1952	Marjorie Jackson, Australia	23.7s
1956	Betty Cuthbert, Australia	23.4s
1960	Wilma Rudolph, United States	24.0s
1964	Edith McGuire, United States	23.0s
1968	Irene Szewinska, Poland	22.5s
1972	Renate Stecher, E. Germany	22.40s
1976	Baerbel Eckert, E. Germany	22.37s*

400-Meter Run

1964	Betty Cuthbert, Australia	52s
1968	Colette Besson, France	52s
1972	Monika Zehrt, E. Germany	51.08s
1976	Irena Szewinska, Poland	49.29s*

800-Meter Run

1928	Linda Radke, Germany	2m. 16.8s
1960	Ludmila Shevcova, USSR	2m. 4.3s
1964	Ann Packer, Great Britain	2m. 1.1s
1968	Madeline Manning, United States	2m. 0.9s
1972	Hildegard Falck, W. Germany	1m. 58.6s
1976	Tatyana Kazankina, USSR	1m. 54.94s*

1,500-Meter Run

1972	Ludmila Bragina, USSR	4m. 01.4s*
1976	Tatyana Kazankina, USSR	4m. 05.48s

400-Meter Relay

1928	Canada	48.4s
1932	United States	47.0s
1936	United States	46.9s
1948	Netherlands	47.5s
1952	United States	45.9s
1956	Australia	44.5s
1960	United States	44.5s
1964	Poland	43.6s
1968	United States	42.8s
1972	West Germany	42.81s
1976	East Germany	42.55s*

1,600-Meter Relay

1972	East Germany	3m. 23s
1976	East Germany	3m. 19.23s*

80-Meter Hurdles

1932	Mildred Didrikson, United States	11.7s
1936	Trebisonda Villa, Italy	11.7s
1948	Francina Blankers-Koen, Netherlands	11.2s
1952	Shirley Strickland de la Hunty, Australia	10.9s
1956	Shirley Strickland de la Hunty, Australia	10.7s
1960	Irina Press, USSR	10.8s
1964	Karen Balzer, Germany	10.5s
1968	Maureen Caird, Australia	10.3s*

100-Meter Hurdles

1972	Annelie Ehrhardt, E. Germany	12.59*
1976	Johanna Schaller, E. Germany	12.77s

High Jump

1928	Ethel Catherwood, Canada	5ft. 3 in.
1932	Jean Shiley, United States	5ft. 5 1-4 in.
1936	Ibolya Csak, Hungary	5ft. 3 in.
1948	Alice Coachman, United States	5ft. 6 1-8 in.
1952	Esther Brand, South Africa	5ft. 5 3-4 in.
1956	Mildred L. McDaniel, United States	5ft. 9 1-4 in.
1960	Iolanda Balas, Romania	6ft. 1-4 in.
1964	Iolanda Balas, Romania	6 ft. 2 7-8 in.
1968	Miloslava Reskova, Czechoslovakia	5ft. 11 3-4 in.
1972	Ulrike Meyfarth, W. Germany	6ft. 3 1-4 in.
1976	Rosemarie Ackermann, E. Germany	6ft. 3 3-4 in.*

Discus Throw

1928	Helena Konopacka, Poland	129ft. 11 7-8 in.
1932	Lillian Copeland, United States	133ft. 2 in.
1936	Gisela Mauermayer, Germany	156ft. 3 3-16 in.
1948	Micheline Ostermeyer, France	137ft. 6 1-2 in.
1952	Nina Romaschkova, USSR	168ft. 8 1-2 in.
1956	Olga Fikotova, Czechoslovakia	176ft. 1 1-2 in.
1960	Nina Ponomareva, USSR	180ft. 8 1-4 in.
1964	Tamara Press, USSR	187ft. 10 1-2 in.
1968	Lia Manolin, Romania	191ft. 2 1-2 in.
1972	Faina Melnik, USSR	218 ft. 7 in.
1976	Evelin Schlaak, E. Germany	226 ft. 4 1-2 in. *

Javelin Throw

1932	Mildred Didrikson, United States	143ft. 4 in.
1936	Tilly Fleischer, Germany	148ft. 2 3-4 in.
1948	Herma Bauma, Austria	149ft. 6 in.
1952	Dana Zatopekova, Czechoslovakia	165ft. 7 in.
1956	Inessa Janzeme, USSR	176ft. 8 in.
1960	Elvira Ozolina, USSR	183ft. 8 in.
1964	Mihaela Penes, Romania	198ft. 7 1-2 in.
1968	Angela Nemeth, Hungary	198ft. 1-2 in.
1972	Ruth Fuchs, E. Germany	209 ft. 7 in.
1976	Ruth Fuchs, E. Germany	216ft. 4 in.*

Shot Put

1948	Micheline Ostermeyer, France	45ft. 1 1-2 in.
1952	Galina Zybina, USSR	50ft. 1 1-2 in.
1956	Tamara Tishkyevich, USSR	54ft. 5 in.
1960	Tamara Press, USSR	56ft. 9 7-8 in.
1964	Tamara Press, USSR	59ft. 6 1-4 in.
1968	Margitta Gummel, E. Germany	64ft. 4 in.
1972	Nadezwda Chizova, USSR	69ft.
1976	Ivanka Christova, Bulgaria	69ft. 5 in.*

Long Jump

1948	Olga Gyarmati, Hungary	18ft. 8 1-4 in.
1952	Yvette Williams, New Zealand	20ft. 5 3-4 in.
1956	E. Krzeskinska, Poland	20ft. 9 3-4 in.
1960	Vyera Krepina, USSR	20ft. 10 3-4 in.
1964	Mary Rand, Great Britain	22ft. 2 1-4 in.
1968	V. Viscopoleanu, Romania	22ft. 4 1-2 in.*
1972	Heidemarie Rosendahl, W. Germany	22ft. 3 in.
1976	Angela Voigt, E. Germany	22 ft. 2 1-2 in.

Pentathlon

1964	Irina Press, USSR	5,246 pts.
1968	Ingred Becker, W. Germany	5,098 pts.
1972	Mary Peters, England	4,801 pts.*
1976	Sigrun Siegl, E. Germany	4,745 pts.

Former point system, 1964-1968

Value of Olympic Medals

An Olympic gold medal is basically silver coated with about six grams of fine gold. It is worth $110. The silver medal is pure silver, and its actual value is about $66. The bronze, which is pure bronze, is worth $16.

Swimming—Men

100-Meter Freestyle

1896	Alfred Hajos, Hungary	1:22.2
1904	Zoltan de Halmay, Hungary (100 yards)	1:02.8
1908	Charles Daniels, U.S.	1:05.6
1912	Duke P. Kahanamoku, U.S.	1:03.4
1920	Duke P. Kahanamoku, U.S.	1:01.4
1924	John Weissmuller, U.S.	59.0
1928	John Weissmuller, U.S.	58.6
1932	Yasuji Miyazaki, Japan	58.2
1936	Ferenc Csik, Hungary	57.6
1948	Wally Ris, U.S.	57.3
1952	Clark Scholes, U.S.	57.4
1956	Jon Henricks, Australia	55.4
1960	John Devitt, Australia	55.2
1964	Don Schollander, U.S.	53.4
1968	Mike Wenden, Australia	52.2
1972	Mark Spitz, U.S.	51.22
1976	Jim Montgomery, U.S.	49.99*

200-Meter Freestyle

1968	Mike Wenden, Australia	1:55.2
1972	Mark Spitz, U.S.	1:52.78
1976	Bruce Furniss, U.S.	1:50.29*

400-Meter Freestyle

1904	C. M. Daniels, U.S. (440 yards)	6:16.2
1908	Henry Taylor, Great Britain	5:36.8
1912	George Hodgson, Canada	5:24.4
1920	Norman Ross, U.S.	5:26.8
1924	John Weissmuller, U.S.	5:04.2
1928	Albert Zorilla, Argentina	5:01.6
1932	Clarence Crabbe, U.S.	4:48.4
1936	Jack Medica, U.S.	4:44.5
1948	William Smith, U.S.	4:41.0
1952	Jean Boiteux, France	4:30.7
1956	Murray Rose, Australia	4:27.3
1960	Murray Rose, Australia	4:18.3
1964	Don Schollander, U.S.	4:12.2
1968	Mike Burton, U.S.	4:09.0
1972	Brad Cooper, Australia	4:00.27
1976	Brian Goodell, U.S.	3:51.93*

1,500-Meter Freestyle

1908	Henry Taylor, Great Britain	22:48.4
1912	George Hodgson, Canada	22:00.0
1920	Norman Ross, U.S.	22:23.2
1924	Andrew Charlton, Australia	20:06.6
1928	Arne Borg, Sweden	19:51.8
1932	Kasuo Kitamura, Japan	19:12.4
1936	Noboru Terada, Japan	19:13.7
1948	James P. McClane, U.S.	19:18.5
1952	Ford Konno, U.S.	18:30.0
1956	Murray Rose, Australia	17:58.9
1960	Jon Konrads, Australia	17:19.6
1964	Robert Windle, Australia	17:01.7
1968	Mike Burton, U.S.	16:38.9
1972	Mike Burton, U.S.	15:52.58
1976	Brian Goodell, U.S.	15:02.40*

400-Meter Medley Relay

1960	United States	4:05.4
1964	United States	3:58.4
1968	United States	3:54.9
1972	United States	3:48.16
1976	United States	3:42.22*

400-Meter Freestyle Relay

1964	United States	3:33.2
1968	United States	3:31.7
1972	United States	3:26.4*

800-Meter Freestyle Relay

1908	Great Britain	10:55.6
1912	Australia	10:11.6
1920	United States	10:04.4
1924	United States	9:53.4
1928	United States	9:36.2
1932	Japan	8:58.4
1936	Japan	8:51.5
1948	United States	8:46.0
1952	United States	8:31.1
1956	Australia	8:23.6
1960	United States	8:10.2
1964	United States	7:52.1
1968	United States	7:52.3
1972	United States	7:35.78
1976	United States	7:23.22*

100-Meter Backstroke

1904	Walter Brack, Germany (100 yds.)	1:16.8
1908	Arno Bieberstein, Germany	1:24.6
1912	Harry Hebner, U.S.	1:21.2
1920	Warren Kealoha, U.S.	1:15.2
1924	Warren Kealoha, U.S.	1:13.2
1928	George Kojac, U.S.	1:08.2
1932	Masaji Kiyokawa, Japan	1:08.6
1936	Adolph Kiefer, U.S.	1:05.9
1948	Allen Stack, U.S.	1:06.4
1952	Yoshi Oyokawa, U.S.	1:05.4
1956	David Thiele, Australia	1:02.2
1960	David Thiele, Australia	1:01.9
1968	Roland Matthes, E. Germany	58.7
1972	Roland Matthes, E. Germany	56.58
1976	John Naber, U.S.	55.49*

200-Meter Backstroke

1964	Jed Graef, U.S.	2:10.3
1968	Roland Matthes, E. Germany	2:09.6
1972	Roland Matthes, E. Germany	2:02.82
1976	John Naber, U.S.	1:59.19*

100-Meter Breaststroke

1968	Don McKenzie, U.S.	1:07.7
1972	Nobutaka Taguchi, Japan	1:04.94
1976	John Hencken, U.S.	1:03.11*

200-Meter Breaststroke

1908	Frederick Holman, Great Britain	3:09.2
1912	Walter Bathe, Germany	3:01.8
1920	Haken Malmroth, Sweden	3:04.4
1924	Robert Skelton, U.S.	2:56.6
1928	Yoshiyuki Tsuruta, Japan	2:48.8
1932	Yoshiyuki Tsuruta, Japan	2:45.4
1936	Tetsuo Hamuro, Japan	2:42.5
1948	Joseph Verdeur, U.S.	2:39.3
1952	John Davies, Australia	2:34.4
1956	Masura Furukawa, Japan	2:34.7
1960	William Mulliken, U.S.	2:37.4
1964	Ian O'Brien, Australia	2:27.8
1968	Felipe Munoz, Mexico	2:28.7
1972	John Hencken, U.S.	2:21.55
1976	David Wilkie, Great Britain	2:15.11*

100-Meter Butterfly

1968	Doug Russell, U.S.	55.9
1972	Mark Spitz, U.S.	54.27*
1976	Matt Vogel, U.S.	54.35

200-Meter Butterfly

1956	William Yorzyk, U.S.	2:18.6
1960	Michael Troy, U.S.	2:12.8
1964	Kevin J. Berry, Australia	2:06.6
1968	Carl Robie, U.S.	2:08.7
1972	Mark Spitz, U.S.	2:00.70
1976	Mike Bruner, U.S.	1:59.23*

200-Meter Individual Medley

1968	Charles Hickcox, U.S.	2:12.0
1972	Gunnar Larsson, Sweden	2:07.2*

400-Meter Individual Medley

1964	Dick Roth, U.S.	4:45.4
1968	Charles Hickcox, U.S.	4:48.4
1972	Gunnar Larsson, Sweden	4.31.98
1976	Rod Strachan, U.S.	4:23.68*

Springboard Diving

	Springboard Diving	Points
1904	Dr. G. E. Sheldon, U.S.	12 2-3
1908	Albert Zuerner, Germany	85.5
1912	Paul Guenther, Germany	6
1920	Louis Kuehn, U.S.	6
1924	Albert White, U.S.	7
1928	Pete Desjardins, U.S.	185.04
1932	Michael Gallitzen, U.S.	161.38
1936	Richard Degener, U.S.	161.57
1948	Bruce Harlan, U.S.	163.64
1952	David Browning, U.S.	205.29

1956	Robert Clothworthy, U.S.	159.56
1960	Gary Tobian, U.S.	170.00
1964	Kenneth Sitzberger, U.S.	159.90
1968	Bernie Wrightson, U.S.	170.15
1972	Vladimir Vasin, USSR	594.09
1976	Phil Boggs, U.S.	619.52

Platform Diving

		Points
1928	Pete Desjardins, U.S.	98.74
1932	Harold Smith, U.S.	124.80
1936	Marshall Wayne, U.S.	113.58
1948	Sammy Lee, U.S.	130.05
1952	Sammy Lee, U.S.	156.28
1956	Joaquin Capilla, Mexico	152.44
1960	Robert Webster, U.S.	165.56
1964	Robert Webster, U.S.	148.58
1968	Klaus Dibiasi, Italy	164.18
1972	Klaus Dibiasi, Italy	504.12
1976	Klaus Dibiasi, Italy	600.51

Swimming—Women

100-Meter Freestyle

1912	Fanny Durack, Australia	1:22.2
1920	Ethelda Bleibtrey, U.S.	1:13.6
1924	Ethel Lackie, U.S.	1:12.4
1928	Albina Osipowich, U.S.	1:11.0
1932	Helene Madison, U.S.	1:06.8
1936	Hendrika Mastenbroek, Holland	1:05.9
1948	Greta Anderson, Denmark	1:06.3
1952	Katalin Szoke, Hungary	1:06.3
1956	Dawn Fraser, Australia	1:02.0
1960	Dawn Fraser, Australia	1:01.2
1964	Dawn Fraser, Australia	59.5
1968	Jan Henne, U.S.	1:00.0
1972	Sandra Neilson, U.S.	58.59
1976	Kornelia Ender, E. Germany	55.65*

200-Meter Freestyle

1968	Debbie Meyer, U.S.	2:10.5
1972	Shane Gould, Australia	2:03.56
1976	Kornelia Ender, E. Germany	1:59.26*

400-Meter Freestyle

1924	Martha Norelius, U.S.	6:02.2
1928	Martha Norelius, U.S.	5:42.8
1932	Helene Madison, U.S.	5:28.5
1936	Hendrika Mastenbroek, Netherlands	5:26.4
1948	Ann Curtis, U.S.	5:17.8
1952	Valerie Gyenge, Hungary	5:12.1
1956	Lorraine Crapp, Australia	4:54.6
1960	Susan Chris von Saltza, U.S.	4:50.6
1964	Virginia Duenkel, U.S.	4:43.3
1968	Debbie Meyer, U.S.	4:31.8
1972	Shane Gould, Australia	4:19.04
1976	Petra Thumer, E. Germany	4:09.89*

800-Meter Freestyle

1968	Debbie Meyer, U.S.	9:24.0
1972	Keena Rothhammer, U.S.	8:53.68
1976	Petra Thumer, E. Germany	8:37.14*

100-Meter Backstroke

1924	Sybil Bauer, U.S.	1:23.3
1928	Marie Braun, Netherlands	1:22.0
1932	Eleanor Holm, U.S.	1:19.4
1936	Dina Senff, Netherlands	1:18.9
1948	Karen Harup, Denmark	1:14.4
1952	Joan Harrison, South Africa	1:14.3
1956	Judy Grinham, Great Britain	1:12.9
1960	Lynn Burke, U.S.	1:09.3
1964	Cathy Ferguson, U.S.	1:07.7
1968	Kaye Hall, U.S.	1:06.2
1972	Melissa Belote, U.S.	1:05.78
1976	Ulrike Richter, E. Germany	1:01.83*

200-Meter Backstroke

1968	Pokey Watson, U.S.	2:24.8
1972	Melissa Belote, U.S.	2:19.19
1976	Ulrike Richter, E. Germany	2:13.43*

100-Meter Breaststroke

1968	Djurdjica Bjedov, Yugoslavia	1:15.8
1972	Cathy Carr, U.S.	1:13.58
1976	Hannelore Anke, E. Germany	1:11.16*

200-Meter Breaststroke

1924	Lucy Morton, Great Britain	3:32.2
1928	Hilde Schrader, Germany	3:12.6
1932	Clare Dennis, Australia	3:06.3
1936	Hideko Maehata, Japan	3:03.6
1948	Nelly Van Vliet, Netherlands	2:57.2
1952	Eva Szekely, Hungary	2:51.7
1956	Ursula Happe, Germany	2:53.1
1960	Anita Lonsbrough, Great Britain	2:49.5
1964	Galina Prozumenschikova, USSR	2:46.4
1968	Sharon Wichman, U.S.	2:44.4
1972	Beverly Whitfield, Australia	2:41.71
1976	Marina Koshevala, USSR	2:33.35*

200-Meter Individual Medley

1968	Claudia Kolb, U.S.	2:24.7
1972	Shane Gould, Australia	2:23.1*

400-Meter Individual Medley

1964	Donna de Varona, U.S.	5:18.7
1968	Claudia Kolb, U.S.	5:08.5
1972	Gail Neall, Australia	5:02.97
1976	Ulrike Tauber, E. Germany	4:42.77*

100-Meter Butterfly

1956	Shelley Mann, U.S.	1:11.0
1960	Carolyn Schuler, U.S.	1:09.5
1964	Sharon Stouder, U.S.	1:04.7
1968	Lynn McClements, Australia	1:05.5
1972	Mayumi Aoki, Japan	1:03.34
1976	Kornelia Ender, E. Germany	1:00.13*

200-Meter Butterfly

1968	Ada Kok, Netherlands	2:24.7
1972	Karen Moe, U.S.	2:15.57
1976	Andrea Pollack, E. Germany	2:11.41*

400-Meter Medley Relay

1960	United States	4:41.1
1964	United States	4:33.9
1968	United States	4:28.3
1972	United States	4:20.7
1976	East Germany	4:07.95*

400-Meter Freestyle Relay

1912	Great Britain	5:52.8
1920	United States	5:11.6
1924	United States	4:58.8
1928	United States	4:47.6
1932	United States	4:38.0
1936	Netherlands	4:36.0
1948	United States	4:29.2
1952	Hungary	4:24.4
1956	Australia	4:17.1
1960	United States	4:08.9
1964	United States	4:03.8
1968	United States	4:02.5
1972	United States	3:55.19
1976	United States	3:44.82*

Springboard Diving

		Points
1920	Aileen Riggin, U.S.	9
1924	Elizabeth Becker, U.S.	8
1928	Helen Meany, U.S.	78.62
1932	Georgia Coleman, U.S.	87.52
1936	Marjorie Gestring, U.S.	89.27
1948	Victoria M. Draves, U.S.	108.74
1952	Patricia McCormick, U.S.	147.30
1956	Patricia McCormick, U.S.	142.36
1960	Ingrid Kramer, Germany	155.81
1964	Ingrid Engel-Kramer, Germany	145.00
1968	Sue Gossick, U.S.	150.77
1972	Micki King, U.S.	450.03
1976	Jenni Chandler, U.S.	506.19

Platform Diving

		Points
1928	Elizabeth B. Pinkston, U.S.	31.60
1932	Dorothy Poynton, U.S.	40.26
1936	Dorothy Poynton Hill, U.S.	33.93
1948	Victoria M. Draves, U.S.	68.87
1952	Patricia McCormick, U.S.	79.37
1956	Patricia McCormick, U.S.	84.85
1960	Ingrid Kramer, Germany	91.28
1964	Lesley Bush, U.S.	99.80
1968	Milena Duchkova, Czech	109.59
1972	Ulrika Knape, Sweden	390.00
1976	Elena Vaytsekhouskaya, USSR	406.59

21st Summer Olympics

Montreal, Quebec, July 17-Aug. 1, 1976

Final Medal Standings

(nations in alphabetical order)

	Gold	Silver	Bronze	Total
Australia	0	1	4	5
Austria	0	0	1	1
Belgium	0	3	3	6
Bermuda	0	0	1	1
Brazil	0	0	2	2
Britain	3	5	5	13
Bulgaria	7	8	9	24
Canada	0	5	6	11
Cuba	6	4	3	13
Czechoslovakia	2	2	4	8
Denmark	1	0	2	3
Germany, East	40	25	25	90
Germany, West	10	12	17	39
Finland	4	2	0	6
France	2	2	5	9
Holland	0	2	3	5
Hungary	4	5	12	21
Iran	0	1	1	2
Italy	2	7	4	13
Jamaica	1	1	0	2
Japan	9	6	10	25

	Gold	Silver	Bronze	Total
Korea, North	1	1	0	2
Korea, South	1	1	4	6
Mexico	1	0	1	2
Mongolia	0	1	0	1
New Zealand	2	1	1	4
Norway	1	1	0	2
Pakistan	0	0	1	1
Poland	8	6	11	25
Portugal	0	2	0	2
Puerto Rico	0	0	1	1
Romania	4	9	14	27
Spain	0	2	0	2
Sweden	4	1	0	5
Switzerland	1	1	2	4
Thailand	0	0	1	1
Trinidad	1	0	0	1
USSR	47	43	35	125
United States	34	35	25	94
Venezuela	0	1	0	1
Yugoslavia	2	3	3	8

Duplicate medals awarded in some events

Olympic Gold Medal Winners

Track and Field — Men

100 Meters — Hasely Crawford, Trinidad. **Time — 0:10.06.**
200 Meters — Donald Quarrie, Jamaica. **Time — 0:20.23.**
400 Meters — Alberto Juantorena, Cuba. **Time — 0:44.26.**
800 Meters — Alberto Juantorena, Cuba. **Time — 1:43.50.**
1,500 Meters — John Walker, New Zealand. **Time — 3:39.17.**
5,000 Meters — Lasse Viren, Finland. **Time — 13:27.76.**
10,000 Meters — Lasse Viren, Finland. **Time — 27:40.38.**
110 - Meter Hurdles — Guy Drut, France. **Time — 0:13.30.**
400 - Meter Hurdles — Edwin Moses, U.S. **Time — 0:47.64.**
400 - Meter Relay — U.S. (Glance, Jones, Hampton, Riddick). **Time — 0:38.33.**
1,600 - Meter Relay — U.S. (Frazier, Brown, Newhouse, Parks). **Time — 2:58.65.**
3,000 - Meter Steeplechase — Anders Garderud, Sweden. **Time — 8:08.2.**
20 - Km. Walk — Daniel Bautista, Mexico. **Time — 1:24:40.6.**
Marathon — Waldemer Cierpinski, E. Germany. **Time — 2:09:55.**
Long Jump — Arnie Robinson, U.S. **27 ft. ½ in.**
Triple Jump — Viktor Saneev, USSR. **50 ft. 8.7 in.**
High Jump — Jacek Wszola, Poland. **7 ft. 4½ in.**
Discus — Mac Wilkins, U.S. **221 ft. 5.4 in.**
Hammer — Yuri Sedykh, USSR. **254 ft. 3¾ in.**
Javelin — Miklos Nemeth, Hungary. **310 ft. 3¾ in.**
Shot Put — Udo Beyer, E. Germany. **69 ft. ¾ in.**
Pole Vault — Tadeusz Slusraski, Poland. **18 ft. ½ in.**
Decathlon — Bruce Jenner, U.S. **8,618 pts.**

Track and Field — Women

100 Meters — Annegret Richter, W. Germany. **Time — 0:11.01.**
200 Meters — Baerbel Eckert, E. Germany. **Time — 0:22.37.**
400 Meters — Irena Szewinska, Poland. **Time — 0:49.29.**
800 Meters — Tatyana Kazankina, USSR. **Time — 1:54.94.**
1,500 Meters — Tatyana Kazankina, USSR. **Time — 4:05.48.**
100-Meter Hurdles — Johanna Schaller, E. Germany. **Time — 0:12.77.**
400 - Meter Relay — E. Germany. **Time — 0:42.55.**
1,600 - Meter Relay — E. Germany. **Time — 3:19.23.**
Long Jump — Angela Voigt, E. Germany. **22 ft. 2½ in.**
High Jump — Rosemarie Ackermann, E. Germany. **6 ft. 3¾ in.**
Javelin — Ruth Fuchs, E. Germany. **216 ft. 4 in.**
Discus — Evelin Schlaak, E. Germany. **226 ft. 4½ in.**
Shot Put — Ivanka Khristova, Bulgaria. **69 ft. 5 in.**
Pentathlon — Sigrun Siegl, E. Germany. **4,745 pts.**

Swimming — Men

100 - Meter Freestyle — Jim Montgomery, U.S. **Time — 0:49.99.**
200 - Meter Freestyle — Bruce Furniss, U.S. **Time — 1:50.29.**
400 - Meter Freestyle — Brian Goodell, U.S. **Time — 3:51.93.**
1,500 - Meter Freestyle — Brian Goodell, U.S. **Time — 15:02.40.**
100 - Meter Breaststroke — John Hencken, U.S. **Time — 1:03.11.**
200 - Meter Breaststroke — David Wilkie, Gr. Britain. **Time — 2:15.11.**
100 - Meter Butterfly — Matt Vogel, U.S. **Time — 0:54.35.**
200 - Meter Butterfly — Mike Bruner, U.S. **Time — 1:59.23.**
100 - Meter Backstroke — John Naber, U.S. **Time — 0:55.49.**
200 - Meter Backstroke — John Naber, U.S. **Time — 1:59.19.**
400 - Meter Individual Medley — Rod Strachan, U.S. **Time — 4:23.68.**
400 - Meter Medley Relay — U.S. (Hencken, Naber, Montgomery, Vogel). **Time — 3:42.22.**
800 - Meter Freestyle Relay — U.S. (Bruner, Furniss, Naber, Montgomery). **Time — 7:23.22.**

Swimming — Women

100 - Meter Freestyle — Kornelia Ender, E. Germany. **Time — 0:55.65.**
200 - Meter Freestyle — Kornelia Ender, E. Germany. **Time — 1:59.26.**
400 - Meter Freestyle — Petra Thumer, E. Germany. **Time — 4:09.89.**
800 - Meter Freestyle — Petra Thumer, E. Germany. **Time — 8:37.14.**
100 - Meter Breaststroke — Hannelore Anke, E. Germany. **Time — 1:11.16.**
200 - Meter Breaststroke — Marina Koshevaia, USSR. **Time — 2:33.35.**
100 - Meter Butterfly — Kornelia Ender, E. Germany. **Time — 1:00.13.**
200 - Meter Butterfly — Andrea Pollack, E. Germany. **Time — 2:11.41.**
100 - Meter Backstroke — Ulrike Richter, E. Germany. **Time — 1:01.83.**
200 - Meter Backstroke — Ulrike Richter, E. Germany. **Time — 2:13.43.**
400 - Meter Individual Medley — Ulrike Tauber, E. Germany. **Time — 4:42.77.**
400 - Meter Freestyle Relay — U.S. (Peyton, Boglioli, Sterkel, Babashoff). **Time — 3:44.82.**
400 - Meter Medley Relay — E. Germany (Richter, Anke, Pollack, Ender). **Time — 4:07.95.**

Archery

Men's Individual — Darrell Pace, U.S.
Women's Individual — Luann Ryon, U.S.

Basketball

Men — U.S.
Women — USSR.

Boxing

Light Flyweight — Jorge Hernandez, Cuba.
Flyweight — Leo Randolph, U.S.
Bantamweight — Yong Jo Gu, No. Korea.
Featherweight — Angel Herrera, Cuba.
Lightweight — Howard Davis, U.S.
Light Welterweight — Ray Leonard, U.S.
Welterweight — Jochen Bąchfeld, E. Germany.
Light Middleweight — Jerzy Rybicki, Poland.
Middleweight — Mike Spinks, U.S.
Light Heavyweight — Leon Spinks, U.S.
Heavyweight — Teofilo Stevenson, Cuba.

Canoeing — Men

500-Meter Kayak Singles — Vasile Diba, Romania.
1,000-Meter Kayak Singles — Rudiger Helm, E. Germany.
500-Meter Kayak Doubles — E. Germany.
1,000-Meter Kayak Doubles — USSR.
1,000-Meter Kayak Fours — USSR.
500-Meter Canadian Singles — Aleksandr Rogov, USSR.
1,000-Meter Canadian Singles — Matija Ljubek, Yugoslavia.
500-Meter Canadian Doubles USSR.
1,000-Meter Canadian Doubles — USSR.

Canoeing — Women

500-Meter Kayak Singles — Carola Zirzow, E. Germany.
500-Meter Kayak Doubles — USSR.

Cycling

Individual Road Race — Bernt Johansson, Sweden.
1,000-Meter Time Trial — Klaus-Jurgen Grunke, E. Germany.
4,000-Meter Individual Pursuit — Gregor Braun, W. Germany.
4,000-Meter Team Pursuit — W. Germany.
Match Sprint — Anton Tkac, Czech.
100-Km. Team — USSR.

Diving — Men

Springboard — Phil Boggs, U.S.
Platform — Klaus Dibiasi, Italy.

Diving — Women

Springboard — Jenni Chandler, U.S.
Platform — Elena Vaytsekhovskaya, USSR.

Equestrian

3-Day Individual — Tad Coffin, U.S.
3-Day Team — U.S.
Individual Grand Prix Dressage — Christine Stueckelberger, Switzerland.
Individual Grand Prix Jumping — Alwin Schockemoehle, W. Germany.
Team Dressage — W. Germany.
Team Jumping — France.

Fencing — Men

Individual Foil — Fabio Dal Zotto, Italy.
Team Foil — W. Germany.
Individual Epee — Alexander Pusch, W. Germany.
Team Epee — Sweden.
Individual Saber — Viktor Krovopouskov, USSR.
Team Saber — USSR.

Fencing — Women

Individual Foil — Ildiko Schwarczenberger, Hungary.
Team Foil — USSR.

Field Hockey

Team Championship — New Zealand.

Gymnastics — Men

All-Around — Nikolai Andrianov, USSR.
Floor Exercise — Nikolai Andrianov, USSR.
Pommeled Horse — Zoltan Magyar, Hungary.
Rings Nikolai Andrianov, USSR.
Vault — Nikolai Andrianov, USSR.
Parallel Bars — Sawao Kato, Japan.
Horizontal Bar — Mitsuo Tsukahara, Japan.
Team Championship — Japan.

Gymnastics — Women

All-Around — Nadia Comaneci, Romania.
Floor Exercise — Nelli Kim, USSR.
Vault — Nelli Kim, USSR.
Uneven Parallel Bars — Nadia Comaneci, Romania.
Balance Beam — Nadia Comaneci, Romania.
Team Championship — USSR.

Team Handball

Men — USSR.
Women — USSR.

Judo

Lightweight — Hector Rodriguez, Cuba.
Light Middleweight — Vladimir Nevzorov, USSR.
Middleweight — Isamu Sonoda, Japan.
Light Heavyweight — Kazuhiro Nimomiya, Japan.
Heavyweight — Sergei Novikov, USSR.
Open — Haruki Uemura, Japan.

Modern Pentathlon

Individual — Janusz Pyciak-Peciak, Poland.
Team — Gt. Britain.

Rowing — Men

Single Sculls — Pertti Karppinen, Finland.
Double Sculls — Norway.
Quadruple Sculls — E. Germany.
Pairs with Coxswain — E. Germany.
Pairs without Coxswain — E. Germany.
Fours with Coxswain — USSR.
Fours without Coxswain — E. Germany.
Eights with Coxswain — E. Germany.

Rowing — Women

Single Sculls — Christine Scheiblich, E. Germany.
Double Sculls — Bulgaria.
Quadruple Sculls — E. Germany.
Pairs without Coxswain — Bulgaria.
Fours with Coxswain — E. Germany.
Eights with Coxswain — E. Germany.

Shooting

Small-bore Rifle Prone — Karlheinz Smieszek, W. Germany.
Small-bore Rifle (3-positions) — Lanny Bassham, U.S.
Rapid Fire Pistol — Norbert Klaar, E. Germany.
Free Pistol — Uwe Potteck, E. Germany.
Moving Target — Alexandr Gazov, USSR.
Trapshooting — Don Haldeman, U.S.
Skeetshooting — Josef Panacek, Czechoslovakia.

Soccer

Team Championship — E. Germany.

Volleyball

Men — Poland.
Women — Japan.

Water Polo

Team Championship — Hungary.

Weight Lifting

Flyweight — Alexandr Voronin, USSR.
Bantamweight — Norair Nourikian, Bulgaria.
Featherweight — Nikolai Kolesnikov, USSR.
Lightweight — Zbigniew Kaczmarek, Poland.
Middleweight — Yordan Mitkov, Bulgaria.
Light Heavyweight — Valery Shary, USSR.
Middle Heavyweight — David Rigert, USSR.
Heavyweight — Valentin Khristov, Bulgaria.
Super Heavyweight — Vasily Alexeev, USSR.

Wrestling — Freestyle

Paperweight — Khassan Issaev, Bulgaria.
Flyweight — Yuji Takada, Japan.
Bantamweight — Vladimir Yumin, USSR.
Featherweight — Jung-Mo Yang, S. Korea.
Lightweight — Pavel Pinigin, USSR.
Welterweight — Date Jiichiro, Japan.
Middleweight — John Peterson, U.S.
Light Heavyweight — Levan Tediashvily, USSR.
Heavyweight — Ivan Yarygin, USSR.
Super Heavyweight — Soslan Andiev, USSR.

Wrestling — Greco-Roman

Paperweight — Alexey Shumakov, USSR.
Flyweight — Vitaly Konstantinov, USSR.
Bantamweight — Pertti Ukkola, Finland.
Featherweight — Kazimer Lipien, Poland.
Lightweight — Suren Nalbandyan, USSR.
Welterweight — Antoly Bykov, USSR.
Middleweight — Momir Petkovic, Yugoslavia.
Light Heavyweight — Valery Rezantsev, USSR.
Heavyweight — Nikolai Balboshin, USSR.
Super Heavyweight — Alexandr Kolchinsky, USSR.

Yachting

Soling — Denmark.
Tempest — Sweden.
Flying Dutchman — W. Germany.
470 Class — W. Germany.
Tornado — Gt. Britain.
Finn — E. Germany.

Winter Olympic Games Champions, 1924-1976

Sites and Unofficial Winners of Games

1924—Chamonix, France (Norway)
1928—St. Moritz, Switzerland (Norway)
1932—Lake Placid, N.Y. (U.S.)
1936—Garmisch-Partenkirchen (Norway)
1948—St. Moritz (Sweden)
1952—Olso, Norway (Norway)
1956—Cortina d'Ampezzo, Italy (USSR)
1960—Squaw Valley, Cal. (USSR)
1964—Innsbruck, Austria (USSR)
1968—Grenoble, France (Norway)
1972—Sapporo, Japan (USSR)
1976—Innsbruck, Austria, (USSR)
1980—Lake Placid, N.Y. (scheduled)

Biathlon (20 km)

	Time
1960—Klas Lestander, Sweden	1:33:21.6
1964—Vladimir Melanin, USSR	1:20:26.8
1968—Magnar Solberg, Norway	1:13:45.9
1972—Magnar Solberg, Norway	1:15:55.50
1976—Nikolai Kruglov, USSR	1:14:12.26

Biathlon Relay (40 km)

	Time
1968—USSR, Norway, Sweden	2:13.02
1972—USSR, Finland, E. Germany	1:51.44
1976—USSR, Finland, E. Germany	1:57.55.64

Bobsledding

4-Man Bob

(Driver in parentheses)	Time
1924—Switzerland (Edward Scherrer)	5:45.54
1928—*United States (William Fiske) (A)	3:20.5
1932—United States (William Fiske)	7:53.68
1936—Switzerland (Pierre Musy)	5:19.85
1948—United States (Edward Rimkus)	5:20.1
1952—Germany (Andreas Ostler)	5:07.84
1956—Switzerland (Frank Kapus)	5:10.44
1964—Canada (Victor Emery)	4:14.46
1968—Italy (Eugenio Monti) (A)	2:17.39
1972—Switzerland (Jean Wicki)	4:43.07
1976—E. Germany (Meinhard Nehmer)	3:40.43

*Five-man bobsled (A) 2 races

2-Man Bob

	Time
1932—United States (Hubert Stevens)	8:14.74
1936—United States (Ivan Brown)	5:29.29
1948—Switzerland (F. Endrich)	5:29.2
1952—Germany (Andreas Ostler)	5:24.54
1956—Italy (Dalla Costa)	5:30.14
1964—Great Britain (Antony Nash)	4:21.90
1968—Italy (Eugenio Monti)	4:41.54
1972—W. Germany (Wolfgang Zimmerer)	4:47.07
1976—E. Germany (Meinhard Nehmer)	3:40.43

Figure Skating

Men's Singles

1908 Ulrich Sachow, Sweden
1920 Gillis Grafstrom, Sweden
1924 Gillis Grafstrom, Sweden
1928 Gillis Grafstrom, Sweden
1932 Karl Schaefer, Austria
1936 Karl Schaefer, Austria
1948 Richard T. Button, U.S.
1952 Richard T. Button, U.S.
1956 Hayes Alan Jenkins, U.S.
1960 David W. Jenkins, U.S.
1964 Manfred Schnelldorfer, Germany
1968 Wolfgang Schwartz, Austria
1972 Ondrej Nepela, Czechoslovakia
1976 John Curry, Great Britain

Women's Singles

1908 Madge Syers, Great Britain
1920 Magda Julin-Mauroy, Sweden
1924 Mrs. Heima von Szabo-Planck, Austria
1928 Sonja Henie, Norway
1932 Sonja Henie, Norway
1936 Sonja Henie, Norway
1948 Barbara Ann Scott, Canada
1952 Jeanette Altwegg, Great Britain
1956 Tenley Albright, U.S.
1960 Carol Heiss, U.S.
1964 Sjoukje Dijkstra, Netherlands
1968 Peggy Fleming, U.S.
1972 Beatrix Schuba, Austria
1976 Dorothy Hamill, U.S.

Pairs

1908 Anna Hubler & Heinrich Burger, Germany
1920 Ludovika & Walter Jakobsson, Finland
1924 Helene Engelman & Alfred Berger, Austria
1928 Andree Joly & Pierre Brunet, France
1932 Andree Joly & Pierre Brunet, France
1936 Maxie Herber & Ernest Baier, Germany
1948 Micheline Lannoy & Pierre Baugniet, Belgium
1952 Ria and Paul Falk, Germany
1956 Elisabeth Schwarz & Kurt Oppelt, Austria
1960 Barbara Wagner & Robert Paul, Canada
1964 Ludmila Beloussova & Oleg Protopopov, USSR
1968 Ludmila Beloussova & Oleg Protopopov, USSR
1972 Irina Rodina & Alexei Ulanov, USSR
1976 Irina Rodina & Aleksandr Zaitzev, USSR

Ice Dancing

1976 Ludmila Pakhomova & Aleksandr Gorschkov, USSR

Alpine Skiing

Men's Downhill

	Time
1948—Henri Oreiller, France	2:55.0
1952—Zeno Colo, Italy	2:30.8
1956—Anton Sailer, Austria	2:52.2
1960—Jean Vuarnet, France	2:06.0
1964—Egon Zimmermann, Austria	2:18.16
1968—Jean Claude Killy, France	1:59.85
1972—Bernhard Russi, Switzerland	1:51.43
1976—Franz Klammer, Austria	1:45.73

Men's Giant Slalom

	Time
1952—Stein Eriksen, Norway	2:25.0
1956—Anton Sailer, Austria	3:00.1
1960—Roger Staub, Switzerland	1:48.3
1964—Francois Bonlieu, France	1:46.7
1968—Jean Claude Killy, France	3:29.28
1972—Gustavo Thoeni, Italy	3:09.62
1976—Heini Hemmi, Switzerland	3:26.97

Men's Slalom

	Time
1948—Edi Reinalter, Switzerland	2:10.3
1952—Othmar Schneider, Austria	2:00.0
1956—Anton Sailer, Austria	194.7 pts.
1960—Ernst Hinterseer, Austria	2:08.9
1964—Josef Stiegler, Austria	2:11.13
1968—Jean Claude Killy, France	1:39.73
1972—Francesco Fernandez Ochoa, Spain	1:49.27
1976—Piero Gros, Italy	2:03.29

Women's Downhill

	Time
1948—Hedi Schlunegger, Switzerland	2:28.3
1952—Trude Jochum-Beiser, Austria	1:47.1
1956—Madeline Bethod, Switzerland	1:40.7
1960—Heidi Biebl, Germany	1:37.6
1964—Christl Haas, Austria	1:55.3
1968—Olga Pall, Austria	1:40.87
1972—Marie Therese Nadig, Switzerland	1:36.68
1976—Rosi Mittermaier, W. Germany	1:46.16

Women's Giant Slalom

	Time
1952—Andrea Mead Lawrence, U.S.	2:06.8
1956—Ossi Reichert, Germany	1:56.5
1960—Yvonne Ruegg, Switzerland	1:39.9
1964—Marielle Goitschel, France	1:52.2
1968—Nancy Greene, Canada	1:51.97
1972—Marie Therese Nadig, Switzerland	1:29.90
1976—Kathy Kreiner, Canada	1:29.13

Women's Slalom

	Time
1948—Gretchen Fraser, U.S.	1:57.2
1952—Andrea Mead Lawrence, U.S.	2:10.6
1956—Renee Colliard, Switzerland	112.3 pts.
1960—Anne Heggtveigt, Canada	1:49.6
1964—Christine Goitschel, France	1:35.11
1968—Marielle Goitschel, France	1:25.86
1972—Barbara Cochran, U.S.	1:31.24
1976—Rosi Mittermaier, W. Germany	1:30.54

Nordic Skiing

Men's Cross-Country Events
15 kilometers (9.3 miles) or equivalent

	Time
1924—Thorleif Haug, Norway	1:14:31
1928—Johan Grottumsbraaten, Norway	1:37:01
1932—Sven Utterstrom, Sweden	1:23:07
1936—Erik-August Larsson, Sweden	1:14:38

1948—Martin Lundstrom, Sweden............ 1:13:50
1952—Hallgeir Brenden, Norway............. 1:01:34
1956—Hallgeir Brenden, Norway............. 49:39.0
1960—Haakon Brusveen, Norway............. 51:55.0
1964—Eero Mantyranta, Finland............. 50:54.1
1968—Harald Groenningen, Norway.......... 47.54.2
1972—Sven-Ake Lundback, Sweden.......... 45:28.24
1976—Nikolai Bajukov, USSR............... 43:58.47
(Note: approx. 18-kilometer course 1924-1952)

30 kilometers (18.6 miles) **Time**

1956—Veikko Hakulinen, Finland............. 1:44:06.0
1960—Sixten Jernberg, Sweden............. 1:51:03.9
1964—Eero Mantyranta, Finland............. 1:30:50.7
1968—Franco Nones, Italy................. 1:35:39.2
1972—Vyacheslav Vedenin, USSR........... 1:36:31.1
1976—Sergei Savaliev, USSR............... 1:30:29.38

50 kilometers (31 miles) **Time**

1924—Thorleif Haug, Norway................ 3:44:32.0
1928—Per Erik Hedlund, Sweden............. 4:52:03.0
1932—Veli Saarinen, Finland................ 4:28:00.0
1936—Elis Viklund, Sweden................. 3:30:11.0
1948—Nils Karlsson, Sweden................ 3:47:48.0
1952—Veikko Hakulinen, Finland............. 3:33:33.0
1956—Sixten Jernberg, Sweden............... 2:50:27.0
1960—Kalevi Hamalainen, Finland............ 2:59:06.3
1964—Sixten Jernberg, Sweden............... 2:43:52.6
1968—Ole Ellefsaeter, Norway............... 2:28:45.8
1972—Paal Tyldum, Norway.................. 2:43:14.7
1976—Ivar Formo, Norway................... 2:37:30.05

40-km. Cross-Country Relay **Time**

1936—Finland, Norway, Sweden............. 2:41:33.0
1948—Sweden, Finland, Norway............. 2:32:08.0
1952—Finland, Norway, Sweden............. 2:20:16.0
1956—USSR, Finland, Sweden............... 2:15:30.0
1960—Finland, Norway, USSR............... 2:18:45.6
1964—Sweden, Finland, USSR............... 2:18:34.6
1968—Norway, Sweden, Finland............. 2:08:33.5
1972—USSR, Norway, Switzerland........... 2:04:47.94
1976—Finland, Norway, USSR............... 2:07:59.72

15-km. Cross-Country & Jumping **Points**

1924—Thorleif Haug, Norway................ 453.800
1928—Johan Grottumsbraaten, Norway........ 427.800
1932—Johan Grottumsbraaten, Norway........ 446.200
1936—Oddbjorn Hagen, Norway............... 430.300
1948—Heikki Hasu, Finland................. 448.800
1952—Simon Slattvik, Norway............... 451.621
1956—Sverre Stenersen, Norway............. 455.000
1960—Georg Thoma, Germany................. 457.952
1964—Tormod Knutsen, Norway............... 469.280
1968—Franz Keller, W. Germany.............. 449.040
1972—Ulrich Wehling, E. Germany............ 413.340
1976—Ulrich Wehling, E. Germany............ 423.390

Ski Jumping (90 meters) **Points**

1924—Jacob T. Thams, Norway............... 227.5
1928—Alfred Andersen, Norway.............. 230.5
1932—Birger Ruud, Norway.................. 228.0
1936—Birger Ruud, Norway.................. 232.0
1948—Petter Hugsted, Norway............... 228.1
1952—A. Bergmann, Norway.................. 226.0
1956—Antti Hyvarinen, Finland.............. 227.0
1960—Helmut Recknagel, Germany............ 227.2
1964—Toralf Engan, Norway................. 230.7
1968—Vladimir Beloussov, USSR............. 231.3
1972—Wojiech Fortuna, Poland............... 219.9
1976—Karl Schnabl, Austria................. 234.8

Ski Jumping (70 meters) **Points**

1964—Veikko Kankkonen, Finland............ 229.9
1968—Jiri Raska, Czechoslovakia............ 216.5
1972—Yukio Kasaya, Japan.................. 244.2
1976—Hans Aschenbach, E. Germany.......... 252.0

Women's Events

5 kilometers (approx. 3.1 miles) **Time**

1964—Claudia Boyarskikh, USSR............. 17:50.5
1968—Toini Gustafsson, Sweden.............. 16:45.2
1972—Galina Koulacova, USSR............... 17:00.5
1976—Helena Takalo, Finland................ 15:48.69

10 kilometers (6.2 miles) **Time**

1952—Lydia Wideman, Finland............... 41:40.0
1956—Lyubov Kosyreva, USSR............... 38:11.0
1960—Maria Gusakova, USSR................. 39:46.6
1964—Claudia Boyarskikh, USSR............. 40:24.3
1968—Toini Gustafsson, Sweden.............. 36:46.5
1972—Galina Koulacova, USSR............... 34:17.82
1976—Raisa Smetanina, USSR................ 30:13.41

15-km. Cross-Country Relay **Time**

1956—Finland, USSR, Sweden............... 1:09:01.0
1960—Sweden, USSR, Finland............... 1:04:21.4
1964—USSR, Sweden, Finland............... 59:20.2
1968—Norway, Sweden, USSR................ 57:30.0
1972—USSR, Finland, Norway................ 48:46.1
1976—USSR, Finland, E. Germany............ 1:07:49.75
(20 km. in 1976)

Ice Hockey

1920 Canada, U.S., Czechoslovakia
1924 Canada, U.S., Great Britain
1928 Canada, Sweden, Switzerland
1932 Canada, U.S., Germany
1936 Great Britain, Canada, U.S.
1948 Canada, Czechoslovakia, Switzerland
1952 Canada, U.S., Sweden
1956 USSR, U.S., Canada
1960 U.S., Canada, USSR
1964 USSR, Sweden, Czechoslovakia
1968 USSR, Czechoslovakia, Canada
1972 USSR, U.S., Czechoslovakia
1976 USSR, Czechoslovakia, W. Germany

Luge

Men's Singles **Time**

1964—Thomas Kohler, Germany.............. 3:26.77
1968—Manfred Schmid, Austria.............. 2:52.48
1972—Wolfgang Scheidel, E. Germany......... 3:27.58
1976—Detlef Guenther, E. Germany........... 3:27.688

Men's Doubles **Time**

1964—Austria.............................. 1:41.62
1968—East Germany........................ 1:35.85
1972—Italy, E. Germany (tie)................ 1:28.35
1976—E. Germany.......................... 1:25.604

Women's Singles **Time**

1964—Ortun Enderlein, Germany.............. 3:24.67
1968—Erica Lechner, Italy................... 2:28.66
1972—Anna M. Muller, E. Germany............ 2:59.18
1976—Margit Schumann, E. Germany.......... 2:50.621

Speed Skating

Men's Events

500 meters (approx. 547 yds.) **Time**

1924—Charles Jewtraw, U.S.................. 0:44.0
1928—Clas Thunberg, Finland &
Bernt Evensen, Norway (tie)............ 0:43.4
1932—John A. Shea, U.S.................... 0:43.4
1936—Ivar Ballangrud, Norway.............. 0:43.4
1948—Finn Helgesen, Norway................ 0:43.1
1952—Kenneth Henry, U.S.................. 0:43.2
1956—Evgeniy Grishin, USSR................ 0:40.2
1960—Evgeniy Grishin, USSR................ 0:40.2
1964—Terry McDermott, U.S................. 0:40.1
1968—Erhard Keller, W. Germany............ 0:40.3
1972—Erhard Keller, W. Germany............ 0:39.44
1976—Evgeny Kulikov, USSR................ 0:39.17

1,000 meters **Time**

1976—Peter Mueller, U.S.................... 1:19.32

1,500 meters **Time**

1924—Clas Thunberg, Finland................ 2:20.8
1928—Clas Thunberg, Finland................ 2:21.1
1932—John A. Shea, U.S.................... 2:57.2
1936—Charles Mathiesen, Norway............ 2:19.2
1948—Sverre Farstad, Norway............... 2:17.6
1952—Hjalmar Anderson, Norway............. 2:20.4
1956—Evgeniy Grishin, USSR................ 2:08.6
1960—Roald Edgar Aas, Norway &
Evgeniy Grishin, USSR (tie)............. 2:10.4
1964—Ants Anston, USSR................... 2:10.3
1968—Cornelis Verkerk, Netherlands.......... 2:03.4
1972—Ard Schenk, Netherlands.............. 2:02.96
1976—Jan Egil Storholt, Norway............. 1:59.38

5,000 meters **Time**

1924—Clas Thunberg, Finland................ 8:39.0
1928—Ivar Ballangrud, Norway.............. 8:50.5
1932—Irving Jaffee, U.S.................... 9:40.8
1936—Ivar Ballangrud, Norway.............. 8:19.6
1948—Reidar Liakleb, Norway............... 8:29.4
1952—Hjalmar Anderson, Norway............. 8:10.6

1956—Boris Shilkov, USSR.................7:48.7
1960—Viktor Kosichkin, USSR................7:51.3
1964—Knut Johannesen, Norway..............7:38.4
1968—F. Anton Maier, Norway...............7:22.4
1972—Ard Schenk, Netherlands..............7:23.61
1976—Sten Stensen, Norway.................7:24.48

10,000 meters	Time
1924—Julius Skutnabb, Finland	18:04.8
1928—Event not held, thawing of ice	
1932—Irving Jaffee, U.S.	19:13.6
1936—Ivar Ballangrud, Norway	17:24.3
1948—Ake Seyffarth, Norway	17:26.3
1952—Hjalmar Anderson, Norway	16:45.8
1956—Sigvard Ericsson, Sweden	16:35.9
1960—Knut Johannesen, Norway	15:46.6
1964—Jonny Nilsson, Sweden	15:50.1
1968—Jonny Hoeglin, Sweden	15:23.6
1972—Ard Schenk, Netherlands	15:01.3
1976—Piet Kleine, Netherlands	14:50.59

Women's Events

500 meters	Time
1960—Helga Haase, Germany	0:45.9
1964—Lydia Skoblikova, USSR	0:45.0
1968—Ludmila Titova, USSR	0:46.1
1972—Anne Henning, U.S.	0:43.44
1976—Sheila Young, U.S.	0:42.76

1,000 meters	Time
1960—Klara Guseva, USSR	1:34.1
1964—Lydia Skoblikova, USSR	1:33.2
1968—Carolina Geijssen, Netherlands	1:32.6
1972—Monika Pflug, W. Germany	1:31.40
1976—Tatiana Averina, USSR	1:28.43

1,500 meters	Time
1960—Lydia Skoblikova, USSR	2:52.2
1964—Lydia Skoblikova,USSR	2:22.6
1968—Kaija Mustonen, Finland	2:22.4
1972—Dianne Holum, U.S.	2:20.85
1976—Galina Stepanskaya, USSR	2:16.58

3,000 meters	Time
1960—Lydia Skoblikova, USSR	5:14.3
1964—Lydia Skoblikova, USSR	5:14.9
1968—Johanna Schut, Netherlands	4:56.2
1972—Stien Baas-Kaiser, Netherlands	4:52.14
1976—Tatiana Averina, USSR	4:45.19

1976 Final Medal Standing

Innsbruck, Austria, Feb. 4-15

	Gold	Silver	Bronze	Total
Austria	2	2	2	6
Canada	1	1	1	3
Czechoslovakia	0	1	0	1
Finland	2	4	1	7
France	0	0	1	1
Germany, East	7	5	7	19
Germany, West	2	5	3	10
Gt. Britain	1	0	0	1
Italy	1	2	1	4
Liechtenstein	0	0	2	2
Netherlands	1	2	3	6
Norway	3	3	1	7
Sweden	0	0	2	2
Switzerland	1	3	1	5
USSR	13	6	8	27
United States	3	3	4	10

Olympic Information

Symbol: Five rings or circles, linked together to represent the sporting friendship of all peoples. The rings also symbolize the 5 continents — Europe, Asia, Africa, Australia, and America. Each ring is a different color — blue, yellow, black, green, and red.

Flag: The symbol of the 5 rings on a plain white background.

Motto: "Citius, Altius, Fortius," Latin meaning "faster, higher, braver," or the modern interpretation "swifter, higher, stronger". The motto was coined by Father Didon, a French educator, in 1895.

Creed: "The most important thing in the Olympic Games is not to win but to take part, just as the most important thing in life is not the triumph but the struggle. The essential thing is not to have conquered but to have fought well."

Oath: An athlete of the host country recites the following at the opening ceremony. "In the name of all competitors I promise that we will take part in these Olympic Games, respecting and abiding by the rules which govern them, in the true spirit of sportsmanship for the glory of sport and the honor of our teams." Both the oath and the creed were composed by Pierre de Coubertin, the founder of the modern Games.

Flame: Symbolizes the continuity between the ancient and modern Games. The modern version of the flame was adopted in 1936. The torch used to kindle the flame is first lit by the sun's rays at Olympia, Greece, and then carried to the site of the Games by relays of runners. Ships and planes are used when necessary.

James E. Sullivan Memorial Trophy Winners

The James E. Sullivan Memorial Trophy, named after the former president of the AAU and inaugurated in 1930, is awarded annually by the AAU to the athlete who "by his or her performance, example and influence as an amateur, has done the most during the year to advance the cause of sportsmanship."

Year	Winner	Sport
1930	Bobby Jones	Golf
1931	Barney Berlinger	Track
1932	Jim Bausch	Track
1933	Glenn Cunningham	Track
1934	Bill Bonthron	Track
1935	Lawson Little	Golf
1936	Glenn Morris	Track
1937	Don Budge	Tennis
1938	Don Lash	Track
1939	Joe Burk	Rowing
1940	Greg Rice	Track
1941	Leslie Mac Mitchell	Track
1942	Cornelius Warmerdam	Track
1943	Gilbert Dodds	Track
1944	Ann Curtis	Swimming
1945	Doc Blanchard	Football
1946	Arnold Tucker	Football
1947	John Kelly Jr.	Rowing
1948	Robert Mathias	Track
1949	Dick Button	Skating
1950	Fred Wilt	Track
1951	Rev. Robert Richards	Track
1952	Horace Ashenfelter	Track
1953	Dr. Sammy Lee	Diving
1954	Mal Whitfield	Track
1955	Harrison Dillard	Track
1956	Patricia McCormick	Diving
1957	Bobby Joe Morrow	Track
1958	Glenn Davis	Track
1959	Parry O'Brien	Track
1960	Rafer Johnson	Track
1961	Wilma Rudolph Ward	Track
1962	James Beatty	Track
1963	John Pennel	Track
1964	Don Schollander	Swimming
1965	Bill Bradley	Basketball
1966	Jim Ryun	Track
1967	Randy Matson	Track
1968	Debbie Meyer	Swimming
1969	Bill Toomey	Track
1970	John Kinsella	Swimming
1971	Mark Spitz	Swimming
1972	Frank Shorter	Track
1973	Bill Walton	Basketball
1974	Rick Wohlhuter	Track
1975	Tim Shaw	Swimming
1976	Bruce Jenner	Track

World Record Fish Caught by Rod and Reel

Source: Saltwater: International Game Fish Association. Freshwater: Field & Stream Magazine.
Records confirmed to June, 1977

Saltwater Fish

The International Game Fish Assn. revised its standards for world records, effective July 1, 1970. Line samples and line tests are now required in order for a world record application to be recognized. Records listed below are based on the new standards.

Species	Weight	Length	Girth	Where caught	Date	Angler
Albacore	74 lbs. 13 oz.	4'2"	34 3/4"	Arguineguin, Canary Is.	Oct. 28, 1973	Olof Idegren
Amberjack	149 lbs.	5'11"	41 3/4"	Bermuda	June 21, 1964	Peter Simons
Barracuda, Great	83 lbs.	6' 1/4"	29"	Lagos, Nigeria	Jan. 13, 1952	K. J. W. Hackett
Bass, Black Sea	8 lbs.	1'10"	19"	Nantucket Sound, Mass.	May 13, 1951	H. R. Rider
Bass, Giant Sea	563 lbs. 8 oz.	7'5"	72"	Anacaba Island, Cal.	Aug. 20, 1968	James D. McAdam Jr.
Bass, Striped	72 lbs.	4'6 1/2"	31"	Cuttyhunk, Mass.	Oct. 10, 1969	Edward J. Kirker
Blackfish (or Tautog)	21 lbs. 6 oz.	2'7 1/2"	23 1/2"	Cape May, N.J.	June 12, 1954	R. N. Sheafer
Bluefish	31 lbs. 12 oz.	3'11"	23"	Hatteras Inlet, N.C.	Jan. 30, 1972	James M. Hussey
Bonefish	19 lbs.	3'3 5/8"	17"	Zululand, S. Africa	May 26, 1962	Brian W. Batchelor
Cobia	110 lbs. 5 oz.	5'3"	34"	Mombasa, Kenya	Sept. 8, 1964	Eric Tinworth
Cod	98 lbs. 12 oz.	5'3"	41"	Isle of Shoals, Mass.	June 8, 1969	Alphonse Bielevich
Dolphin	87 lbs.	5'8"	31 3/4"	Papagallo Gulf, Costa Rica	Sept. 25, 1976	Manual Salazar
Drum, Black	113 lbs. 1 oz.	4'5 1/8"	43 1/2"	Lewes, Del.	Sept. 15, 1975	Gerald Townsend
Drum, Red	90 lbs.	4'7 1/2"	38 1/4"	Rodanthe, N.C.	Nov. 7, 1973	Elvin Hooper
Flounder	30 lbs. 12 oz.	3'2 1/2"	30 1/2"	Vina del Mar, Chile	Nov. 1, 1971	Augusto Nunez Moreno
Jewfish	680 lbs.	7'1 1/2"	66"	Fernandina Beach, Fla.	May 20, 1961	Lynn Joyner
Kawakawa	21 lbs.	2'10"	22"	Kauai, Ha.	Aug. 21, 1975	E. John O'Dell
Mackerel, King	90 lbs.	5'11"	30"	Key West, Fla.	Feb. 16, 1976	Norton Thornton
Marlin, Atlantic Blue	1,142 lbs.	13'9"	80"	Nags Head, N.C.	July 26, 1974	Jack Herrington
Marlin, Black	1,560 lbs.	14'6"	81"	Cabo Blanco, Peru	Aug. 4, 1953	A. C. Glassell Jr.
Marlin, King	78 lbs. 12 oz.	5'5 1/2"	30"	La Romana, Dominican Republic	Nov. 26, 1971	Fernando Viyella
Marlin, Pacific Blue	1,153 lbs.	14'8"	73"	Guam	Aug. 21, 1969	Greg Perez
Marlin, Striped	415 lbs.	11'	52"	Cape Brett, N.Z.	Mar. 31, 1964	B. C. Bain
Marlin, White	174 lbs. 3 oz.	8'8 1/3"	35 1/2"	Vitoria, Brazil	Nov. 1, 1975	Otavio Cunha Reboucas
Permit	50 lbs. 8 oz.	3'8 3/4"	33 3/4"	Key West, Fla.	Mar. 15, 1971	Marshall Earnest
Pollock	46 lbs. 7 oz.	4'2 1/2"	30"	Brielle, N.J.	May 26, 1975	John Tomes Holton
Roosterfish	114 lbs.	5'4"	33"	La Paz, Mex.	June 1, 1960	Abe Sackheim
Runner, Rainbow	33 lbs. 10 oz.	4'7 1/4"	22 1/2"	Clarion Is., Mexico	Mar. 14, 1976	R. A. Mikkelsen
Sailfish, Atlantic	128 lbs. 1 oz.	8'10 1/4"	34 1/4"	Luanda, Angola	Mar. 27, 1974	Harm Steyn
Sailfish, Pacific	221 lbs.	10'9"	....	Santa Cruz Is.	Feb. 12, 1947	C. W. Stewart
Seabass, White	83 lbs. 12 oz.	5'5 1/2"	34"	San Felipe, Mex.	Mar. 31, 1953	L.C. Baumgardner
Seatrout, Spotted	15 lbs. 6 oz.	2'9"	23 3/4"	Jensen Beach, Fla.	May 4, 1969	Michael J. Foremny
Shark, Blue	410 lbs.	11'6"	52"	Rockport, Mass.	Sept. 1, 1960	R.C. Webster
	410 lbs.	11'2"	52 1/2"	Rockport, Mass.	Aug. 17, 1967	Martha Webster
Shark, Hammerhead	703 lbs.	14'4"	63"	Jacksonville Beach, Fla.	July 5, 1975	H. B. Reasor
Shark, Man-Eater or White	2,664 lbs.	16'10"	114"	Ceduna, Australia	Apr. 21, 1959	Alfred Dean
Shark, Porbeagle	465 lbs.	9'3"	56"	Cornwall, Eng.	July 23, 1976	Jorge Potier
Shark, Shortfin Mako	1,061 lbs.	12'2"	79 1/2"	Mayor Island, N.Z.	Feb. 17, 1970	James Penwarden
Shark, Thresher	739 lbs.	8'10"	68"	Tutukaka, N.Z.	Feb. 17, 1975	Brian Galvin
Shark, Tiger	1,780 lbs.	13'10 1/2"	103"	Cherry Grove, S.C.	June 14, 1964	Walter Maxwell
Snook	52 lbs. 6 oz.	4'1 1/2"	26"	La Paz, Mexico	Jan. 9, 1963	Jane Haywood
Swordfish	1,182 lbs.	14'11 1/2"	78"	Iquique, Chile	May 7, 1953	L. Marron
Tanguigue	81 lbs.	5'11 1/2"	29 1/4"	Karachi, Pakistan	Aug. 27, 1960	George E. Rusinak
Tarpon	283 lbs.	7'2 1/2"	....	L. Maracaibo, Venezuela	Mar. 19, 1956	M. Salazar
Tuna, Allison (Yellowfin)	308 lbs.	7'	57"	San Benedicto Isl., Mex.	Jan. 18, 1973	Harold J. Tolson
Tuna, Atlantic Bigeye	353 lbs. 11 oz.	7'5"	58 4/5"	Canary Islands, Spain	Sept. 8, 1976	Dr. M. Margoulies
Tuna, Blackfin	38 lbs.	3'3 1/4"	28 3/4"	Bermuda	June 26, 1970	Archie L. Dickens
	38 lbs.	3'5"	28"	Islamorada, Fla.	May 21, 1973	Elizabeth Jean Wade
Tuna, Bluefin	1,200 lbs.	....	....	Chaleur Bay, N.B., Can.	Sept. 22, 1976	Leslie Vibert
Tuna, Dog-tooth	153 lbs. 8 oz.	....	....	Cooktown, Aust.	Sept. 25, 1975	William Chapman
Tuna, Longtail	60 lbs.	4'8"	30"	Australia	Mar. 17, 1975	N. Noel Webster
Tuna, Pacific Bigeye	435 lbs.	7'9"	63 1/2"	Cabo Blanco, Peru	Apr. 17, 1957	Dr. Russel Lee
Tuna, Skipjack (Oceanic Bonito)	39 lbs. 15 oz.	3'3"	28"	Walker Cay, Bahamas	Jan 21, 1952	F. Dowley
	40 lbs.	3'2 3/4"	27 1/2"	Mauritius	Apr. 19, 1971	Joseph Caboche Jr.
Tunny, Little	27 lbs.	3'3"	22"	Key Largo, Fla.	Apr. 20, 1976	William E. Allison
Wahoo	149 lbs.	6'7 3/4"	37 1/2"	Cat Cay, Bahamas	June 15, 1962	John Pirovano
Weakfish	19 lbs. 8 oz.	3'1"	23 3/4"	Trinidad, W. Indies	Apr. 13, 1962	Dennis Hall
Yellowtail	111 lbs.	5'2"	38"	Bay of Islands, N.Z.	June 11, 1961	A.F. Plim

Freshwater Fish

Species	Weight	Length	Girth	Where caught	Date	Angler
Bass, Largemouth	22 lbs. 4 oz.	32 1/2"	28 1/2"	Montgomery Lake, Ga.	June 2, 1932	George W. Perry
Bass, Redeye	7 lbs. 8 oz.	23"	18"	Lazer Creek, Ga.	Apr. 9, 1975	Jimmy L. Rogers
Bass, Rock	3 lbs.	13 1/2"	10 3/4"	York River, Ont.	Aug. 1, 1974	Peter Gulgin
Bass, Smallmouth	11 lbs. 15 oz.	27"	21 2/3"	Dale Hollow Lake, Ky.	July 9, 1955	David L. Hayes
Bass, Spotted	8 lbs. 10 1/2 oz.	23 1/2"	19 7/8"	Smith Lake, Ala.	Feb. 25, 1972	Billy Henderson
Bass, White	5 lbs. 5 oz.	19 1/2"	17"	Ferguson Lake, Cal.	Mar. 8, 1972	Norman W. Mize
Bass, Yellow	2 lbs. 2 oz.	14"	13"	Lake Monona, Wis.	Jan. 18, 1972	James Thrun
Black Bullhead	8 lbs.	24"	17 3/4"	Lake Waccabuc, N.Y.	Aug. 1, 1951	Kani Evans
Bluegill	4 lbs. 12 oz.	15"	18 1/4"	Ketona Lake, Ala.	Apr. 9, 1950	T.S. Hudson

Species	Weight	Length	Girth	Where caught	Date	Angler
Bowfin	19 lbs. 12 oz.	39"	....	Lake Marion, S.C.	Nov. 5, 1972	M. R. Webster
Buffalo, Bigmouth	56 lbs.	44¾"	33"	Lock Loma L. Mo.	Aug. 19, 1976	W. J. Long
Buffalo, Smallmouth	26 lbs. 10 oz.	34½"	28¼"	Lake Wylie, N.C.	Feb. 19, 1976	J. Gary Hill
Carp	55 lbs. 5 oz.	42"	31"	Clearwater Lake, Minn.	July 10, 1952	Frank J. Ledwein
Catfish, Blue	97 lbs.	57"	37"	Missouri River, S.D.	Sept. 16, 1959	E.B. Elliott
Catfish, Channel	58 lbs.	47½"	29⅛"	Santee-Cooper Res., S.C.	July 7, 1964	W.B. Whaley
Catfish, Flathead	79 lbs. 8 oz.	44"	27"	White River, Ind.	Aug. 13, 1955	Glenn T. Simpson
Catfish, White	10 lbs. 5 oz.	25"	17½"	Raritan R., N.J.	June 23, 1976	Lewis W. Lomerson
Char, Arctic	29 lbs. 11 oz.	39¾"	26"	Arctic River, N.W.T.	Aug. 21, 1968	Jeanne P. Branson
Crappie, Black	5 lbs.	19¼"	18⅝"	Santee-Cooper Res., S.C.	Mar. 15, 1957	Paul E. Foust
Crappie, White	5 lbs. 3 oz.	21"	19"	Enid Dam, Miss.	July 31, 1957	Fred L. Bright
Dolly Varden	32 lbs.	40½"	29¾"	L. Pend Oreille, Ida.	Oct. 27, 1949	N. L. Higgins
Drum, Freshwater	54 lbs. 8 oz.	31½"	29"	Nickajack Lake, Tenn.	Apr. 20, 1972	Benny E. Hull
Gar, Alligator	279 lbs.	93"	....	Rio Grande R., Tex.	Dec. 2, 1951	Bill Valverde
Gar, Longnose	50 lbs. 5 oz.	72¼"	22¼"	Trinity River, Tex.	July 30, 1954	Townsend Miller
Grayling, American	5 lbs. 15 oz.	29⅞"	15⅛"	Katseyedie R., N.W.T.	Aug. 16, 1967	Jeanne P. Branson
Kokanee	6 lbs.	24½"	14½"	Priest Lake, Ida.	June 9, 1975	Jerry Verge
Muskellunge	69 lbs. 15 oz.	64½"	31¾"	St. Lawrence R., N.Y.	Sept. 22, 1957	Arthur Lawton
Perch, White	4 lbs. 12 oz.	19½"	13"	Messalonskee Lake, Me.	June 4, 1949	Mrs. Earl Small
Perch, Yellow	4 lbs. 3½ oz.	....	....	Bordentown, N.J.	May, 1865	Dr. C. C. Abbot
Pickerel, Chain	9 lbs. 6 oz.	31"	14"	Homerville, Ga.	Feb. 17, 1961	Baxley McQuaig Jr.
Pike, Northern	46 lbs. 2 oz.	52½"	25"	Sacandaga Res., N.Y.	Sept. 15, 1940	Peter Dubuc
Redhorse, Silver	4 lbs. 2 oz.	20½"	14"	Gasconade River, Mo.	Oct. 5, 1974	C. Larry McKinney
Salmon, Atlantic	79 lbs. 2 oz.	....	....	Tana R., Norway	1928	Henrik Henriksen
Salmon, Chinook	92 lbs.	58½"	36"	Skeena River, B.C.	July 19, 1959	Heinz Wichmann
Salmon, Chum	24 lbs. 4 oz.	40½"	22[illegible]/8"	Margarita Bay, Alaska	Aug. 19, 1974	Richard Coleman
Salmon, Landlocked	22 lbs. 8 oz.	3'	est.20"	Sebago Lake, Ma.	Aug. 1, 1907	Edward Blakely
Salmon, Silver	31 lbs.	....	....	Cowichan Bay, B.C.	Oct. 11, 1947	Mrs. Lee Hallberg
Sauger	8 lbs. 12 oz.	28"	15"	Lake Sakakawea, N.D.	Oct. 6, 1971	Mike Fischer
Shad, American	9 lbs. 2 oz.	25"	17½"	Enfield, Conn.	Apr. 28, 1973	Edward P. Nelson
Sturgeon, White	360 lbs.	111"	86"	Snake River, Ida.	Apr. 24, 1956	Willard Cravens
Sunfish, Green	2 lbs. 2 oz.	14¾"	14"	Stockton Lake, Mo.	June 18, 1971	Paul M. Dilley
Sunfish, Redear	4 lbs. 8 oz.	16¼"	17¾"	Chase City, Va.	June 19, 1970	Maurice E. Ball
Trout, Brook	14½ lbs.	31½"	11½"	Nipigon R., Ont.	July, 1916	Dr. W. J. Cook
Trout, Brown (record being reviewed.)						
Trout, Cutthroat	41 lbs.	39"	....	Pyramid Lake, Nev.	Dec., 1925	J. Skimmerhorn
Trout, Golden	11 lbs.	28"	16"	Cook's Lake, Wyo.	Aug. 5, 1948	Charles S. Reed
Trout, Lake	65 lbs.	52"	38"	Great Bear Lake, N.W.T.	Aug. 8, 1970	Larry Daunis
Trout, Rainbow						
Stlhd. or Kamloopa	42 lbs. 2 oz.	43"	23½"	Bell Island, Alas.	June 22, 1970	David Robert White
Trout, Sunapee	11 lbs. 8 oz.	33"	17¼"	Lake Sunapee, N.H.	Aug. 1, 1954	Ernest Theoharis
Trout, Tiger	10 lbs.	27"	16¾"	Deerskin River, Wis.	May 23, 1974	Charles J. Mattek
Walleye	25 lbs.	41"	29"	Old Hickory Lake, Tenn.	Aug. 1, 1960	Mabry Harper
Warmouth	2 lbs.	12"	12½"	Sylvania, Ga.	May 4, 1974	Carlton Robbins
Whitefish, Lake	13 lbs.	32¼"	19"	Great Bear Lake, N.W.T.	July 14, 1974	Robert L. Stintsman
Whitefish, Mountain	5 lbs.	19"	14"	Athabasca R., Alta.	June 3, 1963	Orville Welch

The America's Cup

Competition for the America's Cup grew out of the first contest to establish a world yachting championship, one of the carnival features of the London Exposition of 1851. The race, open to all classes of yachts from all over the world, covered a 60-mile course around the Isle of Wight; the prize was a cup worth about $500, donated by the Royal Yacht Squadron of England, known as the "America's Cup" because it was first won by the United States yacht America. Successive efforts of British and Australian yachtsmen have failed to win the famous trophy, which remains in the United States.

On Sept. 18, 1977, the 66-foot 12-meter yacht Courageous won a fourth straight victory over the Australian challenger, Australia, to keep the symbol of world sailing supremacy in the United States. In four races, Australia lost to Courageous by a total of 7 minutes, 48 seconds. The U.S. yacht was designed by Olin Stephens and skippered by Ted Turner.

Winners of the America's Cup

1851 America
1870 Magic defeated Cambria, England, (1-0)
1871 Columbia (first three races) and Sappho (last two races) defeated Livonia, England, (4-1)
1876 Madeline defeated Countess of Dufferin, Canada, (2-0)
1881 Mischief defeated Atalanta, Canada, (2-0)
1885 Puritan defeated Genesta, England, (2-0)
1886 Mayflower defeated Galatea, England, (2-0)
1887 Volunteer defeated Thistle, Scotland, (2-0)
1893 Vigilant defeated Valkyrie II, England, (3-0)
1895 Defender defeated Valkyrie III, England, (3-0)
1899 Columbia defeated Shamrock, England, (3-0)
1901 Columbia defeated Shamrock II, England, (3-0)
1903 Reliance defeated Shamrock III, England, (3-0)
1920 Resolute defeated Shamrock IV, England, (3-2)
1930 Enterprise defeated Shamrock V, England, (4-0)
1934 Rainbow defeated Endeavour, England, (4-2)
1937 Ranger defeated Endeavour II, England, (4-0)
1958 Columbia defeated Sceptre, England, (4-0)
1962 Weatherly defeated Gretel, Australia, (4-1)
1964 Constellation defeated Sovereign, England, (4-0)
1967 Intrepid defeated Dame Pattie, Australia, (4-0)
1970 Intrepid defeated Gretel II, Australia, (4-1)
1974 Courageous defeated Southern Cross, Australia, (4-0)
1977 Courageous defeated Australia, (4-0)

AAU Bobsled Championships in 1977

Lake Placid, N.Y., Feb. 19-20

Four-man

1—Plattsburgh Bobsled Club (Paul Vincent, Dale Lucas, Dick Ashlaw, Louis Pugh). **Time—3:20.05.**
2—Saranac Lake Bobsled Club (Brent Rushlaw, Sean Morgan, John Morgan, Dennis Duprey). **Time—3:20.07.**
3—Hurricane Bobsled Club (Al Turner, John Dieson, Chris Cross, Tony Carlino). **Time—3:21.02.**

Two-man

1—Saranac Lake Bobsled Club (Brent Rushlaw, Dennis Duprey). **Time—4:35.22.**
2—Lake Placid Bobsled Club (Howard Siler, Dave McFayden). **Time—4:35.95.**
3—U.S. Navy (Bob Husher, Dennis Sprenkle). **Time—4:37.72.**

Sports Arenas

The seating capacity of sports arenas can vary depending on the event being presented. The figures below are the normal seating capacity for basketball. (*) indicates hockey seating capacity.

Name and location	Capacity
Allen County Memorial, Ft. Wayne	*8,032
Astrohall, Houston	10,000
Atlantic City Audit, Atlantic City, N.J.	40,000
Baltimore Civic Center	13,043-*11,329
Bismarck Coliseum, N. D.	7,000
Boston Garden	15,320-*15,003
Buffalo Memorial Auditorium	17,900-*16,433(a)
Calgary Corral	*7,000
Capital Center, Landover, Md.	19,035-*18,130
Charlotte Coliseum	11,666-*9,575
Chicago Stadium	17,374-*18,000
Cincinnati Gardens	11,650-*10,606
Cleveland Arena	11,000-*9,300
Cobo Hall, Detroit	11,147
The Coliseum, Richmond Township, Oh.	20,074-*18,544
Convention Center, San Antonio	10,146
Convention Hall, Philadelphia	9,200-*9,500
Cow Palace, San Francisco	14,500
Dallas State Fair Coliseum	*7,513
Denver Coliseum	*9,038
Dorton Arena, Raleigh, N. C.	8,058
Edmonton Coliseum	*15,273
Fairgrounds Coliseum, Indianapolis	9,479
Freedom Hall, Louisville, Ky.	16,613
Greensboro Coliseum	15,500-*13,280
Hampton Coliseum, Va.	10,000-*6,000
Hartford Civic Center	*10,346
HemisFair Arena, San Antonio	10,446
Hersheypark Arena, Pa.	*7,286
Hofheinz Pavilion, Houston	10,218
International Amphitheatre, Chicago	9,000
Jacksonville Coliseum	*7,900
Jefferson County Civic Center, Birmingham, Ala.	*16,753
Kemper Memorial Arena, Kansas City	16,382-15,994
Kiel Auditorium, St. Louis	10,574
Las Vegas Convention Center	9,000
Long Beach Arena, Cal.	11,168
Los Angeles Forum	17,505-*16,005
Los Angeles Sports Arena	15,333-*11,325
Louisiana Superdome	19,203
Lubbock Municipal Coliseum, Tex.	10,400
Macon Coliseum	*8,000
Madison Square Garden, New York	19,694-*17,500
Maple Leaf Gardens, Toronto	17,000-*16,485(a)
Market Square Arena, Indianapolis	16,926-*16,040
McNichols Sports Arena, Denver	17,128-*16,401
Met. Sports Center, Bloomington, Minn.	*15,184
Mid-South Coliseum, Memphis	11,065
Milwaukee Arena	10,938
Mobile Municipal Auditorium	13,100
Montreal Forum	*18,350
Moody Coliseum, Dallas	9,500
Municipal Auditorium, Kansas City	9,929
Myriad, Oklahoma City	*13,494
Nashville Municipal Auditorium	8,000
Nassau Coliseum, Uniondale, N.Y.	15,527-*14,865
New Orleans Municipal Auditorium	9,100
Norfolk Scope, Va.	10,600-*9,364
Oakland Coliseum Arena	12,787-*12,021
Olympia Stadium, Detroit	*16,200 (a)
Olympic Auditorium, Los Angeles	10,500
Omaha Civic Auditorium	9,144
The Omni, Atlanta	15,389-*15,191
Ottawa Civic Center	*9,355
Pacific Coliseum, Vancouver, B.C.	*15,569
Penn Palestra, Philadelphia	9,200
Philadelphia Civic Center	*8,155
Pittsburgh Civic Arena	*16,402
Providence Civic Center	11,619-*10,730
Portland Memorial Coliseum	12,411-*10,500
Quebec Coliseum	*10,000
Reynolds Coliseum, Raleigh, N.C.	12,400
Richmond Coliseum, Va.	10,700-*9,674
Riverfront Coliseum, Cincinnati	*16,820
Roanoke Civic Center, Va.	10,000-*8,372
St. Louis Arena	*18,006
St. Paul Civic Center, Minn.	*15,594
Salt Palace, Salt Lake City	12,201-*10,640
Sam Houston Coliseum, Houston	8,925-*9,300
San Diego Intl. Sports Arena	14,000-*13,039
Seattle Center Coliseum	14,090
Spectrum, Philadelphia	17,920-*17,077
Springfield Civic Center, Mass.	*7,466
The Summit, Houston	15,600-*15,256
Tarrant County Convention Center, Ft. Worth	13,500
Tingley Coliseum, Albuquerque	*12,000
Uline Arena, Washington, D. C.	11,000
Veterans Memorial Audit., Des Moines	15,000
Veterans Memorial Coliseum, New Haven	*8,765
Veterans Memorial Coliseum, Phoenix	13,036-*12,474
Winnipeg Arena	*10,390
Winston-Salem Memorial Coliseum	9,020-*6,100

(a) includes standees

Canadian Intercollegiate Athletic Union Champions

	Basketball	Football	Hockey	Soccer	Swimming, Diving	Volleyball	Wrestling
1965	Acadia	Toronto	Manitoba	—	British Columbia	—	—
1966	Windsor	St. Francis Xavier	Toronto	—	Toronto	—	—
1967	Windsor	Alberta	Toronto	—	Toronto	British Columbia	—
1968	Waterloo Lutheran	Queen's	Alberta	—	Toronto	Ottawa	—
1969	Windsor	Manitoba	Toronto	—	Toronto	Winnipeg	—
1970	British Columbia	Manitoba	Toronto	—	Toronto	Montreal	Alberta
1971	Acadia	Western Ontario	Toronto	—	Toronto	Winnipeg	Alberta
1972	British Columbia	Alberta	Toronto	Alberta	McGill	Winnipeg	Alberta
1973	St. Mary's	St. Mary's	Toronto	Loyola	Toronto	Winnipeg	O.U.A.A.
1974	Guelph	Western Ontario	Waterloo	British Columbia	Toronto	Winnipeg	O.U.A.A.
1975	Waterloo	Otttawa	Alberta	Victoria	Toronto	Sherbrooke	O.U.A.A.
1976	Manitoba	Western Ontario	Toronto	Concordia	Toronto	British Columbia	O.U.A.A.
1977	Acadia		Toronto		Waterloo	Winnipeg	O.U.A.A.

Intercollegiate Rowing Association Regatta

Onondaga Lake, Syracuse, N.Y. (3 miles)

Year	Winner	Time	Year	Winner	Time	Year	Winner	Time
1957	Cornell	15:26.6	1964	California (a)	6:31.1	1971	Cornell (a)	6:06.0
1958	Cornell	17:12.1	1965	Navy	16:51.3	1972	Penn (a)	6:22.6
1959	Wisconsin	18:01.7	1966	Wisconsin	16:03.4	1973	Wisconsin (a)	6:21.0
1960	California	15:57.0	1967	Penn	16:15.9	1974	Wisonsin (a)	6:33.0
1961	California	16:49.2	1968	Penn (a)	6:15.6	1975	Wisconsin (a)	6:08.2
1962	Cornell	17:02.9	1969	Penn (a)	6:30.4	1976	California (a)	6:31.0
1963	Cornell	17:24.0	1970	Washington (a)	——	1977	Cornell (a)	6:32.4

(a) race at 2,000 meters

National Basketball Association, 1976-77

Final Standings

Eastern Conference

Atlantic Division

Club	W	L	Pct.	GB
Philadelphia	50	32	.610	—
Boston	44	38	.537	6
Knicks	40	42	.488	10
Buffalo	30	52	.366	20
Nets	22	60	.268	28

Central Division

Club	W	L	Pct.	GB
Houston	49	33	.598	—
Washington	48	34	.585	1
San Antonio	44	38	.537	5
Cleveland	43	39	.524	6
New Orleans	35	47	.427	14
Atlanta	31	51	.378	18

Western Conference

Midwest Division

Club	W	L	Pct.	GB
Denver	50	32	.610	—
Detroit	44	38	.537	6
Chicago	44	38	.537	6
Kansas City	40	42	.488	10
Indiana	36	46	.439	14
Milwaukee	30	52	.366	20

Pacific Division

Club	W	L	Pct.	GB
Los Angeles	53	29	.646	—
Portland	49	33	.598	4
Golden State	46	36	.561	7
Seattle	40	42	.488	13
Phoenix	34	48	.415	19

NBA Playoff Results

Boston defeated San Antonio 2 games to 0.
Portland defeated Chicago 2 games to 1.
Golden State defeated Detroit 2 games to 1.
Washington defeated Cleveland 2 games to 1.
Philadelphia defeated Boston 4 games to 3.
Houston defeated Washington 4 games to 2.
Portland defeated Denver 4 games to 2.
Los Angeles defeated Golden State 4 games to 3.
Philadelphia defeated Houston 4 games to 2.
Portland defeated Los Angeles 4 games to 0.
Portland defeated Philadelphia 4 games to 2.

Final Statistics

Individual Scoring Leaders
(minimum 70 games played or 1400 points)

	G	FG	FT	Pts	Avg
Maravich, New Orleans	73	886	501	2273	31.1
Knight, Indiana	78	831	413	2075	26.6
Abdul-Jabbar, Los Angeles	82	888	376	2152	26.2
Thompson, Denver	82	824	477	2125	25.9
McAdoo, New York Knicks	72	740	381	1861	25.8
Lanier, Detroit	64	678	260	1616	25.3
Drew, Atlanta	74	689	412	1790	24.2
Hayes, Washington	82	760	422	1942	23.7
Gervin, San Antonio	82	726	443	1895	23.1
Issel, Denver	79	660	445	1765	22.3
Boone, Kansas City	82	747	324	1818	22.2
Kenon, San Antonio	78	706	293	1705	21.9
Barry, Golden State	79	682	359	1723	21.8
Erving, Philadelphia	82	685	400	1770	21.6
Tomjanovich, Houston	81	733	287	1753	21.6
McGinnis, Philadelphia	79	659	372	1690	21.4
Westphal, Phoenix	81	682	362	1726	21.3
Williamson, Indiana	72	618	259	1495	20.8
Dandridge, Milwaukee	70	585	283	1453	20.8
R. Smith, Buffalo	82	702	294	1698	20.7

Field Goal Leaders
(minimum 300 FG made)

	FGM	FGA	Pct
Abdul-Jabbar, Los Angeles	888	1533	.579
Kupchak, Washington	341	596	.572
B. Jones, Denver	501	879	.570
Gervin, San Antonio	726	1335	.544
Lanier, Detroit	678	1269	.534
Gross, Portland	376	711	.529
Nater, Milwaukee	383	725	.528
B. Walton, Portland	491	930	.528
Meriweather, Atlanta	319	607	.526
Gilmore, Chicago	570	1091	.522

Free Throw Leaders
(minimum 125 FT made)

	FTM	FTA	Pct
DiGregorio, Buffalo	138	146	.945
Barry, Golden State	359	392	.916
Murphy, Houston	272	307	.886
Newlin, Houston	269	304	.885
F. Brown, Seattle	168	190	.884
D. Van Arsdale, Phoenix	145	166	.873
J. White, Boston	333	383	.869
Bridgeman, Milwaukee	197	228	.864
C. Russell, Los Angeles	188	219	.858
Van Breda Kolff, New York Nets	195	228	.855

Rebound Leaders
(minimum 70 games or 800 rebounds)

	G	Off	Def	Tot	Avg
B. Walton, Portland	65	211	723	934	14.4
Abdul-Jabbar, Los Angeles	82	266	824	1090	13.3
Malone, Houston	82	437	635	1072	13.1
Gilmore, Chicago	82	313	757	1070	13.0
McAdoo, New York Knicks	72	199	727	926	12.9
Hayes, Washington	82	289	740	1029	12.5
Nater, Milwaukee	72	266	599	865	12.0
McGinnis, Philadelphia	79	324	587	911	11.5
M. Lucas, Portland	79	271	628	899	11.4
Kenon, San Antonio	78	282	597	879	11.3

Assists Leaders
(minimum 70 games or 400 assists)

	G	No	Avg
Buse, Indiana	81	685	8.5
Watts, Seattle	79	630	8.0
Van Lier, Chicago	82	636	7.8
K. Porter, Detroit	81	592	7.3
Henderson, Washington	87	598	6.9
Barry, Golden State	79	475	6.0
J. White, Boston	82	492	6.0
Gale, San Antonio	82	473	5.8
Westphal, Phoenix	81	459	5.7
J. Lucas, Houston	82	463	5.6

Blocked Shots Leaders
(minimum 70 games or 100 blocked shots)

	G	No	Avg
B. Walton, Portland	65	211	3.25
Abdul-Jabbar, Los Angeles	82	261	3.18
Hayes, Washington	82	220	2.68
Gilmore, Chicago	82	203	2.48
C. Jones, Philadelphia	82	200	2.44
G. Johnson, Buffalo	78	177	2.27
Malone, Houston	82	181	2.21
Roundfield, Indiana	61	131	2.15
Paultz, San Antonio	82	173	2.11

Steals Leaders
(minimum 70 games or 125 steals)

	G	No	Avg
Buse, Indiana	81	281	3.47
B. Taylor, Kansas City	72	199	2.76
Watts, Seattle	79	214	2.71
Buckner, Milwaukee	79	192	2.43
Gale, San Antonio	82	191	2.33
B. Jones, Denver	82	186	2.27
Hollins, Portland	76	166	2.18
C. Ford, Detroit	82	179	2.18
Barry, Golden State	79	172	2.18

NBA Champions 1947-1977

	Regular season		Playoffs	
Year	Eastern Conference	Western Conference	Winner	Runner-up
1947	Washington	Chicago	Philadelphia	Chicago
1948	Philadelphia	St. Louis	Baltimore	Philadelphia
1949	Washington	Rochester	Minneapolis	Washington
1950	Syracuse	Minneapolis	Minneapolis	Syracuse
1951	Philadelphia	Minneapolis	Rochester	New York
1952	Syracuse	Rochester	Minneapolis	New York
1953	New York	Minneapolis	Minneapolis	New York
1954	New York	Minneapolis	Minneapolis	Syracuse
1955	Syracuse	Ft. Wayne	Syracuse	Ft. Wayne
1956	Philadelphia	Ft. Wayne	Philadelphia	Ft. Wayne
1957	Boston	St. Louis	Boston	St. Louis
1958	Boston	St. Louis	St. Louis	Boston
1959	Boston	St. Louis	Boston	Minneapolis
1960	Boston	St. Louis	Boston	St. Louis
1961	Boston	St. Louis	Boston	St. Louis
1962	Boston	Los Angeles	Boston	Los Angeles
1963	Boston	Los Angeles	Boston	Los Angeles
1964	Boston	San Francisco	Boston	San Francisco
1965	Boston	Los Angeles	Boston	Los Angeles
1966	Philadelphia	Los Angeles	Boston	Los Angeles
1967	Philadelphia	San Francisco	Philadelphia	San Francisco
1968	Philadelphia	St. Louis	Boston	Los Angeles
1969	Baltimore	Los Angeles	Boston	Los Angeles
1970	New York	Atlanta	New York	Los Angeles

	Atlantic	Central	Midwest	Pacific	Winner	Runner-up
1971	New York	Baltimore	Milwaukee	Los Angeles	Milwaukee	Baltimore
1972	Boston	Baltimore	Milwaukee	Los Angeles	Los Angeles	New York
1973	Boston	Baltimore	Milwaukee	Los Angeles	New York	Los Angeles
1974	Boston	Capital	Milwaukee	Los Angeles	Boston	Milwaukee
1975	Boston	Washington	Chicago	Golden State	Golden State	Washington
1976	Boston	Cleveland	Milwaukee	Golden State	Boston	Phoenix
1977	Philadelphia	Houston	Denver	Los Angeles	Portland	Philadelphia

NBA Scoring Leaders

Year	Scoring champion	Pts	Avg
1947	Joe Fulks, Philadelphia	1,389	23.2
1948	Max Zaslofsky, Chicago	1,007	21.0
1949	George Mikan, Minneapolis	1,698	28.3
1950	George Mikan, Minneapolis	1,865	27.4
1951	George Mikan, Minneapolis	1,932	28.4
1952	Paul Arizin, Philadelphia	1,674	25.4
1953	Neil Johnston, Philadelphia	1,564	22.3
1954	Neil Johnston, Philadelphia	1,759	24.4
1955	Neil Johnston, Philadelphia	1,631	22.7
1956	Bob Pettit, St. Louis	1,849	25.7
1957	Paul Arizin, Philadelphia	1,817	25.6
1958	George Yardley, Detroit	2,001	27.8
1959	Bob Pettit, St. Louis	2,105	29.2
1960	Wilt Chamberlain, Philadelphia	2,707	37.9
1961	Wilt Chamberlain, Philadelphia	3,033	38.4
1962	Wilt Chamberlain, Philadelphia	4,029	50.4
1963	Wilt Chamberlain, San Francisco	3,586	44.8
1964	Wilt Chamberlain, San Francisco	2,948	36.5
1965	Wilt Chamberlain, San Fran., Phila.	2,534	34.7
1966	Wilt Chamberlain, Philadelphia	2,649	33.5
1967	Rick Barry, San Francisco	2,775	35.6
1968	Dave Bing, Detroit	2,142	27.1
1969	Elvin Hayes, San Diego	2,327	28.4
1970	Jerry West, Los Angeles	2,309	31.2
1971	Lew Alcindor, Milwaukee	2,596	31.7
1972	Kareem Abdul-Jabbar (Alcindor), Milwaukee	2,822	34.8
1973	Nate Archibald, Kansas City-Omaha	2,719	34.0
1974	Bob McAdoo, Buffalo	2,261	30.6
1975	Bob McAdoo, Buffalo	2,831	34.5
1976	Bob McAdoo, Buffalo	2,427	31.1
1977	Pete Maravich, New Orleans	2,273	31.1

NBA All Star Team in 1977

First team	Position	Second team
Elvin Hayes, Washington	Forward	Julius Erving, Philadelphia
David Thompson, Denver	Forward	George McGinnis, Philadelphia
Kareem Abdul Jabbar, Los Angeles	Center	Bill Walton, Portland
Pete Maravich, New Orleans	Guard	George Gervin, San Antonio
Paul Westphal, Phoenix	Guard	Jo Jo White, Boston

NBA All-Defensive Team in 1977

First team	Position	Second team
Bobby Jones, Denver	Forward	Jim Brewer, Cleveland
E. C. Coleman, New Orleans	Forward	Jamaal Wilkes, Golden State
Bill Walton, Portland	Center	Kareem Abdul-Jabbar, Los Angeles
Don Buse, Indiana	Guard	Brian Taylor, Kansas City
Norm Van Lier, Chicago	Guard	Don Chaney, Los Angeles

1977 NBA Player Draft

The following are the first round picks of the National Basketball Assn.

Milwakuee	Kent Benson, Indiana
Kansas City	Otis Birdsong, Houston
Milwaukee	Marques Johnson, UCLA
Washington	Greg Ballard, Oregon
Phoenix	Walter Davis, North Carolina
Los Angeles	Kenny Carr, North Carolina State
N.Y Nets	Bernard King, Tennessee
Seattle	Jack Sikma, Illinois Wesleyan
Denver	Tom LaGarde, North Carolina
N.Y. Knicks	Ray Williams, Minnesota
Milwaukee	Ernie Grunfeld, Tennessee
Boston	Cedric Maxwell, North Carolina-Charlotte
Chicago	Tate Armstrong, Duke
Atlanta	Wayne Rollins, Clemson
Los Angeles	Brad Davis, Maryland
Golden State	Rickey Green, Michigan
Washington	Bo Ellis, Marquette
Golden State	Wesley Cox, Louisville
Portland	Rich Laurel, Hofstra
Philadelphia	Glenn Mosley, Seton Hall
Denver	Anthony Roberts, Oral Roberts
Los Angeles	Norm Nixon, Duquesne

NBA Team Statistics in 1976-77

Offense

	Field Goals			Free Throws			Rebounds			Scoring	
Team	Made	Att.	Pct.	Made	Att.	Pct.	Off.	Def.	Tot.	Pts.	Avg.
San Antonio	3711	7657	.485	2010	2522	.797	1110	2550	3660	9432	115.0
Denver	3590	7471	.481	2053	2783	.738	1288	2700	3988	9233	112.6
Portland	3623	7537	.481	1917	2515	.762	1260	2703	3963	9163	111.7
Golden State	3724	7832	.475	1649	2172	.759	1300	2639	3939	9097	110.9
Philadelphia	3511	7322	.480	2012	2732	.736	1293	2752	4045	9034	110.2
Detroit	3764	7792	.483	1442	1960	.736	1169	2495	3664	8970	109.4
N.Y. Knicks	3659	7530	.486	1587	2078	.764	974	2680	3654	8905	108.6
Milwaukee	3668	7840	.468	1553	2072	.750	1220	2519	3739	8889	108.4
Kansas City	3561	7733	.460	1706	2140	.797	1222	2593	3815	8828	107.7
Los Angeles	3663	7657	.478	1437	1941	.740	1177	2628	3805	8763	106.9
Indiana	3522	7840	.449	1714	2297	.746	1409	2584	3993	8758	106.8
Houston	3535	7325	.483	1656	2103	.787	1254	2632	3886	8726	106.4
Washington	3514	7479	.470	1622	2264	.716	1185	2758	3943	8650	105.5
Buffalo	3366	7475	.450	1880	2492	.754	1213	2623	3836	8612	105.0
Phoenix	3406	7249	.470	1791	2345	.764	1059	2493	3552	8603	104.9
New Orleans	3443	7602	.453	1688	2183	.773	1249	2828	4077	8574	104.6
Boston	3462	7775	.445	1648	2181	.756	1241	2966	4207	8572	104.5
Seattle	3439	7639	.450	1646	2386	.690	1355	2433	3788	8524	104.0
Atlanta	3279	7176	.457	1836	2451	.749	1244	2512	3756	8394	102.4
Cleveland	3451	7688	.449	1468	1993	.737	1312	2563	3875	8370	102.1
Chicago	3249	7186	.452	1613	2159	.747	1292	2705	3997	8111	98.9
N.Y. Nets	3096	7222	.429	1673	2274	.736	1157	2547	3704	7865	95.9

Defense

	Field Goals			Free Throws			Rebounds			Scoring		
Team	Made	Att.	Pct.	Made	Att.	Pct.	Off.	Def.	Tot.	Pts.	Avg.	Dif.
Chicago	3306	7095	.466	1425	1907	.747	1055	2559	3614	8037	98.0	+ 0.9
Cleveland	3265	7268	.449	1748	2325	.752	1202	2711	3913	8278	101.0	+ 1.1
N. Y. Nets	3279	7074	.464	1863	2488	.749	1149	2937	4086	8421	102.7	− 6.8
Los Angeles	3515	7781	.452	1510	1990	.759	1348	2625	3973	8540	104.1	+ 2.8
Phoenix	3320	7192	.462	1903	2525	.754	1180	2594	3774	8543	104.2	+ 0.7
Washington	3552	7751	.458	1462	1943	.752	1167	2565	3732	8566	104.5	+ 1.0
Houston	3424	7356	.465	1746	2252	.775	1121	2232	3353	8594	104.8	+ 1.6
Seattle	3394	7339	.462	1863	2474	.753	1257	2651	3908	8651	105.5	− 1.5
Portland	3408	7404	.460	1889	2514	.751	1197	2510	3707	8705	106.2	+ 5.5
Philadelphia	3575	7920	.451	1561	2074	.753	1416	2448	3864	8711	106.2	+ 4.0
Atlanta	3409	7137	.478	1909	2527	.755	1121	2533	3654	8727	106.4	− 4.0
Boston	3559	7904	.450	1616	2180	.741	1110	2753	3863	8734	106.5	− 2.0
Kansas City	3422	7244	.472	1912	2513	.761	1097	2739	3836	8756	106.8	+ 0.9
Denver	3585	7743	.463	1635	2231	.733	1269	2481	3750	8805	107.4	+ 5.2
New Orleans	3486	7712	.452	1833	2448	.749	1318	2781	4099	8805	107.4	− 2.8
Golden State	3567	7584	.470	1699	2282	.745	1256	2640	3896	8833	107.7	+ 3.2
Indiana	3599	7629	.472	1705	2252	.757	1378	2770	4148	8903	108.6	− 1.8
N.Y. Knicks	3577	7610	.470	1752	2327	.753	1163	2716	3879	8906	108.6	...
Buffalo	3786	7917	.478	1404	1859	.755	1268	2721	3989	8976	109.5	− 4.5
Detroit	3561	7539	.472	1933	2543	.760	1317	2637	3954	9055	110.4	− 1.0
Milwaukee	3712	7753	.479	1721	2330	.739	1265	2613	3878	9145	111.5	− 3.1
San Antonio	3935	8075	.487	1512	2059	.734	1329	2687	4016	9382	114.4	+ 0.6

Podoloff Cup Winners

Kareem Abdul-Jabbar of the Los Angeles Lakers was selected as the winner of the Maurice Podoloff Cup (named after the former league commissioner) for Most Valuable Player in the NBA for the 1976-77 season.

1956—Bob Pettit, St. Louis
1957—Bob Cousy, Boston
1958—Bill Russell, Boston
1959—Bob Pettit, St. Louis
1960—Wilt Chamberlain, Philadelphia
1961—Bill Russell, Boston
1962—Bill Russell, Boston
1963—Bill Russell, Boston
1964—Oscar Robertson, Cincinnati
1965—Bill Russell, Boston
1966—Wilt Chamberlain, Philadelphia
1967—Wilt Chamberlain, Philadelphia
1968—Wilt Chamberlain, Philadelphia
1969—Wes Unseld, Baltimore
1970—Willis Reed, New York
1971—Lew Alcindor, Milwaukee
1972—Kareem Abdul-Jabbar (Alcindor), Milwaukee
1973—Dave Cowens, Boston
1974—Kareem Abdul-Jabbar, Milwaukee
1975—Bob McAdoo, Buffalo
1976—Kareem Abdul-Jabbar, Los Angeles
1977—Kareem Abdul-Jabbar, Los Angeles

NBA Rookie of the Year Awards

1954—Don Meineke, Ft. Wayne
1955—Ray Felix, Baltimore
1956—Maurice Stokes, Rochester
1957—Tom Heinsohn, Boston
1958—Woody Sauldsberry, Philadelphia.
1959—Elgin Baylor, Minnesota
1960—Wilt Chamberlain, Philadelphia
1961—Oscar Robertson, Cincinnati
1962—Walt Bellamy, Chicago
1963—Terry Dischinger, Chicago
1964—Jerry Lucas, Cincinnati
1965—Willis Reed, New York
1966—Rick Barry, San Francisco
1967—Dave Bing, Detroit
1968—Earl Monroe, Baltimore
1969—Wes Unseld, Baltimore
1970—Lew Alcindor, Milwaukee
1971—Dave Cowens, Boston;
Geoff Petrie, Portland (tie)
1972—Sidney Wicks, Portland
1973—Bob McAdoo, Buffalo
1974—Ernie DiGregorio, Buffalo
1975—Keith Wilkes, Golden State
1976—Alvan Adams, Phoenix
1977—Adrian Dantley, Buffalo

American Basketball Association, 1968-1976

Champions

Year	Regular Season: Eastern division	Regular Season: Western division	Playoffs: Winner	Playoffs: Runner-up
1968	Pittsburgh	New Orleans	Pittsburgh	New Orleans
1969	Indiana	Oakland	Oakland	Indiana
1970	Indiana	Denver	Indiana	Los Angeles
1971	Virginia	Indiana	Utah	Kentucky
1972	Kentucky	Utah	Indiana	New York
1973	Carolina	Utah	Indiana	Kentucky
1974	New York	Utah	New York	Utah
1975	Kentucky	Denver	Kentucky	Indiana
1976	Denver		New York	Denver

Scoring Leaders

Year	Leader	Pts.	Avg.
1968	Connie Hawkins, Pittsburgh	1,875	26.7
1969	Rick Barry, Oakland	1,190	34.0
1970	Spencer Haywood, Denver	2,519	29.9
1971	Dan Issel, Kentucky	2,480	29.8
1972	Charlie Scott, Virginia	2,524	34.5
1973	Julius Erving, Virginia:	2,268	31.9
1974	Julius Erving, New York	2,299	27.3
1975	George McGinnis, Indiana	2,353	29.7
1976	Julius Erving, New York	2,462	29.3

Most Valuable Player & Rookie of Year

Year	MVP	Rookie
1968	Connie Hawkins, Pittsburgh	Mel Daniels, Indiana
1969	Mel Daniels, Indiana	Warren Armstrong, Oakland
1970	Spencer Haywood, Denver	Spencer Haywood, Denver
1971	Mel Daniels, Indiana	Dan Issel, Kentucky; Charlie Scott, Virginia (tie)
1972	Artis Gilmore, Kentucky	Artis Gilmore, Kentucky
1973	Billy Cunningham, Carolina	Brian Taylor, New York
1974	Julius Erving, New York	Swen Nater, San Antonio
1975	Julius Erving, New York; George McGinnis, Indiana (tie)	Marvin Barnes, St. Louis
1976	Julius Erving, New York	David Thompson, Denver

Chess

Chess dates back to antiquity. Its exact origin is unknown. The strongest players of their time, and therefore regarded by later generations as world champions, were Francois Philidor, France; Alexandre Deschappelles, France; Louis de la Bourdonnais, France; Howard Staunton, England; Adolph Anderssen, Germany and Paul Morphy, United States. In 1866 Wilhelm Steinitz of Czechoslovakia defeated Adolph Anderssen and claimed the title of world champion. The official world champions, since the title was first used follow:

1866-1894 Wilhelm Steinitz, Czech.
1894-1921 Dr. Emanuel Lasker, Germany
1921-1927 Jose R. Capablanca, Cuba
1927-1935 Dr. Alexander A. Alekhine, USSR
1935-1937 Dr. Max Euwe, Netherlands
1937-1946 Dr. Alexander A. Alekhine, USSR
1948-1957 Mikhail Botvinnik, USSR
1957-1958 Vassily Smyslov, USSR
1958-1959 Mikhail Botvinnik, USSR
1960-1961 Mikhail Tal, USSR
1961-1963 Mikhail Botvinnik, USSR
1963-1969 Tigran Petrosian, USSR
1969-1972 Boris Spassky, USSR
1972-1975 Bobby Fischer, U.S. (a)
1975 Anatoly Karpov, USSR

(a) Defaulted championship after refusal to accept International Chess Federation rules for a championship match, April 1975.

United States Champions

Unofficial champions

1857-1871 Paul Morphy
1871-1876 George Mackenzie
1876-1880 James Mason
1880-1889 George Mackenzie
1889-1890 S. Lipschutz
1890 Jackson Showalter
1890-1891 Max Judd

Official champions

1891-1892 Jackson Showalter
1892-1894 S. Lipschutz
1894 Jackson Showalter
1894-1895 Albert Hodges
1895-1897 Jackson Showalter
1897-1909 Harry Pillsbury
1909-1936 Frank Marshall
1936-1944 Samuel Reshevsky
1944-1946 Arnold Denker
1946-1948 Samuel Reshevsky
1948-1951 Herman Steiner
1951-1954 Larry Evans
1954-1957 Arthur Bisguier
1957-1961 Bobby Fischer
1961-1962 Larry Evans
1962-1968 Bobby Fischer
1968-1969 Larry Evans
1969-1972 Samuel Reshevsky
1972-1973 Robert Byrne
1973-1974 Lubomir Kavalek, John Grefe
1974 Walter Browne

Rodeo Championship Standings in 1976

Event	Winner	Money won
All Around	Tom Ferguson, Miami, Oklahoma	$87,908
Saddle Bronc	Monte Henson, Mesquite, Texas	34,383
Bareback Bronc	Joe Alexander, Cora, Wyoming	48,156
Bull Riding	Don Gay, Mesquite, Texas	33,316
Calf Roping	Roy Cooper, Durant, Oklahoma	$37,370
Steer Wrestling	Tom Ferguson, Miami, Oklahoma	48,854
Team Roping	Leo Camarillo, Oakdale, California	30,761

Rodeo Cowboy All Around Champions

Year	Winner	Money won
1960	Harry Tompkins, Dublin, Texas	$32,522
1961	Benny Reynolds, Melrose, Montana	31,309
1962	Tom Nesmith, Bethel, Oklahoma	32,611
1963	Dean Oliver, Boise, Idaho	31,329
1964	Dean Oliver, Boise, Idaho	31,150
1965	Dean Oliver, Boise, Idaho	33,163
1966	Larry Mahan, Brooks, Oregon	40,358
1967	Larry Mahan, Brooks, Oregon	51,996
1968	Larry Mahan, Salem, Oregon	49,129
1969	Larry Mahan, Brooks, Oregon	$57,726
1970	Larry Mahan, Brooks, Oregon	41,493
1971	Phil Lyne, George West, Texas	49,245
1972	Phil Lyne, George West, Texas	60,852
1973	Larry Mahan, Dallas, Texas	64,447
1974	Tom Ferguson, Miami, Oklahoma	66,929
1975	Leo Camarillo, Oakdale, California	50,830
1976	Tom Ferguson, Miami, Oklahoma	87,908

Westminster Kennel Club

Year	Best-in-show	Breed	Owner
1966	Ch. Zeloy Mooremaides Magic	Wire Fox terrier	Marion G. Bunker
1967	Ch. Bardene Bingo	Scottish terrier	E. H. Stuart
1968	Ch. Stingray of Derryabah	Lakeland terrier	Mr. and Mrs. James A. Farrell Jr.
1969	Ch. Glamoor Good News	Skye terrier	Walter & Mrs. Adele F. Goodman
1970	Ch. Arriba's Prima Donna	Boxer	Dr. & Mrs. P. J. Pagano & Dr. Theodore S. Fickles
1971	Ch. Chinoe's Adamant James	English springer spaniel	Dr. Milton Prickett
1972	Ch. Chinoe's Adamant James	English springer spaniel	Dr. Milton Prickett
1973	Ch. Acadia Command Performance	Poodle	Mrs. Jo Ann Sering & Edward B. Jenner
1974	Ch. Gretchenhof Columbia River	German pointer	Dr. Richard Smith
1975	Ch. Sir Lancelot of Barvan	Old English sheepdog	Mr. and Mrs. Ronald Vanword
1976	Ch. Jo-Ni's Red Baron of Crofton	Lakeland terrier	Virginia Dickson
1977	Ch. Dersade Bobby's Girl	Sealyham	Dorothy Wymer

Leonard Brumby Sr. Memorial Trophy

Junior Winner at Westminster Kennel Club

1966—Laura Swyler, Commack, N.Y. **Breed**—Dox.
1967—David L. Brumbaugh, Perry, Ga. **Breed**—Min. Schnauzer.
1968—Cheryl Baker, Kennesaw, Ga. **Breed**—Beagle.
1969—Charles Garvin, Columbus, Oh. **Breed**—Dalmatian.
1970—Pat Hardy, Cincinnati, Oh. **Breed**—Golden Retriever.
1971—Heidi Shellenbarger, Costa Mesa, Cal. **Breed**—Whippet.
1972—Deborah Dagny Von Ahems, Edison Township, N. J. **Breed**—Afghan.
1973—Teresa Nail, Ft. Worth, Tex. **Breed**—Doberman Pinscher.
1974—Leslie Church, St. Louis, Mo. **Breed**—Min. Schnauzer.
1975—Virginia Westfield, Huntington, N.Y. **Breed**—Bulldog.
1976—Cathy Hritzo, Hubbard, Oh. **Breed**—Samoyed.
1977—Randy McAteer, Ocala, Fla. **Breed**—Irish Setter.

Leading American Kennel Club Registrations

Breed	1976	1975
Poodles	126,799	139,750
German Shepherd Dogs	74,723	76,235
Doberman Pinschers	73,615	57,336
Irish Setters	54,917	58,622
Cocker Spaniels	46,862	39,064
Beagles	44,156	45,210
Labrador Retrievers	39,929	36,565
Dachshunds	38,927	40,617
Miniature Schnauzers	36,816	37,786
Golden Retrievers	27,612	22,636
Collies	25,161	24,464
Shetland Sheepdogs	23,950	22,715
Lhasa Apsos	21,145	18,791
Siberian Huskies	20,598	19,678
Pekingese	20,400	20,150
Yorkshire Terriers	20,392	18,954
Brittany Spaniels	20,222	19,188
Great Danes	19,869	19,255
St. Bernards	17,537	22,430
English Springer Spaniels	16,842	15,083
Chihuahuas	16,478	16,494
Old English Sheepdogs	15,364	15,623
Pomeranians	15,241	14,653
Basset Hounds	14,997	15,206
German Shorthaired Pointers	14,269	14,017
Boxers	13,057	12,063
Shih Tzu	12,562	10,452
Boston Terriers	10,806	10,178
Samoyeds	10,147	10,055
Afghan Hounds	10,045	10,412

Dogs Registered by Groups

Group	1976	1975
Sporting Breeds	237,849	221,850
Hound Breeds	125,800	129,450
Working Breeds	318,300	301,699
Terrier Breeds	75,300	76,150
Toy Breeds	103,550	98,150
Non-Sporting Breeds	187,849	195,550
	1,048,648	1,022,849

Purebred Dogs

Six main classes of dogs are recognized: Sporting dogs which include pointers, retrievers, setters, spaniels, weimaraners; the hound group; working dogs which include boxers, collies, doberman pinschers, shepherds, mastiffs; the terrier group; the toy group which includes chihuahuas, toy spaniels, papillions, pekingese, pomeranians, yorkshires; non-sporting group which includes boston terriers, bulldogs, chow chows, dalmatians, poodles. In all, 116 different breeds are recognized and shown in the United States.

Cat Breeds

There are 27 cat breeds recognized: abyssinian, american shorthair, balinese, birman, bombay, burmese, colorpoint shorthair, egyptian mau, exotic shorthair, havana brown, himalayan, japanese bobtail, korat, leopard cat, lilac foreign shorthair, maine coon cat, manx, ocicat, oriental shorthair, persian, rex, russian blue, scottish fold, siamese, sphynx, turkish angora, wirehair shorthair.

81st Annual Boston Marathon

Jerome Drayton of Toronto, Ont. covered the traditional distance of 26 miles 385 yards in 2 hours 14 minutes 46 seconds to win the 1977 Boston Marathon. The leading finishers and their times follow:

1—Jerome Drayton, Toronto, Ont.	**2:14.46**
2—Veli Balli, Turkey	**2:15.44**
3—Brian Maxwell, Berkley, Cal.	**2:17.21**
4—Ronald Wayne, Alamedo, Cal.	**2:18.18**
5—Vincent Fleming, Boston, Mass.	**2:18.37**
6—Tom Fleming, Bloomfield, N.J.	**2:18.46**
7—Gary Tuttle, Ventura, Cal.	**2:19.42**
8—Chris Berk, Palo Alto, Cal.	**2:19.48**
9—Jack Fultz, Franklin, Pa.	**2:20.44**
10—Russell Pate, Columbia, S.C.	**2:21.16**
11—Carl Hatfield, Philippi, W.Va.	**2:21.16**
12—Jeffrey Wells, Dallas, Tex.	**2:21.41**
13—Robert Varsha, Atlanta, Ga.	**2:21.44**
14—Victor Anderson, Australia	**2:21.51**

Leading Women

1—Miki Gorman, Los Angeles, Cal.	**2:48.44**
2—Marilyn T. Bevans, Baltimore, Md.	**2:51.12**
3—Gayle Olinek, Canada	**2:55.27**
4—Ann Forshee, Ann Arbor, Mich.	**2:57.09**

Badminton Championships in 1977

1st World Badminton Championships

Malmo, Sweden, May 3-8

Men's Singles—Flemming Delfs, Denmark def. Svend Pri, Denmark,15-5, 15-6.
Women's Singles—Lene Koppen, Denmark def. Gillian Gilks, England, 12-9, 12-11.
Men's Doubles—Tjun-Tjun & Johan Wahjudi, Indonesia def. Christian and Ade Chandre, Indonesia 15-6, 15-4.
Women's Doubles—Etsuko Toganoo & Emiko Ueno, Japan def. Joke van Beusekom & M. Ridder, Netherlands, 15-10, 15-11.
Mixed Doubles—Steen Skovgaard & Lene Koppen, Denmark def. Derek Talbot & Gillian Gilks, England, 15-12, 18-17.

U. S. National Championships

San Diego, Cal., March 30-April 2

Men's Singles—Chris Kinard, Pasadena, CA def. Charles Coakley, Costa Mesa, CA, 15-6, 15-11.
Women's Singles—Pam Bristol, Flint, MI def. Cheryl Carton, San Diego, CA, 8-11, 11-4, 12-9.
Men's Doubles—Jim Poole, Westminster, CA & Mike Walker, Mahattan Beach, CA def. Gary Higgins & Bob Dickie, Manhattan Beach, CA, 18-17, 15-12.
Women's Doubles—Dianna Oesterhues, Torrance, CA & Janet Wilts, Claremont, CA def. Pam Bristol & Rosine Lemon, Long Lake, N.Y., 18-14, 18-15.
Mixed Doubles—Bruce Pontow, Lombard, IL & Pam Bristol def. Don Paup, Vienna, VA & Rosine Lemon, 15-10, 18-16.
Senior Men's Singles—Jim Poole def. Rod Starkey, La Mesa, CA, 15-11, 15-8.
Senior Men's Doubles—Rod Starkey & Bill Berry, El Cajon, CA def. Bill Goodman, Wellesley, MA & Tom Heden, Millwood, N.Y., 15-11, 15-12.
Senior Ladies Doubles—Rosine Lemon & Carlene Starkey, La Mesa, CA def. Gloria Eli, Swartz Creek, MI & Ket Hoffman, Rochester, MI, 15-8, 15-8.
Senior Mixed Doubles—Carlene & Rod Starkey def. Jim Poole & Helen Tibbetts, Torrance, CA, 17-14, 15-10.
Master Men's Singles—Ed Phillips, Warwick, RI def. Dick Mitchell, San Diego, CA, default.
Master Men's Doubles—Harold Thomas, St. Louis, MO & M. Witte, Honolulu, HI def. Larry Calvert, Pacific Palisades, CA & Bob Lucvano, Los Angeles, CA, 15-9, 15-12.
Master Mixed Doubles—Ed Phillips and Ket Hoffman def. Larry Calvert and Helen Tibbetts, Torrance, CA, 15-6, 15-5.

U. S. National Junior Championships

San Jose, Cal., April 6-9

Boy's Singles—Geoffrey Stensland, Seattle, WA def. David Collis, Hermosa Beach, CA, 15-4, 15-4.
Girl's Singles—Lisa De Rousie, West Los Angeles, CA def. Monica Ortez, Anaheim, CA, 11-5, 11-2.
Boy's Doubles—Bob Gold & Rahul Naidu, Skokie, IL def. Russ Nelson, Tempe, AZ & Danny Rubin, Manhattan Beach, CA, 15-9, 7-15, 15-4.
Girl's Doubles—Denise Corlett, Manhattan Beach, CA & Lisa De Rousie def. Monica Ortez & Valerie Tate, Tempe, AZ, 15-10, 15-8.
Mixed Doubles—Russ Nelson & Lisa De Rousie def. Bob Gold & Monica Ortez, 15-9, 17-14.

All England Championships

Wembley, England, March 23-26

Men's Singles—Flemming Delfs, Denmark def. Liem Swie King, Indonesia, 15-17, 15-11, 15-8.
Women's Singles—Hiroe Yuki, Japan def. Lene Koppen, Denmark, 7-11, 11-3, 11-7.
Men's Doubles—Tjun-Tjun and Johan Wahjudi, Indonesia def. Christian and Ade Chandra, Indonesia, 15-7,18-15.
Women's Doubles—Etsuko Toganoo and Emiko Ueno, Japan def. Margaret Lockwood and Nora Perry, England, 15-13, 15-10.
Mixed Doubles—Derek Talbot and Gillian Gilks, England def. Mike Tredgett and Nora Perry, England, 15-9, 15-9.

Skiing in 1977

U.S. National Alpine Championships

Sun Valley, Ida., Feb. 14-15

Men's Downhill — not held.
Men's Slalom — Gary Adgate. **Time — 106.74.**
Men's Giant Slalom — Phil Mahre. **Time 150.08.**
Combined — Gary Adgate.
Women's Downhill — not held.
Women's Slalom — Christin Cooper. **Time — 105.53.**
Women's Giant Slalom — Becky Dorsey. **Time — 80.42.**
Women's Combined — Christin Cooper.

U.S. National Cross Country Championships

Burke/Lyndon, Vt., Jan. 23-29

Men's 15 km. — Tim Kelley. **Time — 51.39.**
Men's 30 km. — Tim Caldwell. **Time — 1:37.04.**
Men's 50 km. — Stan Dunklee. **Time — 2:37.29.**
Jr. Men's 10 km. — Fritz Koch. **Time — 33.57.**
Jr. Men's 15 km. — Fritz Koch. **Time — 52.23.**
Women's 5 km. — Betsy Haines. **Time — 20.47.**
Women's 7½ km. — Shirley Firth. **Time — 26.33.**
Women's 20 km. — Shirley Firth. **Time — 1:12.02.**
Jr. Women's 5 km. — Beth Paxson. **Time — 20.46.**

The World Cup Winners

Men	Women	Nation's Cup
1967—Jean Claude Killy, France	1967—Nancy Greene, Canada	1967—France
1968—Jean Claude Killy, France	1968—Nancy Greene, Canada	1968—France
1969—Karl Schranz, Austria	1969—Gertrud Gabl, Austria	1969—Austria
1970—Karl Schranz, Austria	1970—Michele Jacot, France	1970—France
1971—Gustavo Thoeni, Italy	1971—Annemarie Proell, Austria	1971—France
1972—Gustavo Thoeni, Italy	1972—Annemarie Proell, Austria	1972—France
1973—Gustavo Thoeni, Italy	1973—Annemarie Proell, Austria	1973—Austria
1974—Piero Gros, Italy	1974—Annemarie Proell, Austria	1974—Austria
1975—Gustavo Thoeni, Italy	1975—Annemarie Proell, Austria	1975—Austria
1976—Ingemar Stenmark, Sweden	1976—Rose Mittermaier, W. Germany	1976—Italy
1977—Ingemar Stenmark, Sweden	1977—Lise-Marie Morerod, Austria	1977—Austria

Kentucky Derby

Churchill Downs, Louisville, Ky.

Inaugurated 1875, Distance 1-1/4 miles; 1-1/2 miles until 1896. 3-yr. olds. Times—seconds in fifths.

Year	Winner	Jockey	Trainer	Wt.	Second	Winner's share	Time
1904	Elwood	F. Prior	C. E. Durnell	117	Ed Tierney	$4,850	2:08.1
1905	Agile	J. Martin	R. Tucker	122	Ram's Horn	4,850	2:10.3
1906	Sir Huon	R. Troxer	P. Coyle	117	Lady Navarre	4,850	2:08.4
1907	Pink Star	A. Minder	W. H. Fizer	117	Zal	4,850	2:12.3
1908	Stone Street	A. Pickens	J. W. Hall	117	Sir Cleges	4,850	2:15.1
1909	Wintergreen	V. Powers	C. Mack	117	Miami	4,850	2:08.1
1910	Donau	F. Herbert	G. Ham	117	Joe Morris	4,850	2:06.2
1911	Meridian	G. Archibald	A. Ewing	117	Governor Gray	4,850	2:05.
1912	Worth	C. H. Shilling	F. M. Taylor	117	Duval	4,850	2:09.2
1913	Donerail	R. Goose	T. P. Hayes	117	Ten Point	5,475	2:04.4
1914	Old Rosebud	J. McCabe	F. D. Weir	114	Hodge	9,125	2:03.2
1915	Regret*	J. Notter	J. Rowe Sr.	112	Pebbles	11,450	2:05.2
1916	George Smith	J. Loftus	H. Hughes	117	Star Hawk	16,600	2:04.3
1917	Omar Khayyam	C. Borel	C. T. Patterson	117	Ticket	9,750	2:04.
1918	Exterminator	W. Knapp	H. McDaniel	114	Escoba	14,700	2:10.4
1919	Sir Barton	J. Loftus	H. G. Bedwell	112	Billy Kelly	20,825	2:09.4
1920	Paul Jones	T. Rice	W. Garth	126	Upset	30,375	2:09.
1921	Behave Yourself	C. Thompson	H. J. Thompson	126	Black Servant	38,450	2:04.1
1922	Morvich	A. Johnson	F. Burlew	126	Bet Mosie	46,775	2:04.3
1923	Zev	E. Sande	D. J. Leary	126	Martingale	53,600	2:05.2
1924	Black Gold	J. D. Mooney	H. Webb	126	Chilhowee	52,775	2:05.1
1925	Flying Ebony	E. Sande	W. B. Duke	126	Captain Hal	52,950	2:07.3
1926	Bubbling Over	A. Johnson	H. J. Thompson	126	Bagenbagggage	50,075	2:03.4
1927	Whiskery	L. McAtee	F. Hopkins	126	Osmand	51,000	2:06.
1928	Reigh Count	C. Lang	B. S. Michell	126	Misstep	55,375	2:10.2
1929	Clyde Van Dusen	L. McAtee	C. Van Dusen	126	Naishapur	53,950	2:10.4
1930	Gallant Fox	E. Sande	J. Fitzsimmons	126	Gallant Knight	50,725	2:07.3
1931	Twenty Grand	C. Kurtsinger	J. Rowe Jr.	126	Sweep All	48,725	2:01.4
1932	Burgoo King	E. James	H. J. Thompson	126	Economic	52,350	2:05.1
1933	Brokers Tip	D. Meade	H. J. Thompson	126	Head Play	48,925	2:06.4
1934	Cavalcade	M. Garner	R. A. Smith	126	Discovery	28,175	2:04.
1935	Omaha	W. Saunders	J. Fitzsimmons	126	Roman Soldier	39,525	2:05.
1936	Bold Venture	I. Hanford	M. Hirsch	126	Brevity	37,725	2:03.3
1937	War Admiral	C. Kurtsinger	G. Conway	126	Pompoon	52,050	2:03.1
1938	Lawrin	E. Arcaro	B. A. Jones	126	Dauber	47,050	2:04.4
1939	Johnstown	J. Stout	J. Fitzsimmons	126	Challedon	46,350	2:03.2
1940	Gallahadion	C. Bierman	R. Waldron	126	Bimelech	60,150	2:05.
1941	Whirlaway	E. Arcaro	B. A. Jones	126	Staretor	61,275	2:01.2
1942	Shut Out	W. D. Wright	J. M. Gaver	126	Alsab	64,225	2:04.2
1943	Count Fleet	J. Longden	G. D. Cameron	126	Blue Swords	60,275	2:04.
1944	Pensive	C. McCreary	B. A. Jones	126	Broadcloth	64,675	2:04.1
1945	Hoop, Jr.	E. Arcaro	I. H. Parke	126	Pot o'Luck	64,850	2:07.
1946	Assault	W. Mehrtens	M. Hirsch	126	Spy Song	96,400	2:06.3
1947	Jet Pilot	E. Guerin	T. Smith	126	Phalanx	92,160	2:06.3
1948	Citation	E. Arcaro	B. A. Jones	126	Coaltown	83,400	2:05.2
1949	Ponder	S. Brooks	B. A. Jones	126	Capot	91,600	2:04.1
1950	Middleground	W. Boland	M. Hirsch	126	Hill Prince	92,650	2:01.3
1951	Count Turf	C. McCreary	S. Rutchick	126	Royal Mustang	98,050	2:02.3
1952	Hill Gail	E. Arcaro	B. A. Jones	126	Sub Fleet	96,300	2:01.3
1953	Dark Star	H. Moreno	E. Hayward	126	Native Dancer	90,050	2:02.
1954	Determine	R. York	W. Molter	126	Hasty Road	102,050	2:03.
1955	Swaps	W. Shoemaker	M. A. Tenney	126	Nashua	108,400	2:01.4
1956	Needles	D. Erb	H. L. Fontaine	126	Fablus	123,450	2:03.2
1957	Iron Liege	W. Hartack	H. A. Jones	126	Gallant Man	107,950	2:02.1
1958	Tim Tam	I. Valenzuela	H. A. Jones	126	Lincoln Road	116,400	2:05.
1959	Tomy Lee	W. Shoemaker	F. Childs	126	Sword Dancer	119,650	2:02.1
1960	Venetian Way	W. Hartack	V. Sovinski	126	Bally Ache	114,850	2:02.2
1961	Carry Back	J. Sellers	J. A. Price	126	Crozier	120,500	2:04.
1962	Decidedly	W. Hartack	H. Luro	126	Roman Line	119,650	2:00.2
1963	Chateaugay	B. Baeza	J. Conway	126	Never Bend	108,900	2:01.4
1964	Northern Dancer	W. Hartack	H. Luro	126	Hill Rise	114,300	2:00.
1965	Lucky Debonair	W. Shoemaker	F. Catrone	126	Dapper Dan	112,000	2:01.1
1966	Kauai King	D. Brumfield	H. Forrest	126	Advocator	120,500	2:02.
1967	Proud Clarion	R. Ussery	L. Gentry	126	Barbs Delight	119,700	2:00.3
1968	Dancer's Image (a)	R. Ussery	H. Forrest	126	Forward Pass	122,600	2:02.1
1969	Majestic Prince	W. Hartack	J. Longden	126	Arts and Letters	113,200	2:01.4
1970	Dust Commander	M. Manganello	D. Combs	126	My Dad George	127,800	2:03.2
1971	Canonero II	G. Avila	J. Arias	126	Jim French	145,500	2:03.1
1972	Riva Ridge	R. Turcotte	L. Laurin	126	No Le Hace	140,300	2:01.4
1973	Secretariat	R. Turcotte	L. Laurin	126	Sham	155,050	1:59.2
1974	Cannonade	A. Cordero	W. C. Stephens	126	Hudson County	274,000	2:04.
1975	Foolish Pleasure	J. Vasquez	L. Jolley	126	Avatar	209,611	2:02.
1976	Bold Forbes	A. Cordero	L. Barrera	126	Honest Pleasure	165,200	2:01.3
1977	Seattle Slew	J. Cruquet	W. H. Turner Jr.	126	Run Dusty Run	214,700	2:02.1

(a) Dancer's Image was disqualified from purse money by order of the Churchill Downs stewards after tests disclosed that he had run with a pain-killing drug, phenylbutazone, in his system. All wagers were paid on Dancer's Image. Forward Pass was awarded first place money.

The Kentucky Derby has been won five times by two jockeys, Eddie Arcaro, 1938, 1941, 1945, 1948 and 1952; and Bill Hartack, 1957, 1960, 1962, 1964 and 1969; and three times by each of three jockeys, Isaac Murphy, 1884, 1890 and 1891; Earle Sande, 1923, 1925 and 1930, and Willie Shoemaker, 1955, 1959, 1965. *Regret was only filly ever to win the Derby.

Belmont Stakes

Elmont, N.Y.; inaugurated 1867; 1 1/2 miles, 3 yr. olds, Time—seconds in fifths.

Year	Winner	Jockey	Trainer	Wt.	Second	Winner's share	Time
1938	Pasteurized	J. Stout	G. M. Odom	126	Dauber	$34,530	2:29.2
1939	Johnstown	J. Stout	J. Fitzsimmons	126	Belay	37,020	2:29.3
1940	Bimelech	F. A. Smith	W. J. Hurley	126	Your Chance	35,030	2:29.3
1941	Whirlaway	E. Arcaro	B. A. Jones	126	Robert Morris	39,770	2:31
1942	Shut Out	E. Arcaro	J. M. Gaver	126	Alsab	44,520	2:29.1
1943	Count Fleet	J. Longden	G. D. Cameron	126	Fairy Manhurst	35,340	2:28.1
1944	Bounding Home	G. L. Smith	M. Brady	126	Pensive	55,000	2:32.1
1945	Pavot	E. Arcaro	O. White	126	Wildlife	52,675	2:30.1
1946	Assault	W. Mehrtens	M. Hirsch	126	Natchez	75,400	2:30.4
1947	Phalanx	R. Donoso	S. Veitch	126	Tide Rips	78,900	2:29.2
1948	Citation	E. Arcaro	H. A. Jones	126	Better Self	77,700	2:28.1
1949	Capot	T. Atkinson	J. M. Gaver	126	Ponder	60,900	2:30.1
1950	Middleground	W. Boland	M. Hirsch	126	Lights Up	61,350	2:28.3
1951	Counterpoint	D. Gorman	S. Veitch	125	Battlefield	82,000	2:29
1952	One Count	E. Arcaro	O. White	126	Blue Man	82,400	2:30.1
1953	Native Dancer	E. Guerin	W. C. Winfrey	126	Jamie K.	82,500	2:28.3
1954	High Gun	E. Guerin	M. Hirsch	126	Fisherman	89,000	2:30.4
1955	Nashua	E. Arcaro	J. Fitzsimmons	126	Blazing Count	83,700	2:29
1956	Needles	D. Erb	H. Fontaine	126	Career Boy	83,600	2:29.4
1957	Gallant Man	W. Shoemaker	J. Nerud	126	Inside Tract	77,300	2:26.3
1958	Cavan	P. Anderson	T. J. Barry	126	Tim Tam	73,440	2:30.1
1959	Sword Dancer	W. Shoemaker	J. E. Burch	126	Bagdad	93,525	2:28.2
1960	Celtic Ash	W. Hartack	T. J. Barry	126	Venetian Way	96,785	2:29.3
1961	Sherluck	B. Baeza	H. Young	126	Globemaster	104,900	2:29.1
1962	Jaipur	W. Shoemaker	W. F. Mulholland	126	Admiral's Voyage	109,550	2:28.4
1963	Chateaugay	B. Baeza	J. P. Conway	126	Candy Spots	101,700	2:30.1
1964	Quadrangle	M. Ycaza	J. E. Burch	126	Roman Brother	110,850	2:28.2
1965	Hail to All	J. Sellers	E. Yowell	126	Tom Rolfe	104,150	2:28.2
1966	Amberoid	W. Boland	L. Laurin	126	Buffle	117,700	2:29.3
1967	Damascus	W. Shoemaker	F. Y. Whiteley Jr.	126	Cool Reception	104,950	2:28.4
1968	Stage Door Johnny	H. Gustines	J. M. Gaver	126	Forward Pass	117,700	2:27.1
1969	Arts and Letters	B. Baeza	J. E. Burch	126	Majestic Prince	104,050	2:28.4
1970	High Echelon	J. L. Rotz	J. W. Jacobs	126	Needles N Pens	115,000	2:34
1971	Pass Catcher	W. Blum	E. Yowell	126	Jim French	97,710	2:30.2
1972	Riva Ridge	R. Turcotte	L. Laurin	126	Ruritania	93,950	2:28
1973	Secretariat	R. Turcotte	L. Laurin	126	Twice A Prince	90,120	2:24
1974	Little Current	M. Rivera	L. Rondinello	126	Jolly Johu	101,970	2:29.1
1975	Avatar	W. Shoemaker	A. T. Doyle	126	Foolish Pleasure	116,160	2:28.1
1976	Bold Forbes	A. Cordero	L. S. Barrera	126	McKenzie Bridge	116,850	2:29
1977	Seattle Slew	J. Cruquet	W. H. Turner Jr.	126	Run Dusty Run	109,080	2:29.3

Preakness

Pimlico, Baltimore, Md.; inaugurated 1873; 1 3-16 miles, 3 yr. olds. Time—seconds in fifths.

Year	Winner	Jockey	Trainer	Wt.	Second	Winner's share	Time
1938	Dauber	M. Peters	R. E. Handlen	126	Cravat	$51,875	1:59.4
1939	Challedon	G. Seabo	L. J. Schaefer	126	Gilded Knight	53,710	1:59.4
1940	Bimelech	F. A. Smith	W. J. Hurley	126	Mioland	53,230	1:58.3
1941	Whirlaway	E. Arcaro	B. A. Jones	126	King Cole	49,365	1:58.4
1942	Alsab	B. James	A. Swenke	126	Requested, Sun Again (tie)	58,175	1:57
1943	Count Fleet	J. Longden	G. D. Cameron	126	Blue Swords	43,190	1:57.2
1944	Pensive	C. McCreary	B. A. Jones	126	Platter	60,075	1:59.1
1945	Polynesian	W. D. Wright	M. Dixon	126	Hoop Jr.	66,170	1:58.4
1946	Assault	W. Mehrtens	M. Hirsch	126	Lord Boswell	96,620	2:01.2
1947	Faultless	D. Dodson	H. A. Jones	126	On Trust	98,005	1:59
1948	Citation	E. Arcaro	H. A. Jones	126	Vulcan's Forge	91,870	2:02.2
1949	Capot	T. Atkinson	J. M. Gaver	126	Palestinian	79,985	1:56
1950	Hill Prince	E. Arcaro	J. H. Hayes	126	Middleground	56,115	1:59.1
1951	Bold	E. Arcaro	P. M. Burch	126	Counterpoint	83,110	1:56.2
1952	Blue Man	C. McCreary	W. C. Stephens	126	Jampol	86,135	1:57.2
1953	Native Dancer	E. Guerin	W. C. Winfrey	126	Jamie K.	65,200	1:57.4
1954	Hasty Road	J. Adams	H. Trotsek	126	Correlation	91,600	1:57.2
1955	Nashua	E. Arcaro	J. Fitzsimmons	126	Saratoga	67,550	1:54.3
1956	Fabius	W. Hartack	H. A. Jones	126	Needles	84,250	1:58.2
1957	Bold Ruler	E. Arcaro	J. Fitzsimmons	126	Iron Liege	65,250	1:56.1
1958	Tim Tam	I. Valenzuela	H. A. Jones	126	Lincoln Road	97,900	1:57.1
1959	Royal Orbit	W. Harmatz	R. Cornell	126	Sword Dancer	136,200	1:57
1960	Bally Ache	R. Ussery	H. J. Pitt	126	Victoria Park	121,000	1:57.3
1961	Carry Back	J. Sellers	J. A. Price	126	Globemaster	126,200	1:57.3
1962	Greek Money	J. L. Rotz	V. W. Raines	126	Ridan	135,800	1:56.1
1963	Candy Spots	W. Shoemaker	M. A. Tenney	126	Chateaugay	127,500	1:56.1
1964	Northern Dancer	W. Hartack	H. Luro	126	The Scoundrel	124,200	1:56.4
1965	Tom Rolfe	R. Turcotte	F. Y. Whiteley Jr.	126	Dapper Dan	128,100	1:56.1
1966	Kauai King	D. Brumfield	H. Forrest	126	Stupendous	129,000	1:55.2
1967	Damascus	W. Shoemaker	F. Y. Whiteley Jr.	126	In Reality	141,500	1:55.1
1968	Forward Pass	I. Valenzuela	H. Forrest	126	Out of the Way	142,700	1:56.4
1969	Majestic Prince	W. Hartack	J. Longden	126	Arts and Letters	129,500	1:55.3
1970	Personality	E. Belmonte	J. W. Jacobs	126	My Dad George	151,300	1:56.1
1971	Canonero II.	G. Avila	J. Arias	126	Eastern Fleet	137,400	1:54
1972	Bee Bee Bee	E. Nelson	D. W. Carroll	126	No Le Hace	135,300	1:55.3
1973	Secretariat	R. Turcotte	L. Laurin	126	Sham	129,900	1:54.2
1974	Little Current	M. Rivera	L. Rondinello	126	Neopolitan Way	156,000	1:56.3
1975	Master Derby	D. McHargue	W. E. Adams	126	Foolish Pleasure	158,100	1:56.2
1976	Elocutionist	J. Lively	P. T. Adwell	126	Play The Red	129,700	1:55
1977	Seattle Slew	J. Cruquet	W. H. Turner Jr.	126	Iron Constitution	138,600	1:54.2

Triple Crown Turf Winners, Jockeys, and Trainers

(Kentucky Derby, Preakness, and Belmont Stakes)

Year	Horse	Jockey	Trainer
1919	Sir Barton	J. Loftus	H. G. Bedwell
1930	Gallant Fox	E. Sande	J. Fitzsimmons
*1935	Omaha	W. Sanders	J. Fitzsimmons
1937	War Admiral	C. Kurtsinger	G. Conway
1941	Whirlaway	E. Arcaro	B. A. Jones
1943	Count Fleet	J. Longden	G. D. Cameron
1946	Assault	Mehrtens	M. Hirsch
1948	Citation	E. Arcaro	H. A. Jones
1973	Secretariat	R. Turcotte	L. Laurin
1977	Seattle Slew	J. Cruquet	W.H. Turner Jr.

American Thoroughbred Records

Dirt Course. Time—seconds in fifths.

Furlongs	Horse, age, weight	Track, state	Date	Time
3	El Macho	Gulfstream, Fla.	Feb. 26, 1974	0:32.1
3½	Deep Sun, 7, 120	Shenandoah Downs, W. Va.	July 11, 1959	0:39
	Crying For More, 7, 128	Shenandoah Downs, W. Va.	Mar. 18, 1972	0:39
4 (½ mile)	Tamran's Jet, 2, 118	Sunland Park, N. M.	Mar. 22, 1968	0:44.4
	Crimson Saint, 2, 119	Oaklawn Park, Ark.	Apr. 1, 1971	0:44.4
	Mighty Mr. A., 3, 116	Sportsman Park, Ill.	Nov. 1, 1971	0:44.4
	Thief of Bagdad, 5, 114	Sportsman Park, Ill.	Nov. 5, 1971	0:44.4
	Argus Ruler, 5, 114	Cahokia Downs, Ill.	Apr. 25, 1973	0:44.4
4½	Kathryn's Doll, 2, 111	Turf Paradise, Ariz.	Apr. 9, 1967	0:50.2
	Dear Ethel, 2, 114	Miles Park, Ky.	July 4, 1967	0:50.2
	Bold Liz, 2, 118	Sunland Park, N.M.	Mar. 19, 1972	0:50.2
	Scott's Poppy, 2, 118	Turf Paradise, Ariz.	Feb. 22, 1975	0:50.2
5	Zip Pocket, 3, 122	Turf Paradise, Ariz.	Apr. 22, 1967	0:55.2
5½	Zip Pocket, 3, 129	Turf Paradise, Ariz.	Nov. 19, 1967	1:01.2
6 (¾ mile)	Grey Papa, 6, 116	Longacres, Wash.	Sept. 4, 1972	1:07.1
6½	Best Hitter, 4, 114	Longacres, Wash.	Aug. 24, 1973	1:13.4
7	Triple Bend, 4, 123	Hollywood, Cal.	May 6, 1972	1:19.4
7½	Aurecolt, 3, 122	Churchill Downs, Ky.	Nov. 12, 1957	1:29
8 (1 mile)	Dr. Fager, 4, 134	Arlington, Ill.	Aug. 24, 1968	1:32.1
8½	Swaps, 4, 130	Hollywood, Cal.	June 23, 1956	1:39
9	Secretariat, 3, 124	Belmont, N.Y.	Sept. 15, 1973	1:45.2
9½	Riva Ridge, 4, 127	Aqueduct, N.Y.	July 4, 1973	1:52.2
10	Noor, 5, 127	Golden Gate, Cal.	June 24, 1950	1:58.1
	Quack, 3, 115	Hollywood, Cal.	July 15, 1972	1:58.1
10½	Tempted, 4, 128	Aqueduct, N.Y.	Oct. 12, 1959	2:09
11	Man o' War, 3, 126	Belmont, N.Y.	June 12, 1920	2:14.1
11½	Theoretic, 6, 111	Sportsman Park, Ill.	Oct. 15, 1973	2:24.1
12 (1½ miles)	Secretariat, 3, 126	Belmont, N.Y.	June 9, 1973	2:24
13	Swaps, 4, 130	Hollywood, Cal.	July 25, 1956	2:38.1
14	Noor, 5, 117	Santa Anita, Cal.	Mar. 4, 1950	2:52.4
15	Pharawell, 5, 119	Gulfstream, Fla.	Apr. 8, 1947	3:13.4
16 (2 miles)	Kelso, 7, 124	Aqueduct, N.Y.	Oct. 31, 1964	3:19.1
18	Fenelon, 4, 119	Belmont, N.Y.	Oct. 4, 1941	3:47
20	Miss Grillo, 6, 118	Pimlico, Md.	Nov. 12, 1948	4:14.3

Leading Money-Winning Horses

As of Mar. 1, 1977

Horse, year foaled	Sts.	1st	2d	3d	Dollars
Kelso, 1957	63	39	12	2	1,977,896
Round Table, 1954	66	43	8	5	1,749,869
Forego, 1970	40	23	6	6	1,655,217
Dahlia, 1970	48	15	3	7	1,543,139
Buckpasser, 1963	31	25	4	1	1,462,014
Allez France, 1970	21	13	3	1	1,386,146
Secretariat, 1970	21	16	3	1	1,316,808
Nashua, 1952	30	22	4	1	1,288,565
Susan's Girl, 1969	63	29	14	11	1,251,667
Carry Back, 1958	62	21	11	11	1,241,165
Foolish Pleasure, 1972	26	16	4	3	1,216,705
Damascus, 1964	32	21	7	3	1,176,781
Cougar, 2nd, 1966	50	20	7	17	1,162,725
Riva Ridge, 1969	30	17	3	1	1,111,347
Fort Marcy, 1964	75	21	18	14	1,109,791
Citation, 1945	45	32	10	2	1,085,760
Native Diver, 1959	81	37	7	12	1,026,500
Royal Glint, 1970	52	21	9	4	1,004,815
Dr. Fager, 1964	22	18	2	1	1,002,642

Annual Leading Money-Winning Horses

Year	Horse	Dollars
1942	Shut Out	238,872
1943	Count Fleet	174,055
1944	Pavot	179,040
1945	Busher	273,735
1946	Assault	424,195
1947	Armed	376,325
1948	Citation	709,470
1949	Ponder	321,825
1950	Noor	346,940
1951	Counterpoint	250,525
1952	Crafty Admiral	277,255
1953	Native Dancer	513,425
1954	Determine	328,700
1955	Nashua	752,550
1956	Needles	440,850
1957	Round Table	600,383
1958	Round Table	662,780
1959	Sword Dancer	537,004
1960	Bally Ache	455,045
1961	Carry Back	565,349
1962	Never Bend	402,969
1963	Candy Spots	604,481
1964	Gun Bow	580,100
1965	Buckpasser	568,096
1966	Buckpasser	669,078
1967	Damascus	817,941
1968	Forward Pass	546,674
1969	Arts and Letters	555,604
1970	Personality	444,049
1971	Riva Ridge	503,263
1972	Droll Roll	471,633
1973	Secretariat	860,404
1974	Chris Evert	551,063
1975	Foolish Pleasure	716,278
1976	Forego	491,701

Leading Jockeys in 1976

Money Won

Jockey	Mts.	Wins	Pct.	Purses
Hawley, S.	1,637	413	.252	$4,546,723
Pincay, L. Jr.	1,435	386	.269	4,377,661
Tejeira, J.	1,414	360	.255	2,555,154
Gall, D.	1,677	353	.210	849,407
Bracciale, V. Jr.	1,604	351	.219	2,223,192
Graell, A.	1,605	346	.216	993,952
McCarron, C. J.	1,360	334	.246	2,133,559
Catalano, W.	1,613	328	.203	1,355,628
Velasquez, J.	1,577	302	.192	4,294,646
Delahoussaye, E.	1,472	292	.198	1,792,904
Fell, J.	1,437	280	.195	1,924,380
Lloyd, J. S.	1,654	280	.169	819,634
Cordero, A. Jr.	1,534	274	.179	4,709,500
Neff, S.	1,685	242	.144	421,488
Cauthen, S.	1,170	240	.205	1,244,423
Snyder, L.	1,419	238	.168	2,008,228
Turcotte, R.	1,550	237	.153	2,903,539
Noguez, A.	1,215	227	.187	714,168
Black, A. S.	1,489	227	.152	1,419,531
Zook, D. J.	1,631	219	.134	387,238

Races Won

Jockey	Mts.	Wins	Pct.	Purses
Cordero, A. Jr.	1,534	274	.179	$4,709,500
Hawley, S.	1,637	413	.252	4,546,723
Pincay, L. Jr.	1,435	386	.269	4,377,661
Velasquez, J.	1,577	302	.192	4,294,646
Shoemaker, W.	1,035	200	.193	3,815,645
Toro, F.	1,303	204	.157	3,171,456
Maple, E.	1,452	192	.132	3,008,998
Turcotte, R.	1,550	237	.153	2,903,539
Vasquez, J.	1,431	185	.129	2,794,478
Tejeira, J.	1,414	360	.255	2,555,154
McHargue, D. G.	1,187	170	.143	2,474,389
Bracciale, V. Jr.	1,604	351	.219	2,223,192
McCarron, C. J.	1,360	334	.246	2,133,559
Snyder, L.	1,419	238	.168	2,008,228
Pierce, D.	1,017	103	.101	1,961,002
Day, P.	1,116	137	.123	1,934,873
Fell, J.	1,437	280	.195	1,924,380
Castaneda, M.	1,236	152	.123	1,862,580
Lively, J.	1,271	189	.149	1,859,664
Cruguet, J.	840	121	.144	1,813,797

Leading Trainers in 1976

Races Won

Trainer	Sts.	Wins	Purses
Van Berg, Jack	2,360	494	$2,972,218
Leatherbury, King	1,486	365	1,691,655
Dutrow, Richard	1,444	275	1,732,608
Vance, David	996	270	1,748,154
Delp, Grover	1,175	256	1,611,311
Hammond, Everett	1,201	212	532,131
Sipp, Burton	1,226	183	531,624
Baird, Dale	1,410	160	285,041
Hazelton, Richard	855	152	845,138
Lenzini, John Jr.	719	139	949,410
Smith, Jere	679	135	1,054,349
Prickett, William	746	131	818,706
Martin, Frank	804	131	1,433,029
Mercer, Henry	672	128	331,174
Hammond, Jerry	700	128	296,393
Imprescia, Dominic	550	125	489,303
Potter, Gordon	525	122	1,042,384
Johnson, Wade	505	121	214,688
Thompson, J. Willard	821	120	722,806
Hild, Glen	972	119	980,048

Money Won

Trainer	Sts.	Wins	Purses
Van Berg, Jack	2,360	494	$2,972,218
Barrera, Lazaro	726	113	2,532,698
Whittingham, Charles	411	67	2,248,783
Vance, David	996	270	1,748,154
Dutrow, Richard	1,444	275	1,732,608
Leatherbury, King	1,486	365	1,691,655
Delp, Grover	1,175	256	1,611,311
Martin, Frank	804	131	1,433,029
Russell, John	218	47	1,402,248
Jolley, Leroy	198	35	1,333,718
Doyle, A. T.	413	54	1,287,866
DiMauro, Stephen	512	57	1,101,420
Stephens, Woodford	305	58	1,067,688
Smith, Jere	679	135	1,054,349
Campo, John	568	79	1,050,137
Potter, Gordon	525	122	1,042,384
McAnally, Ronald	373	57	1,020,487
Davis, Doug Jr.	428	92	1,015,357
Hild, Glen	972	119	980,048
Frankel, Robert	439	93	974,313

Annual Leading Jockey—Money Won

Year	Jockey	Dollars
1942	Arcaro, E.	481,949
1943	Longden, J.	573,276
1944	Atkinson, T.	899,101
1945	Longden, J.	981,977
1946	Atkinson, T.	1,036,825
1947	Dodson, D.	1,429,949
1948	Arcaro, E.	1,686,230
1949	Brooks, S.	1,316,817
1950	Arcaro, E.	1,410,160
1951	Shoemaker, W.	1,329,890
1952	Arcaro, E.	1,859,591
1953	Shoemaker, W.	1,784,187
1954	Shoemaker, W.	1,876,760
1955	Arcaro, E.	1,864,796
1956	Hartack, W.	2,343,955
1957	Hartack, W.	3,060,501
1958	Shoemaker, W.	2,961,693
1959	Shoemaker, W.	2,843,133
1960	Shoemaker, W.	2,123,961
1961	Shoemaker, W.	2,690,819
1962	Shoemaker, W.	2,916,844
1963	Shoemaker, W.	2,526,925
1964	Shoemaker, W.	2,649,553
1965	Baeza, B.	2,582,702
1966	Baeza, B.	2,951,022
1967	Baeza, B.	3,088,888
1968	Baeza, B.	2,835,108
1969	Valasquez, J.	2,542,315
1970	Pincay, L. Jr.	2,626,526
1971	Pincay, L. Jr.	3,784,377
1972	Pincay, L. Jr.	3,225,827
1973	Pincay, L. Jr.	4,093,492
1974	Pincay, L. Jr.	4,251,060
1975	Baeza, B.	3,695,198
1976	Cordero, A. Jr.	4,709,500

Leading Sires in 1976

Sire	Sts.	Wins	Purses
What a Pleasure	804	108	$1,622,159
Round Table	385	70	1,613,214
Exclusive Native	703	123	1,468,845
T. V. Lark	878	114	1,457,119
Northern Dancer	519	90	1,426,047
Gallant Romeo	739	132	1,405,252
Grey Dawn II	827	107	1,208,902
Olden Times	942	145	1,190,507
Dr. Fager	584	87	1,142,800
Crimson Satan	929	139	1,137,742

Sire	Sts.	Wins	Purses
In Reality	596	122	$1,114,744
Cornish Prince	941	113	1,064,606
Delta Judge	588	88	1,060,306
Herbager	632	81	1,007,706
Buckpasser	339	51	1,005,537
Iron Ruler	856	114	1,001,124
Damascus	346	61	998,545
Lt. Stevens	815	136	991,458
The Axe II	813	105	987,364
Creme dela Creme	667	104	975,114

Professional Sports Directory

Baseball

Commissioner's Office
75 Rockefeller Plaza
New York, NY 10019

National League

National League Office
1 Rockefeller Plaza
New York, NY 10019

Atlanta Braves
PO Box 4064
Atlanta, GA 30302

Chicago Cubs
Wrigley Field
Chicago, IL 60613

Cincinnati Reds
100 Riverfront Stadium
Cincinnati, OH 45202

Houston Astros
Astrodome
Houston, TX 77001

Los Angeles Dodgers
Dodger Stadium
1000 Elysian Park Ave.
Los Angeles, CA 90012

Montreal Expos
PO Box 500, Station R
Montreal, Quebec HIV 3P2

New York Mets
William A. Shea Stadium
Roosevelt Ave. & 126th St.
Flushing, NY 11368

Philadelphia Phillies
Philadelphia Veterans Stadium
Broad St. & Pattison Ave.
Philadelphia, PA 19148

Pittsburgh Pirates
600 Stadium Circle
Pittsburgh, PA 15212

St. Louis Cardinals
Busch Memorial Stadium
250 Stadium Plaza
St. Louis, MO 63102

San Diego Padres
PO Box 2000
San Diego, CA 92120

San Francisco Giants
Candlestick Park
San Francisco, CA 94124

American League

American League Office
280 Park Ave.
New York, NY 10017

Baltimore Orioles
Memorial Stadium
Baltimore, MD 21218

Boston Red Sox
24 Jersey St.
Boston, MA 02215

California Angels
Anaheim Stadium
2000 State College Blvd.
Anaheim, CA 92806

Chicago White Sox
Comiskey Park
Dan Ryan & 35th St.
Chicago, IL 60616

Cleveland Indians
Cleveland Stadium
Cleveland, OH 44114

Detroit Tigers
Tiger Stadium
Detroit, MI 48216

Kansas City Royals
Harry S. Truman Sports Complex
PO Box 1969
Kansas City, MO 64141

Milwaukee Brewers
Milwaukee County Stadium
Milwaukee, WI 53214

Minnesota Twins
Metropolitan Stadium
8001 Cedar Ave.
Bloomington, MN 55420

New York Yankees
Yankee Stadium
Bronx, NY 10451

Oakland A's
Oakland-Alameda County
Coliseum
Oakland, CA 94621

Seattle Mariners
PO Box 4100
Seattle, WA 98104

Texas Rangers
Arlington Stadium
PO Box 1111
Arlington, TX 76010

Toronto Blue Jays
Exhibition Stadium
Toronto, Ont.

Basketball

National Basketball Assn.

League Office
Olympic Tower
645 5th Ave.
New York, NY 10022

Atlanta Hawks
100 Techwood Drive NW
Atlanta, GA 30303

Boston Celtics
North Station
Boston, MA 02114

Buffalo Braves
Memorial Auditorium
Buffalo, NY 14202

Chicago Bulls
333 North Michigan Ave.
Chicago, IL 60601

Cleveland Cavaliers
The Coliseum
2923 Streetsboro Rd.
Richfield, OH 44286

Denver Nuggets
P.O. Box 4286
Denver, CO 80204

Detroit Pistons
Cobo Hall
Detroit, MI 48226

Golden State Warriors
Oakland Coliseum Arena
Oakland, CA 94621

Houston Rockets
The Summit
Houston, TX 77046

Indiana Pacers
Market Square Center
151 N. Delaware
Indianapolis, IN 46204

Kansas City Kings
1800 Genessee
Kansas City, MO 64102

Los Angeles Lakers
The Forum
3900 W. Manchester Blvd.
or PO Box 10
Inglewood, CA 90306

Milwaukee Bucks
901 North 4th St.
Milwaukee, WI 53203

New Jersey Nets
Rutgers Univ.
New Brunswick, NJ 08903

New Orleans Jazz
Louisiana Superdome
Box 53213
New Orleans, LA 70153

New York Knickerbockers
Madison Square Garden Center
4 Pennsylvania Plaza
New York, NY 10001

Philadelphia 76ers
The Spectrum
Philadelphia, PA 19148

Phoenix Suns
PO Box 1369
Phoenix, AZ 85001

Portland Trail Blazers
Lloyd Bldg.
700 NE Multnomah St.
Portland, OR 97232

San Antonio Spurs
HemisFair Arena
P.O. Box 530
San Antonio, TX 78292

Seattle SuperSonics
221 West Harrison St.
Seattle, WA 98119

Washington Bullets
Capital Centre
Landover, MD 20786

Hockey

National Hockey League

League Headquarters
920 Sun Life Bldg.
Montreal, Quebec H3B 2W2

League Services
2 Pennsylvania Plaza
New York, NY 10001

Atlanta Flames
100 Techwood Dr., NW
Atlanta, GA 30303

Boston Bruins
150 Causeway St.
Boston, MA 02114

Buffalo Sabres
Memorial Auditorium
Buffalo, NY 14202

Chicago Black Hawks
1800 W. Madison St.
Chicago, IL 60612

Cleveland Barons
The Coliseum
Richfield, OH 44286

Colorado Rockies
McNichols Sports Arena
Denver, CO 80204

Detroit Red Wings
5920 Grand River
Detroit, MI 48208

Los Angeles Kings
PO Box 10
Inglewood, CA 90306

Minnesota North Stars
7901 Cedar Ave. S.
Bloomington, MN 55420

Montreal Canadiens
2313 St. Catherine St., West
Montreal, Quebec H3H 1N2

New York Islanders
1155 Conklin St.
Farmingdale, NY 11735

New York Rangers
Madison Square Garden
4 Pennsylvania Plaza
New York, NY 10001

Philadelphia Flyers
The Spectrum
Pattison Place
Philadelphia, PA 19148

Pittsburgh Penguins
Civic Arena
Pittsburgh, PA 15219

St. Louis Blues
5700 Oakland Ave.
St. Louis, MO 63110

Toronto Maple Leafs
60 Carlton St.
Toronto, Ont. M5B 1L1

Vancouver Canucks
100 North Renfrew St.
Vancouver, B.C. V5K 3N7

Washington Capitals
Capital Centre
Landover, MD 20786

World Hockey Assn.

League Office
415 Yonge St.
Toronto, Ont. M5B 2E7

Birmingham Bulls
1 Civic Center Plaza
Birmingham, AL 35203

Calgary Cowboys
1418 McLedd Trail SE
Calgary, Alta. T2G 2N5

Cincinnati Stingers
Riverfront Coliseum
Cincinnati, OH 45202

Edmonton Oilers
7424 118th Ave.
Edmonton, Alta. T5B 4M9

Houston Aeros
10 Greenway Plaza
Houston, TX 77046

Indianapolis Racers
Market Square Center
Indianapolis, IN 46204

New England Whalers
1 Civic Center Plaza
Hartford, CT 06103

Quebec Nordiques
2025 Ave. Du Colisee
Quebec, Quebec. G1L 4W7

Winnipeg Jets
15-1430 Maroons Rd.
Winnipeg, Man. R3G 0L5

Football

National Football League

NFL League Office
410 Park Avenue
New York, NY 10022

Atlanta Falcons
521 Capitol Ave. SW
Atlanta, GA 30312

Baltimore Colts
Executive Plaza
Hunt Valley, MD 21031

Buffalo Bills
1 Bills Drive
Orchard Park, NY 14127

Chicago Bears
55 E. Jackson
Chicago, IL 60604

Cincinnati Bengals
200 Riverfront Stadium
Cincinnati, OH 45202

Cleveland Browns
Cleveland Stadium
Cleveland, OH 44114

Dallas Cowboys
6116 North Central Expressway
Dallas, TX 75206

Denver Broncos
5700 Logan St.
Denver, CO 80216

Detroit Lions
1200 Featherstone Rd.
Box 4200
Pontiac, MI 48057

Green Bay Packers
1265 Lombardi Ave.
Green Bay, WI 54303

Houston Oilers
P.O. Box 1516
Houston, TX 77001

Kansas City Chiefs
1 Arrowhead Drive
Kansas City, MO 64129

Los Angeles Rams
10271 W. Pico Blvd.
Los Angeles, CA 90064

Miami Dolphins
330 Biscayne Blvd. Bldg.
Miami, FL 33132

Minnesota Vikings
7110 France Ave. So.
Edina, MN 55435

New England Patriots
Schaefer Stadium
Foxboro, MA 02035

New Orleans Saints
944 St. Charles
New Orleans, LA 70130

New York Giants
Giants Stadium
E. Rutherford, NJ 07073

New York Jets
598 Madison Ave.
New York, NY 10022

Oakland Raiders
7811 Oakport St.
Oakland, CA 94621

Philadelphia Eagles
Veterans Stadium
Philadelphia, PA 19148

Pittsburgh Steelers
Three Rivers Stadium
Pittsburgh, PA 15212

St. Louis Cardinals
200 Stadium Plaza
St. Louis, MO 63102

San Diego Chargers
San Diego Stadium
P.O. Box 20666
San Diego, CA 92120

San Francisco 49ers
1255 Post St.
San Francisco, CA 94109

Seattle Seahawks
1200 Westlake Ave. North
Seattle, WA 98109

Tampa Bay Buccaneers
1 Buccaneer Place
Tampa, FL 33607

Washington Redskins
PO Box 17247
Dulles Intl. Airport
Washington, DC 20041

National AAU Volleyball Championships

Honolulu, Hawaii, May 6-8, 1977

Men

Quarterfinals

Multnomah AC defeated Chuck's Cellar, 15-8, 15-8
Maccabi Union defeated Outrigger Canoe Club #1, 12-9, 15-6
Outrigger Cande Club #2 defeated Central YMCA, 15-10, 15-2
Patriots defeated Westside YMCA, 15-8, 15-7
Outrigger #2 defeated Patriots, 7-15, 12-10, 13-9

Semifinals

Maccabi defeated Multnomah AC, 15-6, 15-9
Outrigger #1 defeated Multnomah AC, 15-8, 15-8

Finals

Maccabi defeated Outrigger #1, 15-0, in sudden death game after Outrigger #1 defeated Maccabi, 6-15, 15-12, 14-10
Most Valuable Player—Joe Mica, Maccabi Union

Women

Quarterfinals

Nick's-Beverly Hills #1 defeated Nick's-Beverly Hills #2, 15-8, 13-10
Nick's-Hawaii #1 defeated South Bay Spoilers, 15-5, 15-5
South Bay Spoilers defeated Nick's-Beverly Hills #2, 15-4, 15-11
South Bay Spoilers defeated Dallas Petro White, 16-14, 15-7
Nick's-Beverly Hills #2 defeated Santa Barbara, 12-10, 15-6, 14-12

Semifinals

Nick's Beverly Hills #1 defeated Nick's-Hawaii #1, 15-11, 11-15, 13-11
South Bay Spoilers defeated Nick's-Hawaii #2, 15-7, 15-9

Finals

Nick's-Beverly Hills #1 defeated South Bay Spoilers, 15-6, 12-6
Most Valuable Player—Flora Hymen, South Bay Spoilers.

National AAU Elite Gymnastics Championships in 1977

Rogers, Ark., June 3-5, 1977

Men

Rings — Vic Randazzo, New York AC.
Vault — Guy Spann, Arizona State Univ.
Parallel Bars — Gene Whelan, New York AC.
Horizontal Bar — Gene Whelan.
Floor Exercise — Koji Saito, Gymnastics International.
Pommel Horse — Robert McHattie, Univ. of Minn.
All Around — Koji Saito.
Team Champion — New York AC.

Women

Floor Exercise — Stephanie Willim, Silver Springs, Md
Balance Beam — Stephanie Willim.
Uneven Balance Beam — Stephanie Willim.
Vault — Stephanie Willim.
All Around — Stephanie Willim.
Team Champion — Philadelphia Freedoms.

National Football League

Final 1976 Standings

National Conference

Eastern Division

	W.	L.	T.	Pct.	PF	PA
Dallas	11	3	0	.786	296	194
Washington	10	4	0	.714	291	217
St. Louis	10	4	0	.714	309	267
Philadelphia	4	10	0	.286	165	286
N.Y. Giants	3	11	0	.214	170	250

Central Division

	W.	L.	T.	Pct.	PF	PA
Minnesota	11	2	1	.821	305	176
Chicago	7	7	0	.500	253	216
Detroit	6	8	0	.429	262	220
Green Bay	5	9	0	.357	218	299

Western Division

	W.	L.	T.	Pct.	PF	PA
Los Angeles	10	3	1	.750	351	190
San Francisco	8	6	0	.571	270	190
Atlanta	4	10	0	.286	172	312
New Orleans	4	10	0	.286	253	346
Seattle	2	12	0	.143	229	429

American Conference

Eastern Division

	W.	L.	T.	Pct.	PF	PA
Baltimore	11	3	0	.786	417	246
New England	11	3	0	.786	376	236
Miami	6	8	0	.429	263	264
N.Y. Jets	3	11	0	.214	169	383
Buffalo	2	12	0	.143	245	363

Central Division

	W.	L.	T.	Pct.	PF	PA
Pittsburgh	10	4	0	.714	342	138
Cincinnati	10	4	0	.714	335	210
Cleveland	9	5	0	.643	267	287
Houston	5	9	0	.357	222	273

Western Division

	W.	L.	T.	Pct.	PF	PA
Oakland	13	1	0	.929	350	237
Denver	9	5	0	.643	315	206
San Diego	5	8	0	.429	248	285
Kansas City	5	9	0	.357	290	376
Tampa Bay	0	14	0	.000	125	412

NFC Playoffs — Minnesota 35, Washington 20; Los Angeles 14, Dallas 12; Minnesota 24, Los Angeles 13.
AFC Playoffs — Pittsburgh 40, Baltimore 14; Oakland 24, New England 21; Oakland 24, Pittsburgh 7.
Championship Game — Oakland 32, Minnesota 14.

Oakland Defeats Minnesota in Super Bowl

The Oakland Raiders won their first Super Bowl championship by defeating the Minnesota Vikings 32-14 on Jan. 9, 1977 at the Rose Bowl in Pasadena.

Score by Periods

Oakland	0	16	3	13-32
Minnesota	0	0	7	7-14

Scoring

Oakland—Field goal Mann 24.
Oakland—Casper 1 pass from Stabler (Mann kick).
Oakland—Banaszak 1 run (kick failed).
Oakland—Field goal Mann 40.
Minnesota—S. White 8 pass from Tarkenton (Cox kick).
Oakland—Banaszak 2 run (Mann kick).
Oakland—Brown 75 pass interception (kick failed).
Minnesota—Voigt 13 pass from Lee (Cox kick).

Team Statistics

	Oakland	Minnesota
First downs	21	20
Rushes-Yards	52-266	26-71
Passing yards	163	282
Return yards	134	14
Passes	12-19-0	24-44-2
Punts	5-32.4	7-37.9
Fumbles-Lost	0-0	1-1
Penalties-Yards	4-30	2-25

Attendance—100,421.

Individual Statistics

Oakland rushing — Davis, 16 for 137 yards; van Eeghen, 18 for 73; Garrett, 4 for 19; Banaszak, 10 for 19; Ginn, 2 for 9; Rae, 2 for 9.

Minnesota rushing — Foreman, 17 for 44 yards; S. Johnson, 2 for 9; S. White, 1 for 7; Lee, 1 for 4; Miller, 2 for 4; McClanahan, 3 for 3.

Oakland passing — Stabler, 12 of 19 for 180 yards.

Minnesota passing — Tarkenton, 17 of 35 for 205 yards (two intercepted); Lee, 7 of 9 for 81.

Oakland pass receiving — Biletnikoff, 4 for 79 yards; Casper, 4 for 70; Branch, 3 for 20; Garrett, 1 for 11.

Minnesota pass receiving — S. White, 5 for 77 yards; Foreman, 5 for 62; Voigt, 4 for 49; Miller, 4 for 19; Rashad, 3 for 53; S. Johnson, 3 for 26.

Super Bowl

Year	Winner	Loser	Site
1967	Green Bay Packers, 35	Kansas City Chiefs, 10	Los Angeles Coliseum
1968	Green Bay Packers, 33	Oakland Raiders, 14	Orange Bowl, Miami
1969	New York Jets, 16	Baltimore Colts, 7	Orange Bowl, Miami
1970	Kansas City Chiefs, 23	Minnesota Vikings, 7	Tulane Stadium, New Orleans
1971	Baltimore Colts, 16	Dallas Cowboys, 13	Orange Bowl, Miami
1972	Dallas Cowboys, 24	Miami Dolphins, 3	Tulane Stadium, New Orleans
1973	Miami Dolphins, 14	Washington Redskins, 7	Los Angeles Coliseum
1974	Miami Dolphins, 24	Minnesota Vikings, 7	Rice Stadium, Houston
1975	Pittsburgh Steelers, 16	Minnesota Vikings, 6	Tulane Stadium, New Orleans
1976	Pittsburgh Steelers, 21	Dallas Cowboys, 17	Orange Bowl, Miami
1977	Oakland Raiders, 32	Minnesota Vikings, 14	Rose Bowl, Pasadena

Bert Bell Memorial Trophy

The Bert Bell Memorial Trophy, named after the former NFL commissioner, is awarded annually to the outstanding rookies in a poll conducted by Murray Olderman of Newspaper Enterprise Assn.

1964 Charlie Taylor, Washington, WR
1965 Gale Sayers, Chicago, RB
1966 Tommy Nobis, Atlanta, LB
1967 Mel Farr, Detroit, RB
1968 Earl McCullouch, Detroit, WR
1969 Calvin Hill, Dallas, RB
1970 Raymond Chester, Oakland, TE
1971 AFC: Jim Plunkett, New England, QB
NFC: John Brockington, Green Bay, RB
1972 AFC: Franco Harris, Pittsburgh, RB
NFC: Willie Buchanon, Green Bay, DB
1973 AFC: Boobie Clark, Cincinnati, RB
NFC: Chuck Foreman, Minnesota, RB
1974 Don Woods, San Diego, RB
1975 AFC: Robert Brazile, Houston, LB
NFC: Steve Bartkowski, Atlanta, QB
1976 AFC: Mike Haynes, New England, CB
NFC: Sammy White, Minnesota, WR

National Football League Champions

Year	East Winner W.L.T.	West Winner W.L.T.	Playoff
1933	New York Giants (11-3-0)	Chicago Bears (10-2-1)	Chicago Bears 23, New York 21
1934	New York Giants (8-5-0)	Chicago Bears (13-0-0)	New York 30, Chicago Bears 13
1935	New York Giants (9-3-0)	Detroit Lions (7-3-2)	Detroit 26, New York 7
1936	Boston Redskins (7-5-0)	Green Bay Packers (10-1-1)	Green Bay 21, Boston 6
1937	Washington Redskins (8-3-0)	Chicago Bears (9-1-1)	Wash. 28, Chicago Bears 21
1938	New York Giants (8-2-1)	Green Bay Packers (8-3-0)	New York 23, Green Bay 17
1939	New York Giants (9-1-1)	Green Bay Packers (9-2-0)	Green Bay 27, New York 0
1940	Washington Redskins (9-2-0)	Chicago Bears (8-3-0)	Chicago Bears 73, Wash. 0
1941	New York Giants (8-3-0)	Chicago Bears (10-1-1) (a)	Chicago Bears 37, New York 9
1942	Wash. Redskins (10-1-1)	Chicago Bears (11-0-0)	Wash. 14, Chicago Bears 6
1943	Wash. Redskins (6-3-1) (a)	Chicago Bears (8-1-1)	Chicago Bears 41, Wash. 21
1944	New York Giants (8-1-1)	Green Bay Packers (8-2-0)	Green Bay 14, New York 7
1945	Wash. Redskins (8-2-0)	Cleveland Rams (9-1-0)	Cleveland 15, Washington 14
1946	New York Giants (7-3-1)	Chicago Bears (8-2-1)	Chicago Bears 24, New York 14
1947	Philadelphia Eagles (8-4-0) (a)	Chicago Cardinals (9-3-0)	Chicago Cardinals 28, Phila. 21
1948	Philadelphia Eagles (9-2-1)	Chicago Cardinals (11-1-0)	Phila. 7, Chicago Cardinals 0
1949	Philadelphia Eagles (11-1-0)	Los Angeles Rams (8-2-2)	Philadelphia 14, Los Angeles 0
1950	Cleveland Browns (10-2-0) (a)	Los Angeles Rams (9-3-0) (a)	Cleveland 30, Los Angeles 28
1951	Cleveland Browns (11-1-0)	Los Angeles Rams (8-4-0)	Los Angeles 24, Cleveland 17
1952	Cleveland Browns (8-4-0)	Detroit Lions (9-3-0) (a)	Detroit 17, Cleveland 7
1953	Cleveland Browns (11-1-0)	Detroit Lions (10-2-0)	Detroit 17, Cleveland 16
1954	Cleveland Browns (9-3-0)	Detroit Lions (9-2-1)	Cleveland 56, Detroit 10
1955	Cleveland Browns (9-2-1)	Los Angeles Rams (8-3-1)	Cleveland 38, Los Angeles 14
1956	New York Giants (8-3-1)	Chicago Bears (9-2-1)	New York 47, Chicago Bears 7
1957	Cleveland Browns (9-2-1)	Detroit Lions (8-4-0) (a)	Detroit 59, Cleveland 14
1958	New York Giants (9-3-0) (a)	Baltimore Colts (9-3-0)	Baltimore 23, New York 17 (b)
1959	New York Giants (10-2-0)	Baltimore Colts (9-3-0)	Baltimore 31, New York 16
1960	Philadelphia Eagles (10-2-0)	Green Bay Packers (8-4-0)	Philadelphia 17, Green Bay 13
1961	New York Giants (10-3-1)	Green Bay Packers (11-3-0)	Green Bay 37, New York 0
1962	New York Giants (12-2-0)	Green Bay Packers (13-1-0)	Green Bay 16, New York 7
1963	New York Giants (11-3-0)	Chicago Bears (11-1-2)	Chicago 14, New York 10
1964	Cleveland Browns (10-3-1)	Baltimore Colts (12-2-0)	Cleveland 27, Baltimore 0
1965	Cleveland Browns (11-3-0)	Green Bay Packers (10-3-1) (a)	Green Bay 23, Cleveland 12
1966	Dallas Cowboys (10-3-1)	Green Bay Packers (12-2-0)	Green Bay 34, Dallas 27

(a) Won divisional playoff. (b) Won at 8:15 sudden death overtime period.

Year	Conference	Division	Winner (W-L-T)	Playoff
1967	East	Century	Cleveland (9-5-0)	Dallas 52, Cleveland 14
		Capitol	Dallas (9-5-0)	
	West	Central	Green Bay (9-4-1)	Green Bay 28, Los Angeles 7
		Coastal	Los Angeles (11-1-2) (a)	Green Bay 21, Dallas 17
1968	East	Century	Cleveland (10-4-0)	Cleveland 31, Dallas 20
		Capitol	Dallas (12-2-0)	
	West	Central	Minnesota (8-6-0)	Baltimore 24, Minnesota 14
		Coastal	Baltimore (13-1-0)	Baltimore 34, Cleveland 0
1969	East	Century	Cleveland (10-3-1)	Cleveland 38, Dallas 14
		Capitol	Dallas (11-2-1)	
	West	Central	Minnesota (12-2-0)	Minnesota 23, Los Angeles 20
		Coastal	Los Angeles (11-3-0)	Minnesota 27, Cleveland 7
1970	American	Eastern	Baltimore (11-2-1)	Baltimore 17, Cincinnati 0
		Central	Cincinnati (8-6-0)	Oakland 21, Miami 14
		Western	Oakland (8-4-2)	Baltimore 27, Oakland 17
	National	Eastern	Dallas (10-4-0)	Dallas 5, Detroit 0
		Central	Minnesota (12-2-0)	San Francisco 17, Minnesota 14
		Western	San Francisco (10-3-1)	Dallas 17, San Francisco 10
1971	American	Eastern	Miami (10-3-1)	Miami 27, Kansas City 24
		Central	Cleveland (9-5-0)	Baltimore 20, Cleveland 3
		Western	Kansas City (10-3-1)	Miami 21, Baltimore 0
	National	Eastern	Dallas (11-3-0)	Dallas 20, Minnesota 12
		Central	Minnesota (11-3-0)	San Francisco 24, Washington 20
		Western	San Francisco (9-5-0)	Dallas 14, San Francisco 3
1972	American	Eastern	Miami (14-0-0)	Miami 20, Cleveland 14
		Central	Pittsburgh (11-3-0)	Pittsburgh 13, Oakland 7
		Western	Oakland (10-3-1)	Miami 21, Pittsburgh 17
	National	Eastern	Washington (11-3-0)	Washington 16, Green Bay 3
		Central	Green Bay (10-4-0)	Dallas 30, San Francisco 28
		Western	San Francisco (8-5-1)	Washington 26, Dallas 3
1973	American	Eastern	Miami (12-2-0)	Miami 34, Cincinnati 16
		Central	Cincinnati (10-4-0)	Oakland 33, Pittsburgh 14
		Western	Oakland (9-4-1)	Miami 27, Oakland 10
	National	Eastern	Dallas (10-4-0)	Dallas 27, Los Angeles 16
		Central	Minnesota (12-2-0)	Minnesota 27, Washington 20
		Western	Los Angeles (12-2-0)	Minnesota 27, Dallas 10
1974	American	Eastern	Miami (11-3-0)	Oakland 28, Miami 26
		Central	Pittsburgh (10-3-1)	Pittsburgh 32, Buffalo 14
		Western	Oakland (12-2-0)	Pittsburgh 24, Oakland 13
	National	Eastern	St. Louis (10-4-0)	Minnesota 30, St. Louis 14
		Central	Minnesota (10-4-0)	Los Angeles 19, Washington 10
		Western	Los Angeles (10-4-0)	Minnesota 14, Los Angeles 10
1975	American	Eastern	Baltimore (10-4-0)	Pittsburgh 28, Baltimore 10
		Central	Pittsburgh (12-2-0)	Oakland 31, Cincinnati 28
		Western	Oakland (11-3-0)	Pittsburgh 16, Oakland 10
	National	Eastern	St. Louis (11-3-0)	Dallas 17, Minnesota 14
		Central	Minnesota (12-2-0)	Los Angeles 35, St. Louis 23
		Western	Los Angeles (12-2-0)	Dallas 37, Los Angeles 7

(continued)

(continued)

Year	Conference	Division	Winner (W-L-T)	Playoff
1976	American	Eastern	Baltimore (11-3-0)	Pittsburgh 40, Baltimore 14
		Central	Pittsburg (10-4-0)	Oakland 24, New England 21
		Western	Oakland (13-1-0)	Oakland 24, Pittsburgh 12
	National	Eastern	Dallas (11-3-0)	Minnesota 35, Washington 20
		Central	Minnesota (11-2-1)	Los Angeles 14, Dallas 12
		Western	Los Angeles (10-3-1)	Minnesota 24, Los Angeles 13

National Football Conference Leaders

(National Football League, 1962-1969)

Passing

Player	Atts	Com	YG	TD	Year
Bart Starr, Green Bay	285	178	2,438	9	1962
Y.A. Tittle, N.Y. Giants	367	221	3,145	14	1963
Bart Starr, Green Bay	272	163	2,144	4	1964
Rudy Bukich, Chicago	312	176	2,641	9	1965
Bart Starr, Green Bay	251	156	2,257	3	1966
Sonny Jurgensen, Washington	508	288	3,747	16	1967
Earl Morrall, Baltimore	317	182	2,909	17	1968
Sonny Jurgensen, Washington	422	274	3,102	15	1969
John Brodie, San Francisco	378	223	2,941	24	1970
Roger Staubach, Dallas	211	126	1,882	15	1971
Norm Snead, N. Y. Giants	325	196	2,307	17	1972
Roger Staubach, Dallas	286	179	2,428	23	1973
Sonny Jurgensen, Washington	167	107	1,185	11	1974
Fran Tarkenton, Minnesota	425	273	2,294	25	1975
James Harris, Los Angeles	158	91	1,460	8	1976

Pass-Receiving

Year	Player	Ct.	YG	TD
1962	Bobby Mitchell, Washington	72	1,384	11
1963	Bobby Conrad, Cards, St. Louis	73	967	10
1964	Johnny Morris, Chicago	93	1,200	10
1965	Dave Parks, San Francisco	80	1,344	12
1966	Charlie Taylor, Washington	72	1,119	12
1967	Charlie Taylor, Washington	70	990	9
1968	Clifton McNeil, San Francisco	71	944	7
1969	Dan Abramowicz, New Orleans	73	1,015	7
1970	Dick Gordon, Chicago	71	1,026	13
1971	Bob Tucker, Giants	59	791	4
1972	Harold Jackson, Philadelphia	62	1,048	4
1973	Harold Carmichael, Philadelphia	67	1,116	9
1974	Charles Young, Philadelphia	63	696	3
1975	Chuck Foreman, Minnesota	73	691	9
1976	Drew Pearson, Dallas	58	806	6

Scoring

Player	TD	PAT	FG	Pts	Year
Jim Taylor, Green Bay	19	0	0	114	1962
Don Chandler, New York	0	52	18	106	1963
Lenny Moore, Baltimore	20	0	0	120	1964
Gale Sayers, Chicago	22	0	0	132	1965
Bruce Gossett, Los Angeles	0	29	28	113	1966
Jim Bakken, St. Louis	0	36	27	117	1967
Leroy Kelly, Cleveland	20	0	0	120	1968
Fred Cox, Minnesota	0	43	26	121	1969
Fred Cox, Minnesota	0	35	30	125	1970
Curt Knight, Washington	0	27	29	114	1971
Chester Marcol, Green Bay	0	29	33	128	1972
David Ray, Los Angeles	0	40	30	130	1973
Chester Marcol, Green Bay	0	19	25	94	1974
Chuck Foreman, Minnesota	22	0	0	132	1975
Mark Moseley, Washington	0	31	22	97	1976

Rushing

Year	Player	FG	Atts	TD
1962	Jim Taylor, Green Bay	1,474	272	19
1963	Jimmy Brown, Cleveland	1,863	291	12
1964	Jimmy Brown, Cleveland	1,446	280	7
1965	Jimmy Brown, Cleveland	1,544	289	17
1966	Gale Sayers, Chicago	1,231	229	8
1967	Leroy Kelly, Cleveland	1,205	235	11
1968	Leroy Kelly, Cleveland	1,239	248	16
1969	Gale Sayers, Chicago	1,032	236	8
1970	Larry Brown, Washington	1,125	237	5
1971	John Brockington, Green Bay	1,105	216	4
1972	Larry Brown, Washington	1,216	285	8
1973	John Brockington, Green Bay	1,144	265	3
1974	Larry McCutcheon, Los Angeles	1,109	236	3
1975	Jim Otis, St. Louis	1,076	269	5
1976	Walter Peyton, Chicago	1,390	311	13

American Football Conference Leaders

(American Football League, 1962-1969)

Passing

Player	Atts	Com	YG	TD	Year
Len Dawson, Dallas	310	189	2,749	17	1962
Tobin Rote, San Diego	287	170	2,510	17	1963
Len Dawson, Kansas City	354	199	2,879	18	1964
Jack Hadl, San Diego	348	174	2,798	21	1965
Len Dawson, Kansas City	284	159	2,527	10	1966
Daryle Lamonica, Oakland	425	220	3,228	20	1967
Len Dawson, Kansas City	224	131	2,109	9	1968
Greg Cook, Cincinnati	197	106	1,845	11	1969
Daryle Lamonica, Oakland	356	179	2,516	22	1970
Bob Griese, Miami	263	145	2,089	19	1971
Earl Morrall, Miami	150	83	1,360	11	1972
Ken Stabler, Oakland	260	163	1,997	14	1973
Ken Anderson, Cincinnati	328	213	2,667	18	1974
Ken Anderson, Cincinnati	377	228	3,169	21	1975
Ken Stabler, Oakland	291	194	2,737	27	1976

Pass-Receiving

Year	Player	Ct	YG	TD
1962	Lionel Taylor, Denver	77	908	4
1963	Lionel Taylor, Denver	78	1,101	10
1964	Charlie Hennigan, Houston	101	1,561	8
1965	Lionel Taylor, Denver	85	1,131	6
1966	Lance Alworth, San Diego	73	1,383	13
1967	George Sauer, N.Y. Jets	75	1,189	6
1968	Lance Alworth, San Diego	68	1,312	10
1969	Lance Alworth, San Diego	64	1,003	4
1970	Marlin Briscoe, Buffalo	57	1,036	8
1971	Fred Biletnikoff, Oakland	61	929	9
1972	Fred Biletnikoff, Oakland	58	802	7
1973	Fred Willis, Houston	57	371	1
1974	Lydell Mitchell, Baltimore	72	544	2
1975	Reggie Rucker, Cleveland	60	770	3
	Lydell Mitchell, Baltimore	60	544	4
1976	MacArthur Lane, Kansas City	66	686	1

Scoring

Player	TD	PAT	FG	Pts	Year
Gene Mingo, Denver	4	32	27	137	1962
Gino Cappelletti, Boston	2	35	22	113	1963
Gino Cappelletti, Boston	7	36	25	155	1964
Gino Cappelletti, Boston	9	27	17	132	1965
Gino Cappelletti, Boston	6	35	16	119	1966
George Blanda, Oakland	0	56	20	116	1967
Jim Turner, N.Y. Jets	0	43	34	145	1968
Jim Turner, N.Y. Jets	0	33	32	129	1969
Jan Stenerud, Kansas City	0	26	30	116	1970
Garo Yepremian, Miami	0	33	28	117	1971
Bobby Howfield, N.Y. Jets	0	40	27	121	1972
Roy Gerela, Pittsburgh	0	36	29	123	1973
Roy Gerela, Pittsburgh	0	33	20	93	1974
O. J. Simpson, Buffalo	23	0	0	138	1975
Toni Linhart, Baltimore	0	49	20	109	1976

Rushing

Year	Player	YG	Atts	TD
1962	Cookie Gilchrist, Buffalo	1,096	214	13
1963	Clem Daniels, Oakland	1,098	214	3
1964	Cookie Gilchrist, Buffalo	981	230	6
1965	Paul Lowe, San Diego	1,121	222	7
1966	Jim Nance, Boston	1,458	299	11
1967	Jim Nance, Boston	1,216	269	7
1968	Paul Robinson, Cincinnati	1,023	238	8
1969	Dick Post, San Diego	873	182	6
1970	Floyd Little, Denver	901	209	3
1971	Floyd Little, Denver	1,133	284	6
1972	O.J. Simpson, Buffalo	1,251	292	6
1973	O. J. Simpson, Buffalo	2,003	332	12
1974	Otis Armstrong, Denver	1,407	263	9
1975	O. J. Simpson, Buffalo	1,817	329	16
1976	O. J. Simpson, Buffalo	1,503	290	8

1976 NFL Individual Leaders

National Conference

Passing[1]

	Att	Comp	Pct Comp	Yards Gained	Avg Gain	TDs	Int	Rating Pts
Harris, Los Angeles	158	91	57.6	1460	9.24	8	6	89.8
Landry, Detroit	291	168	57.7	2191	7.53	17	8	89.6
Tarkenton, Minnesota	412	255	61.9	2961	7.19	17	8	89.4
Hart, St. Louis	388	218	56.2	2946	7.59	18	13	81.7
Staubach, Dallas	369	208	56.4	2715	7.36	14	11	79.9
Kilmer, Washington	206	108	52.4	1252	6.08	12	10	70.0
Scott, New Orleans	190	103	54.2	1065	5.61	4	6	64.3
Plunkett, San Francisco	243	126	51.9	1592	6.55	13	16	62.8
Theismann, Washington	163	79	48.5	1036	6.36	8	10	59.9
Douglass, New Orleans	213	103	48.4	1288	6.05	4	8	58.1
Morton, New York	284	153	53.9	1865	6.57	9	20	55.9
Boryla, Philadelphia	246	123	50.0	1247	5.07	9	14	53.5
Dickey, Green Bay	243	115	47.3	1465	6.03	7	14	52.1
Avellini, Chicago	271	118	43.5	1580	5.83	8	15	49.7
Zorn, Seattle	439	208	47.4	2571	5.86	12	27	49.2

Scorers

	TDs	XP	XPA	FG	FGA	Pts
Moseley, Washington	0	31	32	22	34	97
Bakken, St. Louis	0	33	35	20	27	93
Cox, Minnesota	0	32	36	19	31	89
Herrera, Dallas	0	34	34	18	23	88
Dempsey, Los Angeles	0	36	44	17	26	87
Foreman, Minnesota	14	0	0	0	0	84
Szaro, New Orleans	0	25	29	18	23	79
Payton, Chicago	13	0	0	0	0	78
Mike-Mayer, San Francisco	0	26	30	16	28	74

Punting

	No	Yds	Long[2]	Avg
James, Atlanta	101	4253	67	42.1
Jennings, New York	74	3054	61	41.3
Wittum, San Francisco	89	3634	68	40.8
Weaver, Detroit	83	3280	69	39.5
Blanchard, New Orleans	101	3974	63	39.3
Jackson, Los Angeles	77	3006	61	39.0
Bragg, Washington	90	3503	56	38.9
Clabo, Minnesota	69	2678	55	38.8
White, Dallas	70	2690	54	38.4

Pass Receiving

	No	Yds	Avg	TDs
Pearson, Dallas	58	806	13.9	6
Foreman, Minnesota	55	567	10.3	1
Largent, Seattle	54	705	13.1	4
Galbreath, New Orleans	54	420	7.8	1
Rashad, Minnesota	53	671	12.7	3
Harris, St. Louis	52	782	15.0	1
White, Minnesota	51	906	17.8	10
Grant, Washington	50	818	16.4	5
DuPree, Dallas	42	680	16.2	2
Carmichael, Philadelphia	42	503	12.0	5

Punt Returns

	No	Yds	Avg	TDs
Brown, Washington	48	646	13.5	1
Bryant, Los Angeles	29	321	11.1	0
Metcalf, St. Louis	17	188	11.1	0
Johnson, Dallas	45	489	10.9	0
Marshall, Philadelphia	27	290	10.7	0
Tilley, St. Louis	15	146	9.7	0
Athas, New Orleans	35	332	9.5	0
Rhodes, San Francisco	16	142	8.9	0
Leonard, San Francisco	35	293	8.4	1

Interceptions

	No	Yds	Avg	Long[2]	TDs
Jackson, Los Angeles	10	173	17.3	46	3
Perry, Los Angeles	8	79	9.9	43	0
Lavender, Washington	8	77	9.6	28	0
Hunter, Detroit	7	120	17.1	39	1
Brupbacher, Chicago	7	49	7.0	25	0
Wright, Minnesota	7	47	6.7	21	0
Johnson, Detroit	6	206	34.3	76	1
Ellis, Chicago	6	47	7.8	22	1

Kickoff Returns

	No	Yds	Avg	TDs
Bryant, Los Angeles	16	459	28.7	1
Hunter, Detroit	14	375	26.8	0
Baschnagel, Chicago	29	754	26.0	0
McCoy, Green Bay	18	457	25.4	0
Lawrence, Atlanta	21	521	24.8	0
Johnson, Dallas	28	693	24.8	0
Brown, Washington	30	738	24.6	0
Willis, Minnesota	24	552	23.0	0
Latin, St. Louis	16	357	22.3	0

Rushing

	Att	Yds	Avg	TDs
Payton, Chicago	311	1390	4.5	13
Williams, San Francisco	248	1203	4.9	7
McCutcheon, Los Angeles	291	1168	4.0	9
Foreman, Minnesota	278	1155	4.2	13
Thomas, Washington	254	1101	4.3	5
Otis, St. Louis	233	891	3.8	2
Bussey, Detroit	196	858	4.4	3
Jackson, San Francisco	200	792	4.0	1
Kotar, New York	185	731	4.0	3
Cappelletti, Los Angeles	177	688	3.9	1

American Conference

Passing[1]

	Att	Comp	Pct Comp	Yards Gained	Avg Gain	TDs	Int	Rating Pts
Stabler, Oakland	291	194	66.7	2737	9.41	27	17	103.7
Jones, Baltimore	343	207	60.3	3104	9.05	24	9	102.6
Ferguson, Buffalo	151	74	49.0	1086	7.19	9	1	90.0
Griese, Miami	272	162	59.6	2097	7.71	11	12	78.9
Livingston, Kansas City	338	189	55.9	2682	7.93	12	13	77.9
Sipe, Cleveland	312	178	57.1	2113	6.77	17	14	77.1
Anderson, Cincinnati	338	179	53.0	2367	7.00	19	14	77.0
Fouts, San Diego	359	208	57.9	2535	7.06	14	15	75.3
Pastorini, Houston	309	167	54.0	1795	5.81	10	10	68.6
Bradshaw, Pittsburgh	192	92	47.9	1177	6.13	10	9	65.3
Ramsey, Denver	270	128	47.4	1931	7.15	11	13	65.1
Grogan, New England	302	145	48.0	1903	6.30	18	20	60.8
Spurrier, Tampa Bay	311	156	50.2	1628	5.23	7	12	57.1
Namath, New York	230	114	49.6	1090	4.74	4	16	39.7
Todd, New York	162	65	40.1	870	5.37	3	12	33.4
Marangi, Buffalo	232	82	35.3	998	4.30	7	16	30.7

(1) At least 150 passes needed to qualify. Leader based on percentage of completions—touchdown passes—interceptions—and average yards. (2) Longest runback on interception; longest kick punting.

(continued)

(continued)

Scoring

	TDs	XP	XPA	RFG	FGA	Pts
Linhart, Baltimore	0	49	50	20	27	109
Stenerud, Kansas City	0	27	33	21	38	90
Smith, New England	0	42	46	15	25	87
Harris, Pittsburgh	14	0	0	0	0	84
Gerela, Pittsburgh	0	40	43	14	26	82
Bahr, Cincinnati	0	39	42	14	27	81
Turner, Denver	0	36	39	15	21	81
Grogan, New England	13	0	0	0	0	78
Yepremian, Miami	0	29	31	16	23	77
Branch, Oakland	12	0	0	0	0	72

Punting

	No	Yds	Long[2]	Avg
Bateman, Buffalo	86	3678	78	42.8
Wilson, Kansas City	65	2729	62	42.0
Guy, Oakland	67	2785	66	41.6
West, San Diego	38	1548	57	40.7
Patrick, New England	67	2688	52	40.1
Carrell, New York	81	3218	72	39.7
Lee, Baltimore	59	2342	56	39.7
McInally, Cincinnati	76	2999	61	39.5
Green, Tampa Bay	92	3619	56	39.3
Walden, Pittsburgh	76	2982	58	39.2

Pass Receiving

	No	Yds	Avg	TDs
Lane, Kansas City	66	686	10.4	1
Chandler, Buffalo	61	824	13.5	10
Mitchell, Baltimore	60	555	9.3	3
Casper, Oakland	53	691	13.0	10
Burrough, Houston	51	932	18.3	7
Joiner, San Diego	50	1056	21.1	7
Rucker, Cleveland	49	676	13.8	8
White, Kansas City	47	808	17.2	7
Johnson, Houston	47	495	10.5	4
Young, San Diego	47	441	9.4	1

Punt Returns

	No	Yds	Avg	TDs
Upchurch, Denver	39	536	13.7	4
Haynes, New England	45	608	13.5	2
Fuller, San Diego	33	436	13.2	0
Brunson, Kansas City	31	387	12.5	0
Colzie, Oakland	41	448	10.9	0
Johnson, Houston	38	403	10.6	0
Moody, Buffalo	16	166	10.4	1
Bell, Pittsburgh	39	390	10.0	0
Moore, Tampa Bay-Oakland	20	184	9.2	0
Deloplaine, Pittsburgh	17	150	8.8	0

Interceptions

	No	Yds	Avg	Long[2]	TDs
Riley, Cincinnati	9	141	15.7	t53	1
Haynes, New England	8	90	11.3	28	0
Jackson, Denver	7	136	19.4	t46	1
Darden, Cleveland	7	73	10.4	21	0
Edwards, Pittsburgh	6	95	15.8	55	0
Goode, San Diego	6	82	13.7	27	0
Blount, Pittsburgh	6	75	12.5	28	0
McCray, New England	5	182	36.4	t63	2
Greene, Buffalo	5	135	27.0	t101	1
Casanova, Cincinnati	5	109	21.8	t33	2

Kickoff Returns

	No	Yds	Avg	TDs
Harris, Miami	17	559	32.9	0
Phillips, New England	14	397	28.4	0
Perrin, Denver	14	391	27.9	0
Williams, Kansas City	25	688	27.5	0
Jennings, Oakland	16	417	26.1	0
Shelby, Cincinnati	30	761	25.4	1
Holden, Cleveland	19	461	24.3	0
Davis, Miami	26	617	23.7	0
Stevens, Baltimore	30	710	23.7	0
Upchurch, Denver	22	514	23.4	0

Rushing

	Att	Yds	Avg	TDs
Simpson, Buffalo	290	1503	5.2	8
Mitchell, Baltimore	289	1200	4.2	5
Harris, Pittsburgh	289	1128	3.9	14
Bleier, Pittsburgh	220	1036	4.7	5
van Eeghen, Oakland	233	1012	4.3	3
Armstrong, Denver	247	1008	4.1	5
Pruitt, Cleveland	209	1000	4.8	4
Cunningham, New England	172	824	4.8	3
Young, San Diego	162	802	5.0	4
Malone, Miami	186	797	4.3	4

(1) At least 150 passes needed to qualify. Leader based on percentage of completions—touchdown passes—interceptions—and average yards. (2) Longest runback on interception; longest kick punting.

1977 NFL Player Draft

The following are the first round picks of the National Football League

Team	Player	Pos.	College
1—Tampa Bay	Ricky Bell	RB	USC
2—Dallas	Tony Dorsett	RB	Pittsburgh
3—Cincinnati	Eddie Edwards	DE	Miami
4—N.Y. Jets	Marvin Powell	OT	USC
5—N.Y. Giants	Gary Jeter	DT	USC
6—Atlanta	Warren Bryant	G	Kentucky
7—New Orleans	Joe Campbell	DE	Maryland
8—Cincinnati	Wilson Whitley	DT	Houston
9—Green Bay	Mike Butler	DE	Kansas
10—Kansas City	Gary Green	DB	Baylor
11—Houston	Morris Towns	OT	Missouri
12—Buffalo	Phil Dokes	DT	Oklahoma State
13—Miami	A.J. Duhe	DT	LSU
14—Seattle	Steve August	G	Tulsa
15—Chicago	Ted Albrecht	G	California
16—New England	Raymond Clayborn	DB	Texas
17—Cleveland	Robert Jackson	LB	Texas A&M
18—Denver	Steve Schindler	OT	Boston College
19—St. Louis	Steve Pisarkiewicz	QB	Missouri
20—Atlanta	Wilson Faumuina	DT	San Jose State
21—Pittsburgh	Robin Cole	LB	New Mexico
22—Cincinnati	Mike Cobb	TE	Michigan State
23—Los Angeles	Bob Brudzinski	LB	Ohio State
24—San Diego	Bob Rush	C	Memphis State
25—New England	Stanley Morgan	WR	Tennessee
26—Baltimore	Randy Burke	WR	Kentucky
27—Minnesota	Tommy Kramer	QB	Rice
28—Green Bay	Ezra Johnson	DE	Morris Brown

Jim Thorpe Trophy Winners

The winner of the Jim Thorpe Trophy, named after the athletic great, is picked by Murray Olderman of Newspaper Enterprise Assn. in a poll of players from the 28 NFL teams. It goes to the most valuable NFL player and is the oldest and highest professional football award.

Year	Player, Team
1955	Harlon Hill, Chicago Bears
1956	Frank Gifford, N. Y. Giants
1957	John Unitas, Baltimore Colts
1958	Jim Brown, Cleveland Browns
1959	Charley Conerly, N. Y. Giants
1960	Norm Van Brocklin, Philadelphia Eagles
1961	Y. A. Tittle, N. Y. Giants
1962	Jim Taylor, Green Bay Packers
1963	(tie) Jim Brown, Cleveland Browns, and Y. A. Tittle, N. Y. Giants
1964	Lenny Moore, Baltimore Colts
1965	Jim Brown, Cleveland Browns
1966	Bart Starr, Green Bay Packers
1967	John Unitas, Baltimore Colts
1968	Earl Morrall, Baltimore Colts
1969	Roman Gabriel, Los Angeles Rams
1970	John Brodie, San Francisco
1971	Bob Griese, Miami
1972	Larry Brown, Washington
1973	O. J. Simpson, Buffalo
1974	Ken Stabler, Oakland
1975	Fran Tarkenton, Minnesota
1976	Bert Jones, Baltimore

NEA All-NFL Team in 1976

Chosen by team captains, team representatives, and coaches of the 28 NFL teams in a poll conducted by Newspaper Enterprise Assn.

First team	Offense	Second team
Cliff Branch, Oakland	Wide receiver	Roger Carr, Baltimore
Isaac Curtis, Cincinnati	Wide receiver	Charlie Joiner, San Diego
Dave Casper, Oakland	Tight end	Russ Francis, New England
Dan Dierdorf, St. Louis	Tackle	George Kunz, Baltimore
Ron Yary, Minnesota	Tackle	Rayfield Wright, Dallas
Conrad Dobler, St. Louis	Guard	Gene Upshaw, Oakland
Joe DeLameilleure, Buffalo	Guard	John Hannah, New England
Jim Langer, Miami	Center	Tom Banks, St. Louis
Bert Jones, Baltimore	Quarterback	Ken Stabler, Oakland
O.J. Simpson, Buffalo	Running back	Walter Payton, Chicago
Chuck Foreman, Minnesota	Running back	Franco Harris, Pittsburgh
Jim Bakken, St. Louis	Placekicker	Jan Stenerud, Kansas City

First team	Defense	Second team
Jack Youngblood, Los Angeles	End	Coy Bacon, Cincinnati
Tommy Hart, San Francisco	End	Harvey Martin, Dallas
Jerry Sherk, Cleveland	Tackle	Alan Page, Minnesota
Wally Chambers, Chicago	Tackle	Cleveland Elam, San Francisco
Jack Lambert, Pittsburgh	Middle linebacker	Bill Bergey, Philadelphia
Jack Ham, Pittsburgh	Linebacker	Phil Villapiano, Oakland
Chris Hanburger, Washington	Linebacker	Ted Hendricks, Oakland
Monte Jackson, Los Angeles	Corner back	Mike Haynes, New England
Lemar Parrish, Cincinnati	Corner back	Mel Blount, Pittsburgh
Ken Houston, Washington	Strong safety	Tom Casanova, Cincinnati
Cliff Harris, Dallas	Free safety	Glen Edwards, Pittsburgh
Ray Guy, Oakland	Punter	John James, Atlanta

American Football League

Year	Eastern Division	Western Division	Playoff
1960	Houston Oilers (10-4-0)	L. A. Chargers (10-4-0)	Houston 24, Los Angeles 16
1961	Houston Oilers (10-3-1)	San Diego Chargers (12-2-0)	Houston 10, San Diego 3
1962	Houston Oilers (11-3-0)	Dallas Texans (11-3-0)	Dallas 20, Houston 17 (b)
1963	Boston Patriots (8-6-1) (a)	San Diego Chargers (11-3-0)	San Diego 51, Boston 10
1964	Buffalo Bills (12-2-0)	San Diego Chargers (8-5-1)	Buffalo 20, San Diego 7
1965	Buffalo Bills (10-3-1)	San Diego Chargers (9-2-3)	Buffalo 23, San Diego 0
1966	Buffalo Bills (9-4-1)	Kansas City Chiefs (11-2-1)	Kansas City 31, Buffalo 7
1967	Houston Oilers (9-4-1)	Oakland Raiders (13-1-0)	Oakland 40, Houston 7
1968	New York Jets (11-3-0)	Oakland Raiders (12-2-0) (a)	New York 27, Oakland 23
1969	New York Jets (10-4-0)	Oakland Raiders (12-1-1)	Kansas City 17, Oakland 7 (c)

(a) won divisional playoff (b) won at 2:45 of second overtime. (c) Kansas City defeated Jets to make playoffs.

Football Stadiums

See index for major league baseball seating capacity, and college stadiums.

Name, location	Capacity
Joseph Albi Memorial Stadium, Spokane, Wash.	31,820
Arrowhead Stadium, Kansas City, Mo.	78,097
Atlanta-Fulton County Stadium	60,489
Astrodome, Houston, Tex.	50,000
Balboa Stadium, San Diego, Cal.	34,500
Baltimore Memorial Stadium	60,002
Buffalo War Memorial Stadium	46,206
Busch Memorial Stadium, St. Louis	51,392
Candlestick Park, San Francisco, Cal.	61,115
Cleveland Stadium	80,165
Columbus (Ga.) Memorial Stadium	35,000
Cotton Bowl, Dallas, Tex.	72,000
Empire Stadium, Vancouver, British Columbia	32,759
Exhibition Stadium, Toronto, Ontario	39,485
Franklin Field, Philadelphia, Pa.	60,658
Gator Bowl, Jacksonville, Fla.	70,000
Giants Stadium, E. Rutherford, N.J.	76,500
Honolulu Stadium	25,000
John F. Kennedy Stadium, Philadelphia, Pa.	105,000
Robert F. Kennedy Memorial Stadium, Wash., D.C.	55,004
Kezar Stadium, San Francisco, Cal.	59,636
Kingdome, Seattle, Wash.	65,000
Ladd Memorial Stadium, Mobile, Ala.	40,605
Lambeau Field, Green Bay, Wis.	56,267
Legion Field, Birmingham, Ala.	72,000
Los Angeles Memorial Coliseum	90,000
Louisiana Superdome, New Orleans	74,726
Memphis Memorial Stadium	50,000
Metropolitan Stadium, Bloomington, Minn.	48,446
Mile High Stadium, Denver, Col.	63,500
Milwaukee County Stadium	53,000
Mississippi Memorial Stadium, Jackson	46,000
Oakland-Alameda County Coliseum	54,037
Orange Bowl, Miami, Fla.	80,045
Ottawa Stadium, Ottawa, Ontario	27,872
Pontiac Metropolitan Stadium, Mich.	80,638
Portland Civic Stadium, Ore.	33,000
Rich Stadium, Buffalo, N.Y.	80,020
Richmond (Va.) City Stadium	22,009
Riverfront Stadium, Cincinnati, Oh.	56,200
Roanoke (Va.) Victory Stadium	30,000
Roosevelt Stadium, Jersey City, N.J.	25,000
Rose Bowl, Pasadena, Cal.	106,721
Rubber Bowl, Akron, Oh.	35,007
San Diego Stadium	52,568
Schaefer Stadium, Foxboro, Mass.	61,279
Shea Stadium, New York, N.Y.	60,000
Sicks Stadium, Seattle, Wash.	24,420
Soldier Field, Chicago, Ill.	57,455
Sugar Bowl, New Orleans, La.	80,982
Tampa Stadium, Tampa, Fla.	71,000
Texas Stadium, Dallas, Tex.	65,101
Three Rivers Stadium, Pittsburgh, Pa.	50,350
Veterans Stadium, Philadelphia, Pa.	66,052

George Halas Trophy Winners

The Halas Trophy, named after football coach George Halas, is awarded annually to the outstanding defensive player in football in a poll conducted by Murray Olderman of Newspaper Enterprise Assn.

1966—Larry Wilson, St. Louis
1967—Deacon Jones, Los Angeles
1968—Deacon Jones, Los Angeles
1969—Dick Butkus, Chicago
1970—Dick Butkus, Chicago
1971—Carl Eller, Minnesota
1972—Joe Greene, Pittsburgh
1973—Alan Page, Minnesota
1974—Joe Greene, Pittsburgh
1975—Curley Culp, Houston
1976—Jerry Sherk, Cleveland

All-Time Pro Football Records

NFL, AFL, and All-American Football Conference

(as of Sept. 18, 1977)

Leading Lifetime Rushers

Player	League	Yrs	Att	Yards	Avg	Player	League	Yrs	Att	Yards	Avg
Jim Brown	NFL	9	2,359	12,312	5.2	Larry Brown	NFL	8	1,530	5,875	3.8
Joe Perry	AAFC-NFL	16	1,929	9,723	5.0	Steve Van Buren	NFL	8	1,320	5,860	4.3
O.J. Simpson	AFL-NFL	8	1,997	9,626	4.8	Bill Brown	NFL	14	1,649	5,838	3.4
Jim Taylor	NFL	10	1,941	8,597	4.4	Rick Casares	NFL-AFL	12	1,431	5,797	4.1
Leroy Kelly	NFL	10	1,727	7,274	4.2	Mike Garrett	AFL-NFL	9	1,308	5,481	4.2
John Henry Johnson	NFL-AFL	13	1,571	6,803	4.3	Dick Bass	NFL	10	1,218	5,417	4.4
Larry Csonka	AFL-NFL	8	1,446	6,469	4.5	Jim Nance	NFL-AFL	8	1,341	5,401	4.0
Floyd Little	AFL-NFL	9	1,641	6,323	3.8	Calvin Hill	NFL	7	1,145	5,310	4.6
Don Perkins	NFL	8	1,500	6,217	4.1	Hugh McElhenny	NFL	13	1,124	5,231	4.7
Ken Willard	NFL	10	1,622	6,105	3.8	Lenny Moore	NFL	12	1,069	5,174	4.8

Most Yards Gained, Season — 2,003, O.J. Simpson, Buffalo Bills, 1973.
Most Yards Gained, Game — 273, O. J. Simpson, Buffalo vs. Detroit Lions, Nov. 25, 1976.
Most Games, 100 Yards or more, Season — 11, O.J. Simpson, Buffalo Bills, 1973.
Most Games, 100 Yards or more, Career — 58, Jim Brown, Cleveland Browns, 1957-1965.
Most Games, 200 Yards or more, Career — 6, O. J. Simpson, Buffalo Bills, 1969-1976.
Most Touchdowns Rushing, Career — 106, Jim Brown, Cleveland Browns, 1957-1965.
Most Touchdowns Rushing, Season — 19, Jim Taylor, Green Bay Packers, 1962.
Most Touchdowns Rushing, Game — 6, Ernie Nevers, Chicago Cardinals vs. Chicago Bears, Nov. 8, 1929.
Most Rushing Attempts, Season — 332, O.J. Simpson, Buffalo Bills, 1973.
Most Rushing Attempts, Game — 41, Franco Harris, Pittsburgh vs. Cincinnati, Oct. 17, 1976.
Longest run from Scrimmage — 97 yds., Andy Uram, Green Bay vs. Chicago Cardinals, Oct. 8, 1939; Bob Gage, Pittsburgh vs. Chicago Bears, Dec. 4, 1949. (Both scored touchdown).

Leading Lifetime Passers

(Minimum 1,500 attempts)

Player	League	Yrs	Att	Comp	Yds	Pts*	Player	League	Yrs	Att	Comp	Yds	Pts*
Otto Graham	AAFC-NFL	10	2,626	1,464	23,584	86.8	Norm Van Brocklin	NFL	12	2,895	1,553	23,611	75.3
Ken Anderson	NFL	6	1,804	1,042	13,326	84.2	Sid Luckman	NFL	12	1,744	904	14,686	75.0
Sonny Jurgensen	NFL	18	4,262	2,433	32,224	82.8	Don Meredith	NFL	9	2,308	1,170	17,199	74.7
Len Dawson	NFL-AFL	19	3,741	2,136	28,711	82.6	Roman Gabriel	NFL	15	4,495	2,365	29,429	74.5
Fran Tarkenton	NFL	16	5,637	3,186	41,801	82.2	Y.A. Tittle	AAFC-NFL	17	4,395	2,427	33,070	74.4
Bart Starr	NFL	16	3,149	1,808	24,718	80.3	Earl Morrall	NFL	21	2,689	1,379	20,809	74.2
Roger Staubach	NFL	8	1,723	977	13,304	80.0	Frank Albert	AAFC-NFL	7	1,564	831	10,795	73.5
Johnny Unitas	NFL	18	5,186	2,830	40,239	78.2	Daryle Lamonica	AFL-NFL	12	2,601	1,288	19,154	72.9
Frank Ryan	NFL	13	2,133	1,090	16,042	77.7	John Brodie	NFL	17	4,491	2,469	31,548	72.3
Bob Griese	AFL-NFL	10	2,477	1,361	18,099	75.3	Billy Wade	NFL	13	2,523	1,370	18,530	72.2

*Rating points based on performances in the following categories: Percentage of completions, percentage of touchdown passes, percentage of interceptions, and average gain per pass attempt.

Most Yards Gained, Season — 4,007, Joe Namath, New York Jets, 1967.
Most Yards Gained, Game — 554, Norm Van Brocklin, Los Angeles Rams vs. New York Yankees, Sept. 18, 1951 (27 completions in 41 attempts).
Most Touchdowns Passing, Career — 308, Fran Tarkenton, Minnesota Vikings, 1961-65; N.Y. Giants, 1967-71; Minnesota Vikings, 1972-76.
Most Touchdowns Passing, Season — 36, George Blanda, Houston Oilers, 1961 and Y.A. Tittle, N.Y. Giants, 1963.
Most Touchdowns Passing, Game — 7, Sid Luckman, Chicago Bears vs. New York Giants, Nov. 14, 1943; Adrian Burk, Philadelphia Eagles vs. Washington Redskins, Oct. 17, 1954; George Blanda, Houston Oilers vs. New York Titans, Nov. 19, 1961; Y. A. Tittle, New York Giants vs. Washington Redskins, Oct. 28, 1962. Joe Kapp, Minnesota Vikings vs. Baltimore Colts, Sept. 28, 1969.
Most Passing Attempts, Season — 508, Sonny Jurgensen, Washington Redskins, 1967 (288 completions).
Most Passing Attempts, Game — 68, George Blanda, Houston Oilers vs. Buffalo Bills, Nov. 1, 1964 (37 completions).
Most Passes Completed, Season — 288, Sonny Jurgensen, Washington Redskins, 1967 (508 attempts).
Most Passes Completed, Game — 37, George Blanda, Houston Oilers vs. Buffalo Bills, Nov. 1, 1964 (68 attempts).
Most Consecutive Passes Completed — 17, Bert Jones, Baltimore Colts vs. N.Y. Jets, Dec. 15, 1974.

Leading Lifetime Receivers

Player	League	Yrs	No	Yds	Avg	Player	League	Yrs	No	Yds	Avg
Charley Taylor	NFL	12	635	8,952	14.1	Art Powell	AFL-NFL	10	479	8,046	16.8
Don Maynard	AFL-NFL	15	633	11,834	18.7	Jackie Smith	NFL	14	475	7,869	16.6
Ray Berry	NFL	13	631	9,275	14.7	Boyd Dowler	NFL	12	474	7,270	15.4
Lionel Taylor	AFL	9	567	7,195	12.7	Pete Retzlaff	NFL	11	452	7,412	16.4
Lance Alworth	AFL-NFL	11	542	10,266	18.9	Roy Jefferson	NFL	12	451	7,539	16.7
Fred Biletnikoff	AFL-NFL	12	536	8,243	15.4	Carroll Dale	NFL	14	438	8,271	18.9
Bobby Mitchell	NFL	11	521	7,954	15.3	Mike Ditka	NFL	12	427	5,812	13.6
Billy Howton	NFL	12	503	8,459	16.8	Bobby Joe Conrad	NFL	12	422	5,902	14.0
Tom McDonald	NFL	12	495	8,410	17.0	Jerry Smith	NFL	12	420	5,490	13.1
Don Hutson	NFL	11	488	7,991	16.4	Otis Taylor	AFL-NFL	10	410	7,306	17.8

Most Yards Gained, Season — 1,746, Charley Hennigan, Houston Oilers, 1961.
Most Yards Gained, Game — 303, Jim Benton, Cleveland Rams vs. Detroit Lions, Nov. 22, 1945 (10 receptions).
Most Pass Receptions, Season — 101, Charley Hennigan, Houston Oilers, 1964.
Most Pass Receptions, Game — 18, Tom Fears, Los Angeles Rams vs. Green Bay Packers, Dec. 3, 1950 (189 yards).
Most Consecutive Games, Pass Receptions — 105, Dan Abramowicz, New Orleans Saints, 1967-1973; San Francisco 49ers, 1973-1974.
Most Touchdown Passes, Career — 99, Don Hutson, Green Bay Packers, 1935-1945.
Most Touchdown Passes, Season — 17, Don Hutson, Green Bay Packers, 1942; Elroy Hirsch, Los Angeles Rams, 1951; Bill Groman, Houston Oilers, 1961.
Most Touchdown Passes, Game — 5, Bob Shaw, Chicago Cardinals vs. Baltimore Colts, Oct. 2, 1950.
Most Consecutive Games, Touchdown Passes — 11, Elroy Hirsch, Los Angeles Rams, 1950-1951, Buddy Dial, Pittsburgh, 1959-1960.

Leading Lifetime Scorers

Player	League	Yrs	TD	PAT	FG	Total
George Blanda	NFL-AFL	26	9	943	335	2,002
Lou Groza	AAFC-NFL	21	1	810	264	1,608
Fred Cox	NFL	14	0	494	274	1,316
Jim Bakken	NFL	15	0	472	264	1,264
Jim Turner	AFL-NFL	13	0	427	267	1,228
Gino Cappelletti	AFL	11	42	350	176	1,130
Jan Stenerud	AFL-NFL	10	0	314	239	1,031
Bruce Gossett	NFL	11	0	374	219	1,031
Sam Baker	NFL	15	2	428	179	977
Lou Michaels	NFL	13	1	386	187	955*
Bobby Walston	NFL	12	46	365	80	881
Pete Gogolak	AFL-NFL	10	0	344	173	863
Don Hutson	NFL	11	105	172	7	823
Paul Hornung	NFL	9	62	190	66	760
Jim Brown	NFL	9	126	0	0	756
Roy Gerela	AFL-NFL	8	0	267	162	753
Garo Yepremian	NFL	9	0	290	151	743
Tom Davis	NFL	11	0	348	130	738
Don Cockroft	NFL	9	0	288	147	729
Mike Clark	NFL	10	0	325	133	724

*Includes safety.

Most Points, Season — 176, Paul Hornung, Green Bay Packers, 1960 (15 TD's, 41 PAT's, 15 FG's).
Most Points, Game — 40, Ernie Nevers, Chicago Cardinals vs. Chicago Bears, Nov. 28, 1929 (6 TD's, 4 PAT's).
Most Touchdowns, Season — 23, O.J. Simpson, Buffalo Bills, 1975 (16 rushing, 9 pass receptions).
Most Touchdowns, Game — 6, Ernie Nevers, Chicago Cardinals vs. Chicago Bears Nov. 28, 1929 (6 rushing); Dub Jones, Cleveland Browns vs. Chicago Bears, Nov. 25, 1951 (4 rushing, 2 pass receptions); Gale Sayers, Chicago Bears vs. San Francisco 49ers, Dec. 12, 1965 (4 rushing, 1 pass reception, 1 punt return).
Most Points After Touchdown, Season — 64, George Blanda, Houston Oilers, 1961 (65 attempts).
Most Consecutive Points After Touchdown — 234, Tommy Davis, San Francisco 49ers, 1959-1965.
Most Field Goals, Game — 7, Jim Bakken, St. Louis Cardinals vs. Pittsburgh Steelers, Sept. 24, 1967.
Most Field Goals, Season — 34, Jim Turner, New York Jets, 1968 and 1969.
Most Field Goals Attempted, Season — 49, Bruce Gossett, Los Angeles Rams, 1966; Curt Knight, Washington Redskins, 1971.
Most Field Goals Attempted, Game — 9, Jim Bakken, St. Louis Cardinals vs. Pittsburgh Steelers, Sept. 24, 1967 (7 successful).
Most Consecutive Field Goals — 16, Jan Stenerud, Kansas City Chiefs, 1969; Don Cockroft, Cleveland Browns, 1974-75.
Most Consecutive Games, Field Goal — 31, Fred Cox, Minnesota Vikings, 1968-1970.
Longest Field Goal — 63 yds., Tom Dempsey, New Orleans Saints vs. Detroit Lions, Nov, 8, 1970.
Highest Field Goal Percentage, Career (300 attempts) — 67.1, Garo Yepremian, Detroit Lions, 1966-67; Miami Dolphins, 1970-76 (151 FG's in 225 attempts).
Highest Field Goal Completion Percentage, Season (20 attempts) — 88.5, Lou Groza, Cleveland Browns, 1953 (23 FG's in 26 attempts).

Pass Interceptions

Most Passes Had Intercepted, Game — 8, Jim Hardy, Chicago Cardinals vs. Philadelphia Eagles, Sept. 24, 1950 (39 ats).
Most Passes Had Intercepted, Season — 42, George Blanda, Houston Oilers, 1962 (418 attempts).
Most Passes Had Intercepted, Career — 277, George Blanda, Chicago Bears, 1949-1958; Houston Oilers, 1960-1966; Oakland Raiders, 1967-1975 (4,000 attempts).
Most Consecutive Passes Attempted Without Interception — 294, Bart Starr, Green Bay Packers, 1964-1965.
Most Interceptions By, Season — 14, Dick Lane, Los Angeles Rams, 1952.
Most Interceptions By, Career — 79, Emlen Tunnell, New York Giants, 1948-1958; Green Bay Packers, 1959-1961.
Most Consecutive Games, Passes Intercepted By — 8, Tom Morrow, Oakland Raiders, 1962 (4), 1963 (4).
Most Touchdowns Scored via Pass Interceptions, Lifetime — 9, Ken Houston, Housten Oilers, 1967 (2); 1968 (2); 1969; 71 (4).

Punting

Highest Punting Average, Career (300 punts) — 45.10, Sam Baugh, Washington Redskins, 1937-1952 (338 punts).
Highest Punting Average, Season (20 punts) — 51.3, Sam Baugh, Washington Redskins, 1940 (35 punts).
Highest Punting Average, Game (4 punts) — 59.4 Sam Baugh, Washington Redskins vs. Detroit Lions, Oct. 27, 1940 (5 punts).
Longest Punt — 98 yds., Steve O'Neal, New York Jets vs. Denver Broncos, Sept. 21, 1969.

Kickoff Returns

Most Yardage Returning Kickoffs, Career — 6,922 Ron Smith, Chicago Bears, 1965; Atlanta Falcons, 1966-67; Los Angeles Rams, 1968-69; Chicago Bears, 1970-72, San Diego Chargers, 1973; Oakland Raiders, 1974.
Most Yardage Returning Kickoffs, Season — 1,317, Bobby Jancik, Houston Oilers, 1963.
Most Yardage Returning Kickoffs, Game — 294, Wally Triplett, Detroit Lions vs. Los Angeles Rams, Oct. 29, 1950 (4 returns).
Most Touchdowns Scored via Kickoff Returns, Career — 6, Ollie Matson, Chicago Cardinals, 1952 (2), 1954, 1956, 1958 (2); Gale Sayers, Chicago Bears, 1965, 1966 (2), 1967 (3); Travis Williams, Green Bay Packers, 1967 (4), 1969; Los Angeles Rams, 1971.
Most Touchdowns Scored via Kickoff Returns, Season — 4, Travis Williams, Green Bay Packers, 1967; Cecil Turner, Chicago Bears, 1970.
Most Touchdowns Scored via Kickoff Returns, Game — 2, Tim Brown, Philadelphia Eagles vs. Dallas Cowboys, Nov. 6, 1966; Travis Williams, Green Bay Packers vs. Cleveland Browns, Nov. 12, 1967.
Most Kickoff Returns, Career — 275, Ron Smith, Chicago Bears, 1965; Atlanta Falcons, 1966-67; Los Angeles Rams, 1968-69; Chicago Bears, 1970-72, San Diego Chargers, 1973; Oakland Raiders, 1974.
Most Kickoff Returns, Season — 47, Odell Barry, Denver Broncos, 1964; Larry Jones, Washington Redskins, 1975.
Longest Kickoff Return — 106 yds., Al Carmichael, Green Bay Packers vs. Chicago Bears, October 7, 1956 (scored touchdown); Noland Smith, Kansas City vs. Denver, Dec. 17, 1967 (scored touchdown).

Punt Returns

Most Yardage Returning Punts, Career — 2,209, Emlen Tunnell, New York Giants, 1948-1958; Green Bay Packers, 1959-1961.
Most Yardage Returning Punts, Season — 655, Neal Colzie, Oakland Raiders, 1975.
Most Yardage Returning Punts, Game — 205, George Atkinson, Oakland Raiders vs. Buffalo Bills, Sept. 15, 1968.
Most Touchdowns Scored via Punt Returns, Career — 8, Jack Christiansen, Detroit Lions, 1951 (4), 1952 (2), 1954, 1956.
Most Punt Returns, Career — 258, Emlen Tunnell, New York Giants, 1948-1958; Green Bay Packers, 1959-1961.
Most Punt Returns, Season — 54, Rolland Lawrence, Atlanta Falcons, 1976.
Longest Punt Return — 98, Gil LeFebvre, Cincinnati Reds vs. Brooklyn Dodgers, Dec. 3, 1933 (scored touchdown); Charles West, Minnesota Vikings vs. Washington Redskins, Nov. 3, 1968 (scored touchdown); Dennis Morgan, Dallas Cowboys vs. St. Louis Cardinals, Oct. 13, 1974 (scored touchdown).

Miscellaneous Records

Most Fumbles, Season — 17, Dan Pastorini, Houston Oilers, 1973.
Most Fumbles, Game — 7, Len Dawson, Kansas City Chiefs vs. San Diego Chargers, Nov. 15, 1964.
Longest Run with Recovered Fumble — 104 yds., Jack Tatum, Oakland Raiders vs. Green Bay Packers, Sept. 24, 1972.
Longest Winning Streak (regular season) — 17 games, Chicago Bears, 1933-1934.
Longest Undefeated Streak (includes tie games) — 29 games, Cleveland Browns, 1947-1949 (won 27, tied 2).
Most Seasons, Active Player — 26, George Blanda, Chicago Bears, 1949-1958; Houston Oilers, 1960-1966 and Oakland, 67-75.

NFL Attendance

The National Football League drew 11,070,543 fans for the 196 regular season games in 1976, an increase of 857,350 from the previous year.

Pro Football Hall of Fame

Canton, Ohio

Cliff Battles
Sammy Baugh
Chuck Bednarik
Bert Bell
Raymond Berry
Charles Bidwell
Jim Brown
Paul Brown
Roosevelt Brown
Tony Canadeo
Joe Carr
Guy Chamberlin
Jack Christiansen
Dutch Clark
George Connor
Jim Conzelman
Art Donovan
Paddy Driscoll
Bill Dudley
Turk Edwards
Tom Fears
Ray Flaherty
Len Ford
Dr. Daniel Fortmann
Bill George
Frank Gifford
Otto Graham
Red Grange
Forrest Gregg
Lou Groza
Joe Guyon
George Halas
Ed Healey
Mel Hein
Pete Henry
Arnold Herber
Bill Hewitt
Clarke Hinkle
Elroy Hirsch
Cal Hubbard
Lamar Hunt
Don Hutson
Walt Kiesling
Frank (Bruiser) Kinard
Curly Lambeau
Dick (Night Train) Lane
Dante Lavelli
Bobby Layne
Vince Lombardi
Sid Luckman
Link Lyman
Tim Mara
Gino Marchetti
George Marshall
Ollie Matson
George McAfee
Hugh McElhenny
John (Blood) McNally
Mike Michalske
Wayne Millner
Lenny Moore
Marion Motley
Bronco Nagurski
Greasy Neale
Ernie Nevers
Leo Nomellini
Steve Owen
Clarence (Ace) Parker
Jim Parker
Joe Perry
Pete Pihos
Hugh (Shorty) Ray
Dan Reeves
Andy Robustelli
Art Rooney
Gale Sayers
Joe Schmidt
Bart Starr
Ernie Stautner
Ken Strong
Joe Stydahar
Jim Taylor
Jim Thorpe
Y. A. Tittle
George Trafton
Charlie Trippi
Emlen Tunnell
Clyde (Bulldog) Turner
Norm Van Brocklin
Steve Van Buren
Bob Waterfield
Bill Willis
Alex Wojciechowicz

Sports on Television

Source: Nielsen Sports, 1976

	Average Ratings and Viewer Composition			Ages of Men Viewers		
	Household rating	Percent men	Percent women	18-34 (U.S.=40%)	35-49 (25%)	50+ (35%)
Football						
NFL Superbowl	44.4	62	38	40%	27%	33%
ABC-NFL	21.1	66	34	40	27	33
CBS-NFL	17.6	68	32	40	25	35
NBC-NFL	13.5	68	32	40	23	37
College bowl games	19.2	63	37	35	26	39
College All-Star games	12.5	65	35	37	21	42
NCAA reg. season	14.1	69	31	38	21	41
Baseball						
World Series	27.5	58	42	31	23	46
All Star game	27.1	59	41	38	26	36
Regular season	7.9	63	37	31	19	50
Horse racing						
Kentucky Derby	17.5	52	48	25	33	42
Preakness	14.3	51	49	28	18	54
Basketball						
NBA regular season	5.4	64	36	40	22	38
NBA playoffs	6.9	66	34	35	24	41
NBA All Star game	9.3	56	44	44	20	36
NBA championships	11.9	66	34	33	20	47
Bowling						
Pro tour	-	52	48	30	23	47
National Doubles	-	48	52	33	27	40
Auto racing	11.4	54	46	38	29	33
Golf						
Tournaments	6.7	59	41	28	22	50
Tennis						
World Championship	2.9	59	41	47	18	35
World Invitational	3.9	51	49	34	21	45
Multi-sports series						
American Sportsman	6.9	52	48	39	24	37
ABC WW Sports						
Sat.	10.0	57	43	42	23	35
Sun.	12.5	57	43	43	27	30
CBS Sports Spectacular	5.5	54	46	35	23	42

National AAU Karate Championships in 1977

Norfolk, Va., June 24-26, 1977

Men

Novice kata—Jessie Miller.
Intermediate kata—Tom Scarlezzo.
Advanced kata—Domingo Llanos.
Novice kumite—Tony Gutierrez.
Intermediate kumite—John Buese.
Advanced kumite—Ken Ferguson.
Weapons kata—Jerry Serino.

Women

Novice kata—Sherlye Hamlet.
Intermediate kata—Karen Kim.
Advanced kata—Pamela Glaser.
Novice kumite—Patti Booth.
Intermediate kumite—Lea Sukenik.
Advanced kumite—Pam Wansker.
Weapons kata—Ronnie McGinley.

Annual Results of Major Bowl Games

Rose Bowl, Pasadena

1902—Michigan 49, Stanford 0
1916—Wash. State 14, Brown 0
1917—Oregon 14, Pennsylvania 0
1918-19—Service teams
1920—Harvard 7, Oregon 6
1921—California 28, Ohio State 0
1922—Wash. & Jeff. 0, California 0
1923—So. California 14, Penn State 3
1924—Navy 14, Washington 14
1925—Notre Dame 27, Stanford 10
1926—Alabama 20, Washington 19
1927—Alabama 7, Stanford 7
1928—Stanford 7, Pittsburgh 6
1929—Georgia Tech 8, California 7
1930—So. California 47, Pittsburgh 14
1931—Alabama 24, Wash. State 0
1932—So. California 21, Tulane 12
1933—So. California 35, Pittsburgh 0
1934—Columbia 7, Stanford 0
1935—Alabama 29, Stanford 13
1936—Stanford 7, So. Methodist 0
1937—Pittsburgh 21, Washington 0
1938—California 13, Alabama 0
1939—So. California 7, Duke 3
1940—So. California 14, Tennessee 0
1941—Stanford 21, Nebraska 13
1942—Oregon St. 20, Duke 16 (at Durham)
1943—Georgia 9, UCLA 0
1944—So. California 29, Washington 0
1945—So. California 25, Tennessee 0
1946—Alabama 34, So. California 14
1947—Illinois 45, UCLA 14
1948—Michigan 49, So. California 0
1949—Northwestern 20, California 14
1950—Ohio State 17, California 14
1951—Michigan 14, California 6
1952—Illinois 40, Stanford 7
1953—So. California 7, Wisconsin 0
1954—Mich. State 28, UCLA 20
1955—Ohio State 20, So. California 7
1956—Mich. State 17, UCLA 14
1957—Iowa 35, Oregon St. 19
1958—Ohio State 10, Oregon 7
1959—Iowa 38, California 12
1960—Washington 44, Wisconsin 8
1961—Washington 17, Minnesota 7
1962—Minnesota 21, UCLA 3
1963—So. California 42, Wisconsin 37
1964—Illinois 17, Washington 7
1965—Michigan 34, Oregon St. 7
1966—UCLA 14, Mich. State 12
1967—Purdue 14, So. California 13
1968—Southern Cal. 14, Indiana 3
1969—Ohio State 27, Southern Cal 16
1970—Southern Cal 10, Michigan 3
1971—Stanford 27, Ohio State 17
1972—Stanford 13, Michigan 12
1973—So. California 42, Ohio State 17
1974—Ohio State 42, So. California 21
1975—So. California 18, Ohio State 17
1976—UCLA 23, Ohio State 10
1977—So. California 14, Michigan 6

Orange Bowl, Miami

1933—Miami (Fla.) 7, Manhattan 0
1934—Duquesne 33, Miami (Fla.) 7
1935—Bucknell 26, Miami (Fla.) 0
1936—Catholic U. 20, Mississippi 19
1937—Duquesne 13, Miss. State 12
1938—Auburn 6, Mich. State 0
1939—Tennessee 17, Oklahoma 0
1940—Georgia Tech 21, Missouri 7
1941—Miss. State 14, Georgetown 7
1942—Georgia 40, TCU 26
1943—Alabama 37, Boston Col. 21
1944—LSU 19, Texas A&M 14
1945—Tulsa 26, Georgia Tech 12
1946—Miami (Fla.) 13, Holy Cross 6
1947—Rice 8, Tennessee 0
1948—Georgia Tech 20, Kansas 14
1949—Texas 41, Georgia 28
1950—Santa Clara 21, Kentucky 13
1951—Clemson 15, Miami (Fla.) 14
1952—Georgia Tech 17, Baylor 14
1953—Alabama 61, Syracuse 6
1954—Oklahoma 7, Maryland 0
1955—Duke 34, Nebraska 7
1956—Oklahoma 20, Maryland 6
1957—Colorado 27, Clemson 21
1958—Oklahoma 48, Duke 21
1959—Oklahoma 21, Syracuse 6
1960—Georgia 14, Missouri 0
1961—Missouri 21, Navy 14
1962—LSU 25, Colorado 7
1963—Alabama 17, Oklahoma 0
1964—Nebraska 13, Auburn 7
1965—Texas 21, Alabama 17
1966—Alabama 39, Nebraska 28
1967—Florida 27, Georgia Tech 12
1968—Oklahoma 26, Tennessee 24
1969—Penn State 15, Kansas 14
1970—Penn State 10, Missouri 3
1971—Nebraska 17, Louisiana St. 12
1972—Nebraska 38, Alabama 6
1973—Nebraska 40, Notre Dame 6
1974—Penn State 16, Louisiana St. 9
1975—Notre Dame 13, Alabama 11
1976—Oklahoma 14, Michigan 6
1977—Ohio State 27, Colorado 10

Sugar Bowl, New Orleans

1935—Tulane 20, Temple 14
1936—TCU, 3, LSU 2
1937—Santa Clara 21, LSU 14
1938—Santa Clara 6, LSU 0
1939—TCU 15, Carnegie Tech 7
1940—Texas A&M 14, Tulane 13
1941—Boston Col. 19, Tennessee 13
1942—Fordham 2, Missouri 0
1943—Tennessee 14, Tulsa 7
1944—Georgia Tech 20, Tulsa 18
1945—Duke 29, Alabama 26
1946—Oklahoma A&M 33, St. Mary's 13
1947—Georgia 20, No. Carolina 10
1948—Texas 27, Alabama 7
1949—Oklahoma 14. No. Carolina 6
1950—Oklahoma 35, LSU 0
1951—Kentucky 13, Oklahoma 7
1952—Maryland 28, Tennessee 13
1953—Georgia Tech. 24, Mississippi 7
1954—Georgia Tech 42, West Virginia 19
1955—Navy 21, Mississippi 0
1956—Georgia Tech 7, Pittsburgh 0
1957—Baylor 13, Tennessee 7
1958—Mississippi 39, Texas 7
1959—LSU 7, Clemson 0
1960—Mississippi 21, LSU 0
1961—Mississippi 14, Rice 6
1962—Alabama 10, Arkansas 3
1963—Mississippi 17, Arkansas 13
1964—Alabama 12, Mississippi 7
1965—LSU 13, Syracuse 10
1966—Missouri 20, Florida 18
1967—Alabama 34, Nebraska 7
1968—LSU 20, Wyoming 13
1969—Arkansas 16, Georgia 2
1970—Mississippi 27, Arkansas 22
1971—Tennessee 34, Air Force 13
1972—Oklahoma 40, Auburn 22
*1972 (Dec.)—Oklahoma 14, Penn State 0
1973—Notre Dame 24, Alabama 23
1974—Nebraska 13, Florida 10
1975—Alabama 13, Penn State 6
1977 (Jan.)—Pittsburgh 27, Georgia 3
*Penn St. awarded game by forfeit

Cotton Bowl, Dallas

1937—TCU 16, Marquette 6
1938—Rice 28, Colorado 14
1939—St. Mary's 20, Texas Tech 13
1940—Clemson 6, Boston Col. 3
1941—Texas A&M 13, Fordham 12
1942—Alabama 29, Texas A&M 21
1943—Texas 14, Georgia Tech 7
1944—Randolph Field 7, Texas 7
1945—Oklahoma A&M 34, TCU 0
1946—Texas 40, Missouri 27
1947—Arkansas 0, LSU 0
1948—So. Methodist 13, Penn State 13
1949—So. Methodist 21, Oregon 13
1950—Rice 27, No. Carolina 13
1951—Tennessee 20, Texas 14
1952—Kentucky 20, TCU 7
1953—Texas 16, Tennessee 0
1954—Rice 28, Alabama 6
1955—Georgia Tech 14, Arkansas 6
1956—Mississippi 14, TCU 13
1957—TCU 28, Syracuse 27
1958—Navy 20, Rice 7
1959—TCU 0, Air Force 0
1960—Syracuse 23, Texas 14
1961—Duke 7, Arkansas 6
1962—Texas 12, Mississippi 7
1963—LSU 13, Texas 0
1964—Texas 28. Navy 6
1965—Arkansas 10, Nebraska 7
1966—LSU 14, Arkansas 7
1967—Georgia 24, So. Methodist 9
1968—Texas A&M 20, Alabama 16
1969—Texas 36, Tennessee 13
1970—Texas 21, Notre Dame 17
1971—Notre Dame 24, Texas 11
1972—Penn State 30, Texas 6
1973—Texas 17, Alabama 13
1974—Nebraska 19, Texas 3
1975—Penn State 41, Baylor 20
1976—Arkansas 31, Georgia 10
1977—Houston 30, Maryland 21

Liberty Bowl, Memphis

1959—Penn State 7, Alabama 0
1960—Penn State 41, Oregon 12
1961—Syracuse 15, Miami 14
1962—Oregon 6, Villanova 0
1963—Miss. State 16, N. C. State 12
1964—Utah 32, West Virginia 6
1965—Mississippi 13, Auburn 7
1966—Miami (Fla.) 14, Va. Tech 7
1967—N. C. State 14, Georgia 7
1968—Mississippi 34, Va. Tech 17
1969—Colorado 47, Alabama 33
1970—Tulane 17, Colorado 3
1971—Tennessee 14, Arkansas 13
1972—Georgia Tech 31, Iowa State 30
1973—No. Carolina St. 31, Kansas 18
1974—Tennessee 7, Maryland 3
1975—USC 20, Texas A&M 0
1976—Alabama 36, UCLA 6

Sun Bowl, El Paso

1936—Hardin Simmons 14, New Mex. St. 14
1937—Hardin-Simmons 34, Texas Mines 6
1938—West Virginia 7, Texas Tech 6
1939—Utah 26, New Mexico 0
1940—Catholic U. 0, Arizona St. 0
1941—Western Reserve 26, Arizona St. 13
1942—Tulsa 6, Texas Tech 0
1943—Air Force 13, Hardin-Simmons 7
1944—Southwestern (Tex.) 7, New Mexico 0
1945—Southwestern (Tex.) 35, U. of Mex. 0
1946—New Mexico 34, Denver 24
1947—Cincinnati 38, Virginia Tech 6
1948—Miami (O.) 13, Texas Tech 12
1949—West Virginia 21, Texas Mines 12
1950—Texas Western 33, Georgetown 20
1951—West Texas St. 14, Cincinnati 13
1952—Texas Tech 25, Col. Pacific 14
1953—Col. Pacific 26, Miss. Southern 7
1954—Texas Western 37, Miss. Southern 14
1955—Texas Western 47, Florida St. 20
1956—Wyoming 21, Texas Tech 14
1957—Geo. Washington 13, Tex. Western 0
1958—Louisville 34, Drake 20
1959—Wyoming 14, Hardin-Simmons 6
1960—New Mexico St. 28, No. Texas St. 8
1961—New Mexico St. 20, Utah State 13
1962—Villanova 17, Wichita 9
1963—West Texas St. 15, Ohio U. 14
1964—Oregon 21, So. Methodist 14
1965—Georgia 7, Texas Tech 0
1966—Texas Western 13, TCU 12
1967—Wyoming 28, Florida St. 20
1968—UTex El Paso 14, Mississippi 7
1969—Auburn 34, Arizona 10
1969—(Dec.) Nebraska 45, Georgia 6
1970—Georgia Tech. 17, Texas Tech. 9
1971—LSU 33, Iowa State 15
1972—North Carolina 32, Texas Tech 28
1973—Missouri 34, Auburn 17
1974—Mississippi St. 26, North Carolina 24
1975—Pittsburgh 33, Kansas 19
1977—(Jan.) Texas A&M 37, Florida 14

Gator Bowl, Jacksonville

1946—Wake Forest 26, So. Carolina 14
1947—Oklahoma 34, N.C. State 13
1948—Maryland 20, Georgia 20
1949—Clemson 24, Missouri 23
1950—Maryland 20, Missouri 7
1951—Wyoming 20, Wash. & Lee 7
1952—Miami (Fla.) 14, Clemson 0
1953—Florida 14, Tulsa 13
1954—Texas Tech 35, Auburn 13
1955—Auburn 33, Baylor 13
1956—Vanderbilt 25, Auburn 13
1957—Georgia Tech 21, Pittsburgh 14
1958—Tennessee 3, Texas A&M 0
1959—Mississippi 7, Florida 3
1960—Arkansas 14, Georgia Tech 7
1961—Florida 13, Baylor 12
1962—Penn State 30, Georgia Tech 15
1963—Florida 17, Penn State 7
1964—No. Carolina 35, Air Force 0
1965—Florida St. 36, Oklahoma 19
1966—Georgia Tech 31, Texas Tech 21
1967—Tennessee 18, Syracuse 12
1968—Penn State 17, Florida St. 17
1969—Missouri 35, Alabama 10
1969—(Dec.) Florida 14, Tenn. 13
1971—Auburn 35, Mississippi 28
1972—Georgia 7, N. Carolina 3
1973—Auburn 24, Colorado 3
1973—(Dec.) Tex. Tech, 28, Tenn. 19
1974—Auburn 27, Texas 3
1975—Maryland 13, Florida 0
1976—Notre Dame 20, Penn State 9

Bluebonnet Bowl, Houston

1959—Clemson 23, TCU 7
1960—Texas 3, Alabama 3
1961—Kansas 33, Rice 7
1962—Missouri 14, Georgia Tech 10
1963—Baylor 14, LSU 7
1964—Tulsa 14, Mississippi 7
1965—Tennessee 27, Tulsa 6
1966—Texas 19, Mississippi 0
1967—Colorado 31, Miami (Fla.) 21
1968—SMU 28, Oklahoma 27
1969—Houston 36, Auburn 7
1970—Oklahoma 24, Alabama 24
1971—Colorado 29, Houston 17
1972—Tennessee 24, Louisiana St. 17
1973—Houston 47, Tulane 7
1974—N. Carolina St. 31, Houston 31
1975—Texas 38, Colorado 21
1976—Nebraska 27, Texas Tech 24

Peach Bowl, Atlanta

1968—LSU 31, Florida St. 27
1969—West Virginia 14, S. Carolina 3
1970—Arizona St. 48, N. Carolina 26
1971—Mississippi 41, Georgia Tech. 18
1972—N. Carolina St. 49, W. Va. 13
1973—Georgia 17, Maryland 16
1974—Vanderbilt 6, Texas Tech. 6
1975—West Virginia 13, No. Carolina St. 10
1976—Kentucky 21, North Carolina 0

Tangerine Bowl, Orlando

1968—Richmond 49, Ohio 42
1969—Toledo 56, Davidson 33
1970—Toledo 40, William & Mary 12
1971—Toledo 28, Richmond 3
1972—Tampa 21, Kent State 18
1973—Miami, Ohio 16, Florida 7
1974—Miami, Ohio 21, Georgia 10
1975—Miami, Ohio 20, South Carolina 7
1976—Oklahoma St. 49, Brigham Young 21

Fiesta Bowl, Phoenix

1971—Arizona St. 45, Florida St. 38
1972—Arizona St. 49, Missouri 35
1973—Arizona St. 28, Pittsburgh 7
1974—Okla. St. 16, Brigham Young 6
1975—Arizona St. 17, Nebraska 14
1976—Oklahoma 41, Wyoming 7

Heisman Trophy Winners

Awarded annually to the nation's outstanding college football player.

1935	Jay Berwanger, Chicago, HB
1936	Larry Kelley, Yale, E
1937	Clinton Frank, Yale, QB
1938	David O'Brien, Tex. Christian, QB
1939	Nile Kinnick, Iowa, QB
1940	Tom Harmon, Michigan, HB
1941	Bruce Smith, Minnesota, HB
1942	Frank Sinkwich, Georgia, HB
1943	Angelo Bertelli, Notre Dame, QB
1944	Leslie Horvath, Ohio State, QB
1945	Felix Blanchard, Army, FB
1946	Glenn Davis, Army, HB
1947	John Lujack, Notre Dame, QB
1948	Doak Walker, SMU, HB
1949	Leon Hart, Notre Dame, E
1950	Vic Janowicz, Ohio State, HB
1951	Richard Kazmaier, Princeton, HB
1952	Billy Vessels, Oklahoma, HB
1953	John Lattner, Notre Dame, HB
1954	Alan Ameche, Wisconsin, FB
1955	Howard Cassady, Ohio St., HB
1956	Paul Hornung, Notre Dame, QB
1957	John Crow, Texas A & M, HB
1958	Pete Dawkins, Army, HB
1959	Billy Cannon, La. State, HB
1960	Joe Bellino, Navy, HB
1961	Ernest Davis, Syracuse, HB
1962	Terry Baker, Oregon State, QB
1963	Roger Staubach, Navy, QB
1964	John Huarte, Notre Dame, QB
1965	Mike Garrett, USC, HB
1966	Steve Spurrier, Florida, QB
1967	Gary Beban, UCLA, QB
1968	O. J. Simpson, USC, RB
1969	Steve Owens, Oklahoma, RB
1970	Jim Plunkett, Stanford, QB
1971	Pat Sullivan, Auburn, QB
1972	Johnny Rodgers, Nebraska, RB-R
1973	John Cappelletti, Penn State, RB
1974	Archie Griffin, Ohio State, RB
1975	Archie Griffin, Ohio State, RB
1976	Tony Dorsett, Pittsburgh, RB

Outland Awards

Honoring the outstanding interior lineman selected by the Football Writers' Association of America.

1946	George Connor, Notre Dame, T
1947	Joe Steffy, Army, G
1948	Bill Fischer, Notre Dame, G
1949	Ed Bagdon, Michigan St., G
1950	Bob Gain, Kentucky, T
1951	Jim Weatherall, Oklahoma, T
1952	Dick Modzelewski, Maryland, T
1953	J. D. Roberts, Oklahoma, G
1954	Bill Brooks, Arkansas, G
1955	Calvin Jones, Iowa, G
1956	Jim Parker, Ohio State, G
1957	Alex Karras, Iowa, T
1958	Zeke Smith, Auburn, G
1959	Mike McGee, Duke, T
1960	Tom Brown, Minnesota, G
1961	Merlin Olsen, Utah State, T
1962	Bobby Bell, Minnesota, T
1963	Scott Appleton, Texas, T
1964	Steve Delong, Tennessee, T
1965	Tommy Nobis, Texas, G
1966	Loyd Phillips, Arkansas, T
1967	Ron Yary, Southern Cal, T
1968	Bill Stanfill, Georgia, T
1969	Mike Reid, Penn State, DT
1970	Jim Stillwagon, Ohio State, LB
1971	Larry Jacobson, Nebraska, DT
1972	Rich Glover, Nebraska, MG
1973	John Hicks, Ohio State, G
1974	Randy White, Maryland, DE
1975	Leroy Selmon, Oklahoma, DT
1976	Ross Browner, Notre Dame, DE

College Football Teams

Division I

Team	Nickname	Team colors	Conference	Coach	1976 record (W-L-T)
Air Force	Falcons	Blue & Silver	Independent	Ben Martin	4-7-0
Alabama	Crimson Tide	Crimson & White	Southeastern	Paul Bryant	9-3-0
Alcorn State	Braves	Purple & Gold	Southwestern	Marino Casem	8-2-0
Appalachian State	Mountaineers	Black & Gold	Southern	Jim Brakefield	6-4-1
Arizona State	Sun Devils	Maroon & Gold	Western Athletic	Frank Kush	4-7-0
Arizona	Wildcats	Red & Blue	Western Athletic	Tony Mason	5-6-0
Arkansas	Razorbacks	Cardinal & White	Southwest	Lou Holtz	5-5-1
Arkansas State	Indians	Scarlet & Black	Southland	Bill Davidson	5-6-0
Army	Cadets	Black, Gold, Gray	Independent	Homer Smith	5-6-0
Auburn	Tigers	Orange & Blue	Southeastern	Doug Barfield	3-8-0
Ball State	Cardinals	Cardinal & White	Mid-American	Dave McClain	8-3-0
Baylor	Bears	Green & Gold	Southwest	Grant Teaff	7-3-1
Boston College	Eagles	Maroon & Gold	Independent	Joseph Yukica	8-3-0
Bowling Green	Falcons	Orange & Brown	Mid-American	Denny Stolz	6-5-0
Brigham Young	Cougars	Royal Blue & White	Western Athletic	LaVell Edwards	9-3-0
Brown	Bruins	Brown, Cardinal, White	Ivy	John Anderson	8-1-0
California	Golden Bears	Blue & Gold	Pacific-8	Mike White	5-6-0
Central Michigan	Chippewas	Maroon & Gold	Mid-American	Roy Kramer	7-4-0
Cincinnati	Bearcats	Red & Black	Independent	Ralph Staub	8-3-0
Citadel	Bulldogs	Blue & White	Southern	Bobby Ross	6-5-0
Clemson	Tigers	Purple & Orange	Atlantic Coast	Charley Pell	3-6-2
Colgate	Red Raiders	Maroon	Independent	Fred Dunlap	8-2-0
Colorado State	Rams	Green & Gold	Western Athletic	Sarkis Arslanian	6-5-0
Colorado	Buffaloes	Silver & Gold	Big Eight	Bill Mallory	8-4-0
Columbia	Lions	Blue & White	Ivy	Bill Campbell	3-6-0
Cornell	Big Red	Carnelian & White	Ivy	Bob Blackman	2-7-0
Dartmouth	Big Green	Dartmouth Green	Ivy	Jake Crouthamel	6-3-0
Drake	Bulldogs	Blue & White	The Valley	Chuck Shelton	1-10-0
Duke	Blue Devils	Royal Blue & White	Atlantic Coast	Mike McGee	5-5-1
East Carolina	Pirates	Purple & Gold	Independent	Pat Dye	9-2-0
Eastern Michigan	Hurons	Green & White	Mid-American	Ed Chiebek	2-9-0
Florida State	Seminoles	Garnet & Gold	Independent	Bobby Bowden	5-6-0
Florida	Gators	Orange & Blue	Southeastern	Doug Dickey	8-4-0
Fresno State	Bulldogs	Cardinal & Blue	Pacific Coast	Jim Sweeney	5-6-0
Fullerton, Cal. State	Titans	Blue, Orange, White	Pacific Coast	Jim Colletto	3-7-1
Furman	Palidans	Purple & White	Southern	Art Baker	6-4-1
Georgia Tech	Yellow Jackets	Old Gold & White	Independent	Pepper Rodgers	4-6-1
Georgia	Bulldogs	Red & Black	Southeastern	Vince Dooley	10-2-0
Grambling	Tigers	Black & Gold	Southwestern	Eddie Robinson	8-4-0
Harvard	Crimson	Crimson	Ivy	Joe Restic	6-3-0
Hawaii	Rainbow Warriors	Green & White	Independent	to be named	3-8-0
Holy Cross	Crusaders	Royal Purple	Independent	Neil Wheelwright	3-8-0
Houston	Cougars	Scarlet & White	Southwest	Bill Yeoman	10-2-0
Idaho	Vandals	Silver & Gold	Big Sky	Ed Troxel	7-4-0
Illinois State	Redbirds	Red & White	Independent	Charley Cowdrey	5-6-0
Illinois	Fighting Illini	Orange & Blue	Big Ten	Gary Moeller	5-6-0
Indiana State	Sycamores	Blue & White	The Valley	Tom Harp	3-7-0
Indiana	Fightin' Hoosiers	Cream & Crimson	Big Ten	Lee Corso	5-6-0
Iowa State	Cyclones	Cardinal & Gold	Big Eight	Earle Bruce	8-3-0
Iowa	Hawkeyes	Old Gold & Black	Big Ten	Bo Commings	5-6-0
Jackson State	Tigers	Blue & White	Southwestern	Robert C. Hill	5-4-0
Kansas State	Wildcats	Purple & White	Big Eight	Ellis Rainsberger	1-10-0
Kansas	Jayhawks	Crimson & Blue	Big Eight	Bud Moore	6-5-0
Kent State	Golden Flashes	Blue & Gold	Mid-American	Dennis Fitzgerald	8-4-0
Kentucky	Wildcats	Blue & White	Southeastern	Fran Curci	8-4-0
Lamar	Cardinals	Red & White	Southland	Bob Frederick	2-9-0
Long Beach, Cal., State	Forty Niners	Brown & Gold	Pacific Coast	Dave Currey	8-3-0
Louisiana State	Fighting Tigers	Purple & Gold	Southeastern	Charles McClendon	6-4-1
Louisiana Tech	Bulldogs	Red & Blue	Southland	Maxie Lambright	6-5-0
Louisville	Cardinals	Red, Black, White	Independent	Vince Gibson	4-7-0
Marshall	Thundering Herd	Green & White	Southern	Frank Ellwood	4-7-0
Maryland	Terps	Red & White	Atlantic Coast	Jerry Claiborne	11-1-0
McNeese State	Cowboys	Blue & Gold	Southland	Jack Doland	10-2-0
Memphis State	Tigers	Blue & Gray	Independent	Richard Williamson	7-4-0
Miami (Fla.)	Hurricanes	Orange, Green, White	Independent	Lou Saban	3-8-0
Miami (Ohio)	Redskins	Red & White	Mid-American	Dick Crum	3-8-0
Michigan State	Spartans	Green & White	Big Ten	Darryl Rogers	4-6-1
Michigan	Wolverines	Maize & Blue	Big Ten	Bo Schembechler	10-2-0
Minnesota	Gophers	Maroon & Gold	Big Ten	Cal Stoll	6-5-0
Mississippi State	Bulldogs	Maroon & White	Southeastern	Bob Tyler	9-2-0
Mississippi	Rebels	Red & Blue	Southeastern	Ken Cooper	5-6-0
Missouri	Tigers	Old Gold & Black	Big Eight	Al Onofrio	6-5-0
Navy	Midshipmen	Navy Blue & Gold	Independent	George Welsh	4-7-0
Nebraska	Cornhuskers	Scarlet & Cream	Big Eight	Tom Osborne	9-3-1
New Mexico State	Aggies	Crimson & White	The Valley	Jim Bradley	4-6-1
New Mexico	Lobos	Cherry & Silver	Western Athletic	Bill Mondt	4-7-0
North Carolina	Tar Heels	Blue & White	Atlantic Coast	Bill Dooley	9-3-0
North Carolina State	Wolfpack	Red & White	Atlantic Coast	Bo Rein	3-7-1
North Texas State	Mean Green	Green & White	Independent	Hayden Fry	6-5-0
Northeast Louisiana	Indians	Maroon & Gold	Independent	John David Crow	2-9-0
Northern Illinois	Huskies	Cardinal & Black	Mid-American	Pat Culpepper	1-10-0
Northwestern	Wildcats	Purple & White	Big Ten	John Pont	1-10-0
Northwestern State	Demons	Burnt Orange, Purple, White	Independent	A. L. Williams	5-5-0

Team	Nickname	Team colors	Conference	Coach	1976 record (W-L-T)
Notre Dame	Fighting Irish	Gold & Blue	Independent	Dan Devine	9-3-0
Ohio State	Buckeyes	Scarlet & Gray	Big Ten	Woody Hayes	9-2-1
Ohio Univ.	Bobcats	Green & White	Mid-American	Bill Hess	7-4-0
Oklahoma State	Cowboys	Orange & Black	Big Eight	Jim Stanley	9-3-0
Oklahoma	Sooners	Crimson & Cream	Big Eight	Barry Switzer	9-2-1
Oregon State	Beavers	Orange & Black	Pacific-8	Craig Fertig	2-10-0
Oregon	Ducks	Green & Yellow	Pacific-8	Rich Brooks	4-7-0
Pacific	Tigers	Orange & Black	Pacific Coast	Chester Caddas	2-9-0
Penn State	Nittany Lions	Blue & White	Independent	Joe Paterno	7-5-0
Pennsylvania	Red & Blue	Red & Blue	Ivy	Harry Gamble	3-6-0
Pittsburgh	Panthers	Gold & Blue	Independent	Jackie Sherrill	12-0-0
Princeton	Tigers	Orange & Black	Ivy	Bob Casciola	2-7-0
Purdue	Boilermakers	Old Gold & Black	Big Ten	Jim Young	5-6-0
Rice	Owls	Blue & Gray	Southwest	Homer Rice	3-8-0
Richmond	Spiders	Red & Blue	Independent	Jim Tait	5-6-0
Rutgers	Scarlet Knights	Scarlet	Independent	Frank Burns	11-0-0
San Diego State	Aztecs	Scarlet & Black	Independent	Claude Gilbert	10-1-0
San Jose State	Spartans	Gold & White	Pacific Coast	Lynn Stiles	7-4-0
South Carolina	Fighting Gamecocks	Garnet & Black	Independent	Jim Carlen	6-5-0
Southern California	Trojans	Cardinal & Gold	Pacific-8	John Robinson	11-1-0
Southern Illinois	Salukis	Maroon & White	The Valley	Rey Dempsey	7-4-0
Southern Methodist	Mustangs	Red & Blue	Southwest	Ron Meyer	3-8-0
Southern Mississippi	Golden Eagles	Black & Gold	Independent	Bobby Collins	2-9-0
Southern	Jaguars	Blue & Gold	Southwestern	Charlie Bates	8-3-0
Southwestern La.	Ragin' Cajuns	Vermilion & White	Southland	Augie Tamariello	9-2-0
Stanford	Cardinals	Cardinal & White	Pacific-8	Bill Walsh	6-5-0
Syracuse	Orangemen	Orange	Independent	Frank Maloney	3-8-0
Temple	Owls	Cherry & White	Independent	Wayne Hardin	4-6-0
Tennessee	Volunteers	Orange & White	Southeastern	John Majors	6-5-0
Tenn.-Chattanooga	Moccasins	Navy Blue & Gold	Southern	Joe Morrison	6-4-1
Tennessee State	Tigers	Blue & White	Independent	Dan Merritt	7-2-1
Texas-Arlington	Mavericks	Royal Blue & White	Southland	Bud Elliott	5-6-0
Texas-El Paso	Miners	Orange & White	Western Athletic	Bill Michael	1-11-0
Texas A & M	Aggies	Maroon & White	Southwest	Emory Bellard	10-2-0
Texas Christian	Horned Frogs	Purple & White	Southwest	F. A. Dry	0-11-0
Texas Southern	Tigers	Maroon & Gray	Southwestern	Wendell Mosley	2-9-0
Texas Tech	Red Raiders	Scarlet & Black	Southwest	Steve Sloan	10-2-0
Texas	Longhorns	Orange & White	Southwest	Fred Akers	5-5-1
Toledo	Rockets	Blue & Gold	Mid-American	Chuck Stobart	3-8-0
Tulane	Green Wave	Olive Green & Sky Blue	Independent	Larry Smith	2-9-0
Tulsa	Golden Hurricane	Blue, Red, Gold	The Valley	John Cooper	7-4-1
UCLA	Bruins	Navy Blue & Gold	Pacific-8	Terry Donahue	9-2-1
Utah State	Aggies	Navy Blue & White	Independent	Bruce Snyder	3-8-0
Utah	Utes	Crimson & White	Western Athletic	Wayne Howard	3-8-0
Vanderbilt	Commodores	Black & Gold	Southeastern	Fred Pancoast	2-9-0
Villanova	Wildcats	Blue & White	Independent	Dick Bedesem	6-4-1
VMI	Keydets	Red, White, Yellow	Southern	Bob Thalman	5-5-0
Virginia Polytech Inst.	Gobblers	Orange & Maroon	Independent	Jimmy Sharpe	6-5-0
Virginia	Cavaliers	Orange & Blue	Atlantic Coast	Dick Bestwick	2-9-0
Wake Forest	Demon Deacons	Old Gold & Black	Atlantic Coast	Chuck Mills	5-6-0
Washington State	Cougars	Crimson & Gray	Pacific-8	Warren Powers	3-8-0
Washington	Huskies	Purple & Gold	Pacific-8	Don James	5-6-0
West Texas State	Buffaloes	Maroon & White	The Valley	Bill Yung	4-5-2
West Virginia	Mountaineers	Old Gold & Blue	Independent	Frank Cignetti	5-6-0
Western Carolina	Catamounts	Purple & Gold	Southern	Bob Waters	6-4-0
Western Michigan	Broncos	Brown & Gold	Mid-American	Elliot Uzelac	7-4-0
Wichita State	Shockers	Gold & Black	The Valley	Jim Wright	4-7-0
William & Mary	Indians	Green, Gold, Silver	Independent	Jim Root	7-4-0
Wisconsin	Badgers	Cardinal & White	Big Ten	John Jardine	5-6-0
Wyoming	Cowboys	Brown & Yellow	Western Athletic	Bill Lewis	8-4-0
Yale	Bulldogs, Elis	Yale Blue	Ivy	Carmen Cozza	8-1-0

Selected Division 2 and 3 Teams

Akron	Zips	Blue & Gold	Independent	Jim Dennison	10-3-0
Alma	Scots	Maroon & Cream	Michigan	Phil Brooks	5-4-0
Amherst	Lord Jeffs	Purple & White	Little Three	James Ostendarp	3-5-0
Baldwin-Wallace	Yellow Jackets	Brown & Gold	Ohio	Lee J. Tressel	7-3-0
Boise State	Broncos	Orange & Blue	Big Sky	Jim Criner	5-5-1
Boston Univ.	Terriers	Scarlet & White	Yankee	Rick Taylor	3-7-0
Bucknell	Bisons	Orange & Blue	Independent	Bob Curtis	4-5-0
Butler	Bulldogs	Blue & White	Indiana	Bill Sylvester	6-4-0
Carleton	Knights	Maize & Blue	Midwest	Dale Quist	2-6-0
Case Reserve	Spartans	Blue & Gray	Presidents Athletic	Bob DelRosa	3-6-0
Chico State	Wildcats	Cardinal & White	Far Western	Dick Trimmer	5-6-0
Coast Guard	Cadets, Bears	Blue & White	Independent	Bill Hickey	1-8-0
Coe	Kohawks	Crimson & Gold	Midwest	Wayne Phillips	4-4-0
Connecticut	Huskies	Blue & White	Yankee	Walt Nadzak	2-9-0
C.W. Post	Pioneers	Green & Gold	Metropolitan	Dom Anile	8-3-0
Davidson	Wildcats	Red & Black	Southern	Ed Farrell	2-6-1
Dayton	Flyers	Red & Blue	Independent	Rick Carter	3-8-0
Delaware	Fightin' Blue Hens	Blue & Gold	Independent	Harold Raymond	8-3-1
Denison	Big Red	Red & White	Ohio	Keith Piper	1-7-1
De Pauw	Tigers	Old Gold & Black	Indiana	Bob Bergman	2-8-0
Doane	Tigers	Orange & Black	Nebraska Inter.	Joe Glenn	5-5-0

Team	Nickname	Team colors	Conference	Coach	1976 record (W-L-T)
Emory & Henry	Wasps	Blue & Gold	Independent	Jimmy Hughes	4-6-0
Evansville	Purple Aces	Purple & White	Indiana	John Moses	4-6-0
Florida A & M	Rattlers	Orange & Green	Southern IAC	Rudy Hubbard	5-4-2
Idaho State	Bengals	Orange & Black	Big Sky	Bud Hake	1-9-0
John Carroll	Blue Streaks	Blue & Gold	Presidents	Don Stupica	3-6-0
Kalamazoo	Hornets	Orange & Black	Michigan	Ed Baker	3-4-1
Kenyon	Lords	Purple & White	Ohio	Philip Morse	6-3-0
Knox	Siwash	Purple & Gold	Midwest	Joe Campanelli	7-1-1
Lafayette	Leopards	Maroon & White	Independent	Neil Putnam	5-5-0
Lawrence	Vikings	Navy & White	Midwest	Ron Roberts	7-2-0
Lehigh	Engineers	Brown & White	Independent	John Whitehead	6-5-0
Los Angeles State	Diablos	Black & Gold	Cal. Collegiate	Ron Hull	5-3-1
Maine	Black Bears	Blue & White	Yankee	Jack Bicknell	6-5-0
Massachusetts	Minutemen	Maroon & White	Yankee	Richard MacPherson	5-5-0
Michigan Tech	Huskies	Silver & Gold	Northern	Jim Kapp	7-3-0
Middlebury	Panthers	Blue & White	Independent	Mickey Heinecken	6-1-0
Middle Tenn. St.	Blue Raiders	Blue & White	Ohio Valley	Ben Hurt	4-7-0
Montana State	Bobcats	Blue & Gold	Big Sky	Sonny Holland	12-1-0
Montana	Grizzlies	Copper, Silver, Gold	Big Sky	Gene Carlson	4-6-0
Moorhead State	Dragons	Scarlet & White	Northern	Ross Fortier	5-5-0
Morgan State	Bears	Blue & Orange	Mid-Eastern	Henry Lattimore	6-4-0
Mt. Union	Purple Raiders	Purple & White	Ohio	Ken Wable	3-6-0
Muhlenberg	Mules	Cardinal & Gray	Middle Atlantic	Frank Marino	5-3-1
Nevada-Las Vegas	Rebels	Scarlet & Gray	Independent	Tony Knap	8-2-0
New Hampshire	Wildcats	Blue & White	Yankee	William Bowes	8-2-0
Norfolk State	Spartans	Green & Gold	Central	Dick Price	7-5-0
North Dakota State	Bison	Yellow & Green	North Central	Jim Wacker	9-3-0
North Dakota	Sioux	Green & White	North Central	Jerry Olson	1-7-1
Northern Arizona	Lumberjacks	Blue & Gold	Big Sky	Joe Salem	8-3-0
Northern Iowa	Panthers	Purple & Old Gold	North Central	Stan Sheriff	8-3-0
Northern Michigan	Wildcats	Old Gold & Green	Independent	Gil Krueger	11-2-0
Ohio Northern	Polar Bears	Orange & Black	Ohio	A. Wallace Hood	7-2-0
Ohio Wesleyan	Battling Bishops	Red & Black	Ohio	Jack Fouts	3-5-0
Olivet	Comets	Cardinal & White	Michigan	Chuck Cilibraise	0-9-0
Portland State	Vikings	Green & White	Independent	Darrel Davis	8-3-0
Puget Sound	Loggers	Green, Gold, Blue	Independent	Paul Wallrof	6-3-0
Redlands	Bulldogs	Maroon & Gray	So. Cal.	Frank Serrao	10-2-0
Rhode Island	Rams	Blue & White	Yankee	Bob Griffin	3-5-0
Ripon	Redmen	Crimson & White	Midwest	William Connor	6-2-0
Rochester	Yellow Jackets	Yellow & Blue	Independent	Pat Stark	4-4-1
St. Cloud State	Huskies	Red & Black	Northern	Mike Simpson	4-7-0
St. Lawrence	Saints	Scarlet & Brown	ICAC	Ted Stratford	9-2-0
St. Norbert	Green Knights	Green & Gold	Independent	Howie Kolstad	2-8-0
St. Olaf	Oles	Black & Gold	Minn. IAC	Tom Porter	7-3-0
Santa Clara	Broncos	Cardinal & White	Independent	Pat Malley	7-4-0
Slippery Rock	Rockets	Green & White	Pennsylvania	Bob Despirito	7-3-0
So. Carolina State	Bulldogs	Garnet & Blue	Mid-Eastern	Willie Jeffries	10-1-0
So. Dakota State	Jackrabbits	Yellow & Blue	North Central	John Gregory	5-4-1
South Dakota	Coyotes	Vermilion & White	North Central	Bernard Cooper	4-5-1
Southern Oregon	Red Raiders	Red & Black	Evergreen	Scott Johnson	3-6-0
Swarthmore	Little Quakers	Garnet	Middle Atlantic	Tom Lapinski	1-7-1
Tennessee Tech	Golden Eagles	Purple & Gold	Ohio Valley	Don Wade	8-3-0
Thiel	Tomcats	Blue & Gold	President's Athletic	James McCullough	1-6-1
Trenton State	Lions	Blue & Gold	New Jersey State	Eric Hamilton	3-4-1
Tufts	Jumbos	Blue & Brown	Independent	Paul Pawlak	6-2-0
Upsala	Vikings	Blue & Gray	Middle Atlantic	John Hooper	6-3-0
Valparaiso	Crusaders	Brown & Gold	Indiana	Norm Amundsen	2-7-1
Wash. & Jeff.	Presidents	Red & Black	Presidents Athletic	Pat Mondock	6-3-0
Wash. & Lee	Generals	Royal Blue, White	Independent	William McHenry	5-5-0
Wayne State	Tartars	Green & Gold	Great Lakes	Dick Lowry	8-2-0
Weber State	Wildcats	Purple & White	Big Sky	Pete Riehlman	2-9-0
Wesleyan	Cardinals	Red & Black	Little Three	Bill MacDermott	5-3-0
Western Illinois	Leathernecks	Purple & Gold	Independent	Bill Shanahan	7-3-0
Western Kentucky	Hilltoppers	Red & White	Ohio Valley	Jimmy Feix	4-5-1
Wilkes	Colonels	Navy & Gold	Middle Atlantic	Roland Schmidt	3-5-0
Williams	Ephmen	Purple	Little Three	Robert Odell	4-4-0
Wittenberg	Tigers	Red & White	Ohio	Dave Maurer	8-2-0
Wooster	Fighting Scots	Black & Gold	Ohio	Tom Hollman	4-5-0
Youngstown State	Penguins	Red & White	Independent	Bill Narduzzi	4-6-0

National College Football Champions

The NCAA recognizes as unofficial national champion the team selected each year by the AP (poll of writers) and the UPI (poll of coaches). When the polls disagree both teams are listed. The AP poll originated in 1936 and the UPI poll in 1950.

1936—Minnesota
1937—Pittsburgh
1938—Texas Christian
1939—Texas A&M
1940—Minnesota
1941—Minnesota
1942—Ohio State
1943—Notre Dame
1944—Army
1945—Army
1946—Notre Dame
1947—Notre Dame
1948—Michigan
1949—Notre Dame
1950—Oklahoma
1951—Tennessee
1952—Michigan State
1953—Maryland
1954—Ohio State, UCLA
1955—Oklahoma
1956—Oklahoma
1957—Auburn, Ohio State
1958—Louisiana State
1959—Syracuse
1960—Minnesota
1961—Alabama
1962—Southern Cal.
1963—Texas
1964—Alabama
1965—Alabama, Mich. State
1966—Notre Dame
1967—Southern Cal.
1968—Ohio State
1969—Texas
1970—Nebraska, Texas
1971—Nebraska
1972—Southern Cal.
1973—Notre Dame, Alabama
1974—Oklahoma, So. Cal.
1975—Oklahoma
1976—Pittsburgh

College Football Conference Champions

Atlantic Coast

1963—No. Carolina St., No. Carolina
1964—No. Carolina St.
1965—Duke
1966—Clemson
1967—Clemson
1968—No. Carolina St.
1969—So. Carolina
1970—Wake Forest
1971—North Carolina
1972—North Carolina
1973—No. Carolina St.
1974—Maryland
1975—Maryland
1976—Maryland

Ivy League

1963—Dartmouth, Princeton
1964—Princeton
1965—Dartmouth
1966—Dartmouth, Harvard, Princeton
1967—Yale
1968—Yale, Harvard
1969—Princeton, Dartmouth, Yale
1970—Dartmouth
1971—Dartmouth, Cornell
1972—Dartmouth
1973—Dartmouth
1974—Yale, Harvard
1975—Harvard
1976—Yale, Brown

Big Eight

1963—Nebraska
1964—Nebraska
1965—Nebraska
1966—Nebraska
1967—Oklahoma
1968—Kansas, Oklahoma
1969—Missouri, Nebraska
1970—Nebraska
1971—Nebraska
1972—Nebraska
1973—Oklahoma
1974—Oklahoma
1975—Oklahoma, Nebraska
1976—Oklahoma, Colorado Oklahoma State

Big Ten

1963—Illinois
1964—Michigan
1965—Michigan State
1966—Michigan State
1967—Indiana, Purdue, Minn.
1968—Ohio State
1969—Michigan, Ohio State
1970—Ohio State
1971—Michigan
1972—Ohio State, Michigan
1973—Ohio State, Michigan
1974—Ohio State, Michigan
1975—Ohio State
1976—Michigan

Mid-America

1963—Ohio Univ.
1964—Bowling Green
1965—Bowling Green, Miami
1966—Miami, Western Mich.
1967—Toledo, Ohio Univ.
1968—Ohio Univ.
1969—Toledo
1970—Toledo
1971—Toledo
1972—Kent State
1973—Miami
1974—Miami
1975—Miami
1976—Ball State

Missouri Valley

1963—Cincinnati, Wichita
1964—Cincinnati
1965—Tulsa
1966—No. Texas, Tulsa
1967—North Texas
1968—Memphis State
1969—Memphis State
1970—Louisville
1971—Memphis State
1972—Louisville, W. Texas, Drake
1973—No. Texas St., Tulsa
1974—Tulsa
1975—Tulsa
1976—Tulsa, N. Mexico St.

Southeastern

1963—Mississippi
1964—Alabama
1965—Alabama
1966—Alabama, Georgia
1967—Tennessee
1968—Georgia
1969—Tennessee
1970—Louisiana State
1971—Alabama
1972—Alabama
1973—Alabama
1974—Alabama
1975—Alabama
1976—Georgia

Southwest

1963—Texas
1964—Arkansas
1965—Arkansas
1966—Southern Methodist
1967—Texas A & M
1968—Texas, Arkansas
1969—Texas
1970—Texas
1971—Texas
1972—Texas
1973—Texas
1974—Baylor
1975—Texas A&M, Arkansas, Texas
1976—Houston

Pacific Eight

1963—Washington
1964—Oregon St., USC
1965—UCLA
1966—USC
1967—USC
1968—USC
1969—USC
1970—Stanford
1971—Stanford
1972—USC
1973—USC
1974—USC
1975—UCLA, Cal.
1976—USC

Southern

1963—Virginia Tech
1964—West Virginia
1965—West Virginia
1966—East Carolina, William & Mary
1967—West Virginia
1968—Richmond
1969—Richmond, Davidson
1970—William & Mary
1971—Richmond
1972—East Carolina
1973—East Carolina
1974—VMI
1975—Richmond
1976—East Carolina

Western Athletic

1963—New Mexico
1964—New Mexico, Arizona, Utah
1965—Brigham Young
1966—Wyoming
1967—Wyoming
1968—Wyoming
1969—Arizona State
1970—Arizona State
1971—Arizona State
1972—Arizona State
1973—Arizona State, Arizona
1974—Brigham Young
1975—Arizona State
1976—Wyoming, Brigham Young

Pacific Coast

1969—San Diego State
1970—Long Beach State
1971—Long Beach State
1972—San Diego State
1973—San Diego State
1974—San Diego State
1975—San Jose State
1976—San Diego State

Canadian Football League

1976 Final Standings

Eastern Conference

	W	L	T	PF	PA	Pts
Ottawa	9	6	1	411	346	19
Hamilton	8	8	0	269	348	16
Montreal	7	8	1	305	273	15
Toronto	7	8	1	289	354	15

Western Conference

	W	L	T	PF	PA	Pts
Saskatchewan	11	5	0	427	238	22
Winnipeg	10	6	0	384	316	20
Edmonton	9	6	1	311	367	19
British Columbia	5	9	2	308	336	12
Calgary	2	12	2	316	442	6

East semifinal—Hamilton 23, Montreal 0
West semifinal—Edmonton 14, Winnipeg 12
East final—Ottawa 17, Hamilton 15
West final—Saskatchewan 23, Edmonton13
Championship (Grey Cup)—Ottawa 23, Saskatchewan 20

Canadian Football League (Grey Cup)

Winners of Eastern and Western divisions meet in championship game for Grey Cup (donated by Governor-General Earl Grey in 1909). Canadian football features 3 downs, 110-yard field, and each team can have 12 players on field at one time.

1948—Calgary Stampeders 12, Ottawa Rough Riders 7
1949—Montreal Alouettes 28, Calgary Stampeders 15
1950—Toronto Argonauts 13, Winnipeg Blue Bombers 0
1951—Ottawa Rough Riders 21, Saskatchewan Roughriders 14
1952—Toronto Argonauts 21, Edmonton Eskimos 11
1953—Hamilton Tiger-Cats 12, Winnipeg Blue Bombers 6
1954—Edmonton Eskimos 26, Montreal Alouettes 25
1955—Edmonton Eskimos 34, Montreal Alouettes 19
1956—Edmonton Eskimos 50, Montreal Alouettes 27
1957—Hamilton Tiger-Cats 32, Winnipeg Blue Bombers 7
1958—Winnipeg Blue Bombers 35, Hamilton Tiger-Cats 28
1959—Winnipeg Blue Bombers 21, Hamilton Tiger-Cats 7
1960—Ottawa Rough Riders 16, Edmonton Eskimos 6
1961—Winnipeg Blue Bombers 21, Hamilton Tiger-Cats 14
1962—Winnipeg Blue Bombers 28, Hamilton Tiger-Cats 27
1963—Hamilton Tiger-Cats 21, British Columbia Lions 10
1964—British Columbia Lions 34, Hamilton Tiger-Cats 24
1965—Hamilton Tiger-Cats 22, Winnipeg Blue Bombers 16
1966—Saskatchewan Roughriders 29, Ottawa Rough Riders 14
1967—Hamilton Tiger-Cats 24, Saskatchewan Roughriders 1
1968—Ottawa Rough Riders 24, Calgary Stampeders 21
1969—Ottawa Rough Riders 29, Saskatchewan Roughriders 11
1970—Montreal Alouettes 23, Calgary Stampeders 10
1971—Calgary Stampeders 14, Toronto Argonauts 11
1972—Hamilton Tiger-Cats 13, Saskatchewan Roughriders 10
1973—Ottawa Rough Riders 22, Edmonton Eskimos 18
1974—Montreal Alouettes 20, Edmonton Eskimos 7
1975—Edmonton Eskimos 9, Montreal Alouettes 8
1976—Ottawa Rough Riders 23, Saskatchewan Roughriders 20

College Football Stadiums

School	Capacity
Alabama Univ. of (Denny Stad.), University, Ala.	59,000
Arizona State Univ. (Sun Devil), Tempe	51,000
Arizona, Univ. of (Arizona Stad.), Tucson	57,000
Arkansas, Univ. of (Razorback Stad.) Fayetteville	43,500
Auburn Univ. (Jordan Hare Stad.), Auburn, Ala.	62,291
Baylor Univ. Stad., Waco, Texas	48,000
Boston Coll. (Alumni Stad.), Boston, Mass.	32,000
Bowling Green State Univ. (Doyt Perry Field)	23,272
Brigham Young Univ. Stad., Provo, Ut.	30,000
Brown Stad., Providence, R. I.	20,000
Butler Univ. (Butler Bowl), Indianapolis, Ind.	19,500
Cal., Univ. of (Memorial Stad.), Berkeley	77,000
Central Mich. Univ. (Shorts Stad.), Mt. Pleasant	20,000
Cincinnati, Univ. of (Nippert), Oh.	25,692
Citadel (Johnson Hagood Stad.), Charleston, S.C.	22,500
Clemson Univ. (Memorial Stad.), S.C.	43,451
Colorado St. Univ. (Hughes Stad.), Ft. Collins	30,000
Colorado, Univ. of (Folsom Field), Boulder	55,000
Columbia Univ. (Baker Field), N.Y., N.Y.	32,000
Cornell (Schoellkopf Crescent), Ithaca, N.Y.	27,000
Dartmouth Coll. (Memorial Field), Hanover, N.H.	20,816
Delaware, Univ. of (Delaware Stad.), Newark	21,919
Drake Stad., Des Moines, Ia.	18,000
Duke Univ., (Wade Stad.), Durham, N.C.	44,000
E. Carolina Univ. (Ficklen Stad.), Greenville, N.C.	20,000
Eastern Kentucky (Hanger Stad.), Richmond	20,000
Florida State, (Campbell Stad.), Tallahassee	40,500
Florida, Univ. of (Florida Field), Gainesville	62,000
Georgia Inst. of Tech. (Grant Field), Atlanta	58,121
Georgia, Univ. of (Sanford Stad.), Athens	59,200
Harvard Stad., Boston, Mass.	37,289
Hawaii, Univ. of (Aloha Stad.), Honolulu	50,000
Holy Cross (Fitton Field), Worcester, Mass.	25,000
Idaho, Univ. of (Kibbie Stad.), Moscow	18,000
Illinois, Univ. of (Memorial Stad.), Urbana	71,229
Indiana St. (Memorial Stad.), Terre Haute	20,500
Indiana Univ. (Memorial Stad.), Bloomington	52,354
Iowa State Univ. (Cyclone Stad.), Ames	50,000
Iowa, Univ. of (Kinnick Stad.), Iowa City	60,200
Kansas State Univ. Stad., Manhattan	42,000
Kansas, Univ. of (Memorial Stad.), Lawrence	51,500
Kent State Univ. (Dix Stad.), Kent, Oh.	28,748
Kentucky, Univ. of (Commonwealth), Lexington	58,000
La. State Univ. (Tiger Stad.), Baton Rouge	67,720
Louisiana Tech. Univ. (Joe Aillet Stad.), Ruston	23,318
Maryland, Univ. of (Byrd), College Park	45,000
McNeese St. Univ. (Cowboy Stad.), Lake Charles, La.	20,000
Memphis State (Memphis Memorial)	50,164
Michigan State Univ. (Spartan Stad.), E. Lansing	76,000
Michigan, Univ. of (Mich. Stad.), Ann Arbor	101,701
Minnesota, Univ. of (Memorial Stad.), Minneapolis	56,725
Mississippi St. Univ. (Scott Field)	35,000
Mississippi, Univ. of (Hemingway Stad.)	37,500
Missouri, Univ. of (Faurot Field), Columbia	55,000
Nebraska, Univ. of (Memorial Stad.), Lincoln	76,000
New Mexico, Univ. Stad., Albuquerque	30,000
North Carolina St. U. (Carter Stad.), Raleigh	44,000
North Carolina, Univ. of (Kenan Stad.)	47,000
North Texas St. Univ. (Fouts Field), Denton	20,000
Northern Illinois Univ. (Huskie Stad.) DeKalb	20,257
Northwestern Univ. (Dyche Stad.), Evanston, Ill.	48,500
Notre Dame Stad., South Bend, Ind.	59,075
Ohio State Univ. (Ohio Stad.), Columbus	83,112
Oklahoma State (Lewis Stad.), Stillwater	50,588
Oklahoma, Univ. of (Owen Field), Norman	70,286
Old Dominion Univ. (Foreman Field), Norfolk	32,000
Oregon St. Univ. (Parker Stad.), Corvallis	41,000
Oregon, Univ. of (Autzen Stad.), Eugene	41,097
Pacific, Univ. of the (Pacific Memorial), Cal.	31,895
Penn. State Univ. (Beaver Stad.)	57,538
Penn., Univ. of (Franklin Field), Phila.	60,546
Pittsburgh, Univ. of (Pitt. Stad.), Pa.	56,500
Princeton, (Palmer Stad.), Princeton, N.J.	45,725
Purdue, (Ross-Ade Stad.), Lafayette, Ind.	69,250
Rice Stad., Houston, Texas	72,000
Rutgers Stad., New Brunswick, N.J.	23,000
San Jose St. Univ. (Spartan Stad.), Cal.	18,155
So. Carolina, Univ. of (Williams-Brice), Columbia	54,406
So. Illinois Univ. (McAndrew Stad.), Carbondale	20,013
So. Miss., Univ. of (Roberts Stad.), Hattiesburg	36,000
Southwestern La., (Cajun Field), Lafayette	27,000
Stanford Stad., Stanford, Cal.	90,000
Syracuse Univ. (Archbold Stad.), N.Y.	26,388
Tampa, Univ. of (Tampa Stad.), Fla.	47,000
Tenn., Univ. of (Neyland Stad.), Knoxville	80,290
Texas A. & M. Univ. (Kyle Field), College Station	48,000
Texas Christian Univ. (Amon Carter Stad.), Ft. Worth	46,000
Texas-El Paso (Sun Bowl)	30,000
Texas Tech. Univ. (Jones Stad.), Lubbock	47,000
Texas, Univ. of (Memorial Stad.), Austin	80,000
Toledo, Univ. of (Glass Bowl), Oh.	18,210
Trinity Univ. (Alamo Stad.), San Antonio, Tex.	22,500
Tulsa, Univ. of (Skelly Stad.), Okla.	40,235
U. S. Air Force Acad. (Falcon Stad.), Col.	49,068
U. S. Military Academy (Michie Stad.), West Point, N.Y.	41,428
U. S. Naval Academy (Navy-Marine Corps Mem. Stad.), Annapolis, Md.	28,000
Utah State Univ. (Romney Stad.), Logan	20,000
Utah, Univ. of (Robert Rice Stad.), Salt Lake City	30,000
Vanderbilt, (Dudley Stad.), Nashville	34,000
Va. Poly Inst. (Lane Stad.), Blacksburg	40,000
Virginia, Univ. of (Scott Stad.), Charlottesville	25,000
Wake Forest (Groves Stad.), Winston-Salem, N.C.	31,000
Washington State Univ. (Clarence D. Martin)	27,500
Washington, Univ. of (Husky Stad.), Seattle	58,946
West Texas State Univ. (Kimbrough Stad.), Canyon	20,500
West Virginia Univ. (Mountaineer Field)	37,000
Western Illinois Univ. (Hanson Field), Macomb	18,000
Western Kentucky Univ. (L. T. Smith Stad.)	19,250
Western Mich. Univ. (Waldo Stad.), Kalamazoo	24,500
Wichita State Univ. (Cessna Stad.)	30,500
Wisconsin, Univ. of (Camp Randall), Madison	77,280
Wyoming, Univ. of (Memorial), Laramie	27,000
Yale Bowl, New Haven, Conn.	70,874

National AAU Judo Championships in 1977

St. Louis, Mo., Apr. 15-16

Men's Shiai

139 lbs.—Keith Nakasone, San Jose, Cal.
143 lbs.—James Martin, San Francisco, Cal.
152 lbs.—Michael Vincenti, Boston, Mass.
172 lbs.—Steve Cohen, Chicago, Ill.
189 lbs.—Irwin Cohen, Chicago, Ill.
209 lbs.—Leo White, Monterey, Cal.
Over 209 lbs.—Shawn Gibbons, San Jose, Cal.
Open—Shimitchi Otaka, No. Glen, Col.

Women's Shiai

110 lbs.—Lynn Lewis, Peabody, Mass.
120 lbs.—Linda Richardson, Milwaukee, Wis.
130 lbs.—Diane Pierce, Minneapolis, Minn.
142 lbs.—Dolores Brodie, Los Angeles, Cal.
154 lbs.—Christine Penick, Los Angeles, Cal.
166 lbs.—Amy Kublin, Peabody, Mass.
Over 166 lbs.—Margaret Castro, New York, N.Y.
Open—Maureen Braziel, Brooklyn, N.Y.

Men's Kata

Ju no kata—Joel Holloway & Roy Holloway, Oklahoma City, Okla.
Katame no kata—Russell Cockrell & Paul Cameron, Chicago, Ill.
Nage no kata—Wally Barber & Paul Cameron, Chicago, Ill.

Women's Kata

Ju no kata—Linda Stoops & Judy Baker, Lima, Dayton, Oh.
Katame no kata—Robin Brown & Jeaninne Sandlin, Louisville, Ky.
Nage no kata—Muriel Uyemura & Freya Saito, Southfield, Mich.

Notable Sports Personalities

Henry Aaron, b. 1934: Milwaukee-Atlanta outfielder hit record 755 home runs; led NL 4 times.

Kareem Abdul-Jabbar, b. 1947: Milwaukee, L.A. Lakers center; MVP 5 times; leading scorer twice.

Grover Cleveland Alexander, (1887-1950): pitcher won 374 NL games; pitched 16 shutouts, 1916.

Muhammud Ali, b. 1942; current heavyweight champion.

Mario Andretti, b. 1940: U.S. Auto Club national champ 3 times; won Indy 500, 1969.

Earl Anthony, b. 1938: bowler won record $110,833, 1976.

Eddie Arcaro, b. 1916: jockey rode 4,779 winners including the Kentucky Derby 5 times; the Preakness and Belmont Stakes 6 times each.

Henry Armstrong, b. 1912: boxer held feather-, bantam-, lightweight titles simultaneously, 1937-38.

Arthur Ashe, b. 1943: U.S. singles champ, 1968, Wimbledon champ, 1975; won record $306,712, 1975.

Red Auerbach, b. 1917: coached Boston Celtics to 9 NBA championships.

Ernie Banks, b. 1931: Chicago Cubs slugger hit 512 NL homers; twice MVP.

Roger Bannister, b. 1929: Briton ran first sub 4-minute mile, May 6, 1954.

Rick Barry, b. 1944: NBA scoring leader, 1967; ABA, 1969.

Sammy Baugh, b. 1914: Washington Redskins quarterback held numerous records upon retirement after 16 pro seasons.

Elgin Baylor, b. 1934: L.A. Lakers forward; 1st team all-star 10 times.

Bob Beamon, b. 1946: long jumper won 1968 Olympic gold medal with record 29 ft. 2½ in.

Jean Beliveau, b. 1931: Montreal Canadiens center scored 507 goals; twice MVP.

Johnny Bench, b. 1947: Cincinnati Reds catcher; MVP twice; led league in home runs twice, RBIs 3 times.

Patty Berg, b. 1918: won over 80 golf tournaments: AP Woman Athlete-of-the-Year 3 times.

Yogi Berra, b. 1925: N.Y. Yankees catcher; MVP 3 times; played in 14 World Series.

Raymond Berry, b. 1933: Baltimore Colts receiver caught 631 passes.

George Blanda, b. 1927: quarterback, kicker; 26 years as active player, scoring record 2,002 points.

Fanny Blankers-Koen, b. 1918: Dutch track star won 4 1948 Olympic gold medals.

Bjorn Borg, b. 1956: led Sweden to first Davis Cup, 1975; Wimbledon champion, 1976, 1977.

Julius Boros, b. 1920: won U.S. Open, 1952, 1963; PGA champ, 1968.

Jack Brabham, b. 1926: Grand Prix champ 3 times.

Lou Brock, b. 1939: St. Louis Cardinals outfielder stole record 118 bases, 1974; led NL 8 times.

Jimmy Brown, b. 1936: Cleveland Browns fullback ran for record 12,312 career yards; MVP 3 times.

Valery Brumel, b. 1942: Soviet high jumper won 1964 Olympic gold medal; world record holder until 1973.

Don Budge, b. 1915: won numerous amateur and pro tennis titles, "grand slam," 1938.

Maria Bueno, b. 1939: U.S. singles champ 4 times; Wimbledon champ 3 times.

Mike Burton, b. 1947: swimmer won 1968, 1972 Olympic 1,500 meter freestyle.

Dick Butkus, b. 1942: Chicago Bears linebacker twice chosen best NFL defensive player.

Dick Button, b. 1929: figure skater won 1948, 1952 Olympic gold medals; world titlist, 1948-52.

Walter Camp, (1859-1925): Yale football player, coach, athletic director; established many rules; promoted All-America designations.

Roy Campanella, b. 1921: Brooklyn Dodgers catcher; MVP 3 times.

Rod Carew, b. 1945: Minnesota Twins infielder won 6 batting titles.

Don Carter, b. 1930: bowler-of-the-year 6 times.

Billy Casper, b. 1931: PGA Player-of-the-Year 3 times; U.S. Open champ twice.

Wilt Chamberlain, b. 1936: center scored NBA career record 31,419 points; MVP 4 times.

Jim Clark, (1936-1968): world driving champ twice; won Indy 500, 1965.

Bobby Clarke, b. 1949: Philadelphia Flyers center led team to 2 Stanley Cup championships; MVP 3 times.

Roberto Clemente, (1934-1972): Pittsburgh Pirates outfielder won 4 batting titles; MVP, 1966.

Ty Cobb, (1886-1961): Detroit Tigers outfielder had record .367 lifetime batting average, 4,191 hits, 12 batting titles.

Nadia Comaneci, b. 1962: Romanian gymnast won 3 gold medals, achieved 7 perfect scores, 1976 Olympics.

Maureen Connolly, (1934-1969): won tennis "grand slam," 1953; AP Woman-Athlete-of-the-Year 3 times.

Jimmy Connors, b. 1952: U.S. singles champ twice.

James J. Corbett, (1866-1933): heavyweight champion, 1892-97; credited with being the first "scientific" boxer.

Margaret Smith Court, b. 1942: Australian won U.S. singles championship 5 times; Wimbledon champ 3 times.

Bob Cousy, b. 1928: Boston Celtics guard led team to 6 NBA championships; MVP, 1957.

Dave Cowens, b. 1948: Boston Celtics center chosen MVP, 1973.

Stanley Dancer, b. 1927: harness racing driver drove Hambletonian winner 3 times, Little Brown Jug winner 4 times.

Dizzy Dean, (1911-1974): colorful pitcher for St. Louis Cardinals "Gashouse Gang" in the 30s; MVP, 1934.

Jack Dempsey, b. 1895: heavyweight champion, 1919-26.

Joe DiMaggio, b. 1914: N.Y. Yankees outfielder hit safely in record 56 consecutive games, 1941; MVP twice.

Leo Durocher, b. 1906: colorful manager of Dodgers, Giants, and Cubs; won 3 NL pennants.

Gertrude Ederle, b. 1906: first woman to swim English Channel, broke existing men's record, 1926.

Kornelia Ender, b. 1958: E. German swimmer broke 23 world records; won 4 1976 Olympic gold medals.

Julius Erving, b. 1950: MVP and leading scorer in ABA 3 times.

Phil Esposito, b. 1942: scored record 76 goals and 152 points in 1970-71; NHL scoring leader 5 times.

Chris Evert, b. 1954: U.S. and Wimbledon champ twice.

Ray Ewry, (1873-1937): track and field star won 8 gold medals, 1900, 1904, and 1908 Olympics.

Juan Fangio, b. 1911: Argentine World Grand Prix champion 5 times.

Bob Feller, b. 1918: Cleveland Indians pitcher won 266 games; pitched 3 no-hitters, 12 one-hitters.

Mark Fidrych, b. 1954: colorful Detroit Tigers pitcher won 19 games and rookie-of-the-year honors, 1976.

Peggy Fleming, b. 1948: world figure skating champion, 1966-68; gold medalist 1968 Olympics.

Whitey Ford, b. 1928: N.Y. Yankees pitcher won record 10 world series games.

Chuck Foreman, b. 1950: Minnesota Vikings back rushed for 1,155 yds., caught 55 passes, 1976.

Dick Fosbury, b. 1947: high jumper won 1968 Olympic gold medal; developed the "Fosbury Flop."

Jimmy Foxx, (1907-1967): Red Sox, Athletics slugger; MVP 3 times; triple crown, 1933.

A. J. Foyt, b. 1935: won Indy 500 4 times; U.S. Auto Club champ 6 times.

Dawn Fraser, b. 1937: Australian swimmer won Olympics 100-meter freestyle 3 times.

Joe Frazier, b. 1944: heavyweight champion, 1970-73.

Walt Frazier, b. 1945: N.Y. Knicks guard; first team all-star 4 times.

Lou Gehrig, (1903-1941): N.Y. Yankees 1st baseman played record 2,130 consecutive games, MVP, 1936.

Althea Gibson, b. 1927: twice U.S. and Wimbledon singles champ.

Bob Gibson, b. 1935: St. Louis Cardinals pitcher won Cy Young award twice; struck out NL record 3,117 batters.

Frank Gifford, b. 1930: N.Y. Giants back; MVP, 1956.

Pancho Gonzalez, b. 1928: world professional tennis champ, 8 years.

Otto Graham, b. 1921: Cleveland Browns quarterback; all-pro 4 times.

Red Grange, b. 1903: All-America at Univ. of Illinois; played for Chicago Bears, 1925-35.

Joe Greene, b. 1946: Pittsburgh Steelers lineman; twice NFL outstanding defensive player.

Lefty Grove, (1900-1975): pitcher won 300 AL games; 20-game winner 8 times.

Walter Hagen, (1892-1969): won PGA championship 5 times, British Open 4 times.

George Halas, b. 1895: founder-coach of Chicago Bears; won 5 NFL championships.

Bill Hartack, b. 1932: jockey rode 5 Kentucky Derby winners.

Doug Harvey, b. 1930: Montreal Canadiens defenseman; Norris Trophy 7 times.

Bill Haughton, b. 1923: harness racing driver whose horses have won over $22 million.

John Havlicek, b. 1940: Boston Celtics forward scored over 24,000 NBA points.

Carol Heiss, b. 1940: world champion figure skater 5 consecutive years, 1956-60; won 1960 Olympic gold medal.

Sonja Henie, (1912-1969): world champion figure skater 10 consecutive years, 1927-36; Olympic gold medalist, 1928, 1932, 1936.

Graham Hill, (1929-1975): world Grand Prix champ, 1962, 1968.
Ben Hogan, b. 1912: won 4 U.S. Open championships, 2 PGA, 2 Masters.
Willie Hoppe, (1887-1959): won some 50 world billiard titles.
Rogers Hornsby, (1896-1963): NL 2d baseman batted record .424 in 1924; twice won triple crown; batting leader 6 consecutive years, 1920-25.
Paul Hornung, b. 1935: Green Bay Packers runner-placekicker scored record 176 points, 1960.
Gordie Howe, b. 1928: Detroit Red Wings forward holds NHL career records in goals, assists, and points; NHL MVP 6 times, leading scorer 6 times.
Carl Hubbell, b. 1903: N.Y. Giants pitcher; 20-game winner 5 consecutive years, 1933-37.
Bobby Hull, b. 1939: scored 604 NHL; NHL all-star 10 times, WHA all-star 4 times.
James Hunt, b. 1947: Briton won Grand Prix championship, 1976.
Catfish Hunter, b. 1946: pitched perfect game, 1968; 20-game winner 5 times.
Don Hutson, b. 1913: Green Bay Packers receiver caught NFL record 99 touchdown passes.
Reggie Jackson, b. 1946: slugger twice led AL in home runs; MVP, 1973.
Bruce Jenner, b. 1959: decathlon gold medalist, 1976 Olympics.
Jack Johnson, (1878-1946): first black heavyweight champion, 1910-15.
Rafer Johnson, b. 1935: decathlon gold medalist, 1960 Olympics.
Walter Johnson, (1887-1946): Washington Senators pitcher won 414 games.
Bert Jones, b. 1951: Baltimore Colts quarterback; MVP, 1976.
Bobby Jones, (1902-1971): won "grand slam of golf," 1930; U.S. Amateur champ 5 times, U.S. Open champ 4 times.
Deacon Jones, b. 1938: L.A. Rams lineman; twice NFL outstanding defensive player.
Sonny Jurgensen, b. 1934: quarterback named all-pro 5 times; completed record 288 passes, 1967.
Duke Kahanamoku, (1890-1968): swimmer won 1912, 1920 Olympic gold medals in 100-meter freestyle.
Alex Karras, b. 1935: Detroit Lions defensive lineman; all-pro 4 times.
Kipchoge Keino, b. 1940: Kenyan distance runner won 1968, 1972 Olympic gold medals.
Harmon Killebrew, b. 1936: Minnesota Twins slugger led AL in home runs 6 times.
Jean Claude Killy, b. 1943: French skier won 3 1968 Olympic gold medals.
Ralph Kiner, b. 1922: Pittsburgh Pirates slugger led NL in home runs 7 consecutive years, 1946-52.
Billie Jean King, b. 1943: U.S. singles champ 4 times; Wimbledon champ 6 times.
Olga Korbut, b. 1956: Soviet gymnast won 3 1972 Olympic gold medals.
Sandy Koufax, b. 1935: Dodgers pitcher won Cy Young award 3 times; lowest ERA in NL, 1962-66; pitched 4 no-hitters, one a perfect game.
Jack Kramer, b. 1921: twice U.S. singles champ.
Guy Lafleur, b 1951: Montreal Canadiens forward led NHL in scoring, 1976, 1977; MVP, 1977.
Tom Landry, b. 1924: Dallas Cowboys head coach since 1960.
Rod Laver, b. 1938: Australian won tennis "grand slam," 1962, 1969; Wimbledon champ 4 times.
Vince Lombardi, (1913-1970): Green Bay Packers coach led team to 5 NFL championships and victory in first 2 Super Bowl games.
Johnny Longden, b. 1907: jockey rode 6,032 winners.
Joe Louis, b. 1914: heavyweight champion, 1937-49.
Sid Luckman, b. 1916: Chicago Bears quarterback led team to 4 NFL championships; MVP, 1943.
Connie Mack, (1892-1956): Philadelphia Athletics manager, 1901-50; won 9 pennants, 5 championships.
Bill Madlock, b. 1951: NL batting leader, 1975 and 1976.
Mickey Mantle, b. 1931: N.Y. Yankees outfielder; triple crown, 1956; 18 World Series home runs.
Alice Marble, b. 1913: U.S. singles champ 4 times.
Rocky Marciano, (1923-1969): heavyweight champion, 1952-56; retired undefeated.
Roger Maris, b. 1934: N.Y. Yankees outfielder hit record 61 home runs, 1961; MVP, 1960 and 1961.
Christy Mathewson, (1880-1925): N.Y. Giants pitcher won 373 games.
Bob Mathias, b. 1930: decathlon gold medalist, 1948, 1952 Olympics.
Willie Mays, b. 1931: N.Y.-S.F. Giants center fielder hit 660 home runs; twice MVP.
Bob McAdoo, b. 1951: leading NBA scorer, 1974-76; MVP, 1975.
John McGraw, (1873-1934): N.Y. Giants manager led team to 10 pennants, 3 championships.
Debbie Meyer, b. 1952: swimmer won 200-, 400-, and 800-meter freestyle events, 1968 Olympics.
George Mikan, b. 1924: Minneapolis Lakers center selected in a 1950 AP poll as the greatest basketball player of the first half of the 20th century.
Stan Mikita, b. 1940: Chicago Black Hawks center led NHL in scoring 4 times; MVP twice.
Archie Moore, b. 1913: world light-heavyweight champion, 1952-62
Howie Morenz, (1902-1937): Montreal Canadiens forward chosen in a 1950 Canadian press poll as the outstanding hockey player of the first half of the 20th century; MVP 3 times.
Joe Morgan, b. 1943: Cincinnati Reds 2d baseman; MVP, 1975, 1976.
Thurman Munson, b. 1947: N.Y. Yankees catcher; MVP, 1976.
Isaac Murphy, (1856-1896): jockey rode 3 Kentucky Derby winners.
Stan Musial, b. 1920: St. Louis Cardinals star won 7 NL batting titles; MVP 3 times; NL record 3,630 hits.
Bronco Nagurski, b. 1908: Chicago Bears fullback and tackle; gained over 4,000 yds. rushing.
Joe Namath, b. 1943: quarterback passed for record 4,007 yds., 1967.
Ilie Nastase, b. 1946: temperamental Romanian won U.S. singles title, 1972.
Byron Nelson, b. 1912: won 11 consecutive golf tournaments in 1945, ending the year with record 19 victories; twice Masters and PGA titlist.
Ernie Nevers, (1903-1976): Stanford star selected the best college fullback to play between 1919-1969, in a poll of the Football Writers Assn.; played pro football and baseball.
John Newcombe, b. 1943: Australian twice U.S. singles champ; Wimbledon titlist 3 times.
Jack Nicklaus, b. 1940: PGA Player-of-the-Year, 1967, 1972; leading money winner 7 times.
Paavo Nurmi, (1897-1973): Finnish distance runner won 6 Olympic gold medals, 1920, 1924, 1928.
Al Oerter, b. 1936: discus thrower won gold medal at 4 consecutive Olympics, 1956-68.
Barney Oldfield, (1878-1946): turn-of-the-century auto racer.
Bobby Orr, b. 1948: Boston Bruins defenseman; Norris Trophy 8 times; led NHL in scoring twice, assists 5 times.
Mel Ott, (1909-1958): N.Y. Giants outfielder hit 511 home runs; led NL 6 times.
Jesse Owens, b. 1913: track and field star won 4 1936 Olympic gold medals.
Alan Page, b. 1945: Minnesota Vikings lineman; NFL outstanding defensive player, 1973.
Satchel Paige, b. 1906: pitcher starred in Negro leagues, 1924-48; entered major leagues at age 42.
Arnold Palmer, b. 1929: golf's first $1 million winner; won 4 Masters, 2 British Opens.
Jim Palmer, b. 1945: Baltimore Orioles pitcher; Cy Young award 3 times; 20-game winner 6 times.
Floyd Patterson, b. 1935: heavyweight champion, 1956-59, 1960-62.
Pele, b. 1940: Brazilian soccer star has averaged nearly a goal a game during 18-year career.
Bob Pettit, b. 1932: Milwaukee-St. Louis Hawks forward was first NBA player to score 20,000 points; twice league scoring leader.
Richard Petty, b. 1937: NASCAR national champ 6 times; 5-times Daytona 500 winner.
Laffit Pincay Jr., b. 1946: leading money-winning jockey, 1970-74.
Jacques Plante, b. 1929: goalie, 7 Vezina trophies; first goalie to wear a mask in a game.
Gary Player, b. 1935: South African won the Masters, U.S. Open, PGA, and twice the British Open.
Annemarie Proell, b. 1953: Austrian skier won the World Cup championship 5 times.
Willis Reed, b. 1942: N.Y. Knicks center; MVP, 1970; playoff MVP, 1970, 1973.
Maurice Richard, b. 1924: Montreal Canadiens forward scored 544 regular season goals, 82 playoff goals.
Branch Rickey, (1881-1965): executive instrumental in breaking baseball's color barrier, 1947; initiated farm system, 1919.
Oscar Robertson, b. 1938: guard averaged career 25.7 points per game; record 9,887 career assists; MVP, 1964.
Brooks Robinson, b. 1937: Baltimore Orioles 3d baseman played in 4 World Series; MVP, 1964.
Frank Robinson, b. 1935: slugger, MVP in both NL and AL; triple crown winner, 1966; first black manager in majors.
Jackie Robinson, (1919-1972): broke baseball's color barrier with Brooklyn Dodgers, 1947; MVP, 1949.
Sugar Ray Robinson, b. 1920: middleweight champion 4 times, welterweight champion.

Knute Rockne, (1883-1931): Notre Dame football coach, 1918-31; revolutionized game by stressing forward pass.
Pete Rose, b. 1942: Cincinnati Reds star won 3 batting titles; led NL in hits 5 times.
Ken Rosewall, b. 1934: Australian twice U.S. singles champ.
Wilma Rudolph, b. 1940: sprinter won 3 1960 Olympic gold medals.
Bill Russell, b. 1934: Boston Celtics center led team to 11 NBA titles; MVP 5 times; first black coach of major pro sports team.
Babe Ruth, (1895-1948): N.Y. Yankees outfielder hit 60 home runs, 1927; 714 lifetime; led AL 11 times.
Nolan Ryan, b. 1947: Cal. Angels pitcher struck out record 383 batters, 1973; pitched 4 no-hitters.
Jim Ryun, b. 1947: runner set records for the mile and 1,500 meters, 1967.
Gene Sarazen, b. 1902: won PGA championship 3 times, U.S. Open twice; developer of sand wedge.
Gale Sayers, b. 1943: Chicago Bears back twice led NFC in rushing.
Mike Schmidt, b. 1949: Phillies 3d baseman led NL in home runs, 1974-76.
Bob Seagren, b. 1946: pole vaulter won 1968 Olympic gold medal.
Tom Seaver, b. 1944: NL pitcher won Cy Young award 3 times.
Willie Shoemaker, b. 1931: jockey rode 3 Kentucky Derby and 5 Belmont Stakes winners; leading career money winner.
Eddie Shore, b. 1902: Boston Bruins defenseman; MVP 4 times; first-team all-star 7 times.
Al Simmons, (1902-1956): AL outfielder had lifetime .334 batting average.
O.J. Simpson, b. 1947: Buffalo Bills back rushed for record 2,003 yds., 1973; record 273 yds. in a game, 1976; AFC leading rusher 4 times.
George Sisler, (1893-1973): St. Louis Browns 1st baseman had record 257 hits, 1920; batted .340 lifetime.
Sam Snead, b. 1912: PGA and Masters champ 3 times each.
Peter Snell, b. 1938: New Zealand runner won 800-meter race, 1960, 1964 Olympics.
Warren Spahn, b. 1921: Boston-Milwaukee Braves pitcher won 363 games; 20-game winner 13 times; Cy Young award, 1957.
Tris Speaker, (1888-1958): AL outfielder batted .344 over 22 seasons; hit record 793 career doubles.
Mark Spitz, b. 1950: swimmer won 7 1972 Olympic gold medals.
Amos Alonzo Stagg, (1862-1965): coached Univ. of Chicago football team for 41 years, including 5 undefeated seasons; introduced huddle, man-in-motion, and end-around play.
Bart Starr, b. 1934: Green Bay Packers quarterback led team to 5 NFL titles and 2 Super Bowl victories.
Roger Staubach, b. 1942: Navy-Dallas Cowboys quarterback; Heisman Trophy, 1963.
Casey Stengel, (1890-1975): managed Yankees to 10 pennants, 7 championships, 1949-60.
Jackie Stewart, b. 1939: Scot auto racer retired with record 27 Grand Prix victories.
Louise Suggs, b. 1923: U.S. Women's Open champ, 1949, 1952; LPGA titlist, 1957.
John L. Sullivan, (1858-1918): last bareknuckle heavyweight champion, 1882-1892.
Fran Tarkenton, b. 1940: quarterback holds career passing records for touchdowns, completions, yardage.
Gustave Thoeni, b. 1951: Italian 4-time world alpine ski champ.
Jim Thorpe, (1888-1953): football All-America, 1911, 1912; won pentathlon and decathlon, 1912 Olympics; played major league baseball for 6 seasons.
Bill Tilden, (1893-1953): U.S. singles champ 7 times; played on 11 Davis Cup teams.
Y.A. Tittle, b. 1926: N.Y. Giants quarterback; MVP, 1961, 1963.
Bill Toomey, b. 1939: decathlon gold medalist, 1968 Olympics.
Lee Trevino, b. 1939: won the U.S. and British Open championships twice.
Gene Tunney, b. 1897: heavyweight champion, 1926-28.
Wyomia Tyus, b. 1945: sprinter won 1964, 1968 Olympic 100-meter dash.
Johnny Unitas, b. 1933: Baltimore Colts quarterback passed for over 40,000 yds.; MVP, 1957, 1967.
Al Unser, b. 1939: Indy 500 winner, 1970, 1971.
Bobby Unser, b. 1934: Indy 500 winner, 1968, twice U.S. Auto Club national champ.
Norm Van Brocklin, b. 1926: quarterback passed for game record 554 yds., 1951; MVP, 1960.
Honus Wagner, (1874-1955): Pittsburgh Pirates shortstop won 8 NL batting titles.
Joe Walcott, b. 1914: heavyweight champion, 1951-52.
John Walker, b. 1952: New Zealander ran record mile, 3:49.4, Aug. 12, 1975.
Mickey Walker, b. 1901: colorful welter- and middleweight champion of the 20s and 30s.
Johnny Weissmuller, b. 1903: swimmer won 52 national championships, 3 Olympic gold medals; set 67 world records.
Jerry West, b. 1938: L.A. Lakers guard had career average 27 points per game; first team all-star 10 times.
Kathy Whitworth, b. 1939: women's golf leading money winner 4 times; first woman to earn over $300,000.
Ted Williams, b. 1918: Boston Red Sox outfielder won 6 batting titles; last major leaguer to hit over .400: .406 in 1941; .344 lifetime batting average.
Helen Wills, b. 1906: winner of 7 U.S., 8 British, 4 French women's singles titles.
John Wooden, b. 1910: coached UCLA basketball team to 8 national championships.
Mickey Wright, b. 1935: won LPGA championship 4 times, Vare Trophy 5 times; twice AP Woman-Athlete-of-the-Year.
Carl Yastrzemski, b. 1939: Boston Red Sox slugger won 3 batting titles, triple crown, 1967.
Cy Young, (1867-1955): pitcher won record 511 major league games.
Babe Didrikson Zaharias, (1914-1956): track star won 2 1932 Olympic gold medals; won numerous amateur and pro golf tournaments.
Emil Zatopek, b. 1922: Czech distance runner won 5,000- and 10,000-meter and marathon, 1952 Olympics.

AAU Trampoline and Tumbling Championships in 1977

Grandview, Mo., Apr. 8-9

Men

Trampoline — Ron Merriott, Rockford, Ill.
Double Mini-tramp — Ken Kovach, Cleveland, Oh.
Synchronized Trampoline — Bob Bollinger & Ron Merriott, Rockford, Ill.
Tumbling — Dickie Bivins, Newark, N.J.

Women

Trampoline — Shelly Grant, Springfield, Ill.
Double Mini-tramp — Diane Goldsworthy, Rockford, Ill.
Synchronized Trampoline — Leigh Hennessey & Barbara Jenkins, Lafayette, La.
Tumbling — Nancy Quattrochi, Chicago, Ill.

Speed Ice-Skating Championships, 1977

North American Outdoor Championships, Quebec, Canada: Men's Champion: Caeton Bouchure, Canada. Women's Champion: L. Toshack, Canada.

National Outdoor Championships, St. Paul, Minn., Men's Champion: Jim Chapin, St. Louis, Mo. Women's Champion: L. Crowe, St. Louis, Mo.

National Indoor Championships, St. Louis, Mo., Men's Champion: John Montrell, Chicago, Ill. Women's Champion: Celeste Chlapaty, Chicago, Ill.

Table Tennis Championships in 1977

47th U. S. National Open Championship

Hollywood, Cal., June 2-5, 1977

Men's Singles—Jochen Leiss, W. Germany.
Women's Singles—In Seek Bhushan, Columbus, Oh.
Men's Doubles—Jochen Leiss and Peter Stellwag, W. Germany.
Women's Doubles—Lee Eui Ja and Lee Ki Wen, S. Korea.
Mixed Doubles—Jochen Leiss and Judy Bochenski, Portland, Ore.
Men Under 21—Dennis Barish, Northridge, Cal.
Girls Under 17—Kasia Dawidewicz, Aurora, Col.

World Track and Field Records

As of July 6, 1977

*Indicates pending record; a number of new records await confirmation. The International Amateur Athletic Federation, the world body of track and field, announced July 27, 1976, a plan to overhaul the track and field record book. Eliminated are all records in yards except for the mile. Also eliminated are all hand-timed records for distances up to and including 400 meters. The records below meet the new standards except where noted. Records in yards and miles are included although they are no longer officially considered world records.

Men's Records

Running

Event	Record	Holder	Country	Date	Where made
100 yds.	**9.0 s.**	Ivory Crockett	U.S.	May 11, 1974	Knoxville, Tenn.
		Houston McTear	U.S.	May 9, 1975	Winter Park, Fla.
220 yds.	**19.5 s.**	Tommie Smith	U.S.	May 7, 1966	San Jose, Cal.
220 yds.	**19.9 s** (turn)	Don Quarrie	Jamaica	June 7, 1975	Eugene, Ore.
		Steve Williams	U.S.	June 7, 1975	Eugene, Ore.
440 yds.	**44.5 s.**	John Smith	U.S.	June 26, 1972	Eugene, Ore.
880 yds.	**1 m., 44.1 s.**	Rick Wohlhuter	U.S.	June 8, 1974	Eugene, Ore.
1 mile	**3 m., 49.4 s.**	John Walker	New Zealand	Aug. 12, 1975	Goteborg, Sweden
2 miles	**8 m., 13.8 s.**	Brendon Foster	Gr. Britain	Aug. 27, 1973	London
3 miles	**12 m., 47.8 s.**	Emiel Puttemans	Belgium	Sept. 20, 1972	Brussels
6 miles	**26 m., 47.0 s.**	Ron Clarke	Australia	July 14, 1965	Oslo
10 miles	**45 m., 57.2 s.**	Jos Hermens	Netherlands	Sept. 14, 1975	Netherlands
15 miles	**1 hr., 11 min., 52.6 s.**	Pekka Paivarinta	Finland	May 15, 1975	Oulu, Finland

Running — Metric Distances

Event	Record	Holder	Country	Date	Where made
100 meters	**9.96 s.**	Jim Hines	U.S.	Oct. 14, 1968	Mexico City
200 meters	**19.8 s** (turn)	Donald Quarrie	Jamaica	Aug. 3, 1971	Cali, Colombia
400 meters	**43.89 s.**	Lee Evans	U.S.	Oct. 18, 1968	Mexico City
800 meters	**1 m., 43.50 s.**	Alberto Juantorena	Cuba	July 25, 1976	Montreal
1,000 meters	**2 m., 13.9 s.**	Rick Wolhuter	U.S.	July 30, 1974	Oslo
1,500 meters	**3 m., 32.2 s.**	Filbert Bayi	Tanzania	Feb. 2, 1974	Chirstchurch, N.Z.
2,000 meters	**4 m., 51.4 s.**	John Walker	New Zealand	June 30, 1976	Oslo
3,000 meters	**7 m., 35.2 s.**	Brendon Foster	Gr. Britain	Aug. 3, 1974	Gateshead, Eng.
5,000 meters	***13 m., 12.84 s.**	Dick Quax	New Zealand	July 5, 1977	Stockholm
10,000 meters	**27 m., 30.8 s.**	Dave Bedford	Gr. Britain	July 13, 1973	London
20,000 meters	**57 m., 31.6 s.**	Jos Hermens	Netherlands	Sept. 28, 1975	Netherlands
25,000 meters	**1 hr., 14 m., 16.8 s.**	Pekka Paivarinta	Finland	May 15, 1975	Oulu, Finland
30,000 meters	**1 hr., 31 m., 30.4 s.**	Jim Adler	Gr. Britain	Sept. 5, 1970	London
3,000 meter stpl	**8 m., 08 s.**	Anders Garderud	Sweden	July 28, 1976	Montreal

Hurdles

Event	Record	Holder	Country	Date	Where made
120 yards	**13.0 s.**	Rod Milburn	U.S.	June 25, 1971	Eugene, Ore.
		Rod Milburn	U.S.	June 20, 1973	Eugene, Ore.
		Guy Drut	France	Aug. 22, 1975	Berlin, W. Ger.
220 yards	**21.9 s.**	Don Styron	U.S.	Apr. 2, 1960	Baton Rouge
440 yards	**48.7 s.**	Jim Bolding	U.S.	July 24, 1974	Turin, Italy
110 meters	**13.2 s.**	Rod Milburn	U.S.	Sept. 7, 1972	Munich
200 meters	**21.9 s. (not ET)**	Don Styron	U.S.	Apr. 2, 1960	Baton Rouge
200 meters	**22.5 s. (not ET)** (turn)	Martin Lauer	W. Germany	July 7, 1959	Zurich
	(not ET)	Glen Davis	U.S.	Aug. 20, 1960	Bern
400 meters	***47.45 s.**	Edwin Moses	U.S.	June 11, 1977	Los Angeles

Relay Races

Event	Record	Holder	Country	Date	Where made
440 yds. (4x110) (2 turns)	**38.6 s.**	USC (McCullough, Kuller, Simpson, Miller)	U.S.	June 17, 1967	Provo, Utah
830 yds. (4x220)	**1 m., 21.7 s.**	Texas A&M (Rogers, Woods, M. Mills, C. Mills)	U.S.	Apr. 24, 1970	Des Moines
1 mile (4x440)	**3 m., 02.4 s.**	National Team (Ray, Taylor, Peoples, Vinson)	U.S.	July 18, 1975	Durham, N.C.
2 miles (4x880)	**7 m., 10.4 s.**	Chicago TC (Bach, Sparks, Paul, Wohlhuter)	U.S.	May 12, 1973	Durham, N.C.
4 miles (4x1) (mile)	**16 m., 02.8 s.**	Nat'l. Team (Ross, Polhill, Tayler, Quax)	New Zealand	Feb. 3, 1972	Auckland, N.Z.

Relay Races — Metric Distances

Event	Record	Holder	Country	Date	Where made
400 mtrs.	**38.2 s.**	Nat'l. Team (Black, Taylor, Tinker, Hart)	U.S.	Sept. 10, 1972	Munich
800 mtrs. (4x200)	***1 m., 21.4 s.**	Arizona State	U.S.	Apr. 30, 1977	Philadelphia
1,600 mtrs. (4x400)	**2 m., 56.1 s.**	Nat'l. Team (Matthews, Freeman, James, Evans)	U.S.	Oct. 20, 1968	Mexico City
3,200 mtrs. (4x800)	**7 m., 08.6 s.**	Nat'l. Team (Kinder, Adams, Bogatzki, Kemper)	W. Germany	Aug. 13, 1966	Wiesbaden

Field Events

Event	Record	Holder	Country	Date	Where made
High jump	*7 ft., 7 3/4 in.	Vladimir Yashchenko	USSR	July 3, 1977	Richmond, Va.
Long jump	29 ft., 2 1/2 in.	Bob Beamon	U.S.	Oct. 18, 1968	Mexico City
Triple jump	58 ft., 8 1/2 in.	Joao de Oliveira	Brazil	Oct. 15, 1975	Mexico City
Pole vault	18 ft., 8 1/4 in.	Dave Roberts	U.S.	June 22, 1976	Eugene, Ore.
16 lb. shot put	72 ft., 2 1/4 in.	Alexander Baryshnikov	USSR	July 10, 1976	Paris
Discus throw	232 ft., 6 in.	Mac Wilkins	U.S.	May 1, 1976	San Jose, Cal.
Javelin throw	310 ft., 4 in.	Miklos Nemeth	Hungary	July 26, 1976	Montreal
16 lb. hammer throw	260 ft., 2 in.	Walter Schmidt	W. Germany	Aug. 14, 1975	Frankfurt
Decathlon	8,618 pts.	Bruce Jenner	U.S.	July 29-30, 1976	Montreal

Walking

Event	Record	Holder	Country	Date	Where made
20 miles	2 h., 27 m., 38.0 s.	Vittorio Visini	Italy	Nov. 1, 1975	Vicenza, Italy
30 miles	3 h., 48 m., 23.4 s.	Bernd Kannenberg	W. Germany	Nov. 16, 1975	Milan
2 hours	16 mi., 1,270 yds.	Bernd Kannenberg	W. Germany	May 11, 1974	Kassel, W. Germany
30 km	2 h., 12 m., 58.0 s.	Bernd Kannenberg	W. Germany	May 11, 1974	Kassel, W. Germany
50 km	3 hr., 56 m., 51.4 s.	Bernd Kannenberg	W. Germany	Nov. 16, 1975	Milan

Women's Records

Running

Event	Record	Holder	Country	Date	Where made
100 yards	10.0 s.	Chi Cheng	Taiwan	June 13, 1970	Portland, Ore.
220 yards	22.6 s.	Chi Cheng	Taiwan	July 3, 1970	Los Angeles
440 yards	52.2 s.	Kathy Hammond	U.S.	Aug. 12, 1972	Urbana, Ill.
		Debra Sapenter	U.S.	June 29, 1974	Bakersfield, Cal.
880 yards	2 m., 02.0 s.	Judy Pollock	Australia	July 5, 1967	Sweden
		Dixie Willis	Australia	Mar. 3, 1962	Perth, Australia
1 mile	4 m., 29.5 s.	Paolo Cacchi-Pigni	Italy	Aug. 8, 1973	Viareggio, Italy
100 meters	11.01	Annegret Richter	E. Germany	July 25, 1976	Montreal
200 meters	22.2 s.	Irena Szewinska	Poland	June 13, 1974	Potsdam
400 meters	49.29 s.	Irena Szewinska	Poland	July 29, 1976	Montreal
800 meters	1 m., 54.9 s.	Tatyana Kazankina	USSR	July 26, 1976	Montreal
500 meters	3 m., 56 s.	Tatyana Kazankina	USSR	June 28, 1976	USSR
3000 meters	*8 m., 27.1 s.	Ludmila Bragina	USSR	Aug. 7, 1976	College Park, Md.

Hurdles

Event	Record	Holder	Country	Date	Where made
100 meters	12.6 s.	Annelie Ehrhardt	E. Germany	Sept. 8, 1972	Munich
400 meters	56.5 s.	Krystyna Kasperczik	Poland	June 13, 1974	W. Germany

Field Events

Event	Record	Holder	Country	Date	Where made
High jump	6 ft., 5 1/4 in.	Rosemarie Ackermann	E. Germany	May 8, 1976	Dresden
Shot put	72 ft., 2 in.	Helena Fibigerova	Czech.	Sept. 26, 1976	Opova, Czech.
Long jump	22 ft., 11 1/4 in.	Sigrun Siegl	E. Germany	May 19, 1976	Dresden
Discus throw	231 ft., 3 in.	Faina Melnik	USSR	Apr. 24, 1976	USSR
Javelin	226 ft., 9 1/4 in.	Ruth Fuchs	E. Germany	July 10, 1976	Paris
Pentathlon	4,932 pts.	Burglinde Pollak	E. Germany	Sept 22, 1973	Bonn

Relay Races

Event	Record	Holder	Country	Date	Where made
400 mtrs. (4x100)	42.5 s.	National Team	E. Germany	Sept. 8, 1974	Rome
800 mtrs. (4x200)	1 m., 33.8 s.	Nat'l. Team (Tranter, James, Simpson, Peal)	Gt. Britain	Aug. 24, 1968	London
880 yds. (4x220)	1 m., 35.8 s.	(Hoffman, Boyle, Kilborn, Lamy)	Australia	Nov. 9, 1969	Brisbane, Australia
1,600 mtrs. (4x400)	3 m., 19.2 s.	National Team	E. Germany	July 31, 1976	Montreal
1 mile (4x440)	3 m., 30.3 s.	National Team (Krause, Jost, Weinstein, Barth)	W. Germany	July 19, 1975	Durham, N.C.

Evolution of the World Record for the One-Mile Run

The table below shows how the world record for the one-mile has been lowered in the past 113 years.

Year	Individual	Time	Year	Individual	Time
1864	Charles Lawes, Britain	4:56	1934	Glenn Cunningham, U.S.	4:06.8
1865	Richard Webster, Britain	4:36.5	1937	Sydney Wooderson, Britain	4:06.4
1868	William Chinnery, Britain	4:29	1942	Gunder Haegg, Sweden	4:06.2
1868	W. C. Gibbs, Britain	4:28.8	1942	Arne Andersson, Sweden	4:06.2
1874	Walter Slade, Britain	4:26	1942	Gunder Haegg, Sweden	4:04.6
1875	Walter Slade, Britain	4:24.5	1943	Arne Andersson, Sweden	4:02.6
1880	Walter George, Britain	4:23.2	1944	Arne Andersson, Sweden	4:01.6
1882	Walter George, Britain	4:21.4	1945	Gunder Haegg, Sweden	4:01.4
1882	Walter George, Britain	4:19.4	1954	Roger Bannister, Britain	3:59.4
1884	Walter George, Britain	4:18.4	1954	John Landy, Australia	3:58
1894	Fred Bacon, Scotland	4:18.2	1957	Derek Ibbotson, Britain	3:57.2
1895	Fred Bacon, Scotland	4:17	1958	Herb Elliott, Australia	3:54.5
1895	Thomas Conneff, U.S.	4:15.6	1962	Peter Snell, New Zealand	3:54.4
1911	John Paul Jones, U.S.	4:15.4	1964	Peter Snell, New Zealand	3:54.1
1913	John Paul Jones, U.S.	4:14.6	1965	Michel Jazy, France	3:53.6
1915	Norman Taber, U.S.	4:12.6	1966	Jim Ryun, U.S.	3:51.3
1923	Paavo Nurmi, Finland	4:10.4	1967	Jim Ryun, U.S.	3:51.1
1931	Jules Ladoumegue, France	4:09.2	1975	Filbert Bayi, Tanzania	3:51
1933	Jack Lovelock, New Zealand	4:07.6	1975	John Walker, New Zealand	3:49.4

Track and Field Events in 1977

70th Annual Millrose Games

New York, N. Y., Jan. 29, 1977

Men

60 Yds.—Steve Riddick, Philadelphia Pioneer Club. **Time—0:06.**
60-Yd. High Hurdles—Willie Davenport, Baton Rouge TC. **Time—0:07.**
500 Yds.—(tie) Stan Vinson, D. C. Striders and Richard Massey, Howard Univ. **Time—0:56.6.**
600 Yds.—Kevin Price, Adelphi. **Time—1:10.8.**
880 Yds.—Mark Belger, Villanova. **Time—1:50.**
1,000 Yds.—Don Paige, Villanova. **Time—2:09.6.**
One Mile—Eamonn Coghlan, Ireland. **Time—4:00.2.**
2 Miles—Tony Staynings, Western Kentucky. **Time—8:41.4.**
Pole Vault—Earl Bell, Arkansas State. **18 ft. 1/2 in.**
High Jump—Dwight Stones, Desert Oasis TC. **7 ft. 4 1/2 in.**

Women

60 Yds.—Frieda Davy, D. C. Striders. **Time—0:06.7.**
440 Yds.—Rosalyn Bryant, L. A. Mercurettes. **Time—0:53.3.**
880 Yds.—Lorna Ford, Atoms TC. **Time—2:06.5.**
1,500 Meters—Francie Larrieu Lutz, Pacific Coast Club. **Time—4:15.8.**
High Jump—Paula Girvan, Washington, D. C. **5 ft. 10 in.**

9th Annual U. S. Olympic Invitational

New York, N.Y., Feb. 12, 1977

Men

50 Meters—Harvey Glance, Auburn. **Time—0:05.7.**
55-Meter Hurdles—James Walker, Auburn. **Time—0:07.2.**
400 Meters—Kevin Price, Adelphi. **Time—0:48.3.**
500 Meters—Edwin Moses, Morehouse. **Time—1:02.7.**
800 Meters—Mark Belger, Villanova. **Time—1:49.3.**
1,000 Meters—Steve Lacy, Wisconsin. **Time—2:23.9.**
1,500 Meters—John Walker, New Zealand. **Time—3:40.2.**
3,000 Meters—Rod Dixon. **Time—8:05.4.**
1,500-Meter Walk—Todd Scully, Shore AC. **Time—5:48.6**
Pole Vault—Mike Tully, UCLA. **18 ft. 1 1/2 in.**
High Jump—Dwight Stones, Oasis TC. **7 ft. 2 3/4 in.**
Shot Put—Tom Andersson, Maryland. **58 ft. 4 1/4 in.**
35-Lb. Weight Throw—Wayne Durrigan, So.Conn. **64 ft. 1 1/4 in.**

Women

50 Meters—Jeanette Bolden, L.A. Mercurettes. **Time—0:06.2.**
400 Meters—Rosalyn Bryant, L.A. Mercurettes. **Time—0:55.3.**
800 Meters—Robin Campbell, Florida TC. **Time—2:07.4.**
1,500 Meters—Cyndy Poor, Athletes in Action. **Time—4:22.1.**

Toronto Star-Maple Leaf Indoor Games

Toronto, Ont., March 4, 1977

Men

50 Yds.—Steve Riddick, Philadelphia, Pa. **Time—0:05.2**
50-Yd. High Hurdles—Larry Shipp, Baton Rouge, La. **Time—0:05.9.**
440 Yds.—Kevin Price, St. Albans, N.Y. **Time—0:48.8.**
One Mile—Paul Cummings, Phoenix, Ariz. **Time—4:04.1.**
3 Miles—Miruts Yifter, Ethiopia. **Time—13:09.6.**
Triple Jump—Tommy Haynes, Newburgh, N.Y. **55 ft. 3 in.**
Pole Vault—Mike Tully, Westwood, Cal. **18 ft. 1/2 in.**
Pentathlon—Nikolay Avilov, USSR. **4,190 pts.**

Women

50 Yds.—Jeanette Bolden, Los Angeles, Cal. **Time—0:05.8.**
600 Yds.—Robin Campbell, Gainesville, Fla. **Time—1:21.**
2 Miles—Francie Larrieu Lutz, Long Beach, Cal. **Time—9:59.6.**
Shot Put—Nedezhda Chizhova, USSR. **62 ft. 5 3/4 in.**
Long Jump—Diane Jones, Canada. **20 ft. 9 1/4 in.**
High Jump—Debbie Brill, Canada. **6 ft. 1 1/4 in.**

13th Annual NCAA Indoor Track and Field Championships

Detroit, Mich., Mar. 12, 1977. Sponsored by the Detroit News

60 Yds.—Greg Edmond, Houston. **Time—0:06.12.**
60-Yd. High Hurdles—Jeff Lee, Nebraska. **Time—0:07.17.**
440 Yds.—Willie Smith, Auburn. **Time—0:48.28.**
600 Yds.—Mike Solomon, New Mexico. **Time—1:10.01.**
880 Yds.—Mark Belger, Villanova. **Time—1:49.17.**
1,000 Yds.—Kelley Marsh, Ball State. **Time—2:07.89.**
One Mile—Wilson Waigwa, Texas-El Paso. **Time—3:58.97.**
2 Miles—Henry Rono, Washington State. **Time—8:24.83.**
3 Miles—Luis Hernandez, Brigham Young. **Time—13:20.55.**
Long Jump—Charlton Ehizuelen, Illinois. **25 ft. 8 3/4 in.**
Shot Put—Gary England, Alabama, **63 ft. 3/4 in.**
Triple Jump—Ian Campbell, Washington State. **54 ft. 3 in.**
35-Lb. Weight Throw—Scott Neilson, Univ. of Washington. **68 ft. 10 1/2 in.**
Pole Vault—Don Baird, Long Beach State. **17 ft. 4 in.**
High Jump—Greg Joy, Texas-El Paso. **7 ft. 3 1/4 in.**
Team Champion—Washington State.

National AAU Outdoor Track and Field Championships

Los Angeles, Cal., June 9-11, 1977

Men

100 Meters—Don Quarrie, Tobias Striders. **Time—0:10.12.**
200 Meters—Derald Harris, Los Medanos College. **Time—0:20.6.**
400 Meters—Robert Taylor, Philadelphia Pioneers. **Time—0:45.44.**
800 Meters—Mark Belger, Philadelphia Pioneers. **Time—1:45.81.**
1,500 Meters—Steve Scott, unattached. **Time—3:37.29.**
3,000-Meter Steeplechase—James Munyala, Philadelphia Pioneers. **Time—8:21.59.**
5,000 Meters—Marty Liquori, Florida AA. **Time—13:41.58.**
10,000 Meters—Frank Shorter, Colorado TC. **Time—28:19.76.**
110-Meter Hurdles—(tie) James Owens, unattached and Charles Foster, Philadelphia Pioneers. **Time—0:13.49.**
400-Meter Hurdles—Edwin Moses, Atlanta Pioneers. **Time—0:47.45.**
5,000-Meter Walk—Todd Scully, Shore AC. **Time—21:30.14.**
High Jump—Dwight Stones, Desert Oasis TC. **7 ft. 6 1/4 in.**
Pole Vault—Mike Tully, unattached. **18 ft. 2 in.**
Long Jump—Arnie Robinson, Maccabi Union TC. **27 ft. 1/2 in.**
Triple Jump—Milan Tiff, Tobias Striders. **57 ft. 1/4 in.**
Shot Put—Terry Albritton, unattached. **67 ft. 3 1/4 in.**
Discus—Mac Wilkins, unattached. **227 ft.**
Hammer—Emmitt Berry, Maccabi Union TC. **222 ft. 7 in.**
Javelin—Bruce Kennedy, San Jose State. **262 ft. 3 in.**

Women

100 Meters—Evelyn Ashford, Maccabi Union TC. **Time—0:11.14.**
200 Meters—Evelyn Ashford. **Time—0:22.62.**
400 Meters—Sharon Dabney, Clippers TC. **Time—0:51.55.**
800 Meters—Sue Latter, Michigan State Univ. **Time—2:03.75.**
1,500 Meters—Francie Larrieu Lutz, unattached. **Time—4:08.2.**
3,000 Meters—Jan Merrill, Age Group AA. **Time—9:00.19.**
10,000 Meters—Peg Neppel, Iowa State Univ. **Time—33:15.09.**
100-Meter Hurdles—Patty Van Wolvelaere, L.A. Naturite TC. **Time—0:13.15.**
400-Meter Hurdles—Mary Ayers, Prairie View A&M. **Time—0:56.61.**
5,000-Meter Walk—Sue Brodock, Rialto Roadrunners. **Time—24:10.1.**
High Jump—Joni Huntley, unattached. **6 ft. 1 in.**
Long Jump—Jodi Anderson, L. A. Naturite TC. **21 ft. 9 1/4 in.**
Shot Put—Maren Seidler, Mayor Daley YF. **54 ft. 1 1/4 in.**
Discus—Jane Haist, Canada. **193 ft. 6 in.**
Javelin—Kate Schmidt, unattached. **200 ft. 7 in.**

National AAU Indoor Track and Field Championships

New York, N.Y., Feb. 25, 1977

Men

60 Yds.—Steve Riddick, Philadelphia Pioneers. **Time—0:06.1.**
600 Yds.—Fred Sowerby, D.C. Striders. **Time—1:09.8.**
1,000 Yds.—Mike Boit, Kenya. **Time—2:06.9.**
One Mile—Filbert Bayi, Tanzania. **Time—3:59.3.**
3 Miles—Suleiman Nyambui, Tanzania. **Time—13:12.9.**
60-Yd. Hurdles—Larry Shipp, unattached. **Time—0:07.0.**
2-Mile Walk—Todd Scully, Shore AC. **Time—13:02.5.**
High Jump—Paul Underwood, Todias Striders. **7 ft. 2 in.**
Pole Vault—Larry Jessee, Maccabi Union TC. **17 ft. 9 in.**
Long Jump—Tommy Haynes, N.Y. Pioneers. **26 ft. 1/4 in.**
Triple Jump—Tommy Haynes, N.Y. **55 ft. 2 3/4 in.**
Shot Put—Mac Wilkins, unattached. **69 ft. 1 1/4 in.**
35-Lb. Weight Throw—George Frenn, Maccabi Union TC. **69 ft. 2 1/2 in.**
Team Champion—Maccabi Union TC.

Women

60 Yds.—Brenda Morehead, Tennessee State. **Time—0:06.6.**
220 Yds.—Rosalyn Bryant, L.A. Mercurettes. **Time—0:23.4.**
440 Yds.—Lorna Forde, Atoms TC. **Time—0:53.6.**
880 Yds.—Cyndy Poor, Athletes in Action. **Time—2:06.7.**
One Mile—Francie Larrieu Lutz, unattached. **Time—4:43.1.**
2 Miles—Francie Larrieu Lutz. **Time—9:58.2.**
60-Yd. Hurdles—Jane Frederick, Los Angeles TC. **Time—0:07.3.**
One-Mile Walk—Susan Brodock, Rialto Road Runners. **Time—7:05.9.**
High Jump—Joni Huntley, unattached. **6 ft.**
Long Jump—Kathy McMillan, Tennessee State. **21 ft. 4 1/4 in.**
Shot Put—Maren Seidler, Mayor Daley Youth Foundation. **52 ft. 3 3/4 in.**
Team Champion—Los Angeles Mercurettes.

National Interscholastic Outdoor Track and Field Records

Source: National Federation of State High School Associations. Records approved to June, 1977.

Event	Record	Holder	School	Site, year
100 yds	**0:09.0**	Houston McTear	Baker H.S., Baker, Fla.	Winter Park, Fla., 1976
220 yds. (full curve)	**0:20.5**	Dwayne E. Evans	So. Mountain H.S., Phoenix, Ariz.	Glendale, Ariz., 1976
440 yds	**0:45.8**	Ronald E. Ray	Ferguson H.S., Newport News, Va.	Charlottesville, Va., 1972
880 yds	**1:48.8**	Richard J. Joyce	Sierra H.S., Whittier, Cal.	Bakersfield, Cal., 1965
1 mile	**3:58.3**	James Ryun	Wichita East H.S., Wichita, Kan.	Wichita, Kan., 1965
2 mile	**8:41.5**	Steve Prefontaine	Marshfield H.S., Coos Bay, Ore.	Corvallis, Ore., 1969
120 yd. high hurdles	**0:13.2**	Michael Robertson	Winter Pk. H.S., Winter Pk., Fla.	Winter Pk., Fla., 1975
		Dedy Cooper	Ells H.S., Richmond, Cal.	San Diego, Cal., 1975
		Gregory Foster	Proviso E. H.S., Maywood, Ill.	Charleston, Ill., 1976
180-yd. low hurdles	**0:18.1**	Donald Castronovo	Oceanside H.S., Oceanside, N.Y.	Ithaca, N.Y., 1964
		Earl McCullouch	Polytechnic H.S., Long Beach, Cal.	Norwalk, Cal., 1964
High jump	**7 ft. 3 1/4 in.**	Gail Olson	Sycamore H.S., Sycamore, Ill.	Charleston, Ill., 1977
Long jump	**25 ft. 9 1/2 in.**	Gerald Hardeman	Edison H.S., Fresno, Cal.	Porterville, Cal., 1972
Pole vault	**16 ft. 10 in.**	Randy Hall	Calhoun H.S., Pt. Lavaca, Tex.	Klein, Tex., 1977
		Robert Pullard	Los Angeles H.S.	Los Angeles, Cal., 1969
Triple jump	**52 ft. 6 1/4 in.**	David Tucker	San Joaquin Mem. H.S., Fresno, Cal.	Bakersfield, Cal., 1970
Shot put (12 lbs.)	**72 ft. 3 1/4 in.**	Sam Walker	W. W. Samuell H.S., Dallas, Tex.	Corpus Christi, Tex., 1968
Discus	**201 ft. 3 in.**	Christopher James Adams	Los Altos H.S., Los Altos, Cal.	Berkeley, Cal., 1970
Javelin	**254 ft. 11 in.**	Russell Francis	Pleasant Hill H.S., Pleasant Hill, Ore.	Pleasant Hill, Ore., 1971
440-yd. relay	**0:40.2**	Delley, G. Pouncy, J. Pouncy, Shaw	Lincoln H.S., Dallas, Tex.	Austin, Tex., 1970
880-yd. relay	**1:25.4**	Jackson, James, Reed, Hill	White Plains (N.Y.) H.S.	Jamaica, N.Y., 1966
1 mile relay	**3:11.8**	Bouche, Bradley, Brents, Morton	Memorial H.S., Houston, Tex.	Baytown, Tex., 1967
		Anderson, Black, Thompkins, Thompson	Killian H.S., Miami, Fla.	Gainesville, Fla., 1969
2 mile relay	**7:41.9**	Mentz, Jakosa, Bowman, Grant	Proviso West H.S., Hillside, Ill.	Glen Ellyn, Ill., 1965
Sprint medley relay (1 mile)	**3:23.3**	Corson, Brake, Brents, Morton	Memorial H.S., Houston, Tex.	Houston, Tex., 1967

National AAU Weightlifting Championships in 1977

Culver City, Cal., June 11-12, 1977
(Note: weights are in kilograms; one kilogram=2.2 lbs.)

52 kg.—Curt White, Charleston WLC. **187.5 kg.**
56 kg.—Patrick Omori, Nuuanu YMCA. **210 kg.**
60 kg.—Phil Sanderson, unattached. **245 kg.**
67.5 kg.—James Benjamin, Central Ohio. **255 kg.**
75 kg.—David Reigle, York BBC. **290 kg.**
82.5 kg.—Robert Napier, Spoon BBC. **322.5 kg.**
90 kg.—Phil Grippaldi, York BBC. **337.5 kg.**
100 kg.—Mark Cameron, York BBC. **340 kg.**
110 kg.—Ray Blaha, Olympic HC. **337.5 kg.**
Super Heavyweight—Sam Walker, Spoon BBC. **352.5 kg.**

Figure Skating Champions

National Champions

Men	Women	Year
Richard Button	Sonya Klopfer	1951
Richard Button	Tenley Albright	1952
Hayes Jenkins	Tenley Albright	1953
Hayes Jenkins	Tenley Albright	1954
Hayes Jenkins	Tenley Albright	1955
Hayes Jenkins	Tenley Albright	1956
Dave Jenkins	Carol Heiss	1957
Dave Jenkins	Carol Heiss	1958
Dave Jenkins	Carol Heiss	1959
Dave Jenkins	Carol Heiss	1960
Bradley Lord	Laurence Owen	1961
Monty Hoyt	Barbara Roles Pursley	1962
Tommy Litz	Lorraine Hanlon	1963
Scott Allen	Peggy Fleming	1964
Gary Visconti	Peggy Fleming	1965
Scott Allen	Peggy Fleming	1966
Gary Visconti	Peggy Fleming	1967
Tim Wood	Peggy Fleming	1968
Tim Wood	Janet Lynn	1969
Tim Wood	Janet Lynn	1970
John Misha Petkevich	Janet Lynn	1971
Ken Shelley	Janet Lynn	1972
Gordon McKellen Jr.	Janet Lynn	1973
Gordon McKellen Jr.	Dorothy Hamill	1974
Gordon McKellen Jr.	Dorothy Hamill	1975
Terry Kubicka	Dorothy Hamill	1976
Charley Tickner	Linda Fratianne	1977

World Champions

Men	Women
Richard Button, U.S.	Jeannette Altwegg, Gt. Britain
Richard Button, U.S.	Jacqueline du Bief, France
Hayes Jenkins, U.S.	Tenley Albright, U.S.
Hayes Jenkins, U.S.	Gundi Busch, W. Germany
Hayes Jenkins, U.S.	Tenley Albright, U.S.
Hayes Jenkins, U.S.	Carol Heiss, U.S.
Dave Jenkins, U.S.	Carol Heiss, U.S.
Dave Jenkins, U.S.	Carol Heiss, U.S.
Dave Jenkins, U.S.	Carol Heiss, U.S.
Alain Giletti, France	Carol Heiss, U.S.
none	none
Don Jackson, Canada	Sjoukje Dijkstra, Neth.
Don McPherson, Canada	Sjoukje Dijkstra, Neth.
Manfred Schnelldorfer, W. Germany	Sjoukie Dijkstra, Neth.
Alain Calmat, France	Petra Burka, Canada
Emmerich Danzer, Austria	Peggy Fleming, U.S.
Emmerich Danzer, Austria	Peggy Fleming, U.S.
Emmerich Danzer, Austria	Peggy Fleming, U.S.
Tim Wood, U.S.	Gabriele Seyfert, E. Germany
Tim Wood, U.S.	Gabriele Seyfert, E. Germany
Ondrej Nepela, Czech.	Beatrix Schuba, Austria
Ondrej Nepela, Czech.	Beatrix Schuba, Austria
Ondrej Nepela, Czech.	Karen Magnussen, Canada
Jan Hoffman, E. Germany	Christine Errath, E. Germany
Sergei Volkov, USSR	Dianne de Leeuw, Neth.-U.S.
John Curry, Gt. Britain	Dorothy Hamill, U.S.
Vladimir Kovalev, USSR	Linda Fratianne, U.S.

Canadian National Figure Skating Champions

Year	Men	Women
1960	Donald Jackson	Wendy Griner
1961	Donald Jackson	Wendy Griner
1962	Donald Jackson	Wendy Griner
1963	Donald McPherson	Wendy Griner
1964	Charles Snelling	Petra Burka
1965	Donald Knight	Petra Burka
1966	Donald Knight	Petra Burka
1967	Donald Knight	Valerie Jones
1968	Jay Humphrey	Karen Magnussen
1969	Jay Humphrey	Linda Carbonetto
1970	David McGillivray	Karen Magnussen
1971	Toller Cranston	Karen Magnussen
1972	Toller Cranston	Karen Magnussen
1973	Toller Cranston	Karen Magnussen
1974	Toller Cranston	Lynn Nightingale
1975	Toller Cranston	Lynn Nightingale
1976	Toller Cranston	Lynn Nightingale
1977	Ron Shaver	Lynn Nightingale

Lacrosse Championships in 1977

Source: Jack Kelly, U.S. Lacrosse Information

NCAA University Champions—Cornell Univ.
NCAA College Champions—Hobart College
U.S. Intercollegiate Lacrosse Association Champions—Cornell Univ.
U.S. Club Lacrosse Champions—Mt. Washington of Baltimore
Atlantic Coast Conference Champion—Univ. of Maryland
Ivy League Champion—Cornell Univ.
New England Intercollegiate Champion—Univ. of Mass.
Independent College (N.Y.) League Champion—Hobart
Middle Atlantic League Champion—Franklin & Marshall
East Coast League Champion—Univ. of Delaware
South Atlantic League Champion—Washington & Lee Univ.
Mason-Dixon League Champion—UMBC, Towson (tie)
Midwest League Champion—Ohio Wesleyan
Upstate New York League—SUNY-Brockport
Snivley League—Middlebury
Colonial League—Massachusetts Maritime
Knickerbocker League—Dowling (L.I.)
U.S. Junior College Champions—Farmingdale (N.Y.)

NCAA University Championship

At Charlottesville, Va., May 28—Cornell 16, Johns Hopkins 8.

Semi-finals

Cornell 22, Navy 6; Johns Hopkins 22, Maryland 12.

Quarter-finals

Cornell 17, Massachusetts 13; Navy 14, Pennsylvania 12; Maryland 14, Washington & Lee 8; Johns Hopkins 16, North Carolina 9.

NCAA College Championship

At Geneva, N.Y., May 22 — Hobart 23, Washington College 13.

All-Star College Game

At Baltimore, Md., June 9 — North 20, South 15.

Junior College Championship

At Arnold, Md., May 15 — Farmingdale (N.Y.) 11, Nassau C.C. 8.

United States Club Lacrosse Champion

At Baltimore, Md., June 18 — Mt. Washington 12, Long Island A.C. 5.

Lacrosse Coach of the Year

University — Richie Moran, Cornell. College — Jerry Schmidt, Hobart. Junior College — Fred Acee, Farmingdale.

USILA University All America Team in 1977

Goalie: Dan Mackesey, Cornell.
Defense: Tom Keigler, W & L; Don DelGiorno, Penn.; Chris Kane, Cornell.
Midfield: Mike Page, Penn.; Craig Jaeger, Cornell; Bob Henrickson, Cornell; Dave Huntley, Hopkins.
Attack: Eamon McEneaney, Cornell; Mike O'Neill, Hopkins; Jeff Long, Navy; Peter Hollis, Penn.
Note—4 midfield players selected for the three midfield positions, and 4 attack players selected for the 3 attack positions.

USILA College All America Team in 1977

Goalie: Rick Blick, Hobart.
Defense: John Pirro, Roanoke; Gary Clipp, UMBC; Tom Schardt, Hobart.
Midfield: Dave McNaney, Hobart; G.P. Lindsay, Washington; Rick Wey, UMBC.
Attack: John Cheek, Washington; Dave Cottle, Salisbury; Treey Corcoran, Hobart.

USILA University Top Ten Teams in 1977

Rank	University	Rank	University
1	Cornell	6	Navy
2	Johns Hopkins	7	North Carolina
3	Maryland	8	Massachusetts
4	Pennsylvania	9	Army
5	Washington & Lee	10	Virginia

USILA College Division Top Ten Teams in 1977

Rank	College	Rank	College
1	Hobart	6	Cortland State(N.Y.)
2	Washington	7	Towson State(Md.)
3	UMBC	8	Salisbury State(Md.)
4	Roanoke	9	Baltimore
5	Adelphi	10	Ohio Wesleyan

National Hockey League, 1976-77

Final Standings

Clarence Campbell Conference

Lester Patrick Division

Club	W	L	T	Pts	GF	GA
Philadelphia	48	16	16	112	323	213
N.Y. Islanders	47	21	12	106	288	193
Atlanta	34	34	12	80	264	265
N.Y. Rangers	29	37	14	72	272	310

Conn Smythe Division

Club	W	L	T	Pts	GF	GA
St. Louis	32	39	9	73	239	276
Minnesota	23	39	18	64	240	310
Chicago	26	43	11	63	240	298
Vancouver	25	42	13	63	235	294
Colorado	20	46	14	54	226	307

Prince of Wales Conference

Charles F. Adams Division

Club	W	L	T	Pts	GF	GA
Boston	49	23	8	106	312	240
Buffalo	48	24	8	104	301	220
Toronto	33	32	15	81	301	285
Cleveland	25	42	13	63	240	292

James Norris Division

Club	W	L	T	Pts	GF	GA
Montreal	60	8	12	132	387	171
Los Angeles	34	31	15	83	271	241
Pittsburgh	34	33	13	81	240	252
Washington	24	42	14	62	221	307
Detroit	16	55	9	41	183	309

Stanley Cup Playoff Results

N.Y. Islanders defeated Chicago 2 games to 0.
Toronto defeated Pittsburgh 2 games to 1.
Los Angeles defeated Atlanta 2 games to 1.
Buffalo defeated Minnesota 2 games to 0.
N.Y. Islanders defeated Buffalo 4 games to 0.
Philadelphia defeated Toronto 4 games to 2.
Montreal defeated St. Louis 4 games to 0.
Boston defeated Los Angeles 4 games to 2.
Boston defeated Philadelphia 4 games to 0.
Montreal defeated N.Y. Islanders 4 games to 2.
Montreal defeated Boston 4 games to 0.

Leading Scorers

Player, club	G	Goals	Asts	Pts
Lafleur, Montreal	80	56	80	136
Dionne, Los Angeles	80	53	69	122
Shutt, Montreal	80	60	45	105
MacLeish, Philadelphia	79	49	48	97
Perreault, Buffalo	80	39	56	95
Young, Minnesota	80	29	66	95
Ratelle, Boston	78	33	61	94
McDonald, Toronto	80	46	44	90
Sittler, Toronto	73	38	52	90
Clarke, Philadelphia	80	27	62	89
McNab, Boston	80	38	48	86
Goring, Los Angeles	78	30	55	85
Robinson, Montreal	77	19	66	85
Charron, Washington	80	36	46	82
Paiement, Colorado	78	41	40	81
Lysiak, Atlanta	79	30	51	81
Esposito, Rangers	80	34	46	80
D. Potyin, Islanders	80	25	55	80
Turnbull, Toronto	80	22	57	79
Maruk, Cleveland	80	28	50	78

Leading Goalies

(25 or more games)

Goalie, club	G	GA	ShO	Avg
Michel Larocque, Montreal	26	53	4	2.09
Ken Dryden, Montreal	56	117	10	2.14
Glenn Resch, Islanders	46	103	4	2.28
Billy Smith, Islanders	36	87	2	2.50
Don Edwards, Buffalo	25	62	2	2.51
Gerry Desjardins, Buffalo	49	126	3	2.63
Bernie Parent, Philadelphia	61	159	5	2.71
Rogie Vachon, Los Angeles	68	184	8	2.72
Gilles Gilbert, Boston	33	97	1	2.85
Denis Herron, Pittsburgh	34	94	1	2.94
Dunc Wilson, Pittsburgh	45	129	5	2.95
Gerry Cheevers, Boston	45	137	3	3.04
Phil Myre, Atlanta	43	124	3	3.07
Ed Johnston, St. Louis	38	108	1	3.07
Mike Palmateer, Toronto	50	154	4	3.21

NHL Attendance

Club	1977	1976		Increase decrease
Atlanta	490,343	482,494	+	7,849
Boston	470,444	570,287	–	99,843
Buffalo	657,320	657,320		—
Chicago	450,600	563,200	–	112,600
Cleveland	238,543	(a)277,978	–	39,435
Colorado	341,985	(b)315,342	+	26,643
Detroit	385,008	436,370	–	51,362
Los Angeles	497,714	498,556	–	842
Minnesota	363,389	385,347	–	21,958
Montreal	668,214	661,986	+	6,228
N.Y. Islanders	598,551	575,611	+	22,940
N.Y. Rangers	700,000	700,000		—
Philadelphia	683,010	683,010		—
Pittsburgh	401,581	459,639	–	58,058
St. Louis	587,135	684,770	–	97,635
Toronto	658,455	656,296	+	2,159
Vancouver	599,722	618,340	–	18,618
Washington	437,081	394,026	+	43,055
Totals	**9,229,095**	**9,620,572**	–	**391,477**

(a) Oakland; (b) Kansas City.

NHL All Star Team, 1977

First team	Position	Second team
Ken Dryden, Montreal	Goal	Rogie Vachon, Los Angeles
Larry Robinson, Montreal	Defense	Denis Potvin, N.Y. Islanders
Borie Salming, Toronto	Defense	Guy Lapointe, Montreal
Marcel Dionne, Los Angeles	Center	Gil Perreault, Buffalo
Guy Lafleur, Montreal	Right Wing	Lanny McDonald, Toronto
Steve Shutt, Montreal	Left Wing	Rick Martin, Buffalo

Team Scoring Leaders

Atlanta	GP	G	A	Pts.
Tom Lysiak	79	30	51	81
Eric Vail	78	32	39	71
Willi Plett	64	33	23	56
Guy Chouinard	80	17	33	50
Curt Bennett	76	22	25	47

Boston	GP	G	A	Pts.
Jean Ratelle	78	33	61	94
Peter McNab	80	38	48	86
Gregg Sheppard	77	31	36	67
Brad Park	77	12	55	67
Terry O'Reilly	79	14	41	55

Buffalo	GP	G	A	Pts.
Gil Perreault	80	39	56	95
Rene Robert	80	33	40	73
Don Luce	80	26	43	69
Rick Martin	66	36	29	65
Craig Ramsay	80	20	41	61

Chicago	GP	G	A	Pts.
Ivan Boldirev	80	24	38	62
Pit Martin	75	17	36	53
Stan Mikita	57	19	29	48
Dick Redmond	80	22	25	47
Darcy Rota	76	24	22	46

Cleveland	GP	G	A	Pts.
Dennis Maruk	80	28	50	78
Al MacAdam	80	22	41	63
Wayne Merrick	80	18	38	56
Bob Murdoch	57	23	19	42
Rick Hampton	57	16	24	40

Colorado	GP	G	A	Pts.
Wilf Paiement	78	41	40	81
Paul Gardner	60	30	29	59
Gary Croteau	78	24	27	51
Nelson Pyatt	77	23	22	45
Barry Dean	79	14	25	39

Detroit	GP	G	A	Pts.
Walt McKechnie	80	25	34	59
Dennis Polonich	79	18	28	46
Dennis Hextall	78	14	32	46
Nick Libett	80	14	27	41
Michel Bergeron	74	21	12	33

Los Angeles	GP	G	A	Pts.
Marcel Dionne	80	53	69	122
Butch Goring	78	30	55	85
Tommy Williams	80	35	39	74
Mike Murphy	76	25	36	61
Gary Sargent	80	14	40	54

Minnesota	GP	G	A	Pts.
Tim Young	80	29	66	95
Roland Eriksson	80	25	44	69
Glen Sharpley	80	25	32	57
Ernie Hicke	77	30	20	50
Dean Talafous	80	22	27	49

Montreal	GP	G	A	Pts.
Guy Lafleur	80	56	80	136
Steve Shutt	80	60	45	105
Larry Robinson	77	19	66	85
Guy Lapointe	77	25	51	76
Jacques Lemaire	75	34	41	75

N.Y. Islanders	GP	G	A	Pts.
Denis Potvin	80	25	55	80
Bryan Trottier	76	30	42	72
Billy Harris	80	24	43	67
Bob Nystrom	80	29	27	56
J. P. Parise	80	25	31	56

N.Y. Rangers	GP	G	A	Pts.
Phil Esposito	80	34	46	80
Rod Gilbert	78	27	48	75
Ken Hodge	78	21	41	62
Don Murdoch	59	32	24	56
Steve Vickers	75	22	31	53

Philadelphia	GP	G	A	Pts.
Rick MacLeish	79	49	48	97
Bobby Clarke	80	27	62	89
Gary Dornhoefer	79	25	34	59
Mel Bridgman	70	19	38	57
Ross Lonsberry	75	23	32	55

Pittsburgh	GP	G	A	Pts.
Jean Pronovost	79	33	31	64
Pierre Larouche	65	29	34	63
Syl Apps	72	18	43	61
Rick Kehoe	80	30	27	57
Ron Schock	80	17	32	49

St. Louis	GP	G	A	Pts.
Bob MacMillan	80	19	39	58
Garry Unger	80	30	27	57
Larry Patey	80	21	29	50
Red Berenson	80	21	28	49
Claude Larose	80	29	19	48

Toronto	GP	G	A	Pts.
Lanny McDonald	80	46	44	90
Darryl Sittler	73	38	52	90
Ian Turnbull	80	22	57	79
Borje Salming	76	12	66	78
Jack Valiquette	66	15	30	45

Vancouver	GP	G	A	Pts.
Rick Blight	78	28	40	68
Dennis Kearns	80	5	55	60
Don Lever	80	27	30	57
Dennis Ververgaert	79	27	18	45
Garry Monahan	76	18	26	44

Washington	GP	G	A	Pts.
Guy Charron	80	36	46	82
Gerry Meehan	80	28	36	64
Hartland Monahan	79	23	27	50
Ace Bailey	78	19	27	46
Bob Sirois	45	13	22	35

Stanley Cup Champions

1928—New York
1929—Boston
1930—Montreal
1931—Montreal
1932—Toronto
1933—New York
1934—Chicago
1935—Montreal Maroons
1936—Detroit
1937—Detroit
1938—Chicago
1939—Boston
1940—New York
1941—Boston
1942—Toronto
1943—Detroit
1944—Montreal
1945—Toronto
1946—Montreal
1947—Toronto
1948—Toronto
1949—Toronto
1950—Detroit
1951—Toronto
1952—Detroit
1953—Montreal
1954—Detroit
1955—Detroit
1956—Montreal
1957—Montreal
1958—Montreal
1959—Montreal
1960—Montreal
1961—Chicago
1962—Toronto
1963—Toronto
1964—Toronto
1965—Montreal
1966—Montreal
1967—Toronto
1968—Montreal
1969—Montreal
1970—Boston
1971—Montreal
1972—Boston
1973—Montreal
1974—Philadelphia
1975—Philadelphia
1976—Montreal
1977—Montreal

Conn Smythe Trophy (MVP in Playoffs)

1965—Jean Beliveau, Montreal
1966—Roger Crozier, Detroit
1967—Dave Keon, Toronto
1968—Glenn Hall, St. Louis
1969—Serge Sevard, Montreal
1970—Bobby Orr, Boston
1971—Ken Dryden, Montreal
1972—Bobby Orr, Boston
1973—Yvan Cournoyer, Montreal
1974—Bernie Parent, Philadelphia
1975—Bernie Parent, Philadelphia
1976—Reg Leach, Philadelphia
1977—Guy Lafleur, Montreal

NHL Trophy Winners

Ross Trophy
Leading Scorer

1977 Guy Lafleur, Montreal
1976 Guy Lafleur, Montreal
1975 Bobby Orr, Boston
1974 Phil Esposito, Boston
1973 Phil Esposito, Boston
1972 Phil Esposito, Boston
1971 Phil Esposito, Boston
1970 Bobby Orr, Boston
1969 Phil Esposito, Boston
1968 Stan Mikita, Chicago
1967 Stan Mikita, Chicago
1966 Bobby Hull, Chicago
1965 Stan Mikita, Chicago
1964 Stan Mikita, Chicago

Hart Trophy
MVP

1977 Guy Lafleur, Montreal
1976 Bobby Clarke, Philadelphia
1975 Bobby Clarke, Philadelphia
1974 Phil Esposito, Boston
1973 Bobby Clarke, Philadelphia
1972 Bobby Orr, Boston
1971 Bobby Orr, Boston
1970 Bobby Orr, Boston
1969 Phil Esposito, Boston
1968 Stan Mikita, Chicago
1967 Stan Mikita, Chicago
1966 Bobby Hull, Chicago
1965 Bobby Hull, Chicago
1964 Jean Beliveau, Montreal

Norris Trophy
Best Defenseman

1977 Larry Robinson, Montreal
1976 Denis Potvin, N.Y. Islanders
1975 Bobby Orr, Boston
1974 Bobby Orr, Boston
1973 Bobby Orr, Boston
1972 Bobby Orr, Boston
1971 Bobby Orr, Boston
1970 Bobby Orr, Boston
1969 Bobby Orr, Boston
1968 Bobby Orr, Boston
1967 Harry Howell, N.Y. Rangers
1966 Jacques Laperriere, Montreal
1965 Pierre Pilote, Chicago
1964 Pierre Pilote, Chicago

Vezina Trophy
Leading Goalie

1977 Dryden, Larocque, Montreal
1976 Ken Dryden, Montreal
1975 Bernie Parent, Philadelphia
1974 Tony Esposito, Chicago
Bernie Parent, Philadelphia
1973 Ken Dryden, Montreal
1972 Esposito, Smith, Chicago
1971 Giacomin, Villemure, N.Y. Rangers
1970 Tony Esposito, Chicago
1969 Hall, Plante, St. Louis
1968 Worsley, Vachon, Montreal
1967 Hall, De Jordy, Chicago
1966 Hodge, Worsley, Montreal
1965 Sawchuck, Bower, Toronto
1964 Charlie Hodge, Montreal

Calder Trophy
Best Rookie

1977 Willi Plett, Atlanta
1976 Bryan Trottier, N.Y. Islanders
1975 Eric Vail, Atlanta
1974 Denis Potvin, N.Y. Islanders
1973 Steve Vickers, N.Y. Rangers
1972 Ken Dryden, Montreal
1971 Gil Perreault, Buffalo
1970 Tony Esposito, Chicago
1969 Danny Grant, Minnesota
1968 Derek Sanderson, Boston
1967 Bobby Orr, Boston
1966 Brit Selby, Toronto
1965 Roger Crozier, Detroit
1964 Jacques Laperriere, Montreal

Lady Byng Trophy
Sportsmanship

1977 Marcel Dionne, Los Angeles
1976 Jean Ratelle, Boston
1975 Marcel Dionne, Detroit
1974 John Bucyk, Boston
1973 Gilbert Perreault, Buffalo
1972 Jean Ratelle, N.Y. Rangers
1971 John Bucyk, Boston
1970 Phil Goyette, St. Louis
1969 Alex Devecchio, Detroit
1968 Stan Mikita, Chicago
1967 Stan Mikita, Chicago
1966 Alex Devecchio, Detroit
1965 Bobby Hull, Chicago
1964 Ken Wharram, Chicago

Players in the Hockey Hall of Fame

Canadian National Exhibition Park, Toronto, Ont.

Abel, Sid
Adams, Jack
Apps, Syl
Armstrong, George
Bailey, Ace
Bain, Donald
Baker, Hobey
Barry, Marty
Beliveau, Jean
Benedict, Clint (Benny)
Bentley, Doug
Bentley, Max
Blake, Toe
Boon, Dickie
Bouchand, Emile (Butch)
Boucher, Frank
Boucher, George (Buck)
Bower, John
Bowie, Russell
Brimsek, Frank
Broadbent, Punch
Broda, Turk
Burch, Billy
Cameron, Harry
Clancy, King
Clapper, Dit
Cleghorn, Sprague
Colville, Neil
Conacher, Charlie
Connell, Alex
Cook, Bill
Coulter, Art
Cowley, Bill
Crawford, Samuel (Rusty)
Darragh, Jack
Davidson, Allen (Scotty)
Day, Hap
Delvecchio, Alex
Denney, Cy
Drillon, Gordon
Drinkwater, Charles
Dunderdale, Tommy
Durnan, Bill
Dutton, Red
Dye, Babe
Farrell, Arthur
Foyston, Frank
Fredrickson, Frank
Gadsby, Bill
Gardiner, Chuck
Gardiner, Herb
Gardner, Jimmy
Geoffrion, Bernie (Boom Boom)
Gerard, Eddie
Gilmour, Billy
Goodfellow, Ebbie
Goheen, Moose
Grant, Mike
Green, Shorty
Griffis, Silas
Hainsworth, George
Hall, Glenn
Hall, Joe
Harvey, Doug
Hay, George
Hern, Riley
Hextall, Bryan
Holmes, Hap
Hooper, Tom
Horner, Red
Horton, Tim
Howe, Gordie
Howe, Syd
Hutton, John
Hyland, Harry
Irvin, James
Jackson, Busher
Johnson, Moose
Johnson, Ching
Johnson, Tom
Joliat, Aurel
Keats, Gordon
Kelly, Red
Kennedy, Ted
Lach, Elmer
Lalonde, Newsy
Laviolette, Jack
Lehman, Hugh
LeSueur, Percy
Lindsay, Ted
Mackay, Duncan
Mantha, Sylvio
Malone, Joe
Marshall, Jack
Maxwell, Fred
McGee, Frank
McGimsie, Billy
McNamara, George
Moore, Dickie
Moran, Patrick
Morenz, Howie
Mosienko, Bill
Nighbor, Frank
Noble, Reginald
Oliver, Harry
Patrick, Lester
Phillips, Tom
Pilote, Pierre
Pitre, Pit
Pratt, Babe
Primeau, Joe
Pulford, Harvey
Quakenbush, Bill
Rankin, Frank
Rayner, Chuck
Reardon, Ken
Richard, Maurice (Rocket)
Richardson, George
Roberts, Gordon
Ross, Arthur
Russell, Blair
Russell, Ernie
Ruttan, Jack
Sawchuck, Terry
Scanlan, Fred
Schmidt, Milt
Schriner, Sweeney
Seibert, Earl
Seibert, Oliver
Shore, Eddie
Siebert, Babe
Simpson, H. J. (Bullet Joe)
Smith, Alf
Smith, Hooley
Smith, Tommy
Stanley, Barney
Stewart, John (Black Jack)
Stewart, Nels
Stuart, Bruce
Stuart, Hod
Taylor, Fred (Cyclone)
Trihey, Harry
Thompson, Tiny
Vezina, Georges
Walsh, Martin
Walker, Jack
Watson, Harry
Westwick, Harry
Weiland, Cooney
Whitcroft, Fred
Wilson, Phat
Worters, Roy

NCAA Hockey Champions

1951 Michigan
1952 Michigan
1953 Michigan
1954 Rensselaer Poly
1955 Michigan
1956 Michigan
1957 Colorado College
1958 Denver
1959 North Dakota
1960 Denver
1961 Denver
1962 Michigan Tech
1963 North Dakota
1964 Michigan
1965 Michigan Tech
1966 Michigan State
1967 Cornell
1968 Denver
1969 Denver
1970 Cornell
1971 Boston Univ.
1972 Boston Univ.
1973 Wisconsin
1974 Minnesota
1975 Michigan Tech
1976 Minnesota
1977 Wisconsin

NHL Amateur Draft, 1977

First Round Selections

Team	Player	Pos	1976-77 team
Detroit	Dale McCourt	C	St. Catherines
Colorado	Barry Beck	D	New Westminster
Washington	Robert Picard	D	Montreal
Vancouver	Jere Gillis	LW	Sherbrooke
Cleveland	Mike Crombeen	RW	Kingston
Chicago	Doug Wilson	D	Ottawa
Minnesota	Brad Maxwell	D	New Westminster
N. Y. Rangers	Lucien Deblais	RW	Sorel
St. Louis	Scott Campbell	D	London
Montreal	Mark Napler	RW	Birmingham (WHA)
Toronto	John Anderson	RW	Toronto
Toronto	Trevor Johansen	D	Toronto
N.Y. Rangers	Ron Duguay	C	Sudbury
Buffalo	Ric Seiling	RW	St. Catherines
N.Y. Islanders	Mike Bossy	RW	Laval
Boston	Dwight Foster	RW	Kitchener
Philadelphia	Kevin McCarthy	D	Winnipeg
Montreal	Normand Dupont	LW	Montreal

World Hockey Association, 1976-77

Final Standings

East Division

Club	W	L	T	Pts	GF	GA
Quebec	47	31	3	97	353	295
Cincinnati	39	37	5	83	354	303
Indianapolis	36	37	8	80	276	305
New England	35	40	6	76	275	290
Birmingham	31	46	4	66	289	309
*Minnesota	19	18	5	43	136	129

West Division

Club	W	L	T	Pts	GF	GA
Houston	50	24	6	106	320	241
Winnipeg	46	32	2	94	366	291
San Diego	40	37	4	84	284	283
Edmonton	34	43	4	72	243	304
Calgary	31	43	7	69	252	296
Phoenix	28	48	4	60	281	383

*Franchise folded January 20.

East Playoffs — Quebec def. New England 4 games to 1; Indianapolis def. Cincinnati 4 games to 0; Quebec def. Indianapolis 4 games to 1.

West Playoffs — Winnipeg def. San Diego 4 games to 3; Houston def. Edmonton 4 games to 1; Winnipeg def. Houston 4 games to 2.

Championship — Quebec def. Winnipeg 4 games to 3.

Leading Scorers

Player, club	G	Goals	Asts	Pts
Cloutier, Quebec	76	66	75	141
Hedberg, Winnipeg	68	70	61	131
Nilsson, Winnipeg	71	39	85	124
Ftorek, Phoenix	80	46	71	117
Lacroix, San Diego	81	32	82	114
Tardif, Quebec	62	49	60	109
Leduc, Cincinnati	81	52	55	107
C. Bordeleau, Quebec	72	32	75	107
Stoughton, Cincinnati	81	52	52	104
Napier, Birmingham	80	60	36	96
S. Bernier, Quebec	74	43	53	96
Sobchuk, Cincinnati	81	44	51	95
Noris, San Diego	73	35	57	92
Keon, New England	76	27	63	90
Dudley, Cincinnati	77	41	47	88
Webster, New England	70	36	49	85
Ruskowski, Houston	80	24	60	84
P. Bordeleau, Quebec	80	42	41	83
Sullivan, Winnipeg	78	31	52	83
Rogers, New England	78	25	57	82
Lindstrom, Winnipeg	79	44	36	80
Hall, Phoenix	80	38	41	79
Preston, Houston	80	38	41	79
Larose, Cincinnati	81	30	46	76
Mark Howe, Houston	57	23	52	75

Leading Goalies

Goalie, club	G	GA	ShO	Avg
Grahame, Houston	39	107	4	2.74
Caron, Cincinnati	24	61	3	2.83
Raeder, New England	26	69	2	3.12
Rutledge, Houston	42	132	3	3.15
Wakely, San Diego	46	129	3	3.16
Landon, New England	23	59	1	3.17
Daley, Winnipeg	65	206	3	3.24
Dion, Indianapolis	42	128	1	3.36
McLeod, Calgary	66	210	3	3.40
Levasseur, Edmonton	54	166	2	3.40

WHA All-Star Team in 1977

First team	Position	Second team
John Garrett, Birmingham	Goalie	Joe Daley, Winnipeg
Ron Plumb, Cincinnati	Defense	Mark Howe, Houston
Darryl Maggs, Indianapolis	Defense	Paul Popiel, Houston
Robbie Ftorek, Phoenix	Center	Ulf Nilsson, Winnipeg
Anders Hedberg, Winnipeg	Right Wing	Real Cloutier, Quebec
Marc Tardif, Quebec	Left Wing	Rick Dudley, Cincinnati

U.S. National Fencing Champions in 1977

Men's Foil—Michael Marx, Salle Auriol.
Men's Epee—Leonard Dervbinsky, New York Univ.
Men's Sabre—Tom Losonczy, N.Y. Athletic Club.
Women's Foil—Sheila Armstrong, Salle Santelli.

Men's Foil Team—N.Y. Athletic Club.
Men's Epee Team—N.Y. Athletic Club.
Men's Sabre Team—N.Y. Fencers Club.
Women's Foil Team—Salle D'Asaro.

American Bowling Congress Championships in 1977

74th Tournament, Reno, Nev.

Regular Division

Individual

1. Frank Gadaleto, Lansing, Mich. 245, 246, 247 — 738.
2. Dana Bachner, Anchorage, Alas. 247, 232, 253 — 732.
3. Rod Toft, St. Paul, Minn. 225, 233, 265 — 723.

Runners-up — Jerry Perkins, Grand Junction, Col. 720; Henrik Rorije, Las Vegas, Nev. 718; Arsenia Pica, Abingdon, Ill. 714; Bill Baume, Akron, Oh. 707; Dave Roy, Glenwood Springs, Col. 705; Lanson Chien, Metarie, La. 704; Dave Oesch, Kent, Oh. and Bill Stanfield, Grand Rapids, Mich. 701.

All Events

1. Charles (Bud) Debenham, Los Angeles, Cal. 716, 748, 653 — 2117.
2. David Daner, Jamestown, N.Y. 629, 681, 677 — 1987.
3. Pete Trynasty, Seattle, Wash. 667, 638, 647 — 1952.

Runners-up — Rod Toft, St. Paul, Minn. 1949; Warren Servin, Rockford, Ill. 1940; Bill Stanfield, Grand Rapids, Mich. 1938; John Corbin, Springfield, W. Va. 1934; Ron Sommer, Racine, Wis. 1930; Jigger Skillern, Ft. Worth, Tex. 1917; Darrell Christenson, Minneapolis, Minn. and Lou Viet, Milwaukee, Wis. 1915.

Doubles

1. Bob Roy, Glenwood Springs, Col. 200, 215, 257 — 672; Walt Roy, Glenwood Springs, Col. 207, 226, 213 — 646. Aggregate — 1318.
2. Charles (Bud) Debenham, Los Angeles, Cal. 256, 257, 235 — 748; Bud Overbaugh, Los Angeles, Cal. 213, 199, 157 — 569. Aggregate — 1317.
3. Terry Rea, Seattle, Wash. 193, 205, 224 — 622; Tom Anderson, Seattle, Wash. 235, 225, 214 — 674. Aggregate — 1296.

Team

1. Rendel's GMC, Joliet, Ill. — Michael Spiezio 174, 224, 249 — 647; Arnold Weiske 205, 188, 187 — 580; Don Fox, 214, 212, 169 — 595; Ray Marion 214, 211, 197 — 622; Brian Himer 215, 226, 190 — 631. Aggregate — 3075.
2. The Revv Center, Honolulu, Ha. — Earl Onishi 189, 215, 192 — 596; Jim Haitsuka 171, 181, 181 — 533; Earl Hanzawa 201, 205, 179 — 585; Barney Yoshicka 177, 191, 247 — 615; Clifton Kau 257, 180, 278 — 715. Aggregate — 3044.

Classic Division

Individual

1. Mickey Higham, Kansas City, Mo. 279, 266, 256 — 801.
2. Dick Ritger, River Falls, Wis. 246, 210, 269 — 725.
3. Dale Dean, Marietta, Ga. 231, 247, 225 — 703.

Runners-up — Bob Hood, San Mateo, Cal. 693; Wally Wagner, Santa Ana, Cal. 691; Jim Hoepner, Oroville, Cal. and Norm Meyers, St. Louis, Mo. 690; Tom Long, La Mirada, Cal. 689; Emmett Shutes, State College, Pa. and Randy Lightfoot, St. Louis, Mo. 684.

All Events

1. Dick Ritger, River Falls, Wis. 593, 646, 725 — 1964.
2. Bill Spigner, Hamden, Conn. 622, 638, 672 — 1932.
3. (tie) Mickey Higham, Kansas City, Mo. 590, 537, 801 — 1928

Jim Byrnes, Waterbury, Conn. 761, 598, 569 — 1928.

Runners-up — Wally Wagner, Santa Ana, Cal. 1922; George Pappas, Charlotte, N.C. 1921; Jim Roy, Glenwood Springs, Col. 1903; Frank Werman, Los Angeles, Cal. and Don Bell, Scotts Valley, Cal. 1902; Mike Samardzija, Detroit, Mich. 1894.

Doubles

1. (tie) Frank Werman, Los Angeles, Cal. 223, 237, 288 — 748; Randy Neal, Los Angeles, Cal. 163, 204, 222 — 589. Aggregate — 1337. Kevin Gannon, Long Beach, Cal. 258, 227, 197 — 682; Don Bell, Scotts Valley, Cal. 160, 300, 195 — 655. Aggregate — 1337.
3. Mike Samardzija, Detroit, Mich. 233, 214, 201 — 648; Ted Bakatselos, Detroit, Mich. 197, 236, 214 — 647. Aggregate — 1295.

Team

1. Columbia 300 Bowling Balls, San Antonio, Tex. — Don Johnson 215, 189, 214 — 618; John Wilcox 213, 245, 201 — 659; Les Zikes 257, 234, 202 — 693; Tom Hudson 214, 159, 190 — 563; Paul Colwell 217, 193, 179 — 589. Aggregate — 3122.
2. Gus's Gutters, Endicott, N.Y. — Paul Moser 189, 174, 166 — 529; Gus Lampo 190, 198, 197 — 585; Hector Valenzuela 180, 217, 231 — 628; Fred Jaskie 235, 216, 225 — 676; Les Schissler 190, 178, 196 — 564. Aggregate — 2982.

Other Bowling Championships in 1977

7th U.S. Open — Men — Greensboro, N.C. March 9-16; John Petraglia, Staten Island, N.Y., average 218.98, prize $10,000. Women — Milwaukee, Wis., May 15-19; Betty Morris, Stockton, Cal., average 217, prize $6,000.

National Intercollegiate Championships — Reno, Nev., April 5-6; doubles, David Buchanan, Alfred (N.Y.) State and James Fichera, Rochester (N.Y.) Institute of Technology; singles, Jeffrey Bellinger, South Carolina; all events, Ted Schmidt, Hillsborough Community College, Tampa, Fla.

Invitational Tournament of the Americas — Miami, Fla. June 10-16; men's doubles, Miguel Aguilar and Jose Arzu, Guatemala; singles, Jose Arzu, Guatemala; all events, Fernando Barocio, Mexico; women's doubles, Cindy Schuble and Joan Holderness, United States; singles, Joan Holderness, United States; all events, Joan Holderness, United States.

Masters Bowling Tournament Champions

Year	Winner	Runner-up	W-L	Avg
1965	Billy Welu, St. Louis	Don Ellis, Houston	9-1	202-12
1966	Bob Strampe, Detroit	Al Thompson, Cleveland	7-0	219-8
1967	Lou Scalia, Miami	Bill Johnson, New Orleans	7-0	216-9
1968	Pete Tountas, Tucson	Buzz Fazio, Detroit	9-1	220-15
1969	Jim Chestney, Denver	Barry Asher, Costa Mesa, Cal	10-1	223-2
1970	Don Glover, Bakersfield, Cal.	Bob Strampe, Detroit	9-1	215-10
1971	Jim Godman, Lorain, Oh.	Don Johnson, Akron	9-1	229-8
1972	Bill Beach, Sharon, Pa.	Jim Godman, Lorain, Oh.	8-1	220-27
1973	Dave Soutar, Gilroy, Cal.	Dick Ritger, Hartford, Wis.	7-0	218-61
1974	Paul Colwell, Tucson	Steve Neff, Sarasota, Fla.	7-0	234-17
1975	Ed Ressler Jr., Allentown, Pa.	Sam Flanagan, Parkersburg, W. Va.	9-1	213-57
1976	Nelson Burton Jr., St. Louis	Steve Carson, Oklahoma City	7-0	220-79
1977	Earl Anthony, Tacoma, Wash.	Jim Godman, Lorain, Oh.	7-0	218-21

All-Time Records for League and Tournament Play

Type of record	Holder of record	Year	Score	Competition
High team total	Budweiser Beer, St. Louis	1958	3,858	League
High team game	Hook Grip Five, Lodi, N.J.	1950	1,342	League
High doubles total	Nelson Burton Jr., Billy Walden, St. Louis	1970	1,614	Tournament
High doubles game	Jesse Foley and Wendell Cromer, Shreveport, La.	1976	598*	League
High individual total	Albert Brandt, Lockport, N.Y.	1939	886	League
High all events score	Denny Campbell, Chicago	1976	2,314	Tournament

*In 4-person league.

Official Records of Annual ABC Tournaments

Type of record	Holder of record	Year	Score
High team total	Ace Mitchell Shur-Hooks, Akron	1966	3,357
High team game	Falstaff Beer, San Antonio	1958	1,226
High doubles score	John Klares-Steve Nagy, Cleveland	1952	1,453
High doubles game	Tommy Hudson, Akron, Ohio-Les Zikes, Chicago	1976	558
High singles total	Mickey Higham, Kansas City, Mo.	1977	801
High all events score	Jim Godman, Lorain, Oh.	1974	2,184
High team all events	Falstaff Beer, St. Louis, Mo.	1958	9,608
High life-time pin total	Bill Doehrman, Ft. Wayne	1908-1977	107,995

Record Averages for Consecutive Tournaments

No. in row	Holder of record	Span	Games	Average
Two	Jim Godman, Lorain, Oh.	1974-75	18	228.78
Three	Jim Godman, Lorain, Oh.	1974-76	27	222.96
Four	Jim Godman, Lorain, Oh.	1972-76	36	218.41
Five	Jim Godman, Lorain, Oh.	1973-77	45	216.33
Ten	Bob Strampe, Detroit	1961-70	111	211.10

Bowlers with 6 or More Sanctioned 300 Games

Elvin Mesger, Sullivan, Mo.	26
George Billick, Old Forge, Pa.	17
Dick Weber, St. Louis	17
Dave Soutar, Gilroy, Cal.	15
Al Faragalli, Wayne, N.J.	14
Ron Graham, Louisville	14
Don Johnson, Las Vegas	14
Don Carter, Miami, Fla.	13
Ray Bluth, St. Louis	12
Walter Ward, Cleveland	12
*Hank Marino, Milwaukee	11
Frank Clause, Old Forge, Pa.	11
Ed Lubanski, Detroit	11
Pat Patterson, St. Louis	11
Dennis Soper, Tustin, Cal.	11
Casey Jones, Plymouth, Wis.	11
Mike Durbin, Lorain, Oh.	10
Boss Bosco, Akron	9
Al Savas, Milwaukee	9
Lou Foxie, Paterson, N.J.	9
Jerry Woji, Stockton, Cal.	9
Dave Williams, Sebastopal, Cal.	9
Norm Meyers, St. Louis	9
Tom Hennessey, St. Louis	9
George Pappas, Charlotte, N.C.	9
Howard Holmes, Los Angeles	8
Russell Field, San Jose, Cal.	8
Roger Fink, Lodi, Cal.	8
Dennis Wright, Milwaukee	8
Ray Eklund, Milwaukee	8
Walter King, Detroit	8
Junie McMahon, Lodi, N.J.	8
Bud Horn, Los Angeles	8
Joe Donato, Schenectady, N.Y.	7
Eddie Botten, Union City, N.J.	7
Dick Hoover, Akron	7
Ken McKenzie, Dallas	7
Ray Schanen, Milwaukee	7
Wayne Pinkalla, Milwaukee	7
Bob Ramirez, Los Angeles	7
Don McCune, Munster, Ind.	7
Mickey Higham, Kansas City, Mo.	7
Jim Godman, Lorain, Oh.	7
Don Glover, Rosenberg, Tex.	7
Salvatore Bivona, Paterson, N.J.	6
Lou Campi, Dumont, N.J.	6
Ed Davis, Milford, N.J.	6
Don Dubro, St. Louis	6
*Bill Flynn, Cleveland	6
Sam Garofalo, St. Louis	6
Joe Joseph, Lansing, Mich.	6
Pete Kozloski, Plains, Pa.	6
Vince Lucci, Trenton, N.J.	6
Steve Nagy, Cleveland	6
Frank Pollak, Pittsburgh	6
Robert Pinkalla, Milwaukee	6
Harold Schaeffer, St. Louis	6
Harry Smith, Rochester, N.Y.	6
Bob Strampe, Detroit	6
Jerry Tharp, St. Louis	6
George Tomek, Plymouth, Pa.	6
Stephen Tomek, Plymouth, Pa.	6
William Capleton, Prospect Park, N.J.	6
Mark Sutter, St. Louis	6

*Bowled two 300 games in official 3-game-series.

PBA Winter Tour, 1977

Date	Event	Winner	Winner's share
Jan. 4-8	Lite Classic, Torrance, Cal.	Earl Anthony	$10,000
Jan. 11-15	Ford Open, Alameda, Cal.	Steve Jones	8,000
Jan. 16-22	Showboat Invitational, Las Vegas	Mark Roth	14,000
Jan. 25-29	Quaker State Open, Grand Prairie, Tex.	Henry Gonzalez	10,000
Feb. 1-5	Rolaids Open, Florissant, Mo.	Steve Neff	14,000
Feb. 8-12	Midas Open, Gretna, La.	Don Johnson	14,000
Feb. 15-19	King Louis Open, Overland Park, Kan.	Dick Weber	8,000
Feb. 22-26	Miller High Life Open, Milwaukee	Ed Ressler	14,000
Mar. 1-5	Monro-Matic Open, Windsor Locks, Conn.	Tommy Hudson	10,000
Mar. 8-12	AMF Pro Classic, Garden City, N.Y.	Dick Ritger	14,000
Mar. 15-19	Muriel Cigar Open, Cleveland	Roy Buckley	8,000
Mar. 20-26	BPAA U.S. Open, Greensboro, N.C.	Johnny Petraglia	10,000
Mar. 29-Apr. 1	Burger King Open, Miami	Teata Semiz	14,000
Apr. 6-9	Fair Lanes Open, Springfield, Va.	Tommy Hudson	8,000
Apr. 12-16	Toledo Open, Toledo, Oh.	John Denton	7,500
Apr. 18-23	Firestone Tournament of Champions, Akron, Oh.	Mike Berlin	25,000

Leading PBA Averages in 1976

(16 or more tournaments)

Pos.	Name, city	Tournaments	Games	Pinfall	Average
1.	Mark Roth, Staten Island, N.Y.	28	945	204,092	215.970
2.	Earl Anthony, Tacoma, Wash.	28	1,020	219,329	215.028
3.	Larry Laub, San Francisco, Cal.	31	1,013	216,127	213.353
4.	Roy Buckley, Columbus, Oh.	31	965	204,330	211.741
5.	Carmen Salvino, Chicago, Ill.	33	1,061	224,543	211.633
6.	Barry Asher, Costa Mesa, Cal	22	603	127,407	211.289
7.	Butch Soper, Santa Ana, Cal.	32	861	181,892	211.257
8.	Jay Robinson, Los Angeles, Cal.	34	992	209,468	211.157
9.	Gary Dickinson, Ft. Worth, Tex.	33	998	210,619	211.041
10.	Dave Davis, Atlanta, Ga.	24	785	165,605	210.962
11.	George Pappas, Charlotte, N.C.	30	918	193,613	210.907
12.	Tommy Hudson, Akron, Oh.	35	948	199,936	210.903
13.	Tim Harahan, Capistrano Beach, Cal.	17	486	102,465	210.833
14.	Mike Durbin, Chagrin Falls, Oh.	23	655	137,739	210.289
15.	Jim Godman, Lorain, Oh.	31	883	185,426	209.995
16.	Paul Colwell, Tucson, Ariz.	31	853	178,761	209.567

Firestone Tournament of Champions

This is professional bowling's richest tournament and has been held each year since its inception in 1965, in Akron, Oh., the home of the Professional Bowlers Association. First prize is $25,000.

Year	Winner	Year	Winner	Year	Winner	Year	Winner
1965	Billy Hardwick	1969	Jim Godman	1972	Mike Durbin	1975	Dave Davis
1966	Wayne Zahn	1970	Don Johnson	1973	Jim Godman	1976	Marshall Holman
1967	Jim Stefanich	1971	Johnny Petraglia	1974	Earl Anthony	1977	Mike Berlin
1968	Dave Davis						

Leading PBA Averages by Years

Year	Bowler	Tournaments	Average	Year	Bowler	Tournaments	Average
1962	Don Carter, St. Louis, Mo.	25	212.844	1970	Nelson Burton Jr., St. Louis, Mo.	32	214.908
1963	Billy Hardwick, Louisville, Ky.	26	210.346	1971	Don Johnson, Akron, Oh.	31	213.977
1964	Ray Bluth, St. Louis, Mo.	27	210.512	1972	Don Johnson, Akron, Oh.	30	215.290
1965	Dick Weber, St. Louis, Mo.	19	211.895	1973	Earl Anthony, Tacoma, Wash.	29	215.799
1966	Wayne Zahn, Atlanta, Ga.	27	208.663	1974	Earl Anthony, Tacoma, Wash.	28	219.394
1967	Wayne Zahn, Atlanta, Ga.	29	212.342	1975	Earl Anthony, Tacoma, Wash.	30	219.060
1968	Jim Stefanich, Joliet, Ill.	33	211.895	1976	Mark Roth, New York, N.Y.	28	215.970
1969	Bill Hardwick, Louisville, Ky.	33	212.957				

PBA Leading Money Winners

Total winnings are from PBA, ABC Masters, and BPAA All-Star tournaments only, and do not include numerous other tournaments or earnings from special television shows and matches.

Year	Bowler	Total	Year	Bowler	Total	Year	Bowler	Total
1959	Dick Weber	$ 7,672	1965	Dick Weber	$47,674	1971	Johnny Petraglia	$85,065
1960	Don Carter	22,525	1966	Wayne Zahn	54,720	1972	Don Johnson	56,648
1961	Dick Weber	26,280	1967	Dave Davis	54,165	1973	Don McCune	69,000
1962	Don Carter	49,972	1968	Jim Stefanich	67,377	1974	Earl Anthony	99,585
1963	Dick Weber	46,333	1969	Billy Hardwick	64,160	1975	Earl Anthony	107,585
1964	Bob Strampe	33,592	1970	Mike McGrath	52,049	1976	Earl Anthony	110,833

Women's International Bowling Congress Champions

Individual	All events	Year	2-woman teams	5-woman teams
Mary Scruggs, Richmond, Va. 698	Lorrie Koch, Carpentersville, Ill. 1,840	1971	Dorothy Fothergill, N. Attleboro, Mass.-Mildred Martorella, Rochester, N.Y. 1,263	Koenig & Strey Real Estate, Wilmette, Ill. 2,891
D. D. Jacobson, Playa Del Rey, Cal. 737	Mildred Martorella, Rochester, N.Y. 1,877	1972	Judy Roberts-Betty Remmick, Denver, Lakewood, Col. 1,247	Angeltown Creations, Placentia, Cal. 2,838
Bobbie Buffaloe, Costa Messa, Cal. 706	Toni Calvery, Midwest City, Okla. 1,910	1973	Dorothy Fothergill, N. Attleboro, Mass.-Mildred Martorella, Rochester, N.Y. 1,238	Fitzpatrick Chevrolet, Concord, Cal. 2,897
Shirley Garms, Lake Island, Ill. 702	Judy Cook Soutar, Kansas City, Mo. 1,944	1974	Jane Leszczynski, Milwaukee-Carol Miller, Waukesha, Wis. 1,313	Kalicak International Construction, Kansas City, Mo. 2,973
Barbara Leicht, Albany, N.Y. 689	Virginia Park, Whittier, Cal. 1,821	1975	Jennette James, Oyster Bay, Dawn Raddatz, Northport, N.Y. 1,234	Atlanta Bowling Center (Ga.) Buffalo, N.Y. 2,836
Beverly Shonk, Canton, Ohio 686	Betty Morris, Stockton, Cal. 1,866	1976	Georgene Cordes-Shirley Stostrom, Bloomington, Minn.: Eloise Vacco-Debbie Rainone, Cleveland Hts., Oh. (tie). 1,232	PWBA 1, Oklahoma City, Okla. 2,839
Akiko Yamaga, Tokyo 714	Akiko Yamaga 1,895	1977	Ozella Houston-Dorothy Jackson, Detroit, Mich. 1,234	Allgauer's Restaurant Chicago, Ill. 2,818

Sanctioned 300 Games During 1976-77 Season

Jackie Archer, Livonia, Mich.; Maxine Barker, Bay City, Mich.; Sandra Bigley, Port Hueneme, Cal.; Janice Blackburn, Clinton, Mich.; Genny Bosworth, Ripley, W. Va.; Loa Boxberger, Russell, Kan.; Ann Bray, Gary, Ind.; Martha Carlon, Buffalo, N.Y.; Ronnie Connaughton, Richmond Hill, N.Y.; Velda Gooden, Richmond, Cal.; Helen Goodling, Elizabethtown, Pa.; Vesma Grinfelds, San Francisco, Cal.; Carolyn Hallgren, Huntington Beach, Cal.; Jan Hoyer, Ponca City, Okla.; Kay Landin, Montclair, Cal.; Becky Lary, Tulsa, Okla.; Phyllis Majewski, Amsterdam, N.Y.; Julie Mitchell, Augusta, Kan.; Betty Morris, Stockton, Cal.; Bev Ortner, Tucson, Ariz.; M. Carol Pike, Cypress, Cal.; Janet Rohrbaugh, Santa Barbara, Cal.; Pam Rutherford, Oroville, Cal.; Mary Sagasta, Tonawanda, N.Y.; Pat Sjuggerud, Kenosha, Wis.; Arlene Skov, San Jose, Cal.; Joyce Smith, Grand Blanc, Mich.; Audrey Veleta, Palos Hills, Ill.; Gloria Wyckoff, Green Bay, Wis.

Most Sanctioned 300 Games

Betty Morris, Stockton, Cal.	4	Mary Altmeyer, St. Louis, Mo.	2	Norma Rittelmeyer, Dallas, Tex.	2
Beverly Ortner, Tucson, Ariz.	4	Joan McRae, Northridge, Cal.	2	Patricia Robinette, Louisville, Ky.	2
Sylvia Wene Martin, Philadelphia	3	Betty Mivalez, Tujunga, Cal.	2	Jean Worthy, Norwalk, Cal.	2

National Duckpin Bowling Champions in 1977

Men's Singles—Dick Najarian, Cheshire, Conn., 604.
Women's Singles—Linda Rosen, Salisbury, Md., 526.
Men's Doubles—John Garrison-Al Houser, Hamden, Conn., 1042.
Women's Doubles—Denise Przybysz-JoAnn Russell, Baltimore, Md., 882.
Men's Team—Lambis 5, Silver Spring, Md., 2330.
Women's Team—(tie) Craan T. V. Baltimore, Md., Oates Shell, Kings Mountain, N.C., 2080.
Mixed Doubles—Judy and Jim Hardy, Concord, N. C., 957.

College Basketball

Final League Standings

Ivy League

	Conference			All Games		
	W	L	Pct	W	L	Pct
Princeton	13	1	.929	21	4	.840
Pennsylvania	12	2	.857	18	8	.692
Columbia	8	6	.571	16	10	.615
Harvard	6	8	.429	9	16	.360
Brown	5	9	.357	6	20	.231
Cornell	4	9	.308	7	18	.280
Yale	4	9	.308	7	18	.280
Dartmouth	3	11	.214	4	22	.154

East Coast

Eastern Division						
Hofstra	4	1	.800	23	6	.793
Temple	4	1	.800	17	11	.607
LaSalle	3	2	.600	17	12	.586
American	2	3	.400	13	13	.500
St. Joseph's	2	3	.400	13	13	.500
Drexel	0	5	.000	11	13	.485
Western Division						
Lafayette	9	1	.900	21	6	.778
Delaware	7	3	.700	12	13	.480
Lehigh	6	4	.600	12	15	.444
Bucknell	5	5	.500	10	15	.400
West Chester	2	8	.200	11	14	.440
Rider	1	9	.100	8	18	.308

Eastern Independent

Eastern Division						
Rutgers	7	1	.875	18	8	.692
Villanova	6	1	.857	18	8	.692
G. Washington	5	3	.625	14	11	.560
Massachusetts	3	4	.429	16	9	.640
Western Division						
West Virginia	5	5	.500	17	9	.654
Penn St.	5	5	.500	11	14	.440
Duquesne	3	6	.333	12	13	.480
Pittsburgh	0	9	.000	5	20	.250

Atlantic Coast

No. Carolina	9	3	.750	25	4	.862
Clemson	8	4	.667	22	6	.786
Wake Forest	8	4	.667	20	7	.741
Maryland	7	5	.731	19	8	.704
N. Carolina St.	6	6	.500	17	11	.607
Duke	2	10	.166	14	13	.519
Virginia	2	10	.166	12	17	.414

No. Carolina won conference tournament

Big Eight

Kansas St.	11	3	.786	22	7	.759
Missouri	9	5	.643	21	8	.724
Oklahoma	9	5	.643	18	10	.643
Kansas	8	6	.571	18	10	.643
Nebraska	7	7	.500	15	14	.517
Colorado	5	9	.357	11	16	.407
Oklahoma St.	4	10	.286	10	17	.370
Iowa St.	3	11	.214	7	20	.259

Southwest

Arkansas	17	0	1.000	26	1	.963
Houston	16	4	.800	26	7	.788
Texas Tech	14	5	.737	20	9	.690
Texas A&M	9	9	.500	14	14	.500
Texas	8	9	.471	13	13	.500
SMU	7	10	.412	8	19	.296
Baylor	6	12	.333	11	16	.407
Rice	3	14	.176	9	18	.333
TCU	0	17	.000	3	23	.115

Southeastern

	Conference			All Games		
	W	L	Pct	W	L	Pct
Kentucky	16	2	.889	24	3	.889
Tennessee	16	2	.889	22	5	.815
Alabama	14	4	.778	23	4	.852
Florida	10	8	.556	17	9	.654
LSU	8	10	.444	15	12	.556
Auburn	6	12	.333	13	13	.500
Miss. St.	6	12	.333	14	13	.519
Vanderbilt	6	12	.333	10	16	.385
Mississippi	5	13	.278	11	16	.407
Georgia	3	15	.167	9	18	.333

Big Ten

Michigan	16	2	.889	23	3	.885
Minnesota	15	3	.833	24	3	.889
Purdue	13	5	.722	19	8	.704
Iowa	10	8	.556	18	9	.667
Indiana	9	9	.500	14	13	.519
Michigan St.	7	11	.389	10	17	.370
Illinois	6	12	.333	14	16	.467
Wisconsin	5	13	.278	9	17	.346
Northwestern	5	13	.278	7	20	.259
Ohio St.	4	14	.222	9	18	.333

Mid-American

Miami, Oh.	13	3	.866	19	6	.760
Cent. Michigan	12	3	.800	17	9	.653
Toledo	12	4	.750	21	6	.778
N. Illinois	9	6	.600	12	14	.463
W. Michigan	7	8	.466	13	13	.500
Ball St.	7	9	.437	11	14	.444
Bowling Green	5	11	.312	9	18	.333
Kent St.	4	10	.276	8	17	.320
Ohio U.	4	11	.266	9	16	.360
E. Michigan	4	12	.250	9	18	.333

Southern

(a)Va. Military	8	2	.800	25	3	.893
Furman	8	2	.800	18	10	.643
Appalachian	8	4	.667	17	12	.586
Wm. & Mary	7	4	.636	16	14	.533
E. Carolina	3	9	.250	10	18	.357
Davidson	2	8	.200	5	22	.185
Citadel	2	9	.182	8	19	.296
*Tenn-Chatt.	0	0	.000	24	5	.828
*W. Carolina	0	0	.000	8	16	.333
*Marshall	0	0	.000	8	19	.296

*Ineligible for conference championship

(a) Won conference tournament and NCAA Tourney berth

Sun Belt

NC-Charlotte	5	1	.833	23	3	.884
New Orleans	4	2	.667	17	9	.654
S. Alabama	3	3	.500	17	9	.654
Georgia St.	2	4	.333	10	16	.385
S. Florida	2	4	.333	9	18	.333
Jacksonville	2	4	.333	9	18	.333

West Coast Athletic

San Francisco	14	0	1.000	29	1	.967
Santa Clara	9	5	.643	17	10	.630
Nevada-Reno	7	7	.500	15	12	.556
Seattle	7	7	.500	13	14	.481
Portland	6	8	.429	11	15	.423
Pepperdine	5	9	.357	13	13	.500
Loyola	4	10	.286	11	15	.423
St. Mary's	4	10	.286	11	16	.407

Big Sky

	Conference			All Games		
	W	L	Pct	W	L	Pct
Idaho St.	13	1	.928	23	4	.851
Weber St.	11	3	.789	20	8	.713
Gonzaga	7	7	.500	11	16	.409
Montana St.	6	8	.428	12	14	.461
N. Arizona	5	9	.357	12	15	.444
Boise St.	5	9	.357	10	16	.385
Montana	5	9	.357	7	19	.269
Idaho	3	11	.224	5	21	.190

Metro Seven

Louisville	6	1	.857	21	6	.778
Cincinnati	4	2	.667	25	4	.862
Georgia Tech	3	3	.500	18	10	.642
Tulane	3	3	.500	10	17	.371
Memphis St.	3	4	.429	20	8	.714
Florida St.	2	4	.333	16	11	.592
St. Louis	1	5	.167	7	19	.269

Western Athletic

Utah	11	3	.786	21	6	.778
Arizona	10	4	.714	21	5	.808
New Mexico	8	6	.571	19	11	.633
Wyoming	8	6	.571	17	10	.630
Arizona St.	6	8	.429	15	13	.536
Colorado St.	6	8	.429	13	12	.520
Brigham Young	4	10	.286	12	15	.444
Texas-El Paso	3	11	.214	11	15	.423

Pacific-8

UCLA	11	3	.786	23	4	.852
Oregon	9	5	.643	18	9	.667
Wash. St.	8	6	.571	19	8	.704
Oregon St.	8	6	.571	16	13	.552
Washington	8	6	.571	17	10	.630
California	7	7	.500	12	15	.444
Stanford	3	11	.214	11	16	.407
USC	2	12	.143	6	20	.231

Missouri Valley

So. Illinois	8	4	.667	21	6	.778
N. Mexico St.	8	4	.667	17	10	.634
Wichita St.	7	5	.583	18	10	.643
W. Texas St.	7	5	.583	17	13	.567
Drake	5	7	.417	10	17	.370
Bradley	4	8	.333	9	19	.321
Tulsa	3	9	.250	6	21	.222

Ohio Valley

Austin Peay	13	1	.929	24	4	.857
Murray	9	5	.643	17	10	.630
Mid. Tenn.	9	5	.643	19	8	.704
Morehead	9	5	.643	14	10	.583
W. Kentucky	6	8	.429	10	16	.385
E. Tennessee	6	8	.429	12	14	.462
E. Kentucky	3	11	.214	8	16	.333
Tenn. Tech	1	13	.071	7	19	.269

Pacific Coast Athletic

Long Beach St.	9	3	.750	20	7	.741
San Diego St.	9	3	.750	13	15	.464
San Jose St.	8	4	.667	17	11	.607
Fullerton	7	5	.583	16	10	.615
Pacific	5	7	.417	11	14	.444
UC-Santa Barbara	3	9	.250	8	18	.308
Fresno St.	1	11	.083	7	20	.259

Major Independents

Team	W	L
Indiana St.	25	2
Nevada-Las Vegas	25	2
Old Dominion	25	3
Syracuse	25	3
Detroit	24	3
Providence	24	4
Holy Cross	23	5
North Texas St.	21	6
Oral Roberts	21	6
Creighton	21	6
Illinois St.	20	6
Notre Dame	20	6
St. Bonaventure	20	6
Marquette	20	6
Army	19	8
Georgetown, D.C.	19	8
Wis.-Milwaukee	19	8
St. John's, N.Y.	21	9
Pan American	18	8
Seton Hall	17	8
Virginia Tech	18	9
No. Louisana	16	9
Portland St.	16	9
Connecticut	17	10
Fairfield	17	10
Ga. Southern	19	12
Iona	15	10
Dayton	16	11
Oklahoma City	15	11
Richmond	15	11
St. Francis, Pa.	15	11
DePaul	15	11
South Car. St.	13	10
No. Car.-Wilm.	14	11
Northeast La.	15	12
Stetson	15	12
Utah St.	15	12
Colgate	13	11
Navy	13	11
Valparaiso	13	12
Maine	13	12
Rhode Island	13	12
South Carolina	14	13
Catholic, D.C.	13	13
Chicago Loyola	13	13
Fairleigh Dick.	13	13
Niagara	13	13
St. Peter's	13	13
Virginia Com.	13	13
Butler	13	14
Manhattan	13	14
New Hampshire	12	14
St. Francis, N.Y.	12	14
Denver	12	15
Northeastern	11	14
Air Force	11	16
So. Mississippi	10	16
Siena	9	15
Cleveland St.	10	17
Long Island	9	16
Marshall	9	16
Northern Col.	9	16
Centenary	10	18
Xavier (Cinn.)	9	17
Western Carolina	8	16
Hawaii	8	17
Vermont	8	17
Boston Col.	8	18
Baptist	8	19
Robert Morris	7	19
Boston U.	7	19
Samford	7	19
Mercer	7	19
Houston Baptist	7	22
Hardin Simmons	6	21
Fordham	5	21
Buffalo	4	20
Canisius	3	21
Wagner	3	21
North Car. A&T	2	25
Delaware St.	1	25

NCAA Division I Individual Leaders, 1976-77

Scoring

	G	FG	FT	Pts	Avg
Freeman Williams, Portland State	26	417	176	1010	38.8
Anthony Roberts, Oral Roberts	28	402	147	951	34.0
Larry Bird, Indiana State	28	375	168	918	32.8
Otis Birdsong, Houston	36	452	186	1090	30.3
Rich Laurel, Hofstra	30	355	198	908	30.3
Calvin Natt, NE Louisiana	27	307	168	782	29.0
Mike McConathy, Louisiana Tech	26	258	200	716	27.5
Roger Phegley, Bradley	27	272	195	739	27.4
Billy Reynolds, NW Louisiana	26	270	146	686	26.4
Tony Hanson, Connecticut	27	253	196	702	26.0
Bernard King, Tennessee	26	278	116	672	25.8
Matt Hicks, Northern Illinois	27	285	112	682	25.3
Bruce Grimm, Furman	21	184	135	503	24.0
Edgar Jones, Nevada-Reno	27	247	147	641	23.7
Glenn Kolonics, Catholic U.	26	264	83	611	23.5
Gavin Smith, Hawaii	26	252	104	608	23.4
John Gerdy, Davidson	27	264	99	627	23.2
Tommy Harris, Bowling Green	27	267	90	624	23.1
Ron Perry, Holy Cross	25	209	156	574	23.0
Larry Harris, Pittsburgh	27	254	109	617	22.9

Free Throw Percentage

(Min. 2.5 FT Made Per Game)	G	FT	FTA	Pct
Robert Smith, Nevada-Las Vegas	32	98	106	.925
Kevin Kelly, Vermont	25	71	77	.922
Phil Thieneman, Virginia Tech	29	98	107	.916
Ed O'Brien, Seattle	26	89	99	.899
Chris Fagan, Colgate	24	110	123	.894
Joe Desantis, Fairfield	26	116	130	.892
Jeff Jonas, Utah	29	118	133	.887
Chuck Mack, Brown	26	70	79	.886
Kevin Hamilton, Iona	25	68	77	.883
Ron Perry, Holy Cross	25	156	177	.881

Field Goal Percentage

(Min. 5 FG Made Per Game)	G	FG	FGA	Pct
Joe Senser, West Chester	25	130	186	.699
Dave Montgomery, VMI	30	161	247	.652
Sidney Moncrief, Arkansas	28	157	242	.649
Cedric Maxwell, N.C.-Charlotte	31	244	381	.640
Frank Sowinski, Princeton	26	163	258	.632
Calvin Natt, NE Louisiana	27	307	493	.623
Bob Cooper, Providence	29	188	302	.623
Rod Griffin, Wake Forest	26	198	319	.621
Bob Miller, Cincinnati	29	180	291	.619
Ron Brewer, Arkansas	27	199	326	.610
Dave Brown, Iona	25	150	246	.610
Phil Ness, Lafayette	27	197	324	.608
Mike Thompson, Minnesota	27	251	414	.606
Duke Thorpe, Virginia Tech	29	178	295	.603

Rebounds

	G	No	Avg
Glenn Mosley, Seton Hall	29	473	16.31
John Irving, Hofstra	27	440	16.30
Robert Elmore, Wichita State	28	441	15.8
Bob Stephens, Drexel	23	340	14.8
Mark Landsberger, Arizona State	25	359	14.4
Bernard King, Tennessee	26	371	14,3
Larry Bird, Indiana State	28	373	13.3
Bruce King, Iowa	25	332	13.3
Edgar Jones, Nevada-Reno	27	355	13.1
Phil Hubbard, Michigan	30	389	13.0
Matt Hicks, Northern Illinois	27	350	13.0
Wayne Rollins, Clemson	28	359	12.8
Ken Williams, North Texas State	27	345	12.8
Calvin Natt, NE Louisiana	27	340	12.6

National Invitation Tournament Champions

Year	Champion
1938	Temple
1939	Long Island Univ.
1940	Colorado
1941	Long Island Univ.
1942	West Virginia
1943	St. John's
1944	St. John's
1945	DePaul
1946	Kentucky
1947	Utah
1948	St. Louis
1949	San Francisco
1950	CCNY
1951	Brigham Young
1952	LaSalle
1953	Seton Hall
1954	Holy Cross
1955	Duquesne
1956	Louisville
1957	Bradley
1958	Xavier (Ohio)
1959	St. John's
1960	Bradley
1961	Providence
1962	Dayton
1963	Providence
1964	Bradley
1965	St. John's
1966	Brigham Young
1967	Southern Illinois
1968	Dayton
1969	Temple
1970	Marquette
1971	North Carolina
1972	Maryland
1973	Virginia Tech
1974	Purdue
1975	Princeton
1976	Kentucky
1977	St. Bonaventure

NCAA Division II Champions

Year	Champion
1958	South Dakota
1959	Evansville
1960	Evansville
1961	Wittenberg
1962	Mt. St. Mary's
1963	South Dakota St.
1964	Evansville
1965	Evansville
1966	Kentucky Wesleyan
1967	Winston-Salem
1968	Kentucky Wesleyan
1969	Kentucky Wesleyan
1970	Philadelphia Textile
1971	Evansville
1972	Roanoke
1973	Kentucky Wesleyan
1974	Morgan State
1975	Old Dominion
1976	Puget Sound
1977	Tennessee-Chattanooga

NCAA Division I Champions

Year	Champion	Year	Champion	Year	Champion	Year	Champion
1939	Oregon	1949	Kentucky	1959	California	1969	UCLA
1940	Indiana	1950	CCNY	1960	Ohio State	1970	UCLA
1941	Wisconsin	1951	Kentucky	1961	Cincinnati	1971	UCLA
1942	Stanford	1952	Kansas	1962	Cincinnati	1972	UCLA
1943	Wyoming	1953	Indiana	1963	Loyola (Chi.)	1973	UCLA
1944	Utah	1954	La Salle	1964	UCLA	1974	No. Carolina State
1945	Oklahoma A&M	1955	San Francisco	1965	UCLA	1975	UCLA
1946	Oklahoma A&M	1956	San Francisco	1966	Texas Western	1976	Indiana
1947	Holy Cross	1957	North Carolina	1967	UCLA	1977	Marquette
1948	Kentucky	1958	Kentucky	1968	UCLA		

Division 1 Records

(Restricted to games between 4-year colleges.)

Career Scoring Averages

Player, team	Last Year	Games	FG	FT	Pts	Avg
Pete Maravich, LSU	1970	83	1,387	893	3,667	44.2
Austin Carr, Notre Dame	1971	74	1,017	526	2,560	34.6
Oscar Robertson, Cincinnati	1960	88	1,052	869	2,973	33.8
Calvin Murphy, Niagara	1970	77	974	654	2,548	33.1
Frank Selvy, Furman	1954	78	922	694	2,538	32.5
Rick Mount, Purdue	1970	72	910	503	2,323	32.3
Darrell Floyd, Furman	1956	71	868	545	2,281	32.1
Nick Werkman, Seton Hall	1964	71	812	649	2,273	32.0
Willie Humes, Idaho St.	1971	48	565	380	1,510	31.5
Elgin Baylor, Col. Idaho-Seattle	1958	80	956	588	2,500	31.3
William Averitt, Pepperdine	1973	49	615	311	1,541	31.4
Dwight Lamar, SW Louisiana	1973	112	1,445	603	3,493	31.2
Elvin Hayes, Houston	1968	93	1,215	454	2,884	31.0
Bill Bradley, Princeton	1965	83	856	791	2,503	30.2

Season Averages

Player, team	Year	Games	FG	FT	Pts	Avg
Pete Maravich, LSU	1970	31	522	337	1,381	44.5
Pete Maravich, LSU	1969	26	433	282	1,148	44.2
Pete Maravich, LSU	1968	26	432	274	1,138	43.8
Frank Selvy, Furman	1954	29	427	355	1,209	41.7
Johnny Neumann, Mississippi	1971	23	366	191	923	40.1
Billy McGill, Utah	1962	26	394	221	1,009	38.8
Freeman Williams, Portland State	1977	26	417	176	1,010	38.8
Calvin Murphy, Niagara	1968	24	337	242	916	38.2
Austin Carr, Notre Dame	1970	29	444	218	1,106	38.1
Austin Carr, Notre Dame	1971	29	430	241	1,101	38.0
Rick Barry, Miami (Fla.)	1965	26	340	293	973	37.4

Single-Game Scoring

Player, team (opponent)	Year	Pts	Player, Team (opponent)	Year	Pts
Selvy, Furman (Newberry)	1954	100	Floyd, Furman (Morehead St.)	1955	67
Mlkvy, Temple (Wilkes)	1951	73	Maravich, LSU (Tulane)	1969	66
Maravich, LSU (Alabama)	1970	69	Handlan, W. & Lee (Furman)	1951	66
Murphy, Niagara (Syracuse)	1969	68	Zawoluk, St. John's (St. Peter's)	1950	65

Individual Records, Season

Field goal percentage	Alcindor, UCLA, 1967	.667	**Rebounds per game**	Slack, Marshall, 1955	25.6
	Martens, Ab. Christian, 1972	.667	**Rebounds**	Dukes, Seton Hall, 1953	734
	Fleming, Arizona, 1974	.667	**Field goals attempted**	Maravich, LSU, 1970	1,168
Free throw percentage	Boyer, Arkansas, 1962	.993	**Free throws attempted**	Selvy, Furman, 1954	444

Power Boat Racing Champions

APBA Gold Cup Race

Year	Boat	Owner	Driver	Winner's fastest heat MPH	Site
1964	Miss Bardahl	Ole Bardahl	Ron Musson	108.104	Detroit, Mich.
1965	Miss Bardahl	Ole Bardahl	Ron Musson	110.655	Seattle, Wash.
1966	Tahoe Miss.	Harrah's	Mira Slovak	97.861	Detroit, Mich.
1967	Miss Bardahl	Ole Bardahl	Bill Schumacher	104.691	Seattle, Wash.
1968	Miss Bardahl	Ole Bardahl	Bill Schumacher	111.248	Detroit, Mich.
1969	Miss Budweiser	Bernard Little & Tom Friedkin	Bill Sterett	103.587	San Diego, Cal.
1970	Miss Budweiser	Hydroplanes, Inc.	Dean Chenoweth	101.848	San Diego, Cal.
1971	Miss Madison	Miss Madison, Inc.	Jim McCormick	101.522	Madison, Ind.
1972	Atlas Van Lines	Atlas Van Lines	Bill Muncey	103.547	Detroit, Mich.
1973	Miss Budweiser	Hydroplanes, Inc.	Dean Chenoweth	104.046	Tri-Cities, Wash.
1974	Pay'N Pak	David J. Heerensperger	George Henley	112.056	Seattle, Wash.
1975	Pay 'N Pak	David J. Heerensperger	George Henley	113.350	Tri-Cities, Wash.
1976	Miss U.S.	U.S. Racing Team, Inc.	Tom D'Eath	108.021	Detroit, Mich.
1977	Atlas Van Lines	Bill Muncey Industries, Inc.	Bill Muncey	114.869	Tri-Cities, Wash.

World Swimming Records

As of Aug. 31, 1977

Effective June 1, 1969, FINA recognizes only records made over a 50-meter course.

Men's Records

Men's Freestyle

Distance	Time	Holder	Country	Where made	Date
100 Meters	0:49.44	Jonty Skinner	So. Africa	Philadelphia	Aug. 14, 1976
200 Meters	1:50.29	Bruce Furniss	U.S.	Montreal	July 19, 1976
400 Meters	3:51.56	Brian Goodell	U.S.	E. Berlin	Aug., 1977
800 Meters	8:01.54	Bobby Hackett	U.S.	Long Beach, Cal.	June 21, 1976
1,500 Meters	15:02.40	Brian Goodell	U.S.	Montreal	July 20, 1976

Men's Breaststroke

100 Meters	1:02.86	Gerald Morken	W. Germany	Jonkoping, Sweden	Aug. 17, 1977
200 Meters	2:15.11	David Wilkie	Gt. Britain	Montreal	July 24, 1976

Men's Butterfly

100 Meters	0.54,18	Joe Bottom	U.S.	E. Berlin	Aug., 1977
200 Meters	1:59.23	Mike Bruner	U.S.	Montreal	July 18, 1976

Men's Backstroke

100 Meters	0:55.49	John Naber	U.S.	Montreal	July 19, 1976
200 Meters	1:59.19	John Naber	U.S.	Montreal	July 24, 1976

Men's Individual Medley

200 Meters	2:05.31	Graham Smith	Canada	Montreal	Aug. 4, 1977
400 Meters	4:23.68	Rod Strachan	U.S.	Montreal	July 25, 1976

Men's Freestyle Relays

400 M. (4x100)	3:21.11	Babashoff, Bottom, DeMont, Montgomery	U.S.	E. Berlin	Aug., 1977
800 M. (4x200)	7:23.22	Bruner, Furniss, Naber, Montgomery	U.S.	Montreal	July 21, 1976

Men's Medley Relays

400 M. (4x100)	3:42.22	Hencken, Naber Montgomery, Vogel	U.S.	Montreal	July 22, 1976

Women's Records

Women's Freestyle

100 Meters	0:55.65	Kornelia Ender	E. Germany	Montreal	July 19, 1976
200 Meters	1:59.26	Kornelia Ender	E. Germany	Montreal	July 22, 1976
400 Meters	4:08.91	Petra Thumer	E. Germany	Jonkoping, Sweden	Aug. 17, 1977
800 Meters	8:35.04	Petra Thumer	E. Germany	Leipzig	July, 1977
1,500 Meters	16:24.60	Alice Browne	U.S.	Mission Viejo, Cal.	Aug. 21, 1977

Women's Breaststroke

100 Meters	1:10.86	Hannelore Anke	E. Germany	Montreal	July 22, 1976
200 Meters	2:33.35	Marina Koshevaia	USSR	Montreal	July 21, 1976

Women's Butterfly

100 Meters	0:59.78	Christiane Knacke	E. Germany	E. Berlin	Aug., 1977
200 Meters	2:11.22	Rosemarie Gabriel	E. Germany	E. Berlin	June 5, 1976

Women's Backstroke

100 Meters	1:01.51	Ulrike Richter	E. Germany	E. Berlin	June 5, 1976
200 Meters	2:12.47	Brigit Treiber	E. Germany	E. Berlin	June 4, 1976

Women's Individual Medley

200 Meters	2:15.85	Ulrike Tauber	E. Germany	E. Berlin	Aug., 1977
400 Meters	4:42.77	Ulrike Tauber	E. Germany	Montreal	July 24, 1976

Women's Freestyle Relays

400 M. (4x100)	3:44.82	Boglioli, Sterkel, Peyton, Babashoff	U.S.	Montreal	July 25, 1976

Women's Medley Relays

400 M. (4x100)	4:07.95	Richter, Anke, Pollack, Ender	E. Germany	Montreal	July 18, 1976

National AAU Indoor Diving Championships

Austin, Tex., Mar. 30-Apr. 2, 1977

Men

One-Meter Springboard — Robert Cregg, Kimball Divers. **747.05 pts.**
3-Meter Springboard — Phil Boggs, Kimball Divers, **842.220 pts.**
10-Meter Platform — Ken Vosler, unattached. **579.93. pts.**

Women

One-Meter Springboard — Cindy McIngvale, Nautilus Fitness Center. **651.435 pts.**
3-Meter Springboard — Cindy McIngvale. **690.945 pts.**
10-Meter Platform — Melissa Briley, Univ. of Miami. **327.39 pts.**

Swimming Events in 1977

National AAU Short Course Swimming Championships

Canton, Oh., Apr. 6-9, 1977

Men

100-Yd. Freestyle — Jonty Skinner, South Africa. **Time—0:43.92.**
200-Yd. Freestyle — James Montgomery, Gatorade SC. **Time—1:35.67.**
500-Yd. Freestyle — Bruce Furniss, USC. **Time—4:20.25.**
1,650-Yd. Freestyle — Bobby Hackett, Bernal's Gators. **Time—15:01.25.**
100-Yd. Backstroke — John Naber, USC. **Time—4:49.31.**
200-Yd. Backstroke — John Naber. **Time—1:46.56.**
100-Yd. Breaststroke — Scott Spann, Florida Aquatics. **Time—0:56.06.**
200-Yd. Breaststroke — Scott Spann. **Time—2:01.60.**
100-Yd. Butterfly — Joe Bottom, USC. **Time—0:48.42.**
200-Yd. Butterfly — Greg Jagenburg, Foxcatcher. **Time—1:46.50.**
200-Yd. Individual Medley — Scott Spann. **Time—1:49.61.**
400-Yd. Individual Medley — Bruce Furniss. **Time—3:52.07.**
400-Yd. Medley Relay — USC (Naber, Shearin, Pickell, Bottom). **Time—3:20.05.**
400-Yd. Freestyle Relay — Univ. of Tenn.-Holiday Inn (Newton, Sells, Ebuna, Coan). **Time—2:55.58**
800-Yd. Freestyle Relay — USC (Furniss, Greenwood, Pickell, Naber). **Time—6:29.07.**
Team Champion — USC.

Women

100-Yd. Freestyle — Jill Sterkel, El Monte Aquatics. **Time—0:49.88.**
200-Yd. Freestyle — Jill Sterkel. **Time—1:47.89.**
500-Yd. Freestyle — Jennifer Hooker, Mission Viejo. **Time—4:42.61.**
1,650-Yd. Freestyle — Jennifer Hooker. **Time—16:03.24.**
100-Yd. Backstroke — Linda Jezek, Santa Clara SC. **Time—0:56.51.**
200-Yd. Backstroke — Linda Jezek. **Time—2:00.52.**
100-Yd. Breaststroke — Tracy Caulkins, Nashville Aquatics. **Time—1:03.08.**
200-Yd. Breaststroke — Tracy Caulkins. **Time—2:16.97.**
100-Yd. Butterfly — Nancy Hogshead, Amberjax. **Time—0:54.57.**
200-Yd. Butterfly — Alice Browne, Mission Viejo. **Time—1:57.83**
200-Yd. Individual Medley — Nancy Garapick, Halifax Trojans. **Time—2:02.72.**
400-Yd. Individual Medley — Nancy Garapick. **Time—4:19.04.**
400-Yd. Medley Relay — Nashville Aquatics (Pennington, T. Caulkins, Miller, A. Caulkins). **Time—3:47.45.**
400-Yd. Freestyle Relay — El Monte Aquatics (Neilson, Seyfert, Hinderaker, Sterkel). **Time—3:23.15.**
800-Yd. Freestyle Relay — Mission Viejo (Browne, Kramer, Lee, Hooker). **Time—7:19.02.**
Team champion — Mission Viejo.

NCAA Swimming Championships

Cleveland, Oh., Mar. 25-27, 1977

50-Yd. Freestyle — Joe Bottom, USC. **Time—0.19.75.**
100-Yd. Freestyle — Dave Fairbank, Stanford. **Time—0:45.27.**
200-Yd. Freestyle — Bruce Furniss, USC. **Time—1.36.16.**
500-Yd. Freestyle — Tim Shaw, Long Beach State. **Time—4:17.39.**
1,650-Yd. Freestyle — Casey Converse, Al. **Time—14:57.30.**
100-Yd. Breaststroke — Graham Smith, California. **Time—0:55.10.**
200-Yd. Breaststroke — Graham Smith. **Time—2:00.05.**
100-Yd. Butterfly — Joe Bottom. **Time—0:47.77.**
200-Yd. Butterfly — Mike Bruner, Stanford. **Time—2:55.28.**
100-Yd. Backstroke — John Naber, USC. **Time—0:49.36.**
200-Yd. Backstroke — John Naber. **Time—1:46.09.**
200-Yd. Individual Medley — Scott Spann. **Time—1:48.26.**
400-Yd. Individual Medley — Rod Strachan, USC. **Time—3:54.76.**
400-Yd. Medley Relay — Indiana. **Time—3:17.14.**
400-Yd. Freestyle Relay — USC. **Time—6:28.11.**
One-Meter Dive — Matt Shelich, Mich.
3-Meter Dive — Brian Bungum, Indiana.
Team champion — USC.

Contract Bridge Championships in 1976-77

Source: American Contract Bridge League, Memphis, Tenn.

Fall Championships

Pittsburgh, Pa., Nov. 19-28, 1976; attendance, 8,788 tables

Reisinger Open Teams — Malcolm Brachman, Mike Passell, Bobby Goldman, Dallas; Paul Soloway, Eddie Kantar, Billy Eisenberg, Los Angeles.

Blue Ribbon Pairs — Jay Apfelbaum and William Edelstein, Philadelphia.

Life Master Men's Pairs — Roger Bates, Las Vegas and John Mohan, Leucadia, Cal.

Life Master Women's Pairs — Barbara Herr and Barbara Furbeck, Wilmington, Del.

Mixed Pairs — Steve Parker, Gaithersburg, Md. and Peggy Lipsitz, Potomac, Md.

Most Master Points for the Tournament — Paul Soloway, Los Angeles, 198.82 Master Points.

Spring Championships

Pasadena, Cal., Mar. 18-27, 1977; attendance, 12,713 tables

Vanderbilt Knockout Teams — Mark Blumenthal, Schaumburg, Ill.; Mike Lawrence, Berkeley; Fred Hamilton and John Swanson, Los Angeles; Mike Becker, New York; Ron Rubin, Maplewood, N.J.

Men's Teams — Richard Doughty, Baton Rouge, La.; Ron Smith, Flagstaff; Ariz.; Lou Bluhm, Atlanta (plus these players who played only one session each: Sidney Lazard, New Orleans; Les West, Oakland; Irv Kostal, Sherman Oaks; Bruce Ferguson, New Westminister, B.C.)

Women's Knockout Teams — Judi Radin, New York; Jo Morse, Silver Spring, Md.; Betty Adler and Sue Sachs, Baltimore. (Katherine Wei, New York, non-playing captain).

Men's Pairs — Joseph Fox, La Canada; Garey Hayden, Dallas.

Women's Pairs Jacqui Mitchell and Gail Moss, New York.

Open Pairs — Barry Crane, Studio City; Peter Rank, Los Angeles.

Most Master Points for the Tournament — Mark Blumenthal, Schaumburg, Ill., 200 Master Points.

Summer Championships

Chicago, Ill., July 15-24, 1977; attendance 13,171 tables

Spingold Knockout Teams —Curtis Smith, Conroe, Tex.; Dan Morse and Eddie Wold, Houston; Cliff Russell, Miami; Thomas Sanders, Nashville; Lou Bluhm, Atlanta.

Grand National Teams — Bob Hamman and Bobby Wolff, Dallas; Curtis Smith, Conroe, Tex.; Eddie Wold and Dan Morse, Houston.

Master Mixed Teams — Joan DeWitt, Chicago; Sidney Lazard, New Orleans; Nancy Alpaugh, Metairie, La.; Mark Lair, St. Louis.

Life Master Pairs — Alan Sontag, New York; Peter Weichsel, Flushing, N.Y.

Most Master Points for Tournament — Ken Cohen, Philadelphia, 198.10 Master Points.

Auto Racing

Indianapolis 500 Winners

Year	Winner	Chassis	Engine	MPH	Winnings	Runner up
1947	Mauri Rose	Deidt	Offenhauser	116.338	$137,425	Bill Holland
1948	Mauri Rose	Deidt	Offenhauser	119.814	171,075	Bill Holland
1949	Bill Holland	Deidt	Offenhauser	121.327	179,050	Johnnie Parsons
1950	Johnnie Parsons	Kurtis Kraft	Offenhauser	124.002(a)	201,135	Bill Holland
1951	Lee Wallard	Kurtis Kraft	Offenhauser	126.244	207,650	Mike Nazaruk
1952	Troy Ruttman	Kuzma	Offenhauser	128.922	230,100	Jim Rathmann
1953	Bill Vukovich	Kurtis Kraft 500A	Offenhauser	128.740	246,300	Art Cross
1954	Bill Vukovich	Kurtis Kraft 500A	Offenhauser	130.840	269,375	Jim Bryan
1955	Bob Sweikert	Kurtis Kraft 500C	Offenhauser	128.209	270,400	Tony Bettenhausen
1956	Pat Flaherty	Watson	Offenhauser	128.490	282,052	Sam Hanks
1957	Sam Hanks	Epperly	Offenhauser	135.601	300,252	Jim Rathmann
1958	Jimmy Bryan	Epperly	Offenhauser	133.791	305,217	George Amick
1959	Rodger Ward	Watson	Offenhauser	135.857	338,100	Jim Rathmann
1960	Jim Rathmann	Watson	Offenhauser	138.767	369,150	Rodger Ward
1961	A. J. Foyt	Watson	Offenhauser	139.130	400,000	Eddie Sachs
1962	Rodger Ward	Watson	Offenhauser	140.293	426,152	Len Sutton
1963	Parnelli Jones	Watson	Offenhauser	143.137	494,031	Jim Clark
1964	A. J. Foyt	Watson	Offenhauser	147.350	506,625	Rodger Ward
1965	Jim Clark	Lotus	Ford	151.388	628,399	Parnelli Jones
1966	Graham Hill	Lola	Ford	144.317	691,809	Jim Clark
1967	A. J. Foyt	Coyote	Ford	151.207	737,109	Al Unser
1968	Bobby Unser	Eagle	Offenhauser	152.882	809,627	Dan Gurney
1969	Mario Andretti	Hawk	Ford	156.867	805,127	Dan Gurney
1970	Al Unser	P. J. Colt	Ford	155.749	1,000,002	Mark Donohue
1971	Al Unser	P. J. Colt	Ford	157.735	1,001,604	Peter Revson
1972	Mark Donohue	McLaren	Offenhauser	163.465	1,011,846	Al Unser
1973	Gordon Johncock	Eagle	Offenhauser	159.014 (b)	1,011,846	Billy Vukovich
1974	Johnny Rutherford	McLaren	Offenhauser	158.589	1,015,686	Bobby Unser
1975	Bobby Unser	Eagle	Offenhauser	149.213(c)	1,101,322	Johnny Rutherford
1976	Johnny Rutherford	McLaren	Offenhauser	148.725 (d)	1,037,775	A.J. Foyt
1977	A.J. Foyt	Coyote	Ford	161.331	1,116,807	Tom Sneva

(a) 345 miles. (b) 332.5 miles. (c) 435 miles. (d) 255 miles. Race Record—163.465 MPH, Mark Donohue, 1972.

1977 Indianapolis 500 Final Standings

1—A. J. Foyt, Houston, Tex., Coyote-Foyt; 200 laps; 500 miles; 161.331 miles per hour.
2—Tom Sneva, Spokane, Wash., McLaren-Cosworth; 200 laps; 160.930.
3—Al Unser, Albuquerque, N.M., Parnelli-Cosworth; 199 laps; 160.426.
4—Wally Dallenbach, Basalt, Col., Wildcat-DGS; 199 laps; 159.626.
5—Johnny Parsons, Indianapolis, Ind., Wildcat-DGS; 194 laps; 155.324.
6—Tom Bigelow; Whitewater, Wis., Watson-Offenhauser; 192 laps; 154.217.
7—Lee Kunzman, Guttenberg, Ia., Eagle-Offenhauser; 191 laps; 153.510.
8—Roger McCluskey, Tucson, Ariz., Lightning-Offenhauser; 191 laps; 153.181.

World's Land Speed Records—Evolution

Date	Driver	Car	MPH
12/18/98	Chassenloup-Laubat	Jeantaud	39.24
4/29/99	Jenatzy	Jamais Contente Jenatzy	65.79
11/17/02	Augieres	Mars	77.13
11/ 5/03	Duray	Gabron-Brillie	84.73
12/30/04	Barras	Darracq	109.65
1/25/05	Bowden	Mercedes	109.75
1/26/06	Marriott	Stanley (Steam)	127.659
3/16/10	Oldfield	Benz	131.724
4/23/11	Burman	Benz	141.732
2/12/19	DePalma	Packard	149.875
4/27/20	Milton	Dusenberg	155.046
4/28/26	Parry-Thomas	Thomas Spl.	170.624
3/29/27	Seagrave	Sunbeam	203.790
4/22/28	Keech	White Triplex	207.552
3/11/29	Seagrave	Irving-Napier	231.446
2/ 5/31	Campbell	Napier-Campbell	246.086
2/24/32	Campbell	Napier-Campbell	253.96
2/22/33	Campbell	Napier-Campbell	272.109
9/ 3/35	Campbell	Bluebird Special	301.13
11/19/37	Eyston	Thunderbolt 1	311.42
9/16/38	Eyston	Thunderbolt 1	357.5
8/23/39	Cobb	Railton	368.9
9/16/47	Cobb	Railton-Mobil	394.2
8/ 5/63	Breedlove	Spirit of America	407.45
10/27/64	Arfons	Green Monster	536.71
11/15/65	Breedlove	Spirit of America	600.601
10/23/70	Gabelich	Blue Flame	622.407

World Grand Prix Champions

Year	Driver
1950	Nino Farina, Italy
1951	Juan Fangio, Argentina
1952	Alberto Ascari, Italy
1953	Alberto Ascari, Italy
1954	Juan Fangio, Argentina
1955	Juan Fangio, Argentina
1956	Juan Fangio, Argentina
1957	Juan Fangio, Argentina
1958	Mike Hawthorne, England
1959	Jack Brabham, Australia
1960	Jack Brabham, Australia
1961	Phil Hill, United States
1962	Graham Hill, England
1963	Jim Clark, Scotland
1964	John Surtees, England
1965	Jim Clark, Scotland
1966	Jack Brabham, Australia
1967	Denis Hulme, New Zealand
1968	Graham Hill, England
1969	Jackie Stewart, Scotland
1970	Jochen Rindt, Austria
1971	Jackie Stewart, Scotland
1972	Emerson Fittipaldi, Brazil
1973	Jackie Stewart, Scotland
1974	Emerson Fittipaldi, Brazil
1975	Nicki Lauda, Austria
1976	James Hunt, England

American Automobile Assn. National Champions

Year	Driver
1953	Sam Hawks
1954	Jimmy Bryan
1955	Bob Sweikert
1956	Jimmy Bryan
1957	Jimmy Bryan
1958	Tony Bettenhausen
1959	Rodger Ward
1960	A. J. Foyt
1961	A. J. Foyt
1962	Rodger Ward
1963	A. J. Foyt
1964	A. J. Foyt
1965	Mario Andretti
1966	Mario Andretti
1967	A. J. Foyt
1968	Bobby Unser
1969	Mario Andretti
1970	Al Unser
1971	Joe Leonard
1972	Joe Leonard
1973	Roger McCluskey
1974	Bobby Unser
1975	A. J. Foyt
1976	Gordon Johncock

Grand Prix for Formula 1 Cars in 1977

Grand Prix	Winner, car
Argentine	Jody Scheckter, Wolf-Ford
Austrian	Alan Jones, Shadow
Belgian	Gunnar Nilsson, Lotus
British	James Hunt, McLaren
Brazilian	Carlos Reutemann, Ferrari
Dutch	Niki Lauda, Ferrari
French	Mario Andretti, Lotus
Italian	Mario Andretti, Lotus
Monaco	Jody Scheckter, Wolf-Ford
South African	Niki Lauda, Ferrari
Spanish	Mario Andretti, Lotus
Swedish	Jacques Laffite, Ligier-Matra
United States	James Hunt, McLaren
United States (west)	Mario Andretti, Lotus
West German	Niki Lauda, Ferrari

NASCAR Racing in 1977

Winston Cup Grand National Races

Date	Race, site	Winner	Car	Winnings
Jan. 16	Winston Western 500, Riverside, Cal.	David Pearson	Mercury	$11,545
Feb. 20	Daytona 500, Daytona Beach, Fla.	Cale Yarborough	Chevrolet	47,200
Feb. 27	Richmond 400, Richmond, Va.	Cale Yarborough	Chevrolet	10,450
Mar. 13	Carolina 500, Rockingham, N.C.	Richard Petty	Dodge	13,555
Mar. 20	Atlanta 500, Atlanta, Ga.	Richard Petty	Dodge	17,200
Mar. 27	Gwyn Staley 400, N. Wilkesboro, N.C.	Cale Yarborough	Chevrolet	12,350
Apr. 3	Rebel 500, Darlington, S.C.	Darrell Waltrip	Chevrolet	13,870
Apr. 17	Southeastern 500, Bristol, Tenn.	Cale Yarborough	Chevrolet	21,050
Apr. 24	Virginia 500, Martinsville, Va.	Cale Yarborough	Chevrolet	19,350
May 1	Winston 500, Talladega, Ala.	Darrell Waltrip	Chevrolet	20,000
May 7	Music City USA 420, Nashville, Tenn.	Benny Parsons	Chevrolet	7,315
May 15	Mason-Dixon 500, Dover, Del.	Cale Yarborough	Chevrolet	15,400
May 29	World 600, Charlotte, N.C.	Richard Petty	Dodge	62,300
June 12	Napa Riverside 400, Riverside, Cal.	Richard Petty	Dodge	14,400
June 19	Cam2 Motor Oil 400, Brooklyn, Mich.	Cale Yarborough	Chevrolet	15,475
July 4	Firecracker 400, Daytona Beach, Fla.	Richard Petty	Dodge	19,075
July 16	Nashville 420, Nashville, Tenn.	Darrell Waltrip	Chevrolet	7,165
July 31	Coca-Cola 500, Pocono, Pa.	Benny Parsons	Chevrolet	13,700
Aug. 7	Talladega 500, Talladega, Ala.	Donnie Allison	Chevrolet	21,550
Aug. 22	Champion Spark Plug 400, Brooklyn, Mich.	Darrell Waltrip	Chevrolet	13,920
Aug. 28	Volunteer 400, Bristol, Tenn.	Cale Yarborough	Chevrolet	10,450
Sept. 5	Southern 500, Darlington, S.C.	David Pearson	Mercury	17,300
Sept. 11	Capital City 400, Richmond, Va.	Neil Bonnett	Dodge	7,050
Sept. 18	Delaware 500, Dover, Del.	Benny Parsons	Chevrolet	13,900
Sept. 25	Old Dominion 500, Martinsville, Va.	Cale Yarborough	Chevrolet	21,800
Oct. 2	Wilkes 400, No. Wilkesboro, N.C.	Darrell Waltrip	Chevrolet	10,650

Daytona 500 Winners

Year	Driver, car	Avg. MPH
1961	Marvin Panch, Pontiac	149.601
1962	Fireball Roberts, Pontiac	152.529
1963	Tiny Lund, Ford	151.566
1964	Richard Petty, Plymouth	154.334
1965	Fred Lorenzen, Ford (a)	141.539
1966	Richard Petty, Plymouth (b)	160.627
1967	Mario Andretti, Ford	146.926
1968	Cale Yarborough, Mercury	143.251
1969	Lee Roy Yarborough, Ford	160.875
1970	Pete Hamilton, Plymouth	149.601
1971	Richard Petty, Plymouth	144.456
1972	A. J. Foyt, Mercury	161.550
1973	Richard Petty, Dodge	157.205
1974	Richard Petty, Dodge (c)	140.894
1975	Benny Parsons, Chevrolet	153.649
1976	David Pearson, Mercury	152.181
1977	Cale Yarborough, Chevrolet	153.218

(a) 322.5 miles because of rain. (b) 495 miles because of rain. (c) 450 miles.

Leading Daytona 500 Finishers in 1977

	Driver, car	Laps	Winnings
1	Cale Yarborough, Chevrolet	200	$47,200
2	Benny Parsons, Chevrolet	200	30,400
3	Buddy Baker, Ford	199	23,850
4	Coo Coo Marlin, Chevrolet	198	16,875
5	Richard Brooks, Ford	198	17,625
6	A. J. Foyt, Chevrolet	197	$13,600
7	Darrell Waltrip, Chevrolet	193	15,745
8	Jimmy Means, Chevrolet	192	10,985
9	Bob Burcham, Chevrolet	191	12,475
10	James Hylton, Chevrolet	189	11,090

Grand National Champions (NASCAR)

Year	Driver
1951	Herb Thomas
1952	Tim Flock
1953	Herb Thomas
1954	Lee Petty
1955	Tim Flock
1956	Buck Baker
1957	Buck Baker
1958	Lee Petty
1959	Lee Petty
1960	Rex White
1961	Ned Jarrett
1962	Joe Weatherly
1963	Joe Weatherly
1964	Richard Petty
1965	Ned Jarrett
1966	David Pearson
1967	Richard Petty
1968	David Pearson
1969	David Pearson
1970	Bobby Isaac
1971	Richard Petty
1972	Richard Petty
1973	Benny Parsons
1974	Richard Petty
1975	Richard Petty
1976	Cale Yarborough

Motorcycle Racing

Grand National Champion

Year	Champion
1953	Bill Tuman
1954	Joe Leonard
1955	Brad Andres
1956	Joe Leonard
1957	Joe Leonard
1958	Carroll Resweber
1959	Carroll Resweber
1960	Carroll Resweber
1961	Carroll Resweber
1962	Bart Markel
1963	Dick Mann
1964	Roger Reiman
1965	Bart Markel
1966	Bart Markel
1967	Gary Nixon
1968	Gary Nixon
1969	Mert Lawwill
1970	Gene Romero
1971	Dick Mann
1972	Mark Brelsford
1973	Ken Roberts
1974	Ken Roberts
1975	Gary Scott
1976	Jay Springsteen

Golf Records

United States Open

Year	Winner	Year	Winner	Year	Winner	Year	Winner
1896	James Foulis	1916	Chick Evans*	1937	Ralph Guldahl	1959	Billy Casper
1897	Joe Lloyd	1917-18	(Not played)	1938	Ralph Guldahl	1960	Arnold Palmer
1898	Fred Herd	1919	Walter Hagen	1939	Byron Nelson	1961	Gene Littler
1899	Willie Smith	1920	Edward Ray	1940	Lawson Little	1962	Jack Nicklaus
1900	Harry Vardon	1921	Jim Barnes	1941	Craig Wood	1963	Julius Boros
1901	Willie Anderson	1922	Gene Sarazen	1942-45	(Not played)	1964	Ken Venturi
1902	L. Auchterlonie	1923	Bob Jones*	1946	Lloyd Mangrum	1965	Gary Player
1903	Willie Anderson	1924	Cyril Walker	1947	L. Worsham	1966	Billy Casper
1904	Willie Anderson	1925	Willie MacFarlane	1948	Ben Hogan	1967	Jack Nicklaus
1905	Willie Anderson	1926	Bob Jones*	1949	Cary Middlecoff	1968	Lee Trevino
1906	Alex Smith	1927	Tommy Armour	1950	Ben Hogan	1969	Orville Moody
1907	Alex Ross	1928	John Farrell	1951	Ben Hogan	1970	Tony Jacklin
1908	Fred McLeod	1929	Bob Jones*	1952	Julius Boros	1971	Lee Trevino
1909	George Sargent	1930	Bob Jones*	1953	Ben Hogan	1972	Jack Nicklaus
1910	Alex Smith	1931	Wm. Burke	1954	Ed Furgol	1973	Johnny Miller
1911	John McDermott	1932	Gene Sarazen	1955	Jack Fleck	1974	Hale Irwin
1912	John McDermott	1933	John Goodman*	1956	Cary Middlecoff	1975	Lou Graham
1913	Francis Ouimet*	1934	Olin Dutra	1957	Dick Mayer	1976	Jerry Pate
1914	Walter Hagen	1935	Sam Parks Jr.	1958	Tommy Bolt	1977	Hubert Green
1915	Jerome Travers*	1936	Tony Manero				

*Amateur

U. S. Women's Open Golf Champions

Year	Winner	Year	Winner	Year	Winner	Year	Winner
1948	"Babe" Zaharias	1956	Mrs. K. Cornelius	1964	Mickey Wright	1971	JoAnne Carner
1949	Louise Suggs	1957	Betsy Rawls	1965	Carol Mann	1972	Susie Maxwell Berning
1950	"Babe" Zaharias	1958	Mickey Wright	1966	Sandra Spuzich	1973	Susie Maxwell Berning
1951	Betsy Rawls	1959	Mickey Wright	1967	Catherine Lacoste*	1974	Sandra Haynie
1952	Louise Suggs	1960	Betsy Rawls	1968	Susie Maxwell Berning	1975	Sandra Palmer
1953	Betsy Rawls	1961	Mickey Wright	1969	Donna Caponi	1976	JoAnne Carner
1954	"Babe" Zaharias	1962	Marie Lindstrom	1970	Donna Caponi	1977	Hollis Stacy
1955	Fay Crocker	1963	Mary Mills				

*Amateur

Professional Golfers' Association Championships

Year	Winner	Year	Winner	Year	Winner	Year	Winner
1919	Jim Barnes	1934	Paul Runyan	1950	Chandler Harper	1964	Bob Nichols
1920	Jock Hutchison	1935	Johnny Revolta	1951	Sam Snead	1965	Dave Marr
1921	Walter Hagen	1936	Denny Shute	1952	James Turnesa	1966	Al Geiberger
1922	Gene Sarazen	1937	Denny Shute	1953	Walter Burkemo	1967	Don January
1923	Gene Sarazen	1938	Paul Runyan	1954	Melvin Harbert	1968	Julius Boros
1924	Walter Hagen	1939	Henry Picard	1955	Doug Ford	1969	Ray Floyd
1925	Walter Hagen	1940	Byron Nelson	1956	Jack Burke	1970	Dave Stockton
1926	Walter Hagen	1941	Victor Ghezzi	1957	Lionel Hebert	1971	Jack Nicklaus
1927	Walter Hagen	1942	Sam Snead	1958	Dow Finsterwald	1972	Gary Player
1928	Leo Diegel	1944	Bob Hamilton	1959	Bob Rosburg	1973	Jack Nicklaus
1929	Leo Diegel	1945	Byron Nelson	1960	Jay Hebert	1974	Lee Trevino
1930	Tommy Armour	1946	Ben Hogan	1961	Jerry Barber	1975	Jack Nicklaus
1931	Tom Creavy	1947	Jim Ferrier	1962	Gary Player	1976	Dave Stockton
1932	Olin Dutra	1948	Ben Hogan	1963	Jack Nicklaus	1977	Lanny Wadkins
1933	Gene Sarazen	1949	Sam Snead				

Masters Golf Tournament Champions

Year	Winner	Year	Winner	Year	Winner	Year	Winner
1934	Horton Smith	1947	Jimmy Demaret	1958	Arnold Palmer	1968	Bob Goalby
1935	Gene Sarazen	1948	Claude Harmon	1959	Art Wall Jr.	1969	George Archer
1936	Horton Smith	1949	Sam Snead	1960	Arnold Palmer	1970	Billy Casper
1937	Byron Nelson	1950	Jimmy Demaret	1961	Gary Player	1971	Charles Coody
1938	Henry Picard	1951	Ben Hogan	1962	Arnold Palmer	1972	Jack Nicklaus
1939	Ralph Guldahl	1952	Sam Snead	1963	Jack Nicklaus	1973	Tommy Aaron
1940	Jimmy Demaret	1953	Ben Hogan	1964	Arnold Palmer	1974	Gary Player
1941	Craig Wood	1954	Sam Snead	1965	Jack Nicklaus	1975	Jack Nicklaus
1942	Byron Nelson	1955	Cary Middlecoff	1966	Jack Nicklaus	1976	Ray Floyd
1943-1945	(Not played)	1956	Jack Burke	1967	Gay Brewer Jr.	1977	Tom Watson
1946	Herman Keiser	1957	Doug Ford				

Canadian Open Golf Champions

Year	Winner	Year	Winner	Year	Winner	Year	Winner
1942	Craig Wood	1952	John Palmer	1961	Jacky Cupit	1970	Kermit Zarley
1943-44	(Not played)	1953	Dave Douglas	1962	Ted Kroll	1971	Lee Trevino
1945	Byron Nelson	1954	Pat Fletcher	1963	Doug Ford	1972	Gay Brewer
1946	George Fazio	1955	Arnold Palmer	1964	Kel Nagle	1973	Tom Weiskopf
1947	Bobby Locke	1956	Doug Sanders	1965	Gene Littler	1974	Bobby Nichols
1948	C. W. Congdon	1957	George Bayer	1966	Don Massengale	1975	Tom Weiskopf
1949	E. J. Harrison	1958	Wes Ellis Jr.	1967	Billy Casper	1976	Jerry Pate
1950	Jim Ferrier	1959	Doug Ford	1968	Bob Charles	1977	Lee Trevino
1951	Jim Ferrier	1960	Art Wall, Jr.	1969	Tommy Aaron		

Professional Golf Tournaments in 1977

Date	Event	Winner	Score	Prize
Jan. 9	Phoenix Open	Jerry Pate	*277	$40,000
Jan. 16	Tucson Open	Bruce Lietzke	*275	40,000
Jan. 23	Bing Crosby National Pro-Am, Pebble Beach, Cal.	Tom Watson	273	40,000
Jan. 30	Andy Williams-San Diego Open	Tom Watson	269	36,000
Feb. 6	Hawaiian Open, Honolulu	Bruce Lietzke	273	48,000
Feb. 13	Bob Hope Desert Classic, Palm Springs, Cal.	Rik Massengale	337	40,000
Feb. 20	Los Angeles Open	Tom Purtzer	273	40,000
Feb. 27	Jackie Gleason — Inverrary Classic, Ft. Lauderdale, Fla.	Jack Nicklaus	275	50,000
Mar. 6	Florida Citrus Open, Orlando	Gary Koch	274	40,000
Mar. 13	Doral-Eastern Open, Miami, Fla.	Andy Bean	277	40,000
Mar. 20	Tournament Players Championship, Ponte Vedra Beach, Fla.	Mark Hayes	289	60,000
Mar. 27	Heritage Golf Classic, Hilton Head Island, S.C.	Graham Marsh	273	45,000
Apr. 3	Greater Greensboro Open, N.C.	Danny Edwards	276	47,000
Apr. 10	Masters Tournament, Augusta, Ga.	Tom Watson	276	40,000
Apr. 17	Tournament of Champions, Carlsbad, Cal.	Jack Nicklaus	*281	45,000
Apr. 24	New Orleans Open	Jim Simons	273	35,000
May 1	Houston Open	Gene Littler	276	40,000
May 8	Byron Nelson Classic, Dallas, Tex.	Ray Floyd	276	40,000
May 15	Colonial National Tournament, Ft. Worth, Tex.	Ben Crenshaw	272	40,000
May 23	Memorial Tournament, Dublin, Oh.	Jack Nicklaus	281	45,000
May 29	Atlanta Classic	Hale Irwin	273	40,000
June 5	Kemper Open, Charlotte, N.C.	Tom Weiskopf	277	50,000
June 12	Danny Thomas, Memphis Open	Al Geiberger	273	40,000
June 19	U.S. Open, Tulsa, Okla.	Hubert Green	278	45,000
June 26	Western Open, Oak Brook, Ill.	Tom Watson	283	40,000
July 3	Greater Milwaukee Open	Dave Eichelberger	278	26,000
July 10	Quad Cities Open, Coal Valley, Ill.	Mike Morley	267	25,000
July 17	Pleasant Valley Classic, Sutton, Mass.	Ray Floyd	271	50,000
July 24	Canadian Open, Oakville, Ont.	Lee Trevino	280	45,000
July 31	Philadelphia Classic	Jerry McGee	272	40,000
Aug. 7	Sammy Davis Jr. — Greater Hartford Open	Bill Kratzert	265	42,000
Aug. 14	PGA Championship, Pebble Beach, Cal.	*Lanny Wadkins	282	45,000
Aug. 21	Westchester Classic, Harrison, N.Y.	Andy North	272	60,000
Aug. 28	Hall of Fame Classic, Pinehurst, N.C.	Hale Irwin	264	50,000
Sept. 5	World Series of Golf, Akron, Ohio	Lanny Wadkins	267	100,000
Sept. 11	B.C. Open, Endicott, N.Y.	Gil Morgan	270	40,000
Sept. 25	Ohio Kings Island Open, Mason, Oh.	Mike Hill	269	30,000
Oct. 2	Anheuser-Busch Classic, Napa, Cal.	Miller Barber	272	40,000

Women

Date	Event	Winner	Score	Prize
Jan. 16	Colgate Triple Crown, Palm Springs, Cal.	Jane Blalock	143	$15,000
Feb. 20	Orange Blossom Classic, St. Petersburg, Fla.	Judy Rankin	208	7,500
Feb. 27	Bent Tree Classic, Sarasota, Fla.	Judy Rankin	209	15,000
Mar. 27	Kathryn Crosby Tournament, Rancho Santa Fe, Cal.	Sandra Palmer	281	22,500
Apr. 3	Colgate -Dinah Shore Winners Circle Tournament	Kathy Whitworth	289	36,000
Apr. 17	Women's International, Hilton Head Island, S.C.	Sandra Palmer	281	12,000
Apr. 24	American Defender Classic, Raleigh, N.C.	Kathy Whitworth	206	7,500
May 1	Birmingham Classic	Debbie Austin	207	9,000
May 15	Greater Baltimore Classic	Jane Blalock	209	8,250
May 22	Coca-Cola Classic, Jamesburg, N.J.	Kathy Whitworth	202	11,500
May 29	Ladies Keystone Open, Harrisburg, Pa.	Sandra Spuzich	201	7,500
June 5	Talk Tournament, New Rochelle, N.Y.	JoAnne Carner	284	15,000
June 12	LPGA Classic, North Myrtle Beach, S.C.	Chako Higuchi	279	22,500
June 26	Hoosier Classic, Plymouth, Ind.	Debbie Austin	207	7,500
July 3	Peter Jackson Classic, Lachute, Que.	Judy Rankin	212	12,000
July 17	Bordon Classic, Dublin, Oh.	JoAnne Carner	207	12,000
July 24	U.S. Women's Open, Chaska, Minn.	Hollis Stacy	292	11,040
July 31	Pocono Northeast Classic, Mt. Pocono, Pa.	Debbie Austin	213	11,000
Aug. 14	Long Island Charity Classic, Hauppauge, N.Y.	Debbie Austin	279	15,000
Aug. 28	Patty Berg Classic, St. Paul, Minn.	Bonnie Lauer	212	8,250
Sept. 5	Muscular Dystrophy Tournament, Springfield, Ill.	Hollis Stacy	271	15,000
Sept. 11	National Jewish Hospital Open, Denver	JoAnne Carner	210	7,500
Sept. 25	Sarah Coventry Classic, Alamo, Cal.	Jane Blalock	282	15,000

*Won Playoff

British Open Golf Champions

Year	Winner	Year	Winner	Year	Winner	Year	Winner
1908	James Braid	1927	Bob Jones	1947	Fred Daly	1962	Arnold Palmer
1909	J. H. Taylor	1928	Walter Hagen	1948	Henry Cotton	1963	Bob Charles
1910	James Braid	1929	Walter Hagen	1949	Bobby Locke	1964	Tony Lema
1911	Harry Vardon	1930	Bob Jones	1950	Bobby Locke	1965	Peter Thomson
1912	Ted Ray	1931	Tommy Armour	1951	Max Faulkner	1966	Jack Nicklaus
1913	J. H. Taylor	1932	Gene Sarazen	1952	Bobby Locke	1967	Roberto de Vicenzo
1914	Harry Vardon	1933	Denny Shute	1953	Ben Hogan	1968	Gary Player
1915-19	(Not played)	1934	Henry Cotton	1954	Peter Thomson	1969	Tony Jacklin
1920	George Duncan	1935	Alf Perry	1955	Peter Thomson	1970	Jack Nicklaus
1921	Jock Hutchison	1936	Alf Padgham	1956	Peter Thomson	1971	Lee Trevino
1922	Walter Hagen	1937	T. H. Cotton	1957	Bobby Locke	1972	Lee Trevino
1923	Arthur Havers	1938	R. A. Whitcombe	1958	Peter Thomson	1973	Tom Weiskopf
1924	Walter Hagen	1939	Richard Burton	1959	Gary Player	1974	Gary Player
1925	Jim Barnes	1940-45	(Not played)	1960	Ken Nagle	1975	Tom Watson
1926	Bob Jones	1946	Sam Snead	1961	Arnold Palmer	1976	Johnny Miller
						1977	Tom Watson

U.S. Amateur

Year	Winner	Year	Winner	Year	Winner	Year	Winner
1902	Louis James	1921	Jesse Guilford	1939	Bud Ward	1960	Deane Beman
1903	Walter Travis	1922	Jess Sweetser	1940	Dick Chapman	1961	Jack Nicklaus
1904	Chandler Egan	1923	Max Marston	1941	Bud Ward	1962	Labron Harris Jr.
1905	Chandler Egan	1924	Bob Jones	1942-45	(not played)	1963	Deane Beman
1906	Eben Byers	1925	Bob Jones	1946	Ted Bishop	1964	Bill Campbell
1907	Jerome Travers	1926	George Von Elm	1947	Skee Riegel	1965	Robert Murphy Jr.
1908	Jerome Travers	1927	Bob Jones	1948	Willie Turnesa	1966	Gary Cowan
1909	Robert Gardner	1928	Bob Jones	1949	Charles Coe	1967	Bob Dickson
1910	William Fownes Jr.	1929	Harrison Johnston	1950	Sam Urzetta	1968	Bruce Fleisher
1911	Harold Hilton	1930	Bob Jones	1951	Billy Maxwell	1969	Steve Melnyk
1912	Jerome Travers	1931	Francis Ouimet	1952	Jack Westland	1970	Lanny Wadkins
1913	Jerome Travers	1932	Ross Somerville	1953	Gene Littler	1971	Gary Cowan
1914	Francis Ouimet	1933	George Dunlap Jr.	1954	Arnold Palmer	1972	Vinnie Giles
1915	Robert Gardner	1934	Lawson Little	1955	Harvie Ward	1973	Craig Stadler
1916	Chick Evans Jr.	1935	Lawson Little	1956	Harvie Ward	1974	Jerry Pate
1917-18	(not played)	1936	John Fischer	1957	Hillman Robbins	1975	Fred Ridley
1919	Davidson Herron	1937	John Goodman	1958	Charles Coe	1976	Bill Sander
1920	Chick Evans Jr.	1938	Willie Turnesa	1959	Jack Nicklaus	1977	John Fought

Women's U.S. Amateur

Year	Winner	Year	Winner	Year	Winner	Year	Winner
1905	Pauline Mackay	1924	Mrs. D. C. Hurd	1941	Mrs. Frank New	1961	Anne Q. Decker
1906	Harriot Curtis	1925	Glenna Collett	1942-45	(not played)	1962	JoAnne Gunderson
1907	Margaret Curtis	1926	Mrs. G. Stetson	1946	"Babe" Zaharias	1963	Anne Q. Welts
1908	Kate Harley	1927	Mrs. M. Horn	1947	Louise Suggs	1964	Barbara McIntire
1909	Dorothy Campbell	1928	Glenna Collett	1948	Grace Lenczyk	1965	Jean Ashley
1910	Dorothy Campbell	1929	Glenna Collett	1949	Dorothy Porter	1966	JoAnne Carner
1911	Margaret Curtis	1930	Glenna Collett	1950	Beverly Hanson	1967	Lou Dill
1912	Margaret Curtis	1931	Helen Hicks	1951	Dorothy Kirby	1968	JoAnne Carner
1913	Gladys Raven Scroft	1932	Virginia Van Wie	1952	Jackie Pung	1969	Catherine Lacoste
1914	Mrs. H. A. Jackson	1933	Virginia Van Wie	1953	Mary Faulk	1970	Martha Wilkinson
1915	Mrs. C. H. Vanderbeck	1934	Virginia Van Wie	1954	Barbara Romack	1971	Laura Baugh
1916	Alexa Stirling	1935	Glenna C. Vare	1955	Pat Lesser	1972	Mary Budke
1917-18	(not played)	1936	Pamela Barton	1956	Marlene Stewart	1973	Carol Semple
1919	Alexa Stirling	1937	Mrs. J. A. Page	1957	JoAnne Gunderson	1974	Cynthia Hill
1920	Alexa Stirling	1938	Patty Berg	1958	Anne Quast	1975	Beth Daniel
1921	Marion Hollins	1939	Betty Jameson	1959	Barbara McIntire	1976	Donna Horton
1922	Glenna Collett	1940	Betty Jameson	1960	JoAnne Gunderson	1977	Beth Daniel
1923	Edith Cummings						

British Amateur Golf Champions

Year	Winner	Year	Winner	Year	Winner	Year	Winner
1930	Bobby Jones (U.S.)	1946	James Bruen	1957	Reid Jack	1968	Mike Bonallack
1931	E. Martin-Smith	1947	Willie Turnesa	1958	Joseph Carr	1969	Mike Bonallack
1932	J. De Forest	1948	Frank Stranahan (U.S.)	1959	deane Beman (U.S.)	1970	Mike Bonallack
1933	Michael Scott	1949	Sam McCready	1960	Joseph Carr	1971	Steve Melnyk (U.S.)
1934	Lawson Little (U.S.)	1950	Frank Stranahan (U.S.)	1961	Michael Bonallack	1972	Trevor Homer
1935	Lawson Little (U.S.)	1951	Dick Chapman (U.S.)	1962	Richard Davies (U.S.)	1973	Dick Siderowe (U.S.)
1936	H. Thompson	1952	Harvie Ward (U.S.)	1963	Michael Lunt	1974	Trevor Homer
1937	Robert Sweeny	1953	Joseph Carr	1964	Gordon Clark	1975	Vinny Giles (U.S.)
1938	C. Yates (U.S.)	1954	Doug Bachli	1965	Mike Bonallack	1976	Dick Siderowf (U.S.)
1939	Alex Kyle	1955	Joseph Conrad (U.S.)	1966	Bobby Cole	1977	Peter McEvoy
1940-45	(not played)	1956	John Beharrell	1967	Bob Dickson (U.S.)		

PGA Hall of Fame

Established in 1940 to honor those who have made outstanding contributions to the game by their lifetime playing ability.

Anderson, Willie
Armour, Tommy
Barnes, Jim
Boros, Julius
Brady, Mike
Burke, Billy
Burke Jr., Jack
Cooper, Harry
Cruickshank, Bobby
Demaret, Jimmy
Diegel, Leo
Dudley, Edward
Dutra, Olin
Evans, Chick
Farrell, Johnny
Ford, Doug
Ghezzi, Vic
Guldahl, Ralph
Hagen, Walter
Harbert, M. R. (Chick)
Harper, Chandler
Harrison, E. J.
Hogan, Ben
Hutchison Sr., Jock
Jones, Bob
Little, W. Lawson
Mangrum, Lloyd
McDermott, John
McLeod, Fred
Middlecoff, Cary
Nelson, Byron
Ouimet, Francis
Picard, Henry
Revolta, Johnny
Runyan, Paul
Sarazen, Gene
Shute, Denny
Smith, Alex
Smith, Horton
Smith, MacDonald
Snead, Sam
Travers, Jerry
Travis, Walter
Wood, Craig
Zaharias, Mildred (Babe)

PGA Leading Money Winners

Year	Player	Dollars	Year	Player	Dollars	Year	Player	Dollars
1945	Byron Nelson	52,511	1956	Ted Kroll	72,835	1967	Jack Nicklaus	188,988
1946	Ben Hogan	42,556	1957	Dick Mayer	65,835	1968	Billy Casper	205,168
1947	Jimmy Demaret	27,936	1958	Arnold Palmer	42,407	1969	Frank Beard	175,223
1948	Ben Hogan	36,812	1959	Art Wall Jr.	53,167	1970	Lee Trevino	157,037
1949	Sam Snead	31,593	1960	Arnold Palmer	75,262	1971	Jack Nicklaus	244,490
1950	Sam Snead	35,758	1961	Gary Player	64,540	1972	Jack Nicklaus	320,542
1951	Lloyd Mangrum	26,088	1962	Arnold Palmer	81,448	1973	Jack Nicklaus	308,362
1952	Julius Boros	37,032	1963	Arnold Palmer	128,230	1974	Johnny Miller	353,201
1953	Lew Worsham	34,002	1964	Jack Nicklaus	113,284	1975	Jack Nicklaus	323,149
1954	BobToski	65,819	1965	Jack Nicklaus	140,752	1976	Jack Nicklaus	266,438
1955	Julius Boros	65,121	1966	Billy Casper	121,944			

PGA Career Money Winners

(as of January 1, 1977)

Player	Dollars	Player	Dollars	Player	Dollars
Jack Nicklaus	2,808,211	Johnny Miller	1,083,040	Ray Floyd	875,906
Arnold Palmer	1,740,131	Dave Hill	1,038,840	George Archer	853,504
Billy Casper	1,629,538	Hale Irwin	1,012,774	Don January	818,813
Lee Trevino	1,535,615	Julius Boros	996,852	Dan Sikes	800,339
Bruce Crampton	1,373,494	Al Geiberger	989,852	Doug Sanders	770,706
Tom Weiskopf	1,356,186	Frank Beard	964,251	Tommy Aaron	769,769
Gene Littler	1,264,013	Bobby Nichols	916,098	Bob Murphy	756,019
Gary Player	1,216,821	Dave Stockton	909,457	J. C. Snead	755,796
Miller Barber	1,101,544				

LPGA Leading Money Winners

Year	Winner	Dollars	Year	Winner	Dollars	Year	Winner	Dollars
1952	Betsy Rawls	14,505	1961	Mickey Wright	22,236	1969	Carol Mann	49,152
1953	Louise Suggs	19,816	1962	Mickey Wright	21,641	1970	Kathy Whitworth	30,235
1954	Patty Berg	16,011	1963	Mickey Wright	31,269	1971	Kathy Whitworth	41,181
1955	Patty Berg	16,492	1964	Mickey Wright	29,800	1972	Kathy Whitworth	65,063
1956	Marlene Hagge	20,235	1965	Kathy Whitworth	28,658	1973	Kathy Whitworth	82,854
1957	Patty Berg	16,272	1966	Kathy Whitworth	33,517	1974	JoAnne Carner	87,094
1958	Beverly Hanson	12,629	1967	Kathy Whitworth	32,937	1975	Sandra Palmer	94,805
1959	Betsy Rawls	26,774	1968	Kathy Whitworth	48,379	1976	Judy Rankin	150,734
1960	Louise Suggs	16,892						

LPGA Career Money Winners

(as of January 1, 1977)

Player	Dollars	Player	Dollars	Player	Dollars
Kathy Whitworth	636,818	Marlene Hagge	324,771	Betty Burfeindt	187,258
Sandra Haynie	490,337	Betsy Rawls	302,664	Kathy Cornelius	183,203
Judy Rankin	477,899	Jo Ann Prentice	296,725	Murle Breer	180,236
Carol Mann	440,436	Marilynn Smith	289,588	Sandra Spuzich	177,441
Sandra Palmer	417,711	Mary Mills	246,440	Sandra Post	176,472
Jane Blalock	373,929	Clifford Ann Creed	214,388	Susie Berning	171,034
Mickey Wright	333,462	Patty Berg	190,150	Shirley Englehorn	162,863
Donna Caponi Young	332,517	Louise Suggs	189,970	Betsy Cullen	156,844
JoAnne Carner	329,956				

Ryder Cup Matches

United States vs. Great Britain Professional (biennial)
Series Standing — United States 18, Great Britain 3, 1 tie

Series Record

1955 United States 8; Great Britain 4
1957 Great Britain 7; United States 4
1959 United States 8½; Great Britain 3½
1961 United States 14½; Great Britain 9½
1963 United States 23; Great Britain 9
1965 United States 19½; Great Britain 12½

Series Record

1967 United States 23½; Great Britain 8½
1969 United States 16; Great Britain 16
1971 United States 18½; Great Britain 13½
1973 Great Britain 13; United States 10
1975 United States 21; Great Britain 11
1977 United States 12½; Great Britain 7½

International Walker Cup Golf Match

United States vs. Great Britain — Men's Amateur (biennial)
Series Standing — United States, 23, Great Britain 2, 1 tie

Series Record

1955 United States 10; Great Britain 2
1957 United States 10; Great Britain 2
1959 United States 9; Great Britain 3
1961 United States 11; Great Britain 1
1963 United States 9; Great Britain 3
1965 United States 11; Great Britain 11

Series Record

1967 United States 13; Great Britain 7
1969 United States 10; Great Britain 8
1971 Great Britain 13; United States 11
1973 United States 14; Great Britain 10
1975 United States 15½; Great Britain 8½
1977 United States 16; Great Britain 8

International Curtis Cup Golf Match

United States vs. Great Britain — Women's Amateur (biennial)
Series Standing — United States 15, Great Britain 2, 2 ties

Series Record

1954 United States 6; Great Britain 3
1957 Great Britain 5; United States 4
1959 Great Britain 4½; United States 4½
1960 United States 6½; Great Britain 2½
1962 United States 8; Great Britain 1
1964 United States 10½; Great Britain 7½

Series Record

1966 United States 13; Great Britain 5
1968 United States 10½; Great Britain 7½
1970 United States 11½; Great Britain 6½
1972 United States 10; Great Britain 8
1974 United States 13; Great Britain 5
1976 United States 11½; Great Britain 6½

Amateur Softball Association Champions in 1977

Men's major fast pitch— Billard Barbell, Reading, Pa.
Women's major fast pitch— Raybestos Brakettes, Stratford, Conn.
Men's major slow pitch— Nelson Paints, Oklahoma City, Okla.
Women's major slow pitch— Fox Valley Lassies, St. Charles, Ill.
Industrial major slow pitch— Armco, Middletown, Oh.
Men's class A fast pitch— Sawaia, Miami, Ariz.
Women's class A fast pitch— Timber Jills, Everett, Wash.
Men's class A slow pitch— Higgin's Cycle, Greensboro, N.C.
Women's class A slow pitch— Cotters Penn Hills, Verona, Pa.
Modified pitch— Clinica, Miami, Fla.
Church slow pitch— Hickory Hammock, Milton, Fla.
Industrial class A slow pitch— Delta Bucks, Atlanta, Ga.

Boxing Champions by Classes

Recognized by Ring Magazine as of Aug. 1, 1977

Heavyweight	Muhammad Ali, Chicago, Ill.
Light-Heavyweight (175 lbs.)	vacant
Middleweight (160 lbs.)	Carlos Monzon, Argentina
Jr. Middleweight (154 lbs.)	Eddie Gazo, Nicaragua
Welterweight (147 lbs.)	Carlos Palomino, Mexico
Jr. Welterweight (140 lbs.)	Wilfred Benitez, Puerto Rico
Lightweight (135 lbs.)	Roberto Duran, Panama
Junior Lightweight (130 lbs.)	Samuel Serrano, Puerto Rico
Featherweight (126 lbs.)	Alexis Arguello, Nicaragua
Bantamweight (118 lbs.)	Alfonso Zamora, Mexico
Flyweight (112 lbs.)	Miguel Canto, Mexico

As of Aug. 1, 1977, the only universally accepted title holders were in the heavyweight and middleweight divisions. The following are the recognized champions of the World Boxing Association and the World Boxing Council.

	WBA	WBC
Heavyweight	Muhammad Ali, Chicago, Ill.	Muhammad Ali
Light Heavyweight	Victor Galindez, Argentina	Miguel Cuello, Argentina
Middleweights	Carlos Monzon, Argentina	Carlos Monzon
Jr. Middleweight	Eddie Gazo, Nicaragua	Eckhart Dagge, W. Germany
Welterweight	Jose Cuevas, Mexico	Carlos Palomino, Mexico
Jr. Welterweight	Wilfred Benitez, Puerto Rico	Shengsak Muangsurin, Thailand
Lightweight	Roberto Duran, Panama	Esteban DeJesus, Puerto Rico
Jr. Lightweight	Samuel Serrano, Puerto Rico	Alfredo Escalera, Puerto Rico
Featherweight	Rafael Ortega, Panama	Danny Lopez, Los Angeles, Cal.
Bantamweight	Alfonso Zamora, Mexico	Carlos Zarate, Mexico
Flyweight	Gutty Espandas, Mexico	Miguel Canto, Mexico

Ring Champions by Years

*Abandoned title

Heavyweights

1882-1892	John L. Sullivan (a)
1892-1897	James J. Corbett (b)
1897-1899	Robert Fitzsimmons
1899-1905	James J. Jeffries (c)
1905-1906	Marvin Hart
1906-1908	Tommy Burns
1908-1915	Jack Johnson
1915-1919	Jess Willard
1919-1926	Jack Dempsey
1926-1928	Gene Tunney*
1928-1930	Vacant
1930-1932	Max Schmeling
1932-1933	Jack Sharkey
1933-1934	Primo Carnera
1934-1935	Max Baer
1935-1937	James J. Braddock
1937-1949	Joe Louis*
1949-1951	Ezzard Charles
1951-1952	Joe Walcott
1952-1956	Rocky Marciano*
1956-1959	Floyd Patterson
1959-1960	Ingemar Johansson
1960-1962	Floyd Patterson
1962-1964	Sonny Liston
1964-1967	Cassius Clay* (Muhammad Ali) (d)
1970-1973	Joe Frazier
1973-1974	George Foreman
1974	Muhammad Ali

(a) London Prize Ring (bare knuckle champion).

(b) First Marquis of Queensberry champion.

(c) Jeffries abandoned the title (1905) and designated Marvin Hart and Jack Root as logical contenders and agreed to referee a fight between them, the winner to be declared champion. Hart defeated Root in 12 rounds (1905) and in turn was defeated by Tommy Burns (1906) who immediately laid claim to the title. Jack Johnson defeated Burns (1908) and was recognized as champion. He clinched the title by defeating Jeffries in an attempted comeback (1910).

(d) Title declared vacant by the World Boxing Assn. and other groups in 1967 after Clay's refusal to fulfill his military obligation.

Light Heavyweights

1903	Jack Root, George Gardner
1903-1905	Bob Fitzsimmons
1905-1912	Philadelphia Jack O'Brien*
1912-1916	Jack Dillon
1916-1920	Battling Levinsky
1920-1922	Georges Carpentier
1922-1923	Battling Siki
1923-1925	Mike McTigue
1925-1926	Paul Berlenbach
1926-1927	Jack Delaney*
1927-1929	Tommy Loughran*
1930-1934	Maxey Rosenbloom
1934-1935	Bob Olin
1935-1939	John Henry Lewis*
1939	Melio Bettina
1939-1941	Billy Conn*
1941	Anton Christoforidis (won NBA title)
1941-1948	Gus Lesnevich, Freddie Mills
1948-1950	Freddie Mills
1950-1952	Joey Maxim
1952-1960	Archie Moore
1961-1962	Vacant
1962-1963	Harold Johnson
1963-1965	Willie Pastrano
1965-1966	Jose Torres
1966-1968	Dick Tiger
1968-1974	Bob Foster*

Middleweights

1884-1891	Jack "Nonpareil" Dempsey
1891-1897	Bob Fitzsimmons*
1897-1907	Tommy Ryan*
1907-1908	Stanley Ketchel, Billy Papke
1908-1910	Stanley Ketchel
1911-1913	Vacant
1913	Frank Klaus, George Chip
1914-1917	Al McCoy
1917-1920	Mike O'Dowd
1920-1923	Johnny Wilson
1923-1926	Harry Greb
1926-1931	Tiger Flowers, Mickey Walker
1931-1932	Gorilla Jones (NBA)
1932-1937	Marcel Thil
1938	Al Hostak (NBA), Solly Krieger (NBA)
1939-1940	Al Hostak (NBA)
1941-1947	Tony Zale
1947-1948	Rocky Graziano
1948	Tony Zale, Marcel Cerdan
1949-1951	Jake LaMotta
1951	Ray Robinson, Randy Turpin, Ray Robinson*
1953-1955	Carl (Bobo) Olson
1955-1957	Ray Robinson
1957	Gene Fullmer, Ray Robinson, Carmen Basilio
1958	Ray Robinson
1959	Gene Fullmer (NBA); Ray Robinson (N.Y.)
1960	Gene Fullmer (NBA); Paul Pender (New York and Mass.)
1961	Gene Fullmer (NBA); Terry Downes (New York, Mass., Europe)
1962	Gene Fullmer, Dick Tiger (NBA); Paul Pender (New York and Mass.)*
1963	Dick Tiger (universal).
1963-1965	Joey Giardello
1965-1966	Dick Tiger
1966-1967	Emile Griffith
1967	Nino Benvenuti
1967-1968	Emile Griffith
1968-1970	Nino Benvenuti
1970	Carlos Monzon

Welterweights

1892-1894	Mysterious Billy Smith
1894-1896	Tommy Ryan
1896	Kid McCoy (outgrew class)
1900	Rube Ferns, Matty Matthews
1901	Rube Ferns
1901-1904	Joe Walcott
1904-1906	Dixie Kid, Joe Walcott, Honey Mellody
1907-1911	Mike Sullivan
1911-1915	Vacant
1915-1919	Ted Lewis
1919-1922	Jack Britton
1922-1926	Mickey Walker
1926	Pete Latzo
1927-1929	Joe Dundee
1929	Jackie Fields
1930	Jack Thompson, Tommy Freeman
1931	Freeman, Thompson, Lou Brouillard
1932	Jackie Fields
1933	Young Corbett, Jimmy McLarnin
1934	Barney Ross, Jimmy McLarnin
1935-1938	Barney Ross
1938-1940	Henry Armstrong
1940-1941	Fritzie Zivic
1941-1946	Fred Cochrane
1946-1946	Marty Servo*; Ray Robinson (a)
1946-1950	Ray Robinson*
1951	Johnny Bratton (NBA)
1951-1954	Kid Gavilan
1954-1955	Johnny Saxton
1955	Tony De Marco, Carmen Basilio
1956	Carmen Basilio, Johnny Saxton, Carmen Basilio
1957	Carmen Basilio*
1958-1960	Virgil Akins, Don Jordan
1960	Benny Paret
1961	Emile Griffith, Benny Paret
1962	Emile Griffith
1963	Luis Rodriguez, Emile Griffith
1964-1966	Emile Griffith*
1966-1969	Curtis Cokes
1969-1970	Jose Napoles, Billy Backus
1971-1975	Jose Napoles
1975-1976	John Stracey
1976	Carlos Palomino

(a) Robinson gained the title by defeating Tommy Bell in an elimination agreed to by the NY Commission and the NBA. Both claimed Robinson waived his title when he won the middleweight crown from LaMotta in 1951. Gavilan defeated Bratton in an elimination to find a successor.

Lightweights

1896-1899	Kid Lavigne
1899-1902	Frank Erne
1902-1908	Joe Gans
1908-1910	Battling Nelson
1910-1912	Ad Wolgast
1912-1914	Willie Ritchie
1914-1917	Freddie Welsh
1917-1925	Benny Leonard*
1925	Jimmy Goodrich, Rocky Kansas
1926-1930	Sammy Mandell
1930	Al Singer, Tony Canzoneri
1930-1933	Tony Canzoneri
1933-1935	Barney Ross*
1935-1936	Tony Canzoneri
1936-1938	Lou Ambers
1938	Henry Armstrong
1939	Lou Ambers
1940	Lew Jenkins
1941-1943	Sammy Angott
1944	S. Angott (NBA), J. Zurita (NBA)
1945-1951	Ike Williams (NBA: later universal)
1951-1952	James Carter
1952	Lauro Salas, James Carter
1953-1954	James Carter
1954	Paddy De Marco; James Carter
1955	James Carter; Bud Smith
1956	Bud Smith, Joe Brown
1956-1962	Joe Brown
1962-1965	Carlos Ortiz
1965	Ismael Laguna
1965-1968	Carlos Ortiz
1968-1969	Teo Cruz
1969-1970	Mando Ramos
1970	Ismael Laguna
1970-1972	Ken Buchanan
1972	Roberto Duran (WBA)

Featherweights

1892-1900	George Dixon (disputed)
1900-1901	Terry McGovern, Young Corbett*
1901-1912	Abe Attell
1912-1923	Johnny Kilbane
1923	Eugene Criqui, Johnny Dundee
1923-1925	Johnny Dundee*
1925-1927	Kid Kaplan*
1927-1928	Benny Bass, Tony Canzoneri
1928-1929	Andre Routis
1929-1932	Battling Battalino*
1932-1934	Tommy Paul (NBA)
1933-1936	Freddie Miller
1936-1937	Petey Sarron
1937-1938	Henry Armstrong*
1938-1940	Joey Archibald (b)
1942-1948	Willie Pep
1948-1949	Sandy Saddler
1949-1950	Willie Pep
1950-1957	Sandy Saddler*
1957-1959	Hogan (Kid) Bassey
1959-1963	Davey Moore
1963-1964	Sugar Ramos
1964-1969	Vicente Saldivar*
1969	John Famechon
1970	Vicente Saldivar
1970-1972	Kuniaki Shibata
1972	Clemente Sanchez*
1974	Ruben Olivares
1975	Alexis Arguello (WBA)

(b) After Petey Scalzo knocked out Archibald (Dec. 5, 1938) in an overweight match and was refused a title bout, the NBA named Scalzo champion. The NBA title succession was: Petey Scalzo, 1938-1941: Richard Lemos, 1941: Jackie Wilson, 1941-1943: Jackie Callura, 1943: Phil Terranova, 1943-1944: Sal Bartolo, 1944-1946.

History of Heavyweight Championship Bouts

*Title Changed Hands

1889—July 8—John L. Sullivan def. Jake Kilrain, 75, Richburg, Miss. Last championship bare knuckles bout.

***1892**—Sept. 7—James J. Corbett def. John L. Sullivan, 21, New Orleans. Big gloves used for first time.

1894—Jan. 25—James J. Corbett KOd Charley Mitchell, 3, Jacksonville, Fla.

***1897**—March 17—Bob Fitzsimmons def. James J. Corbett, 14, Carson City, Nev.

***1899**—June 9—James J. Jeffries def. Bob Fitzsimmons, 11, Coney Island, N.Y.

1899—Nov. 3—James J. Jeffries def. Tom Sharkey, 25, Coney Island, N.Y.

1900—May 11—James J. Jeffries KOd James J. Corbett, 23, Coney Island, N.Y.

1901—Nov. 15—James J. Jeffries, KOd Gus Ruhlin, 5, San Francisco.

1902—July 25—James J. Jeffries KOd Bob Fitzsimmons, 8, San Francsico.

1903—Aug. 14—James J. Jeffries KOd James J. Corbett, 10, San Francsico.

1904—Aug. 26—James J. Jeffries KOd Jack Monroe, 2, San Francsico.

***1905**—James J. Jeffries retired, July 3—Marvin Hart KOd Jack Root, 12, Reno. Jeffries refereed and presented the title to the victor. Jack O'Brien also claimed the title.

***1906**—Feb. 23—Tommy Burns def. Marvin Hart, 20, Los Angeles.

1906—Nov. 28—Philadelphia Jack O'Brien and Tommy Burns, 20, draw, Los Angeles.

1907—May 8—Tommy Burns def. Jack O'Brien, 20, Los Angeles.

1907—July 4—Tommy Burns KOd Bill Squires, 1, Colma, Cal.

1907—Dec. 2—Tommy Burns KOd Gunner Moir, 10, London.

1908—Feb. 10—Tommy Burns KOd Jack Palmer, 4, London.

1908—March 17—Tommy Burns KOd Jem Roche, 1, Dublin.

1908—April 18—Tommy Burns KOd Jewey Smith, 5, Paris.

1908—June 13—Tommy Burns KOd Bill Squires, 8, Paris.

1908—Aug. 24—Tommy Burns KOd Bill Squires, 13, Sydney, New South Wales.

1908—Sept. 2—Tommy Burns KOd Bill Lang, 2, Melbourne, Australia.

***1908**—Dec. 26—Jack Johnson KOd Tommy Burns, 14, Sydney, Australia. Police halted contest.

1909—May 19—Jack Johnson and Jack O'Brien, 6, draw,

Philadelphia.
1909—June 30—Jack Johnson and Tony Ross, 6, draw, Pittsburgh.
1909—Sept. 9—Jack Johnson and Al Kaufman, 10, draw, San Francisco.
1909—Oct. 16—Jack Johnson KOd Stanley Ketchel, 12, Colma, Cal.
1910—July 4—Jack Johnson KOd Jim Jeffries, 15, Reno, Nev. Jeffries came back from retirement.
1912—July 4—Jack Johnson def. Jim Flynn, 9, Las Vegas, N.M. Contest stopped by police.
1913—Nov. 28—Jack Johnson KOd Andre Spaul, 2, Paris.
1913—Dec. 9—Jack Johnson and Jim Johnson, 10, draw, Paris. Bout called a draw when Jack Johnson declared he had broken his arm.
1914—June 27—Jack Johnson def. Frank Moran, 20, Paris.
***1915**—April 5—Jess Willard KOd Jack Johnson, 26, Havana, Cuba.
1916—March 25—Jess Willard and Frank Moran, 10, draw, New York.
***1919**—July 4—Jack Dempsey KOd Jess Willard, Toledo, Oh. Willard failed to answer bell for 4th round.
1920—Sept. 6—Jack Dempsey KOd Billy Miske, 3, Benton Harbor, Mich.
1920—Dec. 14—Jack Dempsey KOd Bill Brennan, 12, New York.
1921—July 2—Jack Dempsey KOd George Carpentier, 4, Boyle's Thirty Acres, Jersey City, N.J. Carpentier had held the so-called white heavyweight title since July 16, 1914, in a series established in 1913, after Jack Johnson's exile in Europe late in 1912.
1923—July 4—Jack Dempsey def. Tom Gibbons, 15, Shelby, Mont.
1923—Sept. 14—Jack Dempsey KOd Luis Firpo, 2, New York.
***1926**—Sept. 23—Gene Tunney def. Jack Dempsey, 10, Philadelphia.
1927—Sept. 22—Gene Tunney def. Jack Dempsey, 10, Chicago.
1928—July 26—Gene Tunney KOd Tom Heeney, 11, New York; soon afterward he announced his retirement.
***1930**—June 12—Max Schmeling def. Jack Sharkey, 4, New York. Sharkey fouled Schmeling in a bout which was generally considered to have resulted in the election of a successor to Gene Tunney, New York.
1931—July 3—Max Schmeling KOd Young Stribling, 15, Cleveland.
***1932**—June 21—Jack Sharkey def. Max Schmeling, 15, New York.
***1933**—June 29—Primo Carnera KOd Jack Sharkey, 6, New York.
1933—Oct. 22—Primo Carnera def. Paulino Uzcudun, 15, Rome.
1934—March 1—Primo Carnera def. Tommy Loughran, 15, Miami.
***1934**—June 14—Max Baer KOd Primo Carnera, 11, New York.
***1935**—June 13—James J. Braddock def. Max Baer, 15, New York.
***1937**—June 22—Joe Louis KOd James J. Braddock, 8, Chicago.
1937—Aug. 30—Joe Louis def. Tommy Farr, 15, New York.
1938—Feb. 23—Joe Louis KOd Nathan Mann, 3, New York.
1938—April 1—Joe Louis KOd Harry Thomas, 5, New York.
1938—June 22—Joe Louis KOd Max Schmeling, 1, New York.
1939—Jan. 25—Joe Louis KOd John H. Lewis, 1, New York.
1939—April 17—Joe Louis KOd Jack Roper, 1, Los Angeles.
1939—June 28—Joe Louis KOd Tony Galento, 4, New York.
1939—Sept. 20—Joe Louis KOd Bob Pastor, 11, Detroit.
1940—February 9—Joe Louis def. Arturo Godoy, 15, New York.
1940—March 29—Joe Louis KOd Johnny Paychek, 2, New York.
1940—June 20—Joe Louis KOd Arturo Godoy, 8, New York.
1940—Dec. 16—Joe Louis KOd Al McCoy, 6, Boston.
1941—Jan. 31—Joe Louis KOd Red Burman, 5, New York.
1941—Feb. 17—Joe Louis KOd Gus Dorzaio, 2, Philadelphia.
1941—March 21—Joe Louis KOd Abe Simon, 13, Detroit.
1941—April 8—Joe Louis KOd Tony Musto, 9, St. Louis.
1941—May 23—Joe Louis def. Buddy Baer, 7, Washington, D.C., on a disqualification.
1941—June 18—Joe Louis KOd Billy Conn, 13, New York.
1941—Sept. 29—Joe Louis KOd Lou Nova, 6, New York.
1942—Jan. 9—Joe Louis KOd Buddy Baer, 1, New York.
1942—March 27—Joe Louis KOd Abe Simon, 6, New York.
1946—June 19—Joe Louis KOd Billy Conn, 8, New York.
1946—Sept. 18—Joe Louis KOd Tami Mauriello, 1, New York.
1947—Dec. 5—Joe Louis def. Joe Walcott, 15, New York.
1948—June 25—Joe Louis KOd Joe Walcott, 11, New York.
***1949**—June 22-Following Joe Louis' retirement Ezzard Charles def. Joe Walcott, 15, Chicago. NBA recognition only.
1949—Aug. 10—Ezzard Charles KOd Gus Lesnevich, 7, New York.
1949—Oct. 14—Ezzard Charles KOd Pat Valentino, 8, San Francisco; clinched American title.
1950—Aug. 15—Ezzard Charles KOd Freddy Beshore, 14, Buffalo.
1950—Sept. 27—Ezzard Charles def. Joe Louis in latter's attempted comeback, 15, New York; universal recognition.
1950—Dec. 5—Ezzard Charles KOd Nick Barone, 11, Cincinnati.
1951—Jan. 12—Ezzard Charles KOd Lee Oma, 10, New York.
1951—March 7—Ezzard Charles def. Joe Walcott, 15, Detroit.
1951—May 30—Ezzard Charles def. Joey Maxim, light heavyweight champion, 15, Chicago.
***1951**—July 18—Joe Walcott KOd Ezzard Charles, 7, Pittsburgh.
1952—June 5—Joe Walcott def. Ezzard Charles, 15, Philadelphia.
***1952**—Sept. 23—Rocky Marciano KOd Joe Walcott, 13, Philadelphia.
1953—May 15—Rocky Marciano KOd Joe Walcott, 1, Chicago.
1953—Sept. 24—Rocky Marciano KOd Roland LaStarza, 11, New York.
1954—June 17—Rocky Marciano def. Ezzard Charles, 15, New York.
1954—Sept. 17—Rocky Marciano KOd Ezzard Charles, 8, New York.
1955—May 16—Rocky Marciano KOd Don Cockell, 9, San Francisco.
1955—Sept. 21—Rocky Marciano KOd Archie Moore, 9, New York. Marciano retired undefeated, Apr. 27, 1956.
***1956**—Nov. 30—Floyd Patterson KOd Archie Moore, 5, Chicago.
1957—July 29—Floyd Patterson KOd Hurricane Jackson, 10, New York.
1957—Aug. 22—Floyd Patterson KOd Pete Rademacher, 6, Seattle.
1958—Aug. 18—Floyd Patterson KOd Roy Harris, 12, Los Angeles.
1959—May 1—Floyd Patterson KOd Brian London, 11, Indianapolis.
***1959**—June 26—Ingemar Johansson KOd Floyd Patterson, 3, New York.
***1960**—June 20—Floyd Patterson KOd Ingemar Johansson, 5, New York. First heavyweight in boxing history to regain title.
1961—Mar. 13—Floyd Patterson KOd Ingemar Johansson, 6, Miami Beach.
1961—Dec. 4—Floyd Patterson KOd Tom McNeeley, 4, Toronto.
***1962**—Sept. 25—Sonny Liston KOd Floyd Patterson, 1, Chicago.
1963—July 22—Sonny Liston KOd Floyd Patterson, 1, Las Vegas.
***1964**—Feb. 25—Cassius Clay KOd Sonny Liston, 7, Miami Beach.
1965—May 25—Cassius Clay KOd Sonny Liston, 1, Lewiston, Maine.
1965—Nov. 11—Cassius Clay KOd Floyd Patterson, 12, Las Vegas.
1966—Mar. 29—Cassius Clay def. George Chuvalo, 15, Toronto.
1966—May 21—Cassius Clay KOd Henry Cooper, 6, London.
1966—Aug. 6—Cassius Clay KOd Brian London, 3, London.
1966—Sept. 10—Cassius Clay KOd Karl Mildenberger, 12, Frankfurt, Germany.
1966—Nov. 14—Cassius Clay KOd Cleveland Williams, 3, Houston.
1967—Feb. 6—Cassius Clay def. Ernie Terrell, 15, Houston
1967—Mar. 22—Cassius Clay KOd Zora Folley, 7, New York, Clay was stripped of his title by the WBA and others for refusing military service.
***1970**—Feb. 16—Joe Frazier KOd Jimmy Ellis, 5, New York.
1970—Nov. 18—Joe Frazier KOd Bob Foster, 2, Detroit.
1971—Mar. 8—Joe Frazier def. Cassius Clay (Muhammad Ali), 15, New York.
1972—Jan. 15—Joe Frazier KOd Terry Daniels, 4, New Orleans.
1972—May 25—Joe Frazier KOd Ron Stander, 5, Omaha.
***1973**—Jan. 22—George Foreman KOd Joe Frazier, 2, Kingston, Jamaica.
1973—Sept. 1—George Foreman KOd Joe Roman, 1, Tokyo.
1974—Mar. 3—George Foreman KOd Ken Norton, 2, Caracas.
***1974**—Oct. 30—Muhammad Ali KOd George Foreman, 8, Zaire.
1975—Mar. 24—Muhammad Ali KOd Chuck Wepner, 15, Cleveland.

1975—May 16—Muhammad Ali KOd Ron Lyle, 11, Las Vegas.
1975—June 30—Muhammad Ali def. Joe Bugner, 15, Malaysia.
1975—Oct. 1—Muhammad Ali KOd Joe Frazier, 14, Manila.
1976—Feb. 20—Muhammad Ali KOd Jean-Pierre Coopman, 5, San Juan.
1976—Apr. 30—Muhammad Ali def. Jimmy Young, 15, Landover, Md.
1976—May 25—Muhammad Ali KOd Richard Dunn, 5, Munich.
1976—Sept. 28—Muhammad Ali def. Ken Norton, 15, New York.
1977—May 16—Muhammad Ali def. Alfredo Evangelista, 15, Landover, Md.
1977—Sept. 29—Muhammad Ali def. Earnie Shavers, 15, New York.

National AAU Boxing Championships in 1977

Winston-Salem, N.C., May 3-7

106 lbs.—Israel Acosta, Milwaukee, Wis.
112 lbs.—Jerome Coffee, Nashville, Tenn.
119 lbs.—Rocky Lockridge, Tacoma, Wash.
125 lbs.—Johnny Bumphus, Tacoma, Wash.
132 lbs.—Anthony Fletcher, Philadelphia, Pa.
139 lbs.—Thomas Hearns, Detroit, Mich.
147 lbs.—Mike McCallum, Nashville, Tenn.
156 lbs.—Clinton Jackson, Nashville, Tenn.
165 lbs.—Jerome Bennett, USAF.
178 lbs.—Larry Strogen, Shreveport, La.
Heavyweight—Greg Page, Louisville, Ky.
Team championship—Southeastern AAU.

Rifle and Pistol Individual Championships in 1977

Source: National Rifle Association of America

National Outdoor Rifle and Pistol Championships

Pistol—Hershel L. Anderson, Tracy City, Tenn., 2651-128X.
Civilian pistol—Hershel L. Anderson, Tracy City, Tenn., 2651-128X.
Woman pistol—SP5 Kimberly Dyer, USA, Ft. Benning, Ga., 2596-88X.
Senior pistol—Gil Hebard, Knoxville, Ill., 2601-70X.
Police pistol—John L. Farley, Americus, Ga., 2610-108X.
National Guard pistol—SSG James R. Lenardson, NGUS, Eric, Mich., 2641-121X.
Collegiate pistol—Patrick O. McGaugh, West Point, N. Y., 2483-77X.
Smallbore rifle prone—Pvt. Mary E. Stidworthy, NGUS, Prescott, Ariz., 6397-536X.
Service smallbore rifle prone—Pvt. Mary E. Stidworthy, 6397-536X.
Woman smallbore rifle prone—Pvt. Mary E. Stidworthy, 6397-536X.
Collegiate smallbore rifle prone—Kevin B. Richards, Valley Stream, N. Y., 6389-479X.
Senior smallbore rifle prone—Joseph W. Barnes, Branchville, N. J., 6388-463X.
Junior smallbore rifle prone—Oscar L. Hernandez, Miami, Fla., 6390-494X.
Smallbore rifle position—Maj. Lones W. Wigger Jr., USA, Ft. Benning, Ga., 3181-221X.
Service smallbore rifle position—Maj. Lones W. Wigger Jr., 3181-221X.
Civilian smallbore rifle position—Matthew R. Stark, Alexandria, Va., 3163-155X.
Woman smallbore rifle position—SP4 Karen Monez, USA, Ft. Benning, Ga., 3176-188X.
Junior smallbore rifle position—Elaine S. Proffitt, Titusville, Fla., 3146-143X.
Senior smallbore rifle position—Fred W. Cole, Stony Brook, N. Y., 3117-153X.
Collegiate smallbore rifle position—Matthew R. Stark, Alexandria, Va., 3163-155X.
High power rifle—Carl R. Bernosky, Gordon, Pa., 1963-66X.
Match rifle senior—Crighton O. Audette, Springfield, Vt., 1941-59X.
Match rifle woman—Nancy H. Clark, Phoenix, Ariz., 1933-50X.
Match rifle junior—Randy S. Ciavarelli, Plymouth, Ia., 1940-60X.
Match rifle collegiate—Carl R. Bernosky, Gordon, Pa., 1963-66X.
Service rifle champion—CW04 David I. Boyd 2d, USMC, Quantico, Va., 1960-65X.
Service rifle civilian—Chester F. Hamilton, Virginia Beach, Va., 1925-50X.
Service rifle woman—SP5 Diane L. Klimas, USA, Ft. Benning, Ga., 1906-38X.
Service rifle junior—Kevin F. Bulson, Watervliet, N. Y., 1846-34X.
Service rifle senior—Gerritt H. Stekeur, Latham, N. Y., 1888-48X.
Service rifle regular service—CW04 David I. Boyd 2d, 1960-65X.
Service rifle collegiate—Matthew McSheehy, Reading, Mass., 1888-33X.

U.S. NRA International Shooting Championships

English match—David Ross, Houston, Tex., 1785.
Smallbore 3-position—Lanny Bassham, San Antonio, Tex., 3462.
Air rifle—Edward F. Etzel Jr., Morgantown, W.Va., 1163.
Junior air rifle—Kurt H. Fitz-Randolph, El Paso, Tex., 1135.
Ladies air rifle—Karen Monez, Ft. Worth, Tex., 1142.
Ladies standard rifle prone—Margaret Murdock, Topeka, Kan., 1787.
Junior standard rifle prone—Matthew R. Stark, Alexandria, Va., 1753.
Standard rifle 3-position—Boyd Goldsby, Little Rock, Ark., 1710.
Ladies standard rifle 3-position—Margaret Murdock, Topeka, Kan., 1725.
Junior standard rifle 3-position—Gloria Parmentier, Alexandria., Va., 1694.
Free rifle, 300 meter—Lones Wigger, Ft. Benning, Ga., 3413.
Big bore standard rifle—Lones Wigger, 1125.
Free pistol—Darius R. Young, Alberta, Canada, 1650.
Air pistol—Kenneth R. Buster, Billings, Mont., 1155.
Ladies air pistol—Ruby Fox, Parker, Ariz., 1120.
Junior air pistol—Kenneth McNally, Gulfport, Miss., 1075.
Center fire pistol—Michael J. Bonafede, Stafford, Va., 1762.
Rapid fire pistol—Terrence Anderson, New Orleans, La., 1768.
Standard pistol—Bonnie D. Harmon, Ft. Benning, Ga., 1731.
Ladies smallbore pistol—Kimberly S. Dyer, Ft. Benning, Ga., 1747.
Junior smallbore pistol—Mark J. Willis, Annapolis, Md., 1737.
Running boar slow and fast—Louis Theimer, Columbus, Ga., 1693.
Running boar mixed—John Anderson, Phoenix, Ariz., 377.
International skeet—Joseph Clemmons, Ft. Benning, Ga., 295.
Ladies international skeet—Ila N. Hill, Troy, Mich., 277.
Clay pigeon—Harry Skalsky, Chapel Hill, N.C., 290.
Ladies clay pigeon—Audrey Grosch, Minneapolis, Minn., 272.
Junior clay pigeon—Michael D. Coleman, Ackerly, Tex., 284.

National Indoor Rifle and Pistol Championships

Conventional rifle—David J. Cramer, Aliquippa, Pa., 799.
Conventional rifle woman—Elaine S. Proffitt, Titusville, Fla., 798.
International rifle—Roderick M. Fitz-Randolph Jr., El Paso, Tex., 1177.
International rifle woman—Karen E. Monez, Ft. Worth, Tex., 1167.
Conventional pistol—Jan R. Brundin, Quakertown, Pa., 887.
Conventional pistol woman—Kimberly S. Dyer, Ft. Benning, Ga., 866.
International pistol—Steve Reiter, South San Francisco, Cal., 561.
International pistol woman—Norma K. Puryear, North Canton, Oh., 516.

Trotting and Pacing Records

Source: Martin J. Evans, U.S. Trotting Assn., Records to Sept., 1977

Trotting Records

Asterisk (*) denotes record was made against the clock. Times—seconds in fifths.

One mile records (mile track)

All-age — *1:54.4 — Nevele Pride, Indianapolis, Ind., Aug. 31, 1969.
Two-year-old — *1:57.1 — ABC Freight, Inglewood, Cal., Nov. 4, 1976.
Three-year-old — 1:56.2 — Super Bowl, Du Quoin, Ill., Aug. 30, 1972; Steve Lobell, Du Quoin, Ill., Sept. 4, 1976.

(Half-mile track)

All-age — 1:56.4 — Nevele Pride, Saratoga Springs, N.Y., Sept. 6, 1969.
Two-year-old — 2:00.1 — Ayres, Delaware, Oh., 1963.
Three-year-old Colt — 1:58.3 — Songcan, Delaware, Oh., 1972.

(Five Eighth-mile track)

All-Age — 1:57.3 — Dream of Glory, Chicago, Ill., Aug. 21, 1976.
Two-year-old — 2:01 — Starlark Hanover, Wilkes-Barre, Pa., 1973.
Three-year-old — 1:58.2 — Speed In Action, Toronto, Ont., July 25, 1977.

Odd distances

1-1/16 Miles — 2:05.3 — Senator Frost, Inglewood, Cal., Oct. 17, 1959.
1-1/16 Miles, Half-mile Track — 2:07.2 — Nevele Pride, Westbury, N.Y., 1969.
1-3/16 Miles — 2:22.4 — Scotch Victor, Inglewood, Cal., Nov. 6, 1954.
1¼ Miles — 2:30.3 — Pronto Don, Inglewood, Cal., Nov. 24, 1951.
1¼ Miles, Half-mile Track — 2:31.2 — Speedy Scot, Westbury, N.Y., 1964; Noble Victory, Westbury, N.Y., 1966.
1½ Miles — *3:02.1 — Greyhound, Indianapolis, Ind., Sept. 14, 1937.
1½ Miles, Half-mile Track — 3:01.3 — Kash Minbar, Westbury, N.Y., July 30, 1977.
2 Miles — *4:06 — Greyhound, Indianapolis, Ind., Sept. 19, 1939.
2 Miles, Half-mile Track — 4:10.4 — Pronto Don, Westbury, N.Y., Sept. 13, 1951.
Fastest Two Heats — 1:57.2; 1:56.2 — Super Bowl, Du Quoin, Ill., Aug. 29, 1972.
Fastest Two Heats, Half-mile Track — 1:58.4, 2:00.3 — Speedy Rodney, Goshen, N.Y., 1966, and **2:00.4; 1:58.3**, Songcan, Delaware, Oh., 1972.

Pacing Records

One mile records (mile track)

All-age — *1:52 — Steady Star, Lexington, Ky., Oct. 1, 1971.
Two-year-old — 1:54.1 — Jade Prince, Lexington, Ky., Oct. 5, 1976.
Three-year-old — *1:54 — Steady Star, Lexington, Ky., Oct. 7, 1970; **1:54** — B. G.'s Bunny, E. Rutherford, N. J., July 12, 1977.

(Half-mile track)

All-age — 1:55.3 — Adios Butler, Delaware, Oh., Sept. 21, 1961; Albatross, Delaware, Oh., 1972.
Two-year-old — 1:58.4 — Columbia George, Yonkers, N.Y., Nov. 8, 1969; J. D. Skipper, Delaware, Oh., 1972; Ambro Ranger, Delaware, Oh., 1975.
Three-year-old — *1:56.2 — Keystone Ore, Saratoga Springs, N.Y., July 17, 1976.

(Five Eighth-mile track)

All-Age — 1:54.3 — Albatross, Chicago, Ill., 1972.
Two-year-old — 1:57.4 — No No Yankee, Laurel, Md., Aug. 12, 1977.
Three-year-old — 1:54.4 — Governor Skipper, Washington, Pa., Aug. 13, 1977.

Odd Distances

1-1/16 Miles — 2:03.1 — Adios Vic, Inglewood, Cal., Oct. 23, 1965.
1-1/16 Miles, Half-mile Track — 2:06 — Albatross, Westbury, N.Y., 1972.
1⅛ Miles — 2:09.1 — True Duane, Hollywood Park, 1966.
1¼ Miles, Half-mile Track — 2:29.2 — Rambling Willie, Yonkers, N.Y., Aug. 14, 1976.
1½ Miles — 3:05.2 — Right Time, Inglewood, Cal., 1961; and K. D. Senator, E. Boston, Mass., 1963.
1½ Miles, Half-mile Track — 3:01.4 — Handle With Care, Yonkers, N.Y., Aug. 21, 1976.
2 Miles — *4:17 — Dan Patch, Macon, Ga., 1903.
2 Miles, Half-mile Track — 4:08.4 — Irvin Paul, Yonkers, N.Y., June 28, 1962.
Fastest Two Heats — 1:55.1, 1:54.1 — Jade Prince, Lexington, Ky., Oct. 5, 1976 and **1:54.4, 1:54.3** — Taurus Bomber, Springfield, Ill., Aug. 20, 1976.

The Hambletonian (3-year-old trotters)

Du Quoin, Ill.

Year	Winner	Driver	Purse	Year	Winner	Driver	Purse
1946	Chestertown	Thomas Berry	$50,905	1962	A.C.Os Viking	Sanders Russell	$116,312
1947	Hoot Mon	S.F. Palin	46,267	1963	Speedy Scot	Ralph Baldwin	115,549
1948	Demon Hanover	Harrison Hoyt	59,941	1964	Ayres	John Simpson Sr.	115,281
1949	Miss Tilly	Fred Egan	69,791	1965	Egyptian Candor	Del Cameron	122,245
1950	Lusty Song	Del Miller	75,209	1966	Kerry Way	Frank Ervin	122,540
1951	Mainliner	Guy Crippen	95,263	1967	Speedy Streak	Del Cameron	122,650
1952	Sharp Note	Bion Shively	87,637	1968	Nevele Pride	Stanley Dancer	116,190
1953	Helicopter	Harry Harvey	117,118	1969	Lindy's Pride	Howard Bessinger	124,910
1954	Newport Dream	Del Cameron	106,830	1970	Timothy T.	John Simpson Sr.	143,630
1955	Scott Frost	Joe O'Brien	86,863	1971	Speedy Crown	Howard Bessinger	128,770
1956	The Intruder	Ned Bower	98,591	1972	Super Bowl	Stanley Dancer	119,090
1957	Hickory Smoke	John Simpson Sr.	111,126	1973	Flirth	Ralph Baldwin	144,710
1958	Emily's Pride	Flave Nipe	106,719	1974	Christopher T.	Bill Haughton	160,150
1959	Diller Hanover	Frank Ervin	125,284	1975	Bonefish	Stanley Dancer	232,192
1960	Blaze Hanover	Joe O'Brien	144,590	1976	Steve Lobell	Bill Haughton	263,524
1961	Harlan Dean	James Arthur	131,573	1977	Green Speed	Bill Haughton	284,131

Little Brown Jug (3-year-old pacers)

Delaware, Ohio

Year	Winner	Driver	Purse	Year	Winner	Driver	Purse
1954	Adios Harry	Morris MacDonald	$69,332	1966	Romeo Hanover	George Sholty	$74,616
1955	Quick Chief	Billy Haughton	66,608	1967	Best of All	James Hackett	84,778
1956	Noble Adios	John Simpson Sr.	52,666	1968	Rum Customer	Billy Haughton	104,226
1957	Torpid	John Simpson Sr.	73,528	1969	Laverne Hanover	Billy Haughton	109,731
1958	Shadow Wave	Joe O'Brien	65,252	1970	Most Happy Fella	Stanley Dancer	100,110
1959	Adios Butler	Clint Hodgins	76,582	1971	Nansemond	Herve Filion	102,944
1960	Bullet Hanover	John Simpson Sr.	66,510	1972	Strike Out	Keith Waples	104,916
1961	Henry T. Adios	Stanley Dancer	70,069	1973	Melvin's Woe	Joe O'Brien	120,000
1962	Lehigh Hanover	Stanley Dancer	75,038	1974	Ambro Omaha	Billy Haughton	132,630
1963	Overtrick	John Patterson Sr.	68,294	1975	Seatrain	Ben Webster	147,813
1964	Vicar Hanover	Billy Haughton	66,590	1976	Keystone Ore	Stanley Dancer	153,799
1965	Bret Hanover	Frank Ervin	71,447	1977	Gov. Skipper	John Chapman	150,000

Leading Drivers

Races Won

Year	Driver		Year	Driver		Year	Driver		Year	Driver	
1957	Bill Haughton	156	1962	Bob Farrington	203	1967	Bob Farrington	277	1972	Herve Filion	605
1958	Bill Haughton	176	1963	Donald Busse	201	1968	Herve Filion	407	1973	Herve Filion	445
1959	William Gilmour	165	1964	Bob Farrington	312	1969	Herve Filion	394	1974	Herve Filion	637
1960	Del Insko	156	1965	Bob Farrington	310	1970	Herve Filion	486	1975	Daryl Buse	360
1961	Bob Farrington	201	1966	Bob Farrington	283	1971	Herve Filion	543	1976	Herve Filion	445

Money Won

Year	Driver	Dollars	Year	Driver	Dollars	Year	Driver	Dollars
1957	Bill Haughton	586,950	1964	Stanley Dancer	1,051,538	1971	Herve Filion	1,915,945
1958	Bill Haughton	816,659	1965	Bill Haughton	889,943	1972	Herve Filion	2,473,265
1959	Bill Haughton	711,435	1966	Stanley Dancer	1,218,403	1973	Herve Filion	2,233,302
1960	Del Miller	567,282	1967	Bill Haughton	1,305,773	1974	Herve Filion	3,474,315
1961	Stanley Dancer	674,723	1968	Bill Haughton	1,654,172	1975	Carmine Abbatiello	2,275,093
1962	Stanley Dancer	760,343	1969	Del Insko	1,635,463	1976	Herve Filion	2,241,045
1963	Bill Haughton	790,086	1970	Herve Filion	1,647,837			

Harness Horse of the Year

(Chosen by the U.S. Trotting Assn. and the U.S. Harness Writers Assn.)

1948 — Rodney
1949 — Good Time
1950 — Proximity
1951 — Pronto Don
1952 — Good Time
1953 — Hi Lo's Forbes
1954 — Stenographer
1955 — Scott Frost
1956 — Scott Frost
1957 — Torpid
1958 — Emily's Pride
1959 — Bye Bye Byrd
1960 — Adios Butler
1961 — Adios Butler
1962 — Su Mac Lad
1963 — Speedy Scot
1964 — Bret Hanover
1965 — Bret Hanover
1966 — Bret Hanover
1967 — Nevele Pride
1968 — Nevele Pride
1969 — Nevele Pride
1970 — Fresh Yankee
1971 — Albatross
1972 — Albatross
1973 — Sir Dalrae
1974 — Delmonica Hanover
1975 — Savior
1976 — Keystone Ore

Annual Leading Money-Winning Horses

Trotters

Year	Horse	Dollars	Year	Horse	Dollars
1952	Sharp Note	101,625	1965	Dartmouth	252,348
1953	Newport Dream	94,933	1966	Noble Victory	210,696
1954	Katie Key	84,867	1967	Carlisle	231,243
1955	Scott Frost	186,101	1968	Nevele Pride	427,440
1956	Scott Frost	85,851	1969	Lindy's Pride	323,997
1957	Hoot Song	114,877	1970	Fresh Yankee	359,002
1958	Emily's Pride	118,830	1971	Fresh Yankee	293,950
1959	Diller Hanover	149,897	1972	Super Bowl	437,108
1960	Su Mac Lad	159,662	1973	Spartan Hanover	262,023
1961	Su Mac Lad	245,750	1974	Delmonica Hanover	252,165
1962	Duke Rodney	206,113	1975	Savoir	351,385
1963	Speedy Scot	144,403	1976	Steve Lobell	388,770
1964	Speedy Scot	235,710			

Pacers

Year	Horse	Dollars	Year	Horse	Dollars
1952	Good Time	110,299	1965	Bret Hanover	341,784
1953	Keystoner	59,131	1966	Bret Hanover	407,534
1954	Red Sails	66,615	1967	Romulus Hanover	277,636
1955	Adios Harry	98,900	1968	Rum Customer	355,618
1956	Adios Harry	129,912	1969	Overcall	373,150
1957	Torpid	113,982	1970	Most Happy Fella	387,239
1958	Belle Action	167,887	1971	Albatross	558,009
1959	Bye Bye Byrd	199,933	1972	Albatross	459,921
1960	Bye Bye Byrd	187,612	1973	Sir Dalrae	307,354
1961	Adios Butler	180,250	1974	Armbro Omaha	345,146
1962	Henry T. Adios	220,302	1975	Silk Stockings	336,312
1963	Overtrick	208,833	1976	Keystone Ore	539,762
1964	Race Time	199,292			

Leading Money-Winning Horses

(As of January 1, 1977)

Trotters

Horse	Dollars	Horse	Dollars
Une de Mai	$1,660,627	Timothy T.	$894,237
Fresh Yankee	1,294,252	Su Mac Lad	885,095
Bellino II	1,190,255	Nevele Pride	873,238
Savoir	1,185,235	Delmonica Hanover	832,925
Roquepine	956,161	Tidalium Pelo	758,603

Pacers

Horse	Dollars	Horse	Dollars
Albatross	$1,201,470	Handle With Care	$809,689
Rum Customer	1,001,548	Overcall	783,948
Cardigan Bay	1,000,837	Henry T. Adios	706,833
Bret Hanover	922,616	Young Quinn	681,465
Laverne Hanover	868,557	Sir Dalrae	678,314

U.S. National Roller Skating Championship in 1977

Artistic

American Senior Dance — John LaBriola - Debra Coyne, Fountain Valley, Cal.

American Esquire Dance — Joseph Tarvis - Virginia Johnson, Norwood, Mass.

American Free Dance — David Golub - Wendy Galante, East Meadow, N.Y.

International Senior Dance — Dan Littel, Fleurette Arseneault, East Meadow, N.Y.

International Junior Dance — Charles Kirchner - Linda Todd, Cherry Hill, N.J.

American Senior Men's Figures — Tony St. Jacques, Virginia Beach, Va.

American Senior Ladies Figures — Jean O'Laughlin, Waltham, Mass.

American Junior Men's Figures — Gary Schmidt, Cincinnati, Oh.

American Junior Ladies Figures — Rebecca Gardner - Atlanta, Ga.

American Senior Men's Singles — Dean Maynard, San Diego, Cal.

American Senior Ladies Singles — Robbie Coleman, Memphis, Tenn.

American Junior Men's Singles — Gary Schmidt, Cincinnati, Oh.

American Junior Ladies Singles — Shari Ingles, Hillsdale, Mich.

American Senior Pairs — Ray Chappatta-Karen Mejia, Melrose Park, Ill.

American Junior Pairs — Paul Price - Tina Kneisley, Mansfield, Oh.

Speed

Senior Men's — Chris Snyder, Irving, Tex.

Senior Ladies — Marcia Yager, Loveland, Oh.

Junior Men's — Kenneth Sutton, Waukesha, Wis.

Junior Ladies — Gayle Falconer, Olympia, Wash.

Senior Four-Man Relay — Bobby Brewster, Bryant Huntsberry, Dennis Howard, Robin Riggs, Cincinnati, Oh.

Senior Four-Lady Relay — Kaylee Selvidge, Teri Paine, Cheryl Johnson, Gayle Falconer, Olympia, Wash.

Baseball

Major League Pennant Winners, 1901-1977

National League

Year	Winner	Won	Lost	Pct	Manager
1901	Pittsburgh	90	49	.647	Clarke
1902	Pittsburgh	103	36	.741	Clarke
1903	Pittsburgh	91	49	.650	Clarke
1904	New York	106	47	.693	McGraw
1905	New York	105	48	.686	McGraw
1906	Chicago	116	36	.763	Chance
1907	Chicago	107	45	.704	Chance
1908	Chicago	99	55	.643	Chance
1909	Pittsburgh	110	42	.724	Clarke
1910	Chicago	104	50	.675	Chance
1911	New York	99	54	.647	McGraw
1912	New York	103	48	.682	McGraw
1913	New York	101	51	.664	McGraw
1914	Boston	94	59	.614	Stallings
1915	Philadelphia	90	62	.592	Moran
1916	Brooklyn	94	60	.610	Robinson
1917	New York	98	56	.636	McGraw
1918	Chicago	84	45	.651	Mitchell
1919	Cincinnati	96	44	.686	Moran
1920	Brooklyn	93	60	.604	Robinson
1921	New York	94	56	.614	McGraw
1922	New York	93	61	.604	McGraw
1923	New York	95	58	.621	McGraw
1924	New York	93	60	.608	McGraw
1925	Pittsburgh	95	58	.621	McKechnie
1926	St. Louis	89	65	.578	Hornsby
1927	Pittsburgh	94	60	.610	Bush
1928	St. Louis	95	59	.617	McKechnie
1929	Chicago	98	54	.645	McCarthy
1930	St. Louis	92	62	.597	Street
1931	St. Louis	101	53	.656	Street
1932	Chicago	90	64	.584	Grimm
1933	New York	91	61	.599	Terry
1934	St. Louis	95	58	.621	Frisch
1935	Chicago	100	54	.649	Grimm
1936	New York	91	62	.597	Terry
1937	New York	95	57	.625	Terry
1938	Chicago	89	63	.586	Hartnett
1939	Cincinnati	97	57	.630	McKechnie
1940	Cincinnati	100	53	.654	McKechnie
1941	Brooklyn	100	54	.649	Durocher
1942	St. Louis	106	48	.688	Southworth
1943	St. Louis	105	49	.682	Southworth
1944	St. Louis	105	49	.682	Southworth
1945	Chicago	98	56	.636	Grimm
1946	St. Louis	98	58	.628	Dyer
1947	Brooklyn	94	60	.610	Shotton
1948	Boston	91	62	.595	Southworth
1949	Brooklyn	97	57	.630	Shotton
1950	Philadelphia	91	63	.591	Sawyer
1951	New York	98	59	.624	Durocher
1952	Brooklyn	96	57	.627	Dressen
1953	Brooklyn	105	49	.682	Dressen
1954	New York	97	57	.630	Durocher
1955	Brooklyn	98	55	.641	Alston
1956	Brooklyn	93	61	.604	Alston
1957	Milwaukee	95	59	.617	Haney
1958	Milwaukee	92	62	.597	Haney
1959	Los Angeles	88	68	.564	Alston
1960	Pittsburgh	95	59	.617	Murtaugh
1961	Cincinnati	93	61	.604	Hutchinson
1962	San Francisco	103	62	.624	Dark
1963	Los Angeles	99	63	.611	Alston
1964	St. Louis	93	69	.574	Keane
1965	Los Angeles	97	65	.599	Alston
1966	Los Angeles	95	67	.586	Alston
1967	St. Louis	101	60	.627	Schoendienst
1968	St. Louis	97	65	.599	Schoendienst

American League

Year	Winner	Won	Lost	Pct	Manager
1901	Chicago	83	53	.610	Griffith
1902	Philadelphia	83	53	.610	Mack
1903	Boston	91	47	.659	Collins
1904	Boston	95	59	.617	Collins
1905	Philadelphia	92	56	.622	Mack
1906	Chicago	93	58	.616	Jones
1907	Detroit	92	58	.613	Jennings
1908	Detroit	90	63	.588	Jennings
1909	Detroit	98	54	.645	Jennings
1910	Philadelphia	102	48	.680	Mack
1911	Philadelphia	101	50	.669	Mack
1912	Boston	105	47	.691	Stahl
1913	Philadelphia	96	57	.627	Mack
1914	Philadelphia	99	53	.651	Mack
1915	Boston	101	50	.669	Carrigan
1916	Boston	91	63	.591	Carrigan
1917	Chicago	100	54	.649	Rowland
1918	Boston	75	51	.595	Barrow
1919	Chicago	88	52	.629	Gleason
1920	Cleveland	98	56	.636	Speaker
1921	New York	98	55	.641	Huggins
1922	New York	94	60	.610	Huggins
1923	New York	98	54	.645	Huggins
1924	Washington	92	62	.597	Harris
1925	Washington	96	55	.636	Harris
1926	New York	91	63	.591	Huggins
1927	New York	110	44	.714	Huggins
1928	New York	101	53	.656	Huggins
1929	Philadelphia	104	46	.693	Mack
1930	Philadelphia	102	52	.622	Mack
1931	Philadelphia	107	45	.704	Mack
1932	New York	107	47	.695	McCarthy
1933	Washington	99	53	.651	Cronin
1934	Detroit	101	53	.656	Cochrane
1935	Detroit	93	58	.616	Cochrane
1936	New York	102	51	.667	McCarthy
1937	New York	102	52	.662	McCarthy
1938	New York	99	53	.651	McCarthy
1939	New York	106	45	.702	McCarthy
1940	Detroit	90	64	.584	Baker
1941	New York	101	53	.656	McCarthy
1942	New York	103	51	.669	McCarthy
1943	New York	98	56	.636	McCarthy
1944	St. Louis	89	65	.578	Sewell
1945	Detroit	88	65	.575	O'Neill
1946	Boston	104	50	.675	Cronin
1947	New York	97	57	.630	Harris
1948	Cleveland	97	58	.626	Boudreau
1949	New York	97	57	.630	Stengel
1950	New York	98	56	.636	Stengel
1951	New York	98	56	.636	Stengel
1952	New York	95	59	.617	Stengel
1953	New York	99	52	.656	Stengel
1954	Cleveland	111	43	.721	Lopez
1955	New York	96	58	.623	Stengel
1956	New York	97	57	.630	Stengel
1957	New York	98	56	.636	Stengel
1958	New York	92	62	.597	Stengel
1959	Chicago	94	60	.610	Lopez
1960	New York	97	57	.630	Stengel
1961	New York	109	53	.673	Houk
1962	New York	96	66	.593	Houk
1963	New York	104	57	.646	Houk
1964	New York	99	63	.611	Berra
1965	Minnesota	102	60	.630	Mele
1966	Baltimore	97	63	.606	Bauer
1967	Boston	92	70	.568	Williams
1968	Detroit	103	59	.636	Smith

National League

	East					West					
Year	Winner	W	L	Pct	Manager	Winner	W	L	Pct	Manager	Playoff winner
1969	N.Y. Mets	100	62	.617	Hodges	Atlanta	93	69	.574	Harris	New York
1970	Pittsburgh	89	73	.549	Murtaugh	Cincinnati	102	60	.630	Anderson	Cincinnati
1971	Pittsburgh	97	65	.599	Murtaugh	San Francisco	90	72	.556	Fox	Pittsburgh
1972	Pittsburgh	96	59	.619	Virdon	Cincinnati	95	59	.617	Anderson	Cincinnati
1973	N.Y. Mets	82	79	.509	Berra	Cincinnati	99	63	.611	Anderson	New York
1974	Pittsburgh	88	82	.543	Murtaugh	Los Angeles	102	60	.630	Alston	Los Angeles
1975	Pittsburgh	92	69	.571	Murtaugh	Cincinnati	108	54	.667	Anderson	Cincinnati
1976	Philadelphia	101	61	.623	Ozark	Cincinnati	102	60	.630	Anderson	Cincinnati
1977	Philadelphia	100	61	.621	Ozark	Los Angeles	98	64	.605	Lasorda	Los Angeles

American League

Year	East Winner	W	L	Pct	Manager	West Winner	W	L	Pct	Manager	Playoff winner
1969	Baltimore	109	53	.673	Weaver	Minnesota	97	65	.599	Martin	Baltimore
1970	Baltimore	108	54	.677	Weaver	Minnesota	98	64	.605	Rigney	Baltimore
1971	Baltimore	101	57	.639	Weaver	Oakland	101	60	.627	Williams	Baltimore
1972	Detroit	86	70	.551	Martin	Oakland	93	72	.600	Williams	Oakland
1973	Baltimore	97	65	.599	Weaver	Oakland	94	68	.580	Williams	Oakland
1974	Baltimore	91	71	.562	Weaver	Oakland	90	72	.556	Dark	Oakland
1975	Boston	95	65	.594	Johnson	Oakland	98	64	.605	Dark	Boston
1976	New York	97	62	.610	Martin	Kansas City	90	72	.556	Herzog	New York
1977	New York	100	62	.617	Martin	Kansas City	102	60	.630	Herzog	New York

All-Star Baseball Games, 1933-1977

Year	Winner	Score	Location
1933	American	4-2	Chicago
1934	American	9-7	New York
1935	American	4-1	Cleveland
1936	National	4-3	Boston
1937	American	8-3	Washington
1938	National	4-1	Cincinnati
1939	American	3-1	New York
1940	National	4-0	St. Louis
1941	American	7-5	Detroit
1942	American	3-1	New York
1943*	American	5-3	Philadelphia
1944*	National	7-1	Pittsburgh
1945	(not played)		
1946	American	12-0	Boston
1947	American	2-1	Chicago
1948	American	5-2	St. Louis
1949	American	11-7	New York
1950	National (1)	4-3	Chicago
1951	National	8-3	Detroit
1952	National	3-2	Philadelphia
1953	National	5-1	Cincinnati
1954	American	11-9	Cleveland
1955	National(2)	6-5	Milwaukee
1956	National	7-3	Washington
1957	American	6-5	St. Louis
1958	American	4-3	Baltimore
1959	National	5-4	Pittsburgh
1959	American	5-3	Los Angeles
1960	National	5-3	Kansas City
1960	National	6-0	New York
1961	National(3)	5-4	San Francisco
1961	Called-Rain	1-1	Boston
1962	National(3)	3-1	Washington
1962	American	9-4	Chicago
1963	National	5-3	Cleveland
1964	National	7-4	New York
1965	National	6-5	Minnesota
1966	National(3)	2-1	St. Louis
1967	National(4)	2-1	Anaheim
1968*	National	1-0	Houston
1969	National	9-3	Washington
1970*	National(2)	5-4	Cincinnati
1971*	American	6-4	Detroit
1972*	National	4-3	Atlanta
1973*	National	7-1	Kansas City
1974*	National	7-2	Pittsburgh
1975*	National	6-3	Milwaukee
1976*	National	7-1	Philadelphia
1977*	National	7-5	New York

(1) 14 innings, (2) 12 innings, (3) 10 innings, (4) 15 innings *Night game.

Baseball Stadiums

National League

Team	Stadium	Home run distances (ft.) LF	Center	RF	Seating capacity
Atlanta Braves	Atlanta-Fulton County Stadium	330	402	330	51,556
Chicago Cubs	Wrigley Field	355	400	353	37,741
Cincinnati Reds	Riverfront Stadium	330	404	330	51,963
Houston Astros	Astrodome	340	406	340	45,000
Los Angeles Dodgers	Dodger Stadium	330	395	330	56,000
Montreal Expos	Olympic Stadium	330	400	330	60,000
New York Mets	Shea Stadium	341	410	341	55,300
Philadelphia Phillies	Veterans Stadium	330	408	330	58,651
Pittsburgh Pirates	Three Rivers Stadium	335	400	335	50,235
St. Louis Cardinals	Busch Memorial Stadium	330	414	330	50,100
San Diego Padres	San Diego Stadium	330	410	330	48,460
San Francisco Giants	Candlestick Park	335	410	335	58,000

American League

Team	Stadium	LF	Center	RF	Seating capacity
Baltimore Orioles	Memorial Stadium	309	405	309	52,137
Boston Red Sox	Fenway Park	315	420	302	33,513
California Angels	Anaheim Stadium	333	404	333	43,250
Chicago White Sox	Comiskey Park	352	440	352	44,492
Cleveland Indians	Cleveland Stadium	320	400	320	76,713
Detroit Tigers	Tiger Stadium	340	440	325	54,226
Kansas City Royals	Royals Stadium	330	410	330	40,762
Milwaukee Brewers	Milwaukee County Stadium	320	402	315	54,187
Minnesota Twins	Metropolitan Stadium	343	402	330	45,919
New York Yankees	Yankee Stadium	312	417	310	57,145
Oakland A's	Oakland-Alameda County Coliseum	330	400	330	49,649
Seattle Mariners	Kingdome	316	405	316	59,059
Texas Rangers	Arlington Stadium	330	400	330	35,698
Toronto Blue Jays	Exhibition Stadium	330	400	330	40,000

Oh Surpasses Aaron With 756th Homer

Sadaharu Oh hit the 756th home run of his Japanese baseball career making him the most prolific home-run hitter in professional baseball history. The 37-year-old first baseman of the Yomiuri Giants hit his record-breaking homer at Tokyo's Korakuen Stadium, Sept. 3, 1977.

Little League World Series in 1977

Taiwan won the 1977 Little League World Series by defeating El Cajon (Cal.) 7-2, at Williamsport, Pa. on Aug. 27. The victory was Taiwan's 6th world title in 7 attempts since 1969, and its 17th straight victory in World Series competition.

Home Run Leaders

National League

Year		HR
1920	Cy Williams, Philadelphia	15
1921	George Kelly, New York	23
1922	Rogers Hornsby, St. Louis	42
1923	Cy Williams, Philadelphia	41
1924	Jacques Fournier, Brooklyn	27
1925	Rogers Hornsby, St. Louis	39
1926	Hack Wilson, Chicago	21
1927	Hack Wilson, Chicago; Cy Williams, Philadelphia	30
1928	Hack Wilson, Chicago; Jim Bottomley, St. Louis	31
1929	Charles Klein, Philadelphia	43
1930	Hack Wilson, Chicago	56
1931	Charles Klein, Philadelphia	31
1932	Charles Klein, Philadelphia, Mel Ott, New York	38
1933	Charles Klein, Philadelphia	28
1934	Collins, St. Louis; Mel Ott, New York	35
1935	Walter Berger, Boston	34
1936	Mel Ott, New York	33
1937	Mel Ott, New York; Joe Medwick, St. Louis	31
1938	Mel Ott, New York	36
1939	John Mize, St. Louis	28
1940	John Mize, St. Louis	43
1941	Dolph Camilli, Brooklyn	34
1942	Mel Ott, New York	30
1943	Bill Nicholson, Chicago	29
1944	Bill Nicholson, Chicago	33
1945	Tommy Holmes, Boston	28
1946	Ralph Kiner, Pittsburgh	23
1947	Ralph Kiner, Pittsburgh; John Mize, New York	51
1948	Ralph Kiner, Pittsburgh; John Mize, New York	40
1949	Ralph Kiner, Pittsburgh	54
1950	Ralph Kiner, Pittsburgh	47
1951	Ralph Kiner, Pittsburgh	42
1952	Ralph Kiner, Pittsburgh; Hank Sauer, Chicago	37
1953	Ed Mathews, Milwaukee	47
1954	Ted Kluszewski, Cincinnati	49
1955	Willie Mays, New York	51
1956	Duke Snider, Brooklyn	43
1957	Hank Aaron, Milwaukee	44
1958	Ernie Banks, Chicago	47
1959	Ed Mathews, Milwaukee	46
1960	Ernie Banks, Chicago	41
1961	Orlando Cepeda, San Francisco	46
1962	Willie Mays, San Francisco	49
1963	Hank Aaron, Milwaukee, Willie McCovey, San Francisco	44
1964	Willie Mays, San Francisco	47
1965	Willie Mays, San Francisco	52
1966	Hank Aaron, Atlanta	44
	Willie McCovey, San Francisco	44
1967	Hank Aaron, Atlanta	39
1968	Willie McCovey, San Francisco	36
1969	Willie McCovey, San Francisco	45
1970	Johnny Bench, Cincinnati	45
1971	Willie Stargell, Pittsburgh	48
1972	Johnny Bench, Cincinnati	40
1973	Willie Stargell, Pittsburgh	44
1974	Mike Schmidt, Philadelphia	36
1975	Mike Schmidt, Philadelphia	38
1976	Mike Schmidt, Philadelphia	38
1977	George Foster, Cincinnati	52

American League

Year		HR
1920	Babe Ruth, New York	54
1921	Babe Ruth, New York	59
1922	Ken Williams, St. Louis	39
1923	Babe Ruth, New York	41
1924	Babe Ruth, New York	46
1925	Bob Meusel, New York	33
1926	Babe Ruth, New York	47
1927	Babe Ruth, New York	60
1928	Babe Ruth, New York	54
1929	Babe Ruth, New York	46
1930	Babe Ruth, New York	49
1931	Babe Ruth, Lou Gehrig, New York	46
1932	Jimmy Foxx, Philadelphia	58
1933	Jimmy Foxx, Philadelphia	48
1934	Lou Gehrig, New York	49
1935	Jimmy Foxx, Philadelphia, Hank Greenberg, Detroit	36
1936	Lou Gehrig, New York	46
1937	Joe DiMaggio, New York	46
1938	Hank Greenberg, Detroit	58
1939	Jimmy Foxx, Boston	35
1940	Hank Greenberg, Detroit	41
1941	Ted Williams, Boston	37
1942	Ted Williams, Boston	36
1943	Rudy York, Detroit	34
1944	Nick Etten, New York	22
1945	Vern Stephens, St. Louis	24
1946	Hank Greenberg, Detroit	44
1947	Ted Williams, Boston	32
1948	Joe DiMaggio, New York	39
1949	Ted Williams, Boston	43
1950	Al Rosen, Cleveland	37
1951	Gus Zernial, Chicago-Philadelphia	33
1952	Larry Doby, Cleveland	32
1953	Al Rosen, Cleveland	43
1954	Larry Doby, Cleveland	32
1955	Mickey Mantle, New York	37
1956	Mickey Mantle, New York	52
1957	Roy Sievers, Washington	42
1958	Mickey Mantle, New York	42
1959	Rocky Colavito, Cleveland, Harmon Killebrew, Washington	42
1960	Mickey Mantle, New York	40
1961	Roger Maris, New York	61
1962	Harmon Killebrew, Minnesota	48
1963	Harmon Killebrew, Minnesota	45
1964	Harmon Killebrew, Minnesota	49
1965	Tony Conigliaro, Boston	32
1966	Frank Robinson, Baltimore	49
1967	Carl Yastrzemski, Boston, Harmon Killebrew, Minnesota	44
1968	Frank Howard, Washington	44
1969	Harmon Killebrew, Minnesota	49
1970	Frank Howard, Washington	44
1971	Bill Melton, Chicago	33
1972	Dick Allen, Chicago	37
1973	Reggie Jackson, Oakland	32
1974	Dick Allen, Chicago	32
1975	George Scott, Milwaukee; Reggie Jackson, Oakland	36
1976	Graig Nettles, New York	32
1977	Jim Rice, Boston	39

All-time Major League Record (154-game Season)—60—Babe Ruth, New York Yankees (A), 1927. **(162-game Season)—61**—Roger Maris, New York Yankees, 1961. Prior to the 1931 season a batted ball that bounced into the stands was a home run (now a ground-rule double). None of Babe Ruth's record 60 homers bounced into the stands.

Runs Batted In Leaders

National League

Year		RBI
1940	John Mize, St. Louis	137
1941	Dolph Camilli, Brooklyn	120
1942	John Mize, New York	137
1943	Bill Nicholson, Chicago	128
1944	Bill Nicholson, Chicago	122
1945	Dixie Walker, Brooklyn	124
1946	Enos Slaughter, St. Louis	130
1947	John Mize, New York	138
1948	Stan Musial, St. Louis	131
1949	Ralph Kiner, Pittsburgh	127
1950	Del Ennis, Philadelphia	126
1951	Monte Irvin, New York	121
1952	Hank Sauer, Chicago	121
1953	Roy Campanella, Brooklyn	142
1954	Ted Kluszewski, Cincinnati	141
1955	Duke Snider, Brooklyn	136
1956	Stan Musial, St. Louis	109
1957	Hank Aaron, Milwaukee	132
1958	Ernie Banks, Chicago	129

American League

Year		RBI
1940	Hank Greenberg, Detroit	150
1941	Joe DiMaggio, New York	125
1942	Ted Williams, Boston	137
1943	Rudy York, Detroit	118
1944	Vern Stephens, St. Louis	109
1945	Nick Etten, New York	111
1946	Hank Greenberg, Detroit	127
1947	Ted Williams, Boston	114
1948	Joe DiMaggio, New York	155
1949	Ted Williams, Vern Stephens, Boston	159
1950	Walt Dropo, Vern Stephens, Boston	144
1951	Gus Zernial, Chicago-Philadelphia	129
1952	Al Rosen, Cleveland	105
1953	Al Rosen, Cleveland	145
1954	Larry Doby, Cleveland	126
1955	Ray Boone, Detroit, Jack Jensen, Boston	116
1956	Mickey Mantle, New York	130
1957	Roy Sievers, Washington	114
1958	Jack Jensen, Boston	122

Year		RBI
1959	Ernie Banks, Chicago	143
1960	Hank Aaron, Milwaukee	126
1961	Orlando Cepeda, San Francisco	142
1962	Tommy Davis, Los Angeles	153
1963	Hank Aaron, Milwaukee	130
1964	Ken Boyer, St. Louis	119
1965	Deron Johnson, Cincinnati	130
1966	Hank Aaron, Atlanta	127
1967	Orlando Cepeda, St. Louis	111
1968	Willie McCovey, San Francisco	105
1969	Willie McCovey, San Francisco	126
1970	Johnny Bench, Cincinnati	148
1971	Joe Torre, St. Louis	137
1972	Johnny Bench, Cincinnati	125
1973	Willie Stargell, Pittsburgh	119
1974	Johnny Bench, Cincinnati	129
1975	Greg Luzinski, Philadelphia	120
1976	George Foster, Cincinnati	121
1977	George Foster, Cincinnati	149

Year		RBI
1959	Jack Jensen, Boston	112
1960	Roger Maris, New York	112
1961	Roger Maris, New York	142
1962	Harmon Killebrew, Minnesota	126
1963	Dick Stuart, Boston	118
1964	Brooks Robinson, Baltimore	118
1965	Rocky Colavito, Cleveland	108
1966	Frank Robinson, Baltimore	122
1967	Carl Yastrzemski, Boston	121
1968	Ken Harrelson, Boston	109
1969	Harmon Killebrew, Minnesota	140
1970	Frank Howard, Washington	126
1971	Harmon Killebrew, Minnesota	119
1972	Dick Allen, Chicago	113
1973	Reggie Jackson, Oakland	117
1974	Jeff Burroughs, Texas	118
1975	George Scott, Milwaukee	109
1976	Lee May, Baltimore	109
1977	Larry Hisle, Minnesota	119

Batting Champions

National League

Year	Player	Club	Pct.
1912	Henry Zimmerman	Chicago	.372
1913	Jacob Daubert	Brooklyn	.350
1914	Jacob Daubert	Brooklyn	.329
1915	Larry Doyle	New York	.320
1916	Hal Chase	Cincinnati	.339
1917	Edd Roush	Cincinnati	.341
1918	Zack Wheat	Brooklyn	.335
1919	Edd Roush	Cincinnati	.321
1920	Rogers Hornsby	St. Louis	.370
1921	Rogers Hornsby	St. Louis	.397
1922	Rogers Hornsby	St. Louis	.401
1923	Rogers Hornsby	St. Louis	.384
1924	Rogers Hornsby	St. Louis	.424
1925	Rogers Hornsby	St. Louis	.403
1926	Eugene Hargrave	Cincinnati	.353
1927	Paul Waner	Pittsburgh	.380
1928	Rogers Hornsby	Boston	.387
1929	Lefty O'Doul	Philadelphia	.398
1930	Bill Terry	New York	.401
1931	Chick Hafey	St. Louis	.349
1932	Lefty O'Doul	Brooklyn	.368
1933	Charles Klein	Philadelphia	.368
1934	Paul Waner	Pittsburgh	.362
1935	Arky Vaughan	Pittsburgh	.385
1936	Paul Waner	Pittsburgh	.373
1937	Joe Medwick	St. Louis	.374
1938	Ernie Lombardi	Cincinnati	.342
1939	John Mize	St. Louis	.349
1940	Debs Garms	Pittsburgh	.355
1941	Pete Reiser	Brooklyn	.343
1942	Ernie Lombardi	Boston	.330
1943	Stan Musial	St. Louis	.357
1944	Dixie Walker	Brooklyn	.357
1945	Phil Cavarretta	Chicago	.355
1946	Stan Musial	St. Louis	.365
1947	Harry Walker	Philadelphia	.363
1948	Stan Musial	St. Louis	.376
1949	Jackie Robinson	Brooklyn	.342
1950	Stan Musial	St. Louis	.346
1951	Stan Musial	St. Louis	.355
1952	Stan Musial	St. Louis	.336
1953	Carl Furillo	Brooklyn	.344
1954	Willie Mays	New York	.345
1955	Richie Ashburn	Philadelphia	.338
1956	Hank Aaron	Milwaukee	.328
1957	Stan Musial	St. Louis	.351
1958	Richie Ashburn	Philadelphia	.350
1959	Hank Aaron	Milwaukee	.355
1960	Dick Groat	Pittsburgh	.325
1961	Roberto Clemente	Pittsburgh	.351
1962	Tommy Davis	Los Angeles	.346
1963	Tommy Davis	Los Angeles	.326
1964	Roberto Clemente	Pittsburgh	.339
1965	Roberto Clemente	Pittsburgh	329
1966	Matty Alou	Pittsburgh	.342
1967	Roberto Clemente	Pittsburgh	.357
1968	Pete Rose	Cincinnati	.335
1969	Pete Rose	Cincinnati	.348
1970	Rico Carty	Atlanta	.366
1971	Joe Torre	St. Louis	.363
1972	Billy Williams	Chicago	.333
1973	Pete Rose	Cincinnati	.338
1974	Ralph Garr	Atlanta	.353
1975	Bill Madlock	Chicago	.354
1976	Bill Madlock	Chicago	.339
1977	Dave Parker	Pittsburgh	.338

American League

Year	Player	Club	Pct.
1912	Ty Cobb	Detroit	.410
1913	Ty Cobb	Detroit	.390
1914	Ty Cobb	Detroit	.368
1915	Ty Cobb	Detroit	.369
1916	Tris Speaker	Cleveland	.386
1917	Ty Cobb	Detroit	.383
1918	Ty Cobb	Detroit	.382
1919	Ty Cobb	Detroit	.384
1920	George Sisler	St. Louis	.407
1921	Harry Heilmann	Detroit	.394
1922	George Sisler	St. Louis	.420
1923	Harry Heilmann	Detroit	.403
1924	Babe Ruth	New York	.378
1925	Harry Heilmann	Detroit	.393
1926	Henry Manush	Detroit	.378
1927	Harry Heilmann	Detroit	.398
1928	Goose Goslin	Washington	.379
1929	Lew Fonseca	Cleveland	.369
1930	Al Simmons	Philadelphia	.381
1931	Al Simmons	Philadelphia	.390
1932	Dale Alexander	Detroit-Boston	.367
1933	Jimmy Foxx	Philadelphia	.356
1934	Lou Gehrig	New York	.363
1935	Buddy Myer	Washington	.349
1936	Luke Appling	Chicago	.388
1937	Charlie Gehringer	Detroit	.371
1938	Jimmy Foxx	Boston	.349
1939	Joe DiMaggio	New York	.381
1940	Joe DiMaggio	New York	.352
1941	Ted Williams	Boston	.406
1942	Ted Williams	Boston	.356
1943	Luke Appling	Chicago	.328
1944	Lou Boudreau	Cleveland	.327
1945	George Stirnweiss	New York	.309
1946	Mickey Vernon	Washington	.353
1947	Ted Williams	Boston	.343
1948	Ted Williams	Boston	.369
1949	George Kell	Detroit	.343
1950	Billy Goodman	Boston	.354
1951	Ferris Fain	Philadelphia	.344
1952	Ferris Fain	Philadelphia	.327
1953	Mickey Vernon	Washington	.337
1954	Roberto Avila	Cleveland	.341
1955	Al Kaline	Detroit	.340
1956	Mickey Mantle	New York	.353
1957	Ted Williams	Boston	.388
1958	Ted Williams	Boston	.328
1959	Harvey Kuenn	Detroit	.353
1960	Pete Runnels	Boston	.320
1961	Norm Cash	Detroit	.361
1962	Pete Runnels	Boston	.326
1963	Carl Yastrzemski	Boston	.321
1964	Tony Oliva	Minnesota	.323
1965	Tony Oliva	Minnesota	.321
1966	Frank Robinson	Baltimore	.316
1967	Carl Yastrzemski	Boston	.326
1968	Carl Yastrzemski	Boston	.301
1969	Rod Carew	Minnesota	.332
1970	Alex Johnson	California	.328
1971	Tony Oliva	Minnesota	.337
1972	Rod Carew	Minnesota	.318
1973	Rod Carew	Minnesota	.350
1974	Rod Carew	Minnesota	.364
1975	Rod Carew	Minnesota	.359
1976	George Brett	Kansas City	.333
1977	Rod Carew	Minnesota	.388

National League Records in 1977

Final Standings

Eastern Division

Club	W	L	Pct	GB
Philadelphia	101	61	.623	—
Pittsburgh	96	66	.593	5
St. Louis	83	79	.512	18
Chicago	81	81	.500	20
Montreal	75	87	.463	26
New York	64	98	.395	37

Western Division

Club	W	L	Pct	GB
Los Angeles	98	64	.605	—
Cincinnati	88	74	.543	10
Houston	81	81	.500	17
San Francisco	75	87	.463	23
San Diego	69	93	.426	29
Atlanta	61	101	.377	37

National League Playoffs

Oct. 4—Philadelphia 7, Los Angeles 5.
Oct. 5—Los Angeles 7, Philadelphia 1.
Oct. 7—Los Angeles 6, Philadelphia 5.
Oct. 8—Los Angeles 4, Philadelphia 1.

Club Batting

Club	Pct	AB	R	H	HR	SB
Philadelphia	**.279**	5546	847	1548	186	135
Cincinnati	**.274**	5524	802	1513	181	170
Pittsburgh	**.274**	5662	734	1550	133	260
St. Louis	**.270**	5527	737	1490	96	134
Chicago	**.266**	5604	692	1489	111	64
Los Angeles	**.266**	5589	769	1484	191	114
Montreal	**.260**	5675	665	1474	138	88
Houston	**.254**	5530	680	1405	114	187
Atlanta	**.254**	5534	678	1404	139	82
San Francisco	**.253**	5497	673	1392	134	90
San Diego	**.249**	5602	692	1397	120	133
New York	**.244**	5410	587	1319	88	98

Club Pitching

Club	ERA	CG	IP	H	R	BB	SO
Los Angeles	**3.22**	34	1475	1393	582	438	930
Houston	**3.54**	37	1466	1384	650	545	871
Pittsburgh	**3.61**	25	1482	1406	665	485	890
Philadelphia	**3.71**	31	1456	1451	668	482	856
San Francisco	**3.75**	27	1459	1501	711	529	854
New York	**3.77**	27	1434	1378	663	490	911
St. Louis	**3.81**	26	1446	1420	688	532	768
Chicago	**4.01**	16	1468	1500	739	489	942
Montreal	**4.01**	31	1481	1426	736	579	856
Cincinnati	**4.22**	33	1437	1469	725	544	867
San Diego	**4.43**	6	1446	1556	834	673	827
Atlanta	**4.85**	28	1445	1581	895	701	915

Individual Batting

Leaders—450 or more at bats

Player, Club	Pct	AB	R	W	HR	RBI	SB
Parker, Pittsburgh†	**338**	637	107	215	21	88	17
Stennett, Pittsburgh	**.336**	453	53	152	5	51	28
Templeton, St. Louis‡	**.322**	621	94	200	8	79	28
Foster, Cincinnati	**.320**	615	124	197	52	149	6
Griffey, Cincinnati†	**.318**	585	117	186	12	57	17
Simmons, St. Louis‡	**.318**	516	82	164	21	95	2
Rose, Cincinnati‡	**.311**	655	95	204	9	64	16
Hendrick, San Diego	**.311**	541	75	168	23	81	11
Luzinski, Philadelphia	**.309**	554	99	171	39	130	3
Oliver, Pittsburgh†	**.308**	568	75	175	19	82	13
Smith, Los Angeles‡	**.307**	488	104	150	32	87	7

Individual Pitching

Leaders—162 or more innings

Pitcher, Club	W		ERA	G	IP	H	BB	SO
Candelaria, Pitts.†	20	5	**2.34**	33	231	197	50	133
Seaver, Cincinnati	21	6	**2.59**	33	261	199	66	196
Hooton, Los Angeles	12	7	**2.62**	32	223	184	60	153
Carlton, Philadelphia†	23	10	**2.64**	36	283	229	89	198
John, Los Angeles†	20	7	**2.78**	31	220	225	50	123
R. Reuschel, Chicago	20	10	**2.79**	39	252	233	74	166
Richard, Houston	18	12	**2.97**	36	267	212	104	214
Niekro, Houston	13	8	**3.03**	44	181	155	64	101
Rooker, Pittsburgh†	14	9	**3.09**	30	204	196	64	89
Rogers, Montreal	17	16	**3.10**	40	302	272	81	206
Sutton, Los Angeles	14	8	**3.19**	33	240	207	69	150

*Rookie †Bats or pitches lefthanded ‡Switch hitter

Individual Batting (over 100 at-bats) Individual Pitching (over 50 innings)

Atlanta Braves

Batting	Pct	G	AB	R	H	HR	RBI	SB
Bonnell*	**.300**	100	360	41	108	1	45	7
Pocoroba†	**.290**	113	321	46	93	8	44	3
Montanez†	**.287**	136	544	70	156	20	68	1
Matthews	**.283**	148	555	89	157	17	64	22
Burroughs	**.271**	154	579	91	157	41	114	4
Moore*	**.260**	112	361	41	94	5	34	4
Rockett*	**.254**	93	264	27	67	1	24	1
Gilbreath	**.243**	128	407	47	99	8	43	3
Office†	**.241**	124	428	42	103	5	39	2
Paciorek	**.239**	72	155	20	37	3	15	1
Royster	**.216**	140	445	64	96	6	28	28
Asselstine*	**.210**	83	124	12	26	4	17	1
Correll	**.208**	54	144	16	30	7	16	2
Chaney‡	**.201**	74	209	22	42	3	15	0

Batting	Pct	G	AB	R	H	HR	RBI	SB
Campbell*	0	6	**3.03**	65	89	78	33	42
Leon	4	4	**3.95**	31	82	89	25	44
Camp*	6	3	**3.99**	54	79	89	47	51
Niekro	16	20	**4.04**	44	330	315	164	262
Ruthven	7	13	**4.23**	25	151	158	62	84
Messersmith	5	4	**4.41**	16	102	101	39	69
Solomon	6	6	**4.55**	18	89	110	34	54
Hanna*	2	6	**4.95**	17	60	69	34	37
Collins*†	3	9	**5.07**	40	71	82	41	27
Capra	6	11	**5.37**	45	139	142	80	100
Easterly†	2	4	**6.10**	22	59	72	30	37

Chicago Cubs

Batting	Pct	G	AB	R	H	HR	RBI	SB
Gross†	**.322**	115	239	43	77	5	32	0
Ontiveros‡	**.299**	156	546	54	163	10	68	3
Biittner†	**298**	138	493	74	147	12	62	2
Clines	**.293**	101	239	27	70	3	41	1
Morales	**.290**	136	490	56	142	11	69	0
Buckner†	**.284**	122	426	40	121	11	60	7
Trillo	**.280**	152	504	51	141	7	57	3
DeJesus	**.266**	155	624	91	166	3	40	24
Murcer†	**.265**	154	554	90	147	27	89	16
Cardenal	**.239**	100	226	33	54	3	18	5
Mitterwald	**.238**	110	349	40	83	9	43	3
Kelleher	**.230**	63	122	14	28	0	11	0
Swisher	**.190**	74	205	21	39	5	15	0

Batting	Pct	G	AB	R	H	HR	RBI	SB
Sutter	7	3	**1.35**	62	107	69	23	129
R. Reuschel	20	10	**2.79**	39	252	233	74	166
G. Hernandez*†	8	7	**3.03**	67	110	94	28	78
Roberts†	1	1	**3.23**	17	53	55	12	23
Bonham	10	13	**4.35**	34	215	207	82	134
P. Reuschel	5	6	**4.37**	69	107	105	40	62
Krukow*	8	14	**4.40**	34	172	195	61	106
Renko	2	2	**4.59**	13	51	51	21	34
Burris	14	16	**4.72**	39	221	270	67	105

College World Series

Arizona State won the 1977 College World Series by defeating South Carolina 2-1 at Omaha, Neb. It was the 4th NCAA title for Arizona State, which finished the season with a 57-12 record.

Cincinnati Reds

Batting	Pct	G	AB	R	H	HR	RBI	SB
Foster	.320	158	615	124	197	52	149	6
Griffey†	.318	154	585	117	186	12	57	17
Rose‡	.311	162	655	95	204	9	64	16
Driessen†	.300	151	536	75	161	17	91	31
Morgan†	.288	153	521	113	150	22	78	49
Bench	.275	142	494	67	136	31	109	2
Concepcion	.271	156	572	59	155	8	64	29
Geronimo†	.266	149	492	54	131	10	52	10
Lum†	.160	81	125	14	20	5	16	2
Plummer	.137	51	117	10	16	1	7	1

Pitching	W	L	ERA	G	IP	H	BB	SO
Seaver	21	6	2.59	33	261	199	66	196
Borbon	10	5	3.19	73	127	131	24	48
Norman†	14	13	3.38	35	221	200	98	160
Moskau*	6	6	4.00	20	108	116	40	71
Capilla*†	7	8	4.46	24	109	96	61	75
Murray	7	2	4.94	61	102	125	46	42
Billingham	10	10	5.22	36	162	195	56	76
Soto*	2	6	5.31	12	61	60	26	44
Fryman†	5	5	5.40	17	75	83	45	57

Houston Astros

Batting	Pct	G	AB	R	H	HR	RBI	SB
Puhl*	.301	60	229	40	69	0	10	10
Cruz†	.299	157	579	87	173	17	87	44
Johnson	.299	51	144	22	43	10	23	0
Herrmann†	.291	56	158	7	46	1	17	1
Watson	.289	151	554	77	160	22	110	5
Cabell	.282	150	625	101	176	16	68	42
Cedeno	.279	141	530	92	148	14	71	61
Howe	.264	125	413	44	109	8	58	0
Howard‡	.257	87	187	22	48	2	13	11
Ferguson	.257	132	421	59	108	16	61	6
Crawford†	.254	42	114	14	29	2	18	0
Gonzalez*	.245	110	383	34	94	1	27	3
Sperring	.186	58	129	6	24	1	9	0
Metzger‡	.186	97	269	24	50	0	16	2
Fuller	.160	34	100	5	16	2	9	0

Pitching	W	L	ERA	G	IP	H	BB	SO
Sambito†	5	5	2.33	54	89	77	24	67
Forsch	5	8	2.72	42	86	80	28	45
Richard	18	12	2.97	36	267	212	104	214
Niekro	13	8	3.03	44	181	155	64	101
Lemongello*	9	14	3.47	34	215	237	52	83
Andujar	11	8	3.68	26	159	149	64	69
Pentz	5	2	3.83	41	87	76	44	51
Bannister*	8	9	4.03	24	143	138	68	112
McLaughlin	4	7	4.24	46	85	81	34	59
Larson	1	7	5.79	32	98	108	45	44

Los Angeles Dodgers

Batting	Pct	G	AB	R	H	HR	RBI	SB
Smith‡	.307	148	488	104	150	32	87	7
Martinez	.299	67	137	21	41	1	10	3
Garvey	.297	162	646	91	192	33	115	9
Baker	.291	153	533	86	155	30	86	2
Lopes	.283	134	502	85	142	11	53	47
Russell	.278	153	634	84	176	4	51	16
Oates†	.269	60	156	18	42	3	11	1
Grote	.268	60	142	11	38	0	11	0
Lacy	.266	75	169	28	45	6	21	4
Yeager	.256	125	387	53	99	16	55	1
Burke*	.254	83	169	16	43	1	13	13
Cey	.241	153	564	77	136	30	110	3
Hale†	.241	79	108	10	26	2	11	2
Monday†	.230	118	392	47	90	15	48	1

Pitching	W	L	ERA	G	IP	H	BB	SO
Sosa	2	2	1.97	44	64	42	12	47
Hooton	12	7	2.62	32	223	184	60	153
Garman	4	4	2.71	49	63	60	22	29
John†	10	7	2.78	31	220	225	50	123
Sutton	14	8	3.19	33	240	207	69	150
Hough	6	12	3.33	70	127	98	70	105
Rau†	14	8	3.44	32	212	232	49	126
Rhoden	16	10	3.75	31	216	223	63	122

New York Mets

Batting	Pct	G	AB	R	H	HR	RBI	SB
Randle‡	.304	136	513	78	156	5	27	33
Henderson*	.297	99	350	67	104	12	65	6
Boisclair†	.293	127	307	41	90	4	44	6
Kranepool†	.281	108	281	28	79	10	40	1
Hodges†	.265	66	117	6	31	1	5	0
Vail	.262	108	279	29	73	8	35	0
Milner†	.255	131	388	43	99	12	57	6
Staiger	.252	40	123	16	31	2	11	1
Stearns	.251	139	431	52	108	12	55	9
Mazzilli*	.250	159	537	66	134	6	46	22
Millan	.248	91	314	40	78	2	21	1
Youngblood	.244	95	209	17	51	0	12	1
Flynn	.197	126	314	14	62	0	19	1
Harrelson‡	.178	107	269	25	48	1	12	5
Valentine	.153	86	150	13	23	2	13	0

Pitching	W	L	ERA	G	IP	H	BB	SO
Lockwood	4	8	3.38	63	104	87	31	84
Espinosa	10	13	3.42	32	200	188	55	105
Apodaca	4	8	3.43	59	84	83	30	53
Koosman†	8	20	3.49	32	227	195	81	192
Myrick†	2	2	3.62	44	87	86	33	49
Matlack†	7	15	4.21	26	169	175	43	123
Swan	9	10	4.22	26	147	153	56	71
Zachry	10	13	4.25	31	195	207	77	99
Baldwin	1	2	4.43	40	63	62	31	23
Todd*	3	6	4.75	19	72	78	20	39

Montreal Expos

Batting	Pct	G	AB	R	H	HR	RBI	SB
Valentine	.293	127	508	63	149	25	76	13
Cash	.289	153	650	91	188	0	43	21
Carter	.284	154	522	86	148	31	84	5
Perez	.283	154	559	71	158	19	91	4
Cromartie*†	.282	155	620	64	175	5	50	10
Dawson*	.282	139	525	64	148	19	65	21
Unsert	.273	113	289	33	79	12	40	2
Garrett†	.270	68	159	17	43	2	22	2
Parrish	.246	123	402	50	99	11	46	2
Speier	.234	145	548	59	128	5	38	1
Mejias*	.228	73	101	14	23	3	8	1

Pitching	W	L	ERA	G	IP	H	BB	SO
Rogers	17	16	3.10	40	302	272	81	206
Kerrigan	3	5	3.24	66	89	80	33	43
Atkinson*	7	2	3.36	55	83	72	29	56
Stanhouse	10	10	3.42	47	158	147	84	89
McEnaney†	3	5	3.93	69	87	92	22	38
Twitchell	6	10	4.28	34	185	166	74	130
Brown	9	12	4.50	42	186	189	71	89
Bahnsen	8	9	4.82	23	127	142	38	58
Alcala	3	7	4.85	38	117	126	54	73

Philadelphia Phillies

Batting	Pct	G	AB	R	H	HR	RBI	SB
Johnson	.321	78	156	23	50	8	36	1
McCarver†	.320	93	169	28	54	6	30	3
McBride†	.316	128	402	76	127	15	61	36
Luzinski	.309	149	554	99	171	39	130	3
Maddox	.292	139	571	85	167	14	74	22
Hebner†	.285	118	397	67	113	18	62	7
Boone	.284	132	440	55	125	11	66	5
Johnstone†	.284	112	363	64	103	15	59	3
Sizemore	.281	152	519	64	146	4	47	8
Bowa‡	.280	154	624	93	175	4	41	32
Schmidt	.274	154	544	114	149	38	101	15
Martin	.260	116	215	34	56	6	28	6

Pitching	W	L	ERA	G	IP	H	BB	SO
Garber	8	6	2.36	64	103	82	23	78
McGraw†	7	3	2.62	45	79	62	24	58
Carlton†	23	10	2.64	36	283	229	89	198
Brusstar*	7	2	2.66	46	71	64	24	46
Reed	7	5	2.76	60	124	101	37	84
Christenson	19	6	4.07	34	219	229	69	118
Lonborg	11	4	4.10	25	158	157	50	76
Lerch*†	10	6	5.06	32	169	207	75	81
Kaat†	6	11	5.40	35	160	211	40	55

Pittsburgh Pirates

Batting	Pct	G	AB	R	H	HR	RBI	SB
Parker†	.338	159	637	107	215	21	88	17
Stennett	.336	116	453	53	152	5	51	28
Oliver†	.308	154	568	75	175	19	82	13
Robinson	.304	137	507	74	154	26	104	12
Gonzalez	.276	80	181	17	50	4	27	3
Stargell†	.274	63	186	29	51	13	35	0
Ott†	.264	104	311	40	82	7	38	7
Garner	.260	153	585	99	152	17	77	32
Taveras	.252	147	544	72	137	1	29	70
Dyer	.241	94	270	27	65	3	19	6
Moreno*†	.240	150	492	69	118	7	34	53

Pitching	W	L	ERA	G	IP	H	BB	SO
Gossage	11	9	**1.62**	72	133	78	49	151
Candelaria†	20	5	**2.34**	33	231	197	50	133
Tekulve	10	1	**3.06**	72	103	89	33	59
Rooker†	14	9	**3.09**	30	204	196	64	89
Jackson†	5	3	**3.86**	49	91	81	39	41
Reuss†	10	13	**4.11**	33	208	225	71	116
Forster†	6	4	**4.45**	33	87	90	32	58
Kison	9	10	**4.90**	33	193	209	55	122
Jones*	3	7	**5.08**	34	108	118	31	66
Demery	6	5	**5.10**	39	90	100	47	35

St. Louis Cardinals

Batting	Pct	G	AB	R	H	HR	RBI	SB
Templeton‡	**322**	153	621	94	200	8	79	28
Simmons‡	**.318**	150	516	82	164	21	95	2
Scott‡	**.291**	95	292	38	85	3	41	13
Hernandez†	**.291**	161	560	90	163	15	91	7
Mumphrey‡	**.287**	145	463	73	133	2	38	22
Brock†	**.272**	141	489	69	133	2	46	35
Rader†	**.263**	66	114	15	30	1	16	1
Reitz	**.261**	157	587	58	153	17	79	2
Tyson	**.246**	138	418	42	103	7	57	3
Kessinger‡	**.239**	59	134	14	32	0	7	0
Cruz	**.236**	118	339	50	80	6	42	4
Phillips†	**.225**	86	173	22	39	1	12	1
Anderson	**.221**	94	154	18	34	4	17	2

Pitching	W	L	ERA	G	IP	H	BB	SO
Schultz†	6	1	**2.33**	40	85	76	24	66
Carroll	4	2	**2.50**	51	90	77	24	34
Urrea*	7	6	**3.15**	41	140	126	35	81
Rasmussen	11	17	**3.48**	34	233	223	63	120
Forsch	20	7	**3.48**	35	217	210	69	95
Metzger	4	2	**3.68**	75	115	105	50	54
Eastwick	5	9	**3.90**	64	97	114	29	47
Hrabosky†	6	5	**4.40**	65	86	82	41	68
Denny	8	8	**4.50**	26	150	165	62	60
Underwood†	9	11	**5.01**	33	133	148	75	86
Falcone†	4	8	**5.44**	27	124	130	61	75

San Diego Padres

Batting	Pct	G	AB	R	H	HR	RBI	SB
Hendrick	**.311**	152	541	75	168	23	81	11
Richards*†	**.290**	146	525	79	152	5	32	56
Rettenmund	**.286**	107	126	23	36	4	17	1
Winfield	**.275**	157	615	104	169	25	92	16
Ivie	**.272**	134	489	66	133	9	66	3
Rader	**.271**	52	170	19	46	5	27	0
Almon*	**.261**	155	613	75	160	2	43	20
Turner†	**.246**	118	289	43	71	10	48	12
Sutherland	**.243**	80	103	5	25	1	11	0
Tenace	**.233**	147	437	66	102	15	61	5
Champion*	**.229**	150	507	35	116	1	43	3
Kingman	**.222**	114	379	38	84	20	67	5
Roberts	**.220**	82	186	15	41	1	23	2
Ashford*	**.217**	81	249	25	54	3	24	2

Pitching	W	L	ERA	G	IP	H	BB	SO
Fingers	8	9	**3.00**	78	132	123	36	113
Tomlin†	4	4	**3.00**	76	102	98	32	55
Shirley*†	12	18	**3.70**	39	214	215	100	146
Spillner	7	6	**3.73**	76	123	130	60	74
Owchinko*†	9	12	**4.45**	30	170	191	67	101
Griffin	6	9	**4.47**	38	151	144	88	79
Jones†	6	12	**4.59**	27	147	173	36	44
Freisleben	7	9	**4.60**	33	139	140	71	72
Sawyer	7	6	**5.84**	56	111	136	55	45
Wehrmeister*	1	3	**6.04**	30	70	81	44	32
D'Acquisto	1	2	**6.58**	20	52	54	57	54

San Francisco Giants

Batting	Pct	G	AB	R	H	HR	RBI	SB
Alexander*	**.303**	51	119	17	36	5	20	3
Madlock	**.302**	140	533	70	161	12	46	13
Whitfield*†	**.285**	114	326	41	93	7	36	2
McCovey†	**.280**	141	478	54	134	28	86	3
Thomas‡	**.267**	148	506	75	135	8	44	15
Andrews	**.264**	127	436	60	115	0	25	5
Harris‡	**.261**	69	165	28	43	2	14	2
Thomasson†	**.256**	145	446	63	114	17	71	16
Evans†	**.254**	144	461	64	117	17	72	9
Clark*	**.252**	136	413	64	104	13	51	12
Hill	**.250**	108	320	28	80	9	50	0
Elliott*	**.240**	73	167	17	40	7	26	0
Herndon	**.239**	49	109	13	26	1	5	4
Sadek	**.230**	61	126	12	29	1	15	2
Foli	**.221**	117	425	32	94	4	30	2
LeMaster	**.149**	68	134	13	20	0	8	2

Pitching	W	L	ERA	G	IP	H	BB	SO
Lavelle†	7	7	**2.06**	73	118	106	37	93
Heaverlo	5	1	**2.55**	56	99	92	21	58
Halicki	16	12	**3.31**	37	258	241	70	168
Knepper*†	11	9	**3.36**	27	166	151	72	100
Montefusco	7	12	**3.50**	26	157	170	46	110
Moffitt	4	9	**3.58**	64	88	91	39	68
Williams	6	5	**4.01**	55	119	116	60	41
Barr	12	16	**4.77**	38	234	286	56	97
Curtis†	3	3	**5.49**	43	77	95	48	47
McGlothen	2	9	**5.63**	21	80	94	52	42

Leading Pitchers, Earned-Run Average

National League

Year	Pitcher, club	G	IP	ERA
1961	Warren Spahn, Milwaukee	38	263	**3.01**
1962	Sandy Koufax, Los Angeles	28	184	**2.54**
1963	Sandy Koufax, Los Angeles	40	311	**1.88**
1964	Sandy Koufax, Los Angeles	29	223	**1.74**
1965	Sandy Koufax, Los Angeles	43	336	**2.04**
1966	Sandy Koufax, Los Angeles	41	323	**1.73**
1967	Phil Niekro, Atlanta	46	207	**1.87**
1968	Bob Gibson, St. Louis	34	305	**1.12**
1969	Juan Marichal, San Francisco	37	300	**2.10**
1970	Tom Seaver, New York	37	291	**2.81**
1971	Tom Seaver, New York	36	286	**1.76**
1972	Steve Carlton, Philadelphia	41	346	**1.98**
1973	Tom Seaver, New York	36	290	**2.07**
1974	Buzz Capra, Atlanta	39	217	**2.28**
1975	Randy Jones, San Diego	37	285	**2.24**
1976	John Denny, St. Louis	30	207	**2.52**
1977	John Candelaria, Pittsburgh	33	231	**2.34**

American League

Year	Pitcher, club	G	IP	ERA
1961	Dick Donovan, Washington	23	169	**2.40**
1962	Hank Aquirre, Detroit	42	216	**2.21**
1963	Gary Peters, Chicago	41	243	**2.33**
1964	Dean Chance, Los Angeles	46	278	**1.56**
1965	Sam McDowell, Cleveland	42	274	**2.17**
1966	Gary Peters, Chicago	29	204	**2.03**
1967	Joe Horlen, Chicago	35	258	**2.06**
1968	Luis Tiant, Cleveland	34	258	**1.60**
1969	Dick Bosman, Washington	31	193	**2.19**
1970	Diego Segui, Oakland	47	162	**2.56**
1971	Vida Blue, Oakland	39	312	**1.82**
1972	Luis Tiant, Boston	43	179	**1.91**
1973	Jim Palmer, Baltimore	38	296	**2.40**
1974	Catfish Hunter, Oakland	41	318	**2.49**
1975	Jim Palmer, Baltimore	39	323	**2.09**
1976	Mark Fidrych, Detroit	31	250	**2.34**
1977	Frank Tanana, California	31	241	**2.54**

ERA is computed by multiplying earned runs allowed by 9, then dividing by innings pitched.

Cy Young Award Winners

Year	Player, club
1956	Don Newcombe, Dodgers
1957	Warren Spahn, Braves
1958	Bob Turley, Yankees
1959	Early Wynn, White Sox
1960	Vernon Law, Pirates
1961	Whitey Ford, Yankees
1962	Don Drysdale, Dodgers
1963	Sandy Koufax, Dodgers
1964	Dean Chance, Angels
1965	Sandy Koufax, Dodgers
1966	Sandy Koufax, Dodgers

Year	Player, Club
1967	(NL) Mike McCormick, Giants
	(AL) Jim Lonborg, Red Sox
1968	(NL) Bob Gibson, Cardinals
	(AL) Dennis McLain, Tigers
1969	(NL) Tom Seaver, Mets
	(AL) (tie) Dennis McLain, Tigers
	Mike Cuellar, Orioles
1970	(NL) Bob Gibson, Cardinals
	(AL) Jim Perry, Twins
1971	(NL) Ferguson Jenkins, Cubs
	(AL) Vida Blue, A's

Year	Player, club
1972	(NL) Steve Carlton, Phillies
	(AL) Gaylord Perry, Indians
1973	(NL) Tom Seaver, Mets
	(AL) Jim Palmer, Orioles
1974	(NL) Mike Marshall, Dodgers
	(AL) Jim (Catfish) Hunter, A's
1975	(NL) Tom Seaver, Mets
	(AL) Jim Palmer, Orioles
1976	(NL) Randy Jones, Padres
	(AL) Jim Palmer, Orioles

Most Valuable Player

Baseball Writers' Association

National League

Year	Player, Club
1931	Frank Frisch, St. Louis
1932	Charles Klein, Philadelphia
1933	Carl Hubbell, New York
1934	Dizzy Dean, St. Louis
1935	Gabby Hartnett, Chicago
1936	Carl Hubbell, New York
1937	Joe Medwick, St. Louis
1938	Ernie Lombardi, Cincinnati
1939	Bucky Walters, Cincinnati
1940	Frank McCormick, Cincinnati
1941	Dolph Camilli, Brooklyn
1942	Mort Cooper, St. Louis
1943	Stan Musial, St. Louis
1944	Martin Marion, St. Louis
1945	Phil Cavarretta, Chicago
1946	Stan Musial, St. Louis
1947	Bob Elliott, Boston
1948	Stan Musial, St. Louis
1949	Jackie Robinson, Brooklyn
1950	Jim Konstanty, Philadelphia
1951	Roy Campanella, Brooklyn
1952	Hank Sauer, Chicago
1953	Roy Campanella, Brooklyn
1954	Willie Mays, New York
1955	Roy Campenella, Brooklyn
1956	Don Newcombe, Brooklyn
1957	Henry Aaron, Milwaukee
1958	Ernie Banks, Chicago
1959	Ernie Banks, Chicago
1960	Dick Groat, Pittsburgh
1961	Frank Robinson, Cincinnati
1962	Maury Wills, Los Angeles
1963	Sandy Koufax, Los Angeles
1964	Ken Boyer, St. Louis
1965	Willie Mays, San Francisco
1966	Roberto Clemente, Pittsburgh
1967	Orlando Cepeda, St. Louis
1968	Bob Gibson, St. Louis
1969	Willie McCovey, San Francisco
1970	Johnny Bench, Cincinnati
1971	Joe Torre, St. Louis
1972	Johnny Bench, Cincinnati
1973	Pete Rose, Cincinnati
1974	Steve Garvey, Los Angeles
1975	Joe Morgan, Cincinnati
1976	Joe Morgan, Cincinnati

American League

Year	Player, Club
1931	Lefty Grove, Philadelphia
1932	Jimmy Foxx, Philadelphia
1933	Jimmy Foxx, Philadelphia
1934	Mickey Cochrane, Detroit
1935	Henry Greenberg, Detroit
1936	Lou Gehrig, New York
1937	Charley Gehringer, Detroit
1938	Jimmy Foxx, Boston
1939	Joe DiMaggio, New York
1940	Hank Greenberg, Detroit
1941	Joe DiMaggio, New York
1942	Joe Gordon, New York
1943	Spurgeon Chandler, New York
1944	Hal Newhouser, Detroit
1945	Hal Newhouser, Detroit
1946	Ted Williams, Boston
1947	Joe DiMaggio, New York
1948	Lou Boudreau, Cleveland
1949	Ted Williams, Boston
1950	Phil Rizzuto, New York
1951	Yogi Berra, New York
1952	Bobby Shantz, Philadelphia
1953	Al Rosen, Cleveland
1954	Yogi Berra, New York
1955	Yogi Berra, New York
1956	Mickey Mantle, New York
1957	Mickey Mantle, New York
1958	Jackie Jensen, Boston
1959	Nellie Fox, Chicago
1960	Roger Maris, New York
1961	Roger Maris, New York
1962	Mickey Mantle, New York
1963	Elston Howard, New York
1964	Brooks Robinson, Baltimore
1965	Zoilo Versalles, Minnesota
1966	Frank Robinson, Baltimore
1967	Carl Yastrzemski, Boston
1968	Denny McLain, Detroit
1969	Harmon Killebrew, Minnesota
1970	John (Boog)Powell, Baltimore
1971	Vida Blue, Oakland
1972	Dick Allen, Chicago
1973	Reggie Jackson, Oakland
1974	Jeff Burroughs, Texas
1975	Fred Lynn, Boston
1976	Thurman Munson, New York

Rookie of the Year

Baseball Writers' Association

1947—Combined Selection—Jackie Robinson, Brooklyn, 1b
1948—Combined Selection—Alvin Dark, Boston, N. L. ss

National League

Year	Winner
1949	Don Newcombe, Brooklyn, p
1950	Sam Jethroe, Boston, of
1951	Willie Mays, New York, of
1952	Joe Black, Brooklyn, p
1953	Jim Gilliam, Brooklyn, 2b
1954	Wally Moon, St. Louis, of
1955	Bill Virdon, St. Louis, of
1956	Frank Robinson, Cincinnati, of
1957	Jack Sanford, Philadelphia, p
1958	Orlando Cepeda, S.F., 1b
1959	Willie McCovey, S.F., 1b
1960	Frank Howard, Los Angeles, of
1961	Billy Williams, Chicago, of
1962	Ken Hubbs, Chicago, 2b
1963	Pete Rose, Cincinnati, 2b
1964	Richie Allen, Philadelphia, 3b
1965	Jim Lefebvre, Los Angeles, 2b
1966	Tommy Helms, Cincinnati, 2b
1967	Tom Seaver, New York, p
1968	Johnny Bench, Cincinnati, c
1969	Ted Sizemore, Los Angeles, 2b
1970	Carl Morton, Montreal, p
1971	Earl Williams, Atlanta, c
1972	Jon Matlack, New York, p
1973	Gary Matthews, S.F., of
1974	Bake McBride, St. Louis, of
1975	John Montefusco, S.F, p
1976	(tie) Butch Metzger, San Diego, p —Pat Zachry, Cincinnati, p

American League

1949	Roy Sievers, St. Louis, of
1950	Walt Dropo, Boston, 1b
1951	Gil McDougald, New York, 3b
1952	Harry Byrd, Philadelphia, p
1953	Harvey Kuenn, Detroit, ss
1954	Bob Grim, New York, p
1955	Herb Score, Cleveland, p
1956	Luis Aparicio, Chicago, ss
1957	Tony Kubek, New York, if-of
1958	Albie Pearson, Washington, of
1959	Bob Allison, Washington, of
1960	Ron Hansen, Baltimore, ss
1961	Don Schwall, Boston, p
1962	Tom Tresh, New York, if-of
1963	Gary Peters, Chicago, p
1964	Tony Oliva, Minnesota, of
1965	Curt Blefary, Baltimore, of
1966	Tommie Agee, Chicago, of
1967	Rod Carew, Minnesota, 2b
1968	Stan Bahnsen, New York, p
1969	Lou Piniella, Kansas City, of
1970	Thurman Munson, New York, c
1971	Chris Chambliss, Cleveland, 1b
1972	Carlton Fisk, Boston, c
1973	Al Bumbry, Baltimore, of
1974	Mike Hargrove, Texas, 1b
1975	Fred Lynn, Boston, of
1976	Mark Fidrych, Detroit, p

Triple Crown Winners

Players leading league in batting, runs batted in and homers in a single season

Year	Player & Team
1909	Ty Cobb, Detroit Tigers
1922	Rogers Hornsby, St. Louis Cardinals
1925	Rogers Hornsby, St. Louis Cardinals
1933	Jimmy Foxx, Philadelphia Athletics
1933	Chuck Klein, Philadelphia Phillies
1934	Lou Gehrig, New York Yankees
1937	Joe Medwick, St. Louis Cardinals
1942	Ted Williams, Boston Red Sox
1947	Ted Williams, Boston Red Sox
1956	Mickey Mantle, New York Yankees
1966	Frank Robinson, Baltimore Orioles
1967	Carl Yastrzemski, Boston Red Sox

A recent review of baseball statistics indicates that Heinie Zimmerman, formerly credited with winning the triple crown in 1912, did not lead the NL in RBIs that year.

American League Records in 1977

Final Standings

Eastern Division

Club	W	L	Pct.	GB
New York	100	62	.617	—
Boston	97	64	.602	2½
Baltimore	97	64	.602	2½
Detroit	74	88	.457	26
Cleveland	71	90	.441	28½
Milwaukee	67	95	.414	33
Toronto	54	107	.335	45½

Western Division

Club	W	L	Pct.	GB
Kansas City	102	60	.630	—
Texas	94	68	.580	8
Chicago	90	72	.556	12
Minnesota	84	77	.522	17½
California	74	88	.457	28
Seattle	64	98	.395	38
Oakland	63	98	.391	38½

American League Playoffs

Oct. 5 — Kansas City 7, New York 2
Oct. 6 — New York 6, Kansas City 2
Oct. 7 — Kansas City 6, New York 2
Oct. 8 — New York 6, Kansas City 4
Oct. 9 — New York 5, Kansas City 3

Club Batting

Club	Pct.	AB	R	H	HR	SB
Minnesota	**.282**	5639	867	1588	123	105
Boston	**.281**	5510	859	1551	213	66
New York	**.281**	5605	831	1576	184	93
Chicago	**.278**	5633	844	1568	192	42
Kansas City	**.277**	5594	822	1549	146	170
Texas	**.270**	5541	767	1497	135	154
Cleveland	**.269**	5491	676	1476	100	87
Detroit	**.264**	5604	714	1480	166	60
Baltimore	**.261**	5494	719	1433	148	90
Milwaukee	**.258**	5517	639	1425	125	85
Seattle	**.256**	5460	624	1398	133	110
California	**.255**	5410	675	1380	131	159
Toronto	**.252**	5419	605	1367	100	65
Oakland	**.240**	5358	605	1284	117	176

Club Pitching

Club	ERA	CG	IP	H	R	BB	SO
Kansas City	**3.52**	41	1461	1377	651	499	850
Texas	**3.55**	49	1472	1412	657	471	864
New York	**3.61**	52	1449	1395	651	486	758
California	**3.72**	58	1438	1383	695	572	965
Baltimore	**3.74**	65	1451	1414	653	494	737
Oakland	**4.03**	32	1437	1459	749	560	788
Cleveland	**4.10**	45	1452	1441	739	550	876
Boston	**4.11**	40	1428	1555	712	378	758
Detroit	**4.13**	44	1457	1526	751	470	784
Chicago	**4.25**	34	1445	1557	771	516	842
Milwaukee	**4.32**	38	1431	1461	765	566	719
Minnesota	**4.36**	35	1442	1546	776	507	737
Toronto	**4.57**	40	1428	1538	822	623	771
Seattle	**4.83**	18	1433	1508	855	578	785

Individual Batting

Leaders—450 or more at bats

Player, club	Pct	AB	R	H	HR	RBI	SB
Carew, Minnesota†	**.388**	616	128	239	14	100	23
Bostock, Minnesota†	**.336**	593	104	199	14	90	16
Singleton, Baltimore‡	**.328**	536	90	176	24	99	0
Rivers, New York†	**.326**	565	79	184	12	69	22
LeFlore, Detroit	**.325**	652	100	212	16	57	39
Rice, Boston	**.320**	644	104	206	39	114	5
Bumbry, Baltimore†	**.317**	518	74	164	4	41	19
Fisk, Boston	**.315**	536	106	169	26	102	7
Brett, Kansas City†	**.312**	564	105	176	22	88	14
Cowens, Kansas City	**.312**	606	98	189	23	112	16

Individual Pitching

Leaders—162 or more innings

Pitcher, Club	W	L	ERA	G	IP	H	BB	SO
Tanana, California†	15	9	**2.54**	31	241	201	61	205
Blyleven, Texas	14	12	**2.72**	30	235	181	69	182
Ryan, California	19	16	**2.77**	37	299	198	204	341
Guidry, New York†	16	7	**2.82**	31	211	174	65	176
Palmer, Baltimore	20	11	**2.91**	39	319	263	99	193
Leonard, Kansas City	20	12	**3.04**	38	293	246	79	244
Rozema, Detroit*	15	7	**3.10**	28	218	222	34	92
Goltz, Minnesota	20	11	**3.36**	39	303	284	91	186
Perry, Texas	15	12	**3.37**	34	238	239	56	177
Eckersley, Cleveland	14	13	**3.53**	33	247	214	54	191

***Rookie** †**Bats or pitches lefthanded** ‡**Switch hitter**

Individual Batting (over 100 at-bats) Individual Pitching (over 50 innings)

Baltimore Orioles

Batting	Pct	G	AB	R	H	HR	RBI	SB
Singleton†	**.328**	152	536	90	176	24	99	0
Bumbry†	**.317**	133	518	74	164	4	41	19
Skaggs*	**.287**	80	216	22	62	1	24	0
Murray*‡	**.283**	160	611	81	173	27	88	0
Maddox	**.262**	49	107	14	28	2	9	2
DeCinces	**.259**	150	522	63	135	19	69	8
Kelly†	**.256**	120	360	50	92	10	49	25
L. May	**.253**	150	585	75	148	27	99	2
Mora	**.245**	77	233	32	57	13	44	0
Dauer*	**.243**	96	304	38	74	5	25	1
Muser†	**.229**	120	118	14	27	0	7	1
Dempsey	**.226**	91	270	27	61	3	34	2
Garcia†	**.221**	65	131	20	29	2	10	2
Smith‡	**.215**	109	367	44	79	5	29	3
Belanger	**.206**	144	402	39	83	2	30	15

Pitching	W	L	ERA	G	IP	H	BB	SO
F. Martinez†	5	1	**2.70**	41	50	47	27	29
Palmer	20	11	**2.91**	39	319	263	99	193
Drago	6	4	**3.39**	49	61	71	18	35
R. May†	18	14	**3.61**	37	252	243	78	105
Flanagan†	15	10	**3.64**	36	235	235	70	149
Grimsley†	14	10	**3.96**	34	218	230	74	53
D. Martinez*	14	7	**4.10**	42	167	157	64	107
Briles	6	4	**4.18**	30	112	119	30	59
McGregor*†	3	5	**4.42**	29	114	119	30	55

Boston Red Sox

Batting	Pct	G	AB	R	H	HR	RBI	SB
Rice	**.320**	160	644	104	206	39	114	5
Fisk	**.315**	152	536	106	169	26	102	7
Yastrzemski†	**.296**	150	558	99	165	28	102	11
Burleson	**.293**	154	663	80	194	3	52	13
Carbo†	**.289**	86	228	36	66	15	34	1
Evans	**.287**	73	230	39	66	14	36	4
Scott	**.269**	157	584	103	157	33	95	1
Hobson	**.265**	159	593	77	157	30	112	5
Lynn†	**.260**	129	497	81	129	18	76	2
Miller†	**.254**	86	189	34	48	0	24	11
Dillard	**.241**	66	141	22	34	1	13	4
Doyle†	**.240**	137	455	54	109	2	49	2

Pitching	W	L	ERA	G	IP	H	BB	SO
Campbell	13	9	**2.96**	69	140	112	60	114
Aase*	6	2	**3.13**	13	92	85	19	49
Jenkins	10	10	**3.68**	28	193	190	36	105
Paxton*	10	5	**3.83**	29	108	134	25	58
Stanley*	8	7	**3.99**	41	151	176	43	44
Cleveland	11	8	**4.26**	36	190	211	43	85
Lee†	9	5	**4.43**	27	128	155	29	31
Tiant	12	8	**4.52**	32	189	210	51	124
Wise	11	5	**4.78**	26	128	151	28	85
Willoughby	6	2	**4.91**	31	55	54	18	33

California Angels

Batting	Pct	G	AB	R	H	HR	RBI	SB
Bosley*†	**.297**	58	212	19	63	0	19	5
Guerrero	**.283**	86	244	17	69	1	28	0
Flores*	**.278**	104	342	41	95	1	26	12
Chalk	**.277**	149	519	58	144	3	45	12
Mulliniks*†	**.269**	78	271	36	73	3	21	1
Bonds	**.264**	158	592	103	156	37	115	41
Rudi	**.264**	64	242	48	64	13	53	1
Etchebarren	**.254**	80	114	11	29	0	14	3
Remy†	**.252**	154	575	74	145	4	44	41
Bayor	**.251**	154	561	87	141	25	75	26
Jackson	**.243**	106	292	38	71	8	28	3
Grich	**.243**	52	181	24	44	7	23	6
Solaita†	**.241**	116	324	40	78	14	53	1
May†	**.236**	76	199	21	47	2	17	0
Humphrey	**.227**	123	304	17	69	2	34	1

Pitching	W	L	ERA	G	IP	H	BB	SO
Tanana†	15	9	**2.54**	31	241	201	61	205
Ryan	19	16	**2.77**	37	299	198	204	341
LaRoche†	8	7	**3.51**	59	100	79	44	79
D. Miller	6	6	**3.52**	53	115	106	40	58
Hartzell	8	12	**3.57**	41	189	200	38	79
Brett†	13	14	**4.52**	34	225	258	53	80
Barlow	4	2	**4.58**	20	59	53	27	25
Ross	2	4	**5.59**	14	58	83	11	30
Simpson	6	12	**5.83**	27	122	154	62	55

Chicago White Sox

Batting	Pct	G	AB	R	H	HR	RBI	SB
Nordhagen	**.315**	52	124	16	39	4	22	1
L. Johnson	**.302**	118	374	52	113	18	65	1
Garr†	**.300**	134	543	78	163	10	54	12
Gamble†	**.297**	137	408	75	121	31	83	1
Zisk	**.290**	141	531	78	154	30	101	0
Downing	**.284**	69	169	28	48	4	25	1
Orta†	**.282**	144	564	71	159	11	84	4
Soderholm	**.280**	130	460	77	129	25	67	2
Bannister	**.275**	139	560	87	154	3	57	4
Lemon	**.273**	150	553	99	151	19	67	8
Essian	**.273**	114	322	50	88	10	44	1
Brohamer†	**.257**	59	152	26	39	2	20	0
Spencer†	**.247**	128	470	56	116	18	69	1
Kessinger‡	**.235**	39	119	12	28	0	11	2
Stillman†	**.210**	56	119	18	25	3	13	2

Pitching	W	L	ERA	G	IP	H	BB	SO
LaGrow	7	3	**2.45**	66	99	81	35	63
Renko	5	0	**3.57**	8	53	55	17	36
Hamilton†	4	5	**3.63**	55	67	71	33	45
B. Johnson	4	5	**4.01**	29	92	114	38	46
Kravec†	11	8	**4.10**	26	167	161	57	125
Barrios	14	7	**4.13**	33	231	241	58	119
Stone	15	12	**4.52**	31	207	228	80	124
Knapp	12	7	**4.81**	27	146	166	61	103
Wood†	7	8	**4.98**	24	123	139	50	42
Kirkwood	2	1	**5.12**	29	58	69	19	34

Cleveland Indians

Batting	Pct	G	AB	R	H	HR	RBI	SB
Bochte†	**.301**	137	492	64	148	7	51	6
Bell	**.292**	129	479	64	140	11	64	1
Dade	**.291**	134	461	65	134	3	45	16
Pruitt	**.288**	78	219	29	63	2	32	2
Blanks	**.286**	105	322	43	92	6	38	3
Carty	**.280**	127	461	50	129	15	80	1
Kuiper	**.277**	148	610	62	169	1	50	11
Norris*†	**.270**	133	440	59	119	2	37	26
Thornton	**.263**	131	433	77	114	28	70	3
Kendall	**.249**	103	317	18	79	3	39	0
Lowenstein†	**.242**	81	149	24	36	4	12	1
Melton	**.241**	50	133	17	32	0	14	1
Manning†	**.226**	68	252	33	57	5	18	9
Duffy	**.201**	122	334	30	67	4	31	8

Pitching	W	L	ERA	G	IP	H	BB	SO
Hood†	2	1	**3.00**	41	105	87	49	62
Kern	8	10	**3.42**	60	92	85	47	91
Eckersley	14	13	**3.53**	33	247	214	54	191
Bibby	12	13	**3.57**	37	207	197	73	141
Garland	13	19	**3.59**	38	283	281	88	118
Waits†	9	7	**4.00**	37	135	132	64	62
Laxton†	3	2	**4.99**	45	74	64	41	50
Fitzmorris	6	10	**5.41**	29	133	164	53	54
Monge†	1	3	**5.47**	37	51	61	33	29
Dobson	3	12	**6.16**	33	133	155	65	81

Detroit Tigers

Batting	Pct	G	AB	R	H	HR	RBI	SB
LeFlore	**.325**	154	652	100	212	16	57	39
Fuentes‡	**.309**	151	615	83	190	5	51	4
Corcoran*	**.282**	55	103	13	29	3	15	0
Staub†	**.278**	158	623	84	173	22	101	1
Mankowski†	**.276**	94	286	21	79	3	27	1
Wockenfuss	**.274**	53	164	26	45	9	25	0
Thompson†	**.270**	158	585	87	158	31	105	0
Oglivie†	**.262**	132	450	63	118	21	61	9
Kemp*	**.257**	151	552	75	142	18	88	3
May†	**.249**	115	397	32	99	12	46	0
Stanley	**.230**	75	222	30	51	8	23	0
Rodriguez	**.219**	96	306	30	67	10	32	1
Veryzer	**.197**	125	350	31	69	2	28	0

Pitching	W	L	ERA	G	IP	H	BB	SO
Fidrych	6	4	**2.89**	11	81	82	12	42
Rozema*	15	7	**3.10**	28	218	222	34	92
Foucault	7	7	**3.16**	44	74	64	17	58
Hiller†	8	14	**3.56**	45	124	120	61	115
Wilcox	6	2	**3.65**	20	106	96	37	82
Arroyo	8	18	**4.18**	38	209	227	52	60
Sykes*†	5	7	**4.40**	32	133	141	50	58
Crawford†	7	8	**4.79**	37	126	156	50	91
Grilli	1	2	**4.81**	30	73	71	49	49
Roberts†	4	10	**5.16**	22	129	143	41	46
Ruhle	3	5	**5.73**	14	66	83	15	27

Kansas City Royals

Batting	Pct	G	AB	R	H	HR	RBI	SB
Wathan	**.328**	55	119	18	39	2	21	2
Brett†	**.312**	139	564	105	176	22	88	14
Cowens	**.312**	162	606	98	189	23	112	16
LaCock†	**.303**	88	218	25	66	3	29	2
McRae	**.298**	162	641	104	191	21	92	18
Zdeb*	**.297**	105	195	26	58	2	23	6
Poquette†	**.292**	106	342	43	100	2	33	1
Porter†	**.275**	130	425	61	117	16	60	1
Patek	**.262**	154	497	72	130	5	60	53
Otis	**.251**	142	478	85	120	17	78	23
Rojas	**.250**	64	156	8	39	0	10	1
White	**.245**	152	474	59	116	5	50	23
Mayberry†	**.230**	153	543	73	125	23	82	1

Pitching	W	L	ERA	G	IP	H	BB	SO
Leonard	20	12	**3.04**	38	293	246	79	244
Mingori†	2	4	**3.09**	43	64	59	19	19
Gura†	8	5	**3.14**	52	106	108	28	46
Pattin	10	3	**3.59**	31	128	115	37	55
Littell	8	4	**3.60**	48	105	73	55	106
Colborn	18	14	**3.62**	36	239	233	81	103
Splittorff†	16	6	**3.69**	37	229	243	83	99
Bird	11	4	**3.89**	53	118	120	29	83
Hassler†	9	6	**4.21**	29	156	166	75	83

Milwaukee Brewers

Batting	Pct	G	AB	R	H	HR	RBI	SB
Cooper†	**.300**	160	643	86	193	20	78	13
Yount	**.288**	154	605	66	174	4	49	16
Money	**.279**	152	570	86	159	25	83	8
Lezcano	**.273**	109	400	50	109	21	49	6
Joshua†	**.261**	144	536	58	140	9	49	12
Bando	**.250**	159	580	65	145	17	82	4
Brye	**.249**	94	241	27	60	7	28	1
Wohlford	**.248**	129	391	41	97	2	36	17
Moore	**.248**	138	375	42	93	5	45	1
Kirkpatrick†	**.240**	49	125	10	30	0	9	2
Haney	**.228**	63	127	7	29	0	10	0
McMullen	**.228**	63	136	15	31	5	19	0
Quirk†	**.217**	93	221	16	48	3	13	0
Wynn	**.175**	66	194	17	34	1	13	4
Sakata*	**.162**	53	154	13	25	2	12	1

Pitching	W	L	ERA	G	IP	H	BB	SO
McClure†	2	1	**2.54**	68	71	64	34	57
Slaton	10	14	**3.58**	32	221	223	77	104
Castro	8	6	**4.17**	51	69	76	23	28
Haas*	10	12	**4.32**	32	198	195	84	113
Rodriguez	5	6	**4.34**	42	143	126	56	104
Sorensen*	7	10	**4.37**	23	142	147	36	57
Augustine†	12	18	**4.48**	33	209	222	72	68
Caldwell†	5	8	**4.60**	21	94	101	36	38
Hinds*	0	3	**4.75**	29	72	72	40	46
Travers†	4	12	**5.24**	19	122	140	57	49
Beare*	3	3	**6.41**	17	59	63	38	32

Minnesota Twins

Batting	Pct	G	AB	R	H	HR	RBI	SB
Carew†	**.388**	155	616	128	239	14	100	23
Adams†	**.338**	95	269	32	91	6	49	0
Bostock†	**.336**	153	593	104	199	14	90	16
Hisle	**.302**	141	546	95	165	28	119	21
Ford	**.267**	144	453	66	121	11	60	6
Cubbage†	**.264**	129	417	60	110	9	55	1
Chiles†	**.264**	108	261	31	69	3	36	0
Wynegar‡	**.261**	144	532	76	139	10	79	2
Kusick	**.254**	115	268	34	68	12	45	3
Wilfong*†	**.246**	73	171	22	42	1	13	10
Randall	**.239**	103	306	36	73	0	22	1
Smalley‡	**.231**	150	584	93	135	6	56	5
Terrell	**.224**	93	214	32	48	1	20	10
Gorinski*	**.195**	54	118	14	23	3	22	1

Pitching	W	L	ERA	G	IP	H	BB	SO
T. Johnson	16	7	**3.12**	71	147	152	47	87
Goltz	20	11	**3.36**	39	303	284	91	186
Schueler	8	7	**4.40**	52	135	131	61	77
D. Johnson	2	5	**4.56**	30	73	86	23	33
Thormodsgard*	11	15	**4.62**	37	218	236	65	94
Zahn†	12	14	**4.68**	34	198	234	66	88
Burgmeier†	6	4	**5.10**	61	97	113	33	35
Redfern	6	9	**5.19**	30	137	164	66	73

New York Yankees

Batting	Pct	G	AB	R	H	HR	RBI	SB
Piniella	**.330**	103	339	47	112	12	45	2
Rivers†	**.326**	138	565	79	184	12	69	22
Munson	**.308**	149	595	85	183	18	100	5
Johnson	**.296**	56	142	24	42	12	31	0
Chambliss†	**.287**	157	600	90	172	17	90	4
Jackson†	**.286**	146	525	93	150	32	110	17
Randolph	**.274**	147	551	91	151	4	40	13
White‡	**.268**	143	519	72	139	14	52	18
Blair	**.262**	83	164	20	43	4	25	3
Nettles†	**.255**	158	589	99	150	37	107	2
Dent	**.247**	158	477	54	118	8	49	1

Pitching	W	L	ERA	G	IP	H	BB	SO
Lyle†	13	5	**2.17**	72	137	131	33	68
Guidry†	16	7	**2.82**	31	211	174	65	176
Tidrow	11	4	**3.16**	49	151	143	41	83
Figueroa	16	11	**3.58**	32	239	228	75	104
Gullett†	14	4	**3.59**	22	158	137	69	116
Torrez	17	13	**3.93**	35	243	235	86	102
Clay*	2	3	**4.34**	21	56	53	24	20
Hunter	9	9	**4.72**	22	143	137	47	52
Holtzman†	2	3	**5.75**	18	72	105	24	14
Thomas	3	6	**6.09**	16	65	81	29	15

Oakland A's

Batting	Pct	G	AB	R	H	HR	RBI	SB
Page*†	**.307**	145	501	85	154	21	75	42
Sanguillen	**.275**	152	571	42	157	6	58	2
Scott	**.261**	133	364	56	95	0	20	33
North‡	**.261**	56	184	32	48	1	9	17
Jorgensen†	**.246**	66	203	18	50	8	32	3
Tyrone	**.245**	96	294	32	72	5	26	3
E. Williams	**.241**	100	348	39	84	13	38	2
Armas*	**.240**	118	363	26	87	13	53	1
Allen	**.240**	54	171	19	41	5	31	1
Alexander‡	**.238**	90	42	24	10	0	2	26
Gross*†	**.233**	146	485	66	113	22	63	5
Perez	**.233**	116	377	32	88	2	23	1
Newman	**.222**	94	162	17	36	4	15	2
Tabb*†	**.222**	51	144	8	32	6	19	0
Mallory*†	**.214**	64	126	19	27	0	5	12
Picciolo*	**.200**	148	419	35	84	2	22	1
Crawford†	**.184**	59	136	7	25	1	16	0
Murray*	**.179**	90	162	19	29	1	9	12
McKinney	**.177**	86	198	13	35	6	21	0

Pitching	W	L	ERA	G	IP	H	BB	SO
Torrealba†	4	6	**2.62**	41	117	127	38	51
Coleman	4	4	**2.95**	43	128	114	49	55
Giusti	3	3	**3.00**	40	60	54	20	28
Lacey*†	6	8	**3.02**	64	122	100	43	69
Bair*	4	6	**3.47**	45	83	78	57	68
Blue†	14	19	**3.83**	38	280	284	86	157
Langford*	8	19	**4.02**	37	208	223	73	141
Norris	2	7	**4.79**	16	77	77	31	35

Seattle Mariners

Batting	Pct	G	AB	R	H	HR	RBI	SB
Lopez*	**.283**	99	297	39	84	8	34	16
Fosse	**.276**	89	272	28	75	6	32	0
Stanton	**.275**	133	454	56	125	27	90	0
Meyer†	**.273**	159	582	75	159	22	90	11
Stinson‡	**.269**	105	297	27	80	8	32	0
Ru. Jones*†	**.263**	160	597	85	157	24	76	13
Stein	**.259**	151	556	53	144	13	67	3
Baez*	**.259**	91	305	39	79	1	17	6
Cruz*†	**.256**	60	199	25	51	1	7	15
Reynolds*†	**.248**	135	420	41	104	4	28	6
Bernhardt*	**.243**	89	305	32	74	7	30	2
Collins‡	**.239**	120	402	46	96	5	28	25
Braun†	**.235**	139	451	51	106	5	31	8
Jutze	**.220**	42	109	10	24	3	15	0
Milbourne‡	**.219**	86	242	24	53	2	21	3

Pitching	W	L	ERA	G	IP	H	BB	SO
Romo*	8	10	**2.84**	58	114	93	39	105
Montague	8	12	**4.30**	47	182	193	75	98
Abbott	12	13	**4.46**	36	204	212	56	100
Medich	12	6	**4.55**	29	170	181	53	77
House†	5	5	**4.64**	34	97	109	25	45
Wheelock*	6	9	**4.91**	17	88	94	26	47
Pole	7	12	**5.16**	25	122	127	57	51
Kekich†	5	4	**5.60**	41	90	90	51	55
Segui	0	7	**5.68**	40	111	108	43	91
Pagan	1	1	**6.14**	24	66	86	26	30
Mitchell	3	6	**6.45**	14	53	71	23	25

Texas Rangers

Batting	Pct	G	AB	R	H	HR	RBI	SB
Hargrove†	**.305**	153	525	98	160	18	69	2
Sundberg	**.291**	149	453	61	132	6	65	2
Horton	**.289**	140	523	55	151	15	75	2
Wills*‡	**.287**	152	541	87	155	9	62	28
Washington†	**.284**	129	521	63	148	12	68	21
Beniquez	**.269**	123	424	56	114	10	50	26
Harrah	**.263**	159	539	90	142	27	87	27
Henderson‡	**.258**	75	244	23	63	5	23	2
Campaneris	**.254**	150	552	77	140	5	46	27
May†	**.241**	120	340	46	82	7	42	4
J. Ellis	**.235**	49	119	7	28	4	15	0
Grieve	**.225**	79	236	24	53	7	30	1
Mason†	**.187**	58	134	19	25	1	9	1

Pitching	W	L	ERA	G	IP	H	BB	SO
Blyleven	14	12	**2.72**	30	235	181	69	182
Knowles†	5	2	**3.24**	42	50	50	23	14
Perry	15	12	**3.37**	34	238	239	56	177
Devine	11	6	**3.57**	56	106	102	31	67
D. Ellis	12	12	**3.63**	33	213	211	64	106
Alexander	17	11	**3.65**	34	237	221	82	82
Moret†	3	3	**3.75**	18	72	59	38	39
Lindblad†	4	5	**4.18**	42	99	103	29	46
Umbarger†	2	6	**6.32**	15	57	76	32	29

Toronto Blue Jays

Batting	Pct	G	AB	R	H	HR	RBI	SB
Bailor*	**.310**	122	496	62	154	5	32	15
Howell†	**.302**	103	381	41	115	10	44	4
Ewing*†	**.287**	97	244	24	70	4	35	1
A. Woods*†	**.284**	122	440	58	125	6	35	8
Fairly†	**.279**	132	458	60	128	19	64	0
Staggs*	**.258**	72	291	37	75	2	28	5
Velez	**.256**	120	360	50	92	16	62	4
Ault*	**.245**	129	445	44	109	11	64	4
Rader	**.240**	95	312	47	75	13	40	2
Torres	**.240**	91	267	33	64	5	26	1
Scott	**.240**	79	233	26	56	2	15	10
G. Woods*	**.216**	60	227	21	49	0	17	5
Ashby‡	**.210**	124	396	25	83	2	29	0
Garcia	**.208**	41	130	10	27	0	9	0
Bowling*	**.206**	89	194	19	40	1	13	2
Cerone*	**.200**	31	100	7	20	1	10	0
McKay	**.197**	95	274	18	54	3	22	2

Pitching	W	L	ERA	G	IP	H	BB	SO
Vuckovich	7	7	**3.47**	53	148	143	59	123
Willis*†	2	6	**3.95**	43	107	105	38	59
Garvin*†	10	18	**4.19**	34	245	247	85	127
Lemanczyk	13	16	**4.25**	34	252	278	87	105
Jefferson	9	17	**4.31**	33	217	224	83	114
Johnson	2	4	**4.60**	43	86	91	54	54
Murphy	2	2	**4.77**	35	83	107	30	39
Clancy*	4	9	**5.03**	13	77	80	47	44
Byrd*	2	13	**6.21**	17	87	98	68	40
Singer	2	8	**6.75**	13	60	71	39	33

1977 World Series Box Scores

First Game

Yankee Stadium, New York, Oct. 11

Dodgers	ab	r	h	bi	Yankees	ab	r	h	bi
Lopes, 2b. . . .	5	1	0	0	Rivers, cf. . . .	6	0	0	0
Russell, ss. . . .	6	1	1	1	Randolph, 2b. .	5	3	2	1
Smith, rf.	4	0	1	0	Munson, c. . . .	4	1	2	1
Cey, 3b.	3	0	0	1	Jackson, rf. . . .	2	0	1	0
Garvey, 1b. . . .	4	0	1	0	Blair, rf.	2	0	1	1
Baker, lf	4	1	1	0	Chambliss, 1b.	5	0	1	1
Burke, cf	3	0	1	0	Nettles, 3b. . . .	4	0	0	0
Mota, ph.	1	0	0	0	Piniella, lf.	5	0	2	0
Monday, cf	1	0	0	0	Dent, ss.	5	0	2	0
Yeager, c.	3	0	0	0	Gullett, p.	1	0	0	0
Landestoy, pr. .	0	0	0	0	Lyle, p	2	0	0	0
Grote, c.	1	0	0	0					
Sutton, p	2	0	0	0					
Rautzhan, p. . . .	0	0	0	0					
Sosa, p	0	0	0	0					
Lacy, ph.	1	0	1	1					
Garman, p. . . .	0	0	0	0					
Davalillo, ph . . .	1	0	0	0					
Rhoden, p. . . .	0	0	0	0					
Totals.	**39**	**3**	**6**	**3**	**Totals. . . . .**	**41**	**4**	**11**	**4**

None out when winning run scored.

Los Angeles.	2 0 0	0 0 0	0 0 1	0 0 0—3
New York.	1 0 0	0 0 1	0 1 0	0 0 1—4

Left on base—Los Angeles 8, New York 12. Two base hits—Munson, Randolph. Three base hit—Russell. Home run—Randolph (1). Sacrifice—Gullett 2. Sacrifice fly—Cey.

	ip	h	r	er	bb	so
Sutton.	7	8	3	3	1	4
Rautzhan.	1/3	0	0	0	2	0
Sosa.	2/3	0	0	0	0	1
Garman	3	1	0	0	1	3
Rhoden (L, 0-1)	0	2	1	1	1	0
Gullett.	8 1/3	5	3	3	6	6
Lyle (W, 1-0).	3 2/3	1	0	0	0	2

Hit by pitch—by Gullett (Baker), by Sutton (Jackson). Time of game—3:24. Attendance—56,668.

How runs were scored—Two in Dodgers first: Lopes walked. Russell tripled, scoring Lopes. Cey hit a sacrifice fly, scoring Russell.

One in Yankees first: Munson and Jackson singled. Chambliss singled, scoring Munson.

One in Yankees sixth: Randolph hit a home run.

One in Yankees eighth: Randolph walked. Munson doubled, scoring Randolph.

One in Dodgers ninth: Baker singled. Yeager walked. Lacy singled, scoring Baker.

One in Yankees twelfth: Randolph doubled. Blair singled, scoring Raldolph.

Second Game

Yankee Stadium, New York, Oct. 12

Dodgers	ab	r	h	bi	Yankees	ab	r	h	bi
Lopes, 2b.	4	0	0	0	Rivers, cf.	4	0	0	0
Russell, ss	4	1	1	0	Randolph, 2b. .	4	1	1	0
Smith, rf.	3	2	2	2	Munson, c	4	0	1	0
Cey, 3b	4	1	1	2	Jackson, rf. . . .	4	0	0	0
Garvey, 1b. . . .	4	1	2	1	Chambliss, 1b .	4	0	0	0
Baker, lf	4	0	0	0	Nettles, 3b. . . .	2	0	1	0
Monday, cf. . . .	3	0	1	0	Piniella, lf.	3	0	1	0
Burke, cf	1	0	0	0	Dent, ss.	2	0	1	0
Yeager, c	4	1	2	1	Johnson, ph . .	1	0	0	0
Hooton, p	3	0	0	0	Stanley, ss . . .	0	0	0	0
Totals.	**34**	**6**	**9**	**6**	Hunter, p.	0	0	0	0
					Tidrow, p.	1	0	0	0
					Zeber, ph.	1	0	0	0
					Clay, p.	0	0	0	0
					White, ph.	1	0	0	0
					Lyle, p	0	0	0	0
					Totals.	**31**	**1**	**5**	**0**

Los Angeles.	2 1 2	0 0 0	0 0 1—6
New York.	0 0 0	1 0 0	0 0 0—1

Double play — Los Angeles 1. Left on base — Los Angeles 2, Yankees 4. Two-base hit — Smith. Home run — Cey (1), Yeager (1), Smith (1), Garvey (1).

	ip	h	r	er	bb	so
Hooton (W, 1-0)	9	5	1	1	1	8
Hunter (L, 0-1)	2 1/3	5	5	5	0	0
Tidrow.	2 2/3	3	0	0	0	1
Clay	3	0	0	0	1	0
Lyle.	1	1	1	1	0	0

Time of game—2:27. Attendance—56,691.

How runs were scored—Two in Dodgers' first: Smith doubled. Cey hit a home run.

One in Dodgers second: Yeager hit a home run.

Two in Dodgers third: Russell singled. Smith hit a home run.

One in Yankees fourth: Randolph and Munson singled. Jackson grounded into a double play, scoring Randolph.

One in Dodgers ninth: Garvey hit a home run.

Third Game

Dodger Stadium, Los Angeles, Oct. 14

Yankees	ab	r	h	bi	Dodgers	ab	r	h	bi
Rivers, cf.	5	1	3	1	Lopes, 2b	4	0	0	0
Randolph, 2b . .	4	0	0	0	Russell, ss. . . .	4	0	0	0
Munson, c. . . .	5	1	1	1	Smith, rf.	3	1	1	0
Jackson, rf	3	2	1	1	Cey, 3b.	3	0	0	0
Blair, rf.	1	0	0	0	Garvey, 1b . . .	4	1	2	0
Piniella, lf	3	0	2	1	Baker, lf.	4	1	2	3
Chambliss, 1b.	4	0	1	1	Monday, cf . . .	4	0	0	0
Nettles, 3b	4	1	1	0	Yeager, c.	4	0	2	0
Dent, ss	3	0	1	0	John, p	2	0	0	0
Torrez, p.	3	0	0	0	Davalillo, ph . .	1	0	0	0
					Hough, p	0	0	0	0
					Mota, ph.	1	0	0	0
Totals.	**35**	**5**	**10**	**5**	**Totals. . . . .**	**34**	**3**	**7**	**3**

New York.	3 0 0	1 1 0	0 0 0—5
Los Angeles.	0 0 3	0 0 0	0 0 0—3

Error—Baker. Double play—Los Angeles 1. Left on base—Yankees 8, Los Angeles 7. Two-base hit—Rivers 2, Munson, Yeager. Home run—Baker (1). Stolen base—Lopes, Rivers. Sacrifice—Torrez.

	ip	h	r	er	bb	so
Torrez (W, 1-0)	9	7	3	3	3	9
John (L, 0-1)	6	9	5	4	3	7
Hough.	3	1	0	0	0	2

Hit by pitch—by John (Piniella).

Time of game—2:31. Attendance—55,992.

How runs were scored—Three in Yankees first: Rivers doubled. Munson doubled, scoring Rivers. Jackson singled, scoring Munson. Jackson went to second on an error. Piniella singled, scoring Jackson.

Three in Dodgers third: Smith and Garvey singled. Baker hit a home run.

One in Yankees fourth: Nettles and Dent singled. Rivers grounded out, scoring Nettles.

One in Yankees fifth: Jackson walked. Piniella singled. Chambliss singled, scoring Jackson.

Fourth Game

Dodger Stadium, Los Angeles, Oct. 15

Yankees	ab	r	h	bi	Dodgers	ab	r	h	bi
Rivers, cf.	4	0	1	0	Lopes, 2b	2	1	1	2
Randolph, 2b . .	4	0	0	0	Russell, ss. . . .	4	0	0	0
Munson, c	4	0	1	0	Smith, cf	4	0	0	0
Jackson, rf	4	2	2	1	Cey, 3b.	4	0	2	0
Blair, rf	0	0	0	0	Garvey, 1b . . .	4	0	0	0
Piniella, lf	4	1	1	1	Baker, lf.	4	0	0	0
Chambliss, 1b .	3	1	1	0	Lacy, rf	2	0	0	0
Nettles, 3b	3	0	0	1	Yeager, c.	3	0	0	0
Dent, ss	3	0	1	1	Rau, p	0	0	0	0
Guidry, p.	2	0	0	0	Rhoden, p	2	1	1	0
					Mota, ph.	1	0	0	0
					Garman, p. . . .	0	0	0	0
Totals.	**31**	**4**	**7**	**4**	**Totals. . . . .**	**30**	**2**	**4**	**2**

New York.	0 3 0	0 0 1	0 0 0—4
Los Angeles.	0 0 2	0 0 0	0 0 0—2

Double plays—Los Angeles 2. Left on base—Yankees 1, Los Angeles 4. Two base hits—Jackson, Chambliss, Rhoden, Cey. Home runs—Lopes (1), Jackson (1). Stolen base—Lopes. Sacrifice—Guidry.

	ip	h	r	er	bb	so
Guidry (W, 1-0)	9	4	2	2	3	7
Rau (L, 0-1)	1	4	3	3	0	0
Rhoden.	7	2	1	1	0	5
Garman	1	1	0	0	0	0

Time of game—2:07. Attendance 55,995.

How runs were scored—Three in Yankees second: Jackson doubled, Piniella singled, scoring Jackson. Chambliss doubled. Nettles grounded out, scoring Piniella. Dent singled, scoring Chambliss.

Two in Dodgers third: Rhoden doubled. Lopes hit a home run.

One in Yankees sixth: Jackson hit a home run.

Fifth Game

Dodger Stadium, Los Angeles, Oct. 16

Yankees	ab	r	h	bi
Rivers, cf.	4	0	0	0
Randolph, 2b	4	0	1	0
Munson, c	4	1	2	1
Johnson, c	0	0	0	0
Jackson, rf	4	2	2	1
Chambliss, 1b.	4	1	2	0
Nettles, 3b	4	0	2	1
Piniella, lf	4	0	0	0
Dent, ss	4	0	0	1
Gullett, p	1	0	0	0
Clay, p	0	0	0	0
Zeber, ph	1	0	0	0
Tidrow, p	0	0	0	0
White, ph	1	0	0	0
Hunter, p	0	0	0	0
Blair, ph	1	0	0	0
Totals	**36**	**4**	**9**	**4**

Dodgers	ab	r	h	bi
Lopes, 2b	5	1	2	0
Russell, ss.	5	1	2	1
Smith, rf.	4	2	1	2
Cey, 3b.	4	0	0	0
Garvey, 1b	4	2	2	0
Baker, lf.	4	2	3	2
Lacy, rf	3	1	2	1
Burke, cf.	1	0	0	0
Yeager, c.	2	1	1	4
Oates, c.	1	0	0	0
Sutton, p.	4	0	0	0
Totals	**37**	**10**	**13**	**10**

New York	000	000	220	—4
Los Angeles	100	432	00x	—10

Errors—Piniella, Nettles. Left on base—Yankees 5, Los Angeles 5. Two base hits—Garvey, Randolph, Nettles. Three base hit—Lopes. Home runs—Yeager (2), Smith (2), Munson (1), Jackson (2). Sacrifice fly—Yeager.

	ip	h	r	er	bb	so
Gullett (L, 0-1)	4 1/3	8	7	6	1	4
Clay	2/3	2	1	1	0	0
Tidrow	1	2	2	2	0	0
Hunter	2	1	0	0	0	1
Sutton (W, 1-0)	9	9	4	4	0	2

Time of game—2:29. Attendance—55,955.

How runs were scored—One in Dodgers first: Lopes tripled. Russell singled, scoring Lopes.

Four in Dodgers fourth: Garvey doubled. Baker singled, scoring Garvey. Lacy reached first on an error. Yeager hit a home run.

Three in Dodgers fifth: Smith walked. Garvey singled. Baker singled, scoring Smith, Lacy singled, scoring Garvey. Yeager hit a sacrifice fly, scoring Baker.

Two in Dodgers sixth: Russell singled, Smith hit a home run.

Two in Yankees seventh: Jackson and Chambliss singled. Nettles doubled, scoring Jackson. Dent grounded out, scoring Chambliss.

Two in Yankees eighth: Munson hit a home run. Jackson hit a home run.

Sixth Game

Yankee Stadium, New York, Oct. 18

Dodgers	ab	r	h	bi
Lopes, 2b	4	0	1	0
Russell, ss	3	0	0	0
Smith, rf	4	2	1	1
Cey, 3b	3	1	1	0
Garvey, 1b	4	1	2	2
Baker, lf	4	0	1	0
Monday, cf	4	0	1	0
Yeager, c	3	0	1	0
Davalillo, ph	1	0	1	1
Hooton, p	2	0	0	0
Sosa, p	0	0	0	0
Rau, p	0	0	0	0
Goodson, ph	1	0	0	0
Hough, p	0	0	0	0
Lacy, ph	1	0	0	0
Totals	**34**	**4**	**9**	**4**

Yankees	ab	r	h	bi
Rivers, cf	4	0	2	0
Randolph, 2b	4	1	0	0
Munson, c	4	1	1	0
Jackson, rf	3	4	3	5
Chambliss, 1b	4	2	2	2
Nettles, 3b	4	0	0	0
Piniella, lf	3	0	0	1
Dent, ss	2	0	0	0
Torrez, p	3	0	0	0
Totals	**31**	**8**	**8**	**8**

Los Angeles	201	000	001	—4
New York	020	320	01x	—8

Error—Dent. Double plays—Yankees 2. Left on base—Los Angeles 5, Yankees 2. Two base hit—Chambliss. Three base hit—Garvey. Home runs—Chambliss (1), Smith (3), Jackson 3, (5). Sacrifice fly, Piniella.

	ip	h	r	er	bb	so
Hooton (L, 1-1)	3	3	4	4	1	1
Sosa	1 2/3	3	3	3	1	0
Rau	1 1/3	0	0	0	0	1
Hough	2	2	1	1	0	2
Torrez (W, 2-0)	9	9	4	2	2	6

Passed ball—Munson. Time of game—2:19. Attendance—56,407.

How runs were scored—Two in Dodgers first: Smith reached first on an error. Cey walked. Garvey tripled, scoring Smith and Cey.

Two in Yankees second: Jackson walked. Chambliss hit a home run.

Three in Yankees fourth: Munson singled. Jackson hit a home run. Chambliss doubled. Chambliss went to third on a ground out. Piniella hit a sacrifice fly, scoring Chambliss.

Two in Yankees fifth: Rivers singled. Jackson hit a home run.

One in Yankees eighth: Jackson hit a home run.

One in Dodgers ninth: Garvey singled. Baker singled. Davalillo singled, scoring Garvey.

World Series Results, 1903-1977

1903 Boston AL 5, Pittsburgh NL 3
1904 No Series
1905 New York NL 4, Philadelphia AL 1
1906 Chicago AL 4, Chicago NL 2
1907 Chicago NL 4, Detroit AL 0, 1 tie
1908 Chicago NL 4, Detroit AL 1
1909 Pittsburgh NL 4, Detroit AL 3
1910 Philadelphia AL 4, Chicago NL 1
1911 Philadelphia AL 4, New York NL 2
1912 Boston AL 4, New York NL 3, 1 tie
1913 Philadelphia AL 4, New York NL 1
1914 Boston NL 4, Philadelphia AL 0
1915 Boston AL 4, Philadelphia NL 1
1916 Boston AL 4, Brooklyn NL 1
1917 Chicago AL 4, New York NL 2
1918 Boston AL 4, Chicago NL 2
1919 Cincinnati NL 5, Chicago AL 3
1920 Cleveland AL 5, Brooklyn NL 2
1921 New York NL 5, New York AL 3
1922 New York NL 4, New York AL 0, 1 tie
1923 New York AL 4, New York NL 2
1924 Washington AL 4, New York NL 3
1925 Pittsburgh NL 4, Washington AL 3
1926 St. Louis NL 4, New York AL 3
1927 New York AL 4, Pittsburgh NL 0
1928 New York AL 4, St. Louis NL 0
1929 Philadelphia AL 4, Chicago NL 1
1930 Philadelphia AL 4, St. Louis NL 2
1931 St. Louis NL 4, Philadelphia AL 3
1932 New York AL 4, Chicago NL 0
1933 New York NL 4, Washington AL 1
1934 St. Louis NL 4, Detroit AL 3
1935 Detroit AL 4, Chicago NL 2
1936 New York AL 4, New York NL 2
1937 New York AL 4, New York NL 1
1938 New York AL 4, Chicago NL 0
1939 New York AL 4, Cincinnati NL 0
1940 Cincinnati NL 4, Detroit AL 3
1941 New York AL 4, Brooklyn NL 1
1942 St. Louis NL 4, New York AL 1
1943 New York AL 4, St. Louis NL 1
1944 St. Louis NL 4, St. Louis AL 2
1945 Detroit AL 4, Chicago NL 3
1946 St. Louis NL 4, Boston AL 3
1947 New York AL 4, Brooklyn NL 3
1948 Cleveland AL 4, Boston NL 2
1949 New York AL 4, Brooklyn NL 1
1950 New York AL 4, Philadelphia NL 0
1951 New York AL 4, New York NL 2
1952 New York AL 4, Brooklyn NL 3
1953 New York AL 4, Brooklyn NL 2
1954 New York NL 4, Cleveland AL 0
1955 Brooklyn NL 4, New York AL 3
1956 New York AL 4, Brooklyn NL 3
1957 Milwaukee NL 4, New York AL 3
1958 New York AL 4, Milwaukee NL 3
1959 Los Angeles NL 4, Chicago AL 2
1960 Pittsburgh NL 4, New York AL 3
1961 New York AL 4, Cincinnati NL 1
1962 New York AL 4, San Francisco NL 3
1963 Los Angeles NL 4, New York AL 0
1964 St. Louis NL 4, New York AL 3
1965 Los Angeles NL 4, Minnesota AL 3
1966 Baltimore AL 4, Los Angeles NL 0
1967 St. Louis NL 4, Boston AL 3
1968 Detroit AL 4, St. Louis NL 3
1969 New York NL 4, Baltimore AL 1
1970 Baltimore AL 4, Cincinnati NL 1
1971 Pittsburgh NL 4, Baltimore AL 3
1972 Oakland AL 4, Cincinnati NL 3
1973 Oakland AL 4, New York NL 3
1974 Oakland AL 4, Los Angeles NL 1
1975 Cincinnati NL 4, Boston AL 3
1976 Cincinnati NL 4, New York AL 0
1977 New York AL 4, Los Angeles NL 2

All-Time Home Run Leaders

Player	HR	Player	HR	Player	HR	Player	HR	Player	HR
Hank Aaron	755	Lou Gehrig	493	Gil Hodges	370	Roy Sievers	318	Johnny Bench	287
Babe Ruth	714	Willie McCovey	493	Ralph Kiner	369	Reggie Jackson	313	Frank Thomas	286
Willie Mays	660	Stan Musial	475	Carl Yastrzemski	366	Al Simmons	307	Ken Boyer	282
Frank Robinson	586	Billy Williams	426	Joe DiMaggio	361	Rogers Hornsby	302	Ted Kluszewski	279
Harmon Killebrew	573	Duke Snider	407	John Mize	359	Lee May	300	Rudy York	277
Mickey Mantle	536	Willie Stargell	401	Yogi Berra	358	Chuck Klein	300	Willie Horton	277
Jimmy Foxx	534	Al Kaline	399	Dick Allen	351	Tony Perez	296	Roger Maris	275
Ted Williams	521	Frank Howard	382	Ron Santo	342	Jim Wynn	291	Brooks Robinson	268
Ed Mathews	512	Orlando Cepeda	379	John (Boog) Powell	339	Robert Johnson	288	Vic Wertz	266
Ernie Banks	512	Norm Cash	377	Joe Adcock	336	Hank Sauer	288	Bobby Bonds	265
Mel Ott	511	Rocky Colavito	374	Hank Greenberg	331	Del Ennis	288	Bobby Thomson	264

Members of National Baseball Hall of Fame and Museum

The shrine of organized baseball, dedicated June 12, 1939, is located in Cooperstown, N.Y.

Alexander, Grover Cleveland
Anson, Cap
Averill, Earl
Appling, Luke
Baker, Home Run
Bancroft, Dave
Banks, Ernie
Barrow, Edward G.
Beckley, Jake
Bell, Cool Papa
Bender, Chief
Berra, Yogi
Bottomley, Jim
Boudreau, Lou
Bresnahan, Roger
Brouthers, Dan
Brown (Three Finger), Mordecai
Bulkeley, Morgan C.
Burkett, Jesse C.
Campanella, Roy
Carey, Max
Cartwright, Alexander
Chadwick, Henry
Chance, Frank
Charleston, Oscar
Chesbro, John
Clarke, Fred
Clarkson, John
Clemente, Roberto
Cobb, Ty
Cochrane, Mickey
Collins, Eddie
Collins, James
Combs, Earle
Comiskey, Charles A.
Conlan, Jocko
Connolly, Thomas H.
Connor, Roger
Coveleski, Stan
Crawford, Sam
Cronin, Joe
Cummings, Candy
Cuyler, Kiki
Dean, Dizzy
Delahanty, Ed
Dickey, Bill
DiHigo, Martin
DiMaggio, Joe
Duffy, Hugh
Evans, Billy
Evers, John
Ewing, Buck
Faber, Urban
Feller, Bob
Flick, Elmer H.
Ford, Whitey
Foxx, Jimmy
Frick, Ford
Frisch, Frank
Galvin, Pud
Gehrig, Lou
Gehringer, Charles
Gibson, Josh
Gomez, Lefty
Goslin, Goose
Greenberg, Hank
Griffith, Clark
Grimes, Burleigh
Grove, Lefty
Hafey, Chick
Haines, Jesee
Hamilton, Bill
Harridge, Will
Harris, Bucky
Hartnett, Gabby
Heilmann, Harry
Herman, Billy
Hooper, Harry
Hornsby, Rogers
Hoyt, Waite
Hubbard, Cal
Hubbell, Carl
Huggins, Miller
Irvin, Monte
Jennings, Hugh
Johnson, Byron
Johnson, William (Rudy)
Johnson, Walter
Keefe, Timothy
Keeler, William
Kelley, Joe
Kelly, George
Kelly, King
Kiner, Ralph
Klem, Bill
Koufax, Sandy
Lajoie, Napoleon
Landis, Kenesaw M.
Lemon, Bob
Leonard, Buck
Lindstrom, Fred
Lloyd, Pop
Lopez, Al
Lyons, Ted
Mack, Connie
Mantle, Mickey
Manush, Henry
Maranville, Rabbit
Marquard, Rube
Mathewson, Christy
McCarthy, Joe
McCarthy, Thomas
McGinnity, Joe
McGraw, John
McKechnie, Bill
Medwick, Joe
Musial, Stan
Nichols, Kid
O'Rourke, James
Ott, Mel
Paige, Satchel
Pennock, Herb
Plank, Ed
Radbourne, Charlie
Rice, Sam
Rickey, Branch
Rixey, Eppa
Roberts, Robin
Robinson, Jackie
Robinson, Wilbert
Roush, Edd
Ruffing, Red
Rusie, Amos
Ruth, Babe
Schalk, Ray
Sewell, Joe
Simmons, Al
Sisler, George
Spahn, Warren
Spalding, Albert
Speaker, Tris
Stengel, Casey
Terry, Bill
Thompson, Sam
Tinker, Joe
Traynor, Pie
Vance, Dazzy
Waddell, Rube
Wagner, Honus
Wallace, Roderick
Walsh, Ed
Waner, Lloyd
Waner, Paul
Ward, John
Weiss, George
Welch, Mickey
Wheat, Zach
Williams, Ted
Wright, George
Wright, Harry
Wynn, Early
Young, Cy
Youngs, Ross

Major League Baseball Attendance

National League

Club	1977	1976	Change
Atlanta	872,526	818,179	+ 54,347
Chicago	1,439,739	1,026,217	+ 413,522
Cincinnati	2,519,738	2,629,708	− 109,970
Houston	1,108,960	886,146	+ 222,814
Los Angeles	2,955,087	2,386,301	+ 568,786
Montreal	1,433,757	646,704	+ 777,053
New York	1,062,432	1,468,754	− 406,322
Philadelphia	2,700,020	2,480,150	+ 219,870
Pittsburgh	1,237,359	1,025,945	+ 211,414
St. Louis	1,658,674	1,207,036	+ 451,638
San Diego	1,376,269	1,458,478	− 82,209
San Francisco	703,851	626,868	+ 76,983
Totals	**19,068,412**	**16,660,486**	**+ 2,407,926**

American League

Club	1977	1976	Change
Baltimore	1,195,749	1,058,609	+ 137,140
Boston	2,074,549	1,895,846	+ 178,703
California	1,432,633	1,006,774	+ 425,859
Chicago	1,656,135	914,945	+ 741,190
Cleveland	897,255	948,776	− 51,521
Detroit	1,360,056	1,467,020	− 106,964
Kansas City	1,852,599	1,679,766	+ 172,833
Milwaukee	1,114,938	1,012,164	+ 102,774
Minnesota	1,162,726	715,394	+ 447,332
New York	2,103,092	2,012,434	+ 90,658
Oakland	495,578	780,593	− 285,015
Seattle	1,338,523	...	...
Texas	1,250,691	1,164,982	+ 85,709
Toronto	1,701,039	...	...
Totals	**19,635,563**	**14,657,303**	**+ 4,978,260**

Major League Attendance Records

All-time Season Records, Both Leagues—38,703,975 in 1977.
All-time Season Record, One Club—2,955,087—Los Angeles Dodgers, 1977.
Record Attendance, World Series—420,784—1959 Series between Los Angeles Dodgers and Chicago White Sox.
Record Attendance, World Series Game—92,706—fifth game, 1959 Series, Los Angeles, Oct. 6.
Record Attendance, Regular Season Game—84,587—Municipal Stadium, Cleveland, Sept. 12, 1954, in doubleheader between the Indians and Yankees. (Not including pass list of 1,976.)
Attendance, Regular Season Single Game—78,672—Los Angeles Memorial Coliseum, April 18, 1958, in opening game between Los Angeles Dodgers and San Francisco Giants.

Polo Records

National Open

1969—Tulsa Green Hill 11, Milwaukee 10.
1970—Tulsa Green Hill 9, Oak Brook 5.
1971—Oak Brook 8, Green Hill Farm 7.
1972—Milwaukee 9, Tulsa 5.
1973—Oak Brook 9, Willow Bend 4.
1974—Milwaukee 7, Houston 6.
1975—Milwaukee 14, Tulsa-Dallas 6.
1976—Willow Bend 10, Tulsa 5.
1977—Retama 11, Wilson Ranch 7.

Silver Cup

1969—Oak Brook 7, Milwaukee 6.
1970—Oak Brook 9, Tulsa Green Hill 7.
1971—Green Hill Farm 8, Milwaukee 6.
1972—Red Doors Farm 10, Sun Ranch 6.
1973—Houston 6, Willow Bend 4.
1974—Houston 7, Willow Bend 6.
1975—Lone Oak-Bunntyco 8, Tulsa 5.
1976—Wilson Ranch 10, Tulsa 8.

Intercollegiate Championship

1968—Yale 17, Cornell 13
1969—Yale 17, Cornell 16
1970—Yale 22, Cornell 10
1971—Yale 12, Virginia 11
1972—Univ. of Conn. 17, Univ of Virginia 15
1973—Univ. of Conn. 19, Univ. of Virginia 10
1974—Univ. of Conn. 18, Cornell 16
1975—Univ. of Cal.-Davis 15, Yale 12
1976—Xavier Univ. 25, Cornell 12.
1977—Xavier Univ. 13, Univ. of Cal.-Davis 9.

Other Tournaments in 1977

Delegate's Cup—Cajuiles 8, Fairfield 7.
America Cup—Boca Raton 14, Midland 4.
Butler Handicap—San Antonio 8, Dallas-Lone Oak 6.
Continental Cup—Milwaukee 9, Longwood 5.
Gold Cup—Lone Oak 9, Retama 8.
National President's Cup—Birmingham 8, A-Plus Stables 7.

National Skeet Shooting Assn. Championships in 1977

Savannah, Ga., July 31-Aug. 6, 1977

High Overall Championship — 550 targets
Champion — John Shima, San Antonio, Tex., 548.
Women — Conni Place, Pompano Beach, Fla., 544.
Industry — Jimmy Prall, Tulsa, Okla., 541.
Veteran — Tom Sanfilipo, Fairfield, Cal., 528.
Sub-senior — Russell Dorris, Franklin, Tenn., 541.
Senior — K.E. Pletcher, Bellevue, Neb., 533.
Junior — Todd Bender, Fountain Valley, Cal., 538.
Collegiate — John Shima, San Antonio, Tex., 548.

12 Gauge — 250 targets
Champion — Murray Jackson, Conway, S.C., 250.
Women — Lori Higgins, Torrance, Cal., 249.
Industry — Cecil Trammel, Brooks, Ga., 250.
Veteran — R.M. Brame Jr., N. Wilkesboro, N.C., 246.
Sub-senior — Murray Jackson, Conway, S.C., 250.
Senior — Loyd Huval, Baton Rouge, La., 249.
Junior — Gary Winkler, Woodbridge, Va., 249.
Collegiate — Tony West, Wellsville, Kan., 250.

20 Gauge — 100 targets
Champion — Wayne Mayes, Hixson, Tenn., 100.
Women — Barbara Burkhart, San Antonio, Tex., 100.
Industry — Jimmy Prall, Tulsa, Okla., 100.
Veteran — Tom Sanfilipo, Fairfield, Cal., 96.
Sub-senior — Dave Fridl, Chattanooga, Tenn., 100.
Senior — Stan Warber, Grand Rapids, Mich., 99.
Junior — Barry Eschete, Houma, La., 100.
Collegiate — Tony West, Wellsville, Kan., 100.

28 Gauge — 100 targets
Champion — John Shima, San Antonio, Tex., 100.
Women — Joyce Luce, Vernon, Conn., 99.
Industry — Jimmy Prall, Tulsa, Okla., 100.
Veteran — Tom Sanfilipo, Fairfield, Cal., 98.
Sub-senior — Russell Dorris, Franklin, Tenn., 100.
Senior — K.E. Pletcher, Bellevue, Neb., 97.
Junior — Todd Bender, Fountain Valley, Cal., 99.
Collegiate — John Shima, San Antonio, Tex., 100.

.410 Gauge — 100 targets
Champion — Chris Brown, La Grange, Ga., 100.
Women — Conni Place, Pompano Beach, Fla., 100.
Industry — J.O. Stotts, E. Alton, Ill., 98.
Veteran — Henry Alcus, New Orleans, La., 94.
Sub-senior — Charles Wolbach, Birmingham, Ala., 99.
Senior — William Mandel, Toledo, Oh., 97.
Junior — Todd Bender, Fountain Valley, Cal., 97.
Collegiate — Pat Bartel, San Antonio, Tex., 99.

National Water Ski Championships in 1977

Berkeley, Cal., Aug. 17-21, 1977
Source: American Water Ski Association

Men
Open Overall — Ricky McCormick, Winter Haven, Fla., 3,244 points.
Open Slalom — Kris LaPoint, Los Banos, Cal., 51 buoys.
Open Tricks — Ricky McCormick, 6,370 points.
Open Jumping — Ricky McCormick, 165 feet.
Senior Overall — Dr. J. D. Morgan, Pensacola, Fla., 3,075 points.
Senior Slalom — Dr. J. D. Morgan, 51 buoys.
Senior Tricks — Dr. J. D. Morgan, 3,370 points.
Senior Jumping — Ken White, Honolulu, Ha., 130 feet.
Boys' Overall — Sammy Duvall, Irving, Tex., 3,175 points.
Boys' Slalom — Don Morrison, Livermore, Cal., 47 buoys.
Boys' Tricks — Sammy Duvall, 4,910 points.
Boys' Jumping — Sammy Duvall, 135 feet.
Junior Boys' Overall — Carl Roberge, San Diego, Cal., 3,866 points.
Junior Boys' Slalom — Carl Roberge, 57 buoys.
Junior Boys' Tricks — Cory Pickos, Kenosha, Wis., 6,190 points.
Junior Boys' Jumping — Carl Roberge, 112 feet.

Women
Open Overall — Camille Duvall, Irving, Tex., 3,075 points.
Open Slalom — Cathy Marlow, Pinole, Cal., 51½ buoys.
Open Tricks — Pam Folsom, Boynton Beach, Fla., 4,360 points.
Open Jumping — Linda Giddens, Eastman, Ga., 119 feet.
Senior Overall — Thelma Salmas, Newberry Springs, Cal., 3,189 points.
Senior Slalom — Barbara Heddon, Lake Wales, Fla., 45½ buoys.
Senior Tricks — Thelma Salmas, 3,220 points.
Senior Jumping — Thelma Salmas, 95 feet.
Girls' Overall — Karen Crosier, Keystone Hgts., Fla., 2,584 points.
Girls' Slalom — Karen Crosier, 45 buoys.
Girls' Tricks — Karen Crosier, 2,780 points.
Girls' Jumping — Karin Roberge, San Diego, Cal., 103 feet.
Junior Girls' Overall — Kristen Carroll, Oakham, Mass., 2,970 points.
Junior Girls' Slalom — Rhonda Beth Whetsel, Winchester, Tenn., 49 buoys.
Junior Girls' Tricks — Sally Monnier, Rock Falls, Ill., 2,420 points.
Junior Girls' Jumping — Kristen Carroll, 78 feet.

Ten Most Dramatic Sports Events, Nov. 1976-Oct. 1977

Selected by The World Almanac sports staff

—Reggie Jackson hitting 3 home runs in the 6th and final game of the World Series to lead the N.Y. Yankees to victory against the L.A. Dodgers. He hit 5 Series home runs, a new record.

—Seattle Slew winning the Kentucky Derby, Preakness, and Belmont Stakes. He became the 10th horse to win racing's triple crown.

—Lou Brock of the St. Louis Cardinals stealing his 893d base and breaking the modern-day record for career stolen bases. The record was established by Ty Cobb who retired in 1928.

—O.J. Simpson of the Buffalo Bills rushing for 273 yards in a game against Detroit breaking his own NFL record. He rushed for 250 yards in a game in 1973.

—The Portland Trail Blazers upsetting the Philadelphia 76ers in the NBA championship series. Portland won the final 4 games after losing the first 2.

—Virginia Wade winning the women's singles title at Wimbledon. The British star had failed to reach the finals in 15 previous attempts on her home ground.

—A.J. Foyt winning the Indianapolis 500. He became the first man to win the classic auto race 4 times.

—The Cosmos winning the NASL championship by defeating the Seattle Sounders 2-1, before a sellout crowd at Portland, Ore. The game ended a season which saw soccer become a major sport in the U.S.

—Ian Turnbull of the Toronto Maple Leafs scored 5 goals in a game against Detroit. He is the first defenseman in NHL history to score 5 goals in a game.

—Marquette winning the NCAA basketball championship in coach Al McGuire's final game before retirement after 13 years at the school. They defeated North Carolina, 67-59.

U.S. National Squash Racquets Champions

Year	Champion	Year	Champion	Year	Champion
1966	Vic Niederhoffer, N.Y., N.Y.	1970	Anil Nayar, Boston, Mass.	1974	Vic Niederhoffer, N.Y., N.Y.
1967	Samuel Howe 3d, Phil., Pa.	1971	Colin Adair, Canada	1975	Vic Niederhoffer, N.Y., N.Y.
1968	Colin Adair, Canada	1972	Vic Niederhoffer, N.Y., N.Y.	1976	Peter Briggs, N.Y., N.Y.
1969	Anil Nayar, Boston, Mass.	1973	Vic Niederhoffer, N.Y., N.Y.	1977	Sharif Khan, Toronto, Ont.

World Pocket Billiards Champions

1931—Ralph Greenleaf
1932—Ralph Greenleaf
1933—Erwin Rudolph
1934—Erwin Rudolph
1935—Andrew Ponzi
1936—James Caras
1937—Ralph Greenleaf
1938—James Caras
1939—James Caras
1940—Andrew Ponzi
1941—Willie Mosconi, Erwin Rudolph
1942—Irving Crane
1943—Andrew Ponzi
1944—Willie Mosconi
1945—Willie Mosconi
1946—Irving Crane
1947—Willie Mosconi
1948—Willie Mosconi
1949—James Caras
1950—Willie Mosconi
1951—Willie Mosconi
1952—Willie Mosconi
1953—Willie Mosconi
1954—none
1955—Irving Crane, Willie Mosconi
1956-62—none
1963—Luther Lassiter
1964—Luther Lassiter, Arthur Cranfield
1965—Joe Balsis
1966—Luther Lassiter
1967—Luther Lassiter
1968—Irving Crane
1969—Ed Kelly
1970—Irving Crane
1971—Ray Martin
1972—Irving Crane
1973—Lou Butera
1974—Ray Martin
1975—none
1976—none
1977—Allen Hopkins

U.S. Open Pocket Billiards Champions

1966—Irving Crane
1967—James Caras
1968—Joe Balsis
1969—Luther Lassiter
1970—Steve Mizerak
1971—Steve Mizerak
1972—Steve Mizerak
1973—Steve Mizerak
1974—Joe Balsis
1975—Dallas West
1976—Tom Jennings
1977—Tom Jennings

Women's Division

Jean Balukas, 18-year-old high school student from Brooklyn, N.Y., won the women's division of the U.S. Open Pocket Billiards Championship for the 6th straight year on Aug. 14, 1977.

National AAU Wrestling Championships in 1977

Freestyle

105.5 lbs. — Bill Rosado.
114.5 lbs. — Kiyoto Shimizu.
125.5 lbs. — Akira Yamagi.
136.5 lbs. — Jim Humphrey.
149.5 lbs. — Chuck Yagla.
163 lbs. — Stan Dziedzic.
180.5 lbs. — Mark Lieberman.
198 lbs. — Ben Peterson.
220 lbs. — Harold Smith.
Unlimited — Greg Wojciechowski.

Greco-Roman

105.5 lbs. — James Howard.
114.5 lbs. — Enrique Jimenez.
125.5 lbs. — Brian Gust.
136.5 lbs. — Hachiro Oichi.
149.5 lbs. — Dave Schultz.
163 lbs. — Abdul Reheem Ali.
180.5 lbs. — Dan Chandler.
198 lbs. — William Bragg.
220 lbs. — Brad Rheingans.
Heavyweight — Bob Walker.

NCAA Wrestling Champions

Year	Champion	Year	Champion	Year	Champion	Year	Champion	Year	Champion
1960	Oklahoma	1964	Oklahoma State	1968	Oklahoma State	1972	Iowa State	1975	Iowa
1961	Oklahoma State	1965	Iowa State	1969	Iowa State	1973	Iowa State	1976	Iowa
1962	Oklahoma State	1966	Oklahoma State	1970	Iowa State	1974	Oklahoma	1977	Iowa State
1963	Oklahoma	1967	Michigan State	1971	Oklahoma State				

National Rowing Championships in 1977

Cooper River, Collingswood, N.J., July 10, 1977

Senior Fours with Coxswain—Wyandotte BC.
Elite Fours without Coxswain—Potomac BC.
Senior Pairs without Coxswain—West Side RC.
Elite Doubles—New York AC.
Elite Pairs with Coxswain—Univ. of Pennsylvania.
Elite Lightweight Doubles—Malta BC.
Elite Lightweight Fours without Coxswain—Long Beach RA.
Elite Lightweight Pairs—Duluth RC.
Senior Eights—Viking RC.
Elite Fours—New York AC.
Elite Eight—Penn AC.
Elite Singles—Jim Dietz, New York AC.
Team champion—New York AC.

Trapshooting Chamionships in 1977

Source: Trap & Field Magazine

78th Grand American Tournament

Vandalia, Oh., Aug. 15-20, 1977

Grand American Handicap

Men—James Edwards, Fairfield, Oh.
Women—Mildred Paxton, Charleston, W. Va.
Junior—Guy Schwichtenberg, Lester Prairie, Minn.
Sub-junior—Roger Rutan Jr., Mechanicsburg, Oh.
Veteran—Verne Harkins, DeSoto, Ia.
Industry—Cecil Trammell, Brooks, Ga.
Past Trophy Winner—Wayne Hegwood, Jackson, Miss.
Jimmy Robinson Trophy to High Canadian—Larry Ivany, Oshawa, Ont.

Clay Target Championship

Men—Norbert Liette, St. Mary's, Oh.
Women—Susan Nattrass, Waterloo, Ont.
Junior—Lee Kastle, Lakewood, Col.
Sub-junior—Mark Hobbs, Knoxville, Tenn.
Veteran—Armin Lang, Farmington, Ia.
Industry—Art Wheaton, Edina, Minn.

Champion of Champions

Men—Ohmer Webb, Washington, D.C.
Women—Laura Christopher, Brunswick, Oh.
Junior—Storm Mitchell, Murray, Ut.

High-Over-All

Men—Roger Smith, Wichita, Kan.
Women—Loral I. Delaney, Anoka, Minn.
Junior—Martin Wilbur, Salina, Kan.
Veteran—Paul Baker, So. Miami, Fla.
Industry—Jim Hunter, Richmond, Ind.

All-Around Championship

Men—Kay Ohye, New Brunswick, N.J.
Women—Loral I. Delaney, Anoka, Minn.
Junior—Storm Mitchell, Murray, Ut.
Veteran—Armin Lang, Farmington, Ia.
Industry—Jim Hunter, Richmond, Ind.

North American Soccer League in 1977

Final Standings

Atlantic Conference

Northern Division

	W	L	GF	GA	Bonus points	Total points
Toronto Metros	13	13	42	38	37	115
St. Louis Stars	12	14	33	35	32	104
Rochester Lancers	11	15	34	41	33	99
Chicago Stings	10	16	31	43	28	88
Connecticut Bicentennials	7	19	34	65	30	72

Eastern Division

	W	L	GF	GA	Bonus points	Total points
Ft. Lauderdale Strikers	19	7	49	29	47	161
Cosmos	15	11	60	39	50	140
Tampa Bay Rowdies	14	12	55	45	47	131
Washington Diplomats	10	16	32	49	32	92

Playoff winner — Cosmos.

Pacific Conference

Western Division

	W	L	GF	GA	Bonus points	Total points
Minnesota Kicks	16	10	44	36	41	137
Vancouver Whitecaps	14	12	43	46	40	124
Seattle Sounders	14	12	43	34	39	123
Portland Timbers	10	16	39	42	38	98

Southern Division

	W	L	GF	GA	Bonus points	Total points
Dallas Tornado	18	8	56	37	53	161
Los Angeles Aztecs	15	11	65	54	57	147
San Jose Earthquakes	14	12	37	44	35	119
Team Hawaii	11	15	45	59	40	106
Las Vegas Quicksilvers	11	15	38	44	37	103

Total points: Win-6 pts., Loss-0 pts. Bonus points — one point is awarded for each goal scored up to a maximum of 3 per team per game.

Leading Scorers

Player, team	Goals	Assists	Points
Steve David, Los Angeles	26	6	58
Derek Smethurst, Tampa Bay	19	4	42
George Best, Los Angeles	11	18	40
Giorgio Chinaglia, Cosmos	15	8	38
Mike Stojanovic, Rochester	14	5	33
Mickey Cave, Seattle	12	6	30
Alan Willey, Minnesota	14	1	29
Pele, Cosmos	13	3	29
Paul Child, San Jose	13	3	29
Kyle Rote, Dallas	11	6	28
Rodney Marsh, Tampa Bay	8	11	27

Leading Goalkeepers

Player, team	*Minutes	Goals	Average
Ken Cooper, Dallas	2100	21	0.90
Gordon Banks, Ft. Lauderdale	2329	29	1.12
John Jackson, St. Louis	1526	20	1.18
Zeliko Bilecki, Toronto	2239	30	1.21
Geoff Barnett, Minnesota	2165	30	1.25
Tony Chursky, Seattle	2200	31	1.27
Alan Mayer, Las Vegas	1997	31	1.40
Mick Poole, Portland	1932	30	1.40
Mike Hewitt, San Jose	2225	35	1.42
Shep Messing, Cosmos	1737	28	1.45

*At least 1170 minutes of play.

NASL All-Star Team in 1977

First team	Position	Second team
Gordon Banks, Ft. Lauderdale	Goalkeeper	Alan Mayer, Las Vegas
Franz Beckenbauer, Cosmos	Defender	Ray Evans, St. Louis
Mike England, Seattle	Defender	Steve Pecher, Dallas
Bruce Wilson, Vancouver	Defender	Humberto, Las Vegas
Mel Machin, Seattle	Defender	(tie) George Ley, Dallas; Arsene Auguate, Tampa Bay
George Best, Los Angeles	Midfield	Charlie Cooke, Los Angeles
Wolfgang Suhnholz, Las Vegas	Midfield	Vito Dimitrijevic, Cosmos
Alan West, Minnesota	Midfield	Rodney Marsh, Tampa Bay
Steve David, Los Angeles	Forward	Mike Stojanovic, Rochester
Pele, Cosmos	Forward	Steve Wegerle, Tampa Bay
Derek Smethurst, Tampa Bay	Forward	Buzz Parsons, Vancouver

The World Cup

The World Cup, emblematic of international soccer supremacy, was won by West Germany on July 7, 1974, with a 2-1 victory over the Netherlands. By winning the championship, West Germany became the fourth host country to emerge as champion since the trophy was put up in 1930. The next World Cup will be held in 1978 in Argentina. Winners and sites of previous World Cup play follow:

Year	Winner	Site
1930	Uruguay	Uruguay
1934	Italy	Italy
1938	Italy	France
1950	Uruguay	Brazil
1954	W. Germany	Switzerland
1958	Brazil	Sweden
1962	Brazil	Chile
1966	England	England
1970	Brazil	Mexico City
1974	W. Germany	W. Germany

32d Annual Field Archery Championships in 1977

Clemson, S.C., July 18-22, 1977

Freestyle

Professional Men—Dean Pridgen, Kansas City, Kan.
Professional Women—Liz Colombo, Oakdale, Cal.
Open Men—George Gorman, San Antonio, Tex.
Open Women—Janet Boatman, Alden, N.Y.
Amateur Men—Jack Cramer, Gettysburg, Pa.
Amateur Women—Sherilyn Doyle, Taft, Cal.

Barebow

Open Men—James Webb, Keyser, W. Va.
Open Women—Gloria Shelley, Waterbury, Conn.
Amateur Men—Donald Morehead, Wheaton, Ill.
Amateur Women—Judy Albright, Drexel Hill, Pa.

Freestyle—Limited

Professional Men—Jerry Podratz, Shakopee, Minn.
Professional Women—Lucille Shine, Las Vegas, Nev.
Amateur Men—Edwin Eliason, Charlotte, N.C.
Amateur Women—Valerie Gramzow, Creswell, Ore.

Bowhunter

Professional Men—Hugh McConnell, Hilton, Va.
Open Men—James Brown, Marlow Heights, Md.
Open Women—Cay McManus, Evington, Va.
Amateur Men—Philip Dollar, Daytona Beach, Fla.
Amateur Women—Elizabeth Dollar, Daytona Beach, Fla.

Tennis

USTA National Champions

Men's Singles

Year	Champion	Final opponent
1920	Bill Tilden	William Johnston
1921	Bill Tilden	Wallace Johnston
1922	Bill Tilden	William Johnston
1923	Bill Tilden	William Johnston
1924	Bill Tilden	William Johnston
1925	Bill Tilden	William Johnston
1926	Rene Lacoste	Jean Borotra
1927	Rene Lacoste	Bill Tilden
1928	Henri Cochet	Francis Hunter
1929	Bill Tilden	Francis Hunter
1930	John Doeg	Francis Shields
1931	H. Ellsworth Vines	George Lott
1932	H. Ellsworth Vines	Henri Cochet
1933	Fred Perry	John Crawford
1934	Fred Perry	Wilmer Allison
1935	Wilmer Allison	Sidney Wood
1936	Fred Perry	Don Budge
1937	Don Budge	Baron G. von Cramm
1938	Don Budge	C. Gene Mako
1939	Robert Riggs	S. Welby Van Horn
1940	Don McNeill	Robert Riggs
1941	Robert Riggs	F. L. Kovacs
1942	F. R. Schroeder Jr.	Frank Parker
1943	Joseph Hunt	Jack Kramer
1944	Frank Parker	William Talbert
1945	Frank Parker	William Talbert
1946	Jack Kramer	Thomas Brown Jr.
1947	Jack Kramer	Frank Parker
1948	Pancho Gonzales	Eric Sturgess
1949	Pancho Gonzales	F. R. Schroeder Jr.
1950	Arthur Larsen	Herbert Flam
1951	Frank Sedgman	E. Victor Seixas Jr.
1952	Frank Sedgman	Gardnar Mulloy
1953	Tony Trabert	E. Victor Seixas Jr.
1954	E. Victor Seixas Jr.	Rex Hartwig
1955	Tony Trabert	Ken Rosewall
1956	Ken Rosewall	Lewis Hoad
1957	Malcolm Anderson	Ashley Cooper
1958	Ashley Cooper	Malcolm Anderson
1959	Neale A. Fraser	Alejandro Olmedo
1960	Neale A. Fraser	Rod Laver
1961	Roy Emerson	Rod Laver
1962	Rod Laver	Roy Emerson
1963	Rafael Osuna	F. A. Froehling 3d
1964	Roy Emerson	Fred Stolle
1965	Manuel Santana	Cliff Drysdale
1966	Fred Stolle	John Newcombe
1967	John Newcombe	Clark Graebner
1968	Arthur Ashe	Tom Okker
1969	Rod Laver	Tony Roche
1970	Ken Rosewall	Tony Roche
1971	Stan Smith	Jan Kodes
1972	Ilie Nastase	Arthur Ashe
1973	John Newcombe	Jan Kodes
1974	Jimmy Connors	Ken Rosewall
1975	Manuel Orantes	Jimmy Connors
1976	Jimmy Connors	Bjorn Borg
1977	Guillermo Vilas	Jimmy Connors

Men's Doubles

Year	Champions
1920	William Johnston—Clarence Griffin
1921	Bill Tilden—Vincent Richards
1922	Bill Tilden—Vincent Richards
1923	Bill Tilden—Brian Norton
1924	Howard Kinsey—Robert Kinsey
1925	R. Norris Williams—Vincent Richards
1926	R. Norris Williams—Vincent Richards
1927	Bill Tilden—Francis Hunter
1928	George Lott—John Hennessey
1929	George Lott—John Doeg
1930	George Lott—John Doeg
1931	Wilmer Allison—John Van Ryn
1932	H. Ellsworth Vines—Keith Gledhill
1933	George Lott—Lester Stoefen
1934	George Lott—Lester Stoefen
1935	Wilmer Allison—John Van Ryn
1936	Don Budge—C. Gene Mako
1937	Baron G. von Cramm—Henner Henkel
1938	Don Budge—C. Gene Mako
1939	Adrian Quist—John Bromwich
1940	Jack Kramer—Frederick Schroeder Jr.
1941	Jack Kramer—Frederick Schroeder Jr.
1942	Gardnar Mulloy—William Talbert
1943	Jack Kramer—Frank Parker
1944	Don McNeill—Robert Falkenburg
1945	Gardnar Mulloy—William Talbert
1946	Gardnar Mulloy—William Talbert
1947	Jack Kramer—Frederick Schroeder Jr.
1948	Gardnar Mulloy—William Talbert
1949	John Bromwich—William Sidwell
1950	John Bromwich—Frank Sedgman
1951	Frank Sedgman—Kenneth McGregor
1952	Mervyn Rose—E. Victor Seixas Jr.
1953	Rex Hartwig—Mervyn Rose
1954	E. Victor Seixas Jr.—Tony Trabert
1955	Kosei Kamo—Atsushi Miyagi
1956	Lewis Hoad—Ken Rosewall
1957	Ashley Cooper—Neale Fraser
1958	Hamilton Richardson—Alejandro Olmedo
1959	Neale A. Fraser—Roy Emerson
1960	Neale A. Fraser—Roy Emerson
1961	Dennis Ralston—Chuck McKinley
1962	Rafael Osuna—Antonio Palafox
1963	Dennis Ralston—Chuck McKinley
1964	Dennis Ralston—Chuck McKinley
1965	Roy Emerson—Fred Stolle
1966	Roy Emerson—Fred Stolle
1967	John Newcombe—Tony Roche
1968	Robert Lutz—Stan Smith
1969	Fred Stolle—Ken Rosewall
1970	Pierre Barthes—Nicki Pilic
1971	John Newcombe—Roger Taylor
1972	Cliff Drysdale—Roger Taylor
1973	John Newcombe—Owen Davidson
1974	Bob Lutz—Stan Smith
1975	Jimmy Connors—Ilie Nastase
1976	Marty Riessen—Tom Okker
1977	Bob Hewitt—Frew McMillan

Mixed Doubles

Year	Champions
1942	A. Louise Brough — Frederick Schroeder
1943	Margaret Osborne — William Talbert
1944	Margaret Osborne — William Talbert
1945	Margaret Osborne — William Talbert
1946	Margaret Osborne — William Talbert
1947	A. Louise Brough — John Bromwich
1948	A. Louise Brough — Thomas Brown Jr.
1949	A. Louise Brough — Eric Sturgess
1950	Mrs. M. O. duPont — Kenneth MacGregor
1951	Doris Hart — Frank Sedgman
1952	Doris Hart — Frank Sedgman
1953	Doris Hart — E. Victor Seixas Jr.
1954	Doris Hart — E. Victor Seixas Jr.
1955	Doris Hart — E. Victor Seixas Jr.
1956	Mrs. M. O. duPont — Ken Rosewall
1957	Althea Gibson — Kurt Nielsen
1958	Mrs. M. O. duPont — Neale Fraser
1959	Mrs. M. O. duPont — Neale Fraser
1960	Mrs. M. O. duPont — Neale Fraser
1961	Margaret Smith — Robert Mark
1962	Margaret Smith — Fred Stolle
1963	Margaret Smith — Kenneth Fletcher
1964	Margaret Smith — John Newcombe
1965	Margaret Smith — Fred Stolle
1966	Donna Floyd Fales — Owen Davidson
1967	Billie Jean King — Owen Davidson
1968	Mary Ann Eisel — Peter Curtis
1969	Margaret S. Court — Marty Riessen
1970	Margaret S. Court — Marty Riessen
1971	Billie Jean King — Owen Davidson
1972	Margaret S. Court — Marty Riessen
1973	Billie Jean King — Owen Davidson
1974	Pam Teeguarden — Geoff Masters
1975	Rosemary Casals — Dick Stockton
1976	Billie Jean King — Phil Dent
1977	Betty Stove — Frew McMillan

Women's Singles

Year	Champion	Year	Champion	Year	Champion	Year	Champion
1935	Helen Jacobs	1946	Pauline Betz	1957	Althea Gibson	1968	Virginia Wade
1936	Alice Marble	1947	A. Louise Brough	1958	Althea Gibson	1969	Margaret Smith Court
1937	Anita Lizana	1948	Mrs. Margaret O. du Pont	1959	Maria Bueno	1970	Margaret Smith Court
1938	Alice Marble	1949	Mrs. Margaret O. du Pont	1960	Darlene Hard	1971	Billie Jean King
1939	Alice Marble	1950	Mrs. Margaret O. du Pont	1961	Darlene Hard	1972	Billie Jean King
1940	Alice Marble	1951	Maureen Connolly	1962	Margaret Smith	1973	Margaret Smith Court
1941	Mrs. Sarah P. Cooke	1952	Maureen Connolly	1963	Maria Bueno	1974	Billie Jean King
1942	Pauline Betz	1953	Maureen Connolly	1964	Maria Bueno	1975	Chris Evert
1943	Pauline Betz	1954	Doris Hart	1965	Margaret Smith	1976	Chris Evert
1944	Pauline Betz	1955	Doris Hart	1966	Maria Bueno	1977	Chris Evert
1945	Sarah P. Cooke	1956	Shirley J. Fry	1967	Billie Jean King		

Women's Doubles

Year	Champions	Year	Champions
1935	Helen Jacobs — Mrs. Sarah P. Fabyan	1957	A. Louise Brough — Mrs. M. O. du Pont
1936	Mrs. M. G. Van Ryn — Carolin Babcock	1958	Darlene Hard — Jeanne Arth
1937	Mrs. Sarah P. Fabyan — Alice Marble	1959	Darlene Hard — Jeanne Arth
1938	Alice Marble — Mrs. Sarah P. Fabyan	1960	Darlene Hard — Maria Bueno
1939	Alice Marble — Mrs. Sarah P. Fabyan	1961	Darlene Hard — Lesley Turner
1940	Alice Marble — Mrs. Sarah P. Fabyan	1962	Maria Bueno — Darlene Hard
1941	Mrs. S. P. Cooke — Margaret Osborne	1963	Margaret Smith — Robyn Ebbern
1942	A. Louise Brough — Margaret Osborne	1964	Billie Jean Moffit — Karen Susman
1943	A. Louise Brough — Margaret Osborne	1965	Carole C. Graebner — Nancy Richey
1944	A. Louise Brough — Margaret Osborne	1966	Maria Bueno — Nancy Richey
1945	A. Louise Brough — Margaret Osborne	1967	Rosemary Casals — Billie Jean King
1946	A. Louise Brough — Margaret Osborne	1968	Maria Bueno — Margaret S. Court
1947	A. Louise Brough — Margaret Osborne	1969	Francoise Durr — Darlene Hard
1948	A. Louise Brough — Mrs. M. O. du Pont	1970	M. S. Court — Judy Tegart Dalton
1949	A. Louise Brough — Mrs. M. O. du Pont	1971	Rosemary Casals — Judy Tegart Dalton
1950	A. Louise Brough — Mrs. M. O. du Pont	1972	Francoise Durr — Betty Stove
1951	Doris Hart — Shirley Fry	1973	Margaret S. Court — Virginia Wade
1952	Doris Hart — Shirley Fry	1974	Billie Jean King — Rosemary Casals
1953	Doris Hart — Shirley Fry	1975	Margaret Court — Virginia Wade
1954	Doris Hart — Shirley Fry	1976	Linky Boshoff — Ilana Kloss
1955	A. Louise Brough — Mrs. M. O. du Pont	1977	Betty Stove — Martina Navratilova
1956	A. Louise Brough — Mrs. M. O. du Pont		

British Champions, Wimbledon

Inaugurated 1877

Year	Men's singles	Women's singles	Year	Men's singles	Women's singles
1946	Yvon Petra	Pauline Betz	1962	Rod Laver	Karen Hantze Susman
1947	Jack Kramer	Margaret Osborne	1963	Chuck McKinley	Margaret Smith
1948	Bob Falkenburg	A. Louise Brough	1964	Roy Emerson	Maria Bueno
1949	Fred R. Schroeder	A. Louise Brough	1965	Roy Emerson	Margaret Smith
1950	Budge Patty	A. Louise Brough	1966	Manuel Santana	Billie Jean King
1951	Dick Savitt	Doris Hart	1967	John Newcombe	Billie Jean King
1952	Frank Sedgman	Maureen Connolly	1968	Rod Laver	Billie Jean King
1953	Victor Seixas	Maureen Connolly	1969	Rod Laver	Ann Jones
1954	Jaroslav Drobny	Maureen Connolly	1970	John Newcombe	Margaret S. Court
1955	Tony Trabert	A. Louise Brough	1971	John Newcombe	Evonne Goolagong
1956	Lewis Hoad	Shirley Fry	1972	Stan Smith	Billie Jean King
1957	Lewis Hoad	Althea Gibson	1973	Jan Kodes	Billie Jean King
1958	Ashley Cooper	Althea Gibson	1974	Jimmy Connors	Chris Evert
1959	Alex Olmedo	Maria Bueno	1975	Arthur Ashe	Billie Jean King
1960	Neale Fraser	Maria Bueno	1976	Bjorn Borg	Chris Evert
1961	Rod Laver	Angela Mortimer	1977	Bjorn Borg	Virginia Wade

Men's Indoor Champions

Year	Singles	Doubles	Year	Singles	Doubles
1966	Charles Pasarell	Robert Lutz—Stan Smith	1973	Jimmy Connors	Juan Gisbert—Jurgen Fassbender
1967	Charles Pasarell	Arthur Ashe—Charles Pasarell	1974	Jimmy Connors	Jimmy Conners—Frew McMillan
1968	Cliff Richey	Thomas Koch—Tom Okker	1975	Jimmy Connors	Jimmy Connors—Ilie Nastase
1969	Stan Smith	Stan Smith—Robert Lutz	1976	Ilie Nastase	Sherwood Stewart—Fred McNair
1970	Ilie Nastase	Stan Smith—Arthur Ashe	1977	Bjorn Borg	Sherwood Stewart—Fred McNair
1971	Clark Graebner	Juan Gisbert—Manuel Orantes			
1972	Stan Smith	Andres Gimano—Manuel Orantes			

Women's Indoor Champions

Year	Singles	Doubles	Year	Singles	Doubles
1963	Carol Hanks	Carol Hanks—Mary Ann Eisel	1970	Mary Ann E. Curtis	Peaches Bartkowicz—Nancy Richey
1964	Mary Ann Eisel	Mary Ann Eisel—Katherine Hubbell	1971	Billie Jean King	Billie Jean King—Rosemary Casals
1965	Nancy Richey	Carol Hanks Aucamp—Mary Ann Eisel	1972	Virginia Wade	Rosemary Casals—Virginia Wade
1966	Billie Jean King	Billie Jean King—Rosemary Casals	1973	Evonne Goolagong	Olga Morozova—Marina Kroskina
1967	Billie Jean King	Carol Hanks Aucamp—Mary Ann Eisel	1974	Billie Jean King	none
1968	Billie Jean King	Billie Jean King—Rosemary Casals	1975	Martina Navratilova	Billie Jean King—Rosemary Casals
1969	Mary Ann E. Curtis	Mary Ann Eisel—Valerie Ziegenfuss	1976	Virginia Wade	Francoise Durr—Rosemary Casals
			1977	Chris Evert	Martina Navratilova—Betty Stove

WCT-World Series of Tennis in 1977

Dates	Event, city	Singles winner	Doubles winners
Jan. 12-16	Birmingham International Indoor Tennis Classic, Birmingham, Ala.	Jimmy Connors	Wojtek Fibak-Tom Okker
Jan. 24-30	INA-U.S. Pro Indoor Championships, Philadelphia	Dick Stockton	Bob Hewitt-Frew McMillan
Feb. 1-6	United Virginia Bank Tennis Classic, Richmond, Va.	Tom Okker	Wojtek Fibak-Tom Okker
Feb. 8-13	III Torneo International Old Spice de Tenis, Mexico City	Ilie Nastase	Wojtek Fibak-Tom Okker
Feb. 15-20	Rothmans Toronto International Tennis, Toronto	Dick Stockton	Wojtek Fibak-Tom Okker
Mar. 1-6	Copa International Serfin, Monterrey, Mexico	Wojtek Fibak	Ross Case-Wojtek Fibak
Mar. 14-20	St. Louis Tennis Classic, St. Louis	Jimmy Connors	Ilie Nastase-Adriano Panatta
Mar. 22-27	ABN Wereldtennis Toernooi, Rotterdam	Dick Stockton	Wojtek Fibak-Tom Okker
Mar. 29-Apr. 3	WCT-World Series of Tennis Tournament, London	Eddie Dibbs	Ilie Nastase-Adriano Panatta
Apr. 5-10	Championnats Internationaux de Tenis De Monte Carlo, Monte Carlo	Bjorn Borg	Francoise Jauffret-Jan Kodes
Apr. 11-17	River Oaks/Alexander & Alexander Tennis Tournament, Houston	Adriano Panatta	Ilie Nastase-Adriano Panatta
Apr. 18-24	World Championship Tennis Classic, Charlotte, N.C.	Corrado Barazzutti	Tom Okker-Ken Rosewall

WCT-Final Championship Summaries

Singles quarterfinals

Connors defeated Panatta 6-4, 7-5, 6-4.
Dibbs defeated Nastase 6-1, 4-6, 6-2, 6-3.
Gerulaitis defeated Fibak 1-6, 3-6, 6-0, 6-2, 6-3.
Stockton defeated Drysdale 7-5, 6-7, 7-6, 6-2.

Semifinals

Connors defeated Dibbs 6-4, 7-5, 6-1.
Stockton defeated Gerulaitis 7-6, 3-6, 6-7, 6-3, 6-3.

Third place

Dibbs defeated Gerulaitis 7-6, ret.

WCT final

Connors defeated Stockton 6-7, 6-1, 6-4, 6-3.

Doubles quarterfinals

Fibak-Okker defeated Alexander-Drysdale 6-3, 4-6, 5-7, 6-4, 6-4.
Gerulaitis-Panatta defeated Martin-Scanlon 6-4, 3-6, 7-5, 6-2.
Amritraj-Stockton defeated Moore-Rosewall 6-4, 4-6, 4-6, 6-2, 7-5.
Dibbs-Barazzutti defeated Case-Roche 3-6, 6-3, 7-6, 6-4.

Semifinals

Gerulaitis-Panatta defeated Fibak-Okker 6-4, 6-4, 6-3.
Amritraj-Stockton defeated Dibbs-Barazzutti 6-4, 6-2, 6-2.

Third place

Fibak-Okker defeated Dibbs-Barazzutti 7-6, 6-0.

WCT final

Amritraj-Stockton defeated Gerulaitis-Panatta 7-6, 7-6, 4-6, 6-3.

1977 WCT-Caesars Palace Challenge Cup

Round-Robin, $10,000 winner-take-all

Gerulaitis def. Panatta 6-1, 6-4.
Connors def. Rosewall 6-2, 6-2.
Connors def. Panatta 7-6, 6-3.
Gerulaitis def. Rosewall 6-3, 6-2.
Connors def. Gerulaitis 6-4, 6-4.
Panatta def. Rosewall 7-5, 3-6, 6-3.
Orantes def. Nastase 7-5, 3-6, 6-4.
Solomon def. Laver 6-3, 6-4.
Nastase def. Solomon 6-3, 6-3.
Laver def. Orantes 4-6, 7-6, 7-5.
Nastase def. Laver 6-3, 6-1.
Orantes def. Solomon 6-2, 2-6, 6-2.

Semifinal, $50,000 winner-take-all

Connors def. Gerulaitis 5-7, 7-6, 7-6, 6-1.
Nastase def. Orantes 6-2, 2-6, 6-2, 6-1.

Final, $100,000 winner-take-all

Nastase def. Connors 3-6, 7-6, 6-4, 7-5.

National Junior Tennis Champions

Boys' 18 singles

1971 Raul Ramirez
1972 Patrick DuPre
1973 Billy Martin
1974 Ferd Taygan
1975 Howard Schoenfield
1976 Larry Gottfried
1977 Van Winitsky

Boys' 18 doubles

1971 Jim Delaney and Chip Fisher
1972 Steve Mott and Brian Teachar
1973 Billy Martin and Trey Waitke
1974 Francisco Gonzalez and Rocky Maguire
1975 Larry Gottfried and John McEnroe
1976 Larry Gottfried and John McEnroe
1977 Robert Van'tHov and Van Winitsky

Boys' 16 singles

1971 Billy Martin
1972 Bill Maze
1973 Ben McKnown
1974 Walter Redondo
1975 Larry Gottfried
1976 Tim Wilkison
1977 Ramesh Krishnan

Boys' 16 doubles

1971 Billy Martin and Trey Waitke
1972 Bruce Manson and Perry Wright
1973 Nial Brash and Matt Mitchell
1974 Jeff Robbins and Van Winitsky
1975 Tony Giammalua and Billy Scanlon
1976 Murray Robinson and Tim Wilkison
1977 Sean Brawley and David Siegler

Girls' 18 singles

1971 Chris Evert
1972 Ann Kiyomura
1973 Carrie Fleming
1974 Rayni Fox
1975 Beth Norton
1976 Lynn Epstein
1977 Tracy Austin

Girls' 18 doubles

1971 Janet Newberry and Eliza Pande
1972 Marita Redondo and Laurie Tenney
1973 Susan Boyle and Kathy May
1974 Anne Bruning and Barbara Hallquist
1975 Lea Antonoplis and Berta McCallum
1976 Sherry Acker and Anne Smith
1977 Lea Antonoplis and Kathy Jordan

Girls' 16 singles

1971 Carrie Fleming
1972 Marita Redondo
1973 Betsy Nagelson
1974 Zenda Leiss
1975 Lea Antonoplis
1976 Peanut Louie
1977 Linda Siegel

Girls' 16 doubles

1971 Ann Kiyomura and Marita Redondo
1972 Jeanne Evert and Kathy Kendall
1973 Susan Mehmedbasich and Robin Tenney
1974 Sherry Acker and Anne Smith
1975 Lea Antonoplis and Berta McCallum
1976 Lucia Fernandez and Trey Lewis
1977 Tracy Austin and Maria Fernandez

World Team Tennis in 1977

Final Standings

Eastern Division

	Matches W	L	Pct	GB	Games GW	GL	GWA	Sets SW	SL
Boston Lobsters	35	9	.795	—	1181	898	.568	152	68
New York Apples	33	11	.750	2	1151	961	.545	138	82
Indiana Loves	21	23	.477	14	1046	1096	.488	105	115
Cleveland Nets	16	28	.364	19	1026	1068	.490	104	116
Soviets	12	32	.273	23	958	1205	.443	66	154

Western Division

	W	L	Pct	GB	GW	GL	GWA	SW	SL
Phoenix Racquets	28	16	.636	—	1126	1088	.509	117	103
Golden Gaters	25	19	.568	3	1097	1050	.511	118	102
San Diego Friars	21	23	.477	7	1142	1107	.508	110	110
Sea-Port Cascades	18	26	.409	10	1031	1139	.475	102	118
Los Angeles Strings	11	33	.250	17	1018	1165	.466	88	132

Playoff Results

Eastern Division—New York 33, Indiana 21; Indiana 27, New York 25; New York 31, Indiana 15; Boston 30, Cleveland 26; Cleveland 21, Boston 20; Boston 28, Cleveland 21.

Western Division—Phoenix 30, Sea-Port 14; Phoenix 27, Sea-Port 26; San Diego 24, Golden Gaters 22; San Diego 24, Golden Gaters 21.

Eastern Division Finals—New York 29, Boston 21; New York 29, Boston 26.

Western Division Finals—San Diego 29, Phoenix 26; Phoenix 27, San Diego 20; Phoenix 30, San Diego 22.

Championship Series—New York 27, Phoenix 22; New York 28, Phoenix 17.

Final WTT Statistics

Women's Singles

	GW-GL	GWA	SW-SL
Navratilova, Boston	217-126	.633	32-7
Evert, Phoenix	213-134	.614	30-8
Wade, New York	142-122	.538	14-14
King, New York	78-70	.527	10-6
Reid, San Diego	168-169	.499	17-17
Barker, Indiana	179-189	.486	20-21
Holladay, Golden Gaters	189-201	.485	20-24
Turnbull, Cleveland	155-166	.483	15-20
Stove, Sea-Port	173-186	.482	20-19
Casals, Los Angeles	149-163	.478	15-18

Men's Singles

	GW-GL	GWA	SW-SL
Borg, Cleveland	220-161	.577	28-13
Drysdale, San Diego	97-78	.554	10-6
Roche, Boston	185-153	.547	23-13
Laver, San Diego	152-128	.543	17-11
Mayer, New York	208-184	.531	24-16
Gorman, Sea-Port	198-187	.514	23-15
Okker, Golden Gaters	212-202	.512	22-19
Gerulaitis, Indiana	155-152	.505	16-16
Nastase, Los Angeles	97-96	.503	10-9
Walts, Phoenix	176-179	.494	18-14

Women's Doubles

	GW-GL	GWA	SW-SL
Navratilova-Stevens, Boston	237-123	.658	36-3
Wade-King, New York	223-155	.590	29-12
Evert-Shaw, Phoenix	130-107	.549	15-9
Stove-Russell, Sea-Port	195-181	.519	23-15
Guerrant-Reid, San Diego	198-192	.508	19-20
Mappin-Kiyomura, Indiana	93-93	.500	10-9
Barker-Kiyomura, Indiana	119-121	.496	14-11
Morozova-Chmyreva, Soviets	94-99	.487	8-11
Kroshina-Morozova, Soviets	64-69	.481	4-9
Durr-Nagelsen, Golden Gaters	170-212	.445	13-28

Men's Doubles

	GW-GL	GWA	SW-SL
McMillan-Okker, Golden Gaters	218-172	.559	26-10
Mayer-Ruffels, New York	216-179	.547	26-13
Borg-Riessen, Cleveland	205-173	.542	22-13
Stone-Ball, Indiana	114-105	.521	13-8
Laver-Drysdale, San Diego	157-145	.520	16-13
Roche-Emerson, Boston	156-146	.517	17-15
Stone-Gerulaitis, Indiana	83-79	.512	8-9
Case-Walts, Phoenix	190-189	.501	17-19
Nastase-Pasarell, Los Angeles	84-85	.497	8-8
Ralston-Pasarell, Los Angeles	108-112	.491	10-11

Davis Cup Challenge Round

Year	Result
1900	United States 5, British Isles 0
1901	(not played)
1902	United States 3, British Isles 2
1903	British Isles 4, United States 1
1904	British Isles 5, Belgium 0
1905	British Isles 5, United States 0
1906	British Isles 5, United States 0
1907	Australia 3, British Isles 2
1908	Australasia 3, United States 2
1909	Australasia 5, United States 0
1910	(not played)
1911	Australasia 5, United States 0
1912	British Isles 3, Australasia 2
1913	United States 3, British Isles 2
1914	Australasia 3, United States 2
1915-18	(not played)
1919	Australasia 4, British Isles 1
1920	United States 5, Australasia 0
1921	United States 5, Japan 0
1922	United States 4, Australasia 1
1923	United States 4, Australasia 1
1924	United States 5, Australasia 0
1925	United States 5, France 0
1926	United States 4, France 1
1927	France 3, United States 2
1928	France 4, United States 1
1929	France 3, United States 2
1930	France 4, United States 1
1931	France 3, Great Britain 2
1932	France 3, United States 2
1933	Great Britain 3, France 2
1934	Great Britain 4, United States 1
1935	Great Britain 5, United States 0
1936	Great Britain 3, Australia 2
1937	United States 4, Great Britain 1
1938	United States 3, Australia 2
1939	Australia 3, United States 2
1940-45	(not played)
1946	United States 5, Australia 0
1947	United States 4, Australia 1
1948	United States 5, Australia 0
1949	United States 4, Australia 1
1950	Australia 4, United States 1
1951	Australia 3, United States 2
1952	Australia 4, United States 1
1953	Australia 3, United States 2
1954	United States 3, Australia 2
1955	Australia 5, United States 0
1956	Australia 5, United States 0
1957	Australia 3, United States 2
1958	United States 3, Australia 2
1959	Australia 3, United States 2
1960	Australia 4, Italy 1
1961	Australia 5, Italy 0
1962	Australia 5, Mexico 0
1963	United States 3, Australia 2
1964	Australia 3, United States 2
1965	Australia 4, Spain 1
1966	Australia 4, India 1
1967	Australia 4, Spain 1
1968	United States 4, Australia 1
1969	United States 5, Romania 0
1970	United States 5, W. Germany 0
1971	United States 3, Romania 2
1972	United States 3, Romania 2
1973	Australia 5, United States 0
1974	South Africa (default by India)
1975	Sweden 3, Czech. 2
1976	Italy 3, Chile 0

NCAA Tennis Champions

Year	Singles	College	Doubles	College
1967	Bob Lutz	USC	Stan Smith—Bob Lutz	USC
1968	Stan Smith	USC	Stan Smith—Bob Lutz	USC
1969	Joaquin Loyo Mayo	USC	Joaquin Loyo Mayo—Marcelo Lara	USC
1970	Jeff Borowiak	UCLA	Pat Cramer—Luis Garcia	Miami (Fla.)
1971	Jimmy Connors	UCLA	Jeff Borowiak—Haroon Rahim	UCLA
1972	Dick Stockton	Trinity (Tex.)	Sandy Mayer—Roscoe Tanner	Stanford
1973	Sandy Mayer	Stanford	Sandy Mayer—Jim Delaney	Stanford
1974	John Whitlinger	Stanford	John Whitlinger—Jim Delaney	Stanford
1975	Billy Martin	UCLA	Butch Walts—Bruce Manson	USC
1976	Bill Scanlon	Trinity	Peter Fleming—Ferdi Taygan	UCLA
1977	Matt Mitchell	Stanford	Bruce Manson—Chris Lewis	USC

Clay Court Champions

Year	Champion	Year	Champion	Year	Champion	Year	Champion
1954	Bernard Bartzen	1960	Barry MacKay	1966	Cliff Richey	1972	Bob Hewitt
1955	Tony Trabert	1961	Bernard Bartzen	1967	Arthur Ashe	1973	Manuel Orantes
1956	Herbert Flam	1962	Chuck McKinley	1968	Clark Graebner	1974	Jimmy Connors
1957	E. Victor Seixas, Jr.	1963	Chuck McKinley	1969	Zeljko Franulovic	1975	Manuel Orantes
1958	Bernard Bartzen	1964	Dennis Ralston	1970	Cliff Richey	1976	Jimmy Connors
1959	Bernard Bartzen	1965	Dennis Ralston	1971	Zeljko Franulovic	1977	Manuel Orantes

Tennis Championships in 1977

Australian Open (Melbourne) — Men's Singles: Roscoe Tanner def. Guillermo Vilas 6-3, 6-3, 6-3; Men's Doubles: Ashe-Roche def. Pasarell-Van Dillen 6-4, 6-4; Women's Singles: Kerry Reid def. Dianne Fromholtz 7-5, 6-2; Women's Doubles: Fromholtz-Gourlay def. Reid-Nagelsen 5-7, 6-1, 7-5.

Italian Open (Rome) — Men's Singles: Vitas Gerulaitis def. Antonio Zugarelli 6-2, 7-6, 3-6, 7-6; Men's Doubles: Gottfried-Ramirez def. McNair-Stewart 6-7, 7-6, 7-5; Women's Singles: Janet Newberry def. Renata Tomanova 6-3, 7-6; Women's Doubles: Cuypers-Kruger def. Bruning-Walsh 3-6, 7-5, 6-2.

French Open (Paris) — Men's Singles: Guillermo Vilas def. Brian Gottfried 6-0, 6-3, 6-0; Men's Doubles: Gottfried-Ramirez def. Fibak-Kodes 7-6, 4-6, 6-3, 6-4; Women's Singles: Mima Jausovec def. Florenta Mihai 6-2, 6-7, 6-1; Women's Doubles: Marsikova-Teeguarden def. Fox-Gourlay 5-7, 6-4, 6-2.

Women's Collegiates — Singles: Barbara Hallquist, USC; Doubles: Jodi Appelbaum-Terry Salganik, Univ. of Miami.

Leading Tennis Money Winners in 1976

Men

		Tournaments	Other Competition (a)	Total
1.	Jimmy Connors	$303,335	$384,000	$687,335
2.	Ilie Nastase	165,205	411,500	576,705
3.	Raul Ramirez	253,442	212,500	465,942
4.	Bjorn Borg	198,420	226,000	424,420
5.	Arthur Ashe	163,636	210,250	373,886
6.	Manuel Orantes	205,884	156,000	361,884
7.	Harold Solomon	193,182	60,250	253,432
8.	Guillermo Vilas	201,226	49,500	250,726
9.	Eddie Dibbs	171,571	68,250	239,821
10.	Wojtek Fibak	176,539	57,500	234,039

Women

		Tournaments	Other Competition (a)	Total
1.	Chris Evert	$289,165	$54,000	$343,165
2.	Evonne Goolagong	173,285	36,667	209,952
3.	Virginia Wade	126,380	32,833	159,213
4.	Rosemary Casals	102,185	26,500	128,685
5.	Martina Navratilova	96,035	32,500	128,535
6.	Betty Stove	95,025	3,333	98,358
7.	Sue Barker	69,660	22,833	92,493
8.	Francoise Durr	70,830	—	70,830
9.	Billie Jean King	42,970	27,500	70,470
10.	Mona Guerrant	41,910	4,000	45,910

(a)includes challenge matches, share of cup team winnings, and tournaments with less than 8 players

Curling Champions

World Champions

Year	Country, skip	Year	Country, skip	Year	Country, skip
1966	Canada, Ron Northcott	1970	Canada, Don Duguid	1974	United States, Bud Somerville
1967	Scotland, Chuck Hay	1971	Canada, Don Duguid	1975	Switzerland, Otto Danieli
1968	Canada, Ron Northcott	1972	Canada, Crest Melesnuk	1976	United States, Bruce Roberts
1969	Canada, Ron Northcott	1973	Sweden, Kjell Oscarius	1977	Sweden, Ragnar Kamp

U.S. National Champions

Year	State, skip	Year	State, skip	Year	State, skip
1966	North Dakota, Joe Zbacnik	1970	North Dakota, Art Tallackson	1974	Wisconsin, Bud Somerville
1967	Washington, Bruce Roberts	1971	North Dakota, Dale Dalziel	1975	Washington, Ed Risling
1968	Wisconsin, Bud Somerville	1972	North Dakota, Bob LaBonte	1976	Minnesota, Bruce Roberts
1969	Wisconsin, Bud Somerville	1973	Massachusetts, Barry Blanchard	1977	Minnesota, Bruce Roberts

Quarter Horse Racing

The richest horse race in the world, the All American Futurity is run each Labor Day at Ruidoso Downs, New Mexico. It is open to 2-year-old Quarter Horses. The distance of the event was 400 yards through 1972; 440 yards starting in 1973.

Year	Winner	Time	Value to Winner	Jockey	Year	Winner	Time	Value to Winner	Jockey
1962	Hustling Man	20.3	$96,425	C. Detiege	1970	Rocket Wrangler	20.09	$178,488	J. Nicodemus
1963	Goetta	20.40	127,500	C. Smith	1971	Mr. Kid Charge	19.65	200,841	J. Cox
1964	Decketta	20.30	134,030	B. Morris	1972	Possumjet	20.04	336,629	P. Herrera
1965	Savannah Jr.	20.30	192,730	J. Wallace	1973	Time To Thinkrich	21.58	330,000	J. Watson
1966	Go Dick Go	20.27	198,300	B. Nesmith	1974	Easy Date	21.60	330,000	D. Knight
1967	Laico Bird	20.11	228,300	B. Harmon	1975	Bugs Alive in 75	21.98	330,000	J. Burgess
1968	Three Oh's	20.06	160,372	J. Nicodemus	1976	Real Wind	21.70	330,000	G. Sumpter
1969	Easy Jet	20.46	159,840	W. Lovell	1977	Hot Idea	21.75	330,000	T. Lipman

CHRONOLOGY OF THE YEAR'S EVENTS

Reported Month by Month in 3 Categories: National, International, and General — Nov. 1, 1976, to Nov. 1, 1977

NOVEMBER 1976

National

Unemployment and Wholesale Prices Up—Despite a drop in food prices, wholesale prices increased substantially, 0.6% overall, in October, the Labor Department reported **Nov. 4.** Wholesale prices of industrial commodities, generally considered one of the best indicators of basic price trends were up 1%. Unemployment remained on a high plateau in October, the Labor Department reported **Nov. 5,** rising to 7.9% from 7.8% the previous month. More heartening news came **Nov. 19** with a Labor Department report that inflation had continued to abate during October. Consumer prices had registered a 0.3% increase, the smallest since March. The department also reported that consumer prices in the 12-month period ending in October had shown the smallest increase for any such period since that ending April 1973.

Carter Calls Election Mandate—In his first post-election news conference held in Plains, Ga., President-elect Jimmy Carter, **Nov. 4,** called his narrow victory a sufficient mandate to carry out a wide array of government programs and policies he had promised and proposed during the long campaign. "I predict they will be achieved," Carter asserted. In a conciliatory note toward Pres. Gerald R. Ford, Carter indicated that he would work closely with the president during the transition period. Carter said his slim margin of victory was a sign of the nationwide respect and approval of President Ford. In the characteristic Carter style, the president-elect responded in broad terms to a variety of questions. He indicated that a tax cut was a "strong possibility" if the economy remained stagnant through December. He assured foreign governments that they should expect a "substantial amount of continuity" between the Ford administration and his own. Carter also announced that Vice President-elect Walter F. Mondale would "play a larger role in my administration than any other vice president has ever played." Two days later, resting on St. Simons Island, Ga., Carter, **Nov. 6,** said the election was close because Ford had so effectively used the element of fear against him in the campaign, but that he had won because of the wide exposure he had gained during the televised debates. Carter also stated that he would make his White House democratic "with a little 'd' " and would build an administration committed to only excellence in behalf of the nation and unfettered by special interests.

Korean President Linked to Illegal Influence—South Korean Pres. Park Chung Hee and other top Korean officials conceived, originated, and directed illegal attempts to bribe U.S. Congressmen and officials, it was reported **Nov. 8.** A Korean with first-hand knowledge who was cooperating with federal investigators said Park personally had ordered the complex lobbying operation. It had been reported earlier, on **Nov. 6,** that the Justice Department had obtained records of secret Bahamian bank accounts of Park Tong Sun, a South Korean businessman and the central figure in the investigation, showing he had brought large amounts of money into the U.S. during the past 5 years. In further developments, former California Rep. Richard T. Hanna, **Nov. 8,** admitted that while in Congress he had become Park's secret partner in an import-export venture that had earned him from $60,000 to $70,000 over 3 years. But Hanna, like 5 other former or present Congressmen who had admitted accepting money from Park, said he did not think there was an impropriety about the relationship. On **Nov. 22,** it was reported that the Korean CIA had recalled Kim San Keun, said to be the major Korean CIA agent in Washington, in an attempt to limit the federal investigation. However, on **Nov. 30,** government investigators announced that Kim had defied orders to return home and was "voluntarily cooperating" with the government investigation. Kim's cooperation appeared to be the biggest break in the investigation since the FBI had begun its inquiry one year before.

Supreme Court Blocks Abortion Curb—The Supreme Court, **Nov. 8,** refused to stay a Brooklyn Federal District Court ruling barring the federal government from withholding federal funds for elective abortions. The court action deferred, until a formal review in another case, a new federal statute, incorporated by Congress in the fiscal-1977 appropriations bill for the Health, Education, and Welfare Department that would have banned the use of federal funds for an abortion unless it were necessary to save a mother's life. The high court decision was a victory for Planned Parenthood and the New York City Health and Hospitals Corporation who had brought suits against the new federal statute. Planned Parenthood had argued that the statute would discriminate against poor women by denying them their constitutional right to abortion.

Minnesota Governor to Replace Mondale—Minnesota Gov. Wendall R. Anderson, **Nov. 10,** announced that he would take Vice President-elect Walter F. Mondale's Senate seat in the coming Congressional session. Anderson, in turn, would be succeeded by Lt. Gov. Rudy Perpich.

Burns, Carter Clash on Economy—In testimony before the Senate Banking Committee, Federal Reserve Chairman Arthur F. Burns, **Nov. 11,** warned that attempts to stimulate the economy through tax cuts, increased government spending, or a looser money policy might have inflationary consequences. Burns said such steps, those very policies President-elect Jimmy Carter had said he would consider in January 1977 if the economy still appeared to be slow, would be unnecessary as well as dangerous. Burns said that "it seems entirely reasonable to expect a pickup in the tempo of economic activity in the near future" without any special government action. After a week-end flurry over the Burns testimony, Carter, **Nov. 15,** in Plains, Ga., announced that he had received a pledge of support from Burns and that he believed they would "find a substantial degree of compatibility." Carter also said it was likely that Burns would remain as federal reserve chairman until the conclusion of his term in January 1978. On **Nov. 16,** Burns said he was not necessarily opposed to a tax cut and would even support one if he thought it would improve the nation's economy and cut unemployment.

Carter's Church Drops Ban on Blacks—In a 120-66 vote, the congregation of President-elect Carter's church, the Plains Baptist Church, **Nov. 14,** decided to end an 11-year ban against attendance by blacks. The vote was precipitated by the Rev. Clemmon King, a nondenominational black minister from Albany, Ga., who had been barred from the church for the 2 previous Sundays. The congregation also decided to retain its minister, the Rev. Bruce Edwards, who had opposed the ban against blacks. In a third decision, the congregation voted to set up a "watch care committee" to screen all applications for membership, whether white or black, without regard to race. President-elect Carter, who favored all 3 actions and was apparently instrumental in working out a solution to the crisis, said, "I am proud of my church." The Rev. King stated that the decision "vindicates the church" and "vindicates the people of Plains."

Transition Process Underway—In their first meeting since the election, President-elect Jimmy Carter and Pres. Gerald R. Ford, **Nov. 22,** met in the White House. After an hour-and-15-minute talk, the 2 men emerged with renewed pledges of cooperation. Ford said his "administration would cooperate 100% in making certain that the transition would be carried out in the best interest of the American people." The transition process had been underway since **Nov. 5,** when Carter representatives had met with Ford people in the White House to make preliminary plans. On **Nov. 10,** Carter Press Secretary Jody Powell announced that Jack Watson, a 38-year-old Atlanta lawyer who had run the transition planning staff during the campaign, would be the key man in overseeing the transition. Watson had emerged victorious in what was called a "bloodless" post-campaign duel with Hamilton Jordan over control of the transition. Watson, Powell said, would oversee Cabinet appointments, government reorganization, Congressional liaison, budget analysis, and the recruitment of personnel before Carter took office. Hamilton would oversee the assembly of a White House staff prior to the inauguration.

Steel Prices Raised—In a surprise move, the National Steel Corp. and Jones and Laughlin, the nation's 4th and 7th largest steel companies respectively, **Nov. 24,** stated they would raise the price of sheet steel by approximately 6% as of Dec. 1. Sheet steel is used primarily in the automobile, appliance, and construction industries. Immediately following the announcement, the Council on Wage and Price Stability announced, in a sharply worded statement, that it would study the action and demand that the National Steel Corp. provide data on production, costs, profits, and expected sales. Three other leading steel producers, U.S. Steel, Bethlehem Steel Corp., and the Republic Steel Corp., **Nov. 29,** announced that they would also raise prices 6%. Press Secretary Jody Powell stated that President-elect Jimmy Carter was "very" concerned about the potential inflationary effects of the price raises in the United States.

Amy to Attend Public School—Rosalynn Carter, wife of the president-elect, **Nov. 28,** announced that her daughter Amy Carter, 9 years old, would attend the Thaddeus Stevens School, a predominantly black public school in Washington, D.C. About one-third of the school's enrollment is comprised of children of foreign diplomats assigned to the nation's capitol.

International

Chirac Regains Assembly Seat—Former French Prime Minister Jacque Chirac, who had resigned in June in a dispute with Pres. Valery Giscard d'Estaing, **Nov. 14,** regained his National Assembly seat in a bi-election. Chirac, on resigning, had charged that d'Estaing had not given him sufficient authority to deal with France's problems. Capturing 53.7% of the vote, Chirac took an impressive first step toward creating a new power base.

Syrian Troops Take Over Lebanon—Syrian peacekeeping troops, **Nov. 15,** took complete control of Beirut, ending a process that had begun **Nov. 10.** The troops met almost no resistance and were welcomed cautiously by most residents, both Christian and Moslem. Lebanese right-wing Christian leaders had agreed, **Nov. 9,** in a meeting with Lebanese Pres. Elias Sarkis, that Syrian troops, as part of the Arab peace-keeping force, could occupy Christian areas of Beirut and its suburbs. They stated that they had been "reassured" by Sarkis of the necessity of what would be virtual Syrian occupation of Christian strongholds under the Arab peace agreement negotiated late in October. On **Nov. 7,** Sarkis had appealed to all of Lebanon's heavily armed factions to end "bloodshed and ruin" and to greet the Syrian-dominated peace-keeping force with "fraternity and love." He stressed that the 30,000-strong peace-keeping force, dominated by 23,000 Syrians, would be directly under his command. By **Nov. 21,** Syrian troops completed the final phase of occupation, meeting no resistance as they took over the key ports of Tripoli and Saida and dominated all of Lebanon with the exception of a 15-mile wide strip along the Israeli border in southern Lebanon. Israel, **Nov. 23,** reinforcing its prior warnings to Syria and Palestinian guerrillas not to approach the border, paraded tanks and armored personnel carriers on its side of the Lebanese border. On **Nov. 28,** Israeli Prime Minister Yitzhak Rabin reiterated the warning, calling the presence of either Syrian or Palestinian armed troops near the border "intolerable."

Quebec Separatists Oust Liberals—The Quebec movement to separate that province from Canada, the Parti Quebecois, **Nov. 15,** captured 69 seats in the 110-seat Quebec National Assembly, ousting Premier Robert Bourassa's ruling Liberal party. Rene Levesque, a 54-year-old journalist and former Liberal minister, would head the new provincial government. Levesque, in his campaign, had promised his government would make no unilateral move toward independence until a referendum was held and popular support gained for the move. Bourassa, who lost his own Montreal district, had campaigned in favor of Canada's federal system against a separatist threat to Canadian unity. Observers felt the Bourassa defeat signaled voter dissatisfaction with his 6-year rule which had been plagued by a sluggish economy, high unemployment, inflation, labor unrest, and charges of corruption against the Liberal party. Following the stunning separatist victory, both national and local federalist leaders, **Nov. 16,** pressured the new government against breaking away from Canada, warning Levesque he had won a mandate to rule Quebec, not to lead it to independence. At a news conference, Levesque said he could not abandon his long-term goal of independence, but indicated he would govern within the present structures for the next 4 years. He set his immediate goals as financial recovery, economic development, and an honest and open administration.

U.S. Vetoes Vietnam Admission to UN—The U.S., **Nov. 15,** in a 14-1 vote in the Security Council, vetoed the admission of Vietnam into the UN. The U.S. vote was cast on the ground that the Hanoi government had failed to date to give an accounting of 800 American servicemen still listed officially as missing in action in the Vietnam war. U.S. Ambassador to the UN William W. Scranton stated that the U.S. would reconsider its position if Hanoi should decide to demonstrate cooperation on the matter. The chief Vietnam observer at the UN, Dinh Ba Thi, charged the U.S. veto was a "maneuver" and asserted that it was impossible to furnish a "complete list of those missing in action."

Spain Calls for General Elections—In a major step toward elective democracy, the Spanish parliament, **Nov. 18,** approved general elections for 1977 and voted itself out of existence. The move by the largely appointed parliament left over from the Franco regime was a stunning victory for Prime Minister Adolfo Suarez who has been working to slowly dismantle the dictatorial institutions of Franco's Spain.

Israel Re-enters UNESCO—Israel, **Nov. 22**, in Nairobi, Kenya, was restored to full membership in the European grouping of UNESCO (UN Educational, Scientific, and Cultural Organization), which reversed a 2-year-old decision to bar Israel. However, the UNESCO general conference adopted a resolution condemning Israel's education and cultural policies in occupied Arab territories as "cultural assimilation." It was reported that the resolution was the price demanded by Arab and Soviet bloc nations in accepting U.S. and African pressure to return Israel to the European grouping, where most of UNESCO's work is done.

Earthquake Strikes Turkey—A major earthquake, measuring 7.9 on the Richter scale, **Nov. 24**, struck the mountainous area of Turkey near Mt. Ararat in Van province. The quake killed at least 4,000 persons, injured 2,000 more, and left 250,000 persons homeless. The quake area was on the Anatolian fault line. The quake virtually destroyed 4 Turkish towns and 130 villages, leveled 14 Iranian border villages, and also shook portions of Soviet Armenia. Severe cold and snow seriously hampered efforts of Turkish troops and civilian relief workers to reach the devastated area. On **Nov. 28**, Turkey announced drastic emergency measures in Eastern Turkey.

Rhodesian Blacks Accept British Plan.—Ending a month-long deadlock at the Geneva conference on Rhodesian majority rule, 2 Rhodesian black nationalist leaders, **Nov. 26**, accepted a British plan setting Mar. 1, 1978, as the latest independence date for Rhodesia under black rule. The 2 leaders of African National Council (ANC) factions, Robert Mugabe of the Zimbabwe African National Union (ZANU) and Joshua Nkomo of the Zimbabwe African People's Union (ZAPU), who had previously insisted on a Dec. 1, 1977 date, agreed to accept a formula providing for independence prior to Mar. 1 if the transition process were completed earlier. Rhodesian Prime Minister Ian Smith had left the conference **Nov. 3**, after failure to fix a date, stating, "I can't go on sitting here twiddling my thumbs." The break in the deadlock opened the way for formal discussions, beginning **Nov. 29**, on the creation of an interim government for Rhodesia.

General

Hearst Freed From Prison—Federal District Judge William H. Orrick Jr., **Nov. 19**, freed convicted bank robber Patricia Hearst from prison on bail of $1.5 million and placed her in the custody of her parents pending appeal of her conviction. Hearst had been in prison for 14 months. At a brief news conference following her release, Hearst made one statement: "It would be a lot better if I were home right now, and I would like to get this over with so I can go home." On **Nov. 18**, her father, Randolph A. Hearst, president of the **San Francisco Examiner** and chairman of the board of the Hearst Corp. and his twin brother David had signed documents satisfying the $500,000 bail for Hearst to remain free pending a California state trial on an 11-count indictment in a Los Angeles street shooting. Prior to the release, **Nov. 18**, the family had also provided $100,000 in cash and a $900,000-surety bond as a guarantee Hearst would not flee while her appeal for a new trial on the bank robbery was processed.

Reilly Murder Charges Dropped—Charges that Peter A. Reilly had killed his mother in 1973 were dropped, **Nov. 24**, in a Litchfield, Conn., County Superior Court, after the new States' Attorney Dennis Santore announced that he had found new evidence that tended to clear Reilly. Santore had discovered the evidence in the files of his predecessor. On **Nov. 26**, Connecticut Gov. Ella T. Grasso ordered a new investigation into the 1973 murder and an inquiry into the prosecution of Reilly.

Disasters—Heavy flooding caused by torrential rains in East Java, Indonesia, took some 136 lives, it was reported **Nov. 17**; 50 persons were missing and more than 4,000 were evacuated from their homes. . . . All 50 persons aboard died when an Olympic Airways 2-engine prop plane crashed in a snowstorm about 260 miles north of Athens **Nov. 23**. . . . A Soviet Aeroflot TU-104 turbojet, **Nov. 28**, crashed at Moscow's Sheremetyevo Airport, killing all 72 persons aboard.

DECEMBER
National

Carter Gets Good Will Pledge From Brezhnev—Soviet Communist party leader Leonid I. Brezhnev gave President-elect Jimmy Carter a pledge that the USSR would "go out of its way" to avoid any crisis with the U.S. early in the new administration, Carter Press Secretary Jody Powell reported **Dec. 2**. The pledge was brought to Carter by Treasury Secretary William E. Simon who had just returned from Moscow. In a response to Brezhnev, Carter said he would move "aggressively" to get negotiations for a new strategic arms treaty "off dead center."

Economic News Mixed—The labor department, **Dec. 3**, reported that the national unemployment rate in November had risen to its highest level in 1976, 8.1%, up from 7.9% in October. The increase came despite an apparent strong rise in the total number of persons employed. Experts said the rise in unemployment was particularly significant because it resulted in layoffs of adult men, a sign of economic deterioration. However, better economic news came **Dec. 29**, when the commerce department reported that the government's composite index of leading economic indicators revealed the economy was showing renewed expansion. The index of leading economic indicators had risen 1% in November, following a revised increase of 0.6% in October.

Coleman Postpones Air Bag Requirement—Transportation Secretary William T. Coleman Jr., **Dec. 6**, urged automobile makers to take part in a limited program under National Highway Traffic Safety Administration sponsorship to demonstrate air bags for cars, but delayed for at least 2 years the "final decision" on whether to require the safety device on all cars. Although Coleman admitted the bags would be likely to prevent some 12,000 auto deaths a year, he opted for the demonstration project to build public confidence in the devices. Stuart Eizenstat, President-elect Carter's issues director, **Dec. 7**, said he was "disturbed" the Ford administration had issued the decision without giving the incoming administration an opportunity to influence it.

Democrats Set House Leadership—Massachusetts Rep. Thomas P. (Tip) O'Neill Jr., **Dec. 6**, was elected without opposition by House Democrats to be speaker of the House in the 95th Congress. Then, in a stunning one-vote upset on the 3d ballot, Texas Rep. Jim Wright defeated the presumed favorite Phillip Burton of California for the post of House majority leader. Wright had eloquently campaigned that he was the man who could be a bridge between Democratic liberals and conservatives in the House. O'Neill, **Dec. 8**, appointed Indiana Rep. John Brademas House majority whip, replacing Rep. John J. McFall of California. McFall's acceptance of campaign contributions from Korean businessman Park Tong Sun, had led to his downfall. Brademas had also accepted contributions from the Korean businessman, but, unlike McFall, had made a public disclosure of the matter.

Swine Flu Program Suspended—Federal officials, **Dec. 16**, suspended the troubled swine flu program because of growing concern the shots might be linked to an outbreak of 94 cases of paralysis in 14 states. The Federal Center for Disease Control in Atlanta, which ran the program, said the paralysis, known as the Guillain-Barre syndrome, had resulted in 4 fatalities and had involved 51 persons who had received swine flu shots between one to 3 weeks before paralysis.

International

Chirac Forms New Political Movement — Culminating weeks of intense publicity, former French Prime Minister Jacques Chirac, **Dec. 5**, at a mass rally in Paris, dissolved the Gaullist party (Union des Democrates pour la Republique), and transformed it into a new mass movement. At the emotional 50,000-strong gathering, he had himself elected president of the new anti-leftist group, called the Assembly for the Republic. Chirac stated that the purpose of the new party was to call on all the French people to "take hold of ourselves again." "Let us return hope to our country. This appeal should be heard to save Frenchmen from having to support it later, perhaps at a time of drama," Chirac told the rapt assembly. In an indirect response to critics who have compared his new movement to the launching of the fascist parties before World War II, Chirac described it as a "movement of citizens, of free men who want to shape their history with their own hands, and who refuse the fatality of all dictatorships, of fascism as of collectivism."

Japan's Ruling Party Suffers Setback — In Japanese national elections, **Dec. 5**, the ruling conservative Liberal-Democrats suffered severe losses, winning only 249 of 511 seats in the expanded lower house of parliament. They had held 169 of 491 seats in the outgoing house. Prime Minister Takeo Miki commented on the results: "I have accepted the verdict of the people. . . . They have sought a new political direction." He called for a thorough reconstruction of the party and the cleansing of political corruption. Liberal-Democrat party involvement in the Lockheed aircraft bribery scandal, an economic lull following a bad recession, and a vague desire for change were the major factors in the election. In the final tally, the Liberal-Democrats held a razor-thin majority, 258 seats of 511, including 9 conservative independents who had affiliated with the Liberal-Democrats. The biggest winner in the new house was the New Liberal Club, a 5-month-old group of conservatives who had left the ruling party, which they had branded as corrupt. They added 12 seats to the 5 they had held previously. On **Dec. 23**, the Liberal-Democrats named Takeo Fukuda, a 71-year-old long-time professional politician, party president. Fukuda, **Dec. 24**, by a narrow 2-vote margin in the House of Representatives, was elected the new prime minister.

U.S. Philippine Dispute Strains Relations — A public dispute over a U.S.-Philippine agreement for aid to Manila severely strained relations between the 2 nations **Dec. 6**. The state department, **Dec. 3**, had reported that Secretary of State Henry A. Kissinger

Carter Makes Cabinet, Top Appointments; Selections Include 2 Women, 2 Blacks

President-elect Jimmy Carter, **Dec. 3**, announced the first major appointments for his administration, choosing Cyrus R. Vance as his secretary of state and Bert Lance, an old Georgia political ally, as director of the Office of Management and Budget. In making the announcement, Carter said he believed the nation could "be reassured that the first two choices have been superlative." Vance, an establishment figure and Washington pro, served as deputy secretary of defense during the period of increasing U.S. involvement in Vietnam during the mid-1960s. Lance, a Georgia banker, had served under Carter in Georgia and had advised him on his reorganization of the Georgia state government.

Carter, **Dec. 14**, named W. Michael Blumenthal, chief executive of the Bendix Corp., as secretary of the treasury and Rep. Brock Adams (D-Wash.), another Georgian, as secretary of transportation. Carter described both as "superbly qualified" and certain to play major roles in his administration.

On **Dec. 16**, Carter designated Andrew Young U.S. ambassador to the UN. Young, formerly an aide to the Rev. Dr. Martin Luther King Jr., told reporters he supported an aggressive pursuit of black majority rule in Africa. Carter also named Charles L. Schultze, who served on the White House staffs of both Eisenhower and Johnson, to serve as chairman of the Council of Economic Advisers. Also named was Zbigniew Brzezinksi, a Polish-born Columbia University professor, as special presidential assistant for national security affairs.

Carter, **Dec. 18**, gave the post of secretary of interior to another long-time friend, Idaho Gov. Cecil D. Andrus. In making the announcement, Carter expressed some frustration with his search for a woman willing to serve in his cabinet. Nevertheless, **Dec. 20**, Carter named Juanita M. Kreps, a vice president of Duke University and professor of economics, as his commerce secretary. Kreps, regarded as an expert in the problems of the aged, immediately twitted Carter for suggesting he had found few qualified women to serve in his administration. Carter also named Griffin B. Bell, another long-time Georgia friend, as attorney general. The appointment raised an immediate flurry of criticism in civil rights circles because Bell, as a former federal judge, had handed down opinions and rulings on racial matters that had occasionally disturbed civil rights leaders. Carter also designated Minnesota Rep. Robert S. Bergland, a farmer and favorite of Vice President-elect Walter F. Mondale, as secretary of agriculture.

On **Dec. 21**, Carter made 3 more major appointments, naming Patricia Roberts Harris, a black woman and Washington, D.C., attorney, to head the Department of Housing and Urban Development; California Institute of Technology Pres. Harold Brown as secretary of defense; and University of Texas Prof. F. Ray Marshall as secretary of labor.

Completing the major appointments for his administration, Carter, **Dec. 23**, named former Johnson aide Joseph A. Califano to head the Department of Health, Education, and Welfare, and Kennedy confidant Theodore C. Sorensen as director of the Central Intelligence Agency. Carter also named James R. Schlesinger, a Republican who had served under both the Nixon and Ford administrations, to be his special assistant for energy matters. The appointment was the first step toward Schlesinger's eventual elevation as the first secretary of energy and resources. Carter confirmed that he would ask Congress to create the new department in 1977.

and Philippine Foreign Minister Carlos Romulo had reached a tentative agreement to give the Philippines $1 billion in economic and military aid over the next 5 years in return for continued use of Philippine military bases. The unexpected resolution of on-again, off-again negotiations doubled the level of U.S. assistance to Manila. Then, **Dec. 4**, the U.S. learned that Philippine Pres. Ferdinand E. Marcos had rejected the agreement, claiming he wanted more than the $500 million in military aid stipulated in the accord. On **Dec. 6**, Foreign Minister Romulo claimed his government had never agreed to the accord. The state department, however, maintained that Romulo, in fact, had accepted the agreement.

Vietnamese Communists Hold Congress — As the first congress of the Vietnamese Workers party since 1960 convened in Hanoi **Dec. 14**, Vietnamese leaders pledged to follow a "new direction" of development and reconstruction. In a 6-hour address aired over Hanoi radio, Le Duan, first secretary of the party, outlined plans for an extensive expansion of industry and agriculture, foreign trade, and investment. Vietnamese Prime Minister Pham Van Dong, **Dec. 16**, presented the 5-year plan for 1976-1980, which projected a large-scale redistribution of the nation's population. "Work forces in the south will be moved to the north if it is necessary," Dong stated. He projected an increase of 13% to 14% in national income under the plan and an increase in industrial output of as much as 18%. On **Dec. 20**, the congress adjourned after renaming the Workers' party the Communist party and reconfirming Le Duan as the nation's top leader.

Spaniards Vote for Political Reform — In a special referendum, the Spanish people, **Dec. 15**, voted overwhelmingly in favor of a government program to hold free elections for a new parliament next spring. The democratically-elected parliament would have the right to rewrite the laws of Franco Spain. Of those voting, 94.2% answered "yes" to the straightforward question: "Do you approve the political reform bill?"

OPEC Splits for 2-Tier Pricing — Resolving a deadlock over a Saudi Arabian demand for an oil price freeze, the Organization of Petroleum Exporting Countries, **Dec. 17**, in Doha, Qatar, agreed on a price split for the next 6 months. Under the agreement, Saudi Arabia and the United Arab Emirates, the largest oil producers, would raise prices for oil 5% while the other 11 member countries would raise prices 10%. According to 2 OPEC sources, the 11 nations would increase their prices another 5%, for a total of 15%, after July 1, 1977. The decision for a price split came as a surprising fissure in what had been a solid OPEC front over the past few years. Saudi Arabia stated that it would be prepared to increase oil production to hold the world price of oil steady, but warned western nations, particularly the U.S., that it expected a show of "appreciation" in return. The appreciation could be shown, Saudi Arabia said, by responsive measures in both the Arab-Israeli conflict and in so-called "north-south" negotiations between industrialized and developing nations. Experts estimated the OPEC price rises would increase crude oil costs by $10 billion annually.

Soviet Dissident, Chilean Communist Exchanged — Vladimir K. Bukovsky, the Soviet Union's most prominent jailed dissident, and Luis Corvalan Lepe, the jailed head of the Chilean Communist party, **Dec. 18**, were exchanged at Zurich airport, while U.S., USSR, and Chilean ambassadors watched. The exchange had been negotiated over the previous 6 weeks between Chile and the Soviet Union with the U.S. acting as an intermediary. Bukovsky, who had been serving a 7-year-term for anti-Soviet agitation, stated, **Dec. 19**, in Zurich, that prison life had become much harsher after the signing of the Helsinki accord on east-west cooperation. Corvalan, upon his arrival in Moscow **Dec. 23**, said he would work for the restoration of "freedom and democracy" in his country.

Rabin Resigns, Calls for New Elections — Israeli Prime Minister Yitzhak Rabin, in the face of the loss of majority control of the government, **Dec. 20**, called for new elections, dissolved parliament, and resigned office. He would remain as head of a caretaker government until elections were held in late May or early June. On **Dec. 19**, in a move that stunned Israeli politicians, Rabin had ousted the National Religious Party from his shaky government coalition. A week earlier, 9 of 10 of the party's members had abstained in a no-confidence vote that had sought to topple Rabin's government. The vote had come on charges by the United Torah Front that Rabin had desecrated the sabbath by holding a welcoming ceremony after sundown. Rabin had denied the charges. In resigning, Rabin said it was impossible to ignore the defection of members of government when the leadership's ability to run the country was being challenged.

General

Mistrial Declared in Mandel Case—Federal District Court Judge John H. Pratt, **Dec. 7**, in Baltimore, Md., declared a mistrial in the 13-week political corruption trial of Maryland Gov. Marvin Mandel and 4 other defendants. The defense had contended that the defendants could no longer receive a fair trial because members of the jury had learned of alleged attempts to bribe one jury member in order to prevent a conviction. Mandel, who told newsmen that the defense evidence would have "shown there was absolutely nothing to the prosecution's case," immediately returned to the Statehouse to work on the 1977 Maryland budget. The central contention in the government prosecution had been that Mandel, in return for cash and gifts from friends, had favored legislation that enhanced the value of his co-defendants' secret ownership of a Maryland racetrack. The chief prosecutor in the case, Assistant U.S. Attorney Barnet D. Skolnik, **Dec. 8**, identified one of the alleged jury tamperers as a man with Mafia connections.

Bronfman Case Jury Decision: Extortion, Not Kidnapping—A White Plains, N.Y., jury, **Dec. 10**, acquitted Mel Patrick Lynch and Dominic P. Byrne of kidnapping Seagram fortune heir Samuel Bronfman 2d in August 1975, but found the defendants guilty of extortion. The 2 defendants had been charged with grand larceny for extorting a $2.3 million ransom from Edgar Bronfman, chairman of Seagram Co., Ltd. The defense praised the kidnapping verdict as "a victory for justice, but Sam Bronfman said he was "shocked and stunned." "It's a pretty bad system when a guy gets kidnapped, the kidnappers are caught red-handed, and they get off," Bronfman charged. Two jurors indicated to newsmen that they had accepted the defense contention that Bronfman had "masterminded" his own abduction, perhaps for "personal reasons." In his testimony, Bronfman had denied Lynch's claim that the 2 had had a homosexual relationship and that Bronfman had been threatening to disclose Lynch's homosexuality to his employer, the New York City fire department. Lynch and Byrne, **Jan. 6**, were sentenced to 4-to-12 and 3-to-9 year jail terms respectively for the extortion conviction.

Edelin Abortion Conviction Overturned—The Massachusetts Supreme Judicial Court, **Dec. 17**, unanimously overturned the 1975 manslaughter conviction of Dr. Kenneth C. Edelin in one of the nation's most famous abortion cases. Contrary to the original verdict, the court ruled that a doctor can only be convicted of manslaughter if he ends the life of a fetus that is definitely alive outside a woman's body. Edelin had been found guilty of killing a live fetus in a woman's body by holding it in the uterus until it suffocated for lack of oxygen. After the 1975 conviction, many doctors had refused to perform abortions in the middle stages of pregnancy for fear of prosecution.

Daley Dead at 74—Mayor Richard J. Daley, the man who simultaneously ruled Chicago and the Cook County Democratic machine for 2 decades, died, **Dec. 20,** of a heart attack at the age of 74. In 1975, following a stroke, Daley had been overwhelmingly elected to his 6th 4-year term as Chicago mayor. Thousands of Chicagoans lined up to see his body, **Dec. 22,** as Daley was eulogized as a great and powerful man humble before God, his family, and the city he ruled. On **Dec. 28,** the Chicago city council, in a near unanimous vote, chose an intimate friend and neighbor of Daley, Alderman Michael A. Bilandic, as acting mayor. He would serve until a general election could be held. George W. Dunne, another Daley intimate, **Dec. 29,** was chosen by acclamation, in an unexpected show of unity, to succeed Daley as chairman of the Cook County Democratic Committee, the organization through which the Daley machine functioned.

First American Male Saint Elected—A consistory of cardinals, **Dec. 20,** in Rome, Italy, formally approved the canonization of Bishop John Neumann as the first male American Roman Catholic saint. The Bohemian-born Neumann, who died in 1860, had worked among immigrants in upper New York State and later served as the 4th Bishop of Philadelphia. The Medical Board of the Vatican Congregation for the Causes of Saints had previously credited Neumann with 3 miracles.

Carter, Artis Guilty in 2d Trial—After a 9-hour deliberation, a Paterson, N.J., jury, **Dec. 21,** found Rubin "Hurricane" Carter and John Artis guilty in a retrial for 3 murders committed 10 years ago. The new trial had been ordered in March on the grounds that the prosecution had withheld evidence beneficial to the defense in the first trial. Both Carter and Artis had served 9 years of life sentences when they were released on bail in March. In an unusually strong statement following the verdict, Judge Bruno L. Leopizzi warned the jury not to discuss what had happened in the jury room. During the 6-week trial, Alfred P. Bello, one of 2 witnesses at the first trial, who later recanted his identification of Carter and Artis at the scene of the murders, renounced his recantation and again identified the defendants. Arthur D. Bradley, who had also recanted his testimony at the first trial, was not called as a witness. On **Dec. 22,** both Artis and Carter, who had been returned to prison, said they were "shocked" by the guilty verdict. Carter stated, "I have not lost hope. But hope is all we can have. We don't have our freedom anymore." Carter and Artis, **Feb. 9,** received the same sentences imposed after their original trial. Carter would serve 2 consecutive and one concurrent life term; Artis would serve 3 concurrent life terms.

Worst Spill Off U.S. Coast Recorded—The bow of the 640-foot Argo Merchant, a Liberian-flag tanker grounded off Nantucket, **Dec. 22,** broke in half, spilling thick oil into the Atlantic Ocean. The tanker had run aground, **Dec. 15,** 27 miles southeast of Nantucket, and had begun leaking oil into one of the nation's richest commercial fishing areas. Assaulted by a severe storm, the vessel split, **Dec. 21,** and spilled about 5 million gallons of oil. The total spill amounted to about 7.5 million gallons of oil. On **Dec. 22,** a coalition of commercial Massachusetts fishermen and other parties filed a $60-million damage suit against the owners of the tanker. On **Dec. 23,** government sources investigating the spill reported that the Argo Merchant had turned off her electronic navigation equipment, including the depth finder, before she ran aground. Capt. Georgios Papadopoulos, **Dec. 27,** testified in Manhattan Federal District Court in hearings to determine liability that the tanker's gyro compass had not been functioning properly when the ship ran aground.

Carey Pardons 7 Former Attica Inmates—New York State Gov. Hugh Carey, **Dec. 30,** pardoned 7 former Attica inmates who had participated in the 1971 prison uprising at Attica State prison and commuted the sentence of an 8th. After reviewing the case, Carey acted, he said, to "firmly and finally close the book" on an investigation and prosecution which he concluded was such that "we now confront the real possibility that the law itself may well fall into disrespect." Carey also stated that no disciplinary action would be taken against the 20 state troopers and prison guards who had participated in the bloody retaking of the prison.

Disasters—An Egyptair 707, **Dec. 25,** exploded in mid-air and crashed in a predawn mist 5 miles from the main international airport in Bangkok, Thailand, killing 42 passengers, 9 crew members, and 30 workers in a factory where the jetliner crashed. . . An Egyptian liner, the Patria, caught fire and sank, **Dec. 25,** in the Red Sea, claiming the lives of more than 100 Moslems returning home from a pilgrimage to the holy cities of Mecca and Medina. . . An explosion, **Dec. 30,** at the Staric mine in Czechoslovakia's Ostrava coal basin took the lives of 43 miners.

JANUARY

National

Senate Leaders Chosen — Running unopposed, West Va. Sen. Robert C. Byrd, **Jan. 4,** was chosen Democratic Majority leader of the Senate in the 95th Congress. Minnesota Sen. Hubert H. Humphrey had withdrawn as Byrd's last challenger because he did not have "sufficient" votes and didn't want to divide Senate Democrats. Republicans, in a surprise move, elected Tennessee Sen. Howard H. Baker minority leader. Baker defeated Robert P. Griffin of Michigan, who had been in line for the post, in a 19-18 secret ballot vote.

Carter Issues Conflict of Interest Guidelines — Predident-elect Jimmy Carter, **Jan. 4,** presented broad guidelines to limit conflicts of interest in his administration. He personally would avoid such problems, Carter announced, by placing the bulk of his financial holdings in a trust. Under the guidelines, Carter would require all cabinet members as well as other political appointees and career bureaucrats in policy-making positions to make full public disclosures of their financial net worth. Each individual would also pledge that, after leaving office, he would not lobby for at least one year at the agency in which he served. Carter Press Secretary Jody Powell stated that the guidelines were the first step in fulfilling Carter's campaign promise to "restore the confidence of the American people in their own government."

Carter Church Rejects Black — The congregation of the Plains (Ga.) Baptist Church, including President-elect Jimmy Carter, **Jan. 9,** unanimously rejected the membership application of the Rev. Clennon King, a black. "I think you ought to take down that sign that says you are God's church and admit you're just a social club," Clennon charged. Clennon had applied for membership shortly before the presidential election after Carter had stated that he "presumed" his all-white church would accept black members. Shortly thereafter, at Carter's urging, the church had dropped an old ban to exclude blacks and "activists." The rejection had been recommended by the church's watch-care committee on membership on the grounds that King had failed to appear before the committee, that he lived too far from Plains, and also appeared unwilling to carry out the objectives of the church.

Fall in Unemployment Leads Economic News — The government reported, **Jan. 12,** that the national unemployment rate had fallen to 7.9% in December 1976, a decrease of .2% from the November rate. The number of people with jobs rose by 222,000, ending a year in which the number of people employed rose by 3 million. According to Labor Statistics Commissioner Julius Shiskin, the year-end improvement indicated that "the employment situation has broken out of the holding pattern which characterized it during the preceding several months." The labor department reported that the wholesale price index, spurred by an increase in farm prices, rose by .9% in December. However, prices in the key industrial sector had shown the smallest increase in 7 months, signalling a continuation of moderate inflation. Then, on **Jan. 19,** the labor department announced that consumer prices had risen a modest 0.4% in December. The increase, the department reported, capped a year that showed the lowest rate of inflation in consumer prices since 1972.

Ford Delivers Last State of the Union — In his final State of the Union message to Congress, Pres. Gerald R. Ford, **Jan. 12,** offered no specific legislative proposals of his own, but urged Congress and the new administration to adopt "prudent" policies at home. The state of the union was good, Ford said, in a marked contrast with his first message delivered in 1975. Then, as the nation was recovering from Watergate, economic recession, and an energy crisis, Ford had told Congress the state of the union was "not good." "I am proud of the long way we have come together," Ford said. He voiced particular pride in the part he played "in rebuilding confidence in the presidency, confidence in our free system, and confidence in our future." Ford said he was encouraged by the nation's recovery from recession and a "steady return to sound economic growth." He pointed to the need to create productive and permanent jobs, expressing his regret that, despite the creation of 4 million jobs during his presidency, there were still so many people not working. Turning to the international sphere, Ford emphasized that the U.S. must remain first in keeping peace in the world and must never be "second in defense." "The United States would risk the most serious political consequences if the world came to believe that our adversaries have a decisive margin of superiority," Ford warned. Ford admitted that his administration had suffered some disappointments, particularly in failing to make satisfactory progress toward achieving energy independence. He "urgently" asked Congress to create programs to encourage conservation and production of energy to end the nation's vulnerability to foreign suppliers.

Sorensen Withdraws From CIA Post — Acknowledging mounting opposition in the Senate Select Committee on Intelligence, Theodore C. Sorensen, **Jan. 17,** announced that he had asked President-elect Jimmy Carter to withdraw his nomination as CIA director. "It is now clear," Sorensen stated, "that a substantial portion of the United States Senate is not yet ready to accept as director of Central Intelligence an outsider who believes as I believe." Carter, who accepted the decision with an expression of regret, made no attempt to dissuade Sorensen. It had become apparent, **Jan. 15,** that certain senators were objecting to the nomination because Sorensen, a Kennedy confidant, had taken certain classified material when he left the White House staff in 1964 for aid in writing a book on the Kennedy administration. Opposition had also arisen over his inexperience in foreign intelligence, his role in helping Sen. Edward M. Kennedy explain the Chappaquidick incident, his status as a conscientious objector to military service,

Carter, Mondale Inaugurated in Simple Ceremony; Carter Calls for Fresh Beginning for the Nation

In a relatively austere ceremony, Jimmy Carter, dressed in a 3-piece business suit, **Jan. 20,** took the oath of office as the 39th president of the United States. Minutes before, Walter F. Mondale was sworn in as vice president. Following a brief, 17-minute inaugural address, Carter, in a break with inaugural tradition, walked a mile and a half in freezing weather from the Capitol to the White House, accompanied by the cheers of an appreciative crowd. He was joined by his wife Rosalynn, daughter Amy, and other members of his family.

In his inaugural address, more a moralistic sermon than a rallying cry, Carter said, "I have no new dream to set forth today, but rather urge a fresh faith in the old dream." Echoing the populist theme of his campaign, Carter said the ceremonies marked "a new beginning, a new dedication within our government, and a new spirit among us all . . . A president may sense and proclaim that new spirit, but only a people can provide it." He appealed for sacrifice on the part of the American people: "We have learned that 'more' is not necessarily 'better'; that even our great nation has recognized limits, and that we can neither answer all questions nor solve all problems."

Carter also paid tribute to outgoing Pres. Gerald R. Ford, thanking him for "all he has done to heal our land." A tearful Ford rose from his seat to shake hands with the new president.

The religious tone of the inauguration was set in its first official event, an 8 a.m. prayer service conducted in a revivalist spirit at the Lincoln Memorial by the Rev. Martin Luther King Sr. Emphasizing spiritual and moral values, a note that would continue through the day, King made a passionate appeal for compassion for the nation's poor.

In an unusual message cabled to all nations of the world, Carter pledged to the "citizens of the world" that his administration would give priority to shaping "a world order that is more responsive to human aspirations." "We will not seek to dominate or dictate to others," Carter said. In return, the leaders of the world conveyed warm, but cautious, welcomes to the new administration.

The day's festivities ended with 7 "people's inaugural parties," all informal and inexpensive and many of them extremely crowded. Carter and his wife Rosalynn attended each one of them. In the end, the highly touted "people's inaugural" had turned into a 5-day extravaganza which cost $3.3 million. But the emphasis, as promised, was on the nation's ordinary people rather than the very important.

and his position with a law firm representing multinational corporations and foreign governments.

Carter Pardons Vietnam Draft Evaders — In his first major presidential act, Pres. Jimmy Carter, **Jan. 21,** pardoned almost all draft evaders of the Vietnam War era, but made no decision on the status of those who deserted the armed forces during that period. Those pardoned numbered about 10,000, most of them white, middle- and upper-class men who had either fled the country or refused to enter the military service. On the status of deserters, Carter said he would "immediately" initiate a study of a process that might speed review of their cases with a view toward upgrading less-than-honorable discharges. This group, estimated at 100,000, included many black, poor, or disadvantaged young men. The announcement brought mild praise from pro-amnesty groups, but drew many protests, some vehement, from veterans organizations and conservative politicians. William J. Rogers, the national chairman of the 28-million member American Legion, stated that the pardon would be "more divisive than healing."

Carter Calls for Nuclear Test Halt — In his first interview as president, Jimmy Carter, **Jan. 24,** called for a halt to all nuclear testing, including underground tests, "instantly and completely" as part of a broader program to curb the spread of nuclear weapons and ultimately ban them entirely. Carter described a 3-step effort to accomplish the goal: the U.S. and USSR would first "put firm limits" on themselves regarding the number of strategic weapons they held; the 2 nations then would actually reduce their own stockpiles of atomic weapons "to demonstrate to the world we are sincere"; finally, he would seek "reductions including all nations, even those who have a relatively small inventory now." Carter admitted that he did not know whether the Soviet Union would accept his plan, but was optimistic that there would be "fairly rapid ratification" of a new treaty with the USSR on strategic arms limitation.

Severe Cold Grips Nation, Creates Gas Shortage — Bitter cold temperatures in January, exacerbated by a fierce blizzard that roared across the central states to the east coast at month's end, depleted the nation's supply of natural gas, forcing severe curtailment of energy use, closing schools, factories, and businesses, and putting 2 million people out of work at the peak of the crisis. As the situation grew worse, Pres. Jimmy Carter, **Jan. 26,** sent a bill to Congress requesting emergency authorization for federal allocation of natural gas supplies from surplus areas to shortage areas. The legislation also called for suspension until July 31 of federal price ceilings for extra gas sold to interstate pipelines to replenish reserves depleted by the bitter cold in all regions east of the Rocky Mountains. The House and Senate, **Feb. 2,** passed the emergency legislation, giving Carter his first legislative victory. Carter congratulated Congress, but added, "The real problem — our failure to plan for the future or to take energy conservation seriously — started long before this winter and will take much longer to solve."

$31.1-Billion Economic Plan Introduced — The Carter administration, **Jan. 27,** sent to Congress a $31.1-billion economic stimulation plan. The plan, which had been in the works since well before the inauguration, included a $50 rebate on 1976 taxes to each taxpayer and dependent to spur economic growth through greater consumption. The plan, which would cover 2 years, called for $15.5 billion of stimulus in fiscal year 1977, including tax cuts of $13.8 billion and spending of $1.7 billion on jobs programs, and, in fiscal year 1978, tax cuts totaling $8.1 billion and spending of $7.6 billion. During the first year, a total of $11.4 billion would be provided for tax rebates. The same rebate paid to taxpayers would also be paid to poor families filing for federal earned income credit. The plan also proposed a permanent tax reduction, $4 billion annually, for individuals in lower-income brackets. The administration package also would provide permanent tax cuts for business amounting to $2.6 billion per year. Treasury Secretary W. Michael Blumenthal, testifying before the House Budget Committee on the details of the plan, explained, "The tax features of the program have a two-fold purpose: to provide a quick injection of spending into the national economy and also to take the first step in a tax simplification and tax reform program."

International

Israeli Housing Minister Commits Suicide — In a severe blow to the already shaky Labor government, Israeli Housing Minister Abraham Ofer, **Jan. 3,** committed suicide. In the previous 2 days, his name had been linked in the press with an investigation into financial dealings involving a construction company with ties to the Labor party. Ofer left a note denying complicity in any illegal deals. Prime Minister Yitzhak Rabin, **Jan. 5,** at the state funeral for Ofer, said he believed the deceased minister to have been innocent of the embezzlement charges against him in newspaper reports.

Daoud Release Draws Widespread Criticism — The release, **Jan. 11,** by a French court of Abu Daoud, a militant Palestinian leader suspected of having planned the attack on the Israeli team at the 1972 Olympics in Munich, West Germany, encountered harsh criticism in Israel and the West. Daoud was arrested, **Jan. 7,** in Paris, but freed after a French court rejected extradition motions by Israel and West Germany, judging that Israel had no right of extradition and that the West German claim had not been properly formulated. Daoud was immediately expelled from France and flown to Algeria. In protest against the release, Israel, **Jan. 11,** recalled its ambassador to France and Foreign Minister Yigal Allon said the release amounted to "abject surrender to the pressure exercised by Arab countries and the threats of terror organizations." The U.S. expressed "dismay" at the release of Daoud. French Prime Minister Raymond Barre, **Jan. 13,** rejected all allegations that the French court decision had been politically motivated, explaining it was a purely judicial decision. Protest against the release spread **Jan. 14,** with calls from U.S. congressmen and Jewish leaders for a boycott of French goods and travel to France. As attacks on France continued, French Pres. Valery Giscard d'Estaing, **Jan. 17,** blamed West Germany for the release because the West German government had failed to reply through proper channels on its intentions. The French president also denounced "a campaign of insult and vilification against the honor and dignity of France." Judicial authorities in Bavaria, where Munich is the state capital, claimed they had been preparing a dossier to support charges against Daoud and had understood that they had 21 days in which to prepare their case under the French-West German extradition treaty.

Gandhi Relaxes Emergency Rule, Calls Elections — Declaring her "unshakeable faith in the power of the people," Indian Prime Minister Indira Gandhi, **Jan. 18,** in New Delhi, called parliamentary elections for March. The elections, the first since Gandhi imposed a state of emergency on June 26, 1975, signaled a major relaxation of that 19-month-old regime. Just 3 hours prior to the unexpected announcement, Gandhi had freed from prison 2 major political foes, former Deputy Prime Minister Morarji R. Desai and

L. K. Adrani, the leader of the right-wing Hindu nationalist Jan Sangh party. Political observers opined that Gandhi had called elections because of the favorable state of the economy, the desire for an improved image abroad, and the feeling that her Congress party would easily dominate the elections. Two days later, the Indian government ended press censorship and instructed state authorities to "expedite" the release of their political prisoners. The opposition's election campaign opened formally **Jan. 23**, as opposition leader Jaya Prakash Narayan sharply attacked Gandhi: "The choice is nothing less than between democracy and a fascist type of dictatorship." Fifty thousand Indians, **Jan. 30**, gathered in New Delhi for the first anti-government rally permitted since the imposition of the emergency. Desai, the leader of the newly formed Janata or People's party, told the crowd that the "future of India rests upon this election."

Riots Force Sadat to Cancel Price Raises — Following 2 days of angry rioting, Egyptian Pres. Anwar Sadat, **Jan. 19**, cancelled new price increases imposed on food, cooking fuel, and other products **Jan. 17**. The price rises were part of an effort to reduce the large deficit in the national budget and to bolster the economy. Enraged, thousands of students and workers in Cairo and other cities took to the streets, **Jan. 18**, shouting "Down with Sadat." They smashed cars, set fire to police stations, demolished buses, and broke street lamps. Specially-trained police with riot batons and tear gas grenades fanned through the streets to control the rioters. **Al Ahram**, a semi-official newspaper, reported, **Jan. 19**, that 21 persons had been killed, 360 injured, and 439 arrested in Cairo and Alexandria during the 2 days of rioting. The Sadat government, **Jan. 21**, blamed "communists and their allies" for the disorders. It was apparent that the accusation would facilitate an Egyptian appeal to staunchly anti-communist Saudi Arabia and other oil-producing countries for desperately needed financial assistance.

7 Die as Political Violence Sweeps Spain — A wave of political violence **Jan. 23-24**, took 7 lives in Madrid and spread fear throughout Spain. Thousands of workers in Madrid and Barcelona, **Jan. 25**, went on strike to protest the violence. The violence was attributed to a right-wing campaign to undermine the nation's progress toward representative government. The press persistently reported the machinations of the so-called Fascist International in Spain. One male student died **Jan. 23**, when communist-led demonstrators demanding full political amnesty clashed with police. A young woman died in another political demonstration **Jan. 24**, and 5 others died when gunmen invaded the communist-led Workers Commission offices and opened fire. Earlier in the day, Lt. Gen. Emilio Villaescusa Quilis, who headed the military tribunal which had tried major political cases under the Franco regime, was kidnapped, purportedly by the First of October Anti-Fascist Resistance. Since **Dec. 11**, the group also had held Antonio Maria de Oriol y Urquijo, a conservative former justice minister. The timing of the kidnapping raised suspicions that the Anti-Fascist Resistance might be a front for rightist organizations. On **Jan. 26**, the Spanish government announced a ban on public demonstrations, expelled foreigners with "extremist" sympathies, and restricted the use of private arms. The government accused the extremists of trying to "provoke" the armed forces. The government stated that it would continue with plans to hold national elections. Prime Minister Adolfo Suarez, **Jan. 28**, following the shooting deaths of 3 policemen, issued a royal decree suspending constitutional rights for 30 days. On **Jan. 29**, Suarez issued an emotional appeal to the Spanish people to remain calm in the face of terrorism intended to upset "our march toward civilized coexistence."

Mondale Travels to Europe and Japan — On the first leg of a journey to Europe and Japan, U.S. Vice President Walter F. Mondale, **Jan. 23**, in Brussels, Belgium, reassured NATO officials that the new Carter administration would maintain a strong commitment to the Atlantic alliance. Mondale, **Jan. 24**, told the 15-member NATO council that in view of increased Soviet military strength in Europe, the Carter administration was prepared to increase defense spending in NATO. But, Mondale warned, this increased spending would be dependent on further defense spending by other allies. Later in the day, in Bonn, West Germany, Mondale encouraged Chancellor Helmut Schmidt to prod the West German economy into faster growth and to stem the export of nuclear technology to Brazil. However, after nearly 4 hours of talks, it appeared that the 2 nations still disagreed on the 2 issues. Mondale, **Jan. 26**, continued to Rome where he met with Italian Premier Giulio Andreotti and, **Jan. 27**, with Pope Paul VI. Then Mondale flew to Great Britain where he conferred with Prime Minister James Callaghan on the slow economic recovery of the world's industrial democracies. Mondale's next stop was Paris where, **Jan. 29**, in talks with Pres. Valery Giscard d'Estaing, he renewed his plea for a curb in exports of nuclear technology, this time in reference to the sale of a nuclear-processing plant to Pakistan. Beginning the last leg of his world tour, Mondale, **Jan. 30**, flew to Japan where he affirmed continued U.S. political and economic links to Japan and the rest of Asia. On **Feb. 1**, he told the Japanese people, "the U. S. should and will remain an Asian power." Summing up his whirlwind tour, Mondale said he had been delighted with the "warm reception" he had received everywhere and "the candor which characterized our discussions."

Smith Rejects British Rhodesia Proposals — Rhodesian Prime Minister Ian D. Smith, **Jan. 24**, in Salisbury, rejected British proposals for a transition government leading to black rule in 14 months, effectively dashing British attempts to reconvene the Geneva conference on Rhodesia. Smith told Rhodesians that he had acted against the proposals because they allowed for immediate control of the country by a "Marxist-indoctrinated minority." Ivor Richard, the British chairman of the Geneva conference who had presented the proposals to Smith, said he saw no purpose in returning to Geneva until Smith changed his stance.

U.S. Accuses Czechoslovakia of Rights Violations — The U.S. state department, **Jan. 26**, accused Czechoslovakia of violating provisions of the 1975 Helsinki accord on east-west cooperation by its arrest and harassment of human rights activists. It was the first instance in which the U.S., which usually had refrained from commenting on the internal affairs of other countries, publicly accused a nation of violating the Helsinki accord. The accusation stemmed from Czechoslovak government harassment of signers of Charter 77, a call for human rights issued **Jan. 6** and signed by 241 prominent Czechoslovaks.

State Department Supports Sakharov — The U.S. state department, **Jan. 27**, warned the USSR that if it tried to silence political dissident Andrei D. Sakharov, it would be in conflict "with accepted international standards of human rights." The warning followed a recent complaint voiced by Sakharov that Soviet authorities had launched a new campaign to harass and intimidate political dissidents. Specifically, the deputy prosecutor had told Sakharov that he faced criminal charges unless he stopped his "hostile and slanderous" activities. On **Jan. 28**, a group of 4 Soviet writers associated with the dissident movement in Moscow asked western leaders, including U.S. Pres. Jimmy Carter, to give their support to Sakharov. It was reported that Sakharov had sent a letter, dated **Jan. 21**, to Jimmy Carter asking him to "raise your voice" on behalf of persecuted political and religious activists in the Soviet Union and Eastern Europe. Tass, the official Soviet news agency, **Jan. 29**, accused the U.S. state department of engaging in "unsavory play" in issuing a statement in support of Sakharov. Carter, **Jan. 30**, said that although he had not known about the warning prior to its release, it had reflected his attitude. "We're not going to back down on the issue of human rights," Carter asserted.

General

Longet Guilty on Lesser Charge — An Aspen, Col., jury, **Jan. 14**, found Claudine Longet guilty of criminally negligent homicide in the shooting death of her lover, Vladimir "Spider" Sabich, a champion skiier. She had been originally charged with reckless manslaughter, a felony. Accompanied by her ex-husband, singer Andy Williams, Longet showed no emotion as the verdict was read. On **Jan. 31**, Longet was sentenced to serve 30 days in prison "at a time of her own choosing," placed on 2 year's probation, and fined $25.

Gilmore Executed — The nation's 10-year stay on capital punishment ended **Jan. 17**, when Gary Mark Gilmore was executed by a firing squad, by his own choice, at the Utah State Prison, in Point of the Mountain, Utah. Gilmore, 35, had been convicted of the July 1976 slaying of a young hotel manager in Provo, Utah. The much-postponed and disputed execution followed a tension-filled night which culminated when a panel of 3 circuit judges overturned a stay of execution won by death penalty opponents just 7 hours prior to the scheduled execution. Federal District Judge Willis Ritter, in Salt Lake City, had granted a 10-day restraining order to postpone the execution. The tangled events leading to Gilmore's death began **Nov. 10, 1976**, when the Utah Supreme Court had ruled, 4-to-1, that Gilmore, who had made a plea to "die like a man," be executed by firing squad Nov. 15. Gilmore had told the court, "I believe I have been given a fair trial, and I think the sentence was proper, and I am willing to accept it like a man and wish it to be carried out without delay." The execution was postponed for the first time **Nov. 11**, when Utah Gov. Calvin L. Rampton stayed it until the Board of Pardons had time to determine if the punishment was fair. Frustrated and angry at the delay, Gilmore, **Nov. 16**, took an overdose of barbiturates in an apparent suicide pact with his girlfriend, Nicole Barrett. Both were hospitalized, Barrett in a coma. On **Nov. 30**, the pardons board, 2-1, granted Gilmore's plea for execution and, **Dec. 1**, the date was reset for Dec. 6 at sunrise. However, on **Dec. 2**, Bessie Gilmore, the convicted murderer's mother, asked the Supreme Court to block the execution long enough to enable her to seek a full review by the court of the conviction and sentence. The Supreme Court, **Dec. 3**, indefinitely postponed the execution to give it time to consider the case; on **Dec. 13**, the court vacated the stay, sending the case back to the Utah courts.

Legionnaires' Disease Cause Traced — Federal scientists, **Jan. 19**, announced that they believed they had discovered the bacterium that had caused the mysterious legionnaires' disease. The disease had killed 29 persons who had been in Philadelphia during an American Legion convention in July 1976. The bacterium, previously unknown, was discovered by scientists at the Center for Disease Control in Atlanta. However, to date, the scientists had not identified the bacterium, its source, or manner of transmission. They did link the same bacterium to an earlier mysterious outbreak of fatal pneumonia among patients at St. Elizabeth's Hospital, a federal mental institution in Washington, D.C.

Ford Pardons Tokyo Rose — As one of his last official acts, Pres. Gerald R. Ford, **Jan. 20**, pardoned Iva Toguri D'Aquino, widely known as "Tokyo Rose." She had been convicted 27 years earlier for treason for her broadcasts for Japan to American servicemen in the Pacific during World War II. She had served 6½ years in prison. Pressure for the pardon had intensified in 1976 when the California legislature had unanimously applied to Ford for a pardon of D'Aquino, now, at age 60, a clerk in a gift shop in Chicago. As added support, the foreman of the jury that convicted her had admitted that the jurors had been inflamed by anti-Japanese feelings at the end of the war.

Yoshimura Guilty of Illegal Weapons Possession — Wendy Yoshimura, captured with Patricia Hearst in Sept. 1975, **Jan. 20**, was convicted in Alameda County, Cal., court on 3 counts of illegal possession of a machine gun and explosives. The charges originated from the March 1972 discovery of a large cache of explosives in a Berkeley garage. The 3 arrested outside of the garage had all pleaded guilty and served sentences. Yoshimura, who admitted at the trial that she had rented the garage under a false name, had disappeared after the arrests. On **Mar. 17**, Yoshimura was sentenced to serve from one to 15 years in a California state prison. Judge Martin Pulich said she would be resentenced to serve from 16 months to 3 years in July under a new law effective then.

Vatican Bars Women From Priesthood — In a declaration published by the Sacred Congregation for the Doctrine of the Faith, the Vatican, **Jan. 27**, affirmed that the Roman Catholic Church would refuse to ordain women as priests. According to the Vatican declaration, women could not qualify because Jesus was a man and His representatives on earth must bear a "natural resemblance" to him. Vatican spokesman, the Rev. Louis Ligier, at a Rome press conference, stated that the document committed the church for the whole future not simply for the duration of the present pontificate. Support for the stand, as presented in the document — commissioned, revised, and approved by the Pope — went back to the 13th century Pope Innocent III, who had written, "Although the Blessed Virgin Mary surpassed in dignity and in excellence all the Apostles, nevertheless it was not to her but to them that the Lord entrusted the keys to the Kingdom of Heaven."

New Trial Ordered for Boyle — The Pennsylvania Supreme Court, **Jan. 28**, in a 6-1 decision, ordered a new trial for W. A. Boyle, 74, former president of the United Mine Workers. Boyle was convicted 3 years earlier of ordering the murder of UMW insurgent Joseph A. Yablonski, his wife, and daughter. The ailing Boyle, serving 3 consecutive life terms, was in the hospital quarters at Pennsylvania State Penitentiary in Pittsburgh.

Disasters — The Panamanian-registered tanker Grand Zenith sank off Cape Cod, leaving no survivors among the ship's 30 Taiwanese crewmen, it was reported **Jan. 11** by the U.S. and Canadian Coast Guards . . . At least 90 persons died, **Jan. 13**, when a Soviet TU-104 airliner exploded and crashed into the Central Asian city of Alma-Ata . . . At least 46 American sailors and marines died **Jan. 17**, when a launch collided with a Spanish freighter and capsized in the Barcelona, Spain, harbor . . . In the worst rail disaster in Australian history, 82 persons died, **Jan. 18**, when a Sydney-bound commuter train derailed and smashed into the supports of an overhead bridge which collapsed and crushed 2 of the train's wooden cars.

FEBRUARY
National

Carter Gives First Report to the Nation — Seated by the fireside in the White House library, Pres. Jimmy Carter, **Feb. 2**, asked Americans in a nationally televised report to the nation to unite in a spirit of "cooperation and mutual effort" to help him develop "predictable long-range plans that we can be sure we can afford and that we know will work." For the first time, Carter outlined the steps he promised to take during his administration. Carter said he would soon put a "ceiling on the number of people employed by federal government agencies so we can bring the growth of government under control." He promised to "cut down on government regulations," to have them put in plain English, and to see that each new regulation would carry the author's name. He promised further that the code of financial disclosure he had imposed on his top appointees would be a "permanent" rule of government. To "conduct an open administration" as he had promised during the campaign, Carter said he would hold town meetings across the country "where you can criticize, make suggestions, and ask questions." Carter also said his 1977 program would center on development of a national energy policy based on conservation. Also on the agenda would be steps to begin reorganization of the government, a program of "comprehensive tax reform," reform of the welfare system, and a foreign policy that would show continued "concern about the violations of human rights."

Turner Named CIA Head — Pres. Jimmy Carter, **Feb. 7**, nominated Adm. Stansfield Turner to be director of Central Intelligence. A military analyst who had spent a part of his career in weapons systems analysis and the study of strategic deterrence, Turner was commander of allied forces in Southern Europe. Carter described his former Annapolis classmate as having been "so far ahead of us" as a midshipman that "we never considered him a competitor or even a peer." Initial response to the nomination indicated that it would not encounter the kind of criticism that had forced Theodore C. Sorensen, Carter's original choice, to withdraw his name. Turner was confirmed **Feb. 24**.

Frigid Winter Affected Economy — January's cold weather and resulting higher prices for food and fuel hit the economy hard. The labor department, **Feb. 18**, reported that the seasonally adjusted consumer price index had risen sharply, 0.8%, in January. Projected on an annual basis, the increase represented an annual rate of 9.6% compared to 4.8% for all of 1976. Further evidence on the effects of January's cold weather came **Feb. 28**, when the commerce department reported that the composite index that foretells the nation's economic condition had fallen 1.2% in January. This drop in the index of leading indicators was the biggest since January 1975 during the depths of the 1974-75 depression. At the same time, the labor department reported that trade had registered the biggest deficit on record during January, $1.67 billion. Despite the poor figures, economists stated there was no indication of a basic interruption in the cyclical uptrend that had begun in September 1975.

Carter Sends Congress Revised 1978 Budget — Pres. Jimmy Carter, **Feb. 22**, sent to Congress revisions for the fiscal 1978 budget submitted by former Pres. Gerald R. Ford in January. The revisions projected a sizeable increase in spending and deficits for 1977 and 1978 to make room for Carter's economic stimulus package and placed more emphasis than Ford on energy and domestic social problems. The Carter budget also showed a slight decline over the Ford budget of $400 million in defense spending in 1978. Carter set federal spending for 1977 at $417.4 billion, or $6.2 billion more than the Ford budget, and projected a $68 billion deficit, up from Ford's $57.2 billion. For 1978, Carter set total outlays at $459.4 billion, an increase of $19.4 billion over Ford's plan, and a deficit of $57.7 billion as compared to Ford's $47 billion. Although the basic underpinnings of the budget would be largely a Ford product, the revisions, Carter stated in an accompanying message to Congress, were "important first steps toward a federal government that is more effective and responsive to our people's needs." Although Carter's revisions did not reflect many of his expensive campaign promises such as national health insurance and welfare reform, he did scrap Ford proposals to cut food stamps, child nutrition programs, Medicare, and Medicaid.

4 Watergate Burglars Win Settlement — Daniel E. Schultz, attorney for 4 of the men arrested in the 1972 Watergate break-in, said, **Feb. 22**, the 4 men had agreed to an out-of-court settlement that would give them $200,000 from former Pres. Richard M. Nixon's 1972 campaign fund. Bernard L. Barker, Eugenio R. Martinez, Virgilio R. Gonzales, and Frank A. Sturgis, all members of Miami's anti-Castro Cuban exile community, had originally sued for $2 million, charging they had been misled into believing they were acting with government sanction. Schultz said the settlement proved the charge was right because "You don't agree to pay $200,000 unless you're concerned about the outcome."

International

Ethiopian Head of State Killed in Gun Battle— Ethiopian Chief of State Brig. Gen. Tafari Banti and 6 other members of the nation's governing council were killed, **Feb. 3**, in a gun battle amidst a factional dispute in Addis Ababa. The victims were accused of plotting a coup against the government and being allied with the leftist opposition Ethiopian People's Revolutionary Party and the right-wing opposition movement, the Ethiopian Democratic Union. The apparent victor in the power struggle, Lt. Col. Mengistu Haile Mariam, the first vice chairman of the ruling council, **Feb. 4**, addressed a rally estimated at 200,000 people and called for the arming of the people to protect Ethiopia's 28-month-old "Socialist revolution." He urged the people to join in forming a workers' party to continue the social changes begun since the overthrow of Haile Selassie in 1974. Foreign diplomats in Addis Ababa reported, **Feb. 9**, that a wave of arrests had followed the power struggle and that the government had started arming members of the Urban Dwellers Association, which administers local community affairs.

7 Missionaries Killed in Rhodesia—A dozen black guerrillas, **Feb. 6**, killed 7 white Roman Catholic missionaries at a mission station 37 miles northeast of Salisbury, Rhodesia. According to a black nun, who along with other blacks was not harmed, the guerrillas had said, "We want our country." A senior government official stated, "Our reaction is the same as everyone else's — shock and horror." On **Feb. 10**, as the 7 missionaries were buried, the government and Roman Catholic hierarchy argued publicly over the causes of death. Bishop Donal Lamont, a black Jesuit and the church's foremost critic of the Rhodesian government, accused the government of being "remotely responsible" for the killings. Prime Minister Ian Smith, noting Lamont had previously been convicted for failing to report the presence of black insurgents in his diocese, attacked the cleric: "Under those circumstances, I don't think it would surprise anyone that he has resorted to that kind of talk."

Spain, USSR Resume Relations—Spain and the USSR, **Feb. 9,** resumed diplomatic relations. Relations had been broken off 38 years before at the end of the Spanish civil war. Spain also resumed full relations with Hungary and Czechoslovakia. Madrid had resumed ties with Rumania, Bulgaria, Poland, and Yugoslavia in January. The resumption of ties with the Soviet Union and Eastern Europe was considered an important step toward consolidating the position of Premier Adolfo Suarez and easing the status of the Spanish Communist party. On **Feb. 8,** the government had announced a major reform of its restrictive political reform law, eliminating the cabinet's power to deny legality to a political party.

Vance Goes on Middle East Mission—U.S. Secretary of State Cyrus R. Vance, **Feb. 15-21,** visited Israel and 5 Arab nations on a fact-finding mission aimed at breaking the 18-month impasse in Middle East peace discussions. In Jerusalem, **Feb. 16,** Vance told a press conference that the Palestine Liberation Organization had no basis for participation in a conference on the Middle East until it revised its national charter to recognize Israel's right to exist. His statement, in effect an endorsement of the Israeli position, was the first public U.S. call for modification of the PLO covenant. On **Feb. 17,** in a joint news conference with Vance in Cairo, Egyptian Pres. Anwar Sadat, offered a surprise proposal to break the impasse, suggesting the Palestinians form "an official and declared link" with Jordan even before a Geneva peace conference were convened. If carried out, the proposal would make possible Palestinian participation at the conference. However Jordanian King Hussein, **Feb. 18,** told Vance that he was reluctant to form a link with the PLO until key Arab leaders formally joined Sadat in endorsing such a proposal. He also warned Vance against being overly optimistic about an early breakthrough in negotiations. Hussein's negative attitude was echoed, **Feb. 20,** by Syrian Pres. Hafez al-Assad. However, a **Feb. 22-23** meeting in Amman, Jordan, between representatives of Jordan and the PLO ended in a tentative agreement in "principle" on a link between Jordan and a proposed Palestinian state in the West Bank and Gaza Strip.

Sakharov Receives Letter of Support from Carter—Amidst increasing repression of dissidents in the Soviet Union, leading Soviet dissident Andrei D. Sakharov, **Feb. 17,** received a letter of support from U.S. Pres. Jimmy Carter, assuring him of the U.S. commitment to human rights. "Because we are free, we can never be indifferent to the fate of freedom elsewhere," Carter had written. The Soviet Union, **Feb. 18,** warned that such official expressions of sympathy and support for Soviet dissidents could damage relations. In Washington, D.C., Soviet Ambassador Anatoly Dobrynin delivered a message to Acting Secretary of State Arthur A. Hartman, stating that the USSR "resolutely rejects attempts to interfere, under a thought-up pretext of defending human rights, in its internal affairs." The Carter administration stoutly defended the letter and asserted that it had not been an attempt to challenge the Soviet Government. Earlier, following U.S. expression of concern about the arrests of 2 dissidents, Aleksander I. Ginzburg and Yuri Orlov, the USSR had attacked dissidents as pawns of the West. "These unconcealed enemies of socialism," a **Feb. 12 Pravda** editorial had stated, "are just a handful of individuals who do not represent anyone or anything and are far removed from the Soviet people. What is more, they exist only because they are supported, paid, and praised by the West."

Foreign leaders linked to CIA Payments—The CIA made secret payments totaling millions of dollars to Jordan's King Hussein for 20 years, the **Washington Post** reported **Feb. 18.** According to the **Post,** Pres. Jimmy Carter had learned of the payments several days earlier and had ordered them stopped. The report came just as Secretary of State Cyrus R. Vance was conferring with Hussein in Jordan on attempts to overcome the impasse in Middle East peace negotiations. The White House issued a statement praising Hussein as an "outstanding national leader," who had "played a constructive role in reducing tensions in the Middle East." Simultaneously, Presidential Press Secretary Jody Powell said it was administration policy not to confirm or deny "any stories concerning alleged covert activities." Meanwhile, reports from unnamed intelligence sources suggested payments had also been made to other leaders, including Taiwan's Chiang Kai-shek, South Korea's Syngman Rhee, Ngo Dinh Diem of South Vietnam, and Sese Seko Mobuto of Zaire. Carter, **Feb. 23,** while declining to comment "directly on any specific CIA activity," said he had found nothing "illegal or improper" when he had reviewed the more controversial activities of the CIA. "It can be extremely dangerous to our relationship with other nations, to the potential security of our country even in peacetime, for these kinds of operations which are legitimate and proper to be revealed." On **Feb. 25,** Carter confirmed to Congressional leaders that the payments had been made, but said he had found "nothing whatever wrong" with the arrangement with Hussein. Vance, appearing on "Face the Nation" **Feb. 27,** termed the practice of channeling secret funds to foreign leaders as "appropriate." He stated that the things could not be done in "the glare of publicity."

Crosland Dies, Succeeded by Owen—British Foreign Secretary Anthony Crosland died, **Feb. 19,** leaving Prime Minister James Callaghan with no ready solution for his replacement. Callaghan had been planning to move Crosland to the Exchequer in July and bring Chancellor of the Exchequer Denis Healey to the foreign ministry, but Healey was considered indispensable at the Treasury in Britain's struggle against inflation. Consequently, Callaghan, **Feb. 21,** named Dr. David Owen, at 38 the youngest man to hold the post since Anthony Eden in 1935, to head the foreign ministry. Owen, a physician who had been serving as minister of state in the foreign office, was told the job was his permanently, not as a caretaker for Healey or anyone else.

Rabin Re-elected to Lead Labor Party—In a highly charged atmosphere, Israel's Labor party, **Feb. 23,** chose Prime Minister Yitzhak Rabin by a narrow margin to lead the party into the May 17 national elections and be its candidate for a 2d term as head of the government. In the first instance of a challenge to an incumbent, Defense Minister Shimon Peres had waged a tough campaign against Rabin, losing by only 41 of some 3,000 votes. Rabin had received much criticism because of Israel's economic troubles, soaring inflation rate, and heavy tax burdens. The Labor party had also been beset by scandal and divisiveness. On **Feb. 22,** Asher Yadlin, a prominent Labor party leader, had been sentenced to 5 years in prison for taking bribes. He had pleaded guilty, **Feb. 14,** saying he had taken real estate kickbacks under pressure from Labor party leaders, 2 of whom were presently cabinet ministers.

U.S. Aid to Human Rights Violators Reduced—For the first time in memory, it was announced, **Feb. 24**, that U.S. aid to certain foreign countries would be reduced because of human rights violations in those countries. Reporting to the Senate Appropriations Committee on Foreign Operations, Secretary of State Cyrus R. Vance, said the countries included Argentina, Uruguay, and Ethiopia. However, Vance said aid would not be reduced to South Korea and other strategically-placed allies because of overriding security commitments. Vance explained that the "very difficult task" of balancing foreign assistance with human rights considerations had to be handled on a country-by-country basis. He admitted that the U.S. ran the risk of appearing hypocritical by cutting aid to one friendly nation and maintaining it to another, even though both might be equally guilty of human rights violations.

Amin Orders Meeting with Americans in Uganda—Ugandan Pres. Idi Amin, **Feb. 25**, ordered all U.S. citizens in Uganda, some 200 people, mostly missionaries, to meet with him the following Monday and barred them from leaving the country before then. At the same time, he sent a message to U.S. Pres. Jimmy Carter expressing his anger at official U.S. condemnations of recent events in Uganda, chiefly the controversial death of the Ugandan archbishop and reports of widespread killings. Despite a later Ugandan announcement that there was no need for alarm over the meeting, Carter sent word that the U.S. would not tolerate any attempt to use Americans as hostages. An international outcry had mounted over the **Feb. 16** deaths of Janari Luwum, the Anglican archbishop of Uganda and 2 cabinet ministers, allegedly in an auto accident. According to Ugandan radio, the accident had occurred when the 3 had tried to escape after being accused of involvement in an alleged plot against Amin. Church, political leaders, and human rights groups all over the world rejected the official Ugandan version of their deaths. On **Feb. 21**, the Tanzanian government paper, the **Daily News**, reported that Amin had personally killed the archbishop during a torture session. Meanwhile, refugees arriving from Uganda in Tanzania brought reports of widespread killings, predominantly of members of the Christian Lango and Acholi tribes. On **Feb. 26**, Amin stated that he never had any intention of making Americans hostages, but wanted to meet with them, now on Wednesday, to congratulate them on work done in Uganda. Then, after another postponement of the meeting, Amin, **Mar. 1**, cancelled his ban on American departure from Uganda and indefinitely postponed the meeting. U.S. Secretary of State Cyrus R. Vance called the decision a "very positive step."

General

Hustler Editor Guilty on Obscenity Charge—A Cincinnati, Ohio, jury, **Feb. 8**, found Larry Flynt, editor and publisher of **Hustler**, a national men's magazine, guilty of engaging in organized crime and pandering obscenity. He was immediately sentenced to 7 to 25 years in prison and fined $10,000 for the organized crime conviction and given 6 months in jail and a $1,000 fine for the obscenity charge. The magazine, also found guilty on both counts, was fined $10,000 and $1,000 respectively. Organized crime is defined in Ohio statute as the combination of 5 or more persons in an illegal activity for profit. Civil libertarians had watched the trial closely as a major test of the application of community obscenity standards to national publications. Herald Price Fahringer, Flynt's attorney had argued that the Hamilton County (Ohio) prosecutor had no jurisdiction over the editorial and production operation of the magazine — it is published in Columbus, Ohio, printed in Dayton, and distributed from Derby, Conn. Fahringer had maintained that a conviction would mean that no national publication would be safe from obscenity charges brought by a local prosecutor.

Woman, Black Named to Top California Court—Broadening the make-up of the California Supreme Court, California Gov. Edmund G. Brown Jr., **Feb. 12**, named Rose Elizabeth Bird chief justice and Superior Court Judge Wiley Manuel, a black, an associate justice. It was the first time in its history that the court included a woman or a black. The California Trial Lawyers Association, hailed the appointment of Bird, Brown's secretary of agriculture and services, as "one of the most significant acts since the inception of the Brown administration."

Gunman Kills 5 in New Rochelle Shooting Spree—a recently suspended moving company employee, 33-year-old Frederick W. Cowan, **Feb. 14**, killed 5 persons and wounded 5 others in a shooting spree in New Rochelle, N.Y., and then killed himself. Armed with a semi-automatic rifle, Cowan invaded the office-warehouse complex of the Neptune Worldwide Co., and killed 4 co-workers and wounded 2 others. Then he killed one arriving policeman and wounded 3 more. A twice-court-martialed army veteran, Cowan lifted weights and had modeled for body-building magazines. Cowan had been suspended from his job 2 weeks before for being rude to a customer and vowed to "get even" with the supervisor who had disciplined him. He was also known as a gun collector with a fascination for the Nazi period. Police, **Feb. 15**, began investigating a possible link with a militant racist organization believed to be the National States Rights Party.

Sale of Atlantic Oil Leases Voided—U.S. District Court Judge Jack B. Weinstein, **Feb. 17**, voided the government's sale of $1.13 billion in leases for oil and gas drilling rights off the Atlantic Coast. Weinstein also ruled that former Interior Secretary Thomas Kleppe had been guilty in 1976 of consistently violating the National Environmental Protection Act. Weinstein voided the leases because he had concluded that there was considerable evidence that environmental impact statements and public hearings on the matter had been a "charade." "The decision to lease was a foregone conclusion once presidents and those in their administrations, including successive secretaries of interior, decided some years ago that production of Atlantic hydrocarbons should proceed steadily," Weinstein said.

45 Dead in Moscow Hotel Fire—According to an unidentified Soviet medical source, 45 persons died, **Feb. 25**, when a major fire roared through Moscow's 5,250-bed Rossiya Hotel, the world's largest. None of the 200 Americans staying in the hotel were harmed. Soviet officials refused to publish casualty figures or a photograph of the destruction in the news media.

MARCH

National

Economy Recovers From January Cold—The labor department, **Mar. 4**, reported that national unemployment in February had risen to a seasonally adjusted 7.3%. The increase, only 0.2% over the January rate, was lower than many had expected after the plant shutdowns and business decline caused by January's frigid weather. More optimistic news came **Mar. 15**, when the Federal Reserve Board reported that the nation's mines, factories, and utilities had snapped back in late February from the cold-weather slump. The board reported that industrial production had risen a seasonally adjusted 1% in February. The increase had followed a revised decline of 0.8% in January. The labor department reported, **Mar. 18**, that consumer prices advanced 1% in February, the largest increase in nearly 2-1/2 years. By month's end, experts concluded that the economy seemed to have overcome the effects of one of the coldest winters of the century. The experts predicted that the economy was moving toward an annual growth rate of 5% or more and, by year's end, might be within striking distance of a $2 trillion gross national product.

Carter Conducts Radio Call-In—In a first for a U.S. president, Pres. Jimmy Carter, **Mar. 5**, conducted a 2-hour nationwide radio call-in program. On the program, moderated by CBS-TV anchorman Walter Cronkite, Carter answered questions from 42 persons in 26 states. The questions, some hostile, ranged from those of a personal nature to topics of national interest. Reflecting the concerns of ordinary citizens, a great many of the questions centered on taxes and the rising cost of health care. Commenting on the kinds of questions, Carter noted that they were of a sort "you never get in a press conference." On substantive issues, Carter promised a caller a comprehensive tax reform program by Sept. 30. He indicated that he would seek "early" discussions with Cuba on various issues, but warned that restoration of diplomatic recognition would hinge on Cuban respect for human rights and restraint from interference in the Western Hemisphere and Africa. Carter told another caller that he was encouraged by Vietnam's response to steps he had taken toward possible normalization of relations between the 2 countries.

Hanafi Moslems Seize Washington Buildings—Hanafi Moslem gunmen, **Mar. 9**, invaded the B'nai B'rith building in Washington, D.C., and seized several hostages. Several hours later, more Hanafi gunmen took over the District Building and Islamic Center and Mosque, again taking hostages. Maurice Williams, a Howard University reporter, was killed during the invasion of the District Building and another 19 persons were injured during the takeovers. The leader of the gunmen, Hamaas Abdul Khaalis, said the motive was retribution "by the sword" in a "holy war" against rival Black Muslims held responsible for the slayings of 7 Hanafi Moslems in 1973. The gunmen demanded and got the cancellation of New York City and New Jersey performances of a film about the prophet Mohammed. They further demanded, **Mar. 10**, delivery into their hands of 8 convicted murderers, all Moslems serving prison sentences for the 1965 killing of Malcolm X and the murder of the 7 Hanafi followers. Tense negotiations between Khaalis and the ambassadors from Iran, Egypt, and Pakistan, took place at the Hanafi command headquarters at the B'nai B'rith building. The twelve Hanafi gunmen released over 100 hostages and surrendered to police **Mar. 11**. The hostages had been held for a period of 38 hours. The surrender agreement included a provision that Khaalis be released without bail after arraignment, apparently a face-saving gesture. Khaalis, **Mar. 14**, was officially booked for armed kidnapping and released. Eight gunmen were jailed and held on bail of $50,000-$70,000, and 3 others, with no previous arrest records, were released in their own recognizance.

Senate Confirms Warnke as Arms Negotiator—following a 4-day debate, the Senate, **Mar. 10**, in a 58-40 vote, confirmed the controversial nomination of Paul C. Warnke as the nation's chief arms negotiator. The vote, however, fell short of the 67 votes needed to approve any treaty Warnke might negotiate. Pres. Jimmy Carter, at a news conference prior to the vote, had iterated his support for Warnke, stating that opposition would indicate "a lack of confidence in the Senate in my own ability as chief negotiator." Nevertheless, 12 Democrats, including Sen. Henry M. Jackson, a major critic of the Warnke nomination, joined 28 Republicans in opposing the nomination. In a related vote, Warnke was approved as director of the Arms Control and Disarmament Agency by a 70-29 margin. The confirmation followed a long debate and a torrential, conservative-supported, mail campaign against Warnke. Conservative criticism centered on Warnke's history of advocacy of unilateral arms restraints and the fear he would be conciliatory to the USSR. Warnke's attempt to downplay some of his positions at his confirmation hearings had brought charges that he had adopted a line that would secure the post for him.

Congress Nullifies Import of Rhodesian Chrome—the House, **Mar. 14**, and Senate, **Mar. 15**, approved legislation nullifying the Byrd amendment of 1971, thereby barring the import of Rhodesian chrome and chromium products. The amendment had put the U.S. in violation of UN sanctions against Rhodesia, although the U.S. had voted in favor of the economic embargo in 1966 and 1968. Pres. Jimmy Carter, who had committed his prestige to fight for repeal of the amendment, signed the bill into law **Mar. 18**.

Carter Makes First "Meet the People" Trip—Pres. Jimmy Carter, **Mar. 16**, began his "meet the people" program in Clinton, Mass. Speaking at an old-fashioned New England town meeting, Carter told the townspeople," I want the American people, in three or four years, not to look on the federal government as an enemy, but as a friend." He said he would attempt to build an administration that would be responsive to ordinary citizens. Carter then spent the night in the 3-story Victorian home of Edward G. Thompson, a manager for a beer-distributing company.

House Votes to Keep Assassinations Committee—the House, **Mar. 30**, decided to keep the embattled Select Committee on Assassinations in existence for another year. The life of the committee had been jeopardized by a bitter dispute between Texas Democrat Henry B. Gonzalez, the committee's former chairman, and its chief counsel Richard A. Sprague. Gonzalez, accusing Sprague of insubordination and creating disharmony, had attempted to dismiss the counsel. When 11 committee members backed Sprague, Gonzalez, **Mar. 2**, resigned. The decision to extend the life of the committee came after Sprague, advised that his continued presence would probably kill it, resigned. The committee was pursuing investigations into the deaths of Pres. John F. Kennedy and the Rev. Martin Luther King Jr.

Mansfield Named Envoy to Japan-Carter administration officials announced, **Mar. 30**, that former Senate Democratic leader Mike Mansfield had been selected to serve as ambassador to Japan. Prior to his legislative career, Mansfield had been professor of far eastern history at the University of Montana.

International

Major Earthquake Shakes Romania—A major earthquake registering 7.5 on the Richter scale, **Mar. 4**, shook southern and eastern Europe, causing seyere damage in Bucharest, Romania, where it claimed over 1,000 lives, including those of some prominent artists and writers. Another 6,000 persons were injured. Tremors were also reported in the USSR, Hungary, Yugoslavia, Austria, Bulgaria, northern Greece, and central Italy. Worst hit was the center of Bucharest where some buildings collapsed and most of those still standing suffered some damage. Pres. Nicolae Ceaucescu issued a decree mobilizing all state resources for a rescue operation. On **Mar. 6**, as civilian relief teams continued to remove hazards from the city, Rumanian officials revealed that the quake had apparently seriously impaired the nation's industrial capacity. One official estimated that it would take 4 or 5 years to reach prequake production levels. By **Mar. 8,** Romania asked countries sending aid to suspend shipments because the supply of food, drugs, medical equipment, and other materials was sufficient. Romania and the U.S., **Mar. 9,** agreed to collaborate during the critical coming weeks to monitor Romania's geological situation to determine if aftershocks would follow. Romania, **Mar. 11,** sent to the U.S. a list of specific requests for items necessary for its recovery. The requests included new data processing systems for their heavily damaged computer center, instruments for cardiology and other branches of medicine, replacements for destroyed machinery, and spare parts.

Carter Remarks to Rabin Cause Stir—Welcoming Israeli Prime Minister Yitzhak Rabin to the U.S., Pres. Jimmy Carter, **Mar. 7,** told the Israeli leader that in any Middle East settlement Israel should have "defensible borders" as an assurance the agreement would not be violated. It was the first time an American president had endorsed Israel's insistence on defensible borders. The statement caused an immediate stir. White House and state department officials immediately sought to reassure Arab nations, explaining the use of the words "defensible borders" did not indicate a shift in U.S. policy. At a news conference **Mar. 9,** Carter outlined principles for a Middle East settlement. Israel, Carter said, should ultimately withdraw from all Arab lands it had occupied during the 1967 war, with only "some minor adjustments" in the pre-war borders. Carter envisioned an 8-year period during which this settlement would be reached on a step-by-step basis. During the interim period, Carter suggested, Israel could have "defense lines" that "may be extensions of Israeli defense capability beyond the permanent and recognized borders." The Carter administration, again concerned about the possible repercussions of Carter's remarks, **Mar. 10,** contacted representatives of Israel and Arab nations to assure them that Carter's plan was not hard and fast and did not mean an end to American evenhandedness in negotiations. Egyptian Pres. Anwar Sadat, **Mar. 12,** stated that Egypt "will not cede a single inch of Arab land and that our national territory is not open to bargaining; the Israelis must withdraw from all occupied lands." Rabin, **Mar. 12,** on a taped television program, rejected Carter's plan, saying it called for Israel to give up "more territories" than "we want to give." "Without any qualification, Israel will not return to the lines that existed before the 1967 war," Rabin asserted.

Carter Ends Travel Restrictions—Pres. Jimmy Carter, **Mar. 9,** ended restrictions on travel by U.S. citizens to Cuba, Vietnam, North Korea, and Cambodia effective Mar. 18. Carter linked the action to his desire to improve the U.S.'s position on human rights in line with the 1975 Helsinki accords. "I have long been concerned about our nation's stance in prohibiting American citizens to travel to foreign countries," Carter stated. In a further step to ease relations with Cuba, the Carter administration, **Mar. 26,** lifted a ban on the spending of dollars by U.S. visitors in that country.

Pakistan Elections Assailed as Rigged—Following the overwhelming **Mar. 7** victory of Pakistani Prime Minister Zulfikar Ali Bhutto's Pakistan People's party in parliamentary elections, opposition leader Asghar Khan, **Mar. 8,** accused Bhutto of rigging the elections "on a very massive scale." Consequently, Khan announced, the opposition coalition Pakistan

---

Gandhi and Congress Party Defeated in Indian Elections; Desai Elected Prime Minister, Ram Joins New Government

In what was hailed worldwide as a stunning victory for democracy, Indian Prime Minister Indira Gandhi and the ruling Congress party, **Mar. 21,** were soundly defeated in national elections for the lower house of parliament. Gandhi's confidant and son, Sanjay Gandhi, as well as several senior cabinet members associated with India's 20-month-old emergency rule, were also defeated. It was the first time the Congress party, which had held 2/3 of the seats in the last parliament, had been turned out of power since the birth of the Indian state 30 years before.

In a surprise acknowledgement of its defeat, the government revoked emergency rule imposed in June 1975, ending officially what the opposition had called "the blackest period in Indian history."

In the final tally, the Janata or People's party led by Morarji R. Desai, held 271 seats in the 542-seat lower house of parliament; its ally, the Congress for Democracy led by Jagjivan Ram, held 28 seats; the Congress party had 153; the pro-Congress Communist party had 7 seats; and the Marxist (pro-China) Communist party held 22. The remaining seats were divided among minor parties and independents.

On **Mar. 22,** Gandhi, who had held office for 11 years, resigned. "The collective judgment of the people must be respected. My colleagues and I accept their verdict unreservedly and in a spirit of humility," Gandhi said.

The unpopularity of emergency rule and the defection of Jagjivan Ram from Gandhi's cabinet were the major factors in the surprising defeat of the Congress party. Ram, agriculture minister and leader of India's untouchables, had resigned, **Feb. 2,** with a stinging denunciation of emergency rule: "Citizens of the country have been deprived of all their freedoms. . . A fear psychosis has overtaken the whole nation. People are living in a state of constant fear and are silently suffering." He, along with Desai and Jaya Prakash Narayan, another leading opposition figure, had continued that theme throughout the campaign and promised to restore fundamental freedoms. Gandhi and her son, also campaigning for seats in parliament, had increasingly apologized for the excesses of emergency rule as the campaign progressed. Toward the end, Gandhi had stated that "to err is human," and had promised to punish "overzealous officials."

Following several days of negotiations after the elections, Desai, **Mar. 24,** was sworn in as prime minister. The final choice of prime minister had been left to Narayan, considered the spiritual force of the Janata party, and his colleague J.B. Kripalani, another moral leader, to avoid a growing dispute between Desai and Ram over the post. Desai immediately pledged "to drive fear out of the society." He said the government would begin immediately to revoke some of the emergency legislation, including press censorship and changes in the constitution. The government, **Mar. 22,** had already begun to release from prison members of political organizations banned since June 1975.

A minor crisis over the composition of Desai's cabinet was resolved **Mar. 27,** when Ram agreed to become minister of defense, bringing his Congress for Democracy into the new government. The new government coalition held 345 seats to 153 held by the Congress party.

National Alliance would boycott scheduled provincial elections. The Pakistan National Alliance had developed unexpected support in what had turned into a wide open parliamentary campaign. Bhutto ostensibly had nearly squashed all opposition since he took office 5 years before. The newly elected opposition members of parliament, **Mar. 9,** announced that they would not take their seats because the election had been rigged. The 9-party opposition, **Mar. 12,** called on Bhutto to resign and name a caretaker government so that new elections could be held. The air of crisis heightened **Mar. 14,** as the opposition staged large-scale demonstrations in several cities and engaged in hit-and-run battles with large army and police forces. More than 20 persons were killed, **Mar. 18,** in Karachi when police fired on rioters protesting the arrest of 4 opposition leaders, all leading figures in the Pakistan National Alliance. As the violent protests continued **Mar. 19,** the government placed one-third of Karachi under army rule and ordered all residents in the area to stay in their homes. A Pakistan National Alliance spokesman said some 50 persons had been killed and about 400 injured since the previous day. Another 24 opposition leaders were arrested **Mar. 25,** and security forces were ordered to shoot anyone committing arson, looting, and damaging property. On **Mar. 28,** as the rump parliament assembled, Bhutto defended his government and promised to consider lifting the state of emergency in effect since 1971 if the opposition would come to terms with his government.

Zaire Invaded From Angola—The Zaire government reported, **Mar. 10,** that unknown mercenaries had invaded the southern province of Shaba, formerly Katanga, from Angola **Mar. 8.** The mercenaries, described as armed with "heavy weapons," had occupied 3 important mining and communications centers, Kisenge, Dilolo, and Kapanga. The Congolese National Liberation Front (FLNC), **Mar. 11,** in a communique issued from Paris, took responsibility for the invasion, calling it "a national uprising by the Congolese people." The FLNC had been created in 1963 by Katanga secessionists who fled to Angola after the defeat of their movement, led by the late Moise Tshombe. The U.S. government, **Mar. 15,** announced that it was responding to an urgent request from Zaire for spare parts and other equipment necessary to repel the invading forces. The U.S. announced immediate delivery of $1 million of military aid already promised to Zaire, including parachutes, medical supplies, combat rations, and communications equipment. The Carter administration, **Mar. 14,** had expressed concern over the possible effects of the invasion on Zaire's already troubled economy. Answering critics of this aid to a government known to violate human rights, Secretary of State Cyrus R. Vance, **Mar. 16,** stated that the invading forces had created a "dangerous situation" for Zaire's important copper industry which is crucial to the nation's survival. On **Mar. 17,** Zaire flew reinforcement troops to Shaba to stall invading forces approaching Kolwezi, a major copper mining center. Zairian Pres. Mobutu Sese Seko, **Mar. 19,** flew to Kolwezi and expressed confidence the local population would remain loyal to the government. Despite consistently optimistic official Zaire reports of success in repelling the invading forces, there were strong indications that Zairian forces faced fierce opposition. On **Mar. 31,** the Zaire government officially confirmed reports that the invaders had taken Mutshatsha, the government's regional command headquarters in Shaba. The French government disclosed, **Apr. 10,** that it had put a fleet of transports at the disposal of Morocco to airlift men and materiel to Zaire. The U.S., **Apr. 12,** announced it would send $13 million of "nonlethal" military equipment to Zaire, but had denied a request for additional "emergency assistance." Zaire, **Apr. 12,** reported that it had pushed the invaders back 12 miles in heavy fighting, in what appeared to be the first success for Zairian forces. On **Apr. 21,** Zaire reported that Zairian and Moroccan troops had begun a general offensive 3 days before, and, **Apr. 25,** reported that Mutshatsha had been recaptured with little rebel resistance. It was reported, **Apr. 26,** that government troops were moving ahead and meeting little resistance. Mobutu, **Apr. 29,** vowed that he would "hunt down" the retreating rebels.

Druse Chieftain Assassinated—Unknown assailants, **Mar. 16,** shot and killed Kamal Jumblat, the Druse chieftain who had led the leftist-Moslem alliance during the Lebanese civil war. Attacked in his car on a mountain road near Beirut, Jumblat's driver and body guard were also killed. News of the killings sent waves of panic through Beirut; Syrian troops of the Arab peace-keeping force were placed on alert in the city. Moslems in all sections of Beirut fired into the air to express their anger and grief. As Jumblat was buried in his home village of Mukhtara **Mar. 17,** reports of revenge killings mounted. Christian sources reported, **Mar. 18,** that at least 100 Christians had been killed in revenge in the area southeast of Beirut where Jumblat had lived. Syrian troops arrested several persons, including members of Jumblat's Progressive Socialist party, in an attempt to check the reprisal killings. The situation eased **Mar. 20,** when Jumblat's son, Walid Jumblat, toured villages in the troubled area and appealed to members of his sect to cease further violence.

Carter Takes Human Rights Campaign to UN—In a major speech to United Nations members, U.S. Pres. Jimmy Carter, **Mar. 17,** stated that the international body had allowed "its human rights machinery to be ignored and sometimes politicized." To strengthen that machinery, Carter suggested the UN Commission on Human Rights meet more often and move its headquarters from Geneva to New York where "its activities will be in the forefront of our attention." Carter also appealed to the Soviet Union to join in a greater effort "to contain the global arms race." On **Mar. 21,** Soviet Communist party leader Leonid I. Brezhnev accused the U.S. of using the human rights issue to interfere in Soviet internal affairs. It was "unthinkable," Brezhnev stated, that under such circumstances U.S.-Soviet relations could continue to develop normally.

Congolese President, Archbishop Killed—A suicide commando, **Mar. 19,** killed Congolese Pres. Marien Ngouabi in Brazzaville. The group's leader, said to be former Army Captain Barthelemy Kikadidi, escaped. Congo radio reported that Ngouabi had "died fighting with his weapon in his hand" and asserted that former Pres. Alphonse Massamba-Debat was behind the assassination. The Congolese Workers party announced that full power was being delegated to the 11-man military committee. The committee closed the frontiers, imposed an 11-hour night curfew, and banned public meetings of more than 5 persons. On **Mar. 23,** Emile Cardinal Biayenda, Roman Catholic Archbishop of Brazzaville, was kidnapped and murdered. The military committee announced that Massamba-Debat was behind both killings. Massamba-Debat, **Mar. 25,** was convicted and executed for the assassinations and Kikadidi was convicted in absentia.

Chirac Elected Paris Mayor, Leftists Gain—Former French Premier Jacque Chirac, **Mar. 20,** won the

Paris mayoralty, defeating the leftist opposition. However, the leftist coalition of Socialists and Communists made considerable gains in nationwide municipal voting, adding control of 21 major cities to the 33 cities won in first-round elections **Mar. 13.** Chirac's victory bolstered his drive to replace Pres. Valery Giscard d'Estaing as the leader of France's nonleftist parties. Chirac made clear immediately that he would use the power and prestige of the mayoralty to wage a strong campaign to prevent the Socialist-Communist coalition from taking control of the national assembly. The election results gave the leftist coalition control of more than three-quarters of France's major cities.

U.S. Mission to Indochina Returns Optimistic—A White House mission to Indochina to hold talks on Americans still missing in action returned, **Mar. 20,** optimistic about building better relations in the future. The mission, the first to Vietnam since the Communist takeover, received a surprisingly warm welcome in Hanoi **Mar. 16.** The Vietnamese government, **Mar. 18,** handed over 12 black steel caskets containing the remains of American pilots killed during the Vietnam war. Leonard Woodcock, the head of the mission, announced that Hanoi had agreed to set up machinery to discover the fate of other missing Americans. On **Mar. 17,** Vietnamese Prime Minister Pham Van Dong had told the visiting group Pres. Jimmy Carter's "new spirit" could solve all the problems between the 2 countries. On **Mar. 20,** in Vientiane, Laos, Woodcock announced that although no agreement had been reached during the one-day visit "both sides noted that there had been a substantial improvement in the atmosphere between us, and we hope we can build on that in the future." Carter, **Mar. 23,** after meeting with the mission, said he would accept a Vietnamese invitation to hold a new round of negotiations in Paris to try to normalize relations. He said he believed that the Vietnamese "have acted in good faith" in promising to make further efforts to account for missing Americans.

U.S.-Soviet Arms Talks Break Down—Talks on strategic arms limitations between U.S. Secretary of State Cyrus R. Vance and Soviet Communist Party leader Leonid I. Brezhnev in Moscow broke down **Mar. 30.** Brezhnev rejected as "inequitable" both proposals the U.S. had presented in an attempt to break the 2-year impasse in negotiations for a strategic arms limitations treaty. The first U.S. proposal would have reaffirmed the already agreed-to force level of 2,400 missiles and bombers (strategic weapons), while avoiding the disputed issue of whether American low-level cruise missiles and the Soviet Backfire bomber should also be defined as strategic weapons. The 2d U.S. proposal asked for reductions in the force level as well as for constraints on both the cruise missile and Backfire. In rejecting the proposals, Brezhnev offered no counterproposal beyond the previous Soviet call for affirmation of a 2,400-force level which would include the U.S. cruise missile but exclude the Soviet Backfire. In response, U.S. Pres. Jimmy Carter said he was not "discouraged, but indicated he would be "forced to consider" acceleration of American weapons development if the Soviets failed to negotiate "in good faith" in May at another round of talks. In an unusual televised news conference in Moscow, Soviet Foreign Minister Andrei A. Gromyko, **Mar. 31,** accused the U.S. of putting forth false and unrealistic arms control proposals that gave it an unilateral advantage. He further expressed irritation with Carter's public style of casting the U.S. as the innovator and the USSR as the obstructor in arms control negotiations.

General

FDA Announces Saccharin Ban—The Food and Drug Administration, **Mar. 9,** announced that it would propose a ban on the use of saccharin in foods and beverages. The decision was based on the findings of a study sponsored by the Canadian government that large amounts of saccharin fed to laboratory rats caused malignant bladder tumors. The proposed ban of the only artificial sweetener currently allowed in the nation's food supply brought angry criticism from the dietary food industry, individual consumers, and diabetics who routinely use saccharin as a substitute for sugar. If the ban went into effect, all diet soft drinks, artificially sweetened fruits, and sugar substitutes for coffee would disappear from the marketplace. Acting FDA Commissioner Dr. Sherwin Gardner explained that although the findings did not prove saccharin had ever caused cancer in human beings, "we do now have clear evidence that the safety of saccharin does not meet standards for additives established by Congress." Marvin Eisenstadt, executive vice president of Cumberland Packing Corp., the nation's largest maker of low-calorie sweeteners, charged that the "outrageous and harmful action" was based on "flimsy scientific evidence." On **Mar. 10,** the FDA was deluged with complaints demanding that saccharin be allowed to stay on the market. On **Mar. 11,** various doctors and groups representing diabetics argued that the ban could lead to health risks such as obesity, heart disease, and arthritis.

NYC Formulates New Money Plan, Gets Federal Loan—The New York State Emergency Financial Control Board, **Mar. 9,** unanimously approved a surprise New York City plan to raise money needed to pay the city's $983-million short-term debt and again forestall default on the city's financial obligations. Treasury Secretary W. Michael Blumenthal, **Mar. 11,** approved a short-term $255-million federal loan as a key part of the New York City plan. The approval of the loan had been contingent upon the city's ability to devise an adequate "patchwork" plan for paying off its short-term debt. The plan, announced by New York City Mayor Abe Beame, **Mar. 9,** consisted of 8 separate elements, including an expected $410 million from the sale of mortgages on the city-financed Mitchell-Lama housing projects and the willingness of owners of about $250 million in short-term notes to exchange them for new Municipal Assistance Corporation bonds.

Farm Workers, Teamsters Reach Accord—Ending 10 years of discord over organization of agricultural workers in the West, Cesar Chavez's United Farm Workers and the International Brotherhood of Teamsters, **Mar. 11,** in Burlingame, Cal., signed an agreement setting up jurisdiction for each union's attempts to organize workers. Under the accord, the UFW would organize only workers employed under conditions described by the California Agricultural Labor Relations Act. The chief consideration would be the worker's primary area of engagement. The UFW would even have jurisdiction over truck drivers if the employer was primarily engaged in farming.

Chesimard Convicted of Murder—An all-white New Brunswick, N.J., jury, **Mar. 25,** convicted Joanne D. Chesimard of first-degree murder in the 1973 slaying of a New Jersey state trooper. She was immediately sentenced to life in prison. She was found guilty on all 8 counts — 2 counts of murder and 6 counts of assault and related charges in the slaying of one trooper and wounding of another in a shoot-out on the New Jersey Turnpike. Chesimard denounced the jury as "racist," charging, "You have convicted a woman who had her hands in the air." On the stand, Chesimard contended she never handled a gun and had been shot by one of the troopers while she was emerging with her hands raised from the car which had been stopped for a defective tail light.

Disasters—Two earthquakes struck Southern Iran, **Mar. 22** and **23**, killing 167 persons in villages near the Persian Gulf city of Bandar Abbas. . . . Some 30 persons were reported dead **Mar. 25**, in an earthquake that struck Turkey's mountainous Elazig province, damaging homes, schools, and mosques. . . . A total of 581 persons died as a result of the world's worst aviation crash, **Mar. 27**, when a Pan Am Boeing 747 and a KLM Boeing 747 collided and exploded on the foggy single airstrip at Los Rodeos Airport at Santa Cruz de Tenerife in the Canary Islands.

APRIL
National

U.S. Defers Plutonium Programs — President Carter announced, **Apr. 7**, that his administration would "defer indefinitely" all government programs which encouraged the use of plutonium in fueling commercial atomic power plants. The move was justified primarily as a measure to prevent the spread of atomic weapons. Plutonium, because it does not require complex refining and enrichment procedures to reach weapons quality, is far more likely to be used in crude atomic weapons than is uranium. Carter said he would reject a request by Allied General Nuclear Services, a private company, for $500 million in government financing for a pilot commercial nuclear fuel reprocessing plant, which would have recovered plutonium from nuclear fuel plant wastes. Under the Carter plan, the government's fast-breeder reactor demonstration project at Clinch River, Tenn., would receive reduced funding; its future development would center on research rather than commercial implementation. Carter said he would ask for increased U.S. uranium enrichment capacity, in order to eliminate the need for plutonium. In a related development, Carter asked Congress, **Apr. 27**, to grant him power to impose heavy sanctions against any country which received U.S. nuclear fuel or hardware, if it exploded an atomic bomb or violated international safeguards or agreements with the U.S. Under the proposal, nonnuclear-weapons states that had not signed the treaty against the spread of nuclear weapons would be sold U.S. nuclear fuel only if all their nuclear materials and equipment were subject to inspection by the International Atomic Energy Agency.

Carter Drops Tax Rebate Plan — President Carter announced, **Apr. 14**, that he had withdrawn his support for a $50 tax rebate to all individuals, because it was no longer needed to spur the economy and might aggravate inflation. Carter also dropped his request for an increase in tax credits for business investment and for hiring new employees. The tax rebate faced strong opposition in the Senate, and some observers said Carter abandoned it rather than face a damaging political fight. The Senate, **Apr. 21**, voted 74-20, to retain the business tax credits.

Inflation Plan Offered — President Carter, **Apr. 15**, revealed his administration's anti-inflation program, designed to reduce inflation from 6% to 4% by the end of 1979. The plan would rely on overall fiscal and economic policy, and on cooperation from business and labor, rather than on price and wage controls.

Carter Offers Energy Plan; Calls Energy Crisis "Greatest Challenge"

President Carter, in a nationally-televised energy address **Apr. 18**, called for a concerted national effort to put limits on the use of energy. At a joint session of Congress two days later, he outlined a broad legislative program including tax hikes, rebates, incentives, and price increases, designed to change national patterns of energy use, and prevent the shortage of energy supplies from becoming a "national catastrophe."

The national energy program should involve citizens in "the moral equivalent of war," Carter said in his April 18 address, because "with the exception of preventing war," the energy crisis "is the greatest challenge that our country will face during our lifetimes." Sacrifices and changes would be required "in every life." No sector of the economy or interest group would be unfairly affected, Carter said, provided that Congress approved all major components of his plan.

The major components were:

—gasoline taxes would be increased by 5c a year, up to a 50c total, unless consumption fell within specified limits.

—domestically produced oil now under price controls would be subjected to gradually increased excise taxes, until the price of domestic and foreign oil would be equalized.

—the new tax revenues would be returned in rebates to individuals.

—stiff penalties would be imposed on cars that exceeded gasoline consumption limits, and rebates would be paid to buyers of gasoline-efficient cars.

—natural gas prices would be increased to stimulate exploration.

—controls would be set on intrastate natural gas sales.

—taxes would be imposed to curb industrial use of natural gas.

—more atomic power plants would be built, but the breeder reactor program would be indefinitely deferred.

—homeowners and businessmen would be allowed tax credits for installation of solar energy systems in homes.

—building standards would be upgraded to promote efficient energy use.

—federal research on alternate energy sources would be expanded.

—gasoline prices would be decontrolled; and utility rates would be changed to reflect the cost of services.

The overall goals of the plan were to keep the growth in U.S. energy demand under 2% a year; to reduce gasoline demand by 10%; to halve the proportion of imports in the U.S. oil supply; to set up a one-billion-barrel strategic oil reserve; to increase coal output by two-thirds; to insulate all new buildings and most existing homes; and to install solar energy systems in 2 1/2 million houses, all by 1985.

Carter claimed that his program could "lead to an even better life for the people of America," and would not harm living standards.

Administration leaders at first claimed that the program would, on balance, have a positive effect on the economy; but budget director Burt Lance said **Apr. 21**, that the program would have "no significant effect" on economic growth. Some private economists claimed that various provisions of the plan would lead to small increases in both inflation and unemployment.

March consumer prices rose by 0.6% after larger rises in January and February, the labor department reported, **Apr. 21.** Wholesale prices continued their recent sharp rises, with 1.1 monthly increases in both March and April, the labor department reported, **May 5.**

Supreme Court Curbs Transit Aid — By a 4-3 decision, **Apr. 27,** the Supreme Court invalidated a 1974 New Jersey law that would have allowed the Port Authority of New York and New Jersey to use its funds for new mass transit projects. The law, which attempted to repeal a 1962 pledge to bondholders which limited the use of Port Authority funds for mass transit, was overturned as a violation of the clause in the U.S. Constitution which prohibits "imparing the obligation of contracts." While the case only concerned revenues and reserves used to guarantee bonds issued between 1962 and 1973, the dissenting justices said the decision would prevent the use of any funds for mass transit until the year 2007, when the last of the 1973 bonds would be redeemed.

H.E.W. Bars Bias Against Disabled — Health, Education, and Welfare Secretary Joseph Califano signed regulations, **Apr. 28,** barring discrimination against the handicapped by federally-aided schools, hospitals, and other facilities. The rules would protect 35 million disabled people, 10 million alcoholics, and 1.5 million rehabilitated drug addicts. People with heart disease or cancer would be covered as well.

International

German Prosecutor Assassinated—Siegfried Buback, West Germany's chief prosecutor, was murdered, **Apr. 7,** by motorcyclists while riding in his car. Buback had been conducting the government's effort in the trial of 3 left-wing terrorist leaders of the Baader-Meinhof gang. A group called the Ulrike Meinhof Action Committee claimed responsibility for the murder. Police charged, **Apr. 9,** that the crime had been planned by a jailed attorney who had formerly represented the Baader-Meinhof defendants. Of the original 5 defendants, 2 had died in prison. Ulrike Meinhof was found hung in May, 1976, and declared a suicide, and Holger Meins died in a hunger strike in November 1974. A West Berlin Supreme Court judge had been killed in retaliation for Meins' death. The 3 survivors were sentenced, **Apr. 28,** to life imprisonment for the murder of 4 U.S. servicemen in a series of 1972 bombings. The defendants admitted responsibility, but claimed the anti-Vietnam War bombings qualified them for prisoner-of-war status. The 2-year trial was the longest in West German history.

Bonn Approves Brazil Atom Deal—The West German government reported, **Apr. 8,** that it had approved export licenses for sales to Brazil of a pilot uranium reprocessing plant and a demonstration uranium enrichment plant, despite objections by the U.S. that the equipment could be used to produce materials for atomic bombs. The sale was part of a 10-to-15 year agreement between the 2 countries for the sale of up to 8 atomic power plants at a cost of some $5 billion. The deal was the largest export contract in West German history.

Rabin Quits Party Post in Scandal—Israeli Prime Minister Yitzhak Rabin submitted his resignation as Labor Party leader, **Apr. 8,** as a result of a scandal over his U.S. bank accounts, which were illegal under Israeli currency restrictions. He admitted that the accounts had contained $18,000 in the period when he was ambassador to the U.S., and not $2,000, as his wife had publicly claimed. Rabin said he was resigning to avoid further damage to his party, which had been battered by scandals and by discontent with the economic situation. The Finance Ministry fined Rabin the equivalent of $1,500, **Apr. 11;** his wife Leah, who had managed the accounts, was fined $27,000, **Apr. 17.** Defense Minister Shimon Peres, whom Rabin had narrowly defeated at a Labor nominating convention, was chosen by the party's central committee, **Apr. 10,** as its new candidate for prime minister. Rabin, **Apr. 22,** took a leave of absence from his post as prime minister.

Spain Legalizes Communist Party—The government of Spain announced, **Apr. 9,** that the Communist party had been enrolled on the register of political parties eligible to run in upcoming parliamentary elections. The government had ruled that the party was not "subject to an international discipline" or "totalitarian" in aims. The party became the 125th group to be recognized legally. For the 4 decades of rule by Francisco Franco, the party had been portrayed as the chief enemy of Spain.

Soviet Trawlers Seized—The U.S. Coast Guard seized the Soviet fishing ship Taras Shevchenko, **Apr. 9,** and the cargo carried by another Soviet fishing ship, the Antanas Snechkus, **Apr. 10.** The actions had been approved by President Carter after the 2 ships violated the new 200-mile U.S. fishing zone. The U.S. state department warned, **Apr. 11,** that the incidents could cause a "worsening of our bilateral relations" with the USSR. The captain of the first vessel became the first person to be arraigned under the new law, **Apr. 16,** under charges of excessive and illegal catches of two species.

Arms Talks Deadlocked—The USSR reaffirmed its rejection of 2 U.S. strategic arms control proposals, **Apr. 14,** and said they could not even form the basis for further discussions. An editorial in Pravda denied that the Soviet position was a negotiating ploy. Pravda said the Ford Administration had been willing to put limits on cruise missiles with a range of 360 miles or more, but that one of the recent Carter proposals would pose no limits on cruise missiles, while the other would only limit those with a range greater than 1,500 miles. The article contended that the U.S., with its "forward-based nuclear systems" on land and sea near the Soviet Union, would benefit unfairly from the Carter plans.

Carter Backs Young—U.S. ambassador to the UN Andrew Young, whose outspoken statements on world affairs had provoked controversy, was defended, **Apr. 15,** by President Carter. Carter said he agreed with Young's **Apr. 11** assertion that Cuban troops had "stabilized" the situation in Angola. Young also had said that the U.S. was "paranoid" about Communist influence in Africa, and that even Marxist regimes in Africa needed to cooperate economically with the West. Young had apologized to Britain's UN delegate, **Apr. 7,** for having said on British television that Britain had institutionalized racism "more than anyone else in the history of the earth." The state department, **Apr. 15,** labelled "incorrect" Young's assertion the previous day that the South African regime was "illegitimate."

Cuba, U.S. in Fish Pact—The U.S. and Cuba announced, **Apr. 28,** that they had approved a pact governing fishing rights in the waters between Cuba and Florida. The pact was necessitated by the extension by both countries of their territorial waters to 200 miles from the seacoast, which went into effect **Mar. 1.** The pact, arrived at through the first formal direct negotiations between Cuba and the U.S. since 1961, reportedly drew a boundary halfway between the 2 countries, which are 90 miles apart at the closest point. The pact also allowed Cubans to fish in U.S. waters for species in abundant supply, if they obtained permits.

General

Blowout Causes Record North Sea Oil Spill—In the worst oil spill since the start of North Sea operations in 1969, millions of gallons of oil spread over an area of 1300-square-miles, after a pipe blew out on a Phillips Petroleum Co. rig, **Apr. 22.** The blowout, in the Ekofisk field about 160 miles southwest of Norway and 180 miles northwest of Denmark, occurred during a routine maintenance procedure. A crew of Norwegian and American workmen succeeded in capping the well, **Apr. 20,** after earlier attempts failed. Despite the size of the spill, the director of the Norwegian antipollution agency said that harmful effects on fish, birds, and other marine life would be "relatively small."

Saccharine Compromise Offered—The Food and Drug Administration proposed, **Apr. 14,** that the widely-used artificial sweetener saccharine be banned from all commercially prepared diet drinks, foods, and toiletries. Saccharine could still be sold as an over-the-counter drug in drug stores, supermarkets, and restaurants, but manufacturers would have to demonstrate its safety and effectiveness. Recent Canadian tests on animals had confirmed earlier findings that the product could cause bladder cancer. FDA Commissioner Donald Kennedy said continued use of saccharine could cause some 1,200 cases of bladder cancer annually in the U.S. Opponents of the FDA proposal, including the Pharmaceutical Manufacturers Association, the Calorie Control Council, and a majority of consumers in public opinion polls, said that the animal tests were either irrelevant or not conclusive.

Parents Denied Custody of "Moonies"—A 3-judge California State Court of Appeals panel ordered, **Apr. 11,** that 5 young adults be freed from the custody of their parents, who had opposed their membership in Rev. Sun Myung Moon's Unification Church. The parents had charged that their children had been coercively persuaded to join the Church, and had shown emotional and mental deterioration. They sought to "deprogram" their children from church influence, while church lawyers opposed the move on grounds of religious freedom. The appellate judges did not accept a lower court ruling, **Mar. 24,** that parents retained some rights over adult children. They ruled that custody could be granted only if a person were incompetent and unable to care for himself.

Two Convicted in Major Spy Case—Christopher J. Boyce, 23 years old, was convicted in Los Angeles, **Apr. 28,** of 8 counts of espionage and conspiracy to commit espionage, in what prosecutors said was one of the most important spy cases in a decade. Boyce, a former employee of defense contractor TRW Systems, had passed on or sold to Soviet agents the contents of thousands of documents containing data about C.I.A. cryptographic ciphers and information about U.S. spy satellites. Boyce admitted passing the information through an intermediary, Andrew Daulton Lee, over a 2-year period. Boyce claimed he had been blackmailed by Lee, after he had voluntarily disclosed to Lee secret data, indicating that the C.I.A. had withheld or distorted satellite data it was required by agreement to supply to Australia. Lee was convicted, **May 14,** and sentenced to life imprisonment, **July 18.** Boyce received a 40-year sentence, **Sept. 12.**

Disasters—Over 600 people died, **Apr. 1,** when a tornado struck large areas of Bangladesh; 200 of them drowned when a boat capsized in the Meghna River. . . A Southern Airways DC-9 crashed in the village of New Hope, Ga., **Apr. 4,** killing 68 persons. The crash was laid to ingestion of hail by the plane's jet engines. . . Record floods hit parts of West Virginia and Kentucky, **Apr. 5,** leaving thousands homeless. At least 28 persons were killed by rain and windstorms in the area. . . A mountainous region in Western Iran was hit by an earthquake, **Apr. 7,** killing at least 170 people in 4 villages.

MAY

National

Nixon Admits He Let America Down—Former Pres. Richard M. Nixon, **May 4,** in the first of 5 televised talks with David Frost, admitted that he had "let the American people down" by lying, disregarding his constitutional oath, and abetting the Watergate cover-up while he was in the White House. However, throughout the interview, Nixon maintained that he had committed no criminal or impeachable offenses because he had acted from purely political and humanitarian motives. Although at times visibly distraught, Nixon repeatedly refused to concede any of his actions had amounted to obstruction of justice. Preliminary ratings showed that some 45 million persons had watched the interview, making it one of the highest rated news broadcasts ever. A Gallup poll conducted **May 16** indicated that 69% of the viewers still thought Nixon was covering up and 75% believed he was guilty of obstruction of justice and other impeachable offenses.

Unemployment Hits 29-Month Low—The labor department, **May 6,** reported that the national unemployment rate had fallen in April from 7.3% to 7%, the lowest level in 29 months. The total number of persons employed, the department also reported, had hit 90 million for the first time, scoring the 2nd consecutive monthly gain of more than 500,000 jobs. However, the unemployment drop was accompanied by a seasonally adjusted 1.1% rise in the wholesale price index in April, according to a **May 5** labor department report.

Carter Proposes Social Security Tax Hike—In a message delivered to Congress **May 9,** Pres. Jimmy Carter proposed a larger payroll tax on employers to eliminate growing deficits in the Social Security system. Carter also asked for a small tax rise for workers and an experimental diversion of general tax revenues to the Social Security system. Warning Congress that swift action was necessary to "restore the financial integrity of the Social Security system," Carter asserted that his proposals would "eliminate the Social Security deficit for the remainder of this century." The key element of the package would require employers to pay Social Security taxes on an increasingly larger portion of employee earnings until 1981 when taxes would be paid on the entire earnings. Simultaneously, the wage base on which employees are taxed would also increase but would be kept within an upper limit, rising by about $600 every 2 years until 1985. The administration estimated that the additional cost to employers would be $30 billion from 1979 to 1982 and the increase in the wage base for employee tax payments would bring in $4 billion during the same period. Carter also proposed that the tax rate for self-employed persons be raised from 7% to 7.5%. The potentially most controversial proposal, the transfer of general treasury revenue to finance Social Security, would be made available to the Social Security system on a 5-year trial basis only if the national unemployment exceeded 6% and Social Security funds were inadequate. Congressional response to the Carter proposals was sharply divided, especially on the use of general treasury funds.

Carter Signs Jobs Bills—Pres. Jimmy Carter, **May 13,** signed 2 bills which the administration promised would create more than 1 million jobs, chiefly for construction workers and young people. The first bill authorized an expenditure of $4 billion for public works projects and the second appropriated $20 billion to pay for the program and other public service employment.

Gen. Singlaub Reprimanded—Pres. Jimmy Carter, **May 21,** ordered Maj. Gen. John K. Singlaub, serving as chief of staff of American forces in Korea, reassigned for criticizing Pres. Carter's pledge to withdraw ground troops from Korea. Singlaub, a highly respected and much decorated officer, had been quoted by the *Washington Post* as saying that the withdrawal "on the schedule suggested" would "lead to war." Pentagon sources, **May 22,** described Singlaub as "stunned" and reported that he felt he had been "sandbagged" by a reporter who had quoted him by name and taken his remarks out of context.

Carter Signs Tax-Cut Bill—Pres. Jimmy Carter, **May 23,** signed into law a bill to cut taxes and simplify income tax returns. Congress, **May 16,** had given final approval to the legislation, a key component of Pres. Carter's economic stimulus package. The bill was designed to save low-income and middle-income tax payers more than $5 billion in 1977 as part of a $34.2 billion federal tax cut over a period of 28 months. The bill had originally also contained a $50 tax rebate which was later discarded as potentially inflationary. The legislation would simplify most tax filing procedures, eliminate tax payments for some 3 million low-income families, and would reduce by some $2 per week the average payroll deductions of about 50 million Americans who use the revised standard deduction also included in the bill. However, under the new legislation, some 2 million Americans earning more than $13,750 per year and claiming a standard deduction would pay an additional $50 in federal taxes annually.

Supreme Court Rejects Watergate Appeals—The Supreme Court, **May 23,** refused to review appeals from John N. Mitchell, H.R. Haldeman, and John D. Ehrlichman of their convictions in the Watergate cover-up. The decision let stand a Washington, D.C. federal court of appeals ruling which had upheld the convictions in October 1976. The court action ended the extended legal fight over the cover-up convictions, thereby assuring the 3 men would serve their 2½-to-8-year prison sentences.

Some Discriminatory Seniority Plans Backed—In a substantial setback for civil rights advocates, the Supreme Court, **May 31,** in a 7-2 decision, ruled the seniority systems that perpetuate past racial discriminations were not necessary illegal. According to the court, Title VII of the 1964 Civil Rights Act had intended to allow the continued "routine application" of seniority systems "even where the employer's pre-act discrimination in such cases resulted in whites having greater existing seniority rights than Negroes." The decision rejected the views of the Equal Employment Opportunity Commission and justice department that such systems were invalid, positions supported by numerous lower court rulings.

International

U.S.-Vietnamese Talks Make Progress—Ending 2 days of formal negotiations toward normalizing relations, both the U.S. and Vietnam, **May 4,** expressed satisfaction with progress made during the talks in Paris. The U.S. pledged that it would not veto Vietnam's admission to the UN and that it would raise a trade embargo against Vietnam once diplomatic relations were established. The Vietnamese said they would intensify their efforts to provide more information about Americans still listed as missing in action in the Vietnam war. However, both sides made it clear that important problems were still unsolved, chiefly a disagreement on Hanoi's insistence the U.S. has an obligation to contribute to its postwar recovery. Shortly after the talks ended, the U.S. state department, **May 5,** repeated a previous pledge that the U.S. would not offer any economic aid to Vietnam. The state department announcement came on the heels of a House of Representatives vote (266-131) to prohibit any discussion of assistance to Hanoi.

Major Western Leaders Hold Economic Summit—The 7 leaders of the world's major noncommunist industrialized nations, **May 7-8,** at an economic summit in London, agreed to cooperate to combat unemployment and continue their policies of moderate economic growth. Unanimity, however, faltered over U.S. Pres. Jimmy Carter's proposals for halting the spread of nuclear weapons. Joining Carter for the London summit were British Prime Minister James Callaghan, Japanese Prime Minister Takeo Fukuda, West German Chancellor Helmut Schmidt, Canadian Prime Minister Pierre Elliott Trudeau, French Pres. Valery Giscard d'Estaing, and Italian Premier Giulio Andreotti. In a communique issued **May 8,** the 7 leaders said the aim of their centrist approach was to "create jobs while continuing to reduce inflation." The leaders agreed that the stronger U.S., West German, and Japanese economies should spur their own growth to invigorate international trade and lift the troubled British, French, Canadian, and Italian economies out of the current recession. In turn, Britain, Italy, France, and Canada promised to maintain their present stabilization policies to try to check inflation. On specific issues, the 7 leaders agreed not to resort to higher tariffs and protectionism. They agreed to create a multibillion-dollar cushion, through the International Monetary Fund, to help both industrialized and poorer nations cope with trade deficits caused by rising oil prices. The 7 also said they would make a special effort to create jobs for young people in industrialized nations. On the question of a halt to the sale of dangerous nuclear technology, the leaders submitted the problem to a new 7-nation study group for further consideration.

Carter Calls For Palestinian Homeland—In the strongest such statement yet, Pres. Jimmy Carter, **May 9,** in Geneva, following a 3-hour meeting with Syrian Pres. Hafez al-Assad, told reporters that "there must be a resolution of the Palestine problem and a homeland for the Palestinians." Carter had met with Assad as part of continuing American efforts to sound out Middle Eastern leaders on prospects for an Arab-Israeli settlement. The statement was considered significant in light of recent reports that Palestine Liberation Organization leader Yasir Arafat was ready to accept Israel's right to exist if Israel would endorse a Palestinian homeland. In light of Pres. Carter's statement, U.S. Secretary of State Cyrus R. Vance, **May 11,** met in London with Israeli Foreign Minister Yigal Allon to renew the U.S. commitment to a "special relationship" with Israel. He assured Allon that the U.S. would not impose a solution in the Middle East and that any American suggestions for a settlement would be made to the "parties involved." He also promised that Israel would continue to receive the arms it needed as well as "advanced technology."

Carter Calls on NATO to Meet Soviet Threat—Giving the keynote address at a meeting of NATO allies in London, U.S. Pres. Jimmy Carter, **May 10**, told them they must respond strongly to a 12-year Soviet force buildup that was "much stronger than needed for any defense purposes." He said the U.S. would join with Europe to "strengthen the alliance — politically, economically, and militarily" and that NATO would remain "the heart of our foreign policy." He said NATO must begin to develop "a long-term defense program to strengthen the alliance's deterrence and defense in the 1980s." To accomplish this, Carter called for better coordination of national defense programs, a program endorsed by a meeting of NATO foreign ministers **May 11**. On **May 9**, Carter, Schmidt, Giscard d'Estaing, and Callaghan had issued a sharp warning to the USSR against endangering the status quo in Berlin.

Bhutto Announces Referendum in Pakistan—Following 2 months of violent rioting against his victory in the March national elections, Pakistani Prime Minister Zulfikar Ali Bhutto, **May 13**, announced a referendum to decide whether he should retain power. "What we have gone through has been a real nightmare," Bhutto told the National Assembly. The rioting had claimed some 260 lives and forced the imposition of martial law, **Apr. 21**, in Lahore, Karachi, and Hyderabad. The opposition Pakistan National Alliance, however, immediately rejected the referendum, which fell short of their demands that he resign and a new general election be held. Bhutto had tried on several occasions with no success to negotiate with the opposition to end the crisis.

La Pasionaria Ends Spanish Exile—Ending 38 years of exile from her native Spain, La Pasionaria, Dolores Ibarruri, **May 13**, returned to Madrid from Moscow where she had gone after the Spanish civil war. A living Communist legend, the 81-year-old Ibarruri returned just 34 days after Prime Minister Adolfo Suarez's government legalized the Spanish Communist party. A fiery orator, she had rallied the 2nd Spanish Republic against Franco in 1936. Although met by several hundred young Communists, her welcome was restrained, in accordance with an agreement between Suarez and the Communist party to avoid arousing Francoists still entrenched in the bureaucracy and military.

Labor Party Upset in Israeli Elections—In a major upset, Israel's right-wing Likud coalition, **May 17**, in a national election, defeated the Labor party which had governed the nation since its inception in 1948. Although the Likud would hold only 41 seats, a gain of 2, in the 120-seat Knesset, it had emerged as a major political force and its leader Menahem Begin, a hard-line long-time Labor critic, would form a new coalition government. The stunned Labor party won only 34 seats, a drop of 23 from the 1973 election. A big winner in the election was the new Democratic Movement for Change which won 14 seats, apparently siphoning votes away from the Labor party. The Democratic Movement was led by archeologist and army general Yigal Yadin. Defense Minister Shimon Peres, the Labor candidate for prime minister, said the results were "surprising" and "disappointing" and indicated there was a need for "soul-searching within the party." His party attributed the defeat to a reaction against the scandals, corruption, and divisiveness that had wracked the Labor party in recent months. However, Likud, which had taken a strong stand against returning the Israeli-occupied West Bank and Gaza Strip to the Arabs, felt the victory showed disenchantment with the vacillating Labor party regime, particularly in foreign affairs. Begin, as his party's victory became apparent, immediately made statements to allay Arab and U.S. fears his government would take an intransigent pose. He said he would invite major Arab leaders to meet with Israeli officials and negotiate peace.

U.S., USSR, Agree on Framework for SALT Talks—Concluding 3 days of talks in Geneva, U.S. Secretary of State Cyrus R. Vance and Soviet Foreign Minister Andrei A. Gromyko, **May 18**, achieved an agreement on a "framework" for ending a 3-month impasse in negotiations toward a new strategic arms limitations (SALT) treaty. In an official communique issued **May 21**, Vance and Gromyko agreed that progress had been made, but acknowledged that major issues still remained unresolved. Before leaving Geneva, Gromyko stressed that "major, serious difficulties remained" and accused the U.S. of trying to get "unilateral advantages." Far more positive about the talks, Vance outlined the elements of the 3-part "framework": a proposed Soviet-U.S. treaty based on the 1974 Vladivostok agreement (effective until 1985) in which the force level for both sides would be somewhat less than the 2,400 bombers and missile launchers set at Vladivostok; a 3-year protocol to cover controversial issues such as the American cruise missile and the Soviet Backfire bomber; and a general statement of principles to guide negotiations for the next SALT treaty, possibly including further arms reductions. On **May 28**, U.S. Pres. Carter stated that Vance and Gromyko would meet at least twice more before scheduled September talks. But Soviet Communist Party leader Leonid I. Brezhnev, **May 29**, said "no serious movement forward" had been achieved at Geneva and again accused the Carter administration of trying to seek a unilateral advantage.

Podgorny Ousted From Politburo—In a surprise move, Soviet Pres. Nikolai V. Podgorny, **May 24**, was dropped from the Soviet Communist Party Politburo in a vote at a plenary session of the party's central committee. The ouster was generally interpreted as heralding the end of the 74-year-old Podgorny's career.

General

Croation Hijackers Convicted—A Brooklyn, N.Y., federal court jury, **May 5**, convicted 4 Croation nationalists of various charges stemming from the September 1976 hijacking of a TWA jumbo jet to publicize demands for Croation independence from Yugoslavia. A New York City bomb squad officer had been killed by a bomb planted by the nationalists. Zvonko Busic and his wife Julienne were found guilty of air piracy resulting in death, air piracy, and conspiracy. Two other defendants, Pete Matanic and Frane Pesuit, were acquitted of the first charge but found guilty of air piracy and conspiracy. Busic had contended at the trial that he held sole responsibility for the hijacking. A 5th defendant, Mark Vlasic, who had pleaded guilty to reduced New York state charges of attempted kidnaping, was sentenced, **May 12**, in New York State Supreme Court, to 6 to 18 years in prison. Zvonko and Julienne Busic, **July 20**, were sentenced in Brooklyn federal court to mandatory life terms and their 3 accomplices were given 30-year prison terms.

Hearst Placed on 5-Year Probation—California Superior Court Judge E. Talbot Callister, **May 9**, in Los Angeles, ruled that Patricia Hearst would not have to go to prison for her part in a 1974 robbery and shooting incident in Los Angeles and placed her on a 5-year probation. Hearst had pleaded *nolo contendre* to one count of armed robbery and one count of assault with a deadly weapon in an agreement with the prosecution to drop 8 other robbery and assault counts. In letting Hearst go free, Callister disregarded recommendations of the probation department that Hearst should be imprisoned. He stated that Hearst was not a "present or future" threat to society.

Nuclear Power Foes Arrested, Released in N.H.—Some 500 demonstrators arrested for occupying the construction site of a nuclear power plant in Seabrook, N.H., were found guilty of trespass in mass trials, **May 13**, and released on their own recognizance from National Guard Armory prisons pending automatic appeals to county superior court. Some 1,414 demonstrators, called the Clamshell Alliance, had been arrested, **May 1-2**, in the nation's first massive show of civil disobedience in opposition to nuclear plant construction. Many had already bailed themselves out of jail. The remaining 500, in an agreement with the county prosecutor, were sentenced to 15 days in jail, fined $100, and then released. Under the agreement negotiated by the Clamshell Alliance, the organization said it would help the part-time judicial staff with paperwork and scheduling of trials. The confinement of the demonstrators had cost the state an estimated $50,000 a day.

Pan Am Heliport Crash Kills 5—A New York Airways helicopter, **May 16**, at the height of the evening rush hour, keeled over on a broken landing gear at the heliport atop New York City's Pan Am building, causing 5 deaths. As the helicopter fell over, a huge rotor blade snapped off, slashed 4 people to death, and then flew 59 stories down to kill a woman standing on the street a block away. Another 7 persons were injured, 5 of them seriously. New York City Mayor Abe Beame immediately ordered the helicopter service halted pending a Federal Aviation Administration investigation.

Disasters—Fifty Israeli paratroopers and 4 crewmen died, **May 10**, in Israel's worst peacetime military disaster when their helicopter crashed and burned during a military exercise near Jericho on the occupied West Bank . . . . A Soviet Aeroflot jetliner crashed, **May 27**, on its landing approach to Cuba's Havana Airport, killing 56 passengers and 10 crew members . . . . A total of 164 persons died as a result of a fast-spreading fire, **May 28**, at the Beverly Hills Supper Club in Southgate, Ky.; more than 100 others were injured in the fire which was later termed electrical in origin . . . . An Indian express train, **May 31**, crashed into the flood-swollen Beki River in the northeastern state of Assam, taking at least 44 lives and injuring many others.

JUNE
National

Employment At New High—Total employment in the U.S. rose in May to a record high of 90,408,000, the Bureau of Labor Statistics reported, **June 3**. The rise, which brought the 7-month increase in jobs to 2.7 million, helped push the unemployment rate below 7% for the first time in 2½ years, to 6.9%. Manufacturing and construction employment showed particular strength, but the Bureau said these jobs were going to "experienced workers" rather than to the long-term jobless. The labor force, the total of those working or looking for work, rose to a record of 62.2% of the adult population, due largely to a surge of women entering the job market.

Park Tong Sun Named Korean Agent—A former director of the Korean Central Intelligence Agency (KCIA), Kim Hyung Wook, said in Washington, **June 4**, that Korean businessman Park Tong Sun was a KCIA agent. Park was under federal and congressional investigation for allegedly using illegal means to influence American policy toward Korea. Kim implicated South Korean President Park Chung Hee in the scandal, and named several other alleged KCIA agents in the U.S., including Rev. Moon Sun Myung, head of the evangelistic Unification Church. Kim, who had participated with President Park in his 1961 coup, has lived in self-imposed exile in the U.S. since 1973. Kim said that in 1964, Park Tong Sun offered to use his influence in Congress to obtain more military aid for Korea, in exchange for being named sole agent for the sale of U.S. rice in Korea. Most of the allegedly illegal activities occurred between 1971 and 1975, according to Kim.

Ray Flees, Is Caught—James Earl Ray, convicted assassin of Dr. Martin Luther King, Jr., escaped, **June 10**, from Brushy Mountain State Penitentiary in Petros, Tenn., but was recaptured, **June 13**, after one of the most massive manhunts in Tennessee history. Six other prisoners joined Ray in the escape attempt; all were recaptured by **June 14**. Ray had twice before tried to flee the prison; he had been a fugitive from a Missouri prison when arrested in 1968 for the King killing. Penitentiary warden Stonney Lane said, **June 14**, that authorities were "fully convinced there was no outside conspiracy."

Court OKs State Abortion Curb—The Supreme Court ruled, **June 20**, by a 6-3 vote, that states may refuse to spend Medicaid funds for "nontherapeutic," or elective, abortions. Public hospitals in cities and towns may also refuse to fund or permit such abortions, the Court also ruled by a 6-3 vote. An estimated 300,000 women a year had been obtaining abortions under Medicaid, at a total cost of about $50 million. Those states that wished to continue the practice could do so. The ruling was acclaimed by anti-abortion organizations; a spokesman for the National Council of Catholic Bishops said the decision was "to the advantage of the family unit." But Planned Parenthood said the ruling "re-established the poor as second-class patients, unequal to the more affluent in their opportunities for service." The Court majority said that the Constitution's equal protection clause was not violated when a state provided funds for women who choose to bear their children but not to those who choose abortion, since the state has a right to a value judgment favoring childbirth.

Haldeman, Mitchell Jailed—Fifty-year-old H.R. Haldeman, former chief of staff to President Nixon, entered a federal minimum security prison at Lompoc, Cal., **June 21**, to begin a 30-month to 8-year prison sentence for his role in the Watergate burglary cover-up. Former Attorney General John N. Mitchell, 63, entered a federal minimum security prison, **June 22**, at Maxwell Air Force Base near Montgomery, Ala., on an identical sentence in the same case. The two had been convicted in 1975 for conspiracy, obstruction of justice, and perjury. Mitchell, the first former U.S. attorney general to be jailed, was the 25th Watergate defendant to enter prison.

Court OKs Nixon Papers Law—The Supreme Court approved, **June 28**, by a 7-2 vote, a law that directed the government to control Richard Nixon's presidential papers and tape recordings. Nixon had challenged the 1974 law on grounds of separation of powers, protection of privacy, prohibition against bills of attainder, right of association, and privilege for confidential communications. The court majority said that Congress had a right to treat Nixon as "a legitimate class of one" in passing a special law regarding his papers, because the case arose in "a context unique in the history of the presidency," requiring "immediate action," due to the danger that some of the 42 million documents and 880 tapes might be destroyed.

U.S. Mandates Air Bags—Secretary of Transportation Brock Adams ordered, **June 30,** that air bags or automatic lap and shoulder restraints be installed in all standard and luxury cars by the 1982 model year, and in all cars by the 1984 model year. The order would be effective in two months unless vetoed by Congress. Adams said up to 9,000 lives a year could be saved if all cars were equipped with the devices. Air bags would cost $100 to $300 per car, he said, while the lap and shoulder restraints would cost $25 to $100. Consumer groups and insurance companies had lobbied for 8 years to make the devices mandatory.

Carter Drops B-1 Program—President Carter announced in Washington, **June 30,** that he opposed production and deployment of the B-1 strategic bomber, because of its high cost and because he believed it was not necessary to national defense. The bomber, which would have cost over $100 million per plane to produce, with total costs for the entire fleet, including operation and maintenance, of $100 billion, had been the subject of a prolonged national debate; Carter had opposed the bomber in his 1976 presidential campaign. The President said that cruise missiles, which could be deployed on modified versions of existing planes, would serve the same purpose as the B-1: penetration to targets within the Soviet Union. Carter said his decision maintained the strategic "triad" of land, sea, and air-based strategic nuclear forces. Four prototypes of the B-1, already built or under construction, would be used for continued research and development. Executives at the Rockwell International Corp. in Los Angeles said that 8,000 workers would lose their jobs because of the decision to curtail the B-1.

International

U.S., Cuba to Exchange Diplomats—The U.S. state department announced, **June 3,** that the United States and Cuba would station diplomats in each other's capitals for the first time in over 16 years. Between 8 and 10 Americans are to move into the U.S. embassy building in Havana, and a small number of Cubans will occupy the Cuban embassy in Washington. The move would not constitute a full resumption of diplomatic relations. The U.S. staff would fly the Swiss flag, and the Cuban staff would fly the Czechoslovak flag; both staffs would be considered "interest sections" rather than formal missions. An administration official said that "there are elements in both governments that want to put an end to the hostility and estrangement." Among the bars to full diplomatic relations were U.S. claims on over $2 billion in seized property in Cuba, Cuba's refusal to allow imprisoned Americans and Cubans with U.S. relatives to leave the island, and Cuba's demands for an end to the U.S. economic boycott and for Cuban control of the Guantanamo naval base. Cuba announced **June 3** that it would release 10 of its 30 American prisoners at once and review the cases of the other 20.

Seychelles President Ousted—James R.M. Mancham was ousted as president of the Seychelles, **June 5,** while he was attending the Commonwealth Conference in Britain. Some 200 armed men, whose leaders insisted on remaining anonymous, took control of strategic areas on the island of Mahe, where the capital city is located; 2 people were killed in brief fighting. Left-wing Prime Minister France Albert Rene agreed to become president. Mancham, in London, charged that the coup had been aided by the Soviet Union. Rene claimed, **June 8,** that Mancham himself had provoked the coup by asking politicians to agree to postpone the 1979 elections. He said his government would not be "Marxist," but would be "based on some system of socialism which we can evolve for the Seychelles."

Britain Celebrates Jubilee—Queen Elizabeth II led her nation and the Commonwealth, **June 7,** in celebrations to mark the silver jubilee of her accession 25 years before.

Janata Sweeps Indian States Vote—The governing Janata Party won control of 8 of the 10 state governments and one of the 2 union territory governments up for election, **June 10-14.** Nine of the ten had been controlled by Indira Gandhi's Congress Party. A coalition of 5 left-wing parties led by the Communist party (Marxist) won in West Bengal, while a regional party won in Tamil Nadu. Some 20 people had died in violence during the election campaign.

8 Die in Netherlands Anti-Terrorist Raid—Six South Moluccan terrorists and 2 of their hostages were killed, **June 11,** when Dutch marines stormed a train the Moluccans had hijacked, **May 23,** with 56 passengers, near Groningen, the Netherlands. Seven passengers, one terrorist, and 2 marines were hurt; 2 terrorists were taken unharmed. No one was killed in a simultaneous attack on a schoolhouse in nearby Bovensmilde, where 4 terrorists were holding 4 teachers hostage. One teacher and 106 children had been released, **May 27,** after a virus infection swept the school. The terrorists had sought to attract attention to their demands that the Netherlands pressure Indonesia to grant independence to the South Moluccan islands, and demanded that they, as well as 21 South Moluccans jailed in earlier incidents, be flown out of the country.

U.S. Newsmen Detained in Moscow—Los Angeles Times correspondent Robert C. Toth was seized, **June 11,** by plainclothesmen on a Moscow street, and questioned by K.G.B. agents for 13 hours over 5 days about his contacts with Soviet scientists and dissidents. He was given permission to leave the U.S.S.R., **June 16,** after diplomatic protests by the U.S. Toth, who had written articles on Soviet science, was accused in a statement, **June 14,** of "collecting secret information of a political and military nature."

Rosalynn Carter Tours Latin America—President Carter's wife Rosalynn returned, **June 12,** from a 7-nation diplomatic tour of the Caribbean and South America, which she began **May 30.** She had reviewed political and economic questions with heads of state and other officials.

Suarez Wins Spanish Election—In Spain's first free election in 41 years, Prime Minister Adolfo Suarez led the Union of the Democratic Center to victory, **June 15.** Though his party failed to gain a majority in the lower house, capturing only 166 of 350 seats, Suarez was asked by King Juan Carlos, **June 16,** to form a new government. The Democratic Center won 106 of 207 elected Senate seats. Juan Carlos named 41 additional senators, **June 15.** The Socialist Workers Party, led by Felipe Gonzalez, won 118 seats in the lower house, mostly in the large cities and in the Basque and Catalan regions; the Socialists took 28.5% of the popular vote, compared with the Democratic Center's 34.3%. The Communist Party, with 9% of the popular vote, succeeded in winning only 20 lower house seats; one of them went to party leader Santiago Carrillo, and one went to Civil War leader Dolores Ibarruri. The Popular Alliance, led by conservatives associated with the old Franco regime, took 17 seats with 8.2% of the popular vote. Most of the remaining seats were won by Basque and Catalan moderate parties.

Brezhnev Named Soviet President—Communist Party General Secretary Leonid I. Brezhnev was named president of the Soviet Union by the Supreme

Soviet, **June 16**. It was the first time in Soviet history that the party chief also held the post of chief of state. The 70-year-old Brezhnev replaced former President Nikolai V. Podgorny, who had resigned under pressure in May. Brezhnev had previously served as president (officially, Chairman of the Presidium of the Supreme Soviet) from May 1960 to June 1964, and had been a Presidium member for the last several years. Brezhnev said, **June 17**, that his elevation to the presidency was a recognition of the primacy of the Communist Party "in deciding all the key questions of state life." In addition, the state post would give him formal parity with heads of state of non-Communist countries in his diplomatic activities.

Begin Named Israel Prime Minister—Menachem Begin, leader of the major opposition party for the 29 years since the founding of Israel, was voted prime minister, **June 21**, by the nation's Parliament. His new government, which included members of his own Likud bloc as well as members of the National Religious Party and Agudat Israel, was given a vote of confidence by 63 members of the 120 members of Parliament. Former Defense Minister Moshe Dayan, who left the Labor Party to enter Begin's government, became foreign minister. Three of the 15 ministerial places were left vacant, in hopes that the Democratic Movement for Change would join the governing coalition.

Moscow Denounces Eurocommunism—In an authoritative **June 23** editorial in the journal *New Times*, the Soviet leadership denounced Spanish Communist Party leader Santiago Carrillo and called his concept of Eurocommunism an anti-Soviet attempt to split the world communist movement. Carrillo had called for Western European communist parties to reject Soviet domination and Stalinist techniques of gaining and retaining power. The Spanish Communist Party Central Committee responded, **June 26**, with a sharply-worded statement rejecting the use of "anathema and excommunication" by Moscow, and said "the Soviet Union cannot be presented as the ideal model of socialist society."

General

Miami Rights Defeat Stirs Gay Protest—Dade County, Fla. voters, by a more than 2-1 margin, voted, **June 7**, to repeal a county ordinance that prohibited discrimination on the grounds of sexual preference in employment, housing, and public accommodation. The vote had attracted national attention when singer Anita Bryant emerged as leader of the anti-homosexual campaign in Miami. Calling homosexuals "human garbage" and blaming them for natural disasters like the drought in California and the frost in Florida, Bryant formed a group called Save Our Children, which told voters that male homosexual teachers would molest school children if the bill were not repealed. Homosexual-rights leaders in Miami called the molestation issue "totally false," and suggested that Bryant's group should be called "Save Some of Our Children — Discard the Rest." Homosexuals and their supporters responded to the vote with a series of marches and rallies in cities throughout the U.S., **June 26**, with 100,000 participating in San Francisco and tens of thousands in New York.

U.S. Steel Signs Pollution Accord—The United States Steel Corporation entered a consent decree in U.S. District Court in Hammond, Ind., **June 16**, agreeing to install a $70-million water recycling system at its Gary steel plant. The company also agreed to pay a $3.5-million fine for violating air and water pollution standards of the U.S. Environmental Protection Agency and the State of Indiana, and to pay $750,000 for further pollution research. The consent decree ended a 5-year dispute over waste discharge into Lake Michigan and the Grand Calumet River. By Aug. 1, 1980, more than 90% of ammonia, cyanide, and phenols will have to be removed from the up to 775 million gallons of water discharged by the plant each day; limits would be set on oil, grease, sulphates, and chlorides discharged.

EPA OKs Seabrook Plant—The U.S. Environmental Protection Agency approved, **June 17**, a water cooling system for the 2,300-megawatt Seabrook, N.H., nuclear power plant. The Nuclear Regulatory Commission earlier said it would authorize construction on the plant if the system were approved. The plant would draw 1.2 billion gallons of sea water daily in order to cool the reactor core. As a side effect, the water temperature would be raised 39 degrees before being returned to the ocean; cleaning procedures would periodically raise the temperature some 120 degrees.

Disasters—A fire of electrical origin in the Pacha Club in Abidjan, Ivory Coast, killed 41 people, **June 9**. Most of the victims were believed to be French nationals. . . . Carbon monoxide and cyanide fumes from a burning padded cell killed 34 prisoners and 8 visitors in the Maury County Jail in Columbia, Tenn., **June 6**. Andrew J. Zinmer, a 16-year-old prisoner, was charged with arson, **June 27**. The material in the padding had been tested for flammability, but the Tennessee fire marshall's office had known for two years that the tests may not have been "appropriate."

JULY
National

Liddy Granted Early Parole—The U.S. Parole Commission, **July 12**, granted an early release from prison to G. Gordon Liddy, the only one of the Watergate conspirators who refused to tell his story. Liddy, given the longest sentence of all the conspirators, had been in custody since Jan. 30, 1973. The commission made its decision after Pres. Jimmy Carter had commuted Liddy's sentence from 20 to 8 years. On **Sept. 6**, Liddy appeared before a federal magistrate in Williamsport, Pa., to take a pauper's oath, establishing he was too poor to pay a $40,000 fine, a condition for his early release on **Sept. 7**. Liddy, **Sept. 8**, again refused to discuss the 1972 Watergate break-in with reporters.

Carter OKs Admittance of More Indochina Refugees—Pres. Jimmy Carter, **July 15**, approved a state department request to admit an additional 15,000 Indochinese refugees to the U.S. in 1977 and 1978. The number would include some 7,000 "boat people" still living on vessels they had used to escape from Vietnam.

Jaworski to Head Korean Inquiry—Former Watergate Prosecutor Leon A. Jaworski, **July 20**, accepted a House ethics committee invitation to take charge of its investigation of Korean influence-buying. It was hoped Jaworski's presence would revive public confidence in the investigation shaken by the resignation of special counsel Philip A. Lacovara **July 15**. Lacovara had quit with complaints of conflicts and a lack of trust between himself and committee chairman Rep. John J. Flynt Jr. (D, Ga.). Jaworski, **July 21**, said he despised "crooks" of any political stripe and vowed he would pursue investigations of alleged wrongdoing by Democratic Congressmen as vigorously as he had pursued White House Republicans in the Watergate scandal. In the ongoing Korean investigation, Congressional sources had reported, **July 10**, that an ethics committee survey of the House had revealed a more extensive pattern of South Korean favors for senior House members than previously reported. According to the survey, at least 115 Congressmen and former Congressmen had been involved, including former Speaker Carl Albert, the current speaker, Thomas P. O'Neill Jr. (D, Mass.), and House Majority Whip John Brademas (D, Ind.).

GNP Up 6.4% in Second Quarter—The commerce department, **July 21**, reported that the nation's "real" gross national product rose 6.4% during the spring quarter of 1977. Although the growth rate was smaller than the revised 7.5% registered during the first quarter, economists considered it encouraging because it was not concentrated in one sector, and was therefore indicative of stronger, better-balanced growth. Spurred by an increase in the number of jobless women and teenagers, the nation's unemployment rate rose by .2% to 7.1% in June, according to a **July 8** labor department report. However, the number of persons employed increased for the 8th straight month, rising to about 90.6 million.

Urban League Head Attacks Carter—Urban League Executive Director Vernon Jordan, **July 24**, at the league's annual convention in Washington, D.C., charged that the Carter administration had "fallen short on policies, programs, and people." "We expected Mr. Carter to be working as hard to meet the needs of minorities and the poor as he did to get our votes," Jordan said. "But so far, we have been disappointed." Citing specific issues, Jordan stated that despite the administration's assertion that it had done especially well in placing blacks in significant offices, the record had fallen short of black expectations. Jordan asserted that despite Carter's campaign promises, there had been too much talk of balancing the budget and too little effort to create employment, especially for young people. Carter, addressing the same convention **July 25**, said he had "no apologies" for his administration's record of dealing with blacks and urban poor. In his own defense, he cited various jobs and educational programs his administration had formulated.

Record Trade Deficit Set in June—The United States set a record trade deficit of $2.82 billion during June, the commerce department reported **July 27**. The figure, twice that expected by most experts, led to a 19.75-point drop on the stock market. The figure, representing the excess of imports over exports, was twice the May figure and the 13th consecutive monthly deficit. A rise of 26% in oil imports was the major factor behind the June deficit. The deficit was also attributed to the continued slower pace of economic recovery worldwide and resultant reduction in demand for U.S. exports.

Alaska North Slope Oil Reaches Valdez—Despite 6 shutdowns of the 800-mile Trans-Alaska pipeline, Alaska North Slope crude oil, **July 29**, reached Valdez. The oil, which had been in transit for 38½ days, was poured into tankers headed for refineries in California, Washington, and the Middle West.

International

Pakistani Military Seizes Power—The Pakistani army, **July 5**, seized power from Prime Minister Zulfikar Ali Bhutto in a bloodless coup d'etat, imposed martial rule, and promised to hold elections in October. Pakistani radio announced that the coup had been initiated "to fill the vacuum created by political leaders." Army Chief of Staff Gen. Mohammed Zia ul-Haq took over as chief martial law administrator; Pres. Fazal Elahi Choudhry remained head of state. Gen. Zia announced that Bhutto and his cabinet had been taken into "temporary protective custody."

Chinese Pilot Defects to Taiwan—Fan Yuan-yen, a 41-year-old Chinese Air Force pilot, **July 7**, broke away from a routine patrol mission and flew his plane to Taiwan. On arrival in Taipei, he said, "Life on the mainland is too miserable. . . . I cannot stand it any longer." As a defector from the People's Republic of China, he was eligible for a National government award in gold worth about $800,000. On **July 8**, Fan described China as a land of widespread discontent and disillusionment over the frequent purges and political shifts. He also said that China was too weak militarily to launch an attack on Taiwan.

North Korea Shoots Down U.S. Copter—U.S. Pres. Jimmy Carter announced, **July 14**, that North Korea, **July 13**, had apparently shot down a U.S. army helicopter that had inadvertently strayed into North Korean airspace. Three crewmen were killed and a 4th was wounded and captured. Following unusually amicable negotiations at a meeting of the Miltary Armistice Commission, North Korea, **July 16**, turned over the bodies of the 3 crewmen and freed the 4th.

Smith Calls Rhodesian Elections—Rhodesian Prime Minister Ian D. Smith, **July 18**, dissolved parliament and called a general election for Aug. 31. He said he was acting because British proposals for a constitutional settlement for Rhodesia's future government were "unacceptable" and, consequently, he would seek a new mandate for an internal political settlement. British Foreign Minister David Owen, **July 19**, condemned Smith's move, but said it would not put an end to British-American efforts toward a solution of the Rhodesian question.

Carter, Begin Meet on Middle East—Concluding 2 days of talks with Israeli Prime Minister Menahem Begin in Washington, D.C., U.S. Pres. Jimmy Carter, **July 20**, voiced confidence that a Geneva peace conference on the Middle East would be convened as early as October. Carter based his optimistic assessment on his discussions with Begin and a series of earlier talks with Arab leaders. However, just a few hours later, Begin outlined his hitherto secret framework proposals for Geneva talks, excluding any role for the Palestine Liberation Organization, whose participation was a basic demand of all Arab countries.

Bandaranaike Party Ousted in Sri Lanka—Prime Minister Sirimavo Bandaranaike's ruling Sri Lanka Freedom party, **July 21**, suffered a humiliating defeat at the hands of Junius R. Jayawardene's United National party in parliamentary elections. In the final tally, the United National party held 139 seats, up from 19, in the 168-member parliament; the Freedom party held 8 seats, a loss of 73 from the last assembly. Although Bandanaraike held her seat in a close race, all 11 members of her cabinet lost their seats. Bandaranaike's personal rule was generally regarded as the key issue in the election. She had governed the nation under emergency rule since a communist-inspired student rebellion in 1971. Jayawardene had centered his campaign on the poor state of the economy, unemployment, and alleged personal abuses of power by Bandaranaike and her many office-holding relatives.

Teng Rehabilitated—The Chinese government, **July 22**, officially announced that Teng Hsiao-ping, toppled in a 1976 power struggle, had been rehabilitated. It was also announced that his radical opponents, the so-called Gang of Four, had been expelled from the Chinese Communist party. The decisions had been made by the party's central committee. The committee also confirmed Hua Kuo-feng as party chairman, successor to Mao Tse-tung. Teng would resume his posts as party deputy chairman and as deputy prime minister.

Cease-fire Ends Egyptian-Libyan Clashes—Egyptian Pres. Anwar Sadat, **July 24**, ordered Egyptian forces to observe a cease-fire, negotiated by Arab mediators, to end major border clashes between Egypt and Libya. Sadat's announcement came shortly after he had met privately with Algerian Pres. Houari Boumedienne, who had arrived in Cairo unexpectedly from Tripoli where he had conferred with Libyan Pres. Col. Muammar el-Qaddafi. Following a month of minor skirmishes, Egypt, **July 21**, reported that it had beaten back a Libyan armored and aerial attack over the border near the village of Salum. Egypt claimed Libya had lost 40 tanks and 2 airplanes in the clash. On **July 22**, Egyptian military sources announced that Egyptian planes had bombed and strafed a Libyan air base near Tobruk in retaliation for the Libyan raid. As Libya, **July 23**, claimed that Egyptian forces, mounted with heavy armor, had struck deep inside its borders, Palestinian officials reported that mediation efforts by Palestine Liberation Organization head Yasir Arafat had led to a tentative cease-fire. It was also reported that Egyptian officials were privately saying that, although they had not sought the confrontation, they were not determined that it would lead to the overthrow of el-Qaddafi. Sadat, **July 22**, blamed the Libyan leader, whom he called "that very strange person," for a steady 3-year deterioration in relations between the 2 countries. On **July 26**, as the cease-fire seemed to be holding, Sadat announced that the conflict was over.

General

Massive Blackout Stills New York City — A massive power failure sparked by lightning strikes north of the city, **July 13**, about 9:30 in the evening, left some 9 million people without electricity in all 5 New York City boroughs and parts of Westchester county. Although some power was restored 4½ hours later, total restoration was not completed until the evening of **July 14**, 25 hours after the backout hit. Soon after the lights failed, widespread looting and vandalism erupted in primarily black and Hispanic neighborhoods. More than 2,700 persons were arrested and nearly 100 policemen injured. The stock exchanges and office buildings remained deserted **July 14**, as Mayor Abe Beame urged millions of workers to stay home. All New York City subways, the Long Island Railroad, and Conrail were shut down for most of the day. Financial and retail activity was severely disrupted; an estimated **$20** million in retail sales was lost or deferred. Losses to vandalism and looting were estimated at **$1** billion. Con Edison, the immediate butt of public indignation, attributed the failure to an "act of God," but admitted that the protective systems installed after the 1965 blackout had been inadequate in the face of lightning. City and federal officials said they would conduct investigations of Con Edison. The Small Business Administration, **July 15**, gave "disaster status" to the blackout area. The Carter administration, **July 23**, approved an **$11.3** million program of grants and loans to help New York City recover from the looting and vandalism, but, **July 31**, without explanation, denied the city disaster status. The city had bid for **$11.7-million** reimbursements for overtime for the police and other departments. On **Aug. 24**, Con Edison, which was conducting its own investigation of the power failure, for the first time attributed the major blame to human and mechanical failure rather than lightning.

VA Nurses Convicted in Poisonings — A Detroit, Mich., federal jury, **July 13**, convicted 2 Filipino nurses of 5 nonfatal poisonings at the Veterans Administration Hospital in Ann Arbor in 1975. The 2 nurses, Filipina D. Narcisco and Leonora M. Perez, were convicted of acting together to poison one patient and separately to poison 2 persons each by injecting a muscle relaxant into the patients' intravenous medication tubes. Although originally murder charges had also been brought against the nurses, they were later thrown out for lack of evidence. The 2 nurses, **July 14**, stated that they felt "disillusioned and betrayed by American justice." The prosecution, which had offered no motive nor produced any eye witnesses, suggested that the nurses had committed the poisonings to underscore serious understaffing problems at the hospital.

Hanafi Moslems Convicted — An all-black Washington, D.C., Superior Court jury, **July 23**, convicted 12 Hanafi Moslems, who had seized 3 buildings in the city in March, of various charges, including conspiracy, armed kidnapping, and murder in the 2d degree. Maurice Williams, a Howard University reporter was killed in the seizures. Hamaas Abdul Khaalis, the Hanafi leader, and 2 of his followers were convicted of the murder charge. Khaalis was also convicted of 24 counts of armed kidnapping, assault, and conspiracy to commit kidnapping. In all, the 12 Hanafi Moslems were found guilty of 139 counts listed in the 373-count indictment. As the main witness for the defense, Khaalis had contended that not he, but Allah, had directed the siege and that his men had carried arms into the building as "purely a defensive move." U.S. Attorney Earl Silbert commented on the verdict: "This jury has sent a message to all terrorists that this conduct will not be tolerated in the nation's capital or anywhere else in this country." Superior Court Judge Nicholas S. Nunzio, **Sept. 6**, handed down extremely severe sentences to the 12 Moslems. Khaalis was sentenced to serve from 41 to 123 years in prison. The most stringent sentence, 77 years to life in prison, was given to Abdul Muzikir, who was convicted of firing the gun that killed Williams. The other sentences, varying in number of years, were almost as severe as those given to Khaalis and Muzikit.

Brush Fire Sweeps California Community — An explosive brush fire, **July 26**, destroyed more than 185 homes in Santa Barbara, Cal., one of the most scenic residential communities in the U.S. The homes were each worth upward of **$100,000**. The fire started in Montecito, an affluent, residential community in the hills above Santa Barbara, when a box kite became entangled in high-voltage electrical lines.

Judge Halts Work at Kent State Site — Federal Judge Thomas D. Lambros, **July 29**, in Cleveland, Ohio granted a temporary stay to halt construction work at the controversial site of a **$6-million** gymnasium at Kent State University until the case would be heard in federal district court. The site is part of the campus area where 4 students were killed and 9 wounded in a May 1970 confrontation with National Guardsmen in a demonstration over the U.S. invasion of Cambodia. One hundred ninety-four demonstrators who wanted the site preserved as a memorial had been peacefully arrested at the site **July 12**. They were charged with contempt of court for disobeying a **July 11** court order to leave the site.

Disasters — Floods and landslides caused by heavy rains claimed at least 111 lives and left 73 persons missing in and around the South Korean capital of Seoul, it was reported **July 11**. . . . A night-long 7-inch rainfall, **July 20**, caused a massive flash flood in Johnstown, Pa., and its surrounding communities, leaving 68 persons dead, 31 missing, and 2,000 persons homeless. . . . Typhoon Thelma hit southern Taiwan, **July 25**, killing 28 persons, injuring more than 200, and destroying 200,000 homes. A second typhoon hit northern Taiwan, **July 30**, killing 11 persons, including 5 persons crushed to death when a steel bridge support collapsed in downtown Taipei.

AUGUST

National

CIA Mind-Control Program Detailed — Further details of a CIA program to develop mind-control techniques were revealed, **Aug. 1**, by the New York Times. The CIA had reported, **July 15**, that it had uncovered some 2,000 documents relating to the program that had not surfaced during 1975 and 1976 Senate investigations. An additional 10,000 documents were subsequently discovered, the CIA said, **Sept. 2**. Among the newly disclosed information was that the agency had used 3 private medical foundations to channel millions of dollars to universities and hospitals to finance research on LSD, tranquilizers, hypnotism, and methods such as sensory deprivation. Prisoners, mental patients, and private citizens were used for the tests, sometimes without their knowledge. Some 80 institutions, including 44 colleges and universities, were involved at one time or another in aspects of the project, though some researchers had no knowledge of CIA involvement. In addition, apartments were rented in New York and San Francisco, in which men, lured by prostitutes, were unknowingly given mind-affecting drugs and observed for possible behavior changes. The program, most active in the 1950s and 1960s, was finally terminated in 1973, without any apparent success.

Strip Mine Bill Approved — President Carter signed into law, **Aug. 3**, a bill to regulate strip mining of coal, though, he said, he "would have preferred a stricter bill." The bill, sought by environmentalists for 10 years, was the first federal measure to regulate strip mining in all states. Mine operators would be required to restore land to its approximate original contour, replant grass and trees, and prevent siltation and pollution of streams. A federal tax on coal tonnage would pay for the reclamation of lands previously damaged by unrestricted strip mining, and would finance social services in Western strip mine boom towns. States would be required to set up control plans meeting Interior Department standards. Certain farm lands would be barred to strip mining, and blasting near homes and highways would be restricted. The bill would take affect in 1979, with an 18-month extension for 80% of mines, considered "small." The bill was considered less strict than others passed in 1974 and 1975 and vetoed by President Ford.

Energy Department Created — President Carter signed an act, **Aug. 4**, creating a new Energy Department, the first addition to the Cabinet since the Department of Transportation in 1966. His nominee for the post of energy secretary, James Schlesinger, was confirmed by a voice vote in the Senate later that day. House and Senate final votes of approval, **Aug. 2**, were 353-57 and 76-14. Congress refused Carter's request to give the energy secretary power to set natural gas prices. Instead, a new federal energy regulatory commission would set rates for the sale and transportation of natural gas and electricity, and transportation of oil by pipeline. The president could, however, overrule the commission in matters of overriding national importance.

Carter Asks Welfare Reform — President Carter disclosed, **Aug. 6**, his administration's proposals for overhauling the nation's welfare system. It would incorporate a work requirement for many recipients and increase payments and tax benefits for lower- and middle-income workers. Poor people unable to work, including the aged, disabled, and single parents of children under 7, would receive somewhat higher benefits. But single parents (mostly mothers) whose youngest child was between 7 and 14 would have to work part time, or full time, if day care were available. A single parent whose youngest child was 14 or over would have to take a job or lose most of his or her benefits. The bill would create up to 1.4 million public jobs, for those who couldn't find work. Secretary of Labor Ray Marshall said about 28% of adults now on welfare would be placed in these public jobs. Low-wage working parents with family incomes up to $8,500 would get supplemental assistance. Families of four with incomes up to $15,600 would receive tax relief. States and localities would get increased federal assistance of $2.1 billion, to help meet welfare costs. The bill would raise the total cost of welfare aid and public jobs by $2.8 billion a year, and the tax cuts would amount to $3.3 billion a year.

Economic Index Slows — The Commerce Department reported, **Aug. 30**, that its Index of Leading Indicators declined by 0.2% in July, the 3d successive monthly decline of that size. This was the longest consecutive decline since the 1974-75 recession. The unemployment rate declined in July to 6.9% of the work force, the Bureau of Labor Statistics reported, **Aug. 5**, but Julius Shiskin, commissioner of labor statistics, said that day that labor markets had shown "lackluster performance" in the previous few months, especially for black job-seekers. Consumer prices in July showed the smallest monthly rise of the year, increasing only 0.4% the Labor Department reported, **Aug. 19**.

Mandel Found Guilty — Maryland Governor Marvin Mandel and 5 associates were convicted, **Aug. 23**, of 18 counts of mail fraud and racketeering by a federal jury after 113 hours of jury deliberation, the longest on record in a federal criminal case. The governor was found to have used his power to obtain legislation adding 18 days to the racing season at Marlboro Race Track, in which the other defendants had secretly obtained ownership. In exchange, he accepted some $350,000 in cash, loans, investments, goods, and services. The 57-year-old Mandel was the 3d governor in U.S. history to be convicted in office. Mandel was sentenced, **Oct. 7**, to 4 years in jail, and automatically suspended from his powers of office. A 1976 trial on the same charges had ended in a mistrial.

Atlantic Oil Search OKd — A 3-judge U.S. Court of Appeals panel in New York ruled, **Aug. 25**, that a $1 billion 1976 federal sale of oil drilling rights off the northeast shore was valid. The court overruled a February lower court decision which said the Interior Department environmental impact statement had been inadequate. Oil companies which had taken leases on over half a million acres in 93 tracts some 47-90 miles off the Atlantic Coast from Long Island to Maryland, said they hoped to start drilling by the end of the year, though commercial production would not start for another 3 years. The government had estimated that between 400 million to 1.4 billion barrels of oil, and between 2,600 billion to 9,400 billion cubic feet of natural gas might be buried off the coast.

Park Tong Sun Indicted — Korean businessman Park Tong Sun was indicted, **Aug. 23**, by a federal grand jury, on criminal charges related to his alleged bribery of U.S. congressmen on behalf of the South Korean government. The indictment named former Representative Richard Hanna of California as an unindicted co-conspirator. Park denied, **Aug. 24**, in Seoul, South Korea that he was an agent of his government, and he denied having given money to congressmen.

International

ASEAN Economic Accords—The 5 members of

ASEAN (Association of Southeast Asian Nations) signed a series of economic accords, **Aug. 5**, as a step toward a more "viable and cohesive regional organization." Indonesia, the Philippines, Malaysia, Singapore, and Thailand agreed to set aside a $100 million joint fund "to help members bridge temporary international liquidity problems," to give preference to each other in exports of oil and rice, and to reduce tariffs on 71 items by the end of the year.

$10 Billion IMF Fund Set—The U.S., 5 other industrial nations, and 5 oil-exporting nations agreed, **Aug. 6**, to provide $10 billion in loans to a special International Monetary Fund account to help poor countries hurt by the world economic slowdown and oil price rises. The U.S. share, if approved by Congress, would be $1.7 billion.

Panama Canal Agreement Reached—U.S. and Panamanian negotiators announced, **Aug. 10**, that they had reached agreement on the terms of a new Panama Canal treaty, that would return the canal and the Canal Zone to complete Panamanian control by the end of this century. U.S. negotiators Ellsworth Bunker and Sol Linowitz said the accord would strengthen U.S. security and improve ties with Latin America. Dr. Romulo Escobar Bethancourt, chief Panamanian negotiator, said the treaty, which took "13 arduous years" to negotiate, would return to Panama its "full physiognomy as a nation." President Carter, expecting a difficult Senate battle for ratification, obtained endorsements of the treaty from former Secretary of State Henry Kissinger, **Aug. 15**, and former President Ford, **Aug. 16**

U.S., U.K. Set Rhodesia Plan—The U.S. and Britain agreed, **Aug. 13**, on a plan for the peaceful transition to majority rule in Rhodesia, but failed to gain approval from most of the leading figures in the dispute. The plan provided for universal suffrage, a UN-controlled international security force, disbanding of Rhodesian government and guerrilla forces, and a development fund. But British Foreign Secretary David Owen and U.S. Ambassador to the UN Andrew Young were told by guerrilla leaders, in Lusaka talks, **Aug. 28**, that only "those forces that are fighting for change" should control the independence process. South African Prime Minister John Vorster also rejected aspects of the plan, in talks with the 2 western diplomats, **Aug. 29**. Ian Smith, prime minister of the minority white regime in Rhodesia, who had won an overwhelming election victory, **Aug. 21**, over hard line and liberal opposition groups, denounced the U.S.-British plan, **Sept. 2**. At least 11 persons had been killed and 76 wounded, **Aug. 6**, in a terrorist bombing of a Salisbury variety store.

New Chinese Leaders Named—A new 26-member Communist Party Politburo was announced in Peking, **Aug. 21**, after the conclusion of the party's 11th Congress. Its members, and those of the new 333-member Central Committee, included a high proportion of military men, technocrats, and former officials purged during the "cultural revolution" in the 1960s. Party Chairman Hua Kuo-feng and Deputy Chairmen Yen Chien-ying (also defense minister) and Teng Hsiao-ping (also deputy prime minister) appeared to share top power. Hua proclaimed to the Congress, for the first time, that the cultural revolution, the symbol of Mao Tse-tung's radical revolutionary purism and of violent political strife, had been completed with the arrest of Mao's widow, Chiang Ching. A new party constitution, published **Aug. 23**, set economic growth as a major national goal. In another development, Li Hsien-nien, a member of the Politburo's standing committee, said, **Aug. 29**, that China was "quite unhappy" with continued U.S. support of Taiwan. U.S. Secretary of State Cyrus Vance had visited China, **Aug. 22-26**, in an attempt to advance the prospect of full diplomatic relations between the 2 countries.

South Africa Denies A-Bomb—President Carter said, **Aug. 23**, that he had been informed by South Africa that it had no nuclear weapons and had no intention of conducting nuclear tests at any time. The denial came after public charges, by the U.S.S.R., Aug. 9 and 14, that South Africa would have 100 atomic bombs within one year, and by France, Aug. 22, that South Africa was about to explode a nuclear device. The New York Times reported, **Aug. 31**, that U.S. officials had said satellite photos suggested that a South African nuclear test was in preparation.

General

Bombs, Threats Harrass New York—Two terrorist bombs attributed to Puerto Rican extremists exploded in midtown Manhattan, **Aug. 3**, killing one person and injuring 7 more. A series of bomb threats that day led to the evacuation of 100,000 workers from a dozen office buildings around Manhattan, causing millions of dollars in business losses. The F.A.L.N., a Puerto Rican independence group that had been implicated in 60 previous bombings in New York, Chicago, Newark, and Washington, claimed credit for the bombings in 2 telephone calls to a local television station.

Son of Sam Arrested—David Richard Berkowitz, a 24-year-old postal employee believed to be the Son of Sam killer, who murdered 6 young people and wounded 7 others in a year-long series of random nighttime attacks on New York City streets, was arrested, **Aug. 10**, outside his Yonkers, N.Y. home. He was reportedly carrying the .44-caliber Bulldog revolver used in the killings. By **Aug. 24**, he had been formally charged with all of the attacks, which took place between July 29, 1976 and July 31, 1977. Berkowitz had been traced when police checked every car that had been issued a parking ticket near the scene of the final shooting in Brooklyn. One of the cars belonged to Berkowitz, who had been reported to the Yonkers Police Department by several Yonkers residents on suspicion of having sent threatening letters. The string of attacks, all aimed at young women and their companions, usually while the victims sat in parked cars in quiet, residential areas, had terrorized many New Yorkers, forcing police to set up a 300-man task force to investigate every lead. The crimes had no apparent motive; when questioned by police, Berkowitz reportedly said, "It was a command. I had a sign and I followed it." A New York State supreme court judge ruled, Oct. 21, that Berkowitz was fit to stand trial.

S.E.C. Charges New York Bond Deception—The Securities and Exchange Commission, in an 800-page report issued **Aug. 26**, charged that New York City Mayor Abraham Beame, City Comptroller Harrison J. Goldin, 6 New York banks, and the brokerage firm Merrill Lynch, Pierce, Fenner, and Smith all knowingly misled purchasers of New York City bonds in 1974-75, by not informing them of the city's deteriorating financial situation. Five of the banks—Chase Manhattan, Citibank, Morgan Guaranty Trust, Manufacturers Hanover Trust, and Bankers Trust, were accused of selling their own city notes while encouraging other investors to buy. Mayor Beame responded, **Aug. 27**, by calling the report a "political" document.

Disasters—The U.S. Interagency Fire Center said, **Aug. 8**, that it had flown 4,000 firefighters into Western fire areas in the preceding week. Millions of acres of timber, parched by drought and ignited by unusual lightning storms, burned out of control in every state west of the Rocky Mountains early in August. Some 90% of the fires were in central and northern California. Hundreds of millions of dollars in timber losses were feared. . . . Over 200 people were killed in southeastern Indonesia, **Aug. 19,** when a powerful earthquake occurred in the Indian Ocean some 400 miles to the South.

SEPTEMBER
National

American Journalists Linked to CIA—It was reported, **Sept. 11,** that the upcoming issue of *Rolling Stone* would reveal that over the past 25 years some 400 American journalists had secretly shared information with and, in some cases, provided operational assistance to the CIA. The report, written by *Washington Post* reporter Carl Bernstein, named only a few, including *New York Times* foreign affairs columnist C. L. Sulzberger, Joseph Alsop, and the late Stewart Alsop. The article also stated that the *New York Times*, between 1950 and 1960, had allowed "about 10 CIA employees" to pose as clerks or part-time correspondents in some of its foreign bureaus. The *Washington Post*, the *Louisville Courier-Journal*, Copley News Service, ABC, NBC, the Associated Press, United Press International, Reuters, the Hearst newspaper chain, Time, Inc., and *Newsweek*,

---

Lance Resigns in Controversy Over Finances; Carter Defends Judgment in Appointing Lance

Tenaciously defending himself and his record to the end, Bert Lance, **Sept. 21,** finally bowed to pressure over his disputed financial practices and resigned as director of the Office of Management and Budget.

Pres. Jimmy Carter, announcing the resignation at a press conference, stated that he accepted his friend's decision with "regret and sorrow," but believed that Lance had "exonerated himself completely." Carter, who had defended Lance throughout the controversy, also denied that he had made a mistake in judgment in appointing Lance to the office. But Carter did concede that, given the circumstances, Lance had made the right decision "because it would be difficult for him to devote full time to his responsibilities in the future."

In his letter of resignation, Lance had written that his conscience was clear and that he was still convinced that he could continue as an effective budget director. He explained, however, that the "amount of controversy" over his financial exploits and "the continuing nature of it" had forced him to submit his resignation.

Lance, **Sept. 15-17,** had aggressively defended himself in hearings before the Senate Governmental Affairs committee, the committee that had approved his nomination in January. Presenting a point-by-point defense of his personal financial affairs, Lance, **Sept. 15,** maintained he had disclosed the various financial matters now in question to the committee before his confirmation hearings began. He assailed the senators for ignoring the "basic American principles of justice and fair play" and for damaging his reputation with accusations that were "accompanied by prompt and destructive interpretations by certain members of this body."

Lance had first come under attack over news accounts about a **$3.4** million loan he had obtained from the First National City Bank of Chicago shortly after his Georgia bank had established a correspondent relationship with the Chicago bank. The Senate Governmental Affairs committee, **July 25,** accepted Lance's contention that there had been "nothing improper" about his financial dealings and decided against investigating further.

Then, on **Aug. 5,** Comptroller of the Currency John Heimann questioned Lance about a secret memorandum apparently linking a **$2.6** million personal loan from Manufacturers Hanover Trust to the opening of a correspondent relationship between it and the National Bank of Georgia, of which Lance was an official. Use of bank funds as a compensating balance to underpin a personal loan to a bank official is illegal under banking regulations.

The comptrollers' investigation, however, ended **Aug. 18,** with the report that he had found no information to warrant criminal prosecution. But Heiman did criticize Lance's practices as a Georgia bank executive: "This recurring pattern of shifting bank relationships and personal borrowing raises unresolved questions as to what constitutes acceptable banking practice." The report also said overdrafts on the personal accounts of bank officers and their families, a reference to the Lance family's massive overdrafts at the Calhoun First National Bank, "constituted unsafe and unsound banking practices."

Despite the comptrollers' conclusions, questions over Lance's finances continued. On **Aug. 26,** Presidential Press Secretary Jody Powell confirmed that Lance had used a single block of shares as collateral for 2 separate loans from 2 banks. A study by the office of the comptroller revealed, **Sept. 3,** that Lance may have used for political purposes a plane leased or owned by a Georgia bank Lance had once headed.

On **Sept. 6,** the Senate Governmental Affairs committee voted a full-scale investigation, complete with subpoena power, of Lance's financial dealings. Currency Comptroller Heimann, **Sept. 7,** ,stated that Lance and his wife, LaBelle, had received some **$3.5** million in loans or refinancing over a period of 13 years from the Fulton National Bank in Atlanta where Lance's Calhoun bank had maintained a substantial account under a correspondent relationship.

Appearing before the Senate committee, Heimann, **Sept. 8,** stated that Lance and his family had abused their influential positions in overdrawing their accounts. Heimann said he would not have recommended Lance as "well-qualified," as had Acting Comptroller Robert Bloom in January.

Bloom, under intensive questioning by the committee, **Sept. 12,** admitted that he had unintentionally misled the committee when he had written a letter commending Lance. On the same day, Presidential Press Secretary Powell disclosed that 3 presidential aides had read FBI reports critical of Lance's banking practices, but had not shown them to Carter, because of assurances from a senior official in the comptroller's office that such practices were common in small rural banks.

Lance, **Sept. 22,** returned to this hometown of Calhoun, Ga., to be greeted by a cheering crowd of residents who had stood by him during his ordeal. Another Georgian, James T. McIntyre, became acting director of the Office of Management and Budget. As Lance returned home to straighten out his financial problems, justice department officials in Washington, D.C. began reviewing the "Lance affair" to determine if anything had been overlooked. Similar investigations were being conducted by the Securities and Exchange Commission, the Federal Elections Commission, and the Office of the Comptroller of the Currency.

had similar "cover" arrangements, the report alleged. Executives from NBC News, ABC News, the *New York Times*, Associated Press, Times, and *Newsweek*, **Sept. 12**, said they had been unable to find evidence their employees had maintained such confidential relationships with the CIA.

Assessments of Economy Conflict—Secretary of Labor Ray Marshall, **Sept. 13**, said the administration's economic program was not meeting some of its goals. He contended that more fiscal stimulus geared specifically to creating jobs for blacks and young people was necessary. On the same day, Council of Economic Advisers Chairman Charles L. Schultze said the nation's economic recovery was showing few signs of slowing, despite some 3rd quarter slackening in activity. Congress's Joint Economic Committee, **Sept. 25**, issued a pessimistic report on prospects for cutting inflation, fighting unemployment, and balancing the budget by 1981. The Federal Reserve System, attacked for having "systematically obstructed recovery" since the 1974 recession, bore the brunt of the blame.

Americans Arrive From Cuba With Relatives—Under a repatriation accord negotiated between the U.S. and Cuba in August, 29 Americans and 26 of their Cuban relatives, **Sept. 22**, arrived from Havana at Homestead Air Force Base in Florida. The agreement had been reached by Cuban Pres. Fidel Castro and U.S. Sen. Frank Church (D, Ida.), **Aug. 11**. U.S. Pres. Jimmy Carter described the arrival as "the first in what we hope will be a series of similar humanitarian actions on the part of the government of Cuba." The arrangements for the repatriation had been made by the newly established U.S. special interests section in Havana.

International

Bhutto, Arrested, Freed, Re-arrested — Pakistani police, **Sept. 3**, in Lahore, arrested former Prime Minister Zulfikar Ali Bhutto on charges of having conspired to murder a political opponent in 1974. A second murder conspiracy charge was added **Sept. 5**. Gen. Mohammed Zia ul-Haq, head of the military government, **Sept. 6**, stated that he had seen documentary evidence that implicated Bhutto in the murders. He also attacked Bhutto as "an evil genius" who had been "running this country on more or less Gestapo lines, misusing funds, blackmailing people." Bhutto was released on bail **Sept. 13**, but was arrested again, **Sept. 17**, along with 4 former cabinet members under a martial-law regulation designed to protect "the security of Pakistan."

Carter, Torrijos Sign Panama Canal Treaties — In the presence of representatives from 26 other Western Hemisphere nations, U.S. Pres. Jimmy Carter and Panamanian leader Brig. Gen. Omar Torrijos Herrara, **Sept. 7**, in Washington, D.C., signed 2 treaties that, if ratified, would transfer control of the Panama Canal to Panama by the year 2000.

Death in South Africa Stirs Controversy — South African Justice Minister James T. Kruger, **Sept. 12**, announced that Steven Biko, an influential young black leader, had died while in police detention apparently following a hunger strike. The news stunned the black community, especially young activists who considered Biko, the founder of the "black consciousness movement," as their leader. White opponents of South Africa's racial policies, **Sept. 14**, joined black leaders in demands for a judicial inquiry into Biko's death. Demands accelerated **Sept. 16**, when Kruger denied he had said Biko had starved himself to death, and on **Sept. 17**, when he admitted there had been many irregularities in police handling of Biko's death. Some 10,000 persons turned out in Kinwilliamstown, **Sept. 25**. for Biko's funeral. An autopsy report, leaked to reporters **Oct. 25**, revealed that Biko had died of brain damage.

Somalia Claims Major Victory over Ethiopia — The Western Somalia Liberation Front, **Sept. 14**, captured Jijiga, a strategic town at the base of the Ethiopian highlands in the Ogaden region, from Ethiopian units, it was announced **Sept. 18** by diplomatic sources in Addis Ababa, Ethiopia, and Mogadishu, Somalia. Apparently the Somali-backed liberation forces had regrouped since Ethiopian forces, **Sept. 6**, had routed Somali units attacking Jijiga, Harar, and Diredwa, the 3 key cities in the Ogaden. Somalia and Ethiopia had been in a virtual state of war for several months over the Ogaden region in eastern Ethiopia, a Somali-populated area that Somalia claims.

U.S, Canada Sign Gas Pipeline Accord — The U.S. and Canada, **Sept. 20**, in Ottawa, signed an agreement to construct a 2,700-mile pipeline to carry Alaskan natural gas across Canada to the continental U.S. U.S. Pres. Jimmy Carter and Canadian Prime Minister Pierre Elliott Trudeau had announced the accord **Sept. 7**, in Washington, D.C. Carter said the **$10-bil**lion pipeline, expected to be finished by 1981, would save American consumers **$5** billion over the next 20 years and provide new supplies to the gas-short Middle West.

Vietnam Admitted to UN — Sponsored by a record number of countries, Vietnam, **Sept. 20**, at the body's 32nd General Assembly, was admitted to the United Nations. Djibouti was also admitted, bringing UN membership up to 149 nations.

French Leftist Negotiations Break Down — Negotiations among France's leftist parties for a joint political program broke down in Paris **Sept. 23**. Although Communist, Socialist, and Left Radical leaders did not concede their 5-year alliance had collapsed, their statements reflected attempts to blame each other for the breakdown rather than efforts toward reconciliation. The leftist coalition had held a commanding lead in opinion polls since its victories in March municipal elections, but the recent feuding had already started to erode its popularity. The dispute emerged over Communist demands to change the platform for 1978 legislative elections. The chief areas of controversy were the extent of nationalization of industries, wage levels, and defense.

U.S.-British Rhodesia Plan Gains Support — Black Africa's front-line nations, **Sept. 24**, gave qualified support to the latest British-American plan for majority rule in Rhodesia. In a 2-day meeting in Maputo, Mozambique, representatives of Angola, Botswana, Mozambique, Tanzania, and Zambia decided the plan, despite "a lot of negative points," would serve as a "basis for further negotiations." The support was considered a major triumph because it was expected the front-line nations would seek to convince the chief Rhodesian guerrilla groups to accept the plan. The plan, presented to Rhodesian Prime Minister Ian D. Smith, **Sept. 1**, in Salisbury, called for a black majority government to be chosen in a one-man, one-vote election by the end of 1978. It also provided for UN peace-keeping troops to enforce a ceasefire in the guerrilla war and for the white-led Rhodesian army to be replaced by a national force based on the guerrilla forces. Smith, **Sept. 2**, had called key sections of the plan "mad," "crazy," and "insane," but had promised to consider it carefully before responding. On **Sept. 21**, Smith condemned the formula for creating the new Rhodesian army as "an attempt to appease the Russian-oriented terrorists who are operating from Zambia and Mozambique."

Israel Accepts U.S. Plan for Geneva Talks — The Israeli cabinet, **Sept 25**, voted to accept, with conditions, a U.S. proposal for reconvening the Geneva peace talks on the Middle East. The decision, a reversal of a previous rejection, was an apparent concession to U.S. Pres. Carter who had been pressing strongly for a resolution to the diplomatic deadlock stalling the conference. Egypt, Jordan, and Syria, the Arab states directly involved, also accepted the American plan, but rejected several of Israel's conditions centering on the role the Palestinians would assume at the conference. The disputed Israeli conditions stipulated that Palestinians participating at Geneva not be members of the Palestine Liberation Organization and that the Palestinians could not participate as a distinct delegation, but only as part of the Jordanian delegation.

Truce Ends Fighting in Southern Lebanon — A ceasefire arranged by the U.S., **Sept. 26**, ended heavy fighting that had broken out in southern Lebanon, **Sept. 16**, between Palestinian guerrillas and Israeli-backed Lebanese Christian militiamen. Lebanese and Palestinian sources reported, **Sept. 20**, that Israeli mobile units had crossed into Lebanon to help Christian forces in intensified fighting. Lebanese security forces reported **Sept. 21**, that Israeli forces had strengthened their positions and were occupying 6 strategic hilltops. The truce, arranged by the U.S. embassies in Lebanon and Israel, called for withdrawal of Palestinian guerillas to about 6 miles from the Israeli border and their replacement by Lebanese army troops. The Palestinians were also barred from firing into Israel from their new positions.

General

Judge Recalled Over Rape Case —Backed by strong feminist support, Moria Krueger, **Sept. 7**, defeated Dane County Judge Archie Simonson in Wisconsin's first judicial recall election. The election had drawn national attention because Simonson had suggested in court that a teenage boy was reacting "normally" to women's provocative clothing and to sexual permissiveness when he raped a 15-year-old girl. Krueger, one of 4 candidates facing Simonson, became Wisconsin's first elected female judge.

Rudd Surrenders—Radical underground leader Mark Rudd, **Sept. 14**, surrendered at the Manhattan district attorney's office to face numerous misdemeanor charges. He was immediately paroled in his own recognizance pending trial. Rudd, leader of the 1968 Columbia University student revolt, had been sought for 7½ years. He refused to discuss his activities as a fugitive or why he had surrendered. Rudd then flew to Chicago to turn himself in to authorities in Cook County where he faced similar misdemeanor charges stemming from the 1969 "Days of Rage" demonstrations there. On **Oct. 14**, in Manhattan criminal court, Rudd pleaded guilty, by arrangement, to criminal trespassing and was unconditionally discharged.

Koch Wins NYC Democratic Mayoral Primary—Rep. Edward I. Koch, **Sept. 19**, in a runoff for the New York City Democratic nomination for mayor, defeated Mario Cuomo, Gov. Hugh Carey's handpicked candidate. Koch's victory made him a strong favorite to win the election in November. In the **Sept. 8** primary which had drawn a record voter turnout, Koch and Cuomo had defeated 5 other candidates, including the incumbent, Mayor Abe Beame, and former Rep. Bella Abzug.

Disasters—An Ecuadorian airliner, **Sept. 5**, crashed into a mountain peak in the Cajas Mountains 25 miles north of Cuenca and exploded and burned, killing all 33 persons aboard. . . . Torrential rains struck the Kansas City, Mo., area, **Sept. 12**, setting off a devastating flash flood that took the lives of at least 26 persons.

OCTOBER

National

Watergate Sentences Reduced—Federal District Court Judge John J. Sirica, **Oct. 4**, sharply reduced the sentences of 3 principal figures in the Watergate case. Sirica acted after hearing tape-recorded statements in which John N. Mitchell, H. R. Haldeman, and John D. Ehrlichman stated they were guilty of wrongdoing and sorry for what they had done. Sirica reduced the original sentences of 30 months to 8 years to "not less than one year, nor more than 4 years." The 3 men were the only remaining persons convicted in the Watergate affair still serving prison sentences.

Senate Votes Natural Gas Deregulation—In another setback for Pres. Carter's energy program, the Senate, **Oct. 4**, in a 50-46 vote, approved controversial legislation that would free newly discovered natural gas from price controls. The proposal would phase in deregulation of gas produced offshore over 5 years and gas produced onshore over 2 years. The vote followed the end of an 8-day filibuster by liberal Democrats, who, in alliance with the White House, had contended the measure would substantially raise consumer prices without making more gas available. Senate Majority leader Robert C. Byrd, in conjunction with Vice Pres. Walter F. Mondale, forced the end of the filibuster **Oct. 3**, bringing accusations of White House perfidy from the filibuster leaders.

Unemployment Drops Slightly—Despite a labor department report that national unemployment had dropped from 7.1% to 6.9% in September, government officials, **Oct. 7**, stated there was little long-term improvement in the employment situation, particularly for blacks. Sen. William Proxmire (D, Wis.) said the figure indicated the economy was still in a period of "stagflation," i.e. a time when economic growth is stagnant while inflation grows. "The whites are doing pretty well, but the blacks are taking it on the chin," Proxmire said.

Arguments Heard in Bakke Case—In a packed court room, the Supreme Court, **Oct. 12**, heard arguments in the controversial case of the University of California v. Bakke. Allan Bakke, a white man, is contending that he was discriminated against when denied admission to the University of California at Davis medical school while several less qualified blacks and Hispanic Americans were admitted under a special system. In a justice department brief filed with the court, the Carter administration, **Sept. 19**, endorsed the argument that disadvantaged minority groups could constitutionally be given special consideration in university admissions. The brief, however, did not state whether the use of special racial quotas to attain this end were constitutional. Before the Supreme Court, former Watergate Special Prosecutor Archibald Cox, representing the California Board of Regents, argued that openly favoring blacks and other minority group members in professional school admissions was the only way to compensate for past generations of social and educational discrimination. Representing Bakke, Reynold H. Colvin maintained his client was the victim of an unconstitutional quota system which required the admission of a certain number of minority candidates even though they had lower overall ratings than some majority applicants who were rejected. Beyond academic admissions, the Supreme Court's opinion in the case could also affect affirmative action programs that currently require hiring and promotion of blacks and women by private employers in order to make up for past discrimination.

Carter Attacks Oil Industry—Trying to drum up public support for his badly mangled energy program, Pres. Jimmy Carter, **Oct. 13**, at a nationally televised press conference, sharply attacked the American oil industry. Identifying the petroleum lobby as the main source of opposition to his energy program, he accused the oil industry of staging the "biggest rip-off in history." He warned against "potential war profiteering" by the companies in an "impending energy crisis." Carter then indicated that if Congress did not produce energy legislation he considered suitable, he might turn to gasoline rationing or an import tax on foreign oil. He also suggested that he might veto energy legislation adopted by Congress if it "is not a substantial step forward." Senate leaders immediately rejected Carter's accusation that the energy lobby was responsible for Congressional defeats in his energy programs and blamed the White House instead. The major oil companies, in turn, attacked the president for making misleading, grossly exaggerated charges which they claimed made the oil industry the whipping boy for his ravaged energy program. "The president has made an emotional appeal to defend a tax program that is indefensible. . . . His energy program involves the largest peacetime tax increase ever imposed on our citizens," charged John E. Swearingen, chairman of the board of the Standard Oil Co. (Indiana).

U.S., S. Korea Fail to Agree on Park—Following 4 days of talks, the U.S. and South Korea, **Oct. 20**, in Seoul, broke off negotiations on the possibility of U.S. interrogation of Park Tong Sun in connection with his role in the Korean influence-peddling scandal. Because there is no extradition treaty between the U.S. and South Korea, a 3-man justice department team had gone to Seoul in an attempt to seek Korean cooperation in the investigation.

Carter Delays Tax Revision—Pres. Jimmy Carter, **Oct. 27**, announced that he would further delay his tax cut revision proposals, promised for last summer, until Congress adjourned after completing action on his energy and Social Security programs. Carter said his decision was necessitated by the fiscal relationship of the energy, Social Security, and tax programs and the need to integrate potential tax cuts into the fiscal 1979 budget review.

Helms Pleads "No Contest"—Former C.I.A. Director Richard Helms, **Oct. 31**, pleaded *nolo contendere*, or "no contest" to 2 misdeameanor counts of failing to testify fully and accurately at 2 Senate committee hearings in 1973. Helms had twice denied that the C.I.A. had provided money to the opponents of Chilean President Salvadore Allende; it was later revealed that the agency had given over $8 million to Allende's opponents. Helm's plea, which is not an admission of guilt but has the effect of a legal finding of guilt, was the result of intensive bargaining between the justice department and Helms's lawyers. A White House spokesman stated that President Carter felt the plea arrangement "upholds the law but also serves the interests of national security." A public trial of Helms for perjury would have required the release of classified information.

International

Pakistani Elections Cancelled—Pakistan's military leader, Gen. Mohammed Zia ul-Hag, **Oct. 1**, canceled national elections scheduled for Oct. 18 and extended martial law for an indefinite period. Citing Pakistan's state of political turmoil, Zia said elections would only be "an invitation to a new crisis." He also banned all political activity "to allow passions to cool down." He set no new date for elections, but did state that the criminal cases pending against former Prime Minister Zulfikar Ali Bhutto and some of his former aides should be resolved before the people voted. Bhutto, **Oct. 3**, condemned the move and accused Zia of "denying the democratic and constitutional rights of all the people of Pakistan merely because of what he wants to do to a single individual."

Gandhi Arrested, Released—Former Indian Prime Minister Indira Gandhi, **Oct. 3**, was arrested at her New Delhi home on charges of official corruption, but, **Oct. 4**, was released on technical grounds. Terming the arrest "political," Gandhi said it was "an attempt to discredit" her in the eyes of the Indian people and of the world. Four of her former cabinet ministers were also arrested on similar charges. The charges, the product of an intensive police investigation, were less serious than those many had expected the government to bring. She was released by a magistrate who, in an implicit rebuke to the government, deemed that the police had not made a strong enough case against her. Although her arrest and subsequent release seemed to give Gandhi a political boost, her attempt, **Oct. 15**, to gain the presidency of the Congress party at its national convention was rebuffed. The convention was marked by condemnations of her authoritarian rule. However, the 600 convention delegates affirmed their support for Gandhi and several former cabinet ministers in their fight against corruption charges.

Kuznetsov Named First Vice President — After approving its new constitution, the Soviet leadership, **Oct. 7**, named Vasily Kuznetsov, a 76-year-old foreign ministry official, first vice president, a post created by the new constitution. The selection of Kuznetsov was considered a signal that the post would be a ceremonial one and that the leadership had sidestepped the sensitive issue of who would eventually succeed Soviet Communist party leader and president, Leonid I. Brezhnev. The new constitution emphasized economic guarantees, but, like the Soviet Union's 3 previous constitutions, failed to provide a mechanism for judicial review.

Israel Approves Geneva Procedures — The Israeli cabinet, **Oct. 11**, unanimously accepted a secret working paper of procedures to convene a new Geneva conference on the Middle East. The paper was the product of an agreement reached **Oct. 5**, between U.S. Pres. Carter and Israeli Foreign Minister Moshe Dayan. The agreement had considerably eased U.S.-Israeli relations which had been tense since the **Oct. 1** release of a joint U.S.-USSR statement suggesting guidelines for Arab-Israeli negotiations. The Israeli government sharply criticized the statement because it said a new Middle East peace conference should insure "the legitimate rights of the Palestinian people" and establish "normal peaceful relations" in the area. Israel saw the statement as a step toward imposing a settlement from the outside, a move Israel has long opposed. The Carter-Dayan working paper called for the participation of Palestinian Arabs at the opening session as part of a unified Arab delegation. Palestinian Arabs would also be included in a working group to discuss the West Bank and Gaza Strip issues. The Palestinian Liberation Organization, **Oct. 22**, totally rejected the proposal on the ground that it neglected the Palestinian question as a whole.

West German Commandos Free Hostages—A specially-trained West German commando unit, **Oct. 18**, stormed a hijacked Lufthansa airliner standing on a runway in Mogadishu, Somalia, freeing all 86 hostages unharmed and killing 3 of the 4 hijackers. Two West German soldiers were also killed in the attack. The terrorists had killed the pilot enroute during the

5-day, 6,000-mile ordeal that had begun **Oct. 14** when they hijacked the Lufthansa Boeing 737 over the French Riviera and forced it to Dubai, in the United Arab Emirates. Shortly after the rescue raid, 3 imprisoned West German terrorist leaders committed suicide. The 3 dead terrorist leaders, Andreas Baader, founder of the Baader-Meinhof terrorist gang, Jan-Carl Raspe, and Gudrun Ensslin, were among the 13 terrorists whose freedom the hijackers had demanded. During negotiations with the West German government, the hijackers had threatened to kill the hostages as well as West German industrialist Hanns-Martin Schleyer, who had been kidnapped in Cologne, **Sept. 5,** unless their demands were met. Negotiations to free Schleyer had met with no success. Schleyer was found dead, **Oct. 19,** in the trunk of an abandoned car in the eastern French city of Mulhouse. Reflecting the furor in West Germany and abroad, Pres. Walter Scheel, **Oct. 25,** asked western and eastern political leaders to join in a common fight against terrorism.

Czech Dissidents Sentenced—In the biggest dissident trial in Prague in 5 years, 4 prominent dissidents, **Oct. 18,** were sentenced to prison for from 14 to 42 months on charges of subversion. Sentences for 2 of the men, however, were suspended. The harshest prison term, 3 1/2 years, was given to Ota Ornest, a former theater director who allegedly had maintained "conspiratorial links" with foreign diplomats and agents in France and Italy. Journalist Jiri Lederer was sentenced to 3 years on similar charges. The lesser, suspended sentences were imposed on Frantisek Pavlicek, who allegedly slandered the state in articles published abroad, and Vaclav Havel, who allegedly tried to smuggle abroad the banned memoirs of a former government minister. Although all, except Ornest, had been among the first to sign the Charter 77 manifesto calling for respect for human rights in Czechoslovakia, the prosecution had contended the case was purely a matter of subversion.

South Africa Cracks Down on Blacks—In the most severe crackdown in nearly 20 years, the South African government, **Oct. 19,** banned black protest groups, closed down *The World*, the principal black newspaper, and arrested its editor, Percy Qoboza. Beginning with predawn raids, the government arrested at least 50 persons and served an unknown number with orders banning them from political activities and curtailing their freedoms for 5 years. Justice Minister James T. Kruger, in Pretoria, explained that the government had acted to suppress organizations that had used legitimate fronts to promote a revolutionary climate and to create a confrontation between blacks and whites. "The government is determined to insure that peaceful co-existence of peoples in South Africa is not disturbed by small groups of anarchists." The severity of the government action shocked opponents of apartheid. A U.S. rebuke said the U.S. would review the "implications" of the crackdown for overall relations between the 2 countries. Prime Minister John Vorster, **Oct. 20,** responded that any such move was irrelevant because he was more interested in internal security than international standing. U.S. Ambassador William G. Bowdler was recalled to Washington, D.C.,**Oct. 21,** for consultation on what steps the U.S. should take. As the United Nations Security Council debated a proposed move to impose a mandatory embargo on arms sales to South Africa, U.S. Pres. Jimmy Carter indicated the move was "the right decision" and, **Oct. 27,** confirmed the U.S. had decided to support an arms embargo. In a biting attack on the U.S. and Pres. Carter, South African Defense Minister Pieter W. Botha, **Oct. 26,** asserted his nation had a strong enough arms industry to surmount an international embargo.

Thai Military Ousts Civilian Government—A Thai military junta, **Oct. 20,** peacefully overthrew the civilian government it had installed after a coup a year before. Defense Minister Adm. Sa-ngad Chaloryu, identified as the head of the revolutionary party, said the new leadership would aim for elections next year. He indicated that deposed Prime Minister Thanin Kravichen's 12-year reform program for reestablishing democracy had been dilatory. The military junta, **Oct. 21,** announced that elections would be held after the drafting of a revised constitution. Gen. Kriangsak Chamand, supreme commander of the Thai military forces, announced **Oct. 29,** that members of the military would hold key posts in a new government to be announced shortly.

Panamanians Approve Canal Treaties—In a massive voter turnout, Panamanians, **Oct. 23,** approved the Panama Canal treaties by a 2/3's majority in a national plebiscite. The vote followed a national public debate in which the opposition had been given the opportunity to argue against approval. Panamanian leader Gen. Omar Torrijos Herrara stated that the U.S. Senate, in considering ratification of the treaties, would have "to consider this vote if they have respect for the Panamanian people." A week prior to the vote, U.S. Pres. Jimmy Carter and Torrijos, **Oct. 14,** in an attempt to facilitate approval of the treaty, had reached a "statement of understanding" on defense of the canal. They agreed that the U.S. had the right to act against any aggression or threat directed against the canal and that the right of the U.S. to use military force to keep the canal open did not mean it would intervene "in the internal affairs of Panama."

General

Defendant in TV Violence Case Convicted—In a controversial televised trial, a Miami, Fla., jury, **Oct. 6,** convicted 15-year-old Ronny Zamora of premeditated murder. In reaching their verdict, the jury rejected Zamora's contention that years of watching television had left him "involuntarily intoxicated" and caused him to shoot an elderly neighbor. The verdict, however, did not end the debate on the effects of television violence. Several "expert" witnesses had given sharply differing testimony on the subject. Zamora's attorney said at the end of the trial: "The defense we offered was unique, but you have not heard the end of it. It will eventually find its place in the law."

Concorde Ban at JFK Lifted—The Supreme Court, **Oct. 17,** lifted a temporary ban on supersonic Concorde airliner flights to New York City's John F. Kennedy airport. The decision opened up the way for immediate test flights and the beginning of passenger service Nov. 22. New York State Gov. Hugh Carey, who had said the previous week that he didn't think the Supreme Court could stand against the governor, did not challenge the decision. On its first test landing, **Oct. 19,** the British-French Concorde registered an acceptable noise level estimated by the British Aircraft Corp., to be about 2 decibels lower than a subsonic Boeing 707 would have produced. On its first take-off, the more crucial noise-level test, the Concorde, **Oct. 20,** also met the legal noise limit by a wide margin. Concorde operators were jubilant because they had maintained throughout the bitter fight over the Concorde that its noise impact would be comparable to that of the noisiest subsonic jets.

Airliner Hijacked in Nebraska—Thomas Michael Hannan, an alleged bank robber, **Oct. 20,** hijacked a

Frontier Airlines Boeing 737 at Grand Isle, Neb., forced it to Atlanta, Ga., and then, after releasing the remaining 11 passengers unharmed, shot himself to death. He had released all the women, children, and a heart patient on a refueling stop in Kansas City. After the hijacking, he demanded that George David Stewart, being held in an Atlanta jail and identified as his homosexual partner, be freed. He also asked for $3 million, 2 parachutes, and a variety of weapons. Hannan and Stewart were apprehended in September in connection with an Atlanta bank robbery. Hannan had posted a $25,000-bond and was released.

Deaths, Nov. 1, 1976-Nov. 1, 1977

A

Abernathy, Roy, 70; president and chief executive officer of American Motors Corp. 1962-76; Tequestra, Fla., Feb. 28.

Adler, Kurt, 70; opera conductor and chorusmaster at the Metropolitan Opera, 1945-73; Butler, N.J., Sept. 21.

Adrian, Lord Edgar Douglas, 87; physiologist won Nobel Prize in 1932; Cambridge, Eng., Aug. 4.

Allison, Wilmer, 72; tennis star of the 20s and 30s; Austin, Tex., Apr. 20.

Anderson, Eddie (Rochester), 71; gravel-voiced comedian played Jack Benny's valet for 30 years on radio and TV; Los Angeles, Feb. 28.

Arnold, Billy, 66; auto racing driver won the 1930 Indianapolis 500; Oklahoma City, Nov. 10.

Ashbee, Barry, 37; former NFL all-star defenseman; Philadelphia, May 12.

B

Balcon, Sir Michael, 81; British film producer, "Goodbye Mr. Chips", "Tom Jones"; Hartfield, Eng., Oct. 16.

Barbour, George B., 86; geologist explored sites of prehistoric man in China and South Africa; Cincinnati, July 11.

Barnes, George, 56; jazz guitarist; Concord, Cal., Sept. 4.

Barnett, Vince, 75; supporting actor and comic in over 50 films; Encino, Cal., Aug. 10.

Barrett, Edith, 64; stage and film actress; Albuquerque, Feb. 22.

Batchelor, C.D., 89; cartoonist won Pulitzer prize, 1937; Deep River, Conn., Sept. 5.

Becker, Marion Rombauer, 73; co-author, "The Joy of Cooking"; Cincinnati, Dec. 28.

Battalino, Bat, 69; world featherweight boxing champion in the 30s; W. Hartford, Conn., July 25.

Ben-Ami, Jacob, 86; actor, a founder of the Jewish Art Theater; New York, July 22.

Beel, Louis J.M., 74; twice prime minister of the Netherlands; Utrecht, Feb. 11.

Bierman, Bernie, 82; football coach led Univ. of Minnesota to 3 national championships; Laguna Hills, Cal., Mar. 7.

Biggs, E. Power, 70; concert organist; Boston, Mar. 10.

Bissell, Richard, 63; author, playwright, "Pajama Game"; Dubuque, Ia., May 4.

Bliven, Bruce, 87; former editor of the New Republic; Palo Alto, Cal., May 27.

Bloch, Dr. Ernst, 92; Marxist philosopher and spokesman for post-WW2 student radicalism; Tubingen, W. Ger., Aug. 3.

Bolan, Marc, 29; British rock star; London, Sept. 16.

Bolton, Rep. Frances, 91; Ohio congresswoman served 30 years in the House, 1939-69; Lyndhurst, Oh., Mar. 9.

Boyd, Stephen, 49; film and television actor; Los Angeles, June 2.

Brauer, Richard D., 76; mathematician pioneered the development of algebra; Belmont, Mass., Apr. 17.

Britten, Benjamin, 63; British composer famed for operas, "Peter Grimes", "Billy Budd"; Aldernurgh, Eng., Dec. 4.

Brooks, Geraldine, 52; actress appeared on stage, screen, and TV; Riverhead, N.Y., June 19.

Budker, Gersh, 59; Soviet physicist; USSR, July.

Bunn, Alden (Tarheel Slim), 52; blues singer; New York, Aug. 21.

Bustamante, Sir Alexander, 93; Jamaican political leader; Jamaica, Aug. 6.

C

Cabot, Sebastian, 59; character actor starred in TV's, "Family Affair"; Victoria, B.C., Aug. 23.

Cain, James M., 85; crime novelist, "The Postman Always Rings Twice", "Double Indemnity"; University Park, Md., Oct. 27.

Calder, Alexander, 78; American artist known for his mobile structures and "stabiles"; New York, Nov. 11.

Callas, Maria, 53; soprano whose talent and temperamant made her the best known opera star of her time; Paris, Sept. 16.

Cambridge, Godfrey, 43; comedian and actor; Burbank, Cal., Nov. 29.

Caouette, Real, 59; Canadian politician led Social Credit party; Ottawa, Dec. 16.

Carbo, Frankie, 72; underworld boss known as the "czar of boxing"; Miami Beach, Nov. 9.

Carden, Mae, 82; originator and developer of the Carden method of reading instruction; Ridgewood, N.J., Jan. 7.

Carr, John Dickson (aka Carter Dickson), 70; author of 120 mystery novels; master of the locked-room mystery; Greenville, S.C., Feb. 27.

Cassidy, Jack, 49; actor and singer in the theater, films, and TV; Los Angeles, Dec. 12.

Castle, William, 63; producer and director of horror films; Beverly Hills, Cal., May 31.

Clark, Tom C., 77; retired justice of the Supreme Court; New York, June 13.

Clouzot, Henri-Georges, 69; French director of suspense films, "Diabolique"; Paris, Jan. 12.

Cohen, Manuel F., 74; chairman of the SEC, 1964-69; Washington, D.C., June 16.

Cole, Edward N., 67; auto innovator; former president of General Motors; Mendon, Mich., May 2.

Collins, Chuck, 73; one of the "seven mules" on famed 1924 Notre Dame football team; Ridgewood, N.J., Apr. 14.

Coolidge, Albert S., 83; chemist and physicist helped prove the quantum mechanics theory; Concord, Mass., Aug. 31.

Corcoran, Fred, 72; professional golf promoter and executive; White Plains, N.Y., June 23.

Cortez, Ricardo, 77; silent screen star; New York, Apr. 28.

Cotzias, Dr. George C., 58; neurologist; developed L-Dopa therapy for Parkinson's disease; New York, June 13.

Cowan, Louis, 66; former president of the CBS TV network; New York, Nov. 18.

Crane, Roy, 75; cartoonist created, "Captain Easy", "Buzz Sawyer" comic strips; Orlando, Fla., July 7.

Crawford, Joan, 69; actress starred in some 80 films; won Oscar as best actress in 1945, "Mildred Pierce"; New York, May 10.

Crosby, Bing, 74; singer, actor; sold over 300 million records; won Oscar as best actor in 1944, "Going My Way"; Madrid, Oct. 14.

Crosland, Anthony, 58; British foreign secretary; Oxford, Eng., Feb. 19.

D

Dahlberg, Edward, 76; author and critic; Santa Barbara, Cal., Feb. 27.

Daley, Richard J., 74; mayor of Chicago since 1955; Chicago, Dec. 20.

Daves, Delmer, 73; Hollywood screenwriter, director, and producer involved in some 80 films; La Jolla, Cal., Aug. 17.

Desmond, Paul, 52; alto saxophonist with Dave Brubeck quartet for 17 years; New York, May 30.

Devine, Andy, 71; squeaky-voiced supporting actor in some 300 films; Orange, Cal., Feb. 18.

Dodds, Rev. Gil, 58; runner held world indoor mile record; won Sullivan award in 1943; St. Charles, Ill., Feb. 3.

Dresser, David (aka Brett Halliday), 72; author whose work included 50 Michael Shayne detective novels; Montecito, Cal., Feb. 4.

DuBois, Shirley Graham, 69; biographer, playwright, and political activist; widow of W.E.B. DuBois; Peking, Mar. 27.

Dufek, Adm. George J., 74; commander of the navy's Antarctic expeditions, 1955-59; first American to set foot on the South Pole; Bethesda, Md., Feb. 10.

Dunn, Robert W., 81; co-founder of the American Civil Liberties Union; New York, Jan. 21.

E

Earnshaw, George, 76; Philadelphia Athletics pitcher won 20 games in 3 consecutive seasons, 1929-31; Hot Springs, Ark., Dec. 1.

Eden, Sir Anthony, 79; British prime minister during Suez invasion of 1956; former foreign secretary; Wiltshire, Eng., Jan. 14.

Eiseley, Loren, 69; anthropologist, educator, and author; Philadelphia, July 9.

Elder, Ruth, 73; flyer gained fame after an unsuccessful attempt to become the first woman to fly the Atlantic, 1927; San Francisco, Oct. 9.

Erhard, Ludwig, 80; economist led West Germany's economic rise following WW2; Bonn, May 5.

Erskine, Laurie York, 82; author of "Renfrew of the Royal Mounted" adventure series; Mt. Hope, Pa., Nov. 30.

F

Fairfax, Beatrice (Marion C. McCarroll), 84; wrote nationally syndicated "Advice to the Lovelorn" column for 21 years; Allendale, N.J., Aug. 4.

Farrell, Richard (Turk), 43; pitcher won 106 NL games; Great Yarmouth, Eng., June 12.

Faulkner, Lord Brian, 56; Ulster political leader; County Down, Mar. 3.

Ferris, Daniel J., 87; leading figure in amateur athletics for over 70 years; Amityville, N.Y., May 2.

Fieser, Louis, 78; chemist credited with the development of vitamin K and napalm; Cambridge, Mass., July 25.

Finch, Peter, 60; British actor of stage and films; won posthumous best actor Oscar, "Network"; Los Angeles, Jan. 14.

Finklehoffe, Fred F., 67; film and stage producer, playwright, and screenwriter; Springtown, Pa., Oct. 5.

Finley, David, 86; planner and first director of the National Gallery of Art in Washington, D.C.; Washington, D.C., Feb. 1.

Ford, Mary, 53; singer who with husband Les Paul made numerous hit records in the 50s, "How High the Moon"; Los Angeles, Sept. 30.

Foster, Sidney, 59; concert pianist; Boston, Feb. 7.

Foy, Bryan, 80; one of vaudeville's "Seven Little Foys"; produced dozens of Hollywood films including the first all-talking film, "The Lights of New York"; Los Angeles, Apr. 20.

Frisella, Danny, 30; baseball relief pitcher; Phoenix, Jan. 1.

G

Gabin, Jean, 72; French film star for over 40 years; Neuilly, France, Nov. 15.

Gabo, Naum, 87; sculpter pioneered the Constructivism movement in art; Waterbury, Conn., Aug. 23.

Garber, Jan, 82; dance orchestra leader; Shreveport, La., Oct. 5.

Garner, Errol, 53; jazz pianist, composer, "Misty"; Los Angeles, Jan. 2.

Garnett, Tay, 83; Hollywood director, "The Postman Always Rings Twice"; Los Angeles, Oct. 4.

Gilmore, Gary, 36; convicted killer whose execution ended 10-year suspension of capital punishment in the U.S.; Utah, Jan. 17.

Godfrey, Isidore, 76; conductor and music director of the D'Oyly Carte opera for 43 years; Sussex, Eng., Sept. 12.

Goulart, Joao, 58; former president of Brazil; Argentina, Dec. 6.

Granville, E. H., 74; builder of racing aircraft; Madison, N.H., July 18.

Grauer, Ben, 68; NBC radio reporter and personality for 4 decades; New York, May 31.

Gries, Tom, 54; writer and director for films and TV; Pacific Palisades, Cal., Jan. 3.

Gropper, William, 79; left-wing cartoonist and leading artist of the American "social realist" school; Manhasset, N.Y., Jan. 6.

H

Hale, Rep. Robert, 87; Maine congressman, 1943-59; Washington, D.C., Nov. 30.

Halop, Billy, 56; actor portrayed one of the "Dead End Kids", on stage and in films; Hollywood, Cal., Nov. 9.

Hambro, Edvard Isak, 65; Norwegian president of the UN's 25th General Assembly, 1970; Paris, Feb. 1.

Hamer, Fannie Lou, 60; black leader led struggle for civil rights in the South; Mound Bayou, Miss., Mar. 14.

Hansen, Harry, 93; literary critic; editor of The World Almanac, 1949-65; New York, Jan. 2.

Harkness, Richard, 70; newsman on NBC-TV for 30 years; Naples, Fla., Feb. 16.

Hart, Sen. Philip, 64; Michigan Democrat served 18 years in the Senate; Washington, D.C., Dec. 26.

Harvey, Len, 69; boxer held British welterweight, middleweight, light-heavyweight, and heavyweight titles; London, Nov. 28.

Hayes, Margaret, 63; actress appeared on stage, TV, and in films; Miami Beach, Jan. 26.

Hayes, Roland, 89; concert tenor; Boston, Jan. 31.

Heezen, Dr. Bruce C., 53; oceanographer pioneered in mapping the ocean floor; at sea, June 21.

Hagen, Jean, 54; actress appeared on TV and in films; Hollywood, Cal., Aug. 29.

Hellman, Geoffrey T., 70; writer, humorist for the New Yorker for 45 years; New York, Sept. 26.

Hershey, Gen. Lewis, 83; head of the Selective Service System for 3 decades; Angola, Ind., May 20.

Housewright, James T., 55; labor leader led the Retail Clerks International Union; Washington, D.C., Sept. 19.

Howe, Quincy, 76; radio and TV news commentator; New York, Feb. 17.

Hubbard, Cal, 76; football lineman and baseball umpire; only man elected to both professional football and baseball halls of fame; St. Petersburg, Fla., Oct. 17.

Hubley, John, 62; film animator created, "Mr. Magoo"; New Haven, Conn., Feb. 21.

Hull, Henry, 87; actor appeared in 46 films; created Jeeter Lester in Broadway production of "Tobacco Road"; Cornwall, Eng., Mar. 8.

Hull, Lytle, 83; philanthropist helped found the N.Y. Opera Co. and N.Y. City Center; Poughkeepsie, N.Y., Dec. 11.

Hulman, Tony, 76; promoter of the Indianapolis 500; Indianapolis, Oct. 27.

Hutchins, Robert M., 78; educator; founder and president of Center for the Study of Democratic Institutions; Santa Barbara, Cal., May 14.

Hyland, Diana, 41; actress appeared in numerous TV shows; Los Angeles, Mar. 27.

I

Ilyushin, Sergei, 82; Soviet aircraft designer of some 50 planes ranging from dive bombers to passenger jets; Moscow, announced Feb. 9.

Iselin, Philip, 74; president of the N.Y. Jets football team; New York, Dec. 28.

Isaac, Bobby, 43; stock car driver won 37 Grand National races; Hickory, N.C., Aug. 14.

J

Jacobs, Jacob, 86; lyricist, playwright, and actor in the Yiddish theater; New York, Oct. 14.

Johnson, Nunnally, 79; Hollywood screenwriter and producer; Los Angeles, Mar. 25.

Jones, James, 55; novelist, "From Here to Eternity"; Southampton, N.Y., May 9.

Jordan, Henry, 42; defensive lineman on 5 Green Bay Packer championship teams; Milwaukee, Feb. 21.

K

Kamen, Milt, 55; comedian and actor; Beverly Hills, Cal., Feb. 24.

Kantor, MacKinlay, 73; novelist won Pulitzer prize in 1956, "Andersonville"; Sarasota, Fla., Oct. 11.

Kaufman, Sue, 50; novelist, "The Diary of a Mad Housewife"; New York, June 25.

Keita, Mobido, 61; first president of Mali; Mali, May 16.

Kennedy, Walter, 64; former commissioner of the National Basketball Assn.; Stamford, Conn., June 26.

Kenney, Gen. George C., 88; air commander for Gen. MacArthur in the Pacific in WW2; Miami, Aug. 9.

King, Muriel, 76; fashion designer, Danbury, Conn., Mar. 21.

Kleinschmidt, Edward E., 101; inventor of the Teletype machine; Canaan, Conn., Aug. 9.

Knoor, Nathan H., 72; president of Jehovah's Witnesses; Wallkill, N.Y., June 8.

Krantzcke, Karen, 30; Australian tennis player; Tallahassee, Fla., Apr. 10.

L

Laurence, William, 89; science reporter won 2 Pulitzer prizes; only newsman to fly on the atomic bomb mission over Nagasaki; Majorca, Spain, Mar. 19.

Leaf, Munro, 71; author and illustrator of children's books; created "Ferdinand the Bull"; Garrett Park, Md., Dec. 21.

Levitt, Saul, 66; playwright, "The Andersonville Trial"; New York, Sept. 30.

Levy, Dr. David M., 84; child psychiatrist coined the term, "sibling rivalry"; introduced the Roschach test in the U.S., New York, Mar. 1.

Lewis, Ross, 74; editorial cartoonist won Pulitzer prize in 1935; Milwaukee, Aug. 6.

Lhevinne, Rosina, 96; pianist and teacher; Glendale, Cal., Nov. 9.

Lieberson, Goddard, 66; president of Columbia Records introduced LP records to the American public; New York, May 29.

Lilly, Eli, 91; headed drug company; founded philanthropic fund; Indianapolis, Jan. 24.

Lisagor, Peter, 61; journalist; manager of the Washington bureau of the Chicago Daily News; Virginia, Dec. 10.

Loew, Arthur M., 79; headed movie empire for over 3 decades; Glen Cove, N.Y., Sept. 6.

Lollar, Sherman, 53; catcher spent 18 seasons in the major leagues, mostly with the White Sox; Springfield, Mo., Sept. 24.

Lombardi, Ernie, 69; catcher batted .306 in 17-year NL career; MVP in 1938; Santa Cruz, Cal., Sept. 26.

Lowell, Robert, 60; poet won Pulitzer prize in 1947, "Lord Weary's Castle"; New York, Sept. 12.

Lowman, Dr. Charles LeRoy, 97; orthopedic surgeon awarded Medal of Freedom in 1974 for his work with handicapped children; Los Angeles, Apr. 17.

Lowry, Judith, 86; actress played Mother Dexter in TVs "Phyllis"; New York, Nov. 29.

Lunt, Alfred, 84; actor starred on stage for nearly 40 years; appeared with wife Lynn Fontanne in 27 Broadway productions; Chicago, Aug. 3.

Luria, Aleksandr R., 75; Soviet psychologist and brain specialist; USSR, Aug.

Lysenko, Trofim D., 78; Soviet agriculturist dominated science in the USSR during the Stalin era; USSR, Nov. 20.

M

Mainbocher (Main Rosseau Bocher); 86; Paris fashion designer of the 30s; Munich, Dec. 27.

Makarios, Archbishop Michael Christodouros, 63; leader of the Greek community on Cyprus; president of Cyprus since 1960; Cyprus, Aug. 3.

Malraux, Andre, 75; French writer, war hero, and de Gaulle aide; nr. Paris, Nov. 23.

Manchego, Jorge, 55; editor of the United Nations yearbook; New York, Oct. 6.

Mark, Rev. Dr. Julius, 78; national leader of Reform Judiasm; New York, Sept. 6.

Markel, Lester, 83; Sunday editor of the N.Y Times for over 40 years; New York, Oct. 23.
Marriott, John, 83; actor appeared on stage, films, and TV; New York, Apr. 5.
Martini, Nino, 72; lyric tenor in opera, radio, and films; Verona, Italy, Dec. 9.
Marx, Groucho, 86; comedian appeared on stage and in films with the Marx Brothers; TV host, "You Bet Your Life"; Los Angeles, Aug. 20.
Marx, Gummo, 84; a Marx Brother who became the group's business manager and agent; Palm Springs, Cal., Apr. 21.
Matthews, Herbert L., 77; foreign correspondent for the N.Y. Times for 3 decades; Adelaide, Australia, July 30.
McCoy, George B. (The Real), 72; actor pioneered the radio talk show in the 30s; New York, Dec. 22.
McCulloch, Robert, 65; oilman industrialist who bought and shipped London Bridge to Arizona, 1968; Bel Air, Cal., Feb. 25.
Moore, Dr. Barbara, 70s; dietician gained fame in the 50s as long distance walker; England, May 14.
Moran, Lord, 94; physician served Winston Churchill for 25 years; Hampshire, Eng. Apr. 12.
Morehouse, Clifford P., 72; lay leader in the Episcopal church; Sarasota, Fla., Feb. 17.
Morgenstern, Oskar, 75; pioneer in the development of mathematical economics and game theory, Princeton, N.J., July 26.
Mostel, Zero, 62; actor won 3 Tony awards; created role of Tevye, "Fiddler on the Roof"; Philadelphia, Sept. 8.
Moulder, Morgan Moore, 72; Democratic congressman from Missouri, 1949-62; Camdentown, Mo., Nov. 12.
Mowrer, Edgar Ansel, 84; journalist won Pulitzer prize in 1933 for reports on the rise of Hitler; Madeira, Portugal, Mar. 2.
Mueller, Erwin, 76; physicist, first person to see an atom, 1955; Washington, D.C., May 17.
Murtaugh, Danny, 59; baseball manager led the Pittsburgh Pirates to 2 World Series championships; Chester, Pa., Dec. 2.
Musial, Joe, 72; cartoonist pioneered the use of comic books as educational tools; Manhasset, N.Y., June 6.
Mustin, Burt, 94; character actor appeared in over 350 TV shows and 85 films, Glendale, Cal., Jan. 28.

N

Nabokov, Vladimir, 78; Russian-born author, "Lolita," "Ada"; Montreux, Switzerland, July 2.
Nash, John, 84; British landscape painter and illustrator; Colchester, Eng., Sept. 23.
Noyes, Eliot, 66; industrial designer of many family products; New Canaan, Conn., July 17.

O

O'Donnell, Kenneth P., 53; aide and key adviser to JFK; Boston, Sept. 9.
Oppenheimer, George, 77; drama critic and writer, New York, Aug. 14.
Otero, Katherine Stinson, 86; pioneer aviator and stunt flier; Santa Fe, N.M., July 8.

P

Patterson, Russell, 82; illustrator, cartoonist, and designer whose drawings influenced the fashions of the 20s; Atlantic City, N.J., Mar. 17.
Paul, Alice, 92; women's rights leader; Moorestown, N.J., July 9.
Payne, Virginia, 66; actress was voice of radio's, "Ma Perkins," for 27 years; Cincinnati, Feb. 10.
Peer, Dr. Lyndon A., 78; pioneer plastic surgeon, Boca Raton, Fla., Oct. 8.
Piston, Walter, 82; composer won 2 Pulitzer prizes; Belmont, Mass., Nov. 12.
Poindexter, H. R., 41; designer of sets and lighting for the theater; Los Angeles, Sept. 24.
Powers, Francis Gary, 47; U-2 pilot whose capture in 1960 touched off a crisis in Soviet-American relations; Encino, Cal., Aug. 1.
Powers, John R., 84; founder of the world's first modeling agency; Glendale, Cal., July 19.
Presley, Elvis, 42; singer and actor; rock-and-roll king sold over 500 million records in a career spanning 2 decades; Memphis, Aug. 16.
Prevert, Jacques, 77; French poet and screenwriter; Normandy, Apr. 11.
Printemps, Yvonne, 82; French singer starred in operettas and musical reviews; Paris, Jan. 18.
Prinze, Freddie, 22; comedian starred in TVs "Chico and the Man"; Los Angeles, Jan. 29.

R

Rascovich, Mark, 58; author, "The Bedford Incident"; W. Palm Beach, Fla., Dec. 10.
Ray, Man, 86; American painter and photographer helped create the Dadaist movement; Paris, Nov. 18.
Reed, Alan, 69; actor best known as the voice of Fred on TVs "The Flintstones"; Los Angeles, June 14.
Richardson, Rev. Dr. Cyril, 67; scholar of early church history, New York, Nov. 16.
Roberti, Francesco Cardinal, 87; member of the Vatican Curia for many years; Rome, July.
Roberts, Clifford, 84; founder and for 43 years chairman of the Masters golf tournament; Augusta, Ga., Sept. 29.
Rocca, Antonino, 49; bare-footed wrestler; a star attraction for 25 years; New York, Mar. 15.
Rose, Alex, 78; political leader built New York's Liberal party into a major force in city, state, and national politics, New York, Dec. 28.
Rosendahl, Vice Adm. Charles, 84; airship pioneer; Philadelphia, May 14.
Rossellini, Roberto, 71; Italian film director, "Open City"; Rome, June 3.
Russell, Rosalind, 63; actress starred in films and on stage, "Auntie Mame"; Beverly Hills, Cal., Nov. 28.

S

Saypol, Justice Irving H., 71; federal prosecutor in the Rosenberg spy trial; New York, June 30.
Schermerhorn, Willem, 82; Dutch prime minister, 1945-46, played major role in post WW2 reconstruction; Haarlem, The Netherlands, reported Mar. 12.
Schorer, Mark, 69; novelist, literary critic, and biographer, Oakland, Aug. 11.
Schutz, Anton, 83; etcher founded the N.Y. Graphic Society; White Plains, N.Y., Oct. 6.
Scudder, Dr. John, 76; pioneer in the development of blood banks, New York, Dec. 6.
Segal, Alex, 62; pioneering director of live TV drama; Los Angeles, Aug. 23.
Shankar, Uday, 76; Indian dancer popularized Hindu works in the West; Calcutta, Sept. 26.
Sharp, Sir John, 59; British general commanded NATO forces in northern Europe; Norway, Jan. 15.
Shaw, Buck, 77; football coach led Philadelphia Eagles to NFL crown in 1960; Menlo Park, Cal., Mar. 19.
Shipton, Eric, 69; British mountain climber assaulted Mt. Everest 5 times; Salisbury, Eng., Mar. 28.
Shor, Bernard (Toots), 73; colorful New York restaurant owner and host, New York, Jan. 22.
Smart, T. Wayne (Curly), 72; driver and trainer of harness racing horses for 50 years; Delaware, Oh., Nov. 14.
Smith, Robert Paul, 61; novelist and playwright, "The Tender Trap," New York, Jan. 30.
Soper, Dr. Fred L., 83; public health specialist developed techniques for control of yellow fever; Wichita, Kan., Feb. 9.
Speaks, Margaret, 72; soprano soloist on "Voice of Firestone", radio concerts in the 30s and 40s; Blue Mill, Me., July 16.
Stevens, Onslow, 70; character actor of stage and screen; Van Nuys, Cal., Jan. 5.
Stokowski, Leopold, 95; London-born conductor whose career spanned more than 70 years and some 7,000 concerts; Hampshire, Eng., Sept. 13.

T

Taft, Dr. Philip; a leading historian of the American labor movement; E. Providence, R.I., Nov. 17.
Taylor, Dean P., 75; N.Y. Republican served 9 terms in the House, 1942-1960; Albany, N.Y., Oct. 16.
Tcherepnin, Alexander, 78; composer and pianist; Paris, Sept. 29.
Thompson, Danny, 29; infielder for the Texas Rangers baseball team; Rochester, Minn., Dec. 10.

V

Von Braun, Werner, 65; German-born scientist, a pioneer in space travel and rocketry; Alexandria, Va., June 16.
Von Cramm, Baron Gottfried, 66; tennis star of the 30s; Egypt, Nov. 8.

W

Walters, Lou, 81; nightclub impresario founded famed Latin Quarter; Miami, Aug. 15.
Washington, Ned, 75; Hollywood songwriter won 3 Oscars; wrote, "When You Wish Upon a Star", "The Nearness of You"; Los Angeles, Dec. 20.
Waters, Ethel, 80; singer and actress in films and the theater; Chatsworth, Cal., Sept. 1.
Widman Jr., Michael F., 77; labor leader helped unionize the Ford Motor Co. in 1940; Silver Springs, Md., Aug. 14.
Wilcox, Herbert, 85; British film producer and director whose productions won 4 academy awards; London, May 15.
Wilson, Irving W., 87; industrialist headed the Aluminum Co. of America; Pittsburgh, Oct. 16.
Winslow, Ola Elizabeth, 92; biographer won Pulitzer prize in 1941, "Jonathan Edwards"; Damariscotta, Me., Sept. 27.
Wolfe, Bertram, 81; scholar, writer, and expert on Marxism; Palo Alto, Cal., Feb. 22.
Woodham-Smith, Cecil, 80; British biographer and historian; London, Mar. 16.
Wright, Russel, 72; industrial designer popularized modern design in the U.S.; New York, Dec. 22.
Wrigley, Philip, K., 82; owner of the chewing gum company and the Chicago Cubs baseball team; Elkhorn, Wis., Apr. 12.

Y

Yakubovsky, Marshall Ivan I., 64; Soviet commander of Warsaw Pact forces; USSR, announced Dec. 1.

VITAL STATISTICS

Source: Division of Vital Statistics, U.S. Department of Health, Education and Welfare

January-June 1977

Births

During the first half of 1977 there were 1,610,000 births, about 7% more than the number for the same period of 1976. The birth rate for this period, 15.0 per 1,000 population, was 6% higher than the rate for the corresponding period in 1976. The fertility rate was 5% higher, 66.4 per 1,000 women, compared with the 1976 rate of 63.3.

Marriages

Marriages are increasing. During the first half of this year 1,033,000 marriages were reported, 46,000 more than during the first half of 1976. The marriage rate was 9.6 per 1,000 population, 3% higher than the rate for the first 6 months of 1976.

Divorces

Divorces totaled 540,000 in the first half of 1977, less than 1% more than the total for the first half of 1976. In both years, the divorce rate was 5.0 per 1,000 population for the first 6 months.

Deaths

For June 1977 the provisional count of deaths furnished by the 50 states and the District of Columbia totaled 150,000, which amounts to a rate of 8.5 deaths per 1,000 population. Among these 150,000 were 3,700 deaths at ages under 1 year, yielding an infant mortality rate of 13.7 deaths per 1,000 live births.

The provisional death rate for the 12 months ending with May 1977, 874.6 per 100,000 population, was lower than the corresponding rate for the 12 months ending with May 1976, 895.8 per 100,000.

Provisional Statistics

12 months ending with June

	Number		Rate*	
	1977	1976	1977	1976
Live births	3,265,000	3,127,000	15.2	14.6
Deaths	1,887,000	1,910,000	8.8	8.9
Natural increase	1,378,000	1,217,000	6.4	5.7
Marriages	2,179,000	2,132,000	10.1	10.0
Divorces	1,079,000	1,072,000	5.0	5.0
Infant deaths	47,400	48,700	14.5	15.6
Population base (in millions)			215.5	214.0

*Per 1,000 population

Annual Report for the Year 1976 (Provisional Statistics)

Births

The number of births in the United States rose slightly during 1976 while the birth rate and the fertility rate continued to decline. There were an estimated 3,165,000 live births, about 1% more than the final number for 1975.

The birth rate declined from 14.8 births per 1,000 population in 1975 to 14.7 in 1976. The fertility rate of 65.6 births per 1,000 women 15-44 years of age was 1.6% lower than the final rate for 1975.

The increase in the number of births is a result of the increase in the number of women in the child-bearing ages (15-44 years).

During 1976 the growth of the population due to natural increase (the excess of births over deaths) amounted to 1,253,000 persons. The rate of natural increase was 5.8 persons per 1,000 population compared with a final rate of 5.9 for 1975. This decline was due entirely to the decline in the birth rate.

Deaths

An estimated 1,912,000 deaths occurred in the United States during 1976. The provisional death rate was 8.9 per 1,000 population, unchanged from the final rate for 1975.

In 1976 there were approximately 47,800 infant deaths resulting in an estimated infant mortality rate of 15.1 per 1,000 live births. This was the lowest annual rate ever recorded in the United States and represents a decrease of 6.2% from the final rate of 16.1 for 1975. Both the neonatal (under 28 days) and the postneonatal (28 days to 11 months) mortality rates declined in 1976 with the neonatal rate showing a proportionately greater decline than the postneonatal rate.

Marriages and Divorces

Provisional reports indicate that 2,133,000 marriages were performed in 1976, about 20,000 fewer than the 1975 final total of 2,152,662. The number of marriages was lower in 1976 than in any year since 1969. After increasing for 15 years, from 1959 to 1973, the number declined in both 1974 and 1975. In 1976 the provisional marriage rate dropped for the fourth consecutive year. It was 9.9 per 1,000 population, 2% lower than the final rate for 1975. In 10% lower than the 22-year high reached in 1972.

According to provisional estimates, 1,077,000 divorces were granted in 1976, representing an increase of 41,000 or 4% over the final count in 1975. The number of divorces in the United States increased every year after 1962 and more than doubled between 1966 (499,000 divorces) and 1976 (1,077,000 divorces). In recent years the increase has slowed, and the additional number of divorces has been smaller each year since 1971.

While the increase in divorces has been diminishing, it still outspaced population growth, resulting in a higher divorce rate. Estimated from provisional reports, the 1976 divorce rate was 5.0 per 1,000 population, double the 1966 divorce rate of 2.5. The divorce rate has increased every year since 1966, however, the rate of increase has declined in more recent years. The 1976 provisional divorce rate is only 2% higher than the 1975 final rate of 4.9 per 1,000 population.

Births and Deaths in the U.S.

Refers only to events occurring within the U.S., including Alaska and Hawaii beginning in 1960. Excludes fetal deaths. Rates per 1,000 population enumerated as of April 1 for 1955, and 1960; estimated as of July 1 for all other years. (p) provisional. (NA) not available.

	Births				Deaths			
Year	Males	Females	Total number	Rate	Males	Females	Total number	Rate
1955	2,073,719	1,973,576	4,047,295	24.6	872,638	656,079	1,528,717	9.3
1960	2,179,708	2,078,142	4,257,850	23.7	975,648	736,334	1,711,982	9.5
1965	1,927,054	1,833,304	3,760,358	19.4	1,035,200	792,936	1,828,136	9.4
1970	1,915,378	1,816,008	3,731,386	18.4	1,078,478	842,553	1,921,031	9.5
1973	1,608,326	1,528,639	3,136,965	14.9	1,096,795	876,208	1,973,003	9.4
1974	1,622,114	1,537,844	3,159,958	14.9	1,071,627	862,761	1,934,388	9.2
1975	1,613,135	1,531,063	3,144,198	14.8	1,050,819	842,060	1,892,879	8.9
1976(p)	NA	NA	3,165,000	14.7	1,056,420	855,690	1,912,000	8.9

Births and Deaths by States

Source: Division of Vital Statistics, Public Health Service

State	Births 1976^p	Births 1975	Deaths 1976^p	Deaths 1975
Alabama	57,707	57,506	33,986	33,493
Alaska	8,032	7,396	1,665	1,558
Arizona	40,143	39,418	17,805	17,450
Arkansas	33,196	33,632	21,215	21,484
California	331,039	317,606	171,927	171,074
Colorado	41,333	40,623	18,732	17,969
Connecticut	34,946	35,662	26,223	25,728
Delaware	8,291	8,414	4,973	4,908
Dist. of Col.	18,983	19,780	9,127	9,418
Florida	104,742	105,116	91,395	88,784
Georgia	80,229	81,450	41,792	41,828
Hawaii	16,325	15,758	4,719	4,575
Idaho	16,821	15,860	6,326	6,226
Illinois	167,591	166,882	101,417	101,085
Indiana	80,260	82,490	46,712	46,668
Iowa	41,134	41,771	27,636	27,935
Kansas	33,730	32,363	21,212	21,137
Kentucky	56,860	55,990	32,177	32,992
Louisiana	69,388	68,136	34,538	33,810
Maine	14,603	14,771	10,760	10,290
Maryland	45,501	45,807	31,681	31,093
Massachusetts	66,592	69,756	53,719	54,222
Michigan	130,135	132,783	74,866	73,741
Minnesota	56,204	56,780	33,471	33,254
Mississippi	42,431	43,406	22,621	22,385
Missouri	70,802	70,788	49,367	49,986
Montana	12,387	11,815	6,637	6,494
Nebraska	24,068	23,908	14,668	14,755
Nevada	9,622	8,844	4,975	4,821
New Hampshire	11,247	11,073	7,612	7,212
New Jersey	87,643	89,014	63,721	64,029
New Mexico	22,108	20,840	8,237	7,948
New York	235,806	237,683	172,150	169,062
North Carolina	80,390	80,806	45,910	46,014
North Dakota	11,398	11,272	5,762	5,656
Ohio	153,553	158,938	95,223	95,972
Oklahoma	42,372	41,315	26,486	26,413
Oregon	35,633	34,312	20,532	20,184
Pennsylvania	149,457	149,920	121,059	120,242
Rhode Island	11,090	10,957	9,321	9,037
South Carolina	46,554	45,149	23,417	22,978
South Dakota	11,420	11,128	6,568	6,434
Tennessee	65,284	65,752	41,475	40,978
Texas	226,535	224,760	102,447	100,099
Utah	35,965	32,408	7,708	7,854
Vermont	6,604	6,438	4,306	4,324
Virginia	67,007	67,378	39,578	38,874
Washington	49,994	50,424	30,148	30,092
West Virginia	28,440	27,888	19,624	19,650
Wisconsin	65,012	65,000	40,220	39,892
Wyoming	6,784	6,558	3,096	3,028
Total	**3,153,394**	**3,150,555**	**1,910,942**	**1,895,135**

(p) provisional

Marriages and Divorces by States 1976

Source: Division of Vital Statistics, Public Health Service

(Provisional figures: divorces include reported annulments)

State	Marriages	Divorces
Alabama	47,639	24,063
Alaska	4,878	3,207
Arizona	28,312	NA
Arkansas	22,630	17,398
California	150,654	133,672
Colorado	27,144	17,424
Connecticut	22,648	10,546
Delaware	3,941	3,235
Dist. of Col.	4,681	2,805
Florida	86,170	62,571
Georgia	60,207	28,625
Hawaii	9,750	4,714
Idaho	13,105	5,707
Illinois	111,261	50,043
Indiana	56,359	NA
Iowa	25,643	10,803
Kansas	23,416	12,900
Kentucky	34,807	16,784
Louisiana	39,050	NA
Maine	11,345	5,416
Maryland	44,891	15,613
Massachusetts	40,928	16,407
Michigan	83,193	43,109
Minnesota	33,198	13,735
Mississippi	26,450	12,096
Missouri	44,750	25,316
Montana	7,328	4,847
Nebraska	13,386	5,929
Nevada	99,722	10,151
New Hampshire	8,396	4,803
New Jersey	52,281	17,866
New Mexico	12,393	7,089
New York	136,694	53,866
North Carolina	42,548	24,443
North Dakota	5,638	1,864
Ohio	97,929	61,036
Oklahoma	40,677	21,755
Oregon	19,507	16,126
Pennsylvania	88,557	35,695
Rhode Island	6,910	3,289
South Carolina	50,028	9,830
South Dakota	10,755	2,363
Tennessee	53,365	27,801
Texas	156,479	80,235
Utah	14,275	6,170
Vermont	4,292	1,844
Virginia	56,474	21,468
Washington	40,684	26,715
West Virginia	17,145	9,092
Wisconsin	35,972	14,088
Wyoming	5,763	2,825
Total	**2,134,248**	**1,077,000**

(NA) not available.

Marriages, Divorces, and Rates in the U.S.

Source: Division of Vital Statistics, Public Health Service

Data refer only to events occurring within the United States, including Alaska and Hawaii beginning with 1960. Rates per 1,000 population.

Year	Marriages[1] No.	Marriages[1] Rate	Divorces[2] No.	Divorces[2] Rate
1890	570,000	**9.0**	33,461	**0.5**
1895	620,000	**8.9**	40,387	**0.6**
1900	709,000	**9.3**	55,751	**0.7**
1905	842,000	**10.0**	67,976	**0.8**
1910	948,166	**10.3**	83,045	**0.9**
1915	1,007,595	**10.0**	104,298	**1.0**
1920	1,274,476	**12.0**	170,505	**1.6**
1925	1,188,334	**10.3**	175,449	**1.5**
1930	1,126,856	**9.2**	195,961	**1.6**
1935	1,327,000	**10.4**	218,000	**1.7**
1940	1,595,879	**12.1**	264,000	**2.0**
1945	1,612,992	**12.2**	485,000	**[3]3.5**
1950	1,667,231	**11.1**	385,144	**2.6**
1955	1,531,000	**9.3**	377,000	**2.3**
1960	1,523,000	**8.5**	393,000	**2.2**
1965	1,800,000	**9.3**	479,000	**2.5**
1970	2,158,802	**10.6**	708,000	**3.5**
1974	2,229,667	**10.5**	977,000	**4.6**
1975	2,152,662	**10.1**	1,036,000	**4.9**
1976(p)	2,133,000	**9.9**	1,077,000	**5.0**

(1) Includes estimates and marriage licenses for some states for all years. (2) Includes reported annulments. (3)Divorce rates for 1945 based on population including armed forces overseas. (p) provisional.

Wedding Anniversaries

The traditional names for wedding anniversaries go back many years in social usage. As such names as wooden, crystal, silver, and golden were applied it was considered proper to present the married pair with gifts made of these products or of something related. While the list of permissible gifts is extensive, gifts are most appropriate when retaining a suggestion of the originals. Thus the wooden anniversary may call for anything of wood, including furniture, but as the years mount the gifts become more valuable until the 60th or diamond anniversary, calls for diamonds. The traditional list follows, with a few allowable revisions in parentheses.

1st—Paper	6th—Iron	11th—Steel	20th—China	45th—Sapphire
2d—Cotton	7th—Wool (copper)	12th—Silk	25th—Silver	50th—Gold
3d—Leather	8th—Bronze	13th—Lace	30th—Pearl	55th—Emerald
4th—Linen (silk)	9th—Pottery (china)	14th—Ivory	35th—Coral (jade)	60th—Diamond
5th—Wood	10th—Tin (aluminum)	15th—Crystal	40th—Ruby	75th—Diamond

Deaths and Death Rates for Selected Causes

Source: Division of Vital Statistics, Public Health Service
Rates per 100,000 population

1976* Cause of death	Number	Rate
All causes	**1,912,000**	**890.8**
Enteritis and other diarrheal diseases	2,000	0.9
Tuberculosis, all forms	3,290	1.5
Syphilis and its sequelae	250	0.1
Other infective and parasitic diseases	3,630	1.7
Malignant neoplasms, including neoplasms of lymphatic and hematopoietic tissues	374,780	174.6
Diabetes mellitus	35,090	16.3
Meningitis	1,630	0.8
Major cardiovascular diseases	977,410	455.4
Diseases of heart	726,700	388.6
Active rheumatic fever and chronic rheumatic heart disease	13,260	6.2
Hypertensive heart disease with or without renal disease	3,930	1.8
Ischemic heart disease	649,280	302.5
Chronic disease of endocardium and other myocardial insufficiency	4,330	2.0
All other forms of heart disease	49,160	22.9
Hypertension	6,060	2.8
Cerebrovascular diseases	189,000	88.1
Arteriosclerosis	28,760	13.4
Other diseases of arteries arterioles, and capillaries	26,790	12.5

1976* Cause of death	Number	Rate
Acute bronchitis and bronchiolitis	770	0.4
Influenza and pneumonia	62,980	29.3
Influenza	7,800	3.6
Pneumonia	55,180	25.7
Bronchitis, emphysema, and asthma	23,840	11.1
Chronic and unqualified bronchitis	4,490	2.1
Emphysema	17,550	8.2
Asthma	1,800	0.8
Peptic ulcer	6,260	2.9
Hernia and intestinal obstruction	5,940	2.8
Cirrhosis of liver	31,130	14.5
Cholelithiasis, cholecystitis, and cholangitis	2,690	1.3
Nephritis and nephrosis	8,830	4.1
Infections of kidney	3,740	1.7
Hyperplasia of prostate	1,190	0.6
Congenital anomalies	13,780	6.4
Certain causes of mortality in early infancy	24,870	11.6
Symptoms and ill-defined conditions	32,320	15.1
All other diseases	127,100	59.2
Accidents	100,430	46.8
Motor vehicle accidents	45,800	21.3
All other accidents	54,630	25.5
Suicide	25,200	11.7
Homicide	18,970	8.8
All other external causes	4,440	2.1

Due to rounding estimates of death, figures may not add to total. *Provisional.
Data based on a 10% sampling of all death certificates for a 12-month (Jan.-Dec.) period.

Principal Types of Accidental Deaths

Source: Division of Vital Statistics, Public Health Service

Year	All types	Motor vehicle	Falls	Burns	Drown-ing	Fire-arms	Machin-ery	Poison gases	Other poisons
1960	93,806	38,137	19,023	7,645	6,529	2,334	1,951	1,253	1,679
1965	108,004	49,163	19,984	7,347	6,799	2,344	2,054	1,526	2,110
1970	114,638	54,633	16,926	6,718	6,391	2,406	. .	1,620	3,679
1973	115,821	55,511	16,506	6,503	7,152	2,618	. .	1,652	3,683
1974	104,622	46,402	16,339	6,236	6,463	2,513	. .	1,518	4,016
1975	103,030	45,853	14,896	6,071	6,640	2,380	. .	1,577	4,694
Death rates per 100,000 population									
1960	52.1	21.2	10.6	4.2	3.6	1.3	1.1	0.7	0.9
1965	55.7	25.4	10.3	3.8	3.5	1.2	1.1	0.8	0.1
1970	56.4	26.9	8.3	3.3	3.1	1.2	. .	0.8	1.8
1973	55.2	26.5	7.9	3.1	3.4	1.2	. .	0.8	1.7
1974	49.5	22.0	7.7	2.9	3.1	1.2	. .	0.7	1.9
1975	48.4	21.5	7.0	2.8	3.1	1.1	. .	0.7	2.2

Transportation Accident Passenger Death Rates, 1976

Source: National Safety Council

Kind of transportation	Passenger miles (billions)	Passenger deaths	Rate per 100,000,000 pass. miles	1974-1976 aver. death rate
Passenger automobiles and taxis	2,070.0	27,650	1.34	1.41
Passenger automobiles on turnpikes	48.9	300	0.61	0.66
Buses	76.1	130	0.17	0.18
Intercity buses[2]	17.5	2	0.01	0.03
Railroad passenger trains	10.6	5	0.05	0.07
Scheduled air transport planes (domestic)	154.0	4	—	0.06

(1) Drivers of passenger automobiles are considered passengers. (2) Class 1 only, representing 70 per cent of total intercity bus passenger mileage. —Less than 0.005.

Accidental Injuries by Severity of Injury

Source: National Safety Council

1976 Severity of injury	Total*	Motor vehicle	Work	Home	Public non-motor vehicle
Deaths*	100,000	46,700	12,500	24,500	21,500
Disabling injuries*	10,300,000	1,800,000	2,200,000	3,700,000	2,700,000
Permanent impairments	370,000	140,000	80,000	100,000	70,000
Temporary total disabilities	9,900,000	1,650,000	2,100,000	3,600,000	2,600,000
Certain Costs of Accidental Injuries, 1976 ($ billions)					
Total*	$52.8	$24.7	$17.8	$6.3	$5.0
Wage loss	16.1	7.6	3.6	2.9	2.9
Medical expense	6.9	2.1	1.9	1.8	1.2
Insurance administration	8.7	6.1	2.4	0.1	0.1

*Duplication between motor vehicle, work, and home are eliminated in the total column.

Motor Vehicle Traffic Deaths by State

Source: National Safety Council

Place of accidents	Number 1976	Number 1975	Death rate* 1976	Death rate* 1975
Total U.S.†	**46,700**	**46,000**	3.3	3.5
Alabama	1,032	975	3.9	3.9
Alaska	127	114	3.5	4.5
Arizona	737	670	4.4	4.2
Arkansas	535	566	3.7	4.1
California	4,489	4,189	3.2	3.2
Colorado	633	591	3.7	3.6
Connecticut	419	398	2.2	2.2
Delaware	121	127	3.2	3.5
Dist. of Col.	60	74	1.9	2.4
Florida	2,015	2,040	3.1	3.3
Georgia	1,290	1,391	3.1	3.5
Hawaii	149	146	3.5	3.5
Idaho	282	284	4.4	4.8
Illinois	2,073	2,084	3.2	3.4
Indiana	1,262	1,135	3.2	3.0
Iowa	785	674	3.9	3.4
Kansas	563	517	3.5	3.3
Kentucky	874	882	3.3	3.6
Louisiana	967	940	4.5	4.6
Maine	227	226	3.0	3.3
Maryland	677	691	2.6	2.8
Massachusetts	809	884	2.5	3.0
Michigan	1,953	1,811	3.2	3.1
Minnesota	807	777	3.0	3.0
Mississippi	677	612	4.4	4.3
Missouri	1,203	1,075	3.7	3.5
Montana	300	298	4.9	5.2
Nebraska	402	376	3.4	3.4
Nevada	224	220	4.8	4.9
New Hampshire	159	151	2.8	2.9
New Jersey	1,053	1,080	2.0	2.2
New Mexico	549	568	5.2	5.7
New York	2,359	2,458	3.5	3.8
North Carolina	1,521	1,522	3.9	4.2
North Dakota	183	169	3.9	3.8
Ohio	1,930	1,809	2.9	2.8
Oklahoma	838	763	3.4	3.4
Oregon	636	574	3.7	3.6
Pennsylvania	2,025	2,082	2.9	3.3
Rhode Island	121	112	2.1	2.0
South Carolina	820	821	3.7	4.0
South Dakota	224	198	4.1	3.9
Tennessee	1,146	1,145	3.3	3.5
Texas	3,230	3,429	3.6	4.1
Utah	254	275	3.0	3.5
Vermont	117	144	3.4	4.3
Virginia	1,020	1,030	2.8	3.0
Washington	823	771	3.2	3.2
West Virginia	497	486	4.5	4.6
Wisconsin	947	940	3.1	3.3
Wyoming	260	213	6.1	5.8
Puerto Rico	499	490	6.3	7.2

*The death rate is the number of deaths per 100 million vehicle miles. †Includes both traffic and nontraffic motor vehicle deaths.

Deaths in Civil Aviation Accidents

Source: National Safety Council

Includes only U.S. carriers.

Year	Total deaths[1]	Passenger deaths in scheduled flights: Domestic No.	Domestic Rate[2]	International No.	International Rate[2]	General aviation deaths No.	General aviation Rate[2]
1960	1,286	297	0.93	10	0.12	787	0.24
1965	1,279	205	0.38	21	0.12	1,029	0.21
1970	1,454	0	0.00	2	0.01	1,310	0.20*
1974	1,905	158	0.12	262	0.51	1,438	0.18
1975	1,448	113	0.09	0	0.00	1,345	0.16
1976p	1,233	4	—	35	0.10	1,198	0.15

(1) Includes some deaths not shown separately—crew members in scheduled operations and persons not in planes killed in airplane accidents. Excludes deaths in military plane accidents. (2) Rates are the number of deaths per 100,000 passenger miles. General aviation rates (NSC estimate) include deaths of general aviation passengers, pilots, and other crew members. *Rates for this year and subsequent years not comparable with prior years. — less then 0.005. (p) preliminary.

Accidental Deaths by Month and Type, 1975 and 1976

Source: National Safety Council

Month	1976 totals	1975 details by type: All types	Motor vehicle	Falls	Drowning†	Fires, burns*	Ingest. of food, object	Firearms	Poison (solid, liquid)	Poison by gas
Total	**100,000**	**103,030**	**45,853**	**14,896**	**8,000**	**6,071**	**3,106**	**2,380**	**4,694**	**1,577**
January	7,800	8,162	3,191	1,442	260	745	290	237	368	237
February	7,250	7,306	2,949	1,253	250	651	272	167	366	203
March	8,100	8,124	3,405	1,244	400	685	276	185	451	157
April	7,900	7,870	3,412	1,145	480	645	262	176	382	108
May	8,850	9,387	4,145	1,255	1,200	419	243	162	407	100
June	9,100	9,556	4,190	1,198	1,430	343	235	165	416	73
July	9,950	10,093	4,437	1,302	1,590	286	243	158	444	62
August	9,000	9,620	4,460	1,234	1,120	280	270	190	391	61
September	8,100	8,285	4,059	1,184	490	325	223	177	375	109
October	8,200	8,433	4,016	1,336	320	440	240	236	394	91
November	7,750	8,160	3,896	1,096	270	525	284	311	351	173
December	8,000	8,034	3,693	1,207	190	727	268	216	349	203
Average	**8,330**	**8,586**	**3,821**	**1,241**	**667**	**506**	**259**	**198**	**391**	**131**

*Includes deaths resulting from conflagration regardless of nature of injury. †Includes drowning in water transport accidents. Some totals partly estimated.

Accidental Deaths by Age, Sex, and Type, 1975

Source: National Safety Council

	All types	Motor vehicle	Falls	Drowning	Fires, burns	Ingest. of food, object	Firearms	Poison (solid, liquid)	Poison by gas	% Male all types
All ages	**103,030**	**45,853**	**14,896**	**8,000**	**6,071**	**3,106**	**2,380**	**4,694**	**1,577**	**70%**
Under 5	4,948	1,576	197	800	752	504	71	114	38	58%
5 to 14	6,818	3,286	137	1,300	580	77	424	49	81	70%
15 to 24	24,121	15,672	497	2,520	502	223	758	1,332	357	81%
25 to 34	13,823	7,680	428	1,080	500	218	359	1,215	263	81%
35 to 44	9,054	4,289	530	660	461	241	249	638	208	77%
45 to 54	9,993	4,089	1,057	630	757	369	215	545	216	74%
55 to 64	9,650	3,574	1,392	490	845	429	143	381	176	71%
65 to 74	9,220	3,047	2,148	310	795	451	115	233	139	63%
75 & over	15,403	2,640	8,510	210	879	594	46	187	99	47%
Sex										
Male	72,376	33,597	7,696	6,782	3,733	1,829	2,042	3,147	1,165	
Female	30,654	12,256	7,200	1,218	2,338	1,277	338	1,547	412	
Percent male	70%	73%	52%	85%	61%	59%	86%	67%	74%	

Average Lifetime in U.S., 1976

Source: Division of Vital Statistics, Public Health Service

Age interval	Number living[1]	Avg. life expect.[2]	Age interval	Number living[1]	Avg. life expect.[2]
0-1	100,000	72.8	45-50	93,043	31.4
1-5	98,488	72.9	50-55	90,747	27.2
5-10	98,207	69.1	55-60	87,310	23.1
10-15	98,033	64.2	60-65	82,282	19.4
15-20	97,865	59.3	65-70	75,084	16.0
20-25	97,391	54.6	70-75	66,114	12.8
25-30	96,747	49.9	75-80	54,060	10.1
30-35	96,147	45.2	80-85	39,540	7.9
35-40	95,452	40.5	85 and up	25,029	6.0
40-45	94,522	35.9			

(1) Of 100,000 born alive, number living at beginning of age interval. (2) Average number of years of life remaining at beginning of age interval.

Years of Life Expected at Birth

Year	Avg.	Male	Female	Year	Avg.	Male	Female
1960	69.7	66.6	73.1	1976[1]	72.8	NA	NA
1950	68.2	65.6	71.1	1975	72.5	68.7	76.5
1940	62.9	60.8	65.2	1974	71.9	68.1	75.8
1930	59.7	58.1	61.6	1973	71.3	67.6	75.3
1920	54.1	53.6	54.6	1970	70.8	67.1	74.6
1910	47.3	46.3	48.3	1965	70.2	66.8	73.7

Ownership of Life Insurance in the U.S. and Assets of U.S. Life Insurance Companies

Source: American Council of Life Insurance

Legal Reserve Life Insurance Companies
(millions of dollars)

Year	Purchases of life insurance				Insurance in force					Assets
	Ordinary	Group	Industrial	Total	Ordinary	Group	Industrial	Credit	Total	
1940	7,022	747	3,318	11,087	79,346	14,938	20,866	380	115,530	30,802
1950	18,260	6,237	5,492	29,989	149,116	47,793	33,415	3,844	234,168	64,020
1960	56,183	15,328	6,906	78,417	341,881	175,903	39,563	29,101	586,448	119,576
1965	89,643	52,867*	7,302	149,812*	499,638	308,078	39,818	53,020	900,554	158,884
1970	134,802	65,381*	6,612	206,795*	734,730	551,357	38,644	77,392	1,402,123	207,254
1973	175,629	67,703	7,224	250,556	928,192	708,322	40,632	101,154	1,778,300	252,436
1974	198,981	117,790*	6,680	323,451*	1,009,038	827,018	39,441	109,623	1,985,120	263,349
1975	207,052	102,659*	6,741	316,452*	1,083,421	904,695	39,423	112,032	2,139,571	289,304
1976	N/A	N/A	N/A	N/A	1,177,672	1,002,647	39,175	123,569	2,343,063	321,552

*Includes Servicemen's Group Life Insurance $27.4 billion in 1965, $16.8 billion in 1970, $28.8 billion in 1974, and $1.7 billion in 1975. N/A - not available.

Home Accident Deaths

Source: National Safety Council

Year	Total home	Falls	Fires, burns[2]	Suffo., ingested object	Suffo., mech-anical	Poison (solid, liquid)	Poison by gas	Fire-arms	Other
1950	29,000	14,800	5,000	(1)	1,600	1,300	1,250	950	4,100
1955	28,500	14,100	5,400	(1)	1,250	1,150	900	1,100	4,600
1960	28,000	12,300	6,350	1,850	1,500	1,350	900	1,200	2,550
1964	28,000	11,400	6,200	1,400*	1,300	1,700	900	1,200	3.900
1965	28,500	11,700	6,100	1,300	1,200	1,700	1,100	1,300	4,100
1966	29,500	11,900	6,800	1,300	1,100	1,800	1,200	1,400	4,000
1967	29,000	12,000	6,200	1,300	900	2,000	1,100	1,600	3,900
1968	28,000	10,800	6,100	2,000*	1,200*	2,100	1,100	1,300*	3,400*
1969	27,500	10,300	6,000	2,400	1,100	2,400	1,100	1,300	2,900
1970	27,000	9,700	5,600	1,800	1,100	3,000	1,100	1,400	3,300
1971	26,500	9,300	5,600	1,900	1,000	3,000	1,000	1,300	3,400
1972	26,500	9,300	5,500	1,800	900	3,000	1,000	1,400	3,600
1973	26,500	9,200	5,300	1,900	1,100	3,000	1,000	1,500	3,500
1974	26,000	9,000	5,100	1,800	900	3,200	900	1,400	3,700
1975	25,500	8,000	5,000	1,800	800	3,700	1,000	1,300	3,400
1976	24,000	7,700	5,100	1,600	700	3,400	900	1,200	3,400

*Data for this year and subsequent years not comparable with previous years due to classification changes. (1) Included in Other. (2) Includes deaths resulting from conflagration, regardless of nature of injury.

Physical Growth Range for Children from 1 to 18 Years

Source: Division of Health Examination Statistics, U.S. Department of Health, Education and Welfare

Age	Shortest 5%	Median height	Tallest 5%	Lightest 5%	Median weight	Heaviest 5%
			Boys			
1	28.4	30.2	32.0	18.7	23.3	27.8
2	32.1	34.6	37.1	23.3	28.3	33.3
3	35.3	37.8	40.3	27.1	32.5	37.9
4	38.3	40.8	43.3	30.0	36.1	42.2
5	40.3	43.4	46.4	33.0	40.3	47.6
6	42.8	45.9	49.0	36.0	44.7	53.4
7	44.8	48.1	51.4	40.3	50.9	61.5
8	46.9	50.5	54.1	44.4	57.4	70.4
9	48.8	52.8	56.8	48.0	64.4	80.4
10	50.6	54.3	59.2	51.4	71.4	91.4
11	51.9	56.4	60.9	53.3	78.9	102.5
12	53.5	58.6	63.7	60.0	86.0	113.5
13	55.2	61.3	67.4	65.3	98.6	131.9
14	57.5	64.1	70.7	75.5	111.8	148.1
15	61.0	66.9	72.8	88.0	124.3	160.6
16	63.8	68.9	74.0	97.8	133.8	169.8
17	65.2	69.8	74.4	106.5	139.8	174.0
18	65.9	70.2	74.5	110.3	144.8	179.3
			Girls			
1	27.6	29.4	31.2	17.4	21.7	26.0
2	31.6	33.8	36.0	22.3	27.1	31.9
3	35.3	37.5	39.7	26.3	32.3	38.3
4	38.1	40.7	43.3	28.8	36.1	43.4
5	40.6	43.4	46.2	32.2	40.9	49.6
6	42.8	45.9	49.0	35.5	45.7	55.9
7	44.5	47.8	51.1	38.3	51.0	63.7
8	46.4	50.0	53.6	42.0	57.2	72.4
9	48.2	52.2	56.2	45.1	63.6	82.1
10	49.9	54.5	59.1	48.2	71.0	95.0
11	51.9	57.0	62.1	55.4	82.0	108.6
12	54.1	59.5	64.9	63.9	94.4	124.9
13	57.1	62.2	66.8	72.8	105.5	138.2
14	58.5	63.1	67.7	83.0	113.0	144.0
15	59.5	63.8	68.1	89.5	120.0	150.5
16	59.8	64.1	68.4	95.1	123.0	150.1
17	60.1	64.2	68.3	97.9	125.8	153.7
18	60.1	64.4	68.7	96.0	126.2	156.4

This table simply gives a general picture for American children. When used as a standard, the individual variation in children's growth should not be overlooked. In most cases the height-weight relationship is probably a more valid index of weight status than a weight-for-age assessment.

Average Weight of Americans by Height and Age

Source: Society of Actuaries; based on a 4-year study of 5,000,000 persons
The figures represent weights in ordinary indoor clothing and shoes, and heights with shoes.

Men					
Height	20-24	25-29	30-39	40-49	50-59
5'0"	122	128	131	134	136
5'1"	125	131	134	137	139
5'2"	128	134	137	140	142
5'3"	132	138	141	144	145
5'4"	136	141	145	148	149
5'5"	139	144	149	152	153
5'6"	142	148	153	156	157
5'7"	145	151	157	161	162
5'8"	149	155	161	165	166
5'9"	153	159	165	169	170
5'10"	157	163	170	174	175
5'11"	161	167	174	178	180
6'0"	166	172	179	183	185
6'1"	170	177	183	187	189
6'2"	174	182	188	192	194
6'3"	178	186	193	197	199
6'4"	181	190	199	203	205

Women					
Height	20-24	25-29	30-39	40-49	50-59
4'10"	102	107	115	122	125
4'11"	105	110	117	124	127
5'0"	108	113	120	127	130
5'1"	112	116	123	130	133
5'2"	115	119	126	133	136
5'3"	118	122	129	136	140
5'4"	121	125	132	140	141
5'5"	125	129	135	143	148
5'6"	129	133	139	147	152
5'7"	132	136	142	151	156
5'8"	136	140	146	155	160
5'9"	140	144	150	159	164
5'10"	144	148	154	164	169
5'11"	149	153	159	169	174
6'0"	154	158	164	174	180

Pedalcycle Accidents

Since 1935, the number of pedalcycle-motor vehicle deaths doubled to 900 in 1976. The number of pedalcycles in use, 95 million, is 27 times the number in 1935; so the death rate in 1976 was one-thirthteenth the rate in 1935. The proportion of deaths occurring to young adults and adults has steadily increased since 1960. Persons 15 years of age and older accounted for more than one-half the deaths in 1976 compared to one-fifth in 1960.

Leading Cancer Sites 1978

Source: American Cancer Society (all figures rounded to nearest 1,000)

Site	Estimated new cases	Estimated deaths	Warning Signal—see your doctor	Comment
Breast	91,000	34,000	Lump or thickening in the breast, or unusual discharge from nipple.	The leading cause of cancer death in women.
Colon and rectum	102,000	52,000	Change in bowel habits; bleeding.	Considered a highly curable disease when digital and proctoscopic examinations are included in routine checkups.
Lung	102,000	92,000	Persistent cough, or lingering respiratory ailment.	The leading cause of cancer death among men and rising mortality among women.
Oral (including pharynx)	24,000	8,000	Sore that does not heal; difficulty in swallowing.	Many more lives should be saved because the mouth is easily accessible to visual examination by physicians and dentists.
Skin	10,000[1]	6,000	Sore that does not heal, or change in wart or mole.	Skin cancer is readily detected by observation, and diagnosed by simple biopsy,
Uterus	48,000[2]	11,000	Unusual bleeding or discharge.	Uterine cancer mortality has declined 65% during the last 40 years with wider application of the pap test. Postmenopausal women with abnormal bleeding should be checked.
Kidney and bladder	45,000	17,000	Urinary difficulty, bleeding.	Protective measures for workers in high-risk industries are helping to eliminate one of the important causes of these cancers.
Larynx	9,000	3,000	Hoarseness, difficulty in swallowing.	Readily curable if caught early.
Prostate	57,000	21,000	Urinary difficulty.	Occurs mainly in men over 60, the disease can be detected by palpation at regular checkup.
Stomach	23,000	15,000	Indigestion.	A 40% decline in mortality in 25 years, for reasons yet unknown.
Leukemia	22,000	15,000	Leukemia is a cancer of blood-forming tissues and is characterized by the abnormal production of immature white blood cells. Acute lymphocytic leukemia strikes mainly children and is treated by drugs which have extended life from a few months to as much as ten years. chronic leukemia strikes usually after age 25 and progresses less rapidly.	
Lymphomas (including multiple myeloma)	33,000	21,000	These cancers arise in the lymph system and include Hodgkin's disease and lymphosarcoma. Some patients with lymphatic cancers can lead normal lives for many years. Five-year survival rate for Hodgkin's disease increased from 25% to 54% in 20 years.	

(1) Estimated new cases of non-melanoma skin cancer: about 300,000. (2) If carcinoma in situ is included, cases toal over 88,000.

Facts About Cancer

There has been progress against cancer. In the early 1900s few cancer patients had any hope of long-term survival. In the 1930s less than one in 5 were alive at least 5 years after treatment. In the 1950s it was one in 4. Now the ratio is one in 3. The gain from one in 4 to one in 3 currently represents about 58,000 people each year.

For men, the cancer death rate per 100,000 population has increased by over 50% for blacks, and 20% for whites. The increased death rate is mainly the result of lung cancer which rose from 18 deaths per 100,000 in 1950 to 52 deaths per 100,000 in 1974.

For women, since 1950 the death rate has declined 5% for blacks and 10% for whites. This is due mainly to a reduction in deaths caused by cancer of the uterine cervix. However, the lung cancer rate has tripled from 4.0 per 100,000 in 1950 to 12.3 in 1974.

For children, cancer is responsible for more deaths in the 3 to 14-year-old group than any other disease. In 1977, cancer accounted for the deaths of about 3,000 children, about half of them from acute lymphocytic leukemia, a cancer of blood-forming tissues.

More people could be saved. About 115,000 people died of cancer in 1977 who might have been saved by earlier treatment. Of every 6 people who get cancer, 2 will be saved and 4 will die. But of the 4 who will die, one might have been saved with earlier diagnosis and prompt treatment.

Trends in Cancer Death Rates

per 100,000 population

Site	Sex	1953-55	1973-75	Percent changes	Comments
All sites	Male	136.0	160.2	+18	Steady increase mainly due to lung cancer.
	Female	116.4	107.5	−8	Slight decrease.
Bladder	Male	5.1	4.9	−4	Slight fluctuations; overall no change.
	Female	2.1	1.4	*	Some fluctuations, noticeable decrease.
Breast	Male	0.3	0.3	*	Constant rate.
	Female	22.3	23.0	+3	Slight fluctuations; overall no change.
Colon / rectum	Male	19.3	18.6	−4	Slight fluctuations; overall no change.
	Female	18.3	14.9	−19	Slight fluctuations, noticeable of a decrease.
Esophagus	Male	3.7	4.1	*	Slight fluctuations; overall no change in both sexes.
	Female	0.9	1.1	*	
Kidney	Male	2.9	3.7	+28	Steady slight increase.
	Female	1.6	1.7	*	Slight fluctuations; overall no change.
Leukemia	Male	6.8	6.9	+1	Early increase, later leveling off.
	Female	4.7	4.2	−11	Slight early increase, later leveling off and decrease.
Lung	Male	24.0	51.7	+1-15	Steady increase in both sexes due to cigarette smoking.
	Female	4.1	12.3	+200	
Oral	Male	4.6	4.8	*	Slight fluctuations; overall no change.
	Female	1.2	1.6	*	
Ovary	Female	7.4	7.3	−1	Slight fluctuations; overall no change.
Pancreas	Male	7.1	8.5	+20	Steady increase in both sexes, then leveling off. Reasons unknown.
	Female	4.4	5.2	+18	
Prostrate	Male	13.6	13.7	+1	Fluctuations all through period; overall no change.
Skin	Male	2.4	2.6	*	Slight fluctuations; overall no change in both sexes.
	Female	1.5	1.5	*	
Stomach	Male	15.8	7.2	−54	Steady decrease in both sexes. Reasons unknown.
	Female	8.1	3.5	−57	
Uterus	Female	16.6	8.1	−51	Steady decrease.

*Percent changes not listed because they are not meaningful.

The Nation's Hospitals

Source: American Hospital Association

In 1976, there were 7,082 hospitals in the United States registered by the American Hospital Association. These institutions had about 1.43 million beds and reported admitting some 36.8 million inpatients. About $55.7 billion was spent to provide services for both inpatients and outpatients, or a cost of $257 per resident of the nation.

	State hospitals		Beds		Average daily census		Admissions		Expenses ($1,000)	
	Fed.	Non-fed.	Fed.	Non-fed.	Fed.	Non-fed	Fed.	Non-fed.	Fed.	Non-fed.
Alabama	8	138	2,684	22,321	2,212	16,623	37,370	666,969	90,632	691,229
Alaska	9	16	605	966	367	657	17,686	36,986	37,455	55,870
Arizona	17	63	1,753	9,304	1,282	6,840	53,601	307,269	89,285	457,885
Arkansas	4	92	1,942	11,353	1,647	8,033	24,485	398,019	63,547	325,985
California	32	599	11,201	108,208	7,982	73,170	223,776	3,091,352	602,514	5,468,373
Colorado	7	93	1,990	12,736	1,588	9,147	39,923	428,315	100,359	558,544
Connecticut	5	62	1,073	18,462	768	14,784	17,809	438,314	54,429	821,205
Delaware	2	13	379	4,188	299	3,708	6,529	74,734	14,367	144,169
Dist. of Columbia	4	16	4,744	5,868	3,662	4,613	37,391	177,006	211,049	359,621
Florida	14	229	4,233	49,132	3,459	35,328	100,995	1,414,998	233,932	1,893,539
Georgia	10	176	3,026	27,857	2,359	20,415	54,834	861,658	130,907	939,408
Hawaii	1	26	540	3,343	471	2,368	21,065	94,869	42,269	136,907
Idaho	2	50	192	3,476	156	2,308	4,894	128,126	8,885	115,216
Illinois	10	277	6,506	70,806	5,254	54,939	79,426	1,942,994	234,733	3,159,797
Indiana	6	133	2,131	32,731	1,817	25,261	20,489	847,865	61,541	1,086,784
Iowa	3	140	1,632	20,089	1,397	13,889	16,467	555,840	57,818	591,451
Kansas	7	157	2,045	16,138	1,554	11,521	24,495	435,325	66,558	491,957
Kentucky	5	120	1,999	17,433	1,685	13,469	41,293	595,780	84,941	572,282
Louisiana	8	146	2,491	22,235	1,905	15,679	43,559	688,356	101,742	728,658
Maine	2	52	758	6,536	673	4,751	6,442	174,749	20,816	223,592
Maryland	11	70	3,483	21,620	2,697	17,770	50,556	486,012	170,825	940,734
Massachusetts	7	183	3,800	44,529	3,274	35,678	28,239	928,550	117,253	2,104,511
Michigan	9	244	2,827	50,396	2,184	39,635	34,142	1,423,549	99,212	2,410,648
Minnesota	5	184	1,902	29,483	1,537	21,427	22,783	717,605	66,395	928,310
Mississippi	5	106	1,728	15,534	1,461	11,153	29,378	422,519	63,711	368,422
Missouri	8	163	3,404	31,735	2,528	23,756	56,189	902,652	173,264	1,168,213
Montana	6	59	389	4,008	285	2,387	9,167	135,016	16,252	114,640
Nebraska	5	103	990	10,413	735	6,919	21,445	289,005	41,100	326,754
Nevada	4	19	291	2,957	185	1,937	6,983	94,603	15,714	135,766
New Hampshire	2	31	253	4,860	225	3,530	6,301	128,670	15,897	148,314
New Jersey	4	140	2,941	44,704	2,420	35,913	33,358	1,044,905	88,717	1,667,904
New Mexico	11	43	1,029	5,600	721	3,858	31,891	157,872	46,981	190,016
New York	16	378	10,173	141,824	8,564	119,744	97,717	2,727,588	356,974	6,015,583
North Carolina	9	150	3,182	30,882	2,627	23,659	56,936	852,991	128,740	928,991
North Dakota	5	55	401	5,339	282	3,756	12,651	134,187	18,078	143,616
Ohio	6	242	4,634	65,744	3,410	52,581	41,647	1,815,565	146,560	2,551,113
Oklahoma	12	128	1,252	15,871	860	11,111	38,569	466,914	67,129	509,431
Oregon	2	85	992	11,093	807	7,534	15,982	354,730	39,519	437,500
Pennsylvania	11	307	6,866	85,699	5,645	67,599	50,506	1,931,537	215,840	3,112,706
Rhode Island	2	19	513	6,802	337	5,692	10,525	135,420	25,897	271,074
South Carolina	7	81	1,829	15,798	1,415	11,973	49,768	417,167	96,315	432,042
South Dakota	10	60	1,226	4,602	994	3,076	20,939	125,832	39,984	107,997
Tennessee	5	149	2,925	27,618	2,534	21,142	40,462	820,956	99,903	862,847
Texas	25	538	8,867	68,738	7,273	48,074	177,755	2,178,239	391,937	2,343,916
Utah	2	36	541	4,413	379	3,237	12,130	180,814	25,538	184,988
Vermont	1	20	224	3,344	195	2,341	3,933	75,216	10,974	104,734
Virginia	11	118	3,709	28,508	2,775	22,149	68,597	719,745	168,520	895,004
Washington	11	118	2,613	13,682	1,989	9,290	50,339	531,478	113,826	616,323
West Virginia	6	79	1,319	14,508	1,067	11,086	18,183	388,760	48,785	400,773
Wisconsin	3	169	2,196	28,950	1,821	20,692	22,824	767,870	79,876	1,041,996
Wyoming	3	27	551	2,105	450	1,256	5,162	62,693	15,722	54,097
Total U.S.	**380**	**6,702**	**128,974**	**1,304,541**	**102,213**	**987,458**	**1,997,586**	**34,778,184**	**5,313,217**	**50,341,435**

Canadian General and Allied Special Hospitals

1975[1]	Hospitals			Beds			Admissions			Expenses ($1,000)
	Public	Prop.[2]	Fed.	Public	Prop.	Fed.	Public	Prop.	Fed.	Public
Canada	1,043	90	107	151,793	3,898	6,126	3,701,063	24,951	51,618	4,712,358
Newfoundland	47	—	—	3,173	—	—	92,400	—	—	102,833
Prince Edward Is.	9	—	—	745	—	—	24,549	—	—	15,236
Nova Scotia	47	—	3	4,880	—	557	132,845	—	5,231	153,017
New Brunswick	38	—	—	4,429	—	—	121,477	—	—	124,668
Quebec	188	42	10	41,835	2,679	1,622	772,123	11,419	4,127	1,300,184
Ontario	233	46	13	51,218	1,209	1,743	1,412,520	13,351	13,812	1,754,640
Manitoba	80	—	20	6,532	—	683	169,994	—	5,530	203,898
Saskatchewan	135	—	3	7,821	—	110	201,254	—	2,675	166,979
Alberta	145	—	8	14,239	—	896	355,873	—	12,430	384,675
Brit. Columbia	117	1	2	16,769	7	70	413,588	155	1,048	502,489
Yukon	—	1	6	—	3	160	—	26	3,978	—
N.W.T.	4	—	42	152	—	285	4,440	—	2,787	3,739

(1) Preliminary data. (2) Proprietary; privately owned and operated hospitals.

How to Obtain Birth, Marriage, Death Records

The United States government has published a series of inexpensive booklets entitled Where to Write for Birth & Death Records; Where to Write for Marriage Records; Where to Write for Divorce Records; Where to Write for Birth and Death Records of U. S. Citizens who were born or died outside of the U. S. and birth certifications for alien children adopted by U. S. citizens; You May Save Time Proving Your Age and Other Birth Facts. They tell where to write to get a certified copy of an original vital record. Supt. of Documents, Government Printing Office, Washington, DC 20402.

Nursing Care Homes in U.S.

Source: Division of Health Manpower and Facilities Statistics, National Center for Health Statistics (1973 data)

State	Nursing care homes: Homes	Beds	Residents	Full-time personnel	Personal care homes: Homes	Beds
Total	**14,873**	**1,107,358**	**1,011,092**	**559,684**	**6,961**	**220,346**
Alabama	188	13,997	13,350	8,320	9	847
Alaska	8	606	477	238	—	—
Arizona	75	5,969	5,332	3,189	13	461
Arkansas	199	17,070	15,404	7,933	12	882
California	1,618	115,560	100,742	56,159	2,527	35,396
Colorado	179	15,126	13,783	7,425	35	1,544
Connecticut	261	19,438	18,553	9,320	104	3,856
Delaware	34	2,199	2,071	1,472	2	14
District of Columbia	43	2,825	2,434	1,546	29	322
Florida	297	29,304	25,069	16,251	63	5,652
Georgia	285	24,340	23,174	12,759	21	1,596
Hawaii	41	2,105	1,967	1,313	101	621
Idaho	58	4,047	3,693	2,031	6	143
Illinois	786	67,229	60,998	30,030	253	12,922
Indiana	417	29,801	26,798	14,892	78	4,446
Iowa	464	26,734	24,591	10,978	214	8,418
Kansas	305	17,821	16,460	7,856	163	5,068
Kentucky	187	13,118	11,865	6,292	125	5,059
Louisiana	202	16,550	15,666	7,919	10	454
Maine	168	7,667	7,315	4,487	173	1,560
Maryland	175	16,199	15,187	9,315	29	1,556
Massachusetts	754	46,070	43,271	21,548	191	7,788
Michigan	444	38,735	36,860	24,117	133	9,832
Minnesota	441	37,703	34,786	13,775	148	6,958
Mississippi	126	7,494	7,086	4,180	17	392
Missouri	415	29,191	26,827	15,001	87	4,453
Montana	79	3,977	3,765	2,000	26	782
Nebraska	195	14,710	13,325	5,763	56	2,686
Nevada	23	1,201	1,031	763	18	281
New Hampshire	106	5,214	4,925	2,709	24	659
New Jersey	356	28,174	25,857	16,634	193	6,256
New Mexico	43	2,649	2,268	1,509	23	696
New York	691	68,024	63,439	45,461	392	24,864
North Carolina	231	13,890	12,693	6,983	607	8,255
North Dakota	63	4,563	4,338	1,802	44	2,068
Ohio	1,015	58,189	53,305	29,446	148	6,945
Oklahoma	386	28,213	25,270	12,953	31	1,299
Oregon	218	14,157	13,135	6,776	94	4,149
Pennsylvania	666	58,230	53,724	34,471	102	7,733
Rhode Island	113	5,569	5,326	2,357	46	924
South Carolina	110	7,510	7,062	4,468	13	621
South Dakota	114	6,634	6,212	2,633	46	1,161
Tennessee	213	12,473	11,997	7,162	31	2,084
Texas	873	74,430	65,882	35,138	94	6,080
Utah	92	3,941	3,674	1,698	28	615
Vermont	71	3,369	2,974	1,923	30	533
Virginia	198	13,936	12,479	7,755	150	2,796
Washington	327	27,954	25,475	12,151	55	3,193
West Virginia	75	3,510	3,290	2,153	62	1,243
Wisconsin	421	38,104	34,484	15,949	95	13,856
Wyoming	24	1,569	1,403	681	10	327

Active Federal and Non-Federal Doctors (M.D.s) by States

Source: Division of Health Manpower and Facilities Statistics, National Center for Health Statistics (Dec. 31, 1974)

	Total	Non-fed.	Fed.
All areas	**(1) 350,609**	**323,993**	**26,616**
United States	**345,659**	**321,089**	**24,570**
Alabama	3,579	3,333	246
Alaska	426	288	138
Arizona	3,661	3,260	401
Arkansas	2,069	1,892	177
California	44,223	40,526	3,697
Colorado	4,731	4,215	516
Connecticut	6,476	6,230	246
Delaware	843	794	49
D.C.	4,031	3,103	928
Florida	12,801	11,789	1,012
Georgia	6,255	5,652	603
Hawaii	1,386	1,310	76
Idaho	784	738	46
Illinois	17,759	16,835	924
Indiana	5,761	5,586	175
Iowa	3,079	2,942	137
Kansas	3,038	2,798	240
Kentucky	3,957	3,698	259
Louisiana	4,963	4,596	367
Maine	1,304	1,210	103
Maryland	10,333	8,130	2,203
Mass.	13,249	12,546	703
Michigan	12,367	11,987	380
Minnesota	6,529	6,166	363
Mississippi	2,252	2,007	245
Missouri	6,751	6,408	343
Montana	849	767	82
Nebraska	1,971	1,840	131
Nevada	696	643	53
N.H.	1,205	1,135	70
New Jersey	11,963	11,448	515
New Mexico	1,502	1,280	222
New York	44,390	42,830	1,560
North Carolina	6,726	6,240	486
North Dakota	675	600	75
Ohio	15,208	14,633	575
Oklahoma	2,986	2,728	258
Oregon	3,653	3,458	195
Pennsylvania	19,116	18,347	769
Rhode Island	1,710	1,610	100
South Carolina	3,118	2,803	315
South Dakota	609	529	80
Tennessee	5,589	5,244	345
Texas	16,546	14,616	1,930
Utah	1,829	1,697	132
Vermont	884	839	45
Virginia	7,440	6,426	1,014
Washington	5,869	5,295	574
West Virginia	2,109	1,991	118
Wisconsin	6,019	5,713	306
Wyoming	390	347	43
Puerto Rico	2,913	2,745	168
Outlying areas	2,037	159	1,878

(1) Excludes 7,525 physicians with addresses unknown.

Canadian Active Civilian Physicians

Source: Health Programs Branch, Health and Welfare Canada (December 31, 1976)

Province	Number[1]	Population per physician[1]
Newfoundland	779	716
Prince Edward Island	140	871
Nova Scotia	1,404	595
New Brunswick	773	898
Quebec	11,262	558
Ontario	15,251	550
Manitoba	1,769	584
Saskatchewan	1,315	719
Alberta	2,911	641
British Columbia	4,470	562
Yukon	22	955
Northwest Territories	33	1,182
Not specified	1	—
Canada	**40,130**	**581**

(1) Includes interns and residents.

Selected Statistics on State and County Mental Hospitals

Source: National Institute of Mental Health

Year	Total admitted[1]	Net releases[2]	Deaths in hospital	Residents end of year	Expense per patient[3]
1955	178,003	NA	44,384	558,922	$1,116.59
1960	234,791	NA	49,748	535,540	1,702.41
1970	393,174	394,627	30,804	338,592	5,435.38
1973	377,020*	386,962	19,899	248,562	9,207.92
1974	374,554*	389,094	16,597	215,573	11,277.23
1975	376,156	391,345	13,401	193,436	13,634.53

*Includes estimates. NA-not available. (1) Excludes transfers. (2) Net releases alive from hospital is computed by subtracting returns from long-term leave from the total discontinuations. (3) Per average daily resident patient population.

Patients in State and County Mental Hospitals

Source: National Institute of Mental Health. Average daily census 1975

The following data was based on reports of the 313 state and county hospitals. The full-time personnel was estimated at 211,899 and the expenditures $2,641,295,000. The average daily expenditures per patient based on the resident patient population of hospitals reporting expenditures was $37.54.

State	Number	State	Number	State	Number	State	Number
United States	**193,721**	Idaho	228	Missouri	3,214	Pennsylvania	15,126
Alabama	2,735	Illinois	7,183	Montana	954	Rhode Island	1,530
Alaska	123	Indiana	4,374	Nebraska	696	South Carolina	4,272
Arizona	640	Iowa	1,168	Nevada	317	South Dakota	663
Arkansas	408	Kansas	1,283	New Hampshire	1,162	Tennessee	4,111
California	8,727	Kentucky	717	New Jersey	9,606	Texas	7,733
Colorado	1,078	Louisiana	2,712	New Mexico	581	Utah	313
Connecticut	3,093	Maine	812	New York	36,297	Vermont	453
Delaware	903	Maryland	5,093	North Carolina	4,508	Virginia	6,511
District of Columbia	2,735	Massachusetts	5,702	North Dakota	605	Washington	1,227
Florida	6,307	Michigan	5,509	Ohio	9,889	West Virginia	2,801
Georgia	6,922	Minnesota	3,829	Oklahoma	2,316	Wisconsin	1,155
Hawaii	203	Mississippi	3,777	Oregon	1,138	Wyoming	286

Patient Care Episodes in Mental Health Facilities

Source: National Institute of Mental Health

Year	Total all facilities[1]	Inpatient services: State & County mental hospitals	Private mental[2] hospitals	Gen. hosp. psychiatric service (non-VA)	VA psychiatric inpatient services	Federally assisted comm. men. health cen.	Outpatient services: Federally assisted comm. men. health cen.	Other
1975	6,409,447	598,993	165,327	565,696	214,264	246,891	1,584,968	3,033,308
1973	5,248,832	651,857	151,941	475,448	208,416	191,946	982,552	2,586,672
1969	3,572,822	767,115	123,850	535,493	186,913	65,000	291,148	1,603,303
1965	2,636,525	804,926	125,428	519,328	115,843	—	—	1,071,000
1955	1,675,352	818,832	123,231	265,934	88,355	—	—	379,000

(1) In order to present trends on the same set of facilities over this interval, it has been necessary to exclude from this table the following: private psychiatric office practice; psychiatric service modes of all types in hospitals or outpatient clinics of federal agencies other than the VA (e.g., Public Health Service, Indian Health Service, Department of Defense Bureau of Prisons, etc.); inpatient service modes of multiservice facilities not shown in this table; all partial care episodes, and outpatient episodes of VA hospitals. (2) Includes estimates of episodes of care in residential treatment centers for emotionally disturbed children.

Patients in Canadian Mental Hospitals

Average patients per day, 1975[1]

Province	Public hospitals: Mental	Psychiatric	Retardates	Emotionally disturbed children	Other	Total private	Total mental hospitals
Canada	**21,589**	**1,186**	**15,371**	**147**	**1,780**	**894**	**40,967**
Newfoundland	425	—	—	—	—	—	425
Prince Edward Island	272	—	22	—	—	—	294
Nova Scotia	754	513	—	—	—	—	1,267
New Brunswick	983	—	170	—	—	—	1,153
Quebec	9,928	140	2,360	—	345	—	12,773
Ontario	5,033	379	6,798	147	103	894	13,354
Manitoba	891	29	1,149	—	—	—	2,069
Saskatchewan	348	52	1,087	—	—	—	1,487
Alberta	1,486	—	2,038	—	345	—	3,869
British Columbia	1,469	73	1,747	—	987	—	4,276

(1) Preliminary data.

Marriage Information

Source: Compiled by William E. Mariano, Council on Marriage Relations, Inc., 110 E. 42d St., New York, NY 10017 (as of Oct. 1, 1977)

Marriageable age, by states, for both males and females with and without consent of parents or guardians. But in most states, the court has authority, in an emergency, to marry young couples below the ordinary age of consent, where due regard for their morals and welfare so requires. In many states, under special circumstances, blood test and waiting period may be waived.

State	With consent		Without consent		Blood test		Wait for license	Wait after license
	Men	Women	Men	Women	Required	Other state accepted*		
Alabama (b)	17	14	21	18	Yes	Yes	None	None
Alaska	18	16	19	18	Yes	No	3 days	None
Arizona	16(i)	16	18	18	Yes	Yes	None	None
Arkansas	17	16 (j)	18	18	Yes	No	3 days	None
California	—(i)	—(i)	18	18	Yes	Yes	None	None
Colorado	16	16	18	18	Yes	. . .	None	None
Connecticut	16	16(m)	18	18	Yes	Yes	4 days	None
Delaware	18	16(j)	18	18	Yes	Yes	None	24 hrs. (c)
District of Columbia	18	16	21	18	Yes	Yes	3 days	None
Florida	18	16	21	21	Yes	Yes	3 days	None
Georgia	18	16	18	18	Yes	Yes	None (b)	None (k)
Hawaii	16	16	18	18	Yes	Yes	None	None
Idaho	16	16	18	18	Yes	Yes	None (l)	None
Illinois (a)	—(e)	15(e)	18	18	Yes	Yes	None	None
Indiana	17	17	18	18	Yes	No	3 days	None
Iowa	16(e)	16(e)	18	18	Yes	Yes	3 days	None
Kansas	(i)	—(i)	18	18	Yes	Yes	3 days	None
Kentucky	18	16	18	18	Yes	No	3 days	None
Louisiana (a)	18	16	18	18	Yes	No	None	72 hours
Maine	16	16	18	18	No	No	5 days	None
Maryland	18	16	21	18	None	None	48 hours	None
Massachusetts	—(i)	—(i)	18	18	Yes	Yes	3 days	None
Michigan (a)	—	16	18	18	Yes	No	3 days	None
Minnesota	—	16(e)	18	18	None	. . .	5 days	None
Mississippi (b)	17	15	17	15	Yes	. . .	3 days	None
Missouri	15	15	18	18	Yes	Yes	3 days	None
Montana	—(i)	—(i)	18	18	Yes	Yes	5 days	None
Nebraska	18	16	18	18	Yes	Yes	5 days	None
Nevada	18	16	21	18	None	None	None	None
New Hampshire (a)	14(e)	13(e)	18	18	Yes	Yes	5 days	None
New Jersey (a)	—	16	18	18	Yes	Yes	72 hours	None
New Mexico	16	16	21	21	Yes	Yes	None	None
New York	16	14	18	18	Yes	No	None	24 hrs.(g)
North Carolina (a)	16	16	18	18	Yes	Yes	None	None
North Dakota (a)	—(i)	15	18	18	Yes	. . .	None	None
Ohio (a)	18	16	18	18	Yes	Yes	5 days	None
Oklahoma	16	16	18	18	Yes	No	None (f)(h)	. . .
Oregon	18 (e)	15 (e)	18	18	Yes	No	7 days	None
Pennsylvania	16	16	18	18	Yes	Yes	3 days	None
Rhode Island (a) (b)	18	16	18	18	Yes	No	None	None
South Carolina	16	14	18	18	None	None	24 hrs.	None
South Dakota	18	16	18	18	Yes	Yes	None	None
Tennessee (b)	16	16	21	21	Yes	Yes	3 days	None
Texas	16	16	18	18	Yes	Yes	None	None
Utah (a)	—(o)	—(o)	—(o)	—(o)	Yes	Yes	None	None
Vermont (a)	18	16	18	18	Yes	. . .	None	5 days
Virginia (a)	16	16	18	18	Yes	Yes (n)	None	None
Washington	17	17	18	18	(d)	. . .	3 days	None
West Virginia	(i)	16	18	18	Yes	No	3 days	None
Wisconsin	18	16	18	18	Yes	Yes	5 days	None
Wyoming	18	16	21	21	Yes	Yes	None	None
Puerto Rico	16	16	21	21	(f)	None	None	None
Virgin Islands	16	14	21	18	None	None	8 days	None

*__Many states have additional special requirements; contact individual state.__ (a) Special laws applicable to non-residents. (b) Special laws applicable to those under 21 years; Ala., bond required if male is under 21, female under 18. (c) 24 hours if one or both parties resident of state; 96 hours if both parties are non-residents. (d) None, but male must file affidavit. (e) Parental consent plus court's consent required. (f) None, but a medical certificate is required. (g) Marriage may not be solemnized within 10 days from date of blood test. (h) If either under 21, 72 hrs. (i) Statute provides for obtaining license with parental or court consent with no state minimum age. (j) Under 16, with parental and court consent. (k) All those between 19-21 cannot waive 3 day waiting period. (l) if either under 18, wait 3 full days. (m) If under stated age, court consent required. (n) Va. blood test form must be used. (o) Ut. has recently amended its laws to eliminate distinctions of age based on sex. Current ages are not available.

Grounds for Divorce

Source: Compiled by William E. Mariano, Council on Marriage Relations, Inc., 110 E. 42d St., New York, NY 10017 (as of Oct. 1, 1977).

Persons contemplating divorce should study latest decisions or secure legal advice before initiating proceedings since different interpretations or exceptions in each case can change the conclusion reached. *Exceptions are to be noted.

State	Cruelty	Desertion	Non-support	Alcohol	Felony	Impotency	Pregnancy at marriage	Drug addiction	Fraudulent contract	Other causes	Residence time	Time between interlocut'y and final decrees
Alabama	X	X	X	X	X	X	X	X	...	F-I-L-Q-EE	1 year*	None-M
Alaska	X	X	...	X	X	X	...	X	...	D-F-I	1 year	None
Arizona	...	...	...	...	...	...	...	...	...	II	90 days	None
Arkansas	X	X	X	X	X	X	...	...	...	D-I-S-X	3 months*	None
California	...	...	...	...	...	...	...	...	...	I-CC	6 months	6 months
Colorado	...	...	...	...	...	...	...	...	...	II	90 days	None
Connecticut	X	X	X	X	X	...	...	...	X	F-I-II	1 year*	None
Delaware	...	...	...	...	...	...	...	...	...	II	6 months	3 months
Dist. of Columbia	...	X	...	...	X	X	...	...	X	S-T	6 months	None
Florida	...	...	...	...	...	...	...	...	...	I-II	6 months	None
Georgia	X	X	...	X	X	X	X	X	X	I-J-U-II	6 months	A
Hawaii	...	...	...	...	...	...	...	...	...	R-II	1 year	A
Idaho	X	X	X	X	X	...	...	...	...	I-R	6 weeks	None
Illinois	X	X	...	X	X	X	...	X	...	X	6 months*	None
Indiana	...	...	...	...	X	X	...	...	...	I-II	6 months	None
Iowa	...	...	...	...	...	...	...	...	...	EE	1 year*	None-N
Kansas	X	X	...	X	X	X	X	...	X	I-W-X	60 days	None-O
Kentucky	...	...	...	...	...	...	...	...	...	II	180 days	None
Louisiana	...	...	...	...	X	...	...	...	...	R-T	1 year*	None
Maine	X	X	X	X	...	X	...	X	...	R-CC	6 months	None
Maryland	...	X	...	...	X	X	...	...	...	I-S	1 year	None
Massachusetts	X	X	X	X	X	X	...	X	...	DD-II	2 years*	6 months
Michigan	...	...	...	...	...	...	...	...	...	EE	1 year*	None
Minnesota	...	X	...	X	X	...	...	X	...	I-Q-GG-II	1 year*	None-O
Mississippi	X	X	...	X	X	X	X	X	...	I-J-X	1 year*	None-P
Missouri	X	X	...	X	X	X	X	...	...	D-H	1 year	None
Montana	X	X	X	X	X	...	...	...	...	I-CC	1 year	None*
Nebraska	...	...	...	...	...	...	...	...	...	II	1 year	6 months
Nevada	...	...	...	...	...	...	...	...	...	F-I-S	6 weeks	None
New Hampshire	X	X	X	X	X	X	...	...	...	E-Z-AA-BB-CC	1 year*	None
New Jersey	X	X	...	X	X	...	...	X	...	I-S-FF	1 year*	None
New Mexico	X	X	...	...	...	...	...	...	...	F	6 months	None
New York	X	X	...	...	X	...	...	...	...	R-T*	1 year	None
North Carolina	...	...	...	...	...	X	X	...	...	I-L-R	6 months	None
North Dakota	X	X	X	X	X	...	...	X	...	I-CC	1 year	None
Ohio	X	X	...	X	X	X	...	...	X	V-W-X	6 months	None
Oklahoma	X	X	X	X	X	X	X	...	X	F-I-V-W	6 months	None
Oregon	...	...	...	...	...	...	...	...	X	CC	6 months*	90 days
Pennsylvania	X	X	...	...	X	X	...	...	X	D-I-J-S-X	1 year*	None
Rhode Island	X	X	X	X	X	X	...	X	...	G-R	2 years*	6 months
South Carolina	X	X	...	X	...	...	...	X	...	S	1 year	None
South Dakota	X	X	X	X	X	...	...	...	...		1 year*	None
Tennessee	X	X	X	X	X	X	X	X	...	C-X-Y	6 months*	None
Texas	X	X	...	...	X	...	...	...	...	F-I-R-HH	1 year	None-O
Utah	X	X	X	X	X	X	...	...	...	I-Q	3 months	3 mos.*
Vermont	X	X	X	...	X	...	...	...	...	I-S	6 months	3 mos.-K*
Virginia	...	X	...	...	...	...	X	...	...	D-R	1 year	None-P*
Washington	...	...	...	...	...	...	...	...	X	II	6 months	None
West Virginia	X	X	...	X	X	...	...	X	...	I-R	2 years-B*	None
Wisconsin	X	X	X	X	X	...	...	...	...	I-S-T	6 months	None-O
Wyoming	X	X	X	X	X	X	X	...	...	D-I-H	60 days	None

(A) Determined by court order. (B) No minimum residence required in adultery cases. (C) Violence. (D) Indignities. (E) Joining religious order disbelieving in marriage. (F) Incompatibility. (G) Any gross misbehavior or wickedness. (H) Husband being a vagrant. (I) 5-yrs. insanity; permanent insanity in Ut.; incurable insanity in Cal. Exceptions: 1 yr. Wis.; 18 mos. Alas.; 2 yrs. Ga., Ha., Ind., N.J., Nev., Ore., Wash., Wyo.; 3 yrs. Ark., N.C., Fla., Tex., Minn., Col., Kan:, Ha., Md., Miss., W. Va.; 6 yrs. Ida. (J) Consanguinity. (K) Plaintiff, 6 mos.; defendant 2 yrs. to remarry. (L) Crime against nature. (M) Sixty days to remarry. (N) One year to remarry; Ha. one year with minor child. Except Ia., 90 days. (O) Six months to remarry; Kan. 60 days. (P) Adultery cases, remarriage in discretion of court. (Q) Separation for 2 yrs. after decree for same in Ala. and Minn.; 3 yrs. in Ut.; 4 yrs. in N.J.; 18 mos. in N.H.; 5 yrs. in Md. (R) Separation, no cohabitation—5 yrs. Exceptions: La., Va., Wyo., W. Va. 2 yrs.; Tex., Me. 3 yrs.; Nev., N.C. 1 yr.; R.I. 10 yrs. (S) Separation, no cohabitation—3 yrs. Exceptions: Vt., Wash., 2 yrs.; Del., Mo., N.J. 18 mos.; N.Y., Nev., Va., D.C., Wis. 1 yr. (T) Separation for 2 yrs. after decree for Dist. of Col.; 1 yr. for N.Y., Wis., La.; per decree in Ha. (U) Mental incapacity at time of marriage. (V) Procurement of out-of-state divorce. (W) Gross neglect of duty. (X) Bigamy. (Y) Attempted homicide. (Z) Treatment which injures health or endangers reason. (AA) Wife without state for 10 yrs. (BB) Wife in state 2 yrs.; husband never in state and has intent to become citizen of foreign country. (CC) Irreconcilable differences. (DD) Life sentence dissolves marriage. (EE) Breakdown of marriage with no reasonable likelihood of preservation. (FF) Deviate sexual conduct. (GG) Course of conduct detrimental to the marriage relationship of party seeking divorce. (HH) Incompatibility without regard to fault. (II) Marriage irretrievably broken.

Adultery is either grounds for divorce or evidence of irreconcilable differences and a breakdown of the marriage in all states. The plaintiff can invariably remarry in the same state where he or she procured a decree of divorce or annulment. Not so the defendant, who is barred in certain states for some offenses. After a period of time has elapsed even the offender can apply for special permission. The U.S. Supreme Court in a 5 to 4 opinion ruled April 18, 1949, that one-sided quick divorces could be challenged as illegal if notice of the action was not served on the divorced partner within the divorcing states, excepting where the partner was represented at the proceedings. **Enoch Arden Laws:** disappearance and unknown to be alive—Conn., 7 years absence; N.H., 2 years; N.Y., 5 years (called dissolution); Vt., 7 years.

Canadian Marriage Information

Source: Compiled from information provided by the various provincial government departments and agencies concerned.

Marriageable age, by provinces, for both males and females with and without consent of parents or guardians. In some provinces, the court has authority, given special circumstances, to marry young couples below the minimum age. Most provinces waive the blood test requirement and the waiting period varies across the provinces.

Province	With consent		Without consent		Blood test other province		Wait for license	Wait after license
	Men	Women	Men	Women	Required	Accepted		
Newfoundland	—	—	19	19	—	—	—	—
Prince Edward Island	16	16	18	18	Yes	Yes	5 days	None
Nova Scotia	(1)	(1)	19	19	None	None	5 days	None
New Brunswick	14	14	18	18	None	None	5 days	None
Quebec	14	12	18	18	None	—	—	None
Ontario	14	14[2]	18	18	None	—	None[3]	3 days
Manitoba	16	16	18	18	Yes	Yes	None	24 hours
Saskatchewan	15	15	18	18	Yes	Yes	5 days	None
Alberta	18–	18–	18	18	Yes[4]	Yes[5]	None[6]	None
British Columbia	16[7]	16[7]	19	19	None	None	2 days[8]	None
Yukon Territory	15	15	19	19	None	None	None	24 hours
Northwest Territories	15	15	19	19	None	Yes	None	None

(1) There is no statutory minimum age in the province. Anyone under the age of 19 years must have consent for marriage and no person under the age of 16 years may be married without authorization of a Family Court judge and in addition must have the necessary consent of the parent or guardian. (2) Women under 14 years also require a medical certificate as to necessity of marriage to prevent illegitimacy of offspring. (3) Special requirements applicable to non-residents. (4) Applies only to applicants under 60 years of age. (5) This is upon filing of negative lab report indicating blood test was taken within 14 days preceding date of application for license. (6) Exception where consent is required by mail; depending receipt of divorce documents, etc. (7) Persons under 16 years of age (no minimum age specified) may also be married if they have obtained, in addition to the usual consent from parents or guardian, an order from a judge of the Supreme or County Court in this province. (8) Including day of application, e.g., a license applied for on a Monday cannot be issued until Wednesday.

Grounds for Divorce in Canada

Source: Government of Canada Divorce Act

The grounds for divorce in Canada are the same for all the provinces and its territories. There are two cateseries of offense:

A. Marital Offense:
- Adultery
- Sodomy
- Bestiality
- Rape
- Homosexual act
- Subsequent marriage
- Physical cruelty
- Mental cruelty

B. Marriage breakdown by reason of:
- Imprisonment for aggregate period of not less than 3 years
- Imprisonment for not less than 2 years on sentence of death or sentence of 10 years or more
- Addiction to alcohol
- Addiction to narcotics
- Whereabouts of spouse unknown
- Non-consummation
- Separation for not less than 3 years
- Desertion by petitioner for not less than 5 years

Residence time: Domicile in Canada. Time between interlocutory and final decree: normally 3 months before final can be applied for.

Canadian Motor Vehicle Traffic Deaths

Source: Statistics Canada

Province	Number 1975	Number 1974
Newfoundland	104	117
Prince Edward Island	44	42
Nova Scotia	242	268
New Brunswick	230	287
Quebec	1,893	1,882
Ontario	1,800	1,748
Manitoba	203	201
Saskatchewan	286	306
Alberta	527	573
British Columbia	717	844
Yukon	8	8
Northwest Territories	7	14
Total	**6,061**	**6,290**

Birthstones

Source: Jewelry Industry Council

Month	Ancient	Modern
January	Garnet	Garnet
February	Amethyst	Amethyst
March	Jasper	Bloodstone or Aquamarine
April	Sapphire	Diamond
May	Agate	Emerald
June	Emerald	Pearl, Moonstone, or Alexandrite
July	Onyx	Ruby
August	Carnelian	Sardonyx or Peridot
September	Chrysolite	Sapphire
October	Aquamarine	Opal or Tourmaline
November	Topaz	Topaz
December	Ruby	Turquoise or Zircon

U.S. Building Fire Losses by Causes, 1975

Source: National Fire Protection Association

These estimated figures are intended to show the relative order of magnitude of fire losses by cause, and to indicate year-to-year trends. While they are reasonable approximations based on experience in typical states, they should not be taken as exact records for each class. The figures by themselves do not show the relative safety in use of various types of materials, devices, fuels, or services, and they should not be used for that purpose.

Cause	Number of fires		Estimated loss	
Heating and cooking equipment	165,600		$ 222,800,000	
Defective or misused equipment		91,000		$144,700,000
Chimneys and flues		15,600		23,200,000
Hot ashes and coals		12,300		2,000,000
Combustibles near heaters and stoves		46,700		52,900,000
Smoking-related	137,800		166,800,000	
Electrical	150,500		358,100,000	
Fixed wiring and distribution equipment		78,400		193,400,000
Power-consuming appliances		71,100		164,700,000
Trash burning	155,500		5,000,000	
Flammable liquids	61,900		63,400,000	
Open flames and sparks	85,500		175,900,000	
Sparks and embers		17,400		10,200,000
Welding and cutting		14,600		56,400,000
Sparks from machinery		15,100		26,100,000
Thawing pipes		7,900		22,500,000
Other open flames		30,500		60,700,000
Lightning	14,200		36,100,000	
Children and fire	64,200		116,900,000	
Exposure	34,100		21,800,000	
Incendiary and suspicious	144,100		633,900,000	
Spontaneous ignition	11,000		21,900,000	
Gas fires and explosions[1]	9,500		34,900,000	
Fireworks and explosives	3,900		41,100,000	
Miscellaneous known causes	89,300		288,700,000	
Unknown causes	137,300		1,249,300,000	
Total Building Fires	**1,264,400**		**$3,436,600,000**	

(1) Does not include fires originating in heating and cooking equipment.

Annual Fire Losses in the U.S.

Source: Insurance Services Office

Year	Loss	Year	Loss	Year	Loss	Year	Loss
1940	$285,878,697	1955	885,218,000	1970	2,264,000,000	1975	3,560,000,000
1945	484,274,000	1960	1,107,824,000	1973	2,639,000,000	1976	3,558,000,000
1950	648,909,000	1965	1,455,631,000	1974	3,190,000,000	1977, 6 mos.	1,976,000,000

Fire Fighters: Deaths and Injuries

Source: International Association of Fire Fighters
(U.S. and Canadian professional fire fighters)

	In line of duty		Occupational diseases[1]	
Year	Deaths	Injuries	Deaths	Retirement
1970	115	38,583	233	465
1971	106	50,976	N/A	511
1972	100	62,682	133	695
1973	90	62,619	111	702
1974	100	56,296	107	604
1975	108	51,312	88	721

(1) Includes: heart and cardiovascular diseases; lung and respiratory diseases; and other occupational diseases. N/A: not available.

Interpol (International Criminal Police Organization)

The United States is one of 125 countries that are members of Interpol, the International Criminal Police Organization. United States participation in Interpol was authorized by Congress in 1938. Because of the Treasury Department's activities in the suppression of counterfeiting, smuggling, and the narcotics traffic, all of which have international ramifications, that department was designated as U.S. representative to Interpol in 1958, and continued until February 1977. Every second year from February 1, 1977, the U.S. representative to Interpol will rotate between the departments of Justice and Treasury.

Each member nation has one vote at a general assembly of Interpol held annually at a site chosen by the delegates at the previous year's assembly.

Interpol dates from 1914, but World War I brought suspension of all its activities until 1923. The organization's first constitution was drawn up in that year. Files on international criminals were built up gradually to a point where their value to the police of member nations became apparent.

The organization was reconstituted at the end of World War II. The General Secretariat was moved to Paris and is now located in the Parisian suburb of Saint-Cloud. The Secretariat functions as a central depository for fingerprints, photographs, and other records of international criminals. It also operates an international radio network to 64 of the member countries.

Interpol does not employ any investigators as such. Foreign requirements for investigation are referred to the National Central Bureaus, the offices established in each country to handle Interpol coordination. Scotland Yard is the National Central Bureau for the United Kingdom; the Surete in France, the Italiano Di Polizia in Italy, and the Canberra Commonwealth police in Australia serve as the National Central Bureaus for those countries.

In the United States the U.S. National Central Bureau is staffed by U.S. Federal Law Enforcement Agents on loan from the Secret Service, Customs Service, Bureau of Alcohol, Tobacco and Firearms, and the Drug Enforcement Administration. Unless foreign requirements for investigation in the United States involve federal jurisdiction or interest, they are referred to local and state police agencies for investigation.

Federal Bureau of Investigation

The Federal Bureau of Investigation (FBI) is the investigative arm of the Department of Justice, and is located at 9th St. and Pennsylvania Ave., Washington, DC 20535. It investigates all violations of federal laws except those specifically assigned to some other agency by legislative action, such violations including counterfeiting, and internal revenue, postal, and customs violations. It also investigates espionage, sabotage, treason, and other matters affecting internal security, as well as kidnaping, transportation of stolen goods across state lines, and violations of the federal bank and atomic energy laws.

The Identification Division has about 195 million fingerprint cards on file. While this division is of great usefulness in detecting criminals, it serves a wider purpose in recording the fingerprints of many other citizens who voluntarily make this record.

The FBI has 59 field divisions in the principal cities of the country. *Consult telephone directories for location and phone numbers.*

An applicant for the position of Special Agent of the FBI must be a citizen of the U.S. at least 23 and under 35 years old and graduate of a state-accredited resident law school or from a resident 4-year college with a major in accounting with at least one year of practical accounting and/or auditing experience. In addition, applicants with a 4-year resident college degree with a major in certain areas or 3 years specialized experience of a professional, executive, or complex investigative nature are presently being considered on a limited basis. An agent gets 15 weeks of training.

Clarence M. Kelley, former FBI agent and professional law enforcement officer, became Director on July 9, 1973. Federal judge Frank M. Johnson Jr. has been named to replace Kelley in 1978.

U.S. Crime Reports

Source: Federal Bureau of Investigation

Offense	Number 1976 est.	% change over[1] 1975	% change over[1] 1972
Murder	18,780	− 8.3	− 2.2
Rape	56,730	+ 0.4	+17.3
Robbery	420,210	−10.3	+ 8.4
Aggravated assault	490,850	+ 0.6	+21.1
Burglary	3,089,800	− 5.7	+26.2
Larceny-theft	6,270,800	+ 4.2	+46.5
Auto theft	957,600	− 5.0	+ 4.7

[1]Percent by which the rate of crime per 100,000 population changed in 1976 as compared with 1975 and 1972.

Crime in the U.S. Increases Only 1% in 1976

Crime in the U.S., as measured by the Crime Index offenses, increased by 1% in 1976 over 1975. Violent crimes were down 4% with forcible rape reports up 1% and aggravated assault (assault with a dangerous weapons, including the fists) up 1%. Murders decreased 8% and robberies were down 10%. Property crimes went up less than 1%, with burglaries increasing by 5%, larceny-theft up 5%, and auto theft down 4%. Serious crime in cities of 250,000 or more people was up only 0.2%, while crime in suburban areas dropped by 0.4%.

Reported Crime, 1975-76, by Size of Place

Source: 1976 Uniform Crime Reports, Federal Bureau of Investigation

Population group (1976 estimates)	Crime index total	Violent crime	Property crime	Murder and non-negligent man-slaughter	Forcible rape	Robbery	Aggra-vated assault	Burglary-breaking or entering	Larceny -theft
Total all agencies: 9,738 agencies; total population 196,156,000:									
1975	10,530,772	987,385	9,543,387	19,414	53,827	455,646	458,498	3,058,889	5,614,270
1976	10,524,783	939,190	9,585,593	17,491	53,844	410,494	457,361	2,898,722	5,870,818
Percent change		−4.9	+.4	−9.9		−9.9	−.2	−5.2	+4.6
Total cities: 7,448 cities; total population 138,532,000:									
1975	8,575,292	836,944	7,738,348	14,912	42,316	417,845	361,871	2,378,933	4,620,297
1976	8,592,715	794,402	7,798,313	13,538	42,205	378,080	360,579	2,261,639	4,847,325
Percent change	+.2	−5.1	+.8	−9.2	−.3	−9.5	−.4	−4.9	+4.9
59 cities over 250,000; population 42,407,000:									
1975	3,380,858	491,745	2,889,113	9,058	23,619	289,445	169,623	1,008,318	1,530,707
1976	3,386,023	464,535	2,921,448	8,184	22,986	265,556	167,809	969,803	1,626,842
Percent change	+.2	−5.5	+1.1	−9.6	−2.7	−8.3	−1.1	−3.8	+6.3
109 cities, 100,000 to 250,000; population 15,605,000:									
1975	1,198,213	96,981	1,101,232	1,731	5,363	42,896	46,991	334,624	658,569
1976	1,176,816	89,333	1,087,483	1,568	5,466	36,940	45,359	310,022	681,949
Percent change	−1.8	−7.9	−1.2	−9.4	+1.9	−13.9	−3.5	−7.4	+3.6
269 cities, 50,000 to 100,000; population 18,531,000:									
1975	1,152,412	81,373	1,071,039	1,285	4,702	33,795	41,591	314,834	660,161
1976	1,146,555	76,932	1,069,623	1,139	4,835	29,471	41,487	296,612	682,584
Percent change	−.5	−5.5	−.1	−11.4	+2.8	−12.8	−.3	−5.8	+3.4
606 cities, 25,000 to 50,000; population 20,948,000:									
1975	1,129,594	70,479	1,059,115	1,222	3,851	26,345	39,061	288,600	685,526
1976	1,144,514	69,434	1,075,080	1,134	3,902	23,863	40,535	275,188	719,376
Percent change	+1.3	−1.5	+1.5	−7.2	+1.3	−9.4	+3.8	−4.6	+4.9
1,424 cities, 10,000 to 25,000; population 22,302,000:									
1975	1,009,598	56,730	952,868	907	2,843	17,037	35,943	253,958	634,814
1976	1,022,352	55,373	966,979	871	3,028	15,063	36,411	243,243	661,864
Percent change	+1.3	−2.4	+1.5	−4.0	+6.5	−11.6	+1.3	−4.2	+4.3
4,981 cities under 10,000; population 18,738,000:									
1975	704,617	39,636	664,981	709	1,938	8,327	28,662	178,599	450,520
1976	716,455	38,795	677,660	642	1,988	7,187	28,978	166,771	474,710
Percent change	+1.7	−2.1	+1.9	−9.4	+2.6	−13.7	+1.1	−6.6	+5.4
Suburban area: 4,117 agencies; population 69,788,000:									
1975	3,159,545	203,768	2,955,777	3,882	13,503	66,540	119,843	915,798	1,805,744
1976	3,148,443	197,750	2,950,693	3,448	13,669	58,166	122,467	858,263	1,869,546
Percent change	−.4	−3.0	−.2	−11.2	+1.2	−12.6	+2.2	−6.3	+3.5
Rural area: 1,788 agencies; population 25,364,000:									
1975	538,315	44,730	493,585	2,090	3,217	6,137	33,286	210,019	256,803
1976	540,962	42,460	498,502	1,855	3,289	5,166	32,150	201,846	269,013
Percent change	+.5	−5.1	+1.0	−11.2	+2.2	−15.8	−3.4	−3.9	+4.8

Reported Crime in Metropolitan Areas, 1976

Source: 1976 Uniform Crime Reports, Federal Bureau of Investigation

The 28 Standard Metropolitan Statistical Areas listed below are those which appear most frequently among the top 30 cities in per capita reported crime rate for each of 7 kinds of major crime: the 5 listed below plus aggravated assault and auto theft.

The rates are for reported crimes only; they are not an accurate index of crimes actually committed. In many metropolitan areas an unknown number of crimes go unreported by victims. This is especially true of the crimes of rape, burglary, and larceny. Additionally, figures are often distorted for political reasons.

The number in parentheses following the city name indicates the number of categories (including auto theft and aggravated assault) in which the city appears among the top 30.

The numbers in parentheses following crime rate figures give that city's rank in that category of crime. If no number appears, the city is not among the top 30 in that category. The cities are listed in order of the diversity and violence of criminal activity.

	Rate per 100,000 population							
Metropolitan areas	Total[1]	Violent[2]	Property[3]	Murder[4]	Rape	Robbery	Burglary	Larceny
Las Vegas, Nev. (7)	10,237.8 (2)	948.1 (5)	9,289.8 (2)	13.6(29)	60.1 (5)	426.7 (3)	3,091.9 (2)	5,550.8 (2)
Los Angeles-Long Beach, Cal. (5)	7,216.4	951.8 (4)	6,264.6	13.8(27)	57.9 (6)	400.9 (6)	2,271.3(17)	3,113.3
New York, N.Y. (5)	7,852.6(16)	1,437.2 (1)	6,415.4	17.5 (7)	37.2	915.0 (1)	2,263.1(19)	3,057.3
Miami, Fla. (5)	8,520.2 (7)	1,031.8 (2)	7,488.3(12)	13.6(29)	32.4	364.7 (8)	2,263.0(18)	4,714.0(17)
San Francisco-Oakland, Cal. (5)	8,493.8 (9)	802.3 (8)	7,691.5 (8)	12.2	50.4(12)	420.5 (4)	2,458.4 (7)	4,487.1(29)
Detroit, Mich. (4)	7,672.4(21)	960.4 (3)	6,711.9	18.1 (5)	44.0(24)	593.8 (2)	1,906.4	3,765.5
Albuquerque, N.M. (4)	8,565.7 (6)	741.9(12)	7,823.8 (7)	10.5	65.7 (2)	241.9	2,433.3 (9)	4,939.4(10)
Daytona Beach, Fla. (4)	10,582.3 (1)	680.7(17)	9,901.6 (1)	8.6	51.5(10)	187.5	3,180.2 (1)	6,274.5 (1)
Orlando, Fla. (4)	7,721.1(20)	644.4(25)	7,076.8(18)	7.8	49.8(13)	153.6	2,182.6(22)	4,556.4(23)
Memphis, Tenn. (4)	6,317.7	630.6(28)	5,687.0	14.7(19)	57.8 (7)	290.1(17)	2,105.4(27)	3,134.1
Sacramento, Cal. (4)	8,234.5(10)	617.4	7,617.1 (9)	10.4	42.8(27)	243.8	2,397.0(11)	4,599.8(22)
Stockton, Cal. (4)	8,505.6 (8)	562.5	7,943.1 (6)	12.9	34.7	246.2(29)	2,361.0(14)	4,981.1 (8)
Gainesville, Fla. (3)	7,972.7(13)	829.8 (7)	7,142.9(16)	10.0	61.8 (4)	193.0	1,889.7	4,984.5 (7)
W. Palm Beach-Boca Raton, Fla. (3)	7,721.2(19)	775.3 (9)	6,945.9(21)	8.9	27.3	169.2	2,093.3(28)	4,535.5(25)
Lakeland-Winter Haven, Fla. (3)	6,978.9	771.9(11)	6,206.9	13.7(28)	43.9(25)	153.6	1,927.1	3,929.9
Fayetteville, N.C. (3)	6,219.6	722.5(14)	5,497.1	16.3(13)	30.4	222.1	2,115.0(26)	2,997.5
Jacksonville, Fla. (3)	6,719.5	716.4(15)	6,003.1	15.3(16)	46.4(16)	241.2	1,832.1	3,851.7
New Orleans, La. (3)	6,190.5	659.4(20)	5,531.1	19.7 (3)	36.3	297.1(16)	1,529.7	3,335.5
Savannah, Ga. (3)	7,497.4(24)	655.2(21)	6,842.3(24)	14.7(19)	35.0	216.0	2,283.1(16)	4,221.7
Little Rock-N. Lit. Rock, Ark. (3)	7,510.0(23)	649.9(23)	6,860.1(23)	12.5	56.6 (9)	253.3(26)	1,951.3	4,513.0(26)
Fresno, Cal. (3)	8,688.7 (5)	626.1(29)	8,062.6 (5)	12.2	37.7	242.6	2,906.2 (4)	4,460.7(30)
Yakima, Wash. (3)	7,234.8	612.5	6,622.3	7.8	47.0(15)	114.2	1,857.1	4,429.9
Cleveland, Ohio (3)	5,160.9	584.6	4,576.3	15.1(18)	33.4	336.2(10)	1,154.2	2,505.9
Bakersfield, Cal. (3)	8,090.5(11)	532.0	7,558.5(11)	14.1(24)	38.3	191.7	2,383.1(12)	4,662.8(18)
Tucson, Ariz. (3)	9,140.4 (3)	451.1	8,689.2 (3)	9.3	44.3(21)	155.7	2,967.2 (3)	5,191.5 (4)
Houston, Tex. (3)	5,908.7	426.2	5,482.6	16.5(11)	36.4	255.1(24)	1,703.1	3,146.6
Lubbock, Tex. (3)	7,879.1(15)	423.0	7,456.1(13)	14.0(25)	36.5	132.1	2,291.7(15)	4,815.4(14)
Charleston, S.C. (2)	6,369.7	772.7(10)	5,597.1	7.9	57.5 (8)	208.6	1,949.6	3,269.9

(1) Other metro areas among the top 30 in total reported crime (predominantly property crime); Phoenix, Ariz. (4); Ft. Lauderdale-Hollywood, Fla. (12); San Antonio, Tex. (14); Modesto, Cal. (17); Austin, Tex. (18); Denver-Boulder, Col. (22); Ann Arbor, Mich. (25); Corpus Christi, Tex. (26); Riverside-San Bernardino-Ontario, Cal. (27); Columbia, S.C. (28); Portland, Ore. (29); and Dallas-Ft. Worth, Tex. (30).

(2) Violent crime includes murder and non-negligent manslaughter, forcible rape, robbery, and aggravated assault. Other metro areas in the top 30 in violent crime are: Baltimore, Md. (6); Albany, Ga. (13); Flint, Mich. (16); Kansas City, Mo.-Kans. (18); Greenville-Spartanburg, S.C. (19); Pensacola, Fla. (22); St. Louis, Mo. (24); Baton Rouge, La. (26); Wilmington, N.C. (27); and Norfolk, Va. (30).

(3) Property crime includes burglary, larceny and auto theft. Other metro areas in the top 30 are: Phoenix, Ariz. (4); Ft. Lauderdale, Fla. (10); Austin, Tex. (14); Modesto, Cal. (15); Denver-Boulder, Col. (17); Ann Arbor, Mich. (19); Kenosha, Wis. (20); Reno, Nev. (22); Dallas, Tex. (25); Cedar Rapids, Iowa (26); Corpus Christi, Tex. (27); San Antonio, Tex. (28); Riverside-San Bernardino-Ontario, Cal. (29); and Columbia, S.C. (30).

(4) Of the top 30 cities in murder, all but 8 are in the South (16) or in Texas (6).

Crime Rates by State

Source: 1976 Uniform Crime Reports, Federal Bureau of Investigation

(Rates per 100,000 population)

State	Total	Violent	Property	Murder	Rape	Robbery	Assault	Burglary	Larceny	Auto Theft
Alabama	3,808.3	388.8	3,419.5	15.1	21.7	96.0	256.0	1,170.0	1,987.2	262.3
Alaska	6,220.7	540.1	5,680.6	11.3	46.9	124.9	357.1	1,218.1	3,656.8	805.8
Arizona	7,886.4	455.3	7,431.1	7.8	29.7	129.9	287.9	2,366.6	4,642.7	421.8
Arkansas	3,406.7	303.9	3,102.8	10.1	24.2	76.7	192.9	937.5	2,013.9	151.4
California	7,234.0	669.3	6,564.7	10.3	44.7	275.6	338.7	2,174.6	3,745.8	644.3
Colorado	6,782.4	417.0	6,365.4	6.8	33.8	139.7	236.7	1,879.9	4,043.5	442.0
Connecticut	5,004.6	273.2	4,731.4	3.1	14.4	122.9	132.8	1,383.9	2,785.8	561.8
Delaware	6,264.4	321.6	5,942.8	6.2	17.7	128.7	169.1	1,542.6	3,915.8	484.4
Florida	7,016.7	648.3	6,368.4	10.7	36.3	186.4	415.0	1,954.7	4,074.4	339.7
Georgia	4,809.5	423.1	4,386.4	13.9	24.9	142.4	241.9	1,448.4	2,618.3	319.7
Hawaii	6,322.0	229.3	6,092.7	6.2	23.6	133.0	66.5	1,881.6	3,669.0	542.1
Idaho	4,270.5	226.7	4,043.8	5.3	18.7	40.0	162.8	1,036.7	2,776.9	230.2
Illinois	5,055.0	468.8	4,586.3	10.3	21.5	219.5	217.5	1,089.7	2,991.8	504.8
Indiana	4,673.3	315.4	4,357.9	7.1	23.2	128.8	156.3	1,215.6	2,769.9	372.4
Iowa	4,051.4	132.9	3,918.6	2.3	10.7	41.1	78.7	827.1	2,884.6	206.9

State	Total	Violent	Property	Murder	Rape	Robbery	Assault	Burglary	Larceny	Auto theft
Kansas	4,778.4	282.6	4,495.8	4.5	21.9	85.8	170.4	1,325.5	2,938.1	232.3
Kentucky	3,296.8	262.2	3,034.7	10.6	17.8	98.7	135.1	930.2	1,857.7	246.8
Louisiana	4,361.1	472.8	3,888.2	13.2	26.8	124.3	308.5	1,140.6	2,447.0	300.6
Maine	4,084.4	220.0	3,864.4	2.7	9.9	37.9	169.4	1,313.2	2,337.5	213.7
Maryland	5,664.4	633.4	5,031.0	8.5	32.0	295.5	297.4	1,359.9	3,242.2	428.9
Massachusetts	5,820.9	399.2	5,421.7	3.3	17.7	180.2	198.0	1,662.1	2,446.8	1,312.7
Michigan	6,478.2	646.0	5,832.2	11.1	36.1	332.6	266.1	1,668.5	3,550.6	613.1
Minnesota	4,331.1	189.0	4,142.1	2.3	18.3	80.4	87.9	1,122.1	2,672.8	347.1
Mississippi	2,468.3	295.4	2,172.9	12.5	16.3	64.1	202.5	811.3	1,239.4	122.2
Missouri	5,034.1	449.4	4,584.7	9.3	27.1	204.1	208.9	1,403.2	2,794.9	386.6
Montana	4,261.9	180.3	4,081.5	5.0	13.5	35.6	126.2	841.0	2,932.7	307.8
Nebraska	3,561.9	210.5	3,351.4	2.9	20.5	63.0	124.1	684.2	2,433.7	233.5
Nevada	8,306.1	691.0	7,615.1	11.5	47.2	294.9	337.4	2,392.5	4,717.4	505.2
New Hampshire	3,611.3	86.3	3,525.1	3.3	9.7	24.8	48.4	937.5	2,335.3	252.3
New Jersey	5,400.5	396.8	5,003.7	5.2	19.9	200.3	171.4	1,504.2	2,988.9	510.7
New Mexico	6,215.0	554.4	5,660.6	9.7	41.0	124.7	378.9	1,679.5	3,651.5	329.5
New York	6,225.1	868.1	5,357.0	10.9	25.8	529.3	302.1	1,763.5	2,855.2	738.2
N. Carolina	3,881.2	403.4	3,477.8	11.1	15.3	70.6	306.4	1,175.5	2,124.0	178.3
North Dakota	2,514.3	71.9	2,442.5	1.4	5.6	16.2	48.7	478.5	1,804.5	159.4
Ohio	4,948.2	388.7	4,559.5	7.4	25.8	183.8	171.7	1,203.2	2,978.2	378.1
Oklahoma	4,480.9	286.6	4,194.3	6.4	27.0	70.3	182.8	1,317.5	2,570.4	306.4
Oregon	6,358.8	457.4	5,901.4	4.2	35.6	132.7	285.0	1,699.7	3,806.8	394.8
Pennsylvania	3,339.9	294.9	3,045.0	6.1	18.1	138.0	132.8	906.0	1,790.8	348.2
Rhode Island	5,650.2	299.8	5,350.4	2.4	8.5	91.0	197.8	1,414.2	3,050.6	885.5
S. Carolina	4,906.9	599.2	4,307.7	11.6	31.9	105.7	450.0	1,553.6	2,503.2	250.9
South Dakota	2,640.4	186.2	2,454.2	1.7	15.3	23.2	145.9	620.4	1,684.3	149.6
Tennessee	4,258.4	393.3	3,865.1	11.0	25.4	147.5	209.4	1,320.5	2,218.6	325.9
Texas	5,464.4	355.7	5,108.7	12.2	29.4	139.0	175.3	1,547.8	3,209.5	351.3
Utah	4,977.8	220.6	4,757.2	4.5	20.9	69.4	125.8	1,137.9	3,302.0	317.3
Vermont	3,192.2	118.3	3,073.9	5.5	14.9	17.9	80.0	1,022.7	1,853.2	198.1
Virginia	4,203.1	307.7	3,895.4	9.5	22.2	108.2	167.9	1,019.1	2,650.2	226.1
Washington	5,794.0	388.6	5,405.4	4.3	34.3	119.5	230.5	1,642.4	3,414.3	348.7
West Virginia	2,319.7	151.6	2,168.0	6.7	10.3	38.0	96.6	573.1	1,459.0	135.9
Wisconsin	3,900.7	137.7	3,763.0	3.0	11.8	59.3	63.5	843.8	2,696.4	222.8
Wyoming	3,975.1	218.2	3,756.9	6.9	24.9	29.2	157.2	764.6	2,750.3	242.1

Total Arrest Trends by Sex — 1976

Source: 1976 Uniform Crime Reports, Federal Bureau of Investigation

	Males				Females			
	Total		Under 18		Total		Under 18	
	1976	Percent change 1975-76	1976	Percent change 1975-76	1976	Percent change 1975-76	1976	Percent change 1975-76
Total[1]	**5,850,614**	**− 5.6**	**1,387,424**	**− 6.8**	**1,106,466**	**− 1.2**	**380,622**	**− 4.7**
Murder and non-negligent manslaughter	10,163	−18.2	981	−18.5	1,870	−21.6	135	− 8.2
Manslaughter by negligence	2,179	−14.3	229	−26.1	228	−30.3	29	− 40.8
Forcible rape	18,670	− 1.6	3,204	− 3.6	184	− 8.0	56	+ 5.7
Robbery	80,969	−16.8	25,630	−19.5	6,303	−10.6	1,970	− 16.7
Aggravated assault	141,712	− 5.9	23,184	− 4.4	21,663	−4.1	4,523	− 4.3
Burglary—breaking or entering	338,219	−10.5	177,920	−10.7	19,122	− 6.4	9,902	− 7.4
Larceny—theft	580,693	− 4.9	265,201	− 6.5	268,904	− 1.5	104,490	− 6.0
Motor vehicle theft	87,695	− 7.8	47,273	− 9.5	6,865	− 2.3	4,053	− .8
Other assaults	273,180	− 2.5	49,396	+ 1.9	44,714	+ 1.0	12,876	− .1
Arson	11,534	− .8	6,352	+ 2.9	1,446	+ 3.3	652	+ 2.4
Forgery and counterfeiting	34,179	− 6.5	4,154	−13.3	14,709	− .3	1,866	− 2.9
Fraud	92,893	− 2.1	3,010	− .9	53,927	+ 6.7	1,213	+ 2.3
Embezzlement	5,155	−14.8	413	− 2.1	2,445	−17.6	89	− 23.3
Stolen property; offenses	72,003	− 5.7	23,618	− 6.3	8,622	− 4.6	2,151	− 8.2
Vandalism	145,993	− 1.0	92,379	− 3.5	13,104	+ 3.6	7,450	− .1
Weapons; carrying, possessing, etc.	98,438	−10.3	16,482	− 6.8	8,939	− 7.9	1,099	− 7.8
Prostitution and commercialized vice	15,388	+27.6	545	− 3.5	35,413	+ 5.8	1,839	+ 8.0
Sex offenses (except forcible rape and prostitution)	42,706	+ 3.2	7,978	− .3	4,354	+21.1	940	− 8.7
Narcotic drug laws	386,371	− .6	91,431	− 1.0	62,549	+ 1.4	18,128	− .6
Gambling	55,105	+20.9	2,061	+20.3	5,962	+40.4	259	+161.6
Offenses against family, children	48,173	− 1.3	2,719	−23.5	5,760	− 3.0	1,280	−38.2
Driving under the influence	709,297	− 1.3	14,839	+ 8.5	59,610	+ 2.7	1,270	+ 18.5
Liquor laws	245,794	+ 8.1	83,101	+ .8	40,789	+ 9.0	21,701	+ 3.1
Drunkenness	933,259	−10.3	32,057	− 3.7	71,518	− 7.8	4,957	+ 3.6
Disorderly conduct	413,054	−19.6	84,960	−14.9	72,108	− 3.3	18,929	− 1.5
Vagrancy	22,426	−54.1	3,503	+ 2.7	4,153	−20.1	649	+ 3.2
All other offenses (except traffic)	849,970	+ 3.2	189,408	--	165,128	+ 1.6	52,039	+ 1.7

(1) Totals will not add due to deletion of several minor arrest categories.

Police Roster

Police officers and civilian employees in large cities as of Oct. 31, 1976

City	Officer	Civilian
Anchorage, Alas.	120	47
Atlanta, Ga.	1,251	335
Baltimore, Md.	3,455	556
Birmingham, Ala.	619	110
Boston, Mass.	2,301	481
Bridgeport, Conn.	410	20
Buffalo, N.Y.	1,181	244
Chicago, Ill.	13,039	1,795
Cincinnati, Oh.	1,111	193
Cleveland, Oh.	2,031	111
Columbus, Oh.	1,080	239
Dallas, Tex.	2,014	549
Denver, Col.	1,359	297
Detroit, Mich.	5,016	574
Ft. Worth, Tex.	681	149
Fresno, Cal.	317	68
Gary, Ind.	346	59
Hartford, Conn.	463	82
Honolulu, Ha.	1,506	343
Houston, Tex.	2,737	589
Indianapolis, Ind.	1,072	278
Jacksonville, Fla.	982	572
Jersey City, N.J.	998	22
Kansas City, Mo.	1,221	472
Little Rock, Ark.	270	70
Los Angeles, Cal.	7,296	2,761
Louisville, Ky.	729	325
Memphis, Tenn.	1,304	295
Miami, Fla.	821	265
Milwaukee, Wis.	2,083	230
Minneapolis, Minn.	826	103
Newark, N.J.	1,507	133
New Orleans, La.	1,510	503
New York, N.Y.	26,789	3,644
Norfolk, Va.	612	115
Oakland, Cal.	678	286
Oklahoma City, Okl.	620	120
Omaha, Neb.	544	131
Pasadena, Cal.	189	98
Philadelphia, Pa.	9,054	878
Phoenix, Ariz.	1,559	364
Pittsburgh, Pa.	1,398	26
Portland, Ore.	683	166
Rochester, N.Y.	627	123
Sacramento, Cal.	502	158
St. Louis, Mo.	2,068	564
St. Petersburg, Fla.	467	189
San Antonio, Tex.	1,166	239
San Bernardino, Cal.	191	63
San Diego, Cal.	1,067	298
San Francisco, Cal.	1,667	428
San Jose, Cal.	771	179
Santa Ana, Cal.	321	124
Seattle, Wash.	1,030	300
Stockton, Cal.	222	106
Tampa, Fla.	618	132
Toledo, Oh.	204	107
Tucson, Ariz.	510	182
Washington, D.C.	4,340	306
Wichita, Kan.	393	143

1,077 Law Enforcement Officers Killed 1967-1976

Source: Uniform Crime Reports

Responding to disturbance calls	164
Burglaries in progress or pursuing suspect	73
Robberies in progress or pursuing suspect	211
Attempting other arrests	246
Civil disorders	12
Handling, transporting, custody of prisoners	50
Investigating suspicious persons and circumstances	77
Ambush	95
Mentally deranged	37
Traffic stops	112

Geographically for the period of 1967-1976 the 1,077 officers who were slain in the line of duty were divided in this fashion: Northeast 156; North Central 272; South 445; and West 178. Another 26 officers were killed in outlying territories.

Crime Index Trends by Geographic Region 1976 over 1975

(rates per 100,000 population)

Region	Total	Violent	Property	Murder	Rape	Robbery	Assault	Burglary	Larceny	Auto theft
Northeast	+4.6	−2.2	+5.4	− 7.9	−2.9	− 4.1	+0.8	−0.1	+10.7	− 1.1
North Central	−3.1	−8.4	−2.6	− 8.6	−2.9	−15.2	−1.2	−9.6	+ 1.1	− 6.8
South	−1.3	−6.8	−0.7	−11.0	+1.9	−17.0	−0.8	−8.7	+ 5.2	−11.7
West	−0.6	+0.2	−0.7	− 5.6	+3.5	− 4.5	+3.6	−3.3	+ 0.9	− 1.2

(1) Northeast includes New England, New Jersey, New York, and Pennsylvania; North Central extends west through Nebraska and includes Missouri; South extends from Delaware, Maryland, and West Virginia to Oklahoma and Texas.

Canada: Criminal Offenses and Crime Rate

Source: Statistics Canada

	1975		1976[1]		Percent change in rate
	Actual offenses	Rate	Actual offenses	Rate	
Total criminal code	**1,591,058**	**6,978.32**	**1,647,178**	**7,127.60**	**+2.1**
Total homicide	**1,332**	**5.84**	**1,344**	**5.80**	**−0.3**
Murder	4	.02	17	0.10	+500.0
Murder, non-capital	616	2.70	580	2.50	−7.0
Manslaughter	66	.29	46	0.20	−31.0
Infanticide	4	.02	7	0.04	+50.0
Attempted murder	642	2.82	694	3.00	+6.4
Total sexual offenses	**10,918**	**47.89**	**10,647**	**46.10**	**−3.8**
Rape	1,852	8.12	1,834	7.90	−2.2
Indecent assault on female	5,106	22.39	5,283	22.90	+2.1
Indecent assault on male	1,155	5.07	1,119	4.80	−4.5
Other sexual offenses	2,805	12.30	2,411	10.40	−15.3
Total crimes of violence	**135,754**	**595.41**	**137,359**	**594.40**	**−0.2**
Assaults (not indecent)	102,194	448.22	105,273	455.50	+1.6
Robbery	21,310	93.46	20,095	87.00	−7.0
Total property crimes	**1,044,474**	**4,581.03**	**1,069,356**	**4,627.24**	**+1.0**
Breaking and entering	261,287	1,146.00	269,599	1,166.60	+1.8
Theft-motor vehicle	90,914	398.75	88,129	381.30	−4.4
Theft over $200	95,102	417.11	106,217	459.60	+10.2
Theft $200 and under	494,777	2,170.07	501,104	2,168.30	−0.1
Having stolen goods	16,254	71.29	17,759	76.80	+7.7
Fraud	86,140	377.81	86,548	374.50	−0.9
Total other crimes	**410,830**	**1,801.88**	**440,463**	**1,905.90**	**+5.8**
Prostitution	3,409	14.95	2,842	12.30	−18.0
Gaming and betting	3,626	15.90	3,755	16.20	+1.9
Offensive weapons	12,610	55.31	13,544	58.60	+6.0
Other criminal code	391,185	1,715.72	420,322	1,818.80	+6.0
Federal statutes-drugs	55,616	243.93	63,166	273.33	+12.1
Federal statutes-other	44,991	197.33	50,627	219.07	+11.0
Provincial statutes	382,480	1,677.54	369,106	1,597.17	−4.8
Municipal by-laws	65,105	285.55	64,448	278.87	−2.3
Total—all offenses	**2,139,250**	**9,382.67**	**2,194,525**	**9,496.00**	**+1.2**

(1) Preliminary

POSTAL INFORMATION

United States Postal Service

The Postal Reorganization Act, creating a government-owned postal service under the executive branch and replacing the old Post Office Department, was signed into law by President Nixon on Aug. 12, 1970. The service officially came into being on July 1, 1971.

The new U.S. Postal Service is governed by an 11-man Board of Governors. Nine members are appointed to 9-year terms by the president with Senate approval. These 9, in turn, choose a postmaster general, who is no longer a member of the president's cabinet. The board and the new postmaster general choose the 11th member, who serves as deputy postmaster general. A new Postal Rate Commission of 5 members, appointed by the president, recommends postal rates to the governors for their approval.

The first postmaster general under the new system was Winton M. Blount. He resigned Oct. 29, 1971, and was replaced by his deputy, E. T. Klassen, Dec. 7, 1971. Benjamin F. Bailar succeeded him Feb. 16, 1975.

As of June 30, 1976, there was a total of 30,521 post offices throughout the U.S. and possessions.

U.S. Domestic Rates (in effect Dec., 1977)

Domestic includes the U.S., territories and possessions, APO and FPO.

First Class

Letters written, and matter sealed against inspection, 13c for 1st ounce or fraction, 11c for each additional ounce or fraction.

U.S. Postal cards; single 9c; double 18c; private postcards, same.

First class includes written matter, namely letters, postal cards, postcards (private mailing cards) and all other matter wholly or partly in writing, whether sealed or unsealed, except manuscripts for books, periodical articles and music, manuscript copy accompanying proofsheets or corrected proofsheets of the same and the writing authorized by law on matter of other classes. Also matter sealed or closed against inspection, bills and statements of accounts.

Greeting Cards

May be sent first class or single piece third class.

Airmail

At the present time first class mail receives the same service as airmail, as a result of the Postal Service's First Class Mail Service Improvement Program.

Second Class

Single copy mailings by general public 10c for first 2 ounces and 4c for each additional ounce or the 4th class rate, whichever is lower. There are special rates for publications, newspapers, and bulk mailing, consult local postmasters for rates and permit.

Third Class

Third class (limit up to but not including 16 ounces): Mailable matter not in 1st and 2d classes.

Single mailing: Greeting cards (sealed or unsealed), small parcels, printed matter, booklets and catalogs. 14c the first 2 ounces plus 14c for the next 2 ounces, plus 11c for each additional 2 ounces through 15.9 ounces.

Bulk material: books, catalogs of 24 pages or more, seeds, cuttings, bulbs, roots, scions, and plants; subject to a minimum rate, consult postmaster.

Other matter: newsletters, shoppers' guides, advertising circulars. Subject to a minimum rate for which post office should be consulted. Separate rates for some nonprofit organizations. Bulk mailing fee, $40 per calendar year. Apply to postmaster for permit. One-time fee for permit imprint, $20.

Parcel Post—Fourth Class

Fourth class or parcel post (16 ounces and over): merchandise, printed matter, etc., may be sealed, subject to inspection.

On parcels weighing less than 15 lbs. and measuring more than 84 inches, but not more than 100 inches in length and girth combined, the minimum postal charge shall be the zone charge applicable to a 15-pound parcel.

Priority Mail

First class mail of more than 13 ounces and airmail of more than 10 ounces have been merged into a "Priority Mail (Heavy Pieces)" service. The most expeditious handling and transportation available will be used for fastest delivery.

Forwarding Addresses

The mailer, in order to obtain a forwarding address, must endorse the envelope or cover "Address Correction Requested." The destination post office then will determine whether a forwarding address has been left on file and provide it for a fee.

Special Handling

Third and fourth class parcels will be handled and delivered as expeditiously as practicable (but not special delivery) upon payment, in addition to the regular postage: up to 2 lbs., 50c; over 2 lbs. and up to 10 lbs., 70c; over 10 lbs., $1.00. Such parcels must be endorsed, Special Handling.

Special Delivery

First class mail up to 2 lbs. $1.25, over 2 lbs. and up to 10 lbs., $1.50; over 10 lbs. $1.75. All other classes up to 2 lbs. $1.75, over 2 and up to 10 lbs., $1.85, over 10 lbs. $2.15.

Priority Mail

Air parcel post (over 10 ounces to 70 lbs.): packages not to exceed 100 inches in length and girth combined, including written and other matter of the first class, whether sealed or unsealed, fractions of a pound being charged as a full pound, except in the 1 to 5 pound weight category where half-pound weight increments apply.

Rates according to zone apply between the U.S. and Puerto Rico and Virgin Islands.

Parcels weighing less than 15 pounds, measuring over 84 inches but not exceeding 100 inches in length and girth combined are chargeable with a minimum rate equal to that for a 15 pound parcel for the zone to which addressed.

Zones	To 1 lb.	1½	2	2½	3	3½	4	4½	5
1, 2, 3	$1.56	$1.73	$1.89	$2.05	$2.21	$2.37	$2.53	$2.68	$2.83
4	1.58	1.77	1.96	2.15	2.33	2.51	2.69	2.86	3.03
5	1.60	1.84	2.07	2.29	2.50	2.70	2.90	3.09	3.27
6	1.62	1.90	2.18	2.43	2.68	2.91	3.14	3.35	3.56
7	1.64	1.97	2.29	2.59	2.88	3.15	3.41	3.65	3.88
8	1.67	2.07	2.46	2.78	3.09	3.38	3.67	3.94	4.20

Postal Union Mail Special Services

Registration — available to practically all countries. Fee $2.10. The maximum indemnity payable — generally only in case of complete loss (of both contents and wrapper) — is $15.76. To Canada only the fees are $2.10 and $2.30, providing indemnity for loss up to $100 to $200, respectively.

Return receipt — fee is 32c.

Special delivery — available to most countries. Consult post office. Fees: for post cards, letter mail, and airmail "other articles," $1.25 up to 2 pounds; over 2 to 10 pounds, $1.50; over 10 pounds, $1.75. For surface "other articles," $1.75, $1.85, and $2.15, respectively.

Marking — an article intended for special delivery service must have affixed to the cover near the name of the country of destination "EXPRESS" (special delivery) label, obtainable at the post office, or it may be marked on the cover boldly in red "EXPRESS" (special delivery).

Special handling — entitles AO surface packages to priority handling between mailing point and U.S. point of dispatch. Fees: 50c for packages to 2 pounds, 70c for packages over 2 pounds to 10 pounds, and $1.00 for packages over 10 pounds.

Airmail — there is daily air service to practically all countries.

Prepayment of replies from other countries — a mailer who wishes to prepay a reply by letter from another country may do so by sending his correspondent one or more international reply coupons, which may be purchased at United States post offices. One coupon should be accepted in any country in exchange for stamps to prepay a surface letter of the first unit of weight to the U.S.

Domestic Mail Special Services

Registry — all mailable matter prepaid with postage at the first-class or airmail rate may be registered. The mailer is required to declare the value of mail presented for registration.

Insurance — is applicable to 3d and 4th class matter. Matter for sale addressed to prospective purchasers who have not ordered it or authorized its sending will not be insured.

C.O.D.: Unregistered — is applicable to 3d and 4th class matter and sealed domestic mail of any class bearing postage at the 1st class rate. Such mail must be based on bona fide orders or be in conformity with agreements between senders and addressees. **Registered** — for details consult postmaster.

Certified mail — service is available for any matter having no intrinsic value on which 1st class or air mail postage is paid. Receipt is furnished at time of mailing and evidence of delivery obtained. The fee is 60c in addition to postage. Return receipt, restricted delivery, and special delivery are available upon payment of additional fees. No indemnity.

Individual Piece Mailings
(Fourth class catalogs)

Weight lbs.	Local	Zones 1&2	3	4	5	6	7	8
1.5	$0.45	.54	.56	.58	.61	.64	.68	.73
2	.46	.57	.58	.62	.65	.69	.74	.81
2.5	.48	.60	.61	.66	.70	.74	.81	.89
3	.50	.62	.65	.69	.74	.81	.88	.97
3.5	.52	.65	.68	.73	.80	.86	.94	1.05
4	.53	.68	.70	.77	.84	.92	1.02	1.14
4.5	.54	.69	.73	.81	.88	.97	1.09	1.22
5	.56	.72	.76	.84	.93	1.02	1.15	1.30
6	.60	.77	.82	.92	1.02	1.14	1.29	1.46
7	.62	.82	.88	.98	1.10	1.25	1.42	1.62
8	.66	.88	.94	1.06	1.20	1.37	1.56	1.78
9	.69	.93	1.00	1.13	1.29	1.48	1.70	1.96
10	.72	.97	1.05	1.21	1.38	1.58	1.84	2.12

Zone Mileage

1... Up to 50	3... 150-300	5.... 600-1,000	7... 1,400-1,800
2.... 50-150	4... 300-600	6.. 1,000-1,400	8.... over, 1,800

Registered Mail

Indemnity to $100	$2.10
100.01 to 200	2.30
200.01 to 400	2.60
400.01 to 600	2.90
600.01 to 800	3.20
800.01 to 1,000	3.50
1,000.01 to 2,000	3.80
2,000.01 to 3,000	4.10
3,000.01 to 4,000	4.40
4,000.01 to 5,000	4.70
5,000.01 to 6,000	5.00
6,000.01 to 7,000	5.30
7,000.01 to 8,000	5.60
8,000.01 to 9,000	5.90
9,000.01 to 10,000	6.20

Consult postmaster for registry rates above $10,000.

Insured Mail

$0.01 to $15	$0.40
15.01 to 50	.60
50.01 to 100	.80
100.01 to 150	1.00
150.01 to 200	1.20

Liability for insured mail is limited to $200.

C.O.D. Mail

Consult postmaster for fees and conditions of mailing.

Parcel Post Rate Schedule

1 lb., not exceeding	Local	Zones 1 & 2	3	4	5	6	7	8
2	$0.77	$0.90	$0.93	$1.04	$1.15	$1.28	$1.40	$1.48
3	.82	.97	1.02	1.15	1.29	1.46	1.62	1.74
4	.86	1.04	1.10	1.25	1.42	1.63	1.84	2.00
5	.91	1.11	1.19	1.36	1.56	1.81	2.06	2.26
6	.95	1.18	1.27	1.46	1.69	1.98	2.28	2.52
7	1.00	1.25	1.36	1.57	1.83	2.16	2.50	2.78
8	1.04	1.32	1.44	1.67	1.96	2.33	2.72	3.04
9	1.09	1.39	1.53	1.78	2.10	2.51	2.94	3.30
10	1.13	1.46	1.61	1.88	2.23	2.68	3.16	3.56
11	1.18	1.53	1.70	1.99	2.37	2.86	3.38	3.82
12	1.22	1.60	1.78	2.09	2.50	3.03	3.60	4.08
13	1.27	1.67	1.87	2.20	2.64	3.21	3.82	4.34
14	1.31	1.74	1.95	2.30	2.77	3.38	4.04	4.60
15	1.36	1.81	2.04	2.41	2.91	3.56	4.26	4.86
16	1.40	1.88	2.12	2.51	3.04	3.73	4.48	5.12
17	1.45	1.95	2.21	2.62	3.18	3.91	4.70	5.38
18	1.49	2.02	2.29	2.72	3.31	4.08	4.92	5.64
19	1.54	2.09	2.38	2.83	3.45	4.26	5.14	5.90
20	1.58	2.16	2.46	2.93	3.58	4.43	5.36	6.16

Consult postmaster for parcels over 20 pounds or measuring more than 72 inches, length and girth.

Special Fouth Class Rate
(limit 70 lbs.)

First pound or fraction, 30 (23.9c if special rate matter is presorted to 5 digit ZIP code or 24.2c if presorted to 3 digits); each additional pound or fraction through 7 pounds, 11c; each additional pound, 8c. Only following specific articles: books 24 pages or more, at least 22 of which are printed consisting wholly of reading matter or scholarly bibliography containing no advertisement other than incidental announcements of books; 16 millimeter films in final form (except when mailed to or from commercial theaters); printed music in bound or sheet form; printed objective test materials; sound recordings, playscripts, and manuscripts for books, periodicals, and music; printed educational reference charts; loose-leaf pages and binders therefor consisting of medical information for distribution to doctors, hospitals, medical schools, and medical students. Package must be marked "Special 4th Class Rate" stating item contained.

Library Rate (limit 70 lbs.)

First pound or fraction 9c, each additional pound or fraction 4c. Books when loaned or exchanged between schools, colleges, public libraries, and certain non-profit organizations; books, printed music, bound academic theses, periodicals, sound recordings, other library materials, museum materials (specimens, collections), scientific or mathematical kits, instruments or other devices; also catalogs, guides or scripts for some of these materials. Must be marked "Library Rate".

Post Office-Authorized 2-Letter State Abbreviations

Gradually replacing the traditional abbreviations for the states of the United States are the two-letter ones approved by the Post Office Department when it introduced the ZIP Code in 1963. The official list follows, including the District of Columbia, Guam, Puerto Rico, the Canal Zone, and the Virgin Islands (all capital letters are used):

Alabama	AL	Idaho	ID	Montana	MT	Rhode Island	RI
Alaska	AK	Illinois	IL	Nebraska	NE	South Carolina	SC
Arizona	AZ	Indiana	IN	Nevada	NV	South Dakota	SD
Arkansas	AR	Iowa	IA	New Hampshire	NH	Tennessee	TN
California	CA	Kansas	KS	New Jersey	NJ	Texas	TX
Canal Zone	CZ	Kentucky	KY	New Mexico	NM	Utah	UT
Colorado	CO	Louisiana	LA	New York	NY	Vermont	VT
Connecticut	CT	Maine	ME	North Carolina	NC	Virginia	VA
Delaware	DE	Maryland	MD	North Dakota	ND	Virgin Islands	VI
Dist. of Col.	DC	Massachusetts	MA	Ohio	OH	Washington	WA
Florida	FL	Michigan	MI	Oklahoma	OK	West Virginia	WV
Georgia	GA	Minnesota	MN	Oregon	OR	Wisconsin	WI
Guam	GU	Mississippi	MS	Pennsylvania	PA	Wyoming	WY
Hawaii	HI	Missouri	MO	Puerto Rico	PR		

Also approved for use in addressing mail are the following abbreviations:

Alley	Aly	Court	Ct	Grove	Grv	Rural	R
Arcade	Arc	Courts	Cts	Heights	Hts	Square	Sq
Boulevard	Blvd	Crescent	Cres	Highway	Hwy	Street	St
Branch	Br	Drive	Dr	Lane	Ln	Terrace	Ter
Bypass	Byp	Expressway	Expy	Manor	Mnr	Trail	Trl
Causeway	Cswy	Extended	Ext	Place	Pl	Turnpike	Tpke
Center	Ctr	Extension	Ext	Plaza	Plz	Viaduct	Via
Circle	Cir	Freeway	Fwy	Point	Pt	Vista	Vis
		Gardens	Gdns	Road	Rd		

Commemorative Stamps and Regular Postal Issues 1977

Date	Commemorative stamp	Value	From
Jan. 3	Washington at Princeton	13c	Princeton, NJ
Mar. 23	Centennial of Sound Recording	13c	Washington, DC
Apr. 7	Gold Embossed Envelope	15c	Augusta, GA
Apr. 13	Pueblo Indian Art (4 stamps)	13c	Sante Fe, NM
May 20	Lindbergh Flight	13c	Garden City, NY
May 21	Centennial of Colorado Statehood	13c	Denver, CO
June 3	Nonprofit Embossed Envelope	2.1c	Houston, TX
June 6	Butterflies (4 stamps)	13c	Indianapolis, IN
June 13	Marquis de Lafayette	13c	Charleston, SC
July 4	Skilled Hands for Independence (4 stamps)	13c	Cincinnati, OH
July 20	Galveston Courthouse Pictorial Postal Card	9c	Galveston, TX
Aug. 4	50th Anniversary of Peace Bridge	13c	Buffalo, NY
Aug. 6	Herkimer at Oriskany	13c	Herkimer, NY
Sept. 9	First Civil Settlement in Alta California	13c	San Jose, CA
Sept. 30	Drafting the Articles of Confederation	13c	York, PA
Oct. 6	50th Anniversary Year of Talking Pictures	13c	Hollywood, CA
Oct. 7	Surrender at Saratoga	13c	Schuylerville, NY
Oct. 21	Washington at Valley Forge (Christmas)	13c	Valley Forge, PA
Oct. 21	Rural Mailbox (Christmas)	13c	Omaha, NE

Postal Receipts at Large Cities

Fiscal year	Boston	Chicago	Detroit	L.A.	New York	Phila.	St. Louis	Wash., D.C.
1972	$109,178,539	$332,951,729	$85,997,396	$172,644,940	$395,523,484	$120,059,844	$73,246,822	$99,980,611
1973	114,159,472	339,770,450	84,358,518	172,365,582	392,348,195	120,173,378	75,342,257	103,152,177
1974	123,164,661	347,561,637	87,784,811	176,847,940	409,392,651	130,655,216	79,412,843	133,458,807
1975	136,453,079	365,378,795	84,338,282	193,229,077	453,905,277	134,571,376	85,591,774	115,489,343
1976	151,642,227	384,380,826	95,527,250	203,413,409	484,180,727	147,650,431	96,844,188	125,997,649

Other cities for fiscal year 1976: Atlanta, $126,323,319; Baltimore, $80,200,675; Cincinnati, $59,555,300; Cleveland, $92,027,408; Columbus, $71,531,507; Dallas, $125,101,004; Denver, $70,421,633; Houston, $108,229,165; Indianapolis, $73,346,326; Kansas City, $71,980,330; Minneapolis, $97,046,273; Pittsburgh, $78,346,484; San Francisco, $109,333,101; Seattle, $62,928,291.

Air Mail, Parcel Post International Rates

Aerogrammes — 22 cents each to all countries.
Air mail postcards (single) — 21 cents to all countries except Canada and Mexico (14c).

	Air service						Surface parcel post		
	Letters and letter pkgs.		Other articles		Parcel post				
Country	per 1/2 oz. thru 2 oz.	per 1/2 oz. over 2 oz.	First 2 oz.	Each add'l. 2 oz. or fraction	First 4 oz.	Each add'l. 4 oz. or fraction	First 2 lbs.	Each add'l. pound or fraction	Max. wt. for parcel post (surface or air) lbs.
Afghanistan	.31	.26	.86	.42	3.14	1.20	1.90	.57	22
Albania	.31	.26	.73	.29	3.33	.79	1.90	.57	22
Algeria	.31	.26	.73	.29	2.71	.80	1.90	.57	44
Andorra	.31	.26	.73	.29	2.79	.70	1.90	.57	44
Angola	.31	.26	.86	.42	2.93	1.01	1.90	.57	22
Anguilla	.21	.21	.60	.16	1.78	.36	1.90	.57	22
Antigua	.21	.21	.60	.16	1.78	.36	1.75	.50	22
Argentina	.31	.26	.73	.29	2.46	1.07	1.90	.57	44
Aruba	.25	.21	.60	.16	2.08	.45	1.75	.50	44
Ascension Isl.	.25	.21	.73	.29	(4)	—	1.90	.57	22
Australia[3]	.31	.26	.86	.42	2.62	1.21	1.90	.57	44
Austria	.31	.26	.73	.29	2.70	.74	1.90	.57	44
Azores	.31	.26	.73	.29	1.95	.56	1.90	.57	22
Bahamas	.25	.21	.60	.16	2.19	.27	1.75	.50	22
Bahrian	.31	.26	.86	.42	2.42	1.03	1.90	.57	22
Bangladesh	.31	.26	.86	.42	3.46	1.22	1.90	.57	22
Barbados	.25	.21	.60	.16	1.90	.51	1.75	.50	22
Barbuda	.25	.21	.60	.16	1.78	.36	1.75	.50	22
Belgium	.31	.26	.73	.29	2.41	.66	1.90	.57	44
Belize	.25	.21	.60	.16	2.14	.46	1.90	.57	44
Benin	.31	.26	.86	.42	2.36	.85	1.90	.57	44
Bermuda	.25	.21	.60	.16	1.77	.35	1.75	.50	33
Bhutan	.31	.26	.86	.42	(4)	—	....	....	(5)
Bolivia[3]	.31	.26	.73	.29	2.47	.69	1.90	.57	44
Bonaire	.25	.21	.60	.16	2.08	.45	1.75	.50	44
Botswana	.31	.26	.86	.42	2.66	1.27	1.90	.57	22
Brazil	.25	.21	.73	.29	2.94	.79	1.90	.57	44
Br. Virgin Isl.	.25	.21	.60	.16	1.78	.36	1.75	.50	22
Brunei	.31	.26	.86	.42	3.01	1.47	1.90	.57	22
Bulgaria	.31	.26	.73	.29	2.15	.75	1.90	.57	22
Burma[3]	.31	.26	.86	.42	3.30	1.43	1.90	.57	22
Burundi	.31	.26	.86	.42	2.76	1.07	1.90	.57	22
Cameroon	.31	.26	.86	.42	2.79	.92	1.90	.57	22
Canada[3]	(oz.) .17	(addl. oz.) .15	(6)	—	(6)	—	1.75	.50	35
Cape Verde	.31	.26	.86	.42	2.72	.81	1.90	.57	22
Cen. Africa Rep.	.31	.26	.86	.42	2.76	1.07	1.90	.57	44
Chad	.31	.26	.86	.42	2.76	1.07	1.90	.57	44
Chile[3]	.31	.26	.73	.29	2.92	.89	1.90	.57	22
China Rep.	.31	.26	.86	.42	2.46	1.05	1.90	.57	44
China, People's Rep.	.31	.26	.86	.42	3.08	1.37	1.90	.57	44
Colombia	.25	.21	.60	.16	2.86	.50	1.90	.57	44
Comoro Isl.	.31	.26	.86	.42	3.13	1.43	1.90	.57	44
Congo (Brazza.)	.31	.26	.86	.42	2.76	1.07	1.90	.57	44
Corsica	.31	.26	.73	.29	2.98	.66	1.90	.57	44
Costa Rica	.25	.21	.60	.16	2.06	.43	1.75	.50	44
Cuba	.25	.21	.60	.16	(4)	—	....	....	(5)
Curacao	.25	.21	.60	.16	2.08	.45	1.75	.50	44
Cyprus	.31	.26	.73	.29	2.88	.85	1.90	.57	22
Czechoslovakia	.31	.26	.73	.29	2.17	.76	1.90	.57	44
Denmark	.31	.26	.73	.29	2.14	.72	1.90	.57	44
Djibouti	.31	.26	.86	.42	2.89	1.03	1.90	.57	44
Dominica	.25	.21	.60	.16	2.39	.48	1.75	.50	22
Dominican Rep.	.25	.21	.60	.16	2.24	.36	1.75	.50	44
Ecuador	.31	.26	.73	.29	2.78	.48	1.90	.57	44
Egypt	.31	.26	.73	.29	2.32	.92	1.90	.57	44
El Salvador	.25	.21	.60	.16	2.21	.44	1.75	.50	44
Equatorial Guinea	.31	.26	.86	.42	2.82	1.22	1.90	.57	44
Estonia[2]	.31	.26	.86	.42	2.84	.95	1.90	.57	44
Ethiopia	.31	.26	.86	.42	2.83	1.10	1.90	.57	44
Faeroe Isl.	.31	.26	.73	.29	2.14	.72	1.90	.57	44
Falkland Isl.	.31	.26	.73	.29	2.99	.85	1.90	.57	22
Fiji Islands	.31	.26	.86	.42	2.79	.90	1.90	.57	22
Finland	.31	.26	.73	.29	2.17	.79	1.90	.57	44
France incl. Monaco	.31	.26	.73	.29	2.98	.66	1.90	.57	44
French Guiana	.31	.26	.73	.29	2.19	.56	1.90	.57	44
Fr. Polynesia	.31	.26	.86	.42	2.70	.76	1.90	.57	44
Gabon Rep.	.31	.26	.86	.42	2.76	1.07	1.90	.57	44
Gambia	.31	.26	.86	.42	2.39	.76	1.90	.57	22
Germany, incl. Saar.	.31	.26	.73	.29	2.10	.70	1.90	.57	44
Ghana	.31	.26	.86	.42	2.92	.92	1.90	.57	22
Gilbraltar	.31	.26	.73	.29	2.16	.75	1.90	.57	22
Gilbert & Ellice	.31	.26	.86	.42	2.66	1.00	1.90	.57	22
Great Britain	.31	.26	.73	.29	2.08	.66	1.90	.57	44
Greece	.31	.26	.73	.29	2.62	.84	1.90	.57	44
Greenland	.31	.26	.73	.29	2.35	.93	1.90	.57	44
Grenada	.25	.21	.60	.16	2.39	.48	1.75	.50	22
Guadeloupe	.25	.21	.60	.16	2.00	.36	1.75	.50	44

Country	Air service: Letters and letter pkgs. per ½ oz. thru 2 oz.	Air service: Letters and letter pkgs. per ½ oz. over 2 oz.	Air service: Other articles First 2 oz.	Air service: Other articles Each add'l. 2 oz. or fraction	Air service: Parcel post First 4 oz.	Air service: Parcel post Each add'l. 4 oz. or fraction	Surface parcel post First 2 lbs.	Surface parcel post Each add'l. pound or fraction	Max. wt. for parcel post (surface or air) lbs.
Guatemala	.25	.21	.60	.16	2.51	.46	1.75	.50	44
Guinea, Rep. of	.31	.26	.86	.42	2.46	.96	1.90	.57	44
Guinea-Bissau	.31	.26	.86	.42	2.93	1.01	1.90	.57	22
Guyana	.31	.26	.73	.29	2.42	.50	1.90	.57	22
Haiti	.25	.21	.60	.16	2.25	.35	1.75	.50	44
Honduras	.25	.21	.60	.16	2.14	.46	1.75	.50	[1]44
Hong Kong	.31	.26	.86	.42	2.65	1.24	1.90	.57	22
Hungary	.31	.26	.73	.29	2.16	.76	1.90	.57	44
Iceland	.31	.26	.73	.29	2.66	.56	1.90	.57	44
India	.31	.26	.86	.42	2.67	1.27	1.90	.57	[1]44
Indonesia	.31	.26	.86	.42	3.48	1.52	1.90	.57	22
Iran	.31	.26	.86	.42	2.67	.96	1.90	.57	44
Iraq	.31	.26	.86	.42	2.98	.95	1.90	.57	44
Ireland (Eire)	.31	.26	.73	.29	2.06	.66	1.90	.57	22
Israel	.31	.26	.86	.42	2.93	.91	1.90	.57	22
Italy	.31	.26	.73	.29	2.63	.79	1.90	.57	44
Ivory Coast	.31	.26	.86	.42	2.46	.95	1.90	.57	44
Jamaica	.25	.21	.60	.16	2.36	.33	1.75	.50	22
Japan	.31	.26	.86	.42	2.19	.80	1.90	.57	22
Jordan	.31	.26	.86	.42	2.72	.90	1.90	.57	22
Kampuchea (Cambodia)	.31	.26	.86	.42	(4)	—	1.90	.57	(5)
Kenya	.31	.26	.86	.42	2.93	1.10	1.90	.57	22
Korea (Rep. of)	.31	.26	.86	.42	2.25	.85	1.90	.57	22
No. Korea[1]	.31	.26	.86	.42	(4)	—	—	—	(5)
Kuwait	.31	.26	.86	.42	2.39	1.00	1.90	.57	44
Laos	.31	.26	.86	.42	3.35	1.37	1.90	.57	22
Latvia[2]	.31	.26	.86	.42	2.84	.95	1.90	.57	44
Lebanon	.31	.26	.86	.42	2.72	.90	1.90	.57	[1]44
Leeward Islands	.25	.21	.60	.16	1.78	.36	1.75	.50	22
Lesotho	.31	.26	.86	.42	2.66	1.27	1.90	.57	22
Liberia	.31	.26	.86	.42	2.24	.84	1.90	.57	22
Libya	.31	.26	.73	.29	2.70	.85	1.90	.57	44
Liechtenstein	.31	.26	.73	.29	2.39	.67	1.90	.57	44
Lithuania[2]	.31	.26	.86	.42	2.84	.95	1.90	.57	44
Luxembourg	.31	.26	.73	.29	2.47	.65	1.90	.57	44
Macao	.31	.26	.86	.42	3.20	1.24	1.90	.57	22
Madagascar	.31	.26	.86	.42	3.09	1.22	1.90	.57	44
Madeira Isl.	.31	.26	.73	.29	2.10	.72	1.90	.57	22
Malawi	.31	.26	.86	.42	2.66	1.24	1.90	.57	22
Malaysia	.31	.26	.86	.42	3.23	1.42	1.90	.57	22
Maldives, Rep. of	.31	.26	.86	.42	3.59	1.29	1.90	.57	22
Mali	.31	.26	.86	.42	3.46	.82	1.90	.57	44
Malta	.31	.26	.73	.29	2.61	.79	1.90	.57	22
Martinique	.25	.21	.60	.16	2.00	.36	1.75	.50	44
Mauritania	.31	.26	.86	.42	2.36	.79	1.90	.57	44
Mauritius	.31	.26	.86	.42	3.01	1.29	1.90	.57	22
Mexico	(oz.) .17	(addl. oz.) .15	.60	.16	1.77	.35	1.75	.50	44
Montserrat	.25	.21	.60	.16	1.78	.36	1.90	.57	22
Morocco	.31	.26	.73	.29	2.63	.79	1.90	.57	44
Mozambique	.31	.26	.86	.42	3.43	1.28	1.90	.57	22
Namibia (SW Africa)	.31	.26	.86	.42	2.66	1.27	1.90	.57	22
Nauru (Rep.)	.31	.26	.86	.42	2.62	1.21	1.90	.57	22
Nepal	.31	.26	.86	.42	2.66	1.27	1.90	.57	22
Netherlands	.31	.26	.73	.29	2.36	.66	1.90	.57	44
Neth. Antilles	.25	.21	.60	.16	2.08	.45	1.75	.50	44
Nevis	.25	.21	.60	.16	1.78	.36	1.75	.50	22
New Caledonia	.31	.26	.86	.42	2.81	.93	1.90	.57	44
New Guinea, Terr. of	.31	.26	.86	.42	2.72	1.32	1.90	.57	22
New Hebrides	.31	.26	.86	.42	2.65	.93	1.90	.57	44
New Zealand	.31	.26	.86	.42	2.98	1.07	1.90	.57	22
Nicaragua	.25	.21	.60	.16	2.08	.43	1.75	.50	44
Niger	.31	.26	.86	.42	3.45	.80	1.90	.57	44
Nigeria	.31	.26	.86	.42	3.14	.93	1.90	.57	22
Norway	.31	.26	.73	.29	2.14	.72	1.90	.57	44
Oman, Sultanate of	.31	.26	.86	.42	2.42	1.03	1.90	.57	22
Outer Mongolia	.31	.26	.86	.42	(4)	—	1.90	.57	(5)
Pakistan	.31	.26	.86	.42	3.46	1.22	1.90	.57	22
Panama	.25	.21	.60	.16	2.50	.45	1.75	.50	[1]70
Papua New Guinea	.31	.26	.86	.42	2.72	1.32	1.90	.57	22
Paraguay	.31	.26	.73	.29	2.47	.67	1.90	.57	44
Peru	.31	.26	.73	.29	2.88	.60	1.90	.57	44
Philippines	.31	.26	.86	.42	3.03	1.17	1.90	.57	[1]44
Pitcairn	.31	.26	.86	.42	2.89	1.03	1.90	.57	22
Poland	.31	.26	.73	.29	2.61	.75	1.90	.57	44
Portugal	.31	.26	.73	.29	2.05	.64	1.90	.57	22
Portuguese Timor	.31	.26	.86	.42	3.64	1.72	1.90	.57	22
" W. Africa	.31	.26	.86	.42	2.93	1.01	1.90	.57	22
Qatar	.31	.26	.86	.42	2.42	1.03	1.90	.57	22
Reunion	.31	.26	.86	.42	2.89	1.27	1.90	.57	44
Rhodesia	.31	.26	.86	.42	2.66	1.24	1.90	.57	22
Romania	.31	.26	.73	.29	2.42	.79	1.90	.57	22

Country	Air service: Letters and letter pkgs. Per 1/2 oz. thru 2 oz.	Per 1/2 oz. over 2 oz.	Other articles: First 2 oz.	Each add'l. 2 oz. or fraction	Parcel post: First 4 oz.	Each add'l. 4 oz. or fraction	Surface parcel post: First 2 lbs.	Each add'l. pound or fraction	Max. wt. for parcel post (surface or air) lbs.
Rwanda	.31	.26	.86	.42	2.76	1.07	1.90	.57	22
Ryukyu	.31	.26	.86	.42	2.19	.80	1.90	.57	22
Sabah	.25	.25	.60	.16	2.08	.45	1.90	.57	44
St. Christopher	.25	.21	.60	.16	2.39	.48	1.75	.50	22
St. Eustatius	.25	.21	.60	.16	2.08	.45	1.75	.50	44
St. Helena	.31	.26	.86	.42	3.01	1.22	1.90	.57	22
St. Lucia	.25	.21	.60	.16	2.39	.48	1.75	.50	22
St. Pierre, Miquelon	.25	.21	.60	.16	1.72	.35	1.75	.50	44
St. Vincent	.25	.21	.60	.16	2.39	.48	1.75	.50	22
Samoa	.31	.26	.86	.42	2.71	.80	1.90	.57	22
Santa Cruz Isl.	.31	.26	.86	.42	3.10	1.39	1.90	.57	22
Sao Tome & Principe	.31	.26	.86	.42	2.93	1.01	1.90	.57	22
Saudi Arabia	.31	.26	.86	.42	3.10	1.00	1.90	.57	22
Senegal	.31	.26	.86	.42	2.34	.75	1.90	.57	44
Seychelles	.31	.26	.86	.42	2.53	1.12	1.90	.57	22
Sierra Leone	.31	.26	.86	.42	3.09	.81	1.90	.57	22
Singapore	.31	.26	.86	.42	3.23	1.42	1.90	.57	22
Solomon Isl.	.31	.26	.86	.42	3.12	1.39	1.90	.57	22
Somali Rep.	.31	.26	.86	.42	3.23	1.13	1.90	.57	22
South Africa	.31	.26	.86	.42	2.66	1.27	1.90	.57	22
Spain	.31	.26	.73	.29	2.79	.70	1.90	.57	[1]44
Sp. W. Africa	.31	.26	.86	.42	2.81	.81	1.90	.57	[1]44
Sri Lanka (Ceylon)	.31	.26	.86	.42	3.33	1.28	1.90	.57	22
Sudan	.31	.26	.86	.42	3.13	1.01	1.90	.57	22
Surinam	.31	.26	.73	.29	2.24	.53	1.90	.57	44
Swaziland	.31	.26	.86	.42	2.66	1.27	1.90	.57	22
Sweden	.31	.26	.73	.29	2.14	.72	1.90	.57	44
Switzerland	.31	.26	.73	.29	2.39	.67	1.90	.57	44
Syria	.31	.26	.86	.42	2.47	.92	1.90	.57	[1]44
Tanzania	.31	.26	.86	.42	2.99	1.15	1.90	.57	22
Thailand	.31	.26	.86	.42	3.28	1.17	1.90	.57	22
Togo	.31	.26	.86	.42	2.57	.95	1.90	.57	44
Tonga	.31	.26	.86	.42	2.34	.93	1.90	.57	22
Trinidad & Tobago	.31	.26	.60	.16	2.37	.45	1.75	.50	22
Tristan da Cunha	.31	.26	.86	.42	2.83	1.21	1.90	.57	22
Tunisia	.31	.26	.73	.29	2.62	.75	1.90	.57	44
Turkey	.31	.26	.73	.29	2.26	.85	1.90	.57	44
Turks Islands	.25	.21	.60	.16	2.25	.33	1.75	.50	22
Uganda	.31	.26	.86	.42	2.93	1.10	1.90	.57	22
USSR[2]	.31	.26	.86	.42	2.84	.95	1.90	.57	44
United Arab Emir.	.31	.26	.86	.42	2.42	1.03	1.90	.57	22
Upper Volta	.31	.26	.86	.42	2.72	.89	1.90	.57	44
Uruguay	.31	.26	.73	.29	2.93	.90	1.90	.57	44
Vatican City	.31	.26	.73	.29	2.42	.74	1.90	.57	44
Venezuela	.25	.21	.60	.16	2.71	.43	1.90	.57	44
Vietnam	.31	.26	.86	.42	(4)	....	....	....	(5)
Windward Isl.	.25	.21	.60	.16	2.39	.48	1.75	.50	22
Yemen (Aden)	.31	.26	.86	.42	2.81	1.10	....	....	22
Yemen (Sanaa)	.31	.26	.86	.42	3.04	1.55	1.90	.57	44
Yugoslavia	.31	.26	.73	.29	2.17	.79	1.90	.57	44
Zaire	.31	.26	.86	.42	2.76	1.07	1.90	.57	44
Zambia	.31	.26	.86	.42	2.66	1.24	1.90	.57	22

(1) Restrictions apply; consult post office. (2) To facilitate distribution and delivery, include "Union of Soviet Socialist Republics" or "USSR" as part of the address. (3) Small packets weight limit one pound. (4) No air parcel post service. (5) No surface parcel post service. (6) No airmail AO or parcel post to Canada; prepare and prepay all airmail packages as letter mail. (7) The continental China postal authorities will not deliver articles unless addressed to show name of the country as "People's Republic of China"; also, only acceptable spelling of capital is "Peking."

International Mails

Weight and Dimensional Limits and Surface Rates

For air rates and parcel post see pages 972-974

Letters and letter packages: all written matter or correspondence recordings, must be sent as letter mail. Weight limit: 4 lbs. to all countries except Canada, which is 60 lbs. **Surface rates:** Canada and Mexico, 13c first ounce; 11c each additional ounce or fraction up to 13 ounces; eighth-zone priority rates for heavier weights. Countries other than Canada and Mexico, 1 ounce, 18c; over 1 to 2 ounces, 31c; over 2 to 4 ounces, 41c; over 4 to 8 ounces, 82c; over 8 ounces to 1 pound, $1.58; over 1 to 2 pounds, $2.75; and over 2 to 4 pounds, $4.46. **Air rates:** Canada and Mexico, 17c first ounce; 15c each additional ounce or fraction. Central America, Colombia, Venezuela, the Caribbean Islands, Bahamas, Bermuda, and St. Pierre and Miquelon, 25c per half ounce up to and including 2 ounces; 21c each additional half ounce or fraction. All other countries, 31c per half ounce up to and including 2 ounces; 26c each additional half ounce or fraction. Aerogrammes, which can be folded into the form of an envelope and sent by air to all countries, are available at post offices for 22c each.

Note. Mail to Canada bearing postage paid at the surface letter rate will receive airmail service in both the U.S. and Canada during the Postal Service First Class Mail Service Improvement Program.

Postcards. Surface rates to Canada and Mexico, 9c; to all other countries, 12c. By air, Canada and Mexico, 14c; to all other countries, 21c. Maximum size permitted, 6 x 4 1/4 in.; minimum, 5 1/2 x 3 1/2.

Printed matter. To Canada and Mexico, 14c the first 2 ounces, 14c for the next two ounces, plus 11c each add'l. 2 ounces or fraction through 1 pound; $1.15 for 1 to 2 pounds, $1.44 for 2 to 4 pounds. To other countries, 14c the first 2 ounces, 28c 2 to 4 ounces, 50c 4 to 8 ounces, 83c 8 to 16 ounces, $1.15 1 to 2 pounds, $1.44 2 to 4 pounds. To countries admitting regular prints over 4 lbs. 72c for each additional 2 lbs. or fraction. (Consult post office for rates and conditions applying to certain publications mailed by the publishers or by registered news agents.) Book weight limits for most countries is 11 lbs; for exceptions see below.

Consult post office for book rates.

Exceptional weight limits for printed matter. Printed matter may weigh up to 22 lbs. to Argentina, Bolivia, Brazil, Chile, Colombia, Costa Rica, Cuba, Dominican Republic, Ecuador, El Salvador, Guatemala, Haiti, Honduras, Mexico, Nicaragua, Panama, Paraguay, Peru, Spain (including Balearic Islands, Canary Islands, and offices in Northern Africa), Uruguay, and Venezuela. For other countries, limit for books is 11 lbs., all other prints, 4 lbs.

Matter for the blind. Surface rate free; air rates to Canada 17c per oz. (For all other countries, consult postmaster.) Weight limit 15 lbs.

Small packets. Postage rates for small items of merchandise and samples are lower than for letter packages or parcel post; consult post office for weight limits and requirements for customs declarations. Surface rates: Canada and Mexico, 14c the first 2 oz., 14c for the next 2 oz., plus 11c for each add'l 2 oz. or fraction. All other countries, for 4 oz. or less 28c; 4 to 8 oz. 50c; 8 oz. to 1 lb. 83c; 1 to 2 lbs. $1.15. For other rates, see schedule "Air Service Other Articles" under heading of International Rates for Air Mail and Surface Parcel Post, pages 972-974.

International Parcel Post

For rates see pages 972-974

General dimensional limits — greatest length, 3 1/2 feet; greatest length and girth combined, 6 feet.

Prohibited articles. Before sending goods abroad the mailer should satisfy himself that they will not be confiscated or returned because their importation is prohibited or restricted by the country of address.

Packing. Parcels for transmission overseas should be even more carefully packed than those intended for delivery within the continental U.S. Containers should be used which will be strong enough to protect the contents from the weight of other mails, from pressure and friction, climatic changes, and repeated handlings.

Sealing. Registered or insured parcels must be sealed. To some countries the sealing of ordinary (unregistered and uninsured) parcels is optional, and to others compulsory. Consult post office.

Customs declarations and other forms. A parcel post sticker, and at least one customs declaration giving a complete description of the contents, are required for each parcel mailed to another country.

United Nations Postage Stamps Issued in 1977

UN stamps in United States denominations, valid for postage only on mail deposited at UN Headquarters, New York, and UN stamps in Swiss denominations, valid for postage only on mail deposited at the United Nations Office, Geneva, are available at face value from the UN Postal Administration in New York and Geneva and through sales agencies around the world. They may be obtained by mail or automatically through the Customer Deposit Account service, both in New York and Geneva. Revenue from the sale of UN stamps for postage purposes goes to the U.S. Postal Service and the Swiss PTT, respectively; from philatelic sales, revenue goes to the UN.

Date	Stamp	Value
11 Mar.	World Intellectual Property Organization	13c, 31c
22 Apr.	UN Water Conference	13c, 25c
27 May	Security Council	13c, 31c
27 June	Postal card	9c
	Air letter	22c
	Air mails	25c, 31c
19 Sept.	Combat Racism	13c, 25c
18 Nov.	Peaceful Uses of Atomic Energy	13c, 18c

Canadian Postal Rates

(in effect Jan. 1, 1977)

Letter mail and postcards. Up to 1 oz. 12c, over 1 and up to 2 oz. 20c, over 2 and up to 4 oz. 30c, over 4 and up to 6 oz. 40c, over 6 and up to 8 oz. 58c, plus 14c for each additional 2 oz. up to 16 oz.

Parcels (over 1 lb.) **First class** (maximum 66 lb.) parcels receive priority air service. **Fourth class** (maximum 35 lb.) parcels receive surface transmission.

The charges given below are for local (short haul) deliveries. A chart showing the cost for deliveries to all other postal zones may be obtained from your local postmaster.

over/up to	1 lb./2	2/3	3/4	4/5	5/6	6/7	7/8	8/9	9/10	10/15
1st class	$1.25	1.55	1.80	2.10	2.40	2.65	2.95	3.20	3.50	4.05
4th class	.60	.75	.90	1.05	1.15	1.30	1.45	1.60	1.75	1.95

over/up to	15 lb./20	20/25	25/30	30/35	35/40	40/45	45/50	50/55	55/60	60/66
1st class	4.65	5.20	5.75	6.30	6.85	7.45	8.00	8.55	9.15	9.70
4th class	2.15	2.35	2.55	2.75						

Third class. Standard addressed rates (includes greeting cards). Up to 2 oz. 10c, plus 5c for each additional 2 oz. up to a maximum of 1 lb.

Premium Services. Certified mail (proof of delivery service) 60c plus postage. Special Delivery on 1st class mail only 50c plus 1st class postage, with a minimum of 60c per letter. Money order fee (maximum $200) - 35c

To U.S.A., Territories and Possessions

Airmail letters and postcards, up to and including 1 oz. 12c plus 10c for each additional oz. up to 1 lb. Over 1 lb. up to and including 2 lbs. $2.60 plus 65c for each additional lb. up to a maximum of 66 lbs.

Surface parcel post. Up to and including 2 lbs. $1.50 plus 40c for each additional lb. up to a maximum of 35 lbs.

QUICK REFERENCE INDEX

First Class Postal Rates in Brief

(in effect Dec., 1977)

U.S. Domestic

Letters—13c first ounce, 11c each additional ounce.
Postal cards—9c each (up to 4 1/2 x 6 in.). Double cards, 18c. Private cards, 18c.

U.S. International

Letters—(1) Canada and Mexico, 13c first ounce, 11c each addl. ounce to 12 ounces; over 12 ounces to 1 pound, $1.67; over 1 pound to 1 1/2 pounds, $2.07; over 1 1/2 to 2 pounds, $2.46; over 2 to 2 1/2 pounds, $2.78; over 2 1/2 to 3 pounds, $3.09; over 3 to 3 1/2 pounds, $3.38; over 3 1/2 to 4 pounds, $3.67; over 4 to 4 1/2 pounds, $3.94; over 4 1/2 to 5 pounds, $4.20; over 5 pounds, 52c each additional pound or fraction. (2) Countries other than Canada and Mexico, 1 ounce, 18c; over 1 to 2 ounces, 31c; over 2 to 4 ounces, 41c; over 4 to 8 ounces, 82c; over 8 ounces to 1 pound, $1.58; over 1 to 2 pounds, $2.75; and over 2 to 4 pound, $4.46.
Air mail letters—(1) Canada and Mexico, same as domestic surface rates. (2) Cen. America, S. America, the Caribbean Is., Bahamas, Bermuda, and St. Pierre and Miquelon, 25c per half ounce. (3) All other countries, 31c per half ounce.
Aerogrammes—to all countries, 22c each.
Postal cards—to Canada and Mexico 9c each. To all other countries, 12c each.
Air mail postcards—to Canada and Mexico 9c each, to other countries 21c each.

Canada (in effect Jan. 1, 1977)

Domestic—1 oz. 12c; 1-2 oz. 20c; 2-4 oz. 30c; 4-6 oz. 40c; 6-8 oz. 58c; 14c each additional 2 oz.
International—1 oz. 25c; 1-2 oz. 45c; 2-4 oz. 60c; 4-8 oz. $1.20; 8-16 oz. $2.35.
Postcards—25c.
Aerogrammes—25c.